WRITTEN IN MY OWN HEART'S BLOOD

By Diana Gabaldon

(in chronological order)
OUTLANDER
DRAGONFLY IN AMBER
VOYAGER
DRUMS OF AUTUMN
THE FIERY CROSS
A BREATH OF SNOW AND ASHES
AN ECHO IN THE BONE
WRITTEN IN MY OWN HEART'S BLOOD
THE OUTLANDISH COMPANION (NONFICTION)
THE EXILE (GRAPHIC NOVEL)
THE OUTLANDISH COMPANION VOLUME TWO (NONFICTION)

(in chronological order)
LORD JOHN AND THE HELLFIRE CLUB (NOVELLA)
LORD JOHN AND THE PRIVATE MATTER
LORD JOHN AND THE SUCCUBUS (NOVELLA)
LORD JOHN AND THE BROTHERHOOD OF THE BLADE
LORD JOHN AND THE HAUNTED SOLIDER (NOVELLA)
THE CUSTOM OF THE ARMY (NOVELLA)
LORD JOHN AND THE HAND OF DEVILS (COLLECTED NOVELLAS)
THE SCOTTISH PRISONER
A PLAGUE OF ZOMBIES (NOVELLA)

Other Outlander-related novellas
A LEAF ON THE WIND OF ALL HALLOWS
THE SPACE BETWEEN
VIRGINS

DIANA GABALDON

WRITTEN IN MY OWN HEART'S BLOOD

A NOVEL

DELL
NEW YORK

Written in My Own Heart's Blood is a work of fiction. Names, characters, places, and incidents are the product of the author's imagination or are used fictitiously. Any resemblance to actual persons, living or dead, events or locales is entirely coincidental.

2016 Dell Mass Market Edition

Family tree design by Donna Sinisgalli
Title page art from an original photograph by Laura Shreck

Published in the United States by Dell, an imprint of Random House, a division of Penguin Random House LLC, New York.

DELL and the HOUSE colophon are registered trademarks of Penguin Random House LLC.

Originally published in hardcover in the United States by Delacorte Press, an imprint of Random House, a division of Penguin Random House LLC, in 2014.

ISBN 978-1-101-88424-9
ebook ISBN 978-0-440-24644-2

Cover design: Marietta Anastassatos
Cover illustration: © Robert Hunt; symbol of octothorpe © Conrad Altmann

Printed in the United States of America

randomhousebooks.com

20 19 18 17 16 15 14 13

Dell mass market edition: May 2016

This book is dedicated to ALL of the people
(besides me) *who worked like fiends*
to produce it for you.
Especially to

Jennifer Hershey *(editor, U.S.)*
Bill Massey *(editor, U.K.)*
Kathleen Lord *(aka "Hercules"—copy editor)*
Barbara Schnell *(translator and trench-buddy, Germany)*
Catherine MacGregor, Catherine-Ann MacPhee,
and Àdhamh Ó Broin *(Gaelic experts)*
Virginia Norey *(aka "Book Goddess"—designer)*
Kelly Chian, Maggie Hart, Benjamin Dreyer, Lisa Feuer,
and the rest of the Random House Production Team
and
Beatrice Lampe und Petra Zimmermann in München

AN OUTLANDER FAMILY TREE

Key

- = Married
- ≈ Out-of-wedlock affair
- ≠ Divorced
- —— Children
- Foster children
- ······ Stepchildren

FRASER OF LOVAT

Simon, Lord Lovat ≈ Davina Porter

Brian Fraser = Ellen Caitriona Sileas MacKenzie

Janet MacKenzie = Ambrose MacKenzie

Flora MacKenzie

Ian Alastair Robert MacLeod Murray = Janet (Jenny) Flora Arabella Fraser

William Simon Murtagh MacKenzie Fraser

Robert Brian Gordon MacKenzie Fraser

James (Jamie) Alexander Malcolm MacKenzie Fraser

Fergus Claudel Fraser =

James (Young Jamie) Fraser Murray = Joan

Margaret (Maggie) Ellen Murray = [Unknown] Carmichael = Paul Lyle

Katherine (Kitty) Mary Murray = George (Geordie) Silvers

Michael Murray = Lilliane (Lillie)

Janet Ellen Murray

Ian (Young Ian) Fraser Murray ≠ Wakyo'teyehsnonhsa (Works with Her Hands/Emily)

Caitlin Maisri Murray

Matthew Murray

Henry Murray

Caroline Murray

Benjamin Murray

Anthony Brian Montgomery Lyle

Angelica Lyle

Angus Walter (Wally) Edwin Murray Carmichael

Josephine Silvers

Abigail Silvers

Yeksa'a (Iseabail)

MACKENZIE OF LEOCH

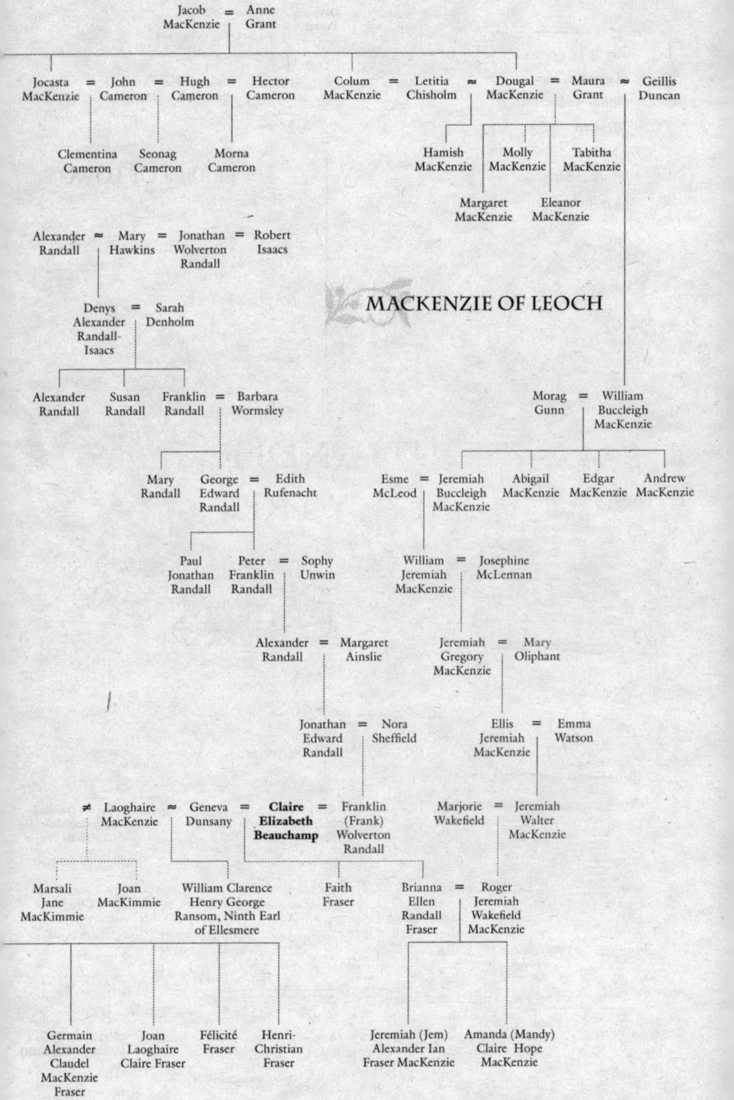

CONTENTS

PART ONE

Nexus

PART TWO

Meanwhile, Back at the Ranch . . .

PART THREE

A Blade Fresh-Made from the Ashes of the Forge

PART FOUR

Day of Battle

PART FIVE

Counting Noses

PART SIX

The Ties That Bind

PART SEVEN

Before I Go Hence

PART EIGHT

Search and Rescue

PART NINE

"Thig crioch air an t-saoghal ach mairidh ceol agus gaol."

PROLOGUE

IN THE LIGHT OF eternity, time casts no shadow.

Your old men shall dream dreams, your young men shall see visions. But what is it that the old women see?

We see necessity, and we do the things that must be done.

Young women don't see—they *are,* and the spring of life runs through them.

Ours is the guarding of the spring, ours the shielding of the light we have lit, the flame that we are.

What have I seen? You are the vision of my youth, the constant dream of all my ages.

Here I stand on the brink of war again, a citizen of no place, no time, no country but my own . . . and that a land lapped by no sea but blood, bordered only by the outlines of a face long-loved.

PART ONE

Nexus

1

A HUNDREDWEIGHT OF STONES

June 16, 1778
The forest between Philadelphia and Valley Forge

IAN MURRAY STOOD with a stone in his hand, eyeing the ground he'd chosen. A small clearing, out of the way, up among a scatter of great lichened boulders, under the shadow of firs and at the foot of a big red cedar; a place where no casual passerby would go, but not inaccessible. He meant to bring them up here—the family.

Fergus, to begin with. Maybe just Fergus, by himself. Mam had raised Fergus from the time he was ten, and he'd had no mother before that. Fergus had known Mam longer than Ian had, and loved her as much. *Maybe more,* he thought, his grief aggravated by guilt. Fergus had stayed with her at Lallybroch, helped to take care of her and the place; he hadn't. He swallowed hard and, walking into the small clear space, set his stone in the middle, then stood back to look.

Even as he did so, he found himself shaking his head. No, it had to be two cairns. His mam and Uncle Jamie were brother and sister, and the family could mourn them here together—but there were others he might bring, maybe, to remember and pay their respects. And those were the folk who would have known Jamie Fraser and loved him well but wouldn't ken Jenny Murray from a hole in the—

The image of his mother *in* a hole in the ground stabbed him like a fork, retreated with the recollection that she wasn't after all in a grave, and stabbed again all the harder for that. He really couldn't bear the vision of them drowning, maybe clinging to each other, struggling to keep—

"A Dhia!" he said violently, and dropped the stone, turning back at once to find more. He'd seen people drown.

Tears ran down his face with the sweat of the summer day; he didn't mind it, only stopping now and then to wipe his nose on his sleeve. He'd tied a rolled kerchief round his head to keep the hair and the stinging sweat out of his eyes; it was sopping before he'd added more than twenty stones to each of the cairns.

He and his brothers had built a fine cairn for their father before he died, at the head of the carved stone that bore his name—all his names, in spite of the expense—in the burying ground at Lallybroch. And then later, at the funeral, members of the family, followed by the tenants and then the servants, would have come one by one to add a stone each to the weight of remembrance.

Fergus, then. Or . . . no, what was he thinking? Auntie Claire must be the first he brought here. She wasn't Scots herself, but she kent fine what a cairn was and would maybe be comforted a bit to see Uncle Jamie's. Aye, right. Auntie Claire, then Fergus. Uncle Jamie was Fergus's foster father; he had a right. And then maybe Marsali and the children. But maybe Germain was old enough to come with Fergus? He was ten, near enough to being a man to understand, to be treated like a man. And Uncle Jamie was his grandsire; it was proper.

He stepped back again and wiped his face, breathing heavily. Bugs whined and buzzed past his ears and hovered over him, wanting his blood, but he'd stripped to a loincloth and rubbed himself with bear grease and mint in the Mohawk way; they didn't touch him.

"Look over them, O spirit of red cedar," he said softly in Mohawk, gazing up into the fragrant branches of the tree. "Guard their souls and keep their presence here, fresh as thy branches."

He crossed himself and bent to dig about in the soft leaf mold. A few more rocks, he thought. In case they might be scattered by some passing animal. Scattered like his thoughts, which roamed restless to and fro among the faces of his family, the folk of the Ridge—God, might he ever go back there? Brianna. Oh, Jesus, Brianna . . .

He bit his lip and tasted salt, licked it away and moved on, foraging. She was safe with Roger Mac and the weans. But, Jesus, he could have used her advice—even more, Roger Mac's.

Who was left for him to ask, if he needed help in taking care of them all?

Thought of Rachel came to him, and the tightness in his chest eased a little. Aye, if he had Rachel . . . She was younger than him, nay more than nineteen, and, being a Quaker, had very strange notions of how things should be, but if he had her, he'd have solid rock under his feet. He hoped he *would* have her, but there were still things he must say to her, and the thought of that conversation made the tightness in his chest come back.

The picture of his cousin Brianna came back, too, and lingered in his mind: tall, long-nosed and strong-boned as her father . . . and with it rose the image of his *other* cousin, Bree's half brother. Holy God, William. And what ought he to do about William? He doubted the man kent the truth, kent that he was Jamie Fraser's son—was it Ian's responsibility to tell him so? To bring him here and explain what he'd lost?

He must have groaned at the thought, for his dog, Rollo, lifted his massive head and looked at him in concern.

"No, I dinna ken that, either," Ian told him. "Let it bide, aye?" Rollo laid his head back on his paws, shivered his shaggy hide against the flies, and relaxed in boneless peace.

Ian worked awhile longer and let the thoughts drain away with his sweat and his tears. He finally stopped when the sinking sun touched the tops of his cairns, feeling tired but more at peace. The cairns rose knee-high, side by side, small but solid.

He stood still for a bit, not thinking anymore, just listening to the fussing of wee birds in the grass and the breathing of the wind among the trees. Then he sighed deeply, squatted, and touched one of the cairns.

"Tha gaol agam oirbh, a Mhàthair," he said softly. *My love is upon you, Mother.* Closed his eyes and laid a scuffed hand on the other heap of stones. The dirt ground into his skin made his fingers feel strange, as though he could maybe reach straight through the earth and touch what he needed.

He stayed still, breathing, then opened his eyes.

"Help me wi' this, Uncle Jamie," he said. "I dinna think I can manage, alone."

2

DIRTY BASTARD

WILLIAM RANSOM, Ninth Earl of Ellesmere, Viscount Ashness, Baron Derwent, shoved his way through the crowds on Market Street, oblivious to the complaints of those rebounding from his impact.

He didn't know where he was going, or what he might do when he got there. All he knew was that he'd burst if he stood still.

His head throbbed like an inflamed boil. Everything throbbed. His hand—he'd probably broken something, but he didn't care. His heart, pounding and sore inside his chest. His foot, for God's sake—what, had he kicked something? He lashed out viciously at a loose cobblestone and sent it rocketing through a crowd of geese, who set up a huge cackle and lunged at him, hissing and beating at his shins with their wings.

Feathers and goose shit flew wide, and the crowd scattered in all directions.

"Bastard!" shrieked the goose-girl, and struck at him with her crook, catching him a shrewd thump on the ear. "Devil take you, *dreckiger Bastard*!"

This sentiment was echoed by a number of other angry voices, and he veered into an alley, pursued by shouts and honks of agitation.

He rubbed his throbbing ear, lurching into buildings as he passed, oblivious to everything but the one word throbbing ever louder in his head. *Bastard.*

"Bastard!" he said out loud, and shouted, "Bastard, bastard, *bastard*!" at the top of his lungs, hammering at the brick wall next to him with a clenched fist.

"Who's a bastard?" said a curious voice behind him. He swung round to see a young woman looking at him with some interest. Her eyes moved slowly down his frame, taking note of the heaving chest, the bloodstains on the facings of his uniform coat, and the green smears of goose shit on his breeches. Her gaze reached his silver-buckled shoes and returned to his face with more interest.

"I am," he said, hoarse and bitter.

"Oh, really?" She left the shelter of the doorway in which she'd been lingering and came across the alley to stand right in front of him. She was tall and slim and had a very fine pair of high young breasts—which were clearly visible under the thin muslin of her shift, because, while she had a silk petticoat, she wore no stays. No cap, either—her hair fell loose over her shoulders. A whore.

"I'm partial to bastards myself," she said, and touched him lightly on the arm. "What kind of bastard are you? A wicked one? An evil one?"

"A sorry one," he said, and scowled when she laughed. She saw the scowl but didn't pull back.

"Come in," she said, and took his hand. "You look as though you could do with a drink." He saw her glance at his knuckles, burst and bleeding, and she caught her lower lip behind small white teeth. She didn't seem afraid, though, and he found himself drawn, unprotesting, into the shadowed doorway after her.

What did it matter? he thought, with a sudden savage weariness. *What did anything matter?*

3

IN WHICH THE WOMEN, AS USUAL, PICK UP THE PIECES

Number 17 Chestnut Street, Philadelphia
The residence of Lord and Lady John Grey

WILLIAM HAD LEFT the house like a thunderclap, and the place looked as though it had been struck by lightning. I certainly felt like the survivor of a massive electrical storm, hairs and nerve endings all standing up straight on end, waving in agitation.

Jenny Murray had entered the house on the heels of William's departure, and while the sight of her was a lesser shock than any of the others so far, it still left me speechless. I goggled at my erstwhile sister-in-law—though, come to think, she still *was* my sister-in-law . . . because Jamie was alive. *Alive.*

He'd been in my arms not ten minutes before, and the memory of his touch flickered through me like lightning in a bottle. I was dimly aware that I was smiling like a loon, despite massive destruction, horrific scenes, William's distress—if you could call an explosion like that "distress"—Jamie's danger, and a faint wonder as to what either Jenny or Mrs. Figg, Lord John's cook and housekeeper, might be about to say.

Mrs. Figg was smoothly spherical, gleamingly black, and inclined to glide silently up behind one like a menacing ball bearing.

"What's *this*?" she barked, manifesting herself suddenly behind Jenny.

"Holy Mother of God!" Jenny whirled, eyes round and hand pressed to her chest. "Who in God's name are you?"

"This is Mrs. Figg," I said, feeling a surreal urge to laugh, despite—or maybe because of—recent events. "Lord John Grey's cook. And, Mrs. Figg, this is Mrs. Murray. My, um . . . my . . ."

"Your good-sister," Jenny said firmly. She raised one black eyebrow. "If ye'll have me still?" Her look was straight and open, and the urge to laugh changed abruptly into an equally strong urge to burst into tears. Of all the unlikely sources of succor I could have imagined . . . I took a deep breath and put out my hand.

"I'll have you." We hadn't parted on good terms in Scotland, but I had loved her very much, once, and wasn't about to pass up any opportunity to mend things.

Her small firm fingers wove through mine, squeezed hard, and, as simply as that, it was done. No need for apologies or spoken forgiveness. She'd never had to wear the mask that Jamie did. What she thought and felt was there in her eyes, those slanted blue cat eyes she shared with her brother. She knew the truth now of what I was, and she knew I loved—and always had loved—her brother with all my heart and soul—despite the minor complications of my being presently married to someone else.

She heaved a sigh, eyes closing for an instant, then opened them and smiled at me, mouth trembling only a little.

"Well, fine and dandy," said Mrs. Figg shortly. She narrowed her eyes and rotated smoothly on her axis, taking in the panorama of destruction. The railing at the top of the stair had been ripped off, and cracked banisters, dented walls, and bloody smudges marked the path of William's descent. Shattered crystals from the chandelier littered the floor, glinting festively in the light that poured through the open front door, the door itself cracked through and hanging drunkenly from one hinge.

"*Merde* on toast," Mrs. Figg murmured. She turned abruptly to me, her small black-currant eyes still narrowed. "Where's his lordship?"

"Ah," I said. This was going to be rather sticky, I saw. While deeply disapproving of most people, Mrs. Figg was devoted to John. She wasn't going to be at all pleased to hear that he'd been abducted by—

"For that matter, where's my brother?" Jenny inquired, glancing round as though expecting Jamie to appear suddenly out from under the settee.

"Oh," I said. "Hmm. Well . . ." Possibly worse than sticky. Because . . .

"And where's my Sweet William?" Mrs. Figg demanded, sniffing the air. "He's been here; I smell that stinky cologne he puts on his linen." She nudged a dislodged chunk of plaster disapprovingly with the toe of her shoe.

I took another long, deep breath and a tight grip on what remained of my sanity.

"Mrs. Figg," I said, "perhaps you would be so kind as to make us all a cup of tea?"

WE SAT IN the parlor, while Mrs. Figg came and went to the cookhouse, keeping an eye on her terrapin stew.

"You don't want to scorch turtle, no, you don't," she said severely to us, setting down the teapot in its padded yellow cozy on her return. "Not with so much sherry as his lordship likes in it. Almost a full bottle—terrible waste of good liquor, that would be."

My insides turned over promptly. Turtle soup—with a lot of sherry—had certain strong and private associations for me, these being connected with Jamie, feverish delirium, and the way in which a heaving ship assists sexual intercourse. Contemplation of which would *not* assist the impending discussion in the slightest. I rubbed a finger between my brows, in hopes of dispelling the buzzing cloud of confusion gathering there. The air in the house still felt electric.

"Speaking of sherry," I said, "or any other sort of strong spirits you might have convenient, Mrs. Figg . . ."

She looked thoughtfully at me, nodded, and reached for the decanter on the sideboard.

"Brandy is stronger," she said, and set it in front of me.

Jenny looked at me with the same thoughtfulness and, reaching out, poured a good-sized slug of the brandy into my cup, then a similar one into her own.

"Just in case," she said, raising one brow, and we drank for a few moments. I thought it might take something stronger than brandy-laced tea to deal with the effect of recent events on my nerves—laudanum, say, or a large slug of straight Scotch whisky—but the tea undeniably helped, hot and aromatic, settling in a soft trickling warmth amidships.

"So, then. We're fettled, are we?" Jenny set down her own cup and looked expectant.

"It's a start." I took a deep breath and gave her a *précis* of the morning's events.

Jenny's eyes were disturbingly like Jamie's. She blinked at me once, then twice, and shook her head as though to clear it, accepting what I'd just told her.

"So Jamie's gone off wi' your Lord John, the British army is after them, the tall lad I met on the stoop wi' steam comin' out of his ears is Jamie's son—well, of course he is; a blind man could see that—and the town's aboil wi' British soldiers. Is that it, then?"

"He's not exactly *my* Lord John," I said. "But, yes, that's essentially the position. I take it Jamie told you about William, then?"

"Aye, he did." She grinned at me over the rim of her teacup. "I'm that happy for him. But what's troubling his lad, then? He looked like he wouldna give the road to a bear."

"What did you say?" Mrs. Figg's voice cut in abruptly. She set down the tray she had just brought in, the silver milk jug and sugar basin rattling like castanets. "William is *whose* son?"

I took a fortifying gulp of tea. Mrs. Figg did know that I'd been married to—and theoretically widowed from—one James Fraser. But that was all she knew.

"Well," I said, and paused to clear my throat. "The, um, tall gentleman with the red hair who was just here—you saw him?"

"I did." Mrs. Figg eyed me narrowly.

"Did you get a good look at him?"

"Didn't pay much heed to his face when he came to the door and asked where you were, but I saw his backside pretty plain when he pushed past me and ran up the stairs."

"Possibly the resemblance is less marked from that angle." I took another mouthful of tea. "Um . . . that gentleman is James Fraser, my . . . er . . . my—" "First husband" wasn't accurate, and neither was "last husband"—or even, unfortunately, "most recent husband." I settled for the simplest alternative. "My husband. And, er . . . William's father."

Mrs. Figg's mouth opened, soundless for an instant. She backed up slowly and sat down on a needlework ottoman with a soft *phumph.*

"William know that?" she asked, after a moment's contemplation.

"He does *now,*" I said, with a brief gesture toward the devastation in the stairwell, clearly visible through the door of the parlor where we were sitting.

"*Merde* on— I mean, Holy Lamb of God preserve us." Mrs. Figg's second husband was a Methodist preacher, and she strove to be a credit to him, but her first had been a French gambler. Her eyes fixed on me like gun sights.

"You his mother?"

I choked on my tea.

"No," I said, wiping my chin with a linen napkin. "It isn't quite *that* complicated." In fact, it was more so, but I wasn't going to explain just how Willie had come about, either to Mrs. Figg or to Jenny. Jamie had to have told Jenny who William's mother was, but I doubted that he'd told his sister that William's mother, Geneva Dunsany, had forced him into her bed by threatening Jenny's family. No man of spirit likes to admit that he's been effectively blackmailed by an eighteen-year-old girl.

"Lord John became William's legal guardian when William's grandfather died, and at that point, Lord John also married Lady Isobel Dunsany, Willie's mother's sister. She'd looked after Willie since his mother's death in childbirth, and she and Lord John were essentially Willie's parents since he was quite young. Isobel died when he was eleven or so."

Mrs. Figg took this explanation in stride but wasn't about to be distracted from the main point at issue.

"James Fraser," she said, tapping a couple of broad fingers on her knee and looking accusingly at Jenny. "How comes he not to be dead? News was he drowned." She cut her eyes at me. "I thought his lordship was like to throw himself in the harbor, too, when he heard it."

I closed my own eyes with a sudden shudder, the salt-cold horror of that news washing over me in a wave of memory. Even with Jamie's touch still joyful on my skin and the knowledge of him glowing in my heart, I relived the crushing pain of hearing that he was dead.

"Well, I can enlighten ye on that point, at least."

I opened my eyes to see Jenny drop a lump of sugar into her fresh tea and nod at Mrs. Figg. "We were to take passage on a ship called *Euterpe*—my brother and myself—out o' Brest. But the blackhearted thief of a captain sailed without us. Much good it did him," she added, frowning.

Much good, indeed. The *Euterpe* had sunk in a storm in the Atlantic, lost with all hands. As I—and John Grey—had been told.

"Jamie found us another ship, but it landed us in Virginia, and we'd to make our way up the coast, partly by wagon, partly by packet boat, keepin' out of the way of the soldiers. Those wee needles ye gave Jamie against the seasickness work a marvel," she added, turning approvingly to me. "He showed me how to put them in for him. But when we came to Philadelphia yesterday," she went on, returning to her tale, "we stole into the city by night, like a pair o' thieves, and made our way to Fergus's printshop. Lord, I thought my heart would stop a dozen times!"

She smiled at the memory, and I was struck by the change in her. The shadow of sorrow still lay on her face, and she was thin and worn by travel, but the terrible strain of her husband Ian's long dying had lifted. There was color in her cheeks again and a brightness in her eyes that I had not seen since I had first known her thirty years before. She had found her peace, I thought, and felt a thankfulness that eased my own soul.

". . . so Jamie taps on the door at the back, and there's no answer, though we can see the light of a fire comin' through the shutters. He knocks again, makin' a wee tune of it—" She rapped her knuckles lightly on the table, *bump-ba-da-bump-ba-da-bump-bump-bump,* and my heart turned over, recognizing the theme from *The Lone Ranger,* which Brianna had taught him.

"And after a moment," Jenny went on, "a woman's voice calls out fierce, 'Who's there?' And Jamie says in the *Gàidhlig,* 'It is your father, my daughter, and a cold, wet, and hungry man he is, too.' For it was rainin' hammer handles and pitchforks, and we were both soaked to the skin."

She rocked back a little, enjoying the telling.

"The door opens then, just a crack, and there's Marsali wi' a horse pistol in her hand, and her two wee lasses behind her, fierce as archangels, each with a billet of wood, ready to crack a thief across his shins. They see the firelight shine on Jamie's face then, and all three of them let out skellochs like to wake the dead and fall upon him and drag him inside and all talkin' at once and greetin', askin' was he a ghost and why was he not drowned, and that was the first we learned that the *Euterpe* had sunk." She crossed herself. "God rest them, poor souls," she said, shaking her head.

I crossed myself, too, and saw Mrs. Figg look sideways at me; she hadn't realized I was a Papist.

"I've come in, too, of course," Jenny went on, "but everyone's talkin' at once and rushin' to and fro in search of dry clothes and hot drinks and I'm just lookin' about the place, for I've never been inside a printshop before, and the smell of the ink and the paper and lead is a wonder to me, and, sudden-like, there's a tug at my skirt and this sweet-faced wee mannie says to me, 'And who are you, madame? Would you like some cider?'"

"Henri-Christian," I murmured, smiling at the thought of Marsali's youngest, and Jenny nodded.

" 'Why, I'm your grannie Janet, son,' says I, and his eyes go round, and he lets out a shriek and grabs me round the legs and gives me such a hug as to make me lose my balance and fall down on the settle. I've a bruise on my bum the size of your hand," she added out of the corner of her mouth to me.

I felt a small knot of tension that I hadn't realized was there relax. Jenny did of course know that Henri-Christian had been born a dwarf—but knowing and seeing are sometimes different things. Clearly they hadn't been, for Jenny.

Mrs. Figg had been following this account with interest, but maintained her reserve. At mention of the printshop, though, this reserve hardened a bit.

"These folk—Marsali is your daughter, then, ma'am?" I could tell what she was thinking. The entire town of Philadelphia knew that Jamie was a Rebel—and, by extension, so was I. It was the threat of my imminent arrest that had caused John to insist upon my marrying him in the wake of the tumult following Jamie's presumed death. The mention of printing in

British-occupied Philadelphia was bound to raise questions as to just *what* was being printed, and by whom.

"No, her husband is my brother's adopted son," Jenny explained. "But I raised Fergus from a wee lad myself, so he's my foster son, as well, by the Highland way of reckoning."

Mrs. Figg blinked. She had been gamely trying to keep the cast of characters in some sort of order to this point, but now gave it up with a shake of her head that made the pink ribbons on her cap wave like antennae.

"Well, where the devil—I mean, where on earth has your brother gone with his lordship?" she demanded. "To this print-shop, you think?"

Jenny and I exchanged glances.

"I doubt it," I said. "More likely he's gone outside the city, using John—er, his lordship, I mean—as a hostage to get past the pickets, if necessary. Probably he'll let him go as soon as they're far enough away for safety."

Mrs. Figg made a deep humming noise of disapproval.

"And maybe he'll make for Valley Forge and turn him over to the Rebels instead."

"Oh, I shouldna think so," Jenny said soothingly. "What would they want with him, after all?"

Mrs. Figg blinked again, taken aback at the notion that anyone might not value his lordship to the same degree that she did, but after a moment's lip-pursing allowed as this might be so.

"He wasn't in his uniform, was he, ma'am?" she asked me, brow furrowed. I shook my head. John didn't hold an active commission. He was a diplomat, though technically still lieutenant colonel of his brother's regiment, and therefore wore his uniform for purposes of ceremony or intimidation, but he was officially retired from the army, not a combatant, and in plain clothes he would be taken as citizen rather than soldier—thus of no particular interest to General Washington's troops at Valley Forge.

I didn't think Jamie was headed for Valley Forge in any case. I knew, with absolute certainty, that he would come back. Here. For me.

The thought bloomed low in my belly and spread upward in a wave of warmth that made me bury my nose in my teacup to hide the resulting flush.

Alive. I caressed the word, cradling it in the center of my heart. Jamie was alive. Glad as I was to see Jenny—and gladder still to see her extend an olive branch in my direction—I really wanted to go up to my room, close the door, and lean against the wall with my eyes shut tight, reliving the seconds after he'd entered the room, when he'd taken me in his arms and pressed me to the wall, kissing me, the simple, solid, warm fact of his presence so overwhelming that I might have collapsed onto the floor without that wall's support.

Alive, I repeated silently to myself. *He's alive.*

Nothing else mattered. Though I did wonder briefly what he'd done with John.

4

DON'T ASK QUESTIONS YOU DON'T WANT TO HEAR THE ANSWERS TO

In the woods, an hour's ride outside Philadelphia

JOHN GREY HAD BEEN quite resigned to dying. Had expected it from the moment that he'd blurted out, *"I have had carnal knowledge of your wife."* The only question in his mind had been whether Fraser would shoot him, stab him, or eviscerate him with his bare hands.

To have the injured husband regard him calmly and say merely, *"Oh? Why?"* was not merely unexpected but . . . infamous. Absolutely infamous.

"Why?" John Grey repeated, incredulous. "Did you say *'Why?'* "

"I did. And I should appreciate an answer."

Now that Grey had both eyes open, he could see that Fraser's outward calm was not quite so impervious as he'd first supposed. There was a pulse beating in Fraser's temple, and he'd shifted his weight a little, like a man might do in the vicinity of a tavern brawl: not quite ready to commit violence but readying himself to meet it. Perversely, Grey found this sight steadying.

"What do you bloody *mean,* 'Why'?" he said, suddenly irritated. "And why aren't you fucking dead?"

"I often wonder that myself," Fraser replied politely. "I take it ye thought I was?"

"Yes, and so did your wife! Do you have the faintest idea what the knowledge of your death *did* to her?"

The dark-blue eyes narrowed just a trifle.

"Are ye implying that the news of my death deranged her to such an extent that she lost her reason and took ye to her bed by force? Because," he went on, neatly cutting off Grey's heated reply, "unless I've been seriously misled regarding your own nature, it would take substantial force to compel ye to any such action. Or am I wrong?"

The eyes stayed narrow. Grey stared back at them. Then he closed his own eyes briefly and rubbed both hands hard over his face, like a man waking from a nightmare. He dropped his hands and opened his eyes again.

"You are not misled," he said, through clenched teeth. "And you *are* wrong."

Fraser's ruddy eyebrows shot up—in genuine astonishment, Grey thought.

"Ye went to her because—from *desire*?" His voice rose, too. "And she let ye? I dinna believe it."

The color was creeping up Fraser's tanned neck, vivid as a climbing rose. Grey had seen that happen before and decided recklessly that the best—the only—defense was to lose his own temper first. It was a relief.

"We thought you were *dead,* you bloody arsehole!" he said, furious. "Both of us! Dead! And we—we—took too much to drink one night—very much too much . . . We spoke of you . . . and . . . Damn you, neither one of us was making love to the other—we were both fucking *you*!"

Fraser's face went abruptly blank and his jaw dropped.

Grey enjoyed one split second of satisfaction at the sight, before a massive fist came up hard beneath his ribs and he hurtled backward, staggered a few steps farther, and fell. He lay in the leaves, completely winded, mouth opening and closing like an automaton's.

All right, then, he thought dimly. *Bare hands it is.*

The hands wrapped themselves in his shirt and jerked him to his feet. He managed to stand, and a wisp of air seeped into his lungs. Fraser's face was an inch from his. Fraser was in fact so close that Grey couldn't see the man's expression—only a close-up view of two bloodshot blue eyes, both of them berserk. That was enough. He felt quite calm now. It wouldn't take long.

"You tell me exactly what happened, ye filthy wee pervert," Fraser whispered, his breath hot on Grey's face and smelling of ale. He shook Grey slightly. "Every word. Every motion. *Everything.*"

Grey got just enough breath to answer.

"No," he said defiantly. "Go ahead and kill me."

FRASER SHOOK HIM violently, so that his teeth clacked painfully together and he bit his tongue. He made a strangled noise at this, and a blow he hadn't seen coming struck him in the left eye. He fell down again, his head exploding with fractured color and black dots, the smell of leaf mold pungent in his nose. Fraser yanked him up and set him on his feet once more, but then paused, presumably deciding how best to continue the process of vivisection.

What with the blood pounding in his ears and the rasp of Fraser's breath, Grey hadn't heard anything, but when he cautiously opened his good eye to see where the next blow was coming from, he saw the man. A rough-looking dirty thug, in a fringed hunting shirt, gawping stupidly from under a tree.

"Jethro!" the man bellowed, taking a tighter hold on the gun he carried.

A number of men came out of the bushes. One or two had the rudiments of a uniform, but most of them were dressed in homespun, though with the addition of the bizarre "liberty" caps, tight-knitted woolen affairs that fitted over the head and ears, which through John's watering eye gave the men the bluntly menacing aspect of animated bombshells.

The wives who had presumably made these garments had knitted such mottoes as LIBERTY or FREEDOM into the bands, though one bloodthirsty abigail had knitted the adjuration KILL! into her husband's hat. The husband in question was, Grey noted, a small and weedy specimen wearing spectacles with one shattered lens.

Fraser had stopped at the sound of the men's approach and now rounded on them like a bear brought to bay by hounds. The hounds stopped abruptly, at a safe distance.

Grey pressed a hand over his liver, which he thought had likely been ruptured, and panted. He was going to need what breath he could get.

"Who're you?" one of the men demanded, jabbing pugnaciously at Jamie with the end of a long stick.

"Colonel James Fraser, Morgan's Rifles," Fraser replied coldly, ignoring the stick. "And you?"

The man appeared somewhat disconcerted but covered it with bluster.

"Corporal Jethro Woodbine, Dunning's Rangers," he said, very gruff. He jerked his head at his companions, who at once spread out in a businesslike way, surrounding the clearing. "Who's your prisoner, then?"

Grey felt his stomach tighten, which, given the condition of his liver, hurt. He replied through clenched teeth, not waiting for Jamie.

"I am Lord John Grey. If it's any business of yours." His mind was hopping like a flea, trying to calculate whether his chances of survival were better with Jamie Fraser or with this gang of yahoos. A few moments before, he had been resigned to the idea of death at Jamie's hands, but, like many ideas, that one was more appealing in concept than in execution.

The revelation of his identity seemed to confuse the men, who squinted and murmured, glancing at him dubiously.

"He ain't got a uniform on," one observed to another, *sotto voce.* "Be he a soldier at all? We got no business with him if he ain't, do we?"

"Yes, we do," Woodbine declared, regaining some of his

self-confidence. "And if Colonel Fraser's taken him prisoner, I reckon he has reason?" His voice went up, reluctantly questioning. Jamie made no reply, his eyes fixed on Grey.

"He's a soldier." Heads swung round to see who had spoken. It was the small man with the shattered spectacles, who had adjusted these with one hand, the better to peer at Grey through his remaining lens. A watery blue eye inspected Grey, then the man nodded, more certain.

"He's a soldier," the man repeated. "I saw him in Philadelphia, sittin' on the porch of a house on Chestnut Street in his uniform, large as life. He's an officer," he added unnecessarily.

"He is not a soldier," Fraser said, and turned his head to fix the spectacled man with a firm eye.

"Saw him," muttered the man. "Plain as day. Had gold braid," he murmured almost inaudibly, dropping his eyes.

"Huh." Jethro Woodbine approached Grey, examining him carefully. "Well, you got anything to say for yourself, Lord Grey?"

"Lord John," Grey said crossly, and brushed a fragment of crushed leaf off his tongue. "I am not a peer; my elder brother is. Grey is my family name. As for being a soldier, I have been. I still bear rank within my regiment, but my commission is not active. Is that sufficient, or do you want to know what I had for breakfast this morning?"

He was purposely antagonizing them, some part of him having decided that he would rather go with Woodbine and bear the inspection of the Continentals than remain here to face the further inspections of Jamie Fraser. Fraser was regarding him through narrowed eyes. He fought the urge to look away.

It's the truth, he thought defiantly. *What I told you is the truth. And now you know it.*

Yes, said Fraser's black gaze. *You think I will live quietly with it?*

"He is not a soldier," Fraser repeated, turning his back deliberately on Grey, switching his attention to Woodbine. "He is my prisoner because I wished to question him."

"About what?"

"That is not your concern, Mr. Woodbine," Jamie said, deep voice soft but edged with steel. Jethro Woodbine, though, was nobody's fool and meant to make that clear.

"I'll be judge of what's my business. Sir," he added, with a notable pause. "How do we know you're who you say you are, eh? You aren't in uniform. Any of you fellows know this man?"

The fellows, thus addressed, looked surprised. They looked uncertainly at one another; one or two heads shook in the negative.

"Well, then," said Woodbine, emboldened. "If you can't prove who you are, then I think we'll take this man back to camp for questioning." He smiled unpleasantly, another thought having evidently occurred to him. "Think we ought to take you, too?"

Fraser stood quite still for a moment, breathing slowly and regarding Woodbine as a tiger might regard a hedgehog: yes, he could eat it, but would the inconvenience of swallowing be worth it?

"Take him, then," he said abruptly, stepping back from Grey. "I have business elsewhere."

Woodbine had been expecting argument; he blinked, disconcerted, and half-raised his stick, but said nothing as Fraser stalked toward the far edge of the clearing. Just under the trees, Fraser turned and gave Grey a flat, dark look.

"We are not finished, sir," he said.

Grey pulled himself upright, disregarding both the pain in his liver and the tears leaking from his damaged eye.

"At your service, sir," he snapped. Fraser glared at him and moved into the flickering green shadows, completely ignoring Woodbine and his men. One or two of them glanced at the corporal, whose face showed his indecision. Grey didn't share it. Just before Fraser's tall silhouette vanished for good, he cupped his hands to his mouth.

"I'm not bloody sorry!" he bellowed.

5

THE PASSIONS OF YOUNG MEN

WHILE FASCINATED to hear about William and the dramatic circumstances under which he had just discovered his paternity, Jenny's true concern was for another young man.

"D'ye ken where Young Ian is?" she asked eagerly. "And did he find his young woman, the Quaker lassie he told his da about?"

I relaxed a little at this; Young Ian and Rachel Hunter were—thank God—*not* on the list of fraught situations. At least not for the moment.

"He did," I said, smiling. "As for where he is . . . I haven't seen him for several days, but he's often gone for longer. He scouts for the Continental army now and then, though since they've been in their winter quarters at Valley Forge for so long, there's been less need for scouting. He spends quite a bit of time there, though, because Rachel does."

Jenny blinked at that.

"She does? Why? Do Quakers not mislike wars and such?"

"Well, more or less. But her brother, Denzell, is an army surgeon—though he's a real physician, not the usual horse-leech or quack-salver the army usually gets—and he's been at Valley Forge since last November. Rachel comes and goes to Philadelphia—she can pass through the pickets, so she carries back food and supplies—but she works with Denny, so she's out there, helping with patients, much more often than she is here."

"Tell me about her," Jenny said, leaning forward intently. "Is she a good lass? And d'ye think she loves Young Ian? From what Ian told me, the lad's desperate in love with her but hadn't spoken to her yet, not knowing how she'd take it—he wasna sure she could deal with him being . . . what he is." Her quick gesture encompassed Young Ian's history and character, from Highland lad to Mohawk warrior. "God kens weel he'll never make a decent Quaker, and I expect Young Ian kens that, too."

I laughed at the thought, though in fact the issue might be serious; I didn't know what a Quaker meeting might think of such a match, but I rather thought they might view the prospect with alarm. I knew nothing about Quaker marriage, though.

"She's a very good girl," I assured Jenny. "Extremely sensible, very capable—and plainly in love with Ian, though I don't think she's told him so, either."

"Ah. D'ye ken her parents?"

"No, they both died when she was a child. She was mostly raised by a Quaker widow and then came to keep house for her brother when she was sixteen or so."

"That the little Quaker girl?" Mrs. Figg had come in with a vase of summer roses, smelling of myrrh and sugar. Jenny inhaled strongly and sat up straight. "Mercy Woodcock thinks the world of her. She comes by Mercy's house every time she's in town, to visit that young man."

"Young man?" Jenny asked, dark brows drawing together.

"William's cousin Henry," I hastened to explain. "Denzell and I carried out a very serious operation on him during the winter. Rachel knows both William and Henry and is very kind about visiting to see how Henry is. Mrs. Woodcock is his landlady."

It occurred to me that I had meant to go check on Henry today myself. There were rumors of a British withdrawal from the city, and I needed to see whether he was fit enough yet to travel. He was doing well when I'd stopped by a week before but at that point had been able to walk only a few steps, leaning on Mercy Woodcock's arm.

And what about Mercy Woodcock? I wondered, with a small jolt at the pit of the stomach. It was clear to me, as it was to John, that there was a serious—and deepening—affection between the free black woman and her aristocratic young lodger. I had met Mercy's husband, very badly wounded, during the exodus from Fort Ticonderoga a year before—and, lacking any communication from or about him, thought it very likely that he had died after being taken prisoner by the British.

Still, the possibility of Walter Woodcock returning miraculously from the dead—people *did,* after all, and a fresh bubble of joy rose under my heart at the thought—was the least of the matter. I couldn't imagine that John's brother, the very firm-minded Duke of Pardloe, would be delighted at hearing that his youngest son meant to marry the widow of a carpenter, whatever her color.

And then there was his daughter, Dottie, speaking of Quakers: she was betrothed to Denzell Hunter, and I did wonder what the duke would think of that. John, who liked a wager, had given me no better than even odds between Dottie and her father.

I shook my head, dismissing the dozen things I could do nothing about. During this minor reverie, Jenny and Mrs. Figg appeared to have been discussing William and his abrupt departure from the scene.

"Where would *he* go to, I wonder?" Mrs. Figg looked worriedly toward the wall of the stairwell, pocked with blood-smeared dents left by William's fist.

"Gone to find a bottle, a fight, or a woman," said Jenny, with the authority of a wife, a sister, and the mother of sons. "Maybe all three."

Elfreth's Alley

IT WAS PAST midday, and the only voices in the house were the distant chitterings of women. No one was visible in the parlor as they passed, and no one appeared as the girl led William up a foot-marked staircase to her room. It gave him an odd feeling, as though he might be invisible. He found the notion a comfort; he couldn't bear himself.

She went in before him and threw open the shutters. He wanted to tell her to close them; he felt wretchedly exposed in the flood of sunlight. But it was summer; the room was hot and airless, and he was already sweating heavily. Air swirled in, heavy with the odor of tree sap and recent rain, and the sun glowed briefly on the smooth top of her head, like the gloss on a fresh conker. She turned and smiled at him.

"First things first," she announced briskly. "Throw off your coat and waistcoat before you suffocate." Not waiting to see whether he would take this suggestion, she turned to reach for the basin and ewer. She filled the basin and stepped back, motioning him toward the washstand, where a towel and a much-used sliver of soap stood on worn wood.

"I'll fetch us a drink, shall I?" And with that, she was gone, bare feet pattering busily down the stairs.

Mechanically, he began to undress. He blinked stupidly at the basin but then recalled that, in the better sort of house, sometimes a man was required to wash his parts first. He'd encountered the custom once before, but on that occasion the whore had performed the ablution for him—plying the soap to such effect that the first encounter had ended right there in the washbasin.

The memory made the blood flame up in his face again, and he ripped at his flies, popping off a button. He was still throbbing all over, but the sensation was becoming more centralized.

His hands were unsteady, and he cursed under his breath, reminded by the broken skin on his knuckles of his unceremonious exit from his father's—no, *not* his bloody father's house. Lord John's.

"You bloody *bastard*!" he said under his breath. "You knew, you knew all along!" That infuriated him almost more than the horrifying revelation of his own paternity. His stepfather, whom he'd loved, whom he'd trusted more than anyone on earth—Lord John bloody Grey—had lied to him his whole life!

Everyone had lied to him.

Everyone.

He felt suddenly as though he'd broken through a crust of frozen snow and plunged straight down into an unsuspected river beneath. Swept away into black breathlessness beneath the ice, helpless, voiceless, a feral chill clawing at his heart.

There was a small sound behind him and he whirled by instinct, aware only when he saw the young whore's appalled face that he was weeping savagely, tears running down his own face, and his wet, half-hard cock flopping out of his breeches.

"Go away," he croaked, making a frantic effort to tuck himself in.

She didn't go away but came toward him, decanter in one hand and a pair of pewter cups in the other.

"Are you all right?" she asked, eyeing him sideways. "Here, let me pour you a drink. You can tell me all about it."

"No!"

She came on toward him, but more slowly. Through his swimming eyes, he saw the twitch of her mouth as she saw his cock.

"I meant the water for your poor hands," she said, clearly trying not to laugh. "I will say as you're a real gentleman, though."

"I'm not!"

She blinked.

"Is it an insult to call you a gentleman?"

Overcome with fury at the word, he lashed out blindly, knocking the decanter from her hand. It burst in a spray of glass and cheap wine, and she cried out as the red soaked through her petticoat.

"You *bastard*!" she shrieked, and, drawing back her arm, threw the cups at his head. She didn't hit him, and they clanged and rolled away across the floor. She was turning toward the door, crying out, "Ned! Ned!" when he lunged and caught her.

He only wanted to stop her shrieking, stop her bringing up whatever male enforcement the house employed. He got a hand on her mouth, yanking her back from the door, grappling one-handed to try to control her flailing arms.

"I'm sorry, I'm sorry!" he kept saying. "I didn't mean—I don't mean—oh, bloody *hell*!" She caught him abruptly in the nose with her elbow and he let go, backing away with a hand to his face, blood dripping through his fingers.

Her face was marked with red where he'd held her, and her eyes were wild. She backed away, scrubbing at her mouth with the back of her hand.

"Get . . . *out*!" she gasped.

He didn't need telling twice. He rushed past her, shouldered his way past a burly man charging up the stairs, and ran down the alley, realizing only when he reached the street that he was in his shirtsleeves, having left coat and waistcoat behind, and his breeches were undone.

"Ellesmere!" said an appalled voice nearby. He looked up in horror to find himself the cynosure of several English officers, including Alexander Lindsay.

"Good Christ, Ellesmere, what happened?" Sandy was by

way of being a friend and was already pulling a voluminous snowy handkerchief from his sleeve. He clapped this to William's nose, pinching his nostrils and insisting that he put his head back.

"Have you been set upon and robbed?" one of the others demanded. "God! This filthy place!"

He felt at once comforted by their company—and hideously embarrassed by it. He was not one of them, not any longer.

"Was it? Was it robbery?" another said, glaring round eagerly. "We'll find the bastards who did it, 'pon my honor we will! We'll get your property back and teach whoever did it a lesson!"

Blood was running down the back of his throat, harsh and iron-tasting, and he coughed but did his best to nod and shrug simultaneously. He *had* been robbed. But no one was ever going to give him back what he'd lost today.

6

UNDER MY PROTECTION

THE BELL OF THE Presbyterian church two blocks away rang for half-two, and my stomach echoed it, reminding me that—what with one thing and another—I hadn't had any tea yet.

Jenny had had a bite with Marsali and the children but declared herself equal to dealing with an egg, if there might be one, so I sent Mrs. Figg to see whether there might, and within twenty minutes we were wallowing—in a genteel fashion—in soft-boiled eggs, fried sardines, and—for lack of cake—flapjacks with butter and honey, which Jenny had never seen before but took to with the greatest alacrity.

"Look how it soaks up the sweetness!" she exclaimed, pressing the spongy little cake with a fork, then releasing it. "Nay like a bannock at all!" She glanced over her shoulder, then leaned toward me, lowering her voice. "D'ye think her in the kitchen might show me the way of it, if I asked?"

A diffident rapping on the damaged front door interrupted her, and as I turned to look, it was shoved open and a long shadow fell across the painted canvas rug, narrowly preceding its owner. A young British subaltern peered into the parlor, looking disconcerted by the wreckage in the foyer.

"Lieutentant Colonel Grey?" he asked hopefully, glancing back and forth between Jenny and me.

"His lordship isn't in just now," I said, attempting to sound self-possessed. I wondered just how many more times I might have to say that—and to whom.

"Oh." The young man looked further disconcerted. "Can you tell me where he is, mum? Colonel Graves sent a message earlier, asking Lieutenant Colonel Grey to attend General Clinton at once, and the general was, er . . . rather wondering why the lieutenant colonel hadn't arrived yet."

"Ah," I said, with a sidewise glance at Jenny. "Well. I'm afraid his lordship was rather urgently called away before he received the colonel's message." That must have been the paper John had received moments before Jamie's dramatic reappearance from a watery grave. He'd glanced at it but then shoved it unread into his breeches' pocket.

The soldier heaved a small sigh at this but was undaunted.

"Yes, mum. If you'll tell me where his lordship is, I'll go fetch him there. I really can't go back without him, you know." He gave me a woeful look, though with a touch of a charming smile. I smiled back, with a small touch of panic in my midsection.

"I'm so sorry, but I really don't *know* where he is right now," I said, standing up in hopes of driving him back toward the door.

"Well, mum, if you'll just tell me where he was heading, I shall go there and seek direction," he said, doggedly standing his ground.

"He didn't tell me." I took a step toward him, but he didn't retreat. This was escalating beyond absurdity into something more serious. I'd met General Clinton briefly at the Mischianza ball a few weeks ago—God, had it been only weeks? It seemed whole lifetimes—and while he'd been quite cordial to me, I didn't think he'd receive a *nolle prosequi* from me with any sort of complaisance. Generals tended to think highly of their own consequence.

"You know, his lordship doesn't hold an active commission," I said, in the faint hope of putting the young man off. He looked surprised.

"Yes, he does, mum. The colonel sent notice of it with the message this morning."

"What? He can't do that—er, can he?" I asked, a sudden dread creeping up my backbone.

"Do what, mum?"

"Just—just tell his lordship that his commission is active?"

"Oh, no, mum," he assured me. "The colonel of Lieutenant Colonel Grey's regiment re-called him. The Duke of Pardloe."

"Jesus H. Roosevelt Christ," I said, sitting down. Jenny snatched up her napkin to muffle what was plainly a laugh; it had been twenty-five years since she'd heard me say that. I gave her a look, but this was no time to be picking up the threads.

"All right," I said, turning to face the young man again and taking a deep breath. "I'd better go with you to see the general." I got to my feet again and only at this point realized that, having been surprised whilst changing, I was still wearing nothing but my shift and dressing gown.

"I'll help ye dress," Jenny said, standing up hurriedly. She gave the soldier a charming smile and gestured at the table, now strewn with toast, marmalade, and a steaming dish of kippers. "Have a bite while ye wait, lad. No point wasting good food."

JENNY POKED HER head out into the corridor and listened, but the faint sound of a fork on china and Mrs. Figg's voice from below indicated that the soldier had accepted her suggestion. She quietly closed the door.

"I'll go with ye," she said. "The town's full of soldiers; ye shouldna go out by yourself."

"I'll be—" I began, but then stopped, unsure. Most of the British officers in Philadelphia knew me as Lady John Grey, but that didn't mean that rank-and-file soldiers shared either that knowledge or the sense of respect that it normally engendered. I also felt like an imposter, but that was rather beside the point; it didn't show.

"Thank you," I said abruptly. "I'd be glad of your company." Unsure as I felt about everything save my conviction that Jamie was coming, I *was* glad of a little moral support—though I wondered whether I might need to warn Jenny of the need for circumspection when I talked to General Clinton.

"I shallna say a word myself," she assured me, grunting slightly as she pulled my laces tight. "D'ye think ye should tell him what's happened to Lord John?"

"No, I definitely don't," I said, exhaling forcefully. "That's . . . tight enough."

"Mmm." She was already deep in the armoire, picking through my gowns. "What about this one? It's got a deep décolletage, and your bosom's still verra good."

"I'm not meaning to seduce the man!"

"Oh, yes, ye are," she said matter-of-factly. "Or at least distract him. If ye're no going to tell him the truth, I mean." One sleek black eyebrow lifted. "If I were a British general and was told that my wee colonel had been abducted by a wicked great Hieland man, I think I might take it amiss."

I couldn't really contradict this piece of reasoning and, with a brief shrug, wriggled my way into the amber silk, which had cream-colored piping in the seams and ruched cream ribbons outlining the edge of the bodice.

"Oh, aye, that's good," Jenny said, tying my laces and stepping back to eye the effect with approval. "The ribbon's near the same color as your skin, so the neck looks even lower than it is."

"One would think you'd spent the last thirty years running a dressmaker's salon or a brothel, rather than a farm," I remarked, nervousness making me rather cross. She snorted.

"I've got three daughters, nine granddaughters, and there's sixteen nieces and great-nieces on Ian's sister's side. It's often much the same sort o' thing."

That made me laugh, and she grinned at me. Then I was blinking back tears, and so was she—the thought of Brianna and of Ian, our lost ones, coming suddenly—and then we were embracing, holding hard to each other to keep grief at bay.

"It's all right," she whispered, hugging me fiercely. "Ye've not lost your lass. She's still alive. And Ian's still wi' me. He'll never go from my side."

"I know," I said, choked. "I know." I let go and straightened up, smudging tears away with a finger, sniffing. "Have you got a handkerchief?"

She had one in her hand, in fact, but reached into the pocket at her waist and pulled out another, freshly washed and folded, which she handed me.

"I'm a grannie," she said, and blew her nose vigorously. "I've *always* got a spare hankie. Or three. Now, what about your hair? Ye canna be going out in the street like *that*."

By the time we'd got my hair done up in something resembling order, corralled in a snood and pinned respectably under a broad-brimmed woven straw hat, I'd come up with at least a rough notion of what to tell General Clinton. *Stick to the truth as far as possible.* That was the first principle of successful lying, though it had been some time since I'd been last obliged to employ it.

Well, then. A messenger had come for Lord John—one had—bringing a note—he did. I had no idea what was in the note—totally true. Lord John had then left with the messenger but without telling me where they were going. Also technically true, the only variance being that it had been a different messenger. No, I hadn't seen in which direction they had gone; no, I didn't know whether they had walked or ridden—Lord John's saddle horse was kept at Davison's livery on Fifth Street, two blocks away.

That sounded good. If General Clinton chose to make inquiries, I was reasonably sure he'd discover the horse still in its stall and thus conclude that John was somewhere in the city. He would also presumably lose interest in me as a source of information and send soldiers round to whatever haunts a man such as Lord John Grey might be supposed to be visiting.

And with any luck at all, by the time the general had exhausted such possibilities as Philadelphia offered, John would be back and could answer his own damned questions.

"And what about Jamie?" Jenny asked, her face showing small signs of anxiety. "He'll not come back into the city, surely?"

"I hope not." I could scarcely draw breath, and not merely

because of the tight lacing. I could feel the thudding of my heart against the placket of the stays.

Jenny gave me a long, considering look, eyes narrowed, and shook her head.

"No, ye don't," she said. "Ye think he'll come straight back here. For you. And ye're right. He will." She considered for a moment longer, her brow furrowed. "I'd best stay here," she said abruptly. "Should he come back whilst ye're wi' the general, he'll need to know what's the state o' things. And I dinna think I trust her in the kitchen not to stab him wi' a toasting fork, should he loom up in her doorway without notice."

I laughed, all too easily envisioning Mrs. Figg's response to a sudden Highlander in her midst.

"Besides," she added, "someone's got to clear up the mess, and I've had a good bit o' practice wi' *that,* too."

THE YOUNG SOLDIER greeted my belated reappearance with relief and, while not actually seizing my arm and hustling me down the pavement, offered me his own arm and then walked in such a fashion that I was urged into a near trot to keep up with him. It was not far to the mansion where Clinton had made his headquarters, but the day was warm and I arrived moist and gasping, with tendrils of hair escaping from under my straw hat and sticking to my neck and cheeks, and tendrils of sweat snaking their tickling slow way down inside my bodice.

My escort delivered me—with an audible sigh of relief—to another soldier in the spacious parquet-floored foyer, and I had a moment to shake the dust from my skirts, straighten and re-pin my hat, and blot my face and neck discreetly with a ladylike lace hankie. I was sufficiently taken up with this that it was a moment before I recognized the man sitting on one of the little gilded chairs on the other side of the foyer.

"Lady John," he said, standing up when he saw that I had noticed him. "Your servant, ma'am." He smiled slightly, though it lent no warmth at all to his eyes.

"Captain Richardson," I said flatly. "How nice." I didn't offer my hand and he didn't bow. There was no point in trying to pretend that we were anything but enemies—and not very cordial ones, either. He'd precipitated my marriage to Lord John by inquiring of John whether he, John, had any personal interest in me, as he, Richardson, was contemplating my immediate arrest on grounds of spying and of passing seditious materials. Both charges were quite true, and while John might not have known that, he took Richardson's word regarding his intentions, told Richardson politely that, no, there was no personal interest—also true as a statement, so far as it went—and two hours later I was standing in his parlor in a daze of shock and grief, mechanically saying, "I do," in response to questions that I neither heard nor comprehended.

I had barely heard Richardson's name at the time, let alone known him by sight. John had introduced me—with cold formality—when Richardson came up to us at the Mischianza, the huge ball thrown for the British officers by the Loyalist ladies of Philadelphia a month before. And only *then* had he told me about Richardson's threats, with a brief admonition to avoid the fellow.

"Are you waiting to see General Clinton?" I inquired politely. If he was, I had half a mind to execute a quiet sneak through the house and out of the back door whilst he was ensconced with the general.

"I am," he replied, adding graciously, "but you must certainly go before me, Lady John. My business will wait."

That had a mildly sinister ring to it, but I merely inclined my head politely, with a noncommittal "Hmm."

It was dawning upon me, like an incipient case of indigestion, that my position with regard to the British army in general, and Captain Richardson in particular, was on the verge of a marked reevaluation. Once it became common knowledge that Jamie wasn't dead—then I was no longer Lady John Grey. I was Mrs. James Fraser again, and while that was certainly cause for ecstatic rejoicing, it also removed any restraint on Captain Richardson's baser urges.

Before I could think of anything useful to say to the man, a lanky young lieutenant appeared to usher me into the general's presence. The drawing room, which had been converted to Clinton's main office, was now in a state of organized disarray, with packing crates lining one wall and bare flagstaffs tied together like a bundle of faggots, the military banners they usually sported being folded briskly into tidy packets by a corporal near the window. I'd heard—the whole city had probably heard—that the British army was withdrawing from Philadelphia. Evidently they were doing so with considerable dispatch.

There were several other soldiers carrying things in and out, but two men were seated, one on either side of the desk.

"Lady John," Clinton said, looking surprised but rising from his desk and coming to bow over my hand. "Your most obedient servant, ma'am."

"Good day to you, sir," I said. My heart had already been beating fast; it speeded up considerably at sight of the man who had risen from his chair and was standing just behind the general. He was in uniform and looked strikingly familiar, but I was sure I'd never seen him before. Who—?

"I am so sorry to have disturbed you, Lady John. I had hoped to surprise your husband," the general was saying. "But I understand that he is not at home?"

"Er . . . no. He's not." The stranger—an infantry colonel, though his uniform seemed to sport even more gold lace than the usual—raised a brow at this. The sudden familiarity of the gesture gave me a slight spinning sensation in the head.

"You're a relative of Lord John Grey's," I blurted, staring at him. He had to be. The man wore his own hair, as John did, though his was dark beneath its powder. The shape of his head—fine-boned and long-skulled—was John's, and so was the set of his shoulders. His features were much like John's, too, but his face was deeply weathered and gaunt, marked with harsh lines carved by long duty and the stress of command. I didn't need the uniform to tell me that he was a lifelong soldier.

He smiled, and his face was suddenly transformed. Apparently he had John's charm, too.

"You're most perceptive, madam," he said, and, stepping forward, smoothly took my limp hand away from the general and kissed it briefly in the continental manner before straightening and eyeing me with interest.

"General Clinton informs me that you are my brother's wife."

"Oh," I said, scrambling to recover my mental bearings. "Then you must be Hal! Er . . . I beg your pardon. I mean, you're the . . . I'm sorry, I know you're a duke, but I'm afraid I don't recall your title, Your Grace."

"Pardloe," he said, still holding my hand and smiling at me. "But my Christian name *is* Harold; do please use it if you like. Welcome to the family, my dear. I had no idea John had married. I understand the event was quite recent?" He spoke with great cordiality, but I was aware of the intense curiosity behind his good manners.

"Ah," I said noncommittally. "Yes, quite recent." It hadn't for an instant occurred to me to wonder whether John had written to tell his family about me, and if he had, they could barely have received the letter by now. I didn't even know who all the members of his family *were*—though I had heard about Hal, he being the father of John's nephew Henry, who—

"Oh, of course, you've come to see Henry!" I exclaimed. "He'll be so pleased to see you! He's doing very well," I assured him.

"I have already seen Henry," the duke assured me in turn. "He speaks with the greatest admiration of your skill in removing pieces of his intestine and reuniting the remnants. Though eager as I naturally was to see my son—and my daughter"—his lips compressed for a moment; apparently Dottie had informed her parents about her engagement—"and delighted as I shall be to meet my brother again, it is actually duty that called me to America. My regiment is newly landed in New York."

"Oh," I said. "Er . . . how nice." John plainly hadn't known that his brother, let alone his regiment, was coming. It occurred dimly to me that I ought to be asking questions and finding out what I could about the general's plans, but it didn't seem the time or place.

The general coughed politely.

"Lady John—do you happen to know the whereabouts of your husband at the moment?"

The shock of meeting Harold, Duke of Pardloe, had quite wiped the reason for my presence out of my mind, but this brought it back with a rush.

"No, I'm afraid I don't," I said, as calmly as possible. "I told your corporal. A messenger came a few hours ago, with a note, and Lord John went off with him. He didn't say where he was going, though."

The general's lips twitched.

"Actually," he said, still polite, "he didn't. Colonel Graves sent the messenger, with a note informing Lord John of his re-commission and directing him to come here at once. He didn't."

"Oh," I said, sounding as blank as I felt. Under the circumstances, it seemed all right to let that show, and I did. "Dear me. In that case . . . he did go off with *someone.*"

"But you don't know with whom?"

"I didn't see him go," I said, neatly avoiding the question. "I'm afraid he didn't leave word as to where he was bound."

Clinton raised a strongly marked black brow and glanced at Pardloe.

"I suppose in that case he will return shortly," the duke said with a shrug. "The matter isn't urgent, after all."

General Clinton looked as though he differed somewhat with this opinion but, with a brief glance at me, said nothing. He clearly had little time to waste, though, and, bowing politely, bade me good day.

I took my leave with alacrity, barely pausing to assure the duke that I was pleased to have met him and to ask where might his brother send word . . . ?

"I have rooms at the King's Arms," Pardloe said. "Shall I—"

"No, no," I said hurriedly, to forestall his offer to see me home. "It's quite all right. Thank you, sir." I bowed to the general, then to Hal, and headed for the door in a whirl of skirts—and emotions.

Captain Richardson was no longer in the foyer, but I hadn't time to wonder where he had gone. I gave the soldier at the door a quick nod and smile and then was out in the open air, breathing as though I'd just escaped from a bathysphere.

Now what? I wondered, swerving to avoid two little boys with a hoop, who were caroming down the street, bouncing off the legs of the soldiers carrying parcels and furniture to a large wagon. The boys must belong to one of Clinton's officers, since the soldiers were tolerating them.

John had spoken fairly often of his brother and had remarked upon Hal's tendency toward ruthless high-handedness. All the current situation needed was a nosey parker with a taste for authority mixing in. I wondered briefly whether William was on good terms with his uncle; if so, perhaps Hal could be diverted and put to good use in talking sense to—no, no, of course not. Hal mustn't know—yet at least—about

Jamie, and he couldn't exchange two words with Willie without finding out—if William *would* talk about it, but then—

"Lady John." A voice behind me stopped me in my tracks, only momentarily but long enough for the Duke of Pardloe to come up beside me. He took me by the arm, detaining me.

"You're a very bad liar," he remarked with interest. "What are you lying about, though, I wonder?"

"I do it better with a little warning," I snapped. "Though, as it happens, I'm *not* lying at the moment."

That made him laugh. He leaned closer, examining my face at close range. His eyes were pale blue, like John's, but the darkness of his brows and lashes gave them a particularly piercing quality.

"Perhaps not," he said, still looking amused. "But if you aren't lying, you aren't telling me everything you know, either."

"I'm not obliged to tell you *anything* I know," I said with dignity, trying to retrieve my arm. "Let go."

He did let go, reluctantly.

"I beg your pardon, Lady John."

"Certainly," I said shortly, and made to go round him. He moved smartly in front of me, blocking my way.

"I want to know where my brother is," he said.

"I should like to know that myself," I replied, trying to sidle past him.

"Where are you going, may I ask?"

"Home." It gave me an odd feeling, still, to call Lord John's house "home"—and yet I had no other. *Yes, you do,* a small, clear voice said in my heart. *You have Jamie.*

"Why are you smiling?" asked Pardloe, sounding startled.

"At the thought of getting home and taking off these shoes," I said, hastily erasing the smile. "They're killing me."

His mouth twitched a little.

"Allow me to offer you the use of my chair, Lady John."

"Oh, no, I really don't—" But he had taken a wooden whistle from his pocket and uttered a piercing blast on it that brought two squat, muscular men—who had to be brothers, such was their resemblance to each other—trotting round the corner, a sedan chair suspended on poles between them.

"No, no, this isn't necessary at all," I protested. "Besides,

John says you suffer from the gout; you'll need the chair yourself."

He didn't like that; his eyes narrowed and his lips compressed.

"I'll manage, madam," he said shortly, and, seizing me by the arm again, dragged me to the chair and pushed me inside, knocking my hat over my eyes as he did so. "The lady is under my protection. Take her to the King's Arms," he instructed Tweedledum and Tweedledee, shutting the door. And before I could say, "Off with his head!" we were jolting down the High Street at a terrific pace.

I seized the door handle, intending to leap out, even at the cost of cuts and bruises, but the bastard had put the locking pin through the outside handle, and I couldn't reach it from the inside. I shouted at the chairmen to stop, but they ignored me completely, pounding along the cobbles as though bringing the news from Aix to Ghent.

I sat back, panting and furious, and jerked the hat off. What did Pardloe think he was doing? From what John had said, and from other remarks made by the duke's children about their father, it was clear to me that he was used to getting his own way.

"Well, we'll bloody see about *that,*" I muttered, stabbing the long, pearl-headed hatpin through the hat brim. The snood that had contained my hair had come off with the hat; I crammed it inside and shook my loose hair out over my shoulders.

We turned in to Fourth Street, which was paved with brick rather than cobbles, and the jolting grew less. I was able to let go my grip on the seat and fumbled with the window. If I could get it open, I might be able to reach the locking pin, and even if the door flew open and decanted me into the street, it would put a stop to the duke's machinations.

The window worked on a sliding-panel arrangement but had no sort of latch by which to get a grip on it; the only way of opening it was by inserting the fingertips into a shallow groove at one side and pushing. I was grimly attempting to do this, in spite of the chair's renewed bucketing, when I heard the duke's voice choke and stop in the midst of some shouted direction to the chairmen.

"St . . . stop. I . . . can't . . ." His words trailed off, the chairmen faltered to a halt, and I pressed my face against the suddenly motionless window. The duke was standing in the middle of the street, a fist pressed into his waistcoat, struggling to breathe. His face was deeply flushed, but his lips were tinged with blue.

"Put me down and open this bloody door this instant!" I bellowed through the glass to one of the chairmen, who was glancing back over his shoulder, a look of concern on his face. They did, and I emerged from the chair in an explosion of skirts, stabbing the hatpin down into the placket of my stays as I did so. I might need it yet.

"Bloody sit down," I said, reaching Pardloe. He shook his head but let me lead him to the chair, where I forced him to sit, my feeling of satisfaction at this reversal of position somewhat tempered by the fear that he might just possibly be about to die.

My first thought—that he was having a heart attack—had vanished the moment I heard him breathe—or try to. The wheezing gasp of someone in the throes of an asthmatic attack was unmistakable, but I seized his wrist and checked his pulse just in case. Hammering but steady, and while he was sweating, it was the normal warm perspiration caused by hot weather rather than the sudden clammy exudation that often accompanied a myocardial infarction.

I touched his fist, still embedded in his midsection.

"Do you have pain here?"

He shook his head, coughed hard, and took his hand away.

"Need . . . pill . . . b . . ." he managed, and I saw that there was a small pocket in the waistcoat that he had been trying to reach into. I put in two fingers and pulled out a small enameled box, which proved to contain a tiny corked vial.

"What—never mind." I pulled the cork, sniffed, and wheezed myself as the sudden fumes of ammonia shot up my nose.

"No," I said definitely, putting the cork back in and shoving vial and box into my pocket. "That won't help. Purse your lips and blow out." His eyes bulged a bit, but he did it; I could feel the slight movement of air on my own perspiring face.

"Right. Now, relax, *don't* gasp for air, just let it come. Blow out, to the count of four. One . . . two . . . three . . . four. In for a count of two, same rhythm . . . yes. Blow out, count of four . . . let it come in, count of two . . . yes, good. Now, don't worry; you aren't going to suffocate, you can keep doing that all day." I smiled encouragingly at him, and he managed to nod. I straightened up and looked round; we were near Locust Street, and Peterman's ordinary was no more than a block away.

"You," I said to one of the chairmen, "run to the ordinary and fetch back a jug of strong coffee. He'll pay for it," I added, with a flip of the hand toward the duke.

We were beginning to draw a crowd. I kept a wary eye out; we were near enough to Dr. Hebdy's surgery that he might come out to see the trouble, and the very last thing I needed was that charlatan to materialize, fleam at the ready.

"You have asthma," I said, returning my attention to the duke. I knelt so that I could see into his face while I monitored his pulse. It was better, noticeably slower, but I thought I could feel the odd condition called "paradoxical pulse," a phenomenon you sometimes saw in asthmatics, wherein the heart rate speeded up during exhalation and dropped during inhalation. Not that I had been in any doubt. "Did you know that?"

He nodded, still pursing his lips and blowing.

"Yes," he managed briefly, before breathing in again.

"Do you see a doctor for it?" A nod. "And did he actually recommend *sal volatile* for it?" I gestured toward the vial in my pocket. He shook his head.

"For fain . . . ting," he managed. "All I . . . had."

"Right." I put a hand under his chin and tilted his head back, examining his pupils, which were quite normal. I could feel the spasm easing, and so could he; his shoulders were beginning to drop, and the blue tinge had faded from his lips. "You don't want to use it when you're having an asthma attack; the coughing and tearing will make matters worse by producing phlegm."

"Whatever are the idle lot of you doing, standing about? Go run and fetch the doctor, lad!" I heard a woman's sharp voice say in the crowd behind me. I grimaced, and the duke saw it; he raised his brows in question.

"You don't want *that* doctor, believe me." I stood up and faced the crowd, thinking.

"No, we don't need a doctor, thank you very much," I said,

as charmingly as possible. "He's just been overtaken by the indigestion—something he ate. He's quite all right now."

"He don't look that good to me, ma'am," said another voice, doubtful. "I think we best fetch the doctor."

"Let him die!" came a shout from the back of the gathering crowd. "Fucking lobster!"

An odd sort of shimmer ran through the crowd at this, and I felt a knot of dread form in my stomach. They hadn't been thinking of him as a British soldier, merely as a spectacle. But now . . .

"I'll get the doctor, Lady John!" To my horror, Mr. Caulfield, a prominent Tory, had forced his way to the front, being tolerably free with his gold-headed walking stick. "Get away, you lice!"

He bent to peer into the sedan chair, lifting his hat to Hal.

"Your servant, sir. Help will be here presently, be assured of that!"

I seized him by the sleeve. The crowd was, thank God, divided. While there were catcalls and insults directed at Pardloe and at me, there were dissenting voices, too, those of Loyalists (or perhaps merely the saner sorts who didn't think attacking a sick man in the street part of their political philosophy) chiming in, with reason, protests—and not a few loud insults of their own.

"No, no!" I said. "Let someone else go for the doctor, please. We daren't leave His Grace here without protection!"

"His Grace?" Caulfield blinked, and carefully unfolding his gold-rimmed *pince-nez* from a little case, put them on his nose and bent to peer into the chair at Pardloe, who gave him a small, dignified nod, though he kept on assiduously with his breathing exercise.

"The Duke of Pardloe," I said hastily, still keeping a grip of Mr. Caulfield's sleeve. "Your Grace, may I present Mr. Phineas Graham Caulfield?" I waved a vague hand between them, then, spotting the chairman coming back at the gallop with a jug, I sprinted toward him, hoping to reach him before he got within earshot of the crowd.

"Thank you," I said, panting as I snatched the jug from him. "We've got to get him away before the crowd turns nasty—nastier," I amended, hearing a sharp *crack!* as a thrown pebble bounced off the roof of the sedan chair. Mr. Caulfield ducked.

"Oy!" shouted the chairman, infuriated at this attack upon his livelihood. "Back off, you lot!" He started for the crowd, fists clenched, and I seized him by the coattails with my free hand.

"Get him—*and* your chair—away!" I said, as forcefully as possible. "Take him to—to—" Not the King's Arms; it was a known Loyalist stronghold and would merely inflame anyone who followed us. Neither did I want to be at the duke's mercy, once inside the place.

"Take us to Number Seventeen Chestnut Street!" I said hurriedly, and, digging one-handed in my pocket, grabbed a coin and thrust it into his hand. "Now!" He didn't pause for thought but took the coin and headed for the chair at the run, fists still clenched, and I trotted after him as fast as my red morocco heels would take me, clutching the coffee. His number was stitched into a band round his sleeve: THIRTY-NINE.

A shower of pebbles was rattling off the sedan chair's sides, and the second chairman—Number Forty—was batting at them as though they were a swarm of bees, shouting, "Fuck OFF!" at the crowd, in a businesslike if repetitious fashion. Mr. Caulfield was backing him up in more genteel fashion, shouting, "Away with you!" and "Leave off at once!" punctuated with pokes of his cane at the more daring children, who were darting forward to see the fun.

"Here," I gasped, leaning into the chair. Hal was still alive, still breathing. He raised one brow at me and nodded toward the crowd outside. I shook my head and thrust the coffee into his hands.

"Drink . . . that," I managed, "and keep breathing." Slamming the door of the chair, I dropped the locking pin into its slot with an instant's satisfaction and straightened up to find Fergus's eldest son, Germain, standing by my side.

"Have ye got a bit of trouble started again, *Grand-mère*?" he asked, unperturbed by the stones—now augmented with clumps of fresh manure—whizzing past our heads.

"You might say so, yes," I said. "Don't—"

But before I could speak further, he turned round and bellowed at the crowd, in a surprisingly loud voice, "THIS'S MY GRANNIE. You touch ONE HAIR on her head and—" Several people in the crowd laughed at this, and I put up a hand to my head. I'd completely forgotten the loss of my hat, and my hair was standing out in a mushroom-like cloud round my head—what wasn't sticking to my sweating face and neck. "And I'll do you BROWN!" Germain yelled. "Aye, I mean YOU, Shecky Loew! And you, too, Joe Grume!"

Two half-grown boys hesitated, clumps of filth in hand. Evidently they knew Germain.

"And my grannie'll tell your da what you've been a-doing, too!" That decided the boys, who stepped back a pace, dropping their clods of dirt and trying to look as though they had no idea where they had come from.

"Come on, *Grand-mère,*" Germain said, grabbing my hand. The chairmen, no slouches on the uptake, had already seized their poles and hoisted the chair. I'd never manage to keep up with them in the high-heeled shoes. As I was kicking them off, I saw plump Dr. Hebdy puffing down the street, in the wake of the hectoring woman who had suggested calling him and who was now sailing toward us on the breeze of her heroism, face set in triumph.

"Thank you, Mr. Caulfield," I said hurriedly, and, snatching up the shoes in one hand, followed the chair, unable to keep my skirts up off the grubby cobbles but not terribly concerned about that. Germain fell back a little, making threatening gestures to discourage pursuit, but I could tell from the sound of the crowd that their momentary hostility had turned to amusement, and though further catcalls followed us, no missiles came in their wake.

The chairmen slowed a little once we'd turned the corner, and I was able to make headway on the flat brick of Chestnut Street, coming up beside the chair. Hal was peering through the side window, looking considerably better. The coffee jug was on the seat beside him, evidently empty.

"Where are we . . . going, madam?" he shouted through the window when he saw me. So far as I could tell over the steady thump of the chairmen's shoes and through the glass of the window, he sounded much better, too.

"Don't worry, Your Grace," I shouted back, jogging along. "You're under my protection!"

7

THE UNINTENDED CONSEQUENCES OF ILL-CONSIDERED ACTIONS

JAMIE SHOVED THROUGH the brush, heedless of ripping brambles and slapping branches. Anything that got in his way could get out of it or be trampled.

He hesitated for no more than an instant when he reached the two horses, hobbled and grazing. He untied them both and, slapping the mare, sent her snorting into the brush. Even if no one made off with the extra horse before the militia let John Grey go, Jamie didn't mean to make it easy for the man to get back to Philadelphia. Whatever must be dealt with there would be done much more easily without the complications of his lordship's presence.

And what *would* be done? he wondered, nudging his heels into his horse's sides and reining its head round toward the road. He noticed with some surprise that his hands were shaking, and squeezed hard on the leather to make it stop.

The knuckles of his right hand throbbed, and a white stab of pain where his missing finger had been ran through his hand, making him hiss through his teeth.

"What the devil did ye *tell* me for, ye wee idiot?" he said under his breath, urging his horse up into a gallop. "What did ye *think* I'd do?"

Just what ye damn well did was the answer. John hadn't resisted, hadn't fought back. *"Go ahead and kill me,"* the wee bugger had said. A fresh spurt of rage curled Jamie's hands as he imagined all too well doing just that. Would he have gone ahead and done it, if that pissant Woodbine and his militia hadn't turned up?

No. No, he wouldn't. Even as he longed momentarily to go back and choke the life out of Grey, he was beginning to answer his own question, reason fighting its way through the haze of fury. Why *had* Grey told him? There was the obvious—the reason he'd hit the man by sheer reflex, the reason he was shaking now. Because Grey had told him the truth.

"We were both fucking you." He breathed hard and deep, fast enough to make him giddy, but it stopped the shaking and he slowed a little; his horse's ears were laid back, twitching in agitation.

"It's all right, *a bhalaich,*" he said, still breathing hard but slower now. "It's all right."

He thought for a moment that he might vomit, but managed not to, and settled back in the saddle, steadier.

He could still touch it, that raw place Jack Randall had left on his soul. He'd thought it so well scarred over that he was safe now, but, no, bloody John Grey had torn it open with five words. "We were both fucking you." And he couldn't blame him for it—oughtn't to, anyway, he thought, reason doggedly fighting back the fury, though he knew only too well how weak a weapon reason was against that specter. Grey couldn't have known what those words had done to him.

Reason had its uses, though. It was reason that reminded him of the second blow. The first had been blind reflex; the second wasn't. Thought of it brought anger, too, and pain, but of a different sort.

"I have had carnal knowledge of your wife."

"You bugger," he whispered, clutching the reins with a reflexive violence that made the horse jerk its head, startled. "Why? Why did ye tell me that, ye bugger!"

And the second answer came belatedly, but as clearly as the first: *Because she'd tell me, the minute she had a chance. And he kent that fine. He thought if I'd do violence when I heard, best I do it to him.*

Aye, she would have told him. He swallowed. *And she* will *tell me.* What might he say—or do—when she did?

He was trembling again and had slowed inadvertently, so the horse was nearly at a walk, head turning from side to side as it snuffed the air.

It's nay her fault. I know *that. It's nay her fault.* They'd thought him dead. He knew what that abyss looked like; he'd lived there for a long while. And he understood what desperation and strong drink could do. But the vision—or the lack of one . . . How did it happen? Where? Knowing it had happened was bad enough; not knowing the how and the why of it from her was almost unbearable.

The horse had stopped; the reins hung slack. Jamie was sitting in the middle of the road, eyes closed, just breathing, trying not to imagine, trying to pray.

Reason had limits; prayer didn't. It took a little while for his mind to relax its grip, its wicked curiosity, its lust to *know*. But, after a bit, he felt he could go on and gathered up the reins again.

All that could wait. But he needed to see Claire before he did anything else. Just now he had no idea what he would say—or do—when he saw her, but he needed to see her, with the same sort of need that a man might feel who'd been cast away at sea, marooned without food or water for weeks on end.

JOHN GREY'S BLOOD was thrumming in his ears so loudly that he barely heard the discussion among his captors, who—having taken the elementary precautions of searching him and tying his hands together in front of him—had gathered into a knot a few yards away and were heatedly hissing at one another like geese in a barnyard, casting occasional hostile glares in his direction.

He didn't care. He couldn't see out of his left eye and he was by now quite certain that his liver was ruptured, but he didn't care about that, either. He'd told Jamie Fraser the truth—the *whole* bloody truth—and felt the same fierce constellation of feelings that attends victory in battle: the bone-deep relief of being alive, the giddy surge of emotion that carries you on a wave much like drunkenness, then ebbs and leaves you staggering light-headed on the beach—and an absolute inability to count the cost 'til later.

His knees experienced much the same post-battle sensations and gave way. He sat down unceremoniously in the leaves and closed his good eye.

After a short interval in which he was aware of nothing much beyond the gradual slowing of his heart, the thrumming noise in his ears began to abate, and he noticed that someone was calling his name.

"Lord Grey!" the voice said again, louder, and close enough that he felt a warmly fetid gust of tobacco-laden breath on his face.

"My name is not Lord Grey," he said, rather crossly, opening his eye. "I told you."

"You said you were Lord John Grey," his interlocutor said, frowning through a mat of grizzled facial hair. It was the large man in the filthy hunting shirt who had first discovered him with Fraser.

"I am. If you bloody have to talk to me, call me 'my lord,' or just 'sir,' if you like. What do you want?"

The man reared back a little, looking indignant.

"Well, since you ask . . . *sir,* first off, we want to know if this elder brother of yours is Major General Charles Grey."

"No."

"No?" The man's unkempt eyebrows drew together. "Do you *know* Major General Charles Grey? Is he kin to you?"

"Yes, he is. He's . . ." Grey tried to calculate the precise degree, but gave it up and flapped a hand. "Cousin of some sort."

There was a satisfied rumble from the faces now peering down at him. The man called Woodbine squatted down next to him, a square of folded paper in his hand.

"Lord John," he said, more or less politely. "You said that you don't hold an active commission in His Majesty's army at present?"

"That's correct." Grey fought back a sudden unexpected urge to yawn. The excitement in his blood had died away now and he wanted to lie down.

"Then would you care to explain these documents, my lord? We found them in your breeches." He unfolded the papers carefully and held them under Grey's nose.

John peered at them with his working eye. The note on top was from General Clinton's adjutant: a brief request for Grey to attend upon the general at his earliest convenience. Yes, he'd seen that, though he'd barely glanced at it before the cataclysmic arrival of Jamie Fraser, risen from the dead, had driven it from his mind. Despite what had occurred in the meantime, he couldn't help smiling. *Alive.* The bloody man was *alive*!

Then Woodbine took the note away, revealing the paper beneath: the document that had come attached to Clinton's note. It was a small piece of paper, bearing a red wax seal and instantly identifiable; it was an officer's warrant, his proof of commission, to be carried on his person at all times. Grey blinked at it in simple disbelief, the spidery clerk's writing wavering before his eyes. But written at the bottom, below the King's signature, was another, this one executed in a bold, black, all-too-recognizable scrawl.

"Hal!" he exclaimed. "You *bastard*!"

"TOLD YOU HE was a soldier," the small man with the cracked spectacles said, eyeing Grey from under the edge of his knitted KILL! hat with an avidity that Grey found very objectionable. "Not just a soldier, neither; he's a spy! Why, we could hang him out o' hand, this very minute!"

There was an outburst of noticeable enthusiasm for this course of action, quelled with some difficulty by Corporal Woodbine, who stood up and shouted louder than the proponents of immediate execution, until those espousing it reluctantly fell back, muttering. Grey sat clutching the commission crumpled in his bound hands, heart hammering.

They bloody could hang him. Howe had done just that to a Continental captain named Hale, not two years before, when Hale was caught gathering intelligence while dressed as a civilian, and the Rebels would like nothing better than a chance to retaliate. William had been present, both at Hale's arrest and his execution, and had given Grey a brief account of the matter, shocking in its starkness.

William. Jesus, William! Caught up in the immediacy of the situation, Grey had had barely a thought to spare for his son. He and Fraser had absquatulated onto the roof and down a drainpipe, leaving William, clearly reeling with the shock of revelation, alone in the upstairs hallway.

No. No, not alone. Claire had been there, and the thought of her steadied him a bit. She would have been able to talk to

Willie, calm him, explain . . . well, possibly not explain, and possibly not calm, either—but at least if Grey was hanged in the next few minutes, William wouldn't be left to face things entirely alone.

"We're taking him back to camp," Woodbine was saying doggedly, not for the first time. "What good would it do to hang him here?"

"One less redcoat? Seems like a good thing to *me*!" riposted the burly thug in the hunting shirt.

"Now, Gershon, I'm not saying as how we shouldn't hang him. I said, not here and now." Woodbine, musket held in both hands, looked slowly round the circle of men, fixing each one with his gaze. "Not here, not now," he repeated. Grey admired Woodbine's force of character and narrowly kept himself from nodding agreement.

"We're taking him back to camp. You all heard what he said; Major General Charles Grey's kin to him. Might be as Colonel Smith will want to hang him in camp—or might even be as he'll want to send this man to General Wayne. Remember Paoli!"

"Remember Paoli!" Ragged cries echoed the call, and Grey rubbed at his swollen eye with his sleeve—tears were leaking from it and irritating his face. Paoli? What the devil was Paoli? And what had it to do with whether, when, or how he should be hanged? He decided not to ask at just this moment and, when they hauled him to his feet, went along with them without complaint.

8

HOMO EST OBLIGAMUS AEROBE

("MAN IS AN OBLIGATE AEROBE")

—HIPPOCRATES

THE DUKE'S FACE WAS dangerously flushed when Number Thirty-Nine ceremoniously opened the sedan chair's door, and not, I thought, from the heat.

"You wanted to see your brother, did you not?" I inquired, before he could gather enough breath to say any of the things on his mind. I gestured toward the house. "This is his house." The fact that John was not presently *in* the house could wait.

He gave me a marked look, but he was still short of breath and wisely saved it, irritably waving off Number Forty's helping hand as he struggled out of the sedan chair. He did pay the chairmen—rather fortunate, as I hadn't any more money with me—and, wheezing, bowed and offered me his arm. I took it, not wanting him to fall on his face in the front garden. Germain, who had kept up with the chair without noticeable effort, followed at a tactful distance.

Mrs. Figg was standing in the front doorway, watching our approach with interest. The broken door was now lying on a pair of trestles next to a camellia bush, having been removed from its hinges, and was presumably awaiting some sort of professional attention.

"May I present Mrs. Mortimer Figg, Your Grace?" I said politely, with a nod in her direction. "Mrs. Figg is his lordship's cook and housekeeper. Mrs. Figg, this is His Grace, the Duke of Pardloe. Lord John's brother."

I saw her lips form the words "*Merde* on toast," but fortunately without sound. She moved nimbly down the steps despite her bulk and took Hal by the other arm, shoring him up, as he was beginning to turn blue again.

"Purse your lips and blow," I said shortly. "Now!" He made an ugly choking noise but did start blowing, though making evil grimaces in my direction.

"What in the name of the everlasting Holy Ghost did you do to him?" Mrs. Figg asked me accusingly. "Sounds like he's about to die."

"Saved his life, to start with," I snapped. "Ups-a-daisy, Your Grace!" and between us we hoicked him up the steps. "Then I saved him from being stoned and beaten by a mob—with Germain's invaluable help," I added, glancing back at Germain, who grinned hugely. I was also in the act of abducting him, but I thought we needn't go into that.

"And I'm about to save his life again, I think," I said, pausing on the porch to pant for a moment myself. "Have we a bedroom we can put him in? William's, perhaps?"

"Will—" the duke began, but then started to cough spasmodically, going a nasty shade of puce. "Wh—wh—"

"Oh, I was forgetting," I said. "Of course, William's your nephew, isn't he? He's not here just now." I looked narrowly at Mrs. Figg, who snorted briefly but said nothing. "Blow, Your Grace."

Inside, I saw that some progress had been made toward restoring order. The debris had been swept into a neat pile by the open doorway, and Jenny Murray was sitting on an ottoman beside it, picking unbroken crystals from the fallen chandelier out of the rubbish and dropping them into a bowl. She lifted an eyebrow at me but rose unhurriedly to her feet, putting the bowl aside.

"What d'ye need, Claire?" she said.

"Boiling water," I said, grunting slightly as we maneuvered Pardloe—he was lean and fine-boned, like John, but a solid man, nonetheless—into a wing chair. "Mrs. Figg? Cups, several cups, and, Jenny, my medicine chest. Don't lose your rhythm, Your Grace—blow . . . two . . . three . . . four—*don't* gasp. Sip the air—you'll get enough, I promise." Hal's face was twitching, shining with sweat, and while he still had control over himself, I could see panic creasing the lines around his eyes as his airways closed.

I fought down a similar sense of panic; it wouldn't serve either of us. The fact was that he *could* die. He was having a severe asthmatic attack, and even with access to epinephrine injections and the facilities of a major hospital, people did die in such circumstances, whether of a heart attack brought on by stress and lack of oxygen or from simple suffocation.

His hands were clenched on his knees, the moleskin breeches crumpled and dark with sweat, and the cords of his neck stood out with strain. With some difficulty, I pried one of his hands loose and grasped it strongly in mine; I had to distract him from the panic darkening his mind, if he was to have any chance at all.

"Look at me," I said, leaning close and looking straight into his eyes. "It's going to be all right. Do you hear me? Nod if you can hear me."

He managed a short nod. He was blowing, but too fast; no more than a wisp of air touched my cheek. I squeezed his hand.

"Slower," I said, my voice as calm as I could make it. "Breathe with me, now. Purse your lips . . . blow . . ." I tapped out a regular count of four on his knee with my free hand, as slow as I dared. He ran out of air between two and three but kept his lips pursed, straining.

"Slow!" I said sharply as his mouth opened, gasping, starving for air. "Let it come by itself; one . . . two . . . blow!" I could hear Jenny hurrying down the stairs with my medicine chest. Mrs. Figg had departed like a great rushing wind in the direction of the cookhouse, where she kept a cauldron boiling—yes, here she came, three teacups looped over the fingers of one hand, a can of hot water wrapped in a towel clutched to her bosom with the other.

". . . three . . . four—joint fir, Jenny—one . . . two . . . blow *out,* two . . . three . . . four—a good handful in each cup—two, yes, that's it . . . blow . . ." Still holding his gaze, willing him to blow—it was all that was keeping his airways open. If he lost his rhythm, he'd lose what little air pressure he had, the airways would collapse, and then—I shoved the thought aside, squeezing his hand as hard as I could, and gave disjoint directions between chanting the rhythm. Joint fir . . . what the bloody hell else did I have?

Not much, was the answer. Bowman's root, jimsonweed—

much too dangerously toxic, and not fast enough. "Spikenard, Jenny," I said abruptly. "The root—grind it." I pointed at the second cup, then the third. ". . . two . . . three . . . four . . ." A large handful of crumbled joint fir (aptly named; it looked like a pile of miniature sticks) had been placed in each cup and was already steeping. I'd give him the first as soon as it had cooled enough to drink, but it took a good half hour of steeping to get a truly effective concentration. "More cups, please, Mrs. Figg—in, one . . . two . . . that's good . . ."

The hand in mine was slick with sweat, but he was gripping me with all the strength he had; I could feel my bones grind, and twisted my hand a bit to ease them. He saw and released the pressure a little. I leaned in, cradling his hand in both of mine—not incidentally taking the opportunity to get my fingers on his pulse.

"You aren't going to die," I said to him, quietly but as forcefully as I could. "I won't let you." The flicker of something much too faint to be a smile passed behind those winter-sharp blue eyes, but he hadn't enough breath even to think of speaking. His lips were still blue and his face paper-white, in spite of the temperature.

The first cup of joint-fir tea helped briefly, the heat and moisture doing as much as the herb; joint fir did contain epinephrine and was the only really good treatment for asthma I had available—but there wasn't enough of the active principle in a cup of the stuff after only ten minutes' brewing. Even the momentary sense of relief steadied him, though. His hand turned, fingers linking with mine, and he squeezed back.

A fighter. I knew one when I saw one and smiled involuntarily.

"Start three more cups, please, Jenny?" If he drank them slowly—and he couldn't do more than sip briefly between gasps—and continuously, we should have got a decent amount of stimulant into him by the end of the sixth, most-concentrated cup. "And, Mrs. Figg, if you would boil three handfuls of the joint fir and half that of spikenard in a pint of coffee for a quarter hour, then let it steep?" If he wasn't going to die, I wanted a concentrated tincture of *Ephedra* easily on hand; this obviously wasn't his first attack, and—if it wasn't his last—there'd be another sometime. And quite possibly sometime soon.

The back of my mind had been ticking through diagnostic possibilities, and now that I was fairly sure he was going to survive the moment, I could spare time to think about them consciously.

Sweat was pouring down the fine-cut bones of his face; I'd got his coat, waistcoat, and leather stock off first thing, and his shirtfront was pasted to his chest, his breeches black-wet in the creases of his groin. No wonder, though, between the heat of the day, his exertions, and the hot tea. The blue tinge was fading from his lips, and there was no sign of edema in face or hands . . . no distention of the blood vessels in his neck, in spite of his effort.

I could hear the crackling rales in his lungs easily without a stethoscope, but he showed no thoracic enlargement; his torso was as trim as John's, a bit narrower through the chest. Probably not a chronic obstructive pulmonary condition, then . . . and I didn't *think* he had congestive heart failure. His color when I met him had been good, and his pulse was presently thumping against my fingers very steadily, fast, but no flutters, no arrhythmia . . .

I became aware of Germain hovering by my elbow, staring interestedly at the duke, who was now sufficiently himself as to lift an eyebrow in the boy's direction, though still unable to speak.

"Mmm?" I said, before resuming my now-automatic counting of breaths.

"I'm only thinking, *Grand-mère,* as how himself there"—Germain nodded at Pardloe—"might be missed. Had I maybe best carry a message to someone, so as they aren't sending out soldiers after him? The chairmen will talk, will they not?"

"Ah." That was a thought, all right. General Clinton, for one, certainly knew that Pardloe was in my company when last seen. I had no idea with whom Pardloe might be traveling or whether he was in command of his regiment. If he *was,* people would be looking for him right now; an officer couldn't be gone from his place for long without someone noticing.

And Germain—an observant lad, if ever there was one—was right about the chairmen. Their numbers meant they were registered with the central chairmen's agency in Philadelphia; it would be the work of a moment for the general's staff to locate numbers Thirty-Nine and Forty and find out where they'd delivered the Duke of Pardloe.

Jenny, who had been tending the array of teacups, stepped in now with the next and knelt by Pardloe, nodding to me that she would see to his breathing while I talked to Germain.

"He told the chairmen to bring me to the King's Arms," I said to Germain, taking him out onto the porch, where we could confer unheard. "And I met him at General Clinton's office in the—"

"I ken where it is, *Grand-mère.*"

"I daresay you do. Have you something in mind?"

"Well, I'm thinkin'—" He glanced into the house, then back at me, eyes narrowed in thought. "How long d'ye mean to keep him prisoner, *Grand-mère*?"

So my motives hadn't escaped Germain. I wasn't surprised; he undoubtedly had heard all about the day's excitements from Mrs. Figg—and, knowing as he did who Jamie was, had probably deduced even more. I wondered if he'd seen William. If so, he likely knew everything. If he didn't, though, there was no need to reveal *that* little complication until it was necessary.

"Until your grandfather comes back," I said. "Or possibly Lord John," I added as an afterthought. I hoped with all my being that Jamie would come back shortly. But it might be that he would find it necessary to stay outside the city and send John in to bring me news. "The minute I let the duke go, he'll be turning the city upside down in search of his brother. Always assuming for the sake of argument that he doesn't drop dead in the process." And the very last thing I wanted was to instigate a dragnet in which Jamie might be snared.

Germain rubbed his chin thoughtfully—a peculiar gesture in a child too young for whiskers, but his father to the life, and I smiled.

"That's maybe not too long," he said. "*Grand-père* will come back directly; he was wild to see ye last night." He grinned at me, then looked through the open doorway, pursing his lips.

"As to himself, ye canna hide where he is," he said. "But if ye were to send a note to the general, and maybe another to the King's Arms, saying as how His Grace was staying with Lord John, they wouldna start searching for him right away. And even if someone was to come here later and inquire, I suppose ye might give him a wee dram that would keep him quiet so ye could tell them he was gone. Or maybe lock him in a closet? Tied up wi' a gag if it should be he's got his voice back by then," he added. Germain was a very logical, thorough-minded sort of person; he got it from Marsali.

"Excellent thought," I said, forbearing to comment on the relative merits of the options for keeping Pardloe incommunicado. "Let me do that now."

Pausing for a quick look at Pardloe, who was doing better though still wheezing strongly, I whipped upstairs and flipped open John's writing desk. It was the work of a moment to mix the ink powder and write the notes. I hesitated briefly over the signature but then caught sight of John's signet on the dressing table; he hadn't had time to put it on.

The thought gave me a slight pang; in the overwhelming joy of seeing Jamie alive, and then the shock of William's advent, Jamie's taking John hostage, and the violence of William's exit—dear Lord, where was William now?—I had pushed John to the back of my mind.

Still, I told myself, he was quite safe. Jamie wouldn't let any harm come to him, and directly he came back into Philadelphia—the chiming of the carriage clock on the mantelpiece interrupted me, and I glanced at it: four o'clock.

"Time flies when you're having fun," I murmured to myself, and, scribbling a reasonable facsimile of John's signature, I lit the candle from the embers in the hearth, dripped wax on the folded notes, and stamped them with the smiling half-moon ring. Maybe John would be back before the notes were even delivered. And Jamie, surely, would be with me as soon as darkness made it safe.

9

A TIDE IN THE AFFAIRS OF MEN

JAMIE WASN'T ALONE on the road. He'd been dimly aware of horses passing by, heard the distant talk of men on foot, but now that he'd come out of his red haze, he was startled to see how many there were. He saw what was plainly a militia company—not marching, but on the move as a body, knots and clumps of men, solitary riders—and a few wagons coming from the city, piled with goods, women and children afoot beside them.

He'd seen a few folk leaving Philadelphia when he'd come in the day before—God, was it only *yesterday*?—and thought to ask Fergus about it, but in the excitement of arrival and the later complications had quite forgotten.

His sense of disturbance increased and he kicked up his horse to a faster pace. It was no more than ten miles to the city; he'd be there long before nightfall.

Maybe just as well if it's dark, he thought grimly. Easier to have things out with Claire alone and undisturbed—and whether the having-out led to beating or bed, he wanted no interference.

The thought was like the striking of one of Brianna's matches. Just the word "bed" and he was aflame with fresh rage.

"Ifrinn!" he said aloud, and slammed his fist against the pommel. All the trouble to calm himself, and all to waste in an instant! God *damn* it—damn him, damn her, John Grey—damn everything!

"Mr. Fraser!"

He jerked as though shot in the back, and the horse slowed at once, snorting.

"Mr. Fraser!" came the loud, wheezy voice again, and Daniel Morgan came trotting up alongside on a small, sturdy bay, grinning all over his big scarred face. "Knew that was you, knew it! Ain't no other rascal that size with that color hair, and if there is one, I don't want to meet him."

"Colonel Morgan," he said, noting auld Dan's unaccustomed uniform with the fresh insignia on the collar. "On your way to a wedding?" He did his best to smile, though the turmoil inside him was like the whirlpools off the rocks of Stroma.

"What? Oh, that," said Dan, trying to look sideways down his own neck. "Pshaw. Washington's a damned stickler for 'proper dress.' The Continental army got more generals than they got private soldiers, these days. An officer lives through more 'n two battles, they make him some kind of general on the spot. Now, gettin' any pay for it, that's a different kettle of fish."

He tipped back his hat and looked Jamie up and down.

"Just come back from Scotland? Heard you went with Brigadier Fraser's body—your kin, I suppose?" He shook his head regretfully. "Cryin' shame. Fine soldier, good man."

"Aye, he was that. We buried him near his home at Balnain."

They continued together, auld Dan asking questions and Jamie replying as briefly as good manners—and his real affection for Morgan—would allow. They hadn't met since Saratoga, where he'd served under Morgan as an officer of his Rifle Corps, and there was a good deal to say. Still, he was glad of the company, and even of the questions; they distracted him and kept his mind from catapulting him again into fruitless fury and confusion.

"I suppose we must part here," Jamie said, after a bit. They were approaching a crossroads, and Dan had slowed his pace a bit. "I'm bound into the city myself."

"What for?" Morgan asked, rather surprised.

"I—to see my wife." His voice wanted to tremble on the word "wife," and he bit it off sharp.

"Oh, yes? Could you maybe spare a quarter hour?" Dan was giving him a sort of calculating look that made Jamie instantly uneasy. But the sun was still high; he didn't want to enter Philadelphia before dark.

"Aye, maybe," he replied cautiously. "To do what?"

"I'm on my way to see a friend—want you to meet him. It's

right close, won't take a moment. Come on!" Morgan veered right, waving at Jamie to follow, which, cursing himself for a fool, he did.

Number 17 Chestnut Street

I WAS SWEATING as freely as the duke was by the time the spasm eased enough for him to breathe without the positive-pressure exercise. I wasn't quite as tired as he was—he lay back in the chair, exhausted, eyes closed, drawing slow, shallow—but free!—breaths—but close. I felt light-headed, too; it's not possible to help someone breathe without doing a lot of it yourself, and I was hyperventilated.

"Here, *a piuthar-chèile.*" Jenny's voice spoke by my ear, and it was only when I opened my eyes in surprise that I realized they'd been closed. She put a small glass of brandy in my hand. "There's nay whisky in the house, but I expect this will help. Shall I give His Grace a dram, too?"

"Yes, you shall," the duke said, with great authority, though he didn't move a muscle or open his eyes. "Thank you, madam."

"It won't hurt him," I said, drawing myself up and stretching my back. "Or you, either. Sit down and have a drink. You, too, Mrs. Figg." Jenny and Mrs. Figg had worked nearly as hard as I had, fetching and grinding and brewing, bringing cool cloths to mop the sweat, spelling me now and then with the counting, and, by combining their not-inconsiderable force of will with mine, helping to keep him alive.

Mrs. Figg had very fixed notions of what was proper, and these didn't include sitting down to share a dram with her employer, let alone a visiting duke, but even she was obliged to admit that the circumstances were unusual. Glass in hand, she perched primly on an ottoman near the parlor door, where she could deal with any potential invasions or domestic emergencies.

No one spoke for some time, but there was a great sense of peace in the room. The hot, still air carried that sense of odd camaraderie that binds people who have passed through a trial together—if only temporarily. I gradually became aware that the air was carrying noises, too, from the street outside.

Groups of people moving hurriedly, shouts from the next block, and a rumble of wagons. And a distant rattle of drums.

Mrs. Figg was aware of it, too; I saw her head rise, the ribbons of her cap atremble with inquisitiveness.

"Baby Jesus, have mercy," she said, setting down her empty glass with care. "Something's coming."

Jenny looked startled and glanced at me, apprehensive.

"Coming?" she said. "What's coming?"

"The Continental army, I expect," said Pardloe. He let his head fall back, sighing. "Dear God. What it is . . . to draw breath." His breath was still short, but not very much constrained. He raised his glass ceremoniously to me. "Thank you, my . . . dear. I was . . . already in your debt for your . . . kind services to my son, but—"

"What do you mean, 'the Continental army'?" I interrupted. I set down my own glass, now empty. My heart rate had calmed after the exertions of the last hour but now abruptly sped up again.

Pardloe closed one eye and regarded me with the other.

"The Americans," he said mildly. "The Rebels. What else . . . would I mean?"

"And when you say, 'coming . . .'" I said carefully.

"I didn't," he pointed out, then nodded at Mrs. Figg. "She did. She's right, though. General Clinton's . . . forces are with . . . drawing from Philadelphia. . . . I daresay Wa . . . Washington is . . . poised to rush in."

Jenny made a small sputtering noise, and Mrs. Figg said something really blasphemous in French, then clapped a broad pink-palmed hand to her mouth.

"Oh," I said, doubtless sounding as blank as I felt. I'd been so distracted during my meeting with Clinton earlier in the day that the logical consequences of a British withdrawal had not occurred to me at all.

Mrs. Figg stood up.

"I best go and be burying the silver, then," she said in a matter-of-fact sort of way. "It'll be under the laburnum bush by the cookhouse, Lady John."

"Wait," I said, raising a hand. "I don't think we need do that *just* yet, Mrs. Figg. The army hasn't yet left the city; the Americans aren't precisely snapping at our heels. And we'll need a few forks with which to eat our supper."

She made a low rumbling noise in her throat but seemed to see the sense in this; she nodded and began to collect the brandy glasses instead.

"What'll you be wanting for supper, then? I got a cold boiled ham, but I was thinking to make a chicken fricassee, William liking that so much." She cast a bleak look at the hallway, where the bloody smudges on the wallpaper had now turned brown. "You think he's coming back for his supper?" William had an official billet somewhere in the town, but frequently spent the night at the house—particularly when Mrs. Figg was making chicken fricassee.

"God knows," I said. I hadn't had time to contemplate the William situation, what with everything else. *Might* he come back, when he'd cooled down, determined to have things out with John? I'd seen a Fraser on the boil, many times, and they didn't sulk, as a rule. They tended to take direct action, at once. I eyed Jenny speculatively; she returned the look and casually leaned her elbow on the table, chin in hand, and tapped her fingers thoughtfully against her lips. I smiled privately at her.

"Where *is* my nephew?" Hal asked, finally able to take note of something other than his next breath. "For that matter . . . where is my brother?"

"I don't know," I told him, putting my own glass on Mrs. Figg's tray and scooping his up to add to it. "I really wasn't lying about that. But I do expect he'll be back soon." I rubbed a hand over my face and smoothed my hair back as well as I could. First things first. I had a patient to tend.

"I'm sure John wants to see you as much as you want to see him. But—"

"Oh, I doubt it," the duke said. His eyes traveled slowly over me, from bare feet to disheveled hair, and the faint look of amusement on his face deepened. "You must tell me how John . . . happened to marry you . . . when there's time."

"A counsel of desperation," I said shortly. "But in the meantime we must get you to bed. Mrs. Figg, is the back bedroom—"

"Thank you, Mrs. Figg," the duke interrupted, "I shan't be . . . requiring . . ." He was trying to struggle up out of the chair and hadn't enough breath to talk. I walked up to him and gave him my best piercing head-matron look.

"Harold," I said in measured tones. "I am not merely your

sister-in-law." The term gave me an odd *frisson,* but I ignored it. "I am your physician. If you don't—what?" I demanded. He was staring up at me with a most peculiar expression on his face, something between surprise and amusement. "You invited me to use your Christian name, didn't you?"

"I did," he admitted. "But I don't think anyone has . . . actually called me Harold since . . . I was three years old." He did smile then, a charming smile quite his own. "The family call me Hal."

"Hal, then," I said, smiling back but refusing to be distracted. "You're going to have a nice refreshing sponge bath, Hal, and then you're going to bed."

He laughed—though he cut it short, as he began to wheeze. He coughed a little, fist balled under his ribs, and looked uneasy, but it stopped, and he cleared his throat and glanced up at me.

"You'd think I *was* . . . three years old. Sister-in-law. Trying to send me . . . to bed without my tea?" He pressed himself gingerly upright, getting his feet under him. I put a hand on his chest and pushed. He hadn't any strength in his legs and fell back into the chair, astonished and affronted. And afraid: he hadn't realized—or at least had not admitted—his own weakness. A severe attack usually left the victim completely drained, and often with the lungs still dangerously twitchy.

"You see?" I said, tempering my tone with gentleness. "You've had attacks like this before, haven't you?"

"Well . . . yes," he said unwillingly, "but . . ."

"And how long were you in bed after the last one?"

His lips compressed.

"A week. But the fool doctor—"

I put a hand on his shoulder and he stopped—as much because he'd temporarily run short of air as because of the touch.

"You. Cannot. Breathe. Yet. On. Your. Own," I said, separating the words for emphasis. "Listen to me, Hal. Look what's happened this afternoon, will you? You had a fairly severe attack in the street; had that crowd on Fourth Street decided to set upon us, you would have been quite helpless—don't argue with me, Hal, I was there." I narrowed my eyes at him. He did the same back at me but didn't argue.

"Then the walk from the street to the door of the house—

a distance of some twenty feet—threw you straight into a full-blown *status asthmaticus;* have you heard that term before?"

"No," he muttered.

"Well, now you have, and now you know what it is. And you were in bed for a week the last time? Was it as bad as this?"

His lips were a thin line and his eyes sparking. I imagined most people didn't speak to a duke—let alone the commander of his own regiment—like this. Be good for him, I thought.

"Bloody doctor . . . said it was my heart." His fist had uncurled and the fingers were slowly rubbing his chest. "Knew it wasn't that."

"I think you're probably right about that," I conceded. "Was this the same doctor who gave you smelling salts? Complete quack, if so."

He laughed, a brief, breathless sound.

"Yes, he is." He paused to breathe for a moment. "Though in . . . justice, he . . . he didn't give me . . . salts. Got them . . . myself. For fainting . . . told you."

"So you did." I sat down beside him and took hold of his wrist. He let me, watching curiously. His pulse was fine; it had slowed and was thumping along very steadily.

"How long have you been subject to fainting spells?" I asked, bending to look closely into his eyes. No sign of petechial hemorrhage, no jaundice, pupils the same size . . .

"A long time," he said, and pulled his wrist abruptly away. "I haven't time to chat about my health, madam. I—"

"Claire," I said, and put a restraining hand on his chest, smiling amiably at him. "You're Hal, I'm Claire—and you aren't going anywhere, Your Grace."

"Take your hand off me!"

"I'm seriously tempted to do just that and let you fall on your face," I told him, "but wait until Mrs. Figg finishes brewing the tincture. I don't want you thrashing about on the floor, gasping like a landed fish, and no way of getting the hook out of your mouth."

I did in fact take my hand off his chest, though, and, rising, I went out into the hall before he could find breath to say anything. Jenny had taken up a stand by the open doorway, looking up and down the street.

"What's going on out there?" I asked.

"I dinna ken," she said, not taking her eyes off a couple of rough-looking men who were lounging down the other side of the street. "But I dinna like the feel of it a bit. D'ye think he's right?"

"That the British army is leaving? Yes. They are. And very likely half the Loyalists in the city with them." I knew exactly what she meant by not liking the feel of things. The air was hot and thick, buzzing with cicadas, and the leaves of the chestnut trees along the street hung limp as dishrags. But *something* was moving in the atmosphere. Excitement? Panic? Fear? All three, I thought.

"Had I best go to the printshop, d'ye think?" she asked, turning to me with a slight frown. "Would Marsali and the weans be safer if I fetched them here, I mean? If there was to be a riot or the like?"

I shook my head.

"I don't think so. They're well-known Patriots. It's the Loyalists who will be in danger, if the British army is leaving. They won't have any protection, and the Rebels may well . . . do things to them. And"—a very unpleasant feeling snaked down my backbone, like a cold, slimy finger—"this is a Loyalist household." *"Without even a door to shut and bolt,"* I might have added, but didn't.

There was a loud thump from the parlor, as of a body hitting the floor, but Jenny didn't turn a hair, nor did I. We'd both had a lot of experience with stubborn men. I could hear him panting; if he started wheezing again, I'd go in.

"Will it put ye in danger, then, to have him here?" she asked, *sotto voce,* with a tilt of her head toward the parlor. "Maybe ye'd best come to the printshop."

I grimaced, trying to evaluate the possibilities. The notes I'd sent with Germain would delay inquiries, and I could put off anyone who did come. But that also meant I could expect no immediate help from the army, if help was needed. And it might be; someone in that hostile crowd on Fourth Street might well have heard where I'd told the chairmen to come. That hostility now showed itself in a different light.

If the Rebels in the city were about to rise and turn upon the defenseless Loyalists—and the currents I sensed beginning to swirl through the streets were dark ones—

"Someone might just show up on your porch wi' a keg of

tar and a bag o' feathers," Jenny observed, preempting my thought in a most unnerving way.

"Well, that wouldn't help His Grace's asthma a bit," I said, and she laughed.

"Had ye maybe better give him back to General Clinton?" she suggested. "I've had soldiers search my house, wi' a wanted man hidin' in the bottom o' my wardrobe and my newborn bairn in his arms. I dinna think it would be a great deal easier on the nerves to have the Sons o' Liberty come in here after His Grace, if half what Marsali told me about them is true."

"It probably is." A gunshot smacked through the heavy air, flat and dull, from somewhere near the river, and we both tensed. It wasn't repeated, though, and after a moment I drew breath again.

"The thing is, he's not stable. I can't risk taking him through streets filled with dust and tree pollen and then leaving him in the care of an army surgeon, or even that quack Hebdy. Were he to have another attack and no one able to get him through it . . ."

Jenny grimaced.

"Aye, ye're right," she said reluctantly. "And ye canna leave him here and go yourself, for the same reason."

"That's right." And Jamie would be coming here, to find me. I wouldn't leave.

"Ken, if Jamie came and didna find ye here, he'd go to the printshop next thing," Jenny observed, making the hair prickle on the back of my neck.

"Will you stop doing that!?"

"What?" she said, startled.

"Reading my mind!"

"Oh, that." She grinned at me, blue eyes creasing into triangles. "Everything ye think shows on your face, Claire. Surely Jamie's told ye that?"

A deep flush burned upward from my low-cut décolletage, and only then did I recall that I was still wearing the amber-colored silk, which was now soaked with sweat, rimed with dust, and altogether rather the worse for wear. And which had very tight stays. I rather hoped that *everything* I was thinking didn't show on my face, because there was quite a bit of information I didn't mean to share with Jenny just yet.

"Well, I canna tell *everything* ye think," she admitted—doing it *again,* dammit!—"but it's easy to tell when ye're thinking about Jamie."

I decided that I really didn't want to hear what I looked like when thinking about Jamie and was about to excuse myself to look in on the duke, who I could hear coughing and swearing breathlessly to himself in German, when my attention was distracted by a boy sprinting down the street as though the devil were after him, his coat on inside out and shirttails streaming.

"Colenso!" I exclaimed.

"What?" Jenny said, startled.

"Not what. Who. Him," I said, pointing at the grubby little creature panting up the walk. "Colenso Baragwanath. William's groom."

Colenso, who always looked as though he should be squatting atop a toadstool, came hurtling toward the door with such violence that Jenny and I both leapt out of the way. Colenso tripped on the doorsill and fell flat on his face.

"Ye look as though Auld Hornie himself was after ye, lad," Jenny said, bending down to hoick him to his feet. "And whatever's become of your breeks?"

Sure enough, the boy was barefoot and wearing only his shirt beneath his coat.

"They took 'em," he blurted, gasping for breath.

"Who?" I said, pulling his coat off and turning it right side out again.

"Them," he said, gesturing hopelessly toward Locust Street. "I put me head into the ordinary, to see was Lord Ellesmere there—he is, sometimes—and there was a knot o' men all buzzin' like a hive o' bees together. They was big lads with 'em, and one of 'em as knew me saw me and raises up a great cry, shoutin' as I'm a-spyin' on 'em and mean to take word back to the army, and then they grabbed me and they called me a turncoat and put me coat on backward and the one man said he'd beat me and teach me not to do such as that and pulled off me breeches and . . . and . . . anyway, I squirmed out of his hand and fell down on the floor and crawled out under the tables and took off a-runnin'." He wiped a sleeve under his runny nose. "His lordship here, ma'am?"

"No," I said. "Why do you want him?"

"Oh, I don't, ma'am," he assured me, with evident sincerity. "Major Findlay wants him. Now."

"Hmm. Well . . . wherever he is at the moment, he'll likely go back to his regular billet this evening. You know where that is, don't you?"

"Yes, ma'am, but I'm not a-goin' back in the street 'thout my breeches!" He looked both horrified and indignant, and Jenny laughed.

"Dinna blame ye a bit, lad," she said. "Tell ye what, though— my eldest grandson's likely got an old pair of breeches he could spare. I'll step round to the printshop," she said to me, "fetch the breeches, and tell Marsali what's ado."

"All right," I said, a little reluctant to see her go. "But hurry back. And tell her not to print *any* of this in the newspaper!"

10

THE DESCENT OF THE HOLY GHOST UPON A RELUCTANT DISCIPLE

DAN MORGAN'S "IT" *WAS* nearby: a ramshackle cabin set in a little elm grove, down a short dirt lane off the main road. There was a big gray gelding hobbled and cropping grass nearby, his tack resting on the porch; he looked up briefly and whinnied at the newcomers.

Jamie ducked under the lintel after Dan and found himself in a dark, shabby room that smelled of cabbage water, grime, and the sharp reek of urine. There was one window, its shutters left open for air, and the sunlight coming in silhouetted the long-skulled head of a large man sitting at the table, who raised his head at the opening of the door.

"Colonel Morgan," he said, in a soft voice touched with the drawl of Virginia. "Have you brought me good news?"

"That's *just* what I brought you, General," auld Dan said, and shoved Jamie ahead of him toward the table. "I found this rascal on the road and bade him come along. This'll be Colonel Fraser, who I've told you of before. Just come back from Scotland, and the very man to take command of Taylor's troops."

The big man had risen from the table and put out a hand, smiling—though he smiled with his lips pressed tight together, as though afraid something might escape. The man was as tall as Jamie himself, and Jamie found himself looking straight into sharp gray-blue eyes that took his measure in the instant it took to shake hands.

"George Washington," the man said. "Your servant, sir."

"James Fraser," Jamie said, feeling mildly stunned. "Your . . . most obedient. Sir."

"Sit with me, Colonel Fraser." The big Virginian gestured toward one of the rough benches at the table. "My horse pulled up lame, and my slave's gone to find another. No notion how long it may take him, as I require a good sturdy beast to bear my weight, and those are thin on the ground these days." He looked Jamie up and down with frank appraisal; they were much of a size. "I don't suppose you have a decent horse with you, sir?"

"Aye, I do." It was clear what Washington expected, and Jamie yielded gracefully. "Will ye do me the honor to take him, General?"

Auld Dan made a disgruntled noise and shifted from foot to foot, clearly wanting to object, but Jamie gave him a brief shake of the head. It wasn't that far to Philadelphia; he could walk.

Washington looked pleased and thanked Jamie with grace in turn, saying that the horse should be returned to him as soon as another suitable mount might be procured.

"But it *is* somewhat necessary that I be nimble at present, Colonel," Washington remarked, with an air of apology. "You're aware, are you, that Clinton is withdrawing from Philadelphia?"

A shock went through Jamie like a hot penny dropped on butter.

"It—he—no, sir. I was not aware."

"I was just about to get to that," Dan said tetchily. "No one lets me get one word in edgewise, I tell you."

"Well, now you've got one," Washington said, amused. "You might get another, if you're quick enough to speak before Lee gets here. Sit down, gentlemen, if you will. I'm expecting—ah, there they are." Sounds from the dooryard indicated a number of horsemen arriving, and within a few moments the cabin was crowded with Continental officers.

They were a creased and weathered lot, for the most part, dressed in motley bits of uniform, these coupled uneasily with hunting shirts or homespun breeches. Even the complete suits of clothes were mud-spattered and worn, and the smell of men who'd been living rough quite overcame the gentler domestic reeks of the cabin.

Among the shuffling and excited greetings, Jamie spotted the source of the urinous smell, though: a thin-faced woman stood with her back pressed into a corner of the room, holding an infant wrapped in a ratty shawl against her bosom, her eyes darting to and fro among the intruders. A dark wet patch showed on the shawl, but it was plain the woman was afraid to move from her place to change the wean and instead shifted mechanically from foot to foot, patting the child to soothe it.

"Colonel Fraser! Well met! Well met!" The voice jerked his attention away, and, to his astonishment, he found his hand being pumped with enthusiasm by Anthony Wayne—known quite openly by now as "Mad Anthony"—whom he had last seen a few weeks before the fall of Ticonderoga.

"Is your wife well, sir, and your Indian nephew?" Wayne was asking, beaming up into Jamie's face. Anthony was short and stocky, with the full cheeks of a chipmunk, but also equipped with a sharp, poking sort of nose over which his eyes did now and then seem to glow with fire. At the moment, Jamie was relieved to see them merely alight with friendly interest.

"All well, sir, I thank ye. And—"

"Tell me, is your wife near at hand?" Wayne moved a little closer and lowered his voice a bit. "I've been having the most damnable time with my gouty foot, and she did wonders with the abscess at the base of my spine while we were at Ti—"

"Colonel Fraser, allow me to make you acquainted with

Major General Charles Lee and with General Nathanael Greene." George Washington's voice drove a smooth Virginia wedge between himself and the base of Mad Anthony's spine, to Jamie's relief.

Besides Washington himself, Charles Lee was the best equipped of the lot, wearing complete uniform from gorget to polished boots. Jamie hadn't met him before but could have picked him out of a crowd as a professional soldier, no matter how he was dressed. An Englishman of the sort who seemed always to be smelling something dubious, but he shook hands cordially enough, with a clipped "Your servant, sir." Jamie knew exactly two things about Charles Lee, both told to him by Young Ian: to wit, that the man had a Mohawk wife—and that the Mohawk called him "Ounewaterika." Ian said it meant "Boiling Water."

Between Mad Anthony and Boiling Water, Jamie was beginning to feel that he should have spurred up and run for it when he met Dan Morgan on the road, but too late for regrets.

"Sit, gentlemen, we have no time to waste." Washington turned to the woman in the corner. "Have you anything to drink, Mrs. Hardman?"

Jamie saw her throat move as she swallowed, squeezing the child so hard that it squealed like a piglet and started to cry. He felt several of the men, doubtless fathers, wince at the sound.

"No, Friend," she said, and he realized she was a Quaker. "Naught but water from the well. Shall I fetch you a bucket?"

"Don't trouble thyself, Friend Hardman," Nathanael Greene said, soft-voiced. "I've two bottles in my saddlebag will do us." He moved slowly toward the woman, not to startle her, and took her gently by the arm. "Come outside. Thee needn't be disturbed by this business." He was a heavy, imposing man, who walked with a noticeable limp, but she seemed reassured by his plain speech and went with him, though looking back with an anxious face, as though fearing that the men might set fire to the place.

A quarter hour later, Jamie wasn't so sure that they might not ignite the cabin by the sheer force of their excitement. Washington and his troops had been bottled up at Valley Forge for the last six months, drilling and preparing, and the generals were on fire to be at the enemy.

Much talk, plans proposed, argued over, put aside, returned

to. Jamie listened with half a mind; the other half was in Philadelphia. He'd heard enough from Fergus to know that the city was divided, with regular clashes between Patriots and Loyalists, these kept under control only by the presence of the British soldiers—but the Loyalists were a minority. The moment the army's protection was withdrawn, the Loyalists would be at the mercy of the Rebels—and Rebels who had been suppressed for months were not likely to be merciful.

And Claire . . . His mouth went dry. Claire was, so far as anyone in Philadelphia knew, the wife of Lord John Grey, a very visible Loyalist. And Jamie himself had just removed John Grey's protection from her, leaving her alone and helpless in a city about to explode.

How long did he have before the British left the city? No one at the table knew.

He took as little part as possible in the conversation, both because he was estimating how fast he could reach Philadelphia on foot—versus the possibility of going out to the privy and stealing back the horse he'd just given Washington—and because he hadn't forgotten what auld Dan had said to General Washington when he'd dragged Jamie in here. The very last thing he wanted was—

"And you, Colonel Fraser," Washington said. Jamie closed his eyes and commended his soul to God. "Will you do me the signal service of accepting command of Henry Taylor's battalion? General Taylor fell ill and died two days ago."

"I . . . am honored, sir," Jamie managed, thinking frantically. "But I have very urgent business . . . in Philadelphia. I should be happy to oblige ye, so soon as my business is accomplished—and I could, of course, bring back word of exactly how matters stand with General Clinton's forces." Washington had been looking severe during the first part of this speech, but the last sentence made Greene and Morgan hum with approval and Wayne nod his little chipmunk head.

"Can you manage your business within three days, Colonel?"

"Yes, sir!" It was no more than ten miles to the city; he could do that in two or three hours. And it wasn't going to take him more than thirty seconds to take Claire out of that house, once he reached it.

"Very well, then. You're appointed to a temporary field rank of General of the Army. That—"

"Ifrinn!"

"I beg your pardon, Colonel?" Washington looked puzzled. Dan Morgan, who'd heard Jamie say "Hell!" in *Gàidhlig* before, shook silently beside him.

"I—thank ye, sir." He swallowed, feeling a dizzy wave of heat pass over him.

"Though the Congress will have to approve your appointment," Washington went on, frowning a little, "and there's no guarantee as to what those contentious, shopkeeping sons of bitches will do."

"I understand, sir," Jamie assured him. He could only hope. Dan Morgan passed him a bottle, and he drank deep, hardly noticing what was in it. Sweating profusely, he sank back on the bench, hoping to avoid any further notice.

Jesus, now what? He'd meant to slip quietly into the city and out again with Claire, then head south to retrieve his printing press, perhaps establish a wee business in Charleston or Savannah until the war was over and they could go home to the Ridge. But he *had* known there was a risk; any man below the age of sixty could be compelled into militia service, and if it came down to it, he was likely a little safer being a general than a commander of militia. Maybe. And a general could resign; that was a heartening thought.

Despite all the talk and the worrying prospects of the immediate future, Jamie found himself paying more attention to Washington's face than to what he said, taking note of how the man talked and carried himself, so that he could tell Claire. He wished that he could tell Brianna; she and Roger Mac had sometimes speculated about what it might be like to meet someone like Washington—though having met a number of famous people himself, he'd told her that the experience was likely to prove a disappointment.

He would admit that Washington knew what he was about, though; he listened more than he talked, and when he said something, it was to the point. And he did give off an air of relaxed authority, though it was clear the present prospect excited him very much. His face was pockmarked, big-featured, and far from handsome, but had a good bit of dignity and presence.

His expression had become very animated, and he went so far as to laugh now and then, showing very bad, stained teeth. Jamie was fascinated; Brianna had told him they were false, made of wood or hippopotamus ivory, and he had a sudden dislocating recollection of his grandfather: the Old Fox had had a set of teeth made of beechwood. Jamie had thrown them on the fire during an argument at Beaufort Castle—and just for an instant he was there, smelling peat smoke and roasting venison, every hair on his body a-prickle with warning, surrounded by kinsmen who might just kill him.

And as suddenly he was back, pressed between Lee and auld Dan, smelling sweat and exhilaration and, despite himself, feeling the rising excitement among them begin to seep into his blood.

It gave him a queer feeling in his wame, to sit nay more than a foot away from a man whom he knew not at all but about whom he maybe kent more than the man himself.

True, he'd sat with Charles Stuart many evenings, knowing—and believing—what Claire had said would happen to him. But still . . . Christ had told doubting Thomas, *"Blessed are those who have not seen but have believed."* Jamie wondered what you called those who *had* seen and were obliged to live with the resultant knowledge. He thought "blessed" was maybe not the word.

IT WAS MORE than an hour before Washington and the others took their leave—an hour during which Jamie thought repeatedly that he might just stand up, flip the table over, and run out the door, leaving the Continental army to make shift without him.

He kent perfectly well that armies moved slowly, save when fighting. And clearly Washington expected that it would be a week or more before the British actually quit Philadelphia. But it was no use talking sense to his body, which as usual had its own measures of importance. He could ignore or suppress hunger, thirst, fatigue, and injury. He couldn't suppress the need to see Claire.

Likely it was what she and Brianna called testosterone poisoning, he thought idly—their term for the obvious things men did that women didn't understand. Someday he must ask her what testosterone was. He shifted uncomfortably on the narrow bench, forcing his mind back to what Washington was saying.

At long last, there came a rap on the door, and a black man put his head in and nodded to Washington.

"Ready, suh," he said, in the same soft Virginia accent as his master.

"Thank you, Caesar." Washington nodded back, then put his hands on the table and rose swiftly. "We are agreed, then, gentlemen? You're coming with me, General Lee. I'll see the rest of you in due course at Sutfin's farm, save you hear otherwise."

Jamie's heart leapt and he made to rise, too, but auld Dan put a hand on his sleeve.

"Set a bit, Jamie," he said. "You'll need to know something about your new command, won't you?"

"I—" he began, but there was no help for it. He sat and waited while Nathanael Greene thanked Mrs. Hardman for her hospitality and begged her to accept a small recompense from the army for her civil reception of them. Jamie would have wagered a good deal that the coins he plucked from his purse were his own and not the army's, but the woman took them, an acceptance too faint to be pleasure showing in her worn face. He saw her shoulders sag with relief as the door closed behind the generals and realized that their presence might have put her and her child in considerable peril, should the wrong people see uniformed Continental officers visiting her house.

She glanced consideringly at him and Dan, but they seemed to trouble her much less, in their rough civilian clothes. Dan had taken off his uniform coat and folded it inside out, laying it on the bench beside him.

"Feel any tongues of fire come down on your head just now, Jamie?" Dan asked, seeing his look.

"What?"

"Then the same day at evening, being the first day of the week, when the doors were shut where the disciples were assembled for fear of the Jews, came Jesus and stood in the midst, and saith unto them, Peace be unto you," Dan quoted, and grinned wide at Jamie's look of astonishment.

"My Abigail's a reading woman, and she reads bits o' the Bible out to me regular, in hopes it'll do some good, though ain't much luck in that direction yet." He took up the rucksack he'd brought in and dredged about in it, coming out with a folded sheaf of dog-eared papers, an inkhorn, and a couple of tattered quills.

"Well, now that the Father, Son, and the Holy Ghost are gone off about their own business, let me write you down the names of your company commanders, what-all you got in the way of militia, and where they all are, 'cuz it ain't like they're all in barracks—or even in the same village. Missus Hardman, might I trouble you, ma'am, for a drop of water for my ink?"

Jamie bent his mind with difficulty to the business at hand, the better to dispatch it quickly, and within a quarter hour was gathering together the lists, made out in Dan's slow, crabbed hand. *Two hours to Philadelphia . . . maybe three . . .*

"Got any money on you to speak of?" Dan asked, pausing by the door.

"Not a penny," Jamie admitted, with a glance at the spot on his belt where his purse was normally fastened. He'd given it to Jenny to keep on the journey, as she delighted in making their small purchases. And this morning he'd been so much on fire to see Claire that he'd left the printshop with nothing but the clothes on his back and the packet of papers for Fergus. He spared an instant to wonder whether things would be different now, had he not been spotted giving the papers to Fergus and followed to Lord John's house by the soldiers—and William—but there was no point in regrets.

Dan pawed in his sack again, came out with a smaller bag and a clinking purse, both of which he tossed to Jamie.

"A bit of food for your journey, and an advance on your general's pay," he said, and chortled with amusement at his own wit. "You'll need to pay hard cash for a uniform these days; ain't a tailor in Philadelphia will take Continentals. And woe betide you if you show up before his worshipfulness George Washington without being dressed proper. He's a stickler for proper uniform, says you can't expect to command respect without lookin' like you deserve it. But I reckon you know all about that."

Dan, who had fought both battles of Saratoga in a hunting shirt, leaving his uniform coat hung over a tree branch in camp because of the heat, smiled broadly at Jamie, the scar on his upper lip where a bullet had torn through his face showing white against the weathered skin.

"Fare thee well, General Fraser!"

Jamie snorted but smiled nonetheless as he stood to shake Dan's hand. Then he turned back to the litter on the table, stowing the papers and purse—and a stray quill that Dan had abandoned, overlooked—into the bag. He was grateful for the food; the scent of jerked meat and journeycake floated out of the canvas depths, and he could feel the hard shape of apples at the bottom. He'd left the printshop without breakfast, too.

He straightened, and a pain like white lightning shot from the middle of his spine down the back of his leg to the sole of his foot. He gasped and collapsed onto a stool, his lower back and right buttock clenched with cramp.

"Jesus, Mary, and Bride—not *now,*" he said between his teeth, and meant it somewhere between prayer and curse. He'd felt something small wrench or tear in his back when he'd hit John Grey, but in the heat of the moment it hadn't seemed important. It hadn't troubled him much walking—he'd barely noticed, with all there was on his mind—but now that he'd sat for a time and the muscles had chilled . . .

He tried rising, carefully, collapsed again. Bent sweating over the table with his fists clenched, he said a number of things in Gaelic that weren't at all prayerful.

"Is thee quite well, Friend?" The woman of the house leaned near, peering nearsightedly at him in concern.

"A . . . moment," he managed, trying to do as Claire told him and breathe through the spasm.

"Like labor pains," she'd told him, amused. He hadn't thought it was funny the first time and didn't now.

The pain eased. He extended his leg, then flexed it back under him, very gingerly. So far, so good. But when he once more tried to rise, his lower back was locked in a vise, and a pain that made him catch his breath stabbed down his buttock.

"Have ye . . . anything like . . . whisky? Rum?" If he could just get to his feet . . . But the woman was shaking her head.

"I'm sorry, Friend. I have not even small beer. Not even milk for the children any longer," she added with a certain bitterness. "The army took my goats away."

She didn't say which army, but he supposed it didn't matter to her. He made a sound of apology, just in case it had been the Continentals or the militia, and subsided, breathing heavily. This had happened three times before—just the same sudden flashing pain, the inability to move. Once, it had taken four days before he could hobble; the other two times, he had got to his feet within two days, and while it had twinged sporadically for weeks, he'd been able to walk, if slowly.

"Is thee ill? I could give thee rhubarb syrup," she offered. He managed to smile at that, shaking his head.

"I thank ye, ma'am. It's no but a clench in my back. When it eases, all will be well." The trouble was that *until* it eased, he was all but helpless, and the dawning realization of that gave him a sense of panic.

"Oh." The woman hesitated for a moment, hovering, but then the baby started to wail and she turned away to fetch it. A little girl—five or six, he thought, a stunted little creature—crawled out from under the bed and stared at him curiously.

"Is thee going to stay to supper?" she asked, in a high, precise voice. She gave him an appraising frown. "Thee looks like thee would eat a lot."

He revised his estimate of the girl's age to eight or nine and smiled at her. He was still sweating with the pain, but it was easing a bit.

"I'll not take your food, *a nighean,*" he assured her. "In fact, there's a good loaf and some jerked meat in yon bag; it's yours." Her eyes went round as pennies, and he amended, "Your family's, I mean."

She glanced eagerly at the bag, swallowing painfully as her mouth watered; he could hear the tiny gulp and it wrung his heart.

"Pru!" she whispered, turning urgently toward the table. "Food!"

Another small girl crawled out and stood beside her sister. They were both plain as fence posts, though they otherwise didn't resemble each other much.

"I heard," the newcomer told her sister, and turned a solemn gaze on Jamie.

"Don't let Mam give thee rhubarb syrup," she advised him. "It makes thee shit like the blazes, and if thee can't get to the privy, it—"

"Prudence!"

Prudence obligingly shut her mouth, though she continued to look Jamie over with interest. Her sister knelt and rummaged under the bed, emerging with the family utensil, this a homely object of brown earthenware, which she presented gravely for his inspection.

"We'll turn our backs, sir, if thee should need to—"

"Patience!"

Red in the face, Mrs. Hardman took the pisspot from her daughter and shooed the little girls to the table, where—with a glance at Jamie to be sure he had meant it—she took the bread and meat and apples from his bag, dividing the food scrupulously into three parts: two large portions for the girls, and a smaller one for herself, put aside for later.

She had left the chamber pot on the floor beside the bed, and as she eased him gingerly onto the corn-shuck mattress, Jamie caught sight of lettering painted in white across the bottom. He squinted to make it out in the dim light, then smiled. It was a Latin motto, encircling a vividly executed bee with a jovial expression and a pronounced wink. *Iam apis potanda fineo ne.*

He'd seen the jest before—the brothel in Edinburgh where he'd once kept a room had been equipped throughout with utensils sporting a variety of Latin tags, most of them prurient, but some merely puns, like this one. It *was* a Latin sentence, if a foolish one—"Drink not the bee now"—but if read phonetically in English, ignoring the spacing, it read, "I am a pisspot and a fine one." He glanced up at Mrs. Hardman in speculation but thought it was likely not her work. The absent Mr. Hardman must be—*or have been,* he thought, given the obvious poverty of the household, and he crossed himself unobtrusively at the thought—an educated man.

The baby had waked and was fussing in her cradle, making small sharp yelps like a fox kit. Mrs. Hardman scooped the child out, pulling a worn nursing chair toward the fire with one foot. She laid the baby momentarily on the bed beside Jamie, opening her blouse with one hand, the other reaching automatically to save an apple that was rolling toward the edge of the table, nudged by a little girl's elbow.

The baby smacked her lips, hungry as her sisters. "And this will be wee Chastity, I make nay doubt?" he said.

Mrs. Hardman gaped at him. "How did thee know the child's name?"

He glanced at Prudence and Patience, who were silently stuffing bread and meat into their mouths as quickly as they could eat. "Well, I havena yet met a lassie named Sobriety or Fortitude," he said mildly. "The wean's sopping; have ye a clean clootie for her?"

There were two worn clouts hung to dry before the fire; she brought one, to find that Jamie had already unpinned the baby's soggy nappie—that's what Claire called them—and wiped the shit from her bottom, holding her tiny ankles in one hand.

"Thee has children, I see." Eyebrows raised, Mrs. Hardman took the soiled clout from him with a nod of thanks and dropped it into a bucket of vinegar and water that stood in the far corner.

"And grandchildren," he said, wiggling a finger in front of wee Chastity's nose. She gurgled and went cross-eyed, kicking her legs enthusiastically. "To say nothing of six nephews and nieces." *And where are Jem and wee Mandy, I wonder? Can she breathe easy now, poor lassie?* He gently tickled the baby's soft pink foot, remembering the strangely beautiful, heart-wrenching blue tinge to Mandy's perfect toes, long-jointed and graceful as a frog's.

"They're just like yours," Claire had told him, drawing a fingernail lightly down the sole of Mandy's foot, making the long big toe spring suddenly away from the others. What had she called that?

He tried it himself, gingerly, and smiled with delight to see it happen to Chastity's chubby toes.

"Babinski," he said to Mrs. Hardman, with a sense of deep satisfaction at recalling the name. "That's what it's called when a wean's great toe does that. A Babinski reflex."

Mrs. Hardman looked astonished—though much more so when he skillfully repinned the new clout and swaddled wee Chastity afresh in her blanket. She took the baby from him and, with an uncertain expression, sank down in the chair and pulled the ratty shawl over the baby's head. Unable to turn over easily, Jamie instead closed his eyes to afford her such privacy as he could.

11

REMEMBER PAOLI!

IT WAS HARD TO wipe away the sweat with his hands tied and impossible to keep the stinging salt out of his wounded eye, so puffed and slitted that he couldn't close it tightly. Water ran down his cheek in a steady flow, dripping off his chin. Blinking in a vain attempt to clear his vision, John Grey missed a fallen branch in his path and fell heavily.

Those behind him on the narrow trail halted abruptly, with sounds of mild collision, jangling weapons and canteens, confusion and impatience. Rough hands seized him and hauled him up again, but the tall, rawboned man deputed to be his escort said only, "Watch your step, me lord," in a mild tone of voice, and gave him a nudge down the path rather than a shove.

Encouraged by this evidence of consideration, he thanked the man and asked his name.

"Me?" The man sounded surprised. "Oh. Bumppo. Natty Bumppo." Adding, after a moment, "Folks mostly call me 'Hawkeye,' though."

"I don't wonder," Grey said, half under his breath. He bowed, as well as he could whilst walking, and nodded at the long rifle that bobbed in a sling at the man's back. "Your servant, sir. I deduce that you are a fine shot, then?"

"Reckon that would be a good deduction, your lordship." Bumppo's voice sounded amused. "Why? D'you want something shot? Or somebody?"

"I'm keeping a list," Grey told him. "I'll let you know when it's complete."

He felt, rather than heard, the other's laugh—the amusement was palpable, but it made little sound.

"Let me guess who's first on your list—the big Scotch fellow what put your light out?"

"He'd be fairly high on the list, yes." Actually, he couldn't decide who he'd rather see shot first: Jamie Fraser or his own bloody brother. Probably Hal, all things considered. Rather ironic, if Hal ended up getting *him* shot. Though his captors seemed quite convinced that hanging was the preferred method.

That reminded him of the uncomfortable bit of conversation that had preceded his being chivvied through the woods on a deer trail bountifully equipped with bramblish bushes, low-hanging branches, ticks, and biting flies the size of the ball of his thumb.

"Would you happen to know what—or possibly who—Paoli is, Mr. Bumppo?" he asked politely, kicking a fir cone out of his way.

"What's Paoli?" The man's voice was filled with astonishment. "Why, man, are you just come to this neck o' the woods?"

"Fairly recently," Grey replied guardedly.

"Oh." Bumppo considered, carefully matching his lengthy stride to Grey's shorter one. "Why, 'twas an infamous attack, to be sure. Your kinsman—Major General Grey, as they said—him and his troops snuck up by night to where General Wayne's men were camped. Grey didn't want to risk a stray flint sparking and giving them away, so he gives the order to take out all the flints from their guns and use the bayonets. Fell upon the Americans and bayoneted near a hundred men in their beds, in cold blood!"

"Really?" Grey tried to reconcile this account with any recent battle *he* knew of, and failed. "And . . . Paoli?"

"Oh. That's the name of the tavern nearby—Paoli's Tavern."

"Ah. Where is it? Geographically, I mean. And when, exactly, did this battle occur?"

Bumppo's prehensile lips pushed out in thought, then withdrew.

"Be up near Malvern, last September. The Paoli Massacre, they calls it," he added with a certain dubiousness.

"Massacre?" Grey echoed. The engagement had taken place before his own arrival, but he'd heard it talked about—briefly, and not in terms of massacre, to be sure. But, then, perceptions of the event were bound to be different, depending upon one's position in the matter. William Howe had spoken of it with approval—as a successful engagement in which a minimal number of British troops had routed an entire American division, with a loss of only seven men.

Bumppo seemed disposed to share Grey's opinion of the rhetorical nature of the name, albeit from yet a third perspective.

"Well, you know how folks will talk," he said, lifting one shoulder. "Ain't what *I'd* call a proper massacre, but, then, ain't many folk seen one, and I have."

"You have?" Glancing up at the tall, bearded ruffian, Grey thought it only too likely.

"Was raised as an Indian," Bumppo said, with visible pride. "By the Mohican, my own folks havin' died when I were just a tadpole. Aye, I've seen a massacre or two."

"Indeed?" Grey said, innate courtesy obliging him to invite the man to elaborate, should he wish to. Besides, it would pass the time; they seemed to have been walking for hours, and no end in sight—not that he was eagerly anticipating the end. . . .

As it was, Mr. Bumppo's reminiscences passed the time to such good effect that Grey was surprised when Corporal Woodbine, in the lead, called the company to a halt at the edge of a fairly sizable encampment. He was glad enough to stop, though; he was wearing city shoes, not suited for the terrain at all, and they had worn through his stockings and rubbed his feet to blood and blisters.

"Scout Bumppo," Woodbine said, with a short nod to Grey's companion. "You'll take the company on to Zeke Bowen's place. I'll deliver the prisoner to Colonel Smith."

This statement gave rise to vocal discontent, from which Grey gathered that the company wished very much to accompany Woodbine, in order not to miss Grey's execution, which they confidently expected to occur within moments of his delivery to the aforesaid Colonel Smith. Woodbine was firm about it, though, and with democratic mutterings and execrations, the militia moved reluctantly off under the guidance of Natty Bumppo.

Woodbine watched them out of sight, then drew himself up, brushing a stray caterpillar from the breast of his shabby coat and straightening his disreputable hat.

"Well, Lieutenant Colonel Grey. Shall we go?"

NATTY BUMPPO'S reminiscences of the proper way to conduct a massacre had left Grey with the feeling that perhaps, by contrast, hanging was not the worst way to die. But while he hadn't personally witnessed any first-rate massacres, he'd seen men hanged, very close to—and the memory of it dried his throat. The leakage from his eye hadn't stopped completely but had lessened; the skin felt raw and inflamed, though, and the swelling gave him the annoying sense that his head was grossly misshapen. Still, he drew himself upright and strode chin out into the ragged canvas tent ahead of Corporal Woodbine.

Colonel Smith looked up from his lap desk, startled at the intrusion—though not quite as startled as Grey.

He'd last seen Watson Smith in his own sister-in-law's drawing room in London two years ago, eating cucumber sandwiches. In the uniform of a captain of the Buffs.

"Mr. Smith," he said, recovering his wits first. He bowed very correctly. "Your servant, sir." He didn't bother trying to keep the edge out of his voice or his expression. He sat down upon a vacant stool without being invited and gave Smith as direct a stare as he could with one operant eye.

Smith's cheeks flushed, but he leaned back a little, gathering his own wits before replying, and returned Grey's stare, with interest. He was not a big man but had broad shoulders and considerable presence of manner—and Grey knew him to be a very competent soldier. Competent enough not to reply directly to Grey but to turn instead to Corporal Woodbine.

"Corporal. How comes this gentleman here?"

"This is Lieutenant Colonel Lord John Grey, sir," Woodbine said. He was near bursting with pride at his capture and placed Grey's King's warrant and Graves's accompanying note on the rickety table with the manner of a butler presenting a roast pheasant with diamond eyes to a reigning monarch. "We caught him in the woods near Philadelphia. Out of uniform. Er . . . as you see, sir." He cleared his throat in emphasis. "*And* he admits to being a cousin of Major General Charles Grey. You know—the Paoli Massacre."

"Really?" Smith picked up the papers but cocked an eyebrow at Grey. "What was he doing there?"

"Having the shit beaten out of him by Colonel Fraser, sir—

he's one of Morgan's officers. He said," Woodbine added, with less certainty.

Smith looked blank.

"Fraser . . . don't believe I know him." Switching his attention to Grey, he addressed him for the first time. "Do *you* know Colonel Fraser . . . Colonel Grey?"

The elaborate hesitation spoke volumes. Well, he hadn't expected anything else. Grey wiped his nose as well as he could on a forearm and sat straight.

"I decline to answer your questions, sir. They are improperly put. You know my name, rank, and regiment. Beyond that, my business is my own."

Smith stared at him, eyes narrowed. Smith's eyes were rather attractive, a pale gray with black brows and lashes, very dramatic. Grey had noticed them when the man came to tea with Minnie.

Woodbine coughed.

"Er . . . Colonel Fraser said the man was his prisoner, sir. But he wouldn't say what for, and when I pressed the matter, he . . . er . . . left. That's when we searched Lord . . . er, the lord colonel here, and found his papers."

"He left," Smith repeated carefully. "And you allowed him to leave, Corporal?"

Woodbine was looking less confident in the virtue of his conduct but wasn't the sort to be easily cowed, Grey saw. He lowered his brow and gave Smith a look of his own.

"Couldn't have stopped him, short of shooting him. Sir," he added flatly. The flesh around Smith's nostrils whitened, and Grey had the distinct impression that the Englishman must find his new command not quite what he'd been used to.

The quarters certainly weren't. While Smith's Continental uniform was smart and well tended, and his wig in good order, his tent, while large, appeared to have been through several campaigns, being worn to the threads in places and patched in others. Not entirely a bad thing, Grey thought, briefly closing his eyes as a faint evening breeze came wafting through the walls of the tent, relieving the stifling heat. He had a noticeable headache, and even such minor relief was welcome.

"Very well, Corporal," Smith said after a moment, having evidently tried and failed to think of something new to ask.

"Well done," he added, offering a belated note of congratulation.

"Thank you, sir." Woodbine hovered, obviously loath to surrender his share of the excitement. "If I may ask, sir—what do you mean to do with the prisoner?"

Grey opened his eye and a half, interested to hear what the answer might be, and found Smith eyeing him in what seemed a faintly carnivorous fashion. The turncoat smiled.

"Oh, I'll think of something, Corporal Woodbine," he said. "You are dismissed. Good night."

SMITH GOT UP and came over to Grey, leaning down to examine his face. Grey could smell his sweat, sharp and musky.

"Do you need a doctor?" he asked dispassionately, but without hostility.

"No," Grey said. Both his head and his side ached deeply, and he felt dizzy, but he doubted there was anything a doctor could do about either condition. And he found that after prolonged contact with Claire and her opinions, he had much less trust in physicians than heretofore—and he hadn't had much to begin with.

Smith nodded and, straightening up, went to a battered campaign chest and dug out two dented pewter cups and a stone bottle of what proved to be applejack. He poured two generous tots, and they sat in silence for a time, sipping.

So close to Midsummer Day, it was still bright light out, though Grey could hear the rattle and shuffle of a camp beginning the evening routine. A mule brayed loudly, and several more answered it in raucous chorus. Wagons, then . . . perhaps artillery? He breathed deeply, nostrils flaring; an artillery company had a distinct smell to it, a sort of distillation of sweat, black powder, and hot metal, much more pungent than the scent of an infantry company with their muskets—the scent of searing iron seeped into an artilleryman's clothes, as well as his soul.

What came to him was not the stink of guns but the smell of roasting meat. It drifted through the tent, and his stomach growled loudly; he'd eaten nothing since the beer that had been his preliminary to a preempted meal. He thought Smith's mouth twitched a little at the noise, but the colonel politely ignored it.

Smith finished his drink, refilled both cups, and cleared his throat.

"I will not plague you with questions, as you don't wish to answer them," he said carefully, "but in the interests of civil conversation, should you wish to make any inquiries of me, I should not take offense."

Grey smiled wryly.

"Very gracious of you, sir. Do you wish to justify your present allegiance to me? I assure you, it's unnecessary."

Small red patches sprang up immediately on Smith's cheekbones.

"That was not my intent, sir," he said stiffly.

"Then I apologize," Grey said, and took another mouthful. The sweet strong cider was assuaging his hunger pangs as well as the pain in his side, though it admittedly wasn't doing much for the dizziness. "What sort of question did you think I might ask? What is the current state of the Continental army? I could deduce that easily enough, I think, from the state of the gentlemen who captured me, and . . . other evidence." He let his eyes roam deliberately around the tent, taking in the chipped pottery utensil under the lopsided cot, the tail of dirty linen straggling out of a portmanteau in the corner; evidently Smith had either no orderly or an inept one. For an instant, Grey felt a pang of nostalgia for Tom Byrd, the best valet he had ever had.

Smith's flush had faded; he gave a small, ironic laugh. "I imagine you could. It's not much of a secret. No, I rather thought you might be curious as to what I propose to do with you."

"Oh, that." Grey put down his cup and rubbed gingerly at his forehead, trying not to touch the swollen area around his eye. "Frankly, I'd forgotten, in the surprise of seeing you. And the pleasure of your kind hospitality," he added, lifting the cup with no irony at all. "Corporal Woodbine and his men appeared to think I should be promptly hanged, both on the charge of spying and on the more serious one of being related to Major General Charles Grey, who I gather is believed to have committed some atrocity at a place called Paoli."

Smith's brow creased.

"Do you deny being a spy?"

"Don't be ridiculous, Smith. I'm a lieutenant colonel. What on earth would I be doing, spying in a deserted wood? Well, deserted until Woodbine and his merry men showed up," he added. His cup was empty; he stared into it, wondering how that had happened. With a small sigh, Smith refilled it.

"Besides, I was carrying no documents of information, no secret writings—no evidence whatever of spying."

"Doubtless you committed to memory whatever information you had gained," Smith said, sounding cynically amused. "I recall that you have a prodigious memory." He gave a small snort that could perhaps have been called a snigger. *"So sayeth Sally, nimble-fingered, as her grip upon his prick did linger . . ."*

In fact, Grey's memory was quite good. Good enough to remember a dinner at which a number of officers from different regiments had been guests. When the gentlemen were at their port, Grey had—upon invitation, and to thunderous applause—recited entirely from memory one of the longer, and very scabrous, odes from Harry Quarry's infamous *Certain Verses Upon the Subject of Eros,* copies of which were still eagerly sought and covertly passed around the circles of society, though the book had been published nearly twenty years before.

"What on earth is there to spy *on*?" he demanded, realizing the logical trap too late. Smith's mouth turned up at one corner.

"You expect me to tell you?" Because the answer, of course, was that Washington's entire force was likely on the move in his immediate vicinity, positioning for the move into Philadelphia—and, very possibly, for an attack on Clinton's withdrawing troops.

Grey dismissed Smith's question as rhetorical and took another tack—though a dangerous one.

"Woodbine gave you a correct assessment of the circumstances in which he discovered me," he said. "Plainly I was not discovered *in flagrante* by Colonel Fraser, as he would simply have done what Corporal Woodbine did and arrested me."

"Are you asserting that Colonel Fraser met you by arrangement, to pass on information?"

Jesus Christ. He'd known this tack was dangerous but

hadn't foreseen *that* possibility—that Jamie Fraser could be suspected of being his confederate. But of course Smith would be particularly sensitive to such a possibility, given his own change of loyalties.

"Certainly not," Grey said, allowing a certain asperity to creep into his tone. "The encounter that Corporal Woodbine witnessed was of a purely personal nature."

Smith, who plainly knew a thing or two about interrogation, cocked a brow at him. Grey knew a thing or two about it, too, and sat back, sipping his applejack insouciantly, as though quite sure his statement had settled matters.

"They *will* probably hang you, you know," Smith said after a suitable pause. He spoke quite casually, eyes on the amber stream as he refilled both cups again. "After what Howe did to Captain Hale? Even more, after Paoli. Charles Grey is your cousin, is he not?"

"Second or third cousin, yes." Grey knew the man, though they didn't move in the same circles, either socially or militarily. Charles Grey was a pig-faced professional killer, rather than a soldier, and while he doubted that the Paoli Massacre had been entirely as described—what sort of idiots would lie on the ground waiting to be bayoneted in their beds? Because he didn't for an instant think a column of infantry was capable of sneaking up in the dark over rough country to within stabbing distance without giving some notice of their presence—he *did* know about Charles's merciless bayonet tactics at Culloden.

"Nonsense," Grey said, with as much confidence as he could summon. "Whatever one may think of the American high command, I doubt it is composed entirely of fools. My execution would yield nothing, whereas my exchange might be of value. My brother does have some small influence."

Smith smiled, not without sympathy.

"An excellent argument, Lord John, and one I'm sure would find favor with General Washington. Unfortunately, the Congress and the King remain at loggerheads over the matter of exchange; at present, there is no mechanism to allow the exchange of prisoners."

That one struck him in the pit of the stomach. He knew all too well that there were no official channels of exchange; he'd been trying to have William exchanged for months.

Smith upended the bottle, dribbling the last amber drops into Grey's cup.

"Are you a Bible-reading man, Colonel Grey?"

Grey looked at him blankly.

"Not habitually. I have read it, though. Some of it. Well . . . bits. Why?"

"I wondered if you were familiar with the concept of a scapegoat." Smith rocked back a little on his stool, gazing at Grey with his lovely deep-set eyes, which seemed to hold a certain sympathy—though perhaps it was just the applejack. "Because I'm afraid that is where your chief value lies, Colonel. It is no secret that the Continental army is in poor condition, lacking money, disillusion and desertion rife. Nothing would hearten and unify the troops more—or send a more potent message to General Clinton—than the trial and very public execution of a high-ranking British officer, a convicted spy and close relation to the infamous 'No Flints' Grey."

He belched softly and blinked, eyes still fixed on Grey.

"You asked what I meant to do with you."

"No, I didn't."

Smith ignored this, leveling a long, knobby finger at him.

"I'm sending you to General Wayne, who, believe me, has 'Paoli' carved upon his heart."

"How very painful for him," Grey said politely, and drained his cup.

12

EINE KLEINE NACHTMUSIK

THE INTERMINABLE DAY was reluctantly ending, the heat at last beginning to fade from the forest along with the waning light. He didn't suppose that he would be taken directly to General Wayne, unless that worthy were close at hand, and he thought not. He could tell from the sounds and the feel of the camp that it was a small one, and plainly Colonel Smith was the senior officer present.

Smith had asked him, *pro forma,* to give his parole—and been substantially taken aback when Grey had courteously refused to do so.

"If I am in fact a duly commissioned British officer," Grey had pointed out, "then clearly it is my duty to escape."

Smith eyed him, the failing light shading his face with sufficient ambiguity that Grey was not sure whether he was fighting an impulse to smile or not. Probably not.

"You're not escaping," he said definitely, and went out. Grey could hear a brief, heated discussion, conducted in low voices outside the tent, as to just what to do with him. A militia camp on the move had no facilities for prisoners. Grey amused himself by composing a mental entertainment in which Smith was obliged to share his narrow cot with Grey, in the interests of keeping his prisoner secure.

In the end, though, a corporal came in, carrying a rusty set of fetters that looked as though they had last seen use during the Spanish Inquisition, and took Grey to the edge of camp, where a soldier who had been a blacksmith in private life banged them into place with a stout hammer, using a flattish rock as an anvil.

He felt the oddest sensations, kneeling on the ground in the twilight, an interested group of militiamen gathered round in a circle to watch. He was forced to lean forward in a crouching posture, hands laid before him, as though he were about to be beheaded, and the hammer blows echoed through the metal, into the bones of his wrists and arms.

He kept his eyes on the hammer, and not only from fear that the smith would miss his aim in the growing dusk and smash one of his hands. Under the influence of intoxication and a growing, deeper fear that he didn't want to acknowledge, he sensed the mingled curiosity and animus surrounding him and felt it as he would a nearby thunderstorm, electricity crawling over his skin, the threat of lightning annihilation so close he could smell its sharp odor, mixed with gunpowder and the heavy tang of the sweat of men.

Ozone. His mind seized on the word, a small escape into rationality. That's what Claire called the smell of lightning.

He'd told her he thought it was from the Greek *ozon,* the neuter present participle of *ozein,* meaning "to smell."

He began to work his way methodically through the complete conjugation; by the time he'd finished, surely they would be done with it. *Ozein,* to smell. I smell . . .

He could smell his own sweat, sharp and sweet. In the old days, it was considered a better death, beheading. To be hanged was shameful, a commoner's death, a criminal's death. Slower. He knew that for a fact.

A final reverberating blow, and a visceral sound of satisfaction from the watching men. He was made prisoner.

THERE BEING NO shelter other than the brushy wigwams and scraps of canvas the militiamen rigged near their fires, he was escorted back to Smith's big, threadbare tent, given supper—which he forced down, not much noticing what he ate—and then tethered to the tent pole with a long, thin rope run through the chain of his irons, with sufficient play as to allow him to lie down or use the utensil.

At Smith's insistence, he took the cot and did lie down with a slight groan of relief. His temples throbbed with each heartbeat, and so did the entire left side of his face, which was now radiating small jolts down into his upper teeth, very unpleasant. The pain in his side had dulled to a deep ache, almost negligible by comparison. Luckily, he was so tired that sleep swamped all discomfort, and he fell into it with a sense of profound gratitude.

He woke in the full dark sometime later, slicked with sweat, heart hammering from some desperate dream. He raised a hand to push the soaked hair off his face and felt the heavy, chafing weight of the fetters, which he'd forgotten about. They clanked, and the dark figure of a sentry silhouetted in the fire glow at the entrance of the tent turned sharply toward him, but then relaxed as he turned over on the cot, clanking further.

Bugger, he thought, still groggy with sleep. *Couldn't even masturbate if I wanted to.* The thought made him laugh, though fortunately it came out as a mere breath of sound.

Another body turned over, rustling, shifting heavily near him. Smith, he supposed, sleeping on a canvas bed sack stuffed with grass; Grey could smell the meadow scent of dry hay, faintly musty in the humid air. The bed sack was standard issue to the British army; Smith must have kept it, along with his tent and other equipment, changing only his uniform.

Why had he turned his coat? Grey wondered vaguely, peering at Smith's humped shape, just visible against the pale canvas. Advancement? Starved as they were for professional soldiers, the Continentals offered rank as inducement; a captain in any European army might become anything from a major to a general in the blink of an eye, whereas the only means of achieving higher rank in England was to find the money to purchase it.

What was rank without pay, though? Grey was no longer a spy, but he had been one, once—and still knew men who labored in those dark fields. From what he'd heard, the American Congress had no money at all and depended upon loans—these unpredictable in amount and erratic in occurrence. Some from French or Spanish sources, though the French wouldn't admit to it, of course. Some from Jewish moneylenders, said one of his correspondents. *Salomon, Solomon . . . some name like that.*

These random musings were interrupted by a sound that made him stiffen. A woman's laughter.

There were women in the camp, wives who had come along to war with their husbands. He'd seen a few when they took him across the campground, and one had brought his supper, glancing suspiciously up at him from under her cap. But he thought he *knew* that laugh—deep, gurgling, and totally unself-conscious.

"Jesus," he whispered under his breath. "Dottie?"

It wasn't impossible. He swallowed, trying to clear his left ear, to listen through the multitude of small sounds outside. Denzell Hunter was a Continental surgeon, and Dottie had—to her brother's, cousin's, and uncle's horror—joined the camp followers at Valley Forge in order to help her fiancé, though she rode into Philadelphia regularly to visit her brother Henry. If Washington's forces were moving—and very plainly they were—it was entirely possible that a surgeon might be anywhere among them.

A high, clear voice, raised in question. An English voice,

and not common. He strained to hear but couldn't make out the words. He wished she'd laugh again.

If it *was* Dottie . . . he breathed deep, trying to think. He couldn't call out to her; he'd felt the avid hostility directed at him from every man in camp—letting the relationship be known would be dangerous for her and Denzell, both, and certainly wouldn't help Grey. And yet he had to risk it—they'd move him in the morning.

Out of sheer inability to think of anything better, he sat up on the cot and began to sing *"Die Sommernacht."* Quietly at first, but gathering strength and volume. As he hit *"In den Kulungen wehn"* at the top of his very resonant tenor voice, Smith sat up like a jack-in-the-box and said, *"What?"* in tones of utter amazement.

"So umschatten mich Gedanken an das Grab
Meiner Geliebten, und ich seh' im Walde
Nur es dämmern, und es weht mir
Von der Blüte nicht her."

Grey went on, reducing his volume somewhat. He didn't want Dottie—if it was Dottie—coming to look, only to let her know he was here. He'd taught her this *lied* when she was fourteen; she sang it often at musicales.

"Ich genoß einst, o ihr Toten, es mit euch!
Wie umwehten uns der Duft und die Kühlung,
Wie verschönt warst von dem Monde,
Du, o schöne Natur!"

He stopped, coughed a little, and spoke into the marked silence before him, slurring his words a bit, as though still drunk. In fact, he discovered, he was.

"Might I have some water, Colonel?"

"Will you sing anymore if I give it to you?" Smith asked, deeply suspicious.

"No, I think I'm finished now," Grey assured him. "Couldn' sleep, you know—too much to drink—but I find a song settles the mind rem-remarkably."

"Oh, does it?" Smith breathed heavily for a moment, but clambered to his feet and fetched the ewer from his basin.

Grey could feel him repressing an urge to douse his prisoner with the contents, but Smith was a man of strong character and merely held the pitcher for him to drink, then put it back and resumed his own bed with no more than a few irritable snorts.

The *lied* had caused some comment in the camp, and a few musical souls took it as inspiration and began singing everything from "Greensleeves"—a very poignant and tender rendition—to "Chester." Grey quite enjoyed the singing, though it was only by exercise of his own strong character that he refrained from shaking his fetters at the end of:

> *"Let tyrants shake their iron rods. And slavery clank her galling chains."*

They were still singing when he fell asleep again, to dream in anxious fragments, the fumes of applejack drifting through the hollow spaces of his head.

Number 17 Chestnut Street

THE BELL OF the Presbyterian church struck midnight, but the city wasn't sleeping. The sounds were more furtive now, muffled by darkness, but the streets were still alive with hurrying feet and the sound of moving wagons—and, in the far distance, I heard a faint cry of "Fire!" being raised.

I stood by the open window, sniffing the air for smoke and watching out for any sign of flames that might spread in our direction. I wasn't aware of Philadelphia having ever burned to the ground like London or Chicago, but a fire that merely engulfed the neighborhood would be just as bad from my point of view.

There was no wind at all; that was something. The summer air hung heavy, damp as a sponge. I waited for a bit, but the cries stopped, and I saw no red glimmer of flames against the half-clouded sky. No trace of fire save the cool green sparks of fireflies, drifting among the shadowed leaves in the front garden.

I stood for a bit, letting my shoulders slump, letting go of my half-formed plans for emergency evacuation. I was exhausted but unable to sleep. Beyond the need to keep an eye on my unsettled patient, and the unsettled atmosphere beyond the quiet room, I was most unsettled in myself. I'd been listening all day, constantly on the alert for a familiar footstep, the sound of Jamie's voice. But he hadn't come.

What if he had learned from John that I had shared his bed on that one drunken evening? Would the shock of that, given without preparation or suitable explanation, be enough to have made him run away—for good?

I felt sudden tears come to my eyes and shut them, hard, to stem the flow, gripping the sill with both hands.

Don't be ridiculous. He'll come as soon as he can, no matter what. You know he will. I did know. But the shocked joy of seeing him alive had wakened nerves that had been numb for a long time, and while I might seem calm externally, on the inside my emotions were at a rolling boil. The steam was building up, and I had no way to release the pressure—save pointless tears, and I wouldn't give way to those.

For one thing, I might not be able to stop. I pressed the sleeve of my dressing gown briefly to my eyes, then turned back resolutely into the darkness of the room.

A small brazier burned near the bed under a tented wet cloth, casting a flickering red glow on Pardloe's sharp-cut features. He was breathing with an audible rasp and I could hear his lungs rattle with each exhalation, but it was a deep breathing, and regular. It occurred to me that I might not have been able to smell the smoke of a fire outside, had there been one: the atmosphere in the room was thick with oil of peppermint, eucalyptus . . . and cannabis. Despite the wet cloth, enough smoke had escaped the brazier to form a hanging cloud of purling wisps, moving pale as ghosts in the darkened air.

I sprinkled more water on the muslin tent and sat down in the small armchair beside the bed, breathing the saturated atmosphere in cautiously but with an agreeable small sense of illicit pleasure. Hal had told me that he was in the habit of smoking hemp to relax his lungs and that it seemed to be effective. He'd said "hemp," and that was undoubtedly what he'd been smoking; the psychoactive form of the plant didn't grow in England and wasn't commonly imported.

I hadn't any hemp leaves in my medical supply but did have a good bit of ganja, which John had acquired from a Philadelphia merchant who had two Indiamen. It was useful in the treatment of glaucoma, as I'd learned when treating Jamie's aunt Jocasta, it relieved nausea and anxiety—and it had occasional non-medicinal uses, as John had informed me, to my private amusement.

Thought of John gave me a small internal qualm, to add to my anxiety over Jamie, and I took a deep, deliberate breath of the sweet, spicy air. Where was *he*? What had Jamie done with him?

"Do you ever make bargains with God?" Hal's voice came quietly out of the half dark.

I must subconsciously have known he wasn't sleeping, for I wasn't startled.

"Everyone does," I said. "Even people who don't believe in God. Do you?"

There was the breath of a laugh, followed by coughing, but it stopped quickly. Perhaps the smoke *was* helping.

"Have you got such a bargain in mind?" I asked, as much from real curiosity as to make conversation. "You aren't going to die, you know. I won't let you."

"Yes, you said that," he replied dryly. After a moment's hesitation, he turned on his side to face me. "I do believe you," he said rather formally. "And . . . I thank you."

"You're quite welcome. I can't let you die in John's house, you know; he'd be upset."

He smiled at that, his face visible in the brazier's glow. We didn't speak for a bit but sat looking at each other, with no particular sense of self-consciousness, both of us calmed by the smoke and the sleepy chirping of crickets outside. The sound of wagon wheels had ceased, but there were still people passing by. Surely I would know Jamie's step, be able to distinguish his, even among so many. . . .

"You're worried about him, aren't you?" he asked. "John."

"No," I said quickly, but I saw one dark brow rise and remembered that he already knew me for a bad liar. "That is . . . I'm sure he's quite all right. But I *would* have expected him home by now. And with so much commotion in the city . . ." I waved a hand toward the window. "You don't know what might happen, do you?"

I heard him draw breath, his chest rattling faintly, and clear his throat.

"And you still decline to tell me where he is."

I lifted one shoulder and let it fall; it seemed pointless to repeat that I didn't know, even though that *was* the truth. Instead, I took up a comb from the table and began to deal slowly with my hair, untangling and smoothing the unruly mass, enjoying the cool feel of it in my hands. After we had bathed Hal and got him put to bed, I'd taken a quarter hour for a somewhat more leisurely wash of my own and had rinsed the sweat and dust from my hair, despite knowing it would take hours to dry in the humid air.

"The bargain I had in mind was not for my own life," he said after a bit. "As such."

"I'm sure John isn't going to die, either, if that's what you—"

"Not John. My son. My daughter. And my grandson. You have grandchildren, I collect? I believe I heard that rather stalwart young man call you 'Grannie' this afternoon, did I not?" His voice held a trace of amusement.

"You did, and I do. You mean Dorothea? Is something the matter with her?" A stab of alarm made me set down the comb. I'd seen Dottie only a few days before, at the house where her brother Henry was staying.

"Aside from the fact that she appears to be on the verge of marrying a Rebel and declares her intent to accompany the man onto battlefields and to live with him under the most insalubrious conditions imaginable?"

He sat up in bed and spoke with evident passion, but I couldn't help smiling at his mode of expression; evidently the Grey brothers shared the same habit of speech. I coughed to hide this, though, and replied as tactfully as possible.

"Um . . . you've seen Dottie, then?"

"Yes, I have," he said shortly. "She was with Henry when I arrived yesterday, and wearing the most extraordinary garment. Evidently the man to whom she considers herself affianced is a Quaker, and she declares that she has become one, as well!"

"So I understand," I murmured. "You . . . er . . . hadn't heard about it?"

"No, I had not! And I have a few things to say to John regarding both his cowardice in not telling me about it and his son's unpardonable machi . . . machinations . . ." The choler in this speech literally choked him, and he had to stop and cough, wrapping his arms round his knees to steady himself against the racking spasms.

I took up the fan I'd left on the table earlier and wafted a bit of smoke from the brazier into his face. He gasped, coughed harder for a moment, and then subsided, wheezing.

"I'd tell you not to excite yourself, if I thought there was the slightest chance of you listening," I remarked, handing him a cup of the boiled tincture of *Ephedra* in coffee. "Drink that. Slowly.

"As for John," I went on, watching him make faces over the bitter taste, "he considered writing to you when he found out what Dottie intended. He didn't, because at the time he thought it might be nothing more than a passing whim and that once she'd seen the reality of Denny's—er, that's her fiancé, Dr. Hunter—of his life, she might think better of it. And if she did, there was no need to alarm you and your wife. He never expected you to turn up here."

Hal coughed once, then drew breath in a tentative fashion.

"I didn't, either," he said, and, putting the cup aside, coughed again and lay back against the heaped pillows. "The War Office decided to send my regiment to support Clinton when the new strategy was decided upon; there wasn't time to write."

"Which new strategy is this?" I asked, only mildly interested.

"To sever the southern colonies from the north, suppress the rebellion there, and thus starve the north into submission. Keep the bloody French out of the West Indies, too," he added as an afterthought. "You think Dottie might change her mind?" He sounded dubious but hopeful.

"Actually, no," I said. I stretched and ran my fingers through my damp hair, which had settled softly on my neck and shoulders, curling light and tickling round my face. "I wondered whether it was you or your wife she took after in terms of willfulness, but the instant I met you, it was clear."

He gave me a narrow look but had the grace to smile.

"She does," he admitted. "So does Benjamin—my eldest son. Henry and Adam are both like my wife in terms of temperament. Which does not mean that they aren't capable of seeking their own way," he added thoughtfully. "Only that they're rather more diplomatic about it."

"I'd like to meet your wife," I said, smiling, too. "Her name is Minnie, John said?"

"Minerva," he said, his smile growing more genuine. "Minerva Cunnegunda, to be exact. Couldn't call her 'Cunny,' could I?"

"Probably not in public, no."

"Wouldn't try it in private, either," he assured me. "She's very demure—to look at."

I laughed, and darted a glance at the brazier. I hadn't thought the active principle in ganja would be very strong, burned as an atmospheric rather than smoked directly. Still, it was obviously having a beneficial effect on Hal's mood as well as his asthma, and I was conscious of a slight feeling of well-being beginning to creep into my own outlook. I was still worried about Jamie—and John—but the worry had lifted from my shoulders and seemed to be floating a little way above my head: still visible, and a dull purple-gray in color, but floating. *Like a lead balloon,* I thought, and gave a small, amused snort.

Hal was lying back, eyes half lidded, watching me with a sort of detached interest.

"You're a beautiful woman," he said, sounding faintly surprised. "Not demure, though," he added, and made a low chuckling noise. "What could John have been thinking?"

I knew what John had been thinking but didn't want to talk about it—for assorted reasons.

"What did you mean earlier," I asked curiously, "about making bargains with God?"

"Ah." His eyelids closed slowly. "When I arrived at General Clinton's office this morning—God, was that only this morning?—he had rather bad news for me—and a letter. Sent some weeks ago from New Jersey, forwarded eventually to him through the army post.

"My eldest son, Benjamin, was captured by the Rebels at the Brandywine," he said, almost dispassionately. Almost; there was enough light for me to see the bulge of his jaw muscle. "There is at present no agreement with the Americans involving the exchange of prisoners, so he remains in captivity."

"Where?" I asked, disturbed at the news.

"I don't know that," he said shortly. "Yet. But I shall discover his whereabouts as quickly as possible."

"Godspeed," I said sincerely. "Was the letter from Benjamin?"

"No." His jaw tightened a little further.

The letter had been from a young woman named Amaranthus Cowden, who informed His Grace the Duke of Pardloe that she was the wife of his son Benjamin—and the mother of Benjamin's son, Trevor Wattiswade Grey, aged three months. *Born after Benjamin was captured,* I thought, and wondered whether Benjamin knew about the baby.

The young Mrs. Grey found herself in difficult circumstances, she wrote, owing to her husband's sad absence, and therefore proposed to go to her relatives in Charleston. She felt some delicacy in approaching His Grace for assistance, but her state was such that she felt she had little choice in the matter and hoped that he would forgive her forwardness and look kindly upon her plea. She enclosed a lock of her son's hair, feeling that His Grace might like to have such a keepsake of his grandson.

"Dear me," I said. I hesitated for a moment, but the same thought must surely have occurred to him. "Do you think she's telling the truth?"

He sighed, a mixture of anxiety and aggravation.

"Almost certainly she is. My wife's maiden name was Wattiswade, but no one outside the family would know that." He nodded toward the wardrobe where Mrs. Figg had hung his uniform. "The letter is in my coat, should you wish to read it."

I waved a hand in polite dismissal.

"I see what you meant about making bargains with God. You want to live to see your grandchild—and your son, of course."

He sighed again, his lean body seeming to diminish slightly. Mrs. Figg had undone his queue—much against his will—brushed out his hair, and tied it in a loose tail that now fell over his shoulder, a soft dark brown shot with streaks of white that glinted red and gold in the fire glow.

"Not precisely. I do want that, of course, but—" He groped for words, quite unlike his earlier elegant loquacity. "You'd die for them, happily. Your family. But at the same time you think, *Christ, I can't die! What might happen to them if I weren't here?*" He gave me a wry and rueful smile. "And you know bloody well that you mostly can't help them anyway; they've got to do it—or not—themselves."

"Unfortunately, yes." A draft of air moved the muslin curtains and stirred the hanging pall of smoke. "Not the grandchildren, though. You can help them." And I suddenly missed Henri-Christian's soft weight, his solid head against my shoulder; I'd saved his life by removing his tonsils and adenoids, and I thanked God that I'd been in time to do it. And Mandy . . . *God, take care of her,* I prayed fiercely. I'd been able to tell Bree what was wrong and that it could be fixed—but *I* couldn't fix her heart defect, and I regretted that lack every day of my life. If I could have done the necessary surgery in this time, they'd all still be here. . . .

The curtains moved again, and the heavy atmosphere drew a clean, sudden breath. I inhaled deeply, catching the faint, sharp scent of ozone. "Rain," I said. "Rain's coming."

The duke didn't reply but turned, lifting his face toward the window. I got up and raised the sash higher, gratefully letting in a cool breeze. I looked out into the night again; clouds were drifting fast across the moon, so the light seemed to pulse rather than flicker, like the beat of a palpitating heart. The streets were dark, with no more than the occasional glow of a moving lantern to mark the muted agitation of the city.

Rain might damp the movement, both of fleeing Loyalists and the army readying itself to depart. Would the cover of the storm make it easier for Jamie to come into the city? A bad storm might hamper him, turning the roads to mud. How far away was he?

The lead balloon had come down on my head. My mood had taken a plunge, whether from fatigue, the oncoming storm, or merely as a natural effect of cannabinol, I didn't know. I shivered, though the air was still hot, unable to keep my brain from projecting vivid images of all the dire possibilities that could befall a man caught between two armies, alone in the night.

Maybe alone. What *had* he done with John? Surely he wouldn't have—

"I was twenty-one when my father died," Hal remarked out of the blue. "Grown. Had my own life, had a wife—" He broke off abruptly, his mouth twisting. "Didn't think I needed him at all, until he suddenly wasn't there."

"What could he have done for you?" I asked, sitting down again. I was curious—but also anxious to avoid my own racing thoughts.

Hal lifted one slender shoulder. The neck of the nightshirt was unbuttoned, both because of the heat and so I could more easily see the pulse in his neck. It fell open, the cloth limp with moisture, and his clavicle showed, high-arched and clean, shadowed sharp against his skin.

"Been there," he said simply. "Listened. Perhaps . . . approved of what I was doing." The last few words came low, barely audible. "Or maybe not. But . . . been there."

"I know what you mean," I said, more to myself than to him. I'd been lucky; I was very young when my parents died, and my uncle had stepped promptly into my life, to be there for me. And casual as his own life had been—he always *was* there. I'd felt his loss acutely when he died, but I'd been married then—a spasm of guilt seized me out of nowhere, thinking of Frank. And another, worse, thinking of Brianna. I'd left her, once—and then she had left me.

That unleashed a jumble of morbid thoughts: of Laoghaire, abandoned by both daughters, unlikely ever to see her grandchildren, now mine. Of Jem and Mandy . . . and Jamie.

Where *was* he? And why wasn't he here? Surely, whatever John might have told him . . .

"Oh, dear," I said hopelessly, under my breath. I could feel the tears prick and well, pressing up against the dam of my determination.

"Do you know, I'm most remarkably hungry," Hal said, sounding surprised. "Is there any food in the house?"

JAMIE'S STOMACH GROWLED, and he coughed to cover the sound, but there was no need. The little girls were curled up like a pair of capped hedgehogs under a tattered quilt by the hearth, back to back and snoring like drunken bumblebees. Mrs. Hardman was on the settle, singing to the baby under her breath. He couldn't make out the words, so he couldn't tell what song it was, but imagined it to be a lullaby. On the other hand, he'd heard Highland women sing their babes asleep often enough with things like *"Nighean Nan Geug,"* which dealt with severed heads and blood-soaked ground. But Mrs. Hardman was a Friend; presumably she'd have no truck with that sort of lullaby. Maybe "The Great Silkie of Sule Skerry," he thought, beginning to relax. Clearly Friends had no objection to carnal relations as such . . .

That reminded him of bloody John Grey, and he grimaced, then stifled a grunt as his back sent a warning shot down his leg, indicating that even that much movement wouldn't be tolerated.

The song was no more music to him than the snoring, but both were gentle sounds, and he eased himself cautiously, checked that knife and pistol were easily to hand, and shut his eyes. He was tired to the bone but doubted he'd sleep. He couldn't even shift himself in the bed without white stabs of pain jabbing him in the backside like the devil's pitchfork.

It had been years since his back had last done this to him. Ached frequently, now and then was stiff in the morning, but it hadn't done this in . . . ten years? He remembered it vividly. It was soon after they'd come to the Ridge, just after he and Ian built the cabin. He'd gone out a-hunting, sprung over a bank in pursuit of a fleeing elk, and found himself lying on his face at the foot of the bank, quite unable to move.

Claire, bless her, had come searching for him—he smiled wryly at thought of it; she'd been so proud of tracking him through the forest. If she hadn't found him . . . well, it would have been the luck of the draw as to whether a painter, bear, or wolf came upon him before his back released its clench and let him move. He supposed he wouldn't have died of cold, though he might well have lost a few toes to frostbite.

She—

A sound brought his head up, fast. His back stabbed viciously, but he set his teeth, ignoring it, and pulled the pistol out from underneath his pillow.

Mrs. Hardman's head jerked up at his movement. She stared at him, wide-eyed, then heard what he had heard and got up hastily. Feet on the path, more than one pair. She turned, looking for the cradle, but he shook his head.

"Keep the bairnie with ye," he said, low-voiced. "Answer when they knock, open if they ask."

He saw her swallow, but she did as he said. There were three or four, he thought, but not bent on mischief. There were feet on the porch, low murmurs, and a bit of laughing. A knock, and Mrs. Hardman called, "Who's there?"

"Friends, missus," said a man's voice, slurred with drink. "Let us in."

She cast a frightened glance at Jamie, but he nodded, and she lifted the latch, opening the door to the night. The first man started to come in but then saw Jamie on the bed and stopped, mouth open.

"Good evenin' to ye," Jamie said, polite, but holding the other man's eyes with his own. The pistol lay in plain sight, under his hand.

"Oh," said the other man, disconcerted. He was young and rather stout, dressed in hunting garb but with a militia badge; he glanced over his shoulder at his companions, who had stopped on the threshold. "I—er—good evening to you, sir. We didn't—er—we thought . . ." He cleared his throat.

Jamie smiled at him, well aware what he thought. Keeping the man in sight from the corner of his eye, he turned to Mrs. Hardman and gestured to her to sit down. She did and bent her head over the child, brushing her lips over Chastity's tiny cap.

"We've nothing to offer ye in the way of food, gentlemen," Jamie said. "But there's cold water from the well, and a bed in the shed, if ye need it."

The other two men stood outside, shuffling awkwardly. There was a strong smell of liquor coming off them, but they hadn't come in a mood to do damage.

"That's all right," the young man said, backing up to his friends. His round face was flushed, as much with embarrassment as with liquor. "We'll just . . . sorry to disturb you. Sir."

The other two bobbed their heads, and all three retreated, shuffling and bumping into one another in their haste to leave. The last one pulled the door to, but not all the way. Mrs. Hardman rose and pushed it to with a small bang, then leaned against it, her eyes closed, the child clasped against her bosom.

"Thank you," she whispered.

"It's all right," he said. "They'll not come back. Put the bairn down and bar the door, aye?"

She did, then turned and leaned against the door, her hands pressed flat against it. She looked at the floor between her feet, breathing audibly for a moment, then slowly straightened.

Her plain jacket was fastened with pins—he didn't know if this was to avoid the vanity of buttons, as the Moravians did, or whether she was simply too poor to have any. Her fingers fiddled nervously with the top pin, and then she suddenly pulled it out and laid it glinting on the shelf. She looked directly at him then, her fingers gripping the head of the next pin. Her long upper lip was pressed down, and a nervous sweat glistened on it.

"Dinna even think about it," he said bluntly. "In my present condition, I couldna swive a dead sheep. To say nothing of which, I'm old enough to be your father, lass—and I'm marrit, forbye."

Her mouth quivered slightly, though he couldn't tell whether with disappointment or relief. Her fingers relaxed, though, and her hand dropped to her side.

"Ye dinna need to pay me for the food, lass," he said. "It was a gift."

"I—yes, I know. I thank thee, Friend." She looked aside, swallowing a little. "I only—I hoped that perhaps—thee might stay. For a time."

"I'm marrit, lass," he repeated gently, then, after an uncomfortable pause, felt compelled to ask, "Do ye have such callers often?" It had been clear to him that the men were strangers to her—but she was not to them. They'd heard of the Quaker woman who lived alone with three young girls.

"I take them to the shed," she blurted, her face going redder than the flames made it. "After the girls are asleep."

"Mmphm," he said, after another pause that lasted much too long. His eyes went to the cradle but then shot away. He wondered how long Mr. Hardman had been gone from home, but it wasn't his business. Nor was it his business how she managed to feed her girls.

"Sleep, lass," he said. "I'll keep watch."

13

MORNING AIR AWASH WITH ANGELS

Next day

JAMIE AWOKE TO THE smell of frying meat and sat up straight in bed, forgetting his back.

"Lord have mercy," said Mrs. Hardman, looking over her shoulder. "I haven't heard a noise like that since the last time my husband, Gabriel, killed a pig." She shook her head and returned to her cookery, pouring batter into an oiled cast-iron spider that sat in the coals, smoking and spitting in a baleful sort of way.

"I beg your pardon, ma'am—"

"Silvia is my name, Friend. And thine?" she asked, raising one brow at him.

"Friend Silvia," he said through clenched teeth. "My name is Jamie. Jamie Fraser." He'd raised his knees in the involuntary jerk that brought him upright, and now he wrapped his arms around them and laid his sweating face against the worn quilt that covered them, trying to stretch his recalcitrant back. The effort shot pain down his right leg and caused an instant sharp cramp in his left calf muscle, which made him grunt and pant until it let go.

"I'm pleased to see thee sit up, Friend Jamie," Silvia Hardman remarked, bringing him a plate filled with sausage, fried onions, and johnnycake. "Your back is some better, I collect?" She smiled at him.

"Somewhat," he managed, and smiled back as well as he could while trying not to groan. "You—have fresh food, I see."

"Yes, God be thanked," she said fervently. "I sent Pru and Patience out to the main road at dawn to watch for wagons coming in to the market in Philadelphia, and they came back with a pound of sausage, two of cornmeal, a sack of oats, and a dozen eggs. Eat up!" She placed the wooden plate on the bed beside him, with a wooden spoon.

Jamie could see Prudence and Patience behind their mother, industriously wiping sausage grease from their empty plates with chunks of johnnycake. Easing himself gingerly around in order to put his back against the wall, he stretched out his legs, picked up the plate, and followed their example.

The food filled him with a surprising sense of well-being, and he put down the empty plate determined upon enterprise.

"I propose to visit your privy, Friend Silvia. But I may need some assistance to rise."

Once on his feet, he found that he could make shift to stagger a few inches at a time, and Prudence and Patience at once rushed up to seize him by the elbows, in the manner of small flying buttresses.

"Don't worry," Prudence advised him, squaring her puny shoulders and looking confidently up at him. "We won't let thee fall."

"I'm sure ye won't," he said gravely. In fact, the little girls had a wiry strength that belied their fragile appearance, and he found their presence an actual help, as they provided something for him to hold on to for balance when it was necessary to stop—as it was every few feet.

"Tell me about the wagons that go into Philadelphia," he said at one such stop, as much to make conversation as because he required the information. "Do they come only in the early morning?"

"Mostly," Patience said. "They go back empty an hour or two before sunset." She set her feet wider, bracing herself. "It's all right," she assured him. "Lean on me. Thee seems summat shaky."

He squeezed her shoulder gently in thanks and let her take a very little of his weight. Shaky, indeed. It was more than half a mile to the main road; it would take over an hour to totter that far, even with the girls' assistance, and the likelihood of his back freezing again and stranding him midway was yet too high to risk it. To say nothing of the risk of arriving in Philadelphia completely unable to move. By tomorrow, though . . .

"And did ye see soldiers on the road?" he asked, essaying a ginger step that shot pain from hip to foot. "Ow!"

"We did," Patience said, taking a tighter grip on his elbow. "Courage, Friend. Thee will prevail. We saw two companies of militia, and one Continental officer on a mule."

"We saw some British soldiers, too, though," Prudence put in, eager not to be overlooked. "They were with a train of carts, going in the other direction."

"The other—away from Philadelphia?" Jamie asked, his heart jumping. Was the evacuation of the British army already begun? "Could you see what was in the carts?"

Prudence shrugged. "Furniture. Trunks and baskets. There were ladies riding atop some of the carts, though mostly they walked alongside. No room," she clarified. "Guard thy shirt-tail, Friend, or thy modesty will be at risk." The morning was cool and breezy, and an errant gust of wind had risen up, bellying his shirt—wonderful on his sweating body, but definitely a risk to maiden eyes.

"Shall I knot the tails between thy legs?" Patience inquired. "I can tie a granny knot, an overhand knot, or a square knot. My daddy taught me!"

"Don't be silly, Patience," her sister said crossly. "If thee knots his shirt, how will he lift it to shit? No one can untie her knots," she confided to Jamie. "She always makes them too tight."

"Oh, I do not, liar!"

"Fie upon thee, sister! I'll tell Mummy what thee said!"

"Where is your father?" Jamie interrupted, wanting to stop the acrimony before they began pulling each other's hair. They did stop and glanced at each other for a moment before replying.

"We don't know," Prudence said, her voice small and sad. "He went a-hunting one day a year ago and didn't come back."

"It might be that Indians took him," Patience said, trying to sound hopeful. "If so, may be that he'll escape one day and come home."

Prudence sighed.

"Maybe," she said flatly. "Mummy thinks the militia shot him."

"Why?" Jamie asked, looking down at her. "Why would they shoot him?"

"For being a Friend," Patience explained. "He wouldn't fight, and so they said he was a Loyalist."

"I see. Was—er, I mean—*is* he?"

Prudence looked at him, grateful for the "is."

"I don't think so. But Mummy says Philadelphia Yearly Meeting told everyone that all Friends should be for the King, as the King would keep peace and the Rebels seek to break it. So"—she shrugged—"people think all Friends are Loyalists."

"Daddy wasn't—*isn't,*" Patience put in. "He used to say all kinds of things about the King, and Mummy would get worried and beg him to hold his tongue. Here's the privy," she announced unnecessarily, letting go of Jamie's elbow in order to open the door. "Don't wipe thyself with the towel; it's for hands. There are corncobs in the basket."

JOHN GREY WOKE feverish and heavy-limbed, with a pounding headache, and a stabbing pain in his left eye when he tried to open it. Both his eyes were crusted and gummy. He'd been dreaming in vivid, fractured swaths, a confusion of images, voices, emotions . . . Jamie Fraser had been shouting at him, face dark with passion, but then something changed, some sort of pursuit began, and he fell back into queasy nightmare. They were running together through a bog, a sucking quagmire that pulled at his steps, and Fraser was struggling just ahead of him, trapped, shouting at him to go back, but he couldn't, his feet were mired fast and he was sinking, flailing madly but unable to get a purchase on anything . . .

"Gaah!" A hand shook him by the shoulder, startling him out of the morass. He pried his good eye open and saw the wavering form of a neat young man in a dark coat and spectacles, peering down at him in an oddly familiar way.

"John Grey?" said the young man.

"I am," he said. He swallowed painfully. "Have I—the honor of your acquaintance, sir?"

The young man flushed a bit.

"Thee has, Friend Grey," he said, low-voiced. "I am—"

"Oh!" Grey said, sitting up in a rush. "Of course, you—oh.

Oh, Jesus." His head, disturbed by the abrupt change of posture, had apparently decided to fly off his shoulders and thump into the nearest wall. The young man . . . *Hunter,* he thought, finding the name turn up with an odd neatness among the chaos inside his skull. *Dr.* Hunter. Dottie's Quaker.

"I think thee had best lie down, Friend."

"I think I had best vomit first."

Hunter snatched the pot out from under the cot just in time. By the time he had administered water—"Drink slowly, Friend, if thee wishes to keep it"—and eased Grey back down on the cot, Colonel Smith was looming up behind him.

"What do you say, Doctor?" Smith was frowning and seemed worried. "Is he in his right mind? He was singing last night, now he's been moaning and saying odd things, and the look of him . . ." Smith grimaced in a fashion that made Grey wonder what the devil he *did* look like.

"He's badly fevered," Hunter said, with a piercing look through his spectacles as he bent to take hold of Grey's wrist. "And thee sees the condition of his eye. It would be dangerous to move him. A further extravasation of blood into the brain . . ."

Smith made a discontented noise and compressed his lips. He nudged Hunter aside and bent over Grey.

"Can you hear me, Colonel?" he asked, speaking in the slow, distinct manner one used with idiots and foreigners.

"Ich bin ein Fisch . . ." Grey murmured beatifically, and closed his eyes.

"His pulse is much disordered," Hunter said warningly, his thumb pressing Grey's wrist. His hand was cool and firm; Grey found the touch comforting. "I really cannot answer for the consequences should he be moved abruptly."

"I see." Smith stood still for a moment; Grey could hear his heavy breathing but forbore opening his eyes. "Very well, then." He gave a short, humorless laugh. "If Mohammed cannot go to the mountain, then the mountain will jolly well have to come here. I'll send a note to General Wayne. Do what you can, please, to see that he's coherent, Doctor?"

HE COULD SEE Denzell Hunter out of his damaged eye; that was reassuring: he wasn't blind. Yet. Hunter had removed his spectacles in order to peer more closely into the injured organ; he had very nice eyes himself, Grey thought—the iris just the light-brown color of the flesh of a ripe olive, with tiny streaks of deep green.

"Look up, please," Hunter murmured.

Grey tried to oblige.

"Ow!"

"No? Look down." This attempt was no more successful, nor could he move the eye to the right or left. It seemed to have solidified in its socket, like a hard-boiled egg. He put this theory to Hunter, who smiled, though in a rather worried way.

"There *is* a great deal of swelling, to be sure. Whatever struck thee did so with a good deal of force." Hunter's fingers moved gently over Grey's face, prodding here and there in a questioning manner. "Does this—"

"Yes, he did. Don't keep asking if it hurts; everything from my scalp to my chin hurts, including my left ear. What you said regarding extravasation of blood into the brain—did you mean it?"

"It's possible." Hunter did smile at that, though. "But since thee has shown no disposition to seizure or unconsciousness—save that due to alcohol—and thee apparently walked for several hours following the injury, I think perhaps the probability is lower. There *is* bleeding beneath the sclera, though." His cool fingertips brushed the puffy lid. "Thy eyeball is crimson, as is the lining of thy eyelid. It's rather . . . dramatic." There was a distinct tone of amusement in this, which Grey found reassuring.

"Oh, good," he said dryly. "How long will it take to go away?"

That made the Quaker grimace and shake his head.

"The blood will take a week to a month to clear; it's essentially the same as mere bruising—the bursting of small blood vessels under the skin. What worries me is thy inability to move the eye. I think thee has a fracture of the bony orbit, which is somehow trapping the orbicularis muscle. I do wish thy wife was here; she has a much greater—"

"My wife," Grey said blankly. "Oh!" Memory and realization collided, and he felt a sudden leap of spirit. "She isn't my wife! Not anymore," he added, and found himself grinning. He leaned forward to whisper into Hunter's astonished ear, "Jamie Fraser isn't dead!"

Hunter stared at him, blinked, put his spectacles back on, and resumed staring, obviously rethinking his appraisal of Grey's brain.

"He's the one who hit me," Grey said helpfully. "It's all right," he added at Hunter's frown. "I was asking for it."

"God be praised," Hunter whispered, breaking into a huge smile—apparently at the news of Fraser's survival rather than Grey's assurance of the morality of his actions. "Ian will be—" He broke off with a gesture indicating his inability to describe Ian Murray's probable emotions.

"And Friend Claire!" he exclaimed, eyes huge behind his spectacles. "Does she know?"

"Yes, but—" Approaching footsteps made Grey hurl himself back onto the cot, with a completely authentic exclamation of pain. He shut his eyes and rolled his head to one side, groaning.

"The mountain seems to be with General Washington," Smith said, plainly disedified. Grey felt him come to a stop by the cot, bumping it with his legs. "Do what you can to see that he's capable of travel by tomorrow, Doctor—we'll load him into one of the wagons, if necessary."

Number 17 Chestnut Street

HIS GRACE WOKE up in the morning red-eyed as a ferret and in roughly the same temper as a rabid badger. Had I a tranquilizing dart, I would have shot him with it without an instant's hesitation. As it was, I prescribed a large slug of brandy to be added to his breakfast coffee and—after a brief struggle with my Hippocratic conscience—added a very small amount of laudanum to it.

I couldn't give him much; it depressed the respiration, among other things. Still, I reasoned, counting the aromatic reddish-brown drops as they plinked into the brandy, it was a more humane way of dealing with him than crowning him with the chamber pot or calling Mrs. Figg to sit on him whilst I tied him to the bedstead and gagged him.

And I did require him to be both immobile and quiet for a short period. Mr. Figg, a preacher of the Methodist Society, was bringing round two young men of the society who were carpenters, to rehang the front door and nail boards over the shutters of the downstairs windows, in case of roving mobs. I'd told Mrs. Figg that of course she might confide our circumstances to her husband—I couldn't very well stop her—but that perhaps he might be persuaded not to mention His Grace's presence, in the interests of protecting Lord John's safety and property—to say nothing of His Grace, who was, after all, Lord John's presumably beloved brother.

Mrs. Figg would cheerfully have handed the duke over to be tarred and feathered, but an appeal on Lord John's behalf would always carry weight with her, and she nodded in sober agreement. So long as His Grace didn't draw attention to himself by shouting out of the upstairs window or hurling things at the workmen, she thought his presence could be concealed.

"What you mean to do with him, though, Lady John?" she asked, glancing warily toward the ceiling. We were standing in the back parlor, conferring in lowered voices while Jenny administered Hal's breakfast and made sure all the brandy-laced coffee was drunk. "And what if the army sends someone round to ask after him?"

I made a helpless gesture.

"I have no idea," I confessed. "I just need to keep him here until either Lord John or my—er, Mr. Fraser—comes. They'll know what to do with him. As for the army, if anyone comes asking after His Grace, I'll . . . um . . . speak to them."

She gave me a look indicating that she'd heard better plans, but nodded reluctantly and went off to fetch her marketing basket. The first thing that happens in a newly occupied city is a shortage of food, and with the Continental army poised to descend on Philadelphia like a plague of locusts, the wagons that normally brought in produce from the countryside would likely be sparse. If either army *was* on the road already, they'd be seizing anything that came along.

At the door, though, Mrs. Figg paused and turned around.

"What about William?" she demanded. "If he comes back . . ." She was obviously torn between hope that he *would* come back—she was worried for him—and consternation at what might happen if he encountered his uncle in captivity.

"I'll speak to him," I repeated firmly, and waved a hand toward the door.

Running upstairs, I found Hal yawning over a nearly empty

breakfast tray and Jenny fastidiously wiping egg yolk off the corner of his mouth. She'd spent the night at the printshop but had come back to help, bringing with her a battered portmanteau filled with possibly useful items.

"His Grace made a good breakfast," she reported, stepping back to examine her work critically. "And he's moved his bowels. I made him do that afore he drank his coffee, just in case. Wasna sure how quick it might be."

Hal frowned at her, though whether in puzzlement or offense, I couldn't tell. His pupils were already noticeably constricted, which gave him a slightly staring look. He blinked at me and shook his head, as though trying to clear it.

"Let me have a quick check of your vital signs, Your Grace," I said, smiling and feeling like Judas. He was my patient—but Jamie was my husband, and I hardened my resolve.

His pulse was slow and quite regular, which reassured me. I took out my stethoscope, unbuttoned his nightshirt, and had a listen: a nice, steady heartbeat, no palpitations, but the lungs were gurgling like a leaky cistern, and his breathing was interrupted by small gasps.

"He'd best have some of the *Ephedra* tincture," I said, straightening up. It was a stimulant and would antagonize the opiate in his system, but I couldn't risk his stopping breathing while asleep. "I'll stay with him; will you go down and get a cup—don't bother heating it, cold will do." I wasn't sure he'd stay conscious long enough to have a cup heated.

"I really must go to see General Clinton this morning," Pardloe said, with surprising firmness, considering his foggy mental state. He cleared his throat and coughed. "There are arrangements to make. . . . My regiment . . ."

"Ah. Er . . . where *is* your regiment just now?" I asked cautiously. If they were in Philadelphia, Hal's adjutant would be starting to look for him in earnest at any minute. He might reasonably have spent the night with a son or daughter, but by now . . . and I didn't know precisely how much distraction value my forged notes might have had.

"New York," he replied. "Or at least I sincerely hope so." He closed his eyes, swayed slightly, then straightened his back with a jerk. "Landed there. I came down to Philadelphia . . . to see Henry . . . Dottie." His face twisted with pain. "Mean . . . to go back with Clinton."

"Of course," I said soothingly, trying to think. *When,* exactly, would Clinton and his troops leave? Assuming Pardloe to be sufficiently recovered that he wouldn't actually die without my attendance, I could give him back as soon as the exodus was under way. At that point, he'd have no way of starting a major search for John and endangering Jamie. But surely Jamie—with or without John—would come back at any moment?

Who did come back was Jenny, with the *Ephedra* tincture—and a hammer in the pocket of her apron and three stout laths under her arm. She handed me the cup without comment and proceeded to nail the laths over the window, in a surprisingly brisk and competent manner.

Hal sipped his *Ephedra* slowly, watching Jenny with bemusement.

"Why is she doing that?" he asked, though not as if he cared particularly what the answer was.

"Hurricanes, Your Grace," she said with a straight face, and zipped out to return the hammer to the carpenters, whose cheerful banging sounded like a battalion of woodpeckers attacking the house.

"Oh," Hal said. He was glancing vaguely round the room, possibly in search of his breeches, which Mrs. Figg had thoughtfully taken away and hidden in the cookhouse. His eye rested on the small pile of Willie's books I had moved to the top of the dressing table. Evidently he recognized one or more, because he said, "Oh. William. Where *is* William?"

"I'm sure Willie's very busy today," I said, and picked up his wrist again. "Perhaps we'll see him later." His heartbeat was slow but still strong. Just as his grip loosened, I caught the empty cup and set it on the table. His head drooped, and I eased him carefully back on the pillow, propped for easier breathing.

"If he comes back . . ." Mrs. Figg had said of Willie, with the obvious implication, *"what then?"*

What indeed?

Colenso had not returned, so presumably he had found William; that was reassuring. But what William was doing—or thinking . . .

14

INCIPIENT THUNDER

"AN ASSIGNMENT BEFITTING *your peculiar situation,"* Major Findlay had said. Findlay didn't know the half of it, William reflected bitterly. Not that his situation wasn't "peculiar," even without his recent discoveries.

He had surrendered at Saratoga, with the rest of Burgoyne's army, in October of '77. The British soldiers and their German allies had been obliged to yield their weapons but were not to be held prisoner; the Convention of Saratoga, signed by Burgoyne and by the Continental general, Gates, had stated that all troops would be allowed to return to Europe, once they had given their parole not to take up arms again in the American conflict.

But ships could not sail during the winter storms, and something had to be done with the captured soldiers. Referred to as the Convention army, they had been marched en masse to Cambridge, Massachusetts, there to await spring and repatriation. All but William and a few like him, who had either connections in America with influence, or connections with Sir Henry, who had succeeded Howe as commander in chief of the American campaign.

William, fortunate fellow, had both; he had served on Howe's personal staff, his uncle was the colonel of a regiment, and his father was an influential diplomat, presently in Philadelphia. He had been released under an exceptional personal parole, as a favor to General Lord Howe, and sent to Lord John. He was, however, still part of the British army, merely precluded from actual fighting. And the army had any number of obnoxious chores that did not involve fighting; General Clinton had been delighted to make use of him.

Deeply galled by his situation, William had begged his father to try to have him exchanged; that would remove the conditions of his parole and allow him to resume full military duties. Lord John had been quite willing to do this, but in January of 1778 there had been a falling-out between General Burgoyne and the Continental Congress over the former's refusal to provide a list of the surrendered soldiers. The Convention of Saratoga had been repudiated by the Congress, which then declared that it would detain the entire Convention army until the convention and the required list were ratified by King George—the Congress knowing damned well that the King would do no such thing, as such an act would be tantamount to acknowledging the independence of the colonies. The upshot of this was that there was at present no mechanism at all for the exchange of prisoners. Any prisoners.

Which left William in a deeply ambiguous position. Technically, he was an escaped prisoner, and in the highly unlikely event that he was recaptured by the Americans and discovered to be one of the Saratoga officers, he would promptly be marched off to Massachusetts to languish for the rest of the war. At the same time, no one was quite sure whether it was appropriate for him to take up arms again, since even though the convention had been repudiated, William had been given a personal parole.

Which had led to William's present invidious situation, in charge of troops assisting the evacuation of Philadelphia's richest Loyalists. The only thing he could think of that might be worse was driving a herd of swine through the eye of a needle.

While the poorer citizens who felt endangered by the proximity of General Washington's militias were obliged to brave the dangers of the road, making their exodus by wagon, handcart, and foot, the wealthier Loyalists were allowed a safer and theoretically more luxurious removal by ship. And not one of them could be brought to understand that there was but *one* ship presently available—General Howe's own ship—and very limited room aboard it.

"No, madam, I'm very sorry, but it's quite impossible to accommodate—"

"Nonsense, young man, my husband's grandfather purchased that tall clock in the Netherlands in 1670. It displays not only the time but also the phases of the moon and a complete table of tides for the Bay of Napoli! Surely you do not expect me to allow such an instrument to fall into the clutches of the Rebels?"

"Yes, madam, I'm afraid I do. No, sir, no servants; only the members of your immediate family and a very small amount of baggage. I'm sure that your bond servants will be perfectly safe following by—"

"But they'll starve!" exclaimed a cadaverous-looking gentleman who was loath to part with his talented cook and a plumply voluptuous housemaid, who, if not talented at sweeping, obviously had other desirable abilities, these clearly on display. "Or be abducted! They are my responsibility! Surely you cannot—"

"I can," said William firmly, with an appreciative sideways glance at the housemaid, "and I must. Corporal Higgins, please see Mr. Hennings's bond servants safely off the quay. No, madam. I agree that the matched armchairs are quite valuable, but so are the lives of the people who will drown if the ship sinks. You may take your carriage clock, yes." He raised his voice and bellowed, "Lieutenant Rendill!"

Rendill, face red and streaming, fought his way through the crowd of pushing, cursing, heaving, shrieking evacuees. Arriving in front of William, who was perched on a box in order to avoid being trampled or pushed into the water by the crowd, the lieutenant saluted but was rudely jostled by several people attempting to gain William's attention and ended with his wig pushed over his eyes.

"Yes, sir?" he said gamely, pushing it back and elbowing a gentleman out of the way as politely as possible.

"Here's a list of General Howe's particular acquaintances, Rendill. Go on board and see if they've all made it—if they haven't . . ." He cast an eloquent glance over the surging throng on the dock, surrounded by mountains of semi-abandoned possessions and trampled baggage, and thrust the list unceremoniously into the lieutenant's hand. "Find them."

"Oh, God," said Rendill. "I mean . . . yes, sir. At once, sir." And, with a hopeless air, he turned and began to swim through the crowd, doing a modified but vigorous form of breaststroke.

"Rendill!"

Rendill obediently turned and made his way resignedly

back into earshot, a stout red porpoise surging his way through shoals of hysterical herring.

"Sir?"

William leaned down and lowered his voice to a level inaudible to the press of people around them, then nodded at the piles of furniture and baggage heaped unsteadily all over the dock—many of them dangerously close to the edge.

"As you pass, tell the fellows on the dock that they should take no great pains to preserve those heaps of things from falling into the river, would you?"

Rendill's perspiring face brightened amazingly.

"Yes, sir!" He saluted and swam off again, radiating renewed enthusiasm, and William, his soul slightly soothed, turned courteously to attend to the complaint of a harried German father with six daughters, all of them carrying what appeared to be their entire lavish wardrobes, anxious round faces peering out between the brims of their wide straw hats and the piles of silk and lace in their arms.

Paradoxically, the heat and incipient thunder in the air suited his mood, and the sheer impossibility of his task relaxed him. Once he'd realized the ultimate futility of satisfying all these people—or even one in ten of them—he stopped worrying about it, took what steps he could to preserve order, and let his mind go elsewhere while he bowed courteously and made noises of reassurance to the phalanx of faces pressing in upon him.

Had he been in a mood for irony, he reflected, there was plenty of it to go round. He was neither fish nor fowl nor good red beef, as the country folk said of an ambiguous cut of meat. Not a full soldier, not a free civilian. And, evidently, neither an Englishman nor an earl . . . and yet . . . how could he possibly not be an Englishman, for God's sake?

Once he had regained enough of his temper to think, he had realized that he was still *legally* the Ninth Earl of Ellesmere, regardless of his paternity. His parents—his real parents—his *theoretically* real parents—had undeniably been married at the time of his birth. At the moment, though, that seemed to make matters worse: how could he go about letting people think and act as though he were the heir of Ellesmere's ancient blood when he knew damned well that he was really the son of—

He choked that thought off, shoving it violently to the back of his mind. "Son of" had brought Lord John vividly to mind, though. He breathed deep of the hot, murky, fish-smelling air, trying to quell the sudden pang that came to him at thought of Papa.

He hadn't wanted to admit it to himself, but he'd been looking through the crowd all day, scanning the faces in search of his fa—yes, dammit, his father! John Grey was as much his father now as he ever had been. *Goddamned liar or not.* And William was growing worried about him. Colenso had reported that morning that Lord John had not returned to his house—and Lord John *should* have returned by now. And if he had, he would have come to find William, he was sure of that. Unless Fraser had killed him.

He swallowed bile at the thought. Why would he? The men had once been friends, good friends.

True, war severed such bonds. But even so—

On account of Mother Claire? He recoiled from that thought, too, but made himself come back to it. He could still see her face, glowing in spite of the uproar, fierce as flame with the joy of seeing Jamie Fraser, and felt a prick of jealousy on behalf of his father. If Fraser felt similarly impassioned, might he . . . but that was nonsense! Surely he must realize that Lord John had only taken her under his protection—and done that for the sake of his good friend!

But, then, they *were* married . . . and his father had always been quite open regarding matters of sex. . . . His face grew even hotter, with embarrassment at the vision of his father enthusiastically bedding the not-quite-ex-Mrs. Fraser. And if Fraser had discovered that—

"No, sir!" he said sharply to the importunate merchant who—he realized belatedly—had just tried to bribe him to admit the merchant's family to Howe's ship. "How dare you? Begone, and think yourself fortunate that I have no time to deal with you as I ought!"

The man shuffled disconsolately away, and William felt a small pang of regret, but there was in fact little he could do. Even had he felt able to stretch a point in the merchant's favor, once a bribe was offered, he had no choice.

Even if it were true, how would Fraser have discovered it?

Surely Lord John wouldn't have been foolish enough to tell him. No, it must be something else that was delaying Papa's return—doubtless the muddle of people leaving Philadelphia; the roads must be choked. . . .

"Yes, madam. I think we have room for you and your daughter," he said to a young mother, very frightened-looking, with a baby clutched against her shoulder. He reached out and touched the infant's cheek; she was awake, but not troubled by the crowd, and regarded him with soft brown long-lashed eyes. "Hallo, sweetheart. Want to go on a boat with your mummy?"

The mother gave a stifled sob of relief.

"Oh, thank you, Lord—it is Lord Ellesmere, is it not?"

"It is," he said automatically, and then felt as though someone had punched him in the belly. He swallowed and his face burned.

"My husband is Lieutenant Beaman Gardner," she said, offering the name in anxious justification of his mercy, and bobbed a short curtsy. "We've met. At the Mischianza?"

"Yes, of course!" he said, bowing, though he didn't recall Mrs. Lieutenant Gardner at all. "Honored to be of service to a brother officer's wife, ma'am. If you will be so good as to go on board directly, please? Corporal Anderson? Escort Mrs. Gardner and Miss Gardner on board."

He bowed again and turned away, feeling as though his insides had been scooped out. *Brother officer. My lord.* And what would Mrs. Lieutenant Gardner have thought if she'd known? What would the lieutenant himself think?

He sighed deeply, closing his eyes for an instant's escape. And when he opened them, found himself face-to-face with Captain Ezekiel Richardson.

"Stercus!" he exclaimed, startled into his uncle Hal's habit of Latin denunciation in moments of extreme stress.

"Indeed," Richardson remarked politely. "May I have a word with you? Yes, just so—Lieutenant!" He beckoned to the nearby Rendill, who was eyeball-to-eyeball with an elderly woman in black bombazine with no fewer than four small dogs yapping at her heels, these held by a long-suffering small black boy. Rendill made a quelling motion to her and turned to Richardson.

"Sir?"

"Relieve Captain Lord Ellesmere, please. I require a moment of his time."

Before William could decide whether to object or not, Richardson had him by the elbow and was towing him out of the scrum and into the lee of a neat little sky-blue boathouse that stood on the riverbank.

William breathed deep with relief as the shade fell upon him but had by then gathered his wits. His first impulse had been to speak sharply to Richardson—followed perhaps by knocking him into the river—but wisdom spoke in his ear, advising otherwise.

It was at Richardson's instigation that William had become for a short time an intelligencer for the army, collecting information in the context of various journeys and delivering this to Richardson. On the last of these missions, though, a journey into the Great Dismal Swamp of Virginia, William had had the misfortune to become lost, be wounded, and suffer a fever that would certainly have killed him had Ian Murray not found and rescued him—in the course of the rescue informing William that he had almost certainly been gulled and sent not into the bosom of British allies but into a nest of Rebels, who would hang him should they discover who he was.

William was of two minds as to whether to believe Murray or not—particularly after the arrival of Jamie Fraser had made it patently clear that Murray was his own cousin but hadn't felt it necessary to apprise him of the fact. But a deep suspicion of Richardson and his motives remained, and it was no friendly face that he turned on the man.

"What do you want?" he said abruptly.

"Your father," Richardson replied, causing William's heart to give a great thump that he thought must be audible to the other. "Where is Lord John?"

"I haven't the slightest idea," William said shortly. "I haven't seen him since yesterday." *The day my bloody life ended.* "What do you want with him?" he asked, not bothering with any semblance of courtesy.

Richardson twitched an eyebrow but didn't otherwise respond to his tone.

"His brother, the Duke of Pardloe, has disappeared."

"The—what?" William stared at him for a moment, uncomprehending. "His brother? Disappeared . . . from where? When?"

"Evidently from your father's house. As to when: Lady John said that he left the house just after tea yesterday afternoon, presumably in search of your father. Have you seen him since then?"

"I haven't seen him at all." William felt a distinct ringing in his ears—probably his brains trying to get out through them. "What—I mean, I had no idea he was in Philadelphia. In the colonies at all, for that matter. When did he arrive?" *Jesus, did he come to deal with Dottie and her Quaker? No, he can't have, he couldn't have had time . . . could he?*

Richardson was squinting at him, probably trying to determine whether he was telling the truth.

"I haven't seen either of them," William said flatly. "Now, if you'll excuse me, Captain . . ." There was a tremendous splash from the direction of the dock and a loud chorus of shock and dismay from the crowd. "Excuse me," William repeated, and turned away.

Richardson seized him by the arm and made an effort to fix William with his gaze. William looked deliberately in the direction of his neglected duty.

"*When* you see either one of them, Captain Ransom, be so good as to send word to me. It would be a great help—to many people."

William jerked his arm free and stalked off without reply. Richardson had used his family name instead of his title—did that mean anything beyond mere rudeness? At the moment, he didn't care. He couldn't fight, he couldn't help anyone, he couldn't tell the truth, and he wouldn't live a lie. God damn it, he was stuck like a hog, mired to the hocks.

He wiped the sweat from his face on his sleeve, squared his shoulders, and strode back into the fray. All there was to do was his duty.

15

AN ARMY ON THE MOVE

WE WERE JUST IN time. No sooner had I closed the bedroom door on Pardloe's gentle snore than a knock came on the newly hung front door below. I hurried downstairs to find Jenny face-to-face with a British soldier, this time a lieutenant. General Clinton was escalating his inquiries.

"Why, no, lad," she was saying, in a tone of mild surprise, "the colonel isn't here. He took tea with Lady John yesterday, but then he went off to look for his brother. His lordship hasn't come back, and"—I saw her lean closer, her voice lowered dramatically—"her ladyship's that worried. Ye'll not have news of him, I suppose?"

This was my cue, and I came down from the landing, rather surprised to find that I was indeed "that worried." Tending Hal had distracted me from the situation temporarily, but by now there was no denying that something had gone seriously wrong.

"Lady John. Lieutenant Roswell, your servant, ma'am." The lieutenant bowed, with a professional smile that didn't hide the slight furrowing of his brow. The army was getting worried, too, and that was bloody dangerous. "Your servant, mum. Have you in fact had no word from Lord John or Lord Melton—oh, I beg your pardon, my lady, I mean from His Grace?"

"D'ye think I'm a liar, lad?" Jenny said tartly.

"Oh! No, mum, not at all," he said, flushing. "But the general will want to know that I spoke with her ladyship."

"Of course," I said soothingly, though my heart was pittering in my throat. "Tell the general that I haven't heard from my husband"—*either of them*—"at all. I'm most disturbed." I wasn't a good liar, but I wasn't lying now.

He grimaced.

"The thing is, mum, the army has begun withdrawing from Philadelphia, and all Loyalists remaining in the city are being advised that they may wish to . . . er . . . make preparations." His lips compressed for a moment as he glanced at the stairwell, with its ruined banister and bloody fist marks. "I . . . see that you have already experienced some . . . difficulty?"

"Och, no," Jenny said, and with a deprecating glance at me, stepped nearer the lieutenant and put her hand on his arm, pushing him gently toward the door. He automatically moved away with her, and I heard her murmur, ". . . no but a wee family quarrel . . . his lordship . . ."

The lieutenant shot me a swift glance, in which surprise mingled with a certain sympathy. But the lines in his forehead eased. He had an explanation to take back to Clinton.

Blood flamed in my cheeks at his look—as though there truly had been a family row, during which Lord John had stamped out, leaving wreckage in his wake and a wife at the mercy of the Rebels. True, it *was* a family row, but the circumstances were more through-the-looking-glass than a matter of mere common scandal.

The White Rabbit shut our new door firmly on Lieutenant Roswell and turned to me, back pressed against it.

"Lord Melton?" she asked, one black eyebrow raised.

"It's one of the duke's titles, one he used before he became Duke of Pardloe. Lieutenant Roswell must have known him some years ago," I explained.

"Oh, aye. Well, lord or duke, how long can we keep him asleep?" she asked.

"The laudanum will keep him out for two or three hours," I replied, glancing at the gilt carriage clock on the mantel, which had somehow escaped the carnage. "But he had a very hard day yesterday and a rather disturbed night; he may well go straight off into a natural sleep as the drug wears off. If no one comes along to knock the house down round our ears," I added, wincing at sounds of a violent altercation somewhere nearby.

Jenny nodded. "Aye. I'd best go along to the printshop now, then, to see what the news in the city is. And perhaps Jamie will ha' gone there," she added hopefully. "Not thinking it safe to come here, I mean, wi' the streets full of soldiers."

A spark of hope at the suggestion flared up like a lit match. Though even as I envisioned the possibility, I knew that if Jamie was in the city at all, he'd be standing before me right now. Possibly enraged, possibly disturbed, but before me.

With the army already beginning its withdrawal, and the concomitant public disturbances, no one would have time or inclination to notice—let alone arrest—a tall Scotsman suspected of nothing more than passing suspicious documents. It wasn't as though there was an all points bulletin out on him—or at least I hoped not. William was the only soldier who knew that Jamie had taken Lord John hostage, and from his manner in leaving, I rather thought that the last thing William would have done was give a full report of the situation to his superiors.

I said as much to Jenny, though agreed that she ought to go back to the printshop, to check on the welfare of Fergus and Marsali's family, as well as to find out what was going on amongst the Rebels in the city.

"Will you be safe in the streets?" I asked, unfolding her cloak and holding it up for her to put on.

"Oh, I expect so," she said briskly. "No one much thinks to look at an auld woman. But I suppose I'd best put away my wee bawbee." The bawbee in question was a small silver chiming watch, with a delicately filigreed cover, which she wore pinned to the bosom of her dress.

"Jamie bought it for me in Brest," she explained, seeing me looking at it as she unpinned it. "I told him it was foolery; I didna need such a thing to ken the time, nay more than he did himself. But he said, no, I must have it, that knowing what o'clock it is gives ye the illusion that ye have some control over your circumstances. Ye ken how he is," she added, putting the watch carefully away in her pocket, "always explaining ye to yourself. Though I will say as he's no often wrong.

"Now, then," she added, turning to me as she opened the door. "I'll come back before him upstairs wakes up, unless I can't, and if I can't, I'll send Germain to say so."

"Why should you not be able to?" I asked, in some surprise.

"Young Ian," she said, equally surprised that I should not have thought of this. "Wi' the army leaving, he may have come back from Valley Forge by now—and ye ken, the poor lad thinks I'm dead."

16

ROOM FOR SECRETS

In the forest,
five miles from Valley Forge

"DO QUAKERS BELIEVE in heaven?" Ian Murray asked.

"Some do," Rachel Hunter replied, pausing to turn over a large toadstool with the toe of her shoe. "No, dog, don't touch that one. See the color of its gills?" Rollo, who had come to sniff at the fungus, dismissed it with a perfunctory sneeze and lifted his snout to the wind in hopes of more promising prey.

"Auntie Claire says dogs canna see colors," Ian remarked. "And what d'ye mean, 'Some do'? Is there a difference of opinion on the matter?" Quaker beliefs puzzled him beyond measure, but he found Rachel's explanations invariably entertaining.

"Perhaps they smell them instead. The dogs, I mean. But to return to thy question, we consider our life here on earth to be a sacrament, lived in the light of Christ. There may be an afterlife, but as no one has come back to say so, it's a matter of speculation, left to each person individually."

They had paused in the shade of a small walnut grove, and the soft green sun that fell flickering through the leaves gave Rachel herself an unearthly glow that any angel might have envied.

"Well, I havena been there, either, so I'll no just say that's wrong," he said, and bent to kiss her just above the ear. A faint rush of tiny gooseflesh stippled her temple for an instant, and the sight touched his heart.

"Why does thee think of heaven?" she asked curiously.

"Does thee think there will be fighting in the city? I haven't known thee overly fearful for thy life before." Valley Forge had been hoaching like a grain sack full of weevils when they left it an hour before, the soldiers salvaging what they could from the camp, molding fresh musket balls and packing cartridges, preparing to march on Philadelphia when the word was given that Clinton's men had withdrawn.

"Och, no. There'll be nay fighting in the city. Washington will try to catch Clinton's men in retreat." He took her hand, small and brown and work-roughened but the fingers reassuringly strong as they turned and clasped his. "Nay, I was thinking of my mam—that I should ha' liked to show her places like this." He gestured toward the little clearing in which they stood, a tiny spring of an improbably deep blue welling up from the rock under their feet, overhung by a yellow wild-rose brier, humming with summer bees. "She had a big yellow rose brier growin' up the wall at Lallybroch; my grandmother planted it." He swallowed a small lump in his throat. "But then I thought, may be as she's happier in heaven with my da than she would be here without him."

Rachel's hand squeezed his, hard.

"She would be with him always, in life or in death," she whispered, and stood a-tiptoe to kiss him back. "And thee will take me someday to see thy grandmother's rose in Scotland."

They stood in silence for a bit, and Ian felt his heart, clenched with a sudden grief at the thought of his mother, ease in Rachel's sympathetic company. He hadn't said it, but what he most regretted was not his inability to show his mother the beauties of America but the fact that he couldn't show her Rachel.

"She'd have liked ye," he blurted. "My mam."

"I hope that she would," Rachel said, though with a tinge of dubiousness. "Did thee tell her about me, in Scotland? That I am a Friend, I mean. Some Catholics find us scandalous."

Ian tried to remember whether he *had* mentioned that to his mother, but couldn't. It made no difference, in any case, and he shrugged, dismissing it.

"I told her I loved ye. That seemed to be enough. Come to think, though—my da asked all kinds of questions about ye; he wanted to know everything he could. He kent ye were a

Quaker, so that means she kent it, too." He took her elbow to help her down from the rock.

She nodded, thoughtful, but as she followed him out of the clearing, he heard her ask behind him, "Does thee think a married couple should be completely in each other's confidence—share not only their histories, I mean, but every thought?"

That sent a qualm skittering down his backbone like a mouse with cold feet, and he took a deep breath. He loved Rachel with every fiber of his being, but he found her apparent ability to read him like a book—if not to actually hear his thoughts, and sometimes he thought for sure she did that, too—unsettling.

He had in fact suggested that they walk together to Matson's Ford and meet Denzell with the wagon there, rather than ride with him from Valley Forge, so that Ian might have sufficient time and solitude in which to share a few necessary things with her. He'd rather be tortured by Abenakis than tell her some of those things, but it was right she should know them, no matter what the result might be.

"Aye. I mean . . . well, so far as one can, I think they maybe should. Not every thought, I dinna mean, but important things. Ahh . . . history, like ye said. Here, come sit for a wee while." There was a big fallen log, half rotted and covered with moss and fuzzy gray lichens, and he led her to it, sitting down beside her in the fragrant shade of a big red cedar.

She didn't say anything, but lifted a brow in question.

"Well." He drew a deep breath, feeling that there wasn't enough air in the whole forest for this. "Did ye ken . . . I've been marrit before?"

Her face flickered, surprise overcome by determination so fast that he'd have missed it if he hadn't been watching so close.

"I did not," she said, and began to pleat the folds of her skirt, one-handed, clear hazel eyes fixed intently on his face. "Thee did say *been* married. Thee isn't now, I suppose?"

He shook his head, feeling a little easier—and very grateful to her. Not every young woman would have taken it so calmly.

"No. I wouldna have spoken to ye—asked ye to marry me, I mean—otherwise."

She pursed her lips a little and her eyes narrowed.

"In point of fact," she said thoughtfully, "thee never *has* asked me to marry thee."

"I didn't?" he said, staggered. "Are ye sure?"

"I would have noticed," she assured him gravely. "No, thee didn't. Though I recall a few very moving declarations, there was no suggestion of marriage among them."

"But—well." Heat had risen in his cheeks. "I—but you . . . ye said . . ." Maybe she was right. She *had* said . . . or had she? "Did ye not say ye loved me?"

Her mouth turned up just a little, but he could see her laughing at him at the back of her eyes.

"Not in so many words. But I did give thee to understand that, yes. Or at least I meant to."

"Oh. Well, then," he said, much happier. "Ye did." And he pulled her into his one sound arm and kissed her with great fervor. She kissed him back, panting a little, her fists curled in the fabric of his shirt, then broke away, looking mildly dazed. Her lips were swollen, the skin around them pink, scraped by his beard.

"Perhaps," she said, and swallowed, pushing him away with one hand flat on his chest, "perhaps thee should finish telling me about not being married, before we go further? Who was thy—thy wife—and what happened to her?"

He let go of her reluctantly but would not surrender her hand. It felt like a small live thing, warm in his.

"Her name is Wakyo'teyehsnonhsa," he said, and felt the accustomed inner shift at the speaking of it, as though the line between his Mohawk self and his white self had momentarily disappeared, leaving him awkwardly suspended somewhere in between. "It means 'Works With Her Hands.'" He cleared his throat. "I called her Emily. Most of the time."

Rachel's small, smooth hand jerked in his.

"Is?" she said, blinking. "Thee said *is*? Thy wife is *alive*?"

"She was a year ago," he said, and, with an effort, didn't cling to her hand but let her take it back. She folded her hands in her lap, fixed her eyes on him, and swallowed; he saw her throat move.

"All right," she said, with no more than a faint tremor in her voice. "Tell me about her."

He took another deep breath, trying to think how to do *that,* but then abandoned the effort and spoke simply.

"D'ye truly want to know that, Rachel? Or do ye only want to ken whether I loved her—or whether I love her now?"

"Start there," she said, lifting one brow. "*Does* thee love her?"

"I—yes," he said, helpless to speak other than the truth to her. Rollo, sensing some disturbance among his pack, got up from his resting place and padded over to Rachel. He sat down by her foot, making his allegiance in the matter clear, and gave Ian a yellow-eyed wolf look over Rachel's knee that bore an uncomfortable resemblance to the look in her own eye. "But . . ."

The brow lifted a fraction of an inch higher.

"She . . . was my refuge," he blurted. "When I left my own family and became a Mohawk, it was as much to be wi' her as because I had to."

"Had to . . . what?" She looked baffled, and he saw her eyes drop a little, tracing the tattooed lines across his cheekbones. "Thee had to become a Mohawk? Why?"

He nodded, feeling momentarily on firmer ground. He could tell her this story; it was only what had happened. Her eyes went round when he explained how he and Uncle Jamie had met Roger Wakefield, not realized who he was and thought him to be the man who had raped his cousin Brianna and got her with child, had come close to killing him, but had thought better of the notion—

"Oh, good," Rachel said, half under her breath. He glanced sidelong at her but couldn't tell if she meant this ironically or not, so he coughed and went on, telling how they had instead given the man to the Tuscarora, who in turn had sold him as a slave to the Mohawk farther north.

"We didna want to risk him ever comin' back to trouble Brianna, aye? Only then—" He swallowed, reliving in memory both the terror of his asking Brianna to marry him and the utter horror when cousin Bree had drawn a picture of the man she loved, the man she was waiting for—and the strong dark features of the man they had given to the Mohawk sprang into view.

"You asked thy cousin to marry thee? Did thee want to?" She looked wary; he supposed she must be thinking that he went about proposing to every third or fourth woman he met and hastened to correct this impression.

"Nay, I mean—well, Brianna's a . . . well, I didna *mind,* ken, we'd ha' got on fine, and she—well . . . I mean, no, not exactly," he added hurriedly, seeing Rachel's graceful brows draw together. The truth was that he'd been seventeen and Brianna several years older; she'd terrified him, but the thought of bedding her had— He choked that thought off as though it were a venomous snake.

"It was Uncle Jamie's idea," he said, with as much an air of casual dismissal as could be assumed on short notice. He lifted one shoulder. "To give the bairn a name, aye? I said I would, for the family honor."

"The family honor," she repeated, giving him a fishy look. "To be sure. But then—"

"But then we found it was Roger Mac—he'd taken back his own name of MacKenzie, is why we didna recognize him—that we'd given to the Indians by mistake, and so we went to retrieve him," he said quickly. By the time he'd finished explaining all the events that had culminated in his volunteering to take the place of a Mohawk killed during Roger's rescue, the washing of his body in the river, the Mohawk women scrubbing him with sand to remove the last trace of his white blood, the plucking of his hair and the tattoos, he thought his marriage to Emily might seem only one more picturesque detail.

But of course it didn't.

"I—" He stopped dead, realizing suddenly that the conversation was about to become even stickier than he'd thought. He glanced at her apprehensively, heart beating in his throat and ears. But she was still looking back; the pinkness round her mouth showing more vividly because she'd gone a little pale—but looking, clear and steady.

"I—wasna a virgin when I wed," he blurted.

The eyebrow went up again.

"Really, I am not quite sure what to ask," she said, examining him in the way he'd seen his auntie Claire appraise some horrible growth—fascinated rather than repelled, but with a firm air of deciding exactly how best to deal with the offending bit. He hoped fervently she didn't mean to cut him out of her life like a wart or amputate him like a gangrenous toe.

"I'll . . . tell ye anything ye want to know," he said bravely. "Anything."

"A generous offer," she said, "and one I shall accept—but I think I must offer thee the same accommodation. Thee does not wish to ask whether I am virgin?"

His mouth fell open, and her shoulders shook briefly.

"Ye're not?" he croaked.

"No, I am," she assured him, still quivering with the effort not to laugh. "But why should thee assume it?"

"Why?" He felt the blood rise in his face. "Because—anyone who looked at ye would know ye on the instant for a—a—a virtuous woman!" he concluded, with a sense of relief at having found a reasonable term.

"I might have been raped," she pointed out. "That would not mean I was not virtuous, would it?"

"I—well. No, I suppose not." He knew that a good many folk *would* think a raped woman was not virtuous—and Rachel knew that. He was on the verge of becoming completely confused, and she knew that, too; he could see her taking pains not to laugh. He squared his shoulders and gave a great sigh, then met her eyes directly.

"D'ye want to hear about every woman whose bed I've shared? Because I'll tell ye, if so. I've never taken a woman unwilling—though they were mostly whores. I'm no poxed, though," he assured her. "Ye should ken that."

She considered that for a moment.

"I think I need not know the details," she said finally. "But should we ever meet a woman thee has bedded, I wish to know it. Thee does not mean to continue fornicating with prostitutes once we are wed, though, does thee?"

"No!"

"Good," she said, but rocked back a little on the log, hands linked around her knees, holding his gaze. "I do wish to hear more about thy wife. Emily."

He could feel the warmth of her leg, her body, close beside him. She hadn't moved away from him when he'd said about sleeping with whores. The silence grew around them, and a jay called somewhere in the wood beyond.

"We loved each other," he said at last, softly, eyes on the ground. "And I wanted her. I—could talk to her. Then, at least."

Rachel drew breath but didn't say anything. He took his courage in his hands and looked up. Her face was carefully expressionless, her eyes intent on his face.

"I dinna ken how to say it," he said. "It wasna the same way I want you—but I dinna mean to make it sound as though . . .

as though Emily didna matter to me. She did," he added, very low-voiced, and glanced down again.

"And . . . she does?" Rachel asked quietly, after a long pause. After a longer one, he nodded, swallowing.

"But," he said, and stopped, searching for the way to go on, because now they were coming to the most perilous part of his confession, the thing that might make Rachel stand up and walk away, dragging his heart behind her through the rocks and brush.

"But?" she said, and her voice was gentle.

"The Mohawk," he began, and had to stop for a breath. "It's the woman's choice, about being married. If a woman should take against her husband for some reason—if he beats her, or he's a lazy sot, or smells too bad when he farts"—he stole a glance and saw the corner of her mouth twitch, which heartened him a little—"she puts his things out o' the longhouse, and he has to go back to live wi' the unmarried men—or find another woman who'll have him at her fire. Or leave altogether."

"And Emily put thee out?" She sounded both startled and a bit indignant. He gave her a wee smile in return.

"Aye, she did. Not because I beat her, though. Because . . . of the bairns."

He felt the tears come to his eyes and clenched his hands in frustration on his knees. Damn, he'd sworn to himself that he wouldn't weep. Either she'd think he made a show of his grief to win her sympathy—or she'd see too deep; he wasn't ready . . . but he had to tell her, he'd started this on purpose to tell her, she had to know. . . .

"I couldna give her children," he blurted. "The first—we had a wee daughter, born too early, who died. I called her Iseabail." He wiped the back of his hand viciously under his nose, swallowing his pain. "After that, she—Emily—she got wi' child again. And again. And when she lost the third . . . her heart toward me died with it."

Rachel made a small sound, but he didn't look at her. Couldn't. Just sat hunched on the log like a toadstool, shoulders drawn up around his ears, and eyes blurred with the tears he couldn't shed.

A small warm hand settled on his.

"And thy heart?" she asked. "Thine died, too?"

He closed his hand on hers and nodded. And then just breathed for a bit, holding on to her hand, until he could speak again without his voice breaking.

"The Mohawk think that the man's spirit fights wi' the woman's, when they . . . lie together. And she willna get with child unless his spirit can conquer hers."

"Oh, I see," Rachel said softly. "So she blamed thee."

He shrugged.

"I canna say she was wrong." He turned a little on the log, to look at her directly. "And I canna say that it would be different—with us. But I did ask Auntie Claire, and she told me about things in the blood . . . well, perhaps ye should ask her to explain it; I wouldna make a decent job of it. But the end of it was that she thought it *might* be different wi' another woman. That I maybe could. Give ye bairns, I mean."

He only realized that Rachel had been holding her breath when she let it out, a sigh that brushed his cheek.

"Do ye—" he began, but she had risen a little, into him, and she kissed him gently on the mouth, then held his head against her breast and took the end of her kerchief and wiped his eyes and then her own.

"Oh, Ian," she whispered. "I do love thee."

17

FREEDOM!

GREY PASSED ANOTHER interminable—though less eventful—day, broken only by watching Colonel Smith write dispatches, which he did at a furious rate, quill scratching with the sound of a scuttling cockroach. This bit of imagery did nothing for Grey's digestion, which, in the aftermath of intoxication, hadn't dealt all that well with the cold grease-caked journeycake and burnt-acorn coffee he'd been given for breakfast.

In spite of physical infelicity and an uncertain future, though, he found himself surprisingly cheerful. Jamie Fraser *was* alive, and he, John, wasn't married. Given those two marvelous facts, the dubious prospects of escape and the much higher probability of being hanged seemed only mildly concerning. He settled himself to wait with what grace he could, sleeping as much as his head allowed, or singing softly to himself—a practice that caused Smith to hunch his shoulders up around his ears and scratch faster.

Messengers came and went with great frequency. If he hadn't already known that the Continentals were not only moving but preparing for a fight, it would have been clear to him within an hour. The hot air was burdened with the scent of molten lead and the whine of a sharpening wheel, and the camp had a sense of rising urgency that any soldier would have felt at once.

Smith made no attempt to keep him from hearing what was said by and to the messengers and subalterns; clearly he didn't expect the information gained to be of any use to Grey. Well . . . neither did Grey, to be honest.

Toward the evening, the tent's door was darkened by a slender female form, though, and Grey raised himself to a sitting position, careful of his tender head, because his heart had begun to beat strongly again and it made his eye throb.

His niece Dottie was in sober Quaker garb, but the soft blue of much-laundered indigo was surprisingly flattering to her English-rose coloring—and she was in amazing fine looks. She nodded to Colonel Smith and set down her tray upon his desk, before glancing over his shoulder at the prisoner. Her blue eyes widened in shock, and Grey grinned at her over the colonel's shoulder. Denzell must have warned her, but he supposed he must look a literal fright, with a grotesquely swollen face and a fixed and glaring crimson eye.

She blinked and swallowed, then said something low-voiced to Smith, with a brief questioning gesture in Grey's direction. He nodded impatiently, already taking up his own spoon, and she wrapped a thick rag around one of the steaming cans on the tray and came across to Grey's cot.

"Dear me, Friend," she said mildly. "Thee seems much injured. Dr. Hunter says thee may eat as much as is comfortable, and he will attend thee later to put a dressing on your eye."

"Thank you, young woman," he said gravely, and, glancing over her shoulder to be sure Smith's back was turned, nodded at her. "Is it squirrel stew?"

"Possum, Friend," she said. "Here, I brought thee a spoon. The stew is boiling; be careful." Putting herself carefully between him and Smith, she placed the rag-wrapped can between his knees and rapidly touched the rags, then the links of his fetters, her eyebrows raised. A horn spoon was produced from the pocket tied at her waist—and a knife with it, which was slipped under his pillow, quick as any conjurer could have managed it.

Her pulse was beating fast in her throat, and perspiration gleamed at her temples. He touched her hand once, softly, and picked up the spoon.

"Thank you," he said again. "Tell Dr. Hunter I look forward to seeing him again."

THE ROPE WAS horsehair and the knife dull, and it was very late and with innumerable small cuts stinging his hands and fingers that Grey rose cautiously from the cot. His heart was pounding; he could feel it thumping briskly behind his injured eye and hoped the eye itself was not going to explode under the impact.

He bent and picked up the tin chamber pot and used it; Smith was a very sound sleeper, thank God; if he roused at all, he would hear the familiar noise, be reassured, and—presumably—fall back asleep, subconsciously ignoring any further small noises as being Grey resettling himself.

Smith's breathing didn't change. He had a small, buzzing snore like a bee working in a flower, a tidy, busy sound that Grey found mildly comical. He lowered himself to his knees, slowly, between the cot and Smith's pallet, fighting a momentary insane impulse to kiss Smith on the ear—he had sweet, small ears, very pink. This vanished in an instant, and he crept on hands and knees to the edge of the tent. He'd threaded the rags and the gauze with which Denzell Hunter had packed his eye through the links of his fetters but still moved with the utmost caution. Being caught would be bad for him; it would be disastrous for Hunter and Dottie.

He'd been listening intently to the sentries for hours. There were two guarding the colonel's tent, but he was fairly sure that both were presently near the front flap, warming themselves at the fire; hot as the day had been, this late at night the forest's blood ran cold. So did his.

He lay down and squirmed as quickly as he could under the edge of the tent, clinging to the canvas to minimize any shaking of the tent itself—though he'd taken pains to jerk on his rope every so often through the evening, so that any shifting of the structure might be put down to his normal movements.

Out! He allowed himself one deep gulp of air—fresh, cold, and leafy—then rose, clutching the padded fetters close against his body, and walked as silently as possible away from the tent. He mustn't run.

He had had a short, sharp, whispered argument with Hunter during the latter's evening visit, seizing the brief moment when Smith had left the tent to visit the latrine. Hunter had insisted that Grey hide in his wagon; he was going into Philadelphia, everyone knew that, there would be no suspicion, and Grey would be safe from patrols. Grey appreciated Hunter's desire to rescue him, but he couldn't possibly put the doctor—let alone Dottie—at risk, and risk it would be. In Smith's place, the first thing he would do was prevent anyone from leaving, the second, search the camp and everything in it.

"There's no time," Hunter had said, briskly tucking in the end of the bandage he had wrapped around Grey's head, "and thee may be right." He glanced over his shoulder; Smith would be back any minute. "I'll leave a bundle of food and clothing in my wagon for thee. If thee chooses to make use of it, I'm glad. If not, God go with thee!"

"Wait!" Grey seized Hunter by the sleeve, making his fetters rattle. "How will I know which wagon is yours?"

"Oh." Hunter coughed, seeming embarrassed. "It . . . has a, um, sign painted on the tailboard. Dottie purchased it from—Now, you must take care, Friend," he said, abruptly raising his voice. "Eat generously but slowly, take no alcohol, and be careful in moving. Do not stand up too quickly."

Colonel Smith came in and, seeing the doctor present, came over to inspect the patient himself.

"Are you feeling better, Colonel?" he inquired politely. "Or are you still suffering from the need to burst into song? If so, might I suggest you do so now and get it out of your system, before I retire for the night?"

Hunter—who had of course heard *"Die Sommernacht"* the night before—made a small noise in his throat but managed to take his leave without losing control.

Grey grinned to himself, recalling Smith's glower—and imagining what the colonel might look like in a few hours, when he woke to discover that his songbird had flown. He made his way around the edge of the camp, avoiding the picket lines of mules and horses—easy to detect by the smell of manure. The wagons were parked nearby: no artillery, he noted.

The sky was overcast, a sickle moon glimmering uneasily between racing clouds, and the air held the scent of impending rain. Fine. There were worse things than being wet and cold, and rain would hamper pursuit, if anyone discovered his absence before daylight.

No abnormal sounds from the camp behind him; none he could hear above the noise of his own heart and breathing. Hunter's wagon was easy to find, even in the flickering dark. He'd thought by "sign" that the doctor meant a name, but it was one of the barn signs that some of the German immigrants painted on their houses and sheds. He smiled when the clouds parted, revealing this one clearly, and he saw why Dottie had chosen it: it was a large circle, in which two comical birds faced each other, beaks open in the manner of lovebirds. *Distlefink.* The word floated into his head; someone, somewhere, had told him the name of that sort of bird, saying it was a symbol of good luck.

"Good," he said under his breath, climbing up into the wagon. "I'll need it."

He found the bundle under the seat, where Hunter had told him, and took a moment to remove the silver buckles from his shoes, tying the flaps together instead with a length of leather lacing that had evidently been meant for his hair. He left the buckles tucked under the seat, put on the shabby coat, which smelled strongly of stale beer and what he thought was old blood, and peered at the knitted cap, which held two journeycakes, an apple, and a small canteen of water. Turning back the edge of the hat, he read by the fitful moonlight, LIBERTY OR DEATH, in bold white letters.

HE WASN'T HEADED in any particular direction; even had the sky been clear, he wasn't sufficiently familiar as to be able to chart his direction by the stars. His only goal was to get as far away from Smith as possible, without running into another militia company or a patrol of Continentals. Once the sun was up, he could orient himself; Hunter had told him that the main road lay south–southwest of the camp, about four miles away.

What the public might make of a man strolling down the main road in fetters was another question, but not one he needed to answer just now. After walking for an hour or so, he found a sheltered spot among the roots of an enormous pine tree and, taking out the knife, hacked off his hair as best he could. He stuffed the shorn locks well back under a root, rubbed his hands in the dirt, and then applied them vigorously to hair and face before donning his Phrygian cap.

Thus suitably concealed, he heaped a thick blanket of fallen dry needles over himself, curled up, and went to sleep to the sound of pattering rain in the trees above, once more a free man.

18

NAMELESS, HOMELESS, DESTITUTE, AND VERY DRUNK INDEED

HOT, DISHEVELED, AND still thoroughly out of temper from his encounter with Richardson, William made his way back through the crowded streets. One more night in a decent bed, at least. Tomorrow he'd leave Philadelphia with the last few companies of the army, following Clinton north—and leaving the remaining Loyalists to fend for themselves. He was torn between relief and guilt at the thought but had little energy left to consider them.

He arrived at his billet to find that his orderly had deserted and had taken with him William's best coat, two pairs of silk stockings, a half bottle of brandy, and the seed-pearl-encrusted double miniature of William's mother, Geneva, and his other mother, her sister, Isobel.

This was so far over the bloody limit of what could be borne that he didn't even swear, merely sank down on the edge of the bed, closed his eyes, and breathed through clenched teeth until the pain in his stomach subsided. It left a raw-edged hollow. He'd had that miniature since he was born, was accustomed to bid it good night before he slept, though since he'd left home he did this silently.

He told himself it didn't matter; he was unlikely to forget what his mothers looked like—there were other paintings, at home at Helwater. He remembered Mama Isobel. And he could see the traces of his real mother in his own face. . . . Involuntarily, he glanced at the shaving mirror that hung on the wall—the orderly had somehow overlooked that in his flight—and felt the hollow inside him fill with hot tar. He no longer saw the curve of his mother's mouth, her dark wavy chestnut hair; he saw instead the too-long, knife-edged nose, the slanted eyes and broad cheekbones.

He stared at this blunt evidence of betrayal for an instant, then turned and stamped out.

"Fuck the resemblance!" he said, and slammed the door behind him.

He didn't care where he was going, but within a few streets he ran into Lindsay and another couple of fellows he knew, all intent on making the most of their last evening in a semicivilized city.

"Come along, young Ellesmere," Sandy said, collaring him firmly and shoving him down the street. "Let's make a few memories to see us through the long winter nights up north, eh?"

Some hours later, viewing the world through the bottom of a beer glass, William wondered rather blearily whether memories counted if you didn't remember them. He'd lost count some time ago of what—and how many of what—he'd drunk.

He thought he'd lost one or two or three of the companions with whom he'd started the evening, too, but couldn't swear to it.

Sandy was still there, swaying in front of him, saying something, urging him to his feet. William smiled vaguely at the barmaid, fumbled in his pocket, and laid his last coin on the table. That was all right, he had more in his trunk, rolled up in his spare pair of stockings.

He followed Sandy outside into a night that seized and clung, the hot air so thick that it was hard to breathe, clogged with the smell of horse droppings, human ordure, fish scales, wilted vegetables, and fresh-slaughtered meat. It was late, and dark; the moon had not yet risen, and he stumbled over the cobbles, lurching into Sandy, a blacker smudge on the night before him.

Then there was a door, a blur of light, and an enveloping hot scent of liquor and women—their flesh, their perfume, the smell more befuddling than the sudden light. A woman in a ribboned cap was smiling at him, greeting him, too old to be a whore. He nodded amiably at her and opened his mouth, only to be mildly surprised by the fact that he'd forgotten how to talk. He closed his mouth and went on nodding; the woman laughed in a practiced way and guided him to a shabby wing chair, where she deposited him as she might leave a parcel to be called for later.

He sat slumped in a daze for some time, the sweat running down his neck under his stock and dampening his shirt. There was a fire burning in a hearth near his legs, a small cauldron of rum punch steaming on the hob, and the scent of it made him queasy. He had the feeling that he was melting like a candle but couldn't move without being sick. He shut his eyes.

Some time later, he slowly became aware of voices near him. He listened for a little, unable to make sense of any words but feeling the flow vaguely soothing, like ocean waves. His stomach had settled now, and with his eyelids at half-mast, he gazed placidly at a shifting sand of light and shadow, pricked with bright colors, like darting tropical birds.

He blinked a few times, and the colors shimmered into coherence: the hair and ribbons and white shifts of women, the red coats of infantry, the blue of an artilleryman moving among them. Their voices had given him the impression of birds, high and trilling, squawking now and then, or scolding like the mockingbirds who lived in the big oak near the plantation house at Mount Josiah. But it wasn't the women's voices that caught his attention.

A pair of dragoons were lounging on the settee nearby, drinking rum punch and eyeing up the women. He thought they'd been talking for some time, but now he could make out the words.

"Ever buggered a girl?" one of the dragoons was saying to his friend. The friend giggled and flushed, shook his head, murmured something that sounded like, "Too dear for *my* purse."

"What you want's a girl that hates it." The dragoon hadn't moved his gaze from the women across the room. He raised his voice, just a little. "They clamp down, trying to get rid of you. But they can't."

William turned his head and looked at the man, repulsed, and making his disgust evident. The man ignored him. He seemed vaguely familiar, dark and heavy-featured, but no one William knew by name.

"Then you take her hand and make her reach back and feel you. God, the squirming—milk you like a dairymaid, she will!" The man laughed loudly, still staring across the room, and for the first time William looked to see the target of this brutish farrago. There were three women standing in a group, two in their shifts, the thin fabric molded damply to their bodies, one in an embroidered petticoat, but it was plain to see who the dragoon's insinuations were meant for: the tallish one in the petticoat, who stood there with her fists clenched, glaring back at the dragoon fit to burn a hole through his forehead.

The madam was standing a little apart, frowning at the dragoon. Sandy had disappeared. The other men present were drinking and talking with four girls at the far end of the room; they hadn't heard this vulgar impertinence. The dragoon's friend was scarlet as his coat, between liquor, amusement, and embarrassment.

The dark dragoon was flushed, too, a livid line across his heavy stubbled jowls where they pressed against the leather of his stock. One hand plucked absently at the sweat-stained crotch of his moleskin breeches. He was having too much fun with his prey to cut the chase short, though.

"Mind, you don't want one who's used to it. You want her

tight." He leaned forward a little, elbows on his knees, eyes intent on the tall girl. "But you don't want one who's never had it before, either. Better if she knows what's coming, eh?"

His friend mumbled something indistinct, glanced at the girl and hastily away. William looked back at the girl, too, and as she made a small involuntary movement—not quite a flinch—the candlelight glowed for an instant on the smooth crown of her head: soft chestnut, with the gloss of a fresh conker. Jesus Christ.

Before he knew it, he was on his feet. He took two swaying paces to the madam's side, touched her shoulder politely, and when she turned a surprised face up to him—all her attention had been on the dragoon, a worried line between her brows—he said slowly, so as not to slur his words, "I'll take that one, please. The—the tall girl. In the petticoat. For the night."

The madam's plucked eyebrows all but vanished into her cap. She looked quickly at the dragoon, who was still so fixed on his prey that he hadn't noticed William at all. His friend had, though; he nudged the dragoon and muttered in his ear.

"Eh? What's that?" The man was already moving, scrambling to his feet. William groped hastily in his pocket, remembering too late that he was penniless.

"What's this, Madge?" The dragoon was with them, dividing a glower between the madam and William. William straightened instinctively—he had six inches on the man—and squared up. The dragoon assessed his size and his age and lifted the corner of his upper lip to show an eyetooth. "Arabella's mine, sir. I'm sure Madge will find another young lady to accommodate you."

"I am before you, sir," William said, and bowed, inclining his head a quarter inch, keeping a close eye on the cullion. Wouldn't put it past the filthy bugger to try to kick him in the balls—the look on his face, he wouldn't stick at it.

"He is, Captain Harkness," the madam said quickly, stepping between the men. "He's already offered for the girl, and as you hadn't made up your mind . . ." She wasn't looking at Harkness; she jerked her chin urgently at one of the girls, who looked alarmed but swiftly vanished through a door at the back. *Gone to fetch Ned,* William thought automatically, and wondered dimly for an instant how he knew the doorkeeper's name.

"Haven't seen the color of his money yet, have you?" Harkness reached into his bosom and pulled out a well-stuffed wallet, from which he withdrew a careless sheaf of paper money. "I'll have her." He grinned unpleasantly at William. "For the night."

William promptly whipped off his silver gorget, took the madam's hand, and pressed the crescent into it.

"For the night," he repeated politely, and without further ado turned and walked across the room, though the floor seemed to undulate slightly beneath his feet. He took Arabella—*Arabella?*—by the arm and steered her toward the back door. She looked appalled—plainly she recognized him—but a quick glance at Captain Harkness decided her that William was the lesser of two weevils, as he'd heard a sailor friend of his father's put it.

He could hear Harkness's shout behind them, but just then the door opened and a very large, tough-looking man walked in. He had but one eye, but that one focused instantly on Harkness. The man advanced on the captain, walking lightly on the balls of his feet, fists half curled. *Ex-boxer,* William thought, pleased. *Put that in your pipe and smoke it, Harkness!*

Then, a hand on the stairwell wall to stop from stumbling, he found himself following a round, agitated bum up the same worn, lye-soap-smelling stairs he had trodden yesterday, wondering what the devil he'd say to her when he reached the top.

HE'D BEEN VAGUELY hoping that it wouldn't be the same room, but it was. It was night now, though, and the windows were open. The warmth of the day lingered in the walls and floor, but there *was* a breeze, spicy with tree sap and the river's breath, that made the single candle flame flicker and bend. The girl waited for him to come in, then closed the door and stood with her back against it, her hand still on the knob.

"I won't hurt you," he blurted. "I didn't mean to, last time." Her hand relaxed a bit, though she continued to look narrowly at him. It was dark where she stood, and he could barely make out the gleam of her eyes. She didn't look friendly.

"You didn't hurt me," she said. "You spoilt my best petticoat, though, *and* a decanter of wine. Cost me a beating and a week's wages, that."

"I'm sorry," he said. "Truly. I'll—I'll pay for the wine and the petticoat." *Using what?* he wondered. It had belatedly occurred to him that the spare stockings in which he kept his cash had vanished with his orderly, and undoubtedly so had the cash. Well, he'd pawn something if he had to, or borrow a bit. "Can't do much about the beating. But I *am* sorry."

She made a small huffing noise through her nose but seemed to accept this. She took her hand off the doorknob and came a little way into the room, so he could see her face in the candlelight. She was very pretty, despite the look of suspicious wariness, and he felt a mild stirring.

"Well." She looked him up and down, much as she'd done when she met him in the alley. "William, you said your name is?"

"Yes." The silence lengthened a heartbeat past comfort, and he asked, almost at random, "Is your name really Arabella?"

That surprised her, and her mouth twitched, though she didn't laugh.

"No. I'm a fancy piece, though, and Madge thinks the fancies should have names like—like—ladies?" She raised a brow, and he wasn't sure whether she was questioning whether ladies had names like Arabella or what he thought of Madge's philosophy.

"I do *know* a couple of Arabellas," he offered. "One of them's six and the other's eighty-two."

"Are they ladies?" She waved a hand, dismissing the question as soon as it was asked. "Of course they are. You wouldn't know them, otherwise. Do you want me to send for wine? Or punch?" She gave him an assessing eye. "Only, if you want to do anything, I really think you'd best stay off the drink. Your choice, though." She put a hand to the tie of her petticoat in tepid invitation but didn't pull it loose. Clearly, she wasn't keen to induce him to "do anything."

He rubbed a hand over his sweating face, imagined he smelled the alcohol oozing from his pores, and wiped it on his breeches.

"I don't want wine, no. Nor do I want to . . . to do . . . well, that's not true," he admitted. "I do want to—very much," he added hurriedly, lest she think him insulting, "but I'm not going to."

She looked at him openmouthed.

"Why not?" she said at last. "You've paid well over the odds for anything you want to do. Including buggery, if that's your pleasure." Her lip curled a little.

He flushed to the scalp.

"You think I would save you from—that, and then do it *myself*?"

"Yes. Often men don't think of something until another mentions it, and then they're all eagerness to try it themselves."

He was outraged.

"You must have a most indifferent opinion of gentlemen, madam!"

Her mouth twitched again, and she gave him a look of such barely veiled amusement that the blood burned in his face and ears.

"Right," he said stiffly. "I take your point."

"Well, that's a novelty," she said, the twitch breaking into a malicious smile. "It's generally the other way round."

He breathed deeply through his nose.

"I . . . it is meant as an apology, if you like." It was a struggle to keep meeting her eye. "For what happened last time."

A faint breeze came in, ruffling the hair about her shoulders and filling the fabric of her shift so it billowed, which afforded him a glimpse of her nipple, like a dark rose in the candlelight. He swallowed and looked away.

"My . . . um . . . my stepfather . . . told me once that a madam of his acquaintance said to him that a night's sleep was the best gift you could give a whore."

"It runs in the family, does it? Frequenting brothels?" She didn't pause for a response to that. "He's right, though. Do you really mean that you intend for me to . . . sleep?" From her tone of incredulity, he might have asked her to engage in some perversion well past buggery.

He kept his temper with some difficulty.

"You can sing songs or stand on your head, if you prefer, madam," he said. "I don't propose to . . . er . . . molest you. Beyond that, your actions are quite up to you."

She stared at him, a small frown between her brows, and he could see that she didn't believe him.

"I . . . would go," he said, feeling awkward again, "but I have some concern that Captain Harkness might be still on the premises, and should he learn that you are alone . . ." And he somehow couldn't face his own dark, empty room. Not to-night.

"I imagine Ned's disposed of *him,*" she said, then cleared her throat. "But don't go. If you do, Madge will send some-body else up." She took off her petticoat, with no display of coquetry or artifice in the motion. There was a screen in the corner; she went behind this, and he heard the splash of her using a chamber pot.

She came out, glanced at him, and with a brief wave at the screen said, "Just there. If you—"

"Uh . . . thank you." He did in fact need to piss fairly badly, but the thought of using her pot, so soon after her own use of it, caused him an unreasonable amount of embarrassment. "I'll be fine." He looked round, found a chair, and sat down in it, ostentatiously thrusting out his boots and leaning back in an attitude of relaxation. He closed his eyes—mostly.

Through slitted lids, he saw her observe him closely for a moment, then she leaned over and blew out the candle. Ghost-like in the darkness, she climbed into her bed—the ropes creaked with her weight—and drew up the quilt. A faint sigh came to him over the sounds of the brothel below.

"Er . . . Arabella?" He didn't expect thanks, exactly, but he did want *something* from her.

"What?" She sounded resigned, obviously expecting him to say that he'd changed his mind about buggery.

"What's your real name?"

There was silence for a minute, as she made up her mind. There was nothing tentative about the young woman, though, and when she did reply, it was without reluctance.

"Jane."

"Oh. Just—the one thing more. My coat—"

"I sold it."

"Oh. Er . . . good night, then."

There was a prolonged moment, filled with the unspoken thoughts of two people, then a deep, exasperated sigh.

"Come and get into bed, you idiot."

HE COULDN'T GET into bed in full uniform. He did keep his shirt on, with some idea of preserving her modesty and his original intent. He lay quite rigid beside her, trying to envision himself as the tomb figure of a Crusader: a marble monument to noble behavior, sworn to a chastity enforced by his stone embodiment.

Unfortunately, it was a rather small bed and William was rather large. And Arabella–Jane wasn't trying at all to avoid touching *him.* Granted, she wasn't trying to arouse him, either, but her mere presence did that without *half* trying.

He was intensely aware of every inch of his body and which of them were in contact with hers. He could smell her hair, a faint scent of soap mingled with the sweetness of tobacco smoke. Her breath was sweet, too, with the smell of burnt rum, and he wanted to taste it in her mouth, share the lingering stickiness. He closed his eyes and swallowed.

Only the fact that he needed desperately to pee made it possible to keep his hands off her. He was in that state of drunkenness where he could perceive a problem but could not analyze a solution to it, and sheer inability to think of two things at once prevented him either speaking to her or laying a hand on hers.

"What's the matter?" she whispered hoarsely. "You're wiggling like you've got tadpoles in your drawers—only you haven't any drawers on, have you?" She giggled, and her breath tickled his ear. He groaned softly.

"Here, now—" Her voice took on a tone of alarm, and she sat up in bed, twisting round to look at him. "You're not going to be sick in my bed! Get up! Get up right this minute!" She pushed at him with small, urgent hands, and he stumbled out of bed, swaying and clutching at furniture to keep from falling.

The window gaped before him, open to the night, a lovely sickle moon pale above. Taking this as the celestial invitation it surely was, he raised his shirt, gripped the window frame, and pissed into the night in a majestically arching rush of blinding bliss.

The sense of relief was so intense that he noticed nothing whatever in its wake, until Arabella–Jane seized him by the arm and pulled him away from the window.

"Get out of sight, for God's sake!" She risked a hasty glance downward, then dodged back, shaking her head. "Oh, well. It's not as though Captain Harkness was ever going to propose you for membership in his favorite club, is it?"

"Harkness?" William swayed toward the window, blinking. There was a remarkable amount of shouting and abuse coming from below, but he was having trouble in focusing his eyes and perceived nothing save the flicker of red uniforms, redder still in the light from the lantern over the establishment's door.

"Never mind. He'll likely think I did it," Arabella–Jane said, a dark note in her voice.

"You're a girl," William pointed out logically. "You couldn't piss out a window."

"Not without making a prime spectacle of myself, no," she agreed. "But 'tisn't unknown for a whore to throw the contents of her chamber pot out on someone, accidental on purpose. Well." She shrugged, went behind the screen, and emerged with the aforementioned receptacle, which she promptly upended out the open window. In response to renewed howls from below, she leaned out and shrieked several insults that a regimental sergeant would have been proud to author, before ducking back in and banging the shutters closed.

"May as well be hanged—or buggered—for a sheep as a lamb," she remarked, taking him by the arm again. "Come back to bed."

"It's only in Scotland that they bugger sheep," William said, obediently following her. "And maybe part of Yorkshire. Northumbria, too, maybe."

"Oh, really? Is Captain Harkness from one of those places, then?"

"Oh, him?" William sat down on the bed rather suddenly, as the room had begun to revolve in a stately manner round him. "No. I'd say maybe Devon, from his—his . . . speech," he concluded, pleased to have found the word.

"So they've got sheep in Devon, too, then, I suppose." Arabella–Jane was unbuttoning his shirt. He raised a hand to stop her, wondered why he should, and left the hand hanging in midair.

"Lot of sheep," he said. "Lot of sheep everywhere in England."

"God save the Queen, then," she murmured, intent on her

work. The last button came free, and a faint draft of air stirred the hairs on William's chest.

He remembered then why he should have been stopping her, but she'd put her head inside the open front of his shirt and licked his nipple before he could make his arrested hand complete its motion, and when he did, it merely settled gently on her head, which was surprisingly warm. So was her breath. So was her hand, which had wrapped itself around his prick in a possessive sort of way.

"No," he said, after what seemed a very long time but could have been no more than seconds. His hand descended and closed—regretfully—over hers where it grasped him. "I . . . I meant it. I won't bother you."

She didn't let go but did sit up and regard him with an air of puzzled impatience, just visible in the lantern light that seeped through the shutters.

"If you bother me, I'll tell you to stop; how's that?" she offered.

"No," he repeated. He was concentrating fiercely now; it seemed exceedingly important that she understand. "Honor. It's my honor."

She made a small sound that might have been impatience or amusement.

"Maybe you should have considered your honor before you came to a whorehouse. Or did someone drag you inside against your will?"

"I came with a friend," he said with dignity. She still hadn't let go but couldn't move her hand, not with his clasped tightly around it. "That's . . . not what I mean. I mean . . ." The words that had come easily a moment before had slipped away again, leaving him blank.

"You could tell me later, once you've had a good think," she suggested, and he was startled to discover that she had *two* hands and knew what to do with the other one, too.

"Unhand my . . ." *Damn, what is the bloody word?* "Unhand my testicles if you please, madam."

"Just as you like," she replied crisply, and, doing so, put her head back inside his damp, smelly shirt, seized one nipple between her teeth, and sucked so hard that it pulled every last word out of his head.

Matters thereafter were unsettled but largely pleasant, though at one point he found himself rearing above her, sweat dripping from his face onto her breasts, muttering, "I'm a bastard, I'm a bastard, I'm a *bastard,* don't you understand?"

She didn't reply to this but stretched up a long white arm, cupped her hand round the back of his head, and pulled him down again.

"That's why." He came gradually to himself, aware that he was talking and evidently had been for some time, in spite of his head being cradled in the curve of her shoulder, his senses aswim in her musk (*like a sweating flower,* he thought dreamily), and her nipple a dark sweet thing an inch or two from his nose. "The only honor I have left is my word. Have to keep it." Then tears came suddenly to his eyes, with recollection of the moments just past. "Why did you make me break my word?"

She didn't answer for a while, and he would have thought she'd fallen asleep, save for the hand that roved over his bare back, gentle as a whisper.

"Ever think that maybe a whore has a sense of honor, too?" she said at last.

Frankly, he hadn't, and opened his mouth to say so, but once more his words had gone missing. He closed his eyes and fell asleep on her breast.

19

DESPERATE MEASURES

SILVIA HARDMAN STOOD regarding Jamie with a lowered brow, her lips pushed out in concentration. Finally she shook her head, sighed, and drew herself up.

"Thee means it, I suppose?"

"I do, Friend Silvia. I must be in Philadelphia as quickly as may be. And to do that, I must reach the road. I must be able to walk tomorrow morning, however haltingly."

"Well, then. Patience, fetch me thy father's special flask. And, Prudence, will thee grind a good measure of mustard seed . . ." She stepped a little closer to the bed, peering nearsightedly at Jamie's back as though to gauge the acreage. "A good handful—no, make it two; thy hands are small." She took a digging stick from the shelf near the door but hesitated before opening it. "Do not touch thy eyes or face, Pru—and by no means touch Chastity without washing thy hands first. Let Patience mind her if she cries."

Chastity was making fretful noises, though freshly fed and changed. Patience, though, had already run out the door, making Jamie wonder where her father's special flask might be. Hidden, apparently.

"Put the wean beside me," he suggested. "I can mind her for a bit."

Silvia did so without hesitation, which pleased him, and he lay face-to-face with wee Chastity, amusing them both by making faces at her. She giggled—and so did Prudence, as the pestle scraped and the hot smell of ground mustard thickened the air. He stuck out his tongue and waggled it; Chastity shook like a small jelly and put out a tiny pink tongue tip in turn, which made *him* laugh.

"What are you all laughing at?" Patience demanded, opening the door. She frowned censoriously from one sister to the other, making them all laugh harder. When Mrs. Hardman came in a few moments later with a large grubby root in her hand, they had reached the point of laughing at absolutely nothing, and she blinked in bewilderment, but then shook her head and smiled.

"Well, they do say laughter is good medicine," she remarked, when the hilarity had run its course, leaving the girls pink-faced and Jamie feeling slightly better—to his surprise. "May I borrow thy knife, Friend James? It is more suited to the purpose than mine."

This was patently true; her knife was a crude iron blade, badly sharpened, the haft bound with string. Jamie had a good ivory case knife, bought in Brest, of hardened steel, with an edge that would shave the hairs off his forearm. He saw her smile with involuntary pleasure at the feel of it in her hand and had a momentary flash of memory—Brianna, delicately unfolding a blade of her Swiss Army knife, an air of pleased satisfaction on her face.

Claire appreciated good tools, too. But she touched tools with immediate thought of what she meant to do with them, rather than simple admiration for elegance and function. A blade in her hand was no longer a tool but an extension of her hand. His own hand closed, thumb rubbing gently against his fingertips, remembering the knife he had made for her, the handle carefully grooved and sanded smooth to fit her hand, to match her grip exactly. Then he closed his fist tight, not wanting to think of her so intimately. Not just now.

Bidding the girls stand well back out of the way, Silvia carefully peeled the root and grated it into a small wooden bowl, keeping her face averted as much as possible from the rising fumes of the fresh horseradish but still with tears streaming down her face. Then, wiping her eyes on her apron and taking up the "special flask"—this being a dark-brown stoneware bottle stained with earth (had the lass just dug it up?)—she cautiously poured a small amount of the very alcoholic contents. What was it? Jamie wondered, sniffing cautiously. Very old applejack? Twice-fermented plum brandy? It had probably started life as some sort of fruit, but it had been some time since that fruit hung on a tree.

Mrs. Hardman relaxed, putting the cork back into the bottle as though relieved that the contents had not in fact exploded upon being decanted.

"Well, then," she said, coming over to pick up Chastity, who squealed and fussed at being removed from Jamie, whom she plainly regarded as a large toy. "That must steep for a few hours. Thee needs heat. Thee should sleep, if thee can. I know thee passed a wakeful night, and tonight may not be much better."

JAMIE HAD STEELED himself to the prospect of drinking horseradish liquor with a mix of trepidation and curiosity. The first of these emotions was momentarily relieved when he discovered that Mrs. Hardman didn't mean him to drink it, but it returned in force when he found himself a moment later facedown on the bed with his shirt rucked up to his oxters and his hostess vigorously rubbing the stuff into his buttocks.

"Have a care, Friend Silvia," he managed, trying to turn his head enough to get his mouth clear of the pillow without either twisting his back or unclenching his bum. "If ye drip that down the crack of my arse, I may be cured wi' a somewhat sudden violence."

A small snort of amusement tickled the hairs in the small of his back, where the flesh was still smarting and tingling from her administrations.

"My grandmother did say this receipt would raise the dead," she said, her voice pitched low in order not to disturb the girls, who were rolled up on the hearth in their blankets like caterpillars. "Perhaps she was less careful in her applications."

"THEE NEEDS HEAT," she'd said. Between the horseradish liniment and the mustard plaster resting on his lower back, he thought he might suffer spontaneous combustion at any moment. He was sure his skin was blistering. *"I know thee passed a wakeful night, and tonight may not be much better."* She'd got that right.

He shifted, trying to turn stealthily onto his side without making noise or dislodging the plaster—she'd bound it to his lower back by means of strips of torn flannel tied round his body, but they had a tendency to slip. The pain when shifting was in fact much less, which encouraged him greatly. On the other hand, he felt as though someone was repeatedly passing a pine torch within inches of his body. And while she *had* been very careful while working the liniment into him from rib cage to knees, a bit of the ferocious liquid had touched his balls, giving him a not-unpleasant sense of remarkable heat between his legs but also an uncontrollable urge to squirm.

He hadn't, while she was working on him, and hadn't said a word. Not after seeing the state of her hands: red as a lobsterback's coat, and a milky blister rising on the side of her thumb. She hadn't said a word, either, just drawn down his shirt when she was done and patted him gently on the backside before going to wash and then smooth a little cooking grease gingerly into her hands.

She was asleep now, too, a hunched form curled up in the corner of the settle, little Chastity's cradle by her foot, safely away from the banked embers of the fire. Now and then one of the glowing chunks of wood split with a loud *crack!* and a small fountain of sparks.

He stretched gingerly, experimenting. Better. But whether he was cured in the morning or not, he was leaving—if he had to drag himself on his elbows to the road. The Hardmans must have their bed back—and he must have his. Claire's bed.

The thought made the heat in his flesh bloom up through his belly, and he did squirm. His thoughts squirmed, too, thinking of her, and he grabbed one, pinning it down like a disobedient dog.

It's nay her fault, he thought fiercely. *She's done me nay wrong.* They'd thought him dead—Marsali had told him so and told him that Lord John had wed Claire in haste following the news of Jamie's death, in order to protect not only her but Fergus and Marsali as well, from imminent arrest.

Aye, and then he took her to his bed! The knuckles of his left hand twinged as he curled his fist. *"Never hit them in the face, lad."* Dougal had told him that a lifetime ago, as they watched a knockdown fight between two of Colum's men in the courtyard at Leoch. *"Hit them in the soft parts."*

They'd hit *him* in the soft parts.

"Nay her fault," he muttered under his breath, turning restlessly into his pillow. What the bloody *hell* had happened, though? How had they done it—why?

He felt as though he was fevered, his mind dazed with the waves of heat that throbbed over his body. And like the half-glimpsed things in fever dreams, he saw her naked flesh, pale and shimmering with sweat in the humid night, slick under John Grey's hand . . .

We were both fucking you*!*

His back felt as though someone had laid a hot girdle on it. With a deep growl of exasperation, he turned onto his side again and fumbled at the bandages holding the scalding plaster to his skin, at last wriggling out of its torrid embrace. He dropped it on the floor and flung back the quilt that covered him, seeking the relief of cool air on body and mind.

But the cabin was filled to the rooftree with the fuggy

warmth of fire and sleeping bodies, and the heat that flamed over him seemed to have rooted itself between his legs. He clenched his fists in the bedclothes, trying not to writhe, trying to calm his mind.

"Lord, let me stand aside from this," he whispered in *Gàidhlig*. "Grant me mercy and forgiveness. Grant me understanding!"

What his mind presented him with instead was a fleeting sense, a memory of cold, as startling as it was refreshing. It was gone in a flash but left his hand tingling with the touch of cold stone, cool earth, and he clung to the memory, closing his eyes, in imagination pressing his hot cheek to the wall of the cave.

Because it was his cave. The place where he'd hidden, where he'd lived, in the years after Culloden. He had throbbed there, too, pulsing with heat and hurt, rage and fever, desolation and the sweet brief consolation of dreams wherein he met his wife again. And he felt in mind the coldness, the dark chill that he'd thought would kill him, finding it now relief in the desert of his thoughts. He envisioned himself pressing his naked, scalded back to the rough damp of the cave wall, willing the coldness to pass into his flesh, to kill the fire.

His rigid body eased a little, and he breathed slower, stubbornly ignoring the ripe reeks of the cabin, the fumes of horseradish and plum brandy and mustard, of cooking and bodies washed infrequently. Trying to breathe the piercing cleanliness of the north wind, the scents of broom and heather.

And what he smelled was . . .

"Mary," he whispered, and his eyes flew open, shocked.

The scent of green onions and cherries, not quite ripe. A cold boiled fowl. And the warm smell of a woman's flesh, faintly acrid with the sweat in her clothes, overlaid by the mild, fatty smell of his sister's lye soap.

He took a deep breath, as though he might capture more of it, but the cool air of the Highlands had fled, and he inhaled a thick gulp of hot mustard, and coughed.

"Aye, all right," he muttered ungraciously to God. "Ye've made your point."

He hadn't sought out a woman, even in his most abject loneliness, living in the cave. But when Mary MacNab had come to him on the eve of his departure for an English prison, he'd found consolation for his grief in her arms. Not as replacement for Claire, never that—but only desperately needing, and gratefully accepting, the gift of touch, of not being alone for a little while. How could he possibly find it wrong that Claire had done the same?

He sighed, wriggling to find a more comfortable position. Little Chastity emitted a faint cry, and Silvia Hardman sat up at once in a rustle of clothes, bending down to the cradle with a sleepy murmur.

For the first time, the child's name struck him. The baby was perhaps three or four months old. How long had Gabriel Hardman been gone? More than a year, he thought, from what the little girls had said. Chastity, indeed. Was the name merely the natural companion to Prudence and Patience—or Mrs. Hardman's private, poignant bitterness, a reproach to her missing husband?

He closed his eyes and sought a sense of coolness in the dark. He thought he had burned long enough.

20

OF CABBAGES AND KINGS

HE WALKED TO THE road just before dawn, declining help from Prudence and Patience, though they insisted upon coming with him, in case he should fall flat on his face, be stricken with sudden paralysis, or step into a gopher's hole and twist an ankle. They had no great opinion of his powers but were well mannered enough to keep a distance of a foot or so on either side, their hands hovering like small white butterflies near his elbows, pale in the half dark.

"There's not so many wagons coming in, these last few days," Patience observed, in a tone somewhere between anxiety and hope. "Thee may not find a suitable conveyance."

"I should be satisfied wi' a dung cart or a wagon filled with cabbages," he assured her, already glancing down the road. "My business is somewhat urgent."

"We know," Prudence reminded him. "We were under the bed when Washington appointed thee." She spoke with a certain reserve, as a Quaker opposed to the practice of war, and he smiled at her small, serious face, long-lipped and kind-eyed like her mother's.

"Washington is nay my greatest concern," he said. "I must see my wife, before . . . before anything else."

"Thee has not seen her in some time?" Prudence asked, surprised. "Why?"

"I was detained upon business in Scotland," he said, deciding not to observe that he'd seen her but two days ago. "Is that a wagon coming, d'ye think?"

It was a drover with a herd of swine, in fact, and they were obliged to scuttle back from the roadside with some haste, in order to avoid being either bitten or trampled. By the time the sun was fully up, though, regular traffic had begun to flow along the road.

Most of this was coming from Philadelphia, as the girls had told him: Loyalist families who could not afford to leave by ship, fleeing the city with what they could carry, some with wagons or handcarts, many with no more than what they could convey on their backs or in their arms. There were also British soldiers in groups and columns, presumably assisting the exodus and protecting the Loyalists from being attacked or looted, should Rebel militia suddenly come out of the wood.

That thought reminded him of John Grey—who had been mercifully absent from his mind for several hours. Jamie ruthlessly pushed him out again, muttering, "Aye, *stay* gone," under his breath. But a reluctant second thought occurred to him—what if Grey had been released by the militia at once and had already made his way back to Philadelphia? On the one hand, he would see to Claire's safety; he could trust the man for that. But on the other . . .

Aye, well. If he walked into the house and found Grey there with her, he'd just take her away with him and say nothing. Unless . . .

"Does thee still suffer from the horseradish, Friend Jamie?"

Patience asked politely. "Thee snorts quite fearful. Perhaps thee had best take my hankie."

In the woods outside Philadelphia

GREY WOKE ABRUPTLY to full daylight and a musket barrel jabbed into his belly.

"Come out of there with your hands up," said a cold voice. He got his good eye sufficiently open as to see that his interlocutor wore a tattered Continental officer's coat over homespun breeches and an open-collared shirt, topped by a slouch hat turned up with a turkey feather through the brim. Rebel militia. Heart in his throat, he crawled stiffly out of his refuge and rose, hands in the air.

His captor blinked at Grey's battered face, then at the fetters, strips of muslin bandage hanging from the rusted links. He withdrew the musket slightly but didn't lower it. Now that Grey was on his feet, he could see several other men, as well, all peering at him with extreme interest.

"Ah . . . where did you escape from?" the officer with the musket asked carefully.

There were two possible answers, and he chose the riskier option. Saying "gaol" would have likely led to them leaving him alone or, at worst, taking him with them but leaving him in irons; either way, he'd still be wearing fetters.

"I was put in irons by a British officer who took me up as a spy," he said boldly. *Entirely true,* he reflected, *so far as it goes.*

A deep hum of interest ran among the men, who pressed closer to look at him, and the prodding musket barrel was withdrawn altogether.

"Indeed," said his captor, who had an educated English voice, with a slight Dorset accent. "And what might be your name, sir?"

"Bertram Armstrong," he replied promptly, using two of his middle names. "And may I have the pleasure of knowing your own name, sir?"

The man pursed his lips a little but answered readily enough.

"I am the Reverend Peleg Woodsworth, Captain of the Sixteenth Pennsylvania, sir. And your company?" Grey saw

Woodsworth's eyes flick toward his liberty cap with its bold motto.

"I haven't yet joined a company, sir," he said, softening his own accent just a little. "I was on my way to do so, in fact, when I ran afoul of a British patrol and shortly thereafter found myself in the straits you see." He raised his wrists a little, clanking. The hum of interest came again, this time with a distinct note of approval.

"Well, then," Woodsworth said, and lifted his musket to his shoulder. "Come along with us, Mr. Armstrong, and I think we might be able to relieve your straits."

21

BLOODY MEN

ONCE THEY REACHED the trace, there were horses, mules, and wagons, as well as militia companies. Rachel was able to ride in a teamster's wagon filled with sacks of barley, Ian and Rollo trotting along beside, as far as Matson's Ford, where they were meant to meet Denzell and Dottie. They waited at the ford until midmorning, but there was no sign of Denzell's wagon, and none of the militia groups crossing there had seen him.

"He'll have had an emergency," Rachel said, lifting one shoulder in resignation. "We'd best go on by ourselves; perhaps we can find a wagon on the main road that will carry us into the city." She wasn't troubled; any doctor's family was used to fending for themselves unexpectedly. And she loved being alone with Ian, talking, looking at his face.

Ian agreed that this was good sense, and they splashed across, shoes in hand, the cold water a relief. Even in the forest, the air was close and hot, restless with prowling thunder that never came close enough to do much good.

"Here," he said to Rachel, and handed her his moccasins,

his rifle, and his belt, with powder horn, shot bag, and dirk. "Stand back a bit, aye?" He could see a scour in the streambed, where a persistent eddy had carved a deep hole, a dark, inviting shadow in the ripples of the creek. He leapt from stone to stone and jumped from the last one, going into the hole with a *PLUNK!* like a dropped boulder. Rollo, belly-deep in the ford and soaked to the shoulders, barked and showered Rachel with water from a huge wagging tail.

Ian's head lunged back into view, streaming water, and he reached a long, skinny arm toward her leg, beckoning her to join him. She didn't retreat but held his rifle out at arm's length and raised one brow, and he dropped his invitation, scrambling out of the hole on hands and knees. He stood up in the ford and shook himself like Rollo, spattering her with icy drops.

"Want to go in?" he asked, grinning as he took back his weapons. He wiped water from his brows and chin with the back of his hand. "It'll cool ye right down."

"I would," she said, smearing the cold droplets over her sweating face with one hand, "if my clothes were as impervious to the elements as thine are." He had on his worn buckskin leggings and breechclout, with a calico shirt so faded that the red flowers on it were nearly the same color as the brown background. Neither water nor sun would make any difference, and he would look just the same wet or dry—while she would look like a drowned rat all day, and an immodest drowned rat at that, shift and dress half transparent with water and sticking to her.

The casual thought coincided with Ian's buckling of his belt, and the movement drew her eye to the flap of his linen breechclout—or, rather, to where it had been before he raised it to pull it over his belt.

She drew in her breath audibly and he looked up at her, surprised.

"Eh?"

"Never mind," she said, her face going hot despite the cool water. But he looked down, following the direction of her gaze, and then looked back, right into her eyes, and she had a strong impulse to jump straight into the water, damage to her wardrobe notwithstanding.

"Are ye bothered?" he said, eyebrows raised, as he plucked at the wet cloth of his breechclout, then dropped the flap.

"No," she said with dignity. "I've seen one before, thee knows. *Many* of them. Just not . . ." *Not one with which I am soon to be intimately acquainted.* "Just not . . . thine."

"I dinna think it's anything out o' the ordinary," he assured her gravely. "But ye can look, if ye like. Just in case. I wouldna want ye to be startled, I mean."

"Startled," she repeated, giving him a look. "If thee thinks I am under any illusions about either the object or the process, after living for months in a military camp . . . I doubt I shall be shocked, when the occasion a—" She broke off, a moment too late.

"Rises," he finished for her, grinning. "I think I'll be verra disappointed if ye're not, ken?"

IN SPITE OF the hot blush, which seemed to run from her scalp straight down into her nether regions, she didn't begrudge him fun at her expense. Anything that made him smile like that was balm to her own spirit.

He'd been deeply oppressed, ever since the dreadful news of the ship's sinking had come, and while he'd borne up with a stoicism she thought natural to both Highlanders and Indians, saying little about it, he hadn't tried to hide his desolation from her, either. She was glad of that, despite her own sadness for Mr. Fraser, for whom she had a deep respect and affection.

She did wonder about Ian's mother and how she might have got on with that lady. At the best, she might have had a mother again herself—and that would have been a great blessing. She hadn't been expecting the best, though; she doubted that Jenny Murray would have been any more pleased at the notion of her son marrying a Friend than a Quaker meeting might be to hear of Rachel's intention of marrying a man of blood—and a Catholic, to boot. She wasn't sure which of those would be more cause for consternation but *was* sure that Ian's tattoos would pale in contrast to his affiliation with the Pope.

"How shall we be wed, d'ye think?" Ian, who had been walking in front of her to push branches out of her way, paused and turned to let her come alongside, the path here being wide enough to walk abreast for a little.

"I don't know," she told him frankly. "I think I cannot in good conscience be baptized Catholic, no more than thee in good conscience could live as a Friend."

"Do Friends marry only other Friends, then?" One side of his mouth curled. "I'd think the choice might be a bit sparse. Or d'ye all end up marrying your cousins?"

"They marry other Friends or they get put out of meeting," she told him, ignoring the gibe about cousins. "With rare exceptions. A marriage between a Friend and a non-Friend might be allowed in case of dire circumstance—after a committee on clearness had conferred with both bride and groom—but it's rare. I fear that even Dorothea may have difficulty, in spite of her very evident sincerity of conversion."

Ian laughed at thought of Denny's fiancée. Lady Dorothea Jacqueline Benedicta Grey was no one's notion of a demure Quaker—though, for that matter, Rachel thought that anyone who supposed female Friends to be demure had never met one.

"Have ye asked Denny what they mean to do?"

"I haven't," she admitted. "To tell the truth, I am somewhat afraid to ask."

Ian's feathery brows shot up.

"Afraid? Why?"

"Both on his account and ours. Thee knows we were put out of our meeting in Virginia—or, rather, he was, and I went with him. It affected him very much, and I know he wishes above all things to marry Dottie properly, before the witness of a meeting to which they both belong."

Ian shot her a quick glance, and she knew he was about to ask if she felt likewise. She hurried on, to forestall him.

"There are other Friends in his same case, though: men who cannot abide the thought of capitulation to the King and who feel obliged to assist the Continental army. 'Fighting Quakers,' they call themselves." She couldn't help smiling at the name; it conjured such incongruous images.

"Some such held meeting now and then at Valley Forge, but they aren't accepted by Philadelphia Yearly Meeting. Denny has to do with them but hasn't joined them as yet."

"Aye?" The trail had narrowed again and Ian moved ahead, turning his head to speak over his shoulder so she would know he attended. She was somewhat distracted herself; the buckskin was drying slowly, molding itself damply to Ian's long, sinewy shanks, and reminding her of his breechclout.

"Yes," she said, recovering her train of thought. "The thing is—is thee familiar with religious disputation, Ian?"

That made him laugh again.

"I thought not," she said dryly. "I am. And the thing is, when a group of . . . of . . . persons who disagree with a central teaching of—"

"Heretics?" he offered helpfully. "Quakers wouldna burn folk, would they?"

"Those who are led of the spirit to follow a different path, let us say," she said, a little tersely. "And, no, they wouldn't. But the point I am making is that when such a group breaks away over some point of doctrine, they are inclined to cling even more rigorously to the rest of their beliefs and be more fierce even than the original group."

Ian's head lifted; so did Rollo's. Both hunters turned to and fro, nostrils flaring, but then shook themselves slightly and resumed walking. "Aye, so?" Ian said, reminding her of her point.

"So even if Denny should become convinced that he should belong to a meeting of Fighting Quakers, they might be that much more reluctant to accept a member such as Dottie. Though, on the other hand, should they be willing to do so, that *might* mean that they would at least consider our marriage. . . ." She tried to sound hopeful about that prospect but in truth thought pigs might fly before any meeting of Friends accepted Ian Murray—or vice versa.

"Is thee attending, Ian?" she asked a little sharply, for man and dog were still moving but with a new wariness. Rollo's ears cocked alertly and Ian shifted his rifle from shoulder to hand. Within a few steps, she heard what they had heard—the distant sounds of wagon wheels and marching feet. An army on the move, and the thought made the fine hairs prickle on her arms, in spite of the heat.

"What?" Ian turned a blank face toward her, then came to himself and smiled. "Well, no. I was wondering what a dire circumstance might be. To Friends."

Rachel had wondered that herself, if only briefly. "Well . . ." she began dubiously. In truth, she had no idea what sort of dire circumstance would make such a marriage thinkable, let alone acceptable.

"I was only thinking," he went on, before she could think of anything. "Uncle Jamie told me how it was when his parents wed. His father stole his mother away from her brothers, and they were obliged to hide where they could, for the MacKenzies of Leoch werena anything ye'd want to face, when roused."

His face was animated, telling the story.

"They couldna be marrit in kirk, for the banns couldna be called, and they'd be discovered the moment they came out of hiding to speak to a priest. So they stayed hidden until Ellen—that would be my grannie, aye?—was big wi' child, and then came out. Her brothers couldna object to the marriage at that point, and so they were wed." He shrugged. "So I was only wondering: would Friends think a coming child a dire circumstance?"

Rachel stared at him.

"If thee thinks that I will lie with thee without marriage, Ian Murray," she said, in measured tones, "thee has no notion just how dire thy own circumstances might become."

BY THE TIME they reached the main road that led to Philadelphia, the sound had grown amazingly—and so had the traffic making it. Normally a busy road, carrying travelers and wagons full of produce to and from the nearby countryside, it was all but choked now, mules braying, children shrieking, harried parents calling out for their offspring, pushing handcarts and barrows full of possessions along the road, often with a resentful pig towed alongside by a rope round its neck or a basket of chickens wobbling atop the pile.

And in, around, and through the struggling knots of civilians fleeing at footpace was the army. Marching columns, two by two, leather straps and gaiters creaking as they sweated through their coats, faces more crimson in the heat than their fading uniforms. Small platoons of cavalry, still fine on their horses, knots of green-clad Hessians, and, here and there, companies of infantry stationed at the side of the road, providing support for officers who were stopping wagons, sometimes commandeering them, sometimes waving them on.

Ian paused in the shadow of the trees, judging the situation. The sun was nearly overhead—plenty of time. And they had nothing that the army would want; no one would stop them.

He was aware of the militia companies, too. They had met several, passing through the woods. These for the most part stayed off the road, making their way carefully through the verges in ones and twos and threes, not hiding, but not drawing attention to themselves, either.

"Look!" Rachel exclaimed, her hand tightening on his arm. "It's William!" She pointed at a tall officer on the far side of the road and looked up at Ian, her face bright as sun on water. "We must speak to him!"

Ian's hand had tightened on her shoulder in response, and he felt the urgency of her flesh—but also the terrible fragility of the bones under it.

"Not you," he said, and lifted his chin toward the plodding ranks of disgruntled troops, sweating and dust-stained. "I dinna want ye anywhere in sight o' them."

Her eyes narrowed just a trifle—but Ian had been married once and took his hand off her shoulder promptly.

"I mean," he said hastily, "I'll go and talk to William. I'll bring him here to ye."

Rachel opened her mouth to reply, but he snooved his way hastily through the screening bushes before she could speak.

"Stay," he said sternly to Rollo, turning back for an instant. The dog, who had not stirred from his comfortable spot at Rachel's feet, twitched one ear.

William was standing by the roadside, looking hot, tired, disheveled, and thoroughly unhappy. As well he might, Ian thought with some sympathy. He kent William had surrendered at Saratoga; he was likely bound for England—if he was lucky—or for a long parole in some rough lodging somewhere far to the north. In either case, his active role as a soldier was over for some time.

His face changed abruptly at sight of Ian. Surprise, the beginnings of indignation, then a quick glance round, decision clamping down upon his features. Ian was surprised for a moment that he could read William's face so easily but then remembered why. Uncle Jamie guarded his own expression in company—but not with Ian. Ian's own face didn't show his knowledge, though, any more than William's now showed more than an irritable acknowledgment.

"Scout," William said, with the briefest of nods. The corporal to whom he had been talking gave Ian a brief, incurious look, then saluted William and plunged back into the trudging stream.

"What the bloody hell do *you* want?" William drew a grubby sleeve across his sweating face. Ian was mildly surprised at this evident hostility; they'd parted on good terms the last time they had seen each other—though there had been little conversation at the time, William having just put a pistol ball through the brain of a madman trying to kill Rachel, Ian, or both, with an ax. Ian's left arm had healed enough to dispense with a sling, but it was still stiff.

"There's a lady who'd like to speak with ye," he said, ignoring William's narrowed eyes. The eyes relaxed a little.

"Miss Hunter?" A small gleam of pleasure lit William's eyes, and Ian's own narrowed slightly. *Aye, well,* he thought, *let her tell him, then.*

William waved to another corporal down the line, who waved back, then he stepped off the road after Ian. A few soldiers glanced at Ian, but he was unremarkable, the double line of dotted tattooing on his cheeks, his buckskin breeches, and his sun-browned skin marking him as an Indian scout—a good many of these had deserted the British army, but there were still a good many left, mostly Loyalists like Joseph Brant, who held land in Pennsylvania and New York; there were also still some ranging parties from the Iroquois nations who had come down to fight at Saratoga.

"William!" Rachel flew across the little clearing and clasped the tall captain's hands, beaming up at him with such joy that he smiled back at her, all irritability vanished. Ian hung back a bit, to give her time. There hadn't been any, really, what with Rollo roaring and tearing at Arch Bug's miserable auld carcass, Rachel sprawled on the floor, frozen with horror, himself lying on the floor pouring blood, and half the street outside screaming bloody murder.

William had pulled Rachel to her feet and thrust her into the arms of the first woman available, who, as it happened, was Marsali.

"Get her out of here!" William had snapped. But Rachel, Ian's nut-brown maiden—her brownness much splattered with blood—had pulled herself together in an instant and, gritting her teeth—Ian had seen her do it, bemused by shock as he lay on the floor, watching things happen as though in a dream—

had stepped over auld Arch's body, fallen to her knees in the mess of brains and blood, wrapped her apron tight about Ian's wounded arm and tied it with her kerchief, and then, with Marsali, had dragged him bodily out of the printshop and into the street, where he'd promptly passed out, waking only when Auntie Claire began stitching his arm.

Ian hadn't had time to thank William, even had he been able to speak, and he meant to convey his own thanks as soon as he might. But clearly Rachel wanted to talk to him first, and he waited, thinking how beautiful she looked, her eyes the clouded hazel of thicket and greenbrier, face clever and quick as flame.

"But thee is tired, William, and thin," she was saying, drawing a finger disapprovingly down the side of his face. "Do they not feed thee? I'd thought it was only the Continentals who went short of rations."

"Oh. I—I haven't had time of late." The happiness that had lit William's face while he talked with Rachel faded noticeably. "We—well, you see." He waved an arm toward the invisible road, where the hoarse chants of the sergeants rang like the calling of disgruntled crows above the shuffle of feet.

"I do see. Where is thee going?"

William rubbed the back of his hand across his mouth and glanced at Ian.

"I suppose he oughtn't to say," Ian said, coming across and touching Rachel's arm, smiling at William in apology. "We're the enemy, *mo nighean donn.*"

William looked sharply at Ian, catching the tone of his voice, then back at Rachel, whose hand he was still holding.

"We are betrothed, William—Ian and I," she said, gently pulling her hand out of his and putting it on Ian's.

William's face changed abruptly, losing its look of happiness altogether. He eyed Ian with something remarkably close to dislike.

"Are you," he said flatly. "I suppose I must wish you every happiness, then. Good day." He turned on his heel, and Ian, surprised, reached out to pull him back.

"Wait—" he said, and then William turned and hit him in the mouth.

He was lying on his back in the leaves, blinking in disbelief, as Rollo hurtled over him and sank his teeth into some soft part of William, judging by the yelp and the brief cry of startlement from Rachel.

"Rollo! *Bad* dog—and thee is a bad dog, too, William Ransom! What the devil does thee mean by this?"

Ian sat up, tenderly fingering his lip, which was bleeding. Rollo had retreated a little under Rachel's scolding but kept a yellow eye fixed on William and a curled lip raised over bared teeth, the faintest rumble of a growl coming from his huge chest.

"Fuirich," Ian said to him briefly, and got to his feet. William had sat down and was examining the calf of his leg, which was bleeding through his torn silk hose, though not badly. When he saw Ian, he scrambled to his feet. His face was bright red and he looked as though he meant to either do murder or burst into tears. *Maybe both,* Ian thought in surprise.

He was careful not to touch William again but stood back a bit—in front of Rachel, just in case the man meant to go off again. He *was* armed, after all; there was a pistol and knife at his belt.

"Are ye all right, man?" Ian asked, in the same tone of mild concern he'd heard his da use now and then on his mam or Uncle Jamie. Evidently it was in fact the right tone to take with a Fraser about to go berserk, for William breathed like a grampus for a moment or two, then got himself under control.

"I ask your pardon, sir," he said, back stiff as a stick of rock maple. "That was unforgivable. I shall . . . leave you. I—Miss Hunter . . . I—" He turned, stumbling a little, and that gave Rachel time to dart round in front of Ian.

"William!" Her face was full of distress. "What is it? Have I—"

He looked down at her, his face contorted, but shook his head.

"You haven't done anything," he said, with an obvious effort. "You . . . you could never do anything that—" He swung round toward Ian, fist clenched on his sword. "But *you,* you fucking bas—you son of a bitch! *Cousin!*"

"Oh," said Ian stupidly. "Ye know, then."

"Yes, I bloody know! You could have fucking told me!"

"Know what?" Rachel looked from him to William and back again.

"Don't you bloody tell her!" William snapped.

"Don't be silly," Rachel said reasonably. "Of course he'll tell me, the minute we're alone. Does thee not wish to tell me thyself? I think perhaps thee might not trust Ian to say it aright." Her eye rested on Ian's lip, and her own mouth twitched. Ian might have taken offense at this, save that William's distress was so apparent.

"It isna really a disgrace—" he began, but then stepped hastily back as William's clenched fist drew back.

"You think not?" William was so furious, his voice was nearly inaudible. "To discover that I am—am—the . . . the get of a Scottish criminal? That I am a fucking *bastard*?"

Despite his resolve to be patient, Ian felt his own dander start to rise.

"Criminal, forbye!" he snapped. "Any man might be proud to be the son of Jamie Fraser!"

"Oh," said Rachel, forestalling William's next heated remark. "That."

"What?" He glared down at her. "What the devil do you mean, *'that'*?"

"We thought it must be the case, Denny and I." She lifted one shoulder, though keeping a close watch on William, who looked as if he were about to go off like a twelve-pound mortar. "But we supposed that thee didn't wish the matter talked about. I didn't know that thee—how could thee not have known?" she asked curiously. "The resemblance—"

"Fuck the resemblance!"

Ian forgot Rachel and hit William on the head with a double-fisted thump that knocked him to his knees, then kicked him in the stomach. Had the kick landed where he'd meant it to, it would have finished the matter right there, but William was a good deal faster than Ian expected him to be. He twisted sideways, caught Ian's foot, and yanked. Ian hit the ground on one elbow, rolled up, and got hold of William's ear. He was dimly aware of Rachel screaming and was momentarily sorry for it, but the relief of fighting was too great to think of anything else, and she disappeared as his fury surged.

There was blood in his mouth and his ears were ringing, but he had one hand on William's throat and the other stabbing forked for his eyes, when hands seized him by the shoulders and jerked him off his cousin's squirming body.

He shook his head to clear it, panting and pulling at whoever was holding him—there were two of the villains. That earned him a thump in the ribs that knocked out what little breath he had.

William wasn't doing much better. He got to his feet, wiping the back of his hand under his nose, which was bleeding profusely. He glanced at the result and grimaced in disgust, wiping the hand on his coat.

"Take him," he said, half breathless but in control of himself. One of his eyes was swelling shut, but the other gave Ian a look of straightforward bloodlust—and, despite the circumstances, Ian was once more startled at seeing one of Uncle Jamie's expressions on another face.

There was a thunderous growl from Rollo. Rachel had the big dog's scruff twisted tight, but Ian kent well enough that she couldn't hold him if he decided to savage William. *"Fuirich, a cu!"* he said, with all the authority he could summon. The soldiers would kill Rollo without a second thought if he lunged for William's throat. The dog eased back down on his haunches but stayed tensed, his lips drawn back from saliva-dripping fangs and a deep, constant growl echoing through his body.

William glanced at Rollo, then turned his back on the dog. He sniffed, hawked, and spat blood to one side, then continued, still breathing heavily. "Take him to the head of the column, to Colonel Prescott. He's under arrest for assaulting an officer; he'll be dealt with at camp this evening."

"What does thee mean, 'dealt with'?" Rachel demanded, pushing her way past the two soldiers holding Ian. "And how dare thee, William Ransom? How—how . . . how *dare* thee?!" She was white-faced with fury, small fists clenched and shaking at her sides, and Ian grinned at her, licking fresh blood from his split lip. She was paying no attention to him, though, all her ire focused on William, who drew himself up to his full height and glared down the steep bridge of his nose at her.

"This is no longer your concern, madam," he said, as coldly as a man who was red as a piece of flannel and shooting sparks out of his ears could manage.

Ian thought Rachel might actually kick William in the shins, and would have paid good money to see that, but her Quaker principles got the better of the situation and she drew herself up to her own not insignificant height—she was as tall as Auntie Claire—and thrust her chin pugnaciously up at William.

"Thee is a coward and a brute," she declared at the top of her voice. Swinging round toward the men holding Ian, she added, "And so are thee brutes and cowards, to be following an order so lacking in justice!"

One of the soldiers sniggered, then coughed as he caught William's bloodshot eye upon him.

"Take him," William repeated. "Now." And, turning on his heel, stalked off. There was a broad stripe of pale road dust down the back of his coat and a good deal of it in his hair.

"Best bugger off, miss," one of the soldiers advised Rachel, not unkindly. "You don't want to be down amongst the troops, like, not on your own."

"I will not bugger off," Rachel said, narrowing her eyes at the man in a way that reminded Ian of a panther about to spring. "What does thee intend to do to this man?" She gestured at Ian, who was getting his own breath back by now.

"Rachel," he began, but was interrupted by the other soldier.

"Assaulting an officer? Probably five hundred lashes. Wouldn't hang him, I don't s'pose," the man added dispassionately. "Seeing as young Galahad's not maimed, I mean."

Rachel went even whiter at this, and Ian jerked hard at his arms, getting his feet solidly under him.

"It'll be all right, *a nighean,*" he said, hoping he sounded reassuring. "Rollo! *Sheas!* But he's right—the camp's nay place for ye, and ye canna do me any good by coming. Go back to the city, aye? Tell Auntie Claire what's happened—she can speak to L—*ungk!*" A third soldier, coming out of nowhere, had hit him in the pit of the stomach with a musket butt.

"What are you lot hangin' about for? Get on! And you—" The soldier turned on Rachel and the dog, glowering. "Shoo." He jerked his head at Ian's captors, who obligingly hauled Ian around.

Ian tried to turn his head to give Rachel a final word, but they jerked him back and firmly down the road.

He stumbled along, in preference to being dragged, thinking furiously. Auntie Claire was his best chance—likely his only one. If she could make Lord John take a hand, either speaking to Willie or directly to this Colonel Prescott . . . He glanced up at the sun. Noon, more or less. And the British on the march carried out routine flogging and other punishment after the evening meal; he'd seen it now and then, and he'd seen his uncle's back now and then, too. A cold worm crawled through his sore belly.

Six hours. Maybe.

He risked another quick glance back. Rachel was running, Rollo loping alongside.

WILLIAM SWABBED HIS face with what was left of his handkerchief. His features felt foreign to him, lumped and swollen, and he explored the inside of his mouth gingerly with his tongue: no teeth missing, a couple maybe loose, and a stinging cut inside his cheek. Not bad. He thought he'd done worse to Murray and was glad of it.

He was still trembling—not with shock but with the urge to rip someone limb from limb. At the same time, he was beginning to *feel* shock, though conscious thought still came in fleeting snatches. What the devil had he done?

A short column of soldiers marched past, a few of them openly staring at him. He gave them a vicious look, and their heads snapped forward so fast he could hear the leather of their stocks creak.

He hadn't done it. Murray had attacked *him*. Where did Rachel Hunter get off, calling *him* a coward and a brute? He felt the tickle of blood crawling down from one nostril and stanched it, snorting into the filthy rag. He saw someone approaching, coming up the road, accompanied by a large dog. He straightened, stuffing the handkerchief into his pocket.

"Speak of the bloody she-devil," he muttered, and coughed, his throat raw with the iron taste of blood.

Rachel Hunter was pale with rage. Apparently she hadn't turned round to apologize for her insults. She had snatched off her cap and held it clutched in one hand—did she mean to throw it at him? he wondered in fogged amazement.

"Miss Hunter—" he began in a rasping voice, and would have bowed, save he was afraid the motion would make his nose bleed again.

"Thee cannot mean it, William!"

"Mean what?" he said, and she gave him a look that might

have singed the small hairs off his body, had he not still been hot himself.

"Do not be obtuse!" she snapped. "What possessed thee, to—"

"What possessed your—your *fiancé*?" he snapped back. "Did I attack him? No!"

"Yes, you did! You struck him in the mouth, without the slightest provocation—"

"And he hit me on the head, without the least warning! If anyone is a coward—"

"Don't you dare call Ian Murray coward, you—you—"

"I'll call him what I bloody like—what he bloody *is*. Just like his goddamned uncle, goddamned Scottish bastard fu—I mean . . ."

"His uncle? Thy *father*?"

"Shut up!" he bellowed, and felt the blood surge into his face, stinging all the raw places. "Don't call him my father!"

She breathed stertorously through her nose for a moment, glaring up at him.

"If thee allow this to be done, William Ransom, I will—I will—"

William could feel the blood pool in his belly and thought he might faint, but not because of her threats.

"You'll what?" he asked, half breathless. "You're a Quaker. You don't believe in violence. Ergo, you can't—or at least won't"—he corrected himself, seeing the dangerous look in her eye—"stab me. You probably won't even strike me. So what did you have in mind?"

She did strike him. Her hand whipped out like a snake and slapped him across the face hard enough to make him stagger.

"So now thee has doomed thy kinsman, repudiated thy father, and caused me to betray my principles. What next?!"

"Oh, bloody hell," he said, and grabbed her arms, pulled her roughly to him, and kissed her. He let go and stepped back quickly, leaving her bug-eyed and gasping.

The dog growled at him. She glared at him, spat on the ground at his feet, then wiped her lips on her sleeve and, turning away, marched off, the dog at her heels casting a red-eyed look at William.

"Is spitting on people a part of your bloody *principles*?" he shouted after her.

She swung round, fists clenched at her sides.

"Is assaulting women part of thine?" she bellowed back, to the amusement of the infantrymen who had been standing still by the road, leaning on their weapons and gaping at the show provided.

Flinging her cap on the ground at his feet, she whirled on her heel and stamped away, before he could say more.

JAMIE CAUGHT SIGHT of a small group of redcoats coming down the road and slumped on the wagon's seat, hat pulled down over his eyes. No one would be looking for him, with the British army on the move, and even were he recognized, probably no one would bother trying to detain or question him in the midst of such an exodus—but the sight of British soldiers would likely put a knot in his tailbone for the rest of his life, and today was no exception.

He turned his head casually away toward the far side of the road as the soldiers passed, but then heard a loud *"Ifrinn!"* in a very familiar voice, and jerked round in reflex to find himself staring straight into his nephew Ian's startled, horrified face.

He was equally startled—and nearly as horrified—to see Ian, hands tied behind his back, smeared with dirt and blood and obviously the worse for wear, being shoved along by two cross-looking British privates, red-faced and sweating in their heavy uniforms.

He stifled his immediate urge to leap off the wagon and stared hard at Ian, willing the lad not to speak. He didn't, just goggled back with his eyes bulging out of his head and his face pale, as though he'd seen a ghost, and walked past, speechless.

"Jesus," Jamie murmured under his breath, realizing. "He thinks he *has* seen my fetch."

"Who thinks what?" asked the driver, though without much interest.

"I think I must get down here, sir, if ye'd be so civil as to stop? Aye, thanks." Without thought of his back, he swung down off the wagon; it twinged, but there was no warning stab of pain down his leg—and if there had been, he would still have gone up the road as fast as he could, because he saw a small figure a little way ahead, running like a rabbit with its tail on fire. The figure was plainly female, it was accompanied by a large dog, and he had the sudden thought that it might be Rachel Hunter.

It was, and he just managed to catch her up, seizing her by the arm as she ran, petticoats kirtled up in her arms and feet hammering the dust.

"Come with me, lass," he said urgently, grabbed her round the waist, and pulled her off the road. She uttered a stifled shriek—and then a much louder one, when she looked up and saw his face.

"No, I'm not dead," he said hurriedly. "Later, aye? Step back on the road wi' me now, or someone's going to come see am I raping ye in the bushes. *Ciamar a tha thu, a choin?*" he added to Rollo, who was sniffing him industriously.

She made an odd gargling noise in her throat and continued to stare, but after an instant blinked and nodded and they were back on the road. Jamie smiled and acknowledged a man who had stopped in the middle of the road, dropping the handles of a barrow he was trundling. The man looked suspiciously at them, but Rachel, after a moment's stunned bewilderment, waved at him with a ghastly smile, and he shrugged and picked up his barrow.

"Wh-what—" she croaked. She looked as though she might collapse or vomit, chest heaving and her face going scarlet and white and scarlet again. She'd lost her cap, and her dark hair was matted with sweat and sticking to her face.

"Later," he said again, but gently. "What's happened to Ian? Where are they taking him?"

Between wrenching gasps, she told him what had happened.

"A mh'ic an diabhail," he said softly, and wondered for a split second what—or who—he meant by that. The thought vanished, though, as he looked up the road. Perhaps a quarter mile back, he could see the large, slow-moving knot of evacuees, a sprawling mass of slow wagons and trudging people, with the neat scarlet columns of soldiers splitting to flow round them, coming on now four abreast.

"Aye, then," he said grimly, and touched Rachel's shoulder. "Dinna fash, lassie. Get your breath and go back after Ian, but dinna get close enough that the soldiers take notice of ye. When he's free, tell him the two of ye must come back to the city straightaway. Go to the printshop. Oh—and best leash the hound wi' your sash. Ye dinna want him to eat anyone."

"Free? But what—what is thee going to do?" She'd got the hair out of her eyes and was calmer, though the whites of her eyes still showed all round. She reminded him of a young badger at bay, baring its teeth in panic, and the thought made him smile a little.

"I mean to have a word with my son," he said, and, leaving her, strode purposefully up the road.

HE MADE OUT William at a considerable distance. The young man was standing at the side of the road, bare-headed, disheveled, and slightly battered, but evidently attempting to look collected; his hands were folded behind his back, and he appeared to be counting the wagons that passed him. He was alone, and Jamie hastened his step to reach the lad before anyone came along to talk to him; he needed privacy for his own conversation.

He was reasonably sure Rachel hadn't told him everything about the recent stramash and wondered whether she herself had been partly the cause of it. She *had* said the trouble began just after she'd told William about her betrothal to Ian. Her account had been slightly confused overall, but he'd got the gist of it well enough, and his jaw tightened as he came up to William and saw the look on his face.

Christ, do I look like that in a temper? he wondered briefly. It was off-putting to speak to a man who looked as though he asked nothing more of the world than the chance to rend someone limb from limb and dance on the pieces.

"Well, rend away, lad," he said under his breath. "And we'll see who dances." He stepped up beside William and took off his hat.

"You," he said baldly, not wishing to call the lad by either title or name, "come aside wi' me. Now."

The look on William's face changed from incipient murder to the same look of startled horror Jamie had just surprised on Ian's. Had matters been otherwise, he'd have laughed. As it was, he gripped William hard by the upper arm, pushed him off-balance, and had him into the shelter of a scrim of saplings before he could set his feet hard.

"You!" William blurted, wrenching loose. "What the devil are you doing here? And where is my—what have you—" He made a convulsive gesture of dismissal. "What are you *doing* here?"

"Talking to you, if ye'll close your mouth for a moment," Jamie said coldly. "Listen to me, lad, because I'm telling ye what you're going to do."

"You're not telling me *anything,*" William began furiously, and cocked a fist. Jamie grabbed him by the upper arm again, and this time dug his fingers hard into the spot Claire had shown him, on the underside of the bone. William let out a strangled "Agh!" and started to pant, his eyes bulging.

"You're going to catch up the men ye sent Ian with and tell them to set him free," Jamie said evenly. "If ye don't, I go down under a flag of truce to the camp where they're taking him, introduce myself, tell the commander who *you* are, and explain the reason for the fight. Ye'll be right there beside me. Do I make myself clear?" he asked, increasing the pressure of his fingers.

"Yes!" The word came out in a hiss, and Jamie let go suddenly, folding his fingers into a fist to hide the fact that they were trembling and twitching from the effort.

"God damn you, sir," William whispered, and his eyes were black with violence. "God damn you to hell." His arm hung limp and must have hurt, but he wouldn't rub it, not with Jamie watching.

Jamie nodded. "Nay doubt," he said quietly, and went into the forest. Once out of sight of the road, he leaned against a tree, feeling sweat stream down his face. His back felt cast in cement. His whole body was trembling, but he hoped that William had been too distrait to notice.

God, should it have come to blows, I couldna take him.

He closed his eyes and listened to his heart, which was thumping like a bodhran. After a little, he heard the sound of hooves on the road, a horse galloping, and, turning to peer through the trees, caught a glimpse of William thundering past, heading in the direction Ian had been taken.

22

THE GATHERING STORM

BY BREAKFAST ON Thursday, I'd come to the firm conclusion that it was the Duke of Pardloe or me. If I stayed in the house, only one of us would remain alive by sundown. Denzell Hunter must have come into the city by now, I reasoned; he'd call in daily at Mrs. Woodcock's house, where Henry Grey was convalescing. A very kind and capable doctor, he could easily manage Hal's recovery—and perhaps his future father-in-law would be grateful for his professional attention.

The thought made me laugh out loud, despite my increasing anxiety.

To Dr. Denzell Hunter
From Dr. C. B. R. Fraser

I am called away to Kingsessing for the day. I surrender His Grace the Duke of Pardloe to your most competent care, in the happy confidence that your religious scruples will prevent your striking him in the head with an ax.

Yours most sincerely,
C.

Postscriptum: I'll bring you back some asafoetida and ginseng root as recompense.

Post-postscriptum: Strongly suggest you don't bring Dottie, unless you possess a pair of manacles. Preferably two.

I sanded this missive, gave it to Colenso for delivery to Mrs. Woodcock's house, and executed a quiet sneak out the front door before Jenny or Mrs. Figg should pop up and demand to know where I was going.

It was barely seven o'clock, but the air was already warming, gradually heating up the city. By noon, the pungent mix of animals, humans, sewage, rotting vegetable matter, resinous trees, river mud, and hot brick would be stifling, but for the moment, the faint scent lent a piquant touch to the gentle air. I was tempted to walk, but even my most utilitarian shoes weren't up to an hour's walk on country roads—and if I waited for sundown and the cooling evening to make my way back, I'd be remarkably late.

Neither was it a good idea for a woman to be alone on the roads, on foot. Day *or* night.

I thought I could manage the three blocks to the livery stable without incident, but at the corner of Walnut I was hailed by a familiar voice from a carriage window.

"Mrs. Fraser? I say, Mrs. Fraser!"

I looked up, startled, to see the hawk-nosed face of Benedict Arnold smiling down at me. His normally fleshy features were gaunt and lined, and his usually ruddy complexion had faded to an indoor pallor, but there was no mistaking him.

"Oh!" I said, and made a quick bob. "How nice to see you, General!"

My heart had sped up. I'd heard from Denny Hunter that Arnold had been appointed military governor of Philadelphia but hadn't expected to see him so soon—if at all.

I should have left it there but couldn't help asking, "How's the leg?" I knew he'd been badly injured at Saratoga—shot in the same leg that had been wounded a short time before, and then crushed by his horse falling with him in the storming of Breymann Redoubt—but I hadn't seen him then. The regular army surgeons had attended him, and from what I knew of their work, I was rather surprised that he was not only alive but still *had* two legs.

His face clouded a bit at that, but he continued to smile.

"Still present, Mrs. Fraser. If two inches shorter than the other. Where are you going this morning?" He glanced automatically behind me, registering my lack of a maid or companion, but didn't seem disturbed by it. He'd met me on the battlefield and knew me—and appreciated me—for what I was.

I knew what he was, too—and what he would become.

The hell of it was that I *liked* the man.

"Ah . . . I'm on my way out to Kingsessing."

"On foot?" His mouth twitched.

"Actually, I had it in mind to hire a gig from the livery stable." I nodded in the general direction of Davison's stable. "Just round the corner there. Lovely to see you, General!"

"Wait a moment, Mrs. Fraser, if you would . . ." He turned his head toward his aide, who was leaning over his shoulder, nodding toward me, and saying something inaudible. Next thing I knew, the carriage door popped open and the aide jumped down, offering me an arm.

"Do come up, ma'am."

"But—"

"Captain Evans here says the livery is closed, Mrs. Fraser. Allow me to put my carriage at your service."

"But—" Before I could think of anything to complete this protest, I was handed up opposite the general and the door firmly shut, Captain Evans hopping nimbly up beside the driver.

"I gather that Mr. Davison was a Loyalist," General Arnold said, eyeing me.

"Was?" I said, rather alarmed. "What's happened to him?"

"Captain Evans says that Davison and his family have left the city."

They had. The carriage had turned in to Fifth Street, and I could see the livery stable, its doors hanging open—one of them pulled entirely off and lying in the street. The stable was empty, as was the stable yard—the wagon, the gig, and the small coach gone with the horses. Sold, or stolen. From the Davisons' house, next to the stable, the tatters of Mrs. Davison's lace curtains fluttered limp in a broken window.

"Oh," I said, and swallowed. I darted a quick look at General Arnold. He'd called me "Mrs. Fraser." Obviously, he didn't know what my current situation was—and I couldn't make up my mind whether to tell him. On impulse, I decided not to. The less official inquiry there was into events at Number 17 Chestnut Street, the better, whether the inquiry was British or American.

"I'm told the British kept quite a clamp on Whigs in the city," he went on, looking me over with interest. "I hope you weren't much troubled, you and the colonel?"

"Oh, no," I said. "Not really." I took a deep breath, groping for some means of diverting the conversation. "But I have been rather short of news—er, American news, I mean. Have there been any . . . remarkable developments of late?"

He laughed at that, but wryly.

"Where shall I start, madam?"

Despite my unease at meeting Benedict Arnold again, I was glad for his courtesy in offering me a ride; the air was thick with moisture and the sky white as a muslin sheet. My shift was moist with perspiration after only a brief walk; I would have been wringing wet—and likely on the verge of heatstroke—by the time I had walked as far as Kingsessing.

The general was excited, both by his new appointment and by the impending military developments. He was not at liberty to tell me what those were, he said—but Washington was on the move. Still, I could see that his excitement was much tempered by regret; he was a natural warrior, and sitting behind a desk, no matter how important and ornate, was no substitute for the bone-deep thrill of leading men into a desperate fight.

Watching him shift in his seat, hands clenching and unclenching on his thighs as he talked, I felt my uneasiness deepen. Not just about him, but about Jamie. They were quite different kinds of men—but Jamie's blood roused at the scent of battle, too. I could only hope he wasn't going to be anywhere in the vicinity of whatever battle might be impending.

The general set me down at the ferry; Kingsessing was on the other side of the Schuylkill. He got out himself to hand me down from the carriage, in spite of his bad leg, and pressed my hand in parting.

"Shall I send the carriage to retrieve you, Mrs. Fraser?" he asked, glancing up at the hazy white sky. "The sky looks untrustworthy."

"Oh, no," I assured him. "I shouldn't be much longer than an hour or two about my business; it won't rain before four o'clock—it never does at this time of year. Or so my son assures me."

"Your son? Do I know your son?" His brow wrinkled; he prided himself on his memory, Jamie had said.

"I don't think you would. Fergus Fraser, he's called; he's my husband's adopted son, really. He and his wife own the printshop on Market Street."

"Indeed?" His face lighted with interest, and he smiled. "A newspaper called . . . *The Onion*? I heard it mentioned in the ordinary where I breakfasted this morning. A Patriot periodical, I gather, and somewhat given to satire?"

"L'Oignon," I agreed, laughing. "Fergus is a Frenchman, and his wife has a sense of humor. They do print other things, though. And they sell books, of course."

"I shall call upon them," Arnold declared. "I'm quite without books, having left such belongings as I possess to follow after me. But really, my dear, how will you get back to Philadelphia?"

"I'm sure I can borrow some form of transportation from the Bartrams," I assured him. "I've been to their gardens several times; they know me." In fact, I intended to walk—I was in no hurry to return to the Chestnut Street house and my cantankerous prisoner (what the devil was I going to do with *him*? Particularly now that the British had left . . .), and it was no more than an hour on foot—but knew better than to tell him that, and we parted with mutual expressions of esteem.

It was only a quarter hour's walk from the ferry to Bartram's Garden, but I took my time about it, as much because my mind was still on General Arnold as because of the heat.

When? I wondered uneasily. When would it begin to happen? Not yet; I was almost sure of that. What was it, what would it be, that turned this gallant, honorable man from patriot to traitor? Who would he talk to, what would plant the deadly seed?

Lord, I thought in a moment of sudden, horrified prayer, *please! Don't let it be something I said to him!*

The very idea made me shudder, in spite of the oppressive heat. The more I saw of how things worked, the less I knew. Roger worried a lot about it, I knew: the *why* of it. Why were a few people able to do this? What effect—conscious or unconscious—did travelers have? And what ought they to do about it if they—we—did?

Knowing what would happen to Charles Stuart and the Rising hadn't stopped him, and it hadn't stopped our being dragged into the tragedy, either. But it had—maybe—saved the lives of a number of men whom Jamie had led from Culloden before the battle. It *had* saved Frank's life, or so I thought. Would I have told Jamie, though, if I'd known what the cost would be to him and me? And if I *hadn't* told him, would we have been dragged into it anyway?

Well, there weren't any bloody answers, no more than there had been the hundreds of other times I'd asked those bloody questions, and I heaved a sigh of relief as the gate to Bartram's Garden came in sight. An hour in the midst of acres of cool greenery was just what I needed.

23

IN WHICH MRS. FIGG TAKES A HAND

JAMIE'S BREATH CAME SHORT, and he found that he was clenching and unclenching his fists as he turned in to Chestnut Street. Not as a means of controlling his temper—he had it well leashed and it would stay that way—but only to let out more of the energy inside him.

He was trembling with it, with the need to see her, touch her, have her tight against him. Nothing else mattered. There'd be words, there needed to be words—but those could wait. Everything could wait.

He'd left Rachel and Ian at the corner of Market and Second, to go on to the printshop to find Jenny, and he spared an instant's quick prayer that his sister and the wee Quaker might get on well together, but this vanished like smoke.

There was a burning just under his ribs that spread through his chest and throbbed in his restless fingers. The city smelled like burning, too; smoke hung under a lowering sky. He noted automatically the signs of looting and violence—a half-burnt wall, the smudge of soot like a giant thumbprint on the plaster, broken windows, a woman's cap snagged on a bush and left to hang limp in the heavy air—and the streets around him were full of people, but not those going about their business. Mostly men, many of them armed, half of them walking warily, glancing about, the rest standing in loose knots of excited conversation.

He didn't care what was happening, providing only that it wasn't happening to Claire.

There it was, Number 17; the neat brick three-story house that he'd rushed into—and out of—three days ago. The sight of it hit him in the pit of the stomach. He'd been in there perhaps five minutes and recalled every second. Claire's hair, half brushed and clouding up around his face as he bent to her, smelling of bergamot, vanilla, and her own green scent. Her warmth and solidness in his arms, his hands; he'd grabbed her by the arse, her lovely round arse so warm and firm under the thin shift, and his palms tingled with the memory of instant lust. And no more than an instant later . . .

He pushed the vision of William out of his mind. William could wait, too.

His knock at the door was answered by the rotund black woman he'd seen on his first arrival, and he greeted her in much the same way, though with not quite the same words.

"Good day to ye, madam. I've come for my wife." He stepped inside, past her open mouth and raised brows, and paused, blinking at the damage.

"What happened?" he demanded, rounding on the housekeeper. "Is she all right?"

"I expect she is, if you're meaning Lady John," the woman said, with a heavy emphasis on the name. "As to all this"—she rotated smoothly on her axis, gesturing toward the gouged, blood-smeared wall, the broken banister, and the iron skeleton of a chandelier, lying drunkenly in a corner of the foyer—"that would be Captain Lord Ellesmere. Lord John's *son.*" She narrowed her eyes and glared at Jamie in a way that made it apparent to him that she knew damned well what had happened in the hallway above when he'd come face-to-face with William—and she was not at all pleased.

He hadn't time to worry about her feelings and pushed past her as politely as possible, heading up the stairs as quickly as his twitching back muscles would allow.

As he reached the top of the stair, he heard a woman's

voice—but not Claire's. To his astonishment, it was his sister's voice, and he approached the farthest bedroom to see her back blocking the doorway. And over her shoulder . . .

He'd felt unreal ever since his conversation with William at the roadside. Now he was convinced that he was hallucinating, because what he *thought* he saw was the Duke of Pardloe, face contorted in annoyance, rising from a chair, clad in nothing but a nightshirt.

"Sit down." The words were spoken quietly, but their effect on Pardloe was instantaneous. He froze, and everything in his face save his eyes went blank.

Leaning forward, Jamie peered over Jenny's shoulder to see a large Highland dag in her hand, its eighteen-inch barrel trained steady on the duke's chest. What he could see of her face was white and set like marble. "Ye heard me," she said, her voice little more than a whisper.

Very slowly, Pardloe—yes, it really was him, Jamie's eyes informed his dazed mind—took two steps backward and lowered himself into the chair. Jamie could smell the gunpowder in the priming pan and thought the duke very likely could, too.

"Lord Melton," Jenny said, moving slightly so as to have him silhouetted against the dim light that filtered through the shutters. "My good-sister said that you're Lord Melton—or were. Is that so?"

"Yes," Pardloe said. He wasn't moving, but Jamie saw that he had sat down with his legs flexed under him; he could be out of the chair in one lunge, if he chose. Very quietly, Jamie edged to the side. He was close enough that Jenny should have sensed him behind her, but he could see why she didn't; her shoulder blades were pressed together in concentration, sharp-edged under the cloth as a pair of hawk's wings.

"It was your men who came to my house," she said, her voice low. "Came more than once, to loot and destroy, to take the food from our mouths. Who took my husband away"—for an instant, the barrel trembled, but then steadied again—"away to the prison where he took the ill that killed him. Move one inch, my lord, and I'll shoot ye in the guts. Ye'll die quicker than he did, but I daresay ye willna think it fast enough."

Pardloe didn't say a word but moved his head a fraction of an inch to indicate that he'd understood her. His hands, which had been clutching the arms of the chair, relaxed. His eyes left the pistol—and saw Jamie. His mouth fell open, his eyes sprang wide, and Jenny's finger whitened on the trigger.

Jamie got a hand under the gun just as it went off in a puff of black smoke, the crack of the firing simultaneous with the explosion of a china figure on the mantelpiece.

Pardloe sat frozen for an instant, then—very carefully—reached up and removed a large shard of porcelain from his hair.

"Mr. Fraser," he said, in a voice that was almost steady. "Your servant, sir."

"Your most obedient, Your Grace," Jamie replied, suffering an insane urge to laugh, and kept from it only by the sure knowledge that his sister would immediately reload and shoot him at point-blank range if he did. "I see ye're acquainted with my sister, Mrs. Murray."

"Your—dear lord, she is." Pardloe's eyes had flicked back and forth between their faces, and he now drew a long, slow breath. "Is your entire family given to irascibility?"

"We are, Your Grace, and I thank ye for the compliment," Jamie said, and laid a hand on Jenny's back. He could feel her heart going like a trip-hammer, and her breath was coming in shallow pants. Putting the pistol aside, he took her hand in both of his. It was cold as ice in spite of the temperature in the room, which was slightly hotter than Hades, with the window shuttered and boarded over.

"Would ye be so amiable as to pour out a dram of whatever's in that decanter, Your Grace?"

Pardloe did and approached warily, holding out the glass—it was brandy; Jamie could smell the hot fumes.

"Don't let him out," Jenny said, getting hold of herself. She glared at Pardloe and took the brandy, then glared at Jamie. "And where in the name of St. Mary Magdalene have *you* been these three days past?"

Before he could answer, heavy footsteps came hastily down the hallway and the black housekeeper appeared in the doorway, breathing audibly and holding a silver-inlaid fowling piece in a manner suggesting that she knew what to do with it.

"The two of you can just sit yourselves down this minute," she said, moving the barrel of the gun back and forth between Pardloe and Jamie in a businesslike fashion. "If you think you're going to take that man out of here, you—"

"I told you—I beg your pardon, madam, but would ye honor me with your name?"

"You—what?" The housekeeper blinked, disconcerted. "I—Mrs. Mortimer Figg, if it's any of your business, and I doubt *that*."

"So do I," Jamie assured her, not sitting down. The duke, he saw, had. "Mrs. Figg, as I said to ye downstairs, I've come for my wife and nothing more. If ye'll tell me where she is, I'll leave ye to your business. Whatever that may be," he added, with a glance at Pardloe.

"*Your* wife," Mrs. Figg repeated, and the barrel swiveled toward him. "Well, now. I'm thinking that perhaps you ought just to sit down and wait until his lordship comes and we see what he has to say about all this."

"Dinna be daft, Jerusha," said Jenny, rather impatiently. "Ye ken Claire's my brother's wife; she told ye that herself."

"Claire?" exclaimed Pardloe, standing up again. He had been drinking from the decanter and still held it carelessly in one hand. "*My* brother's wife?"

"She's no such thing," Jamie said crossly. "She's mine, and I'll thank someone to tell me where the devil she is."

"She's gone to a place called Kingsessing," Jenny said promptly. "To pick herbs and the like. We've been doctoring this *mac na galladh*—" She scowled at Pardloe. "Had I kent who ye were, *a mh'ic an diabhail,* I'd ha' put ground glass in your food."

"I daresay," Pardloe murmured, and took another gulp from the decanter. He turned his attention to Jamie. "I don't suppose that *you* know where my brother is at the moment?"

Jamie stared at him, a sudden feeling of unease tickling the back of his neck. "Is he not here?"

Pardloe made a wide gesture round the room, wordlessly inviting Jamie to look. Jamie ignored him and turned to the housekeeper. "When did ye see him last, madam?"

"Just before he and you skedaddled out the attic window," she replied shortly, and prodded him in the ribs with the barrel of the fowling piece. "What have you done with him, *fils de salope*?"

Jamie edged the barrel gingerly aside with one finger. The fowling piece was primed but not yet cocked.

"I left him in the woods outside the city, two days ago," he said, a sudden feeling of disquiet tightening the muscles at the base of his spine. He backed against the wall, discreetly pressing his arse into it to ease his back. "I expected to find him here—with my wife. Might I inquire how you come to be here, Your Grace?"

"Claire kidnapped him," Jenny said, before Pardloe could speak. The duke's eyes bulged slightly, though whether at the remark or at the fact that Jenny was reloading her pistol, Jamie couldn't tell.

"Oh, aye? What did she want him for, did she say?"

His sister gave him a look.

"She was afraid he'd turn the city upside down looking for his brother and you'd be taken up in the kerfuffle."

"Aye, well, I think I'm safe enough now," he assured Jenny. "Ought ye to turn him loose, d'ye think?"

"No," she said promptly, pounding home her ball and patch. She reached into her apron and came out with a tiny powder horn. "We canna do that; he might die."

"Oh." He considered this for a moment, watching the duke, whose face had assumed a slight purple tinge. "Why is that?"

"He canna breathe properly, and she was afraid if she let him loose before he was quite over it, he'd die in the street, and her conscience wouldna let her do that."

"I see." The urge to laugh was back, but he controlled it manfully. "So ye were about to shoot him in the house, in order to keep him from dyin' in the street."

Her dark-blue eyes narrowed, though she kept her gaze fixed on the powder she was pouring into the priming pan.

"I wouldna really have shot him in the guts," she said, though from the press of her lips it was apparent that she'd have liked nothing more. "I'd just have winged him in the leg. Or maybe shot off a couple o' toes."

Pardloe made a sound that might have been outrage, but, knowing the man as he did, Jamie recognized it as smothered laughter. He hoped his sister wouldn't. He opened his mouth to ask just how long Pardloe had been held captive, but before he could speak, there was a knock at the door below. He glanced at Mrs. Figg, but the housekeeper was still regarding him with narrowed eyes and made no move either to lower the fowling piece or to go downstairs and answer the door.

"Come in!" Jamie shouted, sticking his head out into the

hall, then jerking back into the room before Mrs. Figg should take it into her head that he was attempting to escape and discharge a load of buckshot into his backside.

The door opened, closed, and there was a pause as the caller apparently looked around the devastated entry, then light, quick steps came up the stairs.

"Lord John!" breathed Mrs. Figg, her stern face lightening.

"In here!" called the duke, as the steps reached the landing. An instant later, the slight, bespectacled form of Denzell Hunter appeared in the doorway.

"Merde!" said Mrs. Figg, bringing her shotgun to bear on the newcomer. "I mean, Shepherd of Judea! Who in the name of the Holy Trinity are *you*?"

HUNTER WAS NEARLY as pale as Jenny, Jamie thought. Nonetheless, he didn't blink or pause but walked up to Pardloe and said, "I am Denzell Hunter, Friend Grey. I am a physician, come at the request of Claire Fraser to attend thee."

The duke dropped the decanter, which fell over and disgorged the few drops it still contained onto the braided hearthrug.

"You!" he said, drawing himself abruptly to his full height. He was in fact no taller than Hunter, but it was obvious that he had the habit of command. "You are the skulking fellow who has had the temerity to seduce my daughter, and you dare come here and offer to physic me? Get out of my sight, before I—" At this point, it dawned on Pardloe that he was in his nightshirt and unarmed. Nothing daunted, he seized the decanter from the floor and swung it at Denzell's head.

Denzell ducked, and Jamie got hold of Pardloe's wrist before he could try again. Denny straightened up, fire glinting behind his spectacles.

"I take issue both with thy description of my behavior and thy slur upon thy daughter's reputation," he said sharply. "I can only conceive that the order of thy mind is deranged by illness or drugs, for surely the man who sired and reared such a person as Dorothea could not speak so meanly of her or have so little faith in her strength of character and her virtue as to think that anyone might seduce her."

"I'm sure His Grace didna mean physical seduction," Jamie said hastily, twisting Pardloe's wrist to make him let go of the decanter.

"Is it the act of a gentleman, sir, to induce a young woman to run away with him? Ow! Let go, damn you!" he said, dropping the decanter as Jamie jerked his arm up behind his back. It fell to the hearth and burst in a shower of glass, but the duke disregarded this entirely.

"A gentleman would have sought the approval of the young lady's father, sir, before ever venturing to speak to her!"

"I did," Denzell said more mildly. "Or, rather, I did write to thee at once, apologizing for having been unable to speak with thee in person beforehand, and explaining that Dorothea and I wished to become betrothed and sought thy blessing upon our desire. I doubt thee received my letter before embarking for America, though."

"Oh, thee did, did thee? Your *desire*?" Pardloe snorted, tossing a hank of loosened hair out of his face. "Will you let go of me, you bloody Scotchman! What do you think I'm going to do, strangle him with his own neckcloth?"

"Ye might," Jamie said, easing his grip but keeping hold of Pardloe's wrist. "Jenny, would ye put that pistol somewhere out of His Grace's reach?"

Jenny promptly handed the freshly loaded pistol to Denzell, who took it by reflex, then regarded the thing in his hand in astonishment. "You need it more than I do," she said, and looked grimly at the duke. "If ye shoot him, we'll all swear it was self-defense."

"We will *not,*" said Mrs. Figg indignantly. "If you think I'm going to tell his lordship I let his brother be murdered in cold blood—"

"Friend Jamie," Denny interrupted, holding out the pistol. "I should feel much happier was thee to release Dorothea's father and take charge of this. I think that might increase the civility of our conversation."

"It might," Jamie said dubiously, but let go of Pardloe and took the pistol.

Denny approached the duke, edging glass shards out of the way, and looked carefully into his face.

"I will be pleased to speak and counsel with thee, Friend, and offer any reassurances that lie within my power regarding thy daughter. But thy breathing alarms me, and I would examine thee first."

The duke was in fact making a faint wheezing noise, and Jamie noted that the purple tinge to his face had become more pronounced. At Denzell's remark, this was augmented by a wash of dull red.

"You don't touch me, you qu . . . quack-salver!"

Denzell glanced round and seized upon Jenny as the most likely source of information.

"What did Friend Claire say regarding him, in terms of ailment and treatment?"

"Asthma, and joint fir brewed in coffee. She calls it *Ephedra.*" Jenny replied promptly, turning to add to Pardloe, "Ye ken, I didna have to tell him that. I might ha' let ye strangle, but I suppose that's no a Christian way to carry on. Are Quakers Christians, by the by?" she asked Denny curiously.

"Yes," he replied, advancing cautiously on Pardloe, whom Jamie had forced to sit down by pressing on his shoulder. "We believe the light of Christ is present in all men—though in some cases, perceiving it is somewhat difficult," he added, under his breath but loud enough for Jamie—and the duke—to hear.

Pardloe appeared to be trying to whistle, blowing with pursed lips, meanwhile glaring at Denzell. He gasped in air and managed a few more words.

"I will . . . not be doctored . . . by you, sir." Another pause for blowing and gasping. Jamie noticed Mrs. Figg stir uneasily and take a step toward the door. "I will not . . . leave my . . . daughter in your . . . clutches—" Blow. Gasp. "If you kill me." Blow. Gasp. "Nor risk . . . you sav . . . ing my life . . . and putting . . . me in . . . your . . . debt." The effort involved in getting that one out turned him a ghastly gray, and Jamie was seriously alarmed.

"Has he medicine, Jenny?" he asked urgently. His sister compressed her lips but nodded, and, with a final glare at the duke, scurried out of the room.

With the ginger air of one embracing a crocodile, Denzell Hunter crouched, took hold of the duke's wrist, and peered closely into his eyes, these organs repaying his inspection by narrowing in the most threatening fashion manageable by a man dying of suffocation. Not for the first time, Jamie suffered a reluctant admiration for Pardloe's strength of character—

though he was likewise obliged to admit that Hunter's nearly matched it.

His concentration on the tableau before him was broken by the sound of an excited fist hammering the front door below. The door opened, and he heard his nephew Ian exclaim, "Mam!" in a hoarse voice, concurrent with his sister's astonished "Ian!" Jamie stepped out of the room and, reaching the shattered banister in a few steps, saw his sister engulfed and all but obliterated by her tall son's embrace.

Ian's eyes were closed and his cheeks wet, arms wrapped tight round his small mother, and Jamie felt a sudden lump in his own throat. What would he not give to embrace his daughter that way once more?

A slight motion drew his eye, and he saw Rachel Hunter standing shyly back, smiling at mother and son, her own eyes filled with tears. She dabbed at her nose with a handkerchief, then, happening to glance up, saw Jamie above and blinked.

"Miss Rachel," he said, smiling down at her. He pointed at a jug standing on the occasional table by the door, which he assumed was Pardloe's medicine. "Might ye bring that wee jug up here? Quickly?" He could hear Pardloe's heavy breathing from the room behind him; it didn't seem to be getting worse but was still worrying.

The gasping was momentarily drowned out by the footsteps of Mrs. Figg, appearing behind him with her fowling piece. She peered over the banister at the touching scene below, then at Rachel Hunter, trotting up the stairs, jug in hand.

"And who is *this*?" she demanded of Jamie, not quite brandishing her weapon under his nose.

"Dr. Hunter's sister," he told her, interposing his body between Rachel, who looked taken aback, and the agitated housekeeper. "Your brother wants the stuff in the jug, Miss Rachel."

Mrs. Figg made a low rumbling noise but stepped back and allowed Rachel to pass. With a bleak look down at Jenny and Ian, who had now separated enough to speak and were waving their hands and interrupting each other in excited *Gàidhlig,* she vanished back into the bedroom on Rachel's heels. Jamie hesitated, wanting to rush out the front door and head for Kingsessing, but a sense of morbid responsibility obliged him to follow her.

Denny had pulled up the stool from the dressing table and was still holding Pardloe's wrist, addressing him in calm tones.

"Thee is in no immediate danger, as thee likely knows. Thy pulse is strong and regular, and while thy breathing is clearly compromised, I think—ah, is this the tincture the Scotswoman mentioned? I thank thee, Rachel; will thee pour—" But Rachel, long accustomed to medical situations, was already decanting into the brandy glass some blackish-brown stuff that looked like the contents of a spittoon.

"Shall I—" Denzell's attempt to hold the glass for the duke was preempted by Pardloe's seizing the glass for himself and taking a gulp that all but choked him on the spot. Hunter calmly observed the coughing and spluttering, then handed him a handkerchief.

"I have heard it theorized that such cataclysms of breath as thee is experiencing may be precipitated by violent exercise, a rapid change of temperature, exposure to smoke or dust, or, in some cases, by a surge of violent emotion. In the present instance, I believe I may possibly have caused thy crisis by my appearance, and if so, I ask thy pardon." Denny took the handkerchief and handed Pardloe back the glass, wise enough not to tell him to sip the stuff.

"Perhaps I may make some recompense for this injury, though," he said. "I gather thy brother is not at home, since I can't suppose that he would remain absent from this gathering unless he were dead in the cellar, and I should hope that's not the case. Has thee seen him recently?"

"I have—not." Pardloe's breathing was in fact growing smoother and his face a more normal color, though the expression on it was still feral. "Have you?"

Hunter took off his spectacles and smiled, and Jamie was struck by the kindness of his eyes. He glanced at Rachel; her eyes were hazel, rather than her brother's soft olive brown, and, while good-natured, were much warier. Jamie thought wariness a good thing in a woman.

"I have, Friend. Thy daughter and I discovered him in a militia camp some distance from the city. He had been taken prisoner, and—" Pardloe's exclamation collided with Jamie's, and Hunter patted the air with his hand, begging attention. "We were able to assist his escape, and, since he'd been injured during his capture, I treated him; his injuries were not intrinsically serious."

"When?" Jamie asked. "When did ye see him?" His heart had given a small, disquietingly happy lurch at the news that John Grey was not dead.

"Last night," Denny told him. "We heard of his escape this morning and heard nothing of his recapture as we made our way back to Philadelphia, though I asked each group of regulars or militia we encountered. He will have needed to go with care, both woods and roads being alive with men, but I imagine he'll be with you soon."

Pardloe drew a long, deep breath.

"Oh, God," he said, and closed his eyes.

24

WELCOME COOLNESS IN THE HEAT, COMFORT IN THE MIDST OF WOE

THERE WAS PLENTY OF cool greenery available; the gardens covered the best part of a hundred acres, with trees, bushes, shrubs, vines, and flowers of all descriptions—and the odd exotic fungus thrown in here and there for variety. John Bartram had spent the greater part of a long life combing the Americas for botanical specimens, most of which he had hauled home and induced to grow. I regretted not having met the old gentleman; he had died a year before, leaving his famous garden in the capable hands of his children.

I found Young Mr. Bartram—he was about forty, but so called to distinguish him from his elder brother—in the center of the gardens, sitting under the shade of an immense creeper that covered half the porch of his house, a sketchbook open on the table before him, making careful drawings of a handful of pale, leggy roots that lay on a napkin.

"Ginseng?" I asked, bending to peer at them.

"Yes," he said, not taking his eyes off the delicate line of his pen. "Good morning, Lady John. You're familiar with the root, I see."

"It's fairly common in the mountains of North Carolina, where I . . . used to live." The casual sentence caught in my throat with a sudden unexpectedness. Out of nowhere, I smelled the woods on Fraser's Ridge, pungent with balsam fir and poplar sap, heavy with the musty scent of wood ears and the tang of wild muscats.

"Yes, indeed." Reaching the end of his line, he set down his pen, removed his spectacles, and looked up at me with the bright face of a man who lives for plants and fully expects the world to share his obsession. "These are Chinese ginseng; I want to see whether I might be able to persuade it to grow here—" He waved a hand toward the encompassing acres of lush garden. "The Carolina variety languishes, and the Canadian ginseng stubbornly refuses even to try!"

"How very perverse of it. Though I expect it's too hot," I observed, taking the stool he gestured me to and setting down my basket on the floor. My shift was sticking to me, and I could feel a large splotch of spreading wetness between my shoulder blades, where my hair dripped sweat down my back. "They like cold weather."

The vivid memory of the woods had blossomed into a visceral longing for the Ridge, so immediate that I felt the ghost of my vanished house rise around me, a cold mountain wind thrumming past its walls, and thought that, if I reached down, I could feel Adso's soft gray fur under my fingers. I swallowed, hard.

"It *is* hot," he said, though he himself looked as dry as one of the roots on the table, dappled with shade from his vine. "May I offer you some refreshment, Lady John? I have some iced negus in the house."

"I'd love it," I said, meaning it. "But—iced?"

"Oh, we have quite a large icehouse by the river, Sissy and I," he said proudly. "Let me just tell her . . ."

I *had* had sufficient forethought as to bring a fan with me and now pulled this out of my basket. The sense of longing had turned suddenly into a new—and wonderful—realization. *We could go home.* Jamie had been released from service with the Continental army in order to see his cousin's body back to Scotland. He'd meant, when we returned, to go back to North Carolina, reclaim his printing press, and take up arms on behalf of the revolution via the pen rather than the sword.

That plan had vanished, along with the rest of my life, when he'd been reported drowned. But now . . . A thrill of excitement ran through me and must have shown on my face, for Mr. and Miss Bartram both blinked at me as they came out onto the porch. They were twins, and while their faces bore only a faint similarity of feature, they often shared the same expression and were doing so presently, both looking slightly bewildered but pleased.

I could barely keep myself from sharing my wonderful thought with them, but that wouldn't do, and I managed to sip the negus—port mixed with hot water, sugar, and spices, then chilled to a cold—*truly* cold!—water-beaded delight—and engage in civil admiration of the ongoing improvements to Bartram's Garden, these being already famous for their beauty and variety. Old Mr. Bartram had been planning and planting and extending them for fifty years, and his children had evidently inherited the family mania, as well as the gardens.

". . . and we've improved the river path, and we've just put up a *much* bigger potting shed," Sissy Bartram was saying eagerly. "So many customers wanting potted vines and flowers for their drawing rooms and conservatories! Though I don't know . . ." Her eagerness faded a little, and she made a moue of doubt. "With all this kerfuffle—war is *so* bad for business!"

Mr. Bartram coughed a little. "It does depend on the sort of business," he said mildly. "And I'm afraid we shall have a much increased demand for the medicinals."

"But if the army is leaving . . ." Miss Bartram began hopefully, but her brother shook his head, his face growing sober.

"Does thee not feel it in the air, Sissy?" he said softly. "Something is coming." He lifted his face, as though scenting something on the heavy air, and she reached to put a hand on his arm, silent, listening with him for the sound of distant violence.

"I hadn't realized that you were Friends, Mr. Bartram," I

said, to break the ominous quiet. Both of them blinked and smiled at me.

"Oh," said Miss Bartram. "Father was read out of meeting some years ago. But sometimes the habits of childhood come back when you least expect them." She lifted one plump shoulder, smiling, but with something regretful behind it. "I see you have a list, Lady John?"

That recalled me abruptly to my business, and the next hour was spent in busy exploration, discussion of the merits and drawbacks of various medicinals, the selection of dried herbs from the vast drying sheds, and cutting of fresh ones from the beds. With my sudden realization that we might return to the Ridge quite soon, and Mr. Bartram's very acute observation about the impending demand for medicinals, I bought much more than I had originally intended, replenishing not only my usual stocks (including a pound of dried Chinese joint fir, just in case. What *was* I going to do with the bloody man?), but also a good quantity of Jesuit bark, elecampane, and even lobelia, plus the asafoetida and ginseng I'd promised Denny.

In the end, there was too much for my basket, and Miss Bartram said she would put it up into a package and have one of the assistant gardeners who lived in Philadelphia bring it into the city when he went home in the evening.

"Would you like to see the river path, before you go?" she asked me, with a quick glance skyward. "It's not finished yet, of course, but we have some amazing things put in, and it is wonderfully cool at this time of day."

"Oh, thank you. I really—wait. You wouldn't have fresh arrowhead down there, would you?" I hadn't thought to put that on my list, but if it was available . . .

"Oh, yes!" she cried, beaming. "Masses of it!" We were standing in the largest of the drying sheds, and the late-afternoon light falling through the boards striped the walls with bars of swimming gold, illuminating the constant rain of tiny pollen grains from the drying flowers. There was a scatter of tools on the table, and she plucked a wooden trowel and a stubby knife from the litter without hesitation. "Would you like to dig your own?"

I laughed with pleasure. The opportunity to grub around in the wet mud wasn't an offer that most women would have made—especially to another woman dressed in pale-blue muslin. But Miss Bartram spoke my language. I hadn't had my hands in the earth in months, and the mere suggestion made my fingers tingle.

THE RIVER PATH was lovely, edged with willow and silver birch that cast a flickering shade over banks of nasturtium and azalea and the floating masses of dark-green cress. I felt my blood pressure drop as we strolled, chatting of this and that.

"Do you mind if I ask you something about the Friends?" I asked. "I have a colleague who was read out of meeting—he and his sister—because he volunteered as a surgeon with the Continental army. Since you mentioned your father . . . I wondered, how important a thing is that? Belonging to a meeting, I mean?"

"Oh!" She laughed, rather to my surprise. "I imagine it depends upon the individual—everything does, really, as a Friend. My father, for instance: he *was* read out of meeting, for refusing to acknowledge the divinity of Jesus Christ, but he went right on going to meeting; it made no particular difference to him."

"Oh." That was rather reassuring. "What if—what is a Quaker marriage like? Would one have to belong to a meeting in order to get married?"

She thought that interesting and made low humming noises for a bit.

"Well, a marriage between Friends is . . . between the Friends marrying. No clergyman, I mean, and no specific prayer or service. The two Friends marry *each other,* rather than it being considered a sacrament administered by a priest or the like. But it does need to be done before witnesses—other Friends, you know," she added, a small crease forming between her brows. "And I think that there might be considerable objection if the Friends involved—or one of them—had been formally expelled."

"How interesting—thank you." I wondered how this might affect Denzell and Dorothea; even more, how it might affect Rachel and Ian. "Can a Friend marry a, er, non-Friend?"

"Oh, yes, of course. Though I think they would be put out of meeting as a result," she added dubiously. "But there might be special consideration for dire circumstances. The meeting would appoint a committee of clearness to look into the situation, I suppose."

I hadn't got so far as worrying about dire circumstances, but thanked her, and the conversation went back to plants.

She'd been right about the arrowhead: there *were* masses of it. She smiled happily at my amazement but then left me to my digging, assuring me that I might take some of the lotus and some Sweet Flag rhizomes, as well, if I liked. "And fresh cress, of course!" she added over her shoulder, waving a blithe hand at the water. "All you like!"

She'd thoughtfully brought along a burlap sack for me to kneel on; I spread it carefully, not to crush anything, and kirtled up my skirts out of the way as best I could. There was a faint breeze; there always is, over moving water, and I sighed in relief, both at the coolness and the sudden sense of solitude. The company of plants is always soothing, and after the incessant—well, you couldn't call it sociability, exactly, but at least the incessant *presence* of people requiring to be conversed with, directed, hectored, scolded, conferred with, persuaded, lied to—that I had experienced over the last few days, I found the rooted silence, rushing stream, and rustling leaves balm to the spirit.

Frankly, I thought, my spirit could use a bit of balm. Between—or rather, among—Jamie, John, Hal, William, Ian, Denny Hunter, and Benedict Arnold (to say nothing of Captain Richardson, General Clinton, Colenso, and the whole bloody Continental army), the male of the species had been rather wearing on my nerves of late.

I dug slowly and peaceably, lifting the dripping roots into my basket and packing each layer between mats of watercress. Sweat was running down my face and between my breasts, but I didn't notice it; I was melting quietly into the landscape, breath and muscle turning to wind and earth and water.

Cicadas buzzed heavily in the trees nearby, and gnats and mosquitoes were beginning to collect in uneasy clouds overhead. These were luckily only a nuisance when they flew up my nose or hovered too close to my face; apparently my twentieth-century blood wasn't attractive to eighteenth-century insects, and I was almost never bitten—a great blessing to a gardener. Lulled into mindlessness, I had quite lost track of time and place, and when a pair of large, battered shoes appeared in my field of view, I merely blinked at them for a moment, as I might at the sudden appearance of a frog.

Then I looked up.

"OH," I SAID, a little blankly. Then, "There you are!" I said, dropping my knife and scrambling to my feet in a surge of joyous relief. "Where the bloody hell have you *been*?"

A smile flickered briefly across Jamie's face, and he took my hands, wet and muddy as they were. His were large and warm and solid.

"In a wagon full of cabbages, most recently," he said, and the smile took hold as he looked me over. "Ye look well, Sassenach. Verra bonny."

"You don't," I said frankly. He was grubby, very thin, and he plainly hadn't been sleeping well; he had shaved, but his face was gaunt and shadowed. "What's happened?"

He opened his mouth to reply but then seemed to think better of it. He let go my hands, cleared his throat with a low Scottish noise, and fixed his eyes on mine. The smile had gone.

"Ye went to bed with John Grey, aye?"

I blinked, startled, then frowned at him. "Well, no, I wouldn't say that."

His eyebrows rose.

"He told me ye did."

"Is that what he said?" I asked, surprised.

"Mmphm." Now it was his turn to frown. "He told me he'd had carnal knowledge of ye. Why would he lie about such a thing as that?"

"Oh," I said. "No, that's right. Carnal knowledge is a very reasonable description of what happened."

"But—"

"'Going to bed,' though . . . For one thing, we didn't. It started on a dressing table and ended—so far as I recall—on the floor." Jamie's eyes widened noticeably, and I hastened to correct the impression he was obviously forming. "For another, that phraseology implies that we decided to make love to each other and toddled off hand in hand to do so, and that wasn't what happened at all. Umm . . . perhaps we should sit down?" I gestured toward a rustic bench, standing knee-deep in creamy drifts of ranunculus.

I hadn't had a single thought of that night since learning Jamie was alive, but it was beginning to dawn on me that it might quite possibly seem important to Jamie—and that explaining what *had* happened might be somewhat tricky.

He nodded, rather stiffly, and turned toward the bench. I followed, noting with some concern the set of his shoulders.

"Have you hurt your back?" I asked, frowning as I saw the care with which he sat down.

"What *did* happen?" he asked, ignoring the question. Politely, but with a distinct edge.

I took a deep breath, then blew out my cheeks in a helpless gesture.

He growled. I glanced at him, startled, having never heard such a noise from him before—at least, not aimed at me. Apparently it was somewhat more than important.

"Er . . ." I said cautiously, sitting down beside him. "What did John say, *exactly*? After telling you about the carnal knowledge, I mean?"

"He desired me to kill him. And if ye tell me ye want me to kill *you* rather than tell me what happened, I warn ye, I willna be responsible for what happens *next*."

I looked at him narrowly. He seemed self-possessed, but there was an undeniable tension in his posture.

"Well . . . I remember how it began, at least. . . ."

"Start there," he suggested, the edge more pronounced.

"I was sitting in my room, drinking plum brandy and trying to justify killing myself, if you must know," I said, with an edge of my own. I stared at him, daring him to say something, but he merely cocked his head at me in a "Go on, then" gesture.

"I ran out of brandy and was trying to decide whether I might walk downstairs to look for more without breaking my neck, or whether I'd had enough not to feel guilty about drinking the whole bottle of laudanum instead. And then John came in." I swallowed, my mouth suddenly dry and sticky, as it had been that night.

"He did say there was drink taken," Jamie observed.

"Lots. He seemed nearly as drunk as I was, save that he was still on his feet." I could see John's face in memory, white as bone save for his eyes, which were so red and swollen that they might have been sandpapered. And the expression in those eyes. "He looked the way a man looks just before he throws himself off a cliff," I said quietly, eyes on my folded hands. I took another breath.

"He had a fresh decanter in his hand. He put it down on the dressing table beside me, glared at me, and said, *'I will not mourn him alone tonight.'* " A deep quiver ran through me at the memory of those words.

"And . . . ?"

"And he didn't," I said, a little sharply. "I told him to sit down and he did, and he poured out more brandy and we drank it, and I have not one single notion what we said, but we were talking about you. And then he stood up, and I stood up. And . . . I couldn't bear to be alone and I couldn't bear for *him* to be alone and I more or less flung myself at him because I very much needed someone to touch me just then."

"And he obliged ye, I take it."

The tone of this was distinctly cynical, and I felt a flush rise in my cheeks, not of embarrassment but of anger.

"Did he bugger you?"

I looked at him for a good long minute. He meant it.

"You absolute bastard," I said, as much in astonishment as anger. Then a thought occurred to me. "You said he desired you to kill him," I said slowly. "You . . . didn't, did you?"

He held my eyes, his own steady as a rifle barrel.

"Would ye mind if I did?" he asked softly.

"Yes, I bloody well would," I said, with what spirit I could summon up amongst the growing confusion of my feelings. "But you didn't—I *know* you didn't."

"No," he said, even more softly. "Ye don't know that."

Despite my conviction that he was bluffing, a small chill prickled the hairs on my forearms.

"I should have been within my rights," he said.

"You would not," I said, chill fading into crossness. "You didn't have any rights. You were bloody dead." Despite the crossness, my voice broke a bit on the word "dead," and his face changed at once.

"What?" I said, turning my own face away. "Did you think it didn't *matter*?"

"No," he said, and took my mud-stained hand in his. "But I didna ken it mattered quite that much." His own voice was husky now, and when I turned back to him, I saw that tears stood in his eyes. With an incoherent noise, I flung myself into his arms and clung to him, making foolish hiccuping sobs.

He held me tight, his breath warm on the top of my head, and when I stopped at last, he put me away a little and cupped my face in his hands.

"I have loved ye since I saw you, Sassenach," he said very quietly, holding my eyes with his own, bloodshot and lined with tiredness but very blue. "I will love ye forever. It doesna matter if ye sleep with the whole English army—well, no," he corrected himself, "it would matter, but it wouldna stop me loving you."

"I didn't think it would." I sniffed and he pulled a handkerchief from his sleeve and handed it to me. It was worn white cambric and had the initial "P" embroidered awkwardly in one corner in blue thread. I couldn't imagine where he'd got such a thing but didn't bother asking, under the circumstances.

The bench was not very large, and his knee was within an inch or two of mine. He didn't touch me again, though, and my heart rate was beginning to speed up noticeably. He meant it, about loving me, but that didn't mean the next while was going to be pleasant.

"It was my impression that he told me because he was sure that *you* would tell me," he said carefully.

"So I would have," I said promptly, wiping my nose. "Though I might possibly have waited 'til you'd got home, had a bath, and been fed supper. If there's one thing I know about men, it's that you don't break things like this to them on an empty stomach. When did you last eat?"

"This morning. Sausages. Dinna be changing the subject." His voice was level, but there was a good deal of feeling bubbling under it; he might as well have been a pan of simmering milk. One extra degree of heat and there'd be an eruption and scorched milk all over the stove. "I understand, but I want—I need—to know what happened."

"You understand?" I echoed, sounding surprised even to

my own ears. I hoped he *did* understand, but his manner was more than a little at odds with his words. My hands were no longer cold; they were starting to sweat, and I gripped the skirt over my knees, heedless of mud stains.

"Well, I dinna *like* it," he said, not quite between clenched teeth. "But I understand it."

"You do?"

"I do," he said, eyeing me. "Ye both thought I was dead. And I ken what ye're like when you're drunk, Sassenach."

I slapped him, so fast and so hard that he hadn't time to duck and lurched back from the impact.

"You—you—" I said, unable to articulate anything bad enough to suit the violence of my feelings. "How bloody *dare* you!"

He touched his cheek gingerly. His mouth was twitching.

"I . . . uh . . . didna quite mean that the way it sounded, Sassenach," he said. "Besides, am I no the aggrieved party here?"

"No, you bloody *aren't*!" I snapped. "You go off and get—get drowned, and leave me all alone in the m-midst of spies and s-soldiers and with children—you and Fergus both, you bastards! Leave me and Marsali to-to—" I was so choked with emotion that I couldn't go on. I was damned if I'd cry, though, *damned* if I'd cry any more in front of him.

He reached out carefully and took my hand again. I let him, and let him draw me closer, close enough to see the faint dusting of his beard stubble, to smell the road dust and dried sweat in his clothes, to feel the radiant heat from his body.

I sat quivering, making small huffing sounds in lieu of speech. He ignored this, spreading my fingers out between his own, gently stroking the palm of my hand with a large, callused thumb.

"I didna mean to imply that I think ye a drunkard, Sassenach," he said, making an obvious effort to be conciliatory. "It's only that ye think wi' your body, Claire; ye always have."

With a tremendous effort of my own, I found words.

"So I'm a—a—what are you calling me now? A loose woman? A trollop? A strumpet? And you think that's better than calling me a drunkard?!?"

He gave a small snort of what might have been amusement. I yanked at my hand, but he wouldn't let go.

"I said what I meant, Sassenach," he said, tightening his grip on my hand, and augmenting it with another hand on my forearm, preventing me from rising. "Ye think wi' your body. It's what makes ye a surgeon, no?"

"I—oh." Overcoming my dudgeon momentarily, I was obliged to admit that there was something in this observation.

"Possibly," I said stiffly, looking away from him. "But I don't think that's what you meant."

"Not entirely, no." There was a very slight edge to his voice again, but I wouldn't meet his eyes. "Listen to me."

I sat stubbornly silent for a moment, but he simply held on, and I knew that he was more stubborn by nature than I could be if I worked at it for a hundred years. I was going to hear what he had to say—and I was going to tell him what he wanted to hear—whether I liked it or not.

"I'm listening," I said. He drew breath and relaxed a little but didn't lessen his grip.

"I've taken ye to bed a thousand times at least, Sassenach," he said mildly. "Did ye think I wasna paying attention?"

"Two or three thousand at least," I said, in the interests of strict accuracy, staring at the digging knife I'd dropped on the ground. "And no."

"Well, then. I ken what ye're like in bed. And I see—all too well," he added, his mouth compressing momentarily, "—how this likely was."

"No, you bloody don't," I said warmly.

He made another Scottish noise, this one indicating hesitation.

"I do," he said, but carefully. "When I lost ye, after Culloden—I kent ye weren't dead, but that made it all the worse, if ye ask me . . . eh?"

I had made a noise of my own but gestured briefly at him to go on.

"I told ye about Mary MacNab, aye? How she came to me, in the cave?"

"Several years after the fact," I said rather coldly. "But, yes, you did get round to it eventually." I gave him a look. "I certainly didn't blame you for that—and I didn't ask you for the gory details, either."

"No, ye didn't," he admitted. He rubbed the bridge of his

nose with a knuckle. "Maybe ye weren't jealous. I am." He hesitated. "I'd tell ye, though—how it was—if ye wanted to know."

I looked at him, biting my lip dubiously. *Did* I want to know? If I didn't—and I wasn't at all sure whether I did or not—would he take that as evidence that I didn't care? And I was quite conscious of that brief *"I am."*

I took a deep breath, accepting the implied bargain.

"Tell me," I said. "How it was."

Now he did look away, and I saw his throat move as he swallowed.

"It . . . was tender," he said quietly, after a moment. "Sad."

"Sad," I echoed. "How?"

He didn't look up but kept his eyes fixed on the flowers, following the movements of a big black bumblebee among the furled blooms.

"Both of us mourning things that were lost," he said slowly, brows drawn down in thought. "She said she meant to keep ye alive for me, to let me . . . to let me imagine it was you, I suppose she meant."

"Didn't work quite that way?"

"No." He looked up then, straight on, and his eyes went through me like a rapier through a scarecrow. "There couldna be anyone like you."

It wasn't said with an air of compliment, more one of flat finality—or, even, of resentment.

I lifted a shoulder briefly. There wasn't much response I could make.

"And?"

He sighed and looked back at his knotted hands. He was squeezing the fingers of his narrowed right hand with his left, as though to remind himself of the missing finger.

"It was quiet," he said to his thumb. "We didna talk, really, not once we'd . . . begun." He closed his eyes, and I wondered, with a small twinge of curiosity, just what he saw. I was surprised to realize that curiosity was all I felt—with, perhaps, pity for them. I'd seen the cave in which they'd made love, a cold granite tomb, and I knew how desperate the state of things had been in the Highlands then. Just the promise of a little human warmth . . . *"Both of us mourning things that were lost,"* he'd said.

"It was just the once. It didna last very long; I—it had been a long time," he said, and a faint flush showed across his cheekbones. "But . . . I needed it, verra much. She held me after, and . . . I needed that more. I fell asleep in her arms; she was gone when I woke. But I carried the warmth of her with me. For a long time," he said very softly.

That gave me a quite unexpected stab of jealousy, and I straightened a little, fighting it back with clenched hands. He sensed it and turned his head toward me. He'd felt that flame ignite—and had one to match it.

"And you?" he said, giving me a hard, direct look.

"It wasn't tender," I said with an edge. "And it wasn't sad. It should have been. When he came into my room and said he wouldn't mourn you alone, and we talked, then I got up and went to him, expecting—if I had so much as an expectation; I don't think I had any conscious thoughts. . . ."

"No?" He matched my edge with his own. "Blind drunk, were ye?"

"Yes, I bloody was, and so was he." I knew what he was thinking; he wasn't making any effort to hide it, and I had a sudden, vivid recollection of sitting with him in the corner of a tavern in Cross Creek, his taking my face suddenly between his hands and kissing me, and the warm sweetness of wine passing from his mouth to mine. I sprang to my feet and slapped my hand on the bench.

"Yes, I bloody was!" I said again, furious. "I was drunk every damned day since I heard you were dead."

He drew a deep, deep breath, and I saw his eyes fix on his hands, clenched on his knees. He let it out very slowly.

"And what did he give ye, then?"

"Something to hit," I said. "At least to begin with."

He looked up at me, startled.

"Ye hit him?"

"No, I hit *you,*" I snapped. My fist had curled, without my realization, clenched against my thigh. I remembered that first blow, a blind, frenzied punch into unwary flesh, all the force of my grief behind it. The flex of recoil that took away the sensation of warmth for an instant, brought it back with a smash that flung me onto the dressing table, borne down by a man's weight, his grip tight on my wrists, and me screaming in fury.

I didn't remember the specifics of what came next—or, rather, I recalled certain things very vividly but had no idea of the order in which they happened.

"It was a blur," people say. What they really mean is the impossibility of anyone truly entering such an experience from outside, the futility of explanation.

"Mary MacNab," I said abruptly. "She gave you . . . tenderness, you said. There should be a word for what this was, what John gave me, but I haven't thought of it yet." I needed a word that might convey, encapsulate.

"Violence," I said. "That was part of it." Jamie stiffened and gave me a narrow look. I knew what he was thinking and shook my head. "Not that. I was numb—deliberately numb, because I couldn't bear to feel. He could; he had more courage than I did. And he made me feel it, too. That's why I hit him."

I'd been numb, and John had ripped off the dressing of denial, the wrappings of the small daily necessities that kept me upright and functioning; his physical presence had torn away the bandages of grief and showed what lay below: myself, bloody and unhealed.

I felt the air thick in my throat, damp and hot and itching on my skin. And finally I found the word.

"Triage," I said abruptly. "Under the numbness, I was . . . raw. Bloody. *Skinned.* You do triage, you . . . stop the bleeding first. You stop it. You stop it, or the patient dies. He stopped it."

He'd stopped it by slapping his own grief, his own fury, over the welling blood of mine. Two wounds, pressed together, blood still flowing freely—but no longer lost and draining, flowing instead into another body, and the other's blood into mine, hot, searing, not welcome—but life.

Jamie said something under his breath in Gaelic. I didn't catch most of the words. He sat with his head bent, elbows on his knees and head in his hands, and breathed audibly.

After a moment, I sat back down beside him and breathed, too. The cicadas grew louder, an urgent buzz that drowned out the rush of water and the rustling of leaves, humming in my bones.

"Damn him," Jamie muttered at last, and sat up. He looked disturbed, angry—but not angry at me.

"John, um, *is* all right, isn't he?" I asked hesitantly. To my surprise—and my slight unease—Jamie's lips twisted a little.

"Aye. Well. I'm sure he is," he said, in a tone admitting of a certain doubt, which I found alarming.

"What the bloody hell did you do to him?" I said, sitting up straight.

His lips compressed for an instant.

"I hit him," he said. "Twice," he added, glancing away.

"Twice?" I echoed, in some shock. "Did he fight you?"

"No," he said shortly.

"Really." I rocked back a bit, looking him over. Now that I had calmed down enough to take notice, I thought he was displaying . . . what? Concern? Guilt?

"Why did you hit him?" I asked, striving for a tone of mild curiosity, rather than one of accusation. Evidently I was less than successful with this, as he turned on me like a bear stung in the rump by a bee.

"*Why?* Ye dare to ask me *why*?"

"Certainly I do," I said, discarding the mild tone. "What did he do to make you hit him? And *twice*?" Jamie had no problem with mayhem, but he normally did require a reason.

He made a deeply disgruntled Scottish noise, but he'd promised me honesty a long time ago and hadn't seen fit to break that promise yet. He squared his shoulders and looked at me straight.

"The first was between him and me; it was a blow I've owed him for a good while."

"And you just seized the opportunity to punch him, because it was convenient?" I asked, a bit wary of asking directly what the devil he meant by "between him and me."

"I couldna help it," he said testily. "He said something and I hit him."

I didn't say anything but inhaled through my nose, meaning him to hear it. There was a long moment of silence, weighted with expectation and broken only by the shush of the river.

"He said the two of ye hadna been making love to each other," he finally muttered, looking down.

"No, we weren't," I said, somewhat surprised. "I told you. We were both—oh!"

He did look up at me then, glaring.

"Oh," he said, the word dripping with sarcasm. "Ye were both fucking me, he said."

"Oh, I see," I murmured. "Well. Um. Yes, that's quite true." I rubbed the bridge of my nose. "I see," I said again, and thought I probably did. There was a deep friendship of long standing between Jamie and John, but I was aware that one of the pillars it rested on was a strict avoidance of any reference to John's sexual attraction toward Jamie. If John had lost his composure sufficiently as to kick that pillar out from under the two of them . . .

"And the second time?" I asked, choosing not to ask him to elaborate any further on the first.

"Aye, well, that one was on your account," he said, both voice and face relaxing a little.

"I'm flattered," I said, as dryly as possible. "But you really shouldn't have."

"Well, I ken that now," he admitted, flushing. "But I'd lost my temper already and hadna got it back again. *Ifrinn,*" he muttered, and, stooping, picked up the discarded digging knife and jammed it hard into the bench beside him.

He closed his eyes then, pressed his lips tight, and sat tapping the fingers of his right hand against his leg. He hadn't done that since I'd amputated the remains of his frozen fourth finger, and I was taken aback to see him do it now. For the first time, I began to appreciate the true complexities of the situation.

"Tell me," I said, in a voice not much louder than the cicadas. "Tell me what you're thinking."

"About John Grey. About Helwater." He drew a deep, exasperated breath and opened his eyes, though he didn't look at me. "I managed there. Staying numb, as ye said. I suppose I might have stayed drunk, too, had I been able to afford it." His mouth twisted, and he folded his right hand into a fist, then looked down at it in surprise; he hadn't been able to do that for thirty years. He opened it and put his hand flat on his knee.

"I managed," he repeated. "But then there was Geneva—and I told ye how that was, too, did I not?"

"You did."

He sighed. "And then there was William. When Geneva died and it was my fault, it was a knife in my heart—and then William . . ." His mouth softened. "The bairn cut me wide open, Sassenach. He spilled my guts out into my hands."

I put my hand on his, and he turned it, his fingers curling over mine.

"And that bloody English sodomite bandaged me," he said, so low I could scarcely hear him above the sound of the river. "With his friendship."

He drew breath again and let it out explosively. "No, I didna kill him. I dinna ken if I'm glad of it or not—but I didn't."

I let out my own breath in a deep sigh and leaned against him.

"I knew that. I'm glad."

The haze had thickened into steel-gray clouds, coming purposefully up the river, muttering with thunder. I took a deep, lung-filling whiff of ozone and then another, of his skin. I detected the basic male animal, very appetizing in itself, but he seemed to have acquired a rather unusual—though savory—bouquet in addition: a faint whiff of sausage, the strong bitter scent of cabbage, and . . . yes, mustard, underlaid with something oddly spicy. I sniffed again, repressing the urge to lick him.

"You smell like—"

"I smell like a large plate of *choucroute garnie,*" he interrupted, with a slight grimace. "Give me a moment; I'll have a wash." He made as though to get up and go toward the river, and I reached out and seized him by the arm.

He looked at me for a moment, then drew a deep breath and, reaching slowly out in turn, pulled me against him. I didn't resist. In fact, my own arms went round him in reflex, and we both sighed in unison, in the sheer relief of embrace.

I would have been quite content to sit there forever, breathing the musky, dusty, cabbage-laced smell of him and listening to the thump of his heart under my ear. All the things we'd said—all the things that had happened—hovered in the air around us like the cloud of troubles from Pandora's box, but for this one moment, there was nothing but each other.

After a bit, his hand moved, smoothing the loose, damp curls behind my ear. He cleared his throat and shifted a little, drawing himself up, and I reluctantly let go of him, though I left my hand on his thigh.

"I wish to say something," he said, in the tone of one making a formal statement before a court. My heart had quieted while he held me; now it fluttered in renewed agitation.

"What?" I sounded so apprehensive that he laughed. Only a breath, but he did laugh, and I was able to breathe again. He took my hand firmly and held it, looking into my eyes.

"I don't say that I dinna mind this, because I do. And I don't say that I'll no make a fuss about it later, because I likely will. But what I do say is that there is nothing in this world or the next that can take ye from me—or me from you." He raised one brow. "D'ye disagree?"

"Oh, no," I said fervently.

He breathed again, and his shoulders came down a fraction of an inch.

"Well, that's good, because it wouldna do ye any good if ye did. Just the one question," he said. "Are ye my wife?"

"Of course I am," I said, in utter astonishment. "How could I not be?"

His face changed then; he drew a huge breath and took me into his arms. I embraced him, hard, and together we let out a great sigh, settling with it, his head bending over mine, kissing my hair, my face turned into his shoulder, openmouthed at the neck of his open shirt, our knees slowly giving way in mutual relief, so that we knelt in the fresh-turned earth, clinging together, rooted like a tree, leaf-tossed and multi-limbed but sharing one single solid trunk.

The first drops of rain began to fall.

HIS FACE WAS open now and his eyes clear blue and free of trouble—for the moment, at least. "Where is there a bed? I need to be naked with ye."

I was entirely in sympathy with this proposition, but the question took me momentarily aback. Of course we couldn't go to John's house—or at least not in order to go to bed together. Even if John himself was in no position to object, the thought of what Mrs. Figg would say if I walked into the house with a large Scotsman and immediately ascended the stairs to my bedroom with him . . . and then there was Jenny . . . On the other hand, eager as I was, I really didn't want to be naked with him among the ranunculus, where we might be interrupted at any moment by Bartrams, bumblebees, or rain.

"An inn?" I suggested.

"Is there one where folk wouldna ken ye? A decent one, I mean?"

I knit my brows, trying to think of one. Not the King's Arms, definitely not that. Otherwise . . . I was familiar only with the two or three ordinaries where Marsali bought ale or bread—and people most assuredly knew me there—as Lady John Grey.

It wasn't that Jamie by himself needed to avoid notice anymore—but his supposed death and my marriage to John had been the subject of a tremendous amount of public interest, by reason of its tragedy. For it to become widely known that the presumably deceased Colonel Fraser had suddenly reappeared from the dead to reclaim his wife would be a subject of conversation that would dwarf the withdrawal of the British army from the city. I had a quick flash of memory—our wedding night, witnessed at close quarters by a crowd of raucously drunk Highland clansmen—and imagined a reprise of this experience, with interested commentary by the ordinary's patrons.

I glanced at the river, wondering whether, after all, a nice, sheltering bush—but it was late in the afternoon, cloudy, and the gnats and mosquitoes were hanging in small carnivorous clouds of their own beneath the trees. Jamie stooped suddenly and swept me up in his arms.

"I'll find a place."

THERE WAS A wooden thump as he kicked open the door of the new potting shed, and suddenly we were in a light-streaked darkness smelling of sun-warmed boards, earth, water, damp clay, and plants.

"What, *here*?"

It was abundantly clear that he wasn't seeking privacy for the purpose of further inquiry, discussion, or reproach. For that matter, my own question was largely rhetorical.

He stood me on my feet, turned me about, and began undoing my laces. I could feel his breath on the bare skin of my neck, and the tiny hairs there shivered.

"Are you—" I began, only to be interrupted by a terse "Hush." I hushed. I could hear then what he'd heard: the Bartrams, in conversation with each other. They were some distance away, though—on the back porch of the house, I thought, screened from the river path by a thick hedge of English yew.

"I don't think they can hear us," I said, though I lowered my voice.

"I've done wi' talking," he whispered, and, leaning forward, closed his teeth gently on the nape of my exposed neck.

"Hush," he said again, though mildly. I hadn't actually said anything, and the sound I'd made was too high-pitched to draw the attention of anything save a passing bat. I exhaled strongly through my nose and heard him chuckle deep in his throat.

My stays came loose, and cool air flooded through the damp muslin of my shift. He paused, one hand on the tapes of my petticoats, to reach round with the other and gently lift one breast, heavy and free, thumb rubbing the nipple, hard and round as a cherry stone. I made another sound, this one lower-pitched.

I thought vaguely how fortunate it was that he was left-handed, as that was the hand nimbly engaged in undoing the tapes of my skirts. These fell in a swishing heap round my feet, and I had a sudden vision—as his hand left my breast and the shift whiffed up round my ears—of Young Mr. Bartram suddenly realizing a dire need to pot up a batch of rosemary seedlings. The shock probably wouldn't kill him, but . . .

"May as well be hung for sheep as lambs," Jamie said, having evidently divined my thought from the fact that I'd turned round and was shielding my more private bits in the manner of Botticelli's Venus. "And I'll have ye naked."

He grinned at me, whipped off his own dirt-streaked shirt—he'd thrown off his coat when he set me down—and yanked down his breeks without pausing to undo the flies. He was thin enough to make this possible; the breeches hung on his hipbones, barely staying up by themselves, and I saw the shadow of his ribs beneath his skin as he bent to shed his stockings.

He straightened and I put a hand on his chest. It was damp and warm, and the ruddy hairs prickled into gooseflesh at my touch. I could smell the hot, eager scent of him, even over the agricultural fug of the shed and the lingering smell of cabbage.

"Not so fast," I whispered.

He made a Scottish sound of interrogation, reaching for me, and I dug my fingers into the muscle of his breast.

"I want a kiss first."

He put his mouth against my ear and both hands firmly on my bottom.

"Are ye in a position to make demands, d'ye think?" he whispered, tightening his grasp. I caught the faint barb in *that.*

"Yes, I bloody am," I said, and adjusted my own grip somewhat lower. *He* wouldn't be attracting any bats, I thought.

We were eyeball-to-eyeball, clasped and breathing each other's breath, close enough to see the smallest nuance of expression, even in the dimness. I saw the seriousness that underlay the laughter—and the doubt beneath the bravado.

"I *am* your wife," I whispered, my lips brushing his.

"I ken that," he said, very softly, and kissed me. Softly. Then closed his eyes and brushed his lips across my face, not so much kissing as feeling the contours of cheekbone and brow, of jaw and the tender skin below the ear, seeking to know me again past skin and breath, to know me to the blood and bone, to the heart that beat beneath.

I made a small sound and tried to find his mouth with my own, pressing against him, bare bodies cool and damp, hair rasping sweetly, and the lovely firmness of him rolling between us. He wouldn't let me kiss him, though. His hand gripped the tail of my hair at the base of my neck, cupping my head, the other hand pursuing the same game of blind man's buff.

There was a rattling thump; I had backed into a potting bench, setting a tray of tiny seedling pots to vibrating, the spicy leaves of sweet basil trembling in agitation. Jamie pushed the tray aside with one hand, then grasped me by the elbows and lifted me onto the bench.

"Now," he said, half breathless. "I must have ye now."

He did, and I ceased caring whether there were splinters in the bench or not.

I wrapped my legs round him and he laid me flat and leaned over me, hands braced on the bench, with a sound halfway between bliss and pain. He moved slowly in me and I gasped.

The rain had grown from a patter to a ringing din on the tin roof of the shed, covering any sounds I might make, and a good thing, too, I thought dimly. The air had cooled but was full of moisture; our skins were slick, and heat sprang up where flesh touched flesh. He was slow, deliberate, and I arched my back, urging him. In response, he took me by the shoulders, bent lower, and kissed me lightly, barely moving.

"I willna do it," he whispered, and held tight when I struggled against him, trying vainly to goad him into the violent response I wished—I needed.

"Won't do what?" I was gasping.

"I willna punish ye for it," he said, so softly I could barely hear him, close as he was. "I'll not do that, d'ye hear?"

"I don't frigging *want* you to punish me, you bastard." I grunted with effort, my shoulder joints creaking as I tried to break free of his grasp. "I want you to . . . God, you know what I want!"

"Aye, I do." His hand left my shoulder and cupped beneath my buttock, touching the flesh of our joining, stretched and slippery. I made a small sound of surrender, and my knees loosened.

He pulled back, then came back into me, strongly enough that I gave a small, high-pitched cry of relief.

"Ask me to your bed," he said, breathless, hands on my arms. "I shall come to ye. For that matter—I shall come, whether ye ask it or no. But remember, Sassenach—I am your man; I serve ye as I will."

"Do," I said. "*Please* do. Jamie, I want you so!"

He seized my arse in both hands, hard enough to leave bruises, and I arched up into him, grasping, hands sliding on his sweat-slick skin.

"God, Claire, I need ye!"

Rain was roaring on the tin roof now, and lightning struck close by, blue-white and sharp with ozone. We rode it together, forked and light-blind, breathless, and the thunder rolled through our bones.

25

GIVE ME LIBERTY . . .

AND AS THE SUN set on the third day since he had left his home, Lord John William Bertram Armstrong Grey found himself once more a free man, with a full belly, a swimming head, a badly mended musket, and severely chafed wrists, standing before the Reverend Peleg Woodsworth, right hand uplifted, reciting as prompted:

"I, Bertram Armstrong, swear to be true to the United States of America, and to serve them honestly and faithfully against all their enemies and opposers whatsoever, and to observe and obey the orders of the Continental Congress and the orders of the generals and officers set over me by them."

Bloody hell, he thought. *What next?*

PART TWO

Meanwhile, Back at the Ranch . . .

26

A STEP INTO THE DARK

October 30, 1980
Craigh na Dun

A BLOTCH OF SWEAT darkened the shirt between William Buccleigh's shoulder blades; the day was cool, but it was a steep climb to the top of Craigh na Dun—and the thought of what awaited them at the top was enough to make anybody sweat.

"Ye haven't got to come," Roger said to Buccleigh's back.

"Get stuffed," his great-great-great-great-great-grandfather replied briefly. Buck spoke absentmindedly, though, all his attention, like Roger's, focused on the distant crest of the hill.

Roger could hear the stones from here. A low, sullen buzz, like a hive of hostile bees. He felt the sound move, crawling under his skin, and scratched viciously at his elbow, as though he could root it out.

"Ye've got the stones, aye?" Buck stopped, clinging one-handed to a birch sapling as he looked back over his shoulder.

"I have," Roger said shortly. "D'ye want yours now?"

Buck shook his head and wiped shaggy fair hair off his brow with the back of his free hand.

"Time enough," he said, and began to climb again.

Roger knew the diamonds were there—he knew Buck knew, too—but put a hand into his jacket pocket anyway. Two rough pieces of metal clinked together, the halves of an old brooch Brianna had cut apart with the poultry shears, each half with a scatter of tiny diamonds, barely more than chips. He hoped to God they'd be enough. If not—

The day was only cool, but a bone-deep shudder ran through

him. He'd done it twice—three times, if he counted the first attempt, the one that had almost killed him. It got worse each time. He'd thought he wouldn't make it the last time, coming back on Ocracoke, mind and body shredding in that place that was neither place nor passage. It had only been the feel of Jem in his arms that made him hold on, come through. And it was only the need to find Jem now that would make him do it again.

A hydroelectric tunnel under the Loch Errochty dam

HE MUST BE getting near the end of the tunnel. Jem could tell by the way the air pushed back against his face. All he could see was the red light on the service train's dashboard—did you call it a dashboard on a train? he wondered. He didn't want to stop, because that meant he'd have to get out of the train, into the dark. But the train was running out of track, so there wasn't much else he could do.

He pulled back a bit on the lever that made the train go, and it slowed down. More. Just a little more, and the lever clicked into a kind of slot and the train stopped with a small jerk that made him stumble and grab the edge of the cab.

An electric train didn't make any engine noise, but the wheels rattled on the track and the train made squeaks and clunks as it moved. When it stopped, the noise stopped, too. It was really quiet.

"Hey!" he said out loud, because he didn't want to listen to his heart beating. The sound echoed, and he looked up, startled. Mam had said the tunnel was really high, more than thirty feet, but he'd forgotten that. The idea that there was a lot of empty space hanging over him that he couldn't see bothered him a lot. He swallowed and stepped out of the tiny engine, holding on to the frame with one hand.

"Hey!" he shouted at the invisible ceiling. "Are there any bats up there?"

Silence. He'd kind of been hoping there *were* bats. He wasn't afraid of them—there were bats in the old broch, and he liked to sit and watch them come out to hunt in the summer evenings. But he was alone. Except for the dark.

His hands were sweating. He let go of the metal cab and

scrubbed both hands on his jeans. Now he could hear himself breathing, too.

"Crap," he whispered under his breath. That made him feel better, so he said it again. Maybe he ought to be praying, instead, but he didn't feel like that, not yet.

There was a door, Mam said. At the end of the tunnel. It led into the service chamber, where the big turbines could be lifted up from the dam if they needed fixing. Would the door be locked?

Suddenly he realized that he'd stepped away from the train and he didn't know whether he was facing the end of the tunnel or back the way he'd come. In a panic, he blundered to and fro, hands out, looking for the train. He tripped over part of the track and fell, sprawling. He lay there for a second, saying, "Crap-crap-crap-crap-*crap!*" because he'd skinned both knees and the palm of his hand, but he was okay, really, and now he knew where the track was, so he could follow it and not get lost.

He got up, wiped his nose, and shuffled slowly along, kicking the track every few steps to be sure he stayed with it. He thought he was in front of where the train had stopped, so it didn't really matter which way he was going—either he'd find the train or he'd find the end of the tunnel. And then the door. If it *was* locked, maybe—

Something like an electric shock ran right through him. He gasped and fell over backward. The only thing in his mind was the idea that somebody had hit him with a lightsaber like Luke Skywalker's, and for a minute he thought maybe whoever it was had cut off his head.

He couldn't feel his body, but he could see in his mind his body lying bleeding in the dark and his head sitting right there on the train tracks in the dark, and his head couldn't see his body or even know it wasn't attached anymore. He made a breathless kind of a noise that was trying to be a scream, but it made his stomach move and he felt that, he *felt* it, and suddenly he felt a lot more like praying.

"Deo . . . gratias!" he managed to gasp. It was what Grandda said when he talked about a fight or killing something, and this wasn't quite that sort of thing, but it seemed like a good thing to say anyway.

Now he could feel all of himself again, but he sat up and

grabbed his neck, just to be sure his head was still on. His skin was jumping in the weirdest way. Like a horse's does when a horsefly bites it, but all over. He swallowed and tasted sugared silver and he gasped again, because now he knew what had hit him. Sort of.

This wasn't quite like it had been when they'd all walked into the rocks on Ocracoke. One minute he'd been in his father's arms, and the next minute it was as if he'd been scattered everywhere in little wiggly pieces like the spilled quicksilver in Grannie's surgery. Then he was back together again, and Da was still holding him tight enough to squeeze his breath out, and he could hear Da sobbing and that scared him, and he had a funny taste in his mouth and little pieces of him were still wiggling around trying to get away but they were trapped inside his skin . . .

Yeah. That was what was making his skin jump now, and he breathed easier, knowing what it was. That was okay, then; he was okay; it would stop.

It was stopping already, the twitchy feeling going away. He still felt kind of shaky, but he stood up. Careful, because he didn't know where it was.

Wait—he *did* know. He knew exactly.

"That's weird," he said, out loud without really noticing, because he wasn't scared by the dark anymore; it wasn't important.

He couldn't *see* it, not with his eyes, not exactly. He squinted, trying to think how he *was* seeing it, but there wasn't a word for what he was doing. Kind of like hearing or smelling or touching, but not really any of those.

But he knew where it was. It was right *there,* a kind of . . . shiver . . . in the air, and when he stared at it, he had a feeling in the back of his mind like pretty sparkly things, like sun on the sea and the way a candle flame looked when it shone through a ruby, but he knew he wasn't really *seeing* anything like that.

It went all the way across the tunnel, and up to the high roof, too, he could tell. But it wasn't thick at all; it was thin as air.

He guessed that was why it hadn't swallowed him like the thing in the rocks on Ocracoke had. At least . . . he thought it hadn't and, for an instant, worried that maybe he'd gone sometime else. But he didn't think so. The tunnel felt just the same, and so did he, now that his skin had stopped jumping. When they'd done it, on Ocracoke, he'd known right away it was different.

He stood there for a minute, just looking and thinking, and then shook his head and turned around, feeling with his foot for the track. He wasn't going back through *that,* no matter what. He'd just have to hope the door wasn't locked.

The laird's study,
Lallybroch estate

BRIANNA'S HAND closed on the letter opener, but even as she calculated the distance involved, the obstacle of the desk between Rob Cameron and herself, and the flimsiness of the wooden blade, she was reluctantly concluding that she couldn't kill the bastard. Not yet.

"Where's my son?"

"He's okay."

She stood up suddenly, and he jerked a little in reflex. His face flushed and he hardened his expression.

"He'd bloody well *better* be okay," she snapped. "I said, where is he?"

"Oh, no, hen," he said, rocking back on his heels, affecting nonchalance. "That's no how we're playing it. Not tonight."

God, why didn't Roger keep a hammer or a chisel or something *useful* in his desk drawer? Did he expect her to *staple* this jerk? She braced herself, both hands flat on the desk, to keep from leaping over it and going for his throat.

"I'm not playing," she said through her teeth. "And neither are you. *Where's Jemmy?*"

He leveled a long finger at her.

"You're no longer the boss lady, *Ms.* MacKenzie. I call the shots now."

"Oh, you think so, do you?" she asked, as mildly as she could. Her thoughts were slipping past like grains of sand in an hourglass, a slithering cascade of *what if, how, shall I, no, yes . . .*

"I do, aye." His color, already high, rose higher, and he licked his lips. "Ye're gonna find out what it's like to be on the bottom, hen."

Cameron's eyes were very bright, and his hair was clipped so short that she could see beads of sweat glittering above his ears. Was he high on something? She thought not. He was wearing track pants, and his fingers flicked unconsciously across the front, where a substantial bulge was beginning to show. Her lips tightened at the sight.

Not on your life, buddy.

She widened her gaze as much as possible, to take him in without letting his eyes move from hers. She didn't *think* he was armed, though the pockets of his jacket had stuff in them. He really thought he could make her have sex with him, without a set of manacles and a sledgehammer?

He twirled his finger, pointing to the floor in front of him.

"Come round here, hen," he said softly. "And take your jeans down. Might do ye good to learn what it's like to take it up the arse regularly. Ye've done it to me for months—fair's fair, isn't it?"

Very slowly, she came around the desk but stopped well short of him, keeping out of reach. She fumbled cold-fingered at the button of her fly, unwilling to look down, unwilling to take her eyes off him. Her heart was beating so hard in her ears that she could barely hear his heavy breathing.

The tip of his tongue showed briefly, involuntarily, as she pushed the jeans down over her hips, and he swallowed.

"The knickers, too," he said, half breathless. "Take them off."

"You don't rape people very often, do you?" she said rudely, stepping out of the puddled jeans. "What's your rush?" She bent and picked the heavy denim pants up, shook out the legs, and turned as though to lay them on the desk. Then whipped back, clutching the jeans at the ankle, and lashed them as hard as she could at his head.

The heavy cloth with its zipper and brass fly button struck him full in the face, and he staggered back with a grunt of surprise, clutching at the jeans. She let go of them instantly, leapt onto the desk, and launched herself at him, shoulder-first.

They fell together with a crash that shook the hardwood floor, but she landed on top, kneed him hard in the belly, and then grabbed him by both ears and thumped his head on the floor as hard as she could. He let out a cry of pain, reached for her wrists, and she promptly let go of his ears, leaned backward, and grabbed for his crotch.

Had she been able to get a decent grip on his balls through the soft fabric, she would have crushed them. As it was, she managed a glancing squeeze but one hard enough to make him yelp and convulse, nearly dislodging her from her perch.

She couldn't win a fistfight. Couldn't let him hit her. She scrambled to her feet, looking wildly round the office for something heavy to hit him with, seized the wooden letter box, and smashed it over his head as he started to rise. He didn't fall down but bobbed his head, dazed amongst the cascade of letters, and she kicked him in the jaw as hard as she could, her own teeth clenched. It was a sliding, sweaty impact, but she'd hurt him.

She'd hurt herself, too, had kicked him with her heel, as much as she could, but she felt a burst of pain in the middle of her foot; she'd torn or broken something, but it didn't matter.

Cameron shook his head violently, trying to clear it. He was on his hands and knees now, crawling toward her, reaching for her leg, and she backed up against the desk. With a banshee shriek, she kneed him in the face, squirmed out of his grasp, and ran for the hall, limping heavily.

There were weapons on the walls of the foyer, a few targes and broadswords kept for ornament, but all hung high, to be out of the children's reach. There was a better one easily to hand, though. She reached behind the coat rack and grabbed Jem's cricket bat.

You can't kill him, she kept thinking, dimly surprised at the fact that her mind was still working. *Don't kill him. Not yet. Not 'til he says where Jemmy is.*

"Fucking . . . *bitch*!" He was nearly on her, panting, half blinded by blood running down his forehead, half sobbing through the blood pouring from his nose. "Fuck you, split you open, fuck you up the—"

"Caisteal DOOON!" she bellowed, and, stepping out from behind the coat rack, swung the bat in a scything arc that caught him in the ribs. He made a gurgling noise and folded, arms across his middle. She took a deep breath, swung the bat as high as she could, and brought it down with all her strength on the crown of his head.

The shock of it vibrated up her arms to her shoulders and

she dropped the bat with a *clunk* and stood there gasping, trembling and drenched with sweat.

"Mummy?" said a tiny, quavering voice from the foot of the stair. "Why is you not got pants on, Mummy?"

THANK GOD FOR *instinct* was her first coherent thought. She'd crossed the length of the foyer, snatched Mandy up in her arms, and was patting her comfortingly before any sort of conscious decision to move had been made.

"Pants?" she said, eyeing the limp form of Rob Cameron. He hadn't twitched since he'd fallen, but she didn't think she'd killed him. She'd have to take more-certain steps to neutralize him, and fast. "Oh, pants. I was just getting ready for bed when this naughty man showed up."

"Oh." Mandy leaned out of her arms, peering at Cameron. "Iss Mr. Rob! Iss a burglar? Iss a bad man?"

"Yes, both," Brianna said, deliberately casual. Mandy's speech showed the sibilance it had when she got excited or upset, but the little girl seemed to be recovering pretty fast from the shock of seeing her mother crown a burglar in the front hall while wearing only a T-shirt and underpants. The thought made her want to stomp on Cameron's balls, but she choked it back. No time for that.

Mandy clung to her neck, but Brianna set her firmly on the stairs.

"Mummy wants you to stay here, *a ghraidh*. I have to put Mr. Rob someplace safe, where he can't do anything bad."

"No!" Mandy cried, seeing her mother head toward the crumpled Cameron, but Brianna waved in what she hoped was a reassuring manner, picked up the cricket bat as insurance, and nudged her prisoner in the ribs with a cautious toe. He wobbled but didn't stir. Just in case, she moved round behind him and prodded him rudely between the buttocks with the cricket bat, which made Mandy giggle. He didn't move, and she drew a deep breath for the first time in what seemed like hours.

Going back to the stairs, she gave Mandy the bat to hold and smiled at her. She pushed a strand of sweaty hair behind her ear.

"Okay. We're going to put Mr. Rob in the priest's hole. You go and open the door for Mummy, all right?"

"I hit him?" Mandy asked hopefully, clutching the bat.

"No, I don't think you need to do that, darling. Just open the door."

Her work tote was hanging from the coat rack, the big roll of duct tape easily to hand. She trussed Cameron's ankles and wrists, a dozen turns each, then bent and, clutching him by the ankles, dragged him toward the swinging baize door at the far end of the hall, which separated the kitchen from the rest of the house.

He began to stir as they negotiated the big table in the kitchen, and she dropped his feet.

"Mandy," she said, keeping her voice as calm as possible. "I need to have a grown-up talk with Mr. Rob. Give me the bat. Then you go right on out to the mudroom and wait for me there, okay?"

"Mummy . . ." Mandy was shrinking back against the sink cabinet, eyes huge and fixed on the moaning Cameron.

"*Go,* Mandy. Right now. Mummy will be there before you can count to a hundred. Start counting *now.* One . . . two . . . three . . ." She moved between Cameron and Mandy, motioning firmly with her free hand.

Reluctantly, Mandy moved, murmuring, "Four . . . five . . . six . . . seven . . ." and disappeared through the back kitchen door. The kitchen was warm from the Aga, and despite her lack of clothes, Bree was still streaming with sweat. She could smell herself, feral and acrid, and found that it made her feel stronger. She wasn't sure she'd ever truly understood the term "bloodthirsty" before, but she did now.

"Where's my son?" she said to Cameron, keeping a wary distance in case he tried to roll at her. "Answer me, you piece of crap, or I'll beat the shit out of you and then call the police."

"Yeah?" He rolled slowly onto his side, groaning. "And tell them what, exactly? That I took your boy? What proof of that d'ye have?" His words were slurred; his lip was puffed out on one side, where she'd kicked him.

"Fine," she snapped. "I'll just beat the shit out of you."

"What, beat a helpless man? Fine example for your wee lassie." He rolled onto his back with a muffled grunt.

"As for the police, I can tell them you broke into my house

and assaulted me." She pointed one foot at him, so he could see the livid scratches on her leg. "You'll have my skin cells under your fingernails. And while I'd rather not have Mandy go through it all again, she'd certainly tell them what you were saying in the hallway." *She would, too,* Bree thought. Mandy was a very faithful tape recorder, especially where bad language was concerned.

"Nng." Cameron had closed his eyes, grimacing against the light over the sink, but now opened them again. He was less dazed; she could see the light of calculation back in his eyes. Like most men, she thought, he was probably smarter when he wasn't sexually aroused—and she'd taken care of *that.*

"Aye. And I tell them it was just a wee sex game that got out of hand, and you say it wasn't, and they say, 'Aye, fine, missus, and where's your husband, then?'" The undamaged side of his mouth twisted up. "You're not that swift tonight, hen. But, then, ye're not usually."

His mention of Roger made the blood surge in her ears. She didn't reply but grabbed him by the feet and pulled him roughly through the kitchen and into the back passageway. The grating that covered the priest's hole was hidden by a bench and several boxes of milk bottles, bits of farm equipment awaiting repair, and other items that didn't go anywhere else. She dropped Rob's feet, shoved the bench and boxes aside, and pulled up the grating. There was a ladder leading down into the shadowy space; she pulled this up and slid it behind the bench. *That* little amenity wouldn't be needed.

"Hey!" Rob's eyes widened. Either he hadn't known there really was a priest's hole in the house or he hadn't thought she'd do it. Without a word, she seized him under the arms, dragged him to the hole, and shoved him in. Feetfirst, because if he broke his neck, he couldn't tell her where Jem was.

He fell with a shriek, which was cut short by a heavy thump. Before she could worry that he'd managed to land on his head after all, she heard him moaning and a rustle as he started to stir. A muttering of very bad language further reassured her that he was in good enough shape to answer questions. She fetched the big flashlight from the kitchen drawer and shone it down into the hole. Cameron's face, congested and streaked with blood, glared up at her. He curled up and with some difficulty managed to wriggle into a sitting position.

"You've broken my leg, you fucking bitch!"

"Good," she said coldly, though she doubted it. "Once I get Jem back, I'll take you to a doctor."

He breathed heavily through his nose, making a nasty snuffling noise, and swiped at his face with his bound hands, smearing the blood across one cheek.

"You want him back? You get me out of here, and fast!"

She'd been considering—and discarding—different plans of action, shuffling through them like a mental pack of cards, ever since she'd duct-taped him. And letting him out wasn't one she'd considered. She *had* thought of fetching the .22 rifle the family used to hunt rats and winging him in a few non-essential places—but there was some risk of either disabling him too badly to be of help or killing him accidentally by hitting something vital if he squirmed.

"Think fast," he shouted up at her. "Your wee lass will hit a hundred and be back any second!"

Despite the situation, Brianna smiled. Mandy had very recently been introduced to the idea that numbers were infinite and had been enchanted by the concept. She wouldn't stop counting until she ran out of breath or someone stopped her. Still, she wasn't going to engage in pointless conversation with her prisoner.

"Okay," she said, and reached for the grate. "We'll see how talkative you are after twenty-four hours without food or water, shall we?"

"You bloody bitch!" He tried to surge to his feet but fell over onto his side, writhing impotently. "You—you just think about this, aye? If I'm without food and water, so's your wee lad!"

She froze, the metal edge of the grate digging into her fingers.

"Rob, you're not bright," she said. She was amazed that her voice sounded conversational; waves of horror and relief and renewed horror were rippling across her shoulders, and something primitive in the back of her mind was screaming.

A sullen silence from below, as he tried to work out what he'd just given away.

"Now I know you didn't send Jem back through the stones," she clarified for him. She carefully didn't shriek, *But you sent Roger back to look for him! And he'll never find him. You . . . you . . .* "He's still here, in this time."

Another silence.

"Yeah," he said slowly. "Okay, you know that. But you don't know where he is. And you're not going to, until you turn me loose. I meant it, hen—he'll be thirsty by now. *And* hungry. It'll be a lot worse for him by morning."

Her hand tightened on the grate. "You had better be lying," she said evenly. "For your sake." She shoved the grate back into place and stepped on it, clicking it down into its frame. The priest's hole was literally a hole: a space about six feet by eight, and twelve feet deep. Even if Rob Cameron hadn't been bound hand and foot, he couldn't jump high enough to get hold of the grate, let alone reach the latch that held it down.

Ignoring the furious shouts from below, Brianna went to retrieve her daughter and her jeans.

THE MUDROOM WAS empty, and for an instant she panicked—but then she saw the tiny bare foot sticking out from under the bench, long toes relaxed as a frog's, and her heart rate dropped. A little.

Mandy was curled up under Roger's old mac, thumb half in her mouth, sound asleep. The impulse was to carry her to her bed, let her sleep 'til daylight. Brianna laid a soft hand on her daughter's black curly hair—black as Roger's—and her heart squeezed like a lemon. There was another child to consider.

"Wake up, sweetheart," she said, gently shaking the little girl. "Wake up, honey. We need to go and look for Jem."

It took no little cajoling and the administration of a glass of Coca-Cola—a rare treat, and absolutely unheard of so late at night, how exciting!—to get Mandy into a state of alertness, but once there she was all eagerness to go and hunt for her brother.

"Mandy," Bree said as casually as she could, buttoning her daughter's pink quilted coat, "can you feel Jem? Right now?"

"Uh-huh," Mandy replied offhandedly, and Brianna's heart

leapt. Two nights before, the child had waked screaming from a sound sleep, weeping hysterically and insisting that Jem was gone. She had been inconsolable, wailing that her brother had been eaten by "big wocks!"—an assertion that had terrified her parents, who knew the horrors of those particular rocks all too well.

But then, a few minutes later, Mandy had suddenly calmed. Jem was there, she said. He was there in her head. And she had gone back to sleep as though nothing had happened.

In the consternation that had followed this episode—the discovery that Jem had been taken by Rob Cameron, one of Brianna's fellow employees at the hydroelectric plant, and presumably taken through the stones into the past—there had been no time to recall Mandy's remark about Jem being back in her head, let alone to make further inquiries. But now Brianna's mind was moving at the speed of light, bounding from one horrifying realization to the next, making connections that might have taken hours to make in cooler blood.

Horrifying Realization Number 1: Jem hadn't gone into the past, after all. While by itself this was undeniably a *good* thing, it made Horrifying Realization Number 2 that much worse: Roger and William Buccleigh *had* undoubtedly gone through the stones, searching for Jemmy. She hoped they were in fact in the past and not dead—traveling through whatever sort of thing the stones were was a bloody dangerous proposition—but, if so, that brought her back to Horrifying Realization Number 1: Jem *wasn't* in the past. And if he wasn't there, Roger wasn't going to find him. And since Roger would never give up looking . . .

She pushed Horrifying Realization Number 3 aside with great force, and Mandy blinked, startled.

"Why you making faces, Mummy?"

"Practicing for Halloween." She rose, smiling as best she could, and reached for her own duffel coat.

Mandy's brow creased in thought.

"When's Halloween?"

Cold rippled over Brianna, and not just from the draft through the crack under the back door. *Did they make it?* They thought the portal was most active on the sun feasts and fire feasts—and Samhain was an important fire feast—but they couldn't wait the extra day, for fear that Jem would be taken too far from Craigh na Dun after passing through the stones.

"Tomorrow," she said. Her fingers slipped and fumbled on the fastenings, shaky with adrenaline.

"Goody, goody, goody!" Mandy said, hopping to and fro like a cricket. "Can I wear my mask to look for Jemmy?"

27

NOTHING'S SO HARD BUT SEARCH WILL FIND IT OUT

HE'D FELT THE DIAMONDS explode. For some time, that was the only thought in his mind. *Felt it.* One instant, briefer than a heartbeat, and a pulse of light and heat in his hand and then the throb of something going through him, surrounding him, and then . . .

Not "then," he thought muzzily. *Wasn't any then. Wasn't any* now. *Now there is, though . . .*

He opened his eyes to find that there was a now. He was lying on stones and heather and there was a cow breathing—no, not a cow. He made to rise and managed to turn his head half an inch. It was a man, sitting huddled on the ground. Taking huge, irregular, gasping sobs of breath. *Who . . . ?*

"Oh," he said aloud, or almost. " 'S you." The words came out in a mangle that hurt his throat, and he coughed. That hurt, too. "You . . . okay?" he asked hoarsely.

"No." It came out in a grunt, filled with pain, and alarm got Roger up onto hands and knees, head spinning. He did a bit of gasping himself but crawled as fast as he could toward Buck.

William Buccleigh was curled over, arms crossed, gripping his left upper arm with his right hand. His face was pale and slicked with sweat, lips pressed so tight together that a ring of white showed round his mouth.

"Hurt?" Roger lifted a hand, not sure where or whether to prod. He couldn't see any blood.

"My . . . chest," Buck wheezed. "Arm."

"Oh, Jesus," Roger said, the last remnants of muzziness stripped away by a blast of adrenaline. "Are you having a bloody heart attack?"

"What . . ." Buck grimaced, then something seemed to ease a little. He gulped air. "How would *I* know?"

"It's—never mind. Lie down, will you?" Roger looked wildly round, though even as he did, he realized the sheer pointlessness of doing so. The area near Craigh na Dun was wild and unpopulated in his own time, let alone this one. And even should someone appear out of the stones and heather, the chances of whoever it was being a doctor were remote.

He took Buck by the shoulders and eased him gently down, then bent and put his ear to the man's chest, feeling like an idiot.

"D'ye hear anything?" Buck asked anxiously.

"Not with you talking, no. Shut up." He thought he could make out a heartbeat of some sort but had no idea whether there was anything wrong with it. He stayed bent a moment longer, if only to compose himself.

Always act as if you know what you're doing, even if you don't. He'd been given that bit of advice by a number of people, from performers he'd shared a stage with to academic advisers . . . and, much more recently, by both of his in-laws.

He put a hand on Buck's chest and looked into the man's face. He was still sweating and plainly scared, but there was a little more color in his cheeks. His lips weren't blue; that seemed a good sign.

"Just keep breathing," he advised his ancestor. "Slow, aye?"

He tried to follow that bit of advice himself; his own heart was hammering and sweat was running down his back, in spite of a cold wind that whined past his ears.

"We did it, aye?" Buck's chest was moving more slowly under his hand. He turned his head to look round. "It's . . . different. Isn't it?"

"Yes." In spite of the current situation and the overwhelming worry for Jem, Roger felt a surge of jubilation and relief. It *was* different: from here, he could see the road below—now no more than an overgrown drovers' trace rather than a gray asphalt ribbon. The trees and bushes, they were different, too—there were pines, the big Caledonian pines that looked like giant stalks of broccoli. They *had* made it.

He grinned at Buck. "We made it. Don't die on me now, you bugger."

"Do my best." Buck was gruff but maybe starting to look better. "What happens if ye die out of your time? D'ye just disappear, like ye never were?"

"Maybe ye explode into bits. I don't know, and I don't want to find out. Not while I'm standing next to you, at least." Roger got his feet under him and fought down a wave of dizziness. His own heart was still beating hard enough that he felt it in the back of his head. He breathed as deep as he could and stood up.

"I'll . . . get ye some water. Stay there, aye?"

ROGER HAD BROUGHT a small empty canteen, though he'd worried about what might happen to the metal in transit. Evidently whatever it was that vaporized gemstones wasn't bothered about tin, though; the canteen was intact, and so was the small knife and the silver pocket flask of brandy.

Buck was sitting up by the time Roger came back from the nearest burn with water, and after mopping his face with the water and drinking half the brandy, he declared himself recovered.

Roger wasn't all that sure; the look of the man was a little off-color still—but he was much too anxious about Jem to suggest waiting any longer. They'd talked about it a bit on the drive to Craigh na Dun, agreeing on a basic strategy, at least to start.

If Cameron and Jem had made it through without mishap—and Roger's heart misgave him at that thought, recalling Geillis Duncan's careful collection of news reports involving people found near stone circles, most of them dead—they had to be on foot. And while Jem was a sturdy little boy and capable of walking a good distance, he doubted they could make much more than ten miles in a day over rough country.

The only road was the drovers' track that led near the base of the hill. So one of them would take the direction that would intersect with one of General Wade's good roads that led to Inverness; the other would follow the track west toward the pass that led to Lallybroch and, beyond it, Cranesmuir.

"I think Inverness is the most likely," Roger repeated, probably for the sixth time. "It's the gold he wants, and he knows that's in America. He can't be meaning to walk from the Highlands to Edinburgh to find a ship, not with winter breathing down his neck."

"He won't find a ship anywhere in the winter," Buck objected. "No captain would cross the Atlantic in November!"

"D'ye think he knows that?" Roger asked. "He's an amateur archaeologist, not a historian. And most folk in the twentieth century have trouble thinking anything was ever different in the past, save the funny clothes and no indoor plumbing. The notion that the weather could stop them going anywhere they'd a mind to—he may well think ships run all the time, on a regular timetable."

"Mmphm. Well, maybe he means to hole up in Inverness with the lad, maybe find work, and wait 'til the spring. D'ye want to take Inverness, then?" Buck lifted his chin in the direction of the invisible town.

"No." Roger shook his head and began patting his pockets, checking his supplies. "Jem knows this place." He nodded toward the stones above them. "I brought him here, more than once, to make sure he never came upon it unawares. That means he knows—approximately, at least—how to get home—to Lallybroch, I mean—from here. If he got away from Cameron—and, God, I hope he did!—he'd run for home."

He didn't trouble saying that even if Jem wasn't there, Brianna's relatives were, her cousins and her aunt. He'd not met them, but they knew from Jamie's letters who he was; if Jem wasn't there—and, Lord, how he hoped he was—they'd help him search. As to how much he might try to tell them . . . that could wait.

"Right, then." Buck buttoned his coat and settled the knitted comforter round his neck against the wind. "Three days, maybe, to Inverness and time to search the town, two or three back. I'll meet ye here in six days' time. If ye're not here, I follow on to Lallybroch."

Roger nodded. "And if I've not found them but I've heard some word of them, I'll leave a message at Lallybroch. If . . ." He hesitated, but it had to be said. "If ye find your wife, and things fall out—"

Buck's lips tightened.

"They've already fallen," he said. "But, aye. If. I'll still come back."

"Aye, right." Roger hunched his shoulders, anxious to go, and awkward with it. Buck was already turning away but suddenly about-faced and gripped Roger's hand, hard.

"We'll find him," Buck said, and looked into Roger's eyes, with those bright-moss eyes that were the same as his. "Good luck." He gave Roger's hand one sharp, hard shake and then was off, arms outstretched for balance as he picked his way down through the rocks and gorse. He didn't look back.

28

WARMER, COLDER

"CAN YOU TELL when Jem's at school?"

"Yes. He goes on da bus." Mandy bounced a little on her booster seat, leaning to peer out the window. She was wearing the Halloween mask Bree had helped her make, this being a mouse princess: a mouse face drawn with crayons on a paper plate, with holes pierced for eyes and at either side for pink yarn ties, pink pipe cleaners glued on for whiskers, and a precarious small crown made with cardboard, more glue, and most of a bottle of gold glitter.

Scots celebrated Samhain with hollowed-out turnips with candles in them, but Brianna had wanted a slightly more festive tradition for her half-American children. The whole seat sparkled as though the car had been sprinkled with pixie dust.

She smiled, despite her worry.

"I meant, if you played warmer, colder with Jem, could you do it if he wasn't answering you out loud? Would you know if he was closer or farther away?"

Mandy kicked the back of the seat in meditative fashion. "Maybe."

"Can you try?" They were headed toward Inverness. That was where Jem was supposed to be, spending the night with Rob Cameron's nephew.

"Okay," Mandy said agreeably. She hadn't asked where Rob Cameron was. Brianna spared a thought as to the fate of her prisoner. She really *would* shoot him through the ankles, elbows, knees, or anything else necessary to find out where Jem was—but if there were quieter ways of interrogation, it would be better all round. It wouldn't be good for Jem and Mandy to have their mother sent to prison for life, particularly if Roger— She choked that thought off and stepped harder on the gas.

"Colder," Mandy announced, so suddenly that Brianna nearly stalled the car.

"What? Do you mean we're getting farther away from where Jemmy is?"

"Uh-huh."

Brianna took a deep breath and made a U-turn, narrowly avoiding an oncoming panel truck, which hooted at them in annoyance.

"Right," she said, gripping the wheel with sweaty hands. "We'll go the other way."

THE DOOR WASN'T locked. Jem opened it, heart pounding in relief, and then it pounded harder, as he realized the lights weren't on in the turbine chamber, either.

There was *some* light. The little windows up at the top of the huge space, up where the engineers' room was: there was light coming from there. Just enough so he could see the monsters in the huge room.

"They're just machines," he muttered, pressing his back hard against the wall beside the open door. "Justmachinesjust-machinesjustmachines!" He knew the names of them, the giant pulley hoists that ran overhead with the big hooks dangling, and the turbines, Mam had told him. But he'd been up *there* then, where the light was, and it had been daylight.

The floor under his feet vibrated, and he could feel the knobs on his backbone knocking against the wall as it shook from the weight of the water rushing through the dam under him. Tons of water, Mummy said. Tons and tons and tons of black dark water, all around him, under him . . . If the wall or the floor broke, it—

"Shut up, baby!" he said fiercely to himself, and rubbed his hand hard over his face and wiped it on his jeans. "You got to move. *Go!*"

There were stairs; there had to be stairs. And they were somewhere in here, among the big black humps of the turbines that poked up. They stood higher than the big stones on the hill where Mr. Cameron had taken him. That thought calmed him down some; he was lots more scared of the stones. Even with the deep roaring noise the turbines made—that was making his bones twitch, but it didn't really get *inside* his bones.

The only thing that kept him from going right back into the tunnel and hoping for someone to find him in the morning was the . . . thing in there. He didn't want to be anywhere near that.

He couldn't hear his heart anymore. It was too noisy in the turbine chamber to hear anything. He sure couldn't hear himself think, but the stairs had to be near the windows, and he wobbled that way, keeping as far as he could from the huge black double humps sticking up through the floor.

It was only when he finally found the door, yanked it open, and fell into the lighted staircase that it occurred to him to wonder whether Mr. Cameron was maybe up there, waiting for him.

29

RETURN TO LALLYBROCH

ROGER HAULED HIS WAY laboriously toward the summit of the mountain pass, muttering under his breath (as he had been doing for the last several miles):

"If you had seen this road before it was made,
You would lift up your hands and bless General Wade."

The Irish General Wade had spent twelve years building barracks, bridges, and roads all over Scotland, and if that bit of admiring verse was not in fact carved into a stone on one of the general's roads, it ought to have been, Roger thought. He had picked up one of the general's roads near Craigh na Dun, and it had carried him as swiftly as he could walk to within a few miles of Lallybroch.

These last few miles, though, had not had the benefit of Wade's attention. A rocky trail, pitted with small mud bogs and thickly overgrown with heather and gorse, led up through the steep pass that overlooked—and protected—Lallybroch. The lower slopes were forested with beeches, alders, and stout Caledonian pines, but up this high there was neither shade nor shelter, and a strong, cold wind battered him as he climbed.

Could Jem have come this far by himself, if he'd escaped? Roger and Buck had cast round in the vicinity of Craigh na Dun, hoping that perhaps Cameron had stopped to rest after the strain of the passage, but there had been no sign—not so much as the print of a size-4 trainer in a muddy patch of ground. Roger had come on then by himself, as fast as he could, pausing to knock at the door of any croft he came to—and there weren't many along this way—but he'd made good time.

His heart was pounding, and not only from the exertion of the climb. Cameron had maybe a two-day lead, at the most. If Jem hadn't got away and run for home, though . . . Cameron wouldn't come to Lallybroch, surely. But where *would* he go? Follow the good road, left now ten miles behind, and head west, maybe, into the MacKenzies' territory—but why?

"Jem!" He shouted now and then as he went, though the moors and mountains were empty save for the rustling of rabbits and stoats and silent but for the calling of ravens and the occasional shriek of a seagull winging high overhead, evidence of the distant sea.

"Jem!" he called, as though he could compel an answer by sheer need, and in that need imagined sometimes that he heard a faint cry in response. But when he stopped to listen, it was the wind. Only the wind, whining in his ears, numbing him. He could walk within ten feet of Jem and never see him, and he knew that.

His heart rose, in spite of his anxiety, when he came to the top of the pass and saw Lallybroch below him, its white-harled buildings glowing in the fading light. Everything lay peaceful before him: late cabbages and turnips in orderly rows within the kailyard walls, safe from grazing sheep—there was a small flock in the far meadow, already bedding for the night, like so many woolly eggs in a nest of green grass, like a kid's Easter basket.

The thought caught at his throat, with memories of the horrible cellophane grass that got everywhere, Mandy with her face—and everything else within six feet of her—smeared with chocolate, Jem carefully writing *Dad* on a hard-boiled egg with a white crayon, then frowning over the array of dye cups, trying to decide whether blue or purple was more Dad-like.

"Lord, let him be here!" he muttered under his breath, and hurried down the rutted trail, half sliding on loose rocks.

The dooryard was tidy, the big yellow rose brier trimmed back for the winter, and the step swept clean. He had the sudden notion that if he were simply to open the door and walk in, he would find himself in his own lobby, Mandy's tiny red galoshes flung helter-skelter under the hall tree where Brianna's disreputable duffel coat hung, crusty with dried mud and smelling of its wearer, soap and musk and the faint smell of her motherhood: sour milk, fresh bread, and peanut butter.

"Bloody hell," he muttered, "be weeping on the step, next thing." He hammered at the door, and a huge dog came galloping round the corner of the house, baying like the bloody hound of the Baskervilles. It slid to a stop in front of him but went on barking, weaving its huge head to and fro like a snake, ears cocked in case he might make a false move that would let it devour him with a clear conscience.

He wasn't risking any moves; he'd plastered himself against the door when the dog appeared and now shouted, "Help! Come call your beast!"

He heard footsteps within, and an instant later the door opened, nearly decanting him into the hall.

"Hauld your wheesht, dog," a tall, dark man said in a tolerant tone. "Come ben, sir, and dinna be minding him. He wouldna eat you; he's had his dinner."

"I'm pleased to hear it, sir, and thank ye kindly." Roger pulled off his hat and followed the man into the shadows of the hall. It was his own familiar hall, the slates of the floor just the same, though not nearly as worn, the dark-wood paneling shining with beeswax and polishing. There *was* a hall tree in the corner, though of course different to his; this one was a sturdy affair of wrought iron, and a good thing, too, as it was supporting a massive burden of jackets, shawls, cloaks, and hats, which would have crumpled a flimsier piece of furniture.

He smiled at it, nonetheless, and then stopped dead, feeling as though he'd been punched in the chest.

The wood paneling behind the hall tree shone serene, unblemished. No sign of the saber slashes left by frustrated redcoat soldiers searching for the outlawed laird of Lallybroch after Culloden. Those slashes had been carefully preserved for centuries, were still there, darkened by age but still distinct, when he had owned—would own, he corrected mechanically—this place.

"We keep it so for the children," Bree had quoted her uncle Ian as saying. *"We tell them, 'This is what the English are.'"*

He had no time to deal with the shock; the dark man had shut the door with a firm Gaelic adjuration to the dog and now turned to him, smiling.

"Welcome, sir. Ye'll sup wi' us? The lass has it nearly ready."

"Aye, I will, and thanks to ye," Roger bowed slightly, groping for his eighteenth-century manners. "I—my name is Roger MacKenzie. Of Kyle of Lochalsh," he added, for no respectable man would omit to note his origins, and Lochalsh was far enough away that the chances of this man—who was he? He hadn't the bearing of a servant—knowing its inhabitants in any detail was remote.

He'd hoped that the immediate response would be, *"MacKenzie? Why, you must be the father of wee Jem!"* It wasn't, though; the man returned his bow and offered his hand.

"Brian Fraser of Lallybroch, your servant, sir."

ROGER FELT ABSOLUTELY nothing for a moment. There was a faint clicking that reminded him of the noise a car's starter makes when the battery is dead, and for a disoriented moment he assumed it was being made by his brain. Then his eyes focused on the dog, which, prevented from eating him, had come into the house and was walking down the passage, its toenails clicking on the parquet floor.

Oh. So that's what left those scratches on the kitchen door, he thought, dazed, as the beast reared up and heaved its weight at the swinging door at the end of the passage, then shot through as it opened.

"Are ye quite well, sir?" Brian Fraser was looking at him, thick black brows drawn down in concern. He reached out a hand. "Come into my study and sit. I'll maybe fetch ye a dram?"

"I—thank you," Roger said abruptly. He thought his knees might give way at any second, but he managed to follow the master of Lallybroch into the speak-a-word room, the laird's office and study. His own study.

The shelves were the same, and behind his host's head was the same row of farm ledgers that he'd often thumbed through, conjuring up from their faded entries the phantom life of an earlier Lallybroch. Now the ledgers were new, and Roger felt himself the phantom. He didn't like the feeling at all.

Brian Fraser handed him a small, thick, flat-bottomed glass

half full of spirit. Whisky, and very decent whisky, too. The smell of it began to bring him out of his shock, and the warm burn of it down his gullet loosened the tightness in his throat.

How was he to ask what he so desperately needed to know? *When?!* He glanced over the desk, but there was no half-finished letter, conveniently dated, no planting almanac that he might glance casually through. None of the books on the shelf were of help; the only one he recognized was Defoe's *THE LIFE AND STRANGE SURPRIZING ADVENTURES OF ROBINSON CRUSOE, OF YORK, MARINER,* and that had been published in 1719. He knew he must be later than that; the house itself hadn't yet been built in 1719.

He forced down the rising tide of panic. It didn't matter; it didn't matter if it wasn't the time he'd expected—not if Jem was here. And he must be. He *must* be.

"I'm sorry to disturb your family, sir," he said, clearing his throat as he set down the glass. "But the fact is that I've lost my son and am in search of him."

"Lost your son!" exclaimed Fraser, eyes widening in surprise. "Bride be with ye, sir. How did that come about?"

Just as well to tell the truth where he could, he thought, and, after all, what else could he say?

"He was kidnapped two days ago and carried away—he's no but nine years old. I have some reason to think the man who took him comes from this area. Have ye by chance seen a tall man, lean and dark, traveling with a young red-haired lad, about so tall?" He put the edge of his hand against his own arm, about three inches above the elbow; Jem was tall for his age and even taller for this age—but, then, Brian Fraser was a tall man himself, and *his* son . . .

A fresh shock went through Roger with the thought: Was Jamie here? In the house? And if he was, how old might he be? How old had he been when Brian Fraser die—

Fraser was shaking his head, his face troubled.

"I have not, sir. What's the name of the man who's taken your lad?"

"Rob—Robert Cameron, he's called. I dinna ken his people," he added, falling naturally into Fraser's stronger accent.

"Cameron . . ." Fraser murmured, tapping his fingers on the desk as he searched his memory. The motion flicked something in Roger's memory; it was the ghost of one of Jamie's characteristic gestures when thinking—but Jamie, with his frozen finger, did it with the fingers flat, where his father's came down in a smooth ripple.

He picked up the glass again and took another sip, glancing as casually as he might at Fraser's face, searching for resemblance. It was there but subtle, mostly in the cock of the head, the set of the shoulders—and the eyes. The face was quite different, square in the jaw, broader of brow, and Brian Fraser's eyes were a dark hazel, not blue, but the slanted shape of them, the wide mouth—that was Jamie.

"There're nay many Camerons nearer than Lochaber." Fraser was shaking his head. "And I've heard nothing of a wanderer in the district." He gave Roger a direct look, not accusing but definitely questioning. "Why is it ye think the man came this way?"

"I—he was seen," Roger blurted. "Near Craigh na Dun."

That startled Fraser.

"Craigh na Dun," he repeated, leaning back a little, his eyes gone wary. "Ah . . . and where might ye have come from yourself, sir?"

"From Inverness," Roger replied promptly. "I followed him from there." *Close enough.* He was trying hard not to recall that he'd left on his quest to find Cameron and Jem from the very spot in which he was now sitting. "I—a friend—a kinsman—came with me. I sent him toward Cranesmuir to search."

The news that he apparently wasn't a solitary nutter seemed to reassure Fraser, who pushed back from the desk and stood up, glancing at the window, where a big rose brier curved up gaunt and black against the fading sky.

"Mmphm. Well, bide for a bit, sir, and ye will. It's late in the day, and ye'll make no great distance before dark falls. Sup with us, and we'll gie ye a bed for the night. Mayhap your friend will catch ye up with good news, or one of my tenants may ha' seen something. I'll send round in the morning, to ask."

Roger's legs were quivering with the urge to leap up, rush out, *do* something. But Fraser was right: it would be pointless—and dangerous—to blunder round the Highland mountains in the dark, losing his way, perhaps be caught in a killing storm this time of year. He could hear the wind picking up; the rose brier beat at the glass of the window. It was going to rain soon. *And is Jem out in it?*

"I—yes. I thank you, sir," he said. "It's most kind of ye."

Fraser patted him on the shoulder, went out into the hallway, and called, "Janet! Janet, we've a guest for supper!"

Janet?

He'd risen to his feet without thinking and came out of the office as the kitchen door swung open—and a small, slender shape was momentarily silhouetted against the glow of the kitchen, rubbing her hands on her apron.

"My daughter, Janet, sir," Fraser said, drawing his daughter into the fading light. He smiled fondly at her. "This is Mr. Roger MacKenzie, Jenny. He's lost his wee lad somewhere."

"He has?" The girl paused, halfway through a curtsy, and her eyes went wide. "What's happened, sir?"

Roger explained again briefly about Rob Cameron and Craigh na Dun, but all the time was consumed by the desire to ask the young woman how old she was. Fifteen? Seventeen? Twenty-one? She was remarkably beautiful, with clear white skin that bloomed from the heat of cooking, soft curly black hair tied back from her face, and a trim figure that he tried hard not to stare at—but what was most disturbing was that, despite her obvious femininity, she bore a startling resemblance to Jamie Fraser. *She might be his daughter,* he thought, and then brought himself up short, realizing afresh—and remembering, with a stab of the heart that nearly dropped him to his knees—who Jamie Fraser's daughter really was.

Oh, God. Bree. Oh, Jesus, help me. Will I ever see her again?

He realized that he'd fallen silent and was staring at Janet Fraser with his mouth open. Apparently she was used to this sort of response from men, though; she gave him a demure, slant-eyed smile, said that supper would be on the table in a few moments and maybe Da should show Mr. MacKenzie the way to the necessary? Then she was walking back down the hallway, the big door swung to behind her, and he found he could breathe again.

THE SUPPER WAS plain but plentiful and well cooked, and Roger found that food restored him amazingly. No wonder—he couldn't remember when he'd last eaten.

They ate in the kitchen, with a pair of housemaids called Annie and Senga and a man-of-all-work named Tom McTaggart sharing the table with the family. All of them were interested in Roger and, while giving him great sympathy in the matter of his missing son, were even more interested in where he might come from and what news he might bear.

Here he was at something of a loss, as he had no firm notion what year it was *(Brian died—God,* will *die—when Jamie was nineteen, and if Jamie was born in May of 1721—or was it 1722?—and he was two years younger than Jenny . . .)* and thus no idea what might have been happening in the world of late, but he delayed a bit, explaining his antecedents in some detail—that was good manners, for one thing, and for another, his birthplace in Kyle of Lochalsh was far enough away from Lallybroch that the Frasers were unlikely to have met any of his people.

Then at last he had a bit of luck, when McTaggart told about taking off his shoe to shake out a stone, then seeing one of the pigs wriggle under the fence and head for the kailyard at a trot. He rushed after the pig, of course, and succeeded in catching it—but had dragged it back to the pen only to find that the other pig had likewise wriggled out and was peacefully eating his shoe.

"This was all she left!" he said, pulling half a shredded leather sole out of his pocket and waving it at them reproachfully. "And a rare struggle I had to pull it from her jaws!"

"Why did ye bother?" Jenny asked, wrinkling her nose at the dank object. "Dinna trouble yourself, Taggie. We'll slaughter the pigs next week, and ye can have a bit o' the hide to make yourself a new pair of shoon."

"And I suppose I'm to go barefoot 'til then, am I?" McTaggart asked, disgruntled. "There's frost on the ground in the morn, aye? I could take a chill and be dead of the pleurisy before yon pig's eaten its last bucket o' slops, let alone been tanned."

Brian laughed and lifted his chin toward Jenny. "Did your brother no leave a pair of his outgrown shoon behind when he left for Paris? I mind me he did, and if ye havena given them to the poor, might be as Taggie could manage wi' them for a bit."

Paris. Roger's mind worked furiously, calculating. Jamie had spent not quite two years in Paris at the *université* and had come back . . . when? When he was eighteen, he thought. Jamie would have been—will be—eighteen in May of 1739. So it was now 1737, 1738, or 1739.

The narrowing of uncertainty calmed him a little, and he managed to put his mind to thinking of historical events that had occurred in that gap that he might offer as current news in conversation: absurdly, the first thing that came to mind was that the bottle opener had been invented in 1738. The second was that there had been an enormous earthquake in Bombay in 1737.

His audience was initially more interested by the bottle opener, which he was obliged to describe in detail—inventing wildly, as he had no notion what the thing actually looked like, though there were sympathetic murmurs regarding the residents of Bombay and a brief prayer for the souls of those crushed under falling houses and the like.

"But where *is* Bombay?" asked the younger of the housemaids, wrinkling her brow and looking from one face to another.

"India," said Jenny promptly, and pushed back her chair. "Senga, fetch the cranachan, aye? I'll show ye where India is."

She vanished through the swinging door, and the bustle of removing dishes left Roger with a few moments' breathing space. He was beginning to feel a little easier, getting his bearings, though still agonized with worry for Jem. He did spare a moment's thought for William Buccleigh and how Buck might take the news of the date of their arrival.

Seventeen thirty-something . . . Jesus, Buck himself hadn't even been born yet! But, after all, what difference did that make? he asked himself. *He* hadn't been born yet, either, and had lived quite happily in a time prior to his birth before. . . . Could their proximity to the beginning of Buck's life have something to do with it, though?

He did know—or thought he knew—that you couldn't go back to a time during your own lifetime. Trying to exist physically at the same time as yourself just wasn't on. It had just about killed him once; maybe they'd got too close to Buck's original lifeline, and Buck had somehow recoiled, taking Roger with him?

Before he could explore the implications of *that* unsettling thought, Jenny returned, carrying a large, thin book. This proved to be a hand-colored atlas, with maps—surprisingly accurate maps, in many cases—and descriptions of "The Nations of the World."

"My brother sent it to me from Paris," Jenny told him proudly, opening the book to a double-page spread of the Continent of India, where the starred circle indicating Bombay was surrounded by small drawings of palm trees, elephants, and something that upon close scrutiny turned out to be a tea plant. "He's at the *université* there."

"Really?" Roger smiled, being sure to look impressed. He was, the more so at realization of the effort and expense involved in going from this remote mountain wilderness to Paris. "How long has he been there?"

"Oh, almost two years now," Brian answered. He put out a hand and touched the page gently. "We do miss the lad cruelly, but he writes often. And he sends us books."

"He'll be back soon," Jenny said, though with an air of conviction that seemed somewhat forced. "He said he'd come back."

Brian smiled, though this too was a little forced.

"Aye. I'm sure I hope so, *a nighean.* But ye ken he may have found opportunities that keep him abroad for a time."

"Opportunities? Ye mean that de Marillac woman?" Jenny asked, a distinct edge in her voice. "I dinna like the way he writes about her. Not one bit."

"He could do worse for a wife, lass." Brian lifted one shoulder. "She's from a good family."

Jenny made a very complicated sound in her throat, indicating sufficient respect for her father as to prevent her expressing a fuller opinion of "that woman" while still making that opinion plain. Her father laughed.

"Your brother's no a *complete* fool," he assured her. "I doubt he'd marry a simpleton or a—a—" He'd obviously thought better of saying "whore"—his lips had begun to shape the word—but couldn't think of a substitute in time.

"He would," Jenny snapped. "He'd walk straight into a cob's web wi' his eyes wide open, if the cob had a pretty face and a round arse."

"Janet!" Her father tried to look shocked but failed utterly. McTaggart guffawed openly, and Annie and Senga giggled behind their hands. Jenny glowered at them but then drew herself up with dignity and addressed herself to their guest.

"So, then, Mr. MacKenzie. Is your own wife living, I hope? And is she your wean's mother?"

"Is she—" He felt the question like a blow in the chest but then remembered when he was. The odds of a woman surviving childbirth were no more than even in many places. "Yes. Yes, she's—in Inverness, with our daughter."

Mandy. Oh, my sweet baby. Mandy. Bree. Jem. All at once, the enormity of it struck him. He'd managed so far to ignore it by concentrating on the need to find Jem, but now a cold wind whistled through the holes in his heart left by hurtling odds. The odds were that he would never see any of them again. And they would never know what had happened to him.

"Oh, sir." Jenny whispered it, leaning forward to lay a hand on his arm, her eyes wide with horror at what she'd provoked. "Oh, sir, I'm sorry! I didna mean to—"

"It's all right," he managed, forcing the words through his mangled larynx in a croak. "I'm—" He waved a hand in blind apology and stumbled out. He went straight out through the mudroom at the back of the house and found himself in the night outside.

There was a narrow crack of sullen light just at the tops of the mountains, where the cloud had not quite settled, but the yard about him was deep in shadow, and the wind touched his face with the scent of cold rain. He was shaking, but not from chill, and sat down abruptly on the big stone by the path where they pulled the children's wellies off when it was muddy.

He put his elbows on his knees and his face in his hands, overcome for a moment. Not only for his own situation—but for those in the house. Jamie Fraser was coming home soon. And soon after there would come the afternoon when redcoated soldiers marched into the yard at Lallybroch, finding Janet and the servants alone. And the events would be set in train that would end with the death of Brian Fraser, struck down by an apoplexy while watching his only son flogged—he thought—to death.

Jamie . . . Roger shivered, seeing in mind not his indomitable father-in-law but the lighthearted young man who, among the distractions of Paris, still thought to send books to his sister. Who—

It had begun to rain, with a quiet thoroughness that slicked his face in seconds. At least no one would know if he wept in despair. *I can't stop it,* he thought. *I can't tell them what's coming.*

A huge shape loomed out of the darkness, startling him, and the dog leaned heavily against him, nearly pushing him off the stone he sat on. A large, hairy nose was thrust sympathetically into his ear, whoofling and wetter than the rain.

"Jesus, dog," he said, half-laughing in spite of everything. "God." He put his arms round the big, smelly creature and rested his forehead against its massive neck, feeling inchoate comfort.

He thought of nothing for a little and was inexpressibly relieved. Little by little, though, coherent thought came back. It maybe wasn't true that things—the past—couldn't be changed. Not the big things, maybe, not kings and battles. But maybe—just maybe—the small ones could. If he couldn't come right out and tell the Frasers of Lallybroch what doom was to come upon them, perhaps there was *something* he could say, some warning that might forestall—

And if he did? If they listened? Would that good man in the house die of his apoplexy anyway, some weakness in his brain giving way as he came in from the barn one day? But that would leave his son and his daughter safe—and then what?

Would Jamie stay in Paris and marry the flirtatious Frenchwoman? Would he come home peaceably to live at Lallybroch and mind his estate and his sister?

Either way, he wouldn't be riding near Craigh na Dun in five or six years, pursued by English soldiers, wounded and needing the assistance of a random time traveler who had just stepped out of the stones. And if he didn't meet Claire Randall. . . . *Bree,* he thought. *Oh, Christ. Bree.*

There was a sound behind him—the door of the house opening—and the beam of a lantern fell onto the path nearby.

"Mr. MacKenzie?" Brian Fraser called into the night. "Are ye all right, man?"

"God," he whispered, clutching the dog. "Show me what to do."

30

LIGHTS, ACTION, SIRENS

THE DOOR AT THE top of the staircase *was* locked. Jem pounded on it with his fists, kicked it with his feet, and shouted. He could feel *it* back down there behind him, in the dark, and the feel of it crawled up his back, as if it were coming to get him, and the thought of that scared him so bad that he shrieked like a *ban-sìdhe* and threw himself hard against the door, over and over, and—

The door flew open and he fell flat on a dirty lino floor, all footmarks and cigarette butts.

"What the devil—who are you, laddie, and what in God's name were ye doing in there?"

A big hand grabbed him by the arm and pulled him up. He was out of breath from yelling and almost blubbering from relief, and it took a minute to remember who he was.

"Jem." He swallowed, blinking in the light, and wiped his face on his sleeve. "Jem MacKenzie. My mam's . . ." He went blank, suddenly unable to remember what Mam's first name was. "She works here sometimes."

"I know your mam. No mistaking *that* hair, laddie." The man who'd pulled him up was a security guard; the patch on his shirtsleeve said so. He tilted his head to one side and the other, looking Jem over, light flashing off his bald head, off his glasses. The light was coming from those long tube lights in the ceiling Da said were fluorescent; they buzzed and reminded him of the thing in the tunnel, and he turned round fast and shoved the door shut with a bang.

"Is someone chasin' ye, lad?" The guard reached a hand toward the doorknob, and Jem put his back hard against the door.

"No!" He could feel it back there, behind the door. Waiting. The guard was frowning at him. "I—I just—it's really dark down there."

"Ye were down in the dark? However did ye come to be there? And where's your mother?"

"I don't know." Jem started being scared again. *Really* scared. Because Mr. Cameron had shut him up in the tunnel so he could go somewhere. And he might have gone to Lallybroch.

"Mr. Cameron put me in there," he blurted. "He was supposed to take me to spend the night with Bobby, but instead he took me to Craigh na Dun, and then he took me to his house and locked me in a room overnight, and then the next morning he brought me here and shut me up in the tunnel."

"Cameron—what, Rob Cameron?" The guard crouched down so he could frown right into Jem's face. "Why?"

"I—I don't know." *Don't ever tell anyone,* Da had said. Jem swallowed hard. Even if he wanted to tell, he didn't know how to start. He could say Mr. Cameron took him up the hill at Craigh na Dun, to the stones, and pushed him into one. But he couldn't tell what had happened then, not any more than he could tell Mr. MacLeod—that's what it said on his badge, JOCK MACLEOD—what the shiny thing in the tunnel was.

Mr. MacLeod made a thinking noise in his throat, shook his head, and stood up.

"Well, I'd best be calling your parents to come and fetch ye home, aye? They can say if they maybe want to speak to the polis."

"Please," Jem whispered, feeling his knees turn to water at the thought of Mam and Da coming to get him. "Yes, please."

Mr. MacLeod took him along to a little office where the phone was, gave him a warm can of Coke, and told him to sit down just there and say his parents' telephone number. He sipped the drink and felt lots better right away, watching Mr. MacLeod's thick finger whirl the telephone dial. A pause, and then he could hear ringing on the other end. *Breep-breep . . . breep-breep . . . breep-breep . . .*

It was warm in the office, but he was starting to feel cold around his face and hands. Nobody was answering the phone.

"Maybe they're asleep," he said, stifling a Coke burp. Mr. MacLeod gave him a sideways look and shook his head, pushed down the receiver, and dialed the number again, making Jem say the numbers one at a time.

Breep-breep. . . . breep-breep . . .

He was concentrating so hard on willing somebody to pick up the phone that he didn't notice anything until Mr. MacLeod suddenly turned his head toward the door, looking surprised.

"What—" the guard said, and then there was a blur and a thunking noise like when cousin Ian shot a deer with an arrow, and Mr. MacLeod made an awful noise and fell right out of his chair onto the floor, and the chair shot away and fell over with a crash.

Jem didn't remember standing up, but he was pressed against the filing cabinet, squeezing the can so hard that the bubbly Coke blurped out and foamed over his fingers.

"You come with me, boy," said the man who'd hit Mr. MacLeod. He was holding what Jem thought must be a cosh, though he'd never seen one. He couldn't move, even if he'd wanted to.

The man made an impatient noise, stepped over Mr. MacLeod like he was a bag of rubbish, and grabbed Jem by the hand. Out of sheer terror, Jem bit him, hard. The man yelped and let go, and Jem threw the can of Coke right at his face, and when the man ducked, he tore past him and out of the office and down the long hallway, running for his life.

IT WAS GETTING late; they passed fewer and fewer cars on the road, and Mandy's head began to nod. The mouse-princess mask had ridden up on top of her head, its pipe-cleaner whiskers poking up like antennae. Seeing this in the rearview mirror, Brianna had a sudden vision of Mandy as a tiny radar station, scanning the bleak countryside for Jem's small, pulsing signal.

Could she? She shook her head, not to dispel the notion but to keep her mind from slipping all the way out of reality. The adrenaline of her earlier rage and terror had all drained away;

her hands shook a little on the steering wheel, and the darkness around them seemed vast, a yawning void that would swallow them in an instant if she stopped driving, if the feeble beam of the headlights ceased . . .

"Warm," Mandy murmured sleepily.

"What, baby?" She'd heard but was too hypnotized by the effort of keeping her eyes on the road to take it in consciously.

"Warm . . . *er*." Mandy struggled upright, cross. The yarn ties of her mask were stuck in her hair, and she made a high-pitched cranky noise as she yanked at them.

Brianna pulled carefully onto the verge, set the hand brake, and, reaching back, began to disentangle the mask.

"You mean we're going toward Jem?" she asked, careful to keep her voice from trembling.

"Uh-huh." Free of the nuisance, Mandy yawned hugely and flung out a hand toward the window. "Mmp." She put her head down on her arms and whined sleepily.

Bree swallowed, closed her eyes, then opened them, looking carefully in the direction Mandy had pointed. There was no road . . . but there was, and with a trickle of ice water down her spine, she saw the small brown sign that said: SERVICE ROAD. NO PUBLIC ACCESS. NORTH OF SCOTLAND HYDRO ELECTRIC BOARD. Loch Errochty dam. The tunnel.

"Damn!" said Brianna, and stomped the gas, forgetting the hand brake. The car jumped and stalled, and Mandy sat bolt upright, eyes glazed and wide as a sun-stunned owl's.

"Iss we home yet?"

JEM PELTED DOWN the hallway and threw himself at the swinging door at the end, so hard that he skidded all the way across the landing on the other side and fell down the stairs beyond, bumping and banging and ending up in a dazed heap at the bottom.

He heard the footsteps coming fast toward the door above and, with a small, terrified squeak, scrambled on all fours round the second landing and launched himself headfirst down the next flight, tobogganing on his stomach for a few stairs, then tipping arse over teakettle and somersaulting down the rest.

He was crying with terror, gulping air and trying not to make a noise, stumbling to his feet, and everything hurt, everything—but the door: he had to get outside. He staggered through the half-dark lobby, the only lights shining through the glass window where the receptionist usually sat. The man was coming; he could hear him cursing at the bottom of the stairs.

The main door had a chain looped through the bars. Swiping tears on his sleeve, he ran back in to the reception, looking wildly round. EMERGENCY EXIT—there it was, the red sign over the door at the far end of another small corridor. The man burst into the lobby and saw him.

"Come back here, you little bugger!"

He looked round wildly, grabbed the first thing he saw, which was a rolling chair, and pushed it as hard as he could into the lobby. The man cursed and jumped aside, and Jem ran for the door and flung himself against it, bursting into the night with a scream of sirens and the flash of blinding lights.

"WHASSAT, MUMMY? Mummy, I scared, I SCARED!"

"And you think I'm not?" Bree said under her breath, heart in her mouth. "It's okay, baby," she said aloud, and pressed her foot to the floor. "We're just going to get Jem."

The car slewed to a stop on the gravel, and she leapt out but dithered for a moment, needing urgently to rush toward the building, where sirens and lights were going off over an open door at the side, but unable to leave Mandy alone in the car. She could hear the rush of water down the spillway.

"Come with me, sweetheart," she said, hastily undoing the seat belt. "That's right, here, let me carry you . . ." Even as she spoke, she was looking here, there, from the lights into the darkness, every nerve she had screaming that her son was here, he was *here,* he had to be . . . rushing water . . . her mind filled with horror, thinking of Jem falling into the spillway, or Jem in the service tunnel—God, why hadn't she gone there first? Of course Rob Cameron would have put him there, he had the keys, he . . . but the lights, the sirens . . .

She'd almost made it—at a dead run, impeded only slightly by thirty pounds of toddler—when she saw a big man at the edge of the drive, thrashing through the bushes with a stick or something, cursing a blue streak.

"What do you think you're *doing*?" she bellowed. Mandy, alarmed anew, let out a screech like a scalded baboon, and the man jumped, whirling to face them, stick raised.

"What the bleedin' hell are you doing here?" he said, so taken aback that he spoke almost normally. "You're supposed to be—"

Bree had peeled Mandy off. Setting her daughter down behind her, she prepared to take the man apart with her bare hands, if necessary. Evidently this intent showed, because the man dropped the stick and abruptly vanished into the darkness.

Then flashing lights washed over the drive and she realized that it wasn't her own aspect that had frightened him. Mandy was clinging to her leg, too frightened even to wail anymore. Bree picked her up, patting her gently, and turned to face the two police officers who were advancing cautiously toward her, hands on their batons. She felt wobbly-legged and dreamlike, things fading in and out of focus with the strobing lights. The rush of tons of falling water filled her ears.

"Mandy," she said into her daughter's warm curly hair, her own voice almost drowned out by the sirens. "Can you feel Jem? Please tell me you can feel him."

"Here I am, Mummy," said a small voice behind her. Convinced she was hallucinating, she lifted a restraining hand toward the police officers and pivoted slowly round. Jem was standing on the drive six feet away, dripping wet, plastered with dead leaves, and swaying like a drunk.

Then she was sitting splay-legged on the gravel, a child clutched in each arm, trying hard not to shake, so they wouldn't notice. She didn't start to sob, though, until Jemmy lifted a tearstained face from her shoulder and said, "Where's Daddy?"

31

THE SHINE OF A ROCKING HORSE'S EYES

FRASER DIDN'T ASK BUT poured them each a dram of whisky, warm-smelling and smoke-tinged. There was something comfortable in drinking whisky in company, no matter how bad the whisky. Or the company, for that matter. This particular bottle was something special, and Roger was grateful, both to the bottle and its giver, for the sense of comfort that rose from the glass, beckoning him, a genie from the bottle.

"Slàinte," he said, lifting the glass, and saw Fraser glance at him in sudden interest. Lord, what had he said? *"Slàinte"* was one of the words that had a distinct pronunciation, depending on where you came from—men from Harris and Lewis said *"Slàn-ya,"* while far north it was more like *"Slànj."* He'd used the form he'd grown up with in Inverness; was it strikingly wrong for where he'd said he came from? He didn't want Fraser to think him a liar.

"What is it ye do for yourself, *a chompanaich*?" Fraser asked, having taken a sip, closing his eyes in momentary respect to the drink, then opening them to regard Roger with a kind curiosity—tinged perhaps with a little wariness, lest his visitor be unhinged. "I'm accustomed to know a man's work at once by his dress and manner—not that ye find many folk truly unusual up here." He smiled a bit at that. "And drovers, tinkers, and gypsies dinna take much effort to descry. Clearly you're none of those."

"I have a bit of land," Roger replied. It was an expected question; he was ready with an answer—but found himself longing to say more. To tell the truth—so far as he himself understood it.

"I've left my wife wi' the running of things whilst I came to search for our lad. Beyond that—" He lifted one shoulder briefly. "I was trained as a minister."

"Oh, aye?" Fraser leaned back, surveying him with interest. "I could see ye're an educated man. I was thinkin' maybe a schoolmaster or a clerk—perhaps a lawyer."

"I've been both schoolmaster and clerk," Roger said, smiling. "Havena quite risen—or fallen, maybe—to the practice of law yet."

"And a good thing, too." Fraser sipped, half-smiling.

Roger shrugged. "Law's a corrupt power but one acceptable to men by reason of having arisen from men—it's a way of getting on wi' things, is the best ye can say for it."

"And not a mean thing to say for it, either," Fraser agreed. "The law's a necessary evil—we canna be doing without it—but do ye not think it a poor substitute for conscience? Speakin' as a minister, I mean?"

"Well . . . aye. I do," Roger said, somewhat surprised. "It would be best for men to deal decently with one another in accordance with—well, with God's principles, if ye'll pardon my putting it that way. But what are ye to do, first, if ye have men to whom God is of no account, and, second, if ye have men—and you do, always—who own no power greater than their own?"

Fraser nodded, interested.

"Aye, well, it's true that the best conscience willna avail a man who willna mind it. But what d'ye do when conscience speaks differently to men of goodwill?"

"As in political disputes, you mean? Supporters of the Stuarts versus those of the . . . the House of Hanover?" It was a reckless thing to say, but it might help him to figure out when he was, and he meant to say nothing that might make it look as though he had a personal stake on either side.

Fraser's face underwent a surprising flow of expression, from being taken aback to mild distaste, this then ending in a look of half-amused ruefulness.

"Like that," he agreed. "I fought for the House of Stuart in my youth, and while I'd not say that conscience didna come into it, it didna come very far onto the field wi' me." His mouth quirked at the corner, and Roger felt again the tiny *plop!* of a stone tossed into his depths, the ripples of recognition spreading through him. Jamie did that. Brianna didn't. Jem did.

He couldn't stop to think about it, though; the conversation was teetering delicately on the precipice of an invitation to political disclosure, and that, he couldn't do.

"Was it Sheriffmuir?" he asked, making no effort to disguise his interest.

"It was," Fraser said, openly surprised. He eyed Roger dubiously. "Ye canna have gone yourself, surely . . . did your faither maybe tell ye?"

"No," said Roger, with the momentary twinge that thought of his father always brought. In fact, Fraser was only a few years older than himself, but he knew the other man doubtless took him for a decade younger than he was.

"I . . . heard a song about it. 'Twas two shepherds met on a hillside, talking about the great fight—and arguing who'd won it."

That made Fraser laugh.

"Well they might! We were arguing that before we finished pickin' up the wounded." He took a sip of whisky and washed it meditatively round his mouth, clearly reminiscing. "So, then, how does the song go?"

Roger breathed deep, ready to sing, and then remembered. Fraser had seen his rope scar and been tactful enough not to remark on it, but no need to make the damage obvious. Instead, he chanted the first few lines, tapping his fingers on the desk, echoing the rhythm of the big bodhran that was the song's only accompaniment.

"O cam ye here the fight to shun,
Or herd the sheep wi' me, man?
Or were ye at the Sherra-moor,
Or did the battle see, man?"
I saw the battle, sair and teugh,
And reekin-red ran mony a sheugh;
My heart, for fear, gaed sough for sough,
To hear the thuds, and see the cluds
O' clans frae woods, in tartan duds,
Wha glaum'd at kingdoms three, man.

It went better than he'd thought; the song really *was* more chanted than sung, and he managed the whole of it with no more than the odd choke or cough. Fraser was rapt, glass forgotten in his hand.

"Oh, that's braw, man!" Fraser exclaimed. "Though yon poet's got the devil of an accent. Where's he come from, d'ye ken?"

"Er . . . Ayrshire, I think."

Fraser shook his head in admiration and sat back.

"Could ye maybe write it down for me?" he asked, almost shyly. "I wouldna put ye to the trouble of singin' it again, but I'd dearly love to learn the whole of it."

"I—sure," Roger said, taken aback. Well, what harm could it do to let Robert Burns's poem loose in the world some years in advance of Burns himself? "Ken anyone who can play a bodhran? It's best wi' the drum rattlin' in the background." He tapped his fingers in illustration.

"Oh, aye." Fraser was rustling about in the drawer of his desk; he came out with several sheets of foolscap, most with writing on them. Frowning, he flicked through the papers, picked one, and pulled it from the sheaf, placing it facedown in front of Roger, offering him the blank back side.

There were goose quills, rather tattered from use but well trimmed, in a jar on the desk, and a brass inkstand, which Fraser offered him with a generous sweep of one broad hand.

"My son's friend plays well—he's gone for a soldier, though, more's the pity." A shadow crossed Fraser's face.

"Ach." Roger clicked his tongue in sympathy; he was trying to make out the writing that showed faintly through the sheet. "Joined a Highland regiment, did he?"

"No," Fraser said, sounding a little startled. *Christ, were there Highland regiments yet?* "He's gone to France as a mercenary soldier. Better pay, fewer floggings than the army, he tells his da."

Roger's heart lifted; yes! It was a letter or maybe a journal entry—whatever it was, there was a date on it: 17 . . . was that a 3? Had to be, couldn't be an 8. 173 . . . it might be a 9 or a 0, couldn't tell for sure through the paper—no, it had to be a 9, so 1739. He breathed a sigh of relief. Something October, 1739.

"Probably safer," he said, only half attending to the conversation as he began to scratch out the lines. It was some time since he'd written with a quill, and he was awkward.

"Safer?"

"Aye," he said, "from the point of view of disease, mostly. Most men that die in the army die of some sickness, ken. Comes from the crowding, having to live in barracks, eat army rations. I'd think mercenaries might have a bit more freedom."

Fraser muttered something about "freedom to starve," but it was half under his breath. He was tapping his own fingers on the desk, trying to catch the rhythm as Roger wrote. He was surprisingly rather good; by the time the song was finished, he was singing it softly in a pleasant low tenor and had the drumming down pretty well.

Roger's mind was divided between the task in front of him and the feel of the letter under his hand. The feel of the paper and the look of the ink reminded him vividly of the wooden box, filled with Jamie's and Claire's letters. He had to stop himself from glancing at the shelf where it would be kept when this room was his.

They'd been rationing the letters, reading them slowly—but when Jem was taken, all bets were off. They'd rushed through the whole of the box, looking for any mention of Jem, any indication that he might have escaped from Cameron and found his way to the safety of his grandparents. Not a word about Jem. Not one.

They'd been so distraught that they'd scarcely noticed anything else the letters said, but occasional phrases and images floated up in his mind, quite randomly—some of them distinctly disturbing—Brianna's uncle Ian had died—but scarcely noticeable at the time.

They weren't anything he wanted to think about now, either.

"Will your son be studying the law, then, in Paris?" Roger asked abruptly. He picked up the fresh dram Brian had poured for him and took a sip.

"Aye, well, he'd maybe make a decent lawyer," Fraser admitted. "He could argue ye into the ground, I'll say that for him. But I think he hasna got the patience for law or politics." He smiled suddenly. "Jamie sees at once what he thinks should be done and canna understand why anyone else should think otherwise. And he'd rather pound someone than persuade them, if it comes to that."

Roger laughed ruefully.

"I understand the urge," he said.

"Oh, indeed." Fraser nodded, leaning back a little in his chair. "And I'll no say as that's not a necessary thing to do on occasion. Especially in the Highlands." He grimaced but not without humor.

"So, then. Why do ye think this Cameron has stolen your lad?" Fraser asked bluntly.

Roger wasn't surprised. As well as they'd been getting on together, he'd known Fraser had to be wondering just how much Roger was telling and how truthful he was. Well, he'd been ready for that question—and the answer was at least a version of the truth.

"We lived for a time in America," he said, and felt a pang with the saying of it. For an instant, their snug cabin on the Ridge was around him, Brianna asleep with her hair loose on the pillow beside him and the children's breath a sweet fog above them.

"America!" Fraser exclaimed in astonishment. "Where, then?"

"The colony of North Carolina. A good place," Roger hastened to add, "but not without its dangers."

"Name me one that is," Fraser said, but waved that aside. "And these dangers made ye come back?"

Roger shook his head, a tightness in his throat at the memory.

"No, it was our wee lass—Mandy, Amanda, she's called. She was born with a thing wrong with her heart, and there was no physician there who could treat it. So we came . . . back, and while we were in Scotland, my wife inherited some land, and so we stayed. But . . ." He hesitated, thinking how to put the rest, but knowing what he did of Fraser's antecedents and his history with the MacKenzies of Leoch, the man probably wouldn't be overly disturbed at his story.

"My wife's father," he said carefully, "is a good man—a very good man—but the sort who . . . draws attention. A leader of men, and one that other men . . . Well, he told me once that his own father had said to him that, since he was a large man, other men would try him—and they do."

He watched Brian Fraser's face carefully at this, but, beyond the twitch of an eyebrow, there was no apparent response.

"I'll not go into all the history of it"—*since it hasn't happened yet*—"but the long and the short of it is that my father-in-law was left in possession of a large sum in gold. He doesna regard it as his own property but as something held in trust. Still, there it is. And while it's been kept secret so far as possible . . ."

Fraser made a sympathetic sound, acknowledging the difficulties of secrecy in such conditions.

"So this Cameron learned of the treasure, did he? And thought to extort it from your father-in-law by taking the bairn captive?" Fraser's dark brow lowered at the thought.

"That may be in his mind. But beyond that—my son kens where the gold is hidden. He was with his grandfather when it was put away safe. Only the two of them ken the whereabouts—but Cameron learned that my son knew the place."

"Ah." Brian sat for a moment staring into his whisky, thinking. Finally he cleared his throat and looked up, meeting Roger's eyes. "I maybe shouldna say such a thing, but it may be in your own mind already. If he's taken the boy only because the lad kens where yon treasure is . . . well, was I a wicked man with no scruples, I think I might force the information out of the lad, so soon as I had him alone."

Roger felt the cold slide of the suggestion down into the pit of his belly. It *was* something that had been at the back of his own mind, though he hadn't admitted it to himself.

"Make him tell—and then kill him, you mean."

Fraser grimaced unhappily.

"I dinna want to think it," he said. "But without the lad, what is there to mark him out? A man alone—he could travel as he liked, without much notice."

"Yes," Roger said, and stopped to breathe. "Yes. Well . . . he didn't. I—I know the man, a little. I don't think he'd do that, mur—" His throat closed suddenly, and he coughed violently. "Murder a child," he finished hoarsely. "He wouldn't."

THEY GAVE HIM a room at the end of the hallway on the second floor. When his family would live here, this would be the children's playroom. He undressed to his shirt, put out the candle, and got into bed, resolutely ignoring the shadows in the corners that held the ghosts of giant cardboard building blocks, of dollhouses, six-guns, and chalkboards. The fringed skirt of Mandy's Annie Oakley costume fluttered at the corner of his eye.

He ached from follicles to toenails, inside and out, but the panic engendered by his arrival had passed. How he felt didn't matter, though; the question was—what now? They hadn't gone where they thought, he and Buck, but he had to assume that they *had* ended up in the right place. The place where Jem was.

How else could they have come here? Perhaps Rob Cameron knew more now about how the traveling worked, could control it, and had deliberately brought Jem to this time, in order to frustrate pursuit?

He was too exhausted to keep hold of his thoughts, let alone string them into coherence. He pushed everything out of his mind, so far as he could, and lay still, staring into the dark, seeing the shine of a rocking horse's eyes.

Then he got out of bed, knelt on the cold boards, and prayed.

32

"FOR MANY MEN WHO STUMBLE AT THE THRESHOLD ARE WELL FORETOLD THAT DANGER LURKS WITHIN"

Lallybroch
October 31, 1980

BRIANNA COULDN'T open her own front door. She kept trying, rattling the big iron key all over the escutcheon plate, until the WPC took it from her shaking hand and got it into the keyhole. She hadn't started to shake until the police car turned up the lane to Lallybroch.

"Rather an old lock," the police constable observed, giving

it a dubious look. "Original to the house, is it?" She lifted her head, peering up the white-harled front of the house, pursing her lips at sight of the lintel, with its carved date.

"I don't know. We don't usually lock the door. We've never had burglars." Brianna's lips felt numb, but she thought she'd managed a weak smile. Luckily, Mandy was unable to contradict this bald-faced lie, as she'd seen a toad in the grass by the path and was following it, poking at it with the toe of her shoe to make it hop. Jemmy, glued protectively to Brianna's side, made a low noise in his throat that reminded her startlingly of her father, and she looked down at him, narrowing her eyes.

He made the noise again and looked away.

There was a rattle and click as the lock opened, and the constable straightened up with a pleased sound.

"Aye, that's done it. Now, you're quite sure as you'll be all right, will you, Mrs. MacKenzie?" the woman said, giving her a dubious look. "Out here by yourself, and your man away?"

"He'll be home soon," Brianna assured her, though her stomach went hollow at the words.

The woman eyed her consideringly, then gave a reluctant nod and pushed open the door.

"Well, then, you know best, I expect. I'll just check to see that your phone's in order and all the doors and windows locked, shall I, while you have a look round to be sure everything's as it should be?"

The lump of ice that had formed in her middle during the long hours of questioning shot straight up into her chest.

"I—I—I'm sure everything's fine." But the constable had already gone inside and was waiting impatiently for her. "Jem! Bring Mandy inside and take her up to the playroom, will you?" She couldn't bear to leave the kids outside by themselves, exposed. She could scarcely bear to have them out of her sight. But the *very* last thing she needed was to have Mandy tagging helpfully along, chatting to Constable Laughlin about Mr. Rob in the priest's hole. Leaving the door open, she hurried after the WPC.

"The phone's in there," she said, catching up with Constable Laughlin in the hall and gesturing toward Roger's study. "There's an extension in the kitchen. I'll go and check that and see to the back door." Not waiting for an answer, she strode down the hall and nearly threw herself through the swinging door that led to the kitchen.

She didn't pause to check anything but jerked open the junk drawer and snatched up a big rubber-covered flashlight. Meant to assist farmers lambing at night or searching for lost stock, the thing was a foot long and weighed nearly two pounds.

The .22 rifle was in the mudroom, and for an instant, as she walked through the house, she debated killing him, in a dispassionate way that would probably scare her if she had time to think about it. She had Jem back, after all—but no. Constable Laughlin would certainly recognize the sound of a shot, in spite of the muffling green baize on the kitchen door. And there was apparently more she needed to learn from Rob Cameron. She'd knock him unconscious and tape his mouth.

She stepped into the mudroom and quietly closed the kitchen door behind her. There was a deadbolt, but she couldn't lock it from this side without the key, and her keys were on the table in the foyer, where Constable Laughlin had left them. Instead, she dragged the heavy bench over and jammed it catty-corner between the door and the wall, concentrating on the logistics. Where was the best place to hit someone on the head so as to render them unconscious without fracturing their skull? She had a vague memory of her mother mentioning that once . . . the occiput?

She'd expected an outcry from Cameron at the sound of her entry, but he didn't peep. She could hear footsteps above, the confident stride of an adult going down the hall. Constable Laughlin on her tour of inspection, no doubt checking the first-floor windows, ladder-bearing burglars in mind. She closed her eyes for an instant, envisioning the constable sticking her head into the playroom just as Mandy was regaling her brother with the details of her own adventures the night before.

Nothing to be done about that. She took a deep breath, lifted the grate over the priest's hole, and shone the light down into the shadows. The empty shadows.

For a few moments she went on looking, swinging the torch beam from one side of the priest's hole to the other, then back, then back again . . . her mind simply refusing to believe her eyes.

The light caught the dull gleam of duct tape—two or three discarded wads, flung into a corner. There was a cold feeling at the back of her neck, and she jerked round, flashlight raised—but it was no more than apprehension; no one was there. The outer door was locked, the mudroom windows secure.

The door was locked. She made a small, frightened sound and clapped her hand hard over her mouth. Like the door between mudroom and kitchen, the mudroom's outer door locked with a deadbolt—from the inside. If someone had gone out that way and left the door locked behind him—he had a key to the house. And her rifle was gone.

THEY'RE TOO LITTLE, she kept thinking. *They shouldn't know about things like this; they shouldn't know it's possible.* Her hands were shaking; it took three tries to open the sticky drawer in Mandy's dresser, and after the third failure, she pounded it in fury with the side of her fist, whispering through gritted teeth, "You goddamned fucking bloody buggering *thing*! Don't you *dare* get in my way!" She crashed her fist on top of the dresser, raised her foot, and smashed the sole of her sneaker into the thing so hard that it rocked back and thumped into the wall with a bang.

She grabbed the drawer pulls and yanked. The terrorized drawer shot out, and she snatched the whole thing free and flung it into the opposite wall, where it struck and exploded in a rainbow spray of underpants and tiny striped T-shirts.

She walked over and looked down at the battered drawer, lying upside down on the floor.

"So there," she said calmly. "Teach *you* to get in my way when I have things to think about."

"Like what, Mam?" said a cautious voice from the doorway. She looked up to see Jemmy hovering there, eyes flicking from her to the mistreated drawer and back.

"Oh." She thought of trying to explain the drawer but instead cleared her throat and sat down on the bed, holding out a hand to him. "Come here, *a bhalaich*."

His ginger brows flicked up at the Gaelic endearment, but he came willingly, cuddling into her arm. He hugged her hard, burying his head in her shoulder, and she held him as tightly as she could, rocking back and forth and making the sorts of soft noises she'd made to him when he was tiny.

"It'll be all right, baby," she whispered to him. "It will."

She heard him swallow and felt his small, square back move under her hand.

"Yeah." His voice quivered a little and he sniffed hard, then tried again. "Yeah. But *what's* going to be all right, Mam? What's going on?" He drew away a little then, looking up at her with eyes that held more questions and more knowledge than any nine-year-old should reasonably have.

"Mandy says you put Mr. Cameron in the priest's hole. But he's not there now—I looked."

A cold hand stroked her nape as she remembered the shock of the empty hole.

"No, he's not."

"But you didn't let him out, did you?"

"No. I didn't let him out. He—"

"So somebody else did," he said positively. "Who, do you think?"

"You have a very logical mind," she said, smiling a little, despite herself. "You get it from your Grandda Jamie."

"He said I got it from Grannie Claire," Jem replied, but automatically; he wasn't to be distracted. "I thought maybe it was the man who chased me at the dam—but he couldn't have been here letting Mr. Cameron out at the same time he was chasing me. Could he?" A sudden fear showed in his eyes, and she choked back the overwhelming urge to hunt the man down and kill him like a rabid skunk.

The man had got away at the dam, running off into the dark when the police showed up, but, God help her, she was going to find him one day, and then—but this was not the day. The problem now was to stop him—or Rob Cameron—from getting anywhere near her kids again.

Then she got what Jemmy was saying and felt the chill she'd carried in her heart spread like hoarfrost through her body.

"You mean there has to be another man," she said, surprised at how calm she sounded. "Mr. Cameron, the man at the dam—and whoever let Mr. Cameron out of the priest's hole."

"It could be a lady," Jemmy pointed out. He seemed less scared, talking about it. That was a good thing, because her own skin was rippling with fear.

"Do you know what Grannie called—calls—goose bumps?"

She held out her arm, the fine reddish hairs all standing on end. "Horripilation."

"Horripilation," Jemmy repeated, and gave a small, nervous giggle. "I like that word."

"Me, too." She took a deep breath and stood up. "Go pick out a change of clothes and your PJs, would you, sweetheart? I have to make a couple of phone calls, and then I think we're going to go visit Auntie Fiona."

33

IT'S BEST TO SLEEP IN A HALE SKIN

ROGER WOKE SUDDENLY, but without shock. No sense of abandoned dreams, no half-heard noise, but his eyes were open and he was fully aware. It was perhaps an hour before sunrise. He'd left the shutters open; the room was cold and the clouded sky the color of a black pearl.

He lay motionless, listening to his heart beat, and realized that for the first time in several days it wasn't pounding. He wasn't afraid. The fear and turmoil of the night, the terror of the last few days, had vanished. His body was completely relaxed; so was his mind.

There *was* something floating in his mind. Absurdly, it was a line from "Johnny Cope": *"It's best to sleep in a hale skin; for 'twill be a bluidy morning."* Weirder still, he could hear—could almost feel—himself singing it, in his old voice, full of power and enthusiasm.

"Not that I'm ungrateful," he said to the whitewashed ceiling beams, his morning voice cracked and rough. "But what the hell?"

He wasn't sure whether he was talking to God or to his own unconscious, but the likelihood of getting a straight answer was probably the same in either case. He heard the soft thud of a closing door somewhere below and someone outside whistling through his or her teeth—Annie or Senga, maybe, on the way to the morning milking.

A knock came on his own door: Jenny Murray, tidy in a white pinny, dark curly hair tied back but not yet capped for the day, with a jug of hot water, a pot of soft soap, and a razor for shaving.

"Da says can ye ride a horse?" she said without preamble, looking him up and down in an assessing sort of way.

"I can," he replied gruffly, taking the towel-wrapped jug from her. He needed badly to clear the phlegm from his throat and spit but couldn't bring himself to do that in front of her. Consequently, he just nodded and muttered, *"Taing,"* as he took the razor, instead of asking why.

"Breakfast'll be in the kitchen when you are," she said matter-of-factly. "Bring the jug down, aye?"

AN HOUR LATER, filled to bursting with hot tea, parritch, bannocks with honey, and black pudding, he found himself on an autumn-shaggy horse, following Brian Fraser through the rising mist of early morning.

"We'll go round to the crofts nearby," Fraser had told him over breakfast, spooning strawberry preserves onto a bannock. "Even if no one's seen your lad—and to be honest," his wide mouth twisted in apology, "I think I should ha' heard already if anyone had seen a stranger in the district—they'll pass on the word."

"Aye, thanks very much," he'd said, meaning it. Even in his own time, gossip was the fastest way of spreading news in the Highlands. No matter how fast Rob Cameron might travel, Roger doubted he could outpace the speed of talk, and the thought made him smile. Jenny caught it and smiled back sympathetically, and he thought again what a very pretty lass she was.

The sky was still low and threatening, but impending rain had never yet deterred anyone in Scotland from doing anything and wasn't likely to start now. His throat felt much better for the hot tea, and the odd sense of calm with which he'd waked was still with him.

Something had changed in the night. Maybe it was sleeping

in Lallybroch, among the ghosts of his own future. Perhaps that had settled his mind while he slept.

Maybe it was answered prayer and a moment of grace. Maybe it was no more than Samuel Beckett's bloody existential *I can't go on; I'll go on.* If he had a choice—and he did, Beckett be damned—he'd go with grace.

Whatever had caused it, he wasn't disoriented any longer, thrown off-balance by what he knew about the futures of the people around him. There was still a deep concern about them—and the need to find Jem still filled him. But now it was a quiet, hard thing in his core. A focus, a weapon. Something to brace his back against.

He straightened his shoulders as he thought this and, at the same time, saw Brian's straight, flat back and the broad, firm shoulders under the dark sett of his tartan coat. They were the echo of Jamie's—and the promise of Jem's.

Life goes on. It was his job above all to rescue Jem, as much for Brian Fraser's sake as for his own.

And now he knew what had changed in him and gave thanks to God for what was indeed grace. He'd slept—and waked—in a whole skin. And however bloody the mornings to come, he had direction now, calmness and hope, because the good man who rode before him was on his side.

THEY VISITED MORE than a dozen crofts in the course of the day and stopped a tinker they met along the way, as well. No one had seen a stranger recently, with or without a red-haired lad, but all promised to spread the word and all without exception offered their prayers for Roger and his quest.

They stopped for supper and the night with a family named Murray that had a substantial farmhouse, though nothing to rival Lallybroch. The owner, John Murray, turned out in the course of conversation to be Brian Fraser's factor—the overseer of much of the physical business of Lallybroch's estate—and he lent his grave attention to Roger's story.

An elderly, long-faced man with rawboned, muscular arms, he sucked his teeth consideringly, nodding his head.

"Aye, I'll send one of my lads down in the morn," he said. "But if ye've found nay trace o' this fellow up along the Hieland passes . . . might be as ye should go down to the garrison and tell your tale, Mr. MacKenzie."

Brian Fraser cocked a dark brow, half-frowning at this, but then nodded.

"Aye, that's no a bad thought, John." He turned to Roger. "It's some distance, ken—the garrison's in Fort William, down by Duncansburgh. But we can ask along our way, and the soldiers send messengers regularly betwixt the garrison, Inverness, and Edinburgh. Should they hear a thing about your man, they could get word to us swiftly."

"And they could maybe arrest the fellow on the spot," Murray added, his rather melancholy countenance brightening a bit at the idea.

"Moran taing," Roger said, bowing a little to them both in acknowledgment, then turning to Fraser. "I'll do that, and thanks. But, sir—ye needna go with me. You've business of your own to tend to, and I wouldna—"

"I'll come, and glad to," Fraser interrupted him firmly. "The hay's long since in and naught to do that John canna take care of for me."

He smiled at Murray, who made a small noise, halfway between a sigh and a cough, but nodded.

"Fort William's in the midst of the Camerons' land, forbye," Murray observed absently, gazing off toward the dark fields. They had dined with his family but then come out to the dooryard, ostensibly to share a pipe; it smoldered in Murray's hand, disregarded for the moment.

Brian made a noncommittal sound in his throat, and Roger wondered just what Murray meant. Was it a warning that Rob Cameron might have relatives or allies to whom he was heading? Or was there some tension or difficulty between some of the Camerons and the Frasers of Lovat—or between the Camerons and the MacKenzies?

That presented some difficulty. If there *was* a feud of any importance going on, Roger ought already to know about it. He gave a small, grave "hmp" himself and resolved to approach any Camerons with caution. At the same time . . . *was* Rob Cameron intending to seek refuge or help with the Camerons of this time? Had he maybe come to the past before and had a hiding place prepared among his own clan? That was an evil thought, and Roger felt his stomach tighten as though to resist a punch.

But no; there hadn't been time. If Cameron had only learned about time travel from the guide Roger had written for his children's eventual use, he wouldn't have had time to go to the past, find ancient Camerons, and . . . no, ridiculous.

Roger shook off the tangle of half-formed thoughts as though they were a fishing net thrown over his head. There was nothing more to be done until they reached the garrison tomorrow.

Murray and Fraser were leaning on the fence now, sharing the pipe and chatting casually in Gaelic.

"My daughter bids me ask after your son," Brian Fraser said, with an air of casualness. "Any word?"

Murray snorted, smoke purling from his nostrils, and said something very idiomatic about his son. Fraser grimaced in sympathy and shook his head.

"At least ye ken he's alive," he said, dropping back into English. "Like enough, he'll come home when he's had his fill of fighting. We did, aye?" He nudged Murray gently in the ribs, and the taller man snorted again, but with less ferocity.

"It wasna boredom that led us here, *a dhuine dhubh.* Not you, anyway." He raised one shaggy graying brow, and Fraser laughed, though Roger thought there was a regretful edge in it.

He remembered the story very well: Brian Fraser, a bastard of old Lord Lovat's, had stolen Ellen MacKenzie from her brothers Colum and Dougal, the MacKenzies of Castle Leoch, and had ended up at last with her at Lallybroch, the pair of them more or less disowned by both clans but at least left alone by them. He'd seen the portrait of Ellen, too—tall, red-haired, and undeniably a woman worth the effort.

She'd looked very much like her granddaughter Brianna. By reflex, he closed his eyes, breathed deep of the cold Highland evening, and thought he felt her there at his side. If he opened them again, might he see her standing in the smoke?

I'll come back, he thought to her. *No matter what,* a nighean ruaidh—*I'm coming back. With Jem.*

34

SANCTUARY

IT WAS NEARLY AN hour's drive over the narrow, twisting Highland roads from Lallybroch to Fiona Buchan's new house in Inverness. Plenty of time for Brianna to wonder if she was doing the right thing, if she had any right to involve Fiona and her family in a matter that looked more dangerous by the moment. Plenty of time to get a stiff neck from looking over her shoulder—though if she was being followed, how would she know?

She'd had to tell the kids where Roger was, as gently and briefly as possible. Mandy had put a thumb in her mouth and stared gravely at her, round-eyed. Jem . . . Jem hadn't said anything but had gone white under his freckles and looked as though he was about to throw up. She glanced in the rearview mirror. He was hunched in a corner of the backseat now, face turned to the window.

"He'll come back, honey," she'd said, trying to hug him in reassurance. He'd let her but stood stiff in her arms, stricken.

"It's my fault," he'd said, his voice small and wooden as a puppet's. "I should have got away sooner. Then Dad wouldn't—"

"It's *not* your fault," she'd said firmly. "It's Mr. Cameron's fault and no one else's. You were *very* brave. And Daddy will come back really soon."

Jem had swallowed hard but said nothing in reply. When she'd let him go, he swayed for a moment, and Mandy had come up and hugged his legs.

"Daddy'll come back," she said encouragingly. "For supper!"

"It might take a little bit longer than that," Bree said, smiling in spite of the panic packed like a snowball under her ribs.

She drew a deep breath of relief as the highway opened out

near the airport and she could go faster than 30 mph. Another wary glance in the mirror, but the road was empty behind her. She stepped on the gas.

Fiona was one of the only two people who knew. The other one was in Boston: her mother's oldest friend, Joe Abernathy. But she needed sanctuary for Jem and Mandy, right now. She couldn't stay with them at Lallybroch; the walls were two feet thick in places, yes, but it was a farm manor, not a fortified tower house, and hadn't been built with any notion that the inhabitants might need to repel invaders or stand off a siege.

Being in the city gave her a sense of relief. Having people around. Witnesses. Camouflage. Help. She pulled up in the street outside the Craigh na Dun Bed-and-Breakfast (three AA stars) with the sense of an exhausted swimmer crawling up onto shore.

The timing was good. It was early afternoon; Fiona would have finished the cleaning and it wouldn't yet be time to check in new guests or start the supper.

A little painted bell in the shape of a bluebell tinkled when they opened the door, and one of Fiona's daughters instantly popped an inquiring head out of the lounge.

"Auntie Bree!" she shouted, and at once the lobby was filled with children, as Fiona's three girls pushed one another out of the way to hug Bree, pick up Mandy, and tickle Jem, who promptly dropped to all fours and crawled under the bench where folk left their wraps.

"What—oh, it's you, hen!" Fiona, coming out of the kitchen in a workmanlike canvas apron that said PIE QUEEN on the front, smiled with delight at sight of Bree and enveloped her in a floury hug.

"What's wrong?" Fiona murmured in her ear, under cover of the embrace. She drew back a bit, still holding Bree, and looked up at her, squinting in half-playful worry. "Rog playing away from home, is he?"

"You . . . could say that." Bree managed a smile but evidently not a very good one, because Fiona at once clapped her hands, bringing order out of the chaos in the lobby, and dispatched all the children to the upstairs lounge to watch telly. Jem, looking hunted, was coaxed out from under the bench and reluctantly followed the girls, looking back over his shoulder at his mother. She smiled and made shooing motions at him, then followed Fiona into the kitchen, glancing by reflex over her own shoulder.

THE TEAKETTLE SCREAMED, interrupting Brianna, but not before she'd got to the most salient point of her story. Fiona warmed and filled the pot, purse-lipped with concentration.

"Ye say he took the rifle. Ye've still got your shotgun?"

"Yes. It's under the front seat of my car at the moment."

Fiona nearly dropped the pot. Brianna shot out an arm and grabbed the handle, steadying it. Her hands were freezing, and the warm china felt wonderful.

"Well, I wasn't going to leave it in a house the bastards have a key to, now, was I?"

Fiona set down the pot and crossed herself. *"Dia eadarainn 's an t-olc." God between us and evil.* She sat, giving Brianna a sharp look. "And ye're quite sure as it's bastards, plural?"

"Yes, I bloody am," Bree said tersely. "Even if Rob Cameron managed to grow wings and fly out of my priest's hole—let me tell you what happened to Jem at the dam."

She did, in a few brief sentences, by the end of which Fiona was glancing over her own shoulder at the closed kitchen door. She looked back at Bree, settling herself. In her early thirties, she was a pleasantly rounded young woman with a lovely face and the calm expression of a mother who normally has the Indian sign on her offspring, but at the moment she had a look that Brianna's own mother would have described as "blood in her eye." She said something very bad in English regarding the man who'd chased Jem.

"So, then," she said, picking up a paring knife from the nearby drainboard and examining the edge critically, "what shall we do?"

Bree drew a breath and sipped cautiously at the hot, milky tea. It was sweet, silky, and very comforting—but not nearly as comforting as that "we."

"Well, first—would you let Jem and Mandy stay here while I go do a few things? It might be overnight; I brought their pajamas, just in case." She nodded at the paper sack that she'd set down on one of the chairs.

"Aye, of course." A small frown formed between Fiona's dark brows. "What . . . *sorts* of things?"

"It's—" Brianna began, intending to say, *"better if you don't know,"* but in fact someone *had* better know where she was going and what she was doing. Just in case she didn't come back. A little bubble of what might be either fear or anger rose up through the sense of warmth in her middle.

"I'm going to visit Jock MacLeod in hospital. He's the night watchman who found Jem at the dam. He might know the man who hit him and tried to take Jem. And he *does* know Rob Cameron. He can maybe tell me who Cameron's mates are outside of work or in lodge."

She rubbed a hand down over her face, thinking.

"After that . . . I'll talk to Rob's sister and his nephew. If she's not involved in whatever he's up to, she'll be worried. And if she *is* involved—then I need to know that."

"D'ye think ye'll be able to tell?" Fiona's frown had eased a bit, but she still looked worried.

"Oh, yes," Brianna said, with grim determination. "I'll be able to tell. For one thing, if someone I talk to *is* involved, they're probably likely to try to stop me asking questions."

Fiona made a small noise that could best be spelled as *"eeengh,"* indicating deep concern.

Brianna drank the last of her tea and set down the cup with an explosive sigh.

"And then," she said, "I'm going back to Lallybroch to meet a locksmith and have him change all the locks and install burglar alarms on the lower windows." She looked questioningly at Fiona. "I don't know how long it might take. . . ."

"Aye, that's why ye brought the kids' nighties. Nay problem, hen." She chewed her lower lip, eyeing Brianna.

Bree knew what she was thinking, debating whether to ask or not, and saved her the trouble.

"I don't know what I'm going to do about Roger," she said steadily.

"He'll come back, surely," Fiona began, but Bree shook her head. Horrifying Realization Number 3 couldn't be denied any longer.

"I don't think so," she said, though she bit her lip as if to keep the words from escaping. "He—he can't know that Jem isn't there. And he'd never ab-abandon him."

Fiona was clasping Brianna's hand in both of her own.

"No, no, of course he wouldna do that. But if he and the other fellow go on searching and find no trace . . . eventually, surely he'd think . . ." Her voice died away as she tried to imagine *what* Roger might think under those circumstances.

"Oh, he'll be thinking, all right," Bree said, and managed a small, shaky laugh. The thought of Roger's determination, the growing sense of fear and desperation that must inevitably eat away at it, his fight to keep going—because he would; he'd never give up and come back to tell her Jem was lost for good. For if he didn't find any trace of Jem, what could he think? That Cameron had maybe killed Jem, hidden his body, and gone to America in search of the gold? Or that they had both been lost in that horrifying space between one time and another, never to be found?

"Well, and he'll be praying, too," Fiona said with a brisk squeeze of Bree's hand. "I can help wi' that."

That made tears well, and she blinked hard, scrubbing at her eyes with a paper napkin.

"I can't cry now," she said, in a choked voice. "I *can't.* I haven't got time." She stood up suddenly, pulling her hand free. She sniffed, blew her nose hard on the napkin, and sniffed again.

"Fiona . . . I—I know you haven't told anybody about . . . us," she began, and even she could hear the doubt in her own voice.

Fiona snorted.

"I have not," she said. "I'd be taken off to the booby hatch, and what would Ernie do wi' the girls and all? Why?" she added, giving Brianna a hard look. "What are ye thinking?"

"Well . . . the women who—who dance at Craigh na Dun. Do you think any of them know what it is?"

Fiona sucked in one cheek, thinking.

"One or two o' the older ones might have an idea," she said slowly. "We've been callin' down the sun on Beltane there for as far back as anyone knows. And some things do get passed down, ken. Be strange if nobody ever wondered. But even if someone kent for sure what happens there, they'd not speak—no more than I would."

"Right. I just wondered—could you maybe find out, quietly, if any of the women have ties to Rob Cameron? Or maybe . . . to the Orkneys?"

"To what?" Fiona's eyes went round. "Why the Orkneys?"

"Because Rob Cameron went on archaeological digs there. And I think that's what made him interested in stone circles to start with. I know one man named Callahan, a friend of Roger's—who worked up there with him, and I'll talk to him, too—maybe tomorrow; I don't think I'll have time today. But if there's anyone else who might be connected with things like that . . ." It was more than a long shot, but at the moment she was inclined to look under any stone she could lift.

"I'll call round," Fiona said thoughtfully. "And speak of calling—telephone me if ye're not coming back tonight, aye? Just so as I know ye're safe."

Bree nodded, her throat tight, and hugged Fiona, taking one more moment's strength from her friend.

Fiona saw her down the hall to the front door, pausing at the foot of the stair, and glanced toward the chatter coming from above. Did Bree want to say goodbye to Jem and Mandy? Wordless, Brianna shook her head. Her feelings were too raw; she couldn't hide them sufficiently and didn't want to scare the kids. Instead, she pressed her fingers to her lips and blew a kiss up the stairs, then turned to the door.

"That shotgun—" Fiona began behind her, and stopped. Brianna turned and raised an eyebrow.

"They canna get ballistics off buckshot, can they?"

35

AN GEARASDAN

THEY REACHED Fort William in early afternoon of the second day's travel.

"How large is the garrison?" Roger asked, eyeing the stone walls of the fort. It was modest, as forts went, with only a few buildings and a drill yard within the surrounding walls.

"Maybe forty men, I'd say," Brian replied, turning sideways to allow a pair of red-coated guards carrying muskets to pass him in the narrow entry passage. "Fort Augustus is the only garrison north of it, and that's got maybe a hundred."

That was surprising—or maybe not. If Roger was right about the date, it would be another three years before there was much talk of Jacobites in the Highlands—let alone enough of it to alarm the English crown into sending troops en masse to keep a lid on the situation.

The fort was open, and any number of civilians appeared to have business with the army, judging from the small crowd near one building. Fraser steered him toward another, smaller one with a tilt of his head, though.

"We'll see the commander, I think."

"You know him?" A worm of curiosity tickled his spine. Surely it was too early for—

"I've met him the once. Buncombe, he's called. Seems a decent fellow, for a Sassenach." Fraser gave his name to a clerk in the outer room, and within a moment they were ushered into the commander's office.

"Oh . . ." A small, middle-aged man in uniform with tired eyes behind a pair of half spectacles half-rose, half-bowed, and dropped back into his seat as though the effort of recognition had exhausted him. "Broch Tuarach. Your servant, sir."

Perhaps it had, Roger thought. The man's face was gaunt and lined, and his breath whistled audibly in his lungs. Claire might have known specifically what was up with Captain Buncombe, but it didn't take a doctor to know that something was physically amiss.

Still, Buncombe listened civilly to his story, called in the clerk to make a careful note of Cameron's description and Jem's, and promised that these would be circulated to the garrison and that any patrols or messengers would be advised to ask after the fugitives.

Brian had thoughtfully brought along a couple of bottles in his saddlebags and now produced one, which he set on the desk with a gurgling thump of enticement.

"We thank ye, sir, for your help. If ye'd allow us to present a small token of appreciation for your kindness . . ."

A small but genuine smile appeared on Captain Buncombe's worn face.

"I would, sir. But only if you gentlemen will join me . . . ? Ah, yes." Two worn pewter cups and—after a brief search—a crystal goblet with a chip out of the rim were produced, and the blessed silence of the dram fell upon the tiny office.

After a few moments' reverence, Buncombe opened his eyes and sighed.

"Amazing, sir. Your own manufacture, is it?"

Brian inclined his head with a modest shake.

"Nay but a few bottles at Hogmanay, just for the family."

Roger had himself seen the root cellar from which Brian had chosen the bottle, lined from floor to ceiling with small casks and with an atmosphere to it that would have knocked a moose flat had he stayed to breathe it long. But an instant's thought told him that it was probably wiser not to let a garrison full of soldiers know that you kept any sort of liquor in large quantities on your premises, no matter what terms you were on with their commander. He caught Brian's eye, and Fraser looked aside with a small "mmphm" and a tranquil smile.

"Amazing," Buncombe repeated, and tipped another inch into his glass, offering the bottle round. Roger followed Brian's lead and refused, nursing his own drink while the other two men fell into a sort of conversation he recognized very well. Not friendly but courteous, a trade of information that might be of advantage to one or both—and a careful avoidance of anything that might give the other too *much* advantage.

He'd seen Jamie do it any number of times, in America. It was headman's talk, and there were rules to it. Of course . . . Jamie must have seen his da do it any number of times himself; it was bred in his bones.

He thought Jem maybe had it. He had *something* that made people look at him twice—something beyond the hair, he amended, and smiled to himself.

While Buncombe occasionally directed a question to him, Roger was for the most part able to leave them to it, and he gradually relaxed. The rain had passed, and a beam of sun from the window rested on his shoulders, warming him from without as the whisky warmed him within. He felt for the first time that he might be accomplishing something in his search, rather than merely flailing desperately round the Highlands.

"And they could maybe arrest the fellow," John Murray had remarked, anent the soldiers and Rob Cameron. A comforting thought, that.

The clan angle, though . . . he didn't *think* Cameron could have accomplices here, but—he straightened in his chair. *He* had an accomplice from this time, didn't he? Buck had the gene, and while it was clearly less frequent to travel forward from one's original lifeline—well, Roger *thought* it was less frequent (his own lack of knowledge was an unnerving realization in itself)—Buck had done it. If Cameron was a traveler, he'd got the gene from an ancestor who could also have done it.

Chill was running through his veins like iced wine, killing the whisky's warmth, and a sinister tangle of cold worms came writhing into his mind. Could it be a conspiracy, maybe, between Buck and Rob Cameron? Or Buck and some ancient Cameron from his own time?

He'd never thought Buck was telling the whole truth about himself or his own journey through the stones. Could all this have been a plot to lure Roger away from Lallybroch—away from Bree?

Now the worms were bloody *eating* his brain. He picked up his cup and threw back the rest of the whisky at a gulp to kill them. Buncombe and Fraser both glanced at him in surprise but then courteously resumed their conversation.

In the cold light of his present state of mind, something else now cast new shadows. Brian Fraser. While Roger had taken Fraser's bringing him to the garrison as purely a helpful gesture toward finding Jem, it had another function, didn't it? It displayed Roger to Captain Buncombe, in a context that made it clear that he had no claim of clan obligation or personal friendship on Fraser, just in case Roger turned out not to be what he said he was. And it allowed Fraser to see whether Buncombe recognized Roger or not. Just in case he wasn't what he said he was.

He took a deep breath and pressed his hands on the desktop, concentrating on the feel of the wood grain under his fingers. All right. Perfectly reasonable. How many times had he seen Jamie do the same sort of thing? For these men, the welfare of their own people always came first; they'd protect Lallybroch, or Fraser's Ridge, above all, but that didn't mean they were unwilling to help when help was in their power to give.

And he did believe that Fraser meant to help him. He clung to the thought and found that it floated.

Fraser glanced at him again, and something in the man's face eased at whatever it saw in his own. Brian picked up the bottle and poured another inch into Roger's glass.

"We'll find him, man," he said softly, in Gaelic, before turning to serve Captain Buncombe in turn.

He drank and put everything out of his mind, concentrating on the trivia of the conversation. It was all right. Everything was going to be all right.

He was still repeating this mantra to himself when he heard shouts and whistles from outside. He glanced toward the window, but it showed nothing save a view of the fort's wall. Captain Buncombe looked startled—but Brian Fraser was on his feet, and moving fast.

Roger followed, emerging into the fort's drill yard to see a fine-looking young woman mounted on a large, fine-looking horse and glaring down at a small cluster of soldiers who had gathered round her stirrup, pushing one another, snatching at the reins, and shouting remarks up at her. The horse plainly didn't like it, but she was managing to keep it under control. She was also holding a switch in one hand and, from the look on her face, was plainly choosing a target amongst those presenting themselves.

"Jenny!" Brian roared, and she looked up, startled. The soldiers were startled, too; they turned and, seeing Captain Buncombe come out behind the Scot, instantly melted away, heads down as they hurried off about their business.

Roger was at Brian's shoulder when he grabbed the horse's bridle.

"What in the name of the Blessed Mother are you—" Brian began, furious, but she interrupted him, looking straight at Roger.

"Your kinsman," she said. "William Buccleigh. He sent word to Lallybroch that he's taken bad and will ye come at once. They said he may not live."

IT TOOK A good day and a half to make the journey, even in good weather. Given that it was raining, that the journey back was uphill, and that the latter portion of it involved stumbling around in the dark, hunting for a nearly invisible trail, they covered the distance in a surprisingly short time.

"I'll come in with ye," Brian had said, swinging off his horse in the dooryard. "They're no my tenants, but they know me."

The household—it was a modest crofter's cottage, dull white as a pebble in the light of a gibbous moon—was closed up tight for the night, shutters drawn and the door bolted. Fraser thumped on the door and shouted in Gaelic, though, identifying himself and saying that he'd brought the sick man's kinsman to him, and presently the door swung open, framing a squat, bearded gentleman in shirt and nightcap, who peered at them for a long moment before stepping back with a gruff "Come ben."

Roger's first impression was that the house was crammed to the rafters with odorous humanity. These lay in small snuggled heaps on the floor near the hearth or on pallets by the far wall, and here and there tousled heads poked up like prairie dogs, blinking in the glow of the smoored fire to see what was to do.

Their host—introduced by Fraser as Angus MacLaren—nodded curtly to Roger and gestured toward a bedstead drawn into the center of the room. Two or three small children were sleeping on it, but Roger could just make out the blur of Buck's face on the pillow. Christ, he hoped Buck didn't have anything contagious.

He leaned in close, whispering, "Buck?" so as not to wake anyone who hadn't waked already. He couldn't make out much of Buck's face in the gloom—and it was covered with beard stubble, as well—but his eyes were closed, and he didn't open them in response to Roger's saying his name. Nor in response to Roger's laying a hand on his arm. The arm did feel warm, but given the suffocating atmosphere in the cottage, he thought it likely Buck would feel warm even if he'd been dead for hours.

He squeezed the arm, lightly at first, then harder—and at last Buck gave a strangled cough and opened his eyes. He blinked slowly, not seeming to recognize Roger, then closed them again. His chest heaved visibly, though, and he breathed now with a slow, clearly audible gasping note.

"He says as there's something the matter wi' his heart," MacLaren told Roger, low-voiced. He was leaning over Roger's shoulder, watching Buck intently. "It flutters, like, and when it does, he goes blue and canna breathe or stand up. My second-eldest lad found him out in the heather yesterday afternoon, flat as a squashed toad. We fetched him down and gave him a bit to drink, and he asked would we send someone to Lallybroch to ask after his kinsman."

"Moran taing," said Roger. "I'm that obliged to ye, sir." He turned to Brian, who was lurking behind MacLaren, looking at Buck with a small frown.

"And thank ye, too, sir," Roger said to him. "For all your help. I can't thank ye enough."

Fraser shrugged, dismissing this.

"I imagine ye'll stay with him? Aye. If he's able to travel in the morn, bring him along to Lallybroch. Or send, if there's aught we can do." Fraser nodded to MacLaren in farewell but then paused, squinting through the murk at Buck's face. He glanced at Roger, as though comparing their features.

"Is your kinsman from Lochalsh, as well?" he asked, curious, and looked back at Buck. "He's the look of my late wife's people about him. The MacKenzies of Leoch." Then he noticed the small squat shape of what must be Mrs. MacLaren—glowering under her cap—and he coughed, bowed, and took his leave without waiting for an answer.

Mr. MacLaren went to bolt the door, and the lady of the house turned to Roger, yawned cavernously, then motioned toward the bed, scratching her bottom unself-consciously.

"Ye can sleep wi' him," she said. "Push him oot the bed if he dies, aye? I dinna want ma quilts all spoilt."

HAVING TAKEN OFF his boots, Roger lay down gingerly on the quilt beside Buck—readjusting the position of the small children, who were limp and flexible as cats in sunshine—and spent the remainder of the night listening to his ancestor's irregular snoring, poking him whenever it seemed to stop. Toward dawn, though, he dozed off, to be waked sometime later by the thick warm smell of porridge.

Alarmed by the fact that he'd fallen asleep, he raised up on one elbow to find Buck pale-faced and breathing stertorously through his mouth. He seized his ancestor by the shoulder and shook him, causing Buck to start up in bed, glaring wildly round. Spotting Roger, he punched him solidly in the stomach.

"Bugger off wi' that!"

"I just wanted to be sure you were alive, you bastard!"

"What are ye doing here in the first place?" Buck rubbed a hand through his disheveled hair, looking cross and confused.

"Ye sent for me, fool." Roger was cross, too. His mouth felt as though he'd been chewing straw all night. "How are you, anyway?"

"I—not that well." Buck's face changed abruptly from crossness to a pale apprehension, and he put a hand flat on his chest, pressing hard. "I—it—it doesna feel right."

"Lie down, for God's sake!" Roger squirmed off the bed, narrowly avoiding stepping on a little girl who was sitting on the floor, playing with the buckles of his boots. "I'll get ye some water."

A row of children was watching this byplay with interest, ignored by Mrs. MacLaren and two of the older girls, who were respectively stirring a huge cauldron of parritch and rapidly laying the large table for breakfast, slapping down wooden plates and spoons like cards in a game of old maid.

"If ye need the privy," one of the girls advised him, pausing in her rounds, "ye'd best go now. Robbie and Sandy've gone to tend the kine, and Stuart's no got his shoon on yet." She lifted her chin toward a stripling of twelve or so, who was crawling slowly about on hands and knees, with one worn shoe in one hand, peering under the sparse furniture in search of its mate. "Oh—and since your kinsman's lived the night, Da's gone for the healer."

36

THE SCENT OF A STRANGER

SHE'D BROUGHT Jock MacLeod the traditional hospital present of grapes. And a bottle of eighteen-year-old Bunnahabhain, which had brightened his face—or what could be seen of it behind the bandage that wrapped his head and the bruising that narrowed both eyes to bloodshot slits.

"Oh, I'm a bit peely-wally," he'd told her, wrapping the bottle in his dressing gown and handing it to her to stash in his bedside cabinet, "but no bad, no bad. A wee dunt on the head, is all. I'm only glad the lad got away. D'ye ken how he came to be in the tunnel, lass?"

She'd given him the official version, listened patiently to his speculations, and then asked if he'd maybe recognized the man who hit him?

"Well, I did, then," Jock had said, surprising her. He leaned back on his pillows. "Which is not to say as I know his name. But I've seen him, aye, often. He skippers a boat on the canal."

"What? A charter boat, or one of the Jacobite cruise boats?" Her heart beat faster. The Caledonian Canal, he meant. It ran from Inverness to Fort William and carried a huge amount of water traffic, much of it visible from the road.

"Nice wee motor sailer—must be a charter. I only noticed because my wife's cousin has one like it; we went out wi' him the once. Ten-meter, I think it is."

"You told the police, of course."

"I did, so." He tapped blunt fingers on the coverlet, glancing sideways at her. "I described the man so well as I could—but, ken, he didna really look unusual. I'd know him again—and maybe your wee lad would—but I don't know as the polis would pick him out easy."

She'd brought her Swiss Army knife out of her pocket as she talked, playing with it meditatively, flicking the blades open and shut. She opened the corkscrew, testing the sharp end of it with the ball of her thumb.

"Do you think you could maybe describe him to me? I draw a bit; I could make a stab at a picture."

He grinned at her, eyes disappearing into the bruised flesh. "Pour me a dram, lass, and we'll have a go."

BRIANNA REACHED Lallybroch again in the late afternoon, just in time for her four o'clock appointment with the locksmith. A scrap of white tacked to the door fluttered in the autumn wind; she yanked it off and fumbled it open with chilled fingers.

Had an emergency call in Elgin; won't be back 'til late. Will call by in the morning. Apologies, Will Tranter

She crumpled the note and stuffed it into her jacket pocket, muttering under her breath. Bloody kidnapping rapist bastards walking in and out of her house like it was the public highway and this *wasn't* an emergency?

She hesitated, fingers wrapped around the big antique key in her pocket, looking up at the white-harled front of the house. The sinking sun flashed in the upper windows, glazing them with red, hiding whatever might be behind them. *They had a key.* Did she really want to go in there alone?

She glanced round, self-conscious, but saw nothing out of the ordinary. The home fields lay tranquil, the small flock of sheep already bedding down in the setting sun. She breathed deeply, turning from side to side as she would when hunting with Da in the North Carolina forest, as though she might catch the tang of deer on the breeze.

What was she looking for now? *Exhaust fumes. Rubber, hot metal, unlaid dust in the air, the ghost of a car.* Or maybe something else, she thought, remembering the stink of Rob Cameron's sweat. The scent of a stranger.

But the cold air brought her only the smell of dead leaves,

sheep shit, and a hint of turpentine from the Forestry Commission's pine plantation to the west.

Still. She'd heard her father mention a feeling at the back of his neck when something was wrong, and she felt the hairs on her nape prickle now. She turned away, got back into her car, and drove off, glancing automatically behind her every few minutes. There was a petrol station a few miles up the road; she stopped there to call Fiona and say she'd pick the kids up in the morning, then bought a few snacks and drove back, taking the farm track that circled the far edge of Lallybroch's land and led up into the pine plantation.

At this time of year, it got dark by 4:30 P.M. Up the hillside, the track was no more than a pair of muddy ruts, but she bumped carefully along until she came to one of the clearings where the foresters piled slash for burning. The air was rough with the smell of wood fire, and a big blackened patch of earth and ember still sent up wisps of smoke, but all the fires were out. She drove the car behind a heap of fresh-cut branches, piled ready for the next day, and cut the ignition.

As she came down out of the plantation, carrying the shotgun in one hand, something large shot past her head in total silence, and she stumbled, gasping. An owl; it disappeared, a pale blur in the dark. In spite of her pounding heart, she was glad to see it. White animals were harbingers of good luck in Celtic folklore; she could use any luck going.

"Owls are keepers of the dead, but not just the dead. They're messengers between worlds." For an instant Roger was next to her, solid, warm in the cold night, and she put out a hand by impulse, as though to touch him.

Then he was gone and she was standing alone in the shadow of the pines, looking toward Lallybroch, the shotgun cold in her hand. "I'll get you back, Roger," she whispered under her breath, and curled her left hand into a fist, clenching the copper ring with which he'd married her. "I *will.*" But first she had to make sure the kids were safe.

Night rose up around the house and Lallybroch faded slowly out of sight, a paler blotch against the dark. She checked the safety on the gun and moved silently toward home.

SHE CAME UP the hill behind the broch, as quietly as she could. The wind had come up, and she doubted anyone would hear her steps over the rustling of the gorse and dry broom that grew thick back here.

If they were waiting for her, wanting to do harm, surely they'd be in the house. But if they just wanted to know where she was . . . they might be watching the house instead, and this was the place to do it from. She paused by the wall of the broch and put a hand on the stones, listening. Faint rustling, punctuated by an occasional dovish coo. The bats would have gone out long since, hunting, but the doves were abed.

Pressing her back against the stones, she sidled around the broch, pausing near the door, and reached out a hand, groping for the latch. The padlock was cold in her hand; intact and locked. Letting out her breath, she fumbled the bunch of keys out of her pocket and found the right one by touch.

The sleeping doves erupted in a mad flutter when the wind from the open door whooshed up to the rafters where they roosted, and she stepped hastily back against the wall, out of the way of a pattering rain of panicked incontinence. The doves calmed in a moment, though, and settled down again in a murmurous rustle of indignation at the disturbance.

The upper floors had long since fallen in and the timbers cleared away; the broch was a shell, but a sturdy shell, its outer stones repaired over the years. The stair was built into the wall itself, the stone steps leading up between the inner and outer walls, and she went up slowly, feeling her way one-handed. There was a torch in her pocket but no need to risk using it.

A third of the way up, she took up station by a window slit that commanded a view of the house below. It was cold sitting on the stones, but her jacket was down-filled and she wouldn't freeze. She pulled a bar of Violet Crumble from her pocket and settled down to wait.

She'd called the Hydro Board and asked for a week's leave in order to deal with a family emergency. News of what had happened at the Loch Errochty dam last night had spread, so there'd been no difficulty, save in deflecting the flood of sympathetic exclamations and curious questions—all of which she'd claimed not to be able to answer, owing to the ongoing police inquiry.

The police . . . they *might* be of help. Jock had told them about the man at the dam; they'd be following that up. She'd had to tell them about Rob Cameron. And, with some reluctance, she'd told them about his coming into the house and threatening her, since Mandy would likely blow the gaff about that. She told them about his open disgruntlement over having a woman supervisor and his harassing her at work—though that seemed like a paltry motive for kidnapping a child. She hadn't mentioned most of the physical stuff, the priest's hole, or Cameron's assisted escape, though. Just said she'd hit him—first with the letter box, and then with the cricket bat—and he'd run away. She'd gone with Mandy to find Jem, that being obviously more urgent than calling the police. The police didn't agree with that assessment, but they were British and thus polite about their disapproval.

She'd said Cameron had told her where Jem was. If the police found him, he wasn't going to be in any position to contradict her. She *did* hope they picked him up. It might cause complications, but she'd feel safer if he wasn't wandering around loose. With her rifle. Possibly lurking in her house.

Her hand curled up in the deep pocket of her jacket, fingering the comforting shapes of a dozen shotgun shells.

37

COGNOSCO TE

THE HEALER ARRIVED in midafternoon. He was a short man but not slight; he looked like an amateur wrestler, with shoulders nearly as broad as Roger's own. He didn't introduce himself but nodded politely to Mrs. MacLaren, his eyes flicking round the room in a brief, all-encompassing glance, then focused on Buck, who had fallen into an uneasy sleep and did not wake even to the disturbance caused by the healer's entrance.

"He says his heart—" Roger began awkwardly. The man glanced sharply sideways at him, then flicked a hand in dismissal and, walking over, peered closely at Buck for a moment. All the MacLarens waited in breathless silence, clearly expecting something spectacular.

The man nodded to himself, removed his coat, and turned back his shirtsleeves, displaying sun-browned forearms corded with muscle.

"Well, then," he said, sitting down by the bed and laying a hand on Buck's chest. "Let me—" His face went quite blank and he stiffened, his hand jerking back as though he'd received an electric shock. He gave a quick, hard shake of the head and pulled Buck's shirt open, plunging both hands into the opening and laying them flat on Buck's laboring chest.

"Jesu," he whispered. *"Cognosco te!"*

Quite suddenly the hairs on Roger's body lifted, prickling as though a thunderstorm was coming. The man had spoken in Latin, and what he had said was, *"I know you!"*

THE MACLARENS ALL watched the healer work, with great respect and not a little awe. Roger, who had learned a good bit about the psychology of healing from Claire, was just as impressed. And, to be frank, scared shitless.

The healer had stood motionless for a long moment, hands on Buck's chest, his head thrown back and eyes closed, his face contorted in an expression of the deepest concentration, as though listening to something far, far off. He had murmured what Roger recognized as the Pater Noster—from the looks on the faces of the MacLarens, it might as well have been the Abracadabra. Then, keeping his hands in place, he had raised one thick forefinger and begun to tap, delicately, in a slow, regular rhythm, his finger rebounding each time as though he were striking a piano key.

Thup . . . thup . . . thup. It went on for a long time, so long that everyone in the room began to draw breath again—even Buck, whose labored gasping began to ease, his lungs filling naturally again. Then it was two fingers, *Thup-tup . . . thup-tup . . . thup-tup.* Slow. Regular as a metronome. On and on and on and on . . . Soothing. Hypnotic. And Roger realized that the rhythm was that of a beating heart—his *own* heart. Looking round the room at the wide eyes and slightly open mouths of the adenoidal MacLaren clan, he had the most peculiar sense that *all* their hearts were beating to precisely the same rhythm.

He knew they were breathing as one; he could hear the susurrus of indrawn breath and the sea-foam rush of exhalation. He *knew* it—and was helpless to change his own rhythm, to resist the sense of unity that had formed insensibly among all the people in the cabin, from Angus MacLaren down to little Josephine, round-eyed as the rest in her mother's arms.

All of them were breathing, hearts beating as one—and somehow they were supporting the stricken man, holding him as part of a larger entity, embracing him, bracing him. Buck's injured heart lay in the palm of Roger's hand: he realized it quite suddenly and, just as suddenly, realized that it had been there for some time, resting as naturally in the curve of his palm as rounded river rock, smooth and heavy. And . . . beating, in time with the heart in Roger's chest. What was much stranger was that none of this felt in any way out of the ordinary.

Odd—and impressive—as it was, Roger could have explained this. Mass suggestion, hypnosis, will and willingness. He'd done much the same thing himself any number of times, singing—when the music caught the audience up with him, when he knew they were with him, would follow him anywhere. He'd done it once or twice, preaching; felt the people warm to him and lift him up as he lifted them. It was impressive to see it done so quickly and thoroughly without any sort of warm-up, though—and much more disquieting to feel the effects in his own flesh. What was scaring him, though, was that the healer's hands were blue.

No doubt about it. It wasn't a trick of the light—there wasn't any to speak of, bar the dull glow of the smoored fire. It wasn't a huge thing; no fiery coruscations or neon. But a soft blue tinge had come up between the healer's fingers, crept over the backs of his hands—and now spread in a faint haze *around* his hands, seeming to penetrate Buck's chest.

Roger glanced to one side, then the other, without moving his head. The MacLarens were paying rapt attention but showed no sign of seeing anything startling. *They don't see it.* The hairs on his forearms lifted silently. *Why do* I *see it?*

Thup-tup . . . thup-tup . . . thup-tup . . . Tireless, regular—and yet Roger became aware of some subtle change. Not in the healer's rhythm—that didn't vary at all. But something had shifted. He glanced down involuntarily into his palm, where he still imagined that Buck's heart lay, and was now scarcely surprised to see it there, a ghostly round object, transparent but pulsing gently, regularly. On its own.

Thup-tup . . . . . . thup-tup . . . . . . thup-tup. The healer now was following, not leading. Not slowing the beats but pausing for a longer period between them, letting Buck's heart beat alone between them.

At last, the faint sound stopped, and there was silence in the room for the length of three heartbeats. And then the silence popped like a soap bubble, leaving the onlookers blinking and shaking their heads, as those awakened from dreaming. Roger closed his empty hand.

"He'll be all right," the healer said to Mrs. MacLaren, in a matter-of-fact manner. "Let him sleep as long as he can, give him something to eat when he wakes up."

"Much obliged, sir," Mrs. MacLaren murmured. She patted Josephine, who had fallen asleep with her mouth open, a glimmering trail of saliva falling from the corner of her mouth to her mother's shoulder. "Will I make up a pallet for ye by the fire?"

"Ah, no," the healer said, smiling. He shrugged back into his coat, put on his cloak, and reached for his hat. "I'm staying no great distance away."

He went out, and Roger waited for a moment, just long enough for people to turn back to their own conversations, and then followed, shutting the door quietly behind him.

THE HEALER WAS a little way down the road; Roger saw the man's dark figure kneeling in prayer before a tiny shrine, the ends of his cloak fluttering in the wind. Roger came up to him slowly, hanging back so as not to disturb his devotions—and, on impulse, bowed his own head toward the small statue, so weathered as to be faceless. *Take care of them, please,* he prayed. *Help me get back to them—to Bree.* That was all he had time for, before the healer rose to his feet—but that was all he had to say, in any case.

The healer hadn't heard him; he rose and turned, surprised at seeing Roger but recognizing him at once. He smiled, a little wearily, clearly expecting some medical question of a private nature.

Heart thumping, Roger reached out and grasped the healer's hand. The man's eyes widened with shock.

"Cognosco te," Roger said, very softly. *I know you.*

"WHO ARE YE, then?" Dr. Hector McEwan stood squinting against the wind, his face wary but excited. "The two of ye—who are ye?"

"I think ye maybe ken that better than I do," Roger told him. "That—the light in your hands . . ."

"You could see it." It wasn't a question, and the wary excitement in McEwan's eyes blazed into life, visible even in the dimming light.

"Aye, I could. Where did ye . . ." Roger groped for the best way to ask, but, after all, how many ways were there? "*When* did ye come from?"

McEwan glanced involuntarily over his shoulder toward the croft, but the door was shut, smoke pouring from the hole in the roof. It was beginning to rain, a premonitory pattering among the mounded heather near the path. He moved abruptly, taking Roger's arm.

"Come," he said. "We canna be standing out here, dreich as it is; we'll catch our deaths."

"Dreich" was the word; the rain set to in good earnest and Roger was half soaked in minutes, having come out without hat or cloak. McEwan led the way quickly up a winding path through thickets of dark gorse, emerging onto a stretch of moorland where the remains of a tumbledown croft offered some shelter. The rooftree had been burned, and recently; the smell still lingered. A corner of thatch remained, though, and they huddled inside, close beneath its scanty protection.

"Anno Domini eighteen hundred and forty-one," McEwan

said matter-of-factly, shaking rain from his cloak. He looked up at Roger, one thick brow raised.

"Nineteen hundred and eighty," Roger replied, heart hammering. He cleared his throat and repeated the date; the cold had affected his throat, and the words emerged in a strangled croak. McEwan leaned close at the sound, peering at him.

"What's that?" the man asked sharply. "Your voice—it's broken."

"It's noth—" Roger began, but the healer's fingers were already groping behind his head, undoing his neckcloth in nothing flat. He closed his eyes, not resisting.

McEwan's broad fingers were cold on his neck; he felt the icy touch delicate on his skin as it traced the line of the rope scar, then firmer as the healer prodded gently round his damaged larynx—it gave him an involuntary choking sensation, and he coughed. McEwan looked surprised.

"Do that again," he said.

"What, cough?" Roger said, hoarse as a crow.

"Aye, that." McEwan fitted his hand snugly round Roger's neck, just under the chin, and nodded. "Once, then wait, then do it again." Roger hacked obligingly, feeling a slight pain with each expulsion of breath where the healer's hand pressed. The man's face brightened with interest, and he removed his hand.

"Do you know what a hyoid bone is?"

"If I had to guess, it's something in the throat." Roger cleared his throat hard and rubbed at it, feeling the roughness of the scar under his palm. "Why?" He wasn't sure whether to be offended at the personal intrusion or—something else. His skin tingled slightly where McEwan had touched it.

"It's just *there,*" the healer said, pressing with his thumb, high up under Roger's chin. "And if it had been *here*"—he moved the thumb down an inch—"you'd have been dead, sir. It's a fragile wee bone. Easy to strangle someone by breaking it—with your thumbs *or* a rope." He drew back a little, eyes intent on Roger's; the curiosity was still plain on his face, but the wariness had returned. "Are you and your friend fleeing from . . . something? Someone?"

"No." Roger felt at once very tired, the strain of everything catching up to him, and looked round for something to sit on.

There was nothing but a few dark chunks of rock that had fallen from the cottage's wall when the burning thatch had been pulled down. He pushed two blocks together and sat on one, knees up round his ears. "I—this—" He touched his throat briefly. "It was a long time ago, nothing to do with what we—we—we're looking for my son. He's only nine."

"Oh, dearie me." McEwan's broad face creased in sympathy. "How—"

Roger lifted a hand. "You first," he said, and cleared his throat again. "I'll tell ye everything I know, but . . . you first. Please."

McEwan pursed his lips and glanced aside, thinking, but then shrugged and lowered himself, grunting, to his own rude seat.

"I was a doctor," he said abruptly. "In Edinburgh. I came up to the Highlands to shoot grouse with a friend. Do folk still do that, a hundred years hence?"

"Aye. Grouse are still tasty," Roger said dryly. "It was at Craigh na Dun that ye came through, then?"

"Yes, I—" McEwan halted abruptly, realizing what that question implied. "Dear Lord in heaven, do ye mean to be telling me there are other places? Where . . . *it* happens?"

"Yes." The hairs rippled on Roger's arms. "Four that I know of; likely there are others. How many stone circles are there in the British Isles?"

"I've no idea." McEwan was clearly shaken. He got up and went to the doorway, the jamb of it scorched and the lintel burned almost away. Roger hoped none of the stones above it would fall on the man's head—at least not until he found out more.

Dr. McEwan stayed for a long time, staring out into the rain, which had gone the silvery gray of cat's fur. Finally he shook himself and came back, mouth set in firm decision.

"Aye, nothing to be gained from secrecy. And I hope nothing to be lost by honesty." This last was not quite a question, but Roger nodded and tried to look earnest.

"Well, then. Grouse, as I say. We were on the moor, just below that hill where the standing stones are. All of a sudden a fox shot out of the bracken, right by my foot, and one of the dogs lost his head and chased it. Brewer—that was my friend,

Joseph Brewer—started after it, but he has—he *had,*" McEwan corrected, with an expression of mild irritation that made Roger want to smile, because he was so familiar with the feeling that dealing with the phenomenon caused, "a clubfoot. He managed all right with a special boot, but climbing and chasing . . ." He shrugged.

"So you went after the dog, and . . ." Roger shuddered involuntarily at the memory, and so did McEwan.

"Exactly."

"Did the dog . . . go?" Roger asked suddenly. McEwan looked surprised and vaguely affronted.

"How should I know? It didn't turn up where I did, I can tell ye that much."

Roger made a brief gesture of apology.

"Just curious. We—my wife and I—we've been trying to puzzle out as much as we can, for the sake of the children." "Children" caught in his throat, coming out in no more than a whisper, and McEwan's expression softened.

"Aye, of course. Your son, you said?"

Roger nodded and managed to explain what he could, about Cameron, the letters . . . and, after a moment's hesitation, about the Spaniard's gold, for, after all, he'd have to give a reason for Cameron's taking Jem in the first place, and his sense of Dr. McEwan was one of solid kindness.

"Dearie me," the doctor murmured, shaking his head in dismay. "I'll ask among my patients. Perhaps someone . . ." He trailed off, his face still troubled. Roger had the distinct impression that the sense of trouble wasn't all down to Jem, or even to the staggering discovery that there were other—

He stopped, seeing plainly in his mind's eye the soft blue glow surrounding McEwan's fingers—and the look of surprised delight on his face. *Cognosco te.* I know you. Delight, not just shock. He and Buck weren't the first time travelers this man had known. But the doctor hadn't said as much. Why not?

"How long have you been here?" Roger asked, curious.

McEwan sighed and rubbed a hand over his face.

"Maybe too long," he said, but then pushed that away, straightening up. "Two years, about. Speaking of too long, though . . ." He straightened, pulling the cloak over his shoulders. "It'll be dark in less than an hour. I'll need to go, if I'm to reach Cranesmuir by nightfall. I'll come again tomorrow to tend your friend. We can talk a bit more then."

He turned abruptly, but just as suddenly turned back and, reaching out, took Roger's throat in his hand.

"Maybe," he said, as though to himself. "Just maybe." Then he nodded once, let go, and was gone, his cloak fluttering like bat wings behind him.

38

THE NUMBER OF THE BEAST

AFTER *FRAGGLE ROCK*, the telly went to the evening news, and Ginger reached to turn it off but stopped abruptly as Jem's last year's school picture flashed on the screen. She stared at the television, mouth half open, then looked incredulously at Jem.

"That's you!" she said.

"Ken that fine," he said crossly. "Turn it off, aye?"

"No, I want to see." She blocked him as he lunged for the screen; Ginger was eleven and bigger than him.

"Turn it off!" he said, then, with cunning inspiration, "It'll scare Mandy and she'll howl."

Ginger shot Mandy a quick glance—she had good lungs, did Mandy—then reluctantly turned the TV off.

"Mmphm," she said, and lowered her voice. "Mam told us what happened, but she said we weren't to trouble ye about it."

"Good," Jem said. "Don't." His heart was hammering and he felt sweaty, but his hands were going cold and hot and cold again.

He'd got away by the skin of his teeth, diving under the bushes planted at the top of the spillway and crawling down the concrete edging 'til he found a ladderway that went down into the water. He'd shoogled down it as far as he could and clung on so hard his hands went numb, with the black water rumbling inches under his feet and surging down the spillway past him, drenching him with cold spray. He could still feel his bones shake with it.

He believed he might throw up if he thought about it anymore, so he turned away and went to look into the wee girls' toy chest. It was full of girlie toys, of course, but maybe if they had a ball . . . They did. It was pink but one of the good high-bouncy kind.

"We could go out to the garden, maybe, and have a bit o' catch?" he suggested, bouncing the ball on the floor and catching it.

"It's dark and rainin' like the clappers," Tisha said. "Dinna want to get wet."

"Ach, it's no but a saft drizzle! What are ye, made of sugar?"

"Yes," said Sheena, with a simper. "Sugar and spice 'n everything nice, that's what little girls are made of. Snips and snails and puppy-dog tails—"

"Come play dollies," suggested Tisha, waggling a naked doll invitingly at him. "Ye can have GI Joe if ye want. Or would ye rather Ken?"

"Nay, I'm no playin' dollies," Jem said firmly. "Canna be doing wi' the clothes and all."

"I play dollies!" Mandy muscled her way between Tisha and Sheena, eager hands stretched out for a Barbie in a pink frilly ball gown. Sheena grabbed it away just in time.

"Aye, aye," she soothed Mandy's impending screech, "you can play, sure. Ye have to play nice, though; ye dinna want to spoil her dress. Here, sit down, pet, I'll give ye this one. See her wee comb and brush? Ye can fix her hair."

Jem took the ball and left. The upstairs hall had carpet, but the landing was bare wood. He popped the ball off it and it shot up and hit the ceiling with a smack, just missing the hanging light fixture. It bounced off the floor and he caught it before it could get away, clutching it to his chest.

He listened for a second, to be sure Mrs. Buchan hadn't heard. She was back in the kitchen, though; he could hear the sound of her singing along to the radio.

He was halfway down the stairs when the bell over the front door went, and he looked over the banister to see who it was coming in. Who it was was Rob Cameron, and Jem nearly swallowed his tongue.

JEM PRESSED himself back against the wall of the landing, his heart pounding so loud he could barely hear Mrs. Buchan come out of the kitchen.

Should he go get Mandy? There wasn't any way out of the house but by the stairs; he couldn't drop Mandy out the lounge window, there wasn't a tree or anything . . .

Mrs. Buchan was saying hello and she was sorry if the gentleman was wanting a room, because she was booked full every day this week. Mr. Cameron was being polite, saying, no, thank ye kindly, he was only wondering might he have a wee word . . .

"If ye're selling anything—" she started, and he interrupted her.

"No, missus, nothing like that. It's a few questions I have about the stones at Craigh na Dun."

Jem was gasping for air. His lungs were heaving, but he'd pressed a hand over his mouth so Mr. Cameron wouldn't hear. Mrs. Buchan didn't gasp, but he could hear her take breath, then stop, deciding what to say.

"Stones?" she said, and even he could tell she was faking puzzlement. "I dinna ken anything about stones."

Rob made a polite laugh.

"I apologize, missus. I should have introduced myself, first. My name's Rob Cameron—and—is something wrong, missus?" She'd not only gasped really loud, Jem thought she must have stepped back without looking and hit the wee table in the hall, because there was a thump and an "Ach!" and the splat of picture frames falling over.

"No," Mrs. Buchan said, getting ahold of herself. "No. Had a wee turn, that's all—I've the high blood pressure, ken. Get that wee bit dizzy. Your name's Cameron, is it?"

"Aye. Rob Cameron. I'm cousin by marriage to Becky Wemyss. She told me a bit about the dancing up at the stones."

"Oh." That "oh" meant trouble for Becky Wemyss, thought Jem, who knew a lot about mothers' voices.

"I'm a bit of a scholar of the auld ways, see. I'm writing a wee book . . . Anyway, I wondered if I could maybe talk to you for a few minutes. Becky said ye'd know more about the stones and the dancing than anybody else."

Jem's breathing slowed down, once he realized that Mr. Cameron hadn't come because Mr. Cameron knew Mandy and he were here. Or maybe he did and was trying it on with Mrs. Buchan 'til he could make an excuse to use the loo and come poke round in search of them? He looked apprehensively up the half flight of stairs that led from the landing, but the lounge door above was closed, and while he could hear Mandy's giggling fine through it, probably Mr. Cameron couldn't.

Mrs. Buchan was taking Mr. Cameron back to the kitchen. Her voice when she'd said, "Come ben. I'll tell ye what I can," hadn't sounded at all friendly. Jem wondered whether she might be going to put rat poison in Mr. Cameron's tea.

Maybe Mrs. Buchan didn't have any rat poison, though. He took a step one way, then the other, then back. He really, really wanted to run down the stairs and out the door and keep going. But he couldn't leave Mandy.

His havering stopped at once when the kitchen door opened, but he could hear it was Mrs. Buchan's step, and just hers, coming fast and light.

She turned up the stairs but started back when she saw him on the landing, a hand to her chest. Then she ran up to him and hugged him tight, whispering in his ear.

"Bloody heck, lad. What're you—well, never mind, I was coming to find you. Ye saw him?"

Jem nodded, wordless, and Mrs. Buchan's mouth pressed flat.

"Aye. I'm going to take ye out the door. Go left out the gate. Two houses down is Mrs. Kelleher. Knock and tell her I sent ye to use the phone. Ye call the polis and tell them the man that kidnapped you is here—ye ken the address here?"

He nodded. He'd seen the number when he visited before with Mam and Dad and remembered it because it was 669; Dad had said it should by rights be 666, but that was the number of the beast. Jem had asked whether it was Mr. or Mrs. Buchan that was the beast, and Mam and Dad both laughed like loons.

"Good," said Mrs. Buchan, letting go of him. "Come on, then."

"Mandy—" he started, but she shushed him.

"I'll mind her. Come!"

He ran down the stairs after her, trying not to make any noise, and, at the door, she stood on her toes and held the little bell so it wouldn't ring.

"Run!" she whispered.

He ran.

MRS. KELLEHER WAS an old lady and kind of deaf. Jem was out of breath and so scared that he couldn't put his words together right, so it was a long time before she took him to the telephone, and then the lady at the police station put the phone down on him twice, because she thought he was some bampot wean who'd got hold of the phone and was playing tricks.

"I'm Jeremiah MacKenzie!" he bellowed, next time she answered. "I was kidnapped!"

"Ye were?" said Mrs. Kelleher, very startled. She grabbed the phone away from him. "Who's this?" she demanded of it. Faint squawking—at least the police lady hadn't hung up again. Mrs. Kelleher turned and squinted through her spectacles at him.

"Who was it ye were wanting to call, lad? Ye've got the polis by mistake."

He really wanted to hit something, but he couldn't hit Mrs. Kelleher. He said something very bad in Gaelic, and her mouth fell open. She'd let the phone fall away from her ear, though, and he grabbed it.

"The man that kidnapped me is *here,*" he said, as slow as he could. "I need somebody to come! Before—" Inspiration struck. "Before he hurts my little sister! It's 669 Glenurquhart Road. Come right away!" Then *he* put the phone down, before the lady could ask him questions.

Mrs. Kelleher had plenty of those, and he didn't want to be rude, so he asked could he use the loo and locked the door against her, then hung out the upstairs window, watching for the police.

Nothing happened for what seemed forever. The raindrops started to drip off his hair and eyelashes, but he was afraid of missing anything. He was rubbing the water out of his eyes when all of a sudden the door of 669 flew open and Rob Cameron came running out, jumped in a car, and drove off with the tires squealing.

Jem almost fell out the window but then rushed back and barreled out of the bathroom, nearly knocking Mrs. Kelleher over.

"Thank you, Mrs. Kelleher!" he yelled over his shoulder, taking the stairs three at a time, and shot out the front door.

There was a lot of screaming and crying going on inside the Buchans' house, and he felt his chest go so tight he couldn't breathe.

"Mandy!" He tried to call, but her name came out in a whisper. The front door was hanging open. Inside, there were girls everywhere, but he picked Mandy out of the muddle in the lounge instantly and ran to grab her. She wasn't crying, but she latched on to him like a leech, burying her black curly head in his stomach.

"It's okay," he told her, squeezing the stuffing out of her in relief. "It's okay, Man. I gotcha. I gotcha."

His heart started to slow down a little, and he saw that Mrs. Buchan was sitting on the sofa, holding a towel full of ice cubes to her face. Some of the ice had fallen out and was lying on the rug at her feet. Tisha and Sheena were holding on to their mother and crying, and Ginger was trying to pat her mam's hair and comfort her sisters at the same time, but her face was dead white and tears were running silently down it.

"Mrs. Buchan . . . are ye all right?" Jem asked timidly. He had an awful feeling in the bottom of his stomach. Somehow, he was sure this was his fault.

Mrs. Buchan looked up at him. One side of her face was puffy and the eye on that side was swollen half shut, but the other one had fire in it, and that made him feel a little better.

"Aye, fine, Jem," she said. "Dinna fash, girls! It's well enough; no but a black eye. Quit your caterwauling, will ye? I canna hear myself think." She gave a small, good-natured shake to detach the clinging girls, pushing and patting at them with her free hand. Then there was a knock on the doorjamb, and a man's voice from the front hall.

"Police, here! Anyone to home?"

Jem could have told Mrs. Buchan what happened once you called the police. Questions, and questions, and more questions. And if there were things you couldn't *tell* the police . . . At least Mrs. Buchan wouldn't let them take Jem or her to the police station to answer questions, insisting that she couldn't leave the girls on their own. By the time the police gave up, Mandy and Sheena were both asleep on the couch, curled up together like a pair of kittens, and Ginger and Tisha had made everyone tea, then sat yawning in the corner together, blinking now and then to keep awake.

A few minutes after the police left, *Mr.* Buchan came home for his supper, and all the explaining was to do all over again. There really wasn't much to it: Mrs. Buchan had sat Mr. Cameron down in the kitchen and told him a bit about the dancing—it wasn't secret, most folk who'd lived in Inverness for a long time knew about it—but she'd left the radio playing while they were talking, and all of a sudden the newscaster was saying the name "Robert Cameron" and how Robert Cameron was wanted for questioning in the kidnapping of a local boy, and—

"And then the wee bastard jumps up, and so do I, and he must have thought I meant to stop him—I was betwixt him and the door, anyroad—and he belts me one in the eye, pushes me into the wall, and he's away off!"

Mr. Buchan was giving Jem a hard look now and then and seemed like *he* wanted to start asking questions, but instead he said they'd all go into the town and have a fish supper as it was so late, and everyone started feeling better at once. Jem could see the looks going back and forth between the Buchans, though, and he kind of wondered whether Mr. Buchan maybe meant to drop him and Mandy off at the police station on the way back. Or maybe just leave them by the side of the road.

39

THE GHOST OF A HANGIT MAN

THE HEAVENS OPENED, and Roger was soaked to the skin by the time he got back to the MacLarens' cottage. Amid cries of dismay from Mrs. MacLaren and her ancient mother, he was hastily stripped, wrapped up snug in a ragged quilt, and stood to steam before the fire, where his presence greatly impeded the preparations for supper. Buck, propped up on pillows with the two smallest MacLarens curled up in sleep on the bed beside him, lifted a brow at Roger in inquiry.

Roger moved his hand slightly, in a tell-you-later gesture. He thought Buck looked better; there was color in his face, and he was sitting upright, not slumped into the bedding. For a brief instant, Roger wondered what would happen if he were to lay his own hand on Buck. Would it glow blue?

The thought sent a shiver through him, and Allie, one of the MacLaren daughters, pushed the trailing edge of his quilt away from the fire with a squeak of alarm.

"Take care, sir, do!"

"Aye, do," said Grannie Wallace, pulling the blackened iron spider—this spitting hot grease—well away from his bare legs and making shooing motions. "Take a spark, and ye'll go up like tinder." She was blind in one eye, but the other was sharp as a needle and gave him a piercing look. "Tall as ye are, ye'd likely set the rooftree afire, and then where should we all be, I'd like tae know!"

There was a general titter at that, but he thought the laughter had an uneasy note to it and wondered why.

"Moran taing," Roger said in polite thanks for the advice. He moved a foot or so farther from the hearth, fetching up against the settle on which Mr. Angus MacLaren was sitting,

mending his pipe stem. "Since ye speak of rooftrees—there's a wee croft just over the hill that's been burnt out. Cooking accident, was it?"

The room went silent, and people froze for an instant, all looking at him.

"Evidently not," he said, with an apologetic cough. "I'm sorry to make light—were folk killed, then?"

Mr. MacLaren gave him a brooding sort of look, quite at odds with his earlier geniality, and set the pipe on his knee.

"No by the fire," he said. "What led ye up there, man?"

Roger met MacLaren's eye directly.

"Searching for my lad," he said simply. "I dinna ken where to look—so I look everywhere. Thinkin' what if he's got away, what if he's wandering about by himself . . . maybe taking shelter where he can find it . . ."

MacLaren took a deep breath and sat back, nodding a little.

"Aye, well. Ye'll want to keep well away from that croft."

"Haunted, is it?" Buck asked, and all heads swung round to look at him—then swung back to Mr. MacLaren, waiting for him to give the answer.

"It might be," he said, after a reluctant pause.

"It's cursed," Allie whispered to Roger under her breath.

"Ye didna go in, sir, did ye?" said Mrs. MacLaren, the permanent worry crease deepening between her brows.

"Och, no," he assured her. "What was it happened there?" McEwan hadn't had any hesitation about going into the croft; did he not know whatever they were concerned about?

Mrs. MacLaren made a small "Mmp!" noise and, with a shake of her head, swung the cauldron out on its bracket and began to scoop out boiled neeps with a wooden spoon. Not her place to speak of such goings-on, said her primly sealed mouth.

Mr. MacLaren made a somewhat louder noise and, leaning forward, got ponderously to his feet.

"I'll just be going to check the beasts before supper, ken," he said, and gave Roger an eye. "Perhaps ye'd like to come along and be oot the way o' the lasses and their doings."

"Oh, aye," Roger said, and, with a small bow to Mrs. MacLaren, hitched the quilt up higher over his shoulders and followed his host into the byre. He caught Buck's eye in passing and gave him a brief shrug.

In the usual way, the cattle's quarters were separated from the people's by no more than a stone wall with a large space at the top, allowing the considerable heat—along with floating bits of straw and a strong scent of piss and manure—generated by several large cows to percolate into the ben. The MacLarens' was a snug byre, well kept and piled with clean straw at one end, with three fat, shaggy red cows and a diminutive black bull who snorted fiercely at Roger, nostrils red-black in the dim light and the brass ring in his nose agleam.

The ben of the croft was far from cold—what with nine people crammed into it and a good peat fire on the hearth—but the byre was filled with an encompassing warmth and a sense of peace that made Roger sigh and drop his shoulders, only then realizing that they'd been up round his ears for what seemed hours.

MacLaren made no more than a cursory check of his beasts, scratching the bull between the ears and administering a comforting slap to a cow's flank. Then he led Roger to the far end of the byre with a jerk of his head.

Ever since his conversation with Hector McEwan, Roger had had an uneasy feeling, caused by something he felt he had heard and not understood. And now, as MacLaren turned to speak to him, it was there suddenly, clear in his head. *Cranesmuir.*

"Twa strangers built the croft up there," MacLaren said. "They came from nowhere seemingly; just one day they were there. A man and a woman, but we couldna tell were they man and wife, or maybe a man and his daughter, for he seemed a good bit older than she did. They said they came from the isles—and I think he maybe did, but her speech wasna like any islander I've heard."

"Was she Scots?"

MacLaren looked surprised.

"Oh, aye, she was. She had the *Gàidhlig.* I'd have said she came from somewhere up northwest of Inverness—maybe Thurso—but there again . . . it wasna quite . . . *right.*"

Not quite right. Like someone out of their proper place, pretending.

"What did she look like?" Roger said. His voice was thick; he had to clear his throat and repeat himself.

MacLaren's lips pursed but not in condemnation; it was the

sort of soundless whistle of appreciation one gives at sight of something remarkable.

"Bonny," he said. "Verra bonny, indeed. Tall and straight, but . . . er . . . not so straight in places, if ye take my meaning." He ducked his head, half embarrassed, and Roger realized that his reluctance to talk in front of the womenfolk perhaps wasn't due entirely to the scandalous nature of his story.

"I do," Roger said, lowering his own voice to MacLaren's confidential level. "Did they keep to themselves, then?" If they hadn't, surely the whole district would have known about them and quickly discovered whether they were man and wife.

MacLaren frowned.

"Aye, they did . . . though he was friendly enough; I met him now and again, out on the moor, and we'd have a word, and I'd always come away thinkin' as how he was a good wee fellow, and yet when I came to tell my Maggie about it, I couldna just charge my memory wi' anything he'd *said*."

MacLaren said somehow word got round that the woman was something that wee bit odd—a root doctor, but maybe would give you a bit more than a grass cure, if you found her alone in the house. . . .

There was no light in the byre save the dull glow from the hearth fire next door, but, even so, Roger could see that MacLaren had grown flushed and discomfited. Roger was beginning to feel uncomfortable himself, but not for the same reason.

Cranesmuir. He knew the name, had known it when McEwan said it. The MacLarens had said the healer came from Draighhearnach. Cranesmuir was in the opposite direction—and two miles farther on. Why was he going there tonight?

"There were stories. Always are, about a woman like that." MacLaren cleared his own throat. "But she was good wi' the grass cures—and wi' charms, as well. Or so folk said."

But then the man had gone, MacLaren said. No one knew where; they just didn't see him anymore, and the woman went on as before, but now more of her visitors were men. And the women stopped taking their bairns up there, though they'd go sometimes themselves, quietly, in secret.

And then on the day before Samhain, as the sun was sinking and the great fires being built up for the evening, a woman from nearby had gone up to the lonely croft and run down again, screaming.

"She'd found the door o' the croft standing wide, the woman and her things all gone—and a man hanging from the rooftree, stone dead wi' a rope around his neck."

The shock tightened Roger's own throat. He couldn't speak.

MacLaren sighed, head bent. A cow had come up behind him, nudging gently, and he laid one hand on her back as though seeking support from the animal, who went on placidly chewing her cud.

"It was the priest who said we should cleanse the place with fire, for it had the smell of evil about it, and no one kent the man. We couldna tell was it just a poor fellow as took his life by despair—or was it murder."

"I . . . see." Roger forced the words through the burn in his throat, and MacLaren looked up suddenly at him. He saw the man's mouth drop open, his eyes bulging, and realized that in the warmth he'd let the quilt slide back on his shoulders. MacLaren was looking straight at his throat, where the livid and unmistakable scar of hanging must show plain in the dim red light.

MacLaren backed away, or tried to, but there was nowhere to go. He plastered himself against one beast's shaggy flank, making a low gobbling noise. The cow seemed annoyed by this and brought her hoof down solidly on MacLaren's foot. The consequent anguish and fury at least brought MacLaren out of his fright, and when he had extricated himself—by means of thumps and curses—he turned bravely on Roger, jaw thrust out.

"Why come ye here, *a thaibse*?" he said, fists clenched but his voice low. "Whatever sin I might have done, I did naught to you. I'd nay part in your death—and I said they must bury your body beneath the hearthstone before they fired the place. The priest wouldna have ye in the kirkyard, aye?" he added, evidently fearing that the ghost of the hangit man had come to complain about the unsanctified disposal of his mortal remains.

Roger sighed and rubbed a hand over his face, the stubble rasping against his palm. He could see several curious faces, attracted by MacLaren's cries, peering into the shadows of the byre from the glow of the room beyond.

"Have ye got a rosary in the house, sir?" he said.

IT WAS A long and restless night. Grannie Wallace had snatched the children off Buck's bed, as though fearing he might devour them the moment her back was turned, and put them to bed with her in the trundle, while the older children slept either with their parents or rolled up in quilts by the hearth. Roger shared the pariah's bed with Buck, for while his ability to hold the rosary in his hand, kiss the crucifix, and then lead the family in saying the rosary had—barely—kept Angus MacLaren from throwing him out into the night and pissing on the gateposts to keep him from coming back in, it hadn't made him much more popular.

He doubted Buck had slept much better than himself, for his ancestor had rolled out of bed at first light, declaring an urgent necessity to visit the privy. Roger had as hastily arisen, saying, "I'll help ye," and pulled on a still-damp shirt and breeks.

He was pleased to see that Buck didn't actually appear to need help. He walked stiffly and limped a little, but his shoulders were square and he wasn't gasping or turning blue.

"If they think ye're a vengeful ghost, what the devil do they think *I* am?" Buck inquired, the instant they were clear of the cottage. "And surely to goodness ye could ha' just said the Lord's Prayer once and not dragged everyone through five decades o' the rosary and ruined the supper!"

"Mmphm." Buck had a point there, but Roger had been too much upset at the time to think of that. Besides, he'd wanted to give them time to recover from the shock. "It wasn't ruined," he said crossly. "Only the neeps a bit scorched."

"Only!" Buck echoed. "The place still reeks. And the women hate ye. They'll put too much salt in your porridge, see if they don't. Where d'ye think we're going? It's that way."

He pointed at a path on the left that did indeed lead to the privy, this sitting in plain sight.

Roger made another testy sound but followed. He was off-kilter this morning, distracted. No wonder about why, either.

Now? He wondered, watching the door of the privy close behind Buck. It was a two-seater, but he wasn't minded to broach what he had to say under conditions of *that* much intimacy, no matter how private the subject matter was.

"The healer," he said instead through the door, choosing the simplest place to start. "McEwan. He said he'd come back today to see to ye."

"I don't need seeing to," Buck snapped. "I'm fine!" Roger had known the man long enough to recognize bravado covering fear, and replied accordingly.

"Aye, right. What did it feel like?" he asked curiously. "When he put his hand on you?"

Silence from the privy.

"Did ye feel *anything*?" he asked, after the silence had lengthened well past any time required for natural functions.

"Maybe," said Buck's voice, gruff and reluctant. "Maybe no. I fell asleep whilst he was tapping on my chest like a yaffle after tree grubs. Why?"

"Did you understand what it was he said to ye? When he touched you?" Buck had been a lawyer in his own time; he must have studied Latin.

"Did you?" A slight creak of wood and a rustling of cloth.

"I did. And I said it back to him, just before he left."

"I was asleep," Buck repeated doggedly. Clearly he didn't want to talk about the healer, but he wasn't going to have a choice about that, Roger thought grimly.

"Come out of there, will ye? The MacLarens are all out in the dooryard, crossing their legs." He glanced over his shoulder and was surprised to see that in fact the MacLarens *were* out in the dooryard.

Not all of them—it was only Angus and a tall boy, plainly a MacLaren, too, from the shape of him. He seemed familiar—had he been at the house the evening before? They were bent close together, talking in evident excitement, and the boy was pointing off toward the distant road.

"Come out," Roger repeated, sudden urgency in his voice. "Someone's coming. I hear horses."

The privy door flew open and Buck sprang out like a jack-in-the-box, stuffing his shirt into his breeks. His hair was matted and dirty, but his eyes were alert, and he looked entirely capable; that was reassuring.

The horses had come up over the brow of the hill now—six of them: four of the shaggy Highland ponies called garrons, one indifferent rangy bay, and a startlingly fine chestnut with a flaxen mane. Buck seized Roger's arm with a grip like a horse's bite.

"A Dhia," Buck said, half under his breath. "Who's that?"

40

ANGELS UNAWARE

ROGER HAD NO IDEA who the tall man with the good horse was, but it was crystal clear *what* he was, both from the deferential manner of the MacLarens and from the way in which his companions fell naturally into place a step behind him. The man in charge.

A tacksman of the MacKenzies? he wondered. Most of the men wore a hunting tartan with a sett in green, brown, and white, but Roger wasn't yet familiar enough with the local patterns as to tell whether they came from somewhere close by or not.

The tall man glanced over his shoulder at MacLaren's nod, and his eyes rested on Roger and Buck with an air of casual interest. There was nothing threatening in his manner, but Roger felt himself draw up to his own full height and wished for an instant that he wasn't barefoot and unshaven, breeks flapping unbuckled at his knees.

At least he did have someone at his own back: Buck had fallen a step behind him. He hadn't time to be surprised at that before he came within the stranger's ken.

The man was an inch or two shorter than himself and close to his own age, dark and good-looking in a faintly familiar sort of . . .

"Good morn to ye, sir," the dark man said, with a courteous inclination of the head. "My name is Dougal MacKenzie, of Castle Leoch. And . . . who might you be?"

Dear Jesus bloody hell, he thought. The shock rippled

through him, and he hoped it didn't show on his face. He shook hands firmly.

"I am Roger Jeremiah MacKenzie, of Kyle of Lochalsh," he said, keeping his voice mild and—he hoped—assured, as some compensation for his shabby appearance. His voice sounded nearly normal this morning; if he didn't force it, with luck it wouldn't crack or gurgle.

"Your servant, sir," MacKenzie said with a slight bow, surprising Roger with his elegant manners. He had deep-set hazel eyes, which looked Roger over with frank interest—and a faint touch of what appeared to be amusement—before shifting to Buck.

"My kinsman," Roger said hastily. "William Bu—William MacKenzie." *When?* he thought in agitation. *Was Buck born yet? Would Dougal recognize the name William Buccleigh MacKenzie? But, no, he can't be born yet; you can't exist twice in the same time—can you?!?*

A question from Dougal MacKenzie interrupted this stream of confusion, though Roger missed hearing it. Buck answered, though.

"My kinsman's son was taken," he said, looking Dougal over with exactly—*oh, Jesus, exactly*—the same attitude of insouciant confidence that the other MacKenzie carried. "About a week past, abducted by a man named Cameron. Robert Cameron. Will ye maybe ken such a man?"

Dougal of course did not—not surprising, as Cameron hadn't existed here until a week ago. But he conferred with his men, asked intelligent questions, and expressed an open sympathy and concern that at once comforted Roger and made him feel as though he was about to vomit.

To this point, Dougal MacKenzie had been no more than a name on the historical page, momentarily, if vividly, illustrated by Claire's disjunct memories. Now he sat solid in the early-morning sun beside Roger on the bench outside the MacLarens' cottage, his plaid rough and smelling faintly of piss and heather, two days' stubble rasping as he scratched his jaw in thought.

I like him, God help me. And, God help me, I know what's going to happen to him. . . .

His eyes fixed in helpless fascination on the hollow of Dougal's throat, sun-brown and strong, framed in the open collar of his crumpled shirt. Roger jerked his eyes away, glancing instead at the russet hairs on Dougal's wrist, these catching the sunlight as he motioned toward the east, talking of his brother, chieftain of the clan MacKenzie.

"Colum doesna travel, himself, but he'd be glad to welcome the two of ye, should you find yourselves near Leoch in your search." He smiled at Roger, who smiled back, warmed by it. "Where d'ye mean to go now?"

Roger took a deep breath. Where, indeed?

"South, I think. William found no trace of Cameron in Inverness, so I'm thinking that he might be headed toward Edinburgh, meaning to take ship there."

Dougal pursed his lips, nodding in thought.

"Well, then." He turned to his men, who had sat down on the rocks that lined the path, and called to them. "Geordie, Thomas—we'll lend your beasts to these men; get your bags. Ye'd have little chance of catching up to the villain on foot," he said, turning back to Roger. "He must be mounted himself, and moving fast, or ye'd have found some trace of him."

"I—thank you," Roger managed. He felt a deep chill, in spite of the sun on his face. "You must—I mean—that's very kind. We'll bring them back as soon as we can—or send them, if—if we should be detained anywhere."

"Moran taing," Buck murmured, nodding to Geordie and Thomas, who nodded back, looking dour but philosophical at the prospect of walking back to wherever they'd come from.

Where have *they come from?* Apparently, Angus MacLaren had sent his son off last night before supper, to summon Dougal to come and have a look at his alarming guests. But Dougal and his men had to have been somewhere close at hand . . .

The chink of metal as Jock dumped an obviously heavy bag on the ground beside Dougal gave him a clue. *Quarter Day.* Dougal was collecting the rents for his brother—and likely on his way back to Leoch. A lot of the rents would have been paid in kind—hams, chickens, wool, salt fish—probably Dougal's party was accompanied by one or more wagons, which they'd left behind wherever they'd stayed last night.

Angus MacLaren and his oldest son stood a little to the side, eyes fixed suspiciously on Roger as though he might sprout wings and fly away. Dougal turned to Angus with a smile and said in *Gàidhlig,* "Don't trouble, friend; they're nay more ghosts than the lads and I are."

"Do not forget to entertain strangers," Buck said in the same language, *"for thereby some have entertained angels unawares."*

There was a startled pause at that, everyone staring at him. Then Dougal laughed, and his men followed him. Angus merely made a polite noise in his throat but shifted his weight and visibly relaxed. As though this had been a signal—and perhaps it was—the door opened, and Mrs. MacLaren and Allie came out, with a stack of wooden bowls and a steaming pot of parritch. One of the smaller MacLarens came after, carefully bearing a saltcellar in both hands.

In the general hubbub of serving and eating—the women *had* oversalted his porridge, though not badly—Roger said quietly to Dougal, "Did MacLaren actually send to have you come and see whether I was a ghost?"

Dougal looked surprised but then smiled, one side of his mouth turning up. It was the way Brianna smiled when she wanted to acknowledge a joke she didn't think was funny—or when she saw something funny that she didn't mean to share with the company. A searing pang followed the jolt of recognition, and Roger was obliged to look down for a moment and clear his throat in order to get control of his voice.

"No, man," Dougal said casually, also looking down as he wiped his bowl with a bit of hard journeycake taken from his saddlebag. "He thought I might be of help to ye in your search." He looked up then, straight at Roger's neck, and raised one dark, heavy brow. "Not that the presence of a half-hangit man at your door doesna raise questions, ken?"

"At least a half-hangit man can answer the questions," Buck put in. "Not like him from the croft above, aye?"

That startled Dougal, who put down his spoon and stared at Buck. Who stared back, one fair brow raised.

Holy Lord . . . do they see it? Either of them? It wasn't warm, despite the sun, but Roger felt sweat begin to trickle down his spine. It was more a matter of posture and expression than of feature—and yet the echo of similarity between the two faces was plain as the . . . well, as the long, straight nose on both faces.

Roger could see the thoughts flickering across Dougal's face: surprise, curiosity, suspicion.

"And what have ye to do with him above?" he asked, with a slight lift of his chin in the direction of the burnt-out croft.

"Not a thing, so far as I ken," Buck answered, with a brief shrug. "Only meaning as how if ye want to know what happened to my kinsman, ye can ask him. We've nothing to hide."

Thanks a lot, Roger thought, with a sideways look at his ancestor, who smiled blandly back at him and resumed gingerly eating his salty parritch. *Why the bloody hell did you say* that, *of all things?*

"I was hanged in mistake for another man," he said, as casually as possible, but he heard the voice grate in his throat, tightening, and had to stop to clear it. "In America."

"America," Dougal repeated, in open astonishment. All of them were staring at him now, men-at-arms and MacLarens both. "What took ye to America—and what brought ye back, come to that?"

"My wife has kin there," Roger replied, wondering what the devil Buck was up to. "In North Carolina, on the Cape Fear River." He very nearly named Hector and Jocasta Cameron, before remembering that Jocasta was Dougal's sister. Also that it was Culloden that had sent them to America—and Culloden hadn't happened yet.

And he won't live to see it, he thought, watching Dougal's face as he spoke, feeling a state of bemused horror. Dougal would die, hours before the battle, in the attics of Culloden House near Inverness, with Jamie Fraser's dirk sunk in the hollow of his throat.

He told the story of his hanging and rescue briefly, leaving out the context of the War of the Regulation—and leaving out Buck's role in getting him hanged, too. He could feel Buck there beside him, leaning forward, intent, but didn't look at him. Couldn't look at him without wanting to strangle him. Wanted to strangle him anyway.

He could barely speak by the time he finished, and his heart was thumping in his ears with suppressed rage. Everyone was looking at him, with a range of emotions from awe to sympathy. Allie MacLaren was openly sniffing, her apron hem at her nose, and even her mother looked as though she somewhat regretted the salt. Angus coughed and handed him a stone bottle of what turned out to be beer, and a very grateful beverage it was, too. He muttered thanks and gulped it, avoiding all eyes.

Dougal nodded soberly, then turned to Angus.

"Tell me about the man above," he said. "When did that happen—and what d'ye ken about it?"

MacLaren's face lost a little of its natural high color, and he looked as though he wanted his beer back.

"Six days past, *a ghoistidh.*" He gave a brief, and much less atmospheric, account than he had the night before—but it was the same story.

Dougal looked thoughtful, tapping his fingers gently on his knee.

"The woman," he said. "D'ye ken where she's gone?"

"I . . . uh . . . heard as how she'd gone to Cranesmuir, sir." MacLaren's color had all come back, with interest, and he carefully avoided his wife's hard eye.

"Cranesmuir," Dougal repeated. "Aye, well. Perhaps I'll seek her out, then, and just have a word. What's her name?"

"Isbister," MacLaren blurted. "Geillis Isbister."

Roger didn't actually feel the earth shake under his feet but was surprised that it hadn't.

"Isbister?" Dougal's brows went up. "From the northern isles, is she?"

MacLaren shrugged in elaborate pantomime of ignorance—and unconcern. He looked as though someone had made a serious attempt to boil his head, and Roger saw Dougal's mouth twitch again.

"Aye," he said dryly. "Well, an Orkneywoman maybe won't be hard to find, then, in a place the size of Cranesmuir." He lifted his chin in the direction of his men, and they all rose as one when he stood. So did Roger and Buck.

"Godspeed to ye, gentlemen," he said, bowing to them. "I'll have word put about regarding your wee lad. If I hear anything, where shall I send?"

Roger exchanged glances with Buck, nonplussed. He couldn't ask for word to be sent to Lallybroch, knowing what he knew of the relations between Brian Fraser and his brothers-in-law.

"Do ye ken a place called Sheriffmuir?" he asked, groping for some other place he knew that existed at the present time. "There's a fine coaching inn there—though not much else."

Dougal looked surprised but nodded.

"I do, sir. I fought at Sheriffmuir with the Earl of Mar, and we supped there with him one night, my father and brother and I. Aye, I'll send word there, if there is any."

"Thank you." The words came half choked but clear enough. Dougal gave him a sympathetic nod, then turned to take leave of the MacLarens. Stopped by a sudden thought, though, he turned back.

"I dinna suppose ye really are an angel, are ye?" he asked, quite seriously.

"No," Roger said, smiling as best he could, despite the coldness in his belly. *And it isn't you that's talking to a ghost.*

He stood with Buck, watching the MacKenzies depart, Geordie and Thomas keeping up with little effort, as the horses went slowly on the steep, rocky path.

The phrase *"Blessed are those who have not seen but have believed"* floated through his head. It was maybe not the believing that was the blessing; it was the not having to look. Seeing, sometimes, was bloody awful.

ROGER DELAYED their own departure as long as he decently could, hoping for the return of Dr. McEwan, but as the sun rose high in the sky, it was plain that the MacLarens wanted them gone—and Buck wanted to go.

"I'm fine," he said crossly, and thumped his chest with a fist. "Sound as a drum."

Roger made a skeptical noise in his throat—and was surprised. It hadn't hurt. He stopped himself putting a hand to his own throat; no need to draw attention to it, even if they were leaving.

"Aye, all right." He turned to Angus MacLaren and Stuart, who'd helpfully filled Roger's canteen in the hope of hurrying them on their way and was standing with it dripping in his hands. "I thank ye for your hospitality, sir, and your kindness to my kinsman."

"Och," said MacLaren, a distinct look of relief coming over his face at what was plainly farewell. "That's fine. Nay bother."

"If—if the healer should come along, would ye thank him for us? And say I'll try to come and see him on our way back."

"On your way back," MacLaren repeated, with less enthusiasm.

"Aye. We're bound into Lochaber, to the Cameron lands. If we find nay trace of my son there, though, we'll likely come back this way—perhaps we'll call at Castle Leoch for news."

MacLaren's face cleared at that.

"Och, aye," he said heartily. "Good thought. Godspeed!"

41

IN WHICH THINGS CONVERGE

"NOW, IT'S NOT that I dinna want to be helping your mam," Mr. Buchan said, for the third time. "But I canna be having ructions going on in my house, and criminals coming and goin,' not with my girls there, now, can I?"

Jem shook his head obediently, though Mr. Buchan wasn't looking at him; he was peering into his rearview mirror and looking over his shoulder now and then, like he thought somebody might be following them. It made Jem want to look, too, but he couldn't see behind without getting up on his knees and turning round, and Mandy was passed out asleep, half on his lap.

It was late, and he yawned, forgetting to cover his mouth. He thought of saying, "Excuse me," but he didn't think Mr. Buchan had noticed. He felt a burp coming and did cover his mouth this time, tasting vinegar from the fish and chips. Mr. Buchan had bought an extra fish supper for Mam; it was in a brown-paper bag on the floor by Jem's feet, so as not to get grease on the seat.

"Ken when your da's expected back?" Mr. Buchan asked abruptly, glancing down at him. Jem shook his head, feeling the fish and chips rise up in a queasy ball.

Mr. Buchan's mouth pressed tight, like he wanted to say something he thought he shouldn't.

"Daddy . . ." Mandy murmured, then pushed her head into his ribs, snorted, and went back to sleep. He felt terrible. Mandy didn't even know where Da was; she probably thought he was just at lodge or something.

Mam said Da would come back, as soon as he figured out that Jem wasn't there with Grandda. *But how?* he thought, and had to bite his lip hard not to cry. *How would he know?* It was dark, but there was a glow from the dashboard. If he cried, Mr. Buchan would maybe see.

Headlights flashed in the rearview mirror and he looked up, brushing his sleeve furtively under his nose. He could see a white panel truck coming up behind them. Mr. Buchan said something under his breath and stepped on the gas pedal harder.

BRIANNA HAD SETTLED into the hunter's wait: a state of physical detachment and mental abeyance, mind and body each minding its own business but able to spring into unified action the moment something worth eating showed up. Her mind was on the Ridge, reliving a possum hunt with her cousin Ian. The pungent stickiness and eye-watering smoke of pine-knot torches, a glimpse of glowing eyes in a tree, and a sudden bristling possum like a nightmare in the branches, needle-toothed and gaping threats, hissing and growling like a flatulent motorboat . . .

And then the phone rang. In an instant she was standing, gun in hand, every sense trained on the house. It came again, the short double *brr!* muffled by distance but unmistakable. It was the phone in Roger's study, and even as she thought this, she saw the brief glow of a light inside as the study door was opened, and the ringing phone abruptly stopped.

Her scalp contracted, and she felt a brief kinship with the treed possum. But the possum hadn't had a shotgun.

Her immediate impulse was to go and flush out whoever was in her house and demand to know the meaning of this. Her money was on Rob Cameron, and the thought of flushing him like a grouse and marching him out at the point of a gun made her hand tighten on said gun with anticipation. She had Jem back; Cameron would know she didn't need to keep him alive.

But. She hesitated in the door of the broch, looking down.

But whoever was in the house had answered the phone. *If I was a burglar, I wouldn't be answering the phone in the house I was burgling. Not unless I thought it would wake up the people inside.*

Whoever was in her house already knew no one was home.

"Quod erat demonstrandum," her father's voice said in her mind, with a grim satisfaction. Someone in the house was expecting a call.

She stepped outside, with a deep breath of the fresh cold scent of gorse replacing the dank musk of the broch, her heart beating fast and her mind working faster. *Who would be calling him—them? To say what?*

Maybe someone had been watching earlier, seen her coming down the forestry road. Maybe they were calling to tell Rob she was outside, in the broch. No, that didn't make sense. Whoever was in the house, they'd *been* in there when she arrived. If someone had seen her come, they'd have called the house then.

"Ita sequitur . . ." she murmured. *Thus it follows:* if the call wasn't about her, it must be either a warning that someone—the police, and why?—was coming toward Lallybroch—or news that whoever was on the outside had found the kids.

The metal of the barrel was slick under her sweating palm, and it took a noticeable effort to keep a firm grip on the gun. Even more of an effort not to run toward the house.

Aggravating as it was, she had to wait. If someone had found the kids, she couldn't reach Fiona's house in time to protect them; she'd have to depend on Fiona and Ernie and the City of Inverness police. But if that was the case, whoever was in the house would surely be coming out right away. *Unless that bastard Rob means to hang around in hopes of catching me unawares, and . . .* Despite the gun in her hand, that thought gave her an unpleasant squirm deep inside—one she recognized as the ghostly touch of Stephen Bonnet's penis.

"I killed you, Stephen," she said under her breath. "And I'm glad you're dead. You may have company in hell pretty soon. Make sure the fire's lit for him, okay?"

That restored her nerve, and dropping to her haunches, she duckwalked through the gorse, coming down the hillside at an angle that would bring her out near the kailyard, not by the path, which was visible from the house. Even in the dark, she was taking no chances; there was a rising half-moon, though it showed erratically through scudding cloud.

The sound of a car coming made her lift her head, peering over a tuft of dry broom. She put a hand in her pocket, thumbing through the loose shotgun shells. Fourteen. That should be enough.

Fiona's remark about ballistics flitted through her mind, along with a faint reminder of the possibility of going to prison for wholesale manslaughter. She might risk it, for the satisfaction of killing Rob Cameron—but the unwelcome thought occurred to her that while she didn't need him to locate Jem anymore, she *did* need to find out what the hell was going on. And while the police might track down the man from the dam, if there was some sort of gang involved, Rob was likely the only way of finding out who the others were—and what they wanted.

The headlights jounced down the lane and into the dooryard, and she stood up abruptly. The motion-detecting light had come on, showing her Ernie's white panel truck, unmistakable, with BUCHAN ELECTRICS/FOR ALL YOUR CURRENT NEEDS, CALL 01463 775 4432 on the side, with a drawing of a severed cable, spitting sparks.

"Bloody hell," she said. "Bloody, *bloody* hell!"

The truck's door opened and Jem tumbled out, then turned round to help Mandy, who was no more than a short dark blot in the recesses of the truck.

"GET BACK IN THE TRUCK!" Brianna bellowed, leaping down the slope, skittering on rolling stones and bending her ankles in spongy patches of heather. "JEMMY! GET BACK!"

She saw Jem turn, his face white in the glare of the light, but it was too late. The front door flew open and two dark figures rushed out, running for the truck.

She wasted no more breath but ran for all she was worth. A shotgun was useless at any distance—or maybe not. She skidded to a halt, shouldered the gun, and fired. Buckshot flew into the gorse with a whizzing sound like tiny arrows, but the bang had halted the intruders in their tracks.

"BACK IN THE TRUCK!" she roared, and fired again. The intruders galloped toward the house, and Jem, bless his heart, leapt into the truck like a startled frog and slammed the door. Ernie, who had just got out, stood for a moment gawking up the slope, but then, realizing what had happened, came suddenly to life and dived for his own door.

She ran for Ernie's truck. More headlights jerked her attention toward the lane. Holy Mary, Mother of God, who was this? *Please, God, let it be the police . . .*

The light winked out, then on again almost at once, as the second vehicle roared into the dooryard, moving fast. The people inside the house were hanging out of the drawing room casement, yelling something at the new truck—yes, it was another panel truck, much like Ernie's, save that it said POULTNEY'S, PURVEYOR OF FINE GAME and had a picture of a wild boar.

"Holy Mary, Mother of God, pray for us sinners now and at the hour of our death . . ." She had to get to Ernie's truck before—too late. The FINE GAME truck revved up and rammed Ernie's truck in the side, shunting it several yards. She could hear Mandy's scream above everything, sharp as an augur through her heart.

"Bloody Mother of . . . Jesus H. Roosevelt Christ!" She couldn't take time to circle the dooryard. She ran straight across it, took close aim, and shredded the front tire of the FINE GAME truck with a blast of buckshot.

"STAY IN THE TRUCK!" she shouted, pointing the gun at the windshield. A blur of white as at least two people ducked down out of sight below the dash.

The men—yes, both men—inside the house were yelling at each other, and at the people in the truck, and at her. Useless adjurations and insults, mostly, but one of them was now pointing out to the others that her weapon *was* a shotgun. Useless except at short range.

"You can't cover us all, hen!"

That was Rob Cameron, shouting from the Poultney's truck. She didn't bother replying but ran to get in range of the house, and the drawing room window dissolved in a shower of glass.

Sweat was running down her sides, tickling. She felt as though she were moving in slow motion—but the rest of the world was moving slower. With no sense of hurry, she walked to Ernie's truck and put her back against the door behind which Jem and Mandy were sheltering. A strong waft of fish and malt vinegar floated out as the window cranked down a few inches.

"Mam—"

"Mummy! Mummy!"

"Bloody hell, Brianna! What's going on?"

"A bunch of nutters are trying to kill me and take my kids, Ernie," she said, raising her voice over Mandy's wailing. "What does it look like? How about you start the engine, hmm?"

The other truck was out of effective shotgun range from here, and she could see only one side of it. She heard its door open on the other side and saw a flicker of movement inside the shattered window of the house.

"*Now* would be a good time, Ernie." She wasn't forgetting that one of the bastards had her rifle. She could only hope they didn't know how to use it.

Ernie was frantically turning the key and stomping the gas. She could hear him praying under his breath, but he'd flooded the engine; the starter whirred uselessly. Lower lip tucked under her teeth, she strode round the front of the truck in time to catch one of the people from the FINE GAME truck—to her surprise, this one was a woman, a short, dumpy shape in a balaclava and an old Barbour. She raised the shotgun to her shoulder, and the woman tried to run backward, tripped, and fell on her backside with an audible "Oof!"

She wanted to laugh but then saw Cameron climbing out of the truck, her rifle in hand, and the urge left her.

"Drop it!" She strode toward him, gun at her shoulder. He *didn't* know how to use the rifle; he glanced wildly from her to the gun, as though hoping it would aim itself, then changed his mind and dropped it.

The front door of the house slammed open, and she heard running feet coming fast. She whirled on her heel and ran, too, reaching Ernie's truck barely in time to hold off the two men from the house. One immediately began to sidle round, clearly meaning to circle the other truck and collect his idiot comrades. Rob Cameron was now advancing on her slowly, hands held up to show his non-offensive—*ha*—intent.

"Look, Brianna, we don't mean ye any harm," he said.

She swung the barrel toward him in answer to that, and he took a step back.

"I mean it," he said, an edge in his voice. "We want to talk to you, is all."

"Aye, pull the other one," she said, "it's got bells on. *Ernie?*"

"Mam—"

"Don't you dare open that door until I say so, Jemmy!"

"Mam!"

"Get down on the floor, Jem, right now! Take Mandy!" One of the men from the house and the dumpy woman were moving again; she could hear them. And the second man from the house had disappeared into the dark outside the circle of light. "ERNIE!"

"But, Mam, somebody's coming!"

Everyone froze for an instant, and the sound of an engine advancing down the farm track came clearly through the night. She turned and grabbed the door handle, jerking it open just as Ernie's engine finally coughed into full-throated life. She hurled herself into the seat, her feet narrowly missing Jem's head as he peered up from the footwell, eyes huge in the dim light.

"Let's go, Ernie," she said, very calmly under the circumstance. "Kids, you stay down there."

A rifle butt struck the window near Ernie's head, starring the glass, and he yelped but didn't, God bless him, flood the engine again. Another blow and the glass broke in a cascade of glittering fragments. Brianna dropped her own gun and lunged across Ernie, reaching for the rifle. She got a hand on it, but the man holding it wrenched it free. Grabbing wildly, she scrabbled at the balaclava'd shape, and the woolly helmet came off in her hand, leaving the man beneath openmouthed with shock.

The spotlight went off, plunging the yard into darkness, and bright spots danced in front of her eyes. It popped back on again as the new vehicle roared into the yard, horn blaring. Brianna lifted herself out of Ernie's lap, trying to see out through the windshield, then flung herself toward the other side of the truck.

It was an ordinary car, a dark-blue Fiat, looking like a toy as it circled the yard, horn blatting like a sow in heat.

"Friend, d'ye think?" Ernie asked, his voice strained but not panicked. "Or foe?"

"Friend," she said, breathless, as the Fiat charged three of the intruders who were standing together: the unmasked rifle-wielder, the woman in the Barbour jacket, and whoever the guy who wasn't Rob Cameron was. They scattered like cockroaches into the grass, and Ernie slammed a fist on the dash in exultation.

"That'll show the buggers!"

Bree would have liked to stay and watch the rest of the show, but wherever Cameron was, he was undoubtedly too close.

"*Go,* Ernie!"

He went, with a terrible crunching and screeching of metal. The van lurched badly; the back axle must be damaged. She could only hope a wheel didn't come off.

The blue Fiat was prowling the dooryard; it honked and flashed its lights at Ernie's truck, and a hand waved from the driver's window. Brianna stuck her head out cautiously and returned the wave, then dropped back into her seat, panting. Black spots were swimming in her field of vision and her hair stuck to her face, lank with sweat.

They limped down the lane in first gear, with a horrible grinding noise; from the sound of it, the back wheel well had caved in.

"Mam." Jemmy stuck his head up over the edge of the seat like a prairie dog. "Can I come up now?"

"Sure." She took a deep breath and helped Mandy scramble up after him. The little girl plastered herself at once to Brianna's chest, whimpering.

"It's okay, baby," she whispered into Mandy's hair, clinging to the solid small body as much as Mandy clung to her. "Everything will be fine." She glanced down at Jem, riding between Ernie and herself. He was hunched into himself and shivering visibly in his checked wool jacket, even though it was warm in the cab. She reached out a hand and took him by the back of the neck, shaking him gently. "Okay there, pal?"

He nodded, but without saying anything. She folded her hand over his, clenched into a small fist on his knee, and held it tight—both in reassurance and to stop her own hand shaking.

Ernie cleared his throat.

"I'm sorry, Brianna," he said gruffly. "I didna ken that—I mean, I thought it would be okay to bring the bairns back, and after yon Cameron came to the house and hit Fiona, I—" A trickle of sweat gleamed as it ran down behind his ear.

"He what?" After the events of the last hour, this news registered only as a blip on her personal seismograph, obscured by the bigger shock waves that were only now dying down. But she asked questions, and Jem began to come out of his own shell shock, telling about his part, gradually becoming indignant about Mrs. Kelleher and the police dispatcher. She felt a quiver in the pit of her stomach that wasn't quite laughter but close enough.

"Don't worry about it, Ernie." She brushed off his renewed attempts at apology. Her voice rasped, her throat sore from shouting. "I'd have done the same, I expect. And we'd never have got away without you." They'd never have *been* there without him in the first place, but he knew that as well as she did; no point in rubbing it in.

"Aye, mmphm." He drove in silence for a moment, then remarked conversationally, looking in the rearview mirror, "Yon wee blue motor's following us, ken." His throat moved as he swallowed.

Brianna rubbed a hand over her face, then looked. Sure enough, the Fiat was trundling after them at a discreet distance.

Ernie coughed. "Ehm . . . where d'ye want to go, Bree? Only, I'm none sae sure we'll make it all the way into the town. But there's a petrol station with a garridge bay on the main road—if I was to stop there, they'd have a phone. Ye could call the polis while I deal wi' the van."

"Don't call the polis, Mam," Jemmy said, his nostrils flaring with disgust. "*They're* no help."

"Mmphm," she said noncommittally, and raised an eyebrow at Ernie, who nodded and set his jaw.

She was inclined against calling the police herself—but out of concern lest they be *too* inquisitively helpful. She'd managed to deflect them from the touchy question of just where her husband was last night, telling them he was in London to visit the British Museum Reading Room and that she'd call him as soon as they got home. If the police found out about the shoot-out at the O.K. Corral, there was going to be a lot more scrutiny of her private affairs. And it took no stretch of imagination at all to conclude that the police might really suspect her of having something to do with Roger's disappearance, since she couldn't produce him and couldn't tell them where he was. *Might never be able to.* She swallowed, hard.

The only recourse would be to claim that they'd had a fight and he'd walked out on her—but that would sound pretty flimsy, in light of recent events. And she wouldn't say something like that in front of the kids, regardless.

But stopping at the petrol station was the only thing she could see to do at the moment. If the blue Fiat followed them there, at least she might discover an ally. And if it was the police, incognito . . . well, she'd cross that bridge when she came to it. Adrenaline and shock had both left her now; she felt detached, dreamy, and very, very tired. Jemmy's hand had relaxed in hers, but his fingers were still curled around her thumb.

She leaned back, closing her eyes, and slowly traced the curve of Mandy's spine with her free hand. Her little girl had relaxed into sleep against her chest, her son with his head on her shoulder, the weight of her children's trust heavy on her heart.

THE PETROL STATION was next to a Little Chef café. She left Ernie to talk to the garageman while she extracted the kids. She didn't bother looking over her shoulder; the blue Fiat had fallen back to a respectful distance, not crowding them as they crawled clanking and grinding down the motorway at 20 mph. If the driver didn't mean to talk to her, he'd have driven off and disappeared. Maybe she'd manage a cup of tea before she had to deal with him.

"Can't wait," she muttered. "Get the door, please, Jem?"

Mandy was inert as a bag of cement in her arms but began to stir at the smell of food. Bree gagged at the reek of stale frying oil, burnt chips, and synthetic pancake syrup, but ordered ice cream for Jem and Mandy, with a cup of tea for herself. Surely even this place couldn't ruin tea?

A cup of barely warm water and a PG Tips tea bag convinced her otherwise. It didn't matter; her throat was so tight that she doubted she could swallow even water.

The blessed numbness of shock was lifting, much as she would have preferred to keep it wrapped blanket-like around her. The café seemed too bright, with acres of foot-marked white lino; she felt exposed, like a bug on a grimy kitchen floor. Prickles of apprehension sparked unpleasantly over her scalp, and she kept her eyes fixed on the door, wishing she'd been able to bring the shotgun inside.

She didn't realize that Jem had also been watching the door until he stiffened to attention beside her in the booth.

"Mam! It's Mr. Menzies!"

For a moment, neither the words nor the sight of the man who had just entered the café made any sense. She blinked several times, but he was still there, striding toward them with an anxious face. Jem's school principal.

"Mrs. MacKenzie," he said, and, reaching across the table, shook her hand fervently. "Thank God you're all right!"

"Er . . . thanks," she said feebly. "You—was that *you*? In the blue Fiat?" It was like being keyed up to confront Darth Vader and coming face-to-face with Mickey Mouse.

He actually blushed behind his glasses.

"Ehm . . . well, aye. I—er . . ." He caught Jem's eye and smiled awkwardly. "You're taking good care of your mother, then, Jem?"

"Aye, sir." Jem was quite obviously about to burst with questions. Bree forestalled him with a quelling look and gestured to Lionel Menzies to sit down. He did and took a deep breath, about to say something, but was interrupted by the waitress, a solid, middle-aged woman with thick stockings and a cardigan and an air that indicated that she didn't care whether they were space aliens or cockroaches, so long as they didn't complicate her life.

"Don't order the tea," Bree said, with a nod toward her cup.

"Aye, thanks. I'll have . . . a bacon butty and an Irn-Bru?" he asked tentatively, looking up at the waitress. "With tomato sauce?" She scorned to reply but flipped her pad shut and trundled off.

"Right," Menzies said, squaring his shoulders like one about to face a firing squad. "Tell me the one thing, would you? Was it Rob Cameron there at your house?"

"It was." Bree spoke tersely, recalling belatedly that Cameron was related to Menzies in some way—a cousin or something? "Why?"

He looked unhappy. A pale-faced man with slightly receding curly brown hair and glasses, he wasn't remarkable in any way and yet usually had a presence, a friendliness and quiet air of authority about him that drew the eye and made one feel reassured in his company. This was notably lacking tonight.

"I was afraid that it might be. I heard—on the evening news. That Rob was being looked for by the police"—he lowered his voice, though there was no one within earshot—"in connection with . . . well, with"—he nodded discreetly toward Jem—"taking Jeremiah, here."

"He did!" Jem said, dropping his spoon and sitting up straight. "He did, Mr. Menzies! He said he was going to take me to spend the night with Bobby, only he didn't, he took me up to the rocks and—"

"Jem." Brianna spoke quietly, but it was her Shut Up Right Now voice, and he did, though with an audible snort and a glare at her.

"Yes, he did," she said levelly. "What do you know about it?"

He blinked in surprise.

"I—why, nothing. I can't imagine why he—" He broke off, coughed, and taking his glasses off, pulled a pocket handkerchief out and polished them. By the time he put them back on, he'd pulled himself together.

"You may remember, Rob Cameron's my cousin. And he's in lodge, of course. I was knocked off my perch to hear this about him. So I thought I'd maybe come out to Lallybroch, have a word with you and your husband"—he lifted an eyebrow, but she didn't respond to this obvious hint about Roger, and he went on—"see that Jem was all right—are ye all right, Jem?" he broke off to ask seriously, glancing at the boy.

"Oh, aye, fine," Jem replied airily, though he seemed tense. "Sir," he added belatedly, and licked a smear of chocolate ice cream off his upper lip.

"That's good." Menzies smiled at Jem, and Brianna saw a little of his usual warmth light up behind the glasses. The warmth was still in his eyes, though he was serious when he looked at her. "I wanted to ask if there'd maybe been a mistake, but I'm thinking that there likely wasn't? In light of . . . all that." He tilted his head in the direction of Lallybroch and swallowed.

"Yes, there was," she said grimly, shifting Mandy's weight on her lap, "and Rob Cameron made it."

He grimaced, drew a deep breath, but nodded.

"I'd like to help," he said simply.

"You definitely did," she assured him, wondering what on earth to do with him now. "Ick! Mandy, you're dribbling all over everywhere! Use a napkin, for heaven's sake." She swabbed Mandy's face briskly, ignoring her daughter's cranky whine. *Could* he help? She wanted badly to believe him; she was still shaking internally and all too ready to grab at any offer of assistance.

But he *was* Rob Cameron's relative. And maybe he'd come out to the house to talk, and maybe he'd come for some other reason. He might, after all, have intervened to keep her from blasting Rob into bloody shreds, rather than to save her and the kids from Rob and his masked sidekicks.

"I spoke to Ernie Buchan," Menzies said, nodding toward the plate-glass window. "He, um, seemed to think that you might not want the police involved?"

"No." Bree's mouth was dry; she sipped the lukewarm tea, trying to think. It was getting harder by the moment; her thoughts scattered like drops of quicksilver, wobbling away in a dozen directions. "Not—not just yet. We were at the police station half of last night. I really can't deal with any more questions tonight." She took a deep breath and stared at him directly.

"I don't know what's going on," she said. "I don't know why Rob Cameron should have kidnapped Jemmy—"

"Yes, you d—" Jem started, and she whipped her head round and glared at him. He glared back, red-eyed and clench-fisted, and with a jolt of alarm she recognized the Fraser temper, about to go off with a bang.

"You do so know!" he said, loudly enough that a couple of truckers at the counter turned round to look at him. "I *told* you! He wanted me to—" Mandy, who had started to drop off again, jerked awake and started to wail.

"I want Daddeeeee!"

Jem's face was bright red with fury. At this, it went white.

"Shut up, shut up, shut up!" he shrieked at Mandy, who yelped in terror and screamed louder, trying to scramble up Brianna's body.

"DADDEEE!"

"Jem!" Lionel Menzies was on his feet, reaching for the boy, but Jem was absolutely beside himself, literally hopping up and down with rage. The entire restaurant was gaping at them.

"Go AWAY!" Jem roared at Menzies. "DAMMIT! Don't you touch me! Don't touch my mam!" And, in an excess of passion, he kicked Menzies hard on the shin.

"Jesus!"

"Jem!" Bree had a grip on the struggling, bawling Mandy but couldn't reach Jem before he picked up his dish of ice cream, flung it at the wall, and then ran out of the café, crashing the door open so hard that a man and woman on the verge of entering were forced to leap aside to avoid being knocked over as he rocketed past.

Brianna sat down quite suddenly, as all the blood left her head. *Holy Mary, Mother of God, pray for us . . .*

The room was silent, save for Mandy's sobbing, though this was dying down as her panic subsided. She burrowed into Brianna's chest, burying her face in the padded coat.

"Hush, sweetie," Bree whispered, bending her head so that Mandy's curls brushed her lips. "Hush, now. It's all right. Everything will be all right."

A muffled mumble ended with a tearful ". . . Daddy?"

"Yes," Bree said firmly. "We'll see Daddy soon."

Lionel Menzies cleared his throat. He'd sat down to massage his shin but left off doing this to gesture toward the door. "Had I . . . better go after Jem?"

"No. He's all right . . . I mean . . . he's with Ernie. I can see him." They were in the parking lot, just visible in the glow of light from the neon sign. Jem had cannoned into Ernie, who was coming toward the restaurant, and was clinging to him like a limpet. As Brianna watched, Ernie, an experienced father, knelt down and hugged Jem to him, patting his back and smoothing his hair, talking earnestly to him.

"Mmphm." It was the waitress with Menzie's butty, her

stolid face melted into sympathy. "The wee lassie's tired, nay doubt."

"I'm sorry," Bree said feebly, and nodded at the shattered dish and splotch of chocolate ice cream on the wall. "I'll, um, pay for it."

"Och, dinna fash, lass," the waitress said, shaking her head. "I've had weans. I can see ye've got enough trouble to be goin' on with. Let me fetch ye oot a nice cup o' tea."

She trundled off. Without speaking, Lionel Menzies popped the tab on his can of Irn-Bru and shoved it in her direction. She picked it up and gulped it. The advertising implied that the stuff was made from rusty iron girders salvaged from Glasgow shipyards. Only in Scotland would this have been considered a good selling point, she reflected. But it was about half sugar, and the glucose hit her bloodstream like the elixir of life.

Menzies nodded, seeing her straighten up like a wilting flower revived.

"Where *is* Roger?" he asked softly.

"I don't know," she said, just as softly; Mandy had given a final hiccuping sigh and fallen heavily asleep, face still buried in Brianna's coat. She twitched the quilted fabric aside so Mandy wouldn't suffocate. "And I don't know when he's coming back."

He grimaced, looking unhappy and strangely embarrassed; he was having trouble meeting her eyes.

"I see. Mmphm. Was it—I mean, did he . . . leave because of what Rob . . . er . . . did to Jem?" His voice dropped even lower and she blinked at him. Rising blood sugar had brought her thoughts back into focus, though, and suddenly the penny dropped, and the blood rushed into her face.

He thought Rob had abducted Jemmy in order to—and Jemmy had said, *"You know what he did,"* and she'd shut him up sharp . . . and she'd said she didn't want the police involved . . . oh, dear Lord. She took a deep breath and rubbed a hand over her face, wondering whether it was better to let him think Rob had molested Jemmy—and was now trying to murder her in order to cover that up—or to tell him some halfway believable version of some part of the truth.

"Rob came to my house last night and tried to rape me," she said, leaning over Mandy's head in order to keep her voice low enough to escape the flapping ears of the truckers sitting at the counter, who were glancing covertly over their shoulders at her. "He'd already taken Jem, and Roger had left to try to find him. We thought he'd taken Jem away to . . . to Orkney." *That seems far enough.* "I . . . left messages; I expect Roger'll be back any time now—as soon as he hears that Jemmy's been found." She crossed her fingers under the table.

Menzies's face went blank, all his previous assumptions colliding with new ones.

"He—he—oh." He paused for a moment, mechanically took a swallow of her cold tea, and made a face. "You mean," he said carefully, "that you think Rob took Jem in order to lure your husband away, so that he . . . ehm . . . could—"

"Yes, I do." She seized on this suggestion gratefully.

"But . . . those other people. With the—" He passed a hand vaguely over his head, indicating the balaclavas. "What on earth . . . ?"

"I have *no* idea," she said firmly. She wasn't going to mention the Spanish gold unless or until she had to. The fewer people who knew about that, the better. And as for the other thing . . .

But the mention of "those other people" reminded her of something, and she groped in her capacious pocket, drawing out the balaclava that she'd snatched off the man who'd broken the window with the rifle. She'd caught the barest glimpse of his face amidst the shifting light and shadow and had had no time to think about it. But now she did, and a fresh qualm went through her.

"Do you know a man named Michael Callahan?" she asked, trying to keep her voice casual. Menzies glanced at the balaclava, then at her, eyes widening.

"Of course I do. He's an archaeologist, something to do with ORCA—Orkney Research Centre, I mean. Orkney . . . You're no telling me he was with the people who—"

"Pretty sure. I saw his face for just a second when I pulled this off him. And"—she grimaced in distaste, plucking a tuft of sandy hair from the inside of the balaclava—"apparently that's not all I pulled off him. Rob knows him. He came out to Lallybroch to give us an opinion on some ruins up behind the house, and stayed to supper."

"Oh, dearie me," Menzies murmured, seeming to sink back into his seat. He took off his glasses and massaged his forehead for a bit. She watched him think, feeling increasingly remote.

The waitress hove to and put down a fresh cup of hot, milky tea, already sugared and stirred. Brianna thanked her and sat sipping it, watching the night outside. Ernie had taken Jem off in the direction of the garage, doubtless to check on his van.

"I can see why you don't want trouble," Menzies said carefully at last. He'd eaten half his butty; the rest of it lay on the plate, oozing ketchup in a queasy sort of way. "But really, Mrs.—may I call you Brianna?"

"Bree," she said. "Sure."

"Bree," he said, nodding, and one corner of his mouth twitched.

"Yes, I know what it means in Scots," she said dryly, seeing the thought cross his face. A bree was a storm or a great disturbance.

Lionel's face broke into a half smile.

"Yes. Well . . . what I'm thinking, Bree—I hate to suggest it, but what if Rob's done some harm to Roger? Would it not be worth the questions to get the police to look for him?"

"He hasn't." She felt unutterably tired and wanted only to go home. "Believe me, he hasn't. Roger went with his—his cousin, Buck. And if Rob had managed to hurt them somehow, he'd certainly have gloated about that when he . . . well." She took a breath that went all the way down to her aching feet and shifted her weight, getting a solid hold on Mandy.

"Lionel. Tell you what. Drive us home, will you? If that lot's still lurking around, then we'll go to the police right away. If not—it can wait 'til the morning."

He didn't like it, but he was suffering from the aftereffects of shock and fatigue, too, and after more argument finally agreed, done in by her implacable stubbornness.

Ernie had telephoned for a ride, after being assured that Lionel would see them home. Lionel was tense on the way back to Lallybroch, hands white-knuckled on the steering wheel, but the Fiat's headlights showed the dooryard empty, save for a discarded tire lying in the gravel, shredded rubber spraying out like the wings of some gigantic vulture shot out of the sky.

Both the kids were sound asleep; Lionel carried Jem in, then insisted on searching the house with Bree, nailing up laths across the shattered window in the parlor while she combed the rooms—again—suffering déjà vu.

"Had I not better spend the night?" Lionel asked, hesitating at the door. "I'd be happy to sit up and keep watch, you know."

She smiled, though it took a lot of effort.

"Your wife will already be wondering where you are. No, you've done enough—more than enough for us. Don't worry; I'll . . . take steps in the morning. I just want the kids to be able to have a good night's sleep in their own beds."

He nodded, lips drawn in in worry, and glanced round the foyer, its gleaming walnut paneling serene in the lamplight, even the English saber slashes somehow grown homely and peaceful with age.

"Do you maybe have family—friends—in America?" he asked abruptly. "I mean, it might not be a bad idea to get right away for a bit, aye?"

"Yes," she said. "I was thinking that myself. Thanks, Lionel. Good night."

42

ALL MY LOVE

SHE WAS SHAKING. Had been shaking ever since Lionel Menzies left. With a faint sense of abstraction, she held out her hand, fingers spread, and watched it vibrate like a tuning fork. Then, irritated, made a fist and smacked it hard into the palm of her other hand. Smacked it again and again, clenching her teeth in fury, until she had to stop, gasping for breath, her palm tingling.

"Okay," she said under her breath, teeth still clenched. *"Okay."* The red haze had lifted like a cloud, leaving a pile of cold, icy little thoughts under it.

We have to go.

Where?

And when?

And the coldest of all:

What about Roger?

She was sitting in the study, the wood paneling glowing softly in the candlelight. There was a perfectly good reading lamp, as well as the ceiling fixture, but she'd lit the big candle instead. Roger liked to use that when he wrote late at night, writing down the songs and poems he'd memorized, sometimes with a goose quill. He said it helped him recall the words, bringing back an echo of the time where he'd learned them.

The candle's smell of hot wax brought back an echo of *him.* If she closed her eyes, she could hear him, humming low in his throat as he worked, stopping now and then to cough or clear his damaged throat. Her fingers rubbed softly over the wooden desk, summoning the touch of the rope scar on his throat, passing round to cup the back of his head, bury her fingers in the thick black warmth of his hair, bury her face in his chest . . .

She was shaking again, this time with silent sobs. She curled her fist again, but this time just breathed until it stopped.

"This will *not* do," she said out loud, sniffed deeply, and, clicking on the light, she blew out the candle and reached for a sheet of paper and a ballpoint pen.

WIPING THE TEARS off her face with the back of her hand, she folded the letter carefully. Envelope? No. If anybody found this, an envelope wouldn't stop them. She turned the letter over and, sniffing, wrote *Roger,* in her best parochial-school penmanship.

She groped in her pocket for a Kleenex and blew her nose, feeling obscurely that she should do something more . . . ceremonial? . . . with the letter, but other than putting it in the fireplace and touching a match to it so the north wind would carry it, as her parents had done with her childhood letters to Santa, nothing occurred to her.

In her present state of mind, she found it comforting that Santa had always come through.

She opened the big drawer and was groping at the back for the catch that released the secret hiding place when something else did occur to her. She slammed the big drawer shut and yanked open the wide shallow one in the center, which held pens and paper clips and rubber bands—and a lipstick left in the downstairs powder room by some random dinner guest.

It was pink but a dark pink, and it didn't matter that it clashed with her hair. She applied it hastily by feel, then pressed her lips carefully over the word *Roger.*

"I love you," she whispered, and, touching the pink kiss with one fingertip, opened the big drawer again and pushed the spot that unlocked the hiding place. It wasn't a secret drawer but a space built into the underside of the desk. A sliding panel let you reach up into a shallow hole about six inches by eight.

When Roger discovered it, it had three stamps printed with the head of Queen Victoria in it—unfortunately, all run-of-the-mill late-Victorian postage rather than a helpfully valuable One-Penny Black—and a wispy curl of a child's fine blond hair, faded with age, tied with white thread and a tiny scrap of heather. They'd left the stamps there—who knew, maybe they *would* be valuable by the time another few generations inherited the desk—but she'd put the lock of hair between the pages of her Bible and said a small prayer for the child and his—her?—parents, whenever she came across it.

The letter fit easily into the heart of the old desk. A moment of panic: should she have included locks of the kids' hair? *No,* she thought fiercely. *Don't be morbid. Sentimental, yes. Morbid, no.*

"Lord, let us all be together again," she whispered, pushing down the fear, and, closing her eyes, shut the panel with a little *click.*

If she hadn't opened her eyes right as she withdrew her hand, she'd never have seen it. Just the edge of something hanging down at the back of the big drawer, barely visible. She reached up and found an envelope, far back, attached to the underside of the desk with Scotch tape. This had dried with age; her earlier slamming of the drawer had probably loosened it.

She turned the envelope over with a sense of something happening in a dream and was, dreamlike, not surprised to see the initials *B.E.R.* written on the yellowed envelope. Very slowly, she opened it.

Dearest Deadeye, she read, and felt each tiny hair on her body rise slow and silent, one at a time.

Dearest Deadeye,

You've just left me, after our wonderful afternoon among the clay pigeons. My ears are still ringing. Whenever we shoot, I'm torn between immense pride in your ability, envy of it—and fear that you may someday need it.

What a queer feeling it is, writing this. I know that you'll eventually learn who—and perhaps, what—you are. But I have no idea how you'll come to that knowledge. Am I about to reveal you to yourself, or will this be old news when you find it? If we're both lucky, I may be able to tell you in person, when you're a little older. And if we're very lucky, it will come to nothing. But I daren't risk your life in that hope, and you're not yet old enough that I could tell you.

I'm sorry, sweetheart, that's terribly melodramatic. And the last thing I want to do is alarm you. I have all the confidence in the world in you. But I am your father and thus prey to the fears that afflict all parents—that something dreadful and unpreventable will happen to one's child, and you powerless to protect her.

"What the hell, Daddy?" She rubbed hard at the back of her neck to ease the prickling there.

Men who've lived through war usually don't talk about it, save to other soldiers. Men from my part of the Service don't talk to anyone, and not only because of the Official Secrets Act. But silence eats at the soul. I had to talk to someone, and my old friend Reggie Wakefield became my confessor.

(That's the Reverend Reginald Wakefield, a Church of Scotland minister who lives in Inverness. If you're reading this letter, I'll very likely be dead. If Reggie is still alive and you are of age, go to see him; he has my permission to tell you anything he knows at that point.)

"Of age?" Hastily, she tried to calculate when this had been written. Clay pigeons. Sherman's—the shooting range where he'd taught her to use a shotgun. The shotgun had been a present for her fifteenth birthday. And her father had died soon after her seventeenth birthday.

The Service has nothing directly to do with this; don't go looking in that direction for information. I mention it only because that's where I learned what a conspiracy looks like. I also met a great many people in the war, many of them in high places, and many of them strange; the two overlap more often than one might wish.

Why is this so hard to say? If I'm dead, your mother may have told you already the story of your birth. She promised me that she would never speak of it, so long as I lived, and I'm sure she hasn't. If I'm dead, though, she might—

Forgive me, darling. It's hard to say, because I love your mother and I love you. And you are my daughter forever, but you were sired by another man.

All right, that's out. Seeing it in black and white, my impulse is to rip this paper to bits and burn them, but I won't. You have to know.

Shortly after the war ended, your mother and I came to Scotland. Something of a second honeymoon. She went out one afternoon to pick flowers—and never came back. I searched—everyone searched—for months, but there was no sign, and eventually the police stopped—well, in fact they didn't stop suspecting me of murdering her, damn them, but they grew tired of harassing me. I had begun to put my life back together, made up my mind to move on, perhaps leave Britain—and then Claire came back. Three years after her disappearance, she showed up in the Highlands, filthy, starved, battered—and pregnant.

Pregnant, she said, by a Jacobite Highlander from 1743 named James Fraser. I won't go into all that was said between us; it was a long time ago and it doesn't matter—save for the fact that IF your mother was telling the truth, and did indeed travel back in time, then you may have the ability to do it, too. I hope you don't. But if you should—Lord, I can't believe I'm writing this in all seriousness. But I look at you, darling, with the sun on your ruddy hair, and I see him. I can't deny that.

Well. It took a long time. A very long time. But your mother never changed her story, and though we didn't speak about it after a while, it became obvious that she wasn't mentally deranged (which I had rather naturally assumed to be the case, initially). And I began . . . to look for him.

Now I must digress for a moment; forgive me. I think you won't have heard of the Brahan Seer. Colorful as he was—if, in fact, he existed—he's not really known much beyond those circles with a taste for the more outlandish aspects of Scottish history. Reggie, though, is a man of immense curiosity, as well as immense learning, and was fascinated by the Seer—one Kenneth MacKenzie, who lived in the seventeenth century (maybe), and who made a great number of prophecies about this and that, sometimes at the behest of the Earl of Seaforth.

Naturally, the only prophecies mentioned in connection with this man are the ones that appeared to come true: he predicted, for instance, that when there were five bridges over the River Ness, the world would fall into chaos. In August 1939 the fifth bridge over the Ness was opened, and in September, Hitler invaded Poland. Quite enough chaos for anyone.

The Seer came to a sticky end, as prophets often do (do please remember that, darling, will you?), burnt to death in a spiked barrel of tar at the instigation of Lady Seaforth—to whom he had unwisely prophesied that her husband was having affairs with various ladies while away in Paris. (That one was likely true, in my opinion.)

Amongst his lesser-known prophecies, though, was one called the Fraser Prophecy. There isn't a great deal known about this, and what there is is rambling and vague, as prophecies usually are, the Old Testament notwithstanding. The only relevant bit, I think, is this: "The last of Lovat's line will rule Scotland."

Pause if you will, now, dear, and look at the paper I am enclosing with this letter.

Fumbling and clumsy with shock, she dropped the sheets altogether and had to retrieve them from the floor. It was easy to tell which paper he meant; the paper was flimsier, a photocopy of a handwritten chart—some sort of family tree—the writing not her father's.

Yes. Well. This bit of disturbing information came into my hands from Reggie, who'd had it from the wife of a fellow named Stuart Lachlan. Lachlan had died suddenly, and as his widow was clearing out his desk, she found this and decided to pass it on to Reggie, knowing that he and Lachlan had shared an interest in history and in the Lovat family, they being local to Inverness; the clan seat is in Beauly. Reggie, of course, recognized the names.

You likely know nothing about the Scottish aristocracy, but I knew Simon Lovat, Lord Lovat that is, in the war—he was Commandos, then Special Forces. We weren't close friends but knew each other casually, in the way of business, you might say.

"Whose business?" she said aloud, suspicious. "His, or yours?" She could just see her father's face, with the hidden smile in the corner of his mouth, keeping something back but letting you know it was there.

The Frasers of Lovat have a fairly straightforward line of descent, until we come to Old Simon—well, they're all called Simon—the one they call the Old Fox, who was executed for treason after the Jacobite Rebellion—the '45, they call it. (There's quite a bit about him in my book on the Jacobites; don't know if you'll ever read that, but it's there, should you feel curious.)

"Should I feel curious," she muttered. "Ha." Brianna sensed a definite, if muted, note of accusation there and pressed her lips together, as much annoyed at herself for not having read her father's books yet as at him for mentioning it.

Simon was one of the more colorful Frasers, in assorted ways. He had three wives but was not famous for fidelity. He did have a few legitimate children, and God knows how many illegitimate ones (though two illegitimate sons were acknowledged), but his heir was Young Simon, known as the Young Fox. Young Simon survived the Rising, though attainted and stripped of his property. He eventually got most of it back through the courts, but the struggle took him most of a long life, and while he married, he did so at a very advanced age and had no children. His younger brother, Archibald, inherited, but then died childless, as well.

So Archibald was the "last of Lovat's line"—there's a direct line of descent between him and the Fraser of Lovat who would have been concurrent with the Brahan Seer—but clearly he wasn't the Scottish ruler foreseen.

You see the chart, though. Whoever made it has listed the two illegitimate sons, as well as Young Simon and his brother. Alexander and Brian, born to different mothers. Alexander entered the priesthood and became the abbot of a monastery in France. No known children. But Brian—

She tasted bile and thought she might throw up. *But Brian*—She closed her eyes in reflex, but it didn't matter. The chart was burned on the inside of her eyelids.

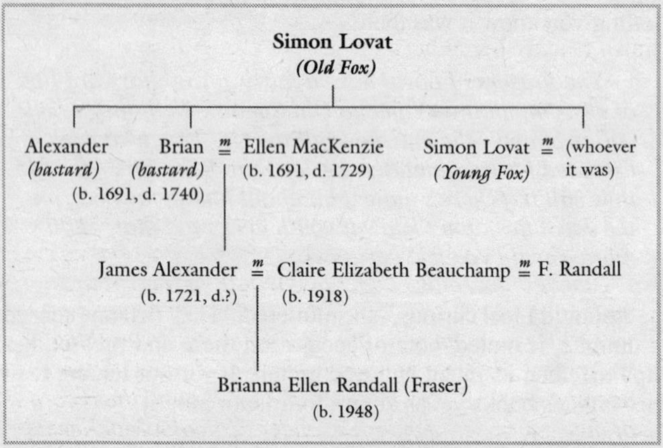

She stood up, pushing back the chair with a screak, and lurched out into the hallway, heart thundering in her ears. Swallowing repeatedly, she went to the lobby and got the shotgun from its place behind the coat rack. She felt a little better with it in hand.

"It isn't right." She hadn't realized that she'd spoken aloud; her own voice startled her. "It's not right," she repeated, in a low, fierce voice. "They left people out. What about Aunt Jenny? She had *six* kids! What about them?"

She was stomping down the hallway, gun in hand, swinging the barrel from side to side as though she expected Rob Cameron—or *somebody,* and the thought made her shudder—to jump out of the parlor or the kitchen or come sliding down the banister. That thought made her look up the stairs—she'd left all the lights on when she came down from tucking in the kids—but the landing was empty and no noise came from above.

A little calmer, she searched the ground floor carefully, testing every door and window. And the priest's hole, whose empty blackness gaped mockingly up at her.

Jem and Mandy were all right. She knew they were. But she still went upstairs, soft-footed, and stood by their beds for a long time, watching the pale glow of the Snow White night-light on their faces.

The longcase clock in the hall below struck the hour, and then a single *bong!* She drew a deep breath and went down to finish reading her father's letter.

The current line of Fraser of Lovat is descended from a collateral branch; presumably the Fraser Prophecy isn't referring to one of them—though there are plenty of heirs in that line.

I don't know who drew this chart, but I do intend to find out. This letter is in case I don't. In case of a number of things.

One of those things being the possibility that your mother's story is true—I still have difficulty believing it, when I wake in the morning beside her and everything is so normal. *But late at night, when I'm alone with the documents . . . Well, why not admit it? I found the record of their marriage. James Alexander Malcolm MacKenzie Fraser and Claire Elizabeth Beauchamp. I'm not sure whether to be grateful or outraged that she didn't marry him using* my *name.*

Forgive me, I'm rambling. It's hard to keep emotion out of it, but I'll try. The essence of what I'm saying is this: if you can indeed go back in time (and possibly return), you are a person of very great interest to a number of people, for assorted reasons. Should anyone in the more shadowed realm of government be halfway convinced that you are what you may be, you would be watched. Possibly approached. (In earlier centuries, the British government pressed men into service. They still do, if less obviously.)

That's a very remote contingency, but it is a real one; I must mention it.

There are private parties who would also have a deep interest in you for this reason—and evidently there is someone who has spotted you and is watching. The chart showing your line of descent, with dates, indicates that much. It also suggests that this person's or persons' interest may be a concern with the Fraser Prophecy. What could be more intriguing to that sort of person than the prospect of someone who is "the last of Lovat's line" and is also a time traveler? These sorts of people—I know them well—invariably believe in mystic powers of all sorts—nothing would draw them more powerfully than the conviction that you hold such power.

Such people are usually harmless. But they can be very dangerous indeed.

If I find whoever drew this chart, I will question them and do my best to neutralize any possible threat to you. But as I say—I know the look of a conspiracy. Nutters of this sort thrive in company. I might miss one.

"Neutralize them," she murmured, the chill in her hands spreading through her arms and chest, crystallizing around her heart. She had no doubt at all what he'd meant by that, the bland matter-of-factness of the term notwithstanding. And had he found him—them?

Don't—I repeat, don't*—go anywhere near the Service or anyone connected with it. At best, they'd think you insane. But if you are indeed what you may be, the last people who should ever know it are the funny buggers, as we used to be known during the war.*

And if worse should come to worst—and you can do it—then the past may be your best avenue of escape. I have no idea how it works; neither does your mother, or at least she says so. I hope I may have given you a few tools to help, if that should be necessary.

And . . . there's him. *Your mother said that Fraser sent her back to me, knowing that I would protect her—and you. She thought that he died immediately afterward. He did not. I looked for him, and I found him. And, like him, perhaps I send you back, knowing—as he knew of me—that he will protect you with his life.*

I will love you forever, Brianna. And I know whose child you truly are.

With all my love,
Dad

43

APPARITION

THE LOCHABER DISTRICT, according to the North of Scotland Hydro Electric Board (as interpreted by Brianna), is a "high glaciated landscape."

"That means it goes up and down a lot," Roger explained to Buck, as they fought their way through what he thought was part of the Locheil Forest, looking for the edge of Loch Lochy.

"Ye don't say?" Buck glanced bleakly over his shoulder at the distant hump of Ben Nevis, then back at Roger. "I'd not noticed."

"Cheer up, it's all downhill for a bit now. And the midgies are all dead wi' the cold. Count your blessings." Roger felt unaccountably cheerful this morning—perhaps only because the walking *was* downhill, after a strenuous week of combing the Cameron clan lands, a bewildering network of corries, tarns, moraines, and Munros, those deceptive summits with their gently rounded tops and their unspeakable slopes. Thank God no one lived on top of them.

Perhaps also because, while they hadn't found Jem or any trace of him, it was progress, of a sort. The Camerons on the whole had been hospitable, after the initial surprise, and they'd had the luck to find a tacksman of Lochiel, the clan chieftain, who'd sent a man to Tor Castle for them. Word had come back a day later: no word of a stranger matching Rob Cameron's description—though, in fact, Rob looked like half the people Roger had met in the last few days—or Jem's, he being a lot more noticeable.

They'd worked their way back along the shores of Loch Arkaig—the fastest way for someone to travel from the Great Glen, if heading for the ocean. But no word of a boat stolen or hired, and Roger began to feel that Cameron had not, after all, sought refuge or help among his ancient clan—a relief, on the whole.

"Blessings, is it?" Buck rubbed a hand over his face. Neither of them had shaved in a week, and he looked as red-eyed and grubby as Roger felt. He scratched his jaw consideringly. "Aye, well. A fox took a shit next to me last night, but I didna step in it this morning. I suppose that'll do, for a start."

The next day and night dampened Roger's mood of optimism somewhat: it rained incessantly, and they spent the night under heaps of half-dry bracken on the edge of a black tarn, emerging at dawn chilled and frowsty, to the shrieks of plovers and killdeer.

He hesitated momentarily as they rode past the place where they might turn toward Cranesmuir; he wanted badly to talk again with Dr. McEwan. His hand found his throat, thumb stroking the scar. *"Maybe,"* the healer had said. *"Just maybe."* But McEwan couldn't aid them in looking for Jem; that visit would have to wait.

Still, he felt his heart rise as they came over the pass and saw Lallybroch below. It was bittersweet, coming home to a home that was not his and might never be again. But it promised refuge and succor, if only temporarily—and it promised hope, at least in these last few minutes before they reached the door.

"Och, it's you!" It was Jenny Fraser who opened the door, her look of wariness changing to one of pleased welcome. Roger heard Buck behind him making a small humming noise of approval at sight of her, and, despite his determination not to hope too much, Roger felt his own spirits rise.

"And this will be your kinsman?" She curtsied to Buck. "Welcome to ye, sir. Come ben; I'll call Taggie to mind the horses." She turned in a flicker of white apron and petticoats, beckoning them to follow. "Da's in the speak-a-word," she called over her shoulder as she headed for the kitchen. "He's something for you!"

"Mr. MacKenzie and . . . this would be also Mr. MacKenzie, aye?" Brian Fraser came out of the study, smiling, and offered Buck his hand. Roger could see him looking Buck over with close attention, a slight frown between his dark brows. Not disapproval—puzzlement, as though he knew Buck from somewhere and was trying to think where.

Roger knew exactly where and felt again that peculiar quiver he'd felt on meeting Dougal MacKenzie. The resemblance between father and son was by no means instantly striking—their coloring was very different, and Roger thought most of Buck's features came from his mother—but there was a fugitive similarity, nonetheless, something in their manner. Men cocksure of their charm—and no less charming for knowing it.

Buck was smiling, making commonplace courtesies, complimenting the house and its estate. . . . The puzzlement faded from Brian's eyes, and he invited them to sit, calling down the hall to the kitchen for someone to bring them a bite and a dram.

"Well, then," Brian said, pulling out the chair from behind his desk in order to sit with them. "As ye havena got the lad with ye, I see he's not found yet. Have ye heard any news of him, though?" He looked from Buck to Roger, worried but hopeful.

"No," Roger said, and cleared his throat. "Not a word. But—your daughter said that you . . . might have heard something?"

Fraser's face changed at once, lighting a little.

"Well, it's nay so much *heard* anything, but . . ." He rose and went to rummage in the desk, still talking.

"A captain from the garrison came by here twa, three days ago, wi' a small party of soldiers. The new man in charge—what was his name, Jenny?" For Jenny had come in with a tray, this holding a teapot, cups, a small bottle of whisky, and a plate of cake. The smell made Roger's stomach rumble.

"Who? Oh, the new redcoat captain? Randall, he said. Jonathan Randall." Her color rose a little, and her father smiled to see it. Roger felt the smile freeze on his own face.

"Aye, he took to you, lass. Wouldna be surprised if he came back one of these days."

"Precious little good it will do him if he does," Jenny snapped. "Have ye lost that thing, *an athair*?"

"No, no, I'm sure I put . . ." Brian's voice trailed off as he scrabbled in the drawer. "Oh. Erm, aye." He coughed, hand in the drawer, and, through his shock, Roger realized what the trouble was. The desk had a secret compartment. Evidently Brian had put the "thing," whatever it was, in the hiding place and was now wondering how to get it out again without revealing the secret to his visitors.

Roger rose to his feet.

"Will ye pardon me, mistress?" he asked, bowing to Jenny. "I'd forgot something in my saddlebag. Come with me, aye?" he added to Buck. "It's maybe in with your things."

Jenny looked surprised but nodded, and Roger blundered out, Buck making little grunts of annoyance at his heels.

"What the devil's wrong wi' you?" Buck said, the minute they were out the door. "Ye went white as a sheet in there, and ye still look like a fish that's been dead a week."

"I feel like one," Roger said tersely. "I know Captain Randall—or, rather, I know a lot of things about him. Leave it that he's the last person I'd want to have any knowledge of Jem."

"Oh." Buck's face went blank, then firmed. "Aye, well. We'll see what it is he brought, and then we'll go and have it out with him if we think he might have the lad."

What it is he brought. Roger fought back all the horrible things that phrase conjured—Jem's ear, a finger, a lock of his hair—because if it had been anything like that, surely the Frasers wouldn't be calm about it. But if Randall had brought some hideous token in a box?

"Why, though?" Buck was frowning, plainly trying to read Roger's expression, which, judging from Buck's own, must be appalling. "Why would this man mean you and the lad ill? He's never met ye, has he?"

"That," Roger said, choking down his feelings, "is an excellent question. But the man is a—do you know what a sadist is?"

"No, but it's plainly something ye dinna want close to your wean. Here, sir! We'll be taking those in, thank ye kindly." They'd come right round the house by now, and McTaggart the hired man was coming down the path from the stable, their saddlebags in either hand.

McTaggart looked surprised but surrendered the heavy bags gladly and went back to his work.

"I ken ye just wanted to get us out of there so to give your man a bit of privacy to work the secret drawer," Buck remarked. "And he kens that fine. Do we need to take in something, though?"

"How do you know about—" Buck grinned at him, and Roger dismissed the question with an irritable gesture. "Yes. We'll give Miss Fraser the cheese I bought yesterday."

"Ah, Mrs. Jenny." Buck made the humming noise again. "I wouldna blame Captain Randall. That skin! And those bubs, come to that—"

"Shut up right this minute!"

Buck did, shocked out of his jocularity.

"What?" he said, in quite a different tone. "What is it?"

Roger unclenched his fist, with an effort.

"It's a bloody long story; I haven't time to tell it to ye now. But it's—something I know from the other end. From my time. In a year or so, Randall's coming back here. And he's going to do something terrible. And, God help me, I don't think I can stop it."

"Something terrible," Buck repeated slowly. His eyes were boring into Roger's own, dark as serpentine. "To that bonnie wee lass? And ye think ye can't *stop* it? Why, man, how can ye—"

"Just shut up," Roger repeated doggedly. "We'll talk about it later, aye?"

Buck puffed out his cheeks, still staring at Roger, then blew out his breath with a sound of disgust and shook his head, but he picked up his saddlebag and followed without further argument.

The cheese—a thing the size of Roger's outstretched hand,

wrapped in fading leaves—was received with pleasure and taken off to the kitchen, leaving Roger and Buck alone once more with Brian Fraser. Fraser had regained his own composure and, picking up a tiny cloth-wrapped parcel from his desk, put it gently in Roger's hand.

Too light to be a finger . . .

"Captain Randall said that Captain Buncombe sent word out wi' all the patrols, and one of them came across this wee bawbee and sent it back to Fort William. None of them ever saw such a thing before, but because of the name, they were thinking it might have to do wi' your lad."

"The name?" Roger untied the cord and the cloth fell open. For an instant, he didn't know what the hell he was seeing. He picked it up; it was light as a feather, dangling from his fingers.

Two disks, made of something like pressed cardboard, threaded onto a bit of light woven cord. One round, colored red—the other was green and octagonal.

"Oh, Jesus," he said. "Oh, Christ Jesus."

J. W. MacKenzie was printed on both disks, along with a number and two letters. He turned the red disk gently over with a shaking fingertip and read what he already knew was stamped there.

RAF

He was holding the dog tags of a Royal Air Force flier. Circa World War II.

44

AMPHISBAENA

"YE CANNA BE SURE those things name your father." Buck nodded at the dog tags, their cord still wrapped round Roger's hand, the tiny disks themselves folded tight in his palm. "How many MacKenzies are there, for God's sake?"

"Lots." Roger sat down on a big lichen-covered boulder. They were at the top of the hill that rose behind Lallybroch; the broch itself stood on the slope just below them, its conical roof a broad black whorl of slates. "But not so bloody many who flew for the Royal Air Force in World War Two. And even fewer who disappeared without a trace. As for those who might be time travelers . . ."

Roger couldn't remember what he'd said when he saw the dog tags or what Brian Fraser had said to him. When he'd started to notice things again, he was sitting in Brian's big wheel-backed chair with a stoneware mug of hot tea cupped between his hands and the entire household crammed into the doorway, regarding him with looks ranging from compassion to curiosity. Buck was squatting in front of him, frowning in what might have been concern or simply curiosity.

"Sorry," Roger had said, cleared his throat, and set the tea undrunk on the desk. His hands throbbed from the heat of the cup. "Rather a shock. I—thank you."

"Is it something to do wi' your wee boy, then?" Jenny Fraser had asked, deep-blue eyes dark with concern.

"I think so, yes." He'd got his wits back now and rose stiffly, nodding to Brian. "Thank ye, sir. I canna thank ye enough for all ye've done for me—for us. I . . . need to think a bit what's to do now. If ye'll excuse me, Mistress Fraser?"

Jenny nodded, not taking her eyes from his face but shooing the maids and the cook away from the door so he could pass through it. Buck had followed him, murmuring reassuring things to the multitude, and come along with him, not speaking until they reached the solitude of the craggy hilltop. Where Roger had explained just what the dog tags were and to whom they had belonged.

"Why two?" Buck asked, reaching out a tentative finger to touch the tags. "And why are they different colors?"

"Two in case one was destroyed by whatever killed you," Roger said, taking a deep breath. "The colors—they're made of pressed cardboard treated with different chemicals—substances, I mean. One resists water and the other resists fire, but I couldn't tell ye which is which."

Speaking of technicalities made it just barely possible to speak. Buck, with unaccustomed delicacy, was waiting for Roger to bring up the unspeakable.

How did the tags turn up here? *And when—and under what circumstances—had they become detached from J(eremiah) W(alter) MacKenzie, Roman Catholic, serial number 448397651, RAF?*

"Claire—my mother-in-law—I told ye about her, did I not?"

"A bit, aye. A seer, was she?"

Roger laughed shortly. "Aye, like I am. Like you are. Easy to be a seer if what you see has already happened."

What's already happened . . .

"Oh, God," he said out loud, and curled over, pressing the fist that held the dog tags hard against his forehead.

"All right, there?" Buck asked after a moment. Roger straightened up with a deep breath.

"Know the expression 'damned if ye do, damned if ye don't'?"

"No, though I wouldna think it was one a minister would use." Buck's mouth twitched into a half smile. "Are ye not dedicated to the notion that there's always one sure way out o' damnation?"

"A minister. Aye." Roger breathed deep again. There was a lot of oxygen on a Scottish hilltop, but somehow there didn't seem quite enough just this minute. "I'm not sure that religion was constructed with time travelers in mind."

Buck's brows rose at that.

"Constructed?" he echoed, surprised. "Who builds God?"

That actually made Roger laugh, which made him feel a little better, if only momentarily.

"We all do," he said dryly. "If God makes man in His image, we all return the favor."

"Mmphm." Buck thought that one over, then nodded slowly. "Wouldna just say ye're wrong about that. But God's *there,* nonetheless, whether we ken quite what He is or not. Isn't He?"

"Yeah." Roger wiped his knuckles under his nose, which had begun to run with the cold wind. "Ever hear of Saint Teresa of Avila?"

"No." Buck gave him a look. "Nor have I heard of a Protestant minister who has to do wi' saints."

"I take advice where I can get it. But St. Teresa once remarked to God, 'If this is how you treat your friends, no wonder you have so few of them.' God's got his own ways."

Buck smiled; it was one of his rare, unwary smiles, and it heartened Roger enough to try to come to grips with the situation.

"Well, Claire—my mother-in-law—she told Brianna and me a good bit. About the things that happened when she went through the stones in 1743, and about things that had happened before that. Things about Captain Randall." And in sentences as brief and unemotional as he could make them, he told the story: Randall's raid on Lallybroch while Brian Fraser was away, his attack on Jenny Murray, and how Jamie Fraser—newly returned from Paris and wondering what to do with his life—had fought for his home and his sister's honor, been arrested and taken to Fort William, where he had been flogged nearly to death.

"Twice," Roger said, pausing for air. He swallowed. "The second time . . . Brian was there. He thought Jamie *was* dead, and he had a stroke—an apoplexy—on the spot. He . . . died." He swallowed again. "Will die."

"Jesus, Mary, and Bride." Buck crossed himself. His face had gone pale. "Your man in the house? He'll be dead in a year or two?"

"Yes." Roger looked down at Lallybroch, pale and peaceful as the sheep that browsed its pastures. "And . . . there's more. What happened later, just before the Rising."

Buck raised a hand.

"I say that's more than enough. I say we go down to Fort William and do for the wicked bugger now. Preemptive action, ye might say. That's a legal term," he explained, with an air of kindly condescension.

"An appealing notion," Roger said dryly. "But if we did—what *would* happen four years from now?"

Buck frowned, not comprehending.

"When Claire came through the stones in 1743, she met—will meet—Jamie Fraser, an outlaw with a price on his head, coming home from France. But if what happened with Captain Randall *doesn't* happen—Jamie won't be there. And if he isn't . . . ?"

"Oh." The frown grew deeper, comprehension dawning. "Oh, aye. I see. No Jamie, no Brianna . . ."

"No Jem or Mandy," Roger finished. "Exactly."

"Oh, God." Buck bent his head and massaged the flesh between his brows with two fingers. "Damned if ye do, damned if ye don't, did ye say? Enough to make your head spin like a top."

"Yes, it is. But I have to do something, nonetheless." He rubbed a thumb gently over the dog tags' surfaces. "I'm going down to Fort William to talk to Captain Randall. I have to know where these came from."

BUCK LOOKED squiggle-eyed at the tags, lips pressed together, then switched the look to Roger.

"D'ye think your lad's with your father, somehow?"

"No." That particular thought hadn't occurred to Roger, and it shook him for a moment. He shrugged it away, though.

"No," he repeated more firmly. "I'm beginning to think that maybe . . . maybe Jem's not here at all." The statement hung there in the air, revolving slowly. He glanced at Buck, who seemed to be glowering at it.

"Why not?" his kinsman asked abruptly.

"A, because we've found no hint of him. And B, because now there's *these.*" He raised the tags, the light cardboard disks lifting in the breeze.

"Ye sound like your wife," Buck said, half amused. "She does that, aye? Layin' things out, A, B, C, and all."

"That's how Brianna's mind works," Roger said, feeling a brief surge of affection for her. "She's very logical."

And if I'm right, and Jem's not here—where is he? Has he gone to another time—or did he not travel at all? As though the word "logical" had triggered it, a whole array of horrifying possibilities opened out before him.

"What I'm thinking—we were both concentrating on the name 'Jeremiah' when we came through, aye?"

"Aye, we were."

"Well . . ." He twirled the cord between his fingers, making the disks spin slowly. "What if we got the wrong Jeremiah? That was my father's name, too. And—and if Rob Cameron *didn't* take Jem through the stones—"

"Why would he not?" Buck interrupted sharply. He transferred the glower to Roger. "His truck was there at Craigh na Dun. He wasn't."

"Plainly he wanted us to *think* he'd gone through. As to why—" He choked on the thought. Before he could clear his throat, Buck finished it for him.

"To get us away, so he'd have your missus to himself." His face darkened with anger—part of it aimed at Roger. "I told her yon man had a hot eye for her."

"Maybe he does," he said shortly. "But think, aye? Beyond whatever he may have had in mind with regard to Brianna—" The mere words conjured up pictures that made the blood shoot up into his head. "Whatever he had in mind," he repeated, as calmly as he could, "he likely also wanted to see whether it was true. About the stones. About whether we—or anyone—really could go through. Seeing's believing, after all."

Buck blew out his cheeks, considering.

"Ye think he was there, maybe? Watching to see if we disappeared?"

Roger shrugged, momentarily unable to speak for the thoughts clotting his brain.

Buck's fists were clenched on his knees. He looked down at the house, then behind him at the rising mountains, and Roger knew exactly what he was thinking. He cleared his throat with a hacking growl.

"We've been gone for two weeks," Roger said. "If he meant Brianna harm . . . he'll have tried." *Jesus. If he—no.* "She'll not have let him harm her or the kids," he went on, as steadily as he could. "If he tried anything, he'll either be in jail or buried under the broch." He lifted his chin toward the tower below, and Buck snorted in reluctant amusement.

"So, then. Aye, I want to rush straight back to Craigh na Dun, too. But think, man. We ken Cameron *went* to the stones after he took Jem. Would he not make Jem touch them, to see? And if he did . . . what if Cameron can't travel but Jem did—to get away from him?"

"Mmphm." Buck thought that one over and gave a reluctant nod. "So ye're maybe thinkin' that if the lad was scairt of Cameron and popped through accidental, he maybe wouldn't try to come straight back?"

"He maybe couldn't." Roger was dry-mouthed and swallowed hard to generate enough saliva to speak. "He didn't have a gemstone. And even with one . . ." He nodded at Buck.

"Ken what happened to you, even with one. It *does* get worse each time. Jemmy might have been too scared to try." *And he might have tried, not made it, and now he's lost for good . . . NO!*

Buck nodded.

"So. Ye think he's maybe with your da, after all?" He sounded dubious in the extreme.

Roger couldn't bear sitting any longer. He stood up abruptly, thrusting the dog tags into the breast pocket of his coat.

"I don't know. But this is the only solid bit of evidence we have. I have to go and see."

45

THE CURE OF SOULS

"YE'RE OUT OF YOUR wee pink mind, ye ken that, aye?"

Roger looked at Buck in amazement.

"Where the devil did you get *that* expression?"

"From your wife," Buck replied. "Who's a verra bonnie lass and a well-spoken one, forbye. And if ye mean to get back to her bed one of these days, ye'll think better of what ye mean to do."

"I've thought," Roger said briefly. "And I'm doing it." The entrance to Fort William looked much as it had when he'd come here with Brian Fraser nearly two weeks earlier, but this time with only a few people hastening in, shawls over their heads, and hats pulled down against the rain. The fort itself now seemed to have a sinister aspect, the gray stones bleak and streaked black with wet.

Buck reined up, grimacing as the horse shook its head and sprayed him with drops from its soaking mane.

"Aye, fine. I'm no going in there. If we have to kill him, it's best if he doesna ken me, so I can get behind him. I'll wait at yonder tavern." He lifted his chin, indicating an establishment called the Peartree, a few hundred feet down the road from the fort, then kicked his horse into motion. Ten feet on, he turned and called over his shoulder, "One hour! If ye're not with me by then, I'm comin' in after ye!"

Roger smiled, despite his apprehension. He waved briefly to Buck and swung off his horse.

Bless me, Lord, he prayed. *Help me to do the right thing—for everyone. Including Buck. And* him.

He hadn't actually stopped praying at any time since Jem had disappeared, though most of it was just the frantic, reflexive *Dear Lord, let it be all right* of everyone facing crisis. Over time, either the crisis or the petitioner wears down, and prayer either ceases or . . . the person praying starts to listen.

He knew that. And he was listening. But he was still taken aback to get an answer.

He had enough experience in the business of prayer to recognize an answer when it showed up, though, however unwelcome. And the pointed reminder, arriving as a random thought in the middle of their mud-spattered, rain-sodden journey—that Jack Randall's soul was in as much danger as Brian Fraser's life—was damned unwelcome.

"Well, then," Buck had said, brightening under the soggy brim of his hat when Roger had shared his disturbance at this insight. "All the more reason to kill him now. Save yon Frasers, and keep the wicked wee sod from going to hell—if he hasn't done something already as would send him there," he'd added as an afterthought. "Two birds wi' one stone, aye?"

Roger had squelched along for a moment before replying.

"Out of sheer curiosity—were you a solicitor or a barrister, when ye did law?"

"Solicitor. Why?"

"No wonder you failed at it. All your talents lie in the other direction. Can ye not have a conversation without arguing?"

"Not wi' *you,*" Buck had said pointedly, and kicked his horse into a trot, sending up thumping clods of mud in his wake.

Roger gave his name and asked the army clerk if he might have a word with Captain Randall, then stood by the peat fire, shaking off as much water as he could before the man came back to lead him to Randall's office.

To his surprise, it was the same office where he and Brian Fraser had had their audience with Captain Buncombe almost two weeks before. Randall was seated behind the desk, quill in hand, but looked up with a courteous expression at Roger's entrance and half rose, with a small bow.

"Your servant, sir. Mr. MacKenzie, is that right? You've come from Lallybroch, I collect."

"Your most obedient, sir," Roger replied, adjusting his accent back to his normal Scots-tinged Oxbridge. "Mr. Brian Fraser was good enough to give me the object that you brought. I wanted both to thank you for your kind assistance—and to ask whether you might be able to tell me where the object was discovered."

He knew about the banality of evil; human monsters came in human shapes. Even so, he was surprised. Randall was a handsome man, rather elegant in bearing, with a lively, interested expression, a humorous curve to his mouth, and warm dark eyes.

Well, he is *human. And perhaps he's not a monster yet.*

"One of my messengers brought it in," Randall replied, wiping his quill and dropping it into a stoneware jar full of such objects. "My predecessor, Captain Buncombe, had sent dispatches to Fort George and Fort Augustus about your son—I am very sorry for your situation," he added rather formally. "A patrol from Ruthven Barracks had brought the ornament in. I'm afraid I don't know where they discovered it, but perhaps the messenger who brought it from Ruthven does. I'll send for him."

Randall went to the door and spoke to the sentry outside. Coming back, he paused to open a cupboard, which revealed a wig stand, a powdering shaker, a pair of hairbrushes, a looking glass, and a small tray with a cut-glass decanter and glasses.

"Allow me to offer you refreshment, sir." Randall poured a cautious inch into each glass and offered one to Roger. He picked up his own, his nostrils flaring slightly at the scent of the whisky. "The nectar of the country, I'm given to understand," he said with a wry smile. "I am told I must develop a taste for it." He took a wary sip, looking as though he expected imminent death to result.

"If I might suggest . . . a bit of water mixed with it is

customary," Roger said, carefully keeping all trace of amusement out of his voice. "Some say it opens the flavor, makes it smoother."

"Oh, really?" Randall put down his glass, looking relieved. "That seems sensible. The stuff tastes as though it's flammable. Sanders!" he shouted toward the door. "Bring some water!"

There was a slight pause, neither man knowing quite what to say next.

"The, um, *thing,*" Randall said. "Might I see it again? It's quite remarkable. Is it a jewel of some kind? An ornament?"

"No. It's a . . . sort of charm," Roger said, fishing the dog tags out of his pocket. He felt an ache in his chest at thought of the small personal rituals that the fliers did—a lucky stone in the pocket, a special scarf, the name of a woman painted on the nose of a plane. Charms. Tiny bits of hopeful magic, protection against a vast sky filled with fire and death. "To preserve the soul." *In memory, at least.*

Randall frowned a little, glancing from the dog tags to Roger's face, then back. He was clearly thinking the same thing Roger was: *And if the charm is detached from the person it was meant to protect . . .* But he didn't say anything, merely touched the green tag gently.

"J. W. Your son's name is Jeremiah, I understand?"

"Yes. Jeremiah's an old family name. It was my father's name. I—" He was interrupted by the entrance of Private MacDonald, a very young soldier, dripping wet and slightly blue with cold, who saluted Captain Randall smartly, then gave way to a rattling cough that shook his spindly frame.

Once recovered, he complied at once with Randall's order to tell Roger all he knew about the dog tags—but he didn't know much. One of the soldiers stationed at Ruthven Barracks had won them in a dice game at a local pub. He did recall the name of the pub—the Fatted Grouse; he'd drunk there himself—and he thought the soldier had said he'd won the bawbee from a farmer come back from the market in Perth.

"Do you recall the name of the soldier who won them?" Roger asked.

"Oh, aye, sir. 'Twas Sergeant McLehose. And now I think—" A broad grin at the recollection showed crooked teeth. "I mind me of the farmer's name, too! 'Twas Mr. Anthony Cumberpatch. It did tickle Sergeant McLehose, bein' foreign and soundin' like 'cucumber patch.'" He sniggered, and Roger smiled himself. Captain Randall cleared his throat, and the sniggering stopped abruptly, Private MacDonald snapping to a sober attention.

"Thank you, Mr. MacDonald," Randall said dryly. "That will be all."

Private MacDonald, abashed, saluted and left. There was a moment's silence, during which Roger became aware of the rain, grown harder now, clattering like gravel on the large casement window. A chilly draft leaked around its frame and touched his face. Glancing at the window, he saw the drill yard below, and the whipping post, a grim crucifix stark and solitary, black in the rain.

Oh, God.

Carefully, he folded up the dog tags again and put them away in his pocket. Then met Captain Randall's dark eyes directly.

"Did Captain Buncombe tell you, sir, that I am a minister?"

Randall's brows rose in brief surprise.

"No, he didn't." Randall was plainly wondering why Roger should mention this, but he was courteous. "My younger brother is a clergyman. Ah . . . Church of England, of course." There was the faintest implied question there, and Roger answered it with a smile.

"I am a minister of the Church of Scotland myself, sir. But if I might . . . will ye allow me to offer a blessing? For the success of my kinsman and myself—and in thanks for your kind help to us."

"I—" Randall blinked, clearly discomfited. "I—suppose so. Er . . . all right." He leaned back a little, looking wary, hands on his blotter. He was completely taken aback when Roger leaned forward and grasped both his hands firmly. Randall gave a start, but Roger held tight, eyes on the captain's.

"Oh, Lord," he said, "we ask thy blessing on our works. Guide me and my kinsman in our quest, and guide this man in his new office. May your light and presence be with us and with him, and your judgment and compassion ever on us. I commend him to your care. Amen."

His voice cracked on the last word, and he let go Randall's hands and coughed, looking away as he cleared his throat.

Randall cleared his throat, too, in embarrassment, but kept his poise.

"I thank you for your . . . er . . . good wishes, Mr. MacKenzie. And I wish you good luck. And good day."

"The same to you, Captain," Roger said, rising. "God be with you."

46

BABY JESUS, TELL ME . . .

Boston, November 15, 1980

DR. JOSEPH ABERNATHY pulled into his driveway, looking forward to a cold beer and a hot supper. The mailbox was full; he pulled out a handful of circulars and envelopes and went inside, tidily sorting them as he went.

"Bill, bill, occupant, junk, junk, more junk, charity appeal, bill, idiot, bill, invitation . . . hi, sweetie—" He paused for a fragrant kiss from his wife, followed by a second sniff of her hair. "Oh, man, are we having brats and sauerkraut for dinner?"

"You are," his wife told him, neatly snagging her jacket from the hall tree with one hand and squeezing his buttock with the other. "I'm going to a meeting with Marilyn. Be back by nine, if the rain doesn't make the traffic too bad. Anything good in the mail?"

"Nah. Have fun!"

She rolled her eyes at him and left before he could ask if she'd bought Bud. He tossed the half-sorted mail on the kitchen counter and opened the refrigerator to check. A gleaming red-and-white six-pack beckoned cheerily, and the warm air was so tangy with the smells of fried sausage and vinegar that he could taste it without even taking the lid off the pan sitting on the stove.

"A good woman is prized above rubies," he said, inhaling blissfully and pulling a can loose from its plastic ring.

He was halfway through the first plate of food and two-thirds of the way into his second beer when he put down the sports section of the *Globe* and saw the letter on top of the spilled pile of mail. He recognized Bree's handwriting at once; it was big and round, with a determined rightward slant—but there was something wrong with the letter.

He picked it up, frowning a little, wondering why it looked strange . . . and then realized that the stamp was wrong. She wrote at least once a month, sending photos of the kids, telling him about her job, the farm—and the letters all had British stamps, purple and blue heads of Queen Elizabeth. This one had an American stamp.

He slowly set down the letter as though it might explode and swallowed the rest of the beer in one gulp. Fortified, he set his jaw and picked it up.

"Tell me you and Rog took the kids to Disneyland, Bree," he murmured, licking mustard off his knife before using it to slit the envelope. She'd talked about doing that someday. "Baby Jesus, tell me this is a photo of Jem shaking hands with Mickey Mouse."

Much to his relief, it *was* a photo of both children at Disneyland, beaming at the camera from Mickey Mouse's embrace, and he laughed out loud. Then he saw the tiny key that had fallen out of the envelope—the key to a bank's safe-deposit box. He set down the photo, went and got another beer, and sat down deliberately to read the brief note enclosed with the photo.

Dear Uncle Joe,

I'm taking the kids to see Grandma and Grandpa. I don't know when we'll be back; could you please see to things while we're gone? (Instructions in the box.)

Thank you for everything, always. I'll miss you. I love you.

Bree

He sat for a long time next to the cold grease congealing on his plate, looking at the bright, happy photo.

"Jesus, girl," he said softly. "What's happened? And what do you mean *you're* taking the kids? Where the hell's Roger?"

PART THREE

A Blade Fresh-Made from the Ashes of the Forge

47

SOMETHING SUITABLE IN WHICH TO GO TO WAR

June 19, 1778
Philadelphia

I WOKE COMPLETELY disoriented, to the splat of water dripping into a wooden bucket, the sharp smells of wood pulp and printer's ink, the softer musk of Jamie's body and frying bacon, the clank of pewter plates, and the loud braying of a mule. The latter noise brought back memory at once, and I sat up, sheet clutched to my bosom.

I was naked, and I was in the loft of Fergus's printshop. When we had left Kingsessing the day before, during a brief pause in the rain, we had found Fergus patiently sheltering in a toolshed near the gates, Clarence the mule and two horses tethered under its eaves.

"You haven't been out here all this time!" I'd blurted upon seeing him.

"Did it take that long?" he inquired, cocking a dark brow at Jamie and giving him the sort of knowing look that Frenchmen appear to be born with.

"Mmphm," Jamie replied ambiguously, and took my arm. "I rode Clarence out, Sassenach, but I asked Fergus to come on a wee bit later wi' a horse for you. The mule canna carry us both, and my back willna stand walking that far."

"What's the matter with your back?" I asked, suspicious.

"Nothing that a night's sleep in a good bed willna cure," he replied, and, stooping so I could put a foot in his hands, tossed me up into the saddle.

It had been past dark when we made it back to the printshop. I'd sent Germain at once to Jenny at Number 17 with word where I was but had gone to bed with Jamie before he came back. I wondered vaguely who else was at the house on Chestnut Street and what they were doing: was Hal still a captive, or had Young Ian decided to release him? If not, had Hal assassinated Denny Hunter, or had Mrs. Figg shot him?

Jamie had told me he'd left Ian in charge of the situation—or situations; there seemed to have been a great deal going on the day before. All of it seemed unreal and dreamlike, both the events I'd participated in and the ones Jamie had told me about on the ride back. The only vividly real recollection I had was of our conversation in the garden—and what followed it, in the potting shed. My flesh still felt the echoes.

Breakfast was plainly preparing below; besides the delectable scent of frying bacon, I could smell toasted yeast bread and fresh honey. My stomach gave a loud gurgle at this, and as though the sound had caused it, the ladder leading up into the loft began to shake. Someone was coming up, moving slowly, and in case it wasn't Jamie, I seized my shift and pulled it hastily over my head.

It wasn't. A pewter tray rose slowly into sight, laid with a plate piled with food, a bowl of porridge, and a pottery mug of something steaming; it couldn't be tea and didn't smell like coffee. As the tray levitated, Henri-Christian's beaming face appeared below it; he was balancing the thing on his head.

I held my breath until he'd stepped off the ladder, and then, as he removed the tray from his head and presented it to me with a ceremonious little bow, applauded.

"Merveilleux!" I told him, and he grinned from ear to ear.

"Félicité wanted to try," he told me proudly, "but she can't do it with a full tray yet. She spills."

"Well, we can't have that. Thank you, sweetheart." I leaned forward to kiss him—his dark wavy hair smelled of woodsmoke and ink—and took the mug. "What's this?"

He looked at it dubiously and shrugged. "It's hot."

"So it is." I cradled the mug in my hands. The loft had been warm the night before, the day's heat trapped under the roof, but it had rained most of the night, and the chilly damp had come through the holes in the roof—four or five vessels placed under the leaks made a symphony of plinking sounds. "Where's *Grand-père*?"

Henri-Christian's face at once went bright red, his lips pressed tight together, and he shook his head vigorously.

"What?" I said, surprised. "Is it a secret?"

"Don't you tell her!" Joanie's shrill voice floated up from the shop below. "*Grand-père* said not to!"

"Oh, a surprise, is it?" I asked, smiling. "Well, perhaps you'd best go down and help your mama, then, so you don't give it away by mistake."

He giggled, hands pressed over his mouth, then reached up over his head, gave a convulsive leap, and flipped over backward, landing adroitly on his hands. He walked on them to the ladder, stocky little legs splayed to keep his balance, and for an instant my heart was in my mouth as he reached the edge and I thought he might try to go down the ladder upside down. He flipped over again, though, landing neatly on the top rung, and scampered out of sight like a squirrel, giggling all the way down.

Smiling, I plumped up the sparse bedding—we had slept on a flattened pallet of worn straw from the stable, which smelled rather strongly of Clarence, and on our half-dried cloaks, covered with a spare sheet and a ragged blanket, though Joanie and Félicité had given us one of their feather pillows, they sharing the other—and sat back against the wall, the tray perched on a keg of ink powder. I was surrounded by stacks of paper, these shielded by oilcloth from the leaks. Some of it was blank reams awaiting the press, some of it pamphlets, circulars, posters, or the guts of unbound books, awaiting delivery to customers or to the bookbinder.

I could hear Marsali's voice below, back in the living quarters behind the shop, raised in maternal command. No male voices but Henri-Christian's, though; Fergus and Germain must have gone out with Clarence the mule to make the morning deliveries of *L'Oignon,* the satirical newspaper started by Fergus and Marsali in North Carolina.

Normally, *L'Oignon* was a weekly paper, but there was a copy on my tray of the special edition for today, with a large cartoon on the first page, showing the British army as a horde of cockroaches, fleeing Philadelphia with tattered flags dragging behind them and trailing ribbon banners filled with speeches of futile threat. A large buckled shoe labeled *General Washington* was squashing some of the more laggard roaches.

There was a large glob of opaque yellow-white honey melting slowly in the middle of the porridge; I stirred it in, poured a bit of cream over it, and settled down to enjoy breakfast in bed, along with an article noting the imminent entrance into Philadelphia of General Arnold, who was taking office as the military governor of the city, welcoming him and praising his military record and gallant exploits at Saratoga.

How long? I thought then, setting down the paper with a small shiver. *When?* I had the feeling that it had been—would be—much later in the war, when circumstance turned Benedict Arnold from patriot to traitor. But I didn't know.

It didn't matter, I told myself firmly. I couldn't change it. And long before that happened, we would be safely back on the Ridge, rebuilding our house and our lives. Jamie was alive. Everything would be all right.

The bell over the shop door below rang, and there was an excited gabble as the children stampeded out of the kitchen. The soft rumble of Jamie's voice floated up over the confusion of shrill greetings, and I caught Marsali's voice among them, stunned.

"Da! What have ye *done*?"

Alarmed, I scrambled out of my nest and went on hands and knees to the edge of the loft to look down. Jamie stood in the middle of the shop, surrounded by admiring children, his loose hair spangled with raindrops, cloak folded over his arm—dressed in the dark blue and buff of a Continental officer.

"Jesus H. Roosevelt *Christ*!" I exclaimed. He looked up and his eyes met mine like those of a guilty puppy.

"I'm sorry, Sassenach," he said apologetically. "I had to."

HE'D COME UP to the loft and pulled the ladder up behind him, to prevent the children coming up. I was dressing quickly—or trying to—as he told me about Dan Morgan, about Washington and the other Continental generals. About the coming battle.

"Sassenach, I *had* to," he said again, softly. "I'm that sorry."

"I know," I said. "I know you did." My lips were stiff. "I—you—I'm sorry, too."

I was trying to fasten the dozen tiny buttons that closed the bodice of my gown, but my hands shook so badly that I couldn't even grasp them. I stopped trying and dug my hairbrush out of the bag he'd brought me from the Chestnut Street house.

He made a small sound in his throat and took it out of my hand. He threw it onto our makeshift couch and put his arms around me, holding me tight with my face buried in his chest. The cloth of his new uniform smelled of fresh indigo, walnut hulls, and fuller's earth; it felt strange and stiff against my face. I couldn't stop shaking.

"Talk to me, *a nighean,*" he whispered into my tangled hair. "I'm afraid, and I dinna want to feel so verra much alone just now. Speak to me."

"Why has it always got to be *you*?" I blurted into his chest.

That made him laugh, a little shakily, and I realized that all the trembling wasn't coming from me.

"It's no just me," he said, and stroked my hair. "There are a thousand other men readying themselves today—more—who dinna want to do it, either."

"I know," I said again. My breathing was a little steadier. "I know." I turned my face to the side in order to breathe, and all of a sudden began to cry, quite without warning.

"I'm sorry," I gasped. "I don't mean—I don't want t-to make it h-harder for you. I—I—oh, Jamie, when I knew you were alive—I wanted so much to go home. To go home with you."

His arms tightened hard round me. He didn't speak, and I knew it was because he couldn't.

"So did I," he whispered at last. "And we will, *a nighean.* I promise ye."

The sounds from below floated up around us: the sounds of children running back and forth between the shop and the kitchen, Marsali singing to herself in Gaelic as she made fresh ink for the press from varnish and lampblack. The door opened, and cool, rainy air blew in with Fergus and Germain, adding their voices to the cheerful confusion.

We stood wrapped in each other's arms, taking comfort

from our family below, yearning for the others we might never see again, at once at home and homeless, balanced on a knife edge of danger and uncertainty. But together.

"You're not going off to war without me," I said firmly, straightening up and sniffing. "Don't even *think* about it."

"I wouldna dream of it," he assured me gravely, went to wipe his nose on his uniform sleeve, thought better of it, and stopped, looking at me helplessly. I laughed—tremulous, but it was a laugh nonetheless—and gave him the handkerchief I'd tucked automatically into my bosom when I fastened my stays. Like Jenny, I *always* had one.

"Sit down," I said, swallowing as I picked up the hairbrush. "I'll plait your hair for you."

He'd washed it this morning; it was clean and damp, the soft red strands cool in my hands and smelling—oddly—of French soap, scented with bergamot. I rather missed the scent of sweat and cabbage that had surrounded me all night.

"Where did you bathe?" I asked curiously.

"At the house on Chestnut Street," he answered, a little tersely. "My sister made me. She said I couldna turn up to be a general smelling like a stale dinner, and there was a tub and hot water to spare."

"Did she?" I murmured. "Um . . . speaking of Chestnut Street . . . how is His Grace, the Duke of Pardloe?"

"Gone before dawn, Jenny said," he said, bending his head to aid in the plaiting. His neck was warm under my fingers. "According to Ian, Denny Hunter said he was well enough to go, provided that he took along a flask of your magic potion. So Mrs. Figg gave him back his breeches—wi' some reluctance, I understand—and he went."

"Went *where*?" I asked. His hair was more heavily traced with silver than it had been. I didn't mind that; I minded that I hadn't been there to see it slowly change, day by day.

"Ian didna ask him. But he said Mrs. Figg told the duke the names of some friends of Lord John's—Loyalists that might be still in the city. And his son's staying in a house here, no? Dinna be worrit on his account, Sassenach." He turned his head to smile sideways at me. "His Grace is a man who's hard to kill."

"I suppose it takes one to know one," I said tartly. I didn't ask why Jamie had gone to Chestnut Street; Hal, Jenny, and all other concerns notwithstanding, I knew he wanted to know whether John had reappeared. Apparently not, and a small chill frosted my heart.

I was groping in my pocket for a ribbon with which to club his queue, when a fresh draft swept through the loft, lifting the oilcloth and fluttering the papers beneath. I turned to see the source of the breeze and beheld Germain, swinging off the pulley rope to come in by the shuttered doors through which bales and kegs could be lowered from the loft to wagons below.

"Bonjour, Grand-père," he said, wiping a cobweb off his face as he landed and bowing to Jamie with great formality. He turned and bowed to me, as well. *"Comment ça va, Grand-mère?"*

"Fi—" I began automatically, but was interrupted by Jamie.

"No," he said definitely. "Ye're not coming."

"Please, Grandda!" Germain's formality disappeared in an instant, replaced by pleading. "I could be a help to ye!"

"I know," Jamie said dryly. "And your parents would never forgive me if ye were. I dinna even want to know what your notion of help involves, but—"

"I could carry messages! I can ride, ye ken that, ye taught me yourself! And I'm nearly twelve!"

"Ye ken how dangerous that is? If a British sharpshooter didna take ye out of the saddle, someone from the militia would club ye over the head to steal the horse. And I can count, ken? Ye're no even eleven yet, so dinna be tryin' it on with me."

Obviously, danger held no fears whatever for Germain. He shrugged, impatient.

"Well, I could be an orderly, then. I can find food anywhere," he added, cunning. He was in fact a very accomplished scrounger, and I looked at him thoughtfully. Jamie intercepted my glance and glowered at me.

"Dinna even think about it, Sassenach. He'd be taken up for theft and hanged or flogged within an inch of his life, and I couldna do a thing to stop it."

"Nobody's ever caught me!" Germain said, his professional pride outraged. "Not once!"

"And they're not going to," his grandfather assured him, fixing him with a steely eye. "When ye're sixteen, maybe—"

"Oh, aye? Grannie Janet says ye were *eight* when ye first went raiding with your da!"

"Lifting cattle's no the same as war, and I wasna anywhere near the fighting," Jamie said. "And your Grannie Janet should keep her mouth shut."

"Aye, I'll tell her ye said so," Germain retorted, disgruntled. "She says ye got bashed on the head with a sword."

"I did. And with luck ye'll live to be an auld man with your brains unscrambled, unlike your grandsire. Leave us, lad, your grannie needs to put her stockings on." He stood up and, lifting the ladder, slid it down from the loft and pushed Germain firmly onto it.

He stood looking sternly down until Germain had reached the floor below, marking his displeasure by skipping the last few rungs and landing with a loud thud.

Jamie sighed, straightened up, and stretched himself gingerly, groaning a little.

"God knows where we'll sleep tonight, Sassenach," he remarked, glancing at our rude couch as he sat down for me to finish clubbing his hair. "For the sake of my back, I hope it's a bit softer than this." He grinned at me suddenly. "Did ye sleep well?"

"Never better," I assured him, smoothing out the ribbon. In fact, I ached in almost every place it was possible to ache, save perhaps the top of my head. For that matter, I'd barely slept, and neither had he; we'd passed the hours of darkness in slow and wordless exploration, finding again each other's body . . . and, toward dawn, had touched each other's soul again. I touched the back of his neck now, gently, and his hand rose to mine. I felt simultaneously wonderful and wretched, and didn't know from moment to moment which feeling was uppermost.

"When will we leave?"

"As soon as ye put your stockings on, Sassenach. And tidy your hair. And do up your buttons," he added, turning and catching sight of my excessive décolletage. "Here, I'll do that."

"I'll need my medicine box," I said, going cross-eyed as I watched his nimble fingers flicking down my chest.

"I brought it," he assured me, and frowned a bit, eyes intent on a recalcitrant button. "It's a bonny bit of furniture. I expect his lordship bought it for ye?"

"He did." I hesitated a moment, rather wishing he had said "John" rather than "his lordship." I also wished I knew where John was—and that he was all right. But this didn't seem the moment to say any of those things.

Jamie leaned forward and kissed the top of my breast, his breath warm on my skin.

"I dinna ken whether I'll have a bed at all tonight," he said, straightening up. "But whether it's feathers or straw, promise ye'll share it with me?"

"Always," I said, and, picking up my cloak, shook it out, swirled it round my shoulders, and smiled bravely at him. "Let's go, then."

JENNY HAD SENT my medicine chest from Chestnut Street and with it the large parcel of herbs from Kingsessing, which had been delivered there the night before. With the forethought of a Scottish housewife, she'd also included a pound of oatmeal, a twist of salt, a package of bacon, four apples, and six clean handkerchiefs. Also a neat roll of fabric with a brief note, which read:

Dear Sister Claire,

You appear to own nothing suitable in which to go to war. I suggest you borrow Marsali's printing apron for the time being, and here are two of my flannel petticoats and the simplest things Mrs. Figg could find amongst your wardrobe.

Take care of my brother, and tell him his stockings need darning, because he won't notice until he's worn holes in the heel and given himself blisters.

Your Good-sister,
Janet Murray

"And just how is it that *you* own something suitable in which to go to war?" I asked, eyeing Jamie in his indigo splendor. His uniform appeared to be complete, from coat with epaulets and a brigadier general's insignia to buff waistcoat and cream silk stockings. Tall and straight, with auburn hair neatly clubbed and ribboned in black, he distinctly drew the eye.

He drew his chin back and looked down his nose at himself.

"Well, the sark and smallclothes were mine already; I had them when I came from Scotland. But when I came back to Philadelphia to find ye yesterday, I found Jenny first, and I told her about General Washington and asked her would she see to it. So she took my measurements and found a tailor and his son who do uniforms and browbeat them into working all night to make the coat and waistcoat—poor wretches," he added, gingerly pulling a loose thread from the edge of his cuff. "How is it that ye don't, Sassenach? Did his lordship think it unseemly for ye to doctor folk and make ye burn your working clothes?"

This was said with the sort of jesting tone that's meant to suggest perfect innocence on the part of the speaker while making it perfectly apparent that malice is intended. *"I don't say that I'll no make a fuss about it later."* I looked pointedly at the medical chest John had given me, then back at him, narrowing my eyes ever so slightly.

"No," I said, with great casualness. "I spilled vitriol on them, making—making ether." The memory made my hands shake slightly, and I had to set down the cup of nettle tea I was drinking.

"Jesus, Sassenach." Jamie spoke under his breath—Félicité and Joan were kneeling at his feet, arguing with each other as they busily burnished his brass shoe buckles—but he met my eyes over their heads, appalled. "Tell me ye werena doing that drunk."

I took a deep breath, at once reliving the experience and trying not to. Standing in the hot, semi-dark shed behind the house, the rounded glass slick in my sweating hands . . . then the flying liquid—it had barely missed my face—and the sickly smell and magically widening, smoking holes that burned straight through my heavy canvas apron and the skirt beneath. I hadn't really cared at the time whether I lived or died—until it looked as though I was going to die in the next few seconds. That made rather a difference. It hadn't convinced me not to commit suicide—but the shock of the near accident did make me think more carefully about how. Slitting one's wrists was one thing; dying in slow, disfiguring agony was another.

"No, I wasn't," I said, and, taking up the cup, managed a deliberate mouthful. "I—it was a hot day. My hands were sweating, and the flask slipped."

He closed his eyes briefly, all too clearly envisioning the scene himself, then reached across Félicité's sleek dark head to cup my cheek.

"Dinna be doing that again, aye?" he said softly. "Don't make it anymore."

To be honest, the thought of making ether again made my palms sweat. It wasn't chemically difficult, but it *was* terribly dangerous. One wrong move, a little too much vitriol, a few degrees of heat too much . . . And Jamie knew as well as I did just how explosive the stuff was. I could see the memory of flames in his eyes, the Big House going up around us. I swallowed.

"I don't want to," I said honestly. "But—without it, Jamie, I can't do things that I can do with it. If I hadn't had it, Aidan would be dead—so would John's nephew Henry."

He compressed his lips and looked as though he considered that Henry Grey might be disposable—but he was fond of little Aidan McCallum Higgins, whose appendix I'd removed on the Ridge with the assistance of my first batch of ether.

"Grannie *has* to help people feel better, *Grand-père,*" Joanie said reproachfully, rising from her spot at Jamie's feet and frowning up at him. "It's her callin', Mam says. She can't just *not.*"

"I ken that fine," he assured her. "But she needna blow herself to kingdom come doing it. After all, who's going to look after all the sick folk, if your grannie's lying about in pieces?"

Félicité and Joanie both thought that image hilarious; I was less amused, but didn't say anything further until they'd taken their rags and vinegar back to the kitchen. We were left in the sleeping part of the living quarters, assembling our bags and bundles for departure, and momentarily alone.

"You said you were afraid," I said quietly, eyes on the spools of coarse thread and twists of silk floss I was stowing in a wooden box with several suture needles. "But that won't stop you doing what you think you have to do, will it? *I'm* afraid *for* you—and that certainly won't stop you, either." I was careful to speak without bitterness, but he was as sensitive to tones of voice this morning as I was.

He paused for a moment, regarding his shining shoe buckles, then lifted his head and looked at me straight.

"Do ye think that because ye've told me the Rebels will win, I am free to walk away?"

"I—no." I slid the box lid shut with a snick, not looking at it. I couldn't look away from him. His face was still, but his eyes held mine, intent. "I know you have to. I know it's part of what you are. You can't stand aside and still be what you are. That was more or less my point, about—"

He interrupted me, stepping forward and seizing me by the wrist.

"And what is it that ye think I am, Sassenach?"

"A bloody *man,* that's what!" I pulled loose and turned away, but he put a hand on my shoulder and turned me back to face him.

"Aye, I *am* a bloody man," he said, and the faintest trace of rue touched his mouth, but his eyes were blue and steady.

"Ye've made your peace with what I am, ye think—but I think ye dinna ken what that means. To be what I am doesna mean only that I'll spill my own blood when I must. It means I must sacrifice other men to the ends of my own cause—not only those I kill as enemies, but those I hold as friends . . . or as kin."

His hand dropped away, and the tension left his shoulders. He turned toward the door, saying, "Come when ye're ready, Sassenach."

I STOOD THERE for an instant, blinking, then ran after him, leaving my half-packed bag behind.

"Jamie!" He was standing in the printshop, Henri-Christian in his arms, bidding goodbye to the girls and Marsali. Germain was nowhere in sight, doubtless sulking. Jamie looked up, startled, then smiled at me.

"I wasna going to leave ye behind, Sassenach. And I didna mean to hurry ye, either. Do ye—"

"I know. I just—I have to tell you something."

All the little heads turned toward me like a nestful of baby birds, soft pink mouths open in curiosity. It occurred to me that I might better have waited until we were on the road, but it had seemed urgent that I tell him now—not only to relieve his anxieties, but to make him know I *did* understand.

"It's William," I blurted, and Jamie's face clouded for an instant, like a breathed-on mirror. Yes, I had understood.

"Come to me, *a bhalaich,*" Marsali said, taking Henri-Christian from Jamie and setting him on the floor. "Oof! Ye weigh more than I do, wee man! Come away now, lassies, Grandda isn't going just yet. Help me fetch out Grannie's things."

The children obediently scampered off behind her, though still looking back at us in frustrated curiosity. Children hate secrets, unless they're the ones keeping them. I glanced after them, then turned back to Jamie.

"I didn't know if they knew about William. I suppose Marsali and Fergus do, since—"

"Since Jenny told them. Aye, they do." He rolled his eyes in brief resignation, then fixed them on my face. "What is it, Sassenach?"

"He can't fight," I said, letting out a half-held breath. "It doesn't matter what the British army is about to do. William was paroled after Saratoga—he's a conventioner. You know about the Convention army?"

"I do." He took my hand and squeezed it. "Ye mean he's not allowed to take up arms unless he's been exchanged—and he hasn't been, is that it?"

"That's it. Nobody *can* be exchanged, until the King and the Congress come to some agreement about it."

His face was suddenly vivid with relief, and I was relieved to see it.

"John's been trying to have him exchanged for months, but there isn't any way of doing it." I dismissed Congress and the King with a wave of my free hand and smiled up at him. "You won't have to face him on a battlefield."

"Taing do Dhia," he said, closing his eyes for an instant. "I've been thinking for days—when I wasna fretting about *you,* Sassenach—" he added, opening his eyes and looking

down his nose at me, "—the third time's the charm. And that would be an evil charm indeed."

"Third time?" I said. "What do you—would you let go my fingers? They've gone numb."

"Oh," he said. He kissed them gently and let go. "Aye, sorry, Sassenach. I meant—I've shot at the lad twice in his life so far and missed him by no more than an inch each time. If it should happen again—ye canna always tell, in battle, and accidents do happen. I was dreaming, during the night, and . . . och, nay matter." He waved off the dreams and turned away, but I put a hand on his arm to stop him. I knew his dreams—and I'd heard him moan the night before, fighting them.

"Culloden?" I said softly. "Has it come back again?" I actually hoped it *was* Culloden—and not Wentworth. He woke from the Wentworth dreams sweating and rigid and couldn't bear to be touched. Last night, he hadn't waked, but had jerked and moaned until I'd got my arms around him and he quieted, trembling in his sleep, head butted hard into my chest.

He shrugged a little and touched my face.

"It's never left, Sassenach," he said, just as softly. "It never will. But I sleep easier by your side."

48

JUST FOR THE FUN OF IT

IT WAS A PERFECTLY ordinary red-brick building. Modest—no pediments, no carved stone lintels—but solid. Ian looked at it warily. The home of Philadelphia Yearly Meeting, the weightiest meeting of the Society of Friends in the Americas. Aye, very solid.

"Will this be like the Vatican?" he asked Rachel. "Or more like an archbishop's palace?"

She snorted.

"Does it look like any sort of palace to thee?" She spoke

normally, but he could see the pulse beat quick in the soft spot just beneath her ear.

"It looks like a bank," he said, and that made her laugh. She cut it short, though, glancing over her shoulder as though afraid someone might come out and scold her for it.

"What do they do in there?" he asked, curious. "Is it a great meetinghouse?"

"It is," she said. "But there is also business to be done, thee knows. The yearly meetings deal with matters of . . . I suppose thee would call it principle. We call it Faith and Practice; there are books, rewritten every so often, to reflect the present sense of the meeting. And queries." She smiled suddenly, and his heart gave a small extra thump. "I think thee would recognize the queries—they're much like thee has described the examination of conscience before thy confession."

"Och, aye," he said agreeably, but declined to pursue the subject. He hadn't been to confession in some years and didn't feel sufficiently wicked at present to trouble about it. "This Faith and Practice—is that where they say ye mustn't join the Continental army, even if ye dinna take up arms?"

He was immediately sorry he'd asked; the question dimmed the light in her eyes, but only momentarily. She drew a deep breath through her nose and looked up at him.

"No, that would be an opinion—a formal opinion. Friends talk over every possible point of consideration before they give an opinion—whether it's a positive one or not." There was the barest hesitation before "not," but he heard it and, reaching out, pulled out her hatpin, gently straightened her straw hat, which had slid a little askew, and pushed the pin back in.

"And if in the end it's not, and we canna find a meeting that will have us, lass—what will we do?"

Her lips pressed together, but she met his eyes straight on.

"Friends are not married *by* their meeting. Or by priest or preacher. They marry each *other*. And we will marry each other." She swallowed. "Somehow."

The small bubbles of misgiving that had been rising through his wame all morning began to pop, and he put a hand over his mouth to stifle a belch. Being nervous took him in the innards; he'd not been able to eat breakfast. He turned a little away, from politeness, and spied two figures coming round the far corner. "Och! There's your brother now, and lookin' gey fine for a Quaker, too."

Denzell was dressed in the uniform of a Continental soldier and looked self-conscious as a hunting dog with a bow tied round its neck. Ian suppressed his amusement, though, merely nodding as his future brother-in-law drew to a stop before them. Denny's betrothed had no such compunctions.

"Is he not *beautiful*?" Dottie crowed, standing back a little to admire him. Denzell coughed and pushed his spectacles up his nose. He was a tidy man, not over-tall, but broad in the shoulder and strong in the forearm. He did look fine in the uniform, Ian thought, and said so.

"I will try not to let my appearance engorge my vanity," Denzell said dryly. "Is thee not also to be a soldier, Ian?"

Ian shook his head, smiling.

"Nay, Denny. I shouldna be any kind of soldier—but I'm a decent scout." He saw Denzell's eyes fix on his face, tracing the double line of tattooed dots that looped across both cheekbones.

"I expect thee would be." A certain tenseness in Denny's shoulders relaxed. "Scouts are not required to kill the enemy, are they?"

"No, we've our choice about it," Ian assured him, straight-faced. "We can kill them if we like—but just for the fun of it, ken. It doesna really count."

Denzell blinked for an instant at that, but Rachel and Dottie both laughed, and he reluctantly smiled.

"Thee is late, Denny," Rachel said, as the public clock struck ten. "Was Henry in difficulty?" For Denzell and Dottie had gone to take farewell of Dottie's brother, Henry, still convalescent from the surgery Denny and Ian's auntie Claire had done.

"Thee might say so," Dottie said, "but not from any physical ill." The look of amusement faded from her face, though a faint gleam still lingered in her eyes. "He is in love with Mercy Woodcock."

"His landlady? Love's no usually a fatal condition, is it?" Ian asked, raising one brow.

"Not if thy name is neither Montague nor Capulet," Denny said. "The difficulty is that while Mercy loves him in return, she may or may not still have a husband living."

"And until she finds out he's dead . . ." Dottie added, lifting one slim shoulder.

"Or alive," Denny said, giving her a look. "There is always the possibility."

"Not much of one," Dottie replied bluntly. "Auntie—I mean Friend—Claire doctored a man called Walter Woodcock who'd been badly wounded at Ticonderoga, and she said he was near death then and taken p-prisoner." She stumbled slightly on the last word, and Ian was reminded suddenly that her eldest brother, Benjamin, was a prisoner of war.

Denzell saw the cloud cross her face and gently took her hand in his.

"Both thy brothers will survive their trials," he said, and warmth touched his eyes behind the glass. "So will we, Dorothea. Men have died from time to time and worms have eaten them—but not for love."

"Hmph!" said Dottie, but gave him a small, grudging smile. "All right, then—go ahead. There's *such* a lot to do before we go."

To Ian's surprise, Denzell nodded, took a folded sheaf of papers from his bosom, and, turning, went up the step to the door of the meetinghouse.

Ian had supposed the place was only a convenient spot to meet—he would be catching up his uncle and Auntie Claire on the road to Coryell's Ferry but had lingered to help with the loading, for Denny, Dottie, and Rachel were driving a wagon filled with medical supplies—but evidently Denny had business with Philadelphia Yearly Meeting.

Was he seeking advice in how to be married as a Quaker even while flouting their . . . what would you call it, edict—no, Rachel had said it was an opinion, but a "weighty" opinion—regarding support of the rebellion?

"He's giving them his witness—his testimony," Dottie said matter-of-factly, seeing the puzzlement in Ian's face. "He wrote it all out. Why he thinks it's right to do what he's doing. He's going to give it to the clerk of the yearly meeting and request that his views be mentioned and discussed."

"D'ye think they will?"

"Oh, yes," Rachel said. "They may disagree with him, but they won't stifle him. And good luck to them if they thought to try," she added, half under her breath. She pulled a handkerchief out of her bosom, very white against the soft brown of her skin, and patted tiny droplets of sweat away from her temples.

Ian felt a sudden and profound longing for her and glanced involuntarily toward the clock tower. He'd need to be on the road soon and hoped there'd be time for a precious hour alone with Rachel first.

Dorothea's eyes were still fixed on the door through which Denny had passed.

"He *is* so lovely," she said softly, as though to herself. Then glanced self-consciously at Rachel. "He felt badly for wearing his uniform to see Henry," she said, a tone of apology in her voice. "But the time was so short . . ."

"Was thy brother upset?" Rachel asked sympathetically. Dottie's brows drew down.

"Well, he didn't *like* it," she said frankly. "But it's not as though he didn't know that we're Rebels; I told him some time ago." Her expression relaxed a little. "And he *is* my brother. He won't disown me."

Ian wondered whether the same was true of her father, but didn't ask. She hadn't mentioned the duke. He wasn't really attending to Dottie's family concerns, though—his mind was busy with thought of the coming battle and all that needed to be done immediately. Ian caught Rachel's eye and smiled, and she smiled back, all worry melting from her face as she met his gaze.

He had concerns himself, certainly, annoyances and worries. At the bottom of his soul, though, was the solid weight of Rachel's love and what she had said, the words gleaming like a gold coin at the bottom of a murky well. *"We will marry each other."*

49

UNCERTAINTY PRINCIPLE

AS JAMIE EXPLAINED to me on the way out of Philadelphia, the problem lay not in finding the British but in catching up to them with enough men and matériel to do some good.

"They left with several hundred wagons and a verra large number of Loyalists who didna feel quite safe in Philadelphia. Clinton canna be protecting them and fighting at the same time. He must make all the speed he can—which means he must travel by the most direct road."

"I suppose he can't very well be legging it cross-country," I agreed. "Have you—meaning General Washington—got any idea how big a force he has?"

He lifted one shoulder and waved off a large horsefly with his hat.

"Maybe ten thousand men. Maybe more. Fergus and Germain watched them assemble to march out, but ye ken it's not easy to judge numbers when they're crawlin' out of the side streets and all."

"Mmm. And . . . um . . . how many men do we have?" Saying *"we"* gave me an odd sensation that rippled through my lower body. Something between tail-curling apprehension and an excitement that was startlingly close to sexual.

It wasn't that I'd never felt the strange euphoria of war before. But it had been a very long time; I'd forgotten.

"Fewer than the British," Jamie said, matter-of-fact. "But we willna ken how many until the militia have gathered—and pray it's not too late when we do."

He glanced aside at me, and I could see him wondering whether to say something further. He didn't speak, though, just gave a little shrug and settled himself in the saddle, putting on his hat again.

"What?" I said, tilting my head to peer up at him from under the brim of my own broad straw. "You were about to ask me something."

"Mmphm. Aye, well . . . I was, but then I realized that if ye did know anything about . . . what might happen in the next few days, ye'd surely have told me."

"I would." In fact, I didn't know whether to regret my lack of knowledge or not. Looking back at those instances where I'd thought I knew the future, I hadn't known nearly enough. Out of nowhere, I thought of Frank . . . and Black Jack Randall, and my hands gripped the reins so strongly that my mare jerked her head with a startled snort.

Jamie looked round, startled, too, but I waved a hand and leaned forward to pat the horse's neck in apology.

"Horsefly," I said, in explanation. My heart was thumping noticeably against the placket of my stays, but I took several deep breaths to quiet it. I wasn't about to mention my sudden thought to Jamie, but it hadn't left me.

I'd thought I knew that Jack Randall was Frank's five-times-great-grandfather. His name was right there, on the genealogical chart that Frank had shown me many times. And, in fact, he *was* Frank's ancestor—on paper. It was Jack's younger brother, though, who had sired Frank's bloodline but then had died before being able to marry his pregnant lover. Jack had married Mary Hawkins at his brother's request and thus given his name and legitimacy to her child.

So many gory details didn't show up on those tidy genealogical charts, I thought. Brianna was Frank's daughter, on paper—and by love. But the long, knife-blade nose and glowing hair of the man beside me showed whose blood ran through her veins.

But I'd thought I *knew.* And because of that false knowledge, I'd prevented Jamie killing Jack Randall in Paris, fearing that if he did, Frank might never be born. What if he *had* killed Randall then? I wondered, looking at Jamie sidelong. He sat tall, straight in the saddle, deep in thought, but with an air now of anticipation; the dread of the morning that had gripped us both had gone.

Anything might have happened; a number of things might

not. Randall wouldn't have abused Fergus; Jamie wouldn't have fought a duel with him in the Bois de Boulogne . . . perhaps I would not have miscarried our first child, our daughter Faith. Likely I would have—miscarriage was usually physiological in basis, not emotional, however romantic novels painted it. But the memory of loss was forever linked to that duel in the Bois de Boulogne.

I shoved the memories firmly aside, turning my mind away from the half-known past to the complete mystery of the waiting future. But just before the images blinked out, I caught the edge of a flying thought.

What about the child? The child born to Mary Hawkins and Alexander Randall—Frank's true ancestor. He was, in all probability, alive now. Right now.

The ripple I'd experienced before came back, this time running from my tailbone up my spine. *Denys.* The name floated up from the parchment of a genealogical chart, calligraphic letters that purported to capture a fact, while hiding nearly everything.

I knew his name was Denys—and he was, so far as I knew, actually Frank's four-times great-grandfather. And that was all I knew—likely all I ever would know. I fervently hoped so. I wished Denys Randall silently well and turned my mind to other things.

50

THE GOOD SHEPHERD

TWELVE. BLOODY. *MILES!* The train of baggage wagons stretched as far as the eye could see in either direction and raised a cloud of dust that nearly obscured the mules negotiating a bend in the road a half mile away. The people trudging beside the wagons on either side were coated with the fine brown stuff—and so was William, though he kept as much distance as he could from the slow-moving cavalcade.

It was mid-afternoon of a hot day, and they'd been on the march since before dawn.

He paused to slap dust from the skirts of his coat and take a mouthful of tin-tasting water from his canteen. Hundreds of refugees, thousands of camp followers, all with packs and bundles and handcarts, with here and there a laden horse or mule that had somehow escaped the army teamsters' rapacity, were strung over the twelve miles between the two main bodies of the army. They spread out in a straggling mass that reminded him of the plague of locusts from the Bible. Was that the book of Exodus? Couldn't recall, but it seemed apposite.

Some of them looked over their shoulders now and then. He wondered if it was fear of pursuit or thoughts of what they'd left behind—the city itself was long out of sight.

Well, if there was any danger of turning to a pillar of salt, it would be owing to sweat, not yearning, he thought, wiping his sleeve across his face for the dozenth time. He was himself eager to shake the dust of Philadelphia from his boots and never think of it again.

If it weren't for Arabella–Jane, he'd likely have forgotten it already. He certainly *wanted* to forget everything else that had happened in the last few days. He twitched his reins and nudged his horse back toward the trudging horde.

It could be worse; nearly *had* been much worse. He'd come close to being dispatched back to England or sent north to join the other conventioners in Massachusetts. Thank Christ that Papa—that is, *Lord John,* he corrected himself firmly—had made him learn German, along with French, Italian, Latin, and Greek. Besides the divisions commanded by Sir Henry and Lord Cornwallis, the army included a huge body of mercenary troops under General von Knyphausen—nearly all of them from Hesse-Kassel, whose dialect William could manage with no trouble.

It had still taken a good deal of persuasion, but in the end he'd landed up as one of Clinton's dozen aides-de-camp, charged with the tedious chore of riding up and down the ponderously moving column, collecting reports, delivering dispatches, and dealing with any small difficulties that developed en route—a more or less hourly occurrence. He kept a running mental note of where the various surgeons and hospital orderlies were; he lived in horror of having to attend the delivery of one of the camp followers' babies—there were at least fifty very pregnant women with the column.

Maybe it was the proximity of these ladies, gravid and pale, their swollen bellies borne like burdens, balanced with the ones on their backs, that made him think of . . .

Surely whores knew how to avoid pregnancy? He didn't recall Arabella–Jane doing anything . . . but he wouldn't have noticed, drunk as he was.

William thought of her whenever he touched the spot on his breast where his gorget should be. If asked, he would have said he put the thing on with his uniform and forgot about it—but from the number of times he found Arabella–Jane in his mind, he was apparently in the habit of fiddling with it constantly.

The loss of the gorget had cost him an unpleasant five-minute analysis of his character, dress, hygiene, and personal failings from Clinton's chief aide, Captain Duncan Drummond, and a ten-shilling fine for being out of proper uniform. He didn't grudge her the cost.

He did find himself keeping an eye out for Captain Harkness. He couldn't recall enough of their encounter to have any idea of Harkness's regiment, but there weren't that many dragoon companies with the present army. He was working his way back along the column now, doing his daily round on Visigoth, a big bay gelding with good wind. The horse wasn't pleased with the slow pace and kept twitching under him, wanting to break into a gallop, but William held him to a steady trot, nodding as he passed each company, looking to the corporals and sergeants to see if any were in difficulty or needed assistance.

"Water's coming!" he called to a particularly wilted-looking group of Loyalist refugees who had stopped on the verge of the road, taking pause in the scant shade provided by a scatter of oak saplings and a handcart precariously piled with their belongings.

This reassurance made the women look up hopefully from under their bonnets, and the gentleman rose to his feet, waving William down.

He reined in and recognized Mr. Endicott, a well-to-do Philadelphia merchant, and his family. He'd been to dinner at their house and had danced with the two older Misses Endicott at several parties.

"Your servant, sir," he said, sweeping off his hat with a bow and nodding in turn to the ladies. "And yours, Mrs. Endicott. Miss Endicott, Miss Sally . . . and your most humble and obedient, Miss Peggy." Miss Peggy Endicott, aged nine, went pink as a young strawberry at being singled out, and her elder sisters exchanged raised brows over her head.

"Is it true, Lord Ellesmere," Endicott said, "that we are closely pursued by the Rebels?" He was holding a large red-flannel handkerchief, with which he wiped a perspiring round face. "The . . . er . . . the ladies find themselves summat worried by the prospect."

"The ladies have no cause for concern, sir," William assured him. "You are under the protection of His Majesty's army, you know."

"Well, yes, we do know that," Mr. Endicott said, rather testily. "Or so we hope, at least; certainly wouldn't be here else, I can tell you. But have you any news of Washington's whereabouts, is what I'd like to know?"

Visigoth shifted his weight and danced a little, eager to be off, but William pulled his head round, clicking his tongue in rebuke.

"Why, yes, sir," he said respectfully. "We have had several deserters from the Rebel camp, come in last night. They say that Washington is gathering his troops, no doubt in hopes of catching up to us—but he has no more than two thousand regulars, with a few scrubby militia companies."

Mr. Endicott looked somewhat reassured at this, but the girls and their mother didn't. Mrs. Endicott plucked at her husband's sleeve and murmured something. He flushed more deeply.

"I said I'll deal with it, madam!" he snapped. He had taken off his wig because of the heat and wore a spotted silk handkerchief tied over his head against the sun; his grizzled hair was cropped short, and tiny bristles stuck out from the edge of the kerchief like the feelers of angry insects.

Mrs. Endicott's lips pressed tight, but she stepped back, jerking her head in a small nod. Miss Peggy, though, emboldened by Captain Ellesmere's particularity, scampered forward and seized hold of his stirrup. Visigoth, startled by the flying scrap of calico at the corner of his vision, shied violently; Peggy shrieked, stumbled back, and went flying. All of the Endicott ladies were shrieking, but William could do nothing about that; he fought the horse's head round and held on grimly while Goth crow-hopped and whirled, then settled down gradually, snorting and jerking at the bit. He could hear passing infantrymen being profanely amused as their column swerved to go round him.

"Is Miss Peggy quite all right?" he inquired, breathing heavily as he finally brought the horse back to the verge. Miss Anne Endicott was standing near the edge of the road, waiting for him; the rest of her family had retreated, and he heard a loud howling coming from behind the handcart.

"Aside from being spanked by Papa for nearly being killed, yes," Miss Endicott replied, looking amused. She drew a little closer, keeping a wary eye on Goth, but the horse was calm enough now, stretching his neck to grab a mouthful of grass.

"I'm sorry to have been the cause of her distress," William said politely, and groped in his pocket, coming out with nothing but a crumpled handkerchief and a stray sixpence. He handed the coin down to Anne, smiling. "Give her that, will you, with my apologies?"

"She will be fine," Anne said, but took the coin. She glanced over her shoulder, then drew a step closer and spoke rapidly, lowering her voice. "I . . . hesitate to ask, Lord Ellesmere . . . but, you see, the cart has broken a wheel, my father cannot fix it, he *won't* abandon our belongings—and my mother is terrified that we will be overtaken and captured by Washington's men." Her dark eyes—very fine dark eyes—fixed on his with a brilliant intensity. "Can you help? Please? That was what my little sister meant to ask you."

"Oh. What exactly is the trouble with—never mind. Let me have a look." It would do Goth no harm to settle for a few minutes. He swung down and tied the horse to one of the saplings, then followed Miss Endicott to the handcart.

It was overflowing with the same higgledy-piggledy assortment of goods he'd seen on the docks two days ago—a tall clock stuck out of heaped clothing and linens, and a homely earthenware chamber pot was stuffed with handkerchiefs, stockings, and what was probably Mrs. Endicott's jewel case.

The sight of this particular mess gave him a sudden pang, though.

These were remnants of a real home, one he'd been a guest in—the rubbish and treasures of people he knew . . . and liked. He'd heard that very clock, with its pierced-work crown, strike midnight just before he'd stolen a kiss from Anne Endicott in the shadows of her father's hallway. He felt the mellow *bong, bong* now, deep in his vitals.

"Where will you go?" he asked quietly, a hand on her arm. She turned to him, flushed and harried, her dark hair coming out of her cap—but still with dignity.

"I don't know," she said, just as quietly. "My aunt Platt lives in a small village near New York, but I don't know that we can travel so far, as we are . . ." She nodded at the unwieldy cart, surrounded by bags and half-wrapped bundles. "Perhaps we can find a safe place closer and wait there while my father goes to make . . . arrangements." Her lips pressed suddenly tight, and he realized that she was holding on to her composure by dint of great effort. And that it was unshed tears that made her eyes so bright. He took her hand and kissed it, gently.

"I'll help," he said.

Easier said than done. While the axle of the cart was intact, one wheel had struck a jagged rock and not merely popped off but had in the process lost the flat-iron tire that encircled the felloes—which in consequence had come apart, being badly glued. The wheel lay in pieces in the grass, and a gaudy orange-and-black butterfly perched on the disjunct hub, lazily fanning its wings.

Mrs. Endicott's fears weren't unfounded. Neither was Mr. Endicott's anxiety—which he was attempting with little success to disguise as irritability. If they were stranded for too long, and left behind . . . even if Washington's regular troops were moving too fast for looting, there were always scavengers on the outskirts of an army—any army.

A respectful period of inspection allowed Mr. Endicott, still red-faced but more settled, to emerge from his domestic imbroglio, followed by Peggy, also red-faced and downcast. William nodded to the merchant and gestured, summoning him to join in contemplation of the wreckage, out of hearing of the women.

"Are you armed, sir?" William asked quietly. Endicott's

face paled noticeably, and his Adam's apple bobbed above his dirt-grimed stock.

"I have a fowling piece that belonged to my father," he said, in a voice so low as to be scarcely audible. "I—it's—not been fired in twenty years." *God,* William thought, appalled. William felt himself naked and edgy without weapons. Endicott had to be fifty, at least, and alone here with four women to protect?

"I'll find you help, sir," William said firmly. Mr. Endicott drew a deep, deep breath. William thought the man might sob if obliged to speak, and turned without haste toward the women, talking as he went.

"There will be a cooper or wainwright somewhere along the column. Ah, and here's the water carrier coming!" He extended a hand to Peggy. "Will you come with me to catch him, Miss Margaret? I'm sure he'll stop for a pretty face." She didn't smile, but she sniffed, wiped her nose on her sleeve, drew herself up, and took his hand. The Endicott ladies were nothing if not courageous.

A bored-looking mule pulled a cart with several barrels of water, passing slowly down the column, the driver pausing when hailed. William waded determinedly into the fray, lifting Peggy in his arms for safety—to her evident delight—and deflected the carrier to the Endicotts' service. Then, with a sweep of his hat to the ladies, he mounted again and made his way down the road in search of a cooper.

The army traveled with the equivalent of several villages' worth of artisans and those men called "supportives": coopers, carpenters, cooks, smiths, farriers, wainwrights, drovers, hauliers, orderlies. To say nothing of the vast swarm of laundresses and sempstresses among the camp followers. It wouldn't take long to find a cooper or a wainwright and persuade him to deal with the Endicotts' trouble. William glanced at the sun; nearly three.

The army was proceeding briskly, but that didn't mean it was moving at any great rate of speed. Clinton had given orders to march an additional two hours per day, though, a strain in the increasing heat. Another two hours before they made camp; with luck, the Endicotts might be whole again by then and able to keep up tomorrow.

A rumble of hooves and catcalls from the infantry caught

his attention and made him glance over his shoulder, heart speeding up. Dragoons, plumes fluttering. He reined up and rode Goth straight at them, glancing from face to face as he passed down their double line. Several of them stared at him, and an officer made irritated motions at him, but he ignored that. A small voice in the back of his mind inquired what he meant to do if he *found* Harkness among them, but he ignored that, too.

He passed the end of the company, circled to the rear, and rode up the other side of the column, looking back over his shoulder at the rank of puzzled faces staring at him, some affronted, some amused. No . . . no . . . no . . . maybe? Would he even recognize the fellow? he wondered. He'd been very drunk. Still, he thought Harkness would recognize *him*. . . .

They were all staring at him by this time, but none with an aspect either of alarm or violence. Their colonel reined up a little and called to him.

"Ho, Ellesmere! Lost something, have you?"

He squinted against the sun and made out the vivid face of Ban Tarleton, red-cheeked and grinning under his flamboyant plumed helmet. He jerked his chin up in invitation, and William wheeled his horse and fell in beside him.

"Not lost, exactly," he said. "Just looking for a dragoon I met in Philadelphia—named Harkness; you know him?"

Ban pulled a face.

"Yes. He's with the Twenty-sixth. Randy bugger, always after women."

"And you aren't?" Ban wasn't a close friend, but William had been out on the randan with him once or twice in London. He didn't drink much, but he didn't need to; he was the sort of man who always seemed a little intoxicated.

Tarleton laughed, face flushed with the heat and red-lipped as a girl.

"Yes. But Harkness doesn't care about anything *but* women. Known him to have three at once, in a brothel."

William considered that one for a moment.

"All right. I can see a use for two, maybe . . . but what's the third one for?"

Ban, who was maybe four years older than William, gave him the sort of pitying look reserved for virgins and confirmed bachelors, then ducked back, laughing, when William punched him in the arm.

"Right," William said. "That aside, I'm looking for a wainwright or a cooper. Any close by?"

Tarleton straightened his helmet and shook his head.

"No, but there's bound to be one or two in that mess." He gestured negligently at the train of baggage wagons. "Which regiment are you with, these days?" He frowned at William, seeming to realize that something was amiss with his dress. "Where's your sword? And your gorget?"

William gritted his teeth—and they really did grit, there being so much coarse dust in the air—and apprised Tarleton of his situation in the minimum number of words. He didn't mention where or under what circumstances he had lost his gorget, and with a brief salute of farewell to the colonel, reined round and went down the column again. He was breathing as though he'd run the length of London Bridge, and pulses of electricity were running down his arms and legs, jolting at the base of his spine.

His anger over his situation had been rekindled by his conversation with Tarleton and—unable to do any bloody thing about any of it—turned his mind to what he wanted to do to Harkness, should he meet the 26th Light Dragoons. He touched his chest by reflex, and his sudden urge to do violence changed at once to an equally sudden rush of desire that made him lightheaded.

Then he recalled his original errand, and hot blood washed through his face. He rode more slowly, calming his mind. Harkness could wait. The Endicotts couldn't.

Thought of the family pained him—and not only because he was ashamed of letting himself be distracted from their difficulty. But in recollecting them now, he realized that for those few moments with the Endicotts, concerned with their troubles, he'd forgotten. Forgotten the burden he'd been carrying like a pound of lead in his chest. Forgotten who he really was.

What would Anne Endicott have done, if she knew? Her parents? Even . . . well, no. He smiled, despite his disquiet. He didn't think Peggy Endicott would mind if he told her he was secretly a cutpurse or a cannibal, let alone a—

Everyone *else* he knew, though . . . The Endicotts were only one Loyalist family who'd welcomed him into their home, and he'd not taken proper leave of any of those who chose to stay in Philadelphia, too ashamed to see them, knowing the truth.

He looked back over his shoulder; the Endicotts were barely visible, now sitting in the grass in a companionable circle, sharing food of some kind. He felt a keen pang at the sight of their companionability. He'd never be part of a decent family, couldn't ever marry a woman even of such modest origins as Anne Endicott.

Her father might well be ruined, might have lost his wealth and business, the family might descend into poverty—but they would remain who they were, firm in their courage and the pride of their name. Not him. His name didn't belong to him.

Well . . . he *could* marry, he grudgingly admitted to himself, making his way gingerly through a group of camp followers. But only a woman who wanted nothing but his title and money would have him, and to wed under such circumstances, knowing that your wife despised you . . . and to know that you passed the taint of your blood to your sons . . .

This morbid train of thought stopped abruptly with the appearance of a small group of artisans, trudging beside a large wagon that undoubtedly held their tools.

He came down on them like a wolf on a flock of startled sheep and ruthlessly cut out a fine, fat wainwright, whom he persuaded by threats and bribery to mount behind him and thus carried his prey back to the Endicotts.

With his spirit soothed by their gratitude, he turned northward again, toward the head of the army, camp, and his supper. Absorbed in thoughts of roast chicken and gravy—he ate with Clinton's staff, and thus ate very well—he didn't notice at once that another horseman had come up alongside him, matching his pace.

"Penny for your thoughts?" said a pleasant, half-familiar voice, and he turned to find himself looking into the smiling face of Denys Randall-Isaacs.

WILLIAM REGARDED Randall-Isaacs with something between annoyance and curiosity. The man had to all effects abandoned him in Quebec City a year and a half before and vanished, leaving him to spend the winter snowbound with nuns and *voyageurs*. The experience had improved both his French and his hunting abilities, but not his temper.

"Captain Randall-Isaacs," he said in acknowledgment, rather coldly. The captain smiled sunnily at him, not at all put off by his tone.

"Oh, just Randall these days," he said. "My father's name, you know. The other bit was a courtesy to my stepfather, but as the old man's passed on now . . ." He lifted one shoulder, leaving William to draw the obvious conclusion: that a Jewish-sounding surname couldn't be an asset to an ambitious officer.

"Surprised to see you here," Randall went on, chummy, as though they'd seen each other at a ball last month. "You were at Saratoga with Burgoyne, weren't you?"

William's hand tightened on the reins, but he patiently explained his peculiar status. For possibly the twentieth time.

Randall nodded, respectful.

"Certainly better than cutting hay in Massachusetts," he said, with a glance at the marching columns they were passing. "Thought of going back to England, though?"

"No," William said, somewhat startled. "Why? For one thing, I doubt I can, by the terms of parole. For another—why should I?" *Why, indeed?* he thought, with a fresh stab. He'd not even begun to think about what awaited him in England, at Helwater, at Ellesmere. In London, for that matter . . . oh, Jesus . . .

"Why, indeed?" Randall said, unconsciously echoing him. The man sounded thoughtful. "Well . . . not much opportunity for distinguishing yourself here, is there?" He glanced very briefly at William's belt, bare of weapons, and away again directly, as though the sight was somehow shameful—which it was.

"And what is it you think I could do there?" William demanded, keeping his temper with some difficulty.

"Well, you *are* an earl," Randall pointed out. William felt the blood rise up his neck, but couldn't say anything. "You have a seat in the House of Lords. Why not use it to accomplish something? Take up politics. Doubt your parole says anything about that—and as long as you weren't going back to rejoin the army, I shouldn't think the travel itself would be a problem."

"I'd never thought of it," William said, striving for politeness. He couldn't think of anything he'd less rather do than be political—unless it was be political while acting a sham.

Randall tilted his head amiably to and fro, still smiling. He was much as he'd been when William had seen him last: dark hair tied back without powder, good-looking rather than handsome, slender without being slight, graceful in movement, with a constant expression of sympathetic geniality. He hadn't changed much—but William had. He was two years older now, much more experienced, and was both surprised and a little gratified to discover that he realized that Randall was playing him like a hand of bezique. Or trying to.

"I suppose there are other possibilities," he said, guiding his horse around an enormous puddle of muddy urine that had collected in a dip in the road.

Randall's horse had paused to add to it. Randall sat as composedly as one can in such a situation, but didn't try to raise his voice over the noise. He picked his way out of the mud and caught William up before continuing the conversation.

"Possibilities?" He sounded genuinely interested, and probably was, William thought—but why? "What were you thinking of doing?"

"You recall Captain Richardson, of course?" William asked casually, but with an eye on Randall's face. One dark brow rose a bit, but otherwise he showed no particular emotion at hearing the name.

"Oh, yes," Randall replied, as casual as William. "Have you seen the good captain recently?"

"Yes, a couple of days ago." William's temper had abated, and he waited with interest to see what Randall might have to say to this.

The captain didn't look taken aback, exactly, but his air of pleasant inconsequence had definitely sharpened into something else. William could actually *see* him wondering whether to ask bluntly what Richardson had wanted or to take another tack, and the perception gave him a small thrill.

"Is Lord John with Sir Henry?" Randall asked. That was enough of a non sequitur to make William blink, but there was no reason not to answer.

"No. Why should he be?"

The brow lifted again.

"You didn't know? The Duke of Pardloe's regiment is in New York."

"It is?" William was more than startled by that, but hastened to collect himself. "How do you know?"

Randall waved a well-manicured hand, as though the answer to this was irrelevant—as perhaps it was.

"Pardloe left Philadelphia this morning with Sir Henry," he explained. "As the duke has recalled Lord John to duty, I thought—"

"He *what*?" William's horse jerked his head and snorted at the exclamation, and William stroked the big neck, using the gesture to avert his face for a moment. His father was *here*?

"I stopped at his lordship's house in Philadelphia yesterday," Randall explained, "and a rather odd Scotchwoman—she must be his lordship's housekeeper, I collect?—told me that his lordship had been gone for several days. But if you haven't seen him . . ."

Randall raised his head, looking ahead. A haze of woodsmoke was already showing above the trees, cook fires, wash fires, and watch fires all marking the growing camp, their tang a pleasant spice in the nostrils. It made William's stomach growl.

"Hup! Hup! At the double, quick . . . march!" A sergeant's bellow came from behind them, and they pulled aside for a double column of infantry, who hadn't needed the exhortation; they were eager for their dinner and the chance to lay down their arms for the night.

The pause gave William room for a moment's thought: ought he to ask Randall to sup with him later, try to draw him out? Or get the hell away from the man as quickly as possible, using his need to wait on Sir Henry as excuse? But what if Lord John really *was* with Sir Henry right this moment? *And* bloody Uncle Hal—all he needed in the present circumstance!

Randall had evidently used the pause for thought, as well, and come to his own decision. He came up close beside William, and after a quick glance to be sure no one was near them, leaned close and spoke in a low voice.

"I say this as a friend, Ellesmere—though I grant you've no reason to trust me, I hope you'll listen. Don't, for God's sake, engage in any enterprise that Richardson suggests. Don't go with him anywhere, no matter what the circumstances. If you can avoid it, don't even talk to him again."

And with that, he reined his horse's head around, spurred up abruptly, and was off down the road at a gallop, heading away from the camp.

51

SCROUNGING

GREY WOULDN'T MIND, if it weren't for the headaches. The ache in his side had faded to something tolerable; he thought a rib might be cracked, but as long as he didn't have to run, that wouldn't be a problem. The eye, though . . .

The injured eye stubbornly refused to move but jerked in its socket, pulling against whatever obstruction held it—an orbicularis muscle? Was that what Dr. Hunter had called it?—in an attempt to focus with its fellow. This was painful and exhausting in itself but also led to double vision and crushing headaches, and he found himself often unable to eat when they halted, wanting only to lie down in darkness and wait for the throbbing to cease.

By the time they stopped to make camp on the evening of the second day of march, he could barely see out of his good eye, and his stomach was heaving with nausea.

"Here," he said, thrusting his hot journeycake at one of his fellows, a tailor from Morristown named Phillipson. "You take it. I can't, not just . . ." He couldn't go on, but pressed the heel of his hand hard against his closed eye. Green and yellow pinwheels and brilliant flashes of light erupted behind his eyelid, but the pressure eased the pain for a moment.

"You save it for later, Bert," Phillipson said, tucking the journeycake into Grey's rucksack. He bent close and peered at Grey's face in the firelight. "You need a patch for that eye," he declared. "Keep you from rubbing at it, at least; it's red as a whore's stocking. Here."

And with that, he took off his own battered felt hat and, whipping a small pair of scissors from his bosom, cut a neat round patch from the brim, rubbed a bit of spruce gum round the edge to make it stick, and then bound it carefully in place over the injured orb with a spotted handkerchief contributed by one of the other militiamen. All of them clustered round to watch, with the kindest expressions of concern, offers of food and drink, suggestions as to which company had a surgeon that might come to let his blood, and so on. Grey, in the weakness of pain and exhaustion, thought he might weep.

He managed to thank them all for their concern, but at last they left off, and after a swig of something unidentifiable but strongly alcoholic from Jacobs's canteen, he sat on the ground, shut his good eye, leaned his head back against a log, and waited for the throbbing in his temples to lessen.

Despite his bodily discomfort, he felt comforted in spirit. The men with him weren't soldiers, and God knew they weren't an army—but they were men, engaged in common purpose and mindful of one another, and that was a thing he knew and loved.

". . . and we bring our needs and desires before thee, O great Lord, and implore thy blessing upon our deeds . . ."

The Reverend Woodsworth was conducting a brief service of prayers. He did this every evening; those who wished might join him; those who didn't occupied themselves in quiet conversation or small tasks of mending or whittling.

Grey had no real idea where they were, save somewhere to the northeast of Philadelphia. Messengers on horseback met them now and then, and confused bits of news and speculation spread like fleas through the group. He gathered that the British army was heading north—clearly to New York—and that Washington had left Valley Forge with his troops and was intending to attack Clinton somewhere en route, but no one knew where. The troops were to muster at a place called Coryell's Ferry, at which point they might, possibly, be told where they were going.

He didn't waste energy on thinking about his own position. He could escape easily enough in the darkness, but there was no point in doing so. Wandering around the countryside in the midst of converging militia companies and regular troops, he ran more risk of ending up back in the custody of Colonel Smith, who would probably hang him out of hand, than he did in remaining with Woodsworth's militia.

The danger might increase when they *did* join Washington's troops—but large armies really couldn't hide from each other, nor did they try to avoid notice. If Washington got anywhere near Clinton, Grey could at that point easily desert—if one considered it desertion—and cross the lines into British hands, risking only being shot by an overenthusiastic sentry before he could surrender and make himself known.

Gratitude, he thought, hearing Mr. Woodsworth's prayer through a haze of growing drowsiness and fading pain. Well, yes, there were a few more things he could count on his list of blessings.

William was still on parole and thus a noncombatant. Jamie Fraser had been released from the Continental army to escort Brigadier Fraser's body back to Scotland. Though he'd returned, he was no longer in the army; he wouldn't be in this fight, either. His nephew Henry was healing, but in no way fit for combat. There was no one likely to be involved in the coming battle—if there was one—over whom he need worry. Though come to think. . . . His hand found the empty pocket of his breeches. *Hal.* Where the bloody hell *was* Hal?

He sighed, but then relaxed, breathing in the scents of woodsmoke, pine needles, and roasted corn. Wherever Hal was, he'd be safe enough. His brother could take care of himself.

The prayers over, one of his companions had started to sing. It was a song he knew, but the words were quite different. His version, picked up from an army surgeon who'd fought with the Colonials during the French and Indian war, went:

Brother Ephraim sold his Cow
And bought him a Commission;
And then he went to Canada
To fight for the Nation;

But when Ephraim he came home
He proved an arrant Coward,
He wouldn't fight the Frenchmen there
For fear of being devour'd.

Dr. Shuckburgh hadn't had much opinion of the colonials, and neither had the composer of the newer version, used as a marching song. He'd heard that one in Philadelphia and hummed along under his breath.

Yankee Doodle came to town,
For to buy a firelock,
We will tar and feather him,
And so we will John Hancock!

His present companions were now singing—with gusto—the latest evolution:

Yankee Doodle went to town
A-riding on a pony,
Stuck a feather in his cap
And called it Macaroni!

He wondered, yawning, whether any of them knew that the word *dudel* meant "simpleton" in German. He doubted Morristown, New Jersey, had ever seen a macaroni, those affected young men who went in for pink wigs and a dozen face patches.

As his headache eased, he began to appreciate the simple pleasure of reclining. The shoes with their makeshift laces fit him badly and, as well as rubbing his heels raw, gave him shooting pains in the shins from the effort of constantly clenching his toes in order to keep the bloody things on. He stretched his legs gingerly, almost enjoying the tenderness in his muscles, so near bliss by contrast with walking.

He was distracted from his catalog of meager blessings by a small, hungry gulp near his ear, followed by a young, low voice.

"Mister . . . if ye're not meanin' to eat that journeycake yourself . . ."

"What? Oh . . . yes. Of course."

He struggled to sit up, one hand pressed protectively over his bad eye, and turned his head to see a boy of eleven or twelve sitting on the log just beside him. He had his hand inside his sack, rummaging for the food, when the boy let out a gasp, and he looked up, vision wavering in the firelight, to discover himself face-to-face with Claire's grandson, fair hair in a tousled halo round his head and a look of horror on his face.

"Hush!" he said in a whisper, and grabbed the child's knee in such a sudden grip that the boy gave a small yelp.

"Why, what's that you've got there, Bert? Caught you a thief?" Abe Shaffstall, distracted from a desultory game of knucklebones, looked over his shoulder, peering shortsightedly at the boy—Christ, what was his name? His father was French; was it Claude? Henri? No, that was the younger boy, the dwarf. . . .

"Tais-toi!" he said under his breath to the boy, and turned to his companions. "No, no—this is a neighbor's son from Philadelphia—er . . . Bobby. Bobby Higgins," he added, grabbing at the first name that offered itself. "What's brought you out here, son?" he asked, hoping that the boy was as quick-witted as his grandmother.

"Lookin' for my grandda," the boy replied promptly, though his eyes shifted uneasily round the circle of faces, now all aimed in his direction as the singing died away.

"My mam sent me with some clothes and food for him, but some wicked fellows in the wood pulled me off my mule and . . . and t-took everything." The boy's voice trembled realistically, and Grey noticed that, in fact, his dirty cheeks showed the tracks of tears.

This provoked a rumble of concern round the circle and the immediate production from pokes and pockets of hard bread, apples, dried meat, and dirty handkerchiefs.

"What's your grandpa's name, son?" Joe Buckman inquired. "What company is he with?"

The boy looked nonplussed at this and shot a quick glance at Grey, who answered for him.

"James Fraser," he said, with a reassuring nod that made his head throb. "He'd be with one of the Pennsylvania companies, wouldn't he, Bobby?"

"Aye, sir." The boy wiped his nose on the proffered handkerchief and gratefully accepted an apple. *"Mer—"* He interrupted himself with an artful coughing fit and amended this to "Thank ye kindly, sir. And you, sir." He handed back the handkerchief and set himself to ravenous consumption, this limiting his replies to nods and shakes of the head. Indistinct mumbles indicated that he had forgotten the number of his grandfather's company.

"No matter, boy," Reverend Woodsworth said comfortingly. "We're all a-going to the same place to muster. You'll find your grandpa with the troops there, surely. You think you can keep up with us, though, a-foot?"

"Oh, aye, sir," Germain—*that was it! Germain!*—said, nodding fast. "I can walk."

"I'll take care of him," Grey said hastily, and that seemed to settle it.

He waited impatiently until everyone had forgotten the boy's presence and begun to ready themselves for sleep, then rose, muscles protesting, and jerked his head at Germain to follow him, muffling an exclamation of pain at the movement.

"Right," he said in a low voice, as soon as they were out of earshot. "What the devil are you doing out here? And where *is* your bloody grandfather?"

"I *was* lookin' for him," Germain replied, unbuttoning his flies to piss. "He's gone to—" He paused, obviously unsure what his relationship with Grey now was. "Beg pardon, my lord, but I dinna ken should I tell ye that or not. I mean . . ." The boy was no more than a silhouette against the darker black of the undergrowth, but even the outline of his body expressed an eloquent wariness. *"Comment se fait-il que vous soyez ici?"*

"How did I come to be here," Grey repeated under his breath. "*Comment,* indeed. Never mind. I'll tell *you* where we're going, shall I? I gather we're bound for a place called Coryell's Ferry to join General Washington. Does that ring a bell?"

Germain's slender shoulders relaxed, and a soft pattering on the earth indicated that apparently it did. Grey joined him, and, finished, they turned back toward the glow of the campfire.

Still in the shelter of the woods, Grey put his hand on Germain's shoulder and squeezed. The boy stopped dead.

"Attendez, monsieur," Grey said, low-voiced. "If the militia learn who I am, they'll hang me. Instantly. My life is in your hands from this moment. *Comprenez-vous?*"

There was silence for an unnerving moment.

"Are you a spy, my lord?" Germain asked softly, not turning round.

Grey paused before answering, wavering between expediency and honesty. He could hardly forget what he'd seen and heard, and when he made it back to his own lines, duty would compel him to pass on such information as he had.

"Not by choice," he said at last, just as softly.

A cool breeze had risen with the setting of the sun, and the forest murmured all around them.

"Bien," Germain said at last. "And thank ye for the food." He turned then, and Grey could see the glint of firelight on one fair brow, arched in inquisitiveness.

"So I am Bobby Higgins. Who are you, then?"

"Bert Armstrong," Grey replied shortly. "Call me Bert."

He led the way then toward the fire and the blanket-humped rolls of sleeping men. He couldn't quite tell, above the rustling of the trees and the snoring of his fellows, but he *thought* the little bugger was laughing.

52

MORPHIA DREAMS

WE SLEPT THAT NIGHT in the public room of an ordinary in Langhorne. Bodies were sprawled on tables and benches, curled *under* the tables, and laid in haphazard arrangements on pallets, folded cloaks, and saddlebags, as far away from the hearth as they could get. The fire was banked, but it still radiated considerable heat. The room was filled with the bitter scents of burning wood and boiling bodies. I estimated the temperature in the room at something like ninety-five degrees Fahrenheit, and the slumbering bodies on display were largely unclad, pale haunches, shoulders, and bosoms glimmering in the sullen glow of the embers.

Jamie had been traveling in shirt and breeches, his new uniform and its dazzling smallclothes carefully folded into a portmanteau until we got within range of the army, so his disrobing was a simple matter of unbuttoning his flies and pulling off his stockings. Mine was complicated by the fact that my traveling stays had leather laces, and over the course of a sweat-drenched day, the knot had tightened into a stubborn nodule that resisted all attempts.

"Are ye no coming to bed, Sassenach?" Jamie was already lying down, having found a remote corner behind the bar counter and spread out our cloaks.

"I've broken a fingernail trying to get this bloody thing loose, and I can't bloody reach it with my teeth!" I said, on the verge of breaking into tears of frustration. I was swaying with weariness, but couldn't bring myself to sleep in the clammy confines of my stays.

Jamie reached up an arm out of the darkness, beckoning.

"Come lie down wi' me, Sassenach," he whispered. "I'll do it."

The simple relief of lying down, after twelve hours in the saddle, was so exquisite that I nearly changed my mind about sleeping in my stays, but he'd meant it. He squirmed down and bent his head to nuzzle at my laces, an arm round my back to steady me.

"Dinna fash," he murmured into my midsection, voice somewhat muffled. "If I canna nibble it loose, I'll prise it wi' my dirk."

He looked up with an inquiring noise, as I'd uttered a strangled laugh at the prospect.

"Just trying to decide whether being accidentally disemboweled would be worse than sleeping in my stays," I whispered, cupping his head. It was warm, the soft hair at his nape damp to the touch.

"My aim's no that bad, Sassenach," he said, pausing in his labors for an instant. "I'd only risk stabbin' ye in the heart."

As it was, he accomplished his goal without recourse to weapons, gently jerking the knot loose with his teeth until he could finish the job with his fingers, opening the heavy seamed canvas stays like a clamshell to expose the whiteness of my shift. I sighed like a grateful mollusk opening at high tide, plucking the fabric out of the creases the stays had made in my flesh. Jamie pushed away the discarded stays but remained where he was, his face near my breasts, rubbing his hands gently over my sides.

I sighed again at his touch; he'd done it by habit, but it was a habit I'd missed for the last four months, and a touch I'd thought never to feel again.

"Ye're too thin, Sassenach," he whispered. "I can feel every rib. I'll find ye food tomorrow."

I had been too much preoccupied in the last few days to think about food, and was much too tired at the moment to be hungry, but made an agreeable sound in response and stroked his hair, tracing the curve of his skull.

"I love you, *a nighean,*" he said, very softly, his breath warm on my skin.

"I love you," I answered just as softly, taking the ribbon from his hair and loosening his plait between my fingers. I pressed his head closer to me, not in invitation, but out of the sudden urgent need to *keep* him close to me, to protect him.

He kissed my breast and turned his head, laying it in the hollow of my shoulder. He took one deep breath, one more, and then was asleep, the relaxing weight of his body against me both protection and trust.

"I love you," I said, almost soundless, my arms wrapped tight about him. "Oh, dear God, I love you."

IT MIGHT HAVE been the sense of overwhelming fatigue, or the smell, the mingling of alcohol and unwashed bodies, that made me dream of the hospital.

I was walking down the little hall beyond the men's ward at the hospital where I'd done my nurse's training, the tiny bottle of morphia grains in my hand. The walls were dingy gray; so was the air. At the end of the hall was the alcohol bath where the syringes were kept.

I lifted one out, cold and slippery, careful not to drop it. But I did drop it; it slid from my hand and shattered on the floor, spraying glass shards that cut my legs.

I couldn't worry about that; I had to get back with the morphine injection—men were calling out behind me, desperate, and somehow it was the sound of the operating tent in France back there, men moaning, screams and hopeless sobbing, and my fingers shook with urgency, groping in the cold steel bath among glass syringes that rattled like bones.

I pulled one out, gripping it so tightly that it, too, broke in my hand, and blood ran down my wrist, but I wasn't conscious of pain. Another, I must have another; they were in dreadful pain and I could stop it, if *only* . . .

Somehow I had a clean syringe and had got the top off the tiny bottle of morphia grains, but my hand was shaking, the grains spilling like salt; Sister Amos would be furious. I needed tweezers, forceps; I couldn't grasp the tiny pellets with my fingers and, in a panic, shook several of them into the syringe, a whole grain, not the quarter grain called for, but I *had* to get to the men, had to stop their pain.

Then I was running back down the endless gray hall toward the cries, shards of glass glinting among the red blood drops on the floor, both as bright as dragonfly wings. But my hand was growing numb, and the last syringe fell from my fingers before I reached the door.

And I woke up with a jolt that seemed to stop my heart. I gulped smoke and the fug of beer and bodies, not knowing where I was.

"Jesus, Sassenach, are ye all right?" Jamie, startled out of sleep, rolled up onto his elbow above me, and I came back into the present with as much of a jolt as my awakening had been. My left arm was numb from the shoulder down, and there were tears on my cheeks; I felt the coolness on my skin.

"I . . . yes. Just a . . . a bad dream." I felt ashamed to confess it, as though it were his privilege alone to suffer nightmares.

"Ah." He lowered himself beside me with a sigh and gathered me to him with one arm. He ran a thumb over my face and, finding wetness, blotted it matter-of-factly with his shirt. "All right now?" he whispered, and I nodded, thankful that I needn't talk about it.

"Good." He stroked the hair off my face and rubbed my back gently, the circles of his hand growing gradually slower until he fell asleep again.

It was deep night, and a deep sleep lay upon the room. The whole of it seemed to breathe in unison, snores and gasps and grunts all fading into something like the waves of a receding tide, rising and falling and bearing me with them, safely back into the depths of sleep.

Only the pins and needles of feeling returning to my dead arm kept me from it, and that only momentarily.

I could still see the blood and the shards of glass and heard against the susurrus of snores the crash of falling crystal, saw the bloody smudges on the wallpaper at Number 17.

Dear Lord, I prayed, listening to Jamie's heart under my ear, slow and steady. *Whatever happens, let him have a chance to talk to William.*

53

TAKEN AT A DISADVANTAGE

WILLIAM LED HIS HORSE down among the rocks to a level place where both of them could drink. It was midafternoon, and after a day spent riding to and fro along the column in the blazing sun, he was parched as a piece of last year's venison jerky.

His present horse was Madras, a cob with a deep chest and a steady, stolid disposition. The horse waded purposefully into the stream, hock-deep, and sank his nose into the water with a blissful snort, shivering his coat against the cloud of flies that appeared instantly out of nowhere whenever they stopped.

William waved a couple of insects away from his own face and took off his coat for a moment's relief from the heat. He was tempted to wade in, too—up to his neck, if the creek was deep enough—but . . . well . . . He looked cautiously over his shoulder, but he was well out of sight, though he could hear the sounds of the baggage train on the distant road. Why not? Just for a moment. It wasn't as though the dispatch he was carrying was urgent; he'd seen it written, and it contained nothing more than an invitation for General von Knyphausen to join General Clinton for supper at an inn with a reputation for good pork. Everyone was wringing with sweat; dampness would be no telltale.

He hastily shucked shoes, shirt, stockings, breeches, and smalls, and walked naked into the purling water, which barely reached his waist but was wet and cool. He closed his eyes in blissful relief—and opened them abruptly a half second later.

"William!"

Madras flung up his head with a startled snort, showering William with droplets, but he barely noticed in the shock of seeing two young women standing on the opposite bank.

"What the devil are *you* doing here?" He tried to squat a little lower in the water without being conspicuous about it. Though a dim voice in the back of his mind wondered aloud why he bothered: Arabella–Jane had already seen anything he had. "And who's that?" he demanded, jerking his chin at the other girl. Both of them were flushed as summer roses, but he thought—he hoped—it was the result of the heat.

"This is my sister, Frances," Jane said, with the elegance of a Philadelphia matron, and gestured to the younger girl. "Curtsy to his lordship, now, Fanny."

Fanny, a very lovely young girl with dark curls peeping out under her cap—what was she, eleven, twelve?—bobbed him a sweet curtsy, blue-and-red-calico petticoats outspread, and dropped long lashes modestly over the big, soft eyes of a young doe.

"Your most humble servant, mademoiselle," he said, bowing with as much grace as possible, which, judging from the expressions on the girls' faces, was probably a mistake. Fanny clapped a hand over her mouth and went much redder from the effort not to laugh.

"I am charmed to meet your sister," he said to Jane, rather coldly. "But I fear you take me at something of a disadvantage, madam."

"Yes, that's a piece of luck," Jane agreed. "I couldn't think how we were to find you in that moil, and when we saw you ride past like the fiend was after you—we'd got a ride on a baggage wagon—I didn't think we'd ever catch you. But we took the chance, and . . . *voilà! Fortuna favet audax,* you know." She wasn't even trying to *pretend* she wasn't laughing at him!

He scrabbled for some cutting rejoinder in Greek, but the only thing that came to his inflamed mind was a humiliating echo from his past, something his father had said to him on the occasion when he'd accidentally fallen into a privy: *"What news from the underworld, Persephone?"*

"Turn your backs," he said curtly. "I'm getting out."

They didn't. Gritting his teeth, he turned his own back on them and deliberately climbed the bank, feeling the itch of four interested eyes focused on his dripping backside. He grabbed his shirt and wrestled his way into it, feeling that even that much shelter would enable him to carry on the conversation in a more dignified manner. Or maybe he'd just tuck his breeches and boots under his arm and leave without further chat.

The sound of heavy splashing whilst he was still enveloped in the folds of his shirt made him whirl round, head popping free just in time to see Madras lunge up out of the creek on the girls' side, lips already reaching for the apple Jane was holding out to him.

"Come back here, sir!" he shouted. But the girls had more apples, and the horse paid no attention whatever—nor did he object when Arabella–Jane took his reins and looped them casually round the trunk of a young willow.

"I noticed that you didn't ask how we came to be here," she said. "Doubtless surprise has deprived you of your usual exquisite manners." She dimpled at him and he eyed her severely.

"I did," he said. "I distinctly recall saying, 'What. The. Devil. Are. You. Doing. Here.'"

"Oh, so you did," she said, without a blush. "Well, not to put too fine a point on the matter, Captain Harkness came back."

"Oh," he said, in a slightly different tone. "I see. You, um, ran away, then?"

Frances nodded solemnly.

William cleared his throat. "Why? Captain Harkness is doubtless *with* the army. Why would you come here, of all places, instead of staying safe in Philadelphia?"

"No, he isn't," Jane said. "He was detained on business in Philadelphia. So we came away. Besides," she added carelessly, "there are *thousands* of women with the army. He'd never find us, even if he was looking—and why should he be?"

That was reasonable. Still . . . he knew what the life of an army whore was like. He also had a strong suspicion that the girls had run out on their contract with the brothel; very few saved enough from their wages to buy their way out, and both of these girls were much too young to have made much money.

To abandon the reasonable comfort of clean beds and regular meals in Philadelphia in order to accommodate filthy, sweating soldiers amidst mud and flies, paid in blows as often as in coin . . . Yet he was obliged to admit that he'd never been buggered by a vicious sod like Harkness and thus had no true basis for comparison.

"I expect you want money, to assist in your escape?" he said, an edge in his voice.

"Well, perhaps," said Jane. Reaching into her pocket, she held up something shiny. "Mostly, I wanted to give this back to you."

His gorget! He took an involuntary step toward her, toes squelching in the mud.

"I—thank you," he said abruptly. He'd felt its lack every time he dressed, and felt even more the weight of his fellow officers' eyes on the empty spot where it should rest. He'd been obliged to explain to Colonel Desplains what had happened—more or less—saying that he'd been robbed in a bawdy house. Desplains had chewed him bloody, but then had given him reluctant leave to appear without a gorget until he might get another in New York.

"What I—we, I mean—*really* want is your protection," Jane said, doing her best to look winsomely earnest, and doing it damned well.

"You *what*?"

"I don't think I should have any difficulty in making a living with the army," she said frankly, "but 'tisn't really what I want for my dear sister, that sort of life."

"Er . . . no. I imagine not," William said warily. "What else did you have in mind?" *"Lady's maid?"* he wanted to suggest sarcastically, but in light of the return of his gorget, he refrained.

"I haven't quite made up my mind," she said, fastening her gaze on the ripples where the creek ran over rocks. "But if you could help us to get safely to New York—and maybe find us a place there . . ."

William ran a hand down his face, wiping away a layer of fresh sweat.

"Don't want much, do you?" he said. On the one hand, if he didn't give her some assurance of help, he wouldn't put it past her to fling his gorget into the water in a fit of pique. And on the other . . . Frances was a lovely child, delicate and pale as a morning-glory blossom. And on the third hand, he hadn't any more time to spare in argument.

"Get on the horse and come across," he said abruptly. "I'll find you a new place with the baggage train. I have to ride a dispatch to von Knyphausen just now, but I'll meet you in General Clinton's camp this evening—no, not this evening, I won't be back until tomorrow. . . ." He fumbled for a moment, wondering where to tell her to find him; he could *not* have two young whores asking for him at General Clinton's headquarters. "Go to the surgeons' tent at sundown tomorrow. I'll—think of something."

54

IN WHICH I MEET A TURNIP

DURING THE NEXT DAY'S ride, we encountered a messenger, sent back from Washington's command with a note for Jamie. He read this leaning against a tree, while I made an unobtrusive visit to a nearby clump of brush.

"What does he say?" I asked, straightening my clothes as I emerged. I was still rather awed that Jamie had actually spoken with George Washington, and the fact that he was frowning at a letter presumably *written* by the future Father of the Country . . .

"Two or three things," he replied with a shrug, and, refolding the note, stuffed it into his pocket. "The only important bit o' news is that my brigade is to be under the command of Charles Lee."

"Do you know Charles Lee?" I got my foot into the stirrup and heaved myself into the saddle.

"I know *of* him." What he knew appeared to be rather problematic, judging from the line between his brows. I raised my own; he glanced at me and smiled.

"I met him, ken, when I first met General Washington. I made it my business to learn a bit more about him since."

"Oh, so you didn't like him," I observed, and he gave me a small snort.

"No, I didn't," he said, nudging his horse into a walk. "He's loud and unmannerly and a sloven—I could see that much for myself—but from what I've heard since, he's also jealous to the bone and doesna trouble to hide it verra well."

"Jealous? Of whom?" Not Jamie, I hoped.

"Of Washington," he answered matter-of-factly, surprising me. "He thought he should have command o' the Continental army and doesna like playin' second fiddle."

"Really?" I'd never once heard of General Charles Lee, which seemed odd, if he had such prominence as to have made that a reasonable expectation. "Why does he think that, do you know?"

"I do. He feels he has a good deal more in the way of military experience than Washington—and that's maybe true: he was in the British army for some time and fought a number of successful campaigns. Still—" He lifted one shoulder and dropped it, dismissing General Lee for the moment. "I wouldna have agreed to do this, had it been Lee who asked me."

"I thought you didn't want to do it, regardless."

"Mmphm." He considered for a moment. "It's true I didna want to do this—I don't now." He looked at me, apologetic. "And I truly dinna want you to be here."

"I'm going to be where you are for the rest of our lives," I said firmly. "If that's a week or another forty years."

"Longer," he said, and smiled.

We rode for a time in silence, but deeply aware of each other. We had been, since that conversation in the gardens at Kingsessing.

"I will love ye forever. It doesna matter if ye sleep with the whole English army—well, no, it would matter, but it wouldna stop me loving you."

"I've taken ye to bed a thousand times at least, Sassenach. Did ye think I wasna paying attention?"

"There couldna be anyone like you."

I hadn't forgotten a word we'd said—and neither had he,

though neither one of us had spoken of it again. We weren't walking on tiptoe with each other, but we were feeling our way . . . finding our way into each other, as we'd done twice before. Once, when I'd returned to find him in Edinburgh—and at the beginning, when we'd found ourselves wed by force and joined by circumstance. Only later, by choice.

"What would you have wanted to be?" I asked, on impulse. "If you hadn't been born the laird of Lallybroch?"

"I wasn't. If my elder brother hadna died, ye mean," he said. A small shadow of regret crossed his face, but didn't linger. He still mourned the boy who had died at eleven, leaving a small brother to pick up the burden of leadership and struggle to grow into it—but he had been accustomed to that burden for a very long time.

"Maybe that," I said. "But what if you'd been born elsewhere, maybe to a different family?"

"Well, I wouldna be who I am, then, would I?" he said logically, and smiled at me. "I may quibble wi' what the Lord's called me to do now and then, Sassenach—but I've nay argument wi' how he made me."

I looked at what he was—the strong, straight body and capable hands, the face so full of everything he was—and had no argument, either.

"Besides," he said, and tilted his head consideringly, "if it had been different, I wouldna have you, would I? Or have had Brianna and her weans?"

If it had been different . . . I didn't ask whether he thought his life as it was had been worth the cost.

He leaned over and touched my cheek.

"It's worth it, Sassenach," he said. "For me."

I cleared my throat.

"For me, too."

IAN AND ROLLO caught us up a few miles from Coryell's Ferry. Darkness had fallen, but the glow of the camp was faintly visible against the sky, and we made our way cautiously in, being stopped every quarter mile or so by sentries who popped unnervingly out of the dark, muskets at the ready.

"Friend or foe?" the sixth of these demanded dramatically, peering at us in the beam of a dark lantern held high.

"General Fraser and his lady," Jamie said, shielding his eyes with his hand and glaring down at the sentry. "Is that friendly enough for ye?"

I muffled a smile in my shawl; he'd refused to stop to find food along the way, and I'd refused to let him consume uncooked bacon, no matter how well smoked. Jenny's four apples hadn't gone far, we'd found no food since the night before, and he was starving. An empty stomach generally woke the fiend that slept within, and this was clearly in evidence at the moment.

"Er . . . yes, sir, General, I only—" The lantern's beam of light shifted to rest on Rollo, catching him full in the face and turning his eyes to an eerie green flash. The sentry made a strangled noise, and Ian leaned down from his horse, his own face—Mohawk tattoos and all—appearing suddenly in the beam.

"Dinna mind us," he said genially to the sentry. "We're friendly, too."

TO MY SURPRISE, there was actually a good-sized settlement at the Ferry, with several inns and substantial houses perched on the bank of the Delaware.

"I suppose that's why Washington chose this as the rendezvous point?" I asked Jamie. "Good staging, I mean, and some supply."

"Aye, there's that," he said, though he spoke abstractedly. He'd risen a little in his stirrups, looking over the scene. Every window in every house was lit, but a large American flag, with its circle of stars, flapped above the door of the largest inn. Washington's headquarters, then.

My chief concern was to get some food into Jamie before he met with General Lee, if the aforementioned indeed had a reputation for arrogance and short temper. I didn't know what it was about red hair, but many years' experience with Jamie, Brianna, and Jemmy had taught me that while most people became irritable when hungry, a redheaded person with an empty stomach was a walking time bomb.

I sent Ian and Rollo with Jamie to find the quartermaster, discover what we might have in the way of accommodation, and unload the pack mule, then followed my nose toward the nearest scent of food.

The dug-in camp kitchens would long since have banked their fires, but I'd been in many army camps and knew how they worked; small kettles would be simmering all night, filled with stew and porridge for the morning—the more so as the army was in hot pursuit of General Clinton. Amazing to think that I had met him socially only a few days before—

I'd been so focused on my quest that I hadn't seen a man come out of the half dark and nearly ran into him. He seized me by the arms and we waltzed a dizzy half-turn before coming to rest.

"*Pardon, madame!* I am afraid I have stepped upon your foot!" said a young French voice, very concerned, and I looked straight into the very concerned face of a very young man. He was in shirtsleeves and breeches, but I could see that his shirtsleeves sported deep, lace-trimmed cuffs. An officer, then, in spite of his youth.

"Well, yes, you have," I said mildly, "but don't worry about it. I'm not damaged."

"Je suis tellement désolé, je suis un navet!" he exclaimed, striking himself in the forehead. He wore no wig, and I saw that despite his age, his hair was receding at a rapid pace. What was left of it was red and inclined to stand on end—possibly owing to his apparent habit of thrusting his fingers through it, which he was now doing.

"Nonsense," I said in French, laughing. "You aren't a turnip at all."

"Oh, yes," he said, switching to English. He smiled charmingly at me. "I once stepped on the foot of the Queen of France. She was much less gracious, *sa Majesté,*" he added ruefully. "*She* called me a turnip. Still, if it hadn't happened—I was obliged to leave the court, you know—perhaps I would never have come to America, so we cannot bemoan my clumsiness altogether, *n'est-ce pas*?"

He was exceedingly cheerful and smelled of wine—not that that was in any way unusual. But given his exceeding Frenchness, his evident wealth, and his tender age, I was beginning to think—

"Have I the, um, honor of addressing—" Bloody hell, what was his actual title? Assuming that he really was—

"Pardon, madame!" he exclaimed, and, seizing my hand, bowed low over it and kissed it. *"Marie Joseph Paul Yves Roch Gilbert du Motier, Marquis de La Fayette, à votre service!"*

I managed to pick "La Fayette" out of this torrent of Gallic syllables and felt the odd little thump of excitement that happened whenever I met someone I knew of from historical accounts—though cold sober realism told me that these people were usually no more remarkable than the people who were cautious or lucky enough *not* to end up decorating historical accounts with their blood and entrails.

I gathered sufficient composure to inform him that I was Madame General Fraser and that I was sure my husband would shortly be along to pay his respects, directly I had located some supper.

"But you must come and dine with me, madame!" he said, and, having not let go of my hand, was in a position to tuck it cozily into his elbow and tow me off toward a large building that looked like an inn of some sort. An inn was precisely what it was, but an inn that had been commandeered by the Rebel forces and was now General Washington's headquarters—as I discovered when *le marquis* led me under a fluttering banner, through the taproom, and into a large back room where a number of officers were sitting at table, presided over by a large man who did not look precisely like the image on a dollar bill, but close enough.

"Mon Général," the marquis said, bowing to Washington and then gesturing to me. "I have the honor to present to you Madame General Fraser, the personification of grace and loveliness!"

The table rose as one, with a screeching of wooden benches, and the men—in fact, there were only six of them—rose and bowed to me in turn, murmuring, "Your servant," and "Your most obedient, ma'am." Washington himself stood up at the head of the table—*My God, he's as tall as Jamie,* I thought—and gave me a very graceful bow, hand on his bosom.

"I am honored by your presence, Mrs. Fraser," he said, in a soft Virginia drawl. "Dare I hope that your husband accompanies you?"

I had a moment's insane impulse to reply, *"No, he sent me to fight instead,"* but managed not to say it.

"He does," I replied instead. "He's . . . er . . ." I gestured helplessly toward the doorway, where—with remarkably good timing—Jamie himself now appeared, brushing pine needles off his sleeve and saying something to Young Ian, behind him.

"There ye are!" he exclaimed, spotting me. "Someone told me ye'd gone off with a strange Frenchman. What—" He stopped abruptly, having suddenly realized that I wasn't merely in the company of a strange Frenchman.

The table fell about laughing, and La Fayette rushed up to Jamie and seized his hand, beaming.

"Mon frère d'armes!" He clicked his heels together, doubtless by reflex, and bowed. "I must apologize for having stolen your lovely wife, sir. Allow me, please, to make recompense by inviting you to dinner!"

I'd met Anthony Wayne before, at Ticonderoga, and was pleased to see him again. I was also delighted to see Dan Morgan, who gave me a hearty buss on both cheeks, and I admitted to a certain thrill at having my hand kissed by George Washington, though noticing the halitosis that accompanied his notorious dental problems. I wondered how I might make an opportunity to inspect his teeth, but gave such speculations up immediately with the arrival of a procession of servants with trays of fried fish, roast chicken, buttermilk biscuits with honey, and an amazing selection of ripe cheeses, these having been—he told me—brought by the marquis himself from France.

"Try this one," he urged me, cutting a slab of an extremely fragrant Roquefort, green-veined and crumbly. Nathanael Greene, who sat on the other side of the marquis, pinched his nose unobtrusively and gave me a small private smile. I smiled back—but in fact I quite liked strong cheese.

I wasn't the only one. Rollo, who had come in—naturally—with Young Ian and was sitting behind him, across the table from me, lifted his head and poked a long, hairy snout between Ian and General Lee, sniffing interestedly at the cheese.

"Good Christ!" Lee apparently hadn't noticed the dog before this and flung himself to one side, nearly ending in Jamie's lap. This action distracted Rollo, who turned to Lee, sniffing him with close attention.

I didn't blame the dog. Charles Lee was a tall, thin man with a long, thin nose and the most revolting eating habits I'd seen since Jemmy had learned to feed himself with a spoon. He not only talked while he ate and chewed with his mouth open, but was given to wild gestures while holding things in his hand, with the result that the front of his uniform was streaked with egg, soup, jelly, and a number of less identifiable substances.

Despite this, he was an amusing, witty man—and the others seemed to give him a certain deference. I wondered why; unlike some of the gentlemen at the table, Charles Lee never attained renown as a Revolutionary figure. He treated *them* with a certain . . . well, it wasn't scorn, certainly—condescension, perhaps?

I was taken up in conversation—mostly with the marquis, who was putting himself out to be charming to me, telling me how much he missed his wife (Good Lord, how old was he? I wondered. He didn't look more than twenty, if that), who had been responsible for the cheese. No, no, not making it herself, but it came from their estate at Chavaniac, which his wife ran most ably in his absence—but now and then caught a glimpse of Jamie. He took part in the conversation, but I could see his eyes flick round the table, appraising, judging. And they rested most often on General Lee, beside him.

Of course, he knew Wayne and Morgan quite well—and he knew what I'd been able to tell him about Washington and La Fayette. God, I hoped what I thought I knew about them was halfway accurate—but we'd find out soon enough if it wasn't.

Port wine was brought—evidently the meal was being hosted by the marquis; I had the distinct feeling that the high command of the Continental army didn't always eat this well. The men had largely avoided talking about the impending battle during the meal, but I could feel the subject looming like an approaching thunderstorm, bright-rimmed black clouds, excitingly shot with flickers of lightning. I began to rearrange my skirts and make gestures of incipient leave-taking, and saw Jamie, seated next to Lee across the table, notice and smile at me.

Lee noticed, too—he'd been gazing in an absent way at my décolletage—and broke off the anecdote he'd been telling Ian, seated on his other side.

"Such a pleasure to make your acquaintance, ma'am," he said cordially. "Your husband obliges us extremely by allowing us the delight of your company. I—"

Lee stopped abruptly in mid-sentence—and mid-bite, staring at Rollo, who had unobtrusively moved closer and was now standing no more than a couple of feet from the general. Given the low bench on which Lee was sitting and Rollo's size, this proximity placed them roughly eye-to-eye.

"Why is that dog looking at me like that?" Lee demanded, swinging round to glare at Ian.

"He's waitin' to see what ye drop next, I expect," Ian said, chewing placidly.

"If I were you, sir," Jamie put in politely, "I'd drop something quickly."

IAN, ROLLO, AND I took our leave of the generals and went out into the dark to find our beds, escorted by an orderly with a lantern. Fires burned high all up and down the bank of the Delaware, and many of the boats on the river had lanterns or open fires as well, the lights reflecting in the water like shoals of glimmering fish.

"Do you know anything about the man who ate beside you?" I asked Ian, in my hesitant Gaelic. He laughed—he and Jamie *always* laughed when I spoke Gaelic—but lifted one shoulder in a negative shrug.

"I do not, but I will find out," he said. "He is an Englishman, I can tell you that much."

He used the word "Sassenach," which gave me a mild shock. It had been a long time since I'd heard a Scot use that word in the way it was meant.

"Yes, he is. Do you think it makes a difference?" Technically, they were *all* still Englishmen—well, bar La Fayette, von Steuben, Kosciuszko, and similar oddities—but it was true that most of the Continental officers had been born and spent their lives in America. Lee hadn't. Ian made a derisory Scottish noise, indicating that it did.

"But I hear that he was adopted into the Kahnyen'kehaka, too," I objected.

Ian was silent for a moment, then took my arm, leaning close to speak in my ear.

"Auntie," he said softly. "D'ye think I ever stopped bein' a Scot?"

55

VESTAL VIRGINS

JAMIE AND I WERE billeted at the home of the Chenowyths, a pleasant—if understandably somewhat anxious—family whose home stood at the end of the single road that ran through Coryell's Ferry. Mrs. Chenowyth was in her wrapper, but greeted me kindly with a candlestick and took me to a small bedroom at the back of the house—this showing the evidence of hasty evacuation by a number of young Chenowyths, these presumably now sharing their parents' room, judging from the sounds of mixed heavy breathing.

The single bed was fairly large, though Jamie's feet would still stick out by a good six inches. There was a washbasin and ewer full of fresh water; I picked this up carefully and drank from it; my throat was dry from too much French wine. I replaced the ewer and sat down on the bed, feeling rather strange.

Possibly it was the wine. Possibly it was the fact that the room had no windows, and Mrs. Chenowyth had thoughtfully closed the door behind her. It was a small room, perhaps ten feet by eight. The air was still and the candle's flame burned high and steady, pure against the bricks of the wall. Perhaps it was the candle that brought to mind Uncle Lamb and the day he'd told me about vestal virgins, showing me a blue chalcedony carving from the temple of Vesta.

"Should a virgin betray her vows," he'd said, waggling his eyebrows at me, *"she'd be whipped, then sealed up alive in a small underground tomb, equipped with a table and chair,*

some water, and a single candle. And there she would die, when the air ran out."

I'd considered that with a sort of morbid relish—I might have been ten—and then asked with interest just *how* a vestal might betray her vows. Which is how I learned what used to be called "the facts of life," Uncle Lamb not being one to shirk any fact that wandered across his path, or mine. And while Uncle Lamb had assured me that the cult of Vesta had long since ceased operations, I had at that point resolved not to be a virgin, just in case. On the whole, a good resolution, though sleeping with men did have the most peculiar side effects.

Ian had brought along my saddlebags, which he'd dumped in the corner of the room before going off with Rollo to find his own sleeping place. I got up and fumbled for my toothbrush and tooth powder, though it seemed quite surreal to be brushing my teeth on what might be the eve of battle. Not *quite* rearranging the deck chairs on the Titanic . . . or at least I hoped not.

I knew that Washington and the marquis were going to survive whatever happened—and spared a thought for the strangeness of now thinking of them as men and not names. The large pores on George Washington's nose as he'd bent over my hand, and the shadowed pits of old smallpox scars across his lower cheeks; the smell of him, starch and sweat, wine and wig powder—for he wore his wig, hot as it was—the sweetly nasty smell of dental decay . . . I picked up my toothbrush, reminded, and set to work with some vigor. He'd smelled of blood, too; I wondered why—bleeding gums, perhaps?

I wriggled my way out of gown, jacket, and stays and stood for a bit flapping my shift, in hopes of admitting a little air. It made the candle flicker but didn't have much effect beyond that, so I blew the candle out and lay down.

I didn't expect to sleep. Adrenaline had been jolting through me like the current in a faulty circuit ever since we'd left Philadelphia, but now it was settling down to a steady humming in my blood. The conversation over dinner had been fairly general, but the atmosphere had been electric with anticipation. Clearly, once Ian and I had left and the plates had been removed . . . It was as close as I had ever been to a council of war, and the vibrations of it were still tingling through me.

There was anxiety tingling, too, to be sure—there had been amongst the men, as well. But given a suitable outlet, anxiety can be transformed into very effective action, and that's plainly what Washington and his generals were now doing, hammering out plans, assigning troops, drawing up strategies . . . I wished I was amongst them. It would be much easier than lying in the pitch dark, staring up into a boring infinity—nasty way to die, that.

I sat up, gulping air, and went hastily to the door. No sounds, no light seeping under the door. I patted round on the floor 'til I located my shoes and the puddle of my cloak and, swinging this over my shoulders, slipped out and made my way silently through the half-dark house, past the smoldering hearth and out.

The door was unbolted and on the latch; perhaps Mr. Chenowyth was out and expected back. I supposed there was some danger of my being locked out, but at this point spending the night in the midst of a military camp in my shift seemed preferable to sleeping—or, rather, not sleeping—in a tomb. Besides, I was sure that one of the small Chenowyths had wee'd in the bed fairly recently.

No one took any notice of me as I walked back along the road. The taverns and ordinaries were crammed full and spilling customers all over the road. Continental regulars in their blue and buff, swaggering about, the envy—they hoped—of the militiamen. Any number of women, too, and not all whores, by any means. But above all . . . air.

The heat of the day had largely gone, and while the air wasn't cold by any means, it wasn't stifling, either. Having escaped entombment, I reveled in the feeling of freedom—and what amounted to invisibility, for tall as I was, with my cloak on and my hair tied back in a plait for bed, I looked much like many of the militiamen in the dark; no one glanced twice at me.

The street and the camp beyond were electric; I recognized the feeling, and it gave me the oddest sense of dislocation—for I recognized it in its various forms from half of the battlefields I'd served near, from France in 1944 to Prestonpans and Saratoga. It wasn't always this way; often the sense of the occasion was one of dread—or worse. I remembered the night before Culloden and felt a wave of cold wash through me so strongly that I staggered and nearly fell against the wall of a building.

"Friend Claire?" said a voice, in amazement.

"Denzell?" Half-blinded by a number of torches being borne past, I blinked at the shape that had manifested before me.

"What is thee doing out here?" he said, alarmed. "Is anything wrong? Is it Jamie?"

"Well, you could say it's Jamie," I said, getting back my composure. "But there's nothing wrong, no. I was just getting a bit of air. What are *you* doing here?"

"I was fetching a pitcher of beer," he said, and took me firmly by the arm, steering me down the street. "Come with me. Thee ought not be in the street with the fighting men. Those that aren't drunk now will be shortly."

I didn't argue. His hand on my arm felt good, steadying me against the strange currents of the night that seemed to carry me willy-nilly into the past—and the future—and back again without warning.

"Where are Rachel and Dottie?" I asked, as we turned right at the end of the street and began to thread our way through the campfires and rows of tents.

"Rachel's gone somewhere with Ian; I didn't inquire. Dottie's in our medical tent, dealing with a case of acute indigestion."

"Oh, dear. What did she eat?"

He laughed softly. "The indigestion isn't hers. A woman named Peabody, who came in complaining of colic pains. Dorothea said she would administer something appropriate, if I would go and fetch her some beer—it being not safe for her to venture to the ordinary alone."

I thought I detected a small note of reproach in his voice, but I made an indeterminate "hmm" in response and he said no more about my wandering the streets *en déshabillé.* Possibly because he hadn't noticed that I was *en déshabillé,* until we entered the Hunters' big medical tent and I took my cloak off.

Denny gave me one brief, shocked look, coughed, and, picking up a canvas apron, managed to hand it to me without looking directly at me. Dottie, who was massaging the massive back of a very large woman seated hunched over on a stool in front of her, grinned at me over the woman's capped head.

"How are you, Auntie. Restless tonight?"

"Very," I replied frankly, putting on the apron. "This is Mrs. Peabody?"

"Yes." Dottie smothered a yawn with her shoulder. "The indigestion seems to be better—I gave her gripe water and peppermint," she added, to Denny. "But she's complaining of pains in her back, as well."

"Hmm." I came over and squatted down in front of the woman, who appeared to be half asleep—until I caught a whiff of her breath, which was eighty proof, at least. I put my hand on her belly to see if I could feel the location of the trouble, when she coughed thickly in a way I'd heard all too often before, choked—and I leapt back just in time.

"Thank you for the apron, Denny," I said mildly, brushing off some of the higher flecks of mud and vomit that had spattered on me. "I don't suppose you brought a birthing stool with you?"

"A birthing stool. To a battle?" he said faintly, his eyes bulging slightly behind his spectacles as he looked at the woman, now swaying ponderously to and fro, like a large bell making up its mind whether to ring or not.

"I rather think it may be one," I said, glancing round. "*If* she's in labor. Can you find a blanket, Dottie? I think we'll have to lay her on the ground; she'll collapse the cot."

It took all three of us to wrestle Mrs. Peabody—who relapsed comfortably into unconsciousness the moment we touched her—onto a blanket spread on the ground under the lantern. There was an almost instant insurgence of moths, as they came fluttering in, attracted not only by the light but by the assorted smells thickening the air.

Mrs. Peabody had lapsed not merely into unconsciousness but into what appeared to be an alcoholic coma. After a certain amount of discussion, we'd turned her onto one side, in case she should vomit again, and the position had allowed her belly to flow away from the rest of her corpulent body, so that it lay on the ground in front of her, gravid and sac-like. She looked like the queen of some order of social insect, ready to deliver in the thousands, but I refrained from mentioning this, as Dottie was still pale.

Denzell had recovered from the shock and was keeping an eye—or rather a hand—on her wrist, keeping track of her pulse. "Amazingly strong," he said at last, letting go, and looked up at me. "Does thee think she is near her time?"

"I really hope *not,*" I said, looking down. "But there's no telling without . . . er . . . closer examination." I took a deep breath and a grip on my more generous instincts. "Would you like me to . . . er . . ."

"I'll go and find clean water," he said, springing to his feet and seizing a bucket.

Given that Dottie was engaged to Denny, I refrained from calling him a coward in her presence and merely waved him off in a reserved manner. Mrs. Peabody made me uneasy on a number of scores. I had no idea whether she might be about to go into labor, or, if she did, how her comatose state might affect it. The level of alcohol in her blood was certainly affecting the child's; would a drunken newborn be able to breathe? It wouldn't vomit, as there wasn't anything in its stomach *to* vomit, but might it void its bowels in utero and aspirate the material? That was a remarkably dangerous thing to happen even in a modern hospital with a full delivery-suite staff attending—most of the babies who did that died of suffocation, lung injury, or infection.

I was very much ashamed to admit to myself that my chief fear, though, was that something would happen during delivery that would require me to remain with mother and/or child for a prolonged period. I could not, by my oath as a physician—and what I conceived my responsibilities to be—abandon a patient in dire need of me.

But I *would* not abandon Jamie. I knew beyond all doubt that he was going into battle, and soon. He wasn't going without me.

A slight noise jerked me out of my hypothetical moral quandary. Dottie had started unpacking and had dropped an amputation saw. She stooped to pick it up and said something under her breath in German that I thought was probably a bad word—John always swore in German; perhaps it was a family habit.

Thought of John added another layer of guilt to my complicated feelings—though the logical part of my brain firmly rejected this as undeserved. Still, the worry for him couldn't be rejected so easily, though I did my best to tuck it away for the present.

"You needn't stay up, Dottie," I said. "I can take care of matters here. Nothing's going to happen immediately, regardless—I can make up the surgical kits."

"No, that's all right," she said, and then yawned involuntarily, gaping so widely that she startled herself and clapped a hand belatedly over her mouth. "Oh, dear. I do beg your pardon, Mrs. Fraser." That made me smile; she had John's elegant manners—perhaps Hal did, too, when he wasn't engaging in undiluted bastardliness.

"Actually," she said, fixing me directly with her striking gaze, "I'm pleased to have a chance to talk with you in privacy."

"Oh?" I said, squatting to put a hand on Mrs. Peabody's belly. I wasn't feeling any movement from the baby, but they usually did go quiet if labor was impending. I could have used my stethoscope to listen for a fetal heartbeat, but it was in one of the boxes or bags that Ian and the orderly had carried off somewhere. Besides, whatever I heard or didn't would make no difference to the immediate protocol.

"Yes." Dottie sat down on a packing case as though it were a throne—like all the Greys I'd met, she had excellent posture. "I want to know the correct way of performing sexual intercourse."

"Oh. Erm . . ."

She glanced down at Mrs. Peabody.

"And whether there is any way of preventing . . . er . . ."

"Pregnancy. To be sure." I cleared my throat. I rather thought the sight of Mrs. Peabody would have put most young women off the idea of childbearing—if not sex—altogether. Dorothea Grey, though, was plainly a young woman of blood and iron.

"Don't mistake me, Auntie," she said earnestly. "Or do I mean Friend Claire? I *do* want children—want them terribly. But if there is any choice about giving birth on a battlefield or a moving ship, say—"

I seized on this last, in part to give myself time to compose something coherent in the way of advice. I'd rather thought Rachel might want to talk about such things at some point, having no mother, but . . .

"A ship? Are you thinking of going home to England, then?"

She grimaced in a way that brought her father vividly before me, and I nearly laughed but fortunately didn't.

"I don't know. I dearly want to see Mama again, of course, and Adam . . . and my . . . well, actually, I doubt I should see any of my friends again." She waved a hand, dismissing the friends. "Not that there aren't any Quakers in society, but they're all very rich, and we won't be."

She bit her lip, but in a way indicating calculation rather than chagrin.

"If I can contrive to make Denny marry me here, so that we arrived in England as husband and wife already, it would be a simple matter to find a London meeting that would welcome us. Whereas here—" She flung out a hand toward the hum of the camp around us. "His involvement in the war would always stand in his way, you see?"

"Even after the war is over?"

She gave me a patient look, too old for her face.

"Papa says that wars take three generations to fade from the ground where they're fought. And from what I've seen, Friends have quite long memories, as well."

"He might just have a point." Mrs. Peabody had begun to snore wetly, but I felt no sense of contraction. I rubbed a hand through my hair and braced my back more comfortably against one of the packing crates set against the wall. "All right. Perhaps . . . a little basic anatomy, to begin with."

I really had no idea how much—if anything—a nobly born young woman might have been told, or found out by other means, so began with female reproductive anatomy, starting with the womb—for surely she knew what that was—and leading outward, part by part.

"You mean it has a *name*?" she exclaimed, charmed, when I got to the clitoris. "I'd always thought of it as just, you know . . . *that* bit." Her tone of voice made it abundantly clear that I needn't explain what *that* bit did, and I laughed.

"To the best of my knowledge, it's the only structure of the human body that appears to have no function whatever save the pleasure of the owner."

"But men . . . don't they . . . ?"

"Well, yes, they do," I said. "And very pleasurable they find theirs, too. But a penis is extremely functional, as well. You, er . . . do know how it . . . works? In terms of intercourse?"

"Denzell won't let me touch his naked member, and I'm *longing* to see it at my leisure—not just the odd glimpse when he, well, you know." Her eyes sparkled at the thought. "But I know what it feels like through his breeches. I was amazed, the first time it went stiff under my hand! However does it do that?"

I explained the concept of hydrostatic pressure as simply as possible, already seeing what was coming next. I cleared my throat and rose to my knees.

"I need to examine Mrs. Peabody for any sign of labor. And while we must be respectful of her privacy—so far as such a thing exists under these conditions"—for Dottie had snorted loudly—"since you're assisting me here, there's no reason why you shouldn't observe what I'm doing, and I'll explain it to you as we go. How things . . . work."

She hummed with interest as I gingerly unveiled Mrs. Peabody's nether regions, which were thickly forested but still identifiably—very identifiably—feminine.

"When the cervix—that's the opening to the womb—when it begins to open in order for the baby to come out, there's often some blood and mucus released, but it's quite harmless. I don't see any sign of it yet, though." That heartened me.

"Oh," said Dottie, rather faintly. But she leaned intently over my shoulder as I carefully inserted my freshly washed hand. "Oh!" Dottie said, in tones of extreme revelation. "*That's* where it goes!"

"Well, yes, it is," I said, trying not to laugh—and failing. "Denzell would have told you, I expect. Did you ask him?"

"No," she said, sitting back a little on her heels but still watching closely as I put a hand on Mrs. Peabody's abdomen and felt the cervix. Softened, but still firm. I began to breathe again.

"No?" I said, only half-attending.

"No." She drew herself up. "I didn't want to seem ignorant. Denny's so—I mean, he's *educated.* I can read, of course, and write, but only letters, and play music, but that's useless. I bustle round after him and help where I can, of course, and he's always so good about explaining things . . . but . . . well, I kept having this vision of our wedding night and him explaining it to me in just the same way he'd tell me how to suck the snot out of a child's nose with a tube or hold the skin together so he could stitch a wound. And . . ." She made a graceful little moue, which had to be her mother's legacy. "And I made up my mind it wasn't going to be that way."

"Very . . . um . . . commendable." I withdrew my hand and wiped it, re-covered Mrs. Peabody, and checked her pulse again—slow, but strong as a tympani; the woman must have the heart of an ox. "How—er—how *do* you want it to be? Bearing in mind," I hastened to add, "that this sort of thing is rather variable." Another thought occurred to me. "Has Denzell ever . . . ? Though I don't suppose you'd know."

Her soft white brow wrinkled in thought.

"I don't know; I never thought of asking him. I just assumed—well, I have brothers. I know *they* have, because they talk about it—whores, I mean—with their friends. I suppose I thought all men . . . but, come to think, perhaps Denny wouldn't go to a prostitute. Do you think he might have?" Her brow furrowed a little, but she didn't seem upset at the thought. Of course, it was probably commonly accepted in the Greys' social circle that men, or soldiers at least, naturally would.

With very vivid memories of my own wedding night—and my stupefaction upon being informed that my bridegroom was a virgin—I temporized a bit.

"Possibly not. Now, being a medical man, plainly he must know the essential mechanics. But there *is* more to it than that."

Her eyes grew brighter and she leaned forward, hands on her knees.

"Tell me."

"RATHER LIKE EGG white mixed with a drop or two of civet. Theoretically good for the skin, though frankly—" I was saying, when I heard the sound of voices just outside the tent.

Rachel and Ian had returned, looking cheerful, flushed, and quite like young people who had just passed the last hour or two doing the sorts of things in which I'd been instructing Dottie. I saw her glance sideways at Rachel, then—very briefly—at Ian's breeches. Her color went up a notch.

Rachel didn't notice, her attention having fixed at once on Mrs. Peabody—well, everyone's attention was fixed on Mrs. Peabody; it was really impossible to look at anything else. She frowned at the supine woman on the ground and then looked at me.

"Where's Denzell?"

"An excellent question. He left a quarter of an hour ago to find water. There's beer, though, if you're thirsty." I nodded at the neglected pitcher.

Ian poured a cup for Rachel, waited while she drank it, then refilled it for himself, eyes still fixed on Mrs. Peabody, who was emitting a remarkable variety of noises, though still out cold.

"Does Uncle Jamie ken where ye are, Auntie?" he asked. "He was lookin' for ye just now. He said he'd put ye somewhere safe to sleep, but ye'd escaped. Again," he added with a broad grin.

"Oh," I said. "He's finished with the generals for the night, then?"

"Aye, he went to make the acquaintance o' some of the militia captains under him, but most had gone to sleep by then, so he went to join ye at the Chenowyths. Mrs. Chenowyth was a bit taken aback to find ye gone," he added delicately.

"I just came out for a little air," I said, defensive. "And then—" I gestured at the patient on the floor, who had now settled down to a rhythmic snore. Her color was looking better; that was heartening. "Er . . . is Jamie put out, do you think?"

Ian and Rachel both laughed at that.

"No, Auntie," Ian said. "But he's dead tired, and he wants ye bad."

"Did he tell you to say that?"

"Not in precisely those words," Rachel said, "but his meaning was plain." She turned to Ian, with a quick squeeze of his arm. "Would thee go and find Denny, Ian? Claire can't leave this woman alone—I think?" she asked, arching a brow at me.

"Not yet," I said. "She doesn't seem to be going into labor immediately"—I crossed my fingers against the possibility—"but she oughtn't to be left alone in this state."

"Aye, of course." Ian yawned suddenly, widely, but then

shook himself back into alertness. "If I come across Uncle Jamie, I'll tell him where ye are, Auntie."

He left, and Rachel poured another cup of beer, which she offered me. It was room temperature—and a warm room, at that—but refreshingly sour and strong. I hadn't really thought I was tired, but the beer revivified me astonishingly.

Dottie, having checked Mrs. Peabody's pulse and breathing, laid a ginger hand on the distended bulge of pregnancy. "Has thee attended a birth before, good-sister?" Dottie asked Rachel, being careful of her plain speech.

"Several," Rachel replied, squatting down by Mrs. Peabody. "This looks somewhat different, though. Has she suffered some injur—oh!" The brewery reek hit her, and she reared back and coughed. "I see."

Mrs. Peabody uttered a loud moan and everyone stiffened. I wiped my hands on my apron, just in case. She relaxed again, though, and after a few moments' contemplative silence to see if Mrs. Peabody would do it again, Dottie took a deep breath.

"Mrs.—I mean, Friend Claire was just telling me some very interesting things. Regarding . . . er . . . what to expect on one's wedding night."

Rachel looked up with interest.

"I should welcome any such instruction myself. I know where the . . . um . . . parts go, because I've seen them go there fairly frequently, but—"

"You *have*?!?" Dottie gawked at her, and Rachel laughed.

"I have. But Ian assures me that he has more skill than the average bull or billy goat, and my observations are limited to the animal world, I'm afraid." A small line showed between her brows. "The woman who cared for me after the death of my parents was . . . very dutiful in informing me of my womanly obligations, but her instructions consisted largely of 'Spread thy legs, grit thy teeth, girl, and let him.'"

I sat down on the packing case and stretched to ease my back, suppressing a groan. God knew how long it might take Ian to find Jamie among the teeming hordes. And I did hope that Denny hadn't been knocked on the head or trampled by a mule.

"Pour me another cup of beer, will you? And have some more yourselves. I suspect we may need it."

". . . AND IF HE says, 'Oh, God, oh, God,' at some point," I advised, "take note of what you were just doing, so you can do it again next time."

Rachel laughed, but Dottie frowned a little, looking slightly cross-eyed.

"Do you—does thee—think Denny would take the Lord's name in vain, even under those circumstances?"

"I've heard him do it on much less provocation than that," Rachel assured her, stifling a burp with the back of her hand. "He tries to be perfect in thy company, thee knows, for fear thee will change thy mind."

"He does?" Dottie looked surprised but rather pleased. "Oh. I wouldn't, thee knows. Ought I to tell him?"

"Not until he says, 'Oh, God, oh, God,' for thee," Rachel said, succumbing to a giggle.

"I wouldn't worry," I said. "If a man says, 'Oh, God,' in that situation, he nearly always means it as a prayer."

Dottie's fair brows drew together in concentration.

"A prayer of desperation? Or gratitude?"

"Well . . . that's up to you," I said, and stifled a small belch of my own.

Approaching male voices outside the tent made us all glance self-consciously at the empty beer pitcher and sit up straight, poking at our slightly disheveled hair, but none of the gentlemen who came in were in any condition to cast stones.

Ian had found Denzell *and* Jamie, and somewhere along the way they had acquired a small, stout companion in a cocked hat, with his hair in a stumpy pigtail. All of them were flushed and, while certainly not staggering, were surrounded by a distinct haze of fermented barleycorn.

"There ye are, Sassenach!" Jamie brightened still further at seeing me, and I felt a small rush of delight at it. "Are ye—who's this?" He had been advancing toward me, hand outstretched, but stopped abruptly at sight of Mrs. Peabody, who was lying with her arms flung out, mouth wide open.

"That's the lady I told ye about, Uncle Jamie." Ian wasn't staggering, either, but was distinctly swaying and took hold of the tent pole to steady himself. "The one that's . . . ehm . . ."

He gestured with his free hand to the gentleman in the cocked hat. "She's his wife."

"Oh? Aye, I see." He edged gingerly around Mrs. Peabody's recumbent form. "She's no dead, is she?"

"No," I said. "I think I would have noticed." He might have been somewhat inebriated, but still caught the faint dubious emphasis I'd placed on "think." He knelt down carefully and put a hand in front of her open mouth.

"Nay, only drunk," he said cheerfully. "Shall we lend ye a hand to take her home, Mr. Peabody?"

"Better lend him a wheelbarrow," Dottie whispered to Rachel, beside me, but luckily no one noticed.

"That would be kindly of you, sir." Surprisingly, Mr. Peabody appeared to be the only sober one of the lot. He knelt and smoothed the damp hair tenderly off his wife's brow. "Lulu? Wake up, darling. Time to be going now."

To my surprise, she opened her eyes and, after blinking several times in confusion, appeared to fix her gaze on her husband.

"There you are, Simon!" she said, and, with a rapturous smile, fell soundly back asleep.

Jamie rose slowly, and I could hear the small bones in his back pop as he eased himself. He was still flushed and smiling, but Ian had been right—he *was* dead tired. I could see the deep lines of weariness in his face and the hollows under his bones.

Ian saw them, too.

"Auntie Claire's in need of her bed, Uncle Jamie," he said, squeezing Jamie's shoulder and giving me a meaning look. "It's been a long night for her. Take her along, aye? Denny and I can help Mr. Peabody."

Jamie gave his nephew a sharp look and then turned the same look on me, but I obligingly yawned widely enough to make my jaw crack—no great effort—and with a final quick look at Mrs. Peabody to be *sure* she was neither dying nor going into labor, I took his arm and towed him determinedly outside, waving briefly in farewell.

Outside, we both drew deep breaths of fresh air, sighed in unison, and laughed.

"It *has* been rather a long night, hasn't it?" I put my forehead against his chest and my arms around him, slowly rubbing the knobs of his vertebrae through his coat. "What happened?"

He sighed again and kissed the top of my head.

"I've command of ten companies of mixed militia from Pennsylvania and New Jersey; the marquis has command of a thousand men—including mine—and is in charge of a plan to go and bite the British army in the arse."

"Sounds like fun." The racket of the camp had died down considerably, but the thick air still held the vibrations of many men, awake or uneasily asleep. I thought I could feel that same expectant vibration pass through Jamie, in spite of his obvious tiredness. "You need sleep, then."

His arm tightened round me and his free hand traveled slowly down my back. I'd left Denny's apron in the tent, and my cloak was over my arm; the thin muslin of my shift might as well have not existed.

"Oh, God," he said, and his big, warm hand cupped my buttock with a sudden urgency. "I need *you,* Sassenach. I need ye bad."

The shift was just as thin in front as in back; I could feel his waistcoat buttons—and a few other things—through it. He did want me bad.

"Do you mind doing it in a crypt that smells of wee?" I asked, thinking of the Chenowyths' back bedroom.

"I've taken ye in worse places, Sassenach."

Before I could say, "Name three," the tent flap opened to disgorge a small procession, this consisting of Denzell, Dottie, Rachel, and Ian, each couple carrying one end of a canvas sheet on which lay the protuberant form of Mrs. Peabody. Mr. Peabody led the way, lantern held high.

We were standing in shadow, and they passed without noticing us, the girls giggling at the occasional stumble, the young men grunting with effort, and Mr. Peabody calling out encouragement as they made their laborious way through the darkness, presumably heading for the Peabody abode.

The tent stood before us, dark and invitingly empty.

"Aye?"

"Oh, yes."

The stretcher bearers had taken the lantern, and the setting moon was the barest sliver above the horizon; the inside of the tent was filled with a soft, dusty black that rose up around us in a fragrantly alcoholic cloud—with a faint tang of vomit—when we stepped inside.

I recalled exactly where things were, though, and we managed to push together four of the packing crates. I spread my cloak on these, he took off his coat and waistcoat, and we lay down precariously in the beery dark together.

"How long do you think we have?" I asked, undoing his flies. His flesh was warm and hard under my hand, and his skin there soft as polished silk.

"Long enough," he said, and brushed my nipple with his thumb, slowly, in spite of his own apparent urgency. "Dinna hurry yourself, Sassenach. There's no telling when we'll have the chance again."

He kissed me lingeringly, his mouth tasting of Roquefort and port. I could feel the vibration of the camp here, too—it ran through both of us like a fiddle string pegged tight.

"I dinna think I've got time to make ye scream, Sassenach," he whispered in my ear. "But I've maybe time to make ye moan?"

"Well, possibly. It's some time 'til dawn, isn't it?"

Whether it was the beer and premarital explanations, the late hour and lure of secrecy—or only Jamie himself and our increasing need to shut out the world and know only each other—he had time, and to spare.

"Oh, God," he said at last, and came down slowly on me, his heart beating heavy against my ribs. "Oh . . . God."

I felt my own pulse throb in hands and bones and center, but couldn't manage any response more eloquent than a faint "Ooh." After a bit, though, I recovered enough to stroke his hair.

"We'll go home again soon," I whispered to him. "And have all the time in the world."

That got me a softly affirmative Scottish noise, and we lay there for a bit longer, not wanting to come apart and get dressed, though the packing cases were hard and the possibility of discovery increasing with each passing minute.

At last he stirred, but not to rise.

"Oh, God," he said softly, in another tone altogether. "Three hundred men." And held me tighter.

56

STINKING PAPIST

THE SUN WASN'T YET above the horizon, but the horse park was busy as an anthill, full of grooms, foragers, teamsters, and farriers, all scurrying about their business in an incongruous soft pink light filled with the sound of hundreds of pairs of steadily champing jaws. William picked up the bay gelding's hoof and held out his hand for the hoof pick his new, small groom was clutching nervously to his chest.

"Now, come here, Zeb," he said coaxingly. "I'll show you how it's done; there's nothing to it."

"Yes, sir." Zebedee Jeffers edged an inch closer, eyes flicking back and forth from the hoof to the towering mass of horseflesh. Jeffers did not like horses. He particularly didn't like Visigoth. William thought it was just as well that Zeb likely didn't know what a Visigoth was.

"All right. See there?" He tapped the pick against the shadow: the edge of a small rock that had trapped itself under the curve of the iron shoe during the night. "It's only a little one, but it feels just like a pebble in your own shoe would feel, and he'll go lame if we don't take care of it. Here, it's not stuck fast; do you want to try?"

"No, sir," Zeb said honestly. Zebedee came from the shore of Maryland and knew about oysters, boats, and fish. Not horses.

"He won't hurt you," William said, with a touch of impatience. He'd be riding back and forth along the columns a dozen times a day, carrying dispatches and gathering reports; both his horses needed to be kept ready, his regular groom, Colenso Baragwanath, was down with a fever, and he hadn't time to find another servant.

"Yes, he will. Sir," Zeb added as an afterthought. "See?" He held out a scrawny arm, displaying what was undoubtedly a festering bite mark.

William suppressed the urge to ask what the devil the boy had been doing to the horse. Visigoth wasn't a bad-tempered horse on the whole, but he could be irritable, and Zeb's nervous fidgeting was enough to try anyone, let alone a tired and hungry horse.

"All right," he said with a sigh, and pried the rock loose with one sharp dig. "Better, then?" he said to the horse, running a hand down the leg and then patting Goth's flank. He felt in his pocket and drew out a bunch of limp carrots, bought the night before from a farmwoman who'd come through camp with baskets of produce on a yoke across her broad shoulders.

"Here. Give him that; make friends with him," he suggested, handing a carrot to Zeb. "Hold it flat on your hand." Before the boy could extend this putative olive branch, though, the horse reached down and snatched it from his fingers with an audible crunch of big yellow teeth. The boy uttered a small shriek and took several steps back, collided with a bucket, and fell over it, arse over teakettle.

Torn between annoyance and an unseemly urge to laugh, William smothered both and went to pick his groom out of a manure pile.

"Tell you what," he said, dusting the boy off with a firm hand, "you see that *all* my dunnage is aboard the baggage wagon, see if Colenso needs anything, and make sure there's something for me to eat tonight. I'll ask Sutherland's groom to tend the horses."

Zeb sagged with relief.

"Thank you, sir!"

"And go see one of the surgeons and have that arm tended to!" William shouted after him, above the rising sound of braying and whickering. The boy's shoulders rose up around his ears and he walked faster, pretending he hadn't heard.

William saddled Goth himself—he always did, not trusting anyone else to check tack that his life might depend on—then left him with his other horse, Madras, and went to find Lord Sutherland's groom. Despite the bustle, he had no trouble finding the string; Sutherland had ten horses, all prime creatures of sixteen hands or so, and at least a dozen grooms to tend them. William was just concluding negotiations with one of these when he caught sight of a familiar face among the throng.

"Shit," he said, under his breath, but Captain Richardson had seen him and was coming toward him, smiling genially.

"Captain Lord Ellesmere. Your servant, sir."

"Yours, sir," William said, as pleasantly as he could. *What did the scoundrel want now?* he wondered. Not that Richardson *was* a scoundrel—or not necessarily one, despite Randall's warning. It might, after all, be Randall who was the scoundrel. But he did hold rather a grudge against Richardson, on Mother Claire's account, as well as his own. The thought of Mother Claire stabbed him unexpectedly, and he forced it back. None of it was *her* fault.

"I'm surprised to see you here, your lordship," Richardson said, glancing round at the roiling camp. The sun was up, and bands of gold lit the fog of dust rising from the mules' rough coats. "You are a conventioneer, are you not?"

"I am," William said coldly. Richardson certainly knew he was. William felt obliged to defend himself, though against what, he wasn't sure. "I cannot fight." He spread his arms slightly. "As you see, I carry no weapons." He made polite motions indicating his immediate need to be elsewhere, but Richardson went on standing there, smiling with that very ordinary face, so unremarkable that his own mother probably couldn't pick him out of a crowd, save for a large brown mole on the side of his chin.

"Ah, to be sure." Richardson drew a little closer, lowering his voice. "That being the case . . . I wonder whether—"

"No," William said definitely. "I am one of General Clinton's aides, and I cannot leave my duty. You will excuse me, sir; I am expected."

He turned on his heel and made off, his heart hammering—and realized rather belatedly that he had left his horse behind. Richardson was still standing at the far side of the horse park, talking to a groom who was taking down the pickets, coiling the rope around one shoulder as he did so. The crowd of horses and mules was swiftly diminishing, but there were enough still near Visigoth to enable William to duck in and pretend to be fiddling with his saddlebags, head bent to hide his face until Richardson should go away.

The conversation had left him with an unsettling image of his erstwhile stepmother as he had last seen her, disheveled and *en déshabillé* but glowing with a radiant life he had never seen. He didn't suppose she was his stepmother anymore, but he'd liked her. Belatedly, it occurred to him that Claire now-Fraser still *was* his stepmother—by a different father. . . . Bloody hell.

He set his teeth, rummaging in the saddlebag for his canteen. Now that that Scotch bugger had returned from his watery grave, throwing everything and everyone into confusion . . . why couldn't he have drowned and never come back?

Never come back.

"You are a stinking Papist, and your baptismal name is James." He froze as though shot in the back. He bloody remembered it. The stables at Helwater, the warm smell of horses and mash, and the prickle of straw that worked its way through his stockings. Cold stone floors. He'd been crying . . . Why? All he recalled was a huge wash of desolation, total helplessness. The end of the world. Mac leaving.

He took a long, slow breath and pressed his lips together. Mac. The word didn't bring back a face; he couldn't remember what Mac had looked like. He'd been big, that was all. Bigger than Grandfather or any of the footmen or the other grooms. *Safety. A sense of constant happiness like a soft, worn blanket.*

"Shit," he whispered, closing his eyes. And had that happiness been a lie, too? He'd been too little to know the difference between a groom's deference to the young master and real kindness. But . . .

"'You are a stinking Papist,'" he whispered, and caught his breath on something that might have been a sob. "'And your baptismal name is James.'"

"It was the only name I had a right to give ye."

He realized that his knuckles were pressed against his chest, against his gorget—but it wasn't the gorget's reassurance that he sought. It was that of the little bumps of the plain wooden rosary that he'd worn around his neck for years, hidden under his shirt where no one would see it. The rosary Mac had given him . . . along with his name.

With a suddenness that shocked him, he felt his eyes swim. *You went away. You left me!*

"Shit!" he said, and punched his fist so hard into the saddlebag that the horse snorted and shied, and a bolt of white-hot pain shot up his arm, obliterating everything.

57

DO NOT GO GENTLE INTO THAT GOOD NIGHT

IAN WOKE JUST BEFORE dawn to find his uncle squatting beside him.

"I'm away to break bread wi' the captains of my companies," Jamie said without preamble. "Ye'll report to Colonel Wilbur as a scout. And will ye see about horses, Ian? I'll need a spare mount, gun-broke, and so will you." He dropped a purse on Ian's chest, smiled, and vanished into the morning mist.

Ian rolled slowly out of his blanket, stretching. He'd chosen his resting spot well away from the main camp, on a small rise of ground near the river. He didn't bother wondering how Uncle Jamie had found him, or waste time in marveling at his uncle's recuperative powers.

He took his time about his preparations, dressed carefully, and found some food, thinking over the things that must be done. He'd dreamed during the night, and the dream was still on him, though he couldn't recall the details. He'd been in thick woods, and something was there with him, hiding among the leaves. He wasn't sure what it was, or even if he'd seen it, but the sense of danger lingered uneasily between his shoulder blades. He'd heard a raven calling in his dream, and that was certainly a warning of some kind—but then the raven had flown past him, and it wasn't a raven at all but a white bird of some kind. Its wing had touched his cheek in flight, and he could still feel the brush of its feathers.

White animals were messengers. Both the Mohawk and the Highlanders said so.

He was an Indian and a Highlander; dreams were not to be dismissed. Sometimes the meaning of a dream floated to the surface of your mind like a drowned leaf rising. He let it go, hoping the dream would return to explain itself, and went about his work, seeing Colonel Wilbur, finding and haggling for two reasonable horses, big enough to bear a large man through battle . . . but the white bird stayed by him all day long, hovering just above his right shoulder, a glimpse now and then in the corner of his eye.

IN THE LATE afternoon, his business done for the moment, he returned to the main camp and found Rachel standing in line with a number of other women at the well in the yard of the Goose and Grapes, two buckets resting at her feet.

"I could take those down to the river for ye," he offered. She was flushed with the heat of the day but looked beautiful, her bare arms brown and the curving muscle of them so neat and delicate that it lifted his heart to look at them.

"I thank thee, Ian, but no." She smiled up at him and reached to tweak one of the two eagle feathers he'd knotted into his hair. "Thy auntie says the boats throw their waste into the river, and half the army is pissing in it, as well, and she's right. I should need to walk a mile upstream to find a clean place from which to draw water. Is thee about thy business, then?"

She spoke with interest but with no sense of concern or disapproval, and he appreciated that.

"I willna kill anyone unless I have to, Rachel," he said softly, and touched her cheek. "I'm signed on as a scout. I shouldna have to."

"But things happen," she said, and looked away, to keep him seeing the sudden shadow in her eyes. "I know."

With an unexpected spurt of impatience, he wanted to ask her: would she rather he kill or *be* killed for the sake of his soul's grace? But he smothered the impulse, and the tinge of anger with it. She loved him, he didn't doubt that. It was maybe a fair question to put to a Quaker, but not to his betrothed.

Her eyes were on his face, interested and thoughtful, and he felt a slight flush rise in his cheeks, wondering just how much of his thoughts showed.

"Thy life's journey lies along its own path, Ian," she said, "and I cannot share thy journey—but I can walk beside thee. And I will."

The woman standing behind them in the line heaved a deep, contented sigh.

"Now, that's a very pretty and right thing to say, sweetheart," she said to Rachel, in approving tones. And, switching her gaze to Ian, looked him skeptically up and down. He was dressed in buckskins, clout, and calico shirt, and, bar the feathers in his hair and the tattoos, didn't look too outlandish, he thought.

"You probably don't deserve her," the woman said, shaking her head doubtfully. "But try, there's a good lad."

HE CARRIED THE water for Rachel, making their way through the sprawl of the camp toward the place where Denzell had set up his medical practice. The tent was still standing, but Denzell's wagon with its painted goldfinches on the tailboard was drawn up beside it, Dottie standing in it, and Denzell handing up parcels and boxes to her.

Rachel stood on tiptoe to kiss his cheek, then vanished into the tent to help with the packing.

"Wilt thee join us later, Ian?" Denny looked up from the pack he was strapping together.

"Anywhere, *a bhràthair,*" Ian said, smiling. "Where are ye bound, then?"

"Oh. Nowhere." Denny took off his spectacles, polishing them absently on the tail of his shirt. "It's not yet First Day, but we may well be engaged in battle then; we thought to hold meeting before supper tonight. We would be pleased if thee feels it good to sit with us, but if not . . ."

"No, I'll come," Ian said quickly. "To be sure. Ah . . . where . . . ?" He waved a hand vaguely, indicating the half-ordered chaos of the camp surrounding them. New companies of militia were still coming in from New Jersey and Pennsylvania to join the Continental soldiers, and while officers had been assigned to receive and organize these and help them find campgrounds, they were swiftly overwhelmed. Men were making camp anywhere they could find open ground, and there was great to-ing and fro-ing in search of water and food, arguments and raised voices, and the sound of industrious shoveling and muttered curses nearby indicated the creation of yet another set of sanitary trenches. A constant small procession of persons who couldn't wait visited a nearby copse in hopes of a private moment. Ian made a mental note to step wary if he walked that way.

"Ye dinna mean to do it here, surely?" People came in and out all day, in need of the doctor's attention, and wouldn't be likely to stop, only because meeting was being held.

"Friend Jamie says he will provide us a refuge," Denny assured him. "We'll go as soon as—who has thee there, Dorothea?"

Dottie was stowing supplies but had paused to talk with a young girl who had climbed up to kneel on the wagon's seat and was addressing Dorothea earnestly.

"It's a woman in childbed, Denny," she called. "Three campfires over!"

"Urgent?" Denny at once began unstrapping the pack he had just done up.

"This child says so." Dottie straightened up and tucked her straggling fair hair back under her cap. "It's her mother's fourth; no trouble with the first three, but given the conditions . . ." She sidled past the baggage to the lowered tailboard, and Ian gave her a hand to hop down.

"She really wanted Mrs. Fraser," Dottie said to Denny, *sotto voce*. "But she'll settle for thee." She dimpled. "Is thee flattered?"

"I see my reputation spreads like pomade on a silken pillow," he replied tranquilly. "And thy use of plain speech inflames me. Thee had best come with me. Will thee watch the wagon, Ian?"

The two of them made off through the maze of wagons, horses, and stray pigs—some enterprising farmer had driven a dozen lean hogs into camp, seeking to sell them to the quartermaster, but the pigs had taken fright at the inadvertent explosion of a musket nearby and run off among the crowd, causing mass confusion. Rollo had run one down and broken its neck; Ian had bled and eviscerated the carcass and—after giving Rollo the heart and lights—stashed it under damp canvas, hidden beneath Denzell's wagon. Should he meet the distraught swineherd, he'd pay him for the beast, but he wasn't letting it out of his sight. He stole a quick glance under the skirting board, but the canvas-covered lump was still there.

Rollo moved a little and made an odd sound, not quite a whine, that shifted Ian's attention at once to the dog.

"How is it, *a choin*?" he asked. Rollo at once licked his hand and panted in a genial fashion, but Ian slid off the wagon tongue and knelt in the leaves, feeling his way over the big, shaggy body, just in case. Palpating, Auntie Claire called it, a word that always made Ian smile.

He found a little tenderness where the dog had been shot the autumn before, in the meat of the shoulder just above the foreleg, but that was always there. And a spot on his spine, a few inches forward of the beast's tail, that made him splay his legs and groan when it was pressed. Maybe Rollo had strained himself taking down the hog.

"None sae young as ye used to be, are ye, *a choin*?" he asked, scratching Rollo's whitened jaw.

"None of us are, *a mac mo pheathar,*" said his uncle Jamie, coming out of the gloaming and sitting down on the stump Dottie had been using to mount the wagon. He was wearing full uniform and looked hot. Ian passed over his canteen and Jamie took it with a nod of thanks, wiping his sleeve across his face.

"Aye, day after tomorrow," he said, in answer to Ian's raised brow. "First light, if not before. Wee Gilbert's got command of a thousand men and permission to go after the rear guard."

"You—I mean us"—Ian corrected himself—"with him?"

Jamie nodded and drank deep. Ian thought he looked a bit tense, but, after all, he was in command of three hundred men—if all of them were going with La Fayette . . .

"I think they're sending me with him in hopes that my ancient wisdom will balance the Seigneur de La Fayette's youthful enthusiasm," Jamie said, lowering the canteen with a sigh. "And it's maybe better than staying back wi' Lee." He grimaced. "Boiling Water thinks it beneath his dignity to marshal no but a thousand men and declined the command."

Ian made a noise indicating amusement at this and faith in his uncle's sagacity. It might be fun, harrying the British rear. He felt a tingle of anticipation at thought of putting on his war paint.

"Where's Denzell gone?" Jamie asked, glancing at the wagon.

"Attending a childbirth over yon," Ian said, lifting his chin in the direction Denzell and Dottie had taken. "He says ye're hosting a Quaker meeting tonight."

Jamie lifted a thick brow glistening with droplets of sweat. "Well, I wasna planning to join in, but I said they might use my tent and welcome. Why, are ye going yourself?"

"Thought I might," Ian said. "I was invited, after all."

"Were ye?" Jamie looked interested. "D'ye think they mean to convert ye?"

"I dinna think that's how Quakers work," Ian said, a little ruefully. "And good luck to them if they do. I think the power o' prayer must have limits."

That made his uncle snort with amusement, but Jamie shook his head. "Never think it, laddie," he advised. "If wee Rachel sets her mind to it, she'll have your sword beaten into a plowshare before ye can say Peter Piper picked a peck o' pickled peppers. Well, twice," he added. "Or maybe three times."

Ian made a dissentient noise through his nose. "Aye, and if I were to try bein' a Friend, who would there be to protect the lot of 'em? Rachel and her brother and Dottie, I mean. Ye ken that, don't ye? That they can only be what they are because you and I are what we are?"

Jamie leaned back a little, purse-lipped, then gave him the ghost of a wry smile.

"I ken that fine. And so does Denzell Hunter; it's why he's here, though it's cost him his home and his meeting. But, mind, they're worth protecting—beyond you bein' in love wi' Rachel, I mean."

"Mmphm." Ian wasn't in the mood to discuss philosophy, and he doubted his uncle was, either. The light was in that long hour before darkfall, when the things of the forest pause and draw breath, slowing for the night. It was a good time to hunt, because the trees slowed first, so you saw the animals still moving among them.

Uncle Jamie kent that. He sat, relaxed, nothing moving save his eyes. Ian saw his gaze flick up and turned his own head to see. Sure enough, a squirrel clung to the trunk of a sycamore, ten feet away. He'd not have seen it, had he not caught the last flick of its tail as it stilled there. He met Jamie's eyes, and they both smiled and sat silent for a while, listening to the racket of the camp, even this beginning to mute itself.

Denzell and Dottie hadn't come back; perhaps the birth was more complicated than Denny had thought. Rachel would be going to Jamie's tent soon, for the meeting.

He wondered about that. You needed a meeting, to counsel the two of you, then to approve and witness the marriage. Might Denny have it in his mind to establish a new Friends meeting, within which he could marry Dottie—and Rachel might wed Ian?

Jamie sighed and stirred, getting ready to rise.

"Ahh . . . Uncle," Ian said, in a casual tone that made his uncle instantly focus attention on him.

"What?" said his uncle warily. "Ye havena got your lass wi' child, have ye?"

"I have not," Ian said, offended—and wondering vaguely how his uncle had known he was thinking of Rachel. "And why would ye think a thing like that, ye evil-minded auld mumper?"

"Because I ken well enough what 'Ahh . . . Uncle' usually means," Jamie informed him cynically. "It means ye've got yourself into some confusion involving a lass and want advice. And I canna think what ye could be confused about wi' regard to wee Rachel. A more straightforward lass I've never met—bar your auntie Claire, that is," he added, with a brief grin.

"Mmphm," Ian said, not best pleased by his uncle's acuity, but obliged to admit the truth of it. "Well, then. It's only . . ." Despite the completely benign intent—the *innocence,* even—of the question that had come into his mind, he felt his face go hot.

Jamie raised his brows.

"Well, if ye must know, then—I've never lain wi' a virgin." Once he'd got it out, he relaxed a little, though his uncle's brows nearly met his hairline. "And, aye, I'm sure Rachel is one," he added defensively.

"I'm sure, too," his uncle assured him. "Most men wouldna consider it a problem."

Ian gave him a look. "Ye ken what I mean. I want her to like it."

"Verra commendable. Have ye had complaints from women before?"

"Ye're in a rare mood, Uncle," Ian said coldly. "Ye ken verra well what I mean."

"Aye, ye mean if ye're paying a woman to bed ye, ye're no likely to hear anything ye dinna like regarding your own performance." Jamie rocked back a little, eyeing him. "Did ye tell Rachel ye're in the habit of consorting wi' whores?"

Ian felt the blood rush to his ears and was obliged to breathe evenly for a moment before replying.

"I told her everything," he said between clenched teeth. "And I wouldna call it a 'habit.'" He did know better than to go on with, *"It's no more than other men do,"* because he kent fine what sort of answer he'd get to *that.*

Fortunately, Jamie seemed to have reined in his jocularity for the moment and was considering the question.

"Your Mohawk wife," he said delicately. "She, er . . ."

"No," Ian said. "The Indians see bedding a bit differently." And, seizing the opportunity to get a bit of his own back, added, "D'ye not recall the time we went to visit the Snowbird Cherokee and Bird sent a couple of maidens to warm your bed?"

Jamie gave him an old-fashioned sort of look that made him laugh.

"Tell me, Ian," he said, after a pause, "would ye be having this conversation with your da?"

"God, no."

"I'm flattered," Jamie said dryly.

"Well, see . . ." Ian had answered by reflex and found himself fumbling for an explanation. "It—I mean . . . it's no that I wouldna talk to Da about things, but if he'd told me anything about . . . it would ha' been to do with him and Mam, wouldn't it? And I couldna . . . well, I couldn't, that's all."

"Mmphm."

Ian narrowed his eyes at his uncle.

"Ye're no going to try and tell me that my mother—"

"Who's my sister, aye? No, I wouldna tell ye anything like

that. I see your point. I'm only thinkin' . . ." He trailed off and Ian gave him a pointed look. The light was fading, but there was still plenty. Jamie shrugged.

"Aye, well. It's only—your auntie Claire was widowed when I wed her, aye?"

"Aye. So?"

"So it was me that was virgin on our wedding night."

Ian hadn't thought he'd moved, but Rollo jerked his head up and looked at him, startled. Ian cleared his throat.

"Oh. Aye?"

"Aye," said his uncle, wry as a lemon. "And I was given any amount of advice beforehand, too, by my uncle Dougal and his men."

Dougal MacKenzie had died before Ian was born, but he'd heard a good bit about the man, one way and another. His mouth twitched.

"Would ye care to pass on any of it?"

"God, no." Jamie stood up and brushed bits of bark from the tails of his coat. "I think ye already ken ye should be gentle about it, aye?"

"Aye, I'd thought of that," Ian assured him. "Nothing else?"

"Aye, well." Jamie stood still, considering. "The only useful thing was what my wife told me on the night. 'Go slowly and pay attention.' I think ye canna go far wrong wi' that." He settled his coat on his shoulders. "*Oidhche mhath,* Ian. I'll see ye at first light—if not somewhat before."

"*Oidhche mhath,* Uncle Jamie."

As Jamie reached the edge of the clearing, Ian called after him.

"Uncle Jamie!"

Jamie turned to look over his shoulder.

"Aye?"

"And was she gentle with ye?"

"God, no," Jamie said, and grinned broadly.

58

CASTRAMETATION

THE SUN WAS LOW in the sky by the time William reached Clinton's camp, and lower still before he'd turned Goth over to Sutherland's grooms. Zeb was nowhere in sight. Perhaps he was with Colenso.

He delivered his cartouche of dispatches to Captain von Munchausen, saw the company clerk, and found the tent he shared with two other young captains, both of the 27th Foot. Randolph Merbling was sitting outside, reading by the last of the sun, but there was no sign of Thomas Evans—nor of Colenso Baragwanath. Nor of Zebedee Jeffers. Nor of William's baggage.

He breathed for a moment, then shook himself like a dog shedding water. He was so tired of being angry that he just couldn't be arsed anymore. He shrugged, borrowed a towel from Merbling, washed his face, and went to find a bite to eat.

He'd made up his mind not to think about anything whatever until he'd had some food and largely succeeded, letting roast chicken, bread, cheese, and beer fill at least some of his empty spaces. As he finished, though, a sudden sharp image punctured his pleasant digestive reverie. A flushed, pretty face, with wary eyes the exact color of the cider he was drinking.

Jane. Bloody hell! What with one thing and another, he'd quite forgotten the whore and her sister. He'd told them to meet him at the surgeon's tent at sundown. . . . Well, the sun wasn't down yet. He was on his feet and on his way, but then had a second thought and, going back to the cook, wangled a couple of loaves and some cheese, just in case.

Castrametation was the science of laying out a proper military camp. Drainage, sanitary trenches, where to put the powder depot to avoid flooding if it rained . . . He'd had a brief course in it once. He'd likely never need to do it himself, but it did help in locating things, if you knew where they were supposed to be. And when in camp, the hospital was meant to be on the opposite side from command headquarters, close to water but on a height, if one was available.

One was, and he found the large green-canvas tent without difficulty. Could have found it with his eyes closed. Surgeons carried the smell of their work around with them, and the whiff of dried blood and the uneasy tang of sickness and recent death were perceptible at a hundred yards. It was worse—much worse—after a battle, but there was always illness and accident, and the stink lingered even on peaceful days, aggravated now by the muggy heat that lay like a wet blanket over the camp.

There were men, and not a few women, clustered round the tent, waiting for attention. He gave them a quick glance, but didn't see Jane. His heart had sped up a little at thought of seeing her, and he felt unaccountably disappointed. No reason why, he told himself. She and her sister would be nothing but trouble to him. They must have grown tired waiting, and—

"You're very late, my lord," said an accusatory voice at his elbow, and he whirled round to see her looking down her nose at him—as well as someone who was shorter than he could do, which wasn't very well. He found himself smiling down at her, absurdly.

"I said sundown," he replied mildly, nodding toward the west, where a thin slice of brilliance still glowed through the trees. "Not down yet, is it?"

"The sun takes a bloody long time to go down out here." She switched her disapproval to the orb in question. "It's much faster in the city."

Before he could argue with this ridiculous assertion, she'd glanced back at him, frowning.

"Why aren't you wearing your gorget?" she demanded, hands on her hips. "I went to a deal of trouble to get it back for you!"

"I'm exceedingly grateful to you, ma'am," he said, striving for gravity. "I thought it might provoke inquiries, though, should I turn up suddenly in the midst of camp wearing it, and

I thought you and your sister might just possibly wish to avoid . . . tedious explanations?"

She sniffed, but not without amusement.

"How thoughtful. Not quite so thoughtful of your servants, though, are you?"

"What do you mean?"

"Come with me." She linked her arm with his and towed him off toward the wood before he could protest. She led him to a small lean-to shelter in the undergrowth, which seemed to have been constructed of an unstuffed army bed sack and two petticoats. Bending down at her invitation, he discovered her sister, Fanny, within, sitting next to a bed sack that had been stuffed with fresh grass, upon which crouched both Colenso and Zeb, both looking bewildered. On sight of him, they crouched further.

"What the devil are you doing here?" he demanded. "And where is my dunnage, Zeb?"

"Back there, sir," Zeb quavered, jerking a thumb toward the growth behind the lean-to. "I couldn't find your tent and I didn't want to leave it, see."

"But I told you—and what about you, Baragwanath? Are you still ill?" William demanded, kneeling down suddenly and thrusting his head into the shelter. Colenso looked bad, pale as a cup of soured milk, and plainly in pain, curled up into himself.

"Oh . . . 'tisn't nothin', sir," he said, swallowing heavily. "Just must have . . . ate . . . something."

"Did you see the surgeon?"

Colenso turned his face into the bed sack, shoulders hunched. Zeb was edging away, apparently thinking of making a run for it.

William grabbed him by the arm; the little groom yelped and he let go. "What's wrong? Did you not have that arm seen to?"

"They're afraid of the surgeons," Jane said sharply.

William drew himself up to his full height and glared down at her.

"Oh? Who told them they should be afraid of the surgeons? And how do they come to be in *your* care, may I ask?"

Her lips pressed tight together, and she glanced involuntarily into the shelter. Fanny was looking out at them, doe eyes huge in the fading light. She swallowed and put a protective hand on Colenso's shoulder. Jane sighed deeply and took William's arm again.

"Come with me."

She led him away a short distance, still within sight of the little shelter but out of earshot.

"Fanny and I were waiting for you when those boys came along together. The bigger one—*what* did you say his name is?"

"Colenso Baragwanath. He's Cornish," William added shortly, seeing a look of amusement flit across her face.

"Really. I hope it isn't catching. Well, he was so ill he couldn't stand, and sank down on the ground near us, making the most horrid noises. The little one—yes, I know he's Zebedee, thank you—was beside himself, half-weeping with confusion. My sister is a most tenderhearted creature," she said, rather apologetically. "She went to help, and I followed." She shrugged.

"We got Colenso into the wood far enough to get his britches down in time, and I gave him a little water." She touched a small wooden canteen that hung from her shoulder, and he wondered briefly where she'd got it. She hadn't had it when he'd met the girls by the creek yesterday.

"I am much obliged to you, ma'am," he said formally. "Now—why is it, exactly, that you did not then take the boys in to see the surgeons?"

For the first time, her composure showed signs of cracking. She turned a little away from him, and he noticed the last rays of the sun polishing the smooth crown of her head with a faint, familiar gleam of chestnut. The sight of it brought back memory of his first meeting with her with the force of a thunderclap—and, with it, the memory of his mingled shame and arousal. Especially the latter.

"Answer me," he said, more roughly than he'd intended, and she turned on him, eyes narrowed at his tone.

"There was a finger lying on the ground by the surgeon's tent," she snapped. "It frightened my sister, and the boys took fright from her."

William rubbed a knuckle down the bridge of his nose, eyeing her.

"A finger." He had himself seen piles of amputated limbs

outside the surgeons' tents at Saratoga, and aside from a quick prayer of gratitude that none of the disconnected arms and legs was his, had experienced no particular qualms. "Whose was it?"

"How should I know? I was too much occupied in keeping your orderly from shitting himself to ask."

"Ah. Yes. Thank you," he said, rather formally. He glanced toward the shelter again and was surprised to see that Fanny had come out and was hovering a little way from her sister, a wary look on her lovely face. Did he look threatening? he wondered. Just in case, he relaxed his posture a bit and smiled at Fanny. She didn't change expression, but continued to stare at him suspiciously.

He cleared his throat and took the sack off his shoulder, holding it out to Jane. "I thought you might have missed your supper. Have the boys—well, Zeb, at least—eaten anything?"

Jane nodded and took the bag with a celerity suggesting that it had been some time since the girls had had a meal. "He ate with the other grooms, he said."

"All right, then. I'll take him in to have his arm seen to and perhaps get a dose for Colenso, while you and your sister refresh yourselves. Then, madam, we can discuss your own situation."

He'd been intensely aware of her physical presence for some moments, but when he said that, she turned the full effect of her eyes on him—*cider,* he thought vaguely, *or sherry wine?*—and seemed somehow to *flow,* shifting in some indefinable way. He hadn't seen her move, but suddenly she was standing near enough to touch, and he smelled the odor of her hair and imagined he felt the warmth of her skin through her clothes. She took his hand briefly, and her thumb moved across the palm, slowly. The palm tingled and the hairs on his arm rippled.

"I'm sure we can come to a reasonable accommodation, my lord," she said, very grave, and let him go.

He dragged Zeb into the surgeon's tent like a recalcitrant colt and stood by, only half-attending, as a young Scottish surgeon with freckles swabbed the boy's wound clean of dirt. Arabella–Jane didn't smell of the whorish scent she'd worn at the brothel, but, by Christ, she smelled good.

"We should cauterize the wound, sir," the young doctor's voice was saying. "It will stop an abscess forming, aye?"

"No!" Zeb jerked away from the doctor and made a dash for the door, knocking into people and sending one woman flying with a shriek. Jolted out of his random thoughts, William made a reflexive dive and knocked the boy flat.

"Come on, Zeb," he said, hauling Zeb to his feet and propelling him firmly back to Dr. MacFreckles. "It won't be that bad. Just a moment or two, and then it's all over."

Zeb appearing patently unconvinced by this, William deposited him firmly on a stool and pulled up his own right cuff.

"Look," he said, displaying the long, comet-shaped scar on his forearm. "*That's* what happens when you get an abscess."

Both Zeb and the doctor peered at the scar, impressed. It had been a splinter wound, he told them, caused by a lightning-struck tree.

"Wandered round the Great Dismal Swamp for three days in a fever," he said. "Some . . . Indians found me and got me to a doctor. I nearly died, and"—he lowered his brows and gave Zeb a piercing look—"the doctor was just about to *cut off my arm,* when the abscess burst and he cauterized it. You might not be so lucky, hey?"

Zeb still looked unhappy, but reluctantly agreed. William gripped him by the shoulders and said encouraging things while the iron was heating, but his own heart was beating as fast as it might have had he been awaiting cautery himself.

Indians. One, in particular. He'd thought he'd exhausted his anger, but there it bloody was again, bursting into bright fresh flame like an ember smashed open with a poker.

Bloody fucking Ian Murray. Fucking Scot and sometime Mohawk. His bloody fucking *cousin,* which made it all that much worse.

And then there was Rachel. . . . Murray had taken him to Dr. Hunter and Rachel. He drew a deep, ragged breath, remembering her worn indigo gown, hanging on its peg in the Hunters' house. Grabbing a handful of the cloth and pressing it to his face, breathing in her scent as though starved of air.

That was where Murray had met Rachel himself. And now she was *betrothed* to that—

"Ow!" Zeb writhed, and William realized belatedly that he was digging his fingers into the boy's shoulder, just like—he let go as though Zeb were a hot potato, feeling the memory of James Fraser's iron grip on his arm and the agonizing pain that had numbed him from shoulder to fingertip.

"Sorry," he said, voice shaking a little with the effort to hide his fury. "Sorry, Zeb." The surgeon was ready with the glowing iron; William took Zeb's arm, as gently as he could, and held it still while the thing was done. Rachel had held his own.

He'd been right; it was quick. The surgeon pressed the hot iron to the wound and counted five, slowly, then took it away. Zeb went stiff as a tent pole and sucked in enough breath to supply three people, but didn't scream.

"It's done," the doctor said, taking the iron away and smiling at Zeb. "Here, I'll put a bit of sweet oil on and bandage it. Ye did well, laddie."

Zeb's eyes were watering, but he wasn't crying. He sniffed deeply and wiped the back of his hand across his face, looking up at William.

"Well done, Zeb," William said, squeezing his shoulder gently, and Zeb managed a tiny smile in return.

By the time they'd returned to the girls and Colenso, William had managed to tamp down the rage—again. Was he never going to be able to get rid of it? *Not 'til you make up your mind what to do about things,* he thought grimly. But there wasn't anything that could be done right now, so he squashed all the sparks in his head firmly into one dense red ball and rolled it to the back of his mind.

"Here, let Fanny do it. He trusts her." Jane took the vial containing the dose Dr. MacFreckles had made up for Colenso and gave it to her sister. Fanny promptly sat down beside Colenso, who was pretending as hard as he could to be asleep, and began stroking his head, murmuring something to him.

William nodded and, gesturing to Jane to accompany him, withdrew far enough to be out of earshot. Rather to his surprise, part of his brain had apparently been analyzing the problem and coming to conclusions while the rest was occupied, for he had a rough plan.

"What I suggest is this," he said, without preamble. "I will make provision for you and your sister to receive regular army rations, as camp followers, and to travel under my protection. Once in New York, I will give you five pounds, and you're on your own. In return . . ."

She didn't quite smile, but a dimple showed in one cheek.

"In return," he repeated more firmly, "you will mind my orderly and my groom, tend their ills, and make sure they're reasonably cared for. You will also be my laundress."

"Your laundress?!" The dimple had disappeared abruptly, replaced by an expression of sheer astonishment.

"Laundress," he repeated doggedly. He knew what she'd been expecting him to propose and was rather surprised himself that he hadn't, but there it was. He couldn't, not with his thoughts of Rachel and of Anne Endicott so fresh in his mind. Not with the deep, smothered rage fueled by the thought that he deserved no woman but a whore.

"But I don't know how to do laundry!"

"How hard can it be?" he asked, as patiently as he could. "You wash my clothes. Don't put starch in my drawers. That's about it, isn't it?"

"But—but—" She looked aghast. "One needs a . . . a kettle! A fork, a paddle, something to stir with . . . Soap! *I* haven't any soap!"

"Oh." That hadn't occurred to him. "Well . . ." He dug in his pocket, found it empty, and tried the other, which held a guinea, tuppence, and a florin. He handed her the guinea. "Buy what you need, then."

She looked at the golden coin in her palm, her face utterly blank. She opened her mouth, then closed it again.

"What's the matter?" he asked impatiently. She didn't answer, but a soft voice behind him did.

"The duffent know how."

He whirled to find Fanny looking up at him from under her cap, her delicate cheeks flushed red by the sunset.

"What did you say?"

Fanny's soft mouth pressed tight and her cheeks grew redder, but she repeated it, dogged. "The . . . duffent . . . know *how.*"

Jane reached Fanny in two steps, putting an arm around her sister's shoulders and glaring at William.

"My sister's tongue-tied," she said, daring him to say anything. "That's why she's afraid of the surgeons. She thinks they will amputate her tongue if they find out."

He drew a deep, slow breath.

"I see. And what she said to me . . . 'She doesn't know

how'? She means you, I collect? What is it, pray, that you don't know how?"

"Muddy," whispered Fanny, now staring at the ground.

"Mud—money?" He stared at Jane. "You don't know how to—"

"I've never *had* any money!" she snapped, and threw the guinea on the ground at his feet. "I know the names of the coins, but I don't know what you can buy with them, except—except—what you can buy in a brothel! My cunt is worth six shillings, all right? My mouth is three. And my arse is a pound. But if someone gave *me* three shillings, I wouldn't know if I could buy a loaf of bread or a horse with them! I've never bought *anything*!"

"You—you mean—" He was so flabbergasted, he couldn't string words into a sentence. "But you have wages. You said—"

"I've been a brothel whore since I was ten years old!" Her fists clenched, knuckles sharp under the skin. "I never *see* my wages! Mrs. Abbott spends them—she says—for my—our—food and clothes. I've never had a penny to my name, let alone spent one. And now you hand me . . . *that*"—she stamped her foot on the guinea, driving it into the ground—"and tell me to buy a kettle?!? Where? How? From whom?!"

Her voice shook and her face was a deal redder than the setting sun could make it. She was furious, but also very near to tears. He wanted to take her in his arms and soothe her, but thought that might be a good way to lose a finger.

"How old is Fanny?" he asked instead. She jerked her head up, panting.

"Fanny?" she said blankly.

"I'm e-lev-en," Fanny's voice said behind him. "You weve her *awone*!"

He turned to see the girl glaring up at him, a stick clutched in her hand. He might have laughed, if not for the expression on her face—and if not for what he'd just realized. He took a step back, so as to see both girls at once, and like magnet and iron, they came together and clung, both staring distrustfully at him.

"How much is her maidenhead worth?" he asked Jane baldly, with a nod at Fanny.

"Ten pounth," Fanny answered automatically, just as Jane

shouted, "She's not for sale! To you or any other bugger!" She pressed Fanny fiercely closer, daring him to make a move toward the girl.

"I don't *want* her," he said through his teeth. "I don't fornicate with children, for God's sake!"

Jane's hard expression didn't alter, and she didn't loosen her grip on her sister.

"Then why did you ask?"

"To verify my suppositions regarding your presence here."

Jane snorted. "Those being?"

"That you ran away. Presumably because your sister has now reached an age where . . . ?" He raised an eyebrow, nodding at Fanny. Jane's lips compressed, but she gave him a tiny, grudging nod.

"Captain Harkness?" he asked. It was a shot in the dark, but well aimed. Harkness hadn't been pleased at being deprived of his prey and, unable to come at William, might well have decided to take his revenge elsewhere.

The light bathed everything in tones of gold and lavender, but he could see Jane's face go pale, nonetheless, and felt a tightening in his loins. If he found Harkness . . . He resolved to go looking tomorrow. The man might be in Philadelphia, as she'd said—but he might not. It would be a welcome focus for his rage.

"Right, then," he said, as matter-of-factly as he could. He stooped and pried the guinea out of the soft earth, realizing as he did so that he'd been a fool to offer it to her. Not because of what she'd told him but because someone like her—or Colenso—would never have such a sum. They'd be suspected of stealing it and very likely would be relieved of it by the first person to see it.

"Just look after the boys, will you?" he said to Jane. "And the both of you keep clear of the soldiers until I can find you simple clothes. Dressed like that"—he gestured at their dust-smudged, sweat-stained finery—"you'll be taken for whores, and soldiers don't take no for an answer."

"I am a whore," Jane said, in a strange, dry voice.

"No," he said, and felt his own voice as oddly separate from himself but very firm. "You're not. You travel under my protection. I'm not a pimp—so you're not a whore. Not until we reach New York."

59

A DISCOVERY IN THE RANKS

THE 16TH PENNSYLVANIA militia company, Captain the Reverend Peleg Woodsworth in command, marched into camp in good order, having paused just outside to tidy themselves, clean their weapons, and wash their faces. Lord John knew no one would take notice but approved of the preparations on grounds of good military discipline, as he explained to Germain.

"Slovenly troops make bad fighters," he said, critically examining a large rent in the sleeve of his filthy black coat. "And soldiers must be in the habit of obeying orders, no matter what those orders are."

Germain nodded. "Aye, that's what my mam says. Doesn't matter whether ye see the point or not, ye do as ye're told, or else."

"Your mother would make an admirable sergeant," Grey assured his orderly. He'd encountered Marsali Fraser once or twice, at her printshop. "Splendid grasp of the essence of command. Speaking of 'or else,' though—what, exactly, do you expect to happen when you go home?"

It was evident that Germain hadn't given much thought to the prospect, but after a moment he uncreased his brow.

"Likely it'll depend how long I've been gone," he said, with a shrug. "If I went back tomorrow, I'd get my ears blistered and my arse, too. But I think if I was to be gone longer than a week, she'd be pleased I wasna deid."

"Ah. Have you heard the story of the Prodigal Son, by chance?"

"No, me lo—er . . . Bert." Germain coughed. "How does it go?"

"It's—" he began automatically, but then stopped dead, feeling as though a stake had been driven through his chest. The company had already begun to fray and straggle; the few men behind him merely skirted him and went past. Germain twisted round to see what he was looking at.

"It's that man who pretends to be a Frenchman. My father doesn't like him."

Grey stared at the gentleman in the suit of very fashionable blue and gray-striped silk, who was likewise staring at Grey, mouth slightly open, ignoring the small knot of Continental officers accompanying him.

"I know a lot of Frenchmen," Grey said, recovering his breath. "But you're right; that's not one of them." He turned his back on the man, mind awhirl, and gripped Germain by the arm.

"Your grandfather has to be in this moil somewhere," he said, forcing resolution into his voice. "Do you see the building over there, with the flag?" He nodded at the limp banner, on the far side of the sprawling camp, but clearly visible. "Go there. That will be the commander in chief's headquarters. Tell one of the officers who you're looking for; they'll find him for you among the militia."

"Oh, they won't have to," Germain assured him. "*Grand-père* will be there."

"Where?"

"With General Washington," Germain said, with the exaggerated patience of those forced to consort with dunces. "He's a general, too; did ye not know that?" Before Grey could respond to this piece of flabbergasting intelligence, Germain had scampered away in the direction of the distant banner.

Grey risked a glance over his shoulder, but Perseverance Wainwright had disappeared, as had the Continental officers, leaving only a couple of lieutenants in conversation.

He thought several blasphemous things in a row, alternating between Jamie Fraser and Percy Wainwright as the recipients of assorted violent assaults of a personal nature. What the fucking *hell* was either of them doing here? His fingers twitched, wanting to strangle someone, but he fought back this useless impulse in favor of deciding what the devil to do now.

He began to walk hastily, with no clear notion where he was going. Percy had seen him, he knew that much. Jamie hadn't, but might at any moment. *A general? What the—no time to worry about that just now.* What might either one of them do about it?

He hadn't seen Percy—ex-lover, ex-brother, French spy, and all-around shit—since their last conversation in Philadelphia, some months before. When Percy had first reappeared in Grey's life, it had been with a last attempt at seduction—political rather than physical, though Grey had an idea that he wouldn't have balked at the physical, either. . . . It was an offer for the British government: the return to France of the valuable Northwest Territory, in return for the promise of Percy's "interests" to keep the French government from making an alliance with the American colonies.

He had—as a matter of duty—conveyed the offer discreetly to Lord North and then expunged it—and Percy—from his mind. He had no idea what, if anything, the First Minister had made of it.

Too late now in any case, he thought. France had signed a treaty with the rebellious colonies in April. It remained to be seen, though, whether that treaty would result in anything tangible in the way of support. The French were notoriously unreliable.

So now what? His instinct toward self-preservation urged him to fade quietly through the camp and disappear as quickly as possible. Germain wouldn't tell Jamie he was here; they'd agreed that much in advance. Two considerations held him back, though: first, the minor matter that he didn't yet know where the British army was or how far away. And second . . . a sense of curiosity about Percy that he himself recognized as dangerously reckless.

He'd kept moving, since to stand still was to be knocked over and trampled, and now found himself walking beside the Reverend Woodsworth. The tall minister's face was suffused with an excitement that kept breaking through the man's normal mien of calm dignity, and Grey couldn't help smiling at it.

"God has brought us safe thus far, Bert," Woodsworth said, looking about him with shining eyes. "And He will grant us victory, I know it!"

"Ah." Grey groped for some reply, and finding—to his surprise—that he was incapable of agreeing with this statement, settled for, "I suppose we cannot presume to divine the

Almighty's intent, but I do trust He will preserve us, in His mercy."

"Very well said, Bert, very well said." And Woodsworth clapped him resoundingly on the back.

60

QUAKERS AND QUARTERMASTERS

JAMIE FOUND NATHANAEL Greene in his tent and still in shirtsleeves, the remains of breakfast on a table before him, frowning at a letter in his hand. He put this down at once upon seeing Jamie and rose to his feet.

"Come in, sir, do! Have you et anything yet today? I've a spare egg going to waste." He smiled, but briefly; whatever had troubled him about the letter still lurked in the creases of his brow. Jamie glanced at it from the corner of his eye; from the blots and ragged edge, it looked a piece of domestic correspondence, rather than an official note.

"I have, I thank ye, sir," Jamie said, with a slight bow of acknowledgment toward the egg, which sat neglected in a little wooden cup with a flowered heart painted on it. "I only wondered, if ye meant to ride out today, might I come with ye?"

"Of course!" Greene looked surprised but pleased. "I should welcome your advice, General."

"Perhaps we might trade wisdom, then," Jamie suggested. "For I should value your own advice, though perhaps on a different matter."

Greene paused, coat half-pulled on.

"Really? Advice on what sort of matter?"

"Marriage."

Greene's face struggled between astonishment, a courteous attempt to suppress the astonishment, and something else. He glanced behind him at the letter lying on the table and settled his coat on his shoulders.

"I could use sound advice on *that* matter myself, General Fraser," he said, with a wry twist of the lips. "Let's be off, then."

They rode out of camp north by northwest—Greene was equipped with a battered compass, and Jamie wished for a moment that he still possessed the gold-plated astrolabe that William had sent from London at the behest of Lord John. That had perished when the Big House burned, though the spurt of dark feeling that went through him now had more to do with the thought of John Grey than with the fire and its aftermath.

Conversation at first dealt only with the business at hand: the location of supply dumps along the probable line of march—and, if necessary, retreat, though no one spoke of that possibility. There was no particular doubt as to where the British army was headed; a body that large, with an enormous baggage train and outlying flocks of camp followers, was limited in its choice of roads.

"Aye, that would do," Jamie said, nodding in agreement at Greene's suggestion of an abandoned farmstead. "D'ye think the well's good?"

"I'm minded to find out," Greene said, turning his horse's head toward the farm. "It's hot as Hades already. Scorch our ears off by noon, I reckon."

It was hot; they'd left off their stocks and waistcoats and were riding in shirtsleeves, coats across their saddlebows, but Jamie felt the linen of his shirt sticking to his back and sweat trickling over his ribs and down his face. Fortunately, the well *was* still good; water glimmered visibly below, and a stone dropped in gave back a satisfactory *plunk!*

"I confess I'm surprised to find you in want of advice regarding marriage, General," Greene said, having first drunk his fill and then upended a bucketful of water luxuriously over his head. He blinked water off his lashes, shook himself like a dog, and handed the bucket to Jamie, who nodded thanks. "I should have thought your own union most harmonious."

"Aye, well, it's not my own marriage I'm worrit for," Jamie said, grunting a little as he pulled up a fresh full bucket—hand over hand, for the windlass had rotted away and he'd been obliged to fetch a rope from his saddlebag. "Will ye ken a young scout named Ian Murray? He's my nephew."

"Murray. Murray . . ." Greene looked blank for a moment, but then comprehension dawned. "Oh, him! Yes, drat him. Your nephew, you say? Thought he was an Indian. Cost me a guinea on that race. My wife won't be happy about that at all. Not that she's happy at the moment, regardless," he added with a sigh. Evidently the letter *had* been domestic.

"Well, I might persuade him to give it ye back," Jamie said, suppressing a smile, "if ye might be able to help him to wed."

He raised the bucket overhead and gave himself over to a moment of joy as the drench of water quenched the heat. He drew one deep, grateful breath of coolness, tasting of the dank stones at the bottom of the well, and likewise shook himself.

"He means to marry a Quaker lass," he said, opening his eyes. "I kent that ye were a Friend yourself, havin' heard ye speak to Mrs. Hardman when we met. So I wondered, maybe, if ye could tell me just what's needed in the way of requirement for such a marriage?"

If Greene had been surprised to find that Ian was Jamie's nephew, this news seemed to knock him speechless. He stood for a moment, pushing his lips in and out, as though they might suck up a word he could spit back out, and at last found one.

"Well," he said. He paused for a bit, considering, and Jamie waited patiently. Greene was a man of fairly strong opinions, but he didn't give them hastily. Jamie did wonder what there was to consider in his question, though—were Quakers even stranger in their customs than he thought?

"Well," Greene said again, and exhaled, settling his shoulders. "I must tell you, General, that I no longer consider myself a Friend, though I was indeed raised in that sect." He shot Jamie a sharp look. "And I must also tell you that the cause of my departure was a mislike of their narrow-minded, superstitious ways. If your nephew means to turn Quaker, sir, I'd recommend you do your best to dissuade him."

"Och. Well, that's part of the difficulty, I gather," Jamie replied equably. "He doesna mean to turn Quaker himself. And I think that a wise decision; he isna suited for it at all."

Greene relaxed a little at that and went so far as to smile, if wryly.

"I'm glad to hear it. But he has no objection to his wife remaining a Friend?"

"I think he's better sense than to suggest otherwise."

That made Greene laugh. "Perhaps he'll manage marriage well enough, then."

"Oh, he'll make a bonny husband for the lass, I've nay doubt. It's the getting them wed that seems a difficulty."

"Ah. Yes." Greene glanced round the homestead, wiping his wet face with a wadded handkerchief. "That might in fact be *very* difficult, if the young woman . . . well. Let me think for a moment. In the meantime . . . the well's good, but we can't store powder here; there's not much roof left, and I'm told this weather often presages thunderstorms."

"There's likely a root cellar at the back," Jamie suggested.

There was. The door had gone and a tangle of spindly, pallid vines had sprouted from a rotted sack of potatoes abandoned in the corner, tendrils crawling in slow desperation toward the light.

"It'll do," Greene decided, and made a penciled note in the small book he carried everywhere. "Let's move on, then."

They let the horses drink, poured more water over themselves, and rode on, gently steaming. Greene was not a chatterer, and there had been no conversation for a mile or two, when he finally reached a conclusion of his mental processes.

"The principal thing to bear in mind regarding Friends," he said, without preliminary, "is that they depend very much upon one another's company and opinion—often to the exclusion of the world outside their meetings." He shot Jamie a glance. "The young woman—is your nephew known to her meeting?"

"Mmphm," Jamie said. "As I understand from her brother, they were both put out of their meeting—in a small place in Virginia when he decided to become a surgeon in the Continental army. Or perhaps he was put out, and she merely went with him; I dinna ken whether it makes a difference."

"Oh, I see." Greene plucked the wet shirt away from his body in hopes of admitting a little air to his skin, but it was a vain hope. The air lay thick as a woolen blanket on the simmering countryside. "A 'fighting Quaker,' as they call it?"

"No, he willna take up arms," Jamie assured Greene, "but apparently his merely being connected with the army offended his meeting." Greene snorted in what appeared to be a personal way, and Jamie cleared his throat. "In fact, Denzell Hunter—Dr. Hunter—also is engaged to be married. Though his path may be somewhat smoother, in that his bride has become a Friend herself."

"Has she a home meeting?" Greene asked sharply. Jamie shook his head.

"No, it appeared to be a . . . private event. The conversion, I mean. I am told that Quakers dinna have either clergy or ritual . . . ?" He left that hanging delicately, and Greene snorted again.

"Nor do they. But I assure you, General, there is nothing truly private in a Friend's life—certainly no spiritual matter. My own father opposed reading, as being a practice likely to separate one from God, and when as a young man I not only read but began to collect works on military strategy, in which I had an interest, I was brought before an examination committee from our meeting and subjected to such questions as to—well, as I say, I am no longer a member of that sect."

He blew out his lips and made small rumbling noises for a bit, frowning at the road ahead—though Jamie saw that, even in his preoccupation, Greene was taking note of their surroundings, with an eye to logistics.

He himself had become aware of a certain vibration in the air and wondered if Greene sensed it. Not quite noise, it was a disturbance that he knew well: a large body of men and horses, too far away to see their dust—but there. They'd found the British army. He slowed a little, looking carefully at the trees ahead in case of British scouts—for the British must surely know by now that they were pursued.

Greene's hearing was less acute, though, or perhaps he was only preoccupied, for he glanced at Jamie in surprise, though he slowed, as well. Jamie raised a hand to stop him speaking and lifted his chin—there was a rider coming toward them, following the road. The sound of hooves was audible, and Jamie's own mount flung up his head and whickered with interest, nostrils flaring.

Both men had come armed; Greene set a hand on the musket balanced across his saddle. Jamie left his rifle in its sling but checked the priming of the pistols in his saddle holsters. Awkward to fire a long gun from horseback.

The rider was coming slowly, though; Jamie's hand on the pistol's grip relaxed, and he shook his head at Greene. They reined up, waiting, and a moment later the rider came in view.

"Ian!"

"Uncle Jamie!" Ian's face blossomed with relief at sight of him, and no wonder. He was dressed like a Mohawk, in buckskin leggings and calico shirt, with feathers in his hair, and a long, hairy gray carcass lay across his saddlebow, blood dripping slowly from it down the horse's leg.

The beast wasn't dead, though; Rollo twitched and raised his head, giving the newcomers a yellow wolf glare, but recognized Jamie's scent and barked once, then let his tongue loll out, panting.

"What's happened to the hound, then?" Jamie rode up alongside and leaned forward to look.

"The numpty fell into a deadfall trap," Ian said, frowning rebuke at the dog. Then he gently scratched the big dog's ruff. "Mind, I'd ha' fallen in it myself, if he hadna gone before me."

"Bad hurt?" Jamie asked. He didn't think so; Rollo was giving General Greene his usual look of appraisal—a look that made most people take a few steps back. Ian shook his head, his hand curled into Rollo's fur to keep him steady.

"Nay, but he's torn his leg and he's lame. I was looking for a safe place to leave him; I've got to report in to Captain Mercer. Though seein' as you're here—oh, good day to ye, sir," he said to Greene, whose horse *had* backed up in response to Rollo and was presently indicating a strong desire to keep going, in spite of his rider's inclination. Ian sketched a salute and turned back to Jamie. "Seein' as you're here, Uncle Jamie, could ye maybe fetch Rollo back to the lines with ye and get Auntie Claire to tend his leg?"

"Oh, aye," Jamie said, resigned, and swung down from the saddle, groping for his soggy handkerchief. "Let me bind his leg first. I dinna want blood all over my breeks, and the horse willna like it, either."

Greene cleared his throat.

"As you mention reporting, Mr. . . . Murray?" he asked, with a sideways glance at Jamie, who nodded. "Perhaps you'd be so good as to give me, as well as Captain Mercer, the benefit of your report?"

"Aye, sir," Ian said agreeably. "The army's divided into three bodies now, wi' a great long line o' baggage wagons in between. Sae far as I could tell—I exchanged words wi' another scout who'd gone all the way up the column—they're headed toward a place called Freehold. The ground's no verra good for attack—folded up like a used napkin, all cut up wi' ravines and bitty creeks—though the other scout told me there's meadows beyond that might do for a fight, and ye could lure them or drive them out there."

Greene asked sharp questions, some of which Ian could answer and some he couldn't, while Jamie tended to the ginger business of binding up the dog's leg—there was a nasty stake wound, though not too deep; he hoped the stake hadn't been poisoned. Indians would do that sometimes, in case a wounded deer or wolverine might spring out of the trap.

Jamie's horse was not enthused at the prospect of carrying a wolf on his back but eventually was persuaded, and with no more than a nervous eye roll backward now and then, they were mounted.

"Fuirich, a choin," Ian said, leaning over and scratching Rollo behind the ears. "I'll be back, aye? *Taing,* Uncle!" And with a brief nod to Greene, he was away, his own horse clearly wanting to put as much distance between himself and Rollo as possible.

"Dear Lord," Greene said, wrinkling his nose at the dog's reek.

"Aye, well," Jamie said, resigned. "My wife says ye get used to any sort of smell after a bit of smelling it. And I suppose she'd know."

"Why, is she a cook?"

"Och, no. A physician. Gangrene, ken, festering bowels and the like."

Greene blinked.

"I see. You have a most interesting family, Mr. Fraser." He coughed and looked after Ian, rapidly vanishing in the distance. "You might be wrong about him never becoming a Quaker. At least he doesn't bow his head to a title."

61

A VISCOUS THREE-WAY

JAMIE CAME BACK from his ride with General Greene looking damp, wrinkled, and completely disheveled but otherwise refreshed—and with Rollo, bloody and disgruntled but not badly hurt.

"He'll be fine," I said, scratching Rollo gently behind the ears. The gash had bled a lot, but wasn't deep. "I don't think I'll stitch it."

"Dinna blame ye a bit, Sassenach," Jamie said, glancing at the dog, who had suffered my cleaning, salving, and bandaging his leg but didn't look at all inclined to stand for more fiddling. "Where are my good stockings?"

"In the portmanteau with your other linen," I replied patiently. "Where they are every morning. Surely you know that?"

"I do," he admitted. "I just like ye to tend to me."

"All right," I said, obligingly pulling them out. "D'you want me to put them on for you?"

"Nay, I can manage that," he said, taking them. "Could ye find my shirt, though?"

"I think I can do that, yes," I replied, taking the shirt out of the same portmanteau and shaking it out. "How was General Greene this morning?"

"Good. I asked him about the Quaker way of marriage," he said, pulling a fresh white shirt—his *only* fresh white shirt, as I pointed out—over his head.

"Evidently the difficulty is with Denzell and Rachel not havin' a home meeting, as it's called. It's no that they canna marry, but to do it in the proper way, it would involve the whole meeting. There's a thing called a Clearness Committee, which meets wi' the bride and groom to counsel them and make sure they're suited and that they've some notion what they're in for." He shrugged into the sleeves and grinned at me. "I couldna help thinking, while he was tellin' me, what a committee like that would have had to say about us when we wed."

"Well, they wouldn't have had any more notion what we were in for than we did," I said, amused. "Do you think they would have thought us well suited?"

"If they'd seen the way I looked at ye, Sassenach, when ye didna see me lookin'—then, aye, they would." He kissed me briefly and looked round for the hairbrush. "Can ye club up my hair for me? I canna be reviewing my troops like this." His hair was tied back carelessly with a leather thong, damp stray wisps sticking to his face.

"Of course. How many of them are you reviewing? And when?" I sat him down on the stool and set to work with the brush. "Have you been burrowing through the countryside headfirst? You have foxtails and leaves in your hair, and those winged seeds that elder trees make. Ooh! To say nothing of *this.*" I carefully removed a tiny green caterpillar that had become entangled in his tresses and showed it to him, perched inquisitively on my forefinger.

"Thalla le Dia," he said to the caterpillar. *Go with God.* And taking it carefully onto his own finger, brought it to the tent flap and loosed it into the grass.

"All of them, Sassenach," he said, returning and sitting down again. "My last two companies came in this morning; they'll have been fed now and rested a bit. I meant to ask," he added, twisting round to look up at me, "would ye come with me, Sassenach, and have a look at them? To see if any should be left back from the fighting or to tend any that might need the odd bit o' repair."

"Yes, of course. When?"

"Come to the parade ground in an hour, if ye would." He passed a hand over the neatly gleaming auburn queue, doubled on itself and ribboned in a club at his nape. "Aye, that's grand. Am I decent otherwise?"

He stood up and brushed bits of discarded leaf from his sleeve. The crown of his head brushed the tent, and he was glowing—with sun, energy, and the suppressed excitement of impending action.

"You look like bloody Mars, god of war," I said dryly, handing him his waistcoat. "Try not to scare your men."

His mouth quirked as he shrugged into the waistcoat, but he spoke seriously, eyes on mine.

"Och, I want them frightened of me, Sassenach. It's the only way I'll have a chance of bringing them out of it alive."

WITH AN HOUR to spare, I took my kit of everyday medical supplies and went out to the big tree where the sick among the camp followers tended to gather. The army surgeons would tend camp followers as well as soldiers, if they had time—but they wouldn't be having time today.

There was the usual assortment of minor ailments and injuries: a deeply embedded splinter (infected, requiring the application of drawing salve, followed by excavation, disinfection, and bandage); a dislocated toe (caused by the patient having kicked a fellow in play, but the work of a moment to reduce); a split lip (requiring one stitch and a little gentian ointment); a badly gashed foot (the result of inattention whilst chopping wood, requiring twenty-eight stitches and a large dressing); one child with an ear infection (an onion poultice and willow-bark tea prescribed); another with the bellyache (peppermint tea and a strong admonition against eating eggs of unknown age out of birds' nests of unknown provenance) . . .

The few patients requiring medicines I put aside until I'd dealt with the injuries. Then—with a wary eye on the sun—I led them off to my tent to dispense packets of willow bark, peppermint, and hemp leaves.

The tent flap was open; surely I had left it closed? I ducked my head into the gloom of the tent and stopped abruptly. A tall figure stood before me, apparently in the act of rifling my medicine chest.

"What the devil are you doing with that?" I asked sharply, and the figure jerked, startled.

My eyes had now become accustomed to the diffuse light, and I saw that the thief—if that's what he was—was a Continental officer, a captain.

"I beg your pardon, madam," he said, giving me a perfunctory bow. "I had heard that there was a supply of medicaments here. I—"

"There is, and they're mine." This seemed a trifle ungracious—though I certainly thought his own attitude rather brusque—and I softened the remark a little. "What is it that you need? I imagine I can spare a little—"

"Yours?" He glanced from the chest—very clearly an expensive professional bit of furniture—to me, and his brows rose. "What are *you* doing with a thing like that?"

Several possible replies flitted through my head, but I'd recovered from the surprise of seeing him sufficiently as not to make any of them. I settled for a neutral "May I ask who you are, sir?"

"Oh." Mildly flustered, he bowed to me. "I beg pardon. Captain Jared Leckie, your servant, ma'am. I am a surgeon with the Second New Jersey."

He eyed me consideringly, clearly wondering who the devil *I* was. I was wearing a canvas apron with capacious pockets over my gown, these pockets presently stuffed with all manner of small instruments, dressings, bottles and jars of ointments and liquids. I'd also taken off my broad-brimmed hat when I came into the tent and, as usual, was not wearing a cap. I *had* bound up my hair, but it had come loose and was coiling damply round my ears. He obviously suspected me of being a laundress, come to collect soiled linen—or possibly something worse.

"I am Mrs. Fraser," I said, drawing myself up with what I hoped was a gracious nod. "Er . . . Mrs. *General* Fraser, that is," I added, seeing that he appeared unimpressed.

His eyebrows shot up, and he looked me openly up and down, his eyes lingering on the top pockets of my apron, these featuring an unwieldy rolled dressing in the act of coming unrolled and trailing down my front and a jar of asafoetida, whose cork was loose, thus allowing the reek of it to waft gently above the other notable smells of the camp. It was known commonly as "devil's dung," and for good reason. I pulled the jar out and pushed the cork in more securely. This gesture seemed somehow to reassure him.

"Oh! The general is a physician, I perceive," he said.

"No," I said, beginning to see that I should have uphill work with Captain Leckie, who appeared young and not overbright. "My husband is a soldier. *I* am a physician."

He stared at me as though I'd told him I was a prostitute. Then he made the mistake of assuming that I was joking and laughed heartily.

At this point, one of my patients, a young mother whose one-year-old son had an ear infection, poked her neatly capped head hesitantly into the tent. Her little boy was in her arms, howling and red-faced.

"Oh, dear," I said. "I'm so sorry to keep you waiting, Mrs. Wilkins. Do bring him in; I'll get the bark for him directly."

Captain Leckie frowned at Mrs. Wilkins and beckoned her closer. She looked nervously at me, but allowed him to lean down and look at little Peter.

"He has a difficult tooth," Leckie said, rather accusingly, after running a large, unwashed thumb through Peter's drooling mouth. "He ought to have the gum slit, to let the tooth come through." He began to fumble in his pocket, where he doubtless had a highly insanitary scalpel or lancet.

"He is teething," I agreed, shaking out a quantity of crumbled willow bark into my mortar. "But he also has an ear infection, and the tooth will come through of its own accord within the next twenty-four hours."

He rounded on me, indignant and astonished.

"Are you contradicting me?"

"Well, yes," I said, rather mildly. "You're wrong. You want to have a good look in his left ear. It's—"

"I, madam, am a diplomate of the Medical College of Philadelphia!"

"I congratulate you," I said, beginning to be provoked. "You're still wrong." Having thus rendered him momentarily speechless, I finished grinding the bark into powder and poured it into a square of gauze, which I folded into a neat packet and handed to Mrs. Wilkins, with instructions as to the brewing of the infusion and how to administer it, as well as how to apply an onion poultice.

She took the packet as though it might explode and, with a hasty glance at Captain Leckie, fled, little Peter's howls receding like a siren in the distance.

I drew a deep breath.

"Now," I said, as pleasantly as possible. "If you're in need of simples, Dr. Leckie, I have a good supply. I can—"

He had drawn himself up like a crane eyeing a frog, beady-eyed and hostile.

"Your servant, ma'am," he said curtly, and stalked past me.

I rolled my eyes up toward the canvas overhead. There was a small gecko-like creature clinging to the cloth, who viewed me with no particular emotion.

"How to win friends and influence people," I remarked to it. "Take note." Then I pushed the tent flap back and beckoned for the next patient to come in.

I HAD TO hurry in order to make my rendezvous with Jamie, who was just about to begin his review when I dashed up, twisting my hair into a mass and pinning it hastily under my broad-brimmed hat. It was a terribly hot day; being in the open sun for only a few minutes had made my nose and cheeks tingle warningly.

Jamie bowed gravely to me and began his advance along the line of men drawn up for review, greeting men, saluting officers, asking questions, giving his aide-de-camp notes of things to be done.

He had Lieutenant Schnell with him as aide-de-camp—a nice German boy from Philadelphia, perhaps nineteen—and a stout gentleman I didn't know but assumed from his uniform to be the captain in charge of whatever companies we were inspecting. I followed them, smiling at the men as I passed, while looking them over sharpish for any overt signs of illness, injury, or disability—I was sure that Jamie could spot excessive drunkenness without my expert opinion.

There were three hundred men, he'd told me, and most of them were quite all right. I kept walking and nodding, but wasn't above beginning to fantasize some dangerous circumstance in which I found Captain Leckie writhing in pain, which I would graciously allay, causing him to grovel and apologize for his objectionable attitude. I was trying to choose between the prospect of a musket ball embedded in his buttock, testicular torsion, and something temporarily but mortifyingly disfiguring, like Bell's palsy, when my eye caught a glimpse of something odd in the lineup.

The man in front of me was standing bolt upright, musket at port arms, eyes fixed straight ahead. This was perfectly correct—but no other man in the line was doing it. Militiamen were more than capable, but they generally saw no point in military punctilio. I glanced at the rigid soldier, passed by—then glanced back.

"Jesus H. Roosevelt Christ!" I exclaimed, and only sheer chance kept Jamie from hearing me, he being distracted by the sudden arrival of a messenger.

I took two hasty steps back, bent, and peered under the brim of the dusty slouch hat. The face beneath was set in fierce lines, with a darkly ominous glower—and was completely familiar to me.

"Bloody effing hell," I whispered, seizing him by the sleeve. "What are you *doing* here?"

"You wouldn't believe me if I told you," he whispered back, not moving a muscle of face or body. "Do walk on, my dear."

Such was my astonishment, I might actually have done it, had my attention not been drawn by a small figure skulking about behind the line, trying to avoid notice by crouching behind a wagon wheel.

"Germain!" I said, and Jamie whirled about, eyes wide.

Germain stiffened for an instant and then turned to flee, but too late; Lieutenant Schnell, living up to his name, sprang through the line and grabbed Germain by the arm.

"Is he yours, sir?" he asked, glancing curiously from Jamie to Germain and back.

"He is," Jamie said, with a tone that had turned many a man's blood to water. "What the devil—"

"I'm an orderly!" Germain said proudly, trying to detach himself from Lieutenant Schnell's grip. "I'm supposed to be here!"

"No, you're not," his grandfather assured him. "And what do ye mean, an orderly? Whose orderly?"

Germain at once glanced in John's direction, then, realizing his mistake, jerked his eyes back, but it was too late. Jamie reached John in a single stride and ripped the hat off his head.

The face was identifiable as that of Lord John Grey, but only by someone who knew him well. He wore a black felt patch over one eye, and the other was all but obscured by dirt and bruises. He'd cut his luxuriant blond hair to roughly an inch in length and appeared to have rubbed dirt into it.

With considerable aplomb, he scratched his head and handed Jamie his musket.

"I surrender to you, sir," he said, in a clear voice. "To you, personally. So does my orderly," he added, putting a hand on Germain's shoulder. Lieutenant Schnell, quite flabbergasted, let go of Germain as though he were red-hot.

"I surrender, sir," Germain said solemnly, and saluted.

I'd never seen Jamie at a complete loss for words, and didn't now, but it was a near thing. He inhaled strongly through his nose, then turned to Lieutenant Schnell.

"Escort the prisoners to Captain McCorkle, Lieutenant."

"Er . . ." I said apologetically. A hard blue eye swiveled in my direction, brow raised.

"He's injured," I said, as mildly as I could, with a brief gesture in John's direction. Jamie's lips compressed for an instant, but he nodded.

"Take the prisoners—and Mrs. Fraser"—I daresay it was merely sensitivity on my part that perceived a certain emphasis on "Mrs. Fraser"—"to my tent, Lieutenant."

With scarcely a breath, he turned on John.

"I accept your surrender, Colonel," he said, with icy politeness. "And your parole. I will attend you later."

And, with that, he turned his back on the three of us, in what could only be described as a marked manner.

"WHAT ON EARTH happened to your eye?" I demanded, peering at it. I had John on the cot in my small medical tent, the flap open to admit as much light as possible. The eye was swollen half shut and surrounded by a sticky black ring where the felt patch had been peeled away, the underlying flesh a lurid palette of green, purple, and ghastly yellow. The eye itself was red as a flannel petticoat and, from the irritated state of the eyelids, had been watering more or less constantly for some time.

"Your husband punched me when I told him I'd bedded you," he replied, with complete composure. "I do hope he didn't take any similarly violent actions upon being reunited with you?"

Had I been capable of a convincing Scottish noise, I might have resorted to one. As it was, I merely glared at him.

"I decline absolutely to discuss my husband with you," I said. "Lie down, blast you."

He eased himself back on the cot, wincing.

"He said he hit you twice," I remarked, watching this. "Where was the second one?"

"In the liver." He gingerly touched his lower abdomen. I pulled up his shirt and inspected the damage, which amounted to further spectacular bruising around the lower ribs, with blue streaks draining down toward the ilial crest, but little more.

"That's not where your liver is," I informed him. "It's on the other side."

"Oh." He looked blank. "Really? Are you sure?"

"Yes, I am," I assured him. "I'm a doctor. Let me look at your eye."

I didn't wait for permission, but he didn't resist, lying back and staring up at the canvas roof while I spread the eyelids as far as possible. The sclera and conjunctiva were badly inflamed, and even the dim light made the eye water profusely. I held up two fingers.

"Two," he said, before I could ask. "And before you start ordering me to look to and fro and up and down . . . I can't. I can see out of it—though it's a bit blurry, and I see everything doubled, which is very disagreeable—but I can't move it at all. Dr. Hunter opined that some muscle or other was trapped by some sort of bone. He didn't feel competent to deal with it."

"I'm flattered that you think I might be."

"I have the fullest confidence in your abilities, Dr. Fraser," he said politely. "Besides, have I any choice?"

"No. Keep quite still, there . . . Germain!" I had caught sight of a telltale flutter of pink calico from the corner of my eye, and the runaway came sidling in, looking vaguely guilty.

"Don't tell me what you have in your shirt," I said, noting a suspicious bulge or two. "I don't want to be an accessory to crime. No, wait—is it alive?"

Germain prodded the bulge, as though not quite sure, but it didn't move, and he shook his head. "No, *Grand-mère*."

"Good. Come here and hold this, will you?"

I handed him my pocket looking glass and, adjusting the tent flap so that a ray of light shone in, then adjusted Germain's hand so that the reflected light shone directly from the mirror into the affected eye. John yelped slightly when the light struck his eye, but obediently clutched the sides of the cot and didn't move, though his eye watered terribly. All the better; it would wash out bacteria and perhaps make it easier to move the eyeball.

Denny was most likely right, I thought, selecting my smallest cautery iron and slipping it gently under the lower lid. It was the best thing I could find for the job, being flat, smooth, and spade-shaped. I couldn't move the globe of the eyeball upward at all; even slight pressure made him go white. I could move it slightly from side to side, and given the sensitivity of John's face just below the eye, I began to form a mental picture of the damage. It was almost certainly what was called a "blowout" fracture, which had cracked the delicate bone of the orbital floor and forced a displaced bit of it—along with part of the inferior rectus muscle—down into the maxillary sinus. The edge of the muscle was caught in the crack, thus immobilizing the eyeball.

"Bloody, bloody-minded, effing *Scot,*" I said, straightening up.

"Not his fault," said John. "I provoked him." He sounded excessively cheerful, and I turned a cold look on him.

"I'm not any more pleased with you," I informed him. "You aren't going to like this, and it will serve you right. How in heaven's name did you—no, don't tell me now. I'm busy."

He folded his hands across his stomach, looking meek. Germain sniggered, but desisted when I gave him a glare of his own.

Tight-lipped, I filled a syringe—Dr. Fentiman's penis syringe, as it happened; how appropriate—with saline solution for irrigation and found my small pair of needle-nosed forceps. I had another peek at the site with my makeshift spatula and prepared a tiny, curved needle with a wet catgut suture, cut very fine. I *might* manage without needing to stitch the inferior rectus—it depended whether the edge of the muscle had frayed very badly, by reason of its long entrapment, and how it survived being dislodged—but best to have the suture handy, in case of need. I hoped the need wouldn't occur;

there was so much swelling . . . but I couldn't wait several days for it to subside.

What was troubling me was not so much the immediate reduction of the fracture and freeing of the muscle but the longer-term possibility of adhesion. The eye should be kept fairly immobile, to aid healing, but doing that might cause the muscle to adhere to the orbit, literally freezing the eye permanently. I needed something slippery with which to dress the site, something biologically inert and non-irritating—in my own time, sterile glycerin drops would have been instantly available, but here . . .

Egg white, perhaps? Probably not, I thought; body heat might coddle it, and then what?

"John!"

A shocked voice behind me made me turn, needle in hand. A very dapper-looking gentleman in a stylish wig and a gray-blue velvet suit was standing just inside the tent flap, staring aghast at my patient.

"What's happened to him?" Percy Beauchamp demanded, spotting me in the background.

"Nothing serious," I said. "Are you—"

"Leave," said John, in a voice I'd never heard him use before. He sat up, fixing the newcomer with as steely a look as could be managed with one badly watering crimson eye. "Now."

"What in God's name are you doing here?" Beauchamp demanded. His accent was English, but English faintly tinged with French. He took a step nearer and lowered his voice. "Surely you have not become a Rebel?"

"No, I bloody haven't! Leave, I said."

"Dear God, you mean you—what the devil *happened* to you?" He'd come close enough now to behold the complete picture: filthy cropped hair, filthy disheveled clothes, filthy stockinged feet with holes in toe and heel, and a distorted visage now directing a glare of bloodshot venom at him.

"Now, look here—" I began, turning on Percy with determined firmness, but Germain stopped me.

"He's the man who was looking for Papa in New Bern last year," Germain said. He'd put down the looking glass and was watching the evolving scene with interest. "*Grand-père* thinks he's a villain."

Percy cast Germain a startled look, but recovered his composure with remarkable speed.

"Ah. The proprietor of distinguished frogs," he said, with a smile. "I recall. Peter and Simon were their names? One yellow and one green."

Germain bowed respectfully.

"Monsieur has an excellent memory," he said, with exquisite politeness. "What do you want with my papa?"

"An excellent question," said John, putting one hand over his injured eye, the better to glare at Monsieur Beauchamp.

"Yes, that *is* a good question," I said mildly. "Do sit down, Mr. Beauchamp—and bloody explain yourself. And, *you,*" I added, taking John firmly by both shoulders, "lie down."

"That can wait," John said shortly, resisting my attempt to flatten him. He swung his legs over the side of the cot. "What are you doing here, Percy?"

"Oh, you know him, do you?" I said, beginning to be provoked.

"Certainly. He's my brother—or was."

"What?" Germain and I exclaimed as one. He looked at me and giggled.

"I thought Hal was your only brother," I said, recovering. I glanced back and forth between John and Percy. There was no resemblance at all between them, whereas John's resemblance to Hal was as marked as if they'd been stamped from the same mold.

"Stepbrother," John said, still more shortly. He got his feet under him, preparing to rise. "Come with me, Percy."

"You're not going anywhere," I said, raising my voice slightly.

"How do you propose to stop me?" John was on his feet, staggering a little as he tried to focus his eyes. Before I could answer, Mr. Beauchamp had lunged forward and grabbed his arm, to keep him from falling. John jerked violently away from him, nearly falling again as he stumbled backward into the cot. He caught his balance and stood glowering at Beauchamp, his fists half clenched.

Beauchamp's gaze was locked with his, and the air between them was . . . electric. *Oh,* I thought, glancing from one to the other, suddenly enlightened. *Oh.*

I must have made some small movement, because Beauchamp's gaze flicked suddenly toward my face. He looked startled at whatever he saw there, then, recovering himself, smiled wryly and bowed.

"Madame," he said. Then, in perfect, accentless English, "He is really my stepbrother, though we haven't spoken in . . . some time. I am here as the guest of the Marquis de La Fayette—amongst other things. Do allow me to take his lordship to meet the marquis. I promise to bring him back in one piece." He smiled at me, warm-eyed and sure of his charm, which was considerable.

"His lordship is a prisoner of war," said a very dry Scottish voice from behind Beauchamp. "And my responsibility. I regret that he must remain here, sir."

Percy Beauchamp whirled round, gaping at Jamie, who was filling the tent flap in a most implacable fashion.

"I *still* want to know what he wants with Papa," Germain said, small blond brows drawn down in a suspicious glower.

"I should like to know that, too, monsieur," Jamie said. He came into the tent, ducking, and nodded toward the stool I had been using. "Pray be seated, sir."

Percy Beauchamp glanced from Jamie to Lord John and back again. His face had gone smooth and blank, though the lively dark eyes were full of calculation.

"Alas," he said, the slight French accent back. "I am engaged to *le marquis*—and General Washington—just now. You will excuse me, I am sure. *Bonjour, Mon Général.*" He marched to the tent flap, head held high, turning at the last moment to smile at John. *"Au revoir, mon frère."*

"Not if I bloody see you first."

NOBODY MOVED FOR the space of nine heartbeats—I counted them—following Percy Beauchamp's dignified exit. Finally, John sat down abruptly on the cot, exhaling audibly. Jamie caught my eye and, with a slight nod, sat down on the stool. Nobody spoke.

"You mustn't hit him again, *Grand-père,*" Germain said earnestly, breaking the silence. "He's a very good man, and I'm sure he won't take Grannie to bed anymore, now that you're home to do it."

Jamie gave Germain a quelling look, but his mouth twitched. From my position behind the cot, I could see the back of John's neck flush a deep pink.

"I'm much obliged to his lordship for his care of your grannie," Jamie told Germain. "But if ye think makin' impertinent remarks regarding your elders is going to save your arse—think again."

Germain shifted uneasily, but rolled his eyes at Lord John in a "worth a try" sort of way.

"I'm obliged to you for your good opinion, sir," John told him. "And I reciprocate the compliment—but I trust you are aware that good intent alone does not absolve one from the consequences of rash conduct."

Jamie was beginning to flush as deeply as John.

"Germain," I said. "Do go away. Oh—see if you can find me some honey, would you?"

All three of them looked at me, startled at this apparent non sequitur.

"It's viscous," I said, with a slight shrug. "And antibacterial."

"Of course it is," John said under his breath in a hopeless sort of way.

"What does 'viscous' mean?" Germain asked, interested.

"Germain," said his grandfather, in a menacing tone, and he hastily disappeared without waiting for enlightenment.

Everyone took a deep breath.

"Lie down *now,*" I said to John, before anything regrettable might be said. "Have you got a moment, Jamie? I need someone to hold the mirror while I fix his eye."

With no more than an instant's hesitation, they both obeyed, not looking at each other. I was nearly ready; when I'd got Jamie positioned and the ray of light focused on the eye, I once more irrigated the eye and socket gently with saline solution, then rinsed my fingers thoroughly with the same stuff.

"I need you both to hold completely still," I said. "I'm sorry, John, but there's no other way to do this, and if we're lucky, it will be quick."

"Aye, I've heard that one before," Jamie muttered, but desisted when I shot a sideways look at him.

I was afraid to use the forceps, for fear of puncturing his eyeball. So I spread the lids of John's affected eye with the fingers of my left hand, wedged the fingertips of my right as deeply into the eye socket as I could, and squeezed.

He made a shocked, strangled sort of noise, and Jamie gasped but didn't drop the mirror.

There are not many things in the world slipperier than a wet eyeball. I tried to squeeze as lightly as I could, but there was no help for it; a light pressure merely allowed the eyeball to pop out of my fingers like an oiled grape. I clenched my teeth and tried again, gripping harder.

On the fourth try, I managed to get a sufficient grip as to allow me to try to rotate the eyeball in its socket. I didn't quite manage it, but at least got a better idea of how it might go.

Five minutes later, John was trembling like a blancmange, hands clenched tight on the rails of the cot, Jamie was praying under his breath in Gaelic, and all three of us were drenched with sweat.

"Once more," I said, drawing breath and wiping sweat from my chin with the back of my hand. I rinsed my fingers again. "If I can't get it this time, we'll have a rest and try again later."

"Oh, God," said John. He closed both eyes briefly, swallowed hard, and opened them as wide as he could. Both eyes were watering badly, and tears washed down his temples.

I felt Jamie move slightly next to me. He refocused the mirror—but I saw that he had also moved nearer to the cot, so that his leg pressed against the rail, just next to John's gripping fingers. I wiggled my wet fingers in preparation, said a brief prayer to St. Claire, patron of sore eyes, and thrust my fingers as deeply into the socket as I could manage.

By this time, I had a very clear mental image of the fracture, a dark line beneath the torn conjunctiva, and the line of the inferior rectus muscle wedged into it. I twisted, a short, sharp jerk, before my fingers slipped—and felt the muscle pop free. John shuddered the full length of his body and gave a little moan.

"Glory be," I said, and laughed from sheer relief. There was a little blood—not much—on my fingers, and I wiped them on my apron. Jamie flinched and looked away.

"Now what?" he asked, carefully not looking at John.

"Now what—Oh." I considered that one for a moment, then shook my head.

"He has to lie down for several hours with the eye covered—a day or two, ideally. If Germain finds me some honey, I'll lubricate the eye socket with a bit of it, to prevent adhesion."

"I mean," Jamie said patiently, "does he require to be kept under a doctor's care?"

"Not all the time," I said, surveying John critically. "Someone—me, I mean—needs to check the eye every so often, but there's really nothing else to be done for it; the swelling and bruises will take care of themselves. Why? What were you planning to do with him?"

Jamie made a small gesture of frustration.

"I *would* hand him over to Washington's staff for interrogation," he said. "But—"

"But I surrendered to you personally," John said helpfully. He glanced at me out of his working eye. "That means I'm his responsibility."

"Aye, thank ye for that," Jamie muttered, giving him an irritable look.

"Well, you aren't going to tell him anything useful, either, are you?" I asked, putting a hand on John's forehead. Slightly warm, but no gross fever. "Such as the nature of the relations between yourself and the recent Mr. Beauchamp?"

Jamie gave a brief snort.

"I ken fine what his relations are wi' that wee sodomite," he said bluntly. He gave John a piercing stare. "Ye dinna mean to tell me what he's doing here, do ye?"

"No," John said cheerfully. "Though it almost certainly wouldn't help you if I did."

Jamie nodded, having evidently expected nothing better, and rose with an air of decision.

"Well, then. I've work to do, and so have you, Sassenach. Wait here for Germain, if ye will, and when ye've finished with the honey, tell Germain he's to be in charge of his lordship. He's no to leave his lordship under any circumstances, save you or I tell him he may—and should Monsieur Beauchamp pay another call, Germain is to be present at any conversation. He speaks French verra fluently," he advised John. "And should ye think of attempting to subvert my grandson's loyalty—"

"Sir!" John said, looking shocked at the mere idea.

"Mmphm," Jamie said darkly, and left.

62

THE MULE DISLIKES YOU

I DIDN'T KNOW QUITE what to say to John, in the wake of recent events. He seemed similarly at a loss, but coped with the social awkwardness by closing his eyes and pretending to be asleep. I couldn't leave him until Germain got back with the honey—assuming he found any, but I had a fair amount of faith in his abilities.

Well, no point in sitting about with my hands folded. I took out my mortar and pestle and set to work grinding gentian root and garlic for antibiotic ointment. This occupied my hands, but unfortunately not my mind, which was scampering in circles like a hamster on a wheel.

I had two main anxieties at the moment, one of which I could do nothing about: that being the escalating sense of oncoming battle. I knew it very well; I couldn't be mistaken. Jamie hadn't told me explicitly, perhaps because he hadn't had written orders yet—but I knew as clearly as if it had been shouted by a town crier. The army would move soon.

I stole a glance at John, who lay like a tomb effigy, hands neatly crossed at his waist. All it wanted was a small dog curled up at his feet. Rollo, snoring under the cot, would have to do, I supposed.

John, of course, was the other anxiety. I had no idea how he'd come to be where he was, but enough people had seen him surrender that his presence would be common knowledge by nightfall. And once it *was* . . .

"I don't suppose you'd consider escaping, if I left for a moment?" I asked abruptly.

"No," he said, not opening his eyes. "I gave my parole. Besides, I wouldn't make it outside the camp," he added.

The silence resumed, broken by the *brumm* of a large bumblebee, which had blundered into the tent, and the more distant shouts and drumbeats of soldiers drilling and the low thrashing noises of daily camp life.

The only good thing—if one chose to regard it that way, and I might as well—was that the rising sense of battle urgency was likely to preclude official curiosity about John. What the devil would Jamie do with him when the army decamped in the morning? I wondered.

"Grand-mère, Grand-mère!" Germain burst into the tent, and Rollo—who had slept through Percy Beauchamp's visit without stirring a whisker—shot out from under the cot with an explosive *WOOF!* that nearly overturned the cot and John with it.

"Hush, dog," I said, seeing him glaring wildly round, and took a restraining grip on his scruff. "And what the he—I mean the dev—I mean what's the matter, Germain?"

"I saw him, Grannie! I saw him! The man who took Clarence! Come quick!" And without waiting for response, he turned and raced out of the tent.

John began to sit up, and Rollo tensed under my hand.

"Sit!" I said to both of them. "And bloody stay!"

THE HAIRS ON my forearms were prickling, even as sweat streamed down my neck. I'd left my hat behind and the sun blazed on my cheeks; I was panting by the time I caught up with Germain, as much from emotion as from heat.

"Where—"

"Just there, Grannie! The big bugger wi' the kerchief round his arm. Clarence must ha' bitten him!" Germain added, with glee.

The bugger in question *was* big: roughly twice my size, with a head like a pumpkin. He was sitting on the ground under the shade of what I thought of as the hospital tree, nursing his kerchief-wrapped arm and glowering at nothing in particular. A small group of people seeking medical treatment—you could tell as much from their hunched and drooping attitudes—was keeping a distance from him, looking warily at him from time to time.

"You'd best keep out of sight," I murmured to Germain,

but, hearing no answer, glanced round to discover that he'd already faded artfully from view, canny child that he was.

I walked up, smiling, to the little group of waiting people—mostly women with children. I didn't know any of them by name, but they clearly knew who and what I was; they bobbed their heads and murmured greetings, but cut their eyes sideways at the man under the tree. *"Take him first before he does something messy"* was the clear message. Just as clear as the sense of badly contained violence that the man was radiating in all directions.

I cleared my throat and walked over to the man, wondering what on earth I was to say to him. *"What have you done with Clarence the mule?"* or *"How dare you rob my grandson and leave him in the wilderness alone, you bloody bastard?"*

I settled for "Good morning. I'm Mrs. Fraser. What happened to your arm, sir?"

"Bleedin' mule bit me to the bone, gaddamn his stinkin' hide," the man replied promptly, and glowered at me under eyebrows ridged with scar tissue. So were his knuckles.

"Let me see it, will you?" Not waiting for permission, I took hold of his wrist—it was hairy and very warm—and unwrapped the kerchief. This was stiff with dried blood, and no wonder.

Clarence—if it was Clarence—actually *had* bitten him to the bone. Horse and mule bites could be serious but usually resulted only in deep bruising; equines had powerful jaws, but their front teeth were designed for tearing grass, and as most bites were through clothing, they didn't often break skin. It could be done, though, and Clarence had done it.

A flap of skin—and a good chunk of flesh—about three inches wide had been partially detached, and I could see past the thin fatty layer to the gleam of tendon and the red membranous covering of the radius. The wound was recent but had stopped bleeding, save for a little oozing at the edges.

"Hmm," I said noncommittally, and turned his hand over. "Can you close your fingers into a fist?" He could, though the ring finger and little finger wouldn't fold in completely. They did move, though; the tendon wasn't severed. "Hmm," I said again, and reached into my bag for the bottle of saline solution and a probe. Saline was a little less painful for disinfection than dilute alcohol or vinegar—and it was somewhat easier to get hold of salt, at least when living in a city—but I kept a tight grip on the enormous wrist as I poured the liquid into the wound.

He made a noise like a wounded bear, and the waiting onlookers took several steps back, as a body.

"Rather a vicious mule," I observed mildly, as the patient subsided, panting. His face darkened.

"Gonna beat the gaddamn bastarding fucker to death, soon as I get back," he said, and bared his yellow teeth at me. "Skin him, I will, and sell his meat."

"Oh, I wouldn't advise that," I said, keeping a grip on my temper. "You don't want to be using that arm violently; it could bring on gangrene."

"It could?" He didn't go pale—it wasn't possible, given the temperature—but I'd definitely got his attention.

"Yes," I said pleasantly. "You've seen gangrene, I daresay? The flesh goes green and putrid—beastly smell—limb rots, dead in days . . . that sort of thing?"

"I seen it," he muttered, eyes now fixed on his arm.

"Well, well," I said soothingly, "we'll do our best here, won't we?" I would normally have offered a patient in such a case a fortifying draft of whatever liquor was available—and, thanks to the marquis, I had quite a good supply of French brandy—but in the present instance, I wasn't feeling charitable.

In fact, my general feeling was that Hippocrates could turn a blind eye for the next few minutes. Do no harm, forsooth. Still, there wasn't a great deal I could do to him, armed with a two-inch suture needle and a pair of embroidery scissors.

I stitched the wound as slowly as I could, taking care to slosh more saline over it periodically and glancing covertly round for assistance. Jamie was with Washington and the high command as they strategized the imminent engagement; I couldn't summon him out to deal with a mule thief.

Ian had vanished on his pony, scouting the British rear guard. Rollo was with Lord John. Rachel had gone off with Denny and Dottie in the Quakers' wagon, to look for supplies in the nearest village. And good luck to them, I thought; General Greene's foragers had spread out like locusts over the face of the earth the moment the army halted, stripping farmsteads and storage barns in their path.

The patient was cursing in a rather monotonous and uninspired fashion, but showed no signs of keeling over in a convenient faint. What I was doing to his arm was unlikely to improve his temper; what if he actually *did* intend to go straight off and beat Clarence to death?

If Clarence was loose, I'd put good odds on the mule to win any such encounter, but he was very likely tied or hobbled. But then . . . a horrid thought struck me. I *knew* where Germain was, and what he was doing—or trying to do.

"Jesus H. Roosevelt Christ," I muttered, bending my head over the teamster's arm to hide an undoubtedly appalled expression. Germain was an extremely talented pickpocket, but stealing a mule out of the middle of a gang of teamsters . . .

What had Jamie said? *"He'd be taken up for theft and hanged or flogged within an inch of his life, and I couldna do a thing to stop it."* Teamsters being what they were, they'd likely just break his neck and be done with it, rather than waiting for any sort of military justice.

I swallowed hard and glanced quickly over my shoulder, to see if I could spot the teamsters' encampment. If I could see Germain . . .

I didn't see Germain. What I saw was Percy Beauchamp, regarding me thoughtfully from the shadow of a nearby tent. Our eyes met, and he instantly came toward me, straightening his coat. Well, I was in no position to look a gift horse—or mule—in the mouth, was I?

"Madame Fraser," he said, and bowed. "Are you in need of some assistance?"

Yes, I bloody did need assistance; I couldn't drag my surgical repairs out much longer. I darted a look at my massive patient, wondering whether he had any French.

Apparently my face was just as transparent as Jamie had always told me it was; Percy smiled at me and said conversationally in French, "I don't think this clot of decaying menstrual blood is capable of understanding more English than it takes to hire the sort of poxed and imbecile whore who would let him touch her, let alone understand the tongue of angels."

The teamster went on muttering, "Shit-fire, shit-fire, fucking shit-ass fucking-ass mule, that gaddamn *hurts* . . ."

I relaxed a little and replied in French. "Yes, I need help—

with the utmost urgency. My grandson is trying to steal the mule this oaf stole from him. Can you retrieve him from the teamsters' camp before someone notices?"

"À votre service, madame," he replied promptly, and, clicking his heels smartly together, bowed and went off.

I TOOK AS long as I could over the final dressing of the wound, worried that should my foul-mouthed patient find Germain among the teamsters, Percy's French manners might be unequal to the occasion. And I couldn't really expect Hippocrates to continue turning a blind eye, were I compelled to do something drastic if the man tried to break Germain's neck.

I heard a familiar loud braying behind me, though, and turned sharply to see Percy, flushed and a trifle disheveled, leading Clarence toward me. Germain sat atop the mule, his face set in lines of vindictive triumph as he glared at my patient.

I stood up hastily, groping for my knife. The teamster, who had been gingerly prodding the fresh bandage round his arm, looked up, startled, then surged to his feet with a roar.

"Shit-*FIRE*!" he said, and started purposefully toward them, fists clenched.

Percy, to his credit, stood his ground, though he paled a little. He handed the reins up to Germain, though, and stepped firmly forward.

"Monsieur . . ." he began. I would have liked to know just what he had in mind to say but didn't find out, as the teamster didn't bother with colloquy, instead driving a hamlike fist into Percy's belly. Percy sat down hard and folded up like a fan.

"Bloody *hell—Germain*!" For Germain, nothing daunted by the sudden loss of support, had gathered up Clarence's reins and tried to lash the teamster across the face with them.

This might possibly have been effective, had he not telegraphed his intention quite so clearly. As it was, the teamster ducked and reached out, clearly intending to grab either the reins or Germain. The crowd around me had realized what was happening by now, and women started screaming. At this point, Clarence decided to become involved and, laying back his ears, curled his lips and snapped at the teamster's face, coming within a toucher of taking off the man's nose.

"SHIT-ASS FUCKING MULE!!" Deeply inflamed, the teamster leapt at Clarence and fixed his teeth in the mule's upper lip, clinging like grim death to his neck. Clarence screamed. The women screamed. Germain screamed.

I didn't scream, because I couldn't breathe. I was elbowing my way through the crowd, fumbling for the slit in my skirt so I could reach my knife. Just as I laid my hand on the hilt, though, a hand came down on my shoulder, halting me in my tracks.

"Pardon me, milady," said Fergus, and, stepping purposefully past me, walked up beside the lunging mass of mule, teamster, and shrieking child, and fired the pistol in his hand.

Everything stopped, for a split second, and then the shouting and screaming started again, everyone surging toward Clarence and his companions to see what had happened. For a long moment, it wasn't apparent what *had* happened. The teamster had let go his grip in astonishment and turned toward Fergus, eyes bulging and blood-tinged saliva running down his chin. Germain, with more presence of mind than I would have had in such a situation, got hold of the reins and was hauling on them with all his strength, trying to turn Clarence's head. Clarence, whose blood was plainly up, was having none of it.

Fergus calmly put the fired pistol back into his belt—I realized at this point that he must have fired into the dirt near the teamster's feet—and spoke to the man.

"If I were you, sir, I would remove myself promptly from this animal's presence. It is apparent that he dislikes you."

The shouting and screaming had stopped, and this made several people laugh.

"Got you there, Belden!" a man near me called. "The mule dislikes you. What you think of that?"

The teamster looked mildly dazed but still homicidal. He stood with his fists clenched, legs braced wide apart and shoulders hunched, glowering at the crowd.

"What I think . . . ?" he began. "*I* think—"

But Percy had managed to get to his feet and, while still somewhat hunched, was mobile. Without hesitation, he walked up and kicked the teamster smartly in the balls.

This went over well. Even the man who appeared to be a friend of Belden's whooped with laughter. The teamster didn't go down but curled up like a dried leaf, clutching himself. Percy wisely didn't wait for him to recover, but turned and bowed to Fergus.

"*À votre service, monsieur.* I suggest that you and your son—and the mule, of course—might withdraw?"

"*Merci beaucoup,* and I suggest you do the same, *tout de suite,*" Fergus replied.

"Hey!" shouted the teamster's friend, not laughing now. "You can't steal that mule!"

Fergus rounded on him, imperious as the French aristocrat Percy had implied he might be.

"I cannot, sir," he said, inclining his head a quarter of an inch in acknowledgment. "Because a man cannot steal that which already belongs to him, is this not so?"

"Is that not . . . is *what* not so?" demanded the man, confused.

Fergus scorned to answer this. Lifting one dark brow, he strode off several paces, turned, and shouted, "Clarence! *Écoutez-moi!*"

With the teamster's collapse, Germain had succeeded in getting Clarence somewhat under control, though the mule's ears were still laid out flat in displeasure. At the sound of Fergus's voice, though, the ears rose slowly upright and swiveled in his direction.

Fergus smiled, and I heard a woman behind me sigh involuntarily. Fergus's smile was remarkably charming. He reached into his pocket and withdrew an apple, which he skewered neatly on his hook.

"Come," he said to the mule, extending his right hand and twiddling the fingers in a head-scratching motion. Clarence came, disregarding Mr. Belden, who had now sat down and was clutching his knees, the better to contemplate his state of inner being. The mule ducked his head to take the apple, nudging Fergus's elbow, and allowed his forehead to be scratched. There was a murmur of interest and approbation from the crowd, and I noticed a few censorious glances being shot at the groaning Mr. Belden.

The sense of being about to faint had left me, and now my

insides began to unclench. With some effort, I slid the knife back into its sheath without stabbing myself in the thigh and wiped my hand on my skirt.

"As for *you, sans cervelle,*" Fergus was saying to Germain, with a low-voiced menace that he'd plainly learned from Jamie, "we have a few things to discuss presently."

Germain turned a rather sickly shade of yellow. "Yes, *Papa,*" he murmured, hanging his head in order to avoid his father's minatory eye.

"Get down," Fergus said to him, and, turning to me, raised his voice. "Madame General, permit me to present this animal personally to General Fraser, in the service of liberty!"

This was delivered in such a tone of ringing sincerity that a few souls applauded. I accepted, as graciously as possible, on behalf of General Fraser. By the conclusion of these proceedings, Mr. Belden had got awkwardly to his feet and stumbled off toward the teamsters' camp, tacitly ceding Clarence to the cause.

I took Clarence's reins, relieved and glad to see him again. Apparently it was mutual, for he nosed me familiarly in the shoulder and made chummy huffing noises.

Fergus, meanwhile, stood for a moment looking down at Germain, then squared his shoulders and turned to Percy, who still looked a little pale but had straightened his wig and regained his self-possession. Percy bowed very formally to Fergus, who sighed deeply, then bowed back.

"And I suppose that we, too, have matters to discuss, monsieur," he said, resigned. "Perhaps a little later?"

Percy's handsome face lighted.

"À votre service . . . seigneur," he said, and bowed again.

63

AN ALTERNATE USE FOR A PENIS SYRINGE

GERMAIN HAD, IN FACT, found some honey, and now that the excitement of recovering Clarence was over, he produced a large chunk of sticky honeycomb, wrapped in a dirty black kerchief, from the recesses of his shirt.

"What are you going to do wi' that, Grannie?" he asked, curious. I'd set the oozing chunk of comb in a clean pottery dish and was again employing the useful penis syringe—carefully sterilized with alcohol—to suck up honey, being careful to avoid bits of wax and noticeable pollen grains. Having been designed for irrigation rather than puncture, the syringe had a blunt, smoothly tapered tip: just the thing for dribbling honey into someone's eye.

"I'm going to lubricate his lordship's bad eye," I said. "Fergus, will you come and steady his lordship's head, please? Put your hand on his forehead. And, Germain, you'll hold his eyelids open."

"I can keep still," John said irritably.

"Be quiet," I said briefly, and sat down on the stool beside him. "No one can keep still while having things poked into their eye."

"You were poking your bloody *fingers* into my eye not an hour since! And I didn't move!"

"You squirmed," I said. "It's not your fault, you couldn't help it. Now, be quiet; I don't want to accidentally stab you in the eyeball with this."

Breathing audibly through his nose, he clamped his mouth

shut and suffered Fergus and Germain to immobilize him. I'd debated whether to dilute the honey with boiled water, but the heat of the day had made it sufficiently thin that I thought it better to use it at full strength.

"It's antibacterial," I explained to the three of them, using my cautery iron again to lift the eyeball and squirting a slow dribble of honey under it. "That means it kills germs."

Fergus and Germain, to whom I had explained germs more than once, nodded intelligently and tried to look as though they believed in the existence of such things, which they didn't. John opened his mouth as though to speak, but then shut it again and exhaled strongly through his nose.

"But the chief virtue of honey in the present instance," I went on, anointing the eyeball generously, "is that it's viscous. Let go now, Germain. Blink, John. Oh, *very* good!" The handling had of course made the eye water, but even dilute honey retains its viscosity; I could see the altered gleam of the light across the sclera, indicating the presence of a thin, soothing—I hoped—layer of honey. Some had overflowed, of course, and amber beads were sliding down his temple toward his ear; I stanched the flow with a handkerchief.

"How does it feel?"

John opened and closed his eye a couple of times, very slowly.

"Everything looks blurry."

"Doesn't matter; you aren't going to be looking out of that eye for a day or two anyway. Does it feel any better?"

"Yes," he said, in a distinctly grudging manner, and the other three of us made approving noises that made him look embarrassed.

"Right, then. Sit up—carefully! Yes, that's it. Close your eye and hold this to catch the drips." And, handing him a clean handkerchief, I unrolled a length of gauze bandage, thumbed a pad of lint carefully into the eye socket, and rolled the bandage round his head a few times, tucking in the ends. He strongly resembled a figure in an old painting titled *The Spirit of '76,* but I didn't mention it.

"All right," I said, exhaling and feeling rather pleased with myself. "Fergus, why don't you and Germain go and find some food? Something for his lordship, and something for the road tomorrow. I rather think it will be a long day."

"This one's been quite long enough already," John said. He was swaying a little, and I pushed him gently back down with little resistance. He stretched his neck to ease it, then settled on the pillow with a sigh. "Thank you."

"It was my pleasure," I assured him. I hesitated, but, with Fergus's departure, I didn't think I'd have a better chance to ask what was in my mind. "I don't suppose *you* know what Percival Beauchamp wants with Fergus, do you?"

The good eye opened and looked at me.

"You mean you don't think he believes Fergus to be the lost heir to a great fortune? No, I don't, either. But if Mr. Fraser will take a bit of unsolicited advice, I'd strongly suggest having as little as possible to do with Monsieur Beauchamp." The eye closed again.

Percy Beauchamp had taken his leave—very gracefully—after Clarence's rescue, explaining that he must attend *le marquis* but adding that he would seek out Fergus on the morrow.

"When things are quieter," he'd added, with a genteel bow.

I regarded John thoughtfully.

"What did he do to you?" I asked. He didn't open his eye, but his lips tightened.

"To me? Nothing. Nothing at all," he repeated, and turned over on his side with his back to me.

64

THREE HUNDRED AND ONE

THREE HUNDRED MEN. Jamie stepped into the darkness beyond the 16th New Jersey's campfire and paused for a moment to let his eyes adjust. Three *hundred* bloody men. He'd never led a band of more than fifty. And never had much in the way of subalterns, no more than one or two men under him.

Now he had ten militia companies, each with its own captain and a few informally appointed lieutenants, and Lee had given him a staff of his own: two aides-de-camp, a secretary—now, *that* he could get used to, he thought, flexing the fingers of his maimed right hand—three captains, one of whom was striding along at his shoulder, trying not to look worrit, ten of his own lieutenants, who would serve as liaison between him and the companies under his command, a cook, an assistant cook—and, of course, he had a surgeon already.

Despite the preoccupations of the moment, the memory of Lee's face when Jamie'd told him exactly why he didn't need an army surgeon assigned to him made him smile.

"Indeed," Lee had said, his long-nosed face going blank. Then he'd gathered his wits and gone red in the face, thinking himself practiced upon. But Jamie had pushed back his cuff and shown Lee his right hand, the old white scars on his fingers like tiny starbursts where the bones had come through, and the broad one, still red but neat, straight, and beautifully knit, running down between the middle finger and the little one, showing where the missing finger had been amputated with such skill that one had to look twice to see why the hand seemed strange.

"Well, General, your wife seems a most accomplished needlewoman," Lee said, now amused.

"Aye, sir, she is," he'd said politely. "And a verra bonny hand with a blade, too."

Lee gave him a sardonic look and spread out the fingers of his own right hand; the outer two were missing.

"So was the gentleman who took these off me. A duel," he added offhandedly, seeing Jamie's raised brows, and curled up his hand again. "In Italy."

He didn't know about Lee. The man had a reputation, but he was a boaster, and the two didn't often go together. On the other hand, he was proud as one of Louis's camels, and arrogance sometimes did mark a man who kent his worth.

The plan to attack the British rear guard, at first intended as a quick strike by La Fayette and a thousand men—Lee scorning such a minor command—had grown more elaborate, as such things always did if you gave commanders time to think about them. Once Washington had decided that the expeditionary force should be five thousand men, Lee had graciously condescended to this more appropriate command—leaving La Fayette in charge of his own smaller force, for the sake of the marquis's *amour-propre,* but with Lee in command overall. Jamie had his doubts, but it wasn't his place to voice them.

He glanced to his left, where Ian and his dog were ambling along, the former whistling to himself and the latter a huge, shaggy shape in the dark, panting from the heat.

"Iain," he said casually in *Gàidhlig,* "did your friends with the feathers have aught to say about Ounewaterika?"

"They had, Uncle," Ian replied in the same language. "Not much, though, for they know him only by repute. He's a most ferocious fighter, or so it's said."

"Mmphm." The Mohawk were certainly ferocious and did set great store by personal courage—but he thought they had a negligible grasp of strategy, tactics, and judgment. He was about to ask about Joseph Brant, who was likely the closest thing to a general—in the formal sense—among the Mohawk, but was interrupted by a tall, gangling form stepping out in front of him.

"I beg your pardon, sir. Might I have a word?" the man said, and, looking right and left at Jamie's companions, added, "A private word."

"Certainly, Captain . . . Woodsworth," he replied, hoping his hesitation in finding the man's name was small enough to pass unnoticed. He'd memorized all the militia captains as he met them—and as many men as he could—but their names wouldn't come easy to him for a bit yet.

After a moment's further hesitation, he nodded to Ian to go on with Captain Whewell to the next fire.

"Tell them what's afoot, Captain," he said, for the next fire was one of Whewell's assigned companies, "but wait for me there, aye?"

"What's afoot?" Woodsworth repeated, sounding alarmed. "What's happening? Are we to go now?"

"Not yet, Captain. Come aside, aye? Else we'll be trampled." For they were standing in the path that led from the fires to a set of hastily dug latrine trenches; he could smell the acrid tang of ordure and quicklime from here.

Leading Woodsworth aside, he acquainted him with the change of commander for the morning, but assured him that this would make no real difference to the militia companies under Jamie's command; they would receive their orders in the normal way.

He thought privately that it wouldn't make a difference in how the companies operated—it might well make a difference as to whether they met battle on the morrow or not, and whether they survived if they did—but there was no telling whether the better odds lay with La Fayette or Lee. Chances were that sheer accident, Fate, or, just possibly, God, would decide.

"Now, sir," he said. "Ye wished to speak wi' me?"

"Oh." Woodsworth inhaled through his nose and straightened himself, hastily retrieving the words of whatever speech he'd composed. "Yes, sir. I wished to inquire after the—er—the disposition made of Bertram Armstrong."

"Bertram . . . what?"

"The man you took from my—er, from the lines earlier today, with the little boy."

Jamie didn't know whether to laugh or be annoyed. *Bertram?*

"The man is well enough disposed for the present, sir. My wife's seen to his eye, and he's been fed."

"Oh." Woodsworth shuffled his feet, but stood his ground. "I'm glad of that, sir. But what I meant—I am concerned for him. There is talk about him."

"I'm sure there is," Jamie said, not bothering to hide the edge in his voice. "And what is your concern, sir?"

"They are saying—the men from Dunning's company—that Armstrong is a government spy, that he is a British officer who concealed himself among us. That they found a commission upon him, and correspondence. I—" He paused and gulped breath, the next words coming out in a rush. "I cannot believe it of him, sir, nor can any of us. We feel that some mistake must have been made, and we—we wish to say that we hope nothing . . . hasty will be done."

"No one has suggested anything of the sort, Captain," Jamie assured him, alarm running down his spine like quicksilver. *Only because they haven't had time.* He'd been able to ignore the thorny problem Grey presented as a prisoner, in the fierce rush of preparation and the fiercer rush of his own feelings, but he couldn't ignore it much longer. He should have notified La Fayette, Lee, *and* Washington of Grey's presence immediately, but had gambled on the confusion of imminent battle to disguise his delay.

His eyes had grown used to the scattered light of stars and fire; he could see Woodsworth's long face, apologetic but determined.

"Yes. I hesitate to speak so frankly, sir, but the sorry fact is that when men's passions run high, regrettable actions—irretrievable actions—may be taken." Woodsworth swallowed audibly. "I should not like to see that."

"Ye think someone might see fit to take such action? Now?" He glanced round at the encircling fires. He could see bodies moving, restless as the flames, dark shadows in the woods—but he caught no sense of riot, no pulse of anger. A murmur of talk, to be sure, voices raised in excitement, bursts of laughter and even singing, but it was the nervous spirit of anticipation, expectation, not the sullen rumble of a mob.

"I am a clergyman, sir." Woodsworth's voice was stronger now, urgent. "I know how men may turn to evil conversation and how quickly such conversation may turn to action. One drink too many, a careless word . . ."

"Aye, ye're right about that," Jamie said. He cursed himself for not having thought of this possibility; he'd let his own feelings cloud his mind. Of course, he'd had no idea when he left Grey that he'd been carrying a commission—but that was no excuse. "I've sent word to General Lee about . . . Mr. Armstrong. Should ye hear any more talk about the man, ye might let it be known that the matter is in official hands. That might prevent anything . . . regrettably informal happening."

Woodsworth's sigh of relief was palpable.

"Yes, sir," he said, with gratitude. "I shall certainly let that be known." He stepped aside, bobbing his head, but then stopped, struck by a thought. "Oh."

"Aye?" Jamie spoke impatiently; he felt assailed from all sides by swarms of tiny, stinging troubles, and was inclined to swat this one.

"I trust you will forgive my persistence, General. But I just thought—the boy who was with Armstrong. Bobby Higgins, he's called."

All Jamie's senses were instantly alert.

"What about him?"

"He—I mean Armstrong—the boy said he was in search of his grandfather, and Armstrong said he knew the man—and that his name was James Fraser. . . ."

Jamie shut his eyes. If no one lynched John Grey before dawn, he might throttle the man himself.

"The boy is indeed my grandson, Captain," he said, as evenly as he could, opening his eyes. *Which means, aye, I ken bloody Bert Armstrong.* And if that small bit of information became generally known, there were going to be a lot of very awkward questions asked, by people in a position to demand answers. "My wife is caring for him."

"Oh. Good. I just wished to—"

"To make known your concern. Aye, Captain. I thank ye. Good night."

Woodsworth bowed and stepped back, murmuring, "Good night," in his turn, and disappeared into a night that was far from good and getting worse by the moment.

Jamie jerked his coat straight and strode on. Three hundred men to inform and command, to rouse, lead, and control. Three hundred lives in his hands.

Three hundred and bloody *one.*

65

MOSQUITOES

JAMIE WALKED INTO the light of the fire quite late, smiled at me, and sat down suddenly.

"Is there food?" he asked.

"There is, sir," said the woman who was stirring it. "And you'll have some, too, ma'am," she added firmly, giving me a look that strongly suggested that I was not looking my very best. I wasn't disposed to care, but accepted with thanks a wooden bowl of something hot and a chunk of bread to eat it with.

I barely noticed what I ate, though I was ravenous. The day had been so filled with activity that I hadn't had time to eat—would not have eaten at all, in fact, had I not brought food for John, at which point he insisted that I sit down for ten minutes and eat with him. Percy Beauchamp had not come back; that was something on the plus side of the ledger, I supposed.

There had been a couple of dozen men from Jamie's companies that I rejected by reason of disfirmity—crippled, asthmatic, collapsed with age—and perhaps three dozen more who were essentially sound but sporting some injury requiring attention, these mostly the result of fistfights or falling down while under the influence of drink. Several of them were *still* under the influence of drink and had been sent off under guard to sleep it off.

I did wonder for a moment how many men normally went into battle drunk. In all honesty, I'd be strongly tempted to do it myself, were I required to do what these men were about to do.

There was still a tremendous bustle, but the earlier sense of exhilaration had transmuted into something more concentrated, more focused and sober. Preparations were being made in earnest.

I'd finished my own, or hoped I had. A small tent for shelter from the blazing sun, packs of medical supplies, surgical kits, each equipped with a jar of wet sutures, a wad of lint for mopping up blood, and a bottle of dilute alcohol—I'd run out of salt and couldn't summon the will to badger or beg more from the commissary officer; I'd try to do it in the morning. And the emergency kit that I carried over my shoulder, no matter what.

I sat close to the fire, but despite that and in spite of the warmth of the night itself, I began to feel chilled and heavy, as though I were slowly ossifying, and only then realized how tired I was. The camp hadn't gone to sleep entirely—there was still talk around the fires, and the occasional rasp of a scythe or a sword being sharpened, but the volume had dropped. The atmosphere had settled with the sinking of the moon, even those souls most excited at the prospect of imminent battle succumbing to sleep.

"Come and lie down," I said softly to Jamie, and rose from my seat with a muffled groan. "It won't be for long, but you need *some* rest—and so do I."

"Aye, all right, but I canna be under canvas," he said, low-voiced, following me. "I feel half smothered; couldna breathe in a tent."

"Well, plenty of room outside," I said, nobly suppressing a twinge at the thought of sleeping on the ground. Fetching a couple of blankets, I followed him, yawning, a little way along the riverbank, until we found a private spot behind the scrim of willows that dragged their leaves in the water.

In fact, it was surprisingly comfortable; there was a thick growth of springy grass on which to spread the blankets, and, so close to the water, the air was at least moving, cool on my skin. I shucked out of my petticoats and took my stays completely off, with a blissful shiver of relief as the coolness stirred gently through my damp shift.

Jamie had stripped to his shirt and was rubbing his face and legs with mosquito ointment, the presence of hordes of these insects accounting for the lack of company near the water. I sat down beside him and helped myself to a small scoop of the mint-smelling grease. Mosquitoes seldom bit me, but that didn't stop them whining past my ears and poking inquisitively into my mouth and nostrils, which I found disconcerting in the extreme.

I lay back, watching as he finished his more thorough anointing. I could feel the distant approach of morning, but longed all the more for whatever brief oblivion I could get before the sun rose and all hell broke loose.

Jamie closed the tin and stretched out beside me with a low groan, black leaf shadows trembling over the paleness of his shirt. I rolled toward him just as he rolled toward me, and we met with a blind and groping kiss, smiling against each other's mouth, wriggling and squirming to find a good way of lying together. Warm as it was, I wanted to be touching him.

He wanted to be touching me, too.

"Really?" I said, astonished. "How can you possibly—you've been up for hours!"

"No, only the last minute or two," he assured me. "I'm sorry, Sassenach. I ken ye're tired and I wouldna ask—but I'm desperate." He let go of my bottom long enough to pull up his shirt, and I rather resignedly started disentangling my shift from my legs.

"I dinna mind if ye fall asleep while I'm about my business," he said in my ear, feeling his way one-handed. "I willna take long about it. I just—"

"The mosquitoes will bite your arse," I said, wiggling my own arse into a better position and opening my legs. "Hadn't I best put some—oh!"

"Oh?" he said, sounding pleased. "Well, it's all right if ye want to stay awake, of course . . ."

I pinched his buttock, hard, and he gave a small yelp, laughed, and licked my ear. The fit was a bit dry, and he fumbled for the tin of mosquito ointment.

"Are you sure—" I began dubiously. "Oh!" He was already applying the half-liquid ointment, with more enthusiasm than dexterity, but the fact of his enthusiasm was more arousing than skill might have been. Having a small amount of oil of peppermint vigorously applied to one's private parts was a rather novel sensation, too.

"Make that noise again," he said, breathing heavily in my ear. "I like it."

He was right; it didn't take long. He lay half on and half off me, panting, his heart beating slow and hard against my breast. I had my legs wrapped round him—I could feel the flutter of tiny insects on my ankles and bare feet as they swarmed, avid for his unprotected bare flesh—and didn't mean to let him go. I squeezed him close, rocking gently, slippery and tingling and . . . I didn't take long, either. My quivering legs relaxed, releasing him.

"Shall I tell you something?" I said, after a bit of mint-scented heavy breathing. "The mosquitoes won't bite your cock."

"I dinna mind if they carry me off to their lair to feed to their bairns," he murmured. "Come here, Sassenach."

I pushed damp hair out of my face and settled contentedly in the hollow of his shoulder, his arm around me. By now, I had reached that sense of accommodation with the humid atmosphere in which I stopped trying to keep track of my own body's boundaries and simply melted into sleep.

I slept without dreaming and without moving, until a touch of cramp in my left foot roused me enough to shift a little. Jamie raised his arm a bit, then replaced it as I settled again, and I became aware that he wasn't asleep.

"You . . . all right?" I murmured, thick-tongued with drowsiness.

"Aye, fine," he whispered, and his hand smoothed the hair from my cheek. "Go back to sleep, Sassenach. I'll wake ye when it's time."

My mouth was sticky, and it took a moment to locate any words.

"You need to sleep, too."

"No," he said, soft but definite. "No, I dinna mean to sleep. So close to the battle . . . I have dreams. I've had them the last three nights, and they get worse."

My own arm was lying across his midsection; at this, I reached up involuntarily, putting my hand over his heart. I knew he'd dreamed—and I had a very good idea what he'd dreamed about, from the things he'd said in his sleep. And the way he'd wakened, trembling. *"They get worse."*

"Shh," he said, and bent his head to kiss my hair. "Dinna fash, *a nighean.* I want only to lie here wi' you in my arms, to keep ye safe and watch ye sleep. I can rise then with a clear mind . . . and go to do what must be done."

66

WAR PAINT

"NESSUN DORMA." *None shall sleep.* It was a song—an aria, Brianna had called it—from an opera she knew; she'd played a part in it at her university, dressed up in Chinese robes. Ian smiled at thought of his cousin, taller than most men, striding up and down on a stage, swishing her silk robes about her; he wished he'd seen that.

He'd thought of her from the moment he'd opened the little deerskin bag that held his paints. She was a painter, Bree, and a good one. She ground her own pigments, and she'd made his red ochre for him, and the black and white from charcoal and dried clay—and made for him, too, a deep green from ground malachite, and a brilliant yellow from the gall of the buffalo she and her mother had killed; no other man had such deep colors to his paint, and he wished for a moment that Eats Turtles and some of his other Mohawk clan brothers could be with him to admire them.

The noise of the distant camp was like the singing of cicadas in the trees near a river: a buzz too loud to think through, but one that went away as you got used to it. *None shall sleep* . . . The women and children, they might sleep—but the whores surely didn't. Not tonight.

He felt a twitch at the thought, but dismissed it. Thought of Rachel, and dismissed her, too, but reluctantly.

He opened the willow-bark box of deer fat and anointed his face and chest and shoulders with it, slowly, focusing his mind. Normally he'd speak to the spirits of the earth as he did this, and then to his own particular saints, Michael and Bride. But he wasn't seeing Michael or Bride; Brianna was still faintly with him, but what he was feeling was a strong sense of his da, which was disconcerting.

It didn't seem respectful to be dismissing his own father. He stopped what he was doing and closed his eyes instead, waiting to see if maybe Da had a thing to tell him.

"I hope ye're no bringing me word of my death, aye?" he said aloud. "Because I dinna mean to die until I've lain wi' Rachel, at least."

"Well, there's a noble goal, to be sure." The dry voice was Uncle Jamie's, and Ian's eyes popped open. His uncle was standing among the trailing fronds of a river willow, dressed in nothing but his shirt.

"Out of uniform, are ye not, Uncle?" he said, though his heart had leapt in his chest like a startled deer mouse. "General Washington willna be pleased." Washington was a great stickler for proper uniform. Officers *must* be dressed suitably at all times; he said the Continentals couldn't be taken seriously as an army, did they come to the field looking and acting like a rabble in arms.

"I'm sorry to interrupt ye, Ian," his uncle said, stepping out from the willow. The moon was nearly down; he was nay more than a ghost, bare-legged in his floating sark. "Who were ye speaking to, though?"

"Oh. My da. He was just . . . there in my mind, ken? I mean, I think of him often, but it's not sae often I feel him *with* me. So I wondered had he come to tell me I'd die this day."

Jamie nodded, not seeming bothered at the thought.

"I doubt it," he said. "Ye're putting on your paint, aye? Getting ready, I mean."

"Aye, I was about to. Ye want some, too?" It was only half said in jest, and Jamie took it that way.

"I would, Ian. But I think General Washington might have me strung up by the thumbs and flogged, should I come before him wi' my troops all marshaled and me wi' war paint on."

Ian made a small sound of amusement and scooped two fingers into the dish of red ochre, which he began to rub on his chest.

"And what are ye doin' out here in your sark, then?"

"Washing," Jamie said, but in a tone indicating that that wasn't all of it. "And . . . talkin' to my ain dead."

"Mmphm. Anyone in particular?"

"My uncle Dougal, and Murtagh, him who was my godfather. They're the two I'd most want with me, in battle." Jamie made a small restless movement. "If I can, I make a wee moment to be alone before a fight. To wash, ken, and pray a bit, and then . . . to just ask if they'll bide with me as I go."

Ian thought this interesting; he hadn't known either man himself—they'd both died at Culloden—but he'd heard stories.

"Bonnie fighters," he said. "Did ye ask my da, too? To go with ye, I mean. Perhaps that's why he's about."

Jamie turned his head sharply toward Ian, surprised. Then relaxed, shaking his head.

"I never had to ask Ian Mòr," he said softly. "He was always . . . just with me." He gestured briefly to the darkness on his right.

Ian's eyes stung and his throat closed. But it was dark; it didn't matter.

He cleared his throat and held out one of the tiny dishes. "Will ye help me, Uncle Jamie?"

"Oh? Aye, surely. How d'ye want it?"

"Red across my forehead—I can do that bit. But black from the wee dots to the chin." He drew a finger across the line of tattooed dots that curved under his cheekbones. "Black's for strength, aye? It declares ye're a warrior. And yellow means ye're no afraid to die."

"Och, aye. Are ye wantin' the yellow today?"

"No." He let the smile show in his voice, and Jamie laughed.

"Mmphm." Jamie dabbed with the rabbit-foot brush, then spread the color evenly with his thumb. Ian closed his eyes, feeling strength come into him with the touch.

"Do ye usually do this alone, Ian? Seems hard, save ye've a looking glass."

"Mostly. Or sometimes we'd do it together, and a clan brother would paint ye. If it's an important thing—a big raid, say, or going to make war on someone—then the medicine man would paint us, and sing."

"Tell me ye dinna want me to sing, Ian," his uncle murmured. "I mean, I'd *try,* but . . ."

"I'll do without, thanks."

Black for the lower face, red on the forehead, and a band of the malachite green following the line of his tattoos, from ear to ear, across the bridge of his nose.

Ian peered at the small dishes of pigment; it was easy to spot the white, and he pointed to it.

"Can ye maybe draw a wee arrow, Uncle? Across my forehead." He drew a finger from left to right, showing where.

"I can, aye." Jamie's head was bent over the paint dishes, hand hovering. "Did ye not tell me once the white is for peace, though?"

"Aye, should ye be going to parley or trade, ye use a good deal of white. But it's for the mourning, too—so if ye go to avenge someone, ye'd maybe wear white."

Jamie's head came up at that, staring at him.

"This one's no for vengeance," Ian said. "It's for Flying Arrow. The dead man whose place I took, when I was adopted." He spoke as casually as he could, but he felt his uncle tighten and look down. Neither one of them was ever going to forget that day of parting, when he'd gone to the Kahnyen'kehaka, and both of them had thought it was forever. He leaned over and put a hand on Jamie's arm.

"That day, ye said to me, *'Cuimhnich,'* Uncle Jamie. And I did." *Remember.*

"So did I, Ian," Jamie said softly, and drew the arrow on his forehead, his touch like a priest's on Ash Wednesday, marking Ian with the sign of the cross. "So did we all. Is that it?"

Ian touched the green stripe gingerly, to be sure it was dry enough.

"Aye, I think so. Ken Brianna made me the paints? I was thinking of her, but then I thought I maybe shouldna take her with me that way."

He felt Jamie's breath on his skin as his uncle gave a small snort and then sat back.

"Ye always carry your women wi' ye into battle, Ian Òg. They're the root of your strength, man."

"Oh, aye?" That made sense—and was a relief to him. Still . . . "I was thinkin' it maybe wasna right to think of Rachel in such a place, though. Her being Quaker and all."

Jamie dipped his middle finger into the deer fat, then delicately into the white clay powder, and drew a wide, swooping "V" near the crest of Ian's right shoulder. Even in the dark, it showed vividly.

"White dove," he said with a nod. He sounded pleased. "There's Rachel for ye."

He wiped his fingers on the rock, then rose and stretched. Ian saw him turn to look toward the east. It was still night, but the air had changed, just in the few minutes they'd sat. His uncle's tall figure was distinct against the sky, where a little before he'd seemed part of the night.

"An hour, nay more," Jamie said. "Eat first, aye?" And, with that, turned and walked away to the stream and his own interrupted prayers.

67

REACHING FOR THINGS THAT AREN'T THERE

WILLIAM WISHED he could stop reaching for things that weren't there. A dozen times today—oftener!—he'd reached for the dagger that should have been on his belt. Once or twice, for one of his pistols. Slapped an impotent hand against his hip, missing his sword, missing the small, solid weight of his shot pouch, the swing of his cartridge box.

And now he lay sweating naked on his cot, hand slapped flat on his chest where he'd reached without thinking for the wooden rosary. The rosary that, if he'd had it, would no longer be the comfort it had been for so many years. The rosary that, if he'd had it, no longer said *"Mac"* to him. If he *did* still have it, he'd have snatched it off and thrown it into the nearest fire. That's likely what James Fraser had done with it after William had thrown the rosary in the bastard's face. But, then, Fraser wasn't the bastard here, was he?

He muttered *"Scheisse!"* and flung himself irritably over. Three feet away, Evans stirred and farted in his sleep, a sudden, muffled sound like distant cannon. On his other side, Merbling went on snoring.

Tomorrow. He'd gone to bed late after an exhausting day and would be up in an hour, maybe, but he lay wide awake, eyes so adapted to the dark that he could see the pale blur of the tent canvas overhead. No chance of sleep, he knew. Even if he'd see no action himself—and he wouldn't—the proximity of battle had him so keyed up that he could have leapt from bed and gone straight for the enemy right now, sword in hand.

There'd be a battle. Maybe not a big one, but the Rebels were yapping at their heels, and tomorrow—today—there would be a meeting. It might put paid to Washington's ambitions, though Sir Henry was firm that this was not his goal. He meant to get his army and the people under its protection to New York; that was all that mattered—though if his officers should choose to demonstrate their military superiority while doing so, he had no great objection.

William had stood at attention behind Sir Henry's chair at dinner, his back against the tent wall, listening attentively while the plans were drawn up. Had in fact had the honor of carrying the formal written orders to von Knyphausen, whose troops were to march to Middletown, while Clinton's brigade would form up at the rear, to engage the Rebels while my lord Cornwallis's escorted the baggage train on to safety. That's why he'd been so late getting to bed.

He yawned suddenly, surprising himself, and settled back, blinking. Maybe he *could* sleep a bit, after all. Thinking of dinner and orders and such mundanities as the color of von Knyphausen's nightshirt—it was pink silk, with purple pansies embroidered round the neck—rather than the oncoming battle had calmed his mind amazingly. Distraction. That's what he needed.

Worth a try, he supposed. . . . He squirmed into the most comfortable attitude he could manage, closed his eyes, and began mentally extracting the square roots of numbers greater than one hundred.

He'd got to the square root of 117 and was muzzily groping for the product of 12 and 6 when he felt the sudden stir of air on his damp skin. He sighed and opened his eyes, thinking that Merbling had got up for a piss, but it wasn't Merbling. A dark figure stood just inside the tent flap. The flap wasn't closed, and the figure was clearly visible against the faint glow from the banked campfires outside. A girl.

He sat up fast, groping one-handed for the shirt he'd tossed to the foot of his cot.

"What the devil are you doing here?" he whispered, as softly as he could.

She'd been hovering, uncertain. But hearing him speak, she came straight for him, and next thing he knew, her hands were on his shoulders, her hair brushing his face. He put up his own hands in reflex and found that she was in her shift, her breasts free and warm under it, a few inches from his face.

She pulled back, and in what seemed like the same motion, skimmed the shift off over her head, shook out her hair, and straddled him, her moist round thighs pressing his.

"Get off!" He grabbed her by the arms, pushing her away. Merbling stopped snoring. Evans's bedclothes rustled.

William stood up, snatched up her shift and his shirt, and, taking her by the arm, marched her out of the tent, as quietly as he could.

"What the devil do you think you're doing? Here, put that on!" He thrust the shift unceremoniously into her arms and hastily pulled his shirt on. They were not in full view of anyone, but might be at any moment.

Her head emerged from the shift like a flower popping out of a snowbank. A rather angry flower.

"Well, what do you *think* I was doing?" she said. She pulled her hair free of the shift and fluffed it violently. "I was trying to do you a kindness!"

"A—what?"

"You're going to fight tomorrow, aren't you?" There was enough light to see the shine of her eyes as she glared at him. "Soldiers always want to fuck before a fight! They need it."

He rubbed a hand hard over his face, palm rasping on his sprouting whiskers, then took a deep breath.

"I see. Yes. Very kind of you." He suddenly wanted to laugh. He also—very suddenly—wanted to take advantage of her offer. But not enough to do it with Merbling on one side and Evans on the other, ears flapping.

"I'm not going to fight tomorrow," he said, and the pang it caused him to say that out loud startled him.

"You're not? Why not?" She sounded startled, too, and more than a little disapproving.

"It's a long story," he said, struggling for patience. "And it's not your business. Now, look. I appreciate the thought, but I told you: you're not a whore, at least not for the time being. And you're not *my* whore." Though his imagination was busy with images of what might have happened had she stolen into his cot and taken hold of him before he was fully awake . . . He put the thought firmly aside and, taking her by the shoulders, turned her round.

"Go back to your own bed now," he said, but couldn't stop himself from patting her very nice arse in farewell. She turned her head and glared at him over her shoulder.

"Coward!" she said. "A man that won't fuck won't fight."

"What?" For an instant, he didn't think she'd really said it, but she had.

"You heard me. Good—fucking—night!"

He reached her in two strides, seized her shoulder, and whirled her round to face him.

"And who gave you that bit of wisdom, may I ask? Your good friend Captain Harkness?" He wasn't truly angry, but the shock of her unexpected arrival was still reverberating in his blood and he *was* annoyed. "Did I save you from buggery so you could throw my circumstances in my face?"

Her chin drew back, and she breathed hard, but not in apparent distress.

"What circumstances?" she demanded.

"I told you—bloody hell. Do you know what the Convention army is?"

"No."

"Well, that's the long story, and I'm not telling you it standing in my shirt in the middle of camp. Now, bugger off and take care of your sister and the lads. That's your job; I'll take care of myself."

She exhaled sharply, with a *puh!* sound.

"Doubtless you *will,*" she said, with the maximum of sarcasm and a pointed glance at his cock, which was poking absurdly at his shirt, making its own urgent preferences known.

"Scheisse," he said again, briefly, then grabbed her in a bear hug that pressed her body against his all the way down and kissed her. She struggled, but after the first moment he realized that the struggle was not meant to procure her release but to provoke him further. He tightened his grip until she stopped, but didn't quit kissing her for some time thereafter.

He finally let go, panting and bedewed with perspiration; the air was like breathing hot tar. She was panting, too. He could take her. Wanted to. Push her down on her knees in the grass beside the tent, pull up her shift, and have her from behind—it wouldn't take more than seconds.

"No," he said, and wiped his mouth on the back of his hand. "No," he said again, more positively. Every nerve in his body wanted her, and had he been sixteen, it would have been long over by this time. But he wasn't, and he had just enough self-control to turn her round again. He gripped her by scruff and buttock to keep her from turning back and held her immobile.

"When we get to New York," he whispered, bending to speak in her ear, "I'll think again."

She stiffened, her buttock rounding hard in his hand, but didn't pull away or try to bite him, which he'd half-expected.

"Why?" she said, in a calm voice.

"That's a long story, too," he said. "Good night, Jane." And, releasing her, stalked away into the dark. Nearby, the drums of reveille began.

PART FOUR

Day of Battle

68

GO OUT IN DARKNESS

IAN HAD BEEN OVER the land briefly the day before, scouting. "And a good thing, too," he said, under his breath. It was the dark of the moon, and he must go canny and keep the road. He wasn't risking his horse's legs over the rough land before he had to, and Bride grant him the sky would be fully light by then.

Still, he was glad of the dark, and the solitude. Not that the land was still; the woods lived at night, and many things came out in the strange dawn hour when the light began to swell. But neither the rustle of hares and voles nor the sleepy call of waking birds demanded his notice or took any notice of him. He had finished his own prayers after Uncle Jamie left him, then departed alone in silence, and the peace of his preparations was still on him.

When he had lived with the Mohawk—particularly when things had gone wrong with Emily—he would leave the longhouse for days, hunting alone with Rollo, until the wilderness had eased his spirit enough to go back, strengthened. He glanced down by reflex, but Rollo had been left behind with Rachel. The wound from the deadfall trap was clean; Auntie Claire had put something on it that helped—but he wouldn't have let Rollo come to a battle like this one offered to be, even had he been whole and a good deal younger than he was.

There was no doubt of the coming battle. He could smell it. His body was rising toward the fight; he could feel the tingling of it—but he treasured this momentary stillness the more for that.

"Won't last long, mind," he said softly to the horse, who

ignored him. He touched the white dove on his shoulder and rode on, still quiet but not alone.

THE MEN HAD lain on their arms all night, by Sir Henry's orders. While one didn't actually lie *on* a musket and cartridge box, there was something about sleeping with a gun touching your body that kept you alert, ready to rouse from sleep in nothing flat.

William had no arms to lie on, and hadn't needed rousing, as he hadn't slept, but was no less alert for the lack. He wouldn't be fighting, and deeply regretted that—but he would be out in it, by God.

The camp was a-bustle, drums rattling up and down the aisles of tents, summoning the soldiers, and the air was full of the smells of baking bread, pork, and hot pease porridge.

There was no visible sign of dawn yet, but he could feel the sun there, just below the horizon, rising with the slow inevitability of its daily dominion. The thought reminded him, vividly, of the whale he had seen on the voyage to America: a dark shadow below the ship's side, easily dismissed as the change of light on the waves—and then, slowly, the growing bulk, the realization and the breathless wonder of seeing it rise, so close, so huge—and suddenly *there.*

He fastened his garters and tugged them tight before buckling his knee bands and pulling on his Hessian boots. At least he had his gorget back, to lend a touch of ceremony to the mundane task of getting dressed. The gorget, of course, reminded him of Jane—was he ever going to be able to wear it *without* thinking of the damned girl?—and of recent events.

He'd regretted not accepting her offer, and still did. He could still smell her scent, musky and soft, like putting his face in thick fur. Her remark still rankled, too, and he snorted, settling his coat on his shoulders. Perhaps he'd think again *before* they reached New York.

These idle thoughts were interrupted by the appearance of another of Sir Henry's aides, Captain Crosbie, who popped his head through the tent flap, clearly in a great flurry.

"Oh, there you are, Ellesmere. Hoped I'd catch you—here."

He tossed a folded note in William's general direction and vanished.

William snorted again and picked it up off the ground. Evans and Merbling had both left, they having actual troops to inspect and command; he envied them bitterly.

It was from General Sir Henry Clinton, and hit him in the stomach like a blow: *. . . in view of your peculiar status, I think it best that you remain with the clerical staff today . . .*

"Stercus!" he said, finding German insufficient to his feelings. *"Excrementum obscaenum! Filius mulieris prostabilis!"*

His chest was tight, blood was pounding in his ears, and he wanted to hit something. It would be useless to appeal to Sir Henry, he knew that much. But to spend the day essentially kicking his heels in the clerks' tent—for what was there for him to *do,* if he wasn't allowed to carry dispatches or even do the lowly but necessary work of shepherding the camp followers and Loyalists? What—was he to fetch the clerks' dinner in, or hold a torch in each hand when it got dark, like a fucking candelabra?

He was about to crumple the note into a wad, when yet another unwelcome head intruded itself, followed by an elegant body: Captain André, dressed for battle, sword at his side and pistols in his belt. William eyed him with dislike, though in fact he was an amiable fellow.

"Oh, there you are, Ellesmere," André said, pleased. "Hoped you hadn't gone off yet. I need you to run me a dispatch, quickly. To Colonel Tarleton—with the British Legion, the new Provincials, green chaps—you know him?"

"I do, yes." William accepted the sealed dispatch, feeling odd. "Certainly, Captain."

"Good man." André smiled and squeezed his shoulder, then strode out, ebullient with the promise of imminent action.

William drew a deep breath, carefully folded Sir Henry's note back into its original shape, and placed it on his cot. Who was to say that he hadn't met André first and, owing to the urgency of his request, left immediately, without reading Sir Henry's note?

He doubted he'd be missed, in any case.

69

SPARROW-FART

IT WAS PERHAPS four o'clock ack emma. Or before sparrow-fart, as the British armed forces of my own time used to put it. That sense of temporal dislocation was back again, memories of another war coming like a sudden fog between me and my work, then disappearing in an instant, leaving the present sharp and vivid as Kodachrome. The army was moving.

No fog obscured Jamie. He was big and solid, his outlines clearly visible against the shredding night. I was awake and alert, dressed and ready, but the chill of sleep still lay upon me, making my fingers clumsy. I could feel his warmth and drew close to him, as I might to a campfire. He was leading Clarence, who was even warmer, though much less alert, ears sagging in sleepy annoyance.

"You'll have Clarence," Jamie told me, putting the mule's reins in my hand. "And these, to make sure ye keep him, if ye should find yourself on your own." "These" were a heavy pair of horse pistols, holstered and strung on a thick leather belt that also held a shot bag and powder horn.

"Thank you," I said, swallowing as I wrapped the reins around a sapling in order to belt the pistols on. The guns were amazingly heavy—but I wouldn't deny that the weight of them on my hips was amazingly comforting, too.

"All right," I said, glancing toward the tent where John was. "What about—"

"I've seen to that," he said, cutting me off. "Gather the rest of your things, Sassenach; I've nay more than a quarter hour, at most, and I need ye with me when we go."

I watched him stride off into the mêlée, tall and resolute, and wondered—as I had so often before—*Will it be today?*

Will this be the last sight I remember of him? I stood very still, watching as hard as I could.

When I'd lost him the first time, before Culloden, I'd remembered. Every moment of our last night together. Tiny things would come back to me through the years: the taste of salt on his temple and the curve of his skull as I cupped his head; the soft fine hair at the base of his neck, thick and damp in my fingers . . . the sudden, magical well of his blood in dawning light when I'd cut his hand and marked him forever as my own. Those things had kept him by me.

And when I'd lost him this time, to the sea, I'd remembered the sense of him beside me, warm and solid in my bed, and the rhythm of his breathing. The light across the bones of his face in moonlight and the flush of his skin in the rising sun. I could hear him breathe when I lay in bed alone in my room at Chestnut Street—slow, regular, never stopping—even though I knew it *had* stopped. The sound would comfort me, then drive me mad with the knowledge of loss, so I pulled the pillow hard over my head in a futile attempt to shut it out—only to emerge into the night of the room, thick with woodsmoke and candle wax and vanished light, and be comforted to hear it once more.

If this time—but he had turned, quite suddenly, as though I'd called his name. He came swiftly up to me, grasped me by the arms, and said in a low, strong voice, "It willna be today, either."

Then he put his arms around me and drew me up on tiptoe into a deep, soft kiss. I heard brief cheers from a few of the men nearby, but it didn't matter. Even if it should be today, I would remember.

JAMIE STRODE toward his waiting companies, loosely assembled near the river. The breath of the water and the mist rising from it comforted him, keeping him wrapped for a little while longer in the peace of the night and the deep sense of his kin, there at his shoulder. He'd told Ian Mòr to stay with Ian Òg, as was right, but had the odd sense that there were three men with him, still.

He'd need the strength of his dead. Three hundred men, and

he'd known them for only days. Always before, when he'd taken men into battle, they were men of his blood, of his clan, men who knew him, trusted him—as he knew and trusted them. These men were strangers to him, and yet their lives were in his hands.

He wasn't worried by their lack of training; they were rough and undisciplined, a mere rabble by contrast with the Continental regulars who'd drilled all winter under von Steuben—the thought of the little barrel-shaped Prussian made him smile—but his troops had always been this kind of men: farmers and hunters, pulled from their daily occupations, armed with scythes and hoes as often as with muskets or swords. They'd fight like fiends for him—with him—if they trusted him.

"How is it, then, Reverend?" he said softly to the minister, who had just blessed his flock of volunteers and was hunched among them in his black coat, arms still half spread like a scarecrow protecting his misty field at dawn. The man's face, always rather stern in aspect, lightened upon seeing him, and he realized that the sky itself had begun to glow.

"All well, sir," Woodsworth said gruffly. "We are ready." He didn't, thank God, mention Bertram Armstrong.

"Good," said Jamie, smiling from face to face, and seeing them all lighten in turn as the dawn touched them. "Mr. Whelan, Mr. Maddox, Mr. Hebden—ye're all well in yourselves this morning, I hope?"

"We are," they murmured, looking shyly gratified that he knew their names. He wished he knew them all, but had had to do the best he could, learning the names and faces of a handful of men in each company. It might give them the illusion that he did know every man by name—he hoped so; they needed to know he cared for them.

"Ready, sir." It was Captain Craddock, one of his three captains, stiff and self-conscious with the importance of the occasion, and Judah Bixby and Lewis Orden, two of Jamie's lieutenants, behind him. Bixby was no more than twenty, Orden maybe a year older; they could barely repress their excitement, and he smiled at them, feeling their joy in their young manhood echo in his own blood.

There were some *very* young men among the militia, he noticed. A couple of half-grown boys, tall and spindly as cornstalks—who were they? Oh, yes, Craddock's sons. He remembered now; their mother had died only a month ago, and so they had come with their father into the militia.

God, let me bring them back safe! he prayed.

And felt—actually felt—a hand rest briefly on his shoulder, and knew who the third man was who walked with him.

Taing, Da, he thought, and blinked, raising his face so the tears in his eyes might be thought due to the brightness of the growing light.

I TIED CLARENCE to a picquet and made my way back into the tent, less troubled, though still keyed up. Whatever was going to happen was going to happen fast, and likely with little warning. Fergus and Germain had gone to find breakfast; I hoped they would show up before I had to leave—because when the time came, I would have to leave, no matter my reservations about abandoning a patient. Any patient.

This particular patient was lying on his back, under the lantern, his working eye half closed, singing to himself in German. He desisted when I came in, and turned his head to see who it was, blinking at sight of my armament.

"Are we expecting imminent invasion and capture?" he asked, sitting up.

"Lie back down. No, this is Jamie being provident." I touched one of the pistols gingerly. "I don't know if they're loaded yet."

"Certainly they are. The man is nothing if not thorough." He eased himself back down, groaning slightly.

"You think you know him awfully well, don't you?" I asked, with an edge that rather surprised me.

"Yes, I do," he answered promptly. He smiled slightly at my expression. "Not nearly as well as you do in some matters, I'm sure—but perhaps better in others. We are both soldiers." He tilted his head, indicating the military racket going on outside.

"If you know him that well," I said, nettled, "you should have known better than to say whatever you did say to him."

"Ah." The smile disappeared and he looked up at the canvas overhead in contemplation. "I did. Know better. I just said it anyway."

"Ah," I replied, and sat down next to the pile of bags and supplies that had made it thus far. Much of this would have to be abandoned. I could take a good deal in Clarence's packs and saddlebags, but not everything. The army had been instructed to abandon almost everything they carried, save weapons and canteens, in the interests of speed.

"Did he tell you what it was?" John asked after a moment, his voice elaborately casual.

"What you said? No, but I could very likely guess." I compressed my lips and didn't look at him, instead lining up bottles on top of a chest. I'd got salt from the innkeeper—not without trouble—and had made up a couple of bottles of crude saline solution, and there was the alcohol . . . I picked up the candle and began to dribble wax carefully over the corks, lest they loosen and the bottles discharge their contents along the way.

I didn't want to pursue the history of John's eye any further. Other considerations aside, any discussion might lead a little too close to Wentworth Prison for comfort. However close a friend Jamie might have considered John during the last few years, I was positive that he'd never told John about Black Jack Randall and what had happened at Wentworth. He'd told his brother-in-law Ian, many years ago—and therefore Jenny must know, too, though I doubted she'd ever spoken of it to Jamie—but no one else.

John would likely assume that Jamie had hit him purely from revulsion at something overtly sexual from John—or from jealousy over me. It was perhaps not quite fair to let him think that—but fairness didn't come into it.

Still, I regretted the trouble between them. Beyond whatever personal awkwardness I found in the present situation, I knew how much John's friendship had meant to Jamie—and vice versa. And while I was more than relieved not to be married to John anymore, I did care for him.

And—while the noise and movement all around urged me to forget everything else but the urgency of departure—I couldn't forget that this might be the last time I ever saw John, too.

I sighed and began to wrap the waxed bottles in towels. I should add whatever I could find room for from my Kingsessing haul, but . . .

"Don't be troubled, my dear," John said gently. "You know it will all come right—provided that we all live long enough."

I gave him a marked look and nodded toward the tent flap, where the clatter and clash of a military camp on the verge of movement was escalating.

"Well, *you'll* likely survive," I said. "Unless you say the wrong thing to Jamie before we leave and he really does break your neck this time."

He glanced—as briefly as possible—toward the pale shaft of dust-filled light, and grimaced.

"You've never had to do it, have you?" I said, seeing his face. "Sit and wait through a battle, wondering if someone you care for will come back."

"Not with regard to anyone other than myself, no," he replied, but I could see that the remark had gone home. He *hadn't* thought of that, and he didn't like the thought one bit. *Welcome to the club,* I thought sardonically.

"Do you think they'll catch Clinton?" I asked, after a moment's silence. He shrugged, almost irritably.

"How should I know? I haven't the slightest idea where Clinton's troops are—I have no idea where Washington is, or where we are, for that matter."

"General Washington would be about thirty yards that way," I said, picking up a basket of bandages and lint, and nodding toward where I'd last seen the commander. "And I would be surprised if General Clinton is very much farther off."

"Oh? And why is that, madam?" he asked, now half amused.

"Because the order came down an hour ago to jettison all unnecessary supplies—though I don't know if he actually said 'jettison,' come to think; that may not be a word in common use now. That's why we were inspecting the men, when we found you—to leave back any who aren't capable of a long forced march on short rations, should that be necessary. Apparently it is.

"But you know what's happening," I added, watching him. "*I* can hear it. You surely can." Anyone with ears or eyes could sense the nervous excitement in camp, see the hasty preparations being made, the small fights and outbreaks of cursing as men got in each other's way, the bawling of officers, only a hair short of eye-rolling, horn-tossing violence, the braying of mules—I hoped no one would steal Clarence before I got back to him.

John nodded, silent. I could see him turning the situation over in his mind, along with the obvious implications.

"Yes, 'jettison' is certainly a word in common use," he said absently. "Though you hear it more in terms of sea cargo. But—" He jerked a little, realizing the further implications of what I'd said, and stared hard at me with his uncovered eye.

"Don't do that," I said mildly. "You'll hurt the other one. And what I am or am not isn't important just now, is it?"

"No," he muttered, and shut the eye for a moment, then opened it, staring upward at the canvas overhead. Dawn was coming; the yellowed canvas was beginning to glow, and the air around us was thick with dust and the odor of dried sweat.

"I know very little that would be of interest to General Washington," he said, "and I would be surprised if he didn't know that little already. I am not a serving officer—or . . . well, I wasn't, until my bloody brother decided to reenter me on the rolls of his bloody regiment. Do you know, he nearly got me *hanged*?"

"No, but it sounds extremely like him," I said, laughing despite my disquiet.

"What do you—oh, God. You've *met* Hal?" He'd reared up on one elbow, blinking at me.

"I have," I assured him. "Lie down, and I'll tell you." Neither of us was going anywhere for a few minutes at least, and I was able to give him the entire story of my adventures with Hal in Philadelphia, while I wound up bandages, put my medical box in good order, and extracted what I thought the most important items from the supplies I'd brought. In an emergency, I might be reduced to what I could carry on my back at a dead run, and I made up a small rucksack with that contingency in mind, whilst regaling John with my opinions of his brother.

"Jesus, if he thinks he's a chance in hell of preventing Dorothea from marrying Dr. Hunter . . . I believe I'd pay good money to overhear the conversation when he meets Denzell," he remarked. "Who would you bet on—given that Hal hasn't got a regiment at his back to enforce his opinions?"

"He likely *has* met him by now. As to odds—Denzell, three to two," I said, after a moment's consideration. "He's got not only God but love—and Dorothea—on his side, and I do think that will outweigh even Hal's brand of . . . of . . . autocratic conviction?"

"I'd call it undiluted bastardliness, myself, but, then, I'm his brother. I'm allowed liberties."

The sound of voices speaking French announced the arrival of Fergus and Germain, and I stood up abruptly.

"I may not—" I began, but he raised a hand, stopping me.

"If not, then goodbye, my dear," he said softly. "And good luck."

70

A SINGLE LOUSE

IT WAS BARELY AN hour past dawn and it would doubtless be another beastly hot day, but for the moment the air was still fresh and both William and Goth were happy. He threaded his way through the boiling mass of men, horses, limbers, and the other impedimenta of war, quietly whistling "The King Enjoys His Own Again."

The baggage wagons were already being readied; a great dust cloud rose, roiling and shot through with gold from the rising sun, from the teamsters' park near von Knyphausen's division, encamped a quarter mile away, on the other side of Middletown. They'd be off directly, heading for Sandy Hook—and Jane, Fanny, Zeb, and Colenso with them, he sincerely hoped. A brief sensory recollection of the skin inside Jane's thighs sparked through his mind and he stopped whistling for an instant, but then shook it out of his head. Work to be done!

No one quite knew where the new British Legion was, though it was assumed to be somewhere in the vicinity of Clinton's division, it being one of his personal regiments, raised only a month ago in New York. That might be chancy, but William was quite willing to wager that he could evade Sir Henry's notice, under the conditions.

"Like picking one louse out of a Frenchie's wig," he murmured, and patted Goth's neck. The horse was fresh and frisky, couldn't wait to reach the open road and break into a gallop. Clinton's division was holding the rear guard at Middletown—enough distance to take the edge off Goth's bounciness. First, though, they'd have to get through the spreading mass of camp followers, struggling out of sleep into a desperate haste. He kept Goth on a short rein, lest he trample a child—there were dozens of the little buggers, swarming over the ground like locusts.

Glancing up from the ground, he caught sight of a familiar form, standing in line for bread, and his heart gave a small leap of pleasure. Anne Endicott, dressed for day but without her cap, dark hair in a thick plait down her back. The sight of it gave him a *frisson* of intimacy, and he barely stopped himself calling out to her. Time enough, after the fight.

71

FOLIE À TROIS

FERGUS HAD BROUGHT me a sausage roll and a cannikin of coffee—real coffee, for a wonder.

"Milord will send for you shortly," he said, handing these over.

"Is he nearly ready?" The food was warm and fresh—and I knew it might be the last I got for some time—but I barely tasted it. "Have I time to dress Lord John's eye again?" The pervading air of haste was clearly perceptible to me, and my skin had started twitching as though I were being attacked by ants.

"I will go and see, milady. Germain?" Fergus tilted his head toward the tent flap, beckoning Germain to go with him.

But Germain, out of what might have been either loyalty to John or fear of finding himself alone with Jamie—who had rather plainly meant what he said regarding the future of Germain's arse—wanted to stay in the tent.

"I'll be fine," John assured him. "Go with your father." He was still pale and sweating, but his jaw and hands had relaxed; he wasn't in severe pain.

"Yes, he will be fine," I said to Germain, but nodded to Fergus, who went out without further comment. "Fetch me some fresh lint, will you? Then you can come and help me while his lordship rests. As for you—" I turned to John. "You lie flat, keep your eye closed, and bloody stay out of trouble, if such a thing is possible."

He swiveled his good eye in my direction, wincing slightly as the movement pulled on the bad one.

"Are you accusing *me* of causing the imbroglio that resulted in my injury, madam? Because I distinctly recall your playing some minor role in its origins." He sounded rather cross.

"I had nothing whatever to do with your ending up *here,*" I said firmly, though I could feel my cheeks flush. "Germain, have you found the lint?"

"Will the honey not draw flies, Grannie?" Germain handed me the requested lint but stood by the cot, frowning down at its occupant. "Ken what they say, aye? Ye catch more flies wi' honey than ye do wi' vinegar. Ye couldna pour vinegar on him, I suppose?"

"Hmmm." He had a point. We were no great distance from the teamsters; I could hear mules snorting and braying, and newly wakened flies, still heavy with sleep, had been buzzing round my ears even as I unwrapped the old bandage. "Right. Not vinegar, but mint might help. Find the tin with the fleur-de-lis, then, and rub ointment on his lordship's face and hands—*don't* get it in his eyes. Then bring the small box—"

"I am certainly capable of rubbing ointment on myself," John interrupted, and extended a hand to Germain. "Here, give it to me."

"Lie still," I said, rather cross myself. "As for what you're capable of, I shudder to think." I had set a small dish of honey to warm near the lantern; I filled my syringe and injected the honey around his bad eye, made a small pad of lint, thumbed it gently into his eye socket, and bound a clean length of gauze round his head to hold it in place, thinking as I did so.

"Germain . . . go and fill the canteen, will you?" It was half full already, but he obligingly took it and went, leaving me alone with John.

"Shall I leave Germain with you?" I asked, stuffing the last few items into my first-aid kit. "And Fergus?" I added hesitantly.

"No," he said, slightly startled. "What for?"

"Well . . . protection. In case Monsieur Beauchamp should come back, I mean." I didn't trust Percy in the slightest. I was also dubious about putting Fergus in close proximity to him, but it had occurred to me that perhaps John might be some protection to *him*.

"Ah." He closed his good eye for a moment, then opened it again. "Now, *that* imbroglio is indeed of my own making," he said ruefully. "But while Germain is admittedly a formidable presence, I shan't need a bodyguard. I rather doubt that Percy intends either to assault or to kidnap me."

"Do you . . . care for him?" I asked curiously.

"Is it your business if I do?" he replied evenly.

I flushed more deeply, but took a few breaths before answering.

"Yes," I said at last. "Yes, I rather think it is. Whatever my role in the origins of this . . . this . . . er . . ."

"Folie à trois?" he suggested, and I laughed. I'd told him what a *folie à deux* was, with reference to Mrs. Figg's and the laundress's shared obsession with starched drawers.

"That will do. But, yes, it is my business—on Jamie's behalf, if not yours." But it was on his behalf, as well. The shock and rush of recent events had prevented my thinking through the situation, but I was quite sure that Jamie had. And now that I was thoroughly awake and undistracted by my own affairs, my thoughts were catching up with uncomfortable rapidity.

"Do you recall a Captain André?" I asked abruptly. "John André. He was at the Mischianza."

"I may have lost a few things over the course of the last few days," he said, with some acerbity, "but neither my memory nor my wits. Yet," he added, in a marked manner. "Of course I know him. A very sociable and artistic young man; he was invited everywhere in Philadelphia. He's on General Clinton's staff."

"Did you know that he's also a spy?" My heart was thumping in my ears, and my stays felt suddenly too tight. Was I about to do something hideously irrevocable?

He blinked, obviously startled.

"No. Why on earth should you think that?" And, a half second later, "And why the devil would you tell me about it, if you do think so?"

"Because," I said, as evenly as I could, "he'll be caught doing it, in another year or two. He'll be found behind the American lines, in civilian clothes, with incriminating documents on his person. And the Americans will hang him."

The words hung in the air between us, visible as though they were written in black smoke. John opened his mouth, then shut it again, clearly nonplussed.

I could hear all the sounds of the camp around us: talk, occasional shouting, and the sounds of horses and mules, the beat of a drum in the distance, summoning men to . . . what? Someone at close range practicing a fife, the shrill note breaking in the same place each time. The constant rumble and shriek of the grinding wheel, frenziedly sharpening metal for the last time. And the increasing buzz of flies.

They were drifting into the tent in small clouds of carnivory; two of them landed on John's forehead, to be irritably brushed away. The tin of bug repellent lay on the cot where Germain had put it down; I reached for it.

"No," he said, rather sharply, and took it from my hand. "I can—I—don't touch me, if you please." His hand trembled, and he had a moment's difficulty in getting the lid off, but I didn't help him. I'd gone cold to the fingertips, in spite of the stifling atmosphere in the tent.

He'd surrendered to Jamie personally, given his parole. It would be Jamie who would eventually have to hand him over to General Washington. Would *have* to; too many people had seen the incident, knew where John was—and, by this time, what he was.

John didn't sit up, but managed to thumb a glob of the mentholated grease from the tin and rub it on his face and neck.

"You didn't have anything in your clothes," I ventured, with a faint hope. "No incriminating documents, I mean."

"I had my warrant of commission in my pocket when the Rebel militia took me, outside Philadelphia," he said, but spoke in an abstract tone, as though it didn't really matter. He rubbed ointment briskly over his hands and wrists. "Not proof of spying in itself—but certainly proof that I was a British officer, out of uniform and arguably behind the American lines at the time. Don't talk anymore, my dear; it's very dangerous."

He snapped the lid onto the tin and held it out to me.

"You'd better go," he said, looking me in the eye and speaking in a low voice. "You must not be found alone with me."

"Grannie?" Germain pushed back the tent flap, red as a beet under his shaggy bangs. "Grannie! Come quick! *Papa* says *Grand-père* wants you!"

He disappeared and I hastily snatched up my equipment, bedizening myself with bags and boxes. I made for the tent flap, but paused for an instant, turning to John.

"I should have asked—does he care for *you*?" I said.

He shut his good eye and his lips compressed for a moment.

"I hope not," he said.

I HURRIED AFTER Germain with my medical satchel full of gurgling bottles slung over my shoulder, a small box of extra instruments and sutures under my arm, Clarence's reins in hand, and a mind so agitated I could hardly see where I was going.

I realized now that I hadn't been telling John anything he didn't know. Well . . . bar the account of Captain André's future fate, and while that was chilling enough, it wasn't of direct importance at the moment.

He'd stopped me speaking, because he'd already known how much danger he stood in—and what the effects were likely to be on Jamie, and on me. *"You must not be found alone with me."*

Because I'd been at one point his wife, he meant. That's what he'd been thinking but hadn't wanted to tell me, until I forced the issue.

If anything happened—well, be blunt about it: if he broke his parole and escaped—I'd very likely be suspected of having a hand in it, but the suspicion would be a great deal more pronounced if anyone could testify to having seen us in private conversation. And Jamie would be suspected of complicity at worst, or, at best, of having a wife who was disloyal both to him and to the cause of independence. . . . I could easily end up in a military prison. So might Jamie.

But if John *didn't* escape . . . or escaped and was recaptured . . .

But the road lay before me, and Jamie was there on his horse, holding the reins of my mare. And it was Jamie with whom I'd cross the Rubicon today—not John.

THE MARQUIS de La Fayette was waiting for them at the rendezvous, face flushed and eyes bright with anticipation. Jamie couldn't help smiling at sight of the young Frenchman, got up regardless in a glorious uniform with red silk facings. He wasn't inexperienced, though, despite his youth and his very obvious Frenchness. He'd told Jamie about the battle at Brandywine Creek a year before, where he'd been wounded in the leg, and how Washington had insisted that he lie beside him and wrapped him in his own cloak. Gilbert idolized Washington, who had no sons of his own, and who clearly felt a deep affection for the wee marquis.

Jamie glanced at Claire, to see if she was appreciating La Fayette's stylish toilette, but her gaze was fixed—with a small frown—on a group of men in the far distance, beyond the Continental regulars drawn up in orderly formations. She wasn't wearing her spectacles; he could see easily at a distance and half-stood in his stirrups to look.

"General Washington and Charles Lee," he told her, sitting back in the saddle. La Fayette, spotting them, as well, swung himself into his own saddle and rode toward the senior officers. "I suppose I'd best go join them. D'ye see Denzell Hunter yet?" He had it in mind to confide Claire to Hunter's care; he didn't mean her to be wandering the battlefield—if there was one—on her own, no matter how helpful she might be there, and was wary of leaving her alone.

Hunter was driving his wagon, though, and that couldn't keep up with the marching men. Clouds of dust rose in the air, stirred by thousands of eager feet; it tickled in his chest, and he coughed.

"No," she said. "Don't worry." And she smiled at him,

brave, though her face was pale despite the heat, and he could feel the flutter of her fear in his own wame. "Are you all right?" She always looked at him in that searching way when he set out to a fight, as though committing his face to memory in case he was killed. He kent why she did it, but it made him feel strange—and he was already unsettled this morning.

"Aye, fine," he said, and taking her hand, kissed it. He should have spurred up and gone, but lingered for a moment, loath to let go.

"Did you—" she began, and then stopped abruptly.

"Put on clean drawers? Aye, though it's like to be wasted effort, ken, when the guns start firin'." It was a feeble enough jest, but she laughed, and he felt better.

"Did I what?" he prompted, but she shook her head.

"Never mind. You don't need anything else to think of now. Just—be careful, will you?" She swallowed visibly, and his heart turned over.

"I will," he said, and took up the reins but looked back over his shoulder, in case Young Ian should be coming. She was safe enough, in the midst of the forming companies, but he'd still be happier with someone to look after her. And if he told her that, she'd likely—

"There's Ian!" she exclaimed, squinting to see. "What's the matter with his horse, I wonder?"

He looked where she was looking and saw the cause at once. His nephew was afoot, leading the halting horse, and both of them were looking crankit.

"Lame," he said. "And badly lamed, too. What's amiss, Ian?" he called.

"Stepped on summat sharp, coming up the bank, and cracked his hoof, right down into the quick." Ian ran a hand down the horse's leg and the animal all but leaned on him, picking up its unshod hoof at once. Sure enough, the crack was visible, and deep enough to make Jamie wince in sympathy. Like having a toenail torn off, he supposed, and having to walk a distance with it.

"Take my horse, Ian," Claire said, and slid off in a flurry of petticoats. "I can ride Clarence. No need for me to be fast, after all."

"Aye, all right," Jamie said, though a bit reluctant. Her mare was a good one, and Ian had to have a mount. "Shift the saddles, then, and, Ian, watch out for Dr. Hunter. Dinna leave your auntie 'til he comes, aye? Goodbye, Sassenach; I'll see ye later in the day." He could wait no longer, and nudged his horse away into the crowd.

Other officers had gathered around Washington; he'd barely be in time. But it wasn't the risk of being conspicuously late that cramped his bowels. It was guilt.

He ought to have reported John Grey's arrest at once. He kent that fine, but had delayed, hoping . . . hoping what? That the ridiculous situation would somehow evaporate? If he *had* reported it, Washington would have had Grey taken into custody and locked up somewhere—or hanged him out of hand, as an example. He didn't think that likely, but the possibility had been enough to keep him from saying anything, counting on the chaos of the impending exodus to keep anyone from noticing.

But what was eating at his insides now was not guilt over duty deferred, or even over exposing Claire to danger by keeping the wee sodomite in his own tent instead of turning him over. It was the fact that he had not thought to revoke Grey's parole this morning when he left. If he had, Grey might easily have escaped in the confusion of leaving, and even if there had been trouble later over it . . . John Grey would be safe.

But it was too late, and with a brief prayer for the soul of Lord John Grey, he reined up beside the Marquis de La Fayette and bowed to General Washington.

72

MORASSES AND IMBROGLIOS

THERE WERE THREE CREEKS running through the land, cutting it up. Where the earth was soft, the water had cut deep and the creek ran at the bottom of a steep ravine, the banks of it thick with saplings and underbrush. A farmer he'd spoken to while scouting the day before had told him the names of them—Dividing Brook, Spotswood Middle Brook, and Spotswood North Brook—but Ian wasn't at all sure he kent for sure which this one was.

The ground here was wide and low; the creek ran out into a sunken, marshy sort of place, and he turned away; bad footing for either man or horse. One of the farmers had called the ravines "morasses," and he thought that a good word. He looked up the creek, searching for good watering places, but the ravine fell too steeply. A man could make shift to scramble down to the water, maybe, but not horses or mules.

Ian felt them before he saw them. The sense of a hunting animal, lying concealed in the wood, waiting for prey to come down to drink. He turned his horse sharply and rode along the creek bank, watching the trees on the other side.

Movement, a horse's head tossing against flies. A glimpse of a face—faces—painted, like his own.

A thrill of alarm shot up his spine and instinct flattened him against the horse's neck, as the arrow whizzed over his head. It stuck, quivering, in a nearby sycamore.

He straightened, his own bow in hand, nocked an arrow in the same movement, and sent it back, aiming blind for the spot where he'd seen them. The arrow shredded leaves as it went but struck nothing—he hadn't expected it to.

"Mohawk!" came a derisory shout from the other side, and a few words in a language he didn't understand but whose intended meaning was clear enough. He made a very Scottish gesture, whose meaning was also clear, and left them laughing.

He paused to yank the arrow out of the sycamore. Fletched with a yaffle's tail feathers, but not a pattern he knew. Whatever they'd been speaking wasn't an Algonquian tongue. Might be something northern like Assiniboine—he'd know, if he got a clear look at them—but might equally be something from nearer to hand.

Very likely working for the British army, though. He kent most of the Indian scouts presently with the Rebels. And while they hadn't been trying to kill him—they could have done so, easily, if they'd really wanted to—this was rougher teasing than might be expected. Perhaps only because they'd recognized him for what he was.

Mohawk! To an English speaker, it was just easier to say than "Kahnyen'kehaka." To any of the tribes who lived within knowledge of the Kahnyen'kehaka, it was either a word to scare children with or a calculated insult. "Man-eater," it meant, for the Kahnyen'kehaka were known to roast their enemies alive and devour the flesh.

Ian had never seen such a thing, but he knew men—old men—who had and would tell you about it with pleasure. He didn't care to think about it. It brought back much too vividly the night the priest had died in Snaketown, mutilated and burned alive—the night that had inadvertently taken Ian from his family and made him a Mohawk.

The bridge lay upstream, perhaps sixty yards from where he was. He paused, but the woods on the other side were silent, and he ventured across, his horse's hooves a careful clopping on the boards. If there were British scouts here, the army was not too far beyond.

There were broad meadows past the woods on the far side, and beyond these the fields of a good-sized farm; he could see a snatch of the buildings through the trees—and the movement of men. He turned hastily, circling a copse and coming out into ground open enough to see.

There were green-coated soldiers on the ridgeline beyond the farm buildings, and he could smell the sulfur of their slow match on the heavy air. Grenadiers.

He wheeled his horse and headed back, to find someone to tell.

WILLIAM FINALLY discovered the cavalry detachment of the British Legion, filling their canteens from a well in the yard of a farmhouse. They had a picket out, though, who gave a warning shout at sight of a lone horseman, and half the company swung round, on the alert. A well-trained company; Banastre Tarleton was a good, energetic officer.

Tarleton himself was standing relaxed in the shade of a big tree, his ornately plumed helmet cradled in one arm, mopping his face with a green silk kerchief. William rolled his eyes briefly at this bit of affectation, but not so Tarleton could see.

He came to a walk and rode up beside Tarleton, leaning down to give him the dispatch.

"From Captain André," he said. "Been busy?" The men had been fighting; he could smell the smoke on them, and a couple of men with what looked like minor wounds were sitting against the barn, uniforms streaked with blood. The barn doors hung open on emptiness, and the yard was trampled and spotted with dung; he wondered for a moment whether the farmer had driven his own stock away, or whether one or another of the armies had taken the animals.

"Not nearly busy enough," Tarleton replied, reading the note. "This may help, though. We're to go reinforce my lord Cornwallis." His face was flushed with the heat, and his leather stock was clearly cutting into his thick, muscular neck, but he looked exceedingly cheerful at the prospect.

"Good," said William, reining up to turn and go, but Tarleton stopped him with a raised hand. He tucked the dispatch away in his pocket, along with the green kerchief.

"Since I see you, Ellesmere—saw a tasty piece last night in camp, in the bread line," he said. Tarleton sucked his lower lip for an instant and released it, red and wet. "*Very* tasty, and a sweet little sister with her, too, though that one's not quite ripe enough for me." William raised his brows, but felt himself tense in thighs and shoulders.

"Made her an offer," Tarleton said, overtly careless but with a swift glance at William's hands. William relaxed them with an effort. "She declined, though—said she was yours?" This last was not quite a question, but not quite not.

"If her name is Jane," William said shortly, "she and her sister are traveling under my protection."

Tarleton's quizzical look flowered into open amusement.

"Your protection," he repeated. His full lips twitched. "I believe she told me that her name was Arabella, though—perhaps we're thinking of different girls."

"No, we're not." William did *not* want to be having this conversation, and gathered up his reins. "Don't fucking touch her."

That was a mistake; Tarleton never passed up a challenge. His eyes sparkled and William saw him set himself, legs spread.

"Fight you for her," he said.

"What, here? Are you insane?" There were bugles in the distance, and not a very far distance, either. To say nothing of Tarleton's troops, many of them clearly listening to this exchange.

"Wouldn't take long," Tarleton said softly, rocking back on his heels. His left fist was loosely curled and he rubbed his right hand flat on the side of his breeches, coat pushed back. He glanced over his shoulder, to the empty barn. "My men wouldn't interfere, but we could go in there, if you're shy." *"Shy"* said with that particular intonation that made it clear that cowardice was meant.

It had been on the tip of William's tongue to say, *"I don't own the girl"*—but to make that admission was to give Tarleton license to go after her. He'd seen Ban with girls often enough; he wasn't violent with them, but he was insistent. Never left without getting what he wanted, one way or another.

And after Harkness . . . His thoughts hadn't caught up with his body; he was on the ground, shucking his coat, before he'd made a conscious decision.

Ban laid his helmet on the ground, grinning, and took off his own coat in a leisurely fashion. The motion attracted all his men at once, and in seconds they were surrounded by a circle of dragoons, whistling and hooting encouragement. The only dissenter was Ban's lieutenant, who had gone a sickly shade of gray.

"Colonel!" he said, and William realized that the man's fear had all to do with taking issue with Ban and not the consequences of what might happen if he didn't. He meant to do his duty, though, and reached out a hand to grip Tarleton's arm. "Sir. You—"

"Let go," Ban said, not taking his eyes off William. "And shut up." The lieutenant's hand dropped away as though someone had punched him in the shoulder.

William felt at once detached, as though he were watching this from somewhere outside himself, above it all—and that part of him wanted to laugh at the ridiculousness of the situation. And some very tiny remnant of conscience was appalled. But the fleshly part of him was grimly exultant, and very much in charge.

He'd seen Ban fight before, and didn't make the mistake of waiting for any sort of signal. The moment the green coat hit the ground, William launched himself and—ignoring a ferocious hook that slammed into his ribs—grabbed Tarleton by both shoulders, jerked him forward, and butted him in the face with a horrid sound of cracking bone.

He let go, pushed Ban hard in the chest, and sent him staggering backward, blood flying from his broken nose and a surprised look on his face that turned immediately to berserk fury. Tarleton dug in his heels and leapt at William like a rabid dog.

William had six inches and forty pounds on Ban, and three older cousins who had taught him to fight. Banastre Tarleton had an unshakable conviction that he was going to win any fight he started.

They were struggling on the ground, so locked that neither was actually able to hit the other effectively, when William dimly heard the lieutenant's voice, full of panic, and a rush all round them. Hands seized him and dragged him away from Tarleton; more hands pushed him frantically toward his horse. There were drums coming down the lane and the sound of marching feet.

He mounted in a daze, a taste of blood in his mouth, and spat by reflex. His coat was thrown across his lap, and someone slapped his horse with a sharp "T'cha!" that nearly unseated William, whose feet were nowhere near the stirrups.

He pressed knees and calves into the horse's sides, urging Goth into a gallop, and burst from the lane directly in front of an infantry column, whose sergeant recoiled with a shout of alarm. Scots. He saw the checkered trews and caps, and heard a few uncouth shouts in what might be Scots or Gaelic, but didn't care. They belonged to a regiment he didn't know—and so their officers wouldn't know him.

Tarleton could give what explanations he liked. William's left ear was ringing, and he shook his head and pressed the flat of his hand against the ear to quiet it.

When he took the hand away, the ringing had eased, and a number of people were singing "Yankee Doodle" instead. He glanced over his shoulder, incredulous, and saw a number of blue-coated Continentals, dragging a number of cannon, making for the distant ridgeline.

Go back and tell the Scots infantry and Tarleton's men? Head south to Cornwallis?

"Hey, redcoat!" A shout from his left made him look in that direction, and just in time. A group of ten or fifteen men in hunting shirts was bearing down on him, most of them armed with scythes and hoes. One man was aiming a musket at him; apparently he was the one who had shouted, for he did so again: "Drop your reins and get off!"

"The devil I will," William replied, and booted Goth, who took off as though his tail were on fire. William heard the boom of the musket, but crouched low over the horse's neck and kept going.

73

PECULIAR BEHAVIOR OF A TENT

WHILE NOT EAGER to be removed to a prison of some sort, John Grey was beginning to wish at least for solitude. Fergus Fraser and his son had insisted on remaining with him until someone came for him. Presumably so they could tell Jamie how he had been disposed of.

He was peculiarly disinterested in the method and means of that disposal, content to await developments. What he wanted solitude for was a contemplation of Percy Wainwright's presence, motives, and possible action. With La Fayette, he'd said. Adviser. John shuddered to think what sort of advice might be given by that . . . and what about his interests in Fergus Fraser?

He glanced at said printer, presently engaged in argument with his precocious offspring.

"You did it!" Germain glowered up at his father, face flushed red with righteous indignation. "Ye told me so yourself, a dozen times or more! How you went to war with *Grand-*

père, and stabbed a man in the leg, and rode on a cannon when the soldiers dragged it back from Prestonpans—and ye weren't even as old as I am now when ye did all that!"

Fergus paused for an instant, regarding his offspring through narrowed eyes, obviously regretting his previous prolixity. He breathed steadily through his nose for a moment, then nodded.

"That was different," he said evenly. "I was milord's employee at the time, not his son. I had a duty to attend him; he had no responsibility to prevent me doing so."

Germain blinked, frowning uncertainly.

"You weren't his son?"

"Of course not," Fergus said, exasperated. "If I told you about Prestonpans, surely I have told you that I was an orphan in Paris when I met your *grand-père.* He hired me to pick pockets for him."

"He did?" John hadn't meant to interrupt, but couldn't help it. Fergus glanced at him, startled; evidently he hadn't really noticed John's presence, focused as he was on Germain. He bowed.

"He did, my lord. We were Jacobites, you understand. He required information. Letters."

"Oh, indeed," John murmured, and took a sip from his flask. Then, recalling his manners, offered it to Fergus, who blinked in surprise, but then accepted it with another bow and took a healthy gulp. Well, it must be thirsty work, pursuing an errant child through an army. He thought briefly of Willie, and thanked God his son was safe—or was he?

He'd known that William would of course have left Philadelphia when Clinton withdrew the army—perhaps as a non-fighting aide-de-camp to a senior officer. But he hadn't thought about that supposition in conjunction with the apparent present fact that General Washington was now in hot pursuit of Clinton and might just possibly catch up with him. In which case, William . . .

These thoughts had distracted him from the ongoing tête-à-tête, and he was jerked out of them by a question directed to him by Germain.

"Me? Oh . . . sixteen. I might have gone to the army earlier," John added apologetically, "had my brother's regiment been formed, but he only raised it during the Jacobite Rising."

He looked at Fergus with new interest. "You were at Prestonpans, were you?" That should have been his own first battle, too—and would have been, save for his happening to meet one Red Jamie Fraser, notorious Jacobite, in a mountain pass two nights before.

"Did you kill anybody?" Germain demanded.

"Not at Prestonpans. Later, at Culloden. I wish I hadn't." He stretched out a hand for the flask. It was nearly empty, and he drained it.

A moment later, he was glad of his celerity; had he not drained the flask already, he might have choked. The tent flap folded back, and Percy Wainwright/Beauchamp stuck his head in, then froze in surprise, dark eyes darting from one to another of the tent's inhabitants. John had an impulse to throw the empty flask at him, but thought better of it, instead saying coldly, "I beg your pardon, sir; I am engaged."

"So I see." Percy didn't look at John. "Mr. Fergus Fraser," he said softly, coming into the tent, hand outstretched. "Your servant, sir. *Comment ça va?*"

Fergus, unable to avoid him, shook his hand with reserve and bowed slightly but said nothing. Germain made a small growling noise in his throat, but desisted when his father gave him a sharp glance.

"I am so pleased finally to have encountered you in private, Monsieur Fraser," Percy said, still speaking French. He smiled as charmingly as possible. "Monsieur—do you know who you are?"

Fergus regarded him thoughtfully.

"Few men know themselves, monsieur," he said. "For my part, I am entirely content to leave such knowledge to God. He can deal with it far better than I could. And having come to this conclusion, I believe that is all I have to say to you. *Pardonnez-moi.*" With that, he shouldered past Percy, taking him off-guard and knocking him off-balance. Germain turned at the tent flap and stuck out his tongue.

"Damned frog!" he said, then disappeared with a small yelp as his father jerked him through the flap.

Percy had lost one of his silver-buckled shoes in trying to stay upright. He brushed dirt and vegetable matter from the bottom of his stocking and screwed his foot back into the shoe, lips compressed and a rather attractive flush showing across his cheekbones.

"Oughtn't you to be with the army?" John inquired. "Surely you want to be there, if Washington does meet Clinton. I imagine your 'interests' would want a full report by an eyewitness, wouldn't they?"

"Shut up, John," Percy said briefly, "and listen. I haven't got much time." He sat down on the stool with a thump, folded his hands on his knee, and looked intently at John, as though evaluating his intelligence. "Do you know a man—a British officer—called Richardson?"

FERGUS MADE HIS way through the shambles left by the exodus of the army, holding Germain firmly by the hand. The camp followers and such men as had been left behind as unfit were setting to the work of salvage, and no one gave the Frasers more than a glance. He could only hope that the horse was where he had left it. He touched the pistol tucked under his shirt, just in case.

"Frog?" he said to Germain, not bothering to keep amusement out of his voice. "Damned *frog,* you said?"

"Well, he *is,* Papa." Germain stopped walking suddenly, pulling his hand free. "Papa, I need to go back."

"Why? Have you forgotten something?" Fergus glanced over his shoulder at the tent, feeling an uneasiness between his shoulder blades. Beauchamp couldn't force him to listen, let alone to do anything he didn't wish to, and yet he had a strong aversion to the man. Well, call it fear; he seldom bothered lying to himself. Though why he should fear a man such as that . . .

"No, but . . ." Germain struggled to choose among several thoughts that were plainly all trying to emerge into speech at once. "*Grand-père* told me I must stay with his lordship and if Monsieur Beauchamp should come, I must listen to anything they said."

"Really? Did he say why?"

"No. But he said it. And, also, I was—I *am*—his lordship's servant, his orderly. I have a duty to attend him." Germain's face was touchingly earnest, and Fergus felt his heart squeeze a little. Still . . .

Fergus had never mastered the Scottish way of making crude but eloquent noises in the throat—he rather envied them—but was not bad with similar communications made via the nose.

"According to what the soldiers said, he is a prisoner of war. Do you mean to accompany him to whatever dungeon or hulk they put him in? Because I think *Maman* would come and hoick you out of it by the scruff of your neck. Come along, she's very worried and waiting to hear that you're safe."

Mention of Marsali had the hoped-for effect; Germain cast down his eyes and bit his lip.

"No, I don't—I mean, I'm not . . . well, but, Papa! I *have* to just go and be sure that Monsieur Beauchamp isn't doing anything bad to him. And maybe see that he has some food before we leave," he added. "You wouldna have him starve, would you?"

"Milord looked reasonably well nourished," Fergus said, but the urgency on Germain's face drew him a reluctant step back toward the tent. Germain at once glowed with relief and excitement, seizing his father's hand again.

"Why do you think Monsieur Beauchamp means his lordship harm?" Fergus asked, holding Germain back for a moment.

"Because his lordship doesna like him, and neither does *Grand-père,*" the boy said briefly. "Come on, Papa! His lordship is unarmed, and who knows what that sodomite has in his pocket?"

"Sodomite?" Fergus stopped dead in his tracks.

"*Oui, Grand-père* says he's a sodomite. Come *on*!" Germain was nearly frantic now and drew his father on by sheer willpower.

Sodomite? Well, that was interesting. Fergus, observant and very much experienced in the ways of the world and of sex, had some time ago drawn his own conclusions regarding milord Grey's preferences but had naturally not mentioned these to Jamie, as the English lord was his father's good friend. Did he know? Regardless, that might make his lordship's relationship with this Beauchamp a good deal more complex, and he approached the tent with a heightened sense of both curiosity and wariness.

He was prepared to clap his hand over Germain's eyes and drag him away, should anything untoward be going on in that tent, but before they came close enough to see through the flap, he saw the canvas quiver in a very odd way, and pulled Germain to a halt.

"Arrête," he said softly. He couldn't conceive of even the most depraved sexual practices causing a tent to behave in that way and, gesturing to Germain to stay put, moved soft-footed to one side, keeping a little distance among the camp debris.

Sure enough, Lord John was wriggling out under the back edge of the tent, cursing quietly in German. Eyes on this peculiar exhibition, Fergus didn't notice that Beauchamp had emerged from the front of the tent until he heard Germain's exclamation and turned to find the boy behind him. He was impressed at Germain's ability to move quietly, but this was not the time for praise. He motioned to his son and withdrew a little farther, taking cover behind a pile of spiled barrels.

Beauchamp, with a high color in his face, walked off briskly, dusting chaff from the elegant skirts of his coat. Lord John, scrambling to his feet, made off in the other direction, toward the woods, not bothering about his own costume, and no wonder. What on earth had the man been doing, dressed in such a way?

"What shall we do, Papa?" Germain whispered.

Fergus hesitated only a moment, glancing after Beauchamp. The man was heading toward a large inn, likely General Washington's erstwhile center of command. If Beauchamp were remaining with the Continental army, he could be found again—if that proved necessary.

"Shall we follow Lord John, Papa?" Germain was vibrating with anxiety, and Fergus put his hand on the boy's shoulder to calm him.

"No," he said, firmly but with some regret—he himself was more than curious. "Clearly his business is urgent, and our presence would be more likely to cause him danger than to help." He didn't add that Lord John was almost certainly headed for the battlefield—if there should be one. Such an observation would only make Germain more eager.

"But—" Germain had his mother's sense of Scottish stubbornness, and Fergus suppressed a smile at seeing his small blond brows draw down in Marsali's exact expression.

"He will be looking either for your *grand-père* or for his compatriots," Fergus pointed out. "Either will take care of him, and in neither case would our presence be useful to him. And your mother will assassinate both of us if we don't return to Philadelphia within the week."

He also didn't mention that the thought of Marsali and the other children alone in the printshop caused him a great uneasiness. The exodus of the British army and a horde of Loyalists hadn't rendered Philadelphia safe, by any means. There were a good many looters and lawless men who had moved in to pick over the leavings of those who had fled—and there were plenty still left with Loyalist sympathies who didn't admit them openly but might easily act upon them under cover of darkness.

"Come," he said more gently, and took Germain by the hand. "We'll need to find some food to eat along the way."

JOHN GREY MADE his way through the wood, stumbling now and then by reason of having only one working eye; the ground wasn't always where he thought it was.

Once away from the campsite, he made no effort to keep out of sight; Claire had packed his eye with cotton lint and wrapped his head in a most professional manner with a gauze bandage to keep the lint in place. It would protect the bad eye while allowing air to dry the skin around it, she said. He supposed it was working—his eyelids weren't as raw and sore as they had been, only rather sticky—but at the moment was only grateful that he looked like a wounded man who'd been left behind by the rushing American army. No one would stop or question him.

Well, no one save his erstwhile comrades of the 16th Pennsylvania, should he have the misfortune to encounter them. God only knew what they'd thought when he surrendered to Jamie. He felt badly about them—they'd been very kind to him and must feel their kindness betrayed by the revelation of his identity, but there hadn't been much bloody choice about it.

There wasn't much choice about this, either.

"They mean to take your son." It was probably the one thing Percy could have said that would have made him attend.

"They who?" he'd said sharply, sitting up. "Take him where? And what for?"

"The Americans. As to what for—you and your brother." Percy had looked him over, shaking his head. "Do you have the slightest notion of your value, John?"

"Value to whom?" He'd stood up then, swaying perilously, and Percy had grabbed his hand to steady him. The touch was warm and firm and startlingly familiar. He withdrew his hand.

"I'm told I have considerable value as a scapegoat, should the Americans decide to hang me." Where was that bloody note from Hal . . . who had it now? Watson Smith? General Wayne?

"Well, that won't do at all, will it?" Percy appeared undisturbed at thought of Grey's imminent demise. "Don't worry. I'll have a word."

"With whom?" he asked, curious.

"General La Fayette," Percy said, adding with a slight bow, "to whom I have the honor of being an adviser."

"Thank you," Grey said dryly. "I am not concerned with the possibility of being hanged—at least not right this minute—but I want to know what the devil you mean about my son, William."

"This would be much easier over a bottle of port," Percy said, with a sigh, "but time doesn't permit, alas. Sit down, at least. You look as though you're going to fall on your face."

Grey sat, with as much dignity as he could muster, and glared up at Percy.

"To put it as simply as possible—and it's not simple, I assure you—there is a British officer named Richardson—"

"I know him," Grey interrupted. "He—"

"I know you do. Be quiet." Percy flapped a hand at him. "He's an American spy."

"He—what?" For an instant, he thought he might really fall on his face, despite the fact of sitting down, and grasped the cot's frame with both hands to prevent this. "He told me that he proposed to arrest Mrs. Fraser for distributing seditious materials. That was what caused me to marry her. I—"

"You?" Percy goggled at him. "*You* married?"

"Certainly," Grey said crossly. "So did you, or so you told me. Go on about bloody Richardson. How long has he been spying for the Americans?"

Percy snorted but obliged.

"I don't know. I became aware of him in the spring of last year, but he may well have been at it before that. Active fellow, I'll give him that. And not content with merely gathering information and passing it on, either. He's what one might call a *provocateur.*"

"He's not the only one who's provoking," Grey muttered, resisting the urge to rub his bad eye. "What's he got to do with William?" He was beginning to have an unpleasant feeling in his abdomen. *He* had given William permission to undertake small intelligence-gathering missions for Captain Richardson, who—

"Put as bluntly as possible, he's tried more than once to lure your son into a position where he might appear to have sympathies with the Rebels. I gather that last year he sent him into the Great Dismal in Virginia, with the intention that he should be captured by a nest of Rebels who have a bastion there—presumably they would let it be known that he had deserted and joined their forces, while actually holding him prisoner."

"What for?" Grey demanded. "Will you bloody sit down? Looking up at you is giving me a headache."

Percy snorted again and sat—not on the conveniently placed stool, but beside Grey on the camp bed, hands on his knees.

"Presumably to discredit your family—Pardloe was making rather inflammatory speeches in the House of Lords at the time, about the conduct of the war." He made a small, impatient gesture that John recognized, a quick flutter of the fingers. "I don't know everything—yet—but what I *do* know is that he's arranged to have your son taken, during the journey to New York. He's not bothering with indirection or politics; things have changed, now that France has come into the war. This is simple abduction, with the intent of demanding your—and Pardloe's—cooperation in the matter of the Northwest Territory—and possibly something else—as the price of the boy's life."

Grey closed his good eye, in an effort to stop his head spinning. Two years before, Percy had abruptly reentered his life, bearing a proposal from certain French "interests"—to wit, that these interests wanted the return of the valuable Northwest Territory, presently held by England, and in return for assistance in achieving that goal would offer their influence to keep France from entering the war on the side of the Americans.

"Things have changed," he repeated, with an edge.

Percy inhaled strongly through his nose.

"Admiral d'Estaing sailed from Toulon with a fleet, in April. If he's not already off New York, he will be shortly. General Clinton may or may not know that."

"Jesus!" He clenched his fists on the bedframe, hard enough to leave marks from the nailheads. So the bloody French *had* now officially entered the war. They'd signed a Treaty of Alliance with America in February, and declared war on England in March, but talk was cheap. Ships and cannon and men cost money.

Suddenly he grasped Percy's arm, squeezing hard.

"And where do you come into this?" he said, voice level and cold. "Why are you telling me all this?"

Percy drew breath, but didn't jerk away. He returned Grey's stare, brown eyes clear and direct.

"Where I come into it doesn't matter," he said. "And there isn't time. You need to find your son quickly. As to why I tell you . . ."

John saw it coming and didn't pull away. Percy smelled of bergamot and petitgrain and the red wine on his breath. John's grip on Percy's arm loosened.

"Pour vos beaux yeux," Percy had whispered against his lips—and laughed, damn him.

74

THE SORT OF THING THAT WILL MAKE A MAN SWEAT AND TREMBLE

WE FOLLOWED IN the wake of the army. Because of the speed of march, the soldiers had been instructed to jettison their nonessential equipment, and I had had to abandon many of my supplies, as well. Still, I was mounted and thus would be able to keep up, even loaded with what I managed to keep. After all, I reasoned, it would do me no good to catch up with the army if I had nothing with which to treat wounds when I did.

I had Clarence packed with as much as he could reasonably be expected to carry. As he was a large mule, this was a substantial amount, including my small tent, a folding camp bed for surgery, and all I could cram in, in terms of bandages, lint, and disinfectant—I had both a small cask of purified saline solution and a couple of bottles of straight ethyl alcohol (these disguised as poison, with large skull-and-crossbones labels painted on). Also a jug of sweet oil for burns, my medicine chest, and bundles of raw herbs, large jars of prepared ointment, and dozens of small bottles and vials of tinctures and infusions. My surgical instruments, stitching needles, and sutures were in their own small box, this in a haversack with extra bandage rolls, to be carried on my person.

I left Clarence tied and went to find out where the hospital tents were to be set up. The camp was milling with noncombatants and support personnel, but I was finally able to locate Denny Hunter, who told me that on the basis of General Greene's reports, the surgeons were to be dispatched to the village of Freehold, where there was a large church that could be used as a hospital.

"The last thing I've heard is that Lee has taken command of the force attacking the British rear and means to encircle the British," he said, polishing his spectacles on the tail of his shirt.

"Lee? But I thought he didn't think it an important command and wouldn't take it." I wouldn't care one way or the other—save that Jamie and his companies would be engaged in that mission, and I had my own doubts about General Lee.

Denzell shrugged, putting his spectacles back on and tucking in his shirttail.

"Apparently Washington decided that a thousand men were insufficient to his purpose and raised the number to five thousand, which Lee considered more appropriate to his . . . sense of his own importance." Denny's mouth twisted a little at this. He looked at my face, though, and touched my arm gently.

"We can but put our trust in God—and hope that the Lord has his eye upon Charles Lee. Will thee come with the girls and me, Claire? Thy mule will bide with us willingly."

I hesitated for no more than a moment. If I rode Clarence, I could take only a fraction of the equipment and supplies he could otherwise carry. And while Jamie had said he wanted me with him, I knew quite well that what he really meant was that he wanted to be assured of where I was, and that I was near at hand if he needed me.

"Thy husband does trust me with thy welfare," Denny said, smiling, having plainly divined what I was thinking.

"Et tu, Brute?" I said rather curtly, and, when he blinked, added more civilly, "I mean—does *everyone* know what I'm thinking, all of the time?"

"Oh, I doubt it," he said, and grinned at me. "If they did, I expect a number of them would take a deal more care in what they said to thee."

I rode in Denny's wagon with Dottie and Rachel, Clarence pacing stolidly along behind, tied to the tailboard. Dottie was flushed with heat and excitement; she had never been near a battle before. Neither had Rachel, but she had helped her brother during a very bad winter at Valley Forge and had much more idea of what the day might hold.

"Does thee think perhaps thee should write to thy mother?"

I heard Rachel ask seriously. The girls were behind Denny and me, sitting in the bed of the wagon and keeping things from bouncing out when we hit ruts and mud bogs.

"No. Why?" Dottie's tone was wary—not quite hostile, but very reserved. I knew she had written to tell her mother that she intended to wed Denzell Hunter, but she hadn't received a reply. Given the difficulties of correspondence with England, though, there was no assurance that Minerva Grey had ever read the letter.

It occurred to me, with a sudden qualm, that I hadn't written a letter to Brianna in several months. I hadn't been able to bear to write about Jamie's death, and there hadn't been time since his return even to think about it.

"It *is* a war, Dottie," Rachel said. "Unexpected things may happen. And thee would not wish thy mother to . . . well . . . to discover that thee had perished without some assurance that she was in thy heart."

"Hmm!" said Dottie, clearly taken aback. Beside me, I felt Denzell shift his weight, bending a little forward as he took a fresh grip on the reins. He glanced aside at me, and his mouth turned up in an expression that was as much grimace as smile, acknowledging that he'd been listening to the girls' talk, too.

"She worries for me," he said very quietly. "Never for herself." He let go the reins with one hand to rub a knuckle under his nose. "She has as much courage as her father and brothers."

"As much pigheadedness, you mean," I said under my breath, and he grinned, despite himself.

"Yes," he said. He glanced over his shoulder and so did I, but the girls had moved to the tailboard and were talking over it to Clarence, brushing flies off his face with the needles of a long pine twig. "Does thee think it a familial lack of imagination? For in the case of the men of her family, it cannot be ignorance of the possibilities."

"No, it certainly can't," I agreed, with a note of ruefulness. I sighed and stretched my legs a little. "Jamie is the same way, and *he* certainly doesn't lack for imagination. I think it's . . ." I made a small helpless gesture. "Perhaps 'acceptance' is the word."

"Acceptance of the fact of mortality?" He was interested and pushed his spectacles back into place. "We have discussed that—Dorothea and I." He nodded back toward the girls. "Friends live in the certain knowledge that this world is temporary and there is nothing to fear in death."

"Some of that, perhaps." In fact, almost everyone in this time had a very matter-of-fact acceptance of mortality; death was a constant presence at everyone's elbow, though they regarded that presence in a variety of ways. "But they—those men—what they do is something different, I think. It's more an acceptance of what they think God made them."

"Really?" He seemed slightly startled by that, and his brows drew together in consideration. "What does thee mean by that? That they believe God has created them deliberately to—"

"To be responsible for other people, I think," I said. "I couldn't say whether it's the notion of *noblesse oblige*—Jamie was a laird, you know, in Scotland—or just the idea that . . . that's what a man does," I ended, rather lamely. Because "that" was plainly not what Denzell Hunter thought a man should do. Though I did wonder a bit. Plainly the question troubled him a little.

As well it might, given his position. I could see that the prospect of battle excited him and that the fact that it did troubled him a great deal.

"You're a very brave man," I said quietly, and touched his sleeve. "I saw that. When you played Jamie's deserter game, after Ticonderoga."

"It wasn't courage, I assure thee," he said, with a short, humorless laugh. "I didn't seek to be brave; I only wanted to prove that I was."

I made a rather disrespectful noise—I wasn't in either Jamie's or Ian's class, but I *had* picked up a few pointers—and he glanced at me in surprise.

"I do appreciate the distinction," I told him. "But I've known a lot of brave men in my time."

"But how can thee know what lies—"

"Be quiet." I waved my fingers at him. "'Brave' covers everything from complete insanity and bloody disregard of other people's lives—generals tend to go in for that sort—to drunkenness, foolhardiness, and outright idiocy—to the sort of thing that will make a man sweat and tremble and throw up . . . and go and do what he thinks he has to do *anyway*.

"Which," I said, pausing for breath and folding my hands

neatly in my lap, "is exactly the sort of bravery you share with Jamie."

"Thy husband does not sweat and tremble," he said dryly. "I've seen him. Or, rather, I have *not* seen him do such things."

"He does the sweating and trembling on the inside, mostly," I replied. "Though he really does often vomit before—or during—a battle."

Denzell blinked, once, and didn't speak for a bit, absorbed—apparently—in steering his way past a large hay wagon whose oxen had suddenly decided they didn't want to go any farther and stopped dead in the middle of the road.

At last he took a breath and let it out explosively.

"I am not afraid to die," he said. "That isn't my difficulty."

"What is?" I asked, curious. "Are you afraid of being maimed and left helpless? I certainly would be."

"No." His throat moved as he swallowed. "It's Dorothea and Rachel. I'm afraid I would lack the courage to see them die without trying to save them, even if that meant killing someone."

I couldn't think of anything to say to this, and we jolted on in silence.

LEE'S TROOPS LEFT Englishtown at about 6 A.M., heading east toward Monmouth Courthouse. Lee arrived at the courthouse at about nine-thirty, to find that the bulk of the British army had left—presumably moving toward Middletown, as that was where the road went.

Lee was prevented from following, though, by the presence of a small but very belligerent rear guard under the command of General Clinton himself. Or so Ian told Jamie, having got close enough to see Clinton's regimental banners. Jamie had communicated this information to Lee, but saw no evidence that it affected either that gentleman's plan of action (always assuming that he had one) or his disinclination to send out more scouts to reconnoiter.

"Go round this lot and see can ye find out where Cornwallis is," Jamie told Ian. "The grenadiers ye saw are likely Hessians, so they'll be close to von Knyphausen."

Ian nodded and took the full canteen Jamie offered him.

"Shall I tell General Lee, if I do? He didna seem much interested in what I had to say."

"Aye, tell him if ye see him before ye see me—tell the marquis, too, should ye come within reach of him—but find me, regardless, aye?"

Ian grinned at him and slung the canteen over his pommel. "Good hunting, *a Bhràthair-mathàr*!"

Jamie had had two companies blooded by midmorning, skirmishing near Monmouth Courthouse, but no one killed yet and only three wounded badly enough to retire. Colonel Owen had requested cover for his artillery—only two cannon, but any artillery was welcome—and Jamie had sent Thomas Meleager's Pennsylvanians to deal with that.

He'd sent one of Captain Kirby's companies to reconnoiter toward what he thought was the creek and kept back the rest, waiting for orders from La Fayette or Lee. La Fayette was somewhere ahead of him, Lee well behind and to the east with the main body of his troops.

The sun stood just short of ten o'clock when a messenger appeared, crouched dramatically in his saddle as though dashing through a hail of bullets, though in fact there was not a British soldier in sight. He pulled his lathered horse to a stop and gasped out his message.

"There's dust clouds in the east—might be more redcoats comin'! And the marky says there's redcoat cannon in the cider orchard, sir, and will you do summat about it, please."

The sweating messenger gulped air, loosening his rein in obvious preparation for dashing off again. Jamie leaned over and seized the horse's bridle to prevent it.

"Where *is* the cider orchard?" he asked calmly. The messenger was young, maybe sixteen, and wild-eyed as his rawboned horse.

"Dunno, sir," he said, and began glancing to and fro, as though expecting the orchard to materialize suddenly out of the meadow they were standing in. A sudden distant boom reverberated in Jamie's bones, and his horse's ears pricked up.

"Never mind, lad," he said. "I hear them. Breathe your horse, or he's like to die under ye before the sun's high."

Letting go the bridle, he waved to Captain Craddock and turned his own horse's head toward the sound of cannon.

THE AMERICAN ARMY had several hours' lead on him, and the British army very much more—but a man alone could move a great deal faster than even a company of light infantry. Neither was John burdened with weapons. Or food. Or water.

You know perfectly well that he's lying to you.

"Oh, be quiet, Hal," Grey muttered to his brother's shade. "I know Percy a great deal better than you do."

I said, *you* know *perfectly well . . .*

"I do. What am I risking if he is lying—and what am I risking if he's *not*?"

Hal was high-handed, but logical. He was also a father; that shut him up.

What he was risking if Percy *was* lying was being shot or hanged out of hand if anyone recognized him. Anyone. If the Americans found him out before he reached the British lines, they'd arrest him for breaking his parole and promptly execute him as a spy. If the British *didn't* recognize him in time, they'd shoot him on sight as Rebel militia. He put a hand in the pocket where he'd wadded the LIBERTY OR DEATH cap and debated the wisdom of throwing it away, but, in the event, kept it.

What he was risking if Percy wasn't lying was Willie's life. No great effort required to call the odds.

It was midmorning, and the air was like treacle, thick and sweet with flowers, sticky with tree sap, and completely unbreathable. His good eye was beginning to itch from the floating pollen grains, and flies were buzzing interestedly round his head, drawn by the scent of honey.

At least the headache had gone away, dispelled by the burst of alarm—and a brief flare of lust, might as well admit it—occasioned by Percy's revelation. He wouldn't begin to speculate as to Percy's motives, but . . .

"'For your beautiful eyes,' indeed!" he muttered, but couldn't help smiling at the impudence. A wise man would not touch Percy Wainwright with a ten-foot pole. Something shorter, though . . .

"Oh, do be quiet, will you?" he murmured to himself, and

made his way down a clay bank to the edge of a tiny creek, where he could throw cold water on his heated face.

IT WAS PERHAPS eight o'clock in the morning when we reached Freehold, where Tennent Church was to be established as the main hospital. It was a large building, set in the midst of a huge, sprawling churchyard, an acre or more of ground whose headstones were as individual as doubtless their owners had been in life. No neat aisles of uniform white crosses here.

I spared a thought for the graves of Normandy and wondered whether those rows upon rows of faceless dead were meant to impose a sort of postmortem tidiness on the costs of war—or whether it was meant rather to underline them, a solemn accounting carried out in endless rows of naughts and crosses.

But I didn't think long. Battle had been joined already—somewhere—and there were already wounded coming in, a number of men sitting in the shade of a large tree next to the church, more coming down the road, some staggering with the help of friends, some being carried on litters—or in someone's arms. My heart lurched at the sight, but I tried not to look for Jamie or Ian; should they be among the early wounded, I'd know it soon enough.

There was a bustle near the church's porch, where the double doors had been flung wide to accommodate passage, and orderlies and surgeons were coming and going in haste—but organized haste, so far.

"Go and see what's happening, why don't you?" I suggested to Denzell. "The girls and I will unload things."

He paused long enough to unhitch his own two mules and hobble them, then hastened into the church.

I found the buckets and dispatched Rachel and Dottie to find a well. The day was already uncomfortably hot; we were going to need a good deal of water, one way or another.

Clarence was showing a strong urge to go join Denny's mules in cropping grass among the headstones, jerking his head against the pull of his tether and uttering loud cries of annoyance.

"All right, all right, all *right,*" I said, hurrying to undo the packing straps and lift his burdens off. "Hold your—oh, dear."

A man was staggering toward me, giving at the knees with every step and lurching dizzily. The side of his face was black, and there was blood down the facing of his uniform. I dropped the bundle of tenting and poles and rushed to catch him by the arm before he should trip over a headstone and fall face-first into the dirt.

"Sit down," I said. He looked dazed and appeared not to hear me, but as I was pulling on his arm, he did go down, letting his knees relax abruptly and nearly taking me with him as he landed on a substantial stone commemorating one Gilbert Tennent.

My patient was swaying as though about to fall over, and yet a hasty check showed me no significant wounds; the blood on his coat was from his face, where the blackened skin had blistered and split. It wasn't just the soot of black powder—the skin had actually been burned to a crisp, the underlying flesh seared, and my patient smelled appallingly like a pork roast. I took a firm grip on my lurching stomach and stopped breathing through my nose.

He didn't respond to my questions but stared hard at my mouth, and he seemed lucid, despite his continued swaying. The penny finally dropped.

"Ex . . . plo . . . sion?" I mouthed with exaggerated care, and he nodded vigorously, then stopped abruptly, swaying so far that I had to grasp him by the sleeve and pull him upright.

Artilleryman, from his uniform. So something big had exploded near him—a mortar, a cannon?—and not only burned his face nearly to the bone but also likely burst both his eardrums and disturbed the balance of his inner ear. I nodded and set his hands to grip the stone he sat on, to keep him in place while I hastily finished unloading Clarence—who was making the welkin ring with frustration; I should have realized at once that the artilleryman was deaf, as he was taking no notice of the racket—hobbled him, and set him loose to join Denny's mules in the shade. I dug what I needed out of the packs and set about to do what little I could for the injured man, this consisting mostly of soaking a towel in saline and applying it to his face like a poultice, to remove as much soot as I could without scrubbing.

I thanked God that I'd had the forethought to bring a jug of sweet oil for burns—and cursed my lack of it for not having asked for aloe at Bartram's Garden.

The girls hadn't yet returned with water; I hoped there was a well somewhere close at hand. Creek water so close to an army couldn't be used without boiling it. That thought led me to look round for a spot where a fire could be lighted and to make a mental note to send the girls to look for wood next.

My mind was jerked from my rapidly expanding mental checklist, though, by Denny's sudden emergence from the church. He wasn't alone; he appeared to be having a passionate argument with another Continental officer. With a brief exclamation of exasperation, I dug in my pocket and found my silk-wrapped spectacles. With these on my nose, the face of Denny's interlocutor sprang into clear focus—Captain Leckie, diplomate of the Medical College of Philadelphia.

My patient tugged at my skirt and, when I turned to him, apologetically opened his mouth and mimed drinking. I held up a finger, adjuring him to wait one moment, and went to see whether Denzell required reinforcement.

My appearance was greeted by an austere look from Captain Leckie, who viewed me rather as he might have looked at something questionable on the bottom of his shoe.

"Mrs. Fraser," he said coldly. "I have just been telling your Quaker friend that there is no room inside the church for cunning-women or—"

"Claire Fraser is the most skillful surgeon I have seen operate!" Denzell said. He was flushed and fairly bristling with anger. "Thee will do thy patients great harm, sir, by not allowing her to—"

"And where did you obtain your training, *Dr.* Hunter, that you are so confident of your own opinion?"

"In Edinburgh," Denny said through his teeth. "Where I was trained by my cousin, John Hunter." Seeing that this made no impact on Leckie, he added, "And his brother, William Hunter—*accoucheur* to the queen."

That took Leckie aback, but unfortunately also got up his nose.

"I see," he said, dividing a faint sneer evenly between us. "I congratulate you, sir. But as I doubt the army requires a man midwife, perhaps you should assist your . . . colleague"—and here he actually flared his nostrils at me, the pompous little swine—"with her seeds and potions, rather than—"

"We haven't time for this," I interrupted firmly. "Dr. Hunter is both a trained physician and a duly appointed surgeon in the Continental army; you can't bloody keep him out. And if my experience of battle—which I venture to suggest may be somewhat more extensive than your own, *sir*—is anything to go on, you'll need every hand you can get." I turned to Denzell and gave him a long, level look.

"Your duty is with those who need you. So is mine. I told you about triage, did I not? I have a tent and my own surgical instruments and supplies. I'll do triage out here, deal with the minor cases, and send in anyone requiring major surgery."

I had a quick look over my shoulder, then turned back to the two fuming men.

"You'd best go inside and be quick about it. They're starting to pile up."

This was not a metaphorical expression. There was a crowd of walking wounded under the trees, a few men lying on make-shift stretchers and sheets of canvas . . . and a small, sinister heap of bodies, these presumably men who had died of their wounds en route to the hospital.

Fortunately, Rachel and Dottie appeared at this moment, each lugging a heavy bucket of water in each hand. I turned my back on the men and went to meet them.

"Dottie, come and put up the tent poles, will you?" I said, taking her buckets. "And, Rachel—you know what arterial bleeding looks like, I imagine. Go and look through those men and bring me anyone who's doing it."

I gave my burnt artilleryman water, then helped him to his feet. As he stood up, I saw behind his legs the epitaph carved into Gilbert Tennent's headstone:

O READER HAD YOU HEARD HIS LAST TESTIMONY YOU WOULD HAVE BEEN CONVINCED OF THE EXTREME MADNESS OF DELAYING REPENTANCE.

"I suppose there are worse places to be doing this," I remarked to the artilleryman, but, unable to hear me, he simply raised my hand and kissed it before swaying off to sit down on the grass, the wet towel pressed to his face.

75

THE CIDER ORCHARD

THE FIRST SHOT took them by surprise, a muffled boom from the cider orchard and a slow roll of white smoke. They didn't run, but they stiffened, looking to him for direction. Jamie said to those near him, "Good lads," then raised his voice. "To my left, now! Mr. Craddock, Reverend Woodsworth—circle them; come into the orchard from behind. The rest—scatter to the right and fire as ye can—" The second crash drowned his words, and Craddock jerked like a puppet with his strings cut and dropped to the ground, blood spraying from the blackened hole in his chest. Jamie's horse shied violently, nearly unseating him.

"Go with the reverend!" he shouted at Craddock's men, who stood there drop-jawed, staring at their captain's body. "Go *now*!" One of the men shook himself, grabbed the sleeve of another, pulled him away, and then they all began to move as a body. Woodsworth, bless him, raised his musket overhead and roared, "To me! Follow me!" and broke into the stork-legged shamble that passed with him for running—but they followed him.

The gelding had settled but was moving uneasily. He was—supposedly—used to the sound of guns, but he didn't like the strong smell of blood. Jamie didn't like it, either.

"Shouldn't we . . . bury Mr. Craddock?" a timid voice suggested behind him.

"He's not *dead,* lackbrain!"

Jamie glanced down. He wasn't—but it wouldn't be more than a few seconds longer.

"Go with God, man," he said quietly. Craddock didn't blink; his eyes were fixed on the sky, not yet dull but sightless.

"Go wi' your fellows," he said to the two lingerers, then

saw that they were Craddock's two sons, maybe thirteen and fourteen, white-faced and staring as sheep. "Say farewell to him," he said abruptly. "He'll still hear ye. Then . . . go." He thought for a moment to send them to La Fayette, but they'd be no safer there. "Run!"

They ran—they were a deal safer running—and with a gesture to Lieutenants Orden and Bixby, he wheeled his horse to the right, following Guthrie's company. The cannon were firing more regularly from the orchard. He saw a ball bounce past, ten feet away, and the air was thickening with smoke. He could still smell Craddock's blood.

He found Captain Moxley and sent him with a full company to look at the farmhouse on the far side of the orchard.

"At a distance, mind. I want to know if the redcoats are in it or if the family's still there. If the family's there, surround the house; go inside if they'll let ye, but don't force your way. If there are soldiers inside and they come out after you, engage them and take the house if ye think ye can. If they stay inside, don't stir them up; send someone back to tell me. I'll be at the back o' the orchard; the north side."

Guthrie was waiting for him, the men lying flat in the long grass behind the orchard. He left the two lieutenants with his horse, which he tied to a fence rail well out of range of the orchard, and scrambled along to the company, keeping low. He dropped to his belly by Bob Guthrie.

"I need to know where the cannon are—exactly where they are, and how many. Send three or four men in from different directions, goin' canny—ye know what I mean? Aye. They're not to do anything; see what they can and come out again, fast."

Guthrie was panting like a dog, stubbled face awash with sweat, but he grinned and nodded and wormed his way off through the grass.

The meadow was dry, brown and brittle in the summer heat; Jamie's stockings prickled with foxtails, and the warm sharp scent of ripe hay was stronger than that of black powder.

He gulped water from his canteen; it was nearly empty. It wasn't yet noon, but the sun was coming down on them like a flatiron. He turned to tell one of the lieutenants who'd been following him to go and find the nearest water, but nothing moved in the grass behind him save hundreds of grasshoppers, whirring up like sparks. Gritting his teeth against the stiffness in his knees, he scrambled up onto hands and feet and scuttled back toward his horse.

Orden was lying ten feet away, shot through one eye. Jamie froze for an instant, and something whirred close past his cheek. It might be a grasshopper and it might not. He was flat to the earth beside the dead lieutenant, heart pounding in his ears before the thought had fully formed.

Guthrie. He daren't raise his head to call out—but had to. He got his feet under him as best he could, shot out of the grass, and ran like a rabbit, to and fro, zigging away from the orchard as best he could while still going in the direction he'd sent Guthrie.

He could hear the shots now: more than one sniper in the orchard, protecting the cannon, and the sound was the flat *crack!* of a rifle. Jaegers? He flung himself down and crawled madly, now shouting for Guthrie.

"Here, sir!" The man popped up suddenly beside him like a groundhog, and Jamie seized Guthrie's sleeve, pulling him back down.

"Get . . . your men back." He gulped air, chest heaving. "Shooting—from the orchard. This side. They'll be picked off."

Guthrie was staring at him, mouth half open.

"Get them!"

Shaken out of his shock, Guthrie nodded like a puppet and started to rise. Jamie grabbed him by the ankle and jerked him flat, pressed him down with a hand on his back.

"Don't . . . stand up." His breathing was slowing and he managed to speak calmly. "We're still in range here. Get your men and retire with your company—back to the ridgeline. Join Captain Moxley; tell him to come round and join me . . ." His mind went blank for a moment, trying to think of some reasonable place for a rendezvous. "South of the farmhouse. With Woodbine's company." He took his hand off Guthrie.

"Aye, sir." The man scuffed up onto hands and knees, reaching for the hat that had fallen off. He glanced back at Jamie, eyes full of earnest concern.

"Are you hit bad, sir?"

"Hit?"

"There's blood all down your face, sir."

"It's nothing. Go!"

Guthrie swallowed, nodded, wiped his face on his sleeve, and made off through the grass, as fast as he could go. Jamie put a hand to his own face, belatedly aware of a slight sting across his cheekbone. Sure enough, his fingers came away bloody. Not a grasshopper, then.

He wiped his fingers on the skirt of his coat and noticed mechanically that the seam of the sleeve had burst at the shoulder, showing the white shirt beneath. He rose a little, cautious, looking round for Bixby, but there was no sign of him. Maybe dead in the long grass, too; maybe not. With luck, he'd seen what was happening and run back to warn the companies coming up. The horse was still where he'd left it, thank God, tethered to a fence, fifty yards away.

He hesitated for a moment, but there wasn't time to lose in looking for Bixby. Woodsworth and his two companies would be coming round the orchard in a few minutes, and right into range of the German rifles. He popped up and ran.

Something tugged at his coat, but he didn't stop, and reached his horse, gasping for air.

"Tiugainn!" he said, swinging up into the saddle. He turned away from the orchard and galloped through a potato field, though it bruised his farmer's heart to see what the armies' passing had done to it already.

I DON'T KNOW when physicians began calling it "the Golden Hour," but surely every battlefield medic from the time of the *Iliad* onward knows about it. From the time of an accident or injury that isn't immediately fatal, the victim's chances of living are best if he receives treatment within an hour of sustaining the injury. After that, shock, continued loss of blood, debility due to pain . . . the chance of saving a patient goes sharply downhill.

Add in blazing temperatures, lack of water, and the stress of running full out through fields and woods, wearing wool homespun and carrying heavy weapons, inhaling powder smoke, and trying either to kill someone or avoid being killed, just prior to being injured, and I rather thought we were looking at a Golden fifteen minutes or so.

Given also the fact that the wounded were having to be carried or to *walk*—probably more than a mile—to a place where they could find assistance . . . I supposed we were doing well to save as many as we were. *If only temporarily,* I added grimly to myself, hearing the screaming from inside the church.

"What's your name, dear?" I said to the young man in front of me. He couldn't be more than seventeen and was precious near to bleeding to death. A bullet had gone through the meat of his upper arm, which would normally be a fortuitous location for a wound. Unfortunately, in this instance the ball had passed through the underside of the arm and nicked the brachial artery, which had been spurting blood in a slow but earnest manner until I'd taken a death grip on his arm.

"Private Adams, ma'am," he replied, though his lips were white and he was shaking. "Billy, they call me," he added politely.

"Pleased to meet you, Billy," I said. "And you, sir . . . ?" For he'd been brought in staggering, leaning on another boy of about his own age—and nearly as white-faced, though I thought he wasn't hurt.

"Horatio Wilkinson, ma'am," he said, dipping his head in an awkward bow—the best he could manage while holding his friend upright.

"Lovely, Horatio," I said. "I've got him now. Would you pour him out a little water, with a splash of brandy in it? Just there." I nodded at the packing case I was using for a table, on which one of my brown bottles marked POISON stood, along with a canteen full of water and wooden cups. "And as soon as he's drunk it, give him that leather strip to bite down on."

I'd have told Horatio to have a tot, too, save that there were only two cups, and the second one was mine. I was sipping water steadily—my bodice was soaked and clung to me like the membrane inside an eggshell, and sweat ran steadily down my legs—and I didn't want to be sharing the germs of assorted soldiers who didn't brush their teeth regularly. Still, I might have to tell him to take a quick gulp direct from the brandy bottle; someone was going to have to apply pressure to Billy Adams's arm while I stitched his brachial artery, and Horatio Wilkinson didn't presently look equal to the task.

"Would you—" I began, but I was holding a scalpel and a

suture needle with a dangling ligature in my free hand, and the sight of these overcame young Mr. Wilkinson. His eyes rolled up in his head and he dropped, boneless, into the gravel.

"Wounded?" said a familiar voice behind me, and I turned my head to see Denzell Hunter looking down at Mr. Wilkinson. He was nearly as pale as Horatio and, with strands of hair come loose and clinging to his cheeks, very much the antithesis of his usual collected self.

"Fainted," I said. "Can you—"

"They are idiots," he said, so pale—with rage, I now realized—that he could barely speak. "Regimental surgeons, they call themselves! A good quarter of them have never seen a man wounded in battle before. And those who have are barely capable of anything in the way of treatment save the crudest amputation. A company of barbers would do better!"

"Can they stop bleeding?" I asked, taking his hand and wrapping it round my patient's upper arm. He automatically pressed his thumb to the brachial artery near the armpit, and the spurting that had started when I took my own hand away stopped again. "Thank you," I said.

"Not at all. Yes, most of them can do that," he admitted, calming down just a little. "But they are so jealous of privilege—and so much affiliated with their own regiments—that some are letting a wounded man die because he is not one of theirs and his own regimental surgeon is otherwise occupied!"

"Scandalous," I murmured, and, "Bite hard now, Private," as I thrust the leather between his teeth and made a quick incision to enlarge the wound enough to find the end of the severed artery. He did bite, and made no more than a low grunting noise as the scalpel sliced into his flesh; perhaps he was sufficiently in shock that he didn't feel it much—I hoped not.

"We haven't a lot of choice," I observed, glancing toward the big shade trees that edged the graveyard. Dottie was minding the victims of heatstroke, giving them water and—as time and buckets permitted—dousing them with it. Rachel was in charge of depressed head fractures, abdominal wounds, and other serious wounds that couldn't be treated by amputation or binding and splinting. In most cases, this amounted to nothing more than comforting them as they died, but she was a good, steady girl, who had seen a great many men die during the winter at Valley Forge; she didn't shrink from the job.

"We have to let them"—I jerked my chin toward the church, my hands being occupied in holding Private Adams's arm and ligating the severed vessel—"do what they're able to do. Not that we could bloody *stop* them."

"No." Denny breathed out, let go of the arm as he saw I had the vessel tied off, and wiped his face on his coat. "No, we can't. I just needed to express my anger where it wouldn't cause more trouble. And to ask if I may have some of thy gentian ointment; I saw thee had two good-sized tubs made up."

I gave him a small, wry laugh.

"Be my guest. That ass Leckie sent an orderly out a little while ago to try to appropriate my stock of lint and bandages. Do you need some, by the way?"

"If thee has them to spare." He cast a bleak eye over the dwindling pile of supplies. "Dr. McGillis has sent an orderly to scavenge the neighborhood for items of use and another to carry word back to camp and bring more."

"Take half," I said, with a nod, and finished wrapping Billy Adams's arm with as miserly a bandage as would still do the job. Horatio Wilkinson had recovered himself a little and was sitting up, though still rather pale. Denny hoisted him to his feet and dispatched him with Billy to sit in the shade for a bit.

I was digging through one of my packs for the gentian ointment when I noticed the approach of another party and straightened up to see what their state of need might be.

None of them appeared to be wounded, though all were staggering. They weren't in uniform and bore no weapons save clubs; no telling whether they were militia, or . . .

"We hear you've some brandy, missus," one of them said, reaching out in a quasi-friendly manner and seizing me by the wrist. "Come and share it with us, eh?"

"Let go of her," Denzell said, in a tone of deep menace that made the man holding my wrist actually let go in surprise. He blinked at Denzell, whom he evidently hadn't noticed before.

"Who the hell're *you*?" he asked, though more in tones of befuddled astonishment than confrontation.

"I'm a surgeon with the Continental army," Denzell said firmly, and moved to stand beside me, thrusting a shoulder between me and the men, all of whom were clearly very drunk. One of them laughed at this, a high *heeheehee* sound, and his fellow giggled and poked him, repeating, "surgeon with the Continental *ar-my.*"

"Gentlemen, thee must go," Denzell said, edging farther in front of me. "We have wounded men who need attention." He stood with his fists loosely curled, in the attitude of a man ready to do battle—though I was fairly sure he wouldn't. I hoped intimidation would do the trick, but glanced at my bottle; it was three-quarters empty—perhaps it would be better to give it to them and hope they went away. . . .

I could see a small party of wounded Continentals coming down the road, two on stretchers, and a few more stumbling, stripped to their bloodied shirts, coats in their hands being dragged in the dust. I reached for the bottle, intending to thrust it at the intruders, but a movement at the corner of my eye made me look toward the shade where the girls were tending prisoners. Both Rachel and Dottie were standing upright, watching the proceedings, and at this point, Dottie, with a strong look of determination on her face, began to walk toward us.

Denny saw her, too; I could see the sudden shift in his posture, a touch of indecision. Dorothea Grey might be a professed Quaker, but her family blood clearly had its own ideas. And I could—rather to my surprise—tell exactly what Denzell was thinking. One of the men had already noticed Dottie and had turned—swaying—in her direction. If she confronted them and one or more of them attacked her . . .

"Gentlemen." I interrupted the hum of interest among our visitors, and three pairs of bloodshot eyes turned slowly toward me. I withdrew one of the pistols Jamie had given me, pointed it into the air, and pulled the trigger.

It went off with a violent jerk and a *blam* that momentarily deafened me, along with a puff of acrid smoke that made me cough. I wiped streaming eyes on my sleeve in time to see the visitors departing hastily, with anxious looks back over their shoulders. I located a spare handkerchief tucked into my stays and wiped a smear of soot from my face, emerging from the damp linen folds to find the doors of the church occupied by several surgeons and orderlies, all goggling at me.

Feeling rather like Annie Oakley, and repressing the urge to try to twirl my pistol—mostly for fear I would drop it; it was nearly a foot long—I re-holstered my weapon and took a deep breath. I felt a trifle light-headed.

Denzell was regarding me with concern. He swallowed visibly and opened his mouth to speak.

"Not now," I said, my own voice sounding muffled, and nodded toward the men coming toward us. "There isn't time."

76

THE DANGERS OF SURRENDER

FOUR BLOODY HOURS. Hours spent slogging through an undulant countryside filled with mobs of Continental soldiers, clots of militia, and more bloody rocks than anyplace required for proper functioning, if you asked Grey. Unable to stand the blisters and shreds of raw skin any longer, he'd taken off his shoes and stockings and thrust them into the pockets of his disreputable coat, choosing to hobble barefoot for as long as he could bear it.

Should he meet anyone whose feet looked his size, he thought grimly, he'd pick up one of the omnipresent rocks and avail himself.

He *knew* he was close to the British lines. He could feel the tremble in the air. The movement of large bodies of men, their rising excitement. And somewhere, no great distance away, the point where excitement was turning to action.

He'd felt the presence of fighting since just past daylight. Sometimes heard shouting and the hollow boom of muskets. *What would I do if I were Clinton?* he'd wondered.

Clinton couldn't outstrip the pursuing Rebels; that was clear. But he would have had time enough to choose decent ground on which to stand and to make some preparation.

Chances were, some part of the army—Cornwallis's brigade, maybe; Clinton wouldn't leave von Knyphausen's Hessians to stand alone—would have taken up some defensible position, hoping to hold off the Rebels long enough for the baggage train to get away. Then the main body would wheel and take up its own position—perhaps occupying a village. He'd walked through two or three such, each with its own church. Churches were good; he'd sent many a scout up a steeple in his day.

Where's William most likely to be? Unarmed and unable to fight, chances were that he was with Clinton. That's where he *should* be. But he knew his son.

"Unfortunately," he muttered. He would, without hesitation, lay down both life and honor for William. That didn't mean he was pleased at the prospect of having to do so.

Granted, the current circumstance was not William's fault. He had to admit—reluctantly—that it was at least in part his own. He'd allowed William to undertake intelligence work for Ezekiel Richardson. He should have looked much more closely into Richardson . . .

The thought of having been gulled by the man was almost as upsetting as what Percy had told him.

He could only hope to run across Richardson in circumstances that would allow him to kill the man unobtrusively. But if it had to be at high noon in full view of General Clinton and his staff—so bloody be it.

He was inflamed in every particular of his being, knew it, and didn't care.

There were men coming, rumbling up the road behind him. Americans, disorderly, with wagons or caissons. He stepped off the road and stood still in the shade of a tree, waiting for them to pass.

It was a group of Continentals, pulling cannon. Fairly small: ten guns, and only four-pounders. Pulled by men, not mules. It was the only artillery he'd seen in the course of the morning, though; was it all Washington possessed?

They didn't notice him. He waited a few minutes, until they were out of sight, and followed in their wake.

HE HEARD MORE cannon, some way to his left, and paused to listen. British, by God! He'd had somewhat to do with artillery, early in his military career, and the rhythm of a working gun crew was embedded in his bones.

Sponge piece!

Load piece!
Ram!
Fire!

A single artillery unit. Ten-pounders, six of them. They had something in range but weren't being attacked; the firing was sporadic, not that of hot combat.

Though, to be fair, any physical effort whatever had to be described as "hot" today. He lunged into a patch of trees, exhaling in relief at the shade. He was ready to expire in his black coat and took it off for a moment's respite. Dare he abandon the bloody thing altogether?

He'd seen a band of militia earlier, shirtsleeved, some with kerchiefs tied over their heads against the sun. Coated, though, he might bluff his way as a militia surgeon—the beastly garment smelled badly enough.

He worked his tongue, bringing a little saliva to his dry mouth. Why the devil had he not thought to bring a canteen when he'd fled? Thirst decided him to make his move now.

Dressed as he was, he might well be shot by any infantryman or dragoon who saw him, before he could speak a word. But while cannon were very effective indeed against a massed enemy, they were almost useless against a single man, as the aim couldn't be adjusted quickly enough to bear, unless the man was fool enough to advance in a straight line—and Grey was not *that* foolish.

Granted, the officer in charge of each gun's crew would be armed with sword and pistol, but a single man approaching an artillery unit on foot could be no conceivable danger; sheer amazement would likely let him get within earshot. And pistols were so inaccurate at anything over ten paces, he wasn't risking much anyway, he reasoned.

He hastened his step as much as he could, a wary eye out. There were a lot of Continental troops in his vicinity now, marching furiously. The regulars would take him for walking wounded, but he daren't try to surrender to the British lines while combat was joined, or he'd be the walking dead in short order.

The artillery in the orchard might be his best chance, hair-raising as it was to walk into the mouths of the guns. With a muffled oath, he put his shoes back on and began to run.

HE RAN HEAD-ON into a militia company, but they were headed somewhere at the trot and gave him no more than a cursory glance. He swerved aside into a hedgerow, where he floundered for a moment before breaking through. He was in a narrow field, much trampled, and on the other side of it was an apple orchard, only the crowns of the trees showing above a heavy cloud of white powder smoke.

He caught a glimpse of movement beyond the orchard and risked a few steps to the side to look—then ducked back hastily out of sight. American militia, men in hunting shirts or homespun, a few shirtless and glistening with sweat. They were massing there, likely planning a rush into the orchard from behind, in hopes of capturing or disabling the guns.

They were making a good deal of noise, and the guns had stopped firing. Plainly the artillerymen knew the Americans were there and would be making preparations to resist. Not the best time to come calling, then . . .

But then he heard the drums. Well in the distance, to the east of the orchard, but the sound carried clearly. British infantry on the march. A better prospect than the artillery in the orchard. Moving, infantry wouldn't be disposed or prepared to shoot a single, unarmed man, no matter how he was dressed. And if he could get close enough to attract the attention of an officer . . . but he'd still have to cross the open ground below the orchard in order to reach the infantry before they'd marched off out of reach.

Biting his lip with exasperation, he shoved through the hedgerow and ran through the clouds of drifting smoke. A shot cracked the air much too near him. He flung himself into the grass by instinct, but then leapt up and ran again, gasping for breath. Christ, there were riflemen in the orchard, defending the cannon! *Jaegers.*

But most of the riflemen must be facing the other way, ready to meet the gathering militia, for no more shots came on this side of the orchard. He slowed down, pressing a hand to the stitch in his side. He was past the orchard now. He could still hear the drums, though they were drawing away . . . keep going, keep going . . .

"Hoy! You there!" He *should* have kept going but, short of

breath and unsure who was calling, paused for an instant, half-turning. Only half, because a solid body hurtled through the air and knocked him down.

He hit the ground on one elbow and was already grappling the man's head with his other hand, wet greasy hair sliding through his fingers. He jabbed at the man's face, squirmed eel-like out from under his weight, kneeing the fellow in the stomach as he moved, and made it lurching to his feet.

"Stop right there!" The voice cracked absurdly, shooting up into a falsetto, and startled him so that he *did* stop, gasping for breath.

"You . . . no-account . . . filthy . . ." The man—no, by God, it was a boy!—who'd knocked him down was getting to his feet. He had a large stone in his hand; his brother—it had to be his brother; they looked like two peas in a pod, both half grown and gawky as turkey poults—had a good-sized club.

Grey's hand had gone to his waist as he'd risen, ready to draw the dagger Percy had given him. He'd seen these boys before, he thought—the sons of the commander of one of the New Jersey militia companies?—and, rather clearly, they'd seen him before, too.

"Traitor!" One of them yelled at him. "Bloody fucking *spy*!" They were between him and the distant infantry company; the orchard was at his back, and the three of them were well within range of any Hessian rifleman who happened to look in their direction.

"Look—" he began, but could see that it was pointless. Something had happened; they were crazed with something—terror, anger, grief?—that made their features shift like water and their limbs tremble with the need to do something immediate and violent. They were boys, but both taller than he was and quite capable of doing him the damage they clearly intended.

"General Fraser," he said loudly, hoping to jar them into uncertainty. "Where is General Fraser?"

77

THE PRICE OF BURNT SIENNA

"COMPANIES ALL present, sir!" Robert MacCammon rushed up, panting. He was a heavyset man, and even the gently rolling fields and meadows were hard on him; the dark stains in his oxters were the size of dinner plates.

"Aye, good." Jamie glanced beyond Major MacCammon and saw Lieutenant Herbert's company emerging from a small wood, glancing cautiously round, their weapons in their hands. They were doing well, untrained as they were, and he was pleased with them.

Lord, let me bring them through it as best I can.

This prayer barely formed in his mind, he turned to look toward the west, and froze. On the slope below him, no more than a hundred yards away, he saw the two Craddock boys, armed with a rock and a stick, respectively, menacing a man whose back was turned to him but whose bare, cropped blond head was instantly recognizable, even without the stained bandage tied round it.

Then he saw Grey put a hand to his waist and knew beyond the shadow of doubt that it was a knife he reached for.

"Craddock!!" he bellowed, and the boys both started. One dropped his rock and stooped to pick it up again, exposing his scrawny neck to Grey. Grey looked at the vulnerable expanse of flesh, glanced bleakly at the older boy, gripping his stick like a cricket bat, then up the slope at Jamie, and let both hands and shoulders drop.

"Ifrinn!" Jamie muttered under his breath. "Stay here," he said briefly to Bixby, and ran down the slope, stumbling and pushing his way through a thick growth of alders that left sticky sap all over his hands.

"Where the devil is your company?" he demanded without preamble, breathing hard as he came up with the boys and Grey.

"Oh. Er . . ." The younger Craddock looked to his brother to answer.

"We couldn't find 'em, sir," the older boy said, and swallowed. "We were looking, when we run into a party of redcoats and had to scamper pretty quick to get away."

"Then we saw *him,*" the younger Craddock said, thrusting out his chin at Grey. "Everybody in camp had said as how he was a redcoat spy, and, sure enough, there he was, makin' for them, waving and callin' out."

"So we thought as how it was our duty to stop him, sir," the older boy put in, anxious not to be eclipsed by his brother.

"Aye, I see." Jamie rubbed the spot between his eyebrows, which felt as though a small, painful knot had formed there. He glanced over his shoulder. Men were still running up from the south, but the rest of Craddock's company was nearly all there, milling anxiously and looking in his direction. No wonder: he could hear British drums, near at hand. Doubtless that was the company the boys had run into—the one Grey had been making for.

"Wenn ich etwas sagen dürfte," Grey said in German, with a glance at the Craddocks. *If I might speak . . .*

"You may not, sir," Jamie replied, with some grimness. There wasn't time—and if these two wee blockheids survived to get back to camp, they'd recount every word that had passed between Grey and him to anyone who would listen. The last thing he could afford was for them to report him involved in foreign confabulation with an English spy.

"I am in search of my son!" Grey switched to English, with another glance at the Craddocks. "I have reason to believe he's in danger."

"So is everyone else out here," Jamie replied with an edge, though his heart jerked in his chest. So that was why Grey had broken his parole. "In danger from whom?"

"Sir! *Sir!*" Bixby's voice was shouting from the other side of the alders, high and urgent. He had to go, and quickly.

"Coming, Mr. Bixby!" he shouted. "Why didn't you kill them?" he asked Grey abruptly, and jerked his head toward the Craddocks. "If you got past them, you could have made it."

One fair brow arched above the handkerchief binding Grey's bad eye.

"You'd forgive me for Claire—but not for killing your . . . men." He glanced at the two Craddocks, spotty as a pair of raisin puddings and—Grey's look implied—likely no brighter.

For a split second, the urge to punch him again surged up from Jamie's bowels, and for the same split second, the knowledge of it showed on John Grey's face. He didn't flinch, and his good eye widened in a pale-blue stare. This time, he'd fight back.

Jamie closed his eyes for an instant, forcibly setting anger aside.

"Go with this man," he said to the Craddocks. "He is your prisoner." He pulled one of the pistols from his belt and presented it to the elder Craddock, who received it with wide-eyed respect. Jamie didn't bother telling the lad it was neither loaded nor primed.

"And you," he said evenly to Grey. "Go with them behind the lines. If the Rebels still hold Englishtown, guide them there."

Grey nodded curtly, lips compressed, and turned to go.

He reached out and caught Grey by the shoulder. The man whipped round, blood in his eye.

"Listen to me," Jamie said, speaking loudly enough to be sure the Craddock boys could hear him. "I revoke your parole." He fixed Grey's single-eyed glare with one of his own. "D'ye understand me? When you reach Englishtown, ye'll surrender yourself to Captain McCorkle."

Grey's mouth twitched, but he said nothing and gave the merest nod of acknowledgment before turning away.

Jamie turned, too, running for his waiting companies, but risked a single glance over his shoulder.

Shooing the Craddocks before him, awkward and flapping as a pair of geese bound for market, Grey was headed smartly to the south, toward the American lines—if the concept of "lines" held any meaning in this goddamned battle.

Grey had certainly understood, and despite the present emergency, a weight lifted from Jamie's heart. With his parole revoked, John Grey was once more a prisoner of war, in the custody of his jailors, officially without freedom of movement. But also without the obligation of honor that would hold him prisoner on his own recognizance. Without parole, his primary duty now was that of any soldier in the hands of his enemy—escape.

"Sir!" Bixby arrived at his shoulder, panting. "There are redcoats—"

"Aye, Mr. Bixby. I hear them. Let's be having them, then."

IF IT WEREN'T for the coloring book, I might not have noticed immediately. In third or fourth grade, Brianna had had a coloring book featuring scenes from the American Revolution. Sanitized, suitably romantic scenes: Paul Revere flying through the night on a galloping horse, Washington crossing the Delaware while exhibiting (as Frank pointed out) a lamentable lack of seamanship . . . and a double-paged spread featuring Molly Pitcher, that gallant woman who had carried water to the heat-stricken troops (left-hand page) and then taken her wounded husband's place to serve his cannon (right-hand page)—at the Battle of Monmouth.

Which, it had dawned on me, was very likely what the battle we were engaged in was going to be called, once anyone got round to naming it. Monmouth Courthouse was only two or three miles from my present location.

I wiped my face once more—this gesture did nothing for the perspiration, which was instantly renewed, but, judging from the state of my three soggy handkerchiefs, was removing a fair amount of dirt from my countenance—and glanced toward the east, where I had been hearing distant cannon fire most of the day. Was she there?

"Well, George Washington certainly is," I murmured to myself, pouring out a fresh cup of water and returning to my work rinsing out bloody cloths in a bucket of salt water. "Why not Molly Pitcher?"

It had been a complicated picture to color, and as Bree had just got to the phase where she insisted that things be colored "real," the cannon could *not* be pink or orange, and Frank had obligingly drawn several crude cannon on a sheet of paper and tried out everything from gray (with shadings of black, blue, blue-violet, and even cornflower) to brown, with tints of burnt sienna and gold, before they finally settled—Frank's opinion as to actual historicity of cannon being diffidently advanced—on black with dark green shadings.

Lacking credentials, I had been relegated to coloring in the grass, though I also got to help with the dramatic shading of Mrs. Pitcher's raggedly streaming clothes, once Brianna got tired of it. I looked up, the smell of crayons strong in my memory, and saw a small group coming down the road.

There were two Continental regulars—and a man in what I recognized as the light-green uniform of Skinner's Greens, a Provincial Loyalist regiment. He was stumbling badly, though supported on both sides by the Continentals. The shorter of these also seemed to be wounded; he had a bloodstained scarf wrapped around one arm. The other was looking from side to side as though on guard, but didn't seem to be wounded.

At first I'd looked at the Provincial, who must be a prisoner. But then I looked more closely at the wounded Continental supporting him. And with Molly Pitcher so clearly and recently in mind, I realized with a small shock that the Continental was a woman. The Continental's coat covered her hips, but I could plainly see the way in which her legs slanted in toward the knee; a man's thighbones run straight up and down, but a woman's width of pelvic basin compels a slightly knock-kneed stance.

It also became clear, by the time they reached me, that the wounded soldiers were related: both were short and thin, with squared-off chins and sloping shoulders. The Provincial was definitely male, though—his face was thickly stubbled—while his . . . sister? They seemed close in age . . . was clear-skinned as an egg and nearly as white.

The Provincial was not. He was red as a blast furnace and nearly as hot to the touch. His eyes were white slits, and his head wobbled on his spindly neck.

"Is he wounded?" I asked sharply, putting a hand under his shoulder to ease him down onto a stool. He went limp the moment his buttocks touched it and would have fallen to the ground had I not tightened my grip. The girl gave a frightened gasp and put out a hand toward him, but she also staggered and would have fallen, had the other man not seized her by the shoulders.

"He took a blow to the head," the male Continental said.

"I—hit him with the hilt of my sword." This admission was made with some embarrassment.

"Help me lay him down." I ran my hand over the Provincial's head, detecting an ugly, contused wound under his hair, but found no crepitation, no sense of a skull fracture. Concussion, likely, but maybe no worse. He began to twitch under my hand, though, and the tip of his tongue protruded from his mouth.

"Oh, dear," I said, under my breath, but not far enough under, for the girl gave a small, despairing cry.

"It's heatstroke," I told her at once, hoping this might sound reassuring. The reality was far from it; once they collapsed and fell into seizures, they usually died. Their core temperature was far above what the systems of the body could tolerate, and seizing like that was often an indication that brain damage had started to occur. Still—

"Dottie!" I bellowed, and made urgent gestures at her, then turned to the sound—but very frightened-looking—Continental soldier. "See that young woman in gray? Drag him over into the shade where she is; she'll know what to do." It was simple. Pour water over him and—if possible—into him. That was the sum total of what *could* be done. Meanwhile . . .

I got hold of the girl by the non-wounded arm and sat her down on the stool, hastily pouring most of what remained in my brandy bottle into a cup. She didn't look as though she had much blood left.

She didn't. When I got the scarf off, I discovered that her hand was missing, and the forearm badly mangled. She hadn't bled to death only because someone had twined a belt round her upper arm and fastened the tourniquet tight with a stick thrust through it. It had been a long time since I'd fainted at sight of anything, and I didn't now, but did have one brief moment when the world shifted under my feet.

"How did you do that, sweetheart?" I asked, as calmly as possible. "Here, drink this."

"I—grenado," she whispered. Her head was turned away, not to see the arm, but I guided the cup to her lips and she drank, gulping the mix of brandy and water.

"She—he picked it up," said a low, choked voice at my elbow. The other Continental was back. "It rolled by my foot and he—she picked it up."

The girl turned her head at his voice, and I saw his anguished look.

"She came into the army because of you, I suppose?" Clearly the arm would have to be amputated; there was nothing below the elbow that could be saved, and to leave it in this state was to doom her to death by infection or gangrene.

"No, I didn't!" the girl said, huffing for breath. "Phil—" She gulped air and twisted her head to look toward the trees. "He tried to make me go with him. Loyalist c-camp . . . follower. Wouldn't." With so little blood remaining in her body, she was having trouble getting enough oxygen. I refilled the cup and made her drink again; she emerged from it spluttering and swaying, but more alert. "I'm a patriot!"

"I—I tried to make her go home, ma'am," the young man blurted. "But wasn't anyone left to look out for her." His hand hovered an inch from her back, wanting to touch her, waiting to catch her if she fell over.

"I see. Him—" I nodded toward Dottie's station under the trees, where the man with heatstroke lay in the shade. "Your brother?"

She hadn't the strength to nod, but closed her eyes briefly in acquiescence.

"Her father died just after Saratoga." The young man looked completely wretched. Christ, he couldn't be more than seventeen, and she looked about fourteen, though she must be older. "Phillip was already gone; he'd broke with his father when he joined the Provincials. I—" His voice broke, and he shut his mouth hard and touched her hair.

"What's your name, dear?" I said. I'd loosened the tourniquet to check that there was still blood flow to the elbow; there was. Possibly the joint could be saved.

"Sally," she whispered. Her lips were white, but her eyes were open. "Sarah." All my amputation saws were in the church with Denzell—I couldn't send her in there. I'd stuck my head in once and nearly been knocked over by the thick smell of blood and excrement—even more by the atmosphere of pain and terror and the sounds of butchery.

There were more wounded coming along the road; someone would have to tend them. I hesitated for no more than a minute.

Both Rachel and Dottie had the necessary resolve to deal

with things and the physical presence to command distraught people. Rachel's manner came from months of experience at Valley Forge, Dottie's more from a habit of autocratic expectation that people would of course do what she wanted them to. Both of them inspired confidence, and I was proud of them. Between them, they were managing as well as could be expected, and—I thought—much better than the surgeons and their assistants in the church, though these were commendably quick about their bloody business.

"Dottie!" I called again, and beckoned. She rose and came at the trot, wiping her face on her apron. I saw her look at the girl—at Sarah—then turn with a brief look at the bodies on the grass, and turn back with a look in which curiosity, horror, and a desperate compassion were blended. So the brother was dead already, or dying.

"Go and get Denzell, Dottie," I said, moving just a little so that she could see the mangled arm. She turned white and swallowed. "Tell him to bring my bow-frame saw and a small tenaculum."

Sarah and the young man made small gasps of horror at the word "saw," and then he moved swiftly, touching her at last, gripping her by her sound shoulder.

"You'll be all right, Sally," he said fiercely. "I'll marry you! Won't make a blind bit of difference to me. I mean—your—your arm." He swallowed, hard, and I realized that he needed water, too, and passed over the canteen.

"Like . . . hell," Sally said. Her eyes were dark and bright as unfired coal in her white face. "I won't—be married for pity. Damn . . . you. Nor guilt. Don't . . . need you!"

The young man's face was blank with surprise—and, I thought, affront.

"Well, what are you going to live on?" he demanded, indignant. "You don't own a thing in this world but that damned uniform! You—you—" He pounded a fist on his leg in frustration. "You can't even whore, with one arm!"

She glared at him, breathing slow and hard. After a moment, a thought crossed her face and she nodded a little and turned to me.

"You reckon the army might . . . pay me . . . a pension?" she asked.

I could see Denzell now, blood-splattered but collected, hurrying across the gravel with the box of surgical instruments. I would have sold my soul for ether or laudanum, but had neither. I took a deep breath of my own.

"I expect they will. They'll give Molly Pitcher one; why not you?"

78

IN THE WRONG PLACE AT THE WRONG TIME

WILLIAM TOUCHED his jaw gingerly, congratulating himself that Tarleton had only managed to hit him in the face once, and it hadn't been in the nose. His ribs, arms, and abdomen were another matter, and his clothes were muddy and his shirt rent, but it wouldn't be apparent to a casual observer that he'd been in a fight. He *might* just get away with it—so long as Captain André didn't happen to mention the dispatch to the British Legion. After all, Sir Henry had had his hands full during the morning, if half what William had heard along his way was true.

A wounded infantry captain on his way back to camp had told of seeing Sir Henry, in command of the rear guard, lead a charge against the Americans, getting so far out to the front that he was nearly captured before the men behind came up to him. William had burned, hearing this—he would have loved to be part of that. But at least he hadn't stayed mewed up in the clerks' tent. . . .

He was no more than a quarter mile along his way back to Cornwallis's brigade when Goth threw a shoe. William said something very bad, pulled up, and swung down to have a look. He found the shoe, but two nails had gone and a quick search didn't turn them up; no chance of hammering it back on with the heel of his boot, which had been his first thought.

He shoved the shoe in his pocket and looked round. Soldiers swarmed in every direction, but there was a company of Hessian grenadiers on the opposite side of the ravine, forming up at the bridgehead. He led Goth across, stepping gingerly.

"Hallo!" he called to the nearest fellow. *"Wo ist der nächste Hufschmied?"*

The man glanced indifferently at him and shrugged. A young fellow, though, pointed across the bridge and called out, *"Zwei Kompanien hinter uns kommen Husaren!" Hussars are coming, two companies behind!*

"Danke!" William called back, and led Goth into the sparse shade of a stand of spindly pines. Well, that was luck. He wouldn't have to walk the horse a long way; he could wait for the farrier and his wagon to come to him. Still, he fretted at the delay.

Every nerve was keyed tight as a harpsichord string; he kept touching his belt, where his weapons would normally be. He could hear the sounds of musket fire in the far distance, but couldn't see a thing. The countryside was folded up like a leporello, rolling meadow diving suddenly into wooded ravines, then springing back out, only to disappear again.

He dug out his handkerchief, so soggy by now that it served only to sluice the sweat from his face. He caught a faint breath of coolness wafting up from the creek, forty feet below, and walked nearer the edge in hopes of more. He drank warm water from his canteen, wishing he could scramble down and drink from the stream, but he daren't; he might get down the steep slope without trouble, but coming back up would be an awkward climb, and he couldn't risk missing the farrier.

"Er spricht Deutsch. Er hat es gehört!" Heard what? He hadn't been paying attention to the grenadiers' sporadic conversation, but these hissed words came to him clearly, and he glanced round to see who it was they were saying spoke German, only to see two of the grenadiers quite close behind him. One of them grinned nervously at him, and he stiffened.

Suddenly two more were there, between him and the bridge. *"Was ist hier los?"* he demanded sharply. *"Was macht Ihr da?" What is this? What are you doing?*

A burly fellow pulled an apologetic face.

"Verzeihung. Ihr seid hier falsch."

I'm in the wrong place? Before William could say anything

more, they closed on him. He elbowed, punched, kicked, and butted wildly, but it didn't last more than a few seconds. Hands pulled his arms behind him, and the burly fellow said once more, *"Verzeihung,"* and, still looking apologetic, bashed him in the head with a rock.

He didn't lose consciousness altogether until he hit the bottom of the ravine.

THERE WAS THE devil of a lot of fighting, Ian thought—but that was about all you could say about it. There was a good deal of movement—particularly among the Americans—and whenever they met with a group of redcoats, there was fighting, often ferocious fighting. But the countryside was so irregular, the armies seldom came together anywhere in large numbers.

He had found his way around several companies of British infantry more or less lying in wait, though, and beyond this vanguard were a goodly number of British, regimental banners in the midst of them. Would it help to know who was in command here? He wasn't sure he could tell, even if he was close enough to make out the details of the banners.

His left arm ached, and he rubbed it absently. The ax wound had healed well, though the scar was still raised and tender—but the arm hadn't yet recovered anything like its full strength, and loosing an arrow at the Indian scouts earlier had left the muscles quivering and jumping, with a burning deep in the bone.

"Best not try that again," he murmured to Rollo—then remembered that the dog wasn't with him.

He looked up and discovered that one of the Indian scouts *was* with him, though. Or at least he thought so. Twenty yards away, an Abenaki warrior sat on a rawboned pony, eyeing Ian thoughtfully. Yes, Abenaki, he was sure of it, seeing the scalp shaved clean from brows to crown and the band of black paint across the eyes, the long shell earrings that brushed the man's shoulders, their nacre glittering in the sun.

Even as he made these observations, he was turning his own mount, seeking shelter. The main body of men was a good two hundred yards distant, standing in open meadow, but there were stands of chestnut and poplar, and perhaps a half mile back the way he'd come, the rolling land dipped into one of the big ravines. Wouldn't do to be trapped in the low ground, but if he had enough lead, it was a good way to disappear. He kicked his horse sharply and they shot off, turning abruptly left as they passed a patch of thick growth—and a good thing, too, because he heard something heavy whiz past his head and go crashing into the growth. Throwing stick? Tomahawk?

It didn't matter; the only important thing was that the man who'd thrown it was no longer holding it. He did look back, though—and saw the second Abenaki come round the grove from the other side, ready to cut him off. The second one shouted something and the other answered—hunting cries. *Beast in view.*

"Cuidich mi, a Dhia!" he said, and jammed his heels hard into his horse's sides. The new mare was a good horse, and they made it out of the open ground, crashed through a small copse of trees and out the other side to find a rail fence before them. It was too close to stop, and they didn't; the horse dropped her hindquarters, bunched, and soared over, back hooves clipping the top rail with a solid *whank!* that made Ian bite his tongue.

He didn't look back but bent low over his horse's neck, and they ran flat out for the curving land he could see before him, dropping down. He turned and ran at an angle, not wanting to hit the edge of the ravine straight on, in case it should be steep just there. . . . No sound from behind save the rumble and clash of the army massing. No yelps, no hunting calls from the Abenaki.

There it was, the thick growth that marked the edge of the ravine. He slowed and now risked a look over his shoulder. Nothing, and he breathed and let the horse slow to a walk, picking their way along the edge, looking for a good way down. The bridge was just visible above him, maybe fifty yards distant, but no one was on it—yet.

He could hear men fighting *in* the ravine—perhaps three hundred yards from where he was—but there was sufficient growth that he was hidden from them. Only a scuffle, from the sounds—he'd heard or seen that a dozen times already today; men on both sides, driven by thirst down to the creeks that had carved the ravines, occasionally meeting and going for one another in a bloody splash among the shallows.

The thought of it reminded him of his own thirst—and the horse's, for the creature was stretching out her neck, nostrils greedily flaring at the scent of water.

He slid off and led the way down to the creek's edge, careful of loose stones and boggy earth—the creek bank here was mostly soft mud, edged with mats of duckweed and small reedbeds. A glimpse of red caught his eye and he tensed, but it was a British soldier, facedown in the mud and clearly dead, his legs swaying in the current.

He shucked his moccasins and edged out into the water himself; the creek was fairly wide here and only a couple of feet deep, with a silty bottom; he sank in ankle-deep. He edged out again and led the horse farther up the ravine, looking for better footing, though the mare was desperate for the water, pushing Ian with her head; she wouldn't wait long.

The sounds of the skirmish had faded; he could hear men up above and some way off, but nothing in the ravine itself anymore.

There, that would do. He let the horse's reins fall, and she lunged for the creek, stood with her forefeet sunk in mud but her hind feet solid on a patch of gravel, blissfully gulping water. Ian felt the pull of the water nearly as much and sank to his knees, feeling the blissful chill as it soaked his clout and leggings, that sensation fading instantly to nothingness as he cupped his hands and drank, and cupped and drank again and again, choking now and then in the effort to drink faster than he could swallow.

At last he stopped—reluctantly—and dashed water over his face and chest; it was cooling, though the bear grease in his paint made the water bead and run off his skin.

"Come on," he said to the horse. "Ye'll burst and ye keep on like that, *amaidan*." It took some struggle, but he got the horse's nose out of the creek, water and bits of green weed sloshing out of the loose-lipped mouth as the horse snorted and shook her head. It was while hauling the horse's head round in order to lead her up the bank that he saw the other British soldier.

This one was lying near the bottom of the ravine, too, but not in the mud. He was lying facedown, but with his head turned to one side, and . . .

"Och, Jesus, *no*!" Ian flung his horse's reins hastily round a tree trunk and bounded up the slope. It was, of course. He'd known it from the first glimpse of the long legs, the shape of the head, but the face made it certain, even masked with blood as it was.

William was still alive; his face twitched under the feet of a half-dozen black flies feeding on his drying blood. Ian put a hand under his jaw, the way Auntie Claire did, but, with no idea how to find a pulse or what a good one should feel like, took it away again. William was lying in the shadow of a big sycamore, but his skin was still warm—it couldn't help but be, Ian thought, even if he was dead, on a day like this.

He'd risen to his feet, thinking rapidly. He'd need to get the bugger onto the horse, but maybe best undress him? Take off the telltale coat, at least? But what if he were to take him back toward the British lines, find someone there to take charge of him, get him to a surgeon? That was closer.

Still need to take the coat off, or the man might die of the heat before he got anywhere. So resolved, he knelt again, and thus saved his own life. The tomahawk chunked into the sycamore's trunk just where his head had been a moment before.

And, a moment later, one of the Abenaki raced down the slope and leapt on him with a shriek that blasted bad breath into his face. That split second of warning, though, was enough that he'd got his feet under him and pushed to the side, heaving the Abenaki's body over his hip in a clumsy wrestling throw that landed the man in the mud four feet away.

The second one was behind him; Ian heard the man's feet in the gravel and weeds and whirled to meet the downward strike, catching the blow on his forearm, grabbing for the knife with his other hand.

He caught it—by the blade, and hissed through his teeth as it cut into his palm—and chopped down on the man's wrist with his half-numbed arm. The knife jarred loose. Hand and knife were slippery with blood; he couldn't get hold of the hilt but had got it away—he turned and threw it as far as he could upstream, and it plunked into the water.

Then they were both on him, punching, kicking, and tearing at him. He staggered backward, lost his balance but not his grip on one of his attackers, and succeeded in falling into the creek with the man atop him. After that, he lost track.

He had one of the Abenaki on his back in the water, was trying earnestly to drown him, while the other rode his own back and tried to get an arm around his neck—and then there was a racket on the other side of the ravine and everything stopped for a moment. A lot of men, moving in a disorganized sort of way—he could hear drums, but there was a noise like the distant sea, incoherent voices.

The Abenaki stopped, too, just for an instant, but that was long enough: Ian twisted, flinging the man off his back, and bounded awkwardly through the water, slipping and sinking in the muddy bottom, but made it to shore and ran for the first thing that met his eye—a tall white oak. He flung himself at the trunk and shinned up, grabbing at branches as they came in reach to pull himself higher, faster, reckless of his wounded hand, the rough bark scraping his skin.

The Indians were after him, but too late; one leapt and slapped at his bare foot but failed to get a grip, and he got a knee over a large branch and clung, panting, to the trunk, ten feet up. Safe? He thought so, but after a moment peered down cautiously.

The Abenaki were casting to and fro like wolves, glancing up at the noise above the rim of the ravine, then up at Ian—then across the creek toward William, and that made Ian's wame curl up. God, what could he do if they should decide to go cut the man's throat? He hadn't even got a stone to throw at them.

The one good thing was that neither of them seemed to have either a gun or a bow; must have left those with their horses, up above. They couldn't do anything but throw stones at *him,* and they seemed disinclined.

More noise from above—a *lot* of men up there; what were they shouting?—and the Abenaki abruptly abandoned Ian. They splashed back across the stream, their leggings clinging with water and streaked with black mud, paused briefly to turn William over and rummage his clothes—evidently he'd already been robbed, for they found nothing—and then untied Ian's horse and with a last mocking call of "Mohawk!" disappeared with the mare into a growth of pussy willows downstream.

IAN HAD DRAGGED himself one-handed up the slope, crawled some distance, and then lay for a while under a fallen log on the edge of a clearing, spots coming and going before his eyes like a swarm of midgies. There was a lot going on nearby, but none of it near enough to cause him immediate concern. He closed his eyes, hoping that would make the spots go away. They didn't, instead turning from black to a horrid constellation of swimming pink and yellow blobs that made him want to vomit.

He hastily opened his eyes again, in time to see several powder-blackened Continental soldiers, stripped to their shirts, some bare to the waist, dragging a cannon down the road. They were followed in short order by more men and another cannon, all staggering with the heat and white-eyed with exhaustion. He recognized Colonel Owen, stumping along between the limbers, sooty face set in unhappy desperation.

Some sense of stirring drew Ian's wandering eye away toward a group of men, and he realized with a faint sense of interest that it was a very large group of men, with a standard hanging limp as an unstuffed haggis against its pole.

That in turn stirred recognition. Sure enough, there was General Lee, long-nosed and frowning but looking very keen, riding out of the mass toward Owen.

Ian was too far away and there was too much noise to hear a word, but the trouble was obvious from Owen's gestures and pointings. One of his cannon was broken, burst, probably from the heat of firing, and another had broken free of its limber and was being dragged with ropes, its metal scraping on the rocks as it juddered along.

A dim sense of urgency was reasserting itself. *William.* He needed to tell someone about William. Plainly it wasn't going to be the British.

Lee's brows drew in and his lips thinned, but he kept his composure. He had bent down from his saddle to listen to Owen; now he nodded, spoke a few words, and straightened up. Owen wiped a sleeve across his face and waved to his men. They picked up their ropes and leaned into the weight, disconsolate, and Ian saw that three or four were wounded, cloths wrapped round heads or hands, one half-hopping with a bloody leg, a hand on one of the cannon for support.

Ian's wame had begun to settle now, and he was desperately

thirsty, despite having drunk his fill at the creek only a short time before. He'd taken no notice where he was going but, seeing Owen's cannon come down the road, knew he must be near the bridge, though it was out of sight. He crawled out of his hiding place and managed to stand up, holding on to the log for a moment while his vision went black and white and black again.

William. He had to find someone to help . . . but first he had to find water. He couldn't manage without it. Everything he'd drunk at the creek had run off him as sweat, and he was parched to the bone.

It took several tries, but he got water at last from an infantryman who had two canteens hanging round his neck.

"What happened to you, chum?" the infantryman asked, eyeing him with interest.

"Had a fight with a British scout," Ian replied, and reluctantly handed back the canteen.

"Hope you won it, then," the man said, and waved without waiting for an answer, moving off with his company.

Ian's left eye was stinging badly and his vision was cloudy; a cut in his eyebrow was bleeding. He groped in the small bag at his waist and found the handkerchief wrapped round the smoked ear he carried. The cloth was a small one, but big enough to tie round his brow.

He wiped his knuckles over his mouth, already longing for more water. What ought he to do? He could see the standard now being vigorously waved, flapping heavily in the thick air, summoning the troops to follow. Plainly Lee was headed over the bridge; he knew where he was going, and his troops with him. No one would—or could—stop to climb down a ravine to aid a wounded British soldier.

Ian shook his head experimentally and, finding that his brains didn't seem to rattle, set off toward the southwest. With luck, he'd meet La Fayette or Uncle Jamie coming up, and maybe get another mount. With a horse, he could get William out of the ravine alone. And whatever else might happen today, he'd settle the hash of those Abenaki bastards.

79

HIGH NOON

ONE OF LA FAYETTE'S men came up at this point with orders to fall back, to rejoin La Fayette's main body near one of the farms between Spotswood South Brook and Spotswood Middlebrook. Jamie was pleased to hear it; there was no reasonable way for half-armed militia companies to lay siege to the artillery entrenched in the orchard, not with rifles guarding the cannon.

"Gather your companies, Mr. Guthrie, and join me on the road up there," Jamie said, pointing. "Mr. Bixby, can ye find Captain Kirby? Tell him the same thing; I'll fetch along Craddock's troops."

Captain Craddock's companies had been badly demoralized by his death, and Jamie had brought them under his own direct command to prevent them scattering like bumblebees.

They made their way across the fields, picking up Corporal Filmer and his men at the farmhouse—it was deserted; no need to leave anyone there—and across the bridge over one of the creeks. He slowed a little as his horse's hooves thudded on the planks, feeling the blessed cool dampness coming up from the water thirty feet below. They should stop, he thought, for water—they hadn't, since early morning, and the canteens would be running dry—but it would take too long for so many men to work their way along the ravine, down to the creek, and back up. He thought they could make it to La Fayette's position; there were wells there.

He could see the road ahead and peeled an eye for lurking British. He wondered, with a moment's irritation, where Ian was; he would have liked to know where the British *were.*

He found out an instant later. A gunshot cracked nearby, and his horse slipped and fell. Jamie yanked his foot free and rolled out of the saddle as the horse hit the bridge with a thud that shook the whole structure, struggled for an instant, neighing loudly, and slid over the edge into the ravine.

Jamie scrambled to his feet; his hand was burning, all the skin taken off his palm when he'd skidded on the splintered boards.

"Run!" he shouted, with what breath he had left, and waved an arm wildly, gathering the men, pointing them down the road toward a growth of trees that would cover them. *"Go!"*

He found himself among them, the surge of men carrying him with them, and they stumbled into cover, gasping and wheezing with the effort of running. Kirby and Guthrie were sorting out their companies, the late Captain Craddock's men were clustering near Jamie, and he nodded, breathless, to Bixby and Corporal Greenhow to count noses.

He could still hear the sound the horse had made, hitting the ground below the bridge.

He was going to vomit; he felt it rising and knew better than to try to hold it back. He made a quick staying motion toward Lieutenant Schnell, who wanted to speak to him, stepped behind a large pine, and let his stomach turn itself out like an emptied sporran. He stayed bent for a moment, mouth open and forehead pressed against the rough bark for support, letting the gush of saliva wash the taste of it from his mouth.

Cuidich mi, a Dhia . . . But his mind had lost all notion of words for the moment, and he straightened up, wiping his mouth on his sleeve. As he came out from behind the tree, though, all thought of what might be going on and what he might have to do about it vanished. Ian had come out of the trees nearby and was making his way across the open space. The lad was afoot and moving slowly, but doggedly. Jamie could see the bruises, even from a distance of forty feet.

"That one of ourn or one of theirn?" a militiaman asked doubtfully, raising his musket to bear on Ian, just in case.

"He's mine," Jamie said. "Don't shoot him, aye? Ian! *Ian!*" He didn't run—his left knee hurt too much to run—but made his way toward his nephew as fast as possible and was relieved to see the glassy look in Ian's eyes shatter and brighten into recognition at sight of him.

"Uncle Jamie!" Ian shook his head as though to clear it and stopped abruptly with a gasp.

"Are ye bad hurt, *a bhalaich*?" Jamie asked, stepping back and looking for blood. There was some, but nothing dreadful. The lad wasn't clutching himself as though wounded in the vitals. . . .

"No. No, it's—" Ian worked his mouth, trying to get up the spit to make words, and Jamie thrust his canteen into Ian's hand. There was pitifully little water left in it, but some, enough, and Ian gulped it.

"William," Ian gasped, lowering the empty canteen. "Your—"

"What about him?" Jamie interrupted. There were more men coming down the road, some of them half-running, looking back. *"What?"* he repeated, grasping Ian's arm.

"He's alive," Ian said at once, correctly gauging both intent and intensity of the question. "Someone hit him on the head and left him in the bottom of yon ravine." He gestured vaguely toward the scouts. "Maybe three hundred yards west o' the bridge, aye? He's no dead, but I dinna ken how bad hurt he may be."

Jamie nodded, making instant calculations.

"Aye, and what happened to *you*?" He could only hope that William and Ian hadn't happened to each other. But if William was unconscious, it couldn't be he who'd taken Ian's horse, and plainly someone had, for—

"Two Abenaki scouts," Ian replied with a grimace. "The buggers have been following me for—"

Jamie was still holding Ian by the left arm and felt the impact of the arrow and the shock of its reverberation through the lad's body. Ian glanced unbelievingly at his right shoulder, where the shaft protruded, and gave at the knees, his weight pulling him from Jamie's grasp as he keeled over.

Jamie launched himself over Ian's body and hit the ground rolling, avoiding the second arrow; he heard it rip the air near his ear. Heard the militiaman's gun speak just above him and then a confusion of screaming and shouting, a group of his men breaking, running toward the source of the arrows, bellowing.

"Ian!" He rolled his nephew onto his back. The lad was conscious, but as much of his face as showed under the paint was white and ghastly, his throat working helplessly. Jamie grasped the arrow; it was lodged in what Claire called the deltoid, the fleshy part of the upper arm, but it didn't budge when he shook it gently.

"I think it's struck the bone," he said to Ian. "No bad, but the tip's stuck fast."

"I think so, too," Ian said faintly. He was struggling to sit up, but couldn't. "Break it off, aye? I canna be going about wi' it sticking out like that."

Jamie nodded, got his nephew sitting unsteadily upright, and broke the shaft between his hands, leaving a ragged stub a few inches long with which to pull the arrow out. There wasn't much blood, only a trickle running down Ian's arm. Claire could see to getting the arrowhead out later.

The shouting and confusion were becoming widespread. A glance showed him more men coming down the road, and he heard a fife signaling in the distance, thin and desperate.

"D'ye ken what's happened up there?" he said to Ian, nodding toward the noise. Ian shook his head.

"I saw Colonel Owen comin' down wi' his cannon all in shambles. He stopped to say a word to Lee and then came on, but he wasna running."

A few men *were* running, though in a heavy, clumsy way—not as though pursuit was close. But he could feel alarm beginning to spread through the men around him and turned to them at once.

"Stay by me," he said calmly to Guthrie. "Keep your men together, and by me. Mr. Bixby—say that to Captain Kirby, as well. Stay by me; dinna move save on my word."

The men from Craddock's company who had run after the Abenaki—he supposed that to be the source of the arrows—had vanished into the woods. He hesitated for an instant, but then sent a small party after them. No Indian he'd ever met would fight from a fixed position, so he doubted he was sending his men into ambush. Perhaps into the face of the oncoming British, but if that was the case, best he knew about it as soon as possible, and at least one or two would likely make it back to tell him.

Ian was getting his feet under him; Jamie bent and gave the lad an arm under his good shoulder and got him standing. His legs shook in their buckskins and sweat ran in sheets down his bare torso, but he stood.

"Was it you who called my name, Uncle Jamie?" he asked.

"Aye, I did when I saw ye come out of the trees." Jamie nodded toward the wood, keeping one eye out for anyone coming back that way. "Why?"

"Not then. Just before this—" He touched the ragged end of the arrow shaft gingerly. "Someone called out behind me; that's what made me move, and a good thing, too. I'd ha' taken this square in the chest otherwise."

Jamie shook his head and felt that faint sense of bemusement that always attended brushes with ghosts—if that's what this was. The only strangeness of it was that it never seemed strange at all.

But there was no time to think of such things; there were calls now of "Retreat! Retreat!" and the men behind him stirred and rippled like wheat in a rising wind.

"Stay by me!" he said, in a loud, firm voice, and the ones nearest him took a grip of their weapons and stood.

William. Thought of his son sparked a flare of alarm in his bones. The arrow that had struck Ian had jolted the vision of William, sprawled and bloody in the mud, out of his head, but now . . . Christ, he couldn't send men after the lad, not with half the army pouring back in this direction, and the British maybe on their heels. . . . A sudden ray of hope: if the British *were* headed this way, they'd maybe come across the lad and care for him.

He wanted badly to go himself. If William was dying . . . but he could in no circumstances leave his men, and particularly not in these circumstances. A terrible urgency seized him.

Christ, if I never speak to him—never tell him—

Now he saw Lee and his aides coming down the road. They were moving slowly, no air of haste about it, but deliberate—and looking back now and then, almost surreptitiously, glancing quickly again to the front, sitting straight in their saddles.

"Retreat!" The cry was springing up now all around them, growing stronger, and men were streaming out of the woods. "Retreat!"

"Stay by me," Jamie said, softly enough that only Bixby and Guthrie heard him—but it was enough. They stiffened, stood by him. Their resolve would help to hold the rest. If Lee came even with him, ordered him . . . then they would have to go. But not 'til then.

"Shit!" said one of the men behind him, surprised. Jamie glanced back, saw a staring face, then whipped round to look where the man was looking. Some of Craddock's men were coming out of the wood, looking pleased with themselves. They had Claire's mare with them, and over her saddle was the limp body of an Indian, his long, greased scalp locks nearly dragging the ground.

"Got him, sir!" One of the men—Mortlake—saluted, grinning white-toothed from the shade of a hat that he didn't think to remove. His face gleamed like oiled leather, and he nodded to Ian in a friendly fashion, jerking his thumb at the mare. "Horse—you?"

"It is," Ian said, and his Scots accent made Mortlake blink. "I thank ye, sir. I think my uncle had best take the horse, though. Ye'll need her, aye?" he added to Jamie, lifting an eyebrow toward the ranks of men behind them.

Jamie wanted to refuse; Ian looked as if he could barely walk. But the lad was right. Jamie would have to lead these men, whether forward or back—and he'd need them to be able to see him. He nodded reluctantly, and the body of the Abenaki was dragged from the saddle and tossed carelessly into the brush. He saw Ian's eyes follow it, dark with dislike, and thought for a split second of the smoked ear his nephew carried in his sporran, and hoped that Ian wouldn't—but, no, a Mohawk took no trophies from another's kill.

"There were two of them, ye said, Ian?"

Ian turned from contemplation of the dead Abenaki and nodded.

"Saw t'other one," Mortlake answered the implied question. "Ran when we shot this villain." He coughed, glancing at the increasing streams of men coming down the road. "Beg pardon, sir, but oughtn't we be moving, too?"

The men were fidgeting, craning their necks to see, murmuring when they spotted Lee, whose aides were spreading out, trying to marshal the swarming men into some kind of orderly retreat but being roundly ignored. Then something, some change of atmosphere, made Jamie turn, and half the men with him.

And here came Washington up the road on Jamie's erstwhile white stallion, galloping, and a look on his big, rough face that would have melted brass.

The incipient panic in the men dissolved at once as they pressed forward, urgent to learn what was afoot. There was chaos in the road. Some companies scattered, stopping abruptly to look round for their fellows, some noticing Washington's sudden appearance, others still coming down the road, colliding with those standing still—and, in the midst of it, Washington pulled his horse up beside Charles Lee's and leaned toward him, flushed like an apple with heat and anger.

"What do you mean by this, sir?!" was all that Jamie heard clearly, the words carried to him by some freak of the heavy air, before noise and dust and smothering heat settled so thickly on the scene that it was impossible to hear anything over the clishmaclaver, save the disquieting echo of musket volleys and the occasional faint popping of grenadoes in the distance.

He didn't try to shout above the noise; it wasn't necessary. His men were going nowhere, as riveted to the spectacle before them as he was.

Lee's long-nosed face was pinched with fury, and Jamie saw him for a brief instant as Punch, the furious puppet in a Punch-and-Judy show. An unhinged urge to laugh bubbled up, as the necessary corollary irresistibly presented itself: George Washington as Judy, the mobcapped shrew who belabored her husband with a stick. For an instant, Jamie feared he had succumbed to the heat and lost his mind.

Once envisioned, though, he couldn't escape the thought, and for an instant he was standing in Hyde Park, watching Punch feed his baby to the sausage machine.

For that was what Washington was very clearly doing. It lasted no more than three or four minutes, and then Washington made a furious gesture of disgust and dismissal and, wheeling his horse, set off at a trot, circling back to pass the troops who had clotted along the roadside, watching in fascination.

Emerging from his own fascination with a jolt, Jamie put a foot in the mare's stirrup and swung up.

"Ian—" he said, and his nephew nodded, putting a hand on his knee—as much to steady himself, he thought, as to reassure his uncle.

"Give me a few men, Uncle Jamie," he said. "I'll see to . . . his lordship."

There was barely time to summon Corporal Greenhow and detail him to take five men and accompany Ian, before Washington came close enough to spot Jamie and his companies. The general's hat was in his hand and his face was afire, anger and desperation subsumed in eagerness, and the whole of his being radiating something Jamie had seldom seen, but recognized. Had felt himself, once. It was the look of a man risking everything, because there was no choice.

"Mr. Fraser!" Washington shouted to him, and his wide mouth stretched wider in a blazing grin. "Follow me!"

80

PATER NOSTER

WILLIAM CAME AWAKE slowly, feeling terrible. His head hurt and he wanted to vomit. He was horribly thirsty, but the thought of drinking anything made his gorge rise and he retched feebly. He was lying in grass and bugs; there were bugs crawling on him. . . . He saw, for one vivid moment, a line of tiny ants climbing busily through the dark hairs on his wrist and tried to dash his hand against the ground to dislodge them. His hand didn't move, though, and his consciousness faded.

It came back with a throbbing rush and jounce. The world was jigging dizzily up and down, and he couldn't breathe. Then he made out the dark things that went in and out of his field of view as being a horse's legs and realized that he was belly-down over a saddle, being carried somewhere. *Where . . . ?*

There was a lot of shouting going on nearby, and the noise hurt his head very much.

"Stop!" shouted an English voice. "What are you doing with him? Stand! Stand or I'll kill you!"

"Leave him! Push him off! Run!" A vaguely familiar voice, Scottish.

Then a confusion of noise and somewhere in it the Scottish voice again, shouting, "Tell my—" But then he hit the ground with a thud that knocked out both wit and wind, and slid back into darkness, headfirst.

IN THE END, it was simplicity itself. John Grey walked down a cattle track, following the hoofprints toward what must be water, and walked straight into a startled group of British soldiers filling their canteens at a muddy ford. Light-headed from thirst and heat, he didn't bother trying to identify or explain himself, just put his hands in the air and gave himself up with an intense feeling of relief.

The soldiers gave him water, at least, and then he was marched off under the guard of a nervous boy with a musket and into the yard of a farmhouse that appeared to be deserted. No doubt the owners had fled upon realizing that they were in the middle of twenty thousand or so armed troops bent on mayhem.

Grey was hustled over to a large wagon half filled with cut grass, made to sit down on the ground with several other captured prisoners—in the shade, thank God—and left there under the guard of two middle-aged privates, armed with muskets, and a nervous child of fourteen or so in a lieutenant's uniform, who twitched every time the sound of a volley echoed off the trees.

This might be his best chance. If he could shock or intimidate the boy into sending him to Cornwallis or Clinton . . .

"Sir!" he barked at the boy, who blinked at him, startled. So did the captured Americans.

"What is your name, sir?" he demanded, in his command voice. That rattled the young lieutenant badly; he took two involuntary steps backward before stopping himself. He flushed, though, and rallied.

"You be quiet!" he said, and, stepping forward, aimed a cuff at Grey's ear.

Grey caught him by the wrist by reflex, but before he could release the boy, one of the privates had taken a stride toward him and brought down the butt of his musket on Grey's left forearm.

"'E said be quiet," the private said mildly. "I'd do it, was I you."

Grey *was* quiet, but only because he couldn't speak. That arm had been broken twice before—once by Jamie Fraser, once by a cannon explosion—and the third time was definitely not the charm. His vision went black for a moment, and everything inside him contracted into a ball of hot lead. Then it started to hurt, and he could breathe again.

"What's that you just said?" the man sitting next him said under his breath, eyebrows raised. "'Tain't English, is it?"

"No," said Grey, and paused for another breath, clutching the arm against his belly. "It's German for 'Oh, shit.'"

"Ah." The man nodded understandingly and—with a wary glance at the guards—brought a small flask out from under his coat and pulled the cork before handing it to Grey. "Try that, friend," he whispered.

The scent of overripe apples surged directly into his brain and very nearly made him vomit. He managed to swallow, though, and handed back the flask with a nod of thanks. Sweat ran down his face in streams, stinging his good eye.

No one spoke. The man who'd given him the applejack was a Continental regular, middle-aged, with a haggard face and only half his teeth remaining. He sat hunched, elbows on his knees, eyes fixed on the distance, where the sound of fighting was. The others were doing the same thing, he realized—all craning toward the battle.

Colonel Watson Smith popped into his mind, doubtless summoned up by the fumes of applejack, but appearing so suddenly that Grey jerked a little, and one of the guards stiffened, giving him a hard look. Grey looked away, though, and the man relaxed.

Shocked with pain, exhausted and thirsty, he lay down, nursing his throbbing arm against his chest. The buzzing of insects filled his ears, and the volley of muskets retreated into the meaningless rumble of distant thunder. He let himself lapse into a not unpleasant catatonia visualizing Smith shirtless, lying on the narrow cot under a lantern, cradling Grey in his arms, stroking his back with a comforting hand. At some point, he drifted into an uneasy sleep, punctuated by the sounds of guns and shouting.

He woke suddenly, with a mouth like cotton, to find that several more prisoners had been delivered and that there was an Indian sitting beside him. Grey's working eye was gummy and bleared, and it took a moment before he recognized the face under the remnants of black and green war paint.

Ian Murray gave him a long, level look that said plainly, *"Don't talk,"* and he didn't. Murray raised an eyebrow at his wounded arm. Grey lifted his good shoulder in a brief shrug and focused his attention on the water cart that had come to a halt on the nearby road.

"You and you, come with me." One of the privates jerked a thumb at two of the prisoners and led them off toward the cart, from which they returned shortly, carrying buckets of water.

The water was blood-warm and tasted of sodden, half-rotted wood, but they drank greedily, spilling it down their clothes in their haste. Grey wiped a wet hand across his face, feeling somewhat more settled in his mind. He flexed his left wrist experimentally; perhaps it was only a brui—no, it wasn't.

He'd drawn in his breath with a hiss, and Murray, as though in response, closed his eyes, steepled his hands together, and began to intone the Pater Noster.

"What in b-buggery is *that*?" the lieutenant demanded, stamping over to him. "Are you talking Indian, sir?"

Ian opened his eyes, regarding the child with a mild stare.

"It's Latin. I'm sayin' my prayers, aye?" he said. "D'ye mind?"

"Do I—" The lieutenant stopped, baffled as much by being addressed in a Scottish accent as by the circumstance. He stole a glance at the privates, who looked off into the distance. He cleared his throat.

"No," he said shortly, and turned away, pretending absorption in the distant cloud of white powder smoke that hung low over the trees.

Murray cut his eyes at Grey and, with a slight nod, began the Pater Noster again. Grey, somewhat puzzled, joined him, stumbling a bit. The lieutenant stiffened, but didn't turn round.

"Do they not know who you are?" Murray asked in Latin at the end of the prayer, not varying his intonation.

"I told them; they don't believe me," Grey replied, adding a random *"Ave Maria"* at the end for verisimilitude.

"*Gratia plena, Dominus tecum.* Shall *I* tell them?"

"I have no idea what comes next. I suppose it couldn't hurt."

"Benedicta tu in mulieribus, et benedictus fructus ventris tui, Jesu," Murray replied, and rose to his feet.

The guards swung round immediately, raising their muskets to their shoulders. Murray ignored this, addressing the lieutenant.

"It's maybe no my business, sir," he said mildly. "But I shouldna like to see ye ruin your career over a wee mistake."

"Be qui—what mistake?" the lieutenant demanded. He had taken off his wig because of the heat but now crammed it back on his head, evidently thinking it might lend him authority. He was mistaken in this impression, as the wig was a good deal too large and immediately slipped sideways over one ear.

"This gentleman," Murray said, gesturing to Grey, who sat up straight and stared impassively at the lieutenant. "I canna imagine what's brought him here or why he should be dressed as he is—but I ken him well. This is Lord John Grey. The, ehm, brother of Colonel Grey, the Duke of Pardloe?" he added delicately.

The hue of the young lieutenant's face changed noticeably. He glanced quickly back and forth between Murray and Grey, frowning, and absently shoved his wig back into place. Grey rose slowly, keeping an eye on the guards.

"That's ridiculous," the lieutenant said, but without force. "Why should Lord John Grey be here, looking like—like *that*?"

"The exigencies of war, Lieutenant," said Grey, keeping his voice level. "I see you belong to the Forty-ninth, which means that your colonel is Sir Henry Calder. I know him. If you will be so kind as to lend me paper and pencil, I will write him a short note, asking him to send an escort to fetch me. You can send the note via the water carrier," he added, seeing a wild look come into the boy's eyes, and hoping to calm him before he panicked and decided that the simplest way out of this imbroglio was to shoot Grey.

One of the privates—the one who had broken Grey's arm—coughed gently.

"We'm goin' to need more men, sir, in any case. Three of us with a dozen prisoners . . . and doubtless more comin'?" The lieutenant looked blank, and the private had another go. "I meantersay . . . might be you'd mean to send for reinforcements anyroad." The man caught Grey's eye and coughed again.

"Accidents happen," Grey said, though with no great charity, and the guards relaxed.

"All right," the lieutenant said. His voice broke on it and he repeated, "All right!" in a gruff baritone, looking belligerently around. No one was foolish enough to laugh.

Grey's knees were wanting to tremble, and he sat down rather abruptly to prevent it. Murray's face—well, the faces of all the prisoners—were carefully blank.

"Tibi debeo," Grey said quietly. *I acknowledge the debt.*

"Deo gratias," Murray murmured, and only then did Grey see the trail of blood that streaked Murray's arm and side, staining his breechclout—and the stub of a broken arrow protruding from the flesh of his right shoulder.

WILLIAM CAME round again lying on something that didn't move, thank God. There was a canteen being pressed to his lips, and he drank, gulping, lips reaching for more water even as it was drawn away.

"Not that fast, you'll be sick," said a familiar voice. "Breathe once, and you can have more." He breathed and forced his eyes open against a glare of light. A familiar face appeared over him, and he reached up a wavering hand toward it.

"Papa . . ." he whispered.

"No, but the next best thing," said his uncle Hal, taking a firm hold on the groping hand and sitting down beside him. "How's the head?"

William closed his eyes and tried to focus on something other than the pain.

"Not . . . that bad."

"Pull the other one, it's got bells on," his uncle murmured, cupping William's cheek and turning his head to the side. "Let's have a look."

"Let's have more water," William managed, and his uncle gave a small snort and put the canteen back to William's lips.

When William stopped to breathe again, his uncle set the canteen down and inquired, in a perfectly normal tone of voice, "Can you sing, do you think?"

His vision was going in and out; there were momentarily two of his uncle, then one, then two again. He closed one eye, and Uncle Hal steadied.

"You want me to . . . *sing*?" he managed.

"Well, perhaps not right this minute," the duke said. He sat back on his stool and began to whistle a tune. "Recognize that, do you?" he asked, breaking off.

"'Lillibulero,'" William said, beginning to feel rather cross. "Why, for God's sake?"

"Knew a chap once who was hit on the head with an ax and lost his ability to make out music. Couldn't tell one note from another." Hal leaned forward, holding up two fingers. "How many fingers am I holding up?"

"Two. Stick them up your nose," William advised him. "Go away, will you? I'm going to be sick."

"Told you not to drink too fast." But his uncle had a basin under his face and a strong hand on his head, bracing him while he heaved and coughed and shot water out of his nose.

By the time he had subsided back onto his pillow—it *was* a pillow, he was lying on a camp cot—he'd recovered enough of his senses to be able to look around and determine that he was in an army tent—probably his uncle's, judging from the battered campaign chest and the sword that lay across it—and the glare of light was coming from the low afternoon sun flooding in through the open tent flap.

"What happened?" he asked, wiping his mouth on the back of his hand.

"What's the last thing you recall?" Uncle Hal countered, handing him the canteen.

"The—er—" His mind was full of confused bits and pieces. The last thing he truly remembered was Jane and her sister, laughing at him as he stood bare-arsed in the creek. He sipped water and put cautious fingers to his head, which seemed to be wrapped in a bandage. It felt sore to the touch. "Taking my horse down to drink at a creek."

Uncle Hal raised one eyebrow. "You were found in a ditch, near a place called Spottiswood or some such thing. Von Knyphausen's troops were holding a bridge there."

William started to shake his head, but thought better of it and closed his eyes against the light.

"Don't remember."

"It will likely come back to you." His uncle paused. "Do you happen to remember where you last saw your father?"

William felt an unnatural calm come over him. He just bloody didn't care anymore, he told himself. The whole world was going to know, one way or another.

"Which one?" he said flatly, and opened his eyes. His uncle was regarding him with interest, but no particular surprise.

"You've met Colonel Fraser, then?" Hal asked.

"I have," William said shortly. "How long have *you* known about it?"

"Roughly three seconds, in the sense of certainty," his uncle replied. He reached up and unfastened the leather stock around his neck, sighing with relief as it came off. "Good Lord, it's hot." The stock had left a broad red mark; he massaged this gently, half-closing his eyes. "In the sense of thinking there was something rather remarkable in your resemblance to the aforesaid Colonel Fraser . . . since I met him again in Philadelphia recently. Prior to that, I hadn't seen him for a long time—not since you were very small, and I never saw him in close conjunction with you then, in any case."

"Oh."

They sat in silence for a bit, gnats and black flies caroming off the canvas and falling onto William's bed like snowflakes. He became aware of the noises of a large camp surrounding them, and it occurred to him that they must be with General Clinton.

"I didn't know you were with Sir Henry," he said at last, breaking the silence. Hal nodded, pulling his worn silver flask out of his coat pocket before tossing the coat itself over the campaign chest.

"I wasn't; I've been with Cornwallis. We—the regiment, that is—arrived in New York about two weeks ago. I came down to Philadelphia to see Henry and John and make inquiries about Benjamin. I arrived just in time to leave the city with the army."

"Ben? What's he done that you're inquiring about?"

"Got married, had a son, and been mug enough to be captured by the Rebels, evidently," his uncle replied lightly. "Thought he might do with a bit of help. If I give you a sip of this, can you keep it down?"

William didn't reply, but reached for the flask. It was filled with good brandy; he breathed it in cautiously, but it seemed not to trouble his wobbly stomach, and he risked a sip.

Uncle Hal watched him for a bit, not speaking. The resemblance between him and Lord John was considerable, and it gave William an odd feeling to see him—something between comfort and resentment.

"Your father," Hal said after a few moments. "Or my brother, if you prefer. Do you recall when you saw him last?"

Resentment sparked abruptly into anger.

"Yes, I bloody do. On the morning of the sixteenth. In his house. With my *other* father."

Hal made a low humming noise, indicating interest.

"That when you found out, was it?"

"It was."

"Did John tell you?"

"No, he bloody didn't!" Blood surged to William's face, making his head throb with a fierce suddenness that made him dizzy. "If I hadn't come face-to-face with the—the fellow, I don't suppose he'd ever have told me!"

He swayed and put out a hand to keep from falling over. Hal grabbed him by the shoulders and eased him back down onto the pillow, where he lay still, teeth clenched, waiting for the pain to ebb. His uncle took the flask from his unresisting hand, sat down again, and took a meditative sip.

"You might have done worse," his uncle observed after a moment. "In the way of sires, I mean."

"Oh, really?" William said coldly.

"Granted, he is a Scot," the duke said judiciously.

"And a traitor."

"And a traitor," Hal agreed. "Damned fine swordsman, though. Knows his horses."

"He was a fucking *groom,* for God's sake! Of course he knows horses!" Fresh outrage made William jerk upright again, despite the thunder in his temples. "What am I bloody going to do?!"

His uncle sighed deeply and put the cork back in the flask.

"Advice? You're too old to be given it and too young to take it." He glanced aside at William, his face very like Papa's. Thinner, older, dark brows beginning to beetle, but with that same rueful humor in the corners of his eyes. "Thought of blowing your brains out?"

William blinked, startled.

"No."

"That's good. Anything else is bound to be an improvement, isn't it?" He rose, stretching, and groaned with the movement. "God, I'm old. Lie down, William, and go to sleep. You're in no condition to think." He opened the lantern and blew it out, plunging the tent into warm gloom.

A rustling as he raised the tent flap, and the searing light of the sinking sun outlined the duke's slender figure as he turned.

"You *are* still my nephew," he said in a conversational tone. "Doubt that's much comfort to you, but there it is."

81

AMONG THE TOMBSTONES

THE SUN WAS LOW and shining directly into my eyes, but the casualties had come so fast that I couldn't take time to move my equipment round. They'd fought all day; it was still going on—I could hear it, close by, but saw nothing when I glanced up, blinking against the sun. Still, the shouts and banging of muskets and what I thought must be grenades—I'd never heard a grenade explode, but something was making a sort of irregular hollow *poong!* that was quite different from the boom of cannon or the slow percussion of musket fire—were loud enough to drown the sounds of groaning and crying from the shade trees and the relentless buzzing of the flies.

I was swaying with weariness and heat and, for my own part, was nearly indifferent to the battle. Until, that is, a young man in militia brown staggered in, blood streaming down his face from a deep cut in his forehead. I had stanched the bleeding and half-wiped his face before I recognized him.

"Corporal . . . Greenhow?" I asked dubiously, and a small spurt of fear penetrated the fog of fatigue. Joshua Greenhow was in one of Jamie's companies; I'd met him.

"Yes, ma'am." He tried to bob his head, but I stopped him, pressing firmly on the wad of lint I'd slapped on his forehead.

"Don't move. General Fraser—have you . . ." My mouth dried, sticky, and I reached automatically for my cup, only to find it empty.

"He's all right, ma'am," the corporal assured me, and reached out a long arm to the table, where my canteen lay. "Or at least he was last time I saw him, and that was no more 'n ten minutes gone." He poured water into my cup, tossed it into his own mouth, breathed heavily for an instant in relief, then poured more, which he handed to me.

"Thank you." I gulped it; it was so warm that it was barely discernible as wet, but it eased my tongue. "His nephew—Ian Murray?"

Corporal Greenhow started to shake his head, but stopped.

"Haven't seen him since about noon, but I haven't seen him dead, either, ma'am. Oh—sorry, ma'am. I meant—"

"I know what you meant. Here, put your hand there and keep the pressure on." I placed his hand on the lint and fished a fresh suture needle threaded with silk out of its jar of alcohol. My hands, steady all day, trembled a little, and I had to stop and breathe for a moment. Close. Jamie was so close. And somewhere in the midst of the fighting I could hear.

Corporal Greenhow was telling me something about the fighting, but I was having trouble attending. Something about General Lee being relieved of his command and—

"Relieved of command?" I blurted. "What the devil for?"

He looked startled by my vehemence, but replied obligingly.

"Why, I don't quite know, ma'am. Was something to do with a retreat and how he oughtn't to have told them to do it, but then General Washington come up on his horse and cursed and swore like the dickens—saving your presence, ma'am," he added politely. "Anyway, I *saw* him! General Washington. Oh, ma'am, it was so . . ." Words failed him, and I handed him the canteen with my momentarily free hand.

"Jesus H. Roosevelt Christ," I murmured under my breath. Were the Americans winning? Holding their own? Had bloody Charles Lee cocked things up after all—or not?

Corporal Greenhow luckily hadn't noticed my language, but was coming to life like a flower in the rain, enthused by his account.

"And so we rushed straight after him, and he was all along the road and the ridgeline, shouting and waving his hat, and all the troops trudging back down . . . why, they all looked up with their eyes staring out of their heads and then they turned round and fell in with us, and the whole army, we just—we just *threw* ourselves on the damned redcoats. . . . Oh, ma'am, it was just *wonderful*!"

"Wonderful!" I echoed dutifully, catching a trickle of blood that threatened to run into his eye. The shadows of the tombstones in the graveyard stretched out long and violet, and the sound of the flies buzzed in my ears, louder than the ringing of the shots that still came—were coming closer—to the frail barrier of the dead. And Jamie with them.

Lord, keep him safe! I prayed in the silence of my heart.

"Did you say something, ma'am?"

JAMIE RUBBED a blood-wet sleeve across his face, the wool rasping his skin, sweat burning in his eyes. It was a church they'd chased the British into—or a churchyard. Men were dodging through the tombstones, vaulting them in hot pursuit.

The British had turned at bay, though, an officer shouting them into a ragged line, and the drill began, the muskets grounded, ramrods drawn . . .

"Fire!" Jamie bellowed, with all the power left in his cracked voice. "Fire on them! Now!"

Only a few men had loaded weapons, but sometimes it took only one. A shot rang out from behind him, and the British officer who was shouting stopped shouting and staggered. He clutched himself, curling up and falling to his knees, and someone shot him again. He jerked backward, then fell over sideways.

There was a roar from the British line, which dissolved at once into a rush, some men pausing long enough to fix their bayonets, others wielding their guns like clubs. The Americans met them, mindless and shrieking, with guns and fists. One militiaman reached the fallen officer, seized him by the legs, and began to drag him away toward the church, perhaps with the notion to take him prisoner, perhaps to get him help. . . .

A British soldier threw himself upon the American, who stumbled backward and fell, loosing his hold on the officer. Jamie was running, shouting, trying to gather the men, but it was no use; they'd lost their wits altogether in the madness of fighting, and whatever their original intent in seizing the British officer, they'd lost that, too.

Leaderless, so had the British soldiers, some of whom were now engaged in a grotesque tug-of-war with two Americans, each grasping the limbs of the dead—for surely he must be now, if he hadn't been killed outright—British officer.

Appalled, Jamie ran in among them, shouting, but his voice failed altogether under strain and breathlessness, and he realized he was making no more than faint cawing noises. He reached the fight, grasped one soldier by the shoulder, meaning to pull him back, but the man rounded on him and punched him in the face.

It was a glancing blow off the side of his jaw but made him lose his grip, and he was knocked off-balance by someone shoving past him to grab some part of the hapless officer's body.

Drums. A drum. Someone in the distance was beating something urgent, a summons.

"Retreat!" someone shouted in a hoarse voice. "Retreat!"

Something happened; a momentary pause—and suddenly it was all different and the Americans were coming past him, hasty but no longer frantic, a few of them carrying the dead British officer. Yes, definitely dead; the man's head lolled like a rag doll's.

Thank God they're not dragging him through the dirt was all he had time to think. Lieutenant Bixby was at his shoulder, blood pouring down his face from an open flap of scalp.

"There you are, sir!" he said, relieved. "Thought you was taken, we did." He took Jamie respectfully by the arm, tugging him along. "Come away, sir, will you? I don't trust those wicked buggers not to come back."

Jamie glanced in the direction Bixby was pointing. Sure enough, the British were retiring, under the direction of a couple of officers who had come forward out of a mass of redcoats forming up in the middle distance. They showed no disposition to come closer, but Bixby was right: there were still random shots being fired, from both sides. He nodded, fumbling in his pocket for his extra kerchief to give the man to stanch his wound.

The thought of wounds made him think of Claire, and he recalled suddenly what Denzell Hunter had said: *"Tennent Church, the hospital's set up there."* Was this Tennent Church?

He was already following Bixby toward the road but glanced back. Yes, the men who had the dead British officer were taking him into the church, and there were wounded men sitting near the door, more of them near a small white—God, that was Claire's tent, was she—

He saw her at once, as though his thought had conjured her, right there in the open. She was standing up, staring open-mouthed, and no wonder—there was a Continental regular on a stool beside her, holding a bloodstained cloth, and more such cloths in a basin at her feet. But why was she out here? She—

And then he saw her jerk upright, clap a hand to her side, and fall.

A SLEDGEHAMMER hit me in the side, making me jerk, the needle dropping from my hands. I didn't feel myself fall but was lying on the ground, black and white spots flashing round me, a sense of intense numbness radiating from my right side. I smelled damp earth and warm grass and sycamore leaves, pungent and comforting.

Shock, I thought dimly, and opened my mouth, but nothing but a dry click came out of my throat. *What* . . . The numbness of the impact began to lessen, and I realized that I had curled into a ball, my forearm pressed by reflex over my abdomen. I smelled burning, and fresh blood, very fresh. *I've been shot, then.*

"Sassenach!" I heard Jamie's bellow over the roaring in my

ears. He sounded far off, but I heard the terror in his voice clearly. I wasn't disturbed by it. I felt very calm.

"Sassenach!" The spots had coalesced. I was looking down a narrow tunnel of light and spinning shadow. At the end of it was the shocked face of Corporal Greenhow, the needle dangling by its thread from the half-sewn gash in his forehead.

PART FIVE

Counting Noses

82

EVEN PEOPLE WHO WANT TO GO TO HEAVEN DON'T WANT TO DIE TO GET THERE

I SWAM DIZZILY TO the surface of consciousness, thinking, *What was it Ernest Hemingway had said, about how one is supposed to pass out from the pain but you don't?* I just had, but he was more or less right; the unconsciousness hadn't lasted more than a few seconds. I was curled into a tight ball, both hands pressed against my right side, and I could feel the blood welling between my fingers, hot and cold and sticky, and it was beginning to hurt . . . very much . . .

"Sassenach! Claire!" I swam out of the fog again and managed to open one eye. Jamie was kneeling by me. He was touching me, had his hands on me, but I couldn't feel it. . . .

Sweat or blood or something ran burning into my eyes. I could hear someone gasping—short, shallow, panting breaths. *Me, or Jamie?* I was cold. *I shouldn't be cold, it was hot as blazes today.* . . . I felt jellied, quivering. And it hurt. A lot.

"Sassenach!"

Hands turned me. I screamed. Tried to. I felt it wrench my throat but couldn't hear it; there was a roaring in my ears. *Shock,* I thought. I couldn't feel my limbs, my feet. I felt the blood leaving my body.

It hurt.

The shock's wearing off, I thought. *Or is it getting worse?* I could see the pain now, going off in bursts like black lightning, jagged and searing.

"Sassenach!"

"What?" I said through clenched teeth. "Auh!"

"Are ye dying?"

"Probably."

Gutshot. The word formed unpleasantly in my mind, and I hoped vaguely that I hadn't spoken it out loud. Even if I had, though . . . surely Jamie could see the wound . . .

Someone was trying to pull my hands away, and I struggled to keep them in place, keep pressing, but my arms had no strength and I saw one hand hanging limp as they lifted it, the nails outlined black with blood, fingers coated scarlet, dripping. Someone rolled me onto my back and I thought I screamed again.

It hurt unspeakably. *Jellied. Impact shock. Cells blasted to shreds and goo. No function . . . organ failure.*

Tightness. Couldn't breathe. Jerking, and someone cursing above me. My eyes were open, I saw color, but the air was thick with pulsing spots.

Shouting. Talk.

I couldn't draw breath. Something tight around my middle. *What's gone? How much?*

God, it hurt. *Oh, God.*

JAMIE COULDN'T take his eyes off Claire's face, lest she die in the second when he looked away. He fumbled for a kerchief, but he'd given it to Bixby, and in desperation seized a fold of her skirt and pressed it hard to her side. She made a horrible sound and he nearly let go, but the ground under her was already darkening with blood and he pressed harder, shouting, "Help! Help me, Rachel! Dottie!"

But no one came, and when he risked a split second's glance around, he saw nothing but clumps of wounded and dead under the trees some distance away and the flickering forms of soldiers, some running, some wandering dazed through the tombstones. If the girls had been nearby, they must have been forced to run when the skirmish rolled through the graveyard.

He felt the slow tickle of Claire's blood running over the back of his hand and shouted again, his dry throat tearing with the effort. *Someone* must hear.

Someone did. He heard running footsteps on the gravel and saw a doctor named Leckie whom he knew racing toward him, white-faced, hurdling a tombstone as he came.

"Shot?" Leckie asked, breathless, collapsing onto his knees beside Jamie. Jamie couldn't speak, but nodded. Sweat was running down his face and the crease of his spine, but his hands seemed frozen to her body; he couldn't pull them away, couldn't let go until Leckie, pawing in one of Claire's baskets, seized a wad of lint and jerked Jamie's hand out of the way in order to clap it in place.

The surgeon elbowed him ruthlessly aside and he scuttled crabwise a foot or two away, then rose to his feet, swaying helplessly. Jamie couldn't look away but became slowly aware that a knot of soldiers had gathered, appalled, shuffling among themselves, not knowing what to do. Jamie gulped air, seized the nearest of these, and sent him running to the church in search of Dr. Hunter. She'd want Denny. If she survived long enough for him to come—

"Sir! General Fraser!" Not even the shouting of his own name made him look away from the spectacle on the ground: the blood, so much of it, soaking her clothes, making a hideous dark red puddle that stained the knees of Leckie's breeches as he knelt over her; her hair, untied and spilling wild, full of grass and bits of leaf from the ground she lay on, her face—oh, Christ, her face.

"Sir!" Someone grabbed his arm to compel his attention. He drove his elbow hard into whoever it was, and the man grunted in surprise and let go.

A gabble of whispers, agitation, people telling the newcomer that it was the general's wife, hurt, shot, dead or dying . . .

"She's not dying!" he turned and bellowed at them. He thought dimly that he must look demented; their blackened faces were aghast. Bixby stepped out and touched his shoulder gingerly, as though he were a lighted grenade that might go off in the next second. He thought he might.

"Can I help, sir?" Bixby said quietly.

"No," he managed to say. "I—he—" He gestured to Leckie, busy on the ground.

"General," said the newcomer, at his other elbow. He turned to find a blue-clad regular, a very young man in a baggy lieutenant's uniform, face set in dogged earnestness. "I dislike to intrude, sir, but as your wife's not dying—"

"Go away!"

The lieutenant flinched, but stood his ground.

"Sir," he said stubbornly. "General Lee has sent me urgently to find you. He requires that you attend him at once."

"Bugger Lee," said Bixby, very rudely, saving Jamie the trouble, and advanced on the newcomer, fists clenched.

The lieutenant was already flushed with heat, but at this grew redder. He ignored Bixby, though, attention focused on Jamie.

"You *must* come, sir."

VOICES . . . I heard words, disjointed, coming out of the fog like bullets, striking randomly.

". . . find Denzell Hunter!"

"General—"

"No!"

"—but you're needed at—"

"No!"

"—orders—"

"NO!"

And another voice, this one stiff with fear.

". . . could be shot for treason and desertion, sir!"

That focused my wandering attention and I heard the reply, clearly.

"Then they'll shoot me where I stand, sir, for I will not leave her side!"

Good, I thought, and, comforted, lapsed into the spinning void again.

"TAKE OFF YOUR coat and waistcoat, lad," Jamie said abruptly. The boy looked completely bewildered, but—stimulated by a menacing movement from Bixby—did as he was told. Jamie took him by the shoulder, turned him round, and said, "Stand still, aye?"

Stooping swiftly, he scooped a handful from the horrifying puddle of bloody mud and, standing, wrote carefully on the messenger's white back with a finger:

I resign my commission. J. Fraser.

He made to fling the remnants of mud away but, after a moment's hesitation, added a smeared and reluctant *Sir* at the top of the message, then clapped the boy on the shoulder.

"Go and show that to General Lee," he said. The lieutenant went pale.

"The general's in a horrid passion, sir," he said. "I dassen't!"

Jamie looked at him. The boy swallowed, said, "Yes, sir," shrugged on his garments, and went at a run, unbuttoned and flapping.

Rubbing his hands heedlessly on his breeches, Jamie knelt again beside Dr. Leckie, who spared him a quick nod. The doctor was pressing a wad of lint and a handful of skirt hard against Claire's side with both hands. The surgeon's hands were red to the elbow, and sweat was running down his face, dripping from his chin.

"Sassenach," Jamie said softly, afraid to touch her. His own clothes were sodden with sweat, but he was cold to the core. "Can ye hear me, lass?"

She'd regained consciousness, and his heart rose into his throat. Her eyes were closed, shut tight in a furious grimace of pain and concentration. She did hear him; the golden eyes opened and fixed on him. She didn't speak; her breath hissed through clenched teeth. She did see him, though, he was sure of that—and her eyes weren't clouded with shock, nor dim with imminent death. Not yet.

Dr. Leckie was looking at her face, too, intent. He let out his own breath, and the tension in his shoulders eased a little, though he didn't relax the pressure of his hands.

"Can you get me more lint, a wad of bandage, anything?" he asked. "I *think* the bleeding is slowing."

Claire's bag lay open a little way behind Leckie. Jamie lunged for it, upended it on the ground, and snatched up a double handful of rolled bandages from the litter. Leckie's hand made a sucking sound as he pulled it away from the sopping wad of cloth and grabbed the fresh bandages.

"You might cut her laces," the doctor said calmly. "I need her stays off. And it will help her to breathe more easily."

Jamie fumbled his dirk free, hands shaking in his haste.

"Un . . . *tie* . . . them!" Claire grunted, scowling ferociously.

Jamie grinned absurdly at hearing her voice, and his hands steadied. So she thought she'd live to need her laces. He gulped air and set himself to undo the knot. Her stay laces were leather and as usual soaked with sweat—but she used a very simple granny knot, and he got it loose with the tip of his dirk.

The knot fell free and he jerked the laces loose, wrenching the stays wide apart. Her bosom rose white as she gasped, and he felt an instant's embarrassment as he saw her nipples stiffen through the sweat-soaked fabric of her shift. He wanted to cover her.

There were flies everywhere, black and buzzing, drawn by the blood. Leckie shook his head to dislodge one that lighted on his eyebrow. They were swarming round Jamie's own ears, but he didn't bother about them, instead brushing them away as they crawled on Claire's body, over her twitching, pallid face, her hands half curled and helpless.

"Here," Leckie said, and, seizing one of Jamie's hands, pushed it down on the fresh compress. "Press hard on that." He sat back on his heels, grabbed another bandage roll, and unfurled it. With some lifting and grunting and a terrible moan from Claire, together they contrived to pass the cingulum round her body, securing the dressing in place.

"Right." Leckie swayed for a moment, then got laboriously to his feet. "The bleeding's mostly stopped—for now," he said to Jamie. "I'll come back when I can." He swallowed and looked directly at Claire's face, wiping his chin on his sleeve. "Good luck to you, ma'am."

And with that, he simply strode off toward the open doors of the church, not looking back. Jamie felt such a rush of fury that he would have gone after the man and dragged him back, could he have left Claire's side. He'd left—just left her, the bastard! Alone, helpless!

"May the devil eat your soul and salt it well first, you whore!" he shouted in *Gàidhlig* after the vanished surgeon. Overcome by fright and the sheer rage of helplessness, he dropped to his knees beside his wife and pounded a fist blindly on the ground.

"Did you just . . . call him a . . . whore?" The whispered words made him open his eyes.

"Sassenach!" He was scrambling for his discarded canteen, lost in the rubble of stuff from her bag. "Here, let me get ye water."

"No. Not . . . yet." She managed to raise one hand halfway, and he stopped dead, canteen in hand.

"Why not?" She was the gray of rotted oats and slick with sweat, trembling like a leaf. He could *see* her lips beginning to crack in the heat, for God's sake.

"I don't . . . know." She worked her mouth a moment before finding the next words. "Don't . . . know where it is." The trembling hand touched the dressing—already showing a stain of blood seeping through. "If it's perf . . . perf'rated the . . . bowel. Drink would . . . kill me. Fast. Intestin'l . . . sh-sh-shock."

He sat down by her slowly and, closing his eyes, breathed deliberately for a few seconds. For the moment, everything had disappeared: the church, the battle, the screams and shouts and the rumble of limber wheels along the rutted road through Freehold. There wasn't anything but her and him, and he opened his eyes to look on her face, to fix it in his mind forever.

"Aye," he said, keeping his voice as steady as he could. "And if that's the case . . . and if it didna kill ye quick . . . I've seen men die gutshot. Balnain died that way. It's long and it's foul, and I willna have ye die like that, Claire. I won't!"

He meant it, truly he did. But his hand squeezed the canteen hard enough to dent the tin. How could he give her the water that might kill her right before his eyes, right . . . *now*?

Not now, he prayed. *Please, don't let it be now!*

"I'm not . . . keen . . . either way," she whispered, after a long pause. She blinked away a green-bellied fly, shining like emerald, that had come to drink her tears. "I need . . . Denny." A soft gasp. "Quick."

"He's coming." He could barely breathe, and his hands hovered over her, afraid to touch anything. "Denny's coming. Hold on!"

The answer to this was a tiny grunt—her eyes were squinched shut and her jaw set hard—but she'd heard him, at least. With the vague recollection that she always said you must cover folk suffering from shock and lift their feet, he took off his coat and put it over her, then took off his waistcoat, rolled it up, and shoved it under her feet. At least the coat covered the blood that had now soaked the whole side of her dress. It terrified him to see that.

Her fists were clenched, both driven hard into her wounded side; he couldn't hold her hand. He put a hand on her shoulder, so she'd know he was there, shut his eyes, and prayed with his whole being.

83

SUNDOWN

THE SUN WAS NEARLY down, and Denzell Hunter was laying out his knives. The air was thick with the sweetness of corn liquor; he'd dipped his instruments in it, and they lay gleaming wetly on the clean napkin Mrs. Macken had put down on the sideboard.

Young Mrs. Macken herself was hovering in the doorway, a hand pressed over her mouth and her eyes big as a cow's. Jamie tried to give her a reassuring smile, but whatever his expression was, it wasn't a smile and appeared to alarm her further, for she retreated into the darkness of her pantry.

She'd likely been alarmed all day, like everyone else in the village of Freehold; she was heavily pregnant and her husband was fighting with the Continentals. And still more alarmed for the last hour, ever since Jamie had pounded on her door. He'd battered six doors before hers. She was the first to answer, and, in poor return for her hospitality, now found a badly injured woman lying on her kitchen table, oozing blood like a fresh-killed deer.

That image unnerved him still further—Mrs. Macken was not the only one in the house who was shaken by events—and he came close and took Claire's hand, as much to reassure himself as her.

"How is it, Sassenach?" he said, low-voiced.

"Bloody awful," she replied hoarsely, and bit her lip to keep from saying more.

"Had ye best have a wee nip?" He moved to pick up the bottle of rough corn liquor from the sideboard, but she shook her head.

"Not quite yet. I don't *think* it struck the bowel—but I'd rather die of blood loss than sepsis or shock, if I'm wrong."

He squeezed her hand. It was cold, and he hoped she would keep talking, though at the same time he knew he ought not to make her talk. She'd need all her strength. He tried as hard as he could to will some of his own strength into her without hurting her.

Mrs. Macken edged into the room, carrying a candlestick with a fresh wax candle; he could smell the sweetness of the beeswax, and the scent of honey reminded him of John Grey. He wondered for an instant whether Grey had made it back to the British lines, but he had no real attention for anything but Claire.

Right this moment, he was busy regretting that he'd ever disapproved of her making ether. He would have given anything he possessed to spare her awareness of the next half hour.

The setting sun washed the room in gold, and the blood seeping through her bandages showed dark.

"ALWAYS CONCENTRATE when you're using a sharp knife," I said weakly. "You might lose a finger, else. My granny used to say that, and my mother, too."

My mother had died when I was five, my granny a few years later—but I hadn't seen her often, as Uncle Lamb spent at least half his time on archaeological expeditions round the world, with me as part of his baggage.

"Did you frequently play with sharp knives as a child?" Denny asked. He smiled, though his eyes stayed fixed on the scalpel he was carefully sharpening on a small oilstone. I could smell the oil, a soft murky scent under the tang of blood and the resinous smell of the unfinished rafters baking overhead.

"Constantly," I breathed, and shifted my position as slowly as I could. I bit my lip hard and managed to ease my back without groaning aloud. It made Jamie's knuckles go white when I did.

He was standing by the window at the moment, clutching the sill as he looked out.

Seeing him there, broad shoulders outlined by the sinking sun, brought back a sudden memory, surprising in its sharpness. Or rather, memories, for the layers of experience came back altogether, in a wodge, and I was seeing Jamie rigid with his fear and grief, the slight black figure of Malva Christie leaning toward him—and remembered feeling both a vague affront and a tremendous sense of peace as I began to leave my body, carried on the wings of fever.

I shook the memory off at once, frightened even to think of that beckoning peace. The fear was reassuring; I wasn't yet so close to death as to find it appealing.

"I'm sure it went through the liver," I said to Denny, gritting my teeth. "That much blood . . ."

"I'm sure thee is right," he said, pressing gently on my side. "The liver is a great mass of densely vascularized tissue," he added, turning to Jamie, who didn't turn from the window but hunched his shoulders against the possibility of being told anything else of a horrifying nature.

"But the excellent thing about a wound to the liver," Denny added cheerfully, "is that the liver, unlike the other organs of the body, will regenerate itself—or so thy wife tells me."

Jamie cast me a brief, haunted look, and went back to staring out the window. I breathed as shallowly as I could, trying to ignore the pain, and trying even harder not to think about what Denny was about to do.

That little exercise in self-discipline lasted about three seconds. If we were all lucky, it would be simple, and quick. He had to widen the bullet's entrance wound enough to see the direction of its track and to insert a probe along it, in hopes of finding the bullet before he had to dig for it. Then a quick—I could only hope—insertion of whichever one of his jawed forceps looked most appropriate. He had three, of different lengths, plus a davier: good for grasping a rounded object, but the jaws were much bigger than the tips of a forceps and would cause more bleeding.

If it wasn't simple or quick, I'd very likely be dead within the next half hour. Denny was entirely correct in what he'd told Jamie: the liver is hugely vascularized, an enormous sponge of tiny blood vessels crossed by very large ones like the hepatic portal vein. That's why the wound, superficially tiny, had bled so alarmingly. None of the major vessels had been damaged—yet—because I would have bled to death in minutes if they had been.

I was trying to breathe shallowly, because of the pain, but had an overwhelming need to draw deep, gasping breaths; I needed oxygen, because of the blood loss.

Sally flitted through my mind, and I seized on thought of her as distraction. She'd survived the amputation, screaming through a leather gag, Gabriel—yes, Gabriel, that was the name of the young man with her—white-eyed as a panicked horse, fighting to hold her steady and not to faint himself. She *had* fainted, luckily, toward the end—*So sucks to you, Ernest,* I thought blearily—and I'd left them both in Rachel's care.

"Where's Rachel, Denny?" I asked, suddenly thinking to wonder. I thought I'd glimpsed her briefly in the churchyard after I'd been shot, but couldn't be sure of anything that had happened in that blur of black and white.

Denny's hand stopped for an instant, the cautery iron he was holding suspended over a tiny brazier he'd set fuming at the end of the sideboard.

"She is searching for Ian, I believe," he said quietly, and laid the iron very gently in the fire. "Is thee ready, Claire?"

Ian, I thought. *Oh, God. He hasn't come back.*

"As I'll ever be," I managed, already imagining the stench of burning flesh. Mine.

If the bullet was resting near one of the large vessels, Denny's probing and grasping could rupture it and I'd hemorrhage internally. The cauterization might cause shock suddenly to set in and assassinate me without warning. Most likely, I'd survive the surgery but die of lingering infection. Consoling thought . . . At least in that case I'd have time to write a brief note to Brianna—and perhaps warn Jamie to be more careful about who he married next time. . . .

"Wait," Jamie said. He didn't raise his voice, but there was enough urgency in it to freeze Denny.

I closed my eyes, rested a hand gingerly on the dressing, and tried to envision just where the damned bullet might be. Was it only *in* the liver, or had it gone all the way through? There was so much trauma and swelling, though, that the pain was generalized over the whole right side of my abdomen; I couldn't pick out a single, vivid line of bright pain leading to the ball.

"What is it, Jamie?" Denny asked, impatient to be about his business.

"Your betrothed," Jamie said, sounding bemused. "Coming up the road with a gang of soldiers."

"Does thee think she is under arrest?" Denny asked, with a fair assumption of calm. I saw his hand tremble slightly as he picked up a linen napkin, though.

"I dinna think so," Jamie said doubtfully. "She's laughing wi' a couple of them."

Denny took his spectacles off and wiped them carefully.

"Dorothea is a Grey," he pointed out. "Any member of her family would pause on the gallows to exchange witty banter with the hangman before graciously putting the noose about his neck with his own hands."

That was so true that it made me laugh, though my humor was cut off at once by a jolt of pain that took my breath away. Jamie looked at me sharply, but I flapped a hand weakly at him, and he went to open the door.

Dorothea popped in, turning to wave over her shoulder and call goodbye to her escort, and I heard Denny sigh in relief as he put his spectacles back on.

"Oh, good," she said, going to kiss him. "I hoped thee hadn't started yet. I've brought a few things. Mrs. Fraser—Claire—how are you? I mean, how is thee?" She put down the large basket she was carrying and came at once to the table I was lying on, to take my hand and gaze sympathetically at me with her big blue eyes.

"I've been slightly better," I said, making an effort not to grit my teeth. I felt clammy and nauseated.

"General La Fayette was most concerned to hear that you'd been hurt," she said. "He has all of his aides telling their rosary beads for you."

"How kind," I said, meaning it, but rather hoping the marquis hadn't sent a complicated greeting that I might need to compose a reply to. Having got this far, I wanted to get the bloody business over with, no matter *what* happened.

"And he sent this," she said, a rather smug look on her face as she held up a squat green-glass bottle. "Thee will want this first, I think, Denny."

"What—" Denny began, reaching for the bottle, but Dorothea had pulled the cork, and the sweet cough-syrup smell of sherry rolled out—with the ghost of a very distinctive herbal scent beneath it, something between camphor and sage.

"Laudanum," said Jamie, and his face took on such a startling look of relief that only then did I realize how frightened he had been for me. "God bless ye, Dottie!"

"It occurred to me that Friend Gilbert might just possibly have a few things that might be useful," she said modestly. "All the Frenchmen I know are dreadful cranks about their health and have enormous collections of tonics and pastilles and clysters. So I went and asked."

Jamie had me half sitting, with his arm braced behind my back and the bottle at my lips, before I could add my own thanks.

"Wait, will you?" I said crossly, putting my hand over the bottle's open mouth. "I haven't any idea how strong this stuff is. You won't do me any good by killing me with opium."

It cost me something to say so; my instinct was to drain the bottle forthwith, if it would stop the beastly pain. That nitwit Spartan who allowed the fox to gnaw his vitals had *nothing* on me. But, come right down to it, I didn't want to die, either of gunshot, fever, or medical misadventure. And so Dottie borrowed a spoon from Mrs. Macken, who watched in grisly fascination from the door while I took two spoonfuls, lay down, and waited an interminable quarter of an hour to judge the effects.

"The marquis sent all sorts of delicacies and things to aid your recovery," Dottie said encouragingly, turning to the basket and starting to lift things out by way of distraction. "Partridge in jelly, mushroom *pâté,* some *terrible*-smelling cheese, and—"

My sudden desire to vomit ceased just as suddenly, and I half-sat up, causing Jamie to emit a cry of alarm and grab me by the shoulders. Just as well that he did; I would have fallen onto the floor. I wasn't attending, though, my attention fixed on Dottie's basket.

"Roquefort," I said urgently. "Is it Roquefort cheese? Sort of gray, with green and blue veins?"

"Why, I don't know," she said, startled by my vehemence. She gingerly plucked a cloth-wrapped parcel out of the basket and held it delicately in front of me. The odor wafting from it was enough, and I relaxed—very slowly—back down.

"Good," I breathed. "Denzell—when you've finished . . . pack the wound with cheese."

Used to me as he was, this still made Denny's jaw drop. He glanced from me to the cheese, plainly thinking that fever must have set in with unusual speed and severity.

"Penicillin," I said, swallowing and waving a hand at the cheese. My mouth felt sticky from the laudanum. "The mold that makes that sort of cheese is a species of *Penicillium.* Use the stuff from the veins."

Denny shut his mouth and nodded, determined.

"I will. But we must begin soon, Claire. The light is going."

The light *was* going, and the sense of urgency in the room was palpable. But Mrs. Macken brought more candles, and Denny assured me that it was a simple operation; he would do quite as well by candlelight.

More laudanum. I was beginning to feel it—a not unpleasant dizzy sensation—and I made Jamie lay me down again. The pain was definitely less.

"Give me a bit more," I said, and my voice didn't seem to belong to me.

I took as deep a breath as I could and eased myself into a good position, looking with distaste at the leather gag that lay beside me. Someone—perhaps Dr. Leckie—had slit my shift up the side earlier in the proceedings. I spread the edges of the opening wide and stretched out my hand to Jamie.

The shadows grew between the smoke-stained rafters. The kitchen fire was banked, but still live, and the glow of it began to show red on the hearth. Looking up at the flickering rafters in my drugged state reminded me too much of the time I had nearly died of bacterial poisoning, and I shut my eyes.

Jamie was holding my left hand, curled on my breast, his other hand gently stroking my hair, smoothing damp wisps of it off my face.

"Better now, *a nighean*?" he whispered, and I nodded—or thought I did. Mrs. Macken murmured some question to Dottie, received an answer, and went out. The pain was still there but distant now, a small, flickering fire that I could shut out by closing my eyes. The thud of my heartbeat was more immediate, and I was beginning to experience . . . not hallucinations, quite. Disconnected images, though—the faces of strangers that faded in and out behind my eyes. Some were looking at me, others seemed oblivious; they smiled and sneered and grimaced but had nothing, really, to do with me.

"Again, Sassenach," Jamie whispered, lifting my head and putting the spoon to my lips, sticky with sherry and the bitter taste of opium. "One more." I swallowed and lay back. If I died, would I see my mother again? I wondered, and experienced an urgent longing for her, shocking in its intensity.

I was trying to summon her face before me, bring her out of the floating horde of strangers, when I suddenly lost my grip on my own thoughts and began to float off into a sphere of dark, dark blue.

"Don't leave me, Claire," Jamie whispered, very close to my ear. "This time, I'll beg. Dinna go from me. Please." I could feel the warmth of his face, see the glow of his breath on my cheek, though my eyes were closed.

"I won't," I said—or thought I said—and went. My last clear thought was that I'd forgotten to tell him not to marry a fool.

THE SKY OUTSIDE was lavender, and Claire's skin was washed with gold. Six candles burned around the room, the flames tall and still in the heavy air.

Jamie stood by her head, a hand on her shoulder as though he could comfort her. In fact, it was the sense of her, still alive under his hand, that was keeping him on his feet.

Denny made a small sound of satisfaction behind his highwayman's mask, and Jamie saw the muscle of his bared forearm tense as he slowly drew the instrument out of Claire's body. Blood gushed from the wound, and Jamie tensed like a cat, ready to spring forward with a pledget, but no spurt followed and the blood died to a trickle, with a final small blurt of blood as the jaws of the instrument emerged, something dark clamped between them.

Denny dropped the ball into the palm of his hand and peered at it, then made an irritable noise; his glasses were fogged with the sweat of his efforts. Jamie snatched them off the Quaker's nose and rubbed them hastily on his shirttail, replacing them before Hunter could blink twice.

"I thank thee," Denny said mildly, returning his attention to the musket ball. He turned it delicately and let out an audible breath.

"Whole," he said. "Thank God."

"Deo gratias," Jamie echoed fervently, and reached out a hand. "Let me see it, will ye?"

Hunter's brows rose, but he dropped the thing in Jamie's hand. It was startlingly warm, warm from her body. Warmer even than the air or Jamie's own sweating flesh, and the feel of it made him fold his fist over it. He stole a look at Claire's chest: rising, falling, though with alarming slowness. Almost as slowly, he opened his hand.

"What is thee looking for, Jamie?" Denny asked, pausing to re-sterilize his beaked probe.

"Marks. A slit, a cross—any mark of tampering." He rolled the ball carefully between his fingers, then relaxed, a small spurt of gratitude making him murmur, *"Deo gratias,"* again.

"Tampering?" There were vertical lines between Denny's brows, deepening as he looked up. "To make the ball fragment, thee means?"

"That—or worse. Sometimes a man will rub something into the marks—poison, say, or . . . or shit. Just in case the wound itself isna fatal, aye?"

Hunter looked shocked, his appalled expression clear even behind the shielding handkerchief.

"If ye mean to kill a man, ye mean him harm," Jamie said dryly.

"Yes, but . . ." Hunter looked down, laying his tool carefully on the towel as though it were made of porcelain, not metal. His breath fluttered the handkerchief tied over his mouth. "But it is one thing, surely, to kill in battle, to shoot at an enemy when it is a matter of one's own life . . . and to form the cold-blooded intent that thy enemy should die a horrible and lingering death . . ."

Claire made a ghastly moaning noise and twitched under his hands as Denny gently squeezed the flesh on either side of the wound. Jamie gripped her by the elbows, to keep her from turning. Denny picked up the jawed thing again.

"Thee wouldn't do it thyself," Hunter said with certainty. His eyes were intent on his delicate probing, a pledget held to catch the blood that dribbled slowly from the wound. Jamie felt the loss of each drop as though it left his own veins, and felt cold; how much could she lose and still live?

"No. It would be a cowardly thing." But he spoke automatically, scarcely attending. She had gone limp; he saw her fingers uncurl, droop, and looked at her face, her throat, searching for a visible pulse. He felt one, in his thumb where it pressed the bone of her arm, but couldn't tell whether it was her heart that beat there or his own.

He was acutely conscious of Denny's breath, audible behind his mask. It stopped for an instant, and Jamie glanced up from his scrutiny of Claire's face to see the Quaker's look of intentness as he drew the thing free once more—this time clutching a tiny clump of something unrecognizable. Denny opened the jaws of his forceps and dropped the clump on the towel, then used the tool to poke at it, trying to spread it, and Jamie saw the prickle of tiny dark threads as the blood soaked away into a bright red stain on the towel. Cloth.

"What does thee think?" Denny asked him, frowning at the thing. "Is it a bit of her shift, or the—the bodice—or material from her stays? For from the hole in her stays, I should think . . ."

Jamie rootled hastily in his sporran, pulled out the little silk bag in which he kept the spectacles he used for reading, and clapped these on his nose.

"Ye've at least two separate bits there," he announced, after an anxious perusal. "Canvas from the stays, and a lighter bit of cloth. See?" He took up a probe and delicately teased the fragments apart. "I think that one bit's her shift."

Denny glanced at the disconsolate pile of bloodstained garments on the floor, and Jamie, at once divining his intent, reached in, stirred about, and pulled out the remnants of her dress.

"It's a clean hole," Denny said, looking at the fabric Jamie spread out on the table. "Maybe . . ." He picked up the forceps and turned back, not finishing.

More probing, deeper, and Jamie gritted his teeth not to cry out in protest. *"The liver is so vascular,"* she'd said, talking Denny through what he must do. *"The risk of hemorrhage . . ."*

"I know," Denny murmured, not looking up. The sweat had plastered the handkerchief to his face, molding itself to nose and lips, so his speech was visible. "I'm being . . . careful."

"Ken that," Jamie said, but so softly he didn't know whether Hunter heard him. *Please. Please let her live. Blessed Mother, save her . . . saveher, saveher, saveher . . .* The words all ran together in an instant and he lost the sense of them, but not the sense of desperate entreaty.

The red stain on the toweling under her had grown to alarming proportions by the time Hunter set down his tool again and sighed, shoulders slumping.

"I think—I hope—I have it all."

"Good. I—what will ye do next?"

He saw Denny smile a little behind the sodden cloth, olive-brown eyes soft and steady over it.

"Cauterize it, bind the wound, and pray, Jamie."

84

NIGHTFALL

IT WAS PAST DARK when Lord John Grey, accompanied by a respectful escort and a slightly damaged Indian, limped into Clinton's camp.

Things were much as might be expected after a battle: strong currents of mingled agitation and exhaustion, the latter prevailing. No carousing amid the tents, no music. Men around the fires and camp kitchens, though, eating, getting themselves sorted, talking it over in low tones. No sense of celebration—more a sense of irritation, of disgruntled surprise. The scent of roast mutton came strongly through the smells of dust, mules, and sweating humanity, and Grey's mouth watered so much that he had to swallow before replying to Captain André's solicitous inquiry as to his immediate desires.

"I need to see my brother," he replied. "I'll attend upon General Clinton and my lord Cornwallis later. When I've washed and changed," he added, shucking the horrible black coat for what he sincerely hoped was the last time.

André nodded understandingly, taking the vile garment from him.

"Of course, Lord John. And . . . um . . . ?" He nodded delicately in the direction of Ian Murray, who was attracting glances, if not stares, from passersby.

"Ah. He'd best come, too."

He followed André through the orderly aisles of tents, hearing the clinking of mess kits and feeling the comfort of the army's stolid routine settle into place around him. Murray paced at his heel, silent. He'd no idea what the man was thinking and was too weary to care.

He did feel Murray's step falter, though, and automatically looked over his shoulder. Murray had turned, all his attention focused on a nearby fire, this an open wood fire, around which sat several Indians. Grey wondered dimly whether these might be friends of Murray's . . . and corrected this impression in the next second, as Murray took three giant strides, grabbed one of the Indians with a forearm round his throat, and punched him in the side with such force as to drive the other's wind out in an audible whoop.

Murray then threw the Indian on the ground, dropped on him with both knees—Grey winced at the impact—and gripped the man by the throat. The other Indians lurched out of the way, laughing and making high-pitched yips of encouragement or derision, Grey couldn't tell which.

He stood there blinking, swaying slightly, and unable either to intervene or to look away. Murray had declined to let one of the field surgeons remove the arrowhead from his shoulder, and fresh blood spattered from the wound as he punched his opponent viciously—and repeatedly—in the face.

The Indian—he had a shaved scalp and dangling earrings of shell; Grey noticed these when Murray ripped one out of the ear and stuffed it into his opponent's mouth—was making a stout attempt at resistance and retaliation, in spite of his being taken at such a disadvantage.

"Do you suppose they are acquainted?" Captain André asked Grey. He had turned back, hearing the outcries, and was now standing beside Grey, watching the affray with interest.

"I think they must be," Grey replied absently. He glanced briefly at the other Indians, none of whom seemed to have any interest in assisting their fellow, though a few of them appeared to be making wagers on the result. They'd plainly been drinking, but seemed no more intoxicated than the average soldier at this time of day.

The combatants were now squirming on the ground, evidently striving for possession of a large knife worn by the man Murray had attacked. The fight was attracting attention from other quarters; a number of men had hurried over from nearby fires and were clustered behind Grey and André, making speculations and hasty bets, offering shouted advice.

Grey was conscious, through his fatigue, of a certain concern for Murray—and not only on Murray's own account. On the off chance that he might at some point in future actually speak with Jamie Fraser again, he didn't want the first subject raised to be the demise of Fraser's nephew while more or less in Grey's custody. He couldn't think what the hell to do about it, though, and thus continued to stand there, watching.

Like most fights, it didn't last very long. Murray gained possession of the knife, by the brutal but effective expedient of bending one of his opponent's fingers backward 'til it broke and grabbing the hilt as the man let go.

As Murray pressed the blade against the other man's throat, it belatedly occurred to Grey that he might really intend to kill him. The men around him certainly thought so; there was a universal gasp as Murray drew the blade across his enemy's throat.

The momentary silence engendered by this was enough for most of the assembled to hear Murray say, with a noticeable effort, "I give you back your life!" He rose off the Indian's body, swaying and staring as though blind drunk himself, and hurled the knife into the darkness—causing considerable consternation and not a little cursing among those in whose direction he'd hurled it.

In the excitement, most of the crowd likely didn't hear the Indian's reply, but Grey and André did. He sat up, very slowly, hands shaking as they pressed a fold of his shirt to the shallow cut across his throat, and said, in an almost conversational tone, "You will regret that, Mohawk."

Murray was breathing like a winded horse, his ribs visible with each gasp. Most of the paint had gone from his face; there were long smears of red and black down his glistening chest, and only a horizontal streak of some dark color remained across his cheekbones—that and a smudge of white on the point of his shoulder, above the arrow wound. He nodded to himself, once, then twice. And, without haste, stepped back into the circle of firelight, picked up a tomahawk that was lying on the ground, and, swinging it high with both hands, brought it down on the Indian's skull.

The sound froze Grey to the marrow and silenced every man present. Murray stood still for a moment, breathing heavily, then walked away. As he passed Grey, he turned his head and said, in a perfectly conversational tone of voice, "He's right. I would have," before disappearing into the night.

There was a sudden, belated stir among the spectators, and André glanced at Grey, but he shook his head. The army took no official notice of what went on among the Indian scouts, save there was an incident involving regulars. And they didn't get more irregular than the gentleman who had just left them.

André cleared his throat.

"Was he your . . . er . . . prisoner, my lord?"

"Ah . . . no. A, erm . . . relation by marriage."

"Oh, I see."

IT WAS FULL dark before the battle ended. William gathered as much from the orderly who'd brought him supper, and he could hear the sounds of a camp slowly reassembling itself as companies of soldiers came in, were dismissed, and scattered to drop their equipment and find food. Nothing like the usual sense of relaxation that lay on a camp after sunset. Everything was agitated and restless—and so was William.

His head ached horribly and someone had stitched his

scalp; the stitches were tender and itching. Uncle Hal hadn't come back, and he'd had no news whatever beyond the orderly's sketchy report, which indicated only that there had been no clear victory over the Americans but that all three parts of Clinton's army had withdrawn in good order, though with considerable casualties.

He wasn't sure he *wanted* any further news, to be honest. There was going to be a moment of reckoning with Sir Henry about that ignored order—though he supposed Sir Henry might just possibly be too preoccupied to realize . . .

Then he heard the sound of footsteps and sat up. His fretting disappeared on the instant when the tent flap lifted and he saw his father—*Lord John,* he corrected himself, but as an absent afterthought. His father seemed surprisingly small, almost fragile, and as Lord John limped slowly into the lantern light, William saw the stained bandage round his head, the makeshift sling, and when William cast his eyes down, he saw, too, the state of his father's bare feet.

"Are you—" he began, shocked, but Lord John interrupted him.

"I'm fine," he said, and tried for a smile, though his face was white and creased with fatigue. "Everything's all right, Willie. As long as you're alive, everything's all right."

He saw his father sway, put out a hand as though to steady himself, and, finding nothing to take hold of, withdraw it and force his body upright. Lord John's voice was hoarse, and his exposed eye bloodshot and exhausted but . . . tender. William swallowed.

"If you and I have things to say to each other, Willie—and of course we do—let it wait until tomorrow. Please. I'm not . . ." He made a vague, wavering gesture that ended nowhere.

The lump in William's throat was sudden and painful. He nodded, hands clenched tight on the bedding. His father nodded, too, drew a deep breath, and turned toward the tent flap—where, William saw, Uncle Hal was hovering, eyes fixed on his brother and brows drawn with worry.

William's heart seized, in a lump more painful than the one in his throat.

"Papa!" His father stopped abruptly, turning to look over his shoulder.

"I'm glad you're not dead," William blurted.

A smile blossomed slowly on his father's battered face.

"Me, too," he said.

IAN MADE HIS way out of the British camp, looking neither to right nor to left. The night was throbbing slowly round him. It was like being trapped inside a huge heart, he thought, feeling the thick walls squeeze him breathless, then draw away to leave him floating and weightless.

Lord John had offered to have an army surgeon tend his wound, but he couldn't bear to stay. He needed to go, to find Rachel, find Uncle Jamie. Had refused the offer of a horse, as well, unsure that he could stay on it. He'd do better walking, he'd told his lordship.

And he was walking all right, though obliged to admit that he didn't feel just that well in himself. His arms were still trembling from the shock of the killing blow. It had come up from his bowels and was still echoing through his bones, couldn't seem to find a way out of his body. Well, it would settle soon enough—this wasn't the first time, though he hadn't killed anyone in a long while, and a longer while since he'd done it with that much violence.

He tried to think who the last one had been, but couldn't. He could hear and see and feel things, but while his senses *worked,* they weren't joined up aright with the things he sensed. Troops were still marching past him into the camp. The battle must have ceased now with the darkness; the soldiers were coming home. He could hear the din they made, marching, their tin cups and canteens jangling against their cartridge boxes—but he heard it clanging long after they'd passed, and he couldn't always tell the light of distant campfires from the glow of fireflies near his feet.

The Scottish overseer. At Saratoga. The man's face was suddenly there in his memory, and just as suddenly his body remembered the feel of the blow. The violent punch of his knife, hard up under the man's back ribs, straight into the kidney. The huge, strange flexing he'd felt in his own body as the man's life surged up and then rushed out.

He wondered for a dazed moment whether butchers felt it—that echo—when they slaughtered a beast. You did, sometimes, when you cut a deer's throat, but usually not if it was just wringing a chicken's neck or crushing a weasel's skull.

"Or maybe ye just get used to it," he said.

"Maybe ye'd best try not to get used to it. Canna be good for your soul, *a bhalaich,* bein' used to that sort of thing."

"No," he agreed. "But ye mean when it's with your hands, aye? It's no the same wi' a gun or an arrow, now, is it?"

"Och, no. I did wonder sometimes, does it make a difference to the man ye kill, as well as yourself?"

Ian's feet blundered into a knee-high growth of thick weed and he realized that he'd stumbled off the road. It was just past the dark of the moon, and the stars still faint overhead.

"Different," he murmured, steering back into the roadway. "How d'ye mean, different? He'd be dead, either way."

"Aye, that's so. I'm thinkin' it's maybe worse to feel it's personal, though. Bein' shot in battle's more like bein' struck by lightning, ken? But ye canna help it bein' personal when ye do a man to death wi' your hands."

"Mmphm." Ian walked a bit farther in silence, the thoughts in his head circling like leeches swimming in a glass, going this way and that.

"Aye, well," he said at last—and realized suddenly that he'd spoken aloud for the first time. "It *was* personal."

The trembling in his bones had eased with the walking. The huge throbbing of the night had shrunk and come to rest in the arrow wound, the ache of it pulsing to the beat of his own heart.

It made him think of Rachel's white dove, though, flying serene above the hurt, and his mind steadied. He could see Rachel's face now, and he could hear crickets chirping. The cannon fire in his ears had stopped and the night grew slowly peaceful. And if his da had more to say on the subject of killing, he chose to keep his silence as they walked toward home together.

JOHN GREY EASED his battered feet into the pan, teeth gritted against the expected sensation, but to his surprise found that it caused him little pain, in spite of the torn skin and ruptured blisters.

"What—that's not hot water, is it?" he asked, leaning forward to look.

"Sweet oil," his brother said, his worn face relaxing a little. "And it had better be warm, not hot, or my orderly will be crucified at dawn."

"I'm sure the man trembles in his boots. Thank you, by the way," he added, gingerly dabbling. He was sitting on Hal's cot, his brother perched on the campaign chest, pouring something out of a canteen into one of the scarred pewter cups that had accompanied him for decades.

"You're welcome," Hal said, handing him the cup. "What the devil happened to your eye? And is your arm broken? I've called for a surgeon, but it may be some time." He waved a hand, encompassing the camp, the recent battle, and the stream of the returning wounded and sun-stricken.

"I don't need one. At first I thought my arm was broken, but I'm fairly sure it's just badly bruised. As for the eye . . . Jamie Fraser."

"Really?" Hal looked surprised and bent forward to peer at Grey's eye, now unwrapped from the bandages and—so far as Grey himself could tell—much improved. The constant watering had stopped, the swelling had gone down quite a bit, and he could, with caution, move it. From the look on Hal's face, though, the redness and bruising had perhaps not quite disappeared.

"Well, first Jamie, and then his wife." He touched the eye lightly. "He punched me, and then she did something excruciating to fix it and put honey in it."

"Having been subject to the lady's notions of medical treatment, I am not even faintly surprised to hear that." Hal lifted his cup in brief salute; Grey did the same and they drank. It was cider, and a dim recollection of applejack and Colonel Watson Smith floated through Grey's mind. Both seemed remote, as though they'd happened years ago rather than days.

"Mrs. Fraser doctored you?" Grey grinned at his brother. "What did she do to *you*?"

"Well . . . saved my life, to be perfectly frank." It was hard to tell in the lantern light, but Grey thought his brother was blushing slightly.

"Oh. In that case, I'm doubly obliged to her." He raised the cup again ceremoniously, then drained it. The cider went down gratefully after a hot day with no food. "How the hell did you fall into her clutches?" he asked curiously, extending the cup for more.

"I was looking for *you,*" Hal said pointedly. "If you'd been where you were *supposed* to be . . ."

"You think I'm supposed to be sitting somewhere waiting for you to turn up without warning and involve me in—do you know you nearly got me *hanged*? Besides, I was busy being kidnapped by James Fraser at the time."

Hal raised one eyebrow and poured more cider. "Yes, you did say he'd punched you. What for?"

Grey rubbed two fingers between his brows. He hadn't really noticed the headache before, only because he'd had it all day. Hal was definitely making it worse, though.

"I couldn't begin to explain it, Hal," he said tiredly. "Can you find me a bed? I think I'm going to die, and if by some unfortunate chance I don't, I'll have to speak to Willie tomorrow about . . . well, never mind." He drank the last of the cider and set down the cup, preparing reluctantly to lift his feet from the soothing oil.

"I know about William," Hal said.

Grey stopped abruptly, looking dubiously at his brother, who shrugged.

"I saw Fraser," he said simply. "In Philadelphia. And when I said something to William this afternoon, he confirmed it."

"Did he?" Grey murmured. He was surprised but somewhat heartened by that. If Willie had calmed down sufficiently as to talk to Hal about the matter, Grey's own conversation with his son might be a trifle less fraught than he'd feared.

"How long have you known?" Hal asked curiously.

"For certain? Since Willie was two or three." He suddenly gave an enormous yawn, then sat blinking stupidly. "Oh—meant to ask. How did the battle go?"

Hal looked at him with something between affront and amusement. "You were bloody *in* it, weren't you?"

"My part of it didn't go that well. But my perspective was somewhat limited by circumstance. That, and having only one working eye," he added, gently prodding the bad one. A good night's sleep . . . Longing for bed made him sway, narrowly catching himself before simply falling into Hal's cot.

"Hard to tell." Hal fished a crumpled towel out of a basket of laundry lurking disreputably in a corner and, kneeling down, lifted Grey's feet out of the oil and blotted them gently. "Hell of a mess. Terrible ground, chopped up by creeks, either farmland or half covered in trees . . . Sir Henry got away with the baggage train and refugees all safe. But as for Washington . . ." He shrugged. "So far as I can tell from what I saw and heard, his troops acquitted themselves well. Remarkably well," he added thoughtfully. He rose to his feet. "Lie down, John. I'll find a bed somewhere else."

Grey was much too tired to argue. He simply fell over and rolled onto his back, not bothering to undress. The bad eye felt gritty, and he wondered dimly whether to ask Hal to find some honey but decided that could wait 'til morning.

Hal took the lantern from its hook and turned toward the tent flap, but paused for an instant, turning back.

"Do you think Mrs. Fraser—by the way, tomorrow I want to know how on earth she came to marry you—do you think she knows about William and James Fraser?"

"Anyone with eyes who'd seen the two of them would know," Grey murmured, eyes half closed. "She never mentioned it, though."

Hal grunted. "Apparently everyone knew—save William. Little wonder he's . . ."

"That's one word for it."

"I hadn't found one yet."

"Does it matter?" Grey's eyes closed all the way. Through the drifting mists of sleep, he heard Hal's quiet voice, by the tent flap.

"I've had word of Ben. They say he's dead."

85

LONG ROAD HOME

JAMIE SAT BY THE tiny window in his shirt and breeches, watching his wife's hair dry.

It was hot as a forge in the tiny spare room Mrs. Macken had given them, and his sweat lay on him in a heavy dew that broke under its own weight and ran down his sides with any movement, but he was careful not to block any faint breath of air that might seep into the room; the air reeked of Roquefort cheese and blood.

He'd soaked her hair with water from the ewer Mrs. Macken had brought and wetted her shift; it clung to her body, the round of her buttock showing pink through the fabric as it dried. It showed the thick wad of the dressing, too, and the bloody stain that spread slow upon the cloth.

Slow. His lips formed the word and he thought it passionately but didn't speak aloud. *Slow!* Stopping altogether would be much better, but he'd settle for slow just now.

Eight pints. That's how much blood she said a human body had. It must vary some, though; clearly a man his size had more than a woman of hers. Single hairs were beginning to rise from the soaking mass, curling as they dried, delicate as an ant's feelers.

He wished he might give her some of his blood; he had plenty. She'd said it was possible, but not in this time. Something to do with things in the blood that mightn't match.

Her hair was a dozen colors, brown, molasses, cream and butter, sugar, sable . . . gleams of gold and silver where the dying light touched it. A broad streak of pure white at her temple, nearly the shade of her skin. She lay on her side facing him, one hand curled against her bosom, the other loose, upturned, so the inside of her wrist showed pure white, too, the blue veins heartbreaking.

She'd said she thought of cutting her wrists when she believed him dead. He didn't think he'd do it that way, if she died. He'd seen it: Toby Quinn with his wrist cut to the bone and all his blood run out across the floor, the room stinking of butchery and the word *"teind"* written on the wall above him in blood, his confession. A tithe to hell, it meant, and he shuddered in spite of the heat and crossed himself.

She'd said it was maybe the blood that had made Young Ian's bairns all die—the blood not matching betwixt him and his Mohawk wife—and that maybe it would be different with Rachel. He said a quick Ave, that it might be so, and crossed himself again.

The hair that lay upon her shoulders was coiling now, sinuous, slow as rising bread. Ought he rouse her to drink again? She needed the water, to help make more blood, to cool her with sweat. But while she slept, the pain was less. A few moments longer, then.

Not now. Please, not now.

She shifted, moaning, and he saw that she was different; restless now. The stain on her bandage had changed color, darkened from scarlet to rust as it dried. He laid a hand softly on her arm and felt the heat.

The bleeding had stopped. The fever had begun.

NOW THE TREES were talking to him. He wished they'd stop. The only thing Ian Murray wanted just now was silence. He was alone for the moment, but his ears buzzed and his head still throbbed with noise.

That always happened for a bit after a fight. You were listening so hard, to start with, for the sounds of the enemy, the direction of the wind, the voice of a saint behind you . . . you began to hear the voices of the forest, like you did hunting. And then you heard the shots and shouting, and when there were moments when that stopped, you heard the blood pounding round your body and beating in your ears, and, all in all, it took some time for the racket to die down afterward.

He had brief flashes of things that had happened during the

day—milling soldiers; the thud of the arrow that struck him; the face of the Abenaki he'd killed by the fire; the look of George Washington on his big white horse, racing up the road, waving his hat—but these came and went in a fog of confusion, appearing as though revealed to him by a stroke of lightning, then disappearing into a buzzing mist.

A wind went whispering through the branches over him, and he felt it on his skin as though he'd been brushed with sandpaper. What might Rachel say, when he told her what he'd done?

He could still hear the sound when the tomahawk caved in the Abenaki's skull. He could still feel it, too, in the bones of his arms, in the bursting pain of his wound.

Dimly, he realized that his feet were no longer keeping to the road; he was stumbling over clumps of grass, stubbing his moccasin-clad toes on rocks. He looked back to find his path—he saw it, plain, a wavering line of black . . . Why was it wavering?

He didn't want silence, after all. He wanted Rachel's voice, no matter what she might say to him.

It came to him dimly that he couldn't go any farther. He was aware of a faint sense of surprise but was not afraid.

He didn't remember falling but found himself on the ground, his hot cheek pressed against the cool prickle of pine needles. Laboriously, he got to his knees and scraped away the thick layer of fallen needles. Then he was lying with his body on damp earth, the blanket of needles half pulled over him; he could do no more and said a brief prayer to the tree, that it might protect him through the night.

And as he fell headlong into darkness, he did hear Rachel's voice, in memory.

"Thy life's journey lies along its own path, Ian," she said, *"and I cannot share thy journey—but I can walk beside thee. And I will."*

His last thought was that he hoped she'd still mean it when he told her what he'd done.

86

IN WHICH ROSY-FINGERED DAWN SHOWS UP MOB-HANDED

GREY WOKE TO THE drums of reveille, not startled by the accustomed rattle but with no clear idea where he was. *In camp.* Well, that much was obvious. He swung his legs out of the cot and sat up slowly, taking stock. His left arm hurt a lot, one of his eyes was stuck shut, and his mouth was so dry he could barely swallow. He'd slept in his clothes, smelled rank, and needed badly to piss.

He groped under the cot, found a utensil, and used it, noting in a rather dreamy way that his urine smelled of apples. That brought back the taste of cider and, with it, full recollection of the day and night before. Honey and flies. Artillery. Jamie, blood down his face. Rifle butt and the crack of bone. William . . . Hal . . .

Almost full recollection. He sat down and remained quite still for a moment, trying to decide whether Hal had really told him that his eldest son, Benjamin, was dead. Surely not. It must have been a shred of nightmare, lingering in his mind. And yet he had the dreadful feeling of doomed certainty that comes down like a curtain on the mind, smothering disbelief.

He stood up, staggering a little, determined to go and find his brother. He hadn't yet found his shoes, though, when the flap was thrown back and Hal came in, followed by an orderly with a basin, a steaming pitcher, and shaving implements.

"Sit down," Hal said, in a completely ordinary voice. "You'll have to wear one of my uniforms, and you're not doing it smelling like that. What the devil happened to your hair?"

Grey had forgotten his hair and flattened a palm on top of his head, surprised at the bristly stubble there.

"Oh. A *ruse de guerre.*" He sat down slowly, eyes on his brother. The bad eye had come open, though it was unpleasantly crusty, and so far as Grey could see, Hal looked much as he usually did. Tired, of course, worn, and a little haunted, but everyone looked like that the day after a battle. Surely if it were true, he'd look different. Worse, somehow.

He would have asked, but Hal didn't linger, going off and leaving John in the hands of the orderly. Before the ablutions were complete, a young Scottish surgeon with freckles appeared, yawning as though he hadn't slept all night, and blinked blearily at Grey's arm. He prodded this in a professional manner, pronounced the bone cracked but not broken, and put it in a sling.

The sling had to be removed almost at once, in order for him to dress—another orderly arrived with a uniform and a tray of breakfast—and by the time he was made tidy and had been forcibly fed, he was wild with impatience.

He would have to wait for Hal to reappear, though; no point going out to scour the camp for him. And he really must talk to his brother before seeking out William. A small dish of honey had been provided with his toast, and he was dipping a dubious finger into it, wondering whether he ought to try dabbing it into his eye, when at last the flap opened again and his brother was with him.

"Did you actually tell me that Ben is dead?" he blurted at once. Hal's face contracted a bit, but his jaw was set.

"No," Hal said evenly. "I told you that I'd had news of Ben, and they *said* he was dead. I don't believe it." He gave John a stare defying him to contradict this belief.

"Oh. Good," Grey said mildly. "Then I don't believe it, either. Who told you, though?"

"That's why I don't believe it," Hal replied, turning to lift the tent flap and peer out—evidently to be sure of not being overheard, and the thought made Grey's belly flutter a little. "It was Ezekiel Richardson who brought me the news, and I wouldn't trust that fellow if he told me I had a hole in the seat of my breeches, let alone something like that."

The flutter in Grey's belly became a full-blown beating of wings.

"Your instincts haven't led you amiss there," he said. "Sit down and have a piece of toast. I have a few things to tell you."

WILLIAM WOKE with a shattering headache and the conviction that he had forgotten something important. Clutching his head, he discovered a bandage wound round it, chafing his ear. He pulled it off impatiently; there was blood on it, but not much and all dried. He recalled vague bits of things from the night before—pain, nausea, his head swimming, Uncle Hal . . . and then an image of his father, white-faced and fragile . . . *"If you and I have things to say to each other . . ."* Christ, had he dreamed that?

He said something bad in German, and a young voice repeated it, rather doubtfully.

"What's that mean, sir?" asked Zeb, who had popped up beside his cot with a covered tray.

"You don't need to know, and don't repeat it," William said, sitting up. "What happened to my head?"

Zeb's brow creased.

"You don't remember, sir?"

"If I did, would I be asking you?"

Zeb's brow creased in concentration, but the logic of this question escaped him, and he merely shrugged, set down the tray, and answered the first one.

"Colonel Grey said you was hit on the head by deserters."

"Desert—oh." He stopped to consider that. British deserters? No . . . there was a reason why German profanity had sprung to his mind. He had a fleeting memory of Hessians, and . . . and what?

"Colenso's got over the shits," Zeb offered helpfully.

"Good to know the day's starting out well for somebody. Oh, Jesus." Pain crackled inside his skull, and he pressed a hand to his head. "Have you got anything to drink on that tray, Zeb?"

"Yes, sir!" Zeb uncovered the tray, triumphantly revealing a dish of coddled eggs with toast, a slice of ham, and a beaker of something that looked suspiciously murky but smelled strongly of alcohol.

"What's in this?"

"Dunno, sir, but Colonel Grey says it's a hair-of-the-dog-what-bit-you sort of thing."

"Oh." So it hadn't been a dream. He shoved that thought aside for the moment and regarded the beaker with a cautious interest. He'd had the first of his father's restoratives when he was fourteen and had mistaken the punch being prepared for Lord John's dinner party as the same sort that ladies had at garden parties. He'd had a few more in the years since and found them invariably effective, if rather startling to drink.

"Right, then," he said, and, taking a deep breath, picked up the beaker and drained it, swallowing heroically without pausing for breath.

"Cor!" said Zeb, admiring. "The cook said he could send some sausages, was you up to eating 'em."

William merely shook his head—being momentarily incapable of speech—and picked up a piece of toast, which he held for a moment, not quite ready to consider actually inserting it into his mouth. His head still hurt, but the restorative had jarred loose a few more bits from the detritus in his brain.

". . . Advice? You're too old to be given it and too young to take it. . . ."

". . . Er spricht Deutsch. Er gehört! . . ." He speaks German. He heard.

"I heard," he said slowly. "What did I hear?"

Zeb appeared to think this another rhetorical question and, instead of trying to answer it, asked one of his own.

"What happened to Goth, sir?" His thin face was solemn, as though he expected to receive bad news.

"Goth," William repeated blankly. "Has something happened to Goth?"

"Well, he's gone, sir," Zeb said, apparently trying to be tactful. "That is—when the regulars took you and the Indian away from the Rebels, you wasn't on him."

"When the . . . what Indian?—what the devil *happened* yesterday, Zeb?"

"How would I know?" Zeb said, affronted. "Wasn't there, was I?"

"No, of course—bloody hell. Is my uncle—the Duke of Pardloe—in camp? I need to talk to him."

Zeb looked dubious.

"Well, I can go and look for him, I s'pose."

"Do, please. Now." William waved him off, then sat still for a moment, trying to stick the jagged fragments of his memory back together. Rebels? Goth . . . He did recall *something* about Goth, but what was it? Had he run into Rebels, who took the horse? But what was this about Indians and deserters, and why did he keep hearing echoes of German speech in the back of his brain?

And who, come to think of it, was the Colonel Grey that Zeb had referred to? He'd assumed it was Uncle Hal—but his father's rank was lieutenant colonel, and he'd also be addressed as "Colonel" in common use. He glanced at the tray and the empty beaker. Uncle Hal certainly knew about the hair of the dog, but . . .

"As long as you're alive, everything's all right."

He put the untouched toast down, a sudden lump in his throat. Again. He'd had the lump last night, when he saw Papa. When he'd said to his father—yes, God damn it, his father!—*"I'm glad you're not dead."*

He maybe wasn't quite ready to talk to Papa—or Papa to him—and he didn't quite agree that everything was all right, but . . .

A shaft of brilliant sunlight lanced into his face as the tent flap was shoved aside, and he sat bolt upright, swinging his legs out of bed to be ready to meet—

But it wasn't either his uncle or his father who appeared out of the eye-watering blur of sunlight. It was Banastre Tarleton, in uniform but wigless and unbuttoned, looking indecently cheerful for someone whose face seemed to have been beaten badly not too long ago.

"Alive, are you, Ellesmere?" Ban spotted the dish and, scooping up a coddled egg in his fingers, gulped it. He licked his buttery fingers, making pleased noises.

"Christ, I'm hungry. Been up since dawn. Killing on an empty stomach leaves you rare sharp-set, I'll say that. Can I have the rest?"

"Be my guest. Who've you been killing for breakfast? Rebels?"

Tarleton looked surprised, arrested with a mouthful of toast. He chewed this imperfectly and bolted the bite before answering with a shower of crumbs.

"No, Washington's troops withdrew to the south, so far as I

know. Hessian deserters. The same lot that crowned you and left you for dead, or so I assume. They had your horse; recognized him." He reached for another egg, and William thrust a spoon into his hand.

"For God's sake, eat like a Christian. Do you *have* my horse?"

"I do. He's lame in the right fore, but I don't think it's bad. Mmm . . . have you got your own cook?"

"No, he's my uncle's. Tell me about the deserters. They knocked me on the head, and my memory's a bit spotty." More than a bit, but chunks of it were beginning to come back pretty fast now.

Between bites, Tarleton gave him the story. A company of mercenaries under von Knyphausen had made up their minds to desert during the battle, but not all the men were of the same mind. Those in favor of desertion had drawn away a bit and were quietly discussing whether it was necessary to kill the dissenters, when William had shown up unexpectedly in their midst.

"That knocked them a bit skew-ways, as you might surmise." Tarleton, having finished the eggs and most of the toast, picked up the beaker and looked disappointed at finding it empty.

"There's probably water in that canteen," William said, motioning toward the battered tin-and-leather object hanging from the tent pole. "So that's it. . . . They looked a bit nervous, but when I asked one of them in German whether there was a farrier nearby—that was it! Goth threw a shoe, that's why he—but then I heard someone whispering, sounding frantic, and he was saying, 'He heard! He knows!' Must've meant he thought I'd overheard them plotting and knew what they were up to."

He breathed out in relief at having this much of the previous day restored to him.

Tarleton nodded. "Imagine so. They *did* kill some of the dissenters—gather a barney broke out after they bashed you on the head and threw you into the ravine—but not all of them."

A few of the mercenaries had escaped and headed for von Knyphausen, who, upon hearing the news, had sent a dispatch to Clinton asking for assistance in dealing with the miscreants.

William nodded at this. It was always better to have matters like desertion or treason dealt with by troops outside the affected companies. And knowing Ban Tarleton, he would have leapt at the chance to track down the deserters and—

"Were you told to kill them?" he asked, striving for casualness.

Tarleton gave him an eggy grin and wiped a few lingering crumbs off his chin.

"Not specifically. Got the impression that as long as I brought a few back to tell the tale, no one much cared how many. And there *was* a hint of *pour encourager les autres* in my orders."

Politely suppressing his shock at the revelation that Tarleton could read, let alone read Voltaire, William nodded.

"I see. My orderly said something rather curious: mentioned that I'd been found by Rebels—with an Indian. D'you know anything about that?"

Tarleton looked surprised, but shook his head.

"Not a thing. Oh—" He'd sat down on the stool and now rocked back a little, hands clasped about one knee, looking pleased with himself. "I *do* know something, though. Recall you asked me about Harkness?"

"Harkness . . . oh, yes!" William's exclamation had less to do with mention of Captain Harkness and more to do with the important thing he'd forgotten, which had just come back to him: Jane and her sister.

He had an immediate impulse to get up and go find her, make sure they were all right. The fugitive Loyalists and camp followers would have been well clear of the actual battle, of course—but the violence and agitation that attended fighting didn't simply stop when the fighting did. And it wasn't only deserters and scavengers who looted, raped, and hunted among the hapless sheep.

He spared a flickering thought for Anne Endicott and her family—but they did at least have a man to protect them, however ill-equipped. Jane and Fanny . . . but surely Zeb would have known, if anything—

"What?" He looked blankly at Tarleton. "What did you say?"

"That knock on the head affected your hearing, too, did it?" Ban took a swig from the canteen. "I said I made inquiries.

Harkness never joined his regiment. For all anyone knows, he's still in Philadelphia."

William's mouth felt dry. He reached for the canteen and took a swallow; the water was warm and tin-tasting, but wet.

"Absent without leave, do you mean?"

"Very much without leave," Tarleton assured him. "Last anyone recalls seeing him, he was promising to go back to some brothel and give some whore a proper seeing-to. Maybe she saw to him, instead!" He laughed heartily at the thought.

William stood up abruptly, then—for something to do—reached to replace the canteen on its nail. The tent flap was down, but a stray beam of dust-filled sunlight still fell through the gap, catching the glitter of metal. His officer's gorget hung from the nail, its silver gleaming in the sun.

"PERCIVAL WAINWRIGHT?" John hadn't seen Hal so disconcerted since the events concerning their father's death—which had also involved Percy, come to think of it.

"In the—very fashionable—flesh. He's apparently an adviser to the Marquis de La Fayette."

"Who's that?"

"A flash young frog with a lot of money," Grey said with a one-shouldered shrug. "Rebel general. Said to be very close to Washington."

"Close," Hal repeated, with a sharp look at Grey. "Close to Wainwright, too, you think?"

"Probably not that way," he replied calmly, though his heart beat a little faster. "I gather you're not altogether surprised that he isn't dead. Percy, I mean." He was vaguely affronted; he'd gone to a lot of trouble to make it appear that Percy had died in prison while awaiting trial for sodomy.

Hal merely snorted. "Men like that never die so conveniently. Why the bloody hell is he telling you this, do you think?"

Grey suppressed the vivid memory of bergamot, red wine, and petitgrain.

"I don't know. But I *do* know he's deeply involved with French interests, and—"

"Wainwright's never been involved with any interests other

than his own," Hal interrupted brusquely. He gave John a sharp look. "You'd do well to remember that."

"I doubt I shall ever see the fellow again," John replied, overlooking the implication that his brother considered him gullible—or worse. He was entirely aware that while Hal was treating Richardson's news of Ben with scorn, and was very likely right to do so, neither of them could completely ignore the possibility that the man had been telling the truth.

Hal verified this assumption by smacking his fist down on the campaign chest, making the pewter cups jump and fall over. He stood abruptly.

"Bloody hell," he muttered. "Stay here!"

"Where are you going?"

Hal paused at the tent flap for an instant. His face was still haggard, but John recognized the battle light in his eyes.

"To arrest Richardson."

"You can't arrest him yourself, for God's sake!" Grey was on his feet, too, reaching for Hal's sleeve.

"Which regiment does he belong to?"

"The Fifth, but he's detached. I told you he was an intelligencer, did I not?" The word "intelligencer" dripped with contempt.

"All right—I'll speak to Sir Henry first."

John had got a grip on Hal's arm and tightened his hold at this. "I should have thought you'd had enough of scandal by now," he said, trying for calmness. "Take a breath and imagine what will likely happen if you do that. Assuming that Sir Henry would take the time to consider your request. Today, for God's sake?" He could hear the army moving outside; there was no danger of pursuit from Washington's troops, but Clinton was not going to hang about. His division, with its baggage and refugees under its wing, would be on the road within the hour.

Hal's arm was hard as marble under John's hand and stayed that way. But he *did* stop, breathing with a slow, deep regularity. At last he turned his head and looked into his brother's eyes. A beam of sunlight threw every line in his face into stark relief.

"Name one thing you think I wouldn't do," he said quietly, "in order not to have to tell Minnie that Ben is dead."

Grey drew one long, deep breath of his own and nodded, letting go.

"Point taken. Whatever you mean to do, I'll help. But first I have to find William. What Percy said—"

"Ah." Hal blinked and his face relaxed a fraction. "Yes, of course. Meet you here in half an hour."

WILLIAM HAD BARELY finished dressing before the message he'd been halfway expecting arrived from Sir Henry, delivered by Lieutenant Foster, whom he knew slightly. Foster grimaced sympathetically when handing it over.

William observed Sir Henry Clinton's personal seal: not a good sign. On the other hand, if he was to be arrested for being absent without leave the previous day, Harry Foster would have brought an armed escort and taken him off without a by-your-leave. That was mildly heartening, and he broke the seal without hesitation.

In the event, it was a terse note advising him that he was relieved of duty until further notice—but that was all. He exhaled, only then realizing that he'd been holding his breath.

But of course Sir Henry wouldn't imprison him—how and where, with the army on the move? Short of putting him in irons and transporting him by wagon . . . Realistically, Clinton couldn't even confine him to quarters; the quarters in question were beginning to shake overhead as his uncle's orderly set to dismantling the tent.

All right, then. He stuffed the note into his pocket, stuffed his feet into his boots, seized up his hat, and went out, feeling not that bad, all things considered. He had a headache, but it was bearable, and he'd managed to eat what breakfast Tarleton had left.

When things settled down and Sir Henry got round to taking official notice of his disobedience of orders, William could fish up Captain André and have him explain about going to find Tarleton, and all would be well. Meanwhile, he'd go down to the camp followers' area and find Jane.

There was a strong bitter smell of fresh cabbage floating over the sprawl of makeshift shelters and human detritus, and a scatter of farm wagons drawn up along the road, with women crowding round them. The army cooks fed the refugees, but rations were sparse—and had doubtless been disrupted by the battle.

He walked along the road, keeping an eye out for Jane or Fanny, but didn't spot either one. His eye attuned for a young girl, though, he did see Peggy Endicott, trudging down the road with a bucket in either hand.

"Miss Peggy! May I offer my assistance, ma'am?" He smiled down at her and was warmed to see her own face—somewhat anxious before—bloom into delight under her cap.

"Captain!" she cried, nearly dropping her buckets in her excitement. "Oh, I'm *so* happy to see you! We were all so worried for you, you know, in the battle, and we all said a prayer for your safety, but Papa told us you would surely prevail over the wicked Rebels and God would see you safe."

"Your lovely prayers were to great effect," he assured her gravely, taking the buckets. One was full of water and the other of turnips, their green tops wilting over the rim. "Are your mama and papa well, then, and your sisters?"

They walked along together, Peggy dancing on her toes and chattering like an affable small parrot. William kept an eye peeled for Jane or Fanny among the laundresses; it was safer near those redoubtable ladies than in some other parts of the camp. There were no kettles boiling this morning, of course, but the scent of lye soap floated on the humid air like scum on a cauldron full of dirty clothes.

There was no sign of Jane and Fanny by the time he'd reached the Endicotts' wagon—still on all four wheels, he was glad to see. He was greeted warmly by all the Endicotts, though the girls and Mrs. Endicott made a great fuss of the lump on his head when he took his hat off to help with the loading of their wagon.

"Nothing, ma'am, the merest bruise," he assured Mrs. Endicott for the ninth time, when she urged him to sit down in the shade and drink some water with the tiniest bit of brandy in it, for they still had some, thank goodness. . . .

Anne, who had maneuvered herself close to him, passing him items to be loaded, leaned in with a tea chest and let her hand brush his—deliberately, he was sure.

"Will you stay in New York, do you think?" she asked, stooping to pick up a portmanteau. "Or perhaps—you must excuse my prying, but people *will* talk—go back to England? Miss Jernigan said that you might."

"Miss . . . oh, of course." He recalled Mary Jernigan, a very flirtatious blond piece with whom he'd danced at a ball in Philadelphia. He glanced over the throng of Loyalist refugees. "Is she here?"

"Yes," Anne replied, a little tersely. "Dr. Jernigan has a brother in New York; they will stay with him for a time." She collected herself—he could see that she was regretting having recalled his attention to Mary Jernigan—and smiled at him, deeply enough as to invoke the dimple in her left cheek. "You needn't take refuge with reluctant relatives, though, need you? Miss Jernigan said that you have a great vast estate awaiting you in England."

"Mmm," he said noncommittally. His father had warned him early on about marriage-minded young women with an eye to his fortune, and he'd met quite a few of them. Still, he *liked* Anne Endicott and her family and was inclined to think they had a real regard for him, as well, despite his position and the pragmatical considerations that must now afflict Anne and her sisters, with their father's affairs so precarious.

"I don't know," he said, taking the portmanteau from her. "I truly have no idea what's to become of me. Who does, in wartime?" He smiled, a little ruefully, and she seemed to feel his sense of uncertainty, for she impulsively laid a hand on his sleeve.

"Well, be assured that you have friends, at least, who care what becomes of you," she said softly.

"Thank you," he said, and turned his face toward the cart, lest she see how much that touched him.

In turning, though, his eye caught a purposeful movement, someone threading toward him through the crowd, and Anne Endicott's soft dark eyes disappeared abruptly from his mind.

"Sir!" It was his groom Colenso Baragwanath, gasping from the effort of running. "Sir, have you—"

"There you are, Baragwanath! What the devil are you doing here, and where have you left Madras? Good news, though: Goth's come back. Colonel Tarleton has him and—what, for God's sake?" For Colenso was squirming as though he had a snake in his breeches, his square Cornish face contorted with information.

"Jane and Fanny're gone, sir!"

"Gone? Gone where?"

"Dunno, sir. But they've gone. I came back to get my jacket and the shelter was still up, but their things were gone and I couldn't find 'em and when I asked the folk who camps near us, they said as the girls had rolled up their bundles and sneaked off!"

William didn't waste time inquiring how one could possibly sneak out of an open camp of several thousand people, let alone why that should be necessary.

"Which way did they go?"

"That way, sir!" Colenso pointed down the road.

William rubbed a hand over his face and stopped abruptly when he inadvertently touched the bruised swelling on his left temple.

"Ouch. Well, bloody hell—oh, I beg your pardon, Miss Endicott." For at this point he became aware of Anne Endicott at his elbow, eyes round with curiosity.

"Who are Jane and Fanny?" she asked.

"Ahh . . . two young ladies who are traveling under my protection," he said, knowing exactly what effect *that* information was likely to have, but there wasn't much help for it. "*Very* young ladies," he added, in the vain hope of improving things. "Daughters of a . . . um, distant cousin."

"Oh," she said, looking distinctly unconvinced. "But they've run off? Whyever should they do such a thing?"

"Damned if I—er, beg pardon, ma'am. I don't know, but I must go and find out. Will you make my excuses to your parents and sisters?"

"I—of course." She made a small, abortive gesture toward him, putting out her hand and then withdrawing it. She looked both startled and slightly affronted. He regretted it, but there wasn't time to do anything about it.

"Your servant, ma'am," he said, and, bowing, left her.

IN THE END, it was half a day, rather than half an hour, before John saw Hal again. He found his brother, quite by chance, standing by the road that led northward, watching the marching columns go past. Most of the camp had already left;

only the cook wagons and laundry kettles were trundling past now, the disorderly sprawl of camp followers spreading out behind them like the plague of lice over the land of Egypt.

"William's gone," he said to Hal without preamble.

Hal nodded, face somber. "So is Richardson."

"Bloody hell."

Hal's groom was standing by, holding two horses. Hal jerked his head at a dark-bay mare and took the reins of his own horse, a light-bay gelding with a blaze and one white stocking.

"Where do you think we're going?" John inquired, seeing his brother turn the gelding's head south.

"Philadelphia," Hal replied, tight-lipped. "Where else?"

Grey could himself think of any number of alternatives, but recognized a rhetorical question when he heard one and contented himself with asking, "Have you got a clean handkerchief?"

Hal gave him a blank look, then rummaged in his sleeve, pulling out a crumpled but unused linen square.

"Apparently. Why?"

"I expect we're going to need a flag of truce at some point. The Continental army lying presently between us and Philadelphia, I mean."

"Oh, that." Hal stuffed the handkerchief back up his sleeve and said no more until they had negotiated their way past the last trailing remnants of the horde of refugees and found themselves more or less alone on the road leading south.

"No one could be sure, in the confusion," he said, as though he'd last spoken ten seconds before. "But it looks very much as though Captain Richardson has deserted."

"What?!"

"Not a bad moment to choose, really," Hal said reflectively. "No one would have noticed he was gone for days, had I not come looking for him. He was in camp last night, though, and unless he's disguised himself as a teamster or a laundress, he's not here any longer."

"The contingency seems remote," Grey said. "William *was* here this morning—both your orderly and his young grooms saw him, and so did a Colonel Tarleton of the British Legion, who breakfasted with him."

"Who? Oh, him." Hal waved off Tarleton as a distraction.

"Clinton values him, but I never trust a man with lips like a girl's."

"Regardless, he seems to have had nothing to do with William's disappearance. The groom Baragwanath thinks that William went off to see about a couple of . . . young women among the camp followers."

Hal glanced at him, one brow raised.

"What sort of young women?"

"Probably the sort you're thinking," John replied, a little tersely.

"At that hour of the morning, after being bashed on the head the night before? And young women, plural? The boy's got stamina, I'll say that for him."

Grey could have said a number of other things about William at this point, but didn't. "So you think Richardson's deserted." That would explain Hal's focus on Philadelphia; if Percy was right and Richardson was in fact an American agent, where else might he go at this point?

"It seems the most likely possibility. Also . . ." Hal hesitated for a moment, but then his mouth firmed. "If I believed that Benjamin was dead, what might I be expected to do?"

"Go and make inquiries into his death," Grey replied, suppressing the queasy feeling the notion induced. "Claim his body, at the least."

Hal nodded. "Ben was—or is—being held at a place in New Jersey called Middletown Encampment. I've not been there, but it's in the middle of Washington's strongest territory, in the Watchung Mountains. Nest of Rebels."

"And you'd be unlikely to undertake that sort of journey with a large armed guard," John observed. "You'd go alone, or perhaps with an orderly, an ensign or two. Or me."

Hal nodded. They rode for a bit, each alone with his thoughts.

"So you're not going to the Watchung Mountains," Grey said at last. His brother sighed deeply and set his jaw.

"Not immediately. If I can catch up with Richardson, I may find out what's really happened—or not happened—to Ben. After that . . ."

"Do you have a plan for proceeding once we reach Philadelphia?" Grey inquired. "Given that it's in the hands of the Rebels?"

Hal's lips compressed. "I will have, by the time we get there."

"I daresay. I have one now, though."

Hal looked at him, thumbing a hank of damp hair behind his ear. His hair was carelessly tied back; he'd not bothered to have it plaited or clubbed this morning, a sure sign of his agitation. "Does it involve anything patently insane? Your better plans always do."

"Not at all. We're certain to encounter the Continentals, as I said. Assuming we aren't shot on sight, we produce your flag of truce"—he nodded at his brother's sleeve, from which the edge of the handkerchief was drooping—"and demand to be taken to General Fraser."

Hal gave him a startled look.

"*James* Fraser?"

"The same." Grey's knotted stomach clenched a little tighter at the thought. At both the thought of speaking to Jamie again—and the thought of telling him that William was missing. "He fought with Benedict Arnold at Saratoga, and his wife is friendly with the man."

"God help General Arnold, in that case," Hal murmured.

"And who else has a better reason for helping us in this matter than does Jamie Fraser?"

"Who indeed?" They rode for some time in silence, Hal apparently lost in thought. It wasn't until they paused to find a creek and water the horses that he spoke again, water streaming down his face where he'd splashed it.

"So you've not only somehow married Fraser's wife, but you've accidentally been raising his illegitimate son for the last fifteen years?"

"Apparently so," Grey said, in a tone that he hoped indicated complete unwillingness to talk about it. For once, Hal took the hint.

"I see," he said, and, with no further questions, wiped his face with the flag of truce and mounted up.

87

MOONRISE

IT HADN'T BEEN a peaceful day. Apparently Jamie had somehow retained sufficient presence of mind last night to write a brief note—though he didn't recall doing so—to La Fayette, explaining what had happened and confiding care of his troops to the marquis. This he had sent with Lieutenant Bixby, with instructions to notify the captains and militia commanders of his companies. After which, he'd forgotten everything but Claire.

Everything had not forgotten him, though. The sun was barely up before a stream of officers appeared at Mrs. Macken's door, in search of General Fraser. Mrs. Macken took every arrival as being the possible bearer of bad news concerning her still-missing husband, and the reek of burnt porridge rose through the house, seeping into the walls like the smell of fear.

Some came with questions, some with news or gossip—General Lee was relieved of duty, was under arrest, had gone to Philadelphia, had turned his coat and joined Clinton, had hanged himself, had challenged Washington to a duel. A messenger arrived from General Washington with a personal note of sympathy and good wishes; another came from La Fayette with an enormous hamper of food and a half-dozen bottles of claret.

Jamie couldn't eat, but gave the food to Mrs. Macken. He retained a couple of bottles of the wine, though, which he'd opened and kept by him through the day, taking occasional gulps to sustain him as he sponged and watched and prayed.

Judah Bixby came and went like a helpful ghost, appearing and disappearing, but always seeming to be there if something was needed.

"The militia companies . . ." Jamie began, but then couldn't think what he'd meant to ask concerning them. "Are they . . . ?"

"Most of them have gone home," Bixby told him, unloading a basket full of beer bottles. "Their enlistment ends on the thirtieth—that's tomorrow, sir," he added gently, "but they mostly set off first thing this morning."

Jamie let out a breath he hadn't known he was holding and felt a small measure of peace.

"I reckon it'll be months before anyone knows was it a victory or not," Bixby remarked. He drew the cork from one bottle, then another, and handed one to Jamie. "But it surely wasn't defeat. Shall we drink to it, sir?"

Jamie was worn out with worry and praying, but managed a smile for Judah and a quick word of thanks to God for the boy.

Once Judah had left, a somewhat longer prayer on behalf of his nephew. Ian hadn't returned, and none of Jamie's visitors had had any word of him. Rachel had come back late the night before, white-faced and silent, and had gone out again at daybreak. Dottie had offered to go with her, but Rachel had refused; the two of them were needed to deal with the wounded still being brought in and those sheltering in the houses and barns of Freehold.

Ian, Jamie thought in anguish, addressing his brother-in-law. *For God's sake, have an eye to our lad, because I canna do it. I'm sorry.*

Claire's fever had risen fast during the night, then seemed to fall a little with the coming of the light; she was conscious now and then and capable of a few words, but for the most part she lay in an uneasy doze, her breath coming in shallow pants punctuated by sudden deep, tearing gasps that woke her—she dreamed that she was being suffocated, she said. He would give her as much water as she would take and douse her hair again, and she would drop back into fever dreams, muttering and moaning.

He began to feel as though he were living in a fever dream himself: trapped in endless repetitions of prayer and water, these broken by visitations from some vanished, alien world.

Perhaps this was purgatory, he thought, and gave a wan smile at memory of himself, waking on Culloden Moor so many years ago, his eyelids sealed with blood, thinking himself dead and grateful for it, even if his immediate prospect was a spell in purgatory—that being a vague, unknown circumstance, probably unpleasant but not one he feared.

He feared the one that might be imminent.

He *had* come to the conclusion that he couldn't kill himself, even if she died. Even could he bring himself to commit a sin of that magnitude, there were people who needed him, and to abandon them would be a greater sin even than the willful destruction of God's gift of life. But to live without her—he watched her breathe, obsessively, counting ten breaths before he would believe she hadn't stopped—that would certainly be his purgatory.

He didn't think he'd taken his eyes off her, and maybe he hadn't, but he came out of his reverie to see that her own eyes were open, a soft smudged black in the white of her face. The light had faded to the final cusp of twilight and all color had washed from the room, leaving them in a luminous dusty haze that wasn't daylight any longer but not yet night. He saw that her hair was nearly dry, curling in masses over the pillow.

"I've . . . decided . . . not to die," she said, in a voice little more than a whisper.

"Oh. Good." He was afraid to touch her, for fear of hurting her, but couldn't bear not to. He laid a hand as lightly as he could over hers, finding it cool in spite of the heat trapped in the small attic.

"I *could,* you know." She closed one eye and looked accusingly at him with the other. "I *want* to; this is . . . bloody horrible."

"I know," he whispered, and brought her hand to his lips. Her bones were frail, and she hadn't the strength to squeeze his hand; her fingers lay limp in his.

She closed her eyes and breathed audibly for a little.

"Do you know why?" she said suddenly, opening her eyes.

"No." He'd thought of making some jesting remark about her needing to write down her receipt for making ether, but her tone was dead serious, and he didn't.

"Because," she said, and stopped with a small grimace that squeezed his heart. "Because," she said through clenched teeth, "I know what it felt . . . like when I . . . thought you were dead, and—" A small gasp for breath, and her eyes locked on his. "And I wouldn't do that to *you.*" Her bosom fell and her eyes closed.

It was a long moment before he could speak.

"Thank ye, Sassenach," he whispered, and held her small, cold hand between his own and watched her breathe until the moon rose.

I COULD SEE the moon through the tiny window; we were in the attic of the house. It was the first breath of the new moon, but the whole of it was visible, a perfect ball of violet and indigo cupped in a sickle of light, luminous among the stars. "The new moon with the old," country folk called it in England. On the Ridge, people called it "holding water."

The fever had left me. It had also left me drained, light-headed, and weak as a newborn mouse. My side was swollen from hip to oxter, hot and tender to the touch, but I was sure this was only surgical trauma. There wasn't any significant infection, only a little inflammation near the surface of the incision.

I felt rather like the new moon: the shadow of pain and death was still clearly visible to me—but only because the light was there to throw it into perspective. On the other hand, there were still small practicalities and indignities to be dealt with. I had to pee, and I couldn't sit up by myself, let alone squat over a chamber pot.

I had no idea what time it was, though with the moon like that, it couldn't be the middle of the night. The house was still, though—Lieutenant Macken had returned safely in late afternoon, bringing with him several other men, but they had been too exhausted for celebration; I could hear faint snoring from the floor below. I couldn't disturb everyone by calling out for Loretta Macken's assistance. With a sigh, I leaned gingerly over the side of the bed and cleared my throat.

"Sassenach? Are ye all right?" A segment of the darkness on the floor moved suddenly and resolved itself into a Jamie-shaped shadow.

"Yes. Are you?"

That got me the breath of a laugh.

"I'll do, Sassenach," he said softly, and I heard the rustle of his movement as he got his feet under him. "I'm glad ye feel well enough to ask. D'ye need water?"

"Er . . . rather the opposite, really," I said.

"Oh? Oh." He stooped, a pale blur in his shirt, to reach under the bed. "D'ye need help?"

"If I didn't, I wouldn't have waked you up," I said, a little testily. "I didn't think I could wait for Mrs. Macken or Dottie, though." He snorted a little and got me under the arms, lifting me into a sitting position.

"Now, then," he murmured. "It's no like ye've not done this—and a good many worse things—for me."

While this was true, it didn't make matters easier.

"You can let go now," I said. "Perhaps leave the room?"

"Perhaps not," he said, still mildly, but with a tone indicating that his mind was made up on the subject. "If I let go, ye'll fall on your face, and ye ken that perfectly well, so stop talkin' and be about your business now, aye?"

It took some time—anything that put pressure on my abdomen, including the act of urinating, hurt remarkably—but the business was accomplished and I was eased back down onto the pillow, gasping. Jamie bent and picked up the chamber pot, clearly intending to hurl the contents out the window in customary Edinburgh fashion.

"No, wait!" I said. "Keep that 'til morning."

He paused.

"What for?" he asked cautiously. Clearly he suspected I might still be unhinged from fever and be contemplating some grossly irrational use of the pot's contents, but he didn't like to say so, in case I had something logical, if bizarre, in mind. I would have laughed, but it hurt too much.

"I need to check, once there's light, to be sure there's no blood," I said. "My right kidney's very sore; I want to be sure there's no damage."

"Ah." He set the utensil down carefully and, to my surprise, opened the door and glided out, moving soft-footed as a hunting fox. I heard one squeak as he stepped on a stair tread, but nothing more until a glow betokened his return with a candlestick.

"Have a look, then," he said, picking up the pot again and bringing it to me. "I kent ye'd just fret about it did ye have to wait for daybreak."

He sounded resigned, but this small thoughtfulness brought me close to tears. He heard the catch in my breathing and leaned close, alarmed, bringing the light up to my face.

"Are ye all right, Sassenach? Is it bad, then?"

"No," I said, and wiped my eyes hastily on a corner of the sheet. "No—it—it's fine. I just—oh, Jamie, I love you!" I did give way to tears, then, snuffling and blubbering like an idiot. "I'm sorry," I said, trying to get hold of myself. "I'm all right, there's nothing wrong, it's just—"

"Aye, I ken fine what it's just," he said, and, setting the candle and pot on the floor, lay down on the bed beside me, balancing precariously on the edge.

"Ye're hurt, *a nighean,*" he said softly, smoothing my hair off my wet cheeks. "And fevered and starved and worn to a shadow. There's no much of ye left, is there, poor wee thing?"

I shook my head and clung to him. "There's not much of you left, either," I managed to say, mumbling wetly into the front of his shirt.

He made a small amused noise and rubbed my back, very gently. "Enough, Sassenach," he said. "I'm enough. For now."

I sighed and fumbled under the pillow for a hankie to blow my nose.

"Better?" he asked, sitting up.

"Yes. Don't go, though." I put a hand on his leg, hard and warm under my hand. "Can you lie with me a minute? I'm awfully cold." I was, though I realized from the damp and salt on his skin that the room was quite hot. But loss of so much blood had left me chilled and gasping; I couldn't get through a sentence without stopping to breathe, and my arms were permanently goose-pimpled.

"Aye. Dinna move; I'll go round." He came round the bed and edged carefully in behind me. It was a narrow bed, barely wide enough to hold us closely pressed together.

I exhaled gingerly and relaxed against him in slow motion, reveling in the feel of his warmth and the solid comfort of his body.

"Elephants," I said, drawing the shallowest possible breath compatible with speaking. "When a female elephant is dying, sometimes a male will try to mate with her."

There was a marked silence behind me, and then a big hand came round and rested assessingly on my forehead.

"Either ye're fevered again, Sassenach," he said in my ear, "or ye have verra perverse fancies. Ye dinna really want me to—"

"No," I said hastily. "Not right this minute, no. And I'm not dying, either. The thought just came to me."

He made an amused Scottish noise and, lifting the hair off my neck, kissed my nape.

"Since ye're no dying," he said, "maybe that will do for the moment?"

I took his hand and placed it on my breast. Slowly I grew warmer, and my chilly feet, pressed against his shins, relaxed. The window now was filled with stars, hazy with the moistness of the summer night, and I suddenly missed the cool, clear, black-velvet nights of the mountains, the stars blazing huge, close enough to touch from the highest ridge.

"Jamie?" I whispered. "Can we go home? Please?"

"Aye," he said softly. He held my hand and the silence filled the room like moonlight, both of us wondering where home might be.

88

A WHIFF OF ROQUEFORT

I HADN'T SEEN ANY of the previous day's flock of visitors, though Jamie had told me about them. This day, though, brought one for me. Mrs. Macken brought him up the stairs, in spite of her advanced state of pregnancy, and showed him into my tiny room with great respect.

He wasn't in uniform and was—for him—quite subfusc, in a coat and breeches of the dull gray that was referred to (with accuracy) as "sad-colored," though he *had* taken the trouble to wear a dove-gray waistcoat with it that flattered his coloring.

"How are you, my dear?" he asked, taking off his hat. Not waiting for an answer, he came down on one knee by the bed, took my hand, and kissed it lightly. His blond hair had been washed, I saw—I smelled his bergamot soap—and trimmed to a uniform length. As that length was roughly an inch, the overall effect reminded me irresistibly of a fuzzy duckling. I laughed, then gasped and pressed a hand to my side.

"Dinna make her laugh!" Jamie said, glowering at John. His tone was cold, but I saw him take in John's aspect, and the corner of his own mouth twitched.

"I know," John said ruefully to me, passing a hand over his head and ignoring Jamie completely. "Isn't it dreadful? I ought really to wear a wig for the sake of public decency, but I couldn't bear it in the heat."

"Don't know that I blame you," I told him, and ran a hand through the damp mass of my own hair, drying on my shoulders. "Though I haven't yet got to the point of wanting to shave my head," I added pointedly, not quite turning my head toward Jamie.

"Don't. It wouldn't suit you at all," John assured me.

"How is your eye?" I asked, gingerly trying to raise myself on the pillow. "Let me have a look at it."

"Stay there," he said, and, leaning over me, opened both eyes wide. "I think it's quite good. It's still a bit tender to the touch and gets the odd twinge when I move it too far up or to the right, but—do you smell French cheese?" He sounded slightly startled.

"Mmm." I was gently prodding the flesh around the orbit, which showed only a slight residual swelling. The sclera was still quite bloodshot, but the bruising was much better. I thumbed down the lower lid to inspect the conjunctiva: a nice slippery pink, no sign of infection. "Does it water?"

"Only in strong sunlight, and not very much," he assured me, straightening up. He smiled at me. "Thank you, my dear."

Jamie didn't say anything, but the way he breathed had a distinctly edgy feel about it. I ignored him. If he chose to make a fuss, I couldn't bloody stop him.

"What are ye doing here?" he asked abruptly. John looked up at him, one brow raised, as though surprised to see him looming on the other side of my bed. John rose slowly to his feet, holding Jamie's eyes with his own.

"What do you think I'm doing?" he asked quietly. There

was no hint of challenge in the question, and I could see Jamie suddenly check his own hostility, frowning slightly as he looked John over, considering.

One side of John's mouth turned up a little.

"Do you think I've come to fight you for the favors of this lady? Or to seduce her from your side?"

Jamie didn't laugh, but the line between his brows smoothed out.

"I don't," he said dryly. "And as ye dinna seem to be much damaged, I doubt ye've come to be doctored."

John gave an amiable bob of the head, indicating that this line of reasoning was correct.

"And I doubt, as well," Jamie continued, an edge creeping into his voice, "that ye've come to continue our previous discussion."

John inhaled slowly, and exhaled even slower, regarding Jamie with a level gaze. "Is it your opinion that anything remains to be said, regarding any part of that discussion?"

There was a marked silence. I glanced from one to the other, Jamie's eyes narrowed and John's eyes wide, both with fixed blue stares. All it lacked was growling and the slow lashing of tails.

"Are you armed, John?" I inquired pleasantly.

He glanced at me, startled. "No."

"Good," I said, grunting slightly as I struggled to sit up. "Then you obviously aren't going to kill *him*"—I nodded at Jamie, standing over me with fists half curled—"and if he didn't break your neck the first time, he isn't going to do it now. Are you?" I inquired, arching a brow at Jamie.

He looked down his nose at me, but I saw the slight relaxation of his mouth. And his hands. "Probably not."

"Well, then." I brushed the hair back from my face. "No point in hitting each other. And harsh language would detract from the pleasant nature of this visit, wouldn't it?"

Neither of them chose to answer this.

"That was not actually a rhetorical question," I said. "But let that go." I turned to John, folding my hands in my lap. "Flattered as I am by the attention, I don't think you came *solely* to inquire after my well-being. So if you'll pardon my vulgar curiosity . . . why *are* you here?"

He finally relaxed and, at my nod, took the stool, linking his fingers round his knee.

"I've come to ask your help," he said directly to Jamie. "But also"—it was slight, but I noticed the hesitation—"to make you an offer. Not as quid pro quo," he added. "The offer is not contingent on your assistance."

Jamie made a Scottish noise indicating deep skepticism but willingness to listen.

John nodded and took a breath before continuing. "You once mentioned to me, my dear, that—"

"Dinna be calling her that."

"Mrs. Fraser," John amended, and, with a polite bow to me, turned his attention to Jamie, "once mentioned that she—and you, I would imagine—had some acquaintance with General Arnold."

Jamie and I exchanged puzzled looks. He shrugged and folded his arms.

"Aye, we do."

"Good. What I—and my brother"—I felt, rather than saw, Jamie's start at mention of Hal—"would ask of you is a note of introduction to Arnold, with your personal request that the general allow us official entrance into the city—and whatever aid he might find it convenient to give us—for the purpose of making a search for my son."

John let out the rest of his breath and sat, head down, not moving. Nobody moved.

At last, Jamie let out a long sigh and sat down on the room's other stool.

"Tell me," he said, resigned. "What's the wee bastard done now?"

THE STORY FINISHED, John inhaled, made to rub his bad eye, and luckily stopped in time.

"I'll put a bit more honey in that before you leave," I told him. "It will ease the grittiness." This non sequitur helped to bridge the awkward gap in the conversation left by Jamie's being struck momentarily speechless.

"Jesus," he said, and rubbed a hand hard over his face. He was still wearing the bloodstained shirt and breeches in which he'd fought; he hadn't shaved in three days, had barely slept or eaten, and looked like something you wouldn't want to meet in broad daylight, let alone a dark alley. He took a deep breath and shook his head like a dog shedding water.

"So ye think the two of them have gone to Philadelphia—William and this Richardson?"

"Probably not together—or at least not to begin with," John said. "William's groom said he left to find a couple of . . . er . . . girls who had gone from the camp. But we strongly suspect that this was a ploy by Richardson, to decoy William out of camp and intercept him on the road."

Jamie made an irascible noise.

"I should *like* to think the lad's no such a fat-heided gomerel as to go off wi' this Richardson. Not after the man sent him into the Great Dismal last year and nearly killed him."

"He told you that?"

"Oh. He didna tell ye that?" Jamie's voice might possibly have held a shade of scorn, had one been listening closely.

"I'm damned sure he didn't tell *you* anything," John replied, with an edge. "He hadn't seen you for years before he met you at Chestnut Street, I'd bet money he hasn't seen you since, and I'm reasonably sure I would have noticed had he mentioned Richardson in the hallway there."

"No," Jamie said briefly. "He told my nephew, Ian Murray. Or at least," he amended, "Ian got it from what he said, raving wi' fever when Ian got him out of the swamp. Richardson sent him wi' a message for some men in Dismal Town—men he said were Loyalists. But half the men in Dismal Town are named Washington."

John's appearance of pugnacity had vanished. He looked pale, and the fading bruises stood out like leprosy against his skin. He took a deep breath, glanced round the room, and, seeing a half-empty bottle of claret on the table, picked it up and drank a quarter of it without stopping.

He set it down, stifled a belch, rose with a brief nod and a "wait a moment," and went out, leaving Jamie and me staring at each other in bafflement.

This was not significantly assuaged by the reappearance of John, followed by the Duke of Pardloe. Jamie said something remarkably creative in *Gàidhlig,* and I gave him a look of startled appreciation.

"And a good day to you, too, General Fraser," Hal said, with a correct bow. Like John, he was dressed in civvies, though with a rather loud mulberry striped waistcoat, and I did wonder where he'd got it from.

"I have resigned my commission," Jamie said coldly. " 'Mr. Fraser' will do. May I ask to what we owe the honor of your presence, Your Grace?"

Hal's lips pressed tight together, but, with a glance at his brother, he obliged with a brief précis of his personal concern with Captain Richardson.

"And I do, of course, wish to retrieve my nephew, William—should he in fact be with Richardson. My brother informs me that you have doubts as to the probability of this being the case?"

"I do," Jamie said shortly. "My son is not a fool, nor a weakling." I caught the faint emphasis on *"my son,"* and so did both Greys, who stiffened slightly. "He wouldna go off on some feeble pretext, nor would he allow someone of whom he was suspicious to take him captive."

"You have a bloody lot of faith in a boy you haven't seen since he was six," Hal observed conversationally.

Jamie smiled, with considerable rue.

"I had the making of him until he was six," he said, and turned his gaze on John. "I ken what he's made of. And I ken who shaped him after that. Tell me I'm wrong, my lord."

There was a marked silence, broken only by Lieutenant Macken's voice below, calling plaintively to his wife about the location of his clean stockings.

"Well, then," Hal said with a sigh. "Where do *you* think William's gone, if he's not with Richardson?"

"He's gone after the girls he spoke of," Jamie said, lifting one shoulder in a shrug. "He told his groom so, did he not? D'ye ken who these lassies are?"

The Greys exchanged looks of muted chagrin, and I coughed, very carefully, holding a pillow to my stomach.

"If that's the case," I said, "then presumably he'll come back, once he's either found them or given up looking for them. Wouldn't he? Would he go AWOL over them—er . . . absent without leave, I mean?"

"He wouldn't have to risk that," Hal said. "He's been relieved of duty."

"What?" John exclaimed, rounding on his brother. "What the devil for?"

Hal sighed, exasperated. "Leaving camp when he was ordered to stay there in the middle of a battle, what else? Getting into a fight with another officer, ending up at the bottom of a ravine with a dent in his skull through being in the wrong place at the wrong time, and in general being a bloody nuisance."

"You're right, he *is* your son," I said to Jamie, amused. He snorted, but didn't look altogether displeased.

"Speaking of nephews," Jamie said to Hal, "ye seem remarkably well informed, Your Grace. Might ye know anything of an Indian scout named Ian Murray?"

Hal looked blank, but John's head turned quickly in Jamie's direction.

"Yes," he said. "I do. He was taken prisoner late on the day of battle and walked with me into camp, whereupon he killed another scout with a tomahawk and walked out again."

"Blood will tell," I murmured, though privately both shocked and worried. "Er . . . was he injured?"

"Aye, he was," Jamie answered brusquely. "He'd been shot wi' an arrow, in the shoulder. I couldna pull it, but I broke the shaft for him."

"And . . . no one's seen him since the night of the battle?" I asked, striving to keep my voice steady. The men exchanged glances, but none of them would meet my eyes.

"I, um, did give him a canteen of water mixed with brandy," John said, a little diffidently. "He wouldn't take a horse."

"Rachel will find him," Jamie said, as firmly as he could. "And I've asked Ian Mòr to watch out for the lad. He'll be all right."

"I trust your faith in your blood will be justified, sir," Hal said with a sigh, evidently meaning it. "But as we can do nothing about Murray, and the question of William's whereabouts is apparently moot for the moment . . . I hesitate to intrude my concerns regarding *my* blood, but I have stringent reasons for finding Captain Richardson, quite apart from anything he may have done or not done with William. And to that end . . ."

"Aye," Jamie said, and the tension in his shoulders relaxed. "Aye, of course, Your Grace. Sassenach, will ye have the goodness not to die whilst I go and ask Mrs. Macken for paper and ink?"

"We have some," John said, reaching into the leather pouch he'd been carrying under his arm. "Allow me." And proceeded to lay out paper, an inkhorn, a small bundle of quills, and a stub of red sealing wax.

Everyone watched as Jamie mixed the ink, trimmed a quill, and began. Knowing how laborious writing was for him and how much he'd hate being watched, I pushed myself up a little more, stifling a groan, and turned to Hal.

"John mentioned that you wanted to make us an offer," I said. "Of course we're happy to help, regardless. But out of curiosity—"

"Oh." Hal blinked but changed gears rapidly, fixing his gaze on me. "Yes. The offer I had in mind has nothing to do with Mr. Fraser's kind accommodation," he said. "John suggested it, as a matter of convenience for all concerned." He turned to his brother, who smiled at me.

"My house on Chestnut Street," John said. "Plainly I shan't be living there for the foreseeable future. And I understand that you had taken refuge with the printer's family in Philadelphia. Given your present fragile state of health"—he nodded delicately at the small heap of bloody dressings in the corner—"clearly it would be more comfortable for you to resume residence at my house. You—"

A deep Scottish noise interrupted him, and he looked up at Jamie, startled.

"The last time I was compelled to accept assistance from your brother, my lord," Jamie said precisely, staring at John, "I was your prisoner and incapable of caring for my own family. Now I am no man's prisoner, nor ever will be again. I shall make provision for my wife."

In dead silence, with all eyes fixed on him, he bent his head to the paper and slowly signed his name.

89

ONE DAY, COCK OF THE WALK—
NEXT DAY, A FEATHER DUSTER

HE'D GONE BY INSTINCT to fetch Madras, but paused to think on the way. If he found the girls, he couldn't bring them both back with him on the horse. He changed direction and plunged into the teamsters' park, emerging a brief time later with an ammunition cart, now sans ammunition, pulled by a large, rugged gray mule with half of one ear missing.

The mule was disinclined to move fast, but still made better time than two girls on foot might. How long a head start did they have? Maybe an hour, from what Zebedee had said, maybe longer.

"Heya!" he shouted, and snapped the whip over the mule's rump. The animal was surly, but not a fool, and lurched into a faster pace—though William suspected that this effort might be as much to outrun the swarming flies as in response to his own urging.

Once solidly in motion, though, the mule seemed able to keep it up without noticeable effort, and they trotted down the road at a tooth-rattling pace, easily passing farm carts, foragers, and a couple of scouting parties. Surely he would catch the girls up in no time.

He didn't. He drove nearly ten miles, by his estimation, before concluding that there was no way the girls could possibly have outrun him, and he turned back, searching carefully along the few farm roads that led off into fields. To and fro he went, inquiring of everyone he saw, growing hotter and more irritated by the moment.

Midway through the afternoon, the army caught up with him, marching columns overtaking the mule, which had slowed to a walk by now. Reluctantly, he turned about and continued with the army to camp. Perhaps Colenso had been wrong; maybe the girls hadn't left at all. In which case, he'd find them once the camp settled for the night.

He did not. He did find Zeb, though, and Colenso with him. Both were adamant that the girls were indeed gone—and William found no trace of them, though he made stubborn inquiries among the laundresses and cooks.

At last, he trudged through the camp in search of either Papa or Uncle Hal. Not that he expected either man to have any notion regarding the girls—but he somehow felt that he could not abandon his search without at least soliciting their help in putting out word of the girls. Two half-grown girls couldn't possibly outstrip an army, and—

He stopped dead in the middle of camp, letting men on their way to supper flow around him.

"Bloody hell," he said, too hot and tired even to make it an exclamation. "Colenso, you left-handed little bugger." And barely containing his exasperation—with himself as much as with his groom—he set off grimly to find Colenso Baragwanath.

Because Colenso *was* a left-handed little bugger. William had noticed that immediately, as he suffered from the same affliction himself. Unlike Colenso, though, William could tell the difference between his right hand and his left—and had a sense of direction. Colenso . . . didn't, and William wanted to kick himself for not remembering that.

"You bloody *idiot,*" he muttered, wiping a sleeve across his sweating, dusty face. "Why didn't you think of that?"

Because it made little sense—once he paused to think about it—for the girls to have run off *ahead* of the army. Even if they were afraid of someone in the army, and even if they meant to reach New York, they would have been better served to have gone the other way, at least temporarily. Let the army march on well ahead, and then make their way wherever they meant to go.

He glanced at the sun, just barely still above the horizon, and heaved a deep, exasperated breath. Whatever else she might be, Jane wasn't a fool. First he'd find some supper, and then Colenso—but he'd give good odds that the morrow would find him on the road back toward Middletown.

HE FOUND THEM, just before noon. They saw him coming, but he'd seen them first: the two of them walking down the side of the road, each with a bundle in either hand. They glanced over their shoulders at the sound of his wheels, saw nothing alarming, turned back—and then Jane whirled round again, her face aghast as she realized who she'd just seen.

She dropped one of her bundles, clutched her younger sister by the wrist, and jerked her off the road. The road led through farmland here, with open fields on either side—but there was a sizable chestnut grove a few hundred yards ahead, and, despite William's shout, the girls ran for this as though the devil himself were after them.

Muttering under his breath, he pulled up, dropped the reins, and leapt out. Long-legged as he was, he failed to catch them before they reached the edge of the wood.

"Stop, for God's sake!" he bellowed. "I'm not going to hurt you!"

Fanny, hearing this, seemed disposed to stop, but Jane yanked her urgently on and they vanished among the rustling leaves.

William snorted and slowed down. Jane could make up her own mind—if she had one, which he was strongly inclined to doubt at the moment—but she hadn't any business to be dragging her little sister off through land that had been a battlefield only two days ago.

Broken trails and big crushed patches marred the fields, from soldiers running or artillery being dragged through it. He could smell death when he drew a deep breath; it made him uneasy. The stink of uncollected corpses swelling in the sun, bursting open, weltering with flies and maggots . . . On the one hand, he hoped the girls wouldn't stumble over such a sight. On the other, if they did, they'd likely come haring back out into his arms, screaming.

And corpses might not be the only things hiding in the folds and furrows of the countryside. His hand went automatically to his waist, groping for the hilt of his knife—which, of course, wasn't there.

"Fucking buggering shit-fucking *hell*!"

As though this had been a signal, a sudden racket broke out in the trees. Not a corpse; he could hear male voices, cursing, cajoling, and high-pitched shrieks. He snatched up a fallen branch and charged into the grove, shouting at the top of his lungs. He could hear them; they could certainly hear him, and the tone of the shouting changed. The girls were still shrieking, but less frantically, and the men—yes, more than one . . . two, three? Not more—were arguing, agitated, fearful. *Not English . . . not speaking English . . .*

"Mistkerle!" he bellowed at the top of his lungs. *Bloody stinking Hessians! "Feiglinge!" Shit-eating cowards!*

A great thrashing of leaves and snapping branches, and, peering through the trees, he saw that the lot of them—judging by the noise, the girls were still with them—were heading for the road.

He stopped yelling and instantly altered his own course, charging back toward the road, crashing heedless through brush and low-hanging branches, half-ripe chestnuts thumping off his head and shoulders. There! He saw a man push out of the trees, stumbling onto the road, and lunge back, grabbing. A louder shriek and Fanny came stumbling out in turn, the man gripping her by the neck.

William veered toward them and burst out running, shouting incoherent curses, brandishing his makeshift club. He must nonetheless have looked frightening in his uniform, for the man holding Fanny let go of her at once, turned, and ran like a rabbit, dust spurting from his feet. Fanny staggered and fell to her knees, but there was no blood, she was all right. . . .

"Jane!" He shouted. "Jane! Where are you?"

"Here! He—" Her voice was cut off suddenly, but he could see where she was, no more than ten feet from him, and dived for the wildly waving branches.

There were two men with her, one with a hand over her mouth, the other struggling to detach the bayonet from a brown Bess musket. William kicked the gun out of his hands, then lunged at the man, and in moments was on the ground, grappling with a burly man who might not know what to do with a bayonet but certainly was acquainted with battle of a more primitive sort.

They rolled to and fro, panting and gouging, twigs breaking with a sound like gunshots, cracking beneath their bodies. He heard dimly a screech from the other man—perhaps Jane had bitten him; good girl!—but had no attention to spare for anything but the man who was trying earnestly to throttle him. He had a grip on the man's wrists, and, with a faint memory of Ban Tarleton, jerked the man closer and butted him in the face.

It worked again; there was a horrible crunch, hot blood spattered his face, and the man's grip relaxed. William squirmed away, his head swimming, only to find himself facing the other man, who had evidently succeeded in freeing the bayonet, for he had a foot of sharpened steel in his hand.

"Here! Here!" Jane popped out of a bush right beside William, startling him, and shoved something into his hand. It was, thank God, a knife. Nothing to rival the bayonet, but a weapon.

Jane was still by him; he grasped her arm and began to walk backward, knife held low and threatening in his other hand. The Hessian—Christ, was it one of the sons of bitches who'd hit him in the head? He couldn't tell; there were spots floating in front of his eyes, and the men had thrown away their telltale green coats. Did all sons of bitches wear green coats? he wondered muzzily.

Then they were on the road, and things became confused. He thought he'd stuck one of the men, and the girls were screaming again, and once he found himself in the roadway, choking on dust, but came up again before one of the bastards could kick him in the face . . . and then there was a shout and the pounding of hooves, and he let go of the man whose arm he was gripping and whirled round to see Rachel Hunter on a mule, coming fast down the road, swinging her bonnet from its strings and shouting, "Uncle Hiram! Cousin Seth! Hurry! Come on! Come on! Help me!"

His mule jerked its head up from the grass and, seeing Rachel's mount, brayed in greeting. This seemed to be the last straw for the deserters, who stood gaping for one stunned moment, then turned and galloped down the road after their vanished fellow.

William stood swaying for a moment, gasping for breath, then dropped his knife and sat down abruptly.

"What," he said, in a voice that sounded petulant even to his own ears, "are *you* doing here?"

Rachel ignored him. She swung down from her mule, landing with a small thump, and led it to William's mule, tethering it to the cart. Only then did she walk over to where William sat, slowly brushing dirt from his knees and counting his limbs.

"You wouldn't happen to have seen a couple of girls, would you?" he asked, tilting his head back to look up at Rachel.

"Yes. They ran into the trees," she said, nodding toward the chestnut grove. "As for what I am doing here, I have been up and down this road three times, looking for thy cousin, Ian Murray." She gave him a hard look as she said this, as though daring him to contradict her assertion regarding his kinship with Murray. Under other circumstances, he might have taken offense, but at the moment he hadn't the energy. "I assume that if thee had seen him, dead or alive, thee would tell me?"

"Yes," he said. There was a swollen knot between his eyes, where he had butted the deserter, and he rubbed this gingerly.

She drew a deep breath, sighed loudly, and wiped her sweating face on her apron, before replacing her bonnet. She looked him over, shaking her head.

"Thee is a rooster, William," Rachel said mournfully. "I saw this in thee before, but now I know it for certain."

"A rooster," he repeated coldly, brushing dirt from his sleeve. "Indeed. A vain, crowing, gaudy sort of fellow—that's what you think me?"

Her brows went up. They were not the level brows of classic beauty; they quirked up at the ends, even when her face was at rest, giving her a look of interested intelligence. When she was *not* at rest, they slanted with a sharp, wicked sort of look. They did this for an instant now, but then relaxed. A little.

"No," she said. "Has thee ever kept chickens, William?"

"Not for some years," he said, examining the hole torn in the elbow of his coat, the hole ripped in the shirt beneath, and the bloody scrape upon his bare elbow. Bloody hell, one of the buggers had come close to taking his arm off with that bayonet. "What with one thing and another, my recent acquaintance with chickens has been limited largely to breakfast. Why?"

"Why, a rooster is a creature of amazing courage," Rachel said, rather reproachful. "He will throw himself into the face of an enemy, even knowing he will die in the attack, and thus buy his hens time to escape."

William's head jerked up.

"My *hens*?" he said, outrage bringing the blood to his face. "*My* hens?" He glanced in the direction Jane and Fanny had taken, then glared back at Rachel. "Do you not realize that they are whores?"

She rolled her eyes at him in exasperation. She bloody rolled her eyes at him!

"I expect I have been living with an army for somewhat longer than thee has thyself," she said, making a decided effort to look down her nose at him. "I am familiar with women who lack both property and protection and are thus reduced to the dreadful expedient of selling their bodies, yes."

"'Dreadful expedient'?" he repeated. "You realize that I—"

She stamped a foot and glared at him.

"Will thee stop repeating everything I say?" she demanded. "I was attempting to pay thee a compliment—while, as thy friend, lamenting the end thy roosterishness will surely bring thee to. Whether thy companions are whores or not—and whether thee pays for their company—is irrelevant to the matter."

"Irre—" William began in indignation, but choked the word off before he could be further accused of repetition. "I don't bloody pay them!"

"Irrelevant," she repeated, doing it herself, by God! "Thee has behaved in exactly the same way on my own behalf, after all."

"You—" He stopped abruptly. "I have?"

She exhaled strongly, eyeing him in a manner suggesting that she would have kicked him in the shins or stamped on his toes if not reminded of her Quaker principles.

"Twice," she said, elaborately polite. "The occasions were so negligible, I suppose—or I was—that thee has forgotten?"

"Remind me," he said dryly, and, ripping a chunk from the torn lining of his coat, used it to wipe the mud—and blood, he saw—from his face.

She snorted briefly, but obliged. "Does thee not recall the odious creature who attacked us in that dreadful place on the road in New York?"

"Oh, that." His belly clenched in recollection. "I didn't exactly do it on your account. Nor did I have much choice in the matter. He bloody tried to cave my head in with an ax."

"Hmph. I think thee has some fatal attraction for ax-wielding maniacs," she said, frowning at him. "That Mr. Bug actually *did* hit thee in the head with an ax. But when thee killed him later, it was to protect Ian and me from a similar fate, was it not?"

"Oh, indeed," he said, a little crossly. "How do you know it wasn't just revenge for his attacking *me*?"

"Thee may be a rooster, but thee is not a vengeful rooster," she said reprovingly. She pulled a kerchief from her pocket and blotted her face, which was growing shiny with perspiration again. "Should we not look for thy . . . companions?"

"We should," he said, with a degree of resignation, and turned toward the grove. "I think they'll run if I go in after them, though."

Rachel made an impatient noise and, pushing past him, stomped into the woods, rustling through the brush like a hungry bear. The thought made him grin, but a sudden yelp wiped the smile off his face. He started after her, but she was already backing out, yanking Jane by one arm, meanwhile trying to avoid the wild swipes Jane was making with her free hand, fingers clawed and slashing toward Rachel's face.

"Stop that!" William said sharply, and, stepping forward, grabbed Jane by the shoulder and jerked her out of Rachel's grasp. She turned blindly on *him,* but he had longer arms than Rachel and could easily hold her at bay.

"Will you quit that?" he said crossly. "No one's going to hurt you. Not now."

She did stop, though she looked back and forth between him and Rachel like a cornered animal, panting and the whites of her eyes showing.

"He's right," Rachel said, edging cautiously toward her. "Thee is quite safe now. What is thy name, Friend?"

"She's called Jane," William said, gradually loosing his hold, ready to grab her again if she bolted. "I don't know her surname."

She didn't bolt, but didn't speak, either. Her dress was torn at the neck, and she put a hand to the torn edge automatically, trying to fit it back in place.

"Have you seen my bundle?" she said, in an almost ordinary voice. "I have a housewife in it. I need a needle."

"I'll look for it," Rachel said soothingly. "Did thee drop it in the wood?"

"Thir!" Fanny spoke quite sharply behind William, and he became aware that she'd been there for a few moments; she'd said it once or twice before.

"What?" he said impatiently, half-turning toward her while trying to keep both Jane and Rachel in view.

"There'th an Indian in there," she said, and pointed toward the woods.

"Ian!"

Rachel ran across the road, fleet as a snipe, and vanished into the trees. William followed hastily, hand on his knife. There was likely more than one Indian in these woods, and if it *wasn't* Murray . . .

But he could tell from Rachel's exclamation of mingled horror and relief from the depths of the wood that it was.

Murray was crumpled into a heap in the deep shadow at the base of a big pine tree, needles half-scuffled over him; evidently he'd tried to disguise himself but had passed out before managing the job.

"He's breathing," Rachel said, and he heard the catch in her voice.

"Good," William said briefly, and, squatting beside her, put a hand on Murray's shoulder to turn him over. The apparently insensible body gave a shriek, contorted violently, and ended on his knees, swaying and glaring wildly round, clutching the shoulder William had seized. Only then did William see the dried blood streaked down the arm and the fresh dribbles running down from the broken shaft of an arrow embedded in the swollen flesh.

"Ian," Rachel said. "Ian, it's me. It's all right now. I have thee." Her voice was steady, but her hand trembled as she touched him.

Murray gulped air, and his bleared gaze seemed to clear, traveling from Fanny and Jane, who had come into the grove after William, pausing briefly with a frown at William's face, then settling and easing as he saw Rachel. He closed his eyes and let out a long breath.

"Taing do Dhia," he said, and sank back on his haunches.

"Water," Rachel said urgently, shaking the empty canteen that lay on the ground beside Ian. "Has thee got any water, William?"

"I have," said Jane, stirring out of her trance and groping for the canteen round her neck. "Will he be all right, do you think?"

Rachel didn't answer but helped Murray to drink, her face pale with anxiety. Murray's own face bore the remnants of war paint, William saw with interest, and a brief ripple raised the hairs on his scalp, wondering whether Murray had killed any of the British soldiers. At least the bugger wasn't sporting any scalps on his belt, British or otherwise.

Rachel was conversing now in low tones with Murray, glancing now and then at William, a certain speculation in her gaze.

William was mildly surprised to find that he knew exactly what she was thinking. Though perhaps it wasn't so surprising; he'd been wondering much the same thing: could Murray ride the mule? Plainly he couldn't walk far. And if he couldn't . . . could Rachel persuade William to take Murray and her into the city in the wagon?

He felt his stomach clench at the thought of going back to Philadelphia.

His own gaze flicked toward Jane—only to discover that she wasn't there. Neither was Fanny.

He was halfway to his feet when he heard Rachel's mule bray in protest, and he made it to the road in seconds, to find Jane engaged in a futile struggle to push Fanny up into the saddle. The younger girl was trying valiantly, clutching at the mule's bristly mane and attempting to get a leg up, but the mule was objecting strenuously to this sort of interference, tossing his head and backing away from Jane, leaving Fanny's legs kicking desperately in the air.

William reached her in three paces and clasped her about the waist.

"Let go, sweetheart," he said calmly. "I've got you." Fanny was surprisingly solid, given her fragile appearance. She smelled sweet, too, though her neck was grubby and her clothes grimed with mud and road dust.

He put her down and turned a firm eye on Jane, who was looking defiant. He'd been acquainted with her long enough now, though, to see that the uplifted chin and tight jaw were covering fear, and, in consequence, spoke more gently than he might have.

"Where were you planning to go?" he asked, in a tone of mild interest.

"I—well, New York," she answered, but uncertainly, and her eyes were darting to and fro, as though expecting some threat to manifest itself from the peaceful countryside.

"Without me? I'm hurt, madam, that you should have conceived a sudden dislike of my company. What have I done to offend you, pray?"

She pressed her lips tight together, but he could see that his jesting tone had settled her a little; she was still red in the face from exertion, but not breathing in that jerky way.

"I think we must part, Lord Ellesmere," she said, with a touchingly absurd attempt at formality. "I—we—shall make our own way now."

He folded his arms, leaned back against the wagon, and looked down his nose at her.

"How?" he inquired. "You haven't any money, you don't have a mount, and you wouldn't get five miles on foot without running into someone else like those German fellows."

"I—have a little money." She smoothed a hand over her skirt, and he saw that there was indeed a bulge where her pocket lay. Despite his intent to remain calm, there was still a spring of anger in him, and it burst forth at this.

"Where did you get it?" he demanded, straightening up and grabbing her by the wrist. "Did I not forbid you to whore?"

She yanked her hand smartly free and took two quick steps back.

"You haven't any right to forbid me to do any damned thing I want!" she snapped, color burning high in her cheeks. "And it's none of your business, but I didn't make this money on my back!"

"What, then? Pimping your sister?"

She slapped him, hard. He shouldn't have said it and knew

it, but the knowledge—and his stinging cheek—only made him angrier.

"I *should* bloody leave you here, you—"

"Good! That's just what I want you to do! You—you—"

Before either of them could decide upon an epithet, Rachel and Ian emerged from the wood, the tall Scot leaning heavily on her. William gave Jane a final glare and went to help, taking Murray's weight on one side. The man stiffened, resisting for a moment, but then yielded; he had to.

"What happened?" William asked, nodding at the broken arrow shaft. "A private quarrel or just bad aim?"

That made Murray's mouth twitch, reluctantly.

"Fortunes of war," he said hoarsely, and sat down at the open tailboard of the wagon. He was breathing like a winded ox, but had possession of himself. He gave William a brief glance.

"What are ye doing here, *a fang Sassunaich*?"

"None of your business, but a good job I was," William replied, just as briefly. He turned to Rachel, having made up his mind on the moment.

"Take the wagon and see the girls somewhere safe."

"That—" Rachel began, but then looked round, startled, as Jane and Fanny ran past her, crossed the road, and dived into the wood. "Where are they going?"

"Oh, bloody hell," William said, already striding across the road. "Wait here."

THEY COULDN'T outrun him, and they had nothing in the way of woodcraft that would enable them to lie hidden. He caught Fanny—again the slower of the two—by the back of her pinafore as she was scrambling over a log. To his astonishment, she squirmed round in his grasp and launched herself at him, scratching at his face and screaming, "Wun, Janie, *wun*!"

"Will you bloody stop that?" he said crossly, holding her at arm's length. "Ow!" For she had sunk her teeth into his wrist, and he dropped her.

She eeled over the log and bounded away like a rabbit, still screaming her head off. He started to follow her, and then thought better. On the one hand, he had a strong impulse to abandon them, but on the other . . . He remembered Mac telling him about plovers one day as they sat near Watendlath Tarn, eating bread and cheese, watching the birds.

"Bugger off, Mac," he said under his breath, and shoved thought of both Helwater and the groom ruthlessly away. But remembered, whether he wanted to or not.

"They run about and call out as though wounded, see?" Mac's arm had been round him, keeping him from going too close to the fluttering bird. *"But it's to draw ye away from their nest, lest ye crush the eggs or damage the young. Look canny, though, and ye'll see them."*

William stood quite still, calming his own breath and looking round, slow and careful, barely moving his head. And there indeed was the plover's nest: alas for Jane, she had worn her pink calico today, and her rosy buttocks rounded smoothly up out of the grass ten feet away, quite like a pair of eggs in a nest, at that.

He walked quietly, without haste. Nobly resisting the strong urge to smack her beguilingly curved behind, he instead laid a hand flat on her back.

"Tag," he said. "You're it."

She wriggled out from under his hand and shot up onto her feet.

"What?" she said. "What the bloody hell do you mean?" She was wild-eyed and nervy, but cross, as well.

"You've never played tag?" he asked, feeling foolish even as he said it.

"Oh," she said, and let out her breath a little. "It's a game. I see. Yes, but not for a long time."

He supposed one *didn't* play tag in a brothel.

"Look," she said tersely, "we want to go. I—I appreciate what you've done for me—for us. But—"

"Sit down," he said, and compelled her to do so, leading her to the log over which her sister had escaped and pressing on her shoulder until she reluctantly sat. He then sat down beside her and took her hand in his. It was very small, cold and damp from the grass where she'd hidden.

"Look," he said, firmly but not—he hoped—unkindly, "I'm not letting you run off. That's flat. If you want to go to New York with the army, I'll take you; I've already said so. If you want to return to Philadelphia—"

"No!" Her terror at the thought was clear now. She pulled desperately at her hand, but he wouldn't let go.

"Is it because of Captain Harkness? Because—"

She gave a cry that might have come from the throat of a wild bird caught in a trap, and he tightened his grip on her wrist. It was fine-boned and slender, but she was surprisingly strong.

"I know you stole the gorget back," he said. "It's all right. No one's going to find out. And Harkness won't touch you again; I promise you that."

She made a small bubbling noise that might have been a laugh or a sob.

"Colonel Tarleton—you know, the green dragoon that made advances to you?—he told me that Harkness was absent without leave, hasn't come back to his regiment. Do you know anything about that?"

"No," she said. "Let me go. Please!"

Before he could answer this, a small, clear voice piped up from the trees a few yards away.

"You'd best tew him, Janie."

"Fanny!" Jane swung round toward her sister, momentarily forgetting that she was pinioned. "Don't!"

Fanny stepped out of the shadows, wary but curiously composed.

"If you don't, I wiw," she said, her big brown eyes fixed on William's face. "He won't thtop." She came a little closer, cautious but not afraid. "If I tew you," she said, "do you pwomise not to take us back?"

"Back where?"

"To Phiwadelphia," she said. "*Or* the army."

He sighed, exasperated, but short of torturing the answer out of one of the girls, clearly no progress would be made unless he agreed. And he was beginning to have a cold feeling under the ribs about just what the answer might be.

"I promise," he said, but Fanny hung back, distrustful.

"Sweaw," she said, folding her arms.

"Sw—oh. Bloody hell. All right, then—I swear on my honor."

Jane made a small, dreary noise that was still a laugh. That stung.

"Do you think I haven't got any?" he demanded, turning on her.

"How would I know?" she countered, sticking out her chin. It wobbled, but she stuck it out. "What does honor look like?"

"For your sake, you'd better hope it looks a lot like me," he told her, but then turned to Fanny. "What do you want me to swear on?"

"Your mudder's head," she said promptly.

"My mother's dead."

"Your favver, den."

He drew a long, deep breath. *Which one?*

"I swear on my father's head," he said evenly.

And so they told him.

"I KNEW HE'D come back," Jane said. She was sitting on the log, hands clasped between her thighs and eyes on her feet. "They always do. The bad ones." She spoke with a sort of dull resignation, but her lips tightened at the memory. "They can't stand to think you've got away without . . . without. I thought it would be me, though."

Fanny was sitting beside her sister, as close as she could get, and now she put her arms around Jane and hugged her, her face in Jane's calico shoulder.

"I'm sowwy," she whispered.

"I know, lovie," Jane said, and patted Fanny's leg. A fierce look came into her face, though. "It's not your fault, and don't ever—*ever*—think so."

William's throat felt thick with disgust at the thought. That beautiful, flower-faced little girl, taken by—

"Her maidenhead's worth ten pound," Jane reminded him. "Mrs. Abbott was saving her, waiting for a rich man with a taste for new-hatched chicks. Captain Harkness offered her twenty." She looked directly at William for the first time. "I wasn't having that," she said simply. "So I asked Mrs. Abbott to send us up together; I said I could help keep Fanny from making a fuss. I knew what he was like, see," she said, and pressed her lips involuntarily together for an instant. "He wasn't the sort to plow you like a bull and have it done. He'd play with you, making you undress a bit at a time and—and do things—while he told you all about what *he* meant to do."

And so it had been easy to come behind him while he was

watching Fanny, with the knife she'd taken from the kitchen hidden in the folds of her petticoats.

"I meant to stab him in the back," she said, looking down again. "I saw a man stabbed that way once. But he saw on Fanny's face what I—it wasn't her fault, she couldn't help it showing," she added quickly. "But he turned round quick and there wasn't any choice."

She'd plunged the knife into Harkness's throat and wrenched it free, intending to stab again. But that hadn't been necessary. "There was blood everywhere." She'd gone pale in the telling, her hands wrapped in her apron.

"I frew up," Fanny added matter-of-factly. "It was a mess."

"I expect it was," William said dryly. He was trying not to envision the scene—the candlelight, the spraying blood, the panicked girls—with remarkably little success. "How did you get away?"

Jane shrugged. "It was my room, and he'd bolted the door. And nobody was surprised when Fanny started screaming," she added, with a trace of bitterness.

There was a basin and pitcher of water, the usual rags for mess; they'd washed themselves hastily, changed clothes, and climbed out the window.

"We found a ride on a farmer's wagon, and . . . you know the rest." She closed her eyes for a moment, as though reliving "the rest," and then opened them and looked up at him, her gaze dark as shadowed water.

"Now what?" she asked.

WILLIAM HAD BEEN asking himself that question for the last several moments of Jane's story. Having met Harkness himself, he had considerable sympathy for Jane's action, but—

"You planned it," he said, giving her a sharp look. Her head was bent, her unbound hair hiding her face. "You took the knife, you had clothes to change into, you knew how to get down from the window and get away."

"Tho?" said Fanny, in a remarkably cold voice for a girl of her age.

"So why kill him?" he asked, transferring his attention to

Fanny, but keeping a wary eye on Jane. "You were going to leave anyway. Why not just escape before he came?"

Jane raised her head and turned it, looking him directly in the eye.

"I wanted to kill him," she said, in a perfectly reasonable voice that chilled him despite the warmth of the day.

"I . . . see."

He saw more than the vision of Jane, with her delicate white wrists, plunging a knife into Captain Harkness's thick red throat while her little sister screamed. He saw Rachel's face, pale among the leaves, six feet away. From her expression, it was apparent that she had heard everything.

He cleared his throat.

"Is, um, Mr. Murray all right?" he asked politely. Jane and Fanny whirled, wide-eyed.

"He fainted," Rachel replied. She was eyeing the younger girls in much the same way that they were looking at her, with a gaze of fascinated horror. "His shoulder is badly inflamed. I came to see if thee had any brandy."

He fumbled in his pocket and withdrew a small silver flask with the Grey family arms engraved upon it.

"Whisky do for you?" he asked, handing it over. Rachel looked surprised; whisky wasn't a popular drink, but Lord John had always had a taste for it and William had taken to it himself—though now, knowing the truth about his disgraceful taint of Scottish blood, he wasn't sure he'd ever be able to drink the stuff again.

"It will, I thank thee." She stood holding it for a moment, clearly wanting to go to Murray but also hesitant to leave. He felt rather grateful to her for that hesitancy; he would as soon not be alone with Jane and Fanny—or, rather, he didn't want to be alone with the decision as to what the devil to do about them.

Rachel appeared to correctly interpret this feeling, for with a brief "I'll bring it right back," she disappeared in the direction of the road.

No one spoke. After that one direct look, Jane had bent her head again and sat quietly, though one hand restlessly smoothed the fabric of her skirt across one round thigh, over and over.

Fanny ran a hand over the crown of Jane's head in a protective gesture, while staring at William with a complete lack of expression. He found it unnerving.

What *was* he to do with them? Of course they couldn't go back to Philadelphia. And he dismissed as unworthy the impulse simply to abandon them to their own devices. But—

"Why not go to New York with the army?" he asked, his voice seeming unnaturally loud, harsh to his own ears. "What made you run yesterday?"

"Oh." Jane looked up slowly, her eyes a little unfocused, as though she had been dreaming. "I saw *him* again. The green dragoon. He'd wanted me to go with him the night before, and I wouldn't. But I saw him again yesterday morning and thought he was looking for me." She swallowed. "I told you—I know the ones who don't give up."

"Very perceptive of you," he said, eyeing her with some respect. "He doesn't. You misliked him on sight, then?" Because he didn't think for an instant that his having forbidden her to ply her trade would have stopped her, had she wanted to.

"It wasn't that," she said, and flicked Banastre Tarleton away with the sort of abrupt gesture one uses to shoo insects. "But he'd come to the brothel before, last year. He didn't go with me then, he chose another girl—but I knew if he spent much time with me, he'd likely remember why I seemed familiar to him. He said I did," she added, "when he came up to me in the bread line."

"I see." He paused. "So you did want to go to New York—but not with the army. Is that right?"

Jane shrugged, angry. "Does it matter?"

"Why the devil shouldn't it matter?"

"When has it *ever* mattered what a whore wants?" She sprang up and stamped across the clearing, leaving him staring after her in astonishment.

"What's wrong with her?" he demanded, turning to Fanny. The younger girl eyed him dubiously, lips pressed together, but then gave a little shrug.

"She thinks you might give her to a conthable or a magithtrate," she said, struggling a bit with "magistrate." "Or maybe to the army. It was a tholdier she killed."

William rubbed a hand over his face. In fact, the thought of delivering Jane to justice *had* flitted through his mind, in the wake of the shock of learning of her crime. The thought hadn't outlasted its birth, though.

"I wouldn't do that," he said to Fanny, striving to sound reasonable. She looked at him skeptically, under level dark brows.

"Why wouldn' you?"

"Excellent question," he said dryly. "And I haven't got an answer. But I suppose I don't need one."

He lifted a brow at her, and she gave a small snort of a laugh. Jane was edging along the far side of the clearing, glancing back toward Fanny every few seconds; her intent was clear—but she wouldn't go without her sister. He was sure of that much.

"Since you're here with me," he observed, "and *not* over there with your sister . . . you don't want to run, and you know she won't go without you. Ergo, I conclude that you don't think I'd give her up to justice."

She shook her head, slow and solemn as an owl.

"Jane says I don' know anyting about men yed, but I *do.*"

He sighed.

"God help me, Frances, you do."

THERE WAS NO further conversation until Rachel returned a few minutes later.

"I can't lift him," she said directly to William, ignoring the girls for the moment. "Will thee help me?"

He rose at once, relieved by the prospect of physical action, but glanced over his shoulder at Jane, still hovering by the far side of the clearing like a hummingbird.

"We'll be heah," Fanny said quietly. He gave her a nod, and went.

He found Murray lying by the side of the road, near the wagon. The man wasn't unconscious, but the influence of the fever upon him was clear; his gaze was bleared and his speech slurring.

"I c'n walk."

"Like hell you can," William said briefly. "Hold on to my arm."

He got the man sitting upright and had a look for himself at the wounded shoulder. The wound itself wasn't that bad; it was apparent no bones were broken and it hadn't bled a lot. On the other hand, the flesh was red and swollen and starting to suppurate. He leaned close and took an unobtrusive sniff—not unobtrusive enough: Rachel noticed.

"There's no gangrene," she said. "I think there will not—I think things will be well, so long as we can get him to a doctor soon. What does thee mean to do about thy girls?" she added abruptly.

He didn't bother telling her again that they weren't *his*. Evidently they were, at least in terms of immediate responsibilities.

"I don't know," he admitted, rising to his feet. He glanced into the woods, but the clearing was far enough in that there was no flicker of garment or movement visible.

"They can't go to Philadelphia, and I can't take them back to the army. The best I can think of just now is to find them some place of refuge in one of the little villages hereabouts and cache them there until I can make some provision to get them to . . . to someplace safer." *Wherever the hell that might be. Canada?* he wondered wildly.

Rachel shook her head decidedly.

"Thee has no notion how people talk in small places—or how quickly news and rumor spread." She glanced down at Murray, who was still sitting upright but swaying, his eyes half closed.

"They have no other profession," she said. "And it would be quickly apparent to anyone what that profession is. They require not only refuge but refuge with people who will not cast them out once that becomes known."

She was brown with the sun—her blue calico bonnet had fallen off in the struggle with Jane and hung back over her shoulders—but her face paled when she looked at Murray. She clenched her fists, closed her eyes for an instant, then opened them, straightening to her full height, and looked William in the eye.

"There is a small settlement of Friends, perhaps two hours' travel from here. No more than three or four farms. I know of it from one of the women who came to Valley Forge with her husband. The girls could be kept safe there, for a while, at least."

"No!" Murray said. "Ye canna be . . ." He paused, eyes going out of focus, and braced himself on his sound arm, still swaying. He swallowed thickly. "No," he repeated. "Not . . . safe."

"It isn't," William agreed. "Three young women on the road, alone? And without even a pistol to defend yourselves?"

"If I had a pistol I would not use it," Rachel pointed out with some asperity. "Nor a cannon, come to that."

Murray laughed—or at least made a noise that might pass for amusement.

"Aye," he managed, and stopped to breathe before getting the next words out. "You take them," he said to William. "I'll . . . do here, fine."

"Thee bloody *won't,*" Rachel said fiercely. She grabbed William's arm and pulled him closer to Murray. "Look at him! Tell him, since he professes not to believe me."

William looked, reluctantly, glancing at Murray's face, pale as suet and slick with an unhealthy sweat. Flies clustered thick on Murray's shoulder; he lacked the strength to brush them away.

"Merde," William muttered under his breath. Then louder, though still with reluctance, "She's right. You need a doctor, if you're to have a chance of keeping your arm."

That thought evidently hadn't struck Murray; death, yes—amputation, no. He turned his head and frowned at the wound.

"Bloody hell," William said, and turned to Rachel.

"All right," he said. "Tell me where this settlement is. I'll take them."

She grimaced, fists balling up at her sides. "Even Friends may not take well to the sudden appearance of a stranger who asks them to give indefinite sanctuary to a murderess. I am not a stranger and can plead the girl's case better than thee can." She drew a breath that swelled her bosom noticeably and looked at Murray, then turned her head to give William a piercing look.

"If I do this, thee must see him safe."

"*I* must?"

"Rachel!" Murray said hoarsely, but she ignored him.

"Yes. We'll have to take the wagon, the girls and I."

William drew a breath of his own, but he could see that she was right. He could also see just what the decision to save Jane was costing her.

"All right," he said tersely. He reached up and took the gorget from his neck and handed it to her. "Give Jane this. She may need it, if they find themselves on their own." Oddly, the removal of the gorget seemed a weight off his mind, as well. Even the possibility of being arrested if anyone in Philadelphia recognized him didn't trouble him overmuch.

He was about to remove his incriminating coat and waistcoat—he'd have to hide those somewhere—when Rachel stepped close to him and laid a hand on his arm.

"This man is my heart and my soul," she said simply, looking up into his face. "And he is thy own blood, whatever thee may presently feel about the fact. I trust thee to see him safe, for all our sakes."

William gave her a long look, thought of several possible replies, and made none of them, but gave a curt nod.

"Where should I take him?" he asked. "To my—to Lady J—I mean, to Mrs. F—I *mean,* God damn it," he amended, feeling the blood rise in his cheeks, "to his aunt?"

Rachel looked at him, startled.

"Thee doesn't know? Of course thee doesn't, how could thee?" She waved off her own denseness, impatient. "His aunt was shot in the course of the battle, outside Tennent Church, where she was tending the wounded."

William's annoyance was doused at once, as though ice water had been poured on his head, flooding his veins.

"Is she dead?"

"By the grace of our Lord, no," she said, and he felt the tightness in his chest relax a little. "Or at least she wasn't yesterday," she amended with a frown. "Though very badly hurt." The tightness returned.

"She is in the Macken house in the village of Freehold—about six miles in that direction." She nodded down the road. "My brother is likely there, as well, or nearby; there are still wounded from the battle there. He can deal with I-Ian's wound." For the first time, her voice lost its steadiness as her eyes went to her betrothed.

Murray's eyes were sunken and glazed with fever, but he had sufficient command of himself to reach out his good hand to her. The movement put weight on the bad arm and he grimaced, but Rachel was kneeling beside him in an instant, arms around him.

William coughed and turned discreetly away to leave them a moment's privacy in which to make their farewells. Whatever his own feelings, they deserved that. He'd seen many wounds go bad, and reckoned Murray's chances as no better than even. On the other hand, the man was apparently both a bloody Scot *and* a Mohawk, and both races were notoriously hard to kill.

He had walked away from the road, and his eye now caught the flutter of pink fabric behind a bush.

"Jane!" he called. "Is that you?"

"Yes," she said. She stepped out into the open, folded her arms, and pointed her chin at him. "What do you mean to do? With me, I mean."

"Miss Hunter is going to take you and Fanny to a safe place," he said, as gently as he could. In spite of her brave façade, she reminded him of a fawn, dappled light coming through the trees mottling her face and gown, making her seem shy and insubstantial, as though she might fade into the forest in the next breath. "I'll send word to you there when I've made some . . . suitable arrangement."

"Her?" Jane shot a surprised glance toward the road. "Why? Why can't you take us? Doesn't she want to stay with her—the Indian?"

"Miss Hunter will have time to explain everything to you on the way." He hesitated, unsure what else to say to her. From the road, he heard the distant murmur of voices, Rachel and Ian Murray. He couldn't make out the words, but it didn't matter; what they were saying to each other was plain. He felt a small, sharp pain under his third waistcoat button and coughed, trying to dislodge it.

"Thank you, thir," said a soft voice behind him, and he turned to find Fanny at his elbow. She took his hand, turned it palm upward, and planted a small, warm kiss in the center.

"I—you're most welcome, Miss Fanny," he said, smiling at her in spite of everything. She nodded to him, very dignified, and walked out to the road, leaving him with Jane.

For a moment, they stood staring at each other.

"I offered you a lot more than a kiss," she said quietly. "You didn't want it. I haven't got anything else to give you in thanks."

"Jane," he said. "It's not—I didn't—" And then stopped,

desperately sorry but helpless to think of anything he could possibly say in reply. "Safe travels, Jane," he said at last, his throat tight. "Goodbye."

90

IT'S A WISE CHILD WHO KNOWS HIS FATHER

IT WAS APPARENT that, while sound, Rachel's mule wasn't up to the weight of two men the size of William and Ian Murray. No matter; they couldn't go any faster than a walk in any case; Murray could ride, and William would walk alongside to make sure the bastard didn't fall off.

Murray managed to get up into the saddle, in spite of having only one functional hand; Rachel had roughly bandaged his wounded arm and put it into a sling torn from her underpetticoat. William didn't offer him assistance, feeling reasonably sure that such an offer would be neither welcomed nor accepted.

Watching the laborious process, though, William was interested to note that while the fabric of the sling was much-laundered and faded, it had been embroidered with small blue and yellow sunbursts along one edge. Did Quaker women commonly wear attractive undergarments beneath their sober gowns?

As they set off at a cautious walk, the sound of the wagon was still audible, though fading into the rush of trees.

"Are ye armed?" Murray asked suddenly.

"Slightly." He still had the knife Jane had pushed into his hand, now wrapped in a handkerchief and tucked in his pocket, as he had no sheath for it. He fingered the wooden handle, wondering whether it was the same knife that she . . . Well, of course it was.

"I'm not. Will ye find me a club?"

"You don't trust me to see you safe?" William asked sarcastically.

Murray's shoulders were slumped and his head thrust forward, nodding a little with the mule's gait, but he turned and gave William a look that was heavy-eyed with fever, but still surprisingly alert.

"Oh, I trust ye fine. It's men like the ones ye just fought I dinna trust."

This was a fair point; the roads were far from safe, and the knowledge gave William a severe pang of conscience on behalf of the women he'd just dispatched, unarmed and unprotected, to drive miles over those very roads with a valuable mule and cart. *I should have gone with them, insisted we all go together . . .*

"My mam always says there's no one more stubborn than my uncle Jamie," Murray observed mildly, "but a Quaker lass wi' her mind made up could give Uncle Jamie a run for his money, I'll tell ye. I couldna have stopped her—and neither could you."

William wasn't in a mood to discuss any of the persons mentioned, nor yet engage in philosophical discussions of relative stubbornness. He put a hand on the bridle and pulled the mule to a halt.

"Stay here. I see something that might do." He'd already seen that there was little in the way of fallen branches near the road; there never was, when an army's foragers had recently passed through. But he saw an orchard of some kind, a little way from the road, with a farmhouse beyond.

As he made his way toward the orchard, he could see that artillery had been hauled through it; there were deep furrows in the ground, and many of the trees had broken limbs, hanging like jackstraws.

There was a dead man in the orchard. American militia, by his hunting shirt and homespun breeches, lying curled among the gnarled roots of a big apple tree.

"Should have culled that one," William said aloud, keeping his voice steady. Old apple trees never yielded much; you took them out after fifteen, twenty years and replanted. He turned away from the body, but not fast enough to avoid seeing the greedy flies rise up in a buzzing cloud from what was left of the face. He walked three paces away and threw up.

No doubt it was the cloying smell of rotting apples that rose above the ghost of black powder; the whole orchard hummed with the noise of wasps gorging themselves on the juices. He unwrapped the handkerchief from Jane's knife and thrust the knife through his belt without looking to see if there were bloodstains on it. He wiped his mouth, then, after a moment's hesitation, went and laid the handkerchief over the Rebel's face. Someone had stripped the body; he had neither weapons nor shoes.

"THIS DO YOU?" He laid a three-foot length of applewood across the saddlebow. He'd broken it at both ends, so it made a serviceable club, about the thickness of his own forearm.

Murray seemed to wake from a doze; he drew himself slowly upright, took hold of the club, and nodded.

"Aye, that'll do," he said softly. His voice sounded thick, and William looked at him sharply.

"You'd best drink some more," he said, handing up the canteen again. It was getting low; probably no more than a quarter full. Murray took it, though moving sluggishly, drank, and gave it back with a sigh.

They walked without conversation for a half hour or so, leaving William time at last to sort through the events of the morning. It was well past noon now; the sun was pressing on his shoulders like a heated flatiron. How far did Rachel say it was to Freehold? Six miles?

"D'ye want me to tell ye, or no?" Murray said suddenly.

"Tell me what?"

There was a brief sound that might have been either amusement or pain.

"Whether ye're much like him."

Possible responses to this came so fast that they collapsed upon themselves like a house of cards. He took the one on top.

"Why do you suppose I should wonder?" William managed, with a coldness that would have frozen most men. Of course, Murray was blazing with such a fever, it would take a Quebec blizzard to freeze him.

"I would, if it was me," Murray said mildly.

That defused William's incipient explosion momentarily.

"Perhaps you think so," he said, not trying to hide his annoyance. "You may know him, but you know nothing whatever about me."

This time, the sound was undeniably amusement: laughter, of a hoarse, creaking sort.

"I helped fish ye out of a privy ten years ago," Murray said. "That was when I first kent it, aye?"

Shock struck William almost dumb, but not quite.

"What—that . . . that place in the mountains—Fraser's Ridge . . . ?!" He'd succeeded, for the most part, in forgetting the incident of the snake in the privy, and with it, most of a miserable journey through the mountains of North Carolina.

Murray took William's choler for confusion, though, and chose to elucidate.

"The way ye came out o' the muck, your eyes bleezin' blue and your face set for murder—that was Uncle Jamie to the life, when he's roused." Murray's head bobbed forward alarmingly. He caught himself and straightened up with a muffled groan.

"If you're going to fall off," William said, with elaborate courtesy, "do it on the other side, will you?"

"Mmphm."

They paced another hundred yards before Murray came to life again, resuming the conversation—if it could be called that—as though there had been no pause.

"So when I found ye in the swamp, I kent who ye were. I dinna recall ye thankin' me for saving your life that time, by the way."

"You can thank *me* for not strapping you into a travois with a dead panther and dragging you for miles through the dirt now," William snapped.

Murray laughed, gasping a little.

"Ye'd likely do it, if ye had a dead panther." The effort of laughing seemed to deprive him of balance, and he swayed alarmingly.

"Fall off and I'll do it anyway," William said, grabbing him by the thigh to steady him. "Dead panther or not." Christ, the man's skin was so hot he could feel it through the buckskin leggings.

Despite his fog, Murray noticed his reaction.

"You lived through the fever," he said, and took a deep breath. "I will, too; dinna fash."

"If by that expression you mean that I ought not to be concerned that you'll die," William said coldly, "I'm not."

"I'm no worrit, either," Murray assured him. The man wobbled slightly, reins held loose in one hand, and William wondered if he could be sunstruck. "Ye promised Rachel, aye?"

"Yes," William said, adding almost involuntarily, "I owe her and her brother my life, as much as I do you."

"Mmphm," Murray said agreeably, and fell silent. He seemed to be going a nasty grayish color under the sun-browned skin. This time he stayed silent for a good five minutes before coming suddenly to life again.

"And ye dinna think I ken much about ye, after listening to ye rave wi' fever for days?"

"I do not," William said. "No more than I think I'll know a great deal about you by the time I get you to Freehold."

"Maybe more than ye think. Stop, aye? I'm going to puke."

"Whoa!" The mule obligingly halted, though it clearly didn't like either the sound or the smell of what was going on behind its head, and kept sidling round in circles, trying to escape it.

William waited 'til it was over, then handed up his canteen without comment. Murray drained it and handed it back. His hand was shaking, and William began to be worried.

"We'll stop as soon as I find water," he said. "Get you into the shade." Neither of them had a hat; he'd left his in the copse, rolled up with his uniform coat under a bush.

Murray didn't reply to this; he was not precisely raving, but seemed to be pursuing a separate conversation in his head.

"I maybe dinna ken ye that well, but Rachel does."

That was undeniably true and gave William an oddly mixed sense of shame, pride, and anger. Rachel and her brother *did* know him well; they'd saved his life and nursed him back to health, had traveled with him for weeks and shared both food and danger.

"She says ye're a good man."

William's heart squeezed a little.

"I'm obliged for her good opinion," he said. The water hadn't helped that much; Murray was definitely swaying in the saddle, his eyes half closed.

"If you die," William said loudly, "I'll marry her."

That worked; Murray's eyelids lifted at once. He smiled, very slightly.

"Ken that," he said. "Ken I'm no going to die? And, besides, ye owe me a life, Englishman."

"I don't. I saved your bloody life, too; I saved the both of you from that maniac—Bug, was he?—with the ax in Philadelphia. We're quits."

Some interminable time later, Murray roused himself again. "I doubt it," he said.

91

KEEPING SCORE

JAMIE SAW THE GREYS out of the house and came back with an air of grim satisfaction. I would have laughed if it hadn't hurt to do it, but settled for smiling at him.

"*Your* son, *your* nephew, *your* wife," I said. "Fraser, three; Grey, nil."

He gave me a startled look, but then his face truly relaxed for the first time in days. "You're feeling better, then," he said, and, coming across the room, bent and kissed me. "Talk daft to me some more, aye?" He sat down heavily on the stool and sighed, but with relief.

"Mind," he said, "I havena the slightest idea how I'm going to keep ye, with no money, no commission, and no profession. But keep ye I will."

"No profession, forsooth," I said comfortably. "Name one thing you can't do."

"Sing."

"Oh. Well, besides that."

He spread his hands on his knees, looking critically at the scars on his maimed right hand.

"I doubt I could make a living as a juggler or a pickpocket, either. Let alone a scribe."

"You haven't got to write," I said. "You have a printing press—Bonnie, by name."

"Well, aye," he admitted, a certain light coming into his eyes. "I do. But she's in Wilmington at the moment." His press had been shipped from Edinburgh in the care of Richard Bell, who was—presumably—keeping her in trust until her real owner should come to repossess her.

"We'll go and get her. And then—" But I stopped, afraid to jinx the future by planning too far. It was an uncertain time for everyone, and no telling what the morrow might bring.

"But first," I amended, reaching out to squeeze his hand, "you should rest. You look as though you're about to die."

"Dinna talk that sort of daft," he said, and laughed and yawned simultaneously, nearly breaking his jaw.

"Lie down," I said firmly. "Sleep—at least until Lieutenant Bixby shows up again with more cheese." The American army had withdrawn to Englishtown, some seven miles away, only an hour's ride. The British army had decamped entirely, but as many of the militia units' enlistments had expired soon afterward, the roads were still very busy with men going home, mostly afoot.

He did lie down on his pallet, with surprisingly little protest—a good indication of just how exhausted he really was—and was asleep in seconds.

I was very tired myself, still very weak and easily exhausted, even by something like the Greys' visit, and I lay back and dozed, stirring to wakefulness every so often when some sound roused me, but Jamie slept deeply, and it eased my heart to hear his soft, regular snore.

I woke some time later, hearing a distant knocking below. As I raised my head blearily off the pillow, I heard a voice shouting, "Hallo, the house!" and snapped into instant alertness. I knew that voice.

I glanced quickly down, but Jamie was dead asleep, curled up like a hedgehog. With excruciating slowness, I managed to swing my legs off the bed and—moving like a geriatric tortoise and clinging to the bed frame—took the two steps that brought me to the window, where I clung to the sill.

There was a handsome bay mule in the dooryard, with a half-naked body laid over the saddle. I gasped—and immediately doubled in pain, but didn't let go the sill. I bit my lip hard, not to call out. The body was wearing buckskins, and his long brown hair sported a couple of bedraggled turkey feathers.

"Jesus H. Roosevelt Christ," I breathed, through gritted teeth. "Please, God, don't let him be—" But the prayer was answered before I'd finished speaking it; the door below opened, and in the next moment William and Lieutenant Macken walked out and lifted Ian off the mule, put his arms about their shoulders, and carried him into the house.

I turned, instinctively reaching for my medical bag—and nearly fell. I saved myself by a grab at the bed frame but let out an involuntary groan that brought Jamie up into a crouch, staring wildly about.

"It's . . . all right," I said, willing my belly muscles into immobility. "I'm fine. It's—Ian. He's come back."

Jamie sprang to his feet, shook his head to clear it, and at once went to the window. I saw him stiffen and, clutching my side, followed him. William had come out of the house and was preparing to mount the mule. He was dressed in shirt and breeches, very grubby, and the sun licked his dark chestnut hair with streaks of red. Mrs. Macken said something from the door, and he turned to answer her. I don't think I made a noise, but something made him look up suddenly and he froze. I felt Jamie freeze, too, as their eyes met.

William's face didn't change, and after a long moment he turned to the mule again, mounted, and rode away. After another long moment, Jamie let out his breath.

"Let me put ye back to bed, Sassenach," he said calmly. "I'll have to go and find Denny to put Ian right."

92

I WILL NOT HAVE THEE BE ALONE

SOMEONE HAD GIVEN HIM laudanum before setting to work on his shoulder. Strange stuff, that. He'd had it before, he thought, a long time ago, though he hadn't known the name at the time. Now Ian lay on his back, blinking slowly as the drug ebbed from his mind, trying to decide where he was and what was real. He was pretty sure most of what he was looking at right now wasn't.

Pain. That was real and something to use as an anchor. It hadn't entirely gone away—he'd been aware of it, but remotely, as a disagreeable muddy green strand like a stream of dirty water meandering through his dreams. Now that he was awake, though, it was becoming more disagreeable by the minute. His eyes didn't want to focus yet, but he forced them to roll about in search of something familiar.

He found it at once.

Girl. Lass. Ifrinn, *what was her*—"Rachel," he croaked, and she rose instantly from what she was doing and came to him, her face worried but alight.

"Rachel?" he said again, uncertain, and she took hold of his good hand, pressing it to her bosom.

"Thee is awake, I see," she said softly, her eyes searching his face. "But still much fevered, from the heat of thy skin. How does thee feel?"

"Better for seein' ye, lass." He tried to lick his dry lips. "Is there maybe water?"

She made a small sound of distress that he'd had to ask, and hurried to bring a cup to his lips. It was perhaps the best thing he'd ever tasted, made better by her holding his head in her hand as he drank—he was very dizzy. He didn't want to stop, but she took the cup away.

"More presently," she promised. "Thee must not drink too much, too fast, or thee will vomit. And between the dirt and the blood, thee has made enough mess already," she said, smiling.

"Mmphm," he said, lying back. He was mostly clean, he discovered. Someone had washed away the last of the deer fat and paint, and a good deal of sweat and blood with it. His shoulder was bound up with a poultice of some kind; it smelled tangy and familiar, but his hazy mind was a long way yet from allowing him to think of the name of the herb.

"Did Auntie Claire bind my arm?" he asked. Rachel glanced at him, her brows furrowing.

"Thy aunt is ill," she said carefully. "Thee remembers I told thee that she was wounded—shot—in the battle?"

"No," he said, feeling blank and confused. He had no recollection of the last couple of days or of battle. "No. What—is she all right, then?"

"Denny removed the ball, and thy uncle Jamie is with her. Both of them say very firmly that she will be well." Her mouth twitched a bit, halfway between a smile and worry. He did his best to smile back.

"Then she'll be fine," he said. "Uncle Jamie's a verra stubborn man. Can I have more water?"

This time he drank more slowly and got more down before she took it away. There was a regular clanging noise somewhere; for a time he had taken it for some phantom of hearing left over from the dreams, but now it ceased for a moment, punctuated by a loud curse.

"What—where are we?" he asked, beginning to be able to look at things again. His wavering sight convinced him that he was indeed in a tiny cow byre; it was new hay he'd been smelling, and the warm scent of fresh cow dung. He was lying on a blanket spread over a mound of hay, but the cow was absent for the moment.

"A place called Freehold. The battle was fought nearby; Washington and the army have withdrawn to Englishtown, but a good many wounded soldiers have been given refuge by the inhabitants here. We currently enjoy the hospitality of the local smith, a gentleman named Heughan."

"Oh." The forge. That was the source of the clanging and cursing. He closed his eyes; that helped with the dizziness, but he could see shadows of his dreams on the inside of his eyelids and opened them again. Rachel was still there; that was good.

"Who won the battle?" he asked.

She shrugged, impatient. "So far as anyone has said anything sensible about it, no one. The Americans are cock-a-hoop at not having been defeated, to be sure—but the British army surely wasn't, either. All I care about is thee. And thee will be fine," she said, and laid her hand gently on his forehead. "*I* say so. And I am as stubborn as any Scot thee cares to name—including thyself."

"I need to tell ye something, lass." He hadn't meant to say that, but the words felt familiar in his mouth, as though he'd said them before.

"Something different?" She had been turning away but paused now, looking wary.

"Different? Did I tell ye things while I was . . ." He tried to wave a hand in illustration, but even his good arm was heavy as lead.

Rachel caught her upper lip between her teeth, regarding him.

"Who is Geillis?" she asked abruptly. "And what in the name of—of goodness did she *do* to thee?"

He blinked, startled and yet relieved to hear the name. Yes, that was what he'd been dreaming—oh, Jesus. The relief departed at once.

"What did I say?" he asked warily.

"If thee doesn't recall it, I don't wish to bring it back to thee." She knelt down by him, skirts rustling.

"I remember what happened—I just want to ken what I said about it."

"What happened," she repeated slowly, watching his face. "In thy dreams, thee means? Or—" She broke off, and he saw her throat move as she swallowed.

"Likely both, lass," he said softly, and managed to reach for her hand. "I spoke of Geillis Abernathy, though?"

"Thee only said 'Geillis,'" she said, and covered his hand with both of hers, holding fast. "Thee was afraid. And thee called out in pain—but of course thee *was* in pain, so . . . but then . . . it—whatever thee saw, it—"

Color rose slowly up her neck and washed her face, and with a slight relapse into the dream, he saw her for an instant as an orchid with a dusky throat into which he could plunge his— He cut that vision off and found that he was breathing fast.

"It seemed that thee experienced something other than pain," she said, frowning.

"Aye, I did," he said, and swallowed. "Can I have a bit more water?"

She gave it to him, but with a fixed look indicating that she didn't mean to be distracted from his story by his physical needs.

He sighed and lay back again. "It was a long time agone, *a nighean,* and nothing to fash about now. I was taken—kidnapped—for a brief time, when I was maybe fourteen or so. I stayed wi' a woman named Geillis Abernathy, on Jamaica, until my uncle found me. It wasna very pleasant, but I wasna damaged, either."

Rachel raised an elegant brow. He loved to watch her do that, but sometimes more than others.

"There were other lads there," he said, "and they were not so lucky." For a long time afterward, he'd been afraid to close his eyes at night, because he saw their faces. But they'd faded away, little by little—and now he felt a spasm of guilt because he'd let them go into darkness.

"Ian," Rachel said softly, and her hand stroked his cheek. He felt the rasp of his beard stubble as she touched him, and a pleasant gooseflesh ran down his jaw and shoulder. "Thee needn't speak of it. I would not bring it back to thee."

"It's all right," he said, and swallowed a little easier. "I'll tell ye—but later. It's an old story, and one ye dinna need to hear just now. But—" He stopped short and she raised the other brow.

"But what I *do* have to tell ye, lass . . ." And he told her. Much of the previous two days' events was still a blur, but he recalled vividly the two Abenaki who had hunted him. And what he'd finally done, in the British camp.

She was silent for so long that he began to wonder whether he'd really waked and had this conversation or was still dreaming.

"Rachel?" he said, shifting uneasily on his bed of prickly hay. The door of the byre was open and there was light enough, but he couldn't read her face at all. Her gaze rested on his own face, though, hazel-eyed and distant, as though she were looking *through* him. He was afraid she was.

He could hear Heughan the smith outside, walking to and fro and making clanking sounds, pausing to apostrophize some uncooperative implement in coarse terms. He could hear his own heart beating, too, an uncomfortable, jerky thump.

Finally a shiver went over Rachel, as though she shook herself awake, and she put a hand on his forehead, smoothing back his hair as she looked into his eyes, her own now soft and fathomless. Her thumb came down and traced the tattooed line across his cheekbones, very slowly.

"I think we can't wait any longer to be married, Ian," she said softly. "I will not have thee face such things alone. These are bad times, and we must be together."

He closed his eyes and all the air went out of him. When he drew breath again, it tasted of peace.

"When?" he whispered.

"As soon as thee can walk without help," she said, and kissed him, lightly as a falling leaf.

93

THE HOUSE ON CHESTNUT STREET

THE HOUSE WAS occupied; there was smoke drifting from the west chimney. The door was locked, though, and bolted to boot.

"I wonder what happened to the old door?" John said to Hal, trying the knob again, just in case. "It used to be green."

"If you knock on this one, you might conceivably get someone to come out and tell you," Hal suggested. They weren't in uniform, but Hal was noticeably on edge, and had been since their call on General Arnold.

The general had been understandably reserved, but civil, and after reading Fraser's letter over three or four times, had agreed to give them passes to remain in the city and to make such inquiries as they saw fit.

"With the understanding," Arnold had said, a flash of his reputed arrogance showing through the façade of governorship, "that if I hear of anything untoward, I'll have you both arrested and ridden out of the city on a rail."

"On a what?" Hal had said incredulously, he having not encountered this peculiarly American method of making guests feel unwelcome.

"A rail," Arnold had repeated, smiling genially. "Long piece of wood? Used for fences, I believe?"

Hal had turned to John, one eyebrow raised, as though inviting him to translate the speech of some Hottentot randomly encountered. John sighed internally, but did so.

"An undesirable person is mounted on the object in question," he said, "straddling it. Whereupon a party of men lift either end and set off through the streets with it, decanting the rider outside the city. I believe tar and feathers are sometimes applied as a preliminary gesture, though the physical effects of the rail are generally presumed to be sufficient."

"Flatten your ball sac like a horse stepped on it," Arnold said, still smiling. "Won't do your arse any good, either."

"I should imagine not," Hal said politely. His color was somewhat higher than usual, but he gave no other indication of offense, which Grey thought a reasonable indication—not that he needed one—of the importance of their mission to Hal.

The sound of the bolt grating free interrupted his recollection. The door swung open, revealing his housekeeper and cook, Mrs. Figg, fowling piece in hand.

"Lord John!" she exclaimed, dropping the gun with a clatter.

"Well, yes," he said, stepping in and picking it up. He smiled, feeling affection well up in his bosom at sight of her—substantial, tidy, and beribboned as always. "It's very good to see you again, Mrs. Figg. Allow me to make you acquainted with my brother, the—"

"We've met," Hal said, a wry edge to his voice. "How do you do, madam?"

"Better than Your Grace, by the looks of you," Mrs. Figg

replied, narrowing her eyes at him. "Still breathing, though, I see." She sounded as though this was not entirely a desirable state of affairs, but Hal smiled broadly at her.

"Did you manage to bury the silver in time?" he asked.

"Certainly," she replied with dignity, and, turning to John, asked, "You come to get it, my lord? I can have it dug up right smart."

"Perhaps not just yet," John said. He looked round, noting the missing banister railing on the upper landing, the smudged and pockmarked wall by the staircase, and— "What's happened to the chandelier?"

Mrs. Figg sighed and shook her head darkly.

"That'd be Master William," she said. "How is he, my lord?"

"I'm afraid I don't know, Mrs. Figg. I was in some hopes that he might have been here—but I gather not?"

She looked disturbed at this.

"No, sir. We've not seen him since—well, since the day you went away yourself." She looked hard at him, taking in everything from the cropped hair to the fading bruises and the undistinguished suit, shook her head and sighed, but then straightened her broad shoulders, determined to be cheerful. "And glad we are to see you, sir! And Your Grace," she added as a definite afterthought. "Go sit yourselves down and I'll have you up a nice cup of tea in two minutes."

"You have tea?" Hal said, brightening.

"We buried the tea chest first thing," she informed him. "But I just brought in a brick for Miss Dottie, so—"

"Dottie's here?"

"To be sure," said Mrs. Figg, pleased to be the bearer of good news. "I'll just step out to the kitchen and fetch her."

This proved to be unnecessary, as the sound of the back door opening betokened Dottie's entrance, carrying an apronful of lumpy objects. These proved to be vegetable marrows from the kitchen garden, which cascaded over the floor in a bouncing flood of green and yellow as she let go the apron in order to leap at her father and embrace him.

"Papa!"

For an instant, Hal's face changed entirely, soft with love, and Grey was surprised and disconcerted to feel tears come to his own eyes. He turned away, blinking, and wandered over to the sideboard, meaning to give them a private moment.

The silver tea service was gone, of course, but his Meissen porcelain plates were in their accustomed spots on the plate rail. He touched the cool gilt-ribboned border of one, feeling oddly disembodied. *And his place shall know him no more.*

But Dottie was talking now to both of them; Grey turned round to her, smiling.

"I'm so glad you're both safe and both *here*!" Her cheeks were flushed, her eyes sparkling—and Grey's heart misgave him at the knowledge that this state of happiness would be quenched within the next minute, as soon as Hal told her the reason for their presence. Before any such doom could fall, though, Dottie had seized the reins of the conversation and driven it off in another direction entirely.

"Since you *are* here—Uncle John, could we possibly use your house? For the wedding, I mean. Please, please?"

"The wedding?" Hal disengaged himself gently and cleared his throat. "*Your* wedding?"

"Of course I mean my wedding, Papa. Don't be silly." She beamed at her uncle, placing a coquettish hand on his sleeve. "May we, Uncle John? We cannot be married in a meeting-house, but we must have witnesses for a proper marriage of Friends, and, really, I'm sure Papa wouldn't want to see me married in the public room of a tavern. Would you?" she appealed, turning to Hal, whose expression had reverted to its earlier guardedness.

"Well, certainly you may, my dear," John said, glancing round his parlor. "Assuming that I retain possession of this place long enough for the marriage to take place. When is the ceremony to be, and how many witnesses will we need to accommodate?"

She hesitated, tapping a fingernail against her teeth.

"I'm not really sure. There will be some of the conscientious Friends who, like Denny, have been put out of meeting for joining the Continental army. And some friends—friends in the lowercase, meaning no disrespect—if any are left in Philadelphia. And . . . family?" She hesitated again, looking at her father sideways, from under her lashes. John suppressed a smile.

Hal closed his eyes and sighed deeply.

"Yes, I'll come to your wedding," he said, opening them with resignation. "And so will Henry, if I have to drag him by the scruff of the neck. I suppose Mrs. Woodcock must be invited, too," he added, with a marked lack of enthusiasm. "But of course Adam . . . and—and Ben—"

John thought for a moment that he must tell her now, but his brother's lips closed, firmed with determination. He didn't look at John, but John caught the *"Not now, for God's sake. Let her be happy for a bit longer,"* as clearly as if it had been spoken aloud.

"No, that's too bad," Dottie said with regret, and met her father's eyes directly. "I'm sorry about Mama. I did write to her, though."

"Did you, sweetheart?" Hal said, sounding almost normal. "That was thoughtful." He tilted his head at her, though, eyes narrowing a bit. "What else?"

"Oh." Her color, which had returned to normal, rose again, and she began absently pleating her apron with one hand. "Well. Did you know that Rachel—Denzell's sister—is affianced to Ian Murray? That's Mr. James—no, no, we don't use 'Mister,' sorry—he's the nephew of James Fraser. You know—"

"I do know," Hal said, in a tone cutting off further amendation. "Who he is, I mean. What are you saying, Dottie? Without embroidery, if you please."

She sniffed at him but didn't appear to be discomposed in the least.

"Well, then. Rachel and Ian wish to be married as soon as they can, and so do Denny and I. As all the witnesses will be present, why not have both marriages at the same time?"

This time, Hal did look at John. Who returned the look, somewhat taken aback.

"Ah . . . well. I suppose that would mean additional guests? Including the aforementioned Mr. Fraser? I'm sure you will excuse my using his title, my dear; I'm accustomed to such social excesses."

"Well, yes. Rachel says that Mrs. Fraser is enough recovered that they will return to Philadelphia tomorrow or next day. And then of course there's Fergus and his wife, Marsali, and perhaps the children, and I don't know if there are other friends who—I don't *think* Ian has any Mohawk relations nearby, but—"

"One, two, three, four, five . . ." John turned and began counting the small gilt chairs that stood rigidly to attention beneath the wainscoting. "I think we shall be somewhat cramped, Dottie, but if—"

Mrs. Figg cleared her throat. The sound was sufficiently impressive that everyone else stopped talking and looked at her.

"Beg pardon, gentlemen," she said, and a faint flush was visible on her round face. "I don't mean to be forward or presuming . . . but so happens that I mentioned to the Reverend Figg about Miss Dottie and Friend Denzell needing a place to be married in."

She cleared her throat, the blush growing deeper beneath her dark skin, so that she bore a surprising resemblance to a just-fired cannonball, Grey thought, charmed by the notion.

"And . . . well, the long and the short of it, ma'am and gentlemen, is that the reverend and his congregation would be pleased was you to consider being married in the new church building, you having been so kind as to contribute to it. 'Tain't anyways fancy, mind, but—"

"Mrs. Figg, you are a marvel." Grey clasped her hands in his, an attention that flustered her to the point of speechlessness. Seeing this, he let go, though this allowed Dottie to swoop in and kiss the housekeeper, exclaiming in gratitude. That was all right, but when Hal took Mrs. Figg by the hand and kissed it, the poor lady was reduced nearly to the point of suffocation and, snatching back her hand, retreated in haste, muttering disjointedly about tea and narrowly avoiding tripping on a marrow.

"Is it all right to be married in a church?" Hal asked Dottie, once Mrs. Figg had retired to a safe distance. "It's not like Jews, is it? We needn't be circumcised in order to attend? Because if so, I think your guest list may be substantially reduced."

"Oh, I'm sure it's not . . ." Dottie began rather vaguely, but her attention was distracted by something seen through the front window. "Goodness, is that . . . ?"

Not bothering to complete her thought, she flew to the unbolted door and yanked it open, revealing a startled William on the stoop.

"Dottie!" he said. "What—" And then caught sight of John and Hal. William's face underwent a lightning shift that made a *frisson* run straight down John's back to his tailbone. He'd seen that exact expression on Jamie Fraser's face a hundred times, at least—but had never before seen it on William's.

It was the look of a man who doesn't like his immediate prospects one bit—but who feels himself entirely capable of dealing with them. William stepped inside, repelling by force of will Dottie's abortive attempt to embrace him. He removed his hat and bowed to Dottie, then, punctiliously, to John and Hal.

"Your servant, ma'am. Sirs."

Hal snorted, looking his nephew over from head to toe. William was dressed much as John and Hal were, in ordinary clothes—though clothes of good cut and quality, John observed; clearly his own.

"And where the devil have *you* been for the last three days, may I ask?"

"No, you mayn't," William replied briefly. "Why are *you* here?"

"Looking for you, for one thing," John replied equably, before Hal could stick his oar in again. He'd put the fowling piece on the mantel, easily within Hal's reach, but was reasonably sure it wasn't loaded. "And for Captain Richardson, for another. Have you seen him recently?"

William's expression of surprise made John heave an internal sigh of relief. "No, I haven't." William glanced shrewdly from one man to the other. "Is that what you were doing at Arnold's headquarters? Looking for Richardson?"

"Yes," John answered, surprised. "How did you—oh. You were watching the place." He smiled. "I did wonder how you happened to appear here so fortuitously. You followed us from General Arnold's."

William nodded and, stretching out a long arm, drew out one of the chairs from the wall. "I did. Sit down. Things need to be said."

"*That* sounds rather ominous," Dottie murmured. "Perhaps I'd best fetch the brandy."

"Please do, Dottie," John said. "Tell Mrs. Figg we want the '57, if you would. If it isn't buried, I mean."

"I think everything of an alcoholic nature is in the well, actually. I'll fetch it."

Mrs. Figg herself arrived at this point with a rattling tea tray, apologizing for the lowly earthenware pot in which the beverage was brewing, and within a few moments, everyone was provided with a steaming cup and a small glass of the '57.

"Thank you, sweetheart," Hal said, accepting a glass from Dottie, then adding pointedly, "You needn't stay."

"I'd rather you did, Dottie," William said quietly, but with an overt stare at Hal. "There are things you ought to know, I think."

With no more than a brief glance at her father, Dottie, who had been picking up the scattered squash, sat down on the ottoman, opposite her cousin.

"Tell me, then," she said simply.

"Nothing out of the way," he assured her, with an assumption of casualness. "I've recently discovered that I am the natural son of one James Fraser, who—"

"Oh," she said, and looked at him with renewed interest. "I *did* think General Fraser reminded me of someone! Of course, that's it! Goodness, Willie, you *do* look like him!"

William looked flabbergasted, but quickly pulled himself together.

"He's a general?" he asked Hal.

"He was," Hal said. "He's resigned his commission."

William made a small, humorless noise. "Has he? Well, so have I."

After a long silent moment, John placed his cup carefully on its saucer with a small clink.

"Why?" he asked mildly, at the same moment that Hal, frowning, said, "Can you do such a thing while technically a prisoner of war?"

"I don't know," William said tersely, and evidently in answer to both questions. "But I've done it. Now, as to Captain Richardson . . ." and he recounted his astonishing encounter with Denys Randall-Isaacs on the road.

"Or, rather, Denys Randall, as he now calls himself. Evidently his stepfather's a Jew, and he wishes to avoid the association."

"Sensible," Hal said briefly. "I don't know him. What else do you know about him, William? What's his connection with Richardson?"

"I haven't the faintest idea," William said, and, draining his cup, reached for the pot and poured another. "There *is* one, obviously, and prior to this, I would have assumed that Randall perhaps worked with, or for, Richardson."

"Perhaps he still does," John suggested, a slight edge in his voice. He'd been a spy himself for some years and was disinclined to take things said by known intelligencers at face value.

That seemed to take William aback for a moment, but he nodded reluctantly.

"All right," he conceded. "But tell me—why the devil are *you* two interested in Richardson?"

They told him.

At the conclusion, Hal was perched anxiously on the ottoman beside Dottie, an arm round her shaking shoulders. She was weeping silently, and he was dabbing at her face with his handkerchief, this now a grubby rag following its service as a flag of truce.

"I don't believe it," he was repeating doggedly, for the sixth or seventh time. "Do you hear me, darling, I do *not* believe it, and I won't have you believe it, either."

"N-no," she said obediently. "No . . . I won't. Oh, *Ben*!"

In some hopes of distracting her, John turned back to William.

"And what business brought you to Philadelphia, may I ask? You can't have come in search of Captain Richardson, because when you left camp, you didn't know he'd disappeared."

"I came on a personal matter," William said, in a tone suggesting that the matter was still personal and was going to remain that way. "But also . . ." He pressed his lips together for a moment, and again John had that odd sense of dislocation, seeing Jamie Fraser. "I was going to leave this here for you, in case you came back to the city. Or ask Mrs. Figg to send it to New York, if . . ." His voice trailed away, as he pulled a letter from the breast of his dark-blue coat.

"But I needn't now," he concluded firmly, and put it away again. "It's only saying what I've already told you." A slight flush touched his cheekbones, though, and he avoided John's eye, turning instead to Hal.

"I'll go and find out about Ben," he said simply. "I'm not a soldier any longer; there's no danger of my being taken up as a spy. And I can travel much more easily than you can."

"Oh, William!" Dottie took the handkerchief from her father and blew her nose with a small, ladylike honk. She looked at him with brimming eyes. "Will you, really? Oh, *thank* you!"

That was not, of course, the end of it. But it was no revelation to Grey that William possessed a stubbornness so obviously derived from his natural father that no one but Hal would even have thought of arguing with him. And even Hal didn't argue long.

In due course, William rose to go.

"Give Mrs. Figg my love, please," he said to John, and, with a small bow to Dottie, "Goodbye, cousin."

John followed him to the door to let him out, but at the threshold put a hand on his sleeve.

"Willie," he said softly. "Give me the letter."

For the first time, William looked a little less than certain. He put his hand to his breast, but left it there, hesitant.

"I won't read it—unless you don't come back. But if you don't . . . I want it. To keep."

William drew breath, nodded, and, reaching into his coat, removed a sealed cover and handed it over. Grey saw that it had been sealed with a thick daub of candle wax and that William hadn't used his signet, preferring instead to stamp it with his thumbprint, firm in the hot wax.

"Thank you," he said through the lump in his throat. "Godspeed. Son."

94

THE SENSE OF THE MEETING

THE METHODIST CHURCH was a modest wooden building with plain glass windows, and, while it did have an altar, might otherwise easily have passed as a Quaker meetinghouse, bar three framed cross-stitched samplers bearing Bible verses that hung on one wall. I heard

Rachel let out her breath as she stopped just inside, looking around.

"No flowers?" Mrs. Figg had said the day before, scandalized. "I understand plain, but *God* made flowers!"

"A Friends' meetinghouse would not have flowers," Rachel had said, smiling. "We think them somewhat pagan, and a distraction to worship. But we are thy guests, and surely a guest must not tell his host how to keep his own house."

Mrs. Figg blinked at the word "pagan," but then made a low humming noise and settled back into benignity.

"Well and good, then," she said. "His lordship has three good rosebushes, and there's sunflowers in every yard in town. Lot of honeysuckle, too," she added thoughtfully. There was; everyone planted honeysuckle by the privy.

As a nod to the Quakers' sensibilities, though, there was only one vase of flowers—a very plain glass vase—between the two wooden benches that had been set at the front of the room, and the faint perfume of honeysuckle and pink cabbage roses mingled with the turpentine smell of hot pine boards and the pungent scents of fairly clean but very hot people.

Rachel and I stepped outside again, joining the rest of what I supposed might be called the wedding party, in the shade under a big lime tree. People were still arriving in ones and twos, and I caught a good many curious looks directed at us—though these were not aimed at the two brides.

"You are being married in . . . *that*?" Hal said, eyeing Dottie's Sunday-best gown of soft gray muslin with a white fichu and a bow at the back of the waist. Dottie raised one smooth blond brow at him.

"Ha," she said. "Mummy told me what *she* wore when you married her in a tavern in Amsterdam. *And* what your first wedding was like. Diamonds and white lace and St. James's Church didn't help all that much, did they?"

"Dorothea," Denzell said mildly. "Don't savage thy father. He has enough to bear."

Hal, who had flushed at Dottie's remarks, went somewhat redder at Denny's and breathed in a menacing rasp, but didn't say anything further. Hal and John were both wearing full dress uniform and far outshone the two brides in splendor. I thought it rather a pity that Hal wouldn't get to walk Dottie down the aisle, but he had merely inhaled deeply when the form of the marriage was outlined to him and said—after being elbowed sharply in the ribs by his brother—that he was honored to witness the event.

Jamie, by contrast, did not wear uniform, but his appearance in full Highland dress made Mrs. Figg's eyes bulge—and not only hers.

"Sweet Shepherd of Judea," she muttered to me. "Is that man wearing a woolen *petticoat*? And what sort of pattern is that cloth? Enough to burn the eyes out your head."

"They call it a *Fèileadh beag,*" I told her. "In the native language. In English, it's usually called a kilt. And the pattern is his family tartan."

She eyed him for a long moment, the color rising slowly in her cheeks. She turned to me with her mouth open to ask a question, then thought better and shut it firmly.

"No," I said, laughing. "He isn't."

She snorted. "Either way, he's like to die of the heat," she predicted, "and so are those two gamecocks." She nodded at John and Hal, glorious and sweating in crimson and gold lace. Henry had also come in uniform, wearing his more modest lieutenant's apparel. He squired Mercy Woodcock on his arm and gave his father a stare daring him to say anything.

"Poor Hal," I murmured to Jamie. "His children are rather a trial to him."

"Aye, whose aren't?" he replied. "All right, Sassenach? Ye look pale. Had ye not best go in and sit down?"

"No, I'm quite all right," I assured him. "I just *am* pale, after a month indoors. It's good to be in the fresh air." I had a stick, as well as Jamie, to lean on but was feeling quite well, bar a slight stitch in my side, and was enjoying the sensations of mobility, if not the sensation of wearing stays and petticoats in hot weather again. It was going to be even hotter, sitting packed together once the meeting began; the Reverend Mr. Figg's congregation was there, of course, it being their church, and the benches were filled with bodies.

The church had no bell, but a few blocks away the bell of St. Peter's began to toll the hour. It was time, and Jamie, I, and the Grey brothers made our way inside and found our places. The air hummed with murmured conversation and curiosity—the more so at the British uniforms and Jamie's plaid, though both he and the Greys had left their swords at home, in deference to the Friends' meeting.

Both curiosity and conversation rose to a much higher pitch when Ian walked in. He wore a new shirt, white calico printed with blue and purple tulips, his buckskins and breechclout, moccasins—and an armlet made of blue and white wampum shells, which I was reasonably sure that his Mohawk wife, Works With Her Hands, had made for him.

"And here, of course, is the best man," I heard John whisper to Hal. Rollo stalked in at Ian's heel, disregarding the further stir *he* caused. Ian sat down quietly on one of the two benches that had been set at the front of the church, facing the congregation, and Rollo sat at his feet, scratched himself idly, then collapsed and lay panting gently, surveying the crowd with a yellow stare of lazy estimation, as though judging them for eventual edibility.

Denzell came in, looking a little pale, but walked up and sat down on the bench beside Ian. He smiled at the congregation, most of whom murmured and smiled back. Denny wore his best suit—he owned two—a decent navy broadcloth with pewter buttons, and while he was both shorter and less ornamental than Ian, did not by any means disappear beside his outlandish brother-in-law-to-be.

"You're no going to be sick, lass?" Jamie said to Rachel. She and Dottie had come in, but hovered near the wall. Rachel's hands were clenched in the fabric of her skirt. She was white as a sheet, but her eyes glowed. They were fastened on Ian, who was looking at no one but her, his own heart in his eyes.

"No," she whispered. "Come with me, Dottie." She held out a hand, and the two girls walked together to the other bench and sat down. Dottie's color was high, and so was her head. Rachel folded her hands in her lap and resumed looking at Ian. I felt Jamie sigh a little and relax. On Jamie's far side, Jenny craned to see round him, then smiled with gratification.

She'd made Rachel's dress herself, for after the exigencies of recent months, Rachel owned nothing that wasn't near rags. And while Jenny was generally in favor of modesty in dress, she knew her way around a bustline. The dress was a pale-green chintz with a small pattern of dark-green curling vines, and fitted like a glove. With her dark-brown hair shining loose on her shoulders and hazel eyes huge in her face, Rachel looked like some denizen of the forest—perhaps a tree nymph.

I was about to share this fancy with Jamie when the Reverend Mr. Figg walked up to the front of the church, turned, and smiled at the congregation.

"Blessings to you all this day, brothers and sisters!" he said, and was answered by a genial rumble of "Blessings to you, brother!" and discreet "Amens."

"Well, now." He glanced from Ian and Denny to the girls, then back to the congregation. "We're gathered here for a wedding today. But the ladies and gentlemen being married belong to the Society of Friends, so it will be a Quaker wedding—and that's maybe a little different from ones you've seen before, so I take the liberty of telling you how it goes."

A little hum of interest and speculation, which he quieted with one hand. Mr. Figg was small and dapper in black suit and high white stock, but had immense presence, and every ear was tuned attentively to his explanations.

"We have the honor to host this meeting—for that's what the Friends call their worship. And for them, a wedding is just a normal part of meeting. There's no priest or minister involved; the lady and the gentleman just . . . marry each other, when they feel like it's the right time."

That caused a ripple of surprise, perhaps a little disapproval, and I could see the color rise in Dottie's cheeks. Mr. Figg turned to smile at the girls, then back to his congregation.

"I think perhaps one of our Quaker friends might tell us a little bit about their notion of meeting, as I'm sure they know more about it than I do." He turned expectantly toward Denzell Hunter—but it was Rachel who rose to her feet. Mr. Figg didn't see her and started with surprise when she spoke behind him, making everyone laugh.

"Good morning," she said, soft-spoken but clear, when the laughter had died down. "I thank you all for your presence here. For Christ said, 'Wherever two or more of you are gathered in my name, there am I.' And that is all the essence of a meeting of Friends: that Christ may make His presence known among us—and within us." She spread her hands a little. "So we gather, and we listen—both to one another and to the light within us. When a person is moved of the spirit to speak, he or she does speak."

"Or sing, if thee likes," Dottie put in, dimpling at John.

"Or sing," Rachel agreed, smiling. "But we do not fear silence, for often God speaks loudest in the quiet of our hearts." And with that, she sat down again, composed.

A moment of shuffling and blinking among the crowd was succeeded in fact by an expectant silence—this broken by Denny, who rose deliberately and said, "I am moved to tell thee how grateful I am for your gracious use of us. For I was put out of meeting, and my sister with me, for my stated intent to join the Continental army. And for the same reason, we are not welcome as members of Philadelphia meeting." He glanced at Rachel, light glinting from his spectacles.

"This is a grievous thing to a Friend," he said quietly. "For our meeting is where our lives and souls abide, and when Friends marry, the whole of their meeting must approve and witness the marriage, for the community itself will support the marriage. I have deprived my sister of this approval and support, and I beg she will forgive me."

Rachel gave an unladylike snort. "Thee followed thy conscience, and if I hadn't thought thee right, I would have said so."

"It was my responsibility to take care of thee!"

"Thee has taken care of me!" Rachel said. "Do I look malnourished? Am I naked?"

A ripple of amusement ran through the congregation, but neither of the Hunters was noticing.

"I took thee from thy home and from the meeting that cared for thee and obliged thee to follow me into violence, into an army full of violent men."

"That would be me, I expect," Ian interrupted, clearing his throat. He looked at Mr. Figg, who seemed somewhat stunned, then at the rapt assemblage on the benches. "I'm no a Friend myself, ye ken. I'm a Highlander and a Mohawk, and they dinna come much more violent than that. By rights, I shouldna wed Rachel, and her brother shouldna let me."

"I should like to see him stop me!" said Rachel, sitting bolt upright with her fists curled on her knees. "Or thee, either, Ian Murray!"

Dottie appeared to be finding the conversation amusing; I could see her struggling not to laugh—and, glancing sideways along the bench in front of me, I could see precisely the same expression on her father's face.

"Well, it's on my account that ye couldna be wed in a proper Quaker meeting," Ian protested.

"No more than on mine," Denny said, grimacing.

"Mea culpa, mea culpa, mea maxima culpa," Jamie murmured in my ear. "D'ye think I should say it's all my fault, for leaving Ian wi' the Indians and bein' a bad example to him?"

"Only if the spirit moves you," I said, not taking my eyes off the show. "Personally, I'd advise you and the spirit to stay out of it."

Mrs. Figg was not disposed to stay out of it. She cleared her throat loudly.

"Now, pardon me for interrupting, but from what I understand, you Friends think a woman's equal to a man, is that right?"

"It is," Rachel and Dottie said firmly together, and everyone laughed.

Mrs. Figg flushed like a ripe black plum, but kept her composure. "Well, then," she said. "If these ladies want to marry with you gentlemen, why do you think you got any business trying to talk them out of it? Have you maybe got your own reservations about the matter?"

A distinctly feminine murmur of approval came from the congregation, and Denny, who was still standing, seemed to be struggling for his own composure.

"Does he have a cock?" came a French-accented whisper from behind me and an unhinged giggle from Marsali in response. "You can't get married without a cock."

This reminiscence of Fergus and Marsali's unorthodox wedding on a Caribbean beach made me stuff my lace handkerchief into my mouth. Jamie shook with suppressed laughter.

"I do have reservations," Denzell said, taking a deep breath. "Though not," he added hastily, with a glance at Dottie, "regarding my desire to wed Dorothea or the honor of my intentions toward her. My reservations—and perhaps Friend Ian's, though I must not speak for him—lie entirely the other way. That is, I—we, perhaps—feel that we must lay bare our failings and limitations as . . . as husbands—" And for the first time, he, too, blushed. "That Dorothea and Rachel may . . . may come to a proper—er . . ."

"That they know what they may be getting into?" Mrs. Figg finished for him. "Well, that's a fine sentiment, Dr. Hunter—"

"Friend," he murmured.

"*Friend* Hunter," she said, with a minimal roll of the eyes. "But I tell you two things. One, your young lady probably knows more about you than you do." More laughter. "And two—speaking as a woman with some experience—I can tell you that nobody knows what being married's going to be like until you find yourself in the midst of it." She sat down with an air of finality, to a hum of approbation.

There was a certain amount of glancing to and fro and a sense of movement on the left side of the church, where several men sat together. I had seen them come in, with women who were plainly their wives; the women had separated, though, and gone to sit on the right side of the church, which made me think that they might be Quakers, though there was nothing in their dress that differentiated them from the other workmen and merchants in the congregation. I could see them come to some sort of silent consensus now, and one of them rose.

"I am William Sprockett," he said formally, and cleared his throat. "We have come to speak in support of Friend Hunter. For we also are Friends who have followed the dictates of our conscience to involvement with rebellion and other matters that a Friend would normally seek to avoid. And in consequence . . . have been read out of meeting."

He paused, brow furrowed, evidently not sure how to go on. A small woman in yellow rose on the other side and spoke clearly.

"What my husband seeks to say, friends, is that a man who would not do as his inner light tells him to is no man. And that while a man of conscience can be mighty inconvenient at times, it don't make him a bad husband." She smiled at Mr. Sprockett and sat down.

"Yes," said Mr. Sprockett gratefully. "As my wife is kind enough to say, going to fight don't unfit us for marriage. So we've all come"—he swept a broad hand around him, indicating his companions and the wives across the aisle—"to approve and witness thy marriage, Friend Hunter."

"And we will support thy marriage, Dorothea," Mrs. Sprockett put in, with a bob of her head. "And thine, Rachel."

Denny Hunter had remained standing while all this colloquy was going on.

"I . . . thank you, Friends," he said, and sat down abruptly, followed more slowly by the Sprocketts.

A hush fell upon the room, and for a little while there was no sound but the remote noise of the streets outside. Here and there a cough, the clearing of a throat, but, overall, silence. Jamie laid a hand on mine, and my fingers turned to intertwine with his. I could feel his pulse in my own fingertips, the solid bones of knuckle and phalanges. His right hand, battered and marked with the scars of sacrifice and labor. Marked also with the signs of my love, the crude repairs done in pain and desperation.

Blood of my blood, bone of my bone . . .

I wondered whether people who are unhappily married think of their own nuptials when they witness a wedding; I thought that those who are happy always do. Jenny's head was bowed, her face calm and inward but peaceful; did she think now of Ian and her wedding day? She did; her head turned a little to one side, she laid a hand lightly on the bench and smiled at the ghost who sat by her side.

Hal and John sat on the bench in front of us, a little to the side, so I could catch glimpses of their faces, so much alike and yet so different. Both of them had been married twice.

It was a slight shock, in fact, to recall that John's second marriage had been to me, for he felt entirely separate from me now, our brief partnership seeming so removed in time as almost to be unreal. And then . . . there was Frank.

Frank. John. Jamie. Sincerity of intention wasn't always enough, I thought, looking at the young people on the benches at the front of the church, none of them now looking at one another but staring at their folded hands, the floor, or sitting with closed eyes. Perhaps realizing that, as Mrs. Figg had said, a marriage is made not in ritual or in words but in the living of it.

A movement pulled me out of my thoughts; Denny had risen to his feet and held out a hand to Dottie, who rose as though mesmerized and, reaching out, clasped both his hands in hers, hanging on for dear life.

"Does thee feel the sense of the meeting clear, Dorothea?" he asked softly, and at her nod, spoke:

"In the presence of the Lord, and before these our Friends, I take thee, Dorothea, to be my wife, promising, with divine assistance, to be unto thee a loving and faithful husband so long as we both shall live."

Her voice was low but clearly audible as, face shining, she replied:

"In the presence of the Lord, and before these our Friends, I take thee, Denzell, to be my husband, promising, with divine assistance, to be unto thee a loving and faithful wife so long as we both shall live."

I heard Hal catch his breath, in what sounded like a sob, and then the church burst into applause. Denny looked startled at this but then broke into a brilliant smile and led Dottie, beaming on his arm, out through the congregation to the back of the church, where they sat close together on the last bench.

People murmured and sighed, smiling, and the church gradually quieted—but not to its former sense of contemplation. There was now a vibrant sense of expectation, tinged perhaps with a little anxiety, as attention focused on Ian and Rachel—no longer looking at each other but down at the floor.

Ian took a breath audible to the back benches, raised his head, and, taking the knife from his belt, laid it on the bench beside him.

"Aye, well . . . Rachel kens I was once married, to a woman of the Wolf clan of the Kahnyen'kehaka. And the Mohawk way of marriage is maybe none so different from the way Friends do it. We sat beside each other before the people, and our parents—they'd adopted me, ken—spoke for us, sayin' what they kent of us and that we were of good character. So far as *they* knew," he added apologetically, and there was a breath of laughter.

"The lass I was to wed had a basket on her lap, filled wi' fruit and vegetables and other bits o' food, and she said to me that she promised to feed me from her fields and care for me. And I—" He swallowed and, reaching out, laid a hand on his knife. "I had a knife, and a bow, and the skins of some otters I'd taken. And I promised to hunt for her and keep her warm wi' my furs. And the people all agreed that we should be married, and so . . . we were."

He stopped, biting his lip, then cleared his throat and went on. "But the Mohawk dinna take each other for as long as they live—but only for as long as the woman wishes. My wife chose to part wi' me—not because I hurt or mistreated her, but for . . . for other reasons." He cleared his throat again, and his hand went to the wampum armlet round his biceps.

"My wife was called Wakyo'teyehsnonhsa, which means 'Works With Her Hands,' and she made this for me, as a love token." Long brown fingers fumbled with the strings, and the strip of woven shells came loose, slithering into his hand. "Now I lay it down, as witness that I come here a free man, that my life and my heart are once more mine to give. And I hope I may be allowed now to give them forever."

The blue and white shells made a soft clicking noise as he laid them on the bench. He let his fingers rest on them for a moment, then took his hand away.

I could hear Hal's breathing, steady now but with a faint rasp. And Jamie's, thick in his throat.

I could feel all sorts of things moving like wraiths in the thick, still air of the church. Sentiment, sympathy, doubt, apprehension . . . Rollo growled very softly in his throat and fell silent, yellow-eyed and watchful at his master's feet.

We waited. Jamie's hand twitched in mine, and I looked up at him. He was looking at Ian, intent, his lips pressed tight, and I knew he was wondering whether to stand up and speak on Ian's behalf, to assure the congregation—and Rachel—of Ian's character and virtue. He caught my glance, though, shook his head very slightly, and nodded toward the front. It was Rachel's part to speak, if she would.

Rachel sat still as stone, face bleached as bone and her eyes on Ian, burning. But she said nothing.

Neither did she move, but something moved in her; I could see the knowledge of it cross her face, and somehow her body changed, straightening and settling. She was listening.

We all listened with her. And the silence kindled slowly into light.

There was a faint throb in the air then, not quite a sound, and people began to look up, called from the silence. A blur appeared between the benches at the front, and a hummingbird materialized, drawn through the open window, a tiny blur of green and scarlet hovering beside the coral trumpets of the native honeysuckle.

A sigh came from the heart of the church, and the sense of the meeting was made clear.

Ian rose, and Rachel came to meet him.

A CODA IN THREE-TWO TIME

DENZELL AND DOROTHEA

IT WAS THE BEST party that Dorothea Jacqueline Benedicta Grey had ever attended. She had danced with earls and viscounts in the most beautiful ballrooms in London, eaten everything from gilded peacock to trout stuffed with shrimp and riding on an artful sea of aspic with a Triton carved of ice brandishing his spear over all. And she'd done these things in gowns so splendid that men blinked when she hove into view.

Her new husband didn't blink. He stared at her so intently through his steel-rimmed spectacles that she thought she could feel his gaze on her skin, from across the room and right through her dove-gray dress, and she thought she might burst with happiness, exploding in bits all over the taproom of the White Camel tavern. Not that anyone would notice if she did; there were so many people crammed into the room, drinking, talking, drinking, singing, and drinking, that a spare gallbladder or kidney underfoot would pass without notice.

Just possibly, she thought, one or two whole people might pass without notice, too—right out of this lovely party.

She reached Denzell with some difficulty, there being a great many well-wishers between them, but as she approached him, he stretched out a hand and seized hers, and an instant later they were outside in the night air, laughing like loons and kissing each other in the shadows of the Anabaptist Meeting House that stood next door to the tavern.

"Will thee come home now, Dorothea?" Denny said, pausing for a momentary breath. "Is thee . . . ready?"

She didn't let go of him but moved closer, dislodging his glasses and enjoying the scent of his shaving soap and the starch in his linen—and the scent of him underneath.

"Are we truly married now?" she whispered. "I am thy wife?"

"We are. Thee is," he said, his voice slightly husky. "And I am thy husband."

She thought he'd meant to speak solemnly, but such an uncontainable smile of joy spread across his face at the speaking that she laughed out loud.

"We didn't say 'one flesh' in our vows," she said, stepping back but keeping hold of his hand. "But does thee think that principle obtains? Generally speaking?"

He settled his glasses more firmly on his nose and looked at her with intense concentration and shining eyes. And, with one finger of his free hand, touched her breast.

"I'm counting on it, Dorothea."

SHE'D BEEN IN his rooms before. But first as a guest, and then as an assistant, coming up to pack a basket with bandages and ointments before accompanying him to some professional call. It was quite different now.

He'd opened all the windows earlier and left them so, careless of flying insects and the butcher's shop down the street. The second floor of the building would have been suffocating after the day's heat—but with the gentle night breeze coming through, the air was like warm milk, soft and liquid on the skin, and the meaty smells of the butcher's shop were now overborne by the night perfume of the gardens at Bingham House, two streets over.

All trace of his profession had been cleared away, and the light of the candle he lit shone serenely on a plainly furnished but comfortable room. Two small wing chairs sat beside the hearth, a single book on the table between them. And, through the open door, a bed fresh-made with a smooth counterpane and plump white pillows beckoned enticingly.

The blood still thrummed through her body like wine, though she'd had very little to drink. Still, she felt unaccountably shy and stood for a moment just inside the door, as though waiting to be invited in. Denny lit two more candles and, turning, saw her standing there.

"Come," he said softly, stretching out a hand to her, and she did. They kissed lingeringly, hands roaming slowly, clothes beginning to loosen. Her hand drifted casually down and touched him through his breeches. He drew breath and would have said something, but wasn't quick enough.

"One flesh," she reminded him, smiling, and cupped her hand. "I want to see thy half of it."

"THEE *HAS* SEEN such things before," Denny said. "I know thee has. Thee has brothers, for one thing. And—and in the course of . . . of treating wounded men . . ." He was lying naked on the bed, and so was she, fondling the object in question, which seemed to be enjoying the attention immensely. His fingers were sliding through her hair, playing with her earlobes.

"I hope thee doesn't think I ever did this to any of my brothers," she said, sniffing him with pleasure. "And those of wounded men aren't generally in a condition to be appreciated at all."

Denny cleared his throat and stretched himself a little, not quite squirming.

"I think thee should allow me to appreciate thy own flesh for a bit," he said. "If thee expects me to be able to make thee a wife tonight."

"Oh." She looked down at his cock and then at herself, surprised. "What do—does thee—mean? Why wouldn't thee be able to?"

"Ah." He looked pleased and eager—he was so young without his glasses—and bounced off the bed, going into the outer room, his bottom pale and tidy in the candlelight. To Dottie's astonishment, he came back with the book she'd noticed on the table and handed it to her. It was bristling with bookmarks, and as she took it, it fell open in her hands, displaying several drawings of a naked man in cross section, his private parts in various stages of operation.

She looked up at Denny in disbelief.

"I thought—I know thee is a virgin; I didn't want thee to be frightened, or unprepared." He was blushing like a rose, and instead of collapsing in howls of laughter, which she badly wanted to do, she shut the book gently and took his face between her hands.

"Is thee a virgin, too, Denny?" she said softly. His blush grew fierce, but he kept her gaze.

"Yes. But—I do know *how.* I'm a physician."

That was too much, and she did laugh, but in small, half-stifled blurts of giggling, which infected him, and in seconds they were in each other's arms on the bed, shaking silently, with occasional snorts and repetitions of "I'm a physician," which sent them into fresh paroxysms.

At last she found herself on her back, breathing heavily, Denny lying on top of her, and a slick of perspiration oiling them. She lifted a hand and touched his chest, and gooseflesh rippled over him, the dark hairs of his body curly and bristling. She was trembling, but not with either fear or laughter.

"Is thee ready?" he whispered.

"One flesh," she whispered back. And they were.

THE CANDLES had burned down nearly to their sockets, and the naked shadows on the wall moved slowly.

"Dorothea!"

"Thee should probably be quiet," she advised him, briefly removing her mouth in order to talk. "I've never done this before. Thee wouldn't want to distract me, now, would thee?" Before he could summon a single word, she had resumed her alarming actions. He groaned—he couldn't help it—and laid his hands gently, helplessly, on her head.

"It's called fellatio, did thee know that?" she inquired, pausing momentarily for breath.

"I did. How . . . I mean . . . Oh. Oh, God."

"What did thee say?" Her face was beautiful, so flushed that the color showed even by candlelight, her lips deep rose and wet . . .

"I said—oh, God."

A smile lit her shadowed face with happiness, and her already firm grip on him tightened. His shadow jerked.

"Oh, *good,*" she said, and with a small, triumphant crow of laughter, bent to slay him with her sharp white teeth.

Ian and Rachel

IAN LIFTED THE GREEN gown off in a whuff of fabric, and Rachel shook her head hard, shedding hairpins in all directions with little pinging sounds. She smiled at him, her dark hair coming damply down in chunks, and he laughed and plucked out a few more of the little wire hoops.

"I thought I should die," she said, running her fingers through her loosened hair, which Jenny had put up before the party at the White Camel tavern. "Between the pins sticking into my head and the tightness of my stays. Unlace me, wilt thee—husband?" She turned her back to him but looked over her shoulder, eyes dancing.

He hadn't thought it possible to be more moved in his feelings or more excited in body—but that one word did both. He wrapped one arm around her middle, making her squeak, pulled the knot of her laces loose, and gently bit the back of her neck, making her squeak much louder. She struggled, and he laughed, holding her tighter as he loosened the laces. She was slim as a willow sapling and twice as springy; she squirmed against him, and the small struggle heated his blood still further. If he had had no self-control, he would have had her pinned to the bed in seconds, stays and shift and stockings be damned.

But he did and let her go, easing the stay straps off her shoulders and the stays themselves over her head. She shook herself again, smoothing down the damp shift over her body, then stood tall, preening for him. Her nipples stood out hard against the limp fabric.

"I won thy wager for thee," she said, passing a hand over the delicate blue satin ribbon threaded through the neck of her shift and fluttering the hem, adorned with embroidered flowers in blue and yellow and rose.

"How did ye hear about that?" He reached for her, pulled

her close, and clasped both hands on her arse, bare under the shift. "Christ, ye've got a sweet round wee bum."

"Blasphemy, on our wedding night?" But she was pleased, he could tell.

"It's not blasphemy, it's a prayer of thanksgiving. And who told ye about the wager?" Fergus had bet him a bottle of stout that a Quaker bride would have plain linen undergarments. He hadn't known, himself, but had had hopes that Rachel wouldn't feel that pleasing her husband was the same thing as making a vain show for the world.

"Germain, of course." She put her own arms around him and clasped him in similar manner, smiling up. "Thine is neither wee nor round, but no less sweet, I think. Does thee need help with thy fastenings?"

He could tell she wanted to, so he let her kneel and unbutton the flies of his breeches. The sight of the top of her dark, disheveled head, bowed earnestly to the task, made him put his hand gently on it, feeling her warmth, wanting the touch of her skin.

His breeches fell and she stood up to kiss him, her hand caressing his standing cock as though by afterthought.

"Thy skin is so soft there," she said against his mouth. "Like velvet!"

Her touch wasn't tentative but very light, and he reached down and wrapped his fingers round hers, showing her the way of it, how to grasp it firmly and work it a bit.

"I like it when thee moans, Ian," she whispered, pressing closer and working it more than a bit.

"I'm not moaning."

"Yes, thee is."

"I'm only breathin' a bit. Here . . . I like that . . . but . . . here." Swallowing, he picked her up—she made a little whoop—and carried her the two steps to the bed. He dropped her onto the mattress—she made a louder whoop—and landed beside her, scooping her into his arms. There was a certain amount of writhing, giggling, and inarticulate noises, and she got him out of his calico shirt, while he had her shift pulled up at the bottom and down at the top but still puddled round her waist.

"I win," she said, wiggling the wadded shift down over her hips and kicking it off.

"Ye think that, do ye?" He bent his head and took her nipple in his mouth. She made a very gratifying noise and clutched his head. He butted her gently under the chin, then lowered his head and sucked harder, flicking his tongue like an adder's.

"I like it when ye moan, Rachel," he said, pausing for breath and grinning down at her. "D'ye want me to make ye scream?"

"Yes," she said, breathless, one hand on her wet nipple. "Please."

"In a bit." He'd paused to breathe, lifting himself above her to let a bit of air in between them—it was a small room, and hot—and she reached up to feel his chest. She rubbed a thumb lightly over his nipple, and the sensation shot straight down to his cock.

"Let me," she said softly, and lifted herself, a hand round his neck, and suckled him, very gently.

"More," he said hoarsely, bracing himself against her weight. "Harder. Teeth."

"Teeth?" she blurted, letting go.

"Teeth," he said breathlessly, rolling onto his back and pulling her on top. She drew breath and lowered her head, hair spilling across his chest.

"Ow!"

"Thee *said* teeth." She sat up anxiously. "Oh, Ian, I'm sorry. I didn't mean to hurt thee."

"I—ye didn't . . . well, ye did, but . . . I mean—do it again, aye?"

She looked at him, dubious, and it occurred to him that when Uncle Jamie told him to go slow and gentle with his virgin, it might not have been all to do with sparing the virgin.

"Here, *mo nighean donn,*" he said, drawing her down beside him. His heart was hammering and he was sweating. He brushed the hair back from her temple and nuzzled her ear. "Slow for a bit, aye? Then I'll show ye what I mean by teeth."

IAN SMELLED OF wine and whisky and musky male skin—he burned astonishingly under her hands and smelled now something like a distant skunk, but in a much better way. She pressed her face into the curve of his shoulder, breathing him in with pleasure. She had his cock in her hand, gripping firmly . . . but curiosity made her loose her hold and grope lower, fingers probing through the thickness of his pubic hair. He breathed out very suddenly when she cupped his scrotum, and she smiled against his shoulder.

"Does thee mind, Ian?" she whispered, rolling the lovely egg-like shapes of his balls in her palm. She'd seen male scrota many times, baggy and wrinkled, and while she wasn't disgusted, had never thought them more than mildly interesting. This was wonderful, drawn up tight, the skin so soft and so hot. Daring, she scooted down a little and felt farther back between his legs.

He had an arm about her shoulders and it tightened, but he didn't tell her to stop, instead spreading his legs a little, allowing her to explore him. She'd wiped men's arses hundreds of time, and the fleeting thought occurred to her that not all of them took great care . . . but his hair was curly and very clean, and her hips moved against him involuntarily as her fingertip slid tentatively between his buttocks. He twitched, tensing involuntarily, and she stopped, feeling him shiver. Then she realized that he was laughing, shaking silently.

"Am I tickling thee?" she asked, raising up on one elbow. The light of the single candle flickered over his face, hollowing his cheeks and making his eyes shine as he smiled up at her.

"Aye, that's one word for it." He ran a hand half roughly up her back and gripped her by the nape. He shook his head slowly, looking at her. His hair had come loose from its binding and spread out dark behind his head. "Here I am, tryin' to go slow, tryin' to be gentle . . . and next thing I ken, ye're squeezin' my balls and stickin' your fingers up my arse!"

"Is that wrong?" she asked, feeling a slight qualm. "I didn't mean to be . . . er, too . . . bold?"

He pulled her down and hugged her close.

"Ye canna be too bold wi' me, lass," he whispered in her ear, and ran his own hand down her back—and down farther. She gasped.

"Shh," he whispered, and went on—slowly. "I thought—ye'd maybe be scairt at first. But ye're no scairt a bit, are ye?"

"I am. I'm t-terrified." She felt the laughter bubble up through her chest, but there was some truth in it, too—and he heard that. His hand stopped moving and he drew back enough to look at her, squinting a little.

"Aye?"

"Well . . . not terrified, exactly. But—" She swallowed, suddenly embarrassed. "I just—this is so nice. But I know when thee—when we—well, it does hurt, the first time. I—I'm somewhat afraid that . . . well, I don't want to stop what we're doing, but I . . . I'd like to get that part over with, so I needn't worry about it."

"Over with," he repeated. His mouth twitched a bit, but his hand was gentle on the small of her back. "Well, then." He eased his other hand down and cupped her, very delicately, between the legs.

She was swollen there, and slippery—had been growing more so ever since he'd lifted her gown off over her head. His fingers moved, one and then two, playing, stroking . . . and . . . and . . .

It took her entirely by surprise, a feeling she knew but bigger, bigger, and then she gave way to it entirely, washed through with ecstasy.

She settled slowly into limpness, throbbing. Everywhere. Ian kissed her lightly.

"Well, that didna take verra long, did it?" he murmured. "Put your hands on my arms, *mo chridhe,* and hold on." He moved over her, agile as a big cat, and eased his cock between her legs, sliding slow but firm. Very firm. She flinched, clenching involuntarily, but the way was slick and her flesh swollen in welcome and no amount of resistance would keep him out.

She realized that her fingers were digging into his arms, but didn't let go.

"Am I hurting ye?" he said softly. He'd stopped moving, his full length inside her, stretching her in a most unnerving way. Something had torn, she thought; it burned a little.

"Yes," she said, breathless. "I don't . . . mind."

He lowered himself very slowly and kissed her face, her nose, her eyelids, lightly. And all the time the awareness of it—*him*—inside her. He pulled back a little and moved. She made a small, breathless noise, not quite protest, a little pain, not *quite* encouragement . . .

But he took it as that and moved more strongly.

"Dinna be worrit, lass," he said, a little breathless, too. "I won't take long, either. Not this time."

ROLLO WAS snoring in the corner, lying on his back for coolness, legs folded like a bug's.

She tasted faintly sweet, of her own musk and a trace of blandness with an animal tang that he recognized as his own seed.

He buried his face in her, breathing deep, and the slight salt taste of blood made him think of trout, fresh-caught and barely cooked, the flesh hot and tender, pink and slick in his mouth. She jerked in surprise and arched up into him, and he tightened his hold on her, making a low *hmmm* of reassurance.

It *was* like fishing, he thought dreamily, hands under her hips. Feeling with your mind for the sleek dark shape just under the surface, letting the fly come down just so . . . She drew her breath in, hard. And then engagement, the sudden sense of startlement, and then a fierce awareness as the line sprang taut, you and the fish so focused on each other that there was nothing else in the world . . .

"Oh, God," he whispered, and ceased to think, only feeling the small movements of her body, her hands on his head, the smell and taste of her, and her feelings washed through him with her murmured words.

"I love thee, Ian. . . ."

And there was nothing else in the world but her.

JAMIE AND CLAIRE

THE LIGHT OF a low yellow half-moon shone through gaps in the trees, glimmering on the dark rushing waters of the Delaware. So late at night, the air was cool by the river, very welcome to faces and bodies heated by dancing, feasting, drinking, and generally being in close proximity to a hundred or so other hot bodies for the last six or seven hours.

The bridal couples had escaped fairly early: Denzell and Dottie very inconspicuously, Ian and Rachel to the raucous shouts and indelicate suggestions of a roomful of festive wedding guests. Once they'd left, the party had settled down to serious merrymaking, the drinking now unhampered by the interruption of wedding toasts.

We'd taken our leave of the Grey brothers—Hal, as father of one of the brides, was hosting the party—sometime after midnight. Hal had been sitting in a chair near a window, very drunk and wheezing slightly from the smoke, but sufficiently composed as to stand and bow over my hand.

"You want to go home," I advised him, hearing the faint squeak of his breathing over the winding-down noises of the party. "Ask John if he's got any more ganja, and if he does, smoke it. It will do you good." And not only in a physical way, I thought.

"I thank you for your kind advice, madam," he said dryly, and, too late, I recalled our conversation the last time he had been exposed to ganja: his worry over his son Benjamin. If he thought of it, too, though, he said nothing, and merely kissed my hand and nodded to Jamie in farewell.

John had stood by his brother's side most of the evening and stood behind him now as we took our leave. His eyes met mine briefly, and he smiled but didn't step forward to take my hand—not with Jamie at my shoulder. I wondered now briefly if I should ever see either of the Greys again.

We hadn't gone back to the printshop but had wandered down by the river, enjoying the coolness of the night air and chatting about the young couples and the excitements of the day.

"I imagine their nights are bein' a bit more exciting still," Jamie remarked. "Reckon the lassies will be sore come morning, poor wee things."

"Oh, it may not be just the girls," I said, and he sniffed with amusement.

"Aye, well, ye may be right about that. I seem to recall wakin' the next morning after our wedding and wondering for a moment whether I'd been in a fight. Then I saw you in the bed wi' me and *knew* I had."

"Didn't slow you down any," I remarked, dodging a pale stone in my path. "I seem to recall being rather rudely awakened next morning."

"Rude? I was verra gentle with ye. More than ye were with me," he added, a distinct grin in his voice. "I told Ian so."

"You told Ian *what*?"

"Well, he wanted advice, and so I—"

"Advice? *Ian?*" To my certain knowledge, the boy had begun his sexual career at the age of fourteen, with a prostitute of similar age in an Edinburgh brothel, and hadn't looked back. Besides his Mohawk wife, there were at least half a dozen other liaisons that I knew of, and I was sure I didn't know them all.

"Aye. He wanted to know how to deal kindly wi' Rachel, her bein' virgin. Something new to him," he added wryly.

I laughed.

"Well, they'll be having an interesting night of it, then—all of them." I told him about Dottie's request in camp, Rachel's advent, and our ad hoc session of premarital counseling.

"Ye told them *what*?" He snorted with amusement. "Ye make *me* say, 'Oh, God,' all the time, Sassenach, and it's mostly not to do wi' bed at all."

"I can't help it if you're naturally disposed to that expression," I said. "You *do* say it in bed with no little frequency. You even said it on our wedding night. Repeatedly. I remember."

"Well, little wonder, Sassenach, wi' all the things ye did to me on our wedding night."

"What I did to *you*?" I said, indignant. "What on earth did I do to you?"

"Ye bit me," he said instantly.

"Oh, I did not! Where?"

"Here and there," he said evasively, and I elbowed him. "Oh, all right—ye bit me on the lip when I kissed ye."

"I don't recall doing that at all," I said, eyeing him. His features were invisible, but the moonglow off the water as he walked cast his bold, straight-nosed profile in silhouette. "I remember you kissing me for quite a long time while you were trying to unbutton my gown, but I'm sure I didn't bite you then."

"No," he said thoughtfully, and ran a hand lightly down my back. "It was later. After I went out to fetch ye some food, and Rupert and Murtagh and the rest all chaffed me. I know, because it was when I drank some o' the wine I'd fetched back, I noticed it burned the cut in my lip. And I bedded ye again before I got round to the wine, so it must ha' been that time."

"Ha," I said. "By that time, you wouldn't have noticed if I'd bitten your head off like a praying mantis. You'd got it properly up your nose and thought you knew everything."

He put an arm round my shoulders, pulled me close, and whispered in my ear, "I'd got it properly up *you, a nighean.* And ye weren't noticing all that much yourself, besides what was goin' on between your legs."

"Rather hard to ignore that sort of carry-on," I said primly.

He gave the breath of a laugh and, stopping under a tree, gathered me in and kissed me. He had a lovely soft mouth.

"Well, I willna deny ye taught me my business, Sassenach," he murmured. "And ye made a good job of it."

"You caught on reasonably quickly," I said. "Natural talent, I suppose."

"If it was a matter of special training, Sassenach, the human race would ha' died out long since." He kissed me again, taking more time over it.

"D'ye think Denny kens what he's about?" he asked, letting go. "He's a virtuous wee man, aye?"

"Oh, I'm sure he knows everything he needs to," I protested. "He's a physician, after all."

Jamie gave a cynical laugh.

"Aye. While he may see the odd whore now and then, it's likely in the way of his profession, not hers. Besides . . ." He moved close and, putting his hands through the pocket slits in my skirt, took a firm and interesting grip on my bottom. "Do they teach ye in medical college how to spread your wife's wee hams and lick her from tailbone to navel?"

"*I* didn't teach you that one!"

"Indeed ye didn't. And you're a physician, no?"

"That—I'm sure that doesn't make any sense. Are you drunk, Jamie?"

"Dinna ken," he said, laughing. "But I'm sure *you* are, Sassenach. Let's go home," he whispered, leaning close and drawing his tongue up the side of my neck. "I want ye to make me say, 'Oh, God,' for ye."

"That . . . could be arranged." I'd cooled down during our walk, but the last five minutes had lit me like a candle, and if

I'd wanted to go home and take off my stays before, I was now wondering whether I could wait that long.

"Good," he said, pulling his hands out of my skirt. "And then I'll see what I can make *you* say, *mo nighean donn.*"

"See if you can make me say, 'Don't stop.'"

PART SIX

The Ties That Bind

95

THE BODY ELECTRIC

Redondo Beach, CA
December 5, 1980

IF SHE HADN'T NEEDED stamps, she wouldn't have stopped in at the post office. She'd have clipped this batch of letters to the mailbox for the postman to collect, or posted them in the corner mailbox when she took the kids down to the beach to look for pelicans.

But she did need stamps; there were at least a dozen more niggling things to deal with: things needing notarization or photocopies or tax returns or . . .

"S-word," she muttered, sliding out of the car. "Bloody F-wording S-word!" This was small relief to her feelings of anxiety and oppression. It really wasn't fair. Who needed the relief of occasional bad language more than a mother of small children?

Maybe she should start using her mother's "Jesus H. Roosevelt Christ!" instead. Jem had incorporated that one into his own collection of expletives before he turned four and had long since taught it to Mandy; they wouldn't be warped by hearing it.

It hadn't been this hard, last time. Well, no, she corrected herself. It had been a lot harder, in the most important respect. But this . . . this . . . this quagmire of pettifogging details—property, bank accounts, leases, notifications . . . She flicked the sheaf of sealed envelopes in her hand against her thigh with irritation. Some days, she would have taken Jem and Mandy by their hands and run, not walked, straight into the stones with no feeling save relief at abandoning all this bloody Stuff.

She hadn't really had much Stuff when she did it the first time. And, of course, she'd had someone to leave it with. Her heart squeezed a little, remembering the day she'd nailed down the lid on the wooden shipping crate that held her family's modest history: the silver passed down through her father's family, cabinet photographs of her mother's parents, the collection of her father's first editions, her mother's World War II Queen Alexandra uniform cap, still with a faint but detectible odor of iodine about it. And taken such pains in writing the note to Roger to go with it: *You told me once that . . . everyone needs a history. This is mine. . . .*

Almost sure then that she'd never see Roger again, let alone the silverware.

She blinked hard and shoved the door of the post office open with so much force that it crashed into the wall, and everyone in the lobby turned to stare at her. Hot-faced, she grabbed the doorframe and closed it with exaggerated care, then crossed the lobby soft-footed, avoiding all eyes.

She shoved the envelopes through the collection-box slot one by one, with a certain feeling of grim satisfaction at each tedious thing disposed of. Preparing to disappear into the past, leaving all Stuff behind, was one thing; preparing to disappear while thinking that you might eventually come *back* and need that Stuff again—or that your children might come back twenty years later, without you . . . She swallowed. That was something else again, as her father was inclined to say. She couldn't just dump it all on Uncle Joe; he didn't—

She turned, glancing across the lobby automatically at her PO box, and stopped, seeing the letter. She felt the hairs rising on her forearm as she strode across the grubby linoleum and reached for the knob, even before her mind had consciously registered the fact that it didn't look like a utility bill, a credit-card application, or any other sort of official mail.

G-H-I-D-E-I . . . the tumblers of the combination lock fell and the heavy little door swung open. And right there in the post office, she smelled heather and peat smoke and the breath of the mountains, so strongly that her eyes blurred and her own breath caught in her throat.

It was a regular white envelope, addressed to her in Joe

Abernathy's round, capable hand. She could feel something inside it, another envelope, this one with a lump on it—a seal of some kind? She made it to her rented car before ripping it open.

It wasn't an envelope but a sheet of paper, folded and sealed with wax, blurs of black ink bleeding through the paper where a quill had scratched too deep. An eighteenth-century letter. She pressed it to her face, inhaling, but the scent of smoke and heather was gone—if it had ever been there. It smelled now only of age and brittle paper; not even the tang of the iron-gall ink was left.

There was a brief note from Uncle Joe, a slip of paper folded next to the letter.

Bree, darlin'—

Hope this catches you in time. It came from the estate agent in Scotland. He said when the new tenant at Lallybroch went to put the furniture in storage, they couldn't get that big old desk through the door of the study. So they called an antiques guy to take the thing apart—very carefully, he assured me. And when they did, they found three Queen Victoria stamps and this.

I didn't read it. If you haven't left yet, let me know if you want the stamps; Lenny Jr. collects them and will give them a good home, if not.

All my love,
Uncle Joe

She folded the note carefully, pressing the creases, tucking it into her handbag. She felt as though she ought to go somewhere else to read the letter, somewhere private and quiet, so she could go to pieces without anyone noticing. The seal was sooty gray candle wax, not sealing wax, and Roger had sealed it with his thumbprint. It wasn't necessary—she'd recognized the writing immediately—but there was no doubt of the tiny hook-shaped scar left when a scaling knife had slipped while he was cleaning a salmon he and Jem had caught in Loch Ness. She'd kissed it while the cut was healing, and a dozen times since.

But she couldn't wait and, hands trembling, opened her pocketknife and carefully pried off the seal, trying not to break it. It was old and brittle; the candle grease had seeped into the paper over the years, making a shadow around the glob of wax, and it shattered in her hand. She clutched the fragments convulsively and turned the folded paper over.

Brianna Randall Fraser MacKenzie, he'd written on the front. *To be kept until called for.*

That made her laugh, but the sound came out as a sob, and she dashed the back of her hand across her eyes, desperate to read.

The very first words made her drop the letter as though it were on fire.

November 15, 1739

She snatched it back up. Lest she somehow miss it, he'd underlined *1739.*

"How in bloody *hell* did you—" she said aloud, and clapped a hand over her mouth, where she kept it as she read the rest.

My Dearest Heart,

I know what you're thinking, and I don't know. My best idea is that I've come in search of Jeremiah and found him—or may have found him—but not the person I thought I was looking for.

I sought help at Lallybroch, where I met Brian Fraser (you would like him, and he, you), and through him—with the assistance of one Captain Jack Randall, of all people—came into possession of a set of RAF identification disks. I recognized the information on them.

We (Buck is still with me) have been searching for Jem since our arrival and have found no sign at all. I won't give up—of course you know that—but as our inquiries have borne no fruit in the northern clan lands, I feel I must follow the one clue I have and see if I can locate the owner of those tags.

I don't know what might happen, and I had to leave you some word, however faint the chance that you'll ever see it.

God bless you and Jem—wherever he is, poor little guy, and I can only hope and pray he's safe—and my sweet Mandy.

I love you. I'll love you forever.

R.

She didn't realize that she was crying, until the tears running down her face tickled her hand.

"Oh, Roger," she said. "Oh, dear *God.*"

IN THE LATE evening, with the kids safely asleep and the sound of the Pacific Ocean washing through the open balcony doors, Brianna took out a bound notebook, brand-new, and a Fisher Space Pen (guaranteed to write upside down, underwater, and in conditions of zero gravity), which she thought entirely appropriate to this particular piece of composition.

She sat down under a good light, paused for a moment, then got up and poured a glass of cold white wine, which she set on the table beside her notebook. She'd been composing bits of this in her mind all day and so began with no difficulty.

There was no telling how old the kids might be when—or if—they read it, so she made no effort to simplify things. It wasn't a simple matter.

A PRACTICAL GUIDE FOR TIME TRAVELERS—
PART II

Right. Dad's written down what we think we know about this, in terms of observation of occurrence, physical effects, and morality. This next part could best be described as preliminary hypotheses of cause: how time travel might work. I'd call it the scientific part, but you can't actually apply the scientific method very far with the scanty data we have available.

Any scientific approach starts with observations, though, and we have enough of those to maybe construct a rough series of hypotheses. Testing those . . .

The idea of testing those made Brianna's hand shake so badly that she was obliged to set down her pen and breathe slowly for two or three minutes, until the black spots stopped swarming in front of her eyes. Gritting her teeth, she wrote:

Hypothesis 1: That the time passages/vortices/whatever the bloody hell they are/ are caused by or occur at the crossing of ley lines. (Defined here as lines of geomagnetic force, rather than the folkloric definition of straight map lines drawn between ancient structures like hill forts, henges, or places of ancient worship, like saints' pools. Supposition is that folkloric lines may be identical or parallel with geomagnetic lines, but no hard evidence to this effect.)

Evidence in Support of Hypothesis: Some. But to start with, we don't know whether the standing stones are part of the vortex thingy or just markers set up when ancient people saw other ancient people step on the grass right . . . there . . . and poof!

"Poof," she muttered to herself, and reached for the glass of wine. She'd planned to drink it as a reward when she'd finished, but at the moment felt more in need of first aid than reward. "I *wish* it was just poof." One sip, two, then she set it down, the citric edge of the wine lingering pleasantly on her tongue.

"Where were we? Oh, poof . . ."

Dad was able to connect a lot of the folkloric leys to standing stone circles. It would theoretically be possible to check the geomagnetic polarity of the rock around standing stone circles; that should actually go some way toward supporting Hypothesis 1, but might be a little difficult to execute. That is, you can measure the earth's magnetic field—Carl Friedrich Gauss figured out how to do it back in 1835 or so—but it isn't the sort of thing individuals do much.

Governments that do geological surveys have the equipment for it; I know the British Geological Survey's Eskdalemuir Observatory does, because I saw a write-up on them. And I quote: "Such observatories can measure and forecast magnetic conditions such as magnetic storms that sometimes affect communications, electric power, and other human activities."

"Other human activities," she muttered. "Riiight . . ."

The army does this sort of thing, too, she wrote as an afterthought. "Yes, I'll get the army right on that. . . ."

The pen hovered over the page as she thought, but she couldn't add anything else useful there, and so went on:

Hypothesis 2: That entering a time vortex with a gemstone (preferably faceted, vide *remarks made by Geillis Duncan to this effect) offers some protection to the traveler in terms of physical effect.*

Query: why facets? We used mostly unfaceted ones coming back through Ocracoke, and we know of other travelers using plain unfaceted ones.

Speculation: Joe Abernathy told me about one of his patients, an archaeologist who told him about some study done on standing stones up in Orkney, where they discovered that the stones have interesting tonal qualities; if you strike them with wooden sticks or other stones, you get a kind of musical note. Any kind of crystal—and all gems have a crystalline interior structure—has a characteristic vibration when struck; that's how quartz watches work.

*So what if the crystal you carry has vibrations that respond to—or stimulate, for that matter—vibrations in the standing stones nearby? And if they did . . . what might be the physical effect? D.B.K.**

She made a swift note at the bottom of the page: **D.B.K.—Don't Bloody Know,* and returned to her writing.

Evidence: There really isn't any, other than the aforesaid remarks from Geillis Duncan (though she may have noted some anecdotal material in her journals, which you'll find in the large safe-deposit box at the Royal Bank of Scotland in Edinburgh. Uncle Joe will have the key or will have made provisions for you to get it).

NB: Grannie Claire traveled the first two times without any stones (though note that she was wearing a gold wedding ring the first time, and a gold and a silver ring on the second journey).

Grannie said that going with a stone seemed slightly easier—but given the subjectivity of the experience, I don't know how much weight to put on that. Doing it with a stone is the most horrible thing I . . .

Maybe better not to say that. She hesitated for some time, but, after all, her own experiences were data, and given how little there was of it . . . She finished the sentence, then went on.

Hypothesis 3: That traveling with a gemstone allows one better control in choosing where/when to emerge.

She stopped, frowning, and crossed out *where.* There wasn't any indication of people traveling *between* sites. Be bloody handy if they could, though. . . . She sighed and went on.

Evidence: Pretty sketchy, owing to lack of data. We know of a few travelers other than ourselves, and of these, five Native Americans (part of a political group called the Montauk Five) traveled with the use of stones. One of these is known to have died in the attempt, one survived and traveled back about 200 years, and another, a man named Robert Springer (aka "Otter-Tooth"), traveled back more than the usual distance, arriving (approximately) 250–260 years prior to his year of departure. We don't know what happened to the two other members of this group; they may have traveled to a different time and we haven't found any mention of them (difficult to track down a time traveler, if you don't know when they may have gone, what their real names are, or what they look like), may have been blown out of the time vortex for unknown reasons, or may have died inside it.

That little possibility unnerved her so much that she set down the pen and took several large swallows of wine before resuming.

By the evidence of Otter-Tooth's journal, these men all did travel with gemstones, and he procured a large opal with which he intended to make the return trip. (This is the stone Jemmy made explode, in North Carolina, presumably because fire opals have a high water content.)

It hadn't—and, thinking back, she couldn't imagine how it hadn't—occurred to her at the time to see whether Jemmy could make water boil by touching it. Well, she could see why it hadn't occurred to her, in retrospect; the last thing she'd wanted was any more dangerous peculiarity near her children, much less dangerous peculiarities being inherent in them.

"I wonder how often it happens that two time travelers marry each other?" she said aloud. No telling what the frequency of the gene—if it was a gene, but that looked to be a decent bet—in the general population was, but it couldn't be *very* common, or people would be walking into Stonehenge and Callanish and going *poof!* on a daily basis. . . . "Somebody would have noticed," she concluded, and sat twiddling the pen for a bit in meditation.

Might she have met and married Roger if it weren't for the time-traveling thing? No, because it was her mother's need to find out what had happened to the men of Lallybroch that had led them to Scotland.

"Well, I'm not sorry," she said aloud to Roger. "In spite of . . . everything."

She flexed her fingers and picked up the pen, but didn't write at once. She hadn't thought further with her hypotheses and wanted them to be clear in her mind, at least. She had vague notions about how a time vortex might be explained in the context of a unified field theory, but if Einstein couldn't do it, she didn't think she was up to it right this minute.

"It has to be in there *somewhere,* though," she said aloud, and reached for the wine. Einstein had been trying to form a theory that dealt both with relativity and electromagnetism, and plainly they were dealing with relativity here—but a sort in which it maybe wasn't the speed of light that was limiting. What, then? The speed of time? The *shape* of time? Did electromagnetic fields crisscrossing in some places warp that shape?

What about the dates? Everything they thought they knew—precious little as it was—indicated that travel was easier, safer, on the sun feasts and fire feasts; the solstices and equinoxes. . . .

A little ripple ran up her back. A few things were known about standing stone circles, and one of the common things was that many had been built with astronomical prediction in mind. Was the light striking a specific stone the signal that the earth had reached some planetary alignment that affected the geomagnetism of that area?

"Huh," she said, and sipped, flipping back over the pages she'd written. "What a hodgepodge." This wouldn't do anyone much good: nothing but disconnected thoughts and things that didn't even qualify as decent speculation.

Still, her mind wouldn't let go of the matter. *Electromagnetism* . . . Bodies had electric fields of their own, she knew that much. Was that maybe why you didn't just disintegrate when you traveled? Did your own field keep you together, just long enough to pop out again? She supposed that might explain the gemstone thing: you *could* travel on the strength of your own field, if you were lucky, but the energy released from the molecular bonds in a crystal might well add to that field, so perhaps . . . ?

"Bugger," she said, her overworked mental processes creaking to a halt. She glanced guiltily at the hallway that led to the kids' room. They both knew that word, but they oughtn't to think their mother did.

She sank back to finish the wine and let her mind roam free, soothed by the sound of the distant surf. Her mind wasn't interested in water, though; it seemed still concerned with electricity.

"I sing the Body Electric," she said softly. *"The armies of those I love engirth me."*

Now, there was a thought. Maybe Walt Whitman had been onto something . . . because if the electric attraction of *the armies of those I love* had an effect on time-traveling, it would explain the apparent effect of fixing your attention on a specific person, wouldn't it?

She thought of standing in the stones of Craigh na Dun, thinking of Roger. Or of standing on Ocracoke, mind fixed fiercely on her parents—she'd read all the letters now; she knew exactly where they were. . . . Would that make a difference? An instant's panic, as she tried to visualize her father's face, more as she groped for Roger's . . .

The expression of the face balks account. The next line

echoed soothingly in her head. *But the expression of a well-made man appears not only in his face;*

It is in his limbs and joints also, it is curiously in the joints of his hips and wrists;
It is in his walk, the carriage of his neck, the flex of his waist and knees—dress does not hide him;
The strong, sweet supple quality he has, strikes through the cotton and flannel;
To see him pass conveys as much as the best poem, perhaps more;
You linger to see his back, and the back of his neck and shoulder-side.

She didn't remember any more, but didn't need to; her mind had calmed.

"I'd know you anywhere," she said softly to her husband, and lifted the remains of her glass. *"Slàinte."*

96

NAY GREAT SHORTAGE OF HAIR IN SCOTLAND

MR. CUMBERPATCH proved to be a tall, ascetic person with an incongruous crop of red curls that sat on his head like a small, inquisitive animal. He had, he said, taken the disks in trade for a sucking pig, along with a tin pan whose bottom had been burnt through but could easy be patched, six horseshoes, a looking glass, and half a dresser.

"Not really a tinker by trade, see?" he said. "Don't travel much. But things come and find me, they do."

Evidently they did. Mr. Cumberpatch's tiny cottage was

crammed to its rafters with items that had once been useful and might be so again, once Mr. Cumberpatch got round to fixing them.

"Sell much?" Buck asked, raising an eyebrow at a disassembled carriage clock that sat on the hearth, its internal organs neatly piled into a worn silver comfit dish.

"Happen," Mr. Cumberpatch said laconically. "See anything ye like?"

In the interests of cooperation, Roger haggled politely for a dented canteen and a canvas bed sack with only a few small charred holes at one end, these the result of some soldier taking his rest too close to a campfire. And received in turn the name and general direction of the person from whom Mr. Cumberpatch had got the disks.

"Flimsy sort of jewel," his host said, with a shrug. "And t'old woman said she wouldn't have it in t'house, all those numbers might be to do with magic, aye? Her not holdin' with sorcery and t'like."

The old woman in question was possibly twenty-five, Roger thought, a tiny, dark-eyed creature like a vole, who—summoned to provide tea—sized them up with a shrewd glance and proceeded to sell them a small, flabby-looking cheese, four turnips, and a large raisin tart, at an extortionate price. But the price included her own observations on her husband's transaction—well worth it, so far as Roger was concerned.

"That ornament—strange thing, no?" she said, narrowing her eyes at the pocket where Roger had replaced it. "Man what sold it to Anthony said he'd had it from a hairy man, one of them as lives on the wall."

"Which wall would this be, missus?" Buck asked, draining his cup and holding it out for more. She gave him a look from her bead-bright eyes, obviously thinking him a simpleton, but they *were* paying customers, after all. . . .

"Why, the Roman one, to be sure," she said. "They say the old king o' the Romes put it up, so as to keep the Scots from coming into England." The thought made her grin, small teeth gleaming. "As though anybody'd want to be a-going *there* in t'first place!"

Further questions elicited nothing more; Mrs. Cumberpatch had no idea what was meant by "a hairy man"; that was what the man said, and she hadn't wondered about it. Declining an offer from Mr. Cumberpatch for his knife, Roger and Buck took their leave, the food wrapped in the bed sack. But as they did so, Roger saw a pottery dish containing a tangle of chains and tarnished bracelets, and a stray gleam of rainy light struck a tiny red glow.

It must have been Cumberpatch's description of the disks as a jewel—a common way to refer to a pendant ornament—that had made his mind sensitive. He stopped and, stirring the dish with a forefinger, drew out a small pendant, blackened, cracked, and with a broken chain—it looked as though it had been in a fire—but set with a fairly large garnet, caked with grime but faceted.

"How much for this?" he said.

IT WAS DARK by four o'clock, and long cold nights to be sleeping out of doors, but Roger's sense of urgency drove them on, and they found themselves benighted on a lonely road, with nothing but a wind-gnarled Caledonian pine for shelter. Starting a fire with tinder and damp pine needles was no joke, but after all, Roger reflected, grimly bashing steel and flint for the hundredth time—and his finger for the twentieth—they had nothing but time.

Buck had, with a forethought born of painful experience, brought a sack of peats, and after a quarter hour of frantic blowing on sparks and thrusting grass-stems and pine needles into the infant flame, they succeeded in getting two of these miserable objects to burn with sufficient heat as to roast—or at least sear—the turnips and warm their fingers, if not the rest of them.

There hadn't been any conversation since they'd left the Cumberpatch establishment: impossible to talk with the cold wind whistling past their ears as they rode, and no breath with which to do it during the struggle with fire and food.

"What'll you do if we find him?" Buck asked suddenly, mid-turnip. "If J. W. MacKenzie really is your father, I mean."

"I've speg"—Roger's throat was clogged from the cold and he coughed and spat, resuming hoarsely—"spent the last three days wondering that, and the answer is, I don't know."

Buck grunted and unwrapped the raisin tart from the bed sack, divided it carefully, and handed Roger half.

It wasn't bad, though Mrs. Cumberpatch couldn't be said to have a light hand with pastry.

"Filling," Roger remarked, thriftily dabbing crumbs off his coat and eating them. "D'ye not want to go, then?"

Buck shook his head. "Nay, I canna think of anything better to do. As ye say—it's the only clue there is, even if it doesna seem to have aught to do with the wee lad."

"Mmphm. And there's the one good thing—we can head straight south to the wall; we needn't waste time looking for the man Cumberpatch got the disks from."

"Aye," Buck said dubiously. "And then what? Walk the length of it, askin' after a hairy man? How many o' those do ye think there might be? Nay great shortage of hair in Scotland, I mean."

"If we have to," Roger said shortly. "But if J. W. MacKenzie—and not just his identity disks—was anywhere in the neighborhood, I'm thinking he would have caused a good bit of talk."

"Mmphm. And how long's this wall, d'ye know?"

"I do, yes. Or, rather," Roger corrected, "I know how long it was when it was built: eighty Roman miles. A Roman mile being just slightly shorter than an English one. No idea how much of it's still there now, though. Most of it, likely."

Buck grimaced. "Well, say we can walk fifteen, twenty miles in a day—the walkin' will be easy, if it's along a bloody wall—that's only four days to cover the lot. Though . . ." A thought struck him and he frowned, pushing his damp forelock back. "That's if we could walk from end to end. If we hit it midway, though, what then? We might cover half and find nothing, and then have to go all the way back to where we started." He looked accusingly at Roger.

Roger rubbed a hand over his face. It was coming on to rain, and the mizzle was misting on his skin.

"I'll think about it tomorrow, aye?" he said. "We'll have plenty of time to make plans on our way." He reached for the canvas bed sack, shook out a limp turnip frond and ate it, then pulled the sack over his head and shoulders. "Want to join me under this, or are ye for bed?"

"Nay, I'm all right." Buck pulled his slouch hat lower and

sat hunched, toes as close to the remnants of the fire as he could get.

Roger drew his knees up and tucked in the ends of the bed sack. The rain made a gentle pittering on the canvas, and in the fatigue of exhaustion and cold, but with the comfort of a full stomach, he allowed himself the further comfort of imagining Bree. He did this only at night but looked forward to it with a greater anticipation than he did supper.

He envisioned her in his arms, sitting between his knees, her head lying back on his shoulder, snug under the canvas with him and her soft hair spangled with raindrops that caught the faint light of the fire. Warm, solid, breathing against his chest, his heart slowing to beat with hers . . .

"I wonder what I'd say to my own father," Buck said suddenly. "Had I ever kent him, I mean." He blinked at Roger from under the shadowed brim of his hat. "Did yours—does he, I mean—know about you?"

Roger suppressed his annoyance at being disturbed in his fantasy, but answered shortly. "Yes. I was born before he disappeared."

"Oh." Buck rocked back a little, looking meditative, but said no more. Roger found, though, that the interruption had made his wife vanish. He concentrated, trying to bring her back, imagining her in the kitchen at Lallybroch, the steam of cooking rising up around her, making wisps of red hair curl round her face and moisture gleam on the long straight bridge of her nose . . .

What he was hearing, though, was her arguing with him about whether he should tell Buck the truth of his begetting.

"Don't you think he has a right to know?" she'd said. *"Wouldn't* you *want to know something like that?"*

"Actually, I don't think I would," he'd said at the time. But now . . .

"Do you know who your father was?" Roger asked suddenly. The question had been in his mind for months, he unsure whether he had any right to ask it.

Buck gave him a baffled, faintly hostile glance.

"What the devil d'ye mean by that? Of course I do—or did. He's dead now." His face twisted suddenly, realizing. "Or—"

"Or maybe he's not, since ye're not born yet. Aye, it gets to ye after a bit, doesn't it?"

Apparently, it had just gotten to Buck. He stood up abruptly and stalked off. He stayed gone for a good ten minutes, giving Roger time to regret saying anything. But at last Buck came out of the dark and sat down again by the smoldering peat. He sat with his knees pulled up, arms locked round them.

"What did ye mean by that?" he asked abruptly. "Did I ken my father, and that."

Roger took in a deep breath of damp grass, pine needles, and peat smoke. "I mean ye werena born to the house ye grew up in. Did ye ken that?"

Buck looked wary and slightly bewildered. "Aye," he said slowly. "Or—not kent it straight out, I mean. My parents didna have any bairns besides me, so I thought there was maybe—well, I thought I was likely a bastard born to my father's sister. She died, they said, about the time I was born, and she wasna marrit, so . . ." He shrugged, one-shouldered. "So, no." He turned his head and looked at Roger, expressionless. "How d'ye come to know, yourself?"

"Brianna's mother." He felt a sharp, sudden longing for Claire and was surprised at it. "She was a traveler. But she was at Leoch, about that time. And she told us what happened." He had the hollow-bellied feel of one about to jump off a precipice into water of unknown depth, but there was no way to stop now.

"Your father was Dougal MacKenzie of Castle Leoch—war chieftain of the clan MacKenzie. And your mother was a witch named Geillis."

Buck's face was absolutely blank, the faint firelight shimmering on the broad cheekbones that were his father's legacy. Roger wanted suddenly to go and take the man in his arms, smooth the hair back from his face, comfort him like a child—like the child he could so plainly see in those wide, stunned green eyes. Instead, he got up and went off into the night, giving his four-times great-grandfather what privacy he could in which to deal with the news.

IT HADN'T HURT. Roger woke coughing, and drops of moisture rolled tickling down his temples, dislodged by the motion. He was sleeping under the empty canvas bed sack rather than on it, valuing its water-resilience more than its potential comfort when stuffed with grass, but he hadn't been able to bear having it over his head.

He put a hand cautiously to his throat, feeling the thickened line of the rope scar cutting across the lower swell of his larynx. He rolled over, lifted himself on one elbow, and cleared his throat experimentally. It didn't hurt this time, either.

"Do you know what a hyoid bone is?" He did; as a result of a number of medical consultations about his damaged voice, he understood the anatomy of his throat quite well. And thus had known what Dr. McEwan meant; his own hyoid was placed slightly higher and farther back than the usual, a fortunate circumstance that had saved his life when he was hanged, as the crushing of that wee bone would have suffocated him.

Had he been dreaming of McEwan? Or of being hanged? Yes, that. He'd had dreams like that often in the months afterward, though they'd grown less frequent in later years. But he remembered looking up through the lacy branches of the tree, seeing—in the dream—the rope tied to the branch above him, and the desperate struggle to scream a protest through the gag in his mouth. Then the ineluctable sliding under him as the horse he sat on was led away . . . but this time it hadn't hurt. His feet had struck the ground and he waked—but waked without the choking or the burning, stabbing sensations that left him gasping and gritting his teeth.

He glanced across; yes, Buck was still there, huddled up under the ragged plaid he'd bought from Cumberpatch. Wise purchase.

He lay back down on his side, hauling the canvas up to shield his face while still allowing him to breathe. He'd admit to a feeling of relief at seeing Buck; he'd half-expected the man to decamp and head straight back to Castle Leoch after hearing the truth about his own family. Though, in justice to Buck, he wasn't a sneak. If he'd made up his mind to do that, he'd likely say so—after punching Roger in the nose for not telling him sooner.

As it was, he'd been there, staring into the ashes of the fire when Roger came back. He hadn't looked up, and Roger hadn't said anything to him but had sat down and taken out needle and thread to mend a rip in the seam of his coat.

After a bit, though, Buck had stirred himself.

"Why wait to tell me now?" he'd asked quietly. His voice held no particular note of accusation. "Why not tell me while we were still near Leoch and Cranesmuir?"

"I hadn't made up my mind to tell ye at all," Roger had said bluntly. "It was just thinking about—well, about what we're doing and what might happen. I thought of a sudden that maybe ye *should* know. And . . ." He hesitated for a moment. "I didn't plan it, but it's maybe better so. Ye'll have time to think, maybe, whether ye want to find your parents before we go back."

Buck had merely grunted in reply to that and said no more. But it wasn't Buck's response that was occupying Roger's mind at the moment.

It hadn't hurt when he'd cleared his throat while talking to Buck, though he hadn't noticed consciously at the time.

McEwan—was it what he'd done, his touch? Roger wished he'd been able to see whether McEwan's hand shed blue light when he'd touched Roger's damaged throat.

And what about that light? He thought that Claire had mentioned something like it once—oh, yes, describing how Master Raymond had healed her, following the miscarriage she'd had in Paris. Seeing her bones glow blue inside her body was how she'd put it, he thought.

Now, that was a staggering thought—was it a familial trait, common to time travelers? He yawned hugely and swallowed once more, experimentally. No pain.

He couldn't keep track of his thoughts any longer. Felt sleep spreading through his body like good whisky, warming him. And let go, finally, wondering what he might say to his father. If . . .

97

A MAN TO DO A MAN'S JOB

Boston, MA
December 8, 1980

GAIL ABERNATHY provided a quick but solid supper of spaghetti with meatballs, salad, garlic bread, and—after a quick, penetrating look at Bree—a bottle of wine, despite Brianna's protests.

"You're spending the night here," Gail said, in a tone brooking no opposition, and pointed at the bottle. "And you're drinking that. I don't know what you've been doing to yourself, girl, and you don't need to tell me—but you need to stop doing it."

"I wish I could." But her heart had risen the moment she walked through the familiar door, and her sense of agitation did subside—though it was far from disappearing. The wine helped, though.

The Abernathys helped more. Just the sense of being with friends, of not being alone with the kids and the fear and uncertainty. She went from wanting to cry to wanting to laugh and back again in the space of seconds, and felt that if Gail and Joe had not been there, she might have had no choice but to go into the bathroom, turn on the shower, and scream into a folded bath towel—her only safety valve in the last few days.

But now there was at least someone to talk to. She didn't know whether Joe could offer anything beyond a sympathetic ear, but at the moment that was worth more to her than anything.

Conversation over dinner was light and kid-oriented, Gail asking Mandy whether she liked Barbies and whether her Barbie had a car, and Joe talking soccer versus baseball—Jem was a hard-core Red Sox fan, being allowed to stay up to ungodly hours to listen to rare radio broadcasts with his mother. Brianna contributed nothing more than the occasional smile and felt the tension slowly leave her neck and shoulders.

It came back, though with less force, when dinner was over and Mandy—half-asleep with her arm in her plate—was carried off to bed by Gail, humming "Jesu, Joy of Man's Desiring" in a voice like a cello. Bree rose to pick up the dirty plates, but Joe waved her back, rising from his chair.

"Leave them, darlin'. Come talk to me in the den. Bring the rest of the wine," he added, then smiled at Jem. "Jem, whyn't you go up and ask Gail can you watch TV in the bedroom?"

Jem had a smudge of spaghetti sauce at the corner of his mouth, and his hair was sticking up on one side in porcupine spikes. He was a little pale from the journey, but the food had restored him and his eyes were bright, alert.

"No, sir," he said respectfully, and pushed back his own chair. "I'll stay with my mam."

"You don't need to do that, honey," she said. "Uncle Joe and I have grown-up things we need to talk about. You—"

"I'm staying."

She gave him a hard look, but recognized instantly, with a combination of horror and fascination, a Fraser male with his mind made up.

His lower lip was trembling, just a little. He shut his mouth hard to stop it and looked soberly from her to Joe, then back.

"Dad's not here," he said, and swallowed. "And neither is Grandda. I'm . . . I'm staying."

She couldn't speak. Joe nodded, though, as soberly as Jem, took a can of Coke from the refrigerator, and led the way to the den. She followed them, clutching the wine bottle and two glasses.

"Bree, darlin'?" Joe turned back for a moment. "Get another bottle from the cupboard over the stove. This is gonna take some talking."

It did. Jemmy was on his second Coke—the question of his going to bed, let alone to sleep, was clearly academic—and the second bottle of wine was one-third down before she'd finished describing the situation—all the situations—and what she thought of doing about them.

"Okay," Joe said, quite casually. "I don't believe I'm saying this, but you need to decide whether to go through some rocks in North Carolina or in Scotland and end up in the eighteenth century either way, is that it?"

"That's . . . most of it." She took a swallow of wine; it seemed to steady her. "But that's the first thing, yes. See, I know where Mama and Da are—were—at the end of 1778, and that's the year we'd go back to, if everything works the way it seems to have worked before. They'll either be back on Fraser's Ridge or on their way there."

Jem's face lightened a little at that, but he didn't say anything. She met his eyes directly.

"I was going to take you and Mandy through the stones on Ocracoke—where we came through before, you remember? On the island?"

"Vroom," he said very softly, and broke into a sudden grin, reliving his first exposure to automobiles.

"Yes," she said, smiling back despite herself. "Then we could go to the Ridge, and I was going to leave you with Grannie and Grandda while I went to Scotland to find Daddy."

Jem's smile faded, and his red brows drew together.

"Pardon my pointing out the obvious," Joe said. "But wasn't there a war going on in 1778?"

"There was," she said tersely. "And, yes, it might be a little bit difficult to get a ship from North Carolina to Scotland, but believe you me, I could do it."

"Oh, I do," he assured her. "It would be easier—and safer, I reckon—than going through in Scotland and searching for Roger with Jem and Mandy to look after at the same time, but—"

"I don't need looking after!"

"Maybe not," Joe told him, "but you got about six years, sixty pounds, and another two feet to grow before you can look after your mama. 'Til you get big enough that nobody can just pick you up and carry you off, she's got to worry about you."

Jem looked as if he wanted to argue the point, but he was at the age where logic did sometimes prevail, and happily this was one of those times. He made a small "mmphm" sound in his throat, which startled Bree, and sat back on the ottoman, still frowning.

"But you can't go to where Grannie and Grandda are," he

pointed out. "'Cuz Dad's not where—I mean when—you thought. He's not in the same time they are."

"Bingo," she said briefly, and, reaching into the pocket of her sweater, carefully withdrew the plastic bag protecting Roger's letter. She handed it to Joe. "Read that."

He whipped his reading glasses out of his own pocket and, with them perched on his nose, read the letter carefully, looked up at her, wide-eyed, then bent his head and read it again. After which he sat quite still for several minutes, staring into space, the letter open on his knee.

At last, he heaved a sigh, folded the letter carefully, and handed it back to her.

"So now it's space *and* time," he said. "You ever watch *Doctor Who* on PBS?"

"All the time," she said dryly, "on the BBC. And don't think I wouldn't sell my soul for a TARDIS."

Jem made the little Scottish noise again, and Brianna looked sideways at him.

"Are you doing that on purpose?"

He looked up at her, surprised. "Doing what?"

"Never mind. When you *are* fifteen, I'm locking you in the cellar."

"What? Why?" he demanded indignantly.

"Because that's when your father and grandfather started getting into real trouble, and evidently you're going to be just like them."

"Oh." He seemed pleased to hear this, and subsided.

"Well, putting aside the possibility of getting hold of a working TARDIS . . ." Joe leaned forward, topping up both glasses of wine. "It's possible to travel farther than you thought, because Roger and this Buck guy just did it. So you think you could do it, too?"

"I've got to," she said simply. "He won't try to come back without Jem, so I have to go find him."

"Do you know *how* he did it? You told me it took gemstones to do it. Did he have, like, a special kind of gem?"

"No." She frowned, remembering the effort of using the kitchen shears to snip apart the old brooch with its scatter of chip-like diamonds. "They each had a few tiny little diamonds—but Roger went through before with a single biggish diamond.

He said it was like the other times we know about; it exploded or vaporized or something—just a smear of soot in his pocket."

"Mmm." Joe took a sip of wine and held it meditatively in his mouth for a moment before swallowing. "Hypothesis one, then: number is more important than size—i.e., you can go farther if you have more stones in your pocket."

She stared at him for a moment, somewhat taken aback.

"I hadn't thought of that," she said slowly. "The first time he tried it, though . . . he had his mother's locket; that had garnets on it. Definitely garnets, plural. But he didn't get through—he was thrown back, on fire." She shuddered briefly, the sudden vision of Mandy flung on the ground, burning . . . She gulped wine and coughed. "So—so we don't know whether he might have gone farther if he *had* gone through."

"It's just a thought," Joe said mildly, watching her. "Now . . . Roger's mentioning Jeremiah here, and it sounds like he means there's somebody besides Jemmy who's got that name. Do you know what he means?"

"I do." A skitter of something between fear and excitement ran down her back with icy little feet, and she took another swallow of wine and a deep breath before telling him about Jerry MacKenzie. The circumstances of his disappearance—and what her mother had told Roger.

"*She* thought he was very likely an accidental traveler. One who—who couldn't get back." She took another quick sip.

"That's my other grandda?" Jemmy asked. His face flushed a little at the thought and he sat forward, hands clutched between his thighs. "If we go where Dad is, will we get to meet him, too?"

"I can't even think about that," she told him honestly, though the suggestion made her insides curl up. Among the million alarming contingencies of the current situation, the possibility of meeting her deceased father-in-law face-to-face was about 999,999th on the list of Things to Be Worried About—but apparently it *was* on the list.

"But what did Roger mean about seeking Jeremiah?" Joe asked, clinging stubbornly to the point.

"We think that's how you . . . steer," Brianna said. "Focusing your thoughts on a particular person who's in the time you want to go to. We don't know that for sure, though," she added, and stifled a small belch. "Each time we—or Mama—did it, it was always two hundred and two years. And it was when Mama went back the first time—though come to think of it," she added, frowning, "she thought it might have been because Black Jack Randall—Daddy's ancestor—was there. He was the first person she met when she came through the stones. She said he looked a lot like Daddy."

"Uh-huh." Joe poured another half glass and stared at it for a moment, as though hypnotized by the soft reddish light glowing in its bowl. "But." He stopped, marshaling his thoughts. "But other people did go farther. This Geillis your mother mentioned, and Buck? Did he—never mind. Roger *and* Buck *did* do it this time, for sure. So it's possible; we just don't know how."

"I was forgetting Geillis," Bree said slowly. She'd seen the woman only once, and very briefly. A tall, slender figure, fair hair flying in the wind of a murderous fire, her shadow thrown onto one of the standing stones, enormous, elongated.

"Now that I think, though . . . I don't believe she had gemstones when she went back. She thought it took . . . er . . . sacrifice." She glanced at Jem, then looked at Joe, lowering her brows with a meaningful look that said, *"Don't ask."* "And fire. And she never came back the other way, though she planned to, with stones." And suddenly a penny that she hadn't known was there dropped. "She told Mama about using stones—not the other way around. So somebody . . . somebody *else* told her."

Joe digested that one for a moment, but then shook his head, dismissing the distraction.

"Huh. Okay, Hypothesis two: focusing your thoughts on a particular person helps you go to where they are. That make sense to you, Jem?" he asked, turning to Jemmy, who nodded.

"Sure. If it's somebody you know."

"Okay. Then—" Joe stopped abruptly, looking at Jem. "If it's somebody you *know*?"

The icy centipede came rippling up Bree's backbone and into her hair, making her scalp contract.

"Jem." Her voice sounded odd to her own ears, husky and half breathless. "Mandy says she can hear you—in her head. Can you . . . hear *her*?" She swallowed, hard, and her voice came clearer. "Can you hear Daddy that way?"

The small red brows drew together in a puzzled frown.

"Sure. Can't you?"

THE DEEP LINE between Uncle Joe's eyebrows hadn't gone away since the night before, Jem saw. He still looked friendly; he nodded at Jem and pushed a cup of hot chocolate across the counter to him, but his eyes kept going back to Mam, and every time they did, the line got deeper.

Mam was buttering Mandy's toast. Jem thought she wasn't as worried as she had been, and felt a little better himself. He'd slept all night, for the first time in a long time, and he thought maybe Mam had, too. No matter how tired he was, he usually woke up every couple of hours, listening out for noises, and then listening harder to be sure Mandy and Mam were still breathing. He had nightmares where they weren't.

"So, Jem," Uncle Joe said. He put down his coffee cup and patted his lips with a paper napkin left over from Halloween; it was black with orange jack-o'-lanterns and white ghosts on it. "Um . . . how far can you . . . er . . . you know, when your sister's not with you?"

"How far?" Jem said uncertainly, and looked at Mam. It hadn't ever occurred to him to wonder.

"If you went in the living room right now," Uncle Joe said, nodding at the door. "Could you tell she was in here, even if you didn't know she was in here?"

"Yeah. I mean, yes, sir. I think so." He stuck his finger in the hot chocolate: still too hot to drink. "When I was in the tunnel, in the train—I knew she was . . . somewhere. It's not like science fiction or anything, I mean," he added, trying to explain. "Not like X-rays or phasers or like that. I just . . ." He struggled for an explanation and finally jerked his head at Mam, who was staring at him with a serious kind of look that bothered him a little. "I mean, if you closed your eyes, you'd still know Mam was here, wouldn't you? It's like that."

Mam and Uncle Joe looked at each other.

"Want toast?" Mandy thrust her half-gnawed piece of buttered toast at him. He took it and had a bite; it was good, squidgy white bread, not the home-baked brown kind Mam made, with gritty bits in it.

"If he could hear her—sense her—from the tunnel while she was at home, he can do it for a good long way," Mam said. "But I don't know for sure that she *was* at home then—I was driving all over with her, looking for Jem. And Mandy could sense him while we were in the car that night. But—" Now *her* eyebrows went together. He didn't like seeing a line there. "She was telling me she was getting colder, when we drove toward Inverness, but I don't know if she meant she couldn't hear him at all, or . . ."

"I don't think I can feel her when I'm at school," Jem said, anxious to be helpful. "But I'm not sure, 'cause I don't think about her at school."

"How far's the school from your place?" Uncle Joe asked. "You want a Pop-Tart, princess?"

"Yes!" Mandy's buttery round face lighted up, but Jem glanced at Mam. Mam looked as if she wanted to kick Uncle Joe under the counter for a second, but then she glanced down at Mandy and her face went all soft.

"All right," she said, and Jem felt a fluttery, excited sort of feeling in his middle. Mam was telling Uncle Joe how far the school was, but Jem wasn't paying attention. They were going to do it. They were really going to do it!

Because the only reason Mam would let Mandy eat Pop-Tarts without a fuss was because she figured she'd never get to eat another one.

"Can I have one, too, Uncle Joe?" he asked. "I like the blueberry ones."

98

THE WALL

HADRIAN'S WALL looked very much as Roger recalled it from a long-ago school trip. A huge thing, standing nearly fifteen feet high and eight feet wide, double stone walls filled with rubble in between, winding off into the distance.

The people were not that much different, either—at least in

terms of speech and livelihood. They raised cattle and goats, and the Northumberland dialect had apparently not developed much since Geoffrey Chaucer's time. Roger and Buck's Highland accents elicited slit-eyed looks of suspicious incomprehension, and they were for the most part reduced to basic gestures and sign language in order to obtain food and—occasionally—shelter.

With a bit of trial and error, Roger did work out an approximate Middle English for *"Hast come here a stranger?"* From the looks of the place—and the looks he and Buck were getting—he would have said the contingency was remote, and so it proved. Three days of walking, and they were still plainly the strangest men anyone near the wall had ever seen.

"Surely a man dressed in RAF uniform would look even more peculiar than we do?" he said to Buck.

"He would," Buck replied logically, "if he was still wearing it."

Roger grunted in chagrin. He hadn't thought of the possibility that Jerry might have discarded his uniform on purpose—or been deprived of it by whomever came across him first.

It was on the fourth day—the wall itself had rather surprisingly changed, being no longer built of stone and rubble but of stacked turves—that they met a man wearing Jerry MacKenzie's flight jacket.

The man was standing at the edge of a half-plowed field, staring morosely into the distance, apparently with nothing on his mind save his hair. Roger froze, hand on Buck's arm, compelling him to look.

"Jesus," Buck whispered, grabbing Roger's hand. "I didn't believe it. That's it! Isn't it?" he asked, turning to Roger, brows raised. "I mean—the way ye described it . . ."

"Yes. It is." Roger felt his throat tighten with excitement—and fear. But there was only the one thing to be done, regardless, and, dropping Buck's hand, he forged through the dead grass and scattered rock toward the farmer, if that's what he was.

The man heard them coming and turned casually—then stiffened, seeing them, and looked wildly round for help.

"Eevis!" he shouted, or so Roger thought. Looking over his shoulder, Roger saw the stone walls of a house, evidently built into the wall.

"Put up your hands," Roger said to Buck, throwing up his own, palm out, to show his lack of threat. They advanced slowly, hands up, and the farmer stood his ground, though watching them as though they might explode if they got too close.

Roger smiled at the man and elbowed Buck in the ribs to make him do likewise.

"Gud morn," he said clearly and carefully. "Hast cum a stranger here?" He pointed to his own coat—and then to the flight jacket. His heart was thumping hard; he wanted to knock the man over and strip it off his back, but that wouldn't do.

"Naow!" said the man quickly, backing away, holding on to the edges of the jacket. "Begone!"

"We mean ye no harm, daftie," Buck said, in as conciliating a tone as he could manage. He patted the air in a soothing manner. "Kenst du dee mann . . . ?"

"What the bloody hell is *that*?" Roger asked, out of the side of his mouth. "Ancient Norse?"

"I don't know, but I heard an Orkneyman say it once. It means—"

"I can tell what it means. Does this look like Orkney to you?"

"No. But if you can tell what it means, maybe he can, too, aye?"

"Naow!" the man repeated, and bellowed, "EEVIS!" again. He began to back away from them.

"Wait!" said Roger. "Look." He fumbled quickly in his pocket and withdrew the little oilcloth packet holding his father's identity disks. He pulled them out, dangling them in the chilly breeze. "See? Where is the man who wore these?"

The farmer's eyes bulged, and he turned and ran clumsily, his clogs hindering him through the clods of the field, shouting, "Eevis! Hellup!" and several other, less comprehensible things.

"Do we want to wait for Eevis to turn up?" Buck said, shifting uneasily. "He may not be friendly."

"Yes, we do," Roger said firmly. The blood was high in his chest and face, and he flexed his hands nervously. Close. They were so close—and yet . . . his spirits went from exhilaration to plunging fear and back within seconds. It hadn't escaped him that there was a strong possibility that Jerry MacKenzie had been killed for that jacket—a possibility that seemed much more likely in view of their interlocutor's precipitate flight.

The man had disappeared into a windbreak of small trees, beyond which some sheds were visible. Perhaps Eevis was a stockman or dairyman?

Then the barking started.

Buck turned to look at Roger.

"Eevis, ye think?"

"Jesus Christ!"

A huge, broad-headed, barrel-chested brown dog with a broad, toothy jaw to match came galloping out of the trees and made for them, its proprietor bringing up the rear with a spade.

They ran for it, circling the house with Eevis on their heels, baying for blood. The broad green bank of the wall loomed up in front of Roger and he leapt for it, jamming the toes of his boots into the turf and scrabbling with fingers, knees, elbows—and likely his teeth, too. He hurled himself over the top and bounced down the far side, landing with a tooth-rattling thud. He was fighting to draw breath when Buck landed on top of him.

"Shit," his ancestor said briefly, rolling off him. "Come on!" He jerked Roger to his feet and they ran, hearing the farmer shouting curses at them from the top of the wall.

They found refuge in the lee of a crag a few hundred yards beyond the wall and collapsed there, gasping.

"The Emp . . . Emperor Had . . . rian kent what the blood . . . y hell he . . . was about," Roger managed, at last.

Buck nodded, wiping sweat from his face. "No . . . very hospitable," he wheezed. He shook his head and gulped air. "What . . . now?"

Roger patted the air, indicating the need for oxygen before he could formulate ideas, and they sat quiet for a bit, breathing. Roger tried to be logical about it, though spikes of adrenaline kept interfering with his thought processes.

One: Jerry MacKenzie had been here. That was all but certain; it was beyond the bounds of probability that there should be *two* displaced travelers wearing RAF flight jackets.

Two: he wasn't here now. Could that be safely deduced? No, Roger concluded reluctantly, it couldn't. He *might* have traded the jacket to Eevis's owner for food or something, in which case he'd likely moved on. But if that were the case, why had the farmer not simply said so, rather than setting the dog on them?

And if he'd stolen the jacket . . . either Jerry was dead and buried somewhere nearby—that thought made Roger's stomach clench and the hairs prickle on his jaw—or he'd been assaulted and stripped but perhaps had escaped.

All right. If Jerry was here, he was dead. And if so, the only way of finding out was to subdue the dog and then beat the information out of Eevis's owner. He didn't feel quite up to it at the moment.

"He's not here," Roger said hoarsely. His breathing was still hard, but regular now.

Buck gave him a quick look, but then nodded. There was a long streak of muddy green down his cheek, smeared moss from the wall that echoed the green of his eyes.

"Aye. What next, then?"

The sweat was cooling on Roger's neck; he wiped it absently with the end of the scarf that had somehow made it over the wall with him.

"I've got an idea. Given the reaction of our friend there"—he nodded in the direction of the farmstead, invisible beyond the green mass of the wall—"I'm thinking that asking for a stranger might be not the wisest thing. But what about the stones?"

Buck blinked at him in incomprehension.

"Stones?"

"Aye. Standing stones. Jerry did travel, we ken that much. What're the odds he came through a circle? And if so . . . they're likely none so far away. And folk wouldn't be threatened, I think, by two dafties asking after stones. If we find the place he likely came through, then we can start to cast out from there and ask at the places nearest to the stones. Cautiously."

Buck tapped his fingers on his knee, considering, then nodded.

"A standing stone isna like to bite the arses out of our breeks. All right, then; let's go."

99

RADAR

Boston
December 9, 1980

JEM FELT NERVOUS. Mam and Uncle Joe were both trying to act as if everything was okay, but even Mandy could tell something was up; she was squirming around in the backseat of Uncle Joe's Cadillac like she had ants in her pants, pulling up her buttoned sweater over her head so her black curls fluffed out of the neckhole like something boiling over.

"Sit *still,*" he muttered to her, but he didn't expect her to, and she didn't.

Uncle Joe was driving, and Mam had a map open in her lap.

"What are you doing, Mandy?" Mam said absently. She was making marks on the map with a pencil.

Mandy unbuckled her seat belt and popped up on her knees. She'd pulled her arms out of her sweater so they flopped around, and now just her face was poking out of the neckhole.

"I'm an ottopus!" she said, and shook herself so the sweater's arms danced. Jem laughed, in spite of himself. So did Mam, but she waved Mandy back down.

"Octopus," she said. "And put your seat belt back on right now. *Octo* means eight in Latin," she added. "Octopuses have eight legs. Or arms, maybe."

"You've only got four," Jem said to Mandy. "Does that make her a tetrapus, Mam?"

"Maybe." But Mam had gone back to her map. "The Common, do you think?" she said to Uncle Joe. "It's a little more than a quarter mile across the longest axis. And we could go down into the Public Garden, if . . ."

"Yeah, good idea. I'll let you and Jem off on Park Street, then drive along Beacon to the end of the Common and back around."

It was cold and cloudy, with just a few flakes of snow in the air. He remembered Boston Common and was kind of glad to see it again, even with the trees leafless and the grass brown and dead. There were still people there; there always were, and their winter hats and scarves looked happy, all different colors.

The car stopped on Park Street, across from the tourist trolleys that stopped every twenty minutes. Dad had taken them all on one once—one of the orange ones, with the open sides. It had been summer then.

"Do you have your mittens, sweetheart?" Mam was already out on the sidewalk, peering through the window. "You stay with Uncle Joe, Mandy—just for a few minutes."

Jem got out and stood with Mam on the sidewalk, putting on his mittens while they watched the gray Caddy pull away.

"Close your eyes, Jem," Mam said quietly, and took his hand, squeezing it. "Tell me if you can feel Mandy in your head."

"Sure. I mean, yes. She's there." He hadn't thought of Mandy as a little red light before the business in the tunnel with the train, but now he did. It kind of made it easier to concentrate on her.

"That's good. You can open your eyes if you want to," Mam said. "But keep thinking about Mandy. Tell me if she gets too far away for you to feel."

He could feel Mandy all the way, until the Caddy pulled up next to them again—though she had got a little fainter, then stronger again.

They did it again, with Uncle Joe and Mandy going all the way down to Arlington Street, on the far side of the Public Garden. He could still do it and was getting kind of cold and bored, standing there on the street.

"She can hear him fine," Uncle Joe reported, rolling down his window. "How 'bout you, sport? You hear your sister okay?"

"Yeah," he said patiently. "I mean—I can tell where she is, kind of. She doesn't talk in my head or anything like that." He was glad she didn't. He wouldn't want Mandy chattering away in his head all the time—and he didn't want her listening to his thoughts, either. He frowned at her; he hadn't actually thought of *that* before.

"You can't hear what I'm thinking, can you?" he demanded, shoving his face in the open window. Mandy was riding up front now and looked up at him, surprised. She'd been sucking her thumb, he saw; it was all wet.

"No," she said, kind of uncertainly. He could see she was sort of scared by this. So was he, but he figured he wouldn't let her—or Mam—know that.

"That's good," he said, and patted her on the head. She hated being patted on the head and swiped at him with a ferocious snarl. He stepped back out of reach and grinned at her.

"If we have to do it again," he said to his mother, "maybe Mandy can stay with you, and I'll go with Uncle Joe?"

Mam glanced uncertainly at him, then at Mandy, but seemed to get what he was really saying and nodded, opening the door for Mandy to bounce out, relieved.

Uncle Joe hummed softly to himself as they turned around, went right, and headed down past the big theater and the Freemasons' building. Jem could see Uncle Joe's knuckles showing through his skin, though, where he was clutching the wheel.

"You nervous, sport?" Uncle Joe said, as they passed the Frog Pond. It was drained for the winter; it looked sort of sad.

"Uh-huh." Jem swallowed. "Are you?"

Uncle Joe glanced at him, kind of startled, then smiled as he turned back to keep his eyes on the road.

"Yeah," he said softly. "But I think it's gonna be okay. You'll take good care of your mom and Mandy, and you'll find your dad. You'll be together again."

"Yeah," Jem said, and swallowed again.

They drove in silence for a little bit, and the snow made little scratchy noises on the windshield, like salt being shaken on the glass.

"Mam and Mandy are gonna be pretty cold," Jem ventured.

"Yeah, this'll be our last try today," Uncle Joe assured him. "Still got her? Mandy?"

He hadn't been paying attention; he'd been thinking about the stone circles. And the thing in the tunnel. And Daddy. His stomach hurt.

"No," he said blankly. "No! I can't feel her!" The idea suddenly panicked him and he stiffened in his seat, pushing back with his feet. "Drive back!"

"Right away, pal," Uncle Joe said, and made a U-turn right

in the middle of the street. "Gloucester Street. Can you remember that name? We need to tell your mom, so she can work out the distance."

"Uh-huh," Jem said, but he wasn't really listening to Uncle Joe. He was listening hard for Mandy. He'd never thought about it at all before this, never paid any attention to whether he could sense her or not. But now it was important, and he balled up his fists and shoved one into his middle, under his ribs, where the hurt was.

Then there she was, just as though she'd always been there, like one of his toenails or something, and he let his breath out in a gasp that made Uncle Joe look sharply at him.

"You got her again?"

Jem nodded, feeling inexpressible relief. Uncle Joe sighed and his big shoulders relaxed, too.

"Good," he said. "Don't let go."

BRIANNA PICKED UP Esmeralda the rag doll from the floor of the Abernathys' guest room and tucked her carefully in next to Mandy. *Four miles*. They'd spent the morning driving round Boston in circles, and now they knew roughly how far the kids' mutual radar went. Jem could sense Mandy at a little over a mile, but she could sense him at nearly four. Jem could sense Brianna, too, but only vaguely and only for a short distance; Mandy could sense her mother almost as far as she could detect Jem.

She should write that down in the guide, she thought, but she'd spent the afternoon in frenzied arrangements, and right now the effort of finding a pencil felt like searching for the source of the Nile or climbing Kilimanjaro. *Tomorrow.*

The thought of tomorrow jolted her out of her exhausted torpor with a zap of adrenaline. Tomorrow, it would start.

They'd talked, after the kids had gone to bed. She and Joe, with Gail listening in the corner, the whites of her eyes showing now and then, but saying not a word.

"It has to be Scotland," she'd explained. "It's December; ships can't sail until the springtime. If we crossed in North Carolina, we couldn't travel from the colonies before April and wouldn't get to Scotland before the summer. And putting aside the fact that I know what ocean travel in the eighteenth century is like and I wouldn't do that with children unless the alternative was being shot . . . I can't wait that long."

She'd taken a gulp of wine and swallowed, but the knot in her throat didn't go down, any more than it had with the last half-dozen swallows. *Anything could happen to him in six months. Anything.* "I—have to find him."

The Abernathys glanced at each other, and Gail's hand touched Joe gently on the knee.

"Of course you do," she said. "You sure about Scotland, though? What about the people that tried to take Jem from you? Won't they be waiting, if you go back?"

Bree laughed—shakily, but a laugh.

"Another reason to go right away," she said. "In the eighteenth century, I can stop looking over my shoulder."

"You haven't seen anybody—" Joe started, frowning, but she shook her head.

"Not in California. And not here. But I keep watching." She'd taken a few other precautions, too, things she'd recalled from her father's brief—and discreet—memoir of his World War II experiences, but no need to go into those.

"And you have some idea how to keep the kids safe in Scotland?" Gail was perched uneasily on the edge of her seat, as though wanting to spring up and go check on the kids. Brianna knew the feeling.

She sighed and wiped a straggle of hair out of her eye.

"There are two people—well, three—there that I think I can trust."

"You think," Joe echoed, sounding skeptical.

"The only people I *know* I can trust are right here," she said simply, and lifted her wineglass to them. Joe looked away and cleared his throat. Then he glanced at Gail, who nodded at him.

"We'll go with you," he said firmly, turning back to Bree. "Gail can mind the kids, and I can make sure nobody bothers you 'til you're set to go."

She bit her lip to quell the rising tears.

"No," she said, then cleared her own throat hard, to kill the quaver in her voice—caused as much by the vision of the two Drs. Abernathy strolling the streets of Inverness as by gratitude. It wasn't that there were *no* black people in the Highlands of Scotland, but they were sufficiently infrequent as to cause notice.

"No," she repeated, and took a deep breath. "We'll go to Edinburgh to start; I can get the things we need there, without attracting attention. We won't go up to the Highlands until everything is ready—and I'll only get in touch with my friends there at the last minute. There won't be time for anyone else to realize we're there, before we—before we go . . . through."

That one word, "through," hit her like a blow in the chest, freighted as it was with memory of the howling void that lay between now and then. Between herself and the kids—and Roger.

The Abernathys hadn't given up easily—or altogether; she was sure there would be another attempt at breakfast—but she had faith in her own stubbornness and, pleading exhaustion, had escaped from their kind worries in order to be alone with her own.

She *was* exhausted. But the bed she'd share with Mandy didn't draw her. She needed just to be alone for a bit, to decompress before sleep would come. She could hear going-to-bed noises on the floor below; taking off her shoes, she padded silently down to the first floor, where a light had been left on in the kitchen and another at the end of the hallway by the den, where Jem had been put to bed on the big couch.

She turned to go and check on him, but her attention was diverted by a familiar metallic *chunk!* The kitchen had a pocket door, slid half across. She stepped up to it and glanced through the opening, to discover Jem standing on a chair next to the counter, reaching to pull a Pop-Tart out of the toaster.

He looked up, wide-eyed at the sound of her step, held the hot pastry for a second too long, and dropped it as it burned his fingers.

"Ifrinn!"

"Don't say that," she told him, coming to retrieve the fallen tart. "We're about to go where people would understand it. Here—do you want some milk with that?"

He hesitated for an instant, surprised, then hopped down like a towhee, both feet together, and landed with a light thud on the tiled floor. "I'll get it. You want some, too?" Suddenly, nothing on earth sounded better than a hot blueberry Pop-Tart with melting white icing and a glass of cold milk. She nodded and broke the hot tart in two, putting each half on a paper towel.

"Couldn't sleep?" she finally said, after they'd eaten their snack in companionable silence. He shook his head, red hair ruffled up in porcupine spikes.

"Want me to read you a story?" She didn't know what made her say that; he was much too old to be read to, though he was always somewhere nearby when she read to Mandy. He gave her a jaundiced look, but then, surprisingly, nodded and scampered up to the third floor, coming back with the new copy of *Animal Nursery Tales* in hand.

He didn't want to lie down right away but sat very close to her on the sofa while she read, her arm round his shoulders and his weight growing warm and heavy against her side as his breathing slowed.

"My dad used to read to me if I woke up and couldn't go back to sleep," she said softly, turning the last page. "Grandpa Frank, I mean. It was a lot like this; everything quiet." And themselves cozy and bonelessly content, alone together in a puddle of warm yellow light, with the night far away.

She felt Jem's sleepy interest rise.

"Was he like Grandda? Grandpa Frank?" She'd told the kids little things about Frank Randall, not wanting him to be forgotten, but she knew he'd never be much more than a faint ghost beside the vivid warmth of their other grandfather—the grandfather they might have back. She felt a sudden small tearing in her heart, a vivid second of understanding for her mother.

Oh, Mama . . .

"He was different," she said softly, her mouth brushing his bright hair. "He was a soldier, though—they had that in common. And he was a writer, a scholar—like Daddy. All of them were—are—alike, though: they'd all take care of people. It's what a good man does."

"Oh." She could feel him falling asleep, struggling to keep a hold on consciousness, the dreams beginning to walk through his waking thoughts. She eased him down into the nest of blankets and covered him, smoothing the cowlick on the crest of his head.

"Could we see him?" Jem said suddenly, his voice drowsy and soft.

"Daddy? Yes, we'll see him," she promised, making her own voice solid with confidence.

"No, *your* daddy . . ." he said, his eyes half open, glazed with sleep. "If we go through the stones, could we see Grandpa Frank?"

Her mouth dropped open, but she still hadn't found an answer when she heard him start to snore.

100

BE THOSE THY BEASTS?

WHILE IT WAS undeniably true that standing stones didn't bite, Roger thought, that didn't mean they weren't dangerous.

It had taken them only a day and a half to find the stone circle. He'd made a quick sketch of standing stones on the back of his hand with a bit of charcoal, to assist communication, and it had worked surprisingly well. While the scattered people they'd found had regarded them with immense curiosity—and not a few private glances accompanied by whirling motions of the forefinger beside the head—no one had found the visitors more than odd, and everyone had known where the stones were.

They'd come across a tiny village, in fact—consisting of a church, a public house, a smithy, and several houses—where the last household they'd approached had even sent one of their younger sons along to guide Buck and Roger to their goal.

And there they were now: a scatter of stumpy, lichened, wind-scored pillars beside a shallow lake filled with reeds. Ageless, harmless, part of the landscape—and the sight of them filled Roger with a fear that shivered as coldly over his skin as though he stood there naked to the wind.

"Can ye hear them?" Buck muttered under his breath, his own eyes fixed on the stones.

"No," Roger muttered back. "Can you?"

"I hope not." But Buck shuddered suddenly, as though something had walked across his grave.

"Be those thy be-asts?" the boy asked, grinning at Roger. He pointed at the stones, explaining—Roger thought—the local legend that the stones were in fact faery cattle, frozen in place when their drover had too much drink betaken and fell into the lake.

"Sooth," the boy assured them solemnly, making a cross over his heart. "Mester Hacffurthe found es whip!"

"When?" Buck asked sharply. "And where liveth Mester Hacffurthe?"

A week ago, maybe twa, said the boy, waving a hand to indicate that the date was not important. And he would take them to Mester Hacffurthe, if they liked to see the thing.

Despite his name, Mester Hacffurthe proved to be a slight, light-haired young man, the village cobbler. He spoke the same impenetrable Northumbrian dialect, but with some effort and the helpful intervention of the boy—whose name, he said, was Ridley—their desire was made clear, and Hacffurthe obligingly fetched the faery whip out from under his counter, laying it gingerly before them.

"Oh, Lord," Roger said at sight of it—and, with a raised brow at Hacffurthe to ask permission, touched the strip carefully. A machine-woven, tight-warped strip some three inches wide and two feet long, its taut surface gleaming even in the dim light of the cobbler's shop. Part of the harness of an RAF flier. They had the right stones, then.

Careful questioning of Mr. Hacffurthe, though, elicited nothing else helpful. He had found the faery lash lying in the shallows of the lake, washing to and fro among the reeds, but had seen nothing else of note.

Roger noticed, though, that Ridley twitched slightly when Mr. Hacffurthe said this. And after they had left the cobbler's house, he paused at the edge of the village, hand in his pocket.

"I thank 'ee, Master Ridley," he said, and pulled out a broad tuppenny piece that made the boy's face light up. Roger put it into Ridley's hand, but, when the boy would have turned to go, laid his own hand on the lad's arm.

"One thing more, Master Ridley," he said, and, with a glance at Buck, drew out the identity disks.

Ridley jerked in Roger's grasp, his round face going pale. Buck made a small sound of satisfaction and took Ridley by his other arm.

"Tell us about the man," Buck suggested pleasantly. "And I might not break thy neck."

Roger shot Buck a glance of annoyance, but the threat was effective. Ridley gulped as though he'd swallowed a mushroom whole, but then began to talk. Between Ridley's dialect and his distress, the tale took some time to piece together, but at last Roger was fairly sure they had the gist of it.

"Let him go," he said, letting go of Ridley himself. He groped in his pocket and came out with another copper penny, which he offered to the boy. Ridley's face flexed between fear and outrage, but after a moment's hesitation, he snatched the penny and made off, glancing over his shoulder as he ran.

"He'll tell his family," Buck observed. "We'd best hurry."

"We had. But not on that account—it's getting dark." The sun was very low, a brilliant band of yellow light showing at the foot of a cold ochre sky. "Come on. We need to take the direction while we can."

So far as Roger had been able to follow Ridley's story, the strangely dressed man (some said he was a faerie, some thought him a northerner, though there was confusion as to whether this meant a Scot, a Norseman, or something else) had had the ill luck to show up at a farm two or three miles from the stones, where he had been set upon by the inhabitants, these being an antisocial clan called Wad.

The Wads had taken everything of apparent value off the man, beaten him, and tossed him into a ravine—one of the Wads had boasted of it to a drover passing through, who had mentioned the stranger in the village.

The village had of course been interested—but not sufficiently so as to go looking for the man. When Hacffurthe the cobbler had found the peculiar strip of cloth, though, rumors had started to fly thick and fast. Excitement had reached a higher pitch this very afternoon, when one of Mester Quarton's cowmen had come into the village to have a boil lanced by Granny Racket and revealed that a stranger with incomprehensible speech had tried to steal a pie from Missus Quarton's sill and was even now held captive whilst Mester Quarton thought what best to do with him.

"What *might* he do?" Roger had asked. Ridley had pushed out his lips portentously and shaken his head.

"Might kill 'un," he said. "Might take 'un's hand off. Mester Quarton don't hold with thievin'."

And that—aside from a vague direction regarding the location of the Quarton farm—was that.

"This side of the wall, two miles west and a little south, below a ridge and along the stream," Roger said grimly, lengthening his stride. "If we can find the stream before full dark . . ."

"Aye." Buck fell in beside him as they turned toward where they'd left the horses. "Suppose Quarton keeps a dog?"

"Everybody here keeps a dog."

"Oh, God."

101

JUST ONE CHANCE

THERE WAS NO MOON. Undeniably a good thing, but it had its drawbacks. The farmhouse and its outbuildings lay in a pocket of darkness so profound that they mightn't have known it was there, had they not seen it before the light was quite gone. They'd waited, though, for full dark and the dousing of the dim candlelight inside the house, and then an extra half hour or so to ensure that the inhabitants—and their dogs—were well asleep.

Roger was carrying the dark lantern, but with the slide still closed; Buck ran into something lying on the ground, let out a startled cry, and fell headlong over it. The something proved to be a large sleeping goose, which let out a startled *whonk!* somewhat louder than Buck's cry, and promptly set about him with beak and thrashing wings. There was a sharp, inquiring bark in the distance.

"Hush!" Roger hissed, coming to his ancestor's aid. "Ye'll wake the dead, let alone them in the house." He dropped his cloak over the goose, which shut up and began waddling around in confusion, a mobile heap of dark cloth. Roger clapped a hand to his mouth, but couldn't help snorting through his nose.

"Aye, right," Buck whispered, getting to his feet. "If ye think I'm getting your cloak back for ye, think again."

"He'll get out of it soon enough," Roger whispered back. "He's no need of it. Meanwhile, where the devil d'ye think they've got him?"

"Someplace that's got a door ye can bolt." Buck rubbed his palms together, brushing off the dirt. "They'd no keep him in the house, though, would they? It's no that big."

It wasn't. You could have fitted about sixteen farmhouses that size into Lallybroch, Roger thought, and felt a sudden sharp pang, thinking of Lallybroch as it was when he had—he would—own it.

Buck was right, though: there couldn't be more than two rooms and a loft, maybe, for the kids. And given that the neighbors thought Jerry—if it was Jerry—was a foreigner at best, a thief and/or supernatural being at worst, it wasn't likely that the Quartons would be keeping him in the house.

"Did ye see a barn, before the light went?" Buck whispered, changing to Gaelic. He had risen onto his toes, as though that might help him see above the tide of darkness, and was peering into the murk. Dark-adapted as Roger's eyes now were, he could at least make out the squat shapes of the small farm buildings. Corncrib, goat shed, chicken coop, the tousled shape of a hayrick . . .

"No," Roger replied in the same tongue. The goose had extricated itself and gone off making disgruntled small honks; Roger bent and retrieved his cloak. "Small place; they likely haven't more than an ox or a mule for the plowing, if that. I smell stock, though . . . manure, ken?"

"Kine," Buck said, heading abruptly off toward a square-built stone structure. "The cow byre. That'll have a bar to the door."

It did. And the bar was in its brackets.

"I don't hear any kine inside," Buck whispered, drawing close. "And the smell's old."

It was near-on winter. Maybe they'd had to slaughter the cow—or cows; maybe they'd driven them to market. But, cow or no, there was *something* inside; he heard a shuffling noise and what might have been a muffled curse.

"Aye, well, there's something inside." Roger raised the dark lantern, groping for the slide. "Get the bar, will you?"

But before Buck could reach for the bar, a shout of "Hoy!" came from inside, and something fell heavily against the door. "Help! Help me! Help!"

The voice spoke English, and Buck changed back at once. "Will ye for God's sake hush your noise?" he said to the man inside, annoyed. "Ye want to have them all down on us? Here, then, bring the light closer," he said to Roger, and drew the bar with a small grunt of effort.

The door swung open as Buck set down the bar, and light shot out of the lantern's open slide. A slightly built young man with flyaway fair hair—*the same color as Buck's,* Roger thought—blinked at them, dazzled by the light, then closed his eyes against it.

Roger and Buck glanced at each other for an instant, then, with one accord, stepped into the byre.

He is, Roger thought. *It's him. I know it's him. God, he's so young! Barely more than a boy.* Oddly, he felt no burst of dizzying excitement. It was a feeling of calm certainty, as though the world had suddenly righted itself and everything had fallen into place. He reached out and touched the man gently on the shoulder.

"What's your name, mate?" he said softly, in English.

"MacKenzie, J. W.," the young man said, shoulders straightening as he drew himself up, sharp chin jutting. "Lieutenant, Royal Air Force. Service Number—" He broke off, staring at Roger, who belatedly realized that, calmness or no, he was grinning from ear to ear. "What's funny?" Jerry MacKenzie demanded, belligerent.

"Nothing," Roger assured him. "Er . . . glad—glad to see you, that's all." His throat was tight, and he had to cough. "Have ye been here long?"

"No, just a few hours. Ye wouldn't have any food on ye, I don't suppose?" He looked hopefully from one man to the other.

"We do," Buck said, "but this isna the time to stop for a bite, aye?" He glanced over his shoulder. "Let's be off."

"Aye. Aye, we should." But Roger spoke automatically, unable to stop looking at J. W. MacKenzie, RAF, aged twenty-two.

"Who *are* you?" Jerry asked, staring back. "Where d'ye come from? God knows ye're not from here!"

Roger exchanged a quick look with Buck. They hadn't planned what to say; Roger hadn't been willing to jinx the enterprise by thinking that they'd really find Jerry MacKenzie, and as for Buck—

"Inverness," Buck said abruptly. He sounded gruff.

Jerry's eyes flicked back and forth between them, and he caught Roger's sleeve.

"Ye know what I mean!" he said, and gulped air, bracing himself. *"When?"*

Roger touched Jerry's hand, cold and dirty, the fingers long like his own. The question caught at his throat and thickened his voice too much to speak.

"A lang way from you," Buck said quietly, and for the first time, Roger caught a note of desolation in his voice. "From now. Lost."

That struck him to the heart. He'd truly forgotten their situation for a little, driven by the urgency of finding this man. But Buck's answer made Jerry's face, already drawn with hunger and strain, go white under the dirt.

"Jesus," Jerry whispered. "Where are we now? And—and when?"

Buck stiffened. Not at Jerry's question, but at a noise from outside. Roger didn't know what had made it, but it wasn't the wind. Buck made a low, urgent noise in his throat, shifting.

"I think it's part of Northumbria now," Roger said. "Look, there's no time. We have to go, before someone hears—"

"Aye, right. Let's go, then." Jerry had a filthy silk scarf round his neck; he tugged the ends straight and shoved them into his shirt.

The air outside was wonderful after the smells of the cow byre, fresh with new-turned earth and dying heather. They made their way as quickly as they could through the yard, skirting the farmhouse. Jerry was lame, he saw, limping badly, and Roger took his arm to help. A shrill yap came from the darkness, some distance away—then another bark, in a deeper tone.

Roger hastily licked a finger and held it up to gauge the

direction of the breeze. A dog barked again, and another echoed it.

"This way," he whispered to his companions, tugging Jerry's arm. He led them away from the house as fast as possible, trying to keep his bearings, and they found themselves stumbling through a plowed field, dirt clods crumbling under their boots.

Buck stumbled and swore under his breath. They lurched from furrow to ridge, half-legged and clumsy, Roger clinging to Jerry's arm to keep him upright; one of Jerry's legs seemed gammy and wouldn't take his weight. *He's been wounded. I saw the medal. . . .*

Then the dogs began to bark, voices suddenly clear—and much closer.

"Jesus." Roger stopped for an instant, breathing hard. Where the bloody hell was the wood they'd hidden in? He'd swear they'd been heading for it, but—the beam from the lantern swung crazily, showing meaningless patches of field. He shut the slide; they'd be better off without it.

"This way!" Buck lurched away and Roger and Jerry followed perforce, hearts thumping. Christ, it sounded like a half-dozen dogs at least had been let loose, all barking. And was that a voice, calling to the dogs? Yes, it bloody was. He couldn't understand a word, but the meaning was as clear as ice water.

They ran, stumbling and panting. Roger couldn't tell where they were; he was following Buck. He dropped the lantern at one point; it fell over with a clank and he heard the oil inside gurgle out of its reservoir. With a soft *whoosh,* it flowered into brilliant flame.

"Shit!" They ran. It didn't matter where, what direction. Just away from the burning beacon and the irate voices—more than one now.

Suddenly they were into a scrim of trees—the low, wind-crabbed grove they'd lurked in earlier. But the dogs were on their track, barking eagerly, and they didn't linger but fought their way through the brush and out again, up a steep hill turfed with heather. Roger's foot sank through the spongy growth into a puddle, soaking him to the ankle, and he nearly lost his balance. Jerry set his feet and yanked Roger upright, then lost his own balance when his knee gave way; they clung together, wobbling precariously for an instant, then Roger lurched forward again and they were out of it.

He thought his lungs would burst, but they kept going—not running any longer; you couldn't run up a hill like this—slogging, planting one foot after another, after another . . . Roger began to see bursts of light at the edges of his vision; he tripped, staggered, and fell, and was hauled to his feet by Jerry.

They were all three half sopping and smeared head to foot with mud and heather scratchings when they lurched at last to the crest of the hill and stopped for a moment, swaying and gasping for air.

"Where . . . are we going?" Jerry wheezed, using the end of his scarf to wipe his face.

Roger shook his head, still short of breath—but then caught the faint gleam of water.

"We're taking you . . . back. To the stones by the lake. Where . . . you came through. Come on!"

They pelted down the far side of the hill, headlong, almost falling, now exhilarated by the speed and the thought of a goal.

"How . . . did you find me?" Jerry gasped, when at last they hit bottom and stopped for breath.

"Found your tags," Buck said, almost brusque. "Followed their trail back."

Roger put a hand to his pocket, about to offer them back—but didn't. It had struck him, like a stone to the middle of his chest, that, having found Jerry MacKenzie against substantial odds, he was about to part from him, likely forever. And that was only if things went *well*. . . .

His father. *Dad?* He couldn't think of this young man, white-faced and lame, nearly twenty years his junior, as his father—not the father he'd imagined all his life.

"Come on." Buck took Jerry's arm now, nearly holding him up, and they began to forge their way across the dark fields, losing their way and finding it again, guided by the light of Orion overhead.

Orion, Lepus. Canis major. He found a measure of comfort in the stars, blazing in the cold black sky. Those didn't change; they'd shine forever—or as close as made no difference—on him and on this man, no matter where each one might end up.

End up. The cold air burned in his lungs. *Bree* . . .

And then he could see them: squatty pillars, no more than blotches on the night, visible only because they showed dark and immobile against the sheet of moving water stirred by the wind.

"Right," he said hoarsely, and, swallowing, wiped his face on his sleeve. "This is where we leave you."

"Ye do?" Jerry panted. "But—but you—"

"When ye came . . . through. Did ye have anything on you? A gemstone, any jewelry?"

"Aye," Jerry said, bewildered. "I had a raw sapphire in my pocket. But it's gone. It's like it—"

"Like it burnt up," Buck finished for him, grim-voiced. "Aye. Well, so?" This last was clearly addressed to Roger, who hesitated. *Bree* . . . No more than an instant, though—he stuck a hand into the leather pouch at his waist, pulled out the tiny oilcloth package, fumbled it open, and pressed the garnet pendant into Jerry's hand. It was faintly warm from his body, and Jerry's cold hand closed over it in reflex.

"Take this; it's a good one. When ye go through," Roger said, and leaned toward him, trying to impress him with the importance of his instructions, "think about your wife, about Marjorie. Think hard; see her in your mind's eye, and walk straight through. Whatever the hell ye do, though, don't think about your son. Just your wife."

"What?" Jerry was gobsmacked. "How the bloody hell do you know my wife's name? And where've ye heard about my son?"

"It doesn't matter," Roger said, and turned his head to look back over his shoulder.

"Damn," said Buck softly. "They're still coming. There's a light."

There was: a single light, bobbing evenly over the ground, as it would if someone carried it. But look as he might, Roger could see no one behind it, and a violent shiver ran over him.

"Thaibhse," said Buck, under his breath. Roger knew that word well enough—spirit, it meant. And usually an ill-disposed one. A haunt.

"Aye, maybe." He was beginning to catch his breath. "And maybe not." He turned again to Jerry. "Either way, ye need to go, man, and now. Remember, think of your wife."

Jerry swallowed, his hand closing tight around the stone.

"Aye. Aye . . . right. Thanks, then," he added awkwardly.

Roger couldn't speak, could give him nothing more than the breath of a smile. Then Buck was beside him, plucking urgently at his sleeve and gesturing at the bobbing light, and they set off, awkward and lumbering after the brief cooldown.

Bree . . . He swallowed, fists clenched. He'd got a stone once, he could do it again. . . . But the greater part of his mind was still with the man they had just left by the lake. He looked over his shoulder and saw Jerry beginning to walk, limping badly but resolute, thin shoulders squared under his pale khaki shirt and the end of his scarf fluttering in the rising wind.

Then it all rose up in him. Seized by an urgency greater than any he'd ever known, he turned and ran. Ran heedless of footing, of dark, of Buck's startled cry behind him.

Jerry heard his footsteps on the grass and whirled round, startled himself. Roger grabbed him by both hands, squeezed them hard enough to make Jerry gasp, and said fiercely, "I love you!"

That was all there was time for—and all he could possibly say. He let go and turned away fast, his boots making a *shoof-shoof* noise in the dry lake grass. He glanced up the hill, but the light had vanished. Likely it had been someone from the farmhouse, satisfied now that the intruders were gone.

Buck was waiting, shrouded in his cloak and holding Roger's; he must have dropped it coming down the hill. Buck shook it out and folded it round Roger's shoulders; Roger's fingers shook, trying to fasten the brooch.

"Why did ye tell him a daft thing like that?" Buck asked, doing it for him. Buck's head was bent, not looking at him.

Roger swallowed hard, and his voice came clear but painful, the words like ice shards in his throat.

"Because he isn't going to make it back. It's the only chance I'll ever have. Come on."

102

POSTPARTUM

THE NIGHT SHIVERED. The *whole* night. The ground and the lake, the sky, the dark, the stars, and every particle of his own body. He was scattered, instantly everywhere and part of everything. And part of *them.* There was one moment of an exaltation too great for fear and then he vanished, his last thought no more than a faint, *I am* . . . voiced more in hope than declaration.

Roger came back to a blurred knowledge of himself, flat on his back under a clear black sky whose brilliant stars seemed pinpoints now, desperately far away. He missed them, missed being part of the night. Missed, with a brief rending sense of desolation, the two men who'd shared his soul for that blazing moment.

The sound of Buck throwing up returned him to a sense of his body. He was lying in cold, wet grass, half soaked, smelling of mud and old manure, chilled to the bone, and bruised in a number of uncomfortable places.

Buck said something horrible in Gaelic and retched again. He was on his hands and knees a few feet away, a blot on the darkness.

"You all right?" Roger croaked, rolling onto his side. He'd remembered, suddenly, the trouble with Buck's heart when they'd made their passage at Craigh na Dun. "If your heart's giving you bother again—"

"If it was, damn-all ye could do about it, is there?" Buck said. He hawked a glob of something nasty into the grass and sat down heavily, wiping his sleeve across his mouth. "Christ, I hate that! Didna ken we'd feel it, this far away."

"Mmphm." Roger sat up slowly. He wondered whether

Buck had felt the same thing he had, but it didn't seem the moment for metaphysical discussion. "He's gone, then."

"Want me to go and make sure of it?" Buck said disagreeably. "God, my head!"

Roger rose to his feet, staggering a little, and went and got Buck under one arm, levering him to his feet.

"Come on," he said. "Let's go find the horses. We'll get away a bit, make a wee camp, get some food into you."

"I'm not hungry."

"*I* bloody am." In fact, he was ravenous. Buck swayed but appeared able to stand on his own. Roger released him and turned briefly to look back at the distant lake and the standing stones. For an instant, he recaptured the sense of being part of them, and then it was gone; the gleaming water and the stones were no more than part of the craggy landscape.

There was no way of knowing what time it was, but the night was still pitch-dark by the time they'd retrieved the horses, made their way to a sheltered spot under a cliff face, found water, made fire, and toasted some bannocks to eat with their dried salt herring.

They didn't talk, both exhausted. Roger pushed away the obvious *"So now what?"* and let his thoughts come randomly as they would; time enough for plans tomorrow.

After a bit, Buck got up abruptly and went off into the dark. He stayed gone for some time, during which time Roger sat gazing into the fire, replaying every moment he'd spent with Jerry MacKenzie in his mind, trying to fix it all. He wished passionately that it had been daylight, that he'd been able to see more of his father's face than the brief glimpses he'd had in the beam of the dark lantern.

Whatever his regrets, though, and the cold knowledge that Jerry wouldn't make it back—or not back to where he'd started from, at least (God, what if he ended up lost in yet another strange time? Was that possible?)—there was the one small, warm thing. He'd said it. And wherever his father had gone, he'd carry that with him.

He wrapped himself in his cloak, lay down by the embers of the fire, and carried it with him into sleep.

WHEN ROGER WOKE in the morning, thickheaded but feeling reasonably okay, Buck had already built up the fire and was frying bacon. The smell of it got Roger into a sitting position, rubbing the last of the sleep from his eyes.

Buck blotted a slice of thick bacon out of the pan with a bannock and handed it to him. He seemed to have recovered from the aftereffects of Jerry's leaving; he was disheveled and unshaven, but clear-eyed, and gave Roger an assessing look.

"Are ye in one piece?" It wasn't asked as a rhetorical question, and Roger nodded, taking the food. He started to say something in reply, but his throat was constricted, and nothing much came out. He cleared his throat hard, but Buck shook his head, indicating that no effort need be made on his part.

"I'm thinking we'll head north again," Buck said, without preamble. "Ye'll want to keep looking for your lad, I suppose—and I want to go to Cranesmuir."

So did Roger, though likely for other reasons. He eyed Buck closely, but his ancestor avoided his eye.

"Geillis Duncan?"

"Wouldn't you?" Buck's tone was belligerent.

"I just did," Roger said dryly. "Aye, of course ye do." This didn't come as a surprise. He chewed his makeshift butty slowly, wondering just how much to tell Buck about Geillis. "Your mother," he began, and cleared his throat again.

When Roger had finished, Buck sat in silence for some time, blinking at the last slice of bacon, drying in the pan.

"Jesus," he said, but not in tones of shock. More a deep interest, Roger thought, with some unease. Buck glanced up at Roger, speculation in his moss-green eyes. "And what d'ye ken about my father, then?"

"More than I can tell ye in a few minutes, and we should be on our way." Roger got up, brushing crumbs off his knees. "I don't want to try explaining our presence to any of those hairy buggers. My Old English isn't what it used to be."

"'Sumer is icumen in,'" Buck said, with a glance at the leafless, wind-blasted saplings precariously rooted in the cliff's crevices. "'Lhude sing cuccu.' Aye, let's go."

103

SOLSTICE

December 19, 1980
Edinburgh, Scotland

A PRACTICAL GUIDE FOR TIME TRAVELERS—
PART II

It's almost time. The winter solstice is day after tomorrow. I keep imagining that I can feel the earth shifting slowly in the dark, tectonic plates moving under my feet and . . . things . . . invisibly lining up. The moon is waxing, nearly a quarter full. Have no idea whether that might be important.

In the morning, we'll take the train to Inverness. I've called Fiona; she'll meet us at the station, and we'll eat and change at her house—then she'll drive us to Craigh na Dun . . . and leave us there. Keep wondering if I should ask her to stay—or at least to come back in an hour, in case one or more of us should still be there, on fire or unconscious. Or dead.

After dithering for an hour, I called Lionel Menzies, too, and asked him to keep an eye on Rob Cameron. Inverness is a small town; there's always the chance that someone will see us coming off the train, or at Fiona's. And word spreads fast. If anything's going to happen, I want warning.

I have these brief lucid moments when everything seems okay and I'm filled with hope, almost trembling with anticipation. Most of the time, I keep thinking I'm insane, and then I'm really shaking.

104

THE SUCCUBUS OF CRANESMUIR

Cranesmuir, Scotland

ROGER AND BUCK stood at the far side of the tiny square in the middle of Cranesmuir, looking up at the fiscal's house. Roger cast a bleak look at the plinth in the middle of the square, with its wooden pillory. At least there were holes for only one miscreant; no crime waves in Cranesmuir.

"The attic, ye said?" Buck was staring intently at the windows of the top story. It was a substantial house, with leaded windows, and even the attic had some, though smaller than the ones in the lower stories. "I can see plants hanging from the ceiling, I think."

"That's what Claire said, aye. That she keeps her . . . her"—the word "lair" came to mind, but he discarded this in favor of—"her surgery up there. Where she makes up her potions and charms." He inspected his cuffs, which were still damp after a hasty sponge bath at the village horse trough to remove the worst stains of travel, and checked to see that his hair ribbon was in order.

The door opened and a man came out—a merchant, maybe, or a lawyer, well dressed, with a warm coat against the mizzle. Buck shifted to one side, peering to get a look before the door closed behind him.

"There's a servant at the door," he reported. "I'll knock, then, and ask if I can see—Mrs. Duncan, is that her name?"

"For the moment, aye," Roger said. He sympathized entirely with Buck's need to see his mother. And in all truth, he was curious to meet the woman himself; she was his five-times great-grandmother—*and* one of the few time travelers he knew about. But he'd also heard enough about her that his feelings were of excitement mixed with considerable unease.

He coughed, fist to his mouth. "D'ye want me to come up with you? If she's to home, I mean."

Buck opened his mouth to reply, then closed it, considered a moment, then nodded.

"Aye, I do," he said quietly. He shot Roger a sidelong look, though, with a gleam of humor in it. "Ye can help keep the conversation going."

"Happy to help," Roger said. "We're agreed, though: ye dinna mean to tell her who ye are. Or what."

Buck nodded again, though his eyes were now fixed on the door, and Roger thought he wasn't attending.

"Aye," he said. "Come on, then," and strode across the square, head up and shoulders squared.

"Mrs. Duncan? Well, I dinna ken, gentlemen," the maid said. "She's to hame the day, but Dr. McEwan's with her just noo."

Roger's heart jumped.

"Is she ill?" Buck asked sharply, and the maid blinked, surprised.

"Och, no. They're takin' tea in the parlor. Would ye like to step in oot the rain and I'll go and see what she says?" She stepped back to let them in, and Roger took advantage of this to touch her arm.

"Dr. McEwan's a friend of ours. Would ye maybe be giving him our names? Roger and William MacKenzie—at his service."

They discreetly shook as much water as possible off their hats and coats, but within a few moments the maid was back, smiling.

"Come up, gentlemen, Mrs. Duncan says, and welcome! Just up the stair there. I'll just be fetching ye a bit o' tea."

The parlor was one floor above, a small room, rather crowded, but warm and colorful. Neither of the men had eyes for the furnishings, though.

"Mr. MacKenzie," Dr. McEwan said, looking surprised but cordial. "And Mr. MacKenzie." He shook hands with them and turned to the woman who had risen from her seat beside the fire. "My dear, allow me to make you acquainted with an erstwhile patient of mine and his kinsman. Gentlemen, Mrs. Duncan."

Roger felt Buck stiffen slightly, and no wonder. He hoped he wasn't staring himself.

Geillis Duncan was maybe not a classic beauty, but that didn't matter. She was certainly good-looking, with creamy-blond hair put up under a lace cap, and—of course—the eyes. Eyes that made him want to close his own and poke Buck in the back to make him do the same, because surely she or McEwan would notice. . . .

McEwan had noticed something, all right, but it wasn't the eyes. He was eyeing Buck with a small frown of displeasure, as Buck took a long stride forward, seized the woman's hand, and boldly kissed it.

"Mrs. Duncan," he said, straightening up and smiling right into those clear green eyes. "Your most humble and obedient servant, ma'am."

She smiled back, one blond brow raised, with an amused look that met Buck's implied challenge—and raised it. Even from where he was standing, Roger felt the snap of attraction between them, sharp as a spark of static electricity. So had McEwan.

"How is your health, Mr. MacKenzie?" McEwan said pointedly to Buck. He pulled a chair into place. "Do sit down and let me examine you."

Buck either didn't hear or pretended not to. He was still holding Geillis Duncan's hand, and she wasn't pulling it away.

"'Twas kind of you to receive us, ma'am," he said. "And certainly we don't mean to disturb your tea. We'd heard of your skill as a healer and meant to call in what you might say is a professional way."

"Professional," she repeated, and Roger was surprised at her voice. It was light, almost girlish. Then she smiled again and the illusion of girlishness vanished. She drew her hand away now, but with a languid air of reluctance, her eyes still fixed on Buck with obvious interest. "Your profession, or mine?"

"Ah, I'm naught but a humble solicitor, ma'am," Buck said, with a gravity so patently mock that Roger wanted to punch him. Then he added, turning to Roger, "and my kinsman here is a scholar and musician. But as ye see, he's suffered a sad accident to his throat, and—"

Now Roger truly wanted to punch him. "I—" he began, but with the cruel whim of fate, his throat chose that moment to constrict, and his protest ended in a gurgle like a rusty pipe.

"We'd heard of ye, mistress, as I said," Buck went on, putting a sympathetic hand on Roger's shoulder and squeezing hard. "And as I say, we wondered . . ."

"Let me see," she said, and came to stand in front of Roger, her face suddenly a few inches from his. Behind her, McEwan was growing red in the face.

"I've seen this man," he told her. "It's a permanent injury, though I was able to offer some small relief. But—"

"Permanent, indeed." She'd undone his neckcloth in seconds and spread his shirt open, her fingers warm and light on his scar. She shifted her gaze and looked directly into his eyes. "But a lucky one, I'd say. You didn't die."

"No," he said, his voice hoarse but at least serviceable again. "I didn't." God, she was unsettling. Claire had described her vividly—but Claire was a woman. She was still touching him, and while her touch was not in any way improper, it was damned intimate.

Buck was growing restive; he didn't like her touching Roger any more than McEwan did. He cleared his throat.

"I wonder, mistress—might ye have any simples, medicines, perhaps? Not only for my kinsman here, but . . . well . . ." He coughed in a way meant to indicate that he harbored more-delicate ailments that he didn't wish to mention before others.

The woman smelled of sex. Very recent sex. It rose from her like incense.

She stayed in front of Roger for a moment, still looking intently into his face, but then smiled and took her hand away, leaving his throat feeling suddenly cool and exposed.

"Of course," she said, switching smile and attention to Buck. "Come up to my wee attic, sir. I'm sure I've something there that will cure what ails ye."

Roger felt gooseflesh ripple across his chest and shoulders, in spite of the good fire on the hearth. Buck and McEwan had both twitched slightly, and she bloody well knew it, though her face was entirely composed. Roger fixed a glare on Buck, willing his ancestor to look at him. Buck didn't but moved to take Geillis's arm, pulling her hand through his elbow. A slow, hot flush burned up the back of his neck.

McEwan made a very small noise in his throat.

Then Buck and Geillis were gone, the sound of their footsteps and animated voices dying away as they climbed the stairs to the attic, leaving Roger and McEwan both silent, each for his own reasons.

ROGER THOUGHT that the good doctor might be about to suffer an apoplexy, if that was the correct medical term for "blow a gasket." Whatever his own feelings about the abrupt departure of Buck and Geillis—and those were vivid—they paled beside the hue of Hector McEwan's face.

The doctor was panting slightly, his complexion puce. Plainly he wanted to follow the errant pair but just as clearly was constrained by the fact that he had no idea what he might conceivably do when he caught up with them.

"It's not what you think," Roger said, commending his soul to God and *hoping* that it wasn't.

McEwan swung round to glare at him. "The devil it's not," he snapped. "You don't know her."

"Plainly not as well as you do, no," Roger said pointedly, and raised one brow.

McEwan said something blasphemous in reply, took up the poker, and stabbed viciously at the smoking bricks of peat in the hearth. He half-turned toward the door, the poker still in his hand, and the look on his face was such that Roger leapt to his feet and grabbed him by the arm.

"Stop, man," he said, keeping his voice pitched as low and evenly as he could, in hopes of soothing McEwan. "Ye'll do yourself no good. Sit down, now. I'll tell ye why it—why he—why the man's interested in her."

"For the same reason every dog in the village is *interested* in a bitch in heat," McEwan said venomously. But he let Roger take the poker from his hand, and while he wouldn't sit down, he did at least take several deep breaths that restored a semblance of calm.

"Aye, tell me, then—for all the good it will do," he said.

It wasn't a situation that allowed for diplomacy or euphemism.

"She's his mother, and he knows it," Roger said bluntly.

Whatever McEwan had been expecting, that wasn't it, and for an instant, Roger was gratified to see the man's face go absolutely blank with shock. Only for an instant, though. It was likely going to be a tricky bit of pastoral counseling, at best.

"Ye know what he is," Roger said, taking the doctor by the arm again and pulling him toward a brocaded wing chair. "Or, rather, what we are. *Cognosco te?*"

"I—" McEwan's voice died, though he opened and closed his mouth a few times, helplessly looking for words.

"Aye, I know," Roger said soothingly. "It's difficult. But ye do know, don't ye?"

"I—yes." McEwan sat down abruptly. He breathed for a moment, blinked once or twice, and looked up at Roger.

"His mother. His *mother*?"

"I have it on good authority," Roger assured him. A thought struck him, though.

"Ah . . . ye did know about her, didn't ye? That she's . . . one of us?"

McEwan nodded. "She's never admitted it. Just—just laughed at me when I told her where I'd come from. And I didn't know for a long time. Not until I—" His lips clamped abruptly into a tight line.

"I'm guessing ye didn't have occasion to heal her of anything," Roger said carefully. "Does she . . . er . . . has it got anything to do with blue light, by chance?"

He was trying hard to avoid the mental picture of Geillis and Dr. McEwan, naked and sweating, both bathed in a faint blue glow. The woman *was* his several-times great-grandmother, whatever else you liked to say about her.

McEwan gave him a bleak look and shook his head.

"Not . . . exactly. She's a very fine herbalist and not bad at diagnosis, but she can't—do that." He twiddled his fingers briefly in illustration, and Roger felt a faint memory of the warmth when McEwan had touched his throat.

The doctor sighed and rubbed a hand over his face.

"No point in evasion, I suppose. I got her with child. And I could—'see' is not quite the right word, but I can't think of a better one. I could see the moment when my . . . seed . . . reached her ovum. The . . . er . . . the fetus. It glowed inside her womb; I could sense it when I touched her."

A certain heat rose in Roger's face. "Forgive me for asking, but—how do you know that happened because she's . . . what she is? Might it not be the case with a normal woman?"

McEwan smiled—very bleakly—at the word "normal," and shook his head.

"I had two children by a woman in Edinburgh, in—in my own time," he said quietly, and looked down at his feet. "That . . . was one of the reasons I didn't try to return."

Roger made a sound in his damaged throat that was meant to be regretful and compassionate, but whether his feelings or his larynx had got the better of him, it emerged as a rather stern "Hrmph!" and McEwan's color began to rise again.

"I know," he said wretchedly. "I don't seek to—to excuse it."

Just as well, Roger thought. *I'd like to see ye try, you—you—* But recriminations would do no one any good just now, and he stifled whatever else he might have said on the subject, instead returning to Geillis.

"Ye said ye got her"—jerking his chin upward, to where the sounds of footsteps and bumpings were audible overhead—"with child. Where *is* the child?"

McEwan drew a long, trembling breath. "I said . . . she is a very fine herbalist . . . ?"

"Jesus, Lord," Roger said. "Did ye know she meant to do it?"

McEwan swallowed audibly, but kept silent.

"My God," Roger said. "My *God.* I know it's not my place to judge you—but if it was, man, you'd burn in hell."

And with that, he went downstairs and out into the streets of Cranesmuir, leaving the lot of them to their own devices.

HE'D MADE SIXTEEN circuits of the village square—it was a small square—before getting a precarious hold on his sense of outrage. He stood in front of the Duncans' front door, fists clenched, taking deep, deliberate breaths.

He had to go back. You didn't walk away from people who were drowning, even if they'd jumped into a quagmire on purpose. And he didn't want to think what might happen if McEwan, left to himself, should be overcome by anguish or fury and rush in on the pair in the attic. He *really* didn't want to think what Buck—or, God forbid, Geillis—might do in that case, and the thought galvanized him.

He didn't trouble knocking. Arthur Duncan was the procurator fiscal; his door was always open. The wee maid poked her head out of an inner door at the sound of his footsteps, but when she saw who he was, she drew it in again, doubtless thinking he'd just stepped out for something.

He nearly sprinted up the stair, a guilty conscience now furnishing him with visions of Hector McEwan hanging from the small chandelier in the parlor, helpless feet kicking in the air.

When he burst in, though, he found McEwan slumped forward in the wing chair, face buried in his hands. He didn't look up at Roger's entrance and wouldn't raise his head even when Roger shook him gently by the shoulder.

"Come on, man," he said gruffly, then cleared his throat. "Ye're still a doctor, aren't ye? Ye're needed."

That made the man look up, startled. His face was mottled with emotion—anger, shame, desolation, lust. Could lust be an emotion? Roger wondered briefly, but dismissed the consideration as academic at the moment. McEwan straightened his shoulders and rubbed both hands hard over his face, as though trying to erase the feelings so plainly displayed there.

"Who needs me?" he said, and rose to his feet with a decent attempt at composure.

"I do," Roger said, and cleared his throat again, with a noise like falling gravel. It felt like gravel, too; strong emotion choked him, literally. "Come outside, aye? I need air, and so do you."

McEwan cast one last look up at the ceiling, where the noises had now ceased, then firmed his lips, nodded, and, taking up his hat from the table, came along.

Roger led the way out of the square and past the last house, then up a cow path, dodging heaps of manure, until they reached a drystane wall that they could sit upon. He sat down himself and gestured to McEwan, who sat obediently. The walk had lent the doctor some semblance of calm, and he turned at once to Roger and spread open his collar—this still flapping loose. Roger felt the ghost of Geillis Duncan's touch on his throat and shivered, but it was cold out, and McEwan took no notice.

The doctor wrapped his fingers loosely around the scar and seemed to listen for a moment, head to one side. Then he pulled his hand back a little and felt delicately up higher with two probing fingers, then lower, a small frown of concentration on his face.

And Roger felt it. The same odd sensation of light warmth. He'd been holding his breath under the doctor's touch, but at this realization he exhaled suddenly—and freely.

"Jesus," he said, and put his own hand to his throat. The word had come freely, too.

"It's better?" McEwan was looking at him intently, his earlier upset subsumed in professional concern.

"It . . . is." The scar was still bumpy under his fingers, but something had changed. He cleared his throat experimentally. A little pain, a little blockage—but noticeably better. He lowered his hand and stared at McEwan. "Thank you. What the bloody hell did you do?"

The tension that had been twanging through McEwan since Roger and Buck had entered the Duncans' house finally eased, just as the tightness in Roger's throat had.

"I don't know that I can tell you with any great precision," he said apologetically. "It's just that I know what a sound larynx should feel like, and I can tell what yours feels like, and . . ." He shrugged a little, helpless. "I put my fingers there and . . . envision the way it *should* feel."

He touched Roger's throat gently again, exploring. "I can tell that it's very slightly better now. But there *is* a good deal of damage. I can't say whether it would ever be completely healed—in all truth, I doubt it. But if I were to repeat the treatment—it seems to need some time between treatments, no doubt for the tissue to heal, just as an external wound would. So far as I can tell, the optimum time between treatments of a serious injury is about a month; Geillis—" And here his face twitched violently; he had forgotten. He mastered himself with an effort, though, and went on, "Geillis thinks that the process may be affected by the phase of the moon, but she is . . ."

"A witch," Roger finished for him.

The look of unhappiness had returned to McEwan's face, and he lowered his head to hide it.

"Perhaps," he said softly. "Surely she is . . . an unusual woman."

"And a good thing for the human race that there aren't more like her," Roger said, but then checked himself. If he could pray for Jack Randall's immortal soul, he couldn't do less for his own great-grandmother, homicidal maniac or not. But the immediate problem was to try to extract the hapless soul before him from her clutches before she could destroy Hector McEwan utterly.

"Dr. McEwan . . . Hector," he said softly, and laid a hand on the doctor's arm. "You need to go right away from this place, and from her. She won't merely bring you great unhappiness or imperil your soul—she may well kill you."

A look of surprise momentarily displaced the unhappiness in McEwan's eyes. He looked aside, pursed his mouth, and glanced back at Roger, sidelong, as though afraid to look at him too directly.

"Surely you exaggerate," he said, but the words had no force. McEwan's own Adam's apple bobbed visibly as he swallowed.

Roger drew a deep, unconstricted breath and felt the cold, damp air fresh in his chest.

"No," he said gently. "I don't. Think about it, aye? And pray, if ye can. There *is* mercy, aye? And forgiveness."

McEwan sighed, too, but not with any sense of freedom in it. He cast his eyes down, fixed them on the muddy lane and the rain-dancing puddles in the low spots.

"I cannot," he said, his voice low and hopeless. "I've . . . tried. I can't."

Roger's hand was still on McEwan's arm. He squeezed, hard, and said, "Then I'll pray for ye. And for her," he added, hoping no reluctance showed in his voice.

"Thank you, sir," the doctor said. "I value that extremely." But his eyes had lifted and turned, as though he had no power over them, toward Cranesmuir and its smoking chimneys, and Roger knew there was no hope.

HE WALKED BACK to Cranesmuir and waited in the square 'til the door of the Duncans' house opened and Buck emerged. The man looked mildly surprised—but not displeased—to see Roger, and nodded at him but didn't speak. They walked together to an ordinary, where they got a room and went upstairs to refresh themselves before supper. The ordinary didn't run to a bath, but hot water, soap, razor, and towels went some way to restore them to a decent state of cleanliness.

Buck hadn't spoken a word more than necessary, but he had an odd expression—half pleased and half ashamed—and kept darting sidelong glances at Roger, as though unsure whether to say something but rather wanting to.

Roger poured a cup of water from the ewer, drank half of it, and set the cup down with an air of resignation.

"Tell me you didn't," he said finally. "Please."

Buck shot him a quick glance, looking both shocked at the words and slightly amused.

"No," he said, after a pause long enough to knot Roger's belly. "No, I didn't. I'm no saying I couldn't have, though," he added. "She . . . wasn't unwilling."

Roger would have said he didn't want to know, but he wasn't quite able to deceive himself.

"Ye tried?"

Buck nodded, then picked up the cup of water and dashed the remnants into his own face, shaking them off with a *whoof* of breath.

"I kissed her," he said. "Put my hand on her breast."

Roger had seen the upper slopes of those breasts as they swelled above her deep-green woolen bodice, round and white as snowdrops—but a lot bigger. By a considerable force of will, he kept himself from asking, *"And what happened then?"*

He didn't have to, though; Buck was obviously reliving the experience and wanted nothing more than to talk about it.

"She put her hand on mine, but she didn't pull my hand away. Not at first. She went on kissing me—" He broke off and looked at Roger, one brow raised. "Have ye kissed many women?"

"I haven't kept count," Roger said, with a slight edge. "Have you?"

"Four besides her," Buck said contemplatively. He shook his head. "That was different."

"I'd expect it would be. Kissing your mother, I mean—"

"Not *that* kind of different." Buck touched his lips with two fingers, lightly as a girl might. "The other kind. Or maybe I dinna mean that, quite. I kissed a whore once, and it wasna like that at all." He patted his lips absently for a moment, then realized what he was doing and drew his hand away, looking momentarily embarrassed. "Ever gone wi' a whore?"

"I have not," Roger said, trying not to sound censorious, but not managing all that well.

Buck shrugged, dismissing it.

"Well, so. She kept my hand on her breast while she took her time about kissin' me. But then . . ." He paused, blushing, and Roger drew himself up. Buck, blushing?

"What, then?" he asked, unable to refrain.

"Well, she drew it down, ken, over her body, very slow, and still kissin' me, and—well, I must have heard her skirts rustle, mustn't I? But I wasna paying attention, because when she took my hand and put it on her . . . erm . . . lady part, I thought I'd pass out from the shock."

"Her—was she—it, I mean—naked?"

"Bare as an egg, and just as bald, too," Buck assured him. "Have ye ever heard of such a thing?"

"I have, aye."

Buck stared at him, green eyes wide.

"Ye mean your wife—"

"I bloody don't," Roger snapped. "Don't ye dare speak of Brianna, *an amaidan,* or I'll gie you your head in your hands to play with."

"You and who else?" Buck said automatically, but waved a hand to calm Roger. "Why did ye not tell me my mother was a whore?"

"I wouldn't tell ye something like that, even if I knew it for a fact, and I didn't," Roger said.

Buck looked at him for a moment in silence, eyes direct. "Ye'll never make a decent minister," he said at last, "if ye can't be honest."

The words were said objectively, without heat—and stung the more on that account, being true. Roger breathed in hard through his nose and out again.

"All right," he said. And told Buck everything he knew, or thought he knew, concerning Gillian Edgars, alias Geillis Duncan.

"Jesus God," Buck said, blinking.

"Aye," Roger said shortly. Buck's description of his encounter with his mother had given Roger a vividly disturbing image of Brianna, and he hadn't been able to dismiss it. He hungered for her, and as a result was acutely aware of Buck's lingering images of Geillis; he saw the man's hand absently cup itself, fingers drawing slowly in, as though he were guddling—Christ, he could smell her on Buck's flesh, pungent and taunting.

"So now ye've met her," Roger said abruptly, looking away. "And now ye ken what she is. Is that enough, do ye think?" He was careful to make the question no more than a question, and Buck nodded, but not in answer, more as though he were having an internal conversation—with himself or with Geillis, Roger didn't know.

"My father," Buck said thoughtfully, without actually answering. "From what he said when we met him at the MacLarens' croft, I thought he maybe didna ken her yet. But he was interested, ye could tell that." He looked suddenly at Roger, a thought having struck him.

"D'ye think it was meeting us that made him—will make him," he corrected, with a grimace, "go and find her?" He glanced down, then back up at Roger. "Would I not exist if we hadn't come to find your wee lad, I mean?"

Roger felt the usual sense of startled creepiness at realizations of this sort, something like having cold fingers suddenly laid against the small of his back.

"Maybe so," he said. "But I doubt ye'll ever know that. Not for sure."

He was glad enough to leave the subject of Geillis Duncan, though Buck's other parent was probably no less dangerous.

"D'ye think ye need to speak with Dougal MacKenzie?" Roger asked carefully. He didn't want to go anywhere near Castle Leoch or the MacKenzies, but Buck had a right to do it if he wanted, and Roger himself had an obligation—two of them, as kin and as priest—to help him if he did. And however such a conversation might work out, he doubted very much that it would be as disconcerting as the meeting with Geillis.

As for dangerous, though . . .

"I don't know," Buck said softly, as though talking to himself. "I dinna ken what I'd say to the man—to either of them."

That alarmed Roger, who sat up straight.

"Ye don't mean ye'd go back to her? To—your mother?"

Buck's mouth curled up on one side.

"Well, we really didna say much to each other," he pointed out.

"Neither did I," Roger said shortly, "to my father."

Buck made an indeterminate noise in his throat, and they fell silent, listening to the growing drum of rain on the slates of the roof. The tiny fire dwindled under the rain coming down the chimney and went out, leaving no more than the faint smell of warmth, and after a bit Roger wrapped himself in his cloak and curled up on one side of the bed, waiting for his body to warm enough for sleep to come.

The air through the cracked window was sharp with cold and the tingling smell of wet bracken and pine bark. No place smelled like the Highlands, and Roger found his heart eased by its harsh perfume. He was nearly asleep when Buck's voice came softly to him through the dark.

"I'm glad ye got to say it, though."

105

NO A VERY GOOD PERSON

ROGER HAD INSISTED on camping outside the town, thinking it better to get Buck as far away from Geillis Duncan as was feasible. For once, it wasn't raining, and they'd managed to gather enough in the way of pine twigs for a decent wood fire; pine would usually burn even if damp, because of the resin.

"I'm no a very good person." The words were quiet and took a moment to register. Roger looked up to see Buck slumped on his rock, a long stick in his hand, poking at the fire in a desultory fashion. Roger rubbed a hand along his jaw. He felt tired, discouraged, and in no mood for more pastoral counseling.

"I've met worse," he said, after a pause. It sounded unconvincing.

Buck looked at him from under the fringe of blond hair. "I wasna looking for contradiction or consolation," he said dryly. "It was a statement of fact. Call it a preface, if ye like."

"All right." Roger stretched, yawning, then settled himself. "A preface to what? An apology?" He saw the question on his ancestor's face and, irritated, touched his throat. "For this."

"Ah, that." Buck rocked back a little and pursed his lips, eyes fixed on the scar.

"Aye, *that*!" Roger snapped, irritation flaring suddenly into anger. "Do you have any notion what it was ye took from me, you bastard?"

"Maybe a bit." Buck resumed poking at the fire, waiting 'til the end of his stick caught, then stubbing it out again in the dirt. He fell silent, then, and for a bit there was no sound but the rattle of wind through the dry bracken. *A ghost walking by,* Roger thought, watching the brown fronds within the circle of firelight stir and then fall still.

"I don't say it as excuse, mind," Buck said at last, eyes still fixed on the fire. "But there's the matter of intent. I didna mean to get ye hanged."

Roger made a low, vicious noise in response to this. It hurt. He was damned tired of it hurting to speak, or sing, or even grunt.

"Bugger off," he said abruptly, standing up. "Just—bugger off. I don't want to look at you."

Buck gave him a long look, as though debating whether to say something, but then shrugged, got up, and disappeared. He was back within five minutes, though, and sat down with the air of someone who had something to say. *Fine,* Roger thought. *Get on with it.*

"Did it not occur to the two of ye, whilst reading those letters, that there's another way for the past to speak to the future?"

"Well, of course," Roger said, impatient. He stabbed his dirk into one of the turnips to test it; still hard as a rock. "We thought of all sorts of things—diaries left under stones, newspaper notices"—he grimaced at that one—"and a number of less-useful notions. But most of those options were either too unsure or too risky; that's why we arranged to use the banks. But . . ."

He trailed off. Buck was looking smugly superior.

"And I suppose you've thought of something better?" Roger said.

"Why, man, it's right under your nose." With a smirk, Buck bent to test his own turnip and, evidently finding the results acceptable, lifted it out of the ashes on the point of his dirk.

"If ye think I'm going to *ask* you—"

"Beyond that—" Buck said, blowing on the hot turnip between phrases, "beyond that—it's the only way for the future to speak to the past."

He gave Roger a straight, hard look, and Roger felt as though he'd been stabbed with a screwdriver.

"What—you?" he blurted. "You mean you—"

Buck nodded, eyes casually on his smoking turnip.

"Can't be you, can it?" He looked up suddenly, green eyes catching the firelight. "You won't go. Ye wouldn't trust me to keep looking."

"I—" The words caught in Roger's throat, but he was well aware that they showed in his face.

Buck's own face twisted in a lopsided smile. "I would keep looking," he said. "But I see how ye'd not believe me."

"It's not that," Roger said, clearing his throat. "It's only—I *can't* leave while Jem might be here. Not when I don't know for sure that I could come back if I left and he . . . wasn't at the other end." He made a helpless gesture. "Go, and know I was maybe abandoning him forever?"

Buck nodded, looking down. Roger saw the other man's throat move, too, and was struck by a pang of realization.

"Your Jem," Roger said softly. "You do know where he is, at least. When, I mean." The question was clear: if Buck was willing to risk the stones again, why would he not do it in search of his own family, rather than to carry a message to Bree?

"Ye're all mine, aren't ye?" Buck said gruffly. "My blood. My . . . sons."

Despite everything, Roger was moved by that. A little. He coughed, and it didn't hurt.

"Even so," he said. He gave Buck a direct look. "Why? Ye

ken it might do for you; it might have done this last time, if McEwan hadn't been there."

"Mmphm." Buck poked his turnip again and put it back into the fire. "Aye. Well, I meant it; I'm no a very good person. No such a waste, I mean, if I didna make it." His lips twisted a little as he glanced up at Roger. "Ye've maybe got a bit more to offer the world."

"I'm flattered," Roger said dryly. "I imagine the world can get on well enough without me, if it came to that."

"Aye, maybe. But maybe your family can't."

There was a long silence while Roger digested that, broken only by the pop of a burning twig and the distant hooting of courting owls.

"What about your own family?" he asked at last, quietly. "Ye seem to think your wife would be happier without ye. Why? What did ye do to her?"

Buck made a short, unhappy noise that might have been meant for a wry laugh.

"Fell in love wi' her." He took a deep breath, looking down into the fire. "Wanted her."

He'd met Morag Gunn just after he'd begun reading law with a solicitor in Inverness. The lawyer had been called to go out to a farm near Essich, to draw up a will for an old man, and had taken his junior along to see the way of it.

"It took three days, for the auld man was that ill, he couldna attend more than a few minutes at a time. So we stayed wi' the family, and I'd go out to help wi' the pigs and the chickens when I wasna needed inside." He shrugged. "I was young and no bad-looking, and I had the trick of makin' women like me. And she did like me—but she was in love wi' Donald McAllister, a young farmer from Daviot."

But Buck had been unable to forget the lass, and whenever he had a day free from the law, would ride out to visit. He came for Hogmanay, and there was *a cèilidh,* and . . .

"And wee Donald had a dram—or two or three or four—too many and was found in a stall wi' his hand down Mary Finlay's bodice. God, the stramash there was!" A rueful smile flickered over Buck's face. "Mary's twa brothers gave Donald laldy and laid him out like a mackerel, and all the lasses were screamin' and the lads shoutin' like it was Judgment Day. And poor wee Morag was off behind the cow byre, greetin' her heart out."

"You, um, comforted her," Roger suggested, not trying to keep the skeptical note out of his voice. Buck shot him a sharp glance, then shrugged.

"Thought it might be my only chance," he said simply. "Aye. I did. She was the worse for drink herself, and that upset. . . . I didna force her." His lips pressed together. "But I didna take no for an answer, either, and after a bit, she gave up sayin' it."

"Aye. And when she woke up next morning and realized . . . ?"

Buck cocked a brow.

"She didna say anything to anyone then. It was two months later when she realized . . ." Buck had arrived at Mr. Ferguson's rooms one day in March to find Morag Gunn's father and three brothers waiting for him, and as soon as the banns could be read, he was a married man.

"So." Buck took a breath and rubbed a hand over his face. "We . . . got on. I was mad in love wi' her, and she kent that and tried to be kind to me. But I knew well enough it was Donald she'd wanted and still did. He was still there, ken, and she'd see him now and then at *cèilidhean* or the cattle sales."

It was knowing that that had made Buck take the opportunity to sail for North Carolina with his wife and small child.

"Thought she'd forget," he said, a little bleakly. "Or at least I wouldna have to see the look in her eyes when she saw him."

But things had gone badly for the MacKenzies in the New World; Buck had failed to establish a practice as a solicitor, they had little money and no land, and they had no one in the way of kinfolk to turn to for help.

"So we came back," Buck said. He rolled the turnip out of the fire and stabbed it with his stick; the black crust broke and oozed white. He stared at the vegetable for a moment, then stamped on it, mashing it into the ashes.

"And Donald was still there, of course. Was he married?"

Buck shook his head, then knuckled the hair out of his eyes.

"It was no good," he said softly. "It was true, what I told ye about how I came to pass through the stones. But once I'd come to myself and discovered how things were—I kent Morag would be best served if I never came back. Either she'd give me up for dead after a time and marry Donald, or, at the worst, her father would have her back, wi' the bairns. They'd live well—her da had inherited the farm, when his auld one died."

Roger's throat felt tight but it didn't matter. He reached out and squeezed Buck's shoulder, hard. Buck gave a small snort, but didn't pull away.

After a bit, though, he heaved a sigh and straightened up, turning to Roger.

"So ye see," he said. "If I go back and tell your wife what's to do—and, with luck, come back to tell you—it's maybe the one good thing I could do. For my family—for yours."

It took some time for Roger to get his voice sufficiently under control as to speak.

"Aye," he said. "Well. Sleep on it. I mean to go up to Lallybroch. Ye'll maybe go and see Dougal MacKenzie at Leoch. If ye think ye still . . . mean it, after . . . there's time enough to decide then."

106

A BROTHER OF THE LODGE

Craigh na Dun, the Scottish Highlands
December 21, 1980

ESMERALDA'S HAIR was much too red. *Somebody will notice. They'll ask questions. You idiot, why are you even thinking about it? They'd notice a Barbie in a polka-dot bikini a heck of a lot faster. . . .* Brianna shut her eyes for an instant to blot out the sight of Mandy's rag dolly with her scarlet fright wig, brilliant with a dye much brighter than anything achievable in the eighteenth century. She tripped on a stone, said, "S-word!" under her breath, and, her eyes having flown open, took a firmer hold of Mandy's free hand, the other being employed to clutch Esmeralda.

She knew bloody well why she was worrying about the doll's hair. If she didn't think of something inconsequential, she was going to turn right around and run down the rocky slope like a panicked hare, dragging Jem and Mandy through the dead gorse.

We're going to do it. We have to. We'll die, we'll all die in there, in the black . . . Oh, God, oh, God . . .

"Mam?" Jemmy looked up at her, small brow furrowed. She made a good attempt—she thought—at a reassuring smile, but it must have looked less than convincing, judging from his alarmed expression.

"It's okay," she said, abandoning the smile and putting what little conviction she could muster into her voice. "It's okay, Jem."

"Uh-huh." He still looked worried, but he turned his face uphill, and his expression smoothed out, intentness replacing concern. "I can hear them," he said softly. "Can ye hear them, Mama?"

That "Mama" made her hand tighten, and he winced, though she didn't think he really noticed. He was listening. She came to a stop, and they all listened. She could hear the rush of the wind and a slight patter as brief rain swept through the brown heather. Mandy was humming to Esmeralda. But Jem's face was turned upward, serious but not frightened. She could just see the pointed top of one of the stones, barely visible above the crest of the hill.

"I can't, honey," she said, letting out just a bit of the huge breath she'd been holding. "Not yet." *What if I can't hear them at all? What if I've lost it? Holy Mary, Mother of God, pray for us* . . . "Let's . . . get a little closer."

She'd been frozen inside for the last twenty-four hours. She hadn't been able to eat or sleep but had kept going, shoving everything aside, tamping it down—refusing to actually believe they were going to do it, yet making the necessary preparations in a state of eerie calmness.

The leather bag hanging from her shoulder clanked a little, reassuring in its solid reality. Weight might be heavy to carry—but it would hold her steady against the pull of wind and water, secure against the earth. Jem had let go of her hand, and she reached compulsively through the slit in her skirt to feel the three hard little lumps in the pocket tied round her waist.

She'd been afraid to try synthetic stones, for fear they wouldn't work—or might explode violently, like the big opal Jemmy had burst into pieces in North Carolina.

Suddenly she was swept by a longing for Fraser's Ridge—and her parents—so intense that tears welled in her eyes. She blinked hard and wiped her eyes on her sleeve, pretending that the wind had made them water. It didn't matter; neither of the kids was noticing. Now both of them were staring upward—and she finally realized, with a small, flat thump of dread, that she could hear the stones; they were humming, and Mandy was humming with them.

She glanced behind her involuntarily, checking to be sure that they hadn't been followed—but they had. Lionel Menzies was coming up the path behind them, climbing fast.

"F-word!" she said aloud, and Jem whirled to see what was going on.

"Mr. Menzies!" he said, and his face broke into a smile of relief. "Mr. Menzies!"

Bree gestured firmly to Jem to stay where he was and took a couple of steps down the steep path toward Menzies, little rocks sliding under her shoes and bouncing downhill toward him.

"Don't be afraid," he said, coming up breathlessly and stopping just below her. "I—I had to come, be sure you were safe. That you—that you—get away." He nodded upward, looking beyond her. She didn't turn to look; she could feel the stones now, humming gently—for the moment—in her bones.

"We're okay," she said, her voice surprisingly steady. "Really. Er . . . thank you," she added, belatedly polite.

His face was pale and a little strained, but quirked into a small smile at that.

"My pleasure," he said, with equal politeness. But he didn't move to turn and go away. She breathed for a moment, realizing that the frozen core had thawed. She was alive again, completely, and thoroughly on the alert.

"Is there some reason why we might *not* be safe?" she asked, watching his eyes behind the glasses. He grimaced slightly and glanced over his shoulder.

"Shit," she said. "Who? Rob Cameron?" She spoke sharply

and heard the creak of gravel under Jem's shoes as he turned sharply, hearing the name.

"Him and his friends, yes." He nodded uphill. "You, um, really should go. Now, I mean."

Brianna said something really bad in Gaelic, and Jemmy gave a nervous giggle. She glared at Menzies.

"And just what were you planning to do if Rob and his band of jerks all turned up after us?"

"What I just did do," he said simply. "Warn you. I'd bloody go if I were you. Your, um, daughter . . . ?"

She whirled round to see Mandy, Esmeralda in the crook of one arm, stumping laboriously up the path.

"Jem!" She took one giant step, seized him by the hand, and they bolted up the hill after Mandy, leaving Lionel Menzies on the path below.

They caught Mandy up right at the edge of the circle, and Bree tried to grab Mandy's hand but missed. She could hear Lionel Menzies coming up behind them. "Mandy!" She grabbed the little girl and stood, panting, surrounded by stones. The hum was higher-pitched and making her teeth itch; she gnashed them once or twice, trying to rid herself of the feeling, and saw Menzies blink. *Good.*

Then she heard the sound of a car's engine below and saw Menzies's face change to a look of acute alarm.

"Go!" he said. "Please!"

She fumbled under her skirt, hands shaking, and finally got hold of all three stones. They were the same kind, small emeralds, though of slightly different cut. She'd chosen them because they reminded her of Roger's eyes. Thought of him steadied her.

"Jem," she said, and put a stone in his hand. "And, Mandy—here's yours. Put them in your pockets, and—"

But Mandy, little fist clutching her emerald, had turned toward the biggest of the standing stones. Her mouth drooped open for a moment, and then suddenly her face brightened as though someone had lit a candle inside her.

"Daddy!" she shrieked, and, yanking her hand out of Brianna's, raced directly toward the cleft stone—and into it.

"Jesus!" Brianna barely heard Menzies's shocked exclamation. She ran toward the stone, tripped over Esmeralda, and fell full length in the grass, knocking out her wind.

"Mama!" Jem paused for a moment beside her, glancing wildly back and forth between her and the stone where his little sister had just vanished.

"I'm . . . okay," she managed, and with that assurance, Jem charged across the clearing, calling back, "I'll get her, Mam!"

She gulped air and tried to shriek after him, but made only a wheezing croak. The sound of feet made her glance fearfully round, but it was only Lionel, who'd run to the edge of the circle, peering down the hillside. In the distance, she could hear car doors slamming. *Doors. More than one . . .*

She staggered to her feet; she'd fallen on the bag and bruised her ribs, but that didn't matter. She limped toward the cleft stone, pausing only to scoop up Esmeralda by reflex. *God, God, God . . .* was the only thought in her head, an agony of unworded prayer.

And suddenly the prayer was answered. Both of them stood in front of her, swaying and white-faced. Mandy threw up; Jem sat down hard on his bottom and slumped there, wavering.

"Oh, God . . ." She ran to them, grabbed them hard against her in spite of the nastiness. Jem clung to her a moment, but then pushed himself away.

"Mam," he said, and his voice was breathless with joy. "Mam, he's *there.* We could feel him. We can find him—we gotta go, Mam!"

"You do." It was Lionel back, breathless and scared, tugging at Brianna's cloak, trying to straighten it for her. "They're coming—three of them."

"Yes, I—" But then realization struck her, and she turned to the children in panic. "Jem, Mandy . . . your stones—where are they?"

"Burned up," Mandy said solemnly, and spat into the grass. "Puh-toody! Yuck." She wiped her mouth.

"What do you mean—"

"Yeah, they are, Mam. See?" Jem turned out the pocket of his breeches, showing her the burnt spot and the smear of carbon black around it, smelling strongly of scorched wool.

Frantic, she fumbled at Mandy's clothes, finding the same scorch mark on the side of her skirt, where the vaporized stone had burned through from her pocket.

"Did it burn you, honey?" she asked, running a hand down Mandy's sturdy little thigh.

"Not much," Mandy reassured her.

"Brianna! For God's sake—I can't—"

"*I* can't!" she shouted, rounding on him, fists clenched. "The kids' stones are *gone*! They can't—they can't go through without them!" She didn't know for sure that this was true, but the thought of letting them try to go into that . . . *that* . . . without the protection of a stone shriveled her stomach, and she nearly wept with fright and exasperation.

"Stones," he repeated, looking blank. "Jewels, do you mean? Gemstones?"

"Yes!"

He stood for an instant with his mouth open, then fell to his knees, yanking at his left hand, and the next instant was whacking his right hand feverishly against a rock that lay half sunk in the grass.

Bree stared at him helplessly for a moment, then ran to the edge of the circle, ducked round a stone, and stood flat against it in the shadow, looking out. By peering sideways, she could just see human forms, halfway up the hill and moving fast.

On the other side of the stone, Menzies gave a grunt of pain or frustration and smacked something hard against the rock, with a small cracking noise.

"Brianna!" he called, urgent, and she rushed back, afraid the children were trying to go through—but it was all right; they were standing in front of Lionel Menzies, who was stooping over Mandy, holding one of her hands.

"Curl up your fist, wee lassie," he said, almost gently. "Aye, that's it. And, Jem—here, put out your hand." Brianna was close enough now to see that it was a small glittering thing he put in Jem's palm—and that Mandy's fist was curled around a large ring, rather battered, with a Masonic emblem carved into its onyx—and the twin of Jem's small diamond winking beside it, an empty socket on the other side.

"Lionel," she said, and he reached out and touched her cheek.

"Go now," he said. "I can't leave until ye go. Once you're gone, though, I'll run for it."

She nodded jerkily, once, then stooped and took the children's hands. "Jem—put that in your other pocket, okay?" She gulped air and turned toward the big cleft stone. The racket of it hammered at her blood and she could feel it pulling, trying to take her apart.

"Mandy," she said, and could barely hear her own voice. "Let's find Daddy. Don't let go."

It was only as the screaming began that she realized she'd not said "Thank you," and then she thought no more.

107

THE BURYING GROUND

SHE LOVED LALLYBROCH in winter. The gorse and broom and heather didn't seem to die so much as simply to fade back into the landscape, the purple heather fading to a soft brown shadow of itself and the broom to a cluster of dry sticks, their long flat pods rattling softly in the wind. Today the air was cold and still, and the soft gray smoke from the chimneys rose straight up to touch the lowering sky.

"Home, we're home!" Mandy said, hopping up and down. "Goody, goody, goody! Can I have a Coke?"

"It isn't home, goofy," Jem said. Only the pink tip of his nose and a flicker of eyelash was visible in the gap between his woolly hat and the muffler round his neck. His breath wisped white. "It's—*then.* They don't have Cokes now. Besides," he added logically, "it's too cold to drink Coke. Your tummy would freeze."

"Huh?"

"Never mind, honey," Brianna said, and tightened her grasp on Mandy's hand. They were standing at the crest of the hill behind the house, near the remains of the Iron Age fort. It had been a laborious haul up the hill, but she'd been reluctant to approach the house from the front, where they would have been visible for a good quarter mile, coming across open ground.

"Can you feel Daddy anywhere nearby?" she asked the

children. She'd automatically looked for Roger's old orange Morris in the drive as they'd crested the hill—and felt a ridiculous plunge of spirits at seeing neither car nor graveled drive. Jem shook his head; Mandy didn't answer, distracted by a faint bleating from below.

"Iss sheep!" she said, delighted. "Let's go see da sheep!"

"It's not sheep," Jem said, rather crossly. "It's goats. They're in the broch. Can we go down now, Mam? My nose is about to fall off."

She was still hesitant, watching the house. Every muscle was straining, pulling toward it. *Home.* But it wasn't her home, not now. *Roger. "The strong, sweet, supple quality he has . . ."*

Of course, she knew that he likely wasn't here; he and Buck would be searching somewhere for Jerry MacKenzie. *And what if they found him?* she thought, with a little thump of something between excitement and fear.

The fear was what was stopping her racing down the hill to hammer on the door and meet whatever of her family happened to be home today. She'd spent the last few days on the road, and the hours on the final walk from where the carter had dropped them, trying to decide—and her mind was still as divided as ever.

"Come on," she said to the kids. She couldn't keep them standing out here in the cold while she made up her mind. "Let's visit the goats first."

The smell of goats struck her the moment she opened the door—pungent, warm, and familiar. Warm, above all; all three humans sighed in relief and pleasure as the animal heat rolled over them, and they smiled at the eager rush and outcry of *mehhs* that greeted their presence.

From the noise that echoed off the stone walls, there might have been fifty goats inside the broch—though Brianna counted only half a dozen nannies, flop-eared and dainty, four or five half-grown, round-bellied kids, and a single robust billy goat who lowered his horns and glowered at them, suspicious and yellow-eyed. All of them shared a rough pen that fenced off half the ground floor of the broch. She glanced up—but instead of the exposed rafters high above that she half-expected to see, there was the intact underside of another floor above.

The kids—her kids, that is, and she smiled at the thought—were already sticking wisps of hay through the fence and playing with the young goats, who were standing on their back legs to peer at the visitors.

"Jemmy, Mandy!" she called. "Take off your hats and mufflers and mittens and put them over by the door, so the goats don't chew on them!" She left Jem to disentangle Mandy from her fuzzy muffler and went up the stair to see what was on the second floor.

Pale winter light from the windows striped the haunches of burlap bags that filled most of the floor space. She breathed in and coughed a little; flour dust was floating in the air, but she smelled the sweetness of dried corn—maize, they called it—and the deeper, nutty smell of ripe barley, as well, and when she nudged her foot against a particularly lumpy sack, she heard the shift and clack of hazelnuts. Lallybroch wouldn't starve this winter.

Curious, she went up one more flight and on the top floor found a good number of small wooden casks arrayed against the wall. It was much colder up here, but the heady aroma of good whisky filled the air with the illusion of warmth. She stood breathing it in for a moment, wanting very badly to be drunk on the fumes, to obliviate her mind, be able not to bloody *think,* if only for a few minutes.

But that was the last thing she could do. In minutes, she'd have to act.

She stepped back onto the narrow stair that wound up between the inner and outer walls of the broch and looked out toward the house, with vivid memories of the last time she had been here, crouched on the stair in the dark with a shotgun in her hands, watching the light of strangers in her house.

There were strangers here now, too, although her own blood. What if . . . She swallowed. If Roger had found Jerry MacKenzie, his father would be only in his early twenties—much younger than Roger himself. And if her own da was here now—

"He can't be," she whispered to herself, and wasn't sure if that was reassurance or regret. She'd met him for the first time in North Carolina, pissing against a tree. He'd been in his forties, she twenty-two.

You couldn't enter your own lifeline, couldn't exist in the same time twice. They thought they knew that for sure. But what if you entered someone else's life twice, at different times?

That was what was turning her blood to ice and making her curled fists tremble. *What happened?* Did one or the other of your appearances change things, perhaps cancel out the other? Would it not happen that way, would she *not* meet Jamie Fraser in North Carolina if she met him now?

But she had to find Roger. No matter what else happened. And Lallybroch was the only place she knew for sure he'd been. She took a deep, deep breath and closed her eyes.

Please, she prayed. *Please help me. Thy will be done, but please show me what to do . . .*

"Mam!" Jemmy came running up the stair, his footsteps loud in the confined stone corridor. "Mam!" He popped into sight, blue eyes round and hair standing half on end with excitement. "Mam, come down! A man's coming!"

"What does he look like?" she asked, urgent, grabbing him by the sleeve. "What color is his hair?"

He blinked, surprised.

"Black, I think. He's at the bottom of the hill—I couldn't see his face."

Roger.

"All right. I'm coming." She felt half choked but no longer frozen. It was happening now, whatever it was, and energy fizzed through her veins.

Even as she hurtled down the stairs behind Jemmy, rationality told her that it wasn't Roger—distance or not, Jemmy would know his father. But she had to see.

"Stay *here,*" she said to the children, with so much command in her voice that they blinked but didn't argue. She threw open the door, saw the man coming up the path, and stepped out to meet him, closing the door firmly behind her.

From the first glance, she saw that it wasn't Roger, but the disappointment was subsumed at once in relief that it wasn't Jamie. And intense curiosity, because it must surely be . . .

She'd run down the path, to get well away from the broch, just in case, and was picking her way through the stones of the family burying ground, eyes on the man coming up the steep, rocky path.

A tall, solid-looking man, his dark hair graying a little but still thick, glossy, and loose on his shoulders. His eyes were on the rough ground, watching his footing. And then he came to his destination and made his way across the hill, to one of the stones in the burying ground. He knelt by it and laid down something he'd been carrying in his hand.

She shifted her weight, uncertain whether to call out or wait 'til he'd finished his business with the dead. But the small stones under her feet shifted, too, rolling down with a *click-clack-click* that made him look up and, seeing her, rise abruptly to his feet, black brows raised.

Black hair, black brows. *Brian Dubh.* Black Brian.

I met Brian Fraser (you would like him, and he, you) . . .

Wide, startled hazel eyes met hers, and for a second that was all she saw. His beautiful deep-set eyes, and the expression of stunned horror in them.

"Brian," she said. "I—"

"A Dhia!" He went whiter than the harled plaster of the house below. "Ellen!"

Astonishment deprived her of speech for an instant—long enough to hear light footsteps scrambling down the hill behind her.

"Mam!" Jem called, breathless.

Brian's glance turned up, behind her, and his mouth fell open at sight of Jem. Then a look of radiant joy suffused his face.

"Willie!" he said. *"A bhalaich! Mo bhalaich!"* He looked back at Brianna and stretched out a trembling hand to her. *"Mo ghràidh . . . mo chridhe . . ."*

"Brian," she said softly, her heart in her voice, filled with pity and love, unable to do anything but respond to the need of the soul that showed so clearly in his lovely eyes. And with her speaking of his name for the second time, he stopped dead, swaying for a moment, and then the eyes rolled up in his head and he fell.

SHE WAS KNEELING in the crunchy dead heather beside Brian Fraser before she'd even thought to move. There was a slight blue tinge to his lips, but he was breathing, and she drew a deep cold breath of relief herself, seeing his chest rise slowly under the worn linen shirt.

Not for the first time, she wished fervently that her mother was there, but turned his head to one side and laid two fingers on the pulse she could see at the side of his neck. Her fingers were cold, and his flesh was startlingly warm. He didn't rouse or stir at her touch, though, and she began to fear that he hadn't just fainted.

He'd died—would die—of a stroke. If there was some weakness in his brain . . . oh, God. Had she just killed him prematurely?

"Don't die!" she said to him aloud. "For God's sake, don't die *here*!"

She glanced hastily toward the house below, but no one was coming. Looking down again, she saw what it was he'd held: a small bouquet of evergreen twigs, tied with red thread. Yew—she recognized the oddly tubular red berries—and holly.

And then she saw the stone. She knew it well, had sat on the ground beside it often, contemplating Lallybroch and those who lay sleeping on its hillside.

Ellen Caitriona Sileas MacKenzie Fraser
Beloved wife and mother
Born 1691, Died in childbed 1729

And below, in smaller letters:

Robert Brian Gordon MacKenzie Fraser
Infant son
Died at birth 1729

And:

William Simon Murtagh MacKenzie Fraser
Beloved son
Born 1716, Died of the smallpox 1727

"Mam!" Jem skidded down the last few feet, almost falling beside her. "Mam, Mam—Mandy says—who is he?" He stared from Brian's pallid face to her own and back again.

"His name's Brian Fraser. He's your great-grandfather." Her hands were trembling, but to her surprise she felt suddenly calm at the speaking of the words, as though she had stepped into the center of a puzzle and found herself to be the missing piece. "What about Mandy?"

"Did I scare him?" Jem squatted down, looking worried. "He looked at me just before he fell down. Is he—dead?"

"Don't worry, I think he's just had a shock. He thought we were . . . somebody else." She touched Brian's cheekbone, feeling the soft prickle of his beard stubble, and smoothed the tumbled hair behind his ear. His mouth twitched a little as she did so, the ghost of a half smile, and her heart jumped. Thank God, he was coming round. "What did Mandy say?"

"Oh!" Jem stood up, fast, eyes wide. "She says she hears Dad!"

108

REALITY IS THAT WHICH, WHEN YOU STOP BELIEVING IN IT, DOESN'T GO AWAY

ROGER TURNED HIS horse's head toward Lallybroch, knowing nowhere else to go. He'd taken leave of Brian Fraser six weeks before and had been sad at what he'd thought was a permanent parting. His heart was eased a little now at the thought of seeing Brian again. Also at the certainty of a sympathetic ear, even though there was little he could openly discuss with him.

He'd have to tell Brian, of course, that he hadn't found Jem. That thought was a thorn in his heart, and one felt at every beat. For the last weeks, he had been able to put the brutal ache of Jemmy's absence aside for a little, hoping that somehow, finding Jerry might also lead to finding Jem. But it hadn't.

What the devil it *did* mean was a complete mystery. Had he

found the only Jeremiah there was to be found here? If he had . . . where *was* Jem?

He wanted to tell Brian that he'd found the man to whom the identity disks belonged—Brian would ask. But how to do so without divulging either Jerry's identity, Roger's relationship with him—or explaining what had happened to him? He sighed, reining his horse around a large puddle in the road. Maybe better to say simply that he'd failed, hadn't found J. W. MacKenzie—though it troubled him to lie outright to such an openhearted man.

And he couldn't discuss Buck, either. Beyond thought of Jem, Buck was the matter lying heaviest on his mind at the moment.

"Ye'll never make a decent minister, if ye can't be honest." He'd tried to be. The honest truths of the situation from his own selfish point of view were that he'd miss Buck's company badly, that he was deeply jealous of the possibility that Buck *might* make it to Brianna, and—not least, he assured himself—that he was terrified that Buck *wouldn't* make it through the stones again. He'd die in the void, or maybe be lost once more, alone in some random time.

The truth for Buck was that while it could be argued (and with no little force) that Buck should remove himself forthwith and permanently from the vicinity of Geillis Duncan, going through the stones was maybe the least desirable means of ensuring such an outcome.

To accept Buck's gallant gesture was a temptation, though. If he *could* make it, tell Bree where Roger was . . . Roger didn't think Buck could come back, though. The effects of travel were cumulative, and Hector McEwan likely wouldn't be standing by next time.

But if Buck was willing to risk the crossing, in spite of the very real danger to his own life, surely it was Roger's obligation to try to persuade him to return to his own wife, rather than to Roger's?

He brushed the back of his hand against his lips, feeling in memory the softness of Morag's brown hair on his cheek when he'd bent to kiss her forehead on the banks of the Alamance. The gentle trust in her eyes—and the fact that she'd bloody saved his own life very shortly thereafter. His fingers rested for an instant on his throat, and he realized, with the flicker of surprise that attends recognition of things already long known, that whatever the bitterness of his regrets about his voice, he'd never for an instant wished that she *hadn't* saved him.

When Stephen Bonnet would have thrown Morag's son overboard, Roger had saved the child from drowning, and that at some risk to his own life. But he didn't think she'd done what she'd done at Alamance in payment of that debt. She'd done it because she didn't want him to die.

Well. He didn't want Buck to die.

Did Morag *want* Buck back? Buck thought not, but he might be wrong. Roger was fairly sure that the man still loved Morag and that his abnegation was due as much to Buck's own sense of personal failure as to what he thought Morag's desires might be.

"Even if that's true," he said aloud, "where do I get off trying to manage people's lives?"

He shook his head and rode on through a light mist that wove shreds of fog through the wet black spikiness of the gorse. It wasn't raining, that was one thing, though the sky bore a burden of cloud that brought it down to shroud the tops of the nearby mountains.

He'd never asked his adoptive father anything about the art of being a priest; it was the last thing he'd ever thought of being. But he'd grown up in the Reverend's house and had seen parishioners come every day to the comfortably shabby study in search of help or advice. He remembered his father (and now felt a new oddness in the word, layered as it was with the freshness of Jerry MacKenzie's physical presence), remembered him sitting down with a sigh to drink tea in the kitchen with Mrs. Graham, shaking his head in response to her questioning look and saying, *"Sometimes there's nothing you can give some of them but a friendly ear and a prayer to be going on with."*

He came to a dead stop in the road, closed his eyes, and tried to find a moment's peace in the chaos of his thoughts. And ended, as every priest since Aaron's time doubtless had, by throwing up his hands and demanding, "What do You *want* of me? What the hell should I *do* about these people?"

He opened his eyes when he said that, but instead of finding an angel with an illuminated scroll standing before him, he was confronted by the beady yellow eyes of a fat seagull sitting in the road a few feet from his horse and not discomposed in the slightest by the presence of a creature a hundred times its size. The bird gave him an old-fashioned sort of look, then spread its wings and flapped off with a piercing *screek!* This echoed from the hillside above, where a few more gulls wheeled slowly, barely visible against the paper-white sky.

The presence of the gull broke his sense of isolation, at least. He rode on in a calmer frame of mind, resolved only not to think about things until he had to.

He thought he was close to Lallybroch; with luck, would reach it well before dark. His belly rumbled at the prospect of tea, and he felt happier. Whatever he could and couldn't tell Brian Fraser, just seeing Brian and his daughter Jenny again would be a comfort.

The gulls cried high overhead, still wheeling, and he looked up. Sure enough: he could just make out the low ruins of the Iron Age hill fort up there, the ruins he'd rebuilt—would rebuild? What if he never got back to—*Jesus, don't even think about it, man, it'll drive you crazier than you are already.*

He nudged the horse and it reluctantly accelerated a bit. It accelerated a lot faster in the next moment, when a crashing noise came from the hillside just above.

"Whoa! Whoa, you eedjit! Whoa, I said!" These adjurations, along with a heave of the reins to bring the horse's head around, had an effect, and they ended facing back the way they'd come, to see a young boy standing, panting, in the middle of the road, his red hair all on end, nearly brown in the muted light.

"Daddy," he said, and his face lit as though touched by a sudden sun. "Daddy!"

ROGER HADN'T ANY memory of leaving his horse or running down the road. Or of anything else. He was sitting in the mud and the mist in a patch of wet bracken with his son hugged tight to his chest, and nothing else mattered in the world.

"Dad," Jem kept saying, gasping with sobs, "Daddy, Daddy . . ."

"I'm here," he whispered into Jem's hair, the tears running down his own face. "I'm here, I'm here. Don't be afraid."

Jem took a shuddering breath, managed to say, "I'm *not* afraid," and cried some more.

At last, a sense of time crept back, along with the sensation of water soaking through the seat of his breeches. He breathed and shuddered a bit himself, smoothed Jem's hair, and kissed his head.

"You smell like a goat," he said, swallowed, brushed at his eyes with the back of a hand, and laughed. "Where the *hell* have you been?"

"In the broch with Mandy," Jem said, as though this was the most natural statement in the world. He gave Roger a faintly accusing look. "Where have *you* been?"

"Mandy?" Roger said blankly. "What do you mean Mandy?"

"My sister," Jem said, with the patience children occasionally show for the denseness of their parents. "*You* know."

"Well . . . where *is* Mandy, then?" In Roger's state of surreal confusion, Mandy might just as well have popped up beside Jem like a mushroom.

Jem's face went momentarily blank with confusion, and he glanced round as though expecting Mandy to materialize out of the moss and heather at any moment.

"I don't know," he said, sounding mildly puzzled. "She ran away to find you, and then Mam fell down and broke something and—"

Roger had let go of Jem but grabbed him again at this, startling the breath out of the boy.

"Your mother's here, *too*?"

"Well, sure," Jem said, sounding mildly annoyed. "I mean—not *here* here. She's up there, in the old fort. She tripped on a rock when we were running to catch Mandy."

"Jesus, Lord," Roger said fervently, taking a stride in the direction of the fort, then halting abruptly. "Wait: you said she broke something—she's hurt?"

Jem shrugged. He was beginning to look worried again, but not very worried. Dad was here; everything would be okay.

"I don't think it's bad," he assured his father. "She couldn't walk, though, so she told me to run and catch Mandy. But I found you first."

"Okay. She's awake, though, she's talking?" He had Jem by

the shoulders, as much to keep him from disappearing—he half-feared he was hallucinating—as to compel an answer.

"Uh-huh." Jem was looking vaguely about, a slight frown on his face. "Mandy's here *someplace*. . . ." Wriggling free, he turned round slowly, face creased in intent concentration.

"Mandy!" Roger shouted up the hill. He cupped his hands around his mouth and yelled again. "BREE!" He scanned the fort and the hillside anxiously for Bree's head popping up above the ruins or any sign of agitation among the vegetation that might be occasioned by a scrambling two-year-old. No head showed, but a breeze had come up and the whole hill seemed alive.

"Mandy ran away down this hill?" he asked, and, at Jem's nod, he glanced behind him. The land flattened out into moor on the other side of the road, and there wasn't a glimpse of anything that might be Mandy on it. Unless she'd fallen down and was lying in a hollow . . .

"You stay *right here*," he said to Jem, squeezing his shoulder hard. "I'm going to go up the hill and look. I'll bring your mother down." He bounded up the gravel trace that was the nearest thing there was to a path, calling out Mandy's name at intervals, torn between overwhelming joy and terrifying panic, lest it not be real, lest he actually had cracked and was simply imagining that Jem was there—he turned at every third step to check that he *was* there, still standing on the road.

Bree. The thought that she was up there, just above him . . . "Mandy!" he shouted again, his voice cracking. But it cracked from emotion, and he realized in a startled instant that he'd been shouting at full volume for minutes now—and it hadn't hurt.

"God bless you, Hector," he said fervently under his breath, and went on, beginning now to zigzag back and forth across the hill, beating through the sticks of dry broom and birch saplings, kicking at gorse and dead ferns in case Mandy should have fallen, maybe knocked herself out on a rock.

He heard the seagulls shriek above, thin and piercing, and looked up, hoping to see Brianna peering over the wall of the fort. She wasn't, but something called again—thin and piercing, but not a gull.

"Daddeeeee . . ."

He whirled, almost losing his footing, and saw Jem running

down the road—and coming round the bend of that road, Buck's horse with Buck atop him, and a wildly squirming bundle with black curly hair cradled precariously in Buck's arm.

He couldn't speak at all by the time he reached them.

"Think ye might have lost something," Buck said gruffly, and handed Mandy carefully down to him. She was a heavy, lively weight in his arms—and smelled of goats.

"Daddy!" she exclaimed, beaming at him as though he'd just come in from work. "Mwah! Mwah!" She kissed him noisily and snuggled into his chest, her hair tickling his chin.

"Where *were* you?" Jem was saying accusingly.

"Where was *you*?" Mandy countered, and stuck her tongue out at him. "Bleah."

Roger was crying again, couldn't stop. Mandy had burrs and foxtails stuck in her hair and in the fabric of her jacket, and he thought she might have wet herself somewhere in the recent past. Buck twitched the reins, as though about to turn and go, and Roger reached out a hand and grabbed his stirrup.

"Stay," he croaked. "Tell me it's real."

Buck made an incoherent noise, and, looking up through his tears, Roger could see that Buck was making an inadequate attempt at hiding his own emotion.

"Aye," Buck said, sounding almost as choked as Roger. He looped his reins and, sliding off into the road, took Jem very gently into his own arms. "Aye, it's real."

109

FROTTAGE

DR. McEWAN WAS a single man and owned a single bed. The bed was presently accommodating four people, and even if two of those people were not full-sized, the general atmosphere was that of the London

Tube in rush hour. Heat, random flesh in all directions, and a distinct shortage of oxygen.

Brianna squirmed, trying to find room to breathe. She was lying on her side, back pressed to the wall, with Mandy squashed into a heavily breathing mass between her parents. Roger balanced precariously on the bed's outer edge with Jem draped bonelessly over him, Jem's legs occasionally twitching spasmodically, prodding Bree in the shins. And Esmeralda was taking up most of the single pillow, red yarn hair getting up everyone's nose.

"Do you know the word 'frottage'?" Bree whispered to Roger. He wasn't asleep; if he had been, he'd have been on the floor by now.

"I do. Why, do ye want to try it now?" He reached carefully across Jem and stroked her bare arm lightly. The fine hairs rose on her forearm; she could see them do it, lifting silently in the dull glow from the hearth.

"I want to do less of it with a two-year-old. Mandy's zonked. Is Jem asleep enough to move?"

"We'll find out. I'm going to suffocate if he's not." Roger edged out from under his son, who emitted a loud "mmmm," but then smacked his lips and subsided. Roger patted him softly, bent to check that he was solidly asleep, and straightened up. "Okay, then."

They'd appeared at McEwan's door well after dark, Brianna supported between Roger and Buck, the children at their heels. The doctor, while clearly surprised at this nocturnal invasion of MacKenzies, had taken it calmly, sitting Bree down in his surgery with her foot in a pan of cold water and then going to call his landlady to find a bit of supper for the children.

"A sprain, and not too bad," he'd assured Brianna, drying her foot with a linen towel and expertly palpating her swollen ankle. He passed a thumb up the problematic tendon and noted her wince. "It will just take time to heal—but I think I can ease the pain a bit . . . if you like?" He glanced toward Roger, brow raised, and Brianna breathed in through her nose.

"It's not *his* ankle," she said, mildly annoyed. "And *I'd* certainly appreciate anything you can do."

Roger nodded, to her further annoyance, and McEwan took her foot onto his knee. Seeing her grip the edges of the stool to keep her balance, Roger knelt behind her and wrapped his arms around her.

"Lean on me," he said quietly in her ear. "Just breathe. See what happens."

She shot him a puzzled look, but he merely brushed her ear with his lips and nodded toward McEwan.

The doctor's head was bent over the foot, which he held lightly in both hands, his thumbs on her instep. He moved them slowly in circles, then pressed firmly. A sharp pain shot up her ankle, but died abruptly before she could gasp.

The doctor's hands were noticeably warm on her chilled flesh, and she wondered at that, since they'd been immersed in the same cold water as her foot. One hand now cupped her heel, and thumb and forefinger massaged the puffy flesh lightly, repeatedly, then a little harder. The sensation hovered unsettlingly somewhere between pain and pleasure.

McEwan looked up suddenly and smiled at her.

"It will take a little time," he murmured. "Relax, if you can."

In fact, she could. For the first time in twenty-four hours, she wasn't hungry. For the first time in days, she was beginning to thaw out completely—and for the first time in months, she wasn't afraid. She let out her breath and eased her head back on Roger's shoulder. He made a low humming noise in his throat and took a firmer hold, settling himself.

She could hear Mandy telling Jem a disjointed story about Esmeralda's adventures, in the back room where the landlady had taken them to eat their soup and bread. Sure that they were safe, she gave herself up to the elemental bliss of her husband's arms and the smell of his skin.

But the expression of a well-made man appears not only
in his face;
It is in his limbs and joints also, it is curiously in the
joints of his hips and wrists . . .

"Bree," Roger whispered to her some moments later. "Bree—look."

She opened her eyes and saw at first the curve of his wrist where it rested on her bosom, the hard elegance of bone and the curve of muscled forearm. But then her focus widened and she started a little. Her toes were glowing with a faint blue light barely visible in the crevices between them. She blinked hard and looked again, to be sure she was really seeing it, but the sound Roger made in his throat assured her that she was—and that he saw it, too.

Dr. McEwan had felt her startlement; he looked up and smiled again, this time joyful. His eyes flicked up toward Roger, then back to her.

"You, too?" he said. "I thought so." He held her foot still for a long moment, until she thought she felt the pulse in his fingers echo in the spaces between the small bones, and then he wrapped a bandage neatly around her ankle and lowered her foot gently to the floor. "Better now?"

"Yes," she said, and found her voice a little husky. "Thank you."

She'd wanted to ask him questions, but he rose and put on his coat.

"Ye'll oblige me greatly by staying here the night," he said firmly, still smiling at her. "I'll find a bed with a friend." And raising his hat to Roger, he bowed and went out, leaving them to put the children to bed.

Not surprisingly, Mandy had put up a fuss at sleeping in a strange bed in a strange room, complaining that Esmeralda thought the surgery smelled funny and was scared of the big wardrobe because there might be kelpies in it.

"Kelpies only live in water, silly," Jem had said, but he also looked a little apprehensively at the enormous dark armoire with its cracked door. So they'd all lain down on the narrow bed together, parents comforted as much as children by sheer physical proximity.

Brianna felt the soft warmth and the haze of exhalation blanketing her bodily exhaustion, a pull on her senses beckoning her toward the well of sleep. But not nearly such a strong pull as her sense of Roger.

It is in his walk, the carriage of his neck, the flex of his
waist and knees; dress does not hide him . . .

She lay for a moment, hand on Mandy's back, feeling the slow beating of the child's heart, watching as Roger scooped

Jem into his arms and turned to lay him down on one of the extra quilts McEwan's landlady had brought up with the soup.

The strong, sweet, supple quality he has, strikes through the cotton and flannel . . .

He was dressed in nothing but shirt and breeks and now paused to shed the homespun breeks, casually scratching his arse in relief, the long linen shirt momentarily rucked up to show the lean curve of a buttock. Then he came to pick up Mandy, smiling over her stertorously breathing body at Bree.

"Leave the bed to the kids, you think? We could make up a pallet with the cloaks—if they've dried out a bit—and quilts in the surgery." He gathered Mandy up like an armful of laundry, and Bree was able to sit up and scoot across the bed, feeling a wonderful movement of air through her perspiration-dampened shift and a brush of soft fabric across her breasts that made her nipples rise.

She turned back the bedding; he moved the children back to the bed, and she covered them and kissed their dreaming faces, kissing Esmeralda for good measure before tucking her into Mandy's arm. Roger turned toward the closed door to the surgery and looked back at Bree over his shoulder, smiling. She could see the shadow of his body through the linen shirt, against the glow of the hearth.

To see him pass conveys as much as the best poem,
perhaps more . . .
You linger to see his back, and the back of his neck and
shoulder-side.

"Wilt bed with me, lass?" he said softly, and put out a hand to her.

"Oh, yes," she said, and came to him.

THE SURGERY WAS cold, after the humid heat of the bedroom, and they came to each other at once, warm limbs and warm lips seeking. The fire in this room had gone out, and they didn't trouble to rebuild it.

Roger had kissed her the moment he saw her on the ground in the fort, grabbing her and lifting her into an embrace that crushed her ribs and nearly bruised her lips. She'd had no objections whatever. But now his mouth was soft and tender and the scruff of his beard light on her skin.

"Fast?" he murmured against her mouth. "Slow?"

"Horizontal," she murmured back, clutching his bottom. "Speed irrelevant." She was standing on one leg, the bad foot elegantly—she hoped—extended behind her. Dr. McEwan's ministrations had eased the throbbing quite a bit, but she still couldn't put weight on it for more than the briefest second.

He laughed—quietly, with a guilty look toward the bedroom door—and, bending suddenly, scooped her up and staggered across the room to the coat rack, where she snagged the hanging cloaks and tossed them onto the floor by the table, that being the cleanest open space visible. He squatted, back creaking audibly and manfully suppressing a groan as he lowered her gently onto the heap.

"Be careful!" she whispered, and not jokingly. "You could put your back out, and then what?"

"Then ye'd get to be on top," he whispered back, and ran a hand up her thigh, her shift rippling up with it. "But I haven't, so ye don't." Then he pulled up his shirt, spread her legs, and came to her with an incoherent noise of deep satisfaction.

"I hope ye meant it about the speed being irrelevant," he said in her ear, a few minutes later.

"Oh. Yes," she said vaguely, and wrapped her arms round his body. "You . . . just . . . stay put." When she could, she let him go, cradling his head and kissing the smooth warm flesh at the side of his neck. She felt the rope scar and gently drew the tip of her tongue along it, making gooseflesh erupt all over his back and shoulders.

"Are you asleep?" he inquired some moments later, suspicious.

She opened one eye halfway. He'd gone back into the bedroom for quilts and was kneeling beside her, spreading one over her. It smelled faintly musty, with a tang of mice, but she didn't care.

"No," she said, and rolled onto her back, feeling wonderful, despite the hard floor, her sprained ankle, and the dawning realization that Dr. McEwan must do operations and amputations on the table. There was a dark stain on the underside, above her head. "Just . . . limp." She stretched out a slow hand to Roger, urging him under the quilt with her. "You?"

"I'm not asleep," he assured her, sliding down close beside her. "And if ye think I'm going to say 'limp,' think again."

She laughed—quietly, with a glance at the door—rolled over, and rested her forehead against his chest.

"I thought I might never see you again," she whispered.

"Aye," he said softly, and his hand stroked her long hair and her back. "Me, too." They were silent for a long moment, each listening to the other's breath—his came easier than it had, she thought, without the small catches—and then he finally said, "Tell me."

She did, baldly and with as little emotion as she could manage. She thought he might be emotional enough for both of them.

He couldn't shout or curse, because of the sleeping children. She could feel the rage in him; he was shaking with it, his fists clenched like solid knobs of bone.

"I'll kill him," he said, in a voice barely pitched above silence, and his eyes met hers, savage and so dark that they seemed black in the dim light.

"It's okay," she said softly, and, sitting up, took both his hands in hers, lifting one and then the other to her lips. "It's okay. We're all right, all of us. And we're here."

He looked away and took a deep breath, then looked back, his hands tightening on hers.

"Here," he repeated, his voice bleak, still hoarse with fury. "In 1739. If I'd—"

"You had to," she said firmly, squeezing back hard. "Besides," she added, a little diffidently, "I sort of thought we wouldn't stay. Unless you've taken a great liking to some of the denizens?"

Expressions flickered across his face, from anger to rue to reluctant acceptance . . . and an even more reluctant humor, as he got a grip of himself. He cleared his throat.

"Aye, well," he said dryly. "There's Hector McEwan, to be sure. But there are a good many other people, too—Geillis Duncan, for one."

A small jolt went through her at the name.

"Geillis Duncan? Well . . . yes, I suppose she *would* be here at this point, wouldn't she? Did you—did you meet her?"

A truly extraordinary expression went over Roger's face at that question.

"I did," he said, avoiding her questioning glance. He turned and waved a hand at the surgery window that looked out onto the square. "She lives just across the way."

"Really?" Brianna got to her feet, clutching a quilt to her bosom, forgot about her bad foot, and stumbled. Roger leapt up and caught her by the arm.

"You *don't* want to meet her," he said, with emphasis. "Sit down, aye? Ye're going to fall."

Brianna eyed him, but allowed him to ease her back down to their nest and to pull a quilt up over her shoulders. It *was* bloody cold in the surgery, now that the warmth of their efforts had faded.

"All right," she said, and shook her hair down to cover her ears and neck. "Tell me why I don't want to meet Geillis Duncan."

To her surprise, he flushed deeply, visible even in the shadows of the surgery. Roger had neither the skin nor the temperament to blush easily, but when he *did* describe—briefly, but vividly—what had happened (or possibly *not* happened) with Buck, Dr. McEwan, and Geillis, she understood it.

"Holy moly," she said, with a glance over her shoulder at the window. "Er . . . when Dr. McEwan said he'd find a bed with a friend . . . ?"

Buck had gone off, saying that he'd take a bed at the ordinary at the foot of the High Street and would see them in the morning. Presumably he'd meant it, but . . .

"She *is* married," Roger said tersely. "Presumably her husband would notice were she inviting strange men to spend the night."

"Oh, I don't know so much," she said, half-teasing. "She's an herbalist, remember? Mama does a good sleeping potion; I imagine Geillis could, too."

The color washed up Roger's face again, and she knew, as clearly as if he'd said so, that he was envisioning Geillis Duncan doing something disgraceful with one or another of her lovers whilst lying beside her snoring husband.

"God," he said.

"You, um, do remember what's going to *happen* to her poor

husband, don't you?" Bree said delicately. The color vanished instantly from Roger's face, and she knew he hadn't.

"That's one of the reasons we can't stay here," she said, gently but firmly. "There are too many things we know. And we *don't* know what trying to interfere might do, but it's a good bet that it's dangerous."

"Yes, but—" he began, but broke off at the look on her face. "Lallybroch. Is that why ye wouldna go there?" For he'd tried to take her down the hill to the house when he'd rescued her from the fort. She'd insisted that they must go to the village for help instead, even though it meant an awkward and painful three-hour ride.

She nodded and felt a small lump come into her throat. It stayed there as she told him about meeting Brian in the burying ground.

"It's not *just* that I'm afraid what meeting them might do to . . . later," she said, and the lump dissolved into tears. "It's . . . oh, Roger, the look on his face when he saw me and thought I was Ellen!

"I—he—he's going to die in a year or two. That beautiful, sweet man . . . and there isn't any-anything we can do to stop it." She gulped and swiped at her eyes. "He—he thinks he's seen his wife and his son, that they're w-waiting for him. And the—oh, God, the *joy* on his face. I couldn't take that away from him, I just couldn't."

He took her in his arms and rubbed her back gently as she sobbed.

"No, of course ye couldn't," he whispered to her. "Dinna fash, Bree. Ye did right."

She sniffed and groped among the cloaks for something to blow her nose on, settling at last for a stained cloth from Dr. McEwan's table. It smelled of some pungent medicine, thank God, not blood.

"But there's Da, too," she said, taking a deep, tremulous breath. "What will happen to him . . . the scars on his back . . . I—can't stand to think about that and us doing nothing, but we—"

"We can't," Roger agreed quietly. "We daren't. God only knows what I may have done already, finding Jerry and sending him—wherever I *did* send him." Taking the cloth, he dipped it in the water bucket and wiped her face, the cold of it soothing on her hot cheeks, though it made her shiver.

"Come lie down," he said, putting an arm round her shoulders. "Ye need rest, *mo chridhe.* It's been a terrible day."

"No," she murmured, easing down and laying her head in the curve of his shoulder, feeling the strength and warmth of his body. "It's been a wonderful day. I have you back."

110

THE SOUNDS THAT MAKE UP SILENCE

ROGER FELT HER begin to relax, and quite suddenly she let go her stubborn hold on consciousness and fell asleep like someone breathing ether. He held her and listened to the tiny sounds that made up silence: the distant hiss of the peat fire in the bedroom, a cold wind rattling at the window, the rustling and breathing of the sleeping kids, the slow beating of Brianna's valiant heart.

Thank you, he said silently to God.

He had expected to fall asleep himself at once; tiredness covered him like a lead blanket. But the day was still with him, and he lay for some time looking up into the dark.

He was at peace, too tired to think coherently of anything. All the possibilities drifted round him in a slow, distant swirl, too far away to be troublesome. Where they might go . . . and how. What Buck might have said to Dougal MacKenzie. What Bree had brought in her bag, heavy as lead. Whether there would be porridge for breakfast—Mandy liked porridge.

The thought of Mandy made him ease out of the quilts to check on the children. To reassure himself that they were really there.

They were, and he stood by the bed for a long time, watching their faces in wordless gratitude, breathing the warm childish smell of them—still tinged with a slight tang of goat.

At last he turned, shivering, to make his way back to his warm wife and the beckoning bliss of sleep. But as he reentered the surgery, he glanced through the window into the night outside.

Cranesmuir slept, and mist lay in her streets, the cobbles beneath gleaming with wet in the half-light of a drowning moon. On the far side of the square, though, a light showed in the attic window of Arthur Duncan's house.

And in the shadow of the square below, a small movement betrayed the presence of a man. Waiting.

Roger closed his eyes, cold rising from his bare feet up his body, seeing in his mind the sudden vision of a green-eyed woman, lazy in the arms of a fair-haired lover . . . and a look of surprise and then of horror on her face as the man vanished from her side. And an invisible blue glow rose in her womb.

With his eyes tight shut, he put a hand on the icy windowpane, and said a prayer to be going on with.

PART SEVEN

Before I Go Hence

111

A DISTANT MASSACRE

September 5, 1778

I FOLDED THE CLOTH into a tidy square and used the tongs to dip it in the steaming cauldron, then stood waving it gently to and fro until the compress should cool enough for me to wring it out and use it. Joanie sighed, fidgeting on her stool.

"Don't rub your eye," I said automatically, seeing her curled fist steal toward the large pink sty on her right eyelid. "Don't fret; it won't take long."

"Yes, it does take long," she said crossly. "It takes *forever*!"

"Dinna be giving your grannie sauce," Marsali told her, pausing in her stride on the way from kitchen to printshop, a cheese roll for Fergus in her hand. "Hauld your wheesht and be grateful."

Joanie groaned and writhed, and stuck her tongue out after her departing mother, but whipped it back into her mouth again and looked rather shamefaced when she caught sight of my raised brow.

"I know," I said, with some sympathy. Holding a warm compress on a sty for ten minutes did feel like forever. Particularly if you'd been doing it six times a day for the last two days. "Maybe you can think of something to pass the time. You could recite me the multiplication tables while I grind valerian root."

"Oh, *Grannie*!" she said, exasperated, and I laughed.

"Here you go," I said, handing her the warm poultice. "Do you know any good songs?"

She exhaled moodily, small nostrils flaring.

"I wish Grandda was here," she said. "*He* could tell me a story." The note of comparative accusation was clear in her voice.

"Spell 'hordeolum' for me and I'll tell you the one about the water horse's wife," I suggested. That made her unaffected eye fly open with interest.

"What's a hordeolum?"

"That's the scientific name for a sty."

"Oh." She seemed unimpressed by this, but her forehead creased a little in concentration, and I could see her lips move as she sounded out the syllables. Both Joanie and Félicité were good spellers; they'd been playing with discarded lead type since they were toddlers and loved stumping each other with new words.

That was a thought; maybe I could get her to spell unusual words for me during the compress treatments. The sty was a big, nasty one; her entire eyelid had been red and swollen in the beginning, the eye no more than a gleaming, resentful slit. Now the sty itself had shrunk to the size of a pea, and at least three-quarters of the eye was visible.

"H," she said, watching me to see if that was right, and I nodded. "O, R, D . . ." I nodded again, and saw her lips move silently. "Hor-de-o-lum," I repeated helpfully, and she nodded, more confident. "E, O, L, U, M!"

"Excellent!" I said, beaming at her. "How about . . ." I cast about for another good one, long but strictly phonetic. "Hepatitis?"

"What's that?"

"Viral infection of the liver. Do you know where your liver is?" I was looking through my medicine chest, but appeared to be out of aloe salve. I should ride over to Bartram's Garden tomorrow, I thought, weather permitting. I was out of almost everything, in the wake of the battle. The usual small twinge came in my side at thought of it, but I pushed it firmly away. It would fade, and so would the thoughts.

Marsali appeared suddenly in the kitchen door, as Joanie was carefully spelling "acanthocytosis," and I looked up from my grinding. She was holding a letter in her hand and looked worried.

"Is it the Indian they call Joseph Brant that Young Ian kens?" she asked.

"I expect he knows quite a few of them," I replied, setting down my pestle. "But I've heard him mention Joseph Brant, yes. The man's Mohawk name starts with a 'T,' I think, but that's as much as I feel sure of. Why?" I felt a slight uneasiness at the name. Ian's Mohawk wife, Emily, had been living in a settlement in New York founded by Brant; Ian had mentioned it, very briefly, when he'd gone up there to visit her last year.

He hadn't said what the purpose of his visit was, and neither Jamie nor I had asked, but I assumed it to have had something to do with his fear that he couldn't sire children, as all his babies with Emily had either been stillborn or miscarried. He'd asked me about the matter, and I'd told him what I could, offering what reassurance I could that he might be able to have children with another woman.

I offered up a quick prayer for Rachel's chances, then returned abruptly to what Marsali was saying.

"They did *what*?"

"This gentleman"—she tapped the letter—"says that Brant and his men fell upon a wee place called Andrustown. No but seven families living there." Her lips pressed tight, and she glanced at Joanie, who was listening with her ears flapping. "They plundered and burnt the place, he says, and massa—er . . . did awa wi' a number of the folk who lived there."

"What's that word, Mam?" Joanie asked brightly. "The one that means 'did awa' with?"

"'Massacred,'" I told her, saving her mother the embarrassment. "It means indiscriminate and brutal slaughter. Here." I handed her the fresh compress, which she applied without protest, frowning in thought.

"Is that different than just killin' someone?"

"Well," I said judiciously, "it depends. You might kill someone by accident, for instance, and that wouldn't be a massacre, though it would certainly be lamentable. You might kill someone who was trying to kill *you,* and that would be self-defense."

"Rachel says ye oughtn't do that," Joanie observed, but merely for the sake of thoroughness. "What about if ye're with an army and have to kill the soldiers on the other side?"

Marsali made a low Scottish noise of disapproval but answered tersely.

"If a man's gone to the army, then killin' is his job," she said. "He does it—mostly—" she added fairly, with a raised brow to me, "to protect his ain family and property. So that's more like self-defense, aye?"

Joanie glanced from her mother to me, still frowning.

"I ken what 'bru-tal' is," she said. "That's bein' mean when ye havena got to. But what's 'in-dis-crim-in-ate'?" She sounded it out carefully, as though about to spell it.

"Without choosing," I said, lifting one shoulder in a shrug. "It means you do something without taking much notice who you do it to and probably without much reason to do it to that particular person."

"Did Cousin Ian's Indian friend have nay reason for burning yon place and killing the folk, then?"

Marsali and I exchanged a glance.

"We dinna ken that," Marsali said. "But it's no a good thing, whatever he meant by it. Now, ye're done. Go along and find Félicité and start in fillin' up the washtub." She took the compress from Joanie and shooed her out.

She stood watching until Joanie had gone out through the back door, then turned to me and handed me the letter.

It was from a Mr. Johansen, apparently one of Fergus's regular correspondents, and the contents were as Marsali had said, though adding a few gruesome details that she hadn't mentioned in Joanie's hearing. It was fairly factual, with only the barest of eighteenth-century ornaments, and the more hair-raising—literally, I thought; some of the Andrustown residents had been scalped, by report—for that.

Marsali nodded as I looked up from the letter.

"Aye," she said. "Fergus wants to publish the account, but I'm nay so sure he ought to. Because of Young Ian, ken?"

"What's because of Young Ian?" said a Scottish voice from the printshop doorway, and Jenny came through, a marketing basket over one arm. Her eyes went to the letter in my hand, and her sharp dark brows rose.

"Has he told ye much about her?" Marsali asked, having explained the letter. "The Indian lass he wed?"

Jenny shook her head and began taking things out of her basket.

"Nay a word, save for his telling Jamie to say he wouldna forget us." A shadow crossed her face at the memory, and I wondered for a moment how it must have been for her and Ian, receiving Jamie's account of the circumstances in which Ian had become a Mohawk. I knew the agony with which he'd written that letter, and doubted that the reading of it had been done with less.

She laid down an apple and beckoned to me for the letter. Having read it through in silence, she looked at me. "D'ye think he's got feelings for her still?"

"I think he does," I answered reluctantly. "But nothing like his feelings for Rachel, surely." I did recall him, though, standing with me in the twilight on the demilune battery at Fort Ticonderoga, when he'd told me about his children—and Emily, his wife.

"He feels guilty about her, does he?" Jenny asked, shrewdly watching my face. I gave her a look, but nodded. She compressed her lips, but then handed the letter back to Marsali.

"Well, we dinna ken whether his wife has anything to do wi' this Brant or his doings, and it's no her that's been massacred. I'd say let Fergus print it, but"—and she glanced at me—"show the letter to Jamie and have him talk to wee Ian about it. He'll listen." Her expression lightened a little then, and a slight smile emerged. "He's got a good wife now, and I think Rachel will keep him to home."

MAIL WAS DELIVERED to the printshop at all hours of the day—and, not infrequently, the night—and by all manner of messengers. Philadelphia gloried in the best postal system in the colonies, this having been established by Benjamin Franklin only three years before; post riders rode regularly between New York and Philadelphia and over thirty other routes through the colonies.

Given the nature of Fergus's business and the nature of the times, though, almost as much mail arrived by older routes: passed along by travelers, merchants, Indians, and soldiers, and shoved under the door in the night watches. Or handed to a member of the family in the street. It was exchanges of that sort during the British occupation of the city that had compelled me to marry John Grey in order to avoid arrest for sedition and spying.

John's own letter, though, arrived sedately in the pouch of a postal rider, properly stamped, and sealed with a blob of yellow wax imprinted with his signet in the shape of a smiling half-moon.

To Mrs. James Fraser, Fraser's Printshop, Philadelphia
From Lord John Grey, Wilbury House, New York

My dear,

I am with my brother and his regiment in New York, and am like to remain here for some time. That being so, I thought I would mention that the Lease of my house on Chestnut Street will run until the End of the Year, and as the Thought of it being left empty to be vandalized or left to ruin distresses me, I conceived the Notion of offering it to you once again.

Not, I hasten to add (lest your intransigent Husband be reading this), as a Domicile but rather as Premises for a Surgery. Acquainted as I am with your peculiar Habit of attracting Persons suffering from Disease, Deformity, or hideous Injury, and being also well acquainted with the Number of Persons presently inhabiting the younger Mr. Fraser's printing Establishment, I believe you may find your medical Adventures more easily accommodated in Chestnut Street than between a Printing Press and a towering Stack of sixpenny Bibles bound in buckram.

As I do not expect you to spend your valuable Time in domestic Labor, I have arranged for Mrs. Figg and a Servant of her choice to remain in my employment for so long as you require them, being paid through my Bank. You will greatly oblige me, my dear, by accepting this Proposition, as it will put my mind at ease regarding the Property. And the Thought of you at work, earnestly administering a Clyster to General Arnold, will greatly enliven the Tedium of my present Condition.

Your most obedient Servant,
John

"What are ye smiling at, Mother Claire?" Marsali inquired, observing me with the letter in hand. She smiled, teasing. "Has someone sent ye a *billet-doux*?"

"Oh, something of the sort," I said, folding it up. "You wouldn't know where Jamie is just now, would you?"

She closed one eye to assist thought, keeping the other on Henri-Christian, who was industriously blacking his father's best boots—and a good deal of himself in the process.

"He said he was going wi' Young Ian to see a man about a horse," she said, "and then to the docks."

"The docks?" I said in surprise. "Did he say why?"

She shook her head. "I could maybe guess, though. That'll do, Henri! *A Dhia,* the state of you! Go find one o' your sisters and tell her to wash your hands for ye, aye?"

Henri looked at his hands, as though astonished to find them completely black.

"Oui, Maman," he said, and, cheerfully wiping them on his breeches, scampered out into the kitchen, bellowing, "Félicité! Come wash me!" at the top of his lungs.

"Why?" I asked, moving closer and lowering my voice slightly—for obviously she'd got rid of Henri-Christian on the little pitchers–big ears principle.

"He's been talking wi' Fergus about going with ye, when ye go back to North Carolina," she said. "If I had to guess, I'd say he's gone to find out what it might cost to move everything"—she made a sweeping gesture, encompassing everything from printing press to loft—"by ship."

"Hmm," I said, as noncommittally as possible, though my heart had leapt—at both the thought of imminent departure for the Ridge and the thought that Fergus and Marsali might come with us. "Do you . . . want to?" I asked cautiously, seeing the line between her brows. She was still a lovely woman, fair and fine-boned, but she was too thin, and the lines of strain sharpened her features.

She shook her head, but in indecision rather than negation.

"I really dinna ken," she admitted. "It's a good bit easier now, wi' the British gone—but they're no so far away, are they? They could come back, and then what?" She glanced uneasily over her shoulder, though the printshop was empty for the moment. Fergus had had to leave home and live furtively on the outskirts of the city, during the last months of the British occupation.

I opened my mouth to tell her that I doubted this. Hal Grey had told me, under the influence of ganja, that the new British strategy was to sever the southern colonies from the North and suppress the rebellion there, thus starving the North into submission. But I closed it without speaking. Best not to mention that until I found out whether Jamie had told Fergus.

Why didn't I bloody *know* what was going to happen? I asked myself in frustration—and not for the first time. Why hadn't I thought to brush up on American history when I had the chance?

Well, because I hadn't expected to end up in America, was the answer. Just went to show, I supposed. Pointless to spend too much time in planning, anyway, given the propensity of life to make sudden left-hand turns without warning.

"It would be wonderful, if you were to come," I said, as mildly as possible, adding craftily, "so nice to have the children nearby."

Marsali snorted, giving me a sideways glance.

"Aye," she said dryly. "Never think I dinna appreciate the value of a grannie. And when ye leave, Grannie Janet will go, too."

"Do you think so?" I hadn't thought of that. "But Jenny loves you and your children—Fergus is as much a son to her as any of the boys she bore."

"Well, that's maybe true," she admitted, with a brief smile that showed me the radiant fifteen-year-old who had married Fergus on a Caribbean beach twelve years before. "But Young Ian's her youngest, ken? And she's had too little of him. Now he's wed, she'll want to be nearby, to help wi' his bairns when they come. And ye ken Rachel will go where Ian does—and Ian will go where Da does."

That was a shrewd assessment, I thought, and gave her a brief nod of agreement and respect.

She sighed deeply and, sitting down in her nursing chair, took up the topmost item in the brimming mending basket, the threaded needle still sticking up from the garment where she'd last put it down. I had no desire to abandon the conversation and, pulling out a stool, sat down beside her and plucked one of Germain's stockings out of the basket. The workbasket, with its housewife, thread balls, and darning egg, was set beside the mending, and I deftly threaded my own needle, feeling pleased that I could still do that without putting on my spectacles.

"What about Fergus?" I asked bluntly. Because plainly Fergus was the crux of the matter, where Marsali was concerned.

"Aye, that's the rub," she said frankly. "I'd go, and happy, but ye ken how it was for him when we stayed on the Ridge."

I did, and grimaced slightly, stretching the heel of the stocking over the darning egg.

"It's been dangerous in the city, this last year," she said, and swallowed at the memory. "Couldna tell ye how many times the soldiers came to arrest him; they broke up the shop, more than once, when they couldna find him. And the Loyalists would come and paint slogans on the front wall sometimes. But the danger didna trouble him—so long as it didna threaten me and the bairns."

"And sometimes even if it does," I muttered. "And I don't mean just Fergus. Bloody men."

Marsali sniffed with amusement.

"Aye. But the thing is—he *is* a man, no? He's got to feel he's worth something. He needs to be able to care for us, and that's a thing he can do—and do well—here. I canna see how he'd make a decent living in the mountains."

"True," I admitted reluctantly. It was a hot day, and stifling in the kitchen, with the cauldron simmering over the hearth. Flies or no flies—and there were an ungodly number of flies in Philadelphia—I got up to open the back door. It wasn't noticeably cooler outside, though at least the fire under the big washtub hadn't yet been lit; the girls were still filling it, trudging to and fro from the well with their buckets.

Henri-Christian was nowhere in sight, but had presumably been scrubbed; a filthy black cloth lay crumpled on the doorstep. I stooped to pick it up and saw a folded bit of paper lying on the ground beside the step. It had no direction on it but looked purposeful, so I picked it up and took it back inside.

"Still," Marsali said, barely waiting for me to sit down. "I'm thinkin' that even if we canna go to the Ridge, it might be as well if we were to go. There must be places in the South that could use a printer, even if they're none sae big as Philadelphia."

"Well, there's Charleston," I said doubtfully, "and Savannah. They're just as hot and ghastly in the summer as Philadelphia is, but the winters are milder, I suppose."

She shot me a brief look over the shift she was mending,

then set it down on her lap, as though having come to a decision.

"It's no the weather that troubles me," she said quietly. And, bending, she groped under the pile of shirts and stockings, emerging with a handful of grubby notes and frayed letters. Handling these gingerly, as though they carried some disease, she placed them on my knee.

"Any printer in these days gets such things poked under his door," she said, watching my face as I read through the first few. "Especially if ye take a stand. We didn't, for as long as we could, but after a time, ye just canna stand in the middle o' the road any longer."

This was said with a simplicity and acceptance that brought tears to my eyes. The more so with the content of the anonymous notes—for they were all unsigned and in a variety of hands, though some were plainly written by the same person—making it quite clear what the price of standing on the Rebel side might be.

"It was worse, maybe," she said, "when the British were here. I thought it might stop when they left, but it didn't."

"I don't imagine all the Loyalists left with them," I said, taking a deep breath in order to control myself. I felt as though I'd been punched in the stomach.

"Only the richer ones," Marsali said cynically. "The ones who thought they'd be dragged from their homes or beaten and robbed, without the army to protect them. But it doesna mean the poorer ones dinna have the same opinions."

"Why do you keep these?" I asked, handing them back with two fingers, as though holding them with tongs. "I think I'd throw them into the fire at once."

"I did, at first," she said, tucking the handful of nastiness carefully back into the bottom of the basket. "But I found I couldna forget what they'd said, and the words would come back to me at night and stop me sleeping." She straightened, shrugged, and took up her needle again.

"I told Fergus, and he said the thing to do was to keep them and read them through several times a day, one after the other. Read them tae each other." A brief, rueful smile touched her mouth. "So we did, after the bairns were asleep—we'd sit by the fire and take turns reading them. And he'd make fun o' them, criticizing the grammar and the lack o' poetry, comparing them one to another, and we'd rank them from best to worst . . . and then we'd put them away and go to sleep in each other's arms."

Her hand rested gently on the mound of mending, as though it were Fergus's shoulder, and I smiled.

"Well," I said, and, clearing my throat, produced the note I'd picked up on the step. "I have no idea whether this is another one for your collection—but I found it on the back step just now."

She took it with a raised brow and looked it over, turning it to and fro.

"It's cleaner than most," she observed. "A decent rag paper, too. It's maybe just a . . ." Her voice died away as she opened it and began to read. I could see that the writing inside was brief; within seconds, the blood drained from her face.

"Marsali." I reached toward her, and she thrust the note into my hand and rose swiftly.

Ladybird, ladybird, the note read, *fly away home. Your house is on fire and your children are gone.*

"Henri-Christian!" Marsali's voice was strong and urgent. "Girls! Where's your wee brother?"

112

DAYLIGHT HAUNTING

I FOUND HENRI-CHRISTIAN in the first place I looked: down the street, playing with the two smallest Phillips girls. The Phillipses had ten children, and even Henri-Christian could blend into their household without causing much notice.

Some parents kept their children from coming anywhere near Henri-Christian—whether from fear that dwarfishness was catching, I supposed, or from the popular superstition that his appearance was the result of his mother having fornicated with the devil. I'd heard that one now and then, though everyone in the neighborhood knew better than to say it anywhere in the hearing of Jamie, Fergus, Ian, or Germain.

The Phillipses were Jewish, though, and apparently felt some kinship with a person whose differences set him apart. Henri-Christian was always welcome at their house. Their maid-of-all-work merely nodded when I asked whether one of the older children would walk home with him later, then went back to her washing; it was laundry day all over Philadelphia, and the humid atmosphere was aggravated by a score of steaming washtubs in the neighborhood, all fuming with the reek of washing soda.

I went back quickly to the printshop to tell Marsali where Henri-Christian was and, having relieved her fears, put on my wide-brimmed hat and announced my intent of going to buy some fish for supper. Marsali and Jenny, armed respectively with a laundry fork and a large paddle for clothes-stirring, gave me marked looks—both of them knew exactly how much I disliked doing laundry—but neither said anything.

I had of course been excused from housework while recuperating and, in all truth, was still not up to the labor of hoicking hot, sodden clothes about. I could have managed hanging out the washing, perhaps, but soothed my conscience on grounds that: 1) fish made an easy supper on laundry day, 2) I needed to walk regularly, in order to regain my strength, and 3) I wanted to talk to Jamie, alone.

The anonymous letter had upset me nearly as much as it had Marsali. It wasn't like the other threats she had shown me: those were all specifically political, and while some were aimed at Marsali (for she had run the newspaper alone while Fergus was in hiding), they were of the run-of-the-mill "Rebel bitch" variety. I'd heard such epithets—along with "Tory whore!" and their German and Yiddish equivalents—commonly in the rougher parts of Philadelphia.

This was different. It had the whiff of a refined and intelligent malice, and I suddenly felt the presence of Jack Randall at my shoulder, so strongly that I came to an abrupt halt and spun round.

The street was busy, but there was no one behind me. No

glimpse of a red coat anywhere, though there were Continental officers here and there, in blue and buff.

"Bugger off, Captain," I said, under my breath. Not quite far enough under: I got a wide-eyed look from a round little woman selling pretzels from a tray round her neck. She glanced over her shoulder to see to whom I was speaking, then turned back to me with a look of concern.

"You are all right, madam?" she said in a heavy German accent.

"Yes," I said, embarrassed. "Yes, quite all right. Thank you."

"Take this," she said kindly, handing me a pretzel. "I think you are hungry." And waving away my fumbling attempt at payment, she went off down the street, wide hips rolling, waving a stick of pretzels stacked like quoits and shouting, *"Brezeln! Heiße Brezeln!"*

Feeling suddenly dizzy, I leaned against the front of a building, closed my eyes, and bit into the pretzel. It was chewy, fresh, and rimed with salt, and I discovered that the woman had been right. I *was* hungry. Starved, in fact.

The pretzel hit my stomach and then my bloodstream, imparting an instant sense of stability and well-being, and the momentary panic I'd felt evaporated so quickly that I could almost believe it hadn't happened. Almost.

It *hadn't* happened in some time. I swallowed the last bit of pretzel and, after checking my pulse—strong and steady—set off again toward the river.

I walked slowly; it was midday, and any great exertion would leave me drenched with sweat and very likely light-headed again. I ought to have brought my walking stick but had recklessly decided to do without it. I hated feeling infirm.

I hated feeling . . . *that,* even more. The sudden sense of threat, irrational fear . . . violation. Flashback, the military called it—would call it—in my time. It hadn't happened to me since Saratoga, though, and I'd almost forgotten about it. Almost.

Completely explainable, of course: I'd been shot, come close to dying, was still physically weak. The last time, I'd been in the dark in the forest near a battlefield, alone, lost, and surrounded by violent men. No wonder it had happened then; the situation was much too close to what it had been when I'd been abducted and assaulted—

"Raped," I said out loud, firmly, to the extreme startlement of a pair of gentlemen passing by. I paid no attention to them. No point in trying to avoid either the word or the memory. It was over; I was safe.

Before that . . . the first time I'd been overtaken by that sense of threat, it was at River Run, in the course of a party. But a party where the sense of imminent violence was palpable. On that occasion, Jamie had been nearby, thank God. He'd seen that I was spooked—literally, he assumed—and had given me a handful of salt with which to lay the ghost that haunted me.

The Highlands always had a practical answer, whether the difficulty was keeping a fire smoored for the night, having your cow run dry, or being haunted.

I touched the corner of my mouth with my tongue, found a stray salt crystal from the pretzel, and nearly laughed. I looked over my shoulder for the woman who'd given me succor, but she'd vanished.

"Just as an angel should, I suppose," I murmured. "Thank you."

There was probably a charm for it in the *Gàidhlig,* I reflected. There were dozens, probably hundreds. I knew only a few, mostly those concerned with health (they gave my Gaelic-speaking patients reassurance), but picked the one that seemed most suitable to the situation and strode firmly along, my feet solid on the cobbles, chanting:

"I trample on thee, thou seizure,
As tramples whale on brine,
Thou seizure of back, thou seizure of body,
Thou foul wasting of chest."

And then I saw Jamie, coming up from the docks, laughing at something Fergus was saying, and the world dropped back into place around me.

JAMIE TOOK ONE look at me, took my arm, and steered me into a small coffeehouse around the corner on Locust Street. At this hour of the day, it was all but deserted, and I attracted relatively little attention. Women did drink coffee—

when any was to be had—but they mostly drank it at home, in company with friends or at small parties and salons. And while there were grander coffeehouses in London and Edinburgh that women might now and then frequent, the Philadelphia coffeehouses tended to be male preserves of business, gossip, and politics.

"What have ye been doing, Sassenach?" Jamie inquired mildly, taking the tray of coffee cups and almond biscuits from the server. "Ye look—" He squinted at me, evidently searching for a term that would be accurate without causing me to pour scalding coffee on him.

"Somewhat indisposed," Fergus said, taking up the sugar tongs. "Here, milady." Without asking, he dropped three large lumps of brown sugar into my cup. "They say that drinking hot beverages will cool you," he added helpfully.

"Well, it does make you sweat more," I said, taking up my spoon. "But if the sweat doesn't evaporate, it certainly won't make you cooler." I estimated the ambient humidity at roughly a thousand percent, but tipped a little of my sweetened coffee into the saucer and blew on it nonetheless. "As to what I've been doing, I was on my way to buy fish for supper. And what have *you* gentlemen been doing?"

Sitting down had made me feel a good bit steadier, and being flanked by Jamie and Fergus made the odd sense of threat I'd experienced in the street fade a bit. But thought of the anonymous letter on the step raised the hairs on the back of my neck, despite the heat.

Jamie and Fergus glanced at each other, and Fergus raised one shoulder.

"Reckoning our assets," Jamie said. "And visiting warehouses and shipping captains."

"Really?" The thought made my heart lift immediately. These sounded like the first concrete steps toward going home. "Have we got any assets to speak of?" Most of our available cash had gone to pay for horses, uniforms, weapons, food for Jamie's men, and other war-related expenses. Theoretically, Congress would reimburse these expenses, but given everything General Arnold had told me about Congress, I rather thought we oughtn't to hold our collective breath in anticipation.

"A bit," Jamie said, smiling at me. He knew very well what I was thinking. "I've found a buyer for the gelding; four pounds."

"That seems a good price," I said uncertainly. "But . . . wouldn't we need the horse, for travel?"

Before he could answer, the door opened and Germain came in, a bundle of broadsheets under one arm and a scowl on his face. The latter disappeared like the morning dew as he spotted us, though, and he came to hug me.

"*Grand-mère!* What are you doing in here? *Maman* said you went to buy fish."

"Oh," I said, suddenly guilty at thought of the laundry. "Yes. I am—er, I mean, I was just on my way. . . . Would you like a bite, Germain?" I offered him the plate of almond biscuits, and his eyes lighted up.

"One," said Fergus firmly. Germain rolled his eyes at me but took a single biscuit, lifting it with two fingers in exaggerated delicacy.

"Papa," he said, consuming the biscuit in two swift bites, "I think perhaps you should go home."

Both of Fergus's strongly marked black brows rose.

"Why?"

"Because," Germain said, licking sugar from the corner of his mouth and eyeing the remaining biscuits, "Grannie Janet told Mr. Sorrel that if he didn't leave off pestering *Maman,* she would stab him with the laundry fork. She might do it, too," he added thoughtfully, dabbing a finger on the plate for crumbs.

Fergus growled. It quite startled me, as I hadn't heard anything like that from him since he'd been a feral eight-year-old pickpocket in Paris.

"Who's Mr. Sorrel?" Jamie asked, in a deceptively mild tone of voice.

"A tavern owner who passes by the shop on his way to and from his work and stops to buy a newspaper—and to ogle my wife," Fergus said tersely. He pushed back his bench, and rose. "Excuse me, milady," he said, bowing to me.

"Had I best come with ye?" Jamie asked, also pushing back from the table. Fergus shook his head, though, and put on his cocked hat.

"No. The man is a coward. One sight of me, and he will be gone." His very white teeth showed in a sudden smile. "If your sister has not disposed of him already."

He went out, leaving the biscuits at the mercy of Germain, who scooped them tidily into his pocket before going to the counter to deposit the new broadsheets, take away the much-read and coffee-spotted ones from yesterday, and collect his money from the proprietress.

"Whilst you were reckoning assets, did Fergus tell you how well he's doing with the printing business?" I asked, pitching my voice low enough as not to reach Germain.

"He did." Jamie passed a coffee cup under his nose and grimaced slightly. The beverage was nominally coffee—a few genuine beans had likely been included in the brew—but contained a high proportion of chicory and a few other ingredients. I picked a small fragment of charred acorn out of my saucer and added more sugar.

The printshop was in fact very profitable; the more so now, as Fergus's chief competitor, a Loyalist, had left town with the departure of the British army.

"There are a good many expenses, though," Jamie explained. "And some of those have increased since the army left." Paper and ink were more difficult to obtain, with the army no longer protecting transport in and out of the city. And the increased danger of the public roads meant that fewer orders of printed books were shipped and, when they were, must either be insured or risk loss.

"And then there's insurance on his premises, which is expensive," Jamie added. He pinched his nose slightly, then drank his coffee in three large gulps. "Marsali doesna like paying that," he said, gasping a little, "but Fergus kent what happened to my place in Edinburgh. And he told me a few things that Marsali doesna ken, too."

"Such as?" I cast a wary eye at Germain, but he was engaged in what was plainly a saucy conversation with a serving girl at the counter. The girl was two or three years older than Germain but clearly amused by him.

"Oh, the odd threat from folk who dinna like something he's printed or who have their noses put out o' joint because he willna print something of theirs. Bit of sabotage, sometimes: his broadsheets stolen from coffeehouses and taverns and scattered in the street—though he said that's got better since Mr. Dunphy left town."

"Dunphy being the Loyalist printer?"

"Aye. Germain!" he called across the shop. "Have ye other places to visit today? Because if so, ye'd best get to them before your news goes stale."

That made the few customers laugh, and Germain's ears went somewhat pink. He gave his grandfather a measured look, but was wise enough not to say anything, and with a few last words to the counter girl, went out, slipping the small cake she'd given him into his pocket with a casual air.

"You don't suppose he's been picking pockets, do you?" I asked, observing the skill with which this maneuver was accomplished. Fergus had taught Germain a good many of his own techniques in that regard, not wanting the skills to be lost.

"God knows, but all the better if he leaves Philadelphia. He willna find so much scope for that particular talent in the mountains." Jamie craned his neck to see out the window, watching Germain go down the street, then sat back, shaking his head.

"The main thing Fergus hasna told Marsali, though, is about yon French popinjay Wainwright."

"What, the fashionable Percival?" I asked, mildly amused. "Is he still around?"

"Aye, he is. Persistent wee sodomite," he observed dispassionately. "He wrote out a detailed account of what he claims is the story of Fergus's parents, wi' the conclusion that Fergus is the heir to some great estate in France. Fergus says if it had been a romantic novel, it would have been criticized as too implausible and nay publisher would touch it." He grinned at the thought, but then sobered. "Still. Fergus says he hasna the slightest intent o' having anything to do with the matter, as even if it were true, he doesna mean to be a pawn for someone else's interests—and if it's not true, still less."

"Hmm." I had taken to simply eating the sugar lumps by now, rather than mixing them into the problematical coffee, and crunched one between my back teeth. "Why is he keeping that from Marsali, though? She knows about Wainwright's earlier approaches, doesn't she?"

Jamie drummed his hand on the table in thought, and I watched in fascination; he had been accustomed for a great while to drumming the two stiff fingers of his right hand when thinking—the middle and ring finger, which had been badly broken, crudely reset, and frequently re-broken, owing to the clumsy way it stuck out. But I had finally amputated the ruined ring finger after he'd had half of it sliced off by a cavalry saber during the first battle of Saratoga. He still drummed his hand, though, as if the finger were still there, though now only the middle finger struck the tabletop.

"She does," he said slowly. "But Fergus said that there began to be that odd wee bit of . . . something . . . in Wainwright's importunities. No *quite* a threat—but just things like an observation that, of course, since Fergus is the heir to the Beauchamp estate—if he is, in fact—then Germain would inherit the title and land after him."

I frowned.

"I can see that being offered as an inducement—but why is it a threat?"

He gavc mc a level look over the coffee debris.

"If Germain would inherit this estate—Wainwright's principals dinna really need Fergus, now, do they?"

"Jesus H. . . . Really?" I said. "You—or, rather, Fergus thinks Wainwright and company might *kill* him and then use Germain to get hold of this property or whatever it is they have in mind?"

Jamie gave the ghost of a shrug.

"Fergus hasna lived as long as he has without having a sense of when someone means him harm. And if he thinks there's summat amiss wi' this Wainwright, I'm inclined to believe him. Besides," he added fairly, "if it makes him more willing to leave Philadelphia and come south with us, I'm no going to persuade him he's wrong."

"Well, there's that." I looked dubiously at the dregs of my coffee and decided against it. "Speaking of Germain, though—or, rather, the children in general—that's actually why I was looking for you." And, in a few words, I described the ladybird note and its effect on Marsali.

Jamie's thick auburn brows drew together, and his face took on a look that his enemies would have recognized. I had last seen it in the light of dawn on a North Carolina mountainside, when he had escorted me through woods and meadows, from one cold body to the next, to show me that the men who had hurt me were dead, to reassure me that they could not touch me.

"That was what made me . . . er . . . indisposed in the street,"

I said, rather apologetically. "It just seemed so . . . evil. But a sort of *delicate* evil, if you know what I mean. It—rather gave me a turn." The dead had their own means of making you remember them, but I felt nothing at the memory of his vengeance beyond a remote sense of relief and an even remoter sense of awe at the supernatural beauty of carnage in such a setting.

"I do know," he said softly, and tapped his missing finger on the table. "And I should like to see that note."

"Why?"

"To see whether the handwriting looks like that in Percy Wainwright's letter, Sassenach," he said, pushing back from the table and handing me my hat. "Are ye ready?"

113

THANKS FOR ALL THE FISH

I HAD BOUGHT A striped bass nearly as long as my arm, along with a mess of crayfish and a gunnysack of oysters from the estuary, and the kitchen smelled delightfully of fresh bread and fish stew. This was a good thing, as stew can always be stretched, and Ian and Rachel, with Rollo in tow, had drifted into the printshop just before supper, so visibly in the throes of wedded bliss that it made one smile—and occasionally blush—to look at them.

Jenny did smile, and I saw her thin shoulders relax a little, seeing Ian's radiant face. I gave the stew a quick stir and came over to stand behind her as she sat by the fire, laying my hands on those shoulders and kneading them gently. I knew bloody well what a day's laundry felt like in the muscles.

She heaved a long, blissful sigh and bent her head to allow me to get my thumbs on her neck.

"D'ye think our wee Quaker lass is wi' child yet?" she murmured to me. Rachel was across the room, chatting with the younger children and very easy with them—though her eyes kept turning to Ian, who was looking at something Fergus had taken out of a drawer in the sideboard.

"They've been married barely a month," I whispered back, though I looked carefully at Rachel.

"It doesna take *that* long," Jenny said. "And plainly the lad kens his job. Look at her." Her shoulders quivered slightly with a suppressed laugh.

"A fine thing for a mother to be thinking about her son," I said under my breath, though I could neither keep the amusement out of my own voice nor say she was wrong. Rachel glowed in the magic light of mingled dusk and hearth fire, and her eyes rested on the lines of Ian's back, even as she admired Félicité's new rag doll.

"He takes after his father," Jenny said, and made a little "hmph" in her throat—still amused, but with a faint tinge of . . . longing? My own eyes went to Jamie, who had come to join Fergus and Ian by the sideboard. Still here, thank God. Tall and graceful, the soft light making shadows in the folds of his shirt as he moved, a fugitive gleam from the long straight bridge of his nose, the auburn wave of his hair. Still mine. Thank God.

"Come cut the bread, Joanie!" Marsali called. "Henri-Christian, stop playin' with that dog and fetch the butter, aye? And, Félicité, put your heid outside and call Germain." The distant sound of boys' voices came from the street, shouts punctuated by the occasional thud of a ball against the front wall of the shop. "And tell those wee heathens I said if they break a windowpane, their fathers will hear about it!"

A brief outbreak of domestic chaos ended with all the adults seated on the benches at table and the children in their own huddle by the hearth with their wooden bowls and spoons. Despite the heat of the evening, the fragrant steam of onions, milk, seafood, and fresh bread enveloped the table in a brief enchantment of anticipation.

The men sat down last, their murmured talk stopping well short of the table, and I gave Jamie a brief, questioning look. He touched my shoulder as he sat down beside me, saying, "Aye, later," under his breath, and nodded at the hearth. *Pas devant les enfants,* then.

Fergus cleared his throat. A small sound, but the children instantly stopped talking. He smiled at them, and their heads bowed over earnestly clasped hands.

"Bless us, O Lord," he said in French, "and these thy gifts, which we are about to receive from thy bounty, through Christ our Lord."

"Amen," everyone murmured, and talk washed over the room like the tide coming in.

"Are ye bound back to the army soon, Ian?" Marsali asked, tucking a damp lock of blond hair back into her cap.

"Aye," he replied, "but not Washington's army. No yet, anyway."

Jamie leaned across me to raise a brow at him.

"Ye've turned your coat, then?" he said. "Or just decided the British pay better?" There was a wry edge to this; he'd not seen a penny of pay and told me frankly that he didn't expect to. Congress wasn't swift about paying anyone, and a temporary general who'd resigned his commission was likely at the bottom of their list.

Ian closed his eyes in momentary bliss, chewing an oyster, then swallowed and opened them, wiping a dribble of milk from his chin.

"No," he said equably, "I'm takin' Dottie up to New York to see her da and Lord John."

That stopped all adult conversation dead, though the children continued to chatter by the hearth. I saw Jenny dart her eyes at Rachel, who looked composed, though considerably less blissful than she had before. She'd known about it, though; there was no surprise on her face.

"Why's that, then?" Jamie asked, in a tone of mild curiosity. "She's not decided Denzell doesna suit her, I hope? For I doubt he's taken to beating her."

That made Rachel laugh—briefly, but out loud, and the company relaxed a bit.

"No," she said. "I believe Dottie to be pleased in her marriage; I know my brother is." The smile lingered in her eyes, though her face grew serious as she glanced at Ian, then turned to Jamie.

"Her eldest brother has died. He was a prisoner of war, held in New Jersey. Her brother Henry received news yesterday confirming his death, but Henry cannot bear the strain of so long a journey yet, especially with the roads so dangerous, and Dottie feels she must go to her father."

Jenny gave her a sharp look, which sharpened a bit further as she turned it on Ian.

"The roads bein' so dangerous," she repeated, with a mild tone that matched Jamie's and fooled no one. Ian grinned at her and took a fresh chunk of bread, which he dunked in his stew.

"Dinna fash, Mam," he said. "There's a wee band o' folk I ken, traveling north. They're agreeable to going by New York. We'll be gey safe wi' them."

"What *sort* of folk?" Jenny asked suspiciously. "Quakers?"

"Mohawk," he said, the grin widening. "Come out wi' me and Rachel after supper, Mam. They'd be that pleased to meet ye."

I could honestly say that, in all the time I'd known her, I'd never before seen Jenny Murray gobsmacked. I could feel Jamie vibrating with suppressed hilarity next to me, and had to look down into my bowl for a moment to regain my own composure.

Jenny was made of stern stuff, though. She took a long moment, took a longer breath, pushed Rollo's nose out of her lap, and then said calmly, "Aye. I'd like that. Pass me the salt, Fergus, aye?"

In spite of the general amusement, I hadn't forgotten what Rachel had said about Dottie's brother Benjamin, and I felt a twist of surprisingly acute pain, as though someone had knotted a length of barbed wire round my heart. *"Do you ever make bargains with God?"* If Hal had offered such a bargain, evidently God had declined it. *Oh, God, Hal . . . I'm sorry.*

"I'm so sorry to hear about Dottie's brother," I said, leaning forward to talk to Rachel. "Do you know what happened?"

She shook her head briefly, and the firelight, now behind her, cast shadow on her face from the curtain of dark hair.

"Henry had had a letter from their brother Adam. He'd had the news from someone on General Clinton's staff, I think he said. All it said was that whoever had written the letter wished to express their regrets as to the death of Captain Benjamin Grey, a British prisoner of war who had been held at Middlebrook Encampment in New Jersey, and would General Clinton's office please relay this sad news to the captain's family.

They'd thought it possible that he was dead—but this seems to put the matter beyond all doubt, alas."

"Middlebrook Encampment is what they call the place in the Watchung Mountains where Washington took his troops after Bound Brook," Fergus remarked with interest. "But the army left there in June of last year. Why would Captain Grey be there, I wonder?"

"Does an army travel wi' its captives?" Jamie asked, raising one shoulder in a shrug. "Save if they're taken when the army's on the move, I mean."

Fergus nodded, conceding the point, but seemed still to be pondering something. Marsali stepped in before he could speak, though, gesturing at Ian with her spoon.

"Speakin' o' why—why are your friends going north?" she asked. "Hasn't anything to do wi' the massacre at Andrustown, has it?"

Jenny turned toward her son, intent. A closed look came over Ian's face, though he answered calmly enough.

"It does, aye. Where did ye hear o' that?"

Marsali and Fergus shrugged in unison, making me smile involuntarily, in spite of my distress over Hal's son.

"The way in which we hear most of the news we print," Fergus amplified. "A letter from someone who heard of the matter."

"And what do your friends have in mind to do about the matter?" Jenny asked.

"More to the point," Jamie said, twisting to address Ian, "what do *you* have in mind to do about it?"

I was watching Rachel, on the other side of the table, rather than Ian, but I saw a look too faint to be called anxiety cross her brow, relaxing in the next instant when Ian replied flatly, "Nothing." Perhaps feeling this too blunt, he coughed and took a gulp of beer.

"I dinna ken anyone who was there, and as I havena any intent to turn my coat and fight for the British wi' Thayendanegea . . . Nay," he finished, setting down his cup. "I'll go as far as New York to see Dottie safe and then come back to wherever Washington might be." He smiled at Rachel, his face shifting abruptly from its usual appealing half-homely expression to a startling attractiveness. "I need my scout's pay, after all; I've a wife to support."

"Ye must come and stay wi' us, then," Marsali said to Rachel. "While Ian's gone, I mean."

I hadn't time to wonder exactly where she planned to put Rachel—Marsali was ingenious and would doubtless find a place—before Rachel shook her head. She wasn't wearing a cap but wore her straight dark hair loose on her shoulders; I could hear the whisper of it against her dress as she moved.

"I shall go with Ian to fetch Dottie. Rollo and I will stay in camp with my brother until Ian returns. I can be useful there." Her long fingers curled and flexed in illustration, and she smiled at me. "Thee knows the joy of useful occupation, Claire, I expect."

Jenny made a nondescript noise in her throat, and Marsali snorted briefly, though without rancor.

"Indeed I do," I said, my eyes on the slice of bread I was buttering. "And which would you rather find useful occupation in, Rachel—boiling laundry, or lancing the boils on Mr. Pinckney's arse?"

She laughed, and the arrival of Henri-Christian with an empty bowl in his hands saved her replying. He set it on the table and yawned sleepily, swaying on his feet.

"Aye, it's late, wee man," his mother said to him, and, picking him up, cradled him in her arms. "Lay your head, *a bhalaich.* Papa will take ye up presently."

More beer was fetched, the little girls collected the empty bowls and put them in the bucket to soak, Germain vanished outside into the gathering dusk for the last few minutes of play with his friends, Rollo curled up to sleep by the fire, and talk became general.

Jamie's hand rested warmly on my thigh, and I leaned against him, laying my head briefly on his shoulder. He looked down at me and smiled, squeezing my leg. I was looking forward to the Spartan comfort of our pallet in the loft, the cooling freedom of shift and nakedness, and the sharing of whispers in the dark—but for the moment was more than content to be where I was.

Rachel was talking across Marsali to Fergus, Marsali humming quietly to Henri-Christian, whose round dark head lolled on her bosom, his eyes almost closed. I looked carefully at Rachel, but it was much too soon to see any signs of pregnancy, even if—And then I stopped, startled, as my eye caught something else.

I'd seen Marsali through her pregnancy with Henri-Christian. And I was seeing a bloom on her cheeks now that wasn't from the warmth of the room: a slight fullness of the eyelids, and a subtle softening and rounding of face and body that I might have recognized earlier, had I been looking for it. Did Fergus know, I wondered? And glanced quickly at the head of the table, to see him looking at Marsali and Henri-Christian, his dark eyes soft with love.

Jamie shifted a little beside me, turning to say something to Ian, on my other side. I turned, too, and saw that Ian's eyes were also fixed on Marsali and Henri-Christian, with a look of wistfulness that smote me to the heart.

I felt his longing, and my own—for Brianna. Roger, and Jem, and Mandy. Safe, I hoped—but not here, and I swallowed a lump in my throat.

"You'd die for them, happily," Hal had said, in the long night watch when I'd kept him breathing. "*Your family. But at the same time you think,* Christ, I *can't* die! What might happen to them if I weren't here?" He'd given me a wry and rueful smile. *"And you know bloody well that you mostly can't help them anyway; they've got to do it—or not—themselves."*

That was true. But it didn't stop you caring.

IT WAS HOT and close in the loft, with the comfortable lingering scents of supper crammed in under the rafters, the more argumentative pungencies of ink, paper, buckram, and leather that had built up all day, and the faintly pervasive scent of mule straw underlying everything. I gasped at the impact as I stepped off the ladder and went at once to open the loading door that looked out onto the cobbled alley behind the shop.

A blast of Philadelphia rushed in, fluttering the stacks of paper: smoke from a dozen nearby chimneys, an acrid stink from the manure pile behind the livery stable down the street, and the intoxicatingly resinous scent of leaves and bark and brush and flowers that was William Penn's legacy. *Leave one acre of trees for every five acres cleared,* he'd advised in his charter, and if Philadelphia had not quite met that ideal, it was still a particularly verdant city.

"God bless you, William," I said, beginning to shed my outer clothes as fast as possible. The evening air might be warm and humid, but it *was* moving, and I couldn't wait to let it move over my skin.

"That's a kind thought, Sassenach," Jamie said, stepping off the ladder into the loft. "Why, though? Is the lad in your mind for some reason?"

"Wh—oh, William," I said, realizing. "I hadn't actually meant your son, but naturally . . ." I fumbled to organize an explanation but gave it up, seeing that he wasn't really attending. "Were you thinking of him?"

"I was, aye," he admitted, coming to help with my laces. "Being wi' the weans and the bairns, and all sae comfortable together . . ." His voice died away and he drew me gently to him, bent his head to mine, and let it rest there with a sigh that stirred the hair near my face.

"You wish he could be part of it," I said softly, reaching up to touch his cheek. "Be part of the family."

"If wishes were horses, then beggars would ride," he said, and let go, with a wry smile visible in the glow from the kitchen below. "And if turnips were swords, I'd hae one by my side."

I laughed, but my eye went to the stack of Bibles where he was accustomed to leave his sword. His dirk was there, his pistols, shot bag, and a scatter of oddments from his sporran, but no sword. I squinted to be sure I was seeing a-right, but I was.

"I sold it," he said matter-of-factly, seeing the direction of my glance. "It's one good thing to be said of war: ye can get a good price for a decent weapon."

I wanted to protest, but didn't. He wore weapons with a lifelong ease, to the point that his knives and guns seemed a part of him, and I didn't like to see him diminished by the loss of any. But without an army commission, he likely wouldn't *need* a sword immediately, and we did certainly need money.

"You can buy another when we reach Wilmington," I said practically, returning his favor by unbuttoning his breeks. They slid off his lean hips and fell, puddling round his feet. "It would be lovely for William to know the truth about Bree and her family sometime. Will you tell him?"

"In the event that he ever comes within speakin' distance of me without trying to kill me?" One corner of his mouth curled ruefully. "Aye, maybe. But I maybe wouldn't tell him *all* the truth."

"Well, perhaps not all at once, no," I agreed. A warm breeze from the window stirred his hair and the tails of his shirt. I fingered the creased linen, warm and damp from his body. "Why don't you take that off?"

He looked me over carefully; I was standing now in nothing but my shift and stockings. A slow smile spread into his eyes.

"Fair's fair," he said. "Take yours off, as well, then."

CLAIRE WAS LOVELY, standing white and naked as a French statue against the deep twilight from the open window, her curly hair a storm cloud round her shoulders. Jamie wanted to stand and look at her, but he wanted a lot more to have his cock inside her.

There were still voices down in the kitchen, though, and he went and pulled the ladder up. Wouldn't do to have Germain or one of the girls scamper up to say good night.

There was a hoot of laughter from Ian and Fergus below, probably at sight of the ladder disappearing, and he grinned to himself, laying it aside. They had their own wives, and if they were foolish enough to sit drinking beer instead of enjoying their beds, it was none of his affair.

Claire was already on their pallet when he turned from the edge of the loft, a pale shadow under the gloom of the ink casks. He eased himself in naked beside her, touched her curving hip; she touched his cock. "I want you," she whispered, and suddenly everything changed.

It was their common magic, but magic nonetheless, the smell of onions and brine on her hands, the taste of butter and beer on her tongue, a tickle of hair on his shoulder, and a sudden rush when she ran a finger down the crack of his arse, which drew him straight up hard between her willing legs.

She made a sound that made him put a hand over her mouth, and he felt her laugh, hot breath against his palm, so he took his hand away and stopped her noises with his mouth, lying full on her for a moment, not moving, trying to wait, not able to wait for the feel of her squirming under him, slick and slippery, rubbing her nipples on his, urging him . . . and then she quivered and made a small noise of surrender that freed him to do as he would, and he did.

JAMIE HEAVED a deep sigh of utter relaxation.

"I have been wanting to do that all day, Sassenach. *Moran taing, a nighean.*"

"So have— Is that a *bat*?" It was: a flittering scrap of detached darkness, ricocheting from one side of the loft to the other. I grabbed Jamie's arm with one hand and pulled a corner of the sheet over my head with the other. It wasn't that I minded bats, as such; a bat whizzing to and fro three feet over my head in the dark, though . . .

"Dinna fash, Sassenach," he said, sounding amused. "It'll go out again directly."

"I'm not so sure of that," I said, slapping something ticklish on my neck. "There are probably any number of insects in here for it to hunt." Clouds of gnats and mosquitoes were inclined to roam in through the open loading window when evening fell, and it was always a Hobson's choice: keep the window closed and die of suffocation, or open it and be chivvied all night by crawling feet and the irritating *sneeeee!* of mosquitoes whining in our ears.

"Ye ought to be pleased about the bat, then," Jamie told me, rolling onto his side and using another bit of sheet to blot a sheen of sweat from his chest. "How many bugs did ye tell me they eat?"

"Well . . . lots," I said. "Don't ask me how I remember this, but according to Brianna's encyclopedia, the average little brown bat can eat up to a thousand mosquitoes in an hour."

"Well, there ye are, then," he said. "I dinna think there can be more than two or three hundred mosquitoes in here just now—it shouldna take him more than a quarter hour to deal wi' those."

It was a definite point, but I was not quite convinced of the virtues of entertaining a resident bat. I did emerge from my makeshift shelter, though, peering upward. "What if more bats come in?"

"Then they'll clear the place in five minutes." He sighed briefly. "D'ye want me to catch him, throw him out, and close the door, Sassenach?"

"No," I said, envisioning Jamie pirouetting around the loft in the dark, either being bitten by a startled bat if he did succeed in catching it or plunging over the edge of the loft in the effort to do so. "No, that's all right. Tell me what you didn't want to say earlier—that will take my mind off it."

"What I—oh, aye." He rolled onto his back, hands clasped on his stomach. "It's only I've been talking wi' Fergus and Ian about coming with us when we leave for the Ridge. Didna want to mention it at table, though. Ian and Fergus should talk it over wi' Rachel and Marsali by themselves first—and I didna want the bairns to hear. They'd go mad with excitement, and Marsali would run me through the heart wi' a meat skewer for stirring them up just before bed."

"She might," I said, amused. "Oh—speaking of Marsali . . . I rather think she's pregnant."

"Is she, now?" He turned his head to me, deeply interested. "Are ye sure?"

"No," I admitted. "I can't be sure without asking her nosy questions and examining her. But I think there's a good chance of it. If so . . . that might affect whether they go with us, mightn't it?"

The prospect of going home was suddenly real, in a way that it hadn't been even a moment before. I could almost feel the breath of the mountains on my bare skin, and gooseflesh rippled fleetingly over my ribs at the thought, in spite of the heat.

"Mmm," Jamie said, though absently. "I suppose it might. D'ye think—if she is wi' child, might the new one be like Henri-Christian?"

"Probably not," I said, though professional caution made me add, "I can't be positive that his type of dwarfism isn't a hereditary condition, because Fergus doesn't know anything about his family. But I think Henri-Christian's is probably a mutation—something that happens just once, a sort of accident."

Jamie gave a small snort.

"Miracles only happen once, too, Sassenach," he said. "That's why all bairns are different."

"I wouldn't argue with that," I said mildly. "But we'll need to be traveling quite soon, won't we? Even if Marsali is pregnant, she won't be more than three or four months along." A small sense of unease crept into my mind. It was early September; snow might begin to close the mountain passes as early as October, though if it was a warm year . . .

"How long will it take, do you think? To get back to the Ridge?"

"Too long to make it before the snow, Sassenach," he said gently, running a hand down my back. "Even if I manage the money and find a ship to take us down to North Carolina—and I'd rather do that—"

"You would?" I blurted, astonished. "*You?* Take a ship? I thought you'd sworn you'd never set foot on one again unless it was the ship taking your coffin back to Scotland."

"Mmphm. Aye, well. If it was only me, then, aye, I'd rather walk to North Carolina barefoot over hot coals. But it's not. It's you, and—"

"Me?" I sat up straight, angry. "What do you mean by that? Ahhh!" I clutched my hair and dived into his lap, for the bat had zoomed within inches of my head; I actually *heard* its faint squeaking and the leathery flap of wings.

Jamie laughed, but with a faint edge to it. As I sat up again, he ran a hand down my right side and rested two fingers over the fresh scar there.

"I mean that, Sassenach," he said, and pressed. Very gently, and I kept myself from flinching at the touch—but the scar was still red and tender.

"I'm fine," I said, as firmly as possible.

"I've been shot, Sassenach," he said, very dryly. "More than once. I ken what it feels like—and how long it takes to get your full strength back. Ye nearly fell over in the street today, and—"

"I hadn't eaten anything; I was hungry, and—"

"I'm no taking ye overland," he said, in a tone that brooked no argument. "And it's not only you—though it's mostly you," he added, in a softer tone, smoothing the hair off my face. "But there are the wee bairns, as well, and now Marsali, if she's wi' child . . . It's a hard journey, lass, and dangerous, forbye. Did ye not say the duke told ye the British mean to take the South now?"

"Hmph," I said, but allowed him to pull me down next to him. "Yes, he did. But I've no idea what that might actually *mean,* in terms of where they are or what they're doing. The only battles I'd actually heard of, beyond Lexington and Concord and Bunker Hill, are Saratoga and Yorktown—that's where it ends, Yorktown," I added. "Obviously a few things must happen in between, though."

"Obviously," he said. "Aye. Well, I'll buy another sword when we get to North Carolina and I've money again."

He did in fact have considerable assets—in North Carolina. But there was no way of retrieving any of the gold hidden in the Spaniard's Cave there—even if he had trusted anyone to do so, no one knew where the cave was, save him and Jemmy—and the aging whisky (almost as valuable as the gold, if brought to the coast for sale) was in the same place.

"I suppose the price of a good sword isn't quite enough for ship's passage for nine people—no, eleven, if Ian and Rachel come, too—is it?"

"No," he said thoughtfully. "I said to Fergus that he might consider selling his press. He doesna own the premises, ken—but the press is his." He made a small gesture, encompassing the building around us. "There's my Bonnie in Wilmington, after all."

"Your—oh, your press. Of course." I hid a smile in his biceps. He invariably spoke of . . . well, her . . . with a certain possessive affection. Come to think, I wasn't sure I'd ever heard him talk about *me* that way. . . .

"Aye. Fergus has his mind set that he'll go on bein' a printer, and I think that's wise. Germain's not yet big enough to plow—and poor wee Henri-Christian never will be."

I suppressed my speculations as to just what Germain's reaction might be if forcibly removed from the environs of a thriving city and plunked down behind a plow. He might remember the Ridge fondly, but that didn't mean he wanted to be a farmer.

"What about Richard Bell?" Bell was the Loyalist who had been forcibly deported from his North Carolina home and sent, penniless and friendless, to England, ending up eventually in Edinburgh, where he had found employment as a printer—and where Jamie had encountered him and made the bargain whereby Richard would bring Bonnie to North Carolina and look after her in return for his passage home.

"I dinna ken," Jamie said reflectively. "I wrote to him, to say we were coming to Wilmington and that we must make some arrangement . . . but I've had no reply." This didn't necessarily mean anything; letters frequently were lost or late. Jamie shrugged a little and shifted, stretching as he resettled himself. "Aye, well; let that bide. We'll see when we see. How's our wee friend?"

"Our—oh." I looked up, scanning the low ceiling, but saw no trace of the bat. I didn't hear any whining mosquitoes, either. "Well done, bat," I said appreciatively.

Jamie laughed, low in his throat.

"Remember sittin' on the stoop and watching the bats come out in the summer evenings on the Ridge?"

"I do," I said softly, and turned on my side to embrace him lightly, hand on the curly hairs of his chest. I did remember. The Ridge. The cabin Jamie and Ian had built for shelter when we first came there, and the white piglet we'd bought, who had become the fearsome white sow, terror of the entire neighborhood. Our friends, Jamie's tenants, Lizzie and the Beardsley twins . . . My heart squeezed at some of the memories.

Malva Christie. Poor doomed child. And the Bugs—Jamie's trusted factor and his wife—who had proven a good deal less than trustworthy. And the Big House, our house, gone up in flames, and our life there with it.

"I'll need to build the new house first thing," he said thoughtfully. He laid his own hand on mine and squeezed it. "And I'll make ye a new garden. Ye can have half the money I got for my sword, to buy seeds."

114

BELIEF IS A WISE WAGER

September 10, 1778
New York

HAL GAVE A MILD snort. "I don't like your going alone," he said.

"I don't like it, either," John said matter-of-factly, corking his hip flask. "But the only person who could effectively go with me is you, and you can't, because of the regiment, so . . . God, I miss Tom Byrd," he said impulsively.

"Your erstwhile valet?" Hal smiled, despite the worry of the situation. "How long has it been since you've seen him? Ten years at least, surely?"

"At least that." Thought of Tom still gave him a slight pang. Tom had left his employment—with deep regret on both sides—in order to marry, and had become a successful publican in Southwark, his wife having inherited a thriving public house from her father. Grey couldn't begrudge him his happiness, but he still sorely missed Byrd, with his sharp eyes, quick mind, and anxious care for Grey's person as well as his clothes.

He glanced down at himself; his current valet managed to keep him decent—a task that he himself admitted to be Sisyphean—but lacked both imagination and conversation.

"You should take Marks, regardless," Hal said, having evidently followed his train of thought without difficulty. "Someone's got to keep you in order." He gave John's uniform a critical look.

"I *can* dress myself, you know," John said mildly. "As for the uniform—" He glanced down and shrugged. "Bit of a brush-off, clean shirt, spare stockings . . . it's not as though I mean to be calling on General Washington."

"We can only hope." Hal's lips pressed together. He'd already expressed his reservations—if anything so violently explicit could be described in such terms—regarding Grey's intent to travel as himself, in uniform.

"I've had quite enough of being arrested as a spy, thank you," John replied. "Beyond the risk of being hanged out-of-hand, the Americans' sense of hospitality . . . though come to think, I'd meant to ask: do you know a Watson Smith? Used to be a captain in the Twenty-second, I think."

Hal frowned in concentration, but his brow cleared almost immediately.

"I do," he said. "A very good officer; did well at Crefeld and Zorndorf." He cocked his head to one side, brows raised. "Why?"

"He's turned his coat; he's now a colonel in the Continental army. I was his involuntary guest for a short time. Nice fellow," Grey added fairly. "Got me drunk on applejack."

"Doubtless with the intent of extracting intelligence from you?" Hal's expression made it clear that he doubted there had been much in that line for Smith to extract.

"No," Grey said thoughtfully. "I don't think so. We just got drunk together. Nice fellow," he repeated. "I was going to express the hope that I wouldn't meet him again—shouldn't like to have to kill him, I mean—but I suppose it isn't beyond belief that I might run into him somewhere." The thought gave him a small, pleasant clench low down in the belly that rather surprised him.

"Anyway," he added, "I'm going in uniform, even if grubby uniform. It won't necessarily keep me from arrest, imprisonment, starvation, and torture, but it *will* save me from being hanged."

"Torture?" Hal gave him a look.

"I had in mind waking up after the applejack," John told him. "And the singing. Have you any idea how many verses the Americans have for 'Yankee Doodle'?"

Hal grunted in response to this and took out a leather folder, from which he extracted a thin sheaf of documents.

"Here are your *bona fides,*" he said, handing them over.

"They *may* help—assuming firstly that you're captured or detained, rather than shot on sight, and secondly that your captors take the time to read them."

Grey didn't trouble to reply to this, being occupied in thumbing through the documents. A copy of his warrant of commission; a note from Hal as Colonel of the Regiment, detaching Lieutenant Colonel John Grey temporarily from service and desiring him to undertake the task of locating and assisting one Mrs. Benjamin Grey (née Amaranthus Cowden), widow of Captain Benjamin Grey, late of the Thirty-fourth Foot; a "To Whom It May Concern" letter from Clinton, formally recognizing Grey's mission and requesting that every courtesy and assistance be provided him in consequence thereof; several bills of exchange drawn on Coutts' bank in New York ("Just in case," Hal told him. "In case of what?" "In case you get knocked over and relieved of your gold, halfwit." "Oh."); and . . . Benedict Arnold's note, granting the Duke of Pardloe and his brother, Lord John Grey, permission to abide temporarily in Philadelphia for the purpose of searching for the duke's nephew.

"Really?" Grey said, raising his brows at this last. "Under what circumstances do you think this might be helpful?"

Hal shrugged and straightened his waistcoat. "The fact that you and I are known to General Arnold is worth something. The note doesn't give his opinion of us, after all."

Grey gave the note a critical eye, but, in fact, Arnold had refrained from personalities and had not codified his threats regarding rails and tar and feathers.

"All right." He closed the folder and put it down, laying his hat on it to ensure against walking off without it. "That's that, then. What's for supper?"

JOHN GREY WAS enjoying a confused but pleasant dream involving spring rain, his dachshund Roscoe, Colonel Watson Smith, and a great deal of mud, when he gradually became aware that the raindrops on his face were real.

He opened his eyes, blinking, to discover his niece, Dottie, holding his pitcher in one hand and sprinkling water from her fingertips onto his face.

"Good morning, Uncle John," she said cheerily. "Rise and shine!"

"The last person injudicious enough to say that to me in the morning came to a most unpleasant end," he said, struggling upright and rubbing the sleeve of his nightshirt across his face.

"Really? What happened to him? Or was it a him?" She dimpled at him and set down the pitcher, wiping her wet fingers on her skirt.

"What an improper question," he said, eyeing her.

"Well, I am a married woman now, you know," she said, sitting down with an air of extreme self-possession. "I am allowed to know that men and women occasionally share a bed, even outwith the bonds of matrimony."

"Outwith? Where did you pick up that barbarous construction? Have you been speaking to Scotchmen?"

"Constantly," she said. "But what happened to the unfortunate person who tried to roust you from your slumbers?"

"Oh, him." He rubbed a hand over his head, still surprised at feeling the hair so short, though it had at least grown enough to fall over and lie somewhat flat, rather than sticking straight up like a shaving brush. "He was scalped by red Indians."

She blinked.

"Well, that will teach him, to be sure," she murmured.

Grey swung his legs out of bed and gave her a pointed look.

"I don't care how married you are, Dottie, you are *not* allowed to help me dress. What the devil are you doing here, anyway?"

"I'm going with you to find B-Ben's widow," she said, and all of a sudden her bright façade collapsed like papier-mâché in the rain. Tears welled up in her eyes, and she clamped a hand hard over her mouth to prevent them falling.

"Oh," Grey said. "Oh, my dear . . ." And pausing only to fling on his banyan—even in emergency, there were limits—he knelt beside her and gathered her into his arms.

"It's all right," he said softly to her, rubbing her back. "Ben may not be dead, after all. We think he's not—your father and I." *We certainly hope he's not,* he thought, but opted for the most positive view of the situation.

"You don't?" She choked, sniffed, and sat up a bit, looking up at him with drowned-cornflower eyes.

"Certainly not," he said firmly, and dug in the pocket of his banyan for a handkerchief.

"But why not?" She accepted the proffered linen—somewhat crumpled but not indecently so—and dabbed at her face. "How could he not be?"

Grey sighed, caught between Scylla and Charybdis, as usual when enmeshed in one of Hal's situations.

"Does your father know you're here?" he asked, as a delaying tactic.

"Don't—I mean, no," she said, clearing her throat and sitting up straighter. "I went to his quarters, but he was out, so I came on here to find you."

"How is it that you're sure Ben's died?" Grey stood up and, tying the belt of his banyan, began looking about for his slippers. He knew that Hal hadn't yet written to Minnie about Ben—wouldn't do so unless forced by dreadful certainty—and even if he had, there was no way in which word could have come back to Dottie so soon. And Hal would not have told his daughter the news until he was sure, no more than he would have told his wife.

"Henry told me," she said. She poured a little water onto the handkerchief and commenced repairs to her complexion. "I went to visit him and Mercy, and he'd just had a letter from Adam, telling him . . . you're *sure* he isn't dead?" she asked anxiously, lowering the handkerchief to gaze at him. "Adam's letter said he'd heard it from someone on General Clinton's staff, telling him for sure that Ben had died at a military camp in New Jersey—Middlebrook, I think he said it was called."

"No, we're not sure," he admitted. "But we have reasonable grounds for doubt, and until those have been completely explored, we will proceed on the assumption that he's not. I do have to find his wife, though," he added. "And child."

Dottie's eyes flew wide.

"A *child*? Ben has a baby?"

"Well, the woman who claims to be his wife has a son, or so she says—and she did say that Ben is the father of her offspring." Seeing that there was little alternative, he apprised her of the letter from Amaranthus Cowden that Hal had received in Philadelphia, and its contents.

"Now, as Ben didn't happen to mention this woman to Hal,

one of the duties I'm to carry out for your father is the determination as to whether she's telling the truth. And if she is, then of course I will bring her back with me, and the family will take care of her and the child."

"What if she's *not* telling the truth?" Dottie's distress was rapidly being subsumed by a combination of hope and curiosity.

"God knows," Grey said frankly. "Would you like to go and ask Marks to see about breakfast for us, Dottie? I may be out of bed, but I'm in no way equipped to conduct hypothetical conversations before I've had a cup of tea."

"Oh. Yes, of course." She rose, though slowly, plainly still thinking about the revelations, and went toward the door, but paused on the threshold and looked back at him.

"I *am* coming with you," she said firmly. "We can talk about it on the way."

HAL WALKED IN as the kippers and mixed grill were being laid out. He halted for a split second as he saw Dottie, but then came on, more slowly, eyeing her.

"Good morning, Papa," she said briskly, rising and coming to kiss his cheek. "Sit down and have a kipper."

He did sit down, still eyeing her, then switched his gaze to John.

"I had nothing to do with it," Grey assured his brother. "She arrived—how did you get here, Dottie?"

"On a horse," she replied patiently, taking a slice of toast.

"And where is your husband?" Hal asked mildly. "Does he know where you are?"

"Denzell is where his duty takes him," she said, rather tersely. "With the Continental army. Mine takes me here. And of course he knows."

"And he had no objection to your traveling alone from Pennsylvania to New York, over roads infested by—"

"I wasn't alone." She took a delicate bite of her toast, chewed, and swallowed. "Ian and some of his Mohawk friends brought me. The Mohawks were traveling to someplace north of here."

"Ian—is that by chance Ian Murray?" Grey asked, but then answered himself. "I suppose it must be; how many Mohawks can there be named Ian? I take it that he survived his wound, then; I'm pleased to hear it. How did you come to—"

"Dorothea," said Hal, in measured tones, staring at Dottie. "Why are you here?"

Dottie returned his stare, her jaw visibly clenched.

"B-because of Ben," she said, unable to keep her voice entirely steady. "Are you— Papa, are you *sure* he's not dead?"

Hal took an audible breath and nodded.

"I'm sure," he said in his best command voice. But John could see his knuckles whiten as he clutched a teaspoon, and felt the knot in his own stomach tighten in response.

Dottie clearly had her own doubts, judging from her glance at her father, but she obligingly nodded. Being Dottie, of course, she didn't stop there.

"How?" she said. "How do you know? Adam and Henry both think . . . the worst."

Hal's mouth opened a fraction of an inch, but nothing came out.

John thought that Hal ought really to have been prepared for this, but, after all, his brother *had* been having a difficult time. And, in all justice, it was hard to be prepared for something like Dottie.

"I suppose you'd better tell her," John said. "If you don't, she'll likely write to Minnie."

Hal shot him a glance full of venom, fully aware that this helpful suggestion had been made with the intent of forcing him to divulge his reasoning to Dottie—but there wasn't much of a choice, and he did so with as much grace as he could.

"But this Captain Richardson *hadn't* done anything to Willie?" Dottie said, frowning a little. "I thought—"

"Not on this occasion," John said briefly, "but given his earlier behavior over the Dismal Swamp and Quebec, we're somewhat suspicious."

"And the man apparently *has* deserted," Hal pointed out.

"You don't know that. He might have been killed by someone and his body concealed," Dottie pointed out logically.

"He was seen leaving the camp," John said patiently. "Alone. And given what we know and surmise about him, I think we have grounds to consider the possibility that he might be an American agent." He was himself fairly well convinced of it, viewing all his experience of Richardson now with the clarity of hindsight. He'd been an intelligencer himself for some years, and every instinct he possessed was presently shouting *Stinking fish!* with regard to Ezekiel Richardson.

"I blame myself extremely," he said apologetically to Hal. "I should have been on to him much sooner. But I was . . . distracted at the time." Distracted. Blown sideways and more than half obliterated by the news of Jamie Fraser's death. Even the memory of it was enough to close his stomach. He put down the forkful of kipper, untasted.

"All right," Dottie said slowly. Her own breakfast was congealing on her plate. So was Hal's. "So you don't believe Ben is dead, because this Richardson told you he *was*—and you think Richardson is a wrong 'un. But that's . . . all?" She looked intently at her father, her young chin trembling slightly, begging reassurance.

Hal closed his eyes for an instant, opened them, and looked at her directly.

"Dorothea," he said softly. "I have to believe that Ben is alive. Because if he isn't, then your mother will die of heartbreak—and I will die with her."

There was a moment of long silence, during which Grey heard the passage of carts in the street and the muffled voices of his valet and a bootblack in the corridor. Dottie made no sound at all, but he felt he could hear, too, the tears that rolled slowly down her cheeks.

115

THE RAVELED SLEEVE OF CARE

September 15, 1778
Philadelphia

I WOKE ABRUPTLY IN the dark, disoriented and alarmed. For a moment, I had no idea where I was or what was happening—only that something was seriously wrong.

I sat up, blinking furiously in an attempt to focus my eyes. Patted round in confusion and found myself naked, legs tangled in a sheet and wisps of straw prickling . . . oh. Loft. Printshop.

Jamie.

That was what was wrong. He lay next to me, but not still. He was on his side, turned away from me, body contorted, knees drawn up, and his arms crossed tight over his chest, head bowed. Shivering violently, though moonlight showed me the gleam of cold sweat on his shoulders. And making the terrible small whimpering noises that betokened the worst of his dreams.

I knew better than to try to wake him suddenly. Not in a small space with a lot of clutter and a steep drop ten feet away.

My own heart was pounding, and I knew his was. I eased myself carefully down beside him, facing his back. I needed to touch him, to bring him slowly to himself—or to enough of himself that he could recover alone. This wasn't the sort of nightmare eased by talking. Or, sometimes, even by waking.

"God, no," he said, in a heartbroken whisper. "God, *no*!"

I mustn't grab or shake him. I clenched my teeth and ran my hand lightly from the slope of his shoulder down to his elbow, and his skin shivered like a horse ridding itself of flies. That was all right, then. I did it again, paused, and again. He took a deep, horrible gasp, choked with fear . . . but the violent shivering eased a little.

"Jamie," I whispered, and, with extreme caution, touched his back very lightly. If he was dreaming about Jack Randall, this might—

"No!" he exclaimed, in a loud, fierce voice, and his legs straightened, every muscle in his body tight against his skin. "Damn you to *hell*!"

I took a deep breath and relaxed, just a bit. Anger was a thousand times better than fear or pain. Anger would leave him, as soon as he woke completely. The other things tended to linger.

"Hush," I said, a little louder but still softly. Germain often slept by the hearth, not wanting to share a bed with his younger siblings. "Hush, Jamie. I'm here." And with some trepidation, I put my arm round him, lightly, and laid my cheek against his back. His skin was hot; he smelled pungently of our lovemaking and even more strongly of fear and rage.

He stiffened, caught his breath—but I felt his awareness come back: instantly, the way it did when he woke to some alarm, ready to leap out of bed, reaching for a weapon. I tightened my hold and pressed my body against his. He didn't move, but I felt the thud of his heart, beating hard and fast.

"Can you hear me?" I asked. "Are you all right?"

After a moment, he drew a deep breath and let it out in a long, quivering sigh.

"Aye," he whispered, and his hand reached back to grasp my thigh, so tightly that I jerked but managed not to squeal. We rested quietly together for a time, until I felt his heart begin to slow and his skin cool, and then I kissed his back and traced the scars that would never fade from his body, over and over with gentle fingers, until they faded from his mind and he slept in my arms.

THE PIGEONS ON the roof of the boardinghouse made a purling noise, like the sea coming in on a pebbled shore, rolling tiny rounded rocks in the surf. Rachel was making a similar noise, snoring very faintly. Ian found it charming and could have lain watching her and listening to her all night—save that she was lying on his left arm, which had gone numb, and he needed urgently to piss.

As gently as possible, he edged out from under her soft weight, but she was a light sleeper and woke at once, yawning and stretching like a young catamount in the candlelight. She was naked, arms and face the color of just-toasted bread, her body white and her privates under their dark-brown bush a wonderful dusky color that wasn't either rose or violet or brown, but reminded him of orchids in the forests of Jamaica.

She stretched her arms above her head, and the movement lifted her startlingly white round breasts and made her nipples slowly rise. He began to slowly rise, too, and hastily turned away, before it became impossible to do what he'd meant to.

"Go back to sleep, lass," he said. "I just—er . . ." He gestured toward the chamber pot under the bed.

She made a pleasant sleepy noise and rolled onto her side, watching him.

"Does thee mind my looking at thee?" she asked, in a soft voice husked by sleep and earlier muffled shrieks.

He glanced at her in astonishment.

"Why would ye want to?" The notion seemed mildly perverse, but in a distinctly arousing fashion. He wanted to turn his back so he *could* piss, but if she wanted to watch him . . .

"It seems an intimacy of the body," she said, looking at him through half-closed eyes. "A trusting, perhaps. That thee consider thy body to be mine, as I consider mine to be thine."

"Do ye?" That idea surprised him, but he didn't object. At all.

"Thee has seen the most hidden parts of me," she pointed out, and, spreading her legs, drew her fingers delicately between them in illustration. "And tasted them, as well. What *did* it taste like?" she asked curiously.

"Fresh-caught trout," he replied, smiling at her. "Rachel—if ye want to watch me piss, ye can. But ye canna do it if ye talk to me like that while I'm trying, aye?"

"Oh." She made a small snort of amusement and rolled over, turning her back and her very round bottom to him. "Go ahead, then."

He sighed, examining his prospects.

"It will take a minute, aye?" Before she could think of anything else outrageous to say to him, he went on, in hopes of distracting her. "Uncle Jamie and Auntie Claire think of leaving Philadelphia soon. To go back to North Carolina, ken? What would ye think of going with them?"

"What?" He heard the rustle of the corn-husk mattress as she turned over quickly. "Where is thee thinking of going, that thee would not take me with thee?"

"Och, I didna mean that, lass," he assured her, with a quick glance over his shoulder. She was propped on her elbows, looking at him accusingly. "I meant we'd both go. To Fraser's Ridge—Uncle Jamie's settlement."

"Oh." That surprised her into silence. He could hear her thinking about it, and smiled to himself.

"Thee does not feel an obligation to the Continental army?" she asked after a moment, cautiously. "To the cause of freedom?"

"I dinna think those are necessarily the same thing, lass," he said, and closed his eyes in relief as everything relaxed at last. He shook himself and put away the pot, giving himself time to form a coherent sentence.

"The Duke of Pardloe told Auntie Claire that after Saratoga the British made a new plan. They mean to try to separate the southern colonies from the northern ones, blockade the South, and try to starve the North into submission."

"Oh." She moved to give him room to lie down beside her, then snuggled into him, her free hand cupping his balls. "Then thee means there will not be fighting in the North, so thee will not be needed as a scout here—but thee might, in the South?"

"Aye, or I might find another use for myself."

"Outside the army, thee means?" She was trying hard to keep hopefulness out of her voice; he could tell from the very sincere way she looked up at him, and he smiled at her, putting his own hand over hers. He was much in favor of bodily intimacy, but would rather not be squeezed like an orange should Rachel be overcome by enthusiasm.

"Perhaps," he said. "I own some land, ken, on the Ridge. Uncle Jamie gave it to me, some years back. 'Twould be hard work, mind, clearing fields and planting and plowing, but farming is mostly peaceful. Bar things like bears and wild pigs and fire and hailstorms, I mean."

"Oh, Ian." Her face had gone soft, and so had her hand, now resting peacefully in his. "I should love to farm with thee."

"Ye'd miss your brother," he reminded her. "And Dottie. Maybe Fergus and Marsali and the weans, too—I dinna think they'd come settle on the Ridge, though Uncle Jamie thinks they'd maybe travel south with us but settle near the coast. Fergus would need a decent-sized city, if he's to make much living as a printer."

A shadow crossed her face at that, but she shook her head.

"I will miss Denzell and Dottie—but I should in any case, for they will go where the army goes. But I will be very happy if thee does not," she added softly, and lifted her face to kiss him.

RACHEL WOKE instantly. She hadn't been soundly asleep, her body still a-hum from lovemaking, and still so attuned to Ian's that when he gasped and stiffened beside her, she sprang at once into awareness and had her hands on his shoulders, meaning to shake him gently out of his dream.

The next moment, she was on the floor in a tangle of bedding, her husband on top of her and his very large hands vised round her throat. She flopped and wriggled, pushed at him in futile panic—and then, as her breath vanished and brilliant red stars flashed in the darkness of her vision, she got hold of herself and brought her knee up as hard as she could.

It was a lucky blow, though it missed its mark; she hit Ian hard in the thigh, and he woke with a start and let go. She struggled out from under him, gasping and wheezing, and crawled as fast as she could to the corner, where she sat quivering with her arms wrapped round her knees, chest heaving and her heart thumping in her ears.

Ian was breathing heavily through his nose, pausing every so often to grunt or to say something brief—and probably very expressive, if she'd had the wit to understand it—in either Gaelic or Mohawk. After a few minutes, though, he got slowly into a sitting position and leaned back against the bedstead.

"Rachel?" he said warily, after a moment's silence. He sounded rational, and her tight-clasped arms loosened a little.

"Here," she said, tentative. "Is thee . . . all right, Ian?"

"Oh, aye," he said mildly. "Who taught ye to do that to a man?"

"Denny," she said, beginning to breathe easier. "He said that discouraging a man from committing the sin of rape wasn't violence."

There was a moment of silence from the vicinity of the bed.

"Oh," said Ian. "I might have a wee chat wi' Denny, one of these days. A philosophical discussion on the meaning of words, like."

"I'm sure he would enjoy it," Rachel said. She was still unnerved by what had happened, but crawled over and sat beside Ian on the floor. The sheet was lying in a pale puddle nearby, and she shook it out and draped it over her nakedness. She offered half of it to Ian, but he shook his head and leaned back a little, groaning as he stretched out his leg.

"Um. Would thee like me to . . . rub it?" she asked tentatively.

He made a small huffing noise that she interpreted as amusement. "Not just now, aye?"

They sat together, shoulders barely touching, for a bit. Her mouth was dry, and it took some time to work up enough spit to speak.

"I thought thee was going to kill me," she said, trying hard to keep her voice from quivering.

"I thought I was, too," Ian said quietly. He groped for her hand in the dark and held it, hard. "Sorry, lass."

"Thee was dreaming," she ventured. "Does—does thee want to tell me about it?"

"God, no," he said, and sighed. He let go her hand and bent his head, folding his arms atop his knees.

She kept quiet, not knowing what to say, and prayed.

"It was the Abenaki," he said eventually, his voice muffled. "The one I killed. In the British camp."

The words were simple and bald, and struck her in the pit of the stomach. She knew; he'd told her when he came back wounded. But to hear it again here, in the dark, with her back scraped from the floor and her throat bruised from his hands . . . She felt as though the deed itself had just happened in front of her, the reverberation of it shocking as a scream in her ear.

She swallowed and, turning to him, put a hand on his shoulder lightly, feeling with her thumb for the fresh, ragged scar where Denzell had cut to remove the arrow.

"Thee strangled the man?" she asked, very quietly.

"No." He breathed deep and sat up slowly. "I choked him, and I cut his throat, just a wee bit, and then I bashed his head in wi' a tomahawk."

He turned to her then and passed a hand lightly over her hair, smoothing it.

"I didna have to," he said. "Not right that moment, I mean. He didna attack me—though he'd tried to kill me before."

"Oh," she said, and tried to swallow, but her mouth had dried afresh. He sighed and bent so that his forehead rested on hers. She felt the warmth of his nearness, the warmth of his breath, smelling of beer and the juniper berries he chewed to clean his teeth. His eyes were open but so shadowed that she couldn't see into them.

"Is thee afraid of me, Rachel?" he whispered.

"I am," she whispered back, and closed her hand on his wounded shoulder, lightly but hard enough for him to feel the hurt of it. "And I am afraid for thee, as well. But there are things I fear much more than death—and to be without thee is what I fear most."

RACHEL REMADE the bed by candlelight and left the candle burning for a bit, saying that she wanted to read, to settle her mind. Ian had nodded, kissed her, and curled up like a dog beside her—the bedstead was too short for him. She glanced at the corner where Rollo slept; *he* was stretched out straight as a knife, head between his paws.

Ian put a hand on her leg and sank into sleep. She could see him doing it, his face going slack and peaceful, the muscles of his shoulders easing. It was why she'd kept the candle lit, so she might watch him sleep for a little and let the sight of him bring her peace, as well.

She'd put on her shift, feeling obscurely exposed, and though it was hot enough to lie above the sheet, she'd pulled it over her legs, too, wanting to be able to feel Ian when she moved in her sleep. She moved a leg toward him now, slowly, and felt the touch of his knee against her calf. His long lashes cast shadows on his cheeks in the candlelight, just above the looping line of his tattoos.

"Thee is my wolf," she'd said to him. *"And if thee hunts at night, thee will come home."*

"And sleep at thy feet," he'd replied.

She sighed, but felt better, and opened her Bible, to read a psalm before blowing out the candle, only to discover that she had absently picked up *Pamela: Or Virtue Rewarded,* from the bedside table. She gave a small snort of amusement and, all sense of distress now driven from her mind, closed the book, put out the candle, and snuggled down beside her sleeping wolf.

Sometime much later, in the empty hours before dawn, she opened her eyes. Not asleep, but certainly not awake, she had a sense of perfect consciousness without thought. And a distinct and vivid sense that she was not alone.

Ian was beside her; his breath touched her face, but she felt quite apart from him. It was only when it happened again that she realized what had wakened her: a tiny, sharp pain in her belly. Like the pain that sometimes came when she started her monthly, but smaller, less an ache than a . . . stab. A stab of awareness.

She blinked and put her hands over her stomach. The rafters were just barely visible overhead, shadowed with the distant coming of the light.

The pain had stopped, but the sense of . . . company? Of presence, rather. That hadn't gone away. It seemed very odd and completely natural—and of course it was, she thought. Natural as the beating of her own heart and the breath in her lungs.

She had a faint impulse to wake Ian, but that passed almost at once. She wanted to keep this for now, be alone with the knowledge—but not alone, she corrected herself, and sank peacefully back to sleep, hands still crossed over her lively womb.

IAN USUALLY WOKE before her, but she always felt him stir and would rise to the edge of wakefulness to enjoy his sleepy warm smell, the small male sounds he made, and the feel of his legs brushing hers as he swung them out of bed and sat up. He'd sit there on the edge for a moment, rubbing his hands through his hair and getting his bearings on the day, and if she cracked her eyes open, she could see his long, lovely back just in front of her, columnar muscles tanned by the sun and sloping gently down to his neat, tight buttocks, white as milk in contrast.

Sometimes he would emit a small, popping fart and look guiltily over his shoulder. She'd shut her eyes instantly and pretend to be still asleep, thinking that she must be completely besotted to find this adorable—but she did.

This morning, though, he sat up, rubbed a hand through his hair, and stiffened. She opened her eyes all the way, instantly alarmed by something in his posture.

"Ian?" she whispered, but he didn't attend.

"A Dhia," he said, very softly. "Ah, no, *a charaid . . .*"

She knew at once. Should have known from the instant she woke. Because Rollo woke when Ian did, stretching and yawning with a groaning creak of jaw muscles and a lazy thump of tail against the wall, before coming to poke a cold nose into his master's hand.

This morning there was only stillness, and the curled form of what used to be Rollo.

Ian rose and went to him swiftly, knelt on the floor beside the body of his dog, and laid a gentle hand on the big furry head. He didn't say anything, or weep, but she heard the sound he made when he breathed, as of something tearing in his chest.

She got out of bed and came to Ian, kneeling beside him, arm about his waist, and *she* was weeping, quite without meaning to.

"Mo chù," Ian said, running his hand lightly over the soft, thick fur. *"Mo chuilean."* There was a catch in his voice when he said, *"Beannachd leat, a charaid." Goodbye, old friend.*

Then he sat back on his heels, took a deep breath, and clasped Rachel's hand very hard. "He waited, I think. Until he kent ye were here for me." He swallowed audibly, and his voice was steady when he spoke again.

"I'll need to bury him. I ken a place, but it's some way. I'll be back by midafternoon, though."

"I'll come with thee." Her nose was running. She reached for the towel by the ewer and blew her nose on one end.

"Ye needn't, *mo ghràidh,*" he said gently, and passed a hand over her hair to smooth it. "It's a long way."

She drew breath and stood up.

"Then we'd best get started." She touched her husband on the shoulder, as lightly as he'd touched Rollo's fur. "I married him, as well as thee."

116

A-HUNTING WE WILL GO

September 15, 1778
First Watchung Mountain

THERE WAS A NEAT mound of droppings by the path, dark and glistening as coffee beans and much the same size. William was leading his mare, owing to her stoutness and the steep nature of the trail, so took the opportunity to stop for a moment and let her breathe. This she did, with an explosive snort and a shake of her mane.

He squatted and scooped up a few of the pellets, sniffing. Very fresh, though not warm, and with the faint oaky tang that meant the deer had been browsing on green acorns. Glancing to his left, he saw the broken brush that marked the animal's passage, and his hand twitched, wanting to wrap itself round his rifle. He could leave the mare tethered . . .

"What about it, owd lass?" he asked the mare, in the accents of the Lake District, where he'd grown up. "Would 'ee carry a carcass, if I shot 'un?"

The mare was maybe fourteen, old enough to be steady; in fact, it would be hard to imagine a steadier mount. She was more like riding a sofa than a horse, with her broad back and sides curved like a hogshead of beer. But he hadn't thought to ask, when he bought her, whether she was used to hunting. Steadiness of gait and a mild temper didn't necessarily mean she'd be fine if he heaved a deer across her back, leaking blood. Still . . .

He lifted his face to the breeze. Perfect. It was straight across the mountainside, toward him, and he imagined he could actually smell the—

Something moved in the wood, snapping twigs, and he heard the unmistakable rustling: the sound of a large herbivorous creature, wrenching mouthfuls of leaves off a tree.

Before he could think twice, he'd got to his feet, slipped the rifle from its sheath as silently as he could, and shucked his boots. Soft-footed as a ferret, he slid into the brush . . .

And, five minutes later, grasped the thrashing stubby antlers of a yearling buck with one hand as he slit the deer's throat with the other, the sound of his shot still echoing off the rocky escarpment above him.

It had happened so fast, it scarcely seemed real, despite the warm-cold feel of the blood soaking into his stockings and the thick smell of it. There was a tick hanging just under the deer's glazing eye, round as a tiny muscat grape. Would it let go at once, he wondered? Or would there be enough blood left for it to go on feeding for some time?

The deer shuddered violently, shoving its antlers hard into his chest, bunched its legs convulsively as though about to make one final leap, and died.

He held it for a few moments, the shredded velvet still on the antlers like rough suede under his sweating palm, the weight of the coarse-haired shoulders growing heavy on his knee.

"Thank you," he whispered, and let go. He remembered that it had been Mac the groom who'd told him that you always thanked a creature that gave you its life—and that it had been James Fraser, some years later, who had killed a huge wapiti in front of him and spoken what he said was a "gralloch prayer" in Gaelic before butchering the beast. But with the deer's blood on his skin and the breeze moving in the wood around him, for once he didn't push those memories away.

He went to check the mare, who was fortunately close to where he'd left her, having merely moved a few yards in order to crop weeds, and who looked at him with tranquil eyes, yellow wildflowers dangling from the corners of her mouth, as though gunshots and the smell of blood were commonplace in her life. Perhaps they were, he thought, and slapped her shoulder companionably.

Here's for you, Ben, he thought a few minutes later, slitting the belly skin. His cousin, nearly six years older than himself, had taken him hunting now and then in the forest near Earlingden, with Viscount Almerding, a friend of Ben's whose preserve it was.

He'd tried not to think of his cousin too much as he'd made his preparations. The greater part of him truly believed that Ben was dead. Gaol fever, according to what Richardson had told his uncle. Not an unusual thing to happen to a prisoner, by any means. And while he was convinced—reluctantly, for it made him burn with shame to have been such a flat as to have been gulled by the man—that Richardson was probably a villain, that didn't necessarily mean that every word from the man's mouth was a lie. Granted, he'd found no other trace of Ben in several weeks of searching.

But there was the small part of his heart that wouldn't give up. And a larger part that would do anything he could to ease the grief of his uncle and father, whatever the truth might prove to be.

"And if you bloody come down to it, what the hell *else* is there for me to do?" he muttered, reaching into the steaming heat of the body and groping for the heart.

At least he'd be welcome when he walked into Middlebrook Encampment, as they called it. A man bearing fresh meat was always welcome.

A half hour later, he'd gutted the carcass and wrapped his canvas bed sack around it to keep off flies. The horse flared her nostrils and snorted in disgust at the smell, but made no great objection when he wrestled it onto her back.

It was late in the afternoon, but this late in the summer it would stay light for some time. Better, he thought, to make his first approach at suppertime. Chances were good that he'd be invited to sit down with someone, and conversation was much easier over food and drink.

He'd gone up to the rocky summit in order to survey the terrain and had to admit that Washington and his engineers had chosen well. From the top of First Watchung Mountain, which he was standing on, the plains before New Brunswick lay clear below. The Continentals could easily keep a beady eye on the British army from their aerie and swoop down to interfere with their movements—and had.

The armies were gone now, though: both of them. The British to New York, Washington's troops to . . . well, wherever they might be at the moment. They weren't *here,* and that was all to the good. But there were people, still, who lived near the encampment.

Ben had been—*was,* he corrected himself fiercely—an officer; an infantry captain, like himself. And captured officers were often billeted upon local householders, under parole. That was the place to begin his inquiries.

"Come on, then, lass," he said to the mare, untying the reins from the sapling he'd wrapped them round. "Let's go and make ourselves welcome."

117

INTO THE BRIAR PATCH

September 16, 1778
Philadelphia

WE'D JUST FINISHED supper and I was wiping Henri-Christian's face with the hem of my apron, when a knock came at the alley door. Jenny, sitting next to me with Félicité on her lap, gave me a quick glance, brows raised. Was this cause for alarm?

I hadn't time to shrug or shake my head; all conversation had ceased on the instant, the children's chatter quelled as though someone had dropped a candle snuffer over them. It was first dark and the door was bolted. Fergus and Jamie exchanged looks and, without a word, both of them rose.

Jamie stood to one side, hand on his dirk—I hadn't realized

until this moment that he wore it all the time now, even at table. I heard the shuffle of feet in the alley. There was more than one man out there, and the hair stirred on my nape. Jamie stood relaxed but watchful, weight on his back foot, ready as Fergus lifted the bar.

"Bonsoir," Fergus said calmly, with an interrogative lift at the end of the phrase. A face hovered pale in the dark, not close enough to recognize.

"Bonsoir, Monsieur Fraser." I blinked in surprise; I knew the voice, but had never heard Benedict Arnold speak French. But of course he could, I thought, recovering. He'd led more than one campaign in Quebec. It was a soldier's French he spoke: rough but serviceable.

"Madame Fraser est ici, monsieur?" he said. *"Votre mère?"*

Fergus glanced reflexively over his shoulder at Jenny, astonished. I coughed and eased Henri-Christian off my lap, smoothing his rumpled hair.

"I rather think the governor means me," I said. The governor turned aside and murmured something to his aide, who nodded and retired into the shadows.

"Mrs. Fraser," Arnold said, sounding relieved. Fergus stood aside, and the governor came in, bowing to Marsali and Jenny, nodding to Jamie, before fixing his attention on me. "Yes, I do mean you, ma'am. I beg pardon for my untimely intrusion, sir," he added, turning to Fergus. "I wasn't sure where Mrs. Fraser was residing and was obliged to make inquiries."

I saw Jamie's mouth tighten briefly at this galling reference to our homelessness, but he bowed courteously.

"And I daresay the matter is urgent, sir, since ye come to make your inquiries in person?"

"It is, rather." The governor turned to me. "I come to beg a favor of you, ma'am, on behalf of a friend." He looked a little better than he had the last time I'd seen him; he'd gained a bit of weight and his color was better, but the lines and smudges of strain and fatigue were still plain in his face. The eyes, though, were as alert as ever.

"This would be a sick friend?" I asked, already glancing toward the ladder that led to the loft where we slept—and where the box holding my modest pharmacopeia was kept when I wasn't holding regular surgery hours.

"A matter of injury, ma'am, rather than illness," Arnold said, and his mouth tightened involuntarily. "Severe injury."

"Oh? Well, then, I'd better—"

Jamie stopped me, a hand on my arm and his eyes on Arnold.

"A moment, Sassenach," he said quietly. "Before I let ye go, I want to know the nature of the injury and the name of the injured man. And I also want to ken why the governor comes to ye under cover of night and hides his intent from his own aide."

The color rose in Arnold's cheeks, but he nodded.

"Fair enough, Mr. Fraser. Do you know a man called Shippen?"

Jamie looked blank and shook his head, but Fergus chimed in.

"I do," he said, looking thoughtfully at Arnold. "He is a wealthy man, and a well-known Loyalist—one of those who chose not to leave the city when the British army withdrew."

"I know one of the Shippen girls," I said, with a vague memory of General Howe's lavish leaving party in May—God, could that possibly be only four months past? "I don't think I've met the father, though. Is he the injured party?"

"No, but he is the friend on whose behalf I ask your help, ma'am." Arnold drew a deep, unhappy breath. "Mr. Shippen's young cousin, a man named Tench Bledsoe, was set upon last night by the Sons of Liberty. They tarred and feathered him, ma'am, and left him on the docks in front of Mr. Shippen's warehouse. He rolled off the dock into the river and by a mercy didn't drown, but crept up the bank and lay in the muddy shallows until a slave hunting crabs found him and ran for help."

"Help," Jamie repeated carefully.

Arnold met his eye and nodded. "Just so, Mr. Fraser," he said bleakly. "The Shippens live within two streets of Dr. Benjamin Rush, but under the circumstances . . ."

The circumstances being that Benjamin Rush was a very visible and outspoken Rebel, active in the Sons of Liberty, and would certainly be familiar with everyone in Philadelphia who held similar sentiments—very likely including the men who had attacked Tench Bledsoe.

"Sit down, Sassenach," Jamie said, gesturing to my stool. I didn't, and he gave me a brief, dark look.

"I dinna mean to stop ye going," he said, a distinct edge in his voice. "I ken well enough that ye will. I just mean to make sure ye come back. Aye?"

"Er . . . yes," I said, and coughed. "I'll just—go and get my things together, then." I sidled through the clump of staring children to the ladder and went up as quickly as I could, hearing Jamie's stern inquisition of Governor Arnold begin behind me.

Severe burns—and the attendant difficulties of hardened tar—and very likely fever and infection already started, after a night lying in river mud. This was going to be messy—and possibly worse. There was no telling how badly the young man had been burned; if we were lucky, it might be only splashes of tar that had reached his skin. If we weren't lucky . . .

I set my jaw and began packing. Linen bandages, a scalpel and small paring knife for debridement . . . leeches? Perhaps; there would certainly be bruising involved—no one submitted meekly to being tarred and feathered. I tied a hasty bandage around the leech jar to keep the lid from coming off in transit. Definitely a jar of honey . . . I held it up to the flicker of light from below: half full, a clouded gold that caught the light through brown glass like candle glow. Fergus kept a tin of turpentine in the shed for cleaning type; I should borrow that, as well.

I didn't worry overmuch about the political delicacies that had made Arnold come to me so surreptitiously. Jamie would take what precautions were possible, I knew. Philadelphia lay in Rebel hands, but it was by no means a safe place—for anyone.

Not for the first time—or the last, I was sure—I was glad that at least my own path lay clear before me. The door below opened and closed with a thump; the governor was gone.

I LOOKED AT the rather grubby sedan chair, inhaled the scent of several dozen previous users, and took a firmer grip on my cane.

"I can walk," I said. "It's not that far."

"Ye're not walking," Jamie replied equably.

"Surely you don't intend to stop me?"

"Aye, I do," he said, still mildly. "I canna stop ye going—

and I wouldna try—but I can, by God, make sure ye dinna fall on your face in the street on your way. Get in, Sassenach. Go slow," he added to the chairmen, as he opened the door of the sedan and gestured to me. "I'm coming, and I dinna want to gallop so soon after supper."

There being no reasonable alternative, I gathered the remnants of my dignity and got in. And with my basket of supplies settled at my feet and the window slid open as far as it would go—the memories of my last claustrophobic ride in a sedan chair were as vivid as the smell of this one—we set off at a stately jog through the quiet nighttime streets of Philadelphia.

The curfew had been eased of late, owing to protests from tavern owners—and, likely, their patrons—but the overall sense of the city was still edgy, and there were no respectable women on the street, no gangs of rowdy apprentices, or any of the slaves who worked for their masters but lived on their own. I saw one whore, standing by the mouth of an alley; she whistled at Jamie and called out an invitation, but halfheartedly.

"Her pimp'll be a-hiding . . . in the alley with a cosh . . . lay you three to one," the chairman behind me remarked, his remarks punctuated by his breathing. "Ain't as safe . . . as when the army was here."

"Think not?" His partner grunted, then found breath to reply. "Army was here . . . when that officer got his . . . throat cut in a whorehouse. Reckon 's why that . . . drab's out here in her shift." He gulped air and went on. "How you mean . . . to settle the bet, then? Go with her yourself?"

"May be as this gentleman'd do us the service," the other said with a brief, gasping laugh.

"It may be that he won't," I said, sticking my head out the window. "But I'll go and look, if you like."

Jamie and the forward man laughed, the other grunted, and we jolted gently round the corner and down the street to where the Shippen house stood, gracious in its own grounds, on a small rise near the edge of town. There was a lighted lantern by the gate, another by the door. I wondered whether that meant we were expected; I hadn't thought to ask Governor Arnold if he had sent word ahead of us. If he hadn't, the next few minutes might be interesting.

"Any notion how long we might be, Sassenach?" Jamie inquired, taking out his purse to pay the chairmen.

"If he's already dead, it won't take long," I replied, shaking my skirts into order. "If he's not, it could well take all night."

"Aye. Wait a bit, then," Jamie told the chairmen, who were staring at me, mouths agape. "If I havena come out in ten minutes, ye're free to go."

Such was his force of personality, they didn't observe that they were quite free to go at once if they wanted, and merely nodded meekly as he took my arm and escorted me up the steps.

We were expected; the door swung wide as Jamie's boots scuffed the scrubbed stone of the stoop, and a young woman peered out, alarm and interest showing in equal measure on her face. Evidently Mr. Bledsoe wasn't dead, then.

"Mrs. Fraser?" She blinked slightly, looking at me sideways. "Er . . . I mean . . . it *is* Mrs. Fraser? Governor Arnold said—"

"It is Mrs. Fraser," Jamie said, a slight edge in his voice. "And I assure ye, young woman, I'm in a position to know."

"This would be *Mr.* Fraser," I informed the young lady, who was looking up at him, clearly bewildered. "I was probably Lady John Grey last time you saw me," I added, trying for a nonchalant matter-of-factness. "But, yes, I'm Claire Fraser. Er . . . still. I mean—again. I understand that your cousin . . . ?"

"Oh, yes! Please—come this way." She stepped back, gesturing toward the rear of the house, and I saw that she was accompanied by a servant, a middle-aged black man, who bowed when I met his gaze and then led the way through a long hallway to the back stair and thence upward.

On the way, our hostess introduced herself belatedly as Margaret Shippen and apologized prettily for the absence of her parents. Her father—she said—was called away on business.

I hadn't been formally introduced to Peggy Shippen before, but I had seen her and knew a bit about her; she'd been one of the organizing lights of the Mischianza, and while her father had prevented her actually attending the ball, all her friends had talked about her at length—and I'd glimpsed her, lavishly dressed, once or twice at other functions I'd attended with John.

Called away on business, was it? I caught Jamie's eye when she'd said that, and he'd raised one shoulder in the briefest of shrugs. More than likely, Edward Shippen wanted to avoid any public linkage with his nephew's misfortune—and, so far as possible, keep talk about the incident to a minimum. It wasn't a safe time or place to make a point of Loyalist leanings in the family.

Miss Shippen led us to a small bedroom on the third floor, where a blackened, man-shaped object lay on the bed. The smell of tar was thick in the air, along with a distinct smell of blood and a sort of constant low moaning noise. This must be Tench Bledsoe—and wherever had he got a name like that? I wondered, gingerly approaching him. So far as I knew, a tench was a rather undistinguished-looking sort of carp.

"Mr. Bledsoe?" I said quietly, setting down my basket on a small table. There was a candlestick on the table, and by the light of the single flame, I could make out his face—or half of it. The other half was obscured by tar, as was a good bit of his head and neck. The clean half was that of a somewhat plain young man with a large, beaky nose, his features contorted in agony, but not at all fish-looking.

"Yes," he gasped, and pressed his lips tight together, as though even the escape of a single word jeopardized the tenuous grip he had on himself.

"I'm Mrs. Fraser," I said, and laid a hand on his shoulder. A fine shudder was running through him like current through a wire. "I've come to help."

He heard me and nodded jerkily. They'd given him brandy; I could smell it under the aromatic reek of pine tar, and a half-full decanter stood on the table.

"Have you any laudanum in the house?" I asked, turning to Peggy. It wouldn't help that much in the long run, but a large dose might get us through the worst of the preliminaries.

She was quite young—no more than eighteen, I thought—but alert and self-possessed, as well as very pretty. She nodded and disappeared, with a murmured word to the servant. *Of course,* I thought, seeing her skirts whisk out of sight. *She couldn't send him for it.* The laudanum would be with the other household simples, in a closet under lock and key.

"What can I do, Sassenach?" Jamie said softly, as though afraid to break the injured man's concentration on his pain.

"Help me undress him." Whoever had attacked him hadn't stripped him; that was lucky. And most of the tar probably hadn't been boiling hot when it was applied; I smelled burnt hair, but not the sickening stench of cooked flesh. Pine tar wasn't like the asphalt road tar of later centuries; it was a by-product of turpentine distillation, and might be soft enough to be daubed without needing to be boiled first.

What *wasn't* fortunate was his leg, as I saw at once when Jamie peeled back the sheet covering him. That was where the smell of blood had come from; it spread in a soggy smear on the bedclothes, black in the candlelight, but copper and scarlet to the nose.

"Jesus H. Roosevelt Christ," I said under my breath. Tench's face was dead white and streaked with sweat and tears, his eyes closed, but he grimaced, hearing that.

Jamie set his jaw and drew his case knife, which was sharp enough to shave the hairs on a man's arm. Sharp enough to slice through shredded stocking and damp breeches, spreading the stiffened fabric aside to show me the damage.

"Who did that to ye, man?" he asked Tench, gripping him by the wrist as the injured man reached a tentative hand downward, seeking the extent of the damage.

"No one," Tench whispered, and coughed. "I—I jumped off the dock when he set my head afire, and landed on one foot in the mud. It stuck well in, and when I fell over . . ."

It was a very nasty compound fracture. Both bones of the lower leg had snapped clean through, and the shattered ends were poking through the skin in different directions. I was surprised that he had survived the shock of it, together with the trauma of the attack—to say nothing of a night and part of a day spent lying in the filthy river shallows afterward. The macerated flesh was swollen, raw, red, and ugly, the wounds deeply infected. I breathed in gently, half-expecting the reek of gangrene, but no. Not yet.

"He set your head afire?" Jamie was saying incredulously. He leaned forward, touching the darkened mass on the left side of the young man's head. "Who?"

"Don't know." Tench's hand floated up, touched Jamie's, but Tench didn't try to pull it away. It rested on Jamie's, as though his touch would tell Tench what he needed to know but couldn't bear to find out for himself.

"Think he . . . Way he spoke. Maybe England, maybe Ireland. He . . . poured pitch over my head and sprinkled feathers on. Others would have left me then, I think. But all of a sudden, he turned back and seized a torch . . ." He coughed, wincing against the spasm, and ended breathlessly, ". . . like he . . . hated me." He sounded astonished.

Jamie was carefully breaking off small chunks of singed hair and matted clumps of mud and tar, revealing the blistered skin underneath.

"It's none sae bad, man," he said, encouraging. "Your ear's still there, no but a wee bit black and crusty round the edges."

That actually made Tench laugh—no more than a breathy gasp—though this was extinguished abruptly when I touched his leg.

"I'll need more light," I said, turning to the servant. "And a lot of bandages." He nodded, avoiding looking at the man on the bed, and left.

We worked for some minutes, murmuring occasional encouragement to Tench. At one point, Jamie pulled the chamber pot out from under the bed, excused himself with a brief word, and took it into the hall; I heard him retching. He came back a few moments later, pale and smelling of vomit, and resumed the delicate work of uncovering what might remain of Tench's face.

"Can ye open this eye, man?" he asked, gently touching the left side. I peered up from my station over his leg, to see that the lid was evidently whole but badly blistered and swollen, the lashes singed off.

"No." Tench's voice had changed, and I moved abruptly up to his head. He sounded almost sleepy, his voice unconcerned. I laid the back of my hand against his cheek; it was cool and clammy. I said something very bad out loud, and his working eye sprang open, staring up at me.

"Oh, there you are," I said, much relieved. "I thought you were going into shock."

"If he hasna been shocked by what's already happened to him, I shouldna think anything would do it, Sassenach," Jamie said, but bent closer to look. "I think he's only worn out from the pain, aye? Sometimes ye canna be bothered to put up with it anymore, but ye're no ready to die, so ye just drift away for a bit."

Tench sighed deeply and gave a small, jerky nod.

"If you could . . . stop for a little while?" he whispered. "Please."

"Aye," Jamie said softly, and, patting his chest, drew the stained sheet up over him. "Rest a bit, *mo charaid.*"

I wasn't at all sure that he wasn't trying to die, but there was a limit to what I could do to prevent him, if that were the case. And there was a much more serious limit to what I could do if he *didn't* die.

On the other hand, I had a vivid understanding of exactly what Jamie meant by "drifting away" and of the symptoms of severe blood loss. There was no telling how much blood Tench *had* lost, lying in the river. The fracture had by some miracle not ruptured either of the main tibial arteries—if it had, he'd have been dead long since—but it had certainly made hash of a number of smaller vessels.

On the other hand . . . the Delaware was a fairly cold river, even in summer. The chill of the water might well have constricted the smaller blood vessels, as well as slowed his metabolism and even perhaps minimized the damage due to burns, both by extinguishing the fire and by cooling the burnt skin. I'd whipped a pro forma tourniquet bandage round the leg above the knee but hadn't tightened it; blood loss at the moment was no more than a slow oozing.

And, in fact, the burns *were* minimal. His shirt had been torn open, but the tar on his chest, hands, and clothes hadn't been hot enough to blister his skin—and while there was certainly visible damage to one side of his face and head, I didn't *think* more than a few square inches of scalp had third-degree burns; the rest was redness and blistering. Painful, of course, but not life-threatening. Whoever had attacked him had likely not meant to kill him—but they stood a good chance of doing so, anyway.

"Pitch-capping, they call it," Jamie said, low-voiced. We had moved away to the window, but he nodded back toward the bed. "I havena seen it before, but I've heard of it." He shook his head, lips tight, then picked up the ewer and offered it to me. "D'ye want water, Sassenach?"

"No—oh, wait. Yes, I do, thank you." The window was firmly closed, in accordance with the custom of the times, and the small room was sweltering. I took the pitcher and nodded to the window. "Can you get that open, do you think?"

He turned to wrestle with the window; it was stuck fast in its frame, the wood swollen with humidity and disuse.

"What about the leg?" he said, back turned to me. "Ye'll have to take it off, no?"

I lowered the pitcher—the water was flat and tasted of earth—and sighed.

"Yes," I said. I'd been fighting that conclusion almost from the moment I'd seen Tench's leg, but hearing Jamie's matter-of-factness made it easier to accept.

"I doubt I could save it in a modern hospital, with blood transfusions and anesthetic—and, *God,* I wish I had ether right now!" I bit my lip, looking at the bed, and watching closely to see whether Tench's chest was still rising and falling. A tiny, treacherous part of me rather hoped it wasn't—but it was.

Feet on the stairs, and both Peggy and the manservant were with us again, armed respectively with a stable lantern and an enormous candelabra, Peggy with a square glass bottle clasped to her chest. Both turned anxious faces toward the bed, then toward me, standing apart by the window. Was he dead?

"No," I said, shaking my head, and saw the same half-regretful relief flit across their faces that I had just experienced. I wasn't without sympathy; no matter what their feelings for the injured man, having him on the premises was a danger to the Shippens.

I came forward and explained in a low voice what had to be done, watching Peggy go the color of a bad oyster in the flickering light. She swayed a little, but swallowed hard and drew herself up.

"Here?" she said. "I don't suppose you could take him to . . . Well, no, I suppose not." She took a deep breath. "All right. What can we do to help?"

The manservant coughed behind her in a meaningful manner, and she stiffened.

"My father would say the same," she informed him coldly.

"Just so, miss," he said, with a deference that wasn't all that deferential. "But he might like to have the chance to say it himself, don't you think?"

She shot him an angry glance, but before she could say anything, there was a grinding screech of wood as the window gave way to Jamie's will, and everyone's eye jerked to him.

"I dinna mean to interrupt," he said mildly, turning round. "But I do believe the governor has come to call."

JAMIE PUSHED PAST Miss Shippen and her servant before either could react. He ran lightly down the back stair and came through the house, startling a kitchen maid. Clearly the governor wasn't going to be admitted by the kitchen door.

He reached the front door just as a firm knock sounded, and pulled it open.

"Miss Margaret!" Arnold pushed past Jamie as though he wasn't there—no small feat—and seized Peggy Shippen's hands in his. "I thought I must come—your cousin? How does he do?"

"He is alive." Peggy swallowed, her face the color of the beeswax candle she was holding. "Mrs. Fraser is—she says—" She swallowed again, and Jamie swallowed with her, out of sympathy, knowing all too well what she was thinking of. Tench Bledsoe's shattered leg bones, red and slimy as an ineptly butchered pig's. The back of his throat was still bitter with the taste of vomit.

"I thank you *so* much for sending Mrs. Fraser to us, sir—I couldn't think what on earth we were to do. My father's in Maryland and my mother with her sister in New Jersey. My brothers . . ." She trailed off, looking distraught.

"No, no, my dear—may I call you so? It is my most fervent concern, to help you—your family, to . . . protect you." He hadn't let go her hands, Jamie noted, and she wasn't pulling them away.

Jamie glanced covertly from Arnold to Peggy Shippen, then turned away a little, drawing back. It wasn't hard for them to ignore him; they were focused on each other.

That made matters plain—or at least plainer. Arnold wanted the girl, and wanted her so nakedly that Jamie was slightly ashamed for the man. You couldn't help lust, but surely a man should have enough control to hide it. *And no just for the sake of decency, either,* he thought, seeing a certain look of cautious calculation come into Peggy's face. It was, he thought, the look of a fisherman who has just seen a fat trout swim right under the lure.

He cleared his throat in a pointed manner, and both of them jerked as though he'd run a drawing pin into them.

"My wife says it will be necessary to amputate the injured

leg," he said. "Quickly. She requires a few things—instruments and the like."

"I need both the large saw and the small lunar one, the set of tenaculae—the long things that look like fishing hooks—and quite a lot of sutures . . ."

He was trying to keep the list in his head, though it made him ill to envision most of the items, thinking of the use they were about to be put to. Beneath the sense of revulsion and pity, though, was wariness—the same wariness he saw at the back of Benedict Arnold's eyes.

"Does she," Arnold said, not quite a question. His eyes flicked back to Peggy Shippen, who bit her lip in a becoming manner.

"Can ye maybe send your coachman to the printshop?" Jamie asked. "I can go with him and fetch back what's needed."

"Yes," Arnold said slowly, but in an abstracted way, the way he did when he was thinking rapidly. "Or . . . no. Let us rather remove Mr. Bledsoe—and Mrs. Fraser, to be sure—to the printshop in my coach. Mrs. Fraser will have access there to everything she requires, and the assistance and support of her family."

"What?" Jamie exclaimed, but Peggy Shippen was already hanging on to Arnold's arm, her face transformed by relief. Jamie seized Arnold by the arm to compel his attention, and the governor's eyes narrowed.

Jamie's intent had been to demand rhetorically whether Arnold was mad, but the split second's delay was enough to change this to a more politic "There's nay room at the shop for such a venture, sir. We live atop one another, and folk come in and out all day. This willna be a simple matter; the man will need to be nursed for some time."

Peggy Shippen made a small moan of anxiety, and it dawned upon Jamie that Tench Bledsoe was a hot potato, as much—or more—for Arnold as for the Shippens. The last thing Arnold could want, as military governor of the city, was public scandal and disorder, the remaining Loyalists in Philadelphia threatened and frightened, the Sons of Liberty seen as secret vigilantes, a law unto themselves.

Arnold must very much want the incident kept quiet. At the same time, he wanted to be the noble knight, riding to the aid of the very young and enchanting Miss Shippen by caring for her cousin while removing the potential danger he posed to her household.

By bringing it to mine, Jamie thought, his wariness beginning to turn to anger.

"Sir," he said formally. "There is no possibility of preventing the matter from being known, should ye bring yon man into my son's shop. And clearly ye ken the danger of that."

The truth of this was evident, and Arnold paused, wrinkling his brow. But Jamie had fought with the man and kent him well enough; Jamie saw that, having made up his mind to relieve Miss Peggy's concern, Arnold meant to do it, come hell or high water.

Evidently Claire was right in what she'd told him about testosterone, and he'd already known that Arnold was a ram, in terms both of balls and hardheadedness.

"Ah, I have it!" Arnold exclaimed triumphantly, and Jamie saw—with grudging admiration—the general emergent. This admiration disappeared with Arnold's next sentence.

"Lord John Grey," he said. "We could transport Mr. Bledsoe to his lordship's house."

"No!" Jamie said by reflex.

"Yes," Arnold said, but in self-congratulation rather than contradiction; he was paying no attention. "Yes, the ideal solution! His lordship and his brother are much in my debt," he explained to Peggy, with a feigned modesty that made Jamie want to hit him. "And as his lordship and Mrs. Fraser—" At this point, he caught sight of Jamie's face and arrested his speech just in time to prevent exactly such a happenstance. He coughed. "The ideal solution," he repeated. "Will you go and tell Mrs. Fraser what we intend, sir?"

"We?" Jamie said. "I intend nothing of the—"

"What the *bloody* hell is going on down here?" Claire's voice came from the stairway behind him, and he swung round to see her leaning on the banister, a-flicker like a ghost in the light from the tin sconce above her. There was blood smudging her apron, blotches black on the pale cloth.

"Nothing, *a nighean,*" he said, fixing Arnold with a firm eye. "Only discussing where Mr. Bledsoe should be."

"I don't care where he *should* be," she snapped, coming

down into the foyer, skirts rustling with agitation. "Where he *will* be is dead, if I can't take care of his leg quickly." Then she noticed the glaring going on betwixt him and Arnold and moved up beside Jamie, looking hard at the governor herself.

"General Arnold," she said, "if you have the slightest concern for Miss Shippen's cousin's life, you'll oblige me by taking my husband promptly to fetch the instruments I need. Hurry!"

Arnold blinked, and Jamie would have smiled had he not been worrit for the lass—she was fierce, but she looked pale, and her fists were clenched in the cloth of her apron. It might have been to keep her from slapping the governor, but he rather thought it was to hide the fact that her hands were trembling—and he realized with a shock that she was afraid.

Not afraid of the circumstance or any future danger—afraid that she couldn't do what she knew she must.

His heart smote him at the thought. He took Arnold firmly by the upper arm, compelling him toward the stair.

"Aye," he said abruptly to Claire. "We'll take the man to Lord John's house, and whilst ye fettle him for the job there, I'll fetch what ye need from the shop. The general will help me to move him."

Arnold's stiff resistance ceased abruptly as he took Jamie's meaning.

"Yes," he said. "Yes, I—" A long moan from above interrupted him, and Claire's face tightened.

"There isn't time," she said, quite calmly. "Miss Shippen—Peggy. Fetch me the largest knife you have in the kitchen, and do it now. Have your servants bring more hot water and cloth for bandages. A strong sewing needle and black thread." Her eyes sought Jamie's, and he let go of the governor at once and went to her.

"Ye're all right, lass?" he said quietly, taking her elbow.

"I am," she said, and squeezed his hand briefly. "This is very bad, though. I don't—I'm sorry, I'll need you to help hold him."

"I'll be fine," he said. "Dinna be worrit. Only do what ye need to do. I promise I willna vomit on him while ye're taking off his leg."

He hadn't actually meant that to be funny, and was surprised—

but pleased—when she laughed. Not much of a laugh, but the tension in her arm relaxed, and her fingers were steady on his.

He could tell the minute they entered the room. He didn't know what it was had changed, but clearly Claire had heard the beating of the wings of Death from the floor below; he could sense them now. Bledsoe was still conscious, but barely so; a slice of white showed as one eyelid lifted at their entrance.

"We're here, man," Jamie whispered, sinking to his knees and grasping Bledsoe's hand. It was cold to the touch and clammy with sweat. "Dinna fash, we're here. It'll be done soon."

There was a strong smell of laudanum in the air, together with the stink of tar and blood and burnt hair. Claire was on the other side of the bed, holding Bledsoe's wrist, her eyes flickering from his slack face to the mangled leg.

"Sepsis," she said, quietly but in a normal voice. "Do you see the red line there?" She gestured at the wounded leg, and Jamie saw it clearly: a streak of an ugly dark-red color that he thought hadn't been there before—or perhaps it had, and he'd not noticed. The sight of it made the fine hairs ripple on his shoulders, and he shifted uneasily.

"Blood poisoning," Claire said. "Bacteria—germs—in the blood. It moves very fast, and if it should get into the body proper . . . there's nothing I can do."

He looked up sharp, hearing a tiny tremor in her voice.

"But before that, ye might? There's a chance?" He tried to sound encouraging, though the thought of the alternative made the gooseflesh that much worse.

"Yes. But it isn't a good one." She swallowed. "The shock of the amputation may well kill him on the spot. And if it doesn't, there's still a great chance of infection."

He stood up then and came round the bed to her, taking her gently but solidly by the shoulders. Her bones were close to the surface, and he thought her feelings were, too.

"If he's got a chance, we must give it to him, Sassenach."

"Yes," she murmured, and he felt the shiver go all through her, though the air was hot and close. "God help me."

"He will," Jamie whispered, folding his arms briefly round her. "So will I."

I WAS STANDING in the wrong place. The fact that I understood what was happening to me didn't help at all.

A trained surgeon is also a potential killer, and an important bit of the training lies in accepting the fact. Your intent is entirely benign—or at least you hope so—but you are laying violent hands on someone, and you must be ruthless in order to do it effectively. And sometimes the person under your hands will die, and knowing that . . . you do it anyway.

I had had them bring more candles, though the air in the room was already suffocating. The miasma of humidity and slowly evaporating sweat made the light of the candelabra fill the chamber with a gentle, romantic glow; just the thing for a dinner party filled with wine, flirtations, and dancing.

The wine could wait, and any surgeon dances with death routinely. The problem was that I'd forgotten the steps and was flirting with panic.

I bent to check Tench's heart rate and respiration. He was breathing shallowly but fast. Lack of oxygen, severe blood loss . . . and I felt my own chest tighten, heaving for air, and stood up, giddy, heart hammering.

"Sassenach." I turned, hand on the bedpost, to see Jamie watching me, eyebrows drawn together. "Are ye all right?"

"Yes," I said, but my voice sounded queer even to my own ears. I shook my head hard, trying to clear it. Jamie came close to me and put his hand on mine, where it rested on the bedpost. It was big and steady, and it helped.

"Ye willna help him, lass, if ye faint in the midst of it," he said, low-voiced.

"I'm not going to faint," I said, made a bit testy by anxiety. "I just—I—I'm fine."

His hand fell away, and after a long, searching look into my face, he nodded soberly and stepped back.

I wasn't going to faint. Or at least I hoped not. But I was trapped there in that close, hot room, smelling blood and tar and the scent of myrrh in the laudanum, feeling Tench's agony. And I could *not* do that. I couldn't, I mustn't.

Peggy hurried in, a maidservant behind her, several large knives clutched to her bosom.

"Will one of these do?" She laid them in a clinking heap at the foot of the bed, then stood back, gazing anxiously at her cousin's pale, slack face.

"I'm sure one will." I stirred the heap gingerly, extracting a couple of possibilities: a carving knife that looked sharp, and a big, heavy knife of the sort used for chopping vegetables. And, with a vivid recollection of what it felt like to sever tendons, I picked up a paring knife with a freshly sharpened, silvered edge.

"Do you butcher your own meat? If you have something like a bone saw . . ."

The servant went as pale as a black man reasonably can, and went out, presumably to acquire one.

"Boiling water?" I asked, brows raised.

"Chrissy is bringing it," Peggy assured me. She licked her lips, uneasy. "Do you—mmm." She broke off, narrowly avoiding saying what she so plainly thought: *"Do you know what you're doing?"*

I did. That was the trouble. I knew much too much about what I was doing—from both sides.

"Everything will be fine," I assured her, with a decent appearance of calm and confidence. "I see we have needles and thread. Would you take the biggest needle—a carpet needle, perhaps—and thread it for me, please? And then a couple of smaller ones, just in case." Just in case I had time and opportunity to actually capture and ligate blood vessels. It was much more likely that the only choice I would have was cautery—a brutal searing of the fresh stump to stanch the bleeding, for Tench didn't have enough blood left to be able to spare any of it.

I needed to be alone in my head, in a calm, clear place. The place from which I could see everything, sense the body under my hand in all its particularities—but not *be* that body.

I was about to disjoint Tench Bledsoe's leg like a chicken's. Throw away his bones and flesh. Sear the stump. And I felt his fear in the pit of my stomach.

Benedict Arnold had come in with an armload of firewood and a silver table knife in one hand—my cautery iron, if there wasn't time to stitch. He set them down on the hearth, and the butler began to poke up the fire.

I closed my eyes for an instant, trying not to breathe through my nose, shutting out the candle glow. Denny Hunter had operated on me by candlelight; I remembered watching through a haze of eyelashes, unable to open my eyes more than a crack, as each of the six big candles was lit, the flames rising up pure and hot—and smelling the small iron heating in the brazier beside them.

A hand touched my waist, and, gulping air, I leaned blindly into Jamie.

"What's wrong, *a nighean*?" he whispered to me.

"Laudanum," I said, almost at random. "You don't—you don't lose consciousness altogether. It makes the pain go away—not stop, just seem not connected to you—but it's *there.* And you . . . you know what's happening to you." I swallowed, forcing down bile.

I felt it. The hard probe jabbing its way into my side, startling. The remarkable sense of cold intrusion, mingled with incongruous faint warm echoes of internal movement, the forceful jabs of a child in the womb.

"You know what's happening," I repeated, opening my eyes. I found his, looking down at me with gentleness.

"I ken that, aye?" he whispered, and cupped my cheek with his four-fingered hand. "Come and tell me what ye need me to do, *mo ghràidh.*"

THE MOMENTARY PANIC was subsiding; I forced it aside, knowing that even to think about it was to slide headfirst back into it. I laid a hand on Tench's injured leg, willing myself to feel it, find the truth of it.

The truth was all too obvious. The lower leg was a complete wreck, mechanically, and so compromised by septicemia that there was no chance of saving it. I was searching desperately for a way to save the knee; having a knee made a tremendous difference in the ability to walk, to manage. But I couldn't do it.

He was far gone from injury, blood loss, and shock; he was a stubborn man, but I could feel his life flickering in his flesh, dying away in the midst of infection, disruption, and pain. I could *not* ask his body to withstand the longer, painstaking surgery that would be necessary to amputate below the knee—even if I felt sure that such an amputation would be sufficient to forestall the advancing septicemia, and I didn't.

"I'm going to take his leg off above the knee," I said to Jamie. I thought I spoke calmly, but my voice sounded odd. "I need you to hold the leg for me and move it as I tell you. Governor"—I turned to Arnold, who stood with a reassuring arm about Peggy's Shippen's waist—"come and hold him down." Laudanum alone wasn't going to be enough.

To his credit, Arnold came instantly and laid a hand against Tench's slack cheek for a moment in reassurance before taking firm hold of his shoulders. His own face was calm, and I remembered the stories I'd heard of his campaigns into Canada: frostbite, injury, starvation . . . No, not a squeamish man, and I felt a small sense of reassurance from the presence of my two helpers.

No, three: Peggy Shippen came up beside me, pale to the lips and with her throat bobbing every few seconds as she swallowed—but jaw set with determination.

"Tell me what to do," she whispered, and clamped her mouth shut hard as she caught sight of the mangled leg.

"Try not to vomit, but if you must, turn away from the bed," I said. "Otherwise—stand there and hand me things as I ask."

There was no further time for thought or preparation. I tightened the tourniquet, grasped the sharpest knife, nodded to my helpers, and began.

A deep incision, fast, around and across the top of the leg, cutting hard down to expose the bone. An army surgeon could lop off a leg in less than two minutes. So could I, but it would be better if I could manage to cut flaps to cover the stump, could seal the major vessels. . . .

"Big needle," I said to Peggy, holding out my hand. Lacking a tenaculum to seize the large blood vessels that snapped back into the flesh when severed, I had to probe for them with the point of the needle and drag them out, anchor them into the raw, exposed flesh, and then ligate them as fast as I could, whipping thread round them with one of the smaller needles and tying it off. Better than cautery, if there was time . . .

Sweat was running into my eyes; I had to dash it away with my bared forearm; my hands were bloody to the wrist.

"Saw," I said, and no one moved. Had I spoken aloud? *"Saw,"* I said, much louder, and Jamie's head twisted toward the implements on the table. Leaning heavily on Tench's leg with one hand, he stretched to grab the saw from the table with the other.

Where was Peggy? On the floor. I saw the bloom of her skirt from the corner of my eye and felt vaguely through the floorboards the steps of a servant coming to haul her out of the way.

I groped for another suture, blind, and the jar of brandy in which I'd stowed them tipped, spilling on the sheet and adding its sweet stickiness to the atmosphere. I heard Jamie gag, but he didn't move; his fingers squeezed the thigh hard above the tourniquet. Tench would have bruises there, I thought idly. If he lived long enough for his capillaries to bleed. . . .

The saw had been made to disjoint hogs. Sturdy, not sharp, and not well kept—half the teeth were bent, and it jumped and skittered in my hand, grating over the bone. I clenched my teeth and pushed, my hand slipping on the handle, greased with blood and sweat.

Jamie made a deep, desperate noise and moved suddenly, taking the saw from my hand and nudging me aside. He gripped Tench's knee and bore down on the saw, driving it into the bone by main force. Three, four, five dragging strokes, and the bone, three-quarters sawn through, made a cracking noise that jolted me into action.

"Stop," I said, and he did, white-faced and pouring sweat. "Lift his leg. Carefully." He did, and I made the cut from below, long, deep strokes of the knife deepening the incision at an angle to make the flap, joining the cut with the upper incision. The sheet was wet and dark with blood—but not too much. Either the tourniquet was holding, or the man had so little blood left to lose . . .

"Saw again," I said urgently, discarding the knife. "Hold steady! Both pieces." There was no more than a thin section of bone remaining; the spongy bone of the marrow showed, blood flowering slowly from the cut surface. I put no pressure on the saw; the last thing I wanted was to crack the bone in some awkward way. It wasn't working, though, and I looked back toward the line of tools, desperate to find something else.

"Rasp," Jamie said, his voice rough with strain. He nodded toward the table. "There."

I seized the rasp, a rat-tailed thing, drenched it with brandy, and, turning it sideways, filed through the last bit of bone, which parted gently. With a ragged edge, but intact, not shattered.

"Is he breathing?" I asked. I was having trouble breathing myself, and couldn't sense the patient's vital signs—save to notice his heart was beating, because blood was pulsing slightly out of the smaller vessels—but Arnold nodded, his head bowed, intent on Tench's face.

"He'll do," he said, his voice firm and loud, and I knew he was speaking as much to Tench as to me. Now I could feel the stir in the upper leg, a violent reflexive urge to move, and Jamie leaned hard on it. My fingers brushed the discarded lower leg, the flesh horribly flaccid and rubbery, and I snatched them back, wiping them convulsively on my apron.

I swiped the bloody apron then across my face and pushed back loosened bits of hair with the back of my hand. It was shaking; they both were.

What the bloody hell are you shaking now *for?* I thought irritably. But I was, and it took much longer than it should have to cauterize the last few small bleeders—adding the ghastly smell of roasting flesh to everything else in the room; I thought even General Arnold might throw up—stitch the flaps, bandage the wound, and, at last, loosen the tourniquet.

"All right," I said, and straightened up. "Now . . ." But if I said anything else, I didn't hear it. The room revolved slowly round me and dissolved into a flicker of black and white spots, and then everything went black.

118

THE SECOND LAW OF THERMODYNAMICS

TENCH LIVED.

"I should have known you would," I said to him. "If you were determined enough to survive all night in the river, plainly a mere amputation wouldn't slow you down."

He hadn't enough strength to laugh—the journey by litter to Chestnut Street had left him white-faced and gasping—but he did twitch his mouth enough to qualify his expression as a smile.

"Oh . . . I'll live," he managed. "Wouldn't . . . give 'em . . . the satis . . . faction . . . of dying." Worn out by this, he closed his eyes, chest heaving. I wiped his face gently with my handkerchief, patted his shoulder, and left him to rest.

I had had the litter bearers take him upstairs, to what had been my bedroom, and I closed the door behind me now with a queerly mixed feeling of triumph and depression.

I had spent the morning with Mrs. Figg and the housemaid, Doreen, packing away what remained of Lord John's furnishings—for many had already been shipped to New York—and rearranging the house to serve as a temporary surgery. Even if we were to leave for North Carolina soon—and the sooner the better—I did have to have someplace to put Tench where he could be looked after in conditions approaching comfort and hygiene. And the patients I had been seeing at the printshop could certainly be taken care of more conveniently here.

At the same time . . . being here again brought back echoes of the numb despair I had lived with all those weeks of believing Jamie dead. I thought the bustle of work and the clean sweep of furnishings would perhaps obviate that distant sense of drowning, but at the moment it was an uneasy swirl around my ankles.

Mental oppression was not the only debilitating condition connected with the new situation. Leaving Number 17 to return to the Shippen house, I had been followed in the street by a gang of young men. Mostly boys, but some big fellows of sixteen or seventeen, big enough to make me uneasy with their glances.

Still more uneasy when they began to draw up close to me, taking a quick step to whisper, "King's whore!" in my ear before falling back, or to try to tread on the hem of my skirt, sniggering.

I thought I had seen one or two of them in the mob when I'd brought Hal here. Perhaps they'd followed me then and, finding that I was married to Lord John, assumed I was a turncoat, a traitor to the Rebel cause. Or possibly, I thought, stiffening my spine, they were just troublemaking pipsqueaks.

I whirled round to face them, gripping my parasol. It wasn't much of a weapon, but no physical weapon would have been of use against so many. Even a twelve-year-old boy was likely stronger than I was at the moment.

"What do you want?" I demanded, using the memory of my matron's voice, whipcrack and steel—or at least I hoped I could still do that.

Some of the little warts blinked and took a step back, but one of the bigger ones took a step toward me, grinning. It took all my control not to recoil.

"I don't know, hinnie," he said, looking me up and down with a lazy insolence. "What does a Loyalist *lady* have that we *might* want?"

"A swift poke in the eye is all I can offer you," I informed him crisply, with a meaningful pointing of my parasol. "Apparently I'm walking too slowly and blocking your progress, gentlemen. Do go on ahead of me." Holding his eye with a menacing stare, I stepped into the street and gestured with my parasol, indicating that they should pass on.

That made some of them giggle, but the big fellow flushed a nasty pink that made his adolescent pimples fluoresce. I stepped back farther into the street, in an imitation of politeness, but actually in hopes of attracting some attention.

I was lucky: a rag-and-bone cart was coming down the road, the horse's hooves clopping on the cobbles, and I moved still farther, blocking the way. The carter, aroused from semi-somnolence, half-stood, peering out from under his hat.

"What the devil are you idle buggers a-doing in the road? Get your fat arses out my way!" He raised his whip in a menacing fashion, and the boys, who had started to advance on me, quickly retreated.

The carter stood up all the way, took off his hat, and bowed to me.

"Good day, your ladyship; I hopes I sees you well. Can I offer you a ride, mayhap?" He was speaking in jest; I didn't think he actually knew I had recently *been* a ladyship. He was certainly surprised when I swept up my skirts and mounted his cart, though.

"Home, James," I said, furling my parasol, "and don't spare the horses."

The recollection made me smile a little, but the smile faded at the thought that the louts who had accosted me certainly lived somewhere nearby. I mightn't be as lucky a second time. And at that thought, a wave of cold terror washed over me and I felt a band of soreness across my middle, the chafing and bruising from hours spent tied facedown across a horse's back, being carried helpless to—

"Stop that!" I said sharply to myself. "Stop it at once. I won't have it." They were teenaged boys. I wasn't afraid of . . . But the first man to rape me had been about sixteen; he'd been apologetic about it. I stepped into a narrow alley between two buildings and threw up.

I'd managed to function. I got back to the Shippens' house and collected my things, then returned to the printshop to eat lunch and pack up the rest of my herbs and medicines; Fergus and Germain would bring them to Chestnut Street on their afternoon delivery round.

No one had molested me on the way back to Chestnut Street. I could have asked Jenny to come with me, but pride prevented me. I would *not* let simpleminded fear stop me doing what needed to be done.

But how long can you keep doing it? And what's the point?

"There's always a point," I muttered. "It's someone's life. That's a point."

A life that could be snatched away, thrown away, frittered on a battlefield . . . How many men had died that way? And it didn't stop, it didn't get better. . . . This was an *early* war, for God's sake. An endless chain of wars lay between my lives: the Revolution here, the Great War at the other end—and constant slaughter in between.

The summer was dying; the air was beginning to have a hint of freshness in the mornings, but in midafternoon it still hung thick and heavy. Too heavy to draw a full breath.

I stood for a moment outside Number 17, feeling unequal to going in and dealing with things. After a moment, I turned down the path that led round the side of the house, out to the tiny garden at the back, and sat down on the bench there, among the roses, feeling most unwell.

I DON'T KNOW how long I had been sitting there, head in my hands, listening to the loud buzzing of bees. But I heard footsteps coming down the path and managed to lift my head.

"Are ye all right, Sassenach?" It was Jamie, the large box of medicines and bandages in his arms. And from the look of alarm on his face, it was reasonably obvious that I didn't look all right. I couldn't muster the energy to try to look all right.

"I just—thought I'd sit down," I said, flapping a hand helplessly.

"I'm glad ye did." He set down the box on the yellowing grass and came to crouch in front of me, examining my face. "What happened?"

"Nothing," I said, and without warning began to cry. Or, rather, to leak. There was nothing of the sobbing, convulsive, racking nature of weeping; tears were just streaking down my cheeks without my approval.

Jamie nudged me over a little and sat down beside me, wrapping his arms around me. He was wearing his old kilt, and the smell of the dusty wool fabric, worn thin with age, made me utterly dissolve.

He tightened his grip and, sighing, pressed his cheek to my head and said small, tender things in Gaelic. And in a little time, the effort to understand them gave me a tenuous grip on myself. I drew a deep breath and he released me, though he kept an arm around me for support.

"Mo nighean donn," he said softly, and smoothed hair out of my face. "Have ye got a hankie?"

That made me laugh. Or rather emit a sort of strangled giggle, but still . . .

"Yes. At least, I think so." I groped in my bosom and withdrew a sturdy square of much-laundered linen, on which I blew my nose several times and then wiped my eyes, trying to think what on earth to offer as an explanation for my disordered state—of mind, as well as body. There wasn't any good way to begin, so I just began.

"Do you ever—well, no. I know you do."

"Likely," he said, smiling a little. "What do I do?"

"See the . . . the void. The abyss." Speaking the words reopened the rent in my soul, and the cold wind came through. A shudder ran through me, in spite of the warmth of the air and Jamie's body. "I mean—it's always there, always yawning at your feet, but most people manage to ignore it, not think about it. I've mostly been able to. You have to, to do medicine." I wiped my nose on my sleeve, having dropped my handkerchief. Jamie pulled a crumpled hankie out of his sleeve and handed it to me.

"Ye dinna mean only death?" he asked. "Because I've seen that often enough. It hasna really scairt me since I was ten or so, though." He glanced down at me and smiled. "And I doubt ye're afraid of it, either. I've seen ye face it down a thousand times and more."

"Facing something down doesn't mean you aren't afraid of it," I said dryly. "Usually quite the opposite. And I *know* you know that."

He made a small sound of agreement in his throat and hugged me gently. I would normally have found this comforting, and the fact that I didn't merely added to my sense of despair.

"It's—it's just . . . *nothing.* And so much endless nothing . . . It's as though nothing you do, nothing you are, can possibly matter, it's all just swallowed up . . ." I closed my eyes, but the darkness behind my eyelids frightened me and I opened them again. "I—" I raised a hand, then let it fall.

"I can't explain," I said, defeated. "It wasn't there—or I wasn't looking at it—after I was shot. It wasn't nearly dying that made me look in, see it yawning there. But being so . . . so bloody *frail*! Being so stinking *afraid*." I clenched my fists, seeing the knobby bones of my knuckles, the blue veins that stood out on the backs of my hands and curved down my wrists.

"Not death," I said at last, sniffing. "Futility. Uselessness. Bloody entropy. Death *matters,* at least sometimes."

"I ken that," Jamie said softly, and took my hands in his; they were big, and battered, scarred and maimed. "It's why a warrior doesna fear death so much. He has the hope—sometimes the certainty—that his death will matter."

"What happens to me between now and then doesna matter to anyone."

Those words swam out of nowhere and struck me in the pit of the stomach, so hard that I could barely breathe. He'd said that to me, from the bottom of despair, in the dungeon of Wentworth Prison, a lifetime ago. He'd bargained for my life then, with what he had—not his life, already forfeit, but his soul.

"It matters to me!" I'd said to him—and, against all odds, had ransomed that soul and brought him back.

And then it had come again, stark and dire necessity, and he'd laid down his life without hesitation for his men and for the child I carried. And that time I had been the one who sacrificed my soul. And it had mattered, for both of us.

It still mattered. And the shell of fear cracked like an egg and everything inside me poured out like blood and water mingled and I sobbed on his chest until there were no more tears and no more breath. I leaned against him, limp as a dishcloth, and watched the crescent moon begin to rise in the east.

"What did you say?" I said, rousing myself after a long while. I felt groggy and disoriented, but at peace.

"I asked, what's entropy?"

"Oh," I said, momentarily disconcerted. When had the concept of entropy been invented? Not yet, obviously. "It's, um . . . a lack of order, a lack of predictability, an inability for a system to do work."

"A system of what?"

"Well, there you have me," I admitted, sitting up and wiping my nose. "Just an ideal sort of system, with heat energy.

The Second Law of Thermodynamics basically says that in an isolated system—one that's not getting energy from somewhere outside, I mean—entropy will always increase. I think it's just a scientific way of saying that everything is going to pot, all of the time."

He laughed, and despite my shattered state of mind, I did, too.

"Aye, well, far be it from me to argue wi' the Second Law of Thermodynamics," he said. "I think it's likely right. When did ye last eat, Sassenach?"

"I don't know," I said. "I'm not hungry." I didn't want to do anything but sit still beside him.

"D'ye see the sky?" he said, a little later. It was a pure deep violet at the horizon, fading into a blue-black immensity overhead, and the early stars burned like distant lamps.

"Hard to miss," I said.

"Aye." He sat with his head tilted back, looking up, and I admired the clean line of his long, straight nose, his soft wide mouth and long throat, as though seeing them for the first time.

"Is it not a void there?" he said quietly, still looking up. "And yet we're no afraid to look."

"There are lights," I said. "It makes a difference." My voice was hoarse, and I swallowed. "Though I suppose even the stars are burning out, according to the Second Law."

"Mmphm. Well, I suppose men can make all the laws they like," he said, "but God made hope. The stars willna burn out." He turned and, cupping my chin, kissed me gently. "And nor will we."

The noises of the city were muted now, though even darkness didn't stifle it entirely. I heard distant voices and the sound of a fiddle: a party, perhaps, from one of the houses down the street. And the bell of St. George's struck the hour with a small, flat *bong*! Nine o'clock. And all's well.

"I'd better go and see to my patient," I said.

119

"ALAS, POOR YORICK!"

September 17, 1778
Middlebrook Encampment, New Jersey

TWO NIGHTS LATER, William stood at the edge of a dark wood, watching a lopsided rising moon shed its light over Middlebrook Encampment. His heart was thumping in his ears and he was breathing fast, his hands clenched around the handle of the spade he'd just stolen.

He'd been correct in his assessment of his welcome. He'd roughened his accent and, posing as a young immigrant from England interested in joining Washington's troops, he'd been invited to join the Hamilton family for supper and given a bed for the night. The next day, he'd walked up to Middlebrook Encampment with the eldest Hamilton son, a man about his own age, where he'd been introduced to a Captain Ronson, one of the few officers still there.

One thing had led to another, and, by degrees, he had steered the conversation to the battle at Brandywine Creek and thence to British prisoners of war . . . and eventually he'd been taken to the small burying ground that lay before him now.

He'd been cautious about Ben, mentioning his name only casually among several others—family acquaintances, he'd said, that he'd heard had been at the battle. Some of the men he talked to hadn't recognized the name at all; two or three said, oh, yes, the English viscount, prisoner, billeted with a family called Tobermory, very civil fellow, shame that he'd died. . . .

And one man, a Lieutenant Corey, had said the same thing but his eyes had flickered slightly when he said it. William was wise enough to abandon the subject at once—but brought up

Captain Benjamin Grey with someone else, much later and out of hearing of Corey.

"Is he buried nearby?" he'd asked, with a decent assumption of casual concern. "I know his family. I should like to be able to write to them, tell them I'd visited, you know. . . ."

It had taken some effort; the burying ground was well outside the encampment, up on a little wooded knoll, and while some of the graves were neatly ranked, others had been dug hastily, and many were unmarked. His companion was not busy, though, and of a helpful complexion; he went and unearthed the adjutant's ledger in which the dead were listed and, with some poking about, eventually led William to a flattened mound with a piece of lath stuck into it, on which GREY had been scratched with a nail.

"Lucky you came before another winter got at it," his companion had remarked, pulling the lath out and examining it critically. He shook his head, reached into his pocket, and, fetching out a lead pencil, reinforced the name with strong, scrubbing strokes before pushing it back into the earth. "Maybe that will last a bit, in case the family should want to set up a stone."

"That's . . . very good of you," William had said, his throat tight. "I'll tell his family of your kindness." But he couldn't weep for a man he theoretically hadn't known and so swallowed his emotions and turned away, finding something commonplace to talk about as they made their way downhill.

He *had* wept in private, later, leaning against the comforting bulk of the mare, whom he'd named Miranda. She wasn't sprightly, but she was a good horse, and merely whuffed a little and shifted her weight to give him support.

He'd been stubbornly insisting to himself that there must be some mistake. Ben *couldn't* be dead. This belief had been sustained by Uncle Hal's complete refusal to believe the news. And it was plausible; whatever Ezekiel Richardson was up to, he meant no good to the Greys.

But here was Ben's grave, silent and muddy, speckled with the first yellowing leaves of September. And all around him lay the decaying bodies of other men, some prisoners, some Continental regulars, some militia . . . equal, and equally alone in death.

He'd eaten dinner that night with the Hamiltons again, replying automatically to their conversation but concerned with his own misery—and the thought of the much greater misery to come when he had to return to New York and tell his father and Uncle Hal. . . .

William had taken leave of the Hamiltons next morning, consigning the remains of the deer to them, and was followed down the narrow road by their good wishes and hopes that they would see him again with General Washington, when the troops came back to Middlebrook to winter. He'd made it several miles down the mountain, dragging his spirit behind him, when he stopped to take a piss.

He'd been hunting once with Ben, and they'd stopped like this; Ben had told him a particularly scabrous joke, and he'd laughed so much that he couldn't piss and Ben had pissed on his shoes, which made them both laugh harder, and . . .

"God damn it," he said aloud, and, buttoning his flies, stamped back to Miranda and swung up into the saddle. "I'm sorry, owd lass," he said, reining her head around to face uphill. "We're going back."

And here he was, wavering between the conviction that this was madness and the stark fact that there wasn't anything else he could do besides go back to New York, and he wouldn't do that until and unless he had no other choice. At least he might be able to salvage a lock of Ben's hair for Aunt Minnie. . . .

That thought made him want to throw up, but he touched the knife at his waist, took a firmer hold of the spade, and made his way gingerly in among the graves.

The moonlight was bright enough to find footing but not to read most of the markers. He had to kneel and run his thumb over several before feeling the letters G-R-E-Y.

"Right," he said out loud. His voice sounded small and choked, and he cleared his throat and spat—to the side, not on the grave. "Right," he said again, more forcefully, and, standing, took up the spade and drove it into the earth.

He'd started close to what he thought should be the head, but dug in from the side—the thought of driving his spade down into Ben's face made his flesh creep. The dirt was soft, damp with recent rain, but it was heavy work, and despite the coolness of the mountain night, he was soaked with sweat before he'd dug a quarter of an hour. If Ben had died of camp fever, as they said—and come to think, was that sensible? He hadn't been held in the stockade with the enlisted men. As an officer, he'd been billeted with the Tobermorys. How had he come to catch camp fever? But still, if he had, then others would have died at the same time; it was a badly infectious sort of plague, he knew that much.

But if *that* were true, then a number of other men would have been buried at the same time, and buried hastily, to prevent contagion from the bodies. (Oh, *there* was a good thought: he might be opening a grave full of teeming pestilence. . . .) Anyway, if that were the case, the graves would be shallow ones.

This one was. His spade struck something harder than dirt, and he stopped abruptly, muscles quivering. He swallowed and resumed shoveling, more cautiously.

The body had been wrapped in a shroud of coarse burlap. He couldn't see, but a ginger probing with his fingers told him as much. Squatting, he dug with his hands, unearthing what he hoped was the head. His stomach was clenched tight and he was breathing through his mouth. The stink was less than he'd expected, but still definitely there.

Oh, God. Ben . . . He'd been nursing the hope that the grave was empty.

Patting and probing, he made out the rounded shape and took a deep breath, feeling for the edge of the shroud. Had it been stitched? No, the edge was loose.

He'd thought of bringing a torch but had dismissed the idea, not wanting to risk detection. On the whole, he was glad he hadn't. He wiped dirt from his hands onto his breeches and peeled the burlap gently back, grimacing as it stuck to the skin beneath. It came loose with a grisly, rasping sound, and he nearly dropped it and ran. But he steeled himself and touched the dead man's face.

It wasn't as awful as he'd thought it might be; the body seemed largely still intact. *How long will a man lie i' the earth ere he rot?* What had the gravedigger said in reply—nine years? Well, then . . . He'd seen *Hamlet* with Ben and Adam, in London. . . .

William fought back an insane urge to laugh and felt gently over the dead features. The nose was broad and stubby, not Ben's sharp beak—but no doubt the process of decay . . . He slid his fingers over the temple, thinking to see if a presentable lock of hair might—and stopped dead, not breathing.

The corpse was missing an ear. Bloody hell, it was missing *both* ears. He felt again, both sides, unable to believe it. But it was true—and the ears had been missing for some time; even with the nasty slack feel of the decaying flesh, the ridges of scar tissue were distinct. A thief.

William sat back on his heels and tilted up his head, letting out a huge breath. He felt dizzy, and the stars made little pinwheels in his vision.

"Jesus," he breathed, flooded with relief, gratitude, and creeping horror. "Oh, Jesus, thank you! And, oh, Christ," he added, looking down at the invisible stranger in Ben's grave, "*now* what?"

120

A CRACKLING OF THORNS

September 18, 1778
Philadelphia

I WAS HAVING A pleasantly incoherent dream involving autumn leaves and fireflies. The fireflies were red, rather than green, and were floating down through the trees like live sparks, and where they brushed against the yellow leaves, the edges browned and curled as the leaves caught fire. Smoke curled upward through the trees, lazy against an evening sky, pungent as tobacco, and I was walking underneath, smoking a cigarette with Frank . . .

I woke muzzily, thinking how nice it was to see Frank again, followed abruptly by *Dreams don't smell, do they?* along with *I don't smoke,* and then—

"Jesus! We're on fire!" I sat up, panicked and wriggling to get out of the sheets. Smoke was already thick in the loft, drifting layers above my head, and Jamie was coughing, grabbing my arm and dragging me free before I could locate all my limbs.

"Quick," he said, hoarse as a crow. "Dinna wait to dress, come down!"

I didn't dress, but did seize my shift and pulled it over my head as I crawled toward the edge of the loft. Jamie had the ladder over the edge as I reached it and was already started down, shouting in a loud, cracked voice.

I could hear the fire. It rattled and crackled, and the ashy smell of burning paper and the stink of singed buckram was thick in the air.

"In the shop," I gasped, catching up with Jamie in the kitchen. "It's in the shop. The Bibles are burning—the type-foundry . . ."

"Get the weans." He ran across the kitchen, shirttails flying, and slammed shut the door that led into the printshop, from which smoke was fuming in clouds. I ran the other way, into the room that served Fergus and Marsali as living and sleeping quarters, with a smaller loft above, where the children and Jenny slept.

That door was shut, thank God. The smoke hadn't yet reached them. I flung it open, shouting, "Fire! Fire! Get up, get up!" and ran for the ladder to the loft, hearing Fergus swear behind me in French and Marsali's confused "What? *WHAT?*"

My hands were sweating and slipped on the smooth wooden rails of the ladder.

"Jenny! Germain!" I bellowed—or tried to. Smoke was drifting here, too, high up under the roof, and I was coughing, my eyes and nose running.

"Jo-hoan!"

There was one small bedstead, two little humps under the bedclothes. I ran to the bed, flinging back the covers. Joan and Félicité were curled together, Félicité's nightdress rucked up to show her little bottom. I grabbed her by the shoulder, shaking her and trying to speak calmly.

"Girls, girls! You have to get up. Right now. Do you hear me, Joan? Wake up!"

Joan's eyelids were fluttering, and she was coughing, turning her head to and fro to escape the smoke, eyes stubbornly closed. Félicité normally slept like the dead, and tonight was no exception; her head wobbled like her rag doll's when I shook her.

"What? What is it?" Jenny was struggling out of the quilts on her pallet in the corner.

"We're on fire!" I shouted. "Hurry—help me!"

I heard a cracking noise from the kitchen and a scream from Marsali. I didn't know what had happened, but in desperation I grabbed Félicité bodily out of bed, still shouting at Joan to wake up, for God's sake!

I felt the vibration of the ladder against the loft and Jamie was there, snatching Joan up out of the bed.

"The lads, where are the lads?" he asked urgently. In the frantic need to wake the girls, I'd forgotten Germain and Henri-Christian. I looked round in an urgent daze; there was a thin mattress on the floor, flattened and dented by bodies, but no sign of the boys.

"Germain! Joan! Henri-Christian!" Marsali's face popped up over the edge of the loft, pale with fear. "Félicité!" In an instant, she was with me, taking Félicité from me. The little girl was coughing and whining, starting to cry.

"It's all right, *a nighean,* it's all right; you're safe, aye?" Marsali was patting her back, coughing herself as the smoke thickened. "Where are the boys?"

Jamie had shoved Jenny onto the ladder and was following her down, Joan draped over his shoulder, small pink feet kicking urgently.

"I'll find them!" I said, pushing Marsali toward the ladder. "Take Félicité down!"

Something in the shop exploded with a loud *whoosh*—probably a barrel of ink, made with varnish and lampblack. Marsali gasped, clutched Félicité hard, and scuttled for the ladder. I began rootling madly through the bits of furniture and boxes and bags in the loft, calling the boys' names between fits of coughing.

The smoke was much worse now; I could barely see. I was kicking my way through blankets, a chamber pot—unfortunately full—and other things, but there was no sign of Henri-Christian or Germain. Even if they'd been overcome by the smoke, surely—

"Sassenach!" Jamie was suddenly there by my elbow. "Come

down, come down! The fire's in the wall; the loft will come down any minute!"

"But—"

He didn't wait for argument, but picked me up bodily and swung me down onto the ladder. I missed my footing and slid the last few feet, knees buckling as I hit the floor. The wall in front of me was alight, plaster shattered and the fire moving, glowing along the edges of the laths. Jamie landed beside me with a thud that shook the floor, seized my arm, and we ran for the kitchen.

I heard a rending crack and then a crash that seemed to happen in slow motion, as the supports to the children's loft gave way and the timbers came down.

"Germain," I gasped. "Henri—"

"Not here," Jamie said, and shook with coughing. "Out, we must get out." The air in the kitchen was a little clearer, but not by much. It was hot enough to sear the hairs inside my nose. Eyes streaming, we made our way across the room to the back door, now standing open, and more or less fell through into the alleyway behind.

Marsali and Jenny were crouched in the privy yard of the house on the other side of the alley, both girls now awake and clinging to them, shrieking.

"Where's Fergus?" Jamie shouted, pushing me toward Marsali. She pointed toward the burning building, screaming something that I couldn't hear over the rumble of the fire. Then there was a second's respite in the noise, and a long, panicked bray split the night air.

"Clarence!" Jamie spun on his heel and ran for the tiny stable, little more than a shed next to the main building. I ran after him, thinking that perhaps the boys had taken refuge there. My bare feet slid on the cobbles, stubbing my toes, but I scarcely noticed, my heart pounding in my ears with fear, lungs laboring to find fresh air.

"Germain!" I heard the shout, faint above the fire, and turned to see a shadow moving just beyond the open door into the kitchen. Smoke was pouring from the door in a thick white column, glowing from the fire beyond. I took a deep gulp of air and dived into the smoke, flailing my arms in a vain effort to dispel enough to see.

One of my flailing arms struck something solid, though,

and Fergus collapsed into me, so far overcome with heat and smoke that he couldn't stand. I grabbed him under the arms and dragged him toward the door with that sort of strength that comes from the absolute determination not to die.

We fell out into the alley, and there were shouts from what proved to be neighbors rushing to help. Hands gripped me and pulled me away. I could hear Fergus, gasping and sobbing, struggling against the helpful hands, desperately croaking his sons' names.

Through streaming eyes, I saw the stable roof alight and Jamie leading Clarence out, the torn-off sleeve of his shirt wrapped round the mule's eyes.

And then I heard a shriek that rose above all the noise, fire, neighbors, Clarence's bray. Marsali stood up straight, eyes and mouth round with horror, looking up.

The loading door that led to the kitchen loft was open, smoke and sparks fuming out, and in the midst of it was Germain, dragging Henri-Christian by the hand.

He shouted something, but no one could hear above the racket. There was a muffled *boom* from the loft as another cask went, and the fire blazed up suddenly as the stacks of paper caught, silhouetting the boys in the doorway.

"Jump! Jump!" Jamie was shouting, and everyone else in the alley was shouting it, too, people shoving one another in the effort to get underneath, to help. Germain looked wildly to and fro; Henri-Christian was panicked, struggling to go back into the loft. The rope used to raise and lower loads to a waiting wagon was there, almost within reach. Germain saw it and let go of Henri-Christian for an instant to reach for it, hanging on to the edge of the doorframe.

He got it, and a gasp went through the crowd. His fair hair was standing on end in the wind from the fire, surrounding his head like flames, and for an instant I thought it *was* on fire.

Henri-Christian, dizzy from the smoke, had fallen against the doorframe and was clinging to it. He was too frightened to move; I could see him shaking his head as Germain pulled at him.

"Throw him, Germain! Throw your brother!" Fergus was shouting as loudly as he could, his voice cracking with the strain, and several other voices joined in. "Throw him!"

I saw Germain's jaw set hard, and he yanked Henri-Christian

loose, picked him up, and clutched him with one arm, wrapping the rope around the other.

"No!" Jamie bellowed, seeing it. "Germain, *don't*!" But Germain bent his head over his brother's, and I thought I saw his lips move, saying, *"Hold on tight!"* And then he stepped out into the air, both hands clinging to the rope, Henri-Christian's stocky legs wrapped round his ribs.

It happened instantly and yet so slowly. Henri-Christian's short legs lost their grip. Germain's grab failed, for the little boy was already falling, arms outstretched, in a half somersault through the smoky air.

He fell straight through the sea of upraised hands, and the sound as his head struck the cobbles was the sound of the end of the world.

121

WALKING ON COALS

September 19, 1778
Philadelphia

EVEN WHEN THE world ends, things bloody go on *happening*. You just don't know what to do about them.

Everything smelled of smoke and burning. The air, my hair, Jamie's skin, the ill-fitting gown someone had given me . . . Even food tasted of ashes. But, then, it would, wouldn't it? I reflected. It didn't matter; I couldn't eat more than the mouthful or two required for politeness.

No one had slept. The printshop had burned to the ground in the small hours; there was nothing to be done but to beat off flying embers and stamp out sparks in an effort to preserve the nearby houses. By a mercy, it hadn't been a windy night.

The neighbors had given us shelter, clothes, food, and abundant sympathy. None of it seemed real, and I hoped in a vague sort of way that this state of things would continue, even though I knew it couldn't.

What did seem real, though, was the small collection of vivid images that had been literally seared on my mind during the night. Henri-Christian's bare feet, dirty-soled and large in comparison with his legs, sticking out from under his mother's skirt as she cradled him, rocking to and fro, wrapped in a grief too dense for any sound to escape it. Germain, letting go the rope in a frantic attempt to fly after his brother, dropping like a rock into Fergus's arms. Fergus clutching Germain so hard against him that it must have bruised them both, his hook gleaming against Germain's soot-streaked back.

The boys had been sleeping on the roof. There was a small trapdoor in the ceiling of the bedroom loft, which no one had remembered in the panic of the fire.

When Germain began finally to talk, sometime toward dawn, he said they had gone out to be cool and to look at the stars. They had fallen asleep and not waked until the slates they lay on began to feel hot—and by then smoke was rolling up through the cracks of the trapdoor. They'd run across the roof to the other side, where a similar trapdoor let them into the printing loft. Half the loft had fallen away and the rest was on fire, but they'd made it through the smoke and rubble to the loading door.

"Why?" he'd cried, passed from one set of arms to another, ignoring all futile words of would-be comfort. "Why didn't I hold on to him?! He was too little; he couldn't hold on."

Only his mother hadn't embraced him. She held Henri-Christian and wouldn't let go until daylight came and sheer exhaustion loosened her grasp. Fergus and Jamie had eased the small, chunky body from her grip and taken him away to be washed and made decent for the long business of being dead. Then Marsali had come to find her eldest son and touched him gently in his deadened sleep, sorrowing.

The Reverend Figg had once more come to our aid, a small neat figure in his black suit and high white stock, offering his church in which to hold the wake.

I was sitting in the church now, in midafternoon, alone, on a bench with my back against a wall, smelling smoke and trembling intermittently with echoes of flame and loss.

Marsali was asleep in a neighbor's bed. I had tucked her in, her daughters curled up on either side of her, Félicité sucking her thumb, round black eyes watchful as those of her rag doll, fortuitously saved from the flames. So few things had survived. I remembered the constant pang of loss after the Big House had burned, reaching for something and realizing that it wasn't there.

Jenny, worn to the gray-white color of weathered bone, had gone to lie down at the Figgs' house, her rosary in her hands, the wooden beads sliding smoothly through her fingers as she walked, her lips moving silently; I doubted that she would stop praying, even in her sleep.

People came and went, bringing things. Tables, extra benches, platters of food. Late-summer flowers, roses and jasmine and early blue asters, and for the first time, tears ran down my cheeks at this scented remembrance of the wedding held here so little time before. I pressed a stranger's handkerchief to my face, though, not wanting anyone to see and feel that they must try to comfort me.

The bench beside me creaked and gave, and I peeped over the edge of my handkerchief to see Jamie beside me, wearing a worn suit that plainly belonged to a chairman—it had a band round the coat sleeve reading "82"—and with his face washed but the whorls of his ears still grimed with soot. He took my hand and held it tight, and I saw the blisters on his fingers, some fresh, some burst and shredded from the efforts to save what could be saved from the fire.

He looked to the front of the church, toward what couldn't be saved, then sighed and looked down to our clasped hands.

"All right, lass?" His voice was hoarse, his throat raw and soot-choked as my own.

"Yes," I said. "Have you had anything to eat?" I already knew he hadn't slept.

He shook his head and leaned back against the wall, closing his eyes, and I felt the relaxation of his body into momentary exhaustion. There were things still to be done, but just for a moment . . . I wanted to dress his hands, but there was nothing to dress them with. I lifted the hand he held and kissed his knuckles.

"What do ye think it's like when ye die?" he asked suddenly, opening his eyes and looking down at me. His eyes were red as an emery bag.

"I can't say I've really thought about it," I replied, taken aback. "Why?"

He rubbed two fingers slowly between his brows; I thought from the look of him that his head must ache.

"I only wondered if it's like this." He made a brief gesture, encompassing the half-empty room, the well-wishers coming and going in whispers, the mourners sitting, blank-faced and sagging like bags of rubbish, stirring—with a visible effort—only when spoken to. "If ye dinna ken what to do, and ye dinna much want to do anything. Or is it like going to sleep and wakin' up in a new, fresh place and wanting to go out at once and see what it's like?"

"According to Father O'Neill, innocents are just in the presence of God immediately. No limbo, no purgatory. Assuming they were properly baptized," I added. Henri-Christian had indeed been baptized, and as he was not yet seven, the Church held that he lacked sufficient sense of reason to commit sins. Ergo . . .

"I've known people in their fifties who had less sense than Henri-Christian," I said, wiping my nose for the thousandth time. My nostrils were as raw as my eyelids.

"Aye, but they've more capacity for causing harm wi' their foolishness." A faint smile touched his mouth. "I thought I was dead on Culloden field; did I ever tell ye that?"

"I don't think you did. Under the circumstances, I suppose it would have been a reasonable assumption, though—were you knocked out?"

He nodded, eyes fixed on the floorboards.

"Aye. If I'd been able to look about, I should have known better, but my eyes were sealed shut wi' the blood. It was all red and dim, so I supposed I was in purgatory and would just have to wait 'til someone came round to chastise me. After a bit, I supposed boredom was meant to be part of the punishment." He glanced at the tiny coffin on its bench at the front of the room. Germain sat by it, one hand on its lid. He hadn't moved at all in the last half hour.

"I've never seen Henri-Christian bored," I said quietly, after a moment. "Not once."

"No," Jamie said softly, and took my hand. "I dinna suppose he ever will be."

Gaelic wakes have their own rhythm. Fergus and Marsali

came in quietly an hour or so later and sat together at first, holding hands near the coffin, but as more people came, the men gradually surrounded Fergus, absorbing him, much as a gang of phagocytes surround a microbe, carrying it along with them, and after a time, as happens normally in such situations, half the men were at one side of the room, talking quietly, and the others outside, unable to bear close quarters and exigent emotion but wanting to lend their presence and sympathy.

The women clustered, first near Marsali, hugging and weeping, then gathering in small clumps with their friends, drifting back to the tables to rearrange things or put out more bread or cakes. Josiah Prentice came with his fiddle, but left it in its case for the time being. Tobacco smoke from the pipes of the men outside drifted through the church in soft blue clouds. It tickled uneasily at the back of my nose, too reminiscent of the fire for comfort.

Jamie left me with a brief squeeze of the hand and went to speak to Ian. I saw them both look at Germain; Ian nodded and moved quietly to his nephew, putting both hands on his shoulders. Rachel hovered nearby, dark eyes watchful.

The bench beside me creaked, and Jenny sat down. Wordless, she put her arm about my shoulder, and equally wordless, I bent my head to hers and we wept for a bit—not only for Henri-Christian but for the babies we each had lost, my stillborn Faith, her infant Caitlin. And for Marsali, now joining us in this sorrowful kinship.

The night drew in, beer and ale were poured, some stronger drink was brought out, and the somber mood of the gathering lifted a little. Still, it was the wake of a child and a life cut short; there couldn't be the sense of shared memory and laughter that there might be for a man who had lived a full life and whose friends had come to share in his death.

Josiah Prentice played his fiddle, but quietly, mixing laments with peaceful tunes and the occasional hymn; there wouldn't be much singing tonight. I wished suddenly and fiercely that Roger were here. He would perhaps have known what to say, in a situation where there was nothing one could say. And even with his ruined voice, he would have known a song to sing, a prayer to offer.

Father O'Neill from St. George's Church had come, tactfully overlooking the unorthodox Quaker marriage of a month before, and stood talking near the door with Fergus and a few other men.

"Poor wee child," Jenny said, her voice roughened by tears but steady now. She was holding my hand, and I hers, and she was looking not at the coffin but at Fergus. "His bairns mean everything to him—and especially our wee man." Her lips trembled, but she pressed them together and straightened her back.

"D'ye think Marsali's breedin'?" she said, very softly, looking at Marsali, with Joan and Félicité clinging to her skirts, Joan's head in her lap. Her mother's hand rested on her hair, gently smoothing it.

"I do," I said, as softly.

She nodded, and her hand twitched, half hidden in the folds of her skirt, making the horns against evil.

More people had come. The Congress was meeting in Philadelphia, and several delegates who did business with Fergus had come. Jonas Phillips and Samuel Adams were both there, chatting by the refreshments table. In a different frame of mind, I might have marveled at being in the same room with two signers of the Declaration of Independence, but, after all, they were only men—though I took it kindly that they'd come.

I looked for Germain every few minutes; now he was standing by the tables with Ian, drinking something from a cup. I blinked and looked again.

"Jesus H— I mean, good Lord. Ian's giving Germain cherry bounce!"

Jenny glanced at Germain's bright red lips, and a quiver of amusement ran through her.

"Canna think of anything better for the lad just now, can you?"

"Well . . . no." I stood up, shaking out my skirts. "D'you want some?"

"I do," she said, and got up with alacrity. "And maybe a wee bite, too. It'll be a long night; we'll need a bit to sustain us, aye?"

It felt better to be up and moving. The fog of grief still numbed sensation, and I didn't look forward to its passing, but at the same time . . . I realized that I *was* hungry now.

The feeling in the room shifted gradually, from the first impact of shock and sorrow, to comforting support for the family, and now to more-general talk. Which was, I realized uneasily, beginning to focus on speculation as to what—or who—had caused the fire.

In the shock and grief of the event, none of us had spoken of it, but even through that numbing fog, the insidious question had hovered like a bat overhead: Why? How? And . . . who?

If anyone. Fire was a common plague in a time when every household had open hearths, and a printshop, with its type forge and its stock of inflammables, was still more vulnerable to simple accident. An open window, a stray breeze, loose papers blowing . . . a spitting ember from a badly smoored fire catching hold . . .

And yet.

The memory of the anonymous letter floated queasily on the surface of my mind. *Your house is on fire and your children are gone . . .*

And the young men who had followed me from Chestnut Street, their stealthy plucking and whispered taunts. God, could I have brought their enmity to Fergus's door?

Jamie had come to stand by me again, steady and solid as a rock, and handed me a fresh cup of cherry bounce. It was like drinking very strong cough syrup, but it was undeniably bracing. Up to the point where you fell down insensible, at least. I saw that Germain had slid slowly down the wall; Rachel knelt next to him and eased him to the ground, then folded her shawl and put it under his head.

The cherry bounce was taking the place of the fog; I thought drunkenness was probably an improvement, on the whole.

"Mrs. Fraser?" A strange voice on my left drew my attention from bemused contemplation of the dark-red depths of my cup. A young man in shabby clothes was standing at my elbow, a small package in his hand.

"She is," Jamie said, giving the young man a searching look. "Are ye needing a physician? Because—"

"Oh, no, sir," the young man assured him, obsequious. "I was told to give this into Mrs. Fraser's hand, that's all." He handed it to me and, with a short bow, turned and left.

Puzzled, and slow with fatigue, grief, and cherry bounce, I fumbled with the string, then gave up and handed the package to Jamie, who reached for his knife, failed to find it—for it had, of course, perished in the fire—and, with a flicker of annoyance, simply broke the string. The wrapping fell open to reveal a small leather purse and a note, folded but unsealed.

I blinked and squinted for a moment, then dipped a hand into my pocket. By a miracle, my spectacles had been downstairs, left behind in the kitchen when I took them off while chopping onions, and Jamie had retrieved them in his hurried foray into the burning house. The stylish handwriting sprang into reassuring clarity.

Mrs. Fraser,

I cannot think my Presence would be welcome and I would not intrude on private Grief. I ask nothing, neither Acknowledgment nor Obligation. I do ask that you would allow me to help in the only way that I can and that you will not reveal the Source of this Assistance to the younger Mr. Fraser. I trust your Discretion, as to the Elder.

It was signed simply, *P. Wainwright (Beauchamp).*

I raised my brows at Jamie and passed him the note. He read it, lips pressed tight together, but glanced at Marsali and the girls, now clustered with Jenny, talking to Mrs. Phillips, all of them crying quietly. Then across the room, to Fergus, flanked by Ian and Rachel. He grimaced very briefly, but his features set in resignation. There was a family to provide for; he couldn't, for the moment, afford pride.

"Well, it probably wasn't him, then," I said, with a sigh, and tucked the little purse into the pocket under my skirt. Numbed as I was, I still felt a vague sense of relief at that. Whatever he might be, might have done, or might intend, I still rather liked the erstwhile Monsieur Beauchamp.

I had no time to consider Percy further, though, for at this point there was a stir among the people near the door, and, looking to see what had caused it, I saw George Sorrel come in.

It was apparent at a glance that the tavern owner had been availing himself of his own wares—possibly as a means of getting up his courage, for he stood swaying slightly, fists clenched at his sides, looking slowly round the room, belligerently meeting the stares that greeted him.

Jamie said something very unsuitable in a house of God under his breath in Gaelic, and started toward the door. Before he could reach it, though, Fergus had turned to see the cause of the stir and had spotted Sorrel.

Fergus was no more sober than Sorrel but was much more upset. He stiffened for an instant, but then pulled himself free of the grasping hands of his supporters and headed for Sorrel without a word, red-eyed as a hunting ferret and just as dangerous.

He hit Sorrel with his fist as the man was opening his mouth. Unsteady as they were, both of them staggered from the impact, and men rushed in to separate them. Jamie reached Sorrel and, grabbing his arm, jerked him out of the scrum.

"I suggest that ye leave, sir," he said, politely, under the circumstances, and turned the man firmly toward the door.

"Don't," Fergus said. He was breathing like a train, sweat pouring down his chalk-white face. "Don't go. Stay—and tell me why. Why have you come here? How dare you come here?" This last was uttered in a cracked shout that made Sorrel blink and take a step backward. He shook his head doggedly, though, and drew himself up.

"I came to—to offer Mrs. Fraser con-condol—to say I was sorry about her son," he said sullenly. "And you ain't a-going to stop me, either, you farting French son of a bitch!"

"You offer my wife nothing," Fergus said, shaking with fury. "Nothing, do you hear? Who is to say you did not set the fire yourself? To kill me, to seize upon my wife? *Salaud!*"

I would have bet money that Sorrel didn't know what a *salaud* was, but it didn't matter; he went the color of beetroot and lunged at Fergus. He didn't reach him, as Jamie managed to grab his collar, but there was a sound of rending cloth and Sorrel jerked to a stop, staggering.

There was a rumble through the room, men and women gathering in a thundercloud of disapproval. I could see Jamie drawing himself up and in, settling himself to haul Sorrel out before someone besides Fergus took a swing at him. A certain shuffling readiness suggested that a number of men had it in mind.

And then Rachel walked between the two men. She was very pale, though a red spot burned in each cheek, and her hands were clenched in the fabric of her skirt.

"Does thee indeed come to offer comfort, friend?" she said to Sorrel, in a voice that shook only a little. "For if that is so, thee ought to offer it to all of those who are met here for the sake of the child. Particularly to his father."

She turned toward Fergus, reaching to put a careful hand on his sleeve.

"Thee will not see thy wife distressed further, I know," she said quietly. "Will thee not go to her now? For while she is grateful for the presence of so many kind folk, it is only thee she wants."

Fergus's face worked, anguish and fury warring with confusion. Seeing him unable to decide what to do or how to do it, Rachel moved closer and took his arm, tucking her hand into the curve of his elbow, and compelled him to turn and to walk with her, the crowd parting in front of them. I saw the curve of Marsali's blond head as she raised it slowly, her face changing as she watched Fergus come.

Jamie took a deep breath and released Sorrel.

"Well?" he said quietly. "Stay or go. As ye will."

Sorrel was still panting a little but had himself in hand now. He nodded jerkily, drew himself up, and straightened his torn coat. Then he walked through the silent crowd, head up, to give his sympathies to the bereaved.

122

HALLOWED GROUND

IN SPITE OF THE neighbors' generosity, there was very little to pack. Nor was there any reason to linger in Philadelphia. Our life there was ended.

There was—there always is—considerable speculation as to the cause of the fire. But after the outburst at the wake, a sense of flat finality had settled over all of us. The neighbors would continue to talk, but among the family there was an unspoken agreement that it made little difference whether the fire had been pure accident or someone's ill design. Nothing would bring Henri-Christian back. Nothing else mattered.

Jamie had taken Fergus to make the arrangements for our travel: not because he needed assistance but as a way of keeping Fergus moving, lest he simply sit down by Henri-Christian's small coffin and never rise again.

Things were both easier and harder for Marsali. She had children to care for, children who needed her badly.

Rachel and I packed what there was to pack, bought food for the journey, and dealt with the final details of leaving. I packed the bits and bobs of my surgery and, with mutual tears and embraces, gave the keys of Number 17 Chestnut Street to Mrs. Figg.

And in the early afternoon of the day following the wake, we borrowed a small cart, hitched up Clarence, and followed Henri-Christian to his grave.

There hadn't been any discussion as to the burial. After the wake, Ian had simply stood up and said, "I know where he must rest."

It was a long way, perhaps two hours' walk outside the city. The heat had broken at last, though, and the air moved gently over us, with the first cool touch of autumn. There was no ceremony to our procession; no Gaelic laments for a life cut short, no professional wailing. Only a small family, walking together for the last time.

We left the road at Ian's signal. Jamie unhitched Clarence and hobbled him to graze, then he and Fergus lifted the coffin and followed Ian into the whisper of the trees, along a small and hidden path made by the hooves of deer, and so upward to a small clearing in the forest.

There were two large cairns there, knee-high. And a smaller one, at the edge of the clearing, under the branches of a red cedar. A flat stone lay against it, the word ROLLO scratched into it.

Fergus and Jamie set down the little coffin, gently. Joanie and Félicité had stopped crying during the long walk, but seeing it there, so small and forlorn, facing the thought of walking away . . . they began to weep silently, clinging hard to each other, and at the sight of them, grief rose in me like a fountain.

Germain was holding hard to his mother's hand, mute and

jaw-set, tearless. Not seeking support, giving it, though the agony showed clear in his eyes as they rested on his brother's coffin.

Ian touched Marsali's arm gently.

"This place is hallowed by my sweat and my tears, cousin," he said softly. "Let us hallow it also by our blood and let our wee lad rest here safe in his family. If he canna go with us, we will abide with him."

He took the *sgian dubh* from his stocking and drew it across his wrist, lightly, then held his arm above Henri-Christian's coffin, letting a few drops fall on the wood. I could hear the sound of it, like the beginning of rain.

Marsali drew a shattered breath, stood straight, and took the knife from his hand.

PART EIGHT

Search and Rescue

123

QUOD SCRIPSI, SCRIPSI

From Mrs. Abigail Bell, Savannah,
the Royal Colony of Georgia
To Mr. James Fraser, Philadelphia,
Colony of Pennsylvania

Dear Mr. Fraser,

I write in response to yours of the 17th inst., apprising my Husband of your return to America, which was forwarded to him by a Friend in Wilmington.

As you will see from the Direction of this Letter, we have removed from Wilmington to Savannah, the political Climate of North Carolina having become increasingly dangerous to Loyalists, particularly to my Husband, given his History and Profession.

I wish to assure you that your Press has been preserved in excellent condition but is not presently in use. My husband contracted a serious Ague soon after our arrival here, and it became evident that his Illness was of the periodic, or relapsing, Kind. He does somewhat better these days but is unable to sustain the difficult Labor of the printing Trade. (I will add, should you think of establishing a Business here, that while the Politics of the Place are a great deal more congenial to those of the Loyalist Persuasion than those of the northern Colonies, a Printer is exposed to much Unpleasantness, whatever his personal Beliefs.)

Your Press is presently stored in the Barn of a Farmer named Simpson, who lives a short Distance outside the

City. I have seen it and assured myself that the Instrument is Clean, Dry (it is packed in Straw), and sheltered from the Weather. Please apprise me of your Desires, should you wish me to sell the Press and forward the Money to you, or should you wish to come and fetch it.

We are most appreciative of your Help and Kindness, and the Girls pray for you and your Family every Day.

Yours most Sincerely,
Abigail Bell

William Ransom,
to His Grace Harold, Duke of Pardloe
September 24, 1778

Dear Uncle Hal,

You will be gratified to know that your paternal Instinct was correct. I am very pleased to tell you that Ben probably isn't dead.

On the other hand, I haven't the slightest Idea where the devil he is or why he's there.

I was shown a Grave at Middlebrook Encampment in New Jersey, purported to be Ben's, but the Body therein is not Ben. (It's probably better if you don't know how that bit of information was ascertained.)

Clearly someone in the Continental army must know something of his whereabouts, but most of Washington's troops who were at the Encampment when he was captured have gone. There is one Man who might possibly yield some Information, but beyond that, the only possible Connection would seem to be the Captain with whom we are acquainted.

I propose therefore to hunt the Gentleman in question and extract what Information he may possess when I find him.

Your most obedient nephew,
William

Lord John Grey,
to Harold, Duke of Pardloe
Charleston, South Carolina
September 28, 1778

Dear Hal,

We arrived in Charleston by ship two days ago, having encountered a Storm off the Chesapeake that blew us out to Sea, delaying us for several days. I'm sure you will not be surprised in the least to learn that Dottie is a much better Sailor than I am.

She also shows Promise as an inquiry Agent. First thing this morning, she discovered the Whereabouts of Amaranthus Cowden by the simple Expedient of stopping a well-dressed Lady on the Street, admiring her Gown, and then asking for the names of the better Dressmakers in the City, on the Assumption (as she later explained to me) that Ben would not have married either a plain Woman or one with no Interest in Fashion.

The third Shop we visited did indeed boast that Miss Cowden (she was *calling herself Mrs. Grey, they said, but they knew her Maiden Name, as she was residing with an Aunt named Cowden) was a Customer, and they were able to describe her to me as a slight young Woman of middle Height, with an excellent Complexion, large brown Eyes, and abundant Hair of a dark-blond Hue. They could not, however, give me her Address, as the Lady had recently decamped to winter with Friends in Savannah. (The Aunt has annoyingly died, I find.)*

Interestingly, she styles herself as a Widow, so apparently she was informed—and by whom? I should like to know—of Ben's presumed Death, sometime after the Date of her Letter to you, as otherwise she would certainly have mentioned it.

I also find it interesting that she should be able to afford the Services of Madame Eulalie—and these to no little Extent; I succeeded in inducing Madame to show me her recent Bills—when her Letter to you professed her to be in financial Difficulties owing to Ben's Capture.

If Ben is indeed dead and both the Death and the Marriage proved, then presumably she would inherit some Property—or at least the Child would. But she can't possibly have taken such Legal Steps in the Time between her Letter to you and the Present; it could easily take that long merely to send a Letter to London—assuming that she had any Idea to whom it should be sent. And assuming also that whoever received it would not immediately have informed you.

Oh—she does possess an Infant, a Boy, and the Child is hers; Madame made her two Gowns and a set of Stays to accommodate the Pregnancy. Naturally, there's no telling whether Benjamin is the child's Father. She clearly has at least met Ben—or possibly Adam; she could have got "Wattiswade" from anyone in the Family—but that's not Proof of either Marriage or Paternity.

All in all, an interesting Woman, your putative Daughter-in-law. Plainly our Path lies now toward Savannah, though this may require somewhat more investigative Effort, as we don't know the Name of the Friends with whom she's taken Refuge, and if she is indeed poverty-stricken, she won't be buying new Gowns.

I hope to convince Dottie that she need not accompany me. She's most determined, but I can see that she pines for her Quaker Physician. And if our Quest should be greatly prolonged . . . I will not allow her to be placed in Danger, I assure you.

Your most affectionate Brother,
John

General Sir Henry Clinton,
Commander in Chief for North America,
to Colonel His Grace Duke of Pardloe, 46th Foot

Sir,

You are hereby ordered and directed to assemble and re-fit your Troops in whatever manner you deem necessary, and then to make Junction with Lieutenant

Colonel Archibald Campbell, to march upon the City of Savannah in the colony of Georgia, and take possession of it in His Majesty's name.

H. Clinton

HAROLD, DUKE OF Pardloe, felt his chest tightening and rang for his orderly.

"Coffee, please," he said to the man. "Brewed very strong, and quickly. And bring the brandy while you're at it."

124

BROUGHT TO YOU BY THE LETTERS Q, E, AND D

IT WAS, OF COURSE, unthinkable that we should sell Clarence.

"Do you think he weighs as much as a printing press?" I asked, looking at him dubiously. His tiny stable next to the shop had survived the fire, and while he wrinkled his nose and sneezed when the wind raised a whiff of ash from the charred remains of the printshop, he didn't seem much affected.

"Substantially more, I think." Jamie scratched his forehead and ran a hand up the length of one long ear. "D'ye think mules suffer from seasickness?"

"Can they vomit?" I tried to recall whether I'd ever seen a horse or mule regurgitate—as opposed to dropping slobbery mouthfuls of whatever they were eating—but couldn't call an instance to mind.

"I couldna say if they *can,*" Jamie said, picking up a stiff brush and beating clouds of dust from Clarence's broad gray back, "but they don't, no."

"Then how would you know if a mule was seasick?" Jamie himself got violently seasick, and I did wonder how he was going to manage if we did go by ship; the acupuncture needles I used to quell his nausea had perished in the fire—with so much else.

Jamie gave me a jaundiced look over Clarence's back.

"Can ye no tell if I'm seasick, even when I'm not puking?"

"Well, yes," I said mildly, "but you aren't covered with hair, and you can talk. You turn green and pour with sweat and lie about, groaning and begging to be shot."

"Aye. Well, bar the turning green, a mule can tell ye verra well if he's feeling peely-wally. And he can certainly make ye want to shoot him."

He ran a hand down Clarence's leg to pick up the mule's left front hoof. Clarence picked it up and set it down again very solidly, exactly where Jamie's own foot had been an instant before. His ears twitched.

"On the other hand," Jamie said to him, "I could make ye walk all the way to Savannah, pullin' a cart behind ye. Think about that, aye?" He came out of the stall and closed the gate, shaking it to be sure it was securely latched.

"Mr. Fraser!" A shout from the end of the alley drew his attention. It was Jonas Phillips, presumably on his way home to a midday dinner from the assembly room, where the Continental Congress was still locked in struggle. Jamie waved back and, with a nod to me, walked down the alley. While I waited for him, I turned my attention to the jumble of items occupying the other half of the stable.

What little room there was besides Clarence's stall was filled with the things the neighbors had managed to salvage from the remains of the printshop. All of it had the sour reek of ash about it, but a few of the items might be salvaged or sold, I supposed.

Mrs. Bell's letter had caused a certain reevaluation of our immediate prospects. Fergus's press had definitely perished in the flames; the derelict carcass was still there, the metal parts twisted in a way suggesting uncomfortably that the thing had died in agony. Fergus hadn't wept; after Henri-Christian, I didn't think anything could ever make him weep again. But he did avert his eyes whenever he came near the ruins.

On the one hand, the loss of the press was terrible—but, on the other, it did save us the problem of hauling it to . . .

Well, that was another problem. Where were we going?

Jamie had assured me that we were going home—back to the Ridge. But it was late September, and even if we found the money to pay the passage for so many people—and Clarence—and were fortunate enough not to be sunk or captured by an English cutter . . . we would part company with Fergus and Marsali in Wilmington, then go up the Cape Fear River into the North Carolina backcountry, leaving Marsali, Fergus, and the children to go on alone to Savannah. I knew that Jamie didn't want to do that. In all honesty, neither did I.

The little family was surviving, but there was no doubt that Henri-Christian's death and the fire had left them all badly wounded. Especially Germain.

You could see it in his face, even in the way he walked, no longer jaunty and bright-eyed, eager for adventure. He walked with his shoulders hunched, as though expecting a blow to come out of nowhere. And while sometimes he would forget for a few moments and revert to his normal swagger and talk, you could see it when the blow of memory did come out of nowhere to send him reeling.

Ian and Rachel had taken it upon themselves to be sure that he didn't slink away by himself; one or the other was always calling on him to come and help carry the marketing or go out to the forest to look for the proper wood for an ax handle or a new bow. That helped.

If Fergus went to Savannah to retrieve Bonnie, Jamie's original press, Marsali would be hampered and preoccupied by advancing pregnancy and the difficulties both of travel with a family and then of establishing a new home, Fergus needing to devote himself to setting up the new business and dealing with whatever the local politics might be. Germain could so easily slip through the cracks in his family and be lost.

I wondered whether Jenny would go with them—or with Ian and Rachel. Marsali could certainly use her help, but I remembered what Marsali had said, and thought she was right: *"Ian's her youngest. . . . And she's had too little of him."* She had; Ian had essentially been lost to her at the age of fourteen, and she hadn't seen him again until he was a grown man—and a Mohawk. I'd seen her now and then, gazing at him as he talked and ate, with a small inward glow on her face.

I poked gingerly through the pile of remnants. Marsali's cauldron had survived unscathed, though covered with soot. A few pewter plates, one half melted—the wooden ones had all burned—and a stack of Bibles, rescued from the front room by some pious soul. A line of washing had been hung out across the alley; what clothes were on it had all survived, though a couple of Fergus's shirts and Joanie's pinafore had been badly singed. I supposed boiling with lye soap might get the stink of fire out of the clothes, but I doubted that any of the family would wear them again.

Clarence, having finished his hay, was methodically rubbing his forehead against the top rail of his gate, making it rattle and thump.

"Itchy, are you?" I scratched him, then poked my head out of the stable. Jamie was still in conversation with Mr. Phillips at the mouth of the alley, though, and I went back to my explorations.

Under a pile of smoke-stained playscripts I found Marsali's small chiming clock, somehow miraculously intact. It had stopped, of course, but emitted one small, sweet silver *bing!* when I picked it up, making me smile.

Perhaps that was a good omen for the journey. And, after all, even if Jamie and I—and Rachel and Ian—were to set out at once for Fraser's Ridge, there was no chance of reaching the mountains of North Carolina before snow had closed the passes for the winter. It would be March, at the earliest, before we could turn inland.

I sighed, clock in hand, envisioning the Ridge in springtime. It would be a good time to arrive, the weather good for planting and building. I could wait.

I heard Jamie's steps come down the cobbled alley and stop. Stepping to the open front of the stable, I saw that he'd paused at the place where Henri-Christian had died. He stood unmoving for a moment, then crossed himself and turned.

The solemnity left his face as he saw me, and he held up a small leather bag, smiling.

"Look, Sassenach!"

"What is it?"

"One of the Phillips boys found it, scavenging about, and brought it to his father. Hold out your hands."

Puzzled, I did so, and he tilted the bag, decanting a small cascade of surprisingly heavy dark-gray chunks of lead—the type for a complete set of . . . I picked one out and squinted at it. "Caslon English Roman?"

"Better than that, Sassenach," he said, and, plucking the letter "Q" from the pile in my hand, he dug his thumbnail into the soft metal, revealing a faint yellow gleam. "Marsali's hoard."

"My God, it is! I'd forgotten all about it." At the height of the British occupation, when Fergus had been obliged to leave home to avoid arrest, sleeping in a different place each night, Marsali had cast a set of type in gold, carefully rubbing each slug with grease, soot, and ink, and had carried the pouch under her apron, in case she and the children should be likewise forced to flee.

"So did Marsali, I expect." His smile faded a bit, thinking of the causes of Marsali's distraction. "She'd buried it under the bricks of the hearth—I suppose when the army left. Sam Phillips found it when they were pulling down the chimney." He nodded toward the charred spot where the printshop had stood. The chimney had been damaged by the wall falling in, so a number of men had taken it down, neatly stacking the bricks, most of which were intact despite the fire and could be sold.

I poured the type carefully back into the pouch and glanced over my shoulder at Clarence.

"I suppose a goldsmith could make me a set of really *big* acupuncture needles. Just in case."

125

SQUID OF THE EVENING, BEAUTIFUL SQUID

Charleston, Royal Colony of South Carolina

LORD JOHN AND HIS niece, Dorothea, ate that night at a small ordinary near the shore, whose air was redolent with the luscious scents of baked fish, eels in wine sauce, and small whole squid, fried crisply in cornmeal. John inhaled deeply with pleasure, handed Dottie to a stool, and sat down himself, enjoying the moment of gustatory indecision.

"It's that moment when you can convincingly imagine the delightful prospect of eating everything the establishment has to offer," he told Dottie. "Momentarily untroubled by the knowledge that one's stomach has a limited capacity and thus one must, alas, choose in the end."

Dottie looked a little dubious, but, thus urged, she took a deep sniff of the atmosphere, to which the scent of fresh-baked bread had just been added as the serving maid came in with a great loaf and a dish of butter with a four-leafed clover—this being the name of the establishment—stamped into its oleaginous surface.

"Oh, that smells wonderful!" she said, her face lighting. "Might I have some, please? And a glass of cider?"

He was pleased to see her nibble hungrily at the bread and take a deep breath of the cider—which was aromatic enough to challenge even the squid, his own reluctantly final choice, though this was accompanied by a dozen fresh-shucked oysters to fill whatever crevices might remain. Dottie had chosen the baked hake, though she had only picked at it so far.

"I came down to the harbor this afternoon while you were resting," he said, tearing off a wodge of bread to counteract the grated horseradish mixed with the oysters' brine. "I asked about and found two or three small boats whose owners are not averse to a quick journey to Savannah."

"How quick?" she asked warily.

"It's little more than a hundred miles by water," he said, shrugging in what he hoped was a casual manner. "Perhaps two days, with a good wind and fair weather."

"Mmm." Dottie cast a skeptical glance at the ordinary's shuttered window. The shutters trembled to a blast of rain and wind. "It's October, Uncle John. The weather is seldom predictable."

"How do you know? Madam—might I have some vinegar for the squid?" The proprietor's wife nodded, bustling off, and he repeated, "How do you know?"

"Our landlady's son is a fisherman. So was her husband. He died in a gale—last October," she finished sweetly, and popped the last bite of bread into her mouth.

"Such squeamish prudence is unlike you, Dottie," he remarked, accepting the vinegar bottle from the proprietress and sousing his crisp squidlings. "Oh, God," he said, chewing. "Ambrosia. Here—have one." He speared one with his fork and passed it across to her.

"Yes. Well . . ." She regarded the squid-laden fork with a distinct lack of enthusiasm. "How long would it take to travel overland?"

"Perhaps four or five days. Again, with good weather."

She sighed, lifted the squid to her mouth, hesitated, and then, with the air of a Roman gladiator facing an oncoming crocodile in the arena, put it into her mouth and chewed. She went white.

"Dottie!" He leapt up, knocking his stool over, and managed to catch her as she wilted toward the floor.

"Gah," she said faintly, and, lunging out of his arms, bolted for the door, retching. He followed and was in time to hold her head as she lost the bread, cider, and the half-chewed squid.

"I'm so sorry," she said a few moments later, as he emerged from the ordinary with a mug and a damp cloth. She was leaning against the most sheltered wall of the building, wrapped in his cloak, and was the color of spoiled suet pudding. "How disgusting of me."

"Think nothing of it," he said amiably. "I've done just the same for all three of your brothers, on occasion—though I somehow doubt from the same cause. How long have you known you were with child?"

"I became certain of it about five minutes ago," she said, swallowing audibly and shuddering. "Dear Lord, I will never eat squid again."

"Had you ever eaten squid before?"

"No. I never want to *see* another squid. Bother, my mouth tastes of sick."

John, who was indeed experienced in such matters, handed her the mug of beer.

"Rinse your mouth with that," he said. "Then drink the rest. It will settle your stomach."

She looked dubious at this but did as he said, and emerged from the cup still pale but much improved.

"Better? Good. I don't suppose you want to go back inside? No, of course not. Let me pay, and I'll take you home." Inside, he asked the landlady to make up a parcel of their abandoned supper—he didn't mind eating cold fried squid, but he did want to eat; he was starving—and held this carefully to windward as they walked back to their lodgings.

"You didn't know?" he asked curiously. "I've often wondered about that. Some women have told me they knew at once, and yet I've heard of others who somehow remained oblivious to their condition until the moment of birth was upon them, incredible as that seems."

Dottie laughed; the cold wind had brought some of the color back to her cheeks, and he was relieved to see her spirits recovered.

"Do lots of women discuss their intimacies with you, Uncle John? That seems somewhat unusual."

"I seem to attract unusual women," he said, rather ruefully. "I also seem to have the sort of face that people feel compelled to tell things to. In another age, perhaps I should have been a confessor, if that's the word. But returning to the point"—he took her elbow to guide her round a large pile of horse droppings—"now that you *do* know . . . what shall we do about it?"

"I don't think anything actually needs to be *done* for about eight months," she said, and he gave her a look.

"You know what I mean," he said. "I doubt you wish to establish residence in Charleston until after your child arrives. Do you wish to return to Philadelphia—or New Jersey, or whatever godforsaken place Denzell happens to be at the moment—or shall I make arrangements to proceed to Savannah and remain there for some time? Or—" Another thought struck him, and he altered the look to one of seriousness.

"Do you want to go home, Dottie? To England, I mean. To your mother?"

Her face went blank with surprise, which gave way to a look of longing that broke his heart. She looked away, blinking back tears, but her voice was steady when she turned back to him.

"No," she said, and swallowed. "I want to be with Denzell. All other considerations aside," she added, managing a smile, "he knows how to deliver a baby. His cousin William is *accoucheur* to the Queen, and Denny studied with him for a time."

"Well, that *will* be helpful," Grey agreed, rather dryly. He had himself delivered a child once—completely against his will—and still had nightmares about it.

It was just as well that Dottie didn't want to return to England, though. He'd suggested the notion on impulse but now realized that it might be more dangerous than any of the other alternatives. Since France had entered the war, all English shipping would be at risk.

"I'm thinking that we ought to go to Savannah, though," Dottie was saying. "We're so close, I mean—and if Ben's wife *is* there . . . she might need our help, mightn't she?"

"Yes," he agreed reluctantly. There was a familial obligation. And, after all, unless he *did* take up residence in Charleston for the next eight months, there seemed no alternative to Dottie's traveling, in whichever direction. Still . . . the thought of her giving birth *here,* him responsible for finding midwives and nurses . . . and then she *and* the child would need to be transported . . .

"No," he said, more definitely. "Amaranthus—assuming she does exist—will have to muddle on by herself a little longer. I'm taking you back to New York."

126

THE OGLETHORPE PLAN

Late November

SAVANNAH, UNLIKE MOST American cities, had been carefully planned by its founder, a man named Oglethorpe. I knew this because Mrs. Landrum, the woman from whom we rented our room, had explained to me that the city was laid out according to "the Oglethorpe plan"—this spoken in portentous tones, for Mrs. Landrum was a relative of the aforesaid Oglethorpe and intensely proud of the city and its civic perfection.

The plan called for six wards—a ward being composed of four civic blocks—for business, and four "tything" blocks for houses, these arrayed around an open square. There were ten houses to a block, and the men of a tything trained together for militia duty.

"Though that's not so important now as it used to be," Mrs. Landrum explained to me. "The Indians are still a bother in the backcountry, but it's years since they troubled to come into the city."

I rather thought Indians were the least of it, but as Mrs. Landrum didn't seem concerned about the war with the British, I didn't bring it up. It was apparent from her references that as not only her family but everyone she knew were Loyalists, plainly this was the proper state of things, and pesky nuisances like this "rebellion, as they're pleased to call it!" would soon be put down and we could get tea at a decent price again.

From my point of view, the most interesting thing about Mr. Oglethorpe's plan—in the course of conversation, it was revealed to me that he'd founded not only Savannah but the whole Province of Georgia—was that each house of a tything was provided with a one-mile tract of farmland outside the city and a five-acre kitchen garden closer in.

"Really," I said, my fingers beginning to itch at the thought of dirt. "Er . . . what do you plant?"

The upshot of this conversation—and many like it—was that I made an arrangement to help with the keeping of the kitchen garden in return for a share of "sass" (as Mrs. Landrum puzzlingly referred to green stuff like kale and turnips), beans, and dried corn, as well as a small plot where I could cultivate medicinal herbs. A secondary consequence of this amiable acquaintance was that Rachel and Ian, whose room was below ours, began referring to their unborn child as Oglethorpe, though this was politely shortened to "Oggy" whenever Mrs. Landrum was in hearing.

And the third and most important effect of Mrs. Landrum's friendship was that I found myself once more a doctor.

We had been in Savannah for a few weeks when Mrs. Landrum came up to our room one afternoon and inquired as to whether I might know anything regarding cures for the toothache, she knowing that I had a way with herbs?

"Oh, I might," I replied, with a surreptitious glance at my medical bag, which had been gathering dust under the bed since our arrival. "Whose tooth is it?"

The tooth had belonged to a gentleman named Murphy from Ellis Ward, the one we lived in. I say "had belonged" because I had the badly broken and infected bicuspid out of Mr. Murphy's head before he could have said Jack Robinson, though he was in such pain that he could barely recall his own name, let alone Jack's.

Mr. Murphy was extremely grateful for his deliverance. Mr. Murphy was also the owner of a very small vacant shop on the other side of Ellis Square. It was the work of a few moments to acquire a small shingle with TEETH EXTRACTED on it. And within twenty-four hours of hanging out my shingle, I was proudly depositing my earnings on the kitchen table—which was also my herbal-preparations counter and Jamie's desk, as it occupied the center of our single room.

"Well done, Sassenach!" Jamie picked up a small jar of honey, taken in payment for a nastily impacted wisdom tooth. He loved honey. I'd also acquired two large speckled turkey eggs (one of them filled the entire palm of my hand), a loaf of reasonably fresh sourdough bread, six pennies, and a small silver Spanish coin.

"I think ye could support the family all on your own, *a nighean,*" he said, dipping a finger in the honey and licking it before I could stop him. "Ian and Fergus and I can all retire and become gentlemen of leisure."

"Good. You can start by making supper," I said, stretching my back. Stays did keep you upright through a long day's work, but I was looking forward to taking them off, eating supper, and lying down, in quick succession.

"Of course, Sassenach." With a small flourish, he drew the knife from his belt, cut a slice off the loaf, drizzled honey on it, and gave it to me. "There ye are."

I raised an eyebrow at him but bit into it. Sweetness flooded my mouth and my bloodstream simultaneously, and I tasted sunlight and flowers. I moaned.

"What did ye say, Sassenach?" He was busily buttering another slice.

"I said, 'Well done,'" I said, and picked up the pot of honey. "We'll make a cook of you yet."

THE BASIC ISSUES of housing and food taken care of, plainly the next order of business was to retrieve Bonnie. Jamie had located the Bell family, and three weeks after our arrival in Savannah, he and Fergus had scraped together enough money to hire a cart and an extra mule from the livery stable where Clarence boarded. We met Richard Bell in the morning, and he came with us to the farm of one Zachary Simpson, the farmer with whom Bonnie boarded.

Mr. Simpson cleared away the last of the hay and pulled away the canvas with the air of a magician producing a rabbit from a hat. From the reaction of three-quarters of his spectators, you'd think he *had:* Jamie and Fergus both gasped audibly, and Richard Bell emitted a hum of satisfaction. I bit my lip and tried not to laugh, but I doubted they'd have noticed if I'd rolled on the floor in paroxysms of mirth.

"Nom de Dieu," Fergus said, stretching out a reverent hand. "She's *beautiful.*"

"Best I've ever seen," Mr. Bell agreed, clearly torn between regard and regret.

"Aye." Jamie was pink with pleasure, trying visibly to retain a modest constraint. "Aye. She's bonnie, no?"

I supposed "she" was—if one was a connoisseur of printing presses, which I wasn't. Still, I confessed some fondness for Bonnie; we'd met before, in Edinburgh. Jamie had been oiling some part of her mechanism when I'd returned to find him after twenty years, and she had been witness to our reunion.

And she had withstood the rigors of disassembly, sea travel, reassembly, and months of being immured in a barn with commendable fortitude. A pale winter sun shone through a crack in the barn's wall, making her wood glow with somber pride, and her metal was—so far as I could see—quite free from rust.

"Well done," I said, giving her a small pat. Mr. Simpson was modestly accepting the applause of the crowd for his feat of preserving Bonnie from harm, and I could see that they'd be some time in getting her onto the cart we'd brought, so I made my way back to the farmhouse. I'd noticed a number of chickens scratching in the yard and had some hopes of acquiring fresh eggs.

Marsali's hoard—and Jenny's novena to St. Bride, Queen of the Sea, plus a modest assist from my acupuncture needles (Clarence luckily proved a good sailor)—had got us safely to Savannah, but the requirements of housing ten people and renting premises suitable for a small printing business had exhausted both the Caslon English Roman gold and the insurance money paid to Fergus for the fire's destruction.

With the need for income somewhat acute, Ian and Jamie had found employment at one of the warehouses on the river. A wise choice, as it turned out: in addition to their pay and the odd damaged cask of salt fish or biscuit, being on the docks all day allowed them first—and cheapest—choice from the fishermen coming in with their catch. We therefore hadn't been starving nor yet threatened with scurvy—the climate was mild enough that plenty of green things grew, even in late November—but I was getting tired of rice and fish and winter kale. A nice dish of scrambled eggs, now . . . possibly with fresh butter . . .

I'd come equipped for trading, with several packets of pins and a bag of salt, and Mrs. Simpson and I amicably concluded a bargain for a basket of eggs and a small tub of butter before the men had got Bonnie out of the barn and were sat on the back stoop, comfortably drinking beer.

"What remarkable chickens those are," I said, stifling a small belch. The beer, of Mrs. Simpson's own production, was tasty but strong. The chickens in question were more than remarkable: they appeared to have no legs but to be trundling round the yard on their bottom sides, pecking at their corn with cheerful imperturbability.

"Oh, aye," said Mrs. Simpson, nodding with pride. "My mother brought those—well, their great-great-grandmothers—with her from Scotland, thirty years a-gone. 'Creepies,' she always called them—but they've got a true name. Scots Dumpy, it is, or so a gentleman from Glasgow told me."

"How very appropriate," I said, taking another sip of beer and peering at the chickens. They did after all *have* legs; just very short ones.

"I breed them for sale," Mrs. Simpson added helpfully. "If might should be ye should find yourself in want of a good hen or two."

"I can't think of anything I'd like better," I said wistfully. The rice paddies and palmettos of Savannah seemed infinitely far away from the clean sharp air of Fraser's Ridge . . . but we were in the South, at least. And come March and good traveling weather, Marsali and Fergus should be safely established, and we could turn our faces toward North Carolina. "Perhaps in a few months . . ." I added *Scots Dumpy chickens* to the mental list I was accumulating and returned to the beer.

The men had got the printing press onto the cart, suitably swathed in canvas and repacked with straw for the journey into town, and now came into the house to resume their own well-earned refreshment.

We sat companionably round Mrs. Simpson's scrubbed kitchen table, drinking beer and eating salted radishes. Jamie and Fergus were glowing with excitement and satisfaction; the looks on their faces warmed me more than the beer. Poor Richard Bell was trying his best to be generous and share their delight, but it was plain that he was low in both body and spirit.

I had met him only a few days before, and that briefly, so had not yet cultivated an acquaintance sufficient as to allow me to make him undress and let me palpate his liver, but I was morally certain that the "relapsing ague" Mrs. Bell had written of was malaria. I couldn't say so with complete certainty without looking at his blood cells under a microscope—and God knew when I might ever have one again—but I'd seen enough people suffering from "the quartan ague" or "the tertian fever" as to have little doubt.

Luckily, I had a small supply of Jesuit bark among the selection of herbs and medicines I'd brought with me. It wouldn't cure him, but I could, with luck, limit the more-severe attacks and relieve some of the symptoms. Thinking of this reminded me suddenly of Lizzie Wemyss. Coming to America as Brianna's bond servant, she also had contracted malaria from the coastal mosquitoes. I'd managed to control the disease in her fairly well, but how had she fared in my absence?

"I'm sorry, what did you say?" My attention was jerked back to the conversation, but I added *LOTS of Jesuit bark* to my mental list before replying.

127

PLUMBING

LIKE PLUMBING, MEDICINE is a profession where you learn early on not to put your fingers in your mouth. I smelled my next patient coming and was reaching for the jar of soft soap and the bottle of raw alcohol before she came through the door. And the instant I saw her, I knew what the problem was.

There were two women, in fact: one was a tall, rather commanding-looking woman, well dressed and wearing a hat rather than the usual bonnet. The other was a small, slight girl who might have been any age between twelve and twenty. She was what they called a mulatto, half black and half white, with *café au lait* skin and snub features. I set her lower age limit at twelve only because she had apparent breasts bubbling over the top of her stays. She was dressed neatly but plainly in blue gingham, and she stank like an open sewer.

The tall woman paused, looking me over consideringly.

"You are a female physician?" she asked, in a tone just short of accusation.

"I am Dr. Fraser, yes," I replied equably. "And you are . . . ?"

She flushed at that and looked disconcerted. Also very dubious. But after an awkward pause, she made up her mind and gave a sharp nod. "I am Sarah Bradshaw. Mrs. Phillip Bradshaw."

"I'm pleased to meet you. And your . . . companion?" I nodded at the young woman, who stood with her shoulders hunched and her head bent, staring at the ground. I could hear a soft dripping noise, and she shifted as though trying to press her legs together, wincing as she did so.

"This is Sophronia. One of my husband's slaves." Mrs. Bradshaw's lips compressed and drew in tight; from the lines surrounding her mouth, she did it routinely. "She—that is—I thought perhaps—" Her rather plain face flamed crimson; she couldn't bring herself to describe the trouble.

"I know what it is," I said, saving her the difficulty. I came round the table and took Sophronia by the hand; hers was small and very callused, but her fingernails were clean. A house slave, then. "What happened to the baby?" I asked her gently.

A small, frightened intake of breath, and she glanced sideways at Mrs. Bradshaw, who gave her another sharp nod, lips still pursed.

"It died in me," the girl said, so softly I could scarcely hear her, even though she was no more than an arm's length from me. "Dey cut it out in pieces." That had likely saved the girl's life, but it surely hadn't helped her condition.

Despite the smell, I took a deep breath, trying to keep my emotions under control.

"I'll need to examine Sophronia, Mrs. Bradshaw. If you have any errands, perhaps you'd like to go and take care of them . . . ?"

She unzipped her lips sufficiently as to make a small, frustrated noise. Quite obviously, she would like nothing better than to leave the girl and never come back. But just as obviously, she was afraid of what the slave might tell me if left alone with me.

"Was the child your husband's?" I asked baldly. I didn't have time to beat around the bush; the poor girl was dripping urine and fecal matter on the floor and appeared ready to die of shame.

I doubted that Mrs. Bradshaw meant to die of that condition, but she plainly felt it almost as acutely as did Sophronia. She went white with shock, then her face flamed anew. She turned on her heel and stamped out, slamming the door behind her.

"I'll take that as a 'yes,' then," I said to the door, and turned to the girl, smiling in reassurance. "Here, sweetheart. Let's have a look at the trouble, shall we?"

Vesicovaginal fistula *and* rectovaginal fistula. I'd known that from the first moment; I just didn't know how bad they might be or how far up the vaginal canal they'd occurred. A fistula is a passage between two things that ought never to be joined and is, generally speaking, a bad thing.

It wasn't a common condition in civilized countries in the twentieth century but more common than one might think. I'd seen it several times in Boston, at a clinic where I gave time once a week to provide medical care to the city's poor. Young girls, much too young to be considering the opposite sex in any serious way, becoming pregnant before their bodies had ripened enough. Prostitutes, some of them. Others just girls who had been in the wrong place at the wrong time. Like this one.

A full-term baby that couldn't be forced out through the birth canal, and days of nonproductive labor, the child's head a battering ram against the tissues of the pelvis, the bladder, the vagina, and the bowel. Until at last the tissues thinned and split, leaving a ragged hole between bladder and vagina, or between vagina and rectum, allowing the body's waste to drip out unhindered through the vagina.

Not a matter of life or death, but revolting, uncontrollable, and bloody uncomfortable, too. Sophronia's inner thighs were swollen, a bright, patchy red, the skin macerated by the constant wetness, the irritating fecal slime. Like a permanent diaper rash, I thought, suppressing a deeply visceral urge to find

Mr. Bradshaw and make a few fistulas in him with a blunt probe.

I talked to her while I made my examinations, soothingly, and after a little she began to answer me, though still in whispers. She was thirteen. Yes, Mr. Bradshaw had took her to his bed. She hadn't minded. He said his wife was mean to him, and she was—all the slaves knew it. Mr. Bradshaw had been nice to her, gentle-like, and when she fell pregnant, he'd taken her from the laundry and put her to kitchen work, where she'd have good food and wouldn't have to break her back with the heavy linens.

"He was sad," she said softly, looking up at the ceiling while I wiped away the filthy trickle between her legs. "When the baby died. He cried."

"Did he," I said, in what I hoped was a neutral voice. I folded a clean towel and pressed it between her legs, throwing the wet one she'd been wearing into my bucket of vinegar and water. "When did the baby die—how long ago, I mean?"

She frowned, the expression barely rippling the pure young skin of her forehead. Could she count? I wondered.

"Be some time before the sausage-makin'," she said uncertainly.

"In the fall, then?"

"Yessum."

And it was mid-December now. I poured water over my dirty hand and dribbled a bit of soap into my palm. I really must try to get a nailbrush, I thought.

Mrs. Bradshaw had come back but hadn't come in; I'd pulled the curtains over the front window, but her shadowed outline was plain on the cloth, the jaunty feathers in her hat stuck up like a silhouette cowlick.

I tapped my foot thoughtfully, then shook myself into order and went to open the door.

"I *might* be able to help," I said without preamble, startling the woman.

"How?" She blinked at me, and, taken unawares, her face was open, troubled but without the pinched look she'd worn earlier.

"Come inside," I said. "It's cold out here in the wind," and guided her in, a hand on her back. She was very thin; I could feel the knobs of her spine, even through her coat and stays.

Sophronia was sitting on the table, hands folded in her lap; when her mistress came in, she bent her head, looking at the floor again.

I explained the nature of the difficulty, so well as I could—neither of them had any grasp of internal anatomy at all; it was simply a matter of holes to them. Still, I managed to get the general point across.

"You know that a wound can be stitched, to hold the skin together while it heals?" I said patiently. "Well, this is much the same kind of thing, but made much harder by the wounds being inside and the tissues being very thin and slippery. It would be very difficult to mend—I'm not *sure* I can do it—but it is at least possible to try."

It was—just. In the late nineteenth century, a physician named J. Marion Sims had more or less invented the entire practice of gynecological surgery, in order to address exactly this condition. It had taken him years to develop the techniques, and I knew them—had done the procedure more than once. The catch was that you really needed good, solid anesthesia in order to have a chance of success. Laudanum or whisky might answer for cruder, swifter operations, but for painstakingly delicate surgery like this, the patient had to be completely unconscious and immobile. I would have to have ether.

I had no idea how I was going to make ether, living in a small rented house with a number of people whom I really didn't want to risk blowing to bits. And the thought of what flammable ether could do—had done—made me break out in a cold sweat. But seeing the faint hope rise in both their faces, I made up my mind to do it.

I gave Sophronia a small jar of beeswax ointment for the skin of her thighs and told them to come back in a week; I would know then whether it was possible. I saw them out, and as they went away down the street, Mrs. Bradshaw reached out unconsciously and touched Sophronia's shoulder in a brief caress of reassurance.

I took a deep breath and resolved that I *would* find a way. Turning to go inside, I glanced the other way down the street and saw a tall young man whose lean ranginess struck me with a sense of instant recognition. I blinked once, and imagination promptly clothed him in scarlet.

"William!" I called, and, picking up my skirts, ran after him.

HE DIDN'T HEAR me at first, and I had time for doubt—but not much; the set of head and shoulders, that long, decisive stride . . . He was thinner than Jamie, and his hair was a dark chestnut, not red, but he had his father's bones. And his eyes: hearing me at last, he turned, and those dark-blue cat eyes widened in surprise.

"Mother Cl—" He cut the word off, his face hardening, but I reached out and took his big hand between my own (rather hoping that I had got all of the slime off).

"William," I said, panting just a bit, but smiling up at him. "You can call me what you like, but I'm no less—and no more—to you than I ever was."

His severe look softened a little at that, and he ducked his head awkwardly.

"I think I must call you Mrs. Fraser, mustn't I?" He detached his hand, though gently. "How do you come to be here?"

"I might ask the same of you—and perhaps with more reason. Where's your uniform?"

"I've resigned my commission," he said, a little stiffly. "Under the circumstances, there seemed little point to my remaining in the army. And I have business that requires somewhat more independence of movement than I should have as one of Sir Henry's aides."

"Will you come and have something hot to drink with me? You can tell me about your business." I'd rushed out without my cloak, and a chilly breeze was fingering me with more intimacy than I liked.

"I—" He caught himself, frowning, then looked at me thoughtfully and rubbed a finger down the long, straight bridge of his nose, just as Jamie did when making up his mind. And just as Jamie did, he dropped his hand and nodded briefly as though to himself.

"All right," he said, rather gruffly. "In fact, my business may be of some . . . importance to you."

Another five minutes saw us in an ordinary off Ellis Square, drinking hot cider, rich with cinnamon and nutmeg. Savannah wasn't—thank God—Philadelphia, in terms of nasty winter weather, but the day was cold and windy, and the pewter cup was delightfully warm in my hands.

"What *does* bring you here, then, Willie? Or should I call you William now?"

"William, please," he said dryly. "It's the only name I feel is rightfully mine, for the moment. I should like to preserve what small dignity I have."

"Mmm," I said noncommittally. "William it is, then."

"As for my business . . ." He sighed briefly and rubbed a knuckle between his brows. He then explained about his cousin Ben, Ben's wife and child, then Denys Randall, and finally—Captain Ezekiel Richardson. *That* name made me sit up straight.

He noticed my reaction and nodded, grimacing.

"That's what I meant when I said my business might have some relevance to you. Pa—Lord John said that it was Richardson's threatening to arrest you as a spy that caused him to, er, marry you." He flushed a little.

"It was," I said, trying not to recall the occasion. In fact, I recalled only snatches of those empty, glaring days when I'd believed Jamie to be dead. One of those snatches, though, was a vivid recollection of standing in the parlor of Number 17, holding a bouquet of white roses, with John beside me and a military chaplain with a book before us—and, standing on John's other side, grave and handsome, William in his captain's uniform and shining gorget, looking so like Jamie that I felt for a dizzying instant that Jamie's ghost had come to watch. Unable to decide whether to faint or to run out of the room shrieking, I'd simply stood frozen, until John had nudged me gently, whispering in my ear, and I'd blurted out, "I do," and collapsed on the ottoman, flowers spilling from my hands.

Caught up in the memory, I'd missed what William was saying and shook my head, trying to focus.

"I've been searching for him for the last three months," he said, putting down his cup and wiping his mouth with the back of his hand. "He's an elusive scoundrel. And I don't know that he's in Savannah at all, for that matter. But the last hint I had of him was in Charleston, and he left there three weeks ago, heading south.

"Now, for all I know, the fellow's bound for Florida or has already taken ship for England. On the other hand . . . Amaranthus is here, or at least I believe so. Richardson seems to take an inordinate interest in the Grey family and its connections, so perhaps . . . Do you know Denys Randall yourself, by the way?"

He was looking at me intently over his cup, and I realized, with a faint sense of amusement mingled with outrage, that he had thrown the name at me suddenly in hopes of surprising any guilty knowledge I might have.

Why, you little scallywag, I thought, amusement getting the upper hand. *You need a bit more practice before you can pull off that sort of thing, my lad.*

I did in fact know something about Denys Randall that William almost certainly didn't know—and that Denys Randall himself might not know—but it wasn't information that would shed any light on the whereabouts and motives of Ezekiel Richardson.

"I've never met him," I said, quite truthfully, and held up my cup toward the serving maid for more cider. "I used to know his mother, Mary Hawkins; we met in Paris. A lovely, sweet girl, but I've had no contact with her for the last . . . thirty . . . no, thirty-four years. I assume from what you tell me that she married a Mr. Isaacs—you said he was a Jewish merchant?"

"Yes. So Randall said—and I can't see why he'd lie about it."

"Nor can I. But what you do know—you think," I corrected, "is that while Denys Randall and Ezekiel Richardson have heretofore appeared to be working together, now they aren't?"

William shrugged, impatient.

"So far as I know. I haven't seen Randall since he warned me about Richardson, but I haven't seen Richardson, either."

I could sense his rising desire to be up and off; he was drumming his fingers softly on the tabletop, and the table itself shuddered slightly when his leg bumped it.

"Where are you staying, William?" I asked impulsively, before he could go. "In—in case I do see Richardson. Or hear anything of Amaranthus, for that matter. I am a doctor; a lot of people come to see me, and everyone talks to a doctor."

He hesitated, but then gave another shrug, this one infinitesimal. "I've taken a room at Hendry's, on River Street."

He stood, tossed some money on the table, and extended a hand to help me up.

"We're staying at Landrum's, one square over from the City

Market," I said on impulse, rising. "If you should—want to call. Or need help. Just in case, I mean."

His face had gone carefully blank, though his eyes were burning like match flames. I felt a chill, knowing from experience the sort of thing that was likely going on behind such a façade.

"I doubt it, Mrs. Fraser," he said politely. And, kissing my hand in brief farewell, he left.

128

GIGGING FROGS

December 22, 1778

JAMIE TOOK A FIRM grip of the back of Germain's shirt and beckoned with his free hand to Ian, who held the torch.

"Look out over the water first, aye?" Jamie whispered, lifting his chin at the black glitter of the submerged marsh. It was broken by clumps of waist-high cordgrass and smaller ones of needlerush, bright green in the torchlight. This was a deep spot, though, with two or three of what the natives of Savannah called "hammocks," though plainly they meant "hummock"—wee islands, with trees like wax myrtle and yaupon holly bushes, though these, too, were of a spiky nature, like everything else in a marsh save the frogs and fish.

Some of the spikier inhabitants of the marsh, though, were mobile and nothing you wanted to meet unexpectedly. Germain peered obediently into the darkness, his gigging spear held tight and high, poised for movement. Jamie could feel him tremble, partly from the chill but mostly, he thought, from excitement.

A sudden movement broke the surface of the water, and

Germain lunged forward, plunging his gig into the water with a high-pitched yell.

Fergus and Jamie let out much deeper cries, each grabbing Germain by an arm and hauling him backward over the mud, as the irate cottonmouth he'd nearly speared turned on him, lashing, yawning mouth flaring white.

But the snake luckily had business elsewhere and swam off with a peeved sinuosity. Ian, safely out of range, was laughing.

"Think it's funny, do ye?" said Germain, scowling in order to pretend he wasn't shaking.

"Aye, I do," his uncle assured him. "Be even funnier if ye were eaten by an alligator, though. See there?" He lifted the torch and pointed; ten feet away, there was a ripple in the water, between them and the nearest hammock. Germain frowned uncertainly at it, then turned his head to his grandfather.

"That's an alligator? How d'ye ken that?"

"It is," Jamie said. His own heart was pounding from the sight of the cottonmouth. Snakes unnerved him, but he wasn't scairt of alligators. Cautious, yes. Scairt, no. "See how the ripples come back from the island there?"

"Aye." Germain squinted across the water. "So?"

"Those ripples are coming toward us side on. The one Ian's pointing at? It's coming at a right angle—right toward us."

It was, though slowly.

"Are alligators good to eat?" Fergus asked, watching it thoughtfully. "A good deal more meat on one than on a frog, *n'est-ce pas*?"

"They are, and there is, aye." Ian shifted his weight a little, gauging the distance. "We canna kill one of those wi' spears, though. I should have brought my bow."

"Should we . . . move?" Germain asked doubtfully.

"Nay, see how big it is first," Ian said, fingering the long knife at his belt. He was wearing a breechclout, and his bare legs were long and steady as a heron's, standing mid-calf in the muddy water.

The four of them watched with great concentration as the ripple came on, paused, came on a little more, slowly.

"Are they stunned by light, Ian?" Jamie asked, low-voiced. Frogs were; they had maybe two dozen bullfrogs in their sack, surprised in the water and killed before they kent what hit them.

"I dinna think so," Ian whispered back. "I've not hunted one before, though."

There was a sudden gleam in the water, a scatter of ripples, and the glow of two small burning orbs, a demon's eyes.

"A Dhia!" Jamie said, making a convulsive sign against evil. Fergus pulled Germain back farther, making a clumsy sign of the cross with his hook. Even Ian seemed taken back a bit; his hand fell from his knife and he stepped back toward the mud, not taking his eyes off the thing.

"It's a wee one, I think," he said, reaching safety. "See, its eyes are nay bigger than my thumbnail."

"Does that matter, if it's possessed?" Fergus asked, suspicious. "Even if we were to kill it, we might be poisoned."

"Oh, I dinna think so," Jamie said. He could see it now as it hung motionless in the water, stubby clawed feet halfway drawn up. It was perhaps two feet long—the toothy jaw maybe six inches. It could give you a nasty bite, nay more. But it wasn't close enough to reach.

"Ken what a wolf's eyes look like in the dark? Or a possum's?" He'd taken Fergus hunting, of course, when he was young, but seldom at night—and such things as you'd hunt at night in the Highlands were usually running from you, not looking at you.

Ian nodded, not taking his eyes off the small reptile.

"Aye, that's true. Wolves' eyes are usually green or yellow, but I've seen them red like that sometimes, by torchlight."

"I would suppose that a wolf could be possessed by an evil spirit as easily as an alligator could," Fergus said, a little testily. It was clear, though, that he wasn't afraid of the thing, either, now that he'd got a good look; they were all beginning to relax.

"He thinks we're stealing his frogs," Germain said, giggling. He was still holding the spear, and even as he spoke, he spotted something and slammed the three-tined sapling into the water with a whoop.

"I got it, I got it!" he shouted, and splashed into the water, heedless of the alligator. He bent to see that his prey was firmly transfixed, let out another small whoop, and pulled up his spear, displaying a catfish of no mean size, belly showing white in its frantic flapping, blood running in trickles from the holes made by the tines.

"More meat on that than on yon wee lizard there, aye?" Ian took the spear, pulled the fish off, and bashed its head with the hilt of his knife to kill it.

Everyone looked, but the alligator had departed, alarmed by the kerfuffle.

"Aye, that's us fettled, I think." Jamie picked up both bags—one half full of bullfrogs, and the other still squirming slightly from the inclusion of a number of shrimp and crayfish netted from the shallows. He held open the one with the frogs for Ian to toss the fish inside, saying a verse from the Hunting Blessing, for Germain: *"Thou shalt not eat fallen fish nor fallen flesh/Nor one bird that thy hand shall not bring down/Be thou thankful for the one/Though nine should be swimming."*

Germain was not paying attention, though; he was standing quite still, fair hair lifting in the breeze, his head turned.

"Look, *Grand-père,*" he said, voice urgent. "Look!"

They all looked and saw the ships, far out beyond the marsh but coming in, heading for the small headland to the south. Seven, eight, nine . . . a dozen at least, with red lanterns at their masts, blue ones at the stern. Jamie felt the hair rise on his body and his blood go cold.

"British men-of-war," Fergus said, his voice empty with shock.

"They are," Jamie said. "We'd best get home."

IT WAS ALMOST dawn before I felt Jamie slide into bed behind me, bringing chilled skin and the smell of brine, cold mud, and marsh plants with him. Also . . .

"What's that smell?" I asked drowsily, kissing the arm he'd put round me.

"Frogs, I expect. God, ye're warm, Sassenach." He cuddled closer, pressing his body into mine, and I felt him pull loose the bow of the ribbon that gathered the neck of my shift.

"Good hunting, then?" I obligingly wiggled my bottom into the hollow of his thighs and he sighed in appreciation, his breath warm on my ear, and slipped a cold hand inside my shift. "Ooh."

"Aye. Germain caught a fine big catfish, and we brought back a sack of crawfish and shrimps—the wee gray ones."

"Mmm. We'll have a good supper, then." His temperature was quickly equalizing with mine, and I was drifting pleasantly back down toward sleep—though quite willing to be roused for the right reasons.

"We saw a wee alligator. And a snake—a water moccasin."

"You didn't catch those, I hope." I knew that snakes and alligators were technically edible, but I didn't think we were quite hungry enough to make the challenges of cooking one worthwhile.

"No. Oh—and a dozen British ships full of soldiers turned up, too."

"That's ni— *What?*" I flipped over in his arms, ending face-to-face.

"British soldiers," he repeated gently. "Dinna fash, Sassenach. I expect it will be all right. Fergus and I already hid the press, and we havena got any silver to bury. That's one thing to be said for poverty," he added reflectively, stroking my bottom. "Ye dinna need to fear bein' plundered."

"That—what the bloody hell are they doing *here*?" I rolled over and sat straight up in bed, pulling my shift up round my shoulders.

"Well, ye did say Pardloe told ye they meant to cut off the southern colonies, aye? I imagine they decided to start here."

"Why here? Why not . . . Charleston? Or Norfolk?"

"Well, I couldna say, not being privy to the British councils of war," he said mildly. "But if I was to guess, I'd say it's maybe that there are a good many troops already in Florida, and they'll be marching up to join this new lot. The Loyalists are thick as fleas on a dog all along the coast of the Carolinas; if the army's secured Florida and Georgia, they'd be well placed to advance northward, picking up local support."

"You have it all figured out, I see." I pressed my back against the wall—there was no headboard—and finished retying the ribbon of my shift. I didn't feel equal to meeting an invasion with my bosom uncovered.

"No," he admitted. "But there are only two things to do, Sassenach: stay or flee. It's the dead of winter in the mountains; we canna get through the passes 'til March, and I'd rather not be stravaiging about the countryside with three bairns, two pregnant women, and nay money. And I doubt they'll burn the city, not if they mean it to be a base for invading the rest of the South." He reached up and ran a soothing hand down my shoulder and arm. "It's not as though ye've not lived in an occupied city before."

"Hmm," I said dubiously, but he did have a point. There *were* some advantages to the situation, the chief one being that if an army already held a city, they wouldn't be attacking it: no fighting in the streets. But, then . . . they didn't hold it yet.

"Dinna fash yourself, lass," he said softly, and twined a finger in my ribbon. "Did I not tell ye when we wed, ye'd have the protection of my body?"

"You did," I admitted, and laid a hand over his. It was big, strong, and capable.

"Then come lie wi' me, *mo nighean donn,* and let me prove it," he said, and pulled the ribbon loose.

FROG LEGS OF that size really did look quite like chicken drumsticks. And tasted very like, too, dredged in flour and egg with a little salt and pepper and fried.

"Why is it that the meat of strange animals is so often described as tasting like chicken?" Rachel asked, neatly snaring another leg out from under her husband's reaching hand. "I've heard people say that of everything from catamount to alligator."

"Because it does," Ian answered, raising a brow at her and stabbing his fork into a platter of catfish chunks, similarly coated and fried.

"Well, if you want to be technical about it," I began, to a chorus of mingled groans and laughter. Before I could launch into an explanation of the biochemistry of muscle fiber, though, there was a rap on the door. We had been making so much noise over supper that I hadn't heard footsteps on the stair and was taken by surprise.

Germain popped up to open the door and gazed up in surprise at two Continental officers, in full uniform.

There was a general scraping of chairs as the men stood up, and Jamie stepped out from behind the table. He'd been working in the warehouse all day, after hunting in the marshes half the night, and was not only barefoot but wearing a badly stained, grimy shirt and a faded plaid so worn that it was thin in spots. Still, no one would have doubted that he was the master of the house. When he inclined his head and said, "Gentlemen? Be welcome," both officers took off their hats, bowed, and came in, murmuring, "Your servant, sir."

"General Fraser," the senior officer said, the title not quite a question, as he eyed Jamie's attire. "I am Major General Robert Howe."

I'd never seen Major General Howe before, but I knew his companion, and my hand tightened on the bread knife. He was wearing a colonel's uniform now, and his face was as blandly forgettable as ever, but I wasn't likely to forget Captain Ezekiel Richardson—lately a captain in His Majesty's army, last seen in Clinton's headquarters in Philadelphia.

"Your humble servant, sir," Jamie said, in a tone quite belying the usual compliment. "I am James Fraser but no longer an officer in any army. I have resigned my commission."

"So I understand, sir." Howe's rather bulging eyes scanned the table, flicking past Jenny, Rachel, Marsali, and the little girls before settling on me. He gave a small nod of inward conviction and bowed to me. "Mrs. Fraser? I trust I see you well, ma'am." Obviously, he'd heard the story behind Jamie's dramatic resignation.

"You do, thank you," I said. "Do watch out for the crayfish there, Colonel." For Richardson was standing just in front of the tin tub in which I'd set the crayfish, covered with water and supplied with a few handfuls of cornmeal, with which they'd purge their nasty little entrails over the next twenty-four hours and become safe to eat.

"Your pardon, ma'am," he said politely, moving aside. Unlike Howe, he was chiefly concerned with the men; I saw his eyes touch for an instant on Fergus's hook, dismiss him, then rest on Ian, with an air of satisfaction. What Jamie called a cold grue went down my back. I knew already what they wanted; this was a high-level press gang.

Jamie recognized their purpose, too.

"My wife is well, thanks be to God, General. I expect she would like her husband to remain in that condition, too."

Well, that was fairly blunt. Howe evidently decided there was no point in further civilities and waded in directly.

"Are you aware, sir, that a number of British troops have

disembarked just outside the city and doubtless mean to invade and capture it?"

"I am," Jamie said patiently. "I watched their ships come in last night. As for capturing the city, I think they're verra well placed to do just that. And if I were you, General—and I thank the Lord that I'm not—I should be gatherin' my men this minute and marching out of the city wi' them. Ken the proverb about livin' to fight another day, do ye? I recommend it as a strategy."

"Do I understand you aright, sir?" Richardson put in, his tone edgy. "You decline to join in the defense of your own city?"

"Aye, we do," Ian put in before Jamie could answer. He eyed the visitors in an unfriendly way, and I saw his right hand drop to his side, reaching for Rollo's head, then his fingers curl up tight, missing it. "It's no our city and we're no disposed to die for it."

I was sitting next to Rachel and felt her shoulders lose a little of their tension. Across the table, Marsali's eyes slid sideways, meeting Fergus's, and I saw a moment of silent marital communication and accord. *"If they don't know who we are, don't tell them."*

Howe, a rather thickset man, opened and closed his mouth several times before finding words.

"I am appalled, sir," he managed finally, his face quite red. "Appalled," he repeated, his second chin quivering with outrage—and, I thought, no little desperation. "That a man known for his bravery in battle, his constancy to the cause of freedom, would cravenly submit to the rule of the bloody tyrant!"

"A choice little short of treason," Richardson put in, nodding severely. I raised my eyebrows at this and stared at him, but he sedulously avoided my eye.

Jamie stood looking at them for a moment, rubbing a forefinger down the bridge of his nose.

"Mr. Howe," he said at last, dropping his hand. "How many men have ye in your command?"

"Why . . . nearly a thousand!"

"How nearly?"

"Six hundred," Richardson said, at the same moment that Howe exclaimed, "Nine hundred, sir!"

"Aye," said Jamie, clearly unimpressed. "Those transports carry three thousand men, easily—well armed, with artillery—and they've an entire Highland regiment wi' them, too; I heard their pipes as they came ashore."

Howe's color faded noticeably. Still, he had grit; he kept his dignity.

"Whatever the odds, sir," he said, "it is my duty to fight and to protect the city entrusted to my care."

"I respect your devotion to your duty, General," Jamie said, quite seriously. "And may God be with ye. But I won't."

"We could physically compel you," Richardson pointed out.

"Ye could," Jamie agreed, unruffled. "But to what end? Ye canna make me command men if I refuse to do it, and what good is an unwilling soldier?"

"This is craven cowardice, sir!" Howe said, but it was clear that this was bluster, and poorly acted bluster, at that.

"Dia eadarainn 's an t-olc," Jamie said quietly, and nodded toward the door. *"God between us and evil,"* he said. "Go with God, gentlemen, but leave my house."

"THEE DID WELL, Jamie," Rachel said quietly, after the sound of the soldiers' footsteps had faded from the stairwell. "No Friend could have spoken more wisely."

He glanced at her, mouth quirking.

"Thank ye, lass," he said. "But I think ye ken I wasna speaking from the same reasons a Friend might have."

"Oh, I do," she said, smiling. "But the effect is the same, and Friends are grateful for whatever they can get. Will thee have the last frog leg?"

A small ripple of laughter ran through the adults, and the children, who had been sitting rigid and white-faced during the soldiers' visit, relaxed as though they were balloons that someone had let the air out of and began zooming around the room in relief. Fearing for the tub of crayfish, Jenny and Marsali marshaled them into some sort of order and marched them off home to bed, Marsali pausing to kiss Fergus and adjuring him to be careful walking home alone.

"The British are not in the city yet, *mon chou,*" he said, kissing her back.

"Aye, well—it never hurts to keep in practice," she said tartly. "Come along, ye wee rattans."

The rest of us sat for a time discussing the immediate future and what little might be done. Jamie was right about the advantages of poverty in such a situation—but at the same time . . .

"They'll take whatever food they find," I said. "At least at first." I gave the shelf behind me a quick glance; it was our pantry and held the sum total of the household's stores: a small crock of lard, cloth bags of oatmeal, flour, rice, beans, and parched corn, a braid of onions and a few dried apples, half a wheel of cheese, a little box of salt and a pepper pot, and the remains of a loaf of sugar. Plus our small stock of candles.

"Aye." Jamie nodded, got up, and fetched his purse, which he turned out on the table. "Fourteen shillings, about. Ian? Fergus?" Ian and Rachel's resources amounted to another nine shillings, Fergus's one guinea, two shillings, and a handful of pennies.

"See what ye can get at the tavern tomorrow, lass," he said, pushing a small pile of coins toward Rachel. "I think I can put aside a cask of salt fish from the warehouse. And you, Sassenach—if ye're quick at the market in the morning, ye might manage to get more rice and beans, maybe a flitch of bacon?" Bits of copper and silver winked on the table before me, the King's stolid countenance chiseled in profile.

"There's no good hiding place in our room," Ian observed, looking around. "Nor here. Auntie's wee surgery, d'ye think?"

"Aye, that's what I was thinking. It's a board floor, and the building's got a good foundation. I'll maybe make a wee hidey-hole tomorrow. I shouldna think there's much in your surgery that soldiers would want?" This last was said questioningly to me.

"Only the medicines that are made with alcohol," I said. I took a deep breath. "Speaking of soldiers—I have to tell you something. It may not be important—but then again . . ." And I told them about Ezekiel Richardson.

"Ye're quite sure of it, Sassenach?" Jamie frowned a little, red brows sparking in the candlelight. "Yon man's got a face that might belong to anyone."

"He's not what you'd call memorable, at all," I admitted. "But, yes, I am sure. He has that mole on the side of his chin;

I remember that. It's more the way he was looking at me, though. He recognized *me,* I'm positive."

Jamie drew breath and blew it out slowly, considering. Then he put his hands flat on the table and looked at Ian.

"Your auntie met my son, William, in the city the other day—by accident," he said, his voice carefully neutral. "Tell them what he said of Richardson, Sassenach, will ye?"

I did, keeping an eye on the pulse in Ian's throat. So was Rachel; she put a hand quietly on his, which he was clenching in a fist on the table. He glanced at her, smiled briefly, and reluctantly unclenched it, lacing his fingers with hers.

"And what's William doing here, then?" Ian asked, obviously working to keep any hint of hostility out of his voice.

"He was looking for Richardson, in fact, but he's also searching for his cousin's wife, a woman named Amaranthus Grey—or perhaps Cowden," I added. "She might be going by her maiden name. I'd meant to ask if either of you had heard any mention of her."

Both Ian and Rachel shook their heads.

"Thee would remember a name like that," Rachel said. "But thee thinks William doesn't know that Richardson is here?"

"I'm sure he doesn't," I said. "Nor that Richardson has gone over to the Rebels. Apparently."

There was silence for a moment. I could hear the faint clicking of the crayfish in the tub behind me and the slight pop as a fault in the candlewick made the flame bob and dance.

"This man Richardson may simply have changed his allegiance," Rachel suggested. "I know of many who have, over the last two years."

"He might," I said slowly, "but the thing is—John thought he was an intelligencer—a spy or secret agent of some sort. And when someone of that stripe turns his coat . . . you have to ask whether he's turned it once or twice. Or not at all. Don't you?"

Jamie laid a hand on the table, thinking.

"Aye, well," he said at last, and, sitting up straight, stretched himself with a sigh. "If there's aught fishy about the man, we'll ken it soon enough."

"We will?" I asked. He gave me a wry smile.

"Aye, Sassenach. He'll come looking for you. Keep your wee knife close to hand, aye?"

129

INVASION

December 29

WE HEARD THE GUNS soon after dawn. Jamie paused in the act of shaving to listen. It was a distant thunder, irregular, muffled by distance. But I had heard artillery close at hand and felt the sound as an echo in my bones, urging instant flight. Jamie had heard artillery at a much closer range than I and set down his razor, planting his hands flat on the washstand. To keep them from trembling, I thought.

"They're firing cannon from the ships in the river," he said quietly. "And regular artillery from the south. God help Howe and his men." He crossed himself and picked up the razor.

"How far away do you think they are?" I had paused in the act of putting on my stockings and now drew one up, slowly fastening my garter. Jamie shook his head.

"No telling from in here. I'll go out in a bit, though, and then I'll see how the wind lies."

"You're going out?" I asked, uneasy at the prospect. "Surely you're not going to work today." Fadler's warehouse, where he worked as a supervisor and senior clerk, was *on* the river.

"I am not," he said briefly. "But I thought I'd go and fetch the bairns and Marsali and my sister. Fergus will be gone to see what's happening, and I dinna want them left alone without a man." His mouth thinned. "Especially not if the soldiers come into the city."

I nodded, at once unable to speak. The thought of the things that happened—could happen—during an invasion . . . I had, thank God, never lived through such an event but had seen too many newsreels and photographs to be under any illusions as to the possibilities. And there had already been reports of a British company come up from Florida under an officer named Major Prevost, raiding the countryside around Sunbury, running off cattle, and burning barns and farmhouses. Sunbury was not nearly far enough away for comfort.

When Jamie left, I rattled around for a few minutes, undecided what to do first, but then pulled myself together and decided to make a quick visit to my surgery. It would be a good idea to take away my more-valuable instruments—not that any of them had great value; there was no black market in amputation saws (at least not yet . . .)—and such drugs and supplies as might be needed if—

I cut that "if" off sharply and looked around our modest room. I had been keeping only a few staples, like flour and butter, and the more perishable items of food here; anything that could be stored for a while was now hidden under the floor of my surgery. If we were about to have Marsali, Jenny, and the children to stay for an indefinite time, though, I'd best bring back a few more things.

I took my biggest basket and knocked at Rachel's door downstairs. She answered at once, already dressed to go out.

"Ian has gone with Fergus," she said, before I could ask. "He says he will not fight with the militia but that Fergus is his brother and it is his duty to see him safe. I can't complain about that."

"I could," I said frankly. "I'd complain like billy-o if I thought it would do any good. Waste of breath, though. Will you come with me down to the surgery? Jamie's gone to get Jenny and Marsali and the children, so I thought I'd best bring back something for them to eat."

"Let me get my basket."

The streets were full of people—most of them in some process of leaving the city, fetching goods, or drawing carts through the streets, though some were clearly bent on looting. I saw two men break a window and crawl through it into a large house off Ellis Square.

We reached the surgery without incident, though, and found two whores standing outside. They were women I knew, and I introduced them to Rachel, who was much less discomposed by the introduction than they were.

"We're wanting to buy pox cures, missus," said Molly, a

sturdy Irish girl. "So many as ye might have to hand and be willin' to part with."

"Are you, um, expecting a—er—rash of the pox? So to speak?" I was unlocking the door as we spoke, calculating whether the current crop of penicillin was likely to be sufficiently potent as to make any difference.

"It don't matter that much whether it works or not, ma'am," said Iris, who was very tall, very thin, and very black. "We'uns plan to sell 'em to the soldiers."

"I see," I said, rather blankly. "Well, then . . ."

I gave them what penicillin I had in liquid form, declining to charge them. I kept the powdered mold and the remnants of Roquefort cheese, though, in case the family might have need of them—and suffered a bolt of vivid fear at the thought of Fergus and Ian, doing God knew what. The artillery had stopped—or the wind had changed—but it started up again as we made our way home, holding our baskets under our cloaks to prevent snatch-and-grab attacks.

Jamie had brought back Marsali and Jenny and the children, all of them carrying what they could in the way of clothes, food, and bedding. There was a long period of total chaos, while things were organized, but at last we sat down to a sort of rough tea, at around three o'clock. Jamie, declining to be involved in the domestic engineering, had exercised his male prerogative of disappearing on vaguely unspecified "business" but, with unerring instinct, reappeared just as the cake was being set out, bearing a large gunnysack full of clams, a barrel of flour, and a modicum of news.

"The fighting's over," he said, looking for someplace to set the clams down.

"I noticed the guns had stopped some time ago. Do you know what's happened?" I took the bag and decanted the clams with a loud clatter into the empty cauldron, then poured a bucket of water over them. They'd keep until supper.

"Exactly what I told General Howe would happen," he said, though not with any sense of pleasure at being right. "Campbell—that's the British Lieutenant Colonel, Archibald Campbell—circled Howe and his men and bagged them up like fish in a net. I dinna ken what he's done wi' them, but I expect there will be troops in the city before nightfall."

The women all looked at one another and relaxed visibly.

This was actually good news. What with one thing and another, the British army was quite good at occupying cities. And while the citizenry might justifiably resent the billeting of troops and the requisitioning of supplies, the underlying fact was that there's nothing for keeping public order like having an army living with you.

"Will we be safe, then, with the soldiers here?" Joanie asked. She was bright-eyed with the adventure, like her siblings, and had been following the adult conversation closely.

"Aye, mostly," Jamie said, but his eye met Marsali's, and she grimaced. We probably would be safe enough, though food might be short for a while, until the army quartermasters got things straightened out. Fergus and Bonnie, though, were another matter.

"Luckily, we hadna started up *L'Oignon* yet," she said, answering Jamie's look. "It's only been printing up handbills and broadsheets and the odd religious tract. I think it will be all right," she said bravely, but she reached to touch Félicité's dark head, as though to reassure herself.

We had the clams made into chowder—rather a watery chowder, as we had very little milk, but we thickened it with crumbled biscuit, and there *was* enough butter—and were setting the table for supper when Fergus and Ian came clattering up the stairs, flushed with excitement and full of news.

"It was a black slave who made the difference," Fergus said, cramming a piece of bread into his mouth. "*Mon Dieu,* I'm famished! We haven't eaten all day. This man wandered into the British camp soon after the fighting began and offered to show them a secret path through the swamp. Lieutenant Colonel Campbell sent a regiment of Highlanders—we could hear the pipes; it reminded me of Prestonpans." He grinned at Jamie, and I could see the scrawny ten-year-old French orphan he'd been, riding on a captured cannon. He swallowed and washed the bite down with water, that being all we had at the moment.

"Highlanders," he continued, "and some other infantry, and they followed the slave through the swamp and got well round General Howe's men, who were all clumped together, for of course they didn't know from which direction the fight might come."

Campbell had then sent another infantry company to Howe's

left, "to make some demonstrations," Fergus said, waving an airy hand and scattering crumbs. "They turned, of course, to meet this, and then the Highlanders fell on them from the other side, and *voilà*!" He snapped his fingers.

"I doubt Howe feels any gratitude to that slave," Ian put in, scooping his bowl into the cauldron of chowder. "But he ought. He didna lose more than thirty or forty men—and had they stood and fought, they'd likely all have been killed, if they hadn't the sense to surrender. And he didna strike me as a man o' sense," he added thoughtfully.

"How long d'ye think they'll stay, the army?" Jenny was slicing bread and handing out the pieces round the table but paused to wipe a forearm across her brow. It was winter, but with the fire going in the small room and so many people crowded in, the temperature was quickly approaching Turkish-bath levels.

All the men exchanged glances. Then Jamie spoke, reluctantly.

"A long time, *a piuthar.*"

130

A SOVEREIGN CURE

IT HAD TO BE done, and it had to be done now. Between Jamie's uneasiness and my own misgivings, I'd put off the question of making ether. But now we were up against it: I simply couldn't do what needed to be done for Sophronia without a dependable general anesthetic.

I'd already decided that I could do the manufacture in the tiny toolshed in Mrs. Landrum's huge kitchen garden. It was outside the city limits, with an acre of open space on every side, this occupied only by winter kale and hibernating carrots. If I blew myself to kingdom come, I wouldn't take anyone else with me.

I doubted that this observation would reassure Jamie to any great extent, though, so I put off mentioning my plans. I'd assemble what I needed and tell him only at the last minute, thus saving him worry. And, after all, if I couldn't obtain the necessary ingredients . . . but I was sure that I could. Savannah was a sizable city, and a shipping port. There were at least three apothecaries in town, as well as several warehouses that imported specialty items from England. *Someone* was bound to have sulfuric acid, otherwise known as oil of vitriol.

The weather was cool but sunny, and seeing a number of red-coated soldiers in the street, I wondered idly whether climatic considerations had had anything to do with the British deciding to switch their theater of operations to the South.

The elder Mr. Jameson—a sprightly gentleman in his seventies—greeted me pleasantly when I entered Jameson's Apothecary. I'd had occasion to make small purchases of herbs from him before, and we got on well. I presented him with my list and browsed among the jars on his shelves while he pottered to and fro in search of my requests. There were three young soldiers on the other side of the shop, gathered in furtive conversation with the younger Mr. Jameson over something he was showing them under his counter. Pox cures, I assumed—or—giving them the benefit of the doubt regarding foresight—possibly condoms.

They concluded their surreptitious purchases and scuttled out, heads down and rather red in the face. The younger Mr. Jameson, who was the grandson of the owner and about the same age as the just-departed soldiers, was also rather pink but greeted me with aplomb, bowing.

"Your servant, Mrs. Fraser! Might I be of assistance?"

"Oh, thank you, Nigel," I said. "Your grandfather has my list. But"—a thought had occurred to me, perhaps jogged by the soldiers—"I wonder whether you might know of a Mrs. Grey. Amaranthus Grey is her name, and I believe her maiden name was . . . oh, what was it? Cowden! Amaranthus Cowden Grey. Have you ever heard that name?"

He wrinkled his very smooth brow in thought.

"What an odd name. Er—meaning no offense, ma'am," he hastily assured me. "I meant . . . rather exotic. Quite unusual."

"Yes, it is. I don't know her," I said, "but a friend of mine said that she lived in Savannah and had urged me to . . . er . . . make her acquaintance."

"Yes, of course." Nigel hmm'd for a bit but shook his head. "No, I'm sorry, ma'am, I don't believe I've ever encountered an Amaranthus Cowden."

"Cowden?" said Mr. Jameson, emerging suddenly from his back room with several bottles in his hands. "Of course we have, boy. Or, rather, not encountered; she's never come in the shop. But we had a request brought by mail, only two or three weeks ago, asking for . . . oh, what was it, my mind is a sieve, Mrs. Fraser, an absolute sieve, I assure you—don't get old, that's my advice—oh, yes. Gould's complexion cream, Villette's gripe water, a box of pastilles to sweeten the breath, and a dozen bars of Savon D'Artagnan French soap. That was it." He beamed at me over his spectacles. "She lives in Saperville," he added, as an afterthought.

"You're a wonder, Granddad," Nigel murmured dutifully, and reached for the bottles his grandfather was holding. "Shall I wrap these, or are we mixing something for the lady?"

"Oh." Mr. Jameson looked down at the bottles in his hands, as though wondering how they'd got there. "Oh, yes! I wanted to ask you, Mrs. Fraser, what it was you had in mind to *do* with oil of vitriol. It's amazingly dangerous, you know."

"Um, yes, I do." I eyed him consideringly; some men would be quite capable of refusing to sell a woman something they thought inappropriate or dangerous, but Mr. Jameson seemed a worldly sort—and he did at least know that I knew the use of medicinal herbs.

"I have it in mind to make ether," I said. The substance was known, I knew—someone or other had discovered it back in the eighth century, or so I was told in medical school—but its use as an anesthetic wouldn't be developed 'til somewhere in the nineteenth century. I wondered idly whether anyone in the intervening eleven hundred years *had* noticed that the stuff put people to sleep, but had inadvertently killed them and thus abandoned further experimentation.

Both Mr. Jamesons looked surprised.

"Ether?" said Nigel, openly puzzled. "Why would you make it yourself?"

"Why would I—what, do you mean that you have the stuff already made up?" I asked, astonished.

Both of them nodded, pleased to be of service.

"Oh, yes," Mr. Jameson said. "We don't always stock it, of course, but with the . . . er . . . army"—he waved a hand, encompassing the recent invasion and occupation—"there are the troop transports, and there will be a great increase of shipping, now that the blockade is not in effect."

"What does the increase of shipping have to do with the sale of ether?" I asked, wondering whether Mr. Jameson might just possibly be right about the effects of advancing age on the brain.

"Why, ma'am," said Nigel. "It's a sovereign cure for the seasickness. Did you not know?"

131

A BORN GAMBLER

I COUNTED MY INSTRUMENTS for the third time and, finding that none of them had escaped since the last count, covered them with a clean linen cloth and patted it lightly in reassurance—whether of the scalpels or myself, I wasn't sure. Silk sutures, gut sutures, needles—the finest embroidery needles obtainable in Savannah. Pledgets, swabs, dressings, rolled bandages. A six-inch willow twig, carefully cleaned of its pith, sanded smooth, and boiled slowly—so as not to crack the wood—to be used as a catheter to stabilize the urethra and bladder and keep urine out of the surgical field. I'd thought of using a larger one for the bowel, but decided that I'd be better using my fingers to manipulate the slippery tissues there—so long as I managed neither to cut nor puncture myself in the process.

Rachel was coming to assist with the surgery, and I'd go through all the instruments and procedures again with her. I'd come down an hour early, though, wanting both to make my final preparations and to spend a little time alone, settling my mind and spirit to the job ahead.

I felt surprisingly calm, considering the complexity and risks of the operation ahead. It could be argued that even if I failed, the poor child couldn't possibly be worse off than she was—but of course she could die as a result of the surgery, from shock, infection, or even accidental hemorrhage. Abdominal surgery was much more serious than trying a transvaginal correction—but given what I had at hand, I thought the chances of achieving a cure were much better that way. And then there was the matter of the curettage that had removed the dead infant; I had no idea what kind of damage that might have inflicted, but if there was any, I might be able to correct it.

I glanced automatically at the shelf where my penicillin factory was working—or at least I hoped it was working, billions of little spores excreting their helpful substance. I hadn't had time in Savannah to establish a good process and test the resultant product; there was, as was so often the case, no guarantee whatever that I *had* usable penicillin in my broth. But I did have a small chunk of very ripe French cheese, acquired at extravagant cost and stirred into a little boiled milk to make a paste; the thick scent of it fought for ascendancy with the pungent smell of ether.

I could hear the early-morning sounds of the city outside, soothing in their ordinariness: the whisk of a broom on pavement, the clop of horse-drawn wagons, a tantalizing smell of hot bread as the baker's boy's quick footsteps passed by. The simple demands of life quickly made routine out of any sort of chaos, and as invasions went, the occupation of Savannah had been reasonably bloodless.

My sense of well-being and calm detachment was interrupted a moment later by the opening of the surgery door.

"May I help—" I began, turning. Then I saw my visitor and altered my remark to a fairly hostile "What do *you* want?"

Captain—no, he was a colonel now; the wages of treason, I supposed—Richardson smiled charmingly at me, then turned and bolted the door. I pulled out a drawer and removed my small amputation saw; it was small enough to handle quickly, and the serrated edge would take his nose off, if my aim was good.

The charming smile broadened into a grin as he saw what I was about, and he bowed. He wasn't wearing a uniform—and no wonder—but was clothed in a decent, rather sober suit, with unpowdered hair tied simply back. No one would have looked at him twice.

"Your most humble servant, ma'am. Have no alarm; I merely wished to make sure we weren't interrupted."

"Yes, that's what I'm alarmed *about,*" I said, taking a firm grip on the saw. "Unbolt that bloody door this minute."

He looked at me for a moment, one eye narrowed in calculation, but then uttered a short laugh and, turning, pulled the bolt. Folding his arms, he leaned against the door.

"Better?"

"Much." I let go the saw but didn't move my hand far from it. "I repeat—what do you want?"

"Well, I thought perhaps the time had come to lay my cards upon your table, Mrs. Fraser—and see whether you might want to play a hand or two."

"The only thing I might be inclined to play with you, Colonel, is mumblety-peg," I said, tapping my fingers on the handle of the saw. "But if you want to show me your cards, go right ahead. You want to be quick about it, though—I have an operation to conduct in less than an hour."

"It shouldn't take that long. May I?" Raising his brows, he gestured at one of the stools. I nodded, and he sat down, looking quite relaxed.

"The essence of the matter, ma'am, is that I am a Rebel—and always have been."

"You—what?"

"I am presently a colonel in the Continental army—but when you first knew me, I was working as an American agent in the guise of a captain in His Majesty's army in Philadelphia."

"I don't understand." I grasped *what* he was telling me but couldn't grasp *why* the hell he should be telling me.

"You are a Rebel yourself, are you not?" One sparse brow lifted in inquiry. He really was the most ordinary-looking man, I thought. If he *was* a spy, he was physically well suited for it.

"I am," I said guardedly. "What about it?"

"Then we're on the same side," he said patiently. "When I cozened Lord John Grey into marrying you, I—"

"You *what*?"

"Surely he told you that I had threatened to have you arrested for distributing seditious materials? At which you're very clumsy, I might add," he added dispassionately. "His lordship assured me that he had no personal interest in you whatever and then most obligingly married you the next day. His lordship is a very gallant man—particularly in view of his own preferences."

He cocked his head, smiling in a conspiratorial manner, and a spear of ice shot through my belly.

"Oh, you do know, then," he observed, watching my face. "I thought you would. He's extremely discreet, but I think you a very perceptive woman, particularly in sexual matters."

"Stand up," I said, in my coldest voice, "and leave. Right now."

He didn't, of course, and I cursed my lack of forethought in not keeping a loaded pistol in the surgery. The saw might serve if he attacked me, but I knew better than to try attacking him.

Besides, what would you do with the body, if you killed him? the logical side of my mind inquired. *He wouldn't fit in the cupboard, let alone the hidey-hole.*

"For the third—and last—time," I said. "What do you bloody want?"

"Your help," he said promptly. "I'd originally had it in mind to use you as an agent in place. You could have been very valuable to me, moving in the same social circles as the British high command. But you seemed too unstable—forgive me, ma'am—to approach immediately. I hoped that as your grief over your first husband faded, you would come to a state of resignation in which I might seek your acquaintance and by degrees achieve a state of intimacy in which you could be persuaded to discover small—and, at first, seemingly innocent—bits of information, which you would pass on to me."

"Just what do you mean by 'intimacy'?" I said, folding my arms. Because while the word in current parlance often meant merely friendship, he hadn't used it with that intonation at all.

"You're a very desirable woman, Mrs. Fraser," he said, looking me over in an objectionably appraising way. "And one who knows her desirability. His lordship obviously wasn't obliging you in that regard, so . . ." He lifted a shoulder, smiling in a deprecating fashion. "But as General Fraser has returned from the dead, I imagine you're no longer susceptible to lures of that kind."

I laughed and dropped my arms.

"You flatter yourself, Colonel," I said dryly. "If not me. Look: why not stop trying to fluster me and tell me what you want me to do and why on earth you think I'd do it."

He laughed, too, which lent some sense of individuality to his face.

"Very well. It may be difficult to believe, but this war will not be won on the battlefield."

"Oh, yes?"

"Yes, I assure you, ma'am. It will be won by spying and by politics."

"A very novel approach, I'm sure." I was trying to place his accent; it was English but a rather flat sort of accent. Not London, not the north . . . educated, but not polished. "I assume you weren't soliciting my assistance in the political line."

"No, actually, I am," he said. "If somewhat indirectly."

"I suggest you try the direct approach," I said. "My patient will be arriving very shortly." The sounds outside had changed; apprentices and housemaids were going past in little groups, bound for work or daily marketing. Calls to and fro, the occasional giggle of a flirtation in passing.

Richardson nodded in acceptance.

"Are you aware of the Duke of Pardloe's opinion of this war?"

I was somewhat taken aback by this. Foolishly, it hadn't occurred to me that Hal might have one, outside the requirements of his service. But if ever I had met a man guaranteed to have opinions, it was Harold, Second Duke of Pardloe.

"What with one thing and another, I've never exchanged views with the duke on political matters. Nor with my—nor with his brother, for that matter."

"Ah. Well, ladies often take no interest in things outside their own sphere of interest—though I rather thought you might have a . . . wider appreciation, shall we say?" He looked pointedly from my canvas apron and tray of instruments to the other appointments of my surgery.

"What about his politics?" I asked shortly, disregarding his implications.

"His Grace is a strong voice in the House of Lords," Richardson said, playing with a frayed thread on the edge of his cuff. "And while he was at first very much in favor of the war, his opinions of late have been noticeably more . . . moderate. He wrote a public letter to the first minister in the fall, urging a consideration of reconciliation."

"And?" I hadn't the slightest idea where he was going with this and was growing impatient.

"Reconciliation is not what we want, ma'am," he said, and, pulling the thread free, flicked it aside. "Such efforts will only delay the inevitable and interfere with the commitment of the citizenry that we desperately need. But the fact that His Grace shows this moderation of outlook is useful to me."

"Jolly good," I said. "Get to the point, if you please."

He ignored this and proceeded about his exposition as though he had all the time in the world.

"Were he fiercely committed to one extreme or the other, he would be difficult to . . . influence. While I don't know His Grace well, everything I know *of* him indicates that he values his sense of honor—"

"He does."

"—almost as much as he values his family," Richardson finished. He looked directly at me, and for the first time I felt a flicker of real fear.

"I have for some time been working to acquire influence—whether direct or otherwise—over such members of the duke's family as are within my reach. With, say, a son—a nephew?—perhaps even his brother in my control, it would then be possible to affect His Grace's public position, in whatever way seemed most advantageous to us."

"If you're suggesting what I think you're suggesting, then I suggest you leave my sight this instant," I said, in what I hoped was a tone of calm menace. Though I spoiled whatever effect there might have been by adding, "Besides, I have absolutely no connection with any of Pardloe's family now."

He smiled faintly, with no sense of pleasantry at all.

"His nephew, William, is in the city, ma'am, and you were seen speaking with him nine days ago. Perhaps you are unaware, though, that both Pardloe and his brother are here, as well?"

"Here?" My mouth hung open for an instant and I closed it sharply. "With the army?"

He nodded.

"I gather that in spite of your recent . . . marital rearrangement? . . . you remain on good terms with Lord John Grey."

"Sufficiently good that I would do nothing whatever to deliver him into your bloody hands, if that's what you had in mind."

"Nothing so crude, ma'am," he assured me, with a brief flash of teeth. "I had in mind only the transmission of information—in both directions. I intend no damage at all to the duke or his family; I only wish to—"

Whatever his intentions, they were interrupted by a tentative knock on the door, which then opened to admit Mrs. Bradshaw's head. She looked apprehensively at me and suspiciously at Richardson, who cleared his throat, stood up, and bowed to her.

"Your servant, ma'am," he said. "I was just taking my leave of Mrs. Fraser. Good day to you." He turned and bowed to me, more elaborately. "Your most humble servant, Mrs. Fraser. I look forward to seeing you again. Soon."

"I'll just bet you do," I said, but far enough under my breath that I doubted he heard me.

Mrs. Bradshaw and Sophronia edged into the room, coming close enough to Richardson on his way out that his face wrinkled up in involuntary revulsion at smelling Sophronia, and he cast a startled glance over his shoulder at me—this causing him to collide heavily with Rachel, hurrying in. He waltzed with her for a step or two, finally getting his balance and making his inelegant escape, pursued by my laughter.

This bit of slapstick had partially dispelled the uneasiness he'd brought to my surgery, and I put him firmly out of my mind. Sufficient to the day was the Richardson thereof, and I had work to do. It was with a sense of confidence that I took Sophronia's small hand between my own and smiled at her downcast face.

"Don't be worried, sweetheart," I said. "I'm going to take care of you."

WITH A MODERN hospital and equipment, I would have done the surgery transvaginally. Given my current resources, though, it would have to be abdominal. With Mrs. Bradshaw anxiously perched on a stool out of the way—she wouldn't leave, and I hoped she wouldn't faint—and Rachel carefully counting drops of ether under her breath, I took my best scalpel and cut into Sophronia's fresh-scrubbed belly. The stretch marks left by her pregnancy were fading but still visible on her very young flesh.

I had makeshift stirrups, should I need them, made by nailing blocks of wood to the table at an angle, and I'd put a wadded towel between her thighs, soaked with the antibacterial lotion I'd scrubbed her with, an alcoholic extraction of crushed garlic mixed with a hot-water extract of lemon balm. It smelled pleasantly kitchen-like and did something to kill the sewage smell—as well as germs, I hoped.

The ether, though, was stronger than anything else, and within ten minutes of starting, I began to feel a slight swimming in my head.

"Mrs. Bradshaw," I called over my shoulder. "Will you open the window, please? And the shutters?" I hoped we wouldn't attract any spectators—but the need for fresh air was imperative.

The vesicovaginal fistula was luckily fairly small and in a reasonably easy position to reach. Rachel was holding a retractor for me with one hand, keeping the other on Sophronia's pulse, and administering more ether every few minutes.

"Are you all right, Rachel?" I asked, trimming back the edges of the fistula in order to get a decent field for stitching—the edges were flattened and macerated, and the tissue would shred and pull apart under any sort of pressure. I'd had some hesitation in asking her to help today; I would have asked Jenny, but she was suffering from what was called the catarrh, and sneezing and coughing were the last things I wanted in a surgical assistant.

"I am," she answered, her voice slightly muffled behind her not-quite-sterile-but-at-least-boiled mask. She'd used one of Ian's handkerchiefs for the purpose; it was an incongruously cheerful calico in dark-pink-and-white checks. Ian's taste in clothing was strongly Mohawk.

"Good. Tell me if you feel at all dizzy." I had no idea what I'd do if she *did* feel dizzy—perhaps Mrs. Bradshaw could take over the dropping bottle for a few minutes. . . .

I spared a quick glance over my shoulder. Mrs. Bradshaw sat on her stool, gloved hands clasped tight in her lap and her face pale as a sheet, but she sat firm.

"It's going well so far," I said to her, trying to sound as reassuring as possible through my own chaste white mask. The masks seemed to unnerve her, and she looked away, swallowing.

It really was going well, though. While it was Sophronia's youth that had caused the problem, that also meant that her tissues were healthy, in good shape, and she had considerable animal vitality. If the surgery was successful, if there was little or no subsequent infection, she'd heal very quickly. If.

"Ifs" hover in the air above your head all the time when you're doing surgery, like a cloud of gnats. For the most part, though, they keep a respectful distance, only buzzing dimly in the background.

Done.

"One down, one to go," I murmured, and, dipping a wad of sterilized gauze into my cheese lotion, I daubed some—not without a qualm—over the newly stitched repair. "Onward."

The bowel repair was easier—though more unpleasant. It was quite cold in the surgery—I hadn't lit a fire, not wanting soot in the air—but I was sweating; beads of perspiration ran tickling down the side of my nose and down my neck from my bound-up hair.

I could feel the girl, though, the life of her echoing in my hands, her heartbeat strong and steady—there was a large blood vessel visible on the surface of the uterus, and I could see it pulsing. She'd been lucky in the one thing: the uterus hadn't been perforated, and looked healthy. I couldn't tell whether there was internal scarring, but when I cupped my hand gently over the organ, it felt normal to me. For a moment, I closed my eyes, feeling deeper, and found what I thought I needed. I opened them again, blotted the ooze of blood from the cut tissues, and reached for a fresh needle.

How long? Anesthesia complications were one of the nasty

little flying "ifs," and that one flew down and perched on my shoulder. I had no clock or pocket watch but had brought a small sandglass borrowed from our landlady.

"How long has it been, Rachel?"

"Twenty minutes." Her voice was soft, and I looked up, but she was still steady, her eyes fixed on the open belly. She was nearly four months' pregnant, her own belly slightly rounded. "Don't worry," I said to her briefly. "It won't happen to you."

"Surely it *could*?" she said, still more softly.

I shook my head.

"Not if I'm with you when you give birth."

She made a small amused sound and picked up the dropping bottle again.

"Thee will be, I assure thee, Claire."

Rachel was shivering slightly by the time I'd finished; I was wringing wet but feeling the glow of at least temporary victory. The fistulas were repaired, the leakage stopped. I irrigated the surgical field with saline solution and the organs glistened, the beautiful deep colors of the body unmarred by smears of fecal matter.

I paused for a moment to admire the neat compactness of the pelvic organs, all in their places. There was a tiny trickle of pale urine from the catheter, staining the towel with a faint yellow shadow. In a modern hospital, I would have left the catheter in during the healing, but it would be difficult to manage without a drainage bag, and the chances of irritation or infection from the device were likely greater than the possible benefits of leaving it. I eased it free of her body, watching. Within a few seconds, the flow of urine ceased, and I let out a breath I hadn't realized I was holding.

I had taken up a fresh needle threaded with silk, to close the incision, when something occurred to me.

"Rachel—do you want to look? Closely, I mean." Sophronia had had ether within the last couple of minutes and was still deeply under; Rachel checked her color and breathing and then came round the table to stand beside me.

I didn't think she'd be disturbed by the blood or the sight of organs, given the things she'd seen in military camps and battlefields. She wasn't, but she *was* disturbed.

"That—" She swallowed and put a hand to her swelling

stomach, very gently. "So beautiful," she whispered. "How the body is made. How such things can be."

"It is," I said, her awe making me lower my own voice.

"To think of her poor infant, though . . . and she no more than a child . . ."

I glanced at Rachel and saw tears standing in her eyes. And I saw the thought cross her face, masked as it was: *It could happen to me.*

"Yes," I said quietly. "Go back to the ether; I'll close the incision now." But as I dipped my hands again in the bowl of alcohol and water, something else occurred to me.

Oh, God, I thought, appalled at the thought. But . . .

"Mrs. Bradshaw," I said. She was sitting with her head bowed, arms wrapped round herself against the chill, perhaps half asleep. When I spoke, though, her head came up sharply.

"Is it over?" she asked. "Does she live?"

"She does," I said. "And, with luck, will continue to do so. But . . ." I hesitated, but I had to ask. And I had to ask this woman.

"Before I sew up the incision . . . I can—do a very minor procedure that will stop Sophronia from becoming pregnant again."

Mrs. Bradshaw blinked.

"You can?"

"Yes. It's a simple thing to do—but, once done, it can't be undone. She'd never be able to have babies." A fresh cloud of "ifs" had formed, buzzing anxiously over my shoulder.

She was thirteen. She was a slave. And had a master who used her. If she were to become pregnant again soon, she might well die during the labor and would almost certainly be seriously damaged. It might never be safe for her to bear a child—but it wasn't safe for any woman, ever. And "never" is a very big word.

Mrs. Bradshaw had drifted slowly toward the table, her eyes twitching toward the exposed, half-draped body, then away, unable either to look or to stay away. I put out a hand, warding her off.

"Don't come closer, please."

"He was sad when the baby died. He cried." I could still hear the sadness in Sophronia's voice; she mourned her child. How

could she not? Could I take away the possibility of another—forever—without even asking her what she felt about it?

And yet . . .

If she bore a child, it, too, would be a slave; it might be taken from her and sold. Even if not, it would likely live and die in slavery.

And yet . . .

"If she wasn't able to bear children . . ." Mrs. Bradshaw said slowly. She stopped speaking, and I could see the thoughts crossing her white, pinched face; her lips had all but disappeared, so tightly were they pressed together. I didn't think she was concerned with the fact that Sophronia's value would be diminished if she couldn't reproduce.

Would the fear of damage due to pregnancy stop Mr. Bradshaw from using the girl?

If she were barren, would he feel no hesitation?

"He didn't hesitate because she was twelve," I said, my words cold as pellets of ice. "Would the chance of killing her next time stop him?"

She stared at me in shock, mouth hanging open. She blinked, swallowed, and looked at Sophronia, limp and helpless, body gaping open on the blood-soaked towels, the floor around her thickly spattered with her fluids.

"I think thee cannot," Rachel said quietly. She looked from me to Mrs. Bradshaw, and it wasn't clear to whom she was speaking: perhaps both of us. She was holding Sophronia's hand.

"She felt her child move within her. She loved it." Rachel's voice broke, and she choked a little. Tears welled and rolled down to disappear into her mask. "She wouldn't . . . she . . ." She stopped, gulping a little, and shook her head, unable to go on.

Mrs. Bradshaw put a hand clumsily over her face, as though to stop me seeing her thoughts.

"I can't," she said, and repeated almost angrily, behind the shield of her hand, "I *can't*. It isn't my fault! I tried—I tried to do the right thing!" She wasn't talking to me; I didn't know if it was to Mr. Bradshaw or God.

The "ifs" were all still there, but so was Sophronia, and I couldn't leave her any longer.

"All right," I said quietly. "Go and sit down, Mrs. Bradshaw. I said I'd take care of her, and I will."

My hands were cold, and the body under them was very warm, pulsing with life. I picked up the needle and put in the first suture.

132

WILL-O'-THE-WISP

SAPERVILLE? WILLIAM WAS beginning to wonder whether Amaranthus Cowden Grey actually existed or whether she was a will-o'-the-wisp created by Ezekiel Richardson. But if so—to what end?

He'd made careful inquiries after receiving Mrs. Fraser's note yesterday; there really was a place called Saperville—a tiny settlement some twenty miles to the southwest of Savannah, in what his interlocutor had told him was "the piney woods," in a tone of voice suggesting that the piney woods were next door to hell, both in terms of remoteness and uncivil conditions. He couldn't conceive what might have made the woman—if she really did exist—go to such a place.

If she *didn't* exist . . . then someone had invented her, and the most likely suspect for such a deception was Ezekiel Richardson. William had been decoyed by Richardson before. The entire experience in the Dismal Swamp still made him grit his teeth in retrospect—the more so when he reflected that, if not for that chain of events, neither he nor Ian Murray would have met Rachel Hunter.

With an effort, he dismissed Rachel from his mind—she wouldn't stay out of his dreams, but he didn't have to think about her while awake—and returned to the elusive Amaranthus.

In purely practical terms, Saperville lay on the other side of Campbell's army, which was still encamped over several acres of ground outside Savannah, while billeting arrangements were made, housing built, and fortifications dug. A large part of the Continental forces that had opposed them had been neatly bagged up and sent north as prisoners, and the chances of the remnants causing trouble for Campbell were minuscule. That didn't mean William could walk straight through the camp without attracting attention. He might not meet with anyone who knew him, but that didn't mean no one would question him. And however innocuous his errand, the last thing he wanted was to have to explain to anyone why he had resigned his commission.

He'd had time, while Campbell was arraying his forces, to take Miranda out of Savannah and board her with a farmer some ten miles to the north. The army foragers might still find her—they certainly would, if the army remained in Savannah for any great time—but for the moment she was safe. All too familiar with military rapacity—he'd seized horses and supplies himself, many times—he wasn't about to take her within sight of the army.

He drummed his fingers on the table, thinking, but reluctantly concluded that he'd best walk to Saperville, making a wide circle around Campbell's men. He wasn't going to find out about bloody Amaranthus sitting here, that was sure.

Resolved, he paid for his meal, wrapped himself in his cloak, and set off. It wasn't raining, that was one good thing.

It was January, though, and the days were still short; the shadows were lengthening by the time he came to the edge of the sea of camp followers that had formed around the army. He made his way past a conclave of red-armed laundresses, their kettles all fuming in the chilly air and the scent of smoke and lye soap hanging over them in a witchy sort of haze.

"Double, double toil and trouble," he chanted under his breath. *"Fire burn and caldron bubble. Fillet of a fenny snake, in the caldron boil and bake. Eye of newt and toe of frog, wool of bat and tongue of dog . . ."* He couldn't recall what came next and abandoned the effort.

Beyond the laundresses, the ground was choppy, the boggy spots interspersed with higher bits of ground, these crowned with stunted trees and low bushes—and quite obviously providing a footing, so to speak, for the whores to ply their own trade.

He gave these a somewhat wider berth and consequently found himself squelching through something that was not quite a bog, but not far off, either. It *was* remarkably beautiful, though, in a chiaroscuro sort of way; the fading light somehow made each barren twig stand out in stark contrast to the air, the swollen buds still sleeping but rounded, balanced on the edge between winter's death and the life of spring. He wished for a moment that he could draw, or paint, or write poetry, but as it was, he could only pause for a few seconds to admire it.

As he did so, though, he felt a permanence form in his heart, a quiet sense that even though he had only these few seconds, he would have them forever, could come back to this place, this time, in his mind.

He was right, though not entirely for the reasons he supposed.

He would have passed right by her, thinking she was a part of the bog, for she was curled over in a tight ball and the hood of her sad-colored cloak covered her head. But she made a tiny sound, a heartbroken whimper that stopped him in his tracks, and he saw her then, crouched in the mud at the foot of a sweet gum.

"Ma'am?" he said tentatively. She hadn't been aware of him; she uncurled suddenly, her white face staring up at him, shocked and tear-streaked. Then she gulped air and leapt to her feet, throwing herself at him.

"Wiyum! Wiyum!" It was Fanny, Jane's sister, alone, daubed with mud, and in a state of complete hysteria. She'd catapulted into his arms; he gripped her firmly, holding her lest she fly to pieces, which she looked very like doing.

"Frances. Frances! It's all right; I'm here. What's happened? Where's Jane?"

At her sister's name, she gave a wail that made his blood go cold and buried her face in his chest. He patted her back and, this failing to help, then shook her a little.

"Frances! Pull yourself together. Sweetheart," he added more gently, seeing her swimming, red-rimmed eyes and swollen face. She'd been weeping for a long time. "Tell me what's happened, so I can help you."

"You can't," she blubbered, and thumped her forehead hard against his chest, several times. "You can't, you can't, nobody can, you *can't*!"

"Well, we'll see about that." He looked around for someplace to sit her down, but there was nothing more solid than clumps of grass and spindly trees in sight. "Come on, it's getting dark. We need to get out of this place, at least." He set her firmly on her feet, took her arm, and compelled her to start walking, on the theory that one can't be hysterical and walk in a straight line at the same time.

In fact, this seemed to be the case. By the time he'd got her back to the camp followers' area, she was sniffling but no longer wailing, and she was looking where she was going. He bought her a cup of hot soup from a woman with a steaming cauldron and made her drink it, though a remnant thought of the fingers of birth-strangled babes made him forgo one for himself.

He handed back the empty cup and, seeing that Fanny was at least superficially calm now, towed her toward the hillock with trees, in search of a seat. She stiffened, though, as they approached, and pulled back with a little mew of fear.

Losing patience, he put a hand under her chin and made her meet his eyes.

"Frances," he said in a level tone. "Tell me what the devil is going on, and do it now. Words of one syllable, if you please."

"Jane," she said, and her eyes began to overflow again. She dashed at them with her cloak-covered forearm, though, and, with a visible effort, managed to tell him.

"It wass a cuwwy."

"A what? Oh, a cully, sorry. At the brothel, you mean. Yes?"

She nodded.

"He wass looking thu the gulls and s-saw J-Jane . . ." She gulped. "He wass a fwend of Captain Hahkness. He wass at da house when he—Captain Hahkness—died. He weckognized huh."

A ball of ice formed in William's entrails at her words.

"The devil he did," he said softly. "What did he do, Fanny?"

The man—a Major Jenkins, she said—had seized Jane by the arm and dragged her off, Fanny running after them. He had taken her all the way into the city, to a house with soldiers standing outside. They wouldn't let Fanny in, so she had stood outside in the street, terrified but determined not to leave, and after a time they had given up trying to drive her away.

The house with soldiers standing outside was very likely

Colonel Campbell's headquarters, William thought, beginning to feel sick. Presumably Jenkins had hauled Jane before some senior officer, if not Campbell himself, to denounce her for Harkness's murder.

Would they even bother giving her a trial? He doubted it. The city was under martial law; the army—or, rather, Lieutenant Colonel Campbell—did as it saw fit, and he doubted very much that Campbell would give a whore accused of murdering a soldier the benefit of any doubt.

"Where is she now?" He forced himself to go on sounding calm, though he felt anything but.

Fanny gulped and wiped her nose on her cloak again. At this point, it scarcely mattered, but by instinct he pulled his handkerchief from his sleeve and handed it to her.

"Dey took her to anovver house. On de edge of da city. Dere's a big tree dere, ousside. I tink dey'll hang her, Wiyum."

William was very much afraid they would. He swallowed the saliva that had collected in his mouth and patted Fanny's shoulder.

"I'll go and see what I can find out. Do you have friends here—someone to stay with?" He motioned at the mass of the encampment, where small fires were beginning to glow amidst the oncoming shades of night. She nodded, pressing her lips together to keep them from trembling.

"All right. Go and find them. I'll come in the morning—at first light. Meet me where I found you, all right?"

"Awright," she whispered, and laid a small white hand on his chest, just over his heart. "Sank you, Wiyum."

HIS ONLY CHANCE was to talk to Campbell. Fanny had told him the house where Jenkins had taken Jane was the big gray house north of Reynolds Square; that was the likeliest place to start.

He paused on the street to brush the worst of the dried mud and bits of vegetation off his cloak. He was only too well aware that he looked like exactly what he'd been pretending to be for the last three months: an unemployed laborer. On the other hand—

As he'd resigned his commission, he was no longer under

Campbell's authority. And no matter how he personally felt about the matter of his title, it was still his, by law. The Ninth Earl of Ellesmere drew himself up to his full height, squared his shoulders, and went to war.

Manner and speech got him past the sentries at the door. The servant who came to take his cloak stared at him in unmitigated dismay, but was afraid to throw him out, and vanished to find someone who would take the responsibility of dealing with him.

There was a dinner party going on; he could hear the clink of silver and china, the glugging of bottles being poured, and the muted rumble of conversation, punctuated by bursts of polite laughter. His hands were sweating; he wiped them unobtrusively on his breeches.

What the devil was he going to say? He'd tried to formulate some line of reasonable argument on his way, but everything seemed to fall to pieces the moment he thought of it. He'd have to say something, though. . . .

Then he heard a voice, raised in question, that made his heart skip a beat. Uncle Hal! He couldn't be mistaken; his uncle and his father both had light but penetrating voices, clear as cut crystal—and sharp as good Toledo steel when they wanted to be.

"Here, you!" He strode down the hall and grabbed a servitor coming out of the dining room with a platter of crab shells in his hands. "Give me that," he ordered, taking the platter from the man's hands, "go back in there, and tell the Duke of Pardloe his nephew would like a word."

The man goggled at him, mouth open, but didn't move. William repeated his request, adding "Please," but also adding a stare meant to indicate that, in the case of resistance, his next step would be to bash the man over the head with the platter. This worked, and the man turned like an automaton and marched back into the dining room—from which, in very short order, his uncle emerged, polished in dress and manner but clearly excited in countenance.

"William! What the devil are you doing with that?" He took the platter from William and shoved it carelessly under one of the gilt chairs ranged along the wall of the foyer. "What's happened? Have you found Ben?"

Christ, he hadn't thought of that. Naturally, Uncle Hal would assume . . . With a grimace, he shook his head.

"I haven't, Uncle, I'm sorry. I think I do know where his wife is, but—"

Hal's face underwent a couple of lightning shifts, from excitement to disappointment to outward calm.

"Good. Where are you staying? John and I will come and—"

"Papa's here, too?" William blurted, feeling like a fool. If he hadn't been so sensitive about his position and thus avoided anyone from the army, he would have learned that the 46th was part of Campbell's force in short order.

"Naturally," Hal said, with a touch of impatience. "Where else would he be?"

"With Dottie, looking for Ben's wife," William riposted smartly. "Is she here, too?"

"No." His uncle looked displeased, but not altogether displeased. "She discovered that she was with child, so John very properly brought her back to New York—and less properly consigned her to the care of her husband. She's presumably wherever Washington's troops are at the moment, unless that bloody Quaker's had the common sense to—"

"Oh, Pardloe." A stout officer in a lieutenant colonel's uniform and an ornate double-curled wig stood in the doorway, looking mildly surprised. "Thought you'd been taken ill, the way you dashed out." Despite the mild tone, there was an undercurrent in the man's voice that drove a two-penny nail into William's spine. This was Archibald Campbell, and from the visible frostiness with which he and Uncle Hal were viewing each other, Uncle Hal's value as a negotiator might not be what his nephew could hope.

Still, Uncle Hal could—and did—introduce William to Campbell, thus relieving him of the worry of producing adequate *bona fides*.

"Your servant, my lord," Campbell said, eyeing him suspiciously. He glanced over his shoulder, moving out of the way of a pair of servants carrying a massive wine cooler. "I fear that dinner has nearly concluded, but if you'd like, I'll have the servants provide a small supper for you in the office."

"No, sir, I thank you," William said, bowing—though the smell of food made his stomach gurgle. "I took the liberty of coming to speak with you about a . . . um . . . an urgent matter."

"Indeed." Campbell looked displeased and wasn't troubling to hide it. "It can't wait until the morning?"

"I don't know that it can, sir." He'd had a look at the big oak on the edge of town, which he thought must be the one Fanny meant. As Jane's corpse wasn't hanging from it, he assumed she was still being held prisoner in the house nearby. But that was no assurance that they didn't mean to execute her at dawn. The army was rather fond of executing prisoners at dawn; start the day off in the right frame of mind . . .

He got hold of his racing thoughts and bowed again.

"It concerns a young woman, sir, who I understand was arrested earlier today, upon suspicion of—of assault. I—"

"Assault?" Campbell's beetling brows shot up toward the furbelows of his wig. "She stabbed a man twenty-six times, then cut his throat in cold blood. If that's your notion of assault, I should hate to see—"

"Who is this young woman, my lord?" Uncle Hal put in, his tone formal and his face impassive.

"Her name is Jane," William began, and stopped, having no idea what her last name might be. "Uh . . . Jane . . ."

"Pocock, she says," put in Campbell. "She's a whore."

"A—" Hal cut his exclamation off one syllable too late. He narrowed his eyes at William.

"She is . . . under my protection," William said, as firmly as he could.

"Really?" drawled Campbell. He gave Uncle Hal a look of amused contempt, and Uncle Hal went white with suppressed fury—most of which was not suppressed at all in the look he turned on William.

"Yes. Really," said William, aware that this was not brilliant but unable to think of anything better. "I wish to speak on her behalf. Provide her with a solicitor," he added, rather wildly. "I'm sure she isn't guilty of the crime of which she's accused."

Campbell actually laughed, and William felt his ears burning with hot blood. He might have said something imprudent had Lord John not appeared at this juncture, as impeccably uniformed as his brother and looking mildly inquisitive.

"Ah, William," he said, as though he'd quite expected to see his son here. His eyes flicked rapidly from face to face, obviously drawing conclusions about the tenor of the conversation, if not its subject. With scarcely a pause, he stepped forward and embraced William warmly.

"You're here! I'm delighted to see you," he said, smiling up at William. "I have remarkable news! Will you excuse us for a moment, sir?" he said to Campbell, and, not waiting for an answer, gripped William by the elbow, yanked open the front door, towed him out onto the wide veranda, and closed the door firmly behind them.

"All right. Tell me what's going on," Lord John said, low-voiced. "And do it fast.

"Jesus," he said, when William had blurted out an only slightly confused account of the situation. He rubbed a hand slowly over his face, thinking, and repeated, "Jesus."

"Yes," William said, still upset but feeling some comfort at his father's presence. "I'd thought to talk to Campbell, but then when Uncle Hal was here, I hoped . . . but he and Campbell seem to be—"

"Yes, their relationship could best be described as one of cordial hatred," Lord John agreed. "Archibald Campbell is highly unlikely to do Hal any sort of favor, unless it was to escort him personally into the next southbound coach for hell." He blew out his breath and shook his head, as though to clear it of wine fumes.

"I don't know, William, I really don't. The girl—she *is* a whore?"

"Yes."

"Did she do it?"

"Yes."

"Oh, God." He looked helplessly at William for a moment, then squared his shoulders. "All right. I'll do what I can, but I don't promise anything. There's a tavern on the square, called Tudy's. Go there and wait—I rather think your presence will not be helpful in this discussion."

IT SEEMED FOREVER but must have been less than an hour when Lord John appeared at Tudy's. One look at his face told William that he hadn't been successful.

"I'm sorry," he said without preliminary, and sat down opposite William. He'd come out without his hat and brushed at the raindrops caught in his hair. "The girl—"

"Her name is Jane," William interrupted. It seemed important that he insist on that, not let everyone just dismiss her as "the whore."

"Miss Jane Eleanora Pocock," his father agreed, with a brief nod. "Apparently she not only committed the crime but has confessed to it. A signed confession, no less. I read it." He rubbed a hand tiredly over his face. "Her only objection was to the statement that she stabbed Harkness twenty-six times and cut his throat. According to her, she only stabbed him once before cutting his throat. People *will* exaggerate these things."

"That's what she told me." William's throat felt tight. His father darted a glance at him but chose not to say anything in response to this. What he thought was all too clear, though.

"She was trying to save her young sister from being defiled by the man," he said, urgently defensive. "And Harkness was a depraved sod who'd used her—Jane, I mean—abominably! I heard him talk about it. It would have turned your stomach to hear him."

"I daresay," Lord John agreed. "Dangerous clients are one of the hazards of that profession. But was there no recourse available to her other than a carving knife? Most brothels that cater to soldiers have some means of rescuing the whores from . . . excessive importunity. And Miss Pocock, from what Colonel Campbell tells me, is a—er—an—"

"Expensive piece. She is. Was."

William reached out blindly for the mug of beer he'd been ignoring, took a huge gulp, and coughed convulsively. His father watched with some sympathy.

William at last drew breath and sat, staring at his fists, clenched on the table.

"She hated him," he said at last, low-voiced. "And the madam wouldn't have kept her sister from him; he'd paid for her maidenhead."

Lord John sighed and covered one of William's fists with his hand, squeezing.

"Do you love the young woman, William?" he asked, very quietly. The tavern wasn't busy, but there were enough men drinking there that no one was noticing them.

William shook his head, helpless.

"I—tried to protect her. To save her from Harkness. I—I bought her for the night. I didn't stop to think that he'd come back—but of course he would," he finished bitterly. "I likely made things worse for her."

"There wouldn't have been a way of making them better, save marrying the girl or killing Harkness yourself," Lord John said dryly. "And I don't recommend murder as a way of settling difficult situations. It tends to lead to complications—but not nearly as many as marriage." He got up and went to the bar, returning with two steaming cups of hot rum punch.

"Drink that," he said, pushing one in front of William. "You look chilled through."

He was; he'd taken a table in a far corner, nowhere near the fire, and a fine, uncontrollable shiver was running through him, enough to ripple the surface of the punch when he wrapped his hand round the pewter cup. The punch was good, though made with preserved lemon peel, sweet, strong, and hot and made with good brandy as well as rum. He hadn't eaten anything in hours, and it warmed his stomach immediately.

They drank in silence—what was there to say? There was no way of saving Jane, bar some sort of physical assault, and he couldn't ask his father or uncle to join or support him in that sort of desperate caper. He didn't think they'd do it, for one thing. He believed in their considerable affection for him but knew quite well that they'd see it as their duty to prevent him committing folly that could well prove fatal.

"It won't have been entirely in vain, you know," Lord John said quietly. "She did save her sister."

William nodded, unable to speak. The thought of seeing Fanny in the morning, only to tell her—and then what? Must he stand beside her and watch Jane be hanged?

Lord John stood up and, without asking, went back to the bar for another pair of drinks. William looked at the gently steaming cup set before him and then at his father.

"You think you bloody know me, don't you?" he said, but with true affection in his voice.

"Yes, I do think that, William," said his father, in the same tone. "Drink your drink."

William smiled and, rising, clapped his father on the shoulder.

"Maybe you do, at that. I'll see you in the morning, Papa."

133

LAST RESORT

I WAS LYING IN bed beside Jamie, drowsily wondering on what grounds I could induce Mrs. Weisenheimer to collect her urine for me. She suffered from gallstones, for which the most effective herbal treatment I had was bearberry. Fortunately, Mr. Jameson had some of the dried leaf in stock. One had to be careful in using it, though, because it contained arbutin, which hydrolyzed to hydroquinone—a very effective urinary antiseptic, but dangerously toxic. On the other hand . . . it was an effective skin lightener, if applied topically.

I yawned and decided that it wasn't worth the bother of making Jamie come to the surgery and talk to Mrs. Weisenheimer in German about her urine. He'd do it if I asked, but I'd never hear the end of it.

I dismissed the idea and rolled over, cuddling against Jamie, who was peacefully asleep on his back, as usual, but who half-woke at my touch, patted me clumsily, curled round me, and fell soundly asleep again at once. Ninety seconds later, there was a knock at the door.

"Ifrinn!" Jamie shot bolt upright, rubbed a hand roughly over his face, and threw back the covers. Groaning, I followed suit less athletically, crawling out of bed and groping blindly for my knitted slippers.

"Let me go. It's probably for me." At this hour of the night, a knock at the door was more likely someone with a medical emergency than one involving salt fish or horses, but given the military occupation of the city, one never knew.

One certainly hadn't anticipated opening the door to find William standing on the other side of it, looking pale and feral.

"Is Mr. Fraser at home?" he said tersely. "I need his help."

FRASER HAD DRESSED at once, taken up a belt with a sheathed dirk and a leather bag upon it, and fastened this round his waist without question. He was wearing Highland dress, William saw, a much-worn, faded plaid. He gathered up a fold of it around his shoulders, nodding toward the door.

"We'd best go down to my wife's surgery," he said softly, nodding toward the thin wall, the laths clearly visible through its plaster. "Ye can tell me there what's to do."

William followed him through the rain-slicked streets, water like cold tears on his cheeks. Inside, he felt parched and dry, cracked leather wrapped around a core of solid terror. Fraser didn't speak on the way but clutched him once by the elbow, pushing him into a narrow space between two buildings, just as an army patrol came round the corner. He pressed hard against the wall, shoulder to shoulder with Fraser, and felt the man's denseness and warmth as a shock.

In the back of his mind was the memory of having been small and lost in the fog on the fells of the Lake District. Cold and terrified, he'd fallen into a rocky hollow and lain there, frozen, hearing ghosts in the mist. And then the overwhelming relief of Mac's finding him, of the enveloping warmth of the groom's arms.

He shoved the memory impatiently aside, but a lingering sense of something that wasn't quite hope remained when the last of the boots trampled out of hearing and Fraser slid from their hiding place, beckoning him to follow.

The small surgery was cold and dark, smelling of herbs and medicines and old blood. There was a sweetish smell, too, strange but familiar, and after a moment's disorientation, he realized that it must be ether; he'd smelled it on Mother Claire and Denzell Hunter when they'd operated on his cousin Henry.

Fraser had locked the door behind them and found a candlestick in the cupboard. He handed this to William, took a tinderbox from the same cupboard, and set the candle alight with a brisk efficiency. The wavering light shone up into his face, and the boldness of his features sprang into view: long straight nose and heavy brows, broad cheekbones and the fine deep modeling of jaw and temple. It was damnably queer to see the resemblance so marked and so close, but at the moment William actually found it an odd comfort.

Fraser set the candlestick on the table and motioned William to one of the two stools, taking the other.

"Tell me, then," he said calmly. "It's safe here; no one will hear. I gather it's a dangerous matter?"

"Life and death," William said, and, with a deep breath, began.

Fraser listened with complete attention, his eyes fixed intently on William's face as he talked. When he had finished, there was a moment of silence. Then Fraser nodded once, as if to himself.

"This young woman," he said. "May I know what she is to you?"

William hesitated, not knowing what to say. What *was* Jane to him? Not a friend, nor yet a lover. And yet . . .

"She—I took her and her sister under my protection," he said. "When they left Philadelphia with the army."

Fraser nodded as though this was a perfectly adequate explanation of the situation.

"D'ye know that your uncle and his regiment are with the occupying army? That he's here, I mean?"

"Yes. I spoke with my—with Lord John and Pardloe. They aren't able to help. I—have resigned my commission," he felt compelled to add. "That hasn't anything to do with why they can't help, only that I'm not subject any longer to military command myself."

"Aye, I saw ye weren't in uniform," he said. He drummed the fingers of his right hand briefly on the tabletop, and William saw with surprise that the ring finger was missing, a thick scar down the back of the hand. Fraser saw him notice.

"Saratoga," he said, with the flicker of something that might have been a smile in other circumstances.

William felt a small shock at the word, things unnoticed at the time suddenly returning to him. Himself kneeling through the night beside Brigadier Simon Fraser's deathbed and a tall man on the other side, a white bandage on his hand, leaning down from the shadows to say something softly in the Scottish tongue to the brigadier, who replied in the same language.

"The brigadier," he said, and stopped abruptly.

"My kinsman," Fraser said. He delicately forbore to add,

"And yours," but William made that connection easily. He felt it as a distant echo of grief, a pebble dropped in water, but that could wait.

"Is the young woman's life worth yours?" Fraser asked. "Because I think that consideration is likely what lies behind your—your other kinsmen's"—the corner of his mouth twitched, though William couldn't tell whether with humor or distaste—"failure to help ye."

William felt hot blood rise in his face, anger supplanting desperation.

"They didn't *fail* me. They couldn't help. Are you saying that you will not help me, either, sir? Or can't? Are you afraid of the venture?"

Fraser gave him a quelling look; William registered this but didn't care. He was on his feet, fists clenched.

"Don't bother, then. I'll do it myself."

"If ye thought ye could, ye'd never have come to me, lad," Fraser said evenly.

"Don't you call me 'lad,' you, you—" William choked off the epithet, not out of prudence but out of inability to choose among the several that sprang at once to his mind.

"Sit down," Fraser said, not raising his voice but infusing it with an air of command that made it unthinkable—or at least uncomfortable—to disobey. William glared at him. His chest was heaving and yet he couldn't draw enough breath to speak. He didn't sit down, but he did uncurl his fists and stand still. At last he managed a jerky nod. Fraser drew a long, visible breath and let it out slowly, white in the chill of the dark little room.

"All right, then. Tell me where she is and what ye ken of the physical situation." He glanced at the shuttered window, where oozing damp showed black between the slats as the rain seeped through. "The night's not long enough."

THEY WENT TO the warehouse where Fraser worked, down by the river. Fraser left William outside to keep watch, unlocked a man door at the side, and slid through it with no sound, reappearing a few minutes later dressed in rough breeches and a shirt that didn't fit him, carrying a small burlap bag and two large black kerchiefs. He handed one of these to William and, folding the other diagonally, tied it round his face, covering nose and mouth.

"Is this truly necessary?" William tied on his own kerchief but felt slightly ridiculous, as though dressing up for some bizarre pantomime.

"Ye can go without if ye like," Fraser advised him, taking a knitted wool cap out of the bag, tucking his hair up under it, and then pulling it down over his eyebrows. "I canna risk being recognized."

"If you think the risk too great—" William began, an edge in his voice, but Fraser stopped him, gripping his arm.

"Ye've a claim to my help," he said, voice low and brusque. "For any venture ye deem worthy. But I've a family who have a claim to my protection. I canna leave them to starve if I'm taken."

William had no chance to reply to this; Fraser had locked the door and was already walking off, beckoning impatiently. He did think about it, though, following the Scot through the mist that rose knee-high in the streets. It had stopped raining; that was one thing in their favor.

"For any venture ye deem worthy." Not a word about Jane's being a whore or about her being a confessed murderess. Perhaps it was that Fraser himself was a criminal and felt some sympathy on that account.

Or maybe it's just that he's willing to take my word that I have to do it. And willing to take the devil of a risk to help me.

But such thoughts could do no good now, and he put them out of his mind. They hurried on, soft-footed and faceless, through the empty squares of Savannah, toward the house by the hanging tree.

"I DINNA SUPPOSE ye ken which room is hers?" Jamie murmured to William. They were loitering under the big live oak, concealed not only by its shadows but by the long beards of Spanish moss that hung from its branches and the mist that drifted under them.

"No."

"Wait here." Fraser disappeared in that unnerving catlike

way of his. Left to his own devices and further unnerved by the silence, William thought to explore the contents of the bag Fraser had left on the ground. These proved to be several sheets of paper and a stoppered vial of what—un-stoppered—proved to be treacle.

He was still puzzling over that when Fraser was back, as suddenly as he'd disappeared.

"There's no but one guard on the house, at the front," he said, moving close enough to whisper into William's ear. "And all the windows are dark, save one upstairs. There's a single candle burning; it must be hers."

"Why do you think that?" William whispered back, startled.

Fraser hesitated for a moment, but then said, even more quietly, "I once spent a night expecting to be hanged the next morning. I wouldna have spent it in darkness, given the choice. Come on."

It was a two-story house and, while fairly large, simply built. Two rooms on the upper floor at the back, two at the front. The shutters of the upper windows were open, and the glow of a candle flickered in the right-hand room at the back. Fraser insisted on circling the house—at a cautious distance, darting from bush to tree to bush—to be sure of the guard's position. The man, armed with a musket slung across his back, was on the veranda that ran across the front of the house. Judging from his build, he was young, probably younger than William. And by his posture, which was careless in the extreme, he wasn't expecting any trouble.

"I don't suppose they thought a whore would have any friends," William said under his breath, getting a brief Scottish grunt in return. Fraser beckoned and led him round the back of the house.

They passed a window that likely belonged to the kitchen; there were no curtains, and he could see the faint light of a smothered hearth deep inside, just visible through the shutters. There'd be a risk that one or more slaves or servants slept in the kitchen, though—and he was pleased to see that Fraser appeared to be going on that assumption. They moved around the next corner of the house, as quietly as possible.

Fraser pressed his ear to the shutters of a large window but appeared to hear nothing. He fitted the blade of his stout knife between the shutters and, with some difficulty, levered the bolt up out of its brackets. He gestured to William to come and lean hard on the shutter, to keep the bolt from falling suddenly, and with a joint effort composed of dumb-show and frantic gestures—that would likely have seemed comic to anyone not involved in performing it—they succeeded in getting the bloody shutters open without too much racket.

The window behind was curtained—all to the good—but a casement, with a thumb latch that wouldn't yield to Jamie's knife. The big Scot was sweating; he pulled his cap off for a moment to wipe his brow, then put it back on, and, taking the treacle from the bag, he un-stoppered the bottle and poured some of the sticky syrup into his hand. This he smeared over a pane of the casement and, taking a sheet of paper, pasted it onto the glass.

William could make no sense of this proceeding, but Fraser drew back his arm and struck the glass a sharp buffet with his fist. It broke with no more than a small cracking noise, and the shattered pieces were removed easily, stuck to the treacled paper.

"Where did you learn that one?" William whispered, deeply impressed, and heard a small chuckle of satisfaction from behind Fraser's mask.

"My daughter told me about it," he whispered in reply, laying glass and paper on the ground. "She read it in a book."

"That's—" William stopped abruptly, and so did his heart. He'd forgotten. "Your . . . daughter. You mean—I have a sister?"

"Aye," Fraser said briefly. "Ye've met her. Come on." He reached through the hole in the glass, undid the catch, and pulled on the window frame. The window swung open, with an unexpected loud screech of unoiled hinges.

"Shit!" William said, under his breath.

Fraser had said something that William assumed was the equivalent sentiment in Gaelic, but he didn't waste time. He shoved William back against the wall and, with a hissed "Stay there!", faded into the night.

William plastered himself against the wall, heart hammering. He could hear rapid footsteps clattering down the wooden steps from the veranda, then muffled thumps on the damp ground.

"Who's there?" the guard shouted, as he rounded the house. Seeing William, he shouldered his musket and took aim. And

Fraser came out of the dark mist like an angry ghost, grabbed the boy by the shoulder, and laid him out with a rock slammed into the back of his skull.

"Hurry," he said, low-voiced, jerking his chin toward the open window as he lowered the guard's limp body to the ground. William wasted no time but heaved himself into the house, squirming across the sill to land almost soundlessly, squatting on the carpet of what must be a parlor, to judge from the dim outlines of the furniture. An unseen clock ticked accusingly, somewhere in the darkness.

Fraser hoisted himself into the open window frame and paused for a moment, listening. But there was no sound in the house save the ticking clock, and he hopped lightly down inside.

"Ye dinna ken whose house this is?" he whispered to William, looking round.

William shook his head. It must be an officer's billet, but he had no idea who the officer might be—probably the major in charge of disciplinary matters. Presumably Campbell had lodged Jane here as an alternative to putting her in the camp's stockade. Thoughtful of him.

His eyes had adapted quickly; there was a dark oblong a few feet away—the door. Fraser saw it, too; his hand rested on William's back for an instant, pushing him toward it.

There was an oval lozenge of glass set into the front door, and enough light came through it to show them the painted canvas floorcloth running down the hall, its diamond pattern black in the colorless light. Near the door, a pool of shadow hid the foot of the staircase, and within seconds they were creeping up the stairs, as quickly and as quietly as two very large men in a hurry could go.

"This way." William was in the lead; he motioned to Fraser as he turned to the left. The blood was beating in his head, and he could scarcely breathe. He wanted to tear off the clinging mask and gulp air, but not yet . . . not yet.

Jane. Had she heard the guard call out? If she was awake, she must have heard them on the stair.

The landing was windowless and very dark, but there was a faint glow of candlelight under Jane's door—he hoped to God it was Jane's door. Running a hand down the doorframe, he felt the knob, and his hand closed round it. It was locked, naturally—but in trying the knob, the heel of his hand brushed the key, still in the lock.

Fraser was behind him; he could hear the man's breathing. Behind the door of the next room, someone was snoring in a reassuringly regular sort of way. So long as the guard stayed out long enough . . .

"Jane," he whispered as loudly as he dared, putting his lips to the crack between the door and its jamb. "Jane! It's me, William. Be quiet!"

He thought he heard a swift intake of breath from the other side of the door, though it might have been only the sound of his own blood racing in his ears. With infinite care, he pulled the door toward him and turned the key.

The candle was standing on a small bureau, its flame flickering wildly in the draft from the open door. There was a strong smell of beer; a broken bottle lay on the floor, brown glass a-glitter in the wavering light. The bed was rumpled, bedclothes hanging half off the mattress . . . Where was Jane? He whirled, expecting to see her cowering in the corner, frightened by his entrance.

He saw her hand first. She was lying on the floor by the bed, beside the broken bottle, her hand flung out, white and half open as though in supplication.

"A Dhia," Fraser whispered behind him, and now he could smell the cut-steel reek of blood, mingled with beer.

He didn't remember falling on his knees or lifting her up in his arms. She was heavy, limp and awkward, all the grace and heat of her gone and her cheek cold to his hand. Only her hair was still Jane, shining in the candlelight, soft against his mouth.

"Here, *a bhalaich.*" A hand touched his shoulder, and he turned without thought.

Fraser had pulled the mask down around his neck, and his face was serious, intent. "We havena much time," he said softly.

They didn't speak. They straightened the bedclothes in silence, put a clean quilt over the worst of the blood, and laid her on it. William wetted his kerchief from the ewer and cleaned the spatters of blood from her face and hands. He hesitated for a moment, then tore the kerchief violently in two and bandaged her torn wrists, then crossed her hands on her breast.

Jamie Fraser was by him then, with a fugitive gleam from the blade of his knife.

"For her sister," he said, and, bending, cut a lock of the shining chestnut hair. He put this into the pocket of the ragged breeches and went quietly out. William heard the brief creak of his footsteps on the stair and understood that he had been left to make his farewell in privacy.

He looked upon her face by candlelight for the first time, and the last. He felt emptied, hollow as a gutted deer. With no notion what to say, he touched one black-bound hand and spoke the truth, in a voice too low for any but the dead to hear.

"I wanted to save you, Jane. Forgive me."

134

LAST RITES

JAMIE CAME HOME just before dawn, white-faced and chilled to the bone. I wasn't asleep. I hadn't slept since he'd left with William, and when I heard his step on the creaking stairs, I scooped hot water from the ever-simmering cauldron into the wooden mug I had ready, half filled with cheap whisky and a spoonful of honey. I'd thought he'd need it, but I hadn't had any idea how much.

"The lassie had cut her wrists wi' a broken bottle," he said, crouching on a stool by the fire, a quilt draped over his shoulders and the warm mug cupped between his big hands. He couldn't stop shivering.

"God rest her soul and forgive her the sin of despair." He closed his eyes and shook his head violently, as though to dispel his memory of what he'd seen in that candlelit room. "Oh, Jesus, my poor lad."

I'd made him go to bed and crawled in to warm him with my body, but I hadn't slept then, either. I didn't feel the need of it. There were things that would need to be done when the day came; I could feel them waiting, a patient throng. William. The dead girl. And Jamie had said something about the girl's young sister. . . . But for the moment, time was still, balanced on the cusp of night. I lay beside Jamie and listened to him breathe. For the moment, that was enough.

BUT THE SUN rose, as it always did.

I was stirring the breakfast porridge when William appeared, bringing with him a mud-smeared young girl who looked like a lightning-blasted tree. William didn't look any better but seemed less likely to fall to bits.

"This is Frances," he said, in a low, hoarse voice, putting a large paw on her shoulder. "These are Mr. and Mrs. Fraser, Fanny." She was so fine-boned that I half-expected her to stagger under the weight of his hand, but she didn't. After a stunned moment, she realized the introduction and gave a jerky nod.

"Sit down, sweetheart," I said, smiling at her. "The porridge is almost ready, and there's toasted bread with honey."

She stared at me, blinking dully. Her eyes were red and swollen, her hair lank under a tattered cap. I thought she was so shocked that she was unable to comprehend anything. William looked as though someone had hit him on the head, stunning him like an ox bound for slaughter. I looked uncertainly at Jamie, not knowing what to do for either of them. He glanced from one to the other, then rose and quietly took the girl into his arms.

"There, *a nighean,*" he said quietly, patting her back. His eyes met Willie's and I saw something pass between them—a question asked and answered. Jamie nodded. "I'll care for her," he said.

"Thank you. She . . . Jane," William said with difficulty. "I want to—to bury her. Decently. But I think I can't . . . claim her."

"Aye," Jamie said. "We'll see to it. Go and do whatever ye need to do. Come back when ye can."

William stood a moment longer, red-rimmed eyes fixed on

the girl's back, then gave me an abrupt bow and left. At the sound of his departing footsteps, Frances gave a small, despairing howl, like an orphaned puppy. Jamie wrapped her closer in his arms, holding her snug against his chest.

"It will be all right, *a nighean,*" he said softly, though his eyes were fixed on the door through which William had gone. "Ye're at home now."

I DIDN'T REALIZE that Fanny was tongue-tied, until I took her to see Colonel Campbell. She hadn't spoken at all until that point, merely shaking her head yes or no, making small motions of refusal or gratitude.

"You kilt my thither!" she said loudly, when Campbell rose from his desk to greet us. He blinked and sat back down.

"I doubt it," he said, eyeing her warily. She wasn't crying, but her face was blotched and swollen, as if someone had slapped her repeatedly. She stood very straight, though, small fists clenched, and glared at him. He looked at me. I shrugged slightly.

"The'th *dead,*" Fanny said. "The wath your prithoner!"

Campbell steepled his hands and cleared his throat.

"May I ask who you are, child? And who your sister is?"

"Her name is Frances Pocock," I put in hastily. "Her sister was Jane Pocock, who I understand . . . died last night, while in your custody. She would like to claim her sister's body, for burial."

Campbell gave me a bleak look.

"I see that news travels fast. And you are, madam?"

"A friend of the family," I said, as firmly as possible. "My name is Mrs. James Fraser."

His face shifted a little; he'd heard the name. That probably wasn't a good thing.

"Mrs. Fraser," he said slowly. "I've heard of you. You dispense pox cures to the city's whores, do you not?"

"Among . . . other things, yes," I said, rather taken aback by this description of my medical practice. Still, it seemed to offer him a logical connection between Fanny and me, for he glanced from one of us to the other, nodding to himself.

"Well," he said slowly. "I don't know where the—er—the body has been—"

"Don't oo call my thither 'the *body*'!" Fanny shouted. "Her name ith Jane!"

Commanders, as a rule, aren't used to being shouted at, and Campbell appeared to be no exception. His square face flushed and he put his hands flat on the desk, preparing to rise. Before he got the seat of his breeches clear of his chair, though, his aide came in and coughed discreetly.

"I beg pardon, sir; Lieutenant Colonel Lord John Grey wishes to see you."

"Does he, indeed." This didn't seem to be welcome news to Campbell, but it was to me.

"You're clearly busy, sir," I said quickly, seizing Fanny by the arm. "We'll come back later." And without waiting to be dismissed, I more or less dragged her out of the office.

Sure enough, John was standing in the anteroom, in full uniform. His face was calmly pleasant and I saw that he was in diplomatic mode, but his expression altered the instant he saw me.

"What are you doing here?" he blurted. "And"—glancing at Fanny—"who the devil is this?"

"Do you know about Jane?" I said, grabbing him by the sleeve. "What happened to her last night?"

"Yes, I—"

"We want to claim her body, for burial. Can you help?"

He detached my hand, courteously, and brushed his sleeve.

"I can, yes. I'm here upon the same errand. I'll send word—"

"We'll wait for you," I said hastily, seeing the aide frown in my direction. "Outside. Come, Fanny!"

Outside, we found a place to wait on an ornamental bench set in the formal front garden. Even in winter, it was a pleasant spot, with several palmetto trees popping out of the shrubbery like so many Japanese parasols, and even the presence of a number of soldiers coming and going didn't much impair the sense of gracious peace. Fanny, though, was in no mood for peace.

"Who wath *that*?" she demanded, twisting to look back at the house. "What doth he want wif Jane?"

"Ah . . . that's William's father," I said carefully. "Lord John Grey is his name. I imagine William asked him to come."

Fanny blinked for a moment, then turned a remarkably penetrating pair of brown eyes on me, red-rimmed and bloodshot but decidedly intelligent.

"He doethn't *wook* wike Wiyum," she said. "Mither Fwather wooks a wot wike Wiyum."

I looked back at her for a moment.

"Really?" I said. "I hadn't noticed that. Do you mind not talking for a bit, Fanny? I need to think."

JOHN CAME OUT about ten minutes later. He paused on the steps, looking around, and I waved. He came down to where we sat and at once bowed very formally to Fanny.

"Your servant, Miss Frances," he said. "I understand from Colonel Campbell that you are the sister of Miss Pocock; please allow me to offer my deepest condolences."

He spoke very simply and honestly, and Fanny's eyes welled up with tears.

"Can I have huh?" she said softly. "Pwease?"

Heedless of his immaculate breeches, he knelt on the ground in front of her and took her hand in his.

"Yes, sweetheart," he said, just as softly. "Of course you can." He patted her hand. "Will you wait here, just for a moment, while I speak with Mrs. Fraser?" He stood and, as an afterthought, pulled a large snowy handkerchief out of his sleeve and handed it to her with another small bow.

"Poor child," he said, taking my hand and tucking it into the curve of his elbow. "Or children—the other girl can't have been more than seventeen." We walked for a few paces, down a small brick walk between empty flower beds, until we were safely out of earshot of both street and house. "I take it that William sought Jamie's help. I thought he might, though I hoped he wouldn't, for both their sakes."

His face was shadowed, and there were blue smudges under his eyes; evidently he'd had a disturbed night, too.

"Where *is* William, do you know?" I asked.

"I don't. He said he had an errand outside the city but would return tonight." He glanced over his shoulder at the house. "I've arranged for . . . Jane . . . to be appropriately tended. She cannot be buried in a churchyard, of course—"

"Of course," I murmured, angry at the thought. He noticed but cleared his throat and went on.

"I know a family with a small private çemetery. I believe I can make arrangement for a quiet burial. Quickly, of course; tomorrow, very early?"

I nodded, getting a grip on myself. It wasn't his fault.

"You've been very good," I said. Worry and the lack of sleep were catching up with me; things seemed oddly non-dimensional, as though trees and people and garden furniture were merely pasted onto a painted backdrop. I shook my head to clear it, though; there were important things to be said.

"I have to tell you something," I said. "I wish I didn't, but there it is. Ezekiel Richardson came to my surgery the other day."

"The devil he did." John had stiffened at the name. "He's not with the army here, surely? I would have—"

"Yes, but not with *your* army." I told him, as briefly as I could, what Richardson now was—or, rather, was revealed to be; God only knew how long he'd been a Rebel spy—and what his intentions were toward Hal and the Grey family in general.

John listened, his face quietly intent, though the corner of his mouth twitched when I described Richardson's plan to influence Hal's political actions.

"Yes, I know," I said dryly, seeing that. "I don't suppose he's ever actually *met* Hal. But the important thing . . ." I hesitated, but he had to know.

"He knows about you," I said. "What you . . . are. I mean that you—"

"What I am," he repeated, expressionless. His eyes had been fastened on my face to this point; now he looked away. "I see." He took a deep breath and let it out slowly.

John was a distinguished soldier and an honorable gentleman, member of an ancient noble family. He was also a homosexual, in a time when that particular attribute was a capital offense. For that knowledge to be in the hands of a man who meant ill to him and his family . . . I wasn't under any illusions about what I'd just done—with three words, I'd shown him that he was standing on a very narrow tightrope over a very deep pit, with Richardson holding the end of the rope.

"I'm sorry, John," I said, very softly. I touched his arm, and he laid his hand briefly over mine, squeezed it gently, and smiled.

"Thank you." He stared at the brick paving under his feet for a moment, then looked up. "Do you know how he came by the—information?" He spoke calmly, but a nerve was jumping just under his injured eye, a tiny twitch. I wanted to put my finger on it, still it. But there was nothing I could do.

"No." I looked back at the distant bench. Fanny was still there, a small, desolate figure, head bent. I turned my gaze back to John; his brow was creased, thinking.

"One last thing. Hal's daughter-in-law, the young woman with the odd name—"

"Amaranthus," he interrupted, and smiled wryly. "Yes, what about her? Don't tell me that Ezekiel Richardson invented her for his own purposes."

"I wouldn't put it past him, but probably not." I told him what I'd learned from Mr. Jameson.

"I told William day before yesterday," I said. "But what with everything"—I waved a hand, encompassing Fanny, Jane, Colonel Campbell, and a few other things—"I doubt he's had time to go to Saperville to look for her. You don't suppose that's the errand he spoke of, do you?" I asked, struck by the thought.

"God knows." He rubbed a hand over his face, then straightened. "I must go. I'll have to tell Hal a few things. Not . . . that, I don't think," he said, seeing my face. "But obviously there are things he needs to know, and know quickly. God bless you, my dear. I'll send word about tomorrow." He took my hand, kissed it very gently, and let go.

I watched him walk away, his back very straight, the scarlet of his coat bright as blood against the grays and faded greens of the winter garden.

WE BURIED JANE on the morning of a dull, cold day. The sky was sodden with low gray clouds, and a raw wind blew in from the sea. It was a small private burying ground, belonging to a large house that stood outside the city.

All of us came with Fanny: Rachel and Ian, Jenny, Fergus

and Marsali—even the girls and Germain. I worried a bit; they couldn't help but feel the echoes of Henri-Christian's death. But death was a fact of life and a common one, and while they stood solemn and pale amongst the adults, they were composed. Fanny was not so much composed as completely numb, I thought; she'd wept all the tears her small body could hold and was white and stiff as a bleached stick.

John came, dressed in his uniform (in case anyone became inquisitive and tried to disturb us, he explained to me in an undertone). The coffin-maker had had only adult coffins to hand; Jane's shrouded body looked so like a chrysalis, I half-expected to hear a dry rattling sound when the men picked it up. Fanny had declined to look upon her sister's face one last time, and I thought that was as well.

There was no priest or minister; she was a suicide, and this was ground hallowed only by respect. When the last of the dirt had been shoveled in, we stood quiet, waiting, the harsh wind flurrying our hair and garments.

Jamie took a deep breath and a step to the head of the grave. He spoke the Gaelic prayer called the Death Dirge, but in English, for the sake of Fanny and Lord John.

Thou goest home this night to thy home of winter,
To thy home of autumn, of spring, and of summer;
Thou goest home this night to thy perpetual home,
To thine eternal bed, to thine eternal slumber.

Sleep thou, sleep, and away with thy sorrow,
Sleep thou, sleep, and away with thy sorrow,
Sleep thou, sleep, and away with thy sorrow,
Sleep, thou beloved, in the Rock of the fold.

The shade of death lies upon thy face, beloved,
But the Jesus of grace has His hand round about thee;
In nearness to the Trinity farewell to thy pains,
Christ stands before thee and peace is in His mind.

Jenny, Ian, Fergus, and Marsali joined in, murmuring the final verse with him.

Sleep, O sleep in the calm of all calm,
Sleep, O sleep in the guidance of guidance,
Sleep, O sleep in the love of all loves,
Sleep, O beloved, in the Lord of life,
Sleep, O beloved, in the God of life!

It wasn't until we turned to go that I saw William. He was standing just outside the wrought-iron fence that enclosed the burying ground, tall and somber in a dark cloak, the wind stirring the dark tail of his hair. He was holding the reins of a very large mare with a back as broad as a barn door. As I came out of the burying ground, holding Fanny's hand, he came toward us, the horse obligingly following him.

"This is Miranda," he said to Fanny. His face was white and carved with grief, but his voice was steady. "She's yours now. You'll need her." He took Fanny's limp hand, put the reins into it, and closed her fingers over them. Then he looked at me, wisps of hair blowing across his face. "Will you look after her, Mother Claire?"

"Of course we will," I said, my throat tight. "Where are you going, William?"

He smiled then, very faintly.

"It doesn't matter," he said, and walked away.

Fanny was staring up at Miranda in complete incomprehension. I gently took the reins from her, patted the horse's jaw, and turned to find Jamie. He was just inside the fence, talking with Marsali; the others had come out already and were standing in a cold little cluster, Ian and Fergus talking with Lord John, while Jenny shepherded the children—all of whom were staring at Fanny.

Jamie was frowning a little, but at last he nodded and, bending forward, kissed Marsali on the forehead and came out. He raised one eyebrow when he saw Miranda, and I explained.

"Aye, well," he said, with a glance at Fanny. "What's one more?" There was an odd tone to his voice, and I looked at him in inquiry.

"Marsali asked me if we'd take Germain," he said, drawing Fanny in against him in a sheltering hug, as if this were a common thing.

"Really?" I glanced over my shoulder at the rest of the family. "Why?" We had all discussed the matter at some length the night before and concluded that we wouldn't wait until spring to leave Savannah. With the city occupied, there was no chance of Fergus and Marsali resuming publication of their newspaper, and with Colonel Richardson lurking behind the scenes, the place was beginning to seem distinctly dangerous.

We would all travel together to Charleston, get Fergus and Marsali established there, and then the rest of us would go on north to Wilmington, where we would begin to equip ourselves for the trip into the mountains when the snows began to melt in March.

"Ye told them, Sassenach," Jamie said, scratching Miranda's forelock with his free hand. "What the war would be, and how long it would last. Germain's of an age when he'll be out and in the thick o' things. Marsali's worrit that he'll come to harm, loose in a city where the sorts of things happen that *do* happen in wartime. God knows the mountains may be no safer"—he grimaced, obviously recalling a few incidents that had taken place there—"but on the whole, he's likely better off not being in a place where he could be conscripted by the militia or pressed into the British navy."

I looked down the gravel path that led to the house; Germain had drifted away from his mother, grandmother, Rachel, and his sisters and joined Ian and Fergus in conversation with Lord John.

"Aye, he kens he's a man," Jamie said dryly, following the direction of my gaze. "Come along, *a leannan,*" he said to Fanny. "It's time we all had breakfast."

135

AMARANTHUS

Saperville
January 15, 1779

SAPERVILLE WAS DIFFICULT to find but, once found, small enough that it was a matter of only three inquiries to discover the residence of a widow named Grey.

"Over there." Hal reined up, nodding toward a house that stood a hundred yards back from the road in the shade of an enormous magnolia tree. He was being casual, but John could see the muscle twitching in his brother's jaw.

"Well . . . I suppose we just go up and knock, then." He turned his own horse's head in at the rutted lane, taking stock of the place as they walked toward it. It was a rather shabby house, the front veranda sagging at one corner where its foundation had given way, and half its few windows boarded over. Still, the place was occupied; the chimney was smoking fitfully, in a way suggesting that it hadn't been recently swept.

The door was opened to them by a slattern. A white woman, but one clothed in a stained wrapper and felt slippers, with wary eyes and a sourly downturned mouth whose corners showed the stains of tobacco chewing.

"Is Mrs. Grey at home?" Hal inquired politely.

"Nobody o' that name here," the woman said, and made to shut the door, this action being prevented by Hal's boot.

"We were directed to this address, madam," Hal said, the politeness diminishing markedly. "Be so good as to inform Mrs. Grey that she has visitors, please."

The woman's eyes narrowed.

"And who in tarnation are you, Mr. Fancy Pants?"

John's estimation of the woman's nerve rose considerably at this, but he thought he ought to intervene before Hal started wheezing.

"This is His Grace the Duke of Pardloe, madam," he said, with maximum politeness. Her face altered at once, though not for the better. Her jaw hardened, but a predatory gleam came into her eye.

"Elle connaît votre nom," he said to Hal. *She knows your name.*

"I know that," his brother snapped. "Madam—"

Whatever he would have said was interrupted by the sudden shrieking of a baby, somewhere upstairs.

"I beg your pardon, madam," Lord John said politely to the slattern, and, seizing her by the elbows, walked her backward into the house, whirled her round, and pushed her into the kitchen. There was a pantry, and he shoved her into this cubbyhole, slammed the door upon her, and, grabbing a bread knife from the table, thrust it through the hasp of the latch as a makeshift bolt.

Hal had meanwhile disappeared upstairs, making enough noise for a company of cavalry. John galloped after him, and by the time he reached the head of the stair, his brother was busily engaged in trying to break down the door of a room from which came the siren shrieks of a baby and the even louder cries of what was probably the baby's mother.

It was a good, solid door; Hal flung himself at it shoulder-first and rebounded as though made of India rubber. Barely pausing, he raised his foot and slammed the flat of his boot sole against the panel, which obligingly splintered but didn't break inward.

Wiping his face on his sleeve, he eyed the door and, catching the flicker of movement through the splintered paneling, called out, "Young woman! We have come to rescue you! Stand well away from the door!

"Pistol, please," he said, turning to John with his hand out.

"I'll do it," John said, resigned. "You haven't any practice with doorknobs."

Whereupon, with an air of assumed casualness, he drew the pistol from his belt, aimed carefully, and shot the doorknob to pieces. The boom of the gun evidently startled the room's inhabitants, for a dead silence fell. He gently pushed the stem of the shattered knob through the door; the remnants of the knob thunked to the floor on the other side, and he pushed the door cautiously open.

Hal, nodding his thanks, stepped forward through the wisps of smoke.

It was a small room, rather grimy, and furnished with no more than a bedstead, dresser, stool, and washstand. The stool was particularly noticeable, as it was being brandished by a wild-eyed young woman, clutching a baby to her breast with her other hand.

An ammoniac reek came from a basket in the corner, piled with dirty clouts; a folded quilt in a pulled-out drawer showed where the baby had been sleeping, and the young woman was less kempt than her mother would have liked to see, her cap askew and her pinny stained. Hal disregarded all matters of circumstance and bowed to her.

"Do I address Miss Amaranthus Cowden?" he said politely. "Or is it Mrs. Grey?"

John gave his brother a disparaging look and turned a cordial smile on the young woman.

"*Viscountess* Grey," he said, and made a leg in courtly style. "Your most humble servant, Lady Grey."

The young woman looked wildly from one man to the other, stool still raised, clearly unable to make head or tail of this invasion, and finally settled on John as the best—if still dubious—source of information.

"Who *are* you?" she asked, pressing her back against the wall. "Hush, darling." For the baby, recovered from shock, had decided to grizzle.

John cleared his throat.

"Well . . . this is Harold, Duke of Pardloe, and I am his brother, Lord John Grey. If our information is correct, I believe we are, respectively, your father-in-law and your uncle by marriage. And, after all," he remarked, turning to Hal, "how many people in the colonies do you think there could possibly *be* named Amaranthus Cowden?"

"She hasn't yet said she *is* Amaranthus Cowden," Hal pointed out. He did, however, smile at the young woman, who reacted as most women did, staring at him with her mouth slightly open.

"May I?" John reached forward and took the stool gently

from her unresisting hand, setting it on the floor and gesturing her to take a seat. "What sort of name is Amaranthus, may I ask?"

She swallowed, blinked, and sat down, clutching the baby.

"It's a flower," she said, sounding rather dazed. "My grandfather's a botanist. It could have been worse," she added more sharply, seeing John smile. "It might have been Ampelopsis or Petunia."

"Amaranthus is a very beautiful name, my dear—if I may call you so?" Hal said, with grave courtesy. He wiggled a forefinger at the baby, who had stopped grizzling and was staring at him warily. Hal pulled his officer's gorget off over his head and dangled the shiny object, close enough for the child to grab—which he did.

"It's too large to choke him," Hal assured Amaranthus. "His father—and his father's brothers—all teethed on it. So did I, come to that." He smiled at her again. She was still white-faced but gave him a wary nod in response.

"What is the little fellow's name, my dear?" John asked.

"Trevor," she said, taking a firmer hold on the child, now completely engrossed in trying to get the demilune gorget—half the size of his head—into his mouth. "Trevor Grey." She looked back and forth between the Grey brothers, a frown puckering her brows. Then she lifted her chin and said, enunciating clearly, "Trevor . . . *Wattiswade* . . . Grey. Your Grace."

"So you are Ben's wife." A little of the tension left Hal's shoulders. "Do you know where Ben is, my dear?"

Her face went stiff, and she clutched the baby tighter.

"Benjamin is dead, Your Grace," she said. "But this is his son, and if you don't mind . . . we should quite like to come with you."

136

UNFINISHED BUSINESS

WILLIAM SHOVED his way through the crowds in the City Market, oblivious to the complaints of those rebounding from his impact.

He knew where he was going and what he meant to do when he got there. It was the only thing left to do before leaving Savannah. After that . . . it didn't matter.

His head throbbed like an inflamed boil. Everything throbbed. His hand—he'd probably broken something, but he didn't care. His heart, pounding and sore inside his chest. He hadn't slept since they'd buried Jane; would likely never sleep again and didn't care.

He remembered where the warehouse was. The place was almost empty; doubtless the soldiers had taken everything the owner hadn't had time to move out of reach. Three men were lounging by the far wall, sitting on the few remaining casks of salt fish and smoking their pipes; the smell of tobacco reached him, a small comfort in the echoing cold fishiness of the building.

"James Fraser?" he said to one of the loungers, and the man pointed with the stem of his pipe toward a small office, a sort of shed attached to the far wall of the warehouse.

The door was open; Fraser was seated at a table covered with papers, writing something by the light that fell through a tiny barred window behind him. He looked up at the sound of William's footsteps and, seeing him, put down his quill and rose slowly to his feet. William came forward, facing him across the table.

"I have come to take my farewell," William said, very formally. His voice was less firm than he liked, and he cleared his throat hard.

"Aye? Where is it that ye mean to go?" Fraser was wearing his plaid, the faded colors muted further by the dimness of the light, but what light there was sparked suddenly from his hair as he moved his head.

"I don't know," William said, gruff. "It doesn't matter." He took a deep breath. "I—wished to thank you. For what you did. Even though—" His throat closed tight; try as he might, he couldn't keep Jane's small white hand out of his thoughts.

Fraser made a slight dismissive motion and said softly, "God rest her, poor wee lass."

"Even so," William said, and cleared his throat again. "But there is one further favor that I wished to ask of you."

Fraser's head came up; he looked surprised but nodded.

"Aye, of course," he said. "If I can."

William turned and pulled the door shut, then turned to face the man again.

"Tell me how I came to be."

The whites of Fraser's eyes flashed in brief astonishment, then disappeared as his eyes narrowed.

"I want to know what happened," William said. "When you lay with my mother. What happened that night? If it *was* night," he added, and then felt foolish for doing so.

Fraser eyed him for a moment.

"Ye want to tell *me* what it was like, the first time ye lay with a woman?"

William felt the blood rush into his head, but before he could speak, the Scot went on.

"Aye, exactly. A decent man doesna speak of such things. Ye dinna tell your friends such things, do ye? No, of course not. So much less would ye tell your . . . father, or a father his . . ."

The hesitation before "father" was brief, but William caught it, no trouble. Fraser's mouth was firm, though, and his eyes direct.

"I wouldna tell ye, no matter who ye were. But being who ye are—"

"Being who I am, I think I have a right to know!"

Fraser looked at him for a moment, expressionless. He closed his eyes for an instant and sighed. Then opened them and drew himself up, straightening his shoulders.

"No, ye haven't. But that's not what ye *want* to know, in any case," he said. "Ye want to know, did I force your mother. I did not. Ye want to know, did I love your mother. I did not."

William let that lie there for a moment, controlling his breathing 'til he was sure his voice would be steady.

"Did she love you?" *It would have been easy to love him.* The thought came to him unbidden—and unwelcome—but with it, his own memories of Mac the groom. Something he shared with his mother.

Fraser's eyes were cast down, watching a trail of tiny ants running along the scuffed floorboards.

"She was verra young," he said softly. "I was twice her age. It was my fault."

There was a brief silence, broken only by their breathing and the distant shouts of men working on the river.

"I've seen the portraits," William said abruptly. "Of my—of the eighth earl. Her husband. Have you?"

Fraser's mouth twisted a little, but he shook his head.

"You know, though—knew. He was fifty years older than she was."

Fraser's maimed hand twitched, fingers tapping lightly against his thigh. Yes, he'd known. How could he *not* have known? He dipped his head, not quite a nod.

"I'm not stupid, you know," William said, louder than he'd intended.

"Didna think ye were," Fraser muttered, but didn't look at him.

"I can count," William went on, through his teeth. "You lay with her just before her wedding. Or was it just after?"

That went home; Fraser's head jerked up and there was a flash of dark-blue anger.

"I wouldna deceive another man in his marriage. Believe that of me, at least."

Oddly enough, he did. And in spite of the anger he still struggled to keep in check, he began to think he perhaps understood how it *might* have been.

"She was reckless." He made it a statement, not a question, and saw Fraser blink. It wasn't a nod, but he thought it was acknowledgment and went on, more confident.

"Everyone says that—everyone who knew her. She was reckless, beautiful, careless . . . she took chances . . ."

"She had courage." It was said softly, the words dropped

like pebbles in water, and the ripples spread through the tiny room. Fraser was still looking straight at him. "Did they tell ye that, then? Her family, the folk who kent her?"

"No," William said, and felt the word sharp as a stone in his throat. For just an instant, he'd seen her in those words. He'd *seen* her, and the knowledge of the immensity of his loss struck through his anger like a lightning bolt. He drove his fist into the table, striking it once, twice, hammering it 'til the wood shook and the legs juddered over the floor, papers flying and the inkwell falling over.

He stopped as suddenly as he'd started, and the racket ceased.

"Are you *sorry*?" he said, and made no effort to keep his voice from shaking. "Are you sorry for it, damn you?"

Fraser had turned away; now he turned sharply to face William but didn't speak at once. When he did, his voice was low and firm.

"She died because of it, and I shall sorrow for her death and do penance for my part in it until my own dying day. But—" He compressed his lips for an instant, and then, too fast for William to back away, came round the table and, raising his hand, cupped William's cheek, the touch light and fierce.

"No," he whispered. "No! I am not sorry." Then he whirled on his heel, threw open the door, and was gone, kilt flying.

PART NINE

"Thig crioch air an t-saoghal ach mairidh ceol agus gaol."

"The world may come to an end, but love and music will endure."

137

IN THE WILDERNESS

A LODGING PLACE

I COULDN'T STOP BREATHING. From the moment we left the salt-marsh miasma of Savannah, with its constant fog of rice paddies, mud, and decaying crustaceans, the air had grown clearer, the scents cleaner—well, putting aside the Wilmington mudflats, redolent with their memories of crocodiles and dead pirates—spicier, and more distinct. And as we reached the summit of the final pass, I thought I might explode from simple joy at the scent of the late-spring woods, an intoxicating mix of pine and balsam fir, oaks mingling the spice of fresh green leaves with the must of the winter's fallen acorns, and the nutty sweetness of chestnut mast under a layer of wet dead leaves, so thick that it made the air seem buoyant, bearing me up. I couldn't get enough of it into my lungs.

"If ye keep gasping like that, Sassenach, ye're like to pass out," Jamie said, smiling as he came up beside me. "How's the new knife, then?"

"Wonderful! Look, I found a huge ginseng root, and a birch gall and—"

He stopped this with a kiss, and I dropped the soggy gunnysack full of plants on the path and kissed him back. He'd been eating wild spring onions and watercress plucked dripping from a creek and he smelled of his own male scent, pine sap, and the bloody tang of the two dead rabbits hanging at his belt; it was like kissing the wilderness itself, and it went on for a bit, interrupted only by a discreet cough a few feet away.

We let go of each other at once, and I took an automatic step back behind Jamie even as he stepped in front of me, hand hovering within reach of his dirk. A split second later, he'd taken a huge stride forward and engulfed Mr. Wemyss in an enormous hug.

"Joseph! *A charaid! Ciamar a tha thu?*"

Mr. Wemyss, a small, slight, elderly man, was swept literally off his feet; I could see a shoe dangling loose from the toes of one stockinged foot as he groped for traction. Smiling at this, I glanced round to see if Rachel and Ian had come into sight yet and spotted instead a small, round-faced boy on the path. He was perhaps four or five, with long fair hair, this flying loose around his shoulders.

"Er . . . Rodney?" I asked, making a hasty guess. I hadn't seen him since he was two or so, but I couldn't think who else might be accompanying Mr. Wemyss.

The child nodded, examining me soberly.

"You be the conjure-woman?" he said, in a remarkably deep voice.

"Yes," I said, rather surprised at this address, but still more surprised at how right my acknowledgment of it felt. I realized at that moment that I had been resuming my identity as we walked, that step by step as we climbed the mountain, smelling its scents and harvesting its plenty, I had sloughed off a few layers of the recent past and become again what I had last been in this place. I had come back.

"Yes," I said again. "I am Mrs. Fraser. You may call me Grannie Fraser, if you like."

He nodded thoughtfully, taking this in and mouthing "Grannie Fraser" to himself once or twice, as though to taste it. Then he looked at Jamie, who had set Mr. Wemyss back on his feet and was smiling down at him with a look of joy that turned my heart to wax.

"Izzat Himself?" Rodney whispered, drawing close to me.

"That is Himself," I agreed, nodding gravely.

"Aidan said he was big," Rodney remarked, after another moment's scrutiny.

"Is he big enough, do you think?" I asked, rather surprised by the realization that I didn't want Rodney to be disappointed in this first sight of Himself.

Rodney gave an odd sideways tilt of his head, terribly

familiar—it was what his mother, Lizzie, did when making a judgment about something—and said philosophically, "Well, he's lot's bigger 'n me, anyway."

"Everything is relative," I agreed. "And speaking of relatives, how is your mother? And your . . . er . . . father?"

I was wondering whether Lizzie's unorthodox marriage was still in effect. Having fallen accidentally in love with identical-twin brothers, she had—with a guile and cunning unexpected in a demure nineteen-year-old Scottish bond servant—contrived to marry them both. There was no telling whether Rodney's father was Josiah or Keziah Beardsley, but I did wonder—

"Oh, Mammy's breedin' again," Rodney said casually. "She says she's a-going to castrate Daddy or Da or both of 'em, if that's what it takes to put a stop to it."

"Ah . . . well, that *would* be effective," I said, rather taken aback. "How many sisters or brothers have you got?" I'd delivered a sister before we'd left the Ridge, but—

"One sister, one brother." Rodney was clearly growing bored with me and stood on his toes to look down the path behind me. "Is that Mary?"

"What?" Turning, I saw Ian and Rachel navigating a horseshoe bend some way below; they vanished into the trees even as I watched.

"You know, Mary 'n Joseph a-flying into Egypt," he said, and I laughed in sudden understanding. Rachel, very noticeably pregnant, was riding Clarence, with Ian, who hadn't troubled to shave for the last several months and was sporting a beard of quasi-biblical dimensions, walking beside her. Jenny was presumably still out of sight behind them, riding the mare with Fanny and leading the pack mule.

"That's Rachel," I said. "And her husband, Ian. Ian is Himself's nephew. You mentioned Aidan—is his family well, too?" Jamie and Mr. Wemyss had started off toward the trailhead, talking sixteen to the dozen about affairs on the Ridge. Rodney took my hand in a gentlemanly way and nodded after them.

"We'd best be going down. I want to tell Mam first, afore *Opa* gets there."

"*Opa* . . . oh, your grandfather?" Joseph Wemyss had married a German lady named Monika, soon after Rodney's birth, and I thought I recalled that *"Opa"* was a German expression for "grandfather."

"Ja," Rodney said, confirming this supposition.

The trail meandered back and forth across the upper slopes of the Ridge, offering me tantalizing glimpses through the trees of the settlement below: scattered cabins among the bright-flowered laurels, the fresh-turned black earth of vegetable gardens—I touched the digging knife at my belt, suddenly dying to have my hands in the dirt, to pull weeds . . .

"Oh, you *are* losing your grip, Beauchamp," I murmured at the thought of ecstatic weed-pulling, but smiled nonetheless.

Rodney was not a chatterbox, but we kept up an amiable conversation as we walked. He said that he and his *opa* had walked up to the head of the pass every day for the last week, to be sure of meeting us.

"Mam and Missus Higgins have a ham saved for ye, for supper," he told me, and licked his lips in anticipation. "And there's honey to have with our corn bread! Daddy found a bee tree last Tuesday sennight and I helped him smoke 'em. And . . ."

I replied, but absentmindedly, and after a bit we both lapsed into a companionable silence. I was bracing myself for the sight of the clearing where the Big House had once stood—and a brief, deep qualm swept through me, remembering fire.

The last time I had seen the house, it was no more than a heap of blackened timbers. Jamie had already chosen a site for a new house and had felled the trees for it, leaving them stacked. Sadness and regret there might be in this return—but there were bright green spikes of anticipation poking through that scorched earth. Jamie had promised me a new garden, a new surgery, a bed long enough to stretch out in—and glass windows.

Just before we came to the spot where the trail ended above the clearing, Jamie and Mr. Wemyss stopped, waiting for Rodney and me to catch up. With a shy smile, Mr. Wemyss kissed my hand and then took Rodney's, saying, "Come along, Roddy, you can be first to tell your mam that Himself and his lady have come back!"

Jamie took my hand and squeezed it hard. He was flushed from the walk, and even more from excitement; the color ran right down into the open neck of his shirt, turning his skin a beautiful rosy bronze.

"I've brought ye home, Sassenach," he said, his voice a little husky. "It willna be the same—and I canna say how things will be now—but I've kept my word."

My throat was so choked that I could barely whisper "Thank you." We stood for a long moment, clasped tight together, summoning up the strength to go around that last corner and look at what had been, and what might be.

Something brushed the hem of my skirt, and I looked down, expecting that a late cone from the big spruce we were standing by had fallen.

A large gray cat looked up at me with big, calm eyes of celadon green and dropped a fat, hairy, very dead wood rat at my feet.

"Oh, *God*!" I said, and burst into tears.

138

FANNY'S FRENULUM

JAMIE HAD SENT word ahead, and preparations had been made for our coming. Jamie and I would stay with Bobby and Amy Higgins; Rachel and Ian with the MacDonalds, a young married couple who lived up the Ridge a way; and Jenny, Fanny, and Germain would bide for the nonce with Widow MacDowall, who had a spare bed.

There was a modest party thrown in our honor the first night—and in the morning we rose and were once more part of Fraser's Ridge. Jamie disappeared into the forest, coming back at nightfall to report that his cache of whisky was safe, and brought a small cask back with him to use as trade goods for what we might need to set up housekeeping, once we had a house to keep again.

As to said house—he'd begun the preparations for building

a new house before we had left the Ridge, selecting a good site at the head of the wide cove that opened just below the ridge itself. The site was elevated but the ground there fairly level, and thanks to Bobby Higgins's industry, it had been cleared of trees, timber for the framing of the house laid in stacks, and an amazing quantity of large stones lugged uphill and piled, ready to be used for the foundation.

For Jamie, the first order of business was to see that his house—or the beginnings of it—was as it should be, and the second was to visit every household on the Ridge, hearing and giving news, listening to his tenants, reestablishing himself as the founder and proprietor of Fraser's Ridge.

My first order of business was Fanny's frenulum. I spent a day or two in organizing the various things we had brought with us, in particular my medical equipment, while visiting with the various women who came to call at the Higginses' cabin—our own first cabin, which Jamie and Ian had built when we first came to the Ridge. But once that was done, I summoned my troops and commenced the action.

"YE MAY PUT the poor lass off drinking whisky for good," Jamie observed, casting a worried look at the cup full of amber liquid sitting on the tray next to my embroidery scissors. "Would it not be easier for her to have the ether?"

"In one way, yes," I agreed, sliding the scissors point-first into a second cup, this one filled with clear alcohol. "And if I were going to do a lingual frenectomy, I'd have to. But there *are* dangers to using ether, and I don't mean merely burning down the house. I'm going to do just a frenotomy, at least for now. That *is* a very simple operation; it will literally take five seconds. And, besides, Fanny says she doesn't want to be put to sleep—perhaps she doesn't trust me." I smiled at Fanny as I said this; she was sitting on the oak settle by the hearth, solemnly taking note of my preparations. At this, though, she looked at me abruptly, her big brown eyes surprised.

"Oh, doh," she said. "I twust oo. I zhust wanna thee."

"Don't blame you a bit," I assured her, handing her the cup of whisky. "Here, then, take a good mouthful of that and hold it in your mouth—let it go down under your tongue—for as long as you can."

I had a tiny cautery iron, its handle wrapped in twisted wool, heating on Amy's girdle. I supposed it didn't matter if it tasted like sausages. I had a fine suture needle, threaded with black silk, too, just in case.

The frenulum is a very thin band of elastic tissue that tethers the tongue to the floor of the mouth, and in most people it is exactly as long as it needs to be to allow the tongue to make all the complex motions required for speaking and eating, without letting it stray between the moving teeth, where it could be badly damaged. In some, like Fanny, the frenulum was too long and, by fastening most of the length of the tongue to the floor of her mouth, prevented easy manipulations of that organ. She often had bad breath because, while she cleaned her teeth nightly, she couldn't use her tongue to dislodge bits of food that stuck between cheek and gum or in the hollows of the lower jaw below the tongue.

Fanny gulped audibly, then coughed violently.

"Tha'th . . . *thtrong*!" she said, her eyes watering. She wasn't put off, though, and at my nod took another sip and sat stoically, letting the whisky seep into her buccal tissues. It would in fact numb the frenulum, at least a bit, and at the same time provide disinfection.

I heard Aidan and Germain calling outside; Jenny and Rachel had come down for the operation.

"I think we'd better do this outside," I said to Jamie. "They'll never all fit in here—not with Oglethorpe." For Rachel's belly had made considerable strides in the last few weeks and was of a size to make men shy nervously away from her lest she go off suddenly, like a bomb.

We took the tray of instruments outside and set up our operating site on the bench that stood by the front door. Amy, Aidan, Orrie, and wee Rob clustered together behind Jamie, who was charged with holding the looking glass—both to direct light into Fanny's mouth to assist me and so that Fanny could indeed watch what was going on.

As Oglethorpe precluded Rachel being called into service as a back brace, though, we reshuffled the staff a bit and ended with Jenny holding the looking glass and Jamie sitting on the bench, holding Fanny on his knee, his arms wrapped comfortingly around her. Germain stood by, holding a stack of clean cloths, solemn as an altar boy, and Rachel sat beside me, the tray between us, so that she could hand me things.

"All right, sweetheart?" I asked Fanny. She was round-eyed as a sun-stunned owl, and her mouth hung open just a little. She heard me, though, and nodded. I took the cup from her limp hand—it was empty, and I handed it to Rachel, who refilled it briskly.

"Mirror, please, Jenny?" I knelt on the grass before the bench, and with no more than a little trial and error, we had a beam of sunlight trained on Fanny's mouth. I took the embroidery scissors from their bath, wiped them, and, with a pledget of cloth, took hold of Fanny's tongue with my left hand and lifted it.

It didn't take even three seconds. I'd examined her carefully several times, making her move her tongue as far as she could, and knew exactly where I thought the point of attachment should be. Two quick snips and it was done.

Fanny made a surprised little noise and jerked in Jamie's arms, but didn't seem to be in acute pain. The wound was bleeding, though, suddenly and profusely, and I hurriedly pushed her head down, so that the blood could run out of her mouth onto the ground and not choke her.

I had another pledget waiting; I dipped this quickly into the whisky and, seizing Fanny's chin, brought her head up and tucked the pledget under her tongue. *That* made her emit a stifled *"Owy!"* but I cupped her chin and shut her mouth, adjuring her sternly to press down on the pledget with her tongue.

Everyone waited breathlessly while I counted silently to sixty. If the bleeding showed no sign of stopping, I'd have to put in a suture, which would be messy, or cauterize the wound, which would certainly be painful.

". . . fifty-nine . . . sixty!" I said aloud, and peering into Fanny's mouth, found the pledget substantially soaked with blood but not overwhelmed by it. I extracted it and put in another, repeating my silent count. This time, the pledget was stained, no more; the bleeding was stopping on its own.

"Hallelujah!" I said, and everyone whooped. Fanny's head bobbed a bit and she smiled, very shyly.

"Here, sweetheart," I said, handing her the half-filled cup.

"Finish that, if you can—just sip it slowly and let it go onto the wound if you can; I know it burns a bit."

She did this, rather quickly, and blinked. If it had been possible to stagger sitting down, she would have.

"I'd best put the lassie to bed, aye?" Jamie stood up, gently holding her against his shoulder.

"Yes. I'll come and see to it that her head stays upright—just in case it should bleed again and run down her throat." I turned to thank the assistants and spectators, but Fanny beat me to it.

"Missus . . . Fraser?" she said drowsily. "I—d-t-dth—" The tip of her tongue was sticking out of her mouth, and she looked cross-eyed toward it, astounded. She'd never been able to stick her tongue out before and now wiggled it to and fro, like a very tentative snake testing the air. "T-th—" She stopped, then, contorting her brow in a fearsome expression of concentration, said, "Th-ank y-y-YOU!"

Tears came to my eyes, but I managed to pat her head and say, "You're very welcome, Frances." She smiled at me then, a small, sleepy smile, and the next instant was asleep, her head on Jamie's shoulder and a tiny drooling line of blood trickling from the corner of her mouth onto his shirt.

139

A VISIT TO THE TRADING POST

BEARDSLEY'S TRADING POST was perhaps no great establishment by comparison to the shops of Edinburgh or Paris—but in the backcountry of the Carolinas, it was a rare outpost of civilization. Originally nothing but a run-down house and small barn, the place had expanded over the years, the owners—or rather, her managers—adding additional structures, some attached to the original buildings, other sheds standing free. Tools, hides, live animals, feed corn, tobacco, and hogsheads of everything from salt fish to molasses were to be found in the outbuildings, while comestibles and dry goods were in the main building.

People came to Beardsley's from a hundred miles—literally—in every direction. Cherokee from the Snowbird villages, Moravians from Salem, the multifarious inhabitants of Brownsville, and—of course—the inhabitants of Fraser's Ridge.

The trading post had grown amazingly in the eight years since I had last set foot in the place. I saw campsites in the forest nearby, and a sort of freelance flea market had sprung up alongside the trading post proper—people who brought small things to trade directly with their neighbors.

The manager of the trading post, a lean, pleasant man of middle years named Herman Stoelers, had wisely welcomed this activity, understanding that the more people who came, the greater the variety of what was available, and the more attractive Beardsley's became overall.

And the wealthier became the owner of Beardsley's trading post—an eight-year-old mulatto girl named Alicia. I wondered whether anyone besides Jamie and myself knew the secret of her birth, but if anyone did, they had wisely decided to keep it to themselves.

It was a two-day trek to the trading post, particularly as we had only Clarence, Jamie having taken Miranda and the pack mule—a jenny named Annabelle—to Salem. But the weather was good, and Jenny and I could walk, accompanied by Germain and Ian, leaving Clarence to carry Rachel and our trade goods. I'd left Fanny with Amy Higgins. She was still shy of talking in front of people; it would take a good deal of practice before she could speak normally.

Even Jenny, sophisticate as she now was after Brest, Philadelphia, and Savannah, was impressed by the trading post.

"I've never seen sae many outlandish-looking people in all my born days," she said, making no effort not to stare as a pair of Cherokee braves in full regalia rode up to the trading post, followed by several women on foot in a mixture of doeskins and European shifts, skirts, breeches, and jackets, these dragging bundles of hides on a travois or carrying huge cloth bundles full of squash, beans, corn, dried fish, or other salables on their heads or backs.

I came to attention, seeing the knobbly bulges of ginseng root protruding from one lady's pack.

"Keep an eye on Germain," I said, shoving him hastily at Jenny, and dived into the throng.

I emerged ten minutes later with a pound of ginseng, having driven a good bargain for a bag of raisins. They were Amy Higgins's raisins, but I would get her the calico cloth she wanted.

Jenny suddenly raised her head, listening.

"Did ye hear a goat just now?"

"I hear several. Do we want a goat?" But she was already making her way toward a distant shed. Evidently we *did* want a goat.

I shoved my ginseng into the canvas bag I'd brought and followed hastily.

"WE DON'T NEED that," a scornful voice said. "Piece o' worthless trash, that is."

Ian looked up from the mirror he was inspecting and squinted at a pair of young men on the other side of the store, engaged in haggling with a clerk over a pistol. They seemed somehow familiar to him, but he was sure he'd never met them. Small and wiry, with yellowish hair cropped short to their narrow skulls and darting eyes, they had the air of stoats: alert and deadly.

Then one of them straightened from the counter and, turning his head, caught sight of Ian. The youth stiffened and poked his brother, who looked up, irritated, and in turn caught sight of Ian.

"What the devil . . . ? Cheese and rice!" the second youth said.

Plainly they knew *him;* they were advancing on him, shoulder to shoulder, eyes gleaming with interest. And seeing them side by side, suddenly he recognized them.

"A Dhia," he said under his breath, and Rachel glanced up.

"Friends of thine?" she said mildly.

"Ye might say so." He stepped out in front of his wife, smiling at the . . . well, he wasn't sure what they *were* just now, but they weren't wee lassies any longer.

He'd thought they were boys when he'd met them: a pair of feral Dutch orphans named—they said—Herman and Vermin, and they *thought* their last name was Kuykendall. In the event, they'd turned out to be in actuality Hermione and Ermintrude. He'd found them a temporary refuge with . . . oh, Christ.

"God, please, no!" he said in Gaelic, causing Rachel to look at him in alarm.

Surely they weren't still with . . . but they were. He saw the back of a very familiar head—and a still more familiar arse—over by the pickle barrel.

He glanced round quickly, but there was no way out. The Kuykendalls were approaching fast. He took a deep breath, commended his soul to God, and turned to his wife.

"Do ye by chance recall once tellin' me that ye didna want to hear about every woman I'd bedded?"

"I do," she said, giving him a deeply quizzical look. "Why?"

"Ah. Well . . ." He breathed deep and got it out just in time. "Ye said ye *did* want me to tell ye if we should ever meet anyone that I . . . er—"

"Ian Murray?" said Mrs. Sylvie, turning round. She came toward him, a look of pleasure on her rather plain, bespectacled face.

"Her," Ian said hastily to Rachel, jerking his thumb in Mrs. Sylvie's direction before turning to the lady.

"Mrs. Sylvie!" he said heartily, seizing her by both hands in case she might try to kiss him, as she had occasionally been wont to do upon their meeting. "I'm that pleased to see ye! And even more pleased to present ye to my . . . er . . . wife." The word emerged in a slight croak, and he cleared his throat hard. "Rachel. Rachel, this is—"

"Friend Sylvie," Rachel said. "Yes, I gathered as much. I'm pleased to know thee, Sylvie." Her cheeks were somewhat flushed, but she spoke demurely, offering a hand in the Friends' manner rather than bowing.

Mrs. Sylvie took in Rachel—and Oglethorpe—at a glance and smiled warmly through her steel-rimmed spectacles, shaking the offered hand.

"My pleasure entirely, I assure you, Mrs. Murray." She gave Ian a sidelong look and a quivering twitch of the mouth that said as clearly as words, "*You?* You *married a* Quaker?"

"It *is* him! Toldja so!" The Kuykendalls surrounded him—

he didn't know how they managed it, there being only two of them, but he *felt* surrounded. Rather to his surprise, one of them seized him by the hand and wrung it fiercely.

"Herman Wurm," he—*he?*—told Ian proudly. "Pleased to meetcha again, sir!"

"Worm?" Rachel murmured, watching them in fascination.

"Aye, Herman, I'm that fettled to see ye doing so . . . er . . . well. And you, too . . ." Ian extended a cautious hand toward what used to be Ermintrude, who responded in a high-pitched but noticeably gruff voice.

"Trask Wurm," the youth said, repeating the vigorous handshake. "It's German."

"'Wurm,' they mean," Mrs. Sylvie put in, pronouncing it *"Vehrm."* She was pink with amusement. "They couldn't ever get the hang of spelling 'Kuykendall,' so we gave it up and settled for something simpler. And as you'd made it *quite* clear that you didn't want them to become prostitutes, we've reached a useful understanding. Herman and Trask provide protection for my . . . establishment." She looked directly at Rachel, who went a shade pinker but smiled.

"Anybody messes with the girls, we'll take care of him right smart," the elder Wurm assured Ian.

"It's not that hard," the other said honestly. "Break just one of them bastards' noses with a hoe handle and the rest of 'em settle right down."

THERE WERE A dozen or so milch goats to choose from in the shed, in varying states of pregnancy. The Higginses had a good billy, though, so I needn't trouble about that. I chose two friendly young unbred nannies, one all brown, the other brown and white, with an odd marking on her side that looked like the rounded fit of two jigsaw-puzzle pieces, one brown and one white.

I pointed out my choices to the young man in charge of the livestock and, as Jenny was still deliberating over her own choice, stepped outside to look over the chickens.

I had some hopes of spotting a Scots Dumpy but found only the usual run of Dominiques and Nankins. Well enough of their kind, but I thought I must wait until Jamie had time to build a chicken coop. And while we could lead the goats home easily enough, I wasn't going to carry chickens for days.

I came out of the chicken yard and looked about, slightly disoriented. That's when I saw him.

At first, I had no idea who he was. None. But the sight of the big, slow-moving man froze me in my tracks and my stomach curled up in instant panic.

No, I thought. *No. He's dead; they're all dead.*

He was a sloppily built man, with sloping shoulders and a protruding stomach that strained his threadbare waistcoat, but big. Big. I felt again the sense of sudden dread, of a big shadow coming out of the night beside me, nudging me, then rolling over me like a thundercloud, crushing me into the dirt and pine needles.

Martha.

A cold swept over me, in spite of the warm sunshine I stood in.

"Martha," he'd said. He'd called me by his dead wife's name and wept into my hair when he'd finished.

Martha. I had to be mistaken. That was my first conscious thought, stubbornly articulated, each word spoken aloud inside my mind, each word set in place like a little pile of stones, the first foundation of a bulwark. *You. Are. Mistaken.*

But I wasn't. My skin knew that. It rippled, a live thing, hairs rising in recoil, in vain defense, for what could skin do to keep such things out?

You. Are. Mistaken!

But I wasn't. My breasts knew that, tingling in outrage, engorged against their will by rough hands that squeezed and pinched.

My thighs knew it, too; the burn and weakness of muscles strained past bearing, the knots where punches and brutal thumbs left bruises that went to the bone, left a soreness that lingered when the bruises faded.

"You are mistaken," I said, whispering but aloud. "Mistaken."

But I wasn't. The deep soft flesh between my legs knew it, slippery with the sudden helpless horror of recollection—and so did I.

I STOOD THERE hyperventilating for several moments before I realized that I was doing it, and stopped with a conscious effort. The man was making his way through the cluster of livestock sheds; he stopped by a pen of hogs and leaned on the fence, watching the gently heaving backs with an air of meditation. Another man employed in the same recreation spoke to him, and he replied. I was too far away to hear what was said, but I caught the timbre of his voice.

"Martha. I know you don't want to, Martha, but you got to. I got to give it to you."

I was not going to be bloody sick. I wasn't. With that decision made, I calmed a little. I hadn't let him or his companions kill my spirit at the time; whyever would I let him harm me now?

He moved away from the pigs, and I followed him. I wasn't sure *why* I was following him but felt a strong compulsion to do so. I wasn't afraid of him; logically, there was no reason to be. At the same time, my unreasoning body still felt the echoes of that night, of his flesh and fingers, and would have liked to run away. I wasn't having that.

I followed him from pigs to chickens, back again to the pigs—he seemed interested in a young black-and-white sow; he pointed her out to the swineherd and seemed to be asking questions, but then shook his head in a dejected fashion and walked away. Too expensive?

I could find out who he is. The thought occurred to me, but I rejected it with a surprising sense of violence. I didn't bloody want to know his name.

And yet . . . I followed him. He went into the main building and bought some tobacco. I realized that I knew he used tobacco; I'd smelled the sour ash of it on his breath. He was talking to the clerk who measured out his purchase, a slow, heavy voice. Whatever he was saying went on too long; the clerk began to look strained, his expression saying all too clearly, *"We're done here; go away. Please go away . . ."* And a full five minutes later, relief was just as clearly marked on the clerk's face as the man turned away to look at barrels full of nails.

I'd known from what he said to me that his wife was dead. From his appearance and the way he was boring everyone he talked to, I thought he hadn't found another. He was plainly poor; that wasn't unusual in the backcountry. But he was also grubby and frayed, unshaven, and unkempt in a way that no man who lives with a woman normally is.

He passed within a yard of me as he went toward the door, his paper twist of tobacco and his bag of nails in one hand, a stick of barley sugar in the other. He was licking this with a large, wet tongue, his face showing a dim, vacant sort of pleasure in the taste. There was a small port-wine stain, a birthmark, on the side of his jaw. He was crude, I thought. Lumpish. And the word came to me: *feckless.*

Christ, I thought, with a mild disgust, this mingled with an unwilling pity that made me even more disgusted. I had had some vague thought—and realized it only now—of confronting him, of walking up to him and demanding to know whether he knew me. But he had looked right at me as he passed me, without a sign of recognition on his face. Perhaps there was enough difference between what I looked like now—clean and combed, decently dressed—and what I had looked like the last time he had seen me: filthy, wild-haired, half naked, and beaten.

Perhaps he hadn't really seen me at all at the time. It had been full dark when he came to me, tied and struggling for breath, trying to breathe through a broken nose. I hadn't seen him.

Are you sure it's really him? Yes, I bloody was. I was sure when I heard his voice and, even more so, having seen him, felt the rhythm of his bulky, shambling body.

No, I didn't want to speak to him. What would be the point? And what would I say? Demand an apology? More than likely, he wouldn't even remember having done it.

That thought made me snort with a bitter amusement.

"What's funny, *Grand-mère*?" Germain had popped up by my elbow, holding two sticks of barley sugar.

"Just a thought," I said. "Nothing important. Is Grannie Janet ready to go?"

"Aye, she sent me to look for ye. D'ye want one of these?" He generously extended a stick of candy toward me. My stomach flipped, thinking of the man's large pink tongue lapping his treat.

"No, thank you," I said. "Why don't you take it home for

Fanny? It would be wonderful exercise for her." Clipping her frenulum hadn't miraculously freed her speech, or even her ability to manipulate food; it just made such things possible, with work. Germain spent hours with her, the two of them sticking out their tongues at each other, wiggling them in all directions and giggling.

"Oh, I got a dozen sticks for Fanny," Germain assured me. "And one each for Aidan, Orrie, and wee Rob, too."

"That's very generous, Germain," I said, slightly surprised. "Er . . . what did you buy them *with*?"

"A beaver skin," he replied, looking pleased with himself. "Mr. Kezzie Beardsley gave it to me for taking his young'uns down to the creek and minding 'em whilst he and Mrs. Beardsley had a lie-down."

"A lie-down," I repeated, my mouth twitching with the urge to laugh. "I see. All right. Let's find Grannie Janet, then."

IT TOOK NO little time to get organized for the journey back to the Ridge. It was a two-day ride; on foot, with goats, it would likely take four. But we had food and blankets, and the weather was fine. No one was in a hurry—certainly not the goats, who were inclined to pause for a quick mouthful of anything in reach.

The peace of the road and the company of my companions did a great deal to settle my disturbed feelings. Rachel's imitation over supper of Ian's expressions on suddenly meeting Mrs. Sylvie and the Wurms did even more, and I fell asleep by the fire within moments of lying down, and slept without dreaming.

140

WOMAN, WILT THOU LIE WITH ME?

IAN COULDN'T TELL whether Rachel was amused, appalled, angry, or all three. This discomfited him. He usually *did* know what she thought of things, because she told him; she wasn't the sort of woman—he'd known a few—who expected a man to read her mind and got fashed when he didn't.

She'd kept her own counsel on the matter of Mrs. Sylvie and the Wurms, though. They'd done their wee bit of business, trading two bottles of whisky for salt, sugar, nails, needles, thread, a hoe blade, and a bolt of pink gingham, and he'd bought her a dilled cucumber that was as long as the span of his outstretched fingers. She'd thanked him for this but hadn't said much else on the way home. She was presently licking the vegetable in a meditative sort of way as she rocked along on Clarence.

It fascinated him to watch her do that, and he nearly walked straight off a steep rocky outcrop doing so. She turned round at his exclamation as he scrabbled for footing, though, and smiled at him, so she maybe wasn't that bothered about Sylvie.

"D'ye no mean to eat that?" he inquired, coming up beside her stirrup.

"I do," she said calmly, "but all in good time." She licked the substantial length of the warty green thing with a long, slow swipe of her tongue and then—holding his eyes—sucked deliberately on the end of it. He walked straight into a springy pine branch, which swiped him across the face with its needles.

He swore, rubbing at his watering eyes. She was laughing!

"Ye did that on purpose, Rachel Murray!"

"Is thee accusing me of propelling thee into a tree?" she inquired, arching one brow. "Thee is an experienced Indian scout, or so I was led to believe. Surely one of those should look where he's going."

She had pulled Clarence to a stop—Clarence was always agreeable to stopping, particularly if there was anything edible in sight—and sat there smiling at Ian, cheeky as a monkey.

"Give me that, aye?" She handed him the pickle willingly, wiping her damp hand on her thigh. He took a large bite, his mouth flooded with garlic and dill and vinegar. Then he jammed the cucumber into one of the saddlebags and extended a hand to her. "Come down here."

"Why?" she asked. She was still smiling, but her body had shifted, leaning toward him but making no effort to get off. He understood *that* sort of conversation and reached up, took her by what was left of her waist, and pulled her off in a flurry of skirts. He paused for an instant to swallow the bite of pickle, then kissed her thoroughly, a hand on her bottom. Her hair smelled of pinecones, chicken feathers, and the soft soap Auntie Claire called shampoo, and he could taste the German sausage they'd had for lunch, under the veil of pickling spice.

Her arms were round his neck, her belly pressed against him, and quite suddenly he felt a small hard shove in his own belly. He looked down in astonishment, and Rachel giggled. He hadn't realized that she wasn't wearing stays; her breasts were bound with a simple band under her shift, but her belly was just *there,* round and firm as a pumpkin under her gown.

"He—or she—is wakeful," she said, putting a hand on her bulge, which was moving slightly as tiny limbs poked experimentally here and there inside her. This was always fascinating in its own way, but Ian was still under the influence of her pickle-sucking.

"I'll rock him back to sleep for ye," he whispered in her ear, and, bending, lifted her in his arms. Nearly eight months gone, she was noticeably heavy, but he managed with no more than a slight grunt and, with a care to low-hanging branches and loose stones, carried her off into the forest, leaving Clarence to graze on a succulent clump of muhly grass.

"I RATHER HOPE that it wasn't the meeting with thy former paramour that caused this outbreak of passion," Rachel remarked a short time later, flicking a wandering wood louse off her husband's forearm, which was just by her face. They were lying on their sides on Ian's plaid, naked and cupped together like spoons in a box. It was cool under the trees, but she seemed never to grow cold these days; the child was like a small furnace—doubtless taking after its father, she thought. Ian's skin was usually warm, but for him the heat of passion was no mere metaphor; he blazed when they lay together.

"She's no my paramour," Ian murmured into her hair, and kissed the back of her ear. "It was only a commercial transaction."

She didn't like hearing that and stiffened a little.

"I did tell ye I'd gone wi' whores." Ian's voice was quiet, but she could hear the slight reproach in it. "Would ye rather I had discarded lovers strewn about the countryside?"

She took a breath, relaxed, and stretched her neck to kiss the back of his long, sun-browned hand.

"No, it's true—thee did tell me," she admitted. "And while there is some small part of me that could wish thee came to me virgin, chaste and untouched . . . honesty obliges me to acknowledge some gratitude for the lessons learned from the likes of Mrs. Sylvie." She wanted to ask whether he'd learned the things he'd just been doing to her from Mrs. Sylvie or perhaps from his Indian wife—but she had no wish to bring any thought of Works With Her Hands between them.

His hand lifted and cupped her breast, playing very gently with her nipple, and she squirmed involuntarily—a slow, insinuating squirm that thrust her buttocks back against him. Her nipples were very large these days and so sensitive that they couldn't bear the rubbing of stays. She squirmed again, and he laughed under his breath and rolled her over to face him so he could take her nipple in his mouth.

"Dinna make noises like that," he murmured against her skin. "The others will be comin' along the trail any time now."

"What—will they think when they see Clarence alone?"

"If anyone asks later, we'll say we were gatherin' mushrooms."

THEY MUSTN'T STAY much longer, she knew that. But she longed to stay like this forever—or at least for five minutes more. Ian lay once more behind her, warm and strong. But his hand was now on her stomach, tenderly stroking the rounded mystery of the child within.

He might have thought she was asleep. Perhaps he didn't mind if she heard him. He spoke in the *Gàidhlig,* though, and while she didn't yet know enough of the tongue to make out all he said, she knew it was a prayer. *"A Dhia"* meant "O God." And of course she knew what it was he prayed for.

"It's all right," she said to him softly, when he had stopped, and put her hand over his.

"What is?"

"That thee should think of thy first child—children. I know thee does. And I know how much thee fears for this one," she added, still more softly.

He sighed deeply, his breath, still scented with dill and garlic, warm on her neck.

"Ye turn my heart to water, lass—and should anything happen to you or to wee Oggy, it would punch a hole in me that would let my life run out."

She wanted to tell him that nothing would happen to them, that she wouldn't let it. But that was taking things upon herself that weren't hers to promise.

"Our lives are in God's hand," she said, squeezing his. "And whatever happens, we will be with thee forever."

DRESSED AGAIN, and as seemly as fingers combed through hair could make them, they reached the trail just as Claire and Jenny made their way around the bend, carrying packs and each leading two milch goats, friendly creatures who set up a loud *mehh* of greeting as they spotted the two strangers.

Rachel saw Ian's mother glance sharply at her son, and then her dark-blue gaze lifted at once to Rachel, perched on Clarence's back. She gave Rachel a smile that said, as plain as words, that she knew exactly what they'd been doing and found it funny. Warm blood rose in Rachel's cheeks, but she kept her composure and inclined her head graciously to Jenny—in spite of the fact that Friends did not bow their heads save in worship.

Still blushing, she'd paid no attention to Claire, but after they had gone far enough ahead of the older women and the goats so as not to be overheard, Ian lifted his chin and gestured over his shoulder with it.

"Does aught seem amiss wi' Auntie Claire, d'ye think?"

"I didn't notice. What does thee mean?"

Ian lifted a shoulder, frowning slightly.

"I canna say, quite. She was herself on the way to the trading post and when we first got there, but when she came back from hagglin' for the goats, she looked . . . different." He struggled to find words to explain what he meant.

"No quite what ye'd say someone looks like if they've seen a ghost—not scairt, I mean. But . . . stunned, maybe? Surprised, or maybe shocked. But then when she saw me, she tried to act as though it was all as usual, and I was busy takin' the bundles out and forgot about it."

He turned his head again, looking over his shoulder, but the trail behind was empty. A faint *mehhhh* filtered down through the trees behind them, and he smiled—but his eyes were troubled.

"Ken—Auntie Claire canna hide things verra well. Uncle Jamie always says she's got a glass face, and it's true. Whatever it is she saw back there . . . I think it's with her, still."

141

THE DEEPEST FEELING ALWAYS SHOWS ITSELF IN SILENCE

IT WAS SOMETIME in the midafternoon of the third day that Jenny cleared her throat in a significant manner. We had paused by a creek where the wild grass grew long and thick and were dabbling our tired feet in the water, watching the hobbled goats disport themselves. One seldom goes to the trouble of hobbling a goat, since they can, if they want to, chew their way free in a matter of seconds. In the present instance, though, there was too much food available for them to want to waste time in eating rope, and the hobbles would keep them within our sight.

"Got something caught in your throat?" I inquired pleasantly. "Luckily there's plenty of water."

She made a Scottish noise indicating polite appreciation of this feeble attempt at wit and, reaching into her pocket, withdrew a very battered silver flask and uncorked it. I could smell the liquor from where I sat—a local forerunner of bourbon, I thought.

"Did you bring that with you from Scotland?" I asked, accepting the flask, which had a crude fleur-de-lis on the side.

"Aye, it was Ian's. He had it from when he and Jamie were soldiering in France; brought it back wi' him when he lost his leg. We'd sit on the wall by his da's house and share a dram, while he was mending; he'd need it, poor lad, after I made him walk up and down the road ten times every day, to learn the use of his peg." She smiled, slanted eyes creasing, but with a wistful turn to her lips.

"I said I wouldna marry him, aye? Unless he could stand up

beside me at the altar on two legs and walk me up the aisle after the vows."

I laughed.

"That's not quite the way *he* told it." I took a cautious sip, but the liquid inside was amazingly good, fiery but smooth. "Where did you get this?"

"A man named Gibbs, from Aberdeenshire. Ye wouldna think they ken anything about whisky-making there, but doubtless he learnt it somewhere else. He lives in a place called Hogue Corners; d'ye ken it?"

"No, but it can't be that far away. It's his own make, is it? Jamie would be interested." I took a second mouthful and handed back the flask, holding the whisky in my mouth to savor.

"Aye, I thought so, too. I have a wee bottle for him in my sack." She sipped and nodded approvingly. "Who was the dirty fat lumpkin that scairt ye at Beardsley's?"

I choked on the whisky, swallowed it the wrong way, and nearly coughed my lungs out in consequence. Jenny put down the flask, kirtled up her skirts, and waded into the creek, sousing her hankie in the cold water; she handed it to me, then cupped water in her hand and poured a little into my mouth.

"Lucky there's plenty of water, as ye said," she remarked. "Here, have a bit more." I nodded, eyes streaming, but pulled up my skirts, got down on my knees, and drank for myself, pausing to breathe between mouthfuls, until I stopped wheezing.

"I wasna in any doubt, mind," Jenny said, watching this performance. "But if I had been, I wouldn't be now. Who is he?"

"I don't bloody know," I said crossly, climbing back on my rock. Jenny wasn't one to be daunted by tones of voice, though, and merely raised one gull-wing-shaped brow.

"I don't," I repeated, a little more calmly. "I—had just seen him somewhere else. I have no idea who he is, though."

She was examining me with the interested air of a scientist with a new microorganism trapped under her microscope.

"Aye, aye. And where was it ye saw the fellow before? Because ye certainly kent him this time. Ye were fair gobsmacked."

"If I thought it would make the slightest bit of difference, I'd tell you it's none of your business," I said, giving her a look. "Give me that flask, will you?"

She gave it to me, watching patiently while I took several tiny sips and made up my mind what to say. At last I drew a deep, whisky-scented breath and gave her back the flask.

"Thank you. I don't know whether Jamie told you that about five years ago a gang of bandits who were terrorizing the countryside came through the Ridge. They burnt our malting shed—or tried to—and hurt Marsali. And they—they took me. Hostage."

Jenny handed back the flask, not speaking, but with a look of deep sympathy in her dark-blue eyes.

"Jamie . . . got me back. He brought men with him, and there was a terrible fight. Most of the gang was killed, but—obviously a few got away in the darkness. That—that man was one of them. No, it's all right, I don't need any more." I'd held the flask like a talisman of courage while I told her but now handed it back. She took a long, meditative swallow.

"But ye didna try to find out his name? Folk there kent him, I could see; they'd have told ye."

"I don't want to know!" I spoke loudly enough that one of the goats nearby emitted a startled *meh-eh-eh!* and bounded over a tussock of grass, evidently not discommoded at all by its hobbles.

"I—it doesn't matter," I said, less loudly but no less firmly. "The—ringleaders—are all dead; so are most of the others. This fellow . . . he . . . well, you can tell by looking at him, can't you? What did you call him—'a dirty fat lumpkin'? That's just what he is. He's no danger to us. I just—want to forget about him," I ended, rather lamely.

She nodded, stifled a small belch, looked startled at the sound, and, shaking her head, corked the flask and put it away.

We sat for a bit in silence, listening to the rush of water and the birds in the trees behind us. There was a mockingbird somewhere nearby, running through its lengthy repertoire in a voice like brass.

After ten minutes or so, Jenny stretched, arching her back and sighing.

"Ye'll remember my daughter Maggie?" she asked.

"I do," I said, smiling a little. "I delivered her. Or, rather, I caught her. You did the work."

"So ye did," she said, splashing one foot in the water. "I'd forgotten."

I gave her a sharp look. If she had, it would be the first thin she ever *had* forgotten, at least to my knowledge, and I didn think she was old enough to have begun forgetting things nov

"She was raped," she said, eyes on the water and her voic very steady. "Not badly—the man didna beat her—but she gc wi' child by him."

"How terrible," I said quietly, after a pause. "It—not a gov ernment soldier, though, surely?" That had been my firs thought—but Maggie would have been no more than a chil during the years of the Rising and Cumberland's clearing c the Highlands, when the British army had burned, plunderec and, yes, indeed, raped their way through any number of vi lages and crofts.

"No, it wasn't," Jenny said thoughtfully. "It was her hus band's brother."

"Oh, God!"

"Aye, that's what I said about it, when she told me." She gr maced. "That was the one good thing about it, though; Geordie– that was the brother—had the same color hair and eyes as he husband, Paul, so the bairn could be passed off easy enough."

"And—did she?" I couldn't help asking. "Pass it off?"

Jenny let out a long sigh and nodded, taking her feet out c the water and tucking them up beneath her petticoat.

"She asked me what to do, poor lassie. I prayed about it– God, I prayed!" she said, with sudden violence, then snorted little. "And I told her not to tell him—tell Paul, I mean. For i she did, what would be the end of it? One of them dead—for Hieland man canna live wi' a man who's raped his wife nearb nor should he—and it might be Paul, as like as not. And eve if he only beat Geordie and drove him off, everyone would gc to know what was behind it, and the poor wee lad—that wa Wally, though of course we didna ken that yet, whilst we wer talking it over—but the bairn branded as a bastard and th child of rape—what would become of it?"

She leaned down and, scooping up a handful of wate threw it over her face. She put her head back, eyes closed an the water running off her high, sharp cheekbones, and shoo her head.

"And the family—Paul and Geordie's? A thing like th would tear them to pieces—and put them at loggerheads w us, nay doubt, for they'd be insisting up and down that Maggi vas lying, rather than believe such a thing. Fat-heided crea-ures, the Carmichaels," she said judiciously. "Loyal enough, ut stubborn as rocks."

"Thus sayeth a Fraser," I remarked. "The Carmichaels must e something special in that line."

Jenny snorted but didn't reply for a moment or two.

"So," she said at last, turning to look at me, "I said to Mag-ie that I'd prayed about it, and it seemed to me that if she ould bear it for the sake of her man and her bairns, she should ay nothing. Try to forgive Geordie if she could, and if she ouldn't, keep away from him—but say nothing. And that's vhat she did."

"What—did Geordie do?" I asked curiously. "Did he—loes he know that Wally is his son?"

She shook her head.

"I dinna ken. He left, a month after the bairn was born—migrated to Canada. No one was surprised at that; everyone ent he was mad in love wi' Maggie and beside himself when he chose Paul. I expect that made it easier."

"Out of sight, out of mind? Yes, I'd suppose so," I said lryly. I thought I shouldn't ask but couldn't help myself. "Did Maggie ever tell Paul—after Geordie left, I mean?"

She shook her head and stood up, a little stiffly, shaking lown her skirts.

"I dinna ken for sure, but I dinna think so. For her to tell im, after so long of keeping silent . . . how would he take hat? And he'd still hate his brother, even if he couldna kill him ight away." Her blue eyes, so like Jamie's, looked at me with ueful amusement. "Ye canna have been marrit to a Hieland nan all these years and not ken how deep they can hate. Come n—we'd best gather these creatures before they burst." And he waded off into the grass, shoes in her hand, calling out a *Gàidhlig* charm for gathering livestock:

"The Three who are above in the City of glory,
Be shepherding my flock and my kine,
Tending them duly in heat, in storm, and in cold,
With the blessing of power driving them down
From yonder height to the sheiling fold."

I THOUGHT about it, after everyone had rolled up their blankets and begun snoring that night. Well . . . I hadr *stopped* thinking about it since I'd seen the man. But in lig of the story that Jenny had told me, my thoughts began to cla ify, much as throwing an egg into a pot of coffee will settle tl grounds.

The notion of saying nothing was of course the first one come to my mind and was still my intent. The only difficulty- well, there were two, to be honest. But the first one was tha irritating as it was to be told so repeatedly, I couldn't deny tl fact that I had a glass face. If anything was seriously troublir me, the people I lived with immediately began glancing at n sideways, tiptoeing exaggeratedly around me—or, in Jamie case, demanding bluntly to know what the matter was.

Jenny had done much the same thing, though she hadr pressed me for details of my experience. Quite plainly, she guessed the outlines of it, though, or she wouldn't have chose to tell me Maggie's story. It occurred to me belatedly to wo der whether Jamie *had* told her anything about Hodgepile attack and its aftermath.

The underlying difficulty, though, was my own response meeting the dirty fat lumpkin. I snorted every time I repeate the description to myself, but it actually helped. He was a ma and not a very prepossessing one. Not a monster. Not . . . n bloody *worth* making a fuss about. God knew how he'd con to join Hodgepile's band—I supposed that most crimin gangs were largely composed of feckless idiots, come to tha

And . . . little as I wanted to relive that experience . . . I di He hadn't come to me with any intent of hurting me, in fa hadn't hurt me (which was not to say that he *hadn't* crushe me with his weight, forced my thighs apart, and stuck his coc into me . . .).

I unclenched my teeth, drew a deep breath, and started ove

He'd come to me out of opportunity—and need.

"Martha," he'd said, sobbing, his tears and snot warm c my neck. *"Martha, I loved you so."*

Could I forgive him on those grounds? Put aside the u pleasantness of what he'd done to me and see him only as tl pathetic creature that he was?

If I could—would that stop him living in my mind, a co stant burr under the blanket of my thoughts?

I put back my head, looking up at the deep black sky swimming with hot stars. If you knew they were really balls of flaming gas, you could imagine them as van Gogh saw them, without difficulty . . . and looking into that illuminated void, you understood why people have always looked up into the sky when talking to God. You need to feel the immensity of something very much bigger than yourself, and there it is—immeasurably vast, and always near at hand. Covering you.

Help me, I said silently.

I never talked to Jamie about Jack Randall. But I knew from the few things he told me—and the disjointed things he said in the worst of his dreams—that this was how he had chosen to survive. He'd forgiven Jack Randall. Over and over. But he was a stubborn man; he could do it. A thousand times, and still one more.

Help me, I said, and felt tears trickle down my temples, into my hair. *Please. Help me.*

142

THINGS COMING INTO VIEW

IT WORKED. NOT EASILY, and often not for more than a few minutes at a time—but the shock faded and, back at home, with the peace of the mountain and the love of family and friends surrounding me, I felt a welcome sense of balance return. I prayed, and I forgave, and I coped.

This was greatly helped by distraction. Summer is the busiest time in an agricultural community. And when men are working with scythes and hoes and wagons and livestock and guns and knives—they hurt themselves. As for the women and children—burns and household accidents and constipation and diarrhea and teething and . . . pinworms.

"There, you see?" I said in a low voice, holding a lighted candle a few inches from the buttocks of Tammas Wilson, aged two. Tammas, drawing the not unreasonable conclusio that I was about to scorch his bum or ram the candle up hi backside, shrieked and kicked, trying to escape. His mothe took a firmer grip on him, though, and pried his buttocks apa again, revealing the tiny white wriggles of female pinworm swarming round his less than ideally immaculate small anus.

"Christ between us and evil," Annie Wilson said, letting g with one hand in order to cross herself. Tammas made a dete mined effort at escape and nearly succeeded in pitching him self headfirst into the fire. I seized him by one foot, thoug and hauled him back.

"Those are the females," I explained. "They crawl out a night and lay eggs on the skin. The eggs cause itching, and sc of course, your wee lad scratches. That's what causes the red ness and rash. But then he spreads the eggs to things h touches"—and, Tammas being two, he touched everythin within reach—"and that's why your whole family is likely in fected."

Mrs. Wilson squirmed slightly on her stool, whether becaus of pinworms or embarrassment, I couldn't tell, and righted Tam mas, who promptly wriggled out of her lap and made for the be containing his two elder sisters, aged four and five. I grabbe him round the waist and lugged him back over to the hearth.

"Bride save us, what shall I do for it?" Annie asked, glanc ing helplessly from the sleeping girls to Mr. Wilson, who— worn out from his day's work—was curled in the other be snoring.

"Well, for the older children and adults, you use this." took a bottle out of my basket and handed it over, rather gin gerly. It wasn't actually explosive, but, knowing its effects, always gave me that illusion.

"It's a tonic of flowering spurge and wild ipecac root. It's *very* strong laxative—that means it will give you the blazin shits," I amended, seeing her incomprehension, "but a fe doses will get rid of the pinworms, provided you can kee Tammas and the girls from respreading them. And for th smaller children—" I handed over a pot of garlic paste, stron enough to make Annie wrinkle her nose, even though it wa corked. "Take a large glob on your finger and smear it roun the child's bumhole—and, er, up inside."

"Aye," she said, looking resigned, and took both pot and ottle. It probably wasn't the worst thing she'd ever done as a nother. I gave her instructions regarding the boiling of bed-ing and strict advice about soap and religious hand-washing, vished her well, and left, feeling a strong urge to scratch my wn bottom.

This faded on the walk back to the Higginses' cabin, hough, and I slid into the pallet beside Jamie with the peace-ul sense of a job well done.

He rolled over drowsily and embraced me, then sniffed.

"What in God's name have ye been doing, Sassenach?"

"You don't want to know," I assured him. "What do I smell ike?" If it was just garlic, I wasn't getting up. If it was feces, hough . . .

"Garlic," he said, luckily. "Ye smell like a French *gigot 'agneau.*" His stomach rumbled at the thought, and I laughed—uietly.

"I think the best you're likely to get is parritch for your break-ast."

"That's all right," he said comfortably. "There's honey for it."

THE NEXT AFTERNOON, there being no pressing nedical calls, I climbed up to the new house site with Jamie. he shield-shaped green leaves and arching stems of the wild trawberries were everywhere, spattering the hillside with iny, sour-sweet red hearts. I'd brought a small basket with ne—I never went anywhere without one in spring or ummer—and had it half filled by the time we reached the learing, with its fine view of the whole cove that lay below he Ridge.

"It seems like a lifetime ago that we came here first," I re-narked, sitting down on one of the stacks of half-hewn tim-ers and pulling off my wide-brimmed hat to let the breeze low through my hair. "Do you remember when we found the trawberries?" I offered a handful of the fruit to Jamie.

"More like two or three. Lifetimes, I mean. But, aye, I re-nember." He smiled, sat down beside me, and plucked one of he tiny berries from the palm of my hand. He motioned at the more or less level ground before us, where he'd laid out rough floor plan with pegs driven into the earth and string ou lining the rooms.

"Ye'll want your surgery in the front, aye? The same as was? That's how I've put it, but it's easy changed, if ye like."

"Yes, I think so. I'll be in there more than anywhere; b nice to be able to look out the window and see what sort hideous emergency is coming."

I'd spoken in complete seriousness, but he laughed an took a few more strawberries.

"At least if they have to come uphill, it will slow ther down a bit." He'd brought up the rough writing desk he'd mad and now put it on his knee, opening it to show me his plan neatly ruled in pencil.

"I'll have my speak-a-word room across the hall from yo like we did before—ye'll see I've made the hallway wider, be cause of the staircase landing—and I think I'd maybe like wee parlor there, between the speak-a-word room and th kitchen. But the kitchen . . . d'ye think we should maybe hav a separate cookhouse, as well, like John Grey did in Philade phia?"

I considered that one for a moment, my mouth puckering bit from the astringent berries. I wasn't surprised that th thought had occurred to him; anyone who'd lived through on house fire, let alone two, would have a very lively awarenes of the dangers.

"Oh, I don't think so," I said at last. "They do that as muc because of the summer heat as for the danger of fire, and that not a problem here. We'll have to have hearths in the hous after all. The danger of fire can't be that much greater if we'r cooking on one of them."

"Surely that depends who's doin' the cooking," Jamie sai cocking an eyebrow at me.

"If you mean anything personal by that remark, you ma retract it," I said coolly. "I may not be the world's best cook but I've never served you cinders."

"Well, ye *are* the only member o' the family who's eve burnt the house down, Sassenach. Ye've got to admit th much." He was laughing and put up a casual hand to intercep the mock blow I aimed at him. His hand completely enclose my fist, and he pulled me effortlessly off my perch and onto his knee.

He put an arm round me and his chin on my shoulder, brushing my hair out of his face with his free hand. He was barefoot and wearing only a shirt and his threadbare green-and-brown working plaid, the one he'd bought from a rag dealer in Savannah. It was rucked up over his thigh; I pulled the fold out from under my bottom and smoothed it down over the long muscle of his leg.

"Amy says there's a Scottish weaver in Cross Creek," I said. "When you next go down, maybe you should commission a new plaid—maybe one in your own tartan, if the weaver's up to a Fraser red."

"Aye, well. There're plenty other things to spend money on, Sassenach. I dinna need to be grand to hunt or fish—and I work the fields in my shirt."

"I could go round day in and day out in a gray flannel petticoat with holes in it and it wouldn't make any difference to *my* work—but you wouldn't want me to do that, would you?"

He made a low Scottish noise of amusement and shifted his weight, settling me more firmly.

"I would not. I like to look at ye now and then in a fine gown, lass, wi' your hair put up and your sweet breasts showin'. Besides," he added, "a man's judged by how well he provides for his family. If I let ye go around in rags, folk would think I was either mean or improvident." It was clear from his tone which of these conditions would be the more frightful sin.

"Oh, they would not," I said, mostly teasing for the sake of argument. "Everyone on the Ridge knows perfectly well that you're neither one. Besides, don't you think I like to look at *you* in all your glory?"

"Why, that's verra frivolous of ye, Sassenach; I should never have expected something like that from Dr. C.E.B.R. Fraser." He was laughing again but stopped abruptly as he turned a little.

"Look," he said into my ear, and pointed down the side of the cove. "Just there, on the right, where the creek comes out o' the trees. See her?"

"Oh, *no*!" I said, spotting the smudge of white moving slowly among the green mats of cress and duckweed. "It can't be, surely?" I couldn't make out details at that distance with out my glasses, but from the way it moved, the object in ques tion was almost certainly a pig. A big pig. A big *white* pig.

"Well, if it's no the white sow, it's a daughter just like hei But my guess is that it's the auld besom herself. I'd know tha proud rump anywhere."

"Well, then." I leaned back against him with a little sigh o satisfaction. "Now I *know* we're home."

"Ye'll sleep under your own roof within a month, *a nighean,*" he said, and I could hear the smile in his voice. "Mind, it may no be more than the roof of a lean-to, to start—but it'll be our own By the winter, though, I'll have the chimneys built, the walls al up, and the roof on; I can be puttin' in the floors and the door while there's snow on the ground."

I put a hand up to cup his cheek, warm and lightly stubbled I didn't fool myself that this was paradise or even a refuge from the war—wars tended not to stay in one place but moved around, much in the manner of cyclones and even more de structive where they touched down. But for however long i lasted, this was home, and now was peace.

We sat in silence for a while, watching hawks circle ove the open ground below and the machinations of the white sow—if indeed it was she—who had now been joined in he foraging by a number of smaller porcine blobs, doubtless thi spring's litter. At the foot of the cove, two men on horseback came into sight from the wagon road, and I felt Jamie's atten tion sharpen, then relax.

"Hiram Crombie and the new circuit rider," he said. "Hiram said he meant to go down to the crossroads and fetch the mar up, so he'd not lose his way."

"You mean so Hiram can make sure he's dour enough fo the job," I said, laughing. "You realize they'll have got out o the habit of thinking you're human, don't you?" Hiram Crom bie was head man of the little group of settlers that Jamie had acquired six years before. All of them were Presbyterians of a particularly rock-ribbed disposition and inclined to regard Pa pists as being deeply perverse, if not actually the spawn o Satan.

Jamie made a small noise, but it was one of tolerant dis missal.

"They'll get used to me again," he said. "And I'd pay mone

o watch Hiram talk to Rachel. Here, Sassenach, my leg's gone ısleep." He helped me off his lap and stood up, shaking his kilt nto place. Faded or not, it suited him, and my heart rose to see ıim looking so much as he should: tall and broad-shouldered, ıead of his household, once more master of his own land.

He looked out over the cove again, sighed deeply, and turned o me.

"Speakin' of hideous emergencies," he said thoughtfully, 'ye do want to see them coming. So ye can be fettled against hem, aye?" His eyes met mine directly. "Would now be a ;ood time to tell me what's coming, d'ye think?"

THERE'S NOTHING wrong," I said, for probably the enth time. I picked at a scab of bark still clinging to the timber sat on. "It's perfectly all right. Really."

Jamie was standing in front of me, the cove and the clouded ky bright behind him, his face shadowed.

"Sassenach," he said mildly. "I'm a great deal more stub-)orn than you are, and ye ken that fine. Now, I know some-hing upset ye when ye went to Beardsley's place, and I know 'e dinna want to tell me about it. Sometimes I ken ye need to ettle your mind about a matter before ye speak, but you've ıad time and more to do that—and I see that whatever it is is vorse than I thought, or ye'd have said by now."

I hesitated, trying to think of something to tell him that)erhaps wasn't quite . . . I looked up at him and decided that, ıo, I couldn't lie to him—and not only because he'd be able to ell immediately that I *was* lying.

"Do you remember," I said slowly, looking up at him, "on)ur wedding night? You told me you wouldn't ask me to tell ,ou things that I couldn't. You said that love had room for se-:rets, but not for lies. I won't lie to you, Jamie—but I really lon't want to tell you."

He shifted his weight from one leg to the other and sighed.

"If ye think *that's* going to relieve my mind, Sassenach . . ." ıe said, and shook his head. "I didna say that, anyway. I do 'emember the occasion—vividly"—and he smiled a little at ne—"and what I said was that there was nothing between us then but respect—and that I thought respect maybe had roor for secrets, but not for lies."

He paused for a moment, then said very gently, "D'ye n think there's more than respect between us now, *mo chridhe*?

I took a very deep breath. My heart was thumping again my stays, but it was just normal agitation, not panic.

"I do," I said, looking up at him. "Jamie . . . please don ask me just now. I truly think it's all right; I've been prayin about it, and—and—I think it will be all right," I ended, rathe lamely. I stood up, though, and took his hands. "I'll tell yo when I think I can," I said. "Can you live with that?"

His lips tightened as he thought. He wasn't a man for faci answers. If he couldn't live with it, he'd tell me.

"Is it a matter that I might need to make preparation for? he asked seriously. "If it might cause a fight of some kind, mean, I should need to be ready."

"Oh." I let out the breath I'd been holding, somewhat re lieved. "No. No, it isn't anything like that. More of a mor question kind of thing."

I could see that he wasn't happy about that; his eyes searche my face, and I saw the troubled look in them, but at last he no ded, slowly.

"I'll live with it, *a nighean*," he said softly, and kissed m forehead. "For now."

143

INTERRUPTUS

THE OTHER MAJOR THINGS requiring healer's attention in summer were pregnancy and birt I prayed every day that Marsali had safely delivere her child. Even though it was already June 1, it would likely b months before we had any news, but I had examined her b fore we parted company—with tears—in Charleston, and all seemed normal.

"Do ye think this one might be . . . like Henri-Christian?" She spoke the name with difficulty and pressed a hand to her swelling belly.

"Probably not," I said, and saw the emotions ripple across her face like wind passing over water. Fear, regret . . . relief.

I crossed myself, with another quick prayer, and walked up the path to the MacDonald cottage, where Rachel and Ian were staying until Ian could build them a place of their own. Rachel was sitting on the bench out front, shelling peas into a basin, the basin sitting comfortably atop her stomach.

"Madainn mhath!" she said, smiling in delight when she saw me. "Is thee not impressed with my linguistic facility, Claire? I can say 'Good morning,' 'Good night,' 'How are you?' and 'Bugger off to St. Kilda' now."

"Congratulations," I said, sitting down next to her. "How does that last one go?"

"Rach a h-Irt," she told me. "I gather 'St. Kilda' is actually a figure of speech indicating some extremely remote location, rather than being specified as the actual destination."

"I wouldn't be at all surprised. Do you try to impose the principles of plain speech on *Gàidhlig,* or is that even possible?"

"I have no idea," she said frankly. "Mother Jenny proposes to teach me the Lord's Prayer in *Gàidhlig.* Perhaps I can tell from that, as presumably one addresses the Creator in the same sort of voice that one uses for plain speech."

"Oh." I hadn't thought about that, but it was sensible. "So you call God 'Thee' when speaking to Him?"

"Of course. Who should be a closer Friend?"

It hadn't occurred to me, but presumably that *was* why one used "thou," "thy," et cetera, in prayer; that was originally the familiar form of the singular pronoun "you," even though common English speech had now moved on and lost the distinction, save for the Friends' plain speech.

"How interesting," I said. "And how is Oggy today?"

"Restless," she said, catching the edge of the basin as a vigorous kick made it bounce, scattering peas. "So am I," she added, as I brushed the spilled peas off her petticoat and poured them back into the pan.

"I don't doubt it," I said, smiling. "Pregnancy actually *does* last forever—until suddenly you go into labor."

"I can't wait," she said fervently. "Neither can Ian."

"Any particular reason?"

A slow, glorious blush rose up from the neck of her shift and suffused her to the hairline.

"I wake him six times a night, rising to piss," she said, avoiding my eye. "And Oggy kicks him, nearly as much as he does me."

"And?" I said invitingly.

The blush deepened slightly.

"He says he can't wait to, er, suckle me," she said diffidently. She coughed and then looked up, the blush fading a little.

"Really," she said, now serious, "he's anxious for the child. Thee knows about his children by the Mohawk woman; he said he'd told thee, making up his mind if it was right for him to marry again."

"Ah. Yes, he would be." I laid a hand on her belly, feeling the reassuring pressure of a thrusting foot and the long curve of a tiny back. The baby hadn't dropped, but Oggy was at least head-down. *That* was a great relief.

"It will be all right," I said, and squeezed her hand. "I'm sure of it."

"I'm not afraid for myself at all," she said, smiling and squeezing back. The smile faded a little as she put her hand on her stomach. "But very much afraid for them."

THE WEATHER being fine—and the smallest Higgins teething—we took a pair of quilts and walked up to the house site after supper, to enjoy the long twilight. And a little privacy.

"You don't think we're likely to be interrupted by a bear or some other form of wildlife, do you?" I asked, shimmying out of the rough gown I wore for foraging.

"No. I spoke wi' Jo Beardsley yesterday; he told me the nearest bear is a good league that way—" He nodded toward the far side of the cove. "And they dinna travel far in the summer, while the eating's good where they are. And painters wouldna trouble wi' people while there are easier things to kill. I'll make a bitty fire, though, just on principle."

"How's Lizzie?" I asked, unfolding the quilts as I watched him assemble a small fire with deft efficiency. "Did Jo say?"

Jamie smiled, eyes on what he was doing.

"He did, at some length. The meat of it bein' that she's well enough but summat inclined to bite pieces out o' him and Kezzie to distract her mind. That's why Jo was out hunting; Kezzie stays in when she's frachetty, because he canna hear her so well." The Beardsley twins were identical, and so alike that the only sure way to tell which you were talking to was that Keziah was hard of hearing, as the result of a childhood infection.

"That's good. No malaria, I mean." I'd visited Lizzie soon after our arrival and found her and the brood thriving—but she'd told me that she'd had a few "spells" of fever during the last year, doubtless owing to lack of the Jesuit bark. I'd left her with most of what I'd brought from Savannah. *I should have thought to ask if they had any at the trading post,* I thought—and pushed away the heavy sense of uneasiness that came with the thought of that place, thinking firmly, *I forgive you.*

The fire built, we sat feeding it sticks and watching the last of the sunset go down in flaming banners of golden cloud behind the black pickets of the farthest ridge.

And with the light of the fire dancing on the stacked timbers and the piles of foundation stones, we enjoyed the privacy of our home, rudimentary as said home might be at the moment. We lay peacefully afterward between our quilts—it wasn't cold but, so high up, the heat of the day vanished swiftly from the air—and watched the flickering lights of chimney sparks and lighted windows, in the few houses visible among the trees of the cove. Before the lights were extinguished for the night, we were asleep.

I woke sometime later from an erotic dream, squirming slowly on the lumpy quilt, limbs heavy with desire. This seemed to happen more frequently as I grew older, as though making love with Jamie ignited a fire that didn't quite die but continued to smolder through the night. If I didn't wake enough to do something about it, I'd wake in the morning stupid and foggy with unslaked dreams and unquiet sleep.

Fortunately, I was awake and, while still very pleasantly drowsy, quite capable of doing something about it, the process made much easier by the presence of the large, warm, pungent-smelling male beside me. He shifted a little as I edged onto my back, making a little space between us, but resumed his regular heavy breathing at once, and I edged my hand downward, encountering tumid warmth. It wouldn't take long.

A few minutes later, Jamie shifted again, and my hand stilled between my thighs. Then his hand slid swiftly under the quilt and touched me in the same place, nearly stopping my heart.

"I dinna mean to interrupt ye, Sassenach," he whispered in my ear. "But would ye like a bit of help wi' that?"

"Um," I said rather faintly. "Ah . . . what did you have in mind?"

In answer, the tip of his tongue darted into my ear, and I let out a small shriek. He snorted with amusement and cupped his hand between my legs, dislodging my own fingers, which had gone rather limp. One large finger stroked me delicately, and I arched my back.

"Ooh, ye're well started, then," he murmured. "Ye're slick and briny as an oyster, Sassenach. Ye hadna finished yet, though?"

"No, I—how long were you *listening*?"

"Oh, long enough," he assured me, and, ceasing operations for a moment, took hold of my disengaged hand and folded it firmly round a very enthusiastic bit of his own anatomy. "Mmm?"

"Oh," I said. "Well . . ." My legs had taken stock of the situation much more quickly than my mind had, and so had he. He lowered his head and kissed me in the dark with a soft, eager thoroughness, then pulled his mouth away long enough to ask, "How do elephants make love?"

Fortunately, he didn't wait for an answer, as I hadn't got one. He rolled over me and slid home in the same movement, and the universe shrank suddenly to a single vivid point.

A few minutes later, we lay under the blazing stars, quilt thrown off and hearts thumping slowly back to normal.

"Did you know," I said, "that your heart actually does stop for a moment at the point of climax? That's why your heart-beat is slow for a minute or two after; the sympathetic nervous system has fired all its synapses, leaving the parasympathetic to run your heart, and the parasympathetic decreases heart rate."

"I noticed it stopped," he assured me. "Didna really care why, as long as it started again." He put his arms over his head and stretched luxuriously, enjoying the cool air on his skin. "Actually, I never cared whether it started again, either."

"There's a man for you," I remarked tolerantly. "No forethought."

"Ye dinna need forethought for *that,* Sassenach. What ye were doing when I interrupted ye, I mean. I admit, if there's a woman involved, ye have to think of all sorts of things, but no for that." He paused for a moment.

"Um. Did I not . . . serve ye well enough earlier, Sassenach?" he asked, a little shyly. "I would ha' taken more time, but I couldna wait, and—"

"No, no," I assured him. "It wasn't that—I mean, I just . . . enjoyed it so much I woke up wanting more."

"Oh. Good."

He relaxed with a deep, contented sigh, closing his eyes. There was a waxing moon and I could see him clearly, though the moonlight washed all color from the scene, leaving him a sculpture in black and white. I ran a hand down his chest and lightly over his still-flat belly—hard physical labor had its price, but also its benefits—and cupped his genitals, warm and damp in my hand.

"Tha ball-ratha sìnte riut," he said, putting a big hand over mine.

"A what?" I said. "A lucky . . . leg?"

"Well, limb, really; leg would be overstating it by a good deal. 'There is a lucky limb stretched against you.' It's the first line of a poem by Alasdair mac Mhaighistir Alasdair. 'To an Excellent Penis,' it's called."

"Thought highly of himself, did Alasdair?"

"Well, he doesna *say* it's his—though I admit that's the implication." He squinted a little, eyes still closed, and declaimed:

"Tha ball-ratha sìnte riut
A choisinn mìle buaidh
Sàr-bodh iallach acfhainneach

Rinn-gheur sgaiteach cruaidh
Ùilleach feitheach feadanach
Làidir seasmhach buan
Beòdha treòrach togarrach
Nach diùltadh bog no cruaidh."

"I daresay," I said. "Do it in English; I believe I've missed a few of the finer points. He can't really have compared his penis to a bagpipe's chanter, can he?"

"Oh, aye, he did," Jamie confirmed, then translated:

"There is a lucky limb stretched against you
That has made a thousand conquests:
An excellent penis that is leathery, well-equipped,
Sharp-pointed, piercing, firm,
Lubricated, sinewy, chanter-like,
Strong, durable, long-enduring,
Vigorous, powerful, joyous,
That would not jilt either soft or hard body."

"Leathery, is it?" I said, giggling. "I don't wonder, after a thousand conquests. What does he mean, 'well-equipped,' though?"

"I wouldna ken. I suppose I must have seen it once or twice—havin' a piss by the side o' the road, I mean—but if so, I wasna greatly struck by its virtues."

"You *knew* this Alasdair?" I rolled over and propped my head on my arm.

"Oh, aye. So did you, though ye maybe didna ken he wrote poetry, you not having much *Gàidhlig* in those days."

I still didn't have a great deal, though now that we were among *Gàidhlig*-speaking people again, it was coming back.

"Where did we know him? In the Rising?"

He was Prince Tearlach's *Gàidhlig* tutor.

"Aye. He wrote a great many poems and songs about the Stuart cause." And now that he reminded me, I thought I *did* perhaps recall him: a middle-aged man singing in the firelight, long-haired and clean-shaven, with a deep cleft in his chin. I'd always wondered how he managed to shave so neatly with a cutthroat razor.

"Hmm." I had distinctly mixed feelings about people like

Alasdair. On the one hand, without them stirring the pot and exciting irrational romanticism, the Cause might easily have withered and died long before Culloden. On the other . . . because of them, the battlefields—and those who had fallen there—were remembered.

Before I could think too deeply on that subject, though, Jamie interrupted my thoughts by idly brushing his penis to one side.

"The schoolmasters made me learn to write wi' my right hand," he remarked, "but luckily it didna occur to anyone to force me to abuse myself that way, too."

"Why call it that?" I asked, laughing. "Abusing yourself, I mean."

"Well, 'masturbate' sounds a great deal more wicked, aye? And if ye're abusing yourself, it sounds less like ye're havin' a good time."

"Strong, durable, long-enduring," I quoted, stroking the object in question lightly. "Perhaps Alasdair meant something like glove leather?"

"Vigorous and powerful it may be, Sassenach, and certainly joyous—but I tell ye, it's no going to rise to the occasion three times in one night. Not at my age." Detaching my hand, he rolled over, scooping me into a spoon shape before him, and in less than a minute was sound asleep.

When I woke in the morning, he was gone.

144

VISIT TO A HAUNTED GARDEN

I BLOODY *KNEW*. From the moment I woke to birdsong and a cold quilt beside me, I knew. Jamie often rose before dawn, for hunting, fishing, or travel—but he invariably touched me before he left, leaving me with a word or a kiss. We'd lived long enough to know how chancy life could be and how swiftly people could be parted forever. We'd never spoken of it or made a formal custom of it, but we almost never parted without some brief token of affection.

And now he'd gone off in the dark, without a word.

"You bloody, bloody *man*!" I said, and thumped the ground with my fist in frustration.

I made my way down the hill, quilts folded under my arm, fuming. Jenny. He'd gone and talked to Jenny. Of course he had; why hadn't I foreseen that?

He'd agreed not to ask me. He hadn't said he wouldn't ask anyone else. And while Jenny clearly loved me, I'd never been under any illusions as to where her ultimate loyalty lay. She wouldn't have voluntarily given up my secret, but if her brother asked her, point-blank, she would certainly have told him.

The sun was spreading warmth like honey over the morning, but none of it was reaching my cold bones.

He knew. And he'd gone a-hunting.

I DIDN'T NEED to look but looked anyway. Jamie's rifle was gone from its place behind the door.

"He came in early," Amy Higgins told me, spooning out a bowl of parritch for me. "We were all in bed still, but he called out soft, and Bobby got up to unbar the door. I would have fed him, but he said he was well enough and away he went. Hunting, he said."

"Of course," I said. The bowl was warm to my hands, and in spite of what I thought—what I *knew*—was going on, the thick grainy smell of it was enticing. And there was honey, and a little cream kept back from the butter-making; Amy allowed these in deference to Bobby's debauched English tastes, though she stuck to the usual virtuously Scottish salt on parritch herself.

Eating settled me, a little. The blunt fact was that there was absolutely nothing I could do. I didn't know the lumpkin's name or where he lived. Jamie might. If he'd talked to Jenny right away, he could easily have sent word to Beardsley's trading post and asked who was the fat man with the port-wine stain on his face. Even if he didn't yet know and was on his way to find out, I had no means of catching up with him—let alone stopping him.

"A Hieland man canna live wi' a man who's raped his wife nearby, nor should he." That's what Jenny had said to me. In warning, I now realized.

"Gak!" It was wee Rob, toddling round the room, who had seized my skirt in both hands and was giving me a toothy smile—all four teeth of it. "Hungy!"

"Hallo, there," I said, smiling back despite my disquiet. "Hungry, you say?" I extended a small spoonful of honeyed parritch in his direction, and he went for it like a starving piranha. We shared the rest of the bowl in companionable silence—Rob wasn't a chatty child—and I decided that I would work in the garden today. I didn't want to go far afield, as Rachel could go into labor at any moment, from the looks of it. And a short spell of solitude amid the soothing company of the vegetable kingdom might lend me a bit of much-needed calm.

It would also get me out of the cabin, I reflected, as Rob, having licked the bowl, handed it back to me, toddled across the cabin, and, lifting his dress, peed in the hearth.

THERE WOULD BE a new kitchen garden near the new house. It was measured and planned, the earth broken, and poles for the deer fence had begun accumulating. But there was little point in walking that far each day to tend a garden when there was not yet a house to live in. I minded Amy's plot in the meantime, sneaking occasional seedlings and propagules into it between the cabbages and turnips—but today I meant to visit the Old Garden.

That's what the people of the Ridge called it, and they didn't go there. I privately called it Malva's Garden, and did.

It was on a small rise behind where the Big House had stood. With the new house rising already in my mind, I passed the bare spot where the Big House had been, without a qualm. There were more exigent things to be qualm about, I thought, and sniggered.

"You are losing your mind, Beauchamp," I murmured, but felt better.

The deer fence had weathered and broken down in spots,

and the deer had naturally accepted the invitation. Most of the bulbs had been pawed up and eaten, and while a few of the softer plants, like lettuce and radishes, had escaped long enough to reseed themselves, the growing plants had been nibbled to scabby white stalks. But a very thorny wild rose brier flourished away in one corner, cucumber vines crawled over the ground, and a massive gourd vine rippled over a collapsed portion of the fence, thick with infant fruits.

A monstrous pokeweed rose from the center of the patch, nearly ten feet high, its thick red stem supporting a wealth of long green leaves and hundreds of purplish-red flower stalks. The nearby trees had grown immensely, shading the plot, and in the diffuse green light the long, nubbly stalks looked like nudibranchs, those colorful sea slugs, gently swaying in currents of air rather than water. I touched it respectfully in passing; it had an odd medicinal smell, well deserved. There were a number of useful things one could do with pokeweed, but eating it wasn't one of them. Which was to say, people *did* eat the leaves on occasion, but the chances of accidental poisoning made it not worth the trouble of preparation unless there was absolutely nothing else to eat.

I couldn't remember the exact spot where she'd died. Where the pokeweed grew? That would be entirely apropos, but maybe too poetic.

Malva Christie. A strange, damaged young woman—but one I'd loved. Who perhaps had loved me, as well as she could. She'd been with child and near her time when her brother—the child's father—had cut her throat, here in the garden.

I'd found her moments later and tried to save the child, performing an emergency cesarean with my gardening knife. He'd been alive when I pulled him from his mother's womb but died at once, the brief flame of his life a passing blue glow in my hands.

Did anyone name him? I wondered suddenly. They'd buried the baby boy with Malva, but I didn't recall anyone mentioning his name.

Adso came stalking through the weeds, eyes intent on a fat robin poking busily for worms in the corner. I kept still, watching, admiring the lithe way in which he sank imperceptibly lower as he came more slowly, creeping on his belly for the last few feet, pausing, moving, pausing again for a long, nerve-racking second, no more than the tip of his tail a-twitch.

And then he moved, too fast for the eye to see, and in a brief and soundless explosion of feathers, it was over.

"Well done, cat," I said, though in fact the sudden violence had startled me a little. He paid no attention but leapt through a low spot in the fence, his prey in his mouth, and disappeared to enjoy his meal.

I stood still for a moment. I wasn't looking for Malva; the Ridge folk said that her ghost haunted the garden, wailing for her child. Just the sort of thing they *would* think, I thought, rather uncharitably. I hoped her spirit had fled and was at peace. But I couldn't help thinking, too, of Rachel, so very different a soul, but a young mother, as well, so near her time, and so nearby.

My old gardening knife was long gone. But Jamie had made me a new one during the winter evenings in Savannah, the handle carved from whalebone, shaped, as the last one had been, to fit my hand. I took it from its sheath in my pocket and nicked my wrist, not stopping to think.

The white scar at the base of my thumb had faded, no more now than a thin line, almost lost in the lines that scored my palm. Still legible, though, if you knew where to look: the letter "J" he had cut into my flesh just before Culloden. Claiming me.

I massaged the flesh near the cut gently, until a full red drop ran down the side of my wrist and fell to the ground at the foot of the pokeweed.

"Blood for blood," I said, the words quiet in themselves but seeming drowned by the rustle of leaves all around. "Rest ye quiet, child—and do no harm."

DO NO HARM. *Well, you tried.* As doctor, as lover, as mother and wife. I said a silent goodbye to the garden and went up the hill, toward the MacDonalds' cottage.

How would Jamie do it? I wondered, and was surprised to find that I did wonder, and wondered in a purely dispassionate way. He'd taken the rifle. Would he pick the man off at a distance, as if he were a deer at water? A clean shot, the man dead before he knew it.

Or would he feel he must confront the man, tell him why he was about to die—offer him a chance to fight for his life? Or just walk up with the cold face of vengeance, say nothing, and kill the man with his hands?

"Ye canna have been marrit to a Hieland man all these years and not ken how deep they can hate."

I really didn't want to know.

Ian had shot Allan Christie with an arrow, as one would put down a rabid dog, and for precisely similar reasons.

I'd seen Jamie's hate flame bright the night he saved me and said to his men, *"Kill them all."*

How was it now for him? If the man had been found on that night, there would have been no question that he would die. Should it be different now, only because time had passed?

I walked in the sun now but still felt cold, the shadows of Malva's Garden with me. The matter was out of my hands; no longer my business, but Jamie's.

I MET JENNY on the path, coming up briskly, a basket on her arm and her face alight with excitement.

"Already?" I exclaimed.

"Aye, Matthew MacDonald came down a half hour ago to say her water's broken. He's gone to find Ian now."

He had found Ian; we met the two young men in the dooryard of the cabin, Matthew bright red with excitement, Ian white as a sheet under his tan. The door of the cabin was open; I could hear the murmur of women's voices inside.

"Mam," Ian said huskily, seeing Jenny. His shoulders, stiff with terror, relaxed a little.

"Dinna fash yourself, *a bhalaich,*" she said comfortably, and smiled sympathetically at him. "Your auntie and I have done this a time or two before. It will be all right."

"Grannie! Grannie!" I turned to find Germain and Fanny, both covered with dirt and with sticks and leaves in their hair, faces bright with excitement. "Is it true? Is Rachel having her baby? Can we watch?"

How did it work? I wondered. News in the mountains seemed to travel through the air.

"Watch, forbye!" Jenny exclaimed, scandalized. "Childbed isna any kind of a place for men. Be off with ye this minute!"

Germain looked torn between disappointment and pleasure at being called a man. Fanny looked hopeful.

"I'm no-t a man," she said.

Jenny and I both looked dubiously at her and then at each other.

"Well, ye're no quite a woman yet, either, are ye?" Jenny said to her. If not, she was close. Tiny breasts were beginning to show when she was in her shift, and her menarche wasn't far off.

"I've s-seen babies bor-n." It was a simple statement of fact, and Jenny nodded slowly.

"Aye. All right, then."

Fanny beamed.

"What do *we* do?" Germain demanded, indignant. "Us men."

I smiled, and Jenny gave a deep chuckle that was older than time. Ian and Matthew looked startled, Germain quite taken aback.

"Your uncle did his part of the business nine months ago, lad, just as ye'll do yours when it's time. Now, you and Matthew take your uncle awa' and get him drunk, aye?"

Germain nodded quite seriously and turned to Ian.

"Do you want Amy's wine, Ian, or shall we use Grandda's good whisky, do ye think?"

Ian's long face twitched, and he glanced at the open cabin door. A deep grunt, not quite a groan, came out and he looked away, paling further. He swallowed and groped in the leather bag he wore at his waist, coming out with what looked like a rolled animal skin of some kind and handing it to me.

"If—" he started, then stopped to gather himself and started again. "When the babe is born, will ye wrap him—or her,"—he added hastily, "in this?"

It was a small skin, soft and flexible, with very thick, fine fur in shades of gray and white. A wolf, I thought, surprised. The hide of an unborn wolf pup.

"Of course, Ian," I said, and squeezed his arm. "Don't worry. It will be all right."

Jenny looked at the small, soft skin and shook her head.

"I doubt, lad, if that will half-cover your bairn. Have ye no seen the size o' your wife lately?"

145

AND YOU KNOW THAT

JAMIE CAME HOME three days later, with a large buck tied to Miranda's saddle. The horse seemed unenthused about this, though tolerant, and she whuffed air through her nostrils and shivered her hide when he dragged the carcass off, letting it fall with a thump.

"Aye, lass, ye've done brawly," he said, clapping her on the shoulder. "Is Ian about, *a nighean*?" He paused to kiss me briefly, glancing up the hill toward the MacDonald cottage. "I could use a bit of help wi' this."

"Oh, he's here," I said, smiling. "I don't know if he'll come skin your deer for you, though. He's got a new son and won't let the baby out of his sight."

Jamie's face, rather tired and worn, broke into a grin.

"A son? The blessing of Bride and Michael be on him! A braw lad?"

"Very," I assured him. "I think he must weigh almost nine pounds."

"Poor lass," he said, with a sympathetic grimace. "And her first, too. Wee Rachel's all right, though?"

"Rather tired and sore, but quite all right," I assured him. "Shall I bring you some beer, while you take care of the horse?"

"A good wife is prized above rubies," he said, smiling. "Come to me, *mo nighean donn*." He reached out a long arm and drew me in, holding me close against him. I put my arms around him and felt the quiver of his muscles, exhausted, and the sheer hard strength still in him, that would hold him up, no matter how tired he might be. We stood quite still for some time, my cheek against his chest and his face against my hair, drawing strength from each other for whatever might come. Being married.

AMID THE GENERAL rejoicing and fuss over the baby—who was still being called Oggy, his parents being spoiled for choice regarding his name—the butchering of the deer, and the subsequent feasting lasting well into the night, it was late morning of the next day before we found ourselves alone again.

"The only thing lacking last night was cherry bounce," I remarked. "I never saw so many people drink so much of so many different things." We were making our way—slowly—up to the house site, carrying several bags of nails, a very expensive small saw, and a plane that Jamie had brought back in addition to the deer.

Jamie made a small amused sound but didn't reply. He paused for a moment to look up at the site, presumably envisioning the outline of the house-to-be.

"D'ye think it should maybe have a third story?" he asked. "The walls would bear it easily enough. Take careful building of the chimneys, though. Keeping them plumb, I mean."

"Do we need that much room?" I asked doubtfully. There had certainly been times in the old house when I'd wished we'd *had* that much room: influxes of visitors, new emigrants, or refugees had often filled the place to the point of explosion—mine. "Providing more space might just encourage guests."

"Ye make it sound like they're white ants, Sassenach."

"Wh—oh, termites. Well, yes, there's a strong superficial resemblance."

Arrived at the clearing, I piled the nails conveniently and went to bathe my face and hands in water from the tiny spring that flowed from the rocks a little way up the hill. By the time I came back, Jamie had stripped off his shirt and was knocking together a pair of rough sawhorses. I hadn't seen him with his shirt off for a long time and paused to enjoy the sight. Beyond the simple pleasure of seeing his body flex and move, whipcord muscles moving easily under his skin, I liked knowing that he felt himself safe here and could ignore his scars.

I sat down on an upturned bucket and watched for a time. The blows of his hammer temporarily silenced the birds, and when he stopped and set the sawhorse on its feet, the air rang empty in my ears.

"I wish you hadn't felt you had to do it," I said quietly.

He didn't reply for a moment but pursed his lips as he squatted and picked up a few stray nails. "When we wed—" he said, not looking at me. "When we wed, I said to ye that I gave ye the protection of my name, my clan—and my body." He stood up then and looked down at me, serious. "Do ye tell me now that ye no longer want that?"

"I—no," I said abruptly. "I just—I wish you hadn't killed him, that's all. I'd—managed to forgive him. It wasn't an easy thing to do, but I did it. Not permanently, but I thought I *could* do it permanently, sooner or later."

His mouth twitched a little.

"And if ye could forgive him, he needn't die, ye're saying? That's like a judge lettin' a murderer go free, because his victim's family forgave him. Or an enemy soldier sent off wi' all his weapons."

"I am not a state at war, and you are not my army!"

He began to speak, then stopped short, searching my face, his eyes intent.

"Am I not?" he said quietly.

I opened my mouth to reply but found I couldn't. The birds had come back, and a gang of house finches chittered at the foot of a big fir that grew at the side of the clearing.

"You are," I said reluctantly, and, standing up, wrapped my arms around him. He was warm from his work, and the scars on his back were fine as threads under my fingers. "I wish you didn't have to be."

"Aye, well," he said, and held me close. After a bit, we walked hand in hand to the biggest pile of barked timber and sat down. I could feel him thinking but was content to wait until he had formed what he wanted to say. It didn't take him long. He turned to me and took my hands, formal as a man about to say his wedding vows.

"Ye lost your parents young, *mo nighean donn,* and wandered about the world, rootless. Ye loved Frank"—his mouth compressed for an instant, but I thought he was unconscious of it—"and of course ye love Brianna and Roger Mac and the weans . . . but, Sassenach—I am the true home of your heart, and I know that."

He lifted my hands to his mouth and kissed my upturned palms, one and then the other, his breath warm and his beard stubble soft on my fingers.

"I have loved others, and I do love many, Sassenach—but you alone hold all my heart, whole in your hands," he said softly. "And you know that."

WE WORKED through the day then, Jamie fitting stones for the foundation, me digging the new garden and foraging through the woods, bringing back pipsissewa and black cohosh, mint and wild ginger to transplant.

Toward late afternoon we stopped to eat; I'd brought cheese and bread and early apples in my basket and had put two stone bottles of ale in the spring to keep cold. We sat on the grass, leaning back against a stack of timber that was shaded by the big fir, tired, eating in companionable silence.

"Ian says he and Rachel will come up tomorrow to help," Jamie said at last, thriftily eating his apple core. "Are ye going to eat yours, Sassenach?"

"No," I said, handing it over. "Apple seeds have cyanide in them, you know."

"Will it kill me?"

"It hasn't so far."

"Good." He pulled off the stem and ate the core. "Have they settled on a name for the wee lad yet?"

I closed my eyes and leaned back into the shade of the big fir, enjoying its sharp, sun-warmed scent.

"Hmm. The last I heard, Rachel was suggesting Fox—for George Fox, you know; he was the founder of the Society of Friends, but naturally they wouldn't call the baby George, because of the king. Ian said he doesn't think highly of foxes, though, and what about Wolf, instead?"

Jamie made a meditative Scottish noise.

"Aye, that's no bad. At least he's not wanting to call the wean Rollo."

I laughed, opening my eyes.

"Do you really think that's what he has in mind? I know people name their children for deceased relatives, but naming one for your deceased dog . . ."

"Aye, well," Jamie said judiciously. "He was a *good* dog."

"Well, yes, but—" A movement down on the far side of the cove caught my eye. People coming up the wagon road. "Look, who's that?" There were four small moving dots, but at this distance I couldn't make out much more than that without my glasses.

Jamie shaded his eyes, peering.

"No one I ken," he said, sounding mildly interested. "It looks like a family, though—they've a couple of bairns. Maybe new folk, wanting to settle. They havena got much in the way of goods, though."

I squinted; they were closer now, and I could make out the disparity of height. Yes, a man and a woman, both wearing broad-brimmed hats, and a boy and girl.

"Look, the lad's got red hair," Jamie said, smiling and raising his chin to point. "He minds me of Jem."

"So he does." Curious now, I got up and rummaged in my basket, finding the bit of silk in which I kept my spectacles when not wearing them. I put them on and turned, pleased as I always was to see fine details spring suddenly into being. Slightly less pleased to see that what I had thought was a scale of bark on the timber near where I'd been sitting was in fact an enormous centipede, enjoying the shade.

I turned my attention back to the newcomers, though; they'd stopped—the little girl had dropped something. Her dolly—I could see the doll's hair, a splotch of color on the ground, even redder than the little boy's. The man was wearing a pack, and the woman had a large bag over one shoulder. She set it down and bent to pick up the doll, brushing it off and handing it back to her daughter.

The woman turned then to speak to her husband, throwing out an arm to point to something—the Higginses' cabin, I thought. The man put both hands to his mouth and shouted, and the wind carried his words to us, faint but clearly audible, called out in a strong, cracked voice.

"Hello, the house!"

I was on my feet, and Jamie stood and grabbed my hand, hard enough to bruise my fingers.

Movement at the door of the cabin, and a small figure that I recognized as Amy Higgins appeared. The tall woman pulled off her hat and waved it, her long red hair streaming out like a banner in the wind.

"Hello, the house!" she called, laughing.

Then I was flying down the hill, with Jamie just before me, arms flung wide, the two of us flying together on that same wind.

AUTHOR'S NOTES

Dams and Tunnels

In the 1950s, a great hydroelectric project was started to bring power to the Highlands, and, in the process, many dams with turbines were built. During the construction of these dams, a good many tunnels were built, a number of them long enough to require a small electric train to transport men and equipment from one end to the other. (If you're interested in this project and its history, I recommend a book called *Tunnel Tigers: A First-Hand Account of a Hydro Boy in the Highlands* by Patrick Campbell, though there are several other good sources.)

Now, Loch Errochty does exist, and it does have a dam. I don't know whether it has a tunnel exactly like the one described in the book, but if it did—that's what it would look like; the tunnel and train are taken from multiple descriptions of the hydroelectric constructions in the Highlands. My description of the dam itself, its spillway, and its turbine room are based on those at the Pitlochry Dam.

Banastre Tarleton and the British Legion

There will likely be a certain amount of quibbling about my inclusion of Colonel Banastre Tarleton in the Battle of Monmouth, as the British Legion of which he was a commander (a regiment of mixed cavalry and artillery) was technically not in existence until after General Clinton's return to New York following the battle. However, the British Legion did consist of two separate parts: cavalry, under the command of Banastre Tarleton, and artillery, and these parts were organized separately. The cavalry unit appears to have been in some stage of organization in early June of 1778, prior to the battle, though the artillery unit (reasonably enough, given the problems of equipping and training) was not organized until late July, after the battle, when Sir Henry Clinton had returned to New York.

Now, there is no report that I can find as to the definite whereabouts of Colonel Tarleton during the month of June 1778. While neither he nor his British Legion is listed in the official order of battle, that listing is admitted by every source I could find to be confused and deficient. Owing to the large number of militia units taking part and the irregular nature of the battle (by eighteenth-century standards), various small groups are known to have been there but were not documented, and others were there but under confusing circumstances (e.g., a portion of Daniel Morgan's Rifle Corps was reported as taking part in the battle, but Morgan himself didn't. I don't know whether his absence was the result of illness, accident, or conflict, but apparently he wasn't there, even though he plainly intended to be).

Now, if *I* were General Clinton, in the throes of imminent departure from Philadelphia, and more or less expecting the possibility of attack by Washington's Rebels, *and* I had this nice new cavalry unit forming up in New York—would I not send word to Colonel Tarleton to bring his men on down, to lend a hand in the evacuation and to have a bit of field experience to meld them together as a new unit? I would, and I can't think that General Clinton was less soldierly than I am.

(Besides, there is this interesting thing called novelistic license. I have one. Framed.)

The Battle of Monmouth

The battle lasted from before daylight 'til after dark: the longest battle of the Revolution. It was also by far the messiest battle of the Revolution.

Owing to the circumstances—Washington's troops trying to catch an enemy army fleeing in three widely separated divisions—neither side could choose its ground, and the ground over which they fought was so chopped up and patchworked with farms, creeks, and forests, they couldn't fight in the usual manner, with lines facing each other, nor was it possible to develop effective flanking maneuvers. Thus it wasn't so much a classic eighteenth-century battle as a very long series of pitched fights between small groups, most of whom had No Idea what was going on anywhere else. And it ended up as one of those indecisive battles that no one wins and where no one has any idea for some time afterward what the actual effects of the battle were or would be.

With two hundred–odd years of historical perspective, the general take on the Battle of Monmouth is that it was important not because the Americans won but because they didn't actually lose.

Washington and his troops had spent the preceding winter at Valley Forge, pulling together what men and resources they had and forming those troops into (they hoped) a real army, with the help of Baron von Steuben (who was actually not a baron but thought it sounded better) and other European officers who lent their services either out of idealism (*vide* the Marquis de La Fayette) or from a sense of personal adventure and ambition. (As the Continental army was a trifle lacking in money, they offered instant promotion as an inducement to experienced officers; a mere captain from a British or German regiment could become a colonel—or occasionally, a general—in the Continental army, no questions asked.)

Consequently, Washington was itching to find an opportunity to try out the new army, and General Clinton provided an excellent opportunity. The fact that the new army did acquit itself very well (bar the occasional snafu such as Lee's botched encircling maneuver and mistaken retreat) was a shot in the arm for the Rebel cause and gave both army and partisans new heart to continue the fight.

Still, in terms both of logistics and results, the battle was One Big Mess. While there is a tremendous amount of material on the battle, and a great many eyewitness reports, the fragmented nature of the conflict prevented anyone from ever having a clear idea as to the overall state of things during the battle, and the staggered arrival of so many companies of militia from Pennsylvania and New Jersey meant that some companies were not documented as having been there, even though they were. (Sources note "several unidentified militia companies from New Jersey," for instance. These are, of course, the companies commanded by General Fraser.)

From a historical perspective, the Battle of Monmouth is also interesting because of the participation of so many well-known Revolutionary figures, from George Washington himself to the Marquis de La Fayette, Nathanael Greene, Anthony Wayne, and Baron von Steuben.

Now, when you include real people in a historical novel, you want to balance a realistic and (insofar as is possible) accurate portrayal of them against the fact that the novel is seldom *about* these people. Therefore, while we do see most of them (and what we do see is based on reasonably accurate biographical information[1]), we see them *en passant,* and only in situations affecting the people who are the real focus of the novel.

In regard to the novelistic license mentioned above: a special embossed seal (stamped by the Temporal Authority) allows me to compress time when necessary. True battle aficionados (or those obsessive souls who feel compelled to construct timelines and then fret about them) will note that Jamie and Claire meet with General Washington and several other senior officers at Coryell's Ferry. Some five days later, we find them making preparations on the day of battle, with little or no description of what was happening to them during the interval. That's because, while there was a tremendous amount of moving around, nothing of dramatic note happened on those five days. While I do strive for historical accuracy, I do also know that a) history is often not very accurate, and b) most people who really care about the logistic minutiae of battles are reading Osprey's Men-at-Arms series or the transcript of the court-martial of General Charles Lee, not novels.

Ergo: While all the officers mentioned were with Washington's army, they were not all at dinner on the same night or in the same place. Commanders (and their troops) came to join Washington from several places over the course of the nine days between Clinton's exodus from Philadelphia and Wash-

---

1 For example, Nathanael Greene's remarks about Quakers are taken from his own letters, as is his reference to his father's discouraging reading as "tending to separate one from God."

ington's catching him near Monmouth Courthouse (the site of Monmouth Courthouse is now the Monmouth Hall of Records, for the benefit of people who choose to read with a map in hand[2]). The general state of the relations among those officers, though, is as shown during that dinner.

Likewise, it seemed unnecessary to depict the mundane events of five days of travel and military conference, just to prove to the meanest intelligence that five days had, in fact, passed. So I didn't.

The Court-Martial of General Charles Lee

Lee's lack of scouting, communications, and (not to put too fine a point on it) leadership led to the massive retreat that nearly scuttled the American attack altogether, this being retrieved by George Washington's personal rallying of the retreating troops. In consequence, General Lee was court-martialed following the battle on charges of disobeying orders, misbehavior before the enemy, and disrespect to the commander in chief; he was convicted and suspended from military command for a year. There would have been a great deal of talk around Philadelphia regarding this—particularly in the household of a printer who published a regular newspaper. However, the Fraser family had other pressing concerns at the time, and so no mention was made of this.

Quaker Plain Speech

The Religious Society of Friends was founded around 1647 by George Fox. As part of the society's belief in the equality of all men before God, they did not use honorific titles (such as "Mr./Mrs.," "General/Colonel/etc.") and used "plain speech" in addressing everyone.

---

2 With regard to maps and distances, etc., it's worth noting that such things as township boundaries did change between the eighteenth century and the twenty-first. Ergo, Tennent Church is now in Manalapan, New Jersey, whereas originally it was in Freehold Township. The church didn't move; the township did.

Now, as any of you who have a second language with Latin roots (Spanish, French, etc.) realize, these languages have both a familiar and a formal version of "you." So did English, once upon a time. The "thee" and "thou" forms that most of us recognize as Elizabethan or Biblical are in fact the English familiar forms of "you"—with "you" used as both the plural familiar form ("all y'all") and the formal pronoun (both singular and plural). As English evolved, the familiar forms were dropped, leaving us with the utilitarian "you" to cover all contingencies.

Quakers retained the familiar forms, though, as part of their "plain speech" until the twentieth century. Over the years, though, plain speech also evolved, and while "thee/thy" remained, "thou/thine" largely disappeared, and the verb forms associated with "thee/thy" changed. From about the mid-eighteenth century onward, plain speech used "thee" as the singular form of "you" (the plural form remained "you," even in plain speech), with the same verb forms normally used for third person singular: e.g., "He knows that/Thee knows that." The older verb endings—"knowest," "doth," etc.—were no longer used.

If you would like to know a whole lot more about the grammatical foundations and usages of Quaker plain speech than most people normally want to, allow me to recommend to you *No Need to be Ashamed of the Plain Language* by Kenneth S. P. Morse

You can find this on the QuakerJane.com website, or Google it (in case that website should no longer be extant).

Scots/Scotch/Scottish

As noted elsewhere (*Lord John and the Brotherhood of the Blade,* see "Author's Notes"), in the eighteenth century (and, indeed, well into the mid-twentieth century), the word "Scotch" and its variants (e.g., "Scotchman") were commonly used (by both English people *and* Scots) to describe an inhabitant of Scotland. The terms "Scottish" and "Scots" were also occasionally used, though less common.

Personally, I don't think political correctness has any place in historical fiction, and therefore those persons in this book who normally would have used "Scotch" do.

Typos and Terminology

Owing to the interesting idiosyncrasies of Scots dialect, some words may appear to be misspelled—but they aren't. For instance, while an English cook may have made her flapjacks on an iron griddle, her Scottish counterpart was frying sausages on a hot girdle. (This occasional transposition of sounds results in such entertaining items as a Scottish dessert known as "creamed crud" ("curd" to the less-imaginative English). It also results in the occasional inattentive reviewer denouncing the occurrence of "typos" in my books. This is not to say that there *aren't* any typos—there always are, no matter how many eyeballs have combed the pages—just that "girdle" isn't one of them.

Besides dialectical idiosyncrasies, there are also the oddities due to obsolete (but entirely accurate) usage. For example, at one point in this book, you will find someone hiding behind a pile of "spiled" barrels. I do *not* mean "spoiled," and it isn't a typo. "Spiled" means that a spile (a small wooden peg or spigot) has been driven into a cask in order to broach it and draw off liquid. So the pile is composed of barrels that have been drained of their contents. (Yes, I could indeed have said "a pile of empty barrels" instead, but what fun would *that* be?)

Bibliography/LibraryThing

Having been an academic for a good long time, I appreciate the virtues of a good bibliography. Having been a reader of novels for a lot longer, I sort of don't think extensive bibliographies belong in them.

Still, one of the side effects of reading historical fiction often is a desire to learn more about events, locations, flora, fauna, etc., described therein. I have a goodish number of references (about 1,500, last time I counted), acquired over the last twenty-odd years of writing historical fiction, and am happy to share the bibliographic information for these.

As it's not convenient to do that individually with a large number of people, I've put my whole reference collection (as of the beginning of 2013, at least) on LibraryThing—this being an online bibliographic site, where people can catalog and share their personal library information. My catalog is public, and you should be able to access all of it using my name as a keyword. (Individual references also include keywords like "medicine," "herbal," "biography," etc.)

ACKNOWLEDGMENTS

It takes me about four years to write one of the Big Books, what with research, travel, and the fact that they are . . . er . . . big. During that time, LOTS of people talk to me and kindly offer advice on everything from How to Reseat an Eyeball to what kind of a mess indigo-dyeing really makes, entertaining trivia (such as the fact that cows do not like daisies. Who knew?), and logistical support (mostly in terms of remembering when the people in my books were born and how far it is from point A to point B and in which direction—I went to a parochial school that stopped teaching geography in the fifth grade, so this is Not One of My Strong Points, and as for personal chronology, I just don't care whether a given character is nineteen or twenty, but apparently lots of people do, and more power to them).

This being the case, I'm sure I'm leaving out dozens of kindly people who have given me useful information and assistance over the last four years and I apologize for not having written down their names at the time—but I surely do appreciate said information and assistance!

Among those whose names I *did* write down, I'd like to acknowledge . . .

. . . My literary agents, Russell Galen and Danny Baror, without whom my books would not be published as successfully and widely as they are, and I would not have the edifying experience of opening cartons of books written in Lithuanian with my name on the front—to say nothing of the Korean edition of *Outlander* with the pink bubbles on the cover.

. . . Sharon Biggs Waller, for information about the Scots Dumpy and for bringing this charming chicken to my attention.

. . . Marte Brengle, for telling me about the forensic reconstruction of George Washington's face, and Dr. Merih O'Donoghue, for notes on his disastrous dental history.

. . . Dr. Merih O'Donoghue and her ophthalmologist friend, for technical commentary and useful gruesome details concerning Lord John's eye. Also for the teaching model of an eyeball, which adorns my bookshelves and gives interviewers who enter my office the willies.

. . . Carol and Tracey of MyOutlanderPurgatory, for their lovely photos of the battlefield at Paoli, which drew my attention to the Rebel rallying cry "Remember Paoli!" and the discovery of Lord John's unpopular cousin.

. . . Tamara Burke, for bits of homestead and farming lore, most particularly for her vivid description of a rooster valiantly defending his hens.

. . . Tamara Burke, Joanna Bourne, and Beth and Matthew Shope, for helpful advice on Quaker marriage customs and absorbing discussions regarding the history and philosophies of the Society of Friends. Any error or license taken with regard to such customs is mine, I hasten to add.

. . . Catherine MacGregor (Gaelic and French, including gruesome lullabies about beheaded lovers), Catherine-Ann MacPhee (Gaelic, phraseology *and* idiom, besides introducing me to the Gaelic poem "To an Excellent Penis" [see below], and Àdhamh Ó Broin, Gaelic tutor for the *Outlander* Starz television production, for emergency help with exclamations. Barbara Schnell, for providing the German and occasional Latin bits (If you want to know how to say "Shit!" in Latin, it's *"Stercus!"*).

. . . Michael Newton, for permission to use his delightful translation of "To an Excellent Penis," from his book *The*

Naughty Little Book of Gaelic (which I recommend highly, for assorted purposes).

. . . Sandra Harrison, who saved me from Grievous Error by informing me that British police cars do not have flashing red lights, only blue ones.

. . . the 3,247 (approximately) French-speakers and scholars who informed me that I had misspelled *"n'est-ce pas"* in an excerpt of this book posted on Facebook.

. . . James Fenimore Cooper, for lending me Natty Bumppo, whose reminiscences of the proper way to conduct a massacre considerably eased Lord John's journey into captivity.

. . . Sandy Parker (aka the Archivist), for faithful tracking and analysis of the *#DailyLines* (these are tiny snippets of whatever I happen to be working on, posted daily on Facebook and Twitter for the purpose of entertaining people during the long time it takes me to finish a book, as well as a constant helpful flow of articles, photos, and useful nits).

. . . The Cadre of Genealogical Nitpickers—Sandy Parker, Vicki Pack, Mandy Tidwell, and Rita Meistrell, who are responsible for the high degree of accuracy in the beautiful family tree you see on pages vi and vii.

. . . Karen L. Henry, for bumblebee-herding and for the "Friday Fun Facts" supplied weekly on her blog, *Outlandish Observations.* (The FFF are a collection of fascinating bits of trivia from the books, explored and expanded upon, with pictures.)

. . . Michelle Moore, for Twitter backgrounds, entertaining tea mugs, and a lot of assorted other things that can best be tactfully called "creative design."

. . . Loretta Moore, faithful and timely mistress of my website.

. . . Nikki and Caitlin Rowe, for designing and maintaining my YouTube Channel (which is frankly not something I ever thought I'd need, but a handy thing to have).

. . . Kristin Matherly, who is the fastest website constructor I've ever seen, for her Random Quote Generator, among many other beautiful and helpful *Outlander*-related sites.

. . . Susan Butler, my assistant, Without Whom Nothing Would Ever Be Mailed, a thousand necessary things would not be done, nor would I ever show up for scheduled events.

. . . Janice Millford, Sherpa of the Everest of email and rider of avalanches.

. . . to my friend Ann Hunt, for lovely writing and golden wishes, to say nothing of virtual flowers and raspberry gin.

. . . the title of Chapter 13 ("Morning Air Awash with Angels") is taken from a line of the poem by Richard Purdy Wilbur, "Love Calls Us to the Things of This World."

. . . and the title of Chapter 117, "Into the Briar Patch," is taken from the American folktale "Brer Rabbit and the Tar Baby" (retold by various authors).

. . . whereas the title of Chapter 123, *"Quod Scripsi, Scripsi,"* is courtesy of Pontius Pilate.

. . . Joey McGarvey, Kristin Fassler, Ashley Woodfolk, Lisa Barnes, and a whole passel of other Highly Competent and Energetic People at Random House.

. . . Beatrice Lampe, Andrea Vetterle, Petra Zimmerman, and a similar passel of helpful publishing people at Blanvalet (the German publisher).

. . . As always, great thanks to those practitioners of Eyeball-Numbing Nitpickery whose time and devotion results in a much better book than this would be without them: Catherine MacGregor, Allene Edwards, Karen Henry, Janet Mc-

Also by DIANA GABALDON

THE COMPANION VOLUMES

THE OUTLANDER GRAPHIC NOVEL

THE LORD JOHN SERIES

Lord John and the Private Matter
Lord John and the Brotherhood of the Blade
Lord John and the Hand of Devils
The Scottish Prisoner

Continue the saga with original eNovellas, engrossing tales to complement the Outlander series.

A Plague of Zombies

The Custom of the Army

A Leaf on the Wind of All Hallows

The Space Between

DianaGabaldon.com
AuthorDianaGabaldon @Writer_DG

Random House Bantam • Dell • Delacorte • Del Rey

THE ETIQUETTE OF WAR
A STARZ ORIGINAL SERIES
OUTLANDER
STARZ

Connaughey, Susan Butler, and especially Barbara Schnell (my invaluable German translator) and Kathleen Lord, copy editor and unsung heroine of the comma and timeline, both of whom always know how far it is from Point A to Point B, even if I would rather not find out.

. . . and my husband, Doug Watkins, who sustains me.

Also by Diana Gabaldon

THE **OUTLANDER** SERIES

DianaGabaldon.com

AuthorDianaGabaldon @Writer_DG

RANDOM HOUSE BALLANTINE • BANTAM • DELL

PRAISE FOR THE OUTLANDER NOVELS

A BREATH OF SNOW AND ASHES

"Time travelers revolutionize colonial America with . . . cliffhangers galore, in Gabaldon's sixth Outlander epic."
—*Kirkus Reviews*

"This compulsively readable mix of authentically set historical fiction and completely satisfying romance maps both violent loss and strong family ties . . . the large scope of the novel allows Gabaldon to do what she does best, paint in exquisite detail the lives of her characters." —*Booklist*

"Essential for every fiction collection." —*Library Journal*

THE FIERY CROSS

"Each and every one of its 979 pages abounds with Ms. Gabaldon's sexy combination of humor, wild adventure and, underlying it all, the redemptive power of true love."
—*Dallas Morning News*

"Fans of the series will be delighted with this novel and there are threads left dangling for another mega epic from the great author." —*Midwest Book Review*

"It is a grand adventure written on a canvas that probes the heart, weighs the soul and measures the human spirit across 10 generations." —CNN

OUTLANDER

"Marvelously entertaining . . . a page-turner of the highest order and a good read from start to finish."
—*Chattanooga Times*

"Absorbing and heartwarming . . . lavishly evokes the land and lore of Scotland." —*Publishers Weekly*

"History comes deliciously alive on the page."
—*New York Daily News*

DRAGONFLY IN AMBER

"A triumph! A powerful tale layered in history and myth. I loved every page." —Nora Roberts

"Compulsively readable." —*Publishers Weekly*

"Diana Gabaldon is a born storyteller . . . the pages practically turn themselves." —*Arizona Republic*

VOYAGER

"Triumphant . . . Her use of historical detail and a truly adult love story confirm Gabaldon as a superior writer."
—*Publishers Weekly*

"An amazing read." —*Arizona Tribune*

"Memorable storytelling." —*Seattle Times*

DRUMS OF AUTUMN

"Unforgettable characters . . . richly embroidered with historical detail . . . I just can't put it down." —*Cincinnati Post*

"Wonderful . . . This is escapist historical fiction at its best." —*San Antonio Express-News*

By Diana Gabaldon

The Outlander Series

Outlander

Dragonfly in Amber

Voyager

Drums of Autumn

The Fiery Cross

A Breath of Snow and Ashes

An Echo in the Bone

Written in My Own Heart's Blood

The Lord John Series

Lord John and the Private Matter

Lord John and the Brotherhood of the Blade

The Custom of the Army (novella)

Lord John and the Hand of Devils (collected novellas)

The Scottish Prisoner

A Plague of Zombies (novella)

Salmagundi*

The Outlandish Companion (nonfiction)

The Exile (graphic novel)

The Outlandish Companion Volume Two (nonfiction)

A Leaf on the Wind of All Hallows (novella)

The Space Between (novella)

Virgins (novella)

"I Give You My Body . . ." (nonfiction)

Seven Stones to Stand or Fall (collected novellas)

---

* a collection of disparate elements

DIANA GABALDON

A BREATH OF SNOW AND ASHES

A DELL BOOK

A BREATH OF SNOW AND ASHES
A Dell Book

PUBLISHING HISTORY
Delacorte Press hardcover edition published October 2005
Dell mass market export edition published September 2006
Dell mass market edition / May 2008

Published by
Bantam Dell
A Division of Random House, Inc.
New York, New York

Library of Congress Catalog Card Number: 2005051948

ISBN 978-0-440-22580-5

Printed in the United States of America

www.bantamdell.com

OPM 30 29 28 27 26 25

This Book Is Dedicated to

CHARLES DICKENS

ROBERT LOUIS STEVENSON

DOROTHY L. SAYERS

JOHN D. MACDONALD

and

P. G. WODEHOUSE

[illegible] who [illegible]

[illegible] new and interesting books, particularly [illegible] works like *Flower of the* [illegible] *in the* [illegible] *of* [illegible] *and Power of the* [illegible] Green Brothers, and [illegible] is, because they [illegible] in Arizona.

[illegible] better [illegible]

ACKNOWLEDGMENTS

My ENORMOUS thanks to . . .

My two marvelous editors, Jackie Cantor and Bill Massey, for insight, support, helpful suggestions (*"What about Marsali?!?!"*), enthusiastic responses, (*"Eeew!"*), and comparing me (favorably, I hasten to add) to Charles Dickens.

My excellent and admirable literary agents, Russell Galen and Danny Baror, who do so much to bring these books to the attention of the world—and put all of my children through college.

Bill McCrea, curator of the North Carolina Museum of History, and his staff, for maps, biographical sketches, general information, and a delightful breakfast in the museum. Love them cheese grits!

The staff of the Moore's Creek Bridge battlefield Visitors' Center, for their kind attention and for supplying me with forty-odd pounds of new and interesting books—particularly gripping works like *Roster of the Patriots in the Battle of Moore's Creek Bridge and Roster of the Loyalists in the Battle of Moore's Creek Bridge*—and for explaining to me what an ice-storm is, because they had just had one. We do not have ice-storms in Arizona.

Linda Grimes, for betting me that I couldn't write an appealing scene about nose-picking. That one is all her fault.

The awe-inspiring and superhuman Barbara Schnell, who translated the book into German as I wrote it, almost neck-and-neck with me, in order to complete it in time for the German premiere.

Silvia Kuttny-Walser and Petra Zimmerman, who have been moving heaven and earth to assist the German debut.

Dr. Amarilis Iscold, for a wealth of detail and advice—and

periodic rolling on the floor with laughter—regarding the medical scenes. Any liberties taken or mistakes made are entirely mine.

Dr. Doug Hamilton, for expert testimony on dentistry, and what one could or could not do with a pair of forceps, a bottle of whisky, and an equine tooth-file.

Dr. David Blacklidge, for helpful advice on the manufacture, use, and dangers of ether.

Dr. William Reed and Dr. Amy Silverthorn, for keeping me breathing through the pollen season so I could finish this book.

Laura Bailey, for expert commentary—with drawings, no less—on period clothing, and in particular, for the useful suggestion of stabbing someone with a corset-busk.

Christiane Schreiter, to whose detective skills (and the goodwill of the librarians of the Braunschweig Library) we owe the German version of Paul Revere's ride.

The Reverend Jay McMillan, for a wealth of fascinating and useful information regarding the Presbyterian church in Colonial America—and to Becky Morgan, for introducing me to the Reverend Jay, and to Amy Jones, for information on Presbyterian doctrine.

Rafe Steinberg, for information on times, tides, and general seafaring issues—particularly the helpful information that the tide turns every twelve hours. Any mistakes in this regard are definitely mine. And if the tide did not turn at 5 A.M. on July 10th, 1776, I don't want to hear about it.

My assistant Susan Butler, for dealing with ten million sticky-notes, photo-copying three copies of a 2500-page manuscript, and FedExing it all over the landscape in a competent and timely fashion.

The untiring and diligent Kathy Lord, who copy-edited this entire manuscript in some impossible time frame, and did not either go blind or lose her sense of humor.

Virginia Norey, Goddess of Book Design, who has once again managed to cram The Whole Thing between two covers and make it not only readable but elegant.

Steven Lopata, for invaluable technical advice re explosions and burning things down.

Arnold Wagner, Lisa Harrison, Kateri van Huystee, Luz,

Suzann Shepherd, and Jo Bourne, for technical advice on grinding pigments, storing paint, and other picturesque tidbits, such as the bit about "Egyptian Brown" being made of ground-up mummies. I couldn't figure out how to work that into the book, but it was too good not to share.

Karen Watson, for her former brother-in-law's notable quote regarding the sensations of a hemorrhoid sufferer.

Pamela Patchet, for her excellent and inspiring description of driving a two-inch splinter under her fingernail.

Margaret Campbell, for the wonderful copy of *Piedmont Plantation*.

Janet McConnaughey, for her vision of Jamie and Brianna playing Brag.

Marte Brengle, Julie Kentner, Joanne Cutting, Carol Spradling, Beth Shope, Cindy R., Kathy Burdette, Sherry, and Kathleen Eschenburg, for helpful advice and entertaining commentary on Dreary Hymns.

Lauri Klobas, Becky Morgan, Linda Allen, Nikki Rowe, and Lori Benton for technical advice on paper-making.

Kim Laird, Joel Altman, Cara Stockton, Carol Isler, Jo Murphey, Elise Skidmore, Ron Kenner, and many, many (many, many) other inhabitants of the Compuserve Literary Forum (now renamed as the Books and Writers Community (http://community.compuserve.com/books), but still the same gathering of eclectic eccentricity, trove of erudition, and source of Really Strange Facts, for their contributions of links, facts, and articles they thought I might find helpful. I always do.

Chris Stuart and Backcountry, for the gift of their marvelous CDs, *Saints and Strangers* and *Mohave River,* to which I wrote quite a bit of this book.

Ewan MacColl, whose rendition of "Eppie Morrie" inspired Chapter 85.

Gabi Eleby, for socks, cookies, and general moral support—and to the Ladies of Lallybroch, for their boundless goodwill, manifested in the form of food boxes, cards, and enormous quantities of soap, both commercial and handmade ("Jack Randall Lavender" is nice, and I quite like the one called "Breath of Snow." The one called "Lick Jamie All Over" was so sweet one of the dogs ate it, though).

Bev LaFrance, Carol Krenz, Gilbert Sureau, Laura Bradbury, Julianne, Julie, and several other nice people whose names I unfortunately forgot to write down, for help with the French bits.

Monika Berrisch, for allowing me to appropriate her persona.

And to my husband, Doug Watkins, who this time gave me the opening lines of the Prologue.

A BREATH OF SNOW AND ASHES

PROLOGUE

TIME IS A LOT of the things people say that God is. There's the always preexisting, and having no end. There's the notion of being all powerful—because nothing can stand against time, can it? Not mountains, not armies.

And time is, of course, all-healing. Give anything enough time, and everything is taken care of: all pain encompassed, all hardship erased, all loss subsumed.

Ashes to ashes, dust to dust. Remember, man, that thou art dust; and unto dust thou shalt return.

And if Time is anything akin to God, I suppose that Memory must be the Devil.

Part One

Rumors of War

1

AN INTERRUPTED CONVERSATION

THE DOG SENSED them first. Dark as it was, Ian Murray felt rather than saw Rollo's head lift suddenly near his thigh, ears pricking. He put a hand on the dog's neck, and felt the hair there ridged with warning.

So attuned as they were to each other, he did not even think consciously, "Men," but put his other hand to his knife and lay still, breathing. Listening.

The forest was quiet. It was hours 'til dawn and the air was still as that in a church, with a mist like incense rising slowly up from the ground. He had lain down to rest on the fallen trunk of a giant tulip tree, preferring the tickle of wood-lice to seeping damp. He kept his hand on the dog, waiting.

Rollo was growling, a low, constant rumble that Ian could barely hear but felt easily, the vibration of it traveling up his arm, arousing all the nerves of his body. He hadn't been asleep—he rarely slept at night anymore—but had been quiet, looking up into the vault of the sky, engrossed in his usual argument with God. Quietness had vanished with Rollo's movement. He sat up slowly, swinging his legs over the side of the half-rotted log, heart beating fast now.

Rollo's warning hadn't changed, but the great head swiveled, following something unseen. It was a moonless night; Ian could see the faint silhouettes of trees and the moving shadows of the night, but nothing more.

Then he heard them. Sounds of passage. A good distance away, but coming nearer by the moment. He stood and stepped softly into the pool of black under a balsam fir. A click of the tongue, and Rollo left off his growling and followed, silent as the wolf who had been his father.

Ian's resting-place overlooked a game trail. The men who followed it were not hunting.

White men. Now that was odd, and more than odd. He couldn't see them, but didn't need to; the noise they made was unmistakable. Indians traveling were not silent, and many of the Highlanders he lived among could move like ghosts in the wood—but he had no doubt whatever. Metal, that was it. He was hearing the jingle of harness, the clink of buttons and buckles—and gun barrels.

A lot of them. So close, he began to smell them. He leaned forward a little, eyes closed, the better to snuff up what clue he could.

They carried pelts; now he picked up the dried-blood cold-fur smell that had probably waked Rollo—but not trappers, surely; too many. Trappers moved in ones and twos.

Poor men, and dirty. Not trappers, and not hunters. Game was easy to come by at this season, but they smelled of hunger. And the sweat of bad drink.

Close by now, perhaps ten feet from the place where he stood. Rollo made a tiny snorting sound, and Ian closed his hand once more on the dog's ruff, but the men made too much noise to hear it. He counted the passing footsteps, the bumping of canteens and bullet boxes, foot-sore grunts and sighs of weariness.

Twenty-three men, he made it, and there was a mule—no, two mules with them; he could hear the creak of laden panniers and that querulous heavy breathing, the way a loaded mule did, always on the verge of complaint.

The men would never have detected them, but some freak of the air bore Rollo's scent to the mules. A deafening bray shattered the dark, and the forest erupted in front of him with a clishmaclaver of crashing and startled shouts. Ian was already running when pistol shots crashed behind him.

"A Dhia!" Something struck him in the head and he fell headlong. Was he killed?

No. Rollo was pushing a worried wet nose into his ear. His head buzzed like a hive and he saw bright flashes of light before his eyes.

"Run! Ruith!" he gasped, pushing at the dog. "Run out! Go!" The dog hesitated, whining deep in his throat. He couldn't see, but felt the big body lunge and turn, turn back, undecided.

"Ruith!" He got himself up onto hands and knees, urging, and the dog at last obeyed, running as he had been trained.

There was no time to run himself, even could he have gained his feet. He fell facedown, thrust hands and feet deep into the leaf mold, and wriggled madly, burrowing in.

A foot struck between his shoulder blades, but the breath it drove out of him was muffled in wet leaves. It didn't matter, they were making so much noise. Whoever had stepped on him didn't notice; it was a glancing blow as the man ran over him in panic, doubtless thinking him a rotted log.

The shooting ceased. The shouting didn't, but he made no sense of it. He knew he was lying flat on his face, cold damp on his cheeks and the tang of dead leaves in his nose—but felt as though very drunk, the world revolving slowly round him. His head didn't hurt much, past the first burst of pain, but he didn't seem able to lift it.

He had the dim thought that if he died here, no one would know. His mother would mind, he thought, not knowing what had become of him.

The noises grew fainter, more orderly. Someone was still bellowing, but it had the sound of command. They were leaving. It occurred to him dimly that he might call out. If they knew he was white, they might help him. And they might not.

He kept quiet. Either he was dying or he wasn't. If he was, no help was possible. If he wasn't, none was needed.

Well, I asked then, didn't I? he thought, resuming his conversation with God, calm as though he lay still on the trunk of the tulip tree, looking up into the depths of heaven above. *A sign, I said. I didna quite expect Ye to be so prompt about it, though.*

2

DUTCH CABIN

March 1773

NO ONE HAD KNOWN the cabin was there, until Kenny Lindsay had seen the flames, on his way up the creek.

"I wouldna ha' seen at all," he said, for perhaps the sixth time. "Save for the dark comin' on. Had it been daylight, I'd never ha' kent it, never." He wiped a trembling hand over his face, unable to take his eyes off the line of bodies that lay at the edge of the forest. "Was it savages, *Mac Dubh?* They're no scalped, but maybe—"

"No." Jamie laid the soot-smeared handkerchief gently back over the staring blue face of a small girl. "None of them is wounded. Surely ye saw as much when ye brought them out?"

Lindsay shook his head, eyes closed, and shivered convulsively. It was late afternoon, and a chilly spring day, but the men were all sweating.

"I didna look," he said simply.

My own hands were like ice; as numb and unfeeling as the rubbery flesh of the dead woman I was examining. They had been dead for more than a day; the rigor of death had passed off, leaving them limp and chilled, but the cold weather of the mountain spring had preserved them so far from the grosser indignities of putrefaction.

Still, I breathed shallowly; the air was bitter with the scent of burning. Wisps of steam rose now and then from the charred ruin of the tiny cabin. From the corner of my eye, I saw Roger kick at a nearby log, then bend and pick up something from the ground beneath.

Kenny had pounded on our door long before daylight, summoning us from warm beds. We had come in haste, even knowing that we were far too late to offer aid. Some of the tenants from the homesteads on Fraser's Ridge had come, too; Kenny's brother Evan stood with Fergus and Ronnie Sinclair in a small knot under the trees, talking together in low-voiced Gaelic.

"D'ye ken what did for them, Sassenach?" Jamie squatted beside me, face troubled. "The ones under the trees, that is." He nodded at the corpse in front of me. "I ken what killed this puir woman."

The woman's long skirt stirred in the wind, lifting to show long, slender feet shod in leather clogs. A pair of long hands to match lay still at her sides. She had been tall—though not so tall as Brianna, I thought, and looked automatically for my daughter's bright hair, bobbing among the branches on the far side of the clearing.

I had turned the woman's apron up to cover her head and upper body. Her hands were red, rough-knuckled with work, and with callused palms, but from the firmness of her thighs and the slenderness of her body, I thought she was no more than thirty—likely much younger. No one could say whether she had been pretty.

I shook my head at his remark.

"I don't think she died of the burning," I said. "See, her legs and feet aren't touched. She must have fallen into the hearth. Her hair caught fire, and it spread to the shoulders of her gown. She must have lain near enough to the wall or the chimney hood for the flames to touch; that caught, and then the whole bloody place went up."

Jamie nodded slowly, eyes on the dead woman.

"Aye, that makes sense. But what was it killed them, Sassenach? The others are singed a bit, though none are burned like this. But they must have been dead before the cabin caught alight, for none o' them ran out. Was it a deadly illness, perhaps?"

"I don't think so. Let me look at the others again."

I walked slowly down the row of still bodies with their cloth-covered faces, stooping over each one to peer again beneath the makeshift shrouds. There were any number of illnesses that could be quickly fatal in these days—with no antibiotics to hand, and no way of administering fluids save by mouth or rectum, a simple case of diarrhea could kill within twenty-four hours.

I saw such things often enough to recognize them easily; any doctor does, and I had been a doctor for more than twenty years. I saw things now and then in this century that I had never encountered in my own—particularly horrible parasitical diseases, brought with the slave trade from the tropics—but it was no parasite that had done for these poor souls, and no illness that I knew, to leave such traces on its victims.

All the bodies—the burned woman, a much older woman, and three children—had been found inside the walls of the flaming house. Kenny had pulled them out, just before the roof fell in, then ridden for help. All dead before the fire started; all dead virtually at the same time, then, for surely the fire had begun to smolder soon after the woman fell dead on her hearth?

The victims had been laid out neatly under the branches of a giant red spruce, while the men began to dig a grave nearby. Brianna stood by the smallest girl, her head bent. I came to kneel by the little body, and she knelt down across from me.

"What was it?" she asked quietly. "Poison?"

I glanced up at her in surprise.

"I think so. What gave you that idea?"

She nodded at the blue-tinged face below us. She had tried to close the eyes, but they bulged beneath the lids, giving the little girl a look of startled horror. The small, blunt features were twisted in a rictus of agony, and there were traces of vomit in the corners of the mouth.

"Girl Scout handbook," Brianna said. She glanced at the men, but no one was near enough to hear. Her mouth twitched, and she looked away from the body, holding out her open hand. *"Never eat any strange mushroom,"* she quoted. *"There are many poisonous varieties, and distinguishing one from another is a job for an expert.* Roger found these, growing in a ring by that log over there."

Moist, fleshy caps, a pale brown with white warty spots, the open gills and slender stems so pale as to look almost phosphorescent in the spruce shadows. They had a pleasant, earthy look to them that belied their deadliness.

"Panther toadstools," I said, half to myself, and picked one gingerly from her palm. "*Agaricus pantherinus*—or that's what they *will* be called, once somebody gets round to naming them properly. *Pantherinus,* because they kill so swiftly—like a striking cat."

I could see the gooseflesh ripple on Brianna's forearm, raising the soft, red-gold hairs. She tilted her hand and spilled the rest of the deadly fungus on the ground.

"Who in their right mind would eat toadstools?" she asked, wiping her hand on her skirt with a slight shudder.

"People who didn't know better. People who were hungry, perhaps," I answered softly. I picked up the little girl's hand, and traced the delicate bones of the forearm. The small belly showed signs of bloat, whether from malnutrition or postmortem changes I couldn't tell—but the collarbones were sharp as scythe blades. All of the bodies were thin, though not to the point of emaciation.

I looked up, into the deep blue shadows of the mountainside above the cabin. It was early in the year for foraging, but there was food in abundance in the forest—for those who could recognize it.

Jamie came and knelt down beside me, a big hand lightly on my back. Cold as it was, a trickle of sweat streaked his neck, and his thick auburn hair was dark at the temples.

"The grave is ready," he said, speaking low, as though he might alarm the child. "Is that what's killed the bairn?" He nodded at the scattered fungi.

"I think so—and the rest of them, too. Have you had a look around? Does anyone know who they were?"

He shook his head.

"Not English; the clothes are wrong. Germans would have gone to Salem, surely; they're clannish souls, and no inclined to settle on their own. These were maybe Dutchmen." He nodded toward the carved wooden clogs on the old woman's feet, cracked and stained with long use. "No books nor writing left, if there was any to begin with. Nothing that might tell their name. But—"

"They hadn't been here long." A low, cracked voice made me look up. Roger had come; he squatted next to Brianna, nodding toward the smoldering remains of the cabin. A small garden plot had been scratched into the earth nearby, but the few plants showing were no more than sprouts, the tender leaves limp and blackened with late frost. There were no sheds, no sign of livestock, no mule or pig.

"New emigrants," Roger said softly. "Not bond servants; this was a family. They weren't used to outdoor labor, either; the women's hands have blisters and fresh scars." His own broad hand rubbed unconsciously over a homespun knee; his palms were as smoothly callused as Jamie's now, but he had once been a tender-skinned scholar; he remembered the pain of his seasoning.

"I wonder if they left people behind—in Europe," Brianna murmured. She smoothed blond hair off the little girl's forehead, and laid the kerchief back over her face. I saw her throat move as she swallowed. "They'll never know what happened to them."

"No." Jamie stood abruptly. "They do say that God protects fools—but I think even the Almighty will lose patience now and then." He turned away, motioning to Lindsay and Sinclair.

"Look for the man," he said to Lindsay. Every head jerked up to look at him.

"Man?" Roger said, and then glanced sharply at the burned remnants of the cabin, realization dawning. "Aye—who built the cabin for them?"

"The women could have done it," Bree said, lifting her chin.

"*You* could, aye," he said, mouth twitching slightly as he cast a sidelong look at his wife. Brianna resembled Jamie in more than coloring; she stood six feet in her stockings and had her father's clean-limbed strength.

"Perhaps they could, but they didn't," Jamie said shortly. He nodded toward the shell of the cabin, where a few bits of furniture still held their fragile shapes. As I watched, the evening wind came down, scouring the ruin, and the shadow of a stool collapsed noiselessly into ash, flurries of soot and char moving ghostlike over the ground.

"What do you mean?" I stood and moved beside him, looking into the house. There was virtually nothing left inside, though the chimney stack still stood, and jagged bits of the walls remained, their logs fallen like jackstraws.

"There's no metal," he said, nodding at the blackened hearth, where the remnants of a cauldron lay, cracked in two from the heat, its contents vaporized. "No pots, save that—and that's too heavy to carry away. Nay tools. Not a knife, not an ax—and ye see whoever built it had that."

I did; the logs were unpeeled, but the notches and ends bore the clear marks of an ax.

Frowning, Roger picked up a long pine branch and began to poke through the piles of ash and rubble, looking to be sure. Kenny Lindsay and Sinclair didn't bother; Jamie had told them to look for a man, and they promptly went to do so, disappearing into the forest. Fergus went with them; Evan Lindsay, his brother Murdo, and the McGillivrays began the chore of collecting stones for a cairn.

"If there *was* a man—did he leave them?" Brianna murmured to me, glancing from her father to the row of bodies. "Did this woman maybe think they wouldn't survive on their own?"

And thus take her own life, and those of her children, to avoid a long-drawn-out death from cold and starvation?

"Leave them and take all their tools? God, I hope not." I crossed myself at the thought, though even as I did so, I doubted it. "Wouldn't they have walked out, looking for help? Even with children . . . the snow's mostly gone." Only the highest mountain passes were still packed with snow, and while the trails and slopes were wet and muddy with runoff, they'd been passable for a month, at least.

"I've found the man," Roger said, interrupting my thoughts. He spoke very calmly, but paused to clear his throat. "Just—just here."

The daylight was beginning to fade, but I could see that he had gone pale. No wonder; the curled form he had unearthed beneath the charred timbers of a fallen wall was sufficiently gruesome as to give anyone pause. Charred to blackness, hands upraised in the boxer's pose so common to those dead by fire, it was difficult even to be sure that it *was* a man—though I thought it was, from what I could see.

Speculation about this new body was interrupted by a shout from the forest's edge.

"We've found them, milord!"

Everyone looked up from contemplation of this new corpse, to see Fergus waving from the edge of the wood.

"Them," indeed. Two men, this time. Sprawled on the ground within the shadow of the trees, found not together, but not far apart, only a short distance from the house. And both, so far as I could tell, probably dead of mushroom poisoning.

"*That's* no Dutchman," Sinclair said, for probably the fourth time, shaking his head over one body.

"He might be," said Fergus dubiously. He scratched his nose with the tip of the hook he wore in replacement of his left hand. "From the Indies, *non*?"

One of the unknown bodies was in fact that of a black man. The other was white, and both wore nondescript clothes of worn homespun—shirts and breeches; no jackets, despite the cold weather. And both were barefoot.

"No." Jamie shook his head, rubbing one hand unconsciously on his own breeches, as though to rid himself of the touch of the dead. "The Dutch keep slaves on Barbuda, aye—but these are better fed than the folk from the cabin." He lifted his chin toward the silent row of women and children. "They didna live here. Besides . . ." I saw his eyes fix on the dead men's feet.

The feet were grubby about the ankles and heavily callused, but basically clean. The soles of the black man's feet showed yellowish pink, with no smears of mud or random leaves stuck between the toes. These men hadn't been walking through the muddy forest barefoot, that much was sure.

"So there were perhaps more men? And when these died, their companions took their shoes—and anything else of value"—Fergus added practically, gesturing from the burned cabin to the stripped bodies—"and fled."

"Aye, maybe." Jamie pursed his lips, his gaze traveling slowly over the earth of the yard—but the ground was churned with footsteps, clumps of grass uprooted and the whole of the yard dusted with ash and bits of charred wood. It looked as though the place had been ravaged by rampaging hippopotami.

"I could wish that Young Ian was here. He's the best of the trackers; he could maybe tell what happened there, at least." He nodded into the wood, where the men had been found. "How many there were, maybe, and which way they've gone."

Jamie himself was no mean tracker. But the light was going fast now; even in the clearing where the burned cabin stood, the dark was rising, pooling under the trees, creeping like oil across the shattered earth.

His eyes went to the horizon, where streamers of cloud were beginning to blaze with gold and pink as the sun set behind them, and he shook his head.

"Bury them. Then we'll go."

One more grim discovery remained. Alone among the dead, the burned man had not died of fire or poison. When they lifted the charred corpse from the ashes to bear him to his grave, something fell free of the body, landing with a small, heavy thunk on the ground. Brianna picked it up, and rubbed at it with the corner of her apron.

"I guess they overlooked this," she said a little bleakly, holding it out. It was a knife, or the blade of one. The wooden hilt had burned entirely away, and the blade itself was warped with heat.

Steeling myself against the thick, acrid stench of burned fat and flesh, I bent over the corpse, poking gingerly at the midsection. Fire destroys a great deal, but preserves the strangest things. The triangular wound was quite clear, seared in the hollow beneath his ribs.

"They stabbed him," I said, and wiped my sweating hands on my own apron.

"They killed him," Bree said, watching my face. "And then his wife—" She glanced at the young woman on the ground, the concealing apron over her head. "She made a stew with the mushrooms, and they all ate it. The children, too."

The clearing was silent, save for the distant calls of birds on the mountain. I could hear my own heart, beating painfully in my chest. Vengeance? Or simple despair?

"Aye, maybe," Jamie said quietly. He stooped to pick up an end of the sheet of canvas they had placed the dead man on. "We'll call it accident."

The Dutchman and his family were laid in one grave, the two strangers in another.

A cold wind had sprung up as the sun went down; the apron fluttered away from the woman's face as they lifted her. Sinclair gave a strangled cry of shock, and nearly dropped her.

She had neither face nor hair anymore; the slender waist narrowed abruptly into charred ruin. The flesh of her head had burned away completely, leaving an oddly tiny, blackened skull, from which her teeth grinned in disconcerting levity.

They lowered her hastily into the shallow grave, her children and mother beside her, and left Brianna and me to build a small cairn over them, in the ancient Scottish way, to mark the place and provide protection from wild beasts, while a more rudimentary resting place was dug for the two barefoot men.

The work finally done, everyone gathered, white-faced and silent, around the new-made mounds. I saw Roger stand close beside Brianna, his arm protectively about her waist. A small shudder went through her, which I thought had nothing to do with the cold. Their child, Jemmy, was a year or so younger than the smallest girl.

"Will ye speak a word, *Mac Dubh*?" Kenny Lindsay glanced inquiringly at Jamie, pulling his knitted bonnet down over his ears against the growing chill.

It was nearly nightfall, and no one wanted to linger. We would have to make camp, somewhere well away from the stink of burning, and that would be hard enough, in the dark. But Kenny was right; we couldn't leave without at least some token of ceremony, some farewell for the strangers.

Jamie shook his head.

"Nay, let Roger Mac speak. If these were Dutchmen, belike they were Protestant."

Dim as the light was, I saw the sharp glance Brianna shot at her father. It was true that Roger was a Presbyterian; so was Tom Christie, a much older man whose dour face reflected his opinion of the proceedings. The question of religion was no more than a pretext, though, and everyone knew it, including Roger.

Roger cleared his throat with a noise like tearing calico. It was always a painful sound; there was anger in it now as well. He didn't protest, though, and he met Jamie's eyes straight on, as he took his place at the head of the grave.

I had thought he would simply say the Lord's Prayer, or perhaps one of the gentler psalms. Other words came to him, though.

"Behold, I cry out of wrong, but I am not heard: I cry aloud, but there is no judgment. He hath fenced up my way that I cannot pass, and He hath set darkness in my paths."

His voice had once been powerful, and beautiful. It was choked now, no more than a rasping shadow of its former beauty—but there was sufficient power in the passion with which he spoke to make all those who heard him bow their heads, faces lost in shadow.

"He hath stripped me of my glory, and taken the crown from my head. He hath destroyed me on every side, and I am gone: and my hope hath He removed like a tree." His face was set, but his eyes rested for a bleak moment on the charred stump that had served the Dutch family for a chopping block.

"He hath put my brethren far from me, and mine acquaintance are verily estranged from me. My kinsfolk have failed, and my familiar friends have forgotten me." I saw the three Lindsay brothers exchange glances, and everyone drew a little closer together, against the rising wind.

"Have pity upon me, have pity upon me, O ye my friends," he said, and his voice softened, so that it was difficult to hear him, above the sighing of the trees. *"For the hand of God has touched me."*

Brianna made a slight movement beside him, and he cleared his throat once more, explosively, stretching his neck so that I caught a glimpse of the rope scar that marred it.

"Oh, that my words were now written! Oh, that they were printed in a book! That they were graven with an iron pen and lead in the rock forever!"

He looked slowly round from face to face, his own expressionless, then took a deep breath to continue, voice cracking on the words.

"For I know that my redeemer liveth, and that He shall stand at the latter day upon the earth: And though after my skin worms destroy this body"—Brianna shuddered convulsively,

and looked away from the raw mound of dirt—*"yet in my flesh shall I see God. Whom I shall see for myself, and mine eyes shall behold."*

He stopped, and there was a brief collective sigh, as everyone let out the breath they had been holding. He wasn't quite finished, though. He had reached out, half-unconsciously, for Bree's hand, and held it tightly. He spoke the last words almost to himself, I thought, with little thought for his listeners.

"Be ye afraid of the sword: for wrath bringeth the punishments of the sword, that ye may know there is a judgment."

I shivered, and Jamie's hand curled round my own, cold but strong. He looked down at me, and I met his eyes. I knew what he was thinking.

He was thinking, as I was, not of the present, but the future. Of a small item that would appear three years hence, in the pages of the *Wilmington Gazette,* dated February 13, 1776.

It is with grief that the news is received of the deaths by fire of James MacKenzie Fraser and his wife, Claire Fraser, in a conflagration that destroyed their house in the settlement of Fraser's Ridge, on the night of January 21 last. Mr. Fraser, a nephew of the late Hector Cameron of River Run Plantation, was born at Broch Tuarach in Scotland. He was widely known in the Colony and deeply respected; he leaves no surviving children.

It had been easy, so far, not to think too much of it. So far in the future, and surely not an unchangeable future—after all, forewarned was forearmed . . . wasn't it?

I glanced at the shallow cairn, and a deeper chill passed through me. I stepped closer to Jamie, and put my other hand on his arm. He covered my hand with his, and squeezed tight in reassurance. No, he said to me silently. No, I will not let it happen.

As we left the desolate clearing, though, I could not free my mind of one vivid image. Not the burned cabin, the pitiful bodies, the pathetic dead garden. The image that haunted me was one I had seen some years before—a gravestone in the ruins of Beauly Priory, high in the Scottish Highlands.

It was the tomb of a noble lady, her name surmounted by the carving of a grinning skull—very like the one beneath the Dutchwoman's apron. Beneath the skull was her motto:

Hodie mihi cras tibi—sic transit gloria mundi.
My turn today—yours tomorrow. Thus passes the glory of the world.

3

KEEP YOUR FRIENDS CLOSE

WE RETURNED TO Fraser's Ridge just before sunset the next day, to discover a visitor waiting. Major Donald MacDonald, late of His Majesty's army, and even more lately of Governor Tryon's personal light-horse guard, was sitting on the front stoop, my cat in his lap and a jug of beer beside him.

"Mrs. Fraser! Your servant, mum," he called genially, seeing me approach. He tried to stand up, but then let out a gasp as Adso, objecting to the loss of his cozy nest, dug his claws into the Major's thighs.

"Do sit, Major," I said, waving him hastily back. He subsided with a grimace, but nobly refrained from flinging Adso into the bushes. I came up onto the stoop beside him and sat down, sighing with relief.

"My husband is just seeing to the horses; he'll be down directly. I see that someone's made you welcome?" I nodded at the beer, which he promptly offered to me with a courtly gesture, wiping the neck of the jug on his sleeve.

"Oh, yes, mum," he assured me. "Mrs. Bug has been most assiduous of my welfare."

Not to seem uncordial, I accepted the beer, which in all truth went down very well. Jamie had been anxious to get back, and we'd been in the saddle since dawn, with only a brief break for refreshment at midday.

"It is a most excellent brew," the Major said, smiling as I exhaled after swallowing, my eyes half-closing. "Your own making, perhaps?"

I shook my head and took another swallow, before handing the jug back to him. "No, it's Lizzie's. Lizzie Wemyss."

"Oh, your bondmaid; yes, of course. Will you give her my compliments?"

"Isn't she here?" I glanced toward the open door behind him, rather surprised. At this time of day, I would have expected Lizzie to be in the kitchen, making supper, but she would surely have heard our arrival and come out. There was no smell of cooking, now that I noticed. She wouldn't have known when to expect us, of course, but . . .

"Mm, no. She is . . ." The Major knitted his brows in the effort of recall, and I wondered how full the jug had been before he got at it; there were no more than a couple of inches left now. "Ah, yes. She went to the McGillivrays' with her father, Mrs. Bug said. To visit her affianced, I believe?"

"Yes, she's engaged to Manfred McGillivray. But Mrs. Bug—"

"—is in the springhoose," he said, with a nod up the hill toward the small shed. "A matter of cheese, I believe she said. An omelette was most graciously proposed for my supper."

"Ah . . ." I relaxed a bit more, the dust of the ride settling with the beer. It was wonderful to come home, though my sense of peace was uneasy, tainted by the memory of the burned cabin.

I supposed that Mrs. Bug would have told him our errand, but he made no reference to it—nor to whatever had brought him up to the Ridge. Naturally not; all business would wait appropriately for Jamie. Being female, I would get impeccable courtesy and small bits of social gossip in the meantime.

I could do social gossip, but needed to be prepared for it; I hadn't a natural knack.

"Ah . . . Your relations with my cat seem somewhat improved," I hazarded. I glanced involuntarily at his head, but his wig had been expertly mended.

"It is an accepted principle of politics, I believe," he said, ruffling his fingers through the thick silver fur on Adso's belly. "Keep your friends close—but your enemies closer."

"Very sound," I said, smiling. "Er . . . I hope you haven't been waiting long?"

He shrugged, intimating that any wait was irrelevant—which it generally was. The mountains had their own time, and a wise man did not try to hurry them. MacDonald was a seasoned soldier, and well-traveled—but he had been born in Pitlochry, close enough to the Highland peaks to know their ways.

"I came this morning," he said. "From New Bern."

Small warning bells went off in the back of my mind. It would have taken him a good ten days to travel from New Bern, if he had come directly—and the state of his creased and mud-stained uniform suggested that he had.

New Bern was where the new royal governor of the colony, Josiah Martin, had taken up his residence. And for MacDonald to have said, "From New Bern," rather than mentioning some later stop on his journey, made it reasonably plain to me that whatever business had impelled this visit, it had originated *in* New Bern. I was wary of governors.

I glanced toward the path that led to the paddock, but Jamie wasn't visible yet. Mrs. Bug was, emerging from the springhouse; I waved to her and she gestured enthusiastically in welcome, though hampered by a pail of milk in one hand, a bucket of eggs in the other, a crock of butter under one arm, and a large chunk of cheese tucked neatly underneath her chin. She negotiated the steep descent with success, and disappeared round the back of the house, toward the kitchen.

"Omelettes all round, it looks like," I remarked, turning back to the Major. "Did you happen to come through Cross Creek, by chance?"

"I did indeed, mum. Your husband's aunt sends you her kind regards—and a quantity of books and newspapers, which I have brought with me."

I was wary of newspapers these days, too—though such events as they reported had undoubtedly taken place several weeks—or months—previously. I made appreciative noises, though, wishing Jamie would hurry up, so I could excuse myself.

My hair smelled of burning and my hands still remembered the touch of cold flesh; I wanted a wash, badly.

"I beg your pardon?" I had missed something MacDonald was saying. He bent politely closer to repeat it, then jerked suddenly, eyes bulging.

"Frigging cat!"

Adso, who had been doing a splendid imitation of a limp dishcloth, had sprung bolt upright in the Major's lap, eyes glowing and tail like a bottlebrush, hissing like a teakettle as he flexed his claws hard into the Major's legs. I hadn't time to react before he had leapt over MacDonald's shoulder and swarmed through the open surgery window behind him, ripping the Major's ruffle and knocking his wig askew in the process.

MacDonald was cursing freely, but I hadn't attention to spare for him. Rollo was coming up the path toward the house, wolflike and sinister in the gloaming, but acting so oddly that I was standing before conscious thought could bring me to my feet.

The dog would run a few steps toward the house, circle once or twice as though unable to decide what to do next, then run back into the wood, turn, and run again toward the house, all the while whining with agitation, tail low and wavering.

"Jesus H. Roosevelt Christ," I said. "Bloody Timmy's in the well!" I flew down the steps and ran for the path, barely registering the Major's startled oath behind me.

I found Ian a few hundred yards down the path, conscious, but groggy. He was sitting on the ground, eyes closed and both hands holding his head, as though to keep the bones of his skull from coming apart. He opened his eyes as I dropped to my knees beside him, and gave me an unfocused smile.

"Auntie," he said hoarsely. He seemed to want to say something else, but couldn't quite decide what; his mouth opened, but then simply hung that way, tongue moving thoughtfully to and fro.

"Look at me, Ian," I said, as calmly as possible. He did—that was good. It was too dark to see whether his pupils were unnaturally dilated, but even in the evening shadow of the pines that edged the trail, I could see the pallor of his face, and the dark trail of bloodstains down his shirt.

Hurried steps were coming after me down the trail; Jamie, followed closely by MacDonald.

"How is it, lad?"

Jamie gripped him by one arm, and Ian swayed very gently toward him, then dropped his hands, closed his eyes, and relaxed into Jamie's arms with a sigh.

"Is he bad?" Jamie spoke anxiously over Ian's shoulder, holding him up as I frisked him for damage. The back of his shirt was saturated with dried blood—but it *was* dried. The tail of his hair was stiff with it, too, and I found the head wound quickly.

"I don't think so. Something's hit him hard on the head and taken out a chunk of his scalp, but—"

"A tomahawk, do you think?"

MacDonald leaned over us, intent.

"No," said Ian drowsily, his face muffled in Jamie's shirt. "A ball."

"Go away, dog," Jamie said briefly to Rollo, who had stuck his nose in Ian's ear, eliciting a stifled squawk from the patient and an involuntary lifting of his shoulders.

"I'll have a look in the light, but it may not be too bad," I said, observing this. "He walked some way, after all. Let's get him up to the house."

The men made shift to get him up the trail, Ian's arms over their shoulders, and within minutes, had him laid facedown on the table in my surgery. Here, he told us the story of his adventures, in a disjoint fashion punctuated by small yelps as I cleaned the injury, clipped bits of clotted hair away, and put five or six stitches into his scalp.

"I thought I was dead," Ian said, and sucked air through his teeth as I drew the coarse thread through the edges of the ragged wound. "Christ, Auntie Claire! I woke in the morning, though, and I wasna dead after all—though I thought my head was split open, and my brains spilling down my neck."

"Very nearly was," I murmured, concentrating on my work. "I don't think it was a bullet, though."

That got everyone's attention.

"I'm not shot?" Ian sounded mildly indignant. One big

hand lifted, straying toward the back of his head, and I slapped it lightly away.

"Keep still. No, you aren't shot, no credit to you. There was a deal of dirt in the wound, and shreds of wood and tree bark. If I had to guess, one of the shots knocked a dead branch loose from a tree, and it hit you in the head when it fell."

"You're quite sure as it wasn't a tomahawk, are ye?" The Major seemed disappointed, too.

I tied the final knot and clipped the thread, shaking my head.

"I don't believe I've ever seen a tomahawk wound, but I don't think so. See how jagged the edges are? And the scalp's torn badly, but I don't believe the bone is fractured."

"It was pitch-dark, the lad said," Jamie put in logically. "No sensible person would fling a tomahawk into a dark wood at something he couldna see." He was holding the spirit lamp for me to work by; he moved it closer, so we could see not only the ragged line of stitches, but the spreading bruise around it, revealed by the hair I had clipped off.

"Aye, see?" Jamie's finger spread the remaining bristles gently apart, tracing several deep scratches that scored the bruised area. "Your auntie's right, Ian; ye've been attacked by a tree."

Ian opened one eye a slit.

"Has anyone ever told ye what a comical fellow ye are, Uncle Jamie?"

"No."

Ian closed the eye.

"That's as well, because ye're not."

Jamie smiled, and squeezed Ian's shoulder.

"Feeling a bit better then, are ye?"

"No."

"Aye, well, the thing is," Major MacDonald interrupted, "that the lad did meet with some sort of banditti, no? Had ye reason to think they might be Indians?"

"No," said Ian again, but this time he opened the eye all the way. It was bloodshot. "They weren't."

MacDonald didn't appear pleased with this answer.

"How could ye be sure, lad?" he asked, rather sharply. "If it was dark, as ye say."

I saw Jamie glance quizzically at the Major, but he didn't interrupt. Ian moaned a little, then heaved a sigh and answered.

"I smelt them," he said, adding almost immediately, "I think I'm going to puke."

He raised himself on one elbow and promptly did so. This effectively put an end to any further questions, and Jamie took Major MacDonald off to the kitchen, leaving me to clean Ian up and settle him as comfortably as I could.

"Can you open both eyes?" I asked, having got him tidied and resting on his side, with a pillow under his head.

He did, blinking a little at the light. The small blue flame of the spirit lamp was reflected twice over in the darkness of his eyes, but the pupils shrank at once—and together.

"That's good," I said, and put down the lamp on the table. "Leave it, dog," I said to Rollo, who was nosing at the strange smell of the lamp—it was burning a mix of low-grade brandy and turpentine. "Take hold of my fingers, Ian."

I held out my index fingers and he slowly wrapped a large, bony hand round each of them. I put him through the drill for neurological damage, having him squeeze, pull, push, and then concluded by listening to his heart, which was thumping along reassuringly.

"Slight concussion," I announced, straightening up and smiling at him.

"Oh, aye?" he asked, squinting up at me.

"It means your head aches and you feel sick. You'll feel better in a few days."

"I could ha' told ye that," he muttered, settling back.

"So you could," I agreed. "But 'concussion' sounds so much more important than 'cracked heid,' doesn't it?"

He didn't laugh, but smiled faintly in response. "Will ye feed Rollo, Auntie? He wouldna leave me on the way; he'll be hungry."

Rollo pricked his ears at the sound of his name, and shoved his muzzle into Ian's groping hand, whining softly.

"He's fine," I said to the dog. "Don't worry. And yes," I

added to Ian, "I'll bring something. Do you think you could manage a bit of bread and milk, yourself?"

"No," he said definitely. "A dram o' whisky, maybe?"

"No," I said, just as definitely, and blew out the spirit lamp.

"Auntie," he said, as I turned to the door.

"Yes?" I'd left a single candlestick to light him, and he looked very young and pale in the wavering yellow glow.

"Why d'ye suppose Major MacDonald wants it to be Indians I met in the wood?"

"I don't know. But I imagine Jamie does. Or will, by now."

4

SERPENT IN EDEN

BRIANNA PUSHED OPEN the door to her cabin, listening warily for the scamper of rodent feet or the dry whisper of scales across the floor. She'd once walked in in the dark and stepped within inches of a small rattlesnake; while the snake had been nearly as startled as she was, and slithered madly away between the hearthstones, she'd learned her lesson.

There was no scuttle of fleeing mice or voles this time, but something larger had been and gone, pushing its way through the oiled skin tacked over the window. The sun was just setting, and there was enough daylight left to show her the woven-grass basket in which she kept roasted peanuts, knocked from its shelf onto the floor and the contents cracked and eaten, a litter of shells scattered over the floor.

A loud rustling noise froze her momentarily, listening. It came again, followed by a loud clang as something fell to the ground, on the other side of the back wall.

"You little *bastard*!" she said. "You're in my pantry!"

Fired with righteous indignation, she seized the broom

and charged into the lean-to with a banshee yell. An enormous raccoon, tranquilly munching a smoked trout, dropped its prey at sight of her, dashed between her legs, and made off like a fat banker in flight from creditors, making loud *birring* noises of alarm.

Nerves pulsing with adrenaline, she put aside the broom and bent to salvage what she could of the mess, cursing under her breath. Raccoons were less destructive than squirrels, who would chew and shred with hapless abandon—but they had bigger appetites.

God knew how long he'd been in here, she thought. Long enough to lick all the butter out of its mold, pull down a cluster of smoked fish from the rafters—and how something so fat had managed the acrobatic feat required for *that* . . . Luckily, the honeycomb had been stored in three separate jars, and only one had been despoiled. But the root vegetables had been dumped on the floor, a fresh cheese mostly devoured, and the precious jug of maple syrup had been overturned, draining into a sticky puddle in the dirt. The sight of this loss enraged her afresh, and she squeezed the potato she had just picked up so hard that her nails sank through its skin.

"Bloody, bloody, beastly, horrible, bloody *beast*!"

"Who?" said a voice behind her. Startled, she whirled and fired the potato at the intruder, who proved to be Roger. It struck him squarely in the forehead and he staggered, clutching the door frame.

"Ow! Christ! Ow! What the hell's going on in here?"

"Raccoon," she said shortly, and stepped back, letting the waning light from the door illuminate the damage.

"He got the maple syrup? Bugger! Did you get the bastard?" Hand pressed to his forehead, Roger ducked inside the lean-to pantry, glancing about for furry bodies.

Seeing that her husband shared both her priorities and her sense of outrage soothed her somewhat.

"No," she said. "He ran. Are you bleeding? And where's Jem?"

"I don't think so," he said, taking the hand gingerly from his forehead and glancing at it. "Ow. You've a wicked arm, girl. Jem's at the McGillivrays'. Lizzie and Mr. Wemyss took him along to celebrate Senga's engagement."

"Really? Who did she pick?" Both outrage and remorse were immediately subsumed in interest. Ute McGillivray, with German thoroughness, had carefully selected partners for her son and three daughters according to her own criteria—land, money, and respectability ranking highest, with age, personal appearance, and charm coming well down the list. Not surprisingly, her children had other ideas—though such was the force of *Frau* Ute's personality that both Inga and Hilda had married men that she approved of.

Senga, though, was her mother's daughter—meaning that she possessed similarly strong opinions and a similar lack of inhibition in expressing them. For months, she had been hovering between two suitors: Heinrich Strasse, a dashing but poor young man—and a Lutheran!—from Bethania, and Ronnie Sinclair, the cooper. A well-off man, by the standards of the Ridge, and to Ute, the fact that Ronnie was thirty years Senga's senior was no bar.

The business of Senga McGillivray's marriage had been a topic of intense speculation on the Ridge for the last several months, and Brianna was aware of several substantial wagers riding on the outcome.

"So who's the lucky man?" she repeated.

"Mrs. Bug doesn't know, and it's driving her mad," Roger replied, breaking into a grin. "Manfred McGillivray came to fetch them yesterday morning, but Mrs. Bug hadn't come down to the Big House yet, so Lizzie left a note pinned to the back door to say where they'd gone—but she didn't think to say who the fortunate bridegroom is."

Brianna glanced at the setting sun; the orb itself had sunk out of sight, though the blazing light through the chestnut trees still lit the dooryard, making the spring grass look deep and soft as emerald velvet.

"I suppose we'll have to wait 'til tomorrow to find out," she said, with some regret. The McGillivrays' place was a good five miles; it would be full dark long before they reached it, and even past the thaw, one didn't wander the mountains at night without a good reason—or at least a better reason than mere curiosity.

"Aye. D'ye want to go up to the Big House for supper? Major MacDonald's come."

"Oh, him." She considered for a moment. She would like to hear any news the Major had brought—and there was something to be said for having Mrs. Bug make supper. On the other hand, she was really in no mood to be sociable, after a grim three days, a long ride, and the desecration of her pantry.

She became aware that Roger was carefully not contributing an opinion. One arm leaning on the shelf where the dwindling stock of winter apples was spread, he idly caressed one of the fruits, a forefinger slowly stroking the round yellow cheek of it. Faint, familiar vibrations were coming off him, suggesting silently that there might be advantages to an evening at home, sans parents, acquaintances—or baby.

She smiled at Roger.

"How's your poor head?"

He glanced at her briefly, the waning rays of the sun gilding the bridge of his nose and striking a flash of green from one eye. He cleared his throat.

"I suppose ye might kiss it," he suggested diffidently. "If ye liked."

She obligingly rose on her tiptoes and did so, gently, brushing back the thick black hair from his brow. There was a noticeable lump, though it hadn't begun to bruise yet.

"Is that better?"

"Not yet. Better try again. Maybe a bit lower?"

His hands settled on the swell of her hips, drawing her in. She was nearly as tall as he was; she'd noticed before what an advantage of fit this was, but the impression struck her forcibly anew. She wriggled slightly, enjoying it, and Roger drew a deep, rasping breath.

"Not quite that low," he said. "Not yet, anyway."

"Picky, picky," she said tolerantly, and kissed him on the mouth. His lips were warm, but the scent of bitter ash and damp earth clung to him—as it did to her—and she shivered a little, drawing back.

He kept a hand lightly on her back, but leaned past her, running a finger along the edge of the shelf where the jug of maple syrup had been overturned. He ran the finger lightly along her lower lip, then his own, and bent again to kiss her, sweetness rising up between them.

"I CAN'T REMEMBER how long it's been since I've seen ye naked."

She closed one eye and looked at him skeptically.

"About three days. I guess it wasn't all that memorable." It had been a great relief to shed the clothes she'd been wearing for the last three days and nights. Even naked and hastily washed, though, she still smelled dust in her hair and felt the grime of the journey between her toes.

"Oh, well, aye. That's not what I mean, though—I mean, it's been a long while since we've made love in the daylight." He lay on his side, facing her, and smiled as he passed a light hand over the deep curve of her waist and the swell of buttock. "Ye've no idea how lovely ye look, stark naked, wi' the sun behind you. All gold, like ye were dipped in it."

He closed one eye, as though the sight dazzled him. She moved, and the sun shone in his face, making the open eye glow like an emerald in the split second before he blinked.

"Mmm." She put out a lazy hand and drew his head in close to kiss him.

She did know what he meant. It felt strange—almost wicked, in a pleasant sort of way. Most often, they made love at night, after Jem was asleep, whispering to each other in the hearth-lit shadows, finding each other among the rustling, secret layers of quilts and nightclothes. And while Jem normally slept as though he'd been poleaxed, they were always half-conscious of the small, heavy-breathing mound beneath the quilt of his trundle bed nearby.

She was oddly just as conscious of Jem now, in his absence. It felt strange to be apart from him; not constantly aware of where he was, not feeling his body as a small, very mobile extension of her own. The freedom was exhilarating, but left her feeling uneasy, as though she had misplaced something valuable.

They'd left the door open, the better to enjoy the flood of light and air on their skins. The sun was nearly down now, though, and while the air still glowed like honey, there was a shadow of chill in it.

A sudden gust of wind rattled the hide tacked over the

window and blew across the room, slamming the door and leaving them abruptly in the dark.

Brianna gasped. Roger grunted in surprise and swung off the bed, going to open the door. He flung it wide, and she gulped in the freshet of air and sunshine, only then aware that she had held her breath when the door closed, feeling momentarily entombed.

Roger seemed to feel the same. He stood in the doorway, bracing himself against the frame, letting the wind stir the dark, curling hairs of his body. His hair was still bound in a tail; he hadn't bothered undoing it, and she had a sudden desire to come behind him, untie the leather thong and run her fingers through the soft, glossy black of it, the legacy of some ancient Spaniard, shipwrecked among the Celts.

She was up and doing it before she had consciously decided to, combing tiny yellow catkins and twigs from his locks with her fingers. He shivered, from her touch or that of the wind, but his body was warm.

"You have a farmer's tan," she said, lifting the hair off his neck and kissing him on the bone at the base of his nape.

"Well, so. Am I not a farmer, then?" His skin twitched under her lips, like a horse's hide. His face, neck, and forearms had paled over the winter, but were still darker than the flesh of back and shoulders—and a faint line still lingered round his waist, demarcating the soft buckskin color of his torso from the startling paleness of his backside.

She cupped his buttocks, enjoying the high, round solidity of them, and he breathed deeply, leaning back a little toward her, so her breasts pressed against his back and her chin rested on his shoulder, looking out.

It was still daylight, but barely. The last long shafts of the sinking sun burst through the chestnut trees, so the tender spring green of their leaves burned with cool fire, brilliant above the lengthening shadows. It was near evening, but it was spring; the birds were still at it, chattering and courting. A mockingbird sang from the forest nearby, in a medley of trills, liquid runs, and odd yowls, which she thought it must have learned from her mother's cat.

The air was growing nippy, and gooseflesh stippled her arms and thighs—but Roger's body against her own was very warm. She wrapped her arms around his waist, the fingers of one hand playing idly with the thicket of his short and curlies.

"What are you looking at?" she asked softly, for his eyes were fixed on the far side of the dooryard, where the trail emerged from the forest. The trailhead was dim, shadowed by a growth of dark pines—but empty.

"I'm watching out for a snake bearing apples," he said, and laughed, then cleared his throat. "Are ye hungry, Eve?" His hand came down to twine with hers.

"Getting there. Are you?" He must be starving; they had had only a hasty snack at midday.

"Aye, I am, but—" He broke off, hesitating, and his fingers tightened in hers. "Ye'll think I'm mad, but—would ye mind if I went to fetch wee Jem tonight, instead of waiting for the morning? It's only, I'd feel a bit better to have him back."

She squeezed his hand in return, her heart lifting.

"We'll both go. It's a great idea."

"Maybe so, but it's five miles to McGillivrays', too. It'll be long dark before we're there." He was smiling, though, and his body brushed against her breasts as he turned to face her.

Something moved by her face, and she drew back sharply. A tiny caterpillar, green as the leaves on which it fed and vibrant against Roger's dark hair, reared itself into an S-shape, looking vainly for sanctuary.

"What?" Roger slid his eyes sideways, trying to see what she was looking at.

"Found your snake. I expect he's looking for an apple, too." She coaxed the tiny worm onto her finger, stepped outside, and squatted to let it crawl onto a grass blade that matched its vivid green. But the grass was in shadow. In only an instant, the sun had gone down, the forest no longer the color of life.

A thread of smoke reached her nose; chimney smoke from the Big House, but her throat closed at the smell of burning. Suddenly her uneasiness was stronger. The light was fading, night coming on. The mockingbird had fallen silent, and the forest seemed full of mystery and threat.

She rose to her feet, shoving a hand through her hair.

"Let's go, then."

"Do ye not want supper, first?" Roger looked quizzically at her, breeches in hand.

She shook her head, chill beginning to creep up her legs.

"No. Let's just go." Nothing seemed to matter, save to get Jem, and be together again, a family.

"All right," Roger said mildly, eyeing her. "I do think ye'd best put on your fig leaf first, though. Just in case we meet an angel with a flaming sword."

5

THE SHADOWS WHICH FIRE THROWS

I ABANDONED IAN and Rollo to the juggernaut of Mrs. Bug's benevolence—let Ian try telling *her* he didn't want bread and milk—and sat down to my own belated supper: a hot, fresh omelette, featuring not only cheese, but bits of salty bacon, asparagus, and wild mushroom, flavored with spring onions.

Jamie and the Major had finished their own meals already, and sat by the fire beneath a companionable fug of tobacco smoke from the Major's clay pipe. Evidently, Jamie had just finished telling Major MacDonald about the gruesome tragedy, for MacDonald was frowning and shaking his head in sympathy.

"Puir gomerels!" he said. "Ye'll be thinking that it was the same banditti, perhaps, who set upon your nephew?"

"I am," Jamie replied. "I shouldna like to think there were two such bands prowling the mountains." He glanced toward the window, cozily shuttered for the night, and I noticed suddenly that he had taken down his fowling piece from over the hearth and was absently wiping the spotless barrel with an oily rag. “Do I gather, *a charaid,* that ye’ve heard some report of similar doings?”

“Three others. At least.” The Major’s pipe threatened to go out, and he drew on it mightily, making the tobacco in the bowl glow and crackle sudden red.

A small qualm made me pause, a bite of mushroom warm in my mouth. The possibility that a mysterious gang of armed men might be roaming at large, attacking homesteads at random, had not occurred to me ’til this moment.

Obviously, it had occurred to Jamie; he rose, put the fowling piece back on its hooks, touched the rifle that hung above it for reassurance, then went to the sideboard, where his dags and the case with its elegant pair of dueling pistols were kept.

MacDonald watched with approval, puffing clouds of soft blue smoke, as Jamie methodically laid out guns, shot pouches, bullet molds, patches, rods, and all the other impedimenta of his personal armory.

“Mmphm,” MacDonald said. “A verra nice piece, that, Colonel.” He nodded at one of the dags, a long-barreled, elegant thing with a scroll butt and silver-gilt fittings.

Jamie gave MacDonald a narrow glance, hearing the “Colonel,” but answered calmly enough.

“Aye, it’s a bonny thing. It doesna aim true at anything over two paces, though. Won it in a horse race,” he added, with a small apologetic gesture at the gun, lest MacDonald think him fool enough to have paid good money for it.

He checked the flint nonetheless, replaced it, and set the gun aside.

“Where?” Jamie said casually, reaching for the bullet mold.

I had resumed chewing, but looked inquiringly at the Major myself.

“Mind, it’s only what I’ve heard,” MacDonald warned, taking the pipe from his mouth for a moment, then hastily putting it back for another puff. “A homestead some distance from Salem, burned to the ground. Folk called Zinzer—Germans.” He sucked hard, cheeks hollowing.

“That was in February, late in the month. Then three weeks later, a ferry, on the Yadkin north of Woram’s Landing—the house robbed, and the ferryman killed. The third—” Here he broke off, puffing furiously, and cut his eyes at me, then back at Jamie.

"Speak, o, friend," Jamie said in Gaelic, looking resigned. "She will have been seeing more dreadful things than you have, by far."

I nodded at this, forking up another bite of egg, and the Major coughed.

"Aye. Well, saving your presence, mum—I happened to find myself in a, er, establishment in Edenton. . . ."

"A brothel?" I put in. "Yes, quite. Do go on, Major."

He did, rather hurriedly, his face flushing dark beneath his wig.

"Ah . . . to be sure. Well, d'ye see, 'twas one of the, er, lasses in the place, told me as she'd been stolen from her home by outlaws who set upon the place one day without warning. She'd no but an auld grannie she lived with, and said they'd kilt the auld woman, and burned the house above her head."

"And who did she say had done it?" Jamie had turned his stool to face the hearth, and was melting lead scrap in a ladle for the bullet mold.

"Ah, mmphm." MacDonald's flush deepened, and the smoke fumed from his pipe with such ferocity that I could barely make out his features through the curling wreaths.

It transpired, with much coughing and circumlocution, that the Major had not really believed the girl at the time—or had been too interested in availing himself of her charms to pay much attention. Putting the story down simply as one of the tales whores often told to elicit sympathy and the odd extra glass of geneva, he had not bothered to ask for further detail.

"But when I heard by chance later of the other burnings . . . well, d'ye see, I've had the luck to be charged by the Governor with keeping an ear to the ground, as it were, in the backcountry, for signs of unrest. And I began to think that this particular instance of unrest was maybe not just sae much of a coincidence as might at first appear."

Jamie and I exchanged glances at that, Jamie's tinged with amusement, mine with resignation. He'd bet me that MacDonald—a half-pay cavalry officer who survived by freelancing—would not only survive Governor Tryon's resignation, but would succeed in worming his way promptly into some position with the new regime, now that Tryon had left to take up a superior position as governor of New York. *"He's a gentleman o' fortune, our Donald,"* he'd said.

The militant smell of hot lead began to permeate the room, competing with the Major's pipe smoke, and quite overpowering the pleasantly domestic atmosphere of rising bread, cooking, dried herbs, scouring rushes, and lye soap that normally filled the kitchen.

Lead melts suddenly; one instant, a deformed bullet or a bent button sits in the ladle, whole and distinct; the next, it's gone, a tiny puddle of metal shimmering dully in its place. Jamie poured the molten lead carefully into the mold, averting his face from the fumes.

"Why Indians?"

"Ah. Well, 'twas what the whore in Edenton said. She said some of those who burned her house and stole her away were Indians. But as I say, at the time I paid her story little mind."

Jamie made a Scottish noise indicating that he took the point, but with skepticism.

"And when did ye meet this lassie, Donald, and hear her story?"

"Near Christmas." The Major poked at the bowl of his pipe with a stained forefinger, not looking up. "Ye mean when was her house attacked? She didna say, but I think . . . perhaps not too long before. She was still . . . fairly, er, fresh." He coughed, caught my eye, caught his breath, and coughed again, hard, going red in the face.

Jamie's mouth pressed tight, and he looked down, flipping open the mold to drop a new-made ball onto the hearth.

I put down my fork, the remnants of appetite vanished.

"How?" I demanded. "How did this young woman come to be in the brothel?"

"Why, they sold her, mum." The flush still stained MacDonald's cheeks, but he had recovered his countenance enough to look at me. "The brigands. They sold her to a river trader, she said, a few days after they'd stolen her. He kept her for a bit, on his boat, but then a man came one night to do business, took a fancy to her, and bought her. He brought her as far as the coast, but I suppose he'd tired of her by then. . . ." His words trailed off, and he stuck the pipe back into his mouth, drawing hard.

"I see." I did, and the half of the omelette I'd eaten lay in a small hard ball in the bottom of my stomach.

"Still fairly fresh." How long did it take, I wondered? How long would a woman last, passed from hand to casual hand, from the splintered planks of a riverboat's deck to the tattered mattress of a hired room, given only what would keep her alive? It was more than possible that the brothel in Edenton had seemed a haven of sorts by the time she reached it. The thought didn't make me feel any more kindly toward MacDonald, though.

"Do you remember her name at least, Major?" I asked, with icy courtesy.

I thought I saw the edge of Jamie's mouth twitch, from the corner of my eye, but kept my stare focused on MacDonald.

He took the pipe from his mouth, exhaled a long stream of smoke, then looked up into my face, his eyes pale blue and very direct.

"In truth, mum," he said, "I just call them all Polly. Saves trouble, ken?"

I was saved from reply—or from something worse—by the return of Mrs. Bug, bearing an empty bowl.

"The laddie's eaten, and now he'll sleep," she announced. Her sharp eyes flicked from my face to my half-empty plate. She opened her mouth, frowning, but then glanced at Jamie, and seeming to pick up some unspoken command from him, shut her mouth again, and picked up the plate with a brief "hmp!"

"Mrs. Bug," said Jamie quietly. "Will ye awa' just now, and ask Arch to come down to me? And, if it's no troubling ye too much, the same word to Roger Mac?"

Her small black eyes went round, then narrowed as she glanced at MacDonald, obviously suspecting that if there were mischief afoot, he was behind it.

"I will," she said, and shaking her head with admonishment at me for my lack of appetite, she put down the dishes and went out, leaving the door on the latch.

"Woram's Landing," Jamie said to MacDonald, resuming

their conversation as though it had not been interrupted. "And Salem. And if it is the same men, Young Ian met them in the forest, a day's travel west of here. Near enough."

"Near enough to be the same? Aye, it is."

"It's early in the spring." Jamie glanced at the window as he spoke; it was dark now, and the shutters closed, but a cool breeze crept through and stirred the threads where I had strung mushrooms to dry, dark wizened shapes that swayed like tiny dancers, frozen against the pale wood.

I knew what he meant by that. The ground in the mountains was impassable during the winter; the high passes still held snow, and the lower slopes had only begun to green and blossom in the last few weeks. If there was an organized gang of marauders, they might only now be moving into the backcountry, after a winter spent lying low in the piedmont.

"It is," MacDonald agreed. "Early enough, perhaps, to have folk on their guard. But before your men come, sir—perhaps we should speak of what brought me?"

"Aye?" Jamie said, squinting carefully as he poured a glittering stream of lead. "Of course, Donald. I should have kent no small matter would bring ye so far. What is it?"

MacDonald smiled like a shark; now we'd come to it.

"Ye've done well wi' your place here, Colonel. How many families it is ye have on your land the noo?"

"Thirty-four," Jamie said. He didn't look up, but turned out another bullet into the ashes.

"Room for a few more, perhaps?" MacDonald was still smiling. We were surrounded by thousands of miles of wilderness; the handful of homesteads on Fraser's Ridge made scarcely a dent in it—and could vanish like smoke. I thought momentarily of the Dutch cabin, and shivered, despite the fire. I could still taste the bitter, cloying smell of burned flesh, thick in the back of my throat, lurking beneath the lighter flavors of the omelette.

"Perhaps," Jamie replied equably. "The new Scottish emigrants, is it? From up past Thurso?"

Major MacDonald and I both stared at him.

"How the devil d'ye ken that?" MacDonald demanded. "I heard it myself only ten days since!"

"Met a man at the mill yesterday," Jamie replied, picking

up the ladle again. "A gentleman from Philadelphia, come into the mountains to collect plants. He'd come up from Cross Creek and seen them." A muscle near his mouth twitched. "Apparently, they made a bit of a stir at Brunswick, and didna feel themselves quite welcome, so they came up the river on flatboats."

"A bit of a stir? What did they do?" I asked.

"Well, d'ye see, mum," the Major explained, "there are a great many folk come flooding off ships these days, straight from the Highlands. Whole villages, packed into the bowels of a ship—and looking as though they've been shat out when they disembark, too. There's nothing for them on the coast, though, and the townsfolk are inclined to point and snigger, seein' them in their outlandish rig—so for the most part, they get straight onto a barge or a flatboat and head up the Cape Fear. Campbelton and Cross Creek at least have folk who can talk to them."

He grinned at me, brushing a smudge of dirt from the skirts of his uniform coat.

"The folk in Brunswick willna be quite accustomed to such rawboned Highlanders, they having seen only such civilized Scotch persons as your husband and his aunt."

He nodded toward Jamie, who gave him a small, ironic bow in return.

"Well, relatively civilized," I murmured. I was not ready to forgive MacDonald for the whore in Edenton. "But—"

"They've barely a word of English among them, from what I hear," MacDonald hurried on. "Farquard Campbell came down to speak wi' them, and brought them north to Campbelton, or I doubt not but they'd be milling about onshore yet, wi' no notion at all where to go or what to do next."

"What's Campbell done wi' them?" Jamie inquired.

"Ah, they're parceled out amongst his acquaintance in Campbelton, but 'twon't suit in the long run, ye can see that, of course." MacDonald shrugged. Campbelton was a small settlement near Cross Creek, centered around Farquard Campbell's successful trading store, and the land around it was entirely settled—mostly by Campbells. Farquard had eight children, many of whom were also married—and as fertile as their father.

"Of course," Jamie said, looking wary. "But they're from the northern coast. They'll be fishermen, Donald, not crofters."

"Aye, but they're willing to make a change, no?" MacDonald gestured toward the door, and the forest beyond. "There's nothing for them left in Scotland. They've come here, and now they must make the best of it. A man can learn to farm, surely?"

Jamie looked rather dubious, but MacDonald was in the full flush of his enthusiasm.

"I've seen many a fisher-lad and plowboy become a soldier, man, and so have you, I'll wager. Farming's no more difficult than soldiering, surely?"

Jamie smiled a little at that; he had left farming at nineteen and fought as a mercenary in France for several years before returning to Scotland.

"Aye, well, that's maybe true, Donald. But the thing about being a soldier is that someone's tellin' ye what to do, from the moment ye rise until ye fall down at night. Who's to tell these poor wee gomerels which end o' the cow to milk?"

"That would be you, I expect," I said to him. I stretched myself, easing my back, stiff from riding, and glanced across at MacDonald. "Or at least I suppose that's what you're getting at, Major?"

"Your charm is exceeded only by your quickness of wit, mum," said MacDonald, bowing gracefully in my direction. "Aye, that's the meat of it. All your folk are Highlanders, sir, and crofters; they can speak to these newcomers in their own tongue, show them what they'll need to know—help them to make their way."

"There are a good many other folk in the colony who have the *Gaidhlig,*" Jamie objected. "And most of them a great deal more convenient to Campbelton."

"Aye, but you've vacant land that needs clearing, and they haven't." Obviously feeling that he had won the argument, MacDonald sat back and took up his neglected mug of beer.

Jamie looked at me, one eyebrow raised. It was perfectly true that we had vacant land: ten thousand acres, but barely twenty of them under cultivation. It was also true that lack of labor was acute in the entire colony, but even more so in the mountains, where the land didn't lend itself to tobacco or rice—the sorts of crops suited to slave labor.

At the same time, though—

"The difficulty is, Donald, how to settle them." Jamie bent to turn out another ball on the hearth, and straightened, brushing back a loose strand of auburn hair behind his ear. "I've land, aye, but little else. Ye canna be loosing folk straight from Scotland into the wilderness, and expect them to claw a living out of it. I couldna even give them the shoon and suit of clothes a bondsman would have, let alone tools. And to feed them and all their wives and weans through the winter? To offer them protection?" He lifted his ladle in illustration, then shook his head and dropped in another lump of lead.

"Ah, protection. Well, since ye've mentioned that, let me proceed to another wee matter of interest." MacDonald leaned forward, lowering his voice confidentially, though there was no one to hear.

"I've said I'm the Governor's man, aye? He's charged me to travel about, over the western part of the colony, and keep an ear to the ground. There are Regulators still unpardoned, and"—he glanced warily to and fro, as though expecting one of these persons to bound out of the fireplace—"ye'll have heard of the Committees of Safety?"

"A bit."

"Ye'll not have one established yet, here in the backcountry?"

"Not that I've heard of, no." Jamie had run out of lead to melt, and now stooped to scoop the new-made balls from the ashes at his feet, the warm light of the fire glowing red on the crown of his head. I sat down beside him on the settle, picking up the shot pouch from the table and holding it open for him.

"Ah," said MacDonald, looking pleased. "I see I've come in good time, then."

In the wake of the civil unrest that surrounded the War of the Regulation a year before, a number of such informal citizens' groups had sprung up, inspired by similar groups in the other colonies. If the Crown was no longer able to assure the safety of the colonists, they argued, then they must take the matter into their own hands.

The sheriffs could no longer be trusted to keep order; the scandals that had inspired the Regulator movement had assured that. The difficulty, of course, was that since the committees were self-appointed, there was no more reason to trust them than the sheriffs.

There were other committees, too. The Committees of Correspondence, loose associations of men who wrote letters to and fro, spreading news and rumor between the colonies. And it was out of these various committees that the seeds of rebellion would spring—were germinating even now, somewhere out in the cold spring night.

As I did now and then—and much more often, now—I reckoned up the time remaining. It was nearly April of 1773 And *on the eighteenth of April, in Seventy-five* . . . as Longfellow so quaintly put it . . .

Two years. But war has a long fuse, and a slow match. This one had been lit at Alamance, and the bright, hot lines of the creeping fire in North Carolina were already visible—for those who knew to look.

The lead balls in the shot pouch I held rolled and clicked together; my fingers had tightened on the leather. Jamie saw it and touched my knee, quick and light, in reassurance, then took the pouch and rolled it up, tucking it into the cartridge box.

"Good time," he repeated, looking at MacDonald. "What d'ye mean by that, Donald?"

"Why, who should lead such a committee other than yourself, Colonel? I had suggested as much to the Governor." MacDonald tried to look modest, and failed.

"Verra obliging of ye, Major," Jamie said dryly. He raised an eyebrow at me. The state of the colony's government must be worse even than he had supposed, for Governor Martin to be not only tolerating the existence of the committees—but clandestinely sanctioning them.

The long-drawn whine of a dog's yawn reached me faintly from the hall, and I excused myself, to go and check on Ian.

I wondered whether Governor Martin had the slightest idea what he was loosing. I rather thought he did, and was making the best of a bad job, by trying to ensure that some, at least, of the Committees of Safety were run by men who had backed the Crown during the War of the Regulation. The fact remained that he could not control—or even know about—many such committees. But the colony was beginning to seethe and bump like a teakettle on the boil, and Martin had no official troops at his command, only such irregulars as MacDonald—and the militia.

Which was why MacDonald was calling Jamie "Colonel," of course. The previous governor, William Tryon, had appointed Jamie—quite against his will—colonel of militia for the backcountry above the Yadkin.

"Hmph," I said to myself. Neither MacDonald nor Martin was a fool. Inviting Jamie to set up a Committee of Safety meant that he would call upon those men who had served under him in the militia—but would commit the government to nothing, in terms of paying or equipping them—and the Governor would be clear of any responsibility for their actions, since a Committee of Safety was not an official body.

The danger to Jamie—and all of us—in accepting such a proposal, though—that was considerable.

It was dark in the hall, with no light but the spill from the kitchen behind me, and the faint glow of the single candle in the surgery. Ian was asleep, but restless, a faint frown of discomfort wrinkling the soft skin between his brows. Rollo raised his head, thick tail swishing to and fro across the floor in greeting.

Ian didn't respond when I spoke his name, or when I set a hand on his shoulder. I shook him gently, then harder. I could see him struggling, somewhere under the layers of unconsciousness, like a man drifting in the underwater currents, yielding to the beckoning depths, then snagged by an unexpected fishhook, a stab of pain in cold-numbed flesh.

His eyes opened suddenly, dark and lost, and he stared at me in incomprehension.

"Hallo there," I said softly, relieved to see him wake. "What's your name?"

I could see that the question made no sense to him at once, and repeated it, patiently. Awareness stirred somewhere in the depths of his dilated pupils.

"Who am I?" he said in Gaelic. He said something else, slurred, in Mohawk, and his eyelids fluttered, closing.

"Wake up, Ian," I said firmly, resuming the shaking. "Tell me who you are."

His eyes opened again, and he squinted at me in confusion.

"Try something easier," I suggested, holding up two fingers. "How many fingers do you see?"

A flicker of awareness sprang up in his eyes.

"Dinna let Arch Bug see ye do that, Auntie," he said drowsily, the hint of a smile touching his face. "That's verra rude, ken."

Well, at least he had recognized me, as well as the "V" sign; that was something. And he must know who he was, if he was calling me Auntie.

"What's your full name?" I asked again.

"Ian James FitzGibbons Fraser Murray," he said, rather crossly. "Why d'ye keep asking me my name?"

"FitzGibbons?" I said. "Where on earth did you get that one?"

He groaned and put two fingers against his eyelids, wincing as he pressed gently.

"Uncle Jamie gave it me—blame him," he said. "It's for his auld godfather, he said. Murtagh FitzGibbons Fraser, he was called, but my mother didna want me named Murtagh. I think I'm going to puke again," he added, taking his hand away.

In the event, he heaved and retched a bit over the basin, but didn't actually vomit, which was a good sign. I eased him back onto his side, white and clammy with sweat, and Rollo stood on his hind legs, front paws braced on the table, to lick his face, which made him giggle between groans and try feebly to push the dog away.

"Theirig dhachaigh, Okwaho," he said. *"Theirig dhachaigh"* meant "go home," in Gaelic, and *Okwaho* was evidently Rollo's Mohawk name. Ian seemed to be having some difficulty choosing among the three languages in which he was fluent, but was obviously lucid, in spite of that. After I had made him answer a few more annoyingly pointless questions, I wiped his face with a damp cloth, let him rinse his mouth with well-watered wine, and tucked him in again.

"Auntie?" he said drowsily, as I was turning for the door. "D'ye think I'll ever see my Mam again?"

I stopped, having no idea how to answer that. In fact, there was no need; he had dropped back into sleep with the suddenness that concussion patients often showed, and was breathing deeply before I could find any words.

6

AMBUSH

IAN WOKE ABRUPTLY, hand closing round his tomahawk. Or what should have been his tomahawk, but was instead a handful of breeches. For an instant, he had no notion at all where he was, and sat up straight, trying to make out shapes in the dark.

Pain shot through his head like heat lightning, making him gasp soundlessly and clutch it. Somewhere in the dark below him, Rollo gave a small, startled *wuff*?

Christ. The piercing smells of his aunt's surgery stabbed the back of his nose, alcohol and burned wick and dried medicine leaves and the foul brews she called penny-syllin. He closed his eyes, put his forehead on his drawn-up knees, and breathed slowly through his mouth.

What had he been dreaming? Some dream of danger, something violent—but no clear image came to him, only the feel of being stalked, something following him through the wood.

He had to piss, badly. Fumbling for the edge of the table he lay on, he eased himself slowly upright, squinting against the flashes of pain in his head.

Mrs. Bug had left him a pot, he remembered her saying so, but the candle had gone out and he'd no mind to crawl round the floor looking for it. Faint light showed him where the door was; she had left it ajar, and a glow spread down the hall from the kitchen hearth. With that as bearing, he made his way to the window, got it open, fumbled free the shutter fastening, and stood in the flood of air from the cool spring night, eyes closed in relief as his bladder eased.

That was better, though with the relief came new awareness of the queasiness of his stomach and the throbbing in his head. He sat down, putting his arms on his knees and his head on his arms, waiting for everything to ease.

There were voices in the kitchen; he could hear them clearly, now that he paid attention.

It was Uncle Jamie and yon MacDonald, and old Arch Bug, as well, with Auntie Claire now and again putting in a word, her English voice sharp by contrast with the gruff mutter of Scots and Gaelic.

"Would ye care, perhaps, to be an Indian agent?" MacDonald was saying.

What was that? he wondered—then it came to him. Aye, of course; the Crown employed men to go out to the tribes, offer them gifts, tobacco, and knives and the like. Tell them silliness about German Geordie, as though the King was like to come and sit down by the council fires at the next Rabbit Moon and speak like a man.

He smiled grimly to think of it. The notion was plain enough; cozen the Indians to fight for the English, when fighting was needed. But why should they think it needed now? The French had yielded, retreated to their northern foothold in Acadia.

Oh. He remembered belatedly what Brianna had told him about the new fighting to come. He'd not known whether to believe her—perhaps she was right, though, in which case . . . he didn't want to think about it. Or about anything.

Rollo padded over to him, sat and leaned heavily against him. He leaned back, resting his head in the thick fur.

An Indian agent had come once, while he lived in Snaketown. A fat wee fellow, shifty-eyed and with a tremble in his voice. He thought the man—Christ, what was his name? The Mohawk had called him Bad Sweat, and that fit; he stank as though with a mortal illness—he thought the man was not accustomed to the Kahnyen'kehaka; he'd not much of their speech, and plainly expected them to take his scalp at any moment, something they had thought hilarious—and one or two would likely have tried it, for a joke, save that Tewaktenyonh said to treat him with respect. Ian had been pressed to interpret for him, a job he'd done, though without much pleasure in it. He would much sooner think himself Mohawk than acknowledge any kinship with Bad Sweat.

Uncle Jamie, though . . . he'd make a better job of it, by far. Would he do it? Ian listened to the voices with a vague sense of interest, but it was clear that Uncle Jamie would not be pressed for a decision. MacDonald might as soon get a grip on a frog in a spring, he thought, hearing his uncle elude commitment.

He sighed, put his arm around Rollo, and eased more of his weight onto the dog. He felt awful. He would have supposed he was dying, save that Auntie Claire had said he'd feel poorly for several days. He was sure she would have stayed if he were dying, not gone and left him with only Rollo for company.

The shutters were still open, and cold air poured over him, chilly and soft at once, the way spring nights were. He felt Rollo raise his nose, sniffing, and utter a low, eager whine. Possum, maybe, or a raccoon.

"Go on, then," he said, straightening up and giving the dog a small push. "I'm fine."

The dog sniffed him suspiciously, and tried to lick the back of his head, where the stitches were, but left off when Ian yelped and covered them with his hands.

"Go, I said!" He cuffed the dog gently, and Rollo snorted, circled once, then sailed over his head and out through the window, hitting the ground outside with a solid thump. A frightful screech rent the air and there was the sound of scrabbling feet and heavy bodies tearing through shrubbery.

Startled voices came from the direction of the kitchen, and he heard Uncle Jamie's step in the hall, an instant before the surgery door pushed in.

"Ian?" called his uncle softly. "Where are ye, lad? What's amiss?"

He stood up, but a sheet of blinding white came down

inside his eyes and he staggered. Uncle Jamie caught him by the arm, and set him down on a stool.

"What is it, lad?" His vision clearing, he could see his uncle in the light from the door, rifle in one hand, his face looking concerned but humorous as he glanced toward the open window. He sniffed deeply. "Not a skunk, I suppose."

"Aye, well, I suppose it's one thing or the other," Ian said, touching his head gingerly. "Either Rollo's gone after a painter, or he's treed Auntie's cat."

"Oh, aye. He'd fare better wi' the painter." His uncle set the rifle down and went to the window. "Shall I close the shutter, or d'ye need the air, lad? You're that bit peaked."

"I feel peaked," Ian admitted. "Aye, leave it, if ye will, Uncle."

"Shall ye rest, Ian?"

He hesitated. His stomach still lurched uneasily and he felt very much that he would like to lie down again—but the surgery made him uneasy, with its strong smells and the glints here and there of tiny blades and other mysterious and painful things. Uncle Jamie seemed to guess the trouble, for he bent and got a hand under Ian's elbow.

"Come along, lad. Ye can sleep upstairs in a proper bed, if ye dinna mind Major MacDonald in the other."

"I dinna mind," he said, "but I'll stay here, I think." He gestured toward the window, not wanting to nod and bother his head again. "Rollo will likely be back soon."

Uncle Jamie didn't argue with him, something he was grateful for. Women fussed. Men just got on with it.

His uncle boosted him unceremoniously back into his bed, covered him up, then began rootling about in the dark, in search of the rifle he had put down. Ian began to feel that perhaps he could do with just a wee bit of fuss, after all.

"Could ye get me a cup o' water, Uncle Jamie?"

"Eh? Oh, aye."

Auntie Claire had left a jug of water close to hand. There was the comfortable sound of glugging liquid, and then the rim of a pottery cup held to his mouth, his uncle's hand at his back to keep him upright. He didn't need it, but didn't object; the touch was warm and comforting. He hadn't realized how chilled he was from the night air, and shivered briefly.

"All right, laddie?" Uncle Jamie murmured, his hand tightening on Ian's shoulder.

"Aye, fine. Uncle Jamie?"

"Mphm?"

"Did Auntie Claire tell ye about—about a war? One coming, I mean. With England."

There was a moment's silence, his uncle's big form gone still against the light from the door.

"She has," he said, and took away his hand. "Did she tell you?"

"No, Cousin Brianna did." He lay down on his side, careful of his tender head. "D'ye believe them?"

There was no hesitation this time.

"Aye, I do." It was said with his uncle's usual dry matter-of-factness, but something in it prickled the hairs on the back of Ian's neck.

"Oh. Well, then."

The goose-down pillow was soft under his cheek, and smelled of lavender. His uncle's hand touched his head, smoothed the ruffled hair back from his face.

"Dinna fash yourself about it, Ian," he said softly. "There's time, yet."

He picked up the gun and left. From where he lay, Ian could see across the dooryard and above the trees where they dropped from the edge of the Ridge, past the slope of Black Mountain, and on into the black sky beyond, thick with stars.

He heard the back door open, and Mrs. Bug's voice, rising high above the others.

"They're no to hame, sir," she was saying, breathless. "And the hoose is dark, no fire in the hearth. Wherever might they go, this time o' night?"

He wondered dimly who was gone, but it didn't seem to matter much. If it was trouble, Uncle Jamie would deal with it. The thought was comforting; he felt like a small boy, safe in bed, hearing his father's voice outside, talking to a tenant in the cold dark of a Highland dawn.

Warmth spread slowly over him beneath the quilt, and he slept.

THE MOON WAS beginning to rise when they set out, and a good thing, too, Brianna thought. Even with the big, lopsided gold orb sailing up out of a cradle of stars and shedding its borrowed radiance over the sky, the trail beneath their feet was invisible. So were their feet, drowned in the absolute black of the forest at night.

Black, but not quiet. The giant trees rustled overhead, small things squealed and snuffled in the dark, and now and then the silent flutter of a bat passed close enough to startle her, as though part of the night had suddenly come loose and taken wing under her nose.

"The Minister's Cat is an apprehensive cat?" Roger suggested, as she gasped and clutched at him in the wake of one such leather-winged visitation.

"The Minister's Cat is an . . . appreciative cat," she replied, squeezing his hand. "Thank you." They'd likely end up sleeping on their cloaks in front of the McGillivrays' fire, instead of cozily tucked up in their own bed—but at least they'd have Jemmy.

He squeezed back, his hand bigger and stronger than hers, very reassuring in the dark.

"It's all right," he said. "I want him, too. It's a night to have your family all together, safe in one place."

She made a small sound in her throat, acknowledgment and appreciation, but wanted to keep up the conversation, as much to keep the sense of connection with him as because it would keep the dark at bay.

"The Minister's Cat was a very eloquent cat," she said delicately. "At the—the funeral, I mean. For those poor people."

Roger snorted; she saw the brief curl of his breath, white on the air.

"The Minister's Cat was a highly embarrassed cat," he said. "Your father!"

She smiled, since he couldn't see her.

"You did really well," she said mildly.

"Mmphm," he said, with another brief snort. "As for eloquence . . . if there was any, it was none of mine. All I did was quote bits of some psalm—I couldna even tell ye which it was."

"It didn't matter. Why did you pick—what you said,

though?" she asked, curious. "I sort of thought you'd say the Lord's Prayer, or maybe the Twenty-Third Psalm—everybody knows that one."

"I thought I would, too," he admitted. "I meant to. But when I came to it . . ." He hesitated, and she saw in memory those raw, cold mounds, and shivered, smelling soot. He tightened his grasp on her hand, and drew her closer, tucking the hand into the crook of his elbow.

"I don't know," he said gruffly. "It just seemed—more suitable, somehow."

"It was," she said quietly, but didn't pursue the subject, choosing instead to steer the conversation into a discussion of her latest engineering project, a hand pump to raise water from the well.

"If I had something to use for pipe, I could get water into the house, easy as anything! I've already got most of the wood I need for a nice cistern, if I can get Ronnie to cooper it for me—so we can shower with rainwater, at least. But hollowing out tree limbs"—the method employed for the small amount of piping used for the pump—"it would take me months to manage enough just to get from the well to the house, let alone the stream. And there's not a chance of getting any rolled copper. Even if we could afford any, which we can't, bringing it up from Wilmington would be—" She threw her free hand up in frustration at the monumental nature of the undertaking.

He considered that for a bit, the chuff of their shoes on the rocky trail a comforting rhythm.

"Well, the ancient Romans did it with concrete; the recipe's in Pliny."

"I know. But it takes a particular kind of sand, which we don't happen to have. Likewise, quicklime, which we likewise don't have. And—"

"Aye, but what about clay?" he interrupted. "Did ye see that plate at Hilda's wedding? The big brown and red one, with the beautiful patterns?"

"Yes," she said. "Why?"

"Ute McGillivray said someone from Salem brought it. I dinna recall the name, but she said he was quite the big noise in potting—or whatever ye call making dishes."

"I'll bet you any amount of money she didn't say that!"

"Well, words to that effect." He went on, undeterred. "The point being that he made it *here;* it wasn't something he'd brought from Germany. So there's clay about that's suitable for firing, eh?"

"Oh, I *see.* Hmm. Well, now, that's an idea, isn't it?"

It was, and an attractive one whose discussion occupied them for most of the rest of the journey.

They had come down off the Ridge and were within a quarter-mile of the McGillivrays' place when she began to have an uneasy feeling down the back of her neck. It *could* be only imagination; after the sights they had seen in that deserted hollow, the dark air of the wood seemed thick with threat, and she had been imagining ambush at every blind bend, tensing with the anticipation of attack.

Then she heard something crack in the trees to her right—a small dry branch breaking, in a way that neither wind nor animal would break it. Real danger had its own taste, vivid as lemon juice, by contrast with the weak lemonade of imagination.

Her hand tightened on Roger's arm in warning, and he stopped at once.

"What?" he whispered, hand on his knife. "Where?" He hadn't heard it.

Damn, why hadn't she brought her gun, or at least her own dirk? All she had was her Swiss Army knife, carried always in her pocket—and what weapons the landscape offered.

She leaned into Roger, pointing, her hand close to his body to be sure he followed the direction of her gesture. Then she stooped, feeling about in the darkness for a rock, or a stick to use as a club.

"Keep talking," she whispered.

"The Minister's Cat is a fraidy cat, is she?" he said, his tone one of fairly convincing teasing.

"The Minister's Cat is a *ferocious* cat," she replied, trying to match his bantering tone, meanwhile fumbling one-handed in her pocket. Her other hand closed on a stone, and she pulled it free of the clinging dirt, cold and heavy in her palm. She rose, all her senses focused on the darkness to their right. "She'll freaking disembowel anything that—"

"Oh, it's you," said a voice in the woods behind her.

She shrieked, and Roger jerked in reflex, spun on his heel to face the threat, grabbed her and thrust her behind him, all in the same motion.

The push sent her staggering backward. She caught a heel in a hidden root in the dark, and fell, landing hard on her backside, from which position she had an excellent view of Roger in the moonlight, knife in hand, charging into the trees with an incoherent roar.

Belatedly, she registered what the voice had said, as well as the unmistakable tone of disappointment in it. A very similar voice, loud with alarm, spoke from the wood on the right.

"Jo?" it said. "What? Jo, what?"

There was a lot of thrashing and yelling going on in the woods to the left. Roger'd got his hands on someone.

"Roger!" she shouted. "Roger, stop! It's the Beardsleys!"

She'd dropped the rock when she fell, and now got to her feet, rubbing the dirt from her hand on the side of her skirt. Her heart was still pounding, her left buttock was bruised, and her urge to laugh was tinged with a strong desire to strangle one or both of the Beardsley twins.

"Kezzie Beardsley, come out of there!" she bellowed, then repeated it, even louder. Kezzie's hearing had improved after her mother had removed his chronically infected tonsils and adenoids, but he was still rather deaf.

A loud rustling in the brush yielded the slight form of Keziah Beardsley, dark-haired, white-faced, and armed with a large club, which he swung off his shoulder and tried abashedly to hide behind him when he saw her.

Meanwhile, much louder rustling and a certain amount of cursing behind her portended the emergence of Roger, gripping the scrawny neck of Josiah Beardsley, Kezzie's twin.

"What in the name of God d'ye wee bastards think ye're up to?" Roger said, shoving Jo across to stand by his brother in a patch of moonlight. "D'ye realize I nearly killed you?"

There was just enough light for Brianna to make out the rather cynical expression that crossed Jo's face at this, before it was erased and replaced with one of earnest apology.

"We're that sorry, Mr. Mac. We heard someone coming, and thought it might be brigands."

"Brigands," Brianna repeated, feeling the urge to laugh rising, but keeping it firmly in check. "Where on earth did you get that word?"

"Oh." Jo looked at his feet, hands clasped behind his back. "Miss Lizzie was a-readin' to us, from that book what Mr. Jamie brought. 'Twas in there. About brigands."

"I see." She glanced at Roger, who met her eye, his annoyance obviously waning into amusement, as well. *"The Pirate Gow,"* she explained. "Defoe."

"Oh, aye." Roger sheathed his dirk. "And why, exactly, did ye think there might be brigands coming?"

Kezzie, with the quirks of his erratic hearing, picked that up and answered, as earnestly as his brother, though his voice was louder and slightly flat, the result of his early deafness.

"We come across Mr. Lindsay, sir, on his way home, and he did tell us what passed, up by Dutchman's Creek. It's true, so, what he said? They was all burned to cinders?"

"They were all dead." Roger's voice had lost any tinge of amusement. "What's that to do with you lot lurking in the woods with clubs?"

"Well, you see, sir, McGillivrays' is a fine, big place, what with the cooper's shop and the new house and all, and being on a road, like—well, if *I* was a brigand, sir, 'tis just the sort of place I might choose," replied Jo.

"And Miss Lizzie's there, with her Pap. And your son, Mr. Mac," Kezzie added pointedly. "Shouldn't want no harm to come to 'em."

"I see." Roger smiled a little crookedly. "Well, thanks to ye, then, for the kind thought. I doubt the brigands will be anywhere near, though; Dutchman's Creek is a long way away."

"Aye, sir," Jo agreed. "But brigands might be anywhere, mightn't they?"

This was undeniable, and sufficiently true as to give Brianna a renewed feeling of chill in the pit of the stomach.

"They might be, but they aren't," Roger assured them. "Come along to the house with us, aye? We're just going to collect wee Jem. I'm sure *Frau* Ute would give ye a bed by the fire."

The Beardsleys exchanged inscrutable looks. They were

nearly identical—small and lithe, with thick dark hair, distinguished only by Kezzie's deafness and the round scar on Jo's thumb—and to see the two fine-boned faces wearing precisely the same expression was a little unnerving.

Whatever information had been exchanged by that look, it had evidently included as much consultation as was required, for Kezzie nodded slightly, deferring to his brother.

"Ah, no, sir," Josiah said politely. "We'll bide, I think." And with no further talk, the two of them turned and crunched off into the dark, scuffling leaves and rocks as they went.

"Jo! Wait!" Brianna called after them, her hand having found something else in the bottom of her pocket.

"Aye, ma'am?" Josiah was back, appearing by her elbow with unsettling abruptness. His twin was no stalker, but Jo was.

"Oh! I mean, oh, there you are." She took a deep breath to slow her heart, and handed him the carved whistle she'd made for Germain. "Here. If you're going to stand guard, this might be helpful. To call for help, if someone *should* come."

Jo Beardsley had plainly never seen a whistle before, but didn't care to admit it. He turned the little object over in his hand, trying not to stare at it.

Roger reached out, took it from him, and blew a healthy blast that shattered the night. Several birds, startled from their rest, shot out of the nearby trees, shrieking, followed closely by Kezzie Beardsley, eyes huge with amazement.

"Blow in that end," Roger said, tapping the appropriate end of the whistle before handing it back. "Squeeze your lips a bit."

"Much obliged, sir," Jo murmured. His normal stoic facade had shattered with the silence, and he took the whistle with the wide-eyed look of a boy on Christmas morning, turning at once to show the prize to his twin. It struck her quite suddenly that neither boy likely ever *had* had a Christmas morning—or any other sort of gift.

"I'll make another one for you," she told Kezzie. "Then the two of you can signal back and forth. If you see any brigands," she added, smiling.

"Oh, yes, ma'am. We'll do that, we surely will!" he assured

her, scarcely glancing at her in his eagerness to examine the whistle his brother had put in his hands.

"Blow it three times, if ye want help," Roger called after them, taking her arm.

"Aye, sir!" came back from the darkness, followed by a belated faint "Thank you, ma'am!"—this in turn followed at once by a fusillade of puffs, gasps, and breathless rattles, punctuated by briefly successful shrill toots.

"Lizzie's been teaching them manners, I see," Roger said. "As well as their letters. D'ye think they'll ever be truly civilized, though?"

"No," she said, with a trace of regret.

"Really?" She couldn't see his face in the dark, but heard the surprise in his voice. "I was only joking. Ye really think not?"

"I do—and no wonder, after the way they grew up. Did you see the way they were with that whistle? No one's ever given them a present, or a toy."

"I suppose not. D'ye think that's what makes boys civilized? If so, I imagine wee Jem will be a philosopher or an artist or something. Mrs. Bug spoils him rotten."

"Oh, as if you don't," she said tolerantly. "And Da, and Lizzie, and Mama, and everyone else in sight."

"Oh, well," Roger said, unembarrassed at the accusation. "Wait 'til he has a bit of competition. Germain's in no danger of spoiling, is he?" Germain, Fergus and Marsali's eldest son, was harried by two small sisters, known to one and all as the hell-kittens, who followed their brother constantly, teasing and pestering.

She laughed, but felt a slight sense of uneasiness. The thought of another baby always made her feel as though she were perched at the top of a roller coaster, short of breath and stomach clenched, poised somewhere between excitement and terror. Particularly now, with the memory of their lovemaking still softly heavy, shifting like mercury in her belly.

Roger seemed to sense her ambivalence, for he didn't pursue the subject, but reached for her hand and held it, his own large and warm. The air was cold, the last vestiges of a winter chill lingering in the hollows.

"What about Fergus, then?" he asked, taking up an earlier

thread of the conversation. “From what I hear, he hadn’t much of a childhood, either, but he seems fairly civilized.”

“My aunt Jenny had the raising of him from the time he was ten,” she objected. “You haven’t met my aunt Jenny, but believe me, she could have civilized Adolf Hitler, if she put her mind to it. Besides, Fergus grew up in Paris, not the back-woods—even if it *was* in a brothel. And it sounds like it was a pretty high-class brothel, too, from what Marsali tells me.”

“Oh, aye? What does she tell you?”

“Oh, just stories that he’s told her, now and then. About the clients, and the wh—the girls.”

“Can ye not say ‘whore,’ then?” he asked, amused. She felt the blood rise in her cheeks, and was pleased that it was dark; he teased her more when she blushed.

“I can’t help it that I went to a Catholic school,” she said, defensive. “Early conditioning.” It was true; she couldn’t say certain words, save when in the grip of fury or when mentally prepared. “Why can you, though? You’d think a preacher’s lad would have the same problem.”

He laughed, a little wryly.

“Not precisely the same problem. It was more a matter of feeling obliged to curse and carry on in front of my friends, to prove I could.”

“What kind of carrying on?” she asked, scenting a story. He didn’t often talk about his early life in Inverness, adopted by his great-uncle, a Presbyterian minister, but she loved hearing the small tidbits he sometimes let fall.

“Och. Smoking, drinking beer, and writing filthy words on the walls in the boys’ toilet,” he said, the smile evident in his voice. “Tipping over dustbins. Letting air out of automobile tires. Stealing sweeties from the Post Office. Quite the wee criminal I was, for a time.”

“The terror of Inverness, huh? Did you have a gang?” she teased.

“I did,” he said, and laughed. “Gerry MacMillan, Bobby Cawdor, and Dougie Buchanan. I was odd man out, not only for being the preacher’s lad, but for having an English father and an English name. So I was always out to show them I was a hard man. Meaning I was usually the one in most trouble.”

"I had no idea you were a juvenile delinquent," she said, charmed at the thought.

"Well, not for long," he assured her wryly. "Come the summer I was fifteen, the Reverend signed me up on a fishing boat, and sent me to sea with the herring fleet. Couldna just say whether he did it to improve my character, keep me out of jail, or only because he couldn't stand me round the house any longer, but it did work. Ye want to meet hard men sometime, go to sea with a bunch of Gaelic fishermen."

"I'll remember that," she said, trying not to giggle and producing a series of small, wet snorts instead. "Did your friends end up in jail, then, or did they go straight, without you to mislead them?"

"Dougie joined the army," he said, a tinge of wistfulness in his voice. "Gerry took over his dad's shop—his dad was a tobacconist. Bobby . . . aye, well, Bobby's dead. Drowned, that same summer, out lobstering with his cousin off Oban."

She leaned closer to him and squeezed his hand, her shoulder brushing his in sympathy.

"I'm sorry," she said, then paused. "Only . . . he isn't dead, is he? Not yet. Not now."

Roger shook his head, and made a small sound of mingled humor and dismay.

"Is that a comfort?" she asked. "Or is it horrible to think about?"

She wanted to keep him talking; he hadn't talked so much in one go since the hanging that had taken his singing voice. Being forced to speak in public made him self-conscious, and his throat tightened. His voice was still rasping, but relaxed as he was now, he wasn't choking or coughing.

"Both," he said, and made the sound again. "I'll never see him again, either way." He shrugged slightly, pushing the thought away. "D'ye think of your old friends much?"

"No, not much," she said softly. The trail narrowed here, and she linked her arm in his, drawing close as they approached the last turn, which would bring them in sight of the McGillivrays'. "There's too much here." But she didn't want to talk about what *wasn't* here.

"Do you think Jo and Kezzie are just playing?" she asked. "Or are they up to something?"

"What should they be up to?" he asked, accepting her change of subject without comment. "I canna think they're lying in wait to commit highway robbery—not at this time of night."

"Oh, I believe them about standing guard," she said. "They'd do anything to protect Lizzie. Only—" She paused. They had come out of the forest onto the wagon road; the far verge fell away in a steep bank, looking at night like a bottomless pool of black velvet—by daylight, it would be a tangled mass of fallen snags, clumps of rhododendron, redbud, and dogwood, overgrown with the snarls of ancient grapevines and creepers. The road made a switchback further on and curved back on itself, arriving gently at the McGillivrays' place, a hundred feet below.

"The lights are still on," she said with some surprise. The small group of buildings—the Old Place, the New Place, Ronnie Sinclair's cooper's shop, Dai Jones's blacksmith's forge and cabin—were mostly dark, but the lower windows of the McGillivrays' New Place were striped with light, leaking through the cracks of the shutters, and a bonfire in front of the house made a brilliant blot of light against the dark.

"Kenny Lindsay," Roger said matter-of-factly. "The Beardsleys said they'd met him. He'll have stopped to share the news."

"Mm. We'd better be careful, then; if they're looking out for brigands, too, they might shoot at anything that moves."

"Not tonight; it's a party, remember? What were ye saying, though, about the Beardsley boys protecting Lizzie?"

"Oh." Her toe stubbed against some hidden obstacle, and she clutched his arm to keep from falling. "Oof! Only that I wasn't sure who they thought they were protecting her from."

Roger tightened his grip on her arm in reflex.

"Whatever d'ye mean by that?"

"Just that if I were Manfred McGillivray, I'd take good care to be nice to Lizzie. Mama says the Beardsleys follow her around like dogs, but they don't. They follow her like tame wolves."

"I thought Ian said it wasn't possible to tame wolves."

"It isn't," she said tersely. "Come on, let's hurry, before they smoor the fire."

THE BIG LOG house was literally overflowing with people. Light spilled from the open door and glowed in the row of tiny arrow-slit windows that marched across the front of the house, and dark forms wove in and out of the bonfire's light. The sounds of a fiddle came to them, thin and sweet through the dark, borne on the wind with the scent of roasting meat.

"I suppose Senga's truly made her choice, then," Roger said, taking her arm for the final steep descent to the crossroad. "Who d'ye bet it is? Ronnie Sinclair or the German lad?"

"Oh, a bet? What are the stakes? Woops!" She stumbled, tripping on a half-buried rock in the path, but Roger tightened his grip, keeping her upright.

"Loser sets the pantry to rights," he suggested.

"Deal," she said promptly. "I think she chose Heinrich."

"Aye? Well, ye may be right," he said, sounding amused. "But I have to tell you, it was five to three in favor of Ronnie, last I heard. *Frau* Ute's a force to be reckoned with."

"She is," Brianna admitted. "And if it was Hilda or Inga, I'd say it was no contest. But Senga's got her mother's personality; nobody's telling *her* what to do—not even *Frau* Ute.

"Where did they get 'Senga,' anyway?" she added. "There are lots of Ingas and Hildas over toward Salem, but I've never heard of another Senga."

"Ah, well, ye wouldn't—not in Salem. It's not a German name, ken—it's Scots."

"Scots?" she said in astonishment.

"Oh, aye," he said, the grin evident in his voice. "It's Agnes, spelt backward. A girl named that is bound to be contrary, don't ye think?"

"You're kidding! Agnes, spelled backward?"

"I wouldna say it's common, exactly, but I've certainly met one or two Sengas in Scotland."

She laughed.

"Do the Scots do that with any other names?"

"Back-spelling?" He considered. "Well, I did go to school with a lass named Adnil, and there was a grocer's lad who got in the messages for old ladies in the neighborhood—his name's pronounced 'Kirry,' but it's spelt 'C-i-r-e.'"

She looked sharply at him, in case he was teasing, but he wasn't. She shook her head.

"I think Mama's right about Scots. So yours spelled backward would be—"

"Regor," he confirmed. "Sounds like something from a Godzilla film, doesn't it? A giant eel, maybe, or a beetle with death-ray eyes." He sounded pleased at the notion.

"You thought about it, didn't you?" she said, laughing. "Which would you rather be?"

"Well, when I was a kid, I thought the beetle with the death-ray eyes would be best," he admitted. "Then I went to sea and started hauling up the occasional Moray eel in my net. Those are not the kind of thing ye'd want to meet in a dark alley, believe me."

"More agile than Godzilla, at least," she said, shuddering slightly at the recollection of the one Moray eel she'd met personally. A four-foot length of spring steel and rubber, fast as lightning and equipped with a mouthful of razors, it had come up from the hold of a fishing boat she'd watched being unloaded in a little port town called MacDuff.

She and Roger had been leaning on a low rock wall, idly watching the gulls hover in the wind, when a shout of alarm from the fishing boat just below had made them look down in time to see fishermen scrambling back from something on deck.

A dark sine wave had flashed through the silver wash of fish on deck, shot under the rail, and landed on the wet stones of the quay, where it had caused similar panic among the fishermen hosing down their gear, writhing and lashing about like a crazed high-tension cable until one rubber-booted man, gathering his self-possession, had rushed up and kicked it back into the water.

"Well, they're no really bad sorts, eels," Roger said judiciously, evidently recalling the same memory. "Ye canna blame them, after all; being dragged up from the bottom of the sea without warning—anyone would thrash about a bit."

"So they would," she said, thinking of themselves. She took his hand, threading her fingers between his, and found his firm, cold grip a comfort.

They were close enough now to catch snatches of laughter

and talk, billowing up into the cold night with the smoke of the fire. There were children running loose; she saw two small forms dart through the legs of the crowd around the fire, black and thin-limbed as Halloween goblins.

That wasn't Jem, surely? No, he was smaller, and surely Lizzie wouldn't—

"Mej," Roger said.

"What?"

"Jem, backward," he explained. "I was just thinking it would be a lot of fun to see Godzilla films with him. Maybe he'd like to be the beetle with death-ray eyes. Be fun, aye?"

He sounded so wistful that a lump came to her throat, and she squeezed his hand hard, then swallowed.

"Tell him Godzilla stories," she said firmly. "It's make-believe anyway. I'll draw him pictures."

He laughed at that.

"Christ, you do, and they'll be stoning ye for trafficking with the devil, Bree. Godzilla looks like something straight out of the Book of Revelation—or so I was told."

"Who told you that?"

"Eigger."

"Who . . . oh," she said, going into mental reverse. "Reggie? Who's Reggie?"

"The Reverend." His great-uncle, his adoptive father. There was still a smile in his voice, but one tinged with nostalgia. "When we went to the monster films together of a Saturday. Eigger and Regor—and ye should have seen the looks on the faces of the Ladies' Altar and Tea Society, when Mrs. Graham let them in without announcing them, and they came into the Reverend's study to find us stamping round and roaring, kicking hell out of a Tokyo built of blocks and soup tins."

She laughed, but felt tears prick at the backs of her eyes.

"I wish I'd known the Reverend," she said, squeezing his hand.

"I wish ye had, too," he said softly. "He would have liked ye so much, Bree."

For the space of a few moments, while he talked, the dark forest and the flaming fire below had faded away; they were in Inverness, cozy in the Reverend's study, with rain on the windows and the sound of traffic going by in the street. It happened so often when they talked like this, between themselves. Then some small thing would fracture the moment—now, it was a shout from the fire as people began to clap and sing—and the world of their own time vanished in an instant.

What if he were gone, she thought suddenly. Could I bring it back, all by myself?

A spasm of elemental panic gripped her, just for a moment, at the thought. Without Roger as her touchstone, with nothing but her own memories to serve as anchor to the future, that time would be lost. Would fade into hazy dreams, and be lost, leaving her no firm ground of reality to stand upon.

She took a deep breath of the cold night air, crisp with woodsmoke, and dug the balls of her feet hard into the ground as they walked, trying to feel solid.

"MamaMamaMAMA!" A small blob detached itself from the confusion round the fire and rocketed toward her, crashing into her knees with enough force to make her grab hold of Roger's arm.

"Jem! There you are!" She scooped him up and buried her face in his hair, which smelled pleasantly of goats, hay, and spicy sausage. He was heavy, and more than solid.

Then Ute McGillivray turned and saw them. Her broad face was creased in a frown, but broke into a beam of delight at seeing them. People turned at her call of greeting, and they were engulfed at once by the crowd, everyone asking questions, expressing gratified surprise at their coming.

A few questions were asked about the Dutch family, but Kenny Lindsay had brought the news of the burning earlier; Brianna was glad of that. People clucked and shook their heads, but by now they had exhausted most of their horrified speculations, and were turning to other matters. The cold of the graves beneath the fir trees still lingered as a faint chill on her heart; she had no wish to make *that* experience real again by talking about it.

The newly engaged couple were seated together on a pair of upturned buckets, holding hands, faces blissful in the glow of the bonfire.

"I win," Brianna said, smiling at sight of them. "Don't they look happy?"

"They do," Roger agreed. "I doubt Ronnie Sinclair is. Is he

here?" He glanced round, and so did she, but the cooper was nowhere in sight.

"Wait—he's in his shop," she said, putting a hand on Roger's wrist and nodding toward the small building on the opposite side of the road. There were no windows on this side of the cooper's shop, but a faint glow showed round the edge of the closed door.

Roger glanced from the darkened shop to the convivial crowd round the fire; a good many of Ute's relations had ridden over with the lucky bridegroom and his friends from Salem, bringing with them an immense barrel of black beer, which was adding to the festivities. The air was yeasty with the tang of hops.

By contrast, the cooper's shop had a desolate, glowering sort of air about it. She wondered whether anyone around the fire had yet missed Ronnie Sinclair.

"I'll go and have a bit of a blether with him, aye?" Roger touched her back in brief affection. "He could maybe use a sympathetic ear."

"That and a stiff drink?" She nodded toward the house, where Robin McGillivray was visible through the open door, pouring what she assumed to be whisky for a select circle of friends.

"I imagine he will have managed that for himself," Roger replied dryly. He left her, making his way around the convivial group by the fire. He disappeared in the dark, but then she saw the door of the cooper's shop open, and Roger silhouetted briefly against the glow from within, his tall form blocking the light before vanishing inside.

"Wanna drink, Mama!" Jemmy was wriggling like a tadpole, trying to get down. She set him on the ground, and he was off like a shot, nearly upsetting a stout lady with a platter of corn fritters.

The aroma of the steaming fritters reminded her that she hadn't had any supper, and she made her way after Jemmy to the table of food, where Lizzie, in her role as almost-daughter-of-the-house, helped her importantly to sauerkraut, sausages, smoked eggs, and something involving corn and squash.

"Where's *your* sweetheart, Lizzie?" she asked, teasing. "Shouldn't you be spooning with him?"

"Oh, him?" Lizzie looked like someone recalling a thing of vague general interest, but no immediate importance. "Manfred, ye mean? He's . . . ower there." She squinted against the glow of the fire, then pointed with her serving spoon. Manfred McGillivray, her own betrothed, was with three or four other young men, all with arms linked, swaying to and fro as they sang something in German. They appeared to have trouble remembering the words, as each verse dissolved into giggles and shoving accusations.

"Here, *Schätzchen*—that's 'sweetheart,' ken, in German," Lizzie explained, leaning down to give Jemmy a bite of sausage. He snapped the tidbit up like a starving seal and chewed industriously, then mumbled, "Wagga gink," and wandered off into the night.

"Jem!" Brianna made to go after him, but was hampered by an oncoming crowd headed for the table.

"Ah, dinna fash yourself about him," Lizzie assured her. "Everyone kens who he is; he'll come to nay harm."

She might still have gone after him, save that she saw a small blond head pop up beside Jem's. Germain, Jem's bosom friend. Germain was two years older, and had a great deal more worldly knowledge than the average five-year-old, thanks in great part to his father's tutelage. She did hope he wasn't picking pockets in the crowd, and made a mental note to frisk him for contraband, later.

Germain had Jem firmly by the hand, so she allowed herself to be persuaded to sit down with Lizzie, Inga, and Hilda, on the bales of straw that had been placed a little way from the fire.

"Und where's *your* sweetheart, then?" teased Hilda. "Yon big bonny black devil?"

"Oh, him?" Brianna said, mimicking Lizzie, and they all broke into rather unladylike roars of laughter; evidently the beer had been making the rounds for some time.

"He's comforting Ronnie," she said, with a nod toward the darkened cooper's shop. "Is your mother upset about Senga's choice?"

"Och, aye," said Inga, rolling her eyes with great expressiveness. "Should ha' heard them at it, her and Senga.

Hammer and tongs, hammer and tongs. Da went out to the fishing, and stayed awa' three days."

Brianna ducked her head to hide a grin. Robin McGillivray liked a peaceful life, something he was never likely to enjoy in the company of his wife and daughters.

"Ah, well," Hilda said philosophically, leaning back a little to ease the strain of her first pregnancy, which was well advanced. "She couldna really say so much, *meine Mutter.* Heinrich's her own cousin's son, after all. Even if he *is* poor."

"But young," Inga added practically. "Da says Heinrich will have time to get rich." Ronnie Sinclair wasn't precisely rich—and he *was* thirty years older than Senga. On the other hand, he did own both his cooper's shop and half of the house in which he and the McGillivrays lived. And Ute, having shepherded both her elder daughters to solid marriages with men of property, had obviously seen the advantages of a match between Senga and Ronnie.

"I can see that it might be a little awkward," Brianna said tactfully. "Ronnie going on living with your family, after—" She nodded at the betrothed couple, who were feeding each other bits of cake.

"Hoo!" Hilda exclaimed, rolling her eyes. "I'm that glad not to be living here!"

Inga nodded vigorous agreement, but added, "Well, but *Mutti* isna the one to be greetin' over spilt milk. She's got an eye out for a wife for Ronnie. Just watch her." She nodded toward the food table, where Ute was chatting and smiling with a group of German women.

"Who d'ye think it is she has picked out?" Inga asked her sister, eyes narrowed as she watched her mother operate. "That wee Gretchen? Or your Archie's cousin, maybe? The walleyed one—Seona?"

Hilda, married to a Scot from Surry County, shook her head at this.

"She'll want a German girl," she objected. "For she'll be thinkin' of what will happen if Ronnie dies, and the wife marries again. If it's a German girl, chances are Mama can bully her into a new marriage with one of her nephews or cousins—keep the property in the family, aye?"

Brianna listened with fascination as the girls discussed the situation, with perfect matter-of-factness—and wondered whether Ronnie Sinclair had the slightest idea that his fate was being decided in this pragmatic fashion. But he'd been living with the McGillivrays for more than a year, she reasoned; he must have some idea of Ute's methods.

Thanking God silently that she was not herself compelled to live in the same house with the redoubtable *Frau* McGillivray, she looked round for Lizzie, feeling a pang of sympathy for her erstwhile bondmaid. Lizzie *would* be living with Ute, once her marriage to Manfred took place next year.

Hearing the name "Wemyss," she returned to the conversation at hand, only to discover that the girls were not discussing Lizzie, but rather her father.

"Auntie Gertrud," declared Hilda, and belched softly, fist to her mouth. "She's a widow-woman herself; she'd be the best for him."

"Auntie Gertrud would have poor wee Mr. Wemyss dead in a year," Inga objected, laughing. "She's twice his size. If she didna kill him from exhaustion, she'd roll over in her sleep and squash him flat."

Hilda clapped both hands to her mouth, but less in shock than to stifle her giggles. Brianna thought she'd had her share of beer, too; her cap was awry and her pale face looked flushed, even by firelight.

"Aye, weel, I think he's no much bothered at the thought. See him?" Hilda nodded past the beer-drinkers, and Brianna had no trouble picking out Mr. Wemyss's head, his hair pale and flyaway as his daughter's. He was in animated conversation with a stout woman in apron and cap, who nudged him intimately in the ribs, laughing.

As she watched, though, Ute McGillivray made her way toward them, followed by a tall blond woman, who hesitated a little, hands folded under her apron.

"Oh, who's that?" Inga craned her neck like a goose, and her sister elbowed her, scandalized.

*"Lass das, du alte Ziege! Mutti'*s looking this way!"

Lizzie had half-risen to her knees, peering.

"Who—?" she said, sounding like an owl. Her attention was momentarily distracted by Manfred, who dropped beside her in the straw, grinning amiably.

"How is it, then, *Herzchen*?" he said, putting an arm round her waist and trying to kiss her.

"Who's that, Freddie?" she said, adroitly eluding his embrace and pointing discreetly toward the blond woman, who was smiling shyly as *Frau* Ute introduced her to Mr. Wemyss.

Manfred blinked, swaying a little on his knees, but answered readily enough.

"Oh. That's *Fraülein* Berrisch. Pastor Berrisch's sister."

Inga and Hilda made little cooing sounds of interest; Lizzie frowned a little, but then relaxed, seeing her father tilt back his head to address the newcomer; *Fraülein* Berrisch was nearly as tall as Brianna herself.

Well, that explains why she's still a Fraülein, Brianna thought with sympathy. The woman's hair was streaked with gray, where it showed beneath her cap, and she had a rather plain face, though her eyes held a calm sweetness.

"Oh, a Protestant, then," Lizzie said, in a dismissive tone that made it clear that the *Fraülein* could hardly be considered as a potential mate for her father.

"Aye, but she's a nice woman, for a' that. Come and dance, Elizabeth." Manfred had clearly lost any interest in Mr. Wemyss and the *Fraülein;* he pulled Lizzie, protesting, to her feet, and propelled her toward the circle of dancers. She went reluctantly, but Brianna saw that by the time they had reached the dance, Lizzie was laughing at something Manfred had said, and he was smiling down at her, the firelight glowing on the handsome planes of his face. They were a nice-looking couple, she thought, better-matched in appearance than Senga and her Heinrich—who was tall, but spindly and rather hatchet-faced.

Inga and Hilda had begun arguing with each other in German, allowing Brianna to devote herself to the wholehearted consumption of the excellent supper. Hungry as she was, she would have enjoyed almost anything, but the tart, crisp sauerkraut and the sausages, bursting with juice and spices, were a rare treat.

It was only as she wiped the last of the juice and grease from her wooden plate with a chunk of corn bread that she cast a glance at the cooper's shop, thinking guiltily that she ought perhaps to have saved some for Roger. He was so kind, taking thought for poor Ronnie's feelings. She felt a rush of pride and affection for him. Maybe she should go over there and rescue him.

She had put down her plate and was sorting out her skirts and petticoats, in preparation for putting this plan into action, when she was forestalled by a pair of small figures who came weaving out of the darkness.

"Jem?" she said, startled. "What's the matter?"

The flames gleamed on Jemmy's hair like freshly minted copper, but the face under it was white, and his eyes enormous dark pools, fixed and staring.

"Jemmy!"

He turned a blank face to her, said "Mama?" in a small, uncertain voice, then sat down suddenly, his legs collapsing under him like rubber bands.

She was dimly aware of Germain, swaying like a sapling in a high breeze, but had no attention to spare for him. She seized Jemmy, lifting his head and shaking him a little.

"Jemmy! Wake up! What's wrong?"

"The wee laddie's dead drunk, *a nighean,*" said a voice above her, sounding amused. "Whatever have ye been givin' him?" Robin McGillivray, rather obviously a little the worse for wear himself, leaned over and prodded Jemmy gently, eliciting nothing more than a soft gurgle. He picked up one of Jemmy's arms, then let it go; it fell, boneless as a strand of boiled spaghetti.

"*I* didn't give him anything," she replied, panic giving way to a rising annoyance, as she saw that Jemmy was in fact merely asleep, his small chest rising and falling with a reassuring rhythm. "Germain!"

Germain had subsided into a small heap, and was singing "Alouette" to himself in a dreamy sort of way. Brianna had taught it to him; it was his favorite song.

"Germain! What did you give Jemmy to drink?"

"*. . . j'te plumerai la tete. . .*"

"*Germain!*" She grabbed him by the arm, and he ceased singing, looking surprised to see her.

"What did you give Jemmy, Germain?"

"He was thirsty, m'dame," Germain said, with a smile of surpassing sweetness. "He wanted a drink." Then his eyes rolled back in his head, and he keeled over backward, limp as a dead fish.

"Oh, Jesus Christ on a piece of *toast*!"

Inga and Hilda looked shocked, but she was in no mood to worry about their sensibilities.

"Where the bloody hell is Marsali?"

"She's no here," Inga said, bending forward to inspect Germain. "She stopped at hame wi' the wee *maedchen*. Fergus is . . ." She straightened up, looking vaguely round. "Well, I saw him a while ago."

"What's the trouble?" The hoarse voice at her shoulder surprised her, and she turned to find Roger looking quizzical, his face relaxed from its usual sternness.

"Your son is a drunkard," she informed him. Then she caught a whiff of Roger's breath. "Following in his father's footsteps, I see," she added coldly.

Disregarding this, Roger sat down beside her and gathered Jemmy up into his lap. Holding the little boy propped against his knees, he patted Jemmy's cheek, gently but insistently.

"Hallo there, Mej," he said softly. "Hallo, then. Ye're all right, are ye?"

Like magic, Jemmy's eyelids floated up. He smiled dreamily at Roger.

"Hallo, Daddy." Still smiling beatifically, his eyes closed and he relaxed into utter limpness, cheek flattened against his father's knee.

"He's all right," Roger told her.

"Well, good," she said, not particularly mollified. "What do you think they've been drinking? Beer?"

Roger leaned forward and sniffed at his offspring's red-stained lips.

"Cherry Bounce, at a guess. There's a vat of it, round by the barn."

"Holy God!" She'd never drunk Cherry Bounce, but Mrs. Bug had told her how to make it: *"Tak' the juice of a bushel o' cherries, dissolve twenty-four pound o' sugar ower it, then ye put it into a forty-gallon cask and fill it up wi' whisky."*

"He's all right." Roger patted her arm. "Is that Germain over there?"

"It is." She leaned over to check, but Germain was peacefully asleep, also smiling. "That Cherry Bounce must be good stuff."

Roger laughed.

"It's terrible. Like industrial-strength cough syrup. I will say it makes ye very cheerful, though."

"Have you been drinking it?" She eyed him narrowly, but his lips appeared to be their usual color.

"Of course not." He leaned over and kissed her, to prove it. "Surely ye dinna think a Scotsman like Ronnie would deal wi' disappointment by drinking Cherry Bounce? When there's decent whisky to hand?"

"True," she said. She glanced at the cooperage. The faint glow from the hearth fire had faded and the outline of the door had disappeared, leaving the building no more than a faint rectangle of black against the darker mass of the forest beyond. "How *is* Ronnie dealing with it?" She glanced round, but Inga and Hilda had taken themselves off to help *Frau* Ute; all of them were clustered round the food table, clearing things away.

"Oh, he's all right, Ronnie." Roger moved Jemmy off his lap, placing him gently on his side in the straw near Germain. "He wasna in love with Senga, after all. He's suffering from sexual frustration, not a broken heart."

"Oh, well, if that's all," she said dryly. "He won't have to suffer much longer; I'm informed that *Frau* Ute has the matter well in hand."

"Aye, she's told him she'll find him a wife. He's what ye might call philosophical about the matter. Though still reeking wi' lust," he added, wrinkling his nose.

"Ew. Do you want anything to eat?" She glanced at the little boys, getting her feet under her. "I'd better get you something before Ute and the girls clear it all away."

Roger yawned, suddenly and immensely.

"No, I'm all right." He blinked, smiling sleepily at her. "I'll go tell Fergus where Germain is, maybe snatch a bite on the way." He patted her shoulder, then stood up, swaying only a little, and moved off toward the fire.

She checked the boys again; both were breathing deeply and regularly, dead to the world. With a sigh, she bundled them close together, piling up the straw around them, and covered them with her cloak. It was growing colder, but winter had gone; there was no feel of frost in the air.

The party was still going on, but it had shifted to a lower gear. The dancing had stopped and the crowd broken up into smaller groups, men gathered in a circle near the fire, lighting their pipes, the younger men disappeared somewhere. All around her, families were settling in for the night, making nests for themselves in the hay. Some were in the house, more in the barn; she could hear the sound of a guitar from somewhere behind the house, and a single voice, singing something slow and wistful. It made her yearn suddenly for the sound of Roger's voice as it had been, rich and tender.

Thinking of that, though, she realized something; his voice had been much better when he came back from consoling Ronnie. Still husky and with only a shadow of its former resonance—but it had come easily, without that choked note in it. Perhaps alcohol relaxed the vocal cords?

More likely, she thought, it simply relaxed Roger; removed some of his inhibitions about the way he sounded. That was worth knowing. Her mother had opined that his voice would improve, if he would stretch it, work with it, but he was shy of using it, wary of pain—whether from the actual sensation of speaking, or from the contrast with the way he had sounded before.

"So maybe I'll make a little Cherry Bounce," she said aloud. Then she looked at the two small forms slumbering in the hay, and contemplated the prospect of waking up alongside three hangovers, come morning. "Well, maybe not."

She bunched up enough hay for a pillow, spread her folded kerchief over it—they'd be picking hay out of their clothes most of tomorrow—and lay down, curling her body round Jem's. If either boy stirred or vomited in his sleep, she'd feel it and rouse.

The bonfire had burned down; only a ragged fringe of flames now flickered over the bed of glowing embers, and the lanterns set around the yard had all gone out or been thriftily extinguished. Guitar and singer had ceased. Without light and noise to keep it at bay, the night came in, spreading wings of cold silence over the mountain. The stars burned bright above, but they were pinpricks, millennia away. She closed her eyes against the immensity of the night, bowing to put her lips against Jem's head, cradling his warmth.

She tried to compose her mind for sleep, but without the distractions of company, and with the scent of burning timber strong in the air, memory stole back, and her normal prayers of blessing became pleas for mercy and protection.

"He hath put my brethren far from me, and mine acquaintance are verily estranged from me. My kinsfolk have failed, and my familiar friends have forgotten me."

I won't forget you, she said silently to the dead. It seemed so pitiful a thing to say—so small and futile. And yet the only thing in her power.

She shivered briefly, tightening her grip on Jemmy.

A sudden rustle of the hay, and Roger slid in behind her. He fumbled a bit, spreading his own cloak over her, then sighed with relief, his body relaxing heavily against hers as his arm came round her waist.

"Been a bloody long day, hasn't it?"

She groaned faintly in agreement. Now that everything was quiet, with no more need to talk, watch, pay attention, every fiber of her muscles seemed about to dissolve with fatigue. There was no more than a thin layer of hay between her and cold, hard ground, but she felt sleep lapping at her like the waves of the tide creeping up a sandy shore, soothing and inexorable.

"'Did you get something to eat?" She put a hand on his leg, and his arm tightened in reflex, holding her close.

"Aye, if ye think beer's food. Many folk do." He laughed, a warm fog of hops on his breath. "I'm fine." The warmth of his body was beginning to seep through the layers of cloth between them, dispelling the night's chill.

Jem always gave off heat when he slept; it was like holding a clay firepot, with him curled against her. Roger was putting out even more heat, though. Well, her mother did say that an alcohol lamp burned hotter than oil.

She sighed and snuggled back against him, feeling warm, protected. The cold immensity of the night had lifted, now that she had her family close, together again, and safe.

Roger was humming. She realized it quite suddenly. There

was no tune to it, but she felt the vibration of his chest against her back. She didn't want to chance stopping him; surely that was good for his vocal cords. He stopped on his own, though, after a moment. Hoping to start him again, she reached back to stroke his leg, essaying a small questioning hum of her own.

"Hmmm-mmmm?"

His hands cupped her buttocks and fastened tight.

"Mmm-hmmm," he said, in what sounded like a combination of invitation and satisfaction.

She didn't reply, but made a slight dissentient motion of the behind. Under normal conditions, this would have caused him to let go. He *did* let go, but only with one hand, and this in order to slide it down her leg, evidently meaning to get hold of her skirt and ruckle it up.

She reached back hastily and grabbed the roving hand, bringing it round and placing it on her breast, as an indication that while she appreciated the notion and under other circumstances would be thrilled to oblige, just this moment she thought—

Roger was usually very good at reading her body language, but evidently this skill had dissolved in whisky. That, or—the thought came suddenly to her—he simply didn't *care* whether she wanted—

"Roger!" she hissed.

He *had* started humming again, the sound now interspersed with the low, bumping noises a teakettle makes, just before the boil. He'd got his hand down her leg and up her skirt, hot on the flesh of her thigh, groping swiftly upward—and inward. Jemmy coughed, jerking in her arms, and she made an attempt to kick Roger in the shin, as a signal of discouragement.

"God, you're beautiful," he murmured into the curve of her neck. "Oh, God, so beautiful. So beautiful . . . so . . . hmmm . . ." The next words were a mumble against her skin, but she *thought* he'd said "slippery." His fingers had reached their goal, and she arched her back, trying to squirm away.

"Roger," she said, keeping her voice low. "Roger, there are *people* around!" And a snoring toddler wedged like a doorstop in front of her.

He mumbled something in which the words "dark" and "nobody'll see" were distinguishable, and then the groping hand retreated—only to grab a handful of her skirts and start shoving them out of the way.

He had resumed the humming, pausing momentarily to murmur, "Love you, love you so much. . . ."

"I love you, too," she said, reaching back and trying to catch his hand. "Roger, *stop that*!"

He did, but immediately reached around her, and grasped her by the shoulder. A quick heave, and she was lying on her back staring up at the distant stars, which were at once blotted out by Roger's head and shoulders as he rolled on top of her in a tremendous rustling of hay and loosened clothing.

"Jem—" She flung out a hand toward Jemmy, who appeared not to have been disturbed by the sudden disappearance of his backstop, but was still curled up in the hay like a hibernating hedgehog.

Roger was, of all things, *singing* now, if one could call it that. Or chanting, at least, the words to a very bawdy Scottish song, about a miller who is pestered by a young woman wanting him to grind her corn. Whereupon he does.

"He flung her down upon the sacks, and there she got her corn ground, her corn ground. . . ." Roger was chanting hotly in her ear, his full weight pinning her to the ground and the stars spinning madly far above.

She'd thought his description of Ronnie as "reeking wi' lust" merely a figure of speech, but evidently not. Bare flesh met bare flesh, and then some. She gasped. So did Roger.

"Oh, God," he said. He paused, frozen for an instant against the sky above her, then sighed in an ecstasy of whisky fumes and began to move with her, humming. It *was* dark, thank God, though not nearly dark enough. The remnants of the fire cast an eerie glow over his face, and he looked for an instant the bonny big, black devil Inga had called him.

Lie back and enjoy it, she thought. The hay made a tremendous rustling—but there were other rustlings nearby, and the sound of the wind soughing through the trees in the cove was nearly enough to drown them all in sibilance.

She had managed to suppress her embarrassment and was indeed beginning to enjoy it, when Roger got his hands under her, lifting.

"Wrap your legs round me," he whispered, and nipped her

earlobe with his teeth. "Wrap them round my back and hammer my arse wi' your heels."

Moved partly by an answering wantonness, and partly by a desire to squeeze the breath out of him like an accordion, she flung her legs apart and swung them high, scissoring them tight across his heaving back. He gave an ecstatic groan and redoubled his efforts. Wantonness was winning; she had nearly forgotten where they were.

Hanging on for dear life and thrilled by the ride, she arched her back and jerked, shuddering against the heat of him, the night wind's touch cool and electric on thighs and buttocks, bared to the dark. Trembling and moaning, she melted back against the hay, her legs still locked around his hips. Boneless and nerveless, she let her head roll to the side, and slowly, languidly, opened her eyes.

Someone was there; she saw movement in the dark, and froze. It was Fergus, come to fetch his son. She heard the murmur of his voice, speaking French to Germain, and the quiet rustle of his footsteps in the hay, moving off.

She lay still, heart pounding, legs still locked in place. Roger, meanwhile, had reached his own quietus. Head hanging so that his long hair brushed her face like cobwebs in the dark, he murmured, "Love you . . . God, I love you," and lowered himself, slowly and gently. Whereupon he breathed, "Thank you," in her ear and lapsed into warm half-consciousness on top of her, breathing heavily.

"Oh," she said, looking up to the peaceful stars. "Don't mention it." She unlocked her stiff legs, and with some difficulty, got herself and Roger disentangled, more or less covered, and restored to blessed anonymity in their hay-lined nest, Jemmy safely stowed between them.

"Hey," she said suddenly, and Roger stirred.

"Mm?"

"What sort of monster was Eigger?"

He laughed, and the sound was low and clear.

"Oh, Eigger was a giant sponge cake. With chocolate icing. He'd fall on the other monsters, and smother them wi' sweetness." He laughed again, hiccuped, and subsided in the hay.

"Roger?" she said softly, a moment later. There was no answer, and she stretched a hand across the slumbering body of her son, to rest light on Roger's arm.

"Sing to me," she whispered, though she knew that he already was asleep.

7

JAMES FRASER, INDIAN AGENT

JAMES FRASER, Indian Agent," I said, closing one eye as though reading it off a screen. "It sounds like a Wild West television show."

Jamie paused in the act of pulling off his stockings, and eyed me warily.

"It does? Is that good?"

"Insofar as the hero of a television show never dies, yes."

"In that case, I'm in favor of it," he said, examining the stocking he'd just pulled off. He sniffed it suspiciously, rubbed a thumb over a thin patch on the heel, shook his head, and tossed it into the laundry basket. "Must I sing?"

"Si—oh," I said, recollecting that the last time I had tried to explain television to him, my descriptions had focused largely on *The Ed Sullivan Show.* "No, I don't think so. Nor yet swing from a trapeze."

"Well, that's a comfort. I'm none sae young as I was, ken." He stood up and stretched himself, groaning. The house had been built with eight-foot ceilings, to accommodate him, but his fists brushed the pine beams, even so. "Christ, but it's been a long day!"

"Well, it's nearly over," I said, sniffing in turn at the bodice of the gown I'd just shed. It smelled strongly, though not disagreeably, of horse and woodsmoke. Air it a bit, I decided, and see whether it could go another little while without washing. "I couldn't have swung on a trapeze even when I *was* young."

"I'd pay money to see ye try," he said, grinning.

"What *is* an Indian agent?" I inquired. "MacDonald seemed to think he was doing you a signal favor by suggesting you for the job."

He shrugged, unbuckling his kilt.

"Nay doubt he thinks he is." He shook the garment experimentally, and a fine sifting of dust and horsehair bloomed on the floor beneath it. He went to the window, opened the shutters, and, thrusting the kilt outside, shook it harder.

"He would be"—his voice came faintly from the night outside, then more strongly, as he turned round again—"were it not for this war of yours."

"Of *mine*?" I said, indignant. "You sound as though you think I'm proposing to start it, single-handed."

He made a small gesture of dismissal.

"Ye ken what I mean. An Indian agent, Sassenach, is what it sounds like—a fellow who goes out and parleys wi' the local Indians, giving them gifts and talking them round, in hopes that they'll be inclined to ally themselves with the Crown's interests, whatever those might happen to be."

"Oh? And what's this Southern Department that MacDonald mentioned?" I glanced involuntarily toward the closed door of our room, but muffled snoring from across the hall indicated that our guest had already collapsed into the arms of Morpheus.

"Mmphm. There's a Southern Department and a Northern Department that deal wi' Indian affairs in the Colonies. The Southern Department is under John Stuart, who's an Inverness man. Turn round, I'll do it."

I turned my back gratefully to him. With expertise born of long experience, he had the lacing of my stays undone in seconds. I sighed deeply as they loosened and fell. He plucked the shift away from my body, massaging my ribs where the boning had pressed the damp fabric into my skin.

"Thank you." I sighed in bliss and leaned back against him. "And being an Inverness man, MacDonald thinks this Stuart will have a natural predisposition to employ other Highlanders?"

"That might depend upon whether Stuart's ever met any of

my kin," Jamie said dryly. "But MacDonald thinks so, aye." He kissed the top of my head in absent affection, then withdrew his hands and began untying the lace that bound his hair.

"Sit," I said, stepping out of my fallen stays. "I'll do it."

He sat on the stool in his shirt, closing his eyes in momentary relaxation as I unbraided his hair. He'd worn it clubbed in a tight queue for riding, bound up for the last three days; I ran my hands up into the warm fiery mass as it unraveled from its plait, and the loosened waves of it spilled cinnamon and gold and silver in the firelight as I rubbed the pads of my fingers gently into his scalp.

"Gifts, you said. Does the Crown supply these gifts?" The Crown, I had noticed, had a bad habit of "honoring" men of substance with offices that required them to come up with large amounts of their own money.

"Theoretically." He yawned hugely, broad shoulders slumping comfortably as I took up my hair brush and set about tidying him. "Oh, that's nice. That's why MacDonald thinks it a favor; there's the possibility of doing well in trade."

"Besides generally excellent opportunities for corruption. Yes, I see." I worked for a few minutes before asking, "Will you do it?"

"I dinna ken. I must think a bit. Ye were mentioning Wild West—Brianna's said such a thing, telling me about cowherds—"

"Cowboys."

He waved off the correction. "And the Indians. That's true, is it—what she says about the Indians?"

"If what she says is that they'll be largely exterminated over the next century or so—yes, she's right." I smoothed his hair, then sat down on the bed facing him and set about brushing my own. "Does that trouble you?"

His brows drew together a little as he considered it, and he scratched absently at his chest, where the curly red-gold hairs showed at the open neck of his shirt.

"No," he said slowly. "Not precisely. It's not as though I should be doing them to death wi' my own hands. But . . . we're coming to it, are we not? The time when I must tread wi' some care, if I'm to walk betwixt the fires."

"I'm afraid we are," I said, an uneasy tightness hovering

between my shoulder blades. I saw what he meant, all too clearly. The battle lines were not clear yet—but they were being drawn. To become an Indian agent for the Crown was to appear to be a Loyalist—all very well for the moment, when the Rebel movement was no more than a radical fringe, with pockets of disaffection. But very, very dangerous, as we grew closer to the point where the disaffected seized power, and independence was declared.

Knowing the eventual outcome, Jamie dare not wait too long to ally himself to the Rebel side—but to do so too early was to risk arrest for treason. Not a good prospect for a man who was already a pardoned traitor.

"Of course," I said diffidently, "if you *were* to be an Indian agent I suppose you might actually persuade some of the Indian tribes into supporting the American side—or staying neutral, at least."

"I might," he agreed, with a certain note of bleakness in his voice. "But putting aside any question as to the honor of such a course—that would help condemn them, no? Would the same thing happen to them in the end, d'ye think, if the English were to win?"

"They won't," I said, with a slight edge.

He glanced sharply at me.

"I do believe ye," he said, with a similar edge. "I've reason to, aye?"

I nodded, my lips pressed together. I didn't want to talk about the earlier Rising. I didn't want to talk about the oncoming Revolution, either, but there was little choice about that.

"I don't know," I said, and took a deep breath. "No one can say—since it didn't happen—but if I were to *guess* . . . then I think the Indians might quite possibly do better under British rule." I smiled at him, a little ruefully.

"Believe it or not, the British Empire did—or will, I should say—generally manage to run its colonies without *entirely* exterminating the native people in them."

"Bar the Hieland folk," he said, very dryly. "Aye, I'll take your word for it, Sassenach."

He stood up, running a hand back through his hair, and I caught a glimpse of the tiny streak of white that ran through it, legacy of a bullet wound.

"You should talk to Roger about it," I said. "He knows a great deal more than I do."

He nodded, but didn't reply, beyond a faint grimace.

"Where do you suppose Roger and Bree went, speaking of Roger?"

"To the MacGillivrays', I suppose," he replied, surprised. "To fetch wee Jem."

"How do you know that?" I asked, equally surprised.

"When there's mischief abroad, a man wants his family safe under his eye, ken?" He raised one brow at me, and reaching to the top of the wardrobe, took down his sword. He drew it halfway from its scabbard, then put it back and set the scabbard gently back in place, the sword loosened, hilt ready to hand.

He'd brought a loaded pistol upstairs with him; that was placed on the washstand by the window. The rifle and fowling piece too had been left loaded and primed, hanging from their hooks above the hearth downstairs. And, with a small ironic flourish, he drew the dirk from its belt sheath and slid it neatly under our pillow.

"Sometimes I forget," I said a little wistfully, watching this. There had been a dirk under the pillow of our wedding couch—and under many a one since then.

"Do ye?" He smiled at that; a little lopsidedly, but he smiled.

"Don't you? Ever?"

He shook his head, still smiling, though it had a rueful tinge. "Sometimes I wish I did."

This colloquy was interrupted by a spluttering snort across the hall, followed at once by a thrashing of bedclothes, violent oaths, and a sharp *thump!* as something—likely a shoe—struck the wall.

"Fucking cat!" bellowed Major MacDonald. I sat, hand pressed across my mouth, as the stomp of bare feet vibrated through the floorboards, succeeded briefly by the crash of the Major's door, which flung open, then shut with a bang.

Jamie too had stood frozen for an instant. Now he moved, very delicately, and soundlessly eased our own door open. Adso, tail arrogantly S-shaped, strolled in. Magnificently ignoring us, he crossed the room, leapt lightly onto the washstand,

and sat in the basin, where he stuck a back leg into the air and began calmly licking his testicles.

"I saw a man once in Paris who could do that," Jamie remarked, observing this performance with interest.

"Are there people willing to pay to watch such things?" I assumed that no one was likely to engage in a public exhibition of that sort merely for the fun of it. Not in Paris, anyway.

"Well, it wasna the man, so much. More his female companion, who was likewise flexible." He grinned at me, his eyes glinting blue in the candlelight. "Like watching worms mate, aye?"

"How fascinating," I murmured. I glanced at the washstand, where Adso was now doing something even more indelicate. "You're lucky the Major doesn't sleep armed, cat. He might have potted you like a jugged hare."

"Oh, I doubt that. Our Donald likely sleeps with a blade—but he kens well enough which side of his bread's buttered. Ye wouldna be likely to give him breakfast, and he'd skewered your cat."

I glanced toward the door. The mattress-heaving and muttered curses across the hall had died down; the Major, with the practiced ease of a professional soldier, was already well on his way back to dreamland.

"I suppose not. You were right about his worming his way into a position with the new governor. Which is the real reason for his desire for your political advancement, I imagine?"

Jamie nodded, but had plainly lost interest in discussing MacDonald's machinations.

"I *was* right, no? That means ye owe me a forfeit, Sassenach."

He eyed me with an air of dawning speculation, which I hoped had not been too much inspired by his memories of the wormlike Parisians.

"Oh?" I regarded him warily. "And, um, *what* precisely . . . ?"

"Well, I havena quite worked out all the details as yet, but I think ye should maybe lie on the bed, to begin with."

That sounded like a reasonable start to the matter. I piled up the pillows at the head of the bed—pausing to remove the dirk—then began to climb onto it. I paused again, though, and instead bent to wind the bedkey, tightening the ropes that supported the mattress until the bedstead groaned and the ropes gave a creaking twang.

"Verra canny, Sassenach," Jamie said behind me, sounding amused.

"Experience," I informed him, clambering over the newly tautened bed on hands and knees. "I've waked up often enough after a night with you, with the mattress folded up round my ears and my arse no more than an inch off the ground."

"Oh, I expect your arse will end up somewhat higher than that," he assured me.

"Oh, you're going to let me be on top?" I had mixed feelings about that. I was desperately tired, and while I enjoyed riding Jamie, all right, I'd been riding a beastly horse for more than ten hours, and the thigh muscles required for both activities were trembling spasmodically.

"Perhaps later," he said, eyes narrowed in thought. "Lie back, Sassenach, and ruckle up your shift. Then open your legs for me, there's a good lass no, a bit wider, aye?" He began—with deliberate slowness—to remove his shirt.

I sighed and shifted my buttocks a little, looking for a position that wouldn't give me cramp if I had to hold it for long.

"If you have in mind what I think you have in mind, you'll regret it. I haven't even bathed properly," I said reproachfully. "I'm desperately filthy and I smell like a horse."

Naked, he raised one arm and sniffed appraisingly.

"Oh? Well, so do I. That's no matter; I'm fond of horses." He'd abandoned any pretense of delay, but paused to survey his arrangements, looking me over with approval.

"Aye, verra good. Now then, if ye'll just put your hands above your head and seize the bedstead—"

"You wouldn't!" I said, and then lowered my voice, with an involuntary glance toward the door. "Not with MacDonald just across the hall!"

"Oh, I would," he assured me, "and the devil wi' MacDonald and a dozen more like him." He paused, though, studying me thoughtfully, and after a moment, sighed and shook his head.

"No," he said quietly. "Not tonight. Ye're still thinking of that poor Dutch bastard and his family, no?"

"Yes. Aren't you?"

He sat down beside me on the bed with a sigh.

"I've been trying verra hard not to," he said frankly. "But the new dead dinna lie easy in their graves, do they?"

I laid a hand on his arm, relieved that he felt the same. The night air seemed restless with the passage of spirits, and I had felt the dragging melancholy of that desolate garden, that row of graves, all through the events and alarums of the evening.

It *was* a night to be securely locked inside, with a good fire on the hearth, and people nearby. The house stirred, shutters creaking in the wind.

"I do want ye, Claire," Jamie said softly. "I need . . . if ye will?"

And had they spent the night before their deaths like this, I wondered? Peaceful and snug betwixt their walls, husband and wife whispering together, lying close in their bed, having no notion what the future held. I saw in memory her long white thighs as the wind blew over her, and the glimpse I'd had of the small curly mat between them, the pudenda beneath its nimbus of brown hair pale as carved marble, the seam of it sealed like a virgin's statue.

"I need, too," I said, just as softly. "Come here."

He leaned close, and pulled the drawstring neatly from the neck of my shift, so the worn linen wilted off my shoulders. I made a grab for the fabric, but he caught my hand, and held it down by my side. One-fingered, he brushed the shift lower, then put out the candle, and in a dark that smelled of wax and honey and the sweat of horses, kissed my forehead, eyes, the corners of my cheeks, my lips and chin, and so continued, slow and soft-lipped, to the arches of my feet.

He raised himself then, and suckled my breasts for a long time, and I ran my hand up his back and cupped his buttocks, naked and vulnerable in the dark.

Afterward, we lay in a pleasantly vermiform tangle, the only light in the room a faint glow from the banked hearth. I was so tired that I could feel my body sinking into the mattress, and desired nothing more than to keep going down, down, into the welcoming dark of oblivion.

"Sassenach?"

"Um?"

A moment's hesitation, then his hand found mine, curling round it.

"Ye wouldna do what she did, would ye?"

"Who?"

"Her. The Dutchwoman."

Snatched back from the edge of sleep, I was muzzy and confused, sufficiently so that even the image of the dead woman, shrouded in her apron, seemed unreal, no more disturbing than the random fragments of reality my brain tossed overboard in a vain effort to keep afloat as I sank down into the depths of sleep.

"What? Fall into the fire? I'll try not," I assured him, yawning. "Good night."

"No. Wake up." He shook my arm gently. "Talk to me, Sassenach."

"Ng." It was a considerable effort, but I pushed away the enticing arms of Morpheus, and flounced over onto my side, facing him. "Mm. Talk to you. About . . . ?"

"The Dutchwoman," he repeated patiently. "If I were to be killed, ye wouldna go and kill your whole family, would ye?"

"What?" I rubbed my free hand over my face, trying to make some sense of this, amid the drifting shreds of sleep. "Whose whole—oh. You think she did it on purpose? Poisoned them?"

"I think maybe so."

His words were no more than a whisper, but they brought me back to full consciousness. I lay silent for a moment, then reached out, wanting to be sure he was really there.

He was; a large, solid object, the smooth bone of his hip warm and live under my hand.

"It might as well have been an accident," I said, voice pitched low. "You can't know for sure."

"No," he admitted. "But I canna keep from seeing it." He turned restlessly onto his back.

"The men came," he said softly, to the beams overhead. "He fought them, and they killed him there, on his own threshold. And when she saw her man was gone I think she told the men she must feed the weans first, before . . . and then she put toadstools into the stew, and fed it to the bairns and her mother. She took the two men with them, but I think it was *that* that was the accident. She only meant to follow him. She wouldna leave him there, alone."

I wanted to tell him that this was a rather dramatic interpretation of what we had seen. But I couldn't very well tell him he was wrong. Hearing him describe what he saw in thought, I saw it, too, all too clearly.

"You don't know," I said at last, softly. "You can't know." *Unless you find the other men,* I thought suddenly, *and ask them.* I didn't say that, though.

Neither of us spoke for a bit. I could tell that he was still thinking, but the quicksand of sleep was once more pulling me down, clinging and seductive.

"What if I canna keep ye safe?" he whispered at last. His head moved suddenly on the pillow, turning toward me. "You and the rest of them? I shall try wi' all my strength, Sassenach, and I dinna mind if I die doing it, but what if I should die too soon—and fail?"

And what answer was there to that?

"You won't," I whispered back. He sighed, and bent his head, so his forehead rested against mine. I could smell eggs and whisky, warm on his breath.

"I'll try not," he said, and I put my mouth on his, soft against mine, acknowledgment and comfort in the dark.

I laid my head against the curve of his shoulder, wrapped a hand round his arm, and breathed in the smell of his skin, smoke and salt, as though he had been cured in the fire.

"You smell like a smoked ham," I murmured, and he made a low sound of amusement and wedged his hand into its accustomed spot, clasped between my thighs.

I let go then, at last, and let the heavy sands of sleep engulf me. Perhaps he said it, as I fell into darkness, or perhaps I only dreamed it.

"If I die," he whispered in the dark, "dinna follow me. The bairns will need ye. Stay for them. I can wait."

Part Two

A Gathering of Shadows

8

VICTIM OF A MASSACRE

From Lord John Grey
To Mr. James Fraser, Esq.

April 14, 1773

My dear friend—

I write you in good Health, and trust that I find you and yours in similar condition.

My Son has returned to England, there to complete his Education. He writes with Delight of his Experiences (I inclose a Copy of his most recent Letter), and assures me of his Well-being. More importantly, my Mother also writes to assure me that he flourishes, though I believe—more from what she does not say than from what she does—that he introduces an unaccustomed Element of Confusion and Upheaval in her Household.

I confess to feeling the Lack of this Element in my own Household. So orderly and well-regulated a Life as mine is these Days, you would be astonished. Still, the Quiet seems oppressive to me, and while I am in Health in terms of Body, I find my Spirit somewhat flagging. I miss William sadly, I fear.

For Distraction from my solitary State, I have of late undertaken a new Employment, that of making Wine. While I admit the Product lacks the Power of your own Distillations, I flatter myself that it is not undrinkable, and if allowed to stand for a Year or two, might eventually be palatable. I shall send you a dozen Bottles later in the Month, by the Hand of my new Servant, Mr. Higgins, whose History you may find interesting.

You will perhaps have heard something of a disreputable Brawl occurring in Boston in March of three Years past, which I have often seen in Newspaper and Broadside called a "Massacre," most irresponsibly—and most inaccurately, to one who has been privy to the actual Occurrence.

I was not present myself, but have spoken to numerous of the Officers and Soldiers who were. If they speak truly, and I believe they do, such a View as is given by the Boston Press of the Matter has been monstrous.

Boston is by all Accounts a perfect Hellhole of republican Sentiment, with so-called "Marching Societies" at large in the Streets in every Weather, these being no more than an Excuse for the Assembly of Mobs, whose chief Sport is the tormenting of the Troops quartered there.

Higgins tells me that no Man would dare go out alone in Uniform, for fear of these Mobs, and that even when in greater Numbers, harassment from the public soon drove them back to their Quarters, save when compelled by Duty to persist.

A Patrol of five Soldiers was so beset one Evening, pursued not only by insults of the grossest Nature, but by hurled Stones, Clods of Earth and Dung, and other such Rubbish. Such was the Press of the Mob around them that the Men feared for their Safety, and thus presented their Weapons, in hopes of discouraging the raucous Attentions rained upon them. So far from accomplishing this Aim, the Action provoked still greater Outrages from the Crowd, and at some Point, a Gun was fired. No one can say for sure whether the Shot was discharged from the Crowd, or from one of the Soldier's Weapons, let alone whether it were by Accident or in Deliberation, but the Effect of it . . .

well, you will have sufficient Knowledge of such Matters to imagine the Confusion of subsequent Events.

In the End, five of the Mob were killed, and while the Soldiers were buffeted and badly handled, they escaped alive, only to be made Scapegoats by the malicious Rantings of the mob's Leaders in the Press, these so styled as to make it seem a wanton and unprovoked Slaughter of Innocents, rather than a Matter of Self-defense against a Mob inflamed by Drink and Sloganeering.

I confess that my Sympathies must lie altogether with the Soldiers; I am sure so much is obvious to you. They were brought to Trial, where the Judge discovered Three to be Innocent, but no Doubt felt it would be Dangerous to his own Situation to free them all.

Higgins, with one other, was convicted of Manslaughter, but pled Clergy and was released after his Branding. The Army of course discharged him, and without means of making a Living and subject to the Opprobrium of the Populace, he found himself in sad Case. He tells me that he was beaten in a Tavern soon after his Release, injuries inflicted therein depriving him of the Sight in one Eye, and in fact, his very Life was threatened on more than one Occasion. So seeking Safety, he took Passage on a Sloop captained by my Friend, Captain Gill, working as a Sailor, though I have seen him sail and I assure you he is not one.

This state of Affairs became soon evident to Captain Gill, who terminated his Employment upon arrival at their first Port. I was in the Town on Business, and encountered Captain Gill, who told me of Higgins's desperate Situation.

I contrived to find the Man, feeling some Pity for a Soldier who appeared to me to have performed his Duty honorably, and thinking it hard that he should suffer by it. Discovering him to be intelligent and of a generally agreeable Character, I engaged him in Service, wherein he has proved most faithful.

I send him with the Wine, in Hopes that your Wife might be so kind as to examine him. The local Physician, one Dr. Potts, has seen him, and declares the Injury to his Eye irretrievable, as indeed it may be. Having some personal Experience of your Wife's skill, however, I wonder whether she might suggest Treatment for his other Ills; Dr. Potts was unable to be of much Help. Tell her, please, that I am her humble Servant, and remain in perpetual Gratitude for her Kindness and Ability.

My warmest Regards to your Daughter, for whom I have sent a small Present, to arrive with the Wine. I trust her Husband will not take Offense at my Familiarity, by Consideration of my long Acquaintance with your Family, and will allow her to accept it.

As always, I remain your Ob't. Servant,
John Grey

9

THE THRESHOLD OF WAR

April 1773

ROBERT HIGGINS WAS a slight young man, so thin as to seem that his bones were barely held together by his clothes, and so pale that it was easy to imagine you could in fact see through him. He was, however, graced with large, candid blue eyes, a mass of wavy, light-brown hair, and a shy manner that caused Mrs. Bug to take him at once under her wing and declare a firm intent to "feed him up," before he should depart back to Virginia.

I quite liked Mr. Higgins myself; he was a sweet-natured boy, with the soft accent of his native Dorset. I did rather wonder, though, whether Lord John Grey's generosity toward him was as unselfish as it seemed.

I had come reluctantly to like John Grey, too, after our shared experience of the measles a few years earlier, and his friendship to Brianna while Roger was held captive by the Iroquois. Still, I remained acutely aware of the fact that Lord John did like men—specifically, Jamie, but certainly other men, as well.

"Beauchamp," I said to myself, laying out trillium roots to dry, "you have a very suspicious mind."

"Aye, ye have," said a voice behind me, sounding amused. "Whom do ye suspect of doing what?"

I jerked in startlement and sent trilliums flying in all directions.

"Oh, it's you," I said crossly. "Why must you sneak up on me like that?"

"Practice," Jamie said, kissing me on the forehead. "I shouldna like to lose my touch at stalking game. Why d'ye talk to yourself?"

"It assures me of a good listener," I said tartly, and he laughed, bending to help me pick up the roots from the floor.

"Who are ye suspecting, Sassenach?"

I hesitated, but was unable to come up with anything but the truth.

"I was wondering whether John Grey's buggering our Mr. Higgins," I said baldly. "Or intends to."

He blinked slightly, but didn't look shocked—which in itself suggested to me that he'd considered the same possibility.

"What makes ye think so?"

"He's a very pretty young man, for the one thing," I said, taking a handful of the roots from him and beginning to spread them out on a sheet of gauze. "And he's got the worst case of piles I've ever seen in a man of his age, for another."

"He let ye *look* at them?" Jamie had flushed up himself at

the mention of buggery; he disliked me being indelicate, but he'd asked, after all.

"Well, it took no little persuasion," I said. "He told me about them readily enough, but he wasn't keen to have me examine them."

"I wouldna care for that prospect, either," Jamie assured me, "and I'm wed to ye. Why on earth would ye want to look at such a thing, beyond morbid curiosity?" He cast a wary glance at my big black casebook, open on the table. "Ye're no drawing pictures of poor Bobby Higgins's backside in there, are ye?"

"No need. I can't imagine a physician in any time who doesn't know what piles look like. The ancient Israelites and Egyptians had them, after all."

"They did?"

"It's in the Bible. Ask Mr. Christie," I advised.

He gave me a sidelong look.

"Ye've been discussing the Bible wi' Tom Christie? Ye're a braver man than I am, Sassenach." Christie was a most devout Presbyterian, and never happier than when hitting someone over the head with a fistful of Sacred Scripture.

"Not me. Germain asked me last week what 'emerods' are."

"What are they?"

"Piles. *Then said they, What shall be the trespass offering which we shall return to him? They answered, Five golden emerods, and five golden mice, according to the number of the lords of the Philistines,*" I quoted, "or something of the sort. That's as close as I can come from memory. Mr. Christie made Germain write out a verse from the Bible as punishment, and having an inquiring sort of mind, Germain wondered what it was he was writing."

"And he wouldna ask Mr. Christie, of course." Jamie frowned, rubbing a finger down the bridge of his nose. "Do I want to know what it was Germain did?"

"Almost certainly not." Tom Christie earned the quitrent on his land by serving as the local schoolmaster, and seemed capable of keeping discipline on his own terms. My opinion was that having Germain Fraser as a pupil was probably worth the entire amount, in terms of labor.

"Gold emerods," Jamie murmured. "Well, there's a

thought." He had assumed the faintly dreamy air he often had just before coming up with some hair-raising notion involving the possibility of maiming, death, or life imprisonment. I found this expression mildly alarming, but whatever the train of thought triggered by golden hemorrhoids, he abandoned it for the moment, shaking his head.

"Well, so. We were speaking of Bobby's backside?"

"Oh, yes. As for why I wanted to look at Mr. Higgins's emerods," I said, returning to the previous point of conversation, "I wanted to see whether the best treatment was amelioration, or removal."

Jamie's eyebrows went up at that.

"Remove them? How? Wi' your wee knife?" He glanced at the case where I kept my surgical tools, and hunched his shoulders in aversion.

"I could, yes, though I imagine it would be rather painful without anesthesia. There was a much simpler method just coming into widespread use, though, when I . . . left." Just for a moment, I felt a deep twinge of longing for my hospital. I could all but smell the disinfectant, hear the murmur and bustle of nurses and orderlies, touch the glossy covers of the research journals bulging with ideas and information.

Then it was gone, and I was estimating the desirability of leeches versus string, with reference to Mr. Higgins's achieving ideal anal health.

"Dr. Rawlings advises the use of leeches," I explained. "Twenty or thirty, he says, for a serious case."

Jamie nodded, showing no particular revulsion at the idea. Of course, he'd been leeched a few times himself, and assured me that it didn't hurt.

"Aye. Ye havena got that many on hand, do ye? Shall I collect the wee lads and set them to gathering?"

Jemmy and Germain would like nothing better than an excuse to go bogging through the creeks with their grandfather, coming back festooned with leeches and mud to the eyebrows, but I shook my head.

"No. Or I mean, yes," I corrected. "At your convenience—but I don't need them immediately. Using leeches would relieve the situation temporarily, but Bobby's hemorrhoids are badly thrombosed—have clots of dried blood in them—" I emended, "and I think he really would be better off if I remove them entirely. I believe I can ligate them—tie a thread very tightly round the base of each hemorrhoid, I mean. That starves them of blood, and eventually, they just dry up and fall off. Very neat."

"Verra neat," Jamie murmured, in echo. He looked mildly apprehensive. "Have ye done it before?"

"Yes, once or twice."

"Ah." He pursed his lips, apparently envisioning the process. "How . . . er, I mean . . . can he shit, d'ye think, while this is going on? It must take a bit of time, surely."

I frowned, tapping a finger on the countertop.

"His chief difficulty is that he *doesn't* shit," I said. "Not often enough, I mean, and not with the proper consistency. Horrible diet," I said, pointing an accusatory finger at him. "He told me. Bread, meat, and ale. No vegetables, no fruit. Constipation is absolutely *rife* in the British army, I don't doubt. I shouldn't be surprised if every man jack of them has piles hanging out of his arse like grape clusters!"

Jamie nodded, one eyebrow raised.

"There are a great many things I admire about ye, Sassenach—especially the delicate manner of your conversation." He coughed, glancing downward. "But if ye say it's costiveness that causes piles—"

"It is."

"Aye, well. It's only—what ye were saying about John Grey. I mean, ye don't think the state of Bobby's arse is to do with . . . mmphm."

"Oh. Well, no, not directly." I paused. "It was more that Lord John said in his letter that he wanted me to—how did he put it?—*I might suggest treatment for his other ills.* I mean, he might possibly know about Bobby's difficulty, without . . . er . . . personal inspection, shall we say? But as *I* say, piles are so commonplace an affliction, why ought he be concerned to the point of asking me to do something about them—unless he thought that they might hamper his own eventual . . . er . . . progress?"

Jamie's face had resumed its normal hue during the discussion of leeches and constipation, but at this point, went red again.

"His—"

"I mean," I said, folding my arms beneath my bosom, "I'm just a trifle put off . . . by the notion that he's sent Mr. Higgins down for repair, you might say." I had been suffering from a niggling feeling of unease regarding the matter of Bobby Higgins's backside, but hadn't put this notion into words before. Now that I had, I realized precisely what was bothering me.

"The thought that I'm meant to be fixing up poor little Bobby, and then sending him home to be—" I pressed my lips tight together, and turned abruptly back to my roots, needlessly turning them.

"I don't like the thought," I said, to the cupboard door. "I'll do what I can for Mr. Higgins, mind. Bobby Higgins hasn't many prospects; no doubt he'd do . . . whatever his Lordship required. But perhaps I'm wronging him. Lord John, I mean."

"Perhaps ye are."

I turned round, to find Jamie sitting on my stool, fiddling with a jar of goose grease that seemed to have his full attention.

"Well," I said uncertainly. "You know him better than I do. If you think he isn't . . ." My words trailed off. Outside, there was a sudden soft thump as a falling spruce cone struck the wooden stoop.

"I ken more about John Grey than I wish I did," Jamie said finally, and glanced at me, a rueful smile in the corner of his mouth. "And he kens a great deal more about me than I like to think on. But"—he leaned forward, setting down the jar, then put his hands on his knees and looked at me—"I ken the one thing beyond doubt. He's an honorable man. He wouldna take advantage of Higgins, nor any other man under his protection."

He sounded very definite about it, and I felt reassured. I did like John Grey. And still . . . the appearance of his letters, regular as clockwork, always gave me a faint sense of unease, like the hearing of distant thunder. There was nothing about the letters themselves to evoke such a response; they were like the man himself—erudite, humorous, and sincere. And he had reason to write, of course. More than one.

"He does still love you, you know," I said quietly.

He nodded, but didn't look at me, his gaze still fixed somewhere beyond the trees that edged the dooryard.

"Would you rather he didn't?"

He paused, then nodded again. This time, though, he did turn to look at me.

"I would, aye. For myself. For him, certainly. But for William?" He shook his head, uncertain.

"Oh, he may have taken William on for your sake," I said, leaning back against the counter. "But I've seen the two of them, remember. I've no doubt he loves Willie for his own sake now."

"No, I dinna doubt that, either." He got up, restless, and beat imaginary dust from the pleats of his kilt. His face was closed, looking inward at something he didn't wish to share with me.

"Do you—" I began, but stopped when he glanced up at me. "No. It doesn't matter."

"What?" He tilted his head to one side, eyes narrowing.

"Nothing."

He didn't move, merely intensified the stare.

"I can see from your face that it's not, Sassenach. What?"

I breathed deeply through my nose, fists wrapped in my apron.

"It's only—and I'm sure it isn't true, it's only a passing thought—"

He made a low Scottish noise, indicating that I had better stop blethering and cough it up. Having enough experience to realize that he wouldn't leave the matter 'til I did, I coughed.

"Did you ever wonder whether Lord John might have taken him because . . . well, William does look terribly like you, and evidently did from an early age. Since Lord John finds you physically . . . attractive . . ." The words died, and I could have cut my throat for speaking them, seeing the look on his face.

He closed his eyes for a moment, to stop me looking in. His fists were curled up so tightly that the veins stood out from knuckle to forearm. Very slowly, he relaxed his hands. He opened his eyes.

"No," he said, complete conviction in his voice. He gave

me a straight, hard look. "And it's no that I canna bear the thought of it, either. I know."

"Of course," I said hastily, eager to leave the subject.

"I know," he repeated more sharply. His two stiff fingers tapped, once, against his leg, and then stilled. "I thought of it, too. When he first told me he meant to wed Isobel Dunsany."

He turned away, staring out through the window. Adso was in the dooryard, stalking something in the grass.

"I offered him my body," Jamie said abruptly, not looking round. The words were steady enough, but I could see from the knotted shoulders how much it cost him to speak them. "In thanks, I said. But it was—" He made an odd convulsive movement, as though trying to free himself from some constraint. "I meant to see, ken, what sort of man he might be, for sure. This man who would take my son for his own."

His voice shook, very slightly, when he said, "take my son," and I moved to him by instinct, wanting somehow to patch the open wound beneath those words.

He was stiff when I touched him, not wanting to be embraced—but he took my hand and squeezed it.

"Could you . . . really tell, do you think?" I was not shocked; John Grey had told me of that offer, years before, in Jamaica. I didn't think he had realized the true nature of it, though.

Jamie's hand tightened on mine, and his thumb traced the outline of mine, rubbing lightly over the nail. He looked down at me, and I felt his eyes search my face—not in question, but in the way one does when seeing anew some object grown familiar—seeing with the eyes what has been seen for a long time only with the heart.

His free hand rose and traced the line of my brows, two fingers resting for an instant on the bone of my cheek, then moved up, back, cool in the warmth of my hair.

"Ye canna be so close to another," he said finally. "To be within each other, to smell their sweat, and rub the hairs of your body with theirs and see nothing of their soul. Or if ye *can* do that . . ." He hesitated, and I wondered whether he thought of Black Jack Randall, or of Laoghaire, the woman he had married, thinking me dead. "Well . . . that is a dreadful thing in itself," he finished softly, and his hand dropped away.

There was silence between us. A sudden rustle came from the grass outside as Adso lunged and disappeared, and a mockingbird began to shriek alarm from the big red spruce. In the kitchen, something was dropped with a clang, and then the rhythmic *shoosh* of sweeping began. All the homely sounds of this life we had made.

Had I ever done that? Lain with a man, and seen nothing of his soul? Indeed I had, and he was right. A breath of coldness touched me, and the hairs rose, silent on my skin.

He heaved a sigh that seemed to come from his feet, and rubbed a hand over his bound hair.

"But he wouldna do it. John." He looked up then, and gave me a crooked smile. "He loved me, he said. And if I couldna give him that in return—and he kent I couldn't—then he'd not take counterfeit for true coin."

He shook himself, hard, like a dog coming out of the water.

"No. A man who would say such a thing is not one who'd bugger a child for the sake of his father's bonny blue eyes, I'll tell ye that for certain, Sassenach."

"No," I said. "Tell me . . ." I hesitated, and he looked at me, one eyebrow up. "If—if he *had* . . . er . . . taken you up on that offer—and you'd found him . . ." I fumbled for some reasonable wording. "Less, um, decent than you might hope—"

"I should have broken his neck there by the lake," he said. "It wouldna have mattered if they'd hanged me; I'd not have let him have the boy.

"But he didn't, and I did," he added with a half-shrug. "And if wee Bobby goes to his Lordship's bed, I think it will be of his own free will."

NO MAN IS really at his best with someone else's hand up his arse. I had noticed this before, and Robert Higgins was no exception to the general rule.

"Now, this won't hurt much at all," I said as soothingly as possible. "All you need to do is to keep quite still."

"Oh, I s'all do that, mum, indeed I will," he assured me fervently.

I had him on the surgery table, wearing only his shirt, and situated foursquare on hands and knees, which brought the area of operation conveniently to eye level. The forceps and ligatures I should need were placed on the small table to my right, with a bowl of fresh leeches alongside, in case of need.

He emitted a small shriek when I applied a wet cloth soaked in turpentine to the area, in order to cleanse it thoroughly, but was as good as his word and didn't move.

"Now, we are going to obtain a very good effect here," I assured him, taking up a pair of long-nosed forceps. "But if the relief is to be permanent, there will have to be a drastic change in your diet. Do you understand me?"

He gasped deeply, as I grasped one of the hemorrhoids and pulled it toward me. There were three, a classic presentation, at nine, two, and five o'clock. Bulbous as raspberries, and quite the same color.

"Oh! Y-yes, mum."

"Oatmeal," I said firmly, transferring the forceps to my other hand without lessening the grip, and taking up a needle threaded with silk thread in my right. "Porridge every morning, without fail. Have you noticed a change for the better in your bowel habits, since Mrs. Bug has been feeding you parritch for breakfast?"

I passed the thread loosely round the base of the hemorrhoid, then delicately pushed the needle up beneath the loop, making a small noose of it, and pulled tight.

"Ahhh . . . oh! Erm . . . tell 'ee truth, mum, it's like shitting house bricks covered with hedgehog skin, makes no matter what I eat."

"Well, it will," I assured him, securing the ligature with a knot. I released the hemorrhoid, and he breathed deeply. "Now, grapes. You like grapes, don't you?"

"No'm. Sets me teeth on edge to bite 'em."

"Really?" His teeth didn't look badly decayed; I should have a closer look at his mouth; he might be suffering from marginal scurvy. "Well, we'll have Mrs. Bug make a nice raisin pie for you; you can eat that with no difficulty. Does

Lord John have a capable cook?" I took aim with my forceps and got hold of the next one. Now accustomed to the sensation, he only grunted a bit.

"Yessum. Be an Indian, he is, named Manoke."

"Hmm." Round, up, tighten, tie off. "I'll write out a receipt for the raisin pie, for you to carry back to him. Does he cook yams, or beans? Beans are quite good for the purpose."

"I b'lieve he does, mum, but his Lordship—"

I had the windows open for ventilation—Bobby was no filthier than the average, but he was certainly no cleaner—and at this point, I heard sounds from the trailhead; voices, and the jingle of harness.

Bobby heard them, too, and glanced wildly at the window, hindquarters tensing as though to spring off the table like a grasshopper. I grasped him by one leg, but then thought better of it. There was no way of covering the window, bar closing the shutters, and I needed the light.

"Go ahead and stand up," I told him, letting go and reaching for a towel. "I'll go and see who it is." He followed this direction with alacrity, scrambling down and reaching hastily for his breeches.

I stepped out onto the porch, in time to greet the two men who led their mules up over the last arduous slope and into the yard. Richard Brown, and his brother Lionel, from the eponymously named Brownsville.

I was surprised to see them; it was a good three-day ride to Brownsville from the Ridge, and there was little commerce between the two settlements. It was at least that far to Salem, in the opposite direction, but the inhabitants of the Ridge went there much more frequently; the Moravians were both industrious and great traders, taking honey, oil, salt fish, and hides in trade for cheese, pottery, chickens, and other small livestock. So far as I knew, the denizens of Brownsville dealt only in cheap trade goods for the Cherokee, and in the production of a very inferior type of beer, not worth the ride.

"Good day, mistress." Richard, the smaller and elder of the brothers, touched the brim of his hat, but didn't take it off. "Is your husband to home?"

"He's out by the hay barn, scraping hides." I wiped my

hands carefully on the towel I was carrying. "Do come round to the kitchen; I'll bring up some cider."

"Don't trouble." Without further ado, he turned and set off purposefully round the house. Lionel Brown, a bit taller than his brother, though with the same spare, almost gangly build and the same tobacco-colored hair, nodded briefly to me as he followed.

They had left their mules, reins hanging, evidently for me to tend. The animals were beginning to amble slowly across the yard, pausing to crop the long grass that edged the path.

"Hmpf!" I said, glaring after the brothers Brown.

"Who are they?" said a low voice behind me. Bobby Higgins had come out and was peering off the corner of the porch with his good eye. Bobby tended to be wary of strangers—and no wonder, given his experiences in Boston.

"Neighbors, such as they are." I lunged off the porch and caught one of the mules by the bridle as he reached for the peach sapling I had planted near the porch. Disliking this interference in his affairs, he brayed ear-splittingly in my face, and attempted to bite me.

"Here, mum, let me." Bobby, already holding the other mule's reins, leaned past to take the halter from me. "Hark at 'ee!" he said to the obstreperous mule. "Hush tha noise, else I take a stick to 'ee, then!"

Bobby had been a foot soldier rather than cavalry, it was clear to see. The words were bold enough, but ill-matched with his tentative manner. He gave a perfunctory yank on the mule's reins. The mule promptly laid back its ears and bit him in the arm.

He screamed and let go both sets of reins. Clarence, my own mule, hearing the racket, set up a loud bray of greeting from his pen, and the two strange mules promptly trotted off in that direction, stirrup leathers bouncing.

Bobby wasn't badly hurt, though the mule's teeth had broken the skin; spots of blood seeped through the sleeve of his shirt. As I was turning back the cloth to have a look at it, I heard footsteps on the porch, and looked up to see Lizzie, a large wooden spoon in hand, looking alarmed.

"Bobby! What's happened?"

He straightened at once, seeing her, assuming nonchalance, and brushed a lock of curly brown hair off his brow.

"Ah, oh! Naught, miss. Bit o' trouble with tha sons o' Belial, like. No fear, it's fine."

Whereupon his eyes rolled up in his head and he fell over in a dead faint.

"Oh!" Lizzie flew down the steps and knelt beside him, urgently patting his cheek. "Is he all right, Mrs. Fraser?"

"God knows," I said frankly. "I think so, though." Bobby appeared to be breathing normally, and I found a reasonable pulse in his wrist.

"Shall we carry him inside? Or should I fetch a burnt feather, do you think? Or the spirits of ammonia from the surgery? Or some brandy?" Lizzie hovered like an anxious bumblebee, ready to fly off in any of several different directions.

"No, I think he's coming round." Most faints last only a few seconds, and I could see his chest lift as his breathing deepened.

"Bit o' brandy wouldn't come amiss," he murmured, eyelids beginning to flutter.

I nodded to Lizzie, who vanished back into the house, leaving her spoon behind on the grass.

"Feeling a bit peaky, are you?" I inquired sympathetically. The injury to his arm was no more than a scratch, and I certainly hadn't done anything of a shocking nature to him—well, not physically shocking. What was the trouble here?

"I dunno, mum." He was trying to sit up, and while he was white as a sheet, seemed otherwise all right, so I let him. "It's only, every now and again, I gets these spots, like, whirring round me head like a swarm o' bees, and then it all goes black."

"Now and again? It's happened before?" I asked sharply.

"Yessum." His head wobbled like a sunflower in the breeze, and I put a hand under his armpit, lest he fall over again. "His Lordship was in hopes you might know summat would stop it."

"His Lord—oh, he knew about the fainting?" Well, of

course he would, if Bobby were in the habit of falling over in front of him.

He nodded, and took a deep, gasping breath.

"Doctor Potts bled me regular, twice a week, but it didn't seem to help."

"I daresay not. I hope he was of somewhat more help with your piles," I remarked dryly.

A faint tinge of pink—he had scarcely enough blood to provide a decent blush, poor boy—rose in his cheeks, and he glanced away, fixing his gaze on the spoon.

"Erm . . . I, um, didn't mention *that* to anybody."

"You didn't?" I was surprised at that. "But—"

"See, 'twas only the riding. From Virginia." The pink tinge grew. "I'd not have let on, save I was in such agony after a week on yon bloody horse—saving your presence, mum—I'd no chance of hiding it."

"So Lord John didn't know about that, either?"

He shook his head vigorously, making the disheveled brown curls flop back over his forehead. I felt rather annoyed—with myself for having evidently misjudged John Grey's motives, and with John Grey, for making me feel a fool.

"Well . . . are you feeling a bit better, now?" Lizzie was not appearing with the brandy, and I wondered momentarily where she was. Bobby was still very pale, but nodded gamely, and struggled to his feet, where he stood swaying and blinking, trying to keep his balance. The "M" branded on his cheek stood out, an angry red against the pallid skin.

Distracted by Bobby's faint, I had ignored the sounds coming from the other side of the house. Now, though, I became aware of voices, and approaching footsteps.

Jamie and the two Browns came into sight round the corner of the house, then stopped, seeing us. Jamie had been frowning slightly; the frown grew deeper. The Browns, by contrast, seemed oddly elated, though in a grim sort of way.

"So it's true, then." Richard Brown stared hard at Bobby Higgins, then turned to Jamie. "You've a murderer on your premises!"

"Have I?" Jamie was coldly polite. "I'd no idea." He bowed to Bobby Higgins with his best French-court manner, then straightened, gesturing to the Browns. "Mr. Higgins, may I present Mr. Richard Brown and Mr. Lionel Brown. Gentlemen, my guest, Mr. Higgins." The words "my guest" were spoken with a particular emphasis that made Richard Brown's thin mouth compress to near invisibility.

"Have a care, Fraser," he said, staring hard at Bobby, as though daring him to evaporate. "Keeping the wrong company can be dangerous, these days."

"I choose my company as I will, sir." Jamie spoke softly, biting off each word between his teeth. "And I do not choose yours. Joseph!"

Lizzie's father, Joseph Wemyss, appeared round the corner, leading the two renegade mules, who now seemed docile as kittens, though either of them dwarfed Mr. Wemyss.

Bobby Higgins, flabbergasted by the proceedings, looked wildly at me for explanation. I shrugged slightly, and kept silence as the two Browns mounted and rode out of the clearing, backs stiff with anger.

Jamie waited 'til they'd disappeared from view, then blew out his breath, rubbing a hand viciously through his hair and muttering something in Gaelic. I didn't follow the finer points, but I gathered that he was comparing the character of our recent visitors to that of Mr. Higgins's piles—to the detriment of the former.

"Beg pardon, sir?" Higgins looked bewildered, but anxious to please.

Jamie glanced at him.

"Let them awa' and bile their heids," he said, dismissing the Browns with a flip of the hand. He caught my eye and turned toward the house. "Come ben, Bobby; I've a thing or two to say to ye."

I FOLLOWED THEM IN, both from curiosity and in case Mr. Higgins should feel faint again; he seemed steady enough, but still very pale. By contrast with Bobby Higgins, Mr. Wemyss—fair-haired and slight as his daughter—looked the picture of ruddy health. Whatever was the matter with

Bobby? I wondered. I stole a discreet look at the seat of his breeches as I followed him, but that was all right; no bleeding.

Jamie led the way into his study, gesturing at the motley collection of stools and boxes he used for visitors, but both Bobby and Mr. Wemyss chose to stand—Bobby for obvious reasons, Mr. Wemyss from respect; he was never comfortable sitting in Jamie's presence, save at meals.

Unhampered by either bodily or social reservations, I settled myself on the best stool and raised one eyebrow at Jamie, who had sat down himself at the table he used as a desk.

"This is the way of it," he said without preamble. "Brown and his brother have declared themselves head of a Committee of Safety, and came to enlist me and my tenants as members of it." He glanced at me, the corner of his mouth curling a little. "I declined, as ye doubtless noticed."

My stomach contracted slightly, thinking of what Major MacDonald had said—and of what I knew. It was beginning, then.

"Committee of Safety?" Mr. Wemyss looked bewildered, and glanced at Bobby Higgins—who was beginning to look substantially less so.

"Have they, so?" Bobby said softly. Strands of curly brown hair had escaped from their binding; he fingered one back behind his ear.

"Ye've heard of such committees before, Mr. Higgins?" Jamie inquired, raising one brow.

"Met one, zur. Close-like." Bobby touched a finger briefly below his blind eye. He was still pale, but beginning to recover his self-possession. "Mobs they be, zur. Like they mules, but more of them—and more wicious." He gave a lopsided smile, smoothing the shirt-sleeve over the bite on his arm.

The mention of mules reminded me abruptly, and I stood up, putting a sudden stop to the conversation.

"Lizzie! Where's Lizzie?"

Not waiting for an answer to this rhetorical question, I went to the study door and shouted her name—only to be met by silence. She'd gone in for brandy; there was plenty, in a jug in the kitchen, and she knew that—I'd seen her reach it down for Mrs. Bug only the night before. She must be in the house. Surely she wouldn't have gone—

"Elizabeth? Elizabeth, where are you?" Mr. Wemyss was right behind me, calling, as I strode down the hall to the kitchen.

Lizzie was lying in a dead faint on the hearth, a limp bundle of clothes, one frail hand flung out as though she had tried to save herself as she fell.

"Miss Wemyss!" Bobby Higgins shouldered his way past me, looking frantic, and scooped her up into his arms.

"Elizabeth!" Mr. Wemyss elbowed his way past me as well, his face nearly as white as his daughter's.

"Do let me *look* at her, will you?" I said, elbowing firmly back. "Put her down on the settle, Bobby, do."

He rose carefully with her in his arms, then sat down on the settle, still holding her, wincing slightly as he did so. Well, if he wanted to be a hero, I hadn't time to argue with him. I knelt and seized her wrist in search of a pulse, smoothing the pale hair off her face with my other hand.

One look had been enough to tell me what was likely the matter. She was clammy to the touch, and the pallor of her face was tinged with gray. I could feel the tremor of oncoming chills that ran through her flesh, unconscious as she was.

"The ague's back, is it?" Jamie asked. He'd appeared by my side, and was gripping Mr. Wemyss by the shoulder, at once comforting and restraining.

"Yes," I said briefly. Lizzie had malaria, contracted on the coast a few years before, and was subject to occasional relapses—though she hadn't had one in more than a year.

Mr. Wemyss took a deep, audible breath, a little color coming back to his face. He was familiar with malaria, and had confidence that I could deal with it. I had, several times before.

I hoped that I could this time. Lizzie's pulse was fast and light under my fingers, but regular, and she was beginning to stir. Still, the speed and suddenness with which the attack had come on was frightening. Had she had any warning? I hoped the concern I felt didn't show on my face.

"Take her up to her bed, cover her, get a hot stone for her feet," I said, rising and addressing Bobby and Mr. Wemyss briskly in turn. "I'll start some medicine brewing."

Jamie followed me down to the surgery, glancing back

over his shoulder to be sure that the others were out of earshot before speaking.

"I thought ye were out of the Jesuit bark?" he asked, low-voiced.

"I am. Damn it." Malaria was a chronic disease, but for the most part, I had been able to keep it under control with small, regular doses of cinchona bark. But I had run out of cinchona during the winter, and no one had yet been able to travel down to the coast for more.

"So, then?"

"I'm thinking."

I pulled open the door of the cupboard, and gazed at the neat ranks of glass bottles therein—many of them empty, or with no more than a few scattered crumbs of leaf or root inside. Everything was depleted, after a cold, wet winter of grippe, influenza, chilblains, and hunting accidents.

Febrifuges. I had a number of things that would help a normal fever; malaria was something else. There was plenty of dogwood root and bark, at least; I had collected immense quantities during the fall, foreseeing the need. I took that down, and after a moment's thought, added the jar containing a sort of gentian known locally as "agueweed."

"Put on the kettle, will you?" I asked Jamie, frowning to myself as I crumbled roots, bark, and weed into my mortar. All I could do was to treat the superficial symptoms of fever and chill. And shock, I thought, better treat for that, too.

"And bring me a little honey, too, please!" I called after him, as he had already reached the door. He nodded and went hurriedly toward the kitchen, his footsteps quick and solid on the oak floorboards.

I began to pound the mixture, still turning over additional possibilities. Some small part of my mind was half-glad of the emergency; I could put off for a little while the necessity of hearing about the Browns and their beastly committee.

I had a most uneasy feeling. Whatever they wanted, it didn't portend anything good, I was sure; they certainly hadn't left on friendly terms. As for what Jamie might feel obliged to do in response to them—

Horse chestnut. That was sometimes used for the tertian ague, as Dr. Rawlings called it. Did I have any left? Glancing quickly over the jars and bottles in the medicine chest, I stopped, seeing one with an inch or so of dried black globules left at the bottom. *Gallberries,* the label read. Not mine; it was one of Rawlings's jars. I'd never used them for anything. But something niggled at my memory. I'd heard or read something about gallberries; what was it?

Half-unconsciously, I picked up the jar and opened it, sniffing. A sharp, astringent smell rose from the berries, slightly bitter. And slightly familiar.

Still holding the jar, I went to the table where my big black casebook lay, and flipped hastily to the early pages, those notes left by the man who had first owned both book and medicine chest, Daniel Rawlings. Where had it been?

I was still flipping pages, scanning for the shape of a half-remembered note, when Jamie came back, a jug of hot water and a dish of honey in hand—and the Beardsley twins dogging his steps.

I glanced at them, but said nothing; they tended to pop up unexpectedly, like a pair of jack-in-the boxes.

"Is Miss Lizzie fearfully sick?" Jo asked anxiously, peering around Jamie to see what I was doing.

"Yes," I said briefly, only half paying attention to him. "Don't worry, though; I'm fixing her some medicine."

There it was. A brief notation, added as an obvious afterthought to the account of treatment of a patient whose symptoms seemed clearly malarial—and who had, I noticed with an unpleasant twinge, died.

I am told by the Trader from whom I procured Jesuit Bark that the Indians use a Plant called Gallberry, which rivals the Bark of Cinchona for bitterness and is thought capital for Use in tertian and quartan Fevers. I have collected some for Experiment and propose to try an Infusion so soon as the Opportunity presents itself.

I picked out one of the dried berries and bit into it. The pungent taste of quinine at once flooded my mouth—accompanied by a copious flood of saliva, as my mouth puckered at the eye-watering bitterness. Gallberry, indeed!

I dived for the open window, spat into the herb bed beneath and went on spitting, to the accompaniment of giggles and snorts from the Beardsleys, who were most diverted at the unexpected entertainment.

"Are ye all right, Sassenach?" Amusement was fighting with worry for dominance of Jamie's face. He poured a bit of water from the jug into a clay beaker, added a dollop of honey as an afterthought, and handed it to me.

"Fine," I croaked. "Don't drop that!" Kezzie Beardsley had picked up the jar of gallberries and was sniffing cautiously at it. He nodded at my admonition, but didn't put the jar down, instead handing it off to his brother.

I took a good mouthful of hot, honeyed water, and swallowed. "Those—they have something like quinine in them."

Jamie's face changed at once, the worry lessening.

"So they'll help the lass?"

"I hope so. There aren't many, though."

"D'ye mean you need more o' these things for Miss Lizzie, Mrs. Fraser?" Jo glanced up at me, dark eyes sharp over the little jar.

"Yes," I said, surprised. "You don't mean you know where to get any, surely?"

"Aye, ma'am," Kezzie said, his voice a little loud, as usual. "Indians got 'em."

"Which Indians?" Jamie asked, his gaze sharpening.

"Them Cherokee," Jo said, waving vaguely over one shoulder. "By the mountain."

This description might have suited half a dozen villages, but evidently it was a specific village that they had in mind, for the two of them turned as one, obviously intending to go directly and fetch back gallberries.

"Wait a bit, lads," Jamie said, snagging Kezzie by the collar. "I'll go along with ye. Ye'll be needing something to trade, after all."

"Oh, we got hides a-plenty, sir," Jo assured him. "'Twas a good season."

Jo was an expert hunter, and while Kezzie still hadn't sufficiently keen hearing to hunt well, his brother had taught him to run traplines. Ian had told me that the Beardsleys' shack was stacked nearly to the rooftree with the hides of beaver, marten, deer, and ermine. The smell of it always clung to them, a faint miasma of dried blood, musk, and cold hair.

"Aye? Well, that's generous of ye, Jo, to be sure. But I'll come, nonetheless." Jamie glanced at me, acknowledging the fact that he had made his decision—but asking for my approval, nonetheless. I swallowed, tasting bitterness.

"Yes," I said, and cleared my throat. "If—if you're going, let me send some things, and tell you what to ask for in trade. You won't leave until morning, surely?"

The Beardsleys were vibrating with impatience to be gone, but Jamie stood still, looking at me, and I felt him touch me, without words or movement.

"No," he said softly, "we'll bide for the night." He turned then to the Beardsleys. "Go up, will ye, Jo, and ask Bobby Higgins to come down. I'll need to speak with him."

"He's up with Miss Lizzie?" Jo Beardsley looked displeased at this, and his brother's face echoed his expression of slit-eyed suspicion.

"What's he a-doin' in her room, then? Don't he know she's betrothed?" Kezzie asked, righteously.

"Her father's with her, too," Jamie assured them. "Her reputation's safe, aye?"

Jo snorted briefly, but the brothers exchanged glances, then left together, slender shoulders set in determination to oust this threat to Lizzie's virtue.

"So you'll do it?" I set down the pestle. "Be an Indian agent?"

"I think I must. If I do not—Richard Brown surely will. I think I canna risk that." He hesitated, then drew close and touched me lightly, fingers on my elbow. "I'll send the lads back at once with the berries ye need. I may need to stay for a day, maybe two. For the talking, aye?" To tell the Cherokee that he was now an agent for the British Crown, he meant—and to make arrangements for word to be spread that the headmen of the mountain villages should come down later to a council for parley and gifts.

I nodded, feeling a small bubble of fear swell under my breastbone. It was starting. No matter how much one knows that something dreadful is going to happen in the future, one somehow never thinks it will be *today*.

"Not—don't stay away too long, will you?" I blurted, not wanting to burden him with my fears, but unable to keep quiet.

"No," he said softly, and his hand rested for an instant in the small of my back. "Dinna fash yourself; I'll not tarry."

The sound of feet descending the stairs echoed in the hall. I supposed Mr. Wemyss had shooed the Beardsleys out, along with Bobby. They didn't stop, but went off without speaking, casting looks of veiled dislike at Bobby, who seemed quite oblivious to them.

"Yon lad said you wanted to speak to me, zur?" He'd regained some color, I was glad to see, and seemed steady enough on his feet. He glanced uneasily at the table, still spread with the sheet I'd put him on, and then at me, but I merely shook my head. I'd finish dealing with his piles later.

"Aye, Bobby." Jamie made a brief gesture toward a stool, as though to invite Bobby to sit, but I cleared my throat in a meaningful manner, and he stopped, then leaned against the table, rather than sitting down himself.

"Those two who came—Brown, they're called. They've a settlement some way away. Ye said ye've heard of the Committees of Safety, aye? So ye'll have some notion what they're about."

"Aye, zur. Tha Browns, zur—did they want me?" He spoke calmly enough, but I saw him swallow briefly, Adam's apple bobbing in his slender throat.

Jamie sighed, and ran a hand through his hair. The sun was slanting through the window now, and struck him directly, making his red hair glow with flame—and picking out here and there a flicker of the silver that was beginning to show among the ruddy strands.

"They did. They kent ye were here; heard of ye, doubtless from someone ye met along the way. Ye'll have told folk where ye were headed, I suppose?"

Bobby nodded, wordless.

"What did they want with him?" I asked, tipping the ground root bark and berries into a bowl and pouring hot water over them to steep.

"They didna make that quite clear," Jamie said dryly. "But

then, I didna give them the chance. I only told them they'd take a guest from my hearth over my dead body—and theirs."

"I thanks 'ee for that, zur." Bobby took a deep breath. "They—knew, I reckon? About Boston? I'd not told anyone *that,* surely."

Jamie's frown deepened slightly.

"Aye, they did. They pretended to think I didna ken; told me I was harboring a murderer unbeknownst, and a threat to the public welfare."

"Well, the first is true enough," Bobby said, touching his brand gingerly, as though it still burned him. He offered a wan smile. "But I dunno as I s'ould be a threat to anyone, these days."

Jamie dismissed that.

"The point is, Bobby, that they do ken ye're here. They'll not come and drag ye away, I think. But I'd ask ye to go canny about the place. I'll make provision to see ye safely back to Lord John, when the time comes, with an escort. I gather ye're no quite finished with him?" he asked, turning to me.

"Not quite," I replied equably. Bobby looked apprehensive.

"Well, then." Jamie reached into the waist of his breeches, and drew out a pistol, which had been hidden by the folds of his shirt. It was, I saw, the fancy gilt-edged one.

"Keep it by ye," Jamie said, handing it to Bobby. "There's powder and shot in the sideboard. Will ye look out for my wife and family, then, whilst I'm gone?"

"Oh!" Bobby looked startled, but then nodded, tucking the pistol away in his own breeches. "I will so, zur. Depend upon it!"

Jamie smiled at him, his eyes warming.

"That's a comfort to me, Bobby. Will ye maybe go and find my son-in-law? I'll need a word with him before I go."

"Aye, zur. Right away!" He squared his shoulders and set off, an expression of determination on his poet's face.

"What do you think they would have done with him?" I asked softly, as the outer door closed behind him. "The Browns."

Jamie shook his head.

"God knows. Hanged him at a crossroad, maybe—or

maybe only beaten him and driven him out of the mountains. They want to make a show of being able to protect the folk, aye? From dangerous criminals and the like," he added, with a twist of the mouth.

"A government derives its powers from the just consent of the governed," I quoted, nodding. "For a Committee of Safety to have any legitimacy, there needs to be an obvious threat *to* the public safety. Clever of the Browns to have reasoned that out."

He gave me a look, one auburn brow raised.

"Who said that? *The consent of the governed.*"

"Thomas Jefferson," I replied, feeling smug. "Or rather, he will say it in another two years."

"He'll steal it from a gentleman named Locke in another two years," he corrected. "I suppose Richard Brown must ha' been decently educated."

"Unlike me, you mean?" I said, unruffled. "If you expect trouble from the Browns, though, should you have given Bobby *that* particular pistol?"

He shrugged.

"I'll need the good ones. And I doubt verra much that he'll fire that one."

"Counting on its deterrent effect?" I was skeptical, but he was likely right.

"Aye, that. But more on Bobby."

"How so?"

"I doubt he'd fire a gun again to save his own life—but he would, maybe, to save yours. And should it come to such a pass, they'll be too close to miss." He spoke with dispassion, but I felt the hairs prickle down my nape.

"Well, that's a comfort," I said. "And just how do you know what he'd do?"

"Talked to him," he said briefly. "The man he shot in Boston was the first he'd ever killed. He doesna want to do it again." He straightened, and moved restlessly toward the counter, where he busied himself in straightening a scatter of small instruments I had laid out for cleaning.

I moved to stand beside him, watching. There was a handful of small cautery irons and scalpels, soaking in a beaker of turpentine. He took them out, one by one, wiped them dry and laid them back in their box, neatly, side by side. The spade-shaped metal ends of the irons were blackened by use; the scalpel blades were weathered to a soft glow, but the sharp edges gleamed, a hairbreadth of bright silver.

"We'll be all right," I said quietly. I meant it to be a reassuring statement, but it came out with a tinge of question.

"Aye, I know," he said. He put the last iron in its box, but didn't replace the lid. Instead, he stood, hands spread flat on the counter, looking straight ahead.

"I dinna want to go," he said softly. "I dinna want to do this."

I wasn't sure whether he was speaking to me, or to himself—but I thought he wasn't referring only to his journey to the Cherokee village.

"Neither do I," I whispered, and moved a little closer, so I felt his breathing. He lifted his hands then and turned toward me, taking me into his arms, and we stood wrapped close, listening to each other's breathing, the bitter smell of the brewing tea seeping through the homely scents of linen, dust, and sun-warmed flesh.

There were still choices to be made, decisions to reach, actions to take. Many of them. But in one day, one hour, one single declaration of intent, we had stepped across the threshold of war.

10

DUTY CALLS

JAMIE HAD SENT BOBBY after Roger Mac, but found himself too restless to wait, and set off himself, leaving Claire to her brewing.

Everything seemed peaceful and beautiful outside. A brown sheep with a pair of lambs stood indolently in her pen, jaws moving in a slow stupor of satisfaction, the lambs hopping awkwardly to and fro like fuzzy grasshoppers behind her. Claire's herb bed was full of leafing greens and sprouting flowers.

The well lid was ajar; he bent to draw it into place and found the boards had warped. He added fixing that to the constant list of chores and repairs that he carried in his head, wishing fervently that he could devote the next few days to digging, hauling manure, shingling, and the like, instead of what he was about to do.

He'd rather bury the old privy pit or castrate pigs than go and ask Roger Mac what he kent about Indians and revolutions. He found it mildly gruesome to discuss the future with his son-in-law, and tried never to do it.

The things Claire told him of her own time seemed often fantastic, with the enjoyable half-real sense of faery tales, and sometimes macabre, but always interesting, for what he learned of his wife from the telling. Brianna tended to share with him small, homely details of machinery, which were interesting, or wild stories of men walking on the moon, which were immensely entertaining, but no threat to his peace of mind.

Roger Mac, though, had a cold-blooded way of talking that reminded him to an uncomfortable degree of the works of the historians he'd read, and had therefore a sense of concrete doom about it. Talking to Roger Mac made it seem all too likely that this, that, or the other frightful happenstance was not only indeed *going* to happen—but would most likely have direct and personal consequences.

It was like talking to a particularly evil-minded fortuneteller, he thought, one you hadn't paid enough to hear something pleasant. The thought made a sudden memory pop up on the surface of his mind, bobbing like a fishing cork.

In Paris. He'd been with friends, other students, drinking in the piss-smelling taverns near the *université.* He'd been fairly drunk himself when someone took a fancy to have his palms read, and he had pushed with the others into the corner where the old woman who did it always sat, scarcely visible amid the gloom and clouds of pipe smoke.

He hadn't intended to do it himself; he had only a few

pennies in his pocket, and didn't mean to waste them on unholy nonsense. He'd said so, loudly.

Whereupon a scraggy claw had shot out of the darkness and seized his hand, sinking long, filthy nails into his flesh. He'd yelped in surprise, and his friends all laughed. They laughed harder when she spat in his palm.

She rubbed the spittle into his skin in a businesslike way, bent close enough that he could smell the ancient sweat of her and see the lice crawling in the grizzled hair that keeked from the edge of her rusty-black shawl. She peered into his hand and a dirty nail traced the lines of it, tickling. He tried to pull his hand away, but she tightened her grip on his wrist, and he found to his surprise that he could not break it.

"T'es un chat, toi," the old woman had remarked, in tones of malicious interest. "You're a cat, you. A little red cat."

Dubois—that was his name, Dubois—had at once begun to miaou and yowl, to the amusement of the others. He himself refused to rise to the bait, and saying only, *"Merci, madame,"* tried again to pull away.

"Neuf," she said, tapping rapid random places on his palm, then seizing a finger and wiggling it by way of emphasis. "You have a nine in your hand. And death," she'd added offhandedly. "You'll die nine times before you rest in your grave."

She'd let go then, amidst a chorus of sarcastic *"aou-la-las!"* from the French students, and laughter from the rest.

He snorted, sending the memory back where it came from, and good riddance to it. The old woman refused to go so easily, though, and called to him through the years, as she'd called through the raucous, beer-filled air of the tavern.

"Sometimes dying doesn't hurt, *mon p'tit chat,*" she'd called after him, mocking. "But more often it does."

"No it doesn't," he muttered, and stopped, appalled, hearing himself. Christ. It wasn't himself he was hearing, but his godfather.

"Don't be afraid, laddie. It doesna hurt a bit, to die." He missed his footing and staggered, caught himself and stood still, a taste of metal on the back of his tongue.

His heart was thumping, suddenly, for no reason, as though he had run miles. He saw the cabin, certainly, and heard the calling of jays in the half-leafed chestnut trees. But he saw even more clearly Murtagh's face, the grim lines of it relaxing into peace and the deep-set black eyes fixed on his, shifting in and out of focus, as though his godfather looked at once at him and at something far beyond him. He felt the weight of Murtagh's body in his arms, growing suddenly heavy as he died.

The vision vanished, as abruptly as it had come, and he found himself standing next to a rain puddle, staring at a wooden duck half-mired in the mud.

He crossed himself, with a quick word for the repose of Murtagh's soul, then bent and retrieved the duck, washing the mud away in the puddle. His hands were trembling, and little wonder. His memories of Culloden were few and fragmentary—but they were beginning to come back.

So far, such things had come to him only in glimpses at the edge of sleep. He'd seen Murtagh there before, and in the dreams that followed.

He hadn't told Claire about them. Not yet.

He pushed open the door of the cabin, but it was empty, the hearth smoored, spinning wheel and loom standing idle. Brianna was likely at Fergus's place, visiting Marsali. Where would Roger Mac be now? He stepped back outside and stood listening.

The thump of an ax came faintly from somewhere in the forest beyond the cabin. It stopped, then, and he heard men's voices, raised in greeting. He turned and headed for the trail that led upslope, half grown over with spring grass, but showing the black smudges of fresh footmarks.

What might the old woman have told him if he'd paid her? he wondered. Had she lied to spite him for his miserliness—or told him the truth, for the same reason?

One of the more disagreeable things about talking to Roger Mac was that Jamie was sure he always told the truth.

He'd forgotten to leave the duck at the cabin. Wiping it on his breeches, he pushed grimly through the sprouting weeds, to hear what fate awaited him.

11

BLOODWORK

I PUSHED THE MICROSCOPE toward Bobby Higgins, who had returned from his errand, his own discomforts forgotten in worry for Lizzie. "See the round pinkish things?" I said. "Those are Lizzie's blood cells. Everyone has blood cells," I added. "They're what make your blood red."

"'Strewth," he muttered, amazed. "I never knew!"

"Well, now you do," I said. "Do you see that some of the blood cells are broken? And that some have little spots in them?"

"I do, mum," he said, screwing up his face and peering intently. "What are 'ey, then?"

"Parasites. Little beasts that get into your blood if a certain kind of mosquito bites you," I explained. "They're called *Plasmodium*. Once you've got them, they go on living in your blood—but every so often, they begin to . . . er . . . breed. When there are too many of them, they burst out of the blood cells, and that's what causes a malarial attack—the ague. The sludge of the broken blood cells sort of silts up, you see, in the organs, and makes you feel terribly sick."

"Oh." He straightened up, making a face of deep aversion at the microscope. "That's . . . that's pure gashly, that is!"

"Yes, it is," I said, succeeding in keeping a straight face. "But quinine—Jesuit bark, you know?—will help stop it."

"Oh, that's good, mum, very good," he said, his face lightening. "However you do come to know such things," he said, shaking his head. "'Tis a wonder!"

"Oh, I know quite a lot of things about parasites," I said casually, taking the saucer off the bowl in which I had been brewing the mix of dogwood bark and gallberries. The liquid was a rich purplish black, and looked slightly viscous, now that it had cooled. It also smelled lethal, from which I deduced that it was about ready.

"Tell me, Bobby—have you ever heard of hookworms?"

He looked at me blankly.

"No, mum."

"Mm. Would you hold this for me, please?" I put a folded square of gauze over the neck of a flask and handed him the bottle to hold while I poured the purple mixture into it.

"These fainting fits of yours," I said, eyes on the stream. "How long have you had them?"

"Oh . . . six months, mebbe."

"I see. Did you by chance notice any sort of irritation—itching, say? Or a rash? Happening maybe seven months ago? Most likely on your feet."

He stared at me, soft blue eyes thunderstruck as though I had performed some feat of mind reading.

"Why, so I did have, mum. Last autumn, 'twas."

"Ah," I said. "Well, then. I think, Bobby, that you may just possibly have a case of hookworms."

He looked down at himself in horror.

"Where?"

"Inside." I took the bottle from him and corked it. "Hookworms are parasites that burrow through the skin—most often through the soles of the feet—and then migrate through the body until they reach your intestines—your, um, innards," I amended, seeing incomprehension cross his face. "The adult worms have nasty little hooked bills, like this"—I crooked my index finger in illustration—"and they pierce the intestinal lining and proceed to suck your blood. That's why, if you have them, you feel very weak, and faint frequently."

From the suddenly clammy look of him, I rather thought he was about to faint *now,* and guided him hastily to a stool, pushing his head down between his knees.

"I don't know for sure that that's the problem," I told him, bending down to address him. "I was just looking at the slides of Lizzie's blood, though, and thinking of parasites, and—well, it came to me suddenly that a diagnosis of hookworms would fit your symptoms rather well."

"Oh?" he said faintly. The thick tail of wavy hair had fallen forward, leaving the back of his neck exposed, fair-skinned and childlike.

"How old are you, Bobby?" I asked, suddenly realizing that I had no idea.

"Twenty-three, mum," he said. "Mum? I think I s'all have to puke."

I snatched a bucket from the corner and got it to him just in time.

"Have I got rid of them?" he asked weakly, sitting up and wiping his mouth on his sleeve as he peered into the bucket. "I could do it more."

"I'm afraid not," I said sympathetically. "Assuming that you have got hookworms, they're attached very firmly, and too far down for vomiting to dislodge them. The only way to be sure about it, though, is to look for the eggs they shed."

Bobby eyed me apprehensively.

"It's not exactly as I'm horrible shy, mum," he said, shifting gingerly. "You know that. But Dr. Potts did give me great huge clysters of mustard water. Surely that would ha' burnt they worms right out? If I was a worm, I s'ould let go and give up the ghost at once, did anyone souse me with mustard water."

"Well, you would think so, wouldn't you?" I said. "Unfortunately not. But I won't give you an enema," I assured him. "We need to see whether you truly do have the worms, to begin with, and if so, there's a medicine I can mix up for you that will poison them directly."

"Oh." He looked a little happier at that. "How d'ye mean to see, then, mum?" He glanced narrowly at the counter, where the assortment of clamps and suture jars were still laid out.

"Couldn't be simpler," I assured him. "I do a process called fecal sedimentation to concentrate the stool, then look for the eggs under the microscope."

He nodded, plainly not following. I smiled kindly at him.

"All you have to do, Bobby, is shit."

His face was a study in doubt and apprehension.

"If it's all the same to you, mum," he said, "I think I'll keep the worms."

12

FURTHER MYSTERIES OF SCIENCE

LATE IN THE AFTERNOON, Roger MacKenzie came back from the cooper's shop to discover his wife deep in contemplation of an object sitting on his dinner table.

"What *is* that? Some type of prehistoric Christmas tinned goods?" Roger extended a ginger forefinger toward a squat jar made of greenish glass and sealed with a cork, the latter covered with a stout layer of red wax. An amorphous chunk of something was visible inside, evidently submerged in liquid.

"Ho ho," said his wife tolerantly, moving the jar out of his reach. "You *think* you're being funny. It's white phosphorus—a present from Lord John."

He glanced at her; she was excited, the tip of her nose gone pink and bits of red hair pulled loose and waving in the breeze; like her father, she was inclined to run her hands through her hair when thinking.

"And you intend to do . . . *what* with it?" he asked, trying to keep any note of foreboding from his voice. He had the vaguest memories of hearing about the properties of phosphorus in his distant school days; he thought either it made you glow in the dark or it blew up. Neither prospect was reassuring.

"Wellll . . . make matches. Maybe." Her upper teeth fastened momentarily in the flesh of her lower lip as she considered the jar. "I know how—in theory. But it might be a little tricky in practice."

"Why is that?" he asked warily.

"Well, it bursts into flame if you expose it to air," she

explained. "That's why it's packed in water. Don't touch, Jem! It's poisonous." Grabbing Jemmy round the middle, she pulled him down from the table, where he had been eyeing the jar with greedy curiosity.

"Oh, well, why worry about that? It will explode in his face before he has a chance to get it in his mouth." Roger picked up the jar for safekeeping, holding it as though it might go off in his hands. He wanted to ask whether she were insane, but had been married long enough to know the price of injudicious rhetorical questions.

"Where d'ye mean to keep it?" He cast an eloquent glance round the confines of the cabin, which in terms of storage boasted a blanket chest, a small shelf for books and papers, another for comb, toothbrushes, and Brianna's small cache of personal belongings, and a pie hutch. Jemmy had been able to open the pie hutch since the age of seven months or so.

"I'm thinking I'd better put it in Mama's surgery," she replied, keeping an absentminded grip on Jem, who was struggling with single-minded energy to get at the pretty thing. "Nobody touches anything in there."

That was true enough; the people who were not afraid of Claire Fraser personally were generally terrified of the contents of her surgery, these featuring fearsomely painful-looking implements, mysterious murky brews, and vile-smelling medicines. In addition, the surgery had cupboards too high for even a determined climber like Jem to reach.

"Good idea," Roger said, anxious to get the jar out of Jem's vicinity. "I'll take it up now, shall I?"

Before Brianna could answer, a knock came at the door, followed immediately by Jamie Fraser. Jem instantly ceased trying to get at the jar and instead flung himself on his grandfather with shrieks of joy.

"How is it, then, *a bhailach*?" Jamie inquired amiably, neatly turning Jem upside down and holding him by the ankles. "A word, Roger Mac?"

"Sure. Ye'll sit, maybe?" He'd told Jamie earlier what he knew—lamentably little—regarding the role of the Cherokee in the upcoming Revolution. Had he come to inquire further? Reluctantly setting down the jar, Roger pulled out a stool and pushed it in his father-in-law's direction. Jamie accepted it with a nod, dexterously transferring Jemmy to a position over one shoulder and sitting down.

Jemmy giggled madly, squirming until his grandfather slapped him lightly on the seat of his breeches, whereupon he subsided, hanging contentedly upside-down like a sloth, his bright hair spilling down the back of Jamie's shirt.

"It's this way, *a charaid,*" Jamie said. "I must be going in the morning to the Cherokee villages, and there is a thing I'd ask ye to do in my place."

"Oh, aye. D'ye want me to see to the barley harvest, then?" The early grain was still ripening. Everyone had his fingers crossed that the weather would keep fair for another few weeks, but the prospects were good.

"No, Brianna can do that—if ye will, lass?" He smiled at his daughter, who raised thick ruddy eyebrows, the twins of his.

"I can," she agreed. "What are you planning to do with Ian, Roger, and Arch Bug, though?" Arch Bug was Jamie's factor, and the logical person to be overseeing the harvest in Jamie's absence.

"Well, I shall take Young Ian with me. The Cherokee ken him well, and he's comfortable wi' their speech. I'll take the Beardsley lads, too, so they can fetch back the berries and bits o' things your mother wants for Lizzie, straightaway."

"I go, too?" Jemmy inquired hopefully.

"Not this time, *a bhailach.* In the autumn, maybe." He patted Jemmy on the bottom, then returned his attention to Roger.

"That being so," he said, "I need ye to go to Cross Creek, if ye will, and collect the new tenants." Roger felt a small surge of excitement—and alarm—at the prospect, but merely cleared his throat and nodded.

"Aye. Of course. Will they—"

"Ye'll take Arch Bug along, and Tom Christie."

A moment of incredulous silence greeted this statement.

"Tom *Christie*?" Bree said, exchanging a glance of bafflement with Roger. "What on earth for?" The schoolmaster was a notably dour sort, and no one's idea of a congenial traveling companion.

Her father's mouth twisted wryly.

"Aye, well. There's the one small thing MacDonald neglected to tell me, when he asked if I'd take them. They're Protestants, the lot."

"Ah," said Roger. "I see." Jamie met his eye and nodded, relieved to be so immediately understood.

"*I* don't see." Brianna patted her hair, frowning, then pulled off the ribbon and began to comb her fingers slowly through it, undoing the tangles as a preliminary to brushing it. "What difference does it make?"

Roger and Jamie exchanged a brief but eloquent glance. Jamie shrugged, and pulled Jem down into his lap.

"Well." Roger rubbed his chin, trying to think how to explain two centuries of Scottish religious intolerance in any way that would make sense to an American of the twentieth century. "Ahh . . . ye recall the civil-rights thing in the States, integration in the South, all that?"

"Of course I do." She narrowed her eyes at him. "Okay. So, which side are the Negroes?"

"The what?" Jamie looked entirely baffled. "Where do Negroes come into the matter?"

"Not quite that simple," Roger assured her. "Just an indication of the depth of feeling involved. Let us say that the notion of having a Catholic landlord is likely to cause our new tenants severe qualms—and vice versa?" he asked, glancing at Jamie.

"What's Negroes?" Jemmy asked with interest.

"Er . . . .dark-skinned people," Roger replied, suddenly aware of the potential quagmire opened up by this question. It was true that the term "Negro" didn't invariably mean also "slave"—but near enough that there was little difference. "D'ye not remember them, from your great-auntie Jocasta's place?"

Jemmy frowned, adopting for an unsettling instant the precise expression his grandfather was wearing.

"No."

"Well, anyway," Bree said, calling the meeting to order with a sharp rap of her hairbrush on the table, "the point is that Mr. Christie is enough of a Protestant to make the new people feel comfortable?"

"Something of the sort," her father agreed, one side of his

mouth curling up. "Between your man here and Tom Christie, at least they'll not think they're entering the devil's realm entirely."

"I see," Roger said again, in a slightly different tone. So it wasn't only his position as son of the house and general right-hand man, was it—but the fact that he was a Presbyterian, at least in name. He raised a brow at Jamie, who shrugged in acknowledgment.

"Mmphm," Roger said, resigned.

"Mmphm," said Jamie, satisfied.

"Stop *doing* that," Brianna said crossly. "Fine. So you and Tom Christie are going to Cross Creek. Why is Arch Bug going?"

Roger became aware, in a subliminally marital way, that his wife was disgruntled at the thought of being left behind to organize the harvest—a filthy, exhausting job at the best of times—whilst he frolicked with a squad of his co-religionists in the romantically exciting metropolis of Cross Creek, population two hundred.

"It will be Arch, mostly, helping them to settle and build themselves shelter before the cold," Jamie said logically. "Ye dinna mean to suggest, I hope, that I send him alone to talk to them?"

Brianna smiled involuntarily at that; Arch Bug, married for decades to the voluble Mrs. Bug, was famous for his lack of speech. He *could* talk, but seldom did so, limiting his conversational contributions to the occasional genial "Mmp."

"Well, they'll likely never realize that Arch is Catholic," Roger said, rubbing his upper lip with a forefinger. "Or is he, come to that? I've never asked him."

"He is," Jamie said, very dryly. "But he's lived long enough to ken when to be silent."

"Well, I can see this is going to be a jolly expedition," Brianna said, raising one brow. "When do you think you'll be back?"

"Christ, I don't know," Roger said, feeling a stab of guilt at the casual blasphemy. He'd have to revise his habits, and quickly. "A month? Six weeks?"

"At least," his father-in-law said cheerfully. "They'll be on foot, mind."

Roger took a deep breath, contemplating a slow march, *en masse,* from Cross Creek to the mountains, with Arch Bug on one side of him and Tom Christie on the other, twin pillars of taciturnity. His eyes lingered wistfully on his wife, envisioning six weeks of sleeping by the roadside, alone.

"Yeah, fine," he said. "I'll . . . um . . . go speak to Tom and Arch tonight, then."

"Daddy go?" Catching the gist of the conversation, Jem scrambled off his grandfather's knee and scampered over to Roger, grabbing him round the leg. "Go with *you,* Daddy!"

"Oh. Well, I don't think—" He caught sight of Bree's face, resigned, and then the green and red jar on the table behind her. "Why not?" he said suddenly, and smiled at Jem. "Great-Auntie Jocasta would love to see you. And Mummy can blow things up to her heart's content without worrying where you are, aye?"

"She can do what?" Jamie looked startled.

"It doesn't *explode,*" Brianna said, picking up the jar of phosphorus and cradling it possessively. "It just burns. Are you sure?" This last was addressed to Roger, and accompanied by a searching look.

"Yeah, sure," he said, affecting confidence. He glanced at Jemmy, who was chanting "Go! Go! Go!", meanwhile hopping up and down like a demented popcorn kernel. "At least I'll have someone to talk to on the way."

13

SAFE HANDS

IT WAS NEARLY DARK when Jamie came in to find me sitting at the kitchen table, head on my arms. I jerked upright at the sound of his footstep, blinking.

"Are ye all right, Sassenach?" He sat down on the opposite

bench, eyeing me. "Ye look as though ye've been dragged through a hedge backward."

"Oh." I patted vaguely at my hair, which did seem to be sticking out a bit. "Um. Fine. Are you hungry?"

"Of course I am. Have ye eaten, yourself?"

I squinted and rubbed my face, trying to think.

"No," I decided at last. "I was waiting for you, but I seem to have fallen asleep. There's stew. Mrs. Bug left it."

He got up and peered into the small cauldron, then pushed the swinging hook back to bring it over the fire to warm.

"What have ye been doing, Sassenach?" he asked, coming back. "And how's the wee lass?"

"The wee lass is what I've been doing," I said, suppressing a yawn. "Mostly." I rose, slowly, feeling my joints protest, and staggered over to the sideboard to cut some bread.

"She couldn't keep it down," I said. "The gallberry medicine. Not that I blame her," I added, cautiously licking my lower lip. After she'd thrown it up the first time, I'd tasted it myself. My tastebuds were still in a state of revolt; I'd never met a more aptly named plant, and being boiled into syrup had merely concentrated the flavor.

Jamie sniffed deeply as I turned.

"Did she vomit on ye?"

"No, that was Bobby Higgins," I said. "He's got hookworms."

He raised his brows.

"Do I want to hear about them whilst I'm eating?"

"Definitely not," I said, sitting down with the loaf, a knife, and a crock of soft butter. I tore off a piece, buttered it thickly, and gave it to him, then took one for myself. My tastebuds hesitated, but wavered on the edge of forgiving me for the gallberry syrup.

"What have *you* been doing?" I asked, beginning to wake up enough to take notice. He seemed tired, but more cheerful than he had been when he'd left the house.

"Talking to Roger Mac about Indians and Protestants." He frowned at the half-eaten chunk of bread in his hand. "Is there something amiss wi' the bread, Sassenach? It tastes odd."

I waved a hand apologetically.

"Sorry, that's me. I washed several times, but I couldn't get it off completely. Perhaps you'd better do the buttering." I pushed the loaf toward him with my elbow, gesturing at the crock.

"Couldna get *what* off?"

"Well, we tried and tried with the syrup, but no good; Lizzie simply couldn't hold it down, poor thing. But I remembered that quinine can be absorbed through the skin. So I mixed the syrup into some goose grease, and rubbed it all over her. Oh, yes, thanks." I leaned forward and took a delicate bite of the buttered bit of bread he held out for me. My tastebuds gave in gracefully, and I realized that I hadn't eaten all day.

"And it worked?" He glanced up at the ceiling. Mr. Wemyss and Lizzie shared the smaller room upstairs, but all was quiet above.

"I think so," I said, swallowing. "The fever finally broke, at least, and she's asleep. We'll keep using it; if the fever doesn't come back in two days, we'll know it works."

"That's good, then."

"Well, and then there was Bobby and his hookworms. Fortunately, I have some ipecacuanha and turpentine."

"Fortunately for the worms, or for Bobby?"

"Well, neither, really," I said, and yawned. "It will probably work, though."

He smiled faintly, and uncorked a bottle of beer, passing it automatically under his nose. Finding it all right, he poured some for me.

"Aye, well, it's a comfort to know I'm leaving things in your capable hands, Sassenach. Ill-smelling," he added, wrinkling his long nose in my direction, "but capable."

"Thanks so much." The beer was better than good; must be one of Mrs. Bug's batches. We sipped companionably for a bit, both too tired to get up and serve the stew. I watched him beneath my lashes; I always did, when he was about to leave on a journey, storing up small memories of him against his return.

He looked tired, and there were small twin lines between his heavy brows, betokening slight worry. The candlelight glowed on the broad bones of his face, though, and cast his shadow clear on the plastered wall behind him, strong and bold. I watched the shadow raise its spectral beer glass, the light making an amber glow in the shadow glass.

"Sassenach," he said suddenly, putting down the glass, "how many times, would ye say, have I come close to dying?"

I stared at him for a moment, but then shrugged and began to reckon, mustering my synapses into reluctant activity.

"Well . . . I don't know what horrible things happened to you before I met you, but after . . . well, you were dreadfully ill at the abbey." I glanced covertly at him, but he seemed not to be bothered at the thought of Wentworth prison, and what had been done to him there that had caused the illness. "Hmm. And after Culloden—you said you had a terrible fever then, from your wounds, and thought you might die, only Jenny forced you—I mean, nursed you, through it."

"And then Laoghaire shot me," he said wryly. "And *you* forced me through it. Likewise, when the snake bit me." He considered for a moment.

"I had the smallpox when I was a wean, but I think I wasna in danger of dying then; they said it was a light case. So only four times, then."

"What about the day I first met you?" I objected. "You nearly bled to death."

"Oh, I did not," he protested. "That was no but a wee scratch."

I lifted one brow at him, and leaning over to the hearth, scooped a ladle of aromatic stew into a bowl. It was rich with the juices of rabbit and venison, swimming in a thick gravy spiced with rosemary, garlic, and onion. So far as my taste-buds were concerned, all was forgiven.

"Have it your way," I said. "But wait—what about your head? When Dougal tried to kill you with an ax. Surely that's five?"

He frowned, accepting the bowl.

"Aye, I suppose you're right," he said, seeming displeased. "Five, then."

I regarded him gently over my own bowl of stew. He was very large, solid, and beautifully formed. And if he was a bit battered by circumstance, that merely added to his charm.

"You're a very hard person to kill, I think," I said. "That's a great comfort to me."

He smiled, reluctant, but then reached out and lifted his glass in salute, touching it first to his own lips, then to mine.

"We'll drink to that, Sassenach, shall we?"

14

PEOPLE OF THE SNOWBIRD

"GUNS," Bird-who-sings-in-the-morning said. "Tell your King we want guns." Jamie suppressed the urge to reply, "Who doesn't?" for a moment, but then gave in to it, surprising the war chief into a blink of startlement, followed by a grin.

"Who, indeed?" Bird was a short man, shaped like a barrel, and young for his office—but shrewd, his affability no disguise to his intelligence. "They all tell you this, all the village war chiefs, eh? Of course they do. What do you tell them?"

"What I can." Jamie lifted one shoulder, let it fall. "Trade goods are certain, knives are likely—guns are possible, but I cannot yet promise them."

They were speaking a slightly unfamiliar dialect of Cherokee, and he hoped he had got right the manner of indicating probability. He did well enough with the usual tongue in casual matters of trade and hunting, but the matters he dealt in here would not be casual. He glanced briefly at Ian, who was listening closely, but evidently what he'd said was all right. Ian visited the villages near the Ridge frequently, and hunted with the young men; he shifted into the tongue of the Tsalagi as easily as he did into his native Gaelic.

"So, well enough." Bird settled himself more comfortably. The pewter badge Jamie had given him as a present glinted on his breast, firelight flickering over the broadly amiable planes of his face. "Tell your King about the guns—and tell him why we need them, eh?"

"You wish me to tell him that, do you? Do you think he will be willing to send you guns with which to kill his own people?" Jamie asked dryly. The incursion of white settlers across the Treaty Line into the Cherokee lands was a sore point, and he risked something by alluding to it directly, rather than addressing Bird's other needs for guns: to defend his village from raiders—or to go raiding himself.

Bird shrugged in reply.

"We can kill them without guns, if we want to." One eyebrow lifted a little, and Bird's lips pursed, waiting to see what Jamie made of this statement.

He supposed Bird meant to shock him. He merely nodded.

"Of course you can. You are wise enough not to."

"Not yet." Bird's lips relaxed into a charming smile. "You tell the King—not yet."

"His Majesty will be pleased to hear that you value his friendship so much."

Bird burst into laughter at that, rocking back and forth, and his brother Still Water, who sat beside him, grinned broadly.

"I like you, Bear-Killer," he said, recovering. "You're a funny man."

"I may be," Jamie said in English, smiling. "Give it time."

Ian gave a small snort of amusement at that, causing Bird to look sharply at him, then away, clearing his throat. Jamie raised one brow at his nephew, who replied with a bland smile.

Still Water was watching Ian narrowly. The Cherokee welcomed them both with respect, but Jamie had noticed at once a particular edge in their response to Ian. They perceived Ian to be Mohawk—and he made them wary. In all honesty, he himself sometimes thought there was some part of Ian that had not come back from Snaketown, and perhaps never would.

Bird had given him an avenue to inquire about something, though.

"You have been much troubled by persons who come into your lands to settle," he said, nodding sympathetically. "You of course do not kill these persons, being wise. But not everyone is wise, are they?"

Bird's eyes narrowed briefly.

"What do you mean, Bear-Killer?"

"I hear of burning, Tsisqua." He held the other man's eyes with his own, careful to give no hint of accusation. "The King hears of houses burning, men killed and women taken. This does not please him."

"Hmp," Bird said, and pressed his lips together. He did not, however, say he had not heard of such things himself, which was interesting.

"Enough of such stories, and the King may send soldiers to protect his people. If he should do that, he will hardly wish to have them face guns that he himself has given," Jamie pointed out logically.

"And what should we do, then?" Still Water broke in hotly. "They come across the Treaty Line, build houses, plant fields, and take the game. If your King cannot keep his people where they belong, how can he protest if we defend our lands?"

Bird made a small flattening gesture with one hand, not looking at his brother, and Still Water subsided, though with bad grace.

"So, Bear-Killer. You will tell the King these things, will you?"

Jamie inclined his head gravely.

"That is my office. I speak of the King to you, and I will take your words to the King."

Bird nodded thoughtfully, then waved a hand for food and beer, and the talk changed firmly to neutral matters. No more business would be done tonight.

IT WAS LATE when they left Tsisqua's house for the small guesthouse. He thought it was well past moonrise, but there was no moon to be seen; the sky glowed thick with cloud, and the scent of rain was live on the wind.

"Oh, God," Ian said, yawning and stumbling. "My bum's gone asleep."

Jamie yawned, too, finding it contagious, but then blinked

and laughed. "Aye, well. Dinna bother waking it up; the rest of ye can join it."

Ian made a derisive noise with his lips.

"Just because Bird says ye're a funny man, Uncle Jamie, I wouldna go believing it. He's only being polite, ken?"

Jamie ignored this, murmuring thanks in Tsalagi to the young woman who had shown them the way to their quarters. She handed him a small basket—filled with corn bread and dried apples, from the smell—then wished them a soft "Good night, sleep well," before vanishing into the damp, restless night.

The small hut seemed stuffy after the cool freshness of the air, and he stood in the doorway for a moment, enjoying the movement of the wind through the trees, watching it snake through the pine boughs like a huge, invisible serpent. A spatter of moisture bloomed on his face, and he experienced the deep pleasure of a man who realizes that it's going to rain and he isn't going to have to spend the night out in it.

"Ask about, Ian, when ye're gossiping tomorrow," he said, ducking inside. "Let it be known—tactfully—that the King would be pleased to know exactly who in hell's been burning cabins—and might be pleased enough to cough up a few guns in reward. They'll not tell ye if it's them that's been doing it—but if it's another band, they might."

Ian nodded, yawning again. A small fire burned in a stone ring, the smoke of it wisping up toward a smoke hole in the roof overhead, and by its light, a fur-piled sleeping platform was visible across one side of the hut, with another stack of furs and blankets on the floor.

"Toss ye for the bed, Uncle Jamie," he said, digging in the pouch at his waist and coming out with a battered shilling. "Call it."

"Tails," Jamie said, setting down the basket and unbelting his plaid. It fell in a warm puddle of fabric round his legs and he shook out his shirt. The linen was creased and grimy against his skin, and he could smell himself; thank God this was the last of the villages. One more night, perhaps, two at the most, and they could go home.

Ian swore, picking up the coin.

"How d'ye do that? Every night ye've said 'tails,' and every night, tails it is!"

"Well, it's your shilling, Ian. Dinna blame me." He sat down on the bed platform and stretched himself pleasurably, then relented. "Look at Geordie's nose."

Ian flipped the shilling over in his fingers and held it to the light of the fire, squinting, then swore again. A tiny splotch of beeswax, so thin as to be invisible unless you were looking, ornamented the aristocratically prominent nose of George III, Rex Britannia.

"How did that get there?" Ian narrowed his eyes suspiciously at his uncle, but Jamie merely laughed and lay down.

"When ye were showing wee Jem how to spin a coin. Remember, he knocked the candlestick over; hot wax went everywhere."

"Oh." Ian sat looking at the coin in his hand for a moment, then shook his head, scraped the wax away with a thumbnail, and put the shilling away.

"Good night, Uncle Jamie," he said, sliding into the furs on the ground with a sigh.

"Good night, Ian."

He'd been ignoring his tiredness, holding it like Gideon, on a short rein. Now he dropped the reins and gave it leave to carry him off, his body relaxing into the comfort of the bed.

MacDonald, he reflected cynically, would be delighted. Jamie had planned on visits only to the two Cherokee villages closest to the Treaty Line, there to announce his new position, distribute modest gifts of whisky and tobacco—this last hastily borrowed from Tom Christie, who had fortunately purchased a hogshead of the weed on a seed-buying trip to Cross Creek—and inform the Cherokee that further largesse might be expected when he undertook ambassage to the more distant villages in the autumn.

He had been most cordially received in both villages—but in the second, Pigtown, several strangers had been visiting; young men in search of wives. They were from a separate band of Cherokee, called the Snowbird band, whose large village lay higher in the mountains.

One of the young men had been the nephew of Bird-who-sings-in-the-morning, headman of the Snowbird band, and had been exigent in pressing Jamie to return with him and his companions to their home village. Taking a hasty private inventory of his remaining whisky and tobacco, Jamie had agreed, and he and Ian had been most royally received there, as agents of His Majesty. The Snowbird had never been visited by an Indian agent before, and appeared most sensible of the honor—and prompt about seeing what advantages might accrue to themselves in consequence.

He thought Bird was the sort of man with whom he could do business, though—on various fronts.

That thought led him to belated recollection of Roger Mac and the new tenants. He'd had no time over the last few days to spare much worry there—but he doubted there was any cause for concern. Roger Mac was capable enough, though his shattered voice made him less certain than he should be. With Christie and Arch Bug, though. . .

He closed his eyes, the bliss of absolute fatigue stealing over him as his thoughts grew more disjointed.

A day more, maybe, then home in time to make the hay. Another malting, two maybe, before the cold weather. Slaughtering . . . could it be time at last to kill the damned white sow? No . . . the vicious creature was unbelievably fecund. What kind of boar had the balls to mate with her? he wondered dimly, and did she eat him, after? Wild boar . . . smoked hams, blood pudding . . .

He was just drifting down through the first layers of sleep when he felt a hand on his privates. Jerked out of drowsiness like a salmon out of a sea-loch, he clapped a hand to the intruder's, gripping tight. And elicited a faint giggle from his visitor.

Feminine fingers wiggled gently in his grasp, and the hand's fellow promptly took up operations in its stead. His first coherent thought was that the lassie would be an excellent baker, so good as she was at kneading.

Other thoughts followed rapidly on the heels of this absurdity, and he tried to grab the second hand. It playfully eluded him in the dark, poking and tweaking.

He groped for a polite protest in Cherokee, but came up with nothing but a handful of random phrases in English and Gaelic, none of them faintly suitable to the occasion.

The first hand was purposefully wriggling out of his grasp, eel-like. Reluctant to crush her fingers, he let go for an instant, and made a successful grab for her wrist.

"Ian!" he hissed, in desperation. "Ian, are ye there?" He couldn't see his nephew in the pool of darkness that filled the cabin, nor tell if he slept. There were no windows, and only the faintest light came from the dying coals.

"Ian!"

There was a stirring on the floor, bodies shifting, and he heard Rollo sneeze.

"What is it, Uncle?" He'd spoken in Gaelic, and Ian answered in the same language. The lad sounded calm, and not as though he'd just come awake.

"Ian, there is a woman in my bed," he said in Gaelic, trying to match his nephew's calm tone.

"There are two of them, Uncle Jamie." Ian sounded amused, damn him! "The other will be down by your feet. Waiting her turn."

That unnerved him, and he nearly lost his grip on the captive hand.

"Two of them! What do they think I am?"

The girl giggled again, leaned over, and bit him lightly on the chest.

"Christ!"

"Well, no, Uncle, they don't think you're Him," Ian said, obviously suppressing his own mirth. "They think you're the King. So to speak. You're his agent, so they're doing honor to His Majesty by sending you his women, aye?"

The second woman had uncovered his feet and was slowly stroking his soles with one finger. He was ticklish and would have found this bothersome, were he not so distracted by the first woman, with whom he was being compelled into a most undignified game of hide-the-sausage.

"Talk to them, Ian," he said between clenched teeth, fumbling madly with his free hand, meanwhile forcing back the questing fingers of the captive hand—which were languidly stroking his ear—and wiggling his feet in a frantic effort to discourage the second lady's attentions, which were growing bolder.

"Erm . . . what d'ye want me to say?" Ian inquired, switching back to English. His voice quivered slightly.

"Tell them I'm deeply sensible of the honor, but—gk!" Further diplomatic evasions were cut off by the sudden intrusion of someone's tongue into his mouth, tasting strongly of onions and beer.

In the midst of his subsequent struggles, he was dimly aware that Ian had lost any sense of self-control and was lying on the floor giggling helplessly. It was filicide if you killed a son, he thought grimly; what was the word for assassinating a nephew?

"Madam!" he said, disengaging his mouth with difficulty. He seized the lady by the shoulders and rolled her off his body with enough force that she whooped with surprise, bare legs flying—Jesus, was she naked?

She was. Both of them were; his eyes adapted to the faint glow of the embers, he caught the shimmer of light from shoulders, breasts, and rounded thighs.

He sat up, gathering furs and blankets round him in a sort of hasty redoubt.

"Cease, the two of you!" he said severely in Cherokee. "You are beautiful, but I cannot lie with you."

"No?" said one, sounding puzzled.

"Why not?" said the other.

"Ah . . . because there is an oath upon me," he said, necessity producing inspiration. "I have sworn . . . sworn . . ." He groped for the proper word, but didn't find it. Luckily, Ian leaped in at this point, with a stream of fluent Tsalagi, too fast to follow.

"Ooo," breathed one girl, impressed. Jamie felt a distinct qualm.

"What in God's name did ye tell them, Ian?"

"I told them the Great Spirit came to ye in a dream, Uncle, and told ye that ye mustn't go with a woman until ye'd brought guns to all the Tsalagi."

"Until I *what*?!"

"Well, it was the best I could think of in a hurry, Uncle," Ian said defensively.

Hair-raising as the notion was, he had to admit it was

effective; the two women were huddled together, whispering in awed tones, and had quite left off pestering him.

"Aye, well," he said grudgingly. "I suppose it could be worse." After all, even if the Crown were persuaded to provide guns, there were a damn lot of Tsalagi.

"Ye're welcome, Uncle Jamie." The laughter was gurgling just below the surface of his nephew's voice, and emerged in a stifled snort.

"What?" he said testily.

"The one lady is saying it's a disappointment to her, Uncle, because you're verra nicely equipped. The other is more philosophical about it, though. She says they might have borne ye children, and the bairns might have red hair." His nephew's voice quivered.

"What's wrong wi' red hair, for God's sake?"

"I dinna ken, quite, but I gather it's not something ye want your bairn to be marked with, and ye can help it."

"Well, fine," he snapped. "No danger of it, is there? Can they not go home now?"

"It's raining, Uncle Jamie," Ian pointed out logically. It was; the wind had brought a patter of rain, and now the main shower arrived, beating on the roof with a steady thrum, drops hissing into the hot embers through the smoke hole. "Ye wouldna send them out in the wet, would ye? Besides, ye just said ye couldna lie wi' them, not that ye meant them to go."

He broke off to say something interrogative to the ladies, who replied with eager confidence. Jamie thought they'd said—they had. Rising with the grace of young cranes, the two of them clambered naked as jaybirds back into his bed, patting and stroking him with murmurs of admiration—though sedulously avoiding his private parts—pressed him down into the furs, and snuggled down on either side of him, warm bare flesh pressed cozily against him.

He opened his mouth, then shut it again, finding absolutely nothing to say in any of the languages he knew.

He lay on his back, rigid and breathing shallowly. His cock throbbed indignantly, clearly meaning to stay up and torment him all night in revenge for its abuse. Small chortling noises came from the pile of furs on the ground, interspersed with hiccuping snorts. He thought it was maybe the first time he'd heard Ian truly laugh since his return.

Praying for fortitude, he drew a long, slow breath, and closed his eyes, hands folded firmly across his ribs, elbows pressed to his sides.

15

STAKIT TO DROON

ROGER WALKED OUT onto the terrace at River Run, feeling pleasantly exhausted. After three weeks of strenuous work, he'd gathered the new tenants from the highways and byways of Cross Creek and Campbelton, become acquainted with all the heads of households, managed to equip them at least minimally for the journey, in terms of food, blankets, and shoes—and got them all collected in one place, firmly overcoming their tendency to panic and stray. They'd start in the morning for Fraser's Ridge, and not a moment too soon.

He looked out over the terrace in satisfaction, toward the meadow that lay beyond Jocasta Cameron Innes's stables. They were all bedded down in a temporary camp there: twenty-two families, with seventy-six individual souls, four mules, two ponies, fourteen dogs, three pigs, and God only knew how many chickens, kittens, and pet birds, bundled into wicker cages for carrying. He had all the names on a list—animals excluded—dog-eared and crumpled in his pocket. He had several other lists there, as well, scribbled over, crossed out, and amended to the point of illegibility. He felt like a walking Book of Deuteronomy. He also felt like a very large drink.

This was luckily forthcoming; Duncan Innes, Jocasta's husband, had returned from his own day's labor and was sitting on the terrace, in company with a cut-glass decanter, from which the rays of the sinking sun struck a mellow amber glow.

"How is it, then, *a charaid*?" Duncan greeted him genially, gesturing toward one of the basketwork chairs. "Ye'll take a dram, perhaps?"

"I will, and thanks."

He sank gratefully into the chair, which creaked amiably beneath his weight. He accepted the glass Duncan handed him, and tossed it back with a brief *"Slàinte."*

The whisky burned through the strictures that bound his throat, making him cough, but seeming suddenly to open things, so that the constant faint sense of choking began to leave him. He sipped, grateful.

"Ready to go, are they?" Duncan nodded toward the meadow, where the smoke of campfires hung in a low golden haze.

"Ready as they'll ever be. Poor things," Roger added with some sympathy.

Duncan raised one shaggy brow.

"Fish out of water," Roger amplified, holding out his glass to accept the proffered refill. "The women are terrified, and so are the men, but they hide it better. Ye'd think I was taking them all to be slaves on a sugar plantation."

Duncan nodded. "Or sell them to Rome to clean the Pope's shoon," he said wryly. "I misdoubt most of them had ever smelt a Catholic before embarking. And from the wrinkled noses, they dinna care so much for the scent now, I think. Do they so much as tak' a dram now and then, d'ye ken?"

"Only medicinally, and only if in actual danger of death, I think." Roger took a slow, ambrosial swallow and closed his eyes, feeling the whisky warm his throat and curl in his chest like a purring cat. "Meet Hiram yet, did you? Hiram Crombie, the head man of this lot."

"The wee sour-drap wi' the stick up his arse? Aye, I met him." Duncan grinned, his drooping mustache lifting at the end. "He'll be at supper with us. Best have another."

"I will, thanks," said Roger, extending his glass. "Though they're none of them much for hedonistic pleasure, so far as I can tell. Ye'd think they were all still Covenanters to the bone. The Frozen Chosen, aye?"

Duncan laughed immoderately at that.

"Well, it's no like it was in my grandsire's day," he said, recovering and reaching across for the decanter. "And thank the Lord for that." He rolled his eyes, grimacing.

"Your grandsire was a Covenanter, then?"

"God, yes." Shaking his head, Duncan poured a goodly measure, first for Roger, then himself. "A fierce auld bastard, he was. Not that he'd no cause, mind. His sister was stakit to droon, ken?"

"Was—Christ." He bit his tongue in penance, but was too interested to pay it much mind. "Ye mean—executed by drowning?"

Duncan nodded, eyes on his glass, then took a good gulp and held it for a moment in his mouth before swallowing.

"Margaret," he said. "Her name was Margaret. Eighteen she was, at the time. Her father and her brother—my grandfather, aye?—they'd fled, after the battle at Dunbar; hid in the hills. The troops came a-hunting them, but she wouldna say where they'd gone—and she had a Bible by her. They tried to make her recant then, but she wouldna do that, either—the women on that side o' the family, ye might as well talk to a stone," he said, shaking his head. "There's no moving them. But they dragged her doon to the shore, her and an auld Covenanter woman from the village, stripped them, and tied them both to stakes at the tide line. Waited there, the crowd o' them, for the water to come in."

He took another swallow, not waiting for the taste of it.

"The auld woman went under first; they'd tied her closer to the water—I suppose thinking Margaret would give in, if she saw the auld woman die." He grunted, shaking his head. "But nay, not a bit of it. The tide rose, and the waves came up ower her. She choked, and she coughed, and her hair loose, hanging over her face, plastered doon like kelp, when the water went out.

"My mither saw it," he explained, lifting his glass. "She was but seven at the time, but she never forgot. After the first wave, she said, there was the space of three breaths, and the wave came ower Margaret again. And then out . . . three breaths . . . and in again once more. And ye couldna see anything then but the swirl of her hair, floating on the tide."

He raised his glass an inch higher, and Roger lifted his own in involuntary toast. "Jesus," he said, and it was no blasphemy.

The whisky burned his throat as it went down and he breathed deep, giving thanks to God for the gift of air. Three breaths. It was the single malt of Islay, and the iodine taste of sea and kelp was strong and smoky in his lungs.

"May God give her peace," he said, his voice rasping.

Duncan nodded, and reached again for the decanter.

"I would suppose she earned it," he said. "Though they"—he pointed with his chin toward the meadow—"they'd say 'twas none of her doing at all; God chose her for salvation and chose the English to be damned; nay more to be said on the matter."

The light was fading and the campfires began to glow in the dimness of the meadow beyond the stables. The smoke of them reached Roger's nose, the scent warm and homelike, but nonetheless adding to the burn in his throat.

"I've no found sae much worth dyin' for, myself," Duncan said reflectively, then gave one of his quick, rare smiles. "But my grandsire, he'd say it only meant I was chosen to be damned. *'By the decree of God, for His everlasting glory, some men and angels are predestined unto everlasting life, and others fore-ordained to everlasting death.'* He'd say that, whenever anyone spoke of Margaret."

Roger nodded, recognizing the statement from the Westminster Confession. When was that—1646? 1647? A generation—or two—before Duncan's grandfather.

"I expect it was easier for him to think her death was God's will, and nothing to do with him," Roger said, not without sympathy. "Ye'll not believe it yourself, then? Predestination, I mean."

He asked with true curiosity. The Presbyterians of his own time did still espouse predestination as a doctrine—but, a bit more flexible in attitude, tended to soft-pedal the notion of predestined damnation, and not to think too much on the idea that every detail of life was so predestined. Himself? God knew.

Duncan lifted his shoulders, the right rising higher and making him seem momentarily twisted. "God knows," he said, and laughed. He shook his head, and drained his glass again.

"Nay, I think I don't. But I wouldna say as much before Hiram Crombie—nor yet yon Christie." Duncan lifted his chin toward the meadow, where he could see two dark figures, walking side by side toward the house. Arch Bug's tall, stooped frame was easy to recognize, as was Tom Christie's shorter, blocky build. He looked pugnacious even in silhouette, Roger thought, making short, sharp gestures as he walked, clearly arguing something with Arch.

"There'd be wicked fights ower it sometimes, in Ardsmuir," Duncan said, watching the progress of the two figures. "The Catholics took it amiss, to be told they were damned. And Christie and his wee band took the greatest pleasure in telling them so." His shoulders shook a little in suppressed laughter, and Roger wondered just how much whisky Duncan had had before he came out to the terrace. He'd never seen the older man so jovial.

"*Mac Dubh* put a stop to it, finally, when he made us all be Freemasons," he added, leaning forward to pour a fresh glass. "But a few men were nearly killed, before that." He lifted the decanter inquiringly in Roger's direction.

Looking forward to a supper including both Tom Christie and Hiram Crombie, Roger accepted.

As Duncan leaned toward him to pour, still smiling, the last of the sun shone across his weathered face. Roger caught a glimpse of a faint white line through Duncan's upper lip, half-visible beneath the hair, and realized quite suddenly why Duncan wore a long mustache—an unusual adornment, in a time when most men were clean-shaven.

He would not have spoken, likely, save for the whisky and the mood of strange alliance between them—two Protestants, amazingly bound to Catholics and bemused at the strange tides of fate that had washed over them; two men left quite alone by the misfortunes of life, and now surprised to find themselves the heads of households, holding the lives of strangers in their hands.

"Your lip, Duncan." He touched his own mouth briefly. "What did that?"

"Och, that?" Duncan touched his own lip, surprised. "Nay, I was born wi' a harelip, or so they said. I dinna recall it, myself; it was mended when I was nay more than a week old."

It was Roger's turn to be surprised.

"Who mended it?"

Duncan shrugged, one-shouldered this time.

"A traveling healer, my mither said. She'd quite resigned

herself to losin' me, she said, because I couldna suck, of course. She and my aunties all took it in turn to drap milk into my mouth from a rag, but she said I'd wasted nearly to a wee skeleton, when this charmer came by the village."

He rubbed a knuckle self-consciously over his lip, smoothing the thick, grizzled hairs of his mustache.

"My faither gave him six herrings and a mull o' snuff, and he stitched it up, and gave my mither a bit o' some ointment to put on the wound. Well, and so . . ." He shrugged again, with a lopsided smile.

"Perhaps I was destined to live, after all. My grandsire said the Lord had chosen me—though God only kens what for."

Roger was conscious of a faint ripple of unease, dulled though it was by whisky.

A Highland charmer who could repair a harelip? He took another drink, trying not to stare, but covertly examining Duncan's face. He supposed it was possible; the scar was just barely visible—if you knew to look—under Duncan's mustache, but didn't extend up into the nostril. It must have been a fairly simple harelip, then, not one of the hideous cases like that one he'd read about—unable to look away from the page for horror—in Claire's big black doctor's book, where Dr. Rawlings had described a child born not only with a split lip, but missing the roof of its mouth, and most of the center of its face, as well.

There had been no drawing, thank God, but the visual picture conjured up by Rawlings's spare description had been bad enough. He closed his eyes and breathed deep, inhaling the whisky's perfume through his pores.

Was it possible? Perhaps. People did *do* surgery now, bloodstained, crude, and agonizing as it was. He'd seen Murray MacLeod, the apothecary from Campbelton, expertly stitch up a man's cheek, laid open when the man was trampled by a sheep. Would it be any more difficult to stitch a child's mouth?

He thought of Jemmy's lip, tender as a blossom, pierced by needle and black thread, and shuddered.

"Are ye cold, then, *a charaid*? Shall we go in?" Duncan got his feet under him, as though to rise, but Roger waved the older man back.

"Ah, no. Goose walking on my grave." He smiled, and accepted another drop to keep the nonexistent evening chill away. And yet he felt the hairs on his arms rise, just a little. *Could there be another one—more—like us?*

There had been, he knew. His own multiple-times great-grandmother, Geillis, for one. The man whose skull Claire had found, complete with silver fillings in its teeth, for another. But had Duncan met another, in some remote Highland village half a century before?

Christ, he thought, freshly unnerved. *How often does it happen? And what happens to them?*

Before they had quite reached the bottom of the decanter, he heard footsteps behind him, and the rustle of silk.

"Mrs. Cameron." He rose at once, the world tilting just a little, and took his hostess's hand, bowing over it.

Her long hand touched his face, as was her habit, her sensitive fingertips confirming his identity.

"Och, there ye are, Jo. Had a good journey wi' the wee lad, did ye?" Duncan struggled to rise, handicapped by whisky and his single arm, but Ulysses, Jocasta's butler, had materialized silently out of the twilight behind his mistress in time to move her wicker chair into place. She sank into it without so much as putting a hand out to see that it was there, Roger noticed; she simply knew it would be.

Roger viewed the butler with interest, wondering who Jocasta had bribed to get him back. Accused—and very likely guilty of—the death of a British naval officer on Jocasta's property, Ulysses had been forced to flee the colony. But Lieutenant Wolff had not been considered a great loss to the navy—and Ulysses was indispensable to Jocasta Cameron. All things might not be possible with gold—but he was willing to bet that Jocasta Cameron hadn't yet met a circumstance she couldn't mend with money, political connections, or guile.

"Oh, aye," she replied to her husband, smiling and putting out a hand to him. "'Twas such fun to show him off, husband! We'd a wonderful luncheon with old Mrs. Forbes and her daughter, and the wee bairn sang a song and charmed them all. Mrs. Forbes had the Montgomery lasses in, as well, and Miss Ogilvie, and we had wee lamb cutlets wi' raspberry sauce and fried apples and—oh, is that you, Mr. Christie? Do come and join us!" She raised her voice a little, and her face, appearing to look expectantly into the gloom over Roger's shoulder.

"Mrs. Cameron. Your servant, madam." Christie stepped up onto the terrace, making a courtly bow that was no less punctilious for the fact that its recipient was blind. Arch Bug followed him, bowing in turn over Jocasta's hand, and making a genial noise in his throat by way of greeting.

Chairs were brought out, more whisky, a plate of savories appeared as by magic, candles were lit—and suddenly it was a party, echoing on a higher plane the sense of slightly nervous festivity taking place in the meadow below. There was music in the distance; the sound of a tin whistle, playing a jig.

Roger let it all wash over him, enjoying the brief sense of relaxation and irresponsibility. Just for tonight, there was no need to worry; everyone was gathered, safe, fed, and prepared for the morrow's journey.

He needn't even trouble to keep up his end of the conversation; Tom Christie and Jocasta were enthusiastically discussing the literary scene in Edinburgh and a book he'd never heard of, with Duncan, looking so mellow that he might slide out of his chair any minute, putting in the occasional remark, and old Arch—where was Arch? Oh, there; gone back toward the meadow, having doubtless thought of some last minute thing he must tell someone.

He blessed Jamie Fraser for his forethought in sending Arch and Tom with him. Between the two of them, they'd saved him from any number of blunders, managed the ten thousand necessary details, and eased the fears of the new tenants regarding this latest leap into the unknown.

He took a deep, contented breath of air scented with the homely smells of campfires in the distance and roasting dinner near at hand—and belatedly recalled the one small detail whose welfare was still his exclusive concern.

Excusing himself, he made his way into the house, and discovered Jem down below in the main kitchen, cozily ensconced in the corner of a settle, eating bread pudding with melted butter and maple syrup on it.

"That's never your dinner, is it?" he asked, sitting down beside his son.

"Uh-huh. Want some, Daddy?" Jem extended a dripping

spoon upward toward him, and he bent hastily to take the offered mouthful before it fell off. It was delicious, bursting-sweet and creamy on the tongue.

"Mmm," he said, swallowing. "Well, let's not tell Mummy or Grannie, shall we? They've this odd prejudice toward meat and vegetables."

Jem nodded, agreeable, and offered him another spoonful. They consumed the bowl together in a companionable silence, after which Jem crawled into his lap, and leaning a sticky face against his chest, fell sound asleep.

Servants bustled to and fro around them, smiling kindly now and then. He should, he thought vaguely, get up. Dinner would be being served in a moment—he saw the platters of roasted duck and mutton being skillfully laid out, bowls mounded with heaps of fluffy, steaming rice soaked with gravy, and a huge sallet of greens being tossed with vinegar.

Filled with whisky, bread pudding, and contentment, though, he lingered, putting off from moment to moment the necessity of parting from Jem and ending the sweet peace of holding his sleeping son.

"Mister Roger? I take him, shall I?" said a soft voice. He looked up from an examination of Jem's hair, which had bits of bread pudding stuck in it, to see Phaedre, Jocasta's body servant, stooping before him, hands held out to receive the boy.

"I wash him, put him to his bed, sir," she said, her oval face as soft as her voice as she looked at Jem.

"Oh. Yes, sure. Thanks." Roger sat up, Jem in his arms, and rose carefully, holding Jem's considerable weight. "Here—I'll carry him up for you."

He followed the slave up the narrow stairs from the kitchen, admiring—in a purely abstract and aesthetic sort of way—the grace of her carriage. How old was she? he wondered. Twenty, twenty-two? Would Jocasta allow her to marry? She must have admirers, surely. But he knew how valuable she was to Jocasta, too—seldom out of her mistress's presence. Not easy to reconcile that with a home and family of her own.

At the top of the stair, she stopped and turned to take Jem from him; he surrendered his limp burden with reluctance, but also with some relief. It was stifling-hot down below, and his shirt was damp with sweat where Jem had pressed against him.

"Mister Roger?" Phaedre's voice stopped him, as he was about to take his leave. She was looking at him over Jem's shoulder, eyes hesitant beneath the white curve of her head scarf.

"Aye?"

The thump of feet coming up the stairs made him move, narrowly avoiding Oscar, charging upstairs with an empty platter under his arm, evidently bound for the summer kitchen, where the fish were being fried. Oscar grinned at Roger as he passed, and blew a kiss toward Phaedre, whose lips tightened at the gesture.

She made a slight motion with her head, and Roger followed her down the hall, away from the bustle of the kitchen. She stopped near the door that led out to the stables, glancing round to be sure they were not overheard.

"I maybe shouldn't say nothin', sir—may be as it *is* nothin'. But I'm thinkin' I should tell you, anyway."

He nodded, shoving back the damp hair at his temple. The door stood open, and there was a little breeze here, thank God.

"We was in the town, sir, this morning, at Mr. Benjamin's warehouse, you know the one? Down by the river."

He nodded again, and she licked her lips.

"Master Jem, he got restless and went to pokin' round, whilst the mistress talked with Mr. Benjamin. I followed him, seein' as he falls into no trouble, and so I was right there when the man come in."

"Aye? Which man was this?"

She shook her head, dark eyes serious.

"I dunno, sir. Was a big man, tall as you. Light-haired; he wasn't wearin' no wig. Was a gentleman, though." By which, he assumed, she meant the man was well-dressed.

"And?"

"He looks round, sees Mr. Benjamin a-talkin' with Miss Jo, and he takes a step to the side, like as he don't want no one takin' notice he there. But then he sees Mr. Jem, and he get a sharp kind of look on his face."

She pulled Jem a little closer, recalling.

"I ain't likin' that look, sir, tell you truly. I see him start toward Jemmy and I go quick and pick the lad up, same as I got him now. The man look surprised, then like he think something's funny; he smile at Jem and ax him who his daddy be?"

She gave a quick smile, patting Jem's back.

"Folk ax him that all the time, sir, downtown, and he speak right up, say his daddy Roger MacKenzie, same as he always do. This man, he laugh and ruffle Jem's hair—they all do that, sir, he gots such pretty hair. Then he say, 'Is he, then, my wee maneen, is he indeed?' "

Phaedre was a natural mimic. She caught the Irish lilt of it perfectly, and the sweat turned cold on Roger's skin.

"And then what happened?" he demanded. "What did he do?" Unconsciously, he glanced over her shoulder through the open door, searching the night outside for danger.

Phaedre hunched her shoulders, shivering slightly.

"He ain't *do* nothin', sir. But he look at Jem real close, and then at me, and he smile, right in my eyes. I ain't likin' that smile, sir, not one bit." She shook her head. "But then I hear Mr. Benjamin lift his voice behind me, callin' out to say does the gentleman want him? And the man turn quick-like on his heel, and be gone out the door, just like *that.*" She clutched Jem with one arm, and snapped the fingers of her free hand briefly.

"I see." The bread pudding had formed a solid mass that lay like iron in his stomach. "Did you say anything to your mistress about this man?"

She shook her head, solemn.

"No, sir. He ain't really done nothin', like I say. But he trouble me, sir, and so I study on it, comin' home, and think finally, well, I best tell you, sir, and I gets the chance."

"Ye did right," he said. "Thank you, Phaedre." He fought the urge to take Jem from her, hold him tight. "Would ye—when ye've got him to bed, will ye stay with him? Just until I come up. I'll tell your mistress I asked you to."

Her dark eyes met his with perfect understanding, and she nodded.

"Aye, sir. I keep him safe." She bobbed the shadow of a curtsy, and went up the stairs toward the room he shared with Jem, humming something soft and rhythmic to the boy.

He breathed slowly, trying to master the overwhelming urge to seize a horse from the stables, ride to Cross Creek, and search the place, going from house to house in the dark until he found Stephen Bonnet.

"Right," he said aloud. "And then what?" His fists curled up involuntarily, knowing quite well what to do, even as his mind acknowledged the futility of such a course.

He fought down rage and helplessness, the last of the whisky lighting his blood, throbbing in his temples. He stepped abruptly through the open door into the night, for it was full dark now. From this side of the house, the meadow was invisible, but he could still smell the smoke of their fires, and catch the faint trill of music on the air.

He'd known Bonnet would come again, one day. Down beside the lawn, the white bulk of Hector Cameron's mausoleum was a pale smear on the night. And safe inside it, hidden in the coffin that waited for Hector's wife, Jocasta, lay a fortune in Jacobite gold, the long-held secret of River Run.

Bonnet knew the gold existed, suspected it was on the plantation. He had tried for it once before, and failed. He was not a careful man, Bonnet—but he *was* persistent.

Roger felt his bones strain in his flesh, urgent with desire to hunt and kill the man who had raped his wife, threatened his family. But there were seventy-six people depending on him—no, seventy-seven. Vengeance warred with responsibility—and, most reluctantly, gave way.

He breathed slow and deep, feeling the knot of the rope scar tighten in his throat. No. He had to go, see the new tenants safe. The thought of sending them with Arch and Tom, while he remained behind to search for Bonnet, was tempting—but the job was his; he couldn't abandon it for the sake of a time-consuming—and likely futile—personal quest.

Nor could he leave Jem unprotected.

He must tell Duncan, though; Duncan could be trusted to take steps for the protection of River Run, to send word to the authorities in Cross Creek, to make inquiries.

And Roger would make sure that Jem was safe away, too, come morning, held before him on his saddle, kept in his sight every inch of the way to the sanctuary of the mountains.

"Who's your daddy?" he muttered, and a fresh surge of rage pulsed through his veins. "God damn it, *I* am, you bastard!"

Part Three

To Every Thing There Is a Season

16

LE MOT JUSTE

August 1773

"YE'RE SMILING TO yourself," Jamie said in my ear. "Nice, was it?"

I turned my head and opened my eyes, finding them on a level with his mouth—which was smiling, too.

"Nice," I said thoughtfully, tracing the line of his wide lower lip with the tip of one finger. "Are you being deliberately modest, or are you hoping to inspire me to raptures of praise by means of classic understatement?"

The mouth widened further, and his teeth closed gently on my questing finger for a moment before releasing it.

"Oh, modesty, to be sure," he said. "If I'd hopes of inspiring ye to raptures, it wouldna be with my words, now, would it?"

One hand ran lightly down my back in illustration.

"Well, the words *help,*" I said.

"They do?"

"Yes. Just now, I was actually trying to rank 'I love you, I like you, I worship you, I have to have my cock inside you,' in terms of their relative sincerity."

"Did I say that?" he said, sounding slightly startled.

"Yes. Weren't you listening?"

"No," he admitted. "I meant every word of it, though." His hand cupped one buttock, weighing it appreciatively. "Still do, come to that."

"What, even the last one?" I laughed and rubbed my forehead gently against his chest, feeling his jaw rest snugly on top of my head.

"Oh, aye," he said, gathering me firmly against him with a sigh. "I will say the flesh requires a bit of supper and a wee rest before I think of doin' it again, but the spirit is always willing. God, ye have the sweetest fat wee bum. Only seeing it makes me want to give it ye again directly. It's lucky ye're wed to a decrepit auld man, Sassenach, or ye'd be on your knees with your arse in the air this minute."

He smelled delectably of road dust and dried sweat and the deep musk of a man who has just enjoyed himself thoroughly.

"Nice to be missed," I said contentedly into the small space beneath his arm. "I missed you, too."

My breath tickled him and his skin shivered suddenly, like a horse shedding flies. He shifted a bit, turning me so that my head fit into the hollow of his shoulder, and sighed in matching content.

"Well, so. I see the place is still standing."

It was. It was late afternoon, the windows open, and the sun came low through the trees to make shifting patterns on the walls and linen sheets, so that we floated in a bower of murmuring shadow leaves.

"The house is standing, the barley is mostly in, and nothing's died," I said, settling myself comfortably to report. Now that we'd taken care of the most important thing, he'd want to know how the Ridge had fared in his absence.

"Mostly?" he said, neatly catching the dicey bit. "What happened? It rained, aye, but the barley should all have been in a week before."

"Not rain. Grasshoppers." I shuddered in memory. A cloud of the nasty goggle-eyed things had come whirring through, just at the end of the barley harvest. I'd gone up to my garden to pick greens, only to discover said greens seething with wedge-shaped bodies and shuffling, clawed feet, my lettuces and cabbages gnawed to ragged nubbins and the morning-glory vine on the palisade hanging in shreds.

"I ran and got Mrs. Bug and Lizzie, and we drove them off with brooms—but then they all rose up in a big cloud and headed up through the wood to the field beyond the Green Spring. They settled in the barley; you could hear the chewing for miles. It sounded like giants walking through rice." Goosebumps of revulsion rose on my shoulders, and Jamie rubbed my skin absently, his hand large and warm.

"Mmphm. Was it only the one field they got, then?"

"Oh, yes." I took a deep breath, still smelling the smoke. "We torched the field, and burnt them alive."

His body jerked in surprise, and he looked down at me.

"What? Who thought of that?"

"I did," I said, not without pride. In cold-blooded retrospect, it was a sensible thing to have done; there were other fields at risk, not only of barley, but of ripening corn, wheat, potatoes, and hay—to say nothing of the garden patches most families depended on.

In actual fact, it had been a decision made in boiling rage—sheer, bloody-minded revenge for the destruction of my garden. I would happily have ripped the wings off each insect and stamped on the remains—burning them had been nearly as good, though.

It was Murdo Lindsay's field; slow in both thought and action, Murdo hadn't had time to react properly to my announcement that I meant to fire the barley, and was still standing on the stoop of his cabin, mouth hanging open, as Brianna, Lizzie, Marsali, Mrs. Bug, and I ran round the field with armsful of faggots, lighting them from torches and hurling the blazing sticks as far as we could out into the sea of ripe, dry grain.

The dry grass went up with a crackle, and then a roar, as the fire took hold. Confused by the heat and smoke of a dozen fires, the grasshoppers flew up like sparks, igniting as their wings caught fire and vanishing into the rising column of smoke and whirling ash.

"Of course, it *would* be just then that Roger chose to arrive with the new tenants," I said, repressing an urge to laugh inappropriately at the memory. "Poor things. It was getting dark, and here they all were, standing in the woods with their bundles and children, watching this—this bally conflagration going on, and all of us dancing round barefoot with our shifts kirtled up, hooting like gibbons and covered with soot."

Jamie covered his eyes with one hand, plainly visualizing the scene. His chest shook briefly, and a wide grin spread beneath the hand.

"Oh, God. They must ha' thought Roger Mac had brought them to hell. Or to a coven meeting, at least."

A bubble of guilty laughter was forcing itself up from under my ribs.

"They did. Oh, Jamie—the looks on their faces!" I lost my grip and buried my own face in his chest. We shook together for a moment, laughing almost soundlessly.

"I *did* try to make them welcome," I said, snorting a little. "We gave them supper, and found them all places to sleep—as many as we could fit in the house, the rest spread between Brianna's cabin, the stable, and the barn. I came down quite late at night, though—I couldn't sleep, for all the excitement—and found a dozen of them praying in the kitchen."

They had been standing in a circle near the hearth, hands linked and heads bowed reverently. All the heads had snapped up at my appearance, eyes showing white in thin, haggard faces. They'd stared at me in total silence, and one of the women had let go the hand of the man beside her to hide her own hand under her apron. In another time and place, I should have thought she was reaching for some weapon—and perhaps she was, at that; I was fairly sure she was making the sign of the horns beneath the shelter of the ragged cloth.

I'd already discovered that only a few of them spoke English. I asked in my halting Gaelic whether they needed anything? They stared at me as though I had two heads, then after a moment, one of the men, a wizened creature with a thin mouth, had shaken his head the barest inch.

"Then they went right back to their praying, leaving me to skulk off back to bed."

"Ye went down in your shift?"

"Well . . . yes. I didn't expect anyone to be awake at that hour."

"Mmphm." His knuckles grazed my breast, and I could tell exactly what he was thinking. My summer night rail was thin, worn linen, and yes, all right, dammit, I supposed one *could* see through it a bit in the light, but the kitchen had been lit only by the ruddy glow of a smoored hearth.

"I dinna suppose ye went down in a proper nightcap, Sassenach?" Jamie asked, running a thoughtful hand through my hair. I'd loosened it to go to bed with him, and it was writhing off merrily in all directions, à la Medusa.

"Of course not. I had it plaited, though," I protested. "Quite respectable!"

"Oh, quite," he agreed, grinning, and pushing his fingers up into the wild mass of my hair, cradled my head in his hands and kissed me. His lips were chapped from wind and sun, but agreeably soft. He hadn't shaved since his departure and his beard was short and curly, springy to the touch.

"Well, so. They're sorted now, I expect? The tenants?" His lips brushed my cheek, and nibbled gently at my ear. I inhaled deeply.

"Ah. Oh. Yes. Arch Bug took them off in the morning; he's got them parceled out with families all over the Ridge, and already working on . . ." My train of thought temporarily derailed, and I closed my fingers by reflex in the muscle of his chest.

"And ye told Murdo I'd make it right with him, of course. About the barley?"

"Yes, of course." My drifting attention snagged momentarily and I laughed. "He just stared at me, and then nodded in a dazed sort of way, and said, oh, just as Himself liked, to be sure. I don't know if he realized even then why I'd burnt his field; perhaps he just thought I'd taken a sudden fancy to set fire to his barley."

Jamie laughed, too—a most unsettling sensation, as he had his teeth fixed in my earlobe.

"Um," I said faintly, feeling the tickle of red beard on my neck and the very warm, firm flesh beneath my palm. "The Indians. How did you manage with the Cherokee?"

"Fine."

He moved suddenly, rolling over on top of me. He was very big, and *very* warm, and he smelled of desire, strong and sharp. The leafy shadows moved across his face and shoulders, dappled the bed and the white skin of my thighs, opened wide.

"I like ye fine, Sassenach," he murmured in my ear. "I can see ye there, half-naked in your shift and your hair down, curling over your breest. . . . I love you. I wor—"

"What was that about a rest and supper?"

His hands were worming themselves under me, cupping my buttocks, squeezing, his breath soft and hot on my neck.

"I *have* to have my—"

"But—"

"Now, Sassenach." He rose up abruptly, kneeling on the bed before me. There was a faint smile on his face, but his eyes were dark blue and intent. He cupped his heavy balls in one hand, the thumb moving up and down his exigent member in a slow and thoughtful manner.

"On your knees, *a nighean,*" he said softly. "Now."

17

THE LIMITS OF POWER

From James Fraser, Esq., Fraser's Ridge
to Lord John Grey of Mount Josiah Plantation

August 14, 1773

My lord—

I write to inform you of my new Office, viz, *that of Indian Agent to the Crown, by Appointment to the Southern Department under John Stuart.*

I was originally of two Minds regarding Acceptance of this Appointment, but found my Views made more singular by Reason of a Visit by Mr. Richard Brown, a distant Neighbor, and his Brother. I expect that Mr. Higgins will already have given you an Account of their so-called Committee of Safety, and its immediate Object of arresting him.

Have you encountered such ad hoc *Bodies in Virginia? I think perhaps your Situation is not so unsettled as is our own, or that in Boston, where Mr. Higgins also reports their Presence. I hope it is not.*

I think a Person of Sense must deplore these committees in Principle. Their stated Purpose is to provide Protection from Vagabonds and Banditti, and to arrest Criminals in those Areas where no Sheriff or Constable is available. With no Law to regulate their Behavior save Self-interest, though, plainly there is Nothing to prevent an irregular Militia from becoming more of a Threat to the Citizenry than the Dangers from which it offers to preserve them.

The Appeal is plain, though, particularly in such Case as we find ourselves here, so remotely situated. The nearest Courthouse is—or was—three days' Ride, and in the constant Unrest that has followed the Regulation, Matters have decayed even from this unsatisfactory State. The Governor and his Council are in constant Conflict with the Assembly, the Circuit Court has effectually ceased to exist, Judges are no longer appointed, and there is no Sheriff of Surry County at present, the latest Holder of that Office having resigned under Threat of having his House fired.

The Sheriffs of Orange and Rowan Counties still boast Office—but their Corruption is so well known that no one may depend upon them, save those whose Interest is invested in them.

We hear frequent reports these Days of House-burnings, Assaults, and similar Alarums in the Wake of the recent War of Regulation. Governor Tryon officially pardoned some of those involved in the Conflict, but did nothing to prevent local Retribution against them; his Successor is still less able to deal with such Events—which are in any Case occurring in the Backcountry, far from his Palace in New Bern and thus the more easily ignored. (In all Justice, the Man doubtless has Troubles nearer at Hand to deal with.)

Still, while Settlers here are accustomed to defend themselves from the normal Threats of the Wilderness, the Occurrence of such random Attacks as these—and the Possibility of Irruption of the Indians, so close to the Treaty Line—is sufficient to unnerve them, and cause them to greet with Relief the Appearance of any Body willing to undertake the Role of public Protection. Hence the Vigilantes of the Committees are welcomed—at least to begin with.

I give you so much Detail by way of explaining my Thoughts regarding the Appointment. My friend Major MacDonald (late of the 32nd Cavalry) had told me that should I ultimately decline to become an Indian Agent, he would approach Mr. Richard Brown, Brown being in the way of doing substantial Trade with the Cherokee, and thus in a position of Acquaintance and presumed Trust that would predispose his Acceptance by the Indians.

My Acquaintance with Mr. Brown and his Brother inclines me to regard this Prospect with Alarm. With such Rise in Influence as such an Appointment would bring, Brown's Stature in this unsettled Region might shortly become so great that no man could easily oppose him in any Venture—and that, I think, is dangerous.

My Son-in-law astutely observes that a Man's sense of Morality tends to decrease as his Power increases, and I suspect that the Brothers Brown possess relatively little of the Former to begin with. It may be mere Hubris on my part, to assume that I have more. I have seen the corrosive Effects of Power upon a Man's Soul—and I have felt its Burden, as you will understand, having borne it so often yourself. Still, if it is a choice between myself and Richard Brown, I suppose I must resort to the old Scottish Adage that the devil you ken is better than the devil you don't.

I am likewise made uneasy at the Thought of the long Absences from Home which my new Duties must require. And yet I cannot in Conscience allow the People under my Dominion to be subject to the Vagaries and possible Injuries of Brown's Committee.

I could of course convene my own such Committee—I think you would urge such a Course—but will not. Beyond the Inconvenience and Expense of such a Move, it would be Tantamount to declaring open War with the Browns, and I think that not prudent, not if I must be frequently away from home, leaving my Family unprotected. This new Appointment, though, will extend my own Influence, and—I trust—put some Limit to the Browns' Ambitions.

So having reached this Decision, I sent Word at once to accept the Appointment, and essayed my first Visit to the Cherokee in the Office of Indian Agent during the last Month. My initial Reception was most Cordial, and I hope my Relations with the Villages will remain so.

I shall visit the Cherokee again in the Autumn. If you should have any Matters of Business that my new Office might assist, send to me regarding them, and rest assured that I shall make every Effort on your Behalf.

To more domestic Matters. Our small Population has nearly doubled, as the Result of an Influx of Settlers newly arrived from Scotland. While most desirable, this Incursion has caused no little Turmoil, the Newcomers being Fisher-folk from the Coast. To these, the Mountain Wilderness is full of Threat and Mystery, such Threats and Mysteries being personified by Pigs and Plowshares.

(With regard to Pigs, I am not sure but that I share their Views. The white Sow has lately taken up Residence beneath the Foundation of my House and there engages in such debauches that our Dinner is disturbed daily by hellish Noises resembling the Sounds of Souls in Torment. These Souls apparently being torn Limb from Limb and devoured by Demons beneath our Feet.)

Since I speak of Matters hellish, I must observe that our Newcomers are also, alas, stern Sons of the Covenant, to whom a Papist such as myself presents himself as one fully furnished with Horns and Tail. You will recall one Thomas Christie, I think, from Ardsmuir? By comparison of these stiff-necked

Gentlemen, Mr. Christie appears the Soul of compassionate Generosity.

I had not thought to thank Providence for the Fact that my Son-in-law is Presbyterian by inclination, but I see now how true it is that the Almighty does indeed have Designs beyond the Ken of us poor mortals. While even Roger MacKenzie is a sadly depraved Libertine by their Lights, the new Tenants are at least able to speak to him without the Necessity of small Gestures and Signs intended to repel Evil, which are the constant Accompaniment to their Conversations with myself.

As for their Behavior with Respect to my Wife, you would think her the Witch of Endor, if not the Great Whore of Babylon. This, because they consider the Furnishments of her Surgery to be "Enchantments," and were appalled at witnessing the Entrance therein of a Number of Cherokee, gaily festooned for visiting, who had come to Trade in such Arcana as Snakes' Fangs and the Gallbladders of Bears.

My wife begs me express her Pleasure at your kind Compliments regarding Mr. Higgins's improved Health—and still more, at your Offer to procure medicinal Substances for her from your Friend in Philadelphia. She bids me send you the enclosed List. As I cast an Eye upon this, I suspect that your supplying of her Desires will do nothing to allay the Suspicions of the Fisher-folk, but pray do not desist on that Account, as I think nothing save Time and Custom will decrease their Fears of her.

My Daughter likewise bids me express her Gratitude for your Present of the Phosphorus. I am not certain that I share this Sentiment, given that her Experiments with the Substance prove frighteningly incendiary to date. Fortunately, none of the Newcomers observed these Experiments, or they would be in no Doubt that Satan is indeed a particular Friend to me and mine.

In happier Vein, I congratulate you upon your latest Vintage, which is indeed drinkable. I send in return a Jug of Mrs. Bug's best Cider, and a Bottle of the barrel-aged Three-year-old, which I flatter myself you will find less corrosive to the Gullet than the last Batch.

Your ob't. servant,
J. Fraser

Postscriptum: I have had Report of a Gentleman who by Description resembles one Stephen Bonnet, this Man appearing briefly in Cross Creek last Month. If it was indeed the Gentleman, his Business is unknown, and he seems to have vanished without Trace; my Uncle-in-law, Duncan Innes, has made Inquiries in the Area, but writes to tell me that these have proved fruitless. Should you hear of anything in this Regard, I pray you will advise me at once.

18

VROOM!

From the Dreambook

Last night I dreamed of running water. Generally, this means I drank too much before I went to bed, but this was different. The water was coming from the faucet in the sink at home. I was helping Mama do the dishes; she was running hot water from the hose-sprayer over the plates, then handing them to me to dry; I could feel the hot china through the dish towel, and feel the mist of water on my face.

Mama's hair was curling up like mad because of the humidity, and the pattern on the plates was the lumpy pink roses of the good wedding china. Mama didn't let me wash that until I was ten or so, for fear I'd drop it, and when I got to wash it at last, I was so proud!

I can still see every last thing in the china cabinet in the living room: Mama's great-grandfather's hand-painted cake stand (he was an artist, she said, and won a competition with that cake stand, a hundred years ago), the dozen crystal goblets that Daddy's mother left him, along with the cut-glass olive dish and the cup and saucer hand-painted with violets and gilt rims.

I was standing in front of it, putting away the china—but we didn't keep the china in that cabinet; we kept it in the shelf over the oven—and the water was overflowing from the sink in the kitchen, and running out across the floor, puddling round my feet. Then it started to rise, and I was sloshing back and forth to the kitchen, kicking up the water so it sparkled like the cut-glass olive dish. The water got deeper and deeper, but nobody seemed to be worried; I wasn't.

The water was warm, hot, in fact, I could see steam rising off it.

That's all there was to the dream—but when I got up this morning, the water in the basin was so cold I had to warm water in a pan on the fire before I washed Jemmy. All the time I was checking the water on the fire, I kept remembering my dream, and all those gallons and gallons of hot, running water.

What I wonder is, these dreams I have about then—they seem so vivid and detailed; more than the dreams I have about now. Why do I see things that don't exist anywhere except inside my brain?

What I wonder about the dreams is—all the new inventions people think up—how many of those things are made by people like me—like us? How many "inventions" are really memories, of the things we once knew? And—how many of us are there?

"IT ISN'T REALLY that hard to have hot, running water. In theory."

"No? I suppose not." Roger only half-heard, concentrated as he was on the object taking shape beneath his knife.

"I mean, it would be a big, horrible job to *do.* But it's simple in concept. Dig ditches or build sluices—and around here, it would probably be sluices. . . ."

"It would?" Here was the tricky bit. He held his breath, chiseling delicate, tiny slivers of wood away, one shaving at a time.

"No metal," Bree said patiently. "If you had metal, you could make surface pipes. But I bet there isn't enough metal in the whole colony of North Carolina to make the piping you'd need to bring water from the creek to the Big House. Let alone a boiler! And if there was, it would cost a fortune."

"Mmm." Feeling that this was perhaps not an adequate response, Roger added hastily, "But there's some metal available. Jamie's still, for instance."

His wife snorted.

"Yeah. I asked him where he got it—he said he won it in a high-stakes game of loo against a ship's captain in Charleston. Think I could travel four hundred miles to bet my silver bracelet against a few hundred feet of rolled copper?"

One more sliver . . . two . . . the smallest scrape with the tip of the knife . . . ah. The tiny circle came free of the matrix. It turned!

"Er . . . sure," he said, belatedly realizing that she'd asked him a question. "Why not?"

She burst out laughing.

"You haven't heard one single word I've said, have you?"

"Oh, sure I have," he protested. "'Ditch,' ye said. And 'water.' I'm sure I remember that one."

She snorted again, though mildly.

"Well, you'd have to do it, anyway."

"Do what?" His thumb sought the little wheel, and set it spinning.

"Gamble. No one's going to let *me* into a high-stakes card game."

"Thank God," he said, in reflex.

"Bless your little Presbyterian heart," she said tolerantly, shaking her head. "You're not any kind of a gambler, Roger, are you?"

"Oh, and you are, I suppose." He said it jokingly, wondering even as he did so why he should feel vaguely reproached by her remark.

She merely smiled at that, wide mouth curving in a way that suggested untold volumes of wicked enterprise. He felt a slight sense of unease at that. She *was* a gambler, though so far . . . He glanced involuntarily at the large, charred spot in the middle of the table.

"That was an accident," she said defensively.

"Oh, aye. At least your eyebrows have grown back."

"Hmpf. I'm nearly there. One more batch—"

"That's what ye said last time." He was aware that he was treading on dangerous ground, but seemed unable to stop.

She took a slow, deep breath, gazing at him through slightly narrowed eyes, like one taking the range before firing off some major piece of artillery. Then she seemed to think better of whatever she had been going to say; her features relaxed and she stretched out her hand toward the object he was holding.

"What's that you've been making?"

"Just a wee bawbee for Jem." He let her take it, feeling the warmth of modest pride. "The wheels all turn."

"Mine, Daddy?" Jemmy had been wallowing on the floor with Adso the cat, who was tolerant of small children. Hearing his name, though, he abandoned the cat, who promptly escaped through the window, and popped up to see the new toy.

"Oh, look!" Brianna ran the little car over the palm of her hand and lifted it, letting all four tiny wheels spin free. Jem grabbed eagerly for it, pulling at the wheels.

"Careful, careful! You'll pull them off! Here, let me show you." Crouching, Roger took the car and rolled it along the hearthstones. "See? Vroom. Vroom-vroom!"

"Broom!" Jemmy echoed. "Lemme do it, Daddy, let me!"

Roger surrendered the toy to Jemmy, smiling.

"Broom! Broom-broom!" The little boy shoved the car enthusiastically, then, losing his grip on it, watched open-mouthed as it zoomed to the end of the hearthstone by itself, hit the edge, and flipped over. Squealing with delight, he scampered after the new toy.

Still smiling, Roger glanced up, to see Brianna looking after Jem, a rather odd expression on her face. She felt his eyes on her, and looked down at him.

"Vroom?" she said quietly, and he felt a small internal jolt, like a punch in the stomach.

"Whatsit, Daddy, what's it?" Jemmy had recaptured the toy and ran up to him, clutching it to his chest.

"It's a . . . a . . ." he began, helpless. It was in fact a crude replica of a Morris Minor, but even the word "car," let alone "automobile," had no meaning here. And the internal combustion engine, with its pleasantly evocative noises, was at least a century away.

"I guess it's a vroom, honey," said Bree, a distinct tone of sympathy in her voice. He felt the gentle weight of her hand, resting on his head.

"Er . . . yeah, that's right," he said, and cleared a thickening in his throat. "It's a vroom."

"Broom," said Jemmy happily, and knelt to roll it down the hearth again. "Broom-broom!"

STEAM. *It would have to be steam- or wind-powered; a windmill would work, maybe, to pump water into the system, but if I want hot water, there would be steam anyway—why not use it?*

Containment is the problem; wood burns and leaks, clay won't hold against pressure. I need metal, that's all there is to it. What would Mrs. Bug do, I wonder, if I took the laundry cauldron? Well, I know what she'd do, and a steam explosion is no comparison; besides, we do need to do *the laundry. I'll have to dream up something else.*

19

MAKING HAY

MAJOR MACDONALD returned on the final day of haymaking. I was just maneuvering my way along the side of the house with an immense basket of bread, when I saw him near the trailhead, tying up his horse to a tree. He lifted his hat to me and bowed, then came across the dooryard, looking curiously round at the preparations taking place.

We had set up trestles under the chestnut trees, with boards laid across them for tables, and a constant stream of women scurried to and fro like ants between the house and yard, fetching food. The sun was setting, and the men would be in soon for a celebratory feast; filthy, exhausted, starving—and exhilarated by the end of their labors.

I greeted the Major with a nod, and accepted with relief his offer to carry the bread to the tables for me.

"Haying, is it?" he said, in answer to my explanation. A nostalgic smile spread across his weathered face. "I remember the haymaking, from when I was a lad. But that was in Scotland, aye? We'd seldom such glorious weather as this for it." He looked up into the blazing deep blue bowl of the August sky above. It really was perfect haying weather, hot and dry.

"It's wonderful," I said, sniffing appreciatively. The scent of fresh hay was everywhere—and so was the hay; there were shimmering mounds of it in every shed, everyone carried bits of it on their clothes, and small trails of scattered straw lay everywhere. Now the smell of cut, dry hay was mingled with the delectable scent of the barbecue that had been simmering underground overnight, the fresh bread, and the heady tang of Mrs. Bug's cider. Marsali and Bree were bringing down jugs of it from the springhouse, where it had been cooling, along with buttermilk and beer.

"I see I've chosen my time well," the Major remarked, viewing all this effort with approval.

"If you came to eat, yes," I said, rather amused. "If you came to talk to Jamie, I rather think you'll have to wait until tomorrow."

He looked at me, puzzled, but had no opportunity to inquire further; I had caught another glimpse of movement at the trailhead. The Major turned, seeing the direction of my glance, and frowned slightly.

"Why, it's that fellow with the brand on his face," he said, wary disapproval in his voice. "I saw him down at Coopersville, but he saw me first, and steered well clear. Will ye have me drive him off, mum?" He set down the bread and was already settling his sword belt on his hip, when I gripped his forearm.

"You'll do no such thing, Major," I said sharply. "Mr. Higgins is a friend."

He gave me a flat look, then dropped his arm.

"As ye like, Mrs. Fraser, of course," he said coolly, and picking up the bread again, went off toward the tables.

Rolling my eyes in exasperation, I went to greet the newcomer. Plainly Bobby Higgins could have joined the Major on the path to the Ridge; just as plainly, he had chosen not to. He had become a little more familiar with mules, I saw; he was riding one and leading another, laden with a promising array of panniers and boxes.

"His Lordship's compliments, mum," he said, saluting me smartly as he slid off. From the corner of my eye, I saw MacDonald watching—and his small start of recognition at the military gesture. So, now he knew Bobby for a soldier, and doubtless would ferret out his background in short order. I repressed a sigh; I couldn't mend matters; they'd have to settle it between themselves—if there was anything to settle.

"You're looking well, Bobby," I said, smiling as I pushed aside my disquiet. "No difficulties with the riding, I hope?"

"Oh, no, mum!" He beamed. "And I's not fallen out once since I left you last!" "Fallen out" meant "fainted," and I congratulated him on the state of his health, looking him over as he unloaded the pack mule with deft efficiency. He did seem much better; pink and fresh-skinned as a child, bar the ugly brand on his cheek.

"Yonder lobsterback," he said, affecting insouciance as he set down a box. "He's known to ye, is he, mum?"

"That's Major MacDonald," I said, carefully not looking in the Major's direction; I could feel his stare boring into my back. "Yes. He . . . does things for the Governor, I believe. Not regular army, I mean; he's a half-pay officer."

That bit of information seemed to ease Bobby's mind a bit. He took a breath, as though to say something, but then thought better of it. Instead, he reached into his shirt and withdrew a sealed letter, which he handed over.

"That's for you," he explained. "From his Lordship. Is Miss Lizzie by any chance about?" His eyes were already searching the flock of girls and women readying the tables.

"Yes, she was in the kitchen last I saw," I replied, a small uneasy feeling skittering down my backbone. "She'll be out in a minute. But . . . you do know she's betrothed, don't you, Bobby? Her fiancé will be coming with the other men for supper."

He met my eyes and smiled with singular sweetness.

"Oh, aye, mum, I know that well enough. On'y thought as I s'ould thank her for her kindness when I last was here."

"Oh," I said, not trusting that smile in the slightest. Bobby was a very handsome lad, blind eye or not—and he had been a soldier. "Well . . . good."

Before I could say more, I caught the sound of male voices, coming through the trees. It wasn't precisely singing; sort of a rhythmic chant. I wasn't sure what it was—there was a lot of Gaelic "Ho-ro!" and the like—but all of them seemed to be bellowing along in a cordial fashion.

Haymaking was a novel concept to the new tenants, who were much more accustomed to rake kelp than scythe grass. Jamie, Arch, and Roger had shepherded them through the process, though, and I had been asked to stitch no more than a handful of minor wounds, so I assumed it had been a success—no hands or feet lopped off, a few shouting matches, but no fistfights, and no more than the usual amount of hay trampled or ruined.

All of them seemed in good spirits as they poured into the dooryard, bedraggled, sweat-soaked, and thirsty as sponges. Jamie was in the thick of them, laughing and staggering as someone pushed him. He caught sight of me, and a huge grin split his sun-browned face. In a stride, he had reached me and swept me into an exuberant embrace, redolent of hay, horses, and sweat.

"Done, by God!" he said, and kissed me soundly. "Christ, I need a drink. And nay, that's no blasphemy, wee Roger," he added, with a glance behind him. "It's heartfelt gratitude and desperate need, aye?"

"Aye. First things first, though, hm?" Roger had appeared behind Jamie, his voice so hoarse that it was barely audible in the general uproar. He swallowed, grimacing.

"Oh, aye." Jamie shot a quick look at Roger, assessing, then shrugged and strode out into the center of the yard.

"Eìsd ris! Eìsd ris!" bellowed Kenny Lindsay, seeing him. Evan and Murdo joined him, clapping their hands and shouting "Hear him!" loudly enough that the crowd began to subside and pay attention.

"I say the prayer from my mouth,
I say the prayer from my heart,
I say the prayer to Thee Thyself,
O, Healing Hand, O Son of the God of salvation."

He didn't raise his voice much above its normal speaking level, but everyone quieted at once, so the words rang clear.

"Thou Lord God of the angels,
Spread over me Thy linen robe;
Shield me from every famine,
Free me from every spectral shape.
Strengthen me in every good,
Encompass me in every strait,
Safeguard me in every ill,
And from every enmity restrain me."

There was a stirring of faint approval in the crowd; I saw a few of the fisher-folk bow their heads, though their eyes stayed fixed on him.

"Be Thou between me and all things grisly,
Be Thou between me and all things mean,
Be Thou between me and all things gruesome
Coming darkly toward me.

"O God of the weak,
O God of the lowly,
O God of the righteous,
O shield of homesteads:
Thou art calling upon us
In the voice of glory,
With the mouth of mercy
Of Thy beloved Son."

I glanced at Roger, who was nodding slightly with approval, as well. Evidently, they'd agreed on it together. Sensible; it would be a prayer familiar in form to the fisher-folk, and nothing specifically Catholic about it.

Jamie spread his arms, quite unconsciously, and the breeze caught the worn damp linen of his shirt as he tilted back his head and raised his face to the sky, open with joy.

"O may I find rest everlasting
In the home of Thy Trinity,
In the Paradise of the godly,
In the Sun-garden of Thy love!"

"Amen!" said Roger, as loudly as he could, and there were gratified murmurs of "amen" round the yard. Then Major MacDonald raised the tankard of cider he was holding, called *"Slàinte!"* and drained it.

Festivity became general after that. I found myself sitting on a cask, Jamie on the grass at my feet, with a platter of food and a constantly refilled mug of cider.

"Bobby Higgins is here," I told him, catching sight of Bobby in the midst of a small group of admiring young ladies. "Do you see Lizzie anywhere?"

"No," he said, stifling a yawn. "Why?"

"He asked for her particularly."

"Then I'm sure he'll find her. Will ye have a bit o' meat,

Sassenach?" He held up a large rib bone, brow cocked inquiringly.

"I've had some," I assured him, and he at once tore into it, addressing himself to the vinegar-spiced barbecue as though he hadn't eaten for a week.

"Has Major MacDonald spoken to you?"

"No," he said, mouth full, and swallowed. "He'll keep. There's Lizzie—wi' the McGillivrays."

I felt reassured by that. The McGillivrays—particularly *Frau* Ute—would certainly discourage any inappropriate attentions to their new intended daughter-in-law. Lizzie was chatting and laughing with Robin McGillivray, who was smiling at her in fatherly fashion, while his son Manfred ate and drank with single-minded appetite. *Frau* Ute, I saw, was keeping a sharp and interested eye on Lizzie's father, who was sitting on the porch nearby, cozily side by side with a tall, rather plain-faced German lady.

"Who's that with Joseph Wemyss?" I asked, nudging Jamie with my knee to direct his attention.

He narrowed his eyes against the sun's glare, looking, then shrugged.

"I dinna ken. She's German; she must ha' come with Ute McGillivray. Matchmaking, aye?" He tilted up his mug and drank, sighing with bliss.

"Do you think so?" I looked at the strange woman with interest. She certainly seemed to be getting on well with Joseph—and he with her. His thin face was alight as he gestured, explaining something to her, and her neatly capped head was bent toward him, a smile on her lips.

I didn't always approve of Ute McGillivray's methods, which tended toward the juggernaut, but I had to admire the painstaking intricacy of her plans. Lizzie and Manfred would marry next spring, and I had wondered how Joseph would fare then; Lizzie was his whole life.

He might, of course, go with her when she married. She and Manfred would simply live in the McGillivrays' large house, and I imagined that they would find room for Joseph, too. Still, he would be torn, not wanting to leave us—and while any able-bodied man could always be of use on a homestead, he was by no means a natural farmer, let alone a gunsmith, like Manfred and his father. If he himself were to wed, though . . .

I gave Ute McGillivray a glance, and saw her watching Mr. Wemyss and his inamorata with the contented expression of a puppet master whose puppets are dancing precisely to her tune.

Someone had left a pitcher of cider beside us. I refilled Jamie's mug, then my own. It was wonderful, a dark, cloudy amber, sweet and pungent and with the bite of a particularly subtle serpent to it. I let the cool liquid trickle down my throat and bloom inside my head like a silent flower.

There was much talk and laughter, and I noticed that while the new tenants still kept to their own family groups, there was now a little more blending, as the men who had been working side by side for the last two weeks maintained their cordial relations, these social courtesies fueled by cider. The new tenants mostly regarded wine as a mocker, strong drink—whisky, rum, or brandy—as raging, but everyone drank beer and cider. Cider was wholesome, one of the women had told me, handing a mug to her small son. I gave it half an hour, I thought, sipping slowly, before they started dropping like flies.

Jamie made a small amused sound, and I looked down at him. He nodded at the far side of the dooryard, and I looked to see that Bobby Higgins had disentangled himself from his admirers, and by some alchemical legerdemain had managed to abstract Lizzie from the midst of the McGillivrays. They were standing in the shadow of the chestnut trees, talking.

I looked back at the McGillivrays. Manfred was leaning against the foundation of the house, head nodding over his plate. His father had curled up beside him on the ground and was snoring peacefully. The girls chatted around them, passing food to and fro over the drooping heads of their husbands, all in various stages of impending somnolence. Ute had moved to the porch, and was talking to Joseph and his companion.

I glanced back. Lizzie and Bobby were only talking, and there was a respectful distance between them. But there was something about the way he bent toward her, and the way she half-turned away from him, then back, swinging a fold of her skirt one-handed . . .

"Oh, dear," I said. I shifted a little, getting my feet under me, but unsure whether I ought really to go and interrupt them. After all, they were in plain sight, and—

"Three things astonish me, nay four, sayeth the prophet." Jamie's hand squeezed my thigh, and I looked down to see that he was also watching the couple under the chestnut trees, his eyes half-closed. "The way of an eagle in the air, the way of a serpent on the rock, the way of a ship in the midst of the sea—and the way of a man with a maid."

"Oh, so I'm not imagining it," I said dryly. "Do you think I'd best do something?"

"Mmphm." He took a deep breath and straightened up, shaking his head vigorously to wake himself. "Ah. No, Sassenach. If wee Manfred willna take the trouble to guard his woman, it's no your place to do it for him."

"Yes, I quite agree. I'm only thinking, if Ute should see them . . . or Joseph?" I wasn't sure what Mr. Wemyss would do; I thought Ute would probably make a major scene.

"Oh." He blinked, swaying a little. "Aye, I suppose ye're right." He turned his head, searching, then spotting Ian, lifted his chin in summons.

Ian had been sprawled dreamily on the grass a few feet away, next to a pile of greasy rib bones, but now rolled over and crawled obligingly to us.

"Mm?" he said. His thick brown hair had fallen half out of its binding, and several cowlicks were sticking straight up, the rest fallen disreputably over one eye.

Jamie nodded in the direction of the chestnut trees.

"Go and ask wee Lizzie to mend your hand, Ian."

Ian glanced blearily down at his hand; there was a fresh scratch across the back of it, though it was long since clotted. Then he looked in the direction Jamie indicated.

"Oh," he said. He remained on hands and knees, eyes narrowed thoughtfully, then slowly rose to his feet, and pulled the binding off his hair. Casually shoving it back with one hand, he strolled in the direction of the chestnut trees.

They were much too far away to hear anything, but we could see. Bobby and Lizzie parted like the waves of the Red

Sea as Ian's tall, gangly form stepped purposefully between them. The three seemed to chat amiably for a moment, then Lizzie and Ian departed for the house, Lizzie giving Bobby a casual wave of the hand—and a brief, backward glance. Bobby stood for a moment looking after her, rocking thoughtfully on his heels, then shook his head and made for the cider.

The cider was taking its toll. I'd expected every man in the place to be laid out cold by nightfall; during haying, men commonly fell asleep in their plates from sheer exhaustion. As it was, there was still plenty of talk and laughter, but the soft twilight glow beginning to suffuse the dooryard showed an increasing number of bodies strewn in the grass.

Rollo was gnawing contentedly on Ian's discarded bones. Brianna sat a little way away; Roger lay with his head in her lap, sound asleep. The collar of his shirt was open, the ragged rope scar still vivid across his neck. Bree smiled at me, her hand gently stroking his glossy black hair, picking bits of hay out of it. Jemmy was nowhere to be seen—neither was Germain, as I ascertained with a quick look around. Luckily the phosphorus was under lock and key, in the top of my highest cupboard.

Jamie laid his own head against my thigh, warm and heavy, and I put my hand on his hair, smiling back at Bree. I heard him snort faintly, and looked in the direction of his gaze.

"For such a wee small lass, yon Lizzie does cause a good deal of trouble," he said.

Bobby Higgins was standing beside one of the tables, drinking cider, and quite evidently unaware that he was being stalked by the Beardsley twins. The two of them were slinking like foxes through the wood, not quite out of sight, converging on him from opposite directions.

One—Jo, probably—stepped out suddenly beside Bobby, startling him into spilling his drink. He frowned, wiping at the wet splotch on his shirt, while Jo leaned close, obviously muttering menaces and warnings. Looking offended, Bobby turned away from him, only to be confronted by Kezzie on the other side.

"I'm not sure it's Lizzie who's causing the trouble," I said defensively. "She only talked to him, after all." Bobby's face was growing noticeably flushed. He set down the mug he'd been drinking from and drew himself up a little, one hand folding into a fist.

The Beardsleys crowded closer, with the evident intention of forcing him into the wood. Glancing warily from one twin to the other, he took a step back, putting a solid tree trunk at his back.

I glanced down; Jamie was watching through half-closed lids, with an expression of dreamy detachment. He sighed deeply, his eyes closed altogether, and he went suddenly and completely limp, the weight of him heavy against me.

The reason for this sudden absquatulation loomed up a second later: MacDonald, ruddy with food and cider, his red coat glowing like a cinder in the sunset light. He looked down at Jamie, peacefully slumbering against my leg, and shook his head. He turned slowly round, surveying the scene.

"Strewth," he said mildly. "I'll tell ye, mum, I've seen battlefields with much less carnage."

"Oh, have you?" His appearance had distracted me, but at the mention of "carnage," I glanced back. Bobby and the Beardsley twins had disappeared, vanished like wisps of mist in the gloaming. Well, if they were beating each other to pulp in the wood, I was sure I'd hear about it before too long.

With a small shrug, MacDonald bent, took Jamie by the shoulders, and eased him off me, laying him down in the grass with surprising gentleness.

"May I?" he asked politely, and upon my nod of assent, sat down beside me on the other side, arms companionably hooked round his knees.

He was neatly dressed, as always, wig and all, but the collar of his shirt was grimy and the skirts of his coat frayed at the hem and spattered with mud.

"A great deal of travel these days, Major?" I asked, making conversation. "You look rather tired, if you'll pardon my mentioning it."

I had surprised him in the middle of a yawn; he swallowed it, blinking, then laughed.

"Aye, mum. I've been in the saddle for the last month, and seen a bed perhaps one night in three."

He did look tired, even in the soft sunset light; the lines of his face were cut deep with fatigue, the flesh beneath his eyes sagging and smudged. He was not a handsome man, but normally had a brash self-assurance that lent him an attractive air. Now he looked what he was: a half-pay soldier pushing fifty, lacking a regiment or regular duty, struggling for any small connections that might hold some hope of advancement.

I wouldn't normally have spoken to him of his business, but sympathy moved me to ask, "Are you working a lot on behalf of Governor Martin these days?"

He nodded, and took another gulp of cider, breathing deeply after it.

"Aye, mum. The Governor has been kind enough to charge me with bringing him news of conditions in the backcountry—and has done me the signal favor of accepting my advice, now and then." He glanced at Jamie, who had curled himself up like a hedgehog and commenced to snore, and smiled.

"With regard to my husband's appointment as Indian Agent, you mean? We do thank you, Major."

He waved a casual hand in dismissal of my thanks.

"Ah, no, mum; that had nothing to do wi' the Governor, save indirectly. Such appointments are the province of the Superintendent of the Southern Department. Though it is of course a matter of interest to the Governor," he added, taking another sip, "to hear news of the Indians."

"I'm sure he'll tell you all about it in the morning," I assured him, with a nod at Jamie.

"Indeed, mum." He hesitated for a moment. "Would ye ken . . . did Mr. Fraser perhaps mention, in his conversations in the villages—was there any mention of . . . burnings?"

I sat up straight, the cider buzz disappearing from my head.

"What's happened? Have there been more?"

He nodded, and rubbed a hand tiredly down his face, scrubbing at the sprout of whiskers.

"Aye, two—but the one was a barn-burning, down below Salem. One o' the Moravian brethren's. And from all I can learn of the matter, 'twas likely some of the Scotch-Irish Presbyterians who've settled in Surry County. There's a wee arsebite of a preacher who's got them riled about the Moravians—Godless heathen that they are—" He grinned suddenly at that, but then sobered again.

"There's been trouble brewing in Surry County for months. To the point that the brethren have been petitioning the Governor to redraw the boundary lines, so as to put them all in Rowan County. The line between Surry and Rowan goes right through their land, ken? And the sheriff in Surry is . . . " He twiddled a hand.

"Perhaps not so keen in the performance of his duty as he might be?" I suggested. "At least where the Moravians are concerned?"

"He's the arsebite's cousin," MacDonald said, and drained his cup. "Ye've had no trouble wi' your new tenants, by the way?" he added, lowering it. He smiled crookedly, looking round the dooryard at the small groups of women, chattering contentedly as their men slept by their feet. "It would appear ye've made them welcome."

"Well, they are Presbyterians, and fairly vehement about it—but they haven't tried to burn the house down yet, at least."

I took a quick glance at the porch, where Mr. Wemyss and his companion still sat, heads close in conversation. I thought Mr. Wemyss was probably the only man still conscious, bar the Major himself. The lady was plainly a German, but not, I thought, a Moravian; they very seldom married outside their community, nor did the women often travel far.

"Unless you think the Presbyterians have formed a gang for the purpose of purging the countryside of Papists and Lutherans—and you *don't* think that, do you?"

He smiled briefly at that, though without much humor.

"No. But then, I was raised Presbyterian myself, mum."

"Oh," I said. "Er . . . a drop more cider, Major?"

He held out his cup without demur.

"The other burning—that seems much like the others," he said, graciously choosing to overlook my remark. "An isolated homestead. A man living alone. But this one was just over the Treaty Line."

This last was said with a significant glance, and I looked

involuntarily at Jamie. He'd told me that the Cherokee were upset about settlers intruding into their territory.

"I shall ask your husband in the morning, of course, mum," MacDonald said, correctly interpreting my glance. "But perhaps ye'd ken whether he's heard any references . . . ?"

"Veiled threats from a Snowbird chief," I confessed. "He wrote to John Stuart about them. But nothing specific. When did this latest burning happen?"

He shrugged.

"No telling. I heard of it three weeks ago, but the man who told me had heard of it a month before that—and he'd not seen it, only heard from someone else."

He scratched thoughtfully at his jaw.

"Someone should go and inspect the place, perhaps."

"Mm," I said, not bothering to hide the skepticism in my voice. "And you think it's Jamie's job, do you?"

"I shouldna be so presumptuous as to instruct Mr. Fraser in his duties, mum," he said, with the hint of a smile. "But I will suggest to him that the situation may be of interest, aye?"

"Yes, you do that," I muttered. Jamie had planned another quick trip to the Snowbird villages, squeezed in between harvesting and the onset of the cold weather. The notion of marching into the village and quizzing Bird-who-sings-in-the-morning about a burned homestead seemed more than slightly risky, viewed from my perspective.

A slight chill made me shiver, and I gulped the rest of my own cider, wishing suddenly that it was hot. The sun was fully set now, and the air had grown cool, but that wasn't what was cooling my blood.

What if MacDonald's suspicions were right? If the Cherokee had been burning homesteads? And if Jamie were to show up, asking inconvenient questions. . . .

I looked at the house, standing solid and serene, its windows glowing with candlelight, a pale bulwark against the darkening woods beyond.

It is with grief that the news is received of the deaths by fire of James MacKenzie Fraser and his wife, Claire Fraser, in a conflagration that destroyed their house. . . .

The fireflies were coming out, drifting like cool green sparks in the shadows, and I looked upward involuntarily, to see a spray of red and yellow ones from the chimney. Whenever I thought of that gruesome clipping—and I tried not to, nor to count the days between now and January 21 of 1776—I had thought of the fire as occurring by accident. Such accidents were more than common, ranging from hearth fires run amok and candlesticks tipped over, to blazes caused by the summer lightning storms. It hadn't consciously occurred to me before that it might be a deliberate act—an act of murder.

I moved my foot enough to nudge Jamie. He stirred in his sleep, reached out one hand, and clasped it warmly round my ankle, then subsided with a contented groan.

"Stand between me and all things grisly," I said, half-under my breath.

"Slàinte," said the Major, and drained his cup again.

20

DANGEROUS GIFTS

PROPELLED BY MAJOR MacDonald's news, Jamie and Ian departed two days later for a quick visit to Bird-who-sings-in-the-morning, and the Major went off on his further mysterious errands, leaving me with Bobby Higgins for assistance.

I was dying to dig into the crates Bobby had brought, but what with one thing and another—the white pig's demented attempt to eat Adso, a goat with infected teats, a strange green mold that had got into the last batch of cheese, the completion of a much-needed summer kitchen, and a stern conversation with the Beardsleys regarding the treatment of guests, among other things—it was more than a week before I found leisure to unpack Lord John's present and read his letter.

September 4, 1773

From Lord John Grey, Mount Josiah Plantation
To Mrs. James Fraser

My dear Madam—

I trust that the Articles you requested will have arrived intact. Mr. Higgins is somewhat nervous of carrying the Oil of Vitriol, as I understand he has had some evil Experience connected with it, but we have packed the Bottle with some Care, leaving it sealed as it came from England.

After examining the exquisite Drawings you sent—do I detect your daughter's elegant Hand in them?—I rode to Williamsburg, in order to consult with a famous Glassmaker who abides there under the nomen (doubtless fabulous) of Blogweather. Mr. Blogweather allowed that the Pelican Retort would be simplicity itself, scarcely a fair Test of his Skill, but was enchanted by the Requirements of the distilling Apparatus, particularly the detachable Coil. He apprehended immediately the Desirability of such a Device in case of Breakage, and has made three of them.

Pray consider these my Gift—a most insignificant Demonstration of my abiding Gratitude for your many Kindnesses, both toward myself and Mr. Higgins.

Your most humble and obedient servant,
John Grey

Postscriptum: I have thus far restrained my sense of vulgar Curiosity, but I do venture to hope that on some future Occasion, you may possibly gratify me by explaining the Purpose to which you intend these Articles be put.

THEY HAD PACKED WITH some care. Pried open, the crates proved to be filled with an immense quantity of straw, the bits of glassware and sealed bottles gleaming within, cradled like roc's eggs.

"You *will* be careful with that, won't 'ee, mum?" Bobby inquired anxiously, as I lifted out a squat, heavy, brown-glass bottle, the cork heavily sealed with red wax. "It's turrible noxious, that stuff."

"Yes, I know." Standing on tiptoe, I boosted the bottle up onto a high shelf, safe from marauding children or cats. "Have you seen it used, then, Bobby?"

His lips drew in tight, and he shook his head.

"Not to say used, mum. But I've seen what it *does.* Was a . . . a lass, in London, what I come to know a bit, whilst we was a-waitin' the ship to carry us to America. Half her face pretty and smooth as a buttercup but t'other side was so scarred you could scarce look at it. Like as it was melted in a fire, but she said 'twas vitriol." He glanced up at the bottle, and swallowed visibly. "Another whore'd thrown it on her, she said, 'cause of jealousy."

He shook his head again, sighing, and reached for the broom to sweep up the scattered straw.

"Well, you needn't worry," I assured him. "I don't propose to throw it at anyone."

"Oh, no, mum!" He was quite shocked. "I s'ould never think that!"

I disregarded this reassurance, involved in delving for more treasure.

"Oh, *look,*" I said, enchanted. I held in my hands the fruit of Mr. Blogweather's artistry: a globe of glass, the size of my head, blown to perfect symmetry and lacking even the hint of a bubble. There was a faint blue tinge to the glass, and I could see my own distorted reflection, wide-nosed and bug-eyed, like a mermaid peering out.

"Aye, mum," said Bobby, dutifully peering at the retort. "It's, er . . . big, in't it?"

"It's perfect. Just perfect!" Rather than being cut off cleanly from the blower's pipe, the neck of the globe had been drawn out into a thick-walled tube about two inches long and an inch in diameter. The edges and interior surface of this had been . . . sanded? Ground? I'd no idea what Mr. Blogweather had done, but the result was a silky, opaque surface that would form a lovely seal when a similarly finished piece was inserted into it.

My hands were damp with excitement and nervousness, lest I drop the precious thing. I clutched a fold of my apron round it, and turned to and fro, debating where best to put it. I hadn't expected one so large; I should need Bree or one of the men to make me a suitable support.

"It has to go over a small fire," I explained, frowning at the little brazier I used for brewing. "But the temperature is important; a charcoal bed may be too hard to keep at a steady heat." I placed the big ball in my cupboard, safely behind a row of bottles. "I think it will have to be an alcohol lamp—but it's bigger than I thought, I'll have to have a good-size lamp to heat it. . . ."

I became aware that Bobby was not listening to my babbling, his attention having been distracted by something outside. He was frowning at something, and I came up behind him, peering through the open window to see what it was.

I should have guessed; Lizzie Wemyss was out on the grass, churning butter under the chestnut trees, and Manfred McGillivray was with her.

I glanced at the pair, engaged in cheerful conversation, then at Bobby's somber countenance. I cleared my throat.

"Perhaps you'd open the other crate for me, Bobby?"

"Eh?" His attention was still fixed on the pair outside.

"Crate," I repeated patiently. "That one." I nudged it with my toe.

"Crate . . . oh! Oh, aye, mum, to be sure." Pulling his gaze from the window, he set about the task, looking glum.

I took the rest of the glassware from the open crate, shaking off the straw and putting globes, retorts, flasks, and coils carefully into a high cupboard—but I kept an eye on Bobby as I did so, pondering this newly revealed situation. I hadn't thought his feelings for Lizzie were more than a passing attraction.

And perhaps it was no more than that, I reminded myself. But if it was . . . Despite myself, I glanced through the window, only to discover that the pair had become a trio.

"Ian!" I exclaimed. Bobby glanced up, startled, but I was already heading for the door, hastily brushing straw from my clothes.

If Ian was back, Jamie was—

He came through the front door just as I barreled into the hallway, and grabbed me round the waist, kissing me with sun-dusty enthusiasm and sandpaper whiskers.

"You're back," I said, rather inanely.

"I am, and there are Indians just behind me," he said, clutching my bottom with both hands and rasping his whiskers fervently against my cheek. "God, what I'd give for a quarter of an hour alone wi' ye, Sassenach! My balls are burst—ah. Mr. Higgins. I, um, didna see ye there."

He let go and straightened abruptly, sweeping off his hat and smacking it against his thigh in an exaggerated pantomime of casualness.

"No, zur," Bobby said morosely. "Mr. Ian's back, as well, is he?" He didn't sound as though this was particularly good news; if Ian's arrival had distracted Lizzie from Manfred—and it had—it did nothing to redirect her attention to Bobby.

Lizzie had abandoned her churn to poor Manfred, who was turning the crank with an air of obvious resentment, as she went laughing off in the direction of the stable with Ian, presumably to show him the new calf that had arrived during his absence.

"Indians," I said, belatedly catching what Jamie had said. "What Indians?"

"A half-dozen of the Cherokee," he replied. "What's this?" He nodded at the trail of loose straw leading out of my surgery.

"Oh, that. That," I said happily, "is ether. Or going to be. We're feeding the Indians, I suppose?"

"Aye. I'll tell Mrs. Bug. But there's a young woman with them that they've fetched along for ye to tend."

"Oh?" He was already striding down the hall toward the kitchen, and I hurried to keep up. "What's the matter with her?"

"Toothache," he said briefly, and pushed open the kitchen door. "Mrs. Bug! *Cá bhfuil tú?* Ether, Sassenach? Ye dinna mean phlogiston, do you?"

"I don't *think* that I do," I said, trying to recall what on earth phlogiston was. "I've told you about anesthesia, though, I know—that's what ether is, a sort of anesthetic; puts people to sleep so you can do surgery without hurting them."

"Verra useful in case of the toothache," Jamie observed. "Where's the woman gone to? Mrs. Bug!"

"So it would be, but it will take some time to make. We'll have to make do with whisky for the moment. Mrs. Bug is in the summer kitchen, I expect; it's bread day. And speaking of alcohol—" He was already out the back door, and I scampered across the stoop after him. "I'll need quite a bit of high-quality alcohol, for the ether. Can you bring me a barrel of the new stuff tomorrow?"

"A barrel? Christ, Sassenach, what d'ye mean to do, bathe in it?"

"Well, as a matter of fact, yes. Or rather not me—the oil of vitriol. You pour it gently into a bath of hot alcohol, and it—"

"Oh, Mr. Fraser! I did think as how I heard someone a-callin'." Mrs. Bug appeared suddenly with a basket of eggs over one arm, beaming. "It's pleased I am to see ye home again safe!"

"And glad to be so, Mrs. Bug," he assured her. "Can we be feeding a half-dozen guests for supper?"

Her eyes went wide for a moment, then narrowed in calculation.

"Sausage," she declared. "And neeps. Here, wee Bobby, come and make yourself useful." Handing me the eggs, she seized Bobby, who had come out of the house after us, by the sleeve and towed him off toward the turnip patch.

I had the feeling of having been caught in some rapidly revolving apparatus like a merry-go-round, and took hold of Jamie's arm in order to steady myself.

"Did you know that Bobby Higgins is in love with Lizzie?" I asked.

"No, but it'll do him little good if he is," Jamie replied callously. Taking my hand on his arm as invitation, he took the eggs from me and set them on the ground, then pulled me in and kissed me again, more slowly, but no less thoroughly.

He let go with a deep sigh of content, and glanced at the new summer kitchen we had erected in his absence: a small framed structure consisting of coarse-woven canvas walls and a pine-branch roof, erected round a stone hearth and chimney—but with a large table inside. Enticing scents of rising dough, fresh-baked bread, oatcakes, and cinnamon rolls wafted through the air from it.

"Now, about that quarter of an hour, Sassenach . . . I believe I could manage wi' a bit less, if necessary. . . ."

"Well, *I* couldn't," I said firmly, though I did allow my hand to fondle him for a thoughtful instant. My face was burning from contact with his whiskers. "And when we do have time, you can tell me *what* on earth you've been doing to bring this on."

"Dreaming," he said.

"What?"

"I kept havin' terrible lewd dreams about ye, all the night long," he explained, twitching his breeks into better adjustment. "Every time I rolled over, I'd lie on my cock and wake up. It was awful."

I burst out laughing, and he affected to look injured, though I could see reluctant amusement behind it.

"Well, *you* can laugh, Sassenach," he said. "Ye havena got one to trouble ye."

"Yes, and a great relief it is, too," I assured him. "Er . . . what sort of lewd dreams?"

I could see a deep blue gleam of speculation at the back of his eyes as he looked at me. He extended one finger, and very delicately ran it down the side of my neck, the slope of my breast where it disappeared into my bodice, and over the thin cloth covering my nipple—which promptly popped up like a puffball mushroom in response to this attention.

"The sort that make me want to take ye straight into the forest, far enough that no one will hear when I lay ye on the ground, lift your skirts, and split ye like a ripe peach," he said softly. "Aye?"

I swallowed, audibly.

At this delicate moment, whoops of greeting came from the trailhead on the other side of the house.

"Duty calls," I said, a trifle breathless.

Jamie drew a deep breath of his own, squared his shoulders, and nodded.

"Well, I havena died of unrequited lust yet; I suppose I shallna do it now."

"Don't suppose you will," I said. "Besides, didn't you tell me once that abstinence makes . . . er . . . things . . . grow firmer?"

He gave me a bleak look.

"If it gets any firmer, I'll faint from a lack of blood to the heid. Dinna forget the eggs, Sassenach."

IT WAS LATE AFTERNOON, but plenty of light left for the job, thank goodness. My surgery was positioned to take advantage of morning light for operations, though, and was dim in the afternoons, so I set up an impromptu theater of operation in the dooryard.

This was an advantage, insofar as everyone wished to watch; Indians always regarded medical treatment—and almost anything else—as a community affair. They were particularly enthusiastic about operations, as these held a high degree of entertainment value. Everyone crowded eagerly around, commenting on my preparations, arguing with each other and talking to the patient, whom I had the greatest difficulty in discouraging from talking back.

Her name was Mouse, and I could only assume that she had been given it for some metaphysical reason, as it certainly wasn't suited either to appearance or personality. She was round-faced, unusually snub-nosed for a Cherokee, and if she wasn't precisely pretty, she had a force of character that is often more attractive than simple beauty.

It was certainly working on the males present; she was the only woman in the Indian party, the others consisting of her brother, Red Clay Wilson, and four friends who had come along, either to keep the Wilsons company, offer protection on the journey—or to vie for Miss Mousie's attention, which seemed to me the most likely explanation of their presence.

Despite the Wilsons' Scottish name, none of the Cherokee spoke any English beyond a few basic words—these including "no," "yes," "good," "bad," and "whisky!" Since the Cherokee equivalent of these terms was the extent of my own vocabulary, I was taking little part in the conversation.

We were at the moment waiting for whisky, in fact, as well as translators. A settler named Wolverhampton, from some nameless hollow to the east, had inadvertently amputated one and a half toes a week before, while splitting logs. Finding this state of things inconvenient, he had proceeded to try to remove the remaining half-digit himself with a froe.

Say what you will regarding general utility; a froe is not a precision instrument. It is, however, sharp.

Mr. Wolverhampton, a burly sort with an irascible temper, lived on his own, some seven miles from his nearest neighbor. By the time he had reached this neighbor—on foot, or what remained of it—and the neighbor had bundled him onto a mule for transport to Fraser's Ridge, nearly twenty-four hours had passed, and the partial foot had assumed the dimensions and appearance of a mangled raccoon.

The requirements of the cleanup surgery, the multiple subsequent debridements to control the infection, and the fact that Mr. Wolverhampton refused to surrender the bottle, had quite exhausted my usual surgical supply. As I needed a keg of the raw spirit for my ether-making in any case, Jamie and Ian had gone to fetch more from the whisky spring, which was a good mile from the house. I hoped they would return while there was still enough light to see what I was doing.

I interrupted Miss Mousie's loud remonstrance with one of the gentlemen, who was evidently teasing her, and indicated by means of sign language that she should open her mouth for me. She did, but went on expostulating by means of rather explicit hand signals, which seemed to be indicating various acts she expected the gentleman in question to perform upon himself, judging from his flushed countenance, and the way his companions were falling about with hilarity.

The side of her face was puffed and obviously tender. She didn't wince or shy away, though, even when I turned her face farther toward the light for a better view.

"Toothache, forsooth!" I said, involuntarily.

"Ooth?" Miss Mouse said, cocking an eyebrow at me.

"Bad," I explained, pointing at her cheek. *"Uyoi."*

"Bad," she agreed. There followed a voluble exposition—interrupted only by my inserting my fingers into her mouth periodically—which I took to be an explanation of what had happened to her.

Blunt trauma, by the look of it. One tooth, a lower canine, had been knocked completely out, and the neighboring bicuspid was so badly broken I would have to extract it. The next to that could be saved, I thought. The inside of her mouth was badly lacerated by the sharp edges, but the gum was not infected. That was heartening.

Bobby Higgins came down from the stable, drawn by the chatter, and was promptly sent back to bring me a file. Miss Mousie grinned lopsidedly at him when he brought it, and he bowed extravagantly to her, making all of them laugh.

"These folk are Cherokee, are they, mum?" He smiled at Red Clay, and made a hand sign, which seemed to amuse the Indians, though they returned it. "I've not met any Cherokee before. It's mostly other tribes near his Lordship's place in Virginia."

I was pleased to see that he was familiar with Indians, and easy in his manner toward them. Hiram Crombie, who appeared at this point, was not.

He stopped dead at the edge of the clearing, seeing the assemblage. I waved cheerily at him, and—with evident reluctance—he advanced.

Roger had told me Duncan's description of Hiram as "that wee sour-drap." It was apt. He was small and stringy, with thin grizzled hair that he wore strained back in a plait so tight that I thought he must find it difficult to blink. His face deeply lined by the rigors of a fisherman's life, he looked about sixty, but was likely much younger—and his mouth was habitually downturned, in the expression of one who has sucked not merely a lemon, but a rotten lemon.

"I was looking for Mr. Fraser," he said, with a wary eye on the Indians. "I had heard he was back." He had a hatchet in his belt, and kept a tight grip on it with one hand.

"He'll be back directly. You've met Mr. Higgins, haven't you?" Evidently he had, and had been unfavorably impressed by the experience. His eyes fixed on Bobby's brand, he made the smallest possible nod of acknowledgment. Nothing daunted, I waved a hand round at the Indians, who were all examining Hiram with much more interest than he showed in them. "May I introduce Miss Wilson, her brother Mr. Wilson, and . . . er . . . their friends?"

Hiram stiffened further, if such a thing was possible.

"Wilson?" he said, in an unfriendly voice.

"Wilson," agreed Miss Mouse cheerily.

"That is my wife's family name," he said, in a tone that made it clear he considered the use of it by Indians to be grossly outrageous.

"Oh," I said. "How nice. Do you think they might be your wife's relatives, perhaps?"

His eyes bulged slightly at that, and I heard a strangled gurgle from Bobby.

"Well, they plainly got the name from a Scottish father or grandfather," I pointed out. "Perhaps . . ."

Hiram's face was working like a nutcracker, emotions from fury to dismay passing in swift succession over it. His right hand curled up, forefinger and little finger protruding in the horns, the sign against evil.

"Great-Uncle Ephraim," he whispered. "Jesus save us." And without further word, he turned on his heel and tottered off.

"Goodbye!" called Miss Mousie in English, waving. He cast a single, haunted glance over his shoulder at her, then fled as though pursued by demons.

THE WHISKY FINALLY arrived, and, a fair amount of it passed out to patient and spectators alike, the operation at last commenced.

The file was normally used on horses' teeth, and thus a little larger than I would have liked, but worked reasonably well. Miss Mouse was inclined to be loud about the discomfort involved, but her complaints grew less with her increasing intake of whisky. By the time I had to draw her broken tooth, I thought, she wouldn't feel a thing.

Bobby, meanwhile, was entertaining Jamie and Ian with imitations of Hiram Crombie's response to the discovery that he might possibly share some family connection with the

Wilsons. Ian, between bursts of laughter, translated the matter for the Indians, who all rolled on the grass in paroxysms of mirth.

"*Do* they have an Ephraim Wilson in their family tree?" I asked, taking a firm grip of Miss Mousie's chin.

"Well, they're not sure of the 'Ephraim,' but aye, they do." Jamie grinned broadly. "Their grandsire was a Scottish wanderer. Stayed long enough to get their grandmother wi' child, then fell off a cliff and was buried by a rockslide. She marrit again, of course, but liked the name."

"I wonder what it was made Great-Uncle Ephraim leave Scotland?" Ian sat up, wiping tears of laughter from his eyes.

"The proximity of people like Hiram, I expect," I said, squinting to see what I was doing. "Do you think—" I realized suddenly that everyone had quit talking and laughing, their attention focused on something across the clearing.

This something was the arrival of another Indian, carrying something in a bundle over his shoulder.

THE INDIAN WAS A gentleman named Sequoyah, somewhat older than the young Wilsons and their friends. He nodded soberly to Jamie, and swinging the bundle off his shoulder, laid it on the ground at Jamie's feet, saying something in Cherokee.

Jamie's face changed, the lingering traces of amusement vanishing, replaced by interest—and wariness. He knelt, and carefully turning back the ragged canvas, revealed a jumble of weathered bones, a hollow-eyed skull staring up from the midst of them.

"Who in bloody hell is *that*?" I had stopped work, and with everyone else, including Miss Mouse, stood staring down at this latest arrival.

"He says it's the auld man who owned the homestead MacDonald told of—the one that burned inside the Treaty Line." Jamie reached down and picked up the skull, turning it gently in his hands.

He heard my small intake of breath, for he glanced at me, then turned the skull over, holding it for me to see. Most of the teeth were missing, and had been missing long enough that the jawbone had closed over the empty sockets. But the two molars remaining showed nothing but cracks and stains—no gleam of silver filling, no empty space where such fillings might have been.

I let my breath out slowly, not sure whether to be relieved or disappointed.

"What happened to him? And why is he *here*?"

Jamie knelt and laid the skull gently back in the canvas, then turned some of the bones over, examining them. He looked up, and with a small motion of the head, invited me to join him.

The bones showed no sign of having been burned, but several of them *did* show signs of having been gnawed by animals. One or two of the long bones had been cracked and split, no doubt to get at the marrow, and many of the smaller bones of hands and feet were missing. All of them had the gray, fragile look of bones that had lain outside for some time.

Ian had relayed my question to Sequoyah, who squatted down next to Jamie, explaining as he jabbed a finger here and there amongst the bones.

"He says," Ian translated, frowning, "that he knew the man a long time. They werena friends, exactly, but now and again, when he was near the man's cabin, he would stop, and the man would share his food. So he would bring things, too, when he came—a hare for the pot, a bit o' salt."

One day, a few months back, he had found the old man's body in the wood, lying under a tree, some distance from his house.

"No one kilt him, he says," Ian said, frowning in concentration at the rapid stream of words. "He just . . . died. He thinks the man was hunting—he had a knife on him, and his gun beside him—when the spirit left him, and he just fell down." He echoed Sequoyah's shrug.

Seeing no reason to do anything with the body, Sequoyah had left it there, and left the knife with it, in case the spirit should require it, wherever it had gone; he did not know where the spirits of white men went, or whether they hunted there. He pointed—there was an old knife, the blade almost rusted away, under the bones.

He had taken the gun, which seemed too good to leave, and as it was on his way, had stopped at the cabin. The old man had owned very little, and what he had was mostly worthless. Sequoyah had taken an iron pot, a kettle, and a jar of cornmeal, which he had carried back to his village.

"He's no from Anidonau Nuya, is he?" Jamie asked, then repeated the question in Cherokee. Sequoyah shook his head, the small ornaments braided into his hair making a tiny chiming sound.

He was from a village some miles west of Anidonau Nuya—Standing Stone. Bird-who-sings had sent word to the nearby towns, in the wake of Jamie's visit, asking if there was anyone who knew of the old man and his fate. Hearing Sequoyah's account, Bird had sent him to collect what was left of the old man, and to bring the remains to Jamie, in proof that no one had killed him.

Ian asked a question, in which I caught the Cherokee word for "fire." Sequoyah shook his head again, and replied with a stream of words.

He had not burned the cabin—why should he do such a thing? He thought no one had done so. After collecting the old man's bones—his face showed his distaste for the procedure—he had gone to look at the cabin again. True, it was burned—but it was clear to him that a tree nearby had been struck by lightning, and had set fire to a good bit of the forest near it. The cabin was only half-burned.

He rose to his feet with an air of finality.

"Will he stay for supper?" I asked, seeing that he seemed about to depart.

Jamie conveyed the invitation, but Sequoyah shook his head. He had done what was required of him; now he had other business. He nodded to the other Indians, then turned to go.

Something struck him, though, and he stopped, turning back.

"Tsisqua says," he said, in the careful way of one who has memorized a speech in an unfamiliar tongue, "you re-member de guns." He nodded then decisively, and went.

THE GRAVE WAS MARKED with a small cairn of stones and a small wooden cross made of pine twigs. Sequoyah hadn't known his acquaintance's name, and we had no idea of his age, nor yet the dates of birth and death. We hadn't known if he was Christian, either, but the cross seemed a good idea.

It was a very small burial service, consisting of myself, Jamie, Ian, Bree and Roger, Lizzie and her father, the Bugs, and Bobby Higgins—who I was fairly sure was in attendance only because Lizzie was. Her father seemed to think so, too, judging from the occasional suspicious glances he cast at Bobby.

Roger read a brief psalm over the grave, then paused. He cleared his throat and said simply, "Lord, we commend to Thy care the soul of this our brother . . ."

"Ephraim," murmured Brianna, eyes cast modestly down.

A subterranean sense of laughter moved through the crowd, though no one actually laughed. Roger gave Bree a dirty look, but I saw the corner of his mouth twitching, as well.

". . . of our brother, whose name Thou knowest," Roger concluded with dignity, and closed the Book of Psalms he had borrowed from Hiram Crombie—who had declined an invitation to attend the funeral.

The light had gone by the time Sequoyah had finished his revelations the night before, and I was obliged to put off Miss Mouse's dental work to the morning. Stewed to the gills, she made no objection, and was helpfully supported off to a bed on the kitchen floor by Bobby Higgins—who might or might not be in love with Lizzie, but who seemed nonetheless most appreciative of Miss Mouse's charms.

Once finished with the tooth-drawing, I had suggested that she and her friends stay for a bit, but they, like Sequoyah, had business elsewhere, and with many thanks and small gifts, had departed by mid-afternoon, smelling strongly of whisky, and leaving us to dispose of the mortal remains of the late Ephraim.

Everyone went back down the hill after the service, but Jamie and I loitered behind, seeking an opportunity to be alone for a few minutes. The house had been full of Indians the night before, with much talk and storytelling by the fire, and by the time we had finally gone to bed, we had simply curled up in each other's arms and fallen asleep, barely exchanging the brief civility of a "good night."

The graveyard was sited on a small rise, some distance from the house, and was a pretty, peaceful place. Surrounded by pines whose golden needles blanketed the earth, and whose murmuring branches provided a constant soft susurrus, it seemed a comforting spot.

"Poor old creature," I said, putting a final pebble on Ephraim's cairn. "How do you suppose he ended up in such a place?"

"God knows." Jamie shook his head. "There are always hermits, men who mislike the society of their fellows. Perhaps he was one o' those. Or perhaps some misfortune drove him into the wilderness, and he . . . stayed." He shrugged a little, and gave me a half-smile.

"I sometimes wonder how any of us came to be where we are, Sassenach. Don't you?"

"I used to," I said. "But after a time, there didn't seem to be any possibility of an answer, so I stopped."

He looked down at me, diverted.

"Have ye, then?" He put out a hand and tucked back a lock of windblown hair. "Perhaps I shouldna ask it, then, but I will. Do ye mind, Sassenach? That ye *are* here, I mean. Do ye ever wish ye were—back?"

I shook my head.

"No, not ever."

And that was true. But I woke sometimes in the dead of night, thinking, *Is now the dream?* Would I wake again to the thick warm smell of central heating and Frank's Old Spice? And when I fell asleep again to the scent of woodsmoke and the musk of Jamie's skin, would feel a faint, surprised regret.

If he saw the thought on my face, he gave no sign of it, but bent and kissed me gently on the forehead. He took my arm, and we walked a little way into the wood, away from the house and its clearing below.

"Sometimes I smell the pines," he said, taking a deep, slow breath of the pungent air. "And I think for an instant I am in Scotland. But then I come to myself and see; there is no kindly bracken here, nor great barren mountains—not the wildness that I kent, but only wilderness that I do not."

I thought I heard nostalgia in his voice, but not sorrow. He'd asked, though; so would I.

"And do you ever wish to be . . . back?"

"Oh, aye," he said, surprising me—and then laughed at the look on my face. "But not enough not to wish more to be here, Sassenach."

He glanced over his shoulder at the tiny graveyard, with its small collection of cairns and crosses, with here and there a larger boulder marking a particular grave.

"Did ye ken, Sassenach, that some folk believe the last person to lie in a graveyard becomes its guardian? He must stand on guard until the next person dies and comes to take his place—only then can he rest."

"I suppose our mysterious Ephraim might be rather surprised to find himself in such a position, when here he'd lain down under a tree all alone," I said, smiling a little. "But I do wonder: what is the guardian of a graveyard guarding—and from whom?"

He laughed at that.

"Oh . . . vandals, maybe; desecraters. Or charmers."

"Charmers?" I was surprised at that; I'd thought the word "charmer" synonymous with "healer."

"There are charms that call for bones, Sassenach," he said. "Or the ashes of a burnt body. Or soil from a grave." He spoke lightly enough, but with no sense of jesting. "Aye, even the dead may need defending."

"And who better to do it than a resident ghost?" I said. "Quite."

We climbed up through a stand of quivering aspen, whose light dappled us with green and silver, and I paused to scrape a blob of the crimson sap from a paper-white trunk. How odd, I thought, wondering why the sight of it gave me pause—and then remembered, and turned sharply to look again at the graveyard.

Not a memory, but a dream—or a vision. A man, battered and broken, rising to his feet amid a stand of aspen, rising for what he knew was the last time, his last fight, baring shattered teeth stained with blood that was the color of the aspens' sap.

His face was painted black for death—and I knew that there were silver fillings in his teeth.

But the granite boulder stood silent and peaceful, drifted all about with yellow pine needles, marking the rest of the man who had once called himself Otter-Tooth.

The moment passed, and vanished. We walked out of the aspens, and into another clearing, this one higher than the rise the graveyard stood on.

I was surprised to see that someone had been cutting timber here, and clearing the ground. A sizable stack of felled logs lay to one side, and nearby lay a tangle of uprooted stumps, though several more, still rooted in the ground, poked through the heavy growth of wood sorrel and bluet.

"Look, Sassenach." Jamie turned me with a hand on my elbow.

"Oh. Oh, my."

The ground rose high enough here that we could look out over a stunning vista. The trees fell away below us, and we could see beyond our mountain, and beyond the next, and the next, into a blue distance, hazed with the breath of the mountains, clouds rising from their hollows.

"D'ye like it?" The note of proprietorial pride in his voice was palpable.

"Of course I like it. What—?" I turned, gesturing at the logs, the stumps.

"The next house will stand here, Sassenach," he said simply.

"The *next* house? What, are we building another?"

"Well, I dinna ken will it be us, or maybe our children—or grandchildren," he added, mouth curling a little. "But I thought, should anything happen—and I dinna think anything *will,* mind, but if it should—well, I should be happier to have made a start. Just in case."

I stared at him for a moment, trying to make sense of this. "Should anything happen," I said slowly, and turned to look to the east, where the shape of our house was just visible among the trees, its chimney smoke a white plume among the soft green of the chestnuts and firs. "Should it really . . . burn down, you mean." Just putting the idea into words made my stomach curl up into a ball.

Then I looked at him again, and saw that the notion scared

him, too. But Jamie-like, he had simply set about to take what action he could, against the day of disaster.

"D'ye like it?" he repeated, blue eyes intent. "The site, I mean. If not, I can choose another."

"It's beautiful," I said, feeling tears prickle at the backs of my eyes. "Just beautiful, Jamie."

HOT AFTER THE CLIMB, we sat down in the shade of a giant hemlock, to admire our future view. And, with the silence broken concerning the dire possibility of the future, found we could discuss it.

"It's not so much the idea of us dying," I said. "Or not entirely. It's that 'no surviving children' that gives me the whim-whams."

"Well, I take your point, Sassenach. Though I'm no in favor of us dying, either, and I mean to see we don't," he assured me. "Think, though. It might not mean they're dead. They might only . . . go."

I took a deep breath, trying to accept that supposition without panic.

"Go. Go back, you mean. Roger and Bree—and Jemmy, I suppose. We're assuming he can—can travel through the stones."

He nodded soberly, arms clasped about his knees.

"After what he did to that opal? Aye, I think we must assume he can." I nodded, recalling what he'd done to the opal: held it, complaining of it growing hot in his hand—until it exploded, shattering into hundreds of needle-sharp fragments. Yes, I thought we must assume he could time-travel, too. But what if Brianna had another child? It was plain to me that she and Roger wanted another—or at least that Roger did, and she was willing.

The thought of losing them was acutely painful, but I supposed the possibility had to be faced.

"Which leaves a choice, I suppose," I said, trying to be brave and objective. "If we're dead, they'd go, because without us, they've no real reason to be here. But if we're *not* dead—will they go anyway? Will we send them away, I mean? Because of the war. It won't be safe."

"No," he said softly. His head was bent, stray auburn hairs lifting from his crown, from the cowlicks he had bequeathed both to Bree and to Jemmy.

"I dinna ken," he said at last, and lifted his head, looking out into the distance of land and sky. "No one does, Sassenach. We must just meet what comes as we can."

He turned and laid his hand over mine, with a smile that had as much of pain in it as joy.

"We've ghosts enough between us, Sassenach. If the evils of the past canna hinder us—neither then shall any fears of the future. We must just put things behind us and get on. Aye?"

I laid a light hand on his chest, not in invitation, but only because I wanted the feel of him. His skin was cool from sweating, but he had helped dig the grave; the heat of his labor glowed in the muscle beneath.

"You were one of my ghosts," I said. "For a long time. And for a long time, I tried to put *you* behind me."

"Did ye, then?" His own hand came to rest lightly on my back, moving unconsciously. I knew that touch—the need of touching only to reassure oneself that the other was actually there, present in flesh.

"I thought I couldn't live, looking back—couldn't bear it." My throat was thick with the memory of it.

"I know," he said softly, his hand rising to touch my hair. "But ye had the bairn—ye had a husband. It wasna right to turn your back on them."

"It wasn't right to turn my back on *you*." I blinked, but tears were leaking from the corners of my eyes. He drew my head close, put out his tongue, and delicately licked my face, which surprised me so much that I laughed in the midst of a sob, and nearly choked.

"I do love thee, as meat loves salt," he quoted, and laughed, too, very softly. "Dinna weep, Sassenach. Ye're here; so am I. There's naught that matters, aside from that."

I leaned my forehead against his cheek, and put my arms around him. My hands rested flat on the planes of his back, and I stroked him from the blade of his shoulder to the tapering small of his back, lightly, always lightly, tracing the whole of him, the shape of him, and not the scars that reamed his skin.

He held me close, and sighed deeply.

"D'ye ken we've been wed this time nearly twice as long as the last?"

I drew back and frowned dubiously at him, accepting the distraction.

"Were we not married in between?"

That took him by surprise; he frowned, too, and ran a finger slowly down the sunburnt bridge of his nose in thought.

"Well, there's a question for a priest, to be sure," he said. "I should think we were—but if so, are we not both bigamists?"

"Were, not are," I corrected, feeling slightly uneasy. "But we weren't, really. Father Anselme said so."

"Anselme?"

"Father Anselme—a Franciscan priest at the Abbey of St. Anne. But perhaps you wouldn't recall him; you were very ill at the time."

"Oh, I recall him," he said. "He would come and sit wi' me at night, when I couldna sleep." He smiled, a little lopsided; that time wasn't something he wished to remember. "He liked ye a great deal, Sassenach."

"Oh? And what about you?" I asked, wanting to distract him from the memory of St. Anne. "Didn't you like me?"

"Oh, I liked ye fine then," he assured me. "I maybe like ye even more now, though."

"Oh, do you, indeed." I sat up a little straighter, preening. "What's different?"

He tilted his head to one side, eyes narrowing a bit in appraisal.

"Well, ye fart less in your sleep," he began judiciously, then ducked, laughing, as a pinecone whizzed past his left ear. I seized a chunk of wood, but before I could bat him over the head with it, he lunged and caught me by the arms. He shoved me flat in the grass and collapsed on top of me, pinning me effortlessly.

"Get off, you oaf! I do *not* fart in my sleep!"

"Now, how would ye ken that, Sassenach? Ye sleep so sound, ye wouldna wake, even to the sound of your own snoring."

"Oh, you want to talk about snoring, do you? You—"

"Ye're proud as Lucifer," he said, interrupting. He was still smiling, but the words were more serious. "And ye're brave. Ye were always bolder than was safe; now ye're fierce as a wee badger."

"So I'm arrogant and ferocious. This does not sound like much of a catalog of womanly virtues," I said, puffing a bit as I strained to wriggle out from under him.

"Well, ye're kind, too," he said, considering. "Verra kind. Though ye are inclined to do it on your own terms. Not that that's bad, mind," he added, neatly recapturing the arm I had extricated. He pinned my wrist over my head.

"Womanly," he murmured, brows knotted in concentration. "Womanly virtues . . ." His free hand crept between us and fastened on my breast.

"Besides that!"

"You're verra clean," he said approvingly. He let go my wrist and ruffled a hand through my hair—which was indeed clean, smelling of sunflower and marigolds.

"I've never seen any woman wash herself sae much as you do—save Brianna, perhaps.

"Ye're no much of a cook," he went on, squinting thoughtfully. "Though ye've never poisoned anyone, save on purpose. And I will say ye sew a neat seam—though ye like it much better if it's through someone's flesh."

"Thanks so much!"

"Tell me some more virtues," he suggested. "Perhaps I've missed one."

"Hmph! Gentleness, patience . . ." I floundered.

"Gentle? Christ." He shook his head. "Ye're the most ruthless, bloodthirsty—"

I darted my head upward, and nearly succeeded in biting him in the throat. He jerked back, laughing.

"No, ye're no verra patient, either."

I gave up struggling for the moment and collapsed flat on my back, tousled hair spread out on the grass.

"So what *is* my most endearing trait?" I demanded.

"Ye think I'm funny," he said, grinning.

"I . . . do . . . not . . ." I grunted, struggling madly. He merely lay on top of me, tranquilly oblivious to my pokings and thumpings, until I exhausted myself and lay gasping underneath him.

"And," he said thoughtfully, "ye like it verra much when I take ye to bed. No?"

"Er . . ." I wanted to contradict him, but honesty forbade. Besides, he bloody well knew I did.

"You are squashing me," I said with dignity. "Kindly get off."

"No?" he repeated, not moving.

"Yes! All right! Yes! Will you bloody get *off*?!"

He didn't get off, but bent his head and kissed me. I was close-lipped, determined not to give in, but he was determined, too, and if one came right down to it . . . the skin of his face was warm, the plush of his beard stubble softly scratchy, and his wide sweet mouth . . . My legs were open in abandon and he was solid between them, bare chest smelling of musk and sweat and sawdust caught in the wiry auburn hair. . . . I was still hot with struggling, but the grass was damp and cool around us. . . . Well, all right; another minute, and he could have me right there, if he cared to.

He felt me yield, and sighed, letting his own body slacken; he no longer held me prisoner, but simply held me. He lifted his head then, and cupped my face with one hand.

"D'ye want to know what it is, really?" he asked, and I could see from the dark blue of his eyes that he meant it. I nodded, mute.

"Above all creatures on this earth," he whispered, "you are faithful."

I thought of saying something about St. Bernard dogs, but there was such tenderness in his face that I said nothing, instead merely stared up at him, blinking against the green light that filtered through the needles overhead.

"Well," I said at last, with a deep sigh of my own, "so are you. Quite a good thing, really. Isn't it?"

21

WE HAVE IGNITION

MRS. BUG HAD MADE chicken fricassee for supper, but that wasn't sufficient to account for the air of suppressed excitement that Bree and Roger brought with them when they came in. They were both smiling, her cheeks were flushed, and his eyes as bright as hers.

So when Roger announced that they had great news, it was perhaps only reasonable that Mrs. Bug should leap directly to the obvious conclusion.

"You're wi' child again!" she cried, dropping a spoon in her excitement. She clapped her hands together, inflating like a birthday balloon. "Oh, the joy of it! And about time, too," she added, letting go her hands to wag a finger at Roger. "And here was me thinkin' as I should add a bit o' ginger and brimstone to your parritch, young man, so as to bring ye up to scratch! But ye kent your business weel enough in the end, I see. And you, *a bhailach,* what d'ye think? A bonny wee brother for ye!"

Jemmy, thus addressed, stared up at her, mouth open.

"Er . . ." said Roger, flushing up.

"Or, of course, it might be a wee sister, I suppose," Mrs. Bug admitted. "But good news, good news, either way. Here, *a luaidh,* have a sweetie on the strength of it, and the rest of us will drink to it!"

Obviously bewildered, but strongly in favor of sweeties, Jem took the proffered molasses drop and stuck it promptly in his mouth.

"But he isn't—" Bree began.

"Nank you, Missus Bug," Jem said hastily, putting a hand

over his mouth lest his mother try to repossess this distinctly forbidden predinner treat on grounds of impoliteness.

"Oh, a wee sweetie will do him nay harm," Mrs. Bug assured her, picking up the fallen spoon and wiping it on her apron. "Call Arch in, *a muirninn,* and we'll tell him your news. Blessed Bride save ye, lass, I thought ye'd never get round to it! Here was all the ladies saying' as they didna ken whether ye'd turned cold to your husband, or was it him maybe, lackin' the vital spark, but as it is—"

"Well, *as* it is," said Roger, raising his voice in order to be heard.

"I'm *not pregnant*!" said Bree, very loudly.

The succeeding silence echoed like a thunderclap.

"Oh," said Jamie mildly. He picked up a serviette and sat down, tucking it into the neck of his shirt. "Well, then. Shall we eat?" He held out a hand to Jem, who scrambled up onto the bench beside him, still sucking fiercely on his molasses drop.

Mrs. Bug, momentarily turned to stone, revived with a marked "Hmpf!" Massively affronted, she turned to the sideboard and slapped down a stack of pewter plates with a clatter.

Roger, still rather flushed, appeared to find the situation funny, judging from the twitching of his mouth. Brianna was incandescent, and breathing like a grampus.

"Sit down, darling," I said, in the tentative manner of one addressing a large explosive device. "You . . . um . . . had some news, you said?"

"Never mind!" She stood still, glaring. "Nobody cares, since I'm not pregnant. After all, what *else* could I possibly do that anybody would think was worthwhile?" She shoved a violent hand through her hair, and encountering the ribbon tying it back, yanked this loose and flung it on the ground.

"Now, sweetheart . . ." Roger began. I could have told him this was a mistake; Frasers in a fury tended to pay no attention to honeyed words, being instead inclined to go for the throat of the nearest party unwary enough to speak to them.

"Don't you 'sweetheart' me!" she snapped, turning on him. "You think so, too! You think everything I do is a waste of time if it isn't washing clothes or cooking dinner or mending your effing socks! And you blame me for not getting pregnant, too, you think it's my fault! Well, it's NOT, and you know it!"

"No! I don't think that, I don't at all. Brianna, please. . . ." He stretched out a hand to her, then thought better of the gesture and withdrew it, clearly feeling that she might take his hand off at the wrist.

"Less EAT, Mummy!" Jemmy piped up helpfully. A long string of molasses-tinged saliva flowed from the corner of his mouth and dripped down the front of his shirt. Seeing this, his mother turned on Mrs. Bug like a tiger.

"Now see what you've done, you interfering old busybody! That was his last clean shirt! And how dare you talk about our private lives with everybody in sight, what possible earthly business of yours is it, you beastly old gossiping—"

Seeing the futility of protest, Roger put his arms round her from behind, picked her up bodily off the floor, and carried her out the back door, this departure accented by incoherent protests from Bree and grunts of pain from Roger, as she kicked him repeatedly in the shins, with considerable force and accuracy.

I went to the door and closed it delicately, shutting off the sounds of further altercation in the yard.

"She gets that from *you,* you know," I said reproachfully, sitting down opposite Jamie. "Mrs. Bug, that smells wonderful. *Do* let's eat!"

Mrs. Bug dished the fricassee in huffy silence, but declined to join us at table, instead putting on her cloak and stamping out the front door, leaving us to deal with the clearing-up. An excellent bargain, if you asked me.

We ate in blissful peace, the quiet broken only by the clink of spoons on pewter and the occasional question from Jemmy as to why molasses was sticky, how did milk get *into* the cow, and when would he get his little brother?

"*What* am I going to say to Mrs. Bug?" I asked, in the brief hiatus between queries.

"Why ought ye to say anything, Sassenach? It wasna you calling her names."

"Well, no. But I'd be willing to bet that Brianna isn't going to apologize—"

"Why should she?" He shrugged. "She was provoked, after all. And I canna think Mrs. Bug has lived sae long without being called a gossiping busybody before. She'll wear herself out, telling Arch all about it, and tomorrow it will be fine again."

"Well," I said uncertainly. "Perhaps so. But Bree and Roger—"

He smiled at me, dark blue eyes crinkling into triangles.

"Dinna feel as though every disaster is yours to fash yourself about, *mo chridhe,*" he said. He reached across and patted my hand. "Roger Mac and the lass must work it out between them—and the lad did appear to have a decent grip on the situation."

He laughed, and I joined him, reluctantly.

"Well, it will be mine to fash about, if she's broken his leg," I remarked, getting up to fetch cream for the coffee. "Likely he'll come crawling back to have it mended."

At this apropos moment, a knock sounded on the back door. Wondering why Roger would knock, I opened it, and stared in astonishment at the pale face of Thomas Christie.

HE WAS NOT ONLY PALE, but sweating, and had a bloodstained cloth wrapped round one hand.

"I wouldna discommode ye, mistress," he said, holding himself stiffly. "I'll just . . . wait upon your convenience."

"Nonsense," I said, rather shortly. "Come into the surgery while there's still some light."

I took care not to catch Jamie's eye directly, but I glanced at him as I bent to push in the bench. He was leaning forward to put a saucer over my coffee, his eyes on Tom Christie with an air of thoughtful speculation that I had last seen in a bobcat watching a flight of ducks overhead. Not urgent, but definitely taking notice.

Christie was taking no notice of anything beyond his injured hand, reasonably enough. My surgery's windows were oriented to east and south, to take best advantage of morning light, but even near sunset, the room held a soft radiance—the setting sun's reflection from the shimmering leaves of the chestnut grove. Everything in the room was suffused with golden light, save Tom Christie's face, which was noticeably green.

"Sit down," I said, shoving a stool hastily behind him. His knees buckled as he lowered himself; he landed harder than he had intended, jarring his hand, and let out a small exclamation of pain.

I put a thumb on the big vein at the wrist, to help slow the bleeding, and unwound the cloth. Given his aspect, I was expecting a severed finger or two, and was surprised to find a simple gash in the meat at the base of the thumb, angled down and running onto the wrist. It was deep enough to gape, and still bleeding freely, but no major vessels had been cut, and he had by great good fortune only nicked the thumb tendon; I could mend that with a stitch or two.

I looked up to tell him this, only to see his eyes roll back in his head.

"Help!" I shouted, dropping the hand and grabbing for his shoulders as he toppled backward.

A crash of overturned bench and the thump of running feet answered my call, and Jamie burst into the room in a heartbeat. Seeing me dragged off my feet by Christie's weight, he seized the man by the scruff of the neck and shoved him forward like a rag doll, pushing Christie's head down between his legs.

"Is he desperate bad?" Jamie asked, squinting at Christie's injured hand, which was resting on the floor, oozing blood. "Shall I lay him on the table?"

"I don't think so." I had a hand under Christie's jaw, feeling for his pulse. "He's not hurt badly; he's only fainted. Yes, see, he's coming round. Keep your head down for a bit, now, you'll be quite all right in a moment." I addressed this latter remark to Christie, who was breathing like a steam engine, but had steadied a little.

Jamie removed his hand from Christie's neck, and wiped it on his kilt with an expression of mild distaste. Christie had broken out in a profuse cold sweat; I could feel my own hand slimy with it, but picked up the fallen cloth and wiped my hand more tactfully with that.

"Would you like to lie down?" I asked, bending to look at

Christie's face. He was still a ghastly color, but shook his head.

"No, mistress. I'm quite all right. Only taken queer for a moment." He spoke hoarsely, but firmly enough, so I contented myself with pressing the cloth hard against the wound to stanch the dripping blood.

Jemmy was loitering in the doorway, wide-eyed, but showing no particular alarm; blood was nothing new to him.

"Shall I fetch ye a dram, Tom?" Jamie said, eyeing the patient warily. "I ken ye dinna hold wi' strong drink, but there's a time for it, surely?"

Christie's mouth worked a little, but he shook his head.

"I . . . no. Perhaps . . . a little wine?"

"*Take a little wine for thy stomach's sake,* eh? Aye, fine. Take heart, man, I'll fetch it." Jamie clapped him encouragingly on the shoulder, and went briskly off, taking Jemmy by the hand as he went out.

Christie's mouth tightened in a grimace. I had noticed before that like some Protestants, Tom Christie regarded the Bible as being a document addressed specifically to himself and confided to his personal care for prudent distribution to the masses. Thus, he quite disliked hearing Catholics—i.e., Jamie—quoting casually from it. I had also noticed that Jamie was aware of this, and took every opportunity to make such quotes.

"What happened?" I asked, as much to distract Christie as because I wished to know.

Christie broke off his glower at the empty doorway and glanced at his left hand—then hastily away, going pale again.

"An accident," he said gruffly. "I was cutting rushes; the knife slipped." His right hand flexed slightly as he said this, and I glanced at it.

"No bloody wonder!" I said. "Here, keep that up in the air." I lifted the injured left hand, tightly wrapped, above his head, let go of it, and reached for the other.

He had been suffering from a condition in the right hand called Dupuytren's contracture—or at least it *would* be called that, once Baron Dupuytren got round to describing it in another sixty or seventy years. Caused by a thickening and shortening of the fibrous sheet that kept the hand's tendons in place when the fingers flexed, the result of it was to draw the ring finger in toward the palm of the hand. In advanced cases, the little finger and sometimes the middle finger as well were involved. Tom Christie's case had advanced quite a bit since I had last had the chance of a good look at his hand.

"Did I tell you?" I demanded rhetorically, pulling gently on the clawed fingers. The middle finger could still be halfway unfolded; the ring and little fingers could barely be lifted away from the palm. "I said it would get worse. No wonder the knife slipped—I'm surprised you could even hold it."

A slight flush appeared under the clipped salt-and-pepper beard, and he glanced away.

"I could have taken care of it easily months ago," I said, turning the hand to look critically at the angle of contracture. "It would have been a very simple matter. Now it will be rather more complicated—but I can still correct it, I think."

Had he been a less stolid man, I should have described him as wriggling with embarrassment. As it was, he merely twitched slightly, the flush deepening over his face.

"I—I do not desire—"

"I don't bloody care what you desire," I told him, putting the clawed hand back in his lap. "If you don't allow me to operate on that hand, it will be all but useless inside six months. You can barely write with it now, am I right?"

His eyes met mine, deep gray and startled.

"I can write," he said, but I could tell that the belligerence in his voice hid a deep uneasiness. Tom Christie was an educated man, a scholar, and the Ridge's schoolteacher. It was to him that many of the Ridge people went for help in the composition of letters or legal documents. He took great pride in this; I knew the threat of loss of this ability was the best lever I had—and it was no idle threat.

"Not for long," I said, and widened my eyes at him to make my meaning clear. He swallowed uneasily, but before he could reply, Jamie reappeared, holding a jug of wine.

"Best listen to her," he advised Christie, setting it on the counter. "I ken what it's like to try to write wi' a stiff finger, aye?" He held up his own right hand and flexed it, looking rueful. "If she could mend *that* wi' her wee knife, I'd lay my hand on the block this instant."

Jamie's problem was almost the reverse of Christie's, though the effect was quite similar. The ring finger had been smashed so badly that the joints had frozen; it could not be bent. Consequently, the two fingers on either side had limited motion, as well, though the joint capsules were intact.

"The difference being that your hand isn't getting any worse," I told Jamie. "His is."

Christie made a small movement, pushing his right hand down between his thighs, as though to hide it.

"Aye, well," he said uncomfortably. "It can bide awhile, surely."

"At least long enough to let my wife mend the other," Jamie observed, pouring out a cup of wine. "Here—can ye hold it, Tom, or shall I—?" He made a questioning gesture, holding the cup as though to feed it to Christie, who snatched his right hand out of the sheltering folds of his clothes.

"I'll manage," he snapped, and took the wine—holding the cup between thumb and forefinger with an awkwardness that made him flush even more deeply. His left hand still hung in the air above his shoulder. He looked foolish, and obviously felt it.

Jamie poured another cup and handed it to me, ignoring Christie. I would have thought it natural tact on his part, were I not aware of the complicated history between the two men. There was always a small barbed edge in any dealings between Jamie and Tom Christie, though they managed to keep an outwardly cordial face on things.

With any other man, Jamie's display of his own injured hand would have been just what it seemed—reassurance, and the offering of fellowship in infirmity. With Tom Christie, it might have been consciously *meant* as reassurance, but there was a threat implied, as well, though perhaps Jamie couldn't help that.

The simple fact was that people came to Jamie for help more often than they did to Christie. Jamie had widespread respect and admiration, despite his crippled hand. Christie was not a personally popular man; he might well lose what social position he had, if he lost his ability to write. And—as I had bluntly noted—Jamie's hand would not get worse.

Christie's eyes had narrowed a little over his cup. He

hadn't missed the threat, whether intended or not. He wouldn't; Tom Christie was a suspicious man by nature, and inclined to see threat where it *wasn't* intended.

"I think that's settled a bit by now; let me take care of it." I took hold of his left hand, gently, and unwrapped it. The bleeding had stopped. I set the hand to soak in a bowl of water boiled with garlic, added a few drops of pure ethanol for additional disinfection, and set about gathering my kit.

It was beginning to grow dark, and I lit the alcohol lamp Brianna had made for me. By its bright, steady flame, I could see that Christie's face had lost its momentary flush of anger. He wasn't as pale as he had been, but looked uneasy as a vole at a convention of badgers, his eyes following my hands as I laid out my sutures, needles, and scissors, all clean and gleaming-sharp in the light.

Jamie didn't leave, but stayed leaning against the counter, sipping his own cup of wine—presumably, in case Christie passed out again.

A fine trembling ran through Christie's hand and arm, braced as they were on the table. He was sweating again; I could smell it, acrid and bitter. It was the scent of that, half-forgotten, but immediately familiar, that finally made me realize the difficulty: it was fear. He was afraid of blood, perhaps; afraid of pain, certainly.

I kept my eyes fixed on my work, bending my head lower to keep him from seeing anything in my face. I should have seen it sooner; I would have, I thought, had he not been a man. His paleness, the fainting . . . not due to loss of blood, but to shock at seeing blood lost.

I stitched up men and boys routinely; mountain farming was rough work, and it was a rare week when I wasn't presented with ax wounds, hoe gouges, spud slashes, hog bites, scalp lacerations sustained while falling over something, or some other minor calamity requiring stitches. By and large, all my patients behaved with complete matter-of-factness, accepting my ministrations stoically, and going right back to work. But nearly all of the men were Highlanders, I realized, and many not only Highlanders but erstwhile soldiers.

Tom Christie was a townsman, from Edinburgh—he had been imprisoned in Ardsmuir as a Jacobite supporter, but had never been a fighting man. He had been a commissary officer. In fact, I realized with surprise, he had likely never even *seen* a real military battle, let alone engaged in the daily physical conflict with nature that Highland farming entailed.

I became aware of Jamie, still standing in the shadows, sipping wine and watching with a faintly ironic dispassion. I glanced up quickly at him; his expression didn't alter, though he met my eyes and nodded, very slightly.

Tom Christie's lip was fixed between his teeth; I could hear the faint whistle of his breath. He couldn't see Jamie, but knew he was there; the stiffness of his back said as much. He might be afraid, Tom Christie, but he had some courage to him.

It would have hurt him less, could he have relaxed the clenched muscles of arm and hand. Under the circumstances, though, I could hardly suggest as much. I could have insisted that Jamie leave, but I was nearly finished. With a sigh of mingled exasperation and puzzlement, I clipped the final knot and laid down the scissors.

"All right, then," I said, swiping the last of the coneflower ointment across the wound and reaching for a clean linen bandage. "Keep it clean. I'll make up some fresh ointment for you; send Malva for it. Then come back in a week and I'll take the stitches out." I hesitated, glancing at Jamie. I felt some reluctance to use his presence as blackmail, but it was for Christie's own good.

"I'll take care of your right hand, then, too, shall I?" I said firmly.

He was still sweating, though the color in his face had begun to come back. He glanced at me, and then, involuntarily, at Jamie.

Jamie smiled faintly.

"Go on, then, Tom," he said. "It's naught to trouble ye. No but a wee nick. I've had worse."

The words were spoken casually, but they might as well have been written in flaming letters a foot high. *I've had worse.*

Jamie's face was still in shadow, but his eyes were clearly visible, slanted with his smile.

Tom Christie had not relaxed his rigid posture. He

matched Jamie's stare, closing his gnarled right hand over the bandaged left.

"Aye," he said. "Well." He was breathing deeply. "I will, then." He rose abruptly, knocking the stool aside, and headed for the door, a little off-balance, like a man the worse for strong drink.

At the door, he paused, fumbling for the knob. Finding it, he drew himself up and turned back, looking for Jamie.

"At least," he said, breathing so hard that he stumbled over the words, "at least it will be an honorable scar. Won't it, *Mac Dubh*?"

Jamie straightened up abruptly, but Christie was already out, stamping down the corridor with a step heavy enough to rattle the pewter plates on the kitchen shelf.

"Why, ye wee pissant!" he said, in a tone somewhere between anger and astonishment. His left hand clenched involuntarily into a fist, and I thought it a good thing that Christie had made such a rapid exit.

I was rather unsure as to exactly *what* had happened—or been happening—but relieved that Christie was gone. I'd felt like a handful of grain, trapped between two grindstones, both of them trying to grind each other's faces, with no heed for the hapless corn in between.

"I've never heard Tom Christie call you *Mac Dubh,*" I observed cautiously, turning to tidy away my surgical leavings. Christie was not, of course, a Gaelic-speaker, but I had never heard him use even the Gaelic nickname that the other Ardsmuir men still called Jamie by. Christie always called Jamie "Mr. Fraser," or simply "Fraser," in moments of what passed for cordiality.

Jamie made a derisive Scottish noise, then picked up Christie's half-full cup and thriftily drained it.

"No, he wouldna—frigging Sassenach." Then he caught a glimpse of my face, and gave me a lopsided smile. "I didna mean you, Sassenach."

I knew he didn't mean me; the word was spoken with a completely different—and quite shocking—intonation; a bitterness that reminded me that "Sassenach" was by no means a friendly term in normal usage.

"Why do you call him that?" I asked curiously. "And just what did he mean by that 'honorable scar' crack?"

He looked down, and didn't answer for a moment, though the stiffened fingers of his right hand drummed soundlessly against his thigh.

"Tom Christie's a solid man," he said at last. "But by God, he is a stiff-necked wee son of a bitch!" He looked up then, and smiled at me, a little ruefully.

"Eight years he lived in a cell wi' forty men who had the Gaelic—and he wouldna lower himself to let a word of such a barbarous tongue pass his lips! Christ, no. He'd speak in English, no matter who it was he spoke to, and if it was a man who had no English, why, then, he'd just stand there, dumb as a stone, 'til someone came along to interpret for him."

"Someone like you?"

"Now and then." He glanced toward the window, as though to catch a glimpse of Christie, but the night had come down altogether, and the panes gave back only a dim reflection of the surgery, our own forms ghostlike in the glass.

"Roger did say that Kenny Lindsay mentioned something about Mr. Christie's . . . pretensions," I said delicately.

Jamie shot me a sharp glance at that.

"Oh, he did, did he? So, Roger Mac had second thoughts about his wisdom in taking on Christie as a tenant, I suppose. Kenny wouldna have said, unless he was asked."

I had more or less got used to the speed of his deductions and the accuracy of his insights, and didn't question this one.

"You never told me about that," I said, coming to stand in front of him. I put my hands on his chest, looking up into his face.

He put his own hands over mine, and sighed, deep enough for me to feel the movement of his chest. Then he wrapped his arms around me, and drew me close, so my face rested against the warm fabric of his shirt.

"Aye, well. It wasna really important, ken."

"And you didn't want to think about Ardsmuir, perhaps?"

"No," he said softly. "I have had enough of the past."

My hands were on his back now, and I realized suddenly what Christie had likely meant. I could feel the lines of the scars through the linen, clear to my fingertips as the lines of a fishnet, laid across his skin.

"Honorable scars!" I said, lifting my head. "Why, that little *bastard*! Is that what he meant?"

Jamie smiled a little at my indignation.

"Aye, he did," he said dryly. "That's why he called me *Mac Dubh*—to remind me of Ardsmuir, so I'd ken for sure what he meant by it. He saw me flogged there."

"That—that—" I was so angry, I could barely speak. "I wish I'd stitched his fucking hand to his balls!"

"And you a physician, sworn to do nay harm? I'm verra much shocked, Sassenach."

He was laughing now, but I wasn't amused at all.

"Beastly little coward! He's afraid of blood, did you know that?"

"Well, aye, I did. Ye canna live in a man's oxter for three years without learning a great many things ye dinna want to know about him, let alone something like that." He sobered a bit, though a hint of wryness still lurked at the corner of his mouth. "When they brought me back from being whipped, he went white as suet, went and puked in the corner, then lay down with his face to the wall. I wasna really taking notice, but I remember thinking that was a bit raw; I was the one was a bloody mess, why was he takin' on like a lass wi' the vapors?"

I snorted. "Don't you go making jokes about it! How dare he? And what does he mean, anyway—I know what happened at Ardsmuir, and those bloody well . . . I mean, those certainly *are* honorable scars, and everyone there knew it!"

"Aye, maybe," he said, all hint of laughter disappearing. "That time. But everyone could see when they stood me up that I'd been flogged before, aye? And no man there has ever said a word to me about those scars. Not 'til now."

That brought me up short.

Flogging wasn't merely brutal; it was shameful—meant to permanently disfigure, as well as to hurt, advertising a criminal's past as clearly as a branded cheek or cropped ear. And Jamie would, of course, prefer to have his tongue torn out by the roots, sooner than reveal to anyone the reasons for his scars, even if that meant leaving everyone with the assumption that he had been flogged for some disgraceful act.

I was so used to Jamie's always keeping his shirt on in anyone else's presence that it had never occurred to me that of course the Ardsmuir men would know about the scars on his back. And yet he hid them, and everyone pretended they did not exist—save Tom Christie.

"Hmph," I said. "Well . . . God damn the man, anyway. Why would he say such a thing?"

Jamie uttered a short laugh.

"Because he didna like me watching him sweat. He wanted a bit of his own back, I expect."

"Hmph," I said again, and folded my arms beneath my bosom. "Since you mention it—why *did* you do that? If you knew he couldn't stand blood and the like, I mean, why stay and watch him like that?"

"Because I kent he wouldna whimper or faint if I did," he replied. "He'd let ye thrust red-hot needles through his eyeballs before he'd squeal in front of me."

"Oh, so you noticed that?"

"Well, of course I did, Sassenach. What d'ye think I was there for? Not that I dinna appreciate your skill, but watching ye stitch up wounds isna really good for the digestion." He cast a brief glance at the discarded cloth, splotched with blood, and grimaced. "D'ye think the coffee's gone cold by now?"

"I'll heat it up." I slid the clean scissors back into their sheath, then sterilized the needle I'd used, ran a fresh silk suture through it, and coiled it up in its jar of alcohol—still trying to make sense of things.

I put everything back into the cupboard, then turned to Jamie.

"You aren't afraid of Tom Christie, are you?" I demanded.

He blinked, astonished, then laughed.

"Christ, no. What makes ye think that, Sassenach?"

"Well . . . the way the two of you act sometimes. It's like wild sheep, butting heads to see who's stronger."

"Oh, that." He waved a hand, dismissive. "I've a harder head by far than Tom, and he kens it well enough. But he's no going to give in and follow me round like a yearling lamb, either."

"Oh? But what do you think you're doing, then? You weren't just torturing him to prove you could, were you?"

"No," he said, and smiled faintly at me. "A man stubborn enough to speak English to Hieland men in prison for eight years is a man stubborn enough to fight beside me for the next eight years; that's what I think. It would be good if he were sure of it, himself, though."

I drew a deep breath and sighed, shaking my head.

"I do *not* understand men."

That made him chuckle, deep in his chest.

"Yes, ye do, Sassenach. Ye only wish ye didn't."

The surgery lay neat again, ready for whatever emergencies the morrow might bring. Jamie reached for the lamp, but I laid a hand on his arm, stopping him.

"You promised *me* honesty," I said. "But are you quite sure you're being honest with yourself? You weren't baiting Tom Christie just because he challenges you?"

He stopped, his eyes clear and unguarded, a few inches from mine. He lifted a hand and cupped the side of my face, his palm warm on my skin.

"There are only two people in this world to whom I would never lie, Sassenach," he said softly. "Ye're one of them. And I'm the other."

He kissed me gently on the forehead, then leaned past me and blew out the lamp.

"Mind," his voice came from the darkness, and I saw his tall form silhouetted against the faint oblong of light from the doorway as he straightened up, "I can be fooled. But I wouldna be doing it on purpose."

ROGER MOVED a little, and groaned.

"I think ye broke my leg."

"Did not," said his wife, calmer now, but still disposed to argument. "But I'll kiss it for you, if you want."

"That'd be nice."

Tremendous rustlings of the corn-shuck mattress ensued

as she clambered into position to execute this treatment, ending with a naked Brianna straddling his chest, and leaving him with a view that caused him to wish they'd taken time to light the candle.

She was in fact kissing his shins, which tickled. Given the circumstances, though, he was inclined to put up with it. He reached up with both hands. Lacking light, Braille would do.

"When I was fourteen or so," he said dreamily, "one of the shops in Inverness had a most daring window display—daring for the times, that is—a lady mannequin wearing nothing but underwear."

"Mm?"

"Aye, a full-length pink girdle, garters, the lot—with matching brassiere. Everyone was shocked. Committees were got up to protest, and calls were made to all the ministers in town. Next day, they took it down, but meanwhile, the entire male population of Inverness had been past that window, taking pains to look casual about it. 'Til this minute, I'd always thought that was the most erotic thing I'd ever seen."

She suspended her operations for a moment, and he thought from the sense of movement that she was looking back over her shoulder at him.

"Roger," she said thoughtfully. "I do believe you're a pervert."

"Yes, but one with really good night vision."

That made her laugh—the thing he'd been striving for since he'd finally got her to stop frothing at the mouth—and he raised himself briefly, planting a light kiss on either side of the looming object of his affections before sinking contentedly back onto the pillow.

She kissed his knee, then put her head down, cheek against his thigh, so the mass of her hair spilled over his legs, cool and soft as a cloud of silk threads.

"I'm sorry," she said softly, after a moment.

He made a dismissive noise, and ran a soothing hand over the round of her hip.

"Och, it's no matter. Too bad, though; I wanted to see their faces when they saw what ye'd done."

She snorted briefly, and his leg twitched at the warmth of her breath.

"Their faces were something to see, anyway." She sounded a little bleak. "And it would have been a real anticlimax, after *that.*"

"Well, you're right about that," he admitted. "But ye'll show them tomorrow, when they're in a frame of mind to appreciate it properly."

She sighed, and kissed his knee again.

"I didn't mean it," she said, after a moment. "Implying it was your fault."

"Aye, ye did," he said softly, still caressing. "It's all right. Ye're probably right." Likely she was. He wasn't going to pretend it hadn't hurt to hear it, but he wouldn't let himself be angry; that would help neither of them.

"You don't know that." She raised up suddenly, looming like an obelisk in silhouette against the pale rectangle of the window. Swinging one leg neatly over his supine body, she slithered down beside him. "It could be me. Or neither of us. Maybe it just isn't the right time, yet."

He put an arm around her and hugged her close in answer.

"Whatever the cause, we'll not blame each other, aye?" She made a small sound of assent and nestled closer. Well enough; there was no way to keep from blaming himself, though.

The facts were clear enough; she'd got pregnant with Jemmy after one night—whether with himself, or Stephen Bonnet, no one knew, but once was all it took. Whereas they'd been trying for the last several months, and Jem was looking more and more like being an only child. Possibly he *did* lack the vital spark, as Mrs. Bug and her chums speculated.

Who's your Daddy? echoed mockingly in the back of his mind—in an Irish accent.

He coughed explosively, and settled back, determined not to dwell on *that* little matter.

"Well, I'm sorry, too," he said, changing the subject. "Ye're maybe right about me acting like I'd rather ye cook and clean than mess about with your wee chemistry set."

"Only because you *would,*" she said without rancor.

"It's not so much the not cooking as it is the setting things on fire I mind."

"Well, you'll love the next project, then," she said, nuzzling his shoulder. "It's mostly water."

"Oh . . . good," he said, though even he could hear the dubious note in his voice. "Mostly?"

"There's some dirt involved, too."

"Nothing that burns?"

"Just wood. A little. Nothing special."

She was running her fingers slowly down his chest. He caught her hand and kissed her fingertips; they were smooth, but hard, callused from the constant spinning she did to help keep them clothed.

"Who can find a virtuous woman?" he quoted, *"for her price is far above rubies. She seeketh wool and flax and worketh willingly with her hands. She maketh herself coverings of tapestry; her clothing is silk and purple."*

"I would *love* to find some dye plant that gives a true purple," she said wistfully. "I miss the bright colors. Remember the dress I wore to the man-on-the-moon party? The black one, with the bands of Day-Glo pink and lime green?"

"That was pretty memorable, aye." Privately, he thought the muted colors of homespun suited her much better; in skirts of rust and brown, jackets of gray and green, she looked like some exotic, lovely lichen.

Seized by the sudden desire to see her, he reached out, fumbling on the table by the bed. The little box was where she'd thrown it when they came back. She'd designed it to be used in the dark, after all; a turn of the lid dispensed one of the small, waxy sticks, and the tiny strip of roughened metal glued to the side was cool to his hand.

A *skritch!* that made his heart leap with its simple familiarity, and the tiny flame appeared with a whiff of sulfur—magic.

"Don't waste them," she said, but smiled in spite of the protest, delighted at the sight as she'd been when she first showed him what she'd done.

Her hair was loose and clean, just washed; shimmering over the pale round of her shoulder, clouds of it lying soft over his chest, cinnamon and amber and roan and gold, sparked by the flame.

"She does not fear the snow for her household, for all her

household are clothed in scarlet," he said softly, his free hand round her, twining a lock near her face round his finger, twisting the tiny strand as he'd seen her spin yarn.

The long lids of her eyes closed halfway, like a basking cat's, but the smile remained on that wide, soft mouth—those lips that hurt, then healed. The light glowed in her skin, bronzed the tiny brown mole beneath her right ear. He could have watched her forever, but the match was burning low. Just before the flame touched his fingers, she leaned forward and blew it out.

And in the smoke-wisped dark, whispered in his ear, "*The heart of her husband doth safely trust in her. She will do him good and not evil all the days of her life.* So there."

22

ENSORCELLMENT

TOM CHRISTIE didn't come back to the surgery, but he did send his daughter, Malva, to get the ointment. The girl was dark-haired, slender, and quiet, but seemed intelligent. She paid close attention as I quizzed her on the look of the wound—so far, so good, a bit of redness, but no suppuration, no reddish streaks up the arm—and gave her instructions on how to apply the ointment and change the dressing.

"Good, then," I said, giving her the jar. "If he should begin a fever, come and fetch me. Otherwise, make him come in a week, to have the stitches taken out."

"Yes, ma'am, I'll do that." She didn't turn and go, though, but lingered, her gaze flickering over the mounds of drying herbs on the gauze racks and the implements of my surgery.

"Do you need something else, dear? Or did you have a question?" She'd seemed to understand my instructions perfectly well—but perhaps she wanted to ask something more personal. After all, she had no mother . . .

"Well, aye," she said, and nodded at the table. "I only wondered—what is it that ye write in yon black book, ma'am?"

"This? Oh. It's my surgical notes, and recipes . . . er . . . receipts, I mean, for medicines. See?" I turned the book round and opened it so that she could see the page where I had drawn a sketch of the damage to Miss Mouse's teeth.

Malva's gray eyes were bright with curiosity, and she leaned forward to read, hands carefully folded behind her back as though afraid she might touch the book by accident.

"It's all right," I said, a little amused by her caution. "You can look through it, if you like." I pushed it toward her, and she stepped back, startled. She glanced up at me, a look of doubt wrinkling her brow, but when I smiled at her, she took a tiny, excited breath, and reached out to turn a page.

"Oh, look!" The page she'd turned to wasn't one of mine, but one of Daniel Rawlings's—it showed the removal of a dead child from the uterus, via the use of assorted tools of dilatation and curettage. I glanced at the page, and hastily away. Rawlings hadn't been an artist, but he had had a brutal knack for rendering the reality of a situation.

Malva didn't seem to be distressed by the drawings, though; she was bug-eyed with interest.

I began to be interested, too, watching covertly as she turned pages at random. She naturally paid most attention to the drawings—but she paused to read the descriptions and recipes, as well.

"Why d'ye write things down that ye've done?" she asked, glancing up with raised eyebrows. "The receipts, aye, I see ye might forget things—but why d'ye draw these pictures and write down the bits about how ye took off a toe wi' the frost-rot? Would ye do it differently, another time?"

"Well, sometimes you might," I said, laying aside the stalk of dried rosemary I'd been stripping of its needles. "Surgery isn't the same each time. All bodies are a bit different, and even though you may do the same basic procedure a dozen times, there will be a dozen things that happen differently—sometimes only tiny things, sometimes big ones.

"But I keep a record of what I've done for several reasons,"

I added, pushing back my stool and coming round the table to stand beside her. I turned another few pages, stopping at the record I kept of old Grannie MacBeth's complaints—a list so extensive that I had alphabetized it for my own convenience, beginning with *Arthritis—all joints,* running through *Dyspepsia, Earache,* and *Fainting,* and then onward for most of two pages, terminating with *Womb, prolapsed.*

"Partly, it's so that I'll know what's been done for a particular person, and what happened—so that if they need treatment later, I can look back and have an accurate description of their earlier state. To compare, you see?"

She nodded eagerly.

"Aye, I see. So ye'd know were they getting better or worse. What else, then?"

"Well, the most important reason," I said slowly, seeking the right words, "is so that another doctor—someone who might come later—so that person could read the record, and see how I'd done this or that. It might show them a way to do something they hadn't done themselves—or a better way."

Her mouth pursed up in interest.

"Ooh! Ye mean someone might learn from this"—she touched a finger to the page, delicately—"how to do what it is ye do? Without 'prenticing himself to a doctor?"

"Well, it's best if you have someone to teach you," I said, amused at her eagerness. "And there are things you can't really learn from a book. But if there's no one to learn from—" I glanced out the window, at the vista of green wilderness swarming over the mountains. "It's better than nothing," I concluded.

"Where did you learn?" she asked, curious. "From this book? I see there's another hand, besides yours. Whose was it?"

I ought to have seen that one coming. I hadn't quite bargained on Malva Christie's quickness, though.

"Ah . . . I learned from a *lot* of books," I said. "And from other doctors."

"Other doctors," she echoed, looking at me in fascination. "D'ye call yourself a doctor, then? I didna ken women ever could be."

For the rather good reason that no women *did* call themselves physicians or surgeons now—nor were accepted as such.

I coughed.

"Well . . . it's a name, that's all. A good many people just say wisewoman, or conjure woman. Or *ban-lichtne,*" I added. "But it's all the same, really. It only matters whether I know something that might help them."

"Ban—" She mouthed the unfamiliar word. "I haven't heard that before."

"It's the Gaelic. The Highland tongue, you know? It means 'female healer' or something like."

"Oh, the Gaelic." An expression of mild derision crossed her face; I expected she had absorbed her father's attitude toward the Highlanders' ancient language. She evidently saw something in *my* face, though, for she instantly erased the disdain from her own features and bent over the book again. "Who was it wrote these other bits, then?"

"A man named Daniel Rawlings." I smoothed a creased page, with the usual sense of affection for my predecessor. "He was a doctor from Virginia."

"Him?" She looked up, surprised. "The same who's buried in the boneyard up the mountain?"

"Ah . . . yes, that's him." And the story of how he came to be there was not something to be shared with Miss Christie. I glanced out of the window, estimating the light. "Will your father be wanting his dinner?"

"Oh!" She stood up straight at that, glancing out the window, too, with a faint look of alarm. "Aye, he will." She cast a last look of longing toward the book, but then brushed down her skirt and set her cap straight, ready to go. "I thank ye, Mrs. Fraser, for showing me your wee book."

"Happy to," I assured her sincerely. "You're welcome to come again and look at it. In fact . . . would you—" I hesitated, but plunged on, encouraged by her look of bright interest. "I'm going to take a growth from Grannie Macbeth's ear tomorrow. Would you like to come along with me, to see how? It would be a help to me, to have another pair of hands," I added, seeing sudden doubt war with the interest in her eyes.

"Oh, aye, Mrs. Fraser—I'd dearly like it!" she said. "It's only my father—" She looked uneasy as she said it, but then seemed to make up her mind. "Well . . . I'll come. I'm sure I can talk him round."

"Would it help if I were to send a note? Or come and speak with him?" I was suddenly quite desirous that she should come with me.

She gave a small shake of the head.

"Nay, ma'am, it'll be all right, I'm sure." She dimpled at me suddenly, gray eyes sparkling. "I'll tell him I've had a keek at your black book, and it's no by way of being spells in it, at all, but only receipts for teas and purges. I'll maybe not say about the drawings, though," she added.

"Spells?" I asked incredulously. "Is that what he thought?"

"Oh, aye," she assured me. "He warned me not to touch it, for fear of ensorcellment."

"Ensorcellment," I murmured, bemused. Well, Thomas Christie *was* a schoolmaster, after all. In fact, he might have been right, I thought; Malva glanced back at the book as I went with her to the door, obvious fascination on her face.

23

ANESTHESIA

I CLOSED MY EYES AND, holding my hand a foot or so in front of my face, wafted it gently toward my nose, like one of the *parfumeurs* I'd seen in Paris, testing a fragrance.

The smell hit me in the face like an ocean wave, and with approximately the same effect. My knees buckled, black lines writhed through my vision, and I ceased to make any distinction between up and down.

In what seemed an instant later, I came to, lying on the floor of the surgery with Mrs. Bug staring down at me in horror.

"Mrs. Claire! Are ye all right, *mo gaolach*? I saw ye fall—"

"Yes," I croaked, shaking my head gingerly as I got up on one elbow. "Put—put the cork in." I gestured clumsily at the large open flask on the table, its cork lying alongside. "Don't get your face near it!"

Face averted and screwed into a grimace of caution, she got the cork and inserted it, at arm's length.

"Phew, what *is* yon stuff?" she said, stepping back and making faces. She sneezed explosively into her apron. "I've never smelt anything like that—and Bride kens I've smelt a good many nasty things in this room!"

"That, my dear Mrs. Bug, is ether." The swimming sensation in my head had almost disappeared, replaced by euphoria.

"Ether?" She looked at the distilling apparatus on my counter in fascination, the alcohol bath bubbling gently away in its great glass bubble over a low flame and the oil of vitriol—later to be known as sulfuric acid—slicking its slow way down the slanted tubing, its malign hot scent lurking below the usual surgery smells of roots and herbs. "Fancy! And what's ether, then?"

"It puts people asleep, so they won't feel pain when you cut them," I explained, thrilled by my success. "And I know exactly who I'm going to use it on first!"

"TOM CHRISTIE?" Jamie repeated. "Have ye told him?"

"I told Malva. She's going to work on him; soften him up a bit."

Jamie snorted briefly at the thought.

"Ye could boil Tom Christie in milk for a fortnight, and he'd still be hard as a grindstone. And if ye think he'll listen to his wee lass prattle about a magic liquid that will put him to sleep—"

"No, she isn't to tell him about the ether. I'll do that," I assured him. "She's just going to pester him about his hand; convince him he needs it mended."

"Mm." Jamie still appeared dubious, though not, it seemed, entirely on Thomas Christie's account.

"This ether ye've made, Sassenach. Might ye not kill him with it?"

I had, in fact, worried considerably about that very possibility. I'd done operations frequently where ether was used, and it was on the whole a fairly safe anesthetic. But homemade ether, administered by hand . . . and people *did* die of anesthetic accidents, even in the most careful settings, with trained anesthetists and all sorts of resuscitating equipment to hand. And I remembered Rosamund Lindsay, whose accidental death still haunted my dreams now and then. But the possibility of having a reliable anesthetic, of being able to do surgery without pain—

"I might," I admitted. "I don't think so, but there's always some risk. Worth it, though."

Jamie gave me a slightly jaundiced look.

"Oh, aye? Does Tom think so?"

"Well, we'll find out. I'll explain it all carefully to him, and if he won't—well, he won't. But I do hope he does!"

The edge of Jamie's mouth curled up and he shook his head tolerantly.

"Ye're like wee Jem wi' a new toy, Sassenach. Take care the wheels dinna come off."

I might have made some indignant reply to this, but we had come in sight of the Bugs' cabin, and Arch Bug was sitting on his stoop, peacefully smoking a clay pipe. He took this from his mouth and made to stand up when he saw us, but Jamie motioned him back.

"Ciamar a tha thu, a charaid?"

Arch replied with his customary "Mmp," infused with a tone of cordiality and welcome. A raised white brow in my direction, and a twiddle of the pipe stem toward the trail indicated that his wife was at our house, if that's who I was looking for.

"No, I'm just going into the woods to forage a bit," I said, lifting my empty basket by way of evidence. "Mrs. Bug forgot her needlework, though—may I fetch it for her?"

He nodded, eyes creasing as he smiled round his pipe. He shifted his lean buttocks courteously to allow me to go past him into the cabin. Behind me, I heard a "Mmp?" of invitation, and felt the boards of the stoop shift as Jamie sat down beside Mr. Bug.

There were no windows, and I was obliged to stand still for a moment to let my eyes adjust to the dimness. It was a small cabin, though, and it took no more than half a minute before I could make out the contents: little more than the bed frame, a blanket chest, and a table with two stools. Mrs. Bug's workbag hung from a hook on the far wall, and I crossed to get it.

On the porch behind me, I heard the murmur of male conversation, featuring the quite unusual sound of Mr. Bug's voice. He could and did talk, of course, but Mrs. Bug talked so volubly that when she was present, her spouse's contribution was generally not much more than a smile and an occasional "mmp" of accord or disagreement.

"Yon Christie," Mr. Bug was saying now, in a meditative tone of voice. "D'ye find him strange, *a Sheaumais*?"

"Aye, well, he's a Lowlander," Jamie said, with an audible shrug.

A humorous "mmp" from Mr. Bug indicated that this was a perfectly sufficient explanation, and was succeeded by the sucking noises of a pipe being encouraged to draw.

I opened the bag, to be sure that the knitting was inside; in fact, it was not, and I was obliged to poke round the cabin, squinting in the dimness. Oh—there it was; a dark puddle of something soft in the corner, fallen from the table and knocked aside by someone's foot.

"Is he stranger than he might be, Christie?" I heard Jamie ask, his own tone casual.

I glanced through the door in time to see Arch Bug nod toward Jamie, though he didn't speak, being engaged in a fierce battle with his pipe. However, he raised his right hand and waggled it, displaying the stumps of his two missing fingers.

"Aye," he said finally, releasing a triumphant puff of white smoke with the word. "He wished to ask me whether it hurt a good deal, when this was done."

His face wrinkled up like a paper bag, and he wheezed a little—high hilarity for Arch Bug.

"Oh, aye? And what did ye tell him, then, Arch?" Jamie asked, smiling a little.

Arch sucked meditatively on his pipe, now fully cooperative, then pursed his lips and blew a small, perfect ring of smoke.

"Weeel, I said it didna hurt a bit—at the time." He paused, blue eyes twinkling. "Of course, that may have been because I was laid out cold as a mackerel from the shock of it. When I came round, it stung a bit." He lifted the hand, looking it over dispassionately, then glanced through the door at me. "Ye didna mean to use an ax on poor old Tom, did ye, ma'am? He says ye're set to mend his hand next week."

"Probably not. May I see?" I stepped out on the porch, bending to him, and he let me take the hand, obligingly switching his pipe to the left.

The index and middle finger had been severed cleanly, right at the knuckle. It was a very old injury; so old that it had lost that shocking look common to recent mutilations, where the mind still sees what *should* be there, and tries vainly for an instant to reconcile reality with expectation. The human body is amazingly plastic, though, and will compensate for missing bits as well as it can; in the case of a maimed hand, the remnant often undergoes a subtle sort of useful deformation, to maximize what function remains.

I felt along the hand carefully, fascinated. The metacarpals of the severed digits were intact, but the surrounding tissues had shrunk and twisted, withdrawing that part of the hand slightly, so that the remaining two fingers and the thumb could make a better opposition; I'd seen old Arch use that hand with perfect grace, holding a cup to drink, or wielding the handle of a spade.

The scars over the finger stumps had flattened and paled, forming a smooth, calloused surface. The remaining finger joints were knobbed with arthritis, and the hand as a whole was so twisted that it really didn't resemble a hand anymore—and yet it was not at all repulsive. It felt strong and warm in mine, and in fact, was oddly attractive, in the same way that a piece of weathered driftwood is.

"It was done with an ax, you said?" I asked, wondering exactly how he had managed to inflict such an injury on himself, given that he was right-handed. A slippage might have gashed an arm or leg, but to take two fingers of the same hand right off like that . . . Realization dawned and my grasp tightened involuntarily. Oh, no.

"Oh, aye," he said, and exhaled a plume of smoke. I looked up, straight into his bright blue eyes.

"Who did it?" I asked.

"The Frasers," he said. He squeezed my hand gently, then withdrew his own and turned it to and fro. He glanced at Jamie.

"Not the Frasers of Lovat," he assured him. "Bobby Fraser of Glenhelm, and his nephew. Leslie, his name was."

"Oh? Well, that's good," Jamie replied, one eyebrow lifted. "I shouldna like to hear it was close kin of mine."

Arch chuckled, almost soundlessly. His eyes still gleamed bright in their webs of wrinkled skin, but there was something in that laugh that made me want suddenly to step back a little.

"No, ye wouldna," he agreed. "Nor me. But this was maybe the year ye would have been born, *a Sheaumais,* or a bit before. And there are no Frasers at Glenhelm now."

The hand itself had not troubled me at all, but the imagined vision of how it had got that way was making me a trifle faint. I sat down beside Jamie, not waiting for invitation.

"Why?" I said bluntly. "How?"

He drew on his pipe, and blew another ring. It struck the remnants of the first and both disintegrated in a haze of fragrant smoke. He frowned a little, and glanced down at the hand, now resting on his knee.

"Ah, well. It was my choice. We were bowmen, see," he explained to me. "All the men of my sept, we were brought up to it, early. I'd my first bow at three, and could strike a grouse through the heart at forty feet by the time I was six."

He spoke with an air of simple pride, squinting a little at a small flock of doves that were foraging under the trees nearby, as though estimating how easily he could have bagged one.

"I did hear my father tell of the archers," Jamie said. "At Glenshiels. Many of them Grants, he said—and some Campbells." He leaned forward, elbows on his knees, interested in the story, but wary.

"Aye, that was us." Arch puffed industriously, smoke wreathing up round his head. "We'd crept down through the bracken in the night," he explained to me, "and hid among the rocks above the river at Glenshiels, under the bracken and the rowans. Ye could have stood a foot away and not seen one of us, so thick as it was.

"A bit cramped," he added confidentially to Jamie. "Ye couldna stand up to take a piss, and we'd had our suppers—with a bit o' beer—before we came up the other side o' the mountain. All squatting like women, we were. Trying like the devil to keep our bowstrings dry in our shirts, too, what wi' the rain coming down and dripping down our necks through the fern.

"But come the dawn," he went on cheerfully, "and we stood on the signal and let fly. I will say 'twas a bonny sight, our arrows hailing down from the hills on the poor sods camped there by the river. Aye, your faither fought there, too, *a Sheaumais,*" he added, pointing the stem of his pipe at Jamie. "He was one o' those by the river." A spasm of silent laughter shook him.

"No love lost, then," Jamie replied, very dryly. "Between you and the Frasers."

Old Arch shook his head, not at all discomposed.

"None," he said. He turned his attention back to me, his manner sobering a little.

"So when the Frasers would capture a Grant alone on their land, it was their habit to give him a choice. He could lose his right eye, or the twa fingers of his right hand. Either way, he wouldna draw a bow again against them."

He rubbed the maimed hand slowly to and fro against his thigh, stretching it out, as though his phantom fingers reached and yearned for the touch of singing sinew. Then he shook his head, as though dismissing the vision, and curled his hand into a fist. He turned to me.

"Ye werena intending to take Christie's fingers straight off, were ye, Mrs. Fraser?"

"No," I said, startled. "Of course not. He doesn't think . . . ?"

Arch shrugged, bushy white brows raised toward his receding hairline.

"I couldna say for sure, but he seemed verra much disturbed at the thought of being cut."

"Hmm," I said. I'd have to speak to Tom Christie.

Jamie had stood up to take his leave, and I followed suit automatically, shaking out my skirts and trying to shake out of my head the mental image of a young man's hand, pinned to the ground, and an ax chunking down.

"No Frasers at Glenhelm, ye said?" Jamie asked thoughtfully, looking down at Mr. Bug. "Leslie, the nephew—he would have been Bobby Fraser's heir, would he?"

"Aye, he would." Mr. Bug's pipe had gone out. He turned it over and knocked the dottle neatly out against the edge of the porch.

"Both killed together, were they? I mind my father telling of it, once. Found in a stream, their heads caved in, he said."

Arch Bug blinked up at him, eyelids lowered, lizardlike, against the sun's glare.

"Weel, ye see, *a Sheaumais,*" he said, "a bow's like a goodwife, aye? Knows her master, and answers his touch. An ax, though—" He shook his head. "An ax is a whore. Any man can use one—and it works as well in either hand."

He blew through the stem of the pipe to clear it of ash, wiped the bowl with his handkerchief, and tucked it carefully away—left-handed. He grinned at us, the remnants of his teeth sharp-edged and yellowed with tobacco.

"Go with God, *Seaumais mac Brian.*"

LATER IN THE WEEK, I went to the Christies' cabin, to take the stitches out of Tom's left hand and explain to him about the ether. His son, Allan, was in the yard, sharpening a knife on a foot-treadled grindstone. He smiled and nodded to me, but didn't speak, unable to be heard above the rasping whine of the grindstone.

Perhaps it was that sound, I thought, a moment later, that had aroused Tom Christie's apprehensions.

"I have decided that I shall leave my other hand as it is," he said stiffly, as I clipped the last stitch and pulled it free.

I set down my tweezers and stared at him.

"Why?"

A dull red rose in his cheeks, and he stood up, lifting his chin and looking over my shoulder, so as not to meet my eye.

"I have prayed about it, and I have come to the conclusion that if this infirmity be God's will, then it would be wrong to seek to change it."

I suppressed the strong urge to say "Stuff and nonsense!", but with great difficulty.

"Sit down," I said, taking a deep breath. "And tell me, if you would, just why you think God wants you to go about with a twisted hand?"

He did glance at me then, surprised and flustered.

"Why . . . it is not my place to question the Lord's ways!"

"Oh, isn't it?" I said mildly. "I rather thought that's what you were doing last Sunday. Or wasn't it you I heard, inquiring as to what the Lord thought He was about, letting all these Catholics flourish like the green bay tree?"

The dull red color darkened substantially.

"I am sure you have misunderstood me, Mistress Fraser." He straightened himself still further, so that he was nearly leaning over backward. "The fact remains that I shall not require your assistance."

"Is it because I'm a Catholic?" I asked, settling back on the stool and folding my hands on my knee. "You think perhaps I'll take advantage of you, and baptize you into the church of Rome when you're off your guard?"

"I have been suitably christened!" he snapped. "And I will thank you to keep your Popish notions to yourself."

"I have an arrangement with the Pope," I said, giving him stare for stare. "I issue no bulls on points of doctrine, and he doesn't do surgery. Now, about your hand—"

"The Lord's will—" he began stubbornly.

"Was it the Lord's will that your cow should fall into the gorge and break her leg last month?" I interrupted him. "Because if it was, then you presumably ought to have left her there to die, rather than fetching my husband to help pull her out, and then allowing me to set her leg. How is she, by the way?"

I could see the cow in question through the window, peacefully grazing at the edge of the yard, and evidently untroubled either by her nursing calf, or by the binding I had applied to support her cracked cannon bone.

"She is well, I thank you." He was beginning to sound a

little strangled, though his shirt was loose at the collar. "That is—"

"Well, then," I said. "Do you think the Lord regards you as less deserving of medical help than your cow? It seems unlikely to me, what with Him regarding sparrows and all that."

He'd gone a sort of dusky purple round the jowls by this point, and clutched the defective hand with the sound one, as though to keep it safe from me.

"I see that you have heard something of the Bible," he began, very pompous.

"Actually, I've read it for myself," I said. "I read quite well, you know."

He brushed this remark aside, a dim light of triumph gleaming in his eye.

"Indeed. Then I am sure you will have read the Letter of St. Paul to Timothy, in which he says, *Let a woman be silent*—"

I had, in fact, encountered St. Paul and his opinions before, and had a few of my own.

"I expect St. Paul ran into a woman who could outargue him, too," I said, not without sympathy. "Easier to try to put a stopper on the entire sex than to win his point fairly. I should have expected better of *you,* though, Mr. Christie."

"But that's blasphemy!" he gasped, clearly shocked.

"It is not," I countered, "unless you're saying that St. Paul is actually God—and if you are, then I rather think *that's* blasphemy. But let's not quibble," I said, seeing his eyes begin to bulge. "Let me . . ." I rose from my stool and took a step forward, bringing me within touching distance of him. He backed up so hastily that he bumped into the table and knocked it askew, sending Malva's workbasket, a pottery jug of milk, and a pewter plate cascading to the floor with a crash.

I bent swiftly and grabbed the workbasket, in time to prevent it being soaked by the flood of milk. Mr. Christie had as swiftly seized a rag from the hearth, and bent to mop up the milk. We narrowly missed bumping heads, but did collide, and I lost my balance, falling heavily against him. He caught hold of my arms by reflex, dropping the rag, then hastily let go and recoiled, leaving me swaying on my knees.

He was on his knees, as well, breathing heavily, but now a safe distance away.

"The truth of it is," I said severely, pointing a finger at him, "you're afraid."

"I am not!"

"Yes, you are." I got to my feet, replaced the workbasket on the table, and shoved the rag delicately over the puddle of milk with my foot. "You're afraid that I'll hurt you—but I won't," I assured him. "I have a medicine called ether; it will make you go to sleep, and you won't feel anything."

He blinked at that.

"And perhaps you're afraid that you'll lose a few fingers, or what use of your hand you have."

He was still kneeling on the hearth, staring up at me.

"I can't absolutely guarantee that you won't," I said. "I don't *think* that will happen—but man proposes, and God disposes, doesn't He?"

He nodded, very slowly, but didn't say anything. I took a deep breath, for the moment out of argument.

"I *think* I can mend your hand," I said. "I can't guarantee it. Sometimes things happen. Infections, accidents—something unexpected. But . . ."

I reached out a hand to him, motioning toward the crippled member. Moving like a hypnotized bird trapped in a serpent's gaze, he extended his arm and let me take it. I grasped his wrist and pulled him to his feet; he rose easily and stood before me, letting me hold his hand.

I took it in both of mine and pressed the gnarled fingers back, rubbing my thumb gently over the thickened palmar aponeurosis that was trapping the tendons. I could feel it clearly, could see in my mind exactly how to approach the problem, where to press with the scalpel, how the calloused skin would part. The length and depth of the Z-shaped incision that would free his hand and make it useful once more.

"I've done it before," I said softly, pressing to feel the submerged bones. "I can do it again, God willing. If you'll let me?"

He was only a couple of inches taller than I; I held his eyes, as well as his hand. They were a clear, sharp gray, and searched my face with something between fear and suspicion—but with something else at the back of them. I became quite suddenly aware of his breathing, slow and steady, and felt the warmth of his breath on my cheek.

"All right," he said at last, hoarsely. He pulled his hand away from mine, not abruptly, but almost with reluctance, and stood cradling it in his sound one. "When?"

"Tomorrow," I said, "if the weather is good. I'll need good light," I explained, seeing the startled look in his eyes. "Come in the morning, but don't eat breakfast."

I picked up my kit, bobbed an awkward curtsy to him, and left, feeling rather queer.

Allan Christie waved cheerfully to me as I left, and went on with his grinding.

"DO YOU THINK he'll come?" Breakfast had been eaten, and no sign yet of Thomas Christie. After a night of broken sleep, in which I dreamed repeatedly of ether masks and surgical disasters, I wasn't sure whether I wanted him to come or not.

"Aye, he'll come." Jamie was reading the *North Carolina Gazette,* four months out of date, while munching the last of Mrs. Bug's cinnamon toast. "Look, they've printed a letter from the Governor to Lord Dartmouth, saying what an unruly lot of seditious, conniving, thieving bastards we all are, and asking General Gage to send him cannon to threaten us back into good behavior. I wonder if MacDonald knows that's public knowledge?"

"Did they really?" I said absently. I rose, and picked up the ether mask I had been staring at all through breakfast. "Well, if he does come, I suppose I'd best be ready."

I had the ether mask Bree had made for me and the dropping bottle laid out ready in my surgery, next to the array of instruments I would need for the surgery itself. Unsure, I picked up the bottle, uncorked it, and waved a hand across the neck, wafting fumes toward my nose. The result was a reassuring wave of dizziness that blurred my vision for a moment. When it cleared, I recorked the bottle and set it down, feeling somewhat more confident.

Just in time. I heard voices at the back of the house, and footsteps in the hall.

I turned expectantly, to see Mr. Christie glowering at me from the doorway, his hand curled protectively into his chest.

"I have changed my mind." Christie lowered his brows still further, to emphasize his position. "I have considered the matter, and prayed upon it, and I shall not allow ye to employ your foul potions upon me."

"You stupid man," I said, thoroughly put out. I stood up and glowered back. "What *is* the matter with you?"

He looked taken aback, as though a snake in the grass at his feet had dared to address him.

"There is nothing whatever the matter with me," he said, quite gruff. He lifted his chin aggressively, bristling his short beard at me. "What is the matter with *you,* madam?"

"And I thought it was only Highlanders who were stubborn as rocks!"

He looked quite insulted at this comparison, but before he could take further issue with me, Jamie poked his head into the surgery, drawn by the sounds of altercation.

"Is there some difficulty?" he inquired politely.

"Yes! He refuses—"

"There is. She insists—"

The words collided, and we both broke off, glaring at each other. Jamie glanced from me to Mr. Christie, then at the apparatus on the table. He cast his eyes up to heaven, as though imploring guidance, then rubbed a finger thoughtfully beneath his nose.

"Aye," he said. "Well. D'ye want your hand mended, Tom?"

Christie went on looking mulish, cradling the crippled hand protectively against his chest. After a moment, though, he nodded slowly.

"Aye," he said. He gave me a deeply suspicious look. "But I shall not be having any of this Popish nonsense about it!"

"Popish?" Jamie and I spoke at the same time, Jamie sounding merely puzzled, myself deeply exasperated.

"Aye, and ye need not be thinking ye can cod me into it, either, Fraser!"

Jamie shot me an "I told ye so, Sassenach" sort of look, but squared himself to give it a try.

"Well, ye always were an awkward wee bugger, Tom," he said mildly. "Ye must please yourself about it, to be sure—but I can tell ye from experience that it does hurt a great deal."

I thought Christie paled a little.

"Tom. Look." Jamie nodded at the tray of instruments: two scalpels, a probe, scissors, forceps, and two suture needles, already threaded with gut and floating in a jar of alcohol. They gleamed dully in the sunlight. "She means to cut into your hand, aye?"

"I know that," Christie snapped, though his eyes slid away from the sinister assemblage of sharp edges.

"Aye, ye do. But ye've not the slightest notion what it's like. I have. See here?" He held up his right hand, the back of it toward Christie, and waggled it. In that position, with the morning sun full on it, the thin white scars that laced his fingers were stark against the deep bronze skin.

"That bloody *hurt,*" he assured Christie. "Ye dinna want to do something like that, and there's a choice about it—which there is."

Christie barely glanced at the hand. Of course, I thought, he would be familiar with the look of it; he'd lived with Jamie for three years.

"I have made my choice," Christie said with dignity. He sat down in the chair and laid his hand palm-up on the napkin. All the color had leached out of his face, and his free hand was clenched so hard that it trembled.

Jamie looked at him under heavy brows for a moment, then sighed.

"Aye. Wait a moment, then."

Obviously, there was no further point in argument, and I didn't bother trying. I took down the bottle of medicinal whisky I kept on the shelf and poured a healthy tot into a cup.

"Take a little wine for thy stomach's sake," I said, thrusting it firmly into his upturned hand. "Our mutual acquaintance, St. Paul. If it's all right to drink for the sake of a stomach, surely to goodness you can take a drop for the sake of a hand."

His mouth, grimly compressed in anticipation, opened in surprise. He glanced from the cup to me, then back. He swallowed, nodded, and raised the cup to his lips.

Before he had finished, though, Jamie came back, holding a small, battered green book, which he thrust unceremoniously into Christie's hand.

Christie looked surprised, but held the book out, squinting to see what it was. *HOLY BIBLE* was printed on the warped cover, *King James Version.*

"Ye'll take help where ye can, I suppose?" Jamie said a little gruffly.

Christie looked at him sharply, then nodded, a very faint smile passing through his beard like a shadow.

"I thank you, sir," he said. He took his spectacles out of his coat and put them on, then opened the little book with great care and began to thumb through it, evidently looking for a suitable inspiration for undergoing surgery without anesthetic.

I gave Jamie a long look, to which he responded with the faintest of shrugs. It wasn't merely a Bible. It was the Bible that had once belonged to Alexander MacGregor.

Jamie had come by it as a very young man, when he was imprisoned in Fort William by Captain Jonathan Randall. Flogged once, and awaiting another, frightened and in pain, he had been left in solitary confinement with no company save his thoughts—and this Bible, given to him by the garrison's surgeon for what comfort it might offer.

Alex MacGregor had been another young Scottish prisoner—one who had died by his own hand, rather than suffer the further attentions of Captain Randall. His name was written inside the book, in a tidy, rather sprawling hand. The little Bible was no stranger to fear and suffering, and if it wasn't ether, I hoped it might still possess its own power of anodyne.

Christie had found something that suited him. He cleared his throat, straightened himself in the chair, and laid his hand on the towel, palm up, in such a forthright manner that I wondered whether he had settled on the passage in which the Maccabees willingly present their hands and tongues for amputation at the hands of the heathen king.

A peek over his shoulder indicated that he was somewhere in the Psalms, though.

"At your convenience, then, Mistress Fraser," Christie said politely.

If he wasn't to be unconscious, I needed a bit of extra preparation. Manly fortitude was all very well, and so was Biblical inspiration—but there are relatively few people capable of sitting motionless while having their hand sliced into, and I didn't think Thomas Christie was one of them.

I had a plentiful supply of linen strips for bandaging. I rolled back his sleeve, then used a few of the strips to bind his forearm tightly to the little table, with an additional band holding back the clawed fingers from the site of operation.

Though Christie seemed rather shocked at the notion of drinking liquor while reading the Bible, Jamie—and, just possibly, the sight of the waiting scalpels—had convinced him that circumstances justified it. He had consumed a couple of ounces by the time I had him properly secured and his palm thoroughly swabbed with raw alcohol, and was looking significantly more relaxed than he had upon entering the room.

This sense of relaxation disappeared abruptly when I made the first incision.

His breath rushed out in a high-pitched gasp and he arched upward out of the chair, jerking the table across the floor with a screech. I grabbed his wrist in time to prevent his ripping the bandages away, and Jamie seized him by both shoulders, pressing him back into the chair.

"Now then, now then," Jamie said, squeezing firmly. "You'll do, Tom. Aye, you'll do."

Sweat had popped out all over Christie's face, and his eyes were huge behind the lenses of his spectacles. He gulped, swallowed, took a quick look at his hand, which was welling blood, then looked away fast, white as a sheet.

"If you're going to vomit, Mr. Christie, do it there, will you?" I said, shoving an empty bucket toward him with one foot. I still had one hand on his wrist, the other pressing a wad of sterilized lint hard onto the incision.

Jamie was still talking to him like one settling a panicked horse. Christie was rigid, but breathing hard, and trembling in every limb, including the one I meant to be working on.

"Shall I stop?" I asked Jamie, giving Christie a quick appraisal. I could feel his pulse hammering in the wrist I grasped. He wasn't in shock—quite—but plainly wasn't feeling at all well.

Jamie shook his head, eyes on Christie's face.

"No. Shame to waste that much whisky, aye? And he'll not want to go through the waiting again. Here, Tom, have another dram; it will do ye good." He pressed the cup to Christie's lips, and Christie gulped it without hesitation.

Jamie had let go of Christie's shoulders as he settled; now he took hold of Christie's forearm with one hand, gripping firmly. With the other, he picked up the Bible, which had fallen to the floor, and thumbed it open.

"The right hand of the Lord is exalted," he read, squinting over Christie's shoulder at the book. "*The right hand of the Lord doeth valiantly.* Well, that's appropriate, no?" He glanced down at Christie, who had subsided, his free hand clenched in a fist against his belly.

"Go on," Christie said, voice hoarse.

"I shall not die, but live, and declare the works of the Lord," Jamie went on, his voice low but firm. *"The Lord hath chastened me sore, but he hath not given me over unto death."*

Christie seemed to find this heartening; his breathing slowed a little.

I couldn't spare time to look at him, and his arm under Jamie's grasp was hard as wood. Still, he was beginning to murmur along with Jamie, catching every few words.

"Open to me the gates of righteousness. . . I will praise thee, for thou hast heard me. . . ."

I had the aponeurosis laid bare, and could clearly see the thickening. A flick of the scalpel freed the edge of it; then a ruthless slice, cutting hard down through the fibrous band of tissue . . . the scalpel struck bone, and Christie gasped.

"God is the Lord which has showed us light; bind the sacrifice with cords, even unto the horns of the altar. . . ." I could hear a tinge of amusement in Jamie's voice as he read that bit, and felt the shift of his body as he glanced toward me.

It did look rather as though I had been sacrificing something; hands don't bleed as profusely as head wounds, but there are plenty of small vessels in the palm, and I was hastily blotting away the blood with one hand as I worked with the other; discarded wads of bloodstained lint littered the table and the floor around me.

Jamie was flipping to and fro, picking out random bits of Scripture, but Christie was with him now, speaking the words along with him. I stole a hasty glance at him; his color was still bad, and his pulse thundering, but the breathing was better. He was clearly speaking from memory; the lenses of his spectacles were fogged.

I had the hindering tissue fully exposed now, and was trimming away the tiny fibers from the surface of the tendon. The clawed fingers twitched, and the exposed tendons moved suddenly, silver as darting fish. I grabbed the feebly wiggling fingers and squeezed them fiercely.

"You mustn't move," I said. "I need both hands; I can't hold yours."

I couldn't look up, but felt him nod, and released his fingers. With the tendons gleaming softly in their beds, I removed the last bits of the aponeurosis, sprayed the wound with a mixture of alcohol and distilled water for disinfection, and set about closing the incisions.

The men's voices were no more than whispers, a low susurrus to which I had paid no attention, engrossed as I was. As I relaxed my attention and began to suture the wound, though, I became aware of them again.

"The Lord is my shepherd, I shall not want. . . ."

I looked up, wiping perspiration from my forehead with my sleeve, and saw that Thomas Christie now held the small Bible, closed and pressed against his body with his free arm. His chin jammed hard into his chest, his eyes tight closed and face contorted with pain.

Jamie still held the bound arm tight, but had his other hand on Christie's shoulder, his own head bent near Christie's; his eyes, too, were closed, as he whispered the words.

"Yea, though I walk through the valley of the shadow of death, I will fear no evil. . . ."

I knotted the last suture, clipped the thread, and in the same movement, cut through the linen bindings with my scissors, and let go the breath I'd been holding. The men's voices stopped abruptly.

I lifted the hand, wrapped a fresh dressing tightly around

it, and pressed the clawed fingers gently back, straightening them.

Christie's eyes opened, slowly. His pupils were huge and dark behind his lenses, as he blinked at his hand. I smiled at him, and patted it.

"Surely goodness and mercy shall follow me all the days of my life," I said softly. *"And I shall dwell in the house of the Lord forever."*

24

TOUCH ME NOT

CHRISTIE'S PULSE WAS a little rapid, but strong. I set down the wrist I had been holding, and put the back of my hand against his forehead.

"You're a bit feverish," I said. "Here, swallow this." I put a hand behind his back to help him sit up in bed, which alarmed him. He sat up in a flurry of bedclothes, drawing in his breath sharply as he jostled the injured hand.

I tactfully affected not to notice his discomposure, which I put down to the fact that he was clad in his shirt and I in my nightclothes. These were modest enough, to be sure, with a light shawl covering my linen night rail, but I was reasonably sure that he hadn't been anywhere near a woman in *dishabille* since his wife died—if then.

I murmured something meaningless, holding the cup of comfrey tea for him as he drank, and then settled his pillows in comfortable but impersonal fashion.

Rather than send him back to his own cabin, I had insisted that he stay the night, so I could keep an eye on him in case of postoperative infection. Intransigent as he was by nature, I didn't by any means trust him to follow instructions and not to be slopping hogs, cutting wood, or wiping his backside with the wounded hand. I wasn't letting him out of sight until the incision had begun to granulate—which it should do by the next day, if all went well.

Still shaky from the shock of surgery, he had made no demur, and Mrs. Bug and I had put him to bed in the Wemysses' room, Mr. Wemyss and Lizzie having gone to the McGillivrays'.

I had no laudanum, but had slipped Christie a strong infusion of valerian and St. John's wort, and he had slept most of the afternoon. He had declined any supper, but Mrs. Bug, who approved of Mr. Christie, had been plying him through the evening with toddies, syllabubs, and other nourishing elixirs—all containing a high percentage of alcohol. Consequently, he seemed rather dazed, as well as flushed, and made no protest as I picked up the bandaged hand and brought the candle close to examine it.

The hand was swollen, which was to be expected, but not excessively so. Still, the bandage was tight, and cutting uncomfortably into the flesh. I snipped it, and holding the honeyed dressing that covered the wound carefully in place, lifted the hand and sniffed at it.

I could smell honey, blood, herbs, and the faintly metallic scent of fresh-severed flesh—but no sweet whiff of pus. Good. I pressed carefully near the dressing, watching for signs of sharp pain or streaks of vivid red in the skin, but bar a reasonable tenderness, I saw only a small degree of inflammation.

Still, he *was* feverish; it would bear watching. I took a fresh length of bandage and wound it carefully over the dressing, finishing with a neat bow at the back of the hand.

"Why do you never wear a proper kerch or cap?" he blurted.

"What?" I looked up in surprise, having temporarily forgotten the man attached to the hand. I put my free hand to my head. "Why should I?"

I sometimes plaited my hair before bed, but hadn't tonight. I had brushed it, though, and it floated loose around my shoulders, smelling pleasantly of the hyssop and nettle-flower infusion I combed through it to keep lice at bay.

"Why?" His voice rose a little. *"Every woman that*

prayeth or prophesieth with her head uncovered dishonoureth her head: for that is even all one as if she were shaven."

"Oh, are we back to Paul again?" I murmured, returning my attention to his hand. "Does it not occur to you that that man had rather a bee in his bonnet when it came to women? Besides, I'm not praying at the moment, and I want to see how this does overnight, before I risk any prophesying about it. So far, though, it seems—"

"Your hair." I looked up to see him staring at me, mouth curved downward in disapproval. "It's . . ." He made a vague movement round his own clipped poll. "It's . . ."

I raised my brows at him.

"There's a great deal of it," he ended, rather feebly.

I eyed him for a moment, then put down his hand and reached for the little green Bible, which was sitting on the table.

"Corinthians, was it? Hmm, oh, yes, here we are." I straightened my back and read the verse: *"Doth not even nature itself teach you, that, if a man have long hair, it is a shame unto him? But if a woman have long hair, it is a glory to her: for her hair is given her for a covering."* I closed the book with a snap and set it down.

"Would you care to step across the landing and explain to my husband how shameful *his* hair is?" I asked politely. Jamie had gone to bed; a faint, rhythmic snoring was audible from our room. "Or do you expect he knows that already?"

Christie was already flushed from drink and fever; at this, an ugly dark red washed him from chest to hairline. His mouth moved, opening and closing soundlessly. I didn't wait for him to decide on something to say, but merely turned my attention back to his hand.

"Now," I said firmly, "you must do exercise regularly, to make sure that the muscles don't contract as they heal. It will be painful at first, but you must do it. Let me show you."

I took hold of his ring finger, just below the first joint, and keeping the finger itself straight, bent the top joint a little inward.

"Do you see? Here, you do it. Take hold with your other hand, and then try to bend just that one joint. Yes, that's it.

Do you feel the pull, down through the palm of your hand? That's just what's wanted. Now, do it with the little finger . . . yes. Yes, that's very good!"

I looked up and smiled at him. The flush had faded a little, but he still looked thoroughly nonplussed. He didn't smile back at me, but glanced hastily away, down at his hand.

"Right. Now, put your hand flat on the table—yes, that's the way—and try to raise your fourth finger and little finger by themselves. Yes, I know it isn't easy. Keep trying, though. Are you hungry, Mr. Christie?"

His stomach had given a loud growl, startling him as much as me.

"I suppose I might eat," he mumbled ungraciously, scowling at his uncooperative hand.

"I'll fetch you something. Keep trying those exercises for a bit, why don't you?"

The house was quiet, settled for the night. Warm as it was, the shutters had been left open, and enough moonlight streamed through the windows that I didn't need to light a candle. A shadow detached itself from the darkness in my surgery, and followed me down the hallway to the kitchen—Adso, leaving off his nocturnal hunt for mice, in hopes of easier prey.

"Hallo, cat," I said, as he slithered past my ankles into the pantry. "If you think you're having any of the ham, think again. I might go as far as a saucer of milk, though." The milk jug was white earthenware with a blue band round it, a squat, pale shape floating in the darkness. I poured out a saucer and put it down on the floor for Adso, then set about assembling a light supper—aware that Scottish expectations of a light meal involved sufficient food to founder a horse.

"Ham, cold fried potatoes, cold fried mush, bread and butter," I chanted under my breath, shoveling it all onto a large wooden tray. "Rabbit dumpling, tomato pickle, a bit of raisin pie for pudding . . . what else?" I glanced down toward the soft lapping noises coming from the shadows at my feet. "I'd give him milk, too, but he wouldn't drink it. Well, we might as well keep on as we've started, I suppose; it will help him to sleep." I reached for the whisky decanter and put that on the tray, as well.

A faint scent of ether floated in the dark air of the hallway as I made my way back toward the stairs. I sniffed suspiciously—had Adso tipped over the bottle? No, it wasn't strong enough for that, I decided, just a few wayward molecules seeping around the cork.

I was simultaneously relieved and regretful that Mr. Christie had refused to let me use the ether. Relieved, because there was no telling how it might have worked—or not. Regretful, because I would have liked very much to add the gift of unconsciousness to my arsenal of skills—a precious gift to bestow on future patients, and one I should very much have liked to give Mr. Christie.

Beyond the fact that the surgery had hurt him badly, it was very much more difficult to operate on a conscious person. The muscles were tensed, adrenaline was flooding through the system, heart rate was vastly speeded up, causing blood to spurt rather than flow. . . . For the dozenth time since the morning, I envisioned exactly what I had done, asking myself whether I might have done better.

To my surprise, Christie was still doing the exercises; his face was sheened with sweat and his mouth set grimly, but he was still doggedly bending the joints.

"That's very good," I said. "Do stop now, though. I don't want you to start bleeding again." I picked up the napkin automatically and blotted the sweat from his temples.

"Is there someone else in the house?" he asked, irritably jerking his head away from my ministrations. "I heard you speaking to someone downstairs."

"Oh," I said, rather embarrassed. "No, just the cat." Prompted by this introduction, Adso, who had followed me upstairs, leapt onto the bed and stood kneading the covers with his paws, big green eyes fixed on the plate of ham.

Christie turned a gaze of deep suspicion from the cat to me.

"No, he is not my familiar," I said tartly, scooping up Adso and dumping him unceremoniously on the floor. "He's a cat. Talking to him is slightly less ridiculous than talking to myself, that's all."

An expression of surprise flitted across Christie's face—perhaps surprise that I had read his mind, or simple surprise at my idiocy—but the creases of suspicion round his eyes relaxed.

I cut up his food with brisk efficiency, but he insisted upon feeding himself. He ate clumsily with his left hand, eyes on his plate and brows knotted in concentration.

When he had finished, he drank off a cup of whisky as though it were water, set down the empty cup, and looked at me.

"Mistress Fraser," he said, speaking very precisely, "I am an educated man. I do not think ye are a witch."

"Oh, you don't?" I said, rather amused. "So you don't believe in witches? But there are witches mentioned in the Bible, you know."

He stifled a belch with his fist and regarded me fishily.

"I did not say I do not believe in witches. I do. I said ye aren't one. Aye?"

"I'm very much obliged to hear it," I said, trying not to smile. He was quite drunk; though his speech was even more precise than usual, his accent had begun to slip. Normally, he suppressed the inflections of his native Edinburgh as much as possible, but it was growing broader by the moment.

"A bit more?" I didn't wait for an answer, but poured a solid tot of whisky into his empty cup. The shutters were open and the room was cool, but sweat still gleamed in the creases of his neck. He was clearly in pain, and wasn't likely to sleep again without help.

He sipped it this time, watching me over the rim of the cup as I tidied up the supper leavings. In spite of whisky and a full stomach, he was increasingly restive, shifting his legs beneath the quilt and twitching his shoulders. I thought he needed the chamber pot, and was debating whether I ought to offer to help him with it, or simply leave promptly so he could manage by himself. The latter, I thought.

I was mistaken, though. Before I could excuse myself, he set down his cup on the table and sat up straight in bed.

"Mistress Fraser," he said, fixing me with a beady eye. "I wish to apologize to ye."

"What for?" I said, startled.

His lips pressed tight.

"For . . . my behavior this morning."

"Oh. Well . . . that's quite all right. I can see how the idea of being put to sleep must seem . . . quite peculiar to you."

"I dinna mean that." He glanced up sharply, then down again. "I meant . . . that I . . . could not keep myself still."

I saw the deepening flush rise up his cheeks again, and had a sudden pang of surprised sympathy. He was truly embarrassed.

I set down the tray and sat down slowly on the stool beside him, wondering what I could say that might assuage his feelings—and not make matters worse.

"But, Mr. Christie," I said. "I wouldn't expect *anyone* to hold still while having their hand taken apart. It's—it's simply not human nature!"

He shot me a quick, fierce glance.

"Not even your husband?"

I blinked, taken aback. Not so much by the words, as by the tone of bitterness. Roger had told me a bit of what Kenny Lindsay had said about Ardsmuir. It had been no secret that Christie had been envious of Jamie's leadership then—but what had that to do with this?

"What makes you say that?" I asked quietly. I took his injured hand, ostensibly to check the bindings—in fact, merely to give me somewhere to look other than into his eyes.

"It's true, aye? Your husband's hand." His beard jutted pugnaciously at me. "He said ye'd mended it for him. *He* didna wriggle and squirm when ye did it, now, did he?"

Well, no, he hadn't. Jamie had prayed, cursed, sweated, cried—and screamed, once or twice. But he hadn't moved.

Jamie's hand wasn't a matter I wanted to discuss with Thomas Christie, though.

"Everyone's different," I said, giving him as straight a look as I could. "I wouldn't expect—"

"Ye wouldna expect any man to do as well as him. Aye, I ken that." The dull red color was burning in his cheeks again, and he looked down at his bandaged hand. The fingers of his good hand were clenched in a fist.

"That's not what I meant," I protested. "Not at all! I've stitched wounds and set bones for a good many men—almost all the Highlanders were terribly brave about—" It occurred to me, that fraction of a second too late, that Christie was *not* a Highlander.

He made a deep growling noise in his throat.

"Highlanders," he said, "hmp!" in a tone that made it clear he would have liked to spit on the floor, had he not been in the presence of a lady.

"Barbarians?" I said, responding to the tone. He glanced at me, and I saw his mouth twist, as he had his own moment of belated realization. He looked away, and took a deep breath—I smelled the gust of whisky as he let it out.

"Your husband . . . is . . . certainly a gentleman. He comes of a noble family, if one tainted by treason." The "r"s of "treason" rolled like thunder—he really was quite drunk. "But he is also . . . also . . ." He frowned, groping for a better word, then gave it up. "One of them. Surely ye ken that, and you an Englishwoman?"

"One of them," I repeated, mildly amused. "You mean a Highlander, or a barbarian?"

He gave me a look somewhere between triumph and puzzlement.

"The same thing, is it not?"

I rather thought he had a point. While I had met Highlanders of wealth and education, like Colum and Dougal MacKenzie—to say nothing of Jamie's grandfather, the treasonous Lord Lovat to whom Christie was referring—the fact was that every single one of them had the instincts of a Viking freebooter. And to be perfectly honest, so did Jamie.

"Ah . . . well, they, um, do tend to be rather . . ." I began feebly. I rubbed a finger under my nose. "Well, they are raised to be fighting men, I suppose. Or is that what you mean?"

He sighed deeply, and shook his head a little, though I thought it was not in disagreement, but simply in dismay at the contemplation of Highland customs and manners.

Mr. Christie was himself well-educated, the son of a self-made Edinburgh merchant. As such, he had pretensions—painful ones—to being a gentleman—but would obviously never make a proper barbarian. I could see why Highlanders both puzzled and annoyed him. What must it have been like, I wondered, for him to find himself imprisoned alongside a horde of uncouth—by his standards—violent, flamboyant,

Catholic barbarians, treated—or mistreated—as one of them?

He had leaned back a little on his pillow, eyes closed and mouth compressed. Without opening his eyes, he asked suddenly, "D'ye ken that your husband bears the stripes of flogging?"

I opened my mouth to reply tartly that I *had* been married to Jamie for nearly thirty years—when I realized that the question implied something about the nature of Mr. Christie's own concept of marriage that I didn't want to consider too closely.

"I know," I said instead, briefly, with a quick glance toward the open door. "Why?"

Christie opened his eyes, which were a little unfocused. With some effort, he brought his gaze to bear on me.

"Ye know why?" he asked, slurring a little. "Wha' he did?"

I felt heat rise in my cheeks, on Jamie's behalf.

"At Ardsmuir," Christie said before I could answer, leveling a finger at me. He poked it at the air, almost in accusation. "He claimed a bit of tartan, aye? Forbidden."

"Aye?" I said, in baffled reflex. "I mean—did he?"

Christie shook his head slowly back and forth, looking like a large, intoxicated owl, eyes fixed now and glaring.

"Not his," he said. "A young lad's."

He opened his mouth to speak further, but only a soft belch emerged from it, surprising him. He closed his mouth and blinked, then tried again.

"It was an act of extra . . . extraordinary . . . nobility and—and courage." He looked at me, and shook his head slightly. "Im—incompre . . . hensible."

"Incomprehensible? How he did it, you mean?" I knew how, all right; Jamie was so bloody-mindedly stubborn that he would see out any action he intended, no matter whether hell itself barred the way or what happened to him in the process. But surely Christie knew *that* about him.

"Not how." Christie's head lolled a little, and he pulled it upright with an effort. "Why?"

"Why?" I wanted to say, *Because he's an effing hero, that's why; he can't help it*—but that wouldn't really have been right. Besides, I didn't know why Jamie had done it; he hadn't told me, and I did wonder why not.

"He'd do anything to protect one of his men," I said instead.

Christie's gaze was rather glassy, but still intelligent; he looked at me for a long moment, unspeaking, thoughts passing slowly behind his eyes. A floorboard in the hall creaked, and I strained my ears for Jamie's breathing. Yes, I could hear it, soft and regular; he was still asleep.

"Does he think that I am one of 'his men'?" Christie asked at last. His voice was low, but full of both incredulity and outrage. "Because I am not, I ass—ashure you!"

I began to think that last glass of whisky had been a grave mistake.

"No," I said with a sigh, repressing the urge to close my eyes and rub my forehead. "I'm sure he doesn't. If you mean that"—I nodded at the little Bible—"I'm sure it was simple kindness. He'd do as much for any stranger—you would yourself, wouldn't you?"

He breathed heavily for a bit, glaring, but then nodded once and lay back, as though exhausted—as well he might be. All the belligerence had gone out of him as suddenly as air from a balloon, and he looked somehow smaller, and rather forlorn.

"I am sorry," he said softly. He lifted his bandaged hand a little, and let it fall.

I wasn't sure whether he was apologizing for his remarks about Jamie, or for what he saw as his lack of bravery in the morning. I thought it wiser not to inquire, though, and stood up, smoothing down the linen night rail over my thighs.

I pulled the quilt up a bit and tugged it straight, then blew out the candle. He was no more than a dark shape against the pillows, his breathing slow and hoarse.

"You did very well," I whispered, and patted his shoulder. "Good night, Mr. Christie."

MY PERSONAL BARBARIAN was asleep, but woke, catlike, when I crawled into bed. He stretched out an arm and gathered me into himself with a sleepily interrogative "mmmm?"

I nestled against him, tight muscles beginning to relax automatically into his warmth.

"Mmmm."

"Ah. And how's our wee Tom, then?" He leaned back a little and his big hands came down on my trapezius, kneading the knots from my neck and shoulders.

"Oh. Oh. Obnoxious, prickly, censorious, and very drunk. Otherwise, fine. Oh, yes. More, please—up a bit, oh, yes. Oooh."

"Aye, well, that sounds like Tom at his best—bar the drunkenness. If ye groan like that, Sassenach, he'll think I'm rubbing something other than your neck."

"I do *not* care," I said, eyes closed, the better to appreciate the exquisite sensations vibrating through my spinal column. "I've had quite enough of Tom Christie for the moment. Besides, he's likely passed out by now, with as much as he's had to drink."

Still, I tempered my vocal response, in the interests of my patient's rest.

"Where did that Bible come from?" I asked, though the answer was obvious. Jenny must have sent it from Lallybroch; her last parcel had arrived a few days before, while I was visiting Salem.

Jamie answered the question I'd really asked, sighing so his breath stirred my hair.

"It gave me a queer turn to see it, when I came to it among the books my sister sent. I couldna quite decide what to do with it, aye?"

Little wonder if it had given him a turn.

"Why did she send it, did she say?" My shoulders were beginning to relax, the ache between them dulling. I felt him shrug behind me.

"She sent it with some other books; said she was turning out the attic and found a box of them, so decided to send them to me. But she did mention hearing that the village of Kildennie had decided to emigrate to North Carolina; they're all MacGregors up near there, ken?"

"Oh, I see." Jamie had once told me that his intention was

one day to find the mother of Alex MacGregor, and give her his Bible, with the information that her son had been avenged. He had made inquiries after Culloden, but discovered that both of the MacGregor parents were dead. Only a sister remained alive, and she had married and left her home; no one knew quite where she was, or even whether she was still in Scotland.

"Do you think Jenny—or Ian, rather—found the sister at last? And she lived in that village?"

He shrugged again, and with a final squeeze of my shoulders, left off.

"It may be. Ye ken Jenny; she'd leave it to me whether to search for the woman."

"And will you?" I rolled over to face him. Alex MacGregor had hanged himself, rather than live as prey to Black Jack Randall. Jack Randall was dead, had died at Culloden. But Jamie's memories of Culloden were no more than fragments, driven from him by the trauma of the battle and the fever he had suffered afterward. He had waked, wounded, with Jack Randall's body lying on top of him—but had no recollection of what had happened.

And yet, I supposed, Alex MacGregor *had* been avenged—whether or not by Jamie's hand.

He thought about that for a moment, and I felt the small stirring as he tapped the two stiff fingers of his right hand against his thigh.

"I'll ask," he said finally. "Her name was Mairi."

"I see," I said. "Well, there can't be more than, oh . . . three or four hundred women named Mairi in North Carolina."

That made him laugh, and we drifted off to sleep, to the accompaniment of Tom Christie's stertorous snores across the hall.

IT MIGHT HAVE BEEN minutes or hours later that I woke suddenly, listening. The room was dark, the fire cold on the hearth, and the shutters rattling faintly. I tensed a little, trying to wake enough to rise and go to my patient—but then heard him, a long wheezing inspiration, followed by a rumbling snore.

It wasn't that that had wakened me, I realized. It was the sudden silence beside me. Jamie was lying stiff beside me, scarcely breathing.

I put out a hand slowly, so he would not be shocked at the touch, and rested it on his leg. He hadn't had nightmares for some months, but I recognized the signs.

"What is it?" I whispered.

He drew breath a little deeper than usual, and his body seemed momentarily to draw in upon itself. I didn't move, but left my hand on his leg, feeling the muscle flex microscopically beneath my fingers, a tiny intimation of flight.

He didn't flee, though. He moved his shoulders in a brief, violent twitch, then let out his breath and settled into the mattress. He didn't speak for a bit, but his weight drew me closer, like a moon pulled near to its planet. I lay quiet, my hand on him, my hip against his—flesh of his flesh.

He stared upward, into the shadows between the beams. I could see the line of his profile, and the shine of his eyes as he blinked now and then.

"In the dark . . ." he whispered at last, "there at Ardsmuir, we lay in the dark. Sometimes there was a moon, or starlight, but even then, ye couldna see anything on the floor where we lay. It was naught but black—but ye could hear."

Hear the breathing of the forty men in the cell, and the shuffles and shifts of their movement. Snores, coughing, the sounds of restless sleep—and the small furtive sounds from those who lay awake.

"It would be weeks, and we wouldna think of it." His voice was coming easier now. "We were always starved, cold. Worn to the bone. Ye dinna think much, then; only of how to put one foot in front of another, lift another stone. . . . Ye dinna really *want* to think, ken? And it's easy enough not to. For a time."

But every now and then, something would change. The fog of exhaustion would lift, suddenly, without warning.

"Sometimes ye kent what it was—a story someone told, maybe, or a letter that came from someone's wife or sister. Sometimes it came out of nowhere; no one said a thing, but ye'd wake to it, in the night, like the smell of a woman lying next to ye."

Memory, longing . . . need. They became men touched by fire—roused from dull acceptance by the sudden searing recollection of loss.

"Everyone would go a bit mad, for a time. There would be fights, all the time. And at night, in the dark . . ."

At night, you would hear the sounds of desperation, stifled sobs or stealthy rustlings. Some men would, in the end, reach out to another—sometimes to be rebuffed with shouts and blows. Sometimes not.

I wasn't sure what he was trying to tell me, nor what it had to do with Thomas Christie. Or, perhaps, Lord John Grey.

"Did any of them ever . . . touch you?" I asked tentatively.

"No. None of them would ever think to touch me," he said very softly. "I was their chief. They loved me—but they wouldna think, ever, to touch me."

He took a deep, ragged breath.

"And did you want them to?" I whispered. I could feel my own pulse begin to throb in my fingertips, against his skin.

"I hungered for it," he said so softly I could barely hear him, close as I was. "More than food. More than sleep—though I wished most desperately for sleep, and not only for the sake of tiredness. For when I slept, sometimes I saw ye.

"But it wasna the longing for a woman—though Christ knows, that was bad enough. It was only—I wanted the touch of a hand. Only that."

His skin had ached with need, 'til he felt it must grow transparent, and the raw soreness of his heart be seen in his chest.

He made a small rueful sound, not quite a laugh.

"Ye ken those pictures of the Sacred Heart—the same as we saw in Paris?"

I knew them—Renaissance paintings, and the vividness of stained glass glowing in the aisles of Notre Dame. The Man of Sorrows, his heart exposed and pierced, radiant with love.

"I remembered that. And I thought to myself that whoever saw that vision of Our Lord was likely a verra lonely man himself, to have understood so well."

I lifted my hand and laid it on the small hollow in the

center of his chest, very lightly. The sheet was thrown back, and his skin was cool.

He closed his eyes, sighing, and clasped my hand, hard.

"The thought of that would come to me sometimes, and I would think I kent what Jesus must feel like there—so wanting, and no one to touch Him."

25

ASHES TO ASHES

JAMIE CHECKED HIS saddlebags once more, though he had done it so often of late that the exercise was little more than custom. Each time he opened the left-hand one, he still smiled, though. Brianna had remade it for him, stitching in loops of leather that presented his pistols, hilt up, ready to be seized in an emergency, and a clever arrangement of compartments that held handy his shot pouch, powder horn, a spare knife, a coil of fishing line, a roll of twine for a snare, a hussif with pins, needles, and thread, a packet of food, a bottle of beer, and a neatly rolled clean shirt.

On the outside of the bag was a small pouch that held what Bree was pleased to call a "first-aid kit," though he was unsure what it was meant to be in aid of. It contained several gauze packets of a bitter-smelling tea, a tin of salve, and several strips of her adhesive plaster, none of which seemed likely to be of use in any imaginable misadventure, but did no harm.

He removed a cake of soap she had added, along with a few more unnecessary fripperies, and carefully hid them under a bucket, lest she be offended.

Just in time, too; he heard her voice, exhorting wee Roger about the inclusion of sufficient clean stockings in his bags.

By the time they came round the corner of the hay barn, he had everything securely buckled up.

"Ready, then, *a charaid*?"

"Oh, aye." Roger nodded, and slung the saddlebags he was carrying on his shoulder off onto the ground. He turned to Bree, who was carrying Jemmy, and kissed her briefly.

"I go with *you,* Daddy!" Jem exclaimed hopefully.

"Not this time, sport."

"Wanna see Indians!"

"Later, perhaps, when ye're bigger."

"I can talk Indian! Uncle Ian tellt me! Wanna go!"

"Not this time," Bree told him firmly, but he wasn't inclined to listen, and began struggling to get down. Jamie made a small rumble in his throat, and fixed him with a quelling eye.

"Ye've heard your parents," he said. Jem glowered, and stuck out his lower lip like a shelf, but ceased his fuss.

"Someday ye must tell me how ye do that," Roger said, eyeing his offspring.

Jamie laughed, and leaned down to Jemmy. "Kiss Grandda goodbye, eh?"

Disappointment generously abandoned, Jemmy reached up and seized him round the neck. He picked the little boy up out of Brianna's arms, hugged him, and kissed him. Jem smelled of parritch, toast, and honey, a homely warm and heavy weight in his arms.

"Be good and mind your mother, aye? And when ye're a wee bit bigger, ye'll come, too. Come and say farewell to Clarence; ye can tell him the words Uncle Ian taught ye." And God willing, they'd be words suitable for a three-year-old child. Ian had a most irresponsible sense of humor.

Or perhaps, he thought, grinning to himself, *I'm only recalling some o' the things I taught Jenny's bairns—including Ian—to say in French.*

He'd already saddled and bridled Roger's horse, and Clarence the pack mule was fully loaded. Brianna was checking the girth and stirrup leathers while Roger slung his saddlebags—more to keep herself busy than because of any need. Her lower lip was caught in her teeth; she was being careful not to seem worried, but was fooling no one.

Jamie took Jem up to pat the mule's nose, in order to give the lass and her man a moment's privacy. Clarence was a good sort, and suffered Jem's enthusiastic patting and mispronounced Cherokee phrases with long-suffering tolerance, but when Jem turned in his arms toward Gideon, Jamie leaned back sharply.

"Nay, lad, ye dinna want to touch yon wicked bugger. He'll take your hand right off."

Gideon twitched his ears and stamped once, impatient. The big stallion was dying to get under way and have another chance at killing him.

"Why do you keep that vicious thing?" Brianna asked, seeing Gideon's long lip wrinkle back to show his yellow teeth in anticipation. She took Jemmy from him, stepping well away from Gideon.

"What, wee Gideon? Oh, we get on. Besides, he's half my trade goods, lass."

"Really?" She gave the big chestnut a suspicious glance. "Are you sure you won't start a war, giving the Indians something like him?"

"Oh, I dinna mean to give him to them," he assured her. "Not directly, at least."

Gideon was a bad-tempered, thrawn-headed reester of a horse, with a mouth like iron and a will to match. However, these unsociable qualities seemed most appealing to the Indians, as did the stallion's massive chest, long wind, and stoutly muscled frame. When Quiet Air, the sachem in one of the villages, had offered him three deerskins for the chance to breed his spotted mare to Gideon, Jamie had realized suddenly that he had something here.

"'Twas the greatest good fortune that I never found the time to castrate him," he said, slapping Gideon familiarly on the withers and dodging by reflex as the stallion whipped his head round to snap. "He earns his keep, and more, standing at stud to the Indian ponies. It's the only thing I've ever asked him to do that he's not balked at."

The lass was pink as a Christmas rose from the morning cold; she laughed at that, though, going an even deeper color.

"What's castrate?" Jemmy inquired.

"Your mother will tell ye." He grinned at her, ruffled Jemmy's hair, and turned to Roger. "Ready, lad?"

Roger Mac nodded and stepped up into his stirrup, swinging aboard. He had a steady old bay gelding named Agrippa, who tended to grunt and wheeze, but was sound enough for all that, and good for a rider like Roger—competent enough, but with an abiding sense of inner reservation about horses.

Roger leaned down from the saddle for a last kiss from Brianna, and they were under way. Jamie'd taken a private—and thorough—leave of Claire earlier.

She was in the window of their bedroom, watching out to wave to them as they rode past, her hairbrush in her hand. Her hair was standing out in a great curly swash round her head, and the early-morning sun caught in it like flames in a thornbush. It gave him a sudden queer feeling to see her thus so disordered, half-naked in her shift. A sense of strong desire, despite what he'd done to her not an hour past. And something almost fear, as though he might never see her again.

Quite without thought, he glanced at his left hand, and saw the ghost of the scar at the base of his thumb, the "C" so faded that it was scarcely visible. He had not noticed it or thought of it in years, and felt suddenly as though there was not air enough to breathe.

He waved, though, and she threw him a mocking kiss, laughing. Christ, he'd marked *her;* he could see the dark patch of the love bite he'd left on her neck, and a hot flush of embarrassment rose in his face. He dug his heels into Gideon's side, causing the stallion to give a squeal of displeasure and turn round to try to bite him in the leg.

With this distraction, they were safe away. He looked back only once, at the trailhead, to see her still there, framed by light. She lifted one hand, as though in benediction, and then the trees hid her from sight.

THE WEATHER WAS FAIR, though cold for as early in the autumn as it was; the horses' breath steamed as they made their way down from the Ridge through the tiny settlement folk now called Cooperville, and along the Great Buffalo

Trail to the north. He kept an eye on the sky; it was much too early for snow, but heavy rains were not uncommon. What clouds there were were mare's tails, though; no cause for worry.

They didn't speak much, each man alone with his thoughts. Roger Mac was easy company, for the most part. Jamie did miss Ian, though; he would have liked to talk over the situation as it stood now with Tsisqua. Ian understood the minds of Indians better than most white men, and while Jamie understood Bird's gesture of sending the hermit's bones well enough—it was meant as a proof of his continuing goodwill toward settlers, if the King should send them guns—he would have valued Ian's opinion.

And while it was necessary that he introduce Roger Mac in the villages, for the sake of future relations . . . Well, he blushed at the thought of having to explain to the man about . . .

Damn Ian. The lad had simply gone in the night, a few days past, him and his dog. He'd done it before, and would doubtless be back as suddenly as he'd gone. Whatever darkness he'd brought back from the north would now and then become too much for him, and he would vanish into the wood, coming back silent and withdrawn, but somewhat more at peace with himself.

Jamie understood it well enough; solitude was in its own way a balm for loneliness. And whatever memory the lad was fleeing—or seeking—in the wood . . .

"Has he ever spoken to you about them?" Claire had asked him, troubled. *"His wife? His child?"*

He had not. Ian did not speak of anything about his time among the Mohawk, and the only token he had brought back from the north was an armlet, made of blue-and-white wampum shells. Jamie had caught a glimpse of it in Ian's sporran once, but not enough to tell the pattern of it.

Blessed Michael defend you, lad, he thought silently toward Ian. *And may the angels mend you.*

With one thing and another, he had no real conversation with Roger Mac until they'd stopped for their noon meal. They ate the fresh stuff the women had sent, enjoying it. Enough for supper left; next day, it would be corn dodgers and anything that came across their path that could be easily caught and cooked. And one day more, and the Snowbird women would have them royally fed, as representatives of the King of England.

"Last time, it was ducks, stuffed wi' yams and corn," he told Roger. "It's manners to eat as much as ye can, mind, no matter what's served, and ye're the guest."

"Got it." Roger smiled faintly, then looked down at the half-eaten sausage roll in his hand. "About that. Guests, I mean. There's a wee problem, I think—with Hiram Crombie."

"Hiram?" Jamie was surprised. "What's to do wi' Hiram?"

Roger's mouth twitched, unsure whether to laugh or not.

"Well, it's only—ye ken everybody's calling the bones we buried Ephraim, aye? It's all Bree's fault, but there it is."

Jamie nodded, curious.

"Well, so. Yesterday Hiram came along to me, and said he'd been studying upon the matter—praying and the like—and had come to the conclusion that if it were true that some of the Indians were his wife's kin, then it stood to reason that some of them must be saved, as well."

"Oh, aye?" Amusement began to kindle in his own breast.

"Yes. And so, he says, he feels called upon to bring these hapless savages the word of Christ. For how else are they to hear it?"

Jamie rubbed a knuckle over his upper lip, torn now between amusement and dismay at the thought of Hiram Crombie invading the Cherokee villages, psalmbook in hand.

"Mmphm. Well, but . . . do ye not believe—Presbyterians, I mean—that it's all predestined? That some are saved, I mean, and some damned, and not a thing to be done about it? Which is why the Papists are all bound for hell in a handbasket?"

"Ah . . . well . . ." Roger hesitated, clearly not quite willing to put the matter so baldly himself. "Mmphm. There may be some difference of opinion among Presbyterians, I imagine. But yes, that's more or less what Hiram and his cohorts think."

"Aye. Well, then, if he thinks some o' the Indians must be saved already, why must they be preached to?"

Roger rubbed a finger between his brows.

"Well, d'ye see, it's the same reason Presbyterians pray

and go to kirk and all. Even if they're saved, they feel they want to praise God for it, and—and learn to do better, so as to live as God wishes them to. In gratitude for their salvation, see?"

"I rather think Hiram Crombie's God might take a dim view of the Indian way of living," Jamie said, with vivid memories of naked bodies in the dimness of ember glow, and the smell of furs.

"Quite," Roger said, catching Claire's dry tone so exactly that Jamie laughed.

"Aye, I see the difficulty," he said, and he did, though he still found it funny. "So Hiram means to go to the Cherokee villages and preach? Is that it?"

Roger nodded, swallowing a bit of sausage.

"To be more exact, he wants you to take him there. And make introduction for him. He wouldna expect ye to interpret the preaching, he says."

"Holy God." He took a moment to contemplate this prospect, then shook his head decidedly. "No."

"Of course not." Roger pulled the cork from a bottle of beer, and offered it to him. "I just thought I should tell ye, so ye can decide best what to say to him when he asks."

"Verra thoughtful of ye," Jamie said, and taking the bottle, drank deeply.

He lowered it, took breath—and froze. He saw Roger Mac's head turn sharply and knew he had caught it, too, borne on the chilly breeze.

Roger Mac turned back to him, black brows furrowed.

"Do ye smell something burning?" he said.

ROGER HEARD THEM first: a raucous caucus of cries and cackles, shrill as witches. Then a clappering of wings as they came in sight, and the birds flew up, mostly crows, but here and there a huge black raven.

"Oh, God," he said softly.

Two bodies hung from a tree beside the house. What was left of them. He could tell that it was a man and a woman, but only by their clothes. A piece of paper was pinned to the man's leg, so crumpled and stained that he saw it only because one edge lifted in the breeze.

Jamie ripped it off, unfolded it enough to read, and threw it on the ground. *Death to Regulators,* it read; he saw the scrawl for an instant, before the wind blew it away.

"Where are the bairns?" Jamie asked, turning sharply to him. "These folk have children. Where are they?"

The ashes were cold, already scattering in the wind, but the smell of burning filled him, clogged his breathing, seared his throat so that words rasped like gravel, meaningless as the scrape of pebbles underfoot. Roger tried to speak, cleared his throat, and spat.

"Hiding, maybe," he rasped, and flung out an arm toward the wood.

"Aye, maybe." Jamie stood abruptly, called into the wood, and, not waiting for an answer, set off into the trees, calling again.

Roger followed, sheering off as they reached the forest's edge, going upslope behind the house, both of them shouting words of reassurance that were swallowed up at once by the forest's silence.

Roger stumbled through the trees, sweating, panting, heedless of the pain in his throat as he shouted, barely stopping long enough to hear if anyone answered. Several times he saw movement from the corner of his eye and swung toward it, only to see nothing but the ripple of wind through a patch of drying sedges, or a dangling creeper, swaying as though someone had passed that way.

He half-imagined he was seeing Jem, playing at hide-and-seek, and the vision of a darting foot, sun gleaming off a small head, lent him strength to shout again, and yet again. At last, though, he was forced to admit that children would not have run so far, and he circled back toward the cabin, still calling intermittently, in hoarse, strangled croaks.

He came back into the dooryard to find Jamie stooping for a rock, which he threw with great force at a pair of ravens that had settled in the hanging tree, edging bright-eyed back toward its burden. The ravens squawked and flapped away—but only so far as the next tree, where they sat watching.

The day was cold, but both of them were soaked with

sweat, hair straggling wet on their necks. Jamie wiped his face with his sleeve, still breathing hard.

"H-how many . . . children?" Roger's own breath was short, his throat so raw that the words were barely a whisper.

"Three, at least." Jamie coughed, hawked, and spat. "The eldest is twelve, maybe." He stood for a moment, looking at the bodies. Then he crossed himself and drew his dirk to cut them down.

They had nothing to dig with; the best that could be managed was a wide scrape in the leaf mold of the forest, and a thin cairn of rocks, as much to spite the ravens as for the sake of decency.

"Were they Regulators?" Roger asked, pausing in the midst of it to wipe his face on his sleeve.

"Aye, but . . ." Jamie's voice trailed away. "It's naught to do wi' that business." He shook his head and turned away to gather more rocks.

Roger thought it *was* a rock at first, half-hidden in the leaves that had drifted against the scorched cabin wall. He touched it, and it moved, bringing him to his feet with a cry that would have done credit to any of the corbies.

Jamie reached him in seconds, in time to help dig the little girl out of the leaves and cinders.

"Hush, *a muirninn,* hush," Jamie said urgently, though in fact the child was not crying. She was maybe eight, her clothes and hair burned away and her skin so blackened and cracked that she might have been made of stone indeed, save for her eyes.

"Oh, God, oh, God." Roger kept saying it, under his breath, long after it became clear that if it was a prayer, it was long past answering.

He was cradling her against his chest, and her eyes opened halfway, regarding him with nothing like relief or curiosity—only a calm fatality.

Jamie had poured water from his canteen onto a handkerchief; he fed the tip of it between her lips to wet them, and Roger saw her throat move in reflex as she sucked.

"Ye'll be all right," Roger whispered to her. "It's all right, *a leannan.*"

"Who has done this, *a nighean*?" Jamie asked, just as gently. Roger saw that she understood; the question stirred the surface of her eyes like wind on a pond—but then passed over, leaving them calm again. She did not speak, no matter what questions they asked, only looked at them with incurious eyes, and went on sucking dreamily at the wet cloth.

"Are ye baptized, *a leannan*?" Jamie asked her at last, and Roger felt a deep jolt at the question. In the shock of finding her, he had not truly taken in her condition.

"Elle ne peut pas vivre," Jamie said softly, his eyes meeting Roger's. She cannot live.

His first instinct was a visceral denial. Of course she could live, she must. But huge patches of her skin were gone, the raw flesh crusted but still oozing. He could see the white edge of a knee bone, and literally see her heart beating, a reddish, translucent bulge that pulsed at the notch of her rib cage. She was light as a corn-dolly, and he became painfully aware that she seemed to float in his arms, like a slick of oil on water.

"Does it hurt, sweetheart?" he asked her.

"Mama?" she whispered. Then she closed her eyes and would say no more, only muttering "Mama?" now and then.

He had thought at first they would take her back to the Ridge, to Claire. But it was more than a day's ride; she wouldn't make it. Not possibly.

He swallowed, realization closing on his throat like a noose. He looked at Jamie, seeing the same sick acknowledgment in his eyes. Jamie swallowed, too.

"Do ye . . . know her name?" Roger could scarcely breathe, and forced the words. Jamie shook his head, then gathered himself, hunching his shoulders.

She had stopped sucking, but still murmured "Mama?" now and then. Jamie took the handkerchief from her lips and squeezed a few drops from it onto her blackened forehead, whispering the words of baptism.

Then they looked at each other, acknowledging necessity. Jamie was pale, sweat beading on his upper lip among the bristles of red beard. He took a deep breath, steeling himself, and lifted his hands, offering.

"No," Roger said softly. "I'll do it." She was his; he could no more surrender her to another than he could have torn off an arm. He reached for the handkerchief, and Jamie put it into his hand, soot-stained, still damp.

He'd never thought of such a thing, and couldn't think now. He didn't need to; without hesitation, he cradled her close and put the handkerchief over her nose and mouth, then clamped his hand tight over the cloth, feeling the small bump of her nose caught snug between his thumb and index finger.

Wind stirred in the leaves above, and a rain of gold fell on them, whispering on his skin, brushing cool past his face. She would be cold, he thought, and wished to cover her, but had no hand to spare.

His other arm was round her, hand resting on her chest; he could feel the tiny heart beneath his fingers. It jumped, beat rapidly, skipped, beat twice more . . . and stopped. It quivered for a moment; he could feel it trying to find enough strength to beat one last time, and suffered the momentary illusion that it would not only do so, but would force its way through the fragile wall of her chest and into his hand in its urge to live.

But the moment passed, as did the illusion, and a great stillness came. Near at hand, a raven called.

THEY HAD ALMOST finished the burying, when the sound of hooves and jingling harness announced visitors—a lot of visitors.

Roger, ready to decamp into the woods, glanced at his father-in-law, but Jamie shook his head, answering his unasked question.

"Nay, they'd no come back. What for?" His bleak gaze took in the smoking ruin of the homestead, the trampled dooryard, and the low mounds of the graves. The little girl still lay nearby, covered with Roger's cloak. He hadn't been able to bear putting her into the ground just yet; the knowledge of her alive was still too recent.

Jamie straightened, stretching his back. Roger saw him glance to see that his rifle was to hand, leaning against a tree trunk. Then he settled himself, leaning on the scorched board he had been using as a shovel, waiting.

The first of the riders came out of the woods, his horse

snorting and tossing its head at the smell of burning. The rider pulled it skillfully round and urged it closer, leaning forward to see who they were.

"So it's you, is it, Fraser?" Richard Brown's lined face looked grimly jovial. He glanced at the charred and steaming timbers, then round at his comrades. "Didn't think you made your money just by selling whisky."

The men—Roger counted six of them—shifted in their saddles, snorting with amusement.

"Have a bit o' respect for the dead, Brown." Jamie nodded at the graves, and Brown's face hardened. He glanced sharply at Jamie, then at Roger.

"Just the two of you, is it? What are you doing here?"

"Digging graves," Roger said. His palms were blistered; he rubbed a hand slowly on the side of his breeches. "What are *you* doing here?"

Brown straightened abruptly in his saddle, but it was his brother Lionel who answered.

"Coming down from Owenawisgu," he said, jerking his head at the horses. Looking, Roger saw that there were four packhorses, laden with skins, and that several of the other horses carried bulging saddlebags. "Smelled the fire and come to see." He glanced down at the graves. "Tige O'Brian, was it?"

Jamie nodded.

"Ye kent them?"

Richard Brown shrugged.

"Aye. It's on the way to Owenawisgu. I've stopped a time or two; taken supper with them." Belatedly, he removed his hat, plastering down wisps of hair over his balding crown with the flat of his hand. "God rest 'em."

"Who's burnt 'em out, if it wasn't you?" one of the younger men in the party called. The man, a Brown by his narrow shoulders and lantern jaw, grinned inappropriately, evidently thinking this a jest.

The singed bit of paper had flown with the wind; it fluttered against a rock near Roger's foot. He picked it up and with a step forward, slapped it against Lionel Brown's saddle.

"Know anything about that, do you?" he asked. "It was pinned to O'Brian's body." He sounded angry, knew it, and didn't care. His throat ached and his voice came out as a strangled rasp.

Lionel Brown glanced at the paper, brows raised, then handed it to his brother.

"No. Write it yourself, did you?"

"What?" He stared up at the man, blinking against the wind.

"Indians," Lionel Brown said, nodding at the house. "Indians done this."

"Oh, aye?" Roger could hear the undercurrents in Jamie's voice—skepticism, wariness, and anger. "Which Indians? The ones from whom ye bought the hides? Told ye about it, did they?"

"Don't be a fool, Nelly." Richard Brown kept his voice pitched low, but his brother flinched a little, hearing it. Brown edged his horse nearer. Jamie stood his ground, though Roger saw his hands tighten on the board.

"Got the whole family, did they?" he asked, glancing at the small body under its cloak.

"No," Jamie said. "We've not found the two elder children. Only the wee lassie."

"Indians," Lionel Brown repeated stubbornly, from behind his brother. "They took 'em."

Jamie took a deep breath, and coughed from the smoke.

"Aye," he said. "I'll ask in the villages, then."

"Won't find 'em," Richard Brown said. He crumpled the note, tightening his fist suddenly. "If Indians took them, they won't keep them near. They'll sell them on, into Kentucky."

There was a general mutter of agreement among the men, and Roger felt the ember that had simmered in his chest all afternoon burst into fire.

"Indians didn't write that," he snapped, jerking a thumb at the note in Brown's hand. "And if it was revenge against O'Brian for being a Regulator, they wouldn't have taken the children."

Brown gave him a long look, eyes narrowed. Roger felt Jamie shift his weight slightly, preparing.

"No," said Brown softly. "They wouldn't. That's why Nelly figured you wrote it yourself. Say the Indians came and stole the little 'uns, but then *you* come along and decide to take what's left. So you fired the cabin, hung O'Brian and his wife, pinned that note, and here you are. How say you to that bit of reasoning, Mr. MacKenzie?"

"I'd ask how ye kent they were hanged, Mr. Brown."

Brown's face tightened, and Roger felt Jamie's hand on his arm in warning, realizing only then that his fists were clenched.

"The ropes, *a charaid,*" Jamie said, his voice very calm. The words penetrated dimly, and he looked. True, the ropes they had cut from the bodies lay by the tree where they had fallen. Jamie was still talking, his voice still calm, but Roger couldn't hear the words. The wind deafened him, and just below the whine of it he heard the intermittent soft thump of a beating heart. It might have been his own—or hers.

"Get off that horse," he said, or thought he had. The wind swept into his face, heavy with soot, and the words caught in his throat. The taste of ash was thick and sour in his mouth; he coughed and spat, eyes watering.

Vaguely, he became aware of a pain in his arm, and the world swam back into view. The younger men were staring at him, with expressions ranging from smirks to wariness. Richard Brown and his brother were both sedulously avoiding looking at him, focused instead on Jamie—who was still gripping his arm.

With an effort, he shook off Jamie's hand, giving his father-in-law the slightest nod by way of reassurance that he wasn't about to go berserk—though his heart still pounded, and the feel of the noose was so tight about his throat that he couldn't have spoken, even had he been able to form words.

"We'll help." Brown nodded at the little body on the ground, and began to swing one leg over his saddle, but Jamie stopped him with a small gesture.

"Nay, we'll manage."

Brown stopped, awkwardly half-on, half-off. His lips thinned and he pulled himself back on, reined around and rode off with no word of farewell. The others followed, looking curiously back as they went.

"It wasna them." Jamie had taken up his rifle and held it, gazing at the wood where the last of the men had disappeared. "They ken something more about it than they'll say, though."

Roger nodded, wordless. He walked deliberately to the hanging tree, kicked aside the ropes, and drove his fist into the trunk, twice, three times. Stood panting, his forehead pressed against the rough bark. The pain of raw knuckles helped, a bit.

A trail of tiny ants was scurrying upward between the plates of bark, bound on some momentous business, all-absorbing. He watched them for a little, until he could swallow again. Then straightened up and went to bury her, rubbing at the bone-deep bruise on his arm.

PART FOUR

Abduction

26

AN EYE TO THE FUTURE

October 9, 1773

ROGER DROPPED HIS saddlebags on the ground beside the pit and peered in.

"Where's Jem?" he said.

His mud-smeared wife looked up at him and brushed a sweat-matted lock of hair out of her face.

"Hello to you, too," she said. "Have a good trip?"

"No," he said. "Where's Jem?"

Her brows rose at that, and she stabbed her shovel into the bottom of the pit, extending a hand for him to help her scramble out.

"He's at Marsali's. He and Germain are playing Vroom with the little cars you made them—or they were when I left him there."

The knot of anxiety he had carried under his ribs for the last two weeks began slowly to relax. He nodded, a sudden spasm of the throat preventing him from speaking, then reached out and pulled her to him, crushing her against him in spite of her startled yelp and mud-stained clothes.

He held her hard, his own heart hammering loud in his ears, and wouldn't—couldn't—let go, until she wriggled out of his embrace. She kept her hands on his shoulders, but cocked her head to one side, one brow raised.

"Yeah, I missed you, too," she said. "What's wrong? What happened?"

"Terrible things." The burning, the little girl's death—these had become dreamlike during their travel, their horror muted to the surreal by the monotonous labor of riding, walking, the constant whine of wind and crunch of boots on gravel, sand, pine needles, mud, the engulfing blur of greens and yellows in which they lost themselves beneath an endless sky.

But now he was home, no longer adrift in the wilderness. And the memory of the girl who had left her heart in his hand was suddenly as real as she had been in the moment she died.

"You come inside." Brianna was peering closely at him, concerned. "You need something hot, Roger."

"I'm all right," he said, but followed her without protest.

He sat at the table while she put the kettle on for tea, and told her everything that had happened, head in his hands, staring down at the battered tabletop, with its homely spills and burn scars.

"I kept thinking there must be something . . . some way. But there wasn't. Even while I—I put my hand over her face—I was sure it wasna really happening. But at the same time—" He sat up, then, looking into the palms of his hands. At the same time, it had been the most vivid experience of his life. He could not bear to think of it, save in the most fleeting way, but knew he could never forget the slightest thing about it. His throat closed suddenly again.

Brianna looked searchingly into his face, saw his hand touch the ragged rope scar on his throat.

"Can you breathe?" she said anxiously. He shook his head, but it wasn't true, he was breathing, somehow, though it felt as though his throat had been crushed in some huge hand, larynx and windpipe mangled into a bloody mass.

He flapped a hand to indicate that he would be all right, much as he doubted it himself. She came round behind him, pulled his hand from his throat, and laid her own fingers lightly over the scar.

"It'll be all right," she said quietly. "Just breathe. Don't think. Just breathe."

Her fingers were cold and her hands smelled of dirt. There was water in his eyes. He blinked, wanting to see the room, the hearth and candle and dishes and loom, to convince himself of where he was. A drop of warm moisture rolled down his cheek.

He tried to tell her that it was all right, he wasn't crying, but she merely pressed closer, holding him across the chest with one arm, the other hand still cool on the painful lump in his throat. Her breasts were soft against his back, and he could feel, rather than hear, her humming, the small tuneless noise she made when she was anxious, or concentrating very hard.

Finally, the spasm began to ease, and the feel of choking left him. His chest swelled with the unbelievable relief of a free breath, and she let go.

"What . . . is it . . . that ye're digging?" he asked, with only a little effort. He looked round at her and smiled, with a lot more. "A bar . . . becue pit for . . . a hippopot . . . amus?"

The ghost of a smile touched her face, though her eyes were still dark with concern.

"No," she said. "It's a groundhog kiln."

He tried for a moment to compose some witty remark about it being a really large hole for killing something as small as a groundhog, but he wasn't up to it.

"Oh," he said instead.

He took the hot mug of catnip tea she placed in his hand and held it near his face, letting the fragrant steam warm his nose and mist on the cold skin of his cheeks.

Brianna poured out a mug for herself, as well, and sat down across from him.

"I'm glad you're home," she said softly.

"Yeah. Me, too." He essayed a sip; it was still scalding. "A kiln?" He'd told her about the O'Brians; he had to, but he didn't want to talk about it. Not now. She seemed to sense this, and didn't press him.

"Uh-huh. For the water." He must have looked confused, for her smile grew more genuine. "I told you there was dirt involved, didn't I? Besides, it was your idea."

"It was?" At this point, almost nothing would surprise him, but he had no memory of having bright ideas about water.

The problem of bringing water to the houses was one of transport. God knew there was plenty of water; it ran in creeks, fell in waterfalls, dripped from ledges, sprang from springs, seeped in boggy patches under the cliffs . . . but making it go where you wanted required some method of containment.

"Mr. Wemyss told *Fraülein* Berrisch—that's his girlfriend;

Frau Ute fixed them up—what I was doing, and she told him that the men's choir over in Salem was working on the same problem, so—"

"The choir?" He tried another cautious sip and found it drinkable. "Why would the choir—"

"That's just what they call them. There's the single men's choir, the single women's choir, the married choir . . . they don't just sing together, though, it's more like a social group, and each choir has particular jobs they do for the community. But anyway"—she flapped a hand—"they're trying to bring water into the town, and having the same problem—no metal for pipes.

"You remember, though—you reminded me about the pottery they do in Salem. Well, they tried making water pipes out of logs, but that's really hard and time-consuming, because you have to bore the middle of the log out with an augur, and you still need metal collars to bind the logs together. And they rot, after a while. But then they had the same idea you had—why not make pipes out of fired clay?"

She was becoming animated, talking about it. Her nose was no longer red from cold, but her cheeks were flushed pink and her eyes bright with interest. She waved her hands when she talked—she got that from her mother, he thought to himself, amused.

". . . so we parked the kids with Mama and Mrs. Bug, and Marsali and I went to Salem—"

"Marsali? But she couldn't be riding, surely?" Marsali was enormously pregnant, to the point that merely being around her made him slightly nervous, for fear she might go into labor at any moment.

"She isn't due for a month. Besides, we didn't ride; we took the wagon, and traded honey and cider and venison for cheese and quilts and—see my new teapot?" Proud, she waved at the pot, a homely squat thing with a red-brown glaze and yellow squiggly shapes painted round the middle. It was one of the uglier objects he'd ever seen, and the sight of it made tears come to his eyes from the sheer joy of being home.

"You don't like it?" she said, a small frown forming between her brows.

"No, it's great," he said hoarsely. He fumbled for a handkerchief and blew his nose to hide his emotion. "Love it. You were saying . . . Marsali?"

"I was saying about the water pipes. But—there's something about Marsali, too." The frown deepened. "I'm afraid Fergus isn't behaving very well."

"No? What's he doing? Having a mad affair with Mrs. Crombie?"

This suggestion was greeted with a withering look, but it didn't last.

"He's gone a lot, for one thing, leaving poor Marsali to mind the children and do all the work."

"Totally normal, for the time," he observed. "Most men do that. Your father does that. I do that; had ye not noticed?"

"I noticed," she said, giving him a faintly evil look. "But what I mean is, most men do the heavy work, like plowing and planting, and let their wives manage the inside stuff, the cooking and the spinning and the weaving, and the laundry, and the preserving, and—well, anyway, all that stuff. But Marsali's doing it all, plus the kids and the outdoor work, and working at the malting floor. And when Fergus is home, he's grumpy and he drinks too much."

This also sounded like normal behavior for the father of three small, wild children and the husband of a very pregnant wife, Roger thought, but didn't say so.

"I'd not have thought Fergus a layabout," he observed mildly. Bree shook her head, still frowning, and poured more tea into his mug.

"No, he's not lazy, really. It's hard for him, with only one hand; he really can't handle some of the heavy chores—but he won't help with the kids, or cook and clean while Marsali does them. Da and Ian help with the plowing, but . . . And he leaves for days on end—sometimes he's picking up little jobs here and there, translating for a traveler—but mostly, he's just gone. And . . ." She hesitated, darting a look at him as though wondering whether to go on.

"And?" he said obligingly. The tea was working; the pain in his throat was almost gone.

She looked down at the table, drawing invisible patterns on the oak with a forefinger.

"She didn't say so . . . but I think he hits her."

Roger felt a sudden weight on his heart. His first reaction was to dismiss the notion out of hand—but he had seen too much, living with the Reverend. Too many families, outwardly content and respectable, where the wives poked fun at their own "clumsiness," brushing away concern at black eyes, broken noses, dislocated wrists. Too many men who dealt with the pressures of providing for a family by resorting to the bottle.

"Damn," he said, feeling suddenly exhausted. He rubbed at his forehead, where a headache was starting.

"Why do you think so?" he asked bluntly. "Has she got marks?"

Bree nodded unhappily, still not looking up, though her finger had stilled.

"On her arm." She wrapped a hand around her forearm, in illustration. "Little round bruises, like fingermarks. I saw when she reached up to get a bucket of honeycomb from the wagon and her sleeve fell back."

He nodded, wishing there was something stronger than tea in his mug.

"Shall I talk to him, then, d'ye think?"

She did look up at him then, her eyes softening, though the look of worry remained.

"You know, most men wouldn't offer to do that."

"Well, it's no my idea of fun," he admitted. "But ye canna let that sort of thing go on, hoping it will cure itself. Someone has to say something."

God knew what, though—or how. He was already regretting the offer, trying to think what the hell he *could* say. "So, Fergus, old man. Hear you're beating your wife. Be a good fellow and stop that, okay?"

He drained the rest of his mug, and got up to look for the whisky.

"We're out," Brianna said, seeing his intent. "Mr. Wemyss had a cold."

He put down the empty bottle with a sigh. She touched his arm delicately.

"We're invited up to the Big House for supper. We could go early." That was a cheering suggestion. Jamie invariably had a bottle of excellent single-malt, secreted somewhere on the premises.

"Aye, all right." He took her cloak from the peg and swung it round her shoulders. "Hey. D'ye think I should mention the business about Fergus to your Da? Or best handle it myself?" He had a sudden, unworthy hope that Jamie would consider it his business and take care of the matter.

That seemed to be what Brianna was afraid of; she was shaking her head, simultaneously fluffing out her half-dried hair.

"No! I think Da would break his neck. And Fergus won't be any good to Marsali if he's dead."

"Mmphm." He accepted the inevitable, and opened the door for her. The big white house glowed on the hill above them, tranquil in the afternoon light, the big red spruce behind it a looming but benign presence; not for the first time, he felt that the tree was somehow guarding the house—and in his present fragile mental state, found that notion a comfort.

They made a short detour, so that he could properly admire the new pit and be told all about the internal workings of a groundhog kiln. He failed to follow these in any detail, only grasping the notion that the point was to make the inside very hot, but he found the flow of Brianna's explanation soothing.

". . . bricks for the chimney," she was saying, pointing at the far end of the eight-foot pit, which at present resembled nothing so much as the resting place for an extremely large coffin. She'd made a nice, neat job of it so far, though; the corners were squared as though done with an instrument of some sort, and the walls painstakingly smoothed. He said as much, and she beamed at him, thumbing a lock of red hair behind her ear.

"It needs to be a lot deeper," she said, "maybe another three feet. But the dirt here is really good for digging; it's soft, but it doesn't crumble too much. I hope I can finish the hole before it starts to snow, but I don't know." She rubbed a knuckle under her nose, squinting dubiously at the hole. "I really need to card and spin enough more wool to weave the fabric for winter shirts for you and Jem, but I'll have to pick and preserve for the next week or so, and—"

"I'll dig it for you."

She stood on tiptoe and kissed him, just under the ear, and he laughed, suddenly feeling better.

"Not for this winter," she said, taking him contentedly by the arm, "but eventually—I'm wondering if I can vent some of the heat from the kiln, and run it under the floor of the cabin. You know what a Roman hypocaust is?"

"I do." He turned to eye the foundation of his domicile, a simple hollow base of fieldstone on which the log walls were built. The notion of central heating in a crude mountain cabin made him want to laugh, but there was really nothing impossible about it, he supposed. "You'd what? Run pipes of warm air through the foundation stones?"

"Yes. Always assuming I can actually make good pipes, which remains to be seen. What do you think?"

He glanced from the proposed project up the hill to the Big House. Even at this distance, a mound of dirt by the foundation was visible, evidence of the white sow's burrowing capabilities.

"I think ye run a great danger of having that big white buggeress transfer her affections to us, if ye make a cozy warm den under our house."

"Buggeress?" she said, diverted. "Is that physically possible?"

"It's a metaphysical description," he informed her. "And ye saw what she tried to do to Major MacDonald."

"That pig really doesn't like Major MacDonald," Bree said reflectively. "I wonder why not?"

"Ask your mother; she's none so fond of him, either."

"Oh, well, that—" She stopped suddenly, lips pursed, and looked thoughtfully at the Big House. A shadow passed the window of the surgery, someone moving inside. "Tell you what. You find Da and have a drink with him, and while you're doing that, I'll tell Mama about Marsali and Fergus. She might have a good idea."

"I don't know that it's a medical problem, exactly," he said. "But anesthetizing Germain would certainly be a start."

27

THE MALTING-FLOOR

I COULD SMELL THE SWEET, musty scent of damp grain on the wind as I made my way up the trail. It was nothing like the heady pungency of the barm mash, the faintly coffeelike toasted smell of malting, nor yet the reek of distilling—but still spoke as strongly of whisky. It was a very fragrant business, making *uisgebaugh,* and the reason why the whisky clearing was located nearly a mile from the Big House. As it was, I often caught a wild faint scent of spirit through my open surgery windows when the wind was right and the mash was making.

The whisky-making had its own cycle, and one that everyone on the Ridge was subconsciously attuned to, whether directly involved in it or not. Which was how I knew without asking that the barley in the malting shed had just begun its germination, and therefore, Marsali would be there, turning and spreading the grain evenly before the malting fire was lit.

The grain must be allowed to germinate, to assure a maximal sweetness—but must not sprout, or the mash would have a bitter taste and be ruined. No more than twenty-four hours must pass after germination began, and I had smelled the fecund damp scent of the grain begin to rise as I foraged in the woods the afternoon before. The time was here.

It was by far the best place to have a private conversation with Marsali; the whisky clearing was the only place she was ever without a cacophonous assortment of children. I often thought that she valued the solitude of the work much more than the share of whisky Jamie gave her for minding the grain—valuable though *that* was.

Brianna told me that Roger had gallantly offered to have a

word with Fergus, but I thought that I should talk to Marsali first, just to find out what was really going on.

What ought I to say? I wondered. A straightforward *"Is Fergus beating you?"* I couldn't quite believe that, despite—or perhaps because of—an intimate knowledge of emergency rooms filled with the debris of domestic disputes.

It wasn't that I thought Fergus incapable of violence; he'd seen—and experienced—any amount of it from an early age, and growing up among Highlanders in the middle of the Rising and its aftermath probably did not inculcate a young man with any deep regard for the virtues of peace. On the other hand, Jenny Murray had had a hand in his upbringing.

I tried and failed to imagine any man who had lived with Jamie's sister for more than a week *ever* lifting his hand to a woman. Besides, I knew by my own observations that Fergus was a very gentle father, and there was usually an easiness between him and Marsali that seemed—

There was a sudden commotion overhead. Before I could so much as glance up, something huge crashed down through the branches in a shower of dust and dead pine needles. I leapt backward and swung my basket up in instinctive defense—but even as I did so, I realized that I was not in fact being attacked. Germain lay flat on the path in front of me, eyes bulging as he struggled for the breath that had been knocked out of him.

"What on *earth*—?" I began, rather crossly. Then I saw that he was clutching something to his chest; a late nest, filled with a clutch of four greenish eggs, which he had miraculously contrived not to break in his fall.

"For . . . *Maman,*" he gasped, grinning up at me.

"*Very* nice," I said. I had had enough to do with young males—well, any age, really; they all did it—to realize the complete futility of reproach in such situations, and since he had broken neither the eggs nor his legs, I merely took the nest and held it while he gulped for air and my heart resumed beating at its normal speed.

Recovered, he scrambled to his feet, disregarding the dirt, pitch, and broken pine needles that covered him from head to toe.

"*Maman*'s in the shed," he said, reaching for his treasure. "You come too, *Grandmère*?"

"Yes. Where are your sisters?" I asked suspiciously. "Are you meant to be watching them?"

"Non," he said airily. "They are at home; that's where women belong."

"Oh, really? And who told you that?"

"I forget." Thoroughly recovered, he hopped ahead of me, singing a song, the refrain of which seemed to be *"Na tuit, na tuit, na tuit, Germain!"*

Marsali was indeed at the whisky clearing; her cap, cloak, and gown hung from a branch of the yellow-leaved persimmon, and a clay firepot full of coals sat nearby, smoking in readiness.

The malting floor had been enclosed now by proper walls, making a shed in which the damp grain could be heaped, first to germinate and then to be gently toasted by a low-burning fire under the floor. The ash and charcoal had been scraped out and oak wood for a new fire laid in the space beneath the stilted floor, but it wasn't yet lit. Even without a fire, the shed was warm; I felt it from several feet away. As the grain germinated, it gave off such heat that the shed fairly glowed with it.

A rhythmic shush and scrape came from within; Marsali was turning the grain with a wooden shovel, making sure it was evenly spread before lighting the malting fire. The door of the shed was open, but there were of course no windows; from a distance, I could see only a dim shadow moving within.

The shushing of the grain had masked our footsteps; Marsali looked up, startled, when my body blocked the light from the doorway.

"Mother Claire!"

"Hallo," I said cheerfully. "Germain said you were here. I thought I'd just—"

"*Maman!* Look, look, see what I have!" Germain pushed past me with single-minded eagerness, thrusting out his prize. Marsali smiled at him, and pushed a damp strand of fair hair back behind her ear.

"Oh, aye? Well, that's grand, no? Let's take it out to the light, shall we, so I can have a proper look."

She stepped out of the shed, sighing in pleasure at the touch of the cool air. She was stripped to her shift, the muslin so wet with sweat that I could see not only the dark rounds of her areolae, but even the tiny bulge of her popped-out navel, where the cloth clung to the massive curves of her belly.

Marsali sat down with another huge sigh of relief, stretching her legs out, bare toes pointed. Her feet were somewhat swollen, and blue veins showed, distended, beneath the transparent skin of her legs.

"Ah, it's good to sit! So then, *a chuisle,* show me what ye've got."

I took the opportunity to circle round behind her, as Germain displayed his prize, and covertly check for bruises or other sinister signs.

She was thin—but Marsali simply *was* thin, bar the bulge of her pregnancy, and always had been. Her arms were slender, but hard with muscle, as were her legs. There were smudges of tiredness beneath her eyes—but she had three small children, after all, besides the discomforts of pregnancy to keep her awake. Her face was rosy and damp, thoroughly healthy-looking.

There were a couple of small bruises on her lower legs, but I dismissed those; pregnant women did bruise easily, and with all the obstructions presented by living in a log cabin and traversing wild mountains, there were few people on the Ridge—male *or* female—not sporting the odd contusion.

Or was I only seeking excuses, not wanting to admit the possibility of what Brianna had suggested?

"One for me," Germain was explaining, touching the eggs, "and one for Joan, and one for Félicité, and one for *Monsieur L'Oeuf.*" He pointed at the melonlike swell of her stomach.

"Ah, now, what a sweet lad," Marsali said, pulling him close and kissing his smudged forehead. "Ye're my wee nestling, to be sure."

Germain's beam of pleasure faded into a look of speculation as he came in contact with his mother's protruding belly. He patted it cautiously.

"When the egg hatches inside, what do you do with the shell?" he inquired. "Can I have it?"

Marsali went pink with suppressed laughter.

"People dinna come in shells," she said. "Thank God."

"You are sure, *Maman*?" He eyed her belly dubiously, then poked it gently. "It *feels* like an egg."

"Well, so it does, but it's not. That's only what Papa and I call a wee one before it's born. *You* were *'Monsieur L'Oeuf'* once, aye?"

"I was?" Germain looked thunderstruck at this revelation.

"Ye were. So were your sisters."

Germain frowned, shaggy blond fringe almost touching his nose.

"No, they weren't. They are *Mademoiselles L'Oeufs.*"

"Oui, certainement," Marsali said, laughing at him. "And perhaps this one is, too—but *Monsieur* is easier to say. Here, look." She leaned back a little and pushed a hand firmly into the side of her mound. Then she seized Germain's hand and put it on the spot. Even from where I stood, I could see the surge of flesh as the baby kicked vigorously in response to being poked.

Germain jerked his hand away, startled, then put it back, looking fascinated, and pushed.

"Hello!" he said loudly, putting his face close to his mother's belly. "*Comment ça va* in there, *Monsieur L'Oeuf*?"

"He's fine," his mother assured him. "Or she. But babies dinna talk right at first. Ye ken that much. Félicité doesna say anything but 'Mama' yet."

"Oh, aye." Losing interest in his impending sibling, he stooped to pick up an interesting-looking stone.

Marsali lifted her head, squinting at the sun.

"Ye should go home, Germain. Mirabel will be wanting milked, and I've a bit to do here yet. Go and help Papa, aye?" Mirabel was a goat, and a sufficiently new addition to the household as still to be interesting, for Germain brightened at the suggestion.

"Oui, Maman. Au'voir, Grandmère!" He took aim and flipped his rock at the shed, missing it, then turned and scampered toward the path.

"Germain!" Marsali called after him. *"Na tuit!"*

"What does that mean?" I asked curiously. "It's Gaelic, is it—or French?"

"It's the Gaelic," she said, smiling. "It means 'Don't fall!'" She shook her head in mock dismay. "That laddie canna stay out of trees to save his life." Germain had left the nest with its eggs; she set it gently on the ground, and I saw then the faint yellowed ovals on the underside of her forearm—faded, but just as Brianna had described them.

"And how *is* Fergus?" I asked, as though it had anything to do with the conversation.

"He's well enough," she replied, a look of wariness closing over her features.

"Really?" I glanced deliberately at her arm, then into her eyes. She flushed, and turned her arm quickly, hiding the marks.

"Aye, he's fine!" she said. "He's no verra good at the milking just yet, but he'll have the way of it soon enough. It's awkward wi' the one hand, to be sure, but he's—"

I sat down on the log beside her, and took hold of her wrist, turning it over.

"Brianna told me," I said. "Did Fergus do this?"

"Oh." She seemed embarrassed, and pulled her wrist away, pressing the forearm against her belly to hide the marks. "Well, aye. Aye, he did."

"Do you want me to speak to Jamie about it?"

A rich tide of color surged into her face, and she sat up in alarm.

"Christ, no! Da would break Fergus's neck! And it wasna his fault, really."

"Certainly it was his fault," I said firmly. I had seen all too many beaten women in Boston emergency rooms, all of whom claimed that it wasn't really their husband's or boyfriend's fault. Granted, the women often *did* have something to do with it, but still—

"But it wasn't!" Marsali insisted. The color had not gone from her face; if anything, it intensified. "I—he—I mean, he grabbed my arm, aye, but 'twas only because I . . . er . . . well, I was tryin' to brain him wi' a stick of wood at the time." She glanced away, blushing fiercely.

"Oh." I rubbed my nose, a little taken aback. "I see. And why were you trying to do that? Was he . . . attacking you?"

She sighed, shoulders slumping a little.

"Oh. No. Weel, it was because Joanie spilled the milk, and he shouted at her, and she cried, and . . ." She shrugged a little, looking uncomfortable. "I just had a wee de'il sittin' on my shoulder, I suppose."

"It's not like Fergus to shout at the children, is it?"

"Oh, no, it's not!" she said quickly. "He hardly ever . . . well, he didna used to, but with so many . . . well, I couldna blame him, this time. It took him a terrible time to milk the goat, and then to have it all spilt and wasted—I would ha' shouted, too, I expect."

Her eyes were fixed on the ground, avoiding mine, and she was fingering the seam of her shift, running a thumb over and over the stitching.

"Small children can certainly be trying," I agreed, with vivid memories of an incident involving a two-year-old Brianna, a phone call that had distracted me, a large bowl of spaghetti with meatballs, and Frank's open briefcase. Frank normally exhibited a saintly degree of patience with Bree—if somewhat less with me—but on that particular occasion his bellows of outrage had rattled the windows.

And now that I recalled the occasion, I actually *had* thrown a meatball at him in a fury verging on hysteria. So had Bree, though she had done it out of glee, rather than vindictiveness. Had I been standing by the stove at the time, it might easily have been the pot I threw. I rubbed a finger under my nose, not sure whether to regret the memory or to laugh at it. I never did get the stains out of the rug.

It was a shame that I couldn't share the memory with Marsali, as she was in ignorance not only of spaghetti and briefcases, but also of Frank. She was still looking down, scuffing at the dead oak leaves with a pointed toe.

"'Twas all my fault, really," she said, and bit her lip.

"No, it wasn't." I squeezed her arm in reassurance. "Things like that are no one's fault; accidents happen, people get upset . . . but it all comes right in the end." So it did, I thought—though often not in any expected way.

She nodded, but the shadow still lay on her face, her lower lip tucked in.

"Aye, it's only . . ." she began, then trailed off.

I sat patiently, careful not to push her. She wanted—

needed—to talk. And I needed to hear it, before deciding what—or if—to tell Jamie. There was something going on between her and Fergus, that was sure.

"I . . . was just thinking of it now, whilst I was shoveling. I wouldna have done it, I don't think, only it minded me so much . . . it was only I felt as though it was the same again. . . ."

"The same as what?" I asked, when it became clear that she had trailed off.

"I spilt the milk," she said, all in a rush. "When I was a wean. I was hungry, and I reached to pull the jug, and it spilled."

"Oh?"

"Aye. And he shouted." Her shoulders hunched a little, as though in memory of a blow.

"Who shouted?"

"I dinna ken, for sure. It might ha' been my father, Hugh—but it might have been Simon—Mam's second husband. I dinna really remember—only bein' so scairt that I wet myself, and that made him angrier." Color flamed in her face, and her toes curled with shame.

"My mother cried, for it was all the food there was, a bit o' bread and milk, and now the milk was gone—but *he* shouted that he couldna bear the noise, for Joan and I were both howling, too . . . and then he slapped my face, and Mam went for him bald-heided, and he pushed her so she fell against the hearth and smacked her face on the chimney—I could see the blood running from her nose."

She sniffed and brushed a knuckle under her own nose, blinking, her eyes still fixed on the leaves.

"He stamped out, then, slammin' the door, and Joanie and I rushed up to Mam, both shriekin' our heids off, for we thought she was deid . . . but she got up onto her hands and knees and told us it was all right, it would be all right—and her swayin' to and fro, with her cap fallen off and strings of bloody snot dripping from her face onto the floor . . . I'd forgot that. But when Fergus started shouting at poor wee Joanie . . . 'twas like he was Simon. Or maybe Hugh. *Him,* whoever he was." She closed her eyes and heaved a deep sigh, leaning forward so her arms cradled the burden of her pregnancy.

I reached out and smoothed the damp strings of hair out of her face, brushing them back from her rounded brow.

"You miss your mother, don't you?" I said softly. For the first time, I felt some sympathy for her mother, Laoghaire, as well as for Marsali.

"Oh, aye," Marsali said simply. "Something terrible." She sighed again, closing her eyes as she leaned her cheek against my hand. I drew her head against me, holding her, and stroked her hair in silence.

It was late afternoon, and the shadows lay long, cold in the oak wood. The heat had left her now, and she shivered briefly in the cooling air, a stipple of gooseflesh coming up on her fine-boned arms.

"Here," I said, standing up and swinging the cloak off my shoulders. "Put this on. You don't want to take a chill."

"Ah, no, it's all right." She straightened up, shaking back her hair, and wiped her face with the back of a hand. "There's no but a bit more to do here, and then I've got to be going home and making up the supper—"

"I'll do it," I said firmly, and tucked the cloak around her shoulders. "You rest a bit."

The air inside the tiny shed was ripe enough to make one light-headed, all by itself, thick with the fecund musk of sprouting grain and the fine sharp dust of barley hulls. The warmth was welcoming after the chill of the air outside, but within moments, my skin was damp beneath dress and shift, and I pulled the gown off over my head and hung it on a nail by the door.

No matter; she was right, there wasn't much to be done. The work would keep me warm, and then I would walk home with Marsali straightaway. I would make supper for the family, letting her rest—and while I was about it, I'd perhaps have a word with Fergus and discover more about what was going on.

Fergus could have been making the supper, I thought, frowning as I dug into the dim heaps of sticky grain. Not that he would think of such a thing, the little French layabout. Milking the goat was as far as he was likely to go in the direction of "women's work."

Then I thought of Joan and Félicité, and felt more charitable toward Fergus. Joan was three, Félicité one and a half—and anyone alone in a house with those two had my complete sympathy, no matter *what* kind of work they were doing.

Joan was outwardly a sweet brown wren of a child, and by herself was even-tempered and biddable—to a point. Félicité was the spitting image of her father, dark, fine-boned, and given to alternate bouts of languishing charm and intemperate passion. Together . . . Jamie referred to them casually as the hell-kits, and if they were at home, it was no wonder that Germain was out wandering in the woods—nor that Marsali found it a relief to be out here by herself, doing heavy labor.

"Heavy" was the operative term, I thought, thrusting the shovel in again and heaving. Sprouting grain was damp grain, and each shovelful weighed pounds. The turned grain was patchy, splotched dark with moisture from the underlying layers. The unturned grain was paler in color, even in the failing light. Only a few mounds of pale grain remained, in the far corner.

I attacked them with a will, realizing as I did so that I was trying very hard not to think of the story Marsali had told me. I didn't want to like Laoghaire—and I didn't. But I didn't want to feel sympathy for her, either, and that was proving harder to avoid.

It hadn't been an easy life for her, apparently. Well, nor had it been for anyone else living in the Highlands then, I thought, grunting as I flung a shovelful of grain to the side. Being a mother was not that easy anywhere—but it seemed she had made a good job of it.

I sneezed from the grain dust, paused to wipe my nose on my sleeve, then went back to shoveling.

It wasn't as though she had tried to steal Jamie from me, after all, I told myself, striving for compassion and high-minded objectivity. Rather the reverse, in fact—or at least she might well see it that way.

The edge of the shovel gritted hard against the floor as I scraped up the last of the grain. I sent the grain flying to the side, then used the flat of the blade to shove some of the new-turned grain into the empty corner and smooth down the highest hillocks.

I knew all the reasons why he said he'd married her—and I believed him. However, the fact remained that the mention of her name conjured up assorted visions—starting with Jamie kissing her ardently in an alcove at Castle Leoch, and ending with him fumbling up her nightgown in the darkness of their marriage bed, hands warm and eager on her thighs—that made me snort like a grampus and feel the blood throb hotly in my temples.

Perhaps, I reflected, I was not really a very high-minded sort of person. Occasionally quite low-minded and grudge-bearing, in fact.

This bout of self-criticism was cut short by the sound of voices and movement outside. I stepped to the door of the shed, squinting against the dazzle of the late afternoon sun.

I couldn't see their faces, nor even tell for sure how many there might be. Some were on horseback, some on foot, black silhouettes with the sinking sun behind them. I caught a movement in the corner of my eye; Marsali was on her feet, backing toward the shed.

"Who are ye, sirs?" she said, chin high.

"Thirsty travelers, mistress," said one of the black forms, edging his horse ahead of the others. "In search of hospitality."

The words were courteous enough; the voice wasn't. I stepped out of the shed, still gripping the shovel.

"Welcome," I said, making no effort to sound welcoming. "Stay where you are, gentlemen; we'll be pleased to bring you a drink. Marsali, will you fetch the keg?"

There was a small keg of raw whisky kept nearby for just such occasions. My heartbeat was loud in my ears, and I was clutching the wooden handle of the shovel so tightly that I could feel the grain of the wood.

It was more than unusual to see so many strangers in the mountains at one time. Now and then, we would see a hunting party of Cherokee—but these men were not Indians.

"No bother, mistress," said another of the men, swinging down off his horse. "I'll help her fetch it. I do think we shall be needing more than one keg, though."

The voice was English, and oddly familiar. Not a cultivated accent, but with a careful diction.

"We have only one keg ready," I said, slowly moving sideways and keeping my eyes on the man who had spoken. He was short and very slender, and moved with a stiff, jerky gait, like a marionette.

He was moving toward me; so were the others. Marsali had reached the woodpile, and was fumbling behind the chunks of oak and hickory. I could hear her breath, harsh in her throat. The keg was hidden in the woodpile. There was an ax lying next to the wood, too, I knew.

"Marsali," I said. "Stay there. I'll come and help you."

An ax was a better weapon than a shovel—but two women against . . . how many men? Ten . . . a dozen . . . more? I blinked, eyes watering against the sun, and saw several more walk out of the wood. I could see these clearly; one grinned at me and I had to steel myself not to look away. His grin broadened.

The short man was coming closer, too. I glanced at him, and a brief itch of recognition tickled me. Who the hell was he? I knew him; I'd seen him before—and yet I hadn't any name to attach to the lantern jaws and narrow brow.

He stank of long-dried sweat, dirt ground into the skin, and the tang of dribbled urine; they all did, and the odor of them floated on the wind, feral as the stink of weasels.

He saw me recognize him; thin lips pulled in for a moment, then relaxed.

"Mrs. Fraser," he said, and the feeling of apprehension deepened sharply as I saw the look in his small, clever eyes.

"I think you have the advantage of me, sir," I said, putting as bold a face on it as I might. "Have we met?"

He didn't answer that. One side of his mouth turned up a little, but his attention was distracted by the two men who had lunged forward to take the keg as Marsali rolled it out of its hiding place. One had already seized the ax I had my eye on, and was about to stave in the top of the cask, when the thin man shouted at him.

"Leave it!"

The man looked up at him, mouth open in heavy incomprehension.

"I said leave it!" the thin man snapped, as the other glanced from the cask to the ax and back in confusion. "We'll take it with us; I'll not have you all befuddled with drink now!"

Turning to me, as though continuing a conversation, he said, "Where's the rest of it?"

"That's all there is," Marsali said, before I could answer. She was frowning at him, wary of him, but also angry. "Take it, then, and ye must."

The thin man's attention shifted to her for the first time, but he gave her no more than a casual glance before turning back to me.

"Don't trouble lying to me, Mrs. Fraser. I know well enough there's more, and I'll have it."

"There is not. Give me that, ye great oaf!" Marsali snatched the ax neatly from the man holding it, and scowled at the thin man. "This is how ye repay proper welcome, is it—by thieving? Well, take what ye came for and leave, then!"

I had no choice but to follow her lead, though alarm bells were ringing in my brain every time I looked at the thin little man.

"She's right," I said. "See for yourselves." I pointed at the shed, the mash tubs and the pot still that stood nearby, unsealed and patently empty. "We're only beginning the malting. It will be weeks yet before there's a new batch of whisky."

Without the slightest change of expression, he took a quick step forward and slapped me hard across the face.

The blow wasn't hard enough to knock me down, but it snapped my head back and left my eyes watering. I was more shocked than hurt, though there was a sharp taste of blood in my mouth, and I could already feel my lip beginning to puff.

Marsali uttered a sharp cry of shock and outrage, and I heard some of the men murmur in interested surprise. They had drawn in, surrounding us.

I put the back of my hand to my bleeding mouth, noticing in a detached sort of way that it was trembling. My brain, though, had withdrawn to a safe distance and was making and discarding suppositions so quickly that they fluttered past, fast as shuffling cards.

Who were these men? How dangerous were they? What were they prepared to do? The sun was setting—how long before Marsali or I was missed and someone came looking for us? Would it be Fergus, or Jamie? Even Jamie, if he came alone . . .

I had no doubt that these men were the same who had burned Tige O'Brian's house, and were likely responsible for the attacks inside the Treaty Line, as well. Vicious, then—but with theft as their major purpose.

There was a copper taste in my mouth; the metal tang of blood and fear. No more than a second had passed in these calculations, but as I lowered my hand, I had concluded that it would be best to give them what they wanted, and hope that they left with the whisky at once.

I had no chance to say so, though. The thin man seized my wrist and twisted viciously. I felt the bones shift and crack with a tearing pain, and sank to my knees in the leaves, unable to make more than a small, breathless sound.

Marsali made a louder sound and moved like a striking snake. She swung the ax from the shoulder with all the power of her bulk behind it, and the blade sank deep in the shoulder of the man beside her. She wrenched it free and blood sprayed warm across my face, pattering like rain upon the leaves.

She screamed, high and thin, and the man screamed, too, and then the whole clearing was in motion, men surging inward with a roar like collapsing surf. I lunged forward and seized the thin man's knees, butted my head hard upward into his crotch. He made a choking wheeze and fell on top of me, flattening me to the ground.

I squirmed out from under his knotted body, knowing only that I had to get to Marsali, get between her and the men—but they were upon her. A scream cut in half by the sound of fists on flesh, and a dull boom as bodies fell hard against the wall of the malting shed.

The clay firepot was in reach. I seized it, heedless of its searing heat, and flung it straight into the group of men. It struck one hard in the back and shattered, hot coals spraying. Men yelled and jumped back, and I saw Marsali slumped against the shed, neck canted over on one shoulder and her eyes rolled back white in her head, legs splayed wide and the shift torn down from her neck, leaving her heavy breasts bare on the bulge of her belly.

Then someone struck me in the side of the head and I flew

sideways, skidding through the leaves and ending boneless, flat on the ground, unable to rise or move or think or speak.

A great calm came over me and my vision narrowed—it seemed very slowly—the closing of some great iris, spiraling shut. Before me, I saw the nest on the ground, inches from my nose, its interwoven sticks slender, clever, the four greenish eggs round and fragile, perfect in its cup. Then a heel smashed down on the eggs and the iris closed.

THE SMELL OF BURNING roused me. I could have been unconscious for no more than moments; the clump of dry grass near my face was barely beginning to smoke. A hot coal glowed in a nest of char, shot with sparks. Threads of incandescence shot up the withered grass blades and the clump burst into flame, just as hands seized me by arm and shoulder, dragging me up.

Still dazed, I flailed at my captor as he lifted me, but was hustled unceremoniously to one of the horses, heaved up, and flung across the saddle with a force that knocked the wind out of me. I had barely the presence of mind to grab at the stirrup leather, as someone smacked the horse's rump and we set off at a bruising trot.

Between dizziness and jostling, everything I saw was fractured, crazed like broken glass—but I caught one last glimpse of Marsali, now lying limp as a rag doll among a dozen tiny fires, as the scattered coals began to catch and burn.

I made some strangled noise, trying to call to her, but it was lost in the clatter of harness and men's voices, speaking urgently, near at hand.

"You crazed, Hodge? You don't want that woman. Put her back!"

"I shan't." The small man's voice sounded cross, but controlled, somewhere near at hand. "She'll show us to the whisky."

"Whisky'll do us no good if we're dead, Hodge! That's Jamie Fraser's *wife,* for Christ's sake!"

"I know who she is. Get on with you!"

"But he—you don't know the man, Hodge! I see him one time—"

"Spare me your memories. Get *on,* I said!"

This last was punctuated by a sudden vicious *thunk,* and a startled sound of pain. A pistol butt, I thought. Square across the face, I added mentally, swallowing as I heard the wet, wheezing gasps of a man with a broken nose.

A hand seized me by the hair and jerked my head round painfully. The thin man's face stared down at me, eyes narrowed in calculation. He seemed only to want to assure himself that I was indeed alive, for he said nothing, and dropped my head again, indifferent as though it were a pinecone he had picked up along the way.

Someone was leading the horse I was on; there were several men on foot, as well. I heard them, calling to one another, half-running to keep up as the horses lurched up a rise, crashing and grunting like pigs through the undergrowth.

I couldn't breathe, save in shallow gasps, and was being jolted unmercifully with each step—but I had no attention to spare for physical discomfort. Was Marsali dead? She had looked it, surely, but I'd seen no blood, and I clung to that small fact for the slim—and temporary—comfort that it was.

Even if she wasn't dead yet, she soon might be. Whether from injury, shock, a sudden miscarriage—oh, God, oh, God, poor little *Monsieur L'Oeuf*—

My hands clenched helpless on the stirrup leathers, desperate. Who might find her—and when?

It had lacked little more than an hour to suppertime when I had arrived at the malting shed. How late was it now? I caught glimpses of the ground juddering past below, but my hair had come loose and streamed across my face whenever I tried to raise my head. There was a growing chill to the air, though, and a still look to the light that told me the sun was near the horizon. Within a few minutes, the light would start to fade.

And then what? How long before a search began? Fergus would notice Marsali's absence when she didn't appear to cook supper—but would he go to look for her, with the little girls in his care? No, he'd send Germain. That caused my heart to lurch and catch in my throat. For a five-year-old boy to find his mother . . .

I could still smell burning. I sniffed, once, twice, again, hoping that I was imagining it. But above the dust and sweat of horse, the tang of stirrup leather, and the whiff of crushed plants, I could distinctly smell the reek of smoke. The clearing, the shed—or both—were well and truly alight now. Someone would see the smoke, and come. But in time?

I shut my eyes tight, trying to stop thinking, seeking any distraction to keep from seeing in my mind's eye the scene that must be taking place behind me.

There were still voices near. The man they called Hodge again. It must be his horse I rode; he was walking near its head, on the far side of the animal. Someone else was expostulating with him, but to no more effect than the first man.

"Spread them out," he was saying tersely. "Divide the men in two groups—you'll 'ave one, the rest go with me. Join again in three days' time at Brownsville."

Bloody hell. He expected pursuit, and meant to frustrate it by splitting his group and confusing the trail. Frantically, I tried to think of something to drop; surely I had *something* to leave as a means of telling Jamie which way I had been taken.

But I wore nothing save shift, stays, and stockings—my shoes had been lost when they dragged me to the horse. The stockings seemed the only possibility; though the garters, with extreme perversity, were for once snugly tied, and quite out of my reach at the moment.

All around me I could hear the noise of men and horses moving, calling and shoving as the main body split. Hodge chirruped to the horse, and we began to move faster.

My floating hair snagged on a twig as we brushed past a bush, held for a second, then broke free with a painful *ping!* as the twig snapped, ricocheting off my cheekbone and narrowly missing my eye. I said something very rude, and someone—Hodge, for a guess—dealt me a censorious smack across the bottom.

I said something much, much ruder, but under my breath and through clenched teeth. My sole comfort was the thought that it would be no great trick to follow a band such as this, leaving as they were a wide trail of broken branches, hoof-prints, and overturned stones.

I'd seen Jamie track things small and sly, as well as large and lumbering—and had seen him check the bark of trees and the twigs of bushes as he went, for scratched bark and betraying tufts of . . . hair.

No one was walking on the side of the horse where my head hung down. Hastily, I began to pluck hairs from my head. Three, four, five—was that enough? I stretched out my hand and dragged it through a yaupon bush; the long, curly hairs drifted on the breeze of the horse's passing, but stayed safely tangled in the jagged foliage.

I did the same thing four times more. Surely he would see at least one of the signs, and would know which trail to follow—if he didn't waste time following the other first. There was nothing I could do about that save pray—and I set in to do that in good earnest, beginning first with a plea for Marsali and *Monsieur L'Oeuf,* whose need was plainly much greater than mine.

We continued upward for quite some time; it was full dark before we reached what seemed to be the summit of a ridge, and I was nearly unconscious, my head throbbing with blood and my stays pushed so hard into my body that I felt each strip of whalebone like a brand against my skin.

I had just enough energy left to push myself backward when the horse stopped. I hit the ground and crumpled at once into a heap, where I sat light-headed and gasping, rubbing my hands, which had swollen from hanging down for so long.

The men were gathered in a small knot, occupied in low-voiced conversation, but too near for me to think of trying to creep away into the shrubbery. One man stood only a few feet away, keeping a steady eye on me.

I looked back the way we had come, half-fearing, half-hoping to see the glow of fire far below. The fire would have drawn attention from someone—someone would know by now what had happened, be even now spreading the alarm, organizing pursuit. And yet . . . Marsali.

Was she already dead, and the baby with her?

I swallowed hard, straining my eyes at the dark, as much to

prevent tears as in hopes of seeing anything. As it was, though, the trees grew thick around us, and I could see nothing at all, save variations on inky blackness.

There was no light; the moon had not yet risen, and the stars were still faint—but my eyes had had more than enough time to adapt, and while I was no cat to see in the dark, I could distinguish enough to make a rough count. They were arguing, glancing at me now and then. Perhaps a dozen men . . . How many had there been, originally? Twenty? Thirty?

I flexed my fingers, trembling. My wrist was badly bruised, but that wasn't what was troubling me at present.

It was clear to me—and therefore presumably to them, as well—that they couldn't head directly for the whisky cache, even were I able to find it at night. Whether Marsali survived to talk or not—I felt my throat close at the thought—Jamie would likely realize that the whisky was the intruders' goal, and have it guarded.

Had things not fallen out as they did, the men would ideally have forced me to lead them to the cache, taken the whisky, and fled, hoping to escape before the theft was discovered. Leaving me and Marsali alive to raise the alarm and describe them? I wondered. Perhaps; perhaps not.

In the panic following Marsali's attack, though, the original plan had fallen apart. Now what?

The knot of men was breaking up, though the argument continued. Footsteps approached.

"I tell you, it won't do," one man was saying heatedly. From the thickened voice, I assumed it was the gentleman with the broken nose, undeterred by his injury. "Kill her now. Leave her here; no one'll find her before the beasts have scattered her bones."

"Aye? And if no one finds her, they'll think she's still with us, won't they?"

"But if Fraser catches up to us, and she's not, who shall he blame . . ."

They stopped, four or five of them surrounding me. I scrambled to my feet, my hand closing by reflex around the nearest thing approaching a weapon—an unfortunately small rock.

"How far are we from the whisky?" Hodge demanded. He

had taken off his hat, and his eyes gleamed, ratlike in the shadow.

"I don't know," I said, keeping a firm grip on my nerves—and the rock. My lip was still tender, puffed from the blow he had dealt me, and I had to form the words carefully. "I don't know where we *are.*"

This was true, though I could have made a reasonable guess. We had traveled for a few hours, mostly upward, and the trees nearby were fir and balsam; I could smell their resin, sharp and clean. We were on the upper slopes, and probably near a small pass that crossed the shoulder of the mountain.

"Kill her," urged one of the others. "She's no good to us, and if Fraser finds her with us—"

"Shut your face!" Hodge rounded on the speaker with such violence that the man, much larger, stepped back involuntarily. That threat disposed of, Hodge ignored him and seized me by the arm.

"Don't play coy with me, woman. You'll tell me what I want to know." He didn't bother with the "or else"—something cold passed across the top of my breast, and the hot sting of the cut followed a second later, as blood began to bloom from it.

"Jesus H. Roosevelt Christ!" I said, more from surprise than pain. I jerked my arm out of his grasp. "I told you, I don't even know where we *are,* you idiot! How do you expect me to tell you where anything else is?"

He blinked, startled, and brought the knife up by reflex, wary, as though he thought I might attack him. Realizing that I wasn't about to, he scowled at me.

"I'll tell you what I *do* know," I said, and was distantly pleased to hear that my voice was sharp and steady. "The whisky cache is about half a mile from the malting shed, roughly northwest. It's in a cave, well-hidden. I could take you there—if we began from the spring where you took me—but that's all I can tell you in the way of direction."

This was true, too. I could find it easily enough—but to give directions? *"Go through a gap in the brush a little way, until you see the cluster of oak where Brianna shot a possum, bear left to a squarish rock with a bunch of adder's-tongue growing over it. . . ."* The fact that the need for my services as a guide was probably all that kept them from killing me on the spot was, of course, a secondary consideration.

It was a very shallow cut; I wasn't bleeding badly at all. My face and hands were ice-cold, though, and small flashing lights came and went at the edges of my vision. Nothing was keeping me upright save a vague conviction that if it came to that, I preferred to die on my feet.

"I tell you, Hodge, you don't want nothing to do with that one—nothing." A larger man had joined the small group round me. He leaned over Hodge's shoulder, looking at me, and nodded. They were all black in the shadow, but this man had a voice tinged with the lilt of Africa—an ex-slave, or perhaps a slave-trader. "That woman—I hear about her. She is a conjure woman. I know them. They are like serpents, conjure wives. You don't touch that one, hear me? She will curse you!"

I managed to give a rather nasty-sounding laugh in answer to this, and the man closest to me took a half-step back. I was vaguely surprised; where had *that* come from?

But I was breathing better now, and the flashing lights were gone.

The tall man stretched his neck, seeing the dark line of blood on my shift.

"You draw her blood? Damn you, Hodge, you done it now." There was a distinct note of alarm in his voice, and he drew back a little, making some sort of sign toward me with one hand.

Without the slightest notion as to what moved me to do it, I dropped the rock, ran the fingers of my right hand across the cut, and in one swift motion, reached out and drew them down the thin man's cheek. I repeated the nasty laugh.

"Curse, is it?" I said. "How's this? Touch me again, and you'll die within twenty-four hours."

The streaks of blood showed dark on the white of his face. He was close enough that I could smell the sourness of his breath, and see the fury gather on his face.

What on earth do you think you are doing, Beauchamp? I thought, utterly surprised at myself. Hodge drew back his fist to strike me, but the large man caught him by the wrist with a cry of fear.

"Don't you do that! You will kill us all!"

"I'll friggin' kill *you* right now, arsebite!"

Hodge was still holding the knife in his other hand; he stabbed awkwardly at the larger man, grunting with rage. The big man gasped at the impact, but wasn't badly stricken—he wrenched at the wrist he held and Hodge gave a high, squealing cry, like a rabbit seized by a fox.

Then the others were all in it, pushing and shouting, grappling for weapons. I turned and ran, but got no more than a few steps before one of them grabbed me, flinging his arms round me and jerking me hard against himself.

"You're not going anywhere, lady," he said, panting in my ear.

I wasn't. He was no taller than I, but a good deal stronger. I lunged against his grip, but he had both arms wrapped tight around me, and squeezed tighter. I stood stiff then, heart pounding with anger and fear, not wanting to give him an excuse to maul me. He was excited; I could feel his heart pounding, too, and smell the reek of fresh sweat over the fetor of stale clothes and body.

I couldn't see what was going on, but I didn't think they were fighting so much as merely shouting at each other now. My captor shifted his weight and cleared his throat.

"Ahh . . . where do you come from, ma'am?" he asked, quite politely.

"What?" I said, no end startled. "Come from? Er . . . ah . . . England. Oxfordshire, originally. Then Boston."

"Oh? I'm from the north myself."

I repressed the automatic urge to reply, "Pleased to meet you," since I wasn't, and the conversation languished.

The fight had stopped, abruptly as it had started. With a lot of token snarling and growling, the rest of them backed down in the face of Hodge's bellowed assertions that he was in command here, and they'd bleedin' well do as he said or take the consequences.

"He means it, too," muttered my captor, still pressing me firmly to his filthy bosom. "You don't want to cross him, lady, believe me."

"Hmph," I said, though I assumed the advice was well-meant. I had been hoping the conflict would be noisy and prolonged, thus increasing the chances of Jamie catching up to us.

"And where is this Hodge from, speaking of origins?" I asked. He still seemed remarkably familiar to me; I was sure I had seen him *somewhere*—but where?

"Hodgepile? Ahhh . . . England, I reckon," said the young man gripping me. He sounded surprised. "Don't he sound like it?"

Hodge? Hodgepile? That rang a bell, certainly, but . . .

There was a good deal of muttering and milling round, but in much too little time, we were off again. This time, thank God, I was allowed to ride astride, though my hands were tied and bound to the saddle.

We moved very slowly; there was a trail of sorts, but even with the faint light shed by a rising moon, the going was difficult. Hodgepile no longer led the horse I rode; the young man who had recaptured me held the bridle, tugging and coaxing the increasingly reluctant horse through the thickets of brush. I could glimpse him now and then, slender, with thick, wild hair that hung past his shoulders and rendered him lion-maned in silhouette.

The threat of immediate death had receded a little, but my stomach was still knotted and the muscles of my back stiff with apprehension. Hodgepile had his way for the moment, but there had been no real agreement among the men; one of those in favor of killing me and leaving my corpse for the skunks and weasels might easily decide to put a quick end to the controversy with a lunge out of the dark.

I could hear Hodgepile's voice, sharp and hectoring, somewhere up ahead. He seemed to be passing up and down the column, bullying, nagging, nipping like a sheepdog, trying to keep his flock on the move.

They *were* moving, though it was clear even to me that the horses were tired. The one I rode was shambling, jerking her head with irritation. God knew where the marauders had come from, or how long they had traveled before reaching the whisky clearing. The men were slowing, too, a gradual fog of fatigue settling on them as the adrenaline of flight and conflict receded. I could feel lassitude stealing upon me, too, and fought against it, struggling to stay alert.

It was still early autumn, but I was wearing only my shift and stays, and we were high enough that the air chilled rapidly after dark. I shivered constantly, and the cut on my chest burned as the tiny muscles flexed beneath the skin. It wasn't at all serious, but what if it became infected? I could only hope that I would live long enough for that to be a problem.

Hard as I tried, I could *not* keep from thinking of Marsali, nor keep my mind from making medical speculations, envisioning everything from concussion with intracranial swelling to burns with smoke inhalation. I could do something—perhaps even an emergency C-section—if I were there. No one else could.

I clenched my hands hard on the edge of the saddle, straining against the rope that bound them. I needed to be there!

But I was not, and might never be.

The quarreling and muttering had all but ceased as the darkness of the forest closed in upon us, but a lingering sense of unease lay heavy on the group. In part, I thought it was apprehension and fear of pursuit, but in much greater part, a sense of internal discord. The fight had not been settled, merely postponed to a more convenient season. A sense of simmering conflict was sharp in the air.

A conflict focused squarely on *me.* Unable to see clearly during the argument, I couldn't be sure which men held which opinions, but the division was clear: one party, headed by Hodgepile, was in favor of keeping me alive, at least long enough to lead them to the whisky. A second group was for cutting their losses, and my throat. And a minority opinion, voiced by the gentleman with the African speech, was for turning me loose, the sooner the better.

Obviously, it would behoove me to cultivate this gentleman, and try to turn his beliefs to my advantage. How? I'd made a start by cursing Hodgepile—and I was still quite startled that I'd done that. I didn't think it would be advisable to start cursing them wholesale, though—ruin the effect.

I shifted in the saddle, which was beginning to chafe me badly. This wasn't the first time I'd had men recoil from me in fear of what they thought I was. Superstitious fear could be an effective weapon—but it was a very dangerous one to use. If I truly frightened them, they'd kill me without a moment's hesitation.

We had crossed into the pass. There were few trees among

the boulders here, and as we emerged onto the far side of the mountain, the sky opened out before me, vast and glowing, fiery with a multitude of stars.

I must have let out a gasp at the sight, for the young man leading my horse paused, lifting his own head skyward.

"Oh," he said softly. He stared for a moment, then was pulled back to earth by the passage of another horse that brushed past us, its rider turning to peer closely at me as it did so.

"Did you have stars like this—where you came from?" my escort asked.

"No," I said, still slightly under the spell of the silent grandeur overhead. "Not so bright."

"No, they weren't," he said, shaking his head, and pulled at the rein. That seemed an odd remark, but I could make nothing of it. I might have engaged him in further conversation—God knew I needed all the allies I could get—but there was a shout from up ahead; evidently, we were making camp.

I was untied and pulled off the horse. Hodgepile pushed his way through the scrum and grasped me by the shoulder.

"You try to run, woman, and you'll wish you 'adn't." He squeezed viciously, fingers digging into my flesh. "I need you alive—I don't need you 'ole."

Still gripping my shoulder, he lifted his knife and pressed the flat of the blade against my lips, jammed the tip of it up my nose, then leaned close enough that I felt the moist warmth of his very repugnant breath on my face.

"The one thing I *won't* cut off is your tongue," he whispered. The knife blade drew slowly out of my nose, down my chin, along the line of my neck, and circled round the curve of my breast. "You take my meaning, do you?"

He waited until I managed a nod, then released me and disappeared into the darkness.

If he meant to unnerve me, he'd managed nicely. I was sweating despite the chill, and still shaking when a tall shadow loomed up beside me, took one of my hands, and pressed something into it.

"My name is Tebbe," he murmured. "You remember that—Tebbe. Remember I was good to you. Tell your spirits they don't hurt Tebbe, he was good to you."

I nodded once more, astonished, and was left again, this time with a lump of bread in my hand. I ate it hastily, observing that while very stale, it had originally been good dark rye bread, of the sort the German women of Salem made. Had the men attacked some house near there, or merely bought the bread?

A horse's saddle had been flung down on the ground near me; a canteen hung from the pommel, and I sank down on my knees to drink from it. The bread and the water—tasting of canvas and wood—tasted better than anything I'd eaten in a long while. I'd noticed before that standing very close to death improves the appetite remarkably. Still, I did hope for something more elaborate as a last meal.

Hodgepile returned a few minutes later, with rope. He didn't bother with further threats, evidently feeling that he'd made his point. He merely tied me hand and foot, and pushed me down on the ground. No one spoke to me, but someone, with a kindly impulse, threw a blanket over me.

The camp settled quickly. No fire was lit, and so no supper was cooked; the men presumably refreshed themselves in the same makeshift way I had, then scattered into the wood to seek their rest, leaving the horses tethered a little way off.

I waited until the comings and goings died down, then took the blanket in my teeth and wriggled carefully away from the spot where I had been placed, making my way inchworm fashion to another tree, a dozen yards away.

I had no thought of escape in doing this; but if one of the bandits in favor of disposing of me should think to take advantage of the darkness in order to achieve their aims, I didn't mean to be lying there like a staked goat. With luck, if anyone came skulking round the spot where I'd been, I would have enough warning to scream for help.

I knew beyond the shadow of a doubt that Jamie would come. My job was to survive until he did.

Panting, sweating, covered with crumbled leaves and with my stockings in rags, I curled up under a big hornbeam, and burrowed back under the blanket. Thus concealed, I had a try at undoing the knots in the rope around my wrists with my teeth. Hodgepile had tied them, though, and had done so with military thoroughness. Short of gnawing gopherlike through the ropes themselves, I was going nowhere.

Military. It was that thought that recalled suddenly to me who he was, and where I had seen him before. Arvin Hodgepile! He had been the clerk at the Crown's warehouse in Cross Creek. I had met him briefly, three years before, when Jamie and I brought the body of a murdered girl to the sergeant of the garrison there.

Sergeant Murchison was dead—and I'd thought Hodgepile was, as well, killed in the conflagration that had destroyed the warehouse and its contents. So, a deserter, then. Either he had had time to escape the warehouse before it went up in flames, or had simply not been there at the time. In either case, he'd been clever enough to realize that he could take this opportunity to disappear from His Majesty's army, leaving his death to be assumed.

What he had been doing since then was clear, too. Wandering the countryside, stealing, robbing, and killing—and collecting a number of like-minded companions along the way.

Not that they appeared to be of one mind just at present. While Hodgepile might be the self-proclaimed leader of this gang at the moment, it was plain to see that he hadn't held the position for long. He wasn't accustomed to command, didn't know how to manage men, save by threat. I'd seen many military commanders in my time, good and bad, and recognized the difference.

I could hear Hodgepile even now, voice raised in distant argument with someone. I'd seen his sort before, vicious men who could temporarily cow those near them by outbursts of unpredictable violence. They seldom lasted long—and I doubted that Hodgepile was going to last much longer.

He wasn't going to last any longer than it took for Jamie to find us. That thought calmed me like a slug of good whisky. Jamie would surely be looking for me by now.

I curled tighter under my blanket, shivering a little. Jamie would need light to track at night—torches. That would make him and his party visible—and vulnerable—if they came within sight of the camp. The camp itself wouldn't be visible; there was no fire lit, and the horses and men were scattered through the wood. I knew sentries had been posted;

I could hear them moving in the wood now and then, talking low-voiced.

But Jamie was no fool, I told myself, trying to drive away visions of ambush and massacre. He would know, from the freshness of the horses' dung, if he were drawing close, and certainly wouldn't be marching right up to the camp, torches blazing. If he had tracked the party this far, he would—

The sound of quiet footsteps froze me. They were coming from the direction of my original resting place, and I cowered under my blanket like a field mouse with a weasel in sight.

The steps shuffled slowly to and fro, as though someone was poking his way through the dried leaves and pine needles, looking for me. I held my breath, though surely no one could hear that, with the night wind sighing through the branches overhead.

I strained my eyes at the darkness, but could make out nothing more than a faint blur moving among the tree trunks, a dozen yards away. A sudden thought struck me—could it be Jamie? If he had come close enough to locate the camp, he would very likely steal in on foot, looking for me.

I drew breath at the thought, straining against my bonds. I wanted urgently to call out, but didn't dare. If it *should* be Jamie, calling to him would expose his presence to the bandits. If I could hear the sentries, they could certainly hear me.

But if it were *not* Jamie, but one of the bandits, seeking to kill me quietly . . .

I let my breath out very slowly, every muscle in my body clenched and trembling. It was cool enough, but I was bathed in sweat; I could smell my own body, the reek of fear mingling with the colder smells of earth and vegetation.

The blur had vanished, the footsteps gone, and my heart was pounding like a kettledrum. The tears I had held back for hours seeped out, hot on my face, and I wept, shaking silently.

The night was immense around me, the darkness filled with threat. Overhead, the stars hung bright and watchful in the sky, and at some point, I slept.

28

CURSES

I WOKE JUST BEFORE DAWN, in a muck sweat and with a throbbing headache. The men were already moving, grumbling about the lack of coffee or breakfast.

Hodgepile stopped beside me, looking down with narrowed eyes. He glanced toward the tree beneath which he had left me the night before and the deep furrow of disturbed leaf mold I had created in worm-crawling toward my present spot. He had very little in the way of lips, but his lower jaw compressed in displeasure.

He pulled the knife from his belt, and I felt the blood drain from my face. However, he merely knelt and cut my bonds, rather than slicing off a finger by way of expressing his emotions.

"We leave in five minutes," he said, and stalked off. I was quivering and faintly nauseated with fear, and so stiff that I could barely stand. I managed to get to my feet, though, and staggered the short distance to a small stream.

The air was damp and I was now chilly in my sweat-soaked shift, but cold water splashed on my hands and face seemed to help a little, soothing the throb behind my right eye. I had just time to make a hasty toilet, removing the rags of my stockings and running wet fingers through my hair, before Hodgepile reappeared to march me off again.

This time, I was put on a horse, but not tied, thank God. I wasn't allowed to hold the reins, though; my mount was on a leading rein, held by one of the bandits.

It was my first chance to get a good look at my captors, as they came out of the wood and shook themselves into rough order, coughing, spitting, and urinating on trees without reference to my presence. Beyond Hodgepile, I counted twelve more men—a baker's dozen of villains.

It was easy to pick out the man called Tebbe; his height aside, he was a mulatto. There was another man of mixed blood—black and Indian, I thought—but he was short and squat. Tebbe didn't glance in my direction, but went about his business with head lowered, scowling.

That was a disappointment; I didn't know what had passed among the men during the night, but evidently Tebbe's insistence that I be released was no longer so insistent. A rust-spotted kerchief bound his wrist; that might have something to do with it.

The young man who had guided my horse the night before was also easy to pick out, by way of his long, bushy hair, but he didn't come near, and avoided looking at me, too. Rather to my surprise, he was an Indian—not Cherokee; perhaps a Tuscarora? I hadn't expected that from his speech, nor his curly hair. Clearly he was mixed-blood, too.

The rest of the gang were more or less white, but a motley crew, nonetheless. Three of them were no more than half-bearded boys in their mid-teens, scruffy and gangling. They *did* look at me, goggling drop-jawed, and nudging one another. I stared at one of them until he met my eye; he went bright scarlet beneath his sparse whiskers, and looked away.

Fortunately, the shift I was wearing was one with sleeves; the thing covered me decently enough from drawstring neck to the hem at mid-calf, but there was no denying that I felt uncomfortably exposed. The shift was damp and clung limply to the curve of my breasts—a sensation I was uncomfortably aware of. I wished I had kept hold of the blanket.

The men swirled slowly round me, loading the horses, and I had the distinct and unpleasant sense of being the center of the mass—in much the same way a bull's-eye lies at the center of a target. I could only hope that I looked aged and cronelike enough for my state of untidiness to be repellent, rather than interesting; my hair was loose, wild, and tangled as witch's moss around my shoulders, and I certainly *felt* as though I had been crumpled up like an old paper bag.

I held myself bolt upright in the saddle, giving an unfriendly glare to anyone who so much as glanced in my direction. One man blinked blearily at my bare leg with a faint look of speculation—only to recoil noticeably when he met my eye.

That gave me a momentary feeling of grim satisfaction—superseded almost immediately by shock. The horses had begun to move, and as mine obediently followed the man in front of me, two more men came into view, standing under a big oak. I knew them both.

Harley Boble was tying the strings on a packsaddle, scowling as he said something to another, larger man. Harley Boble was an erstwhile thieftaker, now evidently turned thief. A thoroughly nasty little man, he was unlikely to be well-disposed toward me, owing to an occurrence at a Gathering some time before.

I wasn't at all pleased to see him here, though I was by no means surprised to find him in such company. But it was the sight of his companion that caused my empty stomach to contract, and my skin to twitch like a horse with flies.

Mr. Lionel Brown, of Brownsville.

He looked up, caught sight of me, and turned hastily away again, shoulders hunching. He must have realized that I had seen him, though, for he turned back to face me, thin features set in a sort of weary defiance. His nose was swollen and discolored, a dark red bulb visible even in the grayish light. He stared at me for a moment, then nodded as though making some reluctant acknowledgment, and turned away again.

I risked a glance back over my shoulder as we entered the trees, but couldn't see him anymore. What was *he* doing here? I hadn't recognized his voice at the time, but clearly it had been he who had argued with Hodgepile about the wisdom of taking me. Little wonder! He wasn't the only one disturbed by our mutual recognition.

Lionel Brown and his brother, Richard, were traders; the founders and patriarchs of Brownsville, a tiny settlement in the hills some forty miles from the Ridge. It was one thing for freebooters like Boble or Hodgepile to roam the countryside, robbing and burning; quite another for the Browns of Brownsville to be providing a base for their depredations. The very last thing in the world Mr. Lionel Brown could wish would be for me to reach Jamie with word of what he had been up to.

And I rather thought he would take steps to prevent me doing so. The sun was coming up, beginning to warm the air, but I felt suddenly cold, as though I had been dropped in a well.

Rays of light shone through the branches, gilding the remnants of the night mist that veiled the trees and silvering the dripping edges of their leaves. The trees were alive with birdsong, and a towhee hopped and scratched in a patch of sun, oblivious of the passing men and horses. It was too early yet for flies and mosquitoes, and the soft morning breeze caressed my face. Definitely one of those prospects where only man was vile.

The morning passed quietly enough, but I was aware of the constant state of tension among the men—though no more tense than I was.

Jamie Fraser, where are *you?* I thought, concentrating fiercely on the forest around us. Every distant rustle or snap of twig might presage rescue, and my nerves began to be distinctly frayed in anticipation.

Where? When? How? I had neither reins nor weapons; if—when—an attack was made on the group, my best—well, the only possible—strategy was to fling myself off the horse and run. As we rode I constantly evaluated each patch of witch-hazel and stand of spruce, spotting footholds, plotting a zigzag path through saplings and boulders.

It wasn't only an attack by Jamie and his men that I was preparing for; I couldn't see Lionel Brown, but I knew he was somewhere nearby. A spot between my shoulder blades clenched in a knot, anticipating a knife.

I kept an eye out for potential weapons: rocks of a useful size, branches that might be seized from the ground. If and when I ran, I meant to let no one stop me. But we pushed on, moving as quickly as the horses' footing allowed, men glancing back constantly over their shoulders, hands on their guns. As for me, I was obliged to relinquish my imaginary grasp on each possible weapon in turn as it slid past, out of sight.

To my intense disappointment, we reached the gorge near midday, without incident.

I had visited the gorge once with Jamie. The cataract fell

sixty feet down a granite cliff face, sparkling with rainbows and roaring with a voice like the archangel Michael. Fronds of red chokeberry and wild indigo fringed the falls, and yellow poplars overhung the river below the cataract's pool, so thick that no more than a fugitive gleam from the water's surface showed between the banks of lush vegetation. Hodgepile, of course, had not been drawn by the scenic beauty of the spot.

"Get off." A gruff voice spoke near my elbow, and I looked down to see Tebbe. "We will swim the horses across. You come with me."

"I'll take her." My heart sprang up into my throat at the sound of a thickly nasal voice. It was Lionel Brown, pushing his way past an overhanging rope of creeper, dark eyes intent on me.

"Not you." Tebbe rounded on Brown, fist closed.

"Not you," I repeated firmly. "I'm going with him." I slid off the horse and promptly took shelter behind the big mulatto's menacing frame, peering out at Brown from beneath the bigger man's arm.

I wasn't under the slightest illusion about Brown's intent. He wouldn't risk assassinating me under Hodgepile's eye, but he could—and would—drown me easily, and claim it was an accident. The river was shallow here, but still fast; I could hear it whooshing past the rocks near shore.

Brown's eyes darted right, then left, thinking whether to try it on—but Tebbe hunched his massive shoulders, and Brown gave it up as a bad job. He snorted, spat to one side, and stamped away, snapping branches.

I might never have a better chance. Not waiting for the sounds of Brown's huffy exit to subside, I slipped a hand over the big man's elbow and squeezed his arm.

"Thank you," I said, low-voiced. "For what you did last night. Are you badly hurt?"

He glanced down at me, apprehension clear in his face. My touching him plainly disconcerted him; I could feel the tension in his arm as he tried to decide whether to pull away from me or not.

"No," he said at last. "I am all right." He hesitated a moment, but then smiled uncertainly.

It was obvious what Hodgepile intended; the horses were being led, one at a time, down a narrow deer trail that edged the escarpment. We were more than a mile from the cataract, but the air was still loud with its noise. The sides of the gorge plunged steeply down to the water, more than fifty feet below, and the opposite bank was equally steep and overgrown.

A thick fringe of bushes hid the edge of the bank, but I could see that the river spread out here, becoming slower as it shallowed. With no dangerous currents, the horses could be taken downstream, to come out at some random point on the opposite shore. Anyone who had succeeded in tracking us to the gorge would lose the trail here, and have no little difficulty in picking it up on the opposite side.

With an effort, I stopped myself looking back over my shoulder for signs of imminent pursuit. My heart was beating fast. If Jamie was nearby, he would wait and attack the group when they entered the water, when they were most vulnerable. Even if he were not yet near, it would be a confusing business, crossing the river. If there were ever a time to attempt an escape . . .

"You shouldn't go with them," I said conversationally to Tebbe. "You'll die, too."

The arm under my hand jerked convulsively. He glanced down at me, wide-eyed. The sclera of his eyes were yellow with jaundice, and the irises broken, giving him an odd, smudgy stare.

"I told him the truth, you know." I lifted my chin toward Hodgepile, visible in the distance. "He'll die. So will all those with him. There's no need for you to die, though."

He muttered something under his breath, and pressed a fist against his chest. He had something on a string there, hanging beneath his shirt. I didn't know whether it might be a cross or some more pagan amulet, but he seemed to be responding well to suggestion so far.

So close to the river, the air was thick with moisture, live with the smell of green things and water.

"The water is my friend," I said, trying for an air of mystery suitable to a conjure woman. I was not a good liar, but I was lying for my life. "When we go into the river, let go your hold. A water horse will rise up to carry me away."

His eyes couldn't get any wider. Evidently, he'd heard of kelpies, or something like them. Even this far from the cataract, the roar of the water had voices in it—if one chose to listen.

"I am not going away with a water horse," he said with conviction. "I know about them. They take you down, drown you, and eat you."

"It won't eat me," I assured him. "You needn't go near it. Just stand clear, once we're in the water. Keep well away."

And if he did, I'd be under the water and swimming for my life before he could say Jack Robinson. I would be willing to bet that most of Hodgepile's bandits couldn't swim; few people in the mountains could. I flexed my leg muscles, readying myself, aches and stiffness dissolved in a flood of adrenaline.

Half the men were over the edge with the horses already—I could delay Tebbe, I thought, until the rest were safely in the water. Even if he wouldn't deliberately connive at my escape, if I slipped his grasp, I thought he wouldn't try to catch me.

He pulled halfheartedly at my arm, and I stopped abruptly.

"Ouch! Wait, I've stepped on a bur."

I lifted one foot, peering at the sole. Given the dirt and resin stains adhering to it, no one could possibly have told whether I had picked up cockleburs, bramble thorns, or even a horseshoe nail.

"We need to go, woman." I didn't know whether it was my proximity, the roar of the water, or the thought of water horses that was disturbing Tebbe, but he was sweating with nerves; his odor had changed from simple musk to something sharp and pungent.

"Just a moment," I said, pretending to pick at my foot. "Nearly got it."

"Leave it. I will carry you."

Tebbe was breathing heavily, looking back and forth from me to the edge of the gorge, where the deer trail disappeared into the growth, as though fearing the reappearance of Hodgepile.

It wasn't Hodgepile who popped out of the bushes, though. It was Lionel Brown, his face set with purpose, two younger men behind him, looking equally determined.

"I'll take her," he said without preamble, grabbing my arm.

"No!" By reflex, Tebbe clutched my other arm and pulled.

An undignified tug-of-war ensued, with Tebbe and Mr. Brown each jerking one of my arms. Before I could be split like a wishbone, Tebbe fortunately changed tactics. Releasing my arm, he seized me instead about the body and clutched me to himself, kicking out with one foot at Mr. Brown.

The result of this maneuver was to cause Tebbe and myself to fall backward into an untidy pile of arms and legs, while Brown also lost his balance, though I didn't realize at first that he had. All I was aware of was a loud yell and stumbling noises, followed by a crash and the rattle of dislodged stones bounding down a rocky slope.

Disengaging myself from Tebbe, I crawled out, to discover the rest of the men grouped round an ominously flattened spot in the bushes fringing the gorge. One or two were hurriedly fetching ropes and yelling contradictory orders, from which I deduced that Mr. Brown had indeed fallen into the gorge, but was not yet certifiably dead.

I rapidly reversed directions, meaning to dive headfirst into the vegetation, but came up instead against a pair of cracked boots, belonging to Hodgepile. He seized me by the hair and yanked, causing me to shriek and lash out at him in reflex. I caught him across the midriff. He oomphed and went open-mouthed, gasping for air, but didn't let go his iron grip on my hair.

Making furious faces in my direction, he let go then, and boosted me toward the edge of the gorge with a knee. One of the younger men was clinging to the bushes, feeling gingerly for footholds on the slope below, one rope tied round his waist and another slung in a coil over his shoulder.

"Frigging mort!" Hodgepile yelled, digging his fingers into my arm as he leaned through the broken bushes. "What d'ye mean by this, you bitch?"

He capered on the edge of the gorge like Rumpelstiltskin, shaking his fist and hurling abuse impartially at his damaged business partner and at me, while the rescue operations commenced. Tebbe had withdrawn to a safe distance, where he stood looking offended.

At length, Brown was hauled up, groaning loudly, and laid

out on the grass. Those men not already in the river gathered round, looking hot and flustered.

"You mean to mend him, conjure woman?" Tebbe asked, glancing skeptically at me. I didn't know whether he meant to cast doubt upon my abilities, or only on the wisdom of my helping Brown, but I nodded, a little uncertainly, and came forward.

"I suppose so." An oath was an oath, though I rather wondered if Hippocrates ever ran into this sort of situation himself. Possibly he did; the ancient Greeks were a violent lot, too.

The men gave way to me easily enough; once having got Brown out of the gorge, it was obvious that they had no notion what to do about him.

I did a hasty triage. Aside from multiple cuts, contusions, and a thick coating of dust and mud, Mr. Lionel Brown had fractured his left leg in at least two places, broken his left wrist, and probably crushed a couple of ribs. Only one of the leg fractures was compound, but it was nasty, the jagged end of the broken thighbone poking through skin and breeches, surrounded by a steadily widening patch of red.

He had unfortunately not severed his femoral artery, since if he had, he would have been dead already. Still, Mr. Brown had probably ceased to be a personal threat to me for the moment, which was all to the good.

Lacking any equipment or medication, bar several filthy neckcloths, a pine branch, and some whisky from a canteen, my ministrations were necessarily limited. I managed—with no little difficulty and quite a lot of whisky—to get the femur roughly straightened and splinted without having Brown die of shock, which I thought no small accomplishment under the circumstances.

It was a difficult job, though, and I was muttering to myself under my breath—something I hadn't realized I was doing, until I glanced up to find Tebbe crouched on his heels on the other side of Brown's body, regarding me with interest.

"Oh, you curse him," he said approvingly. "Yes, that is a good idea."

Mr. Brown's eyes sprang open and bugged out. He was

half off his head with pain, and thoroughly drunk by now, but not quite so drunk as to overlook this.

"Make her stop," he said hoarsely. "Here, Hodgepile—make her stop! Make her take it back!"

" 'Ere, what's this? What did you say, woman?" Hodgepile had simmered down a bit, but his animus was instantly rekindled by this. He reached down and grabbed my wrist just as I was feeling my way over Brown's injured torso. It was the wrist he had twisted so viciously the day before, and a stab of pain shot up my forearm.

"If you must know, I expect I said 'Jesus H. Roosevelt Christ'!" I snapped. "Let go of me!"

"That's what she said when she cursed you! Get her away from me! Don't let her touch me!" Panicked, Brown made to squirm away from me, a very bad idea for a man with freshly broken bones. He went dead-white under the smears of mud, and his eyes rolled back in his head.

"Look at that! He's dead!" one of the onlookers exclaimed. "She's done it! She witched him!"

This caused no little uproar, between the vocal approbation of Tebbe and his supporters, my own protests, and outcries of concern from Mr. Brown's friends and relations, one of whom squatted down by the body, putting an ear to the chest.

"He's alive!" this man exclaimed. "Uncle Lionel! You all right?"

Lionel Brown groaned loudly and opened his eyes, causing further commotion. The young man who had called him Uncle drew a large knife from his belt and pointed it at me. His eyes were open so wide that the whites showed all around.

"You get back!" he said. "Don't you touch him!"

I raised my hands, palms out, in gesture of abnegation.

"Fine!" I snapped. "I won't!" There was, in fact, little more I could do for Brown. He should be kept warm, dry, and well-hydrated, but something told me that Hodgepile would not be open to any such suggestions.

He wasn't. By means of furious and repeated bellows, he quelled the incipient riot, then declared that we were crossing the gorge, and right quickly, too.

"Put 'im on a stretcher, then," he said impatiently, in reply to protests from Brown's nephew. "And as for you—" He rounded on me, glaring. "Did I tell you? No tricks, I said!"

"Kill her," Brown said hoarsely from the ground. "Kill her now."

"Kill her? Not bloody likely, oul' son." Hodgepile's eyes gleamed with malice. "She's no more risk to *me* alive than dead—and a good bit more profit alive. But I'll keep her in line."

The knife was never far from his grasp. He had it out in an instant, and had seized my hand. Before I could so much as draw breath, I felt the blade press down, cutting partway into the base of my forefinger.

"Remember what I told you, do you?" He breathed it, his face was soft with anticipation. "I don't need you whole."

I did remember, and my belly hollowed, my throat dried to silence. My skin burned where he cut, and pain spread in a flash through my nerves; the need to jerk away from the blade was so strong that the muscles of my arm cramped with it.

I could imagine vividly the spurting stump, the shock of broken bone, ripped flesh, the horror of irrevocable loss.

But behind Hodgepile, Tebbe had risen to his feet. His odd, smudgy stare was fixed on me, with an expression of fascinated dread. I saw his hand close in a fist, his throat move as he swallowed, and felt the saliva return to my own. If I was to keep his protection, I must keep his belief.

I fixed my eyes on Hodgepile's, and made myself lean toward him. My skin quivered and jumped, and the blood roared louder in my ears than the voice of the cataract—but I opened my eyes wide. A witch's eyes—or so some said.

Very, very slowly, I lifted my free hand, still wet with Brown's blood. I reached the bloody fingers toward Hodgepile's face.

"I remember," I said, my voice a hoarse whisper. "Do you remember what *I* said?"

He would have done it. I saw the decision flash in his eyes, but before he could press the knife blade down, the bushy-haired young Indian leaped forward, grabbing at his arm with a cry of horror. Distracted, Hodgepile let go his grip, and I pulled free.

In an instant, Tebbe and two more men surged forward, hands on knives and pistol grips.

Hodgepile's thin face was pinched with fury, but the moment of incipient violence had passed. He lowered his own knife, the menace receding.

I opened my mouth to say something that might help defuse the situation further, but was forestalled by a panicked cry from Brown's nephew.

"Don't let her talk! She'll curse us all!"

"Oh, bleedin' 'ell," said Hodgepile, fury transmuted to mere crossness.

I had used several neckcloths to bind Brown's splint. Hodgepile stooped and snatched one from the ground, wadded it into a ball, and stepped forward.

"Open your mouth," he said tersely, and seizing my jaw with one hand, he forced open my mouth and crammed the wadded fabric into it. He glared at Tebbe, who had made a jerky move forward.

"I shan't kill her. But she says not a word more. Not to 'im"—he nodded at Brown, then Tebbe—"not to you. Nor me." He glanced back at me, and to my surprise, I saw a lurking uneasiness in his eyes. "Not to anyone."

Tebbe looked uncertain, but Hodgepile was already tying his own neckcloth round my head, effectively gagging me.

"Not a word," Hodgepile repeated, glaring round at the company. "Now, let's go!"

WE CROSSED THE river. To my surprise, Lionel Brown survived, but it was a lengthy business, and the sun was low by the time we made camp, two miles past the gorge on the farther side.

Everyone was wet, and a fire was kindled without discussion. The currents of dissension and distrust were still there, but had been damped by the river and exhaustion. Everyone was simply too tired for further strife.

They had tied my hands loosely, but left my feet unbound;

I made my way to a fallen log near the fire and sank down, utterly drained. I was damp and chilled, my muscles trembling with exhaustion—I had been forced to walk from the river—and for the first time, I began to wonder whether Jamie would in fact find me. Ever.

Perhaps he had followed the wrong group of bandits. Perhaps he had found and attacked them—and been wounded or killed in the fight. I had closed my eyes, but opened them again, seeking to avoid the visions this thought had conjured up. I still worried about Marsali—but either they had found her in time or they hadn't; either way, her fate had been decided.

The fire was burning well, at least; cold, wet, and eager for hot food, the men had brought an immense pile of wood. A short, silent black man was stoking the fire, while a couple of the teenagers rifled the packs for food. A pot of water was set on the fire with a chunk of salt beef, and the lion-haired young Indian poured cornmeal into a bowl with a lump of lard.

Another bit of lard sizzled on an iron girdle, melting into grease. It smelled wonderful.

Saliva flooded my mouth, absorbed at once into the wad of fabric, and despite discomfort, the smell of food bolstered my spirits a little. My stays, loosened by the travel of the last twenty-four hours, had tightened again as the wet laces dried and shrank. My skin itched beneath the fabric, but the thin ribs of the boning did give me a sense of support, more than welcome at the moment.

Mr. Brown's two nephews—Aaron and Moses, I had learned—limped slowly into camp, a makeshift stretcher sagging between them. They set it gratefully down beside the fire, evoking a loud yell from the contents.

Mr. Brown had survived the river crossing, but it hadn't done him any good. Of course, I *had* told them he should be kept well-hydrated. The thought undid me, tired as I was, and I made a muffled snorting sound behind my gag.

One of the young lads nearby heard me, and reached tentatively for the knot of my gag, but dropped his hand at once when Hodgepile barked at him.

"Leave her!"

"But—don't she need to eat, Hodge?" The boy glanced uneasily at me.

"Not just yet she doesn't." Hodgepile squatted down in front of me, looking me over. "Learned your lesson yet, 'ave you?"

I didn't move. Just sat and looked at him, infusing my gaze with as much scorn as possible. The cut on my finger burned; my palms had begun to sweat—but I stared. He tried to stare back, but couldn't do it—his eyes kept slipping away.

That made him even angrier; a flush burned high on his bony cheeks.

"Stop looking at me!"

I blinked slowly, once, and kept looking, with what I hoped appeared to be interested dispassion. He was looking rather strained, our Mr. Hodgepile was. Dark circles under the eyes, muscle fibers bracketing his mouth like lines carved in wood. Sweat stains wet and hot beneath the armpits. Constant browbeating must take it out of one.

All at once, he stood up, grabbed me by the arm, and yanked me to my feet.

"I'll put you where you can't stare, bitch," he muttered, and marched me past the fire, shoving me ahead of him. A little way outside the camp, he found a tree to his liking. He untied my hands and rebound my wrists, with a loop of line wrapped round my waist and my hands fastened to it. Then he pushed me down into a seated position, fashioned a crude noose with a slipknot, and put it round my neck, tying the free end to the tree.

"So as you won't wander away," he said, pulling the rough hemp snug around my neck. "Shouldn't want you to get lost. Might be eaten by a bear, and then what, eh?" This had quite restored his humor; he laughed immoderately, and was still chuckling when he left. He turned, though, to glance back at me. I sat upright, staring, and the humor abruptly left his face. He turned and strode off, shoulders stiff as wood.

In spite of hunger, thirst, and general discomfort, I actually felt a sense of profound, if momentary, relief. If I was not strictly speaking alone, I was at least unobserved, and even this modicum of privacy was balm.

I was a good twenty yards from the fire ring, out of sight of all the men. I sagged against the tree trunk, the muscles of face and body giving way all at once, and a shiver seized me, though it wasn't cold.

Soon. Surely Jamie would find me soon. Unless—I pushed the dubious thought aside as though it were a venomous scorpion. Likewise any thought of what had happened to Marsali, or might happen if and when—no, *when*—he did find us. I didn't know how he'd manage, but he would. He just *would.*

The sun was nearly down; shadows were pooling under the trees and the light faded slowly from the air, making colors fugitive and solid objects lose their depth. There was rushing water somewhere nearby, and the calling of the occasional bird in the distant trees. These began to fall silent as the evening cooled, replaced by the rising chirp of crickets near at hand. My eye caught the flicker of movement, and I saw a rabbit, gray as the dusk, sitting up on its hind legs under a bush a few feet distant, nose twitching.

The sheer normalcy of it all made my eyes sting. I blinked away the tears, and the rabbit was gone.

The sight of it had restored my nerve a little; I essayed a few experiments, to see the limits of my present bondage. My legs were free—that was good. I could rise up into a sort of ungainly squat, and duck-waddle round the tree. Even better; I would be able to relieve myself in privacy on the far side.

I could not, however, rise entirely to my feet, nor could I reach the knot of the line that circled the tree trunk; the rope either slid or caught on the bark, but in either case, the knot remained frustratingly on the opposite side of the trunk—which had to measure nearly three feet in diameter.

I had about two feet of line between the trunk and the noose about my neck; enough to allow me to lie down, or to turn from side to side. Hodgepile was rather obviously well-acquainted with convenient methods of restraining captives; I thought of the O'Brians' homestead, and the two bodies there. The two elder children missing. A small shudder passed over me again.

Where were they? Sold to one of the Indian tribes as slaves? Taken to a sailors' brothel in one of the coastal towns? Or onto a ship, to be pressed into use on the sugar plantations of the Indies?

I was under no illusions that any of these picturesquely

unpleasant fates lay in store for me. I was much too old, much too obstreperous—and much too notorious. No, the only value I held for Hodgepile was my knowledge of the whisky cache. Once he had got within sniffing distance of that, he would slit my throat without a moment's compunction.

The smell of roasting meat floated through the air, flooding my mouth with fresh saliva—a welcome relief, in spite of the growling of my stomach, since the gag dried my mouth unpleasantly.

A tiny jolt of panic tensed my muscles. I didn't want to think about the gag. Or the ropes around my wrists and neck. It would be too easy to succumb to the panic of confinement, and exhaust myself in futile struggle. I had to preserve my strength; I didn't know when or how I would need it, but need it I surely would. *Soon,* I prayed. *Let it be soon.*

The men had settled to their supper, the contentions of the day sunk in appetite. They were far enough away that I couldn't hear the particulars of their conversation, but only the stray word or phrase borne on the evening breeze. I turned my head to let the breeze smooth the hair from my face, and found that I could see a long, narrow swath of sky above the distant gorge, gone a deep, unearthly blue, as though the fragile layer of atmosphere that covered the earth grew thinner still, and the darkness of space beyond shone through.

The stars began to prick out, one by one, and I managed to lose myself in watching, counting them as they appeared, one by one by one . . . touching them as I might the beads of a rosary, and saying to myself such astronomical names as I knew, comforting in their sound, even though I had no idea whether such names bore any relation to the celestial bodies I saw. Alpha Centauri, Deneb, Sirius, Betelgeuse, the Pleiades, Orion . . .

I succeeded in soothing myself to the extent that I dozed off, only to rouse some time later to find it now full dark. The light of the fire sent a flickering glow through the underbrush, painting my feet, which lay in an open spot, with rosy shadows. I stirred and stretched myself as well as I could, trying to relieve the stiffness in my back, and wondered whether Hodgepile thought himself safe now, to be allowing such a large fire?

A loud groan came to me on the wind—Lionel Brown. I grimaced, but there was nothing I could do for him in my present condition.

I heard shuffling and a murmur of voices; someone was attending to him.

". . . hot as a pistol . . ." one voice said, sounding only mildly concerned.

". . . fetch the woman? . . ."

"No," said a definite voice. Hodgepile. I sighed.

". . . water. No help for *that* . . ."

I was listening so intently, in hopes of hearing what was happening by the fire, that it was some time before I became aware of noises in the brush nearby. Not animals; only bears would make that much noise, and bears didn't giggle. The giggling was subdued, not only muffled but repeatedly interrupted.

There was whispering, too, though I couldn't make out most of the words. The overall atmosphere was so much one of excited juvenile conspiracy, though, that I knew it must be some of the younger members of the gang.

". . . go *on,* then!" I caught, spoken in a vehement tone, and accompanied by a crashing noise, indicating that someone had been pushed into a tree. Another crash, indicating retaliation.

More rustling. Whisper, whisper, snigger, snort. I sat up straight, wondering what in God's name they were up to.

Then I heard, "Her legs aren't tied . . ." and my heart gave a small jump.

"But what if she . . ." mumble, mumble.

"Won't matter. She can't scream."

That came through very clearly, and I jerked my feet back to scramble up—only to be brought up short by the noose around my neck. It felt like an iron bar across my windpipe, and I fell back, seeing blood-red blotches at the corners of my eyes.

I shook my head and gulped air, trying to shake off the dizziness, adrenaline racing through my blood. I felt a hand on my ankle, and kicked out sharply.

"Hey!" he said out loud, sounding surprised. He took his hand off my ankle and sat back a little. My vision was clearing;

I could see him now, but the firelight was behind him; it was one of the young lads, but no more than a faceless, hunched silhouette in front of me.

"Shh," he said, and giggled nervously, reaching out a hand toward me. I made a deep growling noise behind my gag, and he stopped, frozen in mid-reach. There was a rustling in the brush behind him.

This seemed to remind him that his friend—or friends—were watching, and he reached out with renewed resolution, patting me on the thigh.

"Don't you worry, ma'am," he whispered, duck-walking closer on his heels, "I don't mean you no harm."

I snorted, and he hesitated again—but then another rustle from the bush seemed to stiffen his resolve, and he grasped me by the shoulders, trying to make me lie down. I struggled hard, kicking and kneeing at him, and he lost his grip, lost his balance, and fell on his backside.

A muffled explosion of sniggering from the bush brought him up on his feet like a jack-in-the-box. He reached down with decision, seized my ankles, and yanked, jerking me flat. Then he flung himself on top of me, pinning me with his weight.

"Hush!" he said urgently into my ear. His hands were grappling for my throat, and I squirmed and thrashed under his weight, trying to buck him off. His hands closed tight on my neck, though, and I stopped, my vision going black and bloody once again.

"Hush, now," he said more quietly. "You just hush, ma'am, all right?" I was making small choking noises, which he must have taken for assent, for his grip slackened.

"I ain't gonna hurt you, ma'am, I really ain't," he whispered, trying to hold me down with one hand while fumbling about between us with the other. "Would you just be *still,* please?"

I wouldn't, and he finally put a forearm across my throat and leaned on it. Not hard enough to make me black out again, but hard enough to take some of the fight out of me. He was thin and wiry, but very strong, and by dint of simple determination, succeeded in pushing up my shift and wedging his knee between my thighs.

He was breathing nearly as hard as I was, and I could smell the goaty reek of his excitement. His hands had left my throat, and were feverishly grasping at my breasts, in a manner that made it reasonably clear that the only other breast he'd ever touched was likely his mother's.

"Hush, now, don't you be scared, ma'am, it's all right, I ain't . . . oh. Oh, my. I . . . uh . . . oh." His hand was poking about between my thighs, then left off momentarily as he raised himself briefly and wriggled down his breeches.

He collapsed heavily on top of me, hips pumping frantically as he thrust madly away—making no contact save that of friction, as he very obviously had no idea of the way in which female anatomy was constructed. I lay still, astonished into immobility, then felt a warm pulse of liquid under my thighs as he lost himself in panting ecstasy.

All the wiry tension went out of him in a rush, and he subsided on my chest like a limp balloon. I could feel his young heart pounding like a steam hammer, and his temple was pressed against my cheek, damp with sweat.

I found the intimacy of this contact quite as objectionable as the softening presence wedged between my thighs, and rolled abruptly to the side, dumping him off. He came to life suddenly, and scrambled to his knees, yanking at his drooping breeches.

He swayed to and fro for a moment, then dropped to his hands and knees and crawled up close beside me.

"I'm really sorry, ma'am," he whispered.

I made no move, and after a moment, he reached out a tentative hand and patted me gently on the shoulder.

"I'm real sorry," he repeated, still whispering, and then was gone, leaving me lying on my back in a puddle, wondering whether such an incompetent assault could legitimately be termed rape.

Distant rustling in the bushes, accompanied by muffled whoops of young male delight, decided me firmly that it could. Christ, the rest of the obnoxious little beasts would be at me in no time. Panicked, I sat up, mindful of the noose.

The glow from the fire was irregular and flickering, barely enough to make out the trunks of trees and the pale layer of needles and leaf mold on the ground. Enough to see the protrusions of granite boulders through the leaf layer, and the occasional hump of a fallen twig. Not that the lack of potential weapons mattered, given that my hands were still firmly tied.

The weight of the young assailant had made things worse; the knots had pulled tighter during my struggles, and my hands throbbed with lack of circulation. My fingers were beginning to go numb at the tips. Bloody hell. Was I about to lose several fingers to gangrene, as a result of this absurdity?

For an instant, I contemplated the wisdom of behaving compliantly with the next horrible little boy, in hopes that he would remove the gag. If he would, I could at least beg him to loosen the ropes—and then scream for help, in hopes that Tebbe would come and stop further assault, out of fear of my eventual supernatural revenge.

Here he came, a stealthy rustling in the bushes. I gritted my teeth on the gag and looked up, but the shadowy form in front of me wasn't one of the young boys.

The only thought that came to mind when I realized who the new visitor was was, *Jamie Fraser, you bastard, where* are *you?*

I froze, as though not moving might somehow render me invisible. The man moved in front of me, squatting down so as to look into my face.

"Not laughin' so much now, are you?" he said conversationally. It was Boble, the erstwhile thieftaker. "You and your husband thought it was damn funny, didn't you, what them German women did to me? And then Mr. Fraser tellin' me as they meant to make sausage meat of me, and him with a face like a Christian readin' the Bible. Thought that was funny, too, didn't you?"

To be perfectly honest, it had been funny. He was quite correct, though; I wasn't laughing now. He drew back his arm and slapped me.

The blow made my eyes water, but the fire lit him from the side; I could still see the smile on his pudgy face. A cold qualm ran through me, making me shudder. He saw that, and the smile broadened. His canine teeth were short and blunt, so the incisors stood out by contrast, long and yellowed, rodent-like.

"Reckon you'll think this is even funnier," he said, rising to his feet and reaching for his flies. "Hope Hodge don't kill you right away, so you get to tell your husband about it. Bet you he'll enjoy the joke, man with a sense of humor like he's got."

The boy's semen was still damp and sticky on my thighs. I jerked back by reflex, trying to scramble to my feet, but was brought up short by the noose round my neck. My vision went dark for an instant as the rope tightened on my carotids, then cleared, and I found Boble's face inches from mine, his breath hot on my skin.

He seized my chin in his hand and rubbed his face over mine, biting at my lips and rasping the stubble of his beard hard across my cheeks. Then he drew back, leaving my face wet with his saliva, pushed me flat, and climbed on top of me.

I could feel the violence in him, pulsing like an exposed heart, thin-walled and ready to burst. I knew I couldn't escape or prevent him—knew he would hurt me, given the slightest excuse. The only thing to do was be still and endure him.

I couldn't. I heaved under him and rolled to the side, bringing up my knee as he pushed my shift aside. It hit him a glancing blow in the thigh, and he drew back his fist by reflex and punched me in the face, sharp and quick.

Red-black pain bloomed sudden from the center of my face, filled my head, and I went blind, shocked into momentary immobility. *You utter fool,* I thought, with total clarity. *Now he'll kill you.* The second blow struck my cheek and snapped my head to the side. Perhaps I moved again in blind resistance, perhaps I didn't.

Suddenly he was kneeling astride me, punching and slapping, blows dull and heavy as the thump of ocean waves on sand, too remote as yet for pain. I twisted, curling, bringing up my shoulder and trying to shield my face against the ground, and then his weight was gone.

He was standing. He was kicking me and cursing, panting and half-sobbing as his boot thudded into sides and back and thighs and buttocks. I panted in short gasps, trying to breathe. My body jerked and quivered with each blow, skidding on the leaf-strewn ground, and I clung to the sense of the ground below me, trying so hard to sink down, be swallowed by the earth.

Then it stopped. I could hear him panting, trying to speak. "Goddamn . . . goddamn . . . oh, goddamn . . . frig . . . friggin' . . . bitch. . ."

I lay inert, trying to disappear into the darkness that enveloped me, knowing that he was going to kick me in the head. I could feel my teeth shatter, the fragile bones of my skull splinter and collapse into the wet soft pulp of my brain, and I trembled, clenching my teeth in futile resistance against the impact. It would sound like a melon being smashed, dull, sticky-hollow. Would I hear it?

It didn't come. There was another sound, a fast, hard rustling that made no sense. A faintly meaty sound, flesh on flesh in a soft smacking rhythm, and then he gave a groan and warm gouts of fluid fell wet on my face and shoulders, splattering on bare skin where the cloth of my shift had torn away.

I was frozen. Somewhere in the back of my mind, the detached observer wondered aloud whether this was in fact the single most disgusting thing I had ever encountered. Well, no, it wasn't. Some of the things I had seen at L'Hôpital des Anges, to say nothing of Father Alexandre's death, or the Beardsleys' attic . . . the field hospital at Amiens . . . heavens, no, this wasn't even close.

I lay rigid, eyes shut, recalling various nasty experiences of my past and wishing I were in fact in attendance at one of those events, instead of here.

He leaned over, seized my hair, and banged my head several times against the tree, wheezing as he did so.

"Show you . . ." he muttered, then dropped his hand and I heard shuffling noises as he staggered away.

When I finally opened my eyes again, I was alone.

I REMAINED ALONE, a small mercy. Boble's violent attack seemed to have frightened away the boys.

I rolled onto my side and lay still, breathing. I felt very tired, and utterly forlorn.

Jamie, I thought, *where are you?*

I wasn't afraid of what might happen next; I couldn't see any further than the moment I was in, a single breath, a single heartbeat. I didn't think, and wouldn't feel. Not yet. I just lay still, and breathed.

Very slowly I began to notice small things. A fragment of bark caught in my hair, scratchy on my cheek. The give of the thick dead leaves beneath me, cradling my body. The sense of effort as my chest lifted. Increasing effort.

A tiny nerve began to twitch near one eye.

I realized quite suddenly that with the gag in my mouth and my nasal tissues being rapidly congested by blood and swelling, I was in some actual danger of suffocation. I twisted as far onto my side as I could get without strangling, and rubbed my face first against the ground, then—with increasing desperation—dug my heels into the ground and wriggled upward, scraping my face hard against the bark of the tree, trying without success to loosen or dislodge the gag.

The bark rasped lip and cheek, but the kerchief tied round my head was so tight that it cut hard into the corners of my mouth, forcing it open so that saliva leaked constantly into the wad of fabric in my mouth. I gagged at the tickle of sodden cloth in my throat, and felt vomit burn the back of my nose.

You aren't, you aren't, you aren'tyouaren'tyou aren't *going to vomit!* I dragged air bubbling through my bloody nose, tasted thick copper as it slimed down my throat, gagged harder, doubled up—and saw white light at the edge of vision, as the noose went tight around my throat.

I fell back, my head hitting hard against the tree. I hardly noticed; the noose loosened again, thank God, and I managed one, two, three precious breaths of blood-clogged air.

My nose was puffed from cheekbone to cheekbone, and swelling fast. I clenched my teeth on the gag and blew outward through my nose, trying to clear it, if only for a moment. Blood tinged with bile sprayed warm across my chin and splattered on my chest—and I sucked air fast, getting a bit.

Blow, inhale. Blow, inhale. Blow . . . but my nasal passages were almost swollen shut by now, and I nearly sobbed in panic and frustration, as no air came.

Christ, don't cry! You're dead if you cry, for God's sake *don't cry!*

Blow . . . blow . . . I snorted with the last reserve of stale air in my lungs, and got a hair of clearance, enough to fill them once more.

I held my breath, trying to stay conscious long enough to discover a way to breathe—there *had* to be a way to breathe.

I would *not* let a wretch like Harley Boble kill me by simple inadvertence. That wasn't right; it couldn't be.

I pressed myself, half-sitting, up against the tree to ease the strain on the noose around my neck as much as possible, and let my head fall forward, so that the blood from my nose ran down, dripping. That helped, a little. Not for long, though.

My eyelids began to feel tight; my nose was definitely broken, and the flesh all round the upper part of my face was puffing now, swelling with the blood and lymph of capillary trauma, squeezing my eyes shut, further constricting my thread of air.

I bit the gag in an agony of frustration, then, seized by desperation, began to chew at it, grinding the fabric between my teeth, trying to smash it down, compress it, shift it somehow inside my mouth. . . . I bit the inside of my cheek and felt the pain but didn't mind, it wasn't important, nothing mattered but breath, oh, God, I couldn't *breathe,* please help me breathe, please. . . .

I bit my tongue, gasped in pain—and realized that I had succeeded in thrusting my tongue past the gag, reaching the tip of it to the corner of my mouth. By poking as hard as I could with my tongue tip, I had made a tiny channel of air. No more than a wisp of oxygen could ooze through it—but it was air, and that was all that mattered.

I had my head canted painfully to one side, forehead pressed against the tree, but was afraid to move at all, for fear of losing my slender lifeline of air, if the gag should shift when I moved my head. I sat still, hands clenched, drawing long, gurgling, horribly shallow breaths, and wondering how long I could stay this way; the muscles of my neck were already quivering from strain.

My hands were throbbing again—they hadn't ever stopped, I supposed, but I hadn't had attention to spare for them. Now I did, and momentarily welcomed the shooting pains that outlined each nail with liquid fire, for distraction from the deadly stiffness spreading down my neck and through my shoulder.

The muscles of my neck jumped and spasmed; I gasped, lost my air, and arched my body bowlike, fingers dug into the binding ropes as I fought to get it back.

A hand came down on my arm. I hadn't heard him approach. I turned blindly, butting at him with my head. I didn't care who he was or what he wanted, provided he would remove the gag. Rape seemed a perfectly reasonable exchange for survival, at least at the moment.

I made desperate noises, whimpering, snorting, and spewing gouts of blood and snot as I shook my head violently, trying to indicate that I was choking—given the level of sexual incompetence so far demonstrated, he might not even realize that I couldn't breathe, and simply proceed about his business, unaware that simple rape was becoming necrophilia.

He was fumbling round my head. Thank God, thank God! I held myself still with superhuman effort, head swimming as little bursts of fire went off inside my eyeballs. Then the strip of fabric came away and I thrust the wad of cloth out of my mouth by reflex, instantly gagged, and threw up, whooping air and retching simultaneously.

I hadn't eaten; no more than a thread of bile seared my throat and ran down my chin. I choked and swallowed and *breathed,* sucking air in huge, greedy, lung-bursting gulps.

He was saying something, whispering urgently. I didn't care, couldn't listen. All I heard was the grateful wheeze of my own breathing, and the thump of my heart. Finally slowing from its frantic race to keep oxygen moving round my starved tissues, it pounded hard enough to shake my body.

Then a word or two got through to me, and I lifted my head, staring at him.

"Whad?" I said thickly. I coughed, shaking my head to try to clear it. It hurt very much. "*What* did you say?"

He was visible only as a ragged, lion-haired silhouette, bony-shouldered in the faint glow from the fire.

"I said," he whispered, leaning close, "does the name 'Ringo Starr' mean anything to you?"

I WAS BY this time well beyond shock. I merely wiped my split lip gingerly on my shoulder, and said, very calmly, "Yes."

He had been holding his breath; I realized it only when I heard the sigh as he released it, and saw his shoulders slump.

"Oh, God," he said, half under his breath. "Oh, God."

He lunged forward suddenly and caught me against him in a hard embrace. I recoiled, choking as the noose round my neck tightened once again, but he didn't notice, absorbed in his own emotion.

"Oh, God," he said, and buried his face in my shoulder, nearly sobbing. "Oh, God. I knew, I knew you hadda be, I knew it, but I couldn't believe it, oh, God, oh, God, oh, God! I didn't think I'd ever find another one, not ever—"

"Kk," I said. I arched my back, urgently.

"Wha—oh, shit!" He let go and grabbed for the rope around my neck. He scrabbled hold of it and yanked the noose over my head, nearly tearing my ear off in the process, but I didn't mind. "Shit, you okay?"

"Yes," I croaked. "Un . . . tie me."

He sniffed, wiping his nose on his sleeve, and glanced back over his shoulder.

"I can't," he whispered. "The next guy who comes along'll see."

"The *next* guy?" I screamed, as well as I could scream in a strangled whisper. "What do you mean, the next—"

"Well, you know. . . ." It seemed suddenly to dawn on him that I might have objections to waiting tamely like a trussed turkey for the next would-be rapist in the lineup. "Er . . . I mean . . . well, never mind. Who are you?"

"You know damn well who I am," I croaked furiously, shoving him with my bound hands. "I'm Claire Fraser. Who in *bloody* hell are you, what are you doing here, and if you want one more word out of me, you'll bloody well untie me this minute!"

He turned again to glance apprehensively over his shoulder, and it occurred to me vaguely that he was afraid of his so-called comrades. So was I. I could see his profile in silhouette; it was indeed the bushy-haired young Indian, the one I had thought might be a Tuscaroran. Indian . . . some connection clicked into place, deep in the tangled synapses.

"Bloody hell," I said, and dabbed at a trickle of blood that ran from the raw corner of my mouth. "Otter-Toof. Tooth. You're one of his."

"What?!" His head swung back to face me, eyes so wide the whites showed briefly. "Who?"

"Oh, what in hell was his real name? Robert . . . Robert th-something . . ." I was trembling with fury, terror, shock, and exhaustion, groping through the muddled remnants of what used to be my mind. Wreck though I might be, I remembered Otter-Tooth, all right. I had a sudden vivid memory of being alone in the dark, on a night like this, wet with rain and all alone, a long-buried skull cupped in my hands.

"Springer," he said, and gripped my arm eagerly. "Springer—was that it? Robert Springer?"

I had just enough presence of mind to clamp my jaw, thrust out my chin, and hold up my bound hands in front of him. Not another word until he cut me loose.

"Shit," he muttered again, and with another hasty glance behind him, fumbled for his knife. He wasn't skillful with it. If I had needed any evidence that he wasn't a real Indian of the time . . . but he got my hands free without cutting me, and I doubled up with a groan, hands tucked under my armpits as the blood surged into them. They felt like balloons filled and stretched to the point of bursting.

"When?" he demanded, paying no attention to my distress. "When did you come? Where did you find Bob? Where is he?"

"1946," I said, squeezing my arms down tight on my throbbing hands. "The first time. 1968, the second. As for Mr. Springer—"

"The second—did you say the *second* time?" His voice rose in astonishment. He choked it off, looking guiltily back, but the sounds of the men dicing and arguing round the fire were more than loud enough to drown out a simple exclamation.

"Second time," he repeated more softly. "So you did it? You went back?"

I nodded, pressing my lips together and rocking back and forth a little. I thought my fingernails would pop off with each heartbeat.

"What about you?" I asked, though I was fairly sure that I already knew.

"1968," he said, confirming it.

"What year did you turn up in?" I asked. "I mean—how long have you been here? Er . . . now, I mean."

"Oh, God." He sat back on his heels, running a hand back through his long, tangled hair. "I been here six years, as near as I can tell. But you said—second time. If you made it home, why in hell'd you come *back*? Oh—wait. You didn't make it home, you went to another time, but not the one you came from? Where'd you start from?"

"Scotland, 1946. And no, I made it home," I said, not wanting to go into details. "My husband was here, though. I came back on purpose, to be with him." A decision whose wisdom seemed presently in severe doubt.

"And speaking of my husband," I added, beginning to feel as though I might possess a few shreds of sanity after all, "I was *not* joking. He's coming. You don't want him to find you keeping me captive, I assure you. But if you—"

He disregarded this, leaning eagerly toward me.

"But that means you know how it works! You can steer!"

"Something like that," I said, impatient. "I take it that you and your companions *didn't* know how to steer, as you put it?" I massaged one hand with the other, gritting my teeth against the throb of blood. I could feel the furrows the rope had left in my flesh.

"We thought we did." Bitterness tinged his voice. "Singing stones. Gemstones. That's what we used. Raymond said . . . It didn't work, though. Or maybe . . . maybe it did." He was making deductions; I could hear the excitement rising again in his tone.

"You met Bob Springer—Otter-Tooth, I mean. So he *did* make it! And if he made it, maybe the others did, too. See, I thought they were all dead. I thought—thought I was alone." There was a catch in his voice, and despite the urgency of the situation and my annoyance at him, I felt a pang of sympathy.

I knew very well what it felt like to be alone in that way, marooned in time.

In a way, I hated to disillusion him, but there was no point in keeping the truth from him.

"Otter-Tooth is dead, I'm afraid."

He suddenly stopped moving and sat very still. The faint glow of firelight through the trees outlined him; I could see his face. A few long hairs lifted in the breeze. They were the only thing that moved.

"How?" he said at last, in a small, choked voice.

"Killed by the Iroquois," I said. "The Mohawk." My mind was beginning, very slowly, to work again. Six years ago, this man—whoever he was—had come. 1767, that would be. And yet Otter-Tooth, the man who had once been Robert Springer, had died more than a generation earlier. They'd started out together, but ended in different times.

"Shit," he said, though the obvious distress in his voice was mingled with something like awe. "That would have been a real bummer, especially for Bob. He, like, idolized those guys."

"Yes, I expect he was most put out about it," I replied, rather dryly. My eyelids felt thick and heavy. It was an effort to force them open, but I could still see. I glanced at the fire glow, but couldn't see anything beyond the faint movement of shadows in the distance. If there actually was a lineup of men waiting for my services, at least they were tactfully keeping out of sight. I doubted it, and gave silent thanks that I wasn't twenty years younger—there might have been.

"I met some Iroquois—Christ, I went *looking* for 'em, if you can believe that! That was the whole point, see, to find the Iroquois tribes and get them to—"

"Yes, I know what you had in mind," I interrupted. "Look, this is not really the time or place for a long discussion. I think that—"

"Those Iroquois are some nasty tumblers, I tell *you,* man," he said, jabbing me in the chest with a finger for emphasis. "You wouldn't *believe* what they do to—"

"I know. So is my husband." I gave him a glare, which—judging from the way he flinched—was probably rendered highly effective by the state of my face. I hoped so; it hurt a lot to do it.

"Now, what *you* want to do," I said, mustering as much authority into my voice as I could, "is to go back to the fire, wait for a bit, then leave casually, sneak round, and get two horses. I hear a stream down there—" I waved briefly to the right. "I'll meet you there. Once we're safely away, I'll tell you everything I know."

In fact, I probably couldn't tell him anything very helpful, but he didn't know that. I heard him swallow.

"I don't know . . ." he said uncertainly, glancing round again. "Hodge, he's kind of gnarly. He shot one guy, a few days ago. Didn't even say anything, just walked up to him, pulled his gun, and *boom!*"

"What for?"

He shrugged, shaking his head.

"I don't even know, man. Just . . . *boom,* you know?"

"I know," I assured him, holding on to temper and sanity by a thread. "Look, let's not trouble with the horses, then. Let's just go." I lurched awkwardly onto one knee, hoping that I would be able to rise in a few moments, let alone walk. The big muscles in my thighs were knotted hard in the spots where Boble had kicked me; trying to stand made the muscles jump and quiver in spasms that effectively hamstrung me.

"Shit, not now!" In his agitation, the young man seized my arm and jerked me down beside him. I hit the ground hard on one hip and let out a cry of pain.

"You all right there, Donner?" The voice came out of the darkness somewhere behind me. It was casual—obviously one of the men had merely stepped out of camp to relieve himself—but the effect on the young Indian was galvanizing. He flung himself full-length upon me, banging my head on the ground and knocking all the breath out of me.

"Fine . . . really . . . great," he called to his companion, gasping in an exaggerated manner, evidently trying to sound like a man in the throes of half-completed lust. He sounded like someone dying of asthma, but I wasn't complaining. I couldn't.

I'd been knocked on the head a few times, and generally saw nothing but blackness as a result. This time I honestly did see colored stars, and lay limp and bemused, feeling as though I sat tranquilly some distance above my battered body. Then Donner laid a hand on my breast and I came instantly back to earth.

"Let go of me this instant!" I hissed. "What do you think you're doing?"

"Hey, hey, nothing, nothing, sorry," he assured me hastily. He removed the hand, but didn't get off me. He squirmed a bit, and I realized that he was aroused by the contact, whether intended or not.

"Get *off*!" I said, in a furious whisper.

"Hey, I don't mean anything, I mean I wouldn't hurt you or nothing. It's just I haven't had a woman in—"

I grabbed a handful of his hair, lifted my head, and bit his ear, hard. He shrieked and rolled off me.

The other man had gone back toward the fire. At this, though, he turned and called back, "Christ, Donner, is she *that* good? I'll have to give her a try!" This got a laugh from the men by the fire, but luckily it died away and they returned to their own concerns. I returned to mine, which was escape.

"You didn't have to do that," Donner whined in an undertone, holding his ear. "I wasn't going to *do* anything! Christ, you got nice tits, but you're like old enough to be my mother!"

"Shut up!" I said, pushing myself to a sitting position. The effort made my head spin; tiny colored lights flickered like Christmas-tree bulbs at the edge of my vision. In spite of this, some part of my mind was actively working again.

He was at least partly right. We couldn't leave immediately. After drawing so much attention to himself, the others would be expecting him to come back within a few minutes; if he didn't, they'd start looking for him—and we needed more than a few minutes' start.

"We can't go now," he whispered, rubbing his ear reproachfully. "They'll notice. Wait 'til they go to sleep. I'll come get you then."

I hesitated. I was in mortal danger every moment that I spent within reach of Hodgepile and his feral gang. If I had needed any convincing, the encounters of the last two hours had demonstrated that. This Donner needed to go back to the fire and show himself—but I could steal away. Was it worth the risk that someone would come and find me gone, before I had got beyond pursuit? It would be more certain to wait until they slept. But did I dare wait that long?

And then there was Donner himself. If he wanted to talk to me, I certainly wanted to talk to him. The chance of stumbling on another time-traveler . . .

Donner read my hesitation, but misunderstood it.

"You're not going without me!" He grabbed my wrist in sudden alarm, and before I could jerk away, had whipped a bit of the cut line around it. I fought and pulled away, hissing to try to make him understand, but he was panicked at the thought that I might slip away without him, and wouldn't listen. Hampered by my injuries, and unwilling to make enough noise to draw attention, I could only delay but not prevent his determined efforts to tie me up again.

"Okay." He was sweating; a drop fell warm on my face as he leaned over me to check the bindings. At least he hadn't put the noose round my neck again, instead tethering me to the tree with a rope around my waist.

"I shoulda known what you are," he murmured, intent on his job. "Even before you said 'Jesus H. Roosevelt Christ.' "

"What the hell do you mean by that?" I snapped, squirming away from his hand. "Don't bloody do that—I'll suffocate!" He was trying to put the cloth strip back in my mouth, but seemed to pick up the note of panic in my voice, because he hesitated.

"Oh," he said uncertainly. "Well. I guess—" Once again, he looked back over his shoulder, but then made up his mind and dropped the gag on the ground. "Okay. But you be quiet, all right? What I meant—you don't act afraid of men. Most of the women from now do. You oughta act more afraid."

And with that parting shot, he rose and brushed dead leaves from his clothes before heading back to the fire.

THERE COMES A POINT when the body has simply had enough. It snatches at sleep, no matter what menace the future may hold. I'd seen that happen: the Jacobite soldiers who slept in the ditches where they fell, the British pilots who slept in their planes while mechanics fueled them, only to leap to full alert again in time to take off. For that matter, women in long labor routinely sleep between contractions.

In the same manner, I slept.

That kind of sleep is neither deep nor peaceful, though. I came out of it with a hand across my mouth.

The fourth man was neither incompetent nor brutal. He was large and soft-bodied, and he had loved his dead wife. I knew that, because he wept into my hair, and called me by her name at the end. It was Martha.

I CAME OUT of sleep again sometime later. Instantly, fully conscious, heart pounding. But it wasn't my heart—it was a drum.

Sounds of startlement came from the direction of the fire, men rousing in alarm from sleep.

"Indians!" someone shouted, and the light broke and flared, as someone kicked at the fire to scatter it.

It wasn't an Indian drum. I sat up, listening hard. It was a drum with a sound like a beating heart, slow and rhythmic, then trip-hammer fast, like the frantic surge of a hunted beast.

I could have told them that Indians never used drums as weapons; Celts did. It was the sound of a bodhran.

What next? I thought, a trifle hysterically, *bagpipes*?

It was Roger, certainly; only he could make a drum talk like that. It was Roger, and Jamie was nearby. I scrambled to my feet, wanting, needing urgently to *move*. I jerked at the rope around my waist in a frenzy of impatience, but I was going nowhere.

Another drum began, slower, less skilled, but equally menacing. The sound seemed to move—it *was* moving. Fading, coming back full force. A third drum began, and now the thumping seemed to come from everywhere, fast, slow, mocking.

Someone fired a gun into the forest, panicked.

"Hold, there!" Hodgepile's voice came, loud and furious, but to no avail; there was a popcorn rattle of gunfire, nearly drowned by the sound of the drums. I heard a *snick* near my head, and a cluster of needles brushed past me as it fell. It dawned on me that standing upright while guns were blindly fired all round me was a dangerous strategy, and I promptly fell flat, burrowing into the dead needles, trying to keep the trunk of the tree betwixt me and the main body of men.

The drums were weaving, now closer, now farther, the sound unnerving even to one who knew what it was. They were circling the camp, or so it seemed. Should I call out, if they came near enough?

I was saved from the agony of decision; the men were making so much noise round the campfire that I couldn't have been heard if I'd screamed myself hoarse. They were calling out in alarm, shouting questions, bellowing orders—which apparently went ignored, judging from the ongoing sounds of confusion.

Someone blundered through the brush nearby, running from the drums. One, two more—the sound of gasping breath and crunching footsteps. *Donner?* The thought came to me suddenly and I sat up, then fell flat again as another shot whistled past overhead.

The drums stopped abruptly. Chaos reigned around the fire, though I could hear Hodgepile trying to get his men in order, yelling and threatening, nasal voice raised above the rest. Then the drums began again—much closer.

They were drawing in, drawing together, somewhere out in the forest on my left, and the mocking *tip-tap-tip-tap* beating had changed. They were thundering now. No skill, just menace. Coming closer.

Guns fired wildly, close enough for me to see the muzzle flash and smell the smoke, thick and hot on the air. The faggots of the fire had been scattered, but still burned, making a muted glow through the trees.

"There they are! I see 'em!" someone yelled from the fire, and there was another burst of musket-fire, toward the drums.

Then the most unearthly howl rose out of the dark to my right. I'd heard Scots scream going into battle before, but that particular Highland shriek made the hairs on my body prickle from tailbone to nape. *Jamie.* Despite my fears, I sat bolt upright and peered round my sheltering tree, in time to see demons boil out of the wood.

I knew them—knew I knew them—but cowered back at sight of them, blackened with soot and shrieking with the madness of hell, firelight red on the blades of knives and axes.

The drums had stopped abruptly, with the first scream, and now another set of howls broke out to the left, the drummers racing in to the kill. I pressed myself flat back against the tree, heart chokingly huge in my throat, petrified for fear the blades would strike at any random movement in the shadows.

Someone crashed toward me, blundering in the dark—Donner? I croaked his name, hoping to attract his attention, and the slight form turned toward me, hesitated, then spotted me and lunged.

It wasn't Donner, but Hodgepile. He seized my arm, dragging me up, even as he slashed at the rope that bound me to the tree. He was panting hard with exertion, or fear.

I realized at once what he was about; he knew his chances of escape were slight—having me to hostage was his only hope. But I was *damned* if I'd be his hostage. No more.

I kicked at him, hard, and caught him on the side of the knee. It didn't knock him over, but distracted him for a second. I charged him, head down, butted him square in the chest, and sent him flying.

The impact hurt badly, and I staggered, eyes watering from the pain. He was up, and at me again. I kicked, missed, fell heavily on my backside.

"Come *on,* damn you!" he hissed, jerking hard at my bound hands. I ducked my head, pulled back, and yanked him down with me. I rolled and scrabbled in the leaf mold, trying as hard as I could to wrap my legs around him, meaning to get a grip on his ribs and crush the life out of the filthy little worm, but he squirmed free and rolled atop me, punching at my head, trying to subdue me.

He struck me in one ear and I flinched, eyes shutting in reflex. Then the weight of him was suddenly gone, and I opened my eyes to see Jamie holding Hodgepile several inches off the ground. Hodgepile's spindly legs churned madly in a futile effort at escape, and I felt an insane desire to laugh.

In fact, I must actually have laughed, for Jamie's head

jerked round to look at me; I caught a glimpse of the whites of his eyes before he turned his attention to Hodgepile again. He was silhouetted against a faint glow from the embers; I saw him in profile for a second, then his body flexed with effort as he bent his head.

He held Hodgepile close against his chest, one arm bent. I blinked; my eyes were swollen half-shut, and I wasn't sure what he was doing. Then I heard a small grunt of effort, and a strangled shriek from Hodgepile, and saw Jamie's bent elbow go sharply down.

The dark curve of Hodgepile's head moved back—and back. I glimpsed the marionette-sharp nose and angled jaw—angled impossibly high, the heel of Jamie's hand wedged hard beneath it. There was a muffled *pop!* that I felt in the pit of my stomach as Hodgepile's neckbones parted, and the marionette went limp.

Jamie flung the puppet body down, reached for me, and pulled me to my feet.

"You are alive, you are whole, *mo nighean donn*?" he said urgently in Gaelic. He was groping, hands flying over me, trying at the same time to hold me upright—my knees seemed suddenly to have turned to water—and to locate the rope that bound my hands.

I was crying and laughing, snuffing tears and blood, bumping at him with my bound hands, trying awkwardly to thrust them at him so that he could cut the rope.

He quit grappling, and clutched me so hard against him that I yelped in pain as my face was pressed against his plaid.

He was saying something else, urgently, but I couldn't manage to translate it. Energy pulsed through him, hot and violent, like the current in a live wire, and I vaguely realized that he was still almost berserk; he had no English.

"I'm all right," I gasped, and he let me go. The light flared up in the clearing beyond the trees; someone had collected the scattered embers, and thrown more kindling on them. His face was black, his eyes picked out blue in a sudden blaze as he turned his head and the light struck his face.

There was still some struggle going on; no screaming now, but I could hear the grunt and thud of bodies locked in combat. Jamie raised my hands, drew his dirk, and sawed through the rope; my hands dropped like lead weights. He stared at me for an instant, as though trying to find words, then shook his head, cupped a hand for an instant to my face, and disappeared, back in the direction of the fight.

I sank down on the ground, dazed. Hodgepile's body lay nearby, limbs askew. I glanced at it, the picture clear in my mind of a necklace Bree had had as a child, made of linked plastic beads that came apart when you pulled them. Pop-It pearls, they were called. I wished vaguely that I didn't remember that.

The face was lantern-jawed and hollow-cheeked; he looked surprised, eyes wide open to the flickering light. Something seemed oddly wrong, though, and I squinted, trying to make it out. Then I realized that his head was on backward.

It may have been seconds or minutes that I sat there staring at him, arms round my knees and my mind a total blank. Then the sound of soft footsteps made me look up.

Arch Bug came out of the dark, tall and thin and black against the flicker of a growing fire. I saw that he had an ax gripped hard in his left hand; it too was black, and the smell of blood came strong and rich as he leaned near.

"There are some left still alive," he said, and I felt something cold and hard touch my hand. "Will ye have your vengeance now upon them, *a bana-mhaighistear*?"

I looked down and found that he was offering me a dirk, hilt-first. I had stood up, but couldn't remember rising.

I couldn't speak, and couldn't move—and yet my fingers curled without my willing them to, my hand rising up to take the knife as I watched it, faintly curious. Then Jamie's hand came down upon the dirk, snatching it away, and I saw as from a great distance that the light fell on his hand, gleaming wet with blood smeared past the wrist. Random drops shone red, dark jewels glowing, caught in the curly hairs of his arm.

"There is an oath upon her," he said to Arch, and I realized dimly that he was still speaking in Gaelic, though I understood him clearly. "She may not kill, save it is for mercy or her life. It is myself who kills for her."

"And I," said a tall figure behind him, softly. Ian.

Arch nodded understanding, though his face was still in

darkness. Someone else was there beside him—Fergus. I knew him at once, but it took a moment's struggle for me to put a name to the streaked pale face and wiry figure.

"Madame," he said, and his voice was thin with shock. "Milady."

Then Jamie looked at me, and his own face changed, awareness coming back into his eyes. I saw his nostrils flare, as he caught the scent of sweat and semen on my clothes.

"Which of them?" he said. "How many?" He spoke in English now, and his voice was remarkably matter-of-fact, as it might be if he were inquiring as to the number of guests expected for dinner, and I found the simple tone of it steadying.

"I don't know," I said. "They—it was dark."

He nodded, squeezed my arm hard, and turned.

"Kill them all," he said to Fergus, his voice still calm. Fergus's eyes were huge and dark, sunk into his head, burning. He merely nodded, and took hold of the hatchet in his belt. The front of his shirt was splashed, and the end of his hook looked dark and sticky.

In a distant sort of way, I thought I should say something. But I didn't. I stood up straight with the tree against my back and said nothing at all.

Jamie glanced at the dirk he held as though to ensure that it was in good order—it was not; he wiped the blade on his thigh, ignoring the drying blood that gummed the wooden hilt—and went back to the clearing.

I stood quite still. There were more sounds, but I paid no more heed to them than to the rush of wind through the needles overhead; it was a balsam tree, and the breath of it was clean and fresh, falling over me in a wash of fragrant resins, powerful enough to taste on my palate, though little penetrated the clotted membranes of my nose. Beneath the gentle veil of the tree's perfume, I tasted blood, and sodden rags, and the stink of my own weary skin.

Dawn had broken. Birds sang in the distant wood, and light lay soft as wood ash on the ground.

I stood quite still, and thought of nothing but how pleasant it would be to stand neck-deep in hot water, to scrub the skin quite away from my flesh, and let the blood run red and clean down my legs, billowing out in soft clouds that would hide me.

29

PERFECTLY FINE

THEY'D RIDDEN AWAY then. Left them, without burial or word of consecration. In a way, that was more shocking than the killing. Roger had gone with the Reverend to more than one deathbed or scene of accident, helped comfort the bereaved, stood by as the spirit fled and the old man said the words of grace. It was what you did when someone died; turned toward God and at least acknowledged the fact.

And yet . . . how could you stand over the body of a man you'd killed, and look God in the face?

He couldn't sit. The tiredness filled him like wet sand, but he couldn't sit.

He stood, picked up the poker, but stood with it in hand, staring at the banked fire on his hearth. It was perfect, satin-black embers crusted with ash, the red heat smothered just beneath. To touch it would break the embers, make the flame leap up—only to die at once, without fuel. A waste of wood, to throw more on, so late at night.

He put the poker down, wandered from one wall to another, an exhausted bee in a bottle, still buzzing, though his wings hung tattered and forlorn.

It hadn't troubled Fraser. But then, Fraser had ceased even to think of the bandits, directly they were dead; all his thoughts had been for Claire, and that was surely understandable.

He'd led her through the morning light in that clearing, a blood-soaked Adam, a battered Eve, looking upon the knowledge of good and evil. And then he had wrapped her in his plaid, picked her up, and walked away to his horse.

The men had followed, silent, leading the bandits' horses behind their own. An hour later, with the sun warm on their backs, Fraser had turned his horse's head downhill, and led them to a stream. He had dismounted, helped Claire down, then vanished with her through the trees.

The men had exchanged puzzled looks, though no one spoke. Then old Arch Bug had swung down from his mule, saying matter-of-factly, "Well, she'll want to wash then, no?"

A sigh of comprehension went over the group, and the tension lessened at once, dissolving into the small homely businesses of dismounting, hobbling, girth-checking, spitting, having a piss. Slowly, they sought each other, looking for something to say, searching for relief in commonplace.

He caught Ian's eye, but they were yet too stiff with each other for this; Ian turned, clapped a hand round Fergus's shoulder, and hugged him, then pushed him away with a small rude joke about his stink. The Frenchman gave him a tiny smile and lifted the darkened hook in salute.

Kenny Lindsay and old Arch Bug were sharing out tobacco, stuffing their pipes in apparent tranquillity. Tom Christie wandered over to them, pale as a ghost, but pipe in hand. Not for the first time, Roger realized the valuable social aspects of smoking.

Arch had seen him, though, standing aimless near his horse, and come to talk to him, the old man's voice calm and steadying. He had no real idea what Arch said, let alone what he replied; the simple act of conversation seemed to let him breathe again and still the tremors that ran over him like breaking waves.

Suddenly, the old man broke off what he was saying, and nodded over Roger's shoulder.

"Go on, lad. He needs ye."

Roger had turned to see Jamie standing at the far side of the clearing, half-turned away and leaning on a tree, his head bowed in thought. Had he made some sign to Arch? Then Jamie glanced round, and met Roger's eye. Yes, he wanted him, and Roger found himself standing beside Fraser, with no clear memory of having crossed the ground between them.

Jamie reached out and squeezed his hand, hard, and he held on, squeezing back.

"A word, *a cliamhuinn,*" Jamie said, and let go. "I wouldna speak so now, but there may be no good time later, and there's little time to bide." He sounded calm, too, but not like Arch. There were broken things in his voice; Roger felt the hairy bite of the rope, hearing it, and cleared his own throat.

"Say, then."

Jamie took a deep breath, and shrugged a bit, as though his shirt were too tight.

"The bairn. It's no right to ask ye, but I must. Would ye feel the same for him, and ye kent for sure he wasna your own?"

"What?" Roger simply blinked, making no sense whatever of this. "Bai—ye mean Jem?"

Jamie nodded, eyes intent on Roger's.

"Well, I . . . I dinna ken, quite," Roger said, baffled as to what this was about. Why? And why *now,* of all times?

"Think."

He *was* thinking, wondering what the hell? Evidently this thought showed, for Fraser ducked his head in acknowledgment of the need to explain himself further.

"I ken . . . it's no likely, aye? But it's possible. She might be wi' child by the night's work, d'ye see?"

He did see, with a blow like a fist under the breastbone. Before he could get breath to speak, Fraser went on.

"There's a day or two, perhaps, when I might—" He glanced away, and a dull flush showed through the streaks of soot with which he had painted his face. "There could be doubt, aye? As there is for you. But . . ." He swallowed, that "but" hanging eloquent.

Jamie glanced away, involuntarily, and Roger's eyes followed the direction of his gaze. Beyond a screen of bush and red-tinged creeper, there was an eddy pool, and Claire knelt on the far side, naked, studying her reflection. The blood thundered in Roger's ears, and he jerked his eyes away, but the image was seared on his mind.

She did not look human, was the first thing he thought. Her body mottled black with bruises, her face unrecognizable, she looked like something strange and primal, an exotic creature of the forest pool. Beyond appearance, though, it was her attitude that struck him. She was remote, somehow, and still, in the way that a tree is still, even as the air stirs its leaves.

He glanced back, unable not to. She bent over the water, studying her face. Her hair hung wet and tangled down her back, and she skimmed it back with the palm of a hand, holding it out of the way as she surveyed her battered features with dispassionate intentness.

She prodded gently here and there, opening and closing her jaw as her fingertips explored the contours of her face. Testing, he supposed, for loose teeth and broken bones. She closed her eyes and traced the lines of brow and nose, jaw and lip, hand as sure and delicate as a painter's. Then she seized the end of her nose with determination and pulled hard.

Roger cringed in reflex, as blood and tears poured down her face, but she made no sound. His stomach was already knotted into a small, painful ball; it rose up into his throat, pressing against the rope scar.

She sat back on her heels, breathing deeply, eyes closed, hands cupped over the center of her face.

He became suddenly aware that she *was* naked, and he was still staring. He jerked away, blood hot in his face, and glanced surreptitiously toward Jamie in hopes that Fraser had not noticed. He hadn't—he was no longer there.

Roger looked wildly round, but spotted him almost at once. His relief at not being caught staring was superseded at once by a jolt of adrenaline, when he saw what Fraser was doing.

He was standing beside a body on the ground.

Fraser's gaze flicked briefly round, taking note of his men, and Roger could almost feel the effort with which Jamie suppressed his own feelings. Then Fraser's bright blue eyes fastened on the man at his feet, and Roger saw him breathe in, very slowly.

Lionel Brown.

Quite without meaning to, Roger had found himself striding across the clearing. He took up his place at Jamie's right without conscious thought, his attention similarly fixed on the man on the ground.

Brown's eyes were shut, but he wasn't asleep. His face was bruised and swollen, as well as patched with fever, but the expression of barely suppressed panic was plain on his battered features. Fully justified, too, so far as Roger could see.

The sole survivor of the night's work, Brown was still alive only because Arch Bug had stopped young Ian Murray inches away from smashing his skull with a tomahawk. Not from any hesitation about killing an injured man, from cold pragmatism.

"Your uncle will have questions," Arch had said, narrowed eyes on Brown. "Let this one live long enough to answer them."

Ian had said nothing, but pulled his arm from Arch Bug's grasp and turned on his heel, disappearing into the shadows of the forest like smoke.

Jamie's face was much less expressive than his captive's, Roger thought. He himself could tell nothing of Fraser's thoughts from his expression—but scarcely needed to. The man was still as stone, but seemed nonetheless to throb with something slow and inexorable. Merely to stand near him was terrifying.

"How say you, O, friend?" Fraser said at last, turning to Arch, who stood on the far side of the pallet, white-haired and blood-streaked. "Can he be traveling further, or will the journey kill him?"

Bug leaned forward, peering dispassionately at the supine Brown.

"I say he will live. His face is red, not white, and he is awake. You wish to take him with us, or ask your questions now?"

For a brief instant the mask lifted, and Roger, who had been watching Jamie's face, saw in his eyes precisely what he wished to do. Had Lionel Brown seen it, too, he would have leaped off his pallet and run, broken leg or no. But his eyes stayed stubbornly shut, and as Jamie and old Arch were speaking in Gaelic, Brown remained in ignorance.

Without answering Arch's question, Jamie knelt and put his hand on Brown's chest. Roger could see the pulse hammering in Brown's neck and the man's breathing, quick and shallow. Still, he kept his lids squeezed tight shut, though the eyeballs rolled to and fro, frantic beneath them.

Jamie stayed motionless for what seemed a long time—and must have been an eternity to Brown. Then he made a small sound that might have been either a contemptuous laugh or a snort of disgust, and rose.

"We take him. See that he lives, then," he said in English. "For now."

Brown had continued to play possum through the journey to the Ridge, in spite of the bloodthirsty speculations various of the party had made within his hearing on the way. Roger had helped to unstrap him from the travois at journey's end. His garments and wrappings were soaked with sweat, the smell of fear a palpable miasma round him.

Claire had made a movement toward the injured man, frowning, but Jamie had stopped her with a hand on her arm. Roger hadn't heard what he murmured to her, but she nodded and went with him into the Big House. A moment later, Mrs. Bug had appeared, uncharacteristically silent, and taken charge of Lionel Brown.

Murdina Bug was not like Jamie, nor old Arch; her thoughts were plain to see in the bloodless seam of her mouth and the thunderous brow. But Lionel Brown took water from her hand and, open-eyed, watched her as though she were the light of his salvation. She would, Roger thought, have been pleased to kill Brown like one of the cockroaches she ruthlessly exterminated from her kitchen. But Jamie wished him kept alive, so alive he would stay.

For now.

A sound at the door jerked Roger's attention back to the present. Brianna!

It wasn't, though, when he opened the door; only the rattle of wind-tossed twigs and acorn caps. He looked down the dark path, hoping to see her, but there was no sign of her yet. Of course, he told himself, Claire would likely need her.

So do I.

He squashed the thought, but stayed at the door, looking out, wind whining in his ears. She'd gone up to the Big House at once, the moment he came to tell her that her mother was safe. He hadn't said much more, but she had seen something of how matters stood—there was blood on his clothes—and had barely paused to assure herself that none of it was his before rushing out.

He closed the door carefully, looking to see that the draft hadn't wakened Jemmy. He had an immense urge to pick the boy up, and in spite of long-ingrained parental wariness about disturbing a sleeping child, scooped Jem out of his trundle; he had to.

Jem was heavy in his arms, and groggy. He stirred, lifted his head, and blinked, blue eyes glassy with sleep.

"It's okay," Roger whispered, patting his back. "Daddy's here."

Jem sighed like a punctured tire and dropped his head on Roger's shoulder with the force of a spent cannonball. He seemed to inflate again for a moment, but then put his thumb in his mouth and subsided into that peculiarly boneless state common to sleeping children. His flesh seemed to melt comfortably into Roger's own, his trust so complete that it was not necessary even to maintain the boundaries of his body—Daddy would do that.

Roger closed his eyes against starting tears, and pressed his mouth against the soft warmth of Jemmy's hair.

The firelight made black and red shadows on the insides of his lids; by looking at them, he could keep the tears at bay. It didn't matter what he saw there. He had a small collection of grisly moments, vivid from the dawn, but he could look at those unmoved—for now. It was the sleeping trust in his arms that moved him, and the echo of his own whispered words.

Was it even a memory? Perhaps it was no more than a wish—that he had once been roused from sleep, only to sleep again in strong arms, hearing, "Daddy's here."

He took deep breaths, slowing to the rhythm of Jem's breathing, calming himself. It seemed important not to weep, even though there was no one to see or care.

Jamie had looked at him, as they moved from Brown's pallet, the question clear in his eyes.

"Ye dinna think I mind only for myself, I hope?" he had said, low-voiced. His eyes had turned toward the gap in the brush where Claire had gone, half-squinting as though he could not bear to look, but couldn't keep his eyes away.

"For her," he said, so low that Roger scarcely heard. "Would she rather . . . have the doubt, d'ye think? If it came to that."

Roger took a deep breath of his son's hair, and hoped to God he'd said the right thing, there among the trees.

"I don't know," he'd said. "But for you—if there's room for doubt—I say, take it."

If Jamie were disposed to follow that advice, Bree should be home soon.

"I'M FINE," I said firmly. "Perfectly fine."

Bree narrowed her eyes at me.

"Sure you are," she said. "You look like you've been run over by a locomotive. *Two* locomotives."

"Yes," I said, and touched my split lip gingerly. "Well. Yes. Other than that, though . . ."

"Are you hungry? Sit down, Mama, I'll make you some tea, then maybe a little supper."

I wasn't hungry, didn't want tea, and particularly didn't want to sit down—not after a long day on horseback. Brianna was already taking down the teapot from its shelf above the sideboard, though, and I couldn't find the proper words to stop her. All of a sudden, I seemed to have no words at all. I turned toward Jamie, helpless.

He somehow divined my feeling, though he couldn't have read much of anything on my face, given its current state. He stepped forward, though, and took the teapot from her, murmuring something too low for me to catch. She frowned at him, glanced at me, then back, still frowning. Then her face changed a little, and she came toward me, looking searchingly into my face.

"A bath?" she asked quietly. "Shampoo?"

"Oh, yes," I said, and my shoulders sagged in grateful relief. "Please."

I did sit down then, after all, and let her sponge my hands and feet, and wash my hair in a basin of warm water drawn from the cauldron in the hearth. She did it quietly, humming under her breath, and I began to relax under the soothing scrub of her long, strong fingers.

I'd slept—from sheer exhaustion—part of the way, leaning on Jamie's chest. There's no way of achieving real rest on horseback, though, and I found myself now close to nodding off, noticing only in a dreamy, detached sort of way that the water in the basin had turned a grubby, cloudy red, full of grit and leaf fragments.

I'd changed to a clean shift; the feel of the worn linen on my skin was sheer luxury, cool and smooth.

Bree was humming softly, under her breath. What was it . . . "Mr. Tambourine Man," I thought. One of those sweetly silly songs of the sixt—

1968.

I gasped, and Bree's hands gripped my head, steadying me.

"Mama? Are you all right? Did I touch something—"

"No! No, I'm fine," I said, looking down into the swirls of dirt and blood. I took a deep breath, heart pounding. "Perfectly fine. Just—began to doze off, that's all."

She snorted, but took her hands away and went to fetch a pitcher of water for rinsing, leaving me gripping the edge of the table and trying not to shudder.

You don't act afraid of men. You oughta act more afraid. That particularly ironic echo came to me clearly, along with the outline of the young man's head, leonine hair seen silhouetted by the firelight. I couldn't recall his face clearly—but surely I would have noticed that hair?

Jamie had taken my arm, afterward, and led me out from under my sheltering tree, into the clearing. The fire had been scattered during the fight; there were blackened rocks and patches of singed and flattened grass here and there—among the bodies. He had led me slowly from one to another. At the last, he had paused, and said quietly, "Ye see that they are dead?"

I did, and knew why he had shown me—so I need not fear their return, or their vengeance. But I had not thought to count them. Or to look closely at their faces. Even had I been sure how many there were . . . another shiver struck me, and Bree wrapped a warm towel around my shoulders, murmuring words I didn't hear for the questions clamoring in my head.

Was Donner among the dead? Or had he heeded me, when I'd told him that if he were wise, he'd run? He hadn't struck me as a wise young man.

He *had* struck me as a coward, though.

Warm water sluiced around my ears, drowning out the

sound of Jamie's and Brianna's voices overhead; I caught only a word or two, but when I sat back up, with water dripping down my neck, clutching a towel to my hair, Bree was reluctantly moving toward her cloak, hung on the peg by the door.

"Are you *sure* you're all right, Mama?" The worried frown was back between her brows, but this time I could muster a few words of reassurance.

"Thank you, darling; that was wonderful," I said, with complete sincerity. "All I want just now is sleep," I added with somewhat less.

I was still terribly tired, but now completely wakeful. What I did want was . . . well, I didn't know quite what I *did* want, but a general absence of solicitous company was on the list. Besides, I'd caught a glimpse of Roger earlier, bloodstained, white, and swaying with weariness; I wasn't the only victim of the recent unpleasantness.

"Go home, lass," Jamie said softly. He swung the cloak from its peg and over her shoulders, patting her gently. "Feed your man. Take him to bed, and say a prayer for him. I'll mind your mother, aye?"

Bree's gaze swung between us, blue and troubled, but I put on what I hoped was a reassuring expression—it hurt to do it, rather—and after a moment's hesitation, she hugged me tight, kissed my forehead very gently, and left.

Jamie shut the door and stood with his back against it, hands behind him. I was used to the impassive facade he normally used to shield his thoughts when troubled or angry; he wasn't using it, and the expression on his face troubled *me* no end.

"You mustn't worry about me," I said, as reassuringly as I could. "I'm not traumatized, or anything of that sort."

"I mustn't?" he asked guardedly. "Well . . . perhaps I wouldna, if I kent what ye meant by it."

"Oh." I blotted my damp face gingerly, and patted at my neck with the towel. "Well. It means . . . very much injured—or dreadfully shocked. It's Greek, I think—the root word, I mean, 'trauma.'"

"Oh, aye? And you're not . . . shocked. Ye say."

His eyes narrowed, as he examined me with the sort of

critical attention usually employed when contemplating the purchase of expensive bloodstock.

"I'm fine," I said, backing away a little. "Just—I'm all right. Only a bit . . . shaken."

He took a step toward me, and I backed up abruptly, aware belatedly that I was clutching the towel to my bosom as though it were a shield. I forced myself to lower it, and felt blood prickle unpleasantly in patches over face and neck.

He stood very still, regarding me with that same narrow look. Then his gaze dropped to the floor between us. He stood as though deep in thought, and then his big hands flexed. Once, twice. Very slowly. And I heard—heard clearly—the sound of Arvin Hodgepile's vertebrae parting one from another.

Jamie's head jerked up, startled, and I realized that I was standing on the other side of the chair from him, the towel wadded and pressed against my mouth. My elbows moved like rusty hinges, stiff and slow, but I got the towel down. My lips were nearly as stiff, but I spoke, too.

"I am a little shaken, yes," I said very clearly. "I'll be all right. Don't worry. I don't want you to worry."

The troubled scrutiny in his eyes wavered suddenly, like the glass of a window struck by a stone, in the split second before it shatters, and he shut his eyes. He swallowed once, and opened them again.

"Claire," he said very softly, and the smashed and splintered fragments showed clear, sharp and jagged in his eyes. "I have *been* raped. And ye say I must not worry for ye?"

"Oh, God damn it!" I flung the towel on the floor, and immediately wished I had it back again. I felt naked, standing in my shift, and hated the crawling of my skin with a sudden passion that made me slap my thigh to kill it.

"Damn, damn, damn it! I *don't* want you to have to think of that again. I don't!" And yet I had known from the first that this would happen.

I took hold of the chairback with both hands and held tight, and tried to force my own gaze into his, wanting so badly to throw myself upon those glittering shards, to shield him from them.

"Look," I said, steadying my voice. "I don't want—I don't want to make you recall things better left forgotten."

The corner of his mouth actually twitched at that.

"God," he said, in something like wonder. "Ye think I'd forgot any of it?"

"Maybe not," I said, surrendering. I looked at him through swimming eyes. "But—oh, Jamie, I so wanted you to forget!"

He put out a hand, very delicately, and touched the tip of his index finger to the tip of mine, where I clutched the chair.

"Dinna mind it," he said softly, and withdrew the finger. "It's no matter now. Will ye rest a bit, Sassenach? Or eat, maybe?"

"No. I don't want . . . no." In fact, I couldn't decide *what* I wanted to do. I didn't want to do anything at all. Other than unzip my skin, climb out, and run—and that didn't seem feasible. I took a few deep breaths, hoping to settle myself and go back to that nice sense of utter exhaustion.

Should I ask him about Donner? But what was there to ask? *"Did you happen to kill a man with long, tangled hair?"* They'd all looked like that, to some extent. Donner had been—or possibly still was—an Indian, but no one would have noticed that in the dark, in the heat of fighting.

"How—how is Roger?" I asked, for lack of anything better to say. "And Ian? Fergus?"

He looked a little startled, as though he had forgotten their existence.

"Them? The lads are well enough. No one took any hurt in the fight. We had luck."

He hesitated, then took a careful step toward me, watching my face. I didn't scream or bolt, and he took another, coming close enough that I could feel the warmth of his body. Not startled this time, and chilly in my damp shift, I relaxed a little, swaying toward him, and saw the tension in his own shoulders let go slightly, seeing it.

He touched my face, very gently. The blood throbbed just below the surface, tender, and I had to brace myself not to flinch away from his touch. He saw it, and drew back his hand a little, so that it hovered just above my skin—I could feel the heat of his palm.

"Will it heal?" he asked, fingertips moving over the split in my left brow, then down the minefield of my cheek to the scrape on my jaw where Harley Boble's boot had just missed making a solid connection that would have broken my neck.

"Of course it will. You know that; you've seen worse on battlefields." I would have smiled in reassurance, but didn't want to open the deep split in my lip again, and so made a sort of pouting goldfish mouth, which took him by surprise and made *him* smile.

"Aye, I know." He ducked his head a little, shy. "It's only . . ." His hand still hovered near my face, an expression of troubled anxiety on his own. "Oh, God, *mo nighean donn,*" he said softly. "Oh, Christ, your lovely face."

"Can you not bear to look at it?" I asked, turning my own eyes away and feeling a sharp little pang at the thought, but trying to convince myself that it didn't matter. It *would* heal, after all.

His fingers touched my chin, gently but firmly, and drew it up, so that I faced him again. His mouth tightened a little as his gaze moved slowly over my battered face, taking inventory. His eyes were soft and dark in the candlelight, the corners tight with pain.

"No," he said quietly, "I cannot bear it. The sight of ye tears my heart. And it fills me with such rage I think I must kill someone or burst. But by the God who made ye, Sassenach, I'll not lie with ye and be unable to look ye in the face."

"Lie with me?" I said blankly. "What . . . you mean *now*?"

His hand dropped from my chin, but he looked steadily at me, not blinking.

"Well . . . aye. I do."

Had my jaw not been so swollen, my mouth would have dropped open in pure astonishment.

"Ah . . . why?"

"Why?" he repeated. He dropped his gaze then, and made the odd shrugging motion that he made when embarrassed or discomposed. "I—well—it seems . . . necessary."

I had a thoroughly unsuitable urge to laugh.

"Necessary? Do you think it's like being thrown by a horse? I ought to get straight back on?"

His head jerked up and he shot me an angry glance.

"No," he said, between clenched teeth. He swallowed hard and visibly, obviously reining in strong feelings. "Are ye—are ye badly damaged, then?"

I stared at him as best I could, through my swollen lids.

"Is that a joke of some—oh," I said, it finally dawning on me what he meant. I felt heat rise in my face, and my bruises throbbed.

I took a deep breath, to be sure of being able to speak steadily.

"I have been beaten to a bloody pulp, Jamie, and abused in several nasty ways. But only one . . . there was only the one who actually . . . He—he wasn't . . . rough." I swallowed, but the hard knot in my throat didn't budge perceptibly. Tears made the candlelight blur so that I couldn't see his face, and I looked away, blinking.

"No!" I said, my voice sounding rather louder than I intended. "I'm not . . . damaged."

He said something in Gaelic under his breath, short and explosive, and shoved himself away from the table. His stool fell over with a loud crash, and he kicked it. Then he kicked it again, and again, and stamped on it with such violence that bits of wood flew across the kitchen and struck the pie safe with little pinging sounds.

I sat completely still, too shocked and numb to feel distress. Should I not have told him? I wondered vaguely. But he knew, surely. He had asked, when he found me. *"How many?"* he had demanded. And then had said, *"Kill them all."*

But then . . . to know something was one thing, and to be told the details another. I did know that, and watched with a dim sense of guilty sorrow as he kicked away the splinters of the stool and flung himself at the window. It was shuttered, but he stood, hands braced on the sill and his back turned to me, shoulders heaving. I couldn't tell if he was crying.

The wind was rising; there was a squall coming in from the west. The shutters rattled, and the night-smoored fire spouted puffs of soot as the wind came down the chimney. Then the gust passed, and there was no sound but the small sudden *crack!* of an ember in the hearth.

"I'm sorry," I said at last, in a small voice.

Jamie swiveled on his heel at once and glared at me. He wasn't crying, but he had been; his cheeks were wet.

"Don't you dare be sorry!" he roared. "I willna have it, d'ye hear?" He took a giant step toward the table and crashed his fist down on it, hard enough to make the saltcellar jump and fall over. "Don't be sorry!"

I had closed my eyes in reflex, but forced myself to open them again.

"All right," I said. I felt terribly, terribly tired again, and very much like crying myself. "I won't."

There was a charged silence. I could hear chestnuts falling in the grove behind the house, dislodged by the wind. One, and then another, and another, a rain of muffled tiny thumps. Then Jamie drew a deep, shuddering breath, and wiped a sleeve across his face.

I put my elbows on the table and leaned my head on my hands; it seemed much too heavy to hold up anymore.

"Necessary," I said, more or less calmly to the tabletop. "What did you mean, necessary?"

"Does it not occur to you that ye might be with child?" He'd got himself back under control, and said this as calmly as he might have asked whether I planned to serve bacon with the breakfast porridge.

Startled, I looked up at him.

"I'm not." But my hands had gone by reflex to my belly.

"I'm not," I repeated more strongly. "I can't be." I could, though—just possibly. The chance was a remote one, but it existed. I normally used some form of contraception, just to be certain—but obviously . . .

"I am *not,*" I said. "I'd know."

He merely stared at me, eyebrows raised. I wouldn't; not so soon. So soon—soon enough that if it *were* so, and if there were more than one man . . . there would be doubt. The benefit of the doubt; that's what he offered me—and himself.

A deep shudder started in the depths of my womb and spread instantly through my body, making goose bumps break out on my skin, despite the warmth of the room.

"Martha," the man had whispered, the weight of him pressing me into the leaves.

"Bloody, bloody hell," I said very quietly. I spread my hands out flat on the table, trying to think.

"Martha." And the stale smell of him, the meaty press of damp bare thighs, rasping with hair—

"No!" My legs and buttocks pressed together so tightly in revulsion that I rose an inch or two on the bench.

"You might—" Jamie began stubbornly.

"I'm not," I repeated, just as stubbornly. "But even if—you can't, Jamie."

He looked at me, and I caught the flicker of fear in his eyes. That, I realized with a jolt, was exactly what he was afraid of. Or one of the things.

"I mean we can't," I said quickly. "I'm almost sure that I'm not pregnant—but I'm not at all sure that I haven't been exposed to some disgusting disease." That was something else I hadn't thought of until now, and the goose bumps were back in full force. Pregnancy was unlikely; gonorrhea or syphilis weren't. "We—we can't. Not until I've had a course of penicillin."

I was rising from the bench even as I spoke.

"Where are ye going?" he asked, startled.

"The surgery!"

The hallway was dark, and the fire out in my surgery, but that didn't stop me. I flung open the door of the cupboard, and began groping hastily about. A light fell over my shoulder, illuminating the shimmering row of bottles. Jamie had lit a taper and come after me.

"What in the name of God are ye doing, Sassenach?"

"Penicillin," I said, seizing one of the bottles and the leather pouch in which I kept my snake-fang syringes.

"Now?"

"Yes, bloody now! Light the candle, will you?"

He did, and the light wavered and grew into a globe of warm yellow, gleaming off the leather tubes of my homemade syringes. I had a good bit of penicillin mixture to hand, luckily. The liquid in the bottle was pink; many of the *Penicillium* colonies from this batch had been grown in stale wine.

"Are ye sure it will work?" Jamie asked quietly, from the shadows.

"No," I said, tight-lipped. "But it's what I have." The thought of spirochetes, multiplying silently in my bloodstream, second by second, was making my hand shake. I choked down the fear that the penicillin might be defective. It had worked miracles on gross superficial infections. There was no reason why—

"Let me do it, Sassenach." Jamie took the syringe from my hand; my fingers were slippery and fumbling. His were steady, his face calm in candlelight as he filled the syringe.

"Do me first, then," he said, handing it back.

"What—you? But you don't need to—I mean—you hate injections," I ended feebly.

He snorted briefly and lowered his brows at me.

"Listen, Sassenach. If I mean to fight my own fears, and yours—and I do—then I shallna boggle at pinpricks, aye? Do it!" He turned his side to me and bent over, one elbow braced on the counter, and hitched up the side of his kilt, baring one muscular buttock.

I wasn't sure whether to laugh or cry. I might have argued further with him, but a glance at him, standing there bare-arsed and stubborn as Black Mountain, decided me of the futility of that. He'd made up his mind, and we were both going to live with the consequences.

Feeling suddenly and oddly calm, I lifted the syringe, squeezing gently to remove any air bubbles.

"Shift your weight, then," I said, nudging him rudely. "Relax this side; I don't want to break the needle."

He drew in his breath with a hiss; the needle was thick, and there was enough alcohol from the wine to make it sting badly, as I discovered when I took my own injection a minute later.

"Ouch! Ow! Oh, Jesus H. Roosevelt Christ!" I exclaimed, gritting my teeth as I withdrew the needle from my thigh. "Christ, that hurts!"

Jamie gave me a lopsided smile, still rubbing his backside.

"Aye, well. The rest of it won't be worse than this, I expect."

The rest of it. I felt suddenly hollow, and light-headed with it, as though I hadn't eaten for a week.

"You—you're sure?" I asked, putting down the syringe.

"No," he said. "I'm not." He took a deep breath then, and

looked at me, his face uncertain in the wavering candlelight. "But I mean to try. I must."

I smoothed the linen night rail down over my punctured thigh, looking at him as I did it. He'd dropped all his masks long since; the doubt, the anger, and the fear were all there, etched plain in the desperate lines of his face. For once, I thought, my own countenance was less easy to read, masked behind its bruises.

Something soft brushed past my leg with a small *mirp!* and I looked down to see that Adso had brought me a dead vole, no doubt by way of sympathy. I started to smile, felt my lip tingle, and then looked up at Jamie and let it split as I did smile, the taste of blood warm silver on my tongue.

"Well . . . you've come whenever I've needed you; I rather think you'll do it this time, too."

He looked completely blank for an instant, not grasping the feeble joke. Then it struck him, and blood rushed to his face. His lip twitched, and twitched again, unable to decide between shock and laughter.

I thought he turned his back then to hide his face, but in fact, he had only turned to search the cupboard. He found what he was looking for, and turned round again with a bottle of my best muscat wine in his hand, shining dark. He held it to his body with his elbow, and took down another.

"Aye, I will," he said, reaching out his free hand to me. "But if ye think either one of us is going to do this sober, Sassenach, ye're verra much mistaken."

A GUST OF WIND from the open door roused Roger from uneasy sleep. He had fallen asleep on the settle, his legs trailing on the floor, Jemmy snuggled warmly heavy on his chest.

He looked up, blinking and disoriented, as Brianna stooped to take the little boy from his arms.

"Is it raining out?" he said, catching a whiff of damp and ozone from her cloak. He sat up and rubbed a hand over his face to rouse himself, feeling the scruff of a four-day beard.

"No, but it's going to." She laid Jemmy back in his trundle, covered him, and hung up the cloak before coming to Roger. She smelled of the night, and her hand was cold on his flushed cheek. He put his arms round her waist and leaned his head against her, sighing.

He would have been happy to stay that way forever—or at least the next hour or two. She stroked his head gently for a moment, though, then moved away, stooping to light the candle from the hearth.

"You must be starved. Shall I fix you something?"

"No. I mean . . . yes. Please." As the last remnants of grogginess fell away, he realized that he was, in fact, starving. After their stop at the stream in the morning, they hadn't stopped again, Jamie anxious to get home. He couldn't recall when he'd last eaten, but hadn't felt any sense of hunger at all until this minute.

He fell on the bread and butter and jam she brought him, ravenous. He ate single-mindedly, and it was several minutes before he thought to ask, swallowing a final thick, buttery, sweet bite, "How's your mother?"

"Fine," she said, with an excellent imitation of Claire with her stiffest English upper lip. "*Perfectly* fine." She grimaced at him, and he laughed, though quietly, with an automatic glance at the trundle.

"Is she, then?"

Bree raised an eyebrow at him.

"Do *you* think so?"

"No," he admitted, sobering. "But I don't think she's going to tell you if she's not. She'll not want ye worrying."

She made a rather rude glottal noise in response to this notion, and turned her back on him, lifting the long veil of hair off her neck.

"Will you do my laces?"

"You sound just like your father when ye make that noise—only higher-pitched. Have ye been practicing?" He stood up and pulled the laces loose. Undid her stays as well, then on impulse, slid his hands inside the opened gown, resting them on the warm swell of her hips.

"Every day. Have you?" She leaned back against him, and his hands came up, cupping her breasts by reflex.

"No," he admitted. "It hurts." It was Claire's suggestion—

that he try to sing, pitching his voice both higher and lower than normal, in hopes of loosening his vocal cords, perhaps restoring a bit of his original resonance.

"Coward," she said, but her voice was nearly as soft as the hair that brushed his cheek.

"Aye, I am," he said as softly. It did hurt, but it wasn't the physical pain that he minded. It was feeling the echo of his old voice in his bones—the ease and power of it—and then hearing the uncouth noises that emerged with such difficulty now from his throat—croaks and grunts and squeals. Like a pig choking to death on a crow, he thought disparagingly.

"It's them that are cowards," Bree said, still speaking softly, but with steel in her voice. She tensed a little in his arms. "Her face—her poor face! How could they? How could anybody do something like that?"

He had a sudden vision of Claire, naked by the pool, silent as the rocks, her breasts streaked with the blood from her newly set nose. He drew back, nearly jerking his hands away.

"What?" Brianna said, startled. "What's the matter?"

"Nothing." He pulled his hands out of her gown and stepped back. "I—er, is there maybe a bit of milk?"

She looked at him oddly, but went out to the lean-to at the back and brought in a jug of milk. He drank it thirstily, aware of her eyes on him, watchful as a cat's, as she undressed and changed into her night rail.

She sat down on the bed and began to brush out her hair, preparing to plait it for sleep. On impulse, he reached out and took the brush from her. Without speaking, he ran one hand through the thickness of her hair, lifting it, smoothing it back from her face.

"You're beautiful," he whispered, and felt tears come to his eyes again.

"So are you." She lifted her hands to his shoulders and brought him slowly down to his knees before her. She looked searchingly into his eyes—he did his best to look back. She smiled a little, then, and reached to untie the thong that held his own hair back.

It fell around his shoulders in a dusty black tangle, smelling of burned things, stale sweat, and horses. He protested when she took up her hairbrush, but she ignored him, and made him bend his head over her lap, while she picked pine straw and sandburs from his head, slowly working out the snarls. His head bent lower, and lower still, and he found himself at last with his forehead pressed into her lap, breathing in the close scent of her.

He was reminded of medieval paintings, sinners kneeling, heads bowed in confession and remorse. Presbyterians did not confess on their knees—Catholics still did, he thought. In darkness, like this—in anonymity.

"Ye've not asked me what happened," he whispered at last, to the shadows of her thighs. "Did your father tell ye?"

He heard her draw breath, but her voice was calm when she replied.

"No."

She said no more, and the room was quiet, save for the sound of the brush through his hair, and the rising rush of the wind outside.

How would it be for Jamie? Roger wondered suddenly. Would he really do it? Try to . . . He shied away from the thought, unable to contemplate it. Seeing instead a picture of Claire, coming out of the dawn, her face a swollen mask. Still herself, but remote as a distant planet on an orbit departing for the outer reaches of deep space—when might it come in sight again? Stooping to touch the dead, at Jamie's urging, to see for herself the price of her honor.

It wasn't the possibility of a child, he thought suddenly. It was fear—but not of that. It was Jamie's fear that he would lose her—that she would go, swing out into a dark and solitary space without him, unless he could somehow bind her to him, keep her with him. But, Christ, what a risk to take—with a woman so shocked and brutalized, how could he risk it?

How could he not?

Brianna laid down the brush, though she kept a hand gently on his head, stroking it. He knew that fear too well himself—remembered the gulf that once had lain between them, and the courage it had taken to leap over it. For both of them.

He was some kind of a coward, maybe—but not that kind.

"Brianna," he said, and felt the lump in his throat, the scar of the rope. She heard the need in his voice and looked at him as he raised his head, hand lifting toward his face, and he seized it hard, pressing the palm of it against his cheek, rubbing against it.

"Brianna," he said again.

"What? What is it?" Her voice was soft, not to wake the bairn, but full of urgency.

"Brianna, will ye hear me?"

"You know I will. What is it?" Her body was against him, wanting to tend him, and he desired the comfort of her so badly that he would have lain down there on the rug before the fire and buried his head between her breasts—but not yet.

"Only—listen to what I must say. And then—please God—tell me I have done right." *Tell me that you love me, still,* he meant, but could not say it.

"You don't have to tell me anything," she whispered. Her eyes were dark and soft, bottomless with forgiveness not yet earned. And somewhere beyond them, he saw another pair of eyes, staring up at him in drunken bewilderment, changing abruptly into fear as he raised his arm for the killing blow.

"Yes, I do," he said softly. "Put out the candle, aye?"

NOT THE KITCHEN, still strewn with emotional wreckage. Not the surgery, with all its sharp-edged memories. Jamie hesitated, but then nodded toward the stair, raising one eyebrow. I nodded, and followed him up to our bedroom.

It seemed both familiar and strange, as places do when one is away for a time. Perhaps it was only my injured nose that made it smell strange, too; perhaps I only imagined that I could smell it—cold and somehow stale, though everything was swept and dusted. Jamie poked up the fire and light sprang up, wavering in bright swaths over the wooden walls, the scents of smoke and hot resin helping to fill the sense of emptiness in the room.

Neither of us glanced toward the bed. He lit the candlestick on the washstand, then set our two stools near the window, and opened the shutters to the restless night. He'd brought two pewter cups; he filled these and set them on the broad sill, along with the bottles.

I stood just inside the doorway, watching his preparations, feeling thoroughly peculiar.

I was suffering the oddest contradiction of feelings. On the one hand, I felt as though he were a complete stranger. I could not even imagine, let alone recall, a sense of ease in touching him. His body was no longer the comfortable extension of my own, but something foreign, unapproachable.

At the same time, alarming surges of lust ripped through me without warning. It had been happening all day. This was nothing like the slow burn of accustomed desire, nor yet the instant spark of passion. Not even that cyclic and mindless womb-yearning sense of a need to mate that belonged entirely to the body. This was frightening.

He stooped to put another stick on the fire, and I nearly staggered, as all the blood left my head. The light shone on the hair of his arms, the dark hollows of his face—

It was the sheer impersonal sense of a voracious *appetite*—something that possessed me, but was not part of me—that terrified me. It was fear of it that made me avoid his touch, more than the feeling of estrangement.

"Are ye all right, Sassenach?" He had caught sight of my face, and stepped toward me, frowning. I held up a hand to stop him.

"Fine," I said, feeling breathless. I sat down hastily, my knees weak, and picked up one of the cups he had just filled. "Um . . . cheers."

Both his brows went up, but he moved to take his own seat opposite me.

"Cheers," he said quietly, and touched his cup to mine, the wine heavy and sweet-smelling in my hand.

My fingers were cold; so were my toes, and the tip of my nose. That changed, too, without warning. Another minute, and I might be suffused with heat, sweating and flushed. But for the moment, I was cold, and shivered in the rainy breeze from the window.

The wine's aroma was strong enough to make an impact, even on my damaged membranes, and the sweetness was a comfort to nerves and stomach alike. I drank the first cup quickly, and poured another, urgently wanting a small layer of oblivion between reality and myself.

Jamie drank more slowly, but refilled his own cup when I did. The cedar blanket chest, warmed by the fire, was beginning to spread its own familiar fragrance through the room. He glanced at me now and then, but said nothing. The silence between us was not awkward, precisely, but it *was* charged.

I should say something, I thought. But what? I sipped the second cup, racking my brain.

At last, I reached out slowly and touched his nose, where the thin line of the long-healed break pressed white against the skin.

"Do you know," I said, "you've never told me how you came to break your nose. Who set it for you?"

"Och, that? No one." He smiled, touching his nose a little self-consciously. "'Twas only luck that the break was a clean one, for I didna pay it the slightest heed at the time."

"I suppose not. You said—" I broke off, suddenly recalling what he *had* said. When I had found him again, in his printer's shop in Edinburgh, I'd asked him when he'd broken it. He'd answered, *"About three minutes after I last saw ye, Sassenach."* On the eve of Culloden, then—on that rocky Scottish hill, below the ring of standing stones.

"I'm sorry," I said a little weakly. "You probably don't want to think about that, do you?"

He seized my free hand, hard, and looked down at me.

"You may have it," he said. His voice was very low, but he met my eyes straight on. "All of it. Anything that was ever done to me. If ye wish it, if it helps ye, I will live it through again."

"Oh, God, Jamie," I said softly. "No. I don't need to know; all I need is to know that you *did* live through it. That you're all right. But . . ." I hesitated. "Will I tell *you*?" What was done to me, I meant, and he knew it. He did glance away then, though he held my hand in both of his, cradling it and rubbing his palm gently over my bruised knuckles.

"Must you?"

"I think so. Sometime. But not now—not unless you . . . you need to hear." I swallowed. "First."

He shook his head, very slightly, but still didn't look at me. "Not now," he whispered. "Not now."

I took my hand away, and swallowed the rest of the wine in

my cup, rough and warm and musky with the tang of grape skins. I had stopped going hot and cold by turns; now I was only warm throughout, and grateful for it.

"Your nose," I said, and poured another cup. "Tell me, then. Please."

He shrugged slightly.

"Aye, well. There were two English soldiers, come scouting up the hill. I think they didna expect to find anyone—neither had his musket loaded, or I should ha' died there."

He spoke quite casually. A small shiver went over me, but not from cold.

"They saw me, ken, and then one of them saw you, up above. He shouted, and made to go after ye, so I threw myself on him. I didna care at all what happened, so long as ye were safe away, so I went for him bald-heided; plunged my dirk into his side. But his bullet box swung into my way and the knife stuck in it, and—" He smiled, lopsided. "And while I was trying to get it free and keep from bein' killed, his friend came up and swung the stock of his musket into my face."

His free hand had curled up as he spoke, grasping the hilt of a remembered dirk.

I flinched, knowing now exactly what that had felt like. Just hearing about it made my own nose throb. I sniffed, dabbed cautiously at it with the back of my hand, and poured more wine.

"How did you get away?"

"I took the musket from him and clubbed them both to death with it."

He spoke quietly, almost colorlessly, but there was an odd resonance to his voice that made my stomach shift uneasily. It was too fresh, that sight of the blood drops gleaming by dawn light in the hairs of his arm. Too fresh, that undertone of—what was it? satisfaction?—in his voice.

I was suddenly too restless to sit still. A moment before I had been so exhausted that my bones were melting; now I had to move. I stood up, leaning out over the sill. The storm was coming; the wind was freshening, blowing back my newwashed hair, and lightning flickered in the distance.

"I'm sorry, Sassenach," Jamie said, sounding worried. "I shouldna have told ye. Are ye bothered by it?"

"Bothered? No, not by that."

I spoke a little tersely. Why had I asked him about his nose, of all things? Why now, when I had been content to live in ignorance for the last several years?

"What bothers ye, then?" he asked quietly.

What was bothering me was that the wine had been doing its job of anesthetizing me nicely; now I had ruined it. All the images of the night before were back inside my head, thrown into vivid Technicolor by that simple statement, that oh-so-matter-of-fact, *"I took the musket from him and clubbed them both to death with it."* And its unspoken echo, *It is myself who kills for her.*

I wanted to throw up. Instead, I gulped more wine, not even tasting it, swallowing it down as fast as I could. I dimly heard Jamie ask again what bothered me, and swung round to glare at him.

"What bothers me—bothers! What a stupid word! What drives me absolutely *mad* is that I might have been anyone, anything—a convenient warm spot with spongy bits to squeeze—God, I was no more than a *hole* to them!"

I struck the sill with my fist, then, angered by the impotent little thump of it, picked up my cup, turned round, and hurled it against the wall.

"It wasn't that way with Black Jack Randall, was it?" I demanded. "He knew you, didn't he? He saw *you* when he used you; it wouldn't have been the same if you were anyone—he wanted *you.*"

"My God, ye think that was better?" he blurted, and stared at me, eyes wide.

I stopped, panting for breath and feeling dizzy.

"No." I dropped onto the stool and closed my eyes, feeling the room go round and round me, colored lights like a carousel behind my eyes. "No. I don't. I think Jack Randall was a bloody sociopathic, grade-A pervert, and these—these"—I flipped a hand, unable to think of a suitable word—"they were just . . . men."

I spoke the last word with a sense of loathing evident even to me.

"Men," Jamie said, his voice sounding odd.

"Men," I said. I opened my eyes and looked at him. My

eyes felt hot, and I thought they must glow red, like a possum's in torchlight.

"I have lived through a fucking world war," I said, my voice low and venomous. "I have lost a child. I have lost two husbands. I have starved with an army, been beaten and wounded, been patronized, betrayed, imprisoned, and attacked. And I have fucking survived!" My voice was rising, but I was helpless to stop it. "And now should I be shattered because some wretched, pathetic excuses for men stuck their nasty little appendages between my legs and *wiggled* them?!" I stood up, seized the edge of the washstand and heaved it over, sending everything flying with a crash—basin, ewer, and lighted candlestick, which promptly went out.

"Well, I won't," I said quite calmly.

"Nasty little appendages?" he said, looking rather stunned.

"Not yours," I said. "I didn't mean yours. I'm rather fond of yours." Then I sat down and burst into tears.

His arms came round me, slowly and gently. I didn't startle or jerk away, and he pressed my head against him, smoothing my damp, tangled hair, his fingers catching in the mass of it.

"Christ, ye are a brave wee thing," he murmured.

"Not," I said, eyes closed. "I'm not." I grabbed his hand and brought it to my lips, closing my eyes as I did so.

I brushed my battered mouth across his knuckles, blind. They were swollen, as bruised as mine; I touched my tongue to his flesh, tasted soap and dust and the silver taste of scrapes and gashes—marks left by bones and broken teeth. Pressed my fingers to the veins beneath the skin of wrist and arm, softly resilient, and the solid lines of the bones beneath. I felt the tributaries of his veins, wished to enter into his bloodstream, travel there, dissolved and bodiless, to take refuge in the thick-walled chambers of his heart. But I couldn't.

I ran my hand up his sleeve, exploring, clinging, relearning his body. I touched the hair in his oxter and stroked it, surprised at the soft, silky feel of it.

"Do you know," I said, "I don't believe I've ever touched you there before?"

"I dinna believe ye have," he said, with a hint of nervous laughter in his voice. "I would ha' remembered. Oh!" A stipple of gooseflesh burst out over the soft skin there, and I pressed my forehead to his chest.

"The worst of it is," I said, into his shirt, "that I knew *them.* Each one of them. And I'll remember them. And feel guilty that they're dead, because of me."

"No," he said softly, but very firmly. "They are dead because of *me,* Sassenach. And because of their own wickedness. If there is guilt, let it rest upon them. Or on me."

"Not on you alone," I said, my eyes still closed. It was dark in there, and soothing. I could hear my voice, distant but clear, and wondered dimly where the words were coming from. "You're blood of my blood, bone of my bone. You said so. What you do rests on me, as well."

"Then may your vow redeem me," he whispered.

He lifted me to my feet and gathered me to him, like a tailor gathering up a length of fragile, heavy silk—slowly, long-fingered, fold upon fold. He carried me then across the room, and laid me gently on the bed, in the light from the flickering fire.

HE'D MEANT TO be gentle. Very gentle. Had planned it with care, worrying each step of the long way home. She was broken; he must go canny, take his time. Be careful in gluing back her shattered bits.

And then he came to her and discovered that she wished no part of gentleness, of courting. She wished directness. Brevity and violence. If she was broken, she would slash him with her jagged edges, reckless as a drunkard with a shattered bottle.

For a moment, two moments, he struggled, trying to hold her close and kiss her tenderly. She squirmed like an eel in his arms, then rolled over him, wriggling and biting.

He'd thought to ease her—both of them—with the wine. He'd known she lost all sense of restraint when in drink; he simply hadn't realized what she was restraining, he thought grimly, trying to seize her without hurting.

He, of all people, should have known. Not fear or grief or pain—but rage.

She raked his back; he felt the scrape of broken nails, and thought dimly that was good—she'd fought. That was the last of his thought; his own fury took him then, rage and a lust that came on him like black thunder on a mountain, a cloud that hid all from him and him from all, so that kind familiarity was lost and he was alone, strange in darkness.

It might be her neck he grasped, or anyone's. The feel of small bones came to him, knobbled in the dark, and the screams of rabbits, killed in his hand. He rose up in a whirlwind, choked with dirt and the scourings of blood.

Wrath boiled and curdled in his balls, and he rode to her spurs. Let his lightning blaze and sear all trace of the intruder from her womb, and if it burnt them both to bone and ash—then let it be.

WHEN SENSE CAME back to him, he lay with his weight full on her, crushing her into the bed. Breath sobbed in his lungs; his hands clenched her arms so hard he felt the bones like sticks about to snap within his grasp.

He had lost himself. Was not sure where his body ended. His mind flailed for a moment, panicked lest it have been unseated altogether—no. He felt a drop of cold, sudden on his shoulder, and the scattered parts of him drew at once together like shattered bits of quicksilver, to leave him quaking and appalled.

He was still joined to her. He wanted to bolt like a startled quail, but managed to move slowly, loosening his fingers one by one from their death grip on her arms, lifting his body gently away, though the effort of it seemed immense, as though his weight were that of moons and planets. He half-expected to see her crushed and flattened, lifeless on the sheet. But the springy arch of her ribs rose and fell and rose again, roundly reassuring.

Another drop struck him in the back of his neck, and he hunched his shoulders in surprise. Caught by his movement, she looked up, and he met her eyes with shock. She shared it; the shock of strangers meeting one another naked. Her eyes flicked away from his, up toward the ceiling.

"The roof's leaking," she whispered. "There's a wet patch."

"Oh." He had not even realized that it was raining. The room was dark with rainlight, though, and the roof thrummed overhead. The sound of it seemed inside his blood, like the beat of the bodhrana inside the night, like the beat of his heart in the forest.

He shuddered, and for lack of any other notion, kissed her forehead. Her arms came up sudden as a snare and held him fiercely, pulling him down onto her again and he seized her, too, crushing her to him hard enough to feel the breath go out of her, unable to let go. He thought vaguely of Brianna's talk of giant orbs that whirled through space, the thing called gravity—and what was grave about it? He saw that well enough just now: a force so great as to balance some body unthinkably immense in thin air, unsupported—or send two such bodies crashing into each other, in an explosion of destruction and the smoke of stars.

He'd bruised her; there were dark red marks on her arms where his fingers had been. They would be black within the day. The marks of other men bloomed black and purple, blue and yellow, clouded petals trapped beneath the whiteness of her skin.

His thighs and buttocks were strained with effort, and a cramp took him hard, making him groan and twist to ease it. His skin was wet; so was hers, and they slid apart with slow reluctance.

Eyes puffed and bruised, clouded like wild honey, inches from his own.

"How do you feel?" she asked softly.

"Terrible," he replied with complete honesty. He was hoarse, as though he had been screaming—God, perhaps he had been. Her mouth had bled again; there was a red smear on her chin, and the taste of metal from it in his own mouth.

He cleared his throat, wanting to look away from her eyes, but unable to do it. He rubbed a thumb over the smear of blood, clumsily erasing it.

"You?" he asked, and the words were like a rasp in his throat. "How do ye feel?"

She had drawn back a little at his touch, but her eyes were still fixed on his. He had the feeling that she was looking far beyond him, through him—but then the focus of her gaze came back, and she looked directly at him, for the first time since he had brought her home.

"Safe," she whispered, and closed her eyes. She took one huge breath and her body relaxed all at once, going limp and heavy like a dying hare.

He held her, both arms wrapped around her as though to save her from drowning, but felt her sink away all the same. He wished to call out to her not to go, not to leave him alone. She vanished into the depths of sleep, and he yearned after her, wishing her healed, fearing her flight, and bent his head, burying his face in her hair and her scent.

The wind banged the open shutters as it passed, and in the dark outside, one owl hooted and another answered, hiding from the rain.

Then he cried, soundless, muscles strained to aching that he might not shake with it, that she might not wake to know it. He wept to emptiness and ragged breath, the pillow wet beneath his face. Then lay exhausted beyond the thought of tiredness, too far from sleep even to recall what it was like. His only comfort was the small, so fragile weight that lay warm upon his heart, breathing.

Then her hands rose and rested on him, the tears cool on his face, congealing, the white of her clean as the silent snow that covers char and blood and breathes peace upon the world.

30

THE CAPTIVE

IT WAS A STILL, WARM morning; the last of the Indian summer. A woodpecker hammered in the wood nearby, and some insect was making a noise like rasping metal in the tall grass beyond the house. I came downstairs slowly, feeling mildly disembodied—and wishing I were, since the body I had hurt almost everywhere.

Mrs. Bug hadn't come this morning; perhaps she wasn't feeling well. Or perhaps she wasn't sure yet how to deal with seeing me, or what to say to me when she did. My mouth tightened a little, something I realized only because the partially healed split in my lip stung when I did it.

I very consciously relaxed my face and went about getting down the coffee things from the kitchen shelf. There was a trail of tiny black ants running along the edge of the shelf, and a swarm of them over the small tin box in which I kept lump sugar. I flicked them off with a few stern swipes of my apron, and made a mental note to see about finding some avens root for repellant.

That resolve, small as it was, made me feel better and steadier at once. Ever since Hodgepile and his men had turned up at the malting shed, I had been completely at the mercy of someone else, prevented from any sort of independent action. For the first time in days—it seemed much longer—I was able to decide what I was going to do. It seemed a precious liberty.

Very well, I thought. What would I do, then? I would . . . drink some coffee. Eat a bit of toast? No. I felt gingerly with my tongue; several teeth on one side were loose, and my jaw muscles so sore that serious chewing was out of the question. Just coffee, then, and while I drank it, I would decide upon the shape of my day.

Feeling pleased with this plan, I put back the plain wooden cup, and instead ceremoniously set out my sole china cup and saucer, a delicate bit of porcelain Jocasta had given me, hand-painted with violets.

Jamie had poked up the fire earlier and the kettle was boiling; I dipped out enough water to warm the pot, swished it round, and opened the back door in order to toss it out. Fortunately, I looked first.

Ian was sitting cross-legged on the back porch, a small whetstone in one hand, knife in the other.

"Good morn to ye, Auntie," he said cheerfully, and drew the knife across the stone, making the thin, monotonous rasping noise I had heard earlier. "Feeling better, then?"

"Yes, fine," I assured him. He raised one eyebrow dubiously, looking me over.

"Well, better than ye look, I hope."

"Not *that* good," I said tartly, and he laughed. He put down the knife and stone and got to his feet. He was much taller than I; nearly Jamie's height, though thinner. He'd inherited his father's whipcord leanness, as well as the elder Ian's sense of humor—and his toughness.

He took me by the shoulders and turned me into the sunlight, pursing his lips a little as he inspected me at close range. I blinked up at him, imagining what I must look like. I hadn't had the nerve to look into a mirror yet, but I knew the bruising must be going from blacks and reds to a colorful assortment of blues, greens, and yellows. Add in assorted knobbly swellings, flecks of crusty black for the split lip and the scabby bits, and I was undoubtedly quite the picture of health.

Ian's soft hazel eyes peered intently into my face with no apparent surprise or distress, though. At last he let go, and patted my shoulder gently.

"Ye'll do, Auntie," he said. "It's still you, isn't it?"

"Yes," I said. And with no warning at all, tears welled up and overflowed. I knew exactly what he'd meant, and why he'd said it—and it was true.

I felt as though my center had turned unexpectedly to liquid and was gushing out, not from grief, but from relief. I *was* still me. Fragile, battered, sore, and wary—but myself. Only when I recognized that, did I realize how much I had feared that I might not be—that I might emerge from shock and find myself irrevocably altered, some vital part forever missing.

"I'm all right," I assured Ian, hastily wiping my eyes with the edge of my apron. "Just a bit—"

"Aye, I know," he said, and took the pot from me, tossing the water into the grass by the path. "It's a bit strange, aye? Coming back."

I took the coffeepot from him, squeezing his hand hard as I did so. He had come back twice from captivity: rescued from Geillis Duncan's strange compound on Jamaica, only to choose later exile with the Mohawk. He had come to manhood on that journey, and I did wonder what parts of himself might have been left behind on the way.

"Do you want breakfast, Ian?" I asked, sniffing and dabbing gingerly at my swollen nose.

"Of course I do," he said, grinning. "Come and sit yourself down, Auntie—I'll fetch it."

I followed him inside, filled the coffeepot and set it to brew, then sat at the table, the sun on my back through the open door, and watched as Ian rummaged the pantry. My mind felt soggy and incapable of thought, but a sense of peace crept over me, gentle as the wavering light through the chestnut trees. Even the small throbbings here and there seemed pleasant, a sense of healing being quietly accomplished.

Ian spread an armload of random foodstuffs on the table and sat down across from me.

"All right, Auntie?" he asked again, raising one of his father's feathery eyebrows.

"Yes. It's rather like sitting on a soap bubble, though. Isn't it?" I glanced at him as I poured the coffee, but he looked down at the chunk of bread he was buttering. I thought a slight smile touched his lips, but couldn't tell for sure.

"Something like," he said quietly.

The heat of the coffee warmed my hands through the china, and soothed the raw membranes of my nose and palate. I felt as though I had been screaming for hours, but didn't recall actually doing any such thing. Had I, with Jamie the night before?

I didn't quite want to think about the night before; it was part of the soap-bubble feeling. Jamie had been gone when I woke, and I wasn't sure whether I was glad or sorry about that.

Ian didn't talk, but ate his way in a businesslike manner through half a loaf with butter and honey, three raisin muffins, two thick slices of ham, and a jug of milk. Jamie had done the milking, I saw; he always used the blue jug, while Mr. Wemyss used the white one. I wondered vaguely where Mr. Wemyss was—I hadn't seen him, and the house felt empty—but didn't really care. It occurred to me that perhaps Jamie had told both Mr. Wemyss and Mrs. Bug to stay away for a bit, feeling that I might need a little time alone.

"More coffee, Auntie?"

At my nod, Ian rose from the table, reached down the decanter from the shelf, and poured a large slug of whisky into my cup before refilling it.

"Mam always said it's good for what ails ye," he said.

"Your mother is right. Do you want some?"

He sniffed at the aromatic fumes, but shook his head.

"No, I think not, Auntie. I must have a clear head this morning."

"Really? Why?" The porridge in the pot wasn't nine days old—quite—but it had been there for three or four. Of course; no one had been here to eat it. I eyed the cementlike glob adhering to my spoon critically, then decided that it was still soft enough to eat, and doused it with honey.

Ian was dealing with a mouthful of the same substance, and took a moment to clear it from his palate before replying.

"Uncle Jamie means to ask his questions," he answered, giving me a cautious glance as he reached for the bread.

"Does he?" I said, rather blankly, but before I could inquire what he meant by that, the sound of footsteps on the path announced the arrival of Fergus.

He looked as though he had been sleeping in the woods—well, of course, I thought, he had been. Or rather, not sleeping; the men had barely stopped to rest in their pursuit of Hodgepile's gang. Fergus had shaved, but his normally fastidious grooming was sadly lacking, and his handsome face was gaunt, the deep eyes shadowed.

"Milady," he murmured, and unexpectedly bent to kiss my cheek, hand on my shoulder. *"Comment ça va?"*

"Très bien, merci," I replied, smiling gingerly. "How are Marsali and the children? And our hero, Germain?" I had asked Jamie about Marsali on the way back, and had been assured that she was all right. Germain, monkey that he was, had gone straight up a tree when he heard Hodgepile's men approaching. He had seen everything from his perch, and as soon as the men departed, had scrambled down, dragged his semiconscious mother away from the fire, and run for help.

"Ah, Germain," Fergus said, a faint smile momentarily lifting the shadows of fatigue. "*Nous p'tit guerrier.* He says *Grandpère* has promised him a pistol of his own, to shoot bad people with."

Grandpère undoubtedly meant it, I reflected. Germain couldn't manage a musket, being somewhat shorter than the gun itself—but a pistol would do. In my present state of mind, the fact that Germain was only six didn't seem particularly important.

"Have you had breakfast, Fergus?" I pushed the pot toward him.

"Non. Merci." He helped himself to cold biscuit, ham, and coffee, though I noticed that he ate without much appetite.

We all sat quietly, sipping coffee and listening to the birds. Carolina wrens had built a late nest under the eaves of the house and the parent birds swooped in and out, just above our heads. I could hear the high-pitched cheeping of the nestlings begging, and saw a scatter of twigs and a bit of empty eggshell on the floorboards of the porch. They were nearly ready to fledge; just in time, before the real cold weather came.

The sight of the brown-speckled eggshell reminded me of *Monsieur L'Oeuf.* Yes, that's what I would do, I decided, with a small sense of relief at having something firm in mind. I would go and see Marsali later. And perhaps Mrs. Bug, as well.

"Did you see Mrs. Bug this morning?" I asked, turning to Ian. His cabin—little more than a brush-roofed lean-to—lay just beyond the Bugs'; he would have passed them on his way to the house.

"Oh, aye," he said, looking a little surprised. "She was sweeping out as I went by. Offered me breakfast, but I said I'd eat here. I kent Uncle Jamie had a ham, aye?" He grinned, lifting his fourth ham biscuit in illustration.

"So she's all right? I thought she might be ill; she usually comes quite early."

Ian nodded, and took an enormous bite of the biscuit.

"Aye, I expect she's busy, minding the *ciomach.*"

My fragile sense of well-being cracked like the wrens' eggs. A *ciomach* was a captive. In my soggy-minded euphoria, I had somehow managed to forget Lionel Brown's existence.

Ian's remark that Jamie meant to ask questions this morning dropped suddenly into context—as did Fergus's presence. And the knife Ian had been sharpening.

"Where is Jamie?" I asked, rather faintly. "Have you seen him?"

"Oh, aye," Ian said, looking surprised. He swallowed, and gestured toward the door with his chin. "He's just out in the woodshed, makin' new shingles. He says the roof's sprung a leak."

No sooner had he said this than the sound of hammering came from the roof, far above. Of course, I thought. First things first. But then, I supposed Lionel Brown wasn't going anywhere, after all.

"Perhaps . . . I should go and see Mr. Brown," I said, swallowing.

Ian and Fergus exchanged glances.

"No, Auntie, ye shouldn't," Ian said quite calmly, but with an air of authority I wasn't accustomed to seeing in him.

"Whatever do you mean?" I stared at him, but he merely went on eating, though a trifle more slowly.

"Milord says you should not," Fergus amplified, drizzling a spoonful of honey into his coffee.

"He says what?" I asked incredulously.

Neither of them would look at me, but they seemed to draw together, emanating a reluctant sort of stubborn resistance. Either one would do anything I asked, I knew—except defy Jamie. If Jamie thought I ought not to see Mr. Brown, I wasn't going to do it with the assistance of either Ian or Fergus.

I dropped the spoon back into my bowl of porridge, uneaten lumps still adhering to it.

"Did he happen to mention *why* he thinks I ought not to visit Mr. Brown?" I asked calmly, under the circumstances.

Both men looked surprised, then exchanged another look, this one longer.

"No, milady," Fergus said, his voice carefully neutral.

There was a brief silence, during which both of them seemed to be considering. Then Fergus glanced at Ian, deferring to him with a shrug.

"Well, d'ye see, Auntie," Ian said carefully, "we do mean to question the fellow."

"And we will have answers," Fergus said, eyes on the spoon with which he was stirring his coffee.

"And when Uncle Jamie is satisfied that he has told us what he can . . ."

Ian had laid his newly sharpened knife on the table beside his plate. He picked it up, and thoughtfully drew it down the length of a cold sausage, which promptly split open, with an aromatic burst of sage and garlic. He looked up then, and met my eyes directly. And I realized that while I might still be me—Ian was no longer the boy he used to be. Not at all.

"You'll kill him, then?" I said, my lips feeling numb in spite of the hot coffee.

"Oh, yes," Fergus said very softly. "I expect that we shall." He met my eyes now, too. There was a bleak, grim look about him, and his deep-set eyes were hard as stone.

"He—it—I mean . . . it wasn't him," I said. "It couldn't have been. He'd already broken his leg when—" I didn't seem to have enough air to finish my sentences. "And Marsali. It wasn't—I don't think he . . ."

Something behind Ian's eyes changed, as he grasped my meaning. His lips pressed tight for a moment, and he nodded.

"As well for him, then," he said shortly.

"As well," Fergus echoed, "but I think it will not matter in the end. We killed the others—why should he live?" He pushed back from the table, leaving his coffee undrunk. "I think I will go, cousin."

"Aye? I'll come too, then." Ian shoved his plate away, nodding to me. "Will ye tell Uncle Jamie we've gone ahead, Auntie?"

I nodded numbly, and watched them go, vanishing one after the other under the big chestnut tree that overhung the trail leading to the Bugs' cabin. Mechanically, I got up and began slowly to clear away the remains of the makeshift breakfast.

I really wasn't sure whether I minded a lot about Mr. Brown or not. On the one hand, I did disapprove on principle of torture and cold-blooded murder. On the other . . . while it was true enough that Brown had not personally violated or injured me, and he *had* tried to make Hodgepile release me—he'd been all in favor of killing me, later. And I hadn't the slightest doubt that he would have drowned me in the gorge, had Tebbe not intervened.

No, I thought, carefully rinsing my cup and drying it on my apron, perhaps I didn't really mind terribly about Mr. Brown.

Still, I felt uneasy and upset. What I *did* mind about, I realized, were Ian and Fergus. And Jamie. The fact was, killing someone in the heat of battle is a quite different thing from executing a man, and I knew that. Did they?

Well, Jamie did.

"And may your vow redeem me." He had whispered that to me, the night before. It was just about the last thing I recalled him saying, in fact. Well, all right; but I would greatly prefer that he didn't feel in need of redemption to start with. And as for Ian and Fergus . . .

Fergus had fought in the Battle of Prestonpans, at the age of ten. I still remembered the face of the small French orphan, soot-smeared and dazed with shock and exhaustion, looking down at me from his perch atop a captured cannon. *"I killed an English soldier, madame,"* he'd said to me. *"He fell down and I stuck him with my knife."*

And Ian, a fifteen-year-old, weeping in remorse because he thought he had accidentally killed an intruder to Jamie's Edinburgh print shop. God knew what he had done, since; he wasn't talking. I had a sudden vision of Fergus's hook, dark with blood, and Ian, silhouetted in the dark. *"And I,"* he'd said, echoing Jamie. *"It is myself who kills for her."*

It was 1773. And *on the eighteenth of April, in Seventy-five* . . . the shot heard round the world was already being loaded. The room was warm, but I shuddered convulsively. What in the name of God did I think I could shield them from? Any of them.

A sudden roar from the roof above startled me out of my thoughts.

I walked out into the dooryard and looked up, shading my eyes against the morning sun. Jamie was sitting astride the rooftree, rocking to and fro over one hand, which he held curled into his belly.

"What's going on up there?" I called.

"I've got a splinter," came the terse answer, obviously spoken through clenched teeth.

I wanted to laugh, if only as small escape from tension, but didn't.

"Well, come down, then. I'll pull it out."

"I'm no finished!"

"I don't care!" I said, suddenly impatient with him. "Come down this minute. I want to talk to you."

A bag of nails hit the grass with a sudden clank, followed instantly by the hammer.

First things first, then.

TECHNICALLY, I SUPPOSED, it was a splinter. It was a two-inch sliver of cedarwood, and he'd driven it completely under the nail of his middle finger, nearly to the first joint.

"Jesus H. Roosevelt Christ!"

"Aye," he agreed, looking a little pale. "Ye might say that."

The protruding stub was too short to grip with my fingers. I hauled him into the surgery and jerked the sliver out with forceps, before one could say Jack Robinson. Jamie was saying a good deal more than Jack Robinson—mostly in French, which is an excellent language for swearing.

"You're going to lose that nail," I observed, submerging the offended digit in a small bowl of alcohol and water. Blood bloomed from it like ink from a squid.

"To hell wi' the nail," he said, gritting his teeth. "Cut the whole bloody finger off and ha' done with it! *Merde d'chevre!*"

"The Chinese used to—well, no, I suppose they still do, come to think of it—shove splinters of bamboo under people's fingernails to make them talk."

"Christ! *Tu me casses les couilles!*"

"Obviously a very effective technique," I said, lifting his hand out of the bowl and wrapping the finger tightly in a strip of linen. "Were you trying it out, before using it on Lionel Brown?" I tried to speak lightly, keeping my eyes on his hand. I felt his own gaze fix on me, and he snorted.

"What in the name of saints and archangels was wee Ian telling ye, Sassenach?"

"That you meant to question the man—and get answers."

"I do, and I shall," he said shortly. "So?"

"Fergus and Ian seemed to think that—you might be moved to use any means necessary," I said with some delicacy. "They're more than willing to help."

"I imagine they are." The first agony had abated somewhat. He breathed more deeply, and color was beginning to come back into his face. "Fergus has a right. It was his wife attacked."

"Ian seemed . . ." I hesitated, searching for the right word. Ian had seemed so calm as to be terrifying. "You didn't call Roger to help with the—the questioning?"

"No. Not yet." One corner of his mouth tucked in. "Roger Mac's a good fighter, but no the sort to scare a man, save he's truly roused. He's no deceit in him at all."

"Whereas you, Ian, and Fergus . . ."

"Oh, aye," he said dryly. "Wily as snakes, the lot of us. Ye've only to look at Roger Mac to see how safe their time must be, him and the lass. A bit of a comfort, that," he added, the tuck growing deeper. "To ken things will get better, I mean."

I could see that he was trying to change the subject, which was not a good sign. I made a small snorting noise, but it hurt my nose.

"And *you're* not truly roused, is that what you're telling me?"

He made a much more successful snorting noise, but didn't reply. He tilted his head to one side, watching as I laid out a square of gauze and began to rub dried leaves of comfrey into it. I didn't know how to say what was troubling me, but he plainly saw that something was.

"Will you kill him?" I asked baldly, keeping my eyes on the jar of honey. It was made of brown glass, and the light glowed through it as though it were a huge ball of clear amber.

Jamie sat still, watching me. I could feel his speculative gaze, though I didn't look up.

"I think so," he said.

My hands had started to tremble, and I pressed them on the surface of the table to still them.

"Not today," he added. "If I kill him, I shall do it properly."

I wasn't sure I wanted to know what constituted a proper killing, in his opinion, but he told me anyway.

"If he dies at my hand, it will be in the open, before witnesses who ken the truth of the matter, and him standing upright. I willna have it said that I killed a helpless man, whatever his crime."

"Oh." I swallowed, feeling mildly ill, and took a pinch of powdered bloodroot to add to the salve I was making. It had a faint, astringent smell, which seemed to help. "But—you might let him live?"

"Perhaps. I suppose I might ransom him to his brother—depending."

"Do you know, you sound quite like your uncle Colum. He would have thought it through like that."

"Do I?" The corner of his mouth turned up slightly. "Shall I take that as compliment, Sassenach?"

"I suppose you might as well."

"Aye, well," he said thoughtfully. The stiff fingers tapped on the tabletop, and he winced slightly as the movement jarred the injured one. "Colum had a castle. And armed clansmen at his beck. I should have some difficulty in defending this house against a raid, perhaps."

"That's what you mean by 'defending'?" I felt quite uneasy at this; the thought of armed raiders attacking the house had not occurred to me—and I saw that Jamie's forethought in storing Mr. Brown off our premises had perhaps not been entirely for the purpose of sparing my sensibilities.

"One of the things."

I mixed a bit of honey with my powdered herbs, then scooped a small dollop of purified bear grease into the mortar.

"I suppose," I said, eyes on my mixing, "that there's no point in turning Lionel Brown over to the—the authorities?"

"Which authorities did ye have in mind, Sassenach?" he asked dryly.

A good question. This part of the backcountry had not yet formed nor joined a county, though a movement was afoot to that purpose. Were Jamie to deliver Mr. Brown to the sheriff of the nearest county for trial . . . well, no, perhaps not a good idea. Brownsville lay just within the borders of the nearest county, and the current sheriff was in fact named Brown.

I bit my lip, considering. In times of stress, I tended still to respond as what I was—a civilized Englishwoman, accustomed to rely on the sureties of government and law. Well, all right, Jamie had a point; the twentieth century had its own dangers, but some things had improved. *This* was nearly 1774, though, and the colonial government was already showing cracks and fault lines, signs of the collapse to come.

"I suppose we could take him to Cross Creek." Farquard Campbell was a justice of the peace there—and a friend to Jamie's aunt, Jocasta Cameron. "Or to New Bern." Governor Martin and the bulk of the Royal Council were in New Bern—three hundred miles away. "Maybe Hillsborough?" That was the center of the Circuit Court.

"Mmphm."

This noise denoted a marked disinclination to lose several weeks' work in order to haul Mr. Brown before any of these seats of justice, let alone entrust a matter of importance to the highly unreliable—and frequently corrupt—judicial system. I looked up and met his eye, humorous but bleak. If I responded as what I was, so did Jamie.

And Jamie was a Highland laird, accustomed to follow his own laws, and fight his own battles.

"But—" I began.

"Sassenach," he said quite gently. "What of the others?"

The others. I stopped moving, paralyzed by the sudden memory: a large band of black figures, coming out of the wood with the sun behind them. But that group had split in two, intending to meet again in Brownsville, in three days' time—today, in fact.

For the moment, presumably no one from Brownsville yet knew what had happened—that Hodgepile and his men were dead, or that Lionel Brown was now a captive on the Ridge. Given the speed with which news spread in the mountains, though, it would be public knowledge within a week.

In the aftermath of shock, I had somehow overlooked the fact that there were still a number of bandits at large—and while I didn't know who they were, they knew both who I was and where I was. Would they realize that I could not identify them? Or be willing to take that risk?

Obviously, Jamie was not willing to take the risk of leaving the Ridge to escort Lionel Brown anywhere, whether or not he decided to let the man live.

The thought of the others had brought something important back to me, though. It might not be the best time to mention it, but then again, there wasn't going to be a good one.

I took a deep breath, squaring myself for it.

"Jamie."

The tone of my voice jerked him immediately from whatever he'd been thinking; he looked sharply at me, one eyebrow raised.

"I—I have to tell you something."

He paled a little, but reached out at once, grasping my hand. He took a deep breath of his own, and nodded.

"Aye."

"Oh," I said, realizing that he thought I meant that I had suddenly arrived at a point where I needed to tell him the grisly details of my experiences. "Not—not that. Not exactly." I squeezed his hand, though, and held on, while I told him about Donner.

"Another," he said. He sounded slightly stunned. "Another one?"

"Another," I confirmed. "The thing is . . . I, um, I don't remember seeing him . . . seeing him dead." The eerie sense of that dawn returned to me. I had very sharp, distinct memories—but they were disjointed, so fractured as to bear no relation to the whole. An ear. I remembered an ear, thick and cup-shaped as a woodland fungus. It was shaded in the most exquisite tones of purple, brown, and indigo, shadowed in the carved whorls of the inner parts, nearly translucent at the rim; perfect in the light of a sunbeam that cut through the fronds of a hemlock to touch it.

I recalled that ear so perfectly that I could almost reach into my memory and touch it myself—but I had no idea whose ear it had been. Was the hair that lay behind it brown, black, reddish, straight, wavy, gray? And the face . . . I didn't know. If I had looked, I hadn't seen.

He shot me a sharp look.

"And ye think he's maybe not."

"Maybe not." I swallowed the taste of dust, pine needles, and blood, and breathed the comforting fresh scent of buttermilk. "I warned him, you see. I told him you were coming, and that he didn't want you to find him with me. When you attacked the camp—he might have run. He struck me as a coward, certainly. But I don't know."

He nodded, and sighed heavily.

"Can you . . . recall, do you think?" I asked hesitantly. "When you showed me the dead. Did you look at them?"

"No," he said softly. "I wasna looking at anything save you."

His eyes had been on our linked hands. He raised them now, and looked at my face, troubled and searching. I lifted his hand and laid my cheek against his knuckles, closing my eyes for an instant.

"I'll be all right," I said. "The thing is—" I said, and stopped.

"Aye?"

"If he *did* run—where do you suppose he'd go?"

He closed his own eyes and drew a deep breath.

"To Brownsville," he said, in resignation. "And if he did, Richard Brown kens already what's become of Hodgepile and his men—and likely thinks his brother is dead, as well."

"Oh." I swallowed, and changed the subject slightly.

"Why did you tell Ian I wasn't to be allowed to see Mr. Brown?"

"I didna say that. But I think it best if ye dinna see him, that much is true."

"Because?"

"Because ye've an oath upon you," he said, sounding mildly surprised that I didn't understand immediately. "Can ye see a man injured, and leave him to suffer?"

The ointment was ready. I unwrapped his finger, which had stopped bleeding, and tamped as much of the salve under the damaged nail as I could manage.

"Probably not," I said, eyes on my work. "But why—"

"If ye mend him, care for him—and then I decide he must die?" His eyes rested on me, questioning. "How would that be for ye?"

"Well, that *would* be a bit awkward," I said, taking a deep breath to steady myself. I wrapped a thin strip of linen around the nail and tied it neatly. "Still, though . . ."

"Ye wish to care for him? Why?" He sounded curious, but not angry. "Is your oath so strong, then?"

"No." I put both hands on the table to brace myself; my knees seemed suddenly weak.

"Because I'm glad they're dead," I whispered, looking down. My hands were raw, and I fumbled while I worked because my fingers were still swollen; there were deep purple marks still sunk in the skin of my wrists. "And I am very much—" What? Afraid; afraid of the men, afraid of myself. Thrilled, in a horrible sort of way. "Ashamed," I said. "Terribly ashamed." I glanced up at him. "I hate it."

He held out his hand to me, waiting. He knew better than to touch me; I couldn't have borne being touched just then. I didn't take it, not at once, though I longed to. I looked away, speaking rapidly to Adso, who had materialized on the countertop and was regarding me with a bottomless green gaze.

"If I—I keep thinking . . . if I were to see him, help him—Christ, I *don't* want to, I don't at all! But if I could—perhaps that would . . . help somehow." I looked up then, feeling haunted. "Make . . . amends."

"For being glad they are dead—and for wanting him dead, too?" Jamie suggested gently.

I nodded, feeling as though a small, heavy weight had lifted with the speaking of the words. I didn't remember taking his hand, but it was tight on mine. Blood from his finger was seeping through the fresh bandage, but he paid no attention.

"Do you *want* to kill him?" I asked.

He looked at me for a long moment before replying.

"Oh, aye," he said very softly. "But for now, his life is surety for yours. For all of us, perhaps. And so he lives. For now. But I will ask questions—and I shall have answers."

I SAT IN my surgery for some time after he left. Emerging slowly from shock, I had felt safe, surrounded by home and friends, by Jamie. Now I must come to grips with the fact that nothing was safe—not I, not home nor friends—and certainly not Jamie.

"But then, you never are, are you, you bloody Scot?" I said aloud, and laughed, weakly.

Feeble as it was, it made me feel better. I rose with sudden decision and began to tidy my cupboards, lining up bottles in order of size, sweeping out bits of scattered herbs, throwing away solutions gone stale or suspect.

I had meant to go and visit Marsali, but Fergus had told me during breakfast that Jamie had sent her with the children and Lizzie to stay with the McGillivrays, where she would be cared for, and safe. If there was safety in numbers, the McGillivrays' house was certainly the place for it.

Located near Woolam's Creek, the McGillivrays' home place adjoined Ronnie Sinclair's cooper's shop, and enclosed a seething mass of cordial humanity, including not only Robin and Ute McGillivray, their son, Manfred, and their daughter Senga, but also Ronnie, who boarded with them. The usual mob scene was augmented intermittently by Senga McGillivray's fiancé, Heinrich Strasse, and his German relatives from Salem, and by Inga and Hilda, their husbands and children, and their husbands' relatives.

Add in the men who congregated daily in Ronnie's shop, a convenient stopping place on the road to and from Woolam's Mill, and likely no one would even notice Marsali and her family, in the midst of that mob. Surely no one would seek to harm her there. But for me to go and see her . . .

Highland tact and delicacy were one thing. Highland hospitality and curiosity were another. If I stayed peacefully at home, I would likely be left in peace—at least for a while. If I were to set foot near the McGillivrays' . . . I blenched at the thought, and hastily decided that perhaps I would visit Marsali tomorrow. Or the next day. Jamie had assured me she was all right, only shocked and bruised.

The house stood around me in peace. No modern background of furnace, fans, plumbing, refrigerators. No whoosh of pilot lights or hum of compressors. Just the occasional creak of beam or floorboard, and the odd muffled scrape of a wood wasp building its nest up under the eaves.

I looked round the ordered world of my surgery—ranks of

shining jars and bottles, linen screens laden with drying arrowroot and masses of lavender, bunches of nettle and yarrow and rosemary hanging overhead. The bottle of ether, sunlight glowing on it. Adso curled on the countertop, tail neatly tucked around his feet, eyes half-closed in purring contemplation.

Home. A small shiver ran down my spine. I wanted nothing more than to be alone, safe and alone, in my own home.

Safe. I had a day, perhaps two, in which home would still be safe. And then . . .

I realized that I had been standing still for some moments, staring blankly into a box of yellow nightshade berries, round and shiny as marbles. Very poisonous, and a slow and painful death. My eyes rose to the ether—quick and merciful. If Jamie did decide to kill Lionel Brown . . . But no. In the open, he'd said, standing on his feet before witnesses. Slowly, I closed the box and put it back on the shelf.

What then?

THERE WERE ALWAYS chores that could be done—but nothing pressing, with no one clamoring to be fed, clothed, or cared for. Feeling quite odd, I wandered round the house for a bit, and finally went into Jamie's study, where I poked among the books on the shelf there, settling at last on Henry Fielding's *Tom Jones*.

I couldn't think how long it had been since I had read a novel. And in the daytime! Feeling pleasantly wicked, I sat by the open window in my surgery and resolutely entered a world far from my own.

I lost track of time, moving only to brush away roving insects that came through the window, or to absently scratch Adso's head when he nudged against me. Occasional thoughts of Jamie and Lionel Brown drifted through the back of my mind, but I shooed them away like the leafhoppers and midges who landed on my page, drifting in through the window. Whatever was happening in the Bugs' cabin had happened, or would happen—I simply couldn't think about it. As I read, the soap bubble formed around me once more, filled with perfect stillness.

The sun was halfway down the sky before faint pangs of hunger began to stir. It was as I looked up, rubbing my forehead and wondering vaguely whether there was any ham left, that I saw a man standing in the doorway to the surgery.

I shrieked, and leaped to my feet, sending Henry Fielding flying.

"Your pardon, mistress!" Thomas Christie blurted, looking nearly as startled as I felt. "I didna realize that you'd not heard me."

"No. I—I—was reading." I gestured foolishly toward the book on the floor. My heart was pounding, and blood surged to and fro in my body, seemingly at random, so that my face flushed, my ears throbbed, and my hands tingled, all out of control.

He stooped and picked the book up, smoothing its cover with the careful attitude of one who values books, though the volume itself was battered, its cover scarred with rings where wet glasses or bottles had been set down upon it. Jamie had got it from the owner of an ordinary in Cross Creek, in partial trade for a load of firewood; some customer had left it, months before.

"Is there no one here to care for you?" he asked, frowning as he looked around. "Shall I go and fetch my daughter to you?"

"No. I mean—I don't need anyone. I'm quite all right. What about you?" I asked quickly, forestalling any further expressions of concern on his part. He glanced at my face, then hastily away. Eyes fixed carefully in the vicinity of my collarbone, he laid the book on the table and held out his right hand, wrapped in a cloth.

"I beg your pardon, mistress. I wouldna intrude, save . . ."

I was already unwrapping the hand. He'd ripped the incision in his right hand—probably, I realized with a small tightening of the belly, in the course of the fight with the bandits. The wound was no great matter, but there were bits of dirt and debris in the wound, and the edges were red and gaping, raw surfaces clouded with a film of pus.

"You should have come at once," I said, though with no

tone of rebuke. I knew perfectly well why he hadn't—and in fact, I should have been in no state to deal with him, if he had.

He shrugged slightly, but didn't bother replying. I sat him down and went to fetch things. Luckily, there was some of the antiseptic salve left that I'd made for Jamie's splinter. That, a quick alcohol wash, clean bandage . . .

He was turning the pages of *Tom Jones* slowly, lips pursed in concentration. Evidently Henry Fielding would do as anesthetic for the job at hand; I shouldn't need to fetch a Bible.

"Do you read novels?" I asked, meaning no rudeness, but merely surprised that he might countenance anything so frivolous.

He hesitated. "Yes. I—yes." He took a very deep breath as I submerged his hand in the bowl, but it contained only water, soaproot, and a very small amount of alcohol, and he let the breath go with a sigh.

"Have you read *Tom Jones* before?" I asked, making conversation to relax him.

"Not precisely, though I know the story. My wife—"

He stopped abruptly. He'd never mentioned his wife before; I supposed that it was sheer relief at not experiencing agony yet that had made him talkative. He seemed to realize that he must complete the sentence, though, and went on, reluctantly. "My wife . . . read novels."

"Did she?" I murmured, setting about the job of debridement. "Did she like them?"

"I suppose that she must have."

There was something odd in his voice that made me glance up from the job at hand. He caught the glance and looked away, flushing.

"I—did not approve of reading novels. Then."

He was quiet for a moment, holding his hand steady. Then he blurted, "I burnt her books."

That sounded rather more like the response I would have expected of him.

"She couldn't have been pleased about that," I said mildly, and he shot me a startled glance, as though the question of his wife's reaction was so irrelevant as to be unworthy of remark.

"Ah . . . what caused you to alter your opinion?" I asked, concentrating on the bits of debris I was picking out of the wound with my forceps. Splinters and shreds of bark. What had he been doing? Wielding a club of some kind, I thought—a tree branch? I breathed deeply, concentrating on the job to avoid thinking of the bodies in the clearing.

He moved his legs restively; I was hurting him a bit now.

"I—it—in Ardsmuir."

"What? You read it in prison?"

"No. We had no books there." He took a long breath, glanced at me, then away, and fixed his eyes on the corner of the room, where an enterprising spider had taken advantage of Mrs. Bug's temporary absence to set up web-keeping.

"In fact, I have never actually read it. Mr. Fraser, though, was accustomed to recount the story to the other prisoners. He has a fine memory," he added, rather grudgingly.

"Yes, he does," I murmured. "I'm not going to stitch it; it will be better if the wound's left to heal by itself. I'm afraid the scar won't be as neat," I added regretfully, "but I think it will heal up all right."

I spread salve thickly over the injury, and pulled the edges of the wound together as tightly as I could, without cutting off the circulation. Bree had been experimenting with adhesive bandages, and had produced something quite useful in the way of small butterfly shapes, made of starched linen and pine tar.

"So you liked Tom Jones, did you?" I said, returning to the subject. "I shouldn't have thought you'd find him an admirable character. Not much of a moral example, I mean."

"I don't," he said bluntly. "But I saw that fiction"—he pronounced the word gingerly, as though it were something dangerous—"is perhaps not, as I had thought, merely an inducement to idleness and wicked fancy."

"Oh, isn't it?" I said, amused, but trying not to smile because of my lip. "What are its redeeming characteristics, do you think?"

"Aye, well." His brows drew together in thought. "I found it most remarkable. That what is essentially nothing save a confection of lies should somewise still contrive to exert a beneficial effect. For it did," he concluded, sounding still rather surprised.

"Really? How was that?"

He tilted his head, considering.

"It was distraction, to be sure. In such conditions, distraction is not evil," he assured me. "While it is of course more desirable to escape into prayer . . ."

"Oh, of course," I murmured.

"But beyond that consideration . . . it drew the men together. You would not think that such men—Highlanders, crofters—that they would find themselves in particular sympathy with . . . such situations, such persons." He waved his free hand at the book, indicating such persons as Squire Allworthy and Lady Bellaston, I supposed.

"But they would talk it over for hours—whilst we labored the next day, they would wonder why Ensign Northerton had done as he had with regard to Miss Western, and argue whether they themselves would or would not have behaved so." His face lightened a little, recalling something. "And invariably, a man would shake his head and say, 'At least I've never been treated in *that* manner!' He might be starved, cold, covered in sores, permanently separated from his family and customary circumstances—and yet he could take comfort in never having suffered such vicissitudes as had befallen these imaginary beings!"

He actually smiled, shaking his head at the thought, and I thought the smile much improved him.

I'd finished the job, and laid his hand on the table.

"Thank you," I said quietly.

He looked startled.

"What? Why?"

"I'm assuming that that injury was perhaps the result of b-battle done on my behalf," I said. I touched his hand lightly. "I, er . . . well." I took a deep breath. "Thank you."

"Oh." He looked thoroughly taken aback at this, and quite embarrassed.

"I . . . erm . . . hmm!" He pushed back the stool and rose, looking flustered.

I rose, as well.

"You'll need to have fresh salve put on every day," I said, resuming a businesslike tone. "I'll make up some more; you can come, or send Malva to fetch it."

He nodded, but said nothing, having evidently exhausted

his supply of sociability for the day. I saw his eye linger on the cover of the book, though, and on impulse offered it to him.

"Would you like to borrow it? You should really read it for yourself; I'm sure Jamie can't have recalled all the details."

"Oh!" He looked startled, and pursed his lips, frowning, as though suspecting it was a trap of some sort. When I insisted, though, he took the book, picking it up with an expression of guarded avidity that made me wonder how long it had been since he had had any book other than the Bible to read.

He nodded thanks to me, and donned his hat, turning to go. Upon a moment's impulse, I asked, "Did you ever have the chance to apologize to your wife?"

That was a mistake. His face tightened into coldness and his eyes went flat as a snake's.

"No," he said shortly. I thought for a moment that he would put the book down and refuse to take it. But instead, he tightened his lips, tucked the volume more securely under his arm, and left, without further farewell.

31

AND SO TO BED

NO ONE ELSE CAME. By the time night fell, I was beginning to feel rather edgy, starting at noises, searching the deepening shadows under the chestnut trees for lurking men—or worse. I thought I should cook something; surely Jamie and Ian intended coming home for supper? Or perhaps I should go down to the cabin, join Roger and Bree.

But I flinched from the notion of being exposed to any kind of solicitude, no matter how well meant, and while I hadn't yet got up the nerve to look in a mirror, was reasonably sure that the sight of me would frighten Jemmy—or at least lead to a lot of questions. I didn't want to have to try to explain to him what had happened to me. I was fairly sure that Jamie had told Brianna to stay away for a bit, and that was good. I really was in no shape to pretend to be all right. Not quite yet.

Dithering round the kitchen, I picked things up and put them down pointlessly. I opened the drawers of the sideboard and closed them—then opened the second one again, the one where Jamie kept his pistols.

Most of the pistols were gone. Only the gilt-trimmed one that didn't shoot straight was left, with a few loads and a tiny powder horn, the sort made for fancy dueling pistols.

Hands shaking only a little, I loaded it, and poured a bit of powder into the firing pan.

When the back door opened, quite some time later, I was sitting at the table, a copy of *Don Quixote* lying in front of me, pointing the pistol with both hands at the door.

Ian froze momentarily.

"Ye'd never hit anyone wi' that gun at this distance, Auntie," he said mildly, coming in.

"They wouldn't know that, would they?" I set the pistol down, gingerly. My palms were damp, and my fingers ached.

He nodded, taking the point, and sat down.

"Where's Jamie?" I asked.

"Washing. Are ye well, Auntie?" His soft hazel eyes took a casual but careful estimation of my state.

"No, but I'll do." I hesitated. "And . . . Mr. Brown? Did he—tell you anything?"

Ian made a derogatory noise.

"Pissed himself when Uncle Jamie took the dirk from his belt to clean his fingernails. We didna touch him, Auntie, dinna fash yourself."

Jamie came in then, clean-shaven, his skin cold and fresh from the well water, hair damp at his temples. Despite that, he looked tired to death, the lines of his face cut deep and his eyes shadowed. The shadows lifted a bit, though, when he saw me and the pistol.

"It's all right, *a nighean*," he said softly, touching my shoulder as he sat down beside me. "I've men set to watch the house—just in case. Though I dinna expect any trouble for some days yet."

My breath went out in a long sigh.

"You could have told me that."

He glanced at me, surprised.

"I thought ye'd know. Surely ye wouldna think I'd leave ye unprotected, Sassenach?"

I shook my head, momentarily unable to speak. Had I been in any condition to think logically, of course I wouldn't. As it was, I had spent most of the afternoon in a state of quiet—and unnecessary—terror, imagining, remembering. . . .

"I'm sorry, lass," he said softly, and put a large, cold hand on mine. "I shouldna have left ye alone. I thought—"

I shook my head, but put my other hand over his, pressing tight.

"No, you were right. I couldn't have borne any company, beyond Sancho Panza."

He glanced at *Don Quixote,* then at me, brows raised. The book was in Spanish, which I didn't happen to speak.

"Well, some of it was close to French, and I did know the story," I said. I took a deep breath, taking what comfort I could in the warmth of the fire, the flicker of the candle, and the proximity of the two of them, large, solid, pragmatic, and—outwardly, at least—imperturbable.

"Is there any food, Auntie?" Ian inquired, getting up to look. Lacking any appetite myself, and too jittery to focus on anything, I hadn't eaten dinner nor made anything for supper—but there was always food in that house, and without any particular fuss, Jamie and Ian had equipped themselves in short order with the remains of a cold partridge pie, several hard-cooked eggs, a dish of piccalilli, and half a loaf of bread, which they sliced up and toasted over the fire on a fork, buttering the slices and cramming them into me in a manner brooking no argument.

Hot, buttered toast is immensely comforting, even nibbled tentatively with a sore jaw. With food in my stomach, I began to feel much calmer, and capable of inquiring what they had learned from Lionel Brown.

"He put it all on Hodgepile," Jamie told me, loading piccalilli onto a slice of pie. "He would, of course."

"You didn't meet Arvin Hodgepile," I said, with a small shiver. "Er . . . to talk to, I mean."

He shot me a sharp look, but didn't address that matter any further, instead leaving it to Ian to explain Lionel Brown's version of events.

It had started with him and his brother, Richard, establishing their Committee of Safety. This, he had insisted, was intended as public service, pure and simple. Jamie snorted at that, but didn't interrupt.

Most of the male inhabitants of Brownsville had joined the committee—most of the homesteaders and small farmers nearby had not. Still, so far, so good. The committee had dealt with a number of small matters, meting out justice in cases of assault, theft, and the like, and if they had appropriated the odd hog or deer carcass by way of payment for their trouble, there hadn't been too much complaint.

"There's a great deal of feeling still, about the Regulation," Ian explained, frowning as he sliced another piece of bread. "The Browns didna join the Regulation; they'd no need to, as their cousin was sheriff, and half the courthouse ring are Browns, or marrit to Browns." Corruption, in other words, had been on their side.

Regulator sentiment still ran high in the backcountry, even though the main leaders of the movement, such as Hermon Husband and James Hunter, had left the colony. In the aftermath of Alamance, most Regulators had grown more cautious of expressing themselves—but several Regulator families who lived near Brownsville had become vocal in their criticism of the Browns' influence on local politics and business.

"Tige O'Brian was one of those?" I asked, feeling the buttered toast coalesce into a small, hard lump in my stomach. Jamie had told me what had happened to the O'Brians—and I'd seen Roger's face when he'd come back.

Jamie nodded, not looking up from his pie.

"Enter Arvin Hodgepile," he said, and took a ferocious bite. Hodgepile, having neatly escaped the constraints of the British army by pretending to die in the warehouse fire at Cross Creek, had set about making a living in various unsavory ways. And, water having a strong tendency to seek its own level, had ended up with a small gang of like-minded thugs.

This gang had begun simply enough, by robbing anyone they came across, holding up taverns, and the like. This sort of behavior tends to attract attention, though, and with various constables, sheriffs, Committees of Safety, and the like on their trail, the gang had retired from the piedmont where they began, and moved up into the mountains, where they could find isolated settlements and homesteads. They had also begun killing their victims, to avoid the nuisance of identification and pursuit.

"Or most of them," Ian murmured. He regarded the half-eaten egg in his hand for a moment, then put it down.

In his career with the army in Cross Creek, Hodgepile had made various contacts with a number of river traders and coastal smugglers. Some dealt in furs, others in anything that would bring a profit.

"And it occurred to them," Jamie said, drawing a deep breath, "that girls and women and young boys are more profitable than almost anything—save whisky, maybe." The corner of his mouth twitched, but it wasn't a smile.

"Our Mr. Brown insists he'd nothing to do wi' this," Ian added, a cynical note in his voice. "Nor had his brother or their committee."

"But how did the Browns get involved with Hodgepile's gang?" I asked. "And what did they do with the people they kidnapped?"

The answer to the first question was that it had been the happy outcome of a botched robbery.

"Ye recall Aaron Beardsley's auld place, aye?"

"I do," I said, wrinkling my nose in reflex at the memory of that wretched sty, then emitting a small cry and clapping both hands over my abused appendage.

Jamie glanced at me, and put another bit of bread on his toasting fork.

"Well, so," he went on, ignoring my protest that I was full, "the Browns took it over, of course, when they adopted the wee lass. They cleaned it out, stocked it fresh, and went on using it as a trading post."

The Cherokee and Catawba had been accustomed to come

to the place—horrid as it was—when Aaron Beardsley had operated as an Indian trader, and had continued to do business with the new management—a very beneficial and profitable arrangement all round.

"Which is what Hodgepile saw," Ian put in. The Hodgepile gang, with their usual straightforward methods of doing business, had walked in, shot the couple in charge, and begun systematically looting the place. The couple's eleven-year-old daughter, who had fortunately been in the barn when the gang arrived, had slipped out, mounted a mule, and ridden hell-for-leather for Brownsville and help. By good fortune, she had encountered the Committee of Safety, returning from some errand, and brought them back in time to confront the robbers.

There then ensued what in later years would be called a Mexican standoff. The Browns had the house surrounded. Hodgepile, however, had Alicia Beardsley Brown—the two-year-old girl who legally owned the trading post, and who had been adopted by the Browns upon the death of her putative father.

Hodgepile had enough food and ammunition inside the trading post to withstand a siege of weeks; the Browns were disinclined to set fire to their valuable property in order to drive him out, or to risk the girl's life by storming the place. After a day or two during which desultory shots were exchanged, and the members of the committee became increasingly edgy at having to camp in the woods surrounding the trading post, a flag of truce had been waved from the upper window, and Richard Brown had gone inside to parley with Hodgepile.

The result being a wary sort of merger. Hodgepile's gang would continue their operations, steering clear of any settlement under the Browns' protection, but would bring the proceeds of their robberies to the trading post, where they could be disposed of inconspicuously at a good profit, with Hodgepile's gang taking a generous cut.

"The proceeds," I said, accepting a fresh slice of buttered toast from Jamie. "That—you do mean captives?"

"Sometimes." His lips pressed tight as he poured a mug of cider and handed it to me. "And depending upon where they were. When they took captives in the mountains, some of them were sold to the Indians, through the trading post. Those they took from the piedmont, they sold to river pirates, or took to the coast to sell on to the Indies—that would be the best price, aye? A fourteen-year-old lad would bring a hundred pound, at least."

My lips felt numb, and not only from the cider.

"How long?" I said, appalled. "How many?" Children, young men, young women, wrenched from their homes and sold cold-bloodedly into slavery. No one to follow. Even if they were somehow to escape eventually, there would be no place—no one—to return to.

Jamie sighed. He looked unutterably tired.

"Brown doesna ken," Ian said quietly. "He says . . . He says he'd nothing to do with it."

"Like bloody hell he hadn't," I said, a flash of fury momentarily eclipsing horror. "He was *with* Hodgepile when they came here. He knew they meant to take the whisky. And he must have been with them before, when they—did other things."

Jamie nodded.

"He claims he tried to stop them from taking you."

"He did," I said shortly. "And then he tried to make them kill me, to stop me telling you he'd been there. And then he bloody meant to drown me himself! I don't suppose he told you that."

"No, he didn't." Ian exchanged a brief look with Jamie, and I saw some unspoken agreement pass between them. It occurred to me that I might possibly just have sealed Lionel Brown's fate. If so, I was not sure I felt guilty about it.

"What—what do you mean to do with him?" I asked.

"I think perhaps I will hang him," Jamie replied, after a moment's pause. "But I've more questions I want answered. And I must think about how best to manage the matter. Dinna bother about it, Sassenach; ye'll not see him again."

With that, he stood and stretched, muscles cracking, then shifted his shoulders, settling himself with a sigh. He gave me a hand and helped me to my feet.

"Go up to bed, Sassenach, and I'll be up directly. I must just have a wee word with Ian first."

HOT BUTTERED TOAST, cider, and conversation had made me feel momentarily better. I found myself so tired, though, that I could barely drag myself up the stairs, and was obliged to sit on the bed, swaying blearily, in hopes of getting up the strength to take off my clothes. It was a few moments before I noticed that Jamie was hovering in the doorway.

"Erm . . . ?" I said vaguely.

"I didna ken, did ye want me to stay with ye tonight?" he asked diffidently. "If ye'd rest better alone, I could take Joseph's bed. Or if ye'd like, I could sleep beside ye, on the floor."

"Oh," I said blankly, trying to weigh these alternatives. "No. Stay. Sleep with me, I mean." From the bottom of a well of fatigue, I summoned something like a smile. "You can warm the bed, at least."

A most peculiar expression flitted across his face at that, and I blinked, not sure I'd seen it. I had, though; his face was caught between embarrassment and dismayed amusement—with somewhere behind all that the sort of look he might have worn if going to the stake: heroically resigned.

"What on *earth* have you been doing?" I asked, sufficiently surprised as to be shaken out of my torpor.

Embarrassment was getting the upper hand; the tips of his ears were going red, and a flush was visible in his cheeks, even by the dim light of the taper I'd set on the table.

"I wasna going to tell ye," he muttered, avoiding my gaze. "I swore wee Ian and Roger Mac to silence."

"Oh, they've been silent as the grave," I assured him. Though this statement did perhaps explain the occasional odd look on Roger's face, of late. "What's been going on?"

He sighed, scraping the edge of his boot across the floor.

"Aye, well. It's Tsisqua, d'ye see? He meant it as hospitality, the first time, but then when Ian told him . . . well, it wasna the best thing to have said, under the circumstances, only . . . And then the next time we came, and there they were again, only a different pair, and when I tried to make them leave, they said Bird said to say that it was honor to my vow, for what good was a vow that cost nothing to keep? And I will be damned if I ken does he mean that, or is he only thinking that either I'll crack and he'll have the upper hand of me for good, or that I'll get him the guns he wants to put an end to it one way or the other—or is he only having a joke at my expense? Even Ian says he canna tell which it is, and if he—"

"Jamie," I said. "What are you talking about?"

He stole a quick glance at me, then looked away again.

"Ah . . . naked women," he blurted, and went red as a piece of new flannel.

I stared at him for a moment. My ears still buzzed slightly, but there wasn't anything wrong with my hearing. I pointed a finger at him—carefully, because all my fingers were swollen and bruised.

"You," I said, in measured tones, "come here right now. Sit down right there"—I pointed at the bed beside me—"and tell me in words of one syllable *exactly* what you've been doing."

He did, with the result that five minutes later I was lying flat on the bed, wheezing with laughter, moaning with the pain to my cracked ribs, and with helpless tears running down my temples and into my ears.

"Oh, God, oh, God, oh, God," I gasped. "I can't stand it, I really can't. Help me sit up." I extended a hand, yelped with pain as his fingers closed on my lacerated wrist, but got upright at last, bent over with a pillow clutched to my middle, and clutched it tighter each time a gust of recurrent laughter struck me.

"I'm glad ye think it's sae funny, Sassenach," Jamie said very dryly. He'd recovered himself to some extent, though his face was still flushed. "Ye're sure ye're no hysterical?"

"No, not at all." I sniffed, dabbing at my eyes with a damp linen hankie, then snorted with uncontainable mirth. "Oh! Ow, God, that hurts."

Sighing, he poured a cup of water from the flask on the bedside table, and held it for me to drink. It was cool, but flat and rather stale; I thought perhaps it had been standing since before . . .

"All right," I said, waving the cup away and dabbing moisture very carefully from my lips. "I'm fine." I breathed shallowly, feeling my heart begin to slow down. "Well. So. At least now I know why you've been coming back from the Cherokee villages in such a state of—of—" I felt an unhinged giggle rising, and bent over, moaning as I stifled it. "Oh, Jesus H. Roosevelt Christ. And here I thought it was thoughts of me, driving you mad with lust."

He snorted then himself, though mildly. He put down the cup, rose, and turned back the coverlet. Then he looked at me, and his eyes were clear, unguarded.

"Claire," he said, quite gently, "it *was* you. It's always been you, and it always will be. Get into bed, and put the candle out. As soon as I've fastened the shutters, smoored the hearth, and barred the door, I'll come and keep ye warm."

"KILL ME." *Randall's eyes were fever-bright. "Kill me," he said. "My heart's desire."*

He jerked awake, hearing the words echo in his head, seeing the eyes, seeing the rain-matted hair, Randall's face, wet as that of a drowned man.

He rubbed a hand hard over his own face, surprised to feel his skin dry, his beard no more than a shadow. The sense of wet, the itching scurf of a month's whiskers, was still so strong that he got up, moving quietly by instinct, and went to the window, where moonlight shone through the cracks in the shutter. He poured a little water into the basin, moved the bowl into a shaft of light, and looked in, to rid himself of that lingering sense of being someone else, somewhere else.

The face in the water was no more than a featureless oval, but smooth-shaven, and the hair lay loose on his shoulders, not bound up for battle. And yet it seemed the face of a stranger.

Unsettled, he left the water in the bowl, and after a moment, padded softly back to the bed.

She was asleep. He had not even thought of her when he woke, but now the sight of her steadied him. That face he knew, even battered and swollen as it was.

He set his hand on the bedstead, comforted by the solid wood. Sometimes when he woke, the dream stayed with him, and he felt the real world ghostly, faint around him. Sometimes he feared he was a ghost.

But the sheets were cool on his skin, and Claire's warmth a reassurance. He reached for her, and she rolled over, curled herself backward into his arms with a small moan of content, her bum roundly solid against him.

She fell asleep again at once; she hadn't really waked. He had an urge to rouse her, make her talk to him—only to be quite sure she could see him, hear him. He only held her tight, though, and over her curly head he watched the door, as though it might open and Jack Randall stand there, soaked and streaming.

Kill me, he'd said. My heart's desire.

His heart beat slow, echoing in the ear he pressed against the pillow. Some nights, he would fall asleep listening to it, comforted by the fleshy, monotonous thump. Other times, like now, he would hear instead the mortal silence in between the beats—that silence that patiently awaits all men.

He had drawn the quilts up, but now put them back, so that Claire was covered but his own back lay bare, open to the chill of the room, that he might not slip warmly into sleep and risk returning to the dream. Let sleep struggle for him in the cold, and at last pull him off the precipice of consciousness, down to the deeps of black oblivion.

For he did not wish to know what Randall had meant by what he said.

32

HANGING'S TOO GOOD

IN THE MORNING, Mrs. Bug was back in the kitchen, and the air was warm and fragrant with the smells of cooking. She seemed quite as usual, and beyond a brief glance at my face and a "tsk!", not inclined to fuss. Either she had more sensitivity than I'd thought, or Jamie had had a word.

"Here, *a muirninn,* have it while it's hot." Mrs. Bug slid a heap of turkey hash from the platter onto my plate, and deftly topped it with a fried egg.

I nodded thanks and picked up my fork, with a certain lack of enthusiasm. My jaw was still so sore that eating was a slow and painful business.

The egg went down all right, but the smell of burned onion seemed very strong, oily in my nostrils. I separated a small bite of potato and mashed it against the roof of my mouth, squashing it with my tongue in lieu of chewing it, then washing it down with a sip of coffee.

More in hopes of distracting myself than because I truly wanted to know, I asked, "And how is Mr. Brown this morning?"

Her lips tightened, and she smacked down a spatula of fried potatoes as though they were Brown's brains.

"Nowhere near sae badly off as he ought to be," she said. "Hanging's too good for him, and him nay more than a wretched dungheap, crawling wi' maggots."

I spit out the bit of potato I'd been mangling, and took another hasty gulp of coffee. It hit bottom and started back up. I pushed back the bench and ran for the door, reaching it just in time to throw up into the blackberry bush, retching coffee, bile, and fried egg.

I was dimly aware of Mrs. Bug, hovering anxiously in the doorway, and waved her away with one hand. She hesitated for a moment, but then went in again, as I stood up and started toward the well.

The entire inside of my head tasted of coffee and bile, and the back of my nose stung terribly. I felt as though my nose were bleeding again, but when I touched it gingerly, discovered that it wasn't. Careful swilling with water cleansed my mouth, and did a bit to remedy the nasty taste—but nothing to drown the panic that had come in the wake of the nausea.

I had the sudden, distinct, and thoroughly bizarre impression that my skin was missing. My legs felt shaky, and I sat down on the stump where we split kindling, heedless of splinters.

I can't, I thought. *I simply can't.*

I sat on the chopping block, lacking the will to rise. I could feel my womb, very distinctly. A small, round weight at the base of my abdomen, feeling slightly swollen, very tender.

Nothing, I thought, with what determination I could muster. Entirely normal. It always feels that way, at a particular point of my cycle. And after what we had done, Jamie and I . . . well, no bloody wonder if I were still conscious of my interior workings. Granted, we hadn't, the night before; I'd wanted nothing but to be held. On the other hand, I'd nearly ruptured myself, laughing. A small laugh escaped me now, remembering Jamie's confession. It hurt, and I clutched my ribs, but felt a little better.

"Well, bloody hell anyway," I said aloud, and got up. "I've things to do."

Propelled by this bold statement, I fetched my basket and foraging knife, told Mrs. Bug I was off, and set out toward the Christies'.

I'd check Tom's hand, then invite Malva to come out with me in search of ginseng root, and any other useful things we might come across. She was an apt pupil, observant and quick, with a good memory for plants. And I'd meant to teach her how to prepare penicillin colonies. Picking through a collection of damp, moldy garbage would be soothing. I ignored a slight tendency of my gorge to rise at the thought, and lifted my battered face to the morning sun.

And I wasn't going to worry about what Jamie meant to do with Lionel Brown, either.

33

IN WHICH MRS. BUG TAKES A HAND

BY THE NEXT MORNING, I had recovered quite a bit. My stomach had settled, and I felt much more resilient, emotionally; a good thing, as whatever warnings Jamie had given Mrs. Bug about fussing over me had plainly worn off.

Everything hurt less, and my hands had nearly returned to normal, but I was still desperately tired, and it was in fact rather comforting to put my feet up on the settle and be brought cups of coffee—the tea was running very low, and no chance of more likely for several years—and dishes of rice pudding with raisins in.

"And ye're quite sure as your face will go back to lookin' like a face, are ye?" Mrs. Bug handed me a fresh muffin, dripping with butter and honey, and peered dubiously at me, lips pursed.

I was tempted to ask her what the thing on the front of my head looked like now, but was fairly sure I didn't want to hear the answer. Instead, I contented myself with a brief "Yes" and a request for more coffee.

"I kent a wumman up in Kirkcaldy once, as was kicked in the face by a cow," she said, still eyeing me critically as she dished up the coffee. "Lost her front teeth, puir creature, and ever after, her nose pointed off to the side, like *that.*" She pushed her own small round nose sharply to the side with an index finger in illustration, simultaneously tucking her upper lip under the lower one to simulate toothlessness.

I touched the bridge of my own nose carefully, but it was reassuringly straight, if still puffy.

"And then there was William McCrea of Balgownie, him

who fought at Sheriffsmuir with my Arch. Got in the way of an English pike, and cleaved off half his jaw, *and* the best part of his nose! Arch said ye could see straight into his gullet and his brain-box both—but he lived. On parritch, mostly," she added. "And whisky."

"What a very good idea," I said, putting down the nibbled muffin. "I believe I'll go and get some."

Carrying my cup, I escaped as quickly as I could down the hall to my surgery, followed by shouted reminiscences of Dominic Mulroney, an Irishman who'd walked face-first into a church door in Edinburgh and him sober as a sheep at the time. . . .

I shut the door of the surgery behind me, opened the window, and tossed the remains of the coffee out, then took down the bottle from the shelf and filled my cup to the brim.

I had intended to ask Mrs. Bug about Lionel Brown's state of health, but . . . perhaps that could wait. I found that my hands were trembling again, and had to press them flat on the table for a moment to steady them before I could pick up the cup.

I took a deep breath, and a swallow of whisky. Another. Yes, that was better.

Small waves of pointless panic tended still to seize me unawares. I hadn't had one this morning, and had rather hoped they'd gone away. Not quite yet, apparently.

I sipped whisky, dabbed cold sweat from my temples, and looked round for something useful to do. Malva and I had started some fresh penicillin the day before, and had made up fresh tinctures of boneset and troutlilly, and some fresh gentian salve, as well. I ended up thumbing slowly through my big black casebook, sipping whisky and dwelling on pages recounting various horrible complications of childbirth.

I realized what I was doing, but didn't seem able to stop doing it. I was *not* pregnant. I was sure of it. And yet my womb felt tender, inflamed, and my whole being disturbed.

Oh, there was a jolly one; one of Daniel Rawlings's entries, describing a slave woman of middle age, suffering from a recto-vaginal fistula that caused her to leak a constant small stream of fecal matter through the vagina.

Such fistulas were caused by battering during childbirth, and were more common in very young girls, where the strain of prolonged labor often caused such tears—or in older women, where the tissues had grown less elastic. Of course, in older women, the damage was quite likely to be accompanied by complete perineal collapse, allowing uterus, urethra—and possibly the anus for good measure—to sag through the pelvic floor.

"How extremely fortunate that I am not pregnant," I said aloud, closing the book firmly. Perhaps I'd have another go at *Don Quixote.*

On the whole, it was a considerable relief when Malva Christie came and tapped on the door, just before noon.

She gave my face a quick glance, but as she had the day before, merely accepted my appearance without comment.

"How's your father's hand?" I asked.

"Oh, it's fine, ma'am," she replied quickly. "I looked just as ye said, but no red streaks, no pus, and just that tiny bit of redness near where the skin is cut. I made him wiggle his fingers like ye said," she added, a dimple showing briefly in her cheek. "He didna want to, and carried on like I was poking thorns into him—but he did it."

"Oh, well done!" I said, and patted her on the shoulder, which made her pinken with pleasure.

"I think that deserves a biscuit with honey," I added, having noted the delectable aroma of baking that had been wafting down the hall from the kitchen for the last hour. "Come along."

As we entered the hallway and turned toward the kitchen, though, I heard an odd sort of noise from behind us. A peculiar kind of thumping or dragging outside, as though some large animal was lumbering across the hollow boards of the front stoop.

"What's that?" Malva said, looking over her shoulder in alarm.

A loud groan answered her, and a *thud!* that shook the front door as something fell against it.

"Mary, Joseph, and Bride!" Mrs. Bug had popped out of the kitchen, crossing herself. "What's that?"

My heart had begun to race at the noises, and my mouth went dry. Something large and dark blocked the line of light beneath the door, and stertorous breathing was clearly audible, interspersed with groans.

"Well, whatever it is, it's sick or injured," I said. "Stand back." I wiped my hands on my apron, swallowed, walked forward, and pulled open the door.

For a moment, I didn't recognize him; he was no more than a heap of flesh, wild hair, and disheveled garments smeared with dirt. But then he struggled up onto one knee and raised his head, panting, showing me a dead-white face, marked with bruises and glossy with sweat.

"Mr. Brown?" I said, incredulous.

His eyes were glazed; I wasn't sure that he saw me at all, but clearly he recognized my voice, for he lunged forward, nearly knocking me over. I stepped smartly back, but he caught me by the foot and held on, crying, "Mercy! Mistress, have mercy on me, I pray you!"

"What in the name of—let go. Let go, I say!" I shook my foot, trying to dislodge him, but he clung like a limpet, and went on shouting, "Mercy!" in a sort of hoarse, desperate chant.

"Oh, shut your noise, man," Mrs. Bug said crossly. Recovered from the shock of his entrance, she appeared not at all discomposed by his appearance, though substantially annoyed by it.

Lionel Brown did not shut up, but went on imploring me for mercy, despite my attempts to placate him. These were interrupted by Mrs. Bug leaning past me, a large meat-mallet in her hand, and dotting Mr. Brown smartly on the head with it. His eyes rolled back in his head and he dropped on his face without another word.

"I'm that sorry, Mrs. Fraser," Mrs. Bug said, apologetic. "I canna think how he got out, let alone came all this way!"

I didn't know how he'd got out, either, but it was quite clear how he'd come—he'd crawled, dragging his broken leg. His hands and legs were scratched and bloody, his breeches in tatters, and the whole of him covered with smears of mud, stuck full of grass and leaves.

I leaned down and plucked an elm leaf from his hair, trying to think what on earth to do with him. The obvious, I supposed.

"Help me get him into the surgery," I said, sighing as I bent to get him under the arms.

"Ye canna be doing that, Mrs. Fraser!" Mrs. Bug was scandalized. "Himself was verra fierce about it; ye mustna be troubled by this scoundrel, he said, nor even catch sight of the man!"

"Well, I'm afraid it's a bit late not to catch sight of him," I said, tugging at the inert body. "We can't just let him lie on the porch, can we? Help me!"

Mrs. Bug appeared to see no good reason why Mr. Brown ought *not* to continue lying on the porch, but when Malva—who had been pressed flat against the wall, wide-eyed, during the uproar—came to help, Mrs. Bug gave in with a sigh, laying down her weapon and lending a hand.

He had recovered consciousness by the time we got him man-handled onto the surgery table, and was moaning, "Don't let him kill me . . . please don't let him kill me!"

"Would you be quiet?" I said, thoroughly irritated. "Let me look at your leg."

No one had improved on my original rough splinting job, and his journey from the Bugs' cabin hadn't done it any good; blood was seeping through the bandages. I was frankly amazed that he had made it, considering his other injuries. His flesh was clammy and his breath shallow, but he wasn't badly fevered.

"Will you bring me some hot water, please, Mrs. Bug?" I asked, gingerly prodding the fractured limb. "And perhaps a little whisky? He'll need something for shock."

"I will not," Mrs. Bug said, giving the patient a look of intense dislike. "We should just be saving Mr. Fraser the trouble of dealing wi' the gobshite, if he hasna got the courtesy to die by himself." She was still holding her mallet, and raised it in a threatening manner, causing Mr. Brown to cower and cry out, as the movement hurt his broken wrist.

"I'll fetch the water," Malva said, and disappeared.

Ignoring my attempts to deal with his injuries, Mr. Brown seized my wrist with his one good hand, his grip surprisingly strong.

"Don't let him kill me," he said hoarsely, fixing me with bloodshot eyes. "Please, I beg you!"

I hesitated. I hadn't exactly forgotten Mr. Brown's existence, but I had more or less suppressed the knowledge of it over the last day or so. I had been only too glad not to think of him.

He saw my hesitation, and licked his lips, trying again.

"Save me, Mrs. Fraser—I implore you! You are the only one he will listen to!"

With some difficulty, I detached his hand from my wrist.

"Why, exactly, do you think anyone wants to kill you?" I asked carefully.

Brown didn't laugh, but his mouth twisted bitterly at that.

"He says that he will. I don't doubt him." He seemed a little calmer now, and took a deep, shuddering breath. "Please, Mrs. Fraser," he said more softly. "I beg you—save me."

I glanced up at Mrs. Bug, and read the truth in her folded arms and tight lips. She knew.

At this point, Malva hurried in, a beaker of hot water in one hand, the whisky jug in the other.

"What shall I do?" she asked breathlessly.

"Er . . . in the cupboard," I said, trying to focus my mind. "Do you know what comfrey looks like—boneset?" I had hold of Brown's wrist, automatically checking his pulse. It was galloping.

"Aye, ma'am. Shall I put some to steep, then?" She had set down the jug and beaker and was already hunting through the cupboard.

I met Brown's eyes, trying for dispassion.

"You would have killed me, if you could," I said very quietly. My own pulse was going nearly as fast as his.

"No," he said, but his eyes slid away from mine. Only a fraction, but away. "No, I never would!"

"You told H-Hodgepile to kill me." My voice shook on the name and a flush of anger burgeoned suddenly inside me. "You know you did!"

His left wrist was likely broken, and no one had set it; the flesh was puffy, dark with bruising. Even so, he pressed his free hand over mine, urgent with the need to convince me. The smell of him was rank, hot, and feral, like—

I ripped my hand free, revulsion crawling over my skin like a swarm of centipedes. I rubbed my palm hard on my apron, trying not to throw up.

It hadn't been him. I knew that much. Of all the men, it

couldn't have been him; he had broken his leg in the afternoon. There was no way in which he could have been that heavy, inexorable presence in the night, shoving, stinking. And yet I felt he was, and swallowed bile, my head going suddenly light.

"Mrs. Fraser? Mrs. Fraser!" Malva and Mrs. Bug both spoke together, and before I knew quite what was happening, Mrs. Bug had eased me onto a stool, holding me upright, and Malva was pressing a cup of whisky urgently against my mouth.

I drank, eyes closed, trying to lose myself momentarily in the clean, pungent scent and the searing taste of it.

I remembered Jamie's fury, the night he had brought me home. Had Brown been in the room with us then, there was no doubt he would have killed the man. Would he do so now, in colder blood? I didn't know. Brown clearly thought so.

I could hear Brown crying, a low, hopeless sound. I swallowed the last of the whisky, pushed the cup away, and sat up, opening my eyes. To my vague surprise, I was crying, too.

I stood up, and wiped my face on my apron. It smelled comfortingly of butter and cinnamon and fresh applesauce, and the scent of it calmed my nausea.

"The tea's ready, Mrs. Fraser," Malva whispered, touching my sleeve. Her eyes were fixed on Brown, huddled miserably on the table. "Will ye drink it?"

"No," I said. "Give it to him. Then fetch me some bandages—and go home."

I had no idea what Jamie meant to do; I had no idea what I might do, when I discovered his intent. I didn't know what to think, or how to feel. The only thing I did know for certain was that I had an injured man before me. For the moment, that would have to be enough.

FOR A LITTLE WHILE, I managed to forget who he was. Forbidding him to speak, I gritted my teeth and became absorbed in the tasks before me. He sniveled, but kept still. I cleaned, bandaged, tidied, administering impersonal comfort. But as the tasks ended, I was still left with the man, and was conscious of increasing distaste each time I touched him.

At last, I was finished, and went to wash, meticulously

wiping my hands with a cloth soaked in turpentine and alcohol, cleaning under each fingernail despite the soreness. I was, I realized, behaving as though he harbored some vile contagion. But I couldn't stop myself.

Lionel Brown watched me apprehensively.

"What d'ye mean to do?"

"I haven't decided yet." This was more or less true. It hadn't been a process of conscious decision, though my course of action—or lack of it—had been determined. Jamie—damn him—had been right. I saw no reason to tell Lionel Brown that, though. Not yet.

He was opening his mouth, no doubt to plead with me further, but I stopped him with a sharp gesture.

"There was a man with you named Donner. What do you know about him?"

Whatever he'd expected, it wasn't that. His mouth hung open a little.

"Donner?" he repeated, looking uncertain.

"Don't dare to tell me you don't remember him," I said, my agitation making me sound fierce.

"Oh, no, ma'am," he assured me hastily. "I recall him fine—just fine! What"—his tongue touched the raw corner of his mouth—"what d'ye want to know about him?"

The main thing I wanted to know was whether he was dead or not, but Brown almost certainly didn't know that.

"Let's start with his full name," I proposed, sitting down gingerly beside him, "and go from there."

In the event, Brown knew little more for sure about Donner *than* his name—which, he said, was Wendigo.

"What?" I said incredulously, but Brown appeared to find nothing odd in it.

"That's what he said it was," he said, sounding hurt that I should doubt him. "Indian, in't it?"

It was. It was, to be precise, the name of a monster from the mythology of some northern tribe—I couldn't recall which. Brianna's high-school class had once done a unit of Native American myths, with each child undertaking to explain and illustrate a particular story. Bree had done the Wendigo.

I recalled it only because of the accompanying picture she had drawn, which had stuck with me for some time. Done in a reverse technique, the basic drawing done in white crayon, showing through an overlay of charcoal. Trees, lashing to and fro in a swirl of snow and wind, leaf-stripped and needle-flying, the spaces between them part of the night. The picture had a sense of urgency about it, wildness and movement. It took several moments of looking at it before one glimpsed the face amid the branches. I had actually yelped and dropped the paper when I saw it—much to Bree's gratification.

"I daresay," I said, firmly suppressing the memory of the Wendigo's face. "Where did he come from? Did he live in Brownsville?"

He had stayed in Brownsville, but only for a few weeks. Hodgepile had brought him from somewhere, along with his other men. Brown had taken no notice of him; he caused no trouble.

"He stayed with the widow Baudry," Brown said, sounding suddenly hopeful. "Might be he told her something of himself. I could find out for you. When I go home." He gave me a look of what I assumed he meant to be doglike trust, but which looked more like a dying newt.

"Hmm," I said, giving him a look of extreme skepticism. "We'll see about that."

He licked his lips, trying to look pitiful.

"Could I maybe have some water, ma'am?"

I didn't suppose I could let him die of thirst, but I had had quite enough of ministering to the man personally. I wanted him out of my surgery and out of my sight, as soon as possible. I nodded brusquely and stepped into the hall, calling for Mrs. Bug to bring some water.

The afternoon was warm, and I was feeling unpleasantly prickly after working on Lionel Brown. Without warning, a flush of heat rose suddenly upward through my chest and neck and flowed like hot wax over my face, so that sweat popped out behind my ears. Murmuring an excuse, I left the patient to Mrs. Bug, and hurried out into the welcome air.

There was a well outside; no more than a shallow pit, neatly edged with stones. A big gourd dipper was wedged between two of the stones; I pulled it out and, kneeling, scooped up enough water to drink and to splash over my steaming face.

Hot flushes in themselves were not really unpleasant—

rather interesting, in fact, in the same way that pregnancy was; that odd feeling as one's body did something quite unexpected, and not within one's conscious control. I wondered briefly whether men felt that way about erections.

At the moment, a hot flush seemed quite welcome. Surely, I told myself, I couldn't be experiencing hot flushes if I were pregnant. Or could I? I had the uneasy knowledge that the hormonal surges of early pregnancy were quite as capable of causing all kinds of peculiar thermal phenomena as were those of the menopause. I was certainly having the sorts of emotional conniptions that went with being pregnant—or menopausal—or from being raped—

"Don't be ridiculous, Beauchamp," I said out loud. "You know quite well you're not pregnant."

Hearing it gave me an odd feeling—nine parts relief, one part regret. Well, perhaps nine thousand, nine hundred, and ninety-nine parts relief, to one of regret—but it was still there.

The flood of sweat that sometimes followed in the wake of a hot flush, though, was something I could do without. The roots of my hair were soaked, and while the cool water on my face was lovely, waves of heat were still blooming over me, spreading like a clinging veil over chest and face and neck and scalp. Seized by impulse, I tipped half a dipperful of water down the inside of my bodice, exhaling in relief as the wetness soaked the cloth, trickling between my breasts and down over my belly, tickling cool between my legs and dripping to the ground.

I looked a mess, but Mrs. Bug wouldn't mind—and the devil with what bloody Lionel Brown thought. Dabbing at my temples with the end of my apron, I made my way back to the house.

The door stood ajar, as I'd left it. I pushed it open, and the strong pure light of the afternoon shone past me, illuminating Mrs. Bug in the act of pressing a pillow over Lionel Brown's face with all her strength.

I stood blinking for a moment, so surprised that I simply couldn't translate the sight into realization. Then I darted forward with an incoherent cry and grabbed her arm.

She was terribly strong, and so focused on what she was doing that she didn't budge, veins standing out in her forehead and her face nearly purple with effort. I jerked hard on her arm, failed to dislodge her grip, and in desperation shoved her as hard as I could.

She staggered, off-balance, and I snatched the edge of the pillow, yanking it sideways, off Brown's face. She lunged back, intent on completing the job, blunt hands shoving down into the mass of the pillow and disappearing to the wrists.

I drew back a step and flung myself at her bodily. We went over with a crash, hitting the table, upsetting the bench, and ending in a tangle on the floor amid a litter of broken earthenware and the scents of mint tea and a spilled chamber pot.

I rolled, gasped for breath, pain from my cracked ribs paralyzing me for a moment. Then I gritted my teeth, pushing her away and trying to extricate myself from a snarl of skirts—and stumbled to my feet.

His hand hung limp, trailing from the table, and I grabbed his jaw, pulling back his head, and pressed my mouth fervently to his. I blew what little breath I had into him, gasped, and blew again, all the time feeling frantically for some trace of a pulse in his neck.

He was warm, the bones of his jaw, his shoulder felt normal—but his flesh had a terrible slackness, the lips under mine flattening obscenely as I pressed and blew, blood from my split lip splattering everywhere, falling somehow away, so that I was forced to suck frantically to keep them sealed, breathing in hard through the corners of my mouth, fighting my ribs for enough air to blow again.

I felt someone behind me—Mrs. Bug—and kicked out at her. She made an effort to seize my shoulder, but I wrenched aside and her fingers slipped off. I turned round fast and hit her, as hard as I could, in the stomach, and she fell down on the floor with a loud *whoof!* No time to spare for her; I whirled and flung myself once more on Brown.

The chest under my hand rose reassuringly as I blew—but fell abruptly as I stopped. I drew back and pounded hard with both fists, smacking the hard springiness of the sternum with enough force to bruise my own hands further—and Brown's flesh, had he been capable of bruising any longer.

He wasn't. I blew and thumped and blew, until bloody sweat ran down my body in streams and my thighs were slick with it and my ears rang and black spots swam before my eyes with hyperventilating. Finally, I stopped. I stood panting in deep, wheezing gasps, wet hair hanging in my face, my hands throbbing in time to my pounding heart.

The bloody man was dead.

I rubbed my hands on my apron, then used it to wipe my face. My mouth was swollen and tasted of blood; I spat on the floor. I felt quite calm; the air had that peculiar sense of stillness that often accompanies a quiet death. A Carolina wren called in the wood nearby, "Teakettle, teakettle, teakettle!"

I heard a small rustling noise and turned round. Mrs. Bug had righted the bench and sat down on it. She sat hunched forward, hands folded together in her lap, a small frown on her wrinkled round face as she stared intently at the body on the table. Brown's hand hung limp, fingers slightly cupped, holding shadows.

The sheet was stained over his body; that was the source of the chamber pot smell. So, he'd been dead before I began my resuscitation efforts.

Another wave of heat bloomed upward, coating my skin like hot wax. I could smell my own sweat. I closed my eyes briefly, then opened them, and turned back to Mrs. Bug.

"Why on *earth,*" I asked conversationally, "did you do that?"

"SHE'S DONE WHAT?" Jamie stared at me uncomprehendingly, then at Mrs. Bug, who sat at the kitchen table, head bowed, her hands clasped together in front of her.

Not waiting for me to repeat what I'd said, he strode down the hall to the surgery. I heard his footsteps come to a sudden stop. There was an instant's silence, and then a heartfelt Gaelic oath. Mrs. Bug's plump shoulders rose around her ears.

The footsteps came back, more slowly. He came in, and walked to the table where she sat.

"O, woman, how have you dared to lay hands upon a man who was mine?" he asked very softly, in Gaelic.

"Oh, sir," she whispered. She was afraid to look up; she cowered under her cap, her face almost invisible. "I—I didna mean to. Truly, sir!"

Jamie glanced at me.

"She smothered him," I repeated. "With a pillow."

"I think ye do not do such a thing without meaning it," he said, with an edge in his voice that could have sharpened knives. "What were ye about, *a boireannach,* to do it?"

The round shoulders began to quiver with fright.

"Oh, sir, oh, sir! I ken 'twas wrong—only . . . only it was the wicked tongue of him. All the time I had care of him, he'd cower and tremble, aye, when you or the young one came to speak to him, even Arch—but me—" She swallowed, the flesh of her face seeming suddenly loose. "I'm no but a woman, he could speak his mind to me, and he did. Threatening, sir, and cursing most awfully. He said—he said as how his brother would come, him and his men, to free him, and would slaughter us all in our blood and burn the houses over our heids." Her jowls trembled as she spoke, but she found the courage to look up and meet Jamie's eyes.

"I kent ye'd never let that happen, sir, and did my best to pay him no mind. And when he did get under my skin enough, I told him he'd be deid long before his brother heard where he was. But then the wicked wee cur escaped—and I'm sure I've no idea how 'twas done, for I'd have sworn he was in no condition even to rise from the bed, let alone come so far, but he did, and threw himself upon your wife's mercy, and she took him up—I would have dragged his evil carcass away myself, but she wouldna have it—" Here she darted a briefly resentful glance at me, but returned an imploring gaze to Jamie almost at once.

"And she took him to mend, sweet gracious lady that she is, sir—and I could see it in her face, that having tended him so, it was coming to her that she couldna bear to see him killed. And he saw it, too, the gobshite, and when she went out, he jeered at me, saying now he was safe, he'd fooled her into tending him and she'd never let him be killed, and directly he was free of the place, he'd have a score of men down upon us like vengeance itself, and then . . ." She closed her eyes, swaying briefly, and pressed a hand to her chest.

"I couldn't help it, sir," she said very simply. "I really couldn't."

Jamie had been attending to her, a look like thunder on his

brow. At this point, he glanced sharply at me—and evidently saw corroborative evidence upon my own battered features. His lips pressed tight together.

"Go home," he said to Mrs. Bug. "Tell your husband what you have done, and send him to me."

He turned on his heel then, and headed for his study. Not looking at me, Mrs. Bug rose awkwardly to her feet and went out, walking like a blind woman.

"YOU WERE RIGHT. I'm sorry." I stood stiffly in the door of the study, hand on the jamb.

Jamie was sitting with his elbows on his desk, head resting on his hands, but looked up at this, blinking.

"Did I not forbid ye to be sorry, Sassenach?" he said, and gave me a lopsided smile. Then his eyes traveled over me, and a look of concern came over his face.

"Christ, ye look like ye're going to fall down, Claire," he said, getting up hastily. "Come and sit."

He put me in his chair, and hovered over me.

"I'd call Mrs. Bug to bring ye something," he said, "but as I've sent her away . . . shall I bring ye a cup of tea, Sassenach?"

I'd been feeling like crying, but laughed instead, blinking back tears.

"We haven't got any. We haven't had for months. I'm all right. Just rather—rather shocked."

"Aye, I suppose so. Ye're bleeding a bit." He pulled a crumpled handkerchief from his pocket and, bending over, dabbed my mouth, his brows drawn together in an anxious frown.

I sat still and let him, fighting a sudden wave of exhaustion. All at once, I wanted nothing save to lie down, go to sleep, and never wake up again. And if I did wake up, I wanted the dead man in my surgery to be gone. I also wanted the house not to be burned over our heads.

But it isn't time, I thought suddenly, and found that thought—idiotic as it was—obscurely comforting.

"Will it make things harder for you?" I asked, struggling to fight off the weariness and think sensibly. "With Richard Brown?"

"I dinna ken," he admitted. "I've been trying to think. I could wish we were in Scotland," he said a little ruefully. "I'd ken better what Brown might do, were he a Scotsman."

"Oh, really? Say you were dealing with your uncle Colum, for instance," I suggested. "What would he do, do you think?"

"Try to kill me and get his brother back," he replied promptly. "If he kent I had him. And if your Donner *did* go back to Brownsville—Richard knows by now."

He was entirely right, and the knowledge made small fingers of apprehension creep briskly up my back.

The worry evidently showed on my face, for he smiled a little.

"Dinna fash yourself, Sassenach," he said. "The Lindsay brothers left for Brownsville the morning after we came back. Kenny's keeping an eye on the town, and Evan and Murdo are waiting at points along the road, with fresh horses. If Richard Brown and his bloody Committee of Safety should come this way, we'll hear of it in good time."

That was reassuring, and I sat up a little straighter.

"That's good. But—even if Donner did go back, he wouldn't know that you had Lionel Brown captive; you might have killed him d-during the fight."

He flicked a narrow blue glance at me, but merely nodded.

"I could wish I had," he said with a slight grimace. "It would have saved trouble. But then—I'd not have found out what they were doing, and I did need to know that. If Donner's gone back, though, he'll ha' told Richard Brown what happened, and led them back to claim the bodies. He'll see his brother's no among them."

"Whereupon he'll draw the logical conclusion and come here looking for him."

The sound of the back door opening at this point made me jump, heart pounding, but it was succeeded by the soft shuffle of moccasined feet in the hall, announcing Young Ian, who peered inquiringly into the study.

"I've just met Mrs. Bug, hurrying off to her house," he said, frowning. "She wouldna stop and speak to me, and she looked verra queer indeed. What's amiss?"

"What isn't?" I said, and laughed, causing him to glance sharply at me.

Jamie sighed.

"Sit," he said, pushing a stool toward Ian with one foot. "And I'll tell ye."

Ian listened with great attention, though his mouth fell open a little when Jamie reached the point about Mrs. Bug putting the pillow over Brown's face.

"Is he still there?" he asked, at the end of the tale. He hunched a little, looking suspiciously back over his shoulder, as though expecting Brown to come through the surgery door at any moment.

"Well, I hardly think he's going anywhere under his own steam," I observed tartly.

Ian nodded, but got up to look anyway. He came back in a moment, looking thoughtful.

"He's no marks on him," he said to Jamie, sitting down.

Jamie nodded. "Aye, and he's freshly bandaged. Your auntie had just tended him."

They exchanged nods, both obviously thinking the same thing.

"Ye canna tell by looking that he's been killed, Auntie," Ian explained, seeing that I was not yet on their wavelength. "He might have died of himself."

"I suppose you could say that he *did.* If he hadn't tried to terrorize Mrs. Bug . . ." I rubbed a hand—gently—over my forehead, where a headache was beginning to throb.

"How do ye feel—" Ian began, in a worried tone, but I had quite suddenly had more than enough of people asking me how I felt.

"I scarcely know," I said abruptly, dropping my hand. I looked down at my fists, curled in my lap.

"He—he wasn't a *wicked* man, I don't think," I said. There was a splotch of blood on my apron. I didn't know whether it was his or mine. "Just . . . terribly weak."

"Better off dead then," said Jamie matter-of-factly, and without any particular malice. Ian nodded in agreement.

"Well, so." Jamie returned to the point of the discussion. "I was just saying to your auntie, if Brown were a Scot, I should better know how to deal with him—but then it struck me, that while he isna Scottish, he *is* by way of doing business in a

Scottish manner. Him and his committee. They're like a Watch."

Ian nodded, sketchy brows raised.

"So they are." He looked interested. "I've never seen one, but Mam told me—about the one that arrested you, Uncle Jamie, and how she and Auntie Claire went after them." He grinned at me, his gaunt face suddenly transforming to show a hint of the boy he'd been.

"Well, I was younger then," I said. "And braver."

Jamie made a small noise in his throat that might have been amusement.

"They're no verra thrifty about it," he said. "Killing and burning, I mean—"

"As opposed to ongoing extortion." I was beginning to see where he was going with this. Ian had been born after Culloden; he'd never seen a Watch, one of those organized bands of armed men that rode the country, charging fees from the Highland chiefs to protect tenants, land, and cattle—and if the black rent they charged was not paid, promptly seizing goods and cattle themselves. I had. And in all truth, I'd heard of them burning and killing now and then, too—though generally only to create an example and improve cooperation.

Jamie nodded. "Well, Brown's no Scot, as I said. But business is business, isn't it?" A contemplative look had come over his face, and he leaned back a little, hands linked over one knee. "How fast can ye get to Anidonau Nuya, Ian?"

AFTER IAN LEFT, we stayed in the study. The situation in my surgery would have to be dealt with, but I was not quite ready yet to go and face it. Beyond a minor remark to the effect that it was a pity he had not yet had time to build an icehouse, Jamie made no reference to it, either.

"Poor old Mrs. Bug," I said, beginning to get a grip. "I'd no idea he'd been playing on her that way. He must have thought she was a soft touch." I laughed weakly. "*That* was a mistake. She's terribly strong. I was amazed."

I shouldn't have been; I'd seen Mrs. Bug walk for a mile

with a full-grown goat across her shoulders—but somehow one never translates the strength required for daily farm life into a capacity for homicidal fury.

"So was I," Jamie said dryly. "Not that she was strong enough to do it, but that she dared take matters into her own hands. Why did she no tell Arch, if not myself?"

"I suppose it's what she said—she thought it wasn't her place to say anything; you'd given her the job of looking after him, and she'd move heaven and earth to do anything you asked. I daresay she thought she was coping well enough, but when he showed up that way, she . . . just snapped. It does happen; I've seen it."

"So have I," he muttered. A small frown had formed, deepening the crease between his brows, and I wondered what violent incidents he might be recalling. "But I shouldna have thought . . ."

Arch Bug came in so quietly that I didn't hear him; I only realized that he was there when I saw Jamie look up, stiffening. I whirled about, and saw the ax in Arch's hand. I opened my mouth to speak, but he strode toward Jamie, taking no notice of his surroundings. Clearly, for him, there was no one in the room save Jamie.

He reached the desk and laid the ax upon it, almost gently.

"My life for hers, O, chieftain," he said quietly in Gaelic. He stepped back then, and knelt, head bowed. He had braided his soft white hair in a narrow plait and bound it up, so that the back of his neck was left bare. It was walnut-brown and deeply seamed from weather, but still thick and muscular above the white band of his collar.

A tiny noise from the door made me turn from the scene, riveting as it was. Mrs. Bug was there, clinging to the jamb for support, and in obvious need of it. Her cap was askew, and sweaty strands of iron-gray hair stuck to a face the color of cream gone bad.

Her eyes flickered to me when I moved, but then shot back to fix again upon her kneeling husband—and on Jamie, who was now standing, looking from Arch to his wife, then back again. He rubbed a finger slowly up and down the bridge of his nose, eyeing Arch.

"Oh, aye," he said mildly. "I'm to take your head, am I?

Here in my own room and have your wife mop up the blood, or shall I do it in the dooryard, and nail ye up by the hair over my lintel as a warning to Richard Brown? Get up, ye auld fraudster."

Everything in the room was frozen for an instant—long enough for me to notice the tiny black mole in the exact middle of Arch's neck—and then the old man rose, very slowly.

"It is your right," he said, in Gaelic. "I am your tacksman, *a ceann-cinnidh,* I swear by my iron; it is your right." He stood very straight, but his eyes were hooded, fixed on the desk where his ax lay, the sharpened edge a silver line against the dull gray metal of the head.

Jamie drew breath to reply, but then stopped, eyeing the old man narrowly. Something changed in him, some awareness taking hold.

"A ceann-cinnidh?" he said, and Arch Bug nodded, silent.

The air of the room had thickened in a heartbeat, and the hairs prickled on the back of my own neck.

"A ceann-cinnidh," Arch had said. O, chieftain. One word, and we stood in Scotland. It was easy to see the difference in attitude between Jamie's new tenants and his Ardsmuir men—the difference of a loyalty of agreement and one of acknowledgment. This was different still: an older allegiance, which had ruled the Highlands for a thousand years. The oath of blood and iron.

I saw Jamie weigh the present and the past and realize where Arch Bug stood between them. I saw it in his face, exasperation changing to realization—and saw his shoulders drop a little, in acceptance.

"By your word, then, it is my right," he said softly, also in Gaelic. He drew himself up, picked up the ax, and held it out, handle first. "And by that right, I give you back your woman's life—and your own."

Mrs. Bug let out a small sobbing breath. Arch didn't look round at her, but reached out and took the ax, with a grave inclination of the head. He turned then, and walked out without a further word—though I saw the fingers of his maimed hand brush his wife's sleeve, very softly, in passing.

Mrs. Bug straightened herself, hastily tucking up the straggling bits of hair with trembling fingers. Jamie didn't look at her, but sat down again, and took up his quill and a sheet of paper, though I thought he had no intention of writing anything. Not wanting to embarrass her, I affected great interest in the bookshelf, picking up Jamie's little cherrywood snake as though to examine it more closely.

Cap on straight now, she came into the room, and bobbed a curtsy in front of him.

"Will I fetch ye a bit to eat, sir? There's bannocks made fresh." She spoke with great dignity, head upright. He raised his own head from his paper, and smiled at her.

"I should like that," he said. *"Gun robh math agaibh, a nighean."*

She nodded smartly and turned on her heel. At the door, though, she paused, looking back. Jamie raised his brows.

"I was there, ken," she said, fixing him with a direct look. "When the Sassenachs killed your grandsire, there on Tower Hill. There was a lot of blood." She pursed her lips, examining him through narrowed, reddened eyes, then relaxed.

"Ye're a credit to him," she said, and was gone in a whisk of petticoats and apron strings.

Jamie looked at me in surprise, and I shrugged.

"It wasn't necessarily a compliment, you know," I said, and his shoulders began to shake in silent laughter.

"I know," he said at last, and swiped a knuckle beneath his nose. "D'ye ken, Sassenach—sometimes I mourn the auld bastard?" He shook his head. "Sometime I must ask Mrs. Bug if it's true what he said, at the last. What they say he said, I mean."

"What's that?"

"He gave the headsman his fee, and told him to do a good job—'For I shall be very angry indeed if ye don't.'"

"Well, it certainly sounds like something he *would* say," I said, smiling a little. "What do you suppose the Bugs were doing in London?"

He shook his head again, and turned his face to me, lifting his chin so the sun from the window glimmered like water along his jaw and cheekbone.

"God knows. D'ye think she's right, Sassenach? About me being like him?"

"Not to look at," I said, smiling a little. The late Simon,

Lord Lovat, had been short and squat, though powerfully built despite his age. He had also borne a strong resemblance to a malevolent—but very clever—toad.

"No," Jamie agreed. "Thank God. But otherwise?" The light of humor was still in his eyes, but he was serious; he truly wanted to know.

I studied him thoughtfully. There was no trace of the Old Fox in his bold, clean-cut features—those had come mostly from his mother's MacKenzie side—nor yet in the broad-shouldered height of him, but somewhere behind those slanted dark blue eyes, I now and then sensed a faint echo of Lord Lovat's deep-set gaze, glittering with interest and sardonic humor.

"You have something of him," I admitted. "More than a little, sometimes. You haven't the overweening ambition, but . . ." I squinted a bit, considering. "I was going to say that you aren't as ruthless as him," I went on slowly, "but you are, really."

"Am I, then?" He didn't seem either surprised or put out to hear this.

"You can be," I said, and felt somewhere in the marrow of my bones the popping sound of Arvin Hodgepile's neck breaking. It was a warm afternoon, but gooseflesh rippled suddenly up my arms, and then was gone.

"Have I the devious nature, d'ye think?" he asked seriously.

"I don't know, quite," I said with some dubiousness. "You're not a proper twister like he was—but that may be only because you've a sense of honor that he lacked. You don't use people like he did."

He smiled at that, but with less real humor than he'd shown before.

"Oh, but I do, Sassenach," he said. "It's only I try not to let it show."

He sat for a moment, his gaze fixed on the little cherry-wood snake that I held, but I didn't think he was looking at it. At last, he shook his head and looked up at me, the corner of his mouth tucking wryly in.

"If there is a heaven, and my grandsire's in it—and I take leave to doubt that last—he's laughing his wicked auld head off now. Or he would be, if it weren't tucked underneath his arm."

34

THE EXHIBITS IN THE CASE

AND SO IT WAS that several days later, we rode into Brownsville. Jamie, in full Highland regalia, with Hector Cameron's gold-knurled dirk at his waist and a hawk's feather in his bonnet. On Gideon, who had his ears laid back and blood in his eye, as usual.

By his side, Bird-who-sings-in-the-morning, peace chief of the Snowbird Cherokee. Bird, Ian told me, was from the Long Hair clan, and looked it. His hair was not only long and glossily anointed with bear fat, but most resplendently dressed, with a high tail twisted up from the crown of his head and dropping down his back, ending in a dozen tiny braids decorated—like the rest of his costume—with wampum shell beads, glass beads, small brass bells, parakeet feathers, and a Chinese yen; God knew where he'd got that. Slung by his saddle, his newest and most prized possession—Jamie's rifle.

By Jamie's other side, me—Exhibit A. On my mule Clarence, dressed and cloaked in indigo wool—which played up the paleness of my skin and beautifully highlighted the yellow and green of the healing bruises on my face—with my necklace of freshwater pearls about my neck for moral support.

Ian rode behind us with the two braves Bird had brought as retinue, looking more like an Indian than a Scot, with the semicircles of tattooed dots that swooped across his tanned cheekbones, and his own long brown hair greased back from his face and tied in a knot, a single turkey quill thrust through it. At least he hadn't plucked his scalp in the Mohawk fashion; he looked sufficiently menacing without that.

And on a travois behind Ian's horse rode Exhibit B—the corpse of Lionel Brown. We'd put him in the springhouse to keep cool with the butter and eggs, and Bree and Malva had done their best, packing the body with moss to absorb liquids, adding as many strongly aromatic herbs as they could find, then wrapping the unsavory package in a deer's hide, bound with rawhide strips in the Indian fashion. Despite this attention, none of the horses was enthusiastic about being anywhere near it, but Ian's mount was grimly acquiescent, merely snorting loudly every few minutes and shaking his head so his harness rattled, a lugubrious counterpoint to the soft thump of hooves.

We didn't talk much.

Visitors to any mountain settlement were cause for public notice and comment. Our little entourage brought folk popping out of their houses like winkles on pins, mouths agape. By the time we reached Richard Brown's house, which doubled as the local tavern, we had a small band of followers, mostly men and boys.

The sound of our arrival brought a woman—Mrs. Brown, I recognized her—out onto the crudely built stoop. Her hand flew to her mouth, and she rushed back into the house.

We waited in silence. It was a cool, bright autumn day, and the breeze stirred the hair on my neck; I'd worn it pulled back, at Jamie's request, and wore no cap. My face was exposed, the truth written on it.

Did they know? Feeling strangely remote, as though I watched from somewhere outside my own body, I looked from face to face among the crowd.

They couldn't know. Jamie had assured me of it; I knew it, myself. Unless Donner had escaped, and come to tell them all that had happened during that final night. But he hadn't. If he had, Richard Brown would have come to us.

All they knew was what showed on my face. And that was too much.

Clarence felt the hysteria that quivered under my skin like a pool of mercury; he stamped, once, and shook his head as though wanting to dislodge flies in his ears.

The door opened, and Richard Brown came out. There were several men behind him, all armed.

Brown was pale, unkempt, with a sprouting beard and greasy hair. His eyes were red and bleared, and a miasma of beer seemed to surround him. He'd been drinking heavily, and was plainly trying to pull himself together enough to deal with whatever threat we represented.

"Fraser," he said, and stopped, blinking.

"Mr. Brown." Jamie nudged Gideon closer, so he was at eye level with the men on the porch, no more than six feet from Richard Brown.

"Ten days past," Jamie said levelly, "a band of men came upon my land. They stole my property, assaulted my daughter who is with child, burnt my malting shed, destroyed my grain, and abducted and abused my wife."

Half the men had been staring at me already; now all of them were. I heard the small, metallic click of a pistol being cocked. I kept my face immobile, my hands steady on the reins, my eyes fixed on Richard Brown's face.

Brown's mouth began to work, but before he could speak, Jamie raised a hand, commanding silence.

"I followed them, with my men, and killed them," he said, in the same level tone. "I found your brother with them. I took him captive, but did not slay him."

There was a general intake of breath, and uneasy murmurs from the crowd behind us. Richard Brown's eyes darted to the bundle on the travois, and his face went white under the scabby beard.

"You—" he croaked. "Nelly?"

This was my cue. I took a deep breath and nudged Clarence forward.

"Your brother suffered an accident before my husband found us," I said. My voice was hoarse, but clear enough. I forced more air into it, to be heard by everyone. "He was badly injured in a fall. We tended his injuries. But he died."

Jamie let a moment of stunned silence pass, before continuing.

"We have brought him to you, so that you may bury him." He made a small gesture, and Ian, who had dismounted, cut the ropes that held the travois. He and the two Cherokee pulled it to the porch and left it lying in the rutted road, returning silently to their horses.

Jamie inclined his head sharply, and swung Gideon's head around. Bird followed him, pleasantly impassive as the

Buddha. I didn't know whether he understood enough English to have followed Jamie's speech, but it didn't matter. He understood his role, and had carried it out perfectly.

The Browns might have had a profitable sideline in murder, theft, and slavery, but their chief income lay in trade with the Indians. By his presence at Jamie's side, Bird gave clear warning that the Cherokee regarded their relationship with the King of England and his agent as more important than trade with the Browns. Harm Jamie or his property again, and that profitable connection would be broken.

I didn't know everything Ian had said to Bird, when asking him to come—but I thought it quite likely that there was also an unspoken agreement that no formal inquiry would be made on behalf of the Crown into the fate of any captives who might have passed into Indian hands.

This was, after all, a matter of business.

I kicked Clarence in the ribs and wheeled into place behind Bird, keeping my eyes firmly fixed on the Chinese yen that glinted in the middle of his back, dangling from his hair on a scarlet thread. I had an almost uncontrollable urge to look back, and clenched my hands on the reins, digging my fingernails into my palms.

Was Donner dead, after all? He wasn't among the men with Richard Brown; I'd looked.

I didn't know whether I *wanted* him to be dead. The desire to find out more about him was strong—but the desire to be done with the matter, to leave that night on the mountainside behind once and for all, all witnesses safely consigned to the silence of the grave—that was stronger.

I heard Ian and the two Cherokee come into line behind us, and within moments, we were out of sight of Brownsville, though the scent of beer and chimney smoke lingered in my nostrils. I pushed Clarence up beside Jamie; Bird had fallen back to ride with his men and Ian; they were laughing at something.

"Will this be the end of it?" I asked. My voice felt thin in the cold air, and I wasn't sure he'd heard me. But he did. He shook his head slightly.

"There is never an end to such things," he said quietly. "But we are alive. And that is good."

PART FIVE

Great Unexpectations

35

LAMINARIA

SAFELY RETURNED from Brownsville, I took firm steps to resume normal life. And among these was a visit to Marsali, who had returned from her refuge with the McGillivrays. I'd seen Fergus, who had assured me that she was well recovered from her injuries and feeling well—but I needed to see for myself.

The homestead was in good order, I saw, but showing certain signs of dilapidation; a few shingles had blown off the roof, one corner of the stoop was sagging, and the oiled parchment over the single window had split partway up, the flaw hastily mended with a rag stuffed through the hole. Small things, but things that should be dealt with before the snow came—and it was coming; I could feel the touch of it in the air, the brilliant blue sky of late autumn fading into the hazy gray of oncoming winter.

No one rushed out to meet me, but I knew they were home; there was a cloud of smoke and sparks from the chimney, and I thought tartly that at least Fergus seemed able to provide enough wood for the hearth. I called out a cheery "hallooo!" and pushed open the door.

I had the feeling at once. I didn't trust most of my feelings at the moment, but that one went bone-deep. It's the feeling you have, as a doctor, when you walk into an examination room and *know* that something's very wrong. Before you ask the first question, before you've taken the first vital sign. It doesn't happen often, and you'd rather it never did—but there it is. You know, and there's no way round it.

It was the children that told me, as much as anything else.

Marsali sat by the window, sewing, the two girls playing quietly close by her feet. Germain—uncharacteristically indoors—sat swinging his legs at the table, frowning at a ragged but treasured picture book Jamie had brought him from Cross Creek. They knew, too.

Marsali looked up when I came in, and I saw her face tighten in shock at sight of mine—though it was much better than it had been.

"I'm fine," I said briskly, stopping her exclamation. "Only bruises. How are you, though?"

I set down my bag and cupped my hands round her face, turning it gently to the light. One cheek and ear were badly bruised, and there was a fading knot on her forehead—but she wasn't cut, and her eyes looked back at me, clear and healthy. A good color to her skin, no jaundice, no faint scent of kidney dysfunction.

She's all right. It's the baby, I thought, and dropped my hands to her middle without asking. My heart felt cold as I cupped the bulge and lifted gently. I nearly bit my tongue in surprise when a small knee shifted in answer to my touch.

I was terribly heartened at that; I had thought the child might be dead. A quick glance at Marsali's face muted my relief. She was strained between hope and fear, hoping that I would tell her that what she knew to be true wasn't.

"Has the baby moved very much, these last few days?" I asked, keeping my voice calm as I went about fetching out my stethoscope. I'd had it made by a pewtersmith in Wilmington—a small bell with a flat end piece; primitive, but effective.

"Not so much as he did," Marsali answered, leaning back to let me listen to her stomach. "But they don't, do they, when they're nearly ready to come? Joanie lay like the de—like a millstone, all the night before the waters broke."

"Well, yes, often they do do that," I agreed, ignoring what she'd nearly said. "Resting up, I suppose." She smiled in response, but the smile vanished like a snowflake on a griddle as I leaned close and put my ear to the flattened end of the flared metal tube, the wide, bell-shaped opening over her stomach.

It took some time to pick up the heartbeat, and when I did,

it was unusually slow. It was also skipping beats; the hair on my arms rippled with gooseflesh when I heard it.

I went on with the examination, asking questions, making small jokes, pausing to answer questions from the other children, who were crowding round, stepping on each other's feet and getting in the way—and all the time, my mind was racing, envisioning possibilities, all bad.

The child *was* moving—but wrong. Heartbeat was there—but wrong. Everything about that belly felt *wrong* to me. What was it, though? Umbilical cord around the neck was thoroughly possible, and quite dangerous.

I pushed the smock further back, trying for a better listen, and saw the heavy bruising—ugly splotches of healing green and yellow, a few still with deep red-black centers that bloomed like deadly roses over the curve of her belly. My teeth sank into my lip at sight of them; they'd kicked her, the bastards. A wonder she hadn't miscarried on the spot.

Anger swelled suddenly under my breastbone, a huge, solid thing, pushing hard enough to burst it.

Was she bleeding at all? No. No pain, bar tenderness from the bruises. No cramping. No contractions. Her blood pressure seemed normal, so far as I could tell.

A cord accident was still possible—likely, even. But it could be a partially detached placenta, bleeding into the uterus. A ruptured uterus? Or something rarer—a dead twin, an abnormal growth . . . The only thing I knew for sure was that the child needed to be delivered into the air-breathing world, and as soon as possible.

"Where's Fergus?" I said, still speaking calmly.

"I dinna ken," she said, matching my tone of absolute calm. "He's no been home since the day before yesterday. Dinna put that in your mouth, *a chuisle.*" She lifted a hand toward Félicité, who was gnawing a candle stub, but couldn't reach her.

"Hasn't he? Well, we'll find him." I removed the candle stub; Félicité made no protest, aware that something was going on, but not knowing what. In search of reassurance, she seized her mother's leg and began determinedly trying to climb up into Marsali's nonexistent lap.

"No, *bébé,*" Germain said, and clasped his sister round the waist, dragging her backward. "You come with me, *a piuthar.* Want milkie?" he added, coaxing. "We'll go to the spring-hoose, aye?"

"Want Mama!" Félicité windmilled arms and legs, trying to escape, but Germain hoisted her fat little body into his arms.

"You wee lassies come with me," he said firmly, and trundled awkwardly out the door, Félicité grunting and squirming in his grasp, Joanie scampering at his heels—pausing at the door to look back at Marsali, her big brown eyes wide and scared.

"Go on then, *a muirninn,*" Marsali called, smiling. "Take them to see Mrs. Bug. It will be all right.

"He's a sweet lad, Germain," Marsali murmured, folding her hands across her belly as the smile faded.

"Very sweet," I agreed. "Marsali—"

"I know," she said simply. "Might this one live, d'ye think?" She passed a hand gently over her belly, looking down.

I wasn't at all sure, but the child *was* alive for the moment. I hesitated, turning over possibilities in my mind. Anything I did would entail hideous risk—to her, the child, or both.

Why had I not come sooner? I berated myself for taking Jamie's and then Fergus's word that she was all right, but there was no time for self-reproach—and it might not have mattered, either.

"Can you walk?" I asked. "We'll need to go to the Big House."

"Aye, of course." She rose carefully, holding to my arm. She looked around the cabin, as though memorizing all its homely details, then gave me a sharp, clear glance. "We'll talk on the way."

THERE WERE OPTIONS, most of them horrifying to contemplate. If there was danger of a placental abruption, I *could* do an emergency cesarean and possibly save the child—but Marsali would die. To deliver the child slowly, via induction of labor, was to risk the child, but was much safer for Marsali. Of course—and I kept this thought to myself—

induction of labor raised the risk of hemorrhage. If that happened . . .

I could perhaps stop the bleeding and save Marsali—but would be unable to help the infant, who would likely also be in distress. There *was* the ether . . . a tempting thought, but I reluctantly put it aside. It *was* ether—but I'd not used it, had no clear idea of its concentration or effectiveness, nor did I have anything like an anesthetist's training that would allow me to calculate its effects in such a dicey situation as dangerous childbirth. For a minor operation, I could go slowly, judge the patient's respiration, and simply back off if things seemed to be going wrong. If I were in the middle of a cesarean section and things went pear-shaped, there was no way out.

Marsali seemed preternaturally calm, as though she were listening to what was going on inside rather than to my explanations and speculations. As we came near the Big House, though, we met Young Ian, coming down the hillside with a clutch of dead rabbits, dangling by their ears, and she sharpened to attention.

"Ho, cousin! How is it, then?" he asked cheerfully.

"I need Fergus, Ian," she said without preliminary. "Can ye find him?"

The smile faded from his face as he took in Marsali's paleness, and my support of her.

"Christ, the bairn's coming? But why—" He glanced up the pathway behind us, clearly wondering why we had left Marsali's cabin.

"Go and find Fergus, Ian," I cut in. *"Now."*

"Oh." He swallowed, suddenly looking quite young. "Oh. Aye. I will. Directly!" He began to bound off, then whirled back and thrust the rabbits into my hand. Then he leapt off the path and tore down the hillside, rocketing between trees and vaulting fallen logs. Rollo, not wishing to be left out of anything, flashed past in a gray blur and hurtled down the hillside after his master like a falling rock.

"Don't worry," I said, patting Marsali's arm. "They'll find him."

"Oh, aye," she said, looking after them. "If they shouldna find him in time, though . . ."

"They will," I said firmly. "Come on."

I SENT LIZZIE to find Brianna and Malva Christie—I thought I might well need more hands—and sent Marsali to the kitchen to rest with Mrs. Bug, while I readied the surgery. Fresh bedding and pillows, spread on my examination table. A bed would be better, but I needed to have my equipment to hand.

And the equipment itself: the surgical instruments, carefully hidden beneath a clean towel; the ether mask, lined with fresh thick gauze; the dropping bottle—could I trust Malva to administer the ether, if I had to perform emergency surgery? I thought perhaps I could; the girl was very young, and quite untrained, but she had a remarkable coolness about her, and I knew she wasn't squeamish. I filled the dropping bottle, averting my face from the sweet, thick scent that drifted from the liquid, and put a small twist of cotton in the spout, to keep the ether from evaporating and gassing us all—or catching fire. I glanced hastily at the hearth, but the fire was out.

What if labor was prolonged and then things went wrong—if I had to do this at night, by candlelight? I couldn't; ether was hideously inflammable. I shoved away the mental picture of myself performing an emergency cesarean section in the pitch-dark, by feel.

"If you have a moment to spare, this would be a bloody good time to have a look-in," I muttered, addressing this remark collectively to Saints Bride, Raymond, and Margaret of Antioch, all presumably patrons of childbirth and expectant mothers, plus any guardian angels—mine, Marsali's, or the child's—who might be hovering about in the offing.

Evidently, someone was listening. When I got Marsali boosted up onto the table, I was terribly relieved to find that the cervix had begun to dilate—but there was no sign of bleeding. It didn't remove the risk of hemorrhage, by any means, but it did mean the probability was much lower.

Her blood pressure seemed all right, so far as I could tell by looking at her, and the baby's heartbeat had steadied, though the baby had stopped moving, refusing to respond to pokes and shoves.

"Sound asleep, I expect," I said, smiling at Marsali. "Resting up."

She gave me a tiny smile in return, and turned onto her side, grunting like a hog.

"I could use a bit of a rest, myself, after that walk." She sighed, settling her head into the pillow. Adso, seconding this motion, leapt up onto the table, and curled himself into her breasts, rubbing his face affectionately against her.

I would have slung him out, but Marsali seemed to find some comfort in his presence, scratching his ears until he curled up under her chin, purring madly. Well, I'd delivered children in much less sanitary surroundings, cat notwithstanding, and this was likely to be a slow process; Adso would have decamped long before his presence became a hindrance.

I was feeling a bit more reassured, but not to the point of confidence. That subtle feeling of wrongness was still there. On the way, I'd considered the various options available to me; given the slight dilatation of the cervix and the now-steady heartbeat, I thought we might try the most conservative method of inducing labor, so as not to put undue stress upon mother or child. If emergency intervened . . . well, we'd deal with that when and if we had to.

I only hoped the contents of the jar were usable; I'd never had occasion to open it before. *Laminaria,* said the label, written in Daniel Rawlings's flowing script. It was a small jar of dark green glass, corked tight, and very light. When I opened it, a faint whiff of iodine floated out, but no scent of decay, thank goodness.

Laminaria is seaweed. Dried, it's no more than paper-thin slips of brownish-green. Unlike many dried seaweeds, though, *Laminaria* doesn't crumble easily. And it has a most astonishing capacity to absorb water.

Inserted into the opening of the cervix, it absorbs moisture from the mucous membranes—and swells, slowly forcing the cervix further open as it does so, thus eventually causing labor to start. I'd seen *Laminaria* used, even in my own time, though in modern times it was most frequently employed to assist in expelling a dead child from the uterus. I shoved *that* thought well to the back of my mind, and selected a good piece.

It was a simple thing to do, and once done, nothing to do but wait. And hope. The surgery was very peaceful, full of light and the sounds of barn swallows rustling under the eaves.

"I hope Ian finds Fergus," Marsali said after a period of silence.

"I'm sure he will," I replied, distracted by an attempt to light my small brazier using flint and steel. I should have told Lizzie to have Brianna bring matches. "You said Fergus hadn't been home?"

"No." Her voice sounded muffled, and I looked up to see her head bent over Adso, face hidden in his fur. "I've scarce seen him at all, since . . . since the men came to the malting floor."

"Ah."

I didn't know what to say to this. I hadn't realized that Fergus had made himself scarce—though knowing what I did of eighteenth-century men, I supposed I could see why.

"He's ashamed, the wee French gomerel," Marsali said matter-of-factly, confirming my supposition. She turned her face, one blue eye visible above the curve of Adso's head. "Thinks it was his fault, aye? That I was there, I mean. Thinks if he was better able to provide, I shouldna have had to go and tend the malting."

"Men," I said, shaking my head, and she laughed.

"Aye, men. Not that he'd *say* what the trouble is, o' course. Much better go off and brood about it, and leave me to hame wi' three wild bairns!" She rolled her eyes.

"Aye, well, they do that, men," said Mrs. Bug tolerantly, coming in with a lighted taper. "No sense at all to them, but they mean weel. I heard ye clickin' away with that steel like a deathwatch, Mrs. Claire; why would ye no just come and fetch a bit o' fire like a sensible person?" She touched the taper to the kindling in my brazier, which promptly popped into flame.

"Practice," I said mildly, adding sticks to the infant flame. "I have hopes of eventually learning to light a fire in less than a quarter of an hour."

Marsali and Mrs. Bug snorted in simultaneous derision.

"Bless ye, lamb, a quarter-hour's no time at all! Why, often I've spent an hour and more, trying to catch a spark in damp tinder—in Scotland, 'specially, since nothing's ever dry in the winter there. Whyever d'ye think folk go to such trouble, a-smooring the fire?"

This caused a spirited discussion of the best way in which to smoor a fire for the night, including an argument over the proper blessing to be said while doing so, and this lasted long enough for me to have coaxed the brazier into a decent glow and set a small kettle in it for tea-making. Raspberry-leaf tea would encourage contractions.

Mention of Scotland seemed to have reminded Marsali of something, for she raised herself on one elbow.

"Mother Claire—d'ye think Da would mind, if I was to borrow a sheet of paper and some ink? I'm thinkin' it would be as well if I wrote to my mother."

"I think that would be an excellent idea." I went to fetch paper and ink, heart beating a little faster. Marsali was entirely calm; I wasn't. I'd seen it before, though; I wasn't sure whether it was fatalism, religious faith, or something purely physical—but women giving birth seemed very often to lose any sense of fear or misgiving, turning inward upon themselves and exhibiting an absorption that amounted to indifference—simply because they had no attention to spare for anything beyond the universe bounded by their bellies.

As it was, my lingering sense of dread was muted, and two or three hours passed in quiet peace. Marsali wrote to Laoghaire, but also brief notes to each of her children. "Just in case," she said laconically, handing the folded notes to me to put away. I noticed that she didn't write to Fergus—but her eyes darted toward the door every time there was a sound.

Lizzie returned to report that Brianna was nowhere to be found, but Malva Christie turned up, looking excited, and was promptly put to work, reading aloud from Tobias Smollett's *The Adventures of Peregrine Pickle.*

Jamie came in, covered with road dust, and kissed me on the lips and Marsali on the forehead. He took in the unorthodox situation, and gave me the ghost of a raised eyebrow.

"How is it, then, *a muirninn*?" he asked Marsali.

She made a small face and put her tongue out, and he laughed.

"You haven't seen Fergus anywhere, have you?" I asked.

"Aye, I have," he said, looking slightly surprised. "D'ye want him?" This question was addressed to both Marsali and myself.

"We do," I said firmly. "Where is he?"

"Woolam's Mill. He's been interpreting for a French traveler, an artist come in search of birds."

"Birds, is it?" The notion seemed to affront Mrs. Bug, who put down her knitting and sat up straight. "Our Fergus speaks bird-tongue, does he? Well, ye just go and fetch the mannie this minute. Yon Frenchman can mind his own birds!"

Looking rather taken aback at this vehemence, Jamie allowed me to usher him out into the hallway and as far as the front door. Safely out of earshot, he stopped.

"What's to do wi' the lass?" he demanded, low-voiced, and darted a glance back toward the surgery, where Malva's clear, high voice had taken up her reading again.

I told him, as well as I could.

"It may be nothing; I hope so. But—she wants Fergus. She says he's been keeping away, feeling guilty for what happened at the malting floor."

Jamie nodded.

"Well, aye, he would."

"He would? Why, for heaven's sake?" I demanded in exasperation. "It wasn't *his* fault!"

He gave me a look suggesting that I had missed something patently obvious to the meanest intelligence.

"Ye think that makes a difference? And if the lass should die—or mischief come to the child? Ye think he'd not blame himself?"

"He *shouldn't,*" I said. "But rather obviously he does. You don't—" I stopped short, because in fact he *did.* He'd told me so, very clearly, the night he brought me back.

He saw the memory cross my face, and the hint of a smile, wry and painful, showed in his eyes. He reached out and traced the line of my eyebrow, where a healing gash had split through it.

"Ye think I dinna feel that?" he asked quietly.

I shook my head, not in negation, but in helplessness.

"A man's wife is his to protect," he said simply, and turned away. "I'll go fetch Fergus."

THE LAMINARIA HAD been accomplishing its slow, patient work, and Marsali was beginning to have occasional contractions, though we had not really got down to it, yet. The light was beginning to fade when Jamie arrived with Fergus—and Ian, met on the way.

Fergus was unshaven, covered with dust, and plainly hadn't bathed in days, but Marsali's face lighted like the sun when she saw him. I didn't know what Jamie had told him; he looked grim and worried—but at sight of Marsali, he went to her like an arrow to its target, gathering her to him with such fervor that Malva dropped her book on the floor, staring in astonishment.

I relaxed a little, for the first time since I had entered Marsali's house that morning.

"Well," I said, and took a deep breath. "Perhaps we'll have a little food, shall we?"

I left Fergus and Marsali alone, while the rest of us ate, and returned to the surgery to find them with heads close together, talking quietly. I hated to disturb them, but it was necessary.

On the one hand, the cervix had dilated very appreciably, and there was no sign of abnormal bleeding, which was a tremendous relief. On the other . . . the baby's heartbeat was skipping again. Almost certainly a cord problem, I thought.

I was very conscious of Marsali's eyes, fixed on my face as I listened through my stethoscope, and I exerted every ounce of will in order to let nothing show.

"You're doing very well," I assured her, smoothing tumbled hair off her forehead and smiling into her eyes. "I think perhaps it's time to help things along a little."

There were assorted herbs that could assist labor, but most of them were not things I'd use, were there any danger of hemorrhage. At this point, though, I was uneasy enough to want to get things moving as quickly as possible. Raspberry-leaf tea might be a help without being so strong as to induce major or abrupt contractions. Ought I add blue cohosh? I wondered.

"The babe needs to come quickly," Marsali told Fergus, with every appearance of calm. Obviously, I hadn't been as successful in hiding my concern as I'd thought.

She had her rosary with her, and now wound it round her hand, the cross dangling. "Help me, *mon cher.*"

He lifted the hand with the rosary, and kissed it.

"Oui, chérie." He crossed himself then, and set to work.

Fergus had spent the first ten years of his life in the brothel where he'd been born. Consequently, he knew a great deal more about women—in some ways—than any other man I'd ever met. Even so, I was astonished to see him reach for the strings at the neck of Marsali's shift, and draw it down, exposing her breasts.

Marsali didn't seem at all surprised, merely lying back and turning slightly toward him, the hump of her belly nudging him as she did so.

He knelt on a stool beside the bed, and placing a hand tenderly but absently on the bulge, bent his head toward Marsali's breast, lips slightly pursed. Then he appeared to notice me gaping at him, and glanced up over her belly.

"Oh." He smiled at me. "You have not—well, I suppose you would perhaps not have seen this, milady?"

"I can't say that I have." I was torn between fascination and a feeling that I should avert my eyes. "What . . . ?"

"When the birth pangs are slow to start, suckling the woman's breasts encourages the womb to move, thus to hasten the child," he explained, and brushed a thumb unconsciously over one dark-brown nipple, so that it rose, round and hard as a spring cherry. "In the brothel, if one of *les filles* had a difficulty, sometimes another would do such service for her. I have done it for *ma douce* before—when Félicité came. It helps; you will see."

And without more ado, he cupped the breast in both hands and took the nipple into his mouth, sucking gently, but with great concentration, his eyes closed.

Marsali sighed, and her body seemed to relax in the flowing way that a pregnant woman's does, as though she were suddenly boneless as a stranded jellyfish.

I was more than disconcerted, but I couldn't leave, in case anything drastic should happen.

I hesitated for a moment, then pulled out a stool and sat down on it, trying to be inconspicuous. In fact, though, neither of them appeared to be at all concerned with my presence—if they were even aware of me anymore. I did, however, turn away a little, so as not to stare.

I was both astonished and interested by Fergus's technique. He was entirely right; suckling by an infant does cause the uterus to contract. The midwives I had known at L'Hôpital des Anges in Paris had told me that, too; a newly delivered woman should be handed the child at once to nurse, so that the bleeding would slow. None of them had happened to mention use of the technique as a means of inducing labor, though.

"*In the brothel, if one of* les filles *had a difficulty, sometimes another would do such service for her,*" he'd said.

His mother had been one of *les filles,* though he had never known her. I could imagine a Parisian prostitute, dark-haired, likely young, groaning in labor—and a friend kneeling to suckle her tenderly, cupping tender, swollen breasts and whispering encouragement, as the boisterous noises of satisfied customers echoed through the floors and walls.

Had she died, his mother? In childbirth with him or a subsequent child? Throttled by a drunken client, beaten by the madame's enforcer? Or was it only that she hadn't wanted him, hadn't wished to be responsible for a bastard child, and thus she had left him to the pity of the other women, one of the nameless sons of the street, a child of no one?

Marsali shifted on the bed, and I glanced to see that she was all right. She was. She had only moved in order to put her arms about Fergus's shoulders, bending her head to his. She had left off her cap; her yellow hair was loose, bright against the sleek darkness of his.

"Fergus . . . I think I'm maybe going to die," she whispered, her voice barely audible above the wind in the trees.

He released her nipple, but moved his lips delicately over the surface of her breast, murmuring. "You always think you will die, *p'tite puce,* all women think it."

"Aye, that's because a good many of them *do,* too," she

said a little sharply, and opened her eyes. He smiled, eyes still closed, the tip of his tongue flicking gently against her nipple.

"Not you," he said softly, but with great assurance. He passed his hand over her stomach, first gently, then with more strength. I could see the mound firm itself, suddenly drawing up round and solid. Marsali drew a deep, sudden breath, and Fergus pressed the heel of his hand against the base of the mound, hard against her pubic bone, holding it there until the contraction relaxed.

"Oh," she said, sounding breathless.

"Tu . . . non," he whispered, still more softly. "Not you. I will not let you go."

I curled my hands in the stuff of my skirt. That looked like a nice, solid contraction. Nothing horrible seemed to be happening as a result.

Fergus resumed his work, pausing now and then to murmur something ridiculous to Marsali in French. I got up and sidled cautiously round toward the foot of the bed table. No, nothing untoward. I cast a quick look at the counter, to be sure all was in readiness, and it was.

Perhaps it would be all right. There was a streak of blood on the sheet—but it was only a bit of bloody show, quite normal. There was still the child's worrying heartbeat, the possibility of a cord accident—but I could do nothing about that now. Marsali had made her decision, and it was the right one.

Fergus had resumed his suckling. I stepped quietly out into the hall, and swung the door half-closed, to give them privacy. If she did hemorrhage, I could be with her in a second.

I still had the jar of raspberry leaves in my hand. I supposed I might as well go ahead and make the tea—if only to make myself feel useful!

Not finding his wife at home, old Arch Bug had come up to the house with the children. Félicité and Joan were sound asleep on the settle, and Arch was smoking his pipe by the hearth, blowing smoke rings for a rapt Germain. Meanwhile Jamie, Ian, and Malva Christie seemed to be engaged in an amiable literary argument regarding the merits of Henry Fielding, Tobias Smollett, and . . .

"Ovid?" I said, catching the tail end of one remark. "Really?"

"So long as you are secure you will count many friends," Jamie quoted. *"If your life becomes clouded you will be alone.* D'ye not think that's the case for poor Tom Jones and wee Perry Pickle?"

"But surely true friends wouldnae abandon a man, only because he's in some difficulty!" Malva objected. "What sort of friend is that?"

"Rather the common sort, I'm afraid," I said. "Luckily, there *are* a few of the other kind."

"Aye, there are," Jamie agreed. He smiled at Malva. "Highlanders make the truest friends—if only because they make the worst enemies."

She was slightly pink in the face, but realized that she was being teased.

"Hmp," she said, and lifted her nose in order to look down it. "My faither says Highlanders are such fierce fighters because there's sae little of any value *in* the Highlands, and the worst battles are always fought for the lowest stakes."

Everyone dissolved in laughter at that, and Jamie rose to come to me, leaving Ian and Malva to resume their wrangle.

"How is it wi' the lass?" he asked quietly, dipping up hot water from the kettle for me.

"I'm not sure," I said. "Fergus is . . . er . . . helping her."

Jamie's eyebrows went up.

"How?" he asked. "I didna ken there was much a man had to do wi' that business, once he's got it properly begun."

"Oh, you'd be surprised," I assured him. "*I* certainly was!"

He looked intrigued by this, but was prevented from asking further questions by Mrs. Bug's demand that everyone leave off talking about wretched folk who get up to no good in the pages of books, and come sit down to eat.

I sat down to supper, too, but couldn't really eat, distracted as I was by concern for Marsali. The raspberry-leaf tea had finished steeping as we ate; I poured it out and took it to the surgery—rapping cautiously on the door before entering.

Fergus was flushed and breathless, but bright-eyed. He could not be persuaded to come and eat, insisting that he would stay with Marsali. His efforts were showing fruit; she was having regular contractions now, though still fairly far apart.

"It will be fast, once the waters break," Marsali told me. She was a little flushed, too, with a look of inward listening. "It always is."

I checked the heartbeat again—no great change; still bumpy, but not weakening—and excused myself. Jamie was in his study, across the hall. I went in and sat with him, so as to be handy when needed.

He was writing his usual evening note to his sister, pausing now and then to rub the cramp from his right hand before resuming. Upstairs, Mrs. Bug was putting the children to bed. I could hear Félicité whining, and Germain attempting to sing to her.

Across the hall, small shufflings and murmurings, the shifting of weight and the creak of the table. And in the depths of my inner ear, echoing my own pulse, the soft, rapid beat of a baby's heart.

It could so easily end badly.

"What are ye doing, Sassenach?"

I looked up, startled.

"I'm not doing anything."

"Ye're staring fit to see through the wall, and it doesna seem that ye like what ye're looking at."

"Oh." I dropped my gaze, and realized that I had been pleating and repleating the fabric of my skirt between my fingers; there was a large wrinkled patch in the fawn-colored homespun. "Reliving my failures, I suppose."

He looked at me for a moment, then rose and came behind me, putting his hands on the base of my neck, kneading my shoulders with a strong, warm touch.

"What failures?" he asked.

I closed my eyes and let my head nod forward, trying not to groan with the sensations of pain from knotted muscles and the simultaneous exquisite relief.

"Oh," I said, and sighed. "Patients I couldn't save. Mistakes. Disasters. Accidents. Stillbirths."

That last word hung in the air, and his hands paused in their work for a moment, then resumed more strongly.

"There are times, surely, when there's nothing ye could do? You or anyone. Some things are beyond the power of anyone to make right, aye?"

"*You* never believe that, when it's you," I said. "Why should I?"

He paused in his kneading, and I looked up over my shoulder at him. He opened his mouth to contradict me, then realized that he couldn't. He shook his head, sighed, and resumed.

"Aye, well. I suppose it's true enough," he said, with extreme wryness.

"That what the Greeks called *hubris,* do you think?"

He gave a small snort, which might have been amusement.

"I do. And ye ken where *that* leads."

"To a lonely rock under a burning sun, with a vulture gnawing on your liver," I said, and laughed.

So did Jamie.

"Aye, well, a lonely rock under a burning sun is a verra good place to have company, I should think. And I dinna mean the vulture, either."

His hands gave a final squeeze to my shoulders, but he didn't take them away. I leaned my head back against him, eyes closed, taking comfort in his company.

In the momentary silence, we could hear small sounds across the hall, from the surgery. A muffled grunt from Marsali as a contraction came on, a soft French question from Fergus.

I felt that we really ought not to be listening—but neither of us could think of anything to say, to cover the sounds of their private conversation.

A murmur from Marsali, a pause, then Fergus said something hesitant.

"Aye, like we did before Félicité," came Marsali's voice, muffled, but quite clear.

"*Oui,* but—"

"Put something against the door, then," she said, sounding impatient.

We heard footsteps, and the door to the surgery swung open. Fergus stood there, dark hair disheveled, shirt half-buttoned, and his handsome face deeply flushed under the shadow of beard stubble. He saw us, and the most extraordinary look flitted across his face. Pride, embarrassment, and something indefinably . . . French. He gave Jamie a lopsided smile and a one-shouldered shrug of supreme Gallic insouciance—then firmly shut the door. We heard the grating sounds of a small table being moved, and a small thump as it was shoved against the door.

Jamie and I exchanged looks of bafflement.

Giggles came from behind the closed door, accompanied by a massive creaking and rustling.

"He's no going to—" Jamie began, and stopped abruptly, looking incredulous. "Is he?"

Evidently so, judging from the faint rhythmic creaks that began to be heard from the surgery.

I felt a slight warmth wash through me, along with a mild sense of shock—and a slightly stronger urge to laugh.

"Well . . . er . . . I *have* heard that . . . um . . . it does sometimes seem to bring on labor. If a child was overdue, the *maîtresses sage femme* in Paris would sometimes tell women to get their husbands drunk and . . . er-hmm."

Jamie gave the surgery door a look of disbelief, mingled with grudging respect.

"And him with not even a dram taken. Well, if that's what he's up to, the wee bugger's got balls, I'll say that for him."

Ian, coming down the hall in time to hear this exchange, stopped dead. He listened for a moment to the noises proceeding from the surgery, looked from Jamie and me to the surgery door, back, then shook his head and turned around, going back to the kitchen.

Jamie reached out and gently closed the study door.

Without comment, he sat down again, picked up his pen, and began scratching doggedly away. I went over to the small bookshelf, and stood there staring at the collection of battered spines, taking nothing in.

Old wives' tales were sometimes nothing more than old wives' tales. Sometimes they weren't.

I was seldom troubled by personal recollections while dealing with patients; I had neither time nor attention to spare. At the moment, though, I had much too much of both. And a very vivid memory indeed of the night before Bree's birth.

People often say that women forget what childbirth is like,

because if they remembered, no one would ever do it more than once. Personally, I had no trouble at all remembering.

The sense of massive inertia, particularly. That endless time toward the end, when it seems that it never *will* end, that one is mired in some prehistoric tar pit, every small move a struggle doomed to futility. Every square centimeter of skin stretched as thin as one's temper.

You don't forget. You simply get to the point where you don't care what birth will feel like; anything is better than being pregnant for an instant longer.

I'd reached that point roughly two weeks before my due date. The date came—and passed. A week later, I was in a state of chronic hysteria, if one could be simultaneously hysterical and torpid.

Frank was physically more comfortable than I was, but in terms of nerves, there wasn't much to choose between us. Both of us were terrified—not merely of the birth, but of what might come after. Frank being Frank, he reacted to terror by becoming very quiet, withdrawing into himself, to a place where he could control what was happening, by refusing to let anything in.

But I was in no mood to respect anyone's barriers, and broke down in tears of sheer despair, after being informed by a cheerful obstetrician that I was not dilated at all, and "it might be several days—maybe another week."

Trying to calm me, Frank had resorted to rubbing my feet. Then my back, my neck, my shoulders—anything I would let him touch. And gradually, I had exhausted myself and lain quiet, letting him touch me. And . . . and we were both terrified, and terribly in need of reassurance, and neither of us had any words with which to give it.

And he made love to me, slowly and gently, and we fell asleep in each other's arms—and woke up in a state of panic several hours later when my water broke.

"Claire!" I suppose Jamie had called my name more than once; I had been so lost in memory that I had forgotten entirely where I was.

"What?" I swung round, heart pounding. "Has something happened?"

"No, not yet." He studied me for a moment, brow creased, then got up and came to stand by me.

"Are ye all right, Sassenach?"

"Yes. I—I was just thinking."

"Aye, I saw that," he said dryly. He hesitated, then—as a particularly loud moan came through the door—touched my elbow.

"Are ye afraid?" he said softly. "That ye might be wi' child yourself, I mean?"

"No," I said, and heard the note of desolation in my voice as clearly as he did. "I know I'm not." I looked up at him; his face was blurred by a haze of unshed tears. "I'm sad that I'm not—that I never will be again."

I blinked hard, and saw the same emotions on his face that I felt—relief and regret, mingled in such proportion that it was impossible to say which was foremost. He put his arms round me and I rested my forehead on his chest, thinking what comfort it was to know that I had company on this rock, as well.

We stood quietly for some time, just breathing. Then there came a sudden change in the surreptitious noises in the surgery. There was a small cry of surprise, a louder exclamation in French, and then the sound of feet landing heavily on the floor, together with the unmistakable splash of amniotic fluid.

THINGS DID MOVE quickly. Within an hour, I saw the crowning of a black-fuzzed skull.

"He's got lots of hair," I reported, easing the perineum with oil. "Be careful, don't push too hard! Not yet." I spanned the curve of the emerging skull with my hand. "He's got a really big head."

"I wouldna ever have guessed that," said Marsali, red-faced and panting. "Thank ye for telling me."

I barely had time to laugh, before the head eased neatly out into my hands, facedown. The cord *was* round the neck, but not tightly, thank God! I got a finger under it and eased it free, and didn't have to say, "Push!" before Marsali took a breath that went to China and shot the infant into my middle like a cannonball.

It was like being suddenly handed a greased pig, and I fumbled madly, trying to get the little creature turned upright and see whether he—or she—was breathing.

Meanwhile, there were shrieks of excitement from Malva and Mrs. Bug, and heavy footsteps hastening down the hall from the kitchen.

I found the baby's face, hastily cleared the nostrils and mouth, blew a short puff of air into the mouth, snapped a finger against the sole of one foot. The foot jerked back in reflex, and the mouth opened wide in a lusty howl.

"Bon soir, Monsieur L'Oeuf," I said, checking hastily to be sure that it was indeed *Monsieur.*

"Monsieur?" Fergus's face split in an ears-wide grin.

"Monsieur," I confirmed, and hastily wrapping the baby in a flannel, thrust him into his father's arms while I turned my attention to tying and cutting the cord, then tending to his mother.

His mother, thank God, was doing well. Exhausted and sweat-drenched, but likewise grinning. So was everyone else in the room. The floor was puddled, the bedding soaked, and the atmosphere thick with the fecund scents of birth, but no one seemed to notice in the general excitement.

I kneaded Marsali's belly to encourage the uterus to contract, while Mrs. Bug brought her an enormous mug of beer to drink.

"He's all right?" she said, emerging after thirstily engulfing this. "Truly all right?"

"Well, he's got two arms, two legs, and a head," I said. "I hadn't time to count the fingers and toes."

Fergus laid the baby on the table beside Marsali.

"See for yourself, *ma cher,*" he said. He folded back the blanket. And blinked, then leaned closer, frowning.

Ian and Jamie stopped talking, seeing him.

"Is there something amiss, then?" Ian asked, coming over.

Sudden silence struck the room. Malva glanced from one face to another, bewildered.

"Maman?"

Germain stood in the doorway, swaying sleepily.

"Is he here? *C'est Monsieur?*"

Without waiting for answer or permission, he staggered forward and leaned on the bloodstained bedding, mouth a little open as he stared at his newborn brother.

"He looks funny," he said, and frowned a little. "What's wrong with him?"

Fergus had been standing stock-still, as had we all. At this, he looked down at Germain, then glanced back at the baby, then again to his firstborn son.

"Il est un nain," he said, almost casually. He squeezed Germain's shoulder, hard enough to elicit a yelp of startlement from the boy, then turned suddenly on his heel and went out. I heard the opening of the front door, and a cold draft swept down the hall and through the room.

Il est un nain. He is a dwarf.

Fergus hadn't closed the door, and the wind blew out the candles, leaving us in semidarkness, lit only by the glow of the brazier.

36

WINTER WOLVES

LITTLE HENRI-CHRISTIAN appeared to be perfectly healthy; he was simply a dwarf. He was slightly jaundiced, though, with a faint gold cast to his skin that gave his round cheeks a delicate glow, like the petals of a daffodil. With a slick of black hair across the top of his head, he might have been a Chinese baby—bar the huge, round blue eyes.

In a way, I supposed I should feel grateful to him. Nothing less than the birth of a dwarf could have deflected the attention of the Ridge from me and the events of the past month. As it was, people no longer stared at my healing face or stumbled awkwardly to find something to say to me. They had quite a lot to say—to me, to each other, and not infrequently, to Marsali, if neither Bree nor I was in time to stop them.

I supposed they must be saying the same things to Fergus—if they saw him. He had come back, three days following the baby's birth, silent and dark-faced. He had stayed long enough to assent to Marsali's choice of name, and to have a brief, private conversation with her. Then he had left again.

If she knew where he was, she wasn't saying. For the time being, she and the children remained at the Big House with us. She smiled and paid attention to the other children, as mothers must, though she seemed always to be listening for something that wasn't there. Fergus's footsteps? I wondered.

One good thing: she kept Henri-Christian always close to her, carrying him in a sling, or sitting by her feet in his basket of woven rushes. I'd seen parents who had given birth to children with defects; often, their response was to withdraw, unable to deal with the situation. Marsali dealt with it in the other way, becoming fiercely protective of him.

Visitors came, ostensibly to speak to Jamie about something or to get a bit of a tonic or a salve from me—but really in hopes of catching a glimpse of Henri-Christian. It was no surprise, therefore, that Marsali tensed, clutching Henri-Christian to her bosom, when the back door opened and a shadow fell across the threshold.

She relaxed a little, though, seeing that the visitor was Young Ian.

"Hello, coz," he said, smiling at her. "Are ye well, then, and the bairn, too?"

"Verra well," she said firmly. "Come to visit your new cousin, have ye?" I could see that she eyed him narrowly.

"I have, aye, and brought him a wee present, too." He lifted one big hand, and touched his shirt, which bulged a little with whatever was inside it. "Ye're well, too, I hope, Auntie Claire?"

"Hallo, Ian," I said, getting to my feet and putting aside the shirt I'd been hemming. "Yes, I'm fine. Do you want some beer?" I was grateful to see him; I'd been keeping Marsali company while she sewed—or rather, standing guard over her to repel the less-welcome sort of visitor, while Mrs. Bug was tending to the chickens. But I had a decoction of stinging-nettle brewing in the surgery, and needed to check on it. Ian could be trusted to take care of her.

Leaving them with refreshment, I escaped to my surgery and spent a pleasant quarter of an hour alone with the herbs, decanting infusions and separating a heap of rosemary to dry, surrounded by pungent scent and the peacefulness of plants. Such solitude was hard to come by these days, with children popping up underfoot like mushrooms. Marsali was anxious to go back to her own home, I knew—but I was loath to let her go without Fergus there to provide *some* help.

"Bloody man," I muttered under my breath. "Selfish little beast."

Evidently, I wasn't the only one who thought so. As I came back down the hall, reeking of rosemary and ginseng root, I overheard Marsali expressing a similar opinion to Ian.

"Aye, I ken he's taken back, who wouldna be?" she was saying, her voice full of hurt. "But why must he run awa, and leave us alone? Did ye speak to him, Ian? Did he *say* anything?"

So that was it. Ian had been gone on one of his mysterious journeys; he must have encountered Fergus somewhere, and told Marsali about it.

"Aye," he said, after a moment's hesitation. "Just a bit." I hung back, not wanting to interrupt them, but I could see his face, the ferocity of his tattoos at odds with the sympathy that clouded his eyes. He leaned across the table, holding out his arms. "Can I hold him, coz? Please?"

Marsali's back stiffened with surprise, but she handed over the baby, who squirmed and kicked a little in his wrappings, but quickly settled against Ian's shoulder, making little smacking noises. Ian bent his head, smiling, and brushed his lips across Henri-Christian's big round head.

He said something soft to the baby, in what I thought was Mohawk.

"What's that ye said?" Marsali asked, curious.

"A sort of blessing, ye'd call it." He patted Henri-Christian's back, very softly. "Ye call upon the wind to welcome him, the sky to give him shelter, and the water and the earth to yield him food."

"Oh." Marsali's voice was soft. "That's so nice, Ian." But then she squared her shoulders, unwilling to be distracted. "Ye spoke wi' Fergus, ye said."

Ian nodded, eyes closed. His cheek rested lightly on the baby's head. He didn't speak for a moment, but I saw his throat move, the big Adam's apple bobbing as he swallowed.

"I had a child, cousin," he whispered, so softly that I barely heard him.

Marsali heard him. She froze, the needle she had picked up glinting in her hand. Then, moving very slowly, put it down again.

"Did ye, then?" she said just as softly. And rising, went round the table in a quiet rustle of skirts to sit beside him on the bench, close enough that he could feel her there, and laid a small hand against his elbow.

He didn't open his eyes, but drew breath, and with the baby nestled against his heart, began to talk, in a voice hardly louder than the crackle of the fire.

HE WOKE OUT of sleep, knowing that something was deeply wrong. He rolled toward the back of the bed platform, where his weapons lay at hand, but before he could seize knife or spear, he heard again the sound that must have wakened him. It came from behind him; no more than a slight catch of breath, but he heard both pain and fear in it.

The fire burned very low; he saw no more than the dark top of Wako'teqehsnonhsa's head, a red glow outlining it, and the double mound of shoulder and hip beneath the furs. She didn't move or make the sound again, but something in those still dark curves cleft through his heart like a tomahawk striking home.

He gripped her shoulder fiercely, willing her to be all right. Her bones were small and hard through her flesh. He could find no proper words; all the Kahnyen'kehaka had fled out of his head, and so he spoke in the first words that came to him.

"Lass—love—are ye all right, then? Blessed Michael defend us, are ye well?"

She knew he was there, but didn't turn to him. Something—a strange ripple, like a stone thrown in water—went through her, and the breath caught in her throat again, a small dry sound.

He didn't wait, but scrambled naked from the furs, calling for help. People came tumbling out into the dim light of the longhouse, bulky shapes hurrying toward him in a fog of questions. He couldn't speak; didn't need to. Within moments, Tewaktenyonh was there, her strong old face set in grim calm, and the women of the longhouse rushed past him, pushing him aside as they carried Emily away, wrapped in a deer's hide.

He followed them outside, but they ignored him, disappearing into the women's house at the end of the village. Two or three men came out, looked after them, then shrugged, turned, and went back inside. It was cold, and very late, and plainly women's business.

He went inside himself, after a few moments, but only long enough to pull on a few clothes. He couldn't stay in the longhouse, not with the bed empty of her and smelling of blood. There was blood on his skin as well, but he didn't pause to wash.

Outside, the stars had faded, but the sky was still black. It was bone-cold, and very still.

The hide that hung over the door of his longhouse moved, and Rollo slipped through, gray as a ghost. The big dog extended his paws and stretched, groaning with the stiffness of the hour and the cold. Then he shook his heavy ruff, snorted out a puff of white breath, and ambled slowly to his master's side. He sat down heavily, with a resigned sigh, and leaned against Ian's leg.

Ian stood a moment longer, looking toward the house where his Emily was. His face was hot, fevered with urgency. He burned harsh and bright, like a coal, but he could feel the heat seeping out of him into the cold sky, and his heart turning slowly black. Finally, he slapped his palm against his thigh and turned away into the forest, walking fast, the dog padding big and soundless by his side.

"Hail Mary, full of grace . . ." He paid no attention to where he was going, praying under his breath, but aloud, for the comfort of his own voice in the silent dark.

Ought he to be praying to one of the Mohawk spirits, he wondered? Would they be angry that he spoke to his old God, to God's mother? Might they take revenge for such a slight, on his wife and child?

The child is dead already. He had no notion where that knowledge came from, but he knew it was so, as surely as if someone had spoken the words to him aloud. The knowledge was dispassionate, not yet food for grief; only a fact he knew to be true—and was appalled to know it.

On he went into the woods, walking, then running, slowing only when he must, to draw breath. The air was knife-cold and still, smelling of rot and turpentine, but the trees whispered just a little as he passed. Emily could hear them talk; she knew their secret voices.

"Aye, and what good is that?" he muttered, face turned up to the starless void between the branches. "Ye dinna say anything worth knowing. Ye dinna ken how it is with her now, do ye?"

He could hear the dog's feet now and then, rustling among the dead leaves just behind him, thudding softly on patches of bare ground. He stumbled now and then, feet lost in the darkness, fell once bruisingly, stumbled to his feet, and ran clumsily on. He had stopped praying; his mind wouldn't form words any longer, couldn't choose among the fractured syllables of his different tongues, and his breath burned thick in his throat as he ran.

He felt her body against him in the cold, her full breasts in his hands, her small round buttocks thrusting back, heavy and eager as he rammed her, oh, God, he knew he ought not, he knew! And yet he'd done it, night after night, mad for the slippery tight clutch of her, long past the day when he knew he should stop, selfish, mindless, mad and wicked with lust. . . .

He ran, and her trees murmured condemnation above him as he went.

He had to stop, sobbing for breath. The sky had turned from black to the color that comes before the light. The dog nosed at him, whining softly in his throat, amber eyes gone blank and dark in the no-light of the hour.

Sweat poured down his body under the leather shirt, soaked the draggled breechclout between his legs. His privates were chilled, shriveled against his body, and he could smell himself, a rank, bitter scent of fear and loss.

Rollo's ears pricked, and the dog whined again, moving a step away, back, away again, tail twitching nervously. *Come,* he was saying, as clearly as words. *Come now!*

For himself, Ian could have lain down on the frozen leaves, buried his face in the earth, and stayed. But habit pulled at him; he was accustomed to heed the dog.

"What?" he muttered, dragging a sleeve across his wet face. "What is it, then?"

Rollo growled, deep in his throat. He was standing rigid, the hackles slowly rising on his neck. Ian saw it, and some distant tremor of alarm made itself felt through the fog of exhausted despair. His hand went to his belt, found emptiness there, and slapped at it, unbelieving. Christ, he had not so much as a skinning knife!

Rollo growled again, louder. A warning, meant to be heard. Ian turned, looking, but saw only the dark trunks of cedar and pine, the ground beneath them a mass of shadows, the air between them filled with mist.

A French trader who had come to their fire had called such a time, such a light, *l'heure du loup*—the hour of the wolf. And for good reason: it was a hunting time, when the night grows dim, and the faint breeze that comes before the light begins to rise, carrying the scent of prey.

His hand went to the other side of his belt, where the pouch of *taseng* should hang: bear grease steeped with mint leaves, to hide a man's scent while hunting—or hunted. But that side too was empty, and he felt his heart beat quick and hard, as the cold wind dried the sweat from his body.

Rollo's teeth were bared, the growl a continuous rolling thunder. Ian stooped and seized a fallen pine branch from the ground. It was a good length, though flimsier than he would have liked, and unwieldy, clawed with long twigs.

"Home," he whispered to the dog. He had no notion where he was, or where the village lay, but Rollo did. The dog backed slowly, eyes still fixed on the gray shadows—did they move, those shadows?

He was walking faster now, still backward, feeling the slope of the ground through the soles of his moccasins, sensing Rollo's presence from the rustle of the dog's feet, the faint whine that came now and then behind him. There. Yes, a shadow *had* moved! A gray shape, far away and seen too briefly to recognize, but there all the same—and recognizable by its presence alone.

If there was one, there were more. They did not hunt alone. They weren't near yet, though; he turned, beginning almost to run. Not in panic now, despite the fear in the pit of his stomach. A quick, steady lope, the hill-walker's gait that his uncle had shown him, that would devour the steep, endless miles of the Scottish mountains, steady effort without exhaustion. He must save strength to fight.

He observed that thought with a wry twist of the mouth, snapping off the brittle pine twigs from his club as he went. A moment ago, he had wanted to die, and perhaps he would again, if Emily— But not now. If Emily . . . and besides, there was the dog. Rollo wouldn't leave him; they must defend each other.

There was water near; he heard it gurgling under the wind. But carried on the wind came another sound, a long, unearthly howl that brought the sweat out cold on his face again. Another answered it, to the west. Still far away, but they were hunting now, calling to one another. Her blood was on him.

He turned, seeking the water. It was a small creek, no more than a few feet across. He splashed into it without hesitation, splintering the skin of ice that clung to the banks, feeling the cold bite into his legs and feet as it soaked his leggings and filled his moccasins. He stopped for a split second, pulling off the moccasins, lest they be carried away in the current; Emily had made them for him, of moose hide.

Rollo had crossed the stream in two gigantic bounds, and paused on the opposite bank to shake a freezing spray of water from his coat before going on. He held to the bank, though; Ian stayed in the water, splashing shin-deep, staying as long as might be managed. Wolves hunted by wind as much as by ground scent, but no need to make it easy for them.

He had thrust the wet moccasins down the neck of his shirt, and icy trickles ran down chest and belly, soaking his breechclout. His feet were numb; he couldn't feel the rounded stones of the streambed, but now and then his foot slid on one, slippery with algae, and he lurched and stumbled to keep his balance.

He could hear the wolves more clearly; that was good, though—the wind had changed, was toward him now, carrying their voices. Or was it only that they were closer now?

Closer. Rollo was wild, darting to and fro on the far bank, whining and growling, urging him on with brief yips. A deer's path came down to the stream on that side; he stumbled out of the water onto it, panting and shaking. It took several tries to get the moccasins on again. The soaked leather was stiff, and his hands and feet refused to work. He had to put down his club and use both hands.

He had just managed the second one when Rollo suddenly charged down the bank, roaring a challenge. He whirled on the frozen mud, catching up his club, in time to see a gray shape, nearly Rollo's size, on the far side of the water, its pale eyes startlingly near.

He screeched and flung the club in reflex. It sailed across the stream and struck the ground near the wolf's feet, and the thing vanished as though by magic. He stood stock-still for an instant, staring. He had not imagined it, surely?

No, Rollo was raving, bellowing and teeth bared, flecks of foam flying from his muzzle. There were stones at the stream's edge; Ian seized one, another, scraped up a handful, another, stubbing his fingers in haste on the rocks and frozen soil, holding up the front of his shirt to make a bag.

The more-distant wolf howled again; the near one answered, so close that the hairs rose up straight on the back of his neck. He heaved a rock in the direction of the call, turned, and ran, the bundle of rocks clutched hard against his belly.

The sky had lightened into dawn. Heart and lungs strained for blood and air, and yet it seemed as though he ran so slowly that he floated over the forest floor, passing like a drifting cloud, unable to go faster. He could see each tree, each separate needle of a spruce he passed, short and thick, soft silver-green in the light.

His breath came hard, his vision blurred and cleared, as tears of effort clouded his eyes, were blinked away, welled back again. A tree branch lashed his face and blinded him, the scent of it sharp in his nose.

"Red Cedar, help me!" he gasped, the Kahnyen'kehaka coming to his lips as though he had never spoken English or called upon Christ and His mother.

Behind you. It was a small voice, quiet, perhaps no more than the voice of his own instinct, but he whirled at once, stone in hand, and slung it with all his force. Another, and another, and another, as fast as he could fling. There was a crack, a thump, and a yelp, and Rollo slewed and skidded, eager to turn and attack.

"Come-come-come!" He seized the big dog's ruff as he ran, dragging him round, forcing him along.

He could hear them now, or thought he could. The wind that comes at dawn rustled through the trees, and they whispered overhead, calling him this way, then that, guiding him as he ran. He saw nothing but color, half-blind with effort, but felt their embrace, cool in his mind; a prickling touch of spruce and fir, the skin of white aspen, smooth as a woman's, sticky with blood.

Go here, come this way, he thought he heard, and followed the sound of the wind.

A howl came from behind them, followed by short yips, and another of acknowledgment. Close, too close! He flung stones behind him as he ran, not looking, no time to turn and aim.

Then there were no more stones and he dropped the empty flap of shirt, arms pumping as he ran, a harsh panting in his ears that might have been his own breath, or the dog's—or the sound of the beasts behind him.

How many of them? How far to go? He was beginning to stagger, streaks of black and red shooting through his vision. If the village was not nearby, he had no chance.

He lurched sideways, hit the yielding branch of a tree that bent under his weight, then pushed him upright, setting him roughly back on his feet. He had lost his impetus, though, and his sense of direction.

"Where?" he gasped to the trees. "Which way?"

If there was an answer, he didn't hear it. There was a roar and a thud behind him, a mad scuffle punctuated with the growls and yelps of dogs fighting.

"Rollo!" He turned and flung himself through a growth of dead vines, to find dog and wolf squirming and biting in a writhing ball of fur and flashing teeth.

He dashed forward, kicking and shouting, punching wildly, glad at last to have something to hit, to be fighting back, even if it was the last fight. Something ripped across his leg, but he felt only the jar of impact as he rammed his knee hard into the wolf's side. It squealed and rolled away, rounding on him at once.

It leaped, and its paws struck him in the chest. He fell back, struck his head glancingly on something, lost breath for an instant, and came to himself to find his hand braced beneath the slavering jaws, straining to keep them from his throat.

Rollo sprang onto the wolf's back, and Ian lost his grip, collapsing under the weight of reeking fur and squirming flesh. He flung out a hand, seeking anything—a weapon, a tool, a grip to pull himself free—and gripped something hard.

He wrenched it from its bed in the moss and smashed it against the wolf's head. Fragments of bloody teeth flew through the air and struck his face. He struck again, sobbing, and again.

Rollo was whining, a high keening noise—no, it was him. He bashed the rock down once more on the battered skull, but the wolf had stopped fighting; it lay across his thighs, legs twitching, eyes glazing as it died. He pushed it off in a frenzy of revulsion. Rollo's teeth sank into the wolf's outstretched throat, and ripped it out, in a final spray of blood and warm flesh.

Ian closed his eyes and sat still. It didn't seem possible to move, or to think.

After a time, it seemed possible to open his eyes, and to breathe, at least. There was a large tree at his back; he had fallen against the trunk when the wolf struck him; it supported him now. Among the twisted roots was a muddy hole, from which he had wrenched the stone.

He was still holding the stone; it felt as though it had grown to his skin; he couldn't open his hand. When he looked he saw that this was because the stone had shattered; sharp fragments had cut his hand, and the pieces of the stone were glued to his hand by drying blood. Using the fingers of his other hand, he bent back the clenched fingers, and pushed the broken pieces of the stone off his palm. He scraped moss from the tree roots, made a wad of it in his hand, then let the curled fingers close over it again.

A wolf howled, in the middle distance. Rollo, who had lain down by Ian, lifted his head with a soft *wuff!* The howl came again, and seemed to hold a question, a worried tone.

For the first time, he looked at the body of the wolf. For an instant, he thought it moved, and shook his head to clear his vision. Then he looked again.

It was moving. The distended belly rose gently, subsided. It was full light now, and he could see the tiny nubs of pink nipples, showing through the belly fur. Not a pack. A pair. But a pair no more. The wolf in the distance howled again, and Ian leaned to one side and vomited.

Eats Turtles came upon him a little later, sitting with his back against the red-cedar tree by the dead wolf, Rollo's bulk pressed close against him. Turtle squatted down, a short distance away, balanced on his heels, and watched.

"Good hunting, Wolf's Brother," he said finally, in greeting. Ian felt the knot between his shoulder blades relax just a little. Turtle's voice held a quiet tone, but no sorrow. She lived, then.

"She whose hearth I share," he said, careful to avoid speaking her name. To speak it aloud might expose her to evil spirits nearby. "She is well?"

Turtle closed his eyes and raised both brows and shoulders. She was alive, and not in danger. Still, it was not for a man to say what might happen. Ian didn't mention the child. Neither did Turtle.

Turtle had brought a gun, a bow, and his knife, of course. He took the knife from his belt and handed it to Ian, matter-of-factly.

"You will want the skins," he said. "To wrap your son, when he shall be born."

A shock went through Ian, like the shock of sudden rain on bare skin. Eats Turtles saw his face, and turned his head aside, avoiding his eyes.

"This child was a daughter," Turtle said matter-of-factly. "Tewaktenyonh told my wife, when she came for a rabbit skin to wrap the body."

The muscles in his belly tightened and quivered; he thought that perhaps his own skin would burst, but it didn't. His throat was dry, and he swallowed once, painfully, then shook the moss away and held out his wounded hand for the knife. He bent slowly to skin the wolf.

Eats Turtles was poking with interest at the bloodstained remnants of the shattered stone, when the howl of a wolf brought him upright, staring.

It echoed through the forest, that howl, and the trees moved above them, murmuring uneasily at the sound of loss and desolation. The knife drew swiftly down the pale fur of the belly, dividing the two rows of pink nipples.

"Her husband will be nearby," Wolf's Brother said, not looking up. "Go and kill him."

MARSALI STARED at him, scarcely breathing. The sadness in her eyes was still there, but had somehow diminished, overwhelmed with compassion. The anger had left her; she had taken back Henri-Christian, and held the fat bundle of her baby with both arms against her breast, her cheek against the bold round curve of his head.

"Ah, Ian," she said softly. *"Mo charaid, mo chridhe."*

He sat looking down at his hands, clasped loosely in his lap, and seemed not to have heard her. Finally, though, he stirred, like a statue waking. Without looking up, he reached into his shirt and drew out a small, rolled bundle, bound with hair twine, and decorated with a wampum bead.

He undid this, and leaning over, spread the cured skin of an unborn wolf over the baby's shoulders. His big, bony hand smoothed the pale fur, cupping for a moment over Marsali's hand where it held the child.

"Believe me, cousin," he said, very softly, "your husband grieves. But he will come back." Then he rose and left, silent as an Indian.

37

LE MAÎTRE DES CHAMPIGNONS

THE SMALL LIMESTONE cave we used for a stable was home at the moment only to a nanny goat with two brand-new kids. All the animals born in the spring were now large enough to be turned out to forage in the wood with their mothers. The goat was still getting room service, though, in the form of kitchen scraps and a little cracked corn.

It had been raining for several days, and the morning broke cloudy and damp, every leaf dripping and the air thick with the scents of resin and soggy leaf mulch. Luckily, the cloudiness kept the birds subdued; the jays and mockingbirds were quick to learn, and kept a beady eye on the comings and goings of people with food—they dive-bombed me regularly as I made my way up the hill with my basin.

I was on my guard, but even so, a bold jay dropped from a branch in a flash of blue and landed *in* the basin, startling me. Before I could react, it had seized a fragment of corn muffin and darted off, so quickly that I could scarcely believe I'd seen it, save for the racing of my heart. Luckily I hadn't dropped the basin; I heard a triumphant screech from the trees, and hurried to get inside the stable before the jay's friends should try the same tactic.

I was surprised to find that the Dutch door was unbolted at the top and stood an inch or two ajar. There was no danger of the goats escaping, of course, but foxes and raccoons were more than capable of climbing over the lower door, and so both doors were normally bolted at night. Perhaps Mr. Wemyss had forgotten; it was his job to muck out the used straw and settle the stock for the night.

As soon as I pushed open the door, though, I saw that Mr. Wemyss was not to blame. There was a tremendous rustle of straw at my feet, and something big moved in the darkness.

I uttered a sharp yelp of alarm, and this time *did* drop the basin, which fell with a clang, scattering food across the floor and rousing the nanny goat, who started blatting her head off.

"*Pardon,* milady!"

Hand to my thumping heart, I stepped out of the doorway, so the light fell on Fergus, crouched on the floor, with straws sticking out of his hair like the Madwoman of Chaillot.

"Oh, so there you are," I said quite coldly.

He blinked and swallowed, rubbing his hand over a face dark with sprouting whiskers.

"I—yes," he said. He seemed to have nothing further to add to this. I stood glaring down at him for a moment, then shook my head and stooped to retrieve the potato peelings and other fragments that had fallen from the basin. He moved as though to help me, but I stopped him with a shooing gesture.

He sat still, watching me, hands around his knees. It was dim inside the stable, and water dripped steadily from the plants growing out of the cliffside above, making a curtain of falling drops across the open door.

The goat had stopped making noise, having recognized me, but was now stretching her neck through the railing of her pen, blueberry-colored tongue extended like an anteater's, in an effort to reach an apple core that had rolled near the pen. I picked it up and handed it to her, trying to think where to start, and what to say when I did.

"Henri-Christian's doing well," I said, for lack of anything else. "Putting on weight."

I let the remark trail off, bending over the rail to pour corn and scraps into the wooden feed trough.

Dead silence. I waited a moment, then turned round, one hand on my hip.

"He's a very sweet little baby," I said.

I could hear him breathing, but he said nothing. With an audible snort, I went and pushed the bottom half of the door open wide, so that the cloudy light outside streamed in, exposing Fergus. He sat with his face turned stubbornly away. I could smell him at a goodly distance; he reeked of bitter sweat and hunger.

I sighed.

"Dwarves of this sort have got quite normal intelligence. I've checked him thoroughly, and he has all the usual reflexes and responses that he should have. There's no reason why he can't be educated, be able to work—at something."

"Something," Fergus echoed, the word holding both despair and derision. "Something." At last, he turned his face toward me, and I saw the hollowness of his eyes. "With respect, milady—you have never seen the life of a dwarf."

"And you have?" I asked, not so much in challenge as curiosity.

He closed his eyes against the morning light, nodding.

"Yes," he whispered, and swallowed. "In Paris."

The brothel where he had grown up in Paris was a large one, with a varied clientele, famous for being able to offer something for almost any taste.

"The house itself had *les filles, naturellement,* and *les enfants.* They are of course the bread and butter of the establishment. But there are always those who desire . . . the exotic, and will pay. And so now and then the madame would send for those who dealt in such things. *La Maîtresse des Scorpions—avec les flagellantes, tu comprends? Ou Le Maître des Champignons.*"

"The Master of Mushrooms?" I blurted.

"*Oui*. The Dwarf Master."

His eyes had sunk into his head, his gaze turned inward and his face haggard. He was seeing in memory sights and people who had been absent from his thoughts for many years—and was not enjoying the recollection.

"*Les chanterelles,* we called them," he said softly. "The females. The males, they were *les morels.*" Exotic fungi, valued for the rarity of their twisted shapes, the strange savor of their flesh.

"They were not badly treated, *les champignons,*" he said, abstracted. "They were of value, you see. *Le Maître* would buy such infants from their parents—there was one born in the brothel, once, and the madame was delighted at her good fortune—or collect them from the streets."

He looked down at his hand, the long, delicate fingers moving restlessly, pleating the cloth of his breeches.

"The streets," he repeated. "Those who escaped the brothels—they were beggars. I knew one of them quite well—Luc, he was called. We would sometimes assist each other—" The shadow of a smile touched his mouth, and he waved his intact hand in the deft gesture of one picking pockets.

"But he was alone, Luc," he continued matter-of-factly. "He had no protector. I found him one day in the alley, with his throat cut. I told the madame, and she sent the doorkeep out at once to seize the body, and sold it to a doctor in the next *arrondissement.*"

I didn't ask what the doctor had wanted with Luc's body. I'd seen the broad, dried hands of dwarves, sold for divination and protection. And other parts.

"I begin to see why a brothel might seem safe," I said, swallowing heavily. "But still . . ."

Fergus had been sitting with his head braced on his hand, staring at the straw. At this, he looked up at me.

"I have parted my buttocks for money, milady," he said simply. "And thought nothing of it, save when it hurt. But then I met milord, and found a world beyond the brothel and the streets. That my son might return to such places . . ." He stopped abruptly, unable to speak. He closed his eyes again, and shook his head, slowly.

"Fergus. Fergus, dear. You can't think that Jamie—that we—would ever let such a thing happen," I said, distressed beyond measure.

He drew a deep, trembling breath, and thumbed away the

tears that hung on his lashes. He opened his eyes and gave me a smile of infinite sadness.

"No, you would not, milady. But you will not live forever, nor will milord. Nor I. But the child will be a dwarf forever. And *les petits,* they cannot well defend themselves. They will be plucked up by those who seek them, taken and consumed." He wiped his nose on his sleeve and sat up a little.

"If, that is, they should be so fortunate," he added, his voice hardening. "They are not valued, outside the cities. Peasants, they believe the birth of such a child is at best a judgment on the sins of his parents." A deeper shadow crossed his face, his lips drawing tight. "It may be so. My sins—" But he broke off abruptly, turning away.

"At worst—" His voice was soft, head turned away, as though he whispered secrets to the shadows of the cave. "At worst, they are seen as monstrous, children born of some demon who has lain with the woman. People stone them, burn them—sometimes the woman, too. In the mountain villages of France, a dwarf child would be left for the wolves. But do you not know these things, milady?" he asked, suddenly turning back to face me.

"I—I suppose so," I said, and put out a hand to the wall, suddenly feeling the need of some support. I *had* known such things, in the abstract way one thinks of the customs of aborigines and savages—people whom one will never meet, safely distant in the pages of geography books, of ancient histories.

He was right; I knew it. Mrs. Bug had crossed herself, seeing the child, and then made the sign of the horns as protection from evil, pale horror on her face.

Shocked as we had all been, and then concerned with Marsali, and with Fergus's absence, I hadn't been away from the house for a week or more. I had no idea what people might be saying, on the Ridge. Fergus plainly did.

"They'll . . . get used to him," I said as bravely as I could. "People will see that he isn't a monster. It may take some time, but I promise you, they'll see."

"Will they? And if they let him live, what then will he do?" He rose to his feet quite suddenly. He stretched out his left arm, and with a jerk, freed the leather strip that held his hook.

It fell with a soft thump into the straw, and left the narrow stump of his wrist bare, the pale skin creased with red from the tightness of the wrappings.

"Me, I cannot hunt, cannot do a proper man's work. I am fit for nothing but to pull the plow, like a mule!" His voice shook with anger and self-loathing. "If I cannot work as a man does, how shall a dwarf?"

"Fergus, it isn't—"

"I cannot keep my family! My wife must labor day and night to feed the children, must put herself in the way of scum and filth who misuse her, who— Even if I was in Paris, I am too old and crippled to whore!" He shook the stump at me, face convulsed, then whirled and swung his maimed arm, smashing it against the wall, over and over.

"Fergus!" I seized his other arm, but he jerked away.

"What work will he do?" he cried, tears streaming down his face. "How shall he live? *Mon Dieu! Il est aussi inutile que moi!*"

He bent and seized the hook from the ground, and hurled it as hard as he could at the limestone wall. It made a small chiming sound as it struck, and fell into the straw, startling the nanny and her kids.

Fergus was gone, the Dutch door left swinging. The goat called after him, a long *maaaah!* of disapproval.

I held on to the railing of the pen, feeling as though it was the only solid thing in a slowly tilting world. When I could, I bent and felt carefully in the straw until I touched the metal of the hook, still warm from Fergus's body. I drew it out and wiped bits of straw and manure carefully off it with my apron, still hearing Fergus's last words.

"My God! He is as useless as I am!"

38

A DE'IL IN THE MILK

HENRI-CHRISTIAN'S EYES nearly crossed with the effort of focusing on the yarn bobble Brianna dangled over his face.

"I think his eyes might stay blue," she said, peering thoughtfully at him. "What do you think he's looking at?" He lay in her lap, knees drawn up nearly to his chin, the soft blue eyes in question fixed somewhere far beyond her.

"Oh, the wee ones still see heaven, my Mam said." Marsali was spinning, trying out Brianna's new treadle wheel, but spared a quick glance at her newest son, smiling a little. "Maybe there's an angel sitting on your shoulder, aye? Or a saint who stands behind ye."

That gave her an odd feeling, as though someone *did* stand behind her. Not creepy, though—more a mild, warm sense of reassurance. She opened her mouth to say, "Maybe it's my father," but caught herself in time.

"Who's the patron saint of laundry?" she said instead. "That's who we need." It was raining; it had been raining for days, and small mounds of clothing lay scattered about the room or draped over the furniture: damp things in various states of drying, filthy things destined for the wash cauldron as soon as the weather broke, less-filthy things that might be brushed, shaken, or beaten into another few days' wearing, and an ever-growing pile of things needing mending.

Marsali laughed, deftly feeding thread to the bobbin.

"Ye'd have to ask Da about that. He kens more saints than anybody. This is wonderful, this wheel! I've not seen this kind before. However did ye come to think of such a thing?"

"Oh—saw one somewhere." Bree flicked a hand, dismissing it. She had—in a folk-art museum. Building it had been time-consuming—she'd first had to make a crude lathe, as well as soak and bend the wood for the wheel itself—but not terribly difficult. "Ronnie Sinclair helped a lot; he knows what wood will do and what it won't. I can't believe how good you are at that, and this your first time using one like it."

Marsali snorted, likewise dismissing the compliment.

"I've spun since I was five, *a piuthar.* All that's different here is I can sit while I do it, instead of walking to and fro 'til I fall over wi' tiredness."

Her stockinged feet flickered back and forth under the hem of her dress, working the treadle. It made a pleasant *whish-whir* sound—though this was barely audible over the babble at the other side of the room, where Roger was carving yet another car for the children.

Vrooms were a big hit with the small-fry, and the demand for them unceasing. Brianna watched with amusement as Roger fended off Jem's inquisitiveness with a deft elbow, frowning in concentration. The tip of his tongue showed between his teeth, and wood shavings littered the hearth and his clothes, and—of course—one was stuck in his hair, a pale curl against its darkness.

"What's that one?" she asked, raising her voice to reach him. He looked up, his eyes a mossy green in the dim rain-light from the window behind him.

"I think it's a '57 Chevrolet pickup truck," he said, grinning. "Here, then, *a nighean.* This one's yours." He brushed a last shaving from his creation and handed the blocky thing to Félicité, whose mouth and eyes were round with awe.

"Issa vroom?" she said, clutching it to her bosom. "*My* vroom?"

"It's a druck," Jemmy informed her with kindly condescension. "Daddy says."

"A truck is a vroom," Roger assured Félicité, seeing doubt begin to pucker her forehead. "It's just a bigger kind."

"Issa *big* vroom, see!" Félicité kicked Jem in the shin. He yelped and grabbed for her hair, only to be butted in the stomach by Joan, always there to defend her sister.

Brianna tensed, ready to intervene, but Roger broke up the incipient riot by holding Jem and Félicité each at arm's length, glaring Joan into retreat.

"Right, you lot. No fighting, or we put the vrooms away 'til tomorrow."

That quelled them instantly, and Brianna felt Marsali relax, resuming the rhythm of her spinning. The rain hummed on the roof, solid and steady; it was a good day to be inside, despite the difficulty of entertaining bored children.

"Why don't you play something nice and quiet?" she said, grinning at Roger. "Like . . . oh . . . Indianapolis 500?"

"Oh, you're a great help," he said, giving her a dirty look, but he obligingly set the children to work laying out a racetrack in chalk on the big hearthstone.

"Too bad Germain's not here," he said casually. "Where's he gone in the rain and all, Marsali?" Germain's vroom—according to Roger, it was a Jaguar X-KE, though so far as Brianna could tell, it looked exactly like the others: a block of wood with a rudimentary cab and wheels—was sitting on the mantelpiece, awaiting its master's return.

"He's with Fergus," Marsali answered calmly, not faltering in her rhythm. Her lips pressed together, though, and it was easy to hear the note of strain in her voice.

"And how's Fergus, then?" Roger looked up at her, kindly, but intent.

The thread skipped, bounced in Marsali's hand, and wound itself up with a visible slub in it. She grimaced, and didn't reply until the thread was running once more smoothly through her fingers.

"Well, I will say, for a man wi' one hand, he's a bonny wee fighter," she said at last, eyes on the thread and a wry note in her voice.

Brianna glanced at Roger, who raised an eyebrow back at her.

"Who's he been fighting?" she asked, trying to sound casual.

"He doesna often tell me," Marsali said evenly. "Though yesterday it was the husband of a woman who asked him why he didna just strangle Henri-Christian at birth. He took offense," she added, offhand, leaving it unclear as to whether it was Fergus, the husband, or both who had taken offense. Lifting the thread, she bit it sharply off.

"I should think so," Roger murmured. His head was bent,

marking off the starting line, so his hair fell over his forehead, obscuring his face. "Not the only one, though, I take it."

"No." Marsali began winding the thread onto the niddy-noddy, a small, seemingly permanent frown showing between her fair brows. "I suppose it's better than the ones who point and whisper. Those are the ones who think Henri-Christian's the—the devil's seed," she finished bravely, though her voice quivered a little. "I think they'd burn the wee man—and me and the other weans along with him, if they thought they could."

Brianna felt the bottom of her stomach drop, and cuddled the object of discussion in her lap.

"What sort of idiots could *possibly* think such a thing?" she demanded. "Let alone say it out loud!"

"Let alone do it, ye mean." Marsali put aside the yarn and rose, leaning over to take Henri-Christian and put him to her breast. With his knees still curled up, his body was scarcely half the size of a normal baby's—and with his large, round head with its sprout of dark hair, Brianna had to admit that he did look . . . odd.

"Da had a word here and there," Marsali said. Her eyes were closed, and she was rocking slowly back and forth, cradling Henri-Christian close. "If it weren't for that . . ." Her slender throat moved as she swallowed.

"Daddy, Daddy, let's *go*!" Jem, impatient with incomprehensible adult conversation, plucked at Roger's sleeve.

Roger had been looking at Marsali, his lean face troubled. At this reminder, he blinked and glanced down at his thoroughly normal son, clearing his throat.

"Aye," he said, and took down Germain's car. "Well, then, look. Here's the starting line. . . ."

Brianna laid a hand on Marsali's arm. It was thin, but strongly muscled, the fair skin gold from sun, spattered with tiny freckles. The sight of it, so small and brave-looking, clutched at her throat.

"They'll stop," she whispered. "They'll see. . . ."

"Aye, maybe." Marsali cupped Henri-Christian's small round bottom, holding him closer. Her eyes were still closed. "Maybe not. But if Germain's wi' Fergus, he'll maybe be more careful who he fights. I'd rather they didna kill him, aye?"

She bowed her head over the baby, settling into the nursing and plainly disinclined to talk any further. Brianna patted her arm, a little awkwardly, then moved to take the seat by the spinning wheel.

She'd heard the talk, of course. Or some of it. Particularly right after Henri-Christian's birth, which had sent shock waves through the Ridge. Beyond the first overt expressions of sympathy, there had been a lot of muttering, about recent events and what malign influence might have caused them—from the assault on Marsali and the burning of the malting shed, to the kidnapping of her mother, the slaughter in the woods, and the birth of a dwarf. She'd heard one injudicious girl murmur within her hearing something about ". . . witchcraft, what would ye expect?"—but had rounded fiercely to glare at the girl, who had paled and slunk off with her two friends. The girl had glanced back once, though, then turned away, the three of them spitefully sniggering.

But no one had ever treated her or her mother with any lack of respect. It was clear that a number of the tenants were rather afraid of Claire—but they were much more afraid of her father. Time and habituation had seemed to be working, though—until the birth of Henri-Christian.

Working the treadle was soothing; the whir of the spinning wheel faded into the sound of the rain and the bickering of the children.

At least Fergus had come back. When Henri-Christian was born, he had left the house and not come back for several days. *Poor Marsali,* she thought, with a mental scowl at Fergus. Left alone to deal with the shock. And everyone had *been* shocked, her included. Perhaps she couldn't really blame Fergus.

She swallowed, imagining, as she did whenever she saw Henri-Christian, what it would be like to have a child born with some terrible defect. She saw them now and then—children with cleft lips, the misshapen features of what her mother said was congenital syphilis, retarded children—and every time, crossed herself and thanked God that Jemmy was normal.

But then, so were Germain and his sisters. Something like this could come out of the blue, at any time. Despite herself, she glanced at the small shelf where she kept her personal things, and the dark brown jar of *dauco* seeds. She'd been taking them again, ever since Henri-Christian's birth, though she hadn't mentioned it to Roger. She wondered whether he knew; he hadn't said anything.

Marsali was singing softly under her breath. *Did* Marsali blame Fergus? she wondered. Or he her? She hadn't seen Fergus to talk to in some time. Marsali didn't seem critical of him—and she had said she didn't want him killed. Brianna smiled involuntarily at the memory. Yet there was an undeniable sense of distance when she mentioned him.

The thread thickened suddenly, and she trod faster, trying to compensate, only to have it catch and snap. Muttering to herself, she stopped and let the wheel run itself down—only then realizing that someone had been pounding on the door of the cabin for some time, the sound of it lost in the racket inside.

She opened the door to find one of the fisher-folks' children dripping on the stoop, small, bony, and feral as a wild cat. There were several of them among the tenant families, so alike that she had trouble telling them apart.

"Aidan?" she guessed. "Aidan McCallum?"

"Good day, mistress," the little boy said, bobbing his head in nervous acknowledgment of identity. "Is meenister to hame?"

"Mee—oh. Yes, I suppose so. Come in, won't you?" Suppressing a smile, she swung the door wide, beckoning him in. The boy looked quite shocked to see Roger, crouched on the floor, playing Vroom with Jemmy and Joan and Félicité, all industriously screeching and roaring to such effect that they hadn't noticed the newcomer.

"You have a visitor," she said, raising her voice to interrupt the bedlam. "He wants the minister." Roger broke off in mid-vroom, glancing up in inquiry.

"The what?" he said, sitting up, cross-legged, his own car in hand. Then he spotted the boy, and smiled. "Oh. Aidan, *a charaid*! What is it, then?"

Aidan screwed up his face in concentration. Obviously, he had been given a specific message, committed to memory.

"Mither says will ye come, please," he recited, "for to drive out a de'il what's got intae the milk."

THE RAIN WAS FALLING more lightly now, but they were still soaked nearly through by the time they reached the McCallum residence. If it could be dignified by such a term, Roger thought, slapping rain from his hat as he followed Aidan up the narrow, slippery path to the cabin, which was perched in a high and inconvenient notch in the side of the mountain.

Orem McCallum had managed to erect the walls of his shakily built cabin, and then had missed his footing and plunged into a rock-strewn ravine, breaking his neck within a month of arrival on the Ridge, and leaving his pregnant wife and young son to its dubious shelter.

The other men had come and hastily put a roof on, but the cabin as a whole reminded Roger of nothing so much as a pile of giant jackstraws, poised precariously on the side of the mountain and obviously only awaiting the next spring flood to slide down the mountain after its builder.

Mrs. McCallum was young and pale, and so thin that her dress flapped round her like an empty flour sack. *Christ,* he thought, *what did they have to eat?*

"Oh, sir, I do thank ye for coming." She bobbed an anxious curtsy to him. "I'm that sorry to bring ye out in the rain and all—but I just didna ken what else I might do!"

"Not a problem," he assured her. "Er . . . Aidan said, though, that ye wanted a minister. I'm not that, ye know."

She looked disconcerted at that.

"Oh. Well, maybe not exactly, sir. But they do say as how your faither was a minister, and that ye do ken a great deal about the Bible and all."

"Some, yes," he replied guardedly, wondering what sort of emergency might require Bible knowledge. "A . . . um . . . devil in your milk, was it?"

He glanced discreetly from the baby in its cradle to the front of her dress, unsure at first whether she might mean her own breast milk, which would be a problem he was definitely not equipped to deal with. Fortunately, the difficulty seemed to lie with a large wooden pail sitting on the ramshackle table, a muslin cloth draped across it to keep flies out, small stones knotted into the corners as weights.

"Aye, sir." Mrs. McCallum nodded at it, obviously afraid to go nearer. "Lizzie Wemyss, her from the Big House, she brought that to me last night. She said Herself said as I must give it to Aidan, and drink of it myself." She looked helplessly at Roger. He understood her reservations; even in his own time, milk was regarded as a beverage only for infants and invalids; coming from a fishing village on the Scottish coast, she had quite possibly never seen a cow before coming to America. He was sure she knew what milk was, and that it technically was edible, but she had likely never tasted any.

"Aye, that's quite all right," he assured her. "My family all drink milk; it makes the weans grow tall and strong." And wouldn't come amiss to a nursing mother on lean rations, which was undoubtedly what Claire had thought.

She nodded, uncertain.

"Well . . . aye, sir. I wasna quite sure . . . but the lad was hungry, and said he'd drink it. So I went to dip him out a bit, but it—" She glanced at the bucket with an expression of fearful suspicion. "Weel, if it's no a de'il's got into it, it's something else. It's haunted, sir, I'm sure of it!"

He didn't know what made him look at Aidan at that moment, but he surprised a fleeting look of deep interest that vanished immediately, leaving the boy with a preternaturally solemn expression.

So it was with a certain sense of forewarning that he leaned forward and gingerly lifted the cloth. Even so, he let out a yelp and jerked back, the weighted cloth flying sideways to clack against the wall.

The malevolent green eyes that glared at him from the middle of the bucket disappeared and the milk went *gollup!,* a spray of creamy drops erupting from the bucket like a miniature volcano.

"Shit!" he said. Mrs. McCallum had backed away as far as she could get and was staring at the bucket in terror, both hands clapped across her mouth. Aidan had one hand pressed over his own mouth, and was similarly wide-eyed—but a faint fizzing sound was audible from his direction.

Roger's heart was pounding from adrenaline—and a strong desire to wring Aidan McCallum's scrawny neck. He wiped the splattered cream deliberately from his face, then, gritting his teeth, reached gingerly into the bucket of milk.

It took several tries to grab the thing, which felt like nothing so much as a very muscular and animated glob of mucus, but the fourth try succeeded, and he triumphantly pulled a very large and indignant bullfrog out of the bucket, showering milk in every direction.

The frog dug its back legs ferociously into his slippery palm and broke his grip, launching itself in a soaring leap that covered half the distance to the door and made Mrs. McCallum scream out loud. The startled baby woke and added to the uproar, while the cream-covered frog plopped its way rapidly out of the door and into the rain, leaving yellow splotches in its wake.

Aidan prudently followed it out at a high rate of speed.

Mrs. McCallum had sat down on the floor, thrown her apron over her head, and was having hysterics under it. The baby was shrieking, and milk dripped slowly from the edge of the table, punctuating the patter of rain outside. The roof was leaking, he saw; long wet streaks darkened the unbarked logs behind Mrs. McCallum, and she was sitting in a puddle.

With a deep sigh, he plucked the baby out of its cradle, surprising it sufficiently that it gulped and quit screaming. It blinked at him, and stuck its fist in its mouth. He had no idea of its sex; it was an anonymous bundle of rags, with a pinched wee face and a wary look.

Holding it in one arm, he crouched and put the other round Mrs. McCallum's shoulders, patting her gingerly in hopes of getting her to stop.

"It's all right," he said. "It was just a frog, ye know."

She'd been moaning like a banshee and uttering small intermittent screams, and she kept doing that, though the screams became less frequent, and the moaning disintegrated at last into more or less normal crying, though she refused to come out from under the apron.

His thigh muscles were cramped from squatting, and he was wet, anyway. With a sigh, he lowered himself into the puddle beside her and sat, patting her shoulder every now and then so she'd know he was still there.

The baby seemed happy enough, at least; it was sucking its fist, undisturbed by its mother's fit.

"How old's the wean?" he said conversationally, during a brief pause for breath. He knew its age approximately, because it had been born a week after Orem McCallum's death—but it was something to say. And for as old as it was, it seemed terribly small and light, at least by contrast to his memories of Jemmy at that age.

She mumbled something inaudible, but the crying eased off into hiccups and sighs. Then she said something else.

"What's that, Mrs. McCallum?"

"Why?" she whispered from under the faded calico. "Why has God brought me here?"

Well, that was a bloody good question; he'd asked that one fairly often himself, but hadn't got back any really good answers yet.

"Well . . . we trust He's got a plan of some sort," he said a little awkwardly. "We just don't know what it is."

"A fine plan," she said, and sobbed once. "To bring us all this way, to this terrible place, and then take my man from me and leave me here to starve!"

"Oh . . . it's no such a terrible place," he said, unable to refute anything else in her statement. "The woods and all . . . the streams, the mountains . . . it's . . . um . . . very pretty. When it's not raining." The inanity of this actually made her laugh, though it quickly devolved into more weeping.

"What?" He put an arm round her and pulled her a little closer, both to offer comfort, and in order to make out what she was saying, under her makeshift refuge.

"I miss the sea," she said very softly, and leaned her calico-swathed head against his shoulder, as though she was very tired. "I never shall see it again."

She was very likely right, and he could find nothing to say in reply. They sat for some time in a silence broken only by the baby's slobbering over its fist.

"I won't let ye starve," he said at last, softly. "That's all I can promise, but I do. Ye won't starve." Muscles cramped, he got stiffly to his feet, and reached down to one of the small rough hands that lay limply in her lap. "Come on, then. Get up. Ye can feed the wean, while I tidy up a bit."

THE RAIN had ceased by the time he left, and the clouds had begun to drift apart, leaving patches of pale blue sky. He paused at a turn in the steep, muddy path to admire a rainbow—a complete one, that arched from one side of the sky to the other, its misty colors sinking down into the dark wet green of the dripping mountainside across from him.

It was quiet, save for the splat and drip of water from the leaves and the gurgle of water running down a rocky channel near the trail.

"A covenant," he said softly, out loud. "What's the promise, then? Not a pot of gold at the end." He shook his head and went on, grabbing at branches and bushes to keep from sliding down the mountainside; he didn't want to end up like Orem McCallum, in a tangle of bones at the bottom.

He'd talk to Jamie, and also to Tom Christie and Hiram Crombie. Among them, they could put out the word, and ensure the widow McCallum and her children got enough food. Folk were generous to share—but someone had to ask.

He glanced back over his shoulder; the crooked chimney was just visible above the trees, but no smoke came from it. They could gather enough firewood, she said—but wet as it was, it would be days before they had anything that would burn. They needed a shed for the wood, and logs cut, big enough to burn for a day, not the twigs and fallen branches Aidan could carry.

As though the thought had summoned him, Aidan came into view then. The boy was fishing, squatting on a rock beside a pool some thirty feet below, back turned to the trail. His shoulder blades stuck out through the worn fabric of his shirt, distinct as tiny angel wings.

The noise of the water covered Roger's footsteps as he made his way down the rocks. Very gently, he fitted his hand around the skinny, pale neck, and the bony shoulders hunched in surprise.

"Aidan," he said. "A word wi' you, *if* ye please."

THE DARK CAME down on All Hallows' Eve. We went to sleep to the sound of howling wind and pelting rain, and woke on the Feast of All Saints to whiteness and large soft flakes falling down and down in absolute silence. There is no more perfect stillness than the solitude in the heart of a snowstorm.

This is the thin time, when the beloved dead draw near. The world turns inward, and the chilling air grows thick with dreams and mystery. The sky goes from a sharp clear cold where a million stars burn bright and close, to the gray-pink cloud that enfolds the earth with the promise of snow.

I took one of Bree's matches from its box and lit it, thrilling to the tiny leap of instant flame, and bent to put it to the kindling. Snow was falling, and winter had come; the season of fire. Candles and hearth fire, that lovely, leaping paradox, that destruction contained but never tamed, held at a safe distance to warm and enchant, but always, still, with that small sense of danger.

The smell of roasting pumpkins was thick and sweet in the air. Having ruled the night with fire, the jack-o'-lanterns went now to a more peaceful fate as pies and compost, to join the gentle rest of the earth before renewal. I had turned the earth in my garden the day before, planting the winter seeds to sleep and swell, to dream their buried birth.

Now is the time when we reenter the womb of the world, dreaming the dreams of snow and silence. Waking to the shock of frozen lakes under waning moonlight and the cold sun burning low and blue in the branches of the ice-cased trees, returning from our brief and necessary labors to food and story, to the warmth of firelight in the dark.

Around a fire, in the dark, all truths can be told, and heard, in safety.

I pulled on my woolen stockings, thick petticoats, my

warmest shawl, and went down to poke up the kitchen fire. I stood watching wisps of steam rise from the fragrant cauldron, and felt myself turn inward. The world could go away, and we would heal.

39

I AM THE RESURRECTION

November 1773

A HAMMERING ON THE door roused Roger just before dawn. Next to him, Brianna made an inarticulate noise that experience interpreted as a statement that if he didn't get up and answer the door, she would—but he'd regret it, and so would the unfortunate person on the other side.

Resigned, he flung back the quilt and ran a hand through his tangled hair. The air struck cold on his bare legs, and there was an icy breath of snow in the air.

"Next time I marry someone, I'll pick a lass who wakes up cheerful in the morning," he said to the hunched form beneath the bedclothes.

"You do that," said a muffled voice from under the pillow—whose indistinct nature did nothing to disguise its hostile intonation.

The hammering was repeated, and Jemmy—who *did* wake up cheerful in the mornings—popped up in his trundle, looking like a redheaded dandelion gone to seed.

"Somebody's knocking," he informed Roger.

"Oh, are they? Mmphm." Repressing an urge to groan, he rose and went to unbolt the door.

Hiram Crombie stood outside, looking more dour than

usual in the milky half-light. Evidently not a happy riser, either, Roger reflected.

"My wife's auld mither's passed i' the night," he informed Roger without preamble.

"Passed what?" asked Jemmy with interest, poking his disheveled head out from behind Roger's leg. He rubbed one eye with a fist, and yawned widely. "Mr. Stornaway passed a stone—he showed it to me and Germain."

"Mr. Crombie's mother-in-law has died," Roger said, putting a quelling hand on Jem's head, with an apologetic cough toward Crombie. "I'm sorry to hear that, Mr. Crombie."

"Aye." Mr. Crombie appeared indifferent to condolence. "Murdo Lindsay says as ye ken a bit of Scripture for the burying. The wife's wonderin' would ye maybe come and say a word at the grave?"

"Murdo said . . . oh!" The Dutch family, that was it. Jamie had forced him to speak at the graves. "Aye, of course." He cleared his throat by reflex; his voice was desperately hoarse—as usual in the mornings, until he'd had a cup of something hot. No wonder Crombie was looking dubious.

"Of course," he repeated more strongly. "Is there . . . er . . . anything we can do to help?"

Crombie made a small negative gesture.

"The women will have her laid out by now, I expect," he said, with the briefest of glances at the mound Brianna made in the bed. "We'll start the diggin' after breakfast. With luck, we'll have her under before snow falls." He lifted a sharp chin toward an opaque sky the soft gray of Adso's belly fur, then nodded, turned on his heel, and left without further congenialities.

"Daddy—look!" Roger looked down to see Jem, fingers hooked in the corners of his mouth, pulled down to simulate the inverted "U" of Hiram Crombie's customary expression. Small red brows wrinkled in a ferocious scowl, making the resemblance startling. Surprised into laughter, Roger gasped and choked, then coughed until he doubled over, wheezing.

"Are you all right?" Brianna had unearthed herself and was sitting up in bed, squint-eyed with sleep, but looking concerned.

"Aye, fine." The words came out in a thready wheeze,

nearly soundless. He took a breath and hawked deeply, expectorating a repellent glob into his hand, for lack of a handkerchief.

"Eew!" said the tender wife of his bosom, recoiling.

"Lemme see, Daddy!" said his son and heir, jostling for a look. "Eeew!"

Roger stepped outside and wiped his hand in the wet grass by the door. It was cold out, so early, but Crombie was undoubtedly right; snow was on the way again. The air had that soft, muffled feel to it.

"So old Mrs. Wilson is dead?" Brianna had come out after him, a shawl wrapped round her shoulders. "That's too bad. Imagine coming so far, and then dying in a strange place, before you've even had time to settle."

"Well, she had her family with her, at least. I expect she wouldna have wanted to be left alone to die in Scotland."

"Mm." Bree brushed strands of hair off her cheeks; she'd put her hair into a thick plait for sleeping, but a good bit of it had escaped from captivity and was waving up round her face in the cold, humid air. "Should I go up there, do you think?"

"Pay our respects? He said they've laid the old lady out already."

She snorted, white wisps of breath from her nostrils momentarily making him think of dragons.

"It can't be later than seven A.M.; it's still bloody dark out! And I don't believe for a minute that his wife and sister have been laying out the old lady by candlelight. Hiram would balk at the expense of the extra candle, for one thing. No, he felt itchy about asking a favor, so he was trying to get under your skin about your wife being a lazy slattern."

That was perceptive, Roger thought, amused—particularly as she hadn't seen Crombie's eloquent glance at her recumbent form.

"What's a slattern?" Jemmy inquired, picking up instantly on anything vaguely improper-sounding.

"That's a lady who's no lady," Roger informed him. "And a bad housekeeper, to boot."

"That's one of the words that Mrs. Bug will wash out your mouth with soap if she hears you say it," amended his wife with ungrammatical acuity.

Roger was still attired in nothing but a nightshirt, and his legs and feet were freezing. Jem was hopping around barefoot, too, but without the slightest sign of being cold.

"Mummy is not one," Roger said firmly, taking Jem's hand. "Come on, chum, let's nip up to the privy while Mummy makes breakfast."

"Thanks for the vote of confidence," Brianna said, yawning. "I'll take up a jar of honey or something to the Crombies later."

"I go, too," Jemmy announced promptly.

Brianna hesitated for a moment, then looked at Roger and raised her brows. Jem had never seen a dead person.

Roger lifted one shoulder. It would have been a peaceful death, and it was, God knew, a fact of life on the mountain. He didn't suppose that seeing Mrs. Wilson's body would give the child nightmares—though knowing Jem, it *was* quite likely to lead to a number of loud and embarrassing public questions. A bit of preparatory explanation might not be out of place, he reflected.

"Sure," he told Jem. "But first we have to go up to the Big House after breakfast, and borrow a Bible from Grandda."

HE FOUND JAMIE at breakfast, the warm oatmeal smell of fresh parritch wrapping him like a blanket as he stepped into the kitchen. Before he could explain his errand, Mrs. Bug had sat him down with a bowl of his own, a jug of honey, a plate of savory fried bacon, hot toast dripping butter, and a fresh cup of something dark and fragrant that looked like coffee. Jem was next to him, already smeared with honey and buttered to the ears. For a traitorous instant, he wondered whether Brianna was perhaps a bit of a sluggard, though certainly never a slattern.

Then he glanced across the table at Claire, uncombed hair standing on end as she blinked sleepily at him over the toast, and generously concluded that it probably wasn't a conscious choice on Bree's part, but rather the influence of genetics.

Claire roused at once, though, when he explained his errand, between bites of bacon and toast.

"Old Mrs. Wilson?" she asked with interest. "What did she die of, did Mr. Crombie say?"

Roger shook his head, swallowing oatmeal.

"Only that she'd passed in the night. I suppose they found her dead. Her heart, maybe—she must have been at least eighty."

"She was about five years older than I am," Claire said dryly. "She told me."

"Oh. Mmphm." Clearing his throat hurt, and he took a sip of the hot, dark stuff in his cup. It was a brew of roasted chicory and acorns, but not that bad.

"I hope ye didna tell her how old *you* are, Sassenach." Jamie reached across and snared the last piece of toast. Mrs. Bug, ever-vigilant, whisked the plate away to refill it.

"I'm not that careless," Claire said, dabbing a forefinger delicately into a smear of honey and licking it. "They already think I've made some sort of pact with the devil; if I told them my age, they'd be sure of it."

Roger chuckled, but thought privately that she was right. The marks of her ordeal had nearly vanished, bruises faded and the bridge of her nose healed straight and clean. Even unkempt and puffy-eyed from sleep, she was more than handsome, with lovely skin, lushly thick curly hair, and an elegance of feature undreamt of among the Highland fisherfolk. To say nothing of the eyes, sherry-gold and startling.

Add to these natural gifts the twentieth-century practices of nutrition and hygiene—she had all of her teeth, white and straight—and she easily appeared a good twenty years younger than other women of her own age. He found that a comforting thought; perhaps Bree had inherited the art of aging beautifully from her mother, as well. He could always make his own breakfast, after all.

Jamie had finished his own meal and gone to fetch the Bible. He came back, laying it beside Roger's plate.

"We'll go up with ye to the burying," he said, nodding at the book. "Mrs. Bug—can ye maybe put up a wee basket for the Crombies?"

"Done it already," she informed him, and plunked a large

basket on the table before him, covered with a napkin and bulging with goodies. "Ye'll take it, then? I must go tell Arch and fetch my good shawl, and we'll see ye at the graveside, aye?"

Brianna came in then, yawning but well-groomed, and set about making Jem presentable while Claire vanished to find cap and shawl. Roger picked up the Bible, intending to thumb through the Psalms for something suitably somber but uplifting.

"Maybe the Twenty-third?" he said, half to himself. "Nice and short. Always a classic. And it does mention death, at least."

"Are you going to give a eulogy?" Brianna asked, interested. "Or a sermon?"

"Oh, Christ, I hadn't thought of that," he said in dismay. He cleared his throat experimentally. "Is there more coffee?"

He'd been to a great many funerals in Inverness presided over by the Reverend, and was well aware that the paying customers considered such an event a dismal failure unless the preaching went on for at least half an hour. Granted, beggars couldn't be choosers, and the Crombies couldn't expect—

"Why do you have a Protestant Bible, Da?" Bree paused in the act of disentangling a piece of toast from Jemmy's hair, peering over Roger's shoulder.

Surprised, he shut the cover, but she was right; *King James Version,* it said, the letters of the inscription nearly worn away.

"It was given to me," Jamie said. The reply was casual, but Roger glanced up; there was something odd in Jamie's voice. Brianna heard it, too; she shot her father a brief, sharp look, but his face was tranquil as he took a final bite of bacon and wiped his lips.

"D'ye want a dram in your coffee, Roger Mac?" he said, nodding at Roger's cup, as though it were the most natural thing in the world to offer whisky with breakfast.

In fact, the notion sounded really appealing, given the immediate prospects, but Roger shook his head.

"No, thanks; I'll do."

"Are you sure?" Brianna transferred the sharp look to him. "Maybe you should. For your throat."

"It'll be fine," he said shortly. He was worried about his voice himself; he didn't need solicitude from the redheaded contingent, all three of whom were giving him thoughtful looks that he interpreted as casting extreme doubt upon his speaking abilities. Whisky might help his throat, but he doubted it would do much for his preaching—and the last thing he wanted was to show up at a funeral reeking of strong drink in front of a lot of strict teetotalers.

"Vinegar," advised Mrs. Bug, bending to take away his plate. "Hot vinegar's the thing. Cuts the phlegm, aye?"

"I'll bet it would," Roger said, smiling despite his misgivings. "But I think I won't, Mrs. Bug, thanks." He'd awakened with a slight sore throat, and hoped the consumption of breakfast would cure it. It hadn't, and the thought of drinking hot vinegar made his tonsils seize up.

He held out his cup for more chicory coffee, instead, and set his mind to the task ahead.

"Now—does anyone know anything about old Mrs. Wilson?"

"She's dead," Jemmy piped up confidently. Everybody laughed, and Jem looked confused, but then joined the laughter, though plainly having not the slightest idea what was funny.

"Good start, sport." Roger reached out and brushed crumbs from Jemmy's shirtfront. "Might be a point, at that. The Reverend had a decent sermon on something in the Epistles—the wages of sin is death, but the gift of God is eternal life. I heard him give it more than once. What d'ye think?" He raised a brow at Brianna, who frowned in thought and picked up the Bible.

"That would probably work. Does this thing have a concordance?"

"No." Jamie put down his coffee cup. "It's in Romans, chapter six, though." Seeing the looks of surprise turned upon him, he flushed slightly, and jerked his head toward the Bible.

"I had that book in prison," he said. "I read it. Come along, *a bhailach,* are ye ready now?"

THE WEATHER WAS louring, clouds threatening anything from freezing rain to the first snow of the season, and occasional cold gusts of wind catching cloaks and skirts, bellying them out like sails. The men held tight to their hats, and the women huddled deep in their hoods, all walking with their heads down, like sheep pushing stubbornly into the wind.

"Great weather for a funeral," Brianna murmured, pulling her cloak tight around her after one such gust.

"Mmphm." Roger responded automatically, obviously unaware of what she'd said, but registering that she'd spoken. His brow was furrowed, and he seemed tight-lipped and pale. She put a hand on his arm, squeezing in reassurance, and he glanced at her with a faint smile, his face easing.

An unearthly wail cut through the air, and Brianna froze, clutching Roger's arm. It rose to a shriek, then broke in a series of short, jerky gulps, coming down a scale of sobs like a dead body rolling down a staircase.

Gooseflesh prickled down her spine and her stomach clenched. She glanced at Roger; he looked nearly as pale as she felt, though he pressed her hand reassuringly.

"That will be the *bean-treim,*" her father remarked calmly. "I didna ken there was one."

"Neither did I," said her mother. "Who do you suppose it is?" She had startled, too, at the sound of it, but now looked merely interested.

Roger had been holding his breath, too; he let it out now, with a small rattling sound, and cleared his throat.

"A mourning woman," he said. The words emerged thickly, and he cleared his throat again, much harder. "They, um, keen. After the coffin."

The voice rose again out of the wood, this time with a more deliberate sound. Brianna thought there were words in the wailing, but couldn't make them out. *Wendigo.* The word came unbidden into her mind, and she shivered convulsively. Jemmy whimpered, trying to burrow inside his grandfather's coat.

"It's nothing to fear, *a bhailach.*" He patted Jemmy on the back. Jem appeared unconvinced, and put his thumb in his mouth, huddling round-eyed into Jamie's chest as the wailing faded into moans.

"Well, come, then, we'll meet her, shall we?" Jamie turned

aside and began making his way into the forest, toward the voice.

There was nothing to do but follow. Brianna squeezed Roger's arm, but left him, walking close to her father so Jemmy could see her and be reassured.

"It's okay, pal," she said softly. The weather was growing colder; her breath puffed out in wisps of white. The end of Jemmy's nose was red and his eyes seemed a little pink around the edges—was he catching a cold, too?

She put out a hand to touch his forehead, but just then the voice broke out afresh. This time, though, something seemed to have happened to it. It was a high, thready sound, not the robust keening they'd heard before. And uncertain—like an apprentice ghost, she thought in uneasy jest.

An apprentice it proved to be, though not a ghost. Her father ducked under a low pine and she followed him, emerging in a clearing facing two surprised women. Or rather, a woman and a teenaged girl, with shawls wrapped over their heads. She knew them, but what were their names?

"Maduinn mhath, maighistear," the older woman said, recovering from her surprise and dropping into a low curtsy to Jamie. Good morn to you, sir.

"And to you, my mistresses," he replied, also in Gaelic.

"Good morn, Mrs. Gwilty," Roger said in his soft, hoarse voice. "And to you, *a nighean,*" he added, bowing courteously to the girl. Olanna, that was it; Brianna recalled the round face, just like the "O" that began her name. She was Mrs. Gwilty's . . . daughter? Or her niece?

"Ach, bonny boy," the girl crooned, reaching out a finger to touch Jem's rounded cheek. He pulled back a little and sucked harder on his thumb, watching her suspiciously under the edge of his blue woolly bonnet.

The women spoke no English, but Brianna's Gaelic was sufficient by now to allow her to follow the conversation, if not to join fluently in it. Mrs. Gwilty was, she explained, showing her niece the way of a proper *coronach.*

"And a fine job of work you will make of it between you, I'm sure," Jamie said politely.

Mrs. Gwilty sniffed, and gave her niece a disparaging look.

"Mmphm," she said. "A voice like a bat farting, but she is the only woman left of my family, and I shall not live forever."

Roger made a small choking noise, which he hastily developed into a convincing cough. Olanna's pleasant round face, already flushed from the cold, went a blotchy red, but she said nothing, merely cast her eyes down and huddled deeper into her shawl. It was a dark brown homespun, Brianna saw; Mrs. Gwilty's was a fine wool, dyed black—and if it was a trifle frayed around the edges, she wore it still with the dignity of her profession.

"It is sorrowful we are for you," Jamie said, in formal condolence. "She who is gone . . . ?" He paused in delicate inquiry.

"My father's sister," answered Mrs. Gwilty promptly. "Woe, woe, that she should be buried among strangers." She had a lean, underfed face, the spare flesh deeply hollowed and bruised-looking round dark eyes. She turned these deep-set eyes on Jemmy, who promptly grabbed the edge of his bonnet and pulled it down over his face. Seeing the dark, bottomless eyes swivel in her direction, Brianna was hard-pressed not to do the same.

"I hope—that her shade will find comfort. With—with your family being here," Claire said, in her halting Gaelic. It sounded most peculiar in her mother's English accent, and Brianna saw her father bite his lower lip in order not to smile.

"She will not lack company for long." Olanna blurted it out, then, catching Jamie's eye, went beet-red and buried her nose in her shawl.

This odd statement seemed to make sense to her father, who nodded.

"Och, so? Who is it ails?" He looked at her mother in question, but she shook her head slightly. If anyone was sick, they hadn't sought her help.

Mrs. Gwilty's long, seamed upper lip pressed down over dreadful teeth.

"Seaumais Buchan," she remarked with grim satisfaction. "He lies fevered and his chest will kill him before the week is out, but we've beaten him. A fortunate thing."

"What?" said Claire, frowning in bewilderment.

Mrs. Gwilty's eyes narrowed at her.

"The last person buried in a graveyard must stand watch over it, Sassenach," Jamie explained in English. "Until another comes to take his place."

Switching smoothly back to Gaelic, he said, "Fortunate is she, and the more fortunate, in having such *bean-treim* to follow her." He put a hand into his pocket and handed over a coin, which Mrs. Gwilty glanced at, then blinked and looked again.

"Ah," she said, gratified. "Well, we will do our best, the girl and I. Come then, *a nighean,* let me hear you."

Olanna, thus pressed to perform before company, looked terrified. Under her aunt's monitory eye, though, there was no escape. Closing her eyes, she inflated her chest, thrust back her shoulders, and emitted a piercing, "EEEEEEEEEEEEEEeeeeeeeeeeeEEEEEEeeeEEE-uh-Ee-uh-Ee-uh," before breaking off, gasping for breath.

Roger flinched as though the sound were bamboo splinters being shoved under his fingernails and Claire's mouth dropped open. Jemmy's shoulders were hunched up round his ears, and he clung to his grandfather's coat like a small blue bur. Even Jamie looked a little startled.

"Not bad," said Mrs. Gwilty judiciously. "Perhaps it will not be a complete disgrace. I am hearing that Hiram asked you to speak a word?" she added with a disparaging glance at Roger.

"He has," Roger replied, still hoarse, but as firmly as possible. "I am honored."

Mrs. Gwilty did not reply to this, but merely looked him up and down, then, shaking her head, turned her back and raised her arms.

"AaaaaaaaAAAAAAAAaaaaAAAAAAAaaaIIIIeeeeeeee," she wailed, in a voice that made Brianna feel ice crystals in her blood. "Woe, woe, wooooooooooooe! AAaayaaaAAaayaaaAA-haaaaahaaa! Woe is come to the house of Crombie—Woe!"

Dutifully turning her back on them, as well, Olanna joined in with a descant wail of her own. Claire rather untactfully but practically put her fingers in her ears.

"*How* much did you give them?" she asked Jamie in English.

Jamie's shoulders shook briefly, and he hastily ushered her away, a firm hand on her elbow.

Beside Brianna, Roger swallowed, the sound just audible under the noise.

"You should have had that drink," she said to him.

"I know," he said hoarsely, and sneezed.

"HAVE YOU EVEN heard of Seaumais Buchan?" I asked Jamie, as we picked our way across the sodden earth of the Crombies' dooryard. "Who is he?"

"Oh, I've heard of him, aye," he replied, putting an arm round me to help swing me across a fetid puddle of what looked like goat urine. "Oof. God, you're a solid wee thing, Sassenach."

"That's the basket," I replied absently. "I believe Mrs. Bug's put lead shot in it. Or maybe only fruitcake. Who is he, then? One of the fisher-folk?"

"Aye. He's great-uncle to Maisie MacArdle, her who's marrit to him that was a boatbuilder. Ye recall her? Red hair and a verra long nose, six bairns."

"Vaguely. However do you remember these things?" I demanded, but he merely smiled, and offered me his arm. I took it, and we strode gravely through the mud and the scattered straw laid down across it, the laird and his lady come to the funeral.

The door of the cabin was open despite the cold, to let the spirit of the dead go out. Fortunately, it also let a little light come in, as the cabin was crudely built and had no windows. It was also completely packed with people, most of whom had not bathed any time in the preceding four months.

I was no stranger to claustrophobic cabins or unwashed bodies, though, and since I knew that one of the bodies present was probably clean but certainly dead, I had already begun breathing through my mouth by the time one of the Crombie daughters, shawled and red-eyed, invited us in.

Grannie Wilson was laid out on the table with a candle at her head, wrapped in the shroud she had no doubt woven as a new bride; the linen cloth was yellowed and creased with age, but clean and soft in the candlelight, embroidered on the edges with a simple pattern of vine leaves. It had been carefully kept, brought from Scotland at the cost of who knew what pains.

Jamie paused at the door, removing his hat, and murmured formal condolences, which the Crombies, male and female, accepted with nods and grunts, respectively. I handed over the basket of food and nodded back, with what I hoped was a suitable expression of dignified sympathy, keeping an eye on Jemmy.

Brianna had done her best to explain to him, but I had no idea what he might make of the situation—or the corpse. He had been persuaded with some difficulty to emerge from his bonnet, and was looking round now with interest, his cowlick standing on end.

"Is that the dead lady, Grandma?" he whispered loudly to me, pointing at the body.

"Yes, dear," I said, with an uneasy glance at old Mrs. Wilson. She looked perfectly all right, though, done up properly in her best cap with a bandage under her jaw to keep her mouth closed, dry eyelids sealed against the glimmer of the candle. I didn't think Jemmy had ever met the old lady in life; there was no real reason for him to be upset at seeing her dead—and he'd been taken hunting regularly since he could walk; he certainly understood the concept of death. Besides, a corpse was definitely anticlimactic, after our encounter with the *bean-treim*. Still . . .

"We'll pay our respects now, lad," Jamie said quietly to him, and set him on the floor. I caught Jamie's glance at the door, where Roger and Bree were murmuring condolences in their turn, and realized he had been waiting for them to catch up, so that they could watch him, and know what to do next.

He led Jemmy through the press of people, who gave way respectfully, and up to the table, where he laid his hand on the corpse's chest. Oh, so it was that sort of funeral.

At some Highland funerals, it was the custom for everyone to touch the body, so that the dead person should not haunt them. I doubted that Grannie Wilson would have any interest in haunting me, but care never hurt—and I did have an uneasy memory of a skull with silver fillings in its teeth, and my encounter with what might have been its possessor, seen by corpse-light on a black mountain night. Despite myself, I glanced at the candle, but it seemed a perfectly normal thing of brown beeswax, pleasantly fragrant and leaning a little crooked in its pottery candlestick.

Steeling myself, I leaned over and laid my own hand gently on the shroud. An earthenware saucer, holding a piece of bread and a heap of salt, sat on the dead woman's chest, and a small wooden bowl filled with dark liquid—wine?—sat beside her on the table. What with the good beeswax candle, the salt, and the *bean-treim,* it looked as though Hiram Crombie was trying to do right by his late mother-in-law—though I wouldn't put it past him to thriftily reuse the salt after the funeral.

Something seemed wrong, though; an air of uneasiness curled among the cracked boots and rag-wrapped feet of the crowd like the cold draft from the door. At first I had thought it might be due to our presence, but that wasn't it; there had been a brief exhalation of approval when Jamie approached the body.

Jamie whispered to Jemmy, then boosted him up, legs dangling, to touch the corpse. He showed no reluctance, and peered into the dead woman's waxen face with interest.

"What's that for?" he asked loudly, reaching for the bread. "Is she going to eat it?"

Jamie grabbed his wrist, and planted his hand firmly on the shroud instead.

"That's for the sin-eater, *a bhailach.* Leave it, aye?"

"What's a—"

"Later." No one argued with Jamie when he used that tone of voice, and Jemmy subsided, putting his thumb back in his mouth as Jamie set him down. Bree came up and scooped him into her arms, belatedly remembering to touch the corpse herself, and murmur, "God rest you."

Then Roger stepped forward, and there was a stir of interest among the crowd.

He looked pale, but composed. His face was lean and rather ascetic, usually saved from sternness by the gentleness of his eyes and a mobile mouth, ready to laugh. This was no time for laughter, though, and his eyes were bleak in the dim light.

He laid a hand on the dead woman's chest, and bowed his head. I wasn't sure whether he was praying for the repose of her soul, or for inspiration, but he stayed that way for more than a minute. The crowd watched respectfully, with no sound save coughs and the clearing of throats. Roger wasn't the only one catching a cold, I thought—and thought suddenly again of Seaumais Buchan.

"He lies fevered and his chest will kill him before the week is out." So Mrs. Gwilty had said. Pneumonia, perhaps—or bronchitis, or even consumption. And no one had told me.

I felt a slight pang at that, equal parts annoyance, guilt, and unease. I knew the new tenants didn't yet trust me; I had thought that I should allow them to get used to me before I started dropping in on them at random. Many of them would never have seen an English person, before coming to the Colonies—and I was well aware of their attitude toward both Sassenachs and Catholics.

But evidently there was now a man dying virtually on my doorstep—and I hadn't even known of his existence, let alone his illness.

Should I go to see him, as soon as the funeral was over? But where in bloody hell did the man live? It couldn't be very close; I *did* know all the fisher-folk who had settled down the mountain; the MacArdles must be up across the ridge. I stole a look at the door, trying to judge how soon the threatening clouds would cut loose their burden of snow.

There were shufflings and the murmurs of low speech outside; more people had arrived, coming up from the nearby hollows, crowding round the door. I caught the words, *"dèan caithris,"* in a questioning tone, and suddenly realized what was odd about the present occasion.

There was no wake. Customarily, the body would have been washed and laid out, but then kept on display for a day or two, to allow everyone in the area time to come and pay their regards. Listening intently, I caught a distinct tone of disgruntlement and surprise—the neighbors thought this haste unseemly.

"Why isn't there a wake?" I whispered to Jamie. He lifted

one shoulder a fraction of an inch, but nodded toward the door, and the muffled sky beyond.

"There's going to be a great deal of snow by nightfall, *a Sorcha,*" he said. "And likely to go on for days, by the looks of it. I wouldna want to be having to dig a grave and bury a coffin in the midst of that, myself. And should it snow for days, where are they to put the body in the meantime?"

"That's true, *Mac Dubh,*" said Kenny Lindsay, overhearing. He glanced round at the people near us, and edged closer, lowering his voice. "But it's true, too, as Hiram Crombie's no owerfond of the auld bes—er, his good-mother." He raised his chin a fraction, indicating the corpse. "Some say as he canna get the auld woman underground fast enough—before she changes her mind, aye?" He grinned briefly, and Jamie hid his own smile, looking down.

"Saves a bit on the food, too, I suppose." Hiram's reputation as a cheapskate was well-known—which was saying something, among the thrifty but hospitable Highlanders.

A fresh bustle was taking place outside, as new arrivals came. There was a sort of congestion at the door, as someone sought to press inside, though the house was filled shoulder to shoulder, with the only bit of open floor space left under the table on which Mrs. Wilson reposed.

The people near the door gave way reluctantly, and Mrs. Bug surged into the cabin, arrayed in her best cap and shawl, Arch at her shoulder.

"Ye forgot the whisky, sir," she informed Jamie, handing him a corked bottle. Looking round, she at once spotted the Crombies and bowed to them ceremoniously, murmuring sympathy. Bobbing upright, she set her cap straight and looked expectantly round. Clearly, the festivities could now commence.

Hiram Crombie glanced round, then nodded to Roger.

Roger drew himself up slightly, nodded back, and began. He spoke simply for a few minutes, generalities about the preciousness of life, the enormity of death, and the importance of kin and neighbors in facing such things. This all seemed to be going over well with the punters, who were nodding slightly in approval and seemed to be settling down in expectation of decent entertainment.

Roger paused to cough and blow his nose, then shifted into what appeared to be some version of the Presbyterian funeral service—or what he recalled of it, from his life with the Reverend Wakefield.

This too seemed to be acceptable. Bree seemed to relax a little, and put Jemmy down.

It was going well . . . and yet I was still conscious of a faint sense of uneasiness. Part of that, of course, was that I could see Roger. The growing warmth of the cabin was making his nose run; he kept his handkerchief in his hand, dabbing furtively and now and then stopping to blow his nose as discreetly as possible.

Phlegm, though, runs downhill. And as the congestion got worse, it began to affect his vulnerable throat. The choked note in his voice, always present, was getting noticeably worse. He was having to clear his throat repeatedly, in order to speak.

Beside me, Jemmy stirred restively, and from the corner of my eye, I saw Bree put a hand on his head to quiet him. He looked up at her, but her attention was fixed anxiously on Roger.

"We give thanks to God for the life of this woman," he said, and paused to clear his throat—again. I found myself doing it with him in sheer nervous sympathy.

"She is a servant of God, faithful and true, and now praises Him before His throne, with the sa—" I saw sudden doubt flicker across his face as to whether his present congregation countenanced the concept of saints, or would consider such a mention to be Romish heresy. He coughed, and resumed, "With the angels."

Evidently angels were innocuous; the faces around me looked somber, but unoffended. Exhaling visibly, Roger picked up the little green Bible and opened it at a marked page.

"Let us speak together a psalm in praise of Him who—" He glanced at the page and, too late, realized the difficulty of translating an English psalm into Gaelic on the wing.

He cleared his throat explosively, and half a dozen throats among the crowd echoed him in reflex. On my other side, Jamie murmured, "Oh, God," in heartfelt prayer.

Jemmy tugged at his mother's skirt, whispering something, but was peremptorily shushed. I could see Bree yearning toward Roger, body tensed in the urgent desire to help somehow, if only by mental telepathy.

With no alternative in sight, Roger began to read the psalm, haltingly. Half the crowd had taken him at his word when he invited them to "speak together," and were reciting the psalm from memory—several times faster than he could read.

I closed my eyes, unable to watch, but there was no way to avoid hearing, as the congregation ripped through the psalm and fell silent, waiting in dour patience for Roger to stumble his way to the end. Which he did, doggedly.

"Amen," said Jamie loudly. And alone. I opened my eyes to find everyone staring at us, with looks ranging from mild surprise to glowering hostility. Jamie took a deep breath and let it out, very slowly.

"Jesus. Christ," he said very softly.

A bead of sweat ran down Roger's cheek, and he wiped it away with the sleeve of his coat.

"Would anyone wish to say a few words regarding the deceased?" he asked, glancing from face to face. Silence and the whine of the wind answered him.

He cleared his throat, and someone snickered.

"Grannie—" whispered Jemmy, tugging on my skirt.

"Shh."

"But *Grandma*—" The sense of urgency in his voice made me turn and look down at him.

"Do you need to go to the privy?" I whispered, bending down to him. He shook his head, violently enough to make the heavy mop of red-gold hair flop to and fro on his forehead.

"O, God, our Heavenly Father, who art leading us through the changes of time to the rest and blessedness of eternity, be Thou near to us now, to comfort and to uphold."

I glanced up, to see that Roger had laid his hand once more on the corpse, evidently deciding to bring the proceedings to a close. From the relief evident in his face and voice, I thought he must be falling back on some accustomed prayer from the Book of Common Worship, familiar enough to him that he could manage it with fair fluency in Gaelic.

"Make us to know that Thy children are precious in Thy sight. . . ." He stopped, visibly struggling; the muscles of his throat worked, trying vainly to clear the obstruction in silence, but it was no good.

"Err . . . HRRM!" A sound, not quite laughter, ran through the room, and Bree made a small rumbling noise in her own throat, like a volcano getting ready to spew lava.

"Grannie!"

"Shh!"

". . . thy sight. That they . . . live evermore with Thee and that Thy mercy—"

"Grannie!"

Jemmy was wiggling as though a colony of ants had taken up residence in his breeches, an expression of agonized urgency on his face.

"I am the Resurrection and the Life, saith the Lord; he that believeth in Me, though he were dead . . . rr-hm . . . yet shall he live—" With the end in sight, Roger was making a gallant finish, forcing his voice past its limits, hoarser than ever and cracking on every other word, but firm and loud.

"Just a *minute,*" I hissed. "I'll take you out in a—"

"No, Grannie! *Look!*"

I followed his outthrust finger, and for a moment, thought he was pointing at his father. But he wasn't.

Old Mrs. Wilson had opened her eyes.

THERE WAS AN instant's silence, as everyone's eyes fastened at once on Mrs. Wilson. Then there was a collective gasp, and an instinctive stepping back, with shrieks of dismay and cries of pain as toes were trodden on and people squashed against the unyielding rough logs of the walls.

Jamie grabbed Jemmy up off the floor in time to save his being crushed, inflated his lungs, and bellowed, *"Sheas!"* at the top of his voice. Such was his volume that the crowd did indeed freeze momentarily—long enough for him to thrust

Jemmy into Brianna's arms and elbow his way toward the table.

Roger had got hold of the erstwhile corpse, and was lifting her into a sitting position, her hand feebly flapping at the bandage round her jaws. I pushed after Jamie, ruthlessly shoving people out of the way.

"Give her a bit of air, please," I said, raising my voice. The stunned silence was giving way to a rising murmur of excitement, but this quelled as I fumbled to untie the bandage. The room waited in quivering expectation as the corpse worked stiff jaws.

"Where am I?" she said in a quavering voice. Her gaze passed disbelievingly round the room, settling at last on her daughter's face.

"Mairi?" she said dubiously, and Mrs. Crombie rushed forward and fell on her knees, bursting into tears as she gripped her mother's hands.

"A Màthair! A Màthair!" she cried. The old woman set a trembling hand on her daughter's hair, looking as though she were not quite sure she was real.

I, meanwhile, had been doing my best to check the old lady's vital signs, which were not all that vital, but nonetheless fairly good for someone who had been dead a moment before. Respiration very shallow, labored, a color like week-old oatmeal, cold, clammy skin despite the heat in the room, and I couldn't find a pulse at all—though plainly she must have one. Mustn't she?

"How do you feel?" I asked.

She put a trembling hand to her belly.

"I do feel that wee bit poorly," she whispered.

I put my own hand on her abdomen, and felt it instantly. A pulse, where no pulse should be. It was irregular, stumbling, and bumping—but most assuredly there.

"Jesus H. Roosevelt Christ," I said. I didn't say it loudly, but Mrs. Crombie gasped, and I saw her apron twitch, as she doubtless made the horns beneath it.

I hadn't time to bother with apology, but stood and grabbed Roger by the sleeve, pulling him aside.

"She has an aortic aneurysm," I said to him very softly. "She must have been bleeding internally for some time, enough to make her lose consciousness and seem cold. It's going to rupture *very* soon, and then she'll die for real."

He swallowed audibly, his face very pale, but said only, "Do you know how long?"

I glanced at Mrs. Wilson; her face was the same gray as the snow-laden sky, and her eyes were going in and out of focus like the flickering of a candle in a wind.

"I see," Roger said, though I hadn't spoken. He took a deep breath and cleared his throat.

The crowd, which had been hissing amongst themselves like a flock of agitated geese, ceased at once. Every eye in the place was riveted on the tableau before them.

"This our sister has been restored to life, as we all shall be one day by the grace of God," Roger said softly. "It is a sign to us, of hope and faith. She will go soon again to the arms of the angels, but has come back to us for a moment, to bring us assurance of God's love." He paused a moment, obviously groping for something further to say. He cleared his throat and bent his head toward Mrs. Wilson's.

"Did you . . . wish to say anything, O, mother?" he whispered in Gaelic.

"Aye, I do." Mrs. Wilson seemed to be gaining strength—and with it, indignation. A faint pinkness showed in her waxy cheeks as she glared round at the crowd.

"What sort of wake is *this,* Hiram Crombie?" she demanded, fixing her son-in-law with a gimlet eye. "I see nay food laid out, nay drink—and what is this?" Her voice rose in a furious squeak, her eye having fallen on the plate of bread and salt, which Roger had hastily set aside when he lifted her.

"Why—" She looked wildly round at the assembled crowd, and the truth of it dawned upon her. Her sunken eyes bulged. "Why . . . ye shameless skinflint! This is nay wake at all! Ye've meant to bury me wi' nothing but a crust o' bread and a drap o' wine for the sin-eater, and a wonder ye spared *that*! Nay doot ye'll thieve the winding claes from my corpse to make cloots for your snotty-nosed bairns, and where's my good brooch I said I wanted to be buried with?" One scrawny hand closed on her shrunken bosom, catching a fistful of wilted linen.

"Mairi! My brooch!"

"Here it is, Mother, here it is!" Poor Mrs. Crombie, altogether undone, was fumbling in her pocket, sobbing and gasping. "I put it away to be safe—I meant to put it on ye before—before . . ." She came out with an ugly lump of garnets, which her mother snatched from her, cradling it against her breast, and glaring round with jealous suspicion. Clearly she suspected her neighbors of waiting the chance to steal it from her body; I heard an offended inhalation from the woman standing behind me, but had no time to turn and see who it was.

"Now, now," I said, using my best soothing bedside manner. "I'm sure everything will be all right." *Aside from the fact that you're going to die in the next few minutes, that is,* I thought, suppressing a hysterical urge to laugh inappropriately. Actually, it might be in the next few seconds, if her blood pressure rose any higher.

I had my fingers on the thumping big pulse in her abdomen that betrayed the fatal weakening of her abdominal aorta. It had to have begun to leak already, to make her lose consciousness to such a degree as to seem dead. Eventually, she would simply blow a gasket, and that would be it.

Roger and Jamie were both doing their best to soothe her, muttering in English and Gaelic and patting her comfortingly. She seemed to be responding to this treatment, though still breathing like a steam engine.

Jamie's production of the bottle of whisky from his pocket helped still further.

"Well, that's more like it!" Mrs. Wilson said, somewhat mollified, as he hastily pulled the cork and waved the bottle under her nose so she could appreciate the quality of it. "And ye've brought food, too?" Mrs. Bug had bustled her way to the front, basket held before her like a battering ram. "Hmph! I never thought I should live to see Papists kinder than my ain kin!" This last was directed at Hiram Crombie, who had so far been opening and closing his mouth, without finding anything whatever to say in reply to his mother-in-law's tirade.

"Why . . . why . . ." he stammered in outrage, torn between shock, obvious fury, and a need to justify himself before his neighbors. "Kinder than your ain kin! Why, have I not given ye a hame, these twenty years past? Fed and clothed ye as ye were my ain mither? B-borne your wicked tongue and foul t-tempers for *years,* and never—"

Jamie and Roger both leapt in to try to stifle him, but instead interrupted each other, and in the confusion, Hiram was allowed to go on speaking his mind, which he did. So did Mrs. Wilson, who was no slouch at invective, either.

The pulse in her belly was throbbing under my hand, and I was hard put to it to keep her from leaping off the table and dotting Hiram with the bottle of whisky. The neighbors were agog.

Roger took matters—and Mrs. Wilson—firmly into his own hands, seizing her by her scrawny shoulders.

"Mrs. Wilson," he said hoarsely, but loudly enough to drown Hiram's indignant rebuttal of Mrs. Wilson's most recent depiction of his character. "Mrs. Wilson!"

"Eh?" She paused for breath, blinking up at him in momentary confusion.

"Cease. And you, too!" He glared at Hiram, who was opening his mouth again. Hiram shut it.

"I'll no have this," Roger said, and thumped the Bible down on the table. "It's not fitting, and I'll not have it, d'ye hear me?" He glowered from one to the other of the combatants, black brows low and fierce.

The room was silent, bar Hiram's heavy breathing, Mrs. Crombie's small sobs, and Mrs. Wilson's faint, asthmatic wheeze.

"Now, then," Roger said, still glaring round to prevent any further interruptions. He put a hand over Mrs. Wilson's thin, age-spotted one.

"Mrs. Wilson—d'ye not ken that you stand before God this minute?" He darted a look at me, and I nodded; yes, she was definitely going to die. Her head was wobbling on her neck and the glow of anger fading from her eyes, even as he spoke.

"God is near to us," he said, lifting his head to address the congregation at large. He repeated this in Gaelic, and there was a sort of collective sigh. He narrowed his eyes at them.

"We will not profane this holy occasion with anger nor bitterness. Now—sister." He squeezed her hand gently. "Compose your soul. God will—"

But Mrs. Wilson was no longer listening. Her withered mouth dropped open in horror.

"The sin-eater!" she cried, looking wildly round. She grabbed the dish from the table next to her, showering salt down the front of her winding-sheet. "Where is the sin-eater?"

Hiram stiffened as though goosed with a red-hot poker, then whirled and fought his way toward the door, the crowd giving way before him. Murmurs of speculation rose in his wake, only to stop abruptly as a piercing wail rose from outside, another rising behind it as the first one fell.

An awed "oooh!" rose from the crowd, and Mrs. Wilson looked gratified, as the *bean-treim* started in to earn their money in earnest.

Then there was a stirring near the door, and the crowd parted like the Red Sea, leaving a narrow path to the table. Mrs. Wilson sat bolt upright, dead-white and barely breathing. The pulse in her abdomen skittered and jumped under my fingers. Roger and Jamie had hold of her arms, supporting her.

A complete hush had fallen over the room; the only sounds were the howling of the *bean-treim*—and slow, shuffling footsteps, soft on the ground outside, then suddenly louder on the boards of the floor. The sin-eater had arrived.

He was a tall man, or had been, once. It was impossible to tell his age; either years or illness had eaten away his flesh, so that his wide shoulders bowed and his spine had hunched, a gaunt head poking forward, crowned with a balding straggle of graying strands.

I glanced up at Jamie, eyebrows raised. I had never seen the man before. He shrugged slightly; he didn't know him, either. As the sin-eater came closer, I saw that his body was crooked; he seemed caved in on one side, ribs perhaps crushed by some accident.

Every eye was fixed on the man, but he met none of them, keeping his gaze focused on the floor. The path to the table was narrow, but the people shrank back as he passed, careful that he should not touch them. Only when he reached the table did he lift his head, and I saw that one eye was missing, evidently clawed away by a bear, judging from the welted mass of scar tissue.

The other one was working; he halted in surprise, seeing Mrs. Wilson, and glanced round, obviously unsure what to do next.

She wiggled one arm free of Roger's grip and pushed the dish containing the bread and salt toward him.

"Get on, then," she said, her voice high and a little frightened.

"But you're not dead." It was a soft, educated voice, betraying only puzzlement, but the crowd reacted as though it had been the hissing of a serpent, and recoiled further, if such a thing were possible.

"Well, what of it?" Agitation was making Mrs. Wilson tremble even more; I could feel a small constant vibration through the table. "Ye've been paid to eat my sins—be after doing it, then!" A thought occurred to her and she jerked upright, squinting at her son-in-law. "Ye *did* pay him, Hiram?"

Hiram was still flushed from the previous exchanges, but went a sort of puce at this, and clutched his side—clutching at his purse, I thought, rather than his heart.

"Well, I'm no going to pay him *before* he's done the job," he snapped. "What sort of way is that to be carrying on?"

Seeing renewed riot about to break out, Jamie let go his hold on Mrs. Wilson and fumbled hastily in his sporran, emerging with a silver shilling, which he thrust across the table toward the sin-eater—though careful, I saw, not to touch the man.

"Now ye've been paid," he said gruffly, nodding to him. "Best be about your business, sir."

The man looked slowly round the room, and the intake of breath from the crowd was audible, even over the wails of "WOOOOOOOOOOOEEEE to the house of CROMMMM-BIIIEEEEEE" going on outside.

He was standing no more than a foot away from me, close enough that I could smell the sweet-sour odor of him: ancient sweat and dirt in his rags, and something else, some faint aroma that spoke of pustulant sores and unhealed wounds. He turned his head and looked straight at me. It was a soft brown eye, amber in color, and startlingly like my own. Meeting his gaze gave me a queer feeling in the pit of the stomach, as though I looked for a moment into a distorting mirror, and saw that cruelly misshapen face replace my own.

He did not change expression, and yet I felt something nameless pass between us. Then he turned his head away, and reached out a long, weathered, very dirty hand to pick up the piece of bread.

A sort of sigh went through the room as he ate—slowly gumming the bread, for he had few teeth. I could feel Mrs. Wilson's pulse, much lighter now, and fast, like a hummingbird's. She hung nearly limp in the men's grasp, the withered lids of her eyes drooping as she watched.

He wrapped both hands around the cup of wine, as though it were a chalice, and drank it down, eyes closed. He set the empty cup down and looked at Mrs. Wilson, curiously. I supposed he never had met one of his clients alive before, and wondered how long he had fulfilled this strange office.

Mrs. Wilson stared into his eyes, face blank as a child's. Her abdominal pulse was skipping like a stone, a few light beats, a pause, then a thump that struck my palm like a blow, and back to its erratic jumps.

The sin-eater bowed to her, very slowly. Then he turned round, and scampered for the door, with amazing speed for such an infirm specimen.

Several of the boys and younger men near the door rushed out after him, yelling; one or two seized sticks of wood from the fire basket by the hearth. Others were torn; they glanced toward the open door, where shouts and the thumps of thrown stones mingled with the wailing of the *bean-treim*—but their eyes were drawn back ineluctably to Mrs. Wilson.

She looked . . . peaceful, was the only word. It was no surprise whatever to feel the pulse beneath my hand simply stop. Somewhere deeper, in my own depths, I felt the dizzying rush of the hemorrhage begin, a flooding warmth that pulled me into it, made black spots whirl before my eyes, and caused a ringing in my ears. I knew to all intents and purposes she had now died for good. I felt her go. And yet I heard her voice above the racket, very small but calm and clear.

"I forgive ye, Hiram," she said. "Ye've been a good lad."

My vision had gone dark, but I could still hear and sense

things dimly. Something grasped me, pulled me away, and a moment later I came to myself, leaning against Jamie in a corner, his arms supporting me.

"Are ye all right, Sassenach?" he was saying urgently, shaking me a little and patting my cheek.

The black-clad *bean-treim* had come as far as the door. I could see them outside, standing like twin pillars of darkness, falling snow beginning to whirl round them as the cold wind came inside, small hard dry flakes skittering and bouncing in its wake across the floor. The women's voices rose and fell, blending with the wind. By the table, Hiram Crombie was trying to fix his mother-in-law's garnet brooch to her shroud, though his hands shook and his narrow face was wet with tears.

"Yes," I said faintly, then "yes" a little stronger. "Everything is all right now."

Part Six

On the Mountain

40

BIRD-SPRING

March 1774

IT WAS SPRING, and the long months of desolation melted into running water, with streamlets pouring from every hill and miniature waterfalls leaping from stone to stone to stone.

The air was filled with the racket of birds, a cacophony of melody that replaced the lonely calling of geese passing by far overhead.

Birds go one by one in the winter, a single raven hunched brooding in a barren tree, an owl fluffed against the cold in the high, dark shadows of a barn. Or they go in flocks, a massed thunder of wings to bear them up and away, wheeling through the sky like handsful of pepper grains thrown aloft, calling their way in Vs of mournful courage toward the promise of a distant and problematic survival.

In winter, the raptors draw apart unto themselves; the songbirds flee away, all the color of the feathered world reduced to the brutal simplification of predator and prey, gray shadows passing overhead, with no more than a small bright drop of blood fallen back to earth here and there to mark the passing of life, leaving a drift of scattered feathers, borne on the wind.

But as spring blooms, the birds grow drunk with love and the bushes riot with their songs. Far, far into the night, darkness mutes but does not silence them, and small melodious conversations break out at all hours, invisible and strangely intimate in the dead of night, as though one overheard the lovemaking of strangers in the room next door.

I moved closer to Jamie, hearing the clear, sweet song of a

thrush in the great red spruce that stood behind the house. It was still cold at night, but not with the bitter chill of winter; rather with the sweet fresh cold of thawing earth and springing leaves, a cold that sent the blood tingling and made warm bodies seek one another, nesting.

A rumbling snore echoed across the landing—another harbinger of spring. Major MacDonald, who had arrived mud-caked and wind-bitten the night before, bringing unwelcome news of the outside world.

Jamie stirred briefly at the sound, groaned, farted briefly, and lay still. He'd stayed up late, entertaining the Major—if entertainment was the word for it.

I could hear Lizzie and Mrs. Bug in the kitchen below, talking as they banged pots and slammed doors in hopes of rousing us. Breakfast smells began to rise up the stairs, enticing, the bitter smell of roasting chicory spicing the thick warmth of buttered porridge.

The sound of Jamie's breathing had changed, and I knew he was awake, though he still lay with his eyes closed. I didn't know whether this denoted an urge to continue the physical pleasure of sleep—or a marked disinclination to get up and deal with Major MacDonald.

He resolved this doubt at once by rolling over, enveloping me in his arms, and moving his lower body against mine in a manner that made it obvious that, while physical pleasure was what was on his mind, he was quite through sleeping.

He hadn't reached the point of coherent speech yet, though, and nuzzled my ear, making small interrogatory hums in his throat. Well, the Major was still asleep, and the coffee—such as it was—wouldn't be ready for a bit. I hummed back, reached to the bedside table for a bit of almond cream, and commenced a slow and pleasurable rummage through the layers of bedclothes and nightshirt to apply it.

Some small while later, snorts and thumps across the hall denoted the resurrection of Major MacDonald, and the delectable scents of frying ham and potatoes with onions had joined the throng of olfactory stimuli. The sweet smell of almond cream was stronger, though.

"Greased lightning," Jamie said with a drowsy air of satisfaction. He was still in bed, lying on his side to watch me dress.

"What?" I turned from my looking glass to eye him. "Who?"

"Me, I suppose. Or were ye not thunderstruck, there at the end?" He laughed, almost silently, rustling the bedclothes.

"Oh, you've been talking to Bree again," I said tolerantly. I turned back to the glass. "That particular figure of speech is a metaphor for extreme speed, not lubricated brilliance."

I smiled at him in the glass as I brushed knots out of my hair. He had unplaited it while I was anointing him, and subsequent exertions had caused it to explode. Come to think, it did faintly resemble the effects of electrocution.

"Well, I can be fast, too," he said judiciously, sitting up and rubbing a hand through his own hair. "But not first thing in the morning. There are worse ways to wake up, aye?"

"Yes, much worse." Sounds of hawking and spitting came from across the landing, followed by the distinctive sound of someone with very vigorous bladder function employing a chamber pot. "Is he staying long, did he say?"

Jamie shook his head. Rising slowly, he stretched himself like a cat and then came across in his shirt to put his arms around me. I hadn't yet poked up the fire, and the room was chilly; his body was pleasantly warm.

He rested his chin on top of my head, regarding our stacked reflections in the mirror.

"I'll have to go," he said softly. "Tomorrow, perhaps."

I stiffened a little, brush in hand.

"Where? To the Indians?"

He nodded, eyes on mine.

"MacDonald brought newspapers, wi' the text of letters from Governor Martin to various people—Tryon in New York, General Gage—asking help. He's losing his grip upon the colony—insofar as he ever had one—and is seriously thinking of arming the Indians. Though *that* bit of information hasna made it into the newspapers, and a good thing, too."

He released me, and reached for the drawer where his clean shirts and stockings stayed.

"That *is* a good thing," I said, bundling back my hair and hunting for a ribbon to tie it with. We'd seen few newspapers through the winter, but even so, the level of disagreement between the Governor and the Assembly was clear; he'd resorted to a practice of continuous proroguing, repeatedly dismissing the Assembly in order to prevent them passing legislation at odds with his desires.

I could well imagine what the public response would be to the revelation that he contemplated arming the Cherokee, Catawba, and Creek, and inciting them against his own people.

"I'm guessing that he isn't actually going to do that," I said, finding the blue ribbon I was looking for, "because if he had—does, I mean—the Revolution would have got going in North Carolina right now, rather than in Massachusetts or Philadelphia two years from now. But why on earth is he publishing these letters in the newspaper?"

Jamie laughed. He shook his head, pushing back the disheveled hair from his face.

"He's not. Evidently, the Governor's mail is being intercepted. He's no verra pleased about it, MacDonald says."

"I daresay not." Mail was notoriously insecure, and always had been. In fact, we had originally acquired Fergus when Jamie hired him as a pickpocket, in order to steal letters in Paris. "How is Fergus doing?" I asked.

Jamie made a small grimace, pulling on his stockings.

"Better, I think. Marsali says he's staying more to home, which is good. And he's earning a wee bit, teaching French to Hiram Crombie. But—"

"Hiram? *French?*"

"Oh, aye." He grinned at me. "Hiram's set upon the idea that he must go and preach to the Indians, and he thinks he'll be best equipped to manage if he's got some French as well as English. Ian's teaching him a bit of the Tsalagi, too, but there are so many Indian tongues, he'd never learn them all."

"Will wonders never cease," I murmured. "Do you think—"

I was interrupted at this point by Mrs. Bug bellowing up the stairs, "If Certain Persons are wantin' to let a good breakfast be spoilt, I'm sure they're welcome!"

Like clockwork, Major MacDonald's door popped open, and his feet clattered eagerly down the stairs.

"Ready?" I said to Jamie. He seized my hairbrush and tidied himself with a few licks, then came to open the door and bowed, ushering me ceremoniously out.

"What ye said, Sassenach," he said as he followed me down the stair. "About it starting in two years. It's already well begun. Ye know that, aye?"

"Oh, yes," I said, rather grimly. "But I don't want to think about it on an empty stomach."

ROGER STOOD UP straight, measuring. The edge of the kiln pit he stood in came just under his chin. Six feet would be just about at eye level; only a few more inches, then. That was heartening. Setting the shovel against the dirt wall, he stooped, grabbed a wooden bucket full of earth, and heaved it up over the rim.

"Dirt!" he yelled. There was no response to his shout. He rose on his toes, peering balefully round for his so-called assistants. Jemmy and Germain were meant to be taking it in turn to empty the buckets and pass them back down to him, but had a tendency to vanish abruptly.

"Dirt!" he shouted as loudly as he could. The wee buggers couldn't have gone far; it took him less than two minutes to fill a bucket.

This call was answered, but not by the boys. A cold shadow fell over him, and he squinted up to see the silhouette of his father-in-law, stooping to grab the handle of the bucket. Jamie strode two paces and flung the dirt onto the slowly mounting heap, then came back, hopping down into the pit to return it.

"A tidy wee hole ye have here," he said, turning round to survey it. "Ye could barbecue an ox in it."

"I'll need one. I'm starving." Roger wiped a sleeve across his forehead; the spring day was cool and crisp, but he was drenched with sweat.

Jamie had picked up his shovel and was examining the blade with interest.

"I've never seen the like. Is it the lass's work?"

"With a bit of help from Dai Jones, aye." It had taken roughly thirty seconds' work with an eighteenth-century shovel to convince Brianna that improvements could be made. It had taken three months to acquire a chunk of iron that could be shaped to her directions by the blacksmith and to persuade Dai Jones—who was Welsh and thus by definition stubborn—into doing it. The normal spade was made of wood, and looked like nothing so much as a roof shingle attached to a pole.

"May I try?" Enchanted, Jamie drove the pointed end of the new spade into the dirt at his feet.

"Be my guest."

Roger scrambled up out of the deep part of the pit into the shallower end of the kiln. Jamie stood in the part where the fire would go, according to Brianna, with a chimney to be raised over it. Items to be fired would sit in the longer, relatively shallow part of the pit and be covered over. After a week of shoveling, Roger was less inclined to think the distant possibility of plumbing was worth all the labor involved, but Bree wanted it—and like her father, Bree was difficult to resist, though their methods varied.

Jamie shoveled briskly, tossing spadesful of dirt into the bucket, with small exclamations of delight and admiration at the ease and speed with which dirt could be dug. Despite his dim view of the occupation, Roger felt a sense of pride in his wife's implement.

"First the wee matchsticks," Jamie said, making a joke of it, "now shovels. What will she think of next?"

"I'm afraid to ask," Roger said, with a tinge of rue that made Jamie laugh.

The bucket filled, Roger picked it up and took it to empty, while Jamie filled the second. And without spoken agreement, they continued the job, Jamie digging, Roger carrying, finishing in what seemed no time at all.

Jamie climbed out of the pit and joined Roger on the edge, looking down at their handiwork in satisfaction.

"And if it doesna work well as a kiln," Jamie observed, "she can make a root cellar of it."

"Waste not, want not," Roger agreed. They stood looking down into the hole, the breeze chilly through their damp shirts now that they'd stopped moving.

"D'ye think ye might go back, you and the lass?" Jamie

said. He spoke so casually that Roger missed his meaning at first, not catching on until he saw his father-in-law's face, set in the imperturbable calm that—he'd learned to his cost—generally covered some strong emotion.

"Back," he repeated uncertainly. Surely he didn't mean—but of course he did. "Through the stones, do you mean?"

Jamie nodded, seeming to find some fascination in the walls of the pit, where drying grass rootlets hung in tangles, and the jagged edges of stones protruded from the patchy damp dirt.

"I've thought of it," Roger said, after a pause. "*We've* thought. But . . ." He let his voice trail off, finding no good way to explain.

Jamie nodded again, though, as if he had. He supposed Jamie and Claire must have discussed it, even as he and Bree had, playing over the pros and cons. The dangers of the passage—and he did not underestimate those dangers, the more so in light of what Claire had told him about Donner and his comrades; what if he made it through—and Bree and Jem didn't? It didn't bear thinking.

Beyond that, if they all survived the passage, was the pain of separation—and he would admit that it would be painful for him, as well. Whatever its limitations or inconveniences, the Ridge was home.

Against those considerations, though, stood the dangers of the present time, for the four horsemen of the apocalypse rode widely here; it was no trick to catch a glimpse of pestilence or famine from the corner of your eye. And the pale horse and its rider were inclined to show up unexpectedly—and often.

But that's what Jamie meant, of course, he realized belatedly.

"Because of the war, ye mean."

"The O'Brians," Jamie said quietly. "That will happen again, ken? Many times."

It was spring now, not autumn, but the cold wind that touched his bones was the same as the one that had blown brown and golden leaves across the face of the little girl. Roger had a sudden vision of the two of them, Jamie and himself, standing now at the edge of this cavernous hole, like bedraggled mourners at a graveside. He turned his back on the pit, looking instead into the budding green of the chestnut trees.

"Ye know," he said, after a moment's silence, "when I first learned what—what Claire is, what we are, all about it—I thought, 'How fascinating!' To actually see history in the making, I mean. In all honesty, I maybe came as much for that as for Bree. Then, I mean."

Jamie laughed shortly, turning round as well.

"Oh, aye, and is it? Fascinating?"

"More than I ever thought," Roger assured him, with extreme dryness. "But why are ye asking now? I told ye a year ago that we'd stay."

Jamie nodded, pursing his lips.

"Ye did. The thing is—I am thinking I must sell one or more of the gemstones."

That brought Roger up a bit. He'd not consciously thought it, of course—but the knowledge that the gems were there, in case of need . . . He hadn't realized what a sense of security that knowledge had held, until this moment.

"They're yours to sell," he replied, cautious. "Why now, though? Are things difficult?"

Jamie gave him an exceedingly wry look.

"Difficult," he repeated. "Aye, ye could say that." And proceeded to lay out the situation succinctly.

The marauders had destroyed not only a season's whisky in the making, but also the malting shed, only now rebuilding. That meant no surplus of the lovely drink this year to sell or trade for necessities. There were twenty-two more tenant families on the Ridge to be mindful of, most of them struggling with a place and a profession that they could never have imagined, trying merely to keep alive long enough to learn how to stay that way.

"And then," Jamie added grimly, "there's MacDonald—speak o' the devil."

The Major himself had come out onto the stoop, his red coat bright in the morning sun. He was dressed for travel, Roger saw, booted and spurred, and wearing his wig, laced hat in hand.

"A flying visit, I see."

Jamie made a small, uncouth noise.

"Long enough to tell me I must try to arrange the purchase of thirty muskets, with shot and powder—at my own expense, mind—to be repaid by the Crown, eventually," he added, in a cynic tone that made it obvious how remote he considered this eventuality to be.

"Thirty muskets." Roger contemplated that, pursing his own lips in a soundless whistle. Jamie had not been able even to afford to replace the rifle he had given Bird for his help in the matter of Brownsville.

Jamie shrugged.

"And then there are wee matters like the dowry I've promised Lizzie Wemyss—she'll be wed this summer. And Marsali's mother, Laoghaire—" He glanced warily at Roger, unsure how much he might know regarding Laoghaire. More than Jamie would be comfortable knowing, Roger thought, and tactfully kept his face blank.

"I owe a bit to her, for maintenance. We can live, aye, with what we've got—but for the rest . . . I must sell land, or the stones. And I willna give up the land." His fingers drummed restlessly against his thigh, then stopped, as he raised his hand to wave to the Major, who had just spotted them across the clearing.

"I see. Well, then . . ." Plainly, it had to be done; it was foolish to sit on a fortune in gems, merely because they might one day be needed for a far-fetched and risky purpose. Still, the notion made Roger feel slightly hollow, like rappelling down a cliff and having someone cut your safety line.

Jamie blew out his breath.

"Well, so. I'll send one wi' Bobby Higgins to his Lordship in Virginia. He'll get me a good price, at least."

"Aye, that's a—" Roger halted, his attention deflected by the scenario unfolding before him.

The Major, obviously well-breakfasted and cheerful, had come down the steps and was strolling toward them—oblivious of the white sow, who had emerged from her den beneath the foundation and was ambling along the side of the house, bent on her own breakfast. It would be a matter of seconds before she spotted the Major.

"Hoy!" Roger bellowed, and felt something tear in his

throat. The pain was so sharp that it stopped him cold, and he clutched at his throat, struck suddenly mute.

"'Ware the pig!" Jamie was shouting, waving and pointing. The Major thrust his head forward, hand behind his ear—then caught the repeated bellows of "Pig!" and looked wildly round, just in time to see the white sow break into a ponderous trot, scything her tusks from side to side.

He would have been best served by wheeling and sprinting back to the safety of the stoop, but instead panic struck him and he ran—away from the pig, coming straight for Jamie and Roger, who promptly ran in different directions.

Glancing back, Roger saw the Major gaining on the pig with long-legged leaps, his goal evidently the cabin. Between the Major and the cabin, though, lay the open hole of the groundhog kiln, masked by the heavy growth of long spring grass through which the Major bounded.

"Pit!" Roger shouted, only the word came out in a strangled croak. Nonetheless, MacDonald seemed to hear him, for a bright red face turned in his direction, eyes bulging. It must have sounded like "Pig!" for the Major glanced back over his shoulder then to see the sow trot faster, small pink eyes fixed on him with murderous intent.

The distraction proved nearly fatal, for the Major's spurs caught and tangled, and he sprawled headlong in the grass, losing his grip on the laced hat—which he had held throughout the chase—and sending it pinwheeling through the air.

Roger hesitated for an instant, but then ran back to help, with a smothered oath. He saw Jamie running back, too, spade held at the ready—though even a metal shovel seemed pitifully inadequate to deal with a five-hundred-pound hog.

MacDonald was already scrambling to his feet, though; before either of them could reach him, he took off running as though the devil himself were breathing on his coattails. Arms pumping and face set in puce determination, he ran for his life, bounding like a jackrabbit through the grass—and disappeared. One instant he was there, and the next he had vanished, as though by magic.

Jamie looked wide-eyed at Roger, then at the pig, who had stopped short on the far side of the kiln pit. Then, moving gingerly, one eye always on the pig, he sidled toward the pit, glancing sideways, as though afraid to see what lay at the bottom.

Roger moved to stand at Jamie's shoulder, looking down. Major MacDonald had fallen into the deeper hole at the end, where he lay curled up like a hedgehog, arms clasped protectively over his wig—which had remained in place by some miracle, though now much bespattered with dirt and bits of grass.

"MacDonald?" Jamie called down. "Are ye damaged, man?"

"Is she there?" quavered the Major, not emerging from his ball.

Roger glanced across the pit at the pig, now some distance away, snout down in the long grass.

"Er . . . aye, she is." To his surprise, his voice came easy, if a little hoarse. He cleared his throat and spoke a little louder. "Ye needna worry, though. She's busy eating your hat."

41

THE GUN-SMITH

JAMIE ACCOMPANIED MacDonald as far as Coopersville, where he set the Major on the road back to Salisbury, equipped with food, a disreputable slouched hat against the weather, and a small bottle of whisky to fortify his bruised spirits. Then, with an internal sigh, he turned into the McGillivrays' place.

Robin was at work in his forge, surrounded by the smells of hot metal, wood shavings, and gun oil. A lanky young man with a hatchet face was working the leather bellows, though his dreamy expression showed a certain lack of attention to the job.

Robin caught the shadow of Jamie's entrance and glanced up, gave a quick nod, and returned to his work.

He was hammering bar iron into flat bands; the iron cylinder he meant to wrap them round to form a gun barrel was waiting, propped between two blocks. Jamie moved carefully out of range of flying sparks and sat down on a bucket to wait.

That was Senga's betrothed at the bellows . . . Heinrich. Heinrich Strasse. He picked the name unerringly out of the hundreds he carried in his mind, and along with it came automatically all he knew of young Heinrich's history, family, and connections, these appearing in his imagination round the boy's long, dreamy face in a constellation of social affinities, orderly and complex as the pattern of a snowflake.

He always saw people in this way, but seldom thought of it consciously. There was something about the shape of Strasse's face, though, that reinforced the mental imagery—the long axis of forehead, nose, and chin, emphasized by a horsey upper lip, deeply grooved, the horizontal axis shorter, but no less sharply defined by long, narrow eyes and flat dark brows above them.

He could see the boy's origins—the middle of nine children, but the eldest boy, son of an overbearing father and a mother who dealt with this by means of subterfuge and quiet malice—sprouting in a delicate array from the rather pointed top of his head, his religion—Lutheran, but slack about it—a lacy spray under an equally pointed chin, his relation with Robin—cordial, but wary, as befitted a new son-in-law who was also an apprentice—extending like a fanned spike from his right ear, that with Ute—a mix of terror and helpless abashment—from the left.

This notion entertained him very much, and he was obliged to look away, affecting interest in Robin's workbench, in order to keep from staring and rendering the lad uncomfortable.

The gunsmith was not tidy; scraps of wood and metal lay among a jumble of spikes, scribes, hammers, blocks of wood, bits of filthy garnet cloth and sticks of charcoal on the bench. A few papers were weighted down with a spoiled gunstock that had split in the making, their dirty edges fluttering in the hot breath of the forge. He would have taken no notice, save that he recognized the style of the drawing, would have known that boldness and delicacy of line anywhere.

Frowning, he rose and pulled the papers from under the gunstock. Drawings of a gun, executed from different angles—a rifle, there was the cutaway interior of the barrel, the grooves and landings clear—but most peculiar. One drawing showed it whole, reasonably familiar, bar the odd hornlike growths on the barrel. But the next . . . the gun seemed as though someone had broken it over his knee; it was snapped through, stock and barrel pointing downward in opposite directions, joined only by . . . what sort of hinge was that? He closed one eye, considering.

The cessation of clamor from the forge and the loud hiss of hot metal in the sump broke his fascination with the drawings and made him look up.

"Did your lass show ye those?" Robin asked, with a nod at the papers. He pulled the tail of his shirt up from behind his leather apron, and mopped steam from his sweating face, looking amused.

"No. What is she about? Is she wanting ye to make her a gun?" He relinquished the sheets to the gunsmith, who shuffled through them, sniffing with interest.

"Oh, she's no way of paying for that, *Mac Dubh,* unless Roger Mac's discovered a pot o' fairy gold since last week. No, she's only been telling me her notions of improvement in the art of riflery, asking what it might cost to make such a thing." The cynic smile that had been lurking in the corner of Robin's mouth broadened into a grin, and he shoved the papers back at Jamie. "I can tell she's yours, *Mac Dubh.* What other lass would spend her time thinking of guns, rather than gowns and bairns?"

There was more than a little implied criticism in this remark—Brianna had undoubtedly been a good deal more forthright in manner than was becoming—but he let it pass for the moment. He needed Robin's goodwill.

"Well, any woman has her fancies," he observed mildly. "Even wee Lizzie, I suppose—but Manfred will see to that, I'm sure. He'll be in Salisbury just now? Or Hillsboro?"

Robin McGillivray was by no means a stupid man. The abrupt transition of subject made him arch one brow, but he passed no remark. Instead, he sent Heinrich off to the house to fetch them some beer, waiting for the lad to disappear before turning back to Jamie, expectant.

"I need thirty muskets, Robin," he said without preamble. "And I'll need them quickly—within three months."

The gunsmith's face went comically blank with astonishment, but only for a moment. He blinked then, and closed his mouth with a snap, resuming his usual expression of sardonic good humor.

"Starting your own army, are ye, *Mac Dubh*?"

Jamie merely smiled at that without answering. If word got around that he meant to arm his tenantry and muster his own Committee of Safety in answer to Richard Brown's banditry, that would do nay harm and might do good. Letting word get out that the Governor was working secretly to arm the savages, in case he required to suppress an armed rising in the backcountry, and that he, Jamie Fraser, was the agent of such action—that was an excellent way to get himself killed and his house burnt to the ground, to say nothing of what other trouble might ensue.

"How many can ye find for me, Robin? And how fast?"

The gunsmith squinted, thinking, then darted a sideways glance at him.

"Cash?"

He nodded, seeing Robin's lips purse in a soundless whistle of astonishment. Robin kent as well as anyone that he had no money to speak of—let alone the small fortune required to assemble that many guns.

He could see the speculation in Robin's eyes, as to where he might be planning to acquire that sort of money—but the gunsmith said nothing aloud. McGillivray's upper teeth sank into his lower lip in concentration, then relaxed.

"I can find six, maybe seven, betwixt Salisbury and Salem. Brugge"—naming the Moravian gunsmith—"would do one or two, if he kent it was for you. . . ." Seeing the infinitesimal shake of Jamie's head he nodded in resignation. "Aye, well, maybe seven, then. And Manfred and I can manage maybe three more—it's only muskets you're wanting, nothing fancy?" He tilted his head toward Brianna's drawing with a small flash of his earlier humor.

"Nothing fancy," Jamie said, smiling. "That's ten, then." He waited. Robin sighed, settling himself.

"I'll ask about," he said. "But it's no an easy matter. Particularly if ye dinna mean your name to be heard in connection—and I gather ye don't."

"Ye're a man o' rare wit and discretion, Robin," Jamie assured him gravely, making him laugh. It was true, for all that; Robin McGillivray had fought beside him at Culloden, lived three years with him in Ardsmuir; Jamie would trust him with his life—and was. He began to wish the pig had eaten MacDonald after all, but put the unworthy thought from his mind and drank the beer Heinrich brought, chatting of inconsequence and trivia until it was polite to take his leave.

He had ridden Gideon, to bear MacDonald company on his horse, but meant to leave him in Dai Jones's barn. Through a complex bit of bargaining, Gideon would cover John Woolam's spotted mare—to be brought up when Woolam returned from Bear Creek—and when the harvest was in come autumn, Jamie would collect a hundredweight of barley, with a bottle of whisky to Dai for his assistance.

Exchanging a bit of conversation with Dai—he could never decide whether the blacksmith was truly a man of few words, or was it only that he despaired of making the Scots understand his Welsh singsong—Jamie slapped Gideon encouragingly on the neck and left him to eat grain and fettle his loins against the coming of the spotted mare.

Dai had offered him food, but he declined; he was peckish, but looked forward to the peace of the five-mile walk home. The day was fine and pale blue, with the spring leaves murmuring to themselves overhead, and a bit of solitude would be welcome.

The decision had been made when he asked Robin to find him guns. But the situation bore thought.

There were sixty-four villages of the Cherokee; each with its own headman, its own peace chief and war chief. Only five of those villages were within his power to influence—the three villages of the Snowbird people, and two that belonged to the Overhill Cherokee. Those, he thought, would follow the leaders of the Overhill, regardless of his words.

Roger Mac had known relatively little of the Cherokee, or

what their role might be in the looming fight. He had been able to say only that the Cherokee had not acted *en masse;* some villages chose to fight, some did not—some fought for one side, some for another.

Well, so. It was not likely that anything he said or did would turn the tide of war, and that was a comfort. But he could not escape the knowledge that his own time to jump was coming. So far as anyone knew now, he was a loyal subject to His Majesty, a Tory beavering away in Geordie's interest, suborning savages and distributing guns with an eye to suppressing the riotous passions of Regulators, Whigs, and would-be republicans.

At some point, this facade must necessarily crumble to reveal him as a dyed-in-the-wool rebel and a traitor. But when? He wondered idly whether he might have a price on his head this time, and how much it would be.

It might be not so difficult, with the Scots. Grudge-bearing and hardheaded as they were, he was one of them, and personal liking might moderate the sense of outrage at his turning rebel, when the time came.

No, it was the Indians he worried over—for he came to them as the agent of the King. How suddenly to explain his change of heart? And further, do it in such a way that they might share it? Surely they would see this as treachery at worst, grossly suspicious behavior at best. He thought they would not kill him, but how in God's name to induce them to fall in with the cause of rebellion, when they enjoyed a stable and prosperous relation with His Majesty?

Oh, God, and there was John. What could he say to his friend, when the time came? Convince him by logic and rhetoric to change his coat as well? He hissed through his teeth and shook his head in consternation, trying—and failing utterly—to envision John Grey, lifelong soldier, ex-Royal Governor, that very soul of loyalty and honor, suddenly declaring himself for rebellion and republic.

He passed on, fretting in this fashion for some time, but gradually found the walking soothed his mind, and the peace of the day lightened his heart. There would be time before supper to take wee Jem fishing, he thought; the sun was bright, but there was a certain dampness to the air under the trees that was promising for a first hatch of flies on the water. He had a feeling in his bones that the trout would rise near sunset.

In this more pleasant frame of mind, he was glad to meet his daughter, some little way below the Ridge. His heart lifted at sight of her hair, streaming wanton down her back in ruddy glory.

"Ciamar a tha thu, a nighean?" he said, kissing her cheek in greeting.

"Tha mi gu math, mo athair," she said, and she smiled, but he noted a small frown that troubled the smooth flesh of her forehead like the hatch of mayfly on a trout pond.

"I've been waiting for you," she said, taking his arm. "I wanted to talk to you before you go to the Indians tomorrow." And there was that in her tone that drove all thought of fish from his mind upon the instant.

"Oh, aye?"

She nodded, but seemed to have some difficulty in finding words—an occurrence that alarmed him still further. But he could not help her, without some notion what it was about, and so kept pace with her, silent but encouraging. A mockingbird was busy nearby, practicing its repertoire of calls. It was the bird who lived in the red spruce behind the house; he knew because it paused now and then in the midst of its chatter and trilling to give a fine imitation of Adso the cat's midnight yowl.

"When you talked to Roger about the Indians," Brianna said finally, and turned her head to look at him, "did he mention something called the Trail of Tears?"

"No," he said, curious. "What is that?"

She grimaced, hunching her shoulders in a way that seemed disconcertingly familiar.

"I thought maybe he hadn't. He said he'd told you all he knew about the Indians and the Revolution—not that he knows all that much, it wasn't his specialty—but this happened—will happen later, after the Revolution. So he maybe didn't think it was important. Maybe it's not."

She hesitated, as though wanting him to tell her that it wasn't. He only waited, though, and she sighed, looking at her feet as she paced along. She was wearing sandals without stockings, and her long, bare toes were grimed with the soft dust of the wagon road. The sight of her feet always filled him with an odd mixture of pride at their elegant shape and a faint sense of shame at their size—but as he was responsible for both, he supposed he had no grounds for complaint.

"About sixty years from now," she said at last, eyes on the ground, "the American government will take the Cherokee from their land and move them. A long way—to a place called Oklahoma. It's a thousand miles, at least, and hundreds and hundreds of them will starve and die on the way. That's why they called it—will call it—the Trail of Tears."

He was impressed to hear that there should be a government capable of doing such a thing, and said so. She shot him an angry glance.

"They'll do it by cheating. They'll talk some of the Cherokee leaders into agreeing by promising them things and not keeping their bargain."

He shrugged.

"That's how most governments behave," he observed mildly. "Why are ye telling me this, lass? I will—thank God—be safely dead before any of it happens."

He saw a flicker cross her face at mention of his death, and was sorry to have caused her distress by his levity. Before he could apologize, though, she squared her shoulders and went on.

"I'm telling you because I thought you should know," she said. "Not all of the Cherokee went—some of them went farther up into the mountains and hid; the army didn't find them."

"Aye?"

She turned her head and gave him a look from those eyes that were his own, touching in their earnestness.

"Don't you see? Mama told you what would happen—about Culloden. You couldn't stop it, but you saved Lallybroch. And your men, your tenants. Because you knew."

"Oh, Christ," he said, realizing with a shock what she meant. Recollection washed through him in a flood, the terror and desperation and uncertainty of that time—the numb despair that had carried him through that last fatal day. "Ye want me to tell Bird."

She rubbed a hand over her face, and shook her head.

"I don't know. I don't know if you *should* tell him—or if you do, whether he'll listen. But Roger and I talked about it, after you asked him about the Indians. And I kept thinking about it . . . and, well, it just didn't seem *right,* to know and not do anything. So I thought I'd better tell you."

"Aye, I see," he said a little bleakly.

He had noticed before the inclination of persons with tender consciences to ease their discomfort by handing the necessity of taking action on to someone else, but forbore to mention it. She could hardly be telling Bird herself, after all.

As though the situation he faced with the Cherokee were not sufficiently difficult already, he thought wryly—now he must deal with saving unknown future generations of savages? The mockingbird zoomed past his ear, unnervingly close, clucking like a hen, of all things.

It was so incongruous that he laughed. And then realized that there was nothing else to do. Not now.

Brianna was looking at him curiously.

"What are you going to do?"

He stretched himself, slowly, luxuriously, feeling the muscles of his back pull upon his bones, feeling each of them, alive and solid. The sun was coming down the sky, supper was beginning to cook, and for now, for this one last night, he need do nothing. Not yet.

"I'm going fishing," he said, smiling at his lovely, unlikely, problematical daughter. "Fetch the wee lad, aye? I'll get the poles."

James Fraser, Esq. from Fraser's Ridge

To my Lord John Grey, Mount Josiah Plantation,
this 2nd day of April, Anno Domini 1774

My lord,

I depart in the morning to visit the Cherokee, and so leave this with my wife, to be entrusted to Mr. Higgins when he shall next arrive, to be delivered with its accompanying parcel into your hands.

I presume upon your kindness and your solicitude for my family in asking your favor to help in selling the object I entrust to you. I suspect that your connexions might enable you to obtain a better price than I might do myself—and to do so discreetly.

I shall hope upon my return to confide in you the reasons for my action, as well as certain philosophical reflections which you may find of interest. In the meantime, believe me ever

Your most affectionate friend and humble servant,
J. Fraser

42

DRESS REHEARSAL

BOBBY HIGGINS looked uneasily at me over his mug of beer.

"Beg pardon, mum," he said. "But you wouldn't be a-thinking of practicing some type of physic upon me, would you? The worms are gone, I'm sure of it. And the—the other"—he blushed slightly and squirmed upon the bench—"that's quite all right, too. I've et so many beans, I fart quite regular, and not a touch of the fiery knives about it!"

Jamie had frequently remarked upon the transparency of my features, but this was surprising perspicacity on Bobby's part.

"I'm thrilled to hear it," I said, evading his question momentarily. "You look quite in the pink of health, Bobby."

He did; the hollow, wasted look had left him, and his flesh was firm and solid, his eyes bright. The blind one hadn't gone milky, nor did it wander perceptibly; he must have some residual ability to detect light and shape, which strengthened my original diagnosis of a partially detached retina.

He nodded warily, and took a sip of beer, still keeping his eyes fixed on me.

"I'm very well indeed, mum," he said.

"Splendid. You don't happen to know how much you weigh, do you, Bobby?"

The look of wariness vanished, replaced by modest pride.

"Happen I do, mum. I took some fleeces to the river port for his Lordship last month, and was a mercer there what had a scale for weighing out—tobacco or rice, or blocks of indigo as it might be. Some of us fellows got to wagering for sport what this or that might weigh, and . . . well, ten stone four it is, mum."

"Very nice," I said with approval. "Lord John's cook must be feeding you well." I thought he couldn't have weighed more than a hundred and ten pounds when I first saw him; a hundred and forty-four was still on the light side for a man of nearly six feet, but it was a major improvement. And a real stroke of luck, that he should have known his weight exactly.

Of course, if I didn't act fast, he might easily gain a stone or two; Mrs. Bug had set herself to outdo Lord John's Indian cook (of whom we had heard much), and to this end was shoveling eggs, onions, venison, and a slice of leftover pork pie onto Bobby's plate, to say nothing of the basket of fragrant muffins already in front of him.

Lizzie, seated beside me, took one of these and spread it with butter. I noted with approval that she, too, was looking healthier, delicately flushed—though I must remember to take a sample to check the malarial parasites in her blood. That would be an excellent thing to do while she was out. No way of getting an exact weight for her, unfortunately—but she couldn't weigh more than seven stone, small and light-boned as she was.

Now, Bree and Roger at the other end of the scale . . . Roger had to weigh at least a hundred and eighty-five; Bree probably one-fifty. I took a muffin myself, thinking how best to bring up my plan. Roger would do it if I asked, of course, but Bree . . . I'd have to be careful there. She'd had her tonsils out under ether at the age of ten, and hadn't liked the experience. If she found out what I was up to and began expressing her opinions freely, she might arouse alarm in the rest of my guinea pigs.

Enthused by my success at making ether, I had seriously underestimated the difficulty of inducing anyone to let me use it on them. Mr. Christie might well be an awkward bugger, as Jamie on occasion called him—but he was not alone in his resistance to the notion of being rendered suddenly unconscious.

I would have thought that the appeal of painlessness was universal—but not to people who had never experienced it. They had no context in which to place such a notion, and while they presumably didn't all think ether was a Papist plot, they did view an offer to remove pain from them as being in some way contrary to the divine vision of the universe.

Bobby and Lizzie, though, were sufficiently under my sway that I was fairly sure I could coax—or bully—them into a brief trial. If they then reported the experience in a positive light . . . but improved public relations was only the half of it.

The real necessity was to try my ether out on a variety of subjects, taking careful note of the results. The scare of Henri-Christian's birth had shown me how woefully unprepared I was. I needed to have some idea of how much to administer per unit of body weight, how long such-and-such a dose might last, and how deep the resulting stupor might be. The last thing I wanted was to be up to my elbows in someone's abdomen, only to have them come suddenly round with a shriek.

"You're doing it again, mum." Bobby's brow creased as he chewed slowly, eyes narrowed at me.

"What? What am I doing?" I feigned innocence, helping myself to a bit of the pork pie.

"Watching me. Same as a sparrer hawk watches a mouse, just afore she stoops. I'n't she?" he appealed to Lizzie.

"Aye, she is," Lizzie agreed, dimpling at me. "But it's only her way, ken. Ye'd make a big mouse, Bobby." Being Scottish, she pronounced it "moose," which made Bobby laugh and choke over his muffin.

Mrs. Bug paused to pound him helpfully on the back, leaving him purple and gasping.

"Well, wha's amiss wi' him, then?" she asked, coming round to squint critically at Bobby's face. "Ye've no got the shits again, have ye, lad?"

"Again?" I said.

"Oh, no, mum," he croaked. "Perish the thought! 'Twas only eating green apples, the once." He choked, coughed, and sat up straight, clearing his throat.

"Can we please not talk about me bowels, mum?" he asked plaintively. "Not over breakfast, at least?"

I could feel Lizzie vibrating with amusement next to me, but she kept her eyes demurely on her plate, not to embarrass him further.

"Certainly," I said, smiling. "I hope you'll be staying for a few days, Bobby?" He'd come the day before, bearing the usual assortment of letters and newspapers from Lord John—along with a package containing a marvelous present for Jemmy: a musical jack-in-the-box, sent specially from London by the good offices of Lord John's son, Willie.

"Oh, I s'all, mum, yes," he assured me, mouth full of muffin. "His Lordship said I was to see if Mr. Fraser had a letter for me to carry back, so I must wait for him, mustn't I?"

"Of course." Jamie and Ian had gone to the Cherokee a week before; it was likely to be another week before they returned. Plenty of time to make my experiments.

"Is there anything I might do, mum, in the way of service to you?" Bobby asked. "Seeing as I'm here, I mean, and Mr. Fraser and Mr. Ian not." There was a small tone of satisfaction in this; he got on all right with Ian, but there was no doubt that he preferred to have Lizzie's attention to himself.

"Why, yes," I said, scooping up a bit of porridge. "Now that you mention it, Bobby . . ."

By the time I had finished explaining, Bobby still looked healthy, but a good deal less in bloom.

"Put me asleep," he repeated uncertainly. He glanced at Lizzie, who looked a little uncertain, too, but who was much too used to being told to do unreasonable things to protest.

"You'll only be asleep for a moment," I assured him. "Likely you won't even notice."

His face expressed considerable skepticism, and I could see him shifting about for some excuse. I'd foreseen that ploy, though, and now played my trump card.

"It's not only me needing to judge the dose," I said. "I can't operate on someone and give the ether at the same time—or not easily. Malva Christie will be assisting me; she'll need the practice."

"Oh," Bobby said thoughtfully. "Miss Christie." A sort of soft, dreamy expression spread across his face. "Well. I s'ouldn't want to put Miss Christie out, of course."

Lizzie made one of those economical Scottish noises in the back of her throat, managing to convey scorn, derision, and abiding disapproval in the space of two glottal syllables.

Bobby looked up in inquiry, a bit of pie poised on his fork. "Did you say something?"

"Who, me?" she said. "O' course not." She got up abruptly and, carrying her apron before her, neatly shook crumbs into the fire, and turned to me.

"When d'ye mean to do it?" she demanded, adding a belated, "ma'am."

"Tomorrow morning," I said. "It needs to be done on an empty stomach, so we'll do it first thing, before breakfast."

"Fine!" she said, and stamped out.

Bobby blinked after her, then turned to me, bewildered. "Did I say something?"

Mrs. Bug's eye met mine in perfect understanding.

"Not a thing, lad," she said, depositing a fresh spatulaful of scrambled eggs onto his plate. "Eat up. Ye'll need your strength."

BRIANNA, CLEVER WITH her hands, had made the mask to my specifications, woven of oak splits. It was simple enough, a sort of double cage, hinged so that the two halves of it swung apart for the insertion of a thick layer of cotton wool between them, and then back together, the whole thing shaped to fit like a catcher's mask over the patient's nose and mouth.

"Put enough ether on to dampen the cotton wool all

through," I instructed Malva. "We'll want it to take effect quickly."

"Aye, ma'am. Oh, it does smell queer, doesn't it?" She sniffed cautiously, face turned half away as she dripped ether onto the mask.

"Yes. Do be careful not to breathe too much of it yourself," I said. "We don't want you falling over in the midst of an operation."

She laughed, but dutifully held the mask further away.

Lizzie had bravely offered to go first—with the clear intent of deflecting Bobby's attention from Malva to her. This was working; she lay in a languid pose on the table, cap off, and her soft, pale hair displayed to best advantage on the pillow. Bobby sat beside her, earnestly holding her hand.

"All right, then." I had a tiny minute-glass to hand, the best I could do by way of keeping accurate time. "Put it gently over her face. Lizzie, just breathe deeply, and count with me, one . . . two . . . goodness, that didn't take long, did it?"

She'd taken one long breath, rib cage rising high—and then gone limp as a dead flounder as the breath went out. I hastily flipped the glass, and came to take her pulse. All well there.

"Wait for a bit; you can feel it, when they start to come round, a sort of vibration in the flesh," I instructed Malva, keeping one eye on Lizzie and the other on the glass. "Put your hand on her shoulder. . . . There, do you feel it?"

Malva nodded, nearly trembling with excitement.

"Two or three drops then." She added these, her own breath held, and Lizzie relaxed again with a sigh like an escape of air from a punctured tire.

Bobby's blue eyes were absolutely round, but he clung fiercely to Lizzie's other hand.

I timed the period to arousal once or twice more, then let Malva put her under a little more deeply. I picked up the lancet I had ready, and pricked Lizzie's finger. Bobby gasped as the blood welled up, looking back and forth from the crimson drop to Lizzie's angelically peaceful face.

"Why, she don't feel it!" he exclaimed. "Look, she's never moved a muscle!"

"Exactly," I said, with a profound feeling of satisfaction. "She won't feel anything at all, until she comes round."

"Mrs. Fraser says we could cut someone quite open," Malva informed Bobby, self-importantly. "Slice into them, and get at what's ailing—and they'd never feel a thing!"

"Well, not until they woke up," I said, amused. "They'd feel it then, I'm afraid. But it really is quite a marvelous thing," I added more softly, looking down at Lizzie's unconscious face.

I let her stay under whilst I checked the fresh blood sample, then told Malva to take the mask off. Within a minute, Lizzie's eyelids began to flutter. She looked curiously round, then turned to me.

"When are ye going to start it, ma'am?"

Despite assurances from both Bobby and Malva that she had been to all appearances dead as a doornail for the last quarter hour, she refused to believe it, asserting indignantly that she couldn't have been—though at a loss to explain the prick on her finger and the slide of freshly smeared blood.

"You remember the mask on your face?" I asked. "And my telling you to take a deep breath?"

She nodded uncertainly.

"Aye, I do, then, and it felt for a moment as though I were choking—but then ye were all just staring down at me, next thing!"

"Well, I suppose the only way to convince her is to show her," I said, smiling at the three flushed young faces. "Bobby?"

Eager to demonstrate the truth of the matter to Lizzie, he hopped up on the table and laid himself down with a will, though the pulse in his slender throat was hammering as Malva dripped ether on the mask. He drew a deep, convulsive gasp the moment she put it on his face. Frowning a bit, he took another—one more—and went limp.

Lizzie clapped both hands to her mouth, staring.

"Jesus, Joseph, and Mary!" she exclaimed. Malva giggled, thrilled at the effect.

Lizzie looked at me, eyes wide, then back at Bobby. Stooping to his ear, she called his name, to no effect, then picked up his hand and wiggled it gingerly. His arm waggled limply, and she made a soft exclamation and set his hand down again. She looked quite agitated.

"Can he no wake up again?"

"Not until we take away the mask," Malva told her, rather smug.

"Yes, but you don't want to keep someone under longer than you need to," I added. "It's not good for them to be anesthetized too long."

Malva obediently brought Bobby back to the edge of consciousness and put him back under several times, while I made note of times and dosages. During the last of these notes, I glanced up, to see her looking down at Bobby with an intent sort of expression, seeming to concentrate on something. Lizzie had withdrawn to a corner of the surgery, plainly made uneasy by seeing Bobby unconscious, and sat on a stool, plaiting her hair and twisting it up under her cap.

I stood up and took the mask from Malva's hand, setting it aside.

"You did a wonderful job," I told her, speaking quietly. "Thank you."

She shook her head, face glowing.

"Oh, ma'am! It was . . . I've never seen the like. It's such a feeling, is it not? Like as we killed him, and brought him alive again." She spread her hands out, looking at them half-unconsciously, as though wondering how she had done such a marvel, then closed them into small fists, and smiled at me, conspiratorially.

"I think I see why my faither says it's devil's work. Were he to see what it's like"—she glanced at Bobby, who was beginning to stir—"he'd say no one but God has a right to do such things."

"Really," I said, rather dryly. From the gleam in her eye, her father's likely reaction to what we had been doing was one of the chief attractions of the experiment. For an instant, I rather pitied Tom Christie.

"Um . . . perhaps you'd better not tell your father, then," I suggested. She smiled, showing small, sharp white teeth, and rolled her eyes.

"Don't you think it, ma'am," she assured me. "He'd stop me coming, as quick as—"

Bobby opened his eyes, turned his head to one side, and threw up, putting a stop to the discussion. Lizzie gave a cry and hurried to his side, fussing over him, wiping his face and fetching him brandy to drink. Malva, looking slightly superior, stood aside and let her.

"Oh, that's queer," Bobby repeated, for perhaps the tenth time, rubbing a hand across his mouth. "I saw the most terrible thing—just for a moment, there—and then I felt sick, and here it was all over."

"What sort of terrible thing?" Malva asked, interested. He glanced at her, looking wary and uncertain.

"I scarcely know, tell 'ee true, miss. Only as it was . . . dark, like. A form, as you might say; I thought 'twas a woman's. But . . . terrible," he finished, helpless.

Well, that was too bad. Hallucination wasn't an uncommon side effect, but I hadn't expected it with such a brief dose.

"Well, I imagine it was just a bit of nightmare," I said soothingly. "You know, it's a form of sleep, so it's not surprising that you might get the odd bit of dreaming now and then."

To my surprise, Lizzie shook her head at this.

"Oh, no, ma'am," she said. "It's no sleep at all. When ye sleep, ken, ye give your soul up to the angels' keeping, so as no ghoulies shall come near. But this . . ." Frowning, she eyed the bottle of ether, now safely corked again, then looked at me.

"I did wonder," she said, "where does your soul go?"

"Er . . ." I said. "Well, I should think it simply stays with your body. It must. I mean—you aren't dead."

Both Lizzie and Bobby were shaking their heads decidedly.

"No, it doesn't," Lizzie said. "When ye're sleepin', ye're still *there.* When ye do *that*"—she gestured toward the mask, a faint uneasiness on her small features—"ye're not."

"That's true, mum," Bobby assured me. "You're not."

"D'ye think maybe ye go to limbo, wi' the unbaptized babes and all?" Lizzie asked anxiously.

Malva gave an unladylike snort.

"Limbo's no real place," she said. "It's only a notion thought up by the Pope."

Lizzie's mouth dropped open in shock at this blasphemy, but Bobby luckily distracted her by feeling dizzy and requiring to lie down.

Malva seemed inclined to go on with the argument, but beyond repeating, "The Pope . . ." once or twice, simply stood, swaying to and fro with her mouth open, blinking a little. I glanced at Lizzie, only to find her glassy-eyed as well. She gave an enormous yawn and blinked at me, eyes watering.

It occurred to me that I was beginning to feel a trifle lightheaded myself.

"Goodness!" I snatched the ether mask from Malva's hand, and guided her hastily to a stool. "Let me get rid of this, or we'll all be giddy."

I flipped open the mask, pulled the damp wad of cotton wool out of it, and carried it outside at arm's length. I'd opened both the surgery windows, to provide ventilation and save us all being gassed, but ether was insidious. Heavier than air, it tended to sink toward the floor of a room and accumulate there, unless there was a fan or some other device to remove it. I might have to operate in the open air, I thought, were I using it for any length of time.

I laid the cotton-wool pad on a stone to dry out, and came back, hoping that they were all too groggy now to continue their philosophical speculations. I didn't want them following *that* line of thought; let it get around the Ridge that ether separated people from their souls, and I'd never get anyone to let me use it on them, no matter how dire the situation.

"Well, thank you all for helping," I said, smiling as I entered the room, relieved to find them all looking reasonably alert. "You've done something very useful and valuable. You can all go along about your business now, though—I'll tidy up."

Malva and Lizzie hesitated for a moment, neither girl wanting to leave Bobby to the other, but under the impetus of my shooing, drifted toward the door.

"When are ye to be wed, Miss Wemyss?" Malva asked casually—and loudly enough for Bobby to hear—though she certainly knew; everyone on the Ridge did.

"In August," Lizzie replied coolly, lifting her small nose half an inch. "Right after the haying—*Miss* Christie." *And then I shall be Mrs. McGillivray,* her satisfied expression said. *And you*—Miss *Christie*—*without an admirer to your name.* Not that Malva attracted no notice from young men; only that her father and brother were assiduous in keeping them away from her.

"I wish ye great joy of it," Malva said. She glanced at Bobby Higgins, then back at Lizzie, and smiled, demure beneath her starched white cap.

Bobby stayed sitting on the table for a moment, looking after the girls.

"Bobby," I said, struck by the deeply thoughtful expression on his face, "the figure you saw under the anesthetic—did you recognize it?"

He looked at me, then his eyes slid back to the empty doorway, as though unable to keep away.

"Oh, no, mum," he said, in such a tone of earnest conviction that I knew he lied. "Not at all!"

43

DISPLACED PERSONS

THEY HAD STOPPED to water the horses by the edge of the small lake the Indians called Thick Rushes. It was a warm day, and they hobbled the horses, stripped, and waded into the water, spring-fed and gloriously cold. Cold enough to shock the senses and, for a moment at least, drive away Jamie's moody contemplation of the note MacDonald had delivered him from John Stuart, the Indian Superintendent of the Southern Department.

It had been complimentary enough, praising his celerity and enterprise in drawing the Snowbird Cherokee into the British sphere of influence—but had gone on to urge more vigorous involvement, pointing out Stuart's own coup in directing the choice of leaders among the Choctaw and the Chickasaw, at a congress he had himself convened two years before.

. . . The competition and anxiety of the candidates for medals and commissions was as great as can be imagined and equalled the struggles of the most aspiring and ambitious for honours and preferment in great states. I took every step to be informed of characters and filled the vacancies with the most worthy and likely to answer the purposes of maintaining order and the attachment of this nation to the British interest. I urge you to strive for similar good results to be achieved among the Cherokee.

"Oh, aye," he said aloud, popping up among the rushes and shaking water from his hair. "I'm to depose Tsisqua, nay doubt by assassination, and bribe them all to install Pipestone Carver"—the smallest and most self-effacing Indian Jamie had ever seen—"as peace chief. Heugh!" He sank again, in a rush of bubbles, entertaining himself by cursing Stuart's presumption, watching his words rise up in wavering quicksilver balls, to disappear magically at the bright light of the surface.

He rose again, gasping, then gulped air and held his breath.

"What was that?" said a startled voice nearby. "Is it them?"

"No, no," said another, low and urgent. "There are only two; I see them both, over there, do you see?"

He opened his mouth and breathed like a zephyr, striving to hear over the pounding of his heart.

He had understood them, but for an instant, could not put a name to their tongue. Indians, aye, but not Cherokee, they were . . . Tuscarora, that was it.

He hadn't spoken with any Tuscarora for years; most of them had gone north in the wake of the measles epidemic that had destroyed so many—going to join their Mohawk "fathers" in the lands ruled by the Iroquois League.

These two were arguing in whispers, but near enough that he made out most of what they said; they were no more than a few feet from him, hidden by a thick growth of rushes and cattail plants that stood nearly as high as a man's head.

Where was Ian? He could hear distant splashing, at the far end of the lake, and turning his head gently, saw from the corner of his eye that Ian and Rollo were sporting in the water, the dog submerged to his ruff, paddling to and fro. If one didn't know—and the beast didn't sense the intruders and bark—it looked very much like two men swimming.

The Indians had concluded that this was likely the case—two horses, thus two men, and both safely distant. With much creaking and rustling, they began to make their way stealthily in the direction of the horses.

Jamie was half-inclined to let them try to take Gideon and see how far they got with such an enterprise. But they might only make off with Ian's horse and the pack mule—and Claire would be fashit, did he let them take Clarence. Feeling himself very much at a disadvantage, he slithered naked through the reeds, grimacing at the rasp of them on his skin, and crawled up among the cattails, into the mud of the shore.

Had they the wit to look back, they must have seen the cattails shaking—and he hoped Ian *would* see—but they were intent on their errand. He could glimpse them now, skulking in the tall grass at the forest edge, glancing to and fro—but never in the right direction.

Only two, he was sure of that now. Young, from the way they moved, and unsure. He couldn't see if they were armed.

Slimed with mud, he crept further, sinking onto his belly in the rank grasses near the lake, squirming rapidly toward the shelter of a sumac bush. What he wanted was a club, and quickly.

In such circumstances, of course, nothing came to hand but twigs and long-rotted branches. For lack of better, he seized a good-sized stone, but then found what he wanted: a dogwood branch cracked by wind and hanging in reach, still attached to the tree. They were approaching the grazing horses now; Gideon saw them and lifted his head abruptly. He went on chewing, but his ears lay half back in patent suspicion. Clarence, the ever-sociable, took notice and raised his head, as well, ears twitching to alertness.

Jamie seized the chance, and as Clarence emitted a welcoming bray, he ripped the branch from the tree and charged the intruders, roaring, *"Tulach Ard!"* at the top of his voice.

Wide eyes met his, and one man bolted, long hair flying. The other followed, but limping badly, going down on one knee as something gave way. He was up again at once, but too slow; Jamie swept the branch at his legs with a two-handed fury that knocked him flat, and leapt on his back, driving a vicious knee into his kidney.

The man made a strangled noise and froze, paralyzed by pain. Jamie had dropped his rock—no, there it was. He snatched it up and thumped the man solidly behind the ear, for luck. Then he was off and running after the other, who had made for the wood but sheered off, blocked by a rock-bound streamlet in his path. Now the man was bounding through the sedges; Jamie saw him cast a terrified look toward the water, where Ian and Rollo were making their way toward him, swimming like beaver.

The Indian might have made it to the sanctuary of the forest, had one foot not suddenly sunk in soft mud. He staggered sideways, and Jamie was on him, feet sliding in the mud, grappling.

The man was young and wiry and fought like an eel. Jamie, with the advantage of size and weight, managed to push him over, and they fell together and rolled about in the sedges and mud, clawing and thumping. The Indian caught Jamie's long hair and yanked, bringing tears to his eyes; he punched the man hard in the ribs to make him let go, and when he did, butted him in the face.

Their foreheads met with a dull thunk, and blinding pain shot through his head. They fell apart, gasping, and Jamie rolled up onto his knees, head spinning and eyes watering, trying to see.

There was a blur of gray and a shriek of terror. Rollo gave one deep-chested, snarling bark, then settled into a rumbling, continuous growl. Jamie shut one eye, a hand to his throbbing forehead, and made out his opponent lying flat in the mud, Rollo poised over him, black lips drawn back to show all his teeth.

The splash of feet running through the shallows, and Ian was there, gasping for breath.

"Are ye all right, Uncle Jamie?"

He took his hand away and looked at his fingers. No blood, though he would have sworn his head was split open.

"No," he said, "but better than him. Oh, Jesus."

"Did ye kill the other one?"

"Probably not. Oh, God."

Lowering himself to his hands and knees, he crawled a short distance away and threw up. Behind him, he could hear Ian sharply demanding to know who the men were and whether there were others with them, in Cherokee.

"They're Tuscarora," he said. His head still throbbed, but he felt a little better.

"Oh, aye?" Ian was surprised, but at once shifted into the tongue of the Kahnyen'kehaka. The young captive, already terrorized by Rollo, looked as though he might die of fright, seeing Ian's tattoos and hearing him speak Mohawk. Kahnyen'kehaka was of the same family as Tuscarora, and plainly the young man could make out what Ian said, for he replied, stammering with fear. They were alone. Was his brother dead?

Jamie rinsed his mouth with water, splashed it on his face. That was better, though a lump like a duck's egg was swelling over his left eye.

"Brother?"

Yes, the young man said, his brother. If they did not mean to kill him now, might he go and see? His brother was wounded.

Ian glanced at Jamie for agreement, then called Rollo off with a word. The bedraggled captive struggled painfully to his feet, staggering, and set off back along the shore, followed by the dog and the two naked Scots.

The other man was indeed wounded; blood was seeping through a crude bandage round his leg. He had made the bandage of his shirt, and was bare-chested, scrawny, and starved-looking. Jamie glanced from one to the other; neither could be older than twenty, he thought, and likely younger than that, with their faces pinched by hunger and ill-usage, their clothes little more than rags.

The horses had moved off a little, nervous of the fighting, but the clothes the Scots had left hanging from the bushes were still there. Ian pulled on his breeches and went to fetch food and drink from the saddlebags, while Jamie dressed more slowly, interrogating the young man as the latter anxiously examined his brother.

They were Tuscarora, the young man confirmed. His name was a long one, meaning roughly "the gleam of light on water in a spring"; this was his brother, "the goose that encourages the leader when they fly," more simply known as Goose.

"What happened to him?" Jamie pulled his shirt over his head and nodded—wincing at the movement—at the gash in Goose's leg, quite obviously made by something like an ax.

Light on Water took a deep breath and closed his eyes for a moment. He had a substantial knot on his head, as well.

"Tsalagi," he said. "We were two score in number; the rest are dead, or taken. You will not give us to them, Lord? Please?"

"Tsalagi? Which?"

Light shook his head; he could not say. His band had chosen to stay when his village moved north, but they had not prospered; there were not enough men to defend a village and hunt, and without defenders, others stole their crops, took their women.

Growing poorer, they, too, had taken to stealing and to begging to survive through the winter. More had died of cold and sickness, and the remnants moved from place to place, now and then finding a place to settle for a few weeks, but then driven out by the much stronger Cherokee.

A few days past, they had been set upon by a party of Cherokee warriors, who had taken them by surprise, killed most of them, and taken some women.

"They took my wife," Light said, his voice unsteady. "We came to—to take her back."

"They will kill us, of course," said Goose weakly, but with a fair amount of cheerfulness. "But that doesn't signify."

"Of course not," Jamie said, smiling despite himself. "Do you know where they took her?"

The brothers knew the direction taken by the raiders, and had been following, to track them to their village. That way, they said, pointing toward a notch. Ian glanced at Jamie, and nodded.

"Bird," he said. "Or Fox, I should say," for Running Fox

was war chief of the village; a good warrior, though somewhat lacking in imagination—a trait Bird possessed in quantity.

"Shall we help them, then?" Ian said in English. His feathery brows arched in question, but Jamie could see that it was a question in form only.

"Oh, aye, I expect we will." He rubbed gingerly at his forehead; the skin over the lump was already stretched and tender. "Let's eat first, though."

IT WAS NOT a question of whether the thing might be done; only how. Jamie and Ian both dismissed out of hand any suggestion that the brothers might steal back Light's wife.

"They *will* kill ye," Ian assured them.

"We don't mind," Light said stoutly.

"Of course ye don't," said Jamie. "But what of your wife? She'd be left alone, then, and in no better case."

Goose nodded judiciously.

"He's right, you know," he said to his glowering brother.

"We could ask for her," Jamie suggested. "A wife for you, Ian. Bird thinks well of ye; he'd likely give her to you."

He was only half-joking. If no one had yet taken the young woman to wife, the person who had her as slave might be persuaded to give her to Ian, who was deeply respected.

Ian gave a perfunctory smile, but shook his head.

"Nay, we'd best ransom her. Or—" He looked consideringly at the two Indians, industriously eating their way through the remainder of the food in the saddlebags. "Might we ask Bird to adopt them?"

That was a thought, to be sure. For once they had got the young woman back, by whatever means, she and the brothers would be in the same dire case—wandering and hungry.

The brothers frowned, though, and shook their heads.

"Food is a good thing," Goose said, licking his fingers. "But we saw them kill our family, our friends. If we hadn't seen it ourselves, it would be possible. But—"

"Aye, I see," Jamie said, and was struck for an instant by

mild astonishment that he *did* see; evidently, he had spent longer among the Indians than he supposed.

The brothers exchanged glances, obviously communicating something. Decision made, Light made a gesture of respect to Jamie.

"We are *your* slaves," he pointed out with some diffidence. "It is yours to decide what to do with us." He paused delicately, waiting.

Jamie rubbed a hand over his face, considering that perhaps he hadn't spent quite enough time with Indians after all. Ian didn't smile, but seemed to emit a low vibration of amusement.

MacDonald had told him stories of campaigns during the French and Indian War; soldiers who took Indian prisoners commonly either killed them for scalp money or sold them as slaves. Those campaigns lay a scant ten years in the past; the peace since had been frequently uneasy, and God knew the various Indians made slaves of their prisoners, unless they chose—for whatever inscrutable Indian motive—to adopt or kill them, instead.

Jamie had captured the two Tuscarora; ergo, by custom, they were now his slaves.

He understood quite well what Light was suggesting—that *he* adopt the brothers, and doubtless the young woman, too, once he'd rescued her—and how in God's name had he suddenly become responsible for doing that?

"Well, there's nay market for their scalps just now," Ian pointed out. "Though I suppose ye could *sell* the two of them to Bird. Though they're no worth a great deal, scrawny and ill-feckit as they are."

The brothers stared at him, impassive, awaiting his decision. Light belched suddenly, and looked surprised at the sound. Ian *did* laugh at that, a low creaking noise.

"Oh, I couldna do any such thing, and the three of ye ken that perfectly well," Jamie said crossly. "I should have hit ye harder and saved myself trouble," he said to Goose, who grinned at him, with gap-toothed good nature.

"Yes, Uncle," he said, bowing low in deep respect.

Jamie made a displeased sound in response, but the two Indians took no notice.

It would have to be the medals, then. MacDonald had brought him a chest bulging with medals, gilt buttons, cheap brass compasses, steel knife blades, and other bits of attractive rubbish. Since the chiefs derived their power from their popularity, and their popularity increased in direct proportion to their ability to give gifts, the British Indian agents exerted influence by distributing largesse to those chiefs who indicated a willingness to ally themselves to the Crown.

He'd brought only two small bags of such bribery; the rest left at home for future use. What he had on hand would, he was sure, be sufficient to ransom Mrs. Light, but to expend it all in such fashion would leave him empty-handed with respect to the other village chiefs—and that wouldn't do.

Well, and he supposed he must send Ian back, then, to fetch more. But not until he'd arranged the ransom; he wanted Ian's help in that matter.

"Fine, then," he said, standing up. He fought off a wave of dizziness. "But I am *not* adopting them." The last thing he needed just this minute was three more mouths to feed.

44

SCOTCHEE

ARRANGING THE RANSOM was, as he had supposed, a simple matter of bargaining. And in the end, Mrs. Light came fairly cheap, at the price of six medals, four knives, and a compass. Granted, he hadn't seen her until the conclusion of the dealing—if he had, he might have offered even less; she was a small, pockmarked lass of perhaps fourteen, with a slight walleye.

Still, he reflected, there was no accounting for taste, and both Light and Goose had been willing to die for her.

Doubtless she had a kind heart, or some other excellent quality of character, such as a talent and affinity for bed.

He was quite shocked to find himself thinking such a thing, and looked at her more closely. It was in no way obvious—and yet, now that he *did* look—she did radiate that strange appeal, that remarkable gift, held by a few women, that bypassed such superficial appreciations as looks, age, or wit, and caused a man simply to wish to seize her and—

He choked the sprouting image off at the root. He'd known a few such women, most of them French. And had thought more than once that perhaps it was his own wife's French heritage that was responsible for her possession of that most desirable but very dangerous gift.

He could see Bird eyeing the girl thoughtfully, quite obviously regretting that he had let her go for so little. Fortunately, a distraction occurred to drive the matter from his attention—the return of a hunting party, bringing with them guests.

The guests were Cherokee of the Overhill Band, far from their home in the Tennessee mountains. And with them was a man Jamie had often heard of, but never met until this day—one Alexander Cameron, whom the Indians called "Scotchee."

A dark, weathered man of middle-age, Cameron was distinguishable from the Indians only by his heavy beard and the long, inquisitive shape of his nose. He had lived with the Cherokee since the age of fifteen, had a Cherokee wife, and was much esteemed among them. He was also an Indian agent, thick with John Stuart. And his presence here, two hundred miles from home, caused Jamie's own long, inquisitive nose to twitch with interest.

The interest was frankly mutual; Cameron examined him with deep-set eyes in which intelligence and wiliness showed in equal measure.

"The redheided Bear-Killer, och, och!" he exclaimed, shaking Jamie warmly by the hand, and then embracing him in the Indian fashion. "I've heard such tales of ye, ken, and fair dyin' to meet ye to see were they true."

"I doubt it," Jamie said. "The last one I heard myself, I'd done for three bears at once, killin' the last of them high in a tree, where he'd chased me after chewin' off my foot."

Despite himself, Cameron looked down at Jamie's feet,

then looked up and hooted with laughter, all the lines of his face curving in such irresistible merriment that Jamie felt his own laughter bubble up.

It was not, of course, proper to speak of business yet awhile. The hunting party had brought down one of the woods buffaloes, and a great feast was preparing: the liver taken away to be singed and devoured at once, the strap of tender meat from the back roasted with whole onions, and the heart—so Ian told him—to be shared among the four of them: Jamie, Cameron, Bird, and Running Fox, a mark of honor.

After the liver had been eaten, they retired to Bird's house to drink beer for an hour or two, while the women made ready the rest of the food. And in the course of nature, he found himself outside, having a comfortable piss against a tree, when a quiet footfall came behind him, and Alexander Cameron stepped up alongside, undoing the fall of his breeches.

It seemed natural—though plainly Cameron had intended it—to walk about together for a bit then, the cool air of the evening a respite from the smoke inside the house, and speak of things of common interest—John Stuart, for one, and the ways and means of the Southern Department. Indians, for another; comparing the personalities and means of dealing with the various village chiefs, speculating as to who would make a leader, and whether there might be a great congress called within the year.

"Ye'll be wondering, I expect," Cameron said quite casually, "at my presence here?"

Jamie made a slight motion of the shoulders, admitting interest, but indicating a polite lack of inquisition into Cameron's affairs.

Cameron chuckled.

"Aye, well. It's no secret, to be sure. It's James Henderson, is what it is—ye'll ken the name, maybe?"

He did. Henderson had been Chief Justice of the Superior Court in North Carolina—until the Regulation had caused him to leave, climbing out the window of his courthouse and fleeing for his life from a mob bent on violence.

A wealthy man, and one with a due regard for the value of his skin, Henderson had retired from public life and set about increasing his fortune. To which end, he proposed now to buy an enormous tract of land from the Cherokee, this located in Tennessee, and establish townships there.

Jamie gave Cameron an eye, apprehending at once the complexity of the situation. For the one thing, the lands in question lay far, far inside the Treaty Line. For Henderson to instigate such dealings was an indication—had any been needed—of just how feeble the grasp of the Crown had grown of late. Plainly, Henderson thought nothing of flouting His Majesty's treaty, and expected no interference with his affairs as a result of doing so.

That was one thing. For another, though—the Cherokee held land in common, as all the Indians did. Leaders could and did sell land to whites, without such legal niceties as clear title, but were still subject to the *ex post facto* approval or disapproval of their people. Such approval would not affect the sale, which would be already accomplished, but could result in the fall of a leader, and in a good deal of trouble for the man who tried to take possession of land paid for in good faith—or what passed for good faith, in such dealings.

"John Stuart knows of this, of course," Jamie said, and Cameron nodded, with a small air of complacency.

"Not officially, mind," he said.

Naturally not. The Superintendent of Indian Affairs could hardly countenance such an arrangement officially. At the same time, it would be smiled on unofficially, as such a purchase could not help but further the department's goal of bringing the Indians further under the sway of British influence.

Jamie wondered idly whether Stuart profited in any personal way from the sale. Stuart had a good reputation and was not known to be corrupt—but he might well have a silent interest in the matter. Then again, he might have no financial interest himself, and be turning an officially blind eye to the arrangement only in furtherance of the department's purposes.

Cameron, though . . . He couldn't say, of course, but would be most surprised if Cameron had no finger in the pie.

He did not know where Cameron's natural interest lay, whether with the Indians among whom he lived or with the British to whom he had been born. He doubted that anyone did—perhaps not even Cameron. Regardless of his abiding interests, though, Cameron's immediate goals were clear. He wished the sale to be met with approval—or at least indifference—by the surrounding Cherokee, thus keeping his own pet chiefs in good order with their followers, and allowing Henderson to go forward with his plans with no undue harassment by Indians in the area.

"I shall not, of course, say anything for a day or two," Cameron told him, and he nodded. There was a natural rhythm to such business. But of course, Cameron had told him now so that he might be of help when the subject arose in due course.

Cameron took it for granted that he *would* help. There was no explicit promise of a bit of Henderson's pie for himself, but no need; it was the sort of opportunity that was a perquisite of being an Indian agent—the reason that such appointments were considered plums.

Given what Jamie knew of the near future, he had neither expectation nor interest in Henderson's purchase—but the subject did give him a welcome opportunity for a useful *quid pro quo.*

He coughed gently.

"Ye ken the wee Tuscarora lassie I bought from Bird?"

Cameron laughed.

"Aye. And he's most perplexed what ye mean to do with her; he says ye willna take any of the lasses he sends to warm your bed. She's no so much to look at—but still . . ."

"Not that," Jamie assured him. "She's marrit, for the one thing. I brought two Tuscaroran lads with me; she belongs to one of them."

"Oh, aye?" Cameron's nose twitched with interest, scenting a story. Jamie had been waiting for this opportunity since the sight of Cameron first gave him the notion, and he told it well, with the satisfactory outcome that Cameron agreed to take the three displaced young Tuscaroras with him, and sponsor their adoption into the Overhill Band.

"It'll no be the first time," he told Jamie. "There are more and more of them—wee scraps of what were villages, even whole peoples—wandering about the country starved and wretched. Heard of the Dogash, have ye?"

"No."

"Nor are ye like to," Cameron said, shaking his head. "There's no but ten or so of them left. They came to us last winter; offered themselves as slaves, only so that they might survive the cold. No—dinna fash yourself, man," he assured Jamie, catching sight of Jamie's expression. "Your wee lads and the lass won't be slaves; my word on it."

Jamie nodded his thanks, pleased with the business. They had wandered some distance outside the village, and stood talking near the edge of a gorge, where the wood opened suddenly over a vista of mountain ranges, rolling away and away like furrows plowed in some endless field of the gods, their backs dark and brooding beneath a starlit sky.

"How can there ever be people enough to settle such a wilderness?" he said, moved suddenly by the sight of it. And yet the smell of woodsmoke and cooking meat hung heavy in the air. People did inhabit it, few and scattered as they were.

Cameron shook his head in contemplation.

"They come," he said, "and they keep on coming. My ain folk came from Scotland. You have," he added, teeth a brief gleam in his beard. "And dinna mean to go back, I'll warrant."

Jamie smiled at that, but made no answer, though a queer feeling rose in his wame at the thought. He did not mean to go back. Had said goodbye to Scotland at the rail of the *Artemis,* knowing full well it was likely his last sight of the place. And yet, the notion that he would never set foot there again had never fully settled on him 'til this moment.

Calls of "Scotchee, Scotchee" summoned them, and he turned to follow Cameron back to the village, conscious all the time of the glorious, terrifying emptiness behind him—and the more terrifying emptiness within.

THEY SMOKED THAT night, after feasting, in ceremonious observance of Jamie's bargain with Bird, in welcome to

Cameron. When the pipe had gone twice around the fire, they began to tell stories.

Stories of raids, of battles. Exhausted from the day, head still throbbing, mellowed by food and spruce beer, and slightly intoxicated by the smoke, Jamie had meant only to listen. Perhaps it was the thought of Scotland, so casually evoked by Cameron's remark. But at some point, a memory had stirred, and when the next expectant silence fell, he was surprised to hear his own voice, telling them of Culloden.

"And there near a wall I saw a man I knew, named MacAllister, besieged by a horde of enemies. He fought with gun and sword, but both failed him—his blade was broken, his shield shattered upon his breast."

The fume of the pipe reached him and he raised it and drew deep, as though he drank the air of the moor, hazed with rain and the smoke of the day.

"Still they came, his enemies, to kill him, and he seized up a piece of metal, the tongue of a wagon, and with it, killed six"—he held up both hands, fingers stuck up in illustration—"six of them, before he was at last brought down."

Sounds of awe and tongue clicks of approval greeted this recounting.

"And you yourself, Bear-Killer, how many men did you kill in this battle?"

The smoke burned in his chest, behind his eyes, and for an instant he tasted the bitter smoke of cannon fire, not sweet tobacco. He saw—he *saw*—Alistair MacAllister, dead at his feet among the red-clothed bodies, the side of his head crushed in and the round curve of his shoulder shining solid through the cloth of the shirt, so wetly did it cling to him.

He was there, on the moor, the wet and cold no more than a shimmer on his skin, rain slick on his face, his own shirt sopping and steaming on him with the heat of his rage.

And then he no longer stood on Drumossie, and became aware a second too late of the indrawn breaths around him. He saw Robert Talltree's face, the wrinkles all turned up in astonishment, and only then looked down, to see all ten of his fingers flex and fold, and the four fingers of the right extend again, quite without his meaning it. The thumb wavered, indecisive. He watched this with fascination, then, coming finally to his wits, balled his right hand as well as he could and wrapped the left around it, as though to throttle the memory that had been thrust with such unnerving suddenness into the palm of his hand.

He looked up to see Talltree glance sharply at his face, and he saw the dark old eyes harden, then narrow under a frown—and then the old man took the pipe, drank deep, and blew the smoke across him, bowing forward. Talltree did this twice more, and a hum of hushed approval at the honor came from the clustered men.

He took the pipe and returned the honor of the gesture, then passed it to the next man, refusing to speak further.

They didn't push him to, seeming to recognize and respect the shock he felt.

Shock. Not even that. What he felt was the blankest astonishment. Cautiously, unwilling, he stole a keek at that picture of Alistair. God, it was there.

He realized that he was holding his breath, not wanting to breathe the reek of blood and spilled bowels. He breathed, soft smoke and a copper tang of seasoned bodies, and could have wept, swept with sudden longing for the cold, sharp air of the Highlands, pungent with the scents of peat and gorse.

Alexander Cameron said something to him, but he couldn't reply. Ian, seeing the difficulty, leaned forward to answer, and they all laughed. Ian gave him a curious look, but then turned back to the conversation, beginning a story of a famous game of lacrosse he had played among the Mohawk. Leaving Jamie to sit still, wreathed in the smoke.

Fourteen men. And he did not remember a single face. And that random thumb, hovering uncertainly. Whatever did he mean by that? That he had fought yet another, but not made certain of the fellow?

He was afraid even to think of the memory. Unsure what to do with it. But at the same time, conscious of a sense of awe. And despite everything, grateful to have this small thing back.

IT WAS VERY late, and most of the men had gone to their own houses, or lay comfortably asleep around the fire. Ian had left the fire, but hadn't come back. Cameron was still there, smoking his own pipe now, though he shared this with Bird, taking turn and turn about.

"There is a thing I would tell you," Jamie said abruptly, in the midst of a drowsy silence. "Both of you." Bird raised his brows in slow question, drugged with tobacco.

He hadn't known he meant to say it. Had thought to wait, judge his time—if he spoke at all. Perhaps it was the closeness of the house, the dark intimacy of the fireside, or the intoxication of tobacco. Perhaps only the kinship of an exile for those who would suffer the same fate. But he'd spoken; had no choice now but to tell them what he knew.

"The women of my family are . . ." He groped, not knowing the Cherokee word. "Those who see in dreams what is to come." He darted a look at Cameron, who appeared to take this in his stride, for he nodded, and closed his eyes to draw smoke into his lungs.

"Have they the Sight, then?" he asked, mildly interested.

Jamie nodded; it was as good an explanation as any.

"They have seen a thing concerning the Tsalagi. Both my wife and my daughter have seen this thing."

Bird's attention sharpened, hearing this. Dreams were important; for more than one person to share a dream was extraordinary, and therefore most important.

"It grieves me to tell you," Jamie said, and meant it. "Sixty years from this time, the Tsalagi will be taken from their lands, removed to a new place. Many will die on this journey, so that the path they tread will be called . . ." He groped for the word for "tears," did not find it, and ended, "the trail where they wept."

Bird's lips pursed, as though to draw smoke, but the pipe fumed unnoticed in his hands.

"Who will do this?" he asked. "Who *can*?"

Jamie drew a deep breath; here was the difficulty. And yet—so much less difficult than he had thought, now that it came to the matter.

"It will be white men," he said. "But it will not be King George's men."

"The French?" Cameron spoke with a hint of incredulity, but frowned, nonetheless, trying to see how this might come to pass. "Or the Spanish, do they mean? The Spanish are a good deal closer—but none sae many." Spain still held the country south of Georgia, and parts of the Indies, but the English held Georgia firmly; there was little apparent chance of any northward movement by the Spaniards.

"No. Not Spanish, not French." He could wish Ian had stayed, for more than one reason. But the lad had not, and so he would have to struggle with the Tsalagi, which was an interesting tongue, but one in which he could talk fluently only of solid things—and of a very limited future.

"What they tell me—what my women say—" He struggled to find sensible words. "A thing that they see in their dreams, this thing will come to pass, if it concerns many people. But they think it may *not* come to pass, if it concerns a few, or one."

Bird blinked, confused—and no wonder. Grimly, Jamie tried again to explain.

"There are large things, and there are small things. A large thing is a thing like a great battle, or the raising up of a notable chief—though he is one man, he is raised up by the voices of many. If my women dream of these large things, then they will happen. But in any large thing, there are many people. Some say do this; others, do that." He zigzagged his hand to and fro, and Bird nodded.

"So. If many people say, 'Do *this*'"—he stabbed his fingers sharply to the left—"then this happens. But what of the people who said, 'do that'?" And he jerked a thumb back the other way. "These people may choose a different way."

Bird made the hm-hm-*hm!* sound he used when startled.

"So it may be that some will not go?" Cameron asked sharply. "They might escape?"

"I hope so," Jamie said simply.

They sat in silence for a bit, each man staring into the fire, each seeing his own visions—of the future, or the past.

"This wife you have," Bird said at last, deeply contemplative, "did you pay a great deal for her?"

"She cost me almost everything I had," he said, with a wry tone that made the others laugh. "But worth it."

IT WAS VERY late when he went to the guesthouse; the moon had set, and the sky had that look of deep serenity, the stars singing to themselves in endless night. His body ached in every muscle, and he was so tired that he stumbled on the threshold. His instincts were still working, though, and he felt, rather than saw, someone move in the shadows of the sleeping-couch.

God, Bird was still at it. Well, tonight it wouldn't matter; he could lie naked with a covey of young women, and sleep sound. Too exhausted to be annoyed by her presence, he struggled for some polite acknowledgment of the woman. Then she stood up.

The firelight showed him an elderly woman, her hair in grizzled plaits, her dress of white buckskin decorated with paint and porcupine quills. He recognized Calls-in-the-Forest, dressed in her best. Bird's sense of humor had finally got completely out of hand; he had sent Jamie his mother.

All grasp of Tsalagi deserted him. He opened his mouth, but merely gaped at her. She smiled, very slightly, and held out her hand.

"Come and lie down, Bear-Killer," she said. Her voice was kind and gruff. "I've come to comb the snakes from your hair."

She drew him unresisting to the couch, and made him lie down with his head in her lap. Sure enough; she unplaited his hair and spread it out across her knees, her touch soothing to his throbbing head and the painful knot on his brow.

He had no idea how old she might be, but her fingers were muscular and tireless, making small, rhythmic circles in his scalp, on his temples, behind his ears, near to the bone at the base of his skull. She had thrown sweet grass and some other herb on the fire; the chimney hole was drawing well and he could see white smoke rising upward in a wavering pillar, very calm, but a sense of constant movement in it.

She was humming to herself, or rather whispering some song, the words too indistinct to make out. He watched the silent shapes stream upward in the smoke, and felt his body growing heavy, limbs filled with wet sand, his body a sandbag placed in the path of a flood.

"Talk, Bear-Killer," she said very softly, breaking off her

chant. She had a wooden comb in her hand; he felt the teeth of it caress his scalp, rounded with wear.

"I cannot call your words to me," he said, searching for each word in Tsalagi, and thus speaking very slowly. She made a small snorting noise in reply.

"The words don't matter, nor the tongue in which you speak," she said. "Only talk. I will understand."

And so he began haltingly to speak—in Gaelic, as it was the only tongue that didn't seem to require any effort. He understood that he was to speak of what filled his heart, and so began with Scotland—and Culloden. Of grief. Of loss. Of fear.

And in the speaking turned from past to future, where he saw these three specters loom again, cold creatures coming toward him out of the fog, looking through their empty eyes.

Another stood among them—Jack Randall—confusingly on both sides of him. Those eyes were not empty, but alive, intent in a misty face. Had he killed the man, or not? If he had, did the ghost follow at his heels? Or if he had not, was it the thought of vengeance unsatisfied that haunted him, taunted him with its imperfect memory?

But in the speaking, he seemed somehow to rise a little way above his body, and see himself at rest, eyes open, fixed upward, his hair darkly flaming in a halo round his head, streaked with the silver of his age. And here he saw that he merely *was,* in a place between, apart. And quite alone. At peace.

"I hold to no evil in my heart," he said, hearing his voice come slow, from a long way off. "This evil does not touch me. More may come, but not this. Not here. Not now."

"I understand," whispered the old woman, and went on combing his hair as the white smoke rose silent toward the hole to the sky.

45

A TAINT IN THE BLOOD

June 1774

I SAT BACK ON my heels and stretched, tired but pleased. My back ached, my knees creaked like hinges, my fingernails were caked with dirt, and strands of hair stuck to my neck and cheeks—but the new crops of pole beans, onions, turnips, and radishes were planted, the cabbages weeded and culled, and a dozen large peanut bushes had been pulled up and hung to dry on the garden palisades, safe from marauding squirrels.

I glanced up at the sun; still above the chestnut trees. Time enough then before supper for a last chore or two. I stood up and surveyed my small kingdom, debating where best to spend my remaining time. Rooting up the catmint and lemon balm that threatened to engulf the far corner of the garden? Carting baskets of nicely rotted manure up from the heap behind the barn? No, that was man's work.

Herbs? My three French lavender bushes stood knee-high, thick with deep blue swabs on slender stalks, and the yarrow was well in bloom, with lacy umbels of white and pink and yellow. I rubbed a finger under my itching nose, trying to recall whether this was the proper phase of the moon in which to cut yarrow. Lavender and rosemary should be cut in the morning, though, when the volatile oils had risen with the sun; it wasn't as potent if taken later in the day.

Down with the mint, then. I reached for the hoe I had left leaning against the fence, saw a face leering through the palisades, and started back, my heart leaping into my throat.

"Oh!" My visitor had jumped back, too, equally startled. "*Bitte,* ma'am! Didn't mean to fright ye."

It was Manfred McGillivray, peeping shyly through the drooping vines of morning glory and wild yam. He'd come earlier in the day, bringing a canvas-wrapped bundle containing several muskets for Jamie.

"That's all right." I stooped to pick up the hoe I had dropped. "Are you looking for Lizzie? She's in—"

"Ach, no, ma'am. That is, I—do ye think I might have a word, ma'am?" he asked abruptly. "Alone, like?"

"Of course. Come along in; we can talk while I hoe."

He nodded, and went round to let himself in by the gate. What might he want with me? I wondered. He had on a coat and boots, both covered in dust, and his breeches were badly creased. He'd been riding some way, then, not just from his family's cabin—and he hadn't been into the house yet; Mrs. Bug would have dusted him off, forcibly.

"Where have you come from?" I asked, offering him the gourd dipper from my water bucket. He accepted it, drinking thirstily, then wiped his mouth politely on his sleeve.

"Thank ye, ma'am. I've been to Hillsboro, for to fetch the . . . er . . . the things for Mr. Fraser."

"Really? That seems a long way," I said mildly.

A look of profound uneasiness crossed his face. He was a nice-looking boy, tanned and handsome as a young faun under his crop of dark, curly hair, but he looked almost furtive now, glancing back over his shoulder toward the house, as though fearful of interruption.

"I . . . um . . . well, ma'am, that's to do, a bit, with what I meant to speak to ye about."

"Oh? Well . . ." I made a cordial gesture, indicating that he should feel free to unburden himself, and turned away to begin my hoeing, so that he might feel less self-conscious. I was beginning to suspect what he wanted to ask me, though I wasn't sure what Hillsboro had to do with it.

"It's . . . ah . . . well, it's to do with Mrs. Lizzie," he began, folding his hands behind him.

"Yes?" I said encouragingly, nearly sure that I was right in my suppositions. I glanced toward the western end of the garden, where the bees were buzzing happily among the tall yellow umbels of the *dauco* plants. Well, it was better than the eighteenth-century notion of condoms, at least.

"I can't marry her," he blurted.

"What?" I stopped hoeing and straightened up, staring at

him. His lips were pressed tightly together, and I saw now that what I had taken for shyness had been his attempt to mask a deep unhappiness that now showed plainly in the lines of his face.

"You'd better come and sit down." I led him to the small bench Jamie had made me, set beneath the shade of a black gum tree that overhung the north side of the garden.

He sat, head drooping and hands trapped between his knees. I took off my broad-brimmed sun hat, wiped my face on my apron, and pinned up my hair more neatly, breathing in the cool freshness of the spruce and balsam trees that grew on the slope above.

"What is it?" I asked gently, seeing that he did not know how to start. "Are you afraid that perhaps you don't love her?"

He gave me a startled look, then turned his head back to the studied contemplation of his knees.

"Oh. No, ma'am. I mean—I don't, but that's no matter."

"It isn't?"

"No. I mean—I'm sure we *should* grow to be fond of one another, *meine Mutter* says so. And I like her well enough now, to be sure," he added hastily, as though fearing this might sound insulting. "Da says she's a tidy wee soul, and my sisters are verra fond of her indeed."

I made a noncommittal sound. I had had my doubts about this match to begin with, and it was beginning to sound as though they were justified.

"Is there . . . perhaps someone else?" I asked delicately.

Manfred shook his head slowly, and I heard him swallow hard.

"No, ma'am," he said in a low voice.

"You're sure?"

"Aye, ma'am." He drew a deep breath. "I mean—there was. But that's all done with now."

I was puzzled by this. If he had decided to renounce this mysterious other girl—whether out of fear of his mother, or for some other reason—then what was stopping him from going through with the marriage to Lizzie?

"The other girl—is she by chance from Hillsboro?" Things were coming a little clearer. When I had first met him and his family at the Gathering, his sisters had exchanged knowing glances at mention of Manfred's visits to Hillsboro. They had known about it then, even if Ute had not.

"Aye. That's why I went to Hillsboro—I mean, I had to go, for the . . . er . . . But I meant to see . . . Myra . . . and tell her that I would be married to Miss Wemyss and couldna come to see her anymore."

"Myra." So she had a name, at least. I sat back, tapping my foot meditatively. "You meant to—so you didn't see her, after all?"

He shook his head again, and I saw a tear drop and spread suddenly on the dusty homespun of his breeches.

"No, ma'am," he said, his voice half-choked. "I couldn't. She was dead."

"Oh, dear," I said softly. "Oh, I am so sorry." The tears were falling on his knees, making spots on the cloth, and his shoulders shook, but he didn't make a sound.

I reached out and gathered him into my arms, holding him tight against my shoulder. His hair was soft and springy and his skin flushed with heat against my neck. I felt helpless to deal with his grief; he was too old to comfort with mere touch, too young—perhaps—to find any solace in words. There was nothing I could do for the moment save hold him.

His arms went round my waist, though, and he clung to me for several minutes after his weeping was spent. I held him quietly, patting his back and keeping watch through the flickering green shadows of the vine-twined palisades, lest anyone else come looking for me in the garden.

At last he sighed, let go, and sat up. I groped for a handkerchief, and not finding one, pulled off my apron and handed it to him to wipe his face.

"You needn't marry right away," I said, when he seemed to have regained possession of himself. "It's only right that you should take a little time to—to heal. But we can find some excuse to put the wedding off; I'll speak to Jamie—"

But he was shaking his head, a look of sad determination taking the place of tears.

"No, ma'am," he said, low-voiced but definite. "I can't."

"Why not?"

"Myra was a whore, ma'am. She died of the French disease."

He looked up at me then, and I saw the terror in his eyes, behind the grief.

"And I think I've got it."

"YE'RE SURE?" Jamie set down the hoof he had been trimming, and looked bleakly at Manfred.

"*I'm* sure," I said tartly. I had obliged Manfred to show me the evidence—in fact, I had taken scrapings from the lesion to examine microscopically—then took him straight to find Jamie, barely waiting for the boy to do up his breeches.

Jamie looked fixedly at Manfred, plainly trying to decide what to say. Manfred, purple-faced from the double stress of confession and examination, dropped his own eyes before this basilisk gaze, staring at a crescent of black hoof paring that lay on the ground.

"I'm that sorry, sir," he murmured. "I—I didna mean to . . ."

"I shouldna suppose anyone does," Jamie said. He breathed deeply and made a sort of subterranean growling noise that caused Manfred to hunch his shoulders and try to withdraw his head, turtlelike, into the safer confines of his clothing.

"He did do the right thing," I pointed out, trying to put the best face possible on the situation. "Now, I mean—telling the truth."

Jamie snorted.

"Well, he couldna be poxing wee Lizzie, now, could he? That's worse than only going wi' a whore."

"I suppose some men would just keep quiet about it, and hope for the best."

"Aye, some would." He narrowed his eyes at Manfred, evidently looking for overt indications that Manfred might be a villain of this description.

Gideon, who disliked having his feet messed about and was consequently in bad temper, stamped heavily, narrowly missing Jamie's own foot. He tossed his head, and emitted a rumbling noise that I thought was roughly the equivalent of Jamie's growl.

"Aye, well." Jamie left off glaring at Manfred, and grabbed Gideon's halter. "Go along to the house with him, Sassenach. I'll finish here, and then we'll have Joseph in and see what's to do."

"All right." I hesitated, unsure whether to speak in front of Manfred. I didn't want to raise his hopes too much, until I'd had a chance to look at the scrapings under the microscope.

The spirochetes of syphilis were very distinctive, but I didn't think I had a stain that would allow me to see them with a simple light microscope such as mine was. And while I thought my homemade penicillin could likely eliminate the infection, I would have no way of knowing for certain, unless I *could* see them, and then see that they had disappeared from his blood.

I contented myself with saying, "I have got penicillin, mind."

"I ken that well enough, Sassenach." Jamie switched his baleful look from Manfred to me. I'd saved his life with the penicillin—twice—but he hadn't enjoyed the process. With a Scottish noise of dismissal, he bent and picked up Gideon's enormous hoof again.

Manfred seemed a bit shell-shocked, and said nothing on the way to the house. He hesitated at the door to the surgery, glancing uneasily from the gleaming microscope to the open box of surgical tools, and then toward the covered bowls lined up on the counter, in which I grew my penicillin colonies.

"Come in," I said, but was obliged to reach out and take him by the sleeve before he would step across the threshold. It occurred to me that he hadn't been to the surgery before; it was a good five miles to the McGillivrays' place, and *Frau* McGillivray was entirely capable of dealing with her family's minor ills.

I wasn't feeling terribly charitable toward Manfred at the moment, but gave him a stool and asked if he would like a cup of coffee. I thought he could probably use a stiff drink, if he was about to have an interview with Jamie and Joseph Wemyss, but supposed I had better keep him clear-headed.

"No, ma'am," he said, and swallowed, white-faced. "I mean, thank ye, no."

He looked extremely young, and very frightened.

"Roll up your sleeve then, please. I'm going to draw a bit of blood, but it won't hurt much. How did you come to meet the, er, young lady? Myra, that was her name?"

"Aye, ma'am." Tears welled in his eyes at her name; I suppose he really had loved her, poor boy—or thought he had.

He had met Myra in a tavern in Hillsboro. She had seemed kind, he said, and was very pretty, and when she asked the young gunsmith to buy her a glass of geneva, he had obliged, feeling dashing.

"So we drank a bit together, and she laughed at me, and . . ." He seemed rather at a loss to explain how matters had progressed from there, but he had waked up in her bed. That had sealed the matter, so far as he was concerned, and he had seized every excuse to go to Hillsboro thereafter.

"How long did this affair go on?" I asked, interested. Lacking a decent syringe for drawing blood, I'd merely pierced the vein inside his elbow with a fleam, and drained off the welling blood into a small vial.

For the better part of two years, apparently.

"I kent I couldna wed her," he explained earnestly. "*Meine Mutter* would never . . ." He trailed off, assuming the look of a startled rabbit hearing hounds in its immediate vicinity. *"Gruss Gott!"* he said. "My mother!"

I'd been wondering about that particular aspect of the affair myself. Ute McGillivray wasn't going to be at all pleased to hear that her pride and joy, her only son, had contracted a disreputable disease, and furthermore, one which was about to lead to the breaking of his carefully engineered engagement and very likely to a scandal that the entire backcountry would hear about. The fact that it was generally a fatal disease would probably be a secondary concern.

"She'll kill me!" he said, sliding off his stool and rolling his sleeve down hastily.

"Probably not," I said mildly. "Though I suppose—"

At this fraught moment came the sound of the back door opening and voices in the kitchen. Manfred stiffened, dark curls quivering with alarm. Then heavy footsteps started down the hall toward the surgery, and he dived across the room, flung a leg across the windowsill, and was off, running like a deer for the trees.

"Come back here, you ass!" I bellowed through the open window.

"Which ass is that, Auntie?" I turned to see that the heavy footsteps belonged to Young Ian—heavy, because he was carrying Lizzie Wemyss in his arms.

"Lizzie! What's the matter? Here, put her on the table." I could see at once what the matter was: a return of the malarial fever. She was limp, but shivered nonetheless with chill, the contracting muscles shaking her like jelly.

"I found her in the dairy shed," Ian said, laying her gently on the table. "The deaf Beardsley came rushin' out as though the devil was chasing him, saw me, and dragged me in. She was on the floor, wi' the churn overturned beside her."

This was very worrying—she hadn't had an attack for some time, but for a second time, the attack had come upon her too suddenly for her to go for help, causing almost immediate collapse.

"Top shelf of the cupboard," I said to Ian, hastily rolling Lizzie on her side and undoing her laces. "That bluish jar—no, the big one."

He grabbed it without question, removing the lid as he brought it to me.

"Jesus, Auntie! What's that?" He wrinkled his nose at the smell from the ointment.

"Gallberries and cinchona bark in goose grease, among other things. Take some and start rubbing it into her feet."

Looking bemused, he gingerly scooped up a dollop of the purplish-gray cream and did as I said, Lizzie's small bare foot nearly disappearing between the large palms of his hands.

"Will she be all right, d'ye think, Auntie?" He glanced at her face, looking troubled. The look of her was enough to trouble anyone—the clammy color of whey, and the flesh gone slack so that her delicate cheeks juddered with the chills.

"Probably. Close your eyes, Ian." I'd got her clothes loosened, and now pulled off her gown, petticoats, pocket, and stays. I threw a ratty blanket over her before working the shift off over her head—she owned only two, and wouldn't want one spoiled with the reek of the ointment.

Ian had obediently closed his eyes, but was still rubbing the ointment methodically into her feet, a small frown drawing his brows together, the look of concern lending him for a moment a brief but startling resemblance to Jamie.

I drew the jar toward me, scooped up some ointment, and, reaching under the blanket, began to rub it into the thinner skin beneath her armpits, then over her back and belly. I could feel the outlines of her liver distinctly, a large, firm mass beneath her ribs. Swollen, and tender from the way she grimaced at my touch; there was some ongoing damage there, certainly.

"Can I open my eyes now?"

"Oh—yes, of course. Rub more up her legs, please, Ian." Shoving the jar back in his direction, I caught a glimpse of movement in the doorway. One of the Beardsley twins stood there, clinging to the jamb, dark eyes fixed on Lizzie. Kezzie, it must be; Ian had said "the deaf Beardsley" had come to fetch help.

"She'll be all right," I said to him, raising my voice, and he nodded once, then disappeared, with a single burning glance at Ian.

"Who was it ye were shouting at, Auntie Claire?" Ian looked up at me, clearly as much to preserve Lizzie's modesty as from courtesy to me; the blanket was turned back and his big hands were smoothing ointment into the skin above her knee, thumbs gently circling the small rounded curves of her patella, her skin so thin that the pearly bone seemed almost visible through it.

"Who—oh. Manfred McGillivray," I said, suddenly recollecting. "Damn! The blood!" I leapt up and wiped my hands hurriedly on my apron. Thank God, I'd corked the vial; the blood inside was still liquid. It wouldn't keep long, though.

"Do her hands and arms, would you please, Ian? I've got to manage this quickly."

He moved obligingly to do as I said, while I hastily spilled a drop of blood on each of several slides, dragging a clean slide across each one to make a smear. What sort of stain might work on spirochetes? No telling; I'd try them all.

I explained the matter disjointedly to Ian, as I pulled stain bottles out of the cupboard, made up the solutions, and set the slides to soak.

"The pox? Poor lad; he must be nearly mad wi' fright." He eased Lizzie's arm, gleaming with ointment, under the blanket and tucked it gently round her.

I was momentarily surprised at this show of sympathy, but then remembered. Ian had been exposed to syphilis some years before, after his abduction by Geillis Duncan; I hadn't been sure that he had the disease, but had dosed him with the last of my twentieth-century penicillin, just in case.

"Did ye not tell him ye could cure him, though, Auntie?"

"I hadn't the chance. Though I'm not absolutely sure that I can, to be honest." I sat down on a stool, and took Lizzie's other hand, feeling for her pulse.

"Ye're not?" His feathery brows went up at that. "Ye told me I was cured."

"You are," I assured him. "If you ever had the disease in the first place." I gave him a sharp look. "You've never had a sore on your prick, have you? Or anywhere else?"

He shook his head, mute, a dark wave of blood staining his lean cheeks.

"Good. But the penicillin I gave you—that was some that I'd brought from . . . well, from before. That was purified—very strong and certainly potent. I'm never sure, when I use this stuff"—I gestured at the culturing bowls on the counter—"whether it's strong enough to work, or even the right strain. . . ." I rubbed the back of my hand under my nose; the gallberry ointment had a most *penetrating* smell.

"It doesn't always work." I had had more than one patient with an infection that didn't respond to one of my penicillin concoctions—though in those cases, I had often succeeded with another attempt. In a few instances, the person had recovered on his own before the second brew was ready. In one instance, the patient had died, despite applications of two different penicillin mixtures.

Ian nodded slowly, his eyes on Lizzie's face. The first bout of chills had spent itself and she lay quiet, the blanket barely moving over the slight round of her chest.

"If ye're no sure, then . . . ye'd not let him marry her, surely?"

"I don't know. Jamie said he'd speak to Mr. Wemyss, see what he thought of the matter."

I rose and took the first of the slides from its pinkish bath, shook off the clinging drops, and, wiping the bottom of the slide, placed it carefully on the platform of my microscope.

"What are ye looking for, Auntie?"

"Things called spirochetes. Those are the particular kind of germ that causes syphilis."

"Oh, aye." Despite the seriousness of the situation, I smiled, hearing the note of skepticism in his voice. I'd shown him microorganisms before, but—like Jamie—like almost everyone—he simply couldn't believe that something so nearly invisible was capable of harm. The only one who had seemed to accept the notion wholeheartedly was Malva Christie, and in her case, I thought the acceptance was due simply to her faith in me. If I told *her* something, she believed me; very refreshing, after years of assorted Scots looking at me with varying degrees of squiggle-eyed suspicion.

"Has he gone home, d'ye think? Manfred?"

"I don't know." I spoke absently, slowly moving the slide to and fro, searching. I could make out the red blood cells, pale pink discs that floated past my field of view, drifting lazily in the watery stain. No deadly spirals visible—but that didn't mean they weren't there, only that the stain I had used might not reveal them.

Lizzie stirred and moaned, and I looked round to see her eyes flutter open.

"There, lass," Ian said softly, and smiled at her. "Better, is it?"

"Is it?" she said faintly. Still, the corners of her mouth lifted slightly, and she put a hand out from under her blanket, groping. He took it in his, patting it.

"Manfred," she said, turning her head to and fro, eyes half-lidded. "Is Manfred here?"

"Um . . . no," I said, exchanging a quick glance of consternation with Ian. How much had she heard? "No, he was here, but he's—he's gone now."

"Oh." Seeming to lose interest, she closed her eyes again.

Ian looked down at her, still stroking her hand. His face showed deep sympathy—with perhaps a tinge of calculation.

"Shall I maybe carry the lassie up to her bed?" he asked softly, as though she might be sleeping. "And then maybe go and find . . . ?" He tilted his head toward the open window, raising one eyebrow.

"If you would, please, Ian." I hesitated, and his eyes met mine, deep hazel and soft with worry and the shadow of remembered pain. "She'll be all right," I said, trying to infuse a sense of certainty into the words.

"Aye, she will," he said firmly, and stooped to gather her up, tucking the blanket under her. "If I've anything to say about it."

46

IN WHICH THINGS GANG AGLEY

MANFRED MCGILLIVRAY did not come back. Ian did, with a blackened eye, skinned knuckles, and the terse report that Manfred had declared a set intention of going off and hanging himself, and good riddance to the fornicating son of a bitch, and might his rotten bowels gush forth like Judas Iscariot's, the traitorous, stinking wee turd. He then stamped upstairs, to stand silent over Lizzie's bed for a time.

Hearing this, I hoped that Manfred's statement was merely the counsel of temporary despair—and cursed myself for not having told him at once and in the strongest terms that he could be cured, whether it was absolutely true or not. Surely he wouldn't . . .

Lizzie was half-conscious, prostrated with the burning

fevers and shaking agues of malaria, and in no fit state to be told of her betrothed's desertion, nor the cause of it. I would have to make some delicate inquiries, though, so soon as she was fit, because there was the possibility that she and Manfred had anticipated their marriage vows, and if so . . .

"Well, there's the one thing about it," Jamie observed grimly. "The Beardsley twins were making ready to track our poxed lad down and castrate him, but now they've heard he means to hang himself, they've magnanimously decided that will do."

"Thank the Lord for small blessings," I said, sinking down at the table. "They might really do it." The Beardsleys, particularly Josiah, were excellent trackers—and not given to idle threats.

"Oh, they would," Jamie assured me. "They were most seriously sharpening their knives when I found them at it and told them not to trouble themselves."

I suppressed an involuntary smile at the image of the Beardsleys, bent side by side over a grindstone, their lean, dark faces set in identical scowls of vengeance, but the momentary flash of humor faded.

"Oh, God. We'll have to tell the McGillivrays."

Jamie nodded, looking pale at the thought, but pushed back his bench.

"I'd best go straightaway."

"Not 'til ye've had a bite." Mrs. Bug put a plate of food firmly in front of him. "Ye dinna want to be dealing wi' Ute McGillivray on an empty stomach."

Jamie hesitated, but evidently found her argument to have merit, for he picked up his fork and addressed himself to the ragoo'd pork, with grim determination.

"Jamie . . ."

"Aye?"

"Perhaps you *should* let the Beardsleys track Manfred down. Not to hurt him, I don't mean—but we need to find him. He *will* die of it, if he isn't treated."

He paused, a forkful of ragoo halfway to his mouth, and regarded me under lowered brows.

"Aye, and if they find him, he'll die of *that,* Sassenach." He shook his head, and the fork completed its journey. He chewed and swallowed, evidently completing his plan as he did so.

"Joseph's in Bethabara, courting. He'll have to be told, and by rights, I should fetch him to go with me to the McGillivrays'. But . . ." He hesitated, clearly envisioning Mr. Wemyss, that mildest and shyest of men, and no one's notion of a useful ally. "No. I'll go and tell Robin. May be as he'll start searching for the lad himself—or Manfred may have thought better of it and run for home already."

That was a cheering thought, and I saw him off with hope in mind. But he returned near midnight, grim-faced and silent, and I knew that Manfred had not come home.

"You told them both?" I asked, turning back the coverlet for him to crawl in beside me. He smelled of horse and night, cool and pungent.

"I asked Robin to walk outside wi' me, and told him. I hadna the nerve to tell Ute to her face," he admitted. He smiled at me, snuggling under the quilt. "Ye dinna think me too much a coward, I hope, Sassenach."

"No, indeed," I assured him, and leaned to blow out the candle. "Discretion is the better part of valor."

WE WERE ROUSED just before dawn by a thunderous pounding on the door. Rollo, who had been sleeping on the landing, shot down the stair, roaring threats. He was closely followed by Ian, who had been sitting up by Lizzie's bed, keeping watch while I slept. Jamie leapt out of bed and, seizing a loaded pistol from the top of the wardrobe, rushed to join the fray.

Shocked and dazed—I had been asleep for less than an hour—I sat up, heart pounding. Rollo stopped barking for a moment, and I heard Jamie shout, "Who is it?" through the door.

This query was answered by a renewed pounding that echoed up the stairwell and seemed to shake the house, accompanied by an upraised feminine voice that would have done credit to Wagner in one of his more robust moods. Ute McGillivray.

I began to struggle out of the bedclothes. Meanwhile, a confusion of voices, renewed barking, the grate of the bolt being lifted—and then more confused voices, all much louder. I ran to the window and looked out; Robin McGillivray was standing in the dooryard, having evidently just dismounted from one of a pair of mules.

He looked much older, and somehow deflated, as though the spirit had gone out of him, taking all his strength and leaving him flabby. He turned his head away from whatever riot was taking place on the stoop, closing his eyes. The sun was just up now, and the pure clear light showed up all the lines and hollows of exhaustion and a desperate unhappiness.

As though he sensed me looking at him, he opened his eyes and raised his face toward the window. He was red-eyed, disheveled. He saw me, but didn't respond to my tentative wave of greeting. Instead, he turned away, closing his eyes again, and stood, waiting.

The riot below had moved inside, and appeared to be progressing up the stairs, borne on a wave of Scottish expostulations and Germanic shrieks, punctuated by enthusiastic barking from Rollo, always willing to lend his efforts to further the festivities.

I seized my wrapper from its peg, but had barely got one arm into it before the door of the bedchamber was flung open, crashing into the wall so hard that it rebounded and hit her in the chest. Nothing daunted, she slammed it open again and advanced on me like a juggernaut, cap awry and eyes blazing.

"You! *Weibchen!* How you dare, such insult, such lies to say my son about! You I kill, I tear off your hair, *nighean na galladh!* You—"

She lunged at me and I flung myself sideways, narrowly avoiding her grab at my arm.

"Ute! *Frau* McGillivray! Listen to—"

The second grab was more successful; she got hold of the sleeve of my night rail and wrenched, dragging the garment off my shoulder with a rending noise of torn cloth, even as she clawed at my face with her free hand.

I jerked back, and screamed with all my strength, my nerves recalling for one dreadful instant a hand striking at my face, hands pulling at me. . . .

I struck at her, the strength of terror flooding through my limbs, screaming, screaming, some tiny remnant of rationality in my brain watching this, bemused, appalled—but completely unable to stop the animal panic, the unreasoning rage that geysered up from some deep and unsuspected well.

I hit out, hammering blindly, screaming—wondering even as I did so, why, why was I doing this?

An arm grabbed me round the waist and I was lifted off the ground. A fresh spurt of panic ripped through me, and then I found myself suddenly alone, untouched. I was standing in the corner by the wardrobe, swaying drunkenly, panting. Jamie stood in front of me, shoulders braced and elbows raised, shielding me.

He was talking, very calmly, but I had lost the capacity to make sense of words. I pressed my hands back against the wall, and felt some sense of comfort from its solid bulk.

My heart was still hammering in my ears, the sound of my own breathing scaring me, it was so like the gasping sound when Harley Boble had broken my nose. I shut my mouth hard, trying to stop. Holding my breath seemed to work, allowing only small inhalations through my now-functioning nose.

The movement of Ute's mouth caught my eye and I stared at it, trying to fix myself once more in time and space. I was hearing words, but couldn't quite make the jump of comprehension. I breathed, letting the words flow over me like water, taking emotion from them—anger, reason, protest, placation, shrillness, growling—but no explicit meaning.

Then I took a deep breath, wiped my face—I was surprised to find it wet—and suddenly everything snapped back to normal. I could hear, and understand.

Ute was staring at me, anger and dislike clear on her face, but muted by a lurking horror.

"You are mad," she said, nodding. "I see." She sounded almost calm at this point. "Well, then."

She turned to Jamie, automatically twisting up untidy handsful of grizzled blond hair, stuffing them under her enormous cap. The ribbon had been torn; a loop of it dangled absurdly over one eye.

"So, she is mad. I will say so, but still, my son—my son!—

is gone. So." She stood heaving, surveying me, and shook her head, then turned again to Jamie.

"Salem is closed to you," she said curtly. "My family, those who know us—they will not trade with you. Nor anyone else I speak to, to tell them the wicked thing she has done." Her eye drifted back to me, a cold, gelid blue, and her lip curled in a heavy sneer under the loop of torn ribbon.

"You are shunned," she said. "You do not exist, you." She turned on her heel and walked out, forcing Ian and Rollo to sidestep hastily out of her way. Her footfalls echoed heavily on the stair, a ponderous, measured tread, like the tolling of a passing bell.

I saw the tension in Jamie's shoulders relax, little by little. He was still wearing his nightshirt—there was a damp patch between his shoulder blades—and had the pistol still in his hand.

The front door boomed shut below. Everyone stood still, struck silent.

"You wouldn't really have shot her, would you?" I asked, clearing my throat.

"What?" He turned, staring at me. Then he caught the direction of my glance, and looked at the pistol in his hand as though wondering where *that* had come from.

"Oh," he said, "no," and shook his head, reaching up to put it back on top of the wardrobe. "I forgot I had it. Though God kens well enough that I should *like* to shoot the besotted auld besom," he added. "Are ye all right, Sassenach?"

He stooped to look at me, his eyes soft with worry.

"I'm all right. I don't know what—but it's all right. It's gone now."

"Ah," he said softly, and looked away, lashes coming down to hide his eyes. Had he felt it, too, then? Found himself suddenly . . . back? I knew he had sometimes. Remembered waking from sleep in Paris to see him braced in an open window, pressing so hard against the frame that the muscles stood out in his arms, visible by moonlight.

"It's all right," I repeated, touching him, and he gave me a brief, shy smile.

"Ye should have bitten her," Ian was saying earnestly to

Rollo. "She's got an arse the size of a hogshead of tobacco—how could ye miss?"

"Probably afraid of being poisoned," I said, coming out of my corner. "Do you suppose she meant it—or no, she meant it, certainly. But do you suppose she can do it? Stop anyone trading with us, I mean."

"She can stop Robin," Jamie said, a certain grimness returning to his expression. "For the rest . . . we'll see."

Ian shook his head, frowning, and rubbed his knuckled fist gingerly against his thigh.

"I kent I should have broken Manfred's neck," he said with real regret. "We could ha' told *Frau* Ute he fell off a rock, and saved a deal of trouble."

"Manfred?" The small voice made everyone turn as one, to see who had spoken.

Lizzie stood in the doorway, thin and pale as a starveling ghost, her eyes huge and glassy with recent fever.

"What about Manfred?" she said. She swayed dangerously, and put out a hand to the jamb, to save herself falling. "What's happened to him?"

"Poxed and gone," Ian said curtly, drawing himself up. "Ye didna give him your maidenheid, I hope."

IN THE EVENT, Ute McGillivray was not quite able to fulfill her threat—but she did enough damage. Manfred's dramatic disappearance, the breaking of his engagement to Lizzie, and the reason for it was a fearful scandal, and word of it spread from Hillsboro and Salisbury, where he had worked now and then as an itinerant gunsmith, to Salem and High Point.

But thanks to Ute's efforts, the story was even more confused than would be normal for such gossip; some said that he was poxed, others that I had maliciously and falsely accused him of being poxed, because of some fancied disagreement with his parents. Others, more kindly, did not believe Manfred was poxed, but said that doubtless I had been mistaken.

Those who believed him to be poxed were divided as to how

he had achieved that condition, half of them convinced that he had got it from some whore, and a good many of the rest speculating that he had got it from poor Lizzie, whose reputation suffered terribly—until Ian, Jamie, the Beardsley twins, and even Roger took to defending her honor with their fists, at which point people did not, of course, stop talking—but stopped talking where any of her champions might hear directly.

All of Ute's numerous relatives in and around Wachovia, Salem, Bethabara, and Bethania of course believed her version of the story, and tongues wagged busily. All of Salem did not cease trading with us—but many people did. And more than once, I had the unnerving experience of greeting Moravians I knew well, only to have them stare past me in stony silence, or turn their backs upon me. Often enough that I no longer went to Salem.

Lizzie, beyond a certain initial mortification, seemed not terribly upset at the rupture of her engagement. Bewildered, confused, and sorry—she said—for Manfred, but not desolated by his loss. And since she seldom left the Ridge anymore, she didn't hear what people said about her. What *did* trouble her was the loss of the McGillivrays—particularly Ute.

"D'ye see, ma'am," she told me wistfully, "I'd never had a mother, for my own died when I was born. And then *Mutti*—she asked me to call her so when I said I'd marry Manfred—she said I was her daughter, just like Hilda and Inga and Senga. She'd fuss over me, and bully me and laugh at me, just as she did them. And it was . . . just so *nice,* to have all that family. And now I've lost them."

Robin, who had been sincerely attached to her, had sent her a short, regretful note, sneaked out through the good offices of Ronnie Sinclair. But since Manfred's disappearance, neither Ute nor the girls had come to see her, nor sent a single word.

It was Joseph Wemyss, though, who was most visibly affected by the affair. He said nothing, plainly not wishing to make matters worse for Lizzie—but he drooped, like a flower deprived of rain. Beyond his pain for Lizzie, and his distress at the blackening of her reputation, he, too, missed the McGillivrays, missed the joy and comfort of suddenly being part of a large, exuberant family, after so many years of loneliness.

Worse, though, was that while Ute had not been able to carry out her threat entirely, she *had* been able to influence her near relatives—including Pastor Berrisch, and his sister, Monika, who, Jamie told me privately, had been forbidden to see or speak to Joseph again.

"The Pastor's sent her away to his wife's relatives in Halifax," he said, shaking his head sadly. "To forget."

"Oh, dear."

And of Manfred, there was no slightest trace. Jamie had sent word through all his usual avenues, but no one had seen him since his flight from the Ridge. I thought of him—and prayed for him—daily, haunted by pictures of him skulking in the woods alone, the deadly spirochetes multiplying in his blood day by day. Or, much worse, working his way to the Indies on some ship, pausing in every port to drown his sorrows in the arms of unsuspecting whores, to whom he would pass on the silent, fatal infection—and they, in turn . . .

Or sometimes, the nightmare image of a bundle of rotting clothes hanging from a tree limb, deep in the forest, with no mourners save the crows who came to pick the flesh from his bones. And despite everything, I could not find it in my heart to hate Ute McGillivray, who must be thinking the same thoughts.

The sole bright spot in this ruddy quagmire was that Thomas Christie, quite contrary to my expectations, had allowed Malva to continue to come to the surgery, his sole stipulation being that if I proposed to involve his daughter in any further use of the ether, he was to be told ahead of time.

"There." I stood back, gesturing to her to look through the eyepiece of the microscope. "Do you see them?"

Her lips pursed in silent fascination. It had taken no little effort to find a combination of staining and reflected sunlight that would reveal the spirochetes, but I had succeeded at last. They weren't strongly visible, but you could see them, if you knew what you were looking for—and despite my complete conviction in my original diagnosis, I was relieved to see them.

"Oh, yes! Wee spirals. I see them plain!" She looked up at

me, blinking. "D'ye mean seriously to tell me that these bittie things are what's poxed Manfred?" She was too polite to express open skepticism, but I could see it in her eyes.

"I do indeed." I had explained the germ theory of disease a number of times, to a variety of disbelieving eighteenth-century listeners, and in the light of this experience had little expectation of finding a favorable reception. The normal response was either a blank stare, indulgent laughter, or a sniff of dismissal, and I was more or less expecting a polite version of one of these reactions from Malva.

To my surprise, though, she seemed to grasp the notion at once—or at least pretended to.

"Well, so." She put both hands on the counter and peered again at the spirochetes. "These wee beasties cause the syphilis, then. However do they do that? And why is it that the bittie things ye showed me from my teeth don't make me ill?"

I explained, as best I could, the notion of "good bugs" or "indifferent bugs" versus "bad bugs," which she seemed to grasp easily—but my explanation of cells, and the concept of the body being composed of these, left her frowning at the palm of her hand in confusion, trying to make out the individual cells. She shook off her doubt, though, and folding up her hand in her apron, returned to her questions.

Did the bugs cause all disease? The penicillin—why did it work on some of the germs, but not all? And how did the bugs get from one person to another?

"Some travel by air—that's why you must try to avoid people coughing or sneezing on you—and some by water—which is why you mustn't drink from a stream that someone's been using as a privy—and some . . . well, by other means." I didn't know how much she might know about sex in humans—she lived on a farm, clearly she knew how pigs, chickens, and horses behaved—and I was wary of enlightening her, lest her father hear about it. I rather thought he'd prefer her to be dealing with ether.

Naturally, she pounced on my evasion.

"Other means? What other means are there?" With an internal sigh, I told her.

"They do *what*?" she said, incredulous. "Men, I mean.

Like an animal! Whyever would a woman let a man do that to her?"

"Well, they *are* animals, you know," I said, suppressing an urge to laugh. "So are women. As to why one would let them . . ." I rubbed my nose, looking for a tasteful way of putting it. She was moving rapidly ahead of me, though, putting two and two together.

"For money," she said, looking thunderstruck. "*That's* what a whore does! She lets them do such things to her for money."

"Well, yes—but women who aren't whores—"

"The bairns, aye, ye said." She nodded, but was plainly thinking of other things; her small, smooth forehead was wrinkled in concentration.

"How much money do they get?" she asked. "I should want a lot, I think, to let a man—"

"I don't know," I said, somewhat taken aback. "Different amounts, I expect. Depending."

"Depending . . . oh, if he was maybe ugly, ye mean, ye could make him pay more? Or if *she* were ugly . . ." She gave me a quick, interested look. "Bobby Higgins told me of a whore he kent in London, that her looks was spoilt by vitriol." She looked up at the cupboard where I kept the sulfuric acid under lock and key, and shivered, her delicate shoulders quivering with revulsion at the thought.

"Yes, he told me about her, too. Vitriol is what we call a caustic—a liquid that burns. That's why—"

But her mind had already returned to the subject of fascination.

"To think of Manfred McGillivray doing such a thing!" She turned round gray eyes on me. "Well, and Bobby. He must have been, mustn't he?"

"I do believe soldiers are inclined—"

"But the Bible," she said, squinting thoughtfully. "It says ye mustna be whoring after idols. Does that mean men went about sticking their pricks into—did the idols look like women, d'ye think?"

"I'm sure that's not what it means, no," I said hastily. "More a metaphor, you know. Er . . . lusting after something, I think it means, not, er . . ."

"Lust," she said thoughtfully. "That's to want something sinful bad, is it not?"

"Yes, rather." Heat was wavering over my skin, dancing in tiny veils. I needed cool air, quickly, or I'd be flushed as a tomato and drenched with sweat. I rose to go out, but felt I really mustn't leave her with the impression that sex had to do only with money or babies—even though it well might, for some women.

"There *is* another reason for intercourse, you know," I said, speaking over my shoulder as I headed for the door. "When you love someone, you want to give them pleasure. And they want to do the same for you."

"Pleasure?" Her voice rose behind me, incredulous. "Ye mean some women *like* it?"

47

BEES AND SWITCHES

I WAS BY NO means spying. One of my hives had swarmed, and I was looking for the fugitive bees.

New swarms usually didn't travel far, and stopped frequently, often resting for hours in a tree fork or open log, where they formed a ball of humming conference. If they could be located before making up their collective mind about where to settle, they could often be persuaded into a temptingly empty basket hive, and thus hauled back into captivity.

The trouble with bees is that they don't leave footprints. Now I was casting to and fro on the mountainside, nearly a mile from the house, an empty basket hive slung on a rope over my shoulder, trying to follow Jamie's instructions regarding hunting, and think like a bee.

There were huge blooming patches of galax, fire-weed, and other wildflowers on the hillside far above me, but there was a very attractive dead snag—if one was a bee—poking out of the heavy growth some way below.

The basket hive was heavy, and the slope was steep. It was easier to go down than up. I hitched up the rope, which was beginning to rub the skin off my shoulder, and began sidling downward through sumac and hobble-bush, bracing my feet against rocks and grabbing at branches to keep from slipping.

Concentrating on my feet, I didn't take particular notice of where I was. I emerged into a gap in the bushes from which the roof of a cabin was visible, some distance below me. Whose was that? The Christies', I thought. I wiped a sleeve across the sweat dripping from the point of my chin; the day was warm, and I hadn't brought a canteen. Perhaps I would stop and ask for water on the way home.

Making my way at last to the snag, I was disappointed to find no sign of the swarm. I stood still, blotting sweat from my face and listening, in hopes of picking up the bees' telltale deep drone. I heard the hum and whine of assorted flying insects, and the genial racket of a flock of foraging pygmy nuthatches on the slope above—but no bees.

I sighed and turned to make my way around the snag, but then paused, my eye caught by a glimpse of white below.

Thomas Christie and Malva were in the small clearing at the back of their cabin. I had caught the flash of his shirt as he moved, but now he stood motionless, arms crossed.

His attention appeared to be fixed on his daughter, who was cutting branches from one of the mountain ash trees at the side of the clearing. What for? I wondered.

There seemed something very peculiar about the scene, though I couldn't think exactly what. Some attitude of body? Some air of tension between them?

Malva turned and walked toward her father, several long, slender branches in her hand. Her head was bent, her step dragging, and when she handed him the branches, I understood abruptly what was going on.

They were too far away for me to hear them, but he apparently said something to her, gesturing brusquely toward the stump they used as a chopping block. She knelt down by it, bent forward, and lifted up her skirts, exposing her bare buttocks.

Without hesitation, he raised the switches and slashed

them hard across her rump, then whipped them back in the other direction, crisscrossing her flesh with vivid lines that I could see even at such a distance. He repeated this several times, whipping the springy twigs back and forth with a measured deliberation whose violence was the more shocking for its lack of apparent emotion.

It hadn't even occurred to me to look away. I stood stock-still in the shrubbery, too stunned even to brush away the gnats that swarmed around my face.

Christie had thrown down the switches, turned on his heel, and gone into the house before I could do more than blink. Malva sat back on her heels and shook down her skirts, smoothing the fabric gingerly over her bottom as she rose. She was red-faced, but not weeping or distraught.

She's used to it. The thought came unbidden. I hesitated, not knowing what to do. Before I could decide, Malva had settled her cap, turned, and walked into the woods with an air of determination—headed straight toward me.

I ducked behind a big tulip poplar, before I was even aware of making a decision. She wasn't injured, and I was sure she wouldn't like to know that anyone had seen the incident.

Malva passed within a few feet of me, puffing a little on the climb, and snorting through her nose and muttering in a way that made me think she was very angry, rather than upset.

I peered cautiously round the poplar, but caught no more than a glimpse of her cap, bobbing through the trees. There were no cabins up there, and she hadn't carried a basket or any tools for foraging. Perhaps she only wanted to be alone, to recover herself. No surprise, if so.

I waited until she was safely out of sight, then made my own way slowly down the slope. I didn't stop at the Christie cabin, thirsty as I was, and had quite lost interest in errant bees.

I MET JAMIE at a stiled fence, some little distance from home, in conversation with Hiram Crombie. I nodded in greeting, and waited in some impatience for Crombie to finish his business, so I could tell Jamie what I had just witnessed.

Luckily, Hiram showed no inclination to linger; I made him nervous.

I told Jamie at once what I had seen, and was annoyed to find that he didn't share my concern. If Tom Christie thought it necessary to whip his daughter, that was his affair.

"But he might be . . . it might be—perhaps it doesn't stop with a switching. Perhaps he does . . . other things to her."

He shot me a look of surprise.

"Tom? D'ye have any reason to think so?"

"No," I admitted reluctantly. The Christie ménage gave me an uncomfortable feeling, but that was likely only because I didn't get on with Tom. I wasn't so foolish as to think that a tendency toward Bible-thumping meant a person wouldn't engage in wickedness—but in all fairness, it didn't mean he *did,* either. "But surely he shouldn't be whipping her like that—at her age?"

He glanced at me in mild exasperation.

"Ye dinna understand a thing, do ye?" he said, echoing my thought exactly.

"I was about to say just that, to *you,*" I said, giving him look for look. He didn't look away, but held my gaze, his own slowly taking on a wry amusement.

"So it will be different?" he said. "In your world?" There was just enough edge in his voice to remind me forcibly that we were not in my world—nor ever would be. Sudden goose-flesh ran up my arm, lifting the fine blond hairs.

"A man wouldna beat a woman, then, in your time? Not even for good cause?"

And what was I to say to that? I couldn't lie, even if I wanted to; he knew my face much too well.

"Some do," I admitted. "But it's not the same. There—then, I mean—a man who beat his wife would be a criminal. But," I added in fairness, "a man who beat his wife then would most often be using his fists."

A look of astonished disgust crossed his face.

"What sort of man would do that?" he asked incredulously.

"A bad one."

"So I should think, Sassenach. And ye dinna think there's a difference?" he asked. "Ye'd see it the same, if I were to smash your face, rather than only take a tawse to your bum?"

Blood flared abruptly in my cheeks. He once *had* taken a strap to me, and I hadn't forgotten it. I had wanted to kill him at the time—and didn't feel kindly toward him at the memory. At the same time, I wasn't stupid enough to equate his actions with those of a modern-day wife-beater.

He glanced at me, raised one eyebrow, then understood what I was recalling. He grinned.

"Oh," he said.

"Oh, indeed," I said, very cross. I had succeeded in putting that extremely humiliating episode out of mind, and didn't at all like having it recalled.

He, on the other hand, was plainly enjoying the recollection. He eyed me in a manner I found grossly insufferable, still grinning.

"God, ye screamed like a *ban-sidhe.*"

I began to feel a distinct throbbing of blood in my temples.

"I bloody well had cause to!"

"Oh, aye," he said, and the grin widened. "Ye did. Your own fault, mind," he added.

"*My* f—"

"It was," he said firmly.

"You apologized!" I said, completely outraged. "You know you did!"

"No, I didn't. And it was still your fault to begin with," he said, with complete lack of logic. "Ye wouldna have got nearly such a wicked tanning, if ye'd only minded me in the first place, when I told ye to kneel and—"

"Minded you! You think I would have just meekly given in and let you—"

"I've never seen ye do *anything* meek, Sassenach." He took my arm to help me over the stile, but I jerked free, puffing with indignation.

"You beastly *Scot*!" I dropped the hive on the ground at his feet, picked up my skirts, and scrambled over the stile.

"Well, I havena done it again," he protested, behind me. "I promised, aye?"

I whirled round on the other side and glared at him.

"Only because I threatened to cut your heart out if you ever tried!"

"Well, even so. I *could* have—and ye ken that well, Sassenach. Aye?" He'd quit grinning, but there was a distinct glint in his eye.

I took several deep breaths, trying simultaneously to control my annoyance and think of some crushing rejoinder. I failed in both attempts, and with a briefly dignified "Hmph!" turned on my heel.

I heard the rustle of his kilt as he picked up the hive, hopped over the stile, and came after me, catching up within a stride or two. I didn't look at him; my cheeks were still flaming.

The infuriating fact was that I *did* know that. I remembered all too well. He had used his sword belt to such effect that I hadn't been able to sit comfortably for several days—and if he should ever decide to do it again, there was absolutely nothing to stop him.

I was, for the most part, able to ignore the fact that I was legally his property. That didn't alter the fact that it *was* a fact—and he knew it.

"What about Brianna?" I demanded. "Would you feel the same way about it, if young Roger suddenly decided to take his belt or a switch to your daughter?"

He appeared to find something amusing in the notion.

"I think he'd have the devil of a fight on his hands if he tried," he said. "That's a braw wee lassie, no? And she has your notions of what constitutes wifely obedience, I'm afraid. But then," he added, swinging the hive's rope across his shoulder, "ye never ken what goes on in a marriage, do ye? Perhaps she'd be pleased if he tried."

"Pleased?!" I gawked at him in astonishment. "How can you think that any woman would *ever*—"

"Oh, aye? What about my sister?"

I stopped dead in the middle of the path, staring at him.

"What *about* your sister? Surely you aren't telling me—"

"I am." The glint was back, but I didn't think he was joking.

"Ian *beat* her?"

"I do wish ye'd stop calling it that," he said mildly. "It

sounds as though Ian took his fists to her, or blackened her eyes. I gave ye a decent skelping, but I didna bloody ye, for God's sake." His eyes flicked briefly toward my face; everything had healed, at least outwardly; the only trace left was a tiny scar through one eyebrow—invisible, unless one parted the hairs there and looked closely. "Neither would Ian."

I was completely flabbergasted to hear this. I had lived in close proximity with Ian and Jenny Murray for months at a time, and had never seen the slightest indication that he possessed a violent nature. For that matter, it was impossible to imagine anyone trying such a thing on Jenny Murray, who had—if such a thing was possible—an even stronger personality than her brother.

"Well, what *did* he do? And why?"

"Well, he'd only take his belt to her now and then," he said, "and only if she made him."

I took a deep breath.

"If she *made* him?" I asked calmly, under the circumstances.

"Well, ye ken Ian," he said, shrugging. "He's no the one to be doing that sort of thing unless Jenny deviled him into it."

"I never saw anything of that sort going on," I said, giving him a hard look.

"Well, she'd scarcely do it in front of ye, would she?"

"And she would, in front of *you*?"

"Well, not precisely, no," he admitted. "But I wasna often in the house, after Culloden. Now and then, though, I'd come down for a visit, and I'd see that she was . . . brewing for something." He rubbed his nose and squinted against the sun, searching for words. "She'd devil him," he said at last, shrugging. "Pick at him over nothing, make wee sarcastic remarks. She'd—" His face cleared a bit, as he came up with a suitable description. "She'd act like a spoilt wee lassie in need of the tawse."

I found this description completely incredible. Jenny Murray had a sharp tongue, and few inhibitions about using it on anyone, her husband included. Ian, the soul of good nature, merely laughed at her. But I simply couldn't countenance the notion of her behaving in the manner described.

"Well, so. I'd seen that a time or two, as I say. And Ian

would give her an eye, but held his peace. But then the once, I was out hunting, near sunset, and took a small deer on the hill just behind the broch—ye ken the place?"

I nodded, still feeling stunned.

"It was close enough to carry the carcass to the house without help, so I brought it down to the smoke shed and hung it. There was no one about—I found out later the children had all gone to the market in Broch Mhorda, and the servants with them. So I thought the house was empty altogether, and stepped into the kitchen to find a bite and a cup of buttermilk before I left."

Thinking the house empty, he had been startled by noises in the bedchamber overhead.

"What sort of noises?" I asked, fascinated.

"Well . . . shrieks," he said, shrugging. "And giggling. A bit of shoving and banging, with a stool or some such falling over. If it weren't for the yaffling, I should have thought there were thieves in the house. But I kent it was Jenny's voice, and Ian's, and—" He broke off, his ears going pink at the memory.

"So then . . . there was a bit more—raised voices, like—and then the crack of a belt on a bum, and the sort of skelloch ye could hear across six fields."

He took a deep breath, shrugging.

"Well, I was taken back a bit, and couldna think what to do at once."

I nodded, understanding that, at least.

"I expect it would be a bit of an awkward situation, yes. It . . . er . . . went on, though?"

He nodded. His ears were a deep red by now, and his face flushed, though that might only be from heat.

"Aye, it did." He glanced at me. "Mind, Sassenach, if I'd thought he meant harm to her, I should have been up the stairs in an instant. But . . ." He brushed away an inquisitive bee, shaking his head. "There was—it felt—I canna even think how to say it. It wasna really that Jenny kept laughing, because she didna—but that I felt she wanted to. And Ian . . . well, Ian *was* laughing. Not out loud, I dinna mean; it was just . . . in his voice."

He blew out his breath, and swiped his knuckles along his jaw, wiping sweat.

"I stayed quite frozen there, wi' a bit of pie in my hand, listening. I came to myself only when the flies started lighting in my open mouth, and by that time, they'd . . . ah . . . they were . . . mmphm." He hunched his shoulders, as though his shirt were too tight.

"Making it up, were they?" I asked very dryly.

"I expect so," he replied, rather primly. "I left. Walked all the way to Foyne, and stayed the night with Grannie MacNab." Foyne was a tiny hamlet, some fifteen miles from Lallybroch.

"Why?" I asked.

"Well, I had to," he said logically. "I couldna ignore it, after all. It was either walk about and think of things, or else give in and abuse myself, and I couldna verra well do *that*—it was my own sister, after all."

"You mean to say you can't think and engage in sexual activity at the same time?" I asked, laughing.

"Of course not," he said—thus confirming a long-held private opinion of mine—and gave me a look as though I were crazy. "Can you?"

"I *can,* yes."

He raised one eyebrow, plainly unconvinced.

"Well, I'm not saying I *do,* always," I admitted, "but it's possible. Women are used to doing more than one thing at once—they have to, because of the children. Anyway, go back to Jenny and Ian. Why on earth—"

"Well, I did walk about and think of it," Jamie admitted. "I couldna seem to stop thinking of it, to be honest. Grannie MacNab could see I'd something on my mind, and pestered me over the supper until . . . ah . . . well, until I told her about it."

"Really. What did she say?" I asked, fascinated. I'd known Grannie MacNab, a sprightly old person with a highly forthright manner—and a lot of experience with human weakness.

"She cackled like thorns under a pot," he said, one side of his mouth turning up. "I thought she'd fall into the fire wi' merriment."

Recovered to some extent, though, the old lady had wiped

her eyes and explained matters to him, kindly, as though addressing a simpleton.

"She said it was because of Ian's leg," Jamie said, glancing at me to see whether this made sense to me. "She said that such a thing would make no difference to Jenny, but it would to *him.* She said," he added, his color heightening, "that men havena got any idea what women think about bed, but they always think they have, so it causes trouble."

"I knew I liked Grannie MacNab," I murmured. "What else?"

"Well, so. She said it was likely that Jenny was only makin' it clear to Ian—and maybe to herself, as well—that she still thought he was a man, leg or no."

"What? Why?"

"Because, Sassenach," he said, very dryly indeed, "when ye're a man, a good bit of what ye have to do is to draw up lines and fight other folk who come over them. Your enemies, your tenants, your children—your wife. Ye canna always just strike them or take a strap to them, but when ye can, at least it's clear to everyone who's in charge."

"But that's perfectly—" I began, and then broke off, frowning as I considered this.

"And if ye're a man, you're in charge. It's you that keeps order, whether ye like it or not. It's true," he said, then touched my elbow as he nodded toward an opening in the wood. "I'm thirsty. Shall we stop a bit?"

I followed him up a narrow path through the wood to what we called the Green Spring—a bubbling flow of water over pale serpentine stone, set in a cool, shady bowl of surrounding moss. We knelt, splashed our faces, and drank, sighing with grateful relief. Jamie tipped a handful of water down inside his shirt, closing his eyes in bliss. I laughed at him, but unpinned my sweat-soaked kerchief and doused it in the spring, using it to wipe my neck and arms.

The walk to the spring had caused a break in the conversation, and I wasn't sure quite how—or whether—to resume it. Instead, I merely sat quietly in the shade, arms about my knees, idly wriggling my toes in the moss.

Jamie, too, seemed to feel no need of speech for the moment. He leaned comfortably back against a rock, the wet fabric of his shirt plastered to his chest, and we sat still, listening to the wood.

I wasn't sure what to say, but that didn't mean I had stopped thinking about the conversation. In an odd way, I thought I understood what Grannie MacNab had meant—though I wasn't quite sure I agreed with it.

I was thinking more about what Jamie had said, though, regarding a man's responsibility. Was it true? Perhaps it was, though I had never thought of it in that light before. It *was* true that he was a bulwark—not only for me, and for the family, but for the tenants, as well. Was that really how he did it, though? *"Draw up lines, and fight other folk who come over them"?* I rather thought it was.

There were lines between him and me, surely; I could have drawn them on the moss. Which was not to say we did not "come across" each other's lines—we did, frequently, and with varying results. I had my own defenses—and means of enforcement. But he had only beaten me once for crossing his lines, and that was early on. So, had he seen that as a necessary fight? I supposed he had; that was what he was telling me.

But he had been following his own train of thought, which was running on a different track.

"It's verra odd," he said thoughtfully. "Laoghaire drove me mad wi' great regularity, but it never once occurred to me to thrash her."

"Well, how very thoughtless of you," I said, drawing myself up. I disliked hearing him refer to Laoghaire, no matter what the context.

"Oh, it was," he replied seriously, taking no notice of my sarcasm. "I think it was that I didna care enough for her to think of it, let alone do it."

"You didn't care enough to beat her? Wasn't she the lucky one, then?"

He caught the tone of pique in my voice; his eyes sharpened and fixed on my face.

"Not to hurt her," he said. Some new thought came to him; I saw it cross his face.

He smiled a little, got up, and came toward me. He reached down and pulled me to my feet, then took hold of my wrist, which he lifted gently over my head and pinned against the trunk of the pine I had been sitting under, so that I was obliged to lean back flat against it.

"Not to hurt her," he said again, speaking softly. "To own her. I didna want to possess her. You, *mo nighean donn*—you, I would own."

"*Own* me?" I said. "And what, exactly, do you mean by that?"

"What I say." There was still a gleam of humor in his eyes, but his voice was serious. "Ye're mine, Sassenach. And I would do anything I thought I must to make that clear."

"Oh, indeed. Including beating me on a regular basis?"

"No, I wouldna do that." The corner of his mouth lifted slightly, and the pressure of his grip on my trapped wrist increased. His eyes were deep blue, an inch from mine. "I dinna need to—because I *could,* Sassenach—and ye ken that well."

I pulled against his grip, by sheer reflex. I remembered vividly that night in Doonesbury: the feeling of fighting him with all my strength—to no avail whatever. The horrifying feeling of being pinned to the bed, defenseless and exposed, realizing that he could do anything whatever that he liked to me—and would.

I squirmed violently, trying to escape the grip of memory, as much as his grasp on my flesh. I didn't succeed, but did turn my wrist so as to be able to sink my nails into his hand.

He didn't flinch or look away. His other hand touched me lightly—no more than a brush of my earlobe, but that was quite enough. He *could* touch me anywhere—in any way.

Evidently, women *are* capable of experiencing rational thought and sexual arousal simultaneously, because I appeared to be doing precisely that.

My brain was engaged in indignant rebuttal of all kinds of things, including at least half of everything he'd said in the course of the last few minutes.

At the same time, the other end of my spinal cord was not merely shamefully aroused at the thought of physical possession; it was bloody deliriously weak-kneed with desire at the notion, and was causing my hips to sway outward, brushing his.

He was still ignoring the dig of my nails. His other hand

came up and took my free hand before I could do anything violent with it; he folded his fingers around mine and held them captive, down at my side.

"If ye asked me, Sassenach, to free ye—" he whispered, "d'ye think I'd do so?"

I took a deep breath; deep enough that my breasts brushed his chest, he stood so close, and realization welled up in me. I stood still, breathing, watching his eyes, and felt my agitation fade slowly away, mutating into a sense of conviction, heavy and warm in the pit of my belly.

I had thought my body swayed in answer to his—and it did. But his moved unconsciously with mine; the rhythm of the pulse I saw in his throat was the pounding of the heartbeat that echoed in my wrist, and the sway of his body followed mine, barely touching, moving scarcely more than the leaves above, sighing on the breeze.

"I wouldn't ask," I whispered. "I'd tell you. And you'd do it. You'd do as I said."

"Would I?" His grip on my wrist was still firm, and his face so close to mine that I felt his smile, rather than saw it.

"Yes," I said. I had stopped pulling at my trapped wrist; instead, I pulled my other hand from his—he made no move to stop me—and brushed a thumb from the lobe of his ear down the side of his neck. He took a short, sharp breath, and a tiny shudder ran through him, stippling his skin with goose bumps in the wake of my touch.

"Yes, you would," I said again very softly. "Because I own you, too . . . man. Don't I?"

His hand released its grip abruptly and slid upward, long fingers intertwining with mine, his palm large and warm and hard against my own.

"Oh, aye," he said, just as softly. "Ye do." He lowered his head the last half-inch and his lips brushed mine, whispering, so that I felt the words as much as heard them.

"And I ken that verra well indeed, *mo nighean donn.*"

48

WOODEARS

DESPITE HIS DISMISSAL of her worries, Jamie had promised his wife to look into the matter, and found opportunity to speak with Malva Christie a few days later.

Coming back from Kenny Lindsay's place, he met a snake curled up in the dust of the path before him. It was a largish creature, but gaily striped—not one of the venomous vipers. Still, he couldn't help it; snakes gave him the grue, and he did not wish to pick it up with his hands, nor yet to step over it. It might not be disposed to lunge up his kilt—but then again, it might. For its part, the snake remained stubbornly curled among the leaves, not budging in response to his "Shoo!" or the stamping of his foot.

He took a step to the side, found an alder, and cut a good stick from it, with which he firmly escorted the wee beastie off the path and into the wood. Affronted, the snake writhed off at a good rate of speed into a hobble-bush, and next thing, a loud shriek came from the other side of the bush.

He darted round it to find Malva Christie, making an urgent, though unsuccessful, effort to squash the agitated snake with a large basket.

"It's all right, lass, let him go." He seized her arm, causing a number of mushrooms to cascade out of her basket, and the snake decamped indignantly in search of quieter surroundings.

He crouched and scooped up the mushrooms for her, while she gasped and fanned herself with the end of her apron.

"Oh, thank ye, sir," she said, bosom heaving. "I'm that terrified o' snakes."

"Och, well, that's no but a wee king snake," he said, affecting nonchalance. "Great ratters—or so I'm told."

"Maybe so, but they've a wicked bite." She shuddered briefly.

"Ye've no been bitten, have ye?" He stood up and dumped a final handful of fungus into her basket, and she curtsied in thanks.

"No, sir." She straightened her cap. "But Mr. Crombie was. Gully Dornan brought one of those things in a box, to Sunday meeting last, just for mischief, for he kent the text was *For they shall take up poisonous serpents and suffer no harm.* I think he meant to let it out in the midst of the prayin'." She grinned at the telling, clearly reliving the event.

"But Mr. Crombie saw him with the box, and took it from him, not knowing what was in it. Well, so—Gully was shaking of the box, to keep the snake awake, and when Mr. Crombie opened it, the snake came out like a jack-i'-the-box and bit Mr. Crombie on the lip."

Jamie couldn't help smiling in turn.

"Did it, then? I dinna recall hearing about that."

"Well, Mr. Crombie was that furious," she said, trying for tact. "I imagine no one wanted to spread the story, sir, for fear he'd maybe pop with rage."

"Aye, I see," he said dryly. "And that's why he wouldna come to have my wife see to the wound, I suppose."

"Oh, he wouldna do that, sir," she assured him, shaking her head. "Not if he was to have cut off his nose by mistake."

"No?"

She picked up the basket, glancing shyly up at him.

"Well . . . no. Some say may be as your wife's a witch, did ye ken that?"

He felt an unpleasant tightness in his wame, though he was not surprised to hear it.

"She is a Sassenach," he answered, calm. "Folk will always say such things of a stranger, especially a woman." He glanced sideways at her, but her eyes were modestly cast down to the contents of her basket. "Think so yourself, do ye?"

She looked up at that, gray eyes wide.

"Oh, no, sir! Never!"

She spoke with such earnestness that he smiled, despite the seriousness of his errand.

"Well, I suppose ye'd have noticed, so much time as ye spend in her surgery."

"Oh, I should wish nothing but to be just like her, sir!" she assured him, clutching the handle of her basket in worshipful enthusiasm. "She is so kind and lovely, and she kens so much! I want to know all she can teach me, sir."

"Aye, well. She's said often how good it is to have such a pupil as yourself, lass. Ye're a great help to her." He cleared his throat, wondering how best to work round from these cordialities to a rude inquiry as to whether her father was interfering with her. "Ah . . . your Da doesna mind that ye spend so much time with my wife?"

A cloud fell upon her countenance at that, and her long black lashes swept down, hiding the dove-gray eyes.

"Oh. Well. He . . . he doesna say I mustna go."

Jamie made a noncommittal sound in his throat, and gestured her ahead of him back to the path, where he strode along for a bit without further question, allowing her to regain her composure.

"What d'ye think your father will do," he inquired, swishing his stick casually through a patch of toadflax, "once ye've wed and left his house? Is there a woman he might consider? He'd need someone to do for him, I expect."

Her lips tightened at that, to his interest, and a faint flush rose in her cheeks.

"I dinna mean to be wed anytime soon, sir. We'll manage well enough."

Her answer was short enough to cause him to probe a bit.

"No? Surely ye've suitors, lass—the lads swoon after ye in droves; I've seen them."

The flush on her skin bloomed brighter.

"Please, sir, ye'll say no such thing to my faither!"

That rang a small alarm bell in him—but then, she might mean only that Tom Christie was a strict parent, vigilant of his daughter's virtue. And he would have been astonished to the marrow to learn that Christie was soft, indulgent, or in any way delinquent in such responsibilities.

"I shall not," he said mildly. "I was only teasin', lass. Is your father sae fierce, then?"

She did look at him then, very direct.

"Thought ye kent him, sir."

He burst out laughing at that, and after a moment's hesitation, she joined him, with a small titter like the sound of the wee birds in the trees above.

"I do," he said, recovering. "He's a good man, Tom—if a bit dour."

He looked to see the effect of this. Her face was still flushed, but there was a tiny residual smile on her lips. That was good.

"Well, so," he resumed casually, "have ye enough of the woodears there?" He nodded at her basket. "I saw a good many yesterday, up near the Green Spring."

"Oh, did ye?" She glanced up, interested. "Where?"

"I'm headed that way," he said "Come if ye like, I'll show ye."

They made their way along the Ridge, talking of inconsequent things. He led her now and then back to the subject of her father, and noted that she seemed to have no reservations concerning him—only a prudent regard for his foibles and temper.

"Your brother, then," he said thoughtfully, at one point. "Is he content, d'ye think? Or will he be wanting to leave, maybe go down to the coast? I ken he's no really a farmer at heart, is he?"

She snorted a bit, but shook her head.

"No, sir, that he's not."

"What did he do, then? I mean, he grew up on a plantation, did he not?"

"Oh, no, sir." She looked up at him, surprised. "He grew up in Edinburgh. We both did."

He was taken back a bit at that. It was true, both she and Allan had an educated accent, but he had thought it only that Christie was a schoolmaster, and strict of such things.

"How is that, lass? Tom said he'd married here, in the Colonies."

"Oh, so he did, sir," she assured him hastily. "But his wife was not a bond servant; she went back to Scotland."

"I see," he said mildly, seeing her face grow much pinker and her lips press tight. Tom had said his wife had died—

well, and he supposed she had, but in Scotland, after she'd left him. Proud as Christie was, he could hardly wonder that the man hadn't confessed to his wife's desertion. But—

"Is it true, sir, that your grandsire was Lord Lovat? Him they called the Old Fox?"

"Oh, aye," he said, smiling. "I come from a long line of traitors, thieves, and bastards, ken?"

She laughed at that, and very prettily urged him to tell her more of his sordid family history—quite obviously, as a means of avoiding his asking more questions regarding hers.

The "but" lingered in his mind, though, even as they talked, with increasing desultoriness as they climbed through the dark, scented forest.

But. Tom Christie had been arrested two or three days after the Battle of Culloden, and imprisoned for the next ten years, before being transported to America. He did not know Malva's exact age, but he thought she must be eighteen or so—though she often seemed older, her manner was so poised.

She must have been conceived, then, quite soon after Christie's arrival in the Colonies. No great wonder, if the man had seized the first chance he had to marry, after living without a woman for so long. And then the wife had thought better of her bargain, and gone. Christie had told Roger Mac his wife had died of influenza—well, a man had his pride, and God knew Tom Christie had more than most.

But Allan Christie . . . where had *he* come from? The young man was somewhere in his twenties; it was possible that he had been conceived before Culloden. But if so—who was his mother?

"You and your brother," he said abruptly, at the next break in conversation. "Did ye have the same mother?"

"Yes, sir," she said, looking startled.

"Ah," he said, and let the subject drop. Well, now. So Christie had been wed before Culloden. And then the woman, whoever she was, had come to find him in the Colonies. That argued a high degree of determination and devotion, and made him regard Christie with a good deal more interest. But that devotion had not been proof against the hardships of the Colonies—or else she found Tom so changed by time and circumstance that the devotion had been drowned in disappointment, and she had left again.

He could see that, easily—and felt an unexpected bond of sympathy with Tom Christie. He recalled his own feelings, all too well, when Claire came back to find him. The disbelieving joy of her presence—and the bone-deep fear that she would not recognize the man she had known, in the man who stood before her.

Worse, if she had discovered something that made her flee—and well as he knew Claire, he still was not sure that she would have stayed, if he'd told her at once about his marriage to Laoghaire. For that matter, if Laoghaire hadn't shot him and nearly killed him, Claire might well have run away, and been lost for good. The thought of it was a black pit, gaping at his feet.

Of course, had she gone, he *would* have died, he reflected. And never come to this place and got his land, nor seen his daughter, nor held his grandson in his arms. Come to think, perhaps being nearly killed wasn't always a misfortune—so long as you didn't actually die of it.

"Does your arm trouble ye, sir?" He was jerked back from his thoughts to realize that he was standing like a fool, one hand clutching the spot on his upper arm where Laoghaire's pistol ball had gone through and Malva squinting at him in concern.

"Ah, no," he said hastily, dropping his hand. "A midgie bite. The bittie things are out early. Tell me"—he groped for some neutral topic of conversation—"d'ye like it here in the mountains?"

Inane as the question was, she appeared to consider it seriously.

"It's lonely, sometimes," she said, and glanced into the forest, where falling shafts of sunlight splintered on leaves and needles, shrubs and rocks, filling the air with a shattered green light. "But it *is* . . ." she groped for a word. "Pretty," she said, with a small smile at him, acknowledging the inadequacy of the word.

They had reached the small clearing where the water bubbled out over a ledge of what his daughter said was serpentine—the rock whose soft green gave the spring its name; that, and the thick layer of vivid moss that grew around it.

He gestured to her to kneel and drink first. She did, cupping her hands to her face and closing her eyes in bliss at the taste of the cold, sweet water. She gulped, cupped her hands and drank again, almost greedily. She was very pretty herself, he thought in amusement, and the word was much more appropriate to the wee lassie, with that delicate chin and the lobes of her tender pink ears peeping from her cap, than to the spirit of the mountains. Her mother must have been lovely, he thought—and it was fortunate for the lass that she had not taken much of her father's grim looks, save those gray eyes.

She sat back on her heels, breathing deep, and scooted to the side, nodding at him to kneel and take his turn. The day wasn't hot, but it was a steep climb to the spring, and the cold water went down gratefully.

"I've never seen the Highlands," Malva said, dabbing the end of her kerchief over her wet face. "Some say this place is like it, though. D'ye think so yourself, sir?"

He shook the water from his fingers and wiped the back of his hand across his mouth.

"Something like. Some parts. The Great Glen, and the forest—aye, that's verra like this." He pointed his chin up at the trees surrounding them, murmurous and resin-scented. "But there's nay bracken here. And nay peat, of course. And nay heather; that's the biggest difference."

"Ye hear the stories—of men hiding in the heather. Did ye ever do so yourself, sir?" She dimpled slightly, and he didn't know whether she meant to tease, or was only making conversation.

"Now and then," he said, and smiled at her as he rose, brushing pine needles from his kilt. "Stalking the deer, aye? Here, I'll show ye the woodears."

The fungus grew in thick shelves at the foot of an oak, no more than ten feet from the spring. Some of the things had opened their gills already, begun to darken and curl; the ground nearby was scattered with the spores, a dark brown powder that lay upon the glossy crackle of last year's dry leaves. The fresher fungi were still bright, though, deep orange and meaty.

He left her there with a cordial word, and went back down the narrow trail, wondering about the woman who had loved and left Tom Christie.

49

THE VENOM OF THE NORTH WIND

July 1774

BRIANNA DROVE THE sharp end of the spade into the muddy bank and pulled out a chunk of clay the color of chocolate fudge. She could have done without the reminder of food, she thought, flinging it aside into the current with a grunt. She hitched up her soggy shift and wiped a forearm across her brow. She hadn't eaten since mid-morning, and it was nearly teatime. Not that she meant to stop until supper. Roger was up the mountain, helping Amy McCallum rebuild her chimney stack, and the little boys had gone up to the Big House to be fed bread and butter and honey and generally spoiled by Mrs. Bug. She'd wait to eat; there was too much to do here.

"D'ye need help, lass?"

She squinted, shading her eyes against the sun. Her father was standing on the bank above, viewing her efforts with what looked like amusement.

"Do I *look* like I need help?" she asked irritably, swiping the back of a mud-streaked hand across her jaw.

"Ye do, aye."

He'd been fishing; barefoot and wet to mid-thigh. He laid

his rod against a tree and swung the creel from his shoulder, woven reeds creaking with the weight of the catch. Then he grasped a sapling for balance, and started to edge down the slippery bank, bare toes squelching in the mud.

"Wait—take your shirt off!" She realized her mistake an instant too late. A startled look flitted across his face, only for a moment, and then was gone.

"I mean . . . the mud . . ." she said, knowing it was too late. "The washing."

"Oh, aye, to be sure." Without hesitation, he pulled the shirt over his head and turned his back to her, hunting for a convenient branch from which to hang it.

His scars were not really shocking. She'd glimpsed them before, imagined them many times, and the reality was much less vivid. The scars were old, a faint silvered net, moving easily over the shadows of his ribs as he reached upward. He moved naturally. Only the tension in his shoulders suggested otherwise.

Her hand closed involuntarily, feeling for an absent pencil, feeling the stroke of the line that would capture that tiny sense of unease, the jarring note that would draw the observer closer, closer still, wondering what it was about this scene of pastoral grace. . . .

Thou shalt not uncover thy father's nakedness, she thought, and spread her hand flat, pressing it hard against her thigh. But he had turned back and was coming down the bank, eyes on the tangled rushes and protruding stones underfoot.

He slid the last two feet and arrived beside her with a splash, arms flailing to keep his balance. She laughed, as he'd intended, and he smiled. She'd thought for an instant to speak of it, make some apology—but he would not meet her eyes.

"So, then, move it, or go round?" His attention focused on the boulder embedded in the bank, he leaned his weight against it and shoved experimentally.

"*Can* we move it, do you think?" She waded up beside him, retucking the hem of her shift, which she had pulled between her legs and fastened with a belt. "Going round would mean digging another ten feet of ditch."

"That much?" He glanced at her in surprise.

"Yes. I want to cut a notch here, to cut through to that bend—then I can put a small water-wheel here and get a good fall." She leaned past him, pointing downstream. "The next-best place would be down there—see where the banks rise?—but this is better."

"Aye, all right. Wait a bit, then." He made his way back to the bank, scrambled up, and disappeared into the wood, from whence he returned with several stout lengths of fresh oak sapling, still sporting the remnants of their glossy leaves.

"We dinna need to get it out of the creekbed, aye?" he asked. "Only move it a few feet, so ye can cut through the bank beyond it?"

"That's it." Rivulets of sweat, trapped by her thick eyebrows, ran tickling down the sides of her face. She'd been digging for the best part of an hour; her arms ached from heaving shovelsful of heavy mud, and her hands were blistered. With a sense of profound gratitude, she surrendered the spade and stepped back in the creek, stooping to splash cold water on her scratched arms and flushed face.

"Heavy work," her father observed, grunting a little as he briskly finished undermining the boulder. "Could ye not have asked Roger Mac to do it?"

"He's busy," she said, perceiving the shortness of her tone, but not inclined to disguise it.

Her father darted a sharp glance at her, but said no more, merely busying himself with the proper placement of his oak staves. Attracted like iron filings to the magnetism of their grandfather's presence, Jemmy and Germain appeared like magic, loudly wanting to help.

She'd asked them to help, and they'd helped—for a few minutes, before being drawn away by the glimpse of a porcupine high up in the trees. With Jamie in charge, of course, they leaped to the task, madly scooping dirt from the bank with flat bits of wood, giggling, pushing, getting in the way, and stuffing handsful of mud down the back of each other's breeches.

Jamie being Jamie, he ignored the nuisance, merely directing their efforts and finally ordering them out of the creek, so as not to be crushed.

"All right, lass," he said, turning to her. "Take a grip there."

The boulder had been loosened from the confining clay, and now protruded from the bank, oak staves thrust into the mud beneath, sticking up on either side, and another behind.

She seized the one he indicated, while he took the other two.

"On the count of three . . . one . . . two . . . heave!"

Jem and Germain, perched above, chimed in, chanting "One . . . two . . . *heave*!" like a small Greek chorus. There was a splinter in her thumb and the wood rasped against the waterlogged creases of her skin, but she felt suddenly like laughing.

"One . . . two . . . *hea*—" With a sudden shift, a swirl of mud, and a cascade of loose dirt from the bank above, the boulder gave way, falling into the stream with a splash that soaked them both to the chest and made both little boys shriek with joy.

Jamie was grinning ear-to-ear and so was she, wet shift and muddy children notwithstanding. The boulder now lay near the opposite bank of the stream, and—just as she had calculated—the diverted current was already eating into the newly created hollow in the near bank, a strong eddy eating away the fine-grained clay in streams and spirals.

"See that?" She nodded at it, dabbing her mud-spattered face on the shoulder of her shift. "I don't know how far it will erode, but if I let it go for a day or two, there won't be much digging left to do."

"Ye kent that would happen?" Her father glanced at her, face alight, and laughed. "Why, ye clever, bonnie wee thing!"

The glow of recognized achievement did quite a bit to dampen her resentment of Roger's absence. The presence of a bottle of cider in Jamie's creel, keeping cold amongst the dead trout, did a lot more. They sat companionably on the bank, passing the bottle back and forth, admiring the industry of the new eddy pool at work.

"This looks like good clay," she observed, leaning forward to scoop a little of the wet stuff out of the crumbling bank. She squeezed it in her hand, letting grayish water run down her arm, and opened her hand to show him how it kept its shape, showing clearly the prints of her fingers.

"Good for your kiln?" he asked, peering dutifully at it.

"Worth a try." She had made several less-than-successful experiments with the kiln so far, producing a succession of malformed plates and bowls, most of which had either exploded in the kiln or shattered immediately upon removal. One or two survivals, deformed and scorched round the edges, had been pressed into dubious service, but it was precious little reward for the effort of stoking the kiln and minding it for days.

What she needed was advice from someone who knew about kilns and making earthenware. But with the strained relations now existent between the Ridge and Salem, she couldn't seek it. It had been awkward enough, her speaking directly to Brother Mordecai about his ceramic processes—a Popish woman, and speaking to a man she wasn't married to, the scandal!

"Damn wee Manfred," her father agreed, hearing her complaint. He'd heard it before, but didn't mention it. He hesitated. "Would it maybe help was I to go and ask? A few o' the Brethren will still speak to me, and it might be that they'd let me talk wi' Mordecai. If ye were to tell me what it is ye need to know . . . ? Ye could maybe write it down."

"Oh, Da, I love you!" Grateful, she leaned to kiss him, and he laughed, clearly gratified to be doing her a service.

Elated, she took another drink of cider, and rosy visions of hardened clay pipes began to dance in her brain. She had a wooden cistern already built, with a lot of complaint and obstruction from Ronnie Sinclair. She needed help to heave that into place. Then, if she could get only twenty feet of reliable pipe . . .

"Mama, come *look*!" Jem's impatient voice cut through the fog of calculation. With a mental sigh, she made a hasty note of where she had been, and pushed the process carefully into a corner of her mind, where it would perhaps helpfully ferment.

She handed the bottle back to her father, and made her way down the bank to where the boys squatted, expecting to be shown frog spawn, a drowned skunk, or some other wonder of nature appealing to small boys.

"What is it?" she called.

"Look, look!" Jemmy spotted her and popped upright, pointing to the rock at his feet.

They were standing on the Flat Rock, a prominent feature of the creek. As the name suggested, it was a flat shelf of granite, large enough for three men to occupy at once, undercut by the water so that it jutted out over the boiling stream. It was a favorite spot for fishing.

Someone had built a small fire; there was a blackened smudge on the rock, with what looked like the remnants of charred sticks in the center. It was much too small for a cooking fire, but still, she would have thought nothing of it. Her father was frowning at the fire site, though, in a way that made her walk out onto the rock and stand beside him, looking.

The objects in the ashes weren't sticks.

"Bones," she said at once, and squatted down to look closer. "What kind of animal are those from?" Even as she said it, her mind was analyzing and rejecting—squirrel, possum, rabbit, deer, pig—unable to make sense of the shapes.

"They're finger bones, lass," he said, lowering his voice as he glanced at Jemmy—who had lost interest in the fire and was now sliding down the muddy bank, to the further detriment of his breeches. "Dinna touch them," he added—unnecessarily, as she had drawn back her hand in instant revulsion.

"From a human, you mean?" Instinctively, she wiped her hand on the side of her thigh, though she had touched nothing.

He nodded, and squatted beside her, studying the charred remains. There were blackened lumps there, too—though she thought these were the remains of some plant material; one was greenish, maybe a stem of something, incompletely burned.

Jamie bent low, sniffing at the burned remains. Instinctively, Brianna drew a deep breath through her nose in imitation—then snorted, trying to get rid of the smell. It was disconcerting: a reek of char, overlaid with something bitter and chalky—and that in turn overlaid with a sort of pungent scent that reminded her of medicine.

"Where could they have come from?" she asked, also low-voiced—though Jemmy and Germain had begun pelting each other with mudballs, and wouldn't have noticed if she'd shouted.

"I havena noticed anyone missing a hand, have you?" Jamie glanced up, giving her a half-smile. She didn't return it.

"Not walking around, no. But if they aren't walking around—" She swallowed, trying to ignore the half-imagined taste of bitter herbs and burning. "Where's the rest? Of the body, I mean."

That word, "body," seemed to bring the whole thing into a new and nasty focus.

"Where's the rest of that finger, I wonder?" Jamie was frowning at the blackened smudge. He moved a knuckle toward it, and she saw what he had seen: a paler smudge within the circle of the fire, where part of the ashes had been swept away. There were three fingers, she saw, still swallowing repeatedly. Two were intact, the bones gray-white and spectral among the ashes. Two joints of the third were gone, though; only the slender last phalanx remained.

"An animal?" She glanced round for traces, but there were no pawprints on the surface of the rock—only the muddy smudges left by the little boys' bare feet.

Vague visions of cannibalism were beginning to stir queasily in the pit of her stomach, though she rejected the notion at once.

"You don't think Ian—" She stopped abruptly.

"Ian?" Her father looked up, astonished. "Why should Ian do such a thing?"

"I don't think he would," she said, taking hold of common sense. "Not at all. It was just a thought—I'd heard that the Iroquois sometimes . . . sometimes . . ." She nodded at the charred bones, unwilling to articulate the thought further. "Um . . . maybe a friend of Ian's? Uh . . . visiting?"

Jamie's face darkened a little, but he shook his head.

"Nay, there's the smell of the Highlands about this. The Iroquois will burn an enemy. Or cut bits off him, to be sure. But not like that." He pointed at the bones with his chin, in the Highland way. "This is a private business, ken? A witch—or one of their shamans, maybe—might do a thing like that; not a warrior."

"I haven't seen any Indians of any kind lately. Not on the Ridge. Have you?"

He looked at the burned smudge a moment longer, frowning, then shook his head.

"No, nor anyone missing a few fingers, either."

"You're *sure* they're human?" She studied the bones, trying for other possibilities. "Maybe from a small bear? Or a big coon?"

"Maybe," he said flatly, but she could tell he said it only for her sake. He was sure.

"Mama!" The patter of bare feet on the rock behind her was succeeded by a tug at her sleeve. "Mama, we're hungry!"

"Of course you are," she said, rising to meet the demand, but still gazing abstractedly at the charred remnants. "You haven't eaten in nearly an hour. What did you—" Her gaze drifted slowly from the fire to her son, then snapped abruptly, focusing on the two little boys, who stood grinning at her, covered from head to foot in mud.

"*Look* at you!" she said, dismay tempered by resignation. "How could you possibly get that filthy?"

"Oh, it's easy, lass," her father assured her, grinning as he rose to his feet. "Easy cured, too, though." He bent, and seizing Germain by the back of shirt and seat of breeks, heaved him neatly off the rock and into the pool below.

"Me, too, me, too! Me, too, Grandda!" Jemmy was dancing up and down in excitement, spattering clods of mud in all directions.

"Oh, aye. You, too." Jamie bent and grabbed Jem round the waist, launching him high into the air in a flutter of shirt before Brianna could cry out.

"He can't swim!"

This protest coincided with a huge splash, as Jem hit the water and promptly sank like a rock. She was striding toward the edge, prepared to dive in after him, when her father put a hand on her arm to stop her.

"Wait a bit," he said. "How will ye ken whether he swims or not, if ye dinna let him try?"

Germain was already arrowing his way toward shore, his sleek blond head dark with water. Jemmy popped up behind him, though, splashing and spluttering, and Germain dived, turned like an otter, and came up alongside.

"Kick!" he called to Jemmy, churning up a huge spray in illustration. "Go on your back!"

Jemmy ceased flailing, went on his back, and kicked madly. His hair was plastered over his face and the spray of his efforts must have obscured any remnants of vision—but he went on valiantly kicking, to encouraging whoops from Jamie and Germain.

The pool was no more than ten feet across, and he reached the shallows on the opposite bank within seconds, beaching among the rocks by virtue of crashing headfirst into one. He stopped, thrashing feebly in the shallows, then bounced to his feet, showering water, and shoved the wet hair out of his face. He looked amazed.

"I can swim!" he shouted. "Mama, I can *swim*!"

"That's wonderful!" she called, torn between sharing his ecstatic pride, the urge to rush home and tell Roger about it—and dire visions of Jemmy now leaping heedlessly into bottomless ponds and rock-jagged rapids, under the reckless delusion that he could indeed swim. But he'd gotten his feet wet, in no uncertain terms; there was no going back.

"Come here!" She bent toward him, clapping her hands. "Can you swim back to me? Come on, come here!"

He looked blankly at her for an instant, then around him at the rippling water of the pool. The blaze of excitement in his face died.

"I forget," he said, and his mouth curled down, fat with sudden woe. "I forget how!"

"Fall down and kick!" Germain bellowed helpfully, from his perch on the rock. "You can do it, *cousin*!"

Jemmy took one or two blundering steps into the water, but stopped, lip trembling, terror and confusion starting to overwhelm him.

"Stay there, *a chuisle*! I'm coming!" Jamie called, and dove cleanly into the pool, a long pale streak beneath the water, bubbles streaming from hair and breeks. He popped up in front of Jemmy in an explosion of breath and shook his head, flinging strands of wet red hair out of his face.

"Come along then, man," he said, scooting round on his

knees in the shallows, so that his back was to Jemmy. He looked back, patting his own shoulder. "Take hold of me here, aye? We'll swim back together."

And they did, kicking and splashing in ungainly dog paddle, Jemmy's shrieks of excitement echoed by Germain, who had leaped into the water to paddle alongside.

Hauled out onto the rock, the three of them lay puddled, gasping and laughing at her feet, water spreading in pools around them.

"Well, you are cleaner," she said judiciously, moving her foot away from a spreading streamlet. "I'll admit that much."

"Of course we are." Jamie sat up, wringing out the long tail of his hair. "It occurs to me, lass, that there's maybe a better way to do what ye want."

"What I w—oh. You mean the water?"

"Aye, that." He sniffed, and rubbed the back of his hand under his nose. "I'll show ye, if ye come up to the house after supper."

"What's that, Grandda?" Jemmy had got to his feet, wet hair standing up in red spikes, and was looking curiously at Jamie's back. He put out a tentative finger and traced one of the long, curving scars.

"What? Oh . . . that." Jamie's face went quite blank for a moment. "It's . . . ah . . ."

"Some bad people hurt Grandda once," she interrupted firmly, bending down to pick Jemmy up. "But that was a long time ago. He's all right now. You weigh a ton!"

"Papa says *Grandpère* is perhaps a silkie," Germain remarked, viewing Jamie's back with interest. "Like his papa before him. Did the bad people find you in your silkie skin, *Grandpère,* and try to cut it from you? He would then of course become a man again," he explained matter-of-factly, looking up at Jemmy, "and could kill them with his sword."

Jamie was staring at Germain. He blinked, and wiped his nose again.

"Oh," he said. "Aye. Um. Aye, I expect that was the way of it. If your papa says so."

"What's a silkie?" asked Jemmy, bewildered but interested. He wiggled in Brianna's arms, wanting to be put down, and she lowered him back to the rock.

"I don't know," Germain admitted. "But they have fur. What's a silkie, *Grandpère*?"

Jamie closed his eyes against the sinking sun, and rubbed a hand over his face, shaking his head a little. Brianna thought he was smiling, but couldn't tell for sure.

"Ah, well," he said, sitting up straighter, opening his eyes, and throwing back his wet hair. "A silkie is a creature who is a man upon the land, but becomes a seal within the sea. And a seal," he added, cutting off Jemmy, who had been opening his mouth to ask, "is a great sleek beastie that barks like a dog, is as big as an ox, and beautiful as the black of night. They live in the sea, but come out onto the rocks near the shore sometimes."

"Have you seen them, *Grandpère*?" Germain asked, eager.

"Oh, many a time," Jamie assured him. "There are a great many seals who live on the coasts of Scotland."

"Scotland," Jemmy echoed. His eyes were round.

"*Ma mère* says Scotland is a good place," Germain remarked. "She cries sometimes, when she talks of it. I am not so sure I would like it, though."

"Why not?" Brianna asked.

"It's full of giants and water horses and . . . things," Germain replied, frowning. "I don't want to meet any of those. And parritch, *Maman* says, but we have parritch here."

"So we have. And I expect it's time we were going home to eat some." Jamie got to his feet and stretched, groaning in the pleasure of it. The late-afternoon sun washed rock and water with a golden light, gleaming on the boys' cheeks and the bright hairs on her father's arms.

Jemmy stretched and groaned, too, in worshipful imitation, and Jamie laughed.

"Come on, wee fishie. D'ye want a ride home?" He bent so that Jemmy could scramble onto his back, then straightened up, settling the little boy's weight, and put out a hand to take Germain's.

Jamie saw her attention turn momentarily back toward the blackened smudge at the edge of the rock.

"Leave it, lass," he said quietly. "It's a charm of some kind. Ye dinna want to touch it."

Then he stepped off the rock and made for the trail, Jemmy

on his back and Germain clutched firmly by the back of the neck, both boys giggling as they made their way through the slippery mud of the path.

Brianna retrieved her spade and Jamie's shirt from the creekbank, and caught the boys up on the trail to the Big House. A breeze had begun to breathe through the trees, chilly in the damp cloth of her shift, but the heat of walking was enough to keep her from being cold.

Germain was singing softly to himself, still hand in hand with his grandfather, his small blond head tilting back and forth like a metronome.

Jemmy sighed in exhausted bliss, legs wrapped round Jamie's middle, arms about his neck, and leaned his sun-reddened cheek against the scarred back. Then he thought of something, for he raised his head and kissed his grandfather with a loud smacking noise, between the shoulder blades.

Her father jerked, nearly dropping Jem, and made a high-pitched noise that made her laugh.

"Is that make it better?" Jem inquired seriously, pulling himself up and trying to look over Jamie's shoulder into his face.

"Oh. Aye, lad," his grandfather assured him, face twitching. "Much better."

The gnats and midges were out in force now. She beat a cloud of them away from her face, and slapped a mosquito that lit on Germain's neck.

"Ak!" he said, hunching his shoulders, but then resumed singing "Alouette," undisturbed.

Jemmy's shirt was thin, worn linen, cut down from one of Roger's old ones. The cloth had dried to the shape of his body, square-rumped and solid, the breadth of his small, tender shoulders echoing the wide set of the older, firmer ones he clung to. She glanced from the redheads to Germain, walking reed-thin and graceful through shadows and light, still singing, and thought how desperately beautiful men were.

"Who were the bad people, Grandda?" Jemmy asked drowsily, head nodding with the rhythm of Jamie's steps.

"Sassunaich," Jamie replied briefly. "English soldiers."

"English *canaille,*" Germain amplified, breaking off his song. "They are the ones who cut off my papa's hand, too."

"They were?" Jemmy's head lifted in momentary attention, then fell back between Jamie's shoulder blades with a thump that made his grandfather grunt. "Did you kill them with your sword, Grandda?"

"Some of them."

"I will kill the rest, when I am big," Germain declared. "If there are any left."

"I suppose there might be." Jamie hitched Jem's weight a little higher, letting go Germain's hand in order to hold Jemmy's slackening legs tight to his body.

"Me, too," Jemmy murmured, eyelids drooping. "I'll kill them, too."

At the fork in the trail, Jamie surrendered her son to her, sound asleep, and took back his shirt. He pulled it on, brushing disheveled hair out of his face as his head came through. He smiled at her, then leaned forward and kissed her forehead, gently, putting one hand on Jemmy's round, red head where it lay against her shoulder.

"Dinna fash yourself, lass," he said softly. "I'll speak to Mordecai. And your man. Take care of this one."

"THIS IS A *private business,"* her father had said. The general implication being that she should leave it alone. And she might have, save for a couple of things. One, that Roger had come home well after dark, whistling a song he said Amy McCallum had taught him. And two, that other offhand remark her father had made about the fire on the Flat Rock—that there was a smell of the Highlands about it.

Brianna had a very keen nose, and she smelled a rat. She also had recognized—belatedly—what had made Jamie say what he had. The odd smell of the fire, that tang of medicine—it was iodine; the smell of burned seaweed. She'd smelled a fire built of sea wrack on the shore near Ullapool, in her own time, when Roger had taken her up there for a picnic.

There was certainly seaweed on the coast, and it wasn't impossible that someone, sometime, had brought some inland. But it also wasn't impossible that some of the fisher-folk had brought bits of it from Scotland, in the way that some exiles might bring earth in jar, or a handful of pebbles to remind them of the land left behind.

A charm, her father had said. And the song Roger had learned from Amy McCallum was called "The Deasil Charm," he said.

All of which was no particular evidence of anything. Still, she mentioned the small fire and its contents to Mrs. Bug, just from curiosity. Mrs. Bug knew a good deal about Highland charms of all sorts.

Mrs. Bug frowned thoughtfully at her description, lips pursed.

"Bones, ye say? What sort—the bones of an animal, were they, or a man?"

Brianna felt as though someone had dropped a slug down her back.

"A man?"

"Oh, aye. There's some charms that take grave dust, ken, and some the dust of bones, or the ashes of a body." Evidently reminded by the mention of ashes, Mrs. Bug pulled a big pottery mixing bowl from the warm ashes of the hearth, and peered into it. The bread starter had died a few days before, and the bowl of flour, water, and honey had been set out in hopes of snaring a wild yeast from the passing air.

The round little Scotswoman frowned at the bowl, shook her head, and put it back with a brief muttered verse in Gaelic. Naturally, Brianna thought, slightly amused, there *would* be a prayer for catching yeast. Which patron saint was in charge of that?

"What ye said, though," Mrs. Bug said, returning both to her chopping of turnips and to the original subject of conversation. "About it bein' on the Flat Rock. Seaweed, bones, and a flat rock. That's a love charm, lass. The one they call the Venom o' the North Wind."

"What a really peculiar name for a love charm," she said, staring at Mrs. Bug, who laughed.

"Och, now, do I remember it at all?" she asked rhetorically. She wiped her hands upon her apron, and folding them at her waist with a vaguely theatrical air, recited:

"A love charm for thee,
Water drawn through a straw,
The warmth of him thou lovest,
With love to draw on thee.

"Arise betimes on Lord's day,
To the flat rock of the shore
Take with thee the butterbur
And the foxglove.

"A small quantity of embers
In the skirt of thy kirtle,
A special handful of seaweed
In a wooden shovel.

"Three bones of an old man,
Newly torn from the grave,
Nine stalks of royal fern,
Newly trimmed with an ax.

"Burn them on a fire of faggots
And make them all into ashes;
Sprinkle in the fleshy breast of thy lover,
Against the venom of the north wind.

"Go round the rath *of procreation,*
The circuit of the five turns,
And I will vow and warrant thee
That man shall never leave thee."

Mrs. Bug unfolded her hands and took another turnip, quartering it with neat, quick chops and tossing the pieces into the pot. "Ye're not wanting such a thing yourself, I hope?"

"No," Brianna murmured, feeling the small cold feeling continue down her back. "Do you think—would the fisher-folk use a charm like that?"

"Well, as to that, I canna say *what* they'd do—but surely a few would ken that charm; it's weel enough known, though I havena kent anyone myself has done it. There are easier ways to make a lad fall in love wi' ye, lass," she added, pointing a stubby finger at Brianna in admonition. "Cook him up a nice plate o' neeps boiled in milk and served wi' butter, for one."

"I'll remember," Brianna promised, smiling, and excused herself.

She had meant to go home; there were dozens of things needing to be done, from spinning yarn and weaving cloth, to plucking and drawing the half dozen dead geese she had shot and hung in the lean-to. But instead she found her footsteps turning up the hill, along the overgrown trail that led to the graveyard.

Surely it wasn't Amy McCallum who'd made that charm, she thought. It would have taken her hours to walk down the mountain from her cabin, and her with a small baby to tend. But babies could be carried. And no one would know whether she had left her cabin, save perhaps Aidan—and Aidan didn't talk to anyone but Roger, whom he worshipped.

The sun was nearly down, and the tiny cemetery had a melancholy look to it, long shadows from its sheltering trees slanting cold and dark across the needle-strewn ground and the small collection of crude markers, cairns, and wooden crosses. The pines and hemlocks murmured uneasily overhead in the rising breeze of evening.

The sense of cold had spread from her backbone, making a wide patch between her shoulder blades. Seeing the earth grubbed up beneath the wooden marker with *Ephraim* on it didn't help.

50

SHARP EDGES

HE SHOULD HAVE known better. *Did* know better. But what could he have done? Much more important, what was he to do now?

Roger made his way slowly up the mountainside, nearly

oblivious to its beauty. Nearly, but not quite. Desolate in the bleakness of winter, the secluded notch where Amy McCallum's ramshackle cabin perched among the laurels was a blaze of color and life in spring and summer—so vivid that even his worry couldn't stop his noticing the blaze of pinks and reds, interrupted by soft patches of creamy dogwood and carpets of bluets, their tiny blue flowers nodding on slender stems above the torrent of the stream that bounded down beside the rocky trail.

They must have chosen the site in summer, he reflected cynically. It would have seemed charming then. He hadn't known Orem McCallum, but plainly the man hadn't been any more practical than his wife, or they would have realized the dangers of their remoteness.

The present situation wasn't Amy's fault, though; he shouldn't blame her for his own lack of judgment.

He didn't precisely blame himself, either—but he should have noticed sooner what was going on; what was being said.

"Everybody kens ye spend more time up at the notch wi' the widow McCallum than ye do with your own wife."

That's what Malva Christie had said, her little pointed chin raised in defiance. *"Tell my father, and I'll tell everyone I've seen you kiss Amy McCallum. They'll all believe me."*

He felt an echo of the astonishment he'd felt at her words—an astonishment succeeded by anger. At the girl and her silly threat, but much more at himself.

He'd been working at the whisky clearing and, heading back to the cabin for dinner, had rounded a turn in the trail and surprised the two of them, Malva and Bobby Higgins, locked in an embrace. They'd sprung apart like a pair of startled deer, eyes wide, so alarmed as to be funny.

He'd smiled, but before he could either apologize or fade tactfully into the underbrush, Malva had stepped up to him, eyes still wide, but blazing with determination.

"Tell my father," she'd said, *"and I'll tell everyone I've seen you kiss Amy McCallum."*

He'd been so taken aback by her words that he'd scarcely noticed Bobby, until the young soldier had put a hand on her arm, murmuring something to her, drawing her away. She'd turned reluctantly, with a last, wary, meaningful glance at Roger, and a parting shot that left him staggered.

"Everybody kens ye spend more time up at the notch wi' the widow McCallum than ye do with your own wife. They'll all believe me."

God damn it, they would, too, and it was his own bloody fault. Bar one or two sarcastic remarks, Bree hadn't protested his visits; she'd accepted—or seemed to—that *someone* had to go now and then to see the McCallums, make sure they had food and fire, provide a few moments' company, a small respite in the monotony of loneliness and labor.

He'd done such things often, going with the Reverend to call on the aged, the widowed, the ill of the congregation; take them food, stop for a bit to talk—to listen. It was just what you *did* for a neighbor, he told himself; a normal kindness.

But he should have taken more notice. Now he recalled Jamie's thoughtful glance over the supper table, the breath taken as though to say something, when Roger had asked Claire for a salve for wee Orrie McCallum's rash—and then Claire's glance at Brianna, and Jamie's closing his mouth, whatever he'd thought of saying left unspoken.

"They'll all believe me." For the girl to have said that, there must have been talk already. Likely Jamie had heard it; he could only hope that Bree hadn't.

The crooked chimney came in sight above the laurels, the smoke a nearly transparent wisp that made the clear air above the rooftree seem to quiver, as though the cabin were enchanted, might vanish with a blink.

The worst of it was that he knew precisely how it had happened. He had a weakness for young mothers, a terrible tenderness toward them, a desire to take care of them. The fact that he knew exactly *why* he harbored such an urge—the memory of his own young mother, who had died saving his life during the Blitz—didn't help.

It was a tenderness that had nearly cost him his life at Alamance, when that bloody-minded fool William Buccleigh MacKenzie had mistaken Roger's concern for Morag MacKenzie for . . . well, all right, he'd kissed her, but only on the forehead, and for God's sake, she was his own many-times-great-grannie . . . and the thundering idiocy of nearly being killed by your own great-great-etc.-grandfather for molesting his wife . . . it had cost him his voice, and he should have learned his lesson, but he hadn't, not well enough.

Suddenly furious with himself—and with Malva Christie, the malicious little chit—he picked up a stone from the trail and flung it down the mountain, into the stream. It struck another in the water, bounced twice, and vanished into the rushing gurgle.

His visits to the McCallums had to stop, at once. He saw that clearly. Another way would have to be found for them . . . but he had to come once more, to explain. Amy would understand, he thought—but how to explain to Aidan what reputation was, and why gossip was a deadly sin, and why Roger couldn't come anymore to fish or show him how to build things. . . .

Cursing steadily under his breath, he made the last short, steep ascent and came into the ragged, overgrown little dooryard. Before he could call out to announce his presence, though, the door flew open.

"Roger Mac!" Amy McCallum half-fell down the step and into his arms, gasping and weeping. "Oh, you came, you came! I prayed for someone to come, but I didna think anyone would, in time, and he'd die, but ye've come, God be thankit!"

"What is it? What's wrong? Is wee Orrie taken sick?" He got hold of her arms, steadying her, and she shook her head, so violently that her cap slid half off.

"Aidan," she gasped. "It's Aidan."

AIDAN MCCALLUM lay doubled up on my surgery table, white as a sheet, making little gasping groans. My first hope—green apples or gooseberries—vanished with a closer look at him. I was fairly sure what I had here, but appendicitis shares symptoms with a number of other conditions. A classic case does, however, have one striking aspect.

"Can you unfold him, just for a moment?" I looked at his mother, hovering over him on the verge of tears, but it was

Roger who nodded and came to put his hands on Aidan's knees and shoulders, gently persuading him to lie flat.

I put a thumb in his navel, my little finger on his right hipbone, and pressed his abdomen sharply with my middle finger, wondering for a second as I did so whether McBurney had yet discovered and named this diagnostic spot. Pain in McBurney's Spot was a specific diagnostic symptom for acute appendicitis. I pressed Aidan's stomach there, then I released the pressure, he screamed, arched up off the table, and doubled up like a jackknife.

A hot appendix for sure. I'd known I'd encounter one sometime. And with a mixed sense of dismay and excitement, I realized that the time had come for me finally to use the ether. No doubt about it, and no choice; if the appendix wasn't removed, it would rupture.

I glanced up; Roger was supporting little Mrs. McCallum with a hand under her elbow; she clutched the baby close to her chest, wrapped in its bundle. She'd need to stay; Aidan would need her.

"Roger—get Lizzie to come mind the baby, will you? And then run as fast as you can to the Christies'; I'll need Malva to come and help."

The most extraordinary expression flitted across his face; I couldn't interpret it, but it was gone in an instant, and I didn't have time to worry about it. He nodded and left without a word, and I turned my attention to Mrs. McCallum, asking her the questions I needed answered before I cut into her small son's belly.

IT WAS ALLAN Christie who opened the door to Roger's brusque knock. A darker, leaner version of his owl-faced father, he blinked slowly at the question as to Malva's whereabouts.

"Why . . . she's gone to the stream," he said. "Gathering rushes, she said." He frowned. "Why do ye want her?"

"Mrs. Fraser needs her to come and help with—with something." Something moved inside; the back door opening.

Tom Christie came in, a book in his hand, the page he'd been reading caught between two fingers.

"MacKenzie," he said, with a short jerk of the head in acknowledgment. "Did ye say Mrs. Fraser is wanting Malva? Why?" He frowned as well, the two Christies looking exactly like a pair of barn owls contemplating a questionable mouse.

"Only that wee Aidan McCallum's taken badly, and she'd be glad of Malva's help. I'll go and find her."

Christie's frown deepened, and he opened his mouth to speak, but Roger had already turned, hurrying into the trees before either of them could stop him.

He found her fairly quickly, though every moment spent searching seemed an eternity. How long did it take an appendix to burst? She was knee-deep in the stream, skirts kirtled high and her rush basket floating beside her, tethered by an apron string. She didn't hear him at first, deafened by the flow of the water. When he called her name more loudly, her head jerked up in alarm, and she raised the rush knife, gripped tightly in her hand.

The look of alarm faded when she saw who it was, though she kept a wary eye on him—and a good grip on the knife, he saw. His summons was received with a flash of interest.

"The ether? Really, she's going to cut him?" she asked eagerly, wading toward him.

"Yes. Come on; I've already told your father Mrs. Fraser needs you. We needn't stop."

Her face changed at that.

"Ye told him?" Her brow creased for a moment. Then she bit her lip and shook her head.

"I can't," she said, raising her voice above the sound of the stream.

"Yes, ye can," he said, as encouragingly as possible, and stretched out a hand to help her. "Come on; I'll give ye a hand with your things."

She shook her head more decidedly, pink lower lip poking out a bit.

"No. My father—he'll no have it." She glanced in the direction of the cabin, and he turned to look, but it was all right; neither Allan nor Tom had followed him. Yet.

He kicked off his shoes and stepped into the icy creek, the

stones rolling, hard and slippery under his feet. Malva's eyes widened and her mouth fell open as he bent and grabbed her basket, ripped it from her apron string, and tossed it onto the bank. Then he took the knife from her hand, thrust it through his belt, grabbed her round the waist, and picking her up, splashed ashore with her, disregarding the kicking and squealing.

"You're coming with me," he said, grunting as he set her down. "Ye want to walk, or do I carry you?"

He thought she seemed more intrigued than horrified at this proposal, but she shook her head again, backing away from him.

"I can't—truly! He'll—he'll beat me if he finds out I've been meddling wi' the ether."

That checked him momentarily. Would he? Perhaps. But Aidan's life was at stake.

"He won't find out, then," he said. "Or if he does, I'll see to it that he does ye no harm. Come, for God's sake—there's no time to be wasting!"

Her small pink mouth compressed itself in stubbornness. No time for scruples, then. He leaned down to bring his face close to hers and stared her in the eye.

"You'll come," he said, fists curling, "or I tell your father and your brother about you and Bobby Higgins. Say what ye like about me—I don't care. But if ye think your father would beat you for helping Mrs. Fraser, what's he likely to do if he hears ye've been snogging Bobby?"

He didn't know what the eighteenth-century equivalent of snogging was, but plainly she understood him. And if she'd been anywhere near his own size, she would have knocked him down, if he read the dangerous light in those big gray eyes correctly.

But she wasn't, and after an instant's consideration, she bent, dried her legs on her skirts, and shuffled hurriedly into her sandals.

"Leave it," she said briefly, seeing him stoop for the basket. "And give me back my knife."

It might have been simply an urge to keep some influence over her until she was safely in the surgery—surely he wasn't afraid of her. He put a hand to the knife at his belt, though, and said, "Later. When it's done."

She didn't bother arguing, but scampered up the bank ahead of him and headed for the Big House, the soles of her sandals flapping against her bare heels.

I HAD MY fingers on the brachial pulse in Aidan's armpit, counting. His skin was very hot to the touch, maybe a temperature of 101, 102. The pulse was strong, though rapid . . . slowing as he went further under. I could feel Malva counting under her breath, so many drops of ether, so long a pause before the next . . . I lost my own count of the pulse, but it didn't matter; I was taking it into myself, feeling my own pulse begin to beat in the same rhythm, and it was normal, steady.

He was breathing well. The little abdomen rose and fell slightly under my hand, and I could feel the muscles relaxing by the moment, everything except the tense, distended belly, the visible ribs arching high above it as he breathed. I had the sudden illusion that I could push my hand straight through the wall of his abdomen and touch the swollen appendix, could see it in my mind, throbbing malignantly in the dark security of its sealed world. Time, then.

Mrs. McCallum made a small sound when I took up the scalpel, a louder one when I pressed it down into the pale flesh, still gleaming wet with the alcohol I'd swabbed it with, like a fish's belly yielding to the gutting knife.

The skin parted easily, blood welling in that odd, magical way, seeming to appear from nowhere. He had almost no fat beneath it; the muscles were right there, dark red, resilient to the touch. There were other people in the room; I felt them vaguely. I had no attention to spare, though. Every sense I had was focused on the small body under my hands. Someone stood at my shoulder, though—Bree?

"Give me a retractor—yes, that thing." Yes, it was Bree; a long-fingered hand, wet with disinfectant, picked up the claw-shaped thing and put it in my waiting left hand. I missed the services of a good surgical nurse, but we'd manage.

"Hold that, just there." I nosed the blade between the muscle fibers, splitting them easily, and then pinched up the thick soft gleam of the peritoneum, lifted it and sliced it.

His innards were very warm, sucking wet around two probing fingers. Soft squish of intestine, small half-firm lumps of matter felt through their walls, the brush of bone against my knuckle—he was so small, there wasn't much room to feel around. I had my eyes closed, concentrating on touch alone. The cecum *had* to be right under my fingers, that was the curve of the large intestine I could feel, inert but live, like a sleeping snake. Behind? Below? I probed carefully, opened my eyes, and peered closely into the wound. He wasn't bleeding badly, but the wound was still awash. Ought I take the time to cauterize the small bleeders? I glanced at Malva; she was frowning in concentration, her lips moving silently, counting—and she had one hand on the pulse in his neck, keeping track.

"Cautery iron—a small one." A moment's pause; with the flammability of ether in mind, I had doused the hearth and put the brazier across the hall, in Jamie's study. Bree was quick, though; I had it in my hand in seconds. A wisp of smoke rose from his belly and the sizzle of seared flesh struck into the thick warm smell of blood. I glanced up to hand the iron back to Bree, and saw Mrs. McCallum's face, all eyes, staring.

I blotted away the blood with a handful of lint, looked again—my fingers were still holding what I thought . . . all right.

"All right," I said out loud, triumphant. "Got you!" Very carefully, I hooked a finger under the curve of the cecum and pulled a section of it up through the wound, the inflamed appendix sticking out from it like an angry fat worm, purple with inflammation.

"Ligature."

I had it now. I could see the membrane down the side of the appendix and the blood vessels feeding it. Those had to be tied off first; then I could tie off the appendix itself and cut it away. Difficult only because of the small size, but no real problem . . .

The room was so still, I could hear the tiny hisses and pops from the charcoal in the brazier across the hall. Sweat was running down behind my ears, between my breasts, and I became dimly aware that my teeth were sunk in my lower lip.

"Forceps." I pulled the purse-string stitch tight, and taking the forceps, poked the tied-off stump of the appendix neatly up into the cecum. I pressed this firmly back into his belly and took a breath.

"How long, Malva?"

"A bit more than ten minutes, ma'am. He's all right." She took her eyes off the ether mask long enough to dart a quick smile at me, then took up the dropping bottle, lips resuming her silent count.

Closing up was quick. I painted the sutured wound with a thick layer of honey, wrapped a bandage tightly round his body, tucked warm blankets over him and breathed.

"Take off the mask," I said to Malva, straightening up. She made no reply, and I looked at her. She had raised the mask, was holding it in both hands before her, like a shield. But she wasn't watching Aidan anymore; her eyes were fixed on her father, standing rigid in the doorway.

TOM CHRISTIE looked back and forth from the small naked body on the table to his daughter. She took an uncertain step back, still clutching the ether mask. His head twisted, piercing me with a fierce gray look.

"What's to do here?" he demanded. "What are ye doing to that child?"

"Saving his life," I replied tartly. I was still vibrating from the intensity of the surgery, and in no mood for rannygazoo. "Did you want something?"

Christie's thin lips pressed tight, but before he could reply, his son, Allan, pushed his way past into the room, and reaching his sister in a couple of strides, grabbed her by the wrist.

"Come away, ye wee gomerel," he said roughly, jerking at her. "Ye've no business here."

"Let go of her." Roger spoke sharply, and took hold of Allan's shoulder, to pull him away. Allan whirled on his heel and punched Roger in the stomach, short and sharp. Roger made a hollow crowing noise, but didn't crumple. Instead, he slugged Allan Christie in the jaw. Allan reeled backward, knocking over the little table of instruments—blades and retractors clattered over the floor in a swash of falling metal, and the jar of catgut ligatures in alcohol smashed on the boards, spraying glass and liquid everywhere.

A soft thump from the floor made me look down. Amy McCallum, overcome by ether fumes and emotion, had passed out.

I hadn't time to do anything about that; Allan bounced back with a wild swing, Roger ducked, caught the rush of the younger Christie's body, and the two of them staggered backward, hit the sill, and fell out of the open window, entangled.

Tom Christie made a low growling noise and hurried toward the window. Malva, seizing her chance, ran out the door; I heard her footsteps pattering hastily down the hall toward the kitchen—and, presumably, the back door.

"What on *earth* . . . ?" Bree said, looking at me.

"Don't look at me," I said, shaking my head. "I have *no* idea." Which was true; I did, however, have a sinking feeling that my involving Malva in the operation had a lot to do with it. Tom Christie and I had reached something like rapprochement, following my operation on his hand—but that didn't mean he had altered his views on the ungodliness of ether.

Bree drew herself abruptly upright, stiffening. A certain amount of grunting, gasping, and incoherent half-insults outside indicated that the fight was continuing—but Allan Christie's raised voice had just called Roger an adulterer.

Brianna glanced sharply at the huddled form of Amy McCallum, and I said a very bad word to myself. I'd heard a few sidelong remarks about Roger's visits to the McCallums—and Jamie had come close to saying something to Roger about it, but I had dissuaded him from interfering, telling him that I'd take up the matter tactfully with Bree. I hadn't had the chance, though, and now—

With a last unfriendly look at Amy McCallum, Bree strode out the door, plainly intending to take a hand in the fight. I clutched my brow and must have moaned, for Tom Christie turned sharply from the window.

"Are ye ill, mistress?"

"No," I said, a little wanly. "Just . . . look, Tom. I'm sorry if

I've caused trouble, asking Malva to help me. She has a real gift for healing, I think—but I didn't mean to persuade her into doing something you didn't approve of."

He gave me a bleak look, which he then transferred to Aidan's slack body. The look sharpened suddenly.

"Is that child dead?" he asked.

"No, no," I said. "I gave him ether; he's just gone aslee—"

My voice dried in my throat, as I noticed that Aidan had chosen this inconvenient moment to stop breathing.

With an incoherent cry, I shoved Tom Christie out of the way and fell on Aidan, gluing my mouth over his and pressing the heel of my hand hard in the center of his chest.

The ether in his lungs flowed over my face as I took my mouth away, making my head swim. I gripped the edge of the table hard with my free hand, putting my mouth back on his. I could *not* black out, I couldn't.

My vision swam and the room seemed to be revolving slowly round me. I clung doggedly to consciousness, though, urgently blowing into his lungs, feeling the tiny chest under my hand rise gently, then fall.

It couldn't have been more than a minute, but a minute filled with nightmare, everything spinning round me, the feel of Aidan's flesh the only solid anchor in a whirl of chaos. Amy McCallum stirred on the floor beside me, rose swaying to her knees—then fell on me with a shriek, pulling at me, trying to get me off her son. I heard Tom Christie's voice, raised in command, trying to calm her; he must have pulled her away, for suddenly her grip on my leg was gone.

I blew into Aidan once more—and this time, the chest under my hand twitched. He coughed, choked, coughed again, and started simultaneously to breathe and to cry. I stood up, head spinning, and had to hold on to the table to avoid falling.

I saw a pair of figures before me, black, distorted, with gaping mouths that opened toward me, filled with sharp fangs. I blinked, staggering, and took deep gulps of air. Blinked again, and the figures resolved themselves into Tom Christie and Amy McCallum. He was holding her round the waist, keeping her back.

"It's all right," I said, my own voice sounding strange and far off. "He's all right. Let her come to him."

She flung herself at Aidan with a sob, pulling him into her arms. Tom Christie and I stood staring at each other over the wreckage. Outside, everything had gone quiet.

"Did ye just raise that child from the dead?" he asked. His voice was almost conversational, though his feathery brows arched high.

I wiped a hand across my mouth, still tasting the sickly sweetness of the ether.

"I suppose so," I said.

"Oh."

He stared at me, blank-faced. The room reeked of alcohol, and it seemed to sear my nasal lining. My eyes were watering a little; I wiped them on my apron. Finally, he nodded, as though to himself, and turned to go.

I had to see to Aidan and his mother. But I couldn't let him go without trying to mend things for Malva, so far as I could.

"Tom—Mr. Christie." I hurried after him, and caught him by the sleeve. He turned, surprised and frowning.

"Malva. It's my fault; I sent Roger to bring her. You won't—" I hesitated, but couldn't think of any tactful way to put it. "You won't punish her, will you?"

The frown deepened momentarily, then lifted. He shook his head, very slightly, and with a small bow, detached his sleeve from my hand.

"Your servant, Mrs. Fraser," he said quietly, and with a last glance at Aidan—presently demanding food—he left.

BRIANNA DABBED THE wet corner of a handkerchief at Roger's lower lip, split on one side, swollen and bleeding from the impact of some part of Allan Christie.

"It's my fault," he said, for the third time. "I should have thought of something sensible to tell them."

"Shut up," she said, beginning to lose her precarious grip on her patience. "If you keep talking, it won't stop bleeding." It was the first thing she'd said to him since the fight.

With a mumbled apology, he took the handkerchief from her and pressed it to his mouth. Unable to keep still, though, he got up and went to the open door of the cabin, looking out.

"He's not still hanging around, is he? Allan?" She came to look over his shoulder. "If he is, leave him alone. I'll go—"

"No, he's not," Roger interrupted her. Hand still pressed to his mouth, he nodded toward the Big House, at the far end of the sloped clearing. "It's Tom."

Sure enough, Tom Christie was standing on the stoop. Just standing, apparently deep in thought. As they watched, he shook his head like a dog shedding water, and set off with decision in the direction of his own place.

"I'll go and talk to him." Roger tossed the handkerchief at the table.

"Oh, no, you won't." She grabbed him by the arm as he turned toward the door. "You stay out of it, Roger!"

"I'm not going to fight him," he said, patting her hand in what he plainly thought a reassuring manner. "But I've got to talk to him."

"No, you don't." She tightened her grip on his arm, and pulled, trying to bring him back to the hearth. "You'll just make it worse. Leave them alone."

"No, I won't," he said, irritation beginning to show on his face. "What do ye mean, I'll make it worse? What d'ye think I am?"

That wasn't a question she wanted to answer right this minute. Vibrating with emotion from the tension of Aidan's surgery, the explosion of the fight, and the niggling bur of Allan's shouted insult, she barely trusted herself to speak, let alone be tactful.

"Don't go," she repeated, forcing herself to lower her voice, speak calmly. "Everyone's upset. At least wait until they've settled down. Better yet, wait 'til Da comes back. He can—"

"Aye, he can do everything better than I can, I know that fine," Roger replied caustically. "But it's me that promised Malva she'd come to no harm. I'm going." He yanked at his sleeve, hard enough that she felt the underarm seam give way.

"Fine!" She let go, and slapped him hard on the arm. "Go! Take care of everybody in the world but your own family. Go! Bloody *go*!"

"What?" He stopped, scowling, caught between anger and puzzlement.

"You heard me! Go!" She stamped her foot, and the jar of

dauco seeds, left too near the edge of the shelf, fell off and smashed on the floor, scattering tiny black seeds like pepper grains. "Now look what you've done!"

"What *I've*—"

"Never mind! Just never mind. Get out of here." She was puffing like a grampus with the effort not to cry. Her cheeks were hot with blood and her eyeballs felt red, bloodshot, so hot that she felt she might sear him with a look—certainly she wished she could.

He hovered, clearly trying to decide whether to stay and conciliate his disgruntled wife, or rush off in chivalrous protection of Malva Christie. He took a hesitant step toward the door, and she dived for the broom, making stupid, high-pitched squeaks of incoherent rage as she swung it at his head.

He ducked, but she got him on the second swing, catching him across the ribs with a *thwack.* He jerked in surprise at the impact, but recovered fast enough to catch the broom on the next swing. He yanked it out of her hand, and with a grunt of effort, broke it over his knee with a splintering crack.

He threw the pieces clattering at her feet and glared at her, angry but self-possessed.

"What in the name of God is the matter with you?"

She drew up tall and glared back.

"What I said. If you're spending so much time with Amy McCallum that it's common talk you're having an affair with her—"

"I'm *what*?" His voice broke with outrage, but there was a shifty look in his eyes that gave him away.

"So you've heard it, too—haven't you?" She didn't feel triumphant at having caught him out; more a sense of sick fury.

"You can't possibly think that's true, Bree," he said, his voice pitched uncertainly between angry repudiation and pleading.

"I know it isn't true," she said, and was furious to hear her own voice as shaky and cracked as his was. "That's not the effing *point,* Roger!"

"The point," he repeated. His black brows were drawn down, his eyes sharp and dark beneath them.

"The point," she said, gulping air, "is that you're always *gone.* Malva Christie, Amy McCallum, Marsali, Lizzie—you even go help Ute McGillivray, for God's sake!"

"Who else is to do it?" he asked sharply. "Your father or your cousin might, aye—but they've to be gone to the Indians. I'm here. And I'm not always gone," he added, as an afterthought. "I'm home every night, am I not?"

She closed her eyes and clenched her fists, feeling the nails dig into her palms.

"You'll help any woman but me," she said, opening her eyes. "Why is that?"

He gave her a long, hard look, and she wondered for an instant whether there was such a thing as a black emerald.

"Maybe I didn't think ye needed me," he said. And turning on his heel, he left.

51

THE CALLING

THE WATER LAY CALM as melted silver, the only movement on it the shadows of the evening clouds. But the hatch was about to rise; you could feel it. Or perhaps, Roger thought, what he felt was the expectation in his father-in-law, crouched like a leopard on the bank of the trout pool, pole and fly at the ready for the first sign of a ripple.

"Like the pool at Bethesda," he said, amused.

"Oh, aye?" Jamie answered, but didn't look at him, his attention fixed on the water.

"The one where an angel would go down into the pool and trouble the water now and then. So everyone sat about waiting, so as to plunge in the minute the water began to stir."

Jamie smiled, but still didn't turn. Fishing was serious business.

That was good; he'd rather not have Jamie look at him. But he'd have to hurry if he meant to say something; Fraser was already paying out the line to make a practice cast or two.

"I think—" He stopped himself, correcting. "No, I don't think. I know. I want—" His air ran out in a wheeze, annoying him; the last thing he wanted was to sound in any way doubtful about what he was saying. He took a huge breath, and the next words shot out as though fired from a pistol. "I mean to be a minister."

Well, then. He'd said it out loud. He glanced upward, involuntarily, but sure enough, the sky hadn't fallen. It was hazed and riffled with mare's tails, but the blue calm of it showed through and the ghost of an early moon floated just above the mountain's shoulder.

Jamie glanced thoughtfully at him, but didn't seem shocked or taken aback. That was some small comfort, he supposed.

"A minister. A preacher, d'ye mean?"

"Well . . . aye. That, too."

The admission disconcerted him. He supposed he *would* have to preach, though the mere notion of it was terrifying.

"That, *too*?" Fraser repeated, looking at him sideways.

"Aye. I mean—a minister does preach, of course." Of course. What about? How? "But that's not—I mean, that's not the main thing. Not why I—I have to do it." He was getting flustered, trying to explain clearly something that he could not even explain properly to himself.

He sighed, and rubbed a hand over his face.

"Aye, look. Ye recall Grannie Wilson's funeral, of course. And the McCallums?"

Jamie merely nodded, but Roger thought perhaps a flicker of understanding showed in his eyes.

"I've done . . . a few things. A bit like that, when it was needed. And—" He twitched a hand, unsure even how to begin describing things like his meeting with Hermon Husband on the banks of the Alamance, or the conversations had with his dead father, late at night.

He sighed again, made to toss a pebble into the water, and

stopped himself, just in time, when he saw Jamie's hand tense round his fishing pole. He coughed, feeling the familiar choke and rasp in his throat, and closed his hand around the pebble.

"The preaching, aye, I suppose I'll manage. But it's the other things—oh, God, this sounds insane, and I do believe I may be. But it's the burying and the christening and the—the—maybe just being able to *help,* even if it's only by listening and praying."

"Ye want to take care of them," Jamie said softly, and it wasn't a question, but rather an acceptance.

Roger laughed a little, unhappily, and closed his eyes against the sparkle of the sun off the water.

"I don't want to do it," he said. "It's the last thing I thought of, and me growing up in a minister's house. I mean, I ken what it's like. But someone *has* to do it, and I am thinking it's me."

Neither of them spoke for a bit. Roger opened his eyes and watched the water. Algae coated the rocks, wavering in the current like locks of mermaids' hair. Fraser stirred a little, drawing back his rod.

"Do Presbyterians believe in the sacraments, would ye say?"

"Yes," Roger said, surprised. "Of course we do. Have ye never—" Well, no. He supposed in fact Fraser never *had* spoken to anyone not a Catholic, regarding such matters. "We do," he repeated. He dipped a hand gently in the water, and wiped it across his brow, so the coolness ran down his face and down his neck inside his shirt.

"It's Holy Orders I mean, ken?" The drowned fly swam through the water, a tiny speck of red. "Will ye not need to be ordained?"

"Oh, I see. Aye, I would. There's a Presbyterian academy in Mecklenburg County. I'll go there and speak with them about it. Though I'm thinking it willna take such a time; I've the Greek and Latin already, and for what it's worth"—he smiled, despite himself—"I've a degree from Oxford University. Believe it or not, I was once thought an educated man."

Jamie's mouth twitched at the corner as he drew back his arm and snapped his wrist. The line sailed out, a lazy curve, and the fly settled. Roger blinked; sure enough—the surface of the pool was beginning to pucker and shiver, tiny ripples spreading out from the rising hatch of mayflies and damselflies.

"Have ye spoken to your wife about it?"

"No," he said, staring across the pool.

"Why not?" There was no tone of accusation in the question; more curiosity. Why, after all, should he have chosen to talk to his father-in-law first, rather than his wife?

Because you know what it is to be a man, he thought, *and she doesn't.* What he said, though, was another version of the truth.

"I don't want her to think me a coward."

Jamie made a small "hmph" noise, almost surprise, but didn't reply at once, concentrating on reeling in his line. He took the sodden fly from the hook, then hesitated over the collection on his hat, finally choosing a delicate green thing with a curving wisp of black feather.

"D'ye think she would?" Not waiting for an answer, Fraser stood and whipped the line up and back, sending the fly out to drift down over the center of the pool, lighting like a leaf on the water.

Roger watched as he brought it in, playing it over the water in a jerky dance. The Reverend had been a fisherman. All at once, he saw the Ness and its sparkling riffles, running clear brown over the rocks, Dad standing in his battered waders, reeling in his line. He was choked with longing. For Scotland. For his father. For one more day—just one—of peace.

The mountains and the green wood rose up mysterious and wild around them, and the hazy sky unfurled itself over the hollow like angel's wings, silent and sunlit. But not peaceful; never peace, not here.

"Do you believe us—Claire and Brianna and me—about the war that's coming?"

Jamie laughed shortly, gaze fixed on the water.

"I've eyes, man. It doesna take either prophet or witch to see it standing on the road."

"That," said Roger, giving him a curious look, "is a very odd way of putting it."

"Is it, so? Is that no what the Bible says? *When ye shall see the abomination of desolation, standing where it ought not, then let them in Judaea flee to the mountains?*"

Let him who readeth understand. Memory supplied the missing part of the verse, and Roger became aware, with a small sense of cold in the bone, that Jamie did indeed see it standing on the road, and recognized it. Nor was he using figures of speech; he was describing, precisely, what he saw—because he had seen it before.

The sound of small boys yelling in joy drifted across the water, and Fraser turned his head a little, listening. A faint smile touched his mouth, then he looked down into the moving water, seeming to grow still. The ropes of his hair stirred against the sunburned skin of his neck, in the same way that the leaves of the mountain ash moved above.

Roger wanted suddenly to ask Jamie whether he was afraid, but kept silence. He knew the answer, in any case.

It doesn't matter. He breathed deep, and felt the same answer, to the same question, asked of himself. It didn't seem to come from anywhere, but was just there inside him, as though he had been born with it, always known it.

It doesn't matter. You will do it anyway.

They stayed for some time in silence. Jamie cast twice more with the green fly, then shook his head and muttered something, reeled it in, changed it for a Dun Fly, and cast again. The little boys charged past on the other bank, naked as eels, giggling, and disappeared through the bushes.

Really odd, Roger thought. He felt all right. Still having not the slightest idea what he meant to do, exactly, still seeing the drifting cloud coming toward them, and now knowing much more about what lay within it. But still all right.

Jamie had a fish on the line. He brought it in fast, and jerked it shining and flapping onto the bank, where he killed it with a sharp blow on a rock before tucking it into his creel.

"D'ye mean to turn Quaker?" Jamie asked seriously.

"No." Roger was startled by the question. "Why do you ask that?"

Jamie made the odd little half-shrugging gesture that he sometimes used when uncomfortable about something, and didn't speak again until he'd made the new cast.

"Ye said ye didna want Brianna to think ye coward. I've

fought by the side of a priest before." One side of his mouth turned up, wry. "Granted, he wasna much of a swordsman, the Monsignor, and he couldna hit the broad side of a barn wi' a pistol—but he was game enough."

"Oh." Roger scratched the side of his jaw. "Aye, I take your meaning. No, I can't fight with an army, I don't think." Saying it, he felt a sharp pang of regret. "But take up arms in defense of—of those who need it . . . I can square that with my conscience, aye."

"That's all right, then."

Jamie reeled in the rest of the line, shook water from the fly, and stuck the hook back into his hat. Laying the line aside, he rummaged in the creel and pulled out a stoneware bottle. He sat down with a sigh, pulled the cork with his teeth, spat it into his hand, and offered Roger the bottle.

"It's a thing Claire says to me, now and again," he explained, and quoted: *"Malt does more than Milton can, to justify God's ways to man."*

Roger lifted an eyebrow.

"Ever read Milton?"

"A bit. She's right about it."

"Ye ken the next lines?" Roger lifted the bottle to his lips. *"Ale, man, ale's the stuff to drink, For fellows whom it hurts to think."*

A subterranean laugh moved through Fraser's eyes.

"This must be whisky, then," he said. "It only smells like beer."

It was cool and dark and pleasantly bitter, and they passed the bottle to and fro, not saying much of anything, until the ale was gone. Jamie put the cork thriftily back in, and tucked the empty bottle away in the creel.

"Your wife," he said thoughtfully, rising and hitching the strap of the creel onto his shoulder.

"Aye?" Roger picked up the battered hat, bestrewn with flies, and gave it to him. Jamie nodded thanks, and set it on his head.

"She has eyes, too."

52

M-I-C-

FIREFLIES LIT THE GRASS, the trees, and floated through the heavy air in a profusion of cool green sparks. One lighted on Brianna's knee; she watched it pulse, on-off, on-off, and listened to her husband telling her he meant to be a minister.

They were sitting on the stoop of their cabin as the dusk thickened into night. Across the big clearing, the whoops of small children at play sounded in the bushes, high and cheerful as hunting bats.

"You . . . uh . . . could say something," Roger suggested. His head was turned, looking at her. There was enough light yet to see his face, expectant, slightly anxious.

"Well . . . give me a minute. I sort of wasn't expecting this, you know?"

That was true, and it wasn't. Certainly, she hadn't consciously thought of such a thing, yet now that he'd stated his intentions—and he had, she thought; he wasn't asking her permission—she wasn't at all surprised. It was less a change than a recognition of something that had been there for some time—and in a way, it was a relief to see it and know it for what it was.

"Well," she said, after a long moment of consideration, "I think that's good."

"Ye do." The relief in his voice was palpable.

"Yes. If you're helping all these women because God told you to, that's better than doing it because you'd rather be with them than with me."

"Bree! Ye can't think that, that I—" He leaned closer, looking anxiously into her face. "Ye don't, do you?"

"Well, only sometimes," she admitted. "In my worse moments. Not most of the time." He looked so anxious that she reached up and cupped her hand to the long curve of his cheek; the stubble of his beard was invisible in this light, but she could feel it, soft and tickling against her palm.

"You're sure?" she said softly. He nodded, and she saw his throat move as he swallowed.

"I'm sure."

"Are you afraid?"

He smiled a little at that.

"Yeah."

"I'll help," she said firmly. "You tell me how, and I'll help."

He took a deep breath, his face lightening, though his smile was rueful.

"I don't know how," he said. "How to do it, I mean. Let alone what *you* might do. That's what scares me."

"Maybe not," she said. "But you've *been* doing it, anyway, haven't you? Do you need to do anything formal about this, though? Or can you just announce you're a minister, like those TV preachers, and start taking up the collection right away?"

He smiled at the joke, but answered seriously.

"Bloody Romanist. Ye always think no one else has any claim to sacraments. We do, though. I'm thinking I'll go to the Presbyterian Academy, see what I need to do about ordination. As for taking up the collection—I expect this means I'll never be rich."

"I sort of wasn't expecting that, anyway," she assured him gravely. "Don't worry; I didn't marry you for your money. If we need more, I'll make it."

"How?"

"I don't know. Not selling my body, probably. Not after what happened to Manfred."

"Don't even joke about that," he said. His hand came down over hers, large and warm.

Aidan McCallum's high, piercing voice floated through the air, and a sudden thought struck her.

"Your—your, um, flock . . ." The word struck her funny bone, and she giggled, despite the seriousness of the question. "Will they mind that I'm a Catholic?" She turned to him suddenly, another thought coming rapidly in its wake. "You don't—you aren't asking me to convert?"

"No, I'm not," he said quickly, firmly. "Not in a million years. As for what they might think—or say—" His face twitched, caught between dismay and determination. "If they're not willing to accept it, well . . . they can just go to hell, that's all."

She burst out laughing, and he followed her, his laugh cracked, but without restraint.

"The Minister's Cat is an irreverent cat," she teased. "And how do you say *that* in Gaelic?"

"I've no idea. But the Minister's Cat is a relieved cat," he added, still smiling. "I didn't know what ye might think about it."

"I'm not totally sure what I *do* think about it," she admitted. She squeezed his hand lightly. "But I see that you're happy."

"It shows?" He smiled, and the last of the evening light glowed briefly in his eyes, a deep and lambent green.

"It shows. You're sort of . . . lighted up inside." Her throat felt tight. "Roger—you won't forget about me and Jem, will you? I don't know that I can compete with God."

He looked thunderstruck at that.

"No," he said, his hand tightening on hers, hard enough to make her ring cut into her flesh. "Not ever."

They sat silent for a little, the fireflies drifting down like slow green rain, their silent mating song lighting the darkening grass and trees. Roger's face was fading as the light failed, though she still saw the line of his jaw, set in determination.

"I swear to ye, Bree," he said. "Whatever I'm called to now—and God knows what that is—I was called to be your husband first. Your husband and the father of your bairns above all things—and that I always shall be. Whatever I may do, it will not ever be at the price of my family, I promise you."

"All I want," she said softly to the dark, "is for you to love me. Not because of what I can do or what I look like, or because I love you—just because I am."

"Perfect, unconditional love?" he said just as softly. "Some would tell ye only God can love that way—but I can try."

"Oh, I have faith in you," she said, and felt the glow of him reach her own heart.

"I hope ye always will," he said. He raised her hand to his lips, kissed her knuckles in formal salutation, his breath warm on her skin.

As though to test the resolution of his earlier declaration, Jem's voice rose and fell on the evening breeze, a small, urgent siren. "DadddeeeDaaaddeeeDAAADDDEEE . . ."

Roger sighed deeply, leaned over, and kissed her, a moment's soft, deep connection, then rose to deal with the emergency of the moment.

She sat for a bit, listening. The sound of male voices came from the far end of the clearing, high and low, demand and question, reassurance and excitement. No emergency; Jem wanted to be lifted into a tree too high for him to climb alone. Then laughter, mad rustling of leaves—oh, good grief, Roger was in the tree, too. They were all up there, hooting like owls.

"What are ye laughing at, *a nighean*?" Her father loomed out of the night, smelling of horses.

"Everything," she said, scooching over to make room for him to sit beside her. It was true. Everything seemed suddenly bright, the candlelight from the windows of the Big House, the fireflies in the grass, the glow of Roger's face when he told her his desire. She could still feel the touch of his mouth on hers; it fizzed in her blood.

Jamie reached up and fielded a passing firefly, holding it for a moment cupped in the dark hollow of his hand, where it flashed on and off, the cool light seeping through his fingers. Far off, she heard a brief snatch of her mother's voice, coming through an open window; Claire was singing "Clementine."

Now the boys—and Roger—were howling at the moon, though it was no more than a pale sickle on the horizon. She felt her father's body shake with silent laughter, too.

"It reminds me of Disneyland," she said on impulse.

"Oh, aye? Where's that?"

"It's an amusement park—for children," she added, knowing that while there were such things as amusement parks in places like London and Paris, these were purely adult places. No one ever thought of entertaining children now, beyond their own games and the occasional toy.

"Daddy and Mama took me there every summer," she said, slipping back without effort to the hot, bright days and warm California nights. "The trees all had little sparkling lights in them—the fireflies reminded me."

Jamie spread his palm; the firefly, suddenly free, pulsed to itself once or twice, then spread its wings with a tiny whir and lifted into the air, floating up and away.

"Dwelt a miner, forty-niner, and his daughter, Clementine . . ."

"What was it like, then?" he asked curiously.

"Oh . . . it was wonderful." She smiled to herself, seeing the brilliant lights of Main Street, the music and mirrors and beautiful, beribboned horses of King Arthur's Carrousel. "There were . . . rides, we called them. A boat, where you could float through the jungle on a river, and see crocodiles and hippopotamuses and headhunters . . ."

"Headhunters?" he said, intrigued.

"Not real ones," she assured him. "It's all make-believe—but it's . . . well, it's a world to itself. When you're there, the real world sort of disappears; nothing bad can happen there. They call it 'The Happiest Place on Earth'—and for a little while, it really seems that way."

"Light she was, and like a fairy, and her shoes were number nine, Herring boxes without topses, sandals were for Clementine."

"And you'd hear music everywhere, all the time," she said, smiling. "Bands—groups of musicians playing instruments, horns and drums and things—would march up and down the streets, and play in pavilions. . . ."

"Aye, that happens in amusement parks. Or it did, the once I was in one." She could hear a smile in his voice, as well.

"Mm-hm. And there are cartoon characters—I told you about cartoons—walking around. You can go up and shake hands with Mickey Mouse, or—"

"With what?"

"Mickey Mouse." She laughed. "A big mouse, life-size—human-size, I mean. He wears gloves."

"A giant rat?" he said, sounding slightly stunned. "And they take the weans to play with it?"

"Not a rat, a mouse," she corrected him. "And it's really a person dressed up like a mouse."

"Oh, aye?" he said, not sounding terribly reassured.

"Yes. And an enormous carrousel with painted horses, and a railroad train that goes through the Rainbow Caverns, where there are big jewels sticking out of the walls, and colored streams with red and blue water . . . and orange-juice bars. Oh, orange-juice bars!" She moaned softly in ecstatic remembrance of the cold, tart, overwhelming sweetness.

"It was nice, then?" he said softly.

"Thou art lost and gone forever, Dreadful sor-ry . . . Clementine."

"Yes," she said, sighed, and was silent for a moment. Then she leaned her head against his shoulder, and wrapped her hand around his arm, big and solid.

"You know what?" she said, and he made a small interrogatory noise in reply.

"It *was* nice—it was great—but what I really, really loved about it was that when we were there, it was just the three of us, and everything was perfect. Mama wasn't worrying about her patients, Daddy wasn't working on a paper—they weren't ever silent or angry with each other. Both of them laughed—we all laughed, all the time . . . while we were there."

He made no reply, but tilted his head so it rested against hers. She sighed again, deeply.

"Jemmy won't get to go to Disneyland—but he'll have that. A family that laughs—and millions of little lights in the trees."

Part Seven

Rolling Downhill

53

PRINCIPLES

*From Fraser's Ridge, North Carolina,
on the Third day of July, Anno Domini 1774,
James Fraser, Esq.*

*To his Lordship, John Grey, at Mount Josiah
Plantation, in the colony of Virginia*

My Dear Friend,

I cannot begin to express our Gratitude for your kind Behavior in sending a Draft drawn upon your own Bank, as advance Payment against the eventual Sale of the Objects I confided to your disposition. Mr. Higgins, in delivering this Document, was of course most tactful—and yet, I gathered from his anxious Demeanor and his efforts at Discretion that you may perhaps believe us to be in dire Straits. I hasten to assure you that this is not the Case; we will do well enough, so far as Matters of Victuals, Clothes, and the Necessities of Life.

I said that I would tell you the Details of the Affair, and I see that I must, if only to disabuse you of the Vision of rampant Starvation among my family and tenants.

Beyond a small legal Obligation requiring Cash, I have a Matter of Business in Hand, involving the acquisition of a Number of Guns. I had been in Hopes of acquiring these through the good offices of a Friend, but find that this Arrangement will no longer answer; I must look further abroad.

I and my Family are invited to a Barbecue in honor of Miss Flora MacDonald, the Heroine of the Rising—you are familiar with the Lady, I believe? I recall your telling me once of your meeting with her in London, whilst she was imprisoned there—to take place next month at my aunt's Plantation, River Run. As this Affair will be attended by a great many Scots, some coming from considerable Distances, I am in Hopes that with Cash in Hand, I may make Arrangements to procure the requisite Weapons via other Avenues. In re which, should your own Connexions suggest any such useful Avenues, I should be grateful to hear of them.

I write quickly, as Mr. Higgins has other Errands, but my Daughter bids me send herewith a box of Matchsticks, her own Invention. She has schooled Mr. Higgins most carefully in their Use, so if he does not burst inadvertently into Flame on the way back, he will be able to demonstrate them to you.

Your humble and ob't. servant,
James Fraser

P.S. I require thirty Muskets, with as much Powder and Ammunition as may be possible. These need not be of the latest Manufacture, but must be well-kept and functional.

"'OTHER AVENUES?'" I said, watching him sand the letter before folding it. "You mean smugglers? And if so, are you sure that Lord John will understand what you mean?"

"I do, and he will," Jamie assured me. "I ken a few smugglers myself, who bring things in through the Outer Banks. He'll know the ones who come through Roanoke, though—and there's more business there, because of the blockade in Massachusetts. Goods come in through Virginia, and go north overland."

He took a half-burned beeswax taper from the shelf and held it to the coals in the hearth, then dripped soft brown wax in a puddle over the seam of the letter. I leaned forward and pressed the back of my left hand into the warm wax, leaving the mark of my wedding ring in it.

"Damn Manfred McGillivray," he said, with no particular heat. "It will be three times the cost, and I must get them from a smuggler."

"Will you ask about him, though? At the barbecue, I mean?" Flora MacDonald, the woman who had saved Charles Stuart from the English after Culloden, dressing him in her maid's clothes and smuggling him to a rendezvous with the French on the Isle of Skye, was a living legend to the Scottish Highlanders, and her recent arrival in the colony was the subject of vast excitement, news of it coming even as far as the Ridge. Every well-known Scot in the Cape Fear valley—and a good many from farther away—would be present at the barbecue to be held in her honor. No better place to spread the word for a missing young man.

He glanced up at me, surprised.

"Of course I will, Sassenach. What d'ye think I am?"

"I think you're very kind," I said, kissing him on the forehead. "If a trifle reckless. And I notice you carefully didn't tell Lord John why you need thirty muskets."

He gave a small snort, and swept the grains of sand carefully off the table into the palm of his hand.

"I dinna ken for sure myself, Sassenach."

"Whatever do you mean by that?" I asked, surprised. "Do you not mean to give them to Bird, after all?"

He didn't answer at once, but the two stiff fingers of his right hand tapped gently on the tabletop. Then he shrugged, reached to the stack of journals and ledgers, and pulled out a paper, which he handed to me. A letter from John Ashe, who had been a fellow commander of militia during the War of the Regulation.

"The fourth paragraph," he said, seeing me frown at a recounting of the latest contretemps between the Governor and the Assembly. I obligingly skimmed down the page, to the indicated spot, and felt a small, premonitory shiver.

"A Continental Congress is proposed," I read, *"with delegates to be sent from each colony. The lower house of the Connecticut Assembly has moved already to propose such men, acting through Committees of Correspondence. Some gentlemen with whom you are well-acquainted propose that*

North Carolina shall do likewise, and will meet to accomplish the matter in mid-August. I could wish that you would join us, friend, for I am convinced that your heart and mind must lie with us in the matter of liberty; surely such a man as yourself is no friend to tyranny.

"*Some gentlemen with whom you are well-acquainted,*" I repeated, putting down the letter. "Do you know who he means?"

"I could guess."

"Mid-August, he says. Before the barbecue, do you think, or after?"

"After. One of the others sent me the date of the meeting. It's to be in Halifax."

I put down the letter. The afternoon was still and hot, and the thin linen of my shift was damp, as were the palms of my hands.

"One of the others," I said. He shot me a quick glance, with a half-smile, and picked up the letter.

"In the Committee of Correspondence."

"Oh, naturally," I said. "You might have told me." Naturally, he would have found a means of inveigling himself into the North Carolina Committee of Correspondence—the center of political intrigue, where the seeds of rebellion were being sown—meanwhile holding a commission as Indian agent for the British Crown and ostensibly working to arm the Indians, in order to suppress precisely those seeds of rebellion.

"I am telling ye, Sassenach," he said. "This is the first time they've asked me to meet wi' them, even in private."

"I see," I said softly. "Will you go? Is it—is it time?" Time to make the leap, declare himself openly as a Whig, if not yet a rebel. Time to change his public allegiance, and risk the brand of treason. Again.

He sighed deeply and rubbed a hand through his hair. He'd been thinking; the short hairs of several tiny cowlicks were standing on end.

"I don't know," he said finally. "It's two years yet, no? The fourth of July, 1776—that's what Brianna said."

"No," I said. "It's two years until they declare independence—but, Jamie, the fighting will have started already. That will be much too late."

He stared at the letters on the desk, and nodded bleakly.

"Aye, it will have to be soon, then."

"It would be likely safe enough," I said hesitantly. "What you told me about Henderson buying land in Tennessee: if no one's stopping him, I can't see anyone in the government being agitated enough to come up here and try to force us out. And surely not if you were only known to have *met* with the local Whigs?"

He gave me a small, wry smile.

"It's no the government I'm worrit by, Sassenach. It's the folk nearby. It wasna the Governor who hanged the O'Brians and burnt their house, ken? Nor was it Richard Brown, nor Indians. That wasna done for the sake of law nor profit; it was done for hate, and verra likely by someone who knew them."

That made a more pronounced chill skitter down my spine. There was a certain amount of political disagreement and discussion on the Ridge, all right, but it hadn't reached the stage of fisticuffs yet, let alone burning and killing.

But it would.

I remembered, all too well. Bomb shelters and ration coupons, blackout wardens and the spirit of cooperation against a dreadful foe. And the stories from Germany, France. People reported on, denounced to the SS, dragged from their houses—others hidden in attics and barns, smuggled across borders.

In war, government and their armies were a threat, but it was so often the neighbors who damned or saved you.

"Who?" I said baldly.

"I could guess," he said, with a shrug. "The McGillivrays? Richard Brown? Hodgepile's friends—if he had any. The friends of any of the other men we killed? The Indian ye met—Donner?—if he's still alive. Gerald Forbes? He's a grudge against Brianna, and she and Roger Mac would do well to remember it. Hiram Crombie and his lot?"

"Hiram?" I said dubiously. "Granted, he doesn't like you very much—and as for me—but . . ."

"Well, I do doubt it," he admitted. "But it's possible, aye? His people didna support the Jacobites at all; they'll no be pleased at an effort to overthrow the King from this side of the water, either."

I nodded. Crombie and the rest would of necessity have taken an oath of loyalty to King George, before being allowed to travel to America. Jamie had—of necessity—taken the same oath, as part of his pardon. And must—of an even greater necessity—break it. But when?

He'd stopped drumming his fingers; they rested on the letter before him.

"I do trust ye're right, Sassenach," he said.

"About what? What will happen? You know I am," I said, a little surprised. "Bree and Roger told you, too. Why?"

He rubbed a hand slowly through his hair.

"I've never fought for the sake of principle," he said, reflecting, and shook his head. "Only necessity. I wonder, would it be any better?"

He didn't sound upset, merely curious, in a detached sort of way. Still, I found this vaguely disturbing.

"But there is principle to it, this time," I protested. "In fact, it may be the first war ever fought over principle."

"Rather than something sordid like trade, or land?" Jamie suggested, raising one eyebrow.

"I don't say trade and land haven't anything to do with it," I replied, wondering precisely how I'd managed to become a defender of the American Revolution—an historical period I knew only from Brianna's school textbooks. "But it goes well beyond that, don't you think? *We hold these truths to be self-evident, that all men are created equal, that they are endowed by their Creator with certain unalienable Rights, that among these are Life, Liberty, and the pursuit of Happiness.*"

"Who said that?" he asked, interested.

"Thomas Jefferson will say it—on behalf of the new republic. The Declaration of Independence, it's called. Will be called."

"All men," he repeated. "Does he mean Indians, as well, do ye think?"

"I can't say," I said, rather irritated at being forced into this position. "I haven't met him. If I do, I'll ask, shall I?"

"Never mind." He lifted his fingers in brief dismissal. "I'll ask him myself, and I have the opportunity. Meanwhile, I'll ask Brianna." He glanced at me. "Though as to principle, Sassenach—"

He leaned back in his chair, folded his arms over his chest, and closed his eyes.

"As long as but a hundred of us remain alive," he said pre-

cisely, *"never will we on any conditions be brought under English rule. It is in truth not for glory, nor riches, nor honours that we are fighting, but for freedom—for that alone, which no honest man gives up but with life itself."*

"The Declaration of Arbroath," he said, opening his eyes. He gave me a lopsided smile. "Written some four hundred years ago. Speaking o' principles, aye?"

He stood up then, but still remained standing by the battered table he used as a desk, looking down at Ashe's letter.

"As for my own principles . . ." he said, as though to himself, but then looked at me, as though suddenly realizing that I was still there.

"Aye, I think I mean to give Bird the muskets," he said. "Though I may have cause to regret it, and I find them pointing at me, two or three years hence. But he shall have them, and do with them what seems best, to defend himself and his people."

"The price of honor, is it?"

He looked down at me, with the ghost of a smile.

"Call it blood money."

54

FLORA MACDONALD'S BARBECUE

River Run Plantation
August 6, 1774

WHATEVER DID ONE SAY to an icon? Or an icon's husband, for that matter?

"Oh, I shall faint, I know I shall." Rachel Campbell was fluttering her fan hard enough to create a perceptible breeze. "Whatever shall I say to her?"

"'Good day, Mrs. MacDonald'?" suggested her husband, a faint smile lurking at the corner of his withered mouth.

Rachel hit him sharply with her fan, making him chuckle as he dodged away. For all he was thirty-five years her senior, Farquard Campbell had an easy, teasing way with his wife, quite at odds with his usual dignified demeanor.

"I shall faint," Rachel declared again, having evidently decided upon this as a definite social strategy.

"Well, ye must please yourself, of course, *a nighean,* but if ye do, it will have to be Mr. Fraser picking you up from the ground; my ancient limbs are scarcely equal to the task."

"Oh!" Rachel cast a quick glance at Jamie, who smiled at her, then hid her blushes behind her fan. While plainly fond of her own husband, she made no secret of her admiration for mine.

"Your humble servant, madam," Jamie gravely assured her, bowing.

She tittered. I shouldn't like to wrong the woman, but she definitely tittered. I caught Jamie's eye, and hid a smile behind my own fan.

"And what will *you* say to her, then, Mr. Fraser?"

Jamie pursed his lips and squinted thoughtfully at the brilliant sun streaming through the elm trees that edged the lawn at River Run.

"Oh, I suppose I might say that I'm glad the weather has kept fine for her. It was raining the last time we met."

Rachel's jaw dropped, and so did her fan, bouncing on the lawn. Her husband bent to pick it up for her, groaning audibly, but she had no attention to spare for him.

"You've *met* her?" she cried, eyes wide with excitement. "When? Where? With the prin—with *him*?"

"Ah, no," Jamie said, smiling. "On Skye. I'd gone wi' my father—a matter of sheep, it was. We chanced to meet Hugh MacDonald of Armadale in Portree—Miss Flora's stepfather, aye?—and he'd brought the lass into the town with him, for a treat."

"Oh!" Rachel was enchanted. "And was she beautiful and gracious as they say?"

Jamie frowned, considering.

"Well, no," he said. "But she'd a terrible grippe at the time, and no doubt would have looked much improved without the red nose. Gracious? Well, I wouldna say so, really. She snatched a bridie right out of my hand and ate it."

"And how old were you both at the time?" I asked, seeing Rachel's mouth sag in horror.

"Oh, six, maybe," he said cheerfully. "Or seven. I doubt I should remember, save I kicked her in the shin when she stole my bridie, and she pulled my hair."

Recovering somewhat from the shock, Rachel was pressing Jamie for further reminiscences, a pressure he was laughingly deflecting with jokes.

Of course, he had come prepared to this occasion; all over the grounds, there were stories being exchanged—humorous, admiring, longing—of the days before Culloden. Odd, that it should have been the defeat of Charles Stuart, and his ignominious flight, that made a heroine of Flora MacDonald and united these Highland exiles in a way that they could never have achieved—let alone sustained—had he actually won.

It struck me suddenly that Charlie was likely still alive, quietly drinking himself to death in Rome. In any real way, though, he was long since dead to these people who had loved or hated him. The amber of time had sealed him forever in that one defining moment of his life—*Bliadha Tearlach;* "Charlie's Year," it meant, and even now, I heard people call it that.

It was Flora's coming that was causing this flood of sentiment, of course. How strange for her, I thought, with a pang of sympathy—and for the first time, wondered what on earth I might say to her myself.

I had met famous people before—not the least of them the Bonnie Prince himself. But always before, I had met them when they—and I—were in the midst of their normal lives, not yet past the defining events that would make them famous, and thus still just people. Bar Louis—but then, he was a king. There are rules of etiquette for dealing with kings, since after all, no one ever does approach them as normal people. Not even when—

I snapped my own fan open, hot blood bursting through my face and body. I breathed deeply, trying not to fan quite as frantically as Rachel, but wanting to.

I had not once, in all the years since it happened, ever specifically recalled those two or three minutes of physical intimacy with Louis of France. Not deliberately, God knew, and not by accident, either.

Yet suddenly, the memory of it had touched me, as suddenly as a hand coming out of the crowd to seize my arm. Seize my arm, lift my skirts, and penetrate me in a way much more shockingly intrusive than the actual experience had been.

The air around me was suffused with the scent of roses, and I heard the creak of the dress cage as Louis's weight pressed upon it, and heard his sigh of pleasure. The room was dark, lit by one candle; it flickered at the edge of vision, then was blotted out by the man between my—

"Christ, Claire! Are ye all right?" I hadn't actually fallen down, thank God. I had reeled back against the wall of Hector Cameron's mausoleum, and Jamie, seeing me go, had leapt forward to catch hold of me.

"Let go," I said, breathless, but imperative. "Let go of me!"

He heard the note of terror in my voice, and slackened his grip, but couldn't bring himself to let go altogether, lest I fall. With the energy of sheer panic, I pulled myself upright, out of his grasp.

I still smelled roses. Not the cloying scent of rose oil—fresh roses. Then I came to myself, and realized that I was standing next to a huge yellow brier rose, trained to climb over the white marble of the mausoleum.

Knowing that the roses were real was comforting, but I felt as though I stood still on the edge of a vast abyss, alone, separate from every other soul in the universe. Jamie was close enough to touch, and yet it was as though he stood an immeasurable distance away.

Then he touched me and spoke my name, insistently, and just as suddenly as it had opened, the gap between us closed. I nearly fell into his arms.

"What is it, *a nighean*?" he whispered, holding me against his chest. "What's frightened ye?" His own heart was thumping under my ear; I'd scared him, too.

"Nothing," I said, and an overwhelming wave of relief went over me, at the realization that I was safely in the present; Louis had gone back into the shadows, an unpleasant but harmless memory once more. The staggering sense of violation, of loss and grief and isolation, had receded, no more than a shadow on my mind. Best of all, Jamie was there; solid and physical and smelling of sweat and whisky and horses . . . and *there.* I hadn't lost him.

Other people were clustering round, curious, solicitous. Rachel fanned me earnestly, and the breeze of it felt soothing; I was drenched with sweat, wisps of hair clinging damply to my neck.

"Quite all right," I murmured, suddenly self-conscious. "Just a bit faint . . . hot day . . ."

A chorus of offers to fetch me wine, a glass of syllabub, lemon shrub, a burned feather, were all trumped by Jamie's production of a flask of whisky from his sporran. It was the three-year-old stuff, from the sherry casks, and I felt a qualm as the scent of it reached me, remembering the night we had got drunk together after he had rescued me from Hodgepile and his men. God, was I about to be hurled back into *that* pit?

But I wasn't. The whisky was merely hot and consoling, and I felt better with the first sip.

Flashback. I'd heard colleagues talk about it, arguing as to whether this was the same phenomenon as shell shock, and if it was, whether it truly existed, or should be dismissed as simply "nerves."

I shuddered briefly, and took another sip. It most assuredly existed. I felt much better, but I had been shaken to the core, and my bones still felt watery. Beyond the faint echoes of the experience itself was a much more unsettling thought. It had happened once before, when Ute McGillivray attacked me. Was it likely to happen again?

"Shall I carry ye inside, Sassenach? Perhaps ye should lie down a bit."

Jamie had shooed away the well-wishers, had a slave fetch me a stool, and was now hovering over me like an anxious bumblebee.

"No, I'm all right now," I assured him. "Jamie . . ."

"Aye, lass?"

"You—when you—do you . . ."

I took a deep breath—and another sip of whisky—and tried again.

"Sometimes, I wake up during the night and see you—struggling—and I think it's with Jack Randall. Is it a dream that you have?"

He stared down at me for a moment, face blank, but trouble moving in his eyes. He glanced from side to side, but we were quite alone now.

"Why?" he asked, low-voiced.

"I need to know."

He took a breath, swallowed, and nodded.

"Aye. Sometimes it's dreams. That's . . . all right. I wake, and ken where I am, say a wee prayer, and . . . it's all right. But now and then—" He shut his eyes for a moment, then opened them. "I *am* awake. And yet I am there, with Jack Randall."

"Ah." I sighed, feeling at once terribly sad for him, and at the same time somewhat reassured. "Then I'm not losing my mind."

"Ye think so?" he said dryly. "Well, I'm that glad to hear it, Sassenach."

He stood very close, the cloth of his kilt brushing my arm, so that I should have him for support, if I suddenly went faint again. He looked searchingly at me, to be sure that I wasn't going to keel over, then touched my shoulder and with a brief "Sit still" went off.

Not far; just to the tables set up under the trees at the edge of the lawn. Ignoring the slaves arranging food for the barbecue, he leaned across a platter of boiled crayfish and picked up something from a tiny bowl. Then he was back, leaning down to take my hand. He rubbed his fingers together, and a pinch of salt sprinkled into my open palm.

"There," he whispered. "Keep it by ye, Sassenach. Whoever it is, he'll trouble ye no more."

I closed my hand over the damp grains, feeling absurdly comforted. Trust a Highlander to know precisely what to do about a case of daylight haunting! Salt, they said, kept a ghost in its grave. And if Louis was still alive, the other man, whoever he had been, that pressing weight in the dark, was surely dead.

There was a sudden rush of excitement, as a call came

from the river—the boat had been sighted. As one, the crowd drew itself up on tiptoe, breathless with anticipation.

I smiled, but felt the giddy contagion of it touch me nonetheless. Then the pipes began to skirl, and my throat at once was tight with unshed tears.

Jamie's hand tightened on my shoulder, unconsciously, and I looked up to see him rub his knuckles hard across his upper lip, as he, too, turned toward the river.

I looked down, blinking to control myself, and as my vision cleared, I saw the grains of salt on the ground, carefully scattered before the gates of the mausoleum.

SHE WAS MUCH smaller than I'd thought. Famous people always are. Everyone—dressed in their best, and an absolute sea of tartan—pressed close, awed past courtesy. I caught a glimpse of the top of her head, dark hair dressed high with white roses, and then it disappeared behind the thronged backs of well-wishers.

Her husband, Allan, was visible. A stoutly handsome man with gray-streaked black hair tied neatly back, he was standing—I assumed—behind her, bowing and smiling, acknowledging the flood of Gaelic compliment and welcome.

Despite myself, I felt the urge to rush forward and stare, with everyone else. I held firm, though. I was standing with Jocasta on the terrace; Mrs. MacDonald would come to us.

Sure enough; Jamie and Duncan were pushing their way firmly through the crowd, forming a flying wedge with Jocasta's black butler, Ulysses.

"That's really her?" Brianna murmured at my shoulder, eyes fixed with interest on the seething multitude, from which the men had now extracted the guest of honor, escorting her from the dock, up the lawn, toward the terrace. "She's smaller than I thought. Oh, it's too bad Roger isn't here—he'd just die to see her!" Roger was spending a month at the Presbyterian Academy at Charlotte, having his qualifications for ordination examined.

"He may get to see her another time," I murmured back. "I hear they've bought a plantation near Barbecue Creek, by

Mount Pleasant." And they would stay in the colony for at least another year or two, but I didn't say that out loud; so far as the people here knew, the MacDonalds had immigrated permanently.

But I had seen the tall memorial stone on Skye—where Flora MacDonald had been born, and would someday die, disillusioned with America.

It wasn't the first time I'd met someone and known their fate, of course—but it was always unsettling. The crowd opened and she stepped out, small and pretty, laughing up at Jamie. He had a hand under her elbow, guiding her up onto the terrace, and made a gesture of introduction toward me.

She looked up, expectant, met my gaze dead on, and blinked, her smile momentarily fading. It was back in an instant, and she was bowing to me and I to her, but I did wonder what she had seen in my face?

But she turned at once to greet Jocasta, and introduce her grown daughters, Anne and Fanny, a son, a son-in-law, her husband—by the time she had accomplished the confusion of introduction, she was perfectly in command of herself, and greeted me with a charming, gentle smile.

"Mrs. Fraser! I am so much obliged to meet you at last. I have heard such stories of your kindness and skill, I confess I am in awe to be in your presence."

It was said with so much warmth and sincerity—she seizing me by the hands—that I found myself responding, in spite of a cynical wonder as to who she'd been talking to about me. My reputation in Cross Creek and Campbelton was notorious, but not universally lauded, by any means.

"I had the honor of Dr. Fentiman's acquaintance at the subscription ball held for us in Wilmington—so kind, so amazingly kind of everyone! We have been so well treated, since our arrival—and he was quite in raptures regarding your—"

I should have liked to hear what had enraptured Fentiman—our relations were still marked by a certain wariness, though we had reached a rapprochement—but at this point, her husband spoke in her ear, desiring her to come and meet Farquard Campbell and some other prominent gentlemen, and with a regretful grimace, she squeezed my hands and departed, the brilliant public smile back in place.

"Huh," Bree remarked, *sotto voce.* "Lucky for her she's still got most of her teeth."

That was in fact exactly what I'd been thinking, and I laughed, converting it into a hasty coughing fit as I saw Jocasta's head turn sharply toward us.

"So that's her." Young Ian had come up on my other side, and was watching the guest of honor with an expression of deep interest. He was dressed in kilt, waistcoat, and coat for the occasion, his brown hair done up in a proper queue, and he looked quite civilized, bar the tattoos that looped across his cheekbones and over the bridge of his nose.

"That's her," Jamie agreed. "*Fionnaghal*—the Fair One." There was a surprising note of nostalgia in his voice, and I glanced at him in surprise.

"Well, it's her proper name," he said mildly. "*Fionnaghal.* It's only the English call her Flora."

"Did you have a crush on her when you were little, Da?" Brianna asked, laughing.

"A what?"

"A *tendresse,*" I said, batting my eyelashes delicately at him over my fan.

"Och, dinna be daft!" he said. "I was seven years old, for God's sake!" Nonetheless, the tips of his ears had gone quite pink.

"I was in love when I was seven," Ian remarked, rather dreamily. "Wi' the cook. Did ye hear Ulysses say as she's brought a looking glass, Uncle? Given to her by Prince *Tearlach,* with his arms upon the back. Ulysses put it in the parlor, wi' two of the grooms to stand guard over it."

Sure enough, those people who weren't in the swirling crowd surrounding the MacDonalds were all pressing through the double doors into the house, forming a line of animated chatter down the hall to the parlor.

"Seaumais!"

Jocasta's imperious voice put a stop to the teasing. Jamie gave Brianna an austere look, and went to join her. Duncan was detained in conversation with a small knot of prominent men—I recognized Gerald Forbes, the lawyer, as well as

Cornelius Harnett and Colonel Moore—and Ulysses was nowhere in sight—most likely dealing with the backstage logistics of a barbecue for two hundred people—thus leaving Jocasta temporarily marooned. Her hand on Jamie's arm, she sailed off the terrace, heading for Allan MacDonald, who had become detached from his wife by the press of people round her, and was standing under a tree, looking vaguely affronted.

I watched them go across the lawn, amused by Jocasta's sense of theatrics. Her body servant, Phaedre, was dutifully following—and could plainly have guided her mistress. That wouldn't have had at all the same effect, though. The two of them together made heads turn—Jocasta tall and slender, graceful despite her age and striking with her white hair piled high and her blue silk gown, Jamie with his Viking height and crimson Fraser tartan, both with those bold MacKenzie bones and catlike grace.

"Colum and Dougal would be proud of their little sister," I said, shaking my head.

"Oh, aye?" Ian spoke absently, not attending. He was still watching Flora MacDonald, now accepting a bunch of flowers from one of Farquard Campbell's grandchildren, to general applause.

"Not jealous, are you, Mama?" Brianna teased, seeing me glance in the same direction.

"Certainly not," I said with a certain amount of complacence. "After all, I have all *my* teeth, too."

I HAD MISSED him in the initial crush, but Major MacDonald was among the revelers, looking very flash in a brilliantly scarlet uniform coat and a new hat, lavish with gold lace. He removed this object and bowed low to me, looking cheerful—no doubt because I was unaccompanied by livestock, Adso and the white sow being both safely on Fraser's Ridge.

"Your servant, mum," he said. "I saw that ye had a word with Miss Flora—so charming, is she not? And a canty, handsome woman, as well."

"Indeed she is," I agreed. "Do you know her, then?"

"Oh, aye," he said, a look of profound satisfaction spreading across his weathered face. "I should not dare to the presumption of friendship—but believe I may stake a modest claim to acquaintancy. I accompanied Mrs. MacDonald and her family from Wilmington, and have had the great honor to assist in settling them in their present situation."

"Did you really?" I gave him an interested eye. The Major wasn't the type to be awed by celebrity. He *was* the type to appreciate its uses. So was Governor Martin, evidently.

The Major was watching Flora MacDonald now with a proprietary eye, noting with approval the way in which people clustered round her.

"She has most graciously agreed to speak today," he told me, rocking back a little on his bootheels. "Where would be the best place, do you think, mum? From the terrace, as being the point of highest elevation? Or perhaps near the statue on the lawn, as being more central and allowing the crowd to surround her, thus increasing the chance of everyone hearing her remarks?"

"I think she'll have a sunstroke, if you put her out on the lawn in this weather," I said, tilting my own broad-brimmed straw hat to shade my nose. It was easily in the nineties, in terms both of temperature and humidity, and my thin petticoats clung soddenly to my lower limbs. "What sort of remarks is she going to make?"

"Just a brief address upon the subject of loyalty, mum," he said blandly. "Ah, there is your husband, talking to Kingsburgh; if you'll excuse me, mum?" Bowing, he straightened, put his hat back on, and strode down the lawn to join Jamie and Jocasta, who were still with Allan MacDonald—styled "Kingsburgh," in the Scottish fashion, for the name of his estate on Skye.

Food was beginning to be brought out: tureens of powsowdie and hotchpotch—and an enormous tub of soup à la Reine, a clear compliment to the guest of honor—platters of fried fish, fried chicken, fried rabbit; venison collops in red wine, smoked sausages, Forfar bridies, inky-pinky, roast turkeys, pigeon pie; dishes of colcannon, stovies, turnip purry, roasted apples stuffed with dried pumpkin, squash, corn, mushroom pasties; gigantic baskets overflowing with fresh baps, rolls, and other breads . . . all this, I was well aware, merely as prelude to the barbecue whose succulent aroma was drifting through the air: a number of hogs, three or four beeves, two deer, and, the *pièce de résistance,* a wood bison, acquired God knew how or where.

A hum of pleasant anticipation rose around me, as people began metaphorically to loosen their belts, squaring up to the tables with a firm determination to do their duty in honor of the occasion.

Jamie was still stuck fast to Mrs. MacDonald, I saw; he was helping her to a dish of what looked from the distance to be broccoli salad. He looked up and saw me, beckoned me to join them—but I shook my head, gesturing with my fan toward the buffet tables, where the guests were setting to in the businesslike manner of grasshoppers in a barley field. I didn't want to lose the opportunity of inquiring about Manfred McGillivray, before the stupor of satiety settled over the crowd.

I made my way purposefully into the fray, accepting tidbits offered to me by assorted servants and slaves, pausing to chat with any acquaintance I saw, particularly those from Hillsboro. Manfred had spent a great deal of time there, I knew, taking commissions for guns, delivering the finished products, and doing small jobs of repair. That was the most likely place for him to go, I thought. But no one I talked to had seen him, though most knew him.

"Nice lad," one gentleman told me, pausing momentarily in his potations. "And sore missed, too. Besides Robin, there's few gunsmiths closer than Virginia."

I knew that, and knowing, wondered whether Jamie was having any luck in locating the muskets he needed. Perhaps Lord John's smuggling connections would be necessary.

I accepted a small pie from a passing slave's tray, and wandered on, munching and chatting. There was much talk about a series of fiery articles that had appeared recently in the *Chronicle,* the local newspaper, whose proprietor, one Fogarty Simms, was spoken of with considerable sympathy.

"A rare plucked 'un, is Simms," said Mr. Goodwin, shaking his head. "But I doubt me he'll stand. I spoke with him last week, and he told me he's in some fear of his skin. There've been threats, aye?"

From the tone of the gathering, I assumed that Mr. Simms must be a Loyalist, and this appeared to be true, from the various accounts I was given. There was talk, apparently, of a rival paper setting up, this to support the Whiggish agenda, with its incautious talk of tyranny and the overthrow of the King. No one knew quite who was behind the new venture, but there was talk—and much indignation at the prospect—that a printer was to be brought down from the north, where folk were notably given to such perverse sentiments.

The general consensus was that such persons wanted their backsides kicked, to bring them to their senses.

I hadn't sat down to eat formally, but after an hour of moving slowly through fields of champing jaws and wandering herds of hors d'oeuvre trays, I felt as though I'd sat through a French royal banquet—those occasions lasting so long that chamber pots were discreetly placed beneath the guests' chairs, and where the occasional guest giving way and sliding beneath the table was discreetly ignored.

The present occasion was less formal, but not much less prolonged. After an hour's preliminary eating, the barbecue was raised steaming from the pits near the stable, and brought to the lawns on wooden trestles, mounted on the shoulders of slaves. The sight of immense sides of beef, pork, venison, and buffalo, gleaming with oil and vinegar and surrounded by the smaller charred carcasses of hundreds of pigeons and quail, was greeted with applause by the guests, all by this time drenched with the sweat of their efforts, but nothing daunted.

Jocasta, seated by her guest, looked deeply gratified by the sound of her hospitality being so warmly accepted, and leaned toward Duncan, smiling, putting a hand on his arm as she said something to him. Duncan had left off looking nervous—the effect of a quart or two of beer, followed by most of a bottle of whisky—and seemed to be enjoying himself, too. He smiled broadly at Jocasta, then essayed a remark to Mrs. MacDonald, who laughed at whatever he said.

I had to admire her; she was besieged on all sides by people wanting a word, but she kept her poise admirably, being kind and gracious to everyone—though this meant sitting sometimes for ten minutes, a forkful of food suspended in air as she listened to some interminable story. At least she was in the shade—and Phaedre, dressed in white muslin, stood dutifully behind her with a huge fan made of palmetto fronds, making a breeze and keeping off the flies.

"Lemon shrub, ma'am?" A wilting slave, gleaming with sweat, offered me yet another tray, and I took a glass. I was dripping with perspiration, my legs aching and my throat dried with talking. At this point, I didn't care what was in the glass, provided it was wet.

I changed my opinion instantly upon tasting it; it was lemon juice and barley water, and while it *was* wet, I was much more inclined to pour it down the neck of my gown than to drink it. I edged unobtrusively toward a laburnum bush, intending to pour the drink into it, but was forestalled by the appearance of Gerald Forbes, who stepped out from behind it.

He was as startled to see me as I was to see him; he jerked back, and glanced hastily over his shoulder. I looked in the same direction, and caught sight of Robert Howe and Cornelius Harnett, making off in the opposite direction. Clearly, the three of them had been conferring secretly behind the laburnum bush.

"Mrs. Fraser," he said, with a short bow. "Your servant."

I curtsied in return, with a vague murmur of politeness. I would have slithered past him, but he leaned toward me, preventing my exit.

"I hear that your husband is collecting guns, Mrs. Fraser," he said, his voice at a low and rather unfriendly pitch.

"Oh, really?" I was holding an open fan, as was every other woman there. I waved it languidly before my nose, hiding most of my expression. "Who told you such a thing?"

"One of the gentlemen whom he approached to that end," Forbes said. The lawyer was large and somewhat overweight; the unhealthy shade of red in his cheeks might be due to that, rather than to displeasure. Then again . . .

"If I might impose so far upon your good nature, ma'am, I would suggest that you exert your influence upon him, so as to suggest that such a course is not the wisest?"

"To begin with," I said, taking a deep breath of hot, damp air, "just what course do you think he's embarked upon?"

"An unfortunate one, ma'am," he said. "Putting the best complexion upon the matter, I assume that the guns he seeks are intended to arm his own company of militia, which is legitimate, though disturbing; the desirability of that course would rest upon his later actions. But his relations with the Cherokee are well-known, and there are rumors about that the weapons are destined to end in the hands of the savages, to the end that they may turn upon His Majesty's subjects who presume to offer objection to the tyranny, abuse, and corruption so rife among the officials who govern—if so loose a word may be employed to describe their actions—this colony."

I gave him a long look over the edge of my fan.

"If I hadn't already known you were a lawyer," I remarked, "that speech would have done it. I *think* that you just said that you suspect my husband of wanting to give guns to the Indians, and you don't like that. On the other hand, if he's wanting to arm his own militia, that might be all right—providing that said militia acts according to *your* desires. Am I right?"

A flicker of amusement showed in his deep-set eyes, and he inclined his head toward me in acknowledgment.

"Your perception astounds me, ma'am," he said.

I nodded, and shut the fan.

"Right. And what *are* your desires, may I ask? I won't ask why you think Jamie ought to take heed of them."

He laughed, his heavy face, already flushed with the heat, going a deeper shade of red beneath his neat tie-wig.

"I desire justice, ma'am; the downfall of tyrants and the cause of liberty," he said. "As must any honest man."

. . . freedom alone—which any honest man surrenders only with his life. The line echoed in my head, and must have shown on my face, for he looked keenly at me.

"I esteem your husband deeply, ma'am," he said quietly. "You will tell him what I have said?" He bowed and turned away, not waiting for my nod.

He hadn't guarded his voice when speaking of tyrants and liberty; I saw heads nearby turn, and here and there, men drew together, murmuring as they watched him go.

Distracted, I took a mouthful of lemon shrub, and was then obliged to swallow the nasty stuff. I turned to find Jamie; he was still near Allan MacDonald, but had moved a little aside, and was in private conversation with Major MacDonald.

Things were moving faster than I had thought. I had thought republican sentiment was still a minority in this part of the colony, but for Forbes to speak so openly in a public gathering, it was obviously gaining ground.

I turned back to look after the lawyer, and saw two men confront him, their faces tight with anger and suspicion. I was too far away to hear what was said, but their postures and expressions were eloquent. Words were exchanged, growing in heat, and I glanced toward Jamie; the last time I had attended a barbecue like this at River Run, in the prelude to the War of the Regulation, there had been a fistfight on the lawn, and I rather thought such an occurrence might be about to happen again. Alcohol, heat, and politics made for explosions of temper in any gathering, let alone one composed largely of Highlanders.

Such an explosion might have happened—more men were gathering round Forbes and his two opponents, fists curling in readiness—had the boom of Jocasta's large gong not sounded from the terrace, making everyone look up in startlement.

The Major was standing on an upturned tobacco hogshead, hands raised in the air, beaming at the multitudes, face shining red with heat, beer, and enthusiasm.

"Ceud mile fàilte!" he called, and was greeted by enthusiastic applause. "And we wish a hundred thousand welcomes to our honored guests!" he continued in Gaelic, sweeping a hand toward the MacDonalds, who were now standing side by side near him, nodding and smiling at the applause. From their demeanor, I rather thought they were accustomed to this sort of reception.

A few more introductory remarks—half-drowned in the enthusiastic cheers—and Jamie and Kingsburgh lifted Mrs. MacDonald carefully up onto the barrel, where she swayed a little, but regained her balance, grabbing the heads of both men for stability, and smiling at the laughter of the audience.

She beamed at the crowd, who beamed back, *en masse,* and immediately quieted themselves in order to hear her.

She had a clear, high voice, and was obviously accustomed to speaking in public—a most unusual attribute in a woman of the time. I was too far away to hear every word, but had no trouble picking up the gist of her speech.

After graciously thanking her hosts, the Scottish community who had welcomed her family so warmly and generously, and the guests, she commenced an earnest exhortation against what she called "factionalism," urging her hearers to join in suppressing this dangerous movement, which could not but cause great unrest, threatening the peace and prosperity that so many of them had achieved in this fair land, they having risked everything to attain it.

And she was, I realized with a small shock, exactly right. I'd heard Bree and Roger arguing the point—why any of the Highlanders, who had suffered so much under English rule, should have fought on the English side, as many of them eventually would.

"Because," Roger had said patiently, "they had something to lose, and damn little to gain. And—of all people—they knew exactly what it was like to fight *against* the English. Ye think folk who lived through Cumberland's cleansing of the Highlands, made it to America, and rebuilt their lives from nothing were eager to live through all that *again*?"

"But surely they'll want to fight for freedom," Bree had protested. He looked at her cynically.

"They *have* freedom, a great deal more than they've ever seen in Scotland. They risk losing it in the event of a war—and they know that very well. And then, of course," he'd added, "nearly all of them have sworn an oath of loyalty to the Crown. They'd not break it lightly, surely not for something that looked like one more wild-eyed—and doubtless short-lived—political upheaval. It's like—" His brow had furrowed as he looked for a suitable analogy.

"Like the Black Panthers, or the civil-rights movement. Anyone could see the idealistic point—but a lot of middle-class people found the whole thing threatening or frightening and just wished it would go away, so life could be peaceful."

The trouble, of course, was that life never *was* peaceful—and this particular wild-eyed movement wasn't *going* to go away. I could see Brianna on the far side of the crowd, eyes narrowed in thoughtful speculation as she listened to Flora MacDonald's high, clear voice, talking of the virtues of loyalty.

I heard a low sort of "Hmph!" just to the side, behind me, and turning, saw Gerald Forbes, his heavy features set in disapproval. He had reinforcements now, I saw; three or four other gentlemen stood close beside him, glancing to and fro but trying not to look as though they were. Gauging the mood of the crowd, I thought they were outnumbered by roughly two hundred to one, and the two hundred were growing steadily more entrenched in their opinions as the drink took hold and the speech went on.

Looking away, I caught sight again of Brianna, and realized that she was now looking at Gerald Forbes, too—and he was looking back. Both taller than the people around them, they stared at each other over the heads of the intervening crowd, he with animosity, she with aloofness. She had rejected his suit a few years before, and had done so without tact. Forbes certainly hadn't been in love with her—but he was a man with a fair degree of self-esteem, and not the sort to suffer such a public slight with philosophical resignation.

Brianna turned away, coolly, as though she had taken no notice of him, and spoke to the woman beside her. I heard him grunt again, say something in a low tone to his compatriots—and then the knot of them were leaving, rudely turning their backs on Mrs. MacDonald, who was still speaking.

Gasps and murmurs of indignation followed them, as they shoved their way through the thick-packed crowd, but no one offered to stop them, and the offense of their leaving was drowned by the outburst of prolonged applause that greeted the conclusion of the speech—this accompanied by the starting up of bagpipes, the random firing of pistols into the air, organized cheering of "Hip, hip, huzzay!" led by Major MacDonald, and such a general hullabaloo that no one would have noticed the arrival of an army, let alone the departure of a few disaffected Whigs.

I found Jamie in the shade of Hector's mausoleum, combing out his hair with his fingers, preparatory to retying it.

"That went with a bang, didn't it?" I asked.

"Several of them," he said, keeping a wary eye on one obviously inebriated gentleman in the act of trying to reload his musket. "Watch that man, Sassenach."

"He's too late to shoot Gerald Forbes. Did you see him leave?"

He nodded, deftly knotting the leather thong at his nape.

"He couldna have come much closer to an open declaration, save he'd got up on the barrel next to Fionnaghal."

"And that would have made him an *excellent* target." I squinted at the red-faced gentleman, presently spilling gunpowder on his shoes. "I don't think he has any bullets."

"Oh, well, then." Jamie dismissed him with a wave of the hand. "Major MacDonald's in rare form, no? He told me he's arranged for Mrs. MacDonald to give such speeches here and there about the colony."

"With himself as impresario, I take it." I could just catch the gleam of MacDonald's red coat among the press of well-wishers on the terrace.

"I daresay." Jamie didn't seem pleased at the prospect. In fact, he seemed rather sober, his face shadowed by dark thoughts. His mood would not be improved by hearing about my conversation with Gerald Forbes, but I told him anyway.

"Well, it couldna be helped," he said with a small shrug. "I'd hoped to keep the matter quiet, but wi' things as they are wi' Robin McGillivray, I've no real choice save to ask where I may, though that lets the matter be known. And talked about." He moved again, restless.

"Are ye well, Sassenach?" he asked suddenly, looking at me.

"Yes. But *you* aren't. What is it?"

He smiled faintly.

"Och, it's nothing. Nothing I didna ken already. But it's different, no? Ye think ye're ready, and then ye meet it face to face, and would give anything to have it otherwise."

He looked out at the lawn, lifting his chin to point at the crowd. A sea of tartan flowed across the grass, the ladies' parasols raised against the sun, a field of brightly colored flowers. In the shade of the terrace, a piper played on, the sound of his *piobreachd* a thin, piercing descant to the hum of conversation.

"I kent I should have to stand one day against a good many of them, aye? To fight friends and kin. But then I found myself standing there, wi' Fionnaghal's hand upon my head like a blessing, face to face wi' them all, and watching her words fall upon them, see the resolve growing in them . . . and all of a sudden, it was as though a great blade had come down from heaven between them and me, to cleave us forever apart. The day is coming—and I can not stop it."

He swallowed, and looked down, away from me. I reached out to him, wanting to help, wanting to ease him—and knowing that I couldn't. It was, after all, by my doing that he found himself here, in this small Gethsemane.

Nonetheless, he took my hand, not looking at me, and squeezed it hard, so the bones pressed together.

"Lord, that this cup might pass from me?" I whispered.

He nodded, his gaze still resting on the ground, the fallen petals of the yellow roses. Then he looked at me, with a small smile but such pain in his eyes that I caught my breath, stricken to the heart.

Still, he smiled, and wiping his hand across his forehead, examined his wet fingers.

"Aye, well," he said. "It's only water, not blood. I'll live."

Perhaps you won't, I thought suddenly, appalled. To fight on the winning side was one thing; to survive, quite another.

He saw the look on my face, and released the pressure on my hand, thinking he was hurting me. He was, but not physically.

"But not my will be done, but Thine," he said very softly. "I chose my way when I wed ye, though I kent it not at the time. But I chose, and cannot now turn back, even if I would."

"Would you?" I looked into his eyes as I asked, and read the answer there. He shook his head.

"Would you? For you have chosen, as much as I."

I shook my head, as well, and felt the small relaxation of his body as his eyes met mine, clear now as the brilliant sky. For the space of a heartbeat, we stood alone together in the universe. Then a knot of chattering girls drifted within earshot, and I changed the subject to something safer.

"Have you heard anything about poor Manfred?"

"Poor Manfred, is it?" He gave me a cynical look.

"Well, he may be an immoral young hound, and have

caused any amount of trouble—but that doesn't mean he ought to die for it."

He looked as though he might not be in complete agreement with this sentiment, but let the matter lie, saying merely that he'd asked, but so far without result.

"He'll turn up, though," he assured me. "Likely in the most inconvenient place."

"Oh! Oh! Oh! That I should live to see such a day! I thank ye, sir, thank ye indeed!" It was Mrs. Bug, flushed with heat, beer, and happiness, fanning herself fit to burst. Jamie smiled at her.

"So, were ye able to hear everything, then, *mo chridhe*?"

"Oh, indeed I was, sir!" she assured him fervently. "Every word! Arch found me a lovely place, just by one of they tubs o' wee flowers, where I could hear and not be trampled." She had nearly died of excitement when Jamie had offered to bring her down to the barbecue. Arch was coming, of course, and would go on to do errands in Cross Creek, but Mrs. Bug hadn't been off the Ridge since their arrival several years before.

Despite my disquiet over the profoundly Loyalist atmosphere that surrounded us, her bubbling delight was infectious, and I found myself smiling, Jamie and myself taking it in turns to answer her questions: she hadn't seen black slaves close-to before, and thought them exotically beautiful—did they cost a great deal? And must they be taught to wear clothes and speak properly? For she had heard that Africa was a heathen place where folk went entirely naked and killed one another with spears, like as one would do with a boar, and if one wanted to speak of naked, that statue of the soldier laddie on the lawn was shocking, did we not think? And him wi' not a stitch behind his shield! And whyever was that woman's heid at his feet? And had I looked—her hair was made to look as if 'twere snakes, of all horrid things! And who was Hector Cameron, whose tomb this was?—and made all of white marble, same as the tombs in Holyrood, imagine! Oh, Mrs. Innes's late husband? And when had she married Mr. Duncan, whom she had met, and such a sweet, kind-eyed man as he was, such a shame as he had lost his arm, was that in a battle of some type? And—oh, look! Mrs. MacDonald's husband—

and a fine figure of man he was, too—was going to talk, as well!

Jamie gave the terrace a bleak look. Sure enough, Allan MacDonald was stepping up—merely onto a stool; no doubt the hogshead seemed extreme—and a number of people—far fewer than had attended his wife, but a respectable number—were clustering round attentively.

"Will ye no come and hear him?" Mrs. Bug was already in flight, hovering above the ground like a hummingbird.

"I'll hear well enough from here," Jamie assured her. "You go along then, *a nighean.*"

She bumbled off, buzzing with excitement. Jamie gingerly touched both hands to his ears, testing to be sure they were still attached.

"It was kind of you to bring her," I said, laughing. "The dear old thing probably hasn't had such fun in half a century."

"No," he said, grinning. "She likely—"

He stopped abruptly, frowning as he caught sight of something over my shoulder. I turned to look, but he was already moving past me, and I hurried to catch up.

It was Jocasta, white as milk, and disheveled in a way I had never seen her. She swayed unsteadily in the side doorway, and might have fallen, had Jamie not come up and taken quick hold of her, one arm about her waist to support her.

"Jesus, Auntie. What's amiss?" He spoke quietly, not to draw attention, and was moving her back inside the house even as he spoke.

"Oh, God, oh, merciful God, my head," she whispered, hand spread over her face like a spider, so that her fingers barely touched the skin, cupping her left eye. "My eye."

The linen blindfold that she wore in public was creased and blotched with moisture; tears were leaking out from under it, but she wasn't crying. Lacrimation: one eye was watering terribly. Both eyes were tearing, but much worse on the left; the edge of the linen was soaked, and wetness shone on that cheek.

"I need to look at her eye," I said to Jamie, touching his elbow, and looking round in vain for any of the servants. "Get her to her sitting room." That was closest, and all the guests were either outside or traipsing through the parlor to see the Prince's looking glass.

"No!" It was almost a scream. "No, not there!"

Jamie glanced at me, one brow raised in puzzlement, but spoke soothingly to her.

"Nay, Auntie, it's all right. I'll bring ye to your own chamber. Come, then." He stooped, and lifted her in his arms as though she were a child, her silk skirts falling over his arm with the sound of rushing water.

"Take her; I'll be right there." I'd spotted the slave named Angelina passing through the far end of the hall, and hurried to catch her up. I gave my orders, then rushed back toward the stairs—pausing momentarily to glance into the small sitting room as I did so.

There was no one there, though the presence of scattered punch cups and the strong scent of pipe tobacco indicated that Jocasta had likely been holding court there earlier. Her workbasket stood open, some half-knitted garment dragged out and left to dangle carelessly down the side like a dead rabbit.

Children perhaps, I thought; several balls of thread had been pulled out, too, and lay scattered on the parquet floor, trailing their colors. I hesitated—but instinct was too much for me, and I hastily scooped up the balls of thread and dropped them back into the workbasket. I stuffed the knitting in on top, but jerked my hand back with an exclamation.

A small gash on the side of my thumb was welling blood. I put it in my mouth and sucked hard to apply pressure to the wound; meanwhile, I groped more cautiously in the depths of the basket with my other hand, to see what had cut me.

A knife, small but businesslike. Likely used to cut embroidery threads; there was a tooled-leather sheath for it, loose in the bottom of the basket. I slipped the knife back into its sheath, seized the needle case I'd come for, and closed the folding tabletop of the workbasket before hurrying for the stairs.

Allan MacDonald had finished his brief speech; there was a loud clatter of applause outside, with shouts and whoops of Gaelic approval.

"Bloody Scots," I muttered under my breath. "Don't they *ever* learn?"

But I hadn't time to consider the implications of the MacDonalds' rabble-rousing. By the time I reached the top of the stair, one slave was close behind me, puffing under the weight of my medicine box, and another was at the bottom, starting more cautiously up with a pan of hot water from the kitchen.

Jocasta was bent double in her big chair, moaning, lips pressed into invisibility. Her cap had come off and both hands moved restlessly to and fro through her disordered hair, as though looking helplessly for something to seize. Jamie was stroking her back, murmuring to her in Gaelic; he looked up with obvious relief as I came in.

I had long suspected that the cause of Jocasta's blindness was glaucoma—rising pressure inside the eyeball that if untreated eventually damages the optic nerve. Now I was quite sure of it. More than that, I knew what form of the disease she had; she was plainly having an acute attack of closed-angle glaucoma, the most dangerous type.

There was no treatment for glaucoma now; the condition itself wouldn't be recognized for some time. Even if there had been, it was far too late; her blindness was permanent. There was, however, something I could do about the immediate situation—and I was afraid I'd have to.

"Put some of this to steep," I said to Angelina, grabbing the jar of goldenseal from my box and thrusting it into her hands. "And you"—I turned to the other slave, a man whose name I didn't know—"set the water to boil again, fetch me some clean rags, and put them in the water."

Even as I talked, I'd got out the tiny spirit lamp I carried in my case. The fire had been allowed to burn down on the hearth, but there were still live coals; I bent and lit the wick, then opened the needle case I'd taken from the sitting room and abstracted the largest needle in it, a three-inch length of steel, used for mending carpets.

"You aren't . . ." Jamie began, then broke off, swallowing.

"I have to," I said briefly. "There's nothing else. Hold her hands."

He was nearly as pale as Jocasta, but he nodded and took

hold of the clutching fingers, pulling her hands gently away from her head.

I lifted away the linen bandage. The left eye bulged noticeably beneath its lid, vividly bloodshot. Tears welled up round it and overflowed in a constant stream. I could *feel* the pressure inside the eyeball, even without touching it, and clenched my teeth in revulsion.

No help for it. With a quick prayer to Saint Clare—who was, after all, patroness of sore eyes, as well as my own patron saint—I ran the needle through the flame of the lamp, poured pure alcohol onto a rag, and wiped the soot from the needle.

Swallowing a sudden excess of saliva, I spread the eyelids of the affected eye apart with one hand, commended my soul to God, and shoved the needle hard into the sclera of the eye, near the edge of the iris.

There was a cough and a splattering on the floor nearby, and the stink of vomit, but I had no attention to spare. I withdrew the needle carefully, though as fast as I could. Jocasta had stiffened abruptly, frozen stiff, hands clawed over Jamie's. She didn't move at all, but made small, shocked panting sounds, as though afraid to move enough even to breathe.

There was a trickle of fluid from the eye, vitreous humor, faintly cloudy, just thick enough to be distinguishable as it flowed sluggishly across the wet surface of the sclera. I was still holding the eyelids apart; I plucked a rag from the goldenseal tea with my free hand, squeezed out the excess liquid, careless of where it went, and touched it gently to her face. Jocasta gasped at the touch of the warmth on her skin, pulled her hands free, and grasped at it.

I let go then, and allowed her to seize the warm rag, pressing it against her closed left eye, the heat of it some relief.

Light feet pounded up the stairs again, and down the hall; Angelina, panting, a handful of salt clutched to her bosom, a spoon in her other hand. I brushed the salt from her damp palm into the pan of warm water, and set her to stir it while it dissolved.

"Did you bring laudanum?" I asked her quietly. Jocasta was lying back in her chair, eyes closed—but rigid as a statue, her eyelids squeezing tight, fists clenched in knots on her knees.

"I couldna find the laudanum, missus," Angelina murmured to me, with a frightened glance at Jocasta. "I dinna ken who could be takin' it—hain't nobody got the key but Mr. Ulysses and Miz Cameron herself."

"Ulysses let you into the simples closet, then—so he knows that Mrs. Cameron is ill?"

She nodded vigorously, setting the ribbon on her cap aflutter.

"Oh, yes, missus! He be bleezin', if he find out and I hain't told him. He say come fetch him quick, she want him—otherwise, I tell Miz Cameron she hain't to worry none, he take care every single thing."

Jocasta let out a long sigh at this, her clenched fists relaxing a little.

"God bless the man," she murmured, eyes closed. "He *will* take care of everything. I should be lost without him. Lost."

Her white hair was soaked at the temples, and sweat dripped from the ends of the tendrils that lay over her shoulder, making spots on the dark blue silk of her gown.

Angelina unlaced Jocasta's gown and stays and got them off. Then I had Jamie lay her down on the bed in her shift, with a thick layer of towels tucked round her head. I filled one of my rattlesnake syringes with the warm salt water, and with Jamie gingerly holding the lids of her eye apart, I was able to gently irrigate the eye, in hopes of perhaps preventing infection to the puncture wound. The wound itself showed as a tiny scarlet spot on the sclera, a small conjunctival bleb above it. Jamie couldn't look at it without blinking, I saw, and smiled at him.

"She'll be all right," I said. "You can go, if you like."

Jamie nodded, turning to go, but Jocasta's hand shot out to stop him.

"No, be staying, *a chuisle*—if ye will." This last was strictly for form's sake; she had him clutched by the sleeve, hard enough to turn her fingers white.

"Aye, Auntie, of course," he said mildly, and put his hand over hers, squeezing in reassurance. Still, she didn't let go until he had sat down beside her.

"Who else is there?" she asked, turning her head fretfully from side to side, trying to hear the telltale sounds of breathing and movement that would inform her. "Have the slaves gone?"

"Yes, they've gone back to help with the serving," I told her. "It's only me and Jamie left."

She closed her eyes and drew a deep, shuddering breath, only then beginning to relax a little.

"Good. I must tell ye a thing, Nephew, and no one else must hear. Niece"—she lifted a long white hand toward me—"go and be seeing as we're truly alone."

I went obediently to look out into the hall. No one was visible, though there were voices coming from a room down the hall—laughter, and tremendous rustlings and thumpings, as young women chattered and rearranged their hair and clothing. I pulled my head back in and closed the door, and the sounds from the rest of the house receded at once, muffled into a distant rumble.

"What is it, then, Auntie?" Jamie was still holding her hand, one big thumb gently stroking the back of it, over and over, in the soothing rhythm I'd seen him use on skittish animals. It was less effective on his aunt than on the average horse or dog, though.

"It was him. He's here!"

"Who's here, Auntie?"

"I don't know!" Her eyes rolled desperately to and fro, as though in a vain attempt to see through not only darkness, but walls, as well.

Jamie raised his brows at me, but he could see as well as I that she wasn't raving, incoherent as she sounded. She realized what she sounded like; I could see the effort in her face as she pulled herself together.

"He's come for the gold," she said, lowering her voice. "The Frenchman's gold."

"Oh, aye?" Jamie said cautiously. He darted a glance at me, one eyebrow raised, but I shook my head. She wasn't having hallucinations.

Jocasta sighed with impatience and shook her head, then stopped abruptly, with a muffled "Och!" of pain, putting both hands to her head as though to keep it on her shoulders.

She breathed deeply for a moment or two, her lips pressed tight together. Then she slowly lowered her hands.

"It started last night," she said. "The pain in my eye."

She'd waked in the night to a throbbing in her eye, a dull pain that spread slowly to the side of her head.

"It's come before, ken," she explained. She had pushed herself up to a sitting position now, and was beginning to look a little better, though she still held the warm cloth to her eye. "It began when I started to lose my sight. Sometimes it would be one eye, sometimes both. But I kent what was coming."

But Jocasta MacKenzie Cameron Innes was not a woman to allow mere bodily indisposition to interfere with her plans, let alone interrupt what promised to be the most scintillating social affair in Cross Creek's history.

"I was that disgusted," she said. "And here Miss Flora MacDonald coming!"

But the arrangements had all been made; the barbecued carcasses were roasting in their pits, hogsheads of ale and beer stood ready by the stables, and the air was full of the fragrance of hot bread and beans from the cookhouse. The slaves were well-trained, and she had full faith that Ulysses would manage everything. All she must do, she'd thought, was to stay on her feet.

"I didna want to take opium or laudanum," she explained. "Or I'd fall asleep for sure. So I made do wi' the whisky."

She was a tall woman, and thoroughly accustomed to an intake of liquor that would have felled a modern man. By the time the MacDonalds arrived, she'd had the better part of a bottle—but the pain was getting worse.

"And then my eye began to water so fierce, everyone would ha' seen something was wrong, and I didna want *that.* So I came into my sitting room; I'd taken care to put a wee bottle of laudanum in my workbasket, in case the whisky should be not enough.

"Folk were swarming thick as lice outside, trying to catch a glimpse or a word with Miss MacDonald, but the sitting room was deserted, so far as I could tell, what wi' my head pounding and my eye fit to explode." She said this last quite casually, but I saw Jamie flinch, the memory of what I'd done with the needle obviously still fresh. He swallowed and wiped his knuckles hard across his mouth.

Jocasta had quickly abstracted the bottle of laudanum, swallowed a few gulps, and then sat for a moment, waiting for it to take effect.

"I dinna ken if ye've ever had the stuff, Nephew, but it gives ye an odd feeling, as though ye might be starting to dissolve at the edges. Take a drop too much, and ye begin to see things that aren't there—blind or not—and hear them, too."

Between the effects of laudanum and liquor and the noise of the crowd outside, she hadn't noticed footsteps, and when the voice spoke near her, she'd thought for a moment that it was a hallucination.

"*'So here ye are, lass,'* he said," she quoted, and her face, already pale, blanched further at the memory. "*'Remember me, do ye?'*"

"I take it ye did, Aunt?" Jamie asked dryly.

"I did," she replied just as dryly. "I'd heard that voice twice before. Once at the Gathering where your daughter was wed—and once more than twenty years ago, in an inn near Coigach, in Scotland."

She lowered the wet cloth from her face and put it unerringly back into the bowl of warm water. Her eyes were red and swollen, raw against the pale skin, and looking terribly vulnerable in their blindness—but she had command of herself once more.

"Aye, I did ken him," she repeated.

She had recognized the voice at once as one known—but for a moment, could not place it. Then realization had struck her, and she had clutched the arm of her chair for support.

"Who are ye?" she'd demanded, with what force she could summon. Her heart was pounding in time to the throbbing in her head and eye, and her senses swimming in whisky and laudanum. Perhaps it was the laudanum that seemed to transform the sound of the crowd outside into the sound of a nearby sea, the noise of a slave's footsteps in the hall to the thump of the landlord's clogs on the stairs of the inn.

"I was there. Truly there." Despite the sweat that still ran down her face, I saw gooseflesh pebble the pale skin of her shoulders. "In the inn at Coigach. I smelt the sea, and I heard the men—Hector and Dougal—I could *hear* them! Arguing together, somewhere behind me. And the man wi' the mask—I could *see* him," she said, and a ripple went up the back of my own neck as she turned her blind eyes toward me. She spoke with such conviction that for an instant, it seemed she *did* see.

"Standing at the foot of the stair, just as he'd been twenty-five years ago, a knife in his hand and his eyes upon me through the holes in his mask."

And, "Ye ken well enough who I am, lass," he'd said, and she had seemed to see his smile, though dimly she had known she only heard it in his voice; she'd never seen his face, even when she had her sight.

She was sitting up, half doubled over, arms crossed over her breast as though in self-defense and her white hair wild and tangled down her back.

"He's come back," she said, and shook with a sudden convulsive shudder. "He's come for the gold—and when he finds it, he will kill me."

Jamie laid a hand on her arm, in an attempt to calm her.

"No one will kill ye while I'm here, Aunt," he said. "So this man came to ye in your sitting room, and ye kent him from his voice. What else did he say to ye?"

She was still shivering, but not so badly. I thought it was as much reaction to massive amounts of laudanum and whisky as from fear.

She shook her head in the effort of recollection.

"He said—he said he had come to take the gold to its rightful owner. That we'd held it in trust, and while he didna grudge me what we'd spent of it, Hector and me—it wasna mine, had never been mine. I should tell him where it was, and he would see to the rest. And then he put his hand on me." She ceased clutching herself, and held out one arm toward Jamie. "On my wrist. D'ye see the marks there? D'ye see them, Nephew?" She sounded anxious, and it occurred to me suddenly that she might doubt the existence of the visitor herself.

"Aye, Auntie," Jamie said softly, touching her wrist. "There are marks."

There were; three purplish smudges, small ovals where fingers had gripped.

"He squeezed, and then twisted my wrist so hard I thought it had snapped. Then he let go, but he didna step back. He stayed over me, and I could feel the heat of his breath and the stink of tobacco on my face."

I had hold of her other wrist, feeling the pulse beat there. It was strong and rapid, but every once in a while would skip a beat. Hardly surprising. I did wonder how often she took laudanum—and how much.

"So I reached down into my workbasket, took my wee knife from its sheath, and went for his balls," she concluded.

Taken by surprise, Jamie laughed.

"Did ye get him?"

"Yes, she did," I said, before Jocasta could answer. "I saw dried blood on the knife."

"Well, that will teach him to terrorize a helpless blind woman, won't it?" Jamie patted her hand. "Ye did well, Auntie. Did he go, then?"

"He did." The recounting of her success had steadied her a lot; she pulled her hand from my grip, in order to push herself up straighter against the pillows. She pulled away the towel still draped around her neck, and dropped it on the floor with a brief grimace of distaste.

Seeing that she was plainly feeling better, Jamie glanced at me, then rose to his feet.

"I'll go and see is anyone limping about the place, then." At the door, he paused, though, turning back to Jocasta.

"Auntie. Ye said ye'd met this fellow *twice* before? At the inn in Coigach where the men brought the gold ashore—and at the Gathering four years ago?"

She nodded, brushing back the damp hair from her face.

"I did. 'Twas on the last day. He came into my tent, while I was alone. I kent someone was there, though he didna speak at first, and I asked who was it? He gave a bit of a laugh, then, and said, 'It's true what they said, then—you're blind entirely?'"

She had stood up, facing the invisible visitor, recognizing the voice, but not quite knowing yet why.

"'So ye dinna ken me, Mrs. Cameron? I was a friend to your husband—though it's been a good many years since last we met. On the coast of Scotland—on a moonlicht nicht.'"

She licked dry lips at the memory.

"So then it came to me, all on the sudden. And I said, 'Blind I may be, but I ken ye well, sir. What d'ye want?' But he was gone. And the next instant, I heard Phaedre and Ulysses talking as they came toward the tent; he'd seen them, and fled away. I asked them, but they'd been ta'en up wi' their arguing, and hadna seen him leave. I kept someone by me all the time, then, until we left—and he didna come near me again. Until now."

Jamie frowned and rubbed a knuckle slowly down the long, straight bridge of his nose.

"Why did ye not tell me then?"

A trace of humor touched her ravaged face, and she wrapped her fingers round her injured wrist.

"I thought I was imagining things."

PHAEDRE HAD found the bottle of laudanum where Jocasta had dropped it, under her chair in the sitting room. Likewise, a trail of tiny blood spots that I had missed in my hurry. These disappeared before reaching the door, though; whatever wound Jocasta had inflicted on the intruder had been minor.

Duncan, summoned discreetly, had hurried in to comfort Jocasta—only to be sent directly out again, with instructions to see to the guests; neither injury nor illness was going to mar such an occasion!

Ulysses met with a slightly more cordial reception. In fact, Jocasta sent for him. Peering into her room to check on her, I found him sitting by the bed, holding his mistress's hand, with such an expression of gentleness on his usually impassive face that I was quite moved by it, and stepped quietly back into the hall, not to disturb them. He saw me, though, and nodded.

They were talking in low voices, his head in its stiff white wig bending toward hers. He seemed to be arguing with her, in a most respectful fashion; she shook her head, and gave a small cry of pain. His hand tightened on hers, and I saw that he had taken off his white gloves; her hand lay long and frail, pallid in his powerful dark grasp.

She breathed deeply, steadying herself. Then she said something definite, squeezed his hand, and lay back. He rose, and stood for a moment beside the bed, looking down at her. Then he drew himself up, and taking his gloves from his pocket, came out into the hall.

"If you will fetch your husband, Mrs. Fraser?" he said, low-voiced. "My mistress wishes me to tell him something."

THE PARTY WAS still in full swing, but had shifted to a lower, digestive sort of gear. People greeted Jamie or me as we followed Ulysses into the house, but no one stopped us.

He led us downstairs to his butler's pantry, a tiny room that lay off the winter kitchen, its shelves crammed with silver ornaments, bottles of polish, vinegar, blacking, and bluing, a housewife with needles, pins, and threads, small tools for mending, and what looked like a substantial private stock of brandy, whisky, and assorted cordials.

He removed these from their shelf, and reaching back into the empty space where they had stood, pressed upon the wood of the wall with both white-gloved hands. Something clicked, and a small panel slid aside with a soft rasping sound.

He stood aside, silently inviting Jamie to look. Jamie raised one eyebrow and leaned forward, peering into the recess. It was dark and shadowy in the butler's pantry, with only a dim light filtering in from the high basement windows that ran around the top of the kitchen walls.

"It's empty," he said.

"Yes, sir. It should not be." Ulysses's voice was low and respectful, but firm.

"What *was* there?" I asked, glancing out of the pantry to be sure we were not overheard. The kitchen looked as though a bomb had gone off in it, but only a scullion was there, a half-witted boy who was washing pots, singing softly to himself.

"Part of an ingot of gold," Ulysses replied softly.

The French gold Hector Cameron had brought away from

Scotland, ten thousand pounds in bullion, cast in ingots and marked with the royal fleur-de-lis, was the foundation of River Run's wealth. But it would not do, of course, for that fact to be known. First Hector, and then, after Hector's death, Ulysses, had taken one of the gold bars and scraped bits of the soft yellow metal into a small, anonymous heap. This could then be taken to the river warehouses—or for additional safety, sometimes as far as the coastal towns of Edenton, Wilmington, or New Bern—and there carefully changed, in small amounts that would cause no comment, into cash or warehouse certificates, which could safely be used anywhere.

"There was about half of the ingot left," Ulysses said, nodding toward the cavity in the wall. "I found it gone a few months ago. Since then, of course, I have contrived a new hiding place."

Jamie looked into the empty cavity, then turned to Ulysses.

"The rest?"

"Safe enough, last time I checked, sir." The bulk of the gold was concealed inside Hector Cameron's mausoleum, hidden in a coffin and guarded, presumably, by his spirit. One or two of the slaves besides Ulysses might know about it, but the very lively fear of ghosts was enough to keep everyone away. I remembered the line of salt spread on the ground in front of the mausoleum, and shivered a little, in spite of the stifling heat in the basement.

"I could not, of course, make shift to look today," the butler added.

"No, of course not. Duncan knows?" Jamie nodded toward the recess, and Ulysses nodded.

"The thief might have been anyone. So many people come to this house. . . . " The butler's massive shoulders moved in a small shrug. "But now that this man from the sea has come again—it puts a different face upon the matter, does it not, sir?"

"Aye, it does." Jamie contemplated the matter for a moment, tapping two fingers softly against his leg.

"Well, then. Ye'll need to stay for a bit, Sassenach, will ye not? To look after my aunt's eye?"

I nodded. Provided no infection resulted from my crude intervention, there was little or nothing I could do for the eye itself. But it should be watched, kept clean and irrigated, until I could be sure it was healed.

"We'll stay, then, for a bit," he said, turning to Ulysses. "I'll send the Bugs back to the Ridge, to mind things and see to the haying. We'll stay, and watch."

THE HOUSE WAS full of guests, but I slept in Jocasta's dressing room, so that I might keep an eye on her. The easing of pressure in her eye had relieved the excruciating pain, and she had fallen soundly asleep, her vital signs reassuring enough that I felt I could sleep, too.

Knowing I had a patient, though, I slept lightly, waking at intervals to tiptoe into her room. Duncan was sleeping on a pallet at the foot of her bed, dead to the world from the exhaustions of the day. I could hear his heavy breathing, as I lit a taper from the hearth and came to stand by the bed.

Jocasta was still soundly asleep, lying on her back, arms crossed gracefully over the coverlet and her head thrown back, sternly long-nosed and aristocratic as the tomb figures in the chapel of St. Denys. All she wanted was a crown, and a small dog of some kind crouched at her feet.

I smiled at the thought, thinking as I did how odd it was: Jamie slept in exactly that fashion, lying flat on his back, hands crossed, straight as an arrow. Brianna didn't; she was a wild sleeper, and had been from a child. Like me.

The thought gave me a small, unexpected feeling of pleasure. I knew I had given her some parts of me, of course, but she resembled Jamie so strongly, it was always something of a surprise to notice one.

I blew out the taper, but didn't at once return to bed. I had taken Phaedre's cot in the dressing room, but it was a hot, airless little space. The hot day and the consumption of alcohol had left me cotton-mouthed, with a vague headache; I picked up the carafe from Jocasta's bedside, but it was empty.

No need to relight the taper; one of the sconces in the hallway was still burning, and a dim glow outlined the door. I pushed it open quietly and looked out. The corridor was lined with bodies—servants sleeping by the doors of the bedrooms—and the air throbbed gently with the snoring and heavy breathing of a great many people sunk in slumber of varying degrees.

At the end of the corridor, though, one pale figure stood upright, looking out through the tall casement window toward the river.

She must have heard me, but didn't turn around. I came to stand beside her, looking out. Phaedre was undressed to her shift, her hair free of its cloth and falling in a soft thick mass around her shoulders. Rare for a slave to have such hair, I thought; most women kept their hair very short under turban or headcloth, lacking both time and tools for dressing it. But Phaedre was a body servant; she would have some leisure—and a comb, at least.

"Would you like your bed back?" I asked, low-voiced. "I'll be up for a while—and can sleep on the divan."

She glanced at me, and shook her head.

"Oh, no, ma'am," she said softly. "Thankee kindly; I ain't sleepy." She saw the carafe I carried, and reached for it. "I fetch you some water, ma'am?"

"No, no, I'll do it. I'd like the air." Still, I stood beside her, looking out.

It was a beautiful night, thick with stars that hung low and bright over the river, a faint silver thread that wound its way through the dark. There was a moon, a slender sickle, riding low on its way below the curve of the earth, and one or two small campfires burned in the trees beside the river.

The window was open, and bugs were swarming in; a small cloud of them danced around the candle in the sconce behind us, and tiny winged things brushed my face and arms. Crickets sang, so many of them that their song was a high, constant sound, like a bow drawn over violin strings.

Phaedre moved to shut it—to sleep with a window open was considered most unhealthy, and likely *was,* given the various mosquito-borne diseases in this swampish atmosphere.

"I thought I heard something. Out there," she said, nodding toward the dark below.

"Oh? Probably my husband," I said. "Or Ulysses."

"Ulysses?" she said, looking startled.

Jamie, Ian, and Ulysses had organized a system of patrol,

and were doubtless out somewhere in the night, gliding round the house and keeping an eye on Hector's mausoleum, just in case. Knowing nothing of the disappearing gold nor Jocasta's mysterious visitor, though, Phaedre wouldn't be aware of the increased vigilance, save in the indirect way in which slaves always knew things—the instinct that had doubtless roused her to look out the window.

"They're just keeping an eye out," I said, as reassuringly as I could. "With so many people here, you know." The MacDonalds had gone to Farquard Campbell's plantation to spend the night, and a goodly number of guests had gone with them, but there were still a lot of people on the premises.

She nodded, but looked troubled.

"It just feel like something ain't right," she said. "Don't know what 'tis."

"Your mistress's eye—" I began, but she shook her head.

"No. No. I don't know, but there something in the air; I be feelin' it. Not just tonight, I don't mean—something goin' on. Something coming." She looked at me, helpless to express what she meant, but her mood communicated itself to me.

It might be in part simply the heightened emotions of the oncoming conflict. One could in fact feel that in the air. But there might be something else, too—something subterranean, barely sensed, but there, like the dim form of a sea serpent, glimpsed for only a moment, then gone, and so put down to legend.

"My grannie, she taken from Africa," Phaedre said softly, staring out at the night. "She talk to the bones. Say they tell her when bad things comin'."

"Really?" In such an atmosphere, quiet save the night sounds, so many souls adrift around us, there seemed nothing unreal about such a statement. "Did she teach you to . . . talk to bones?"

She shook her head, but the corner of her mouth tucked in, a small, secret expression, and I thought she might know more about it than she was willing to say.

One unwelcome thought had occurred to me. I didn't see how Stephen Bonnet could be connected to present events—

surely he was not the man who had spoken to Jocasta out of her past, and just as surely, stealthy theft was not his style. But he did have some reason to believe there might be gold somewhere at River Run—and from what Roger had told us of Phaedre's encounter with the big Irishman in Cross Creek . . .

"The Irishman you met, when you were out with Jemmy," I said, changing my grip on the slick surface of the carafe, "have you ever seen him again?"

She looked surprised at that; clearly Bonnet was the farthest thing from her mind.

"No, ma'am," she said. "Ain't seen him again, ever." She thought for a moment, big eyes hooded. She was the color of strong coffee with a dash of cream, and her hair—there had been a white man in her family tree at some time, I thought.

"No, ma'am," she repeated softly, and turned her troubled gaze back to the quiet night and the sinking moon. "All I know—something ain't right."

Out by the stables, a rooster began to crow, the sound out of place and eerie in the dark.

55

WENDIGO

August 20, 1774

THE LIGHT IN THE morning room was perfect.

"We began with this room," Jocasta had told her great-niece, raising her face to the sun that poured through the open double doors to the terrace, lids closed over her blind eyes. "I wanted a room to paint in, and chose this spot, where the light would come in, bright as crystal in the morning, like still water in the afternoon. And then we built the house around it." The old woman's hands, still long-fingered and strong, touched the easel, the pigment pots, the brushes, with affectionate regret, as she might caress the statue of a long-dead lover—a passion recalled, but accepted as forever gone.

And Brianna, sketching block and pencil in hand, had drawn as quickly, as covertly as she could, to catch that fleeting expression of grief outlived.

That sketch lay with the others in the bottom of her box, against the day when she might try it in more finished form, try to catch that merciless light, and the deep-carved lines of her aunt's face, strong bones stark in the sun she could not see.

For now, though, the painting at hand was a matter of business, rather than love or art. Nothing suspicious had happened since Flora MacDonald's barbecue, but her parents meant to stay for a little longer, just in case. With Roger still in Charlotte—he had written to her; the letter was secreted in the bottom of her box, with the private sketches—there was no reason why she shouldn't stay, too. Hearing of her continued presence, two or three of Jocasta's acquaintances, wealthy planters, had commissioned portraits of themselves or their families; a welcome source of income.

"I will never understand how ye do that," Ian said, shaking his head at the canvas on her easel. "It's wonderful."

In all honesty, she didn't understand how she did it, either; it didn't seem necessary. She'd said as much in answer to similar compliments before, though, and realized that such an answer generally struck the hearer either as false modesty or as condescension.

She smiled at him, instead, letting the glow of pleasure she felt show in her face.

"When I was little, my father would take me walking on the Common, and we'd see an old man there often, painting with an easel. I used to make Daddy stop so I could watch, and he and the old man would chat. I mostly just stared, but once I got up the nerve to ask him how he did that and he looked down at me and smiled, and said, 'The only trick, sweetie, is to see what you're looking at.'"

Ian looked from her to the picture, then back, as though comparing the portrait with the hand that had made it.

"Your father," he said, interested. He lowered his voice, glancing toward the door into the hallway. There were voices, but not close. "Ye dinna mean Uncle Jamie?"

"No." She felt the familiar small ache at the thought of her first father, but put it aside. She didn't mind telling Ian about him—but not here, with slaves all over the place and a constant flow of visitors who might pop in at any moment.

"Look." She glanced over her shoulder to be sure no one was near, but the slaves were talking loudly in the foyer, arguing over a misplaced boot scraper. She lifted the cover of the small compartment that held spare brushes, and reached under the strip of felt that lined it.

"What do you think?" She held the pair of miniatures out for his inspection, one in either palm.

The look of expectation on his face changed to outright fascination, and he reached slowly for one of the tiny paintings.

"I will be damned," he said. It was the one of her mother, her hair long and curling loose on bare shoulders, the small firm chin raised with an authority that belied the generous curve of the mouth above.

"The eyes—I don't think those are quite right," she said, peering into his hand. "Working so small . . . I couldn't get the color, exactly. Da's were much easier."

Blues just *were* easier. A tiny dab of cobalt, highlighted with white and that faint green shadow that intensified the blue while vanishing itself . . . well, and that was Da, too. Strong, vivid, and straightforward.

To get a brown with true depth and subtlety, though, let alone something that even approximated the smoky topaz of her mother's eyes—always clear, but changing like the light on a peat-brown trout stream—that needed more underpainting than was really possible in the tiny space of a miniature. She'd have to try again sometime, with a larger portrait.

"Are they like, do you think?"

"They're wonderful." Ian looked from one to the other, then he put the portrait of Claire gently back into its place. "Have your parents seen them yet?"

"No. I wanted to be sure they were right, before I showed them to anybody. But if they are—I'm thinking I can show them to the people who come to sit, and maybe get commissions for more miniatures. Those I could work on at home, on the Ridge; all I'd need is my paint box and the little ivory discs. I could do the painting from the sketches; I wouldn't need the sitter to keep coming."

She made a brief, explanatory gesture toward the large canvas she was working on, which showed Farquard Campbell, looking rather like a stuffed ferret in his best suit, surrounded by numerous children and grandchildren, most of these mere whitish blobs at the moment. Her strategy was to have their mothers drag the small ones in one at a time, to have each child's limbs and features hastily sketched into the appropriate blob before natural wriggliness or tantrums obtruded.

Ian glanced at the canvas, but his attention returned to the miniatures of her parents. He stood looking at them, a slight smile on his long, half-homely face. Then, feeling her eyes on him, he glanced up, alarmed.

"Oh, no, ye don't!"

"Oh, come on, Ian, let me just sketch you," she coaxed. "It won't hurt, you know."

"Och, that's what you think," he countered, backing away as though the pencil she had taken up might be a weapon. "The Kahnyen'kehaka think to have a likeness of someone gives ye power over them. That's why the medicine society wear false faces—so the demons causing the illness willna have their true likeness and willna ken who to hurt, aye?"

This was said in such a serious tone that she squinted at him, to see whether he was joking. He didn't seem to be.

"Mmm. Ian—Mama explained to you about germs, didn't she?"

"Aye, she did, o' course," he said, in a tone exhibiting no conviction at all. "She showed me things swimmin' about, and said they were livin' in my teeth!" His face showed momentary repugnance at the notion, but he left the matter to return to the subject at hand.

"There was a traveling Frenchman came to the village once, a natural philosopher—he'd drawings he'd made of birds and animals, and that astonished them—but then he made the mistake of offering to make a likeness of the war chief's wife. I barely got him out in one piece."

"But you aren't a Mohawk," she said patiently, "and if you were—you're not afraid of me having power over you, are you?"

He turned his head and gave her a sudden queer look that went through her like a knife through butter.

"No," he said. "No, of course not." But his voice had little more conviction than when discussing germs.

Still, he moved to the stool she kept for sitters, set in good light from the open doors that led to the terrace, and sat down, chin lifted and jaw set like one about to be heroically executed.

Suppressing a smile, she took up the sketching block and drew as quickly as she could, lest he change his mind. He was a difficult subject; his features lacked the solid, clear-cut bone structure that both her parents and Roger had. And yet it was in no way a soft face, even discounting the stippled tattoos that curved from the bridge of his nose across his cheeks.

Young and fresh, and yet the firmness of his mouth—it was slightly crooked, she saw with interest; how had she never noticed that before?—belonged to someone much older, bracketed by lines that would cut much deeper with age, but were already firmly entrenched.

The eyes . . . she despaired of getting those right. Large and hazel, they were his one claim to beauty, and yet, beautiful was the last thing you would call them. Like most eyes, they weren't one color at all, but many—the colors of autumn, dark wet earth and crackling oak leaves, and the touch of setting sun on dry grass.

The color was a challenge, but one she could meet. The expression, though—it changed in an instant from something so guilelessly amiable as to seem almost half-witted to something you wouldn't want to meet in a dark alley.

The expression at present was somewhere between these two extremes, but shifted suddenly toward the latter as his attention focused on the open doors behind her, and the terrace beyond.

She glanced over her shoulder, startled. Someone was there; she saw the edge of his—or her—shadow, but the person who threw it was keeping out of sight. Whoever it was began to whistle, a tentative, breathy sound.

For an instant, everything was normal. Then the world shifted. The intruder was whistling "Yellow Submarine."

All the blood rushed from her head, and she swayed, grabbing the edge of an occasional table to keep from falling. Dimly, she sensed Ian rising like a cat from his stool, seizing one of her palette knives, and sliding noiselessly out of the room into the hallway.

Her hands had gone cold and numb; so had her lips. She tried to whistle a phrase in reply, but nothing but a little air emerged. Straightening up, she took hold of herself, and sang the last few words instead. She could barely manage the tune, but there was no doubt of the words.

Dead silence from the terrace; the whistling had stopped.

"Who are you?" she said clearly. "Come in."

The shadow lengthened slowly, showing a head like a lion's, light shining through the curls, glowing on the terrace stones. The head itself poked cautiously into sight around the corner of the door. It was an Indian, she saw, with astonishment, though his dress was mostly European—and ragged—bar a wampum necklet. He was lean and dirty, with close-set eyes, which were fixed on her with eagerness and something like avidity.

"You alone, man?" he asked, in a hoarse whisper. "Thought I heard voices."

"You can see I am. Who on earth are you?"

"Ah . . . Wendigo. Wendigo Donner. Your name's Fraser, right?" He had edged all the way into the room now, though still glancing warily from side to side.

"My maiden name, yes. Are you—" She stopped, not sure how to ask.

"Yeah," he said softly, looking her up and down in a casual way that no man of the eighteenth century would have employed to a lady. "So are you, aren't you? You're her daughter, you have to be." He spoke with a certain intensity, moving closer.

She didn't think he meant her harm; he was just very interested. Ian didn't wait to see, though; there was a brief darkening of the light from the door, and then he had

Donner from behind, the Indian's squawk of alarm choked off by the arm across his throat, the point of the palette knife jabbing him under the ear.

"Who are ye, arsebite, and what d'ye want?" Ian demanded, tightening the arm across Donner's throat. The Indian's eyes bulged, and he made small mewling noises.

"How do you expect him to answer you, if you're choking him?" This appeal to reason caused Ian to relax his grip, albeit reluctantly. Donner coughed, rubbing his throat ostentatiously, and shot Ian a resentful look.

"No need for that, man, I wasn't doin' nothin' to her." Donner's eyes went from her to Ian and back. He jerked his head toward Ian. "Is he . . . ?"

"No, but he knows. Sit down. You met my mother when she—when she was kidnapped, didn't you?"

Ian's feathery brows shot up at this, and he took a firmer grip on the palette knife, which was flexible but had a definite point.

"Yeah." Donner lowered himself gingerly onto the stool, keeping a wary eye on Ian. "Man, they nearly got me. Your mother, she told me her old man was gnarly and I didn't want to be there when he showed up, but I didn't believe her. Almost, I didn't. But when I heard those drums, man, I bugged out, and a damn good thing I did, too." He swallowed, looking pale. "I went back, in the morning. Jeez, man."

Ian said something under his breath, in what Brianna thought was Mohawk. It sounded unfriendly in the extreme, and Donner evidently discerned enough of the meaning to make him scoot his stool a little farther away, hunching his shoulders.

"Hey, man, I didn't do nothin' to her, okay?" He looked pleadingly at Brianna. "I didn't! I was gonna help her get away—ask her, she'll tell you! Only Fraser and his guys showed up before I could. Christ, why would I hurt her? She's the first one I found back here—I needed her!"

"The first one?" Ian said, frowning. "The first—"

"The first . . . traveler, he means," Brianna said. Her heart was beating fast. "What did you need her for?"

"To tell me how to get—back." He swallowed again, his hand going to the wampum ornament around his neck.

"You—did you come through, or were you born here? I'm figuring you came through," he added, not waiting for an answer. "They don't grow 'em as big as you now. Little bitty girls. Me, I like a big woman." He smiled, in what he plainly intended to be an ingratiating manner.

"I came," Brianna said shortly. "What the hell are you doing here?"

"Trying to get close enough to talk to your mother." He glanced uneasily over his shoulder; there were slaves in the kitchen garden, their voices audible. "I hid out with the Cherokee for a while, then I figured to come down and talk to her at Fraser's Ridge when it was safe, but the old lady there told me you were all down here. Heck of a long way to walk," he added, looking vaguely resentful.

"But then that big black dude ran me off twice, when I tried to get in before. Guess I didn't meet the dress code." His face flickered, not quite managing a smile.

"I been sneaking around for the last three days, trying to catch a glimpse of her, find her alone outside. But I saw her talking to you, out on the terrace, and heard you call her Mama. Seeing how big you are, I figured you must be . . . well, I figured if you didn't pick up on the song, no harm done, huh?"

"So ye want to go back where ye came from, do ye?" Ian asked. Plainly he thought this was an excellent idea.

"Oh, yeah," Donner said fervently. "*Oh,* yeah!"

"Where did you come through?" Brianna asked. The shock of his appearance was fading, subsumed by curiosity. "In Scotland?"

"No, is that where you did it?" he asked eagerly. Scarcely waiting for her nod, he went on. "Your mother said she came and then went back and came again. Can you-all go back and forth, like, you know, a revolving door?"

Brianna shook her head violently, shuddering in recollection.

"God, no. It's horrible, and it's so dangerous, even with a gemstone."

"Gemstone?" He pounced on that. "You gotta have a gemstone to do it?"

"Not absolutely, but it seems to be some protection. And it

may be that there's some way to use gemstones to—to steer, sort of, but we don't really know about that." She hesitated, wanting to ask more questions, but wanting still more to fetch Claire. "Ian—could you go get Mama? I think she's in the kitchen garden with Phaedre."

Her cousin gave the visitor a flat, narrow look, and shook his head.

"I'll not leave ye alone wi' this fellow. You go; I'll watch him."

She would have argued, but long experience with Scottish males had taught her to recognize intractable stubbornness when she saw it. Besides, Donner's eyes were fixed on her in a way that made her slightly uncomfortable—he was looking at her hand, she realized, at the cabochon ruby in her ring. She was reasonably sure she could fight him off, if necessary, but still . . .

"I'll be right back," she said, hastily stabbing a neglected brush into the pot of turps. "Don't go anywhere!"

I WAS SHOCKED, but less so than I might have been. I had felt that Donner was alive. Hoped he was, in spite of everything. Still, seeing him face to face, sitting in Jocasta's morning room, struck me dumb. He was talking when I came in, but stopped when he saw me. He didn't stand up, naturally, nor yet offer any observations on my survival; just nodded at me, and resumed what he'd been saying.

"To stop whitey. Save our lands, save our people."

"But you came to the wrong time," Brianna pointed out. "You were too late."

Donner gave her a blank look.

"No, I didn't—1766, that's when I was supposed to come, and that's when I came." He pounded the heel of his hand violently against the side of his head. "Crap! What was *wrong* with me?"

"Congenital stupidity?" I suggested politely, having regained my voice. "That, or hallucinogenic drugs."

The blank look flickered a little, and Donner's mouth twitched.

"Oh. Yeah, man. There was some of that."

"But if you came to 1766—and meant to"—Bree objected—"what about Robert Springer—Otter-Tooth? According to the story Mama heard about him, he meant to warn the native tribes against white men and prevent them colonizing the place. Only he arrived too *late* to do that—and even so, he must have arrived forty or fifty years before you did!"

"That wasn't the plan, man!" Donner burst out. He stood up, rubbing both hands violently through his hair in agitation, making it stand out like a bramble bush. "Jeez, no!"

"Oh, it wasn't? What the bloody hell *was* the plan, then?" I demanded. "You did have one."

"Yeah. Yeah, we did." He dropped his hands, glancing round as though fearing to be overheard. He licked his lips.

"Bob did want to do what you said—only the rest said, nah, that wouldn't work. Too many different groups, too much pressure to trade with the whiteys . . . just no way it would fly, you know? We couldn't stop it all, just maybe make it better."

The official plan of the group had been somewhat less ambitious in scope. The travelers would arrive in the 1760s, and over the course of the next ten years, in the confusion and reshuffling, the movement of tribes and villages attendant upon the end of the French and Indian War, would infiltrate themselves into various Indian groups along the Treaty Line in the Colonies and up into the Canadian territories.

They would then use such persuasive powers as they had gained to sway the Indian nations to fight on the British side in the oncoming Revolution, with the intent of insuring a British victory.

"See, the English, they act like the Indians are sovereign nations," he explained, with a glibness suggesting this was a theory learned by rote. "They won, they'd go on doing trade and like that, which is okay, but they wouldn't be trying to push the Indians back and stomp 'em out. The colonists"—he waved scornfully toward the open door—"greedy sons o' bitches been shoving their way into Indian lands for the last hundred years; *they* ain't going to stop."

Bree raised her brows, but I could see that she found the

notion intriguing. Evidently, it wasn't quite as insane as it sounded.

"How could you think you'd succeed?" I demanded. "Only a few men to—oh, my God," I said, seeing his face change. "Jesus H. Roosevelt Christ—you weren't the only ones, were you?"

Donner shook his head, wordless.

"How many?" Ian asked. He sounded calm, but I could see that his hands were clenched on his knees.

"I dunno." Donner sat down abruptly, slumping into himself like a bag of grain. "There were like, two or three hundred in the group. But most of 'em couldn't hear the stones." His head lifted a little, and he glanced at Brianna. "Can you?"

She nodded, ruddy brows drawn together.

"But you think there were more . . . travelers . . . than you and your friends?"

Donner shrugged, helpless.

"I got the idea there were, yeah. But Raymond said only five at a time could pass through. So we trained in, like, cells of five. We kept it secret; nobody in the big group knew who could travel and who couldn't, and Raymond was the only one who knew all of 'em."

I had to ask.

"What did Raymond look like?" A possibility had been stirring in the back of my mind, ever since I'd heard that name.

Donner blinked, having not expected that question.

"Jeez, I dunno," he said helplessly "Short dude, I think. White hair. Wore it long, like we all did." He raked a hand through his knotted locks in illustration, brows furrowed in the search for memory.

"A rather . . . wide . . . forehead?" I knew I oughtn't to prompt him, but couldn't help myself, and drew both index fingers across my own brow in illustration.

He stared at me in confusion for a moment.

"Man, I don't remember," he said, shaking his head helplessly. "It was a long time ago. How would I remember something like that?"

I sighed.

"Well, tell me what happened, when you came through the stones."

Donner licked his lips, blinking in the effort of recall. It wasn't just native stupidity, I saw; he didn't like thinking about it.

"Yeah. Well, there were five of us, like I said. Me, and Rob, and Jeremy and Atta. Oh, and Jojo. We came through on the island, and—"

"What island?" Brianna, Ian, and I all chorused together.

"Ocracoke," he said, looking surprised. "It's the northmost portal in the Bermuda Triangle group. We wanted to be as close as we could get to—"

"The Ber—" Brianna and I began, but broke off, looking at each other.

"You know where a number of these portals are?" I said, striving for calm.

"How many are there?" Brianna chimed in, not waiting for his answer.

The answer, in any event, was confused—no surprise there. Raymond had told them that there were many such places in the world, but that they tended to occur in groups. There was such a group in the Caribbean, another in the Northeast, near the Canadian border. Another in the Southwestern desert—Arizona, he thought, and down through Mexico. Northern Britain and the coast of France, as far as the tip of the Iberian peninsula. Probably more, but that's all he'd mentioned.

Not all of the portals were marked with stone circles, though those in places where people had lived for a long time tended to be.

"Raymond said those were safer," he said, shrugging. "I dunno why."

The spot on Ocracoke hadn't been bounded by a full circle of stones, though it *was* marked. Four stones, he said. One of them had marks on it Raymond said were African—maybe made by slaves.

"It's kind of in the water," he said, shrugging. "A little stream runs through it, I mean. Ray said he didn't know about water, whether that made any difference, but he thought it might. But we didn't know what *kind* of difference. You guys know?"

Brianna and I shook our heads, round-eyed as a pair of owls. Ian's brow, already furrowed, drew further down at this, though. Had he heard something, during his time with Geillis Duncan?

The five of them—and Raymond—had driven as far as they could; the road that led down the Outer Banks was a poor one, which tended to wash away in storms, and they were obliged to leave the car several miles away from the spot, struggling through the scrub pines of the coastal forest and patches of unexpected quicksand. It was late fall—

"Samhain," Brianna said softly, but softly enough that Donner was not distracted from the flow of his story.

Late fall, he said, and the weather was bad. It had been raining for days, and the footing was uncertain, slippery and boggy by turns. The wind was high, and the storm surge pounded the beaches; they could hear it, even in the secluded spot where the portal lay.

"We were all scared—maybe all but Rob—but it was way exciting, man," he said, beginning to show a glimmer of enthusiasm. "The trees were just about layin' down flat, and the sky, it was green. The wind was so bad, you could taste salt, all the time, because little bits of ocean were flying through the air, mixed with the rain. We were, like, soaked through to our choners."

"Your what?" Ian said, frowning.

"Underpants—you know, drawers. Smallclothes," Brianna said, flapping an impatient hand. "Go on."

Once arrived at the place, Raymond had checked them all, to see that they carried the few necessities they might need—tinderboxes, tobacco, a little money of the time—and then given each one a wampum necklet, and a small leather pouch, which he said was an amulet of ceremonial herbs.

"Oh, you know about that," he said, seeing the expression on my face. "What kind did you use?"

"I didn't," I said, not wanting him to wander from his story. "Go on. How did you plan to hit the right time?"

"Oh. Well." He sighed, hunching on his stool. "We didn't. Ray said it would be just about two hundred years, give or take a couple. It wasn't like we could steer—that's what I was hoping you guys would know. How to get to a specific time. 'Cuz, boy, I'd sure like to go back and get there *before* I got messed up with Ray and them."

They had, at Raymond's direction, walked a pattern among the stones, chanting words. Donner had no idea what the words meant, nor even what the language was. At the conclusion of the pattern, though, they had walked single file toward the stone with African markings, passing carefully to the left of it.

"And, like—pow!" He smacked a fist into the palm of his other hand. "First guy in line—he's *gone,* man! We were just freaked out. I mean, that's what was s'posed to happen, but . . . gone," he repeated, shaking his head. "Just . . . *gone.*"

Agog at this evidence of effectiveness, they had repeated the pattern and the chant, and at each repetition, the first man to pass the stone had vanished. Donner had been the fourth.

"Oh, God," he said, going pale at the memory. "Oh, God, I never felt anything like that before and I hope I never do again."

"The amulet—the pouch you had," Brianna said, ignoring his pallor. Her own face was intense, blazing with interest. "What happened to that?"

"I dunno. I maybe dropped it, maybe it went someplace else. I passed out, and when I came to, it wasn't with me." The day was warm and close, but he began to shiver. "Jojo. He was with me. Only he was dead."

That statement struck me like a knife blow, just under the ribs. Geillis Duncan's notebooks had held lists of people found near stone circles—some alive, some dead. I hadn't needed anything to tell me that the journey through the stones was a perilous passage—but this reminder made me feel weak in the knees, and I sat down on Jocasta's tufted ottoman.

"The others," I said, trying to keep my voice steady. "Did they . . . "

He shook his head. He was still clammy and shivering, but sweat glazed his face; he looked very unwell.

"Never saw 'em again," he said.

He didn't know what had killed Jojo; didn't pause to look, though he had a vague notion that there might have been burn marks on his shirt. Finding his friend dead, and none of the others nearby, he had stumbled off in a panic through scrub forest and salt marsh, collapsing after several hours of wandering, lying in the sand dunes among stiff grass all night. He had starved for three days, found and eaten a nest of turtle eggs, eventually made his way to the mainland on a stolen canoe, and thereafter had drifted haplessly, working here and there at menial jobs, seeking refuge in drink when he could afford it, falling into company with Hodgepile and his gang a year or so past.

The wampum necklets, he said, were to allow the conspirators to identify each other should they meet at some point—but he had never seen anybody else wearing one.

Brianna wasn't paying attention to this rambling part of the story, though; she had jumped ahead.

"Do you think Otter-Tooth—Springer—screwed up your group by deliberately trying to go to a different time?"

He looked at her, mouth hanging open a little.

"I never thoughta that. He went first. He went first," he repeated, in a wondering sort of way.

Brianna began to ask another question, but was interrupted by the sound of voices in the hall, coming toward the morning room. Donner was on his feet in an instant, eyes wide with alarm.

"Crap," he said. "It's him. You gotta help me!"

Before I could inquire exactly why he thought so, or who "him" was, the austere form of Ulysses appeared in the doorway.

"You," he said to the cowering Donner, in awful tones. "Did I not tell you to begone, sirrah? How dare you to enter Mrs. Innes's house and pester her relations?"

He stepped aside, then, with a nod to whomever stood beside him, and a small, round, cross-looking gentleman in a rumpled suit peered in.

"That's him," he said, pointing an accusatory finger. "That's the blackguard what stole my purse at Jacobs's ordinary this morning! Took it right out my pocket whilst I was eatin' ham for breakfast!"

"It wasn't me!" Donner made a poor attempt at a show of outrage, but guilt was written all over his face, and when Ulysses seized him by the scruff of the neck and unceremoniously rummaged his clothing, the purse was discovered, to the outspoken gratification of the owner.

"Thief!" he cried, shaking his fist. "I been a-following of

you all the morning. Damn' tick-bellied, louse-ridden, dog-eatin' savage—oh, I do beg pardon, ladies," he added, bowing to me and Brianna as an afterthought before resuming his denunciation of Donner.

Brianna glanced at me, eyebrows raised, but I shrugged. There was no way of preserving Donner from the righteous wrath of his victim, even had I really wanted to. At the gentleman's behest, Ulysses summoned a pair of grooms and a set of manacles—the sight of which made Brianna grow somewhat pale—and Donner was marched off, protesting that he hadn't done it, he'd been framed, wasn't him, he was a friend of the ladies, really, man, ask 'em! . . . to be conveyed to the gaol in Cross Creek.

There was a deep silence in the wake of his removal. At last, Ian shook his head as though trying to rid himself of flies, and putting down the palette knife at last, picked up the sketching block, where Brianna had made Donner try to draw the pattern he said the men had walked. A hopeless scrawl of circles and squiggles, it looked like one of Jemmy's drawings.

"What kind of name is Weddigo?" Ian asked, putting it down.

Brianna had been clutching her pencil so tightly that her knuckles were white. She unfolded her hand and put it down, and I saw that her hands were shaking slightly.

"Wendigo," she said. "It's an Ojibway cannibal spirit that lives in the wood. It howls in storms and eats people."

Ian gave her a long look.

"Nice fellow," he said.

"Wasn't he, just." I felt more than a little shaken myself. Apart from the shock of Donner's appearance and revelations, and then his arrest, small jolts of memory—vivid images of my first meeting with him—kept shooting uncontrollably through my mind, despite my efforts to shut them out. I could taste blood in my mouth, and the stink of unwashed men drowned the scent of flowers from the terrace.

"I suppose it's what one would call a *nom de guerre*," I said, with an attempt at nonchalance. "He can't have been christened that, surely."

"Are you all right, Mama?" Bree was frowning at me. "Shall I get something? A glass of water?"

"Whisky," Ian and I said in unison, and I laughed, despite the shakiness. By the time it arrived, I was in command of myself again.

"What do you think will happen to him, Ulysses?" I asked, as he held the tray for me. The butler's stolidly handsome face showed nothing beyond a mild distaste for the recent visitor; I saw him frown at the scumbled bits of dirt that Donner's shoes had left on the parquet floor.

"I suppose they will hang him," he said. "Mr. Townsend—that was the gentleman's name—had ten pound in the purse he stole." More than enough to merit hanging. The eighteenth century took a dim view of thievery; as little as a pound could incur a capital sentence.

"Good," said Ian, with obvious approval.

I felt a small lurch of the stomach. I disliked Donner, distrusted him, and to be honest, really didn't feel that his death would be a great loss to humanity, by and large. But he was a fellow traveler; did that impose any obligation on our part to help him? More importantly, perhaps—did he have any more information that he hadn't told us yet?

"Mr. Townsend has gone to Campbelton," the butler added, offering the tray to Ian. "To ask Mr. Farquard to attend to the case promptly, as he is bound for Halifax, and wishes to give his witness at once." Farquard Campbell was a justice of the peace—and likely the only thing approaching a judge within the county, since the Circuit Court had ceased to operate.

"They won't hang him before tomorrow, though, I don't suppose," Brianna said. She didn't normally drink whisky, but had taken a glass now; the encounter had shaken her, too. I saw she had turned the ring around upon her finger, rubbing the big ruby absentmindedly with her thumb.

"No," said Ian, looking at her suspiciously. "Ye dinna mean to—" He glanced at me. "No!" he said in horror at the indecision he saw on my face. "Yon fellow's a thief and a blackguard, and if ye didna see him burning and killing wi' your own eyes, Auntie, ye ken well enough he did it. For God's sake, let them hang him and have done!"

"Well . . ." I said, wavering. The sound of footsteps and voices in the hall saved me answering. Jamie and Duncan had been in Cross Creek; now they were back. I felt an overwhelming flood of relief at sight of Jamie, who loomed up in the doorway, sunburned and ruddy, dusty from riding.

"Hang who?" he inquired cheerfully.

JAMIE'S OPINION WAS the same as Ian's; let them hang Donner, and good riddance. He was reluctantly persuaded that either Brianna or I must talk to the man at least once more, though, to be sure there was nothing further he could tell us.

"I'll speak to the gaoler," he said without enthusiasm. "Mind, though"—he pointed a monitory finger at me—"neither of ye is to go anywhere near the man, save Ian or I am with ye."

"What do you think he'd do?" Brianna was ruffled, annoyed at his tone. "He's about half my size, for heaven's sake!"

"And a rattlesnake is smaller yet," her father replied. "Ye wouldna walk into a room with one of those, only because ye outweigh him, I hope?"

Ian snickered at that, and Brianna gave him an elbow, hard in the ribs.

"Anyway," Jamie said, ignoring them, "I've a bit of news. And a letter from Roger Mac," he said. He pulled it out of his shirt, smiling at Bree. "If ye're no too distracted to read it?"

She lit up like a candle and grabbed it. Ian made a teasing snatch at it, and she slapped his hand away, laughing, and ran out of the room to read it in privacy.

"What sort of news?" I asked. Ulysses had left the tray and decanter; I poured a tot into my empty glass and gave it to Jamie.

"Someone's seen Manfred McGillivray," he replied. *"Slàinte."* He drained the glass, looking contented.

"Oh, aye? Where?" Ian looked less than pleased at this news. For myself, I was thrilled.

"In a brothel, where else?"

Unfortunately, his informant had not been able to supply the exact location of said brothel—having likely been too drunk at the time to know precisely where he was, as Jamie cynically observed—but had been reasonably sure that it was in Cross Creek or Campbelton. Also unfortunately, the sighting was several weeks old. Manfred might well have moved on.

"It's a start, though," I said, hopeful. Penicillin was effective, even against more advanced cases of syphilis, and I had some brewing in the winter kitchen, even now. "I'll go with you, when you go to the gaol. Then after we've spoken with Donner, we can go look for the brothel."

Jamie's look of contentment lessened appreciably.

"What? Why?"

"I dinna think Manfred would be still there, Auntie," Ian said, patently amused. "I doubt he'd have the money, for one thing."

"Oh, ha ha," I said. "He might have said where he was staying, mightn't he? Besides, I want to know whether he was showing any symptoms." In my own time, it might be ten, twenty, or even thirty years after the appearance of the initial chancre before further syphilitic symptoms developed; in this time, though, syphilis was a much more fulminant disease—a victim could die within a year of infection. And Manfred had been gone for more than three months; God knew how long since he had first contracted the infection.

Jamie looked distinctly unenthused about the idea of searching for brothels; Ian seemed rather more interested.

"I'll help look," he volunteered. "Fergus can come, too; he kens a great deal about whores—they'd likely talk to him."

"Fergus? Fergus is here?"

"He is," Jamie said. "That was the other bit of news. He's payin' his respects to my aunt at the moment."

"Why is he here, though?"

"Well, ye heard the talk at the barbecue, aye? About Mr. Simms, the printer, and his troubles? It seems they've got worse, and he thinks of selling up, before someone burns his shop to the ground and him in it. It struck me that perhaps it would suit Fergus and Marsali, better than the farming. So I sent word for him to come down, and maybe have a word wi' Simms."

"That's a brilliant idea!" I said. "Only . . . what would Fergus use for money to buy it?"

Jamie coughed and looked evasive.

"Aye, well. I imagine some sort of bargain might be struck. Particularly if Simms is anxious to sell up."

"All right," I said, resigned. "I don't suppose I want to know the gory details. But Ian—" I turned to him, fixing him with a beady eye. "Far be it from me to offer you moral advice. But you are *not*—repeat, not—to be questioning whores in any deeply personal manner. Do I make myself clear?"

"Auntie!" he said, pretending shock. "The idea!" But a broad grin spread across his tattooed face.

56

TAR AND FEATHERS

IN THE EVENT, I let Jamie go alone to the gaol to make arrangements for seeing Donner. He had assured me that this would be simpler without my presence, and I had several errands in Cross Creek. Besides the usual salt, sugar, pins, and other household goods needing replenishment, I urgently needed more cinchona bark for Lizzie. The gallberry ointment worked to treat malarial attacks, but was not nearly so effective as Jesuit bark in preventing them.

The British trade restrictions were having their effect, though. There was, of course, no tea to be found—I had expected that; there had been none for nearly a year—but neither was there any sugar, save at an exorbitant price, and steel pins were not to be found at all.

Salt, I could get. With a pound of this in my basket, I made my way up from the docks. The day was hot and humid; away from the slight breeze off the river, the air was motionless and thick as treacle. The salt had solidified in its burlap bags, and the merchant had had to chip off lumps of it with a chisel.

I wondered how Ian and Fergus were coming with their

researches; I had a scheme in mind regarding the brothel and its inhabitants, but first, we had to find it.

I hadn't mentioned the idea to Jamie. If anything came of it, that would be time enough. A side street offered shade, in the form of a number of large elms that had been planted so as to overhang the street. I stepped into the welcome shadow of one of these, and found myself at the edge of the fashionable district—about ten houses, all told—of Cross Creek. From where I stood, I could see Dr. Fentiman's fairly modest abode, distinguished by a small hanging shingle decorated with a caduceus. The doctor was not in when I called, but his servant, a neat, plain young woman with badly crossed eyes, admitted me and showed me to the consulting room.

This was a surprisingly cool and pleasant room, with large windows and a worn canvas cloth on the floor, painted in blue and yellow chequers, and furnished with a desk, two comfortable chairs, and a chaise longue on which patients might recline for examination. He had a microscope standing on the desk, through which I peered with interest. It was a fine one, though not quite so good as my own, I thought with some complacency.

I was possessed of a strong curiosity about the rest of his equipment, and was debating with myself as to whether it would be an abuse of the doctor's hospitality to snoop through his cupboards, when the doctor himself arrived, borne on the wings of brandywine.

He was humming a little tune to himself, and carrying his hat under one arm, his battered medical case in the crook of the other. Seeing me, he dropped these carelessly on the floor and hastened to grasp me by the hand, beaming. He bowed over my hand and pressed moistly fervent lips to my knuckles.

"Mrs. Fraser! My dear lady, I am so pleased to see you! You are in no physical distress, I trust?"

I was in some danger of being overwhelmed by the fumes of alcohol on his breath, but kept as cordial a countenance as possible, unobtrusively wiping my hand upon my gown, whilst assuring him that I was entirely well, as were all the members of my immediate family.

"Oh, splendid, splendid," he said, plumping down quite

suddenly upon a stool and giving me an enormous grin, revealing tobacco-stained molars. His oversize wig had slid round sideways, causing him to peer out from under it like a dormouse under a tea cozy, but he seemed not to have noticed. "Splendid, splendid, splendid."

I took his rather vague wave as invitation and sat down, as well. I had brought a small present in order to sweeten the good doctor, and now removed this from my basket—though in all truth, I rather thought he was so well-marinated as to require little more attention before I broached the subject of my errand.

He was, however, thrilled with my gift—a gouged-out eyeball, which Young Ian had thoughtfully picked up for me following a fight in Yanceyville, hastily preserved in spirits of wine. Having heard something of Doctor Fentiman's tastes, I thought he might appreciate it. He did, and went on saying, "Splendid!" at some length.

Eventually trailing off, he blinked, held the jar up to the light, and turned it round, viewing it with great admiration.

"Splendid," he said once more. "It will have a most particularly honorable place in my collection, I do assure you, Mrs. Fraser!"

"You have a collection?" I said, affecting great interest. I'd heard about his collection.

"Oh, yes, oh, yes! Would you care to see it?"

There was no possibility of refusal; he was already up and staggering toward a door at the back of his study. This proved to lead into a large closet, the shelves of which held thirty or forty glass containers, filled with alcoholic spirits—and a number of objects which could indeed be described as "interesting."

These ranged from the merely grotesque to the truly startling. One by one, he brought out a big toe sporting a wart the size and color of an edible mushroom, a preserved tongue which had been split—apparently during the owner's lifetime, as the two halves were quite healed—a cat with six legs, a grossly malformed brain ("Removed from a hanged murderer," as he proudly informed me. "I shouldn't wonder," I murmured in reply, thinking of Donner and wondering what *his* brain might look like), and several infants, presumably stillborn, and exhibiting assorted atrocious deformities.

"Now, *this,*" he said, lifting down a large glass cylinder in trembling hands, "is quite the prize of my collection. There is a most distinguished physician in Germany, a *Herr Doktor* Blumenbach, who has a world-renowned collection of skulls, and he has been pursuing me—nay, absolutely *pestering* me, I assure you!—in an effort to persuade me to part with it."

"This" was the defleshed skulls and spinal column of a double-headed infant. It was, in fact, fascinating. It was also something that would cause any woman of childbearing age to swear off sex immediately.

Grisly as the doctor's collection was, though, it offered me an excellent opportunity for approaching my true errand.

"That is truly amazing," I said, leaning forward as though to examine the empty orbits of the floating skulls. They were separate and complete, I saw; it was the spinal cord that had divided, so that the skulls hung side by side in the fluid, ghostly white and leaning toward each other so that the rounded heads touched gently, as though sharing some secret, only separating when a movement of the jar caused them momentarily to float apart. "I wonder what causes such a phenomenon?"

"Oh, doubtless some dreadful shock to the mother," Doctor Fentiman assured me. "Women in an expectant condition are fearfully vulnerable to any sort of excitement or distress, you know. They must be kept quite sequestered and confined, well away from any injurious influences."

"I daresay," I murmured. "But you know, some malformations—that one, for instance?—I believe are the result of syphilis in the mother."

It was; I recognized the typical malformed jaw, the narrow skull, and the caved-in appearance of the nose. This child had been preserved with flesh intact, and lay curled placidly in its bottle. By the size and lack of hair, it had likely been premature; I hoped for its own sake that it had not been born alive.

"Shiphi—syphilis," the doctor repeated, swaying a little. "Oh, yes. Yes, yes. I got that particular little creature from a, um . . ." It occurred to him belatedly that syphilis was perhaps not a topic suitable to discuss with a lady. Murderer's brains and two-headed children, yes, but not venereal disease. There was a jar in the closet that I was reasonably sure contained the scrotum of a Negro male who had suffered from elephantiasis; I noticed he hadn't shown me *that* one.

"From a prostitute?" I inquired sympathetically. "Yes, I suppose such misfortunes must be common among such women."

To my annoyance, he slithered away from the desired topic.

"No, no. In fact—" He darted a look over his shoulder, as though fearing to be overheard, then leaned near me and whispered hoarsely, "I received that specimen from a colleague in London, some years ago. It is reputed to be the child of a foreign nobleman!"

"Oh, dear," I said, taken aback. "How . . . interesting."

At this rather inconvenient point, the servant came in with tea—or rather, with a revolting concoction of roasted acorns and chamomile, stewed in water—and the conversation turned ineluctably toward social trivia. I was afraid that the tea might sober him up before I could inveigle him back in the right direction, but luckily the tea tray also included a decanter of fine claret, which I dispensed liberally.

I had a fresh try at drawing him back into medical subjects, by leaning over to admire the jars left out on his desk. The one nearest me contained the hand of a person who had had such an advanced case of Dupuytren's contracture as to render the appendage little more than a knot of constricted fingers. I wished Tom Christie could see it. He had avoided me since his surgery, but so far as I knew, his hand was still functional.

"Isn't it remarkable, the variety of conditions that the human body displays?" I said.

He shook his head. He had discovered the state of his wig and turned it round; his wizened countenance beneath it looked like that of a solemn chimpanzee—bar the flush of broken capillaries that lit his nose like a beacon.

"Remarkable," he echoed. "And yet, what is quite as remarkable is the resilience a body may show in the face of quite terrible injury."

That was true, but it wasn't at all the line I wished to work upon.

"Yes, quite. But—"

"I am very sorry not to be able to show you one specimen—it would have been a notable addition to my collection, I assure you! But alas, the gentleman insisted upon taking it with him."

"He—what?" Well, after all, I had in my time presented various children with their appendixes or tonsils in a bottle, following surgery. I supposed it wasn't entirely unreasonable for someone to wish to retain an amputated limb.

"Yes, most astonishing." He took a meditative sip of claret. "A testicle, it was—I trust you will pardon my mentioning it," he added belatedly. He hesitated for an instant, but in the end, simply couldn't resist describing the occurrence. "The gentleman had suffered a wound to the scrotum, a most unfortunate accident."

"Most," I said, feeling a sudden tingle at the base of my spine. Was this Jocasta's mysterious visitor? I had been keeping off the claret, in the interests of a clear head, but now poured a tot, feeling it needed. "Did he say how this unfortunate incident transpired?"

"Oh, yes. A hunting accident, he said. But they all say that, don't they?" He twinkled at me, the end of his nose bright red. "I expect it was a *duello*. The work of a jealous rival, perhaps!"

"Perhaps." A *duello*? I thought. But most duels of the time were fought with pistols, not swords. It really was good claret, and I felt a little steadier. "You—er—removed the testicle?" He must have, if he had been contemplating adding it to his ghastly collection.

"Yes," he said, and was not too far gone to give a small sympathetic shudder at the memory. "The gun-shot had been seriously neglected; he said it had occurred some days previous. I was obliged to remove the injured testicle, but fortunately preserved the other."

"I'm sure he was pleased about that." *Gun-shot? Surely not,* I was thinking. *It can't be* . . . and yet . . . "Did this happen quite recently?"

"Mmm, no." He tilted back in his chair, eyes crossing

slightly with the effort of recall. "It was in the spring, two years ago—May? Perhaps May."

"Was the gentleman named Bonnet, by chance?" I was surprised that my voice sounded quite casual. "I believe I had heard that a Stephen Bonnet was involved in some such . . . accident."

"Well, you know, he would not give his name. Often patients will not, if the injury is one that might cause public embarrassment. I do not insist in such cases."

"But you do remember him." I found that I was sitting on the edge of my chair, claret cup clenched in my fist. With a little effort, I set it down.

"Mm-hmm." Damn, he was getting sleepy; I could see his lids begin to droop. "A tall gentleman, well-dressed. He had a . . . a most beautiful *horse*. . . ."

"A bit more tea, Doctor Fentiman?" I urged a fresh cup upon him, willing him to stay awake. "Do tell me more about it. The surgery must have been quite delicate?"

In fact, men never like to hear that the removal of testicles is a simple matter, but it is. Though I would admit that the fact of the patient's being conscious during the whole procedure had likely added to the difficulty.

Fentiman regained a bit of his animation, telling me about it.

" . . . and the ball had gone straight *through* the testicle; it had left the most perfect hole. . . . You could look quite through it, I assure you." Plainly he regretted the loss of this interesting specimen, and it was with some difficulty that I got him to tell me what had become of the gentleman to whom it belonged.

"Well, that was odd. It was the horse, you see . . ." he said vaguely. "Lovely animal . . . long hair, like a woman's, so unusual . . ."

A Friesian horse. The doctor had recalled that the planter Phillip Wylie was fond of such horses, and had said as much to his patient, suggesting that as the man had no money—and would not be capable of riding comfortably for some time, in any case—he might think of selling his animal to Wylie. The man had agreed to this, and had requested the doctor to make inquiry of Wylie, who was in town for the Court Sessions.

Doctor Fentiman had obligingly gone out to do so, leaving his patient cozily tucked up on the chaise with a draught of tincture of laudanum.

Phillip Wylie had professed himself most interested in the horse ("Yes, I'll wager he was," I said, but the doctor didn't notice), and had hastened round to see it. The horse was present, but the patient was not, having absconded on foot in the doctor's absence—taking with him half a dozen silver spoons, an enameled snuffbox, the bottle of laudanum, and six shillings, which happened to be all the money the doctor had in the house.

"I cannot imagine how he managed it," Fentiman said, eyes quite round at the thought. "In such condition!" To his credit, he appeared more distressed at the notion of his patient's condition than his own loss. He was a terrible drunkard, Fentiman, I thought; I'd never seen him completely sober—but not a bad doctor.

"Still," he added philosophically, "all's well as ends well, is it not, my dear lady?"

By which he meant that Phillip Wylie had purchased the horse from him for a price sufficient to more than compensate for his losses, and leave him with a tidy profit.

"Quite," I said, wondering just how Jamie would take this news. He had won the stallion—for it must of course be Lucas—from Phillip Wylie in the course of an acrimonious card game at River Run, only to have the horse stolen by Stephen Bonnet a few hours later.

On the whole, I expected that Jamie would be pleased that the stallion was back in good hands, even if they weren't his. As for the news about Bonnet . . . *"A bad penny always turns up,"* had been his cynical opinion, expressed when Bonnet's body had failed to be discovered after Brianna had shot him.

Fentiman was openly yawning by now. He blinked, eyes watering, patted about his person in search of a handkerchief, then bent to rummage in his case, which he had dropped on the floor near his chair.

I had pulled out my own handkerchief and leaned across to hand it to him, when I saw them in the open case.

"What are those?" I asked, pointing. I could see what they were, of course; what I wanted to know was where he'd got them. They were syringes, two of them, lovely little syringes, made of brass. Each one was composed of two bits: a plunger with curled handles, and a cylindrical barrel, drawn out at the narrowed end into a very long, blunt-tipped needle.

"I—why—that is . . . ah . . ." He was terribly taken aback, and stammered like a schoolboy caught sneaking cigarettes behind the toilets. Then something occurred to him, and he relaxed.

"Ears," he declared, in ringing tones. "For cleansing ears. Yes, that is what they are, indubitably. Ear clysters!"

"Oh, are they really?" I picked one up; he tried to stop me, but his reflexes were delayed, and he succeeded only in grabbing at the ruffle of my sleeve.

"How ingenious," I said, working the plunger. It was a little stiff, but not bad at all—particularly not when the alternative was a makeshift hypodermic composed of a leather tube with a rattlesnake's fang attached. Of course a blunt tip wouldn't do, but it would be a simple matter to cut it to a sharp angle. "Where did you get them? I should like very much to order one myself."

He stared at me in abject horror, jaw agape.

"I—er—I really do not think . . ." he protested feebly. Just then, in a perfect miracle of bad timing, his housemaid appeared in the doorway.

"Mr. Brennan's come; it's his wife's time," she said briefly.

"Oh!" Doctor Fentiman leapt to his feet, slammed shut his case, and snatched it up.

"My apologies, dear Mrs. Fraser . . . must go . . . matter of great urgency—so pleasant to have seen you!" He rushed out, case clutched to his bosom, stepping on his hat in his haste.

The maid picked up the crushed chapeau with an air of resignation, and punched it indifferently back into shape.

"Will you be wanting to leave now, ma'am?" she inquired, with an intonation making it clear that I ought to be leaving, whether I wanted to or not.

"I will," I said, rising. "But tell me"—I held out the brass syringe on the palm of my hand—"do you know what this is, and where Doctor Fentiman got it?"

It was difficult to tell in which direction she was looking, but she bent her head as though to examine it, with no more interest than had it been a two-day old smelt offered her for sale in the market.

"Oh, that. Aye, ma'am, it's a penis syringe. I b'lieve he had it sent him from Philadelphia."

"A, um, penis syringe. I see," I said, blinking a little.

"Yes, ma'am. It's for treating of the drip, or the clap. The doctor does a deal of business for the men what goes to Mrs. Silvie's."

I took a deep breath.

"Mrs. Silvie's. Ah. And would you know where Mrs. Silvie's . . . establishment is?"

"Behind Silas Jameson's ordinary," she replied, giving me for the first time a faintly curious look, as though wondering what sort of blockhead didn't know *that*. "Will you be needing anything else, ma'am?"

"Oh, no," I said. "That will do nicely, thank you!" I made to hand her back the penis syringe, but then was struck by impulse. The doctor had two, after all.

"Give you a shilling for it," I said, meeting the eye that seemed most likely to be pointed in my direction.

"Done," she said promptly. She paused for a moment, then added, "If you're going to use it on your man, best be sure he's dead drunk first."

MY PRIMARY MISSION was thus accomplished, but now I had a new possibility to explore, before mounting an assault on Mrs. Silvie's house of ill-repute.

I had planned to visit a glassmaker and attempt to explain by means of drawings how to make the barrel and plunger for a hypodermic syringe, leaving up to Bree the problem of making a hollow needle and attaching it. Unfortunately, while the single glassblower operating in Cross Creek was capable of producing any manner of everyday bottles, jugs, and cups, a glance at his stock had made it obvious that my requirements were well beyond his capabilities.

But now I needn't worry about that! While metal syringes lacked some desirable qualities of glass, they also had an undeniable advantage, insofar as they wouldn't break—and while a disposable needle was nice, I could simply sterilize the entire item after each use.

Doctor Fentiman's syringes had very thick, blunt-tipped needle ends. It would be necessary to heat them, and draw the tips out much further in order to narrow them. But any idiot with a forge could do that, I thought. Then to cut the brass tip at an angle and file the point smooth enough to puncture skin cleanly . . . child's play, I thought blithely, and narrowly refrained from skipping down the sandy walk. Now, all I required was a good stock of cinchona bark.

My hopes of obtaining the bark were dashed, though, as soon as I turned into the main street and glimpsed Mr. Bogues's apothecary's shop. The door stood open, letting in flies, and the usually immaculate stoop was marred with such a multitude of muddy footprints as to suggest that some hostile army had descended upon the shop.

The impression of sacking and looting was furthered by the scene inside; most of the shelves were empty, scattered with remnants of dried leaf and broken pottery. The Bogueses' ten-year-old daughter, Miranda, stood mournful watch over a small collection of jars and bottles and an empty tortoiseshell.

"Miranda!" I said. "Whatever has happened?"

She brightened at sight of me, small pink mouth momentarily reversing its downward droop.

"Mrs. Fraser! D'you want some horehound? We've nearly a pound of that left—and it's cheap, only three farthings the ounce."

"I'll have an ounce," I said, though in fact I had plenty growing in my own garden. "Where are your parents?"

The mouth went down again, and the lower lip quivered.

"Mama's in the back, packing. And Papa's gone to sell Jack to Mr. Raintree."

Jack was the apothecary's wagon horse, and Miranda's particular pet. I bit the inside of my lip.

"Mr. Raintree's a very kind man," I said, striving for what comfort there might be. "And he has a nice pasture for his horses, and a warm stable; I think Jack might be happy there. He'll have friends."

She nodded, mouth pinched tight, but two fat tears escaped to roll down her cheeks.

With a quick glance behind me, to assure that no one was coming in, I stepped round the counter, sat down on an upturned keg, and drew her onto my lap, where she melted at once, clinging to me and crying, though making an obvious effort not to be heard in the living quarters behind the shop.

I patted her and made small soothing noises, feeling an unease beyond mere sympathy for the girl. Clearly the Bogueses were selling up. Why?

So infrequently as I came down the mountain, I had no idea what Ralston Bogues's politics might be these days. Not being Scottish, he hadn't come to the barbecue in Flora MacDonald's honor. The shop had always been prosperous, though, and the family decently off, judging by the children's clothes—Miranda and her two little brothers always had shoes. The Bogueses had lived here all of Miranda's life, at least, and likely longer. For them to be leaving in this manner meant that something serious had happened—or was about to.

"Do you know where you're going?" I asked Miranda, who was now sitting on my knee, sniffing and wiping her face on my apron. "Perhaps Mr. Raintree can write to you, to tell you how Jack is faring."

She looked a little more hopeful at that.

"Can he send a letter to England, do you think? It's a terrible long way."

England? It *was* serious.

"Oh, I should think so," I said, tucking wisps of hair back under her cap. "Mr. Fraser writes a letter every night, to his sister in Scotland—and that's much further away even than England!"

"Oh. Well." Looking happier, she scrambled off my lap and smoothed down her dress. "Can I write to Jack, do you think?"

"I'm sure Mr. Raintree will read the letter to him if you do," I assured her. "Can you write well, then?"

"Oh, yes, ma'am," she said earnestly. "Papa says I read and write better than he ever did when he was my age. *And* in Latin. He taught me to read all the names of the simples, so I could fetch him what he wanted—see that one?" She pointed with some pride to a large china apothecary's jar, elegantly decorated with blue and gold scrolls. "*Electuary Limonensis*. And that one is *Ipecacuanha*!"

I admired her prowess, thinking that at least I now knew her father's politics. The Boegueses must be Loyalists, if they were returning to England. I would be sorry to see them go, but knowing what I knew of the immediate future, I was glad that they would be safe. At least Ralston would likely have got a decent price for his shop; a short time hence, Loyalists would have their property confiscated, and be lucky to escape arrest—or worse.

"Randy? Have you seen Georgie's shoe? I've found one under the chest, but—oh, Mrs. Fraser! Your pardon, ma'am, I didn't know anyone was here." Melanie Bogues's sharp glance took in my position behind the counter, her daughter's pink-rimmed eyes, and the damp spots on my apron, but she said nothing, merely patting Miranda's shoulder as she passed.

"Miranda tells me you're leaving for England," I said, rising and moving unobtrusively out from behind the counter. "We'll be sorry to see you go."

"That's kind of you, Mrs. Fraser." She smiled unhappily. "We're sorry to go, as well. And I'm not looking forward to the voyage, I can tell you!" She spoke with the heartfelt emotion of someone who had made such a voyage before and would strongly prefer to be boiled alive before doing it again.

I sympathized very much, having done it myself. Doing it with three children, two of them boys under five . . . the imagination boggled.

I wanted to ask her what had caused them to make such a drastic decision, but couldn't think how to broach the matter in front of Miranda. Something had happened; that was clear. Melanie was jumpy as a rabbit, and somewhat more harried than even packing up a household containing three children might account for. She kept darting glances over her shoulder, as though fearing something sneaking up on her.

"Is Mr. Bogues—" I began, but was interrupted by a shadow falling across the stoop. Melanie started, hand to her chest, and I whirled round to see who had come.

The doorway was filled by a short, stocky woman, dressed in a very odd combination of garments. For an instant, I thought she was an Indian, for she wore no cap, and her dark hair was braided—but then she came into the shop, and I saw that she was white. Or rather, pink; her heavy face was flushed with sunburn and the tip of her pug nose was bright red.

"Which one of you is Claire Fraser?" she demanded, looking from me to Melanie Bogues.

"I am," I said, repressing an instinctive urge to take a step backward. Her manner wasn't threatening, but she radiated such an air of physical power that I found her rather intimidating. "Who are you?" I spoke from astonishment, rather than rudeness, and she did not seem offended.

"Jezebel Hatfield Morton," she said, squinting intently at me. "Some geezer at the docks tellt me that you was headin' here." In marked contrast to Melanie Bogues's soft English accent, she had the rough speech I associated with people who had been in the backcountry for three or four generations, speaking to no one in the meantime save raccoons, possums, and one another.

"Er . . . yes," I said, seeing no point in denying it. "Did you need help of some kind?"

She didn't look it; had she been any healthier, she would have burst the seams of the man's shirt she was wearing. Melanie and Miranda were staring at her, wide-eyed. Whatever danger Melanie had been afraid of, it wasn't Miss Morton.

"Not to say help," she said, moving further into the shop. She tilted her head to one side, examining me with what looked like fascination. "I was thinkin' you might know where'bouts that skunk Isaiah Morton be, though."

My mouth dropped open, and I shut it quickly. Not Miss Morton, then—*Mrs.* Morton. The *first* Mrs. Isaiah Morton, that is. Isaiah Morton had fought with Jamie's militia company in the War of the Regulation, and he had mentioned his first wife—breaking out in a cold sweat as he did so.

"I . . . ah . . . believe he's working somewhere upcountry," I said. "Guilford? Or was it Paleyville?"

Actually, it was Hillsboro, but that scarcely mattered, since at the moment, he wasn't *in* Hillsboro. He was, in fact, in

Cross Creek, come to take delivery of a shipment of barrels for his employer, a brewster. I'd seen him at the cooper's shop barely an hour earlier, in company with the *second* Mrs. Morton and their infant daughter. Jezebel Hatfield Morton did not look like the sort of person to be civilized about such things.

She made a low noise in her throat, indicative of disgust.

"He's a dang slippery little weasel. But I'll kotch up to him yet, don't you trouble none about that." She spoke with a casual assurance that boded ill for Isaiah.

I thought silence was the wiser course, but couldn't stop myself asking, "Why do you want him?" Isaiah possessed a certain uncouth amiability, but viewed objectively, he scarcely seemed the sort to inflame one woman, let alone two.

"Want him?" She looked amused at the thought, and rubbed a solid fist under her reddened nose. "I don't want him. But ain't no man runs out on *me* for some whey-faced trollop. Once I kotch up to him, I mean to stave his head in and nail his fly-bit hide to my door."

Spoken by another person, this statement might have passed for rhetoric. As spoken by the lady in question, it was an unequivocal declaration of intent. Miranda's eyes were round as a frog's, and her mother's nearly so.

Jezebel H. Morton squinted at me, and scratched thoughtfully beneath one massive breast, leaving the fabric of her shirt pasted damply to her flesh.

"I heerd tell as how you saved the little toad-sucker's life at Alamance. That true?"

"Er . . . yes." I eyed her warily, watching for any offensive movement. She was blocking the door; if she made for me, I would dive across the counter and dash through the door into the Bogueses' living quarters.

She was wearing a large pig-sticker of a knife, unsheathed. This was thrust through a knotted wampum belt that was doing double duty, holding up a kilted mass of what I thought might originally have been red flannel petticoats, hacked off at the knee. Her very solid legs were bare, as were her feet. She had a pistol and powder horn slung from the belt, as well, but made no move to reach for any of her weapons, thank God.

"Too bad," she said dispassionately. "But then, if he'd died,

I'd not have the fun of killin' him, so I s'pose it's as well. Don't worry me none; if'n I don't find him, one of my brothers will."

Business apparently disposed of for the moment, she relaxed a bit, and looked around, noticing for the first time the empty shelves.

"What-all's goin' on here?" she demanded, looking interested.

"We're selling up," Melanie murmured, attempting to shove Miranda safely behind her. "Going to England."

"That so?" Jezebel looked mildly interested. "What happened? They kill your man? Or tar and feather him?"

Melanie went white.

"No," she whispered. Her throat moved as she swallowed, and her frightened gaze went toward the door. So that was the threat. I felt suddenly cold, in spite of the sweltering heat.

"Oh? Well, if you care whether they do, maybe you best move on down to Center Street," she suggested helpfully. "They're fixin' to make roast chicken out of *somebody,* sure as God made little green apples. You can smell hot tar all over town, and they's a boiling of folks comin' forth from the taverns."

Melanie and Miranda uttered twin shrieks, and ran for the door, shoving past the unflappable Jezebel. I was moving rapidly in the same direction, and narrowly avoided a collision, as Ralston Bogues stepped through the door, just in time to catch his hysterical wife.

"Randy, you go mind your brothers," he said calmly. "Be still, Mellie, it's all right."

"Tar," she panted, clutching him. "She said—she said—"

"Not me," he said, and I saw that his hair dripped and his face shone pale through its sweat. "They're not after me. Not yet. It's the printer."

Gently, he disengaged his wife's hands from his arm, and stepped round the counter, casting a brief glance of curiosity at Jezebel.

"Take the children, go to Ferguson's," he said, and pulled a fowling piece from its hiding place beneath the counter. "I'll come so soon as I may." He reached into a drawer for the powder horn and cartridge box.

"Ralston!" Melanie spoke in a whisper, glancing after Miranda's retreating back, but the entreaty was no less urgent for its lack of volume. "Where are you going?"

One side of his mouth twitched, but he didn't reply.

"Go to Ferguson's," he repeated, eyes fixed on the cartridge in his hand.

"No! No, don't go! Come with us, come with me!" She seized his arm, frantic.

He shook her off, and went doggedly about the business of loading the gun.

"Go, Mellie."

"I will not!" Urgent, she turned to me. "Mrs. Fraser, tell him! Please, tell him it's a waste—a terrible waste! He mustn't go."

I opened my mouth, unsure what to say to either of them, but had no chance to decide.

"I don't imagine Mistress Fraser will think it a waste, Mellie," Ralston Bogues said, eyes still on his hands. He slung the strap of the cartridge box over his shoulder and cocked the gun. "Her husband is holding them off right now—by himself."

He looked up at me then, nodded once, and was gone.

JEZEBEL WAS RIGHT: you *could* smell tar all over town. This was by no means unusual in the summertime, especially near the warehouse docks, but the hot thick reek now took on an atmosphere of threat, burning in my nostrils. Tar—and fear—aside, I was gasping from the effort to keep up with Ralston Bogues, who was not precisely running, but was moving as fast as it was possible to go without breaking into a lope.

Jezebel had been right about the people boiling out of taverns, too; the corner of Center Street was choked with an excited crowd. Mostly men, I saw, though there were a few women of the coarser type among them, fishwives and bond servants.

The apothecary hesitated when he saw them. A few faces turned toward him; one or two plucked at their neighbors' sleeves, pointing—and with not very friendly expressions on their faces.

"Get away, Bogues!" one man yelled. "It's not your business—not yet!"

Another stooped, picked up a stone, and hurled it. It clacked harmlessly on the wooden walk, a few feet short of Bogues, but it drew more attention. Bits of the crowd were beginning to turn, surging slowly in our direction.

"Papa!" said a small, breathless voice behind me. I turned to see Miranda, cap lost and pigtails unraveling down her back, her face the color of beetroot from running.

There wasn't time to think about it. I picked her up and swung her off her feet, toward her father. Taken off guard, he dropped the gun and caught her under the arms.

A man lunged forward, reaching for the gun, but I swooped down and got it first. I backed away from him, clutching it to my chest, daring him with my eyes.

I didn't know him, but he knew me; his eyes flicked over me, hesitating, then he glanced back over his shoulder. I could hear Jamie's voice, and a lot of others, all trying to shout each other down. The breath was still whistling in my chest; I couldn't make out any words. The tone of it was argument, though; confrontation, not bloodshed. The man wavered, glanced at me, away—then turned and shoved his way back into the gathering crowd.

Bogues had had the sense to keep hold of his daughter, who had her arms wrapped tightly round his neck, face buried in his shirt. He darted his eyes at me, and made a small gesture, as though to take back the gun. I shook my head and held it tighter. The stock was warm and slick in my hands.

"Take Miranda home," I said. "I'll—do something."

It was loaded and primed. One shot. The best I could do with that was to create a momentary distraction—but that *might* help.

I pushed my way through the crowd, the gun pointed carefully down not to spill the powder, half-hidden in my skirts. The smell of tar was suddenly much stronger. A cauldron of the stuff lay overturned in front of the printer's shop, a black sticky puddle smoking and reeking in the sun.

Glowing embers and blackened chunks of charcoal were

scattered across the street, under everyone's feet; a solid citizen whom I recognized as Mr. Townsend was kicking the bejesus out of a hastily built fire, thwarting the attempts of a couple of young men to rebuild it.

I looked for Jamie and found him precisely where Ralston Bogues had said he was—in front of the door to the printer's shop, clutching a tar-smeared broom and with the light of battle in his eye.

"That your man?" Jezebel Morton had caught up, and was peering interestedly over my shoulder. "Big 'un, ain't he?"

Tar was spattered all over the front of the shop—and Jamie. A large glob was stuck in his hair, and I could see the flesh of his arm reddened where a long string of hot tar had struck. Despite this, he was grinning. Two more tar-daubed brooms lay on the ground nearby, one broken—almost certainly over someone's head. At least for the moment, he was having fun.

I didn't at once see the printer, Fogarty Simms. Then a frightened face showed briefly at the window, but ducked out of sight as a rock flung from the crowd crashed into the window frame, cracking the glass.

"Come out, Simms, you slinkin' coward!" bellowed a man nearby. "Or shall we smoke you out?"

"Smoke him! Smoke him!" Enthusiastic shouts came from the crowd, and a young man near me bent, scrabbling after a burning brand scattered from the fire. I stamped viciously on his hand as he grasped it.

"Jesus *God*!" He let go and fell to his knees, clutching his hand between his thighs, open-mouthed and gasping with pain. "Oh, oh, Jesus!"

I edged away, shouldering my way through the press. Could I get near enough to give Jamie the gun? Or would that make matters worse?

"Get away from the door, Fraser! We've no quarrel with you!"

I recognized that cultivated voice; it was Gerald Forbes, the lawyer. He wasn't dressed in his usual natty suiting, though; he wore rough homespun. So it wasn't an impromptu attack—he'd come prepared for dirty work.

"Hey! You speak for yourself, Forbes! *I've* a quarrel with

him!" That was a burly man in a butcher's apron, red-faced and indignant, sporting a swollen and empurpled eye. "Look what he did to me!" He waved a meaty hand at the eye, then at the front of his clothing, where a tar-clotted broom had quite evidently caught him square in the chest. He shook a massive fist at Jamie. "You'll pay for this, Fraser!"

"Aye, but I'll pay ye in the same coin, Buchan!" Jamie feinted, broom held like a lance. Buchan yelped and skittered backward, face comically alarmed, and the crowd burst into laughter.

"Come back, man! Ye want to play savage, ye'll need a bit more paint!" Buchan had turned to flee, but was blocked by the crowd. Jamie lunged with the broom, smudging him neatly on the seat of his breeches. Buchan leaped in panic at the jab, causing more laughter and hoots of derision as he shoved and stumbled out of range.

"The rest of ye want to play savage, too, do ye?" Jamie shouted. He swiped his broom through the steaming puddle and swung it hard in a wide arc before him. Droplets of hot tar flew through the air, and men yelled and pushed to get out of the way, stepping on each other and knocking each other down.

I was shoved to one side and fetched up hard against a barrel standing in the street. I would have fallen, save for Jezebel, who caught me by the arm and hauled me up, with no apparent effort.

"Yon feller's right rumbustious," she said with approval, eyes fixed on Jamie. "I could admire me a man like that!"

"Yes," I said, nursing a bruised elbow. "So could I. Sometimes."

Such sentiments appeared not to be universal.

"Give him up, Fraser, or wear feathers with him! Frigging Tories!"

The shout came from behind me, and I turned to see that the speaker had come prepared; he clutched a feather pillow in one hand, the end of it already ripped open, so that down feathers flew in spurts with each gesture.

"Tar and feather 'em all!"

I turned again at the shout from above, and looked up in time to see a young man fling wide the shutters in the upper story of the house on the other side of the street. He was trying to stuff a feather bed through the window but was being substantially impeded in this endeavor by the housewife whose property it was. This lady had leaped on his back and was beating him about the head with a spurtle, uttering shrieks of condemnation.

A young man near me started clucking like a chicken, flapping his elbows—to the intense amusement of his friends, who all began to do it, too, drowning out any attempts at reason—not that there was much of that.

A chant started up at the far side of the street.

"Tory, Tory, Tory!"

The tenor of the situation was changing, and not for the better. I half-lifted the fowling piece, unsure what to do, but knowing that I must do *something.* Another moment, and they'd rush him.

"Give me the gun, Auntie," said a soft voice at my shoulder, and I whirled round to find Young Ian there, breathing hard. I gave it to him without the slightest hesitation.

"Reste d'retour!" Jamie shouted in French. "*Oui, le tout!* Stay back, all of you!" He might have been shouting at the crowd, but he was looking at Ian.

What the devil did he—then I caught sight of Fergus, elbowing viciously to keep his place near the front of the crowd. Young Ian, who had been about to raise the gun, hesitated, holding it close.

"He's right, stay back!" I said urgently. "Don't fire, not yet." I saw now that a hasty shot might do more harm than good. Look at Bobby Higgins and the Boston Massacre. I didn't want any massacres taking place in Cross Creek—particularly not with Jamie at the center of them.

"I won't—but I'm no going to let them take him, either," Ian muttered. "If they go for him—" He broke off, but his jaw was set, and I could smell the sharp scent of his sweat, even above the reek of tar.

A momentary distraction had intervened, thank God. Yells from above made half the crowd turn to see what was happening.

Another man—evidently the householder—had popped up in the window above, jerking the first man back and punching him. Then the struggling pair disappeared from view, and within a few seconds, the sounds of altercation ceased and the woman's shrieks died away, leaving the feather bed hanging in limp anticlimax, half in and half out of the window.

The chant of "Tory Tory Tory!" had died out during the fascination with the conflict overhead, but was now starting up again, punctuated by bellows for the printer to come out and give himself up.

"Come out, Simms!" Forbes bellowed. I saw that he had equipped himself with a fresh broom, and was edging closer to the print shop's door. Jamie saw him, too, and I saw his mouth twist with derision.

Silas Jameson, the proprietor of a local ordinary, was behind Forbes, crouched like a wrestler, his broad face wreathed in a vicious grin.

"Come out, Simms!" he echoed. "What kind of man takes shelter beneath a Scotsman's skirts, eh?"

Jameson's voice was loud enough that everyone heard that, and most laughed—including Jamie.

"A wise one!" Jamie shouted back, and shook the end of his plaid at Jameson. "This tartan's sheltered many a poor lad in its time!"

"And many a lassie, too, I'll wager!" shouted some ribald soul in the crowd.

"What, d'ye think I've your wife under my plaid?" Jamie was breathing hard, shirt and hair pasted to him with sweat, but still grinning as he seized the hem of his kilt. "Ye want to come and have a look for her, then?"

"Is there room under there for me, too?" called one of the fishwives promptly.

Laughter rolled through the crowd. Fickle as any mob, their mood was changing back from threat to entertainment. I took a deep, trembling breath, feeling sweat roll down between my breasts. He was managing them, but he was walking a razor's edge.

If he'd made up his mind to protect Simms—and he had—then no power on earth would make him give the printer up. If the mob wanted Simms—and they did—they'd have to go through Jamie. And they *would,* I thought, any minute.

"Come out, Simms!" yelled a voice from the Scottish Lowlands. "Ye canny be hidin' up Fraser's backside all day!"

"Better a printer up my arse than a lawyer!" Jamie shouted back, waving his broom at Forbes in illustration. "They're smaller, aye?"

That made them roar; Forbes was a beefily substantial sort, while Fogarty Simms was a pinched starveling of a man. Forbes went very red in the face, and I saw sly looks being cast in his direction. Forbes was in his forties, never married, and there was talk . . .

"I wouldna have a lawyer up my backside at all," Jamie was shouting happily, poking at Forbes with his broom. "He'd steal your shite and charge ye for a clyster!"

Forbes's mouth opened, and his face went purple. He backed up a step, and seemed to be shouting back, but no one could hear his response, drowned as it was by the roar of laughter from the crowd.

"And then he'd sell it back to ye for night soil!" Jamie bellowed, the instant he could be heard. Neatly reversing his broom, he jabbed Forbes in the belly with the handle.

The crowd whooped in glee, and Forbes, no kind of a fighter, lost his head and charged Jamie, his own broom held like a shovel. Jamie, who had quite obviously been waiting for some such injudicious move, stepped aside like a dancer, tripped Forbes, and smacked him across the shoulders with the tar-smeared broom, sending him sprawling into the cooling tar puddle, to the raucous delight of the whole street.

"Here, Auntie, hold this!" The fowling piece was thrust suddenly back into my hands.

"What?" Completely taken aback, I whirled round to see Ian moving fast behind the crowd, beckoning to Fergus. In seconds, unnoticed by the crowd—whose attention was riveted on the fallen Forbes—they had reached the house where the feather bed hung from the window.

Ian stooped and cupped his hands; as though they had rehearsed it for years, Fergus stepped into this improvised stirrup and launched himself upward, swiping at the feather bed with his hook. It caught; he dangled for a moment, grabbing frantically with his sound hand at the hook, to keep it from coming off.

Ian sprang upward and seized Fergus round the waist, yanking downward. Then the fabric of the bed gave way under their combined weight, Fergus and Ian tumbled to the ground, and a perfect cascade of goose feathers poured out on top of them, only to be caught at once by the thick, damp air and whirled up into a delirious snowstorm that filled the street and plastered the surprised mob with clumps of sticky down.

The air seemed filled with feathers; they were everywhere, tickling eyes and nose and throat, sticking to hair and clothes and lashes. I wiped a bit of down from a watering eye and stepped hastily back, away from the half-blind people staggering near me, yelling and bumping into one another.

I had been watching Fergus and Ian, but when the featherstorm struck, I—unlike everyone else in the street—looked back at the print shop, in time to see Jamie reach through the door, seize Fogarty Simms by the arm, and snatch him out of the shop like a winkle on a pin.

Jamie gave Simms a shove that sent him staggering, then whirled back to snatch up his broom and cover the printer's escape. Ralston Bogues, who had been lurking in the shadow of a tree, popped out, a club in his hand, and ran after Simms to protect him, glancing back and brandishing the club to discourage pursuers.

This action had not gone totally unnoticed; though most of the men were distracted, batting and clawing at the bewildering cloud of feathers that surrounded them, a few had seen what was going on, and raised a halloo, yelping like hounds as they tried to push through the crowd in pursuit of the fleeing printer.

If ever there was a moment . . . I'd shoot above their heads and they'd duck, giving Simms time to get away. I raised the gun with decision, reaching for the trigger.

The fowling piece was snatched from my grasp so deftly that I didn't realize for an instant that it was gone, but stood staring in disbelief at my empty hands. Then a bellow came from behind me, loud enough to stun everyone nearby into silence.

"Isaiah Morton! You gonna *die,* boy!"

The fowling piece went off by my ear with a deafening *bwoom!* and a cloud of soot that blinded me. Choking and coughing, I scrubbed at my face with my apron, recovering sight in time to see the short, pudgy figure of Isaiah Morton a block away, running as fast as his legs would carry him. Jezebel Hatfield Morton was after him in an instant, ruthlessly flattening anyone in her way. She leapt nimbly over a besmeared and befeathered Forbes, who was still on his hands and knees, looking dazed, then pushed through the remnants of the mob and hared down the street, short flannel petticoats flying, moving at a surprising rate of speed for someone of her build. Morton careened round a corner and disappeared, implacable Fury close on his tail.

I felt a trifle dazed myself. My ears were still ringing, but I looked up at a touch on my arm.

Jamie was squinting down at me, one eye closed, as though unsure he was seeing what he thought he was seeing. He was saying something I couldn't make out, but the gestures he was making toward my face—coupled with a telltale twitching of the corner of his mouth—made his probable meaning *quite* clear.

"Ha," I said coldly, my own voice sounding tinny and far off. I swiped at my face again with the apron. "*You* should talk!"

He looked like a piebald snowman, with black splotches of tar on his shirt, and clumps of white goose down clinging to his brows, his hair, and the stubble of his beard. He said something else, but I couldn't hear him clearly. I shook my head and twisted a finger in my ear, indicating temporary deafness.

He smiled, took me by the shoulders, and leaned his head forward until his forehead met mine with a small *thunk!* I could feel him trembling slightly, but wasn't sure whether it was laughter or exhaustion. Then he straightened up, kissed my forehead, and took me by the arm.

Gerald Forbes sat in the middle of the street, legs splayed and careful hair disheveled. He was black with tar from the shoulder to the knee on one side. He'd lost a shoe, and helpful parties were trying to pick the feathers off him. Jamie led me in a wide circle round him, nodding pleasantly as we passed.

Forbes looked up, glowering, and said something muffled,

heavy face twisting in dislike. On the whole, I thought it was just as well I couldn't hear him.

IAN AND FERGUS had gone off with the majority of the rioters, no doubt to commit mayhem elsewhere. Jamie and I retired to the Sycamore, an inn on River Street, to seek refreshment and make repairs. Jamie's hilarity gradually subsided as I picked tar and feathers off him, but was significantly quenched by hearing an account of my visit to Dr. Fentiman.

"Ye do *what* with it?" Jamie had flinched slightly during my recounting of the tale of Stephen Bonnet's testicle. When I reached a description of the penis syringes, he crossed his legs involuntarily.

"Well, you work the needlelike bit down in, of course, and then flush a solution of something like mercuric chloride through the urethra, I suppose."

"Through the, er . . ."

"Do you want me to show you?" I inquired. "I left my basket at the Bogueses', but I can get it, and—"

"No." He leaned forward and planted his elbows firmly on his knees. "D'ye suppose it burns much?"

"I can't think it's at all pleasant."

He shuddered briefly.

"No, I shouldna think so."

"I don't think it's really effective, either," I added thoughtfully. "Pity to go through something like that, and not be cured. Don't you think?"

He was watching me with the apprehensive air of a man who has just realized that the suspicious-looking parcel sitting next to him is ticking.

"What—" he began, and I hurried to finish.

"So you won't mind going round to Mrs. Sylvie's and making the arrangements for me to treat the girls, will you?"

"Who is Mrs. Sylvie?" he asked suspiciously.

"The owner of the local brothel," I said, taking a deep breath. "Dr. Fentiman's maid told me about her. Now, I realize that there might be more than one brothel in town, but I think that Mrs. Sylvie must certainly know the competition, if there is any, so she can tell you—"

Jamie drew a hand down over his face, pulling down his lower eyelids so that the bloodshot appearance of his eyes was particularly emphasized.

"A brothel," he repeated. "Ye want me to go to a brothel."

"Well, I'll go with you if you like, of course," I said. "Though I think you might manage better alone. I'd do it myself," I added, with some asperity, "but I think they might not pay any attention to me."

He closed one eye, regarding me through the other, which looked as though it had been sandpapered.

"Oh, I rather think they would," he said. "So this is what ye had in mind when ye insisted on coming to town with me, is it?" He sounded a trifle bitter.

"Well . . . yes," I admitted. "Though I really did need cinchona bark. Besides," I added logically, "if I hadn't come, you wouldn't have found out about Bonnet. Or Lucas, for that matter."

He said something in Gaelic, which I interpreted roughly as an indication that he could have lived quite happily in ignorance of either party.

"Besides, you're quite accustomed to brothels," I pointed out. "You had a room in one, in Edinburgh!"

"Aye, I did," he agreed. "But I wasna marrit, then—or rather I was, but I—aye, well, I mean it quite suited me, at the time, to have folk think that I—" He broke off and looked at me pleadingly. "Sassenach, d'ye honestly want everyone in Cross Creek to think that I—"

"Well, they won't think that if I go with you, will they?"

"Oh, God."

At this point, he dropped his head into his hands and massaged his scalp vigorously, presumably under the impression that this would help him figure out some means of thwarting me.

"Where is your sense of compassion for your fellow man?" I demanded. "You wouldn't want some hapless fellow to be facing a session with Dr. Fentiman's syringe, just because you—"

"As long as I'm no required to face it myself," he assured

me, raising his head, "my fellow man is welcome to the wages of sin, and serve him just right, too."

"Well, I'm rather inclined to agree," I admitted. "But it isn't only them. It's the women. Not just the whores; what about all the wives—*and* the children—of the men who get infected? You can't let all of them die of the pox, if they can be saved, surely?"

He had by this time assumed the aspect of a hunted animal, and this line of reasoning did not improve it.

"But—the penicillin doesna always work," he pointed out. "What if it doesna work on the whores?"

"It's a possibility," I admitted. "But between trying something that might not work—and not trying at all . . ." Seeing him still looking squiggle-eyed, I dropped the appeal to reason and resorted to my best weapon.

"What about Young Ian?"

"What about him?" he replied warily, but I could see that my words had caused an instant vision to spring up in his mind. Ian was not a stranger to brothels—thanks to Jamie, inadvertent and involuntary as the introduction had been.

"He's a good lad, Ian," he said, stoutly. "He wouldna . . ."

"He might," I said. "And you know it."

I had no idea of the shape of Young Ian's private life—if he had one. But he was twenty-one, unattached, and so far as I could see, a completely healthy young male of the species. Hence . . .

I could see Jamie coming reluctantly to the same conclusions. He had been a virgin when I married him, at the age of twenty-three. Young Ian, owing to factors beyond everyone's control, had been introduced to the ways of the flesh at a substantially earlier age. And that particular innocence could not be regained.

"Mmphm," he said.

He picked up the towel, rubbed his hair ferociously with it, then flung it aside, and gathered back the thick, damp tail, reaching for a thong to bind it.

"If it were done when 'tis done, 'twere well it were done quickly," I said, watching with approval. "I think I'd best come, too, though. Let me fetch my box."

He made no response to this, merely setting grimly about

the task of making himself presentable. Luckily he hadn't been wearing his coat or waistcoat during the contretemps in the street, so was able to cover the worst of the damage to his shirt.

"Sassenach," he said, and I turned to find him regarding me with a bloodshot glint.

"Yes?"

"Ye'll pay for this."

MRS. SYLVIE'S establishment was a perfectly ordinary-looking two-storied house, small and rather shabby. Its shingles were curling up at the ends, giving it a slight air of disheveled surprise, like a woman taken unawares with her hair just out of rollers.

Jamie made disapproving Scottish noises in his throat at sight of the sagging stoop and overgrown yard, but I assumed that this was merely his way of covering discomfiture.

I was not quite sure what I had been expecting Mrs. Sylvie to be—the only madam of my acquaintance having been a rather elegant French émigré in Edinburgh—but the proprietor of Cross Creek's most popular bawdy house was a woman of about twenty-five, with a face as plain as piecrust, and extremely prominent ears.

In fact, I had momentarily assumed her to be the maid, and only Jamie's greeting her politely as "Mrs. Sylvie" informed me that the madam herself had answered the door. I gave Jamie a sideways look, wondering just how he came to be acquainted with her, but then looked again and realized that he had noted the good quality of her gown and the large brooch upon her bosom.

She looked from him to me, and frowned.

"May we come in?" I said, and did so, not waiting for an answer.

"I'm Mrs. Fraser, and this is my husband," I said, gesturing toward Jamie, who was looking pink around the ears already.

"Oh?" Mrs. Sylvie said warily. "Well, it'll be a pound extra, if it's the two of you."

"I beg your—oh!" Hot blood flooded my face as I belatedly

grasped her meaning. Jamie had got it instantly, and was the color of beetroot.

"It's quite all right," she assured me. "Not the usual, to be sure, but Dottie wouldn't mind a bit, she being summat partial to women, you see."

Jamie made a low growling noise, indicating that this was my idea and it was up to me to be carrying it out.

"I'm afraid we didn't make ourselves clear," I said, as charmingly as possible. "We . . . er . . . we merely wish to interview your—" I stopped, groping for an appropriate word. Not "employees," surely.

"Girls," Jamie put in tersely.

"Um, yes. Girls."

"Oh, you do." Her small bright eyes darted back and forth between us. "Methody, are you? Or Bright Light Baptists? Well, that'll be *two* pound, then. For the nuisance."

Jamie laughed.

"Cheap at the price," he observed. "Or is that per girl?"

Mrs. Sylvie's mouth twitched a little.

"Oh, per girl, to be sure."

"Two pound per soul? Aye, well, who would put a price on salvation?" He was openly teasing now, and she—having plainly made out that we were neither potential clients nor door-to-door missionaries—was amused, but taking care not to seem so.

"I would," she replied dryly. "A whore knows the price of everything but the value of nothing—or so I've been told."

Jamie nodded at this.

"Aye. What's the price of one of your girls' lives, then, Mrs. Sylvie?"

The look of amusement vanished from her eyes, leaving them just as bright, but fiercely wary.

"Do you threaten me, sir?" She drew herself up tall, and put her hand on a bell that stood on the table near the door. "I have protection, sir, I assure you. You would be well-advised to leave at once."

"If I wished to damage ye, woman, I should scarcely bring my wife along to watch," Jamie said mildly. "I'm no so much a pervert as all that."

Her hand, tight on the bell's handle, relaxed a bit.

"You'd be surprised," she said. "Mind," she said, pointing a finger at him, "I don't deal in such things—never think it—but I've seen them."

"So have I," said Jamie, the teasing tone gone from his voice. "Tell me, have ye maybe heard of a Scotsman called *Mac Dubh*?"

Her face changed at that; clearly she had. I was bewildered, but had the sense to keep quiet.

"I have," she said. Her gaze had sharpened. "That was you, was it?"

He bowed gravely.

Mrs. Sylvie's mouth pursed briefly, then she seemed to notice me again.

"Did he tell you?" she asked.

"I doubt it," I said, giving him an eye. He sedulously avoided my glance.

Mrs. Sylvie uttered a short laugh.

"One of my girls went with a man to the Toad"—naming a low sort of dive near the river, called the Toad and Spoon—"and he dealt badly with her. Then dragged her out to the taproom and offered her to the men there. She said she knew she was dead—you know it is possible to be raped to death?" This last was addressed to me, in a tone that mingled aloofness with challenge.

"I do," I said, very shortly. A brief qualm ran through me and my palms began to sweat.

"A big Scotsman was there, though, and he took issue with the proposal, apparently. It was him alone, though, against a mob—"

"Your specialty," I said to Jamie, under my breath, and he coughed.

"—but he suggested that they deal cards for the girl. Played a game of brag, and won."

"Really?" I said politely. Cheating at cards was another of his specialties, but one I tried to discourage his using, convinced that it would get him killed one day. No wonder he hadn't told me about this particular adventure.

"So he picked up Alice, wrapped her in his plaid, and brought her home—left her at the door."

She looked at Jamie with grudging admiration.

"So. Have you come to claim a debt, then? You have my thanks, for what they may be worth."

"A great deal, madam," he said quietly. "But no. We've come to try to save your girls from worse than drunken rapparees."

Her thin brows arched high in question.

"From the pox," I said baldly. Her mouth fell open.

For all her relative youth, Mrs. Sylvie was a hard customer, and no easy sell. While fear of the pox was a constant factor in the life of a whore, talk of spirochetes cut no ice with her, and my proposition that I inject her staff—there were only three girls, it appeared—with penicillin met with a firm refusal.

Jamie allowed the wrangling to go on until it became clear we had reached a stone wall. Then he came in on a different tack.

"My wife isna proposing such a course only from the goodness of her heart, ken?" he said. By now, we had been invited to sit, in a neat little parlor adorned with gingham curtains, and he leaned forward gingerly, so as not to strain the joints of the delicate chair he was sitting on.

"The son of a friend came to my wife, saying he'd contracted the syphilis from a whore in Hillsboro. She saw the sore; there is no question but that the lad is poxed. He panicked, though, before she was able to treat him, and ran. We have been looking for him ever since—and heard just yesterday that he had been seen here, in your establishment."

Mrs. Sylvie lost control of her face for an instant. It was back in a moment, but there was no mistaking the look of horror.

"Who?" she said hoarsely. "A Scotch lad? What did he look like?"

Jamie exchanged a brief, quizzical glance with me, and described Manfred McGillivray. By the time he had finished, the young madam's face was white as a sheet.

"I had him," she said. "Twice. Oh, Jesus." She took a couple of deep breaths, though, and rallied.

"He was clean, though! I made him show me—I always do."

I explained that while the chancre healed, the disease remained in the blood, only to emerge later. After all, had she not known of whores who contracted syphilis, without any exhibition of a previous sore?

"Yes, of course—but they can't have taken proper care," she said, jaw set stubbornly. "I always do, and my girls, too. I insist upon it."

I could see denial setting in. Rather than admit she might be harboring a deadly infection, she would insist it was not possible, and within moments would have talked herself into believing it and would throw us out.

Jamie could see it, too.

"Mrs. Sylvie," he said, interrupting her flow of justifications. She looked at him, blinking.

"Have ye a deck of cards in the house?"

"What? I—yes, of course."

"Bring them, then," he said with a smile. "Gleek, loo, or brag, your choice."

She gave him a long, hard look, her mouth pressed tight. Then it relaxed a little.

"Honest cards?" she asked, and a small gleam showed in her eye. "And for what stakes?"

"Honest cards," he assured her. "If I win, my wife injects the lot of ye."

"And if you lose?"

"A cask of my best whisky."

She hesitated a moment longer, eyeing him narrowly, estimating the odds. There was still a blob of tar in his hair, and feathers on his coat, but his eyes were deep blue and guileless. She sighed, and put out a hand.

"Done," she said.

"DID YOU CHEAT?" I asked, grasping his arm to keep from stumbling. It was well after dark by now, and the streets of Cross Creek were not lighted, save by starlight.

"Didna have to," he said, and yawned hugely. "She may be a good whore, but she's no hand at cards. She should have chosen loo; that's mostly luck, while brag takes skill. Easier to cheat at loo, though," he added, blinking.

"What, exactly, constitutes a good whore?" I asked curiously. I had never considered the question of qualifications anent that profession, but supposed there must be some, beyond possession of the requisite anatomy and a willingness to make it available.

He laughed at that, but scratched his head, considering.

"Well, it helps if she has a genuine liking for men, but doesna take them verra serious. And if she likes to go to bed, that's as well, too. Ouch." I had stepped on a rock, and tightening my grip on his arm, had got him on the patch of skin burned by tar earlier in the day.

"Oh, sorry. Is it bad? I have a bit of balm I can put on it, when we get to the inn."

"Och, no. Just blisters; it will bide." He rubbed his arm gingerly, but shrugged off the discomfort, and taking me by the elbow, led me round the corner, toward the main street. We had decided earlier that since we might be late, we would stay at McLanahan's King's Inn, rather than make the long drive back to River Run.

The smell of hot tar still permeated this end of town, and the evening breeze swirled feathers into small drifts at the side of the road; now and then, a down feather floated past my ear like a slow-moving moth.

"I wonder, are they still picking the feathers off Gerald Forbes?" Jamie said, a grin in his voice.

"Maybe his wife will just put a bolster cover on him and use him as a pillow," I suggested. "No, wait, he hasn't got a wife. They'll have to—"

"Call him a rooster, and put him out in the yard to serve the hens," Jamie suggested, giggling. "He's a fine cock-a-doodle, if no much in the way of a cock."

He wasn't drunk—we had drunk weak coffee with Mrs. Sylvie, after the injections—but he was desperately tired; we both were, and suddenly in the state of exhaustion where the lamest joke seems immensely funny, and we staggered, bumping together and laughing at worse and worse jokes until our eyes teared.

"What's that?" Jamie said suddenly, drawing a deep, startled breath through his nose. "What's burning?"

Something substantial; there was a glow in the sky, visible

over the roofs of the nearby houses, and the sharp scent of burning wood suddenly overlaid the thicker smell of hot tar. Jamie ran toward the corner of the street, with me hot on his heels.

It was Mr. Simms's print shop; well ablaze. Evidently his political enemies, balked of their prey, had decided to vent their animosity on his premises.

A knot of men was milling in the street, much as they had earlier in the day. Again, there were calls of "Tory!" and a few were brandishing torches. More men were running down the street toward the scene of the fire, shouting. I caught a bellow of "Goddamn Whigs!" and then the two groups collided in a flurry of shoving and punching.

Jamie grabbed my arm and propelled me back the way we had come, out of sight around the corner. My heart was pounding, and I was short of breath; we ducked under a tree and stood panting.

"Well," I said, after a short silence, filled with the shouts of the riot, "I suppose Fergus will have to find a different occupation. There's an apothecary's shop going cheap, I know."

Jamie made a small sound, not quite a laugh.

"He'd do better to go into partnership wi' Mrs. Sylvie," he said. "There's a business not subject to politics. Come on, Sassenach—we'll go the long way round."

When at length we reached the inn, we found Young Ian fidgeting on the porch, watching out for us.

"Where in the name of Bride have you *been*?" he demanded severely, in a manner that made me think suddenly of his mother. "We've been combin' the town for ye, Uncle Jamie, and Fergus sure ye'd been caught up in the collieshangie yonder and maimed or killed." He nodded toward the print shop; the blaze was beginning to die, though there was still enough light from it to see his face, set in a disapproving frown.

"We've been doing good deeds," Jamie assured him piously. "Visiting the sick, as Christ commands us."

"Oh, aye?" Ian responded, with considerable cynicism. "He said ye should visit those in prison, too. Too bad ye didna start wi' that."

"What? Why?"

"Yon bugger Donner's escaped, that's for why," Ian informed him, seeming to take a grim pleasure in imparting bad news. "During the fight this afternoon. The gaoler came to join in the fun, and left the door on the latch; the bugger just walked out and awa'."

Jamie inhaled deeply, then let his breath out slowly, coughing slightly from the smoke.

"Aye, well," he said. "So we're down by one print shop and one thief—but four whores to the good. D'ye think that a fair exchange, Sassenach?"

"Whores?" Ian exclaimed, startled. "What whores?"

"Mrs. Sylvie's," I said, peering at him. He looked shifty, though perhaps it was only the light. "Ian! You didn't!"

"Well, of course he did, Sassenach," Jamie said, resigned. "Look at him." A guilty expression was spreading over Ian's features like an oil slick on water, easy to make out, even by the flickering, ruddy light of the dying fire.

"I found out about Manfred," Ian offered hastily. "He went downriver, meaning to find a ship in Wilmington."

"Yes, we found that out, too," I said a little testily. "Who was it? Mrs. Sylvie or one of the girls?"

His large Adam's apple bobbed nervously.

"Mrs. Sylvie," he said in a low voice.

"Right," I said. "Fortunately, I have some penicillin left—and a nice, dull syringe. Inside with you, Ian, you abandoned wretch, and down with your breeks."

Mrs. McLanahan, emerging onto the porch to inquire whether we would like a bit of late supper, overheard this and gave me a startled look, but I was well past caring.

Sometime later, we lay at last in the haven of a clean bed, safe from the upheavals and turmoils of the day. I had pried the window open, and the faintest of breezes disturbed the heaviness of the thick, hot air. Several soft gray flecks drifted in, feathers or bits of ash, spiraling like snowflakes toward the floor.

Jamie's arm lay across me, and I could make out the soft, glaucous shapes of the blisters that covered most of his forearm. The air was harsh with burning, but the smell of tar lay like an abiding threat beneath. The men who had burned Simms's shop—and come so close to burning Simms, and likely Jamie, as well—were rebels in the making, men who would be called patriots.

"I can hear ye thinking, Sassenach," he said. He sounded peaceful, on the verge of sleep. "What is it?"

"I was thinking of tar and feathers," I said softly, and very gently touched his arm. "Jamie—it's time."

"I know," he answered just as softly.

Some men went by in the street outside, singing drunkenly, with torches; the flickering light flowed across the ceiling and was gone. I could feel Jamie watch it go, listening to the raucous voices as they faded down the street, but he said nothing, and after a bit, the big body that cradled me began to relax, sinking once again toward sleep.

"What are you thinking?" I whispered, not sure whether he could still hear me. He could.

"I was thinking that ye'd make a really good whore, Sassenach, were ye at all promiscuous," he replied drowsily.

"What?" I said, quite startled.

"But I'm glad ye're not," he added, and began to snore.

57

THE MINISTER'S RETURN

September 4, 1774

ROGER STEERED CLEAR of Coopersville on his way home. It wasn't that he feared Ute McGillivray's wrath, but he didn't want to tarnish the happiness of his homecoming with coldness nor confrontation. Instead, he took the long way round, winding his way gradually up the steep slope toward the Ridge, pushing through overgrown parts where the forest had taken back the path, and fording small streams.

His mule splashed out of the last of these at the base of the trail, shaking itself and scattering droplets from its belly. Pausing to wipe sweat from his face, he spotted a movement on a large stone by the bank. Aidan, fishing, affecting not to have seen him.

Roger reined Clarence up alongside and watched for a moment, saying nothing. Then he asked, "Are they biting well?"

"Tolerable," Aidan replied, squinting hard at his line. Then he looked up, a huge grin splitting his face from ear to ear, and flinging down his pole, sprang up, reaching with both hands, so that Roger could grasp his skinny wrists and swing him up onto the saddle in front of him.

"Ye're back!" he exclaimed, throwing his arms about Roger and burying his face happily in Roger's chest. "I waited for ye. Are ye a real minister now, then?"

"Almost. How'd ye know I'd be along today?"

Aidan shrugged. "I've been waitin' the best part of a week, have I no?" He looked up into Roger's face, round-eyed and quizzical. "Ye dinna look any different."

"I'm not," Roger assured him, smiling. "How's the belly?"

"Prime. Ye want to see my scar?" He leaned back, pulling up his ratty shirttail to display a neat red four-inch weal across the pallid skin.

"Well done," Roger approved. "Taking care of your Mam and wee Orrie, then, now ye're mended, I suppose."

"Oh, aye." Aidan puffed his narrow chest. "I brought home *six* trout for supper last night, and the biggest one the size of me arm!" He stuck out a forearm in illustration.

"Ah, get on wi' ye."

"I *did,* then!" Aidan said indignantly, then twigged that he was being teased, and grinned.

Clarence was becoming restive, wanting home, and turned in little circles, stamping his feet and twitching at the reins.

"Best go. Ye want to ride up wi' me?"

Aidan looked tempted, but shook his head.

"Nah, then. I promised Mrs. Ogilvie as I should come tell her, the minute ye came."

Roger was surprised at that.

"Oh, aye? Why's that?"

"She's had a wean last week, what she wants ye to baptize."

"Oh?" His heart rose a little at that, and the bubble of happiness he carried inside him seemed to expand a little. His first christening! Or rather—his first official baptism, he thought, with a small pang at the memory of the small O'Brian girl he had buried without a name. He wouldn't be able to do it until after his ordination, but it was something to look forward to.

"Tell her I'll be glad to christen the wean," he said, lowering Aidan to the ground. "Have her send to tell me when. And dinna forget your wee fish!" he called.

Aidan grabbed up his pole and the string of silvery fish—none of them longer than the length of a hand—and plunged off into the wood, leaving Roger to turn Clarence's head toward home.

He smelled smoke from a good way down the trail. Stronger than chimney smoke. With all the talk he had heard on his way, regarding the recent events in Cross Creek, he couldn't help a small feeling of uneasiness, and urged Clarence on with a nudge of the heels. Clarence, scenting home even through the smoke, took the hint with alacrity, and trotted briskly up the steep incline.

The smell of smoke grew stronger, mixed with an odd musty sort of scent that seemed vaguely familiar. A visible haze grew among the trees, and when they burst out of the undergrowth into the clearing, he was nearly standing in his stirrups with agitation.

The cabin stood, weathered and solid, and relief dropped him back in the saddle with a force that made Clarence grunt in protest. Smoke rose around the house in thick swirls, though, and the figure of Brianna, swathed like a Muslim with a scarf around her head and face, was dimly visible in the midst of it. He dismounted, took a breath to call out to her, and immediately suffered a coughing fit. The damned groundhog kiln was open, belching smoke like hell's chimney, and now he recognized the musty scent—scorched earth.

"Roger! Roger!" She'd seen him, and came running, skirts and scarf ends flying, leaping a stack of cut turves like a mountain goat to hurl herself into his arms.

He grabbed her and held on, thinking that nothing in life had ever felt better than the solid weight of her against him and the taste of her mouth, in spite of the fact that she'd plainly eaten onions for lunch.

She emerged beaming and wet-eyed from the embrace, long enough to say, "I love you!" then grabbed his face and kissed him again. "I missed you. When did you shave last? I love you."

"Four days ago, when I left Charlotte. I love you, too. Is everything all right?"

"Sure. Well, actually no. Jemmy fell out of a tree and knocked out a tooth, but it was a baby tooth and Mama says she doesn't think it will hurt the permanent one coming in. And Ian got exposed to syphilis, maybe, and we're all disgusted with him, and Da was nearly tarred and feathered in Cross Creek, and we met Flora MacDonald, and Mama stuck a needle in Aunt Jocasta's eye, and—"

"Eugh!" Roger said in instinctive revulsion. "Why?"

"So it wouldn't burst. And I got paid six pounds in painting commissions!" she concluded triumphantly. "I bought some fine wire and silk to make paper screens with, and enough wool for a winter cloak for you. It's green. The biggest thing, though, is we met another—well, I'll tell you about that later; it's complicated. How did it go with the Presbyterians? Is it all right? Are you a minister?"

He shook his head, trying to decide which part of this cataract to respond to, and ended up choosing the last bit, only because he could remember it.

"Sort of. Have you been taking lessons in incoherence from Mrs. Bug?"

"How can you be sort of a minister? Wait—tell me in a minute, I have to open it up some more."

With that, she was flitting back across the broken ground toward the gaping hole of the kiln. The tall clay-brick chimney stack rose at one end, looking like a headstone. The scorched turves that had covered it in operation were scattered round it, and the general impression was that of an enormous, smoking grave from which something large, hot, and doubtless demonic had just arisen. Had he been Catholic, he would have crossed himself.

As it was, he advanced carefully toward the edge, where Brianna was kneeling, reaching across with her shovel to remove another layer of turves from the willow-work frame that arched across the top of the pit.

Looking down through a roiling haze of smoke, he could see irregularly shaped objects, lying on the earthen shelves that lined the pit. A few he could make out as being bowls or platters. Most of them, though, were vaguely tubular objects, two or three feet long, tapered and rounded at one end, the other slightly flared. They were a dark pinkish color, streaked and darkened with smoke, and looked like nothing so much as a collection of giant barbecued phalluses, a notion that he found nearly as disturbing as the story of Jocasta's eyeball.

"Pipes," Brianna said proudly, pointing her shovel at one of these objects. "For water. Look—they're perfect! Or they will be, if they don't crack while they're cooling."

"Terrific," Roger said, with a decent show of enthusiasm. "Hey—I brought ye a present." Reaching into the side pocket of his coat, he brought out an orange, which she seized with a cry of delight, though she paused for an instant before digging her thumb into the peel.

"No, you eat it; I've got another for Jem," he assured her.

"I love you," she said again, fervently, juice running down her chin. "What about the Presbyterians? What did they say?"

"Oh. Well, basically, it's all right. I have got the university degree, and enough Greek and Latin to impress them. The Hebrew was a bit lacking, but if I mug that up in the meantime—Reverend Caldwell gave me a book." He patted the side of his coat.

"Yes, I can just see you preaching in Hebrew to the Crombies and Buchanans," she said grinning. "So? What else?"

There was a fleck of orange pulp stuck to her lip, and he bent on impulse and kissed it off, the tiny burst of sweetness rich and tart on his tongue.

"Well, they examined me as to doctrine and understanding, and we talked a great deal; prayed together for discernment." He felt somewhat shy talking to her about it. It had been a remarkable experience, like returning to a home he'd never known he'd missed. To confess his calling had been joyful; to do it among people who understood and shared it . . .

"So I'm provisionally a minister of the Word," he said, looking down at the toes of his boots. "I'll need to be ordained before I can administer sacraments, but that will have to wait until there'a Presbytery Session held somewhere. In the meantime, I can preach, teach, and bury."

She was looking at him, smiling, but a little wistfully.

"You're happy?" she said, and he nodded, unable to speak for a moment.

"Very happy," he said at last, his voice hardly audible.

"Good," she said softly, and smiled a little more genuinely. "I understand. So now you're sort of handfast with God, is that it?"

He laughed, and felt his throat ease. God, he'd have to do something about that; he couldn't be preaching drunk every Sunday. Talk of giving scandal to the faithful . . .

"Aye, that's it. But I'm properly married to *you*—I'll not forget it."

"See that you don't." Her smile now was wholehearted. "Since we *are* married . . ." She gave him a very direct look, one that went through him like a mild electric shock. "Jem's at Marsali's, playing with Germain. And I've never made love to a minister before. It seems kind of wicked and depraved, don't you think?"

He took a deep breath, but it didn't help; he still felt giddy and light-headed, doubtless from the smoke.

"Behold, thou art fair, my beloved, yea, pleasant," he said, *"and our bed is green. The joints of thy thighs are like jewels, the work of the hands of a cunning workman. Thy navel is like a round goblet, which wanteth not liquor: thy belly is like an heap of wheat set about with lilies."* He reached out and touched her, gently.

"Thy two breasts are like two young roes that are twins."

"They are?"

"It's in the Bible," he assured her gravely. "It must be so, aye?"

"Tell me more about my navel," she said, but before he could, he saw a small form bounding out of the woods and haring toward them. Aidan, now fishless and panting.

"Mrs. Ogil . . . vie says . . . come *now*!" he blurted. He gasped a little, recovering enough breath for the rest of the message. "The wean—she's poorly, and they want her christened, in case she should die."

Roger clapped a hand to his other side; *The Book of Common Worship* that they'd given him in Charlotte was a small, reassuring weight in his pocket.

"Can you?" Brianna was looking at him worriedly. "Catholics can—I mean, a lay person can baptize somebody if it's an emergency."

"Yes, in that case—yes," he said, more breathless than he'd been a moment before. He glanced at Brianna, smudged with soot and dirt, her garments reeking of smoke and baked clay rather than myrrh and aloes.

"D'ye want to come?" He urgently wanted her to say yes.

"Wouldn't miss it for the world," she assured him, and discarding the filthy scarf, shook out her hair, bright as banners on the wind.

IT WAS THE Ogilvies' first child, a tiny girl who Brianna—with the experience of long motherhood—diagnosed as suffering from a vicious colic, but basically in good health. The frighteningly young parents—they both looked about fifteen—were pathetically grateful for everything: Brianna's reassurances and advice, her offer to have Claire visit (for they were much too scared to think of approaching the laird's wife themselves, leave alone the stories they had heard of her) with medicine and food, and most of all, for Roger's coming to baptize the baby.

That a real minister—for they could not be convinced otherwise—should appear in this wilderness, and condescend to come confer the blessing of God upon their child—they were overwhelmed by their good fortune.

Roger and Brianna stayed for some time, and left as the sun was going down, glowing with the faintly self-conscious pleasure of doing good.

"Poor things," Brianna said, voice trembling between sympathy and amusement.

"Poor wee things," Roger agreed, sharing her sentiments. The christening had gone beautifully; even the screaming, purple-faced infant had suspended operations long enough for him to pour the water on her bald head and claim heaven's protection for her soul. He felt the greatest joy in it, and immense humility at having been allowed to perform the ceremony. There was only the one thing—and his feelings were still confused between embarrassed pride and deep dismay.

"Her name—" Brianna said, and stopped, shaking her head.

"I tried to stop them," he said, trying to control his voice. "I did *try*—you're my witness. Elizabeth, I said. Mairi. Elspeth, perhaps. You heard me!"

"Oh, now," she said, and her voice trembled. "I think Rogerina is a perfectly *beautiful* name." Then she lost control, sat down in the grass, and laughed like a hyena.

"Oh, God, the poor wee lassie," he said, trying—and failing—not to laugh himself. "I've heard of Thomasina, and even Jamesina, but . . . oh, God."

"Maybe they'll call her Ina for short," Brianna suggested, snuffling and wiping her face on her apron. "Or they can spell it backward—Aniregor—and call her Annie."

"Oh, *you're* a great comfort," Roger said dryly, and reached down to haul her to her feet.

She leaned against him and put her arms round him, still vibrating with laughter. She smelled of oranges and burning, and the light of the setting sun rippled in her hair.

Finally, she stopped, and lifted her head from his shoulder.

"I am my beloved's, and my beloved is mine," she said, and kissed him. "You did good, Reverend. Let's go home."

Part Eight

The Call

58

LOVE ONE ANOTHER

ROGER TOOK THE deepest breath he could, and shouted as loudly as he could. Which was not very damn loud. Again. And again. It hurt. It was aggravating, too; the feeble, choked sound of it made him want to shut up and never open his mouth again. He breathed, shut his eyes, and screamed with all his might, or tried to.

A searing flash of pain shot down inside his throat on the right, and he broke off, gasping. All right. He breathed gingerly for a moment, swallowing, then did it again.

Jesus, that hurt.

He rubbed a sleeve across his watering eyes and braced himself for another go. As he inflated his chest, fists curling, he heard voices, and let the breath out.

The voices were calling to each other, not far from him, but the wind was away and he couldn't make out the words. Likely hunters, though. It was a fine fall day, with air like blue wine and the forest restless with dappled light.

The leaves had just begun to turn, but some were already falling, a silent, constant flicker at the edge of vision. Any movement could look like game in such surroundings, he knew that well. He drew breath to call out, hesitated, and said, "Shit," under his breath. Great. He'd rather be shot in mistake for a deer than embarrass himself by calling out.

"Ass," he said to himself, drew breath, and shouted, "Halloooo!" at the top of his voice—reedy and without volume as it was. Again. Again. And yet again. By the fifth time, he was beginning to think he'd rather be shot than go on trying to make them hear him, but at last a faint "Halloooo!" drifted back to him on the crisp, light air.

He stopped, relieved, and coughed, surprised not to be bringing up blood; his throat felt like raw meat. But he essayed a quick hum, then, cautiously, a rising arpeggio. An octave. Just barely, and it was a strain that sent shooting pains through his larynx—but a full octave. The first time he'd managed that much of a range in pitch since the injury.

Encouraged by this small evidence of progress, he greeted the hunters cheerfully when they came in view: Allan Christie and Ian Murray, both with long rifles in hand.

"Preacher MacKenzie!" Allan greeted him, grinning, like an incongruously friendly owl. "What are you doing out here all on your owney-o? Rehearsing your first sermon?"

"As a matter of fact, yes," Roger said pleasantly. It was true, in a way—and there was no other good explanation for what he was doing out in the woods by himself, lacking weapons, snare, or fishing pole.

"Well, best make it good," Allan said, wagging his head. "Everyone will be coming. Da's had Malva hard at it from dawn to dusk, sweeping and cleaning."

"Ah? Well, do tell her I appreciate it, will ye?" After a good deal of thought, he'd asked Thomas Christie whether the Sunday services might be held in the schoolmaster's home. It was no more than a rude cabin, like most on the Ridge, but since lessons were held there, the main room was somewhat more commodious than the average. And while Jamie Fraser would certainly have allowed the use of the Big House, Roger felt that his congregation—what a daunting word—might well be uneasy at holding their services in the house of a Papist, accommodating and tolerant though said Papist might be.

"Ye're coming, are ye not?" Allan was asking Ian. Ian looked surprised at the invitation, and rubbed an uncertain knuckle beneath his nose.

"Och, well, but I was baptized Romish, eh?"

"Well, ye're a Christian, at least?" Allan said with some impatience. "Or no? Some folk do say as how ye turned pagan, with the Indians, and didna turn back."

"Do they?" Ian spoke mildly, but Roger saw his face

tighten a little at that. He noticed with interest that Ian didn't answer the question, though, instead asking him, "Will your wife come to hear ye, cousin?"

"She will," he said, mentally crossing his fingers against the day, "and wee Jem, too."

"How's this?" Bree had asked him, fixing him with a look of rapt intensity, chin slightly lifted, lips just a fraction of an inch apart. *"Jackie Kennedy. That about right, do you think, or shall I aim for Queen Elizabeth reviewing the troops?"* Her lips compressed, the chin drew in a bit, and her mobile face altered from rapt attention to dignified approbation.

"Oh, Mrs. Kennedy, by all means," he'd assured her. He'd be pleased if she kept a straight face, let alone anyone else's.

"Aye, well, I'll come along then—if ye dinna think anyone would take it amiss," Ian added formally to Allan, who dismissed the notion with a hospitable flap of the hand.

"Oh, everyone will be there," he repeated. The notion made Roger's stomach contract slightly.

"Out after deer, are ye?" he asked with a nod toward the rifles, in hopes of turning the conversation toward something other than his own impending debut as a preacher.

"Aye," Allan answered, "but then we heard a painter screech, off this way." He nodded, indicating the wood just around them. "Ian said if there's a painter about, the deer will be long gone."

Roger shot a narrow glance at Ian, whose unnaturally blank expression told him more than he wanted to know. Allan Christie, born and raised in Edinburgh, *might* not know a panther's scream from a man's, but Ian most assuredly did.

"Too bad if it's frightened away the game," he said, lifting one brow at Ian. "Come on, then; I'll walk back with ye."

HE'D CHOSEN "Love thy neighbor as thyself" as the text for his first sermon. "An oldie but a goodie," as he'd told Brianna, causing her to fizz slightly. And having heard at least a hundred variations on that theme, he was reasonably sure of having sufficient material to go on for the requisite thirty or forty minutes.

A standard church service was a great deal longer—several readings of psalms, discussion of the lesson of the day, intercessions for members of the congregation—but his voice wouldn't take that yet. He was going to have to work up to the full-bore service, which could easily run three hours. He'd arranged with Tom Christie, who was an elder, to do the readings and the earliest prayers, to start with. Then they'd see how things went.

Brianna was sitting modestly off to one side now, watching him—not like Jackie Kennedy, thank God, but with a hidden smile that warmed her eyes whenever he met her gaze.

He'd brought notes, in case he should dry up or inspiration fail, but found that he didn't need them. He'd had a moment's breathlessness, when Tom Christie, who had read the lesson, snapped shut his Bible and looked significantly at him—but once launched, he felt quite at home; it was a lot like lecturing at university, though God knew the congregation was more attentive by far than his university students usually were. They didn't interrupt with questions or argue with him, either—at least not while he was talking.

He was intensely conscious for the first few moments of his surroundings: the faint fug of bodies and last night's fried onions in the air, the scuffed boards of the floor, scrubbed and smelling of lye soap, and the close press of people, ranged on benches, but so many that they crammed into every bit of standing space, as well. Within a few minutes, though, he lost all sense of anything beyond the faces in front of him.

Allan Christie hadn't exaggerated; everyone had come. It was nearly as crowded as it had been during his last public appearance, presiding at old Mrs. Wilson's untimely resurrection.

He wondered how much that occasion had to do with his present popularity. A few people were watching him covertly, with a faint air of expectation, as though he might turn water into wine for an encore, but for the most part, they appeared satisfied with the preaching. His voice was hoarse, but loud enough, thank God.

He believed in what he was saying; after the start he found himself talking more easily, and without the need of concentrating on his speech was able to glance from one person to another, making it seem he spoke to each one personally—meanwhile making fleeting observations in the back of his mind.

Marsali and Fergus hadn't come—no surprise there—but Germain was present; he sat with Jem and Aidan McCallum next to Brianna. All three boys had poked each other excitedly and pointed at him when he began to speak, but Brianna had quelled this behavior with some muttered threat of sufficient force to reduce them to simple squirming. Aidan's mother sat on his other side, looking at Roger with a sort of open adoration that made him uneasy.

The Christies had the place of honor in the center of the first bench: Malva Christie, demure in a lacy cap, her brother sitting protectively on one side, her father on the other, apparently unaware of the occasional looks shot her way by some of the young men.

Rather to Roger's surprise, Jamie and Claire had come, as well, though they stood at the very back. His father-in-law was calmly impassive, but Claire's face was an open book; she clearly found the proceedings amusing.

". . . and if we are truly considering the love of Christ as it is . . ." It was instinct, honed by innumerable lectures, that made him aware that something was amiss. There was some slight disturbance in the far corner, where several half-grown lads had congregated. A couple of the numerous McAfee boys, and Jacky Lachlan, widely known as a limb of Satan.

No more than a nudge, the glint of an eye, some sense of subterranean excitement. But he sensed it, and kept glancing back at that corner with a narrowed eye, in hopes of keeping them subdued. And so happened to be looking when the serpent slithered out between Mrs. Crombie's shoes. It was a largish king snake, brightly striped with red, yellow, and black, and it seemed fairly calm, all things considered.

"Now, ye may say, 'Who's my neighbor, then?' And a good question, coming to live in a place where half the folk ye meet are strangers—and plenty of them more than a bit strange, too."

A titter of appreciation ran through the congregation at that. The snake was casting about in a leisurely sort of way, head raised and tongue flickering with interest as it tested the air. It must be a tame snake; it wasn't bothered by the crush of people.

The reverse was not true; snakes were rare in Scotland, and most of the immigrants were nervous of them. Beyond the natural association with the devil, most folk couldn't or wouldn't distinguish a poison snake from any other, since the only Scottish snake, the adder, *was* venomous. They'd have fits, Roger thought grimly, were they to look down and see what was gliding silently along the floorboards by their feet.

A strangled giggle, cut short, rose from the corner of guilty parties, and several heads in the congregation turned, uttering a censorious "Shoosh!" in unison.

". . . when I was hungry, ye gave me to eat; when I was thirsty, ye gave me to drink. And who d'ye ken here who would ever turn away even . . . even a Sassenach, say, who came to your door hungry?"

A ripple of amusement, and slightly scandalized glances at Claire, who was rather pink, but with suppressed laughter, he thought, not offense.

A quick glance down; the snake, having paused for a rest, was on the move again, snooving its way gently round the end of a bench. A sudden movement caught Roger's eye; Jamie had seen the snake, and jerked. Now he was standing rigid, eyeing it as though it were a bomb.

Roger had been sending up brief prayers, in the interstices of his sermon, suggesting that heavenly benevolence might see fit to shoo the snake quietly out the open door at the back. He intensified these prayers, at the same time unobtrusively unbuttoning his coat to allow for freer action.

If the damned thing came toward the front of the room instead of the back, he'd have to dive forward and try to catch it before it got out in full sight of everyone. That would cause a disturbance, but nothing to what might happen if . . .

". . . now ye'll have noticed what Jesus said, when He spoke to the Samaritan woman at the well . . ."

The snake was still wrapped halfway round the bench leg, making up its mind. It was no more than three feet from his father-in-law. Jamie was watching it like a hawk, and a visible gloss of sweat had appeared on his brow. Roger was aware that his father-in-law had a fixed dislike of snakes—and no wonder, given that a big rattler had nearly killed him three years before.

Too far now for Roger to reach the thing; there were three benches of bodies between him and the snake. Bree, who could have dealt with it, was right away on the far side of the room. No help for it, he decided, with an inward sigh of resignation. He'd have to stop the proceedings, and in a very calm voice, call upon someone dependable—who? He cast hastily round, and spotted Ian Murray, who was within reach, thank God, to grasp the thing and take it out.

He was opening his mouth to do just this, in fact, when the snake, bored with the scenery in its view, slid rapidly round the bench and headed straight along the back row.

Roger's eye was on the snake, so he was as surprised as anyone—including the snake, no doubt—when Jamie suddenly stooped and snatched it from the floor, whipping the startled serpent under his plaid.

Jamie was a large man, and the stir of his movement made several people look over their shoulders to see what had happened. He shifted, coughed, and endeavored to look passionately interested in Roger's sermon. Seeing that there was nothing to look at, everyone turned back, settling themselves more comfortably.

". . . Now, we come across the Samaritans again, do we not, in the story of the Good Samaritan? Ye'll most of ye ken that one, but for the weans who may not have heard it yet—" Roger smiled at Jem, Germain, and Aidan, who all wriggled like worms and made small, ecstatic squeaks at the thrill of being singled out.

From the corner of his eye, he could see Jamie, standing frozen and pale as his best linen sark. Something was moving about inside said sark, and the barest hint of bright scales showed in his clenched hand—the snake was evidently trying to escape up his arm, being restrained from popping through the neck of the shirt only by Jamie's desperate grip on its tail.

Jamie was sweating badly; so was Roger. He saw Brianna frown a little at him.

". . . and so the Samaritan told the innkeeper to mind the poor fellow, bind up his wounds, and feed him, and he'd stop to settle the account on his way back from his business. So . . ."

Roger saw Claire lean close to Jamie, whispering something. His father-in-law shook his head. At a guess, Claire had noticed the snake—she could scarcely fail to—and was urging Jamie to go outside with it, but Jamie was nobly refusing, not wanting to further disrupt the sermon, as he couldn't go out without pushing past a number of other standees.

Roger paused to wipe his face with the large handkerchief Brianna had provided for the purpose, and under cover of this, saw Claire reach into the slit of her skirt and draw out a large calico pocket.

She appeared to be arguing with Jamie in a whisper; he was shaking his head, looking like the Spartan with the fox at his vitals.

Then the snake's head appeared suddenly under Jamie's chin, tongue flicking, and Jamie's eyes went wide. Claire stood instantly on tiptoe, seized it by the neck, and whipping the astonished reptile out of her husband's shirt like a length of rope, crammed the writhing ball headfirst into her pocket and jerked shut the drawstring.

"Praise the Lord!" Roger blurted, to which the congregation obligingly chorused "Amen!" though looking a little puzzled at the interjection.

The man next to Claire, who had witnessed this rapid sequence of events, stared at her bug-eyed. She stuffed the pocket—now heaving with marked agitation—back into her skirt, dropped her shawl over it, and giving the gentleman beside her a "What are *you* looking at, mate?" sort of stare, faced front and adopted a look of pious concentration.

Roger made it somehow to the end, sufficiently relieved at having the snake in custody that even leading the final hymn—an interminable back-and-forth "line hymn" in which he was obliged to chant each line, this echoed by the congregation—didn't disconcert him too much, though he had almost no voice left and what there was creaked like an unoiled hinge.

His shirt was clinging to him and the cool air outside was a balm as he stood shaking hands, bowing, accepting the kind words of his flock.

"A grand sermon, Mr. MacKenzie, grand!" Mrs. Gwilty assured him. She nudged the wizened gentleman who accompanied her, who might be either her husband or her father-in-law. "Was it no the grand sermon, then, Mr. Gwilty?"

"Mmphm," said the wizened gentleman judiciously. "No bad, no bad. Bit short, and ye left out the fine story aboot the harlot, but nay doot ye'll get the way of it in time."

"Nay doubt," Roger said, nodding and smiling, wondering, *What harlot?* "Thank ye for coming."

"Oh, wouldna have missed it for the world," the next lady informed him. "Though the singing wasna quite what one might have hoped for, was it?"

"No, I'm afraid not. Perhaps next time—"

"I never did care for Psalm 109, it's that dreary. Next time, perhaps ye'll give us one o' the mair sprightly ones, aye?"

"Aye, I expect—"

"DaddyDaddyDaddy!" Jem cannoned into his legs, clutching him affectionately round the thighs and nearly knocking him over.

"Nice job," said Brianna, looking amused. "What was going on in the back of the room? You kept looking back there, but I couldn't see anything, and—"

"Fine sermon, sir, fine sermon!" The older Mr. Ogilvie bowed to him, then walked off, his wife's hand in his arm, saying to her, "The puir lad canna carry a tune in his shoe, but the preaching wasna sae bad, all things considered."

Germain and Aidan joined Jemmy, all trying to hug him at once, and he did his best to encompass them, smile at everyone, and nod agreeably to suggestions that he speak louder, preach in the Gaelic, refrain from Latin (what Latin?) and Popish references, try to look more sober, try to look happier, try not to twitch, and put in more stories.

Jamie came out, and gravely shook his hand.

"Verra nice," he said.

"Thanks." Roger struggled to find words. "You—well. Thanks," he repeated.

"Greater love hath no man," Claire observed, smiling at him from behind Jamie's elbow. The wind lifted her shawl, and he could see the side of her skirt moving oddly.

Jamie made a small amused sound.

"Mmphm. Ye might drop by, maybe, and have a word wi'

Rab McAfee and Isaiah Lachlan—perhaps a short sermon on the text, *'He who loveth his son chasteneth him betimes?'* "

"McAfee and Lachlan. Aye, I'll do that." Or perhaps he'd just get the McAfees and Jacky Lachlan alone and see to the chastening himself.

He saw off the last of the congregation, took his leave of Tom Christie and his family with thanks, and headed for home and luncheon, his own family in tow. Normally, there would be another service in the afternoon, but he wasn't up to that yet.

Old Mrs. Abernathy was a little way before them on the path, being assisted by her friend, the slightly less-ancient Mrs. Coinneach.

"A nice-looking lad," Mrs. Abernathy was remarking, her cracked old voice floating back on the crisp fall air. "But nervous, och! Sweating rivers, did ye see?"

"Aye, well, shy, I suppose," Mrs. Coinneach replied comfortably. "I expect he'll settle, though, in time."

ROGER LAY IN bed, savoring the lingering sense of the day's accomplishments, the relief of disasters averted, and the sight of his wife, the light from the embers glowing through the thin linen of her shift as she knelt by the hearth, touching her skin and the ends of her hair with light, so that she looked illuminated from within.

The fire banked for the night, she rose and peered at Jemmy, curled up in his trundle and looking deceptively angelic, before coming to bed.

"You look contemplative," she said, smiling as she climbed onto the mattress. "What are you thinking about?"

"Trying to think what on earth I might have said that Mr. MacNeill could possibly have thought was Latin, let alone a Catholic reference," he replied, companionably making room for her.

"You didn't start singing 'Ave Maria' or anything," she assured him. "I would have noticed."

"Mm," he said, and coughed. "Don't mention the singing, aye?"

"It'll get better," she said firmly, and turned, pushing and squirming, to make a nest for herself. The mattress was stuffed with wool, much more comfortable—and a hell of a lot quieter—than corn shucks, but very prone to lumps and odd hollows.

"Aye, maybe," he said, though thinking, *Maybe. But it will never be what it was.* No point in thinking of that, though; he'd grieved as much as he meant to. It was time to make the best of things and get on.

Comfortable at last, she turned to him, sighing in contentment as her body seemed to melt momentarily and remold itself around him—one of her many small, miraculous talents. She had put her hair in a thick plait for sleeping, and he ran his hand down its length, recalling the snake with a brief shudder. He wondered what Claire had done with it. Likely set it free in her garden to eat mice, pragmatist that she was.

"Did you figure out which harlot story it was you left out?" Brianna murmured, moving her hips against his in a casual but definitely nonaccidental sort of way.

"No. There are a terrible lot of harlots in the Bible." He took the tip of her ear very gently between his teeth and she drew a deep, sudden breath.

"Whassa harlot?" said a small, sleepy voice from the trundle.

"Go to sleep, mate—I'll tell ye in the morning," Roger called, and slid a hand down over Brianna's very round, very solid, very warm hip.

Jemmy would almost certainly be asleep in seconds, but they contented themselves with small, secret touches beneath the bedclothes, waiting to be sure he was *soundly* asleep. He slept like the dead, once firmly in dreamland, but had more than once roused from the drowsy foreshore at very awkward moments, disturbed by his parents' unseemly noises.

"Is it like you thought it would be?" Bree asked, putting a thoughtful thumb on his nipple and rotating it.

"Is what—oh, the preaching. Well, bar the snake . . ."

"Not just that—the whole thing. Do you think . . ." Her eyes searched his, and he tried to keep his mind on what she was saying, rather than what she was doing.

"Ah . . ." His hand clamped over hers, and he took a deep

breath. "Yeah. Ye mean am I still sure? I am; I wouldna have done such a thing if I weren't."

"Dad—Daddy—always said it was a great blessing to have a calling, to *know* that you were meant to be something in particular. Do you think you've always had a—a calling?"

"Well, for a time, I had the fixed notion that I was meant to be a deep-sea diver," he said. "Don't laugh; I mean it. What about you?"

"Me?" She looked surprised, then pursed her lips, thinking. "Well, I went to a Catholic school, so we were all urged to think about becoming priests or nuns—but I was pretty sure I didn't have a religious vocation."

"Thank God," he said, with a fervency that made her laugh.

"And then for quite a while, I thought I should be a historian—that I wanted to be one. And it *was* interesting," she said slowly. "I could do it. But—what I really wanted was to build things. To make things." She pulled her hand out from under his and waggled her fingers, long and graceful. "But I don't know that that's a calling, really."

"Do ye not think motherhood is a calling, of sorts?" He was on delicate ground here. She was several days late, but neither of them had mentioned it—or was going to, yet.

She cast a quick glance over her shoulder at the trundle bed, and made a small grimace, whose import he couldn't read.

"Can you call something that's accidental for most people a calling?" she asked. "I don't mean it isn't important—but shouldn't there be some choice involved?"

Choice. Well, Jem had been thoroughly an accident, but this one—if there was one—they'd chosen, all right.

"I don't know." He smoothed the long rope of her braid against her spine, and she pressed closer in reflex. He thought she felt somehow riper than usual; something about the feel of her breasts. Softer. Bigger.

"Jem's asleep," she said softly, and he heard the surprisingly deep, slow breathing from the trundle. She put her hand back on his chest, the other somewhat lower.

A little later, drifting toward dreamland himself, he heard

her say something, and tried to rouse enough to ask her what it was, but managed only a small interrogative "Mm?"

"I've always thought I *do* have a calling," she repeated, looking upward at the shadows in the beamed ceiling. "Something I was meant to do. But I don't know yet what it is."

"Well, ye definitely weren't meant to be a nun," he said drowsily. "Beyond that—I couldna say."

THE MAN'S FACE *was in darkness. He saw an eye, a wet shine, and his heart beat in fear. The bodhrana were talking.*

There was wood in his hand, a tipper, a club—it seemed to change in size, immense, yet he handled it lightly, part of his hand, it beat the drumhead, beat in the head of the man whose eyes turned toward him, shining with terror.

Some animal was with him, something large and half-seen, brushing eager past his thighs into the dark, urgent for blood, and he after it, hunting.

The club came down, and down, and upanddown, upanddown, upanddown with the waggle of his wrist, the bodhran live and talking in his bones, the thud that shivered through his arm, a skull breaking inward with a wet, soft sound.

Joined for that instant, joined closer than man and wife, hearts one, terror and bloodlust both yielding to that soft, wet thud and the empty night. The body fell, and he felt it go away from him, a rending loss, felt earth and pine needles rough against his cheek as he fell.

The eyes shone wet and empty, and the face slack-lipped in firelight, one he knew, but he knew not the name of the dead, and the animal was breathing in the night behind him, hot breath on his nape. Everything was burning: grass, trees, sky.

The bodhrana were talking in his bones, but he could not make it out what they said, and he beat the ground, the soft limp body, the burning tree in a rage that made sparks fly, to make the drums leave his blood, speak clearly. Then the tipper flew free, his hand struck the tree and burst into flame.

He woke with his hand on fire, gasping. He brought his knuckles to his mouth by instinct, tasting silver blood. His heart was hammering so that he could scarcely breathe, and he fought the notion, trying to slow his heart, keep breathing, keep panic at bay, stop his throat closing up and strangling him.

The pain in his hand helped, distracting him from the thought of suffocation. He'd thrown a punch in his sleep, and hit the log wall of the cabin square. Jesus, it felt like his knuckles had burst. He pressed the heel of his other hand against them, hard, gritting his teeth.

Rolled onto his side and saw the wet shine of eyes in the ghost of firelight and would have screamed, if he'd had any breath.

"Are you all right, Roger?" Brianna whispered, voice urgent. Her hand touched his shoulder, his back, the curve of his brow, quickly seeking injury.

"Yeah," he said, fighting for breath. "Bad . . . dream." He wasn't dreaming of suffocation; his chest was tight, every breath a conscious effort.

She threw back the covers and rose in a rustle of sheets, pulling him up.

"Sit up," she said, low-voiced. "Wake all the way up. Breathe slow; I'll make you some tea—well, something hot, at least."

He hadn't any breath to protest. The scar on his throat was a vise. The first agony in his hand had subsided; now it began to throb in time to his heart—fine, that was all he needed. He fought back the dream, the sense of drums beating in his bones, and in the struggle, found his breath start to ease. By the time Brianna brought him a mug of hot water poured over something foul-smelling, he was breathing almost normally.

He declined to drink whatever it was, whereupon she thriftily used it to bathe his scraped knuckles instead.

"Do you want to tell me about the dream?" She was heavy-eyed, still yearning for sleep, but willing to listen.

He hesitated, but he could feel the dream hovering in the night-still air, just behind him; to keep silent and lie back in the dark was to invite its return. And perhaps she should know what the dream had told him.

"It was a muddle, but to do with the fight—when we went to bring Claire back. The man—the one I killed—" The word stuck in his throat like a bur, but he got it out. "I was smashing in his head, and he fell, and I saw his face again. And suddenly I realized I'd seen him before; I—I know who he was." The faint horror of knowing the man showed in his voice, and her heavy lashes rose, her eyes suddenly alert.

Her hand covered his injured knuckles, lightly, questioning.

"Do ye recall a wretched little thieftaker named Harley Boble? We met him, just the once, at the Gathering at Mount Helicon."

"I remember. Him? You're sure? It was dark, you said, and all confused—"

"I'm sure. I didn't know, when I hit him, but I saw his face when he fell—the grass was on fire, I saw it clearly—and I saw it again, just now, in the dream, and the name was in my mind when I woke up." He flexed his hand slowly, grimacing. "It seems a lot worse, somehow, to kill someone ye know." And the knowledge of having killed a stranger was quite bad enough. It obliged him to think of himself as one capable of murder.

"Well, you *didn't* know him, at the time," she pointed out. "Didn't recognize him, I mean."

"No, that's true." It was, but didn't help. The fire was smoored for the night, and the room was chilly; he noticed the gooseflesh on her bare forearms, the gold hairs rising. "You're cold; let's go back to bed."

The bed still held a faint warmth, and it was unutterable comfort to have her curl close to his back, the heat of her body penetrating his bone-deep chill. His hand still throbbed, but the pain had dulled to a negligible ache. Her arm settled firmly round him, a loose fist curled under his chin. He bent his head to kiss her own knuckles, smooth and hard and round, felt her warm breath on his neck, and had the oddest momentary recollection of the animal in his dream.

"Bree . . . I did *mean* to kill him."

"I know," she said softly, and tightened her arm around him, as though to save him falling.

59

FROGGY GOES A-COURTING

From Lord John Grey
Mount Josiah Plantation

My dear Friend,

I write in some Perturbation of Spirit.

You will recall Mr. Josiah Quincy, I am sure. I should not have provided him with a Letter of Introduction to you, had I had any Notion of the eventual Outcome of his Efforts. For I am sure that it is by his Action that your Name is associated with the so-called Committee of Correspondence in North Carolina. A Friend, knowing of my Acquaintance with you, showed me a Missive yesterday, purporting to originate from this Body, and containing a List of its presumed Recipients. Your Name was among these, and the Sight of it in such Company caused me such Concern as to compel me to write at once to inform you of the Matter.

I should have burned the Missive at once, was it not apparent that it was only one of several Copies. The Others are doubtless in transit through various of the Colonies. You must move at once to disassociate yourself from any such Body, and take Pains that your Name does not appear in Future in such Contexts.

For be warned: the Mail is not safe. I have received more than one official Document—even some bearing royal Seals!—that not only show Signs of having been opened, but that in some Cases are blatantly marked with the Initials or Signatures of those Men who have intercepted and inspected them. Such Inspection may be imposed either by Whig or Tory, there is no telling, and I hear that Governor Martin himself is now having his Mail directed to his Brother in New York, thus to be brought to him by private Messenger—one of these was a recent Guest at my table—as he cannot trust its secure Delivery within North Carolina.

I can only hope that no incriminating Document containing your Name falls into the Hands of Persons with the Power to arrest or instigate other Proceedings against the Speakers of such Sedition as appears in it. I apologize most sincerely, if my Inadvertence in introducing Mr. Quincy should in any way have endangered or inconvenienced you, and I will, I assure you, lend my every Effort to correct the Situation so far as may be in my Power.

Meanwhile, I offer you the Services of Mr. Higgins, should you require secure Delivery of any Document, not merely Letters addressed to myself. He is completely trustworthy, and I will send him regularly to you, in case you may require him.

Still, I am in Hopes that the Situation overall may yet be retrieved. I think those Hotheads who urge Rebellion must be for the most Part ignorant of the Nature of War, or surely they would not risk its Terrors and Hardships, nor yet think lightly of shedding Blood or the Sacrifice of their own Lives for the sake of so Small a Disagreement with their Parent.

Feeling in London at present is that the Matter will amount to no more than "a few bloody Noses," as Lord North puts it, and I trust it may be so.

This News has also a personal Aspect; my son William has purchased a Lieutenant's Commission, and will join his Regiment almost immediately. I am of course proud of him—and yet, knowing the Dangers and Hardships of a Soldier's Life, I confess that I should have preferred him to adopt another Course, either devoting himself to the Conduct of his considerable Estates, or, if he felt this too tame a Life, perhaps entering the Realm of Politics or Commerce—for he has much natural Ability to add to the Power of his Resources, and might well achieve some Influence in such Spheres.

Those Resources are of course still within my Control, until William shall attain his Majority. But I could not gainsay him, so exigent was his Desire—and so vivid my Memories of myself at that Age, and my Determination to serve. It may be that he will have his Fill of Soldiering quickly, and adopt another Course. And I will admit that the military Life has many Virtues to recommend it, stern as these Virtues may sometimes be.

On a less alarming Note—

I find myself returned unexpectedly to the Role of Diplomat. Not, I hasten to add, on behalf of His Majesty, but rather on behalf of Robert Higgins, who begs that I will employ what small Influence I possess in advancing his Prospects for Marriage.

I have found Mr. Higgins a good and faithful Servant, and am pleased to offer what Assistance I may; I hope you will find yourself similarly disposed, for as you will see, your Advice and Counsel is most urgently desired and, in fact, quite indispensable.

There is some small Delicacy involved in this Matter, and upon this Point, I would beg your Consideration; your Discretion I of course trust implicitly. It would appear that Mr. Higgins has formed some Attachment to two young Ladies, both resident on Fraser's Ridge. I have pointed out to him the Difficulty of fighting on two Fronts, as it were, and advised him to concentrate his Forces so as to provide the best chance of Success in his Attack upon a single Object—with, perhaps, the Possibility of falling back to regroup, should his initial Essay fail.

The two Ladies in question are Miss Wemyss and Miss Christie, both possessed of Beauty and Charm in Abundance, according to Mr. Higgins, who is most eloquent in their Praises. Pressed to choose between them, Mr. Higgins protested that he could not—but after some little Discussion on the matter, has at length settled upon Miss Wemyss as his first Choice.

This is a practical Decision, and the Reasons for his Choice concern not only the Lady's undoubted Attractions, but a more mundane Consideration: viz, *that the Lady and her Father are both Bond Servants, indentured to you. I am, by Reason of Mr. Higgins's devoted Service, offering to purchase both Indentures, should this be agreeable to you, upon Miss Wemyss's Agreement to wed Mr. Higgins.*

I should not wish to deprive you thus of two valued Servants, but Mr. Higgins feels that Miss Wemyss will not wish to leave her Father. By the same Token, he hopes that my offering to free Father and Daughter from Servitude (for I have agreed that I would do so, provided that Mr. Higgins's Employment with me shall continue) would be sufficient Inducement to overcome any Objections which Mr. Wemyss might present on Account of Mr. Higgins's lack of Connexions and personal Property, or such other small Impediments to the Marriage as might present themselves.

I collect that Miss Christie, while equally attractive, has a Father who may be somewhat more difficult of Persuasion, and her social Situation is somewhat higher than that of Miss Wemyss. Still, should Miss Wemyss or her father decline Mr. Higgins's Offer, I will do my Best, with your Assistance, to devise some Inducement that might appeal to Mr. Christie.

What think you of this Plan of Attack? I beg you to consider the Prospects carefully, and if you feel that the Proposal might be received favorably, to broach the Matter to Mr. Wemyss and his Daughter—if possible, with such Discretion as not to prejudice a secondary Expedition, should that prove necessary.

Mr. Higgins is most sensible of his inferior Position, viewed as a potential Groom, and thus most conscious of the Favor he seeks, as is

Your most humble and obedient Servant,
John Grey

". . . such other small Impediments to the Marriage as might present themselves," I read, over Jamie's shoulder. "Like being a convicted murderer with a brand on his cheek, no family, and no money, do you think he means?"

"Aye, like that," Jamie agreed, straightening out the sheets of paper and tapping the edges straight. He was clearly amused by Lord John's letter, but his brows had drawn together, though I didn't know whether this was a sign of concern over Lord John's news about Willie, or merely concentration on the delicate question of Bobby Higgins's proposal.

The latter, evidently, for he glanced upward, toward the room that Lizzie and her father shared. No sound of movement came through the ceiling, though I'd seen Joseph go upstairs a little earlier.

"Asleep?" Jamie asked, eyebrows raised. He looked involuntarily at the window. It was mid-afternoon, and the yard was cheerfully awash in mellow light.

"Common symptom of depression," I said, with a small shrug. Mr. Wemyss had taken the dissolution of Lizzie's betrothal hard—much more so than had his daughter. Frail-looking to begin with, he had noticeably lost weight, and had withdrawn into himself, speaking only when spoken to, and becoming increasingly hard to rouse from sleep in the mornings.

Jamie struggled momentarily with the concept of depression, then dismissed it with a brief shake of the head. He tapped the stiff fingers of his right hand thoughtfully on the table.

"What d'ye think, Sassenach?"

"Bobby's a lovely young man," I said dubiously. "And Lizzie obviously likes him."

"And if the Wemysses were still indentured, Bobby's proposal would likely have some appeal," Jamie agreed. "But they're not." He had given Joseph Wemyss his papers of indenture some years earlier, and Brianna had hastily freed Lizzie from her own bond nearly as soon as it was made. That was not a matter of public knowledge, though, since Joseph's presumed status as a bondsman protected him from service in the militia. Likewise, as a bondmaid, Lizzie benefited from

Jamie's overt protection, as she was considered his property; no one would dare to trouble her or treat her with open disrespect.

"Perhaps he'd be willing to engage them as paid servants," I suggested. "Their combined salary would likely be a good deal less than the price of two indentures." We paid Joseph, but his salary was only three pounds a year, though with room, board, and clothing supplied.

"I will suggest as much," Jamie said, but with an air of dubiousness. "But I'll have to speak with Joseph." He glanced upward once more, and shook his head.

"Speaking of Malva . . ." I said, glancing across the hall and lowering my voice. She was in the surgery, straining liquid from the bowls of mold that provided our supply of penicillin. I had promised to send more to Mrs. Sylvie, with a syringe; I hoped she would use it.

"Do you think Tom Christie would be receptive, if Joseph isn't? I think both girls are rather partial to Bobby."

Jamie made a mildly derisive noise at the thought.

"Tom Christie marry his daughter to a murderer, and a penniless murderer at that? John Grey doesna ken the man at all, or he wouldna be suggesting such a thing. Christie's proud as Nebuchadnezzar, if not more so."

"Oh, as proud as all that, is he?" I said, amused despite myself. "Who do you think he *would* find suitable, here in the wilderness?"

Jamie lifted one shoulder in a shrug.

"He hasna honored me with his confidences in the matter," he said dryly. "Though he doesna let his daughter walk out wi' any of the young lads hereabouts; I imagine none seems worthy to him. I shouldna be surprised at all, if he were to contrive some means of sending her to Edenton or New Bern to make a match, and he can contrive a way to do it. Roger Mac says he's mentioned such a course."

"Really? He's getting quite thick with Roger these days, isn't he?"

A reluctant smile crossed his face at that.

"Aye, well. Roger Mac takes the welfare of his flock to heart—with an eye to his own, nay doubt."

"Whatever do you mean by that?"

He eyed me for a moment, evidently judging my capacity for keeping secrets.

"Mmphm. Well, ye mustna mention it to Brianna, but Roger Mac has it in mind to make a match between Tom Christie and Amy McCallum."

I blinked, but then considered. It wasn't really a bad idea, though not one that would have occurred to me. Granted, Tom was likely more than twenty-five years older than Amy McCallum, but he was still healthy and strong enough to provide for her and her sons. And she plainly needed a provider. Whether she and Malva could share a house was another question; Malva had had the running of her father's house since she could manage it. She was amiable, certainly, but I rather thought she had as much pride as her father, and wouldn't take kindly to being supplanted.

"Mmm," I said dubiously. "Perhaps. What do you mean about Roger's own welfare, though?"

Jamie raised one thick eyebrow.

"Have ye not seen the way the widow McCallum looks at him?"

"No," I said, taken aback. "Have you?"

He nodded.

"I have, and so has Brianna. She bides her time for the moment—but mark my words, Sassenach: if wee Roger doesna see the widow safely marrit soon, he'll find hell nay hotter than his own hearth."

"Oh, now. Roger isn't looking *back* at Mrs. McCallum, is he?" I demanded.

"No, he is not," Jamie said judiciously, "and that's why he's still in possession of his balls. But if ye think my daughter is one to stand—"

We had been speaking in low voices and, at the sound of the surgery door opening, stopped abruptly. Malva poked her head into the study, her cheeks flushed and wispy tendrils of dark hair floating round her face. She looked like a Dresden figurine, despite the stains on her apron, and I saw Jamie smile at her look of eager freshness.

"Please, Mrs. Fraser, I've strained off all the liquid and bottled it—ye did say that we must feed the slops left over to the pig at once . . . did ye mean the big white sow that lives under the house?" She looked rather doubtful at the prospect, and no wonder.

"I'll come and do it," I said, rising. "Thank you, dear. You go along to the kitchen and ask Mrs. Bug for a bit of bread and honey before you go home, why don't you?"

She curtsied and went off toward the kitchen; I could hear Young Ian's voice, teasing Mrs. Bug, and saw Malva stop for an instant to pat her cap, twirl a wisp of hair around her finger to make it curl against her cheek, and straighten her slender back before going in.

"Well, Tom Christie may propose all he likes," I murmured to Jamie, who had come out into the hall with me and seen her go, "but yours isn't the only daughter with a mind of her own and strong opinions."

He gave a small, dismissive grunt and went back to his study, while I continued across the hall, to find a large basin of soggy garbage, the remnants of the latest batch of penicillin-making, neatly collected and standing on the counter.

Opening the window at the side of the house, I peered out and down. Four feet below was the mound of dirt that marked the white sow's den beneath the foundation.

"Pig?" I said, leaning out. "Are you at home?" The chestnuts were ripe and falling from the trees; she might well be out in the wood, gorging herself on chestnut mast. But no; there were hoofmarks in the soft soil, leading in, and the sound of stertorous breathing was audible below.

"Pig!" I said, louder and more peremptorily. Hearing the stirring and scraping of an enormous bulk beneath the floorboards, I leaned out and dropped the wooden basin neatly into the soft dirt, spilling only a little of its contents.

The thump of its landing was followed at once by the protrusion of an immense white-bristled head, equipped with a large and snuffling pink nose, and followed by shoulders the width of a hogshead of tobacco. With eager grunts, the rest of the sow's great body followed, and she fell upon the treat at once, curly tail coiled tightly with delight.

"Yes, well, just you remember who's the source from whom all blessing flows," I told her, and withdrew, taking pains to shut the window. The sill showed considerable splintering and gouging—the result of leaving the slop basin too long on the counter; the sow was an impatient sort, who was quite willing to try to come into the house and claim her due, if it wasn't forthcoming promptly enough to suit.

While partly occupied with the pig, my mind had not yet left the question of Bobby Higgins's proposal, with all its potential complications. To say nothing of Malva. Granted, she was undoubtedly sensible of Bobby's blue eyes; he was a very handsome young man. But she wasn't insensible to Young Ian's charms, either, less striking as they might be.

And what would Tom Christie's opinion of Ian as a son-in-law be, I wondered. He wasn't *quite* penniless; he had ten acres of mostly uncleared land, though no income to speak of. Were tribal tattoos more socially acceptable than a murderer's brand? Probably—but then, Bobby was a Protestant, while Ian was at least nominally Catholic.

Still, he was Jamie's nephew—a fact that might cut both ways. Christie was intensely jealous of Jamie; I knew that. Would he see an alliance between his family and ours as a benefit, or as something to be avoided at all costs?

Of course, if Roger succeeded in getting him to marry Amy McCallum, that might distract his mind a bit. Brianna hadn't said anything to me about the widow—but now that I thought back, I realized that the fact that she hadn't said *anything* might be an indication of suppressed feeling.

I could hear voices and laughter from the kitchen; obviously, everyone was having fun. I thought to go and join them, but glancing into Jamie's study, saw that he was standing by his desk, hands clasped behind him, looking down at Lord John's letter, a small frown of abstraction on his face.

His thoughts weren't with his daughter, I thought, with a small, queer pang—but with his son.

I came into the study and put my arm round his back, leaning my head against his shoulder.

"Have you thought, perhaps, of trying to convince Lord John?" I said, a little hesitantly. "That the Americans may possibly have a point, I mean—convert him to your way of thinking." Lord John himself would not be fighting in the coming conflict; Willie well might, and on the wrong side. Granted, fighting on either side was likely to be as dangerous—but the fact remained that the Americans would win, and the only conceivable way of swaying Willie was through his putative father, whose opinions he respected.

Jamie snorted, but put an arm around me.

"John? D'ye recall what I told ye about Highlanders, when Arch Bug came to me wi' his wee ax?"

"They live by their oath; they will die by it, too."

I shivered a little, and pressed closer, finding some comfort in his solidness. He was right; I had seen it myself, that brutal tribal fealty—and yet it was so hard to grasp, even when I saw it right under my nose.

"I remember," I said.

He nodded at the letter, his eyes still fixed on it.

"He is the same. Not all Englishmen are—but he is." He looked down at me, ruefulness tinged with begrudging respect. "He is the King's man. It wouldna matter if the Angel Gabriel appeared before him and told him what will pass; he wouldna abandon his oath."

"Do you think so?" I said, emboldened. "I'm not so sure."

His brows went up in surprise, and I went on, hesitating as I groped for words.

"It's—I do know what you mean; he's an honorable man. But that's just it. I don't think he *is* sworn to the King—not in the same way Colum's men swore to him, nor the way your men from Lallybroch swore to you. What matters to him—what he'd sell his life for—it's honor."

"Well, aye—it is," he said slowly, brows knit in concentration. "But for a soldier, such as he is, honor lies in his duty, no? And that comes from his fealty to the King, surely?"

I straightened and rubbed a finger beneath my nose, trying to put into words what I thought.

"Yes, but that's not quite what I mean. It's the *idea* that matters to him. He follows an ideal, not a man. Of all the people you know, he may be the only one who *would* understand—this will be a war fought about ideals; maybe the first."

He closed one eye and regarded me quizzically out of the other.

"Ye've been talking to Roger Mac. Ye'll never have thought that on your own, Sassenach."

"I gather you have, too," I said, not bothering to refute the implied insult. Besides, he was right. "So you understand?"

He made a small Scottish noise, indicating dubious agreement.

"I did ask him what about the Crusades, did he not think that was fought for an ideal? And he was obliged to admit that ideals were involved, at least—though even there he said it was money and politics, and I said it always was, and surely it would be now, as well. But, aye, I understand," he added hastily, seeing my nostrils flare. "But with regard to John Grey—"

"With regard to John Grey," I said, "you do have a chance of convincing him, because he's both rational and idealistic. You'd have to convince him that honor doesn't lie in following the King—but in the ideal of freedom. But it's possible."

Jamie made another Scottish noise, this one deep-chested and filled with uneasy doubt. And finally, I realized.

"*You* aren't doing it for the sake of ideals, are you? Not for the sake of—of liberty. Freedom, self-determination, all that."

He shook his head.

"No," he said softly. "Nor yet for the sake of being on the winning side—for once. Though I expect that will be a novel experience." He gave me a sudden rueful smile, and, caught by surprise, I laughed.

"Why, then?" I asked, more gently.

"For you," he said without hesitation. "For Brianna and the wee lad. For my family. For the future. And if that is not an ideal, I've never heard of one."

JAMIE DID HIS best in the office of ambassador, but the effect of Bobby's brand proved insuperable. While admitting that Bobby was a nice young man, Mr. Wemyss was unable to countenance the notion of marrying his daughter to a murderer, no matter what the circumstances that had led to his conviction.

"Folk would take against him, sir, ye ken that fine," he said, shaking his head in response to Jamie's arguments.

"They dinna stop to ask the why and wherefore, if a man's condemned. His eye—he did nothing, I am sure, to provoke such a savage attack. How could I expose my dear Elizabeth to the possibility of such reprisals? Even if she should escape herself, what of her fate—and that of her children—if he is knocked over in the street one day?" He wrung his hands at the thought.

"And if he should one day lose his Lordship's patronage, he could not look for decent employment elsewhere, not with yon mark of shame upon his face. They would be beggared. I have been left in such straits myself, sir—and would not for the world risk my daughter's sharing such a fate again."

Jamie rubbed a hand over his face.

"Aye. I understand, Joseph. A pity, but I canna say as ye're wrong. For what the observation be worth, I dinna believe that Lord John would cast him off, though."

Mr. Wemyss merely shook his head, looking pale and unhappy.

"Well, then." Jamie pushed himself back from his desk. "I'll have him in, and ye can give him your decision." I rose, as well, and Mr. Wemyss sprang up in panic.

"Oh, sir! Ye will not leave me alone with him!"

"Well, I scarcely think he'll try to knock ye down or pull your nose, Joseph," Jamie said mildly.

"No," Mr. Wemyss said dubiously. "Nooo . . . I suppose not. But still, I should take it *very* kindly if you would—would remain while I speak with him? And you, Mrs. Fraser?" He turned pleading eyes upon me. I looked at Jamie, who nodded in resignation.

"All right," he said. "I'll go and fetch him, then."

"I AM SORRY, sir." Joseph Wemyss was nearly as unhappy as Bobby Higgins. Small in stature and shy in manner, he was unaccustomed to conducting interviews, and kept glancing at Jamie for moral support, before returning his attention to his daughter's importunate suitor.

"I *am* sorry," he repeated, meeting Bobby's eyes with a sort of helpless sincerity. "I like ye, young man, and so does

Elizabeth, I am sure. But her welfare, her happiness, is my responsibility. And I cannot think . . . I really do not suppose . . ."

"I should be kind to her," Bobby said anxiously. "You know I should, zur. She should have a new gown once a year, and I should sell anything I have to keep her in shoes!" He, too, glanced at Jamie, presumably in hopes of reinforcement.

"I'm sure Mr. Wemyss has the highest regard for your intentions, Bobby," Jamie said as gently as possible. "But he's right, aye? It is his duty to make the best match he can for wee Lizzie. And perhaps . . ."

Bobby swallowed hard. He had groomed himself to the nines for this interview, and wore a starched neckcloth that threatened to choke him, with his livery coat, a pair of clean woolen breeches, and a pair of carefully preserved silk stockings, neatly darned in only a few places.

"I know I ha'n't got a great deal of money," he said. "Nor property. But I have got a good situation, zur! Lord John pays me ten pound a year, and has been so kind as to say I may build a small cottage on his grounds, and 'til it is ready, we might have quarters in his house."

"Aye, so ye said." Mr. Wemyss looked increasingly wretched. He kept looking away from Bobby, perhaps in part from natural shyness and unwillingness to refuse him eye-to-eye—but also, I was sure, to avoid seeming to look at the brand upon his cheek.

The discussion went on for a bit, but to no effect, as Mr. Wemyss could not bring himself to tell Bobby the real reason for his refusal.

"I—I—well, I will think further." Mr. Wemyss, unable to bear the tension any longer, got abruptly to his feet and nearly ran out of the room—forcing himself to a stop at the door, though, to turn and say, "Mind, I do not think I shall change my mind!" before disappearing.

Bobby looked after him, nonplussed, then turned to Jamie. "Have I hopes, zur? I know you will be honest."

It was a pathetic plea, and Jamie himself glanced away from those large blue eyes.

"I do not think so," he said. It was said kindly, but definitely, and Bobby sagged a little. He had slicked down his wavy hair with water; now dried, tiny curls were popping up from the thick mass, and he looked absurdly like a newborn lamb that has just had its tail docked, shocked and dismayed.

"Does she—do ye know, zur, or ma'am"—turning to me—"are Miss Elizabeth's affections given elsewhere? For if that was to be the case, sure I would bide. But if not . . ." He hesitated, glancing toward the door where Joseph had so abruptly disappeared.

"D'ye think I might have some chance of overcoming her father's objections? Perhaps—perhaps if I was to find some way of coming by a bit o' money . . . or if it was to be a question of religion . . ." He looked a little pale at this, but squared his shoulders resolutely. "I—I think I should be willing to be baptized Romish had he required it. I meant to tell him so, but forgot. Would ye maybe say so to him, zur?"

"Aye . . . aye, I will," Jamie said reluctantly. "Ye've quite made up your mind as it's Lizzie, then, have ye? Not Malva?"

Bobby was taken back by that.

"Well, to be honest, zur—I'm that fond of them both, I'm sure I should be happy with either one. But—well, truth to tell, I be mortal feared of Mr. Christie," he confessed, blushing. "And I think he don't like you, zur, while Mr. Wemyss does. If you could . . . speak for me, zur? Please?"

In the end, even Jamie was not proof against this guileless begging.

"I'll try," he conceded. "But I promise ye nothing, Bobby. How long will ye stay now, before ye go back to Lord John?"

"His Lordship's given me a week for my wooing, zur," Bobby said, looking much happier. "But I suppose ye'll be going yourself tomorrow or next day?"

Jamie looked surprised.

"Going where?"

Bobby looked surprised in turn.

"Why . . . I don't rightly know, zur. But I thought *you* must."

After a bit more cross-talk, we succeeded in disentangling the tale. He had, it seemed, fallen in with a small group of travelers on the road, farmers driving a herd of pigs to market. Given the nature of pigs as traveling companions, he hadn't stayed with them for more than one night, but over supper, in the course of casual talk, had heard them make reference to a meeting of sorts and speculate as to who might come to it.

"Your name was mentioned, zur—'James Fraser,' they said, and they mentioned the Ridge, too, so as I was sure 'twas you they meant."

"What sort of meeting was it?" I asked curiously. "And where?"

He shrugged, helpless.

"Took no notice, ma'am. Only they said 'twas Monday next."

Neither did he recall the names of his hosts, having been too much occupied in trying to eat without being overcome by the presence of the pigs. He was plainly too occupied at the moment with the results of his unsuccessful courtship to give much mind to the details, and after a few questions and confused answers, Jamie sent him off.

"Have you any idea—" I began, but then saw that his brows were furrowed; he obviously did.

"The meeting to choose delegates for a Continental Congress," he said. "It must be that."

He had had word after Flora MacDonald's barbecue that the initial meeting place and time were to be abandoned, the organizers fearing interference. A new place and time would be established, John Ashe had told him—word would be sent.

But that was before the contretemps in downtown Cross Creek.

"I suppose a note might have gone astray," I suggested, but the suggestion was a feeble one.

"One might," he agreed. "Not six."

"Six?"

"When I heard nothing, I wrote myself, to the six men I know personally within the Committee of Correspondence. No answer from any of them." His stiff finger tapped once against his leg, but he noticed, and stilled it.

"They don't trust you," I said, after a moment's silence, and he shook his head.

"Little wonder, I suppose, after I rescued Simms and tarred Gerald Forbes in the public street." Despite himself, a small smile flitted across his face at the memory. "And poor wee Bobby didna help, I expect; he would have told them he carried letters betwixt me and Lord John."

That was probably true. Friendly and garrulous, Bobby *was* capable of keeping a confidence—but only if you told him explicitly which confidence to keep. Otherwise, anyone who shared a meal with him would know all his business by the time the pudding came.

"Can you do anything else to find out? Where the meeting is, I mean?"

He blew out his breath in mild frustration.

"Aye, maybe. But if I did, and went there—there's a great chance they would put me out. If not worse. I think the risk of such a breach isna worth it." He glanced at me, with a wry expression. "I suppose I should have let them roast the printer."

I disregarded that, and came to stand beside him.

"You'll think of something else," I said, trying to be encouraging.

The big hour candle stood on his desk, half-burned, and he touched it. No one seemed ever to notice that the candle was never consumed.

"Perhaps . . ." he said meditatively. "I may find a way. Though I should hate to take another for the purpose."

Another gem, he meant.

I swallowed a small lump in my throat at the thought. There were two left. One each, if Roger, or Bree, and Jemmy—but I choked that thought off firmly.

"What does it profit a man to gain the world," I quoted, "if he lose his soul? It won't do us any good to be secretly rich, if *you* get tarred and feathered." I didn't like that thought any better, but it wasn't one I could avoid.

He glanced at his forearm; he had rolled up his sleeves for writing, and the fading burn still showed, a faint pink track among the sunbleached hairs. He sighed, went round his desk, and picked a quill from the jar.

"Aye. Perhaps I'd best write a few more letters."

60

THE PALE HORSEMAN RIDES

ON THE TWENTIETH of September, Roger preached a sermon on the text *God hath chosen the weak things of the world to confound the things which are mighty.* On the twenty-first of September, one of those weak things set out to prove the point.

Padraic and Hortense MacNeill and their children hadn't come to church. They always did, and their absence aroused comment—enough that Roger asked Brianna next morning if she might walk round and visit, to see that there was nothing wrong.

"I'd go myself," he said, scraping the bottom of his porridge bowl, "but I've promised to ride with John MacAfee and his father to Brownsville; he means to offer for a girl there."

"Does he mean you to make them handfast on the spot if she says yes?" I asked. "Or are you just there to keep assorted Browns from assassinating him?" There had been no open violence since we had returned Lionel Brown's body, but there were occasional small clashes, when a party from Brownsville happened to meet men from the Ridge now and then in public.

"The latter," Roger said with a small grimace. "Though I've some hopes that a marriage or two betwixt the Ridge and Brownsville might help to mend matters, over time."

Jamie, reading a newspaper from the most recent batch, looked up at that.

"Oh, aye? Well, it's a thought. Doesna always work out just so, though." He smiled. "My uncle Colum thought to mend just such a matter wi' the Grants, by marrying my mother to the Grant. Unfortunately," he added, turning over a page, "my mother wasna inclined to cooperate. She snubbed Malcolm Grant, stabbed my uncle Dougal, and eloped wi' my father, instead."

"Really?" Brianna hadn't heard that particular story; she looked enchanted. Roger gave her a sidelong glance, and coughed, ostentatiously removing the sharp knife with which she'd been cutting up sausages.

"Well, be that as it may," he said, pushing back from the table, knife in hand. "If ye wouldn't mind having a look-in on Padraic's family, just to see they're all right?"

In the event, Lizzie and I came along with Brianna, meaning to call on Marsali and Fergus, whose cabin was a little way beyond the MacNeills'. We met Marsali on the way, though, coming back from the whisky spring, and so there were four of us when we came to the MacNeills' cabin.

"Why are there so many flies, of a sudden?" Lizzie slapped at a large bluebottle that had landed on her arm, then waved at two more, circling round her face.

"Something's dead nearby," Marsali said, lifting her nose to sniff the air. "In the wood, maybe. Hear the crows?"

There were crows, cawing in the treetops nearby; looking up, I saw more circling, black spots against the brilliant sky.

"Not in the wood," Bree said, her voice suddenly strained. She was looking toward the cabin. The door was tightly shut, and a mass of flies milled over the hide-covered window. "Hurry."

The smell in the cabin was unspeakable. I saw the girls gasp and clamp their mouths tight shut, as the door swung open. Unfortunately, it was necessary to breathe. I did so, very shallowly, as I moved across the dark room and ripped down the hide that had been tightly nailed across the window.

"Leave the door open," I said, ignoring a faint moan of complaint from the bed at the influx of light. "Lizzie—go and start a smudge fire near the door and another outside the window. Start it with grass and kindling, then add something—damp wood, moss, wet leaves—to make it smoke."

Flies had begun to come in within seconds of my opening the window, and were whizzing past my face—deerflies, bluebottles, gnats. Drawn by the smell, they had been clustered on the sun-warmed logs outside, seeking entrance, avid for food, desperate to lay their eggs.

The room would be a buzzing hell in minutes—but we needed light and air, and would just have to deal with the flies as best we might. I pulled off my kerchief and folded it into a makeshift flyswatter, slapping to and fro with it as I turned to the bed.

Hortense and the two children were there. All naked, their pallid limbs glimmering with the sweat of the sealed cabin. They were clammy white where the sunlight struck, legs and bodies streaked with reddish-brown. I hoped that it was only diarrhea, and not blood.

Someone had moaned; someone moved. Not dead then, thank God. The bedcoverings had been thrown to the floor in a tangled heap—that was fortunate, as they were still mostly clean. I thought we had better burn the straw mattress, as soon as we got them off it.

"Do *not* put your fingers in your mouth," I murmured to Bree, as we began to work, sorting the feebly twitching heap of humanity into its component parts.

"You have *got* to be kidding," she said, speaking through her teeth while smiling at a pale-faced child of five or six, who lay half-curled in the exhausted aftermath of a diarrhetic attack. She worked her hands under the little girl's armpits. "Come on, lovey, let me lift you."

The child was too weak to make any protest at being moved; her arms and legs hung limp as string. Her sister's state was even more alarming; no more than a year old, the baby didn't move at all, and her eyes were sunk deep, a sign of severe dehydration. I picked up the tiny hand and gently pinched the skin between thumb and forefinger. It stayed for a moment, a tiny peak of grayish skin, then slowly, slowly, began to disappear.

"Bloody fucking hell," I said softly to myself and bent swiftly to listen, hand on the child's chest. She wasn't dead—I could barely feel the bump of her heart—but wasn't far from it. If she were too far gone to suck or drink, there was nothing that would save her.

Even as the thought passed through my mind, I was rising, looking about the cabin. No water; a hollowed gourd lay on its side by the bed, empty. How long had they been like this, with nothing to drink?

"Bree," I said, my voice level but urgent. "Go and get some water—quickly."

She had laid the older child on the floor, and was wiping the filth from her body; she glanced up, though, and the sight of my face made her drop the rag she was using and stand up at once. She grabbed the kettle I thrust into her hand and vanished; I heard her footsteps, running across the dooryard.

The flies were settling on Hortense's face; I flapped the kerchief close to shoo them away. The cloth skimmed her nose, but her slack features barely twitched. She was breathing; I could see her belly, distended with gas, moving slightly.

Where was Padraic? Hunting, perhaps.

I caught a whiff of something under the overwhelming stench of voided bowels and leaned over, sniffing. A sweet, pungently fermented scent, like rotted apples. I put a hand under Hortense's shoulder and pulled, rolling her toward me. There was a bottle—empty—under her body. A whiff of it was enough to tell me what it had contained.

"Bloody, bloody fucking hell," I said, under my breath. Desperately ill and with no water to hand, she had drunk applejack, either to quench her thirst or to soothe the pain of the cramps. A logical thing to do—save that alcohol was a diuretic. It would leach even more water from a body that was already seriously dehydrated, to say nothing of further irritating a gastrointestinal tract that scarcely needed it.

Bloody Christ, had she given it to the children, too?

I stooped to the elder child. She was limp as a rag doll, head lolling on her shoulders, but there was still some resilience to her flesh. A pinch of the hand; the skin stayed peaked, but returned to normal faster than the baby's had.

Her eyes had opened when I pinched her hand. That was good. I smiled at her, and brushed the gathering flies away from her half-open mouth. The soft pink membranes were dry and sticky-looking.

"Hallo, darling," I said softly. "Don't worry now. I'm here."

And was that going to help? I wondered. Damn it all; if only I had been a day earlier!

I heard Bree's hurrying steps and met her at the door.

"I need—" I began, but she interrupted me.

"Mr. MacNeill's in the woods!" she said. "I found him on the way to the spring. He's—"

The kettle in her hands was still empty. I seized it with a cry of exasperation.

"Water! I need water!"

"But I—Mr. MacNeill, he's—"

I thrust the kettle back into her hands and shoved past her.

"I'll find him," I said. "Get water! Give it to them—the baby first! Make Lizzie help you—the fires can wait! Run!"

I heard the flies first, a buzzing noise that made my skin crawl with revulsion. Out in the open, they had found him quickly, attracted by the smell. I took a hasty gulp of air and shoved through the buckbrush to where Padraic lay, collapsed in the grass beneath a sycamore.

He wasn't dead. I saw that at once; the flies were a cloud, not a blanket—hovering, lighting, flicking away again as he twitched.

He lay curled on the ground, wearing only a shirt, a water jug lying near his head. I knelt by him, peering as I touched him. His shirt and legs were stained, as was the grass where he lay. The excrement was very watery—most had soaked into the soil by now—but there was some solid matter. He'd been stricken later than Hortense and the children, then; his guts hadn't been griping long, or there would be mostly water, tinged with blood.

"Padraic?"

"Mrs. Claire, thank the Lord ye've come." His voice was so hoarse I could scarcely make out words. "My bairnies. Have ye got my bairnies safe?"

He raised himself on one elbow, shaking, sweat plastering strands of gray hair to his cheeks. His eyes cracked open, trying to see me, but they were swelled to mere slits by the bites of deerflies.

"I have them." I put a hand on him at once, squeezing to force reassurance into him. "Lie down, Padraic. Wait a moment while I tend them, then I'll see to you." He was very ill, but not in immediate danger; the children were.

"Dinna mind me," Padraic muttered. "Dinna . . . mind . . ."

He swayed, brushed at the flies that crawled on his face and chest, then groaned as cramp seized his belly again, doubling as though some massive hand had crushed him in its grip.

I was already running back to the house. There were splashes of water in the dust of the path—good, Brianna had come this way, hurrying.

Amoebic dysentery? Food poisoning? Typhoid? Typhus? Cholera—please God, not that. All of those, and a lot more, were currently lumped together simply as "the bloody flux" in this time, and for obvious reasons. Not that it mattered in the short term.

The immediate danger of all the diarrhetic diseases was simple dehydration. In the effort to expel whatever microbial invader was irritating the gut, the gastrointestinal tract simply flushed itself repeatedly, depleting the body of the water necessary to circulate blood, to eliminate wastes, to cool the body by means of sweat, to maintain the brain and membranes—the water necessary to maintain *life.*

If one could keep a patient sufficiently hydrated by means of intravenous saline and glucose infusions, then the gut would, most likely, heal itself eventually and the patient would recover. Without intravenous intervention, the only possibility was to administer fluids by mouth or rectum as quickly and as constantly as possible, for as long as it took. If one could.

If the patient couldn't keep down even water—I didn't think the MacNeills were vomiting; I didn't recall *that* smell among the others in the cabin. Probably not cholera, then; that was something.

Brianna sat on the floor by the elder child, the little girl's head in her lap, pressing a cup against her mouth. Lizzie knelt by the hearth, face red with exertion as she kindled the fire. The flies were settling on the motionless body of the woman on the bed, and Marsali crouched over the limp form of the baby on her lap, frantically trying to rouse it to drink.

Spilled water streaked her skirt. I could see the tiny head lolled back on her lap, water dribbling down a slack and horribly flattened cheek.

"She can't," Marsali was saying, over and over. "She can't, she can't!"

Disregarding my own advice about fingers, I ruthlessly thrust an index finger into the baby's mouth, prodding the palate for a gag reflex. It was there; the baby choked on the water in its mouth and gasped, and I felt the tongue close hard against my finger for an instant.

Sucking. She was an infant, still breastfed—and suckling is the first of the instincts for survival. I whirled to look at the woman, but a glance at her flat breasts and sunken nipples was enough; even so, I grabbed one breast, squeezing my fingers toward the nipple. Again, again—no, no droplets of milk showed on the brownish nipples, and the breast tissue was flabby in my hand. No water, no milk.

Marsali, grasping what I was about, seized the neck of her blouse and ripped it down, pressing the child to her own bared breast. The tiny legs were limp against her dress, toes bruised and curled like wilted petals.

I was tipping back Hortense's face, dribbling water into her open mouth. From the corner of my eye, I saw Marsali rhythmically squeezing her breast with one hand, an urgent massage to make the milk let down, even as my own fingers moved in an echo of the motion, massaging the unconscious woman's throat, urging her to swallow.

Her flesh was slick with sweat, but most of it was mine. Trickles of perspiration were running down my back, tickling between my buttocks. I could smell myself, a strange metallic scent, like hot copper.

The throat moved in sudden peristalsis, and I took my hand away. Hortense choked and coughed, then her head rolled to the side and her stomach heaved, sending its meager contents rocketing back up. I wiped the trace of vomit from her lips, and pressed the cup to her mouth again. Her lips didn't move; the water filled her mouth and dribbled down her face and neck.

Among the buzzing of the flies, I heard Lizzie's voice behind me, calm but abstracted, as though she spoke from a long way off.

"Can ye stop cursing, ma'am? It's only that the weans can hear ye."

I jerked round at her, only then realizing that I had in fact been repeating "Bloody fucking *hell*!" out loud, over and over as I worked.

"Yes," I said. "Sorry." And turned back to Hortense.

I got some water down her now and then, but not enough. Not nearly enough, given that her bowels were still trying to rid themselves of whatever troubled them. Bloody flux.

Lizzie was praying.

"Hail Mary, full of grace, the Lord is with thee . . ."

Brianna was murmuring something under her breath, urgent sounds of maternal encouragement.

"Blessed is the fruit of thy womb, Jesus . . ."

My thumb was on the pulse of the carotid artery. I felt it bump, skip, and go on, jerking along like a cart with a missing wheel. Her heart was beginning to fail, arrhythmic.

"Holy Mary, Mother of God . . ."

I slammed my fist down on the center of her chest, and then again, and again, hard enough that the bed and the pale splayed body quivered under the blows. Flies rose in alarm from the soaked straw, buzzing.

"Oh, no," said Marsali softly behind me. "Oh, no, no, please." I had heard that tone of disbelief before, of protest and appeal denied—and knew what had happened.

"Pray for us sinners . . ."

As though she, too, had heard, Hortense's head rolled suddenly to one side, and her eyes sprang open, staring toward the place where Marsali sat, though I thought she saw nothing. Then the eyes closed and she doubled suddenly, onto one side, legs drawn up nearly to her chin. Her head wrenched back, body tight in spasm, and then she suddenly relaxed. She would not let her child go alone. Bloody flux.

"Now and at the hour of our death, amen. Hail Mary, full of grace . . ."

Lizzie's soft voice went on mechanically, repeating her words of prayer as mindlessly as I had said mine earlier. I held Hortense's wrist, checking for the pulse, but it was mere formality. Marsali curled over the tiny body in grief, rocking it against her breast. Milk dripped from the swollen nipple, coming slowly, then faster, falling like white rain on the small still face, futilely eager to nourish and sustain.

The air was still stifling, still thick with odor and flies and the sound of Lizzie's prayers—but the cabin seemed empty, and curiously silent.

There was a shuffling noise outside; the sound of something being dragged, a grunt of pain and dreadful exertion. Then the soft sound of falling, a gasp of breath. Padraic had made it back to his own doorstep. Brianna looked to the door, but she still held the older girl in her arms, still alive.

I set down the limp hand that I held, carefully, and went to help.

61

A NOISOME PESTILENCE

THE DAYS WERE growing shorter, but light still came early. The windows at the front of the house faced east, and the rising sun glowed on the scrubbed white oak of my surgery floor. I could see the brilliant bar of light advancing across the hand-hewn boards; had I had an actual timepiece, I could have calibrated the floor like a sundial, marking the seams between the boards in minutes.

As it was, I marked them in heartbeats, waiting through the moments until the sun should have reached the counter where my microscope stood ready, slides and beaker beside it.

I heard soft footsteps in the corridor, and Jamie pushed the door open with his shoulder, a pewter mug of something hot held in each hand, wrapped with rags against the heat.

"Ciamar a tha thu, mo chridhe," he said softly, and handed one to me, brushing a kiss across my forehead. "How is it, then?"

"It could be worse." I gave him a smile of gratitude, though it was interrupted by a yawn. I didn't need to tell him that Padraic and his elder daughter still lived; he would have known at once by my face if anything dire had happened. In fact, bar any complications, I thought both would recover; I had stayed with them all night, rousing them hourly to drink a concoction of honeyed water, mixed with a little salt, alternating with a strong infusion of peppermint leaf and dogwood bark to calm the bowels.

I lifted the mug—goosefoot tea—closing my eyes as I inhaled the faint, bitter perfume, and feeling the tight muscles of my neck and shoulders relax in anticipation.

He had seen me twist my head to ease my neck; Jamie's hand came down on my nape, large and wonderfully warm from holding the hot tea. I gave a small moan of ecstasy at the touch, and he laughed low in his throat, massaging my sore muscles.

"Should ye not be abed, Sassenach? Ye'll not have slept at all the night."

"Oh, I did . . . a bit." I had dozed fitfully, sitting up by the open window, roused periodically by the startling touch on my face of the moths that flew in, drawn to the light of my candle. Mrs. Bug had come at dawn, though, fresh and starched, ready to take over the heavy nursing.

"I'll go lie down in a bit," I promised. "But I wanted to have a quick look first." I waved vaguely toward my microscope, which stood assembled and ready on the table. Next to it were several small glass bottles, plugged with twists of cloth, each containing a brownish liquid. Jamie frowned at them.

"Look? At what?" he said. He lifted his long, straight nose, sniffing suspiciously. "Is that shit?"

"Yes, it is," I said, not bothering to stifle a jaw-cracking yawn. I had—as discreetly as possible—collected samples from Hortense and the baby and, later, from my living patients, as well. Jamie eyed them.

"Exactly *what,*" he inquired cautiously, "are ye looking for?"

"Well, I don't know," I admitted. "And in fact, I may not find anything—or anything I can recognize. But it's possible that it was either an amoeba or a bacillus that made the MacNeills sick—and I think I *would* recognize an amoeba; they're quite big. Relatively speaking," I added hastily.

"Oh, aye?" His ruddy brows drew together, then lifted. "Why?"

That was a better question than he knew.

"Well, partly for the sake of curiosity," I admitted. "But also, if I do find a causative organism that I can recognize, I'll know a bit more about the disease—how long it lasts, for instance, and whether there are any complications to look out for specially. And how contagious it is."

He glanced at me, cup half-raised to his mouth.

"Is it one *you* can catch?"

"I don't know," I admitted. "Though I'm fairly sure it is. I've been vaccinated against typhus and typhoid—but this doesn't look like either one of those. And there are no vaccines for dysentery or *Giardia* poisoning."

The brows drew together and stayed that way, knotted as he sipped his tea. His fingers gave my neck a final squeeze and dropped away.

I sipped cautiously at my own tea, sighing in pleasure as it gently scalded my throat and ran hot and comforting down into my stomach. Jamie lounged on his stool, long legs thrust out. He glanced down into the steaming cup between his hands.

"D'ye think this tea is hot, Sassenach?" he asked.

I raised my own brows at that. Both cups were still wrapped in rags, and I could feel the heat seeping through to my palms.

"I do," I said. "Why?"

He lifted the mug and took a mouthful of tea, which he held for a moment before swallowing; I could see the long muscles move in his throat.

"Brianna came into the kitchen whilst I was brewing the pot," he said. "She took down the basin, and the pannikin of soap—and then she took a dipper of water steaming from the kettle, and poured it over her hands, one and then the other." He paused a moment. "The water was boiling when I took it off the fire a moment before."

The mouthful of tea I had taken went down crooked, and I coughed.

"Did she burn herself?" I said, when I had got my breath back.

"She did," he said, rather grimly. "She scrubbed herself from fingertips to elbows, and I saw the blister on the side of her hand where the water fell." He paused for a moment, and his eyes met mine over the mugs, dark blue with worry.

I took another sip of my un-honeyed tea. The room was cool enough, just past dawn, that my hot breath made tiny wisps of steam as I sighed.

"Padraic's baby died in Marsali's arms," I said quietly. "She held the other child. She knows it's contagious." And knowing, could not touch or pick up her own child without doing her best to wash away her fear.

Jamie moved uneasily.

"Aye," he began. "But still . . ."

"It's different," I said, and put a hand on his wrist, as much for my own comfort as his.

The transient coolness of the morning air touched face and mind alike, dispelling the warm tangle of dreams. The grass and trees were still lit with a chilly dawn glow, blue-shadowed and mysterious, and Jamie seemed a solid point of reference, fixed in the shifting light.

"Different," I repeated. "For her, I mean." I took a breath of the sweet morning air, smelling of wet grass and morning glories.

"I was born at the end of a war—the Great War, they called it, because the world had never seen anything like it. I told you about it." My voice held a slight question, and he nodded, eyes fixed on mine, listening.

"The year after I was born," I said, "there was a great epidemic of influenza. All over the world. People died in hundreds and thousands; whole villages disappeared in the space of a week. And then came the other, my war."

The words were quite unconscious, but hearing them, I felt the corner of my mouth twitch with irony. Jamie saw it and a faint smile touched his own lips. He knew what I meant—that odd sense of pride that comes of living through a terrible conflict, leaving one with a peculiar feeling of possession. His wrist turned, his fingers wrapping tight around my own.

"And she has never seen plague or war," he said, beginning to understand. "Never?" His voice held something odd. Nearly incomprehensible, to a man born a warrior, brought up to fight as soon as he could lift a sword; born to the idea that he must—he would—defend himself and his family by violence. An incomprehensible notion—but a rather wonderful one.

"Only as pictures. Films, I mean. Television." That one he would never understand, and I could not explain. The way in which such pictures focused on war itself; bombs and planes and submarines, and the thrilling urgency of blood shed on purpose; a sense of nobility in deliberate death.

He knew what battlefields were really like—battlefields, and what came after them.

"The men who fought in those wars—and the women—they didn't die of the killing, most of them. They died like this—" A lift of my mug toward the open window, toward the peaceful mountains, the distant hollow where Padraic MacNeill's cabin lay hidden. "They died of illness and neglect, because there wasn't any way to stop it."

"I have seen that," he said softly, with a glance at the stoppered bottles. "Plague and ague run rampant in a city, half a regiment dead of flux."

"Of course you have."

Butterflies were rising among the flowers in the dooryard, cabbage whites and sulfur yellows, here and there the great, lazy sail of a late tiger swallowtail out of the shadow of the wood. My thumb still rested on his wrist, feeling his heartbeat, slow and powerful.

"Brianna was born seven years after penicillin came into common use. She was born in America—not this one"—I nodded toward the window again—"but *that* one, that will be. There, it isn't usual for lots of people to die of contagious illness." I glanced at him. The light had reached his waist, and glowed on the metal cup in his hand.

"Do you remember the first person you knew of who had died?"

His face went blank with surprise, then sharpened, thinking. After a moment, he shook his head.

"My brother was the first who was important, but I kent others before him, surely."

"I can't remember, either." My parents, of course; their deaths had been personal—but born in England, I had lived in the shadow of cenotaphs and memorials, and people just beyond the bounds of my own family died regularly; I had a sudden vivid memory, of my father putting on a homburg and dark coat to go to the baker's wife's funeral. Mrs. Briggs, her name had been. But she hadn't been the first; I knew already about death and funerals. How old had I been then—four, perhaps?

I was very tired. My eyes felt grainy from lack of sleep, and the delicate early light was brightening to full sun.

"I think Frank's was the first death Brianna ever experienced personally. Maybe there were others; I can't be sure. But the point is—"

"I see the point." He reached to take the empty cup from my hand, and set it on the counter, then drained his own and set it down, too.

"But it's no herself she fears for, aye?" he asked, his eyes penetrating. "It's the wean."

I nodded. She would have known, of course, in an academic sort of way, that such things were possible. But to have a child die suddenly before you, from something like a simple case of diarrhea . . .

"She's a good mother," I said, and yawned suddenly. She was. But it would never have struck her in any visceral way that something so negligible as a germ could suddenly snatch away her child. Not until yesterday.

Jamie stood up suddenly, and pulled me to my feet.

"Go to bed, Sassenach," he said. "That will wait." He nodded at the microscope. "I've never known shit spoil with keeping."

I laughed, and collapsed slowly against him, my cheek pressed against his chest.

"Maybe you're right." Still, I didn't push away. He held me, and we watched the sunlight grow, creeping slowly up the wall.

62

AMOEBA

I TURNED THE MIRROR of the microscope a fraction of an inch further, to get as much light as I could.

"There." I stepped back, motioning Malva to come and look. "Do you see it? The big, clear thing in the middle, lobed, with the little flecks in it?"

She frowned, squinting one-eyed into the ocular, then drew in her breath in a gasp of triumph.

"I see it plain! Like a currant pudding someone's dropped on the floor, no?"

"That's it," I said, smiling at her description in spite of the general seriousness of our investigation. "It's an amoeba—one of the bigger sorts of microorganisms. And I very much think it's our villain."

We were looking at slides made from the stool samples I had retrieved from all the sick so far—for Padraic's family was not the only one affected. There were three families with at least one person ill with a vicious bloody flux—and in all of the samples I had looked at so far, I had found this amoebic stranger.

"Is it really?" Malva had looked up when I spoke, but now returned to the eyepiece, absorbed. "However can something so small cause such *a stramash* in something so big as a person?"

"Well, there *is* an explanation," I said, swishing another slide gently through the dye bath and setting it to dry. "But it would take me a bit of time to tell you, all about cells—you remember, I showed you the cells from the lining of your mouth?"

She nodded, frowning slightly, and ran her tongue along inside her cheek.

"Well, the body makes all kinds of different cells, and there are special kinds of cells whose business it is to fight bacteria—the small, roundish sorts of things, you remember those?" I gestured at the slide, which being fecal matter, had the usual vast quantities of *Escherichia coli* and the like.

"But there are millions of different sorts, and sometimes a microorganism comes along that the special cells aren't able to deal with. You know—I showed you the *Plasmodium* in Lizzie's blood?" I nodded toward the stoppered vial on the counter; I had taken blood from Lizzie only a day or two before, and shown the malarial parasites in the cells to Malva. "And I do think that this amoeba of ours may well be one like that."

"Oh, well. Will we give the sick folk the penicillin, then?" I smiled a little at the eager "we," though there was little enough to smile at in the situation overall.

"No, I'm afraid penicillin isn't effective against amoebic dysentery—that's what you call a very bad flux, a dysentery. No, I'm afraid we've nothing much to be going on with save herbs." I opened the cupboard and ran an eye over the ranks of bottles and gauze-wrapped bundles, puzzling.

"Wormwood, for a start." I took the jar down and handed it to Malva, who had come to stand beside me, looking with interest into the mysteries of the cupboard. "Garlic, that's generally useful for infections of the digestive tract—but it makes quite a good poultice for skin things, as well."

"What about onions? My grannie would steam an onion, and put it to my ear, when I was a wee bairn and had the earache. It smelt something dreadful, but it did work!"

"It can't hurt. Run out to the pantry, then, and fetch . . . oh, three big ones, and several heads of garlic."

"Oh, at once, ma'am!" She set down the wormwood and dashed out, sandals flapping. I turned back to the shelves, trying to calm my own sense of urgency.

I was torn between the urge to be with the sick, nursing them, and the need to make medicines that *might* be of help. But there were other people who could do the nursing, and no one but me who knew enough to try to compound an antiparasitic remedy.

Wormwood, garlic . . . agrimony. And gentian. Anything with a very high content of copper or sulfur—oh, rhubarb. We were past the growing season, but I'd had a fine crop and had put up several dozen bottles of the boiled pulp and syrup, as Mrs. Bug liked it for pies, and it provided some vitamin C for the winter months. That would make a splendid base for the medicine. Add perhaps slippery elm, for its soothing effects on the intestinal tract—though such effects were likely to be so slight as to be unnoticeable against the ravages of such a virulent onslaught.

I began pounding wormwood and agrimony in my mortar, meanwhile wondering where the bloody hell the thing had come from. Amoebic dysentery was normally a disease of the tropics, though God knew, I'd seen any number of peculiar tropical diseases on the coast, brought in with the slave and sugar trade from the Indies—and not a few further inland, too, since any such disease that wasn't instantly fatal tended to become chronic and move along with its victim.

It wasn't impossible that one of the fisher-folk had contracted it during the journey from the coast, and while being one of the fortunate persons who suffered only a mild infection, was now carrying the encysted form of the amoeba around in his or her digestive tract, all ready to shed infective cysts right and left.

Why this sudden outbreak? Dysentery was almost always spread via contaminated food or water. What—

"Here, ma'am." Malva was back, breathless from her hurry, several large brown onions in hand, crackling and glossy, and a dozen garlic heads bundled in her apron. I set her to slicing them up, and had the happy inspiration of telling her to stew them in honey. I didn't know whether the antibacterial effect of honey would be likewise effective against an amoeba, but it couldn't hurt—and might conceivably make the mixture a little more palatable; it was shaping up to be more than a trifle eye-watering, between the onions, the garlic, and the rhubarb.

"Phew! What are you guys *doing* in here?" I looked up

from my macerating to see Brianna in the door, looking deeply suspicious, nose wrinkled against the smell.

"Oh. Well . . ." I'd become habituated to it myself, but in fact, the air in the surgery was fairly thick with the smell of fecal samples, now augmented by waves of onion fumes. Malva looked up, eyes streaming, and sniffed, wiping her nose on her apron.

"We're magking bedicine," she informed Bree, with considerable dignity.

"Is anyone else fallen sick?" I asked anxiously, but she shook her head and edged into the room, fastidiously avoiding the counter where I had been making slides of fecal material.

"No, not that I've heard. I took some food over to the McLachlans' this morning, and they said only the two little ones had it. Mrs. Coinneach said she'd had diarrhea a couple of days ago, but not bad, and she's all right now."

"They're giving the little ones honey water?"

She nodded, a small frown between her eyebrows.

"I saw them. They look pretty sick, but nothing like the MacNeills." She looked rather sick herself, at the memory, but shook it off, turning to the high cupboard.

"Can I borrow a little sulfuric acid, Mama?" She'd brought an earthenware cup with her, and the sight of it made me laugh.

"Ordinary people borrow a cup of sugar," I told her, nodding at it. "Of course. Be careful with it, though—you'd best put it in one of those vials with a waxed cork. You do *not* want to chance tripping and spilling it."

"I definitely don't," she assured me. "I only need a few drops, though; I'm going to dilute it down pretty far. I'm making paper."

"Paper?" Malva blinked, red-eyed, and sniffed. "How?"

"Well, you squish up anything fibrous you can get your hands on," Bree told her, making squishing motions with both hands in illustrations. "Old bits of used paper, old rags of cloth, bits of yarn or thread, some of the softer sorts of leaves or flowers. Then you soak the mash for days and days in water and—if you happen to have some—dilute sulfuric acid." One long finger tapped the square bottle affectionately.

"Then once the mash is all digested down to a sort of pulp, you can spread a thin layer of it on screens, press out the water, let it dry, and hey-presto, paper!"

I could see Malva mouthing "hey-presto" to herself, and turned away a little, so she couldn't see me smile. Brianna uncorked the big square bottle of acid and, very carefully, poured a few drops into her cup. Immediately, the hot smell of sulfur rose like a demon amidst the miasma of feces and onions.

Malva stiffened, eyes still streaming but wide.

"What is that?" she said.

"Sulfuric acid," Bree said, looking at her curiously.

"Vitriol," I amended. "Have you seen—er, smelled it before?"

She nodded, put the sliced onions into a pot, and put the lid neatly on.

"Aye, I have." She came to look at the green glass bottle, dabbing at her eyes. "My mother—she died when I was young—she had some of that. I remember the smell of it, and how she'd say as I mustn't touch it, ever. Brimstone, folk called the smell—a whiff o' brimstone."

"Really? I wonder what she used it for." I *did* wonder, and with a certain sense of unease. An alchemist or an apothecary might have the stuff; the only reason that I knew of for a common citizen to keep it was as a means of aggression—to throw at someone.

But Malva only shook her head, and turning, went back to the onions and garlic. I'd caught the look on her face, though; a queer expression of hostility and longing that rang a small, unsuspected bell somewhere inside me.

Longing for a mother long dead—and the fury of a small girl, abandoned. Bewildered and alone.

"What?" Brianna was watching *my* face, frowning slightly. "What's wrong?"

"Nothing," I said, and put a hand on her arm, just to feel the strength and joy of her presence, the years of her growth. Tears stung my eyes, but that could be put down to onions. "Nothing at all."

I WAS GETTING terribly tired of funerals. This was the third, in as many days. We had buried Hortense and the baby together, then the older Mrs. Ogilvie. Now it was another child, one of Mrs. MacAfee's twins. The other twin, a boy, stood by his sister's grave, in a shock so profound that he looked like a walking ghost himself, though the disease hadn't touched him.

We were later than intended—the coffin hadn't been quite ready—and the night was rising around us. All the gold of the autumn leaves had faded into ash, and white mist was curling through the dark wet trunks of the pines. One could hardly imagine a more desolate scene—and yet it was in a way more fitting than the bright sunshine and fresh breeze that had blown when we buried Hortense and little Angelica.

"The Lord is my shepherd. He leadeth me beside—" Roger's voice cracked painfully, but no one seemed to notice. He struggled for a moment, swallowing hard, and went on, doggedly. He held the little green Bible in his hands, but wasn't looking at it; he was speaking from memory, and his eyes went from Mr. MacDuff, standing alone, for his wife and his sister were both sick, to the little boy beside him—a little boy about Jemmy's age.

"Though I walk . . . though I walk through the valley of death, I shall . . . shall fear no evil—" His voice was trembling audibly, and I saw that tears were running down his face. I looked for Bree; she was standing a little way behind the mourners, Jem half-swaddled in the folds of her dark cloak. The hood of it was drawn up, but her face was visible, pale in the gloaming, Our Lady of Sorrows.

Even Major MacDonald's red coat was muted, charcoal-gray in the last vestiges of light. He had arrived in the afternoon, and helped to carry up the little coffin; he stood now, hat somberly tucked beneath his arm, wigged head bowed, his face invisible. He, too, had a child—a daughter, somewhere back in Scotland with her mother.

I swayed a little, and felt Jamie's hand under my elbow. I had been without sleep for most of the last three days, and had taken precious little food. I didn't feel either hungry or tired, though; I felt remote and unreal, as though the wind blew through me.

The father uttered a cry of inconsolable grief, and sank suddenly down upon the heap of dirt thrown up by the grave. I felt Jamie's muscles contract in instinctive compassion toward him, and pulled away a little, murmuring, "Go."

I saw him cross swiftly to Mr. MacAfee, bend to whisper to him, put an arm around him. Roger had stopped talking.

My thoughts would not obey me. Try as I might to fix them on the proceedings, they strayed away. My arms ached; I had been pounding herbs, lifting patients, carrying water . . . I felt as though I were doing all these things over and over, could feel the repetitive thud of pestle in mortar, the dragging weight of fainting bodies. I was seeing in vivid memory the slides of *Entameba,* greedy pseudopodia flowing in slow-motion appetite. Water, I heard water flowing; it lived in water, though only the cystic form was infective. It was passed on by means of water. I thought that very clearly.

Then I was lying on the ground, with no memory of falling, no memory of ever being upright, the smell of fresh, damp dirt and fresh, damp wood strong in my nose, and a vague thought of worms. There was a flutter of motion before my eyes; the small green Bible had fallen and lay on the dirt in front of my face, the wind turning over its pages, one by one by one in a ghostly game of *sortes Virgilianae*—where would it stop? I wondered dimly.

There were hands and voices, but I could not pay attention. A great amoeba floated majestically in darkness before me, pseudopodia flowing slowly, slowly, in welcoming embrace.

63

MOMENT OF DECISION

FEVER ROLLED ACROSS my mind like a thunderstorm, jagged forks of pain crackling through my body in bursts of brilliance, each a lightning bolt that glowed for a vivid moment along some nerve or plexus, lighting up the hidden hollows of my joints, burning down the length of muscle fibers. A merciless brilliance, it struck again, and again, the fiery sword of a destroying angel who gave no quarter.

I seldom knew whether my eyes were open or closed, nor whether I woke or slept. I saw nothing but a roiling gray, turbulent and shot with red. The redness pulsed in veins and patches, shrouded in the cloud. I seized upon one crimson vein and followed its path, clinging to the track of its sullen glow amid the buffeting of thunder. The thunder grew louder as I penetrated deeper and deeper into the murk that boiled around me, becoming hideously regular, like the beating of a kettledrum, so that my ears rang with it, and I felt myself a hollow skin, tight-stretched, vibrating with each crash of sound.

The source of it was now before me, throbbing so loudly that I felt I must shout, only to hear some other sound—but though I felt my lips draw back and my throat swell with effort, I heard nothing but the pounding. In desperation, I thrust my hands—if they were my hands—through the misty gray and seized some warm, moist object, very slippery, that throbbed, convulsing in my hands.

I looked down and knew it all at once to be my own heart.

I dropped it in horror, and it crawled away in a trail of reddish slime, shuddering with effort, the valves all opening and closing like the mouths of suffocating fish, each popping open with a hollow click, closing again with a small, meaty thud.

Faces sometimes appeared in the clouds. Some seemed familiar, though I could put no name to them. Others were the faces of strangers, the half-seen, unknown faces that flit sometimes through the mind on the verge of sleep. These looked at me with curiosity or indifference—then turned away.

The others, the ones I knew, bore looks of sympathy or worry; they would seek to fix my gaze with theirs, but my glance slid guiltily off, giddily away, unable to gain traction. Their lips moved, and I knew they spoke to me, but I heard nothing, their words drowned by the silent thunder of my storm.

I FELT quite odd—but, for the first time in uncountable days, not ill. The fever clouds had rolled back; still grumbling softly somewhere near, but for the moment, gone from sight. My eyes were clear; I could see the raw wood in the beams overhead.

In fact, I saw the wood with such clarity that I was struck with awe at the beauty of it. The loops and whorls of the polished grain seemed at once static and alive with grace, the colors of it shimmering with smoke and the essence of the earth, so that I could see how the beam was transformed and yet held still the spirit of the tree.

I was so entranced by this that I reached out my hand to touch it—and did. My fingers brushed the wood with delight at the cool surface and the grooves of the axmarks, wing-shaped and regular as a flight of geese along the beam. I could hear the beating of powerful wings, and at the same time, feel the flex and swing of my shoulders, the vibration of joy through my forearms as the ax fell on the wood. As I explored this fascinating sensation, it occurred to me, dimly, that the beam was eight feet above the bed.

I turned—with no sense whatever of effort—and saw that I lay upon the bed below.

I lay on my back, the quilts rumpled and scattered, as

though I had tried at some point to throw them off but lacked the strength to do so. The air in the room was strangely still, and the blocks of color in the fabric glowed through it like jewels at the bottom of the sea, rich but muted.

By contrast, my skin was the color of pearls, bloodless pale and shimmering. And then I saw that this was because I was so thin that the skin of face and limb pressed hard upon the bone, and it was the gleam of bone and cartilage below that gave that luster to my face, smooth hardness shining through transparent skin.

And such bones as they were! I was filled with wonder at the marvel of their shaping. My eyes followed the delicacy of the arching ribs, the heartbreaking beauty of the sculptured skull with a sense of awed astonishment.

My hair was tumbled, matted, and snarled . . . and yet I felt myself drawn to it, tracing its curves with eye and . . . finger? For I had no consciousness of moving, and yet I felt the softness of the strands, the cool silk of brown and the springing vibrancy of silver, heard the hairs chime softly past each other, a rustle of notes cascading like a harp's.

My God, I said, and heard the words, though no sound stirred the air, *you are so lovely!*

My eyes were open. I looked deep and met a gaze of amber and soft gold. The eyes looked through me, to something far beyond—and yet they saw me, too. I saw the pupils dilate slightly, and felt the warmth of their darkness embrace me with knowledge and acceptance. *Yes,* said those knowing eyes. *I know you. Let us go.* I felt a sense of great peace, and the air around me stirred, like wind rushing through feathers.

Then some sound turned me toward the window and I saw the man who stood there. I had no name for him, and yet I loved him. He stood with his back turned to the bed, arms braced on the sill, and his head sunk on his chest, so the dawn light glowed red on his hair and traced his arms with gold. A spasm of grief shook him; I felt it, like the temblors of a distant quake.

Someone moved near him. A dark-haired woman, a girl. She came close, touched his back, murmuring something to him. I saw the way she looked at him, the tender inclination of her head, the intimacy of her body swaying toward him.

No, I thought, with great calm. *That won't do.*

I looked once more at myself lying on the bed, and with a feeling that was at once firm decision and incalculable regret, I took another breath.

64

I AM THE RESURRECTION, PART 2

I STILL SLEPT FOR long periods, waking only briefly to take nourishment. Now the fever dreams were gone, though, and sleep was a lake of deep black water, where I breathed oblivion and drifted past the waving waterweed, mindless as a fish.

I would float sometimes just below the surface, aware of people and things in the air-breathing world, but incapable of joining them. Voices spoke near me, muffled and meaningless. Now and then some phrase would penetrate the clear liquid around me and float into my head, where it would hang like a tiny jellyfish, round and transparent, yet pulsating with some mysterious inner meaning, its words a drifting net.

Each phrase hung for a time in my purview, folding and unfolding in its curious rhythms, and then drifted quietly up and away, leaving silence.

And in between the small jellyfish came open spaces of clear water, some filled with radiant light, some the darkness of utter peace. I drifted upward and downward, suspended between the surface and the depths, at the whim of unknown currents.

"Physician, look." Fizz. A stirring there, some dormant spore of consciousness, disturbed by carbonation, splits and blooms. Then a stab as sharp as metal, *Who is calling me?* "Physician, look."

I opened my eyes.

It was no great shock, for the room was filled with twilight, still light, like being underwater, and I had no sense of disruption.

"O Lord Jesus Christ, Thou great Physician: Look with Thy gracious favor upon this Thy servant; give wisdom and discretion to those who minister to her in her sickness; bless all the means used for her recovery . . ."

The words flowed past me in a whispering stream, cool on my skin. There was a man before me, dark head bent over a book. The light in the room embraced him and he seemed part of it.

"Stretch forth Thy hand," he whispered to the pages, in a voice that cracked and broke, "and according to Thy will, restore her to health and strength, that she may live to praise Thee for Thy goodness and Thy grace; to the glory of Thy holy name. Amen."

"Roger?" I said, groping for his name. My own voice was hoarse from disuse; speaking was an intolerable effort.

His eyes were closed in prayer; they sprang open, unbelieving, and I thought how vivid they were, the green of wet serpentine and summer leaves.

"Claire?" His voice cracked like a teenaged boy's, and he dropped the book.

"I don't know," I said, feeling the dreamlike sense of submergence threatening to engulf me again. "Am I?"

I COULD LIFT a hand for a moment or two, but was too weak even to lift my head, let alone sit up. Roger helpfully dragged me semi-upright against piled pillows, and put his hand at the back of my head to prevent wobbling, holding a cup of water to my dry lips. It was the odd feel of his hand on the bare skin of my neck that began a dim process of realization. Then I felt the warmth of his hand, vivid and immediate, at the back of my head, and jerked like a gaffed salmon, sending the cup flying.

"What? What?" I spluttered, clutching my head, too shocked to formulate a complete sentence, and oblivious to the cold water soaking through the sheets. "WHAT?!"

Roger looked nearly as shocked as I felt. He swallowed, searching for words. "I . . . I . . . I thought you knew," he stammered, voice breaking. "Didn't you . . . ? I mean . . . I thought . . . look, it'll grow!"

I could feel my mouth working, vainly trying different shapes that might approximate words, but there was no connection between tongue and brain—there was room for nothing but the realization that the accustomed soft, heavy weight of my hair was gone, replaced by a fuzz of bristles.

"Malva and Mrs. Bug cut it off, day before yesterday," Roger said, all in a rush. "They—we weren't here, Bree nor I, we wouldn't have let them, of course we wouldn't—but they thought it's what you do for someone with a terrible fever, it *is* what people do now. Bree was furious with them, but they thought—they truly thought they were helping save your life—oh, God, Claire, don't look like that, please!"

His face had disappeared in a starburst of light, a curtain of shimmering water suddenly coming down to protect me from the gaze of the world.

I wasn't conscious of crying, at all. Grief simply burst from me, like wine spraying from a wineskin stabbed with a knife. Purple-red as bone marrow, splattering and dripping everywhere.

"I'll fetch Jamie!" he croaked.

"NO!" I seized him by the sleeve, with more strength than I would have imagined I possessed. "God, no! I don't want him to see me like this!"

His momentary silence told me, but I kept stubborn hold of his sleeve, unable to think how else to prevent the unthinkable. I blinked, water sliding over my face like a stream over rock, and Roger wavered once more into visibility, blurred around the edges.

"He's . . . er . . . he's seen you," Roger said gruffly. He looked down, not wanting to meet my eyes. "It. Already. I mean—" He waved a hand vaguely in the vicinity of his own black locks. "He saw it."

"He did?" This was nearly as much a shock as the initial discovery. "What—what did he say?"

He took a deep breath and looked back up, like someone fearing to see a Gorgon. Or the anti-Gorgon, I thought bitterly.

"He didn't say anything," Roger said quite gently, and put a hand on my arm. "He—he just cried."

I was still crying, too, but in a more orthodox fashion now. Less of the gasping note. The sense of bone-deep cold had passed, and my limbs felt warm now, though I still felt a disconcertingly chilly breeze on my scalp. My heart was slowing again, and a faint sense that I was standing outside my body came over me.

Shock? I thought, dimly surprised as the word formed itself in my mind, rubbery and melting. I supposed that one *could* suffer true physical shock as the result of emotional wounds—of course one could, I knew that. . . .

"Claire!" I became aware that Roger was calling my name with increasing urgency, and shaking my arm. With immense effort, I brought my eyes to focus on him. He was looking truly alarmed, and I wondered, vaguely, whether I had started to die again. But no—it was too late for that.

"What?"

He sighed—with relief, I thought.

"You looked funny for a moment." His voice was cracked and husky; he sounded as though it hurt him to talk. "I thought—d'ye want another drink of water?"

The suggestion seemed so incongruous that I nearly laughed. But I *was* terribly thirsty—and all at once, a cup of cold water seemed the most desirable thing in the world.

"Yes." The tears continued to flow down my face, but now seemed almost soothing. I made no attempt to stop them—that seemed much too difficult—but blotted my face with a corner of the damp sheet.

It was beginning to dawn on me that I might not have made the wisest—or at least not the easiest—choice, when I decided not to die. Things outside the limits and concerns of my own body were starting to come back. Troubles, difficulties, dangers . . . sorrow. Dark, frightening things, like a swarm of bats. I didn't want to look too closely at the images that lay in a disorderly pile at the bottom of my brain—things I had jettisoned in the struggle to stay afloat.

But if I had come back, I had come back to be what I was—and I was a doctor.

"The . . . sickness." I blotted the last of the tears and let Roger wrap his hands around mine, helping me to hold the new cup. "Is it still—?"

"No." He spoke gently, and guided the rim of the cup to my lips. What was it? I wondered vaguely. Water, but with something in it—mint and something stronger, more bitter . . . angelica?

"It's stopped." Roger held the cup, letting me sip slowly. "No one's fallen sick in the last week."

"A week?" I bobbled the cup, spilling a little down my chin. "How long have I—"

"Just about that." He cleared his throat. Roger's eyes were intent on the cup; he skimmed a thumb lightly along my chin, removing the drops I had spilled. "You were among the last to fall sick."

I took a long breath, then drank a bit more. The liquid had a soft, sweet taste, too, floating over the bitter tang . . . honey. My mind located the word and I felt a sense of relief at having located this small missing piece of reality.

I knew from his manner that some of the sick had died, but asked no more for the moment. Deciding to live was one thing. Rejoining the world of the living was a struggle that would take strength I didn't have right now. I had pulled up my roots, and lay like a wilted plant; sinking them back into the earth was beyond me for the moment.

The knowledge that people I knew—perhaps had loved—had died seemed an equal grief to the loss of my hair—and either was more than I could cope with.

I drank two further cups of honey-sweetened water, despite the underlying bitterness, then lay back with a sigh, my stomach feeling like a small, cold balloon.

"Ye want to take a bit of rest," Roger advised me, putting down the cup on the table. "I'll fetch Brianna, aye? But you sleep if ye want to."

I hadn't strength to nod, but managed a twitch of the lips that seemed to pass muster as a smile. I reached up a trembling hand and brushed it gingerly over the top of my shorn head. Roger flinched, very slightly.

He rose, and I saw how thin and strained he looked—he would have been helping tend the sick all week, I supposed, not only me. And bury the dead. He was licensed to conduct funerals.

"Roger?" It was a terrible effort to speak; so terribly hard to find the words, separate them from the tangle in my head. "Have you eaten anything recently?"

His face changed then, a look of relief lightening the lines of strain and worry.

"No," he said, cleared his throat again, and smiled. "Not since last night."

"Oh. Well," I said, and lifted one hand, heavy as lead. "Do. Get something. Won't you?"

"Yes," he said. "I will." Instead of leaving, though, he hesitated, then took several rapid strides back, bent over the bed, and seizing my face between his palms, kissed me on the forehead.

"You're beautiful," he said fiercely, and with a final squeeze of my cheeks, left.

"What?" I said faintly, but the only answer was the bellying of the curtain as the breeze came in, scented with apples.

IN POINT of fact, I looked like a skeleton with a particularly unflattering crew cut, as I learned when I finally gained sufficient strength as to force Jamie to bring me a looking glass.

"I dinna suppose ye'd think of wearing a cap?" he suggested, diffidently fingering a muslin specimen that Marsali had brought me. "Only until it grows out a bit?"

"I don't suppose I bloody would."

I had some difficulty in saying this, shocked as I was by the horrifying vision in the glass. In fact, I had a strong impulse to seize the cap from his hands, put it on and pull it down to my shoulders.

I had rejected earlier offers of a cap from Mrs. Bug—who had been volubly congratulating herself on my survival as the obvious result of her fever treatment—and from Marsali, Malva, and every other woman who'd come to visit me.

This was simple contrariness on my part; the sight of my unrestrained hair outraged their Scottish sense of what was proper in a woman, and they'd been trying—with varying degrees of subtlety—to force me into a cap for years. I was damned if I'd let circumstance accomplish it for them.

Having now seen myself in a mirror, I felt somewhat less adamant about it. And my scalped head did feel a bit chilly. On the other hand, I realized that if I were to give in, Jamie would be terribly alarmed—and I thought I'd frightened him quite enough, judging by the hollow look of his face and the deep smudges under his eyes.

As it was, his face had lightened considerably when I rejected the cap he was holding, and he tossed it aside.

I carefully turned the looking glass over and set it on the counterpane, repressing a sigh.

"Always good for a laugh, I suppose, seeing the expressions on people's faces when they catch sight of me."

Jamie glanced at me, the corner of his mouth twitching.

"Ye're verra beautiful, Sassenach," he said gently. Then he burst out laughing, snorting through his nose and wheezing. I raised one eyebrow at him, picked up the glass and looked again—which made him laugh harder.

I leaned back against the pillows, feeling a bit better. The fever had quite gone, but I still felt wraithlike and weak, barely able to sit up unassisted, and I fell asleep almost without warning, after the least exertion.

Jamie, still snorting, took my hand, raised it to his mouth, and kissed it. The sudden warm immediacy of the touch rippled the fair hairs of my forearm, and my fingers closed involuntarily on his.

"I love you," he said very softly, his shoulders still trembling with laughter.

"Oh," I said, suddenly feeling quite a lot better. "Well, then. I love you, too. And it *will* grow, after all."

"So it will." He kissed my hand again, and set it gently on the quilt. "Have ye eaten?"

"A bit," I said, with what forbearance I could muster. "I'll have more later."

I had realized many years before why "patients" are called that; it's because a sick person is generally incapacitated, and thus obliged to put up with any amount of harassment and annoyance from persons who are *not* sick.

The fever had broken and I had regained consciousness two days before; since then, the invariable response of everyone who saw me was to gasp at my appearance, urge me to wear a cap—and then try to force food down my throat. Jamie, more sensitive to my tones of voice than were Mrs. Bug, Malva, Brianna, or Marsali, wisely desisted after a quick glance at the tray by the bed to see that I actually *had* eaten something.

"Tell me what's happened," I said, settling and bracing myself. "Who's been ill? How are they? And who—" I cleared my throat. "Who's died?"

He narrowed his eyes at me, obviously trying to guess whether I would faint, die, or leap out of bed if he told me.

"Ye're sure ye feel well enough, Sassenach?" he asked dubiously. "It's news that wilna spoil with keeping."

"No, but I have to hear sooner or later, don't I? And knowing is better than worrying about what I *don't* know."

He nodded, taking the point, and took a deep breath.

"Aye, then. Padraic and his daughter are well on the mend. Evan—he's lost his youngest, wee Bobby, and Grace is still ill, but Hugh and Caitlin didna fall sick at all." He swallowed, and went on. "Three of the fisher-folk have died; there's maybe a dozen still ailing, but most are on the mend." He knit his brows, considering. "And then there's Tom Christie. He's still bad, I hear."

"Is he? Malva didn't mention it." But then, Malva had refused to tell me anything when I'd asked earlier, insisting that I must just rest, and not worry myself.

"What about Allan?"

"No, he's fine," Jamie assured me.

"How long has Tom been sick?"

"I dinna ken. The lass can tell ye."

I nodded—a mistake, as the light-headedness had not left me yet, and I was obliged to shut my eyes and let my head fall back, illuminated patterns flashing behind my lids.

"That's very odd," I said, a little breathlessly, hearing

Jamie start up in response to my small collapse. "When I close my eyes, often I see stars—but not like stars in the sky. They look just like the stars on the lining of a doll's suitcase—a portmanteau, I mean—that I had as a child. Why do you suppose that is?"

"I havena got the slightest idea." There was a rustle as he sat back down on the stool. "Ye're no still delirious, are ye?" he asked dryly.

"Shouldn't think so. *Was* I delirious?" Breathing deeply and carefully, I opened my eyes and gave him my best attempt at a smile.

"Ye were."

"Do I want to know what I said?"

The corner of his mouth twitched.

"Probably not, but I may tell ye sometime, anyway."

I considered closing my eyes and floating off to sleep, rather than contemplate future embarrassments, but rallied. If I was going to live—and I was—I needed to gather up the strands of life that tethered me to the earth, and reattach them.

"Bree's family, and Marsali's—they're all right?" I asked only for form's sake; both Bree and Marsali had come to hover anxiously over my prostrate form, and while neither one would tell me anything they thought might upset me in my weakened condition, I was reasonably sure that neither one could have kept it secret if the children were seriously ill.

"Aye," he said slowly, "aye, they're fine."

"What?" I said, picking up the hesitation in his voice.

"They're fine," he repeated quickly. "None of them has fallen ill at all."

I gave him a cold look, though careful not to move too much while doing it.

"You may as well tell me," I said. "I'll get it out of Mrs. Bug if you don't."

As though mention of her name had invoked her, I heard the distinctive thump of Mrs. Bug's clogs on the stair, approaching. She was moving more slowly than usual, and with a care suggesting that she was laden with something.

This proved to be true; she negotiated sideways through the door, beaming, a loaded tray in one hand, the other wrapped round Henri-Christian, who clung to her, monkey-like.

"I've brought ye a wee bit to eat, *a leannan,*" she said briskly, nudging the barely touched bowl of parritch and plate of cold toast aside to make room for the fresh provisions. "Ye're no catching, are ye?"

Barely waiting for my shake of the head, she leaned over the bed and gently decanted Henri-Christian into my arms. Undiscriminatingly friendly as always, he butted his head under my chin, nuzzled into my chest, and began mouthing my knuckles, his sharp little baby teeth making small dents in my skin.

"Hallo, what's happened here?" I frowned, smoothing the soft brown licks of baby hair off his rounded brow, where the yellowing stain of an ugly bruise showed at his hairline.

"The spawn of the de'il tried to kill the poor wean," Mrs. Bug informed me, mouth pulled tight. "And would have done, too, save for Roger Mac, bless him."

"Oh? Which spawn was this?" I asked, familiar with Mrs. Bug's methods of description.

"Some of the fishers' weans," Jamie said. He put out a finger and touched Henri-Christian's nose, snatched it away as the baby grabbed for it, then touched his nose again. Henri-Christian giggled and grabbed his own nose, entranced by the game.

"The wicked creatures tried to drown him," Mrs. Bug amplified. "Stole the puir wee laddie in his basket and set him adrift in the creek!"

"I shouldna think they meant to drown him," Jamie said mildly, still absorbed in the game. "If so, they wouldna have troubled wi' the basket, surely."

"Hmph!" was Mrs. Bug's response to this piece of logic. "They didna mean to do him any good," she added darkly.

I had been taking a quick inventory of Henri-Christian's physique, finding several more healing bruises, a small scabbed cut on one heel, and a scraped knee.

"Well, you've been bumped about a bit, haven't you?" I said to him.

"Ump. Heeheehee!" said Henri-Christian, vastly entertained by my explorations.

"Roger saved him?" I asked, glancing up at Jamie.

He nodded, one side of his mouth turning up a little.

"Aye. I didna ken what was going on, 'til wee Joanie rushed up to me, shouting as they'd taken her brother—but I got there in time to see the end of the matter."

The boys had set the baby's basket afloat in the trout pool, a wide, deep spot in the creek, where the water was fairly quiet. Made of stoutly woven reeds, the basket had floated—long enough for the current to push it toward the outfall from the pool, where the water ran swiftly through a stretch of rocks, before plunging over a three-foot fall, down into a tumbling churn of water and boulders.

Roger had been building a rail fence, within earshot of the creek. Hearing boys shouting and Félicité's steam-whistle shrieks, he had dropped the rail he was holding and rushed down the hill, thinking that she was being tormented.

Instead, he had burst from the trees just in time to see Henri-Christian, in his basket, tip slowly over the edge of the outfall and start bumping crazily from rock to rock, spinning in the current and taking on water.

Running down the bank and launching himself in a flat dive, Roger had landed full-length in the creek just below the fall, in time for Henri-Christian, bawling with terror, to drop from his sodden basket, plummet down the fall, and land on Roger, who grabbed him.

"I was just in time to see it," Jamie informed me, grinning at the memory. "And then to see Roger Mac rise out o' the water like a triton, wi' duckweed streaming from his hair, blood runnin' from his nose, and the wee lad clutched tight in his arms. A terrible sight, he was."

The miscreant boys had followed the basket's career, yelling along the banks, but were now struck dumb. One of them moved to flee, the others starting up like a flight of pigeons, but Roger had pointed an awful finger at them and bellowed, *"Sheas!"* in a voice loud enough to be heard over the racket of the creek.

Such was the force of his presence, they *did* stay, frozen in terror.

Holding them with his glare, Roger had waded almost to the shore. There, he squatted and cupped a handful of water, which he poured over the head of the shrieking baby—who promptly quit shrieking.

"I baptize thee, Henri-Christian," Roger had bellowed, in his hoarse, cracked voice. "In the name of the Father, and the Son, and the Holy Ghost! D'ye hear me, wee bastards? His name is *Christian*! He belongs to the Lord! Trouble him again, ye lot of scabs, and Satan will pop up and drag ye straight down screaming—TO HELL!"

He stabbed an accusing finger once more at the boys, who this time did break and run, scampering wildly into the brush, pushing and falling in their urge to escape.

"Oh, dear," I said, torn between laughter and dismay. I looked down at Henri-Christian, who had lately discovered the joys of thumb-sucking and was absorbed in further study of the art. "That must have been impressive."

"It impressed *me,* to be sure," Jamie said, still grinning. "I'd no notion Roger Mac had it in him to preach hellfire and damnation like that. The lad's a great roar to him, cracked voice and all. He'd have a good audience, did he do it for a Gathering, aye?"

"Well, that explains what happened to his voice," I said. "I wondered. Do you think it *was* only mischief, though? Them putting the baby in the creek?"

"Oh, it was mischief, sure enough," he said, and cupped a big hand gently round Henri-Christian's head. "Not just boys' mischief, though."

Jamie had caught one of the fleeing boys as they hurtled past him, grabbing him by the neck and quite literally scaring the piss out of the lad. Walking the boy firmly into the wood, he'd pinned him hard against a tree and demanded to know the meaning of this attempted murder.

Trembling and blubbering, the boy had tried to excuse it, saying that they hadn't meant any harm to the wean, truly! They'd only wanted to see him float—for their parents all said he was demon-born, and everyone kent that those born of Satan floated, because the water would reject their wickedness. They'd taken the baby in his basket and put that into the water, because they were afraid to touch him, fearing his flesh would burn them.

"I told him I'd burn him myself," Jamie said with a certain

grimness, "and did." He'd then dismissed the smarting lad, with instructions to go home, change his breeks, and inform his confederates that they were expected in Jamie's study before supper to receive their own share of retribution—or else Himself would be coming round to their houses after supper, to thrash them before their parents' eyes.

"Did they come?" I asked, fascinated.

He gave me a look of surprise.

"Of course. They took their medicine, and then we went to the kitchen and had bread and honey. I'd told Marsali to bring the wee lad, and after we'd eaten, I took him on my knee, and had them all come and touch him, just to see."

He smiled lopsidedly.

"One of the lads asked me was it true, what Mr. Roger said, about the wean belonging to the Lord? I told him I certainly wouldna argue with Mr. Roger about that—but whoever else he belonged to, Henri-Christian belongs to me, as well, and best they should remember it."

His finger trailed slowly down Henri-Christian's round, smooth cheek. The baby was nearly asleep now, heavy eyelids closing, a tiny, glistening thumb half in, half out of his mouth.

"I'm sorry I missed that," I said softly, so as not to wake him. He'd grown much warmer, as sleeping babies did, and heavy in the curve of my arm. Jamie saw that I was having difficulty holding him, and took him from me, handing him back to Mrs. Bug, who had been bustling quietly round the room, tidying, all the while listening with approval to Jamie's account.

"Oh, 'twas something to see," she assured me in a whisper, patting Henri-Christian's back as she took him. "And the lads all poking their fingers out to touch the bairnie's wee belly, gingerlike, as if they meant to prod a hot potato, and him squirmin' and giggling like a worm wi' the fits. The wicked little gomerels' eyes were big as sixpences!"

"I imagine they were," I said, amused.

"On the other hand," I remarked *sotto voce* to Jamie as she left with the baby, "if their parents think he's demon-born, and you're his grandfather . . ."

"Well, you're his grannie, Sassenach," Jamie said dryly. "It might be you. But aye, I'd prefer not to have them dwell on that aspect of the matter."

"No," I agreed. "Though—do any of them know, do you think, that Marsali isn't your daughter by blood? They must know about Fergus."

"It wouldna much matter," he said. "They think wee Henri's a changeling, in any case."

"How do you know that?"

"People talk," he said briefly. "Are ye feeling well in yourself, Sassenach?"

Relieved of the baby's weight, I had put back the covers a bit to let in air. Jamie stared at me in disapproval.

"Christ, I can count all your ribs! Right through your shift!"

"Enjoy the experience while you can," I advised him tartly, though I felt a sharp pang of hurt. He seemed to sense this, for he took my hand, tracing the lines of the deep blue veins that ran across the back of it.

"Dinna fash yourself, Sassenach," he said, more gently. "I didna mean it that way. Here, Mrs. Bug's brought ye something tasty, I expect." He lifted the lid off a small covered dish, frowned at the substance in it, then stuck a cautious finger in and licked it.

"Maple pudding," he announced, looking happy.

"Oh?" I had no appetite at all yet, but maple pudding sounded at least innocuous, and I made no objection as he scooped up a spoonful, guiding it toward my mouth with the concentration of a man flying an airliner.

"I *can* feed myself, you kn—" He slipped the spoon between my lips, and I resignedly sucked the pudding off it. Amazing revelations of creamy sweetness immediately exploded in my mouth, and I closed my eyes in minor ecstasy, recalling.

"Oh, God," I said. "I'd forgotten what good food tastes like."

"I *knew* ye hadn't been eating," he said with satisfaction. "Here, have more."

I insisted upon taking the spoon myself, and managed half the dish; Jamie ate the other half, at my urging.

"You may not be as thin as I am," I said, turning my hand

over and grimacing at the sight of my protruding wrist bones, "but you haven't been eating a lot, either."

"I suppose not." He scraped the spoon carefully round the bowl, retrieving the last bits of pudding, and sucked the spoon clean. "It's been . . . busy."

I watched him narrowly. He was being patently cheerful, but my rusty sensibilities were beginning to come back. For some unknowable span of time, I'd had neither energy nor attention for anything that lay outside the fever-racked shell of my body; now I was seeing the small familiarities of Jamie's body, voice and manner, and becoming reattuned to him, like a slack violin string being tightened in the presence of a tuning fork.

I could feel the vibration of some strain in him, and I was beginning to think it wasn't all due to my recent near-demise.

"What?" I said.

"What?" He raised his eyebrows in question, but I knew him too well for that. The question alone gave me confidence that I was right.

"What aren't you telling me?" I asked, with what patience I could muster. "Is it Brown again? Have you got news of Stephen Bonnet? Or Donner? Or has the white sow eaten one of the children and choked to death?"

That made him smile, at least, though only for a moment.

"Not that," he said. "She went for MacDonald, when he called a few days ago, but he made it onto the porch in time. Verra agile the Major is, for a man of his age."

"He's younger than you are," I objected.

"Well, I'm agile, too," he said logically. "The sow hasna got me yet, has she?"

I felt a qualm of unease at his mention of the Major, but it wasn't news of political unrest or military rumblings that was troubling Jamie; he would have told me that at once. I narrowed my eyes at him again, but didn't speak.

He sighed deeply.

"I am thinking I must send them away," he said quietly, and took my hand again.

"Send who away?"

"Fergus and Marsali and the weans."

I felt a sharp, sudden jolt, as though someone had struck

me just below the breastbone, and found it suddenly difficult to draw breath.

"What? Why? And—and *where*?" I managed to ask.

He rubbed his thumb lightly over my knuckles, back and forth, his eyes focused on the small motion.

"Fergus tried to kill himself, three days ago," he said very quietly.

My hand gripped his convulsively.

"Holy God," I whispered. He nodded, and I saw that he was unable to speak for the moment; his teeth were set in his lower lip.

Now it was I who took his hand in both of mine, feeling coldness seep through my flesh. I wanted to deny it, reject the notion utterly—but couldn't. It sat there between us, an ugly thing like a poisonous toad that neither of us wished to touch.

"How?" I said at last. My voice seemed to echo in the room. I wanted to say, "Are you *sure*?" but I knew he was.

"With a knife," he replied literally. The corner of his mouth twitched again, but not with humor. "He said he would have hanged himself, but he couldna tie the rope with one hand. Lucky, that."

The pudding had formed a small, hard ball, like rubber, that lay in the bottom of my stomach.

"You . . . found him? Or was it Marsali?"

He shook his head.

"She doesna ken. Or rather, I expect she does, but she's no admitting it—to either of them."

"He can't have been badly wounded, then, or she'd have to know for sure." My chest still hurt, but the words were coming more easily.

"No. I saw him go past, whilst I was scraping a deer's hide up on the hill. He didna see me, and I didna call out—I dinna ken what it was that struck me queer about him . . . but something did. I went on wi' my work for a bit—I didna want to go far from the house, in case—but it niggled at me." He let go of my hand and rubbed his knuckles underneath his nose.

"I couldna seem to let go of the thought that something was amiss, and finally I put down my work and went after him, thinking myself all kinds of a fool for it."

Fergus had headed over the end of the Ridge, and down the

wooded slope that led to the White Spring. This was the most remote and secluded of the three springs on the Ridge, called "white" because of the large pale boulder that stood near the head of the pool.

Jamie had come down through the trees in time to see Fergus lie down by the spring, sleeve rolled up and coat folded beneath his head, and submerge his handless left arm in the water.

"I should maybe ha' shouted then," he said, rubbing a distracted hand through his hair. "But I couldna really believe it, ken?"

Then Fergus had taken a small boning knife in his right hand, reached down into the pool, and neatly opened the veins of his left elbow, blood blooming in a soft, dark cloud around the whiteness of his arm.

"I shouted *then,*" Jamie said. He closed his eyes, and scrubbed his hands hard over his face, as though trying to erase the memory of it.

He had run down the hill, grabbed Fergus, jerked him to his feet, and hit him.

"You *hit* him?"

"I did," he said shortly. "He's lucky I didna break his neck, the wee bastard." Color had begun to rise in his face as he talked, and he pressed his lips tight together.

"Was this after the boys took Henri-Christian?" I asked, my memory of the conversation in the stable with Fergus vividly in mind. "I mean—"

"Aye, I ken what ye mean," he interrupted. "And it was the day after the lads put Henri-Christian in the creek, aye. It wasna only that, though—not only all the trouble over the wee laddie being a dwarf, I mean." He glanced at me, his face troubled.

"We talked. After I'd bound up his arm and brought him round. He said he'd been thinking of it for some time; the thing wi' the bairn only pushed him into it."

"But . . . how *could* he?" I said, distressed. "To leave Marsali, and the children—how?"

Jamie looked down, hands braced on his knees, and sighed. The window was open, and a soft breeze came in, lifting the hairs on the crown of his head like tiny flames.

"He thought they would do better without him," he said flatly. "If he was dead, Marsali could wed again—find a man who could care for her and the weans. Provide for them. Protect wee Henri."

"He thinks—thought—he couldn't?"

Jamie glanced sharply at me.

"Sassenach," he said, "he kens damn well he can't."

I drew breath to protest this, but bit my lip instead, finding no immediate rebuttal.

Jamie stood up and moved restlessly about the room, picking things up and putting them down.

"Would you do such a thing?" I asked, after a bit. "In the same circumstances, I mean."

He paused for a moment, his back to me, hand on my hairbrush.

"No," he said softly. "But it's a hard thing for a man to live with."

"Well, I see that . . ." I began, slowly, but he swung round to face me. His own face was strained, filled with a weariness that had little to do with lack of sleep.

"No, Sassenach," he said. "Ye don't." He spoke gently, but with such a tone of despair in his voice that tears came to my eyes.

It was as much sheer physical weakness as emotional distress, but I knew that if I gave way to it, the end would be complete soggy disintegration, and no one needed that just now. I bit my lip hard and wiped my eyes with the edge of the sheet.

I heard the thump as he knelt down beside me, and I reached out blindly for him, pulling his head against my breast. He put his arms round me and sighed deeply, his breath warm on my skin through the linen of my shift. I stroked his hair with one trembling hand, and felt him give way suddenly, all the tension going out of him like water running from a jug.

I had the oddest feeling, then—as though the strength he had clung to had now been let go . . . and was flowing into me. My tenuous grip on my own body firmed as I held his, and my heart ceased wavering, taking up instead its normal solid, tireless beating.

The tears had retreated, though they were precariously near the surface. I traced the lines of his face with my fingers, ruddy bronze and lined with sun and care; the high forehead with its thick auburn brows, and the broad planes of his cheek, the long straight nose, straight as a blade. The closed eyes, slanted and mysterious with those odd lashes of his, blond at the root, so deep an auburn at the tips as to seem almost black.

"Don't you know?" I said very softly, tracing the small, neat line of his ear. Tiny, stiff blond hairs sprouted in a tiny whorl from the tagus, tickling my finger. "Don't *any* of you know? That it's *you.* Not what you can give, or do, or provide. Just you."

He took a deep, shuddering breath, and nodded, though he didn't open his eyes.

"I know. I said that to him, to Fergus," he said very softly. "Or at least I think I did. I said a terrible lot of things."

They had knelt together by the spring, embracing, wet with blood and water, locked together as though he could hold Fergus to the earth, to his family, by force of will alone, and he had no notion at all what he had said, lost in the passion of the moment—until the end.

"You must continue, for their sakes—though you would not for your own," he had whispered, Fergus's face pressed into his shoulder, the black hair wet with sweat and water, cold against his cheek. *"Tu comprends, mon enfant, mon fils? Comprends-tu?"*

I felt his throat move as he swallowed.

"See, I kent ye were dying," he said very softly. "I was sure ye'd be gone when I came back to the house, and I should be alone. I wasna speaking to Fergus then, I think, so much as to myself."

He raised his head then, and looked at me through a blur of tears and laughter.

"Oh, God, Claire," he said, "I would have been so angry, if ye'd died and left me!"

I wanted to laugh or cry, or both, myself—and had I still harbored regrets regarding the loss of eternal peace, I would have surrendered them now without hesitation.

"I didn't," I said, and touched his lip. "I won't. Or at least

I'll try not." I slid my hand behind his head and drew him back to me. He was a good deal larger and heavier than Henri-Christian, but I felt I could hold him forever, if necessary.

It was early afternoon, and the light just beginning to shift, slanting in through the tops of the west-facing windows so that the room filled with a clean, bright light that glowed on Jamie's hair and the worn creamy linen of his shirt. I could feel the knobs at the top of his spine, and the yielding flesh in the narrow channel between shoulder blade and backbone.

"Where will you send them?" I asked, and tried to smooth the whorled hair of the cowlick on his crown.

"To Cross Creek, maybe—or to Wilmington," he replied. His eyes were half-closed, watching the shadows of leaves flicker on the side of the armoire he had built me. "Wherever seems best for the printing trade."

He shifted a little, tightening his grip on my buttocks, then frowned.

"Christ, Sassenach, ye havena got any bum left at all!"

"Well, never mind," I said with resignation. "I'm sure *that* will grow back soon enough."

65

MOMENT OF DECLARATION

JAMIE MET THEM near Woolam's Mill, five men on horseback. Two were strangers; two were men from Salisbury that he knew—ex-Regulators named Green and Wherry; avid Whigs. The last was Richard Brown, whose face was cold, save for his eyes.

He silently cursed his love of conversation. If not for that, he would have parted from MacDonald as usual, at Coopersville. But they had been talking of poetry—poetry, for God's sake!—and amusing each other in declamation.

Now here he stood in the empty road, holding two horses, while MacDonald, whose guts were in disagreement with him, busied himself deep in the wood.

Amos Green tipped him a nod, and would have passed, but Kitman Wherry reined up; the strangers did likewise, staring curiously.

"Where are Thou bound, friend James?" Wherry, a Quaker, asked pleasantly. "Does Thee come to the meeting at Halifax? For Thee are welcome to ride with us, and that be so."

Halifax. He felt a trickle of sweat run down the crease of his back. The meeting of the Committee of Correspondence to elect delegates to the Continental Congress.

"I am seeing a friend upon his road," he replied courteously, with a nod toward MacDonald's horse. "I will follow, though; perhaps I shall catch ye up along the way." *Fat chance of that,* he thought, carefully not looking at Brown.

"I'd not be so sure of your welcome, Mr. Fraser." Green spoke civilly enough, but with a certain coldness in his manner that made Wherry glance at him in surprise. "Not after what happened in Cross Creek."

"Oh? And would ye see an innocent man burnt alive, or tarred and feathered?" The last thing he wished was an argument, but something must be said.

One of the strangers spat in the road.

"Not so innocent, if that's Fogarty Simms you're speakin' of. Little Tory pissant," he added as an afterthought.

"That's the fellow," Green said, and spat in agreement. "The committee in Cross Creek set out to teach him a lesson; seems Mr. Fraser here was in disagreement. Quite a scene it was, from what I hear," he drawled, leaning back a little in his saddle to survey Jamie from his superior height. "Like I said, Mr. Fraser—you ain't all that popular, right this minute."

Wherry was frowning, glancing to and fro between Jamie and Green. "To save a man from tar and feathers, no matter what his politics, seems no more than common humanity," he said sharply.

Brown laughed unpleasantly.

"Might seem so to you, I reckon. Not to other folk. You know a man by the company he keeps. And beyond that, there's your auntie, eh?" he said, redirecting his speech to Jamie. "And the famous Mrs. MacDonald. I read that speech she gave—in the final edition of Simms's newspaper," he added, repeating the unpleasant laugh.

"My aunt's guests have naught to do wi' me," Jamie said, striving for simple matter-of-factness.

"No? How 'bout your aunt's husband—your uncle, would he be?"

"Duncan?" His incredulity plainly showed in his voice, for the strangers exchanged glances, and their manner relaxed a little. "No, he's my aunt's fourth husband—and a friend. Why d'ye speak of him?"

"Why, Duncan Innes is cheek-by-jowl with Farquard Campbell, and a good many other Loyalists. The two of 'em have been putting money enough to float a ship into pamphlets preachin' reconciliation with Mother England. Surprised you didn't know that, Mr. Fraser."

Jamie was not merely surprised but thunderstruck at this revelation, but hid it.

"A man's opinions are his own," he said with a shrug. "Duncan must do as he likes, and I shall do the same."

Wherry was nodding agreement with this, but the others were regarding him with expressions ranging from skepticism to hostility.

Wherry was not unaware of his companions' responses.

"What *is* thy opinion, then, friend?" he asked politely.

Well, he'd known it was coming. Had now and then tried to imagine the circumstances of his declaration, in situations ranging from the vaingloriously heroic to the openly dangerous, but as usual in such matters, God's sense of humor trumped all imagination. And so he found himself taking that final step into irrevocable and public commitment to the rebel cause—just incidentally being required to ally himself with a deadly enemy in the process—standing alone in a dusty road, with a uniformed officer of the Crown squatting in the bushes directly behind him, breeches round his ankles.

"I am for liberty," he said, in a tone indicating mild astonishment that there could be any question regarding his position.

"Are you so?" Green looked hard at him, then lifted his

chin in the direction of MacDonald's horse, where MacDonald's regimental sword hung from the saddle, gilt and tassels gleaming in the sun. "How come you to be in company with a redcoat, then?"

"He is a friend," Jamie replied evenly.

"A redcoat?" One of the strangers reared back in his saddle as though stung by a bee. "How come redcoats *here*?" The man sounded flabbergasted, and looked hastily to and fro, as though expecting a company of the creatures to burst from the wood, muskets firing.

"Only the one, so far as I know," Brown assured him. "Name's MacDonald. He's not a real soldier; retired on half-pay, works for the Governor."

His companion didn't seem noticeably reassured.

"What are you doing with this MacDonald?" he demanded of Jamie.

"As I said—he is a friend." The attitude of the men had changed in an instant, from skepticism and mild hostility to open offense.

"He's the Governor's spy, is what he is," Green declared flatly.

This was no more than the truth, and Jamie was reasonably sure that half the backcountry knew it; MacDonald made no effort to hide either his appearance nor his errands. To deny the fact was to ask them to believe Jamie a dunce, duplicitous, or both.

There was a stirring among the men now, glances exchanged, and the smallest of motions, hands touching knife hilts and pistol grips.

Very fine, Jamie thought. Not satisfied with the irony of the situation, God had now decided that he should fight to the death against the allies he had declared himself to moments earlier, in defense of an officer of the Crown he had just declared himself against.

As his son-in-law was fond of remarking—great.

"Bring him out," Brown ordered, nudging his horse to the forefront. "We'll see what he has to say for himself, this friend of yours."

"And then might be we'll learn him a lesson he can carry back to the Governor, eh?" One of the strangers took off his hat and tucked it carefully beneath the edge of his saddle, preparing.

"Wait!" Wherry drew himself up, trying to quell them with a hand, though Jamie could have told him he was several minutes past the point where such an attempt might have had any effect. "You cannot lay violent hands upon—"

"Can't we, though?" Brown grinned like a death's head, eyes fixed on Jamie, and began to undo the leather quirt coiled and fastened to his saddle. "No tar to hand, alas. But a good beating, say, and send 'em both squealing home to the Governor stark naked—that'd answer."

The second stranger laughed, and spat again, so the gob landed juicily at Jamie's feet.

"Aye, that'll do. Hear you held off a mob by yourself in Cross Creek, Fraser—only five to two now, how you like them odds?"

Jamie liked them fine. Dropping the reins he held, he turned and flung himself between the two horses, screeching and slapping hard at their flanks, then dived headlong into the brush at the roadside, scrabbling through roots and stones on hands and knees as fast as he could.

Behind him, the horses were rearing and wheeling, whinnying loudly and spreading confusion and fright through the other men's mounts; he could hear cries of anger and alarm, as they tried to gain control of the plunging horses.

He slid down a short slope, dirt and uprooted plants spraying up around his feet, lost his balance and fell at the bottom, bounded up and dashed into an oak copse, where he plastered himself behind a screen of saplings, breathing hard.

Someone had had wit—or fury—enough to jump off his horse and follow on foot; he could hear crashing and cursing near at hand, over the fainter cries of the commotion on the road. Glancing cautiously through the leaves, he saw Richard Brown, disheveled and hatless, looking wildly round, pistol in hand.

Any thought he might have had of confrontation vanished; he was unarmed, save a small knife in his stocking, and it was clear to him that Brown would shoot him instantly, claiming self-defense when the others eventually caught up.

Up the slope, toward the road, he caught a glimpse of red.

Brown, turning in the same direction, saw it, too, and fired. Whereupon Donald MacDonald, having thoughtfully hung up his coat in a tree, stepped out of cover behind Richard Brown in his shirtsleeves, and hit Brown over the head with a solid length of tree branch.

Brown fell on his knees, momentarily stunned, and Jamie slipped out of the copse, beckoning to MacDonald, who ran heavily to meet him. Together they made their way deeper into the forest, waiting by a stream until prolonged silence from the road indicated that it might be safe to go back for a look.

The men were gone. So was MacDonald's horse. Gideon, the whites of his eyes showing and ears laid flat, rolled back his upper lip and squealed fiercely at them, big yellow teeth bared and slobber flying. Brown and company had wisely thought twice about stealing a rabid horse, but had tied him up to a tree and managed to spoil his harness, which hung in bits around his neck. MacDonald's sword lay in the dust, torn from its scabbard, blade broken in two.

MacDonald picked up the pieces, viewed them for a moment, then, shaking his head, tucked them through his belt.

"D'ye think Jones could mend it?" he asked. "Or better to go down to Salisbury?"

"Wilmington or New Bern," Jamie said, wiping a hand across his mouth. "Dai Jones hasna the skill to mend a sword, but ye'll find few friends in Salisbury, from what I hear." Salisbury had been at the heart of the Regulation, and antigovernment sentiment still ran high there. His own heart had gone back to its usual way of beating, but he still felt weak-kneed in the aftermath of flight and anger.

MacDonald nodded bleakly, then glanced at Gideon.

"Is yon thing safe to ride?"

"No."

In Gideon's present state of agitation, Jamie wouldn't risk riding him alone, let alone double-mounted and with no bridle. They'd left the rope on his saddle, at least. He got a loop over the stallion's head without being bitten, and they set off without comment, returning to the Ridge on foot.

"Verra unfortunate," MacDonald observed thoughtfully at one point. "That they should have met us together. D'ye think it's dished your chances of worming your way into their councils? I should give my left ball to have an eye and an ear in that meeting they spoke of, I'll tell ye that for nothing!"

With a dim sense of wonder, Jamie realized that having made his momentous declaration, overheard by the man whose cause he sought to betray, and then nearly killed by the new allies whose side he sought to uphold—neither side had believed him.

"D'ye ever wonder what it sounds like when God laughs, Donald?" he asked thoughtfully.

MacDonald pursed his lips and glanced at the horizon, where dark clouds swelled just beyond the shoulder of the mountain.

"Like thunder, I imagine," he said. "D'ye not think so?"

Jamie shook his head.

"No. I think it's a verra small, wee sound indeed."

66

THE DARK RISES

I HEARD ALL THE sounds of the household below, and the rumble of Jamie's voice outside, and felt entirely peaceful. I was watching the sun shift and glow on the yellowing chestnut trees outside, when the sound of feet came marching up the stairs, steady and determined.

The door flung open and Brianna came in, wind-tousled and bright-faced, wearing a steely expression. She halted at the foot of my bed, leveled a long forefinger at me, and said, "You are not allowed to die."

"Oh?" I said, blinking. "I didn't think I was going to."

"You tried!" she said, accusing. "You know you did!"

"Well, not to say tried, exactly . . ." I began weakly. If I hadn't exactly tried to die, though, it was true that I hadn't quite tried not to, and I must have looked guilty, for her eyes narrowed into blue slits.

"Don't you dare do that again!" she said, and wheeling in a sweep of blue cloak, stomped out, pausing at the door to say, "BecauseIloveyouandIcan'tdowithoutyou," in a strangled voice, before running down the stairs.

"I love you too, darling!" I called, the always-ready tears coming to my eyes, but there was no reply, save the sound of the front door closing.

Adso, drowsing in a puddle of sun on the counterpane at my feet, opened his eyes a fraction of an inch at the noise, then sank his head back into his shoulders, purring louder.

I lay back on the pillow, feeling a good deal less peaceful, but somewhat more alive. A moment later, I sat up, put back the quilts, and swung my legs out of bed. Adso abruptly quit purring. "Don't worry," I told him. "I'm not going to keel over; your supply of milk and scraps is perfectly safe. Keep the bed warm for me."

I had been up, of course, and even allowed on short, intensely supervised excursions outside. But no one had let me try to go anywhere alone since before I fell ill, and I was reasonably sure they wouldn't let me do it now.

I therefore stole downstairs in stockinged feet, shoes in hand, and instead of going through the front door, whose hinges squeaked, or through the kitchen, where Mrs. Bug was working, I slipped into my surgery, opened the window, and—having checked to be sure the white sow was not hanging about below—climbed carefully out.

I felt quite giddy at my escape, a rush of spirits that sustained me for a little way down the path. Thereafter, I was obliged to stop every few hundred feet, sit down, and gasp a bit while my legs recovered their strength. I persevered, though, and at last came to the Christie cabin.

No one was in sight, nor was there any response to my tentative "Hallo!", but when I knocked at the door, I heard Tom Christie's voice, gruff and dispirited, bid me enter.

He was at the table, writing, but from the looks of him, ought still to have been in bed. His eyes widened in surprise at sight of me, and he hastily tried to straighten the grubby shawl round his shoulders.

"Mrs. Fraser! Are you—that is—what in the name of God . . ." Deprived of speech, he pointed at me, eyes round as saucers. I had taken off my broad-brimmed hat when I entered, forgetting momentarily that I looked like nothing so much as an excited bottle brush.

"Oh," I said, passing a self-conscious hand over my head. "That. You ought to be pleased; I'm not going about outraging the public by a wanton display of my flowing locks."

"You look like a convict," he said bluntly. "Sit down."

I did, being rather in need of the stool he offered me, owing to the exertions of the walk.

"How are you?" I inquired, peering at him. The light in the cabin was very bad; he had been writing with a candle, and had put it out upon my appearance.

"How am I?" He seemed both astonished and rather put out at the inquiry. "You have walked all the way here, in a dangerously enfeebled condition, to ask after my health?"

"If you care to put it that way," I replied, rather nettled by that "dangerously enfeebled." "I don't suppose you would care to step out into the light, so that I can get a decent look at you, would you?"

He drew the ends of the shawl protectively across his chest.

"Why?" He frowned at me, peaked brows drawing together so that he looked like an irritable owl.

"Because I want to know a few things regarding your state of health," I replied patiently, "and examining you is likely the best way of finding them out, since you don't seem able to tell me anything."

"You are most unaccountable, madam!"

"No, I am a doctor," I countered. "And I want to know—" A brief wave of giddiness came over me, and I leaned on the table, holding on 'til it passed.

"You are insane," he stated, having scrutinized me for a moment. "You are also still ill, I believe. Stay there; I shall call my son to go and fetch your husband."

I flapped a hand at him and took a deep breath. My heart was racing, and I was a trifle pale and sweaty, but essentially all right.

"The fact of the matter, Mr. Christie, is that while I've

certainly *been* ill, I wasn't ill with the same sickness that's been afflicting people on the Ridge—and from what Malva was able to tell me, I don't think you were, either."

He had risen to go and call Allan; at this, he froze, staring at me with his mouth open. Then he slowly lowered himself back into his chair.

"What do you mean?"

Having finally got his attention, I was pleased to lay out the facts before him; I had them neatly to hand, having given them considerable thought over the last few days.

While several families on the Ridge had suffered the depredations of amoebic dysentery, I hadn't. I had had a dangerously high fever, accompanied by dreadful headache and—so far as I could tell from Malva's excited account—convulsions. But it certainly wasn't dysentery.

"Are you certain of this?" He was twiddling his discarded quill, frowning.

"It's rather hard to mistake bloody flux for headache and fever," I said tartly. "Now—did you have flux?"

He hesitated a moment, but curiosity got the better of him.

"No," he said. "It was as you say—a headache fit to split the skull, and fever. A terrible weakness, and . . . and extraordinarily unpleasant dreams. I had no notion that it was not the same illness afflicting the others."

"No reason you should, I suppose. You didn't see any of them. Unless—did Malva describe the illness to you?" I asked only from curiosity, but he shook his head.

"I do not wish to hear of such things; she does not tell me. Still, why have you come?" He tilted his head to one side, narrowing his eyes. "What difference does it make whether you and I suffered an ague, rather than a flux? Or anyone else, for that matter?" He seemed rather agitated, and got up, moving about the cabin in an unfocused, bumbling sort of way, quite unlike his usual decisive movements.

I sighed, rubbing a hand over my forehead. I'd got the basic information I came for; explaining why I'd wanted it was going to be uphill work. I had enough trouble getting Jamie, Young Ian, and Malva to accept the germ theory of disease, and that was with the evidence visible through a microscope to hand.

"Disease is catching," I said a little tiredly. "It passes from one person to another—sometimes directly, sometimes by means of food or water shared between a sick person and a healthy one. All of the people who had the flux lived near a particular small spring; I have some reason to think that it was the water of that spring that carried the amoeba—that made them ill.

"You and I, though—I haven't seen you in weeks. Nor have I been near anyone else who's had the ague. How is it that we should both fall ill of the same thing?"

He stared at me, baffled and still frowning.

"I do not see why two persons cannot fall ill without seeing each other. Certainly I have known such illnesses as you describe: gaol fever, for instance, spreads in close quarters—but surely not all illnesses behave in the same fashion?"

"No, they don't," I admitted. I wasn't in a fit state to try to get across the basic notions of epidemiology or public health, either. "It's possible, for instance, for some diseases to be spread by mosquitoes. Malaria, for one." Some forms of viral meningitis, for another—my best guess as to the illness I'd just recovered from.

"Do you recall being bitten by a mosquito any time recently?"

He stared at me, then uttered a brief sort of bark I took for laughter.

"My dear woman, everyone in this festering climate is bitten repeatedly during the hot weather." He scratched at his beard, as though by reflex.

That was true. Everyone but me and Roger. Now and then, some desperate insect would have a go, but for the most part, we escaped unbitten, even when there were absolute plagues of the creatures and everyone around us was scratching. As a theory, I suspected that blood-drinking mosquitoes had evolved so closely with mankind through the years that Roger and I simply didn't smell right to them, having come from too far away in time. Brianna and Jemmy, who shared my genetic material but also Jamie's, were bitten, but not as frequently as most people.

I didn't recall having been bitten any time recently, but it was possible that I had been and had simply been too busy to notice.

"Why does it matter?" Christie asked, seeming now merely baffled.

"I don't know. I just—need to find things out." I'd also needed both to get away from the house and to make some move to reclaim my life by the most direct means I knew—the practice of medicine. But that wasn't anything I meant to share with Tom Christie.

"Hmph," he said. He stood looking down at me, frowning and undecided, then suddenly extended a hand—the one I had operated on, I saw; the "Z" of the incision had faded to a healthy pale pink, and the fingers lay straight.

"Come outside, then," he said, resigned. "I will see you home, and if ye insist upon asking intrusive and bothersome questions regarding my health along the way, I suppose I cannot stop you."

Startled, I took his hand, and found his grip solid and steady, despite the haggard look of his face and the slump of his shoulders.

"You needn't walk me home," I protested. "You ought to be in bed, by the looks of you!"

"So should you," he said, leading me to the door with a hand beneath my elbow. "But if ye choose to risk your health and your life by undertaking such inappropriate exertion—why, so can I. Though you must," he added sternly, "put on your hat before we go."

WE MADE IT back to the house, stopping frequently for rest, and arrived panting, dripping with sweat, and generally exhilarated by the adventure. No one had missed me, but Mr. Christie insisted upon delivering me inside, which meant that everyone observed my absence *ex post facto,* and in the irrational way of people, at once became very annoyed.

I was scolded by everyone in sight, including Young Ian, frog-marched upstairs virtually by the scruff of the neck, and thrust forcibly back into bed, where, I was given to understand, I should be lucky to be given bread and milk for my supper. The most annoying aspect of the whole situation was Thomas Christie, standing at the foot of the stairs with a mug of beer in his hand, watching as I was led off, and wearing the only grin I had ever seen on his hairy face.

"What in the name of God possessed ye, Sassenach?" Jamie jerked back the quilt and gestured peremptorily at the sheets.

"Well, I felt quite well, and—"

"Well! Ye're the color of bad buttermilk, and trembling so ye can scarcely—here, let me do that." Making snorting noises, he pushed my hands away from the laces of my petticoats, and had them off me in a trice.

"Have ye lost your mind?" he demanded. "And to sneak off like that without telling anyone, too! What if ye'd fallen? What if ye got ill again?"

"If I'd told anyone, they wouldn't have let me go out," I said mildly. "And I *am* a physician, you know. Surely I can judge my own state of health."

He gave me a look, strongly suggesting that he wouldn't trust me to judge a flower show, but merely gave a louder than usual snort in reply.

He then picked me up bodily, carried me to the bed, and placed me gently into it—but with enough demonstration of restrained strength as to let me know that he would have preferred to drop me from a height.

He then straightened up, giving me a baleful look.

"If ye didna look as though ye were about to faint, Sassenach, I swear I would turn ye over and smack your bum for ye."

"You can't," I said, rather faintly. "I haven't got one." I was in fact a little tired . . . well, to be honest, my heart was beating like a kettledrum, my ears were ringing, and if I didn't lie down flat at once, I likely *would* faint. I did lie down, and lay with my eyes closed, feeling the room spin gently round me, like a merry-go-round, complete with flashing lights and hurdy-gurdy music.

Through this confusion of sensations, I dimly sensed hands on my legs, then a pleasant coolness on my heated body. Then something warm and cloudlike enveloped my head, and I flailed my hands about wildly, trying to get it off before I smothered.

I emerged, blinking and panting, to discover that I was

naked. I glanced at my pallid, sagging, skeletal remains, and snatched the sheet up over myself. Jamie was bending to collect my discarded gown, petticoat, and jacket from the floor, adding these to the shift he had folded over his arm. He picked up my shoes and stockings and added these to his bag.

"You," he said, pointing a long accusatory finger at me, "are going nowhere. You are not allowed to kill yourself, do I make myself clear?"

"Oh, so that's where Bree gets it," I murmured, trying to stop my head from swimming. I closed my eyes again.

"I seem to recall," I said, "a certain abbey in France. And a very stubborn young man in ill health. And his friend Murtagh, who took his clothes in order to prevent his getting up and wandering off before he was fit."

Silence. I opened one eye. He was standing stock still, the fading light from the window striking sparks in his hair.

"Whereupon," I said conversationally, "if memory serves, you promptly climbed out a window and decamped. Naked. In the middle of winter."

The stiff fingers of his right hand tapped twice against his leg.

"I was four-and-twenty," he said at last, sounding gruff. "I wasna meant to have any sense."

"I wouldn't argue with *that* for an instant," I assured him. I opened the other eye and fixed him with both. "But you do know why I did it. I had to."

He drew a very deep breath, sighed, and set down my clothes. He came and sat down on the bed beside me, making the wooden frame creak and groan beneath his weight.

He picked up my hand, and held it as though it were something precious and fragile. It was, too—or at least it *looked* fragile, a delicate construct of transparent skin and the shadow of the bones within it. He ran his thumb gently down the back of my hand, tracing the bones from phalange to ulna, and I felt an odd, small tingle of distant memory; the vision of my own bones, glowing blue through the skin, and Master Raymond's hands, cupping my inflamed and empty womb, saying to me through the mists of fever, "Call him. Call the red man."

"Jamie," I said very softly. Sunlight flashed on the metal of my silver wedding ring. He took hold of it between thumb and forefinger, and slid the little metal circlet gently up and down my finger, so loose that it didn't even catch on the bony knuckle.

"Be careful," I said. "I don't want to lose it."

"Ye won't." He folded my fingers closed, his own hand closing large and warm around mine.

He sat silent for a time, and we watched the bar of sun creep slowly across the counterpane. Adso had moved with it, to stay in its warmth, and the light tipped his fur with a soft silver glow, the fine hairs that edged his ears tiny and distinct.

"It's a great comfort," he said at last, "to see the sun come up and go down. When I dwelt in the cave, when I was in prison, it gave me hope, to see the light come and go, and know that the world went about its business."

He was looking out the window, toward the blue distance where the sky darkened toward infinity. His throat moved a little as he swallowed.

"It gives me the same feeling, Sassenach," he said, "to hear ye rustling about in your surgery, rattling things and swearin' to yourself." He turned his head, then, to look at me, and his eyes held the depths of the coming night.

"If ye were no longer there—or somewhere—" he said very softly, "then the sun would no longer come up or go down." He lifted my hand and kissed it, very gently. He laid it, closed around my ring, upon my chest, rose, and left.

I SLEPT LIGHTLY now, no longer flung into the agitated world of fever dreams, nor sucked down into the deep well of oblivion as my body sought the healing of sleep. I didn't know what had wakened me, but I *was* awake, quite suddenly, alert and fresh-eyed, with no interval of drowsiness.

The shutters were closed, but the moon was full; soft light striped the bed. I ran a hand over the sheet beside me, lifted my hand far above my head. My arm was a slender pale stem, bloodless and fragile as a toadstool's stalk; my fingers flexed gently and spread, a web, a net to catch the dark.

I could hear Jamie breathing, in his accustomed spot on the floor beside the bed.

I brought my arm down, stroked my body lightly with both hands, assessing. A tiny swell of breast, ribs I could count, one, two, three, four, five, and the smooth concavity of my stomach, slung like a hammock between the uprights of my hipbones. Skin, and bones. Not much else.

"Claire?" There was a stirring in the dark beside the bed, and Jamie's head rose up, a presence more sensed than seen, so dark was the shadow there by contrast with the moonlight.

A large dark hand groped across the quilt, touched my hip.

"Are ye well, *a nighean*?" he whispered. "D'ye need anything?"

He was tired; his head lay on the bed beside me, his breath warm through my shift. If he hadn't been warm, his touch, his breath, perhaps I wouldn't have had the courage, but I felt cold and bodiless as the moonlight itself, and so I closed my spectral hand on his and whispered, "I need you."

He was quite still for a moment, slowly making sense of what I'd said.

"I'll not trouble your sleep?" he said, sounding doubtful. I pulled on his wrist in answer, and he came, rising up from the pool of dark on the floor, the thin lines of moonlight rippling over him like water.

"Kelpie," I said softly.

He snorted briefly in answer, and awkwardly, gingerly, eased himself beneath the quilt, the mattress giving under his weight.

We lay very shyly together, barely touching. He was breathing shallowly, clearly trying to make as little obtrusion of his presence as possible. Aside from a faint rustling of sheets, the house was silent.

Finally, I felt one large finger nudge gently against my thigh.

"I missed ye, Sassenach," he whispered.

I rolled onto my side facing him, and kissed his arm in answer. I wanted to move closer, lay my head in the curve of his shoulder, and lie in the circle of his arm—but the idea of my short, bristly hair against his skin kept me from it.

"I missed you, too," I said, into the dark solidness of his arm.

"Will I take ye, then?" he said softly. "D'ye want it, truly?" One hand caressed my arm; the other went downward, starting the slow, steady rhythm to ready himself.

"Let me," I whispered, stilling his hand with my own. "Lie still."

I made love to him at first like a sneak thief, hasty strokes and tiny kisses, stealing scent and touch and warmth and salty taste. Then he put a hand on the back of my neck, pressing me closer, deeper.

"Dinna hurry yourself, lass," he said in a hoarse whisper. "I'm no going anywhere."

I let a quiver of silent amusement pass through me and he drew in a deep, deep breath as I closed my teeth very gently round him and slid my hand up under the warm, musky weight of his balls.

Then I rose up over him, light-headed at the sudden movement, needing urgently. We both sighed deeply as it happened, and I felt the breath of his laughter on my breasts as I bent over him.

"I missed ye, Sassenach," he whispered again.

I was shy of his touching me, changed as I was, and leaned with my hands on his shoulders, keeping him from pulling me down to him. He didn't try, but slid his hand curled between us.

I felt a brief pang at the thought that the hair on my privates was longer than that on my head—but the thought was driven out by the slow pressure of the big knuckle pressing deep between my legs, rocking gently back and forth.

I seized his other hand and brought it to my mouth, sucked his fingers hard, one by one, and shuddered, gripping his hand with all my strength.

I was still gripping it sometime later, as I lay beside him. Or rather, holding it, admiring the unseen shapes of it, complex and graceful in the dark, and the hard, smooth layer of callus on palms and knuckles.

"I've the hands of a bricklayer," he said, laughing a little as I passed my lips lightly over the roughened knuckles and the still-sensitive tips of his long fingers.

"Calluses on a man's hands are deeply erotic," I assured him.

"Are they, so?" His free hand passed lightly over my shorn head and down the length of my back. I shivered and pressed closer to him, self-consciousness beginning to be forgotten. My own free hand roamed down the length of his body, toying with the soft, wiry bush of his hair, and the damply tender, half-hard cock.

He arched his back a little, then relaxed.

"Well, I'll tell ye, Sassenach," he said. "If I havena got calluses *there,* it's no fault of yours, believe me."

67

THE LAST LAUGH

IT WAS AN OLD musket, made perhaps twenty years before, but well-kept. The stock was polished with wear, the wood beautiful to the touch, and the metal of the barrel mellow and clean.

Standing Bear clutched it in ecstasy, running awed fingers up and down the gleaming barrel, bringing them to his nose to sniff the intoxicating perfume of oil and powder, then beckoning his friends to come and smell it, too.

Five gentlemen had received muskets from the beneficent hand of Bird-who-sings-in-the-morning, and a sense of delight ran through the house, spreading in ripples through the village. Bird himself, with twenty-five muskets still to give, was drunk with the sense of inestimable wealth and power, and thus in a mood to welcome anyone and anything.

"This is Hiram Crombie," Jamie said to Bird, in Tsalagi, indicating Mr. Crombie, who had stood by him, white-faced with nerves, throughout the preliminary talk, the presentation of the muskets, the summoning of the braves, and the general rejoicing over the guns. "He has come to offer his friendship, and to tell you stories of the Christ."

"Oh, your Christ? The one who went to the lower world and came back? I always wondered, did he meet Sky-woman there, or Mole? I am fond of Mole; I would like to know what he said." Bird touched the stone pendant at his neck, a small red carving of Mole, the guide to the underworld.

Mr. Crombie's brow was furrowed, but luckily he had not yet developed any sense of ease in Tsalagi; he was still in the stage of mentally translating each word into English, and Bird was a rapid speaker. And Ian had found no occasion to teach Hiram the word for Mole.

Jamie coughed.

"I am sure he will be happy to tell you all the stories he knows," he said. "Mr. Crombie," he said, switching momentarily to English, "Tsisqua offers you welcome."

Bird's wife Penstemon's nostrils flared delicately; Crombie was sweating with nervousness, and smelled like a goat. He bowed earnestly, and presented Bird with the good knife he had brought as a present, slowly reciting the complimentary speech he had committed to memory. Reasonably well, too, Jamie thought; he'd mispronounced only a couple of words.

"I come to b-bring you great joy," he finished, stammering and sweating.

Bird looked at Crombie—small, stringy, and dripping wet—for a long, inscrutable moment, then back at Jamie.

"You're a funny man, Bear-Killer," he said with resignation. "Let us eat!"

It was autumn; the harvest was in and the hunting was good. And so the Feast of the Guns was a notable occasion, with wapiti and venison and wild pig raised steaming from pits and roasted over roaring fires, with overflowing platters of maize and roasted squash and dishes of beans spiced with onion and coriander, dishes of pottage, and dozen upon dozen of small fish rolled in cornmeal, fried in bear grease, their flesh crisp and sweet.

Mr. Crombie, very stiff to begin with, began to unbend under the influence of food, spruce beer, and the flattering attention paid him. A certain amount of the attention, Jamie thought, was due to the fact that Ian, a wide grin on his face, stayed by his pupil for a time, prompting and correcting, 'til Hiram should feel more at ease in the tongue, and able to manage on his own. Ian was extremely popular, particularly with the young women of the village.

For himself, he enjoyed the feasting very much; relieved of responsibility, there was nothing to do save to talk and listen and eat—and in the morning he would go.

It was an odd feeling, and one he was not sure he had ever had before. He had had many leavetakings, most regretful—a few taken with a sense of relief—some that wrenched the heart from his chest and left him aching. Not tonight. Everything seemed strangely ceremonious, something consciously done for the last time, and yet there was no sadness in it.

Completion, he supposed, was the sense of it. He had done what he could do, and now must leave Bird and the others to make their own way. He might come again, but never again by duty, in his role as the agent of the King.

That was a peculiar thought in itself. He had never lived without the consciousness of allegiance—whether willing or not, witting or not—to a king, whether that be German Geordie's house or the Stuarts. And now he did.

For the first time, he had some glimmer of what his daughter and his wife had tried to tell him.

Hiram was trying to recite one of the psalms, he realized. He was doing a good job of it, because he had asked Ian to translate it, and had then carefully committed it to memory. However . . .

"Oil runs down over the head and the beard . . ."

Penstemon cast a wary glance at the small pot of melted bear grease that they were using as a condiment, and narrowed her eyes at Hiram, plainly intending to snatch the dish from him if he tried to pour it over his head.

"It's a story of his ancestors," Jamie said to her, with a brief shrug. "Not his own custom."

"Oh. Hm." She relaxed a little, though continuing to keep a close eye on Hiram. He was a guest, but not all guests could be trusted to behave well.

Hiram did nothing untoward, though, and with many

protests of sufficiency, and awkward compliments toward his hosts, was persuaded to eat until his eyes bulged, which pleased them.

Ian would stay for a few days, to be sure that Hiram and Bird's people were in some sort of mutual accord. Jamie was not quite sure that Ian's sense of responsibility would overcome his sense of humor, though—in some ways, Ian's sense of humor tended toward the Indians'. A word from Jamie might therefore not come amiss, just by way of precaution.

"He has a wife," Jamie said to Bird, with a nod toward Hiram, now engaged in close discourse with two of the older men. "I think he would not welcome a young woman in his bed. He might be rude to her, not understanding the compliment."

"Don't worry," said Penstemon, overhearing this. She glanced at Hiram, and her lip curled with scorn. "Nobody would want a child from *him.* Now, a child from *you,* Bear-Killer . . ." She gave him a long look beneath her lashes, and he laughed, saluting her with a gesture of respect.

It was a perfect night, cold and crisp, and the door was left open that the air might come in. The smoke from the fire rose straight and white, streaming toward the hole above, its moving wraiths like spirits ascending in joy.

Everyone had eaten and drunk to the point of a pleasant stupor, and there was momentary silence and a pervading sense of peace and happiness.

"It is good for men to eat as brothers," Hiram observed to Standing Bear, in his halting Tsalagi. Or rather, tried to. And after all, Jamie reflected, feeling his ribs creak under the strain, it was really a very minor difference between "as brothers" and "their brothers."

Standing Bear gave Hiram a thoughtful look, and edged slightly farther away from him.

Bird observed this, and after a moment's silence, turned to Jamie.

"You're a very funny man, Bear-Killer," he repeated, shaking his head. "You win."

To Mr. John Stuart,
Superintendent of the Southern
Department of Indian Affairs

From Fraser's Ridge,
on the First Day of November,
Anno Domini 1774,
James Fraser, Esq.

My dear sir,

This is to notify you of my Resignation as Indian Agent, as I find that my personal Convictions will no longer allow me to perform my Office on behalf of the Crown in good Conscience.

In thanks for your kind Attention and many Favors, and wishing you well in future, I remain

Your most humble Servant,
J. Fraser

PART NINE

The Bones of Time

68

SAVAGES

ONLY TWO LEFT. The pool of liquid wax glowed with the light of the flaming wick above it, and the jewels slowly came into view, one green, one black, glowing with their own inner fire. Jamie dipped the feather end of a quill gently into the melted wax and scooped the emerald up, raising it into the light.

He dropped the hot stone into the handkerchief I held waiting, and I rubbed it quickly, to get off the wax before it should harden.

"Our reserves are getting rather low," I said, in uneasy jest. "Let's hope there aren't any more expensive emergencies."

"I shallna touch the black diamond, regardless," he said definitely, and blew out the wick. "That one is for you."

I stared at him.

"What do you mean by that?"

He shrugged a little, and reached to take the emerald in its handkerchief from me.

"If I should be killed," he said very matter-of-factly. "Ye'll take it and go. Back through the stones."

"Oh? I don't know that I would," I said. I didn't like talking about any contingency that involved Jamie's death, but there was no point in ignoring the possibilities. Battle, disease, imprisonment, accident, assassination . . .

"You and Bree were going about forbidding *me* to die," I said. "I'd do the same thing, if I had the faintest hope of your paying the least attention."

He smiled at that.

"I always mind your words, Sassenach," he assured me

gravely. "But ye do tell me that man proposes and God disposes, and should He see fit to dispose of *me*—ye'll go back."

"Why would I?" I said, nettled—and unsettled. The memories of his sending me back through the stones on the eve of Culloden were not ones I ever wished to recall, and here he was, prying open the door to that tightly sealed chamber of my mind. "I'd stay with Bree and Roger, wouldn't I? Jem, Marsali and Fergus, Germain and Henri-Christian and the girls—everyone's here. What is there to go back to, after all?"

He took the stone from its cloth, turning it over between his fingers, and looked thoughtfully at me, as though making up his mind whether to tell me something. Small hairs began to prickle on the back of my neck.

"I dinna ken," he said at last, shaking his head. "But I've seen ye there."

The prickling ran straight down the back of my neck and down both arms.

"Seen me *where*?"

"There." He waved a hand in a vague gesture. "I dreamt of ye there. I dinna ken where it was; I only know it was *there*—in your proper time."

"How do you know that?" I demanded, my flesh creeping briskly. "What was I doing?"

His brow furrowed in the effort of recollection.

"I dinna recall, exactly," he said slowly. "But I knew it was *then,* by the light." His brow cleared suddenly. "That's it. Ye were sitting at a desk, with something in your hand, maybe writing. And there was light all round ye, shining on your face, on your hair. But it wasna candlelight, nor yet firelight or sunlight. And I recall thinking to myself as I saw ye, *Oh, so that's what electric light is like.*"

I stared at him, open-mouthed.

"How can you recognize something in a dream that you've never seen in real life?"

He seemed to find that funny.

"I dream of things I've not seen all the time, Sassenach—don't you?"

"Well," I said uncertainly. "Yes. Sometimes. Monsters, odd plants, I suppose. Peculiar landscapes. And certainly *peo-*

ple that I don't know. But surely that's different? To see something you know about, but haven't seen?"

"Well, what I saw may not be what electric light *does* look like," he admitted, "but that's what I said to myself when I saw it. And I was quite sure that ye were in your own time.

"And after all," he added logically, "I dream of the past; why would I not dream of the future?"

There was no good answer to a thoroughly Celtic remark of that nature.

"Well, *you* would, I suppose," I said. I rubbed dubiously at my lower lip. "How old was I, in this dream of yours?"

He looked surprised, then uncertain, and peered closely at my face, as though trying to compare it with some mental vision.

"Well . . . I dinna ken," he said, sounding for the first time unsure. "I didna think anything about it—I didna notice that ye had white hair, or anything of the sort—it was just . . . you." He shrugged, baffled, then looked down at the stone in my hand.

"Does it feel warm to your touch, Sassenach?" he asked curiously.

"Of course it does," I said, rather crossly. "It's just come out of hot wax, for heaven's sake." And yet the emerald *did* seem to pulse gently in my hand, warm as my own blood and beating like a miniature heart. And when I handed it to him, I felt a small, peculiar reluctance—as though it did not want to leave me.

"Give it to MacDonald," I said, rubbing my palm against the side of my skirt. "I hear him outside, talking to Arch; he'll be wanting to be off."

MACDONALD HAD come pelting up to the Ridge in the midst of a rainstorm the day before, weathered face nearly purple with cold, exertion, and excitement, to inform us that he had found a printing establishment for sale in New Bern.

"The owner has already left—somewhat involuntarily," he told us, dripping and steaming by the fire. "His friends seek to sell the premises and equipment promptly, before they might be seized or destroyed, and thus provide him with funds to reestablish himself in England."

By "somewhat involuntarily," it turned out, he meant that the print shop's owner was a Loyalist, who had been kidnapped off the street by the local Committee of Safety and shoved willy-nilly onto a ship departing for England. This form of impromptu deportation was becoming popular, and while it was more humane than tar and feathers, it did mean that the printer would arrive penniless in England, and owing money for his passage, to boot.

"I happened to meet wi' some of his friends in a tavern, tearin' their hair over his sad fate and drinking to his welfare—whereupon I told them that I might be able to put them in the way of an advantage," the Major said, swelling with satisfaction. "They were all ears, when I said that ye might—just might, mind—have ready cash."

"What makes ye think I do, Donald?" Jamie asked, one eyebrow cocked.

MacDonald looked surprised, then knowing. He winked and laid a finger beside his nose.

"I hear the odd bit, here and there. Word has it that ye've got a wee cache of gems—or so I hear, from a merchant in Edenton whose bank dealt wi' one."

Jamie and I exchanged looks.

"Bobby," I said, and he nodded in resignation.

"Well, as for me, mum's the word," MacDonald said, observing this. "Ye can rely upon my discretion, to be sure. And I doubt the matter's widely known. But then—a poor man doesna go about buying muskets by the dozen, now, does he?"

"Oh, he might," Jamie said, resigned. "Ye'd be surprised, Donald. But as it is . . . I imagine a bargain might be struck. What are the printer's friends asking—and will they offer insurance, in case of fire?"

MACDONALD HAD been empowered to negotiate on behalf of the printer's friends—they being anxious to get the problematical real estate sold before some patriotic soul came and burned it down—and so the bargain was concluded on the spot. MacDonald was sent hurtling back down the mountain to change the emerald into money, conclude payment on the printer's shop, leaving the residue of the money with Fergus for ongoing expenses—and let it be known as quickly as possible in New Bern that the premises were shortly to be under new management.

"And if anyone asks about the politics of the new owner . . ." Jamie said. To which MacDonald merely nodded wisely, and laid his finger alongside his red-veined nose once more.

I was reasonably sure that Fergus had no personal politics to speak of; beyond his family, his sole allegiance was to Jamie. Once the bargain was made, though, and the frenzy of packing begun—Marsali and Fergus would have to leave at once, to have any chance of making it to New Bern before winter set in in earnest—Jamie had had a serious talk with Fergus.

"Now, it'll no be like it was in Edinburgh. There's no but one other printer in the town, and from what MacDonald says, he's an elderly gentleman, and sae much afraid o' the committee and the Governor both, he willna print a thing but books of sermons and handbills advertising horseraces."

"Très bon," said Fergus, looking even happier, if such a thing was possible. He'd been going about lit up like a Chinese lantern since hearing the news. "We will have all of the newspaper and broadsheet business, to say nothing of the printing of scandalous plays and pamphlets—there is nothing like sedition and unrest for the printing business, milord, you know that yourself."

"I do know that," Jamie said very dryly. "Which is why I mean to beat the need for care into your thick skull. I dinna wish to hear that ye've been hanged for treason, nor yet tarred-and-feathered for no being treasonous enough."

"Oh, la." Fergus waved an airy hook. "I know well enough how this game is played, milord."

Jamie nodded, still looking dubious.

"Aye, ye do. But it's been some years; ye may be out of practice. And ye'll not know who's who in New Bern; ye dinna want to find yourself buying meat from the man ye've savaged in the morning's paper, aye?"

"I'll mind that, Da." Marsali sat by the fire, nursing Henri-Christian, and taking close heed. If anything, she looked happier than Fergus, upon whom she looked adoringly. She switched the look of adoration to Jamie, and smiled. "We'll take good care, I promise."

Jamie's frown softened as he looked at her.

"I'll miss ye, lass," he said softly. Her look of happiness dimmed, but didn't go out entirely.

"I'll miss ye, too, Da. All of us will. And Germain doesna want to leave Jem, o' course. But . . ." Her eyes drifted back to Fergus, who was making a list of supplies, whistling "Alouette" under his breath, and she hugged Henri-Christian closer, making him kick his legs in protest.

"Aye, I know." Jamie coughed, to cover his emotion, and wiped a knuckle underneath his nose. "Now then, wee Fergus. Ye'll have a bit of money left over; be sure to bribe the constable and the watch first of all. MacDonald's given me the names o' the Royal Council, and the chief Assemblymen—he'll be of help wi' the council, as he's the Governor's man. Be tactful, aye? But see he's taken care of; he's been a great help in the matter."

Fergus nodded, head bent over his paper.

"Paper, ink, lead, bribes, shammy leather, brushes," he said, writing busily, and resumed absently singing, *"Alouette, gentil alouette . . ."*

IT WAS impossible to get a wagon up to the Ridge; the only approach was by the narrow trail that wound up the slope from Coopersville—one of the factors that had led to the development of that minor crossroads into a small hamlet, as itinerant peddlers and other travelers tended to stop there, making brief forays on foot upward into the mountain.

"Which is all very well for discouraging hostile invasion onto the Ridge," I told Bree, panting as I set down a large canvas-wrapped bundle of candlesticks, chamber pots, and other small household belongings at the side of the trail. "But it unfortunately makes it rather difficult to get *off* the bloody Ridge, too."

"I suppose it never occurred to Da that anyone would want to leave," Bree said, grunting as she lowered her own burden—Marsali's cauldron, packed with cheeses, sacks of flour, beans, and rice, plus a wooden box full of dried fish and a string bag of apples. "This thing weighs a *ton.*"

She turned and bellowed, "GERMAIN!" up the trail behind us. Dead silence. Germain and Jemmy were meant to be shepherding Mirabel the goat down to the wagon. They had left the cabin with us, but had been dropping steadily behind.

Neither a call nor a *mehhhh* came from the trail, but Mrs. Bug came into view, trundling slowly under the weight of Marsali's spinning wheel, which she bore on her back, and holding Mirabel's halter in one hand. Mirabel, a small, neat white goat with gray markings, blatted happily at sight of us.

"I found the puir wee lassie tethered to a bush," Mrs. Bug said, setting down the spinning wheel with a wheeze and wiping her face with her apron. "No sign o' the lads, the wicked wee creatures."

Brianna made a low growling noise that boded ill for either Jemmy or Germain, if she caught them. Before she could stomp back up the trail, though, Roger and Young Ian came down, each carrying one end of Marsali's loom, collapsed for the occasion into a large bundle of heavy timbers. Seeing the traffic jam in the road, though, they stopped, setting down their burden with sighs of relief.

"What's amiss, then?" Roger asked, glancing from face to face, and settling on the goat with a frown. "Where are Jem and Germain?"

"Dollars to donuts the little fiends are hiding somewhere," Bree said, smoothing tumbled red hair out of her face. Her plait had come undone, and straggling wisps of hair were sticking damply to her face. I was momentarily grateful for my short thicket of curls; no matter what it looked like, it was certainly convenient.

"Shall I go and look?" Ian asked, emerging from the wooden pudding basin he'd been carrying upside down on his head. "They'll no have gone far."

Sounds of hasty feet from below made everyone turn

expectantly in that direction—but it was not the boys, but Marsali, breathless and wide-eyed.

"Henri-Christian," she gasped, her eyes flicking rapidly round the group. "Have ye got him, Mother Claire? Bree?"

"I thought *you* had him," Bree said, catching Marsali's sense of urgency.

"I did. Wee Aidan McCallum was minding him for me, whilst I loaded things into the wagon. But then I stopped to feed him"—a hand went briefly to her bosom—"and they were both vanished! I thought perhaps . . ." Her words died away as she began scanning the bushes along the trail, her cheeks flushed with exertion and annoyance.

"I'll strangle him," she said through gritted teeth. "And where's Germain, then?" she cried, catching sight of Mirabel, who had taken advantage of the stop to nibble tasty thistles by the path.

"This is beginning to have the look of a plan about it," Roger observed, obviously amused. Ian, too, seemed to be finding something funny in the situation, but vicious glares from the frazzled females present wiped the smirks off their faces.

"Yes, do go and find them, please," I said, seeing that Marsali was about to either burst into tears or go berserk and throw things.

"Aye, do," she said tersely. "And beat them, while ye're at it."

"YE KEN where they are?" Ian asked, shading his eyes to look up a trough of tumbled rock.

"Aye, likely. This way." Roger pushed through a tangle of yaupon and redbud, with Ian after him, and emerged onto the bank of the small creek that paralleled the trail here. Below, he caught a glimpse of Aidan's favorite fishing place near the ford, but there was no sign of life down there.

Instead, he turned upward, making his way through thick dry grass and loose rocks along the creekbank. Most of the leaves had fallen from the chestnuts and poplars, and lay in slippery mats of brown and gold underfoot.

Aidan had shown him the secret place some time ago; a shallow cave, barely three feet high, hidden at the top of a steep slope overgrown by a thicket of oak saplings. The oaks were bare now, and the cave's opening easily visible, if you knew to look for it. It was particularly noticeable at the moment, because smoke was coming out of it, slipping veil-like up the face of the rock above, leaving a sharp scent in the cold, dry air.

Ian raised one eyebrow. Roger nodded, and made his way up the slope, making no effort to be quiet about it. There was a mad scuffle of noises inside the cave, thumpings and low cries, and the veil of smoke wavered and stopped, replaced by a loud hiss and a puff of dark gray from the cave mouth as someone threw water on the fire.

Ian, meanwhile, had made his way silently up the side of the rockface above the cave, seeing a small crevice from which a tiny plume of smoke issued. Clinging one-handed to a dogwood that grew out of the rock, he leaned perilously out, and cupping a hand near his mouth, let out a frightful Mohawk scream, directed into the crevice.

Terror-stricken shrieks, much higher-pitched, issued from the cave, followed in short order by a tumble of little boys, pushing and tripping over each other in their haste.

"Ho, there!" Roger snagged his own offspring neatly by the collar as he rushed past. "The jig's up, mate."

Germain, with Henri-Christian's sturdy form clutched to his midsection, was attempting to escape down the slope, but Ian leapt past him, springing pantherlike down the rocks, and grabbed the baby from him, bringing him to a reluctant stop.

Only Aidan remained at large. Seeing his comrades in captivity, he hesitated at the edge of the slope, obviously wanting to flee, but nobly gave in, coming back with dragging step to share their fate.

"Right, lads; sorry, it's not on." Roger spoke with some sympathy; Jemmy had been upset for days at the prospect of Germain's leaving.

"But we do not want to go, Uncle Roger," Germain said, employing his most effective look of wide-eyed pleading. "We will stay here; we can live in the cave, and hunt for our food."

"Aye, sir, and me and Jem, we'll share our dinners wi' them," Aidan piped up in anxious support.

"I brought some of Mama's matches, so they've got a fire to keep warm," Jem chipped in eagerly, "and a loaf of bread, too!"

"So ye see, Uncle—" Germain spread his hands gracefully in demonstration, "we shall be no trouble to anyone!"

"Oh, nay trouble, is it?" Ian said, with no less sympathy. "Tell your mother that, aye?"

Germain put his hands behind him, clutching his buttocks protectively by reflex.

"And what were ye thinking, dragging your wee brother up here?" Roger said a little more severely. "He can barely walk yet! Two steps out of there"—he nodded at the cave—"and he'd be tumbling down the burn and his neck broken."

"Oh, no, sir!" Germain said, shocked. He fumbled in his pocket and drew out a piece of string. "I should tie him up, when I was not there, so he shouldna wander or fall. But I couldna be leaving him; I promised *Maman,* when he was born, I said I would never leave him."

Tears were beginning to trickle down Aidan's thin cheeks. Henri-Christian, totally confused, began to howl in sympathy, which made Jem's lower lip tremble, as well. He wriggled out of Roger's grasp, ran to Germain, and clutched him passionately about the middle.

"Germain can't go, Daddy, please don't make him go!"

Roger rubbed his nose, exchanged brief looks with Ian, and sighed.

He sat down on a rock, and motioned to Ian, who was having a certain amount of difficulty in deciding which way up to hold Henri-Christian. Ian gave him the baby with a noticeable air of relief, and Henri-Christian, feeling the need of security, seized Roger's nose with one hand and his hair with the other.

"Look, *a bhailach,*" he said, detaching Henri-Christian's grasp with some difficulty. "Wee Henri-Christian needs his mother to feed him. He's barely got teeth, for God's sake—he canna be living up here in the wild, eating raw meat wi' you savages."

"He has too got teeth!" Aidan said stoutly, extending a bitten forefinger in proof. "Look!"

"He eats pap," Germain said, but with some uncertainty to his tone. "We would mash up biscuits for him with milk."

"Henri-Christian needs his mother," Roger repeated firmly, "and your mother needs *you.* Ye dinna expect her to manage a wagon and two mules *and* your sisters, all the way to New Bern alone, do ye?"

"But Papa can help," Germain protested. "The girls mind him, when they mind no one else!"

"Your papa's gone already," Ian informed him. "He's ridden ahead, to find a place for ye all to live, once ye've got there. Your mother's to follow on, wi' all your things. Roger Mac's right, *a bhailach*—your mother needs ye."

Germain's small face paled a little. He looked helplessly down at Jemmy, still clinging to him, then up the hill at Aidan, and gulped. The wind had come up, and blew his blond fringe back from his face, making him look very small and fragile.

"Well, then," he said, and stopped, swallowing. Very gently, he put his arms round Jemmy's shoulders and kissed the top of his round red head.

"I'll come back, cousin," he said. "And you will come and visit me by the sea. You'll come, too," he assured Aidan, looking up. Aidan sniffed, nodding, and made his way slowly down the slope.

Roger reached out a free hand and gently detached Jemmy. "Get on my back, *mo chuisle,*" he said. "It's a steep slope; I'll take ye down pick-a-back."

Not waiting to be asked, Ian leaned down and picked up Aidan, who wrapped his legs round Ian's middle, hiding his tear-streaked face in Ian's buckskin shirt.

"D'ye want to ride, too?" Roger asked Germain, standing up carefully under the weight of his double burden. "Ian can carry ye, if ye like."

Ian nodded and held out a hand, but Germain shook his head, blond hair flying.

"*Non,* Uncle Roger," he said, almost too softly to hear. "I'll walk." And turning round, began to make his way gingerly down the precipitous slope.

69

A STAMPEDE OF BEAVERS

October 25, 1774

THEY HAD BEEN walking for an hour before Brianna began to realize that they weren't after game. They'd cut the trail of a small herd of deer, with droppings so fresh that the pellets were still patchy with moisture, but Ian ignored the sign, pushing up the slope in single-minded determination.

Rollo had come with them, but after several fruitless attempts to draw his master's attention to promising scents, abandoned them in disgust and bounded off through the flurrying leaves to do his own hunting.

The climb was too steep to permit conversation, even had Ian seemed inclined. With a mental shrug, she followed, but kept gun in hand and an eye on the brush, just in case.

They had left the Ridge at dawn; it was well past noon when they paused at last, on the bank of some small and nameless stream. A wild grapevine wrapped itself round the trunk of a persimmon that overhung the bank; animals had taken most of the grapes, but a few bunches still hung out over the water, out of reach for any but the most daring of squirrels—or a tall woman.

She shucked her moccasins and waded into the stream, gasping at the icy shock of the water on her calves. The grapes were ripe to bursting, so purple as to be nearly black, and sticky with juice. The squirrels hadn't got to them, but the wasps had, and she kept a cautious eye on the dagger-bellied foragers as she twisted the tough stem of a particularly succulent bunch.

"So, do you want to tell me what we're really looking for?" she asked, back turned to her cousin.

"No," he said, a smile in his voice.

"Oh, a surprise, is it?" She popped the stem, and turned to toss the grapes to him.

He caught the bunch one-handed, and set them down on the bank beside the ragged knapsack in which he carried provisions.

"Something o' the sort."

"As long as we aren't just out for a walk, then." She twisted off another bunch, and sloshed ashore, to sit down beside him.

"No, not that." He flipped two grapes into his mouth, crushed them, and spat the skins and pips with the ease of long custom. She nibbled hers more daintily, biting one in half and flicking the seeds out with a fingernail.

"You ought to eat the skins, Ian; they have vitamins."

He raised one shoulder in skepticism, but said nothing. Both she and her mother had explained the concept of vitamins—numerous times—to little or no effect. Jamie and Ian had reluctantly been obliged to admit the existence of germs, because Claire could show them teeming seas of microorganisms in her microscope. Vitamins, however, were unfortunately invisible and thus could be safely ignored.

"Is it much farther, this surprise?" The grape skins were, in fact, very bitter. Her mouth puckered involuntarily as she bit into one. Ian, industriously eating and spitting, noticed and grinned at her.

"Aye, a bit farther."

She cast an eye at the horizon; the sun was coming down the sky. If they were to turn back now, it would be dark before they reached home.

"How *much* farther?" She spit the mangled grape skin into her palm and flicked it away into the grass.

Ian glanced at the sun, too, and pursed his lips.

"Well . . . I should think we'll reach it by midday tomorrow."

"We'll *what*? Ian!" He looked abashed, and ducked his head.

"I'm sorry, coz. I ken I should have told ye before—but I thought ye maybe wouldn't come, if I said how far."

A wasp lighted on the bunch of grapes in her hand, and she slapped it irritably away.

"You *know* I wouldn't. Ian, what were you thinking? Roger will have a fit!"

Her cousin seemed to find the notion funny; his mouth turned up at the corner.

"A fit? Roger Mac? I shouldna think so."

"Well, all right, he won't throw a fit—but he'll be worried. And Jemmy will miss me!"

"No, they'll be all right," Ian assured her. "I told Uncle Jamie we'd be gone three days, and he said he'd bring the wean up to the Big House. With your Mam and Lizzie and Mrs. Bug to fuss him, wee Jem won't even notice you're gone."

This was likely true, but did nothing to assuage her annoyance.

"You told *Da*? And he just said fine, and both of you thought it was perfectly all right to—to—lug me off into the woods for three days, without telling me what was going on? You—you—"

"High-handed, insufferable, beastly *Scots,*" Ian said, in such a perfect imitation of her mother's English accent that she burst out laughing, despite her annoyance.

"Yes," she said, wiping spluttered grape juice off her chin. "Exactly!"

He was still smiling, but his expression had changed; he wasn't teasing anymore.

"Brianna," he said softly, with that Highland lilt that made of her name something strange and graceful. "It's important, aye?"

He wasn't smiling at all now. His eyes were fixed on hers, warm, but serious. His hazel eyes were the only feature of any beauty about Ian Murray's face, but they held a gaze of such frank, sweet openness that you felt he had let you look inside his soul, just for an instant. She had had occasion before to wonder whether he was aware of this particular effect—but even if he was, it was difficult to resist.

"All right," she said, and waved away a circling wasp, still cross but resigned. "All *right*. But you still should have told me. And you won't tell me, even now?"

He shook his head, looking down at the grape he was thumbing loose from its stem.

"I can't," he said simply. He flipped the grape into his mouth and turned to open his bag—which, now that she noticed, bulged suspiciously. "D'ye want some bread, coz, or a bit of cheese?"

"No. Let's go." She stood up and brushed dead leaves from her breeches. "The sooner we get there, the sooner we'll be back."

THEY STOPPED an hour before sunset, while enough light remained to gather wood. The bulging knapsack had proved to contain two blankets, as well as food and a jug of beer—welcome, after the day's walking, which had been mostly uphill.

"Oh, this is a good batch," she said approvingly, sniffing at the neck of the jug after a long, aromatic, hop-edged swallow. "Who made it?"

"Lizzie. She caught the knack of it from *Frau* Ute. Before the . . . er . . . mphm." A delicate Scottish noise encompassed the painful circumstances surrounding the dissolution of Lizzie's betrothal.

"Mmm. That was too bad, wasn't it?" She lowered her lashes, watching him covertly to see whether he would say anything further about Lizzie. Lizzie and Ian had seemed fond of each other once—but first he had gone to the Iroquois, and then she had been engaged to Manfred McGillivray when he returned. Now that both of them were free once more . . .

He dismissed her comment about Lizzie with nothing more than a shrug of agreement, though, concentrating on the tedious process of fire-making. The day had been warm and an hour of daylight remained, but the shadows under the trees were already blue; the night would be chilly.

"I'm going to have a look at the stream," she announced, plucking a coiled line and hook from the small pile of effects Ian had unloaded from his bag. "It looked like there's a trout pool just below the bend, and the flies will be rising."

"Oh, aye." He nodded, but paid her little attention, patiently scraping the pile of kindling a little higher before striking the next shower of sparks from his flint.

As she made her way around the bend of the little creek, she saw that it wasn't merely a trout pool—it was a beaver pond. The humped mound of the lodge was reflected in still water, and on the far bank she could see the agitated judderings of a couple of willow saplings, evidently in the process of being consumed.

She moved slowly, a wary eye out. Beavers wouldn't trouble her, but they *would* make a dash for the water if they saw her, not only splashing, but smacking the water with their tails in alarm. She'd heard it before; it was amazingly loud, sounding like a fusillade of gunshots, and guaranteed to scare every fish within miles into hiding.

Gnawed sticks littered the near bank, the white inner wood chiseled as neatly as any carpenter could do, but none was fresh, and she heard nothing nearby but the sigh of wind in the trees. Beavers were not stealthy; none was close.

With a cautious eye on the far bank, she baited the hook with a small chunk of cheese, whirled it slowly overhead, picked up speed as she let the line out, then let it fly. The hook landed with a small *plop!* in the middle of the pond, but the noise wasn't sufficient to alarm the beavers; the willow saplings on the far bank continued to shake and heave under the assault of industrious teeth.

The evening hatch was rising, just as she'd told Ian. The air was soft, cool on her face, and the surface of the water dimpled and glimmered like gray silk shaken in light. Small clouds of gnats drifted in the still air under the trees, prey for the rising of the carnivorous caddis flies, stone flies, and damselflies breaking free of the surface, new-hatched and ravenous.

It was a pity that she hadn't a casting rod or tied flies—but still worth a try. Caddis flies weren't the only things that rose hungry at twilight, and voracious trout had been known to strike at almost anything that floated in front of them—her father had once taken one with a hook adorned with nothing more than a few knotted strands of his own bright hair.

That was a thought. She smiled to herself, brushing back a wisp of hair that had escaped from its plait, and began to draw the line slowly back toward shore. But there were likely more than trout here, and cheese was—

A strong tug came on the line, and she jerked in surprise. A snag? The line jerked back, and a thrill from the depths shot up her arm like electricity.

The next half hour passed without conscious thought, in the single-minded pursuit of finny prey. She was wet to mid-thigh, rashed with mosquito bites, and her wrist and shoulder ached, but she had three fat fish gleaming in the grass at her feet, a hunter's sense of profound satisfaction—and a few more crumbs of cheese left in her pocket.

She was drawing back her arm to throw the hook again, when a sudden chorus of squeaks and hisses shattered the evening calm, and a stampede of beavers broke from cover, trundling down the opposite bank of the pond like a platoon of small, furry tanks. She stared at them open-mouthed, and took a step back in reflex.

Then something big and dark appeared among the trees behind the beavers, and further reflex shot adrenaline through her limbs as she whirled to flee. She would have been into the trees and away in an instant, had she not stepped on one of her fish, which slid under her foot like greased butter and dumped her unceremoniously on her backside. From which position she was ideally placed to see Rollo race from the trees in a long, low streak and launch himself in an arching parabola from the top of the bank. Graceful as a comet, he soared through the air and landed in the pond among the beavers, with a splash like a fallen meteor.

IAN LOOKED up at her, open-mouthed. Slowly, his eyes traveled from her dripping hair, over her sopping, mud-smeared clothes, and down to the fish—one slightly squashed—that dangled from a leather string in her hand.

"The fish put up a good fight, did they?" he asked, nodding at the string. The corners of his mouth began to twitch.

"Yes," she said, and dropped them on the ground in front of him. "But not nearly as good a fight as the beavers."

"Beavers," he said. He rubbed a knuckle meditatively down the bridge of his long, bony nose. "Aye, I heard them slapping. Ye've been fighting beavers?"

"I've been rescuing your wretched *dog* from beavers," she said, and sneezed. She sank to her knees in front of the new-made fire and closed her eyes in momentary bliss at the touch of heat on her shivering body.

"Oh, Rollo's back, then? Rollo! Where are ye, hound?" The big dog slunk reluctantly out of the shrubbery, tail barely twitching in response to his master's call.

"What's this I hear about beavers, then, *a madadh*?" Ian said sternly. In response, Rollo shook himself, though no more than a fine mist of water droplets rose from his coat. He sighed, dropped to his belly, and put his nose morosely on his paws.

"Maybe he was only after fish, but the beavers didn't see it that way. They ran from him on shore, but once he was in the water—" Brianna shook her head, and wrung out the soggy tail of her hunting shirt. "I tell you what, Ian—*you* clean those damn fish."

He was already doing so, gutting one with a single neat slice up the belly and a scoop of the thumb. He tossed the entrails toward Rollo, who merely let out another sigh, and seemed to flatten against the dead leaves, ignoring the treat.

"He's no hurt, is he?" Ian asked, frowning at his dog.

She glared at him.

"No, he isn't. I expect he's embarrassed. You could ask whether *I'm* hurt. Do you have any idea what kind of *teeth* beavers have?"

The light was nearly gone, but she could see his lean shoulders shaking.

"Aye," he said, sounding rather strangled. "I have. They, um, didna bite ye, did they? I mean—I should think it would be noticeable, if ye'd been gnawed." A small wheeze of amusement escaped him, and he tried to cover it with a cough.

"No," she said, rather coldly. The fire was going well, but not nearly well enough. The evening breeze had come up, and was reaching through the soaked fabric of shirt and breeches to fondle her backside with ice-cold fingers.

"It wasn't so much the teeth as the tails," she said, shuffling round on her knees to present her back to the fire. She rubbed a hand gingerly over her right arm, where one of the muscular paddles had struck flat on her forearm, leaving a reddened bruise that stretched from wrist to elbow. For a few moments, she'd thought the bone was broken.

"It was like being hit with a baseball bat—er . . . with a club, I mean," she amended. The beavers hadn't attacked her directly, of course, but being in the water with a panicked wolf-dog and half a dozen sixty-pound rodents in a state of extreme agitation had been rather like walking through an automated car wash on foot—a maelstrom of blinding spray and thrashing objects. A chill struck her and she wrapped both arms around herself, shivering.

"Here, coz." Ian stood up and skinned the buckskin shirt off over his head. "Put this on."

She was much too cold and battered to refuse the offer. Retiring modestly behind a bush, she stripped off the wet things and emerged a moment later, clad in Ian's buckskin, one of the blankets wrapped around her waist sarong-style.

"You don't eat enough, Ian," she said, sitting down by the fire again, and eyeing him critically. "All your ribs show."

They did. He'd always been lean to the point of thinness, but in his younger years, his teenage scrawniness had seemed quite normal, merely the result of his bones outstripping the growth of the rest of him.

Now he had reached his full growth and had had a year or two to let his muscles catch up. They had—she could see every sinew in his arms and shoulders—but the knobs of his spine bulged against the tanned skin of his back, and she could see the shadows of his ribs like rippled sand underwater.

He raised a shoulder, but made no reply, intent on skewering the cleaned fish on peeled willow twigs for broiling.

"And you don't sleep very well, either." She narrowed her eyes at him across the fire. Even in this light, the shadows and hollows in his face were obvious, despite the distraction of the Mohawk tattoos that looped across his cheekbones. The shadows had been obvious to everyone for months; her mother had wanted to say something to Ian, but Jamie had told her to let the lad be; he would speak when he was ready.

"Oh, well enough," he murmured, not looking up.

Whether he was ready now or not, she couldn't say. But he'd brought her here. If he wasn't ready, he could bloody well get that way fast.

She had—of course—wondered all day about the mysterious goal of their journey, and why *she* was his necessary companion. For a matter of hunting, Ian would have taken one of the men; good as she was with a gun, several of the men on the Ridge were better, including her father. And any one of them would be better suited than she to something like digging out a bear's den or packing home meat or hides.

They were in the Cherokee lands at the moment; she knew Ian visited the Indians frequently, and was on good terms with several villages. But if it had been a matter of some formal arrangement to be made, surely he would have asked Jamie to accompany him, or Peter Bewlie, with his Cherokee wife to interpret.

"Ian," she said, with the tone in her voice that could bring almost any man up short. "Look at me."

His head jerked up, and he blinked at her.

"Ian," she said, a little more gently, "is this to do with your wife?"

He stayed frozen for a moment, eyes dark and unfathomable. Rollo, in the shadows behind him, suddenly raised his head and let out a small whine of inquiry. That seemed to rouse Ian; he blinked and looked down.

"Aye," he said, sounding quite matter-of-fact. "It is."

He adjusted the angle of the stick he had driven into the earth by the fire; the pale flesh of the fish curled and sizzled, browning on the green wood.

She waited for him to say more, but he didn't speak—just broke off the edge of a piece of half-cooked fish and held it out to the dog, clicking his tongue in invitation. Rollo rose and sniffed Ian's ear in concern, but then deigned to take the fish, and lay down again, licking the hot tidbit delicately before scooping it up with his tongue, gathering enough spirit then to engulf the discarded heads and fish guts as well.

Ian pursed his lips a little, and she could see the thoughts flickering half-formed across his face, before he made up his mind to speak.

"I did once think of marrying you, ye ken."

He gave her a quick, direct glance, and she felt an odd little jolt of realization. He'd thought about it, all right. And while she had no doubt that his offer then had been made from the purest of motives . . . he was a young man. She hadn't until this moment realized that he would of course have contemplated every detail of what that offer entailed.

His eyes held hers in wry acknowledgment of the fact that he had indeed imagined the physical details of sharing her bed—and had not found the prospect in any way objectionable. She resisted the impulse to blush and look away; that would discredit them both.

She was suddenly—and for the first time—aware of him *as* a man, rather than as an endearing young cousin. And aware of the heat of his body that had lingered in the soft buckskin when she pulled it on.

"It wouldn't have been the worst thing in the world," she said, striving to match his matter-of-fact tone. He laughed, and the stippled lines of his tattoos lost their grimness.

"No," he said. "Maybe not the best—that would be Roger Mac, aye? But I'm glad to hear I wouldna have been the worst, either. Better than Ronnie Sinclair, d'ye think? Or worse than Forbes the lawyer?"

"Ha, bloody ha." She refused to be discomposed by his teasing. "You would have been at least third on the list."

"Third?" That got his attention. "What? Who was second?" He actually seemed miffed at the notion that someone might precede him, and she laughed.

"Lord John Grey."

"Oh? Oh, well. Aye, I suppose he'd do," Ian admitted grudgingly. "Though of course, he—" He stopped abruptly, and darted a cautious look in her direction.

She felt an answering stab of caution. Did Ian know about John Grey's private tastes? She thought he must, from the odd expression on his face—but if not, it was no place of hers to be revealing Lord John's secrets.

"Have you met him?" she asked curiously. Ian had gone with her parents to rescue Roger from the Iroquois, before

Lord John had appeared at her aunt's plantation, where she had met the nobleman herself.

"Oh, aye." He was still looking wary, though he had relaxed a little. "Some years ago. Him and his . . . son. Stepson, I mean. They came to the Ridge, traveling through to Virginia, and stopped a bit. I gave him the measle." He grinned, quite suddenly. "Or at least he *had* the measle. Auntie Claire nursed him through it. Ye've met the man yourself, though?"

"Yes, at River Run. Ian, the fish is on fire."

It was, and he snatched the stick from the flames with a small Gaelic exclamation, waving scorched fingers to cool them. Extinguished in the grass, the fish proved to be quite edible, if a little crispy round the edges, and a tolerably good supper, with the addition of bread and beer.

"Did ye meet Lord John's son, then, at River Run?" he asked, resuming their conversation. "Willie, his name is. A nice wee lad. He fell into the privy," he added thoughtfully.

"Fell in the privy?" she said, laughing. "He sounds like an idiot. Or was he just quite small?"

"No, a decent size for his age. And sensible enough, for an Englishman. See, it wasna quite his fault, ken. We were looking at a snake, and it came up the branch toward us, and . . . well, it was an accident," he concluded, handing Rollo another piece of fish. "Ye've not seen the lad yourself, though?"

"No, and I think you are deliberately changing the subject."

"Aye, I am. D'ye want a bit more beer?"

She raised an eyebrow at him—he needn't think he was going to escape that easily—but nodded, accepting the jug.

They were quiet for a bit, drinking beer and watching the last of the light fade into darkness as the stars came out. The scent of the pine trees strengthened, their sap warmed from the day, and in the distance she heard the occasional gunshot warning slap of a beaver's tail on the pond—evidently the beavers had posted sentries, in case she or Rollo should sneak back after dark, she thought wryly.

Ian had wrapped his own blanket round his shoulders against the growing chill, and was lying flat in the grass, staring upward into the vault of heaven overhead.

She didn't make any pretense of not watching him, and was quite sure he was aware of it. His face was quiet for the moment, minus its usual animation—but not guarded. He was thinking, and she was content to let him take his time; it was autumn now and night would be long enough for many things.

She wished she had thought to ask her mother more about the girl Ian called Emily—the Mohawk name was something multisyllabic and unpronounceable. Small, her mother had said. Pretty, in a neat, small-boned sort of way, and very clever.

Was she dead, Emily the small and clever? She thought not. She'd been in this time long enough to have seen many men deal with the death of wives. They showed loss and grief—but they didn't do what Ian had been doing.

Could he be taking her to *meet* Emily? That was a staggering thought, but one she rejected almost immediately. It would be a month's journey, at least, to reach the Mohawks' territory—probably more. But then . . .

"I wondered, ken?" he said suddenly, still looking up at the sky. "D'ye feel sometimes . . . wrong?" He glanced at her helplessly, not sure whether he'd said what he meant—but she understood him perfectly.

"Yes, all the time." She felt a sense of instant, unexpected relief at the admission. He saw the slump of her shoulders, and smiled a little, crookedly.

"Well . . . maybe not *all* the time," she amended. "When I'm out in the woods, alone, it's fine. Or with Roger, by ourselves. Though even then . . ." She saw Ian's eyebrow lift, and hurried to explain. "Not that. Not being with him. It's just that we . . . we talk about what was."

He gave her a look in which sympathy was mingled with interest. Plainly, he would like to know about "what was," but put that aside for the moment.

"The woods, aye?" he said. "I see that. When I'm awake, at least. Sleeping, though . . ." He turned his face back toward the empty sky and the brightening stars.

"Are you afraid—when the dark comes on?" She'd felt that now and then; a moment of deep fear at twilight—a sense of abandonment and elemental loneliness as night rose from the earth. A feeling that sometimes remained, even when she had gone inside the cabin, the bolted door secure behind her.

"No," he said, frowning a little at her. "You are?"

"Just a little," she said, waving it away. "Not all the time. Not now. But what is it about sleeping in the woods?"

He sat up, and rocked back a little, big hands linked around one knee, thinking.

"Aye, well . . ." he said slowly. "Sometimes I think of the auld tales—from Scotland, aye? And ones I've heard now and then, living wi' the Kahnyen'kehaka. About . . . things that may come upon a man while he sleeps. To lure away his soul."

"Things?" Despite the beauty of the stars and the peace of the evening, she felt something small and cold slide down her back. "*What* things?"

He took a deep breath and blew it out, brows puckered.

"Ye call them *sidhe* in the Gaelic. The Cherokee call them the Nunnahee. And the Mohawk have names for them, too—more than one. But when I heard Eats Turtles tell of them, I kent at once what they were. It's the same—the Old Folk."

"Fairies?" she said, and her incredulity must have been clear in her voice, for he glanced up sharply at her, a glint of irritation in his eyes.

"No, I ken what *you* mean by that—Roger Mac showed me the wee picture ye drew for Jem, all tiny things like dragonflies, prinking in the flowers. . . ." He made an uncouth noise in the back of his throat. "Nay. These things are . . ." He made a helpless gesture with one big hand, frowning at the grass.

"Vitamins," he said suddenly, looking up.

"Vitamins," she said, and rubbed a hand between her brows. It had been a long day; they had likely walked fifteen or twenty miles and fatigue had settled like water in her legs and back. The bruises from her battle with the beavers were beginning to throb.

"I see. Ian . . . are you sure that your head isn't still a bit cracked?" She said it lightly, but her real anxiety lest it be true must have shown in her voice, for he gave a low, rueful chuckle.

"No. Or at least—I dinna think so. I was only—well, d'ye see, it's like that. Ye canna see the vitamins, but you and

Auntie Claire ken weel that they're there, and Uncle Jamie and I must take it on faith that ye're right about it. I ken as much about the—the Old Ones. Can ye no believe me about *that*?"

"Well, I—" She had begun to agree, for the sake of peace between them—but a feeling swept over her, sudden and cold as a cloud-shadow, that she wished to say nothing to acknowledge the notion. Not out loud. And not here.

"Oh," he said, catching sight of her face. "So ye *do* know."

"I don't *know,* no," she said. "But I don't know it's not, either. And I don't think it's a good idea to talk about things like that, in a wood at night, a million miles away from civilization. All right?"

He smiled a little at that, and nodded in acceptance.

"Aye. And it's no what I meant to say, really. It's more . . ." His feathery brows knitted in concentration. "When I was a bairn, I'd wake in my bed, and I'd ken at once where I was, aye? There was the window"—he flung out a hand—"and there was the basin and ewer on the table, wi' a blue band round the top, and *there*"—he pointed toward a laurel bush—"was the big bed where Janet and Michael were sleepin', and Jocky the dog at the bed fit, farting like a beetle, and the smell of peat smoke from the fire and . . . well, even if I should wake at midnight and the house all still around me, I should ken at once where I was."

She nodded, the memory of her own old room in the house on Furey Street rising around her, vivid as a vision in the smoke. The striped wool blanket, itchy under her chin, and the mattress with the indentation of her body in the middle, cupping her like a huge, warm hand. Angus, the stuffed Scottie with the ragged tam-o'-shanter who shared her bed, and the comforting hum of her parents' conversation from the living room below, punctuated by the baritone sax of the theme music from *Perry Mason.*

Most of all, the sense of absolute security.

She had to close her eyes, and swallow twice before answering.

"Yes. I know what you mean."

"Aye. Well. For some time after I left home, I might find myself sleeping rough, wi' Uncle Jamie in the heather, or here and there in inns and pothouses. I'd wake wi' no notion where I was—and still, I'd ken I was in Scotland. It was all right." He paused, lower lip caught between his teeth as he struggled to find the right words.

"Then . . . things happened. I wasna in Scotland any longer, and home was . . . gone." His voice was soft, but she could hear the echo of loss in it.

"I would wake, with no idea where I might be—or who."

He was hunched over now, big hands hanging loose between his thighs as he gazed into the fire.

"But when I lay wi' Emily—from the first time. I knew. Kent who I was again." He looked up at her then, eyes dark and shadowed by loss. "My soul didna wander while I slept—when I slept wi' her."

"And now it does?" she asked quietly, after a moment.

He nodded, wordless. The wind whispered in the trees above. She tried to ignore it, obscurely afraid that if she listened closely, she might hear words.

"Ian," she said, and touched his arm, very lightly. "Is Emily dead?"

He sat quite still for a minute, then took a deep, shuddering breath, and shook his head.

"I dinna think so." He sounded very doubtful, though, and she could see the trouble in his face.

"Ian," she said very softly. "Come here."

He didn't move, but when she scooted close and put her arms around him, he didn't resist. She pulled him down with her, insisting that he lie beside her, his head pillowed in the curve between shoulder and breast, her arm around him.

Mother instinct, she thought, wryly amused. Whatever's wrong, the first thing you do is pick them up and cuddle them. And if they're too big to lift . . . and if his warm weight and the sound of his breathing in her ear kept the voices in the wind at bay, so much the better.

She had a fragmentary memory, a brief vivid image of her mother standing behind her father in the kitchen of their house in Boston. He lay back in a straight chair, his head against her mother's stomach, eyes closed in pain or exhaustion, as she rubbed his temples. What had it been? A headache? But her mother's face had been gentle, the lines of her own day's stress smoothed away by what she was doing.

"I feel a fool," Ian said, sounding shy—but didn't pull away.

"No, you don't."

He took a deep breath, squirmed a little, and settled cautiously into the grass, his body barely touching hers.

"Aye, well. I suppose not, then," he murmured. He relaxed by wary degrees, his head growing heavier on her shoulder, the muscles of his back yielding slowly, their tension subsiding under her hand. Very tentatively, as though expecting her to slap him away, he lifted one arm and laid it over her.

It seemed the wind had died. The firelight shone on his face, the dark dotted lines of his tattoos standing out against the young skin. His hair smelled of woodsmoke and dust, soft against her cheek.

"Tell me," she said.

He sighed, deeply.

"Not yet," he said. "When we get there, aye?"

He would not say more, and they lay together, quiet in the grass, and safe.

Brianna felt sleep come, the waves of it gentle, lifting her toward peace, and did not resist. The last thing she recalled was Ian's face, cheek heavy on her shoulder, his eyes still open, watching the fire.

WALKING ELK WAS *telling a story. It was one of his best stories, but Ian wasn't paying proper attention. He sat across the fire from Walking Elk, but it was the flames he was watching, not his friend's face.*

Very odd, he thought. He'd been watching fires all his life, and never seen the woman in them, until these winter months. Of course, peat fires had no great flame to speak of, though they had a good heat and a lovely smell . . . oh. Aye, so she was *there, after all, the woman. He nodded slightly, smiling. Walking Elk took this as an expression of approval at his performance and became even more dramatic in his gestures, scowling horrendously and lurching to and fro with bared teeth, growling in illustration of the glutton he had carefully tracked to its lair.*

The noise distracted Ian from the fire, drawing his attention to the story again. Just in time, for Walking Elk had reached the climax, and the young men nudged each other in anticipation. Walking Elk was short and heavily built—not so much unlike a glutton himself, which made his imitations that much more entertaining.

He turned his head, wrinkling up his nose and growling through his teeth, as the glutton caught the hunter's scent. Then he changed in a flash, became the hunter, creeping carefully through the brush, pausing, squatting low—and springing upward with a sharp yelp, as his buttock encountered a thorny plant.

The men around the fire whooped as Walking Elk became the glutton, who looked at first astonished at the noise, and then thrilled to have seen its prey. It leaped from its lair, uttering growls and sharp yips of rage. The hunter fell back, horrified, and turned to run. Walking Elk's stubby legs churned the pounded earth of the longhouse, running in place. Then he threw up his arms and sprawled forward with a despairing "Ay-YIIIIII!" as the glutton struck him in the back.

The men shouted encouragement, slapping their palms on their thighs, as the beleaguered hunter managed to roll onto his back, thrashing and cursing, grappling with the glutton that sought to tear out his throat.

The firelight gleamed on the scars that decorated Walking Elk's chest and shoulders—thick white gouges that showed briefly at the gaping neck of his shirt as he writhed picturesquely, arms straining upward against his invisible enemy. Ian found himself leaning forward, his breath short and his own shoulders knotted with effort, though he knew what was coming next.

Walking Elk had done it many times, but it never failed. Ian had tried it himself, but couldn't do it at all. The hunter dug his heels and shoulders into the dirt, his body arched like a bow at full stretch. His legs trembled, his arms shook—surely they would give way at any moment. The men by the fire held their breath.

Then it came: a soft, sudden click. *Distinct and somehow muffled, it was exactly the sound made by the breaking of a neck. The snap of bone and ligament, muffled in flesh and fur. The hunter stayed arched a moment, unbelieving, and then slowly, slowly, lowered himself to the ground and sat up, staring at the body of his enemy, clutched limp in his hands.*

He cast up his eyes in prayerful thanks, then stopped, wrinkling his nose. He glanced down, face screwed into a grimace, and rubbed fastidiously at his leggings, soiled by the odorous voidings of the glutton. The hearth rocked with laughter.

A small bucket of spruce beer was making the rounds; Walking Elk beamed, his face shining with sweat, and accepted it. His short, thick throat worked industriously, sucking the sharp drink down as though it was water. He lowered the bucket at last and looked about in dreamy satisfaction.

"You, Wolf's Brother. Tell us a story!" He threw the half-empty bucket across the fire; Ian caught it, only sloshing a little over his wrist. He sucked the liquid from his sleeve, laughed, and shook his head. He took a quick mouthful of beer and passed the bucket to Sleeps with Snakes, beside him.

Eats Turtles, on his other side, poked Ian in the ribs, wanting him to talk, but he shook his head again and shrugged, jerking his chin toward Snake.

Snake, nothing loath, set the bucket neatly before him and leaned forward, the firelight dancing on his face as he began to talk. He was no actor like Walking Elk, but he was an older man—perhaps thirty—and had traveled much in his youth. He had lived with the Assiniboin and the Cayuga, and had many stories from them, which he told with great skill—if less sweat.

"Will you talk later, then?" Turtle said in Ian's ear. "I want to hear more tales of the great sea and the woman with green eyes."

Ian nodded, a little reluctant. He had been very drunk the first time, or he would never have spoken of Geillis Abernathy. It was only that they had been drinking trader's rum, and the spinning sensation it caused in his head was very like that caused by the stuff she'd *given him to drink, though the taste was different. That caused a giddiness that made his eyes blur, so candle flames streaked and ran like water, and the flames of the fire seemed to overflow and leap the hearthstones, glimmering all round her lavish room, small separate blazes springing up in all the rounded surfaces of silver and glass, gems and polished wood—flickering brightest behind green eyes.*

He glanced around. There were no shining surfaces here. Clay pots, rough firewood, and the smooth poles of bed frames, grinding stones and woven baskets; even the cloth and furs of their clothes were soft dull colors that drowned the light. It must have been only the memory of those times of light-glazed dizziness that had brought her to mind.

He seldom thought of the Mistress—that was how the slaves and the other boys spoke of her; she needed no more name than that, for no one could imagine another of her sort. He did not value his memories of her, but Uncle Jamie had told him not to hide from them, and he obeyed, finding it good counsel.

He stared intently into the fire, only half-hearing Snake's recounting of the story about Goose and how he had outwitted the Evil One to bring tobacco to the People and save Old Man's life. Was it her, then, the witch Geillis, that he saw in the fire?

He thought it was not. The woman in the fire gave him a warm feeling when he saw her that ran from his heated face down through his chest and curled up low and hot in his belly. The woman in the fire had no face; he saw her limbs, her curving back, a sweep of long, smooth hair, twisting toward him, gone in a flicker; he heard her laugh, soft and breathy, far away—and it was not Geillis Abernathy's laugh.

Still, Turtle's words had brought her to his mind, and he could see her there. He sighed to himself and thought what story he might tell, when it came his turn. Perhaps he would tell about Mrs. Abernathy's twin slaves, the huge black men who did her every bidding; he had once seen them kill a crocodile, and carry it up from the river between them to lay it at her feet.

He didn't mind so much. He had found—after that first drunken telling—that to speak of her in such a way caused him to think of her in the same way—as though she was a story, interesting but unreal. Perhaps she had happened, as perhaps Goose had brought tobacco to Old Man—but it did not seem so much as though she had happened to him.

And after all, he had no scars, like Walking Elk's, that would remind either his hearers or himself that he spoke truth.

In truth, he was growing bored with drinking and stories. The real truth was that he longed to escape to the furs and cool darkness of his bed platform, shed his clothes, and curl his hot nakedness around his wife. Her name meant "Works with Her Hands," but in the privacy of bed, he called her Emily.

Their time was growing short; in two moons more, she would leave, to go to the women's house, and he would not see her. Another moon before the child came, one more after that for cleansing . . . The thought of two months spent cold and alone, without her next to him at night, was enough to make him reach for the beer as it came around, and drink deep.

Only the bucket was empty. His friends giggled as he held it upside down above his open mouth, a single amber drop splattering on his surprised nose.

A small hand reached over his shoulder and took the bucket from his grasp, as its partner reached over his other shoulder, holding a full one.

He took the bucket and twisted, smiling up at her. Works with Her Hands smiled smugly back; it gave her great pleasure to anticipate his wants. She knelt behind him, the curve of her belly pressing warm against his back, and swatted away Turtle's hand as he reached for the beer.

"No, let my husband have it! He tells much better stories when he's drunk."

Turtle closed one eye, fixing her with the other. He was swaying slightly.

"Is it that he tells better stories when he's drunk?" he asked. "Or do we just think *they're better, because* we're *drunk?"*

Works with Her Hands ignored this philosophical inquiry and proceeded to make room for herself at the hearth, swinging her solid little bum deftly back and forth like a battering ram. She settled comfortably next to Ian, folding her arms atop her mound.

Other young women had come in with her, bringing more beer. They nudged their way in among the young men, murmuring, poking, and laughing. He'd been wrong, Ian thought, watching them. The firelight shone on their faces, glanced from their teeth, caught the moist shine of eyes and the soft dark flesh inside their mouths as they laughed. The fire gleamed on their faces more than it had ever shone from the crystal and silver of Rose Hall.

"So, husband," Emily said, lowering her eyelids demurely. "Tell us about this woman with green eyes."

He took a thoughtful swallow of beer, then another.

"Oh," he said. "She was a witch, and a very wicked woman—but she did make good beer."

Emily's eyes flew open wide, and everyone laughed. He looked into her eyes and saw it, clearly; the image of the fire behind him, tiny and perfect—welcoming him in.

"But not as good as yours," he said. He lifted the bucket in salute, and drank deep.

70

EMILY

BRIANNA WOKE IN the morning stiff and sore, but with one clear thought in mind. *Okay. I know who I am.* She had no clear idea *where* she was, but that didn't matter. She lay still for a moment, feeling oddly peaceful, despite the urge to get up and pee.

How long had it been, she wondered, since she *had* wakened alone and peaceful, with no company but her own thoughts? Really, not since she had stepped through the stones, she thought, in search of her family. And found them.

"In spades," she murmured, stretching gingerly. She groaned, staggered to her feet, and shuffled into the brush to pee and change back into her own clothes before returning to the blackened fire ring.

She unplaited her draggled hair, and began groggily combing her fingers through it. There was no sign of Ian or the dog nearby, but she wasn't concerned. The wood around her was filled with the racket of birds, but not alarm calls, just the daily business of flutter and feeding, a cheerful chatter that didn't alter when she rose. The birds had been watching her for hours; they weren't concerned, either.

She never woke easily, but the simple pleasure of not being dragged from sleep by the insistent demands of those who did made the morning air seem particularly sweet, in spite of the bitter tang of ashes from the dead fire.

Mostly awake, she wiped a handful of dew-wet poplar leaves over her face by way of a morning toilette, then squatted by the fire ring and began the chore of fire-starting. They had no coffee to boil, but Ian would be hunting. With luck, there'd be something to cook; they'd eaten everything in the knapsack, save a heel of bread.

"Heck with this," she muttered, whacking flint and steel together for the dozenth time, and seeing the spatter of sparks wink out without catching. If Ian had only told her they were camping, she would have brought her fire-striker, or some matches—though on second thought, she was not sure that would be safe. The things could easily burst into flame in her pocket.

"How did the Greeks do it?" she said aloud, scowling at the tiny mat of charred cloth on which she was attempting to catch a spark. "They must have had a way."

"The Greeks had what?"

Ian and Rollo were back, having captured, respectively, half a dozen yams and a blue-gray waterbird of some kind—a small heron? Rollo refused to allow her to look at it, and took his prey off to devour under a bush, its long, limp yellow legs dragging on the ground.

"The Greeks had what?" Ian repeated, turning out a pocket

full of chestnuts, red-brown skins gleaming from the remnants of their prickly hulls.

"Had stuff called phosphorus. You ever heard of it?"

Ian looked blank, and shook his head.

"No. What is it?"

"Stuff," she said, finding no better word to hand. "Lord John sent me some, so I could make matches."

"Matches between whom?" Ian inquired, regarding her warily.

She stared at him for a moment, her morning-sodden mind making slow sense of the conversation.

"Oh," she said, having at last discovered the difficulty. "Not that kind of match. Those fire-starters I made. Phosphorus burns by itself. I'll show you, when we get home." She yawned, and gestured vaguely at the small pile of unlit kindling in the fire ring.

Ian made a tolerant Scottish noise and took up the flint and steel himself.

"I'll do it. Do the nuts, aye?"

"Okay. Here, you should put your shirt back on." Her own clothes had dried, and while she missed the comfort of Ian's buckskin, the worn thick wool of her fringed hunting shirt was warm and soft on her skin. It was a bright day, but chilly so early in the morning. Ian had discarded his blanket while starting the fire, and his bare shoulders were pebbled with gooseflesh.

He shook his head slightly, though, indicating that he'd put on his shirt in a bit. For now . . . his tongue stuck out of the corner of his mouth in concentration as he struck flint and steel again, then disappeared as he muttered something under his breath.

"What did you say?" She paused, a half-hulled nut in her fingers.

"Oh, it's no but a—" He'd struck once more and caught a spark, glowing like a tiny star on the square of char. Hastily, he touched a wisp of dry grass to it, then another, and as a tendril of smoke rose up, added a bark chip, more grass, a handful of chips, and finally a careful crisscross of pine twigs.

"No but a fire charm," he finished, grinning at her over the infant blaze that had sprung up before him.

She applauded briefly, then proceeded to cut the skin of the chestnut she was holding, crosswise, so it wouldn't burst in the fire.

"I haven't heard that one," she said. "Tell me the words."

"Oh." He didn't blush easily, but the skin of his throat darkened a little. "It's . . . it's no the Gaelic, that one. It's the Kahnyen'kehaka."

Her brows went up, as much at the easy sound of the word on his tongue as at what he'd said.

"Do you ever think in Mohawk, Ian?" she asked curiously.

He shot her a glance of surprise, almost, she thought, of fright.

"No," he said tersely, and rose off his heels. "I'll fetch a bit of wood."

"I have some," she said, holding him with a stare. She reached behind her and thrust a fallen pine bough into the kindling fire. The dry needles burst in a puff of sparks and were gone, but the ragged bark began to catch and burn at the edges.

"What is it?" she said. "What I said, about thinking in Mohawk?"

His lips pressed tight together, not wanting to answer.

"You asked me to come," she said, not sharp with him, but firm.

"So I did." He took a deep breath, then looked down at the yams he was burying in the heating ashes to bake.

She worked on the nuts slowly, watching him make up his mind. Loud chewing sounds and intermittent puffs of blue-gray feathers drifted out from under Rollo's bush, behind him.

"Did ye dream last night, Brianna?" he asked suddenly, his eyes still on what he was doing.

She wished he had brought something coffeelike to boil, but still, she was sufficiently awake by now as to be able to think and respond coherently.

"Yes," she said. "I dream a lot."

"Aye, I ken that. Roger Mac told me ye write them down sometimes."

"He did?" That was a jolt, and one bigger than a cup of coffee. She'd never *hidden* her dreambook from Roger, but they didn't really discuss it, either. How much of it had he read?

"He didna tell me anything about them," Ian assured her, catching the tone of her voice. "Only that ye wrote things down, sometimes. So I thought, maybe, those would be important."

"Only to me," she said, but cautiously. "Why . . . ?"

"Well, d'ye see—the Kahnyen'kehaka set great store by dreams. More even than Highlanders." He glanced up with a brief smile, then back at the ashes where he had buried the yams. "What did ye dream of last night, then?"

"Birds," she said, trying to recall. "Lots of birds." Reasonable enough, she thought. The forest around her had been live with birdsong since well before dawn; of course it would seep into her dreams.

"Aye?" Ian seemed interested. "Were the birds alive, then?"

"Yes," she said, puzzled. "Why?"

He nodded, and picked up a chestnut to help her.

"That's good, to dream of live birds, especially if they sing. Dead birds are a bad thing, in a dream."

"They were definitely alive, and singing," she assured him, with a glance up at the branch above him, where some bird with a bright yellow breast and black wings had lighted, viewing their breakfast preparations with interest.

"Did any of them talk to ye?"

She stared at him, but he was clearly serious. And after all, she thought, why *wouldn't* a bird talk to you, in a dream?

She shook her head, though.

"No. They were—oh." She laughed, unexpectedly recalling. "They were building a nest out of toilet paper. I dream about toilet paper all the time. That's a thin, soft kind of paper that you use to wipe your, er, behind with," she explained, seeing his incomprehension.

"Ye wipe your arse with *paper*?" He stared at her, jaw dropped in horror. "Jesus God, Brianna!"

"Well." She rubbed a hand under her nose, trying not to laugh at his expression. He might well be horrified; there were no paper mills in the Colonies, and aside from tiny amounts of handmade paper such as she made herself, every sheet had to be imported from England. Paper was hoarded and treasured; her father, who wrote frequently to his sister in Scotland, would write a letter in the normal fashion—but then would turn the paper sideways, and write additional lines perpendicularly, to save space. Little wonder that Ian was shocked!

"It's very cheap then," she assured him. "Really."

"Not as cheap as a cob o' maize, I'll warrant," he said, narrow-eyed with suspicion.

"Believe it or not, most people then won't have cornfields to hand," she said, still amused. "And I tell you what, Ian—toilet paper is *much* nicer than a dry corncob."

"'Nicer,'" he muttered, obviously still shaken to the core. "Nicer. Jesus, Mary, and Bride!"

"You were asking me about dreams," she reminded him. "Did you dream last night?"

"Oh. Ah . . . no." He turned his attention from the scandalous notion of toilet paper with some difficulty. "Or at least if I did, I dinna recall it."

It came to her suddenly, looking at his hollowed face, that one reason for his sleeplessness might be that he was afraid of what dreams might come to him.

In fact, he seemed afraid now that she might press him on the subject. Not meeting her eye, he picked up the empty beer jug and clicked his tongue for Rollo, who followed him, blue-gray feathers sticking to his jaws.

She had cut the last of the chestnut skins and buried the gleaming marrons in the ashes to bake with the yams, by the time he came back.

"Just in time," she called, seeing him. "The yams are ready."

"Just in time, forbye," he answered, smiling. "See what I've got?"

What he had was a chunk of honeycomb, thieved from a bee tree and still chilled enough that the honey ran slow and thick, drizzled over the hot yams in glorious blobs of gold sweetness. Garnished with roasted, peeled, sweet chestnuts and washed down with cold creek water, she thought it was possibly the best breakfast she'd eaten since leaving her own time.

She said as much, and Ian lifted one feathery brow in derision.

"Oh, aye? And what would ye eat then that's better?"

"Oooh . . . chocolate donuts, maybe. Or hot chocolate, with marshmallows in it. I really miss chocolate." Though it was hard to miss it much at the moment, licking honey off her fingers.

"Och, get on wi' ye! I've had chocolate." He squinched his eyes and pinched his lips in exaggerated distaste. "Bitter, nasty stuff. Though they did charge a terrible lot of money just for a wee cup of it, in Edinburgh," he added practically, unsquinching.

She laughed.

"They put sugar in it, where I come from," she assured him. "It's sweet."

"Sugar in your chocolate? That's the most decadent thing I've ever heard of," he said severely. "Even worse than the arse-wiping paper, aye?" She saw the teasing glint in his eye, though, and merely snorted, nibbling the last shreds of orange yam flesh from the blackened skin.

"Someday I'll get hold of some chocolate, Ian," she said, discarding the limp peel and licking her fingers like a cat. "I'll put sugar in it and feed it to you, and see what you think then!"

It was his turn to snort, good-naturedly, but he made no further remarks, concentrating instead on licking his own hands clean.

Rollo had appropriated the remnants of honeycomb, and was noisily gnawing and slurping at the wax, with complete enjoyment.

"That dog must have the digestion of a crocodile," Brianna said, shaking her head. "Is there anything he won't eat?"

"Well, I've no tried him on nails, yet." Ian smiled briefly, but didn't take up the conversation. The unease that had lain upon him when he talked of dreams had disappeared over breakfast, but seemed now to have returned. The sun was well up, but he made no move to rise. He merely sat, arms wrapped about his knees, gazing thoughtfully into the fire as the rising sun stole the light from the flames.

In no great hurry to start moving herself, Brianna waited patiently, eyes fixed on him.

"And what would you eat for breakfast when you lived with the Mohawk, Ian?"

He looked at her then, and his mouth tucked in at one corner. Not a smile, but a wry acknowledgment. He sighed, and laid his head on his knees, face hidden. He sat slumped that way for a bit, then slowly straightened up.

"Well," he said, in a matter-of-fact tone of voice. "It was to do wi' my brother-in-law. At least to start."

IAN MURRAY thought that before too long, he would be obliged to do something about his brother-in-law. Not that "brother-in-law" was precisely the word for it. Still, Sun Elk was the husband of Looking at the Sky, who was in turn the sister of his own wife. By the notions of the Kahnyen'kehaka this implied no relation between the men beyond that of clansmen, but Ian still thought of Sun Elk with the white part of his mind.

That was the secret part. His wife had English, but they did not speak it, even when most private. He spoke no word of Scots or English aloud, had heard not a syllable of either tongue in the year since he had chosen to stay, to become Kahnyen'kehaka. It was assumed he had forgotten what he had been. But each day he found some moment to himself, and, lest he lose the words, would silently name the objects around him, hearing their English names echo in the hidden white part of his mind.

Pot, he thought to himself, squinting at the blackened earthenware warming in the ashes. In fact he was not alone at the moment. He was, however, feeling distinctly alien.

Corn, he thought, leaning back against the polished tree trunk that formed one upright of the longhouse. Several clusters of dried maize hung above him, festively colored by comparison with the sacks of grain sold in Edinburgh—and yet *corn* nonetheless. *Onions,* he thought, eyes passing down the braided chain of yellow globes. *Bed. Furs. Fire.*

His wife leaned toward him, smiling, and the words ran

suddenly together in his mind. *Blackravenblackhairshining-breastbudsthighssoroundohyesohyesohEmily* . . .

She set a warm bowl in his hand, and the rich aroma of rabbit and corn and onion rose up into his nose. *Stew,* he thought, the slippery flow of words coming to a sudden halt as his mind focused on food. He smiled at her, and laid his hand over hers, holding it for a moment, small and sturdy under his, curved around the wooden bowl. Her smile deepened; then she pulled away, rising up to go and fetch more food.

He watched her go, appreciating the sway of her walk. Then his eye caught Sun Elk—watching, too, from the doorway of his own apartment.

Bastard, Ian thought, very clearly.

"SEE, WE GOT on well enough to start," Ian explained. "He's a bonny man, for the most part, Sun Elk."

"For the most part," Brianna echoed. She sat still, watching him. "And which part was that?"

Ian rubbed a hand through his hair, making it stand up like the bushy quills on a porcupine.

"Well . . . the friend part. We *were* friends, to begin with, aye? Brothers, in fact; we were of the same clan."

"And you stopped being friends because of—of your wife?"

Ian sighed deeply.

"Well, ye see . . . the Kahnyen'kehaka, they've a notion of marriage that—it's like what ye see in the Highlands, often enough. That is, the parents have a good deal to do wi' arranging it. Often enough, they've watched the weans as they grew, and seen if maybe there was a lad and a lassie that seemed well-matched. And if they were—and if they came from the proper clans—now, that bit's different, see?" he added, breaking off.

"The clans?"

"Aye. In the Highlands, ye'd mostly marry within your own clan, save it was to make an alliance wi' another. Among the Iroquois nations, though, ye canna ever marry someone from your own clan, and ye can only marry someone from particular clans, not just any other."

"Mama said the Iroquois reminded her a lot of Highlanders," Brianna said, mildly amused. "Ruthless, but entertaining, was how she put it, I think. Bar some of the torturing, maybe, and the burning your enemies alive."

"Your mother's no heard some of Uncle Jamie's stories about his grandsire, then," he replied with a wry smile.

"What, Lord Lovat?"

"No, the other—*Seaumais Ruaidh*—Red Jacob, him Uncle Jamie's named for. A wicked auld bugger, my Mam always said; he'd put any Iroquois to shame for pure cruelty, from all I've heard of him." He dismissed this tangent with a wave of the hand, though, returning to his explanation.

"Well, so, when the Kahnyen'kehaka took me, and named me, I was adopted to the Wolf clan, aye?" he said, with an explanatory nod at Rollo, who had consumed the honeycomb, dead bees and all, and was now meditatively licking his paws.

"Very appropriate," she murmured. "What clan was Sun Elk?"

"Wolf, of course. And Emily's mother and grandmother and sisters were Turtle. But what I was saying—if a lad and lassie from properly different clans seemed maybe suited to each other, then the mothers would speak—they call all the aunties 'mother,' too," he added. "So there might be a good many mothers involved in the matter. But if all the mothers and grandmothers and aunties were to agree that it would be a good match . . ." He shrugged. "They'd marry."

Brianna rocked back a little, arms around her knees.

"But you didn't have a mother to speak for you."

"Well, I did wonder what my Mam would ha' said, if she'd been there," he said, and smiled, despite his seriousness.

Brianna, having met Ian's mother, laughed at the thought.

"Aunt Jenny would be a match for any Mohawk, male *or* female," she assured him. "But what happened, then?"

"I loved Emily," he said very simply. "And she loved me."

This state of affairs, which rapidly became apparent to everyone in the village, caused considerable public comment. Wakyo'teyehsnonhsa, Works with Her Hands, the girl Ian called Emily, had been widely expected to marry Sun Elk, who had been a visitor to her family's hearth since childhood.

"But there it was." Ian spread his hands and shrugged. "She loved me, and she said so."

When Ian had been taken into the Wolf clan, he had been given to foster parents, as well—the parents of the dead man in whose stead he had been adopted. His foster mother had been somewhat taken aback by the situation, but after discussing the matter with the other women of the Wolf clan, had gone to speak formally with Tewaktenyonh, Emily's grandmother—and the most influential woman in the village.

"And so we married." Dressed in their best, and accompanied by their parents, the two young people had sat together on a bench before the assembled people of the village, and exchanged baskets—his containing the furs of sable and beaver, and a good knife, symbolizing his willingness to hunt for her and protect her; hers filled with grain and fruit and vegetables, symbolizing her willingness to plant, gather, and provide for him.

"And four moons later," Ian added, "Sun Elk wed Looking at the Sky, Emily's sister."

Brianna raised one eyebrow.

"But . . . ?"

"Aye, but."

IAN HAD THE gun Jamie had left with him, a rare and valued item among the Indians, and he knew how to use it. He also knew how to track, to lie in ambush, to think like an animal—other things of value that Uncle Jamie had left with him.

In consequence, he was a good hunter, and rapidly gained respect for his ability to bring in meat. Sun Elk was a decent hunter—not the best, but capable. Many of the young men would joke and make remarks, denigrating each other's skills and making fun; he did it himself. Still, there was a tone to Sun Elk's jests to Ian that now and then made one of the other men glance sharply at him, then away with the faintest of shrugs.

He had been inclined to ignore the man. Then he had seen Sun Elk look at Wakyo'teyehsnonhsa, and everything became at once clear to him.

She had been going to the forest with some other girls, one day in late summer. They carried baskets for gathering; Wakyo'teyehsnonhsa had an ax through her belt. One of the other girls had asked her whether she meant to find wood for another bowl like the one she had made for her mother; Works With Her Hands had said—with a quick, warm look toward Ian, who lounged nearby with the other young men—that no, she wished to find a good red cedar, for wood to make a cradleboard.

The girls had giggled and embraced Wakyo'teyehsnonhsa; the young men had grinned and prodded Ian knowingly in the ribs. And Ian had caught a glimpse of Sun Elk's face, hot eyes fixed on Emily's straight back as she walked away.

Within one moon, Sun Elk had moved into the longhouse, husband to his wife's sister, Looking at the Sky. The sisters' compartments were across from each other; they shared a hearth. Ian had seldom seen Sun Elk look at Emily again—but he had seen him look carefully away, too many times.

"There is a person who desires you," he said to Emily one night. It was long past the hour of the wolf, deep night, and the longhouse slept around them. The child she carried obliged her to rise and make water; she had come back to their furs skin-chilled and with the fresh smell of pines in her hair.

"Oh? Well, why not? Everyone else is asleep." She had stretched luxuriously and kissed him, the small bulge of her belly smooth and hard against his.

"Not me. I mean—of course this person desires you, too!" he'd said hastily, as she drew back a bit, offended. He wrapped his arms about her in quick illustration. "I mean—there is someone else."

"Hmf." Her voice was muffled, her breath warm against his chest. "There are many who desire me. I am very, very good with my hands." She gave him a brief demonstration, and he gasped, causing her to chuckle with satisfaction.

Rollo, who had accompanied her outside, crawled under the bed platform and curled up in his accustomed spot, chewing noisily at an itching spot near his tail.

A little later, they lay with the furs thrown back. The hide that hung over their doorway was pulled back, so the heat of the fire could come in, and he could see the shine of light on the moist gold skin of her shoulder, where she lay turned away from him. She reached back and put one of her clever hands on his, took his palm, and pressed it against her belly. The child inside had begun to stir; he felt a soft, sudden push against his palm, and his breath stilled in his throat.

"You shouldn't worry," Emily said very softly. "This person desires only you."

He had slept well.

In the morning, though, he had sat by the hearth eating cornmeal mush, and Sun Elk, who had already eaten, walked by. He stopped and looked down at Ian.

"This person dreamed about you, Wolf's Brother."

"Did you?" Ian said pleasantly. He felt the warmth rise up his throat, but kept his face relaxed. The Kahyen'kehaka set great store by dreams. A good dream would have everyone in the longhouse discussing it for days. The look on Sun Elk's face didn't indicate that his dream about Ian had been a good one.

"That dog—" He nodded at Rollo, who lay sprawled inconveniently in the doorway of Ian's compartment, snoring. "I dreamed that it rose up over your couch, and seized you by the throat."

That was a menacing dream. A Kahnyen'kehaka who believed such a dream might decide to kill the dog, lest it be a foretelling of ill fortune. But Ian was not—not quite—Kahnyen'kehaka.

Ian raised both brows, and went on eating. Sun Elk waited for a moment, but as Ian said nothing, eventually nodded and turned away.

"Ahkote'ohskennonton," Ian said, calling his name. The man turned back, expectant.

"This person dreamed of you, too." Sun Elk glanced sharply at him. Ian didn't speak further, but let a slow and evil smile grow upon his face.

Sun Elk stared at him. He kept smiling. The other man turned away with a snort of disgust, but not before Ian had seen the faint look of unease in Sun Elk's eyes.

"WELL, SO." Ian took a deep breath. He closed his eyes briefly, then opened them. "Ye ken the child died, aye?"

He spoke with no emotion at all in his voice. It was that dry, controlled tone that seared her heart, and choked her so that she could do no more than nod in reply.

He couldn't keep it up, though. He opened his mouth as though to speak, but the big, bony hands clenched suddenly on his knees, and instead, he rose abruptly to his feet.

"Aye," he said. "Let's go. I'll—I'll tell ye the rest, walking."

And he did, his back resolutely turned, as he led her higher up the mountain, then across a narrow ridge, and down the path of a stream that fell in a series of small, enchanting waterfalls, each encircled with a mist of miniature rainbows.

Works with Her Hands had conceived again. That child was lost just after her belly began to swell with life.

"They say, the Kahnyen'kehaka," Ian explained, his voice muffled as he shoved his way through a screen of brilliant red creeper, "that for a woman to conceive, her husband's spirit does battle with hers, and must overcome it. If his spirit isna strong enough"—his voice came clear as he ripped a handful of creeper down, breaking the branch it hung from, and cast it viciously away—"then the child canna take root in the womb."

After this second loss, the Medicine Society had taken the two of them to a private hut, there to sing and beat drums and to dance in huge painted masks, meant to frighten away whatever evil entities might be hampering Ian's spirit—or unduly strengthening Emily's.

"I wanted to laugh, seeing the masks," Ian said. He didn't turn round; yellow leaves spangled the shoulders of his buckskin and stuck in his hair. "They call it the Funny-Face Society, too—and for a reason. Didna do it, though."

"I don't . . . suppose Em-Emily laughed." He was going so fast that she was pressed to keep up with him, though her legs were nearly as long as his own.

"No," he said, and uttered a short, bitter laugh himself. "She didna."

She had gone into the medicine hut beside him silent and gray, but had come out with a peaceful face, and reached for him in their bed that night with love. For three months, they had made love with tenderness and ardor. For another three, they had made love with a sense of increasing desperation.

"And then she missed her courses again."

He had at once ceased his attentions, terrified of causing a further mishap. Emily had moved slowly and carefully, no longer going into the fields to work, but staying in the longhouse, working, always working, with her hands. Weaving, grinding, carving, boring beads of shell for wampum, hands moving ceaselessly, to compensate for the waiting stillness of her body.

"Her sister went to the fields. It's the women who do, ken?" He paused to slash an outreaching brier with his knife, tossing the severed branch out of the way so it wouldn't snap back and hit Brianna in the face.

"Looking at the Sky brought us food. All the women did, but her most of all. She was a sweet lass, Karònya."

There was a slight catch in his voice at this, the first in his harsh recitation of facts.

"What happened to her?" Brianna hastened her step a little as they came out onto the top of a grass-covered bank, so that she drew up nearly even with him. He slowed a little, but didn't turn to look at her—kept his face forward, chin raised as though confronting enemies.

"Taken." Looking at the Sky had been in the habit of staying later in the fields than the other women, gathering extra corn or squash for her sister and Ian, though she had a child of her own by then. One evening, she did not return to the longhouse, and when the villagers had gone out to search for her, neither she nor the child was anywhere to be found. They had vanished, leaving only one pale moccasin behind, tangled in the squash vines at the edge of a field.

"Abenaki," Ian said tersely. "We found the sign next day; it was full dark before we began to search in earnest."

It had been a long night searching, followed by a week of the same—a week of growing fear and emptiness—and Ian had returned to his wife's hearth at dawn on the seventh day, to learn that she had miscarried once more.

He paused. He was sweating freely from walking so fast, and wiped a sleeve across his chin. Brianna could feel the sweat trickling down her own back, dampening the hunting shirt, but disregarded it. She touched his back, very gently, but said nothing.

He heaved a deep sigh, almost of relief, she thought—perhaps that the dreadful tale was nearly done.

"We tried a bit longer," he said, back to the matter-of-fact tone. "Emily and I. But the heart had gone out of her. She didna trust me any longer. And . . . Ahkote'ohskennonton was there. He ate at our hearth. And he watched her. She began to look back."

Ian had been shaping wood for a bow one day, concentrating on the flow of the grain beneath his knife, trying to see those things in the swirls that Emily saw, to hear the voice of the tree, as she had told him. It wasn't the tree that spoke behind him, though.

"Grandson," said a dry old voice, lightly ironic.

He dropped the knife, narrowly missing his own foot, and swung round, bow in hand. Tewaktenyonh stood six feet away, one eyebrow lifted in amusement at having sneaked up on him unheard.

"Grandmother," he said, and nodded in wry acknowledgment of her skill. Ancient she might be, but no one moved more softly. Hence her reputation; the children of the village lived in respectful dread of her, having heard that she could vanish into air, only to rematerialize in some distant spot, right before the guilty eyes of evil-doers.

"Come with me, Wolf's Brother," she said, and turned away, not waiting for his response. None was expected.

She was already out of sight by the time he had laid the half-made bow under a bush, taken up his fallen knife, and whistled for Rollo, but he caught her up with no difficulty.

She had led him away from the village, through the forest, to the head of a deer trail. There she had given him a bag of salt and an armlet of wampum and bade him go.

"And you went?" Brianna asked, after a long moment of silence. "Just—like that?"

"Just like that," he said, and looked at her for the first time since they had left their campsite that morning. His face was gaunt, hollow with memories. Sweat gleamed on his cheekbones, but he was so pale that the dotted lines of his tattoos stood out sharp—perforations, lines along which his face might come apart.

She swallowed a few times before she could speak, but managed a tone much like his own when she did.

"Is it much farther?" she asked. "Where we're going?"

"No," he said softly. "We're nearly there." And turned to walk again before her.

HALF AN HOUR later, they had reached a place where the stream cut deep between its banks, widening into a small gorge. Silver birch and hobblebush grew thick, sprouting from the rocky walls, smooth-skinned roots twisting through the stones like fingers clawing at the earth.

The notion gave Brianna a slight prickle at the neck. The waterfalls were far above them now, and the noise of the water had lessened, the creek talking to itself as it purled over rocks and shushed through mats of cress and duckweed.

She thought the going might be easier above, on the lip of the gorge, but Ian led her down into it without hesitation, and she followed likewise, scrambling over the tumble of boulders and tree roots, hampered by her long gun. Rollo, scorning this clumsy exertion, plunged into the creek, which was several feet deep, and swam, ears clamped back against his head so that he looked like a giant otter.

Ian had recovered his self-possession in the concentration of navigating the rough ground. He paused now and then, reaching back to help her down a particularly tricky fall of rock, or over a tree uprooted in some recent flood—but he didn't meet her eyes, and the shuttered planes of his face gave nothing away.

Her curiosity had reached fever pitch, but clearly he had done speaking for the moment. It was just past midday, but the light under the birches was a shadowed gold that made everything seem somehow hushed, almost enchanted. She could make no sensible guess as to the purpose of this expedition, in light of what Ian had told her—but the place was one where almost anything seemed possible.

She thought suddenly of her first father—of Frank Randall—

and felt a small, remembered warmth at the thought. She would like so much to show him this place.

They had taken holidays often in the Adirondacks; different mountains, different trees—but something of the same hush and mystery in the shadowed glades and rushing water. Her mother had come sometimes, but more often it was just the two of them, hiking far up into the trees, not talking much, but sharing a deep content in the company of the sky.

Suddenly, the sound of the water rose again; there was another fall nearby.

"Just here, coz," Ian said softly, and beckoned her to follow with a turn of the head.

They stepped out from under the trees and she saw that the gorge dropped suddenly away, the water falling twenty feet or more into a pool below. Ian led her past the head of the falls; she could hear the water rushing past below, but the top of the bank was thick with sedges, and they had to push their way through, tramping down the yellowing stems of goldenrod and dodging the panicked whir of grasshoppers rocketing up underfoot.

"Look," Ian said, glancing back, and reached to part the screen of laurel in front of her.

"Wow!"

She recognized it immediately. There was no mistaking it, in spite of the fact that much of it was invisible, still buried in the crumbling bank on the far side of the gorge. Some recent flood had raised the level of the creek, undercutting the bank so that a huge block of stone and dirt had fallen away, revealing its buried mystery.

The raked arches of ribs rose huge from the dirt, and she had the impression of a scatter of things half-buried in the rubble at the foot of the bank: enormous things, knobbed and twisted. They might be bones or simply boulders—but it was the tusk that caught her eye, jutting from the bank in a massive curve, intensely familiar, and the more startling for its very familiarity.

"Ye ken it?" Ian asked eagerly, watching her face. "Ye've seen something like it?"

"Oh, yes," she said, and though the sun was warm on her back, she shivered, gooseflesh pebbling her forearms. Not from fear, but sheer awe at sight of it, and a kind of incredulous joy. "Oh, yes. I have."

"What?" Ian's voice was still pitched low, as though the creature might hear them. "What is it?"

"A mammoth," she said, and found that she was whispering, too. The sun had passed its zenith; already the bottom of the creekbed lay in shadow. Light struck the stained curve of ancient ivory, and threw the vault of the high-crowned skull that held it into sharp relief. The skull was fixed in the soil at a slight angle, the single visible tusk rising high, the eye socket black as mystery.

The shiver came again, and she hunched her shoulders. Easy to feel that it might at any moment wrench itself free of the clay and turn that massive head toward them, empty-eyed, clods of dirt raining from tusks and bony shoulders as it shook itself and began to walk, the ground vibrating as long toes struck and sank in the muddy soil.

"That's what it's called—mammoth? Aye, well . . . it *is* verra big." Ian's voice dispelled the illusion of incipient movement, and she was able finally to take her eyes off it—though she felt she must glance back, every second or so, to be sure it was still there.

"The Latin name is *Mammuthus,*" she said, clearing her throat. "There's a complete skeleton in a museum in New York. I've seen it often. And I've seen pictures of them in books." She glanced back at the creature in the bank.

"A museum? So it's not a thing ye've got where—when"—he stumbled a bit—"where ye come from? Not alive then, I mean?" He seemed rather disappointed.

She wanted to laugh at the picture of mammoths roaming Boston Common, or wallowing on the bank of the Cambridge River. In fact, she had a moment's pang of disappointment that they *hadn't* been there; it would have been so wonderful to see them.

"No," she said regretfully. "They all died thousands and thousands of years ago. When the ice came."

"Ice?" Ian was glancing back and forth between her and the mammoth, as though afraid one or the other might do something untoward.

"The Ice Age. The world got colder, and sheets of ice

spread down from the north. A lot of animals went extinct—I mean, they couldn't find food, and all died."

Ian was pale with excitement.

"Aye. Aye, I've heard such stories."

"You have?" She was surprised at that.

"Aye. But ye say it's real." He swung his head to look at the mammoth's bones once more. "An animal, aye, like a bear or a possum?"

"Yes," she said, puzzled by his attitude, which seemed to alternate between eagerness and dismay. "Bigger, but yes. What else would it be?"

"Ah," he said, and took a deep breath. "Well, d'ye see, that's what I needed ye to tell me, coz. See, the Kahnyen'kehaka—they have stories of . . . things. Animals that are really spirits. And if ever I saw a thing that might *be* a spirit—" He was still looking at the skeleton, as though it might walk out of the earth, and she saw a slight shiver pass through him.

She couldn't prevent a similar shiver, looking at the massive creature. It towered above them, grim and awful, and only her knowledge of what it was kept her from wanting to cower and run.

"It's real," she repeated, as much to reassure herself as him. "And it's dead. *Really* dead."

"How d'ye know these things?" he asked, intently curious. "It's auld, ye say. You'd be much further away from—that"—he jerked his chin at the giant skeleton—"in your own time than we are now. How can ye ken more about it than folk do now?"

She shook her head, smiling a little, and helpless to explain.

"When did you find this, Ian?"

"Last month. I came up the gorge"—he gestured with his chin—"and there it was. I near beshit myself."

"I can imagine," she said, stifling an urge to laugh.

"Aye," he said, not noticing her amusement in his desire to explain. "I should have been sure that it was Rawenniyo—a spirit, a god—save for the dog."

Rollo had climbed out of the stream, and having shaken the water from his fur, was squirming on his back in a patch of crushed turtlehead, tail wagging in pleasure, and clearly oblivious to the silent giant in the cliff above.

"What do you mean? That Rollo wasn't afraid of it?"

Ian nodded.

"Aye. He didna behave as though there were anything there at all. And yet . . ." He hesitated, darting a glance at her. "Sometimes, in the wood. He—he *sees* things. Things I canna see. Ken?"

"I ken," she said, a ripple of unease returning. "Dogs do see . . . things." She remembered her own dogs; in particular, Smoky, the big Newfoundland, who would sometimes in the evening suddenly raise his head, listening, hackles rising as his eyes followed . . . something . . . that passed through the room and disappeared.

He nodded, relieved that she knew what he was talking about.

"They do. I ran, when I saw that"—he nodded at the cliff—"and ducked behind a tree. But the dog went on about his business, paying it no mind. And so I thought, well, just maybe it's no what I think, after all."

"And what did you think?" she asked. "A Rawenniyo, you said?" As the excitement of seeing the mammoth began to recede, she remembered what they were theoretically doing here. "Ian—you said what you wanted to show me had to do with your wife. Is this—" She gestured toward the cliff, brows raised.

He didn't answer directly, but tilted his head back, studying the jut of the giant tusks.

"I heard stories, now and then. Among the Mohawk, I mean. They'd speak of strange things that someone found, hunting. Spirits trapped in the rock, and how they came to be there. Evil things, for the most part. And I thought to myself, if that should be what this is . . ."

He broke off and turned to her, serious and intent.

"I needed ye to tell me, aye? Whether that's what it is or no. Because if it was, then perhaps what I've been thinking is wrong."

"It's not," she assured him. "But what on earth have you been thinking?"

"About God," he said, surprising her again. He licked his lips, unsure how to go on.

"Yeksa'a—the child. I didna have her christened," he said. "I couldna. Or perhaps I could—ye can do it yourself, ken, if there's no priest. But I hadna the courage to try. I—never saw her. They'd wrapped her already. . . . They wouldna have liked it, if I'd tried to . . ." His voice died away.

"Yeksa'a," she said softly. "Was that your—your daughter's name?"

He shook his head, his mouth twisting wryly.

"It only means 'wee girl.' The Kahnyen'kehaka dinna give a name to a child when it's born. Not until later. If . . ." His voice trailed off, and he cleared his throat. "If it lives. They wouldna think of naming a child unborn."

"But you did?" she asked gently.

He raised his head and took a breath that had a damp sound to it, like wet bandages pulled from a fresh wound.

"Iseabaìl," he said, and she knew it was the first—perhaps would be the only—time he'd spoken it aloud. "Had it been a son, I would ha' called him Jamie." He glanced at her, with the shadow of a smile. "Only in my head, ken."

He let out all his breath then with a sigh and put his face down upon his knees, back hunched.

"What I am thinking," he said after a moment, his voice much too controlled, "is this. Was it me?"

"Ian! You mean your fault that the baby died? How could it be?"

"I left," he said simply, straightening up. "Turned away. Stopped being a Christian, being Scots. They took me to the stream, scrubbed me wi' sand to take away the white blood. They gave me my name—Okwaho'kenha—and said I was Mohawk. But I wasna, not really."

He sighed deeply again, and she put a hand on his back, feeling the bumps of his backbone press through the leather of his shirt. He didn't eat nearly enough, she thought.

"But I wasna what I had been, either," he went on, sounding almost matter-of-fact. "I tried to be what they wanted, ken? So I left off praying to God or the Virgin Mother, or Saint Bride. I listened to what Emily said, when she'd tell me about *her* gods, the spirits that dwell in the trees and all. And when I went to the sweat lodge wi' the men, or sat by the hearth and heard the stories . . . they seemed as real to me as Christ and His saints ever had."

He turned his head and looked up at her suddenly, half-bewildered, half-defiant.

"I am the Lord thy God," he said. *"Thou shalt have no other gods before me.* But I did, no? That's mortal sin, is it not?"

She wanted to say no, of course not. Or to protest weakly that she was not a priest, how could she say? But neither of those would do; he was not looking for easy reassurance, and a weak-minded abnegation of responsibility would not serve him.

She took a deep breath and blew it out. It had been a good many years since she'd been taught the Baltimore Catechism, but it wasn't the sort of thing you forget.

"The conditions of mortal sin are these," she said, reciting the words precisely from memory. "First, that the action be grievously wrong. Secondly, that you know the action is wrong. And thirdly—that you give full consent to it."

He was watching her intently.

"Well, it was wrong, and I suppose I kent that—aye, I *did* ken that. Especially—" His face darkened further, and she wondered what he was recalling.

"But . . . how should I serve a God who would take a child for her father's sins?" Without waiting for an answer, he glanced toward the cliff face, where the remains of the mammoth lay frozen in time. "Or was it them? Was it not my God at all, but the Iroquois spirits? Did they ken I wasna really Mohawk—that I held back a part of myself from them?"

He looked back at her, dead serious.

"Gods are jealous, are they no?"

"Ian . . ." She swallowed, helpless. But she had to say something.

"What you did—or didn't do—that wasn't wrong, Ian," she said firmly. "Your daughter . . . she was half-Mohawk. It wasn't wrong to let her be buried according to her mother's ways. Your wife—Emily—she would have been terribly upset, wouldn't she, if you'd insisted on baptizing the baby?"

"Aye, maybe. But . . ." He closed his eyes, hands clenched hard into fists on his thighs. "Where is she, then?" he whispered, and she could see tears trembling on his lashes. "The others—they were never born; God will have them in His hand. But wee Iseabail—she'll not be in heaven, will she? I canna bear the thought that she—that she might be . . . lost, somewhere. Wandering."

"Ian . . ."

"I hear her, greeting. In the night." His breath was coming in deep, sobbing gasps. "I canna help, I canna find her!"

"Ian!" The tears were running down her own cheeks. She gripped his wrists fiercely, squeezed as hard as she could. "Ian, listen to me!"

He drew a deep, trembling breath, head bent. Then he nodded, very slightly.

She rose onto her knees and gathered him tight against her, his head cradled on her breasts. Her cheek pressed against the top of his head, his hair warm and springy against her mouth.

"Listen to me," she said softly. "I had another father. The man who raised me. He's dead now." For a long time now, the sense of desolation at his loss had been muted, softened by new love, distracted by new obligations. Now it swept over her, newly fresh, and sharp as a stab wound in its agony. "I know—I know he's in heaven."

Was he? Could he be dead and in heaven, if not yet born? And yet he was dead to her, and surely heaven took no heed of time.

She lifted her face toward the cliff, but spoke to neither bones nor God.

"Daddy," she said, and her voice broke on the word, but she held her cousin hard. "Daddy, I need you." Her voice sounded small, and pathetically unsure. But there was no other help to be had.

"I need you to find Ian's little girl," she said, as firmly as she could, trying to summon her father's face, to see him there among the shifting leaves at the clifftop. "Find her, please. Hold her in your arms, and make sure that she's safe. Take—please take care of her."

She stopped, feeling obscurely that she should say something else, something more ceremonious. Make the sign of the cross? Say "amen"?

"Thank you, Daddy," she said softly, and cried as though

her father were newly dead, and she bereft, orphaned, lost, and crying in the night. Ian's arms were wrapped around her, and they clung tight together, squeezing hard, the warmth of the late sun heavy on their heads.

She stood still within his arms when she stopped crying, her head resting on his shoulder. He patted her back, very gently, but didn't push her away.

"Thank you," he whispered in her ear. "Are ye all right, Brianna?"

"Uh-huh." She straightened and stood away from him, swaying a little, as though she were drunk. She felt drunk, too, her bones gone soft and malleable, everything around her faintly out of focus, save for certain things that caught her eye: a brilliant patch of pink lady's slipper, a stone fallen from the cliff face, its surface streaked red with iron. Rollo, almost sitting on Ian's foot, big head pressed anxiously against his master's thigh.

"Are *you* all right, Ian?" she asked.

"I will be." His hand sought Rollo's head, and gave the pointed ears a cursory rub of reassurance. "Maybe. Just . . ."

"What?"

"Are ye . . . are ye sure, Brianna?"

She knew what he was asking; it was a question of faith. She drew herself up to her full height, wiping her nose on her sleeve.

"I'm a Roman Catholic and I believe in vitamins," she declared stoutly. "And I knew my father. Of course I'm sure."

He took a deep, sighing breath and his shoulders slumped as he let it out. He nodded then, and the lines of his face relaxed a little.

She left him sitting on a rock, and made her way down to the stream to splash cold water on her face. The shadow of the cliff fell across the creek and the air was cold with the scents of earth and pine trees. In spite of the chill, she remained there for a while, on her knees.

She could still hear the voices murmuring in trees and water, but paid no attention to them. Whoever they were, they were no threat to her or hers—and not at odds with the presence that she felt so strongly nearby.

"I love you, Daddy," she whispered, closing her eyes, and felt at peace.

Ian must be better, too, she thought, when she made her way at length back through the rocks to where he sat. Rollo had left him to investigate a promising hole at the foot of a tree, and she knew the dog wouldn't have left Ian, had he considered his master to be in distress.

She was about to ask him whether their business here was complete, when he stood up, and she saw that it wasn't.

"Why I brought ye here," he said abruptly. "I wanted to know about that—" He nodded at the mammoth. "But I meant to ask ye a question. Advice, like."

"Advice? Ian, I can't give you any advice! How could I tell you what to do?"

"I think ye're maybe the only one who can," he said with a lopsided smile. "You're my family, you're a woman—and ye care for me. Yet ye ken more even than Uncle Jamie, perhaps, because of who—or what"—his mouth twisted a little—"ye are."

"I don't know more," she said, and looked up at the bones in the rock. "Only—different things."

"Aye," he said, and took a deep breath.

"Brianna," he said very softly. "We're no wed—we never shall be." He looked away for an instant, then back. "But if we *had* been marrit, I should have loved ye and cared for ye, so well as I could. I trust you, that ye'd have done the same by me. Am I right?"

"Oh, Ian." Her throat was still thick, raspy with grief; the words came out in a whisper. She touched his face, cool-skinned and bony, and traced the line of tattooed dots with a thumb. "I love you now."

"Aye, well," he said still softly. "I ken that." He lifted a hand and put it over her own, big and hard. He pressed her palm against his cheek for a moment, then his fingers closed over hers and he brought their linked hands down, but didn't let go.

"So tell me," he said, his eyes not leaving hers. "If ye love me, tell me what I shall do. Shall I go back?"

"Back," she repeated, searching his face. "Back to the Mohawk, you mean?"

He nodded.

"Back to Emily. She loved me," he said quietly. "I ken that. Did I do wrong, to let the old woman send me away? Ought I to go back, maybe fight for her, if I had to? Perhaps see if she would come away wi' me, back to the Ridge."

"Oh, Ian." She felt the same sense of helplessness as before, though this time it came without the burden of her own grief. But who was she to tell him anything? How could she be responsible for making that decision for him—for saying to him, stay, or go?

His eyes stayed steady on her face, though, and it came over her—she was his family. And so the responsibility lay in her hands, whether she felt adequate to it or not.

Her chest felt tight, as though she might burst if she took a deep breath. She took it anyway.

"Stay," she said.

He stood looking into her eyes for a long time, his own deep hazel, gold-flecked and serious.

"You could fight him—Ahk . . ." She fumbled for the syllables of the Mohawk name. "Sun Elk. But you can't fight her. If she's made up her mind that she doesn't want to be with you anymore . . . Ian, you can't change it."

He blinked, dark lashes cutting off his gaze, and kept his eyes closed, whether in acknowledgment or denial of what she'd said, she didn't know.

"But it's more than that," she said, her voice growing firmer. "It isn't only her, *or* him. Is it?"

"No," he said. His voice sounded distant, almost uncaring, but she knew it wasn't that.

"It's them," she said more softly. "All the mothers. The grandmothers. The women. The—the children." Clan and family and tribe and nation; custom, spirit, tradition—the strands that wrapped Works with Her Hands and held her to the earth, secure. And above all, children. Those loud small voices that drowned the voices of the wood, and kept a soul from wandering through the night.

No one knew the strength of such bonds better than one who had walked the earth without them, outcast and alone. She had, and he had, and they both knew the truth.

"It's them," he echoed softly, and opened his eyes. They

were dark with loss, the color of shadows in the deepest wood. "And them." He turned his head, to look upward, into the trees beyond the creek, above the bones of the mammoth that lay trapped in the earth, stripped to the sky and mute to all prayer. He turned back, raised a hand, and touched her cheek.

"I'll stay, then."

THEY CAMPED FOR the night on the far side of the beaver pond. The litter of wood chips and debarked saplings made good kindling for their fire.

There was little to eat; no more than a hatful of bitter fox-grapes and the heel of bread, so hard by now that it had to be dunked in water to chew. It didn't matter; neither one of them was hungry, and Rollo had disappeared to hunt for himself.

They sat silently, watching the fire die down. There was no need to keep it going; the night was not cold, and they would not linger in the morning—home was too near.

At last, Ian stirred a bit, and Brianna glanced at him.

"What was your father's name?" he asked very formally.

"Frank—er . . . Franklin. Franklin Wolverton Randall."

"An Englishman, then?"

"Very," she said, smiling in spite of herself.

He nodded, murmuring "Franklin Wolverton Randall" to himself, as though to commit it to memory, then looked at her seriously.

"If ever I find myself in a church again, then, I shall light a candle to his memory."

"I expect . . . he'd like that."

He nodded, and leaned back, back braced against a long-leaf pine. The ground nearby was littered with the cones; he picked up a handful and tossed them, one by one, into the fire.

"What about Lizzie?" she asked after a little while. "She's always been fond of you." To put it mildly: Lizzie had wilted and pined for weeks, when he had been lost to the Iroquois. "And now that she's not marrying Manfred . . ."

He tilted back his head, eyes closed, and rested it against the trunk of the pine.

"I've thought of it," he admitted.

"But . . . ?"

"Aye, but." He opened his eyes and gave her a wry look. "I'd ken where I was, if I woke beside her. But where I'd be is in bed wi' my wee sister. I think I'm maybe not so desperate as that. Yet," he added as an obvious afterthought.

71

BLACK PUDDING

I WAS IN THE middle of a black pudding when Ronnie Sinclair appeared in the yard, carrying two small whisky casks. Several more were bound in a neatly corrugated cascade down his back, which made him look like some exotic form of caterpillar, balanced precariously upright in mid-pupation. It was a chilly day, but he was sweating freely from the long walk uphill—and cursing in a similar vein.

"Why in the name of Bride did Himself build the frigging house up here in the godforsaken clouds?" he demanded without ceremony. "Why not where a bloody wagon could reach the yard?" He set the casks down carefully, then ducked his head through the straps of the harness to shed his wooden carapace. He sighed in relief, rubbing at his shoulders where the straps had dug.

I ignored the rhetorical questions, and kept stirring, tilting my head toward the house in invitation.

"There's fresh coffee made," I said. "And bannocks with honey, too." My own stomach recoiled slightly at the thought of eating. Once spiced, stuffed, boiled, and fried, black pudding was delicious. The earlier stages, involving as they did arm-deep manipulations in a barrel of semi-coagulated pig's blood, were substantially less appetizing.

Sinclair, though, looked happier at mention of food. He wiped a sleeve across his sweating forehead and nodded to me, turning toward the house. Then he stopped and turned back.

"Ah. I'd forgot, missus. I've a wee message for yourself, as well." He patted gingerly at his chest, then lower, probing around his ribs until he at length found what he was looking for and extracted it from the layers of his sweat-soaked clothing. He pulled out a damp wad of paper and held it out to me in expectation, ignoring the fact that my right arm was coated with blood nearly to the shoulder, and the left in scarcely better case.

"Put it in the kitchen, why don't you?" I suggested. "Himself's inside. I'll come as soon as I've got this lot sorted. Who—" I started to ask whom the letter was from, but tactfully altered this to, "Who gave it to you?" Ronnie couldn't read—though I saw no marks on the outside of the note, in any case.

"A tinker on his way to Belem's Creek handed it to me," he said. "He didna say who gave it him—only that it was for the healer."

He frowned at the wadded paper, but I saw his eyes slide sideways toward my legs. In spite of the chill, I was barefoot and stripped to my chemise and stays, no more than a smeared apron wrapped around my waist. Ronnie had been looking for a wife for some little time, and in consequence had formed the unconscious habit of appraising the physical attributes of every woman he encountered, without regard to age or availability. He noticed my noticing, and hastily jerked his gaze away.

"That was all?" I asked. "The healer? He didn't give my name?"

Sinclair rubbed a hand through thinning ginger hair, so two spikes stood up over his reddened ears, increasing his naturally sly, foxy look.

"Didna have to, did he?" Without further attempts at conversation, he disappeared into the house, in search of food and Jamie, leaving me to my sanguinary labors.

The worst part was cleaning the blood: swishing an arm through the dark, reeking depths of the barrel to collect the threads of fibrin that formed as the blood began to clot. These clung to my arm and could then be pulled out and rinsed away—repeatedly. At that, it was slightly less nasty than the job of washing out the intestines to be used for the sausage casings; Brianna and Lizzie were doing that, down at the creek.

I peered at the latest results; no fibers visible in the clear red liquid that dripped from my fingers. I dunked my arm again in the water cask that stood beside the blood barrel, balanced on boards laid across a pair of trestles under the big chestnut tree. Jamie and Roger and Arch Bug had dragged the pig—not the white sow, but one of her many offspring from a prior year—into the yard, clubbed it between the eyes with a maul, then swung it up into the branches, slit the throat, and let the blood drain into the barrel.

Roger and Arch had then taken the disemboweled carcass away to be scalded and the bristles scraped off; Jamie's presence was required to deal with Major MacDonald, who had appeared suddenly, puffing and wheezing from the climb up to the Ridge. Between the two, I thought Jamie would much have preferred to deal with the pig.

I finished washing my hands and arms—wasted labor, but necessary to my peace of mind—and dried off with a linen towel. I shoveled double handsful into the barrel from the waiting bowls of barley, oatmeal, and boiled rice, smiling slightly at memory of the Major's plum-red face, and Ronnie Sinclair's complaints. Himself had picked his building site on the Ridge with a great deal of forethought—precisely *because* of the difficulties involved in reaching it.

I ran my fingers through my hair, then took a deep breath and plunged my clean arm back into the barrel. The blood was cooling rapidly. Doused by the cereal, the smell was less immediate now than the metallic reek of fresh, hot blood. The mixture was still warm to the touch, though, and the grains made graceful swirls of white and brown, pale whirlpools drawn down into the blood as I stirred.

Ronnie was right; it hadn't been necessary to identify me further than "the healer." There wasn't another closer than Cross Creek, unless one counted the shamans among the Indians—which most Europeans wouldn't.

I wondered who had sent the note, and whether the matter was urgent. Probably not—at least it was not likely to be a matter of imminent childbirth or serious accident. Word of such events was likely to arrive in person, carried urgently by a friend or relative. A written message entrusted to a tinker couldn't be counted on to be delivered with any sort of promptitude; tinkers wandered or stayed, depending on what work they found.

For that matter, tinkers and tramps seldom came so far as the Ridge, though we had seen three within the last month. I didn't know whether that was the result of our growing population—Fraser's Ridge boasted nearly sixty families now, though the cabins were scattered over ten miles of forested mountain slopes—or something more sinister.

"It's one of the signs, Sassenach," Jamie had told me, frowning after the departing form of the last such temporary guest. "When there is war in the air, men take to the roads."

I thought he was right; I remembered wanderers on the Highland roads, carrying rumors of the Stuart Rising. It was as though the tremors of unrest jarred loose those who were not firmly attached to a place by love of land or family, and the swirling currents of dissension bore them onward, the first premonitory fragments of a slow-motion explosion that would shatter everything. I shivered, the light breeze touching cold through my shift.

The mass of gruel had reached the necessary consistency, something like a very thick, dark-red cream. I shook clumps of clotted grain from my fingers and reached with my clean left hand for the wooden bowl of minced and sauteed onions, standing ready. The strong smell of the onions overlaid the scent of butchery, pleasantly domestic.

The salt was ground, so was the pepper. All I needed now . . . as if on cue, Roger appeared around the corner of the house, a large basin in his hands, filled with fine-chopped pork fat.

"Just in time!" I said, and nodded toward the barrel. "No, don't dump it in, it has to be measured—roughly." I'd used ten double handsful of oatmeal, ten of rice, ten of barley. Half that total, then—fifteen. I shook back the hair from my eyes again, and carefully scooped up a double handful of the basin's content, dropping it into the barrel with a splat.

"All right, are you?" I asked. I gestured toward a stool with my chin, beginning to work the fat into the mixture with my fingers. Roger was still a trifle pale and tight around the mouth, but he gave me a wry smile as he sat.

"Fine."

"You didn't have to do it, you know."

"Yes, I did." The note of wryness in his voice deepened. "I only wish I'd done it better."

I shrugged, one-shouldered, and reached into the basin he held out for me.

"It takes practice."

Roger had volunteered to kill the pig. Jamie had simply handed him the maul and stood back. I had seen Jamie kill pigs before; he said a brief prayer, blessed the pig, then crushed the skull with one tremendous blow. It had taken Roger five tries, and the memory of the squealing raised gooseflesh on my shoulders even now. Afterward, he had set down the maul, gone behind a tree, and been violently sick.

I scooped another handful. The mix was thickening, developing a greasy feel.

"He should have shown you how."

"I shouldn't think there's anything technically difficult about it," Roger said dryly. "Straightforward enough, after all, to bash an animal on the head."

"Physically, perhaps," I agreed. I scooped more fat, working with both hands now. "There's a prayer for it, you know. For slaughtering an animal, I mean. Jamie should have told you."

He looked faintly startled.

"No, I didn't know." He smiled, a little better now. "Last rites for the pig, aye?"

"I don't think it's for the pig's benefit," I said tartly. We lapsed into silence for a few moments, as I creamed the rest of the fat into the grain mixture, pausing to flick away occasional bits of gristle. I could feel Roger's eyes on the barrel, watching the curious alchemy of cookery, that process of making the transfer of life from one being to another palatable.

"Highland drovers sometimes drain a cup or two of blood

from one of their beasts, and mix it with oatmeal to eat on the road," I said. "Nutritious, I suppose, but less tasty."

Roger nodded, abstracted. He had set down the nearly empty basin and was cleaning dried blood from under his nails with the point of his dirk.

"Is it the same as the one for deer?" he asked. "The prayer. I've seen Jamie say that one, though I didn't catch all of the words."

"The gralloch prayer? I don't know. Why don't you ask him?"

Roger worked industriously on a thumbnail, eyes fixed on his hand.

"I wasn't sure if he thought it right for me to know it. Me not being a Catholic, I mean."

I looked down into the mixture, hiding a smile.

"I don't think it would make a difference. That particular prayer is a lot older than the Church of Rome, if I'm not mistaken."

A flicker of interest lit Roger's face, the buried scholar coming to the surface.

"I did think the Gaelic was a very old form—even older than what you hear these days—I mean . . . now." He flushed a little, realizing what he had said. I nodded, but didn't say anything.

I remembered what it was like, that feeling that one was living in an elaborate make-believe. The feeling that reality existed in another time, another place. I remembered, and with a small shock, realized that it *was* now only memory—for me, time had shifted, as though my illness had pushed me through some final barrier.

Now was my time, reality the scrape of wood and slick of grease beneath my fingers, the arc of the sun that set the rhythm of my days, the nearness of Jamie. It was the other world, of cars and ringing telephones, of alarm clocks and mortgages, that seemed unreal and remote, the stuff of dreams.

Neither Roger nor Bree had made that transition, though. I could see it in the way they behaved, hear it in the echoes of their private conversations. Likely it was because they had each other; they could keep the other time alive, a small shared world between them. For me, the change was easier. I had lived here before, had come this time on purpose, after all—and I had Jamie. No matter what I told him of the future, he could never see it as other than a fairy tale. Our small shared world was built of different things.

I worried now and then about Bree and Roger, though. It was dangerous to treat the past as they sometimes did—as picturesque or curious, a temporary condition that could be escaped. There was no escape for them—whether it was love or duty, Jemmy held them both, a small redheaded anchor to the present. Better—or safer, at least—if they could wholly accept this time as theirs.

"The Indians have it, too," I said to Roger. "The gralloch prayer, or something like it. That's why I said I thought it older than the Church."

He nodded, interested.

"I think that kind of thing is common to all primitive cultures—anyplace where men kill to eat."

Primitive cultures. I caught my lower lip between my teeth, forbearing to point out that primitive or not, if his family were to survive, he personally would very likely be obliged to kill for them. But then I caught sight of his hand, idly rubbing at the dried blood between his fingers. He knew that already. *"Yes, I did,"* he'd said, when I'd told him he need not.

He looked up then, caught my eye, and gave me a faint, tired smile. He understood.

"I think maybe . . . it's that killing without ceremony seems like murder," he said slowly. "If you have the ceremony—some sort of ritual that acknowledges your necessity . . ."

"Necessity—and also sacrifice." Jamie's voice came softly from behind me, startling me. I turned my head sharply. He was standing in the shadow of the big red spruce; I wondered how long he'd been there.

"Didn't hear you come out," I said, turning up my face to be kissed as he came to me. "Has the Major gone?"

"No," he said, and kissed my brow, one of the few clean spots left. "I've left him wi' Sinclair for a bit. He's exercised about the Committee of Safety, aye?" He grimaced, then turned to Roger.

"Aye, ye've the right of it," he said. "Killing's never a pleasant business, but it's needful. If ye must spill blood, though, it's right to take it wi' thanks."

Roger nodded, glancing at the mixture I was working, up to my elbows in spilled blood.

"Ye'll tell me the proper words for the next time, then?"

"Not too late for this time, is it?" I said. Both men looked slightly startled. I raised an eyebrow at Jamie, then Roger. "I did say it wasn't for the pig."

Jamie's eyes met mine with a glint of humor, but he nodded gravely.

"Well enough."

At my direction, he took up the heavy jar of spices: the ground mixture of mace and marjoram, sage and pepper, parsley and thyme. Roger held out his hands, cupped, and Jamie poured them full. Then Roger rubbed the herbs slowly between his palms, showering the dusty, greenish crumbs into the barrel, their pungent scent mingling with the smell of the blood, as Jamie spoke the words slowly, in an ancient tongue come down from the days of the Norsemen.

"Say it in English," I said, seeing from Roger's face that while he spoke the words, he did not recognize them all.

"O Lord, bless the blood and the flesh of this the creature that You gave me," Jamie said softly. He scooped a pinch of the herbs himself, and rubbed them between thumb and forefinger, in a rain of fragrant dust.

"Created by Your hand as You created man,
Life given for life.
That me and mine may eat with thanks for the gift,
That me and mine may give thanks for Your own
sacrifice of blood and flesh,
Life given for life."

The last crumbs of green and gray disappeared into the mixture under my hands, and the ritual of the sausage was complete.

"THAT WAS GOOD of ye, Sassenach," Jamie said, drying my clean, wet hands and arms with the towel afterward. He nodded toward the corner of the house, where Roger had disappeared to help with the rest of the butchering, looking somewhat more peaceful. "I did think to tell him before, but I couldna see how to do it."

I smiled and moved close to him. It was a cold, windy day, and now that I had stopped working, the chill drove me closer to seek his warmth. He wrapped his arms around me, and I felt both the reassuring heat of his embrace, and the soft crackle of paper inside his shirt.

"What's that?"

"Oh, a bittie letter Sinclair's brought," he said, drawing back a bit to reach into his shirt. "I didna want to open it while Donald was there, and didna trust him not to be reading it when I went out."

"It's not your letter, anyway," I said, taking the smudged wad of paper from him. "It's mine."

"Oh, is it? Sinclair didna say, just handed it to me."

"He would!" Not unusually, Ronnie Sinclair viewed me—all women, for that matter—as simply a minor appendage of a husband. I rather pitied the woman he might eventually induce to marry him.

I unfolded the note with some difficulty; it had been worn so long next to sweaty skin that the edges had frayed and stuck together.

The message inside was brief and cryptic, but unsettling. It had been scratched into the paper with something like a sharpened stick, using an ink that looked disturbingly like dried blood, though it was more likely berry juice.

"What does it say, Sassenach?" Seeing me frowning at the paper, Jamie moved to the side to look. I held it out to him.

Far down, in one corner, scratched in faint and tiny letters, as though the sender had hoped by this means to escape notice, was the word "Faydree." Above, in bolder scratchings, the message read

YU
CUM

"IT MUST BE HER," I said, shivering as I drew my shawl closer. It was cold in the surgery, despite the small brazier glowing in the corner, but Ronnie Sinclair and MacDonald were in the kitchen, drinking cider and waiting while the sausages boiled. I spread the note open on my surgery table, its minatory summons dark and peremptory above the timid signature. "Look. Who else could it be?"

"She canna write, surely?" Jamie objected. "Though I suppose it might be that someone wrote it for her," he amended, frowning.

"No, she could have written this, I think." Brianna and Roger had come into the surgery, too; Bree reached out and touched the ragged paper, one long finger gently tracing the staggered letters. "I taught her."

"You did?" Jamie looked surprised. "When?"

"When I stayed at River Run. When you and Mama went to find Roger." Her wide mouth pressed thin for a moment; it wasn't an occasion she wished much to remember.

"I taught her the alphabet; I meant to teach her to read and write. We did all the letters—she knew how they sounded, and she could draw them. But then one day she said she couldn't anymore, and she wouldn't sit down with me." She glanced up, a troubled frown between her thick, red brows. "I thought maybe Aunt Jocasta found out, and stopped her."

"More likely Ulysses. Jocasta would have stopped *you,* lass." Jamie's frown matched hers as he glanced at me. "Ye do think it's Phaedre, then? My aunt's body slave?"

I shook my head, and bit one corner of my lip in doubt.

"The slaves at River Run do say her name like that—Faydree. And I certainly don't know anyone else by that name."

Jamie had questioned Ronnie Sinclair—casually, to give no occasion for alarm or gossip—but the cooper knew no more than he had told me: the note had been handed to him by a tinker, with the simple direction that it was "for the healer."

I leaned over the table, lifting a candle high to look at the note once more. The "F" of the signature had been made with a hesitant, repeated stroke—more than one try before the writer had committed herself to signing it. The more evidence, I thought, of its origin. I didn't know whether it was against the law in North Carolina to teach a slave to read or write, but it was certainly discouraged. While there were marked exceptions—slaves educated to their owners' ends, like Ulysses himself—it was on the whole a dangerous skill, and one a slave would go some way to conceal.

"She wouldn't have risked sending word like this, unless it was a serious matter," Roger said. He stood behind Bree, one hand on her shoulder, looking down at the note she held flattened on the table. "But what?"

"Have you heard from your aunt lately?" I asked Jamie, but I knew the answer before he shook his head. Any word from River Run that reached the Ridge would have been a matter of public knowledge within hours.

We had not gone to the Gathering at Mt. Helicon this year; there was too much to do on the Ridge and Jamie wished to avoid the heated politics involved. Still, Jocasta and Duncan had meant to be there. Anything wrong would surely have been a matter of general gossip, which would have reached us long since.

"So it is not only serious, but a private matter to the slave, too," Jamie said. "Otherwise, my aunt would have written, or Duncan sent word." His two stiff fingers tapped once, softly, against his thigh.

We stood around the table, staring at the note as though it were a small white slab of dynamite. The scent of boiling sausages filled the cold air, warm and comforting.

"Why you?" Roger asked, looking up at me. "Do you think it might be a medical matter? If she were ill, say—or pregnant?"

"Not illness," I said. "Too urgent." It was a week's ride to River Run at least—in good weather, and barring accident. Heaven knew how long it had taken the note to make its way up to Fraser's Ridge.

"But if she was pregnant? Maybe." Brianna pursed her lips, still frowning at the paper. "I think she thinks of Mama as a friend. She'd tell you before she'd tell Aunt Jocasta, I think."

I nodded, but reluctantly. Friendship was too strong a word; people situated as Phaedre and I could not be friends.

Liking was constrained by too many things—suspicion, mistrust, the vast chasm of difference that slavery imposed.

And yet there was a certain feeling of sympathy between us, that much was true. I had worked with her, side by side, planting herbs and harvesting them, making simples for the stillroom, explaining their uses. We had buried a dead girl together and plotted to protect a runaway slave accused of her murder. She had a certain talent with the sick, did Phaedre, and some knowledge of herbs. Any minor matter, she could deal with herself. But something like an unexpected pregnancy . . .

"What does she think I could do, though, I wonder?" I was thinking out loud, and my fingertips felt cold in contemplation. An unexpected child born to a slave would be of no concern to an owner—to the contrary, it would be welcomed as additional property; but I had heard stories of slave women who killed a child at birth, rather than have the babe brought up in slavery. Phaedre was a house slave, though, well-treated, and Jocasta did not separate slave families, I knew that. If it were that, Phaedre's situation was surely not so dire—and yet, who was I to judge?

I blew out a cloud of smoky breath, uncertain.

"I just can't see why—I mean, she couldn't possibly expect that I'd help her to get rid of a child. And for anything else . . . why me? There are midwives and healers much closer. It just doesn't make sense."

"What if—" Brianna said, and stopped. She pursed her lips in speculation, looking from me to Jamie and back. "What if," she said carefully, "she was pregnant, but the father was . . . someone it shouldn't be?"

A wary but humorous speculation sprang up in Jamie's eyes, increasing the resemblance between him and Brianna.

"Who, lass?" he said. "Farquard Campbell?"

I laughed out loud at the thought, and Brianna snorted with mirth, white wisps of breath floating round her head. The notion of the very upright—and quite elderly—Farquard Campbell seducing a house slave was . . .

"Well, no," Brianna said. "Though he *does* have all those children. But I just thought suddenly—what if it was Duncan?"

Jamie cleared his throat, and avoided catching my eye. I

bit my lip, feeling my face start to go red. Duncan had confessed his chronic impotence to Jamie before Duncan's wedding to Jocasta—but Brianna didn't know.

"Oh, I shouldna think it likely," Jamie said, sounding a trifle choked. He coughed, and fanned smoke from the brazier away from his face. "What gives ye that notion, lass?"

"Nothing about Duncan," she assured him. "But Aunt Jocasta *is*—well, old. And you know what men can be like."

"No, what?" asked Roger blandly, making me cough with the effort to suppress a laugh.

Jamie eyed her with a certain amount of cynicism.

"A good deal better than you do, *a nighean.* And while I wouldna wager much on some men, I think I should feel safe in laying odds that Duncan Innes isna the man to be breaking his marriage vows with his wife's black slave."

I made a small noise, and Roger lifted one eyebrow at me.

"Are you all right?"

"Fine," I said, sounding strangled. "Just—fine." I put a corner of the shawl over my no-doubt purple face and coughed ostentatiously. "It's . . . smoky in here, isn't it?"

"Maybe so," Brianna conceded, addressing Jamie. "It might not be that at all. It's just that Phaedre sent the note to 'the healer,' probably because she didn't want to use Mama's name, in case anybody saw the note before it got here. I just thought, maybe it wasn't really Mama she wants—maybe it's you."

That sobered both Jamie and me, and we glanced at each other. It was a definite possibility, and one that hadn't occurred to either of us.

"She couldn't send a note direct to you without rousing all kinds of curiosity," Bree went on, frowning at the note. "But she could say 'the healer' without putting a name on it. And she'd know that if Mama came, you'd probably come with her, at this time of year. Or if you didn't, Mama could send for you openly."

"It's a thought," Jamie said slowly. "But why in God's name might she want *me*?"

"Only one way to find out," said Roger, practical. He looked at Jamie. "Most of the outside work is done; the crops and the hay are in, the slaughtering's finished. We can manage here, if you want to go."

Jamie stood still for a moment, frowning in thought, then crossed to the window and raised the sash. A cold wind blew into the room, and Bree pinned the fluttering note to the table to keep it from taking wing. The coals in the small brazier smoked and flamed higher, and the bunches of dried herbs rustled uneasily overhead.

Jamie thrust his head out the window and breathed in deeply, eyes closed like one savoring the bouquet of fine wine.

"Cold and clear," he announced, drawing in his head and closing the window. "Clear weather for three days, at least. We could be off the mountain by that time, and we ride briskly." He smiled at me; the tip of his nose was red with the cold. "In the meantime, d'ye think those sausages are ready yet?"

72

BETRAYALS

A SLAVE I DIDN'T recognize opened the door to us, a broad-built woman in a yellow turban. She eyed us severely, but Jamie gave her no chance to speak, pushing rudely past her into the hall.

"He's Mrs. Cameron's nephew," I felt obliged to explain to her, as I followed him.

"I can see *that,*" she muttered, in a lilt that came from Barbados. She glared after him, making it evident that she detected a family resemblance in terms of high-handedness, as well as physique.

"I'm his wife," I added, overcoming the reflexive urge to shake her hand, and bowing slightly instead. "Claire Fraser. Nice to meet you."

She blinked, disconcerted, but before she could reply, I had whisked past her, following Jamie toward the small drawing room where Jocasta was inclined to sit in the afternoons.

The door to the drawing room was closed, and as Jamie set his hand on the knob, a sharp yelp came from inside—the prelude to a barrage of frenzied barking as the door swung wide.

Stopped in his tracks, Jamie paused, hand on the door, frowning at the small brown bundle of fur that leaped to and fro at his feet, eyes bulging in hysteria as it barked its head off.

"What is *that*?" he said, edging his way into the room as the creature made abortive dashes at his boots, still yapping.

"It's a wee dog, what d'ye think?" Jocasta said acerbically. She lifted herself from her chair, frowning in the direction of the noise. "*Sheas,* Samson."

"Samson? Oh, to be sure. The hair." Smiling despite himself, Jamie squatted and extended a closed fist toward the dog. Throttling back to a low growl, the dog extended a suspicious nose toward his knuckles.

"Where's Delilah?" I asked, edging into the room behind him.

"Ah, ye've come, as well, Claire?" Jocasta's face swiveled in my direction, lit by a smile. "A rare treat, to have the both of ye. I dinna suppose Brianna or the bittie lad have come along—no, I would have heard them." Dismissing that, she sat down again, and waved toward the hearth.

"As for Delilah, the lazy creature's asleep by the fire; I can hear her snoring."

Delilah was a large whitish hound of indeterminate breed but plentiful skin; it drooped around her in folds of relaxation as she lay on her back, paws curled over a freckled belly. Hearing her name, she snorted briefly, opened one eye a crack, then closed it again.

"I see ye've had a few changes since I was last here," Jamie observed, rising to his feet. "Where is Duncan? And Ulysses?"

"Gone. Looking for Phaedre." Jocasta had lost weight; the high MacKenzie cheekbones stood out sharp, and her skin looked thin and creased.

"Looking for her?" Jamie glanced sharply at her. "What's become of the lass?"

"Run away." She spoke with her usual self-possession, but her voice was bleak.

"Run away? But—are you sure?" Her workbox had been upset, the contents spilled on the floor. I knelt and began to tidy the confusion, picking up the scattered reels of thread.

"Weel, she's gone," Jocasta said with some acerbity. "Either she's run, or someone's stolen her. And I canna think who would have the gall or the skill to snatch her from my house, and no one seeing."

I exchanged a quick glance with Jamie, who shook his head, frowning. Jocasta was rubbing a fold of her skirt between thumb and forefinger; I could see small worn spots in the nap of the fabric near her hand, where she had done it repeatedly. Jamie saw it, too.

"When did she go, Auntie?" he asked quietly.

"Four weeks past. Duncan and Ulysses have been gone for two."

That fitted well enough with the arrival of the note. No telling how long before her disappearance the note had actually been written, given the vagaries of delivery.

"I see Duncan took pains to leave ye some company," Jamie observed. Samson had abandoned his watchdog role, and was sniffing assiduously at Jamie's boots. Delilah rolled onto her side with a luxurious groan and opened two luminous brown eyes, through which she regarded me with utmost tranquillity.

"Oh, aye, they're that." Half-grudgingly, Jocasta leaned out from her chair and located the hound's head, scratching behind the long, floppy ears. "Though Duncan meant them for my protection, or so he said."

"A sensible precaution," Jamie said mildly. It was; we had had no further word of Stephen Bonnet, nor had Jocasta heard the voice of the masked man again. But lacking the concrete reassurance of a corpse, either one could presumably pop up at any time.

"Why would the lassie run, Aunt?" Jamie asked. His tone was still mild, but persistent.

Jocasta shook her head, lips compressed.

"I dinna ken at all, Nephew."

"Nothing's happened of late? Nothing out of the ordinary?" he pressed.

"Do ye not think I should have said at once?" she asked sharply. "No. I woke late one morning, and couldna hear her about my room. There was nay tea by my bed, and the fire had gone out; I could smell the ashes. I called for her, and there was no answer. Gone, she was—vanished without a trace." She tilted her head toward him with a grim sort of "so there" expression.

I raised a brow at Jamie and touched the pocket I wore at my waist, containing the note. Ought we to tell her?

He nodded, and I drew the note from my pocket, unfolding it on the arm of her chair, as he explained.

Jocasta's look of displeasure faded into one of puzzled astonishment.

"Whyever should she send for you, *a nighean*?" she asked, turning to me.

"I don't know—perhaps she was with child?" I suggested. "Or had contracted a—disease of some sort?" I didn't want to suggest syphilis openly, but it was a possibility. If Manfred had infected Mrs. Sylvie, and she had then passed the infection on to one or more of her customers in Cross Creek, who then had visited River Run . . . but that would mean, perhaps, that Phaedre had had some kind of relationship with a white man. *That* was something a slave woman would go to great lengths to keep secret.

Jocasta, no fool, was rapidly coming to similar conclusions, though her thoughts ran parallel to mine.

"A child, that would be no great matter," she said, flicking a hand. "But if she had a lover . . . aye," she said thoughtfully. "She might have gone off with a lover. But then, why send for you?"

Jamie was growing restive, impatient with so much unprovable speculation.

"Perhaps she might think ye meant to sell her, Aunt, if ye discovered such a thing?"

"To *sell* her?"

Jocasta broke out laughing. Not her usual social laughter, nor even the sound of genuine amusement; this was shocking—

loud and crude, almost vicious in its hilarity. It was her brother Dougal's laugh, and the blood ran momentarily cold in my veins.

I glanced at Jamie, to find him looking down at her, face gone blank. Not in puzzlement; it was the mask he wore to hide strong feeling. So he'd heard that grisly echo, too.

She seemed unable to stop. Her hands clutched the carved arms of her chair and she leaned forward, face turning red, gasping for breath between those unnerving deep guffaws.

Delilah rolled onto her belly and uttered a low *"wuff"* of unease, looking anxiously round, unsure what the matter was, but convinced that something wasn't right. Samson had backed under the settee, growling.

Jamie reached out and took her by the shoulder—not gently.

"Be still, Aunt," he said. "Ye're frightening your wee dogs."

She stopped, abruptly. There was no sound but the faint wheeze of her breathing, nearly as unnerving as the laughter. She sat still, bolt upright in her chair, hands on the arms, the blood ebbing slowly from her face and her eyes gone dark and bright, fixed as though on something that only she could see.

"Sell her," she murmured, and her mouth creased as though the laughter were about to break out of her again. She didn't laugh, though, but stood up suddenly. Samson yapped once, in astonishment.

"Come with me."

She was through the door before either of us could say anything. Jamie lifted an eyebrow at me, but motioned me through the door before him.

She knew the house intimately; she made her way down the hall toward the door to the stables with no more than an occasional touch of the wall to keep her bearings, walking as fast as though she could see. Outside, though, she paused, feeling with one extended foot for the edge of the brick-laid path.

Jamie stepped up beside her and took her firmly by the elbow.

"Where d'ye wish to go?" he asked, a certain resignation in his tone.

"To the carriage barn." The peculiar laughter had left her, but her face was still flushed, her strong chin lifted with an air of defiance. Who was she defying? I wondered.

The carriage barn was shadowed and tranquil, dust motes drifting gold in the stir of air from the opened doors. A wagon, a carriage, a sledge, and the elegant two-wheeled trap sat like large, placid beasts on the straw-covered floor. I glanced at Jamie, whose mouth curled slightly as he looked at me; we had taken temporary refuge in that carriage, during the chaos of Jocasta's wedding to Duncan, almost four years before.

Jocasta paused in the doorway, one hand braced on the jamb and breathing deeply, as though orienting herself. She made no move to enter the barn herself, though, but instead nodded toward the depths of the building.

"Along the back wall, *an mhic mo peather*. There are boxes there; I want the large chest made of wickerwork, the one as high as your knee, with a rope tied round it."

I had not really noticed during our earlier excursion into the carriage barn, but the back wall was stacked high with boxes, crates, and bundles, piled two and three deep. With such explicit direction, though, Jamie made short work of finding the desired container, and dragged it out into the light, covered with dust and bits of straw.

"Shall I carry it into the house for ye, Auntie?" he asked, rubbing a finger under a twitching nose.

She shook her head, stooping and feeling for the knot of the rope that bound it.

"No. I shallna have it the house. I swore I should not."

"Let me." I laid a hand on hers to still her fumbling, then took charge of the knot myself. Whoever had tied it had been thorough, but not skilled; I had it loose within a minute, and the catch undone.

The wicker chest was filled with pictures. Bundles of loose drawings, done in pencil, ink, and charcoal, neatly tied with faded ribbons of colored silk. Several bound sketch-books. And a number of paintings: a few large unframed squares, and two smaller boxes of miniatures, all framed, stacked on edge like a deck of cards.

I heard Jocasta sigh, above me, and looked up. She stood still, eyes closed, and I could tell that she was inhaling deeply, breathing in the smell of the pictures—the smell of oils and charcoal, gesso, paper, canvas, linseed and turpentine, a full-bodied ghost that floated out of its wicker casket, transparently vivid against the background scents of straw and dust, wood and wicker.

Her fingers curled, thumb rubbing against the tips of her other fingers, unconsciously rolling a brush between them. I had seen Bree do that, now and then, looking at something she wanted to paint. Jocasta sighed again, then opened her eyes and knelt down beside me, reaching in to run her fingers lightly over the cache of buried art, searching.

"The oils," she said. "Fetch those out."

I had already taken out the boxes of miniatures. Jamie squatted on the other side of the casket, lifting the bundles of loose drawings and the sketchbooks, so that I could pull out the larger oils, laid on edge along the side of the container.

"A portrait," she said, head on one side to listen to the flat, hollow sound as I laid each one against the side of the wicker box. "An old man."

It was plain which one she meant. Two of the large canvases were landscapes, three, portraits. I recognized Farquard Campbell, much younger than his present age, and what must be a self-portrait of Jocasta herself, done perhaps twenty years before. I had no time to look at these, though, interesting as they were.

The third portrait looked to have been done much more recently than the others, and showed the effects of Jocasta's failing eyesight.

The edges were blurred, the colors muddy, shapes just slightly distorted, so that the elderly gentleman who looked out of the clouded oil seemed somehow disturbing, as though he belonged to some race not quite human, in spite of the orthodoxy of his wig and high white stock.

He wore a black coat and waistcoat, old-fashioned in style, with the folds of a tartan plaid draped over his shoulder, caught up with a brooch whose golden gleam was echoed by the ornamental knurl atop the dirk the old man held, his fingers bent and gnarled with arthritis. I recognized that dirk.

"So that is Hector Cameron." Jamie recognized it, too. He looked at the painting with fascination.

Jocasta reached out a hand, touching the surface of the paint as though to identify it by touch.

"Aye, that's him," she said dryly. "Never saw him in life, did ye, Nephew?"

Jamie shook his head.

"Once perhaps—but I was nay more than a babe at the time." His gaze traced the old man's features with deep interest, as though looking for clues to Hector Cameron's character. Such clues were evident; the man's force of personality fairly vibrated from the canvas.

He had strong bones, the man in the portrait, though the flesh hung from them in the infirmity of age. The eyes were still sharp, but one was half-closed—it might have been only a drooping eyelid caused by a small stroke, but the impression was that of an habitual manner of looking at the world; one eye always narrowed in cynical appraisal.

Jocasta was searching through the contents of the chest, fingers darting lightly here and there, like hunting moths. She touched one box of miniatures, and lifted it with a small grunt of satisfaction.

She ran a finger slowly along the edge of each miniature, and I saw that the frames were patterned differently; squares and ovals, smooth gilded wood, tarnished silver laid in a rope border, another studded with tiny rosettes. She found one she recognized, and plucked it from the box, handing it absently to me as she went back to her search.

The miniature was also of Hector Cameron—but this portrait done many years before the other. Dark wavy hair lay loose on his shoulders, a small ornamental braid down one side sporting two grouse's feathers, in the ancient Highland style. The same solid bones were there, but the flesh was firm; he had been handsome, Hector Cameron.

It *was* an habitual expression; whether by inclination or accident of birth, the right eye was narrowed here, as well, though not as much as in the older portrait.

My scrutiny was interrupted by Jocasta, who laid a hand on my arm.

"Is this the lass?" she asked, thrusting another of the miniatures at me.

I took it, puzzled, and gasped when I turned it over. It was Phaedre, done when the girl was in her early teens. Her usual cap was missing; she wore a simple kerchief bound over her hair that threw the bones of her face into bold relief. Hector Cameron's bones.

Jocasta nudged the box of paintings with her foot.

"Give those to your daughter, Nephew. Tell her to paint them over—it would be shame to waste the canvas." Without waiting for response, she set off back toward the house alone, hesitating only briefly at the fork in the path, steering by scent and memory.

THERE WAS A profound silence in the wake of Jocasta's departure, broken only by the singing of a mockingbird in a nearby pine.

"I will be damned," Jamie said at last, taking his eyes off the figure of his aunt as she vanished into the house, alone. He didn't look shocked, so much as deeply bemused. "Did the girl know, d'ye think?"

"Almost certainly," I said. "The slaves would surely have known; some must have been here when she was born; they'd have told her, if she wasn't quick enough to have worked it out herself—and I certainly think she is."

He nodded, and leaned back against the wall of the carriage house, looking meditatively down his long nose at the wicker chest of paintings. I felt a strong reluctance to go back to the house, myself. The buildings were beautiful, a mellow gold in the late-fall sun, and the grounds were peaceful, well-ordered. The sound of cheerful voices came from the kitchen garden, several horses grazed contentedly in the paddock nearby, and far away down the distant silver river, a small boat came down, a four-oared piretta, its oars stroking the surface, brisk and graceful as a water strider.

"Where every prospect pleases, and only man is vile," I

remarked. Jamie gave me a brief glance of incomprehension, then returned to his thoughts.

So Jocasta would by no means sell Phaedre, and thought Phaedre knew it. I wondered exactly why. Because she felt some duty to the girl, as the child of her husband? Or as a subtle form of revenge on that long-dead husband, keeping his illegitimate daughter as a slave, a body servant? I supposed that the two were not entirely exclusive, come to that—I had known Jocasta long enough to realize that her motives were rarely simple.

There was a chill in the air, with the sun low in the sky. I leaned against the carriage house beside Jamie, feeling the stored warmth of the sun soak from its bricks into my body, and wished that we could step into the old farm wagon and drive posthaste back to the Ridge, leaving River Run to deal with its own legacies of bitterness.

But the note was in my pocket, crackling when I moved. *YU CUM.* Not an appeal I could dismiss. But I *had* come—and now what?

Jamie straightened suddenly, looking toward the river. I looked, too, and saw that the boat had drawn into the dock there. A tall figure sprang up onto the dock, then turned to help another out of the boat. The second man was shorter, and moved in an odd fashion, off-kilter and out of rhythm.

"Duncan," I said at once, seeing this. "And Ulysses. They're back!"

"Aye," Jamie said, taking my arm and starting toward the house. "But they havena found her."

RUNAWAY or STOLEN on the 31st of October, a Negro Wench, twenty-two years of Age, above middling Height and comely in Appearance, with a Scar on the left Forearm in the shape of an Oval, caused by a Burn. Dressed in an indigo Gown, with a green-striped Apron, white Cap, brown Stockings, and leather Shoes. No missing Teeth. Known by the Name of "FAYDREE." Communicate Particulars to D. Innes, River Run Plantation, in the vicinity of Cross Creek. Substantial Reward will be paid for good Information.

I smoothed the crumpled broadsheet, which also sported a crude drawing of Phaedre, looking vaguely cross-eyed. Duncan had emptied his pockets and dropped a handful of these sheets on the table in the hall when he had come in the afternoon before, exhausted and dispirited. They had, he said, posted the bills in every tavern and public house between Campbelton and Wilmington, making inquiries as they went—but to no avail. Phaedre had vanished like the dew.

"May I have the marmalade, please?" Jamie and I were taking breakfast alone, neither Jocasta nor Duncan having appeared this morning. I was enjoying it, despite the gloomy atmosphere. Breakfast at River Run was normally a lavish affair, extending even to a pot of real tea—Jocasta must be paying her pet smuggler an absolute fortune for it; there was none to be found between Virginia and Georgia, to the best of my knowledge.

Jamie was frowning at another of the broadsheets, deep in thought. He didn't take his eyes off it, but his hand roamed vaguely over the table, settled on the cream jug, and passed it across to me.

Ulysses, showing little sign of his long journey beyond a certain heaviness of the eyes, stepped silently forward, took the cream jug, replaced it neatly, and set the pot of marmalade beside my plate.

"Thank you," I said, and he graciously inclined his head.

"Will you require further bloaters, madam?" he inquired. "Or more ham?"

I shook my head, my mouth being full of toast, and he glided off, picking up a loaded tray by the door, this presumably intended for Jocasta, Duncan, or both.

Jamie watched him go, with a sort of abstracted expression.

"I have been thinking, Sassenach," he said.

"I would never have guessed it," I assured him. "About what?"

He looked momentarily surprised, but then smiled, realizing.

"Ye kent what I told ye, Sassenach, about Brianna and the widow McCallum? That she wouldna scruple long to act, if Roger Mac were to be taking heed where he shouldn't?"

"I do," I said.

He nodded, as though verifying something to himself.

"Well, the lass comes by it honestly enough. The MacKenzies of Leoch are proud as Lucifer, all of them, and black jealous with it. Ye dinna want to cross one—still less to betray one."

I regarded him warily over my cup of tea, wondering where this was leading.

"I thought their defining trait was charm, allied with cunning. And as for betrayal, both your uncles were past hands at it."

"The two go together, do they not?" he asked, reaching across to dip a spoon in the marmalade. "Ye must beguile someone before ye can betray them, no? And I am inclined to think that a man who would betray is all the quicker to resent betrayal himself. Or a woman," he added delicately.

"Oh, really," I said, sipping with pleasure. "Jocasta, you mean." Put in those terms, I could see it. The MacKenzies of Leoch had powerful personalities—I did wonder what Jamie's maternal grandfather, the notorious Red Jacob, had been like—and I'd noted small commonalities of behavior between Jocasta and her elder brothers before.

Colum and Dougal had had an unshakable loyalty to each other—but to no one else. And Jocasta was essentially alone, separated from her family since her first marriage at fifteen. Being a woman, it was natural that the charm should be more apparent in her—but that didn't mean the cunning wasn't there. Nor yet the jealousy, I supposed.

"Well, plainly she knew that Hector betrayed her—and I do wonder whether she painted that portrait of Phaedre as a means of indicating to the world at large that she knew it, or merely as a private message to Hector—but what has that got to do with the present situation?"

He shook his head.

"Not Hector," he said. "Duncan."

I stared at him, absolutely open-mouthed. All other considerations aside, Duncan was impotent; he had told Jamie so, on the eve of his wedding to Jocasta. Jamie smiled crookedly, and reaching across the table, put a thumb under my chin and pushed my mouth gently shut.

"It's a thought, Sassenach, is all I'm saying. But I think I must go and have a word wi' the man. Will ye come?"

DUNCAN WAS IN the small room he used as a private office, tucked away above the stables, along with the tiny rooms that housed the grooms and stable-lads. He was slumped in a chair, looking hopelessly at the untidy stacks of papers and undusted ledgers that had accumulated on every horizontal surface.

He looked desperately tired, and a great deal older than when I had last seen him, at Flora MacDonald's barbecue. His gray hair was thinning, and when he turned to greet us, the light of the sun shone across his face, and I saw the thin line of the harelip scar Roger had mentioned, hidden in the luxuriant growth of his mustache.

Something vital seemed to have gone out of him, and when Jamie delicately broached the subject upon which we had come, he made no attempt at all to deny it. In fact, he seemed glad, rather than otherwise, to have it out.

"Ye did lie wi' the lass, then, Duncan?" Jamie asked directly, wanting to have the fact established.

"Well, no," he said vaguely. "I should have liked to, o' course—but what wi' her sleeping in Jo's dressing room . . ." At this reference to his wife, his face flushed a deep, unhealthy red.

"I mean, ye've had carnal knowledge of the woman, have ye not?" Jamie said, keeping a grip on his patience.

"Oh, aye." He gulped. "Aye. I did."

"How?" I asked bluntly.

The flush deepened, to such a degree that I feared he might have an apoplexy on the spot. He breathed like a grampus for a bit, though, and finally, his complexion began to fade back to something like normal.

"She fed me," he said at last, rubbing a hand tiredly across his eyes. "Every day."

Jocasta rose late and breakfasted in her sitting room, attended by Ulysses, to make plans for the day. Duncan, who had risen before dawn every day of his life, usually in the expectation of a dry crust or at most, a bit of drammach—oatmeal mixed with water—woke now to find a steaming pot of tea beside his bed, accompanied by a bowl of creamy parritch, liberally garnished with honey and cream, toast drenched in butter, eggs fried with ham.

"Sometimes a wee fish, rolled in cornmeal, crisp and sweet," he added, with mournful reminiscence.

"Well, that's verra seductive, to be sure, Duncan," Jamie said, not without sympathy. "A man's vulnerable when he's hungry." He gave me a wry glance. "But still . . ."

Duncan had been grateful to Phaedre for her kindness, and had—being a man, after all—admired her beauty, though in a purely disinterested sort of way, he assured us.

"To be sure," Jamie said with marked skepticism. "What happened?"

Duncan had dropped the butter, was the answer, whilst struggling to butter his toast one-handed. Phaedre had hastened to retrieve the pieces of the fallen dish, and then hurried to fetch a cloth and wipe the streaks of butter from the floor—and then from Duncan's chest.

"Well, I was in my nightshirt," he murmured, starting to go red again. "And she was—she had—" His hand rose and made vague motions in the vicinity of his chest, which I took to indicate that Phaedre's bodice had displayed her bosom to particular advantage while in such close proximity to him.

"And?" Jamie prompted ruthlessly.

And, it appeared, Duncan's anatomy had taken note of the fact—a circumstance admitted with such strangulated modesty that we could barely hear him.

"But I thought you couldn't—" I began.

"Oh, I couldna," he assured me hastily. "Only at night, like, dreaming. But not waking, not since I had the accident. Perhaps it was being so early i' the morning; my cock thought I was still asleep."

Jamie made a low Scottish noise expressing considerable doubt as to this supposition, but urged Duncan to continue, with a certain amount of impatience.

Phaedre had taken notice in her turn, it transpired.

"She was only sorry for me," Duncan said frankly. "I could

tell as much. But she put her hand on me, soft. So soft," he repeated, almost inaudibly.

He had been sitting on his bed—and had gone on sitting there in dumb amazement, as she took away the breakfast tray, lifted his nightshirt, climbed on the bed with her skirts neatly tucked above her round brown thighs, and with great tenderness and gentleness, had welcomed back his manhood.

"Once?" Jamie demanded. "Or did ye keep doing it?"

Duncan put his head in his hand, a fairly eloquent admission, under the circumstances.

"How long did this . . . er . . . liaison go on?" I asked more gently.

Two months, perhaps three. Not every day, he hastened to add—only now and then. And they had been very careful.

"I wouldna ever have wanted to shame Jo, ken," he said very earnestly. "And I kent weel I shouldna be doing it, 'twas a great sin, and yet I couldna keep from—" He broke off, swallowing. "It's all my fault, what's happened, let the sin be on me! Och, my puir darling lass . . ."

He fell silent, shaking his head like an old, sad, flea-ridden dog. I felt terribly sorry for him, regardless of the morality of the situation. The collar of his shirt was turned awkwardly under, strands of his grizzled hair trapped beneath his coat; I gently pulled them out and straightened it, though he took no heed.

"D'ye think she's dead, Duncan?" Jamie asked quietly, and Duncan blanched, his skin going the same gray as his hair.

"I canna bring myself to think it, *Mac Dubh,*" he said, and his eyes filled with tears. "And—and yet . . ."

Jamie and I exchanged uneasy glances. And yet. Phaedre had taken no money when she disappeared. How could a female slave travel very far without detection, advertised and hunted, lacking a horse, money, or anything beyond a pair of leather shoes? A man might possibly make it to the mountains, and manage to survive in the woods, if he were tough and resourceful—but a girl? A house slave?

Someone had taken her—or else she was dead.

None of us wanted to voice that thought, though. Jamie heaved a great sigh, and taking a clean handkerchief from his sleeve, put it in Duncan's hand.

"I shall pray for her, Duncan—wherever she may be. And for you, *a charaid* . . . and for you."

Duncan nodded, not looking up, the handkerchief clutched tight. It was clear that any attempt at comfort would be futile, and so at last we left him sitting there, in his tiny, landlocked room, so far from the sea.

We made our way back slowly, not speaking, but holding hands, feeling the strong need to touch each other. The day was bright, but there was a storm coming up; ragged clouds were streaming in from the east, and the breeze came in gusts that whirled my skirts about like a twirling parasol.

The wind was less on the back terrace, sheltered as it was by its waist-high wall. Looking up from here, I could just see the window that Phaedre had been looking out of when I'd found her there, the night of the barbecue.

"She told me that something wasn't right," I said. "The night of Mrs. MacDonald's barbecue. Something was troubling her then."

Jamie shot me an interested glance.

"Oh, aye? But she didna mean Duncan, surely?" he objected.

"I know." I shrugged helplessly. "She didn't seem to know what was wrong herself—she just kept saying, 'Something ain't right.'"

Jamie took a deep breath and blew it out again, shaking his head.

"In a way, I suppose I hope that whatever it was, it had to do with her going. For if it wasna to do with her and Duncan . . ." He trailed off, but I had no difficulty in finishing the thought.

"Then it wasn't to do with your aunt, either," I said. "Jamie—do you really think Jocasta might have had her killed?"

It should have sounded ridiculous, spoken aloud like that. The horrible thing was that it didn't.

Jamie made that small, shrugging gesture he used when very uncomfortable about something, as though his coat was too tight.

"Had she her sight, I should think it—possible, at least," he said. "To be betrayed by Hector—and she blamed him already, for the death of her girls. So her daughters are dead, but there is Phaedre, alive, every day, a constant reminder of insult. And then to be betrayed yet again, by Duncan, *with* Hector's daughter?"

He rubbed a knuckle under his nose. "I should think any woman of spirit might be . . . moved."

"Yes," I said, imagining what I might think or feel under the same circumstances. "Certainly. But to murder—that *is* what we're talking about, isn't it? Couldn't she simply have sold the girl?"

"No," he said thoughtfully. "She couldn't. We made provision to safeguard her money when she wed—but not the property. Duncan is the owner of River Run—and all that goes with it."

"Including Phaedre." I felt hollow, and a little sick.

"As I said. Had she her sight, I shouldna be astonished at all by the thought. As it is . . ."

"Ulysses," I said, with certainty, and he nodded reluctantly. Ulysses was not only Jocasta's eyes, but her hands, as well. I didn't think he would have killed Phaedre at his mistress's command—but if Jocasta had poisoned the girl, for instance, Ulysses might certainly have helped to dispose of the body.

I felt an odd air of unreality—even with what I knew of the MacKenzie family, calmly discussing the possibility of Jamie's aged aunt having murdered someone . . . and yet . . . I *did* know the MacKenzies.

"*If* my aunt had any hand at all in the matter," Jamie said. "After all, Duncan said they were discreet. And it may be the lass was taken off—perhaps by the man my aunt recalls from Coigach. It could be he'd think Phaedre might help him to the gold, no?"

That was a somewhat happier thought. And it *did* fit with Phaedre's premonition—if that's what it was—which had occurred the same day that the man from Coigach came.

"I suppose all we *can* do is pray for her, poor thing," I said. "I don't suppose there's a patron saint of abducted persons, is there?"

"Saint Dagobert," he replied promptly, causing me to stare at him.

"You're making that up."

"Indeed I am not," he said with dignity. "Saint Athelais is another one—and perhaps better, now I think. She was a young Roman lass, who was abducted by the Emperor Justinian, who wished to have his way wi' her, and she vowed to chastity. But she escaped and went off to live with her uncle in Benevento."

"Good for her. And Saint Dagobert?"

"A king of some sort—Frankish? Anyway, his guardian took against him as a child, and had him kidnapped away to England, so the guardian's son might reign instead."

"Where do you learn these things?" I demanded.

"From Brother Polycarp, at the Abbey of St. Anne," he said, the corner of his mouth tucking back in a smile. "When I couldna sleep, he'd come and tell me stories of the saints, hours on end. It didna always put me to sleep, but after an hour or so of hearing about holy martyrs having their breasts amputated or being flogged wi' iron hooks, I'd close my eyes and make a decent pretense of it."

Jamie took my cap off and set it on the ledge. The air blew through my inch of hair, ruffling it like meadow grass, and he smiled as he looked at me.

"Ye look like a boy, Sassenach," he said. "Though damned if I've ever seen a lad with an arse like yours."

"Thanks so much," I said, absurdly pleased. I had eaten like a horse in the last two months, slept well and deeply through the nights, and knew I was much improved in looks, hair notwithstanding. Never hurt to hear it, though.

"I want ye verra much, *mo nighean donn,*" he said softly, and curled his fingers round my wrist, letting the pads rest gently on my pulse.

"So the MacKenzies of Leoch are all prone to black jealousy," I said. I could feel my pulse, steady under his fingers. "Charming, cunning, and given to betrayal." I touched his lip, ran my thumb lightly along it, the tiny prickles of beard pleasant to the touch. "All of them?"

He looked down, fixing me suddenly with a dark blue gaze in which humor and ruefulness were mingled with a good many other things I couldn't read.

"Ye think I am not?" he said, and smiled a little sadly. "God and Mary bless ye, Sassenach." And bent to kiss me.

WE COULD NOT tarry at River Run. The fields down here on the piedmont had long since been harvested and turned under, the remnants of dried stalks flecking the fresh dark earth; snow would fly soon in the mountains.

We had discussed the matter round and round—but came to no useful conclusion. There was nothing further we could do to help Phaedre—except to pray. Beyond that, though . . . there was Duncan to think of.

For it had occurred to both of us that if Jocasta *had* found out about his liaison with Phaedre, her wrath was not likely to be limited to the slave girl. She might bide her time—but she would not forget the injury. I'd never met a Scot who *would.*

We took our leave of Jocasta after breakfast the next day, finding her in her private parlor, embroidering a table runner. The basket of silk threads sat in her lap, the colors carefully arrayed in a spiral, so that she could choose the one she wanted by touch, and the finished linen fell to one side, five feet of cloth edged with an intricate design of apples, leaves, and vines—or no, I realized, when I picked up the end of the cloth to admire it. Not vines. Black-eyed serpents, coiling slyly, slithering, green and scaly. Here and there one gaped to show its fangs, guarding scattered red fruit.

"Garden of Eden," she explained to me, rubbing the design lightly betwixt her fingers.

"How beautiful," I said, wondering how long she'd been working on it. Had she begun it before Phaedre's disappearance?

A bit of casual talk, and then Josh the groom appeared to say that our horses were ready. Jamie nodded, dismissing him, and stood.

"Aunt," he said to Jocasta matter-of-factly, "I should take it verra much amiss were any harm to come to Duncan."

She stiffened, fingers halting in their work.

"Why should any harm come to him?" she asked, lifting her chin.

Jamie didn't reply at once, but stood regarding her, not without sympathy. Then he leaned down, so that she could feel his presence close, his mouth near her ear.

"I know, Aunt," he said softly. "And if ye dinna wish anyone else to share that knowledge . . . then I think I shall find Duncan in good health when I return."

She sat as though turned to salt. Jamie stood up, nodding toward the door, and we took our leave. I glanced back from the hallway, and saw her still sitting like a statue, face as white as the linen in her hands and the little balls of colored thread all fallen from her lap, unraveling across the polished floor.

73

DOUBLE-DEALING

WITH MARSALI GONE, the whisky-making became more difficult. Among us, Bree and Mrs. Bug and I had managed to get off one more malting before the weather became too cold and rainy, but it was a near thing, and it was with great relief that I saw the last of the malted grain safely decanted into the still. Once set to ferment, the stuff became Jamie's responsibility, as he trusted no one else with the delicate job of judging taste and proof.

The fire beneath the still had to be kept at exactly the right level, though, to keep fermentation going without killing the mash, then raised for the distillings once fermentation was complete. This meant that he lived—and slept—beside the still for the few days necessary for each batch to come off. I generally brought him supper and stayed until the dark came, but it was lonely without him in my bed, and I was more than pleased when we poured the last of the new making into casks.

"Oh, that smells good." I sniffed beatifically at the inside of an empty cask; it was one of the special casks Jamie had obtained through one of Lord John's shipping friends—

charred inside like a normal whisky cask, but previously used to store sherry. The sweet mellow ghost of the sherry mingled with the faint scent of char and the hot, raw reek of the new whisky were together enough to make my head spin pleasantly.

"Aye, it's a small batch, but no bad," Jamie agreed, inhaling the aroma like a perfume connoisseur. He lifted his head and eyed the sky overhead; the wind was coming up strong, and thick clouds were racing past, dark-bellied and threatening.

"There's only the three casks," he said. "If ye think ye might manage one, Sassenach, I'll take the others. I should like to have them safe, rather than dig them out of a snowbank next week."

A half-mile walk in a roaring wind, carrying or rolling a six-gallon cask, was no joke, but he was right about the snow. It wasn't quite cold enough for snow yet, but it would be soon. I sighed, but nodded, and between us, we managed to lug the casks slowly up to the whisky cache, hidden among rocks and ragged grapevines.

I had quite regained my strength, but even so, every muscle I had was trembling and jerking in protest by the time we had finished, and I made no objection at all when Jamie made me sit down to rest before heading back to the house.

"What do you plan to do with these?" I asked, nodding back toward the cache. "Keep, or sell?"

He wiped a flying strand of hair out of his face, squinting against a blast of flying dust and dead leaves.

"I'll have to sell one, for the spring seed. We'll keep one to age—and I think perhaps I can put the last to good purpose. If Bobby Higgins comes again before the snow, I shall send a half-dozen bottles to Ashe, Harnett, Howe, and a few others—a wee token of my abiding esteem, aye?" He grinned wryly at me.

"Well, I've heard of worse bona fides," I said, amused. It had taken him a good deal of work to worm his way back into the good graces of the North Carolina Committee of Correspondence, but several members had begun answering his letters again—cautiously, but with respect.

"I shouldna think anything important will happen over the winter," he said thoughtfully, rubbing his cold-reddened nose.

"Likely not." Massachusetts, where most of the uproar had been taking place, was now occupied by a General Gage, and the latest we had heard was that he had fortified Boston Neck, the narrow spit of land that connects the city to the mainland—which meant that Boston was now cut off from the rest of the colony, and under siege.

I felt a small pang, thinking of it; I had lived in Boston for nearly twenty years, and was fond of the city—though I knew I would not recognize it now.

"John Hancock—he's a merchant there—is heading the Committee of Safety, Ashe says. They've voted to recruit twelve thousand militia, and are looking to purchase five *thousand* muskets—with the trouble I had to find thirty, good luck to them, is all I can say."

I laughed, but before I could reply, Jamie stiffened.

"What's that?" His head turned sharply, and he laid a hand on my arm. Silenced abruptly, I held my breath, listening. The wind stirred the drying leaves of wild grapevines with a papery rustle behind me, and in the distance a murder of crows passed, squabbling in shrill cries.

Then I heard it, too: a small, desolate, and very human sound. Jamie was already on his feet, making his way with care between the fallen rocks. He ducked beneath the lintel made by a leaning slab of granite, and I made to follow him. He stopped abruptly, nearly making me run into him.

"Joseph?" he said incredulously.

I peered around him as best I could. To my equal astonishment, it *was* Mr. Wemyss, sitting hunched on a boulder, a stone jug between his bony knees. He'd been crying; his nose and eyes were red, making him look even more like a white mouse than usual. He was also extremely drunk.

"Oh," he said, blinking in dismay at us. "Oh."

"Are ye . . . quite well, Joseph?" Jamie came closer, extending a hand gingerly, as though afraid that Mr. Wemyss might crack into pieces if touched.

This instinct was sound; when he touched the little man, Mr. Wemyss's face crumpled like paper, and his thin shoulders began to shake uncontrollably.

"I am so sorry, sir," he kept saying, quite dissolved in tears. "I'm *so* sorry!"

Jamie gave me a "do something, Sassenach" look of appeal, and I knelt swiftly, putting my arms round Mr. Wemyss's shoulders, patting his slender back.

"Now, now," I said, giving Jamie a "now *what*?" sort of look over Mr. Wemyss's matchstick shoulder in return. "I'm sure it will be all right."

"Oh, no," he said, hiccuping. "Oh, no, it can't." He turned a face streaming with woe toward Jamie. "I can't bear it, sir, truly I can't."

Mr. Wemyss's bones felt thin and brittle, and he was shivering. He was wearing only a thin shirt and breeches, and the wind was beginning to whine through the rocks. Clouds thickened overhead, and the light went from the little hollow, suddenly, as though a blackout curtain had been dropped.

Jamie unfastened his own cloak and wrapped it rather awkwardly round Mr. Wemyss, then lowered himself carefully onto another boulder.

"Tell me the trouble, Joseph," he said quite gently. "Is someone dead, then?"

Mr. Wemyss sank his face into his hands, head shaking to and fro like a metronome. He muttered something, which I understood to be "Better if she were."

"Lizzie?" I asked, exchanging a puzzled glance with Jamie. "Is it Lizzie you mean?" She'd been perfectly all right at breakfast; what on earth—

"First Manfred McGillivray," Mr. Wemyss said, raising his face from his hands, "and then Higgins. As though a degenerate and a murderer were not bad enough—now this!"

Jamie's brows shot up and he looked at me. I shrugged slightly. The gravel was jabbing sharply into my knees; I rose stiffly and brushed it away.

"Are you saying that Lizzie is, er . . . in love with someone . . . unsuitable?" I asked carefully.

Mr. Wemyss shuddered.

"Unsuitable," he said, in a hollow tone. "Jesus Christ. Unsuitable!"

I'd never heard Mr. Wemyss blaspheme before; it was unsettling.

He turned wild eyes on me, looking like a crazed sparrow, huddled in the depths of Jamie's cloak.

"I gave up everything for her!" he said. "I sold myself—and gladly!—to save her from dishonor. I left home, left Scotland, knowing I should never see it more, that I should leave my bones in the soil of the strangers. And yet I've said nay word of reproach to her, my dear wee lassie, for how should it be her fault? And now . . ." He turned a hollow, haunted gaze on Jamie.

"My God, my God. What shall I do?" he whispered. A blast of wind thundered through the rocks and whipped the cloak around him, momentarily obliterating him in a shroud of gray, as though distress had quite engulfed him.

I kept tight hold of my own cloak, to prevent it being torn off me; the wind was strong enough that I nearly lost my footing. Jamie squinted against the spray of dust and fine gravel that blasted us, setting his teeth in discomfort. He wrapped his arms around himself, shivering.

"Is the lass with child, then, Joseph?" he said, obviously wanting to get to the bottom of things and go home.

Mr. Wemyss's head popped out of the folds of cloak, fair hair tousled into broomstraw. Blinking reddened eyes, he nodded, then excavated the jug and, raising it in trembling hands, took several gulps. I saw the single "X" marked on the jug; with his characteristic modesty, he had taken a jug of the raw new whisky, not the cask-aged higher quality.

Jamie sighed, reached out a hand, and taking the jug from him, took a healthy gulp himself.

"Who?" he said, handing it back. "Is it my nephew?"

Mr. Wemyss stared at him, owl-eyed.

"Your nephew?"

"Ian Murray," I put in helpfully. "Tall brown-haired lad? Tattoos?"

Jamie gave me a look suggesting that I was perhaps not being quite so helpful as I thought, but Mr. Wemyss went on looking blank.

"Ian Murray?" Then the name appeared to penetrate through the alcoholic fog. "Oh. No. Christ, if it were! I should bless the lad," he said fervently.

I exchanged another look with Jamie. This looked like being serious.

"Joseph," he said with just a touch of menace. "It's cold." He wiped his nose on the back of his hand. " Who's debauched your daughter? Give me his name, and I'll see him wed to her in the morning or dead at her feet, whichever ye like. But let's do it inside by the fire, aye?"

"Beardsley," Mr. Wemyss said, in a tone suggesting visions of utter despair.

"Beardsley?" Jamie repeated. He raised one eyebrow at me. It wasn't what I would have expected—but hearing it came as no great shock, either.

"Which Beardsley was it?" he asked, with relative patience. "Jo? Or Kezzie?"

Mr. Wemyss heaved a sigh that came from the bottoms of his feet.

"She doesn't know," he said flatly.

"Christ," said Jamie involuntarily. He reached for the whisky again, and drank heavily.

"Ahem," I said, giving him a meaningful look as he lowered the jug. He surrendered it to me without comment, and straightened himself on his boulder, shirt plastered against his chest by the wind, his hair whipped loose behind him.

"Well, then," he said firmly. "We'll have the two of them in, and find out the truth of it."

"No," said Mr. Wemyss, "we won't. They don't know, either."

I had just taken a mouthful of raw spirit. At this, I choked, spluttering whisky down my chin.

"They *what*?" I croaked, wiping my face with a corner of my cloak. "You mean . . . *both* of them?"

Mr. Wemyss looked at me. Instead of replying, though, he blinked once. Then his eyes rolled up into his head and he fell headlong off the boulder, poleaxed.

I MANAGED to restore Mr. Wemyss to semiconsciousness, but not to the point of his being able to walk. Jamie was therefore obliged to carry the little man slung across his shoulders like a deer carcass; no mean feat, considering the broken ground that lay between the whisky cache and the new malting floor, and the wind that pelted us with bits of gravel, leaves, and flying pinecones. Clouds had boiled up over the shoulder of the mountain, dark and dirty as laundry suds, and were spreading rapidly across the sky. We were going to get drenched, if we didn't hurry.

The going became easier once we reached the trail to the house, but Jamie's temper was not improved by Mr. Wemyss's suddenly coming to at this point and vomiting down the front of his shirt. After a hasty attempt at swabbing off the mess, we reorganized our strategy, and made our way with Mr. Wemyss precariously balanced between us, each firmly gripping one elbow as he slipped and stumbled, his spindly knees giving way at unexpected moments, like Pinocchio with his strings cut.

Jamie was talking to himself volubly in Gaelic under his breath during this phase of the journey, but desisted abruptly when we came into the dooryard. One of the Beardsley twins was there, catching chickens for Mrs. Bug before the storm; he had two of them, held upside down by the legs like an ungainly bouquet of brown and yellow. He stopped when he saw us, and stared curiously at Mr. Wemyss.

"What—" began the boy. He got no further. Jamie dropped Mr. Wemyss's arm, took two strides, and punched the Beardsley twin in the stomach with sufficient force that he doubled over, dropped the chickens, staggered back, and fell down. The chickens flapped off in a cloud of scattered feathers, squawking.

The boy writhed about on the ground, mouth opening and closing in a vain search for air, but Jamie paid no attention. He stooped, seized the lad by the hair, and spoke loudly and directly into his ear—in case it was Kezzie, I supposed.

"Fetch your brother. To my study. Now."

Mr. Wemyss had been watching this interesting tableau, one arm draped across my shoulders for support and his mouth hanging open. It continued to hang open as he turned his head, following Jamie as he strode back toward us. He blinked, though, and shut it, as Jamie seized his other arm and, removing him neatly from me, propelled him into the house without a backward glance.

I gazed reproachfully at the Beardsley on the ground.

"How *could* you?" I said.

He made soundless goldfish mouths at me, his eyes completely round, then managed a long *heeeeee* sound of inhalation, his face dark purple.

"Jo? What's the matter, are ye hurt?" Lizzie came out of the trees, a pair of chickens clutched by the legs in either hand. She was frowning worriedly at—well, I supposed it *was* Jo; if anyone could tell the difference, it would surely be Lizzie.

"No, he's not hurt," I assured her. "Yet." I pointed a monitory finger at her. "You, young lady, go and put those chickens in their coop and then—" I hesitated, glancing at the boy on the ground, who had recovered enough breath to gasp and was gingerly sitting up. I didn't want to bring her into my surgery, not if Jamie and Mr. Wemyss were going to be eviscerating the Beardsleys right across the hall.

"I'll go with you," I decided hastily, gesturing her away from Jo. "Shoo."

"But—" She cast a bewildered glance at Jo—yes, it was Jo; he ran a hand through his hair to get it out of his face, and I saw the scarred thumb.

"He's fine," I said, turning her toward the chicken coop with a firm hand on her shoulder. "Go."

I glanced back, to see that Jo Beardsley had made it to his feet and, with a hand pressed to his tender middle, was making off toward the stable, presumably to fetch his twin as ordered.

I glanced back at Lizzie, giving her a narrow eye. If Mr. Wemyss had the right end of the stick and she *was* pregnant, she was evidently one of those fortunate persons who doesn't suffer from morning sickness or the usual digestive symptoms of early pregnancy; she was, in fact, very healthy-looking.

That in itself should have alerted me, I supposed, pale and green-stick as she normally was. Now that I looked carefully, there seemed to be a soft pink glow about her, and her pale blond hair was shiny where it peeped out under her cap.

"How far along are you?" I asked, holding back a branch

for her. She gave me a quick look, gulped visibly, then ducked under the branch.

"About four months gone, I think," she said meekly, not looking at me. "Um . . . Da told ye, did he?"

"Yes. Your poor father," I said severely. "Is he right? *Both* of the Beardsleys?"

She hunched her shoulders a little, head bowed, but nodded, almost imperceptibly.

"What—what will Himself do to them?" she asked, her voice small and tremulous.

"I really don't know." I doubted that Jamie himself had formed any specific notions—though he *had* mentioned having the miscreant responsible for Lizzie's pregnancy dead at her feet if her father wished it.

Now that I thought, the alternative—having her wed by morning—was likely to be somewhat more problematic than simply killing the twins would be.

"I don't know," I repeated. We had reached the coop, a stoutly built edifice that sheltered under a spreading maple. Several of the hens, slightly less stupid than their sisters, were roosting like huge, ripe fruits in the lower branches, heads buried in their feathers.

I pulled open the door, releasing a gust of ripe ammonia from the dark interior, and holding my breath against the stink, pulled the hens from the tree and tossed them brusquely inside. Lizzie ran into the woods nearby, snatching chickens out from under bushes and rushing back to shove them in. Large drops were beginning to plummet from the clouds, heavy as pebbles, making small, audible splats as they struck the leaves above.

"Hurry!" I slammed the door behind the last of the squawking chickens, threw the latch, and seized Lizzie by the arm. Borne on a whoosh of wind, we ran for the house, skirts whirling up round us like pigeons' wings.

The summer kitchen was nearest; we burst through the door just as the rain came down with a roar, a solid sheet of water that struck the tin roof with a sound like anvils falling.

We stood panting inside. Lizzie's cap had come off in flight, and her plait had come undone, so that her hair straggled over her shoulders in strands of shining, creamy blond; a noticeable change from the wispy, flyaway look she usually shared with her father. If I had seen her without her cap, I should have known at once. I took time to recover my breath, trying to decide what on earth to say to her.

She was making a great to-do over tidying herself, panting and pulling at her bodice, smoothing her skirts—all the while trying not to meet my eye.

Well, there was one question that had been niggling at me since Mr. Wemyss's shocking revelation; best to get that one out of the way at once. The initial roar of the rain had slackened to a regular drumbeat; it was loud, but conversation was at least possible.

"Lizzie." She looked up from her skirt-settling, slightly startled. "Tell me the truth," I said. I put my hands on either side of her face, looking earnestly into her pale blue eyes. "Was it rape?"

She blinked, the look of absolute amazement that suffused her features more eloquent than any spoken denial could have been.

"Oh, no, ma'am!" she said just as earnestly. "Ye couldna think Jo or Kezzie would do such a thing?" Her small pink lips twitched slightly. "What, did ye think they maybe took it in turns to hold me down?"

"No," I said tartly, releasing her. "But I thought I'd best ask, just in case."

I hadn't really thought so. But the Beardsleys were such an odd mix of the civil and the feral that it was impossible to say definitely *what* they might or might not do.

"But it *was* . . . er . . . both of them? That's what your father said. Poor man," I added, with a tone of some reproach.

"Oh." She cast down her pale lashes, pretending to find a loose thread on her skirt. "Ummm . . . well, aye, it was. I do feel something terrible about shaming Da so. And it wasna really that we did it a-purpose . . ."

"Elizabeth Wemyss," I said, with no little asperity, "rape aside—and we've ruled that out—it is not possible to engage in sexual relations with two men without meaning to. One, maybe, but not two. Come to that . . ." I hesitated, but vulgar curiosity was simply too much. "Both at *once*?"

She did look shocked at that, which was something of a relief.

"Oh, no, ma'am! It was . . . I mean, I didna ken that it . . ." She trailed off, quite pink in the face.

I pulled two stools out from under the table and pushed one toward her.

"Sit down," I said, "and tell me about it. We aren't going anywhere for a bit," I added, glancing through the half-open door at the downpour outside. A silver haze rose knee-high over the yard, as the raindrops struck the grass in small explosions of mist, and the sharp smell of it washed through the room.

Lizzie hesitated, but took the stool; I could see her making up her mind to it that there was really nothing to do now but explain—assuming that the situation *could* be explained.

"You, um, said you didn't know," I said, trying to offer her an opening. "You mean—you thought it was only one twin, but they, er, fooled you?"

"Well, aye," she said, and took a huge breath of the chilly air. "Something like that. See, 'twas when you and Himself went to Bethabara for the new goat. Mrs. Bug was down wi' the lumbago, and it was only me and Da in the house—but then he went down to Woolam's for to fetch the flour, and so it was just me."

"To Bethabara? That was six months ago! And you're four months gone—you mean all this time you've been—well, never mind. What happened, then?"

"The fever," she said simply. "It came back."

She had been gathering firewood when the first malarial chill struck her. Recognizing it for what it was, she had dropped the wood and tried to reach the house, only to fall halfway there, her muscles going slack as string.

"I lay upon the ground," she explained, "and I could feel the fever comin' for me. It's like a great beast, aye? I can feel it seize me in its jaws and bite—'tis like my blood runs hot and then cold, and the teeth of it sink into my bones. I can feel it set in then, to try to break them in twa, and suck the marrow." She shuddered in memory.

One of the Beardsleys—she thought it was Kezzie, but had been in no state of mind to ask—had discovered her lying in a disheveled heap in the dooryard. He'd run to fetch his brother, and the two of them had raised her, carried her between them into the house, and fetched her upstairs to her bed.

"My teeth were clackin' so hard together I thought they'd break, surely, but I told them to fetch the ointment, wi' the gallberries, the ointment ye'd made."

They had rummaged through the surgery cupboard until they found it, and then, frantic as she burned hotter and hotter, had stripped off her shoes and stockings and begun to rub the ointment into her hands and feet.

"I told them—I told them they must rub it all over," she said, her cheeks going a deep peony. She looked down, fiddling with a strand of hair. "I was—well, I was quite oot my mind wi' the fever, ma'am, truly I was. But I kent I needed my medicine bad."

I nodded, beginning to understand. I didn't blame her; I'd seen the malaria overpower her. And so far as that went, she'd done the right thing; she did need the medicine, and couldn't have managed to apply it herself.

Frantic, the two boys had done as she'd said, got her clothes awkwardly off, and rubbed the ointment thoroughly into every inch of her naked body.

"I was goin' in and oot a bit," she explained, "wi' the fever dreams walkin' oot my heid and about the room, so it's all a bit mixed, what I recall. But I do think one o' the lads said to the other as he was getting the ointment all over, and would spoil his shirt, best take it off."

"I see," I said, seeing vividly. "And then . . ."

And then she had quite lost track of what was happening, save that whenever she drifted to the surface of the fever, the boys were still there, talking to her and each other, the murmur of their voices a small anchor to reality and their hands never leaving her, stroking and smoothing and the sharp smell of gallberries cutting through the woodsmoke from the hearth and the scent of beeswax from the candle.

"I felt . . . safe," she said, struggling to express it. "I dinna remember much in particular, only opening my eyes once and seein' his chest right before my face, and the dark curlies all round his paps, and them wee and brown and wrinkled, like raisins." She turned her face to me, eyes still rounded at the memory. "I can still see that, like as it was right in front o' me this minute. That's queer, no?"

"Yes," I agreed, though in fact it was not; there was something about high fever that blurred reality but at the same time could sear certain images so deeply into the mind that they never left. "And then . . . ?"

Then she had begun to shake violently with chills, which neither more quilts nor a hot stone at her feet had helped. And so one of the boys, in desperation, had crawled under the quilts beside her and held her against him, trying to drive out the cold from her bones with his own heat—which, I thought cynically, must have been considerable, at that point.

"I dinna ken which it was, or if it was the same one all night, or if they changed now and then, but whenever I woke, he was there, wi' his arms about me. And sometimes he'd put back the blanket and rub more ointment down my back and, and, round . . ." She stumbled, blushing. "But when I woke in the morning, the fever was gone, like it always is on the second day."

She looked at me, pleading for understanding.

"D'ye ken how that is, ma'am, when a great fever's broken? 'Tis the same every time, so I'm thinking it may be so for everyone. But it's . . . peaceful. Your limbs are sae heavy ye canna think of moving, but ye dinna much care. And everything ye see—all the wee things ye take nay notice of day by day—ye notice, and they're beautiful," she said simply. "I think sometimes that will be how it is when I'm dead. I shall just wake, and everything will be like that, peaceful and beautiful—save I shall be able to move."

"But you woke this time, and couldn't," I said. "And the boy—whichever it was—he was still there, with you?"

"It was Jo," she said, nodding. "He spoke to me, but I didna pay much mind to what he said, and I dinna think he did, either."

She bit her lower lip momentarily, the small teeth sharp and white.

"I—I hadna done it before, ma'am. But I came close, a time or two wi' Manfred. And closer still wi' Bobby Higgins. But Jo hadna ever even kissed a lass, nor his brother had, either. So ye see, 'twas really my fault, for I kent well enough what was happening, but . . . we were both slippery wi' the ointment, still, and naked under the quilts, and it . . . happened."

I nodded, understanding precisely and in detail.

"Yes, I can see how it happened, all right. But then it . . . er . . . went on happening, I suppose?"

Her lips pursed up and she went very pink again.

"Well . . . aye. It did. It—it feels sae *nice,* ma'am," she whispered, leaning a little toward me as though imparting an important secret.

I rubbed a knuckle hard across my lips.

"Um, yes. Quite. But—"

The Beardsleys had washed the sheets at her direction, and there were no incriminating traces left by the time her father returned, two days later. The gallberries had done their work, and while she was still weak and tired, she told Mr. Wemyss only that she had had a mild attack.

Meanwhile, she met with Jo at every opportunity, in the deep summer grass behind the dairy shed, in the fresh straw in the stable—and when it rained, now and then on the porch of the Beardsleys' cabin.

"I wouldna do it inside, for the stink o' the hides," she explained. "But we put an old quilt on the porch, so as I shouldna have splinters in my backside, and the rain comin' down just a foot away . . ." She looked wistfully through the open door, where the rain had softened into a steady whisper, the needles trembling on the pine trees as it fell.

"And what about Kezzie? Where was he, while all this was going on?" I asked.

"Ah. Well, Kezzie," she said, taking a deep breath.

They had made love in the stable, and Jo had left her lying on her cloak in the straw, watching as he rose and dressed himself. Then he had kissed her and turned to the door. Seeing that he had forgotten his canteen, she called softly after him.

"And he didna answer, nor turn round," she said. "And it came to me sudden, as he didna hear me."

"Oh, I see," I said softly. "You, um, couldn't tell the difference?"

She gave me a direct blue look.

"I can *now,*" she said.

In the beginning, though, sex was so new—and the brothers

both sufficiently inexperienced—that she hadn't noticed any differences.

"How long . . . ?" I asked. "I mean, do you have any idea when they, er . . . ?"

"Not for certain," she admitted. "But if I was to guess about it, I think the first time it was Jo—no, I ken for sure that was Jo, for I saw his thumb—but the second time, it was likely Kezzie. They share, ken?"

They *did* share—everything. And so it was the most natural thing in the world—to all three of them, evidently—that Jo should wish his brother to share in this new marvel.

"I ken it seems . . . strange," she said, shrugging a little. "And I suppose I ought to have said something, or done something—but I couldna think what. And really"—she raised her eyes to me, helpless—"it didna seem *wrong* at all. They're different, aye, but at the same time, they're sae close to each other . . . well, it's just as if I was touching the one lad, and talking to him—only he's got the twa bodies."

"Twa bodies," I said, a little bleakly. "Well, yes. There's just the difficulty, you see, the two bodies part." I eyed her closely. Despite the history of malaria and her fine-boned build, she had definitely filled out; she had a plump little bosom swelling over the edge of her bodice, and, while she was sitting on it so I couldn't tell for sure, very likely a bottom to match. The only real wonder was that it had taken her three months to fall pregnant.

As though reading my mind, she said, "I took the seeds, aye? The ones you and Miss Bree take. I had a store put by, from when I was betrothed to Manfred; Miss Bree gave me them. I meant to gather more, but I didna always remember, and—" She shrugged again, putting her hands across her belly.

"Whereupon you proceeded to say nothing," I observed. "Did your father find out by accident?"

"No, I told him," she said. "I thought I best had, before I began to show. Jo and Kezzie came with me."

This explained Mr. Wemyss's resort to strong drink, all right. Perhaps we should have brought the jug back with us.

"Your poor father," I said again, but abstractedly. "Had the three of you worked out any sort of plan?"

"Well, no," she admitted. "I hadna told the lads I was in a family way 'til this morning, either. They seemed taken back a bit," she added, biting her lip again.

"I daresay." I glanced outside; it was still raining, but the downpour had slackened momentarily, dimpling the puddles on the path. I rubbed a hand over my face, feeling suddenly rather tired.

"Which one will you choose?" I asked.

She gave me a sudden, startled look, the blood draining from her cheeks.

"You can't have them both, you know," I said gently. "It doesn't work that way."

"Why?" she said, trying for boldness—but her voice trembled. "It's no harming anyone. And it's no one's business but ours."

I began to feel the need of a stiff drink myself.

"Hoho," I said. "Try telling your father that. Or Mr. Fraser. In a big city, perhaps you could get away with it. But here? Everything that happens is everybody's business, and you know it. Hiram Crombie would stone you for fornication as soon as look at you, if he found out about it." Without waiting for a reply, I got to my feet.

"Now, then. We'll go back to the house and see whether they're both still alive. Mr. Fraser may have taken matters into his own hands, and solved the problem for you."

THE TWINS WERE still alive, but didn't look as though they were particularly glad of the fact. They sat shoulder to shoulder in the center of Jamie's study, pressed together as though trying to reunite into a single being.

Their heads jerked toward the door in unison, looks of alarm and concern mingling with joy at seeing Lizzie. I had her by the arm, but when she saw the twins, she pulled loose and hurried to them with a small exclamation, putting an arm about each boy's neck to draw him to her bosom.

I saw that one of the boys had a fresh black eye, just beginning to puff and swell; I supposed it must be Kezzie, though I didn't know whether this was Jamie's notion of fairness, or merely a convenient means of ensuring that he could tell which twin was which while talking to them.

Mr. Wemyss was also alive, though he didn't look any more pleased about it than the Beardsleys. He was red-eyed, pale, and still slightly green about the gills, but was at least upright and reasonably sober, seated beside Jamie's table. There was a cup of chicory coffee in front of him—I could smell it—but it seemed so far untouched.

Lizzie knelt on the floor, still clinging to the boys, the three heads drawn together, like the lobes of a clover leaf, as they murmured to one another.

"Are ye hurt?" she was saying, and "Are ye all right?" they were asking, an absolute tangle of hands and arms meanwhile searching, patting, stroking, and embracing. They reminded me of nothing so much as a tenderly solicitous octopus.

I glanced at Jamie, who was viewing this behavior with a jaundiced eye. Mr. Wemyss emitted a low moan, and buried his head in his hands.

Jamie cleared his throat with a low Scottish noise of infinite menace, and the proceedings in the middle of the room stopped as though hit with some sort of paralyzing death ray. Very slowly, Lizzie turned her head to look at him, chin held high, her arms still locked protectively about the Beardsleys' necks.

"Sit down, lass," Jamie said with relative mildness, nodding toward an empty stool.

Lizzie rose, and turned, her eyes still fixed on him. She made no move to take the offered stool, though. Instead, she walked deliberately round behind the twins and stood between them, putting her hands upon their shoulders.

"I'll stand, sir," she said, her voice high and thin with fear, but filled with determination. Like clockwork, each twin reached up and grasped the hand upon his shoulder, their faces assuming similar expressions of mingled apprehension and steadfastness.

Jamie wisely decided not to make an issue of it, instead nodding to me in an offhand way. I took the stool myself, surprisingly glad to sit down.

"The lads and I have been talking wi' your father," he said, addressing Lizzie. "I take it it's true, what ye told your Da? Ye are with child, and ye dinna ken which is the father?"

Lizzie opened her mouth, but no words came out. Instead, she bobbed her head in an awkward nod.

"Aye. Well, then, ye'll need to be wed, and the sooner the better," he said, in a matter-of-fact tone of voice. "The lads couldna quite decide which of them it should be, so it's up to you, lass. Which one?"

All six hands tightened in a flash of white knuckles. It was really quite fascinating—and I couldn't help feeling sorry for the three of them.

"I can't," Lizzie whispered. Then she cleared her throat and tried again. "I can't," she repeated more strongly. "I don't—I don't want to choose. I love them both."

Jamie looked down at his clasped hands for a moment, lips pursing as he thought. Then he raised his head and looked at her, very levelly. I saw her draw herself upright, lips pressed together, trembling but resolute, determined to defy him.

Then, with truly diabolical timing, Jamie turned to Mr. Wemyss.

"Joseph?" he said mildly.

Mr. Wemyss had been sitting transfixed, eyes on his daughter, pale hands wrapped round his coffee cup. He didn't hesitate, though, or even blink.

"Elizabeth," he said, his voice very soft, "do you love *me*?"

Her facade of defiance broke like a dropped egg, tears welling from her eyes.

"Oh, Da!" she said. She let go the twins and ran to her father, who stood up in time to clasp her tightly in his arms, cheek pressed to her hair. She clung to him, sobbing, and I heard a brief sigh from one of the twins, though I couldn't tell which one.

Mr. Wemyss swayed gently with her, patting and soothing her, his murmured words indistinguishable from her sobs and broken utterances.

Jamie was watching the twins—not without sympathy. Their hands were knotted together, and Kezzie's teeth were fixed in his lower lip.

Lizzie separated herself from her father, sniffling and

groping vaguely for a handkerchief. I pulled one from my pocket, got up, and gave it to her. She blew her nose hard, and wiped her eyes, trying not to look at Jamie; she knew very well where the danger lay.

It was, however, a fairly small room, and Jamie was not a person who could be easily ignored, even in a large one. Unlike my surgery, the windows of the study were small and placed high in the wall, which gave the room under normal circumstances a pleasant dim coziness. At the moment, with the rain still coming down outside, a gray light filled the room and the air was chill.

"It's no a matter of whom ye love, now, lass," Jamie said very gently. "Not even your father." He nodded toward her stomach. "Ye've a child in your belly. Nothing else matters, but to do right by it. And that doesna mean painting its mother a whore, aye?"

Her cheeks flamed, a patchy crimson.

"I'm not a whore!"

"I didna say ye were," Jamie replied calmly. "But others will, and it gets around what ye've been up to, lass. Spreading your legs for two men, and married to neither of them? And now with a wean, and ye canna name its father?"

She looked angrily away from him—and saw her own father, head bowed, his own cheeks darkening in shame. She made a small, heartbroken sound, and buried her face in her hands.

The twins stirred uneasily, glancing at each other, and Jo got his feet under him to rise—then caught a look of wounded reproach from Mr. Wemyss, and changed his mind.

Jamie sighed heavily and rubbed a knuckle down the bridge of his nose. He stood then, stooped to the hearth, and pulled two straws from the basket of kindling. Holding these in his fist, he held them out to the twins.

"Short straw weds her," he said with resignation.

The twins gaped at him, open-mouthed. Then Kezzie swallowed visibly, closed his eyes, and plucked a straw, gingerly, as though it might be attached to something explosive. Jo kept his eyes open, but didn't look at the straw he'd drawn; his eyes were fixed on Lizzie.

Everyone seemed to exhale at once, looking at the straws.

"Verra well, then. Stand up," Jamie said to Kezzie, who held the short one. Looking dazed, he did so.

"Take her hand," Jamie told him patiently. "Now, d'ye swear before these witnesses"—he nodded at me and Mr. Wemyss—"that ye take Elizabeth Wemyss as your wife?"

Kezzie nodded, then cleared his throat and drew himself up. "I do, so," he said firmly.

"And do you, ye wee besom, accept Keziah—ye *are* Keziah?" he asked, squinting dubiously at the twin. "Aye, all right, Keziah. Ye'll take him as your husband?"

"Aye," Lizzie said, sounding hopelessly confused.

"Good," Jamie said briskly. "You're handfast. Directly we find a priest, we'll have it properly blessed, but ye're married." He looked at Jo, who had risen to his feet.

"And you," he said firmly, "ye'll leave. Tonight. Ye'll not come back 'til the child is born."

Jo was white to the lips, but nodded. He had both hands pressed to his body—not where Jamie had hit him, but higher, over his heart. I felt a sharp answering pain in the same place, seeing his face.

"Well, then." Jamie took a deep breath, his shoulders slumping a little. "Joseph—have ye still got the marriage contract ye drew for your daughter and young McGillivray? Fetch it out, aye, and we'll change the name."

Looking like a snail poking its head out after a thunderstorm, Mr. Wemyss nodded cautiously. He looked at Lizzie, still standing hand in hand with her new bridegroom, the two of them resembling Lot and Mrs. Lot, respectively. Mr. Wemyss patted her softly on the shoulder, and hurried out, his feet tapping on the stairs.

"You'll need a fresh candle, won't you?" I said to Jamie, tilting my head meaningfully toward Lizzie and the twins. The stub in his candlestick had half an inch to go, but I thought it only decent to give them a few moments of privacy.

"Oh? Oh, aye," he said, catching my meaning. He coughed. "I'll, ah, come and get it."

The moment we entered my surgery, he closed the door, leaned against it, and let his head fall, shaking it.

"Oh, God," he said.

"Poor things," I said, with some sympathy. "I mean—you do have to feel sorry for them."

"I do?" He sniffed at his shirt, which had dried but still had a distinct stain of vomit down the front, then straightened up, stretching 'til his back creaked. "Aye, I suppose I do," he admitted. "But—oh, God! Did she tell ye how it happened?"

"Yes. I'll tell you the gory details later." I heard Mr. Wemyss's feet coming down the stairs. I took down a fresh pair of candles from the array that hung near the ceiling and held them out, stretching the long wick that joined them. "Do you have a knife handy?"

His hand went automatically to his waist, but he wasn't wearing his dirk.

"No. There's a penknife on my desk, though."

He opened the door just as Mr. Wemyss reached the office. Mr. Wemyss's exclamation of shock reached me simultaneously with the smell of blood.

Jamie pushed Mr. Wemyss unceremoniously aside, and I rushed in after him, heart in my throat.

The three of them were standing by the desk, close together. A spray of fresh blood stained the desk, and Kezzie was holding my bloodied handkerchief wrapped round his hand. He looked up at Jamie, his face ghostly in the guttering light. His teeth were gritted tight together, but he managed a smile.

A small movement caught my eye, and I saw Jo, carefully holding the blade of Jamie's penknife over the candle flame. Acting as though no one was there, he took his brother's hand, pulled off the handkerchief, and pressed the hot metal against the raw oval of the wound on Kezzie's thumb.

Mr. Wemyss made a small choking noise, and the smell of seared flesh mixed with the scent of rain. Kezzie drew breath deeply, then let it out, and smiled crookedly at Jo.

"Godspeed, Brother," he said, his voice a little loud and flat.

"Much happiness to you, Brother," Jo said—in the same voice.

Lizzie stood between them, small and disheveled, her reddened eyes fixed on Jamie. And smiled.

74

SO ROMANTIC

BRIANNA DROVE THE little car slowly up the slope of the quilt over Roger's leg, across his stomach, and into the center of his chest, where he captured both the car and her hand, giving her a wry grin.

"That's a really good car," she said, pulling her hand loose and rolling comfortably onto her side beside him. "All four wheels turn. What kind is it? A Morris Minor, like that little orange thing you had in Scotland? That was the cutest thing I ever saw, but I never understood how you managed to squeeze into it."

"With talcum powder," he assured her. He lifted the toy and set a front wheel spinning with a flick of his thumb. "Aye, it *is* a good one, isn't it? It isn't really meant to be a particular model, but I suppose I was remembering that Ford Mustang of yours. Remember driving down out of the mountains that time?" His eyes softened with memory, the green of them nearly black in the dim light of the banked fire.

"I do. I nearly drove off the road when you kissed me at eighty-five miles per hour."

She moved closer to him by reflex, nudging him with a knee. He rolled obligingly to face her, and kissed her again, meanwhile running the car swiftly backward down the length of her spine and over the curve of her buttocks. She yelped and squirmed against him, trying to escape the tickling wheels, then punched him in the ribs.

"Cut that out!"

"I thought ye found speed erotic. Vroom," he murmured, steering the toy up her arm—and suddenly down the neck of her shift. She grabbed for the car, but he snatched it away, then plunged his hand under the covers, running the wheels down her thigh—then madly up again.

A furious wrestling match for possession of the car ensued, which ended with both of them on the floor in a tangle of bedding and nightclothes, gasping for breath and helpless with giggling.

"Ssh! You'll wake up Jemmy!" She heaved and wriggled, trying to get out from under Roger's weight. Secure in his fifty pounds' advantage, he merely relaxed on top of her, pinning her to the floor.

"You couldn't wake him with cannon fire," Roger said, with a certainty born of experience. It was true; once past the stage of waking to be fed every few hours, Jem had always slept like a particularly comatose log.

She subsided, puffing hair out of her eyes and biding her time.

"Do you think you'll ever go anywhere at eighty-five miles per hour again?"

"Only if I fall off the edge of a very deep gorge. Ye're naked, did ye know that?"

"Well, so are you!"

"Aye, but I started out that way. Where's the car?"

"I have no idea," she lied. It was, in fact, under the small of her back, and very uncomfortable, but she wasn't about to give him any further advantages. "What do you want it for?"

"Oh, I was going to explore the terrain a bit," he said, raising himself on one elbow and walking his fingers slowly across the upper slope of one breast. "I suppose I could do it on foot, though. Takes more time, but ye do enjoy the scenery more. They say."

"Mmm." He could hold her down with his weight, but couldn't restrain her arms. She extended one index finger, and placed the nail of it precisely on his nipple, making him breathe in deeply. "Did you have a long journey in mind?" She glanced at the small shelf near the bed, where she kept her contraceptive materials.

"Long enough." He followed her glance, then looked back to meet her eyes, a question in his own.

She wriggled to make herself more comfortable, unobtrusively dislodging the miniature car.

"They say a journey of a thousand miles begins with a single step," she said, and raising her head, put her mouth on his nipple, and closed her teeth gently. A moment later, she let go.

"Be quiet," she said reproachfully. "You'll wake up Jemmy."

"WHERE ARE your scissors? I'm cutting it off."

"I'm not telling you. I like it long." She pushed the soft dark hair back from his face and kissed the end of his nose, which appeared to disconcert him slightly. He smiled, though, and kissed her briefly back before sitting up, swiping the hair out of his face with one hand.

"That can't be comfortable," he said, eyeing the cradle. "Surely I should move him to his own bed?"

Brianna glanced up at the cradle from her position on the floor. Jemmy, aged four, had long since graduated to a trundle bed, but now and then insisted upon sleeping in his cradle for old times' sake, wedging himself stubbornly into it, despite the fact that he couldn't get all four limbs and his head inside at once. He was invisible at the moment, save for two chubby bare legs sticking straight up in the air at one end.

He was getting so big, she thought. He couldn't quite read yet, but knew all his letters, and could count to a hundred and write his name. And he knew how to load a gun; his grandfather had taught him.

"Do we tell him?" she asked suddenly. "And if so, when?"

Roger must have been thinking something along the same lines, for he appeared to understand exactly what she meant.

"Christ, how do you tell a kid something like that?" he said. He rose and picked up a handful of bedding, shaking it in apparent hopes of finding the leather string with which he bound his hair.

"Wouldn't you tell a kid if he were adopted?" she objected, sitting up and running both hands through her own bountiful hair. "Or if there's some family scandal, like his father's not dead, he's in prison? If you tell them early, it doesn't mean all that much to them, I don't think; they're comfortable with it as they get older. If they find out later, it's a shock."

He gave her a wry, sidelong look. "You'd know."

"So would you." She spoke dryly, but she felt the echo of it, even now. Disbelief, anger, denial—and then the sudden collapse of her world as she began, against her will, to believe. The sense of hollowness and abandonment—and the sense of black rage and betrayal at discovering how much of what she had taken for granted was a lie.

"At least for you, it wasn't a choice," she said, squirming into a more comfortable position against the edge of the bed. "Nobody knew about you; nobody *could* have told you what you were—but didn't."

"Oh, and ye think they should have told you about the time travel early on? Your parents?" He lifted one black brow, cynically amused. "I can see the notes coming home from your school—*Brianna has a most creative imagination, but should be encouraged to recognize situations where it is not appropriate to employ it.*"

"Ha." She kicked away the remaining tangle of clothes and bedding. "I went to a Catholic school. The nuns would have called it lying, and put a stop to it, period. Where's my shift?" She had wriggled completely out of it in the struggle, and while she was still warm from their struggle, she felt uncomfortably exposed, even in the dim shadows of the room.

"Here it is." He plucked a wad of linen from the mess and shook it out. "Do you?" he repeated, looking up at her with one brow raised.

"Think they should have told me? Yes. And no," she admitted reluctantly. She reached for the shift and pulled it over her head. "I mean—I see why they didn't. Daddy didn't believe it, to start with. And what he *did* believe . . . well, whatever it was, he did ask Mama to let me think he was my real father. She gave him her word; I guess I don't think she should have broken it, no." To the best of her knowledge, her mother had broken her word only once—unwillingly, but to staggering effect.

She smoothed the worn linen over her body and fished for the ends of the drawstring that gathered the neck. She was covered now, but felt just as much exposed as if she were still naked. Roger was sitting on the mattress, methodically shaking out the blankets, but his eyes were still fixed on her, green and questioning.

"It was still a lie," she burst out. "I had a right to know!"

He nodded slowly.

"Mmphm." He picked up a rope of twisted sheet and began unwinding it. "Aye, well. I can see telling a kid he's adopted or his dad's in prison. This is maybe more along the lines of telling a kid his father murdered his mother when he found her screwing the postie and six good friends in the kitchen, though. Maybe it doesn't mean that much to him if you tell him early on—but it's definitely going to get the attention of his friends when he starts telling *them*."

She bit her lip, feeling unexpectedly cross and prickly. She hadn't thought her own feelings were still so near the surface, and didn't like either the fact that they were—or that Roger could see that they were.

"Well . . . yes." She glanced at the cradle. Jem had moved; he was curled up like a hedgehog now, with his face pressed to his knees, and nothing visible save the curve of his bottom under his nightshirt, rising over the edge of the cradle like the moon rising above the horizon. "You're right. We'd have to wait until he's old enough to realize that he can't tell people; that it's a secret."

The leather thong fell out of a shaken quilt. He bent to pick it up, dark hair falling round his face.

"Would ye want to tell Jem someday that I'm not his real father?" he asked quietly, not looking at her.

"Roger!" All her crossness disappeared in a flood of panic. "I wouldn't do that in a hundred million years! Even if I thought it was true," she added hastily, "and I don't. Roger, I don't! I know you're his father." She sat down beside him, gripping his arm urgently. He smiled, a little crookedly, and patted her hand—but he wouldn't meet her eyes. He waited a moment, then moved, gently disengaging himself in order to tie up his hair.

"What ye said, though. Has he not got a right to know who he is?"

"That's not—it's different." It was; and yet it wasn't. The act that had resulted in her own conception hadn't been rape—but it had been just as unintended. On the other hand, there had been no doubt, either: both—well, all three—of her parents had known that she was Jamie Fraser's child, beyond doubt.

With Jem . . . she looked again at the cradle, instinctively wanting to find some stamp, some undeniable clue to his paternity. But he looked like her, and like her father, in terms both of coloring and feature. He was big for his age, long-limbed and broad-backed—but so were both of the men who might have fathered him. And both, damn them, had green eyes.

"I'm not telling him that," she said firmly. "Not ever, and neither are you. You *are* his father, in any way that matters. And there wouldn't be any good reason for him to even know that Stephen Bonnet exists."

"Save that he *does* exist," Roger pointed out. "And *he* thinks the wean is his. What if they should meet someday? When Jem's older, I mean."

She had not grown up with the habit of crossing herself at moments of stress as her father and cousin did—but she did it now, making him laugh.

"I am not being funny," she said, sitting up straight. "It's not happening. And if it did—if I ever saw Stephen Bonnet anywhere near my child, I'd . . . well, next time, I'll aim higher, that's all."

"Ye're determined to give the lad a good story for his classmates, aren't you?" He spoke lightly, teasing, and she relaxed a little, hoping that she had succeeded in easing any doubt he might have about what she might tell Jemmy regarding his paternity.

"Okay, but he does have to know the rest, sooner or later. I don't want him to find out by accident."

"You didna find out by accident. Your mother *did* tell you." *And look where we are now.* That bit went unspoken, but rang loud inside her head, as he gave her a long, straight look.

If she hadn't felt compelled to come back, go through the stones to find her real father—none of them would be here now. They'd be safe in the twentieth century, perhaps in Scotland, perhaps in America—but in a place where children didn't die of diarrhea and sudden fevers.

In a place where sudden danger didn't lurk behind every

tree and war wasn't hiding under the bushes. A place where Roger's voice still sang pure and strong.

But maybe—just maybe—she wouldn't have Jem.

"I'm sorry," she said, feeling choked. "I know it's my fault—all of it. If I hadn't come back . . ." She reached out, tentatively, and touched the ragged scar that circled his throat. He caught her hand and pulled it down.

"Christ," he said softly, "if I could have gone anywhere to find either of my parents—including hell—Brianna, I would have done it." He looked up, his eyes bright green, and squeezed her hand hard. "If there's anyone in this world who understands that, hen, it's me."

She squeezed back with both hands, hard. Relief that he didn't blame her loosened the cords of her body, but sorrow for his own losses—and hers—still filled throat and chest, heavy as wet feathers, and it hurt to breathe.

Jemmy stirred, rose suddenly upright, then fell back, still sound asleep, so that one arm flopped out of the cradle, limp as a noodle. She'd frozen at his sudden movement, but now relaxed and rose to try to tuck the arm back in. Before she could reach the cradle, though, a knock came at the door.

Roger grabbed hastily for his shirt with one hand, his knife with the other.

"Who is it?" she called, heart thumping. People didn't pay calls after dark, save in emergency.

"It's me, Miss Bree," said Lizzie's voice through the wood. "Can we come in, please?" She sounded excited, but not alarmed. Brianna waited to be sure that Roger was decently covered, then lifted the heavy bolt.

Her first thought was that Lizzie looked excited, too; the little bondmaid's cheeks were flushed as apples, the color visible even in the darkness of the stoop.

"We" was herself and the two Beardsleys, who bowed and nodded, murmuring apologies for the lateness of the hour.

"Not at all," Brianna said automatically, glancing around for a shawl. Not only was her linen shift thin and ratty, it had an incriminating stain on the front. "Er, come in!"

Roger came forward to greet the unexpected guests, magnificently disregarding the fact that he was wearing nothing but a shirt, and she scuttled hastily into the dark corner behind her loom, groping for the ancient shawl she kept there as comfort for her legs while working.

Safely wrapped in this, she kicked a log to break the fire, and stooped to light a candle from the fiery coals. In the wavering glow of the candlelight, she could see that the Beardsleys were dressed with unaccustomed neatness, their hair combed and firmly plaited, each with a clean shirt and a leather vest; they didn't own coats. Lizzie was dressed in her best, too—in fact, she was wearing the pale peach woolen dress they had made for her wedding.

Something was up, and it was fairly obvious what, as Lizzie buzzed earnestly into Roger's ear.

"Ye want me to *marry* you?" Roger said, in tones of astonishment. He glanced from one twin to the other. "Er . . . to whom?"

"Aye, sir." Lizzie bobbed a respectful curtsy. "It's me and Jo, sir, if ye'd be sae kind. Kezzie's come to be witness."

Roger rubbed a hand over his face, looking baffled.

"Well . . . but . . ." He gave Brianna a pleading look.

"Are you in trouble, Lizzie?" Brianna asked directly, lighting a second candle and putting it in the sconce by the door. With more light, she could see that Lizzie's eyelids were reddened and swollen, as though she had been crying—though her attitude was one of excited determination, rather than fear.

"Not to say trouble, exactly. But I—I'm wi' child, aye." Lizzie crossed her hands on her belly, protective. "We—we wanted to be marrit, before I tell anyone."

"Oh. Well . . ." Roger gave Jo a disapproving look, but appeared no more than half-convinced. "But your father—won't he—"

"Da would want us to be marrit by a priest," Lizzie explained earnestly. "And so we will be. But ye ken, sir, it'll be months—maybe years—before we can find one." She cast down her eyes, blushing. "I—I should like to be marrit, with proper words, ken, before the babe comes."

"Yes," he said, eyes drawn ineluctably to Lizzie's midsection. "I grasp that. But I dinna quite understand the rush, if ye take my meaning. I mean, ye won't be noticeably more pregnant tomorrow than ye are tonight. Or next week."

Jo and Kezzie exchanged glances over Lizzie's head. Then Jo put his hand on Lizzie's waist and drew her gently to him.

"Sir. It's only—we want to do right by each other. But we'd like it to be private, see? Just me and Lizzie, and my brother."

"Just us," Kezzie echoed, drawing close. He looked earnestly at Roger. "Please, sir?" He seemed to have injured his hand somehow; there was a handkerchief wound round it.

Brianna found the three of them touching almost beyond bearing; they were so innocent, and so young, the three scrubbed faces turned earnestly up to Roger in supplication. She moved closer and touched Roger's arm, warm through the cloth of his sleeve.

"Do it for them," she said softly. "Please? It's not a marriage, exactly—but you can make them handfast."

"Aye, well, but they ought to be counseled . . . her father . . ." His protests trailed off as he glanced from her toward the trio, and she could see that he was as much touched by their innocence as she was. And, she thought, privately amused, he was also very much drawn by the thought of performing his first wedding, unorthodox as it might be. The circumstances would be romantic and memorable, here in the quiet of the night, vows exchanged by the light of fire and candle, with the memory of their own lovemaking warm in the shadows and the sleeping child a silent witness, both blessing and promise for the new marriage to be made.

Roger sighed deeply, then smiled at her in resignation, and turned away.

"Aye, all right, then. Let me put my breeches on, though; I'm not conducting my first wedding bare-arsed."

ROGER HELD A spoon of marmalade over his slice of toast, staring at me.

"They *what*?" he said, in a strangled tone.

"Oh, she *didn't*!" Bree clapped a hand to her mouth, eyes wide above it, removing it at once to ask, "*Both* of them?"

"Evidently so," I said, suppressing a most disgraceful urge to laugh. "You really married her to Jo last night?"

"God help me, I did," Roger muttered. Looking thoroughly

rattled, he put the spoon in his coffee cup and stirred mechanically. "But she's handfast with Kezzie, too?"

"Before witnesses," I assured him, with a wary glance at Mr. Wemyss, who was sitting across the breakfast table, mouth open and apparently turned to stone.

"Do you think—" Bree said to me, "I mean—both of them at *once*?"

"Er, she said not," I replied, cutting my eyes toward Mr. Wemyss as an indication that perhaps this was not a suitable question to be considering in his presence, fascinating as it was.

"Oh, God," Mr. Wemyss said, in a voice from the sepulchre. "She is damned."

"Holy Mary, Mother of God." Mrs. Bug, saucer-eyed, crossed herself. "May Christ have mercy!"

Roger took a gulp of his coffee, choked, and put it down, spluttering. Brianna pounded him helpfully on the back, but he motioned her away, eyes watering, and pulled himself together.

"Now, it's maybe not so bad as it seems," he said to Mr. Wemyss, trying to find a bright side to look on. "I mean, one could maybe make a case that the twins are one soul that God's put into two bodies for purposes of His own."

"Aye, but—two bodies!" Mrs. Bug said. "Do ye think—both at *once*?"

"I don't know," I said, giving up. "But I imagine—" I glanced at the window, where the snow whispered at the closed shutter. It had begun to snow heavily the night before, a thick, wet snow; by now, there was nearly a foot of it on the ground, and I was reasonably sure that everyone at the table was imagining exactly what I was: a vision of Lizzie and the Beardsley twins, tucked up cozily in a warm bed of furs by a blazing fire, enjoying their honeymoon.

"Well, I don't suppose there's actually much anybody can *do* about it," Bree said practically. "If we say anything in public, the Presbyterians will probably stone Lizzie as a Papist whore, and—"

Mr. Wemyss made a sound like a stepped-on pig's bladder.

"Certainly no one will say anything." Roger fixed Mrs. Bug with a hard look. "Will they?"

"Well, I'll have to tell Arch, mind, or I'll burst," she said frankly. "But no one else. Silent as the grave, I swear it, de'il take me if I lie." She put both hands over her mouth in illustration, and Roger nodded.

"I suppose," he said dubiously, "that the marriage I performed isna actually valid as such. But then—"

"It's certainly as valid as the handfasting Jamie did," I said. "And besides, I think it's too late to force her to choose. Once Kezzie's thumb heals, no one will be able to tell . . ."

"Except Lizzie, probably," Bree said. She licked a smear of honey from the corner of her mouth, regarding Roger thoughtfully. "I wonder what it would be like if there were two of you?"

"We'd both of us be thoroughly bamboozled," he assured her. "Mrs. Bug—is there any more coffee?"

"Who's bamboozled?" The kitchen door opened in a swirl of snow and frigid air, and Jamie came in with Jem, both fresh from a visit to the privy, ruddy-faced, their hair and lashes thick with melting snowflakes.

"You, for one. You've just been done in the eye by a nineteen-year-old bigamist," I informed him.

"What's a bigamiss?" Jem inquired.

"A very large young lady," Roger said, taking a piece of buttered toast and thrusting it into Jem's mouth. "Here. Why don't ye take that, and . . ." His voice died away as he realized that he couldn't send Jem outside.

"Lizzie and the twins came round to Roger's last night, and he married her to Jo," I told Jamie. He blinked, water from the melting snow on his lashes running down his face.

"I will be damned," he said. He took a long breath, then realized he was still covered with snow, and went to shake himself at the hearth, bits of snow falling into the fire with a sputter and hiss.

"Well," he said, coming back to the table and sitting down beside me, "at least your grandson will have a name, Joseph. It's Beardsley, either way."

This ridiculous observation seemed actually to comfort Mr. Wemyss a bit; a small bit of color came back to his cheeks, and he allowed Mrs. Bug to put a fresh bannock on his plate.

"Aye, I suppose that's something," he said. "And I really cannot see—"

"Come *look,*" Jemmy was saying, tugging impatiently on Bree's arm. "Come see, Mama!"

"See what?"

"I wrote my name! Grandda showed me!"

"Oh, you did? Well, good for you!" Brianna beamed at him, then her brow furrowed. "What—just now?"

"Yes! Come see afore it's covered up!"

She looked at Jamie under lowered brows.

"Da, you *didn't.*"

He took a piece of fresh toast from the platter, and spread it neatly with butter.

"Aye, well," he said, "there's got to be *some* advantage still to being a man, even if no one pays a bit of heed to what ye say. Will ye pass the marmalade, Roger Mac?"

75

LICE

JEM PUT HIS elbows on the table, chin on his fists, following the path of the spoon through the batter with the intent expression of a lion watching an appetizing wildebeest on its way to the water hole.

"Don't even think about it," I said, with a glance at his grubby fingers. "They'll be done in a few minutes; you can have one then."

"But I like 'em raw, Grandma," he protested. He widened his dark-blue eyes in wordless pleading.

"You oughtn't to eat raw things," I said sternly. "They can make you sick."

"You do, Grandma." He poked a finger at my mouth,

where a smudge of brownish batter remained. I cleared my throat and wiped the incriminating evidence on a towel.

"You'll spoil your supper," I said, but with the acuity of any jungle beast, he sensed the weakening of his prey.

"Promise I won't. I'll eat everything!" he said, already reaching for the spoon.

"Yes, that's what I'm afraid of," I said, relinquishing it with some reluctance. "Just a taste, now—leave some for your daddy and grandda."

He nodded, wordless, and licked the spoon with a long, slow swipe of the tongue, closing his eyes in ecstasy.

I found another spoon and set about dropping the cookies onto the tin sheets I used for baking. We ended in a dead heat, the sheets full and the bowl quite empty, just as footsteps came down the hallway toward the door. Recognizing Brianna's tread, I snatched the empty spoon from Jemmy and rubbed a quick towel across his smudgy mouth.

Bree stopped in the doorway, her smile turning to a look of suspicion.

"What are you guys doing?"

"Making molasses cookies," I said, lifting the sheets in evidence, before sliding them into the brick oven set in the wall of the fireplace. "Jemmy's been helping me."

One neat red brow arched upward. She glanced from me to Jemmy, who was wearing a look of sublimely unnatural innocence. I gathered my own expression was no more convincing.

"So I see," she said dryly. "How much batter did you eat, Jem?"

"Who, me?" Jemmy said, eyes going wide.

"Mmm." She leaned forward, and picked a speck out of his wavy red hair. "What's this, then?"

He frowned at it, crossing his eyes slightly in the attempt to focus.

"A real big louse?" he suggested brightly. "Reckon I got it from Rabbie McLeod."

"Rabbie McLeod?" I said, uneasily aware that Rabbie had been curled up on the kitchen settle a few days ago, his unruly black curls flowing into Jemmy's bright locks as the boys slept, waiting for their fathers. I recalled thinking at the time how charming the little boys looked, curled up head to head, their faces soft with dreaming.

"Has Rabbie got lice?" Bree demanded, flicking the bit of batter away from her as though it were indeed a loathsome insect.

"Oh, aye, he's crawlin'," Jemmy assured her cheerfully. "His Mam says she's gonna get his daddy's razor and shave off ever bit of his hair, him and his brothers and his daddy and his uncle Rufe too. She says they got lice hoppin' all over their bed. She's tired of bein' ate up alive." Quite casually, he lifted a hand to his head and scratched, fingers raking through his hair in a characteristic gesture I had seen all too often before.

Bree and I exchanged a brief look of horror, then she seized Jemmy by the shoulders, dragging him over to the window.

"Come here!"

Sure enough. Exposed to the brilliant light bouncing off the snow, the tender skin behind his ears and on the back of his neck showed the characteristic pinkness caused by scratching for lice, and a quick inspection of his head revealed the worst: tiny nits clinging to the base of the hairs, and a few reddish-brown adult lice, half the size of rice grains, who scrambled madly away into the thickets. Bree caught one and cracked it between her thumbnails, tossing the remains into the fire.

"Eugh!" She rubbed her hands on her skirt, then pulled off the ribbon that tied back her hair, scratching vigorously. "Have I got them?" she asked anxiously, thrusting the crown of her head toward me.

I ruffled quickly through the thick mass of auburn and cinnamon, looking for the telltale whitish nits, then stepped back, bending my own head.

"No, have I?"

The backdoor opened, and Jamie stepped in, looking only mildly surprised to find Brianna picking through my hair like a crazed baboon. Then his head jerked up, sniffing the air.

"Is something burning?"

"I got 'em, Grandda!"

The exclamation reached me together with the scent of

singeing molasses. I jerked upright and banged my head on the edge of the dish shelf, hard enough to make me see stars.

These cleared just in time for me to see Jemmy, standing on tiptoe as he reached into the smoking oven in the wall of the hearth, well over his head. His eyes were squinched shut with concentration, his face turned away from the waves of heat coming off the brick, and he had a towel wound clumsily round the groping hand.

Jamie reached the boy with two strides, jerking him back by the collar. He reached into the oven bare-handed and yanked out a tin sheet of smoking cookies, flinging the hot sheet away with such force that it struck the wall. Small brown discs flew off and scattered over the floor.

Adso, who had been perched in the window, helping with the louse hunt, saw what looked like prey and pounced fiercely on a fleeing cookie, which promptly burned his paws. Uttering a startled yowl, he dropped it and raced under the settle.

Jamie, shaking his scorched fingers and making extremely vulgar remarks in Gaelic, had seized a stick of kindling in his other hand and was poking into the oven, trying to extract the remaining cookie-sheet amid clouds of smoke.

"What's going—hey!"

"Jemmy!"

Roger's cry coincided with Bree's. Coming in on Jamie's heels, Roger's expression of bewilderment had changed at once to alarm at sight of his offspring crouched on the floor, industriously collecting cookies, and oblivious of the fact that his trailing towel was smoldering in the ashes of the cookfire.

Roger lunged for Jemmy, colliding with Bree on the same course. The two of them cannoned into Jamie, who had just maneuvered the second sheet of cookies to the edge of the oven. He reeled, staggering off balance, and the sheet clanged into the hearth, scattering lumps of smoking, molasses-scented charcoal. The cauldron, knocked askew, swung and shifted perilously on its hook, splashing soup into the coals and sending up clouds of hissing, savory steam.

I didn't know whether to laugh or run out of the door, but settled for snatching up the towel, which had burst into flames, and beating it out on the stone-flagged hearth.

I stood up, panting, to find that my family had now managed to extricate itself from the fireplace. Roger had a squirming Jemmy in a death grip against his chest, while Bree frisked the child for burns, flames, and broken bones. Jamie, looking rather annoyed, was sucking on a blistered finger, waving smoke away from his face with his free hand.

"Cold water," I said, addressing the most immediate exigency. I grasped Jamie by the arm, pulled the finger out of his mouth, and stabbed it into the washbowl.

"Is Jemmy all right?" I asked, turning to the Happy Families tableau by the window. "Yes, I see he is. Do put him down, Roger, the child has lice."

Roger dropped Jemmy like a hot potato, and—in the usual adult reaction to hearing the word "lice"—scratched himself. Jemmy, unaffected by the recent commotion, sat down on the floor and began to eat one of the cookies he had kept clutched in his hand throughout.

"You'll spoil your—" Brianna began automatically, then caught sight of the spilled cauldron and the puddled hearth, glanced at me, and shrugged. "Got any more cookies?" she asked Jemmy. Mouth full, he nodded, reached into his shirt, and handed her one. She viewed it critically, but took a bite anyway.

"Not bad," she said, through crumbs. "Hm?" She held the remnant out to Roger, who wolfed it one-handed, using the other to poke through Jemmy's hair.

"It's going round," he said. "At least, we saw half a dozen lads near Sinclair's, all shaved like convicts. Shall we have to shave your head, then?" he asked, smiling at Jemmy and ruffling the boy's hair.

The boy's face lighted up at the suggestion.

"Will I be bald like Grandma?"

"Yes, even balder," I assured him tartly. I had in fact got a good two-inch crop at the moment, though the curliness made it look shorter, little waves and swirls hugging the curves of my skull.

"Shave his *head*?" Brianna looked aghast. She turned to me. "Isn't there any other good way to get rid of lice?"

I looked consideringly at Jemmy's head. He had the same thick, slightly wavy hair as his mother and grandfather. I glanced at Jamie, who grinned at me, one hand in the washbowl. He knew from experience just how long it took to nit-comb that sort of hair; I'd done it for him many times. He shook his head.

"Shave him," he said. "Ye'll not get a lad that size to sit still long enough to comb."

"We *could* use lard," I suggested dubiously. "You plaster his head with lard or bear grease and leave it for a few days. It suffocates the lice. Or at least you hope so."

"Ack." Brianna viewed her son's head with disfavor, obviously envisioning the havoc he could wreak on clothes and linens, if allowed to roam at large while plastered with lard.

"Vinegar and a fine-comb will get out the big ones," I said, coming to peer down at the fine white line of the parting through Jemmy's ruddy hair. "It doesn't get the nits, though; you have to scrape those off with your fingernails—or else wait 'til they hatch and comb them out."

"Shave him," Roger said, shaking his head. "Ye never get all the nits; you have to do it over again every few days, and if ye miss a few that grow big enough to hop . . ." He grinned and flicked a cookie crumb off his thumbnail; it bounced off Bree's skirt and she slapped it away, glowering at Roger.

"You're a big help!" She bit her lip, frowning, then nodded reluctantly. "All right, then, I suppose there's no help for it."

"It will grow back," I assured her.

Jamie went upstairs to fetch his razor; I went to the surgery to get my surgical scissors and a bottle of oil of lavender for Jamie's burned finger. By the time I came back, Bree and Roger had their heads together over what looked like a newspaper.

"What's that?" I asked, coming to peer over Brianna's shoulder.

"Fergus's maiden effort." Roger smiled up at me, and moved the paper so I could see. "He sent it up with a trader who left it at Sinclair's for Jamie."

"Really? That's wonderful!"

I craned my neck to see, and a small thrill went through me at sight of the bold headline across the top of the page:

THE NEW BERN UNION

Then I looked closer.

"Onion?" I said, blinking. "*The Onion*?"

"Well, he explains that," Roger said, pointing to an ornately embellished *Remarks by the Proprietor* in the center of the page, the legend upheld by a couple of floating cherubim. "It's to do with onions having layers—complexity, you see—and the . . . er"—his finger ran down the line—*"the Pungency and Savor of the Reasoned Discourse always to be exercised herein for the compleat Information and Amusement of our Purchasers and Readers."*

"I notice he makes a distinction between purchasers and readers," I remarked. "Very French of him!"

"Well, yes," Roger agreed. "There's a distinctly Gallic tone to some of the pieces, but you can see that Marsali must have had a hand in it—and, of course, most of the advertisements were written by the people who placed them." He pointed to one small item, headed, *Lost, a hat. If found in good condition, please return to the subscriber, S. Gowdy, New Bern. If not in good condition, wear it yourself.*

Jamie arrived with his razor in time to hear this, and joined in the laughter. He poked a finger down the page, at another item.

"Aye, that's good, but I think the 'Poet's Corner' is maybe my favorite. Fergus couldna have done it, I dinna think; he's no ear for rhyme at all—was it Marsali, d'ye think, or someone else?"

"Read it out loud," Brianna said, reluctantly relinquishing the paper to Roger. "I'd better clip Jemmy before he gets away and spreads lice all over Fraser's Ridge."

Once resigned to the prospect, Brianna didn't hesitate, but tied a dishcloth round Jemmy's neck and set to with the scissors in a determined fashion that sent strands of red-gold and auburn falling to the floor like shimmering rain. Meanwhile, Roger read out, with dramatic flourishes,

"On the late Act against retailing
Spirituous Liquors, etc.—
Tell me—can it be understood,
This Act intends the Publick Good?
No truly; I deny it:

For if, as all allow, 'tis best,
Of Evils Two, to chose the least,
Then my Opinion's right.
Suppose on Search—it should appear,
Ten Bunters dy'd in every year—
—By drinking to Excess
Should thousands innocent be led
Into Despair, and lose their Bread,
Such folly to redress?
I'd not be thought t'encourage sin,
Or be an Advocate of Gin;
But humbly do conceive,
This scheme, tho' drawn with nicest care
Don't with Almighty Justice square
If Scriptures we believe
When Sodom's Sin for Vengeance call'd
Ten righteous had its Doom forestall'd
And mov'd e'en God to Pity.
But now Ten bare-fac'd Debauchees
Some private Epicures displease,
And ruin half a City."

"I'd not be thought t'encourage sin/Or be an Advocate of Gin," Bree repeated, giggling. "You notice he—or she—doesn't mention whisky. What's a Bunter, though? Oops, hold still, baby!"

"A harlot," Jamie said absently, stropping his razor while still reading over Roger's shoulder.

"What's a harlot?" Jemmy asked, his radar naturally picking up the single indelicate word in the conversation. "Is it Richie's sister?"

Richard Woolam's sister Charlotte was a most attractive young person; she was also a most devout Quaker. Jamie exchanged glances with Roger, and coughed.

"No, I shouldna think it, lad," he said. "And for God's sake, don't say so, either! Here, are ye ready to be shaved?" Not waiting for an answer, he picked up the shaving brush and lathered Jemmy's polled head, to the accompaniment of delighted squeals.

"Barber, barber, shave a pig," Bree said, watching. "How many hairs to make a wig?"

"Lots," I replied, sweeping up the drifts of fallen hair and throwing them into the fire, hopefully to the destruction of all resident lice. It *was* rather a pity; Jemmy's hair was beautiful. Still, it would grow again—and the clipping showed off the lovely shape of his head, roundly pleasing as a cantaloupe.

Jamie hummed tunelessly under his breath, drawing the razor over the skin of his grandson's head with as much delicacy as if he had been shaving a honeybee.

Jemmy turned his head slightly, and I caught my breath, struck by a fleeting memory—Jamie, his hair clipped short against his skull in Paris, readying himself to meet Jack Randall; readying himself to kill—or be killed. Then Jemmy turned again, squirming on his stool, and the vision vanished—to be replaced by something else.

"Whatever is that?" I leaned forward to look, as Jamie drew his razor down with a flourish and flicked away the last dollop of lather into the fire.

"What?" Bree leaned in beside me, and her eyes widened at sight of the small brown blotch. It was about the size of a farthing, quite round, just above the hairline toward the back of his head, behind the left ear.

"What is it?" she asked, frowning. She touched it gently, but Jemmy scarcely noticed; he was squirming even more, wanting to get down.

"I'm fairly sure it's all right," I assured her, after a quick inspection. "It looks like what's called a nevus—it's something like a flat mole, usually quite harmless."

"But where did it come from? He wasn't born with it, I know!" she protested.

"Babies very seldom have any sort of mole," I explained, untying my dishcloth from round Jemmy's neck. "All right, yes, you're done! Go and be good now—we'll have supper as soon as I can manage. No," I added, turning back to Bree, "moles usually start to develop around three years of age—though of course people can get more as they grow older."

Freed from restraint, Jemmy was rubbing his naked head with both hands, looking pleased and chanting, "Char-lotte the Har-lot, Char-lotte the Har-lot," quietly under his breath.

"You're sure it's all right?" Brianna was still frowning, worried. "It isn't dangerous?"

"Oh, aye, it's nothing," Roger assured her, glancing up from the newspaper. "I've had one just like that myself, ever since I was a kid. Just . . . here." His face changed abruptly as he spoke, and his hand rose, very slowly, to rest on the back of his head—just above the hairline, behind the left ear.

He looked at me, and I saw his throat move as he swallowed, the jagged rope scar dark against the sudden paleness of his skin. The down hairs rose silently on my arms.

"Yes," I said, answering the look, and hoping my voice didn't shake too noticeably. "That sort of mark is . . . often hereditary."

Jamie said nothing, but his hand closed on mine, squeezing tight.

Jemmy was on his hands and knees now, trying to coax Adso out from under the settle. His neck was small and fragile, and his shaven head looked unearthly white and shockingly naked, like a mushroom poking out of the earth. Roger's eyes rested on it for a moment; then he turned to Bree.

"I do believe perhaps I've picked up a few lice myself," he said, his voice just a tiny bit too loud. He reached up, pulled off the thong that bound his thick black hair, and scratched his head vigorously with both hands. Then he picked up the scissors, smiling, and held them out to her. "Like father, like son, I suppose. Give us a hand here, aye?"

[illegible] and [illegible] instead.

[illegible] setting [illegible] and [illegible] like [illegible] charred [illegible] the [illegible], and his [illegible] to [illegible] the [illegible]

[illegible] and [illegible]

[illegible] with [illegible] and [illegible]

[illegible] and [illegible] and [illegible]

[illegible] his [illegible] the [illegible] with [illegible] and [illegible] her [illegible]

Part Ten

Where's Perry Mason When You Need Him?

76

DANGEROUS CORRESPONDENCE

*From Mount Josiah Plantation in the Colony of Virginia,
Lord John Grey to Mr. James Fraser, Esq.,
Fraser's Ridge, North Carolina,
upon the Sixth of March, Anno Domini 1775*

Dear Mr. Fraser—

What in the Name of God are you about? I have known you in the course of our long Acquaintance to be many Things—Intemperate and Stubborn being two of them—but have always known you for a Man of Intelligence and Honor.

Yet despite explicit Warnings, I find your Name upon more than one List of suspected Traitors and Seditionists, associated with illegal Assemblies, and thus subject to Arrest. The Fact that you are still at Liberty, my Friend, reflects nothing more than the Lack of Troops at present available in North Carolina—and that may change rapidly. Josiah Martin has implored London for Help, and it will be forthcoming, I assure you.

Was Gage not more than sufficiently occupied in Boston, and Lord Dunsmore's Virginia troops still in process of Assembly, the Army would be upon you within a few Months. Do not delude yourself; the King may be misguided in his Actions, but the Government perceives—if belatedly—the Level of Turmoil in the Colonies, and is moving as rapidly as may be to suppress it, before greater Harm can ensue.

Whatever else you may be, you are no Fool, and so I must assume you realize the Consequences of your Actions. But I would be less than a Friend did I not put the Case to you bluntly: you expose your Family to the utmost Danger by your Actions, and you put your own Head in a Noose.

For the Sake of whatever Affection you may yet bear me, and for the Sake of those dear Connexions between your Family and myself—I beg you to renounce these most dangerous Associations while there is still Time.

John

I read the letter through, then looked up at Jamie. He was sitting at his desk, papers strewn in every direction, scattered with the small brown fragments of broken sealing wax. Bobby Higgins had brought a good many letters, newspapers, and packages—Jamie had put off reading Lord John's letter 'til the last.

"He's very much afraid for you," I said, putting the single sheet of paper down on top of the rest.

Jamie nodded.

"For a man of his parts to refer to the King's actions as possibly 'misguided' is verra close to treason, Sassenach," he observed, though I *thought* he was joking.

"These lists he mentions—do you know anything about that?"

He shrugged at that, and poked through one of the untidy piles with a forefinger, pulling out a smeared sheet that had obviously been dropped in a puddle at some point.

"Like that, I suppose," he said, handing it over. It was unsigned, and nearly illegible, a misspelt and vicious denunciation of various *Outrages and Debached Persons*—here listed—whose speech, action, and appearance was a threat to all who valued peace and prosperity. These, the writer felt, should be *shown whats what,* presumably by being beaten, skinned alive, *rold in bolling Tar and plac'd on a Rail,* or in particularly pernicious cases, *Hanged outright from there own Rooftrees.*

"Where did you pick *that* up?" I dropped it on the desk, using two fingers.

"In Campbelton. Someone sent it to Farquard, as Justice of the Peace. He gave it to me, because my name is on it."

"It is?" I squinted at the straggling letters. "Oh, so it is. *J. Frayzer.* You're sure it's you? There are quite a few Frasers, after all, and not a few named John, James, Jacob, or Joseph."

"Relatively few who could be described as a *Red-haired dejenerate Pox-ridden Usuring Son of a Bitch who skulks in Brothels when not drunk and comitting Riot in the Street,* I imagine."

"Oh, I missed that part."

"It's in the exposition at the bottom." He gave the paper a brief, indifferent glance. "I think Buchan the butcher wrote it, myself."

"Always assuming that 'usuring' is a word, I don't see where he gets that bit; you haven't any money to lend."

"I wouldna suppose a basis in truth is strictly required, under the circumstances, Sassenach," he said very dryly. "And thanks to MacDonald and wee Bobby, there are a good many folk who think I *do* have money—and if I am not inclined to lend it to them, why then, plainly it's a matter of my having put my fortune all in the hands of Jews and Whig speculators, as I am intent upon ruining trade for my own profit."

"What?"

"That was a somewhat more literary effort," he said, shuffling through the pile and pulling out an elegant parchment sheet, done in a copperplate hand. This one had been sent to a newspaper in Hillsboro, and was signed, *A Friend to Justice;* and while it didn't name Jamie, it was clear who the subject of the denunciation was.

"It's the hair," I said, looking critically at him. "If you wore a wig, they'd have a much harder time of it."

He lifted one shoulder in a sardonic shrug. The commonly held view of red hair as an indicator of low character and moral coarseness, if not outright demonic possession, was by no means limited to anonymous ill-wishers. The knowledge of that view—together with personal disinclination—had quite a bit to do with the fact that he never *did* wear either wig or powder, even in situations where a proper gentleman would.

Without asking, I reached for a stack of the papers and began to leaf through them. He made no move to stop me, but sat quietly watching, listening to the thrum of the rain.

A heavy spring storm was washing down outside, and the air was cold and damp, thick with the green scents of the forest insinuating themselves through the crevices of door and window. I sometimes had the sudden feeling, hearing the wind coming through the trees, that the wilderness outside meant to come in, march through the house, and obliterate it, erasing all trace of us.

The letters were a mixed bag. Some were from the members of the North Carolina Committee of Correspondence, with bits of news, most of it from the north. Continental Association Committees had sprung up in New Hampshire and New Jersey, these bodies now beginning to virtually take over the functions of government, as the royal governors lost their grip on assemblies, courts, and Customs, the remnants of organization falling ever deeper into disarray.

Boston was still occupied by Gage's troops, and some of the letters continued the appeals for food and supplies to be sent to the succor of her citizens—we had sent two hundredweight of barley during the winter, which one of the Woolams had undertaken to get into the city, along with three wagonloads of other foodstuffs contributed by the inhabitants of the Ridge.

Jamie had picked up his quill, and was writing something, slowly, to accommodate the stiffness of his hand.

Next up was a note from Daniel Putnam, circulated through Massachusetts, noting the rising of militia companies in the countryside, and asking for arms and powder. It was signed by a dozen other men, each one bearing witness to the truth of the situation in his own township.

A Second Continental Congress was proposed, to meet in Philadelphia, the date yet undecided.

Georgia had formed a Provincial Congress, but as the Loyalist letter-writer—plainly assuming Jamie to be like-minded—triumphantly noted, *There is no Sense of Grievance toward Great Britain here, as elsewhere; Loyalist Sentiment is so strong that only five Parishes of twelve have sent anyone to this upstart and illegal Congress.*

A much-bedraggled copy of the *Massachusetts Gazette,* dated February 6, containing a letter, circled in ink and titled *The Rule of Law and the Rule of Men.* It was signed *Novanglus*—which I took to be a sort of hog-Latin for "new Englishman"—and to be a response to previous letters by a Tory who signed himself *Massachusettensis,* of all things.

I had no idea who Massachusettensis might be, but I recognized a few phrases from Novanglus's letter, from long-ago bits of Bree's schoolwork—John Adams, in good form.

"A government of laws, not of men," I murmured. "What sort of pen name would you use, if you were going to write this sort of thing?" Glancing up, I caught sight of him, looking sheepish to a degree.

"You've been doing it *already*?"

"Well, just the odd bittie letter here or there," he said defensively. "No pamphlets."

"Who are you?"

He shrugged, deprecating.

"*Scotus Americanus,* but only 'til I think of something better. There are a few others using that name, that I ken."

"Well, that's something. The King will have a harder time picking you out of the crowd." Muttering "Massachusettensis" to myself, I picked up the next document.

A note from John Stuart, much affronted by Jamie's abrupt resignation, noting that the *most illegal and prodigal Congress, as they call it* of Massachusetts had formally invited the Stockbridge Indians to enlist in the service of the colony, and informing Jamie that should any of the Cherokee follow suit, he, John Stuart, would take the greatest pleasure in personally ensuring that he, Jamie Fraser, was hanged for treason.

"And I don't suppose John Stuart even knows you have red hair," I observed, laying it aside. I felt a trifle shaky, in spite of my attempts to joke about it. Seeing it all laid out in black and white solidified the clouds that had been gathering round us, and I felt the first chilling drop of icy rain on my skin, despite the woolen shawl around my shoulders.

There was no hearth in the study; only a small brazier that we used for heat. It was burning now in the corner, and Jamie rose, picked up a stack of letters, and began to feed them to the fire, one by one.

I had a sudden rush of déjà vu, and saw him standing by the hearth in the drawing room of his cousin Jared's house in Paris, feeding letters to the fire. The stolen letters of Jacobite conspirators, rising in white puffs of smoke, the gathering clouds of a storm long past.

I remembered what Fergus had said, in answer to Jamie's instructions: *"I remember how this game is played."* So did I, and spicules of ice began to form in my blood.

Jamie dropped the last flaming fragment into the brazier, then sanded the page he had been writing, shook the sand off, and handed it to me. He had used one of the sheets of the special paper Bree had made by pressing a digested pulp of rags and plant matter between silk screens. It was thicker than the usual, with a soft, glossy texture, and she had mixed berries and tiny leaves into the pulp, so that here and there a small red stain spread like blood beneath the shadow of a leaf's silhouette.

From Fraser's Ridge, in the Colony of North Carolina,
this 16th day of March, Anno Domini 1775,
James Fraser to Lord John Grey, of Mount
Josiah Plantation,
in the Colony of Virginia

My dear John—

It is too late.

Our continued Correspondence cannot but prove a Danger to you, but it is with the greatest Regret that I sever this Link between us.

Believe me ever

Your most humble and affectionate Friend,
Jamie

I read it in silence, and handed it back. As he poked about in search of the sealing wax, I noticed a small wrapped parcel on the corner of his desk that had been hidden by the drifts of paper.

"What's this?" I picked it up; it was amazingly heavy for its size.

"A present from his Lordship, for wee Jemmy." He lit the beeswax taper from the brazier and held it over the seam of the folded letter. "A set of lead soldiers, Bobby says."

77

THE EIGHTEENTH OF APRIL

ROGER CAME AWAKE quite suddenly, with no notion what had wakened him. It was full dark, but the air had the still, inward feel of the small hours; the world holding its breath, before dawn comes on a rising wind.

He turned his head on the pillow and saw that Brianna was awake, too; she lay looking upward, and he caught the brief flicker of her eyelids as she blinked.

He moved a hand to touch her, and hers closed over it. An adjuration to silence? He lay very still, listening, but heard nothing. An ember broke in the hearth with a muffled crack and her hand tightened. Jemmy flung himself over in bed with a rustle of quilts, let out a small yelp, and fell silent. The night was undisturbed.

"What is it?" he said, low-voiced.

She didn't turn to look at him; her eyes were fixed now on the window, a dark gray rectangle, barely visible.

"Yesterday was the eighteenth of April," she said. "It's here." Her voice was calm, but there was something in it that made him move closer, so they lay side by side, touching from shoulder to foot.

Somewhere to the north of them, men were gathering in the cold spring night. Eight hundred British troops, groaning and cursing as they dressed by candlelight. Those who had gone to bed rousing to the beat of the drum passing by the houses and warehouses and churches where they quartered, those who hadn't, stumbling from dice and drink, the warm hearths of taverns, the warm arms of women, hunting lost boots and seizing weapons, turning out by twos and threes and fours, clanking and mumbling through the streets of frozen mud to the muster point.

"I grew up in Boston," she said, her voice softly conversational. "Every kid in Boston learned that poem, somewhere along the line. I learned it in fifth grade."

"Listen, my children, and you shall hear/Of the midnight ride of Paul Revere." Roger smiled, envisioning her in the uniform of Saint Finbar's parochial school, blue overall jumper, white blouse, and knee socks. He'd seen her fifth-grade school photograph once; she looked like a small, fierce, disheveled tiger that some maniac had dressed in doll's clothes.

"That's the one. *On the eighteenth of April, in Seventy-five/Hardly a man is now alive/Who remembers that famous day and year.*"

"Hardly a man," Roger echoed softly. Someone—who? A householder, eavesdropping on the British commanders quartered in his house? A barmaid, bringing mugs of pokered hot rum to a couple of sergeants? There was no keeping of secrets, not with eight hundred men on the move. It was all a matter of time. Someone had sent word from the occupied city, word that the British meant to seize the stored arms and powder in Concord, and at the same time, arrest Hancock and Samuel Adams—the founder of the Committee of Safety, the inflammatory speaker, the leaders of *this treasonous rebellion*—reported to be in Lexington.

Eight hundred men to capture two? Good odds. And a silversmith and his friends, alarmed at the news, had set out into that cold night. Bree continued:

"He said to his friend, 'If the British march
By land or sea from the town tonight,

Hang a lantern aloft in the belfry arch
Of the North Church tower as a signal light—
One if by land, and two if by sea;
And I on the opposite shore will be,
Ready to ride and spread the alarm
Through every Middlesex village and farm,
For the country folk to be up and to arm.' "

"They don't write poems like *that* anymore," Roger said. But in spite of his cynicism, he couldn't bloody help seeing it: the steam of a horse's breath, white in darkness, and across the black water, the tiny star of a lantern, high above the sleeping town. And then another.

"What happened next?" he said.

"Then he said 'Good-night!' and with muffled oar
Silently rowed to the Charlestown shore,
Just as the moon rose over the bay,
Where swinging wide at her moorings lay
The Somerset, *British man-of-war;*
A phantom ship, with each mast and spar
Across the moon like a prison bar,
And a huge black hulk, that was magnified
By its own reflection in the tide."

"Well, that's not too bad," he said judiciously. "I like the bit about the *Somerset.* Rather a painterly description."

"Shut up." She kicked him, though without real violence. "It goes on about his friend, who *wanders and watches, with eager ears*—" Roger snorted, and she kicked him again. *"Till in the silence around him he hears/The muster of men at the barrack door/The sound of arms, and the tramp of feet/And the measured tread of the grenadiers/Marching down to their boats on the shore."*

He had visited her in Boston in the spring. In mid-April, the trees would have no more than a haze of green, their branches still mostly bare against pale skies. The nights were still frigid, but the cold was somehow touched with life, a freshness moving through the icy air.

"Then there's a boring part about the friend climbing the

stairs of the church tower, but I like the next verse." Her voice, already soft, dropped a little, whispering.

"Beneath, in the churchyard, lay the dead,
In their night encampment on the hill,
Wrapped in silence so deep and still
That he could hear, like a sentinel's tread,
The watchful night-wind, as it went
Creeping along from tent to tent,
And seeming to whisper, 'All is well!'
A moment only he feels the spell
Of the place and the hour, and the secret dread
Of the lonely belfry and the dead;
For suddenly all his thoughts are bent
On a shadowy something far away,
Where the river widens to meet the bay—
A line of black that bends and floats
On the rising tide like a bridge of boats."

"Then there's a lot of stuff with old Paul killing time waiting for the signal," she said, abandoning the dramatic whisper for a more normal tone of voice. "But it finally shows up, and then . . .

"A hurry of hoofs in a village street,
A shape in the moonlight, a bulk in the dark,
And beneath, from the pebbles, in passing, a spark
Struck out by a steed flying fearless and fleet;
That was all! And yet, through the gloom and the light,
The fate of a nation was riding that night;
And the spark struck out by that steed, in his flight,
Kindled the land into flame with its heat."

"That's actually pretty good." His hand curved over her thigh, just above the knee, in case she might kick him again, but she didn't. "Do you remember the rest?"

"So he goes along by the Mystic River," Brianna said, ignoring him, "and then there are three verses, as he passes through the townships:

"It was twelve by the village clock
When he crossed the bridge into Medford town.
He heard the crowing of the cock,
And the barking of the farmer's dog,
And felt the damp of the river fog,
That rises after the sun goes down.

"It was one by the village clock,
When he galloped into Lexington.
He saw the gilded weathercock
Swim in the moonlight as he passed,
And the meeting-house windows, blank and bare,
Gaze at him with a spectral glare,
As if they already stood aghast
At the bloody work they would look upon.

"*It was two by the village clock*—and yes, I hear the clock chiming in the first lines, be quiet!" He had in fact drawn breath, but not to interrupt, only because he'd suddenly realized he'd been holding it. "*It was two by the village clock,*" she repeated,

"When he came to the bridge in Concord town.
He heard the bleating of the flock,
And the twitter of birds among the trees,
And felt the breath of the morning breeze
Blowing over the meadow brown.
And one was safe and asleep in his bed
Who at the bridge would be first to fall,
Who that day would be lying dead,
Pierced by a British musket ball.

"*You know the rest.*" She stopped abruptly, her hand tight on his.

From one moment to the next, the character of the night had changed. The stillness of the small hours had ceased, and a breath of wind moved through the trees outside. All of a sudden, the night was alive again, but dying now, rushing toward dawn.

If not actively twittering, the birds were wakeful; something called, over and over, in the nearby wood, high and sweet. And above the stale, heavy scent of the fire, he breathed the wild clean air of morning, and felt his heart beat with sudden urgency.

"Tell me the rest," he whispered.

He saw the shadows of men in the trees, the stealthy knocking on doors, the low-voiced, excited conferences—and all the while, the light growing in the east. The lap of water and creak of oars, the sound of restless kine lowing to be milked, and on the rising breeze the smell of men, stale with sleep and empty of food, harsh with black powder and the scent of steel.

And without thinking, pulled his hand from his wife's grasp, rolled over her, and pulling up the shift from her thighs, took her hard and fast, in vicarious sharing of that mindless urge to spawn that attended the imminent presence of death.

Lay on her trembling, the sweat drying on his back in the breeze from the window, heart thumping in his ears. For the one, he thought. The one who would be the first to fall. The poor sod who maybe hadn't swived his wife in the dark and taken the chance to leave her with child, because he had no notion what was coming with the dawn. This dawn.

Brianna lay still under him; he could feel the rise and fall of her breath, powerful ribs that lifted even under his weight.

"You know the rest," she whispered.

"Bree," he said very softly. "I would sell my soul to be there now."

"Shh," she said, but her hand rose, and settled on his back in what might be benediction. They lay still, watching the light grow by degrees, keeping silence.

THIS SILENCE WAS broken a quarter of an hour later, by the sound of rushing footsteps and a pounding at the door. Jemmy popped out of his blankets like a cuckoo from a clock, eyes round, and Roger heaved himself up, hurriedly brushing down his nightshirt.

It was one of the Beardsleys, face pinched and white in the gray light. He paid no attention to Roger, but cried out to

Brianna, "Lizzie's having the baby, come quick!", before dashing off in the direction of the Big House, where the figure of his brother could be seen gesticulating wildly on the porch.

Brianna flung on her clothes and burst out of the cabin, leaving Roger to deal with Jemmy. She met her mother, similarly disheveled but with a neatly packed medical kit slung over her shoulder, hurrying toward the narrow path that led past spring house and stable, into the distant woods where the Beardsleys' cabin lay.

"She should have come down last week," Claire gasped. "I told her . . ."

"So did I. She said . . ." Brianna gave up the attempt to speak. The Beardsley twins had long outdistanced them, sprinting through the wood like deer, whooping and yelling—whether from sheer excitement at their impending fatherhood, or to let Lizzie know help was on the way, she couldn't tell.

Claire had worried about Lizzie's malaria, she knew. And yet the yellow shadow that so often hung over her erstwhile bondmaid had all but disappeared during her pregnancy; Lizzie bloomed.

Nonetheless, Brianna felt her stomach clench in fear as they came into sight of the Beardsleys' cabin. The hides had been moved outside, stacked round the tiny house like a barricade, and the smell of them gave her a moment's terrible vision of the MacNeills' cabin, filled with death.

The door hung open, though, and there were no flies. She forced herself to hang back an instant, to let Claire go in first, but hurried in on her heels—to find that they were too late.

Lizzie sat up in a blood-smeared bower of furs, blinking with amazed stupefaction at a small, round, blood-smeared baby, who was regarding her with the exact same expression of open-mouthed astonishment.

Jo and Kezzie were clutching each other, too excited and afraid to speak. From the corner of her eye, Brianna saw their mouths opening and closing in syncopation, and wanted to laugh, but instead followed her mother to the bedside.

"He just popped out!" Lizzie was saying, glancing momentarily at Claire, but then jerking her fascinated gaze back to the baby, as though she expected him—yes, it was a him, Brianna saw—to disappear as suddenly as he had arrived.

"My back hurt something dreadful, all last night, so I couldna sleep, and the lads took it in turns to rub me, but it didna really help, and then when I got up to go to the privy this morning, all the water burst forth from betwixt my legs—just as ye said it would, ma'am!" she said to Claire. "And so I said to Jo and Kezzie they must run fetch ye, but I didna ken quite what to do next. So I set about to mix up batter for to make hoecake for breakfast"—she waved at the table, where a bowl of flour sat with a jug of milk and two eggs—"and next thing, I had this terrible urge to—to—" She blushed, a deep, becoming peony color.

"Well, I couldna even reach the chamber-pot. I just squatted there by the table, and—and—pop! There he was, right on the ground beneath me!"

Claire had picked the new arrival up, and was cooing reassurances to him, while deftly checking whatever it was one checked about new babies. Lizzie had made a blanket in preparation, carefully knitted of lamb's wool, dyed with indigo. Claire glanced at the pristine blanket, then pulled a length of stained, soft flannel from her kit. Wrapping the baby in it, she handed him to Brianna.

"Hold him a moment while I deal with the cord, will you, darling?" she said, pulling scissors and thread from her kit. "Then you can clean him off a bit—there's a bottle of oil in here—while I take care of Lizzie. And you lot," she added, glancing sternly at the Beardsleys, "go outside."

The baby moved suddenly inside his wrappings, startling Brianna with the sudden vivid recollection of tiny, solid limbs pushing from inside: a kick to the liver, the liquid swell and shift as head or buttocks pressed up in a hard, smooth curve beneath her ribs.

"Hallo, little guy," she said softly, cuddling him against her shoulder. He smelled strongly and strangely of the sea, she thought, and oddly fresh against the acrid pungency of the hides outside.

"Ooh!" Lizzie gave a startled squeal, as Claire kneaded her belly, and there was a juicy, slithering sort of sound. Brianna remembered that vividly, too; the placenta, that liverish, slippery afterthought of birth, almost soothing as it passed over the much-abused tissues with a sense of peaceful completion. All over, and the stunned mind began to comprehend survival.

There was a gasp from the doorway, and she looked up to see the Beardsleys, side by side and saucer-eyed.

"Shoo!" she said firmly, and flipped a hand at them. They promptly disappeared, leaving her to the entertaining task of cleaning and oiling the flailing limbs and creased body. He was a small baby, but round: round-faced, very round-eyed for a newborn—he hadn't cried at all, but was plainly awake and alert—and with a round little belly, from which the stump of his umbilical cord protruded, dark purple and fresh.

His look of astonishment had not faded; he goggled up at her, solemn as a fish, though she could feel the huge smile on her own face.

"You are so cute!" she told him. He smacked his lips in a thoughtful sort of way, and crinkled his brow.

"He's hungry!" she called over her shoulder. "Are you ready?"

"Ready?" Lizzie croaked. "Mother of God, how can ye be ready for something like *this*?", which made Claire and Brianna both laugh like loons.

Nonetheless, Lizzie reached for the little blue-wrapped bundle and put it uncertainly to her breast. There was a certain amount of fumbling and increasingly anxious grunts from the baby, but at last a suitable connection was established, making Lizzie utter a brief shriek of surprise, and everyone breathed a sigh of relief.

At this point, Brianna became aware that there had been conversation going on outside for some time—a mutter of male voices, deliberately pitched low, in a confusion of speculation and puzzlement.

"I imagine you can let them in now. Then put the griddle in the fire, if you would." Claire, beaming fondly at mother and child, was mixing the neglected batter.

Brianna poked her head out of the cabin door, to find Jo, Kezzie, her own father, Roger, and Jemmy, clustered in a knot a little distance away. They all glanced up when they saw her, with expressions ranging from vaguely shamefaced pride to simple excitement.

"Mama! Is the baby here?" Jem rushed up, pushing to get past her into the cabin, and she grabbed him by the collar.

"Yes. You can come see him, but you have to be quiet. He's very new, and you don't want to scare him, all right?"

"Him?" one of the Beardsleys asked, excited. "It's a boy?"

"I told ye so!" his brother said, nudging him in the ribs. "I said I saw a wee prick!"

"You don't say things like 'prick' in front of ladies," Jem informed him severely, turning to frown at him. "And Mama says be quiet!"

"Oh," said the Beardsley twin, abashed. "Oh, aye, to be sure."

Moving with an exaggerated caution that made her want to laugh, the twins tiptoed into the cabin, followed by Jem, Jamie's hand firm on his shoulder, and Roger.

"Is Lizzie all right?" he asked softly, pausing to kiss her briefly in passing.

"A little overwhelmed, I think, but fine."

Lizzie was in fact sitting up, soft blond hair now combed and shining around her shoulders, glowing with happiness at Jo and Kezzie, who knelt at her bedside, grinning like apes.

"May the blessing of Bride and of Columba be on you, young woman," Jamie said formally in Gaelic, bowing to her, "and may the love of Christ sustain you always in your motherhood. May milk spring from your breasts like water from the rock and may you rest secure in the arms of your"—he coughed briefly, glancing at the Beardsleys—"husband."

"If you can't say 'prick,' why can you say 'breasts'?" Jemmy inquired, interested.

"Ye can't, unless it's a prayer," his father informed him. "Grandda was giving Lizzie a blessing."

"Oh. Are there any prayers with pricks in them?"

"I'm sure there are," Roger replied, carefully avoiding Brianna's eye, "but ye don't say them out loud. Why don't ye go and help Grannie with the breakfast?"

The iron griddle was sizzling with fat, and the fragrant smell of fresh batter filled the room as Claire began to pour spoonfuls onto the hot metal.

Jamie and Roger, having presented their compliments to Lizzie, had stepped back a bit, to give the little family a moment to themselves—though the cabin was so small, there was barely room for everyone to fit inside.

"You are so beautiful," Jo—or possibly Kezzie—whispered, touching her hair with an awed forefinger. "Ye look like the new moon, Lizzie."

"Did it hurt ye very much, sweetheart?" murmured Kezzie—or maybe Jo—stroking the back of her hand.

"Not so much," she said, stroking Kezzie's hand, then lifting her palm to cup Jo's cheek. "Look. Is he no the bonniest wee creature ye've ever seen?" The baby had drunk his fill and fallen asleep; he let go the nipple with an audible *pop!* and rolled back in his mother's arm like a dormouse, mouth a little open.

The twins made identical soft sounds of awe, and looked doe-eyed at their—well, what else could one say? Brianna thought—their son.

"Oh, such dear wee fingers!" Kezzie—or Jo—breathed, touching the little pink fist with a dirty forefinger.

"Is he all there?" Jo—or Kezzie—asked. "Ye've looked?"

"I have," Lizzie assured him. "Here—d'ye want to hold him?" Not pausing for assent, she put the bundle into his arms. Whichever twin it was looked at once thrilled and terrified, and glanced wildly at his brother for support.

Brianna, enjoying the tableau, felt Roger close behind her.

"Aren't they sweet?" she whispered, reaching back for his hand.

"Oh, aye," he said, a smile in his voice. "Enough to make ye want another, isn't it?"

It was an innocent remark; she could tell he had meant nothing by it—but he heard the echo, even as she did, and coughed, letting go her hand.

"Here—that's for Lizzie." Claire was handing a plate of fragrant cakes, drizzled with butter and honey, to Jem. "Is anyone else hungry?"

The general stampede in response to this enabled Brianna to hide her feelings, but they were still there—and painfully clear, if still tangled.

Yes, she *did* want another baby, thank you, she thought

fiercely at Roger's oblivious back. In the instant of holding the newborn child, she wanted it with a yearning of flesh that surpassed hunger or thirst. And she would have loved to blame him for the fact that it hadn't happened yet.

It had taken a true leap of faith, across the vertiginous abyss of knowledge, for her to put aside her *dauco* seeds, those fragile pellets of protection. But she'd done it. And nothing. Lately, she'd been thinking uneasily of what Ian had told her about his wife and their struggles to conceive. True, she had suffered no miscarriage, and was profoundly grateful for that. But the part he had told her, where their lovemaking became more mechanical and desperate—*that* was beginning to loom like a specter in the distance. It hadn't gotten that bad yet—but more often than not, she turned into Roger's arms, thinking, *Now? Will it be this time?* But it never was.

The twins were becoming more comfortable with their offspring, their dark heads pressed close together, tracing the chubby outlines of his sleeping features and wondering aloud who he most resembled, of all idiotic things.

Lizzie was single-mindedly devouring her second plate of hoecakes, accompanied by grilled sausages. The smell was wonderful, but Brianna wasn't hungry.

It was a good thing that they knew for sure, she told herself, watching Roger take his turn to hold the baby, his dark, lean face softening. If there had still been any doubt that Jemmy was Roger's child, he would have blamed himself as Ian did, thought there was something wrong with him. As it was . . .

Had something happened to *her*? she wondered uneasily. Had Jemmy's birth damaged something?

Jamie was holding the new baby now, one big hand cradling the round little head, smiling down with that look of soft affection so peculiar—and endearing—to men. She did long to see that look on Roger's face, holding his own newborn child.

"Mr. Fraser." Lizzie, filled at last with sausages, put aside her empty plate and leaned forward, looking earnestly up at Jamie. "My father. Does—does he know?" She couldn't help glancing at the empty doorway behind him.

Jamie looked momentarily disconcerted.

"Ah," he said, and handed the baby carefully to Roger,

clearly taking advantage of the pause to try to think of some less-hurtful way to phrase the truth.

"Aye, he kens the babe was on the way," he said carefully. "I told him."

And he had not come. Lizzie's lips pressed together, and a shadow of unhappiness crossed the new-moon glow of her face.

"Had we—had I—one of us—best go and tell him, sir?" one of the twins asked hesitantly. "That the child's here, I mean, and . . . and that Lizzie's all right."

Jamie hesitated, clearly uncertain whether that would be a good idea or not. Mr. Wemyss, pale and ill-looking, had not referred to his daughter, his putative sons-in-law, or his theoretical grandchild since the imbroglio surrounding Lizzie's multiple weddings. Now that the grandchild was a concrete fact, though . . .

"Whatever he thinks he *ought* to do," Claire said, her face slightly troubled, "he'll *want* to know that they're all right, surely."

"Oh, aye," Jamie agreed. He glanced dubiously at the twins. "I'm just no entirely sure it should be Jo or Kezzie to tell him, though."

The twins exchanged a long glance, in which some decision seemed to be reached.

"It should, sir," one of them said firmly, turning to Jamie. "The baby's ourn, but it's his blood, too. That's a link between us; he'll know that."

"We don't want him to be crosswise with Lizzie, sir," his brother said, more soft-spoken. "It hurts her. Might be the baby would . . . ease things, d'ye think?"

Jamie's face betrayed nothing other than a studied attention to the matter at hand, but Brianna saw him dart a quick glance at Roger before returning his gaze to the bundle in Roger's arm, and she hid a smile. He had certainly not forgotten his own acrimonious first response to Roger, but it had been Roger's claiming of Jem that had established the first—and very fragile—link in the chain of acceptance that she thought now bound Roger nearly as close to Jamie's heart as she herself.

"Aye, then," Jamie said, still reluctant. He very much disliked being involved in this situation, she could tell—but hadn't yet succeeded in figuring out any way of dealing with it. "Go and tell him. Just the one of ye, though! And should he come, t'other of ye keep well out of his sight, d'ye hear me?"

"Oh, aye, sir," both of them assured him in unison. Jo—or Kezzie—frowned a little at the bundle, and hesitantly extended his arms. "Should I—"

"No, don't." Lizzie was sitting bolt upright, her arms braced to keep her weight off her tender nether parts. Her small fair brow was set in a frown of determination. "Tell him we're well, aye. But if he wants to see the bairn—he'll come, and welcome. But if he'll no set foot upon my threshold . . . well, then, he's no welcome to see his grandson. Tell him," she repeated, easing herself back upon her pillows.

"Now give my bairnie to me." She held out her arms, and clutched the sleeping baby to her, closing her eyes against any possibility of argument or reproach.

78

THE UNIVERSAL BROTHERHOOD OF MAN

BRIANNA LIFTED THE waxed cloth covering one of the big earthenware basins, and sniffed, taking pleasure in the musty, turned-earth smell. She stirred the pale mess with a stick, lifting it out periodically in order to assess the texture of the pulp that dripped from it.

Not bad. Another day, and it would be dissolved enough to press. She considered whether to add more of the dilute sulfuric acid solution, but decided against it, and instead reached into the bowl at her side, filled with the limp petals of dogwood and redbud flowers gathered for her by Jemmy and

Aidan. She scattered a handful of these delicately over the grayish pulp, stirred them in, then covered the bowl again. By tomorrow, they'd be no more than faint outlines, but still visible as shadows in the finished sheets of paper.

"I'd always heard that paper mills stank." Roger made his way through the bushes toward her. "Perhaps they use something else in the making?"

"Be glad I'm not tanning hides," she advised him. "Ian says the Indian women use dog turds for that."

"So do European tanners; they just call the stuff 'pure.'"

"Pure what?"

"Pure dog turds, I suppose," he said with a shrug. "How's it going?"

Coming up beside her, he looked with interest at her own small paper factory: a dozen big, fired-clay basins, each filled with scraps of used paper, worn-out scraps of silk and cotton, flax fibers, the soft pith of cattail reeds, and anything else she could get her hands on that might be useful, torn to shreds or ground small in a quern. She'd dug out a small seep, and laid one of her broken water pipes as a catch basin, to provide a convenient water supply; nearby, she'd built a platform of stone and wood, on which stood the framed silk screens in which she pressed the pulp.

There was a dead moth floating in the next bowl, and he reached to take it out, but she waved him away.

"Bugs drown in it all the time, but as long as they're soft-bodied, it's okay. Enough sulfuric acid"—she nodded at the bottle, stoppered with a bit of rag—"and they all just become part of the pulp: moths, butterflies, ants, gnats, lacewings . . . wings are the only things that won't dissolve all the way. Lacewings look sort of pretty embedded in the paper, but not roaches." She fished one of these out of a bowl and flicked it away into the bushes, then added a little more water from the gourd dipper, stirring.

"I'm not surprised. I stamped on one of them this morning; he flattened out, then popped back up and strolled off, smirking." He paused a moment; he wanted to ask her something, she could tell, and she made an interrogative hum to encourage him.

"I was only wondering—would ye mind taking Jem up to

the Big House after supper? Perhaps the two of ye spending the night?"

She looked at him in astonishment.

"What are you planning to do? Throw a stag party for Gordon Lindsay?" Gordon, a shy boy of about seventeen, was betrothed to a Quaker girl from Woolam's Mill; he'd been round the day before to "thig"—beg small bits of household goods in preparation for his marriage.

"No girls popping out of cakes," he assured her, "but it's definitely men only. It's the first meeting of the Fraser's Ridge Lodge."

"Lodge . . . what, Freemasons?" She squinted dubiously at him, but he nodded. The breeze had come up, and it whipped his black hair up on end; he smoothed it back with one hand.

"Neutral ground," he explained. "I didna want to suggest holding meetings in either the Big House or Tom Christie's place—not wanting to favor either side, ye might say."

She nodded, seeing that.

"Okay. But why Freemasons?" She knew nothing whatever about Freemasons, save that they were some sort of secret society and that Catholics weren't allowed to join.

She mentioned this particular point to Roger, who laughed.

"True," he said "The Pope forbade it about forty years ago."

"Why? What does the Pope have against Freemasons?" she asked, interested.

"It's rather a powerful body. A good many men of power and influence belong—and it crosses international lines. I imagine the Pope's actual concern is competition in terms of power-broking—though if I recall aright, his stated reason was that Freemasonry is too much like a religion itself. Oh, that, and they worship the devil."

He laughed.

"Ye did know your father started a Lodge at Ardsmuir, in the prison there?"

"Maybe he mentioned it; I don't remember."

"I did bring up the Catholic thing with him. He gave me one of those looks of his and said, 'Aye, well, the Pope wasna in Ardsmuir Prison, and I was.'"

"Sounds reasonable to me," she said, amused. "But then, I'm not the Pope. Did he say why? Da, I mean, not the Pope."

"Sure—as a means of uniting the Catholics and Protestants imprisoned together. One of the principles of Freemasonry being the universal brotherhood of man, aye? And another being that ye don't talk religion or politics in Lodge."

"Oh, you don't? What do you do in Lodge, then?"

"I can't tell you. Not worshipping the devil, though."

She raised her eyebrows at him, and he shrugged.

"I can't," he repeated. "When ye join, you take an oath not to talk outside the Lodge about what's done there."

She was mildly miffed at that, but dismissed it, going back to add more water to one bowl. It looked as though someone had thrown up in it, she thought critically, and reached for the acid bottle.

"Sounds pretty fishy to me," she remarked. "And kind of silly. Isn't there something about secret handshakes, that sort of thing?"

He merely smiled, not bothered by her tone.

"I'm not saying there isn't a bit of stage business involved. It's more or less medieval in origin, and it's kept quite a bit of the original trappings—rather like the Catholic Church."

"Point taken," she said dryly, picking up a ready bowl of pulp. "Okay. So, is it Da's idea to start a Lodge here?"

"No, mine." His voice lost its humorous tone, and she looked at him sharply.

"I need a way to give them common ground, Bree," he said. "The women have it—the fishers' wives sew and spin and knit and quilt wi' the others, and if they privately think you or your mother or Mrs. Bug are heretics damned to hell, or goddamned Whigs, or whatever, it seems to make no great difference. But not the men."

She thought of saying something about the relative intelligence and common sense of the two sexes, but feeling that this might be counterproductive just at the moment, nodded understanding. Besides, he obviously had no notion of the kind of gossip that went on in sewing circles.

"Hold that screen steady, will you?"

He obligingly grasped the wooden frame, pulling taut the edges of the finely drawn wire threaded through it, as instructed.

"So," she said, spooning the thin gruel of the pulp onto the silk, "do you want me to provide milk and cookies for this affair tonight?"

She spoke with considerable irony, and he smiled across the screen at her.

"That'd be nice, aye."

"I was joking!"

"I wasn't." He was still smiling, but with complete seriousness behind his eyes, and she realized suddenly that this wasn't a whim. With an odd small twist of the heart, she saw her father standing there.

One had known the care of other men from his earliest years, a part of the duty of his birthright; the other had come to it later, but both felt that burden to be the will of God, she had no doubt at all—both accepted that duty without question, would honor it, or die in trying. She only hoped it wouldn't come to that—for either of them.

"Give me one of your hairs," she said, looking down to hide what she felt.

"Why?" he asked, but was plucking a strand from his head even as he spoke.

"The paper. The pulp shouldn't be spread any thicker than a hair." She laid the black thread at the edge of the silk screen, then spread the creamy liquid thin and thinner, so it flowed past the hair but did not cover it. It flowed with the liquid, a sinuous dark line through the white, like the tiny crack on the surface of her heart.

79

ALARMS

L'OIGNON–INTELLIGENCER

A MARRIAGE IS ANNOUNCED. The NEW BERN INTELLIGENCER, founded by Jno. Robinson, has ceased publication with the removal of its founder to Great Britain, but we assure its Customers that this Newspaper shall not vanish altogether, as its Premises, Stock, and Subscription Lists have been acquired by the Proprietors of THE ONION, that esteemed, popular, and Preeminent Journal. The New Periodical, Much Improved and Expanded, will henceforth appear as the L'OIGNON–INTELLIGENCER, distributed upon a Weekly Basis, with Extra Editions as events demand, these provided at a modest cost of One Penny. . . .

To Mr. and Mrs. James Fraser, of the Ridge,
North Carolina, from Mr. and Mrs. Fergus Fraser,
Thorpe Street, New Bern

Dear Father and Mother Claire:

I write to acquaint you with the latest Change in our Fortunes. Mr. Robinson, who had owned the other Newspaper in the town, found himself removed to Great Britain. Literally removed, as some Persons unknown, disguised as Savages, invaded his Shop in the early Hours of the Morning, and pulled him from his Bed, hurrying him to the Harbor and there thrusting him aboard a Ship, clad only in his Nightclothes and Cap.

The Captain promptly cast off his Tethers and made Sail, leaving the Town in some Uproar, as you may imagine.

Within a Day of Mr. Robinson's abrupt Departure, though, we were visited by two separate Parties (I cannot write their Names, being discreet as you will appreciate). One of these was a Member of the local Committee of Safety—which everyone knows was behind Mr. Robinson's Removal, but no one says so. He was civil in his Speech, but his manner was not so much. He wished, he said, to assure himself that Fergus did not share the Willfully Wrongheaded Sentiments so oft expressed by Mr. Robinson, regarding recent Events and Particulars.

Fergus told him with a very straight face that he would not chuse to share so much as a Glass of Wine with Mr. Robinson (which he could not, Mr. Robinson being Methody and against Drink), and the Gentleman took this to mean what he wished, and went away satisfied, and gave Fergus a Purse of Money.

Next thing comes another Gentleman, fat and most Important in the Affairs of the Town, and a Member of the Royal Council, though I did not know it at the time. His Errand was the Same—or rather, the Opposite: he wished to inquire whether Fergus was inclined to acquire Mr. Robinson's Assets, so to continue his work on behalf of the King—that being the printing of some Letters, and the Suppression of Others.

Fergus says to this Gentleman, most grave, that he has always found Much to admire in Mr. Robinson (chiefly his horse, which is gray and very amiable, and the curious Buckles on his Shoes), but adding that we have barely Means to buy Ink and Paper, and so he feared we must resign ourselves to the Acquisition of Mr. Robinson's Shop by a Person of no great Sensitivity in Politickal Matters.

I was myself in Terror, a State not improved when the Gentleman uttered a Laugh and took a fat Purse from his Pocket, remarking that one must not "spoil the ship for a happeny's worth of tar." He seemed to think this most amusing, and laughed quite immoderate, then patted Henri-Christian on the Head and went away.

So our Prospects are at once enlarged and alarming. I am fair sleepless, thinking on the Future, but Fergus is so much Improved in Spirits that I cannot regret it.

Pray for us, as we pray for you always, my Dear Parents.

Your Obedient and Loving Daughter,
Marsali

"You taught him well," I remarked, trying to keep my voice casual.

"Evidently so." Jamie looked slightly worried, but much more amused. "Dinna fash yourself over it, Sassenach. Fergus has some skill at this game."

"It is not a game," I said, with enough vehemence that he looked at me in surprise.

"It's not," I repeated, a little more calmly.

He raised his brows at me, and pulling a small sheaf of papers from the mess on his desk, handed them across.

WEDNESDAY MORNING
NEAR 10 OF THE CLOCK—WATERTOWN

To all the friends of American liberty be it known that this morning before break of day, a brigade, consisting of about 1,000 to 1,200 men landed at Phip's Farm at Cambridge and marched to Lexington, where they found a company of our colony militia in arms, upon whom they fired without any provocation and killed six men and wounded four others. By an express from Boston, we find another brigade are now upon their march from Boston supposed to be about 1,000. The Bearer, Israel Bissell, is charged to alarm the country quite to Connecticut and all persons are desired to furnish him with fresh horses as they may be needed. I have spoken with several persons who have seen the dead and wounded. Pray let the delegates from this colony to Connecticut see this.

J. Palmer, one of the Committee of Safety.

They know Col. Foster of Brookfield one of the Delegates.

Beneath this message was a list of signatures, though most were done in the same handwriting. The first read *A true copy taken from the original per order of the Committee of Correspondence for Worcester—April 19, 1775. Attest. Nathan Baldwin, Town Clerk.* All the others were preceded by similar statements.

"I will be damned," I said. "It's the Lexington Alarm." I glanced up at Jamie, wide-eyed. "Where did you get it?"

"One of Colonel Ashe's men brought it." He shuffled to the end of the last sheet, pointing out John Ashe's endorsement. "What is the Lexington Alarm?"

"That." I looked at it with fascination. "After the battle at Lexington, General Palmer—he's a general of militia—wrote this and sent it through the countryside by an express rider, to bear witness to what had happened; to notify the militias nearby that the war had started.

"Men along the way took copies of it, endorsed them to swear that they were true copies, and sent the message along to other townships and villages; there were probably hundreds of copies made at the time, and quite a few survived. Frank had one that someone gave him as a present. He kept it in a frame, in the front hall of our house in Boston."

Then a quite extraordinary shudder went through me, as I realized that the familiar letter I was looking at had in fact been written only a week or two before—not two hundred years.

Jamie was looking a little pale, too.

"This—it's what Brianna told me would happen," he said, a tone of wonder in his voice. "Upon the nineteenth of April, a fight in Lexington—the start of the war." He looked straight at me, and I saw that his eyes were dark, with a combination of awe and excitement.

"I did believe ye, Sassenach," he said. "But . . ."

He didn't finish the sentence, but sat down, reaching for his quill. With slow deliberation, he signed his name at the foot of the page.

"Ye'll make me a fair copy, Sassenach?" he said. "I'll send it on."

80

THE WORLD TURNED UPSIDE DOWN

COLONEL ASHE'S MAN had also brought word of a congress to be held in Mecklenberg County, to take place in mid-May, with the intent to declare the county's official independence from the King of England.

Aware of the fact that he was still viewed with skepticism by not a few leaders of what had now suddenly become "the rebellion," despite the stout personal support of John Ashe and a few other friends, Jamie made up his mind to attend this congress and speak openly in support of the measure.

Roger, absolutely blazing with suppressed excitement at this, his first chance to witness recorded history in the making, was to go with him.

A few days before their scheduled departure, though, everyone's attention was distracted from the prospect of history by the more immediate present: the entire Christie family arrived suddenly at the front door, soon after breakfast.

Something had happened; Allan Christie was flushed with agitation, Tom grim and gray as an old wolf. Malva had clearly been crying, and her face went red and white by turns.

I greeted her, but she looked away from me, lips trembling, as Jamie invited them into his study, gesturing them to sit.

"What is it, Tom?" He glanced briefly at Malva—plainly she was the focus of this family emergency—but gave his attention to Tom, as patriarch.

Tom Christie's mouth was pressed so tight that it was barely visible in the depths of his neatly clipped beard.

"My daughter finds herself with child," he said abruptly.

"Oh?" Jamie cast another brief glance at Malva—who stood with capped head bowed, looking down at her clasped hands—then looked at me with a raised eyebrow. "Ah. Well . . . there's a good bit of it going about, to be sure," he said, and smiled kindly, in an effort to ease the Christies, all of whom were quivering like beads on a tight-pulled wire.

I was myself less than startled to hear the news, though naturally concerned. Malva had always attracted a great deal of attention from young men, and while both her brother and father had been vigilant in preventing any open courting, the only way of keeping young men away altogether would have been to lock her in a dungeon.

Who had the successful suitor been? I wondered. Obadiah Henderson? Bobby, perhaps? One of the McMurchie brothers? Not—please God—both of them, I hoped. All of these—and not a few others—had been obvious in their admiration.

Tom Christie received Jamie's attempt at pleasantry with stony silence, though Allan made a poor attempt at a smile. He was nearly as pale as his sister.

Jamie coughed.

"Well, so. Is there some way in which I might help, then, Tom?"

"She says," Christie began gruffly, with a piercing look at his daughter, "that she will not name the man, save in your presence." He turned the look on Jamie, thick with dislike.

"In my presence?" Jamie coughed again, clearly embarrassed at the obvious implication—that Malva thought her male relatives would either beat her or proceed to do violence upon her lover, unless the presence of the landlord constrained them. Personally, I thought that particular fear was probably well founded, and gave Tom Christie a narrow look of my own. Had he already tried, and failed, to beat the truth out of her?

Malva was not making any attempt at divulging the name of the father of her child, Jamie's presence notwithstanding. She merely pleated her apron between her fingers, over and over, eyes fixed on her hands.

I cleared my throat delicately.

"How—um—how far gone are you, my dear?"

She didn't answer directly, but pressed both hands, shaking, against her apron front, smoothing down the cloth so that the round bulge of her pregnancy was suddenly visible, smooth and melonlike, surprisingly large. Six months, perhaps; I was startled. Clearly, she'd delayed telling her father for as long as she possibly could—and hidden it well.

The silence was well beyond awkward. Allan shifted uncomfortably on his stool, and leaned forward to murmur reassuringly to his sister.

"It'll be all right, Mallie," he whispered. "Ye've got to say, though."

She took a huge gulp of air at that, and raised her head. Her eyes were reddened, but still very beautiful, and wide with apprehension.

"Oh, sir," she said, but then stopped dead.

Jamie was by now looking nearly as uncomfortable as the Christies, but did his best to keep his air of kindness.

"Will ye not tell me, then, lass?" he said, as gently as possible. "I promise ye'll not suffer for it."

Tom Christie made an irritable noise, like some beast of prey disturbed at its meal, and Malva went very pale indeed, but her eyes stayed fixed on Jamie.

"Oh, sir," she said, and her voice was small but clear as a bell, ringing with reproach. "Oh, sir, how can ye say that to me, when ye ken the truth as well as I do?" Before anyone could react to that, she turned to her father, and lifting a hand, pointed directly at Jamie.

"It was him," she said.

I HAVE NEVER been so grateful for anything in life as for the fact that I was looking at Jamie's face when she said it. He had no warning, no chance to control his features—and he didn't. His face showed neither anger nor fear, denial or surprise; nothing save the open-mouthed blankness of absolute incomprehension.

"What?" he said, and blinked, once. Then realization flooded into his face.

"WHAT?" he said, in a tone that should have knocked the little trollop flat on her lying little bottom.

She blinked then, and cast down her eyes, the very picture of virtue shamed. She turned, as though unable to bear his gaze, and stretched out a tremulous hand toward me.

"I'm *so* sorry, Mrs. Fraser," she whispered, tears trembling becomingly on her lashes. "He—we—we didna mean to hurt ye."

I watched with interest from somewhere outside my body, as my arm lifted and drew back, and felt a sense of vague approval as my hand struck her cheek with enough force that she stumbled backward, tripped over a stool, and fell, her petticoats tumbled up to her waist in a froth of linen, woolstockinged legs sticking absurdly up in the air.

"Can't say the same, I'm afraid." I hadn't even thought of saying anything, and was surprised to feel the words in my mouth, cool and round as river stones.

Suddenly, I was back in my body. I felt as though my stays had tightened during my temporary absence; my ribs ached with the effort to breathe. Liquid surged in every direction; blood and lymph, sweat and tears—if I did draw breath, my skin would give way and let it all spurt out, like the contents of a ripe tomato, thrown against a wall.

I had no bones. But I had will. That alone held me upright and saw me out the door. I didn't see the corridor or realize that I had pushed open the front door of the house; all I saw was a sudden blaze of light and a blur of green in the dooryard and then I was running, running as though all the demons of hell coursed at my heels.

In fact, no one pursued me. And yet I ran, plunging off the trail and into the wood, feet sliding in the layers of slippery needles down the runnels between stones, half-falling down the slope of the hill, caroming painfully off fallen logs, wrenching free of thorns and brush.

I arrived breathless at the bottom of a hill and found myself in a dark, small hollow walled by the towering black-green of rhododendrons. I paused, gasping for breath, then sat down abruptly. I felt myself wobble, and let go, ending on my back among the dusty layers of leathery mountain laurel leaves.

A faint thought echoed in my mind, under the sound of my gasping breath. *The guilty flee, where no man pursues.* But *I* surely wasn't guilty. Nor was Jamie; I knew that. Knew it.

But Malva was certainly pregnant. Someone was guilty.

My eyes were blurred from running and the sunlight starred into fractured slabs and streaks of color—dark blue, light blue, white and gray, pinwheels of green and gold as the cloudy sky and the mountainside spun round and round above me.

I blinked hard, unshed tears sliding down my temples.

"Bloody, bloody, fucking hell," I said very softly. "Now what?"

JAMIE STOOPED without thought, seized the girl by the elbows, and hauled her unceremoniously to her feet. Her one cheek bore a crimson patch where Claire had struck her, and for an instant, he had a strong urge to give her one to match on the other side.

He hadn't the chance either to quell that desire or to execute it; a hand seized his shoulder to yank him round, and it was reflex alone that made him dodge aside as Allan Christie's fist glanced off the side of his head, catching him painfully on the tip of the ear. He pushed the young man hard in the chest with both hands, then hooked a heel behind his calf as he staggered, and Allan dropped on his backside with a thud that shook the room.

Jamie stepped back, a hand to his throbbing ear, and glared at Tom Christie, who was standing staring at him like Lot's wife.

Jamie's free left hand was clenched in a fist, and he raised it a little, in invitation. Christie's eyes narrowed further, but he made no move toward Jamie.

"Get up," Christie said to his son. "And keep your fists to yourself. There's nay need for that now."

"Isn't there?" cried the lad, scrambling to his feet. "He's

made a whore of your daughter, and you'll let him stand? Well, and ye'll play coward, auld man, I'll not!"

He lunged at Jamie, wild-eyed, hands grabbing for his throat. Jamie stepped to the side, shifted weight back on one leg, and hooked the lad in the liver with a vicious left that drove his wame into his backbone and doubled him over with a *whoof.* Allan stared up at him, open-mouthed and the whites of his eyes showing all round, then subsided onto his knees with a thud, mouth opening and closing like a fish's.

It might have been comical under other circumstances, but Jamie felt no disposition to laugh. He wasted no more time on either of the men, but swung round on Malva.

"So, what mischief is this ye're about, *nighean na galladh*?" he said to her. It was a serious insult, and Tom Christie knew what it meant, Gaelic or not; Jamie could see Christie stiffen, in the corner of his eye.

The girl herself was already in tears, and burst into sobs at this.

"How can ye speak to me so?" she wailed, and clutched her apron to her face. "How can ye be so cruel?"

"Oh, for God's sake," he said crossly. He shoved a stool in her direction. "Sit, ye wee loon, and we'll hear the truth of whatever ye think ye're up to. Mr. Christie?" He glanced at Tom, nodded toward another stool, and went to take his own chair, ignoring Allan, who had collapsed onto the floor and was curled up on his side like a kitten, holding his belly.

"Sir?"

Mrs. Bug, hearing the racket, had come out from her kitchen, and was standing in the doorway, eyes wide under her cap.

"Will ye . . . be needin' anything, sir?" she asked, making no pretense of not staring from Malva, red-faced and sobbing on her stool, to Allan, white and gasping on the floor.

Jamie thought that he needed a strong dram—or maybe two—but that would have to wait.

"I thank ye, Mrs. Bug," he said politely, "but no. We'll bide." He lifted his fingers in dismissal, and she faded reluctantly from view. She hadn't gone far, though, he knew, just round the edge of the door.

He rubbed a hand over his face, wondering what it was

about young girls these days. It was a full moon tonight; perhaps they truly did run lunatic.

On the other hand, the wee bitch had undoubtedly been playing the loon with *someone;* with her apron up like that, the bairn was showing plainly, a hard round swell like a calabash under her thin petticoat.

"How long?" he asked Christie, with a nod toward her.

"Six months gone," Christie said, and sank reluctantly onto the offered stool. He was dour as Jamie had ever seen him, but in control of himself, that was something.

"It was when the sickness came late last summer; when I was here, helping to nurse his wife!" Malva burst out, lowering her apron and staring reproachfully at her father, full lip a-tremble. "And not just the once, either!" She switched her gaze back to Jamie, wet-eyed and pleading. "Tell them, sir, please—tell them the truth!"

"Oh, I mean to," he said, giving her a black look. "And ye'll do the same, lass, I assure ye."

The shock of it was beginning to fade, and while his sense of irritation remained—in fact, it was growing by the moment—he was beginning to think, and furiously.

She was pregnant by someone grossly unsuitable; that much was clear. Who? Christ, he wished Claire had stayed; she listened to the gossip on the Ridge and she took interest in the lass; she'd know which young men were likely prospects. He'd seldom noticed young Malva particularly himself, save she was always about, helping Claire.

"The first time was when Herself was so ill as we despaired of her life," Malva said, snapping him back to attention. "I told ye, Faither. It wasna rape—only Himself being off his heid wi' the sorrow of it, and me, as well." She blinked, a pearly tear sliding down the unmarked cheek. "I came down from her room late at night, to find him in here, sitting in the dark, and grieving. I felt so sorry for him. . . ." Her voice shook, and she stopped, swallowing.

"I asked could I fetch him a wee bite, maybe something to drink—but he'd drink taken already, there was whisky in a glass before him. . . ."

"And I said no, thank ye kindly, and that I'd be alone,"

Jamie broke in, feeling the blood begin to surge in his temples at her recounting. "Ye left."

"No, I didn't." She shook her head; the cap had come half off when she fell and she hadn't settled it again; dark tendrils of hair hung down, framing her face. "Or rather, ye did say that to me, that ye'd be alone. But I couldn't bear to see ye in such straits, and—I know 'twas forward and unseemly, but I did pity ye so much!" she burst out, looking up and then immediately dropping her gaze again.

"I . . . I came and touched him," she whispered, so low that he had trouble hearing her. "Put my hand on his shoulder, like, only to comfort him. But he turned then, and put his arms round me, all of a sudden and grasped me to him. And—and then . . ." She gulped, audibly.

"He . . . he took me. Just . . . there." The toe of one small buskin stretched out, pointing delicately at the rag rug just in front of the table. Where there was, in fact, a small and ancient brown stain, which might have been blood. It *was* blood—Jemmy's, left when the wee lad had tripped on the rug and bumped his nose so it bled.

He opened his mouth to speak, but was so choked by outraged amazement that nothing emerged but a sort of gasp.

"So ye've not the balls to deny it, eh?" Young Allan had recovered his breath; he was swaying on his knees, hair hanging in his face, and glaring. "Balls enough to do it, though!"

Jamie gave Allan a quelling look, but didn't bother replying to him. He turned his attention instead to Tom Christie.

"Is she mad?" he inquired. "Or only clever?"

Christie's face might have been carved in stone, save for the pouchy flesh quivering beneath his eyes, and the eyes themselves, bloodshot and narrowed.

"She's not mad," Christie said.

"A clever liar, then." Jamie narrowed his own eyes at her. "Clever enough to ken no one would believe a tale of rape."

Her mouth opened in horror.

"Oh, no, sir," she said, and shook her head so hard the dark curls danced by her ears. "I should *never* say such a thing of ye, never!" She swallowed, and timidly raised her eyes to meet his—swollen with weeping, but a soft dove gray, guileless with innocence.

"Ye needed comfort," she said, softly but clearly. "I gave it ye."

He pinched the bridge of his nose hard betwixt thumb and forefinger, hoping the sensation would wake him from what was plainly nightmare. This failing to occur, he sighed and looked at Tom Christie.

"She's with child by someone, and not by me," he said bluntly. "Who might it have been?"

"It *was* you!" the girl protested, letting her apron fall as she sat bolt upright on her stool. "There's no one else!"

Christie's eyes slid reluctantly toward his daughter, then came back to meet Jamie's. They were the same dove gray, but they'd never possessed any trace of either guilelessness or innocence.

"I know of no one," he said. He took a deep breath, squaring his stocky shoulders. "She says it wasn't just the once. That ye had her a dozen times or more." His voice was nearly colorless, but not from lack of feeling, rather, from the grip he had upon his feelings.

"Then she's lied a dozen times or more," Jamie said, keeping his own voice under as much control as Christie's.

"Ye know I have not! Your wife believes me," Malva said, and a steely note had entered her voice. She lifted a hand to her cheek, where the flaming color had subsided but where the print of Claire's fingers was still clear, livid in outline.

"My wife has better sense," he said coldly, but was conscious all the same of a sinking sensation at the mention of Claire. Any woman might find such an accusation shock enough to make her flee—but he did wish that she'd stayed. Her presence, stoutly denying any misbehavior by him and personally rebuking Malva's lies, would have helped.

"Does she?" The vivid color had faded from the girl's face altogether, but she had stopped weeping. She was white-faced, her eyes huge and brilliant. "Well, I've sense, as well, sir. Sense enough to prove what I say."

"Oh, aye?" he said skeptically. "How?"

"I've seen the scars on your naked body; I can describe them."

That declaration brought everyone up short. There was silence for a moment, broken by Allan Christie's grunt of satisfaction. He rose to his feet, one hand still pressed to his middle, but an unpleasant smile upon his face.

"So, then?" he said. "Nay answer to that one, have ye?"

Irritation had long since given way to a monstrous anger. Under that, though, was the barest thread of something he would not—not yet—call fear.

"I dinna put my scars on display," he said mildly, "but there are a number of folk who've seen them, nonetheless. I havena lain with any of *them,* either."

"Aye, folk speak sometimes of the scars on your back," Malva shot back. "And everyone kens the great ugly one up your leg, that ye took at Culloden. But what of the crescent-shaped one across your ribs? Or the wee one on your left hurdie?" She reached a hand behind her, cupping her own buttock in illustration.

"Not in the center, quite—a bit down, on the outer side. About the size of a farthing." She didn't smile, but something like triumph blazed in her eyes.

"I havena got—" he began, but then stopped, appalled. Christ, he did. A spider's bite, taken in the Indies, that festered for a week, made an abscess, then burst, to his great relief. Once healed, he'd never thought of it again—but it was there.

Too late. They'd seen the realization cross his face.

Tom Christie closed his eyes, jaw working under his beard. Allan grunted again with satisfaction, and crossed his arms.

"Want to show us she's wrong?" the young man inquired sarcastically. "Take down your breeks, and gie us a look at your backside, then!"

With a good deal of effort, he kept himself from telling Allan Christie what he could do with his own backside. He took a long, slow breath, hoping that by the time he let it out again, some useful thought would have come to him.

It didn't. Tom Christie opened his eyes with a sigh.

"So," he said flatly. "I suppose ye'll not intend to put aside your wife and marry her?"

"I should never do such a thing!" The suggestion filled him with fury—and something like panic at the mere notion of being without Claire.

"Then we'll draw a contract." Christie rubbed a hand over his face, shoulders slumped with exhaustion and distaste.

"Maintenance for her and the bairn. Formal acknowledgment of the child's rights as one of your heirs. Ye can decide, I suppose, if ye wish to take it for your wife to rear, but that—"

"Get out." He rose, very slowly, and leaned forward, hands on the table, eyes fixed on Christie's. "Take your daughter and leave my house."

Christie stopped speaking and looked at him, black-browed. The girl had started grieving again, making whimpering noises into her apron. He'd the odd feeling that time had stopped, somehow; they would all just be trapped here forever, himself and Christie staring each other down like dogs, unable to look down but knowing that the floor of the room had vanished beneath their feet and they hung suspended over some dreadful abyss, in the endless moment before the fall.

It was Allan Christie who broke it, of course. The movement of the young man's hand going to his knife freed Jamie's gaze from Christie's, and his fingers tightened, digging into the wood of the table. An instant before, he'd felt bodiless; now blood hammered in his temples and pulsed through his limbs and his muscles trembled with an urgent need to damage Allan Christie. And wring his sister's neck to stop her noise, as well.

Allan Christie's face was black with anger, but he'd sense enough—barely, Jamie thought—not to draw the knife.

"I should like nothing better, wee man, than to gie ye your heid in your hands to play with," he said softly. "Leave now, before I do it."

Young Christie licked his lips and tensed himself, knucklebones going white on the hilt—but his eyes wavered. He glanced at his father, who sat like a stone, grim-jowled and square. The light had changed; it shone from the side and through the grizzled tufts of Christie's beard, so his own scar showed, a thin pink rope that curled like a snake above his jaw.

Christie straightened slowly, pushing himself up with his hands on his thighs, then shook his head suddenly like a dog shaking off water and stood up. He gripped Malva by the arm, lifted her from her stool, and pushed her before him, weeping and stumbling on the way out.

Allan followed them, making occasion to brush so near to Jamie as he left that Jamie could smell the younger man's stink, ripe with fury. Young Christie cast a single angry glance back over his shoulder, hand still on his knife—but left. Their tread in the hall made the floorboards tremble under Jamie's feet, and then came the heavy slam of the door.

He looked down, then, vaguely surprised to see the battered surface of his table and his own hands still flattened there as if they'd grown to it. He straightened up and his fingers curled, the stiff joints painful as they made themselves into fists. He was drenched with sweat.

Lighter footsteps came down the hall then, and Mrs. Bug came in with a tray. She set it down before him, curtsied to him, and went out. The single crystal goblet that he owned was stood on it, and the decanter that held the good whisky.

He felt obscurely that he wanted to laugh, but couldn't quite remember how it was done. The light touched the decanter and the drink within glowed like a chrysoberyl. He touched the glass gently in acknowledgment of Mrs. Bug's loyalty, but that would have to wait. The devil was loose in the world and there'd be hell to pay, surely. Before he did aught else, he must find Claire.

AFTER A TIME, the drifting clouds boiled up into thunderheads, and a cold breeze moved over the top of the hollow, shaking the laurels overhead with a rattling like dry bones. Very slowly, I got to my feet and began to climb.

I had no sure destination in mind; didn't care, really, if I were wet or not. I only knew that I couldn't go back to the house. As it was, I came to the trail that led to the White Spring, just as rain began to fall. Huge drops splattered on the leaves of pokeweed and burdock, and the firs and pines let go their long-held breath in a fragrant sigh.

The patter of drops on leaves and branches was punctuated by the muffled thud of heavier drops striking deep into soft earth—hail was coming with the rain, and suddenly there were tiny white particles of ice bouncing crazily on the packed needles, peppering my face and neck with stinging cold.

I ran, then, and took shelter beneath the drooping branches of a balsam fir that overhung the spring. The hail pocked the water and made it dance, but melted on impact, disappearing at once into the dark water. I sat still, arms wrapped around myself against the chill, shivering.

You could almost understand, said the part of my mind that had begun talking somewhere on the journey up the hill. *Everyone thought you were dying—including you. You know what happens . . . you've seen it.* People under the terrible strain of grief, those dealing with the presence of overwhelming death—I'd seen it. It was a natural seeking of solace; an attempt to hide, only for a moment, to deny death's coldness by taking comfort in the simple warmth of bodily contact.

"But he didn't," I said stubbornly, out loud. "If he *had,* and that was it—I could forgive him. But God damn it, he *didn't*!"

My subconscious subsided in the face of this certainty, but I was aware of subterranean stirrings—not suspicions, nothing strong enough to be called doubts. Only small, cool observations that poked their heads above the surface of my own dark well like spring peepers, high, thin pipings that were barely audible individually but that together might eventually form a racket of sound to shake the night.

You're an old woman.

See how the veins stand out on your hands.

The flesh has fallen away from your bones; your breasts sag.

If he were desperate, needing comfort . . .

He might reject her, but could never turn away from a child of his blood.

I closed my eyes and fought a rising sense of nausea. The hail had passed, succeeded by heavy rain, and cold steam began to rise from the ground, vapor drifting upward, disappearing like ghosts into the downpour.

"No," I said aloud. "No!"

I felt as though I had swallowed several large rocks, jagged and dirt-covered. It wasn't just the thought that Jamie might—but that Malva had most certainly betrayed me. Had betrayed me if it were true—and still more, if it were not.

My apprentice. My daughter of the heart.

I was safe from the rain, but the air was thick with water; my garments grew damp and hung heavy on me, clammy on my skin. Through the rain, I could see the big white stone that stood at the head of the spring, that gave the pool its name. Here it was that Jamie had shed his blood in sacrifice, and dashed it on that rock, asking the help of the kinsman he had slain. And here it was that Fergus had lain down, opening his veins in despair for his son, his blood blooming dark in the silent water.

And I began to realize why I had come here, why the place had called me. It was a place to meet oneself, and find truth.

The rain passed, and the clouds broke. Slowly, the light began to fade.

IT WAS NEARLY dark when he came. The trees were moving, restless with twilight and whispering among themselves; I didn't hear his footsteps on the sodden trail. He was just there, suddenly, at the edge of the clearing.

He stood searching; I saw his head lift when he saw me, and then he strode round the pool and ducked under the overhanging branches of my shelter. He'd been out for some time, I saw; his coat was wet and the cloth of his shirt plastered to his chest with rain and sweat. He'd brought a cloak with him, bundled under his arm, and he unfolded this and wrapped it round my shoulders. I let him.

He sat quite close to me then, arms wrapped about his knees, and stared into the darkening pool of the spring. The light had reached that point of beauty, just before all color fades, and the hairs of his eyebrows arched auburn and perfect over the solid ridges of his brows, each hair distinct, like the shorter, darker hairs of his sprouting beard.

He breathed long and deep, as though he had been walking for some time, and rubbed away a drop of moisture that dripped from the end of his nose. Once or twice, he took a shorter breath, as though about to say something, but didn't.

The birds had come out briefly after the rain. Now they were going to their rest, cheeping softly in the trees.

"I do hope you were planning to say something," I said finally, politely. "Because if you don't, I'll probably start screaming, and I might not be able to stop."

He made a sound somewhere between amusement and dismay, and sank his face into the palms of his hands. He stayed that way for a moment, then rubbed his hands hard over his face and sat up, sighing.

"I have been thinking all the time I was searching for ye, Sassenach, what in God's name I should say when I found ye. I thought of one thing and another—and . . . there seemed nothing whatever I could say." He sounded helpless.

"How is that?" I asked, a distinct edge in my voice. "I could think of a few things to say, I daresay."

He sighed, and made a brief gesture of frustration.

"What? To say I was sorry—that's not right. I am sorry, but to say so—it sounds as though I've done something to be sorry for, and that I have not. But I thought to start off so would make ye maybe think . . ." He glanced at me. I was keeping a tight grip on both my face and my emotions, but he knew me very well. The instant he'd said, "I'm sorry," my stomach had plunged toward my feet.

He looked away.

"There's naught I can say," he said quietly, "that doesna sound as though I try to defend or excuse myself. And I willna do that."

I made a small sound, as though someone had punched me in the stomach, and he glanced sharply at me.

"I won't do it!" he said fiercely. "There is no way to deny such a charge that doesna carry the stink of doubt about it. And nothing I can say to you that doesna sound like some groveling apology for—for—well, I willna apologize for something I havena done, and if I did, ye'd only doubt me more."

I was beginning to breathe a little easier.

"You don't seem to have a lot of faith in my faith in you."

He gave me a wary look.

"If I hadna got quite a lot of it, Sassenach, I wouldna be here."

He watched me for a moment, then reached out and touched my hand. My fingers turned at once and curved to meet his, and our hands clasped tight. His fingers were big and cold and he held mine so tightly that I thought my bones would break.

He took a deep breath, almost a sob, and his shoulders, tight in his sodden coat, relaxed all at once.

"Ye didna think it true?" he asked. "Ye ran away."

"It was a shock," I said. And I'd thought, dimly, that if I stayed, I might just kill her.

"Aye, it was," he said very dryly. "I expect I might have run away myself—if I could."

A small twinge of guilt was added to the overload of emotions; I supposed my hasty exit couldn't have helped the situation. He didn't reproach me, though, but merely said again, "Ye didna think it true, though?"

"I don't."

"Ye don't." His eyes searched mine. "But ye did?"

"No." I pulled the cloak closer round me, settling it on my shoulders. "I didn't. But I didn't know why."

"And now ye do."

I took a deep, deep breath of my own and let it go, then turned to face him, straight on.

"Jamie Fraser," I said, with great deliberation. "If you could do such a thing as that—and I don't mean lying with a woman, I mean doing it and lying to me about it—then everything I've done and everything I've been—my whole life—has been a lie. And I am not prepared to admit such a thing."

That surprised him a little; it was nearly dark now, but I saw his eyebrows rise.

"What d'ye mean by that, Sassenach?"

I waved a hand up the trail, where the house lay invisible above us, then toward the spring, where the white stone stood, a blur in the dark.

"I don't belong here," I said softly. "Brianna, Roger . . . they don't belong here. Jemmy shouldn't be here; he should be watching cartoons on television, drawing pictures of cars and airplanes with crayons—not learning to shoot a gun as big as he is and cut the entrails from a deer."

I lifted my face and closed my eyes, feeling the damp settle on my skin, heavy on my lashes.

"But we are here, all of us. And we're here because I loved you, more than the life that was mine. Because I believed you loved me the same way."

I took a deep breath, so that my voice wouldn't tremble, opened my eyes and turned to him.

"Will you tell me that's not true?"

"No," he said after a moment, so softly I could barely hear him. His hand tightened harder on mine. "No, I willna tell ye that. Not ever, Claire."

"Well, then," I said, and felt the anxiety and fury and fear of the afternoon run out of me like water. I rested my head on his shoulder, and breathed the rain and sweat on his skin. He smelled acrid, pungent with the musk of fear and curdled anger.

It was entirely dark by now. I could hear sounds in the distance, Mrs. Bug calling to Arch from the stable where she'd been milking the goats, and his cracked old voice hallooing back. A bat flittered past, silent and hunting.

"Claire?" Jamie said softly.

"Hm?"

"I've got to tell ye something."

I froze. After a moment, I carefully detached myself from him and sat upright.

"Don't do that," I said. "It makes me feel as though I've been punched in the stomach."

"I'm sorry."

I wrapped my arms around myself, trying to swallow the sudden feeling of nausea.

"You said you wouldn't start off by saying you were sorry, because it felt as though there must be something to be sorry for."

"I did," he said, and sighed.

I felt the movement between us as the two stiff fingers of his right hand thrummed against his leg.

"There isna any good way," he said finally, "of telling your wife ye've lain wi' someone else. No matter what the circumstances. There's just not."

I felt suddenly dizzy, and short of breath. I closed my eyes momentarily. He didn't mean Malva; he'd made that clear.

"Who?" I said as evenly as possible. "And when?"

He stirred uneasily.

"Oh. Well . . . when ye . . . when ye were . . . gone, to be sure."

I managed to take a short breath.

"Who?" I said.

"Just the once," he said. "I mean—I hadna the slightest intention of—"

"Who?"

He sighed, and rubbed hard at the back of his neck.

"Christ. The last thing I want is to upset ye, Sassenach, by sounding as though it—but I dinna want to malign the puir woman by makin' it seem that she was—"

"WHO?" I roared, seizing him by the arm.

"Jesus!" he said, thoroughly startled. "Mary MacNab."

"Who?" I said again, blankly this time.

"Mary MacNab," he repeated, and sighed. "Can ye let go, Sassenach? I think ye've drawn blood."

I had, my fingernails digging hard enough into his wrist as to pierce the skin. I flung his hand away, and folded my own into fists, wrapping my arms around my body by way of stopping myself from strangling him.

"Who. The. Hell. Is. Mary. MacNab?" I said, through my teeth. My face was hot, but cold sweat prickled along my jaw and rolled down my ribs.

"Ye ken her, Sassenach. She was wife to Rab—him that died when his house was burnt. They had the one bairn, Rabbie; he was stable-lad at Lallybroch when—"

"Mary MacNab. Her?" I could hear the astonishment in my own voice. I did recall Mary MacNab—barely. She'd come to be a maid at Lallybroch after the death of her nasty husband; a small, wiry woman, worn with work and hardship, who seldom spoke, but went about her business like a shadow, never more than half-noticed in the rowdy chaos of life at Lallybroch.

"I scarcely noticed her," I said, trying—and failing—to remember whether she had been there on my last visit. "But I gather you did?"

"No," he said, and sighed. "Not like ye mean, Sassenach."

"Don't call me that," I said, my voice sounding low and venomous to my own ears.

He made a Scottish noise in his throat, of frustrated resignation, rubbing his wrist.

"Aye. Well, see, 'twas the night before I gave myself up to the English—"

"You never told me that!"

"Never told ye what?" He sounded confused.

"That you gave yourself up to the English. We thought you'd been captured."

"I was," he said briefly. "But by arrangement, for the price on my head." He flipped a hand, dismissing the matter. "It wasna important."

"They might have hanged you!" And a good thing, too, said the small, furiously hurt voice inside.

"No, they wouldn't." A faint tinge of amusement showed in his voice. "Ye'd told me so, Sass—mmphm. I didna really care, though, if they did."

I had no idea what he meant by saying I'd told him so, but I certainly didn't care at the moment.

"Forget that," I said tersely. "I want to know—"

"About Mary. Aye, I ken." He rubbed a hand slowly through his hair. "Aye, well. She came to me, the night before I—I went. I was in the cave, ken, near Lallybroch, and she brought me supper. And then she . . . stayed."

I bit my tongue, not to interrupt. I could feel him gathering his thoughts, searching for words.

"I tried to send her away," he said at last. "She . . . well, what she said to me . . ." He glanced at me; I saw the movement of his head. "She said she'd seen me with ye, Claire—and that she kent the look of a true love when she saw it, for all she'd not had one herself. And that it wasna in her mind to make me betray that. But she would give me . . . some small thing. That's what she said to me," he said, and his voice had grown husky, "'some small thing, that maybe ye can use.'"

"It was—I mean, it wasna . . ." He stopped, and made that odd shrugging motion of his, as though his shirt were tight across his shoulders. He bowed his head for a moment on his knees, hands linked round them.

"She gave me tenderness," he said finally, so softly that I barely heard him. "I—I hope I gave her the same."

My throat and chest were too tight to speak, and tears prickled behind my eyes. I remembered, quite suddenly, what he had said to me the night I mended Tom Christie's hand, about the Sacred Heart—*"so wanting—and no one to touch him."* And he had lived in a cave for seven years, alone.

There was no more than a foot of space between us, but it seemed an unbridgeable gulf.

I reached across it and laid my hand on his, the tips of my fingers on his big, weathered knuckles. I took a breath, then two, trying to steady my voice, but it cracked and broke, nonetheless.

"You gave her . . . tenderness. I know you did."

He turned to me, suddenly, and my face was pressed into his coat, the cloth of it damp and rough on my skin, my tears blooming in tiny warm patches that vanished at once into the chill of the fabric.

"Oh, Claire," he whispered into my hair. I reached up, and could feel wetness on his cheeks. "She said—she wished to keep ye alive for me. And she meant it; she didna mean to take anything for herself."

I cried then, holding nothing back. For empty years, yearning for the touch of a hand. Hollow years, lying beside a man I had betrayed, for whom I had no tenderness. For the terrors and doubts and griefs of the day. Cried for him and me and for Mary MacNab, who knew what loneliness was—and what love was, as well.

"I would have told ye, before," he whispered, patting my back as though I were a small child. "But it was . . . it was the once." He shrugged a little, helpless. "And I couldna think how. How to say it, that ye'd understand."

I sobbed, gulped air, and finally sat up, wiping my face carelessly on a fold of my skirt.

"I understand," I said. My voice was thick and clogged, but fairly steady now. "I do."

And I did. Not only about Mary MacNab and what she had done—but why he'd told me now. There was no need; I would never have known. No need but the need for absolute honesty between us—and that I must know it was there.

I had believed him, about Malva. But now I had not only certainty of mind—but peace of heart.

We sat close together, the folds of my cloak and skirts flowing over his legs, his simple presence a comfort. Somewhere nearby, a very early cricket began to chirp.

"The rain's past, then," I said, hearing it. He nodded, with a small sound of assent.

"What shall we do?" I said at last. My voice sounded calm.

"Find out the truth—if I can."

Neither of us mentioned the possibility that he might not. I shifted, gathering the folds of my cloak.

"Will we go home, then?"

It was too dark to see now, but I felt him nod as he got to his feet, putting down a hand to help me.

"Aye, we will."

THE HOUSE was empty when we returned, though Mrs. Bug had left a covered dish of shepherd's pie on the table, the floor swept, and the fire neatly smoored. I took off my wet cloak and hung it on the peg, but then stood, unsure quite what to do next, as though I stood in a stranger's house, in a country where I did not know the custom.

Jamie seemed to feel the same way—though after a moment, he stirred, fetched down the candlestick from the shelf over the hearth, and lit it with a spill from the fire. The wavering glow seemed only to emphasize the odd, echoing quality of the room, and he stood holding it for a minute, at a loss, before finally setting it down with a thump in the middle of the table.

"Are ye hungry, S . . . Sassenach?" He had begun to speak by habit, but then interrupted himself, looking up to be sure the name was once more allowed. I did my best to smile at him, though I could feel the corners of my mouth tremble.

"No. Are you?"

He shook his head, silent, and dropped his hand from the dish. Looking round for something else to do, he took up the poker and stirred the coals, breaking up the blackened embers and sending a swirl of sparks and soot up the chimney and out onto the hearth. It would ruin the fire, which would need to be rebuilt before bed, but I said nothing—he knew that.

"It feels like a death in the family," I said at last. "As though something terrible has happened, and this is the shocked bit, before you begin to send round and tell all the neighbors."

He gave a small, rueful laugh, and put the poker down.

"We'll not need to. They'll all ken well enough by daybreak what's happened."

Rousing at last from my immobility, I shook out my damp skirts and came to stand beside him by the fire. The heat of it seared at once through the wet cloth; it should have been comforting, but there was an icy weight in my abdomen that wouldn't melt. I put a hand on his arm, needing the touch of him.

"No one will believe it," I said. He put a hand over mine, and smiled a little, his eyes closed, but shook his head.

"They'll all believe it, Claire," he said softly. "I'm sorry."

81

BENEFIT OF THE DOUBT

"IT ISN'T FREAKING TRUE!"

"No, of course not." Roger watched his wife warily; she was exhibiting the general symptoms of a large explosive device with an unstable timing mechanism, and he had the distinct feeling that it was dangerous to be in her vicinity.

"That little *bitch*! I want to just grab her and choke the truth out of her!" Her hand closed convulsively on the neck of the syrup bottle, and he reached to take it from her before she should break it.

"I understand the impulse," he said, "but on the whole—better not."

She glared at him, but relinquished the bottle.

"Can't *you* do something?" she said.

He'd been asking himself that since he'd heard the news of Malva's accusation.

"I don't know," he said. "But I thought I'd go and talk to the Christies, at least. And if I can get Malva alone, I will." Thinking of his last tête-à-tête with Malva Christie, though, he had an uneasy feeling that she wouldn't be easily shaken from her story.

Brianna sat down, scowling at her plate of buckwheat cakes, and began slathering them with butter. Her fury was beginning to give way to rational thought; he could see ideas darting behind her eyes.

"If you can get her to admit that it's not true," she said slowly, "that's good. If not, though—the next best thing is to find out who's been with her. If some guy will admit in public that he *could* be the father—that would cast a lot of doubt on her story, at least."

"True." Roger poured syrup sparingly over his own cakes, even in the midst of uncertainty and anxiety enjoying the thick dark smell of it and the anticipation of rare sweetness. "Though there would still be those who'd be convinced Jamie's guilty. Here."

"I saw her kissing Obadiah Henderson in the woods," Bree said, accepting the bottle. "Late last fall." She shuddered fastidiously. "If it was him, no wonder she doesn't want to say."

Roger eyed her curiously. He knew Obadiah, who was large and uncouth, but not at all bad looking and not stupid. Some women would consider him a decent match; he had fifteen acres, which he farmed competently, and was a good hunter. He'd never seen Bree so much as speak to the man, though.

"Can you think of anybody else?" she asked, still frowning.

"Well . . . Bobby Higgins," he replied, still wary. "The Beardsley twins used to eye her now and then, but of course . . ." He had a nasty feeling that this line of inquiry was going to culminate in her adjuring *him* to go and ask awkward questions of any putative fathers—a process that struck him as likely being both pointless and dangerous.

"Why?" she demanded, cutting viciously into her stack of pancakes. "Why would she *do* it? Mama's always been so kind to her!"

"One of two reasons," Roger replied, and paused for a moment, closing his eyes, the better to savor the decadence of melted butter and velvet-smooth maple syrup on fresh, hot buckwheat. He swallowed, and reluctantly opened his eyes.

"Either the real father is someone she doesn't want to marry—for whatever reason—or she's decided to try to get hold of your father's money or property, by getting him to settle a sum on her or, failing that, on the child."

"Or both. I mean, she doesn't want to marry whoever it is, *and* wants Da's money—not that he has any."

"Or both," he agreed.

They ate in silence for a few minutes, forks scraping on

the wooden plates, each absorbed in thought. Jem had spent the night at the Big House; in the wake of Lizzie's marriage, Roger had suggested that Amy McCallum take over Lizzie's work as housemaid, and since she and Aidan had moved in, Jem spent even more time over there, finding solace for the loss of Germain in Aidan's companionship.

"It isn't true," she repeated stubbornly. "Da simply *wouldn't* . . ." But he saw the faint doubt at the back of her eyes—and a slight glaze of panic at the thought.

"No, he wouldn't," he said firmly. "Brianna—you can't possibly think there's any truth to it?"

"No, of course not!" But she spoke too loudly, too definitely. He laid down his fork and looked at her levelly.

"What's the matter? Do ye know something?"

"Nothing." She chased the last bite of pancake round her plate, speared and ate it.

He made a skeptical sound, and she frowned at the sticky puddle left on her plate. She always poured too much honey or syrup; he, more sparing, always ended with a clean plate.

"I don't," she said. She bit her lower lip, though, and put the tip of her finger into the puddle of syrup. "It's only . . ."

"What?"

"Not Da," she said slowly. She put the tip of her finger in her mouth and sucked the syrup off. "And I don't *know* for sure about Daddy. It's only—looking back at things I didn't understand at the time—now I see—" She stopped abruptly, and closed her eyes, then opened them, fixing him directly.

"I was looking through his wallet one day. Not snooping, just having fun, taking all the cards and things out and putting them back. There was a note tucked away, between the dollar bills. It was asking him to meet somebody for lunch—"

"Innocent enough."

"It started out with *Darling—*, and it wasn't my mother's handwriting," she said tersely.

"Ah," he said, and after a moment, "how old were you?"

"Eleven." She drew small patterns on the plate with the tip of her finger. "I just put the note back and kind of blotted it out of my mind. I didn't want to think about it—and I don't think I ever did, from that day to this. There were a few other things, things I saw and didn't understand—it was mostly the way things were between them, my parents . . . Every now and then, *something* would happen, and I never knew what, but I always knew something was really wrong."

She trailed off, sighed deeply, and wiped her finger on her napkin.

"Bree," he said gently. "Jamie's an honorable man, and he loves your mother deeply."

"Well, see, that's the thing," she said softly. "I would have sworn Daddy was, too. And did."

IT WASN'T IMPOSSIBLE. The thought kept returning, to niggle Roger uncomfortably, like a pebble in his shoe. Jamie Fraser *was* an honorable man, he *was* deeply uxorious—and he had been in the depths of despair and exhaustion during Claire's illness. Roger had feared for him nearly as much as for Claire; he'd gone hollow-eyed and grim-jawed through the hot, endless days of reeking death, not eating, not sleeping, held together by nothing more than will.

Roger had tried to speak to him then, of God and eternity, reconcile him with what seemed the inevitable, only to be repulsed with a hot-eyed fury at the mere idea that God might think to take his wife—this followed by complete despair as Claire lapsed into a stupor near death. It wasn't impossible that the offer of a moment's physical comfort, made in that void of desolation, had gone further than either party intended.

But it was early May now, and Malva Christie was six months gone with child. Which meant that she'd got that way in November. The crisis of Claire's illness had been in late September; he remembered vividly the smell of burnt-over fields in the room when she'd wakened from what looked like certain death, her eyes huge and lambent, startlingly beautiful in a face like an androgynous angel's.

Right, then, it frigging *was* impossible. No man was perfect, and any man might yield in extremis—once. But not repeatedly. And not Jamie Fraser. Malva Christie was a liar.

Feeling more settled in mind, Roger made his way down the creekside toward the Christies' cabin.

Can't you do something? Brianna had asked him, anguished.

Damn little, he thought, but he had to try. It was Friday; he could—and would—preach an ear-blistering sermon on the evils of gossip, come Sunday. Knowing what he did of human nature, though, any benefit derived from that was likely to be short-lived.

Beyond that—well, Lodge meeting was Wednesday night. It had been going really well, and he hated to jeopardize the fragile amity of the newborn Lodge by risking unpleasantness at a meeting . . . but if there was a chance of it helping . . . would it be useful to encourage both Jamie and the two Christie men to attend? It would get the matter out in the open, and no matter how bad, open public knowledge was always better than the festering weed of whispered scandal. He thought Tom Christie would observe the proprieties and be civil, notwithstanding the delicacy of the situation—but he wasn't all that sure of Allan. The son shared his father's features and his sense of self-righteousness, but lacked Tom's iron will and self-control.

But now he was at the cabin, which seemed deserted. He heard the sound of an ax, though, the slow *klop!* of kindling being split, and went round to the back.

It was Malva, who turned at his greeting, her face wary. There were lavender smudges beneath her eyes, he saw, and the bloom of her skin was clouded. Guilty conscience, he hoped, as he greeted her cordially.

"If ye've come to try to get me to take it back, I won't," she said flatly, ignoring his greeting.

"I came to ask if ye wanted someone to talk to," he said. That surprised her; she set down the ax, and wiped her face with her apron.

"To talk to?" she said slowly, eyeing him. "What about?"

He shrugged and offered her a very slight smile.

"Anything ye like." He let his accent relax, broadening toward her own Edinburgh tinge. "I doubt ye've been able to talk to anyone of late, save your Da and brother—and they might not be able to listen just the noo."

A matching small smile flitted across her features, and disappeared.

"No, they don't listen," she said. "But it's all right; I've naught much to say, ken? I'm a hoor; what else is there?"

"I dinna think ye're a hoor," Roger said quietly.

"Oh, ye don't?" She rocked back a little on her heels, surveying him mockingly. "What else would ye call a woman that spreads her legs for a marrit man? Adulteress, of course—but hoor, as well, or so I'm told."

He thought she meant to shock him with deliberate coarseness. She did, rather, but he kept it to himself.

"Mistaken, maybe. Jesus didna speak harshly to the woman who *was* a harlot; it's no my business to be doing it to someone who isn't."

"And if ye've come to quote the Bible to me, save your breath to cool your parritch with," she said, a look of distaste pulling down the delicate corners of her mouth. "I've heard a deal more of it than I care to."

That, he reflected, was probably true. Tom Christie was the sort who knew a verse—or ten—for every occasion, and if he didn't beat his daughter physically, had almost certainly been doing it verbally.

Not sure what to say next, he held out his hand.

"If ye'll give me the hatchet, I'll do the rest."

One eyebrow raised, she put it into his hand and stepped back. He put up a chunk of kindling and split it clean in two, stooped for another. She watched for a moment, then sat down, slowly, on a smaller stump.

The mountain spring was still cool, touched with the last winter breath of the high snows, but the work warmed him. He didn't by any means forget she was there, but he kept his eyes on the wood, the bright grain of the fresh-split stick, the tug of it as he pulled the ax blade free, and found his thoughts move back to his conversation with Bree.

So Frank Randall had been—perhaps—unfaithful to his wife, on occasion. In all justice, Roger wasn't sure he could be blamed, knowing the circumstances of the case. Claire had disappeared completely, without trace, leaving Frank to hunt desperately, to mourn, and then, at last, to begin to put the pieces of his life back together and move on. Whereupon the missing wife pops back up, distraught, mistreated—and pregnant by another man.

Whereupon Frank Randall, whether from a sense of honor, of love, or simply of—what? curiosity?—had taken her back. He recalled Claire's telling them the story, and it was clear that she hadn't particularly *wanted* to be taken back. It must have been damned clear to Frank Randall, too.

Little wonder, then, if outrage and rejection had led him occasionally—and little wonder, too, that the echoes of the hidden conflicts between her parents had reached Brianna, like seismic disturbances that travel through miles of earth and stone, jolts from an upwelling of magma, miles deep beneath the crust.

And little wonder, he realized with a sense of revelation, that she'd been so upset by his friendship with Amy McCallum.

He realized, quite suddenly, that Malva Christie was crying. Silently, without covering her face. Tears ran down her cheeks and her shoulders quivered, but her lower lip was caught hard between her teeth; she made no sound.

He cast down the ax and went to her. Put an arm gently round her shoulders, and cradled her capped head, patting her.

"Hey," he said softly. "Don't worry, aye? It's going to be all right."

She shook her head, and the tears washed down her face.

"Can't be," she whispered. "Can't be."

Beneath his pity for her, Roger was aware of a sense of growing hope. Whatever reluctance he might have to exploit her desperation was well overcome by a determination to get to the bottom of her trouble. Mostly for the sake of Jamie and his family—but for her own, as well.

He mustn't push too hard, though, mustn't rush. She had to trust him.

So he patted her, rubbed her back as he did for Jem when he woke with nightmare, said small soothing things, all meaningless, and felt her begin to yield. Yield, but in a strangely physical fashion, as though her flesh were somehow opening, blossoming slowly under his touch.

Strange, and at the same time, oddly familiar. He'd felt it now and then with Bree, when he'd turned to her in the dark, when she hadn't time to think but responded to him with her body alone. The physical recollection jarred him, and he drew back a little. He meant to say something to Malva, but the sound of a footfall interrupted him, and he looked up to see Allan Christie coming toward him out of the trees, fast, with a face like black thunder.

"Get away from her!"

He straightened, heart pounding as he realized quite suddenly what this might look like.

"What d'ye mean, slinkin' round like a rat after a rind o' cheese?" Allan cried. "D'ye think since she's shamed, she's meat for any whoreson bastard that cares to take her?"

"I came to offer counsel," Roger said as coolly as he could manage. "And comfort, if I might."

"Oh, aye." Allan Christie's face was flushed, the tufts of his hair standing on end like the bristles on a hog about to charge. "Comfort me with apples and stay me with raisins, is it? Ye can stick your comfort straight up your arse, MacKenzie, and your goddamned stiff prick, too!"

Allan's hands were clenched at his sides, trembling with rage.

"Ye're no better than your wicked good-father—or perhaps"—he rounded suddenly on Malva, who had stopped crying, but was sitting white-faced and frozen on her stump—"perhaps it was him, too? Is that it, ye wee bitch, did ye take them both? Answer me!" His hand shot out to slap her, and Roger caught his wrist by reflex.

Roger was so angry that he could barely speak. Christie was strong, but Roger was bigger; he would have broken the young man's wrist, if he could. As it was, he dug his fingers hard into the space between the bones, and was gratified to see Christie's eyes pop and water from the pain of it.

"Ye'll not speak to your sister that way," he said, not loudly, but very clearly. "Nor to me." He shifted his grip suddenly and bent Christie's wrist sharply backward. "D'ye hear me?"

Allan's face went white and the breath hissed out of him. He didn't answer, but managed to nod. Roger released his hold, almost flinging the younger man's wrist away, with a sudden feeling of revulsion.

"I do not wish to hear that ye've abused your sister in any way," he said, as evenly as he could. "If I do—ye'll regret it. Good day, Mr. Christie. Miss Christie," he added, with a brief bow to Malva. She didn't respond, only stared at him from eyes gray as storm clouds, huge with shock. The memory of them followed him as he strode from the clearing and plunged into the darkness of the wood, wondering whether he'd made things better, or much, much worse.

THE NEXT MEETING of the Fraser's Ridge Lodge was on Wednesday. Brianna went as usual to the Big House, taking Jemmy and her workbasket, and was surprised to find Bobby Higgins seated at the table, finishing his supper.

"Miss Brianna!" He half-rose at sight of her, beaming, but she waved him back to his seat, and slid into the bench opposite.

"Bobby! How nice to see you again! We thought—well, we thought you wouldn't come again."

He nodded, looking rueful.

"Aye, happen I might not, at least not for a bit. But his Lordship had some things, things come in from England, and he says to me as I shall bring 'em." He ran a piece of bread carefully round the inside of his bowl, sopping up the last of Mrs. Bug's chicken gravy.

"And then . . . well, I did wish to come on my own account. For to see Miss Christie, aye?"

"Oh." She glanced up and caught Mrs. Bug's eye. The older woman rolled her eyes, helpless, and shook her head. "Um. Yes, Malva. Er . . . is my mother upstairs, Mrs. Bug?"

"Nay, *a nighean.* She was called to Mr. MacNeill; he's bad wi' the pleurisy." Barely pausing for breath, she whipped off her apron and hung it on its hook, reaching for her cloak with the other hand. "I'll be along, then, *a leannan;* Arch will be wanting his supper. If there's aught wanting, Amy's about." And with the briefest of farewells, she vanished, leaving Bobby staring after her in puzzlement at this uncharacteristic behavior.

"Is something amiss?" he asked, turning back to Brianna with a small frown.

"Ahh . . . well." With a few uncharitable thoughts toward Mrs. Bug, Brianna girded up her loins and told him, grimacing inwardly at the sight of his sweet young face as it turned white and rigid in the firelight.

She couldn't bring herself to mention Malva's accusation,

only told him that the girl was with child. He'd hear about Jamie, soon enough, but please God, not from her.

"I see, miss. Aye . . . I see." He sat for a moment, staring at the bit of bread in his hand. Then he dropped it into his bowl, rose suddenly, and rushed outside; she heard him retching into the blackberry bushes outside the back door. He didn't come back.

It was a long evening. Her mother was plainly spending the night with Mr. MacNeill and his pleurisy. Amy McCallum came down for a little while, and they made awkward conversation over their sewing, but then the maid escaped upstairs. Aidan and Jemmy, allowed to stay up late and play, wore themselves out and fell asleep on the settle.

She fidgeted, abandoned her sewing, and paced up and down, waiting for Lodge to finish. She wanted her own bed, her own house; her parents' kitchen, normally so welcoming, seemed strange and uncomfortable, and she a stranger in it.

At long, long last, she heard footsteps and the creak of the door, and Roger came in, looking bothered.

"There you are," she said with relief. "How was Lodge? Did the Christies come?"

He shook his head.

"No. It . . . went all right, I suppose. A bit of awkwardness, of course, but your father carried it off as well as anyone might, in the circumstances."

She grimaced, imagining it.

"Where is he?"

"He said he thought he'd go and walk by himself for a bit—maybe do a little night fishing." Roger put his arms round her and hugged her close, sighing. "Did ye hear the ruckus?"

"No! What happened?"

"Well, we'd just had a wee blether on the universal nature of brotherly love, when a clishmaclaver broke out, over by your kiln. Well, so, everyone streamed out to see what was to do, and here's your cousin Ian and wee Bobby Higgins, rolling in the dirt and trying to kill each other."

"Oh, dear." She felt a spasm of guilt. Probably someone had told Bobby everything, and he had gone in search of Jamie, meeting Ian instead, and thrown Malva's accusations of Jamie at him. If she'd told him herself . . .

"What happened?"

"Well, Ian's bloody dog took a hand, for the one thing—or a paw. Your father barely stopped him tearing out Bobby's throat, but it did stop the fight. We dragged them apart, then, and Ian tore free and loped off into the woods, with the dog beside him. Bobby's . . . well, I cleaned him up a bit, then gave him Jemmy's trundle for the night," he said apologetically. "He said he couldna stay up here—" He looked round at the shadowed kitchen; she'd already smoored the fire and carried the little boys up to bed; the room was empty, lit only by a faint hearth glow.

"I'm sorry. Will ye sleep here, then?"

She shook her head emphatically.

"Bobby or no Bobby, I want to go home."

"Aye, all right. You go on, then; I'll fetch Amy down to bar the door."

"No, that's okay," she said quickly. "I'll get her." And before he could protest, she was down the hall and up the stair, the empty house strange and silent below.

82

NOT THE END OF THE WORLD

THERE IS A great deal of satisfaction in wresting weeds out of the earth. Backbreaking and endless as the chore may be, there is a tiny but unassailable sense of triumph in it, feeling the soil give suddenly, yielding the stubborn root, and the foe lying defeated in your hand.

It had rained recently and the earth was soft. I ripped and tore with ferocious concentration; dandelions, fireweed, rhododendron sprouts, bunchgrass, muhly, smartweed, and the creeping mallow known locally as "cheese." Paused for an instant, narrow-eyed at a bull thistle, and prised it from the ground with a vicious stab of my pruning knife.

The grapevines that ran up the palisades had just begun their spring rush, and sprouts and ruffles of a delicate green tinged with rust cascaded from the woody stems, eager tendrils curling like my own new-grown hair—God damn her, she'd taken my hair on purpose to disfigure me! The shade they cast provided refuge for immense bushy growths of the pernicious thing I called "jewelweed," not knowing its real name, for the tiny white flowers that winked like diamond clusters in the feathery green fronds. It was likely a fennel of some sort, but formed neither a useful bulb nor edible seeds; pretty, but useless—and thus the sort of thing that spreads like wildfire.

There was a small swishing sound, and a ball of rags came to rest by my foot. This was followed immediately by the rush of a much larger body, and Rollo swept past me, snatching the ball adroitly and galloping away, the wind of his passage stirring my skirts. Startled, I looked up, to see him bounding toward Ian, who'd come soft-footed into the garden.

He made a small gesture of apology, but I sat back on my heels and smiled at him, making an effort to quell the vicious sentiments surging to and fro in my bosom.

Evidently, the quelling wasn't all that successful, for I saw him frown a little, and hesitate, looking at my face.

"Did you want something, Ian?" I said shortly, dropping the facade of welcome. "If that hound of yours knocks over one of my hives, I'll make a rug of him."

"Rollo!" Ian snapped his fingers at the dog, who leapt gracefully over the row of bee gums and basket hives that sat at the far end of the garden, trotted up to his master, dropped the ball at his feet, and stood genially panting, yellow wolf-eyes fixed with apparent interest on me.

Ian scooped up the ball, and turning, flung it out through the open gate, Rollo after it like the tail of a comet.

"I did want to ask ye something, Auntie," he said, turning back to me. "It would wait, though."

"No, that's all right. Now's as good a time as any." Getting awkwardly to my feet, I waved him to the little bench Jamie had made for me in a shady nook beneath a flowering dogwood that overhung the corner of the garden.

"So?" I settled myself beside him, brushing crumbs of dirt from the bottom of my skirt.

"Mmphm. Well . . ." He stared at his hands, linked over his knee, big-knuckled and bony. "I . . . ah . . ."

"You haven't been exposed to syphilis again, have you?" I asked, with a vivid memory of my last interview with an awkward young man in this garden. "Because if you have, Ian, I swear I will use Dr. Fentiman's syringe on you and I won't be gentle with it. You—"

"No, no!" he said hastily. "No, of course not, Auntie. It's about—about Malva Christie." He tensed as he said it, in case I should lunge for the pruning knife, but I merely drew a deep breath and let it out again, slowly.

"What about her?" I said, my voice deliberately even.

"Well . . . no really her, exactly. More what she said—about Uncle Jamie." He stopped, swallowing, and I drew another slow breath. Disturbed as I was by the situation myself, I'd scarcely thought about its impact on anyone else. But Ian had idolized Jamie from the time he was a tiny boy; I could well imagine that the widespread suggestions that Jamie might have feet of clay were deeply upsetting to him.

"Ian, you mustn't worry yourself." I put a consoling hand—dirt-stained as it was—on his arm. "It will . . . work itself out, somehow. Such things always do." They did—generally with the maximum of uproar and catastrophe. And if Malva's child should by some horrid cosmic joke be born with red hair . . . I closed my eyes for a moment, feeling a wave of dizziness.

"Aye, I suppose they will," Ian said, sounding uncertain in the extreme. "It's only—what they're sayin', about Uncle Jamie. Even his own Ardsmuir men, folk that should know better! That he must have—well, I'll no repeat any of it, Auntie—but . . . I canna bear to hear it!"

His long, homely face was twisted with unhappiness, and it suddenly occurred to me that he might be having his own doubts about the matter.

"Ian," I said, with as much firmness as I could muster, "Malva's child could not possibly be Jamie's. You do believe that, don't you?"

He nodded, very slowly, but wouldn't meet my eyes.

"I do," he said softly, and then swallowed hard. "But, Auntie . . . it could be mine."

A bee had lighted on my arm. I stared at it, seeing the veins in its glassy wings, the dust of yellow pollen that clung to the minuscule hairs of its legs and abdomen, the gentle pulsing of its body as it breathed.

"Oh, Ian," I said as softly as he'd spoken himself. "Oh, Ian."

He was strung tight as a marionette, but when I spoke, a little of the tension left the arm under my hand, and I saw that he had closed his eyes.

"I'm sorry, Auntie," he whispered.

Wordless, I patted his arm. The bee flew off, and I wished passionately that I could exchange places with it. It would be so wonderful, simply to be about the business of gathering, single-minded in the sun.

Another bee lighted on Ian's collar, and he brushed it absently away.

"Well, so," he said, taking a deep breath and turning his head to look at me. "What must I do, Auntie?"

His eyes were dark with misery and worry—and something very like fear, I thought.

"Do?" I said, sounding as blank as I felt. "Jesus H. Roosevelt Christ, Ian."

I hadn't meant to make him smile, and he didn't, but he did seem to relax very slightly.

"Aye, I've done it already," he said, very rueful. "But—it's done, Auntie. How can I mend it?"

I rubbed my brow, trying to think. Rollo had brought back his ball, but seeing that Ian was in no mood to play, dropped it by his feet and leaned against his leg, panting.

"Malva," I said finally. "Did she tell you? Before, I mean."

"Ye think I scorned her, and that's what made her accuse Uncle Jamie?" He gave me a wry look, absently scratching Rollo's ruff. "Well, I wouldna blame ye if ye did, Auntie, but no. She said not a word to me about the matter. If she had, I should ha' marrit her at once."

The hurdle of confession overcome, he was talking more easily now.

"You didn't think of marrying her *first*?" I said, with perhaps a slight tinge of acerbity.

"Ah . . . no," he said, very sheepish. "It wasna precisely a matter of—well, I wasna thinking at all, Auntie. I was drunk. The first time, anyway," he added as an afterthought.

"The first—? How many— No, don't tell me. I don't want to know the gory details." I shut him up with a brusque gesture, and sat up straight, struck by a thought. "Bobby Higgins. Was that—"

He nodded, lowering his lashes so I couldn't see his eyes. The blood had come up under his tan.

"Aye. That was why—I mean, I didna really wish to marry her, to begin with, but still, I would have asked, after we . . . but I put it off a bit, and—" He scrubbed a hand across his face, helpless. "Well, I didna want her to wife, but I couldna keep from wanting her, nonetheless, and I ken well enough how awful it must seem—but I've got to tell the truth, Auntie, and that's it." He took a gulp of air, and continued.

"I'd—wait for her. In the woods, when she came to gather. She'd not speak when she saw me, only smile, and raise her skirts a bit, then turn quick and run and . . . God, I should be after her like a dog after a bitch in heat," he said bitterly. "But then one day I came late, and she wasna there where we usually met. But I heard her laughing, far off, and when I went to see . . ."

He twisted his hands hard enough to dislocate a finger, grimacing, and Rollo whined softly.

"Let us just say that yon bairn might well be Bobby Higgins's, too," he said, biting off the words.

I felt suddenly exhausted, as I had when recovering from my illness, as though it was too much effort even to breathe. I leaned back against the palisades, feeling the cool papery rustle of grape leaves against my neck, fanning softly over my heated cheeks.

Ian bent forward, head in his hands, the dappled green shadows playing over him.

"What shall I do?" he asked at last, voice muffled. He sounded as tired as I felt. "I dinna mind saying that I—that the child might be mine. But would it help, d'ye think?"

"No," I said bleakly. "It wouldn't." Public opinion would not be changed in the slightest; everyone would simply assume that Ian was lying for his uncle's sake. Even if he were to marry the girl, it wouldn't—

A thought struck me and I pulled myself upright again.

"You said you didn't want to marry her, even before you knew about Bobby. Why?" I asked curiously.

He lifted his head from his hands with a helpless gesture.

"I dinna ken how to say it. She was—well, she was bonnie enough, aye, and a proper spirit to her, as well. But she . . . I dinna ken, Auntie. It was only that I always had the feeling, lying wi' her—that I dare not fall asleep."

I stared at him.

"Well, that would be off-putting, I imagine."

He had dismissed that, though, and was frowning, digging the heel of his moccasin into the soil.

"There's no means of telling which of two men has fathered a bairn, is there?" he asked abruptly. "Only—if it's mine, I should want it. I would wed her for the child's sake, no matter what else. If it's mine."

Bree had told me the bare bones of his history; I knew about his Mohawk wife, Emily, and the death of his daughter, and I felt the small presence of my own first child, Faith, stillborn but always with me.

"Oh, Ian," I said softly, and touched his hair. "You might be able to tell, by the way the child looked—but probably not, or not right away."

He nodded, and sighed. After a moment, he said, "If I say it's mine, and I wed her—folk might still talk, but after a time . . ." His voice died away. True, talk might eventually die down. But there would still be those who thought Jamie responsible, others who would call Malva a whore, a liar, or both—which she bloody well *was,* I reminded myself, but not a nice thing to hear about one's wife. And what might Ian's life be like, married under such circumstances, to a woman he could not trust and—I thought—did not especially like?

"Well," I said, rising to my feet and stretching, "don't do anything drastic just yet awhile. Let me talk with Jamie; you don't mind if I tell him?"

"I wish ye would, Auntie. I dinna think I could face him, myself." He still sat on the bench, bony shoulders slumped. Rollo lay on the ground at his feet, the big wolf head resting on

Ian's moccasined foot. Moved with pity, I put my arms round Ian, and he leaned his head against me, simply, like a child.

"It isn't the end of the world," I said.

The sun was touching the edge of the mountain, and the sky burned red and gold, the light of it falling in blazing bars through the palisades.

"No," he said, but there was no conviction in his voice.

83

DECLARATIONS

Charlotte, Mecklenberg County
May 20, 1775

THE ONE THING ROGER HAD NOT envisioned about the making of history was the sheer amount of alcohol involved. He should have, he thought; if there was anything a career in academia had taught him, it was that almost all worthwhile business was conducted in the pub.

The public houses, taverns, ordinaries, and pothouses in Charlotte were doing a roaring business, as delegates, spectators, and hangers-on seethed through them, men of Loyalist sentiments collecting in the King's Arms, those of rabidly opposing views in the Blue Boar, with shifting currents of the unallied and undecided eddying to and fro, purling through the Goose and Oyster, Thomas's ordinary, the Groats, Simon's, Buchanan's, Mueller's, and two or three nameless places that barely qualified as shebeens.

Jamie visited all of them. And drank in all of them, sharing beer, ale, rum punch, shandy, cordial, porter, stout, cider, brandywine, persimmon beer, rhubarb wine, blackberry wine, cherry bounce, perry, merry brew, and scrumpy. Not all of them were alcoholic, but the great majority were.

Roger confined himself largely to beer, and found himself glad of his restraint, when he happened to meet with Davy Caldwell in the street, turning from a fruiterer's stall with a handful of early apricots.

"Mr. MacKenzie!" Caldwell cried, his face lighting with welcome. "I had nay thought to meet you here, but what blessing that I have!"

"Blessing indeed," Roger said, shaking the minister's hand with cordial fervor. Caldwell had married him and Brianna, and had examined him at the Presbyterian Academy regarding his own calling, some months before. "How d'ye do, Mr. Caldwell?"

"Och, for myself, well enough—but my heart misgives me for the fate of my poor brethren!" Caldwell shook his head in dismay, gesturing at a group of men crowding into Simon's ordinary, laughing and talking. "What is to come of this, I ask ye, Mr. MacKenzie—what's to come?"

Roger was, for an unbalanced instant, tempted to tell him what was to come of it, exactly. As it was, though, he gestured to Jamie—who had been stopped by an acquaintance in the street—to go along without him, and turned away to walk a bit with Caldwell.

"Have ye come for the conference, then, Mr. Caldwell?" he asked.

"I have that, Mr. MacKenzie, I have that. Little hope have I that my words will make the slightest difference, but it is my duty to speak as I find, and so I shall."

What Davy Caldwell found was a shocking condition of human slothfulness, for which he blamed the entire current situation, convinced that unreflective apathy and "a stupid concern with personal comfort" on the part of the colonists both tempted and provoked the exercise of tyrannical powers on the part of Crown and Parliament.

"It's a point, sure," Roger said, aware that Caldwell's impassioned gestures were attracting a certain amount of notice, even amongst the crowds in the street, most of them reasonably argumentative themselves.

"A point!" Caldwell cried. "Aye, it is, and *the* point entirely.

The ignorance, disregard of moral obligation, and the supreme love of ease of the groveling sluggard corresponds exactly—exactly!—with a tyrant's appetite and cynicism."

He glowered at one gentleman who had subsided against the side of a house, taking a brief respite from the noonday heat with his hat over his face.

"The spirit of God must redeem the slothful, fill the human frame with activity, poise, and libertarian consciousness!"

Roger wondered, rather, whether Caldwell would view the escalating war as the result of God's intervention—but upon reflection, thought that he likely would. Caldwell was a thinker, but a staunch Presbyterian, and thus a believer in predestination.

"The slothful encourage and facilitate oppression," Caldwell explained, with a scornful gesture toward a family of tinkers enjoying an alfresco luncheon in the yard of a house. "Their own shame and sinking spirits, their own pitiful compliance and submission—these become self-made chains of slavery!"

"Oh, aye," Roger said, and coughed. Caldwell was a famous preacher, and rather inclined to want to keep in practice. "Will ye take a whet, Mr. Caldwell?" It was a warm day, and Caldwell's rather round, cherubic face was becoming very red.

They went into Thomas's ordinary, a fairly respectable house, and sat down with tankards of the house beer—for Caldwell, like most, did not regard beer as being in any way "drink," like rum or whisky. What else, after all, would one drink? Milk?

Out of the sun, and with a cooling draught to hand, Davy Caldwell became less heated in his expressions, as well as his countenance.

"Praise God for the fortune of meeting ye here, Mr. MacKenzie," he said, breathing deep after lowering his tankard. "I had sent a letter, but doubtless ye will have left home before it could come. I wished to inform ye of the gladsome news—there is to be a Presbytery."

Roger felt a sudden leap of the heart.

"When? And where?"

"Edenton, early next month. The Reverend Doctor McCorkle is coming from Philadelphia. He'll remain for a time, before departing on his further journey—he is going to the Indies, to encourage the efforts of the church there. I am, of course, presuming to know your mind—I apologize for the forwardness of my address, Mr. MacKenzie—but is it still your desire to seek ordination?"

"With all my heart."

Caldwell beamed, and grasped him strongly by the hand. "Give ye joy of it, dear man—great joy."

He then plunged into a close description of McCorkle, whom he had met in Scotland, and speculations regarding the state of religion in the colony—he spoke of Methodism with some respect, but considered the New Light Baptists "somewhat unregulated" in their effusions of worship, though doubtless well-meaning—and surely sincere belief was an improvement over unbelief, whatever the form it might take. In due course, though, he came back round to their present circumstances.

"Ye've come with your father-in-law, have ye?" he asked. "I thought I saw him, in the road."

"I have, and ye did," Roger assured him, fumbling in his pocket for a coin. The pocket itself was full of coiled horsehair; with his academic experience as guide, he had made provision against possible boredom by bringing the makings of a new fishing line.

"Ah." Caldwell looked at him keenly. "I've heard things of late—is it true, he's turned Whig?"

"He is a firm friend to liberty," Roger said, cautious, and took a breath. "As am I." He'd not had occasion to say it out loud before; it gave him a small, breathless feeling, just under the breastbone.

"Aha, aha, very good! I had heard of it, as I say—and yet there are a great many who say otherwise: that he is a Tory, a Loyalist like his relations, and that this protestation of support for the independency movement is but a ruse." It wasn't phrased as a question, but Caldwell's bushy eyebrow, cocked like a swell's hat, made it clear that it was.

"Jamie Fraser is an honest man," Roger said, and drained his tankard. "And an honorable one," he added, setting it down. "And speaking of the same, I think I must go and find him."

Caldwell glanced around; there was an air of restlessness around them, of men calling their accounts and settling up.

The official meeting of the convention was to begin at two o'clock, at MacIntyre's farmhouse. It was past noon now, delegates, speakers, and spectators would be slowly gathering, girding themselves for an afternoon of conflict and decision. The breathless feeling came back.

"Aye, then. Give him my regards, if ye will—though perhaps I may see him myself. And may the Holy Spirit penetrate the encrustations of habit and lethargy, and convert the souls and rouse the consciences of those who gather here today!"

"Amen," said Roger, smiling in spite of the glances from the men—and not a few women—around them.

He found Jamie in the Blue Boar, in the company of a number of men in whom the Holy Spirit had already been hard at work on the encrustations, judging from the volume. The chatter near the door died away, though, as he made his way through the room—not in cause of his own presence, but because there was something more interesting going on near the center.

To wit: Jamie Fraser and Gerald Forbes, both red with heat, passion, and a gallon or two of mixed spirits, head to head over a table, and hissing like snakes in the Gaelic.

Only a few of the spectators were Gaelic speakers; these were hastily translating the high points of the dialogue for the rest of the crowd.

Gaelic insult was an art, and one at which his father-in-law excelled, though Roger was obliged to admit that the lawyer was no slouch at it, himself. The translations rendered by the onlookers fell far short of the original; nonetheless, the taproom was rapt, with occasional admiring whistles or whoops from the spectators, or laughter as a particularly pungent point was made.

Having missed the beginning, Roger had no idea how the conflict had begun, but so far into it as they were, the exchange was focused on cowardice and arrogance, Jamie's remarks aimed at Forbes's leading the attack on Fogarty Simms as a low-minded and cowardly attempt to make himself look the big man at the price of a defenseless man's life, Forbes—shifting into English here, as he realized that they had become the cynosure of the room—taking the view that Jamie's presence here was an unwarrantable affront to those who truly held the ideals of liberty and justice, as everyone knew he was in truth the King's man, but he, the puffed-up cock o' the walk, thought that he could pull the wool over everyone's eyes long enough to betray the whole boiling, but if he, Fraser, thought he, Forbes, was fool enough to be gulled by antic tricks in the public street and a lot of talk with nay more substance than the shrieking of gulls, he, Fraser, had best think again!

Jamie slapped a hand flat on the table, making it boom like a drum, and rattling the cups. He rose, glaring down at Forbes.

"Do ye libel my honor, sir?" he cried, also shifting to English. "For if ye do, let us go out, and we shall settle the matter at once, yea or nay!"

Sweat was streaming down Forbes's broad, flushed face, and his eyes were gleaming with anger, but even overheated as he was, Roger saw belated caution pluck at his sleeve. Roger hadn't seen the fight in Cross Creek, but Ian had told him the details, meanwhile laughing his head off. The last thing Gerald Forbes could desire was a duel.

"Have ye honor to libel, sir?" Forbes demanded, standing in turn, and drawing himself up as though about to address the jury. "Ye come here acting the great one, carousing and showing away like a sailor come ashore with prize money in his pocket—but have we any evidence that your words are more than puffery? Puffery, I say, sir!"

Jamie stood, both hands braced on the tabletop, surveying Forbes through narrowed eyes. Roger had once seen that expression focused on himself. It had been followed rapidly by the sort of mayhem customary in a Glasgow pub on Saturday night—only more so. The only thing to be thankful for was that Forbes had clearly not heard any whiff of Malva Christie's accusation, or there would be blood on the floor already.

Jamie straightened slowly, and his left hand went toward his waist. There were gasps, and Forbes paled. But Jamie had reached for his sporran, not his dirk, and plunged his hand inside.

"As to that . . . *sir* . . ." he said in a low, even voice that carried through the room, "I have made myself clear. I am for liberty, and to that end, I pledge my name, my fortune"—here he withdrew his hand from his sporran and slammed it on the table; a small purse, two golden guineas, and a jewel—"and my sacred honor."

The room was silent, all eyes focused on the black diamond, which shimmered with a baleful light. Jamie paused for the space of three heartbeats, then drew breath.

"Is there any man here who gives me the lie?" he said. It was ostensibly addressed to the room at large, but his eyes were fixed on Forbes. The lawyer had gone a mottled red and gray, like a bad oyster, but said nothing.

Jamie paused again, looked once round the room, then picked up purse, money, and jewel, and stalked out the door. Outside, the town clock chimed two, the strokes slow and heavy in the humid air.

L'OIGNON–INTELLIGENCER

Upon the 20th of this month, a Congress met in Charlotte, composed of Delegates from Mecklenberg County, for the purpose of discussion upon the issue of current Relations with Great Britain. After due Deliberation, a Declaration was proposed and accepted, whose Provisions are Herewith Shown:

1. *That whosoever directly or indirectly abetted or in any way, form or manner countenanced to unchartered & dangerous invasion of our rights as claimed by G. Britain is an enemy to this County—to America & to the inherent & inaliable rights of man.*
2. *We the Citizens of Mecklenburg County do hereby desolve the political bands which have connected us to the Mother Country & hereby absolve ourselves from all allegiance to the British crown & abjure all political connection, contract or association with that nation who have wantonly trampled on our rights & liberties & inhumanely shed the innocent blood of American patriots at Lexington.*
3. *We do hereby declare ourselves a free and independent people—are & of right ought to be a sovereign & self-governing association, under the controul of no power other than that of our God & the general government of the congress, to the maintainence of which independence civil & religious*

we solemnly pledge to each other our mutual cooperation, our lives, our fortunes & our most sacred honor.

4. *As we now acknowledge the existence & controul of no law or legal officers, civil or military, within this County, we do hereby ordain & adopt as a rule of life, all, each & every of our former laws—wherein nevertheless the crown of Great Britain never can be considered as holding rights, privileges, immunities, or authority therein.*
5. *It is also further decreed that all, each & every military officer in this County is hereby reinstated in his former command & authority, he acting conformably to these regulations. And that every member present of this delegation shall henceforth be a civil officer, viz. a Justice of the peace in the character of a "Committee-man" to issue process, hear & determine all matters of controversy according to sd. adopted laws—to preserve peace, union & harmony in sd. County & to use every exertion to spread the love of country & fire of freedom throughout America until a more general & organized government be established in this province. A selection from the members present shall constitute a Committee of public safety for sd. County.*
6. *That a copy of these resolutions be transmitted by express to the President of the Continental Congress assembled in Philadelphia, to be laid before that body.*

84

AMONG THE LETTUCES

SOME IDIOT—OR child—had left the gate of my garden open. I hurried up the path, hoping that it hadn't been that way for long. If it had been open overnight, the deer would have eaten every lettuce, onion, and bulb plant in the plot, to say nothing of ruining the—

I jerked, letting out a small cry. Something like a red-hot hat pin had stabbed me in the neck, and I smacked the place by reflex. An electric jab in the temple made my vision go white, then blur with water, and a fiery stab in the crook of my elbow—bees.

I blundered off the path, suddenly aware that the air was full of them, frenzied and stinging. I plunged through the brush, barely able to see for the watering of my eyes, aware too late of the low-pitched thrum of a hive at war.

Bear! God damn it, a bear had got in! In the half-second between the first sting and the next, I had glimpsed one of the bee gums lying on its side in the dirt just inside the gate, combs and honey spilling out of it like entrails.

I ducked under branches and flung myself into a patch of pokeweed, gasping and cursing incoherently. The sting on my neck throbbed viciously, and the one on my temple was already puffing up, pulling at the eyelid on that side. I felt something crawling on my ankle, and batted it away by reflex before it could sting.

I wiped tears away, blinking. A few bees sailed past through the yellow-flowered stems above me, aggressive as Spitfires. I crawled a little farther, trying at once to get away, slap at my hair, and shake out my skirts, lest any more of them be trapped in my clothes.

I was breathing like a steam engine, shaking with adrenaline and fury.

"Bloody hell . . . frigging bear . . . God damn it . . ."

My strong impulse was to rush in screaming and flapping my skirts, in hopes of panicking the bear. An equally strong impulse of self-preservation overcame it.

I scrambled to my feet, and keeping low in case of enraged bees, thrust my way through the brush uphill, meaning to circle the garden and come down on the other side, away from the ravaged hives. I could get back to the path that way and down to the house, where I could recruit help—preferably armed—to drive away the monster before it destroyed the rest of the hives.

No point in keeping quiet, and I crashed through bushes and stumbled over logs, panting with rage. I tried to see the bear, but the growth of grapevines over the palisades was too thick to show me anything but rustling leaves and sun shadows. The side of my face felt as though it were on fire, and jolts of pain shot through the trigeminal nerve with each heartbeat, making the muscles twitch and the eye water terribly.

I reached the path just below the spot where the first bee had stung me—my gardening basket lay where I'd dropped it, tools spilled out. I grabbed the knife I used for everything from pruning to digging roots; it was a stout thing, with a six-inch blade, and while it might not impress the bear, I felt better for having it.

I glanced at the open gate, ready to run—but saw nothing. The ruined hive lay just as I'd seen it, the wax combs broken and squashed, the smell of honey thick in the air. But the combs were not scattered; shattered pillars of wax still stuck to the exposed wooden base of the hive.

A bee zoomed menacingly past my ear and I ducked, but didn't run. It was quiet. I tried to stop panting, trying to hear over the thunder of my own racing pulse. Bears weren't quiet; they didn't need to be. I should hear snufflings and gulping noises, at least—rustlings of broken foliage, the lap of a long tongue. I didn't.

Cautiously, I moved sideways up the path, a step at a time, ready to run. There was a good-size oak, about twenty feet away. Could I make that, if the bear popped out?

I listened as hard as I could, but heard nothing beyond the soft rustle of the grapevines and the sound of angry bees, now dropped to a whining hum as they gathered thick on the remnants of their combs.

It was gone. Had to be. Still wary, I edged closer, knife in hand.

I smelled the blood and saw her in the same instant. She was lying in the salad bed, her skirt flown out like some gigantic, rusty flower blooming amid the young lettuces.

I was kneeling by her, with no memory of reaching her, and the flesh of her arm was warm when I grasped her wrist—such small, fragile bones—but slack, there was no pulse—*Of course not,* said the cold small watcher inside, *her throat is cut, there's blood everywhere, but you can see the artery isn't pumping; she's dead.*

Malva's gray eyes were open, blank with surprise, and her

cap had fallen off. I clutched her wrist harder, as though I must be able to find the buried pulse, to find some trace of life . . . and did. The bulge of her belly moved, very slightly, and I dropped the flaccid arm at once and seized my knife, scrabbling for the hem of her skirt.

I acted without thought, without fear, without doubt—there wasn't anything but the knife and the pressure, the flesh parting and the faint possibility, the panic of absolute *need* . . .

I slit the belly from navel to pubis, pushing hard through slack muscle, nicked the womb but no matter, cut quick but careful through the wall of the womb, dropped the knife, and thrust my hands into the depths of Malva Christie, still blood-warm, and seized the child, cupping, turning, wrenching hard in my frenzy to pull it free, bring it out from sure death, bring it into the air, help it breathe. . . . Malva's body flopped and heaved as I jerked, limp limbs flailing with the force of my yanking.

It came free with the suddenness of birth, and I was swiping blood and mucus from the tiny sealed face, blowing into its lungs, gently, gently, you have to blow gently, the alveoli of the lungs are like cobwebs, so small, compressing its chest, no more than a hand's span, two fingers pressing, no more, and felt the tiny spring of it, delicate as a watch spring, felt the movement, small squirms, a faint instinctive struggling—and felt it fade, that flicker, that tiny spark of life, cried out in anguish and clutched the tiny, doll-like body to my breast, still warm, still warm.

"Don't go," I said, "don't go, don't go, please don't go." But the vibrancy faded, a small blue glow that seemed to light the palms of my hands for an instant, then dwindle like a candle flame, to the coal of a smoldering wick, to the faintest trace of brightness—then everything was dark.

I was still sitting in the brilliant sun, crying and blood-soaked, the body of the little boy in my lap, the butchered corpse of my Malva beside me, when they found me.

85

THE STOLEN BRIDE

A WEEK PASSED AFTER Malva's death, and there was no slightest hint of who had killed her. Whispering, sidelong glances, and a palpable fog of suspicion hung about the Ridge, but despite Jamie's every effort, no one could be located who knew—or would say—anything at all useful.

I could see the tension and frustration building up in Jamie, day by day, and knew it must find an outlet. I had no idea what he might do, though.

After breakfast on the Wednesday, Jamie stood glowering at the window in his study, then slammed down his fist on the table, with a suddenness that made me jump.

"I have reached the mortal limit of endurance," he informed me. "One moment more of this, and I shall run mad. I must do something, and I will." Without waiting for any response to this statement, he strode to the office door, flung it open, and bellowed, "Joseph!" into the hall.

Mr. Wemyss appeared out of the kitchen, where he had been sweeping the chimney at Mrs. Bug's direction, looking startled, pale, soot-smudged, and generally unkempt.

Jamie ignored the black footprints on the study floor—he had burned the rug—and fixed Mr. Wemyss with a commanding gaze.

"D'ye want that woman?" he demanded.

"Woman?" Mr. Wemyss was understandably bewildered. "What—oh. Are you—might you be referring to *Fraülein* Berrisch?"

"Who else? D'ye want her?" Jamie repeated.

It had plainly been a long time since anyone had asked Mr.

Wemyss what he wanted, and it took him some time to gather his wits from the shock of it.

Brutal prodding by Jamie forced him past deprecating murmurs about the *Fraülein*'s friends no doubt being the best judge of her happiness, his own unsuitability, poverty, and general unworthiness as a husband, and into—at long last—a reckless admission that, well, if the *Fraülein* should not be terribly averse to the prospect, perhaps . . . well . . . in a word . . .

"Aye, sir," he said, looking terrified at his own boldness. "I do. Very much!" he blurted.

"Good." Jamie nodded, pleased. "We'll go and get her, then."

Mr. Wemyss was open-mouthed with astonishment; so was I. Jamie swung round to me, issuing orders with the confidence and *joie de vivre* of a sea-captain with a fat prize in view.

"Go and find Young Ian for me, will ye, Sassenach? And tell Mrs. Bug to put up food, enough for a week's travel for four men. And then fetch Roger Mac; we'll need a minister."

He rubbed his hands together in satisfaction, then clapped Mr. Wemyss on the shoulder, causing a small puff of soot to rise from his clothes.

"Go fettle yourself, Joseph," he said. "And comb your hair. We're going to go and steal ye a bride."

". . . AND PUT A pistol to his breest, his breest," Young Ian chanted, "Marry me, marry me, minister, or else I'll be your priest, your priest—or else I'll be your priest!"

"Of course," Roger said, dropping the song, in which a bold young man named Willie rides with his friends to abduct and forcibly marry a young woman who proves bolder yet, "we'll hope ye prove a wee bit more capable than Willie upon the night, aye, Joseph?"

Mr. Wemyss, scrubbed, dressed, and fairly vibrating with excitement, gave him a glance of complete incomprehension. Roger grinned, tightening the strap of his saddlebag.

"Young Willie obliges a minister to marry him to the young woman at gunpoint," he explained to Mr. Wemyss, "but then, when he takes his stolen bride to bed, she'll have none of him—and his best efforts will not avail to force her."

"And so return me, Willie, to my hame, as virgin as I came, I came—as virgin as I came!" Ian caroled.

"Now, mind," Roger said warningly to Jamie, who was heaving his own saddlebags over Gideon's back. "If the *Fraülein* is at all unwilling . . ."

"What, unwilling to be wed to Joseph?" Jamie clapped Mr. Wemyss on the back, then bent to give him a foot up and fairly heaved the smaller man into the saddle. "I canna see any woman of sense turning from such an opportunity, can you, *a charaid*?"

He took a quick look round the clearing, to see all was well, then ran up the steps and kissed me in quick farewell, before running down again to mount Gideon, who for once seemed amenable and made no effort to bite him.

"Keep well, *mo nighean donn,*" he said, smiling into my eyes. And then they were gone, thundering out of the clearing like a gang of Highland raiders, Ian's ear-splitting whoops ringing from the trees.

ODDLY ENOUGH, the departure of the men seemed to ease things slightly. The talk, of course, went merrily on—but without Jamie or Ian there to serve as a lightning-rod, it merely crackled to and fro like St. Elmo's fire; spitting, fizzing, and making everyone's hair stand on end, but essentially a harmless phenomenon, unless touched directly.

The house felt less an embattled fortress, and more the eye of a storm.

Also, with Mr. Wemyss out of the house, Lizzie came to visit, bringing little Rodney Joseph, as the baby was called—Roger having set his face firmly against the young fathers' enthusiastic suggestions of Tilgath-pileser and Ichabod. Wee Rogerina had come out of it all right, being now commonly known as Rory, but Roger declined entirely to hear of a child being christened anything that might result in his being known to the world at large as Icky.

Rodney seemed a very congenial child, in part because he had never quite lost that air of round-eyed astonishment that made him seem agog to hear what you had to say. Lizzie's astonishment at his birth had mutated into an enchantment that might have completely eclipsed Jo and Kezzie, were it not for the fact that they shared it.

Either one of them would—unless forcibly stopped—spend half an hour discussing Rodney's bowel habits with the intensity heretofore reserved for new snares and the peculiar things found inside the stomachs of animals they had killed. Pigs, it seemed, really would eat anything; so would Rodney.

A few days after the men's departure on their bride-stealing expedition, Brianna had come up from her cabin with Jemmy to visit, and Lizzie likewise had brought Rodney. The two of them joined Amy McCallum and me in the kitchen, where we were spending a pleasant evening sewing by the light of the fire, admiring Rodney, keeping a negligent eye on Jemmy and Aidan—and after a certain amount of cautious exploration, devoting ourselves wholeheartedly to a rundown of the male population of the Ridge, viewed in the light of suspects.

I, of course, had a more personal and painful interest in the topic, but all three of the young women were solidly on the side of justice—i.e., the side that refused even to contemplate the notion that either Jamie or I might have had anything to do with the murder of Malva Christie.

For myself, I found such open speculation rather a comfort. I had, of course, been engaging in private conjecture nonstop—and an exhausting business it was, too. Not only was it unpleasant to visualize every man I knew in the role of cold-blooded murderer—the process obliged me continuously to reimagine the murder itself, and relive the moment when I had found her.

"I'd really hate to think it might have been Bobby," Bree said, frowning as she pushed a wooden darning egg into the heel of a sock. "He seems just such a nice boy."

Lizzie drew down her chin at this, pursing her lips.

"Oh, aye, he's a sweet lad," she said. "But what ye might call warm-blooded."

All of us looked at her.

"Well," she said mildly, "I didna let him, but he tried hard enough. And when I said no, he did go off and kick a tree."

"My husband would do that sometimes, if I refused him,"

Amy said, thoughtful. "But I'm sure he wouldna have cut my throat."

"Well, but Malva didn't refuse whoever it was," Bree pointed out, squinting as she threaded her darning needle. "That was the problem. He killed her because she was pregnant, and he was afraid she'd tell everyone."

"Ho!" Lizzie said, triumphant. "Well, then—it canna have been Bobby at all, can it? For when my Da turned him awa'—" A brief shadow crossed her face at mention of her father, who still had not spoken a word to her nor acknowledged the birth of little Rodney. "Did he not think of speiring for Malva Christie? Ian said he meant to. And if she were with child by him—well, then, her father would be obliged to agree, would he not?"

Amy nodded, finding this convincing, but Bree had objections.

"Yes—but she was insisting that it *wasn't* his baby. And he threw up in the blackberry bushes when he heard that she was"—her lips compressed momentarily—"well, he wasn't happy at all. So he might have killed her out of jealousy, don't you think?"

Lizzie and Amy hmm'd dubiously at this—both of them were fond of Bobby—but were obliged to admit the possibility.

"What I wonder about," I said a little hesitantly, "is the older men. The married ones. Everyone knows about the young men who were interested in her—but I've certainly seen more than one married man glance at her in passing."

"I nominate Hiram Crombie," Bree said at once, stabbing her needle into the heel of the sock. Everyone laughed, but she shook her head.

"No, I'm serious. It's always the really religious, very uptight ones that turn out to have secret drawers full of women's underwear, and slink around molesting choirboys."

Amy's jaw dropped.

"Drawers full of women's underwear?" she said. "What . . . shifts and stays? Whatever would he do wi' them?"

Brianna flushed at that, having forgotten her audience. She coughed, but there was no good way out.

"Er . . . well. I was thinking more of French women's underwear," she said weakly. "Um . . . lacy sorts of things."

"Oh, French," Lizzie said, nodding wisely. Everyone knew about the notorious reputation of French ladies—though I doubted that any woman on Fraser's Ridge save myself had ever seen one. In the interests of covering Bree's lapse, though, I obligingly told them about La Nestlé, the King of France's mistress, who had had her nipples pierced and appeared at court with her breasts exposed, sporting gold hoops through them.

"Another few months o' this," Lizzie said darkly, looking down at Rodney, who was nursing fiercely at her breast, tiny fists clenched with effort, "and I shall be able to do the same. I'll tell Jo and Kezzie to fetch me back some hoops when they sell their hides, aye?"

In the midst of the laughter at this, the sound of a knock at the front door passed unnoticed—or would have, if not for Jemmy and Aidan, who had been playing in Jamie's study, rushing into the kitchen to tell us about it.

"I'll get it." Bree set down her darning, but I was already on my feet.

"No, I'll go." I waved her back, picked up a candlestick, and went down the dark hallway, heart beating fast. Visitors after dark were almost always an emergency of one kind or another.

So was this one, though not any kind I might have expected. For a moment, I didn't even recognize the tall woman who stood swaying on the stoop, white-faced and gaunt. Then she whispered, "*Frau* Fraser? I may—may I komm?" and fell into my arms.

The noise of it brought all the young women rushing to help, and we had Monika Berrisch—for it was indeed Mr. Wemyss's putative bride—laid on the settle, covered with quilts, and plied with hot toddy in nothing flat.

She recovered quickly—there was nothing wrong with her, really, save exhaustion and hunger—she said she hadn't eaten in three days—and within a short time, was able to sit up eating soup, and explain her astonishing presence.

"It was my late husband's sister," she said, closing her eyes in momentary bliss at the aroma of split-pea soup with ham. "She did not want me, effer, and when her husband had the bad accident and lost his wagon, so there was not so much money to keep us all, she did not want me more."

She had, she said, yearned for Joseph, but had not had either the strength nor yet the means to withstand her family's opposition and insist upon returning to him.

"Oh?" Lizzie was examining her in a close, but not unfriendly manner. "What happened, then?"

Fraülein Berrisch turned large, gentle eyes on her.

"I could not bear it more," she said simply. "I wish so much to be with Joseph. My late husband's sister, she wish me to be gone, so she will give a small bit of money. So I came," she concluded, with a shrug, and took another small, greedy spoonful of soup.

"You . . . walked?" Brianna said. "From Halifax?"

Fraülein Berrisch nodded, licking the spoon, and put out a foot from under the quilts. Her shoes had worn entirely through at the sole; she had wrapped them with random scraps of leather and strips of fabric torn from her shift, so her feet looked like bundles of filthy rags.

"Elizabeth," she said, looking earnestly at Lizzie. "I hope you do not mind I komm. Your father—he is hier? I hope so much he does not mind, too."

"Umm, no," I said, exchanging a glance with Lizzie. "He isn't here—but I'm sure that he'll be delighted to see you!"

"Oh?" Her gaunt face, which had shown alarm at hearing that Mr. Wemyss was not here, grew radiant when we told her where he was.

"Oh," she breathed, clasping the spoon to her bosom as though it were Mr. Wemyss's head. "Oh, *mein Kavalier*!" Beaming with joy, she looked round at all of us—and for the first time, noticed Rodney, snoozing in his basket at Lizzie's feet.

"But who is this?" she cried, and leaned forward to look at him. Not quite asleep, Rodney opened round, dark eyes and regarded her with a solemn, sleepy interest.

"This is my wee bairnie. Rodney Joseph, he's called—for my Da, ken?" Lizzie hoisted him out of his basket, chubby knees pulled up under his chin, and laid him gently in Monika's arms.

She cooed over him in German, face alight.

"Granny lust," Bree muttered to me, out of the side of her

mouth, and I felt laughter bubble up under my stays. I hadn't laughed since before Malva's death, and found it balm to the spirit.

Lizzie was explaining earnestly to Monika the estrangement resulting from her unorthodox marriage, to which Monika was nodding, clicking her tongue in sympathetic understanding—and I did wonder how much of it she grasped—and talking baby-talk to Rodney all at once.

"Fat chance of Mr. Wemyss staying estranged," I said out of the side of my own mouth. "Keep his new wife from her new grandson? Ha!"

"Yes, what's a little matter of dual sons-in-law?" Bree agreed.

Amy was regarding the tender scene with a slight sense of wistfulness. She reached out and put an arm round Aidan's skinny shoulders.

"Well, they do say, the more, the merrier," she said.

86

PRIORITIES

THREE SHIRTS, AN extra pair of decent breeches, two pair of stockings, one lisle, one silk—wait, where were the silk ones?

Brianna stepped to the door and called to her husband, who was industriously laying segments of clay pipe into the trench he had dug, assisted by Jemmy and Aidan.

"Roger! What have you done with your silk stockings?"

He paused, frowning, and rubbed his head. Then, handing the shovel to Aidan, he came across to the house, leaping over the open trench.

"I wore them last Sunday to preach, no?" he asked, reaching her. "What did I . . . oh."

"Oh?" she said suspiciously, seeing his face change from puzzlement to guilt. "What's 'oh'?"

"Ahh . . . well, you'd stayed to home with Jem and his stomachache"—a tactically helpful ailment, greatly exaggerated in order to keep her from having to sit through two hours of staring and whispering—"so when Jocky Abernathy asked me would I care to go fishing with him . . ."

"Roger MacKenzie," she said, fixing him with a look of wrath, "if you put your good silk stockings in a creel full of smelly fish and forgot them—"

"I'll just nip up to the house and borrow a pair from your Da, shall I?" he said hurriedly. "I'm sure mine will turn up, somewhere."

"So will your head," she said. "Probably under a rock!"

That made him laugh, which was not what she had intended, but which had the effect of easing her temper.

"I'm sorry," he said, leaning forward to kiss her forehead. "It's probably Freudian."

"Oh? And what does leaving your stockings wrapped around a dead trout symbolize?" she demanded.

"Generalized guilt and divided loyalties, I imagine," he said, still joking, but not so much. "Bree—I've been thinking. I really don't think I should go. I don't need to—"

"Yes, you do," she said, as firmly as possible. "Da says so, Mama says so, *and so do I*."

"Oh, well, then." He smiled, but she could see the uneasiness under his humor—the more so because she shared it. Malva Christie's murder had caused an uproar on the Ridge—alarm, hysteria, suspicion, and finger-pointing in every direction. Several young men—Bobby Higgins among them—had simply disappeared from the Ridge, whether from a sense of guilt, or merely from a sense of self-preservation.

There had been accusations enough to go around; even she herself had come in for her share of gossip and suspicion, some of her unguarded remarks about Malva Christie having been repeated. But by far the greatest weight of suspicion rested squarely on her parents.

Both of them were doing their best to go about their daily business, grimly ignoring the gossip and the pointed looks—but it was getting harder; anyone could see that.

Roger had gone at once to visit the Christies—had gone every day since Malva's death save for his hasty expedition to Halifax—had buried the girl with simplicity and tears—and had since worn himself out with being reasonable and soothing and firm to everyone else on the Ridge. He had immediately put aside his plan to go to Edenton for ordination, but Jamie, hearing of it, had insisted.

"You've done everything here you could possibly do," Brianna said, for the hundredth time. "There's nothing else you can do to help—and it might be years before you have another chance."

She knew how urgently he wished to be ordained, and would have done anything to further that wish. For herself, she wished that she could see it; but without a great deal of talk, they had agreed that it was best for her and Jem to go to River Run, and wait there for Roger to make the trip to Edenton and then return. It couldn't do a candidate for ordination any good to turn up with a Catholic wife and child.

The guilt of leaving, though, with her parents standing in the eye of the whirlwind . . .

"You have to go," she repeated. "But maybe I—"

He stopped her with a look.

"No, we've done that." His argument was that her presence couldn't affect public opinion, which was probably true. She realized that his real reason—shared by her parents—was a desire to get her and Jem away from the situation on the Ridge, out of the uproar and safe, preferably before Jem realized that a good many of the neighbors thought that one, if not both, of his grandparents was a cold-blooded murderer.

And, to her private shame, she was eager to go.

Someone had killed Malva—and her baby. Every time she thought of it, the possibilities swam before her, the litany of names. And every time, she was forced to see her cousin's name among them. Ian had not run away, and she couldn't—could *not*—think that it had been him. And yet every day she was obliged to see Ian, and to contemplate the possibility.

She stood staring into the bag she was packing, folding and refolding the shirt in her hands, looking for reasons to go, reasons to stay—and knowing that no reason had any power at all, not now.

A dull *thunk!* from outside jerked her from her mire of indecision.

"What—" She reached the door in two steps, fast enough to see Jem and Aidan disappearing into the woods like a pair of rabbits. On the edge of the trench lay the cracked pieces of the pipe segment they had just dropped.

"You little *snot*-rags!" she bellowed, and grabbed for a broom—intending what she didn't know, but violence seemed the only outlet for the frustration that had just erupted like a volcano, searing through her.

"Bree," Roger said softly, and put a hand on her back. "It's not important."

She jerked away and rounded on him, the blood roaring in her ears.

"Do you have any idea how long it takes to make one of those? How many firings it takes to get one that's not cracked? How—"

"Yes, I do know," he said, his voice level. "And it's still not important."

She stood trembling, breathing hard. Very gently, he reached out and took the broom from her, standing it neatly back in its place.

"I need—to go," she said, when she could form words again, and he nodded, his eyes tinged with the sadness he had carried ever since the day of Malva's death.

"Aye, ye do," he said quietly.

He came behind her, put his arms around her, his chin resting on her shoulder, and gradually she stopped shaking. Across the clearing, she saw Mrs. Bug come down the path from the garden with an apron full of cabbages and carrots; Claire had not set foot in her garden since . . .

"Will they be all right?"

"We'll pray that they will," he said, and tightened his arms around her. She was comforted by his touch, and didn't notice until later that he had not in fact reassured her that they would.

87

JUSTICE IS MINE, SAYETH THE LORD

I POKED AT THE LAST package from Lord John, trying to work up enough enthusiasm to open it. It was a small wooden crate; perhaps more vitriol. I supposed I should make a fresh batch of ether—but then, what was the point? People had stopped coming to my surgery, even for the treatment of minor cuts and bruises, let alone the odd appendectomy.

I ran a finger through the dust on the counter, and thought that I should at least take care of that; Mrs. Bug kept the rest of the house spotless, but wouldn't come into the surgery. I added dusting to the long list of things that I should do, but made no move to go and find a dust cloth.

Sighing, I got up and went across the hall. Jamie was sitting at his desk, twiddling a quill and staring at a half-finished letter. He put down the quill when he saw me, smiling.

"How is it, Sassenach?"

"All right," I said, and he nodded, accepting it at face value. His face showed the lines of strain, and I knew that he was no more all right than I was. "I haven't seen Ian all day. Did he say he was going?" To the Cherokee, I meant. Little wonder if he wanted to get away from the Ridge; I thought it had taken a good deal of fortitude for him to stay as long as he had, bearing the stares and murmurs—and the outright accusations.

Jamie nodded again, and dropped the quill back into its jar.

"Aye, I told him to go. No purpose to him staying any longer; there'd only be more fights." Ian didn't say anything about the fights, but had more than once turned up to supper with the marks of battle on him.

"Right. Well, I'd better tell Mrs. Bug before she starts the supper." Still, I made no motion to get up, finding some small sense of comfort in Jamie's presence, some surcease from the constant memory of the small, bloody weight in my lap, inert as a lump of meat—and the sight of Malva's eyes, so surprised.

I heard horses in the yard, several of them. I glanced at Jamie, who shook his head, brows raised, then rose to go and meet the visitors, whoever they were. I followed him down the hall, wiping my hands on my apron and mentally revising the supper menu to accommodate what sounded like at least a dozen guests, from the whickering and murmuring I heard in the dooryard.

Jamie opened the door, and stopped dead. I looked over his shoulder, and felt terror seize me. Horsemen, black against the sinking sun, and in that moment, I was back in the whisky clearing, damp with sweat and clad in nothing but my shift. Jamie heard my gasp, and put back a hand, to keep me away.

"What d'ye want, Brown?" he said, sounding most unfriendly.

"We've come for your wife," said Richard Brown. There was an unmistakable note of gloating in his voice, and hearing it, the down hairs on my body rippled with cold, and black spots floated in my field of vision. I stepped back, hardly feeling my feet, and took hold of the doorjamb to my surgery, clinging to it for support.

"Well, ye can just be on your way, then," Jamie replied, with the same unfriendly tone. "Ye've nothing to do with my wife, nor she with you."

"Ah, now, there you're wrong, *Mister* Fraser." My vision had cleared, and I saw him urge his horse up closer to the stoop. He leaned down, peering through the door, and evidently saw me, for he smiled, in a most unpleasant fashion.

"We've come to arrest your wife, for the dastard crime of murder."

Jamie's hand tensed where he gripped the door, and he drew himself slowly to his fullest height, seeming to expand as he did so.

"Ye'll leave my land, sir," he said, and his voice had

dropped to a level just above the rustlings of horses and harness. "And ye'll go now."

I felt, rather than heard, footsteps behind me. Mrs. Bug, coming to see what was afoot.

"Bride save us," she whispered, seeing the men. Then she was gone, running back through the house, light-footed as a deer. I should follow her, I knew, escape through the back door, run up into the forest, hide. But my limbs were frozen. I could barely breathe, let alone move.

And Richard Brown was looking at me over Jamie's shoulder, open dislike mingling with triumph.

"Oh, we'll leave," he said, straightening up. "Hand her over, and we'll be gone. Vanished like the morning dew," he said, and laughed. Dimly, I wondered whether he was drunk.

"By what right do you come here?" Jamie demanded. His left hand rose, rested on the hilt of his dirk in plain threat. The sight of it galvanized me, finally, and I stumbled down the hall, toward the kitchen where the guns were kept.

". . . Committee of Safety." I caught those words in Brown's voice, raised in threat, and then was through into the kitchen. I grabbed the fowling piece from its hooks above the hearth, and wrenching open the drawer of the sideboard, hastily bundled the three pistols there into the large pockets of my surgical apron, made to hold instruments while I worked.

My hands were shaking. I hesitated—the pistols were primed and loaded; Jamie checked them every night—should I take the shot pouch, the powder horn? No time. I heard Jamie's voice and Richard Brown's, shouting now at the front of the house.

The sound of the back door opening jerked my head up, and I saw an unfamiliar man pause in the doorway, looking round. He saw me and started toward me, grinning, hand out to seize my arm.

I lifted a pistol from my apron and shot him, point-blank. The grin didn't leave his face, but took on a slightly puzzled air. He blinked once or twice, then put a hand to his side, where a reddening spot was beginning to spread on his shirt. He looked at his blood-smeared fingers, and his jaw dropped.

"Well, goddamn!" he said. "You shot me!"

"I did," I said, breathless. "And I'll bloody do it again, if you don't get out of here!" I dropped the empty pistol on the floor with a crash, and scrabbled one-handed in my apron pocket for another, still holding the fowling piece in a death grip.

He didn't wait to see if I meant it, but whirled and crashed into the door frame, then stumbled through it, leaving a smear of blood on the wood.

Wisps of black-powder smoke floated in the air, mingling oddly with the scent of roasting fish, and I thought for an instant that I might throw up, but managed despite my nausea to set down the fowling piece for a moment and bar the door, my hands shaking so that it took several tries.

Sudden sounds from the front of the house drove nerves and everything else from my mind, and I was running down the hall, gun in hand, before I had made a conscious decision to move, the heavy pistols in my apron banging against my thighs.

They'd dragged Jamie off the porch; I caught a brief glimpse of him in the midst of a surging melee of bodies. They'd stopped shouting. There wasn't any noise at all, save for small grunts and the impact of flesh, the scuffling of myriad feet in the dust. It was deadly earnest, that struggle, and I knew at once that they meant to kill him.

I leveled the fowling piece at the edge of the crowd farthest from Jamie, and pulled the trigger. The crash of the gun and the startled screams seemed to come together, and the scene before me flew apart, the knot of men dissolving, peppered with bird shot. Jamie had kept hold of his dirk; with a little room around him now, I saw him drive it into one man's side, wrench it back and lash sideways in the same motion, scoring a bloody furrow across the forehead of a man who had fallen back a little.

Then I caught a glimpse of metal to one side and by reflex shrieked "DUCK!" an instant before Brown's pistol fired. There was a small *tchoong* past my ear, and I realized, in a very calm sort of way, that Brown had fired at me, not Jamie.

Jamie had, however, ducked. So had everyone else in the yard, and men were now scrambling to their feet, confused, the impetus of the attack dispersed. Jamie had dived toward the porch; he was up and stumbling toward me, striking viciously with the hilt of his dirk at a man who grabbed at his sleeve, so the man fell back with a cry.

We might have rehearsed it a dozen times. He took the steps of the porch in one leap and flung himself into me, carrying us both through the door, then spun on his heel and slammed the door, throwing himself against it and holding it against the frenzied impact of bodies for the instant it took me to drop the fowling piece, seize the bolt, and lift it into place.

It fell into its hooks with a thunk.

The door vibrated to the blows of fists and shoulders, and the shouting had started up again, but with a different sound. No gloating, no taunting. Cursing still, but with a set, malign intent.

Neither of us paused to listen.

"I barred the kitchen door," I gasped, and Jamie nodded, diving into my surgery to secure the bolts of the inside shutters there. I heard the crash of breaking glass in the surgery behind me as I ran into his study; the windows there were smaller, and not glass, placed high in the wall. I slammed the shutters to and bolted them, then ran back into the suddenly darkened hallway to find the gun.

Jamie had it already; he was in the kitchen, grabbing things, and as I started toward the kitchen door, he came out of it, hung about with shot pouches, powder horns, and the like, fowling piece in his hand, and with a jerk of the head, motioned me before him up the stairs.

The rooms above were still filled with light; it was like bursting up from underwater, and I gulped the light as though it were air, dazzled and eyes watering as I rushed to bolt the shutters in the boxroom and Amy McCallum's room. I didn't know where Amy and her sons were; I could only be grateful that they weren't in the house at the moment.

I ran into the bedroom, gasping. Jamie was kneeling by the window, methodically loading guns and saying something under his breath in Gaelic—prayer or cursing, I couldn't tell.

I didn't ask if he was hurt. His face was bruised, his lip was split, and blood had run down his chin onto his shirt, he was covered with dirt and what I assumed to be smears of other peoples' blood, and the ear on the side closest me was swollen. But he was steady in his movements, and anything short of a fractured skull would have to wait.

"They mean to kill us," I said, and didn't mean it as a question.

He nodded, eyes on his work, then handed me a spare pistol to load.

"Aye, they do. Good job the weans are all safe away, isn't it?" He smiled at me suddenly, bloody-toothed and fierce, and I felt steadier than I had for a long time.

He'd left one side of the shutter ajar. I moved carefully back behind him and peered out, the loaded pistol primed and in my hand.

"No bodies lying in the dooryard," I reported. "I suppose you didn't kill any of them."

"Not for want of trying," he replied. "God, what I'd give for a rifle!" He rose cautiously to his knees, the barrel of the fowling piece protruding over the sill, and surveyed the state of the attack.

They had withdrawn for the moment; a small group was visible under the chestnut trees at the far side of the clearing, and they'd taken the horses down toward Bree and Roger's cabin, safely out of range of flying bullets. Brown and his minions were clearly planning what to do next.

"What do you suppose they would have done, if I'd agreed to go with them?" I could feel my heart again, at least. It was going a mile a minute, but I could breathe, and some feeling was coming back into my extremities.

"I should never ha' let ye go," he replied shortly.

"And quite possibly Richard Brown knows that," I said. He nodded; he'd been thinking along the same lines. Brown had never intended actually to arrest me; only to provoke an incident in which we could both be killed under circumstances dubious enough as to prevent wholesale retaliation by Jamie's tenants.

"Mrs. Bug got out, did she?" he asked.

"Yes. If they didn't catch her outside the house." I narrowed my eyes against the brilliant afternoon sun, searching for a short, broad figure in skirts among the group by the chestnut trees, but I saw only men.

Jamie nodded again, hissing gently through his back teeth

as he swiveled the gun barrel slowly through an arc that covered the dooryard.

"We'll see, then" was all he said. "Come that wee bit closer, man," he murmured, as one man started cautiously across the yard toward the house. "One shot; that's all I ask. Here, Sassenach, take this." He pushed the fowling piece into my hands, and selected his favorite of the pistols, a long-barreled Highland dag with a scroll butt.

The man—it was Richard Brown, I saw—stopped some distance away, pulled a handkerchief from the waist of his breeches, and waved it slowly overhead. Jamie snorted briefly, but let him come on.

"Fraser!" he called, coming to a stop at a distance of forty yards or so. "Fraser! D'ye hear me?"

Jamie sighted carefully and fired. The ball struck the ground a few feet in front of Brown, raising a sudden puff of dust from the path, and Brown leapt in the air as though stung by a bee.

"What's the matter with you?" he yelled indignantly. "Have ye never heard of a flag o' truce, you horse-stealin' Scotcher?"

"If I wanted ye dead, Brown, ye'd be coolin' this minute!" Jamie shouted back. "Speak your piece." What he did want was plain: he wanted them wary of coming closer to the house; it was impossible to hit anything accurately with a pistol at forty yards, and not that easy with a musket.

"You know what I want!" Brown called. He took off his hat, wiping sweat and dirt from his face. "I want that goddamn murderous witch of yours."

The answer to that was another carefully aimed pistol ball. Brown jumped again, but not so high.

"Look you," he tried again, with a conciliating note in his voice. "We ain't going to hurt her. We mean to take her to Hillsboro for trial. A fair trial. That's all."

Jamie handed me the second pistol to reload, took another, and fired.

You had to give Brown credit for persistence, I thought. Of course, it had probably dawned on him that Jamie either couldn't or wouldn't actually hit him, and he doggedly stood his ground through two more shots, yelling that they meant to take me to Hillsboro, and surely to God if I were innocent, Jamie should *want* a trial, shouldn't he?

It was hot upstairs, and sweat was trickling down between my breasts. I blotted the fabric of my shift against my chest.

With no answer save the whine of pistol balls, Brown threw up his hands in exaggerated pantomime of a reasonable man tried beyond endurance, and stamped back to his men beneath the chestnut trees. Nothing had changed, but seeing the narrow back of him made me breathe a little easier.

Jamie was still crouched in the window, pistol at the ready, but seeing Brown go back, he relaxed and sat back on his heels, sighing.

"Is there water, Sassenach?"

"Yes." The bedroom ewer was full; I poured him a cup and he drank it thirstily. We had food, water, and a fair amount of shot and powder. I did not, however, foresee a long siege ahead.

"What do you suppose they'll do?" I didn't go near the window, but by standing to one side, I could see them clearly, gathered in conference under the trees. The air was still and heavy, and the leaves above them hung like damp rags.

Jamie came to stand behind me, dabbing at his lip with the tail of his shirt.

"Fire the house as soon as it's dark, I suppose," he said matter-of-factly. "I would. Though I suppose they might try draggin' Gideon out and threatening to put a ball through his head, and I didna give ye up." He seemed to think this last was a joke, but I failed to see the humor in it.

He saw my face and put a hand behind my back, drawing me close for a moment. The air was hot and sticky, and we were both wringing wet, but the nearness of him was a comfort, nonetheless.

"So," I said, taking a deep breath. "It all depends on whether Mrs. Bug got away—and who she's told."

"She'll ha' gone for Arch, first thing." Jamie patted me gently, and sat down on the bed. "If he's to home, he'll run for Kenny Lindsay; he's nearest. After that . . ." He shrugged, and closed his eyes, and I saw that his face was pale under the sunburn and the smears of dirt and blood.

"Jamie—are you hurt?"

He opened his eyes and gave me a small, one-sided smile, trying not to stretch his torn lip.

"No, I've broken my bloody finger again, is all." He raised a shoulder in deprecation, but let me lift his right hand to look.

It was a clean break; that was all that could be said for it. The fourth finger was stiff, the joints fused from being so badly broken long ago, in Wentworth Prison. He couldn't bend it, and it therefore stuck out awkwardly; this wasn't the first time he'd snapped it.

He swallowed as I felt gently for the break, and closed his eyes again, sweating.

"There's laudanum in the surgery," I said. "Or whisky." I knew he would refuse, though, and he did.

"I'll want a clear head," he said, "whatever happens." He opened his eyes and gave me the ghost of a smile. The room was sweltering and airless, despite the open shutter. The sun was more than halfway down the sky, and the first shadows were gathering in the corners of the room.

I went down to the surgery to fetch a splint and bandage; it wouldn't help a lot, but it was something to do.

The surgery was dark, with the shutters closed, but with the windows broken, air came through them, making the room seem oddly exposed and vulnerable. I walked in like a mouse, quiet, stopping abruptly, listening for danger, whiskers twitching. Everything was quiet, though.

"*Too* quiet," I said aloud, and laughed. Moving with purpose and ignoring the noise, I set my feet down firmly and opened cupboard doors with abandon, banging instruments and rattling bottles as I looked out for what I needed.

I stopped into the kitchen before returning upstairs. Partly to reassure myself that the back door *was* firmly bolted, and partly to see what bits of food Mrs. Bug might have left out. He hadn't said so, but I knew the pain of the broken finger was making Jamie mildly nauseated—and in him, food generally quelled that sort of disturbance, and made him feel more settled.

The cauldron was still over the coals, but the fire, untended, had burned down so far that the soup had luckily not boiled away. I poked up the embers and put on three sticks of fat pine, as much by way of thumbing my nose at the besiegers outside as from the long-ingrained habit of never letting a fire die. Let them see the spray of sparks from the chimney, I thought, and imagine us sitting peacefully down to eat by our hearth. Or better yet, imagine us sitting by the blazing fire, melting lead and molding bullets.

In this defiant frame of mind, I went back upstairs, equipped with medical supplies, an alfresco lunch, and a large bottle of black ale. I couldn't help but notice, though, the echo of my footsteps on the stair, and the silence that settled quickly back into place behind me, like water when one steps out of it.

I heard a shot, just as I approached the head of the stair, and took the last steps so fast that I tripped and would have fallen headlong, save for reeling into the wall.

Jamie appeared from Mr. Wemyss's room, fowling piece in hand, looking startled.

"Are ye all right, Sassenach?"

"Yes," I said crossly, wiping spilled soup off my hand with my apron. "What in the name of God are you shooting at?"

"Nothing. I only wanted to make the point that the back of the house is nay safer than the front, if they thought of creeping up that way. Just to ensure that they *do* wait for dark to fall."

I bound up his finger, which seemed to help a little. The food, as I'd hoped, helped considerably more. He ate like a wolf, and rather to my surprise, so did I.

"The condemned ate a hearty meal," I observed, picking up crumbs of bread and cheese. "I'd always thought being in danger of death would make one too nervous to eat, but apparently not."

He shook his head, took a swallow of ale, and passed me the bottle.

"A friend once told me, 'The body has nay conscience.' I dinna ken that that's entirely so—but it is true that the body doesna generally admit the possibility of nonexistence. And if ye exist—well, ye need food, that's all." He grinned one-sided at me, and tearing the last of the sweet rolls in half, gave one to me.

I took it, but didn't eat it immediately. There was no sound outside, save the buzzing of cicadas, though the air had a sultry thickness to it that often presaged rain. It was early in the summer for storms, but one could only hope.

"You've thought of it, too, haven't you?" I said quietly.

He made no pretense of misunderstanding me.

"Well, it *is* the twenty-first o' the month," he said.

"It's *June,* for heaven's sake! And the wrong year, as well. That newspaper clipping said January, of 1776!" I was absurdly indignant, as though I had somehow been cheated.

He found that funny.

"I was a printer myself, Sassenach," he said, laughing through a mouthful of sweet roll. "Ye dinna want to believe everything ye read in the newspapers, aye?"

When I looked out again, only a few men were visible under the chestnut trees. One of them saw my movement; he waved his arm slowly to and fro above his head—then drew the edge of his hand flat across his throat.

The sun was just above the treetops; two hours, perhaps, to nightfall. Two hours surely was enough time for Mrs. Bug to have summoned help, though—always assuming she had found anyone who would come. Arch might have gone to Cross Creek—he went once a month; Kenny might be hunting. As for the newer tenants . . . without Roger to keep them in order, their suspicion and dislike of me had become blatant. I had the feeling that they might come if summoned—but only to cheer as I was dragged away.

If anyone *did* come—what then? I didn't want to be dragged away, much less shot or burnt alive in the ashes of my house—but I didn't want anyone else injured or killed in an effort to prevent it, either.

"Come away from the window, Sassenach," Jamie said. He held out a hand to me, and I went, sitting on the bed beside him. I felt all at once exhausted, the adrenaline of emergency having burned away, leaving my muscles feeling like heat-softened rubber.

"Lie down, *a Sorcha,*" he said softly. "Lay your head in my lap."

Hot as it was, I did so, finding it a comfort to stretch out, even more to hear his heart, thumping slow and solid above my ear, and feel his hand, light on my head.

All the weapons were laid out, ranged on the floor beside the window, all loaded, primed, and ready for use. He'd taken his sword down from the armoire; it stood by the door, a last resort.

"There's nothing we can do now, is there?" I said after a little. "Nothing but wait."

His fingers moved idly through the damp curls of my hair; it fell to just above my shoulders now, long enough—barely—to tie back or pin up.

"Well, we might say an Act of Contrition," he said. "We did that, always, the night before a battle. Just in case," he added, smiling down at me.

"All right," I said after a pause. "Just in case."

I reached up and his good hand closed round mine.

"Mon Dieu, je regrette . . ." he began, and I remembered that he said this prayer in French, harking back to those days as a mercenary in France; how often had he said it then, a necessary precaution, cleansing the soul at night in expectation of the possibility of death in the morning?

I said it, too, in English, and we fell silent. The cicadas had stopped. Far, far away, I thought I heard a sound that might be thunder.

"Do you know," I said after a long while, "I'm sorry for a great many things and people. Rupert, Murtagh, Dougal . . . Frank. Malva," I added softly, with a catch in my throat. "But speaking only for myself . . ." I cleared my throat.

"I don't regret anything," I said, watching the shadows creep in from the corners of the room. "Not one bloody thing."

"Nor do I, *mo nighean donn,*" he said, and his fingers stilled, warm against my skin. "Nor do I."

I WOKE FROM a doze with the smell of smoke in my nostrils. Being in a state of grace is all very well, but I imagine even Joan of Arc had qualms when they lit the first brand. I sat bolt upright, heart pounding, to see Jamie at the window.

It wasn't quite dark yet; streaks of orange and gold and rose lit the sky to the west, and touched his face with a fiery light. He looked long-nosed and fierce, the lines of strain cut deep.

"Folk are coming," he said. His voice was matter-of-fact, but his good hand was clenched hard round the edge of the shutter, as though he would have liked to slam and bolt it.

I came to stand by him, combing my fingers hastily through my hair. I could still make out figures under the chestnut trees, though they now were no more than silhouettes. They'd built a bonfire there, at the far edge of the dooryard; that's what I'd smelled. There were more people coming into the dooryard, though; I was sure I made out the squat figure of Mrs. Bug among them. The sound of voices floated up, but they weren't talking loudly enough to make out words.

"Will ye plait my hair, Sassenach? I canna manage, wi' this." He gave his broken finger a cursory glance.

I lit a candle, and he moved a stool to the window, so he could keep watch while I combed his hair and braided it into a tight, thick queue, which I clubbed at the base of his neck and tied with a neat black ribbon.

I knew his reasons were twofold: not only to appear well-groomed and gentlemanly, but to be ready to fight if he had to. I was less worried about someone seizing me by the hair as I attempted to cleave them in half with a sword, but supposed that if this were my last appearance as the lady of the Ridge, I should not appear unkempt.

I heard him mutter something under his breath, as I brushed my own hair by candlelight, and turned on my stool to look at him.

"Hiram's come," he informed me. "I hear his voice. That's good."

"If you say so," I said dubiously, recollecting Hiram Crombie's denunciations in church a week before—thinly veiled remarks clearly aimed at us. Roger hadn't mentioned them; Amy McCallum had told me.

Jamie turned his head to look at me, and smiled, an expression of extraordinary sweetness coming over his face.

"Ye're verra lovely, Sassenach," he said as though surprised. "But, aye, it's good. Whatever he thinks, he wouldna countenance Brown hanging us in the dooryard, nor yet setting the house afire to drive us out."

There were more voices outside; the crowd was growing quickly.

"Mr. Fraser!"

He took a deep breath, took the candle from the table, and threw open the shutter, holding the candle near his face so they could see him.

It was almost full dark, but several of the crowd were holding torches, which gave me uneasy visions of the mob coming to burn Dr. Frankenstein's monster—but did at least allow me to make out the faces below. There were at least thirty men—and not a few women—there, in addition to Brown and his thugs. Hiram Crombie was indeed there, standing beside Richard Brown, and looking like something out of the Old Testament.

"We require ye to come down, Mr. Fraser," he called. "And your wife—if ye please."

I caught sight of Mrs. Bug, plump and clearly terrified, her face streaked with tears. Then Jamie closed the shutters, gently, and offered me his arm.

JAMIE HAD WORN both dirk and sword, and had not changed his clothes. He stood on the porch, bloodstained and battered, and dared them to harm us further.

"Ye'll take my wife over my dead body," he said, raising his powerful voice enough to be heard across the clearing. I was rather afraid they would. He'd been right—so far—about Hiram not countenancing lynching, but it was clear that public opinion was not in our favor.

"Thou shalt not suffer a witch to live!" someone shouted from the back of the crowd, and a stone whistled through the air, bouncing off the front of the house with a sharp report, like a gunshot. It struck no more than a foot from my head, and I flinched, instantly regretting it.

Angry murmurs had risen from the moment Jamie had opened the door, and this encouraged them. There were shouts of "Murderers!" and "Heartless! Heartless!" and a number of Gaelic insults that I didn't try to understand.

"If she didn't do it, *breugaire,* who did?" someone bellowed. "Liar" it meant.

The man Jamie had slashed across the face with his dirk was in the forefront of the crowd; the open wound gaped, still oozing, and his face was a mask of dried blood.

"If 'twasn't her, 'twas him!" he shouted, pointing at Jamie. *"Fear-siûrsachd!"* Lecher.

There was an ugly rumble of agreement at that, and I saw Jamie shift his weight and set his hand to his sword, ready to draw if they charged him.

"Be still!" Hiram's voice was rather shrill, but penetrating. "Be still, I tell ye!" He pushed Brown aside and came up the steps, very deliberately. At the top, he gave me a look of revulsion, but then turned to the crowd.

"Justice!" one of Brown's men yelled, before he could speak. "We want justice!"

"Aye, we do!" Hiram shouted back. "And justice we shall have, for the puir raped lass and her bairn unborn!"

A satisfied growl greeted this, and icy terror ran down my legs, so that I feared my knees would give way.

"Justice! Justice!" Various people were taking up the chant, but Hiram stopped them, raising both hands as though he were bloody Moses parting the Red Sea.

"*Justice is mine,* sayeth the Lord," Jamie remarked, in a voice just loud enough to be generally heard. Hiram, who had evidently been about to say the same thing, gave him a furious look, but couldn't very well contradict him.

"And justice you'll have, Mister Fraser!" Brown said very loudly. He lifted his face, narrow-eyed and malicious with triumph. "I wish to take her for trial. Anyone accused is entitled to that, nay? If she is innocent—if *you* are innocent—how can you refuse?"

"Certainly a point," Hiram observed, very dry. "If your wife be clean o' the crime, she's naught to fear. How say ye, sir?"

"I say that should I surrender her to the hands of this man, she willna live to stand a trial," Jamie replied hotly. "He holds me to blame for the death of his brother—and some of ye here will ken well enough the truth o' *that* affair!" he added, lifting his chin to the crowd.

Here and there, heads nodded—but they were few. No more than a dozen of his Ardsmuir men had been on the expedition that rescued me; in the wake of gossip following it, many of the new tenants would have known only that I had been abducted, assaulted in some scandalous fashion, and that men had died on my account. The mind of the times being what it was, I was well aware that an obscure sense of blame attached to the victim of any sexual crime—unless the woman died, in which case she became at once a spotless angel.

"He will slaughter her out of hand, for the sake of revenge upon me," Jamie said, raising his voice. He changed abruptly to Gaelic, pointing at Brown. "Look at yon man, and see the truth of the matter writ upon his face! He has no more to do with justice than with honor, and he would not recognize honor by the smell of its arse!"

That made a few of them laugh, in sheer surprise. Brown, disconcerted, looked round to see what they were laughing at, which made more of them laugh.

The mood of the assembly was still against us, but they were not yet with Brown—who was, after all, a stranger. Hiram's narrow brow creased in consideration.

"What would ye offer by way of guarantee for the woman's safety?" Hiram asked Brown.

"A dozen hogsheads of beer and three dozen prime hides," Brown replied promptly. "Four dozen!" His eagerness gleamed in his eyes, and it was all he could do to keep his voice from shaking with the lust to take me. I had a sudden, unpleasant conviction that while my death was his ultimate goal, he didn't intend that it should be a quick one, unless circumstances demanded it.

"It would be worth far more than that to ye, *breugaire,* to have your revenge upon me with her death," Jamie said evenly.

Hiram glanced from one to the other, unsure what to do. I looked out into the crowd, keeping my face impassive. In truth, it was not difficult to do; I felt completely numb.

There were a few friendly faces, glancing anxiously to

Jamie, to see what to do. Kenny and his brothers, Murdo and Evan, stood in a tight group, hands on their dirks and faces set. I didn't know whether Richard Brown had chosen his timing, or merely been lucky. Ian was gone, hunting with his Cherokee friends. Arch was plainly gone, as well, or he would be visible—Arch and his ax would be uncommonly handy just now, I thought.

Fergus and Marsali were gone—they, too, would have helped to stem the tide. But the most important absence was Roger's. He alone had been keeping the Presbyterians more or less under control since the day of Malva's accusation, or at least keeping a lid on the simmering pot of gossip and animosity. He might have cowed them now—had he been here.

The conversation had devolved from high drama to a three-way wrangle among Jamie, Brown, and Hiram, the former two adamant in their positions, and poor Hiram, quite unsuited to the task, trying to adjudicate. Insofar as I had feelings to spare, I felt rather sorry for him.

"Take him!" a voice called suddenly. Allan Christie pushed his way to the front of the crowd, and pointed at Jamie. His voice trembled and broke with emotion. "It's him debauched my sister, him that kilt her! If ye'll put someone to the trial, take him!"

There was a subterranean rumble of agreement at that, and I saw John MacNeill and young Hugh Abernathy draw close together, glancing uneasily from Jamie to the three Lindsay brothers, and back again.

"Nay, it's her!" a woman's voice called in contradiction, high and shrill. One of the fishers' wives; she stabbed a finger at me, face pinched with malevolence. "A man might kill a lass he'd got wi' child—but no man would do sich wickedness as to steal a babe unborn frae the womb! No but a witch would do that—and she found wi' the puir wee corpse in her hands!"

A higher susurrus of condemnation greeted that. The men might possibly give me the benefit of doubt—no woman would.

"By the name of the Almighty!" Hiram was losing his grip on the situation, and becoming panicky. The situation was perilously close to degenerating into riot; anyone could feel the currents of hysteria and violence in the air. He cast his eyes up to heaven, looking for inspiration—and found some.

"Take them both!" he said suddenly. He looked at Brown, then Jamie. "Take them both," he repeated, testing the notion and finding it good. "Ye'll go along, to see that nay harm comes to your wife," he said reasonably to Jamie. "And if it should be proved that she is innocent . . ." His voice died away on that, as it dawned on him that what he was saying was that if I were proven innocent, Jamie must be guilty, and what a good idea it would be to have him on the spot to be hanged instead.

"She is innocent; so am I." Jamie spoke without heat, doggedly repeating it. He had no real hope of convincing anyone; the only doubt among the crowd was whether he or I was the guilty party—or whether we had plotted together to destroy Malva Christie.

He turned suddenly to face the crowd, and cried out to them in Gaelic.

"If you will deliver us into the stranger's hand, then our blood be upon your heads, and you will answer for our lives upon the Day of Judgment!"

A sudden hush fell on the crowd at that. Men glanced uncertainly at their neighbors, measured Brown and his cohort with doubtful eyes.

They were known to the community, but strangers—Sassenachs—in the Scottish sense. So was I, and a witch, to boot. Lecher, rapist, and Papist murderer he might be—but Jamie at least was not a stranger.

The man I had shot was grinning at me evilly over Brown's shoulder; evidently, I had no more than grazed him, worse luck. I gave him stare for stare, sweat gathering between my breasts, moisture slick and hot beneath the veil of my hair.

A murmur was rising among the crowd; argument and disputation, and I could see the Ardsmuir men begin to make their way slowly toward the porch, pushing through the mob. Kenny Lindsay's eyes were fixed on Jamie's face, and I felt Jamie take a deep breath beside me.

They would fight for him, if he called them. But there were too few of them, and poorly armed, by contrast with Brown's mob. They would not win—and there were women and children in the crowd. To call his men would provoke only bloody riot, and leave the deaths of innocents upon his conscience. That was not a burden he could bear; not now.

I saw him come to this conclusion, and his mouth tighten. I had no idea what he might be about to do, but he was forestalled. There was a disturbance at the edge of the crowd; people turned to look, then froze, stricken silent.

Thomas Christie came through the crowd; in spite of the darkness and wavering torchlight, I knew at once it was him. He walked like an old man, hunched and halting, looking at no one. The crowd gave way before him at once, deeply respectful of his grief.

The grief was plainly marked on his face. He had let his beard and hair go untrimmed, uncombed, and both were matted. His eyes were pouched and bloodshot, the lines from nose to mouth black furrows through his beard. His eyes were alive, though, alert and intelligent. He walked through the crowd, past his son, as though he were alone, and came up the steps onto the porch.

"I will go with them to Hillsboro," he said quietly to Hiram Crombie. "Let them both be taken, if ye will—but I will travel with them, as surety that no further evil may be done. Surely justice is mine, if it be anyone's."

Brown looked much taken aback by this declaration; plainly it wasn't what he'd had in mind at all. But the crowd was in instant sympathy, murmuring agreement at the proposed solution. Everyone had the greatest compassion and respect for Tom Christie in the wake of his daughter's murder, and the general feeling seemed to be that this gesture was one of the greatest magnanimity.

It was, too, as he had in all likelihood just saved our lives—at least for the moment. From the look in his eye, Jamie would strongly have preferred simply to take his chances on killing Richard Brown, but realized that beggars could not be choosers, and acquiesced as gracefully as possible, with a nod of the head.

Christie's gaze rested on me for a moment, then turned to Jamie.

"If it will suit your convenience, Mr. Fraser, perhaps we

will leave in the morning? There is no reason why you and your wife should not rest in your own beds."

Jamie bowed to him.

"I thank ye, sir," he said with great formality. Christie nodded back, then turned and went back down the steps, completely ignoring Richard Brown, who was looking at once irritated and confounded.

I saw Kenny Lindsay close his eyes, shoulders slumping in relief. Then Jamie put his hand under my elbow, and we turned, going into our house for what might be the final night spent under its roof.

88

IN THE WAKE OF SCANDAL

THE RAIN THAT HAD threatened arrived in the night, and the day dawned gray, bleak, and wet. Mrs. Bug was in a similar state, sniffling into her apron and repeating over and over, "Oh, if only Arch had been here! But I couldna find anyone save Kenny Lindsay, and by the time he'd run for MacNeill and Abernathy—"

"Dinna fash yourself for it, *a leannan,*" Jamie said, and kissed her affectionately on the brow. "It may be for the best. No one was damaged, the house is still standing"—he cast a wistful eye toward the rafters, every beam shaped by his own hand—"and it may be we'll have this wretched matter settled soon, God willing."

"God willing," she echoed fervently, crossing herself. She sniffed and wiped her eyes. "And I've packed a wee bit of food, that ye shouldna starve on the way, sir."

Richard Brown and his men had sheltered under the trees as best they could; no one had offered them hospitality, which was as damning an indication of their unpopularity as could be imagined, Highland standards being what they were in such matters. And as clear an indication of our own unpopularity, that Brown should be permitted to take us into custody.

In consequence, Brown's men were soaking wet, ill-fed, sleepless, and short-tempered. I hadn't slept, either, but I was at least full of breakfast, warm, and—for the moment—dry, which made me feel a little better, though my heart felt hollow and my bones filled with lead as we reached the head of the trail and I looked back across the clearing at the house, with Mrs. Bug standing waving on the porch. I waved back, and then my horse plunged into the darkness of the dripping trees.

It was a grim journey, and silent for the most part. Jamie and I rode close together, but couldn't speak of anything important, in hearing of Brown's men. As for Richard Brown, he was seriously out of countenance.

It was reasonably clear that he had never intended to take me anywhere for trial, but had merely seized upon the pretext as a means of revenging himself on Jamie for Lionel's death—and God knew what he would have done, I reflected, had he known what had really happened to his brother, and Mrs. Bug there within arm's length of him. With Tom Christie along, though, there was nothing he could do; he was obliged to take us to Hillsboro, and he did so with bad grace.

Tom Christie rode like a man in a dream—a bad dream—his face closed and inward-looking, speaking to no one.

The man Jamie had slashed was not there; I supposed he had gone home to Brownsville. The gentleman I had shot was still with us, though.

I couldn't tell how bad the wound was, nor yet whether the bullet had gone into him or merely grazed his side. He wasn't incapacitated, but it was plain from the way he hunched to one side, his face contorting now and then, that he was in pain.

I hesitated for some time. I had brought a small medical kit with me, as well as saddlebags and bedroll. Under the circumstances, I felt relatively little sense of compassion for the man. On the other hand, instinct was strong—and as I said to Jamie in an undertone when we stopped to make camp for the evening, it wouldn't help matters if he died of infection.

I steeled myself to offer to examine and dress the wound, as soon as the opportunity should occur. The man—his name seemed to be Ezra, though under the circumstances, no formal introductions had been made—was in charge of distributing bowls of food at supper, and I waited under the pine where Jamie and I had taken shelter, intending to speak kindly to him when he brought our food.

He came over, a bowl in each hand, shoulders hunched under a leather coat against the rain. Before I could speak, though, he grinned nastily, spat thickly in one bowl, and handed it to me. The other he dropped at Jamie's feet, spattering his legs with dried-venison stew.

"Oops," he said mildly, and turned on his heel.

Jamie contracted sharply, like a big snake coiling, but I got hold of his arm before he could strike.

"Never mind," I said, and raising my voice just a little, said, "Let him rot."

The man's head snapped round, wide-eyed.

"Let him rot," I repeated, staring at him. I'd seen the flush of fever in his face when he came near, and smelled the faint sweet scent of pus.

Ezra looked completely taken back. He hurried back to the sputtering fire, and refused to look in my direction.

I was still holding the bowl he'd given me, and was startled to have it taken from my hand. Tom Christie threw the contents of the bowl into a bush, and handed me his own, then turned away without speaking.

"But—" I started after him, meaning to give it back. We wouldn't starve, thanks to Mrs. Bug's "wee bit of food," which filled one entire saddlebag. Jamie's hand on my arm stopped me, though.

"Eat it, Sassenach," he said softly. "It's kindly meant."

More than kind, I thought. I was aware of hostile eyes upon me, from the group around the fire. My throat was tight, and I had no appetite, but I took my spoon from my pocket and ate.

Beneath a nearby hemlock tree, Tom Christie had wrapped himself in a blanket and lain down alone, his hat pulled down over his face.

IT RAINED ALL the way to Salisbury. We found shelter in an inn there, and seldom had a fire seemed so welcome. Jamie had brought what cash we had, and in consequence, we could afford a room to ourselves. Brown posted a guard on the stair, but that was merely for show; after all, where would we go?

I stood in front of the fire in my shift, my wet cloak and gown spread over a bench to dry.

"You know," I observed, "Richard Brown hasn't thought this out at all." Not surprising, that, since he hadn't actually intended to take me or us to trial. "Who, exactly, does he mean to hand us over to?"

"The sheriff of the county," Jamie replied, untying his hair and shaking it out over the hearth, so that droplets of water sizzled and popped in the fire. "Or failing that, a justice of the peace, perhaps."

"Yes, but what then? He's got no evidence—no witnesses. How can there be any semblance of a trial?"

Jamie looked at me curiously.

"Ye've never been tried for anything, have ye, Sassenach?"

"You know I haven't."

He nodded.

"I have. For treason."

"Yes? And what happened?"

He ran a hand through his damp hair, considering.

"They made me stand up, and asked my name. I gave it, the judge muttered to his friend for a bit, and then he said, 'Condemned. Imprisonment for life. Put him in irons.' And they took me out to the courtyard and had a blacksmith hammer fetters onto my wrists. The next day we began walking to Ardsmuir."

"They made you *walk* there? From Inverness?"

"I wasna in any great hurry, Sassenach."

I took a deep breath, trying to stem the sinking feeling in the pit of my stomach.

"I see. Well . . . but surely—wouldn't m-murder"—I could just about say it without stammering, but not quite, yet—"be a matter for a jury trial?"

"It might, and certainly I shall insist upon it—if things go so far. Mr. Brown seems to think they may; he's telling everyone in the taproom the story, making us out to be monsters of depravity. Which I must say is no great feat," he added ruefully, "considering the circumstances."

I pressed my lips tight together, to avoid giving a hasty answer. I knew he knew that I had had no choice—he knew that I knew he had had nothing to do with Malva in the first place—but I could not help but feel a sense of blame in both directions, for this desperate muddle in which we found ourselves. Both for what had happened afterward, and for Malva's death itself—though God knew I would give anything to have her alive again.

He was right about Brown, I realized. Cold and wet, I'd paid little attention to the noises from the taproom below, but I could hear Brown's voice, echoing up the chimney, and from the random words that came through, it was apparent that he was doing exactly what Jamie said—blackening our characters, making it out that he and his Committee of Safety had undertaken the ignoble but necessary job of apprehending us and committing us to justice. And, just incidentally, carefully prejudicing any potential jury members by making sure the story spread abroad in all its scandalous detail.

"Is there anything to be done?" I asked, having listened to as much of this nonsense as I could stomach.

He nodded, and pulled a clean shirt from his saddlebag.

"Go down for supper, and look as little like depraved murderers as possible, *a nighean.*"

"Right," I said, and with a sigh, withdrew the ribbon-trimmed cap I had packed.

I SHOULDN'T HAVE been surprised. I had lived long enough to have a fairly cynical view of human nature—and lived long enough in this time to know how directly public opinion expressed itself. And yet I was still shocked, when the first stone hit me in the thigh.

We were some distance south of Hillsboro. The weather continued wet, the roads muddy, and the travel difficult. I think Richard Brown would have been pleased to relinquish us to the sheriff of Rowan county—if such a person had been available. The office, he was informed, was currently unfilled, the last occupant having decamped hurriedly overnight and no one yet found willing to replace him.

A matter of politics, I gathered, the recent sheriff having leaned toward independency, whilst the majority of persons in the county were still strongly Loyalist. I didn't learn the specifics of the incident that had triggered the recent sheriff's hasty departure, but the taverns and inns near Hillsboro were buzzing like hornets' nests in the wake of it.

The Circuit Court had ceased to meet some months before, Brown was informed, the justices who attended it feeling it too dangerous to appear in the present unsettled state of things. The sole justice of the peace he was able to discover felt similarly, and declined point-blank to take custody of us, informing Brown that it was more than his life was worth, to be involved in anything even faintly controversial at the moment.

"But it's nothing to do with politics!" Brown had shouted at him, frustrated. "It's murder, for God's sake—black murder!"

"Anything and everything's political these days, sir," the JP, one Harvey Mickelgrass, informed him sadly, shaking his head. "I should not venture to address even a case of drunk and disorderly, for fear of having my house pulled down around my ears and my wife left widowed. The sheriff attempted to sell his office, but could find no one willing to purchase it. No, sir—you will have to go elsewhere."

Brown would by no means take us to Cross Creek or Campbelton, where Jocasta Cameron's influence was strong, and where the local justice was her good friend, Farquard Campbell. And so we headed south, toward Wilmington.

Brown's men were disedified; they had expected a simple lynching and house-burning, perhaps the odd bit of looting—not this long-drawn-out and tedious plodding from place to place. Their spirits were further lowered when Ezra, who had been clinging to his horse in a dogged daze of fever, fell suddenly into the road and was picked up dead.

I didn't ask to examine the body—and wouldn't have been given leave in any case—but I rather thought from the lolling looks of him that he had simply lost consciousness, tumbled off, and broken his neck.

Not a few of the others cast looks of open fear toward me in the wake of this occurrence, though, and their sense of enthusiasm for the venture diminished visibly.

Richard Brown was not deterred; he would, I was sure, have shot us without mercy long since, had it not been for Tom Christie, silent and gray as the morning fog on the roads. He said little, and that little confined to necessities. I should have thought him moving mechanically, in the numb haze of grief—had I not turned one evening as we camped by the road, to see his eyes fixed upon me, with a look of such naked anguish in them that I glanced hastily away, only to see Jamie, sitting beside me, watching Tom Christie with a very thoughtful expression.

For the most part, though, he kept his face impassive—what could be seen of it, under the shade of his leather slouch hat. And Richard Brown, prevented by Christie's presence from doing us active harm, took every opportunity to spread his version of the tale of Malva's murder—perhaps as much to harrow Tom Christie in the hearing of it, over and over again, as for its effect on our reputations.

At any rate, I should not have been surprised when they stoned us, in a small, nameless hamlet south of Hillsboro—but I was. A young boy had seen us on the road, stared as we rode by—then vanished like a fox, scampering down a bank with the news. And ten minutes later, we rode around a bend in the road and into a fusillade of stones and shrieks.

One struck my mare on the shoulder and she shied violently. I kept my seat narrowly, but was off-balance; another hit me in the thigh, and another high in the chest, knocking the breath from me, and when one more bounced painfully off my head, I lost my grip on the reins, and as the horse, panicked, curvetted and spun, I flew off, landing on the ground with a bone-shaking thud.

I should have been terrified; in fact, I was furious. The stone that had hit me in the head had glanced off—thanks to the thickness of my hair and the cap I wore—but with the infuriating sting of a slap or a pinch, rather than true impact. I was on my feet by reflex, staggering, but caught sight of a jeering boy on the bank above me, hooting and dancing in triumph. I lunged, caught him by the foot and jerked.

He yelped, slipped, and fell on top of me. We crashed to the ground together, and rolled in a tangle of skirts and cloak. I was older, heavier, and completely berserk. All the fear, misery, and uncertainty of the last weeks came to an instant boil, and I punched his sneering face, twice, as hard as I could. I felt something crack in my hand, and pain shot up my arm.

He bellowed, and wriggled to escape—he was smaller than I was, but strong with panic. I struggled to keep a grip on him, got him by the hair—he struck out at me, flailing, and knocked off my cap, getting one hand in my hair and yanking hard.

The pain reignited my fury and I jammed a knee into him, anywhere I could, again, and once more, blindly seeking his soft parts. His mouth opened in a soundless "O" and his eyes bulged; his fingers relaxed and let go of my hair, and I reared up over him and slapped him as hard as I possibly could.

A big rock struck my shoulder with a numbing blow and I was knocked sideways by the impact. I tried to hit him again, but couldn't lift my arm. Panting and sobbing, he writhed free of my cloak and scrambled away on hands and knees, nose bleeding. I whirled on my knees to look after him, and looked straight into the eyes of a young man, his face intent and blazing with excitement, rock at the ready.

It hit me in the cheekbone and I swayed, my vision gone blurry. Then something very large hit me from behind, and I found myself flat on my face, pressed into the ground, the weight of a body on top of mine. It was Jamie; I could tell by the breathless "Holy Mother." His body jerked as the stones hit him; I could hear the horrifying thud of them into his flesh.

There was a lot of shouting going on. I heard Tom Christie's hoarse voice, then the firing of a single shot. More yelling, but of a different character. One or two soft thumps, stones striking earth nearby, a last grunt from Jamie as one slammed into him.

We lay pressed flat for a few moments, and I became aware of the uncomfortably spiky plant squashed under my cheek, the scent of its leaves harsh and bitter in my nose.

Then Jamie sat up, slowly, drawing in his breath with a catch, and I rose in turn on a shaky arm, nearly falling. My cheek was puffed and my hand and shoulder throbbed, but I had no attention to spare for that.

"Are you all right?" Jamie had got halfway to his feet, then sat down again, suddenly. He was pale, and a trickle of blood ran down the side of his face from a cut in his scalp, but he nodded, a hand pressed to his side.

"Aye, fine," he said, but with a breathlessness that told me he likely had cracked ribs. "Ye're all right, Sassenach?"

"Fine." I managed to get to my feet, trembling. Brown's men were scattered, some chasing the horses who had fled in the melee, others cursing, gathering up scattered bits of belongings from the road. Tom Christie was vomiting into the bushes by the road. Richard Brown stood under a tree, watching, his face white. He glanced at me sharply, then away.

We stopped at no more taverns on the way.

89

A MOONLICHT FLICHT

WHEN YE GO TO hit someone, Sassenach, ye want to do it in the soft parts. Faces have too many bones. And then there's the teeth to be thinkin' of."

Jamie spread her fingers, gently pressing the scraped, swollen knuckles, and air hissed between her own teeth.

"Thanks so much for the advice. And you've broken your hand *how* many times, hitting people?"

He wanted to laugh; the vision of her pounding that wee boy in a fury of berserk rage, hair flying in the wind and a look of blood in her eye, was one he would treasure. He didn't, though.

"Your hand's not broken, *a nighean.*" He curled her fingers, cupping her loose fist with both of his.

"How would you know?" she snapped. "*I'm* the doctor here."

He stopped trying to hide his smile.

"If it were broken," he said, "ye'd be white and puking, not red-faced and crankit."

"Crankit, my arse!" She pulled her hand free, glaring at him as she nursed it against her bosom. She was in fact only slightly flushed, and most attractive, with her hair curling out in a wild mass round her head. One of Brown's men had picked up her fallen cap after the attack, timidly offering it to her. Enraged, she had snatched it from him and stuffed it violently into a saddlebag.

"Are ye hungry, lass?"

"Yes," she admitted grudgingly, as aware as he was that folk with broken bones generally had little appetite immediately, though they ate amazingly, once the pain had backed a bit.

He rummaged in the saddlebag, blessing Mrs. Bug as he came out with a handful of dried apricots and a large wrapped wedge of goat's cheese. Brown's men were cooking something over their fire, but he and Claire had not touched any food but their own, not since the first night.

How much longer might this farce go on? he wondered, breaking off a bit of cheese and handing it to his wife. They had food for perhaps a week, with care. Long enough, maybe, to reach the coast, and the weather held good. And what then?

It had been plain to him from the first that Brown had no plan, and was attempting to deal with a situation that had been out of his control since the first moment. Brown had ambition, greed, and a respectable sense of revenge, but almost no capacity of forethought, that much was clear.

Now, here he was, saddled with the two of them, forced to travel on and on, the unwelcome responsibility dragging like a worn-out shoe tied to a dog's tail. And Brown the hindered dog, snarling and turning in circles, snapping at the thing that hampered him, and biting his own tail in consequence. Half his men had been wounded by the flung stones. Jamie thoughtfully touched a large, painful bruise on the point of his elbow.

He himself had had no choice; now Brown hadn't, either.

His men were growing restive; they had crops to tend, and hadn't bargained for what they must see now as a fool's errand.

It would be a simple matter to escape by himself. But then what? He could not leave Claire in Brown's hands, and even were he able to get her safe away, they could not return to the Ridge with matters as they were; to do so would be to find themselves straight back in the pot.

He sighed, then caught his breath and let it out gingerly. He didn't think his ribs were cracked, but they hurt.

"Ye've a bit of ointment, I expect?" he said, nodding at the bag that held her bits of medicine.

"Yes, of course." She swallowed her bite of cheese, reaching for the bag. "I'll put some on that cut on your head."

He let her do that, but then insisted upon anointing her hand in turn. She objected, insisting that she was perfectly fine, needed no such thing, they should save the ointment in case of future need—and yet she let him take her hand and smooth the sweet-smelling cream into her knuckles, the small fine bones of her hand hard under his fingers.

She so hated being helpless in any way—but the armor of righteous fury was wearing off, and while she kept a fierce face for Brown and the rest, he knew she was afraid. Not without reason, either.

Brown was uneasy, unable to settle. He moved to and fro, talking aimlessly with one man or another, needlessly checking the hobbled horses, pouring a cup of chicory coffee and holding it undrunk until it grew cold, then flinging it into the weeds. And all the time, his restless gaze returned to them.

Brown was hasty, impetuous, and half-baked. He was not entirely stupid, Jamie thought. And clearly he had realized that his strategy of spreading gossip and scandal concerning his prisoners in order to endanger them had severe defects, so long as he was himself obliged to continue in close proximity to said prisoners.

Their simple meal finished, Jamie lay down, carefully, and Claire curled herself into him spoonwise, wanting comfort.

Fighting was an exhausting business, and so was fear; she was asleep in moments. Jamie felt the pull of sleep, but would not yield to it yet. He occupied himself instead in reciting some of the poems Brianna had told him—he quite liked the one about the silversmith in Boston, riding to spread the alarm to Lexington, which he considered a handsome piece.

The company was beginning to settle for the night. Brown was still a-fidget, sitting staring darkly at the ground, then leaping to his feet to stride up and down. By contrast, Christie had barely stirred, though he made no move to go to bed. He sat on a rock, his supper barely touched.

A flicker of movement near Christie's boot; a wee small mouse, making feints toward the neglected plate that sat on the ground, filled with bounty.

It had occurred to Jamie a couple of days before, in the vague way that one recognizes a fact unconsciously known for some time, that Tom Christie was in love with his wife.

Poor bugger, he thought. Surely Christie did not believe that Claire had had aught to do with the death of his daughter; if so, he would not be here. Did he think that Jamie, though . . . ?

He lay in the shelter of the darkness, watching the fire play across Christie's haggard features, his eyes half-hooded, giving no hint of his thoughts. There were men who could be read like books; Tom Christie wasn't one of them. But if ever he had seen a man being eaten alive before his eyes . . .

Was it the fate of his daughter, alone—or also the desperate need of a woman? He'd seen that need before, that gnawing at the soul, and knew it personally. Or *did* Christie think that Claire had killed wee Malva, or been in some way involved? There would be a quandary for an honorable man.

The need of a woman . . . the thought brought him back to the moment, and the awareness that the sounds he had been listening for in the wood behind him were now there. He had known for the past two days that they were followed, but last night they had camped in an open meadow, with no cover at all.

Moving slowly, but with no attempt at furtiveness, he rose, covered Claire with his cloak, and stepped into the wood, like one called by nature.

The moon was pale and hunchbacked and there was little light beneath the trees. He closed his eyes to damp the fire shadow and opened them again to the dark world, that place of shapes that lacked dimension and air that held spirits.

It was no spirit that stepped out from behind the blur of a pine tree, though.

"Blessed Michael defend us," he said softly.

"The blessed host of angels and archangels be with ye, Uncle," said Ian, in the same soft tone. "Though I am thinking that a few thrones and dominations wouldna come amiss, either."

"Well, I wouldna argue, if Divine Intervention chose to take a hand," Jamie said, heartened most amazingly by his nephew's presence. "I'm sure I've no notion how else we shall escape this foolish coil."

Ian grunted at that; Jamie saw his nephew's head turn, checking the faint glow of the camp. Without discussion, they moved further into the wood.

"I canna be gone for long, without they come after me," he said. "First, then—is all well wi' the Ridge?"

Ian lifted a shoulder.

"There's talk," he said, the tone of his voice indicating that "talk" covered everything from auld wives' gossip to the sort of insult that must be settled by violence. "No one killed yet, though. What shall I do, Uncle Jamie?"

"Richard Brown. He's thinking, and God only kens what *that* will lead to."

"He thinks too much; such men are dangerous," Ian said, and laughed. Jamie, who had never known his nephew to read a book willingly, gave him a look of disbelief, but dismissed questions in favor of the pressing concerns of the moment.

"Aye, he is," he said dryly. "He's been spreading the story in pothouses and inns as we go—at a guess, in hopes of rousing public indignation to the point that some poor fool of a constable can be pushed into taking us off his hands, or better yet, that a mob might be stirred up to seize us and hang us out of hand, thus resolving his difficulty."

"Oh, aye? Well, if that's what he had in mind, Uncle, it's working. Ye wouldna countenance some of the things I've heard, following in your tracks."

"I know." Jamie stretched gently, easing his painful ribs. It was only the mercy of God that it hadn't been worse—that, and Claire's rage, which had interrupted the attack, as everyone stopped to watch the engrossing spectacle of her hatcheling her assailant like a bundle of flax.

"It's come home to him, though, that if ye mean to pin

a target on someone, it's wise to step away smartly thereafter. He's thinking, as I say. Should he go off, then, or send someone . . ."

"I'll follow, aye, and see what's to do."

He sensed rather than saw Ian's nod; they stood in black shadow, the faint haze of moonlight like fog in the space between the trees. The lad moved, as though to go, then hesitated.

"Ye're sure, Uncle, as it wouldna be better to wait a bit, then creep away? There's nay bracken, but there's decent cover in the hills nearby; we could be safe hidden by dawn."

It was a great temptation. He felt the pull of the dark wild forest, above all, the lure of freedom. If he could but walk away into the greenwood, and stay there . . . But he shook his head.

"It wouldna do, Ian," he said, though he let regret show in his voice. "We should be fugitives, then—and doubtless wi' a price on our heads. With the countryside already roused against us—broadsides, posted bills? The public would do Brown's work for him, promptly. And then, to run would seem an admission of guilt, forbye."

Ian sighed, but nodded agreement.

"Well, then," he said. He stepped forward and embraced Jamie, squeezing hard for an instant, and then was gone.

Jamie let out a long, tentative breath against the pain of his injured ribs.

"God go with ye, Ian," he said to the dark, and turned back.

When he lay down again beside his wife, the camp was silent. The men lay like logs, wrapped in their blankets. Two figures, though, remained by the embers of the dying fire: Richard Brown and Thomas Christie, each alone on a rock with his thoughts.

Ought he to wake Claire, tell her? He considered for a moment, his cheek against the warm softness of her hair, and reluctantly decided no. It might hearten her a little to know of Ian's presence—but he dare not risk rousing Brown's suspicion; and if Brown were to perceive by any change in Claire's mood or face that something had happened . . . no, best not. At least not yet.

He glanced along the ground at Christie's feet, and saw the faint pale scurry of movement in the dark; the mouse had brought friends to share her feast.

90

FORTY-SIX BEANS TO THE GOOD

AT DAWN, RICHARD BROWN was gone. The rest of the men seemed grim, but resigned, and under the command of a squatty, morose sort of fellow named Oakes, we resumed our push south.

Something had changed in the night; Jamie had lost a little of the tension that had infused him since our departure from the Ridge. Stiff, sore, and disheartened as I was, I found this change some comfort, though wondering what had caused it. Was it the same thing that had caused Richard Brown to leave on his mysterious errand?

Jamie said nothing, though, beyond inquiring after my hand—which was tender, and so stiff that I couldn't immediately flex my fingers. He continued to keep a watchful eye on our companions, but the lessening of tension had affected them, too; I began to lose my fear that they might suddenly lose patience and string us up, Tom Christie's dour presence notwithstanding.

As though in accord with this more relaxed atmosphere, the weather suddenly cleared, which heartened everyone further. It would have been stretching things to say that there was any sense of rapprochement, but without Richard Brown's constant malevolence, the other men at least became occasionally civil. And as it always did, the tedium and hardships of travel wore everyone down, so that we rolled down the rutted roads like a pack of marbles, occasionally caroming off one another, dusty, silent, and united in exhaustion, if nothing else, by the end of each day.

This neutral state of affairs changed abruptly in Brunswick. For a day or two before, Oakes had been plainly anticipating something, and when we reached the first houses, I could see him beginning to draw great breaths of relief.

It was therefore no surprise when we stopped to refresh ourselves at a pothouse on the edge of the tiny, half-abandoned settlement, to find Richard Brown awaiting us. It *was* a surprise when, without more than a murmured word from Brown, Oakes and two others suddenly seized Jamie, knocking the cup of water from his hand and slamming him against the wall of the building.

I dropped my own cup and flung myself toward them, but Richard Brown grabbed my arm in a viselike grip and dragged me toward the horses.

"Let go! What are you doing? Let go, I say!" I kicked him, and had a good go at scratching out his eyes, but he got hold of both my wrists, and shouted for one of the other men to help. Between the two of them, they got me—still screaming at the top of my lungs—on a horse in front of another of Brown's men. There was a deal of shouting from Jamie's direction, and general hubbub, as a few people came out of the pothouse, staring. None of them seemed disposed to interfere with a large group of armed men, though.

Tom Christie was shouting protests; I glimpsed him hammering on the back of one man, but to no avail. The man behind me wrapped an arm round my middle and jerked it tight, knocking out what breath I had left.

Then we were thundering down the road, Brunswick—and Jamie—disappearing in the dust.

My furious protests, demands, and questions brought no response, of course, beyond an order to be quiet, this accompanied by another warning squeeze of the restraining arm around me.

Shaking with rage and terror, I subsided, and at that point, saw that Tom Christie was still with us, looking shaken and disturbed.

"Tom!" I shouted. "Tom, go back! Don't let them kill him! Please!"

He looked in my direction, startled, rose in his stirrups, and looked back toward Brunswick, then turned toward Richard Brown, shouting something.

Brown shook his head, reined his mount in so that Christie

could come up alongside, and leaning over, yelled something at him that must have passed for explanation. Christie clearly didn't like the situation, but after a few impassioned exchanges, he subsided, scowling, and dropped back. He pulled his horse's head aside and circled back to come within speaking distance of me.

"They will not kill nor harm him," he said, raising his voice to be heard over the rumble of hooves and rattle of harness. "Brown's word of honor upon it, he says."

"And you *believe* him, for God's sake?"

He looked disconcerted at that, glanced again at Brown, who had spurred up to ride ahead, then back at Brunswick. Indecision played across his features, but then his lips firmed and he shook his head.

"It will be all right," he said. But he would not meet my eyes, and in spite of my continued entreaties to him to go back, to stop them, he slackened his pace, falling back so that I couldn't see him anymore.

My throat was raw from screaming, and my stomach hurt, bruised and clenched in a knot of fear. Our speed had slowed, now that we had left Brunswick behind, and I concentrated on breathing; I wouldn't speak until I was sure I could do so without my voice trembling.

"Where are you taking me?" I asked finally. I sat stiff in the saddle, enduring an unwanted intimacy with the man behind me.

"New Bern," he said, with a note of grim satisfaction. "And then, thank God, we'll be shut of you at last."

THE JOURNEY to New Bern passed in a blur of fear, agitation, and physical discomfort. While I did wonder what was about to happen to me, all such speculations were drowned by my anxiety about Jamie.

Tom Christie was plainly my only hope of finding out anything, but he avoided me, keeping his distance—and I found *that* as alarming as anything else. He was clearly troubled, even more so than he had been since Malva's death, but he no longer bore a look of dull suffering; he was actively agitated.

I was terribly afraid that he knew or suspected Jamie was dead, but would not admit it—either to me, or to himself.

All of the men clearly shared my captor's urge to be rid of me as soon as possible; we stopped only briefly, when absolutely necessary for the horses to rest. I was offered food, but could not eat. By the time we reached New Bern, I was completely drained from the sheer physical exertion of the ride, but much more so from the constant strain of apprehension.

Most of the men remained at a tavern on the outskirts of the town; Brown and one of the other men took me through the streets, accompanied by a silent Tom Christie, arriving at last at a large house of whitewashed brick. The home, as Brown informed me with a sense of lively pleasure, of Sheriff Tolliver—also, the town gaol.

The sheriff, a darkly handsome sort, viewed me with a sort of interested speculation, mingled with a growing disgust as he heard the crime of which I was accused. I made no attempt at rebuttal or defense; the room was going in and out of focus, and all my attention was required to keep my knees from giving way.

I barely heard most of the exchange between Brown and the sheriff. At the last, though, just before I was led away into the house, I found Tom Christie suddenly beside me.

"Mrs. Fraser," he said, very low. "Believe me, he is safe. I would not have his death on my conscience—nor yours." He was looking at me directly, for the first time in . . . days? weeks? . . . and I found the intensity of his gray eyes both disconcerting and oddly comforting.

"Trust in God," he whispered. "He will deliver the righteous out of all his dangers." And with a sudden hard and unexpected squeeze of my hand, he was gone.

AS EIGHTEENTH-CENTURY gaols went, it could have been worse. The women's quarters consisted of a small room at the back of the sheriff's house, which had likely been a storeroom of sorts originally. The walls were roughly plastered, though some escape-minded former occupant had chipped away a large chunk of the plaster, before discovering that beneath it lay a layer of lath, and beneath *that* an impenetrable wall of baked-clay brick, which confronted me at once with its bland impenetrability when the door was opened.

There was no window, but an oil dip burned on a ledge by the door, casting a faint circle of light that illuminated the daunting bare patch of brick, but left the corners of the room in deep shadow. I couldn't see the night-soil bucket, but knew there was one; the thick, acrid tang of it stung my nose, and I automatically began breathing through my mouth as the sheriff pushed me into the room.

The door closed firmly behind me, and a key grated in the lock.

There was a single, narrow bedstead in the shadows, occupied by a large lump under a threadbare blanket. The lump took its time, but eventually stirred and sat up, resolving itself into a small, plump woman, capless and frowsy with sleep, who sat blinking at me like a dormouse.

"Ermp," she said, and rubbed her eyes with her fists, like a small child.

"So sorry to disturb you," I said politely. My heart had slowed a bit by now, though I was still shaking and short of breath. I pressed my hands flat against the door to stop them trembling.

"Think nothing of it," she said, and yawned suddenly, like a hippopotamus, showing me a set of worn but serviceable molars. Blinking and smacking her lips absently, she reached down beside her, pulled out a battered pair of spectacles, and set them firmly on her nose.

Her eyes were blue, and hugely magnified by the lenses, enormous with curiosity.

"What's your name?" she asked.

"Claire Fraser," I said, watching her narrowly, in case she too might already have heard all about my supposed crime. The bruise on my breast left by the stone that had struck me there was still visible, beginning to yellow above the edge of my gown.

"Oh?" She squinted, as though trying to place me, but evidently failed, for she shrugged away the effort. "Got any money?"

"A bit." Jamie had forced me to take almost all the money—

not a great deal, but there was a small weight of coin at the bottom of each of the pockets tied around my waist, and a couple of proclamation notes tucked inside my stays.

The woman was a good deal shorter than I, and pillowy in aspect, with large, drooping breasts and several comfortable rolls corrugating her uncorseted middle; she was in her shift, with her gown and stays hung from a nail in the wall. She seemed harmless—and I began to breathe a little more easily, beginning to grasp the fact that at least I was safe for the moment, no longer in danger of sudden, random violence.

The other prisoner made no offensive moves toward me, but hopped down off the bed, bare feet thumping softly in what I realized now was a matted layer of moldy straw.

"Well, call the old bizzom and send for some Holland, then, why don't you?" she suggested cheerfully.

"The . . who?"

Instead of answering, she trundled to the door and banged on it, shouting, "Mrs. Tolliver! Mrs. Tolliver!"

The door opened almost immediately, revealing a tall, thin woman, looking like an annoyed stork.

"Really, Mrs. Ferguson," she said. "You are the most dreadful nuisance. I was just coming to pay my respects to Mrs. Fraser, in any case." She turned her back on Mrs. Ferguson with magisterial dignity and inclined her head a bare inch toward me.

"Mrs. Fraser. I am Mrs. Tolliver."

I had a split second in which to decide how to react, and chose the prudent—if galling—course of genteel submission, bowing to her as though she were the Governor's lady.

"Mrs. Tolliver," I murmured, careful not to meet her eyes. "How kind of you."

She twitched, sharp-eyed, like a bird spotting the stealthy progress of a worm through the grass—but I had firm control of my features by now, and she relaxed, detecting no sarcasm.

"You are welcome," she said with chilly courtesy. "I am to see to your welfare, and acquaint you with our custom. You will receive one meal each day, unless you wish to send to the ordinary for more—at your own expense. I will bring you a basin for washing once each day. You'll carry your own slops. And—"

"Oh, stuff your custom, Maisie," said Mrs. Ferguson, butting into Mrs. Tolliver's set speech with the comfortable assumption of long acquaintance. "She's got some money. Fetch us a bottle of geneva, there's a good girl, and then if you must, you can tell her what's what."

Mrs. Tolliver's narrow face tightened in disapproval, but her eyes twitched toward me, bright in the dim light of the rush dip. I ventured a hesitant gesture toward my pocket, and her lower lip sucked in. She glanced over her shoulder, then took a quick step toward me.

"A shilling, then," she whispered, hand held open between us. I dropped the coin into her palm, and it disappeared at once beneath her apron.

"You've missed supper," she announced in her normal disapproving tones, stepping backward. "However, as you've just come, I shall make an allowance and bring you something."

"How kind of you," I said again.

The door closed firmly behind her, shutting out light and air, and the key turned in the lock.

The sound of it set off a tiny spark of panic, and I stamped on it hard. I felt like a dried skin, stuffed to the eyeballs with the tinder of fear, uncertainty, and loss. It would take no more than a spark to ignite that and burn me to ashes—and neither I nor Jamie could afford that.

"She drinks?" I asked, turning back to my new roommate with an assumption of coolness.

"Do you know anyone who doesn't, given the chance?" Mrs. Ferguson asked reasonably. She scratched her ribs. "Fraser, she said. You aren't the—"

"I am," I said, rather rudely. "I don't want to talk about it."

Her eyebrows shot up, but she nodded equably.

"Just as you like," she said. "Any good at cards?"

"Loo or whist?" I asked warily.

"Know a game called brag?"

"No." Jamie and Brianna played it now and then, but I had never acquainted myself with the rules.

"That's all right; I'll teach you." Reaching under the mattress, she pulled out a rather limp deck of pasteboards and fanned them expertly, waving them gently under her nose as she smiled at me.

"Don't tell me," I said. "You're in here for cheating at cards?"

"Cheat? Me? Not a bit of it," she said, evidently unoffended. "Forgery."

Rather to my own surprise, I laughed. I was still feeling shaky, but Mrs. Ferguson was definitely proving a welcome distraction.

"How long have you been in here?" I asked.

She scratched at her head, realized that she wasn't wearing a cap, and turned to pull one out of the rumpled bedding.

"Oh—a month, just about." Putting on the crumpled cap, she nodded at the doorpost beside me. Turning to look, I saw that it was crosshatched with dozens of small nicks, some old and dark with dirt, some freshly scratched, showing raw yellow wood. The sight of the marks made my stomach plunge again, but I took a deep breath and turned my back on them.

"Have you had a trial yet?"

She shook her head, light glinting off her spectacles.

"No, praise God. I hear from Maisie that the court's shut down; all the justices gone into hiding. Hasn't been anybody tried in the last two months."

This was not good news. Evidently the thought showed on my face, for she leaned forward and patted my arm sympathetically.

"I wouldn't be in a hurry, dearie. Not in your shoes, I wouldn't. If they've not tried you, they can't hang you. And while I have met those as say the waiting's like to kill them, I've not seen anybody die of it. And I *have* seen them die at the end of a rope. Nasty business, that is."

She spoke almost negligently, but her own hand rose, as though by itself, and touched the soft white flesh of her neck. She swallowed, the tiny bump of her Adam's apple bobbing.

I swallowed, too, an unpleasantly constricted feeling in my own throat.

"But I'm innocent," I said, wondering even as I said it how I could sound so uncertain.

" 'Course you are," she said stoutly, giving my arm a

squeeze. "You stick to it, dearie—don't you let 'em bully-whack you into admitting the least little thing!"

"I won't," I assured her dryly.

"One of these days, a mob's like to come *here,*" she said, nodding. "String up the sheriff, if he don't look sharp. He's not popular, Tolliver."

"I can't imagine why not—a charming fellow like that." I wasn't sure how I felt about the prospect of a mob storming the house. Stringing up Sheriff Tolliver was all very well, so far as that went—but with the memory of the hostile crowds in Salisbury and Hillsboro fresh in mind, I wasn't sure at all that they'd stop with the sheriff. Dying at the hands of a lynch mob wasn't at all preferable to the slower sort of judicial murder I likely faced. Though I supposed there was always a possibility of escaping in the riot.

And go where, if you did? I wondered.

With no good answer to that question, I shoved it to the back of my mind and turned my attention back to Mrs. Ferguson, who was still holding out the cards invitingly.

"All right," I said. "But not for money."

"Oh, no," Mrs. Ferguson assured me. "Perish the thought. But we must have some sort of stake to make it interesting. We'll play for beans, shall we?" She set down the cards, and digging under the pillow, withdrew a small pouch, from which she poured a handful of small white beans.

"Splendid," I said. "And when we're finished, we'll plant them, shall we, and hope for a giant beanstalk to spring up and burst through the roof, so we can escape up it."

She burst into giggles at that, which somehow made me feel very slightly better.

"From your mouth to God's ear, dearie!" she said. "I'll deal first, shall I?"

BRAG APPEARED to be a form of poker. And while I had lived with a cardsharp long enough to know one when I saw one, Mrs. Ferguson appeared to be playing honestly—for the moment. I was forty-six beans to the good, by the time Mrs. Tolliver returned.

The door opened without ceremony, and she came in, holding a three-legged stool and a chunk of bread. This latter appeared to be both my supper and her ostensible excuse for visiting the cell, for she shoved it at me with a loud, "This will have to keep you 'til tomorrow, Mrs. Fraser!"

"Thank you," I said mildly. It was fresh, and appeared to have been hastily dragged through bacon drippings, in lieu of butter. I bit into it without hesitation, having sufficiently recovered from shock now as to feel very hungry indeed.

Mrs. Tolliver, glancing over her shoulder to be sure the coast was clear, shut the door quietly, put down the stool, and drew a squat bottle from her pocket, blue glass and filled with some clear liquid.

She pulled the cork from it, tilted it, and drank deeply, her long, lean throat moving convulsively.

Mrs. Ferguson said nothing, but watched the process with a sort of analytic attention, light glinting from her spectacles, as though comparing Mrs. Tolliver's behavior with that of previous occasions.

Mrs. Tolliver lowered the bottle and stood for a moment grasping it, then handed it abruptly to me and sat down suddenly on the stool, breathing heavily.

I wiped the neck of the bottle as inconspicuously as possible on my sleeve, then took a token sip. It was gin, all right—heavily flavored with juniper berries to hide the poor quality, but powerfully alcoholic.

Mrs. Ferguson took a healthy guzzle in her turn, and so we continued, passing the bottle from hand to hand, exchanging small cordialities with it. Her first thirst slaked, Mrs. Tolliver became almost affable, her frosty manner thawing substantially. Even so, I waited until the bottle was nearly empty before asking the question foremost in my mind.

"Mrs. Tolliver, the men who brought me—did you happen to hear them say anything about my husband?"

She put a fist to her mouth to stifle a belch.

"Say anything?"

"About where he is," I amended.

She blinked a little, looking blank.

"I didn't hear," she said. "But I suppose they may have told Tolly."

Mrs. Ferguson handed down the bottle to her—we were sitting side by side on the bed, that being the only place to sit in the small room—nearly falling off the bed in the process.

"S'pose you could ask him, could you, Maisie?" she said.

An uneasy look came into Mrs. Tolliver's eyes, glazed as they were.

"Oh, no," she said, shaking her head. "He doesn't talk to me about such things. Not my business."

I exchanged a glance with Mrs. Ferguson, and she shook her head slightly; best not to press the matter now.

Worried as I was, I found it difficult to abandon the subject, but plainly there was nothing to be done. I gathered what shreds of patience I had, estimating how many bottles of gin I could afford before my money ran out—and what I might accomplish with them.

I LAY STILL that night, breathing the damp, thick air with its scents of mold and urine. I could smell Sadie Ferguson next to me, too: a faint miasma of stale sweat, overlaid with a strong perfume of gin. I tried to close my eyes, but every time I did, small waves of claustrophobia washed over me; I could feel the sweating plaster walls draw closer, and gripped my fists in the cloth of the mattress ticking, to keep from throwing myself at the locked door. I had a nasty vision of myself, pounding and shrieking, my nails torn and bloody from clawing at the unyielding wood, my cries unheard in the darkness—and no one ever coming.

I thought it a distinct possibility. I had heard more from Mrs. Ferguson regarding Sheriff Tolliver's unpopularity. If he were to be attacked and dragged from his home by a mob—or to lose his nerve and run—the chances of him or his wife remembering the prisoners were remote.

A mob might find us—and kill us, in the madness of the moment. Or not find us, and fire the house. The storeroom was clay brick, but the adjoining kitchen was timber; damp or not, the place would burn like a torch, leaving nothing but that bloody brick wall standing.

I took an especially deep breath, smell notwithstanding, exhaled, and shut my eyes with decision.

Sufficient unto the day is the evil thereof. That had been one of Frank's favorite expressions, and by and large, a good sentiment.

Depends a bit on the day, though, doesn't it? I thought in his direction.

Does it? You tell me. The thought was there, vivid enough that I might have heard it—or only imagined it. If I had imagined it, though, I had imagined also a tone of dry amusement that was particularly Frank's.

Fine, I thought. *Reduced to having philosophical arguments with a ghost. It's been a worse day than I thought.*

Imagination or not, the thought had succeeded in wrenching my attention off the single-minded track of worry. I felt a sense of invitation—or temptation, perhaps. The urge to talk to him. The need to escape into conversation, even if one-sided . . . and imaginary.

No. I won't use you that way, I thought, a little sadly. *Not right that I should only think of you when I need distraction, and not for your own sake.*

And do you never think of me, for my own sake? The question floated in the darkness of my eyelids. I could see his face, quite clearly, the lines of it curved in humor, one dark eyebrow raised. I was dimly surprised; it had been so long since I thought of him in any focused way that I should have long since forgotten exactly what he looked like. But I hadn't.

And I suppose that's the answer to your question, then, I thought silently to him. *Good night, Frank.*

I turned onto my side, facing the door. I felt a little calmer now. I could just make out the outlines of the door, and being able to see it lessened that feeling of being buried alive.

I closed my eyes again, and tried to concentrate on the processes of my own body. That often helped, bringing me a sense of quiet, listening to the purling of blood through my vessels and the subterranean gurglings of organs all carrying peacefully on without the slightest need of my conscious direction. Rather like sitting in the garden, listening to the bees hum in their hives—

I stopped *that* thought in its tracks, feeling my heart jolt in memory, electric as a bee sting.

I thought quite fiercely about my heart, the physical organ, its thick soft chambers and delicate valves—but what I felt was a soreness there. There were hollow places in my heart.

Jamie. A gaping, echoing hollow, cold and deep as the crevasse of a glacier. Bree. Jemmy. Roger. And Malva, like a tiny, deep-drilled sore, an ulcer that wouldn't heal.

I had managed so far to ignore the rustlings and heavy breathings of my companion. I couldn't ignore the hand that brushed my neck, then slipped down my chest and rested lightly, cupped around my breast.

I stopped breathing. Then, very slowly, exhaled. Entirely without my intent, my breast settled into her cupped palm. I felt a touch on my back; a thumb, gently tracing the groove of my spine through my shift.

I understood the need of human comfort, the sheer hunger for touch. I had taken it, often, and given it, part of the fragile web of humanity, constantly torn, constantly made new. But there was that in Sadie Ferguson's touch that spoke of more than simple warmth, or the need of company in the dark.

I took hold of her hand, and lifting it from my breast, squeezed the fingers gently shut, and put it firmly away from me, folded back against her own bosom.

"No," I said softly.

She hesitated, moved her hips so that her body curved behind me, thighs warm and round against mine, offering encompassment and refuge.

"No one would know," she whispered, still hopeful. "I could make you forget—for a bit." Her hand stroked my hip, gentle, insinuating.

If she could, I thought wryly, I might be tempted. But that pathway was not one I could take.

"No," I said more firmly, and shifted, rolling onto my back, as far away as I could get—which was roughly an inch and a half. "I'm sorry—but no."

She was silent for a moment, then sighed heavily.

"Oh, well. Perhaps a bit later."

"No!"

The noises from the kitchen had ceased, and the house

settled into silence. It wasn't the silence of the mountains, though, that cradle of boughs and whispering winds and the vast deep of the starry sky. It was the silence of a town, disturbed by smoke and the fogged dim glow of hearth and candle; filled with slumbering thoughts unleashed from waking reason, roaming and uneasy in the dark.

"Could I hold you?" she asked wistfully, and her fingers brushed my cheek. "Only that."

"No," I said again. But I reached for her hand, and held it. And so we fell asleep, hands chastely—and firmly—linked between us.

WE WERE ROUSED by what I thought at first was the wind, moaning in the chimney whose back bulged into our cubbyhole. The moaning grew louder, though, broke into a full-throated scream, then stopped abruptly.

"Ye gods and little fishes!" Sadie Ferguson sat up, eyes wide and blinking, groping for her spectacles. "What was that?"

"A woman in labor," I said, having heard that particular pattern of sounds fairly often. The moaning was starting up again. "And *very* near her time." I slid off the bed and shook my shoes, dislodging a small roach and a couple of silverfish who had taken shelter in the toes.

We sat for nearly an hour, listening to the alternate moaning and screaming.

"Shouldn't it stop?" Sadie said, swallowing nervously. "Shouldn't the child be birthed by now?"

"Perhaps," I said absently. "Some babies take longer than others." I had my ear pressed to the door, trying to make out what was going on on the other side. The woman, whoever she was, was in the kitchen, and no more than ten feet away from me. I heard Maisie Tolliver's voice now and then, muffled and sounding doubtful. But for the most part, only the rhythmic panting, moaning, and screaming.

Another hour of it, and my nerves were becoming frayed. Sadie was on the bed, the pillow pressed down hard over her head, in hopes of blocking the noise.

Enough of this, I thought, and when next I heard Mrs. Tolliver's voice, I banged on the door with the heel of my shoe, shouting, "Mrs. Tolliver!" as loudly as I could, to be heard over the noise.

She did hear me, and after a moment, the key grated in the lock and a wave of light and air fell into the cell. I was momentarily blinded by the daylight, but blinked and made out the shape of a woman on her hands and knees by the hearth, facing me. She was black, bathed in sweat, and, raising her head, howled like a wolf. Mrs. Tolliver started as though someone had run a pin into her from behind.

"Excuse me," I said, pushing past her. She made no move to stop me, and I caught a strong blast of juniper-scented gin fumes as I brushed by her.

The black woman sank down on her elbows, panting, her uncovered rear in the air. Her belly hung like a ripe guava, pale in the sweat-soaked shift that clung to it.

I asked sharp questions in the brief interval before the next howl, and ascertained that this was her fourth child and that she had been laboring since her water had broken the night before. Mrs. Tolliver contributed the information that she was also a prisoner, and a slave. I might have guessed that, from the purplish weals on her back and buttocks.

Mrs. Tolliver was of little other use, swaying glassy-eyed over me, but had managed to provide a small pile of rags and a basin of water, which I used to mop the woman's sweating face. Sadie Ferguson poked her bespectacled nose cautiously out of the cell, but drew back hastily when the next howl broke forth.

It was a breech birth, which accounted for the difficulty, and the next quarter-hour was hair-raising for all concerned. At length, though, I eased a small baby into the world, feet first, slimy, motionless, and the most unearthly shade of pale blue.

"Oh," said Mrs. Tolliver, sounding disappointed. "It's dead."

"Good," said the mother, in a hoarse, deep voice, and closed her eyes.

"Damned if he is," I said, and turned the child hastily face-down, tapping its back. No movement, and I brought the sealed, waxy face to my own, covered nose and mouth with my own mouth, and sucked hard, then turned my head to spit away the mucus and fluid. Face slimy and the taste of silver in my mouth, I blew gently into him, paused, holding him, limp and slippery as a fresh fish, blew—and saw his eyes open, a deeper blue than his skin, vaguely interested.

He took a startled, gasping breath and I laughed, a sudden wellspring of joy bubbling up from my depths. The nightmare memory of another child, a flicker of life blinking out between my hands, faded away. This child was well and truly lit, burning like a candle with a soft, clear flame.

"Oh!" said Mrs. Tolliver, again. She leaned forward to look, and an enormous smile spread across her face. "Oh, oh!"

The baby started crying. I cut the cord, wrapped him in some of the rags, and with some reservation, handed him to Mrs. Tolliver, hoping she wouldn't drop him in the fire. Then I turned my attention to the mother, who was drinking thirstily from the basin, water spilling down her front and soaking the already wet shift further.

She lay back and allowed me to tend her, but without speaking, rolling her eyes occasionally toward the child with a brooding, hostile look.

I heard footsteps coming through the house, and the sheriff appeared, looking surprised.

"Oh, Tolly!" Mrs. Tolliver, smeared with birth fluids and reeking of gin, turned to him happily, holding out the baby to him. "Look, Tolly, it's alive!"

The sheriff looked quite taken aback, and his brow furrowed as he looked at his wife, but then he seemed to catch the scent of her happiness, above the gin. He leaned forward and touched the little bundle gently, his stern face relaxing.

"That's good, Maisie," he said. "Hallo, little fellow." He caught sight of me, then, kneeling on the hearth, doing my best to clean up with a rag and what was left of the water.

"Mrs. Fraser brought the child," Mrs. Tolliver explained eagerly. "It was laid catty-wumpus, but she brought it so cleverly, and made it breathe—we thought 'twas dead, it was so still, but it wasn't! Isn't that wonderful, Tolly?"

"Wonderful," the sheriff repeated a little bleakly. He gave me a hard look, then transferred the same look to the new mother, who gazed back with a sullen indifference. He beckoned me to my feet, then, and with a curt bow, gestured me back into the cell and shut the door.

Only then did I recall what it was he thought I'd done. Little wonder if my juxtaposition with a newborn child made him a trifle nervous, I supposed. I was wet and filthy, and the cell seemed particularly hot and airless. Nonetheless, the miracle of birth was still tingling through my synapses, and I sat down on the bed, still smiling, a wet rag in my hand.

Sadie was regarding me with respect, mingled with a slight revulsion.

"That's the messiest business I ever did see," she said. "Heavens above, is it always like that?"

"More or less. Haven't you ever seen a child born? You've never had one yourself?" I asked curiously. She shook her head vigorously, and made the sign of the horns, which made me laugh, giddy as I was.

"Had I ever been disposed to let a man near me, the thought of *that* would dissuade me," she assured me fervently.

"Oh, yes?" I said, belatedly recalling her overtures of the night before. It *wasn't* merely comfort she'd been offering, then. "And what about *Mister* Ferguson?"

She gave me a demure look, blinking through her spectacles.

"Oh, he was a farmer—*much* older than I. Dead of the pleurisy, these five years gone."

And totally fictitious, I was inclined to think. But a widow had a great deal more freedom than did a maid or a wife, and if ever I saw a woman capable of taking care of herself . . .

I had been paying no attention to the sounds in the kitchen, but at this point, there was a heavy crash and the sheriff's voice, cursing. No sound of the child or Mrs. Tolliver.

"Taking the black bitch back to her quarters," Sadie said, with such a hostile intonation that I glanced at her in amazement.

"Didn't you know?" she said, seeing my surprise. "She's killed her babies. They can hang her, now she's borne this one."

"Oh," I said a little blankly. "No. I didn't know." The noises in the kitchen receded, and I sat staring at the rush dip, the sense of life still moving in my hands.

91

A REASONABLY NEAT SCHEME

WATER LAPPED JUST under Jamie's ear, the mere sound of it making him feel queasy. The reek of decaying mud and dead fish didn't help, nor did the dunt he'd taken when he fell against the wall.

He shifted, trying to find some position that would ease head, stomach, or both. They'd trussed him like a boiled fowl, but he managed with some effort to roll onto his side and bring his knees up, which helped a bit.

He was in a dilapidated boat shed of some sort; he'd seen it in the last of the twilight, when they'd brought him down to the shore—he'd thought at first they meant to drown him—and carried him inside, dropping him on the floor like a sack of flour.

"Hurry up, Ian," he muttered, shifting again, in increasing discomfort. "I'm a great deal too old for this sort of nonsense."

He could only hope his nephew had been close enough when Brown moved to have been able to follow, and to have some notion where he was now; certainly the lad would be looking. The shore where the shed stood was open, no cover, but there was plenty among the brush below Fort Johnston, standing on the headland a little way above him.

The back of his head throbbed dully, giving him a nasty taste in the back of the mouth, and a disquieting echo of the shattering headaches he used to suffer in the wake of an ax wound that had cracked his skull, many years before. He was shocked at how easily the recollection of those headaches came back; it had happened a lifetime ago, and he had thought even the memory of it dead and buried. His skull clearly had a much more vivid memory of its own, though, and was determined to make him sick by way of revenge for his forgetfulness.

The moon was up, and bright; the light shone soft through the cracks between the crude boards of the wall. Dim as it was, it seemed to shift, wavering in a disturbingly qualmish fashion, and he shut his eyes, concentrating grimly on what he might do to Richard Brown, and he got the man alone someday.

Where in the name of Michael and all the saints had he taken Claire, and why? Jamie's only comfort was that Tom Christie had gone with them. He was fairly sure that Christie wouldn't let them kill her—and if Jamie could find him, Christie would lead him to her.

A sound reached him above the nauseating lapping of the tide. Faint whistling—then singing. He could just make out the words, and smiled a little, in spite of everything. *"Marry me, marry me, minister—or else I'll be your priest, your priest—or else I'll be your priest."*

He shouted, though it hurt his head, and within a few moments, Ian, the dear wee lad, was beside him, cutting through the ropes. He rolled over, unable for a moment to make his cramped muscles work, then managed to get his hands under him and rise enough to vomit.

"All right, Uncle Jamie?" Ian sounded vaguely amused, damn him.

"I'll do. D'ye ken where Claire is?" He got to his feet, swaying, and was fumbling at his breeches; his fingers felt like sausages, and the broken one was throbbing, the pins and needles of returning circulation stabbing through the jagged ends of bone. All discomfort was forgotten for an instant, though, in the rush of overwhelming relief.

"Jesus, Uncle Jamie," Ian said, impressed. "Aye, I do. They've taken her to New Bern. There's a sheriff there that Forbes says might take her."

"Forbes?" He swung round in his astonishment, and nearly fell, saving himself with a hand on the creaking wood wall. "Gerald Forbes?"

"The very same." Ian caught him with a hand beneath his elbow to steady him; the flimsy board had cracked under his weight. "Brown went here and there and talked to this one and that—but it was Forbes he did business with at last, in Cross Creek."

"Ye heard what they said?"

"I heard." Ian's voice was casual, but with an underlying excitement—and no little pride in his accomplishment.

Brown's aim was simple at this point—to rid himself of the encumbrance the Frasers had become. He knew of Forbes and his relations with Jamie, owing to all the gossip after the tar incident in the summer of last year, and the confrontation at Mecklenberg in May. And so he offered to hand the two of them over to Forbes, for what use the lawyer might make of the situation.

"So he strode to and fro a bit, thinking—Forbes, I mean—they were in his warehouse, ken, by the river, and me hiding behind the barrels o' tar. And then he laughs, as though he's just thought of something clever."

Forbes's suggestion was that Brown's men should take Jamie, suitably bound, to a small landing that he owned, near Brunswick. From there, he would be taken onto a ship headed for England, and thus safely removed from interference in the affairs of either Forbes or Brown—and, incidentally, rendered unable to defend his wife.

Claire, meanwhile, should be committed to the mercies of the law. If she were to be found guilty, well, that would be the end of her. If not, the scandal attendant upon a trial would both occupy the attention of anyone connected to her and destroy any influence they might have—thus leaving Fraser's Ridge ripe for the pickings, and Gerald Forbes a clear field toward claiming leadership of the Scottish Whigs in the colony.

Jamie listened to this in silence, torn between anger and a reluctant admiration.

"A reasonably neat scheme," he said. He was feeling steadier now, the queasiness disappearing with the cleansing flow of anger through his blood.

"Oh, it gets better, Uncle," Ian assured him. "Ye recall a gentleman named Stephen Bonnet?"

"I do. What about him?"

"It's Mr. Bonnet's ship, Uncle, that's to take ye to England."

Amusement was beginning to show in his nephew's voice again. "It seems Lawyer Forbes has had a verra profitable partnership with Bonnet for some time—him and some merchant friends in Wilmington. They've shares in both the ship and its cargoes. And since the English blockade, the profits have been greater still; I take it that our Mr. Bonnet is a most experienced smuggler."

Jamie said something extremely foul in French, and went quickly to look out of the shed. The water lay calm and beautiful, a moon path stretching silver out to sea. There was a ship out there; small and black and perfect as a spider on a sheet of paper. Bonnet's?

"Christ," he said. "When will they come in, d'ye think?"

"I dinna ken," Ian said, sounding unsure for the first time. "Is the tide coming in, would ye say, Uncle? Or going out?"

Jamie glanced down at the water rippling under the boathouse, as though it might offer some clue.

"How would I know, for God's sake? And what difference would it make?" He rubbed a hand hard over his face, trying to think. They'd taken his dirk, of course. He had a *sgian dhu,* carried in his stocking, but somehow doubted that its three-inch blade would offer much help in the present situation.

"What have ye got by way of weapons, Ian? Ye dinna have your bow with ye, I don't suppose?"

Ian shook his head regretfully. He had joined Jamie in the door of the boathouse, and the moon showed the hunger in his face as he eyed the ship.

"I've two decent knives, a dirk, and a pistol. There's my rifle, but I left it with the horse." He jerked his head toward the dark line of the distant wood. "Shall I fetch it? They might see me."

Jamie thought for a moment, tapping his fingers against the jamb of the door, 'til the pain of the broken one made him stop. The urge to lie in wait for Bonnet and take him was a physical thing; he understood Ian's hunger, and shared it. But his rational mind was busy reckoning the odds, and would insist upon presenting them, little as the vengefully animal part of him wished to know them.

There was not yet any sign of a boat coming from the ship. Always assuming that the ship out there was indeed Bonnet's—

and that, they didn't know for sure—it might still be hours before anyone came to fetch him away. And when they did, what odds that Bonnet himself would come? He was the ship's captain; would he come on such an errand, or send minions?

With a rifle, if Bonnet *were* in the boat, Jamie would wager any amount that he could shoot the man from ambush. If he were in the boat. If he were recognizable in the dark. And while he could hit him, he might not kill him.

If Bonnet were not in the boat, though . . . then it would be a matter of waiting 'til the boat came close enough, leaping aboard, and overpowering whoever was aboard—how many would come on such an errand? Two, three, four? They must all be killed or disabled, and then it would be a matter of rowing the damn boat back out to the ship—where all aboard would doubtless have noticed the stramash taking place on shore, and be prepared either to drop a cannonball through the bottom of the boat or to wait for them to haul alongside and then pick them off from the rail with small-arms fire, like sitting ducks.

And if they should somehow succeed in getting aboard without notice—then searching the goddamn ship for Bonnet himself, hunting him down, and killing him, without attracting undue notice from the crew . . .

This laborious analysis ran through his mind in the time it took to breathe, and was as quickly dismissed. If they were to be captured or killed, Claire would be alone and defenseless. He could not risk it. Still, he thought, trying to comfort himself, he could find Forbes—and would, when the time came.

"Aye, well, then," he said, and turned away with a sigh. "Have ye but the one horse, Ian?"

"Aye," Ian said with a matching sigh. "But I ken where we can maybe steal another."

92

AMANUENSIS

TWO DAYS PASSED. Hot, damp days in the sweltering dark, and I could feel various kinds of mold, fungus, and rot trying to take hold in my crevices—to say nothing of the omnivorous, omnipresent cockroaches, who seemed determined to nibble my eyebrows the moment the light was put out. The leather of my shoes was clammy and limp, my hair hung lank and dirty, and—like Sadie Ferguson—I took to spending most of my time in my shift.

When Mrs. Tolliver appeared and ordered us to come assist with the washing, therefore, we abandoned the latest game of loo—she was winning—and nearly pushed each other over in our haste to oblige.

It was much hotter in the yard, with the laundry fire roaring, and quite as damp as it had been in the cell, with the thick clouds of moisture boiling off the big kettle of clothes and plastering strands of hair to our faces. Our shifts already clung to our bodies, the grubby linen almost transparent with sweat—laundry was heavy work. There were, however, no bugs, and if the sun shone blinding, and fierce enough to redden my nose and arms—well, it shone, and that was something to be grateful for.

I asked Mrs. Tolliver about my erstwhile patient and her child, but she merely pressed her lips tight and shook her head, looking pinched and severe. The sheriff had been absent the night before; there had been no sound of his booming voice in the kitchen. And from the green-gilled looks of Maisie Tolliver herself, I diagnosed a long and solitary night with the gin bottle, followed by a fairly ghastly dawn.

"You'll feel much better if you sit in the shade and sip . . . water," I said. "Lots of water." Tea or coffee would be better, but these substances were more costly than gold in the colony, and I doubted a sheriff's wife would have any. "If you have any ipecacuanha . . . or perhaps some mint . . ."

"I thank you for your valuable opinion, Mrs. Fraser!" she snapped, though she swayed, rather, and her cheeks were pale and glossy with sweat.

I shrugged, and bent my attention to the task of levering a wad of sopping, steaming clothes from the filthy suds with a five-foot wooden laundry spoon, so worn with use that my sweaty hands slipped on the smooth wood.

We got the lot laboriously washed, rinsed, scaldingly wrung, and hung upon a line to dry, then sank gasping into the thin line of shade afforded by the side of the house, and took turns passing a tin dipper back and forth, gulping lukewarm water from the well bucket. Mrs. Tolliver, disregarding her elevated social position, sat down, too, very suddenly.

I turned to offer her the dipper, only to see her eyes roll back into her head. She didn't so much fall as dissolve backward, subsiding slowly into a heap of damp, checked gingham.

"Is she dead?" Sadie Ferguson inquired with interest. She glanced to and fro, obviously estimating the chances of making a run for it.

"No. Bad hangover, possibly aggravated by a slight case of sunstroke." I'd got hold of her pulse, which was light and fast, but quite steady. I was myself debating the wisdom of abandoning Mrs. Tolliver to the dangers of aspirating her own vomit and absconding, even barefoot and in my shift, but was forestalled by male voices coming round the corner of the house.

Two men—one was Tolliver's constable, whom I'd seen briefly when Brown's men had delivered me to the gaol. The other was a stranger, very well dressed, with silver coat buttons and a silk waistcoat, rather the worse for sweat stains. This gentleman, a heavyset sort of about forty, frowned at the scene of dissipation before him.

"Are these the prisoners?" he asked in tones of distaste.

"Aye, sir," the constable said. "Leastwise, the two in their shifts is. 'Tother one's the sheriff's wife."

Silver Buttons's nostrils pinched in briefly in receipt of this intelligence, then flared.

"Which is the midwife?"

"That would be me," I said, straightening up and trying for an air of dignity. "I am Mrs. Fraser."

"Are you," he said, his tone indicating that I might have said I was Queen Charlotte, for all it mattered to him. He looked me up and down in a disparaging fashion, shook his head, then turned to the sweating constable.

"What is she charged with?"

The constable, a rather dim young man, pursed his lips at this, looking dubiously back and forth between us.

"Ahh . . . well, one of 'em's a forger," he said, "and 'tother's a murderess. But as to which bein' which . . ."

"I'm the murderess," Sadie said bravely, adding loyally, "She's a very fine midwife!" I looked at her in surprise, but she shook her head slightly and compressed her lips, adjuring me to keep quiet.

"Oh. Hmm. All right, then. Have you a gown . . . madam?" At my nod, he said briefly, "Get dressed," and turned to the constable, taking out a vast silk handkerchief from his pocket, with which to wipe his broad pink face. "I'll take her, then. You'll tell Mr. Tolliver."

"I will, sir," the constable assured him, more or less bowing and scraping. He glanced down at the unconscious form of Mrs. Tolliver, then frowned at Sadie.

"You, there. Take her inside and see to her. Hop!"

"Oh, yes, sir," Sadie said, and gravely pushed up her sweat-fogged spectacles with one forefinger. "Right away, sir!"

I had no opportunity to speak with Sadie, and barely time enough to struggle into my bedraggled gown and stays and seize my small bag before being escorted into a carriage—rather bedraggled itself, but once of good quality.

"Would you mind telling me who you are, and where you're taking me?" I inquired, after we had rattled through two or three cross streets, my companion gazing out the window with an abstracted sort of frown.

My question roused him, and he blinked at me, only then seeming to realize that I was not in fact an inanimate object.

"Oh. Beg pardon, madam. We are going to the Governor's Palace. Have you not a cap?"

"No."

He grimaced, as though he'd expected nothing else, and resumed his private thoughts.

They'd finished the place, and very nicely, too. William Tryon, the previous governor, had built the Governor's Palace, but had been sent to New York before construction had been finished. Now the enormous brick edifice with its graceful spreading wings was complete, even to the lawns and ivy beds that lined the drive, though the stately trees that would eventually surround it were mere saplings. The carriage pulled up on the drive, but we did not—of course—enter by the imposing front entrance, but rather scuttled round the back and down the stairs to the servants' quarters in the basement.

Here I was hastily shoved into a maid's room, handed a comb, basin, ewer, and a borrowed cap, and urged to make myself look less like a slattern, as quickly as possible.

My guide—Mr. Webb was his name, as I learned from the cook's respectful greeting to him—waited with obvious impatience while I made my hasty ablutions, then grasped my arm and urged me upstairs. We ascended by a narrow back stair to the second floor, where a very young and frightened-looking maidservant was waiting.

"Oh, you've come, sir, at last!" She bobbed a curtsy to Mr. Webb, giving me a curious glance. "Is this the midwife?"

"Yes. Mrs. Fraser—Dilman." He nodded at the girl, giving only her surname, the English fashion for house servants. She curtsied to me in turn, then beckoned me toward a door that stood ajar.

The room was large and gracious, furnished with a canopied bed, a walnut commode, armoire, and armchair, though the air of elegant refinement was somewhat impaired by a heap of mending, a ratty sewing basket overturned and spilling its threads, and a basket of children's toys. In the bed was a large mound, which—given the evidence to hand—I rather supposed must be Mrs. Martin, the Governor's wife.

This proved to be the case when Dilman curtsied again, murmuring my name to her. She was round—very round, given her advanced state of pregnancy—with a small, sharp nose and a nearsighted way of peering that reminded me irresistibly of Beatrix Potter's Mrs. Tiggy-Winkle. In terms of personality, not quite so much.

"Who the devil is this?" she demanded, poking a frowsy, capped head out of the bedclothes.

"Midwife, mum," Dilman said, bobbing again. "Have you slept well, mum?"

"Of course not," Mrs. Martin said crossly. "This beastly child's kicked my liver black and blue, I've puked all night, I've sweated through my sheets, and I have a shaking ague. I was told there was no midwife to be found within the county." She gave me a dyspeptic look. "Where did you discover this person, the local prison?"

"Actually, yes," I said, unslinging my bag from my shoulder. "How far gone are you, how long have you been ill, and when's the last time you moved your bowels?"

She looked marginally more interested, and waved Dilman out of the room.

"What did she say your name was?"

"Fraser. Are you experiencing any symptoms of early labor? Cramping? Bleeding? Intermittent pain in the back?"

She gave me a sideways look, but did begin to answer my questions. From which, in the fullness of time, I eventually was able to diagnose an acute case of food poisoning, likely caused by a leftover slice of oyster pie, consumed—with quite a lot of other edibles—in a fit of pregnancy-induced greed the day before.

"I have not an ague?" She withdrew the tongue she had allowed me to inspect, frowning.

"You have not. Not yet, anyway," honesty compelled me to add. It was no wonder she thought she had; I had learned in the course of the examination that a particularly virulent sort of fever was abroad in the town—and in the palace. The Governor's secretary had died of it two days before, and Dilman was the only upstairs servant still on her feet.

I got her out of bed, and helped her to the armchair, where she subsided, looking like a squashed cream cake. The room was hot and stuffy, and I opened the window in hopes of a breeze.

"God's teeth, Mrs. Fraser, do you mean to kill me?" She clutched her wrapper tight around her belly, hunching her shoulders as though I had admitted a howling blizzard.

"Probably not."

"But the miasma!" She waved a hand at the window, scandalized. In all truth, mosquitoes *were* a danger. But it was still several hours 'til sunset, when they would begin to rise.

"We'll close it in a bit. For the moment, you need air. And possibly something light. Could you stomach a bit of dry toast, do you think?"

She thought that one over, tasting the corners of her mouth with a tentative tongue tip.

"Perhaps," she decided. "And a cup of tea. Dilman!"

Dilman dismissed to fetch the tea and toast—how long was it since I had even seen real tea? I wondered—I settled down to take a more complete medical history.

How many earlier pregnancies? Six, but a shadow crossed her face, and I saw her glance involuntarily at a wooden puppet, lying near the hearth.

"Are your children in the palace?" I asked, curious. I had heard no sign of any children, and even in a place the size of the palace, it would be difficult to hide six of them.

"No," she said with a sigh, and put her hands on her belly, holding it almost absently. "We sent the girls to my sister in New Jersey, a few weeks ago."

A few more questions, and the tea and toast arrived. I left her to eat it in peace, and went to shake out the damp, crumpled bedclothes.

"Is it true?" Mrs. Martin asked suddenly, startling me.

"Is what true?"

"They say you murdered your husband's pregnant young mistress, and cut the baby from her womb. Did you?"

I put the heel of my hand against my brow and pressed, closing my eyes. How on earth had she heard that? When I thought I could speak, I lowered my hands and opened my eyes.

"She wasn't his mistress, and I didn't kill her. As for the rest—yes, I did," I said as calmly as I could.

She stared at me for a moment, her mouth hanging open. Then she shut it with a snap and crossed her forearms over her belly.

"Trust George Webb to choose me a proper midwife!" she said—and much to my surprise, began to laugh. "He doesn't know, does he?"

"I would assume not," I said with extreme dryness. "I didn't tell him. Who told you?"

"Oh, you are quite notorious, Mrs. Fraser," she assured me. "Everyone has been talking of it. George has no time for gossip, but even he must have heard of it. He has no memory for names, though. I do."

A little color was coming back into her face. She took another nibble of toast, chewed, and swallowed gingerly.

"I was not sure that it was you, though," she admitted. "Not until I asked." She closed her eyes, grimacing doubtfully, but evidently the toast hit bottom, for she opened them and resumed her nibbling.

"So now that you *do* know . . . ?" I asked delicately.

"I don't know. I've never known a murderess before." She swallowed the last of the toast and licked the tips of her fingers before wiping them on the napkin.

"I am *not* a murderess," I said.

"Well, of course you'd say so," she agreed. She took up the cup of tea, surveying me over it with interest. "You don't look depraved—though I must say, you don't look quite respectable, either." She raised the fragrant cup and drank, with a look of bliss that made me conscious that I hadn't eaten anything since the rather meager bowl of unsalted, unbuttered porridge provided for breakfast by Mrs. Tolliver.

"I'll have to think about it," Mrs. Martin said, setting down her cup with a clink. "Take that back to the kitchen," she said, waving at the tray, "and have them send me up some soup, and perhaps a few sandwiches. I do believe my appetite has come back!"

WELL, NOW bloody what? I had been whisked so abruptly from gaol to palace that I felt like a sailor decanted onto land after months at sea, staggering and off-balance. I went obediently down to the kitchen, as instructed, obtained a tray—with a most delectable-smelling bowl of soup—and took it back to Mrs. Martin, walking like an automaton. By the time she dismissed me, my brain had begun to function again, if not yet at full capacity.

I was in New Bern. And, thanks be to God and Sadie Ferguson, out of Sheriff Tolliver's noisome gaol. Fergus and Marsali were in New Bern. Ergo, the obvious—in fact, the only—thing to do was plainly to escape and find my way to them. They could help me to find Jamie. I clung firmly to Tom Christie's promise that Jamie wasn't dead and to the notion that he *was* findable, because nothing else was tolerable.

Escaping from the Governor's Palace, though, proved more difficult than I had anticipated. There were guards posted at all the doors, and my attempt to talk my way past one of them failed utterly, leading to the abrupt appearance of Mr. Webb, who took me by the arm and escorted me firmly up the stairs to a hot, stuffy little garret, where he locked me in.

It was better than the gaol, but that was all that could be said for it. There was a cot, a chamber pot, a basin, ewer, and chest of drawers, the latter containing meager bits of clothing. The room showed signs of recent occupancy—but not immediately recent. A film of fine summer dust lay over everything, and while the ewer was full of water, it had obviously been there for some time; a number of moths and other small insects had drowned in it, and a film of the same fine dust floated on the surface.

There was also a small window, painted shut, but determined banging and heaving got it open, and I breathed a heady lungful of hot, muggy air.

I stripped off, removed the dead moths from the pitcher, and washed, a blissful experience that made me feel immensely better, after the last week of unalloyed grime, sweat, and filth. After a moment's hesitation, I helped myself to a worn linen shift from the chest of drawers, unable to bear the thought of putting my own filthy, sweat-soaked chemise back on.

I could do only so much without soap or shampoo, but even so, felt much improved, and stood by the window, combing out my wet hair—there had been a wooden comb on the chest, though no looking glass—and surveying what I could see from my perch.

There were more guards, posted round the edge of the

property. Was that usual? I wondered. I thought perhaps it was not; they seemed uneasy, and very alert; I saw one challenge a man who approached the gate, presenting his weapon in rather belligerent fashion. The man seemed startled and backed up, then turned and walked away fast, glancing backward as he went.

There were a number of uniformed guards—I thought they were perhaps Marines, though I wasn't sufficiently familiar with uniforms as to be sure of it—clustered round six cannon, these situated on a slight rise before the palace, commanding the town and the harbor's edge.

There were two nonuniformed men among them; leaning out a bit, I made out the tall, heavyset figure of Mr. Webb, and a shorter man beside him. The shorter man was strolling along the line of cannon, hands folded beneath his coattails, and the Marines, or whatever they were, were saluting him. At a guess, this was the Governor, then: Josiah Martin.

I watched for a little while, but nothing of interest happened, and I found myself overwhelmed with sudden sleepiness, borne down by the strains of the last month and the hot, still air that seemed to press upon me like a hand.

I lay down on the cot in my borrowed shift, and fell instantly asleep.

I SLEPT until the middle of the night, when I was again called to attend Mrs. Martin, who seemed to be having a relapse of her digestive difficulties. A slightly pudgy, long-nosed man in nightshirt and cap lurked in the doorway with a candle, looking worried; I took this to be the Governor. He looked hard at me, but made no move to interfere, and I had no time to take much notice of him. By the time the crisis had passed, the Governor—if indeed it was he—had disappeared. The patient now safely asleep, I lay down like a dog on the rug beside her bed, with a rolled-up petticoat as pillow, and went thankfully back to sleep.

It was full daylight when I woke again, and the fire was out. Mrs. Martin was out of bed, calling fretfully into the passage for Dilman.

"Wretched girl," she said, turning back as I got awkwardly to my feet. "Got the ague, I suppose, like the rest. Or run away."

I gathered that while several servants were down with the fever, a good many of the others had simply decamped out of fear of contagion.

"You're quite sure I have not got the tertian ague, Mrs. Fraser?" Mrs. Martin squinted at herself in her looking glass, putting out her tongue and surveying it critically. "I do believe I look yellow."

In fact, her complexion was a soft English pink, though rather pale from throwing up.

"Keep off the cream cakes and oyster pie in hot weather, don't eat anything larger than your head at one sitting, and you should be quite all right," I said, suppressing a yawn. I caught a look at myself in the glass, over her shoulder, and shuddered. I was nearly as pale as she was, with dark circles under my eyes, and my hair . . . well, it was almost clean, that was all that could be said for it.

"I should be let blood," Mrs. Martin declared. "That is the proper treatment for a plethory; dear Dr. Sibelius always says so. Three or four ounces, perhaps, to be followed by the black draught. Dr. Sibelius says he finds the black draught answer very well in such cases." She moved to an armchair and reclined, her belly bulging under her wrapper. She pulled up the sleeve of the wrapper, extending her arm in languorous fashion. "There is a fleam and bowl in the top left drawer, Mrs. Fraser. If you would oblige me?"

The mere thought of letting blood first thing in the morning was enough to make *me* want to vomit. As for Dr. Sibelius's black draught, that was laudanum—an alcoholic tincture of opium, and not *my* treatment of choice for a pregnant woman.

The subsequent acrimonious discussion over the virtues of blood-letting—and I began to think, from the anticipatory gleam in her eye, that the thrill of having a vein opened by a murderess was what she actually desired—was interrupted by the unceremonious entry of Mr. Webb.

"Do I disturb you, mum? My apologies." He bowed perfunctorily to Mrs. Martin, then turned to me. "You—put on your cap and come with me."

I did so without protest, leaving Mrs. Martin indignantly unperforated.

Webb ushered me down the gleamingly polished front stair this time, and into a large, gracious, book-lined room. The Governor, now properly wigged, powdered, and elegantly suited, was seated behind a desk overflowing with papers, dockets, scattered quills, blotters, sand-shakers, sealing wax, and all the other impedimenta of an eighteenth-century bureaucrat. He looked hot, bothered, and quite as indignant as his wife.

"What, Webb?" he demanded, scowling at me. "I need a secretary, and you bring me a midwife?"

"She's a forger," Webb said baldly. That stopped whatever complaint the Governor had been going to bring forth. He paused, mouth slightly open, still frowning at me.

"Oh," he said in an altered tone. "Indeed."

"*Accused* of forgery," I said politely. "I haven't been tried, let alone convicted, you know."

The Governor's eyebrows went up, hearing my educated accent.

"Indeed," he said again, more slowly. He looked me up and down, squinting dubiously. "Where on earth did you get her, Webb?"

"From the gaol." Webb cast me an indifferent glance, as though I might be some unprepossessing yet useful bit of furniture, like a chamber pot. "When I made inquiries for a midwife, someone told me that this woman had done prodigies with a slave, another prisoner, having a difficult lying-in. And as the matter was urgent, and no other cunning woman to be found . . ." He shrugged, with a faint grimace.

"Hmmmm." The Governor pulled a handkerchief from his sleeve and dabbed thoughtfully at the plump flesh beneath his chin. "Can you write a fair hand?"

I supposed it would be a poor forger who couldn't, but contented myself with saying, "Yes." Fortunately, it was true; in my own time, I had scribbled ball-point prescriptions with the best of them, but now I had trained myself to write clearly with a quill, so that my medical records and case notes should be legible, for the benefit of whoever should read them after me. Once again, I felt a sharp pang at the thought of Malva—but there was no time to think of her.

Still eyeing me speculatively, the Governor nodded toward a straight-backed chair and a smaller desk at the side of the room.

"Sit." He rose, scrabbled among the papers on his desk, and deposited one in front of me. "Let me see you make a fair copy of that, if you please."

It was a brief letter to the Royal Council, outlining the Governor's concerns regarding recent threats to that body, and postponing the next scheduled meeting of the council. I chose a quill from the cut-glass holder on the desk, found a silver penknife by it, trimmed the quill to my liking, uncorked the inkwell, and set about the business, deeply aware of the scrutiny of the two men.

I didn't know how long my imposture might hold up—Mrs. Governor could blow the gaff at any time—but for the nonce, I thought I probably had a better chance of escape as an accused forger than as an accused murderer.

The Governor took my finished copy, surveyed it, and laid it on the desk with a small grunt of satisfaction.

"Good enough," he said. "Make eight further copies of that, and then you can go on with these." Turning back to his own desk, he shuffled together a large sheaf of correspondence, which he deposited in front of me.

The two men—I had no notion of Webb's office, but he was obviously the Governor's close friend—returned to a discussion of current business, ignoring me completely.

I went about my assigned task mechanically, finding the scratch of the quill, the ritual of sanding, blotting, and shaking, soothing. Copying occupied a very small part of my mind; the rest was free to worry about Jamie, and to think how best to engineer an escape.

I could—and doubtless should—make an excuse after a bit to go and see how Mrs. Martin did. If I could make shift to do so unaccompanied, I would have a few moments of unobserved freedom, during which to make a surreptitious dash for the nearest exit. So far, though, every door I'd seen had been guarded. The Governor's Palace had a very well-stocked simples closet, alas; it would be hard to invent a need for anything from an apothecary—and even then, unlikely that they'd let me go alone to fetch it.

Waiting for nightfall seemed the best notion; at least if I did get out of the palace, I would have several hours before my absence was noted. If they locked me in again, though . . .

I scratched away assiduously, turning over various unsatisfactory plans, and trying very hard not to envision Jamie's body turning slowly in the wind, hanging from a tree in some lonely hollow. Christie had given me his word; I clung to that, having nothing else to cling to.

Webb and the Governor murmured together, but their talk was of things I had no notion of, and for the most part, it washed over me like the sound of the sea, meaningless and soothing. After some time, though, Webb came over to instruct me in the sealing and direction of those letters to be sent. I thought of asking why he didn't lend a hand himself in this clerical emergency, but then saw his hands—both badly twisted with arthritis.

"You write a very fair hand, Mrs. Fraser," he unbent enough to say, at one point, and gave me a brief, wintry smile. "It is unfortunate that you should have been the forger, rather than the murderess."

"Why?" I asked, rather astonished at that.

"Why, you are plainly literate," he said, surprised in turn at my astonishment. "If convicted of murder, you could plead benefit of clergy, and be let off with a public whipping and branding in the face. Forgery, though—" He shook his head, pursing his lips. "Capital crime, no pardon possible. If convicted of forgery, Mrs. Fraser, I am afraid you must be hanged."

My feelings of gratitude toward Sadie Ferguson underwent an abrupt reappraisal.

"Indeed," I said as coolly as possible, though my heart had given a convulsive leap and was now trying to burrow out of my chest. "Well, we'll hope that justice is served then, and I am released, won't we?"

He made a choked sound that I thought passed for a laugh. "To be sure. If only for the Governor's sake."

After that, we resumed work silently. The gilded clock behind me struck noon, and as though summoned by the sound, a servant whom I took to be the butler came in, to inquire whether the Governor would receive a delegation of the town's citizens?

The Governor's mouth compressed a bit, but he nodded in resignation, and a group of six or seven men came in, all attired in their best coats, but plainly tradesmen, rather than merchants or lawyers. None I recognized, thank God.

"We have come, sir," said one, who introduced himself as George Herbert, "to ask the meaning of this movement of the cannon."

Webb, sitting next to me, stiffened a little, but the Governor seemed to have been prepared for this.

"The cannon?" he said with every evidence of innocent surprise. "Why—the mountings are being repaired. We shall fire a royal salute—as usual—in honor of the Queen's birthday, later in the month. Upon inspecting the cannon in anticipation of this, though, it was discovered that the wood of the caissons had rotted away in spots. Firing the cannon is of course impossible until repairs shall be effected. Would you wish to inspect the mountings for yourself, sir?"

He half-rose from his seat as he said this, as though personally to escort them outside, but spoke with such a tinge of irony to his courtesy that they flushed and muttered refusals.

There was a bit more back and forth, in the name of courtesy, but the delegation then left, exhibiting only marginally less suspicion than that with which they'd come in. Webb closed his eyes and exhaled audibly, as the door closed behind them.

"God damn them," said the Governor very softly. I didn't think he meant it to be heard, and pretended I hadn't, busying myself with the papers and keeping my head lowered.

Webb got up and went to the window that overlooked the lawn, presumably to assure himself that the cannon were where he thought they should be. By craning a bit, I could see past him; sure enough, the six cannon had been removed from their mountings and lay on the grass, harmless logs of bronze.

From the subsequent conversation—salted with strong remarks regarding rebellious dogs who had the temerity to put the question to a Royal Governor as though he were a bootblack, by God!—I gathered that in fact, the cannon had been removed because of a very real fear that the townspeople might seize them and turn them upon the palace itself.

It dawned on me, listening to all this, that things had gone further and moved faster than I had expected. It was mid-July, but of 1775—nearly a year before a larger and more forceful version of the Mecklenberg Declaration would flower into an official declaration of independence for the united Colonies. And yet here was a Royal Governor, in obvious fear of open revolt.

If what we had seen on our journey south from the Ridge had not been enough to convince me that war was now upon us, a day spent with Governor Martin left no doubt.

I did go up in the afternoon—accompanied by the watchful Webb, alas—to check my patient, and to make inquiries regarding anyone else who might be ill. Mrs. Martin was torpid and low in spirits, complaining of the heat and the pestilential, wretched climate, missing her daughters, and suffering severely from a lack of personal service, having been obliged to brush her own hair in the absence of Dilman, who had vanished. She was, however, in good health, as I was able to report to the Governor, who asked me of it upon my return.

"Would she stand a journey, do you think?" he asked, frowning a bit.

I considered for a moment, then nodded.

"I think so. She's a bit wobbly, still, from the digestive upset—but she should be quite well again by tomorrow. I see no difficulties with the pregnancy—tell me, had she any trouble with previous confinements?"

The Governor's face flushed rosily at that, but he shook his head.

"I thank you, Mrs. Fraser," he said with a slight inclination of the head. "You will excuse me, George—I must go and speak to Betsy."

"Is he thinking of sending his wife away?" I asked Webb, in the wake of the Governor's departure. Despite the heat, a small qualm of uneasiness stirred beneath my skin.

For once, Webb seemed quite human; he was frowning after the Governor, and nodded absently.

"He has family in New York and New Jersey. She'll be safe

there, with the girls. Her three daughters," he explained, catching my eye.

"Three? She said she'd had six—ah." I stopped abruptly. She said she had borne six children, not that she had six living children.

"They have lost three small sons to the fevers here," Webb said, still looking after his friend. He shook his head, sighing. "It hasn't been a fortunate place for them."

He seemed then to recover himself, and the man disappeared back behind the mask of the chilly bureaucrat. He handed me another sheaf of papers, and went out, not bothering to bow.

93

IN WHICH I IMPERSONATE A LADY

I ATE SUPPER ALONE in my room; the cook seemed still to be functioning, at least, though the atmosphere of disorder in the house was a palpable thing. I could feel the uneasiness, bordering on panic—and had the thought that it wasn't fear of fever or ague that had caused the servants to leave, but more likely that sense of self-preservation that causes rats to flee a sinking ship.

From my tiny window, I could see a small portion of the town, apparently serene in the gathering twilight. The light was very different here from that in the mountains—a flat, dimensionless light that limned the houses and the fishing boats in the harbor with a hard-edged clarity, but faded into a haze that hid the farther shore completely, so that I looked beyond the immediate prospect into featureless infinity.

I shook off the notion, and took from my pocket the ink,

quill, and paper I had abstracted from the library earlier. I had no idea whether or how I might get a note out of the palace—but I did have a little money, still, and if the opportunity offered . . .

I wrote quickly to Fergus and Marsali, telling them briefly what had happened, urging Fergus to make inquiries for Jamie in Brunswick and Wilmington.

I thought myself that if Jamie *was* alive, that he was most likely in the Wilmington gaol. Brunswick was a tiny settlement, dominated by the looming presence of the log-built Fort Johnston, but the fort was a militia garrison; there would be no good reason to take Jamie there—though if they *had* . . . the fort was under the command of a Captain Collet, a Swiss emigrant who knew him. At least he would be safe there.

Who else did he know? He had a good many acquaintances on the coast, from the days of the Regulation. John Ashe, for one; they had marched side by side to Alamance, and Ashe's company had camped next to ours every night; we had entertained him at our campfire many times. And Ashe was from Wilmington.

I had just finished a brief plea to John Ashe, when I heard footsteps coming down the hallway toward my room. I folded it hastily, not worrying about smearing, and thrust it with the other note into my pocket. There was no time to do anything with the contraband ink and paper, save push it under the bed.

It was Webb, of course, my customary jailer. Evidently, I was now considered the general dogsbody of the establishment; I was escorted to Mrs. Martin's room and desired to pack her things.

I might have expected complaint or hysteria, but in fact, she was not only dressed but pale-faced and composed, directing and even assisting the process with a sense of clear-minded order.

The reason for her self-possession was the Governor, who came in midway through the packing, his face drawn with worry. She went at once to him, and put her hands affectionately on his shoulders.

"Poor Jo," she said softly. "Have you had any supper?"

"No. It doesn't matter. I'll have a bite later." He kissed her briefly on the forehead, his look of worry lightening a little as he looked at her. "You're quite well now, Betsy? You're sure of it?" I realized suddenly that he was Irish—Anglo-Irish, at least; he had no hint of an accent, but his unguarded speech held a faint lilt.

"Entirely recovered," she assured him. She took his hand and pressed it to her bulge, smiling. "See how he kicks?"

He smiled back, raised her hand to his lips, and kissed it.

"I'll miss you, darling," she said very softly. "You will take very great care?"

He blinked rapidly, and looked down, swallowing.

"Of course," he said gruffly. "Dear Betsy. You know I could not bear to part with you, unless—"

"I do know. That's why I fear so greatly for you. I—" At this point, she looked up, and realized suddenly that I was there. "Mrs. Fraser," she said in quite a different tone. "Go down to the kitchen, please, and have a tray prepared for the Governor. You may take it to the library."

I bobbed slightly, and went. Was this the chance I had been waiting for?

The halls and stairway were deserted, lit only by flickering tin sconces—burning fish oil, by the smell. The brick-walled kitchen was, of course, in the basement, and the eerie silence in what should ordinarily be a hive of activity made the unlighted kitchen stairway seem like the descent into a dungeon.

There was no light in the kitchen now save the hearth fire, burning low—but it *was* burning, three servants clustered near it despite the smothering heat. They turned at my footsteps, startled and faceless in silhouette. With steam rising from the cauldron behind them, I had the momentary delusion that I was facing Macbeth's three witches, met in dreadful prophecy.

"Double, double, toil and trouble," I said pleasantly, though my heart beat a little faster as I approached them. "Fire burn, and cauldron bubble."

"Toil and trouble, *that* be right," said a soft female voice, and laughed. Closer now, I could see that they had appeared faceless in the shadows because they were all black; slaves, likely, and thus unable to flee the house.

Unable also to carry a message for me. Still, it never hurt to be friendly, and I smiled at them.

They smiled shyly back, looking at me with curiosity. I had not seen any of them before—nor they me, though "downstairs" being what it was, I thought it likely they knew who I was.

"Governor be sendin' his lady away?" asked the one who had laughed, moving to fetch down a tray from a shelf in response to my request for something light.

"Yes," I said. I realized the value of gossip as currency, and related everything that I decently could, as the three of them moved efficiently about, dark as shadows, their darting hands slicing, spreading, arranging.

Molly, the cook, shook her head, her white cap like a sunset cloud in the fire's glow.

"Bad times, bad times," she said, clicking her tongue, and the other two murmured assent. I thought, from their attitude, that they liked the Governor—but then, as slaves, their fate was inextricably linked with his, regardless of their feelings.

It occurred to me, as we chatted, that even if they could not reasonably flee the house altogether, they might at least leave the premises now and again; someone had to do the marketing, and there seemed to be no one else left. In fact, this proved to be the case; Sukie, the one who had laughed, went out to buy fish and fresh vegetables in the mornings, and tactfully approached, was not averse to delivering my notes to the printshop—she said she knew where it was, the place with all the books in the window—for a small consideration.

She tucked away the paper and money in her bosom, giving me a knowing look, and winked. God knew what she thought it was, but I winked back, and hefting the loaded tray, made my way back up into the fishy-smelling realms of light.

I found the Governor alone in the library, burning papers. He nodded absently at the tray I set on the desk, but did not touch it. I wasn't sure what to do, and after a moment's awkward standing about, sat down at my accustomed place.

The Governor thrust a final sheaf of documents into the fire, then stood looking bleakly after them, as they blackened and curled. The room had cooled a little, with the setting sun, but the windows were tightly shut—of course—and rivulets of condensing moisture rolled down the ornamental panes of glass. Blotting a similar condensation from my cheeks and nose, I got up and threw open the window closest to me, drawing in a deep gulp of the evening air, cloyingly warm, but fresh, and sweet with honeysuckle and roses from the garden, undercut with dankness from the distant shore.

Woodsmoke, too; there were fires burning outside. The soldiers who guarded the palace had watch fires burning, evenly spaced around the perimeter of the grounds. Well, that would help with the mosquitoes—and we would not be completely surprised, if an attack should come.

The Governor came to stand behind me. I expected him to tell me to shut the window, but he merely stood, looking out across his lawns and the long, graveled drive. The moon had risen, and the dismounted cannon were dimly visible, lying in the shadows like dead men in a row.

After a moment, the Governor moved back to his desk, and calling me over, handed me a sheaf of official correspondence for copying, another for sorting and filing. He left the window open; I thought that he wished to hear, if anything should happen.

I wondered where the omnipresent Webb was. There was no sound from elsewhere in the Palace; presumably Mrs. Martin had finished her packing alone, and gone to bed.

We worked on, through the intermittent chiming of the clock, the Governor getting up now and then to commit another batch of papers to the fire, taking my copies and bundling them into large leather folders that he bound with tape, stacking them on his desk. He had taken off his wig; his hair was brown, short but curly—rather like my own had been, after the fever. Now and then he paused, head turned, listening.

I had faced a mob, and knew what he was listening for. I didn't know what to hope for, at this point, or to fear. And so I worked on, welcoming the work for the numbing distraction it was, though my hand had grown desperately cramped, and I had to pause every few moments to rub it.

The Governor was writing now; he shifted in his chair, grimacing with discomfort in spite of the cushion. Mrs. Martin had told me that he suffered from a fistula. I doubted very much that he'd let me treat it.

He eased himself onto one buttock, and rubbed a hand

down his face. It was late, and he was plainly tired, as well as uncomfortable. I was tired, too, stifling yawns that threatened to dislocate my jaw and left my eyes watering. He kept doggedly working, though, with occasional glances at the door. Who was he expecting?

The window at my back was still open, and the soft air caressed me, warm as blood, but moving enough to stir the wisps of hair on my neck and make the candle flame waver wildly. It bent to one side and flickered, as though it would go out, and the Governor reached quickly to shelter it with a cupped hand.

The breeze passed and the air fell still again, save for the sound of crickets outside. The Governor's attention seemed focused on the paper before him, but suddenly his head turned sharply, as though he had seen something dart past the open door.

He looked for a moment, then blinked, rubbed his eyes, and returned his attention to the paper. But he couldn't keep it there. He glanced again at the empty doorway—I couldn't help looking, too—then back, blinking.

"Did you . . . see someone pass, Mrs. Fraser?" he asked.

"No, sir," I said, nobly swallowing a yawn.

"Ah." Seeming somehow disappointed, he took up his quill, but didn't write anything, just held it between his fingers, as though he had forgotten it was there.

"Were you expecting anyone, Your Excellency?" I asked politely, and his head jerked up, surprised to be directly addressed.

"Oh. No. That is . . ." His voice died away as he glanced once more at the doorway that led to the back of the house.

"My son," he said. "Our darling Sam. He—died here, you know—late last year. Only eight years old. Sometimes . . . sometimes I think I see him," he ended quietly, and bent his head once more over his paper, lips pressed tight.

I moved impulsively, meaning to touch his hand, but his tight-lipped air prevented me.

"I am sorry," I said quietly, instead. He didn't speak, but gave one quick, short nod of acknowledgment, not raising his head. His lips tightened further, and he went back to his writing, as did I.

A little later, the clock struck the hour, then two. It had a soft, sweet chime, and the Governor stopped to listen, a distant look in his eyes.

"So late," he said, as the last chime died away. "I have kept you intolerably late, Mrs. Fraser. Forgive me." He motioned to me to leave the papers I was working on, and I rose, stiff and aching from sitting so long.

I shook my skirts into some order and turned to go, realizing only then that he had made no move to put away his ink and quills.

"You should go to bed, too, you know," I said to him, turning and pausing at the door.

The palace was still. Even the crickets had ceased, and only the soft snore of a sleeping soldier in the hall disturbed the quiet.

"Yes," he said, and gave me a small, tired smile. "Soon." He shifted his weight to the other buttock, and picked up his quill, bending his head once more over the papers.

NO ONE WOKE me in the morning, and the sun was well up when I stirred on my own. Listening to the silence, I had a momentary fear that everyone had decamped in the night, leaving me locked in to starve. I rose hastily, though, and looked out. The red-coated soldiers were still patrolling the grounds, just as usual. I could see small groups of citizens outside the perimeter, mostly strolling past in twos or threes, but sometimes stopping to stare at the palace.

Then I began to hear small thumps and homely noises on the floor below, and felt relieved; I was not entirely abandoned. I was, however, extremely hungry by the time the butler came to let me out.

He brought me to Mrs. Martin's bedchamber, but to my surprise it was empty. He left me there, and within a few moments, Merilee, one of the kitchen slaves, came in, looking apprehensive at being in this unfamiliar part of the house.

"Whatever is going on?" I asked her. "Where is Mrs. Martin, do you know?"

"Well, I know *that,*" she said, in a dubious tone indicating that it was the only thing she *did* know for certain. "She lef' just afore dawn this mornin'. That Mr. Webb, he took her away, secret-like, in a wagon with her boxes."

I nodded, perplexed. It was reasonable that she should have left quietly; I imagined the Governor didn't want to give any indication that he felt threatened, for fear of provoking exactly the violence he feared.

"But if Mrs. Martin is gone," I said, "why am I here? Why are *you* here?"

"Oh. Well, I know that, too," Merilee said, gaining a bit of confidence. "I s'posed to hep you dress, ma'am."

"But I don't need any . . ." I began, and then saw the garments laid out on the bed: one of Mrs. Martin's day gowns, a pretty printed floral cotton, done in the newly popular "polonaise" fashion, complete with voluminous petticoats, silk stockings, and a large straw hat to shade the face.

Evidently, I was meant to impersonate the Governor's wife. There was no real point in protesting; I could hear the Governor and the butler talking in the hall, and after all—if it got me out of the palace, so much the better.

I was only two or three inches taller than Mrs. Martin, and my lack of a bulge made the gown hang lower. There was no hope of my fitting into any of her shoes, but my own were not completely disreputable, in spite of all my adventures since leaving home. Merilee cleaned them and rubbed them with a bit of grease to make the leather shine; they were at least not so crude as to draw attention immediately.

With the broad-brimmed hat slanting forward to hide my face, and my hair twisted up and firmly pinned under a cap beneath it, I was probably a reasonable approximation, at least to people who did not know Mrs. Martin well. The Governor frowned when he saw me, and walked slowly round me, tugging here and there to adjust the fit, but then nodded, and with a small bow, offered me his arm.

"Your servant, mum," he said politely. And with me slumping slightly to disguise my height, we went out the front door, to find the Governor's carriage waiting in the drive.

94

ABSQUATULATION

JAMIE FRASER OBSERVED the quantity and quality of books in the window of the printshop—*F. Fraser, Proprietor*—and allowed himself a momentary sense of pride in Fergus; the establishment, though small, was apparently thriving. Time, however, was pressing, and he pushed through the door without stopping to read the titles.

A small bell over the door rang at his entrance, and Germain popped up behind the counter like an ink-smeared jack-in-the-box, emitting a whoop of joy at sight of his grandfather and his uncle Ian.

"Grandpère, Grandpère!" he shouted, then dived under the flap in the counter, clutching Jamie about the hips in ecstasy. He'd grown; the top of his head now reached Jamie's lower ribs. Jamie ruffled the shiny blond hair gently, then detached Germain and told him to fetch his father.

No need; aroused by the shouting, the whole family came boiling out from the living quarters behind the shop, exclaiming, yelling, squealing, and generally carrying on like a pack of wolves, as Ian pointed out to them, Henri-Christian riding on his shoulders in red-faced triumph, clinging to his hair.

"What has happened, milord? Why are you here?" Fergus disengaged Jamie easily from the riot and drew him aside, into the alcove where the more expensive books were kept—and those not suitable for public display.

He could see from the look on Fergus's face that some news had come down from the mountains; while surprised to see him, Fergus was not astonished, and his pleasure covered a worried mind. He explained the matter as quickly as he could, stumbling now and then over his words from haste and weariness; one of the horses had broken down some forty miles from town, and unable to find another, they had walked for two nights and a day, taking it in turns to ride, the other trotting alongside, clinging to the stirrup leathers.

Fergus listened with attention, wiping his mouth with the handkerchief he had taken from his collar; they had arrived in the middle of dinner.

"The sheriff—that would be Mr. Tolliver," he said. "I know him. Shall we—"

Jamie made an abrupt gesture, cutting him short.

"We went there to begin with," he said. They had found the sheriff gone, and no one in the house save a very drunken woman with a face like a discontented bird, collapsed and snoring on the settle with a small Negro baby clutched in her arms.

He had taken the baby and thrust it into Ian's arms, bidding him grimly to mind it while he sobered the woman enough to talk. He had then dragged her out into the yard and poured buckets of well water over her until she gasped and blinked, then dragged her dripping and stumbling back into the house, where he obliged her to drink water poured over the black, burned dregs of chicory coffee he had found in the pot. She had vomited profusely and disgustingly, but regained some vague sense of language.

"At first, all she could say was that all of the female prisoners were gone—run off or hanged." He said nothing of the fright that had lanced through his belly at that last. He had shaken the woman thoroughly, though, demanding particulars, and eventually, after further applications of water and vile coffee, got them.

"A man came, the day before yesterday, and took her away. That was all she knew—or all she remembered. I made her tell me what she could of how he looked—it wasna Brown, nor yet Gerald Forbes."

"I see." Fergus glanced behind him; his family were all gathered round Ian, pestering and caressing him. Marsali, though, was looking toward the alcove, worry on her face, obviously wanting to come and join the conversation, but detained by Joan, who was tugging on her skirt.

"Who would take her, I wonder?"

"Joanie, *a chuisle,* will ye not leave go? Help Félicité for a moment, aye?"

"But, Mama—"

"Not *now*. In a moment, aye?"

"I dinna ken," Jamie said, the frustration of helplessness welling up like black bile at the back of his throat. A sudden, more horrible thought struck him. "God, d'ye suppose it might have been Stephen Bonnet?"

The woman's slurred description had not sounded like the pirate—but she had been far from certain in it. Could Forbes have learned of his own escape, and determined simply to reverse the roles in the drama he had conceived—deport Claire forcibly to England, and try to pin the guilt of Malva Christie's death to Jamie's coat?

He found it hard to breathe, and had to force air into his chest. If Forbes had given Claire to Bonnet, he would slit the lawyer from wishbone to cock, rip the guts from his belly, and strangle him with them. And the same for the Irishman, once he laid hands upon him.

"Papi, Pa-pee . . ." Joan's singsong voice penetrated dimly through the red cloud that filled his head.

"What, *chérie*?" Fergus lifted her with the ease of long practice, balancing her fat little bottom on his left arm, to leave his right hand free.

She put her arms round his neck and hissed something into his ear.

"Oh, did you?" he said, plainly abstracted. "*Très bien*. Where did you put it, *chérie*?"

"With the naughty-lady pictures."

She pointed at the upper shelf, where several volumes lay, leather-bound but discreetly untitled. Glancing in the direction she indicated, Jamie saw a smudged paper sticking out from between two of the books.

Fergus clicked his tongue in displeasure, and smacked her lightly on the bottom with his good hand.

"You know you are not to climb up there!"

Jamie reached over and pulled the paper out. And felt all the blood leave his head, at sight of the familiar writing on it.

"What?" Fergus, alarmed at his appearance, set Joanie down. "Sit, milord! Run, *chérie,* get the smelling bottle."

Jamie waved a hand, speechless, trying to indicate that he was all right, and succeeded at last in finding his tongue.

"She's in the Governor's Palace," he said. "Christ be thanked, she's safe."

Seeing a stool pushed under the shelf, he pulled it out and sat on it, feeling exhaustion pulse through the quivering muscles of thigh and calf, ignoring the confusion of question and explanation, how Joanie had found the note pushed under the door—anonymous submissions to the newspaper often were delivered in this fashion, and the children knew they were to bring such things to their father's attention. . . .

Fergus read the note, his dark eyes assuming the expression of interested intent that he always had when contemplating the abstraction of something difficult and valuable.

"Well, that is good," he said. "We will go and fetch her. But I think first you must eat a little, milord."

He wished to refuse, to say that there was not a moment to be lost, that he could eat nothing in any case; his wame was knotted, hurting him.

But Marsali was already hurrying the girls back to the kitchen, calling out things about hot coffee and bread, and Ian following her, Henri-Christian still wrapped lovingly about his ears, Germain yapping eagerly at his heels. And he knew that should it come to a fight, he had nothing left to fight with. Then the succulent sizzle and scent of eggs frying in butter reached him, and he was up and moving toward the back, like iron drawn by a magnet.

Over their hasty meal, various plans were offered and rejected. At length, he reluctantly accepted Fergus's suggestion that either Fergus or Ian should go openly to the palace, asking to see Claire, saying that he was a kinsman, wishing to assure himself of her welfare.

"They have no reason to deny her presence, after all," Fergus said, shrugging. "If we can see her, so much the better; but even if not, we will learn whether she is still there, and perhaps where she is likely to be within the palace."

Fergus clearly wished to undertake the errand, but yielded when Ian pointed out that Fergus was widely known in New Bern, and it might be suspected that he was merely hunting scandal for the newspaper.

"For I am pained to say, milord," Fergus said apologetically, "that the matter—the crime—is known here already. There are broadsheets . . . the usual nonsense. *L'Oignon* was obliged to print something regarding the matter, of course, to keep our countenance, but we did so in a most repressive fashion, mentioning only the bald facts of the matter." His long, mobile mouth compressed briefly, in illustration of the repressive nature of his article, and Jamie smiled faintly.

"Aye, I see," he said. He pushed back from the table, pleased to feel some strength returned to his limbs, and heartened anew by food, coffee, and the comforting knowledge of Claire's whereabouts. "Well, then, Ian, comb your hair. Ye dinna want the Governor to think ye a savage."

JAMIE INSISTED UPON going with Ian, despite the danger of being recognized. His nephew eyed him narrowly.

"Ye're no going to do anything foolish, Uncle Jamie?"

"When was the last time ye kent me to do anything foolish?"

Ian gave him an old-fashioned look, held up one hand, and began to fold the fingers down, one by one.

"Oh, well, let me reckon, then . . . Simms the printer? Tarring Forbes? Roger Mac told me what ye did in Mecklenberg. And then there was—"

"Ye would have let them kill wee Fogarty?" Jamie inquired. "And if we're mentioning fools, who was it got his arse pricked for wallowing in mortal sin with—"

"What I mean is," Ian said severely, "ye're no going to walk into the Governor's Palace and try to take her by force, no matter what happens. Ye'll wait quietly wi' your hat on until I come back, and then we'll see, aye?"

Jamie pulled down the brim of his hat, a floppy, weathered felt affair such as a pig farmer might wear, with his hair tucked up beneath it.

"What makes ye think I wouldn't?" he asked, as much from curiosity as natural contention.

"The look on your face," Ian replied briefly. "I want her back as much as you do, Uncle Jamie—well," he amended, with a wry grin, "perhaps not *quite* sae much—but I mean to have her back, nonetheless. You"—he poked his uncle emphatically in the chest—"bide your time."

And leaving Jamie standing under a heat-stricken elm, he strode purposefully toward the gates of the palace.

Jamie took several deep breaths, trying to maintain a sense of annoyance with Ian as an antidote to the anxiety that wrapped itself round his chest like a snake. As the annoyance had been purely manufactured, it evaporated like steam from a kettle, leaving the anxiety squirming and writhing.

Ian had reached the gate, and was in palaver with the guard who stood there, musket at the ready. Jamie could see the man shaking his head emphatically.

This was nonsense, he thought. The need of her was a physical thing, like the thirst of a sailor becalmed for weeks on the sea. He'd felt that need before, often, often, in their years apart. But why now? She was safe; he knew where she was—was it only the exhaustion of the past weeks and days, or perhaps the weakness of creeping age that made his bones ache, as though she had in fact been torn from his body, as God had made Eve from Adam's rib?

Ian was arguing, making persuasive gestures toward the guard. The sound of wheels on gravel drew his attention from them; a carriage was coming down the drive, a small open conveyance with two people and a driver, drawn by a team of nice dark bays.

The guard had pushed Ian back with the barrel of his musket, gesturing him to keep away while the guard and his fellow opened the gates. The carriage rattled through without stopping, turned into the street, and came past him.

He had never seen Josiah Martin, but thought the plump, self-important-looking gentleman must surely be the— His eye caught the merest glimpse of the woman, and his heart clenched like a fist. Without an instant's thought, he was pelting after the carriage, as hard as he could run.

In his prime, he could not have outrun a team of horses. Even so, he came within a few feet of the carriage, would have called, but had no breath, no sight, and then his foot struck a misplaced cobble and he fell headlong.

He lay stunned and breathless, vision dark and his lungs afire, hearing only the receding clatter of hooves and carriage wheels, until a strong hand seized his arm and jerked.

"We'll avoid notice, he says," Ian muttered, bending to get

his shoulder under Jamie's arm. "Your hat's flown off, did ye notice *that*? Nay, of course not, nor the whole street staring, ye crack-brained gomerel. God, ye weigh as much as a three-year bullock!"

"Ian," he said, and paused to gulp for breath.

"Aye?"

"Ye sound like your mother. Stop." Another gulp of air. "And let go my arm; I can walk."

Ian gave a snort that sounded even more like Jenny, but did stop, and did let go. Jamie picked up his fallen hat and limped toward the printshop, Ian following in urgent silence through the staring streets.

SAFELY AWAY FROM the palace, we trotted sedately through the streets of New Bern, provoking only mild interest from the citizenry, some of whom waved, a few of whom called out vaguely hostile things, most of whom simply stared. At the edge of town, the groom turned the team onto the main road, and we bowled pleasantly along, apparently bound for an outing in the countryside, an illusion bolstered by the wicker picnic hamper visible behind us.

Once past the congestion of heavy wagons, cattle, sheep, and the other traffic of commerce, though, the groom whipped up, and we were flying again.

"Where are we going?" I shouted over the noise of the team, holding on to my hat to prevent it blowing off. I had thought we were merely providing a diversion, so that no one would notice Mrs. Martin's quiet removal until she was safely out of the colony. Evidently, though, we were *not* merely out for a picnic.

"Brunswick!" the Governor shouted back.

"Where?"

"Brunswick," he repeated. He looked grim, and grimmer still as he cast a last look back toward New Bern. "God damn them," he said, though I was sure he meant this observation only for himself. He turned round then, and settled himself, leaning slightly forward, as though to speed the carriage, and said no more.

95

THE *CRUIZER*

I WOKE EVERY MORNING, just before dawn. Worn out from worry and the Governor's late hours, I slept like the dead, through all the thumps and rattlings and bell-ringings of the watch, shouts from boats nearby, occasional musket-fire from the shore, and the whine of the offshore wind as it passed through the rigging. But in that moment before the light, the silence woke me.

Today? was the single thought in my mind, and I seemed to hang bodiless for a moment, just above my pallet beneath the forecastle. Then I drew breath, heard my heart beating, and felt the gentle heave of the deck beneath me. Would turn my face to the shore, watching, as the light began to touch the waves and reach toward land. We had first gone to Fort Johnston, but had stayed there barely long enough for the Governor to meet with local Loyalists who had assured him how unsafe it was, before retreating further.

We had been aboard His Majesty's sloop *Cruizer* for nearly a week, anchored off Brunswick. Lacking any troops save the Marines aboard the sloop, Governor Martin was unable to seize back control of his colony, and was reduced to writing frenzied letters, attempting to keep up some semblance of a government in exile.

Lacking anyone else to fill the office, I remained in my role as *ad hoc* secretary, though I had moved up from mere copyist to amanuensis, taking down some letters by dictation when Martin grew too tired to write himself. And cut off from land and information alike, I spent every spare moment watching the shore.

Today, a boat was coming, out of the fading dark.

One of the watch hailed it, and an answering "halloo"

came up, in tones of such agitation that I sat up abruptly, groping for my stays.

Today, there would be news.

The messenger was already in the Governor's cabin, and one of the Marines barred my way—but the door was open, and the man's voice clearly audible.

"Ashe's done it, sir, he's moving against the fort!"

"Well, God damn him for a treasonous dog!"

There was a sound of footsteps, and the Marine stepped hastily out of the way, just in time to avoid the Governor, who came popping out of his cabin like a jack out of the box, still attired in a billowing nightshirt and minus his wig. He seized the ladder and scampered up it like a monkey, affording me an unwanted view from below of his chubby bare buttocks. The Marine caught my eye and quickly averted his own gaze.

"What are they doing? Do you see them?"

"Not yet." The messenger, a middle-aged man in the dress of a farmer, had followed the Governor up the ladder; their voices floated down from the rail.

"Colonel Ashe ordered all the ships in Wilmington Harbor to take on troops yesterday and float them down to Brunswick. They were mustering just outside the town this morning; I heard the roll calls whilst I was doing the morning milking—nigh onto five hundred men, they must have. When I saw that, sir, I slipped away down to the shore and found a boat. Thought you ought to know, Your Excellence." The man's voice had lost its agitation now, and taken on a rather self-righteous tone.

"Oh, yes? And what do you expect me to do about it?" The Governor sounded distinctly cranky.

"How should I know?" said the messenger, replying in like vein. "*I* ain't the Governor, now, am I?"

The Governor's response to this was drowned out by the striking of the ship's bell. As it died away, he strode past the companionway, and looking down, saw me below.

"Oh, Mrs. Fraser. Will you fetch me some tea from the galley?"

I hadn't much choice, though I would have preferred to stay and eavesdrop. The galley fire had been banked for the night in its small iron pot, and the cook was still abed. By the time I had poked up the fire, boiled water, brewed a pot of tea, and assembled a tray with teapot, cup, saucer, milk, and toast, butter, biscuits, and jam, the Governor's informant had gone; I saw his boat heading for the shore, a dark arrowhead against the slowly brightening surface of the sea.

I paused for a moment on deck and rested my tea tray on the rail, looking inland. It was just light now, and Fort Johnston was visible, a blocky log building that stood exposed on top of a low rise, surrounded by a cluster of houses and outbuildings. There was a fair amount of activity around it; men were coming and going like a trail of ants. Nothing that looked like an imminent invasion, though. Either the commander, Captain Collet, had decided to evacuate—or Ashe's men had not yet begun their march from Brunswick.

Had John Ashe received my message? If he had . . . would he have acted? It wouldn't have been a popular thing to do; I couldn't blame him if he had decided that he simply couldn't afford to be seen aiding a man widely suspected of being a Loyalist—let alone one accused of such a hideous crime.

He might have, though. With the Governor marooned at sea, the Council disbanded, and the court system evaporated, there was no effective law in the colony now—save for the militias. If Ashe chose to storm the Wilmington jail and remove Jamie, he would have faced precious little opposition.

And if he had . . . if Jamie were free, he would be looking for me. And surely he would hear quickly where I was. If John Ashe came to Brunswick and Jamie were free, he would surely come with Ashe's men. I looked toward shore, seeking movement, but saw only a boy driving a cow desultorily along the road to Brunswick. But the shadows of the night were still cold around my feet; it was barely dawn.

I took a deep breath, and noticed the aromatic scent of the tea, mixed with the shore's morning breath—the smell of tide flats and piney scrub. I hadn't drunk tea in months, if not years. Thoughtfully, I poured a cup, and sipped it slowly, watching the shore.

WHEN I ARRIVED in the surgeon's cabin, which the Governor had taken for his office, he was dressed, and alone.

"Mrs. Fraser." He nodded briefly to me, scarcely looking up. "I am obliged. Will you write, please?"

He had been writing himself, already; quills and sand and blotter were scattered about the desk, and the inkwell stood open. I picked out a decent quill and a sheet of paper, and began to write as per his dictation, with a sense of growing curiosity.

The note—dictated between bites of toast—was to a General Hugh MacDonald, and referred to the General's safe arrival upon the mainland with a Colonel McLeod. Receipt of the General's report was acknowledged, and request made for continuing information. Mention was also made of the Governor's request for support—which I knew about—and assurances he had received regarding the arrival of that support, which I didn't.

"Enclosure, a letter of credit—no, wait." The Governor darted a look in the direction of the shore—to no particular avail, as the surgeon's cabin boasted no porthole—and scowled in concentration. Evidently, it had occurred to him that in light of recent events, a letter of credit issued by the Governor's office was possibly worth less than one of Mrs. Ferguson's forgeries.

"Enclosure, twenty shillings," he amended with a sigh. "If you will make the fair copy at once, Mrs. Fraser? These, you may do at your leisure." He pushed across an untidy stack of notes, done in his own crabbed hand.

He got up then, groaning as he stretched, and went up, no doubt to peer over the railing at the fort again.

I made the copy, sanded it, and set it aside, wondering who on earth *this* MacDonald was, and what he was doing? Unless Major MacDonald had undergone a change of name and an extraordinary promotion of late, it couldn't be he. And from the tone of the Governor's remarks, it appeared that General MacDonald and his friend McLeod were traveling alone—and on some particular mission.

I flipped quickly through the waiting stack of notes, but saw nothing else of interest; just the usual administrative trivia. The Governor had left his writing desk on the table, but it was closed. I debated trying to pick the lock and rummage through his private correspondence, but there were too many people about: seamen, Marines, ship's boys, visitors—the place was seething.

There was a sense of nervous tension aboard, as well. I'd noticed many times before how a sense of danger communicates itself among people in a confined setting: hospital emergency room, surgical suite, train car, ship; urgency flashes from one person to the next without speech, like the impulse down a neuron's axon to the dendrites of another. I didn't know whether anyone beyond the Governor and myself knew about John Ashe's movements yet—but the *Cruizer* knew that something was up.

The sense of nervous anticipation was affecting me, too. I was fidgeting, toe tapping absently, fingers moving restlessly up and down the shaft of the quill, unable to concentrate enough to write with it.

I stood up, with no idea what I meant to do; only the fixed notion that I would suffocate with impatience if I stayed below any longer.

On the shelf beside the door to the cabin stood the usual half-tidy clutter of shipboard, jammed behind a rail: a candlestick, extra candles, a tinderbox, a broken pipe, a bottle with a twist of flax stopping it, a bit of wood that someone had tried to carve and made a mess of. And a box.

The *Cruizer* had no surgeon aboard. And surgeons tended to take their personal implements with them, unless they died. This must be a kit belonging to the ship itself.

I glanced out the door; there were voices nearby, but no one in sight. I hastily flipped open the box, wrinkling my nose at the scent of dried blood and stale tobacco. There wasn't much there, and what there was was thrown in higgledy-piggledy, rusted, crusted, and of little use. A tin of Blue Pills, so labeled, and a bottle, not labeled, but recognizable, of black draught—laudanum, that is. A dried-up sponge and a sticky cloth stained with something yellow. And the one thing certain to be in any surgeon's kit of the times—blades.

There were footsteps coming down the companionway, and I heard the Governor's voice, talking to someone. Without pausing to consider the wisdom of my conduct, I grabbed a small jointing knife and thrust it down the front of my stays.

I slammed shut the lid of the box. There was no time to sit down again, though, before the Governor arrived, with another visitor in tow.

My heart was hammering in my throat. I pressed my palms, damp with sweat, against my skirt, and nodded to the new arrival, who was regarding me, open-mouthed, behind the Governor.

"Major MacDonald," I said, hoping that my voice wouldn't tremble. "Fancy meeting *you* here!"

MACDONALD'S MOUTH snapped shut and he drew himself more firmly upright.

"Mrs. Fraser," he said, bowing warily. "Your servant, mum."

"You know her?" Governor Martin glanced from MacDonald to me and back, frowning.

"We've met," I said, nodding politely. It had occurred to me that it might not profit either of us for the Governor to think there was some connection between us—if indeed there was one.

The same thought had clearly struck MacDonald; his face betrayed nothing beyond faint courtesy, though I could see the thoughts darting to and fro behind his eyes like a swarm of gnats. I was entertaining a similar swarm, myself—and knowing that my own face was naturally revealing, I cast down my eyes demurely, and murmuring an excuse about refreshment, made off toward the galley.

I threaded my way through clumps of seamen and Marines, mechanically acknowledging their salutes, mind working furiously.

How? How was I going to speak to MacDonald alone? I *had* to find out what he knew about Jamie—if anything. Would he tell me, if he did know anything? But yes, I thought, he would; soldier he might be, but MacDonald was also a confirmed gossip—and he was plainly dying of curiosity at the sight of me.

The cook, a chubby young free black named Tinsdale, who

wore his hair in three stubby braids that stuck out of his head like the horns of a triceratops, was at work in the galley, dreamily toasting bread over the fire.

"Oh, hullo," he said amiably, seeing me. He waved the toasting fork. "Want a bit of toast, Mrs. Fraser? Or is it the hot water, again?"

"Love some toast," I said, seized by inspiration. "But the Governor has company; he wants coffee sent. And if you have a few of those nice almond biscuits to go with it . . ."

Armed with a loaded coffee tray, I made my way toward the surgeon's cabin a few minutes later, heart pounding. The door was open for air; evidently it wasn't a secret meeting.

They were huddled together over the small desk, the Governor frowning at a wad of papers, these clearly having traveled some distance in MacDonald's dispatch case, judging from the creases and stains upon them. They appeared to be letters, written in a variety of hands and inks.

"Oh, coffee," the Governor said, looking up. He seemed vaguely pleased, plainly not recalling that he hadn't ordered any. "Splendid. Thank you, Mrs. Fraser."

MacDonald hastily picked up the papers, making room for me to set the tray down on the desk. The Governor had one in his hand; he kept hold of this, and I caught a quick glimpse of it as I bent to place the tray in front of him. It was a list of some sort—names on one side, numbers beside them.

I managed to knock a spoon to the floor, enabling a better look as I stooped for it. *H. Bethune, Cook's Creek, 14. Jno. McManus, Boone, 3. F. Campbell, Campbelton, 24?*

I darted a look at MacDonald, who had his eyes fixed on me. I dropped the spoon on the desk, then took a hasty step back, so that I stood directly behind the Governor. I pointed a finger at MacDonald, then in rapid succession clutched my throat, tongue protruding, grabbed my stomach with crossed forearms, then jabbed the finger again at him, then at myself, all the while giving him a minatory stare.

MacDonald viewed this pantomime with subdued fascination, but—with a veiled glance at the Governor, who was stirring his coffee with one hand, frowning at the paper he held in the other—gave me a tiny nod.

"How many can you be quite sure of?" the Governor was saying, as I curtsied and backed out.

"Oh, at least five hundred men, sir, even now," MacDonald replied confidently. "A great many more to come, as word spreads. Ye should see the enthusiasm with which the General has been received so far! I cannot speak for the Germans, of course, but depend upon it, sir, we shall have all the Highlanders of the backcountry, and not a few of the Scotch–Irish, too."

"God knows I hope you are right," the Governor said, sounding hopeful, but still dubious. "Where is the General now?"

I would have liked to hear the answer to that—and a good many other things—but the drum was beating overhead for mess, and thundering feet were already pounding down the decks and companionways. I couldn't lurk about eavesdropping in plain sight of the mess, so was obliged to go back up top, hoping that MacDonald had indeed got my message.

The captain of the *Cruizer* was standing by the rail, his first mate beside him, both scanning the shore with their telescopes.

"Is anything happening?" I could see more activity near the fort, people coming and going—but the shore road was still empty.

"Can't say, ma'am." Captain Follard shook his head, then lowered the telescope and shut it, reluctantly, as though afraid something might happen if he didn't keep his eyes fixed on the shore. The first mate didn't move, still squinting fixedly toward the fort on its bluff.

I remained there by his side, staring silently toward the shore. The tide shifted; I had been on the ship long enough to feel it, a barely perceptible pause, the sea taking breath as the invisible moon yielded its pull.

There is a tide in the affairs of men. . . . Surely Shakespeare had stood upon a deck, at least once, and felt that same faint shift, deep in the flesh. A professor had told me once, in medical school, that the Polynesian seafarers dared their vast journeys through the trackless sea because they had learned to sense the currents of the ocean, the shifts of wind and tide, registering these changes with that most delicate of instruments—their testicles.

It didn't take a scrotum to feel the currents that were swirling round us now, I reflected, with a sideways glance at the first mate's securely fastened white breeches. I could feel them in the pit of my stomach, in the damp of my palms, in the tenseness of the muscles at the back of my neck. The mate had lowered his telescope, but still looked toward the shore, almost absently, his hands resting on the rail.

It occurred to me suddenly that if something drastic were to happen on land, the *Cruizer* would at once lift sail and head out to sea, carrying the Governor to safety—and me farther from Jamie. Where on earth might we end up? Charlestown? Boston? Either was as likely. And no one on that seething shore would have any notion where we had gone.

I'd met displaced persons during the war—my war. Driven or taken from their homes, their families scattered, their cities destroyed, they thronged refugee camps, stood in lines besieging embassies and aid stations, asking, always asking for the names of the vanished, describing the faces of the loved and lost, grasping at any scrap of information that might lead them back to whatever might be left. Or, failing that, preserve for a moment longer what they had once been.

The day was warm, even on the water, and my clothes clung to me with humid damp, but my muscles convulsed and my hands on the rail shook with sudden chill.

I might have seen them all for the last time, not knowing it: Jamie, Bree, Jemmy, Roger, Ian. That's how it happened: I had not even said goodbye to Frank, had had no faintest inkling when he left that last night that I would never see him alive again. What if—

But no, I thought, steadying myself with a tighter grip on the wooden rail. We would find each other again. We had a place to return to. Home. And if I remained alive—as I most firmly intended to do—I *would* go back home.

The mate had shut his telescope and left; I hadn't noticed his departure, absorbed in morbid thoughts, and was quite startled when Major MacDonald hove to alongside me.

"Too bad the *Cruizer* has nay long-range guns," he said with a nod at the fort. "'Twould put a crimp in the plans o' those wee heathen, eh?"

"Whatever those plans might be," I replied. "And speaking of plans—"

"I've a kind of a griping in the wame," he interrupted blandly. "The Governor suggested that ye might possibly have some sort of medicine to soothe it."

"Did he indeed?" I said. "Well, come down to the galley; I'll brew you a cup of something that will set you right, I expect."

"DID YE KEN, he thought ye were a forger?" MacDonald, hands wrapped around a mug of tea, jerked his head in the direction of the main cabin. The Governor was nowhere in sight, and the cabin's door closed.

"I did, yes. Does he know better now?" I asked with a sense of resignation.

"Well, aye." MacDonald looked apologetic. "I supposed he knew already, or I wouldna have said. Though if I hadn't," he added, "he would have kent it sooner or later. The story's spread all the way to Edenton by now, and the broadsheets . . ."

I flapped a hand, dismissing this.

"Have you seen Jamie?"

"I have not." He glanced at me, curiosity warring with wariness. "I'd heard . . . aye, well, I've heard a great many things, and all different. But the meat of the matter is that ye've both been arrested, aye? For the murder of Miss Christie."

I nodded briefly. I wondered whether one day I would grow used to that word. The sound of it was still like a punch in the stomach, short and brutal.

"Need I tell you that there is no truth to it?" I said bluntly.

"Not the slightest need, mum," he assured me, with a fair assumption of confidence. But I sensed the hesitation in him, and saw the sideways glance, curious and somehow avid. Perhaps one day I'd get used to that, too.

My hands were cold; I wrapped them round my own mug, taking what comfort I could in its heat.

"I need to get word to my husband," I said. "Do you know where he is?"

MacDonald's pale blue eyes were fixed on my face, his own showing no more now than courteous attention.

"No, mum. But you do, I assume?"

I gave him a sharp look.

"Don't be coy," I advised him shortly. "You know as well as I do what's going on on shore—probably much better."

"Coy." His thin lips pursed in brief amusement. "I dinna believe anyone's called me that before. Aye, I know. And so?"

"I think that he *may* be in Wilmington. I tried to send word to John Ashe, and asked him to get Jamie out of the gaol in Wilmington, if possible—if he was there—and to tell him where I was. But I don't know—" I waved a hand in frustration toward the shore.

He nodded, native caution at odds with his obvious desire to ask me for the gory details of Malva's death.

"I shall be going back through Wilmington. I'll make such inquiries as may be possible. If I find Mr. Fraser—shall I tell him anything, beyond your present situation?"

I hesitated, thinking. I had been holding a constant conversation with Jamie, ever since they took him away from me. But none of what I said to him in the wide black nights or the lonely dawns seemed appropriate to confide to MacDonald. And yet . . . I couldn't forgo the opportunity; God knew when I might have another.

"Tell him that I love him," I said softly, my eyes on the tabletop. "I always will."

MacDonald made a small sound that made me look up at him.

"Even though he—" he began, then stopped himself.

"He didn't kill her," I said sharply. "And neither did I. I told you so."

"Of course not," he said hurriedly. "No one could imagine . . . I only meant . . . but of course, a man's but a man, and . . . mmphm." He broke off and looked away, the color high in his face.

"He didn't do that, either," I said through my teeth.

There was a marked silence, during which we avoided each other's gaze.

"Is General MacDonald a kinsman of yours?" I asked abruptly, needing either to change the course of the conversation or to leave.

The Major glanced up, surprised—and relieved.

"Aye, a distant cousin. The Governor's mentioned him?"

"Yes," I said. It was the truth, after all; Martin simply hadn't mentioned the General to *me.* "You're, um, assisting him, are you? It sounded as though you've been having some success."

Relieved to have escaped the social awkwardness of dealing with the question as to whether I were a murderess, and Jamie only a philanderer, or he a murderer and I his scorned and deluded dupe, MacDonald was only too eager to take the offered bait.

"Great success, indeed," he said heartily. "I've gathered pledges from many of the most prominent men in the colony; they stand ready to do the Governor's bidding at the slightest word!"

Jno. McManus, Boone, 3. Prominent men. I happened to know Jonathan McManus, whose gangrenous toes I had removed the winter before. He likely *was* the most prominent man in Boone, if by that, MacDonald meant that the other twenty inhabitants all knew him for a drunkard and a thief. It was also probably true that he had three men who would go to fight with him if called: his one-legged brother and his two feeble-minded sons. I took a sip of tea to hide my expression. Still, MacDonald had Farquard Campbell on his list; had Farquard really made a formal commitment?

"I gather the General is not presently anywhere near Brunswick, though," I said, "given the, er, present circumstances?" If he was, the Governor would be much less nervous than he was.

MacDonald shook his head.

"No. But he is not ready to muster his forces yet; he and McLeod do but discover the readiness of the Highlanders to rise. They will not call muster until the ships come."

"Ships?" I blurted. "What ships?"

He knew he oughtn't to speak further, but couldn't resist. I saw it in his eyes; after all, what danger could there be in telling me?

"The Governor has asked for aid from the Crown in subduing the factionalism and unrest that runs rampant in the colony. And has received assurances that it will be forthcoming—should he be able to raise enough support on the ground to reinforce the government troops who will arrive by ship.

"That is the plan, ye see," he went on, warming to it. "We are notified"—*Oh, "we" indeed,* I thought—"that my Lord Cornwallis begins to gather troops in Ireland, who will take ship shortly. They should arrive in the early autumn, and join wi' the General's militia. Between Cornwallis on the coast and the General comin' doon frae the hills—" He closed thumb and fingers in a pinching movement. "They'll crush the Whiggish whoresons like a pack o' lice!"

"Will they?" I said, endeavoring to sound impressed. Possibly they would; I had no idea, nor did I much care, being in no position to see far beyond the present moment. If I ever got off this frigging boat and out of the shadow of a noose, I'd worry about it.

The sound of the main cabin's door opening made me look up. The Governor was closing it behind him. Turning, he saw us, and came to inquire as to MacDonald's presumed indisposition.

"Oh, I am a great deal better," the Major assured him, hand pressed to the waistcoat of his uniform. He belched in illustration. "Mrs. Fraser is a capital hand at such things. Capital!"

"Oh, good," Martin said. He seemed a trifle less harassed than he had earlier. "You will be wanting to go back, then." He signaled to the Marine standing at the foot of the companionway, who knuckled his forehead in acknowledgment and disappeared up the ladder.

"The boat will be ready for you in a few minutes' time." With a nod at MacDonald's half-drunk tea, and a punctilious bow to me, the Governor turned and went into the surgeon's cabin, where I could see him standing beside the desk, frowning at the heap of crumpled papers.

MacDonald hastily swallowed the rest of his tea, and with a lift of the eyebrows, invited me to accompany him to the upper deck. We were standing on deck, waiting as a local fishing boat made its way out to the *Cruizer* from shore, when he suddenly laid a hand on my arm.

This startled me; MacDonald was not a casual toucher.

"I will do my utmost to discover your husband's whereabouts, mum," he said. "It occurs to me, though—" He hesitated, eyes on my face.

"What?" I said cautiously.

"I said I had heard considerable speculation?" he said delicately. "Regarding . . . erm . . . the unfortunate demise of Miss Christie. Would it not be . . . desirable . . . that I know the truth of the matter, so that I might put any ill-natured rumors firmly to rest, should I encounter them?"

I was torn between anger and laughter. I should have known that curiosity would be too much for him. But he was right; given the rumors I had heard—and I knew they were but a fraction of those circulating—the truth was certainly more desirable. On the other hand, I was entirely sure that the telling of the truth would do nothing to quell the rumors.

And still. The urge to be justified was a strong one; I understood those poor wretches who cried their innocence from the gallows—and I bloody hoped I wasn't going to be one.

"Fine," I said crisply. The first mate was back by the rail, keeping an eye on the fort, and within earshot, but I supposed it didn't matter whether he heard.

"The truth is this: Malva Christie was got with child by *someone,* but rather than name the real father, insisted that it was my husband. I know this to be false," I added, fixing him with a gimlet stare. He nodded, mouth a little open.

"A few days later, I went out to tend my garden and found the little—Miss Christie lying in my lettuce patch with her throat freshly cut. I thought . . . there was some chance that I might save her unborn child. . . ." Despite my assumption of bravado, my voice trembled a little. I stopped, clearing my throat. "I couldn't. The child was born dead."

Much better not to say *how* it was born; that weltering image of severed flesh and dirt-smeared blade was not one I wished the Major to have in mind, if it could be prevented. I had told no one—not even Jamie—about the faint flicker of life, that tingle that I still held secret in the palms of my hands. To say that the child had been born alive was to arouse immediate suspicion that I had killed it, and I knew as much. Some would think that anyway; Mrs. Martin plainly had.

MacDonald's hand was still resting on my arm, his gaze on my face. For once, I blessed the transparency of my countenance; no one watching my face ever doubted what I said.

"I see," he said quietly, and gently squeezed my arm.

I took a deep breath, and told him the rest—circumstantial details might convince some hearers.

"You know that there were bee gums at the edge of my garden? The murderer kicked two of them over in fleeing; he must have been stung several times—I was, when I came into the garden. Jamie—Jamie had no stings. It wasn't him." And under the circumstances, I had not been able to find out which man—or woman? For the first time, it occurred to me that it could have been a woman—*had* been stung.

At this, he gave a deep "hum!" of interest. He stood for a moment in contemplation, then shook his head, as though waking from a dream, and let go my arm.

"I thank ye, mum, for telling me," he said formally, and bowed to me. "Be assured, I will speak in your behalf, whenever the occasion shall arise."

"I appreciate that, Major." My voice was husky, and I swallowed. I hadn't realized how much it would hurt to speak of.

The wind stirred around us, and the reefed sails rustled in their ropes overhead. A shout from below announced the presence of the boat that would carry MacDonald back to the shore.

He bowed low over my hand, breath warm on my knuckles. For an instant, my fingers tightened on his; I was surprisingly reluctant to let him go. But let him go I did, and watched him all the way to the shore; a diminishing silhouette against the brightness of the water, back straight with resolution. He didn't look back.

The mate moved at the rail, sighing, and I glanced at him, then at the fort.

"What are they doing?" I asked. Some of the antlike forms seemed to be dropping lines from the walls to their fellows on the ground; I saw the ropes, fine as spiderwebs from this distance.

"I do believe the fort's commander is preparing to remove the cannon, madam," he said, snapping shut his brass telescope with a click. "If you will excuse me, I need to go inform the captain."

96

GUNPOWDER, TREASON, AND PLOT

IF THE GOVERNOR'S attitude toward me was altered by the news that I was not in fact a forger but rather a notorious—if merely accused—murderess, I had no opportunity to find out. He, like the rest of the officers and half the men aboard, rushed to the rail, and the rest of the day passed in a flurry of observation, speculation, and largely fruitless activity.

The lookout at the masthead called down periodic observations—men were leaving the fort, carrying things . . . the fort's weaponry, it looked like.

"Are they Collet's men?" the Governor bellowed, shading his eyes to look aloft.

"Can't say, sir," came the unhelpful reply from above.

At last, the *Cruizer*'s two launches were sent ashore, with orders to collect what information they could. They came back several hours later, with the news that Collet had abandoned the fort, in the face of threats, but had taken pains to remove the guns and powder, lest these fall into rebel hands.

No, sir, they had not spoken with Colonel Collet, who was—by rumor—on his way upriver with his militia forces. They had sent two men down the road toward Wilmington; it was true that a large force was gathering in the fields outside the town, under Colonels Robert Howe and John Ashe, but no word of what was planned.

"No word of what's planned, God's ballocks!" muttered the Governor, having been ceremoniously informed of this by Captain Follard. "They mean to burn the fort, what else would Ashe be planning, for the love of Jesus?"

His instincts were quite sound; just before sunset, the

scent of smoke came across the water, and we could just make out the antlike scurrying of men, piling heaps of flammable debris around the base of the fort. It was a simple, square building, made of logs. And despite the dampness of the humid air, it *would* burn, eventually.

It took them no little time to get the fire going, though, with neither powder nor oil to hasten its burning; as night fell, we could clearly see flaming torches, streaming in the breeze as they were carried to and fro, passed from hand to hand, dipping to touch off a pile of kindling, coming back a few minutes later, as the kindling went out.

Around nine o'clock, someone found a few barrels of turpentine, and the blaze took a sudden, lethal hold of the fort's log walls. Sheets of wavering flame rose pure and brilliant, orange and crimson billows against the night-black sky, and we heard scraps of cheering and snatches of ribald song, borne with the smell of smoke and the tang of turpentine on the offshore breeze.

"At least we needn't worry about the mosquitoes," I observed, waving a cloud of whitish smoke away from my face.

"Thank you, Mrs. Fraser," said the Governor. "I had not considered that particular positive aspect of the matter." He spoke with some bitterness, his fists resting impotently on the rail.

I took the hint, and said no more. For myself, the leaping flames and the column of smoke that rose wavering toward the stars were cause for celebration. Not for any benefit that the burning of Fort Johnston might be to the rebel cause—but because Jamie might be there, by one of the campfires that had sprung up on the shore below the fort.

And if he was . . . he would come tomorrow.

HE DID. I was awake well before dawn—in fact, I had not slept—and standing at the rail. There was little of the usual boat traffic this morning, in the wake of the fort's burning; the bitter smell of wood ash mingled with the marshy smell of the nearby mud flats, and the water was still and oily-looking. It was a gray day, heavily overcast, and a deep bank of haze hung over the water, hiding the shore.

I kept watching, though, and when a small boat came out of the haze, I knew at once that it was Jamie. He was alone.

I watched the long, smooth reach of his arms and the pull of the oars, and felt a sudden deep, calm happiness. I had no notion what might happen—and all the horror and anger connected with Malva's death still lurked at the back of my mind, a great dark shape under very thin ice. But he was *there.* Near enough now to see his face, as he looked back over his shoulder toward the ship.

I lifted a hand to wave; his eyes were already fixed on me. He didn't stop rowing, but turned round and came on. I stood clinging to the rail, waiting.

The rowboat passed out of sight for a moment, under the lee of the *Cruizer,* and I heard the watch hail him, the deep half-audible answer, and felt something that had been knotted inside me for a long time let go at the sound of his voice.

I stood rooted, though, not able to move. Then there were footsteps on deck, and a murmur of voices—someone going to fetch the Governor—and I turned blindly, into Jamie's arms.

"Knew you'd come," I whispered into the linen of his shirt. He reeked of fire: smoke and pinesap and scorched cloth, and the bitter tang of turpentine. Reeked of stale sweat and horses, the weariness of a man who has not slept, who has labored all night, the faint yeasty smell of long hunger.

He held me close, ribs and breath and warmth and muscle, then put me away from him a little and looked down into my face. He had been smiling since I saw him. It lit his eyes, and without a word, he pulled the cap off my head and threw it over the rail. He ran his hands through my hair, fluffing it out into abandon, then cupped my head in his hands and kissed me, fingers digging into my scalp. He had a three-day beard, which rasped my skin like sandpaper, and his mouth was home and safety.

Somewhere behind him, one of the Marines coughed, and said loudly, "You wished to see the Governor, I believe, sir?"

He let go, slowly, and turned.

"I do indeed," he said, and put out a hand to me. "Sassenach?"

I took it, and followed the Marine, heading for the companionway. I glanced back over the rail, to see my cap bobbing in the swell, puffed with air and tranquil as a jellyfish.

The momentary illusion of peace vanished directly, though, once we were below.

The Governor had been up most of the night, as well, and didn't look much better than Jamie, though he was not, of course, besmeared with soot. He was, however, unshaven, bloodshot, and in no mood to be trifled with.

"Mr. Fraser," he said with a short nod. "You are James Fraser, I collect? And you dwell in the mountain backcountry?"

"I am the Fraser, of Fraser's Ridge," Jamie said courteously. "And I have come for my wife."

"Oh, have you." The Governor gave him a sour look and sat down, gesturing indifferently at a stool. "I regret to inform you, sir, that your wife is a prisoner of the Crown. Though perhaps you were aware of this?"

Jamie ignored this bit of sarcasm and took the proffered seat.

"In fact, she is not," he said. "It is true, is it not, that you have declared martial law upon the colony of North Carolina?"

"It is," Martin said shortly. This was rather a sore point, since while he *had* declared martial law, he was in no position actually to enforce it, but was obliged to float impotently offshore, fuming, until and unless England chose to send him reinforcements.

"Then in fact, all customary legal usage is suspended," Jamie pointed out. "You alone have control over the custody and disposition of any prisoners—and my wife has in fact been in your custody for some little time. Ye therefore have also the power to release her."

"Hm," said the Governor. Plainly he hadn't thought of that, and wasn't sure of its ramifications. At the same time, the notion that he was in control of anything at all at the moment was likely soothing to his inflamed spirits.

"She has not been committed for trial, and in fact, there

has been no evidence whatever adduced against her," Jamie said firmly.

I found myself uttering a silent prayer of thanks that I had told MacDonald the gory details *after* his visit with the Governor—it might not be what a modern court called evidence, but being found with a knife in my hand and two warm, bloody corpses was very damned circumstantial.

"She is accused, but there is no merit to the charge. Surely, having had her acquaintance for even so short a time as you have, ye will have drawn your own conclusions as to her character?" Not waiting for an answer to this, he pressed on.

"When accusation was made, we did not resist the attempt to bring my wife—or myself, for I also have been accused in the matter—to trial. What better indication is there that we should hold such conviction of her innocence as to wish for a speedy trial to establish it?"

The Governor had narrowed his eyes, and appeared to be thinking intently.

"Your arguments are not entirely lacking in virtue, sir," he said at last, with formal courtesy. "However, I understand that the crime of which your wife stands accused was a most heinous one. For me to release her must necessarily cause public outcry—and I have had rather enough of public unrest," he added, with a bleak look at the scorched cuffs of Jamie's coat.

Jamie took a deep breath and had another go.

"I quite understand Your Excellency's reservations," he said. "Perhaps some . . . surety might be offered, which would overcome them?"

Martin sat bolt upright in his chair, receding jaw thrust out.

"What do you suggest, sir? Have you the impertinence, the—the—unspeakable bloody face to try to *bribe* me?" He slapped both hands down on the desk and glared from Jamie to me and back. "God damn it, I should hang the two of you, out of hand!"

"Very nice, Mr. Allnutt," I muttered to Jamie under my breath. "At least we're already married."

"Oh, ah," he replied, giving me a brief glance of incomprehension before returning his attention to the Governor, who was muttering "Swing them from the bloody yardarm . . . the infernal cheek of it, the creatures!"

"I had no such intent, sir." Jamie kept his voice level, his eyes direct. "What I offer is a bond, against my wife's appearance in court to answer the charge against her. When she does so appear, it would be returned to me."

Before the Governor could respond to this, he reached into his pocket and withdrew something small and dark, which he set on the desk. The black diamond.

The sight of it stopped Martin in mid-sentence. He blinked, once, his long-nosed face going almost comically blank. He rubbed a finger slowly across his upper lip, considering.

Having seen a great deal of the Governor's private correspondence and accounts by now, I was well aware that he had few private means, and was obliged to live far beyond his modest income in order to maintain the appearances necessary for a Royal Governor.

The Governor in turn was well aware that in the current state of unrest, there was little chance of my being brought to trial in any sort of timely manner. It could be months—and possibly years—before the court system was restored to anything like routine function. And for however long it took, he would have the diamond. He couldn't in honor simply sell the thing—but could most assuredly borrow a substantial sum against it, in the reasonable expectation that he might redeem it later.

I saw his eyes flicker toward the sooty marks on Jamie's coat, narrowing in speculation. There was also a good possibility of Jamie's being killed or arrested for treason—and I saw the impulse to do just that pop momentarily into his mind—which would leave the diamond perhaps in legal limbo, but certainly in Martin's possession. I had to force myself to keep on breathing.

But he wasn't stupid, Martin—nor was he venal. With a small sigh, he pushed the stone back toward Jamie.

"No, sir," he said, though his voice had now lost its earlier outrage. "I will not accept this as bond for your wife. But the notion of surety . . ." His gaze went to the stack of papers on his desk, and returned to Jamie.

"I will make you a proposition, sir," he said abruptly. "I have an action in train, an operation by which I hope to raise a considerable body of the Scottish Highlanders, who will march from the backcountry to the coast, there to meet with troops sent from England, and in the process, to subdue the countryside on behalf of the King."

He paused for breath, eyeing Jamie closely to assess the effect of his speech. I was standing close behind Jamie, and couldn't see his face, but didn't need to. Bree, joking, called it his "brag face"; no one looking at him would ever know whether he held four aces, a full house, or a pair of threes. I was betting on the pair of threes, myself—but Martin didn't know him nearly as well as I did.

"General Hugh MacDonald and a Colonel Donald McLeod came into the colony some time ago, and have been traversing the countryside, rallying support—which they have gained in gratifying numbers, I am pleased to say." His fingers drummed briefly on the letters, then stopped abruptly as he leaned forward.

"What I propose, then, sir, is this: you will return to the backcountry, and gather such men as you can. You will then report to General MacDonald and commit your troops to his campaign. When I receive word from MacDonald that you have arrived—with, let us say, two hundred men—then, sir, I will release your wife to you."

My pulse was beating fast, and so was Jamie's; I could see it throbbing in his neck. Definitely a pair of threes. Obviously, MacDonald hadn't had time to tell the Governor—or hadn't known—just how widespread and acrimonious the response had been to Malva Christie's death. There were still men on the Ridge who would follow Jamie, I was sure—but many more who would not, or who would, but only if he repudiated me.

I was trying to think logically about the situation, as a means of distracting myself from the crushing disappointment of realizing that the Governor was not going to let me go. Jamie must go without me, leave me here. For an overwhelming instant, I thought I could not bear it; I would run mad, scream and leap across the desk to claw Josiah Martin's eyes out.

He glanced up, caught a glimpse of my face, and started back, half-rising from his chair.

Jamie put back a hand and gripped my forearm, hard.

"Be still, *a nighean,*" he said softly.

I had been holding my breath without realizing it. Now I let it out in a gasp, and made myself breathe slowly.

Just as slowly, the Governor—a wary gaze still fixed on me—lowered himself back into his seat. Clearly, the accusation against me had just become a lot more likely, in his mind. *Fine,* I thought fiercely, to keep from crying. *See how easily you sleep, with me never more than a few feet away from you.*

Jamie drew a long, deep breath, and his shoulders squared beneath his tattered coat.

"You will give me leave, sir, to consider your proposal," he said formally, and letting go of my arm, rose to his feet.

"Do not despair, *mo chridhe,*" he said to me in Gaelic. "I will see you when the morning comes."

He lifted my hand to his lips and kissed it, then, with the barest of nods to the Governor, strode out, without looking back.

There was an instant's silence in the cabin, and I heard his feet going away, climbing the ladder of the companionway. I didn't pause to consider, but reached down into my stays and withdrew the small knife I had taken from the surgeon's kit.

I jabbed it down with all my strength, so that it stuck in the wood of the desk and stood there, quivering before the Governor's astonished eyes.

"You fucking *bastard,*" I said evenly, and left.

97

FOR THE SAKE OF ONE WHO IS

I WAS WAITING AT the rail again before dawn the next day. The smell of ashes was strong and acrid on the wind, but the smoke had gone. An early-morning haze still shrouded the shore, though, and I felt a small thrill of *déjà vu,* mingled with hope, as I saw the small boat come out of the mist, pulling slowly toward the ship.

As it grew closer, though, my hands tightened on the rail. It wasn't Jamie. For a few moments, I tried to convince myself that it was, that he had merely changed his coat—but with each stroke of the oars, it became more certain. I closed my eyes, stinging with tears, all the while telling myself that it was absurd to be so upset; it meant nothing.

Jamie would be here; he'd said so. The fact that someone else was coming early to the ship had nothing to do with him or me.

It did, though. Opening my eyes and wiping them on my wrist, I looked again at the rowboat, and felt a start of disbelief. It couldn't be. It was, though. He looked up at the watch's hail, and saw me at the rail. Our eyes met for an instant, then he bowed his head, reaching to the oars. Tom Christie.

The Governor was not amused at being roused from his bed at dawn for the third day running; I could hear him below, ordering one of the Marines to tell the fellow, whoever he was, to wait to a more reasonable hour—this followed by a peremptory slam of the cabin door.

I was not amused, either, and in no mood to wait. The Marine at the head of the companionway refused to allow me below, though. Heart pounding, then, I turned and made my way to the stern, where they had put Christie to wait the Governor's pleasure.

The Marine there hesitated, but after all, there were no orders to prevent me speaking with visitors; he let me pass.

"Mr. Christie." He was standing at the rail, staring back at the coast, but turned at my words.

"Mrs. Fraser." He was very pale; his grizzled beard stood out nearly black. He had trimmed it, though, and his hair, as well. While he still looked like a lightning-blasted tree, there was life in his eyes once more when he looked at me.

"My husband—" I began, but he cut me off.

"He is well. He awaits you on the shore; you will see him presently."

"Oh?" The boil of fear and fury inside me reduced itself slightly, as though someone had turned down the flame, but a sense of impatience was still steaming. "Well, what in bloody hell is going on, will you tell me that?"

He looked at me for a long moment in silence, then licked his lips briefly, and turned to look over the rail at the smooth gray swell. He glanced back at me and drew a deep breath, obviously bracing himself for something.

"I have come to confess to the murder of my daughter."

I simply stared at him, unable to make sense of his words. Then I assembled them into a sentence, read it from the tablet of my mind, and finally grasped it.

"No, you haven't," I said.

The faintest shadow of a smile seemed to stir in his beard, though it vanished almost before I had seen it.

"You remain contrary, I see," he said dryly.

"Never mind what I remain," I said, rather rudely. "Are you insane? Or is this Jamie's latest plan? Because if so—"

He stopped me with a hand on my wrist; I started at the touch, not expecting it.

"It is the truth," he said very softly. "And I will swear to it by the Holy Scriptures."

I stood looking at him, not moving. He looked back, directly, and I realized suddenly how seldom he had ever met my eyes; all through our acquaintance, he had glanced away, avoided my gaze, as though he sought to escape any real acknowledgment of me, even when obliged to speak to me.

Now that was gone, and the look in his eyes was nothing I had ever seen before. The lines of pain and suffering cut deep around them, and the lids were heavy with sorrow—but the eyes themselves were deep and calm as the sea beneath us. That sense he had carried through our nightmare journey south, that atmosphere of mute horror, numb pain, had left him, replaced by resolve and something else—something that burned, far down in his depths.

"Why?" I said at last, and he let go his grip on my wrist, stepping back a pace.

"D'ye remember once"—from the reminiscent tone of his voice, it might have been decades before—"ye asked me, did I think ye a witch?"

"I remember," I replied guardedly. "You said—" Now I remembered that conversation, all right, and something small and icy fluttered at the base of my spine. "You said that you believed in witches, all right—but you didn't think I was one."

He nodded, dark gray eyes fixed on me. I wondered whether he was about to revise that opinion, but apparently not.

"I believe in witches," he said with complete matter-of-fact seriousness. "For I've kent them. The girl was one, as was her mother before her." The icy flutter grew stronger.

"The girl," I said. "You mean your daughter? Malva?"

He shook his head a little, and his eyes took on a darker hue. "No daughter of mine," he said.

"Not—not yours? But—her eyes. She had your eyes." I heard myself say it, and could have bitten my tongue. He only smiled, though, grimly.

"And my brother's." He turned to the rail, put his hands on it, and looked across the stretch of sea, toward land. "Edgar was his name. When the Rising came, and I declared for the Stuarts, he would have none of it, saying 'twas folly. He begged me not to go." He shook his head slowly, seeing something in memory, that I knew was not the wooded shore.

"I thought—well, it doesna matter what I thought, but I went. And asked him, would he mind my wife, and the wee lad." He drew a deep breath, let it slowly out. "And he did."

"I see," I said very quietly. He turned his head sharply at the tone of my voice, gray eyes piercing.

"It was not his fault! Mona was a witch—an enchantress." His lips compressed at the expression on my face. "Ye don't believe me, I see. It is the truth; more than once, I caught her at it—working her charms, observing times—I came once to the roof o' the house at midnight, searching for her. I saw her there, stark naked and staring at the stars, standing in the center of a pentacle she'd drawn wi' the blood of a strangled dove, and her hair flying loose, mad in the wind."

"Her hair," I said, looking for some thread to grasp in this, and suddenly realizing. "She had hair like mine, didn't she?"

He nodded, looking away, and I saw his throat move as he swallowed.

"She was . . . what she was," he said softly. "I tried to save her—by prayer, by love. I could not."

"What happened to her?" I asked, keeping my voice as low as his. With the wind as it was, there was little chance of our being overheard here, but this was not the sort of thing I thought anyone should hear.

He sighed, and swallowed again.

"She was hangit," he said, sounding almost matter-of-fact about it. "For the murder of my brother."

This, it seemed, had happened while Tom was imprisoned at Ardsmuir; she had sent him word, before her execution, telling him of Malva's birth, and that she was confiding care of the children to Edgar's wife.

"I suppose she thought that funny," he said, sounding abstracted. "She'd the oddest sense of humor, Mona had."

I felt cold, beyond the chill of the early-morning breeze, and hugged my elbows.

"But you got them back—Allan and Malva."

He nodded; he had been transported, but had the good fortune to have his indenture bought by a kind and wealthy man, who had given him the money for the children's passage to the Colonies. But then both his employer and the wife he had taken here had died in an epidemic of the yellow fever, and casting about for some new opportunity, he had heard of Jamie Fraser's settling in North Carolina and that he would help those men he had known in Ardsmuir to land of their own.

"I would to God I had cut my own throat before I came," he said, turning back abruptly to me. "Believe me in that."

He seemed entirely sincere. I didn't know what to say in response, but he seemed to require none, and went on.

"The girl . . . she was nay more than five years old when I first saw her, but already she had it—the same slyness, the charm—the same darkness of soul."

He had tried to the best of his ability to save Malva, as well—to beat the wickedness out of her, to constrain the streak of wildness, above all, to keep her from working her wiles upon men.

"Her mither had that, too." His lips tightened at the thought. "Any man. It was the curse of Lilith that they had, the both of them."

I felt a hollowness in the pit of my stomach, as he came back now to the matter of Malva.

"But she was with child . . ." I said.

His face paled further, but his voice was firm.

"Aye, she was. I do not think it wrong to prevent yet another witch from entering the world."

Seeing my face, he went on before I could interrupt.

"Ye ken she tried to kill ye? You and me, both."

"What do you mean? Tried to kill me, how?"

"When ye told her about the invisible things, the—the germs. She took great interest in that. She told me, when I caught her wi' the bones."

"What bones?" I asked, a sliver of ice running down my back.

"The bones she took from Ephraim's grave, to work her charms upon your husband. She didna use them all, and I found them in her workbasket later. I beat her, badly, and she told me then."

Accustomed to wander alone in the woods in search of food plants and herbs, she had been doing so during the height of the dysentery epidemic. And in her wanderings, had come upon the isolated cabin of the sin-eater, that strange, damaged man. She had found him near death, burning with fever and sunk in coma, and while she stood there undecided whether to run for help, or only run, he had in fact died.

Whereupon, seized by inspiration—and bearing my careful teachings in mind—she had taken mucus and blood from the body and put it into a little bottle with a bit of broth from the kettle on the hearth, nurturing it inside her stays with the warmth of her own body.

And had slipped a few drops of this deadly infusion into my food, and that of her father, in the hope that if we fell sick, our deaths would be seen as no more than a part of the sickness that plagued the Ridge.

My lips felt stiff and bloodless.

"You're sure of this?" I whispered. He nodded, making no effort to convince me, and that alone gave me conviction that he spoke the truth.

"She wanted—Jamie?" I asked.

He closed his eyes for a moment; the sun was coming up, and while the brilliance of it was behind us, the gleam off the water was bright as silver plate.

"She . . . wanted," he said at last. "She lusted. Lusted for wealth, for position, for what she saw as freedom, not seeing it as license—never seeing!" He spoke with sudden violence, and I thought it was not Malva alone who had never seen things as he did.

But she had wanted Jamie, whether for himself or only for his property. And when her love charm failed, and the epidemic of sickness came, had taken a more direct way toward what she wanted. I could not yet find a way to grasp that—and yet I knew it was true.

And then, finding herself inconveniently with child, she had come up with a new scheme.

"Do you know who the father really was?" I asked, my throat tightening again—I thought it always would—at the memory of the sunlit garden and the two neat, small bodies, ruined and wasted. Such a waste.

He shook his head, but would not look at me, and I knew that he had some idea, at least. He would not tell me, though, and I supposed it didn't matter just now. And the Governor would be up soon, ready to receive him.

He, too, heard the stirrings down below, and took a deep breath.

"I could not let her destroy so many lives; could not let her go on. For she was a witch, make no mistake; that she failed to kill either you or me was no more than luck. She would have killed someone, before she finished. Perhaps you, if your husband clung to you. Perhaps him, in the hope of inheriting his property for the child." He took a ragged, painful breath.

"She was not born of my loins, and yet—she was my daughter, my blood. I could not . . . could not allow . . . I was responsible." He stopped, unable to finish. In this, I thought, he told the truth. And yet . . .

"Thomas," I said firmly, "this is twaddle, and you know it."

He looked at me, surprised, and I saw that tears stood in his eyes. He blinked them back and answered fiercely.

"Say you so? You know nothing, nothing!"

He saw me flinch, and looked down. Then, awkwardly, he reached out and took my hand. I felt the scars of the surgery I had done, the flexible strength of his gripping fingers.

"I have waited all my life, in a search . . ." He waved his free hand vaguely, then closed his fingers, as though grasping the thought, and continued more surely, "No. In hope. In hope of a thing I could not name, but that I knew must exist."

His eyes searched my face, intent, as though he memorized my features. I raised a hand, uncomfortable under this scrutiny, intending, I suppose, to tidy my mad hair—but he caught my hand and held it, surprising me.

"Leave it," he said.

Standing with both hands in his, I had no choice.

"Thomas," I said, uncertain. "Mr. Christie . . ."

"I became convinced that it was God I sought. Perhaps it was. But God is not flesh and blood, and the love of God alone could not sustain me.

"I have written down my confession." He let go, and poked a hand into his pocket, fumbling a little, and pulled out a folded paper, which he clutched in his short, solid fingers.

"I have sworn here that it was I who killed my daughter, for the shame she had brought upon me by her wantonness." He spoke firmly enough, but I could see the working of his throat above the wilted stock.

"You didn't," I said positively. "I know you didn't."

He blinked, gazing at me.

"No," he said, quite matter-of-fact. "But perhaps I should have.

"I have written a copy of this confession," he said, tucking the document back into his coat, "and have left it with the newspaper in New Bern. They will publish it. The Governor will accept it—how can he not?—and you will go free."

Those last four words struck me dumb. He was still gripping my right hand; his thumb stroked gently over my knuckles. I wanted to pull away, but forced myself to keep still, compelled by the look in his eyes, clear gray and naked now, without disguise.

"I have yearned always," he said softly, "for love given and returned; have spent my life in the attempt to give my love to those who were not worthy of it. Allow me this: to give my life for the sake of one who is."

I felt as though someone had knocked the wind from me. I hadn't any breath, but struggled to form words.

"Mr. Chr—Tom," I said. "You mustn't. Your life has—has value. You can't throw it away like this!"

He nodded, patient.

"I know that. If it did not, this would not matter."

Feet were coming up the companionway, and I heard the Governor's voice below, in cheerful conversation with the Captain of Marines.

"Thomas! Don't do this!"

He only looked at me, and smiled—had I ever seen him smile?—but did not speak. He raised my hand and bent over it; I felt the prickle of his beard and the warmth of his breath, the softness of his lips.

"I am your servant, madam," he said very softly. He squeezed my hand and released it, then turned and glanced toward the shore. A small boat was coming, dark against the glitter of the silver sea. "Your husband is coming for you. *Adieu,* Mrs. Fraser."

He turned and walked away, back steady in spite of the swell that rose and fell beneath us.

PART ELEVEN

In the Day of Vengeance

98

TO KEEP A GHOST AT BAY

JAMIE GROANED, STRETCHED, and sat down heavily on the bed.

"I feel as though someone's stepped on my cock."

"Oh?" I opened one eye to look at him. "Who?"

He gave me a bloodshot look.

"I dinna ken, but it feels as though it was someone heavy."

"Lie down," I said, yawning. "We haven't got to leave right away; you can rest a bit more."

He shook his head.

"Nay, I want to be home. We've been gone too long as it is." Nonetheless, he didn't get up and finish dressing, but continued to sit on the swaybacked inn bed in his shirt, big hands hanging idle between his thighs.

He looked tired to death, in spite of just having risen, and no wonder. I didn't think he could have slept at all for several days, what with his search for me, the burning of Fort Johnston, and the events attending my release from the *Cruizer.* Remembering, I felt a pall settle over my own spirits, in spite of the joy in which I had wakened, realizing that I was free, on land, and with Jamie.

"Lie down," I repeated. I rolled toward him, and put a hand on his back. "It's barely dawn. At least wait for breakfast; you can't travel without rest *or* food."

He glanced at the window, still shuttered; the cracks had begun to pale with the growing light, but I was right; there was no sound below of fires being stoked or pots banged in preparation. Capitulating suddenly, he collapsed slowly sideways, unable to repress a sigh as his head settled back on the pillow.

He didn't protest when I flung the ratty quilt over him, nor yet when I curved my body to fit round him, wrapping an arm about his waist and laying my cheek against his back. He still smelled of smoke, though both of us had washed hastily the night before, before falling into bed and a dearly bought oblivion.

I could feel how tired he was. My own joints still ached with fatigue—and from the lumps in the flattened, wool-stuffed mattress. Ian had been waiting with horses when we came ashore, and we had ridden as far as we could before darkness fell, finally fetching up at a ramshackle inn in the middle of nowhere, a crude roadside accommodation for wagoneers on their way to the coast.

"Malcolm," he'd said, with the slightest of hesitations, when the innkeeper had asked his name. "Alexander Malcolm."

"And Murray," Ian had said, yawning and scratching his ribs. "John Murray."

The innkeeper had nodded, not particularly caring. There was no reason why he should associate three nondescript, bedraggled travelers with a notorious case of murder—and yet I had felt panic well up under my diaphragm when he glanced at me.

I had sensed Jamie's hesitation in giving the name, his distaste for reassuming one of the many aliases he had once lived under. More than most men, he valued his name—I only hoped that given time, it would once more *have* value.

Roger might help. He would be a full-fledged minister by now, I thought, smiling at the thought. He had a true gift for soothing the divisions among the inhabitants of the Ridge, easing acrimony—and having the additional authority of being an ordained minister, his influence would be increased.

It would be good to have him back. And to see Bree and Jemmy again—I had a moment's longing for them, though we would see them soon; we meant to go through Cross Creek and collect them on the way. But of course, neither Bree nor Roger had any notion what had happened in the last three weeks—nor what life might now be like, in the wake of it.

The birds were in full voice in the trees outside; after the constant screeching of gulls and terns that formed the background of life on the *Cruizer,* the sound of them was tender, a homely conversation that made me long suddenly for the Ridge. I understood Jamie's strong urge to be home—even knowing that what we would find there was not the same life we had left. The Christies would be gone, for one thing.

I hadn't had the chance to ask Jamie about the circumstances of my rescue; I had finally been put ashore just before sunset, and we had ridden off at once, Jamie wanting to put as much distance as possible between me and Governor Martin—and, perhaps, Tom Christie.

"Jamie," I said softly, my breath warm in the folds of his shirt. "Did you make him do it? Tom?"

"No." His voice was soft, too. "He came to Fergus's printshop, the day after ye left the palace. He'd heard that the gaol had burned—"

I sat up in bed, shocked.

"What? Sheriff Tolliver's house? No one told me that!"

He rolled onto his back, looking up at me.

"I dinna suppose anyone ye've spoken to in the last week or two would know," he said mildly. "No one was killed, Sassenach—I asked."

"You're sure of it?" I asked with uneasy thoughts of Sadie Ferguson. "How did it happen? A mob?"

"No," he said, yawning. "From what I hear, Mrs. Tolliver got stinking drunk, stoked her laundry fire too high, then lay down in the shade and fell asleep. The wood collapsed, the embers set fire to the grass, it spread to the house, and . . ." He flipped a hand in dismissal. "The neighbor smelt smoke, though, and rushed over in time to drag Mrs. Tolliver and the bairn safe away. He said there was no one else in the place."

"Oh. Well . . ." I let him persuade me to lie down again, my head resting in the hollow of his shoulder. I couldn't feel strange with him, not after spending the night pressed close against him in the narrow bed, each of us aware of the other's every small movement. Still, I was very conscious of him.

And he of me; his arm was round me, his fingers unconsciously exploring the length of my back, lightly reading the shapes of me like braille as he talked.

"So, then, Tom. He kent about *L'Oignon,* of course, and so went there, when he found ye'd disappeared from the gaol. By then, of course, ye'd gone from the palace, as well—it had taken him some time to part company wi' Richard Brown, without rousing their suspicions.

"But he found us there, and he told me what he meant to do." His fingers stroked the back of my neck, and I felt the tightness there begin to relax. "I told him to bide; I should have a go at getting ye back on my own—but if I could not . . ."

"So you know he didn't do it." I spoke with certainty. "Did he tell you he had?"

"He only said that he had kept silent while there was any chance of ye being tried and acquitted—but that had ye ever seemed in urgent danger, then he'd meant to speak up at once; that's why he insisted upon coming with us. I, ah, didna wish to ask him questions," he said delicately.

"But he didn't do it." I prodded, insistent. "Jamie, you *know* he didn't!"

I felt the rise of his chest under my cheek as he breathed.

"I know," he said softly.

We were silent for a bit. There was a sudden, muffled rapping outside, and I jerked—but it was only a woodpecker, hunting insects in the wormy timbers of the inn.

"Will they hang him, do you think?" I asked at last, staring up at the splintered beams above.

"I expect they will, aye." His fingers had resumed their half-unconscious motion, smoothing strands of my hair behind my ear. I lay still, listening to the slow thump of his heart, not wanting to ask what came next. But I had to.

"Jamie—tell me that he didn't do it—that he didn't make that confession—for me. Please." I didn't think I could bear that, not on top of everything else.

His fingers stilled, just touching my ear.

"He loves you. Ye ken that, aye?" He spoke very quietly; I heard the reverberation of the words in his chest, as much as the words themselves.

"He said he did." I felt a tightness in the throat, recalling that very direct gray look. Tom Christie was a man who said what he meant, and meant what he said—a man like Jamie, in that regard at least.

Jamie was quiet for what seemed a long time. Then he sighed, and turned his head so his cheek rested against my hair; I heard the faint rasp of his whiskers.

"Sassenach—I would have done the same, and counted my life well lost, if it saved ye. If he feels the same, then ye've done nay wrong to him, to take your life from his hand."

"Oh, dear," I said. "Oh, dear." I didn't want to think of any of it—not Tom's clear gray look and the calling of gulls, not the lines of affliction that carved his face into pieces, not the thought of what he had suffered, in loss, in guilt, in suspicion—in fear. Nor did I want to think of Malva, going unwitting to that death among the lettuces, her son heavy and peaceful in her womb. Nor the dark rusty blood drying in gouts and splashes among the leaves of the grapevines.

Above all, I didn't want to think that I had had any part in this tragedy—but that was inescapable.

I swallowed, hard.

"Jamie—can it ever be made right?"

He held my hand now, in his other hand, stroking his thumb gently back and forth under my fingers.

"The lass is dead, *mo chridhe.*"

I closed my hand on his thumb, stilling it.

"Yes, and someone killed her—and it wasn't Tom. Oh, God, Jamie—who? Who was it?"

"I dinna ken," he said, and his eyes grew deep with sadness. "She was a lass who craved love, I think—and took it. But she didna ken how to give it back again."

I took a deep breath and asked the question that had lain unspoken between us since the murder.

"You don't think it was Ian?"

He nearly smiled at that.

"If it had been, *a nighean,* we'd know. Ian could kill; he couldna let you or me suffer for it."

I sighed, shifting my shoulders to ease the knot between them. He was right, and I felt comforted, on Ian's account—and still more guilty, on Tom Christie's.

"The man who fathered her child—if that wasn't Ian, and I so hope it wasn't—or someone who wanted her and killed her from jealousy when he found she was pregnant—"

"Or someone already wed. Or a woman, Sassenach."

That stopped me cold. "A woman?"

"She took love," he repeated, and shook his head. "What makes ye think it was only the young men she took it from?"

I closed my eyes, envisioning the possibilities. If she had had an affair with a married man—and they had looked at her, too, only more discreetly—yes, he might have killed her to keep it undiscovered. Or a scorned wife . . . I had a brief, shocking glimpse of Murdina Bug, face contorted with effort as she pressed the pillow over Lionel Brown's face. Arch? God, no. Once again, with a sense of utter hopelessness, I turned away from the question, seeing in mind the myriad faces of Fraser's Ridge—one of them hiding a murderer's soul.

"No, I know it can't be fixed for them—not Malva, or Tom. Or—or even Allan." For the first time, I spared a thought for Tom's son, so suddenly bereft of his family and in such dreadful circumstances. "But the rest . . ." The Ridge, I meant. Home. The life we had had. Us.

It had grown warm under the quilt, lying together—too warm, and I felt the heat of a hot flush wash over me. I sat up abruptly, throwing off the quilt, and leaned forward, lifting the hair off my neck in hopes of an instant's coolness.

"Stand up, Sassenach."

Jamie rolled out of bed, stood up, and took me by the hand, pulling me to my feet. Sweat had already broken out on my body like dew, and my cheeks were flushed. He bent and, taking the hem of my shift in both hands, stripped it off over my head.

He smiled faintly, looking at me, then bent and blew softly over my breasts. The coolness was a tiny but blessed relief, and my nipples rose in silent gratitude.

He opened the shutters for more air, then stepped back and pulled off his own shirt. Day had broken fully now, and the flood of pure morning light glimmered on the lines of his pale torso, on the silver web of his scars, the red-gold dusting of hair on his arms and legs, the rust and silver hairs of his sprouting beard. Likewise on the darkly suffused flesh of his genitals in their morning state, standing stiff against his belly and gone the deep, soft color one would find in the heart of a shadowed rose.

"As to putting things right," he said, "I canna say—though I mean to try." His eyes moved over me—stark naked, slightly salt-encrusted, and noticeably grimy about the feet and ankles. He smiled. "Shall we make a start, Sassenach?"

"You're so tired you can barely stand up," I protested. "Um—with certain exceptions," I added, glancing down. It was true; there were dark hollows under his eyes, and while the lines of his body were still long and graceful, they were also eloquent of deep fatigue. I felt as though I'd been run over by a steamroller myself, and *I* hadn't been up all night burning down forts.

"Well, seeing as we've a bed to hand, I didna plan to stand up for it," he replied. "Mind, I may never get back on my feet again, but I think I might be able to stay awake for the next ten minutes or so, at least. Ye can pinch me if I fall asleep," he suggested, smiling.

I rolled my eyes at him, but didn't argue. I lay down upon the grubby but now-cool sheets, and with a small tremor in the pit of my stomach, opened my legs for him.

We made love like people underwater, heavy-limbed and slow. Mute, able to speak only through crude pantomime. We had barely touched one another in this way since Malva's death—and the thought of her was still with us.

And not only her. For a time, I tried to focus only on Jamie, fixing my attention on the small intimacies of his body, so well known—the tiny white cicatrice of the triangular scar at his throat, the whorls of auburn hair and the sunburned skin beneath—but I was so tired that my mind refused to cooperate, and persisted in showing me instead random bits of memory or, even more disturbing, imagination.

"It's no good," I said. My eyes were shut tight, and I was clinging to the bedclothes with both hands, sheets knotted in my fingers. "I can't."

He made a small sound of surprise, but at once rolled away, leaving me damp and trembling.

"What is it, *a nighean*?" he said softly. He didn't touch me, but lay close.

"I don't know," I said, close to panic. "I keep seeing—I'm sorry, I'm sorry, Jamie. I see other people; it's like I'm making love to other m-men."

"Oh, aye?" He sounded cautious, but not upset. There was a whish of fabric, and he drew the sheet up over me. That helped a little, but not much. My heart was pounding hard in my chest, I felt dizzy and couldn't seem to take a full breath; my throat kept closing.

Bolus hystericus, I thought, quite calmly. *Do stop, Beauchamp.* Easier said than done, but I did stop worrying that I was having a heart attack.

"Ah . . ." Jamie's voice was cautious. "Who? Hodgepile and—"

"No!" My stomach clenched in revulsion at the thought. I swallowed. "No, I—I hadn't even thought of that."

He lay quietly beside me, breathing. I felt as though I were literally coming apart.

"Who is it that ye see, Claire?" he whispered. "Can ye tell me?"

"Frank," I said, fast, before I could change my mind. "And Tom. And—and Malva." My chest heaved, and I felt that I would never have air enough to breathe again.

"I could—all of a sudden, I could feel them all," I blurted. "Touching me. Wanting to come in." I rolled over, burying my face in the pillow, as though I could seal out everything.

Jamie was silent for a long time. Had I hurt him? I was sorry that I'd told him—but I had no defenses anymore. I could not lie, even for the best of reasons; there was simply no place to go, nowhere to hide. I felt beset by whispering ghosts, their loss, their need, their desperate love pulling me apart. Apart from Jamie, apart from myself.

My entire body was clenched and rigid, trying to keep from dissolution, and my face was pushed so deep into the pillow, trying to escape, that I felt I might suffocate, and was obliged to turn my head, gasping for breath.

"Claire." Jamie's voice was soft, but I felt his breath on my face and my eyes popped open. His eyes were soft, too, shadowed with sorrow. Very slowly, he lifted a hand and touched my lips.

"Tom," I blurted. "I feel as though he's already dead, because of me, and it's so terrible. I can't bear it, Jamie, I really can't!"

"I know." He moved his hand, hesitated. "Can ye bear it if I touch ye?"

"I don't know." I swallowed the lump in my throat. "Try it and see."

That made him smile, though I'd spoken with complete seriousness. He put his hand gently on my shoulder and turned me, then gathered me against him, moving slowly, so that I might pull back. I didn't.

I sank into him, and clung to him as though he was a floating spar, the only thing keeping me from drowning. He was.

He held me close and stroked my hair for a long time.

"Can ye weep for them, *mo nighean donn*?" he whispered into my hair at last. "Let them come in."

The mere idea made me go rigid with panic again. "I can't."

"Weep for them," he whispered, and his voice opened me deeper than his cock. "Ye canna hold a ghost at bay."

"I can't. I'm afraid," I said, but I was already shaking with grief, tears wet on my face. "I can't!"

And yet I did. Gave up the struggle and opened myself, to memory and sorrow. Sobbed as though my heart would break—and let it break, for them, and all I could not save.

"Let them come, and grieve them, Claire," he whispered. "And when they've gone, I'll take ye home."

99

OLD MASTER

River Run

IT HAD RAINED HARD the night before, and while the sun had come out bright and hot, the ground was soggy and steam seemed to rise from it, adding to the thickness of the air. Brianna had put her hair up, to keep it off her neck, but wisps escaped constantly, clinging damply to forehead and cheeks, always in her eyes. She wiped a strand away crossly with the back of her hand; her fingers were smeared with the pigment she was grinding—and the humidity wasn't doing *that* any good, making the powder clump and cling to the sides of the mortar.

She needed it, though; she had a new commission, due to start this afternoon.

Jem was hanging round, too, bored and poking his fingers into everything. He was singing to himself, half under his breath; she paid no attention, until she happened to catch a few words.

"*What* did you say?" she asked, rounding on him incredulously. He couldn't have been singing "Folsom Prison Blues"—could he?

He blinked at her, lowered his chin to his chest, and said—in the deepest voice he could produce—"Hello. I'm Johnny Cash."

She narrowly stopped herself laughing out loud, feeling her cheeks go pink with the effort of containment.

"Where did you get that?" she asked, though she knew perfectly well. There was only one place he *could* have gotten it, and her heart rose up at the thought.

"Daddy," he said logically.

"Has Daddy been singing?" she asked, trying to sound casual. He had to have been. And, just as obviously, had to have been trying Claire's advice, to shift the register of his voice so as to loosen his frozen vocal cords.

"Uh-huh. Daddy sings a lot. He teached me the song about Sunday morning, and the one about Tom Dooley, and . . . and lots," he ended, rather at a loss.

"Did he? Well, that's—put that down!" she said, as he idly picked up an open pouch of rose madder.

"Oops." He looked guiltily at the blob of paint that had erupted from the leather pouch and landed on his shirt, then at her, and made a tentative move toward the door.

"Oops, he says," she said darkly. "Don't you move!" Snaking out a hand, she grabbed him by the collar and applied a turpentine-soaked rag vigorously to the front of his shirt, succeeding only in producing a large pink blotch rather than a vivid red line.

Jem was silent during this ordeal, head bobbing as she pulled him to and fro, swabbing.

"What are you doing in here, anyway?" she demanded

crossly. "Didn't I tell you to go find something to do?" There was no shortage of things to do at River Run, after all.

He hung his head and muttered something, in which she made out the word "scared."

"Scared? Of what?" A little more gently, she pulled the shirt off over his head.

"The ghost."

"What ghost?" she asked warily, not sure yet how to handle this. She was aware that all of the slaves at River Run believed implicitly in ghosts, simply as a fact of life. So did virtually all of the Scottish settlers in Cross Creek, Campbelton, and the Ridge. And the Germans from Salem and Bethania. So, for that matter, did her own father.

She could not simply inform Jem that there was no such thing as a ghost—particularly as she was not entirely convinced of that herself.

"*Maighistear àrsaidh*'s ghost," he said, looking up at her for the first time, his dark blue eyes troubled. "Josh says he's been walkin'."

Something skittered down her back like a centipede. *Maighistear àrsaidh* was Old Master—Hector Cameron. Involuntarily, she glanced toward the window. They were in the small room above the stable block where she did the messier bits of paint preparation, and Hector Cameron's white marble mausoleum was clearly visible from here, gleaming like a tooth at the side of the lawn below.

"What makes Josh say that, I wonder?" she said, stalling for time. Her first impulse was to observe that ghosts didn't walk in broad daylight—but the obvious corollary to that was that they *did* walk by night, and the last thing she wanted to do was give Jem nightmares.

"He says Angelina saw him, night before last. A *big* ol' ghost," he said, stretching up, hands clawed, and widening his eyes in obvious imitation of Josh's account.

"Yeah? What was he doing?" She kept her tone light, only mildly interested, and it seemed to be working; Jem was more interested than scared, for the moment.

"Walkin'," Jem said with a small shrug. What else did ghosts do, after all?

"Was he smoking a pipe?" She'd caught sight of a tall

gentleman strolling under the trees on the lawn below, and had an idea.

Jem looked somewhat taken aback at the notion of a pipe-smoking ghost.

"I dunno," he said dubiously. "Do ghosts smoke pipes?"

"I sort of doubt it," she said. "But Mr. Buchanan does. See him down there on the lawn?" She moved aside, gesturing toward the window with her chin, and Jem rose up on his toes to look out over the sill. Mr. Buchanan, an acquaintance of Duncan's who was staying at the house, was in fact smoking a pipe at this very moment; the faint aroma of his tobacco reached them through the open window.

"I think probably Angelina saw Mr. Buchanan walking around in the dark," she said. "Maybe he was in his nightshirt, going out to the necessary, and she just saw the white and *thought* he was a ghost."

Jem giggled at the thought. He seemed willing to be reassured, but hunched his skinny shoulders, peering closely at Mr. Buchanan.

"Josh says Angelina says the ghost was comin' out of old Mr. Hector's tomb," he said.

"I expect Mr. Buchanan just walked round it, and she saw him coming along the side, and *thought* he was coming out of it," she said, carefully avoiding any question as to why a middle-aged Scottish gentleman should be walking round tombs in his nightshirt; obviously, that wasn't a notion that struck Jemmy as odd.

It did occur to her to ask just what Angelina was doing outside in the middle of the night seeing ghosts, but on second thought, better not. The most likely reason for a maid's stealing out at night wasn't something a boy of Jemmy's age needed to hear about, either.

Her lips tightened a little at the thought of Malva Christie, who had perhaps gone to a rendezvous of her own in Claire's garden. Who? she wondered for the thousandth time, even as she automatically crossed herself, with a brief prayer for the repose of Malva's soul. Who had it been? If ever there were a ghost that should walk . . .

A small shiver passed over her, but that in turn gave her a new idea.

"I think it was Mr. Buchanan Angelina saw," she said firmly. "But if you ever *should* be afraid of ghosts—or anything else—you just make the sign of the cross, and say a quick prayer to your guardian angel."

The words gave her a slight sense of dizziness—perhaps it was *déjà vu*. She thought that someone—her mother? her father?—had said exactly that to her, sometime in the distant past of her childhood. What she had been afraid of? She no longer remembered that, but did remember the sense of security that the prayer had given her.

Jem frowned uncertainly at that; he knew the sign of the cross, but wasn't so sure about the angel prayer. She rehearsed it with him, feeling slightly guilty as she did so.

It was only a matter of time before he did something overtly Catholic—like make the sign of the cross—in front of someone who mattered to Roger. For the most part, people either assumed that the minister's wife was Protestant, as well—or knew the truth, but were in no position to make a fuss about it. She was aware of a certain amount of muttering amongst Roger's flock, particularly in the wake of Malva's death and the talk about her parents—she felt her lips press tight again, and consciously relaxed them—but Roger steadfastly refused to hear any such remarks.

She felt a deep pang of longing for Roger, even with the worrying thought of potential religious complications fresh in her mind. He'd written; Elder McCorkle had been delayed, but should be in Edenton within the week. A week more, maybe, before the Presbytery Session convened—and then he'd be coming to River Run for her and Jem.

He was so happy at the thought of his ordination; surely once he *was* ordained, they couldn't defrock him—if that's what happened to miscreant ministers—for having a Catholic wife, could they?

Would she convert, if she had to, for Roger to be what he so clearly wanted—and needed—to be? The thought made her feel hollow, and she put her arms round Jemmy for reassurance. His skin was damp and still baby-soft, but she could feel the hardness of his bones pressing through, giving promise of a size that would likely one day match his father and grandfather. His father—there was a small, glowing thought that calmed all her anxieties, and even soothed the ache of missing Roger.

Jemmy's hair had long since grown again, but she kissed the spot behind his left ear where the hidden mark was, making him hunch his shoulders and giggle at the tickle of her breath on his neck.

She sent him off then, to take the paint-stained shirt to Matilda the laundress to see what might be done, and went back to her grinding.

The mineral smell of the malachite in her mortar seemed vaguely wrong; she lifted it and sniffed, even as she did so aware that that was ridiculous: ground stone couldn't go bad. Maybe the mixture of turpentine and the fumes from Mr. Buchanan's pipe was affecting her sense of smell. She shook her head, and scraped the soft green powder carefully out into a vial, to be mixed with walnut oil or used in an egg tempera later.

She cast an appraising eye over the selection of boxes and pouches—some supplied by Aunt Jocasta, others courtesy of John Grey, sent specially from London—and the vials and drying trays of the pigments she'd ground herself, to see what else might be needed.

This afternoon, she'd only be making preliminary sketches—the commission was for a portrait of Mr. Forbes's ancient mother—but she might have only a week or two to finish the job before Roger's return; she couldn't waste—

A wave of dizziness made her sit down suddenly, and black spots flickered through her vision. She put her head between her knees, breathing deep. That didn't help; the air was raw with turps, and thick with the meaty, decaying animal smells of the stables below.

She lifted her head, and grabbed for the edge of the table. Her insides seemed to have turned abruptly to a liquid substance that shifted with her movement like water in a bowl, sloshing from belly to throat and back, leaving the bitter yellow smell of bile at the back of her nose.

"Oh, God."

The liquid in her belly rushed up her throat, and she had barely time to seize the washbasin from the table and dump the water on the floor before her stomach turned inside out in the frantic effort to empty itself.

She set the basin down, very carefully, and sat panting, staring at the wet blotch on the floor, as the world beneath her shifted on its axis and settled at a new, uneasy angle.

"Congratulations, Roger," she said out loud, her voice sounding faint and uncertain in the close, damp air. "I *think* you're going to be a daddy. Again."

SHE SAT STILL for some time, cautiously exploring the sensations of her body, looking for certainty. She hadn't been sick with Jemmy—but she remembered the oddly altered quality of her senses; that odd state called synesthesia, where sight, smell, taste, and even sometimes hearing occasionally and weirdly took on characteristics of each other.

It had gone away as abruptly as it had happened; the tang of Mr. Buchanan's tobacco was much stronger, but now it was only the mellow burning of cured leaves, not a mottled green-brown thing that writhed through her sinuses and rattled the membranes of her brain like a tin roof in a hailstorm.

She had been concentrating so hard on her bodily sensations and what they might or might not mean that she hadn't really noticed the voices in the next room. That was Duncan's modest lair, where he kept the ledgers and accounts of the estate and—she thought—went to hide, when the grandeur of the house became too much for him.

Mr. Buchanan was in there with Duncan now, and what had started out as a genial thrum of conversation was now showing signs of strain. She got up, relieved to feel only a slight residual clamminess now, and picked up the basin. She had the natural human inclinations toward eavesdropping, but lately, she had been careful not to hear anything but what she must.

Duncan and her aunt Jocasta were stout Loyalists, and nothing she could say by way of tactful urging or logical argument would sway them. She had overheard more than one of Duncan's private conversations with local Tories that made her heart go small with apprehension, knowing as she did what would be the outcome of the present events.

Here in the piedmont, in the heart of the Cape Fear country, most of the solid citizens *were* Loyalists, convinced that the violence taking place to the north was an overblown rumpus that might be unnecessary, and if it was not, had little to do with them—and that what was most needed here was a firm hand to rein in the wild-eyed Whigs, before their excesses provoked a ruinous retaliation. Knowing that exactly such a ruinous retaliation was coming—and to people she liked, or even loved—gave her what her father called the grue: a cold sense of oppressive horror, coiling through the blood.

"When, then?" Buchanan's voice came clearly as she opened the door, sounding impatient. "They will not wait, Duncan. I must have the money by Wednesday week, or Dunkling will sell the arms elsewhere; ye ken it's a seller's market the noo. For gold, he'll wait—but not for long."

"Aye, I ken that fine, Sawny." Duncan sounded impatient—and very uneasy, Brianna thought. "If it can be done, it will be."

"IF?" Buchanan cried. "What is this 'if'? 'Til now, it's been, oh, aye, Sawny, nay difficulty, to be sure, Sawny, tell Dunkling it's on, oh, of *course,* Sawny—"

"I said, Alexander, that if it can be done, it will." Duncan's voice was low, but suddenly had a note of steel in it that she had never heard before.

Buchanan said something rude in the Gaelic, and suddenly the door of Duncan's office burst open and the man himself popped out, in so great a huff that he barely saw her, and gave her no more than a brusque nod in passing.

Which was just as well, she thought, since she was standing there holding a bowl full of vomit.

Before she could move to dispose of it, Duncan came out in turn. He looked hot, cross—and extremely worried. He did, however, notice her.

"How d'ye fare, lass?" he asked, squinting at her. "Ye're that bit green; have ye eaten aught amiss?"

"I think so. But I'm all right now," she said, hastily turning to put the basin back in the room behind her. She set it on the floor and closed the door on it. "Are you, er, all right, Duncan?"

He hesitated for an instant, but whatever was bothering him was too overwhelming to keep it bottled up. He glanced about, but none of the slaves was up here at this time of day. He leaned close, nonetheless, and lowered his voice.

"Have ye by chance . . . seen anything peculiar, *a nighean*?"

"Peculiar, how?"

He rubbed a knuckle under his drooping mustache, and glanced round once more.

"Near Hector Cameron's tomb, say?" he asked, his voice pitched only just above a whisper.

Her diaphragm, still sore from vomiting, contracted sharply at that, and she put a hand to her middle.

"Ye have, then?" Duncan's expression sharpened.

"Not me," she said, and explained about Jemmy, Angelina, and the supposed ghost.

"I thought perhaps it was Mr. Buchanan," she finished, nodding toward the stair down which Alexander Buchanan had vanished.

"Now, there's a thought," Duncan muttered, rubbing distractedly at his grizzled temple. "But no . . . surely not. He couldna—but it's a thought." Brianna thought that he looked very slightly more hopeful.

"Duncan—can you tell me what's wrong?"

He took a deep breath, shaking his head—not in refusal, but in perplexity—and let it out again, his shoulders slumping.

"The gold," he said simply. "It's gone."

SEVEN THOUSAND pounds in gold bullion was a substantial amount, in all senses of the word. She had no idea how much such a sum might weigh, but it had completely lined Jocasta's coffin, standing chastely next to Hector Cameron's in the family mausoleum.

"What do you mean 'gone'?" she blurted. "*All* of it?"

Duncan clutched her arm, features contorted in the urge to shush her.

"Aye, all of it," he said, looking round yet again. "For God's sake, lass, keep your voice down!"

"When did it go? Or rather," she amended, "when did you find it gone?"

"Last night." He looked round yet again, and jerked his chin toward his office. "Come in, lass; I'll tell ye about it."

Duncan's agitation subsided a little as he told her the story; by the time he had finished, he had regained a certain amount of outward calm.

The seven thousand pounds was what was left of the original ten thousand, which in turn was one-third of the thirty thousand sent—too late, but sent nonetheless—from Louis of France in support of Charles Stuart's doomed attempt on the thrones of England and Scotland.

"Hector was careful, aye?" Duncan explained. "He lived as a rich man, but always within such means as a place like this"—he waved his one hand around, indicating the grounds and messuages of River Run—"might provide. He spent a thousand pound acquiring the land and building the house, then over the years, another thousand in slaves, cattle, and the like. And a thousand pound he put to the bankers—Jo said he couldna bear the thought of all that money sitting, earning nay interest"—he gave her a small, wry smile—"though he was too clever to attract attention by putting it all out. I suppose he meant, maybe, to invest the rest, a bit at a time—but he died before that was done."

Leaving Jocasta as a very wealthy widow—but even more cautious than her husband had been about attracting undue attention. And so the gold had sat, safe in its hiding place, save for the one ingot being gradually whittled away and disposed of by Ulysses. Which had disappeared, she remembered with a qualm. *Someone* knew there was gold here.

Perhaps whoever had taken that ingot had guessed that there was more—and hunted, quietly, patiently, until they found it.

But now—

"Ye'll have heard about General MacDonald?"

She'd heard the name frequently of late, in conversation—he was a Scottish general, more or less retired, she'd assumed—who had been staying here and there, the guest of various prominent families. She *hadn't* heard of his purpose, though.

"He means to raise men—three thousand, four—among the Highlanders, to march to the coast. The Governor's sent for aid; troopships are coming. So the General's men will come down through the Cape Fear valley"—he made a graceful swooping gesture with his hand—"meet the Governor and his troops—and pincer the rebel militias that are a-building."

"And you meant to give him the gold—or no," she corrected herself. "You meant to give him arms and powder."

He nodded and chewed his mustache, looking unhappy.

"A man named Dunkling; Alexander knows him. Lord Dunsmore is gathering a great store of powder and arms in Virginia, and Dunkling is one of his lieutenants—and willing to give up some of that store, in return for gold."

"Which is now gone." She took a deep breath, feeling sweat trickle down between her breasts, further dampening her shift.

"Which is now gone," he agreed bleakly. "And I'm left to wonder what about this ghost of wee Jem's, aye?"

Ghost, indeed. For someone to have entered a place like River Run, teeming with people, and to have moved several hundred pounds by weight of gold, completely unnoticed . . .

The sound of feet on the stairs caused Duncan to jerk his head sharply toward the door, but it was only Josh, one of the black grooms, his hat in his hand.

"Best we be going, Miss Bree," he said, bowing respectfully. "If ye be wanting the light, like?"

For her drawings, he meant. It was a good hour's trip into Cross Creek to lawyer Forbes's house, and the sun was rising fast toward noon.

She glanced at her green-smeared fingers, and recalled the hair straggling untidily down from its makeshift bun; she'd have to tidy herself a bit first.

"Go, lass." Duncan waved her toward the door, his lean face still creased with worry but lightened a little by having shared it.

She kissed him affectionately on the forehead and went down after Josh. She *was* worried, and not only about missing gold and prowling ghosts. General MacDonald, indeed. For if he meant to raise fighting men among the Highlanders, one of the natural places for him to go was to her father.

As Roger had noted to her sometime earlier, *"Jamie can walk the tightrope between Whigs and Tories better than any man I know—but when push comes to shove . . . he'll have to jump."*

The push had come at Mecklenberg. But shove, she thought, was named MacDonald.

100

A TRIP TO THE SEASIDE

GERALD FORBES, THINKING it prudent to be absent from his usual haunts for a time, had removed to Edenton, with the excuse of taking his aged mother to visit her even more aged sister. He had enjoyed the long journey, in spite of his mother's complaints about the clouds of dust raised by another carriage that preceded them.

He had been loath to sacrifice his sight of that carriage—a small, well-sprung affair, whose windows were sealed and heavily curtained. But he had always been a devoted son, and at the next post stop, he went to speak to the driver. The other coach obligingly dropped back, following them at a convenient distance.

"Whatever are ye lookin' at, Gerald?" his mother demanded, looking up from fastening her favorite garnet brooch. "That's the third time ye've had a peek out thon window."

"Not a thing, Mam," he said, inhaling deeply. "Only taking pleasure in the day. Such beautiful weather, is it not?"

Mrs. Forbes sniffed, but obligingly settled her spectacles on her nose and leaned to peer out.

"Aye, weel, it's fair enough," she admitted dubiously. "Hot, though, and damp enough to wring buckets from your shirt."

"Never mind, *a leannan,*" he said, patting her black-clad shoulder. "We'll be in Edenton afore ye know. It'll be cooler there. Nothing like a sea-breeze, so they say, to put the roses in your cheeks!"

101

NIGHTWATCH

Edenton

THE REVEREND MCMILLAN'S house was on the water. A blessing in the hot, muggy weather. The offshore breeze in the evening swept everything away—heat, hearth smoke, mosquitoes. The men sat on the big porch after supper, smoking their pipes and enjoying the respite.

Roger's enjoyment was spiced by the guilty awareness that Mrs. Reverend McMillan and her three daughters were sweating to and fro, washing dishes, clearing away, sweeping floors, boiling up the leftover ham bones from supper with lentils for tomorrow's soup, putting children to bed, and generally slaving away in the stuffy, sweltering confines of the house. At home, he would have felt obliged to help with such work, or face Brianna's wrath; here, such an offer would have been received with drop-jawed incredulity, followed by deep suspicion. Instead, he sat peacefully in the cool evening breeze, watching fishing boats come in across the water of the sound and sipping something that passed for coffee, engaged in pleasant male conversation.

There was, he thought, occasionally something to be said for the eighteenth-century model of sexual roles.

They were talking over the news from the south: the flight of Governor Martin from New Bern, the burning of Fort Johnston. The political climate of Edenton was strongly Whiggish, and the company was largely clerical—the Reverend Doctor McCorkle, his secretary Warren Lee, the Reverend Jay McMillan, Reverend Patrick Dugan, and four "inquirers" awaiting ordination besides Roger—but there were still currents of political disagreement flowing beneath the outwardly cordial surface of the conversation.

Roger himself said little; he didn't wish to offend McMillan's hospitality by contributing to any argument—and something inside him wished for quiet, to contemplate tomorrow.

Then the conversation took a new turn, though, and he found himself paying rapt attention. The Continental Congress had met in Philadelphia two months before, and given General Washington command of the Continental army. Warren Lee had been in Boston shortly thereafter, and was giving the company a vivid account of the battle at Breed's Hill, at which he had been present.

"General Putnam, he brought up wagonloads of dirt and brush, to the neck of the Charlestown peninsula—you said you knew it, sir?" he asked, courteously turning toward Roger. "Well, Colonel Prescott, he's there already, with two militia comp'nies from Massachusetts, and parts of another from Connecticut—was mebbe a thousand men in all, and dear Lord, was they a stench from the camps!"

His soft Southern accent—Lee was a Virginian—held a slight touch of amusement, but this faded as he went on.

"General Ward, he'd give orders to fortify this one hill, Bunker Hill, they call it, for an old redoubt atop. But Colonel Prescott, he goes up it and don't care so much for the looks, him and Mr. Gridley, the engineer. So they leave a detachment there, and go on to Breed's Hill, what they think is maybe better to the purpose, bein' closer to the harbor.

"Now, this is all at night, mind. I was with one of the Massachusetts companies, and we marched right smart, then spent the whole night through, 'twixt midnight and dawn, diggin' trenches and raising up six-foot walls about the perimeter.

"Come the dawn, and we skulked down behind our fortifications, and just in time, too, for there's a British ship in the harbor—the *Lively,* they said—and she opens fire the minute the sun's up. Looked right pretty, for the fog was still on the water and the cannon lit it up in red flashes. Did no harm, though; most all the balls fell short into the harbor—did see one whaleboat at the docks hit, though; stove it like kindling. The crew, they'd hopped out like fleas when the *Lively* took to firing. From where I was, I could just see 'em, hoppin' up and down on the dock, a-shakin' their fists—then the *Lively* let off another broadside, and they all fell flat or run like rabbits."

The light was nearly gone, and Lee's young face invisible in the shadows, but the amusement in his voice made a small rumble of laughter run among the other men.

"They was some firin' from a little battery up on Copp's Hill, and one or two of the other ships, they let off a pop or two, but they could see 'twan't no earthly use and ceased. Then come in some fellows from New Hampshire to join up with us, and that was purely heartening. But General Putnam, he sends a good many men back to work on the fortifications at Bunker, and the New Hampshire folk, they're crouched way down on the left, where they's got no cover beyond rail fences stuffed with mown grass. Lookin' at 'em down there, I was pleased as punch to have four feet of solid earthwork in front of me, I tell you, gentlemen."

The British troops had set out across the Charles River, bold as brass under the midday sun, with the warships behind them and the batteries on shore all providing covering fire.

"We didn't fire back, of course. Had no cannon," Lee said with an audible shrug.

Roger, listening intently, couldn't keep from asking a question at this point.

"Is it true that Colonel Stark said, 'Don't fire until you see the whites of their eyes'?"

Lee coughed discreetly.

"Well, sir. I couldn't say for sure as no one said that, but I didn't hear it myself. Mind, I *did* hear one colonel call out, 'Any whoreson fool wastes his powder afore the bastards are close enough to kill is gonna get his musket shoved up his arse butt-first!'"

The assembly erupted into laughter. An inquiry from Mrs. McMillan, who had come out to offer further refreshment, as to the source of this merriment shut them all up sharp, though, and they listened with a fair assumption of sober attention to the rest of Lee's account.

"Well, so, then, on they come, and I will say 'twas a daunting sight. They'd several regiments, and all in their different colors, fusiliers and grenadiers, Royal Marines, and a proper boiling of light infantry, all comin' on over the ground like a horde of ants, and just as mean.

"I wouldn't make great claim to bravery myself, gentlemen, but I would say the fellows standin' with me had some nerve. We did let 'em come, and the first ranks weren't no more than ten feet away when our volley cut into them.

"They rallied, came back on, and we cut them down again—like ninepins. And the officers—there was a powerful lot of the officers went; they were on their horses, see? I—I shot one such. He keeled over, but he didn't fall off—his horse carried him away. Kind of lolling, with his head loose. But he didn't fall."

Lee's voice had lost some of its color, and Roger saw the burly form of the Reverend Doctor McCorkle lean toward his secretary, touching his shoulder.

"They rallied a third time, and came on. And . . . we were most of us out of ammunition. They came on over the earthworks and through the fences. With their bayonets fixed."

Roger was sitting on the steps of the porch, Lee above him and several feet away, but could hear the young man swallow.

"We fell back. That's how they say it. We ran, is what we did. So'd they."

He swallowed again.

"A bayonet—it makes a terrible sound, goin' into a man. Just—terrible. I can't say how it is, describe it properly. Heard it, though, and more'n once. Was a good many run straight through the body that day—skewered and then the steel pulled out, and they left to die on the ground, floppin' like fish."

Roger had seen—handled—eighteenth-century bayonets, often. A seventeen-inch triangular blade, heavy and brutal, with a blood groove down one side. He thought, quite suddenly, of the furrowed scar that ran up Jamie Fraser's thigh, and rose to his feet. Murmuring a brief excuse, he left the porch, and walked down the shore, pausing only for a moment to shed his shoes and stockings.

The tide was going out; sand and shingle were wet and cool under his bare feet. The breeze rattled faintly among palmetto leaves behind him, and a line of pelicans flew down the shore, solemn against the last of the light. He walked a little way into the surf, small rippling waves that tugged at his heels, sucking the sand away beneath him, making him shift and sway to keep his balance.

Far out on the water of Albemarle Sound, he could see lights; fishing boats, with small fires built in sandboxes aboard, to light the torches the fishermen swung over the side. These seemed to float in the air, swinging to and fro, their reflections in the water winking slowly in and out like fireflies.

The stars were coming out. He stood looking up, trying to empty his mind, his heart, open himself to the love of God.

Tomorrow, he would be a minister. *Thou art a priest forever,* said the ordination service, quoting from the Bible, *after the order of Melchizedek.*

"Are you afraid?" Brianna had asked him, when he'd told her.

"Yeah," he said softly, aloud.

He stood until the tide left him, then followed it, walking into the water, wanting the rhythmic touch of the waves.

"Will you do it anyway?"

"Yeah," he said, more softly still. He had no idea what he was agreeing to, but said it, anyway. Far down the beach behind him, the breeze brought him now and then a snatch of laughter, a few words from the Reverend McMillan's porch. They had moved on, then, from the talk of war and death.

Had any of them ever killed a man? Lee, perhaps. The Reverend Doctor McCorkle? He snorted a little at the thought, but did not dismiss it. He turned and walked a little further, until the only sounds were those of the waves and the offshore wind.

Soul-searching. It was what squires used to do, he thought, smiling a little wryly at the thought. The night before he became a knight, a young man would keep vigil in church or chapel, watching through the dark hours, lighted only by the glow of a sanctuary lamp, praying.

For what? he wondered. Purity of mind, singleness of purpose. Courage? Or perhaps forgiveness?

He hadn't meant to kill Randall Lillington; that had been almost accident, and what wasn't had been self-defense. But he had been hunting when he did it, had gone out looking for Stephen Bonnet, meaning to kill him in cold blood. And Harley Boble; he could still see the shine of the thieftaker's eyes, feel the echo of the blow, the shards of the man's skull reverberating through the bones of his own arm. He'd meant that, yes. Could have stopped. Didn't.

Tomorrow, he would swear before God that he believed in the doctrine of predestination, that he had been meant to do what he had done. Perhaps.

Maybe I don't believe that, so much, he thought, doubt stealing in. *But maybe I do. Christ—oh, sorry*—he apologized mentally—*can I be a proper minister, with doubts? I think everyone's got them, but if I've got too many—maybe ye'd best let me know now, before it's too late.*

His feet had gone numb, and the sky was ablaze with a glory of stars, thick in the black velvet night. He heard the crunch of footsteps among the shingle and the sea wrack nearby.

It was Warren Lee—tall and gangly by starlight, the Reverend Doctor McCorkle's secretary, erstwhile militiaman.

"Thought I'd take a bit of air," Lee said, his voice hardly audible above the hiss of the sea.

"Aye, well, there's a lot of it, and it's free," Roger said as amiably as he could. Lee chuckled briefly in response, but luckily didn't seem disposed to talk.

They stood for some time, watching the fishing boats. Then, by unspoken consent, turned to go back. The house was dark, the porch deserted. A single candle burned in the window, though, lighting them home.

"That officer, the one I shot," Lee blurted suddenly. "I pray for him. Every night."

Lee shut up abruptly, embarrassed. Roger breathed slow and deep, feeling the jerk of his own heart. Had he ever prayed for Lillington, or Boble?

"I will, too," he said.

"Thank you," said Lee very softly, and side by side, they made their way back up the beach, pausing to pick up their shoes, going back barefooted, sand drying on their feet.

They had sat down on the steps to brush it off before going in, when the door behind them opened.

"Mr. MacKenzie?" said the Reverend McMillan, and something in his voice pulled Roger to his feet, heart pounding. "You have a visitor."

He saw the tall silhouette behind McMillan, and knew, even before Jamie Fraser's pale, fierce face appeared, eyes black in the candlelight.

"He's taken Brianna," Jamie said without preamble. "Ye'll come."

102

ANEMONE

FEET TRAMPLED BACK and forth overhead, and she could hear voices, but most of the words were too muffled to make out. There was a chorus of jovial shouts on the side nearest shore, and cordial feminine shrieks in reply.

The cabin had a wide, paned window—did you call it a window on a ship, she wondered, or had it some special nautical name?—that ran behind the bunk, raked back with the angle of the stern. It was made in small, thick panes, set in leading. No hope there of escape, but it did offer the possibility of air, and perhaps information regarding their whereabouts.

Repressing a qualm of nauseated distaste, she clambered across the stained and rumpled sheets of the bed. She pressed close to the window and pushed her face into one of the open panes, taking deep breaths to dispel the aromas of the cabin, though the smell of the harbor was no great improvement, rife as it was with the smell of dead fish, sewage, and baking mud.

She could see a small dock, and moving figures on it. A fire was burning on the shore outside a low, whitewashed building roofed with palmetto leaves. It was too dark to see what, if anything, lay beyond the building. There must be at least a small town, though, judging from the noise of the people on the dock.

There were voices outside the cabin door, coming closer.

". . . meet him on Ocracoke, the dark o' the moon," said one, to which the other replied in an indistinct mumble, before the door flew open.

"Care to join the party, sweetheart? Or have ye started without me?"

She whirled on her knees, heart hammering in her throat. Stephen Bonnet stood inside the door to the cabin, a bottle in one hand and a slight smile on his face. She took a deep breath to quell the shock, and nearly gagged on the stale scent of sex that wafted from the sheets under her knees. She scrambled off the bed, heedless of her clothes, and felt a rip at the waist as her knee caught in her skirt.

"Where are we?" she demanded. Her voice sounded shrill, panicked to her own ears.

"On the *Anemone,*" he said patiently, still smiling.

"You know that isn't what I mean!" The neck of her gown and chemise had torn in the struggle when the men pulled her from her horse, and most of one breast was exposed; she put up a hand, pushing the fabric back in place.

"Do I?" He set the bottle on the desk, and reached to unfasten the stock from his neck. "Ah, that's better." He rubbed at the dark red line across his throat, and she had a sudden, piercing vision of Roger's throat, with its ragged scar.

"I wish to know what this town is called," she said, deepening her voice and fixing him with a gimlet eye. She didn't expect that what worked on her father's tenants would work on him, but the assumption of an air of command helped to steady her a bit.

"Well, that's an easily gratified wish, to be sure." He waved a casual hand toward the shore. "Roanoke." He shucked his coat, tossing it carelessly over the stool. The linen of his shirt was crumpled, and clung damply to his chest and shoulders. "Ye'd best take off the gown, darlin'; it's hot."

He reached for the strings that tied his shirt, and she moved abruptly away from the bed, glancing round the cabin, searching the shadows for something that could be used as a weapon. Stool, lamp, logbook, bottle . . . there. A piece of wood showed among the rubble on the desk, the blunt end of a marlinespike.

He frowned, attention fastened momentarily on a knot in

the string. She took two long steps and seized the marlinespike, yanking it off the desk in a shower of rubbish and clanging oddments.

"Stand back." She held the thing like a baseball bat, gripped in both hands. Sweat streamed down the hollow of her back, but her hands felt cold and her face went hot and cold and hot again, ripples of heat and terror rolling down her skin.

Bonnet looked at her as though she had gone mad.

"Whatever will ye be after doing with that, woman?" He left off fiddling with his shirt and took a step toward her. She took one back, raising the club.

"Don't fucking touch me!"

He stared at her, eyes fixed wide, pale green and unblinking above a small, odd smile. Still smiling, he took another step toward her. Then another, and the fear boiled off in a surge of rage. Her shoulders bunched and lifted, ready.

"I mean it! Stand back or I'll kill you. I'll know who this baby's father is, if I die for it!"

He had raised a hand, as though to grasp the club and jerk it away from her, but at this, he stopped abruptly.

"Baby? You are with child?"

She swallowed, her breath still thick in her throat. The blood hammered in her ears, and the smooth wood was slick with sweat from her palms. She tightened her grip, trying to keep the rage alive, but it was already dying.

"Yes. I think so. I'll know for sure in two weeks."

His sandy eyebrows lifted.

"Hm!" With a short grunt, he stepped back, surveying her with interest. Slowly, his eyes traveled over her, appraising her one bared breast.

The sudden spurt of rage had drained away, leaving her breathless and empty-bellied. She kept hold of the marlinespike, but her wrists quivered, and she lowered it.

"Is that the way of it, then?"

He leaned forward and reached out, quite without lascivious intent now. Startled, she froze for an instant, and he weighed the breast in one hand, kneading thoughtfully, as though it were a grapefruit he meant to buy at market. She gasped and hit at him one-handed with the club, but she had lost what readiness she had, and the blow bounced off his shoulder, rocking him but having little other effect. He grunted and stepped back, rubbing at his shoulder.

"Could be. Well, then." He frowned, and tugged at the front of his breeches, adjusting himself without the slightest embarrassment. "Lucky we're in port, I suppose."

She made no sense whatever of this remark, but didn't care; apparently he had changed his mind upon hearing her revelation, and the feeling of relief made her knees go weak and her skin prickle with sweat. She sat down, quite suddenly, upon the stool, the club clanking to the floor beside her.

Bonnet had put his head out into the corridor, and was bellowing for someone named Orden. Whoever Orden was, he didn't come into the cabin, but within a few moments, a voice mumbled interrogatively outside.

"Fetch me down a whore from the docks," Bonnet said, in the casual tone of one ordering a fresh pint of bitter. "Clean, mind, and fairly young."

He shut the door then, and turned to the table, scrabbling through the debris until he unearthed a pewter cup. He poured a drink, quaffed half of it, and then—seeming belatedly to realize that she was still there—offered her the bottle with a vague "Eh?" of invitation.

She shook her head, wordless. A faint hope had sprung up in the back of her mind. He did have some faint streak of gallantry, or at least decency; he had come back to rescue her from the burning warehouse, and he had left her the stone for what he assumed to be his child. Now he had abandoned his advances, upon hearing that she was with child again. Perhaps he would let her go, then, particularly if she was of no immediate use to him.

"So . . . you don't want me?" she said, edging her feet under her, ready to leap up and run, as soon as the door opened to admit her replacement. She hoped she *could* run; her knees were still trembling with reaction.

Bonnet glanced at her, surprised.

"I've split your quim once already, sweetheart," he said, and grinned. "I recall the red hair—a lovely sight, sure—but it wasn't so memorable an experience otherwise that I can't be waitin' to repeat it. Time enough, darlin', time enough." He chucked her negligently under the chin, and gulped more of his drink. "For now, though, LeRoi's needing a bit of a gallop."

"Why am I here?" she demanded.

Distracted, he pulled once more at the crotch of his breeches, quite unself-conscious of her presence.

"Here? Why, because a gentleman paid me to take ye to London-town, darlin'. Didn't ye know?"

She felt as though someone had hit her in the stomach, and sat down on the bed, folding her arms protectively across her midsection.

"What gentleman? And for God's sake—why?"

He considered for a moment, but evidently concluded that there was no reason not to tell her.

"A man named Forbes," he said, and threw back the rest of his drink. "Know him, do you?"

"I most certainly do," she said, amazement vying with fury. "That bloody *bastard*!" So they were Forbes's men, the masked bandits that had stopped her and Josh, dragged them from their horses, and shoved them both into a sealed carriage, bumping over unseen roads for days on end, until they reached the coast, and then been pulled out, disheveled and reeking, and bundled aboard the ship.

"Where's Joshua?" she asked abruptly. "The young black man who was with me?"

"Was there?" Bonnet looked quizzical. "If they brought him aboard, I imagine they've put him in the hold with the other cargo. A bonus, I suppose," he added, and laughed.

Her fury at Forbes had been tinged with relief at finding out he was the motive behind her abduction; Forbes might be a low-down, sneaking scoundrel, but he wouldn't be intending to murder her. That laugh of Stephen Bonnet's, though, made a cold qualm run through her, and she felt suddenly light-headed.

"What do you mean, a bonus?"

Bonnet scratched his cheek, gooseberry eyes roaming over her in approval.

"Oh, well, then. Mr. Forbes only wanted ye out of the way, he said. Whatever did ye do to the man, darlin'? But he's paid your fare already, and I've the impression that he's no great interest in where ye end up."

"Where I end up?" Her mouth had been dry; now saliva was pouring from her membranes, and she had to swallow repeatedly.

"Well, after all, darlin', why bother takin' ye all the way to London, where ye'd be of no particular use to anyone? Besides, it rains quite a bit in London; I'm sure ye wouldn't like it."

Before she could draw breath to ask any more questions, the door opened, and a young woman slid through, closing it behind her.

She was likely in her twenties, though with a missing molar that showed when she smiled. She was plump and plain-faced, brown-haired, and clean by local standards, though the scent of her sweat and waves of freshly applied cheap cologne wafted across the cabin, making Brianna want to throw up again.

"Hallo, Stephen," the newcomer said, standing on tiptoe to kiss Bonnet's cheek. "Give us a drink to be starting with, eh?"

Bonnet grabbed her, gave her a deep and lingering kiss, then let her go and reached for the bottle.

Coming down onto her heels, she looked at Brianna with detached professional interest, then back at Bonnet, and scratched at her neck.

"You'll have the two of us, Stephen, or shall it be me and her to start? It's a quid more, either way."

Bonnet didn't bother answering, but thrust the bottle into her hand, whipped off the kerchief that hid the swell of her heavy breasts, and began at once to undo his flies. He dropped the breeches on the floor, and without ado, seized the woman by the hips and pressed her against the door.

Guzzling from the bottle she held in one hand, the young woman snatched up her skirts with the other, whisking skirt and petticoat out of the way with a practiced motion that bared her to the waist. Brianna caught a glimpse of sturdy thighs and a patch of dark hair, before they were obscured by Bonnet's buttocks, blond-furred and clenched with effort.

She turned her head away, cheeks burning, but morbid fascination compelled her to glance back. The whore was standing balanced on her toes, squatting slightly to accommodate him, gazing placidly over his shoulder as he thrust and grunted. One hand still held the bottle; the other stroked

Bonnet's shoulders in a practiced way. She caught Brianna's eye on her, and winked, still saying, "Ooh, yes . . . oh, YES! That's good, love, so good . . ." in her client's ear.

The cabin door quivered with each meaty thump of the whore's backside, and Brianna could hear laughter in the corridor outside, both male and female; evidently Orden had brought back enough to supply crew as well as captain.

Bonnet heaved and grunted for a minute or two, then gave a loud groan, his movements suddenly jerky and uncoordinated. The whore put a helpful hand on his buttocks and pulled him close, then relaxed her grip as his body went limp, leaning heavily against her. She supported him for a moment, patting his back matter-of-factly, like a mother burping a baby, then pushed him off.

His face and neck were flushed dark red, and he was breathing heavily. He nodded to the whore, and stooped, fumbling for his breeches. He stood up with them and waved toward the littered desk.

"Help yourself to your pay, darlin', but give me back the bottle, aye?"

The whore pouted slightly, but took a final deep gulp of the liquor and handed him the bottle, now no more than a quarter full. She pulled a wadded cloth from the pocket at her waist and clapped it between her thighs, then shook down her skirts and minced across to the desk, poking delicately among the litter for scattered coins, which she picked out with two fingers, dropping them one by one into the depths of her pocket.

Bonnet, clothed once more, went out without a backward glance at the two women. The air in the cabin was hot and thick with the scent of sex, and Brianna felt her stomach clench. Not with revulsion, but with panic. The strong male reek had triggered an instinctive flush of response that tingled across her breasts and gripped her inwardly; for a brief, disorienting moment, she felt Roger's skin, slick with sweat against her own, and her breasts tingled, swollen and wanting.

She pressed both lips and legs tight together, and curled her hands into fists, breathing shallowly. The last thing she could stand right now, she thought—the *very* last thing—was to think of Roger and sex, while anywhere within miles of Stephen Bonnet. She resolutely pushed the thought aside, and edged closer to the whore, searching for some remark with which to open conversation.

The whore sensed the movement, and glanced at Brianna, taking in both the torn dress and its quality, but then dismissed her in favor of finding more coins. Once she had her pay, the woman would leave, going back to the docks. It was a chance to get word to Roger and her parents. Not much, perhaps, but a chance.

"You . . . um . . . know him well?" she said.

The whore glanced at her, eyebrows lifted.

"Who? Oh, Stephen? Aye, he's a good 'un, Stephen." She shrugged. "Don't take more than two or three minutes, no bones about the money, never wants nothin' but a simple swive. He's rough now and then, but he don't hit unless you cross him, and no one's fool enough to do that. Not more than once, anyroad." Her gaze lingered for a moment on Brianna's torn dress, one brow lifting sardonically.

"I'll remember that," Brianna said dryly, and pulled the edge of her ripped chemise up higher. She glimpsed a glass bottle amid the rubble on the desk, filled with a clear liquid, containing a small round object. She leaned closer to look at it, frowning. It couldn't be . . . but it was. A round, fleshy object, rather like a hard-boiled egg, a pinkish-gray in color—with a neat round hole drilled completely through it.

She crossed herself, feeling faint.

"I was that surprised," the whore went on, eyeing Brianna with open curiosity. "He's never had two girls together, so far as I know, and he's not one as wants someone to watch while he's at his pleasure."

"I'm not—" Brianna began, but then stopped, not wanting to offend the woman.

"Not a whore?" The young woman grinned broadly, exposing the black gap of her missing tooth. "I might ha' guessed as much, chickie. Not as it would make no never mind to Stephen. He sows as he likes, and I can see as how he might like you. Most men would." She looked at Brianna with dispassionate assessment, nodding at her disheveled hair, flushed face, and tidy figure.

"I expect they like you, too," Brianna said politely, with a faint feeling of surreality. "Er . . . what's your name?"

"Hepzibah," the woman said with an air of pride. "Or Eppie, for short, like." There were coins still on the desk, but the whore left them alone. Bonnet might be generous, but evidently the whore didn't want to take advantage of him—more likely a sign of fear than of friendship, Brianna thought. She took a deep breath and pressed on.

"What a lovely name. Pleased to meet you, Eppie." She held out a hand. "My name is Brianna Fraser MacKenzie." She gave all three names, hoping the whore would remember at least one of them.

The woman glanced at the extended hand in puzzlement, then gingerly shook it, dropping it like a dead fish. She pulled up her skirt, and began to clean herself with the rag, fastidiously wiping away all trace of the recent encounter.

Brianna leaned closer, bracing herself against the odors of the stained rag, the woman's body, and the hot smell of liquor on her breath.

"Stephen Bonnet kidnapped me," she said.

"Oh, aye?" said the whore, indifferent. "Well, he takes as he likes, does Stephen."

"I want to get away," Brianna said, keeping her voice low, with a glance at the cabin door. She could hear the sound of feet on the deck overhead, and hoped voices wouldn't carry through the heavy planks.

Eppie wadded up the rag and dropped it on the desk. She rummaged in her pocket, coming out with a small bottle stoppered with a plug of wax. She still held her skirts up, and Brianna could see the silvery streaks of stretch marks across her plump belly.

"Well, give him what he wants, then," the whore advised, taking out the plug and pouring a bit of the bottle's contents—a surprisingly mild scent of rosewater—into her hand. "Chances are he'll tire of ye in a few days and put ye ashore." She wiped the rosewater lavishly over her pubic hair, then sniffed critically at her hand and made a face.

"No. I mean, that's not what he kidnapped me for. I don't think," she added.

Eppie recorked the bottle, and dropped both it and the rag into her pocket.

"Oh, he means to ransom you?" Eppie eyed her with a

little more interest. "Still, I've never known scruples interfere with the man's appetite. He'd take a virgin's maidenhead and sell her back to her father before her belly started swelling." She pursed her lips, a belated thought coming to her.

"So how did you talk him out of havin' you, then?"

Brianna put a hand on her stomach.

"I told him I was pregnant. That stopped him. I wouldn't have thought—a man like that—but it did. Perhaps he's better than you think?" she asked with a wisp of hope.

Eppie laughed at that, small eyes squeezing half-shut with hilarity at the thought.

"Stephen? God, no!" She sniffed with amusement, and smoothed down her skirts.

"No," she went on, more matter-of-factly, "best story you could tell, though, if you don't want him at you. He called me down to him once, then put me off when he saw I'd a cake in the oven—when I joked him about it, he said he'd once taken a whore with her belly the size of a cannonball, and right in the midst of it, she give a groan and the blood come spurting out of her fit to drench the room. Put him right off, he said, and no wonder. Left our Stephen with a horror of swiving girls what are up the spout. He's takin' no chances, see."

"I see." A trickle of sweat ran down Brianna's cheek, and she wiped it away with the back of her hand. Her mouth felt dry, and she sucked the inside of her cheek for moisture. "The woman—what happened to her?"

Hepzibah looked blank for a moment.

"Oh, the whore? Why, she died, of course, poor cow. Stephen said as how he was struggling to get into his wet breeches, all soused with blood like they were, and he looked up and saw her layin' still as stone on the floor, but with her belly still wriggling and twitching like a bag full o' snakes. Said it come to him sudden that the babe meant to come out and take its revenge on him, and he fled the house right then in his shirt, leavin' his breeches behind."

She chortled at this amusing vision, then snorted and settled herself, brushing down her skirts. "But then, Stephen's Irish," she added tolerantly. "They take morbid fancies, the Irish, especially when they're gone in drink." The tip of her tongue came out and passed reminiscently over her lower lip, tasting the lingering traces of Bonnet's liquor.

Brianna leaned closer, holding out her hand.

"Look."

Hepzibah glanced into her hand, then looked again, riveted. The thick gold band with its big cabochon ruby winked and glowed in the lantern light.

"I'll give it to you," Brianna said, lowering her voice, "if you'll do something for me."

The whore licked her lips again, a sudden look of alertness coming into her heavy face.

"Aye? Do what?"

"Get word to my husband. He's in Edenton, at the Reverend McMillan's house—anyone will know where it is. Tell him where I am, and tell him—" She hesitated. What should she say? There was no telling how long the *Anemone* would stay here, or where Bonnet would choose to go next. The only clue she had was what she had overheard in his conversation with his mate, just before he came in.

"Tell them I think he has a hiding place on Ocracoke. He means to rendezvous with someone there at the dark of the moon. Tell him that."

Hepzibah cast an uneasy glance at the cabin door, but it stayed shut. She looked back at the ring, longing for it warring in her face with an obvious fear of Bonnet.

"He won't know," Brianna urged. "He won't find out. And my father will reward you."

"He's a rich man, then, your father?" Brianna saw the look of calculation in the whore's eyes, and felt a moment's misgiving—what if she should simply take the ring and betray her to Bonnet? Still, she hadn't taken more money than her due; perhaps she was honest. And there was no choice, after all.

"Very rich," she said firmly. "His name is Jamie Fraser. My aunt is rich, too. She has a plantation called River Run, just above Cross Creek in North Carolina. Ask for Mrs. Innes—Jocasta Cameron Innes. Yes, if you don't find Ro—my husband, send word there."

"River Run." Hepzibah repeated it obediently, eyes still fixed on the ring.

Brianna twisted it off and dropped it into the whore's palm

before she could change her mind. The woman's hand closed tight around it.

"My father's name is Jamie Fraser; my husband is Roger MacKenzie," she repeated. "At the Reverend McMillan's house. Can you remember?"

"Fraser and MacKenzie," Hepzibah repeated uncertainly. "Oh, aye, to be sure." She was already moving toward the door.

"Please," Brianna said urgently.

The whore nodded but without looking at her, then sidled through the door, shutting it behind her.

The ship creaked and swayed underfoot, and she heard the rattle of wind through the trees on the shore, over the shouts of drunken men. Her knees gave way then and she sat down on the bed, careless of the sheets.

THEY LEFT WITH the tide; she heard the anchor chain rumble and felt the ship quicken, taking life as her sails took wind. Glued to the window, she watched the dark green mass of Roanoke recede. A hundred years before, the first English colony had landed here—and disappeared without trace. The governor of the colony, returning from England with supplies, had found everyone gone, leaving no clue save the word "Croatan" carved into the trunk of a tree.

She wasn't even leaving that much. Heartsick, she watched until the island sank into the sea.

No one came for some hours. Empty-bellied, she grew nauseated, and threw up in the chamber pot. She could not bear the thought of lying down on those revolting sheets, but instead pulled them off, remade the bed with only the quilts, and lay down.

The windows were open, and the fresh air of the sea stirred her hair and lifted the clamminess from her skin, making her feel a little better. She was unbearably conscious of her womb, a small, heavy, tender weight, and what was likely happening inside it: that orderly dance of dividing cells, a sort of peaceful violence, implacably wresting lives and wrenching hearts.

When had it happened? She tried to think back, remember.

It might have been the night before Roger left for Edenton. He had been excited, almost exalted, and they had made love with lingering joy, spiced by longing, for they both knew the morrow would bring separation. She had fallen asleep in his arms, feeling loved.

But then she had waked alone, in the middle of the night, to find him sitting by the window, bathed in the light of a gibbous moon. She had been reluctant to disturb his private contemplation, but he had turned, feeling her eyes on him, and something in his look had made her get out of bed and go to him, taking his head against her bosom, holding him.

He had risen then, laid her on the floor, and had her again, wordless and urgent.

Catholic that she was, she had found it terribly erotic, the notion of seducing a priest on the eve of his ordination, stealing him—if only for a moment—from God.

She swallowed, hands clasped over her belly. *Be careful what you pray for.* The nuns at school had always told the children that.

The wind was growing cold, chilling her, and she pulled the edge of one quilt—the cleanest—over her. Then, concentrating fiercely, she began very carefully to pray.

103

PUT TO THE QUESTION

GERALD FORBES SAT IN the parlor of the King's Inn, enjoying a glass of hard cider and the feeling that all was right with the world. He had had a most fruitful meeting with Samuel Iredell and his friend, two of the most prominent rebel leaders in Edenton—and an even more fruitful meeting with Gilbert Butler and William Lyons, local smugglers.

He had a great fondness for jewels, and in private celebration of his elegant disposal of the threat of Jamie Fraser, he had bought a new stickpin, topped with a beautiful ruby. He contemplated this with quiet satisfaction, noting the lovely shadows that the stone cast on the silk of his ruffle.

His mother was safely planted at her sister's house, he had an appointment for luncheon with a local lady, and an hour to spare beforehand. Perhaps a stroll to stimulate appetite; it was a beautiful day.

He had in fact pushed back his chair and begun to rise when a large hand planted itself in the center of his chest and shoved him back into it.

"What—?" He looked up in indignation—and took great care to keep that expression on his face, despite a sudden deep qualm. A tall, dark man was standing over him, wearing a most unfriendly expression. MacKenzie, the chit's husband.

"How dare you, sir?" he said, belligerent. "I must demand apology!"

"You demand what ye like," MacKenzie said. He was pale under his tan, and grim. "Where is my wife?"

"How should I know?" Forbes's heart was beating fast, but with glee as much as trepidation. He lifted his chin and made to rise. "You will excuse me, sir."

A hand on his arm stopped him, and he turned, looking into the face of Fraser's nephew, Ian Murray. Murray smiled, and Forbes's sense of self-satisfaction diminished slightly. They said the boy had lived with the Mohawk, become one of them—that he dwelt with a vicious wolf who spoke to him and obeyed his commands, that he had cut a man's heart out and eaten it in some heathen ritual.

Looking at the lad's homely face and disheveled dress, though, Forbes was not impressed.

"Remove your hand from my person, sir," he said with dignity, straightening in his chair.

"No, I think I won't," Murray said. The hand tightened on his arm like the bite of a horse, and Forbes's mouth opened, though he made no sound.

"What have ye done with my cousin?" Murray said.

"I? Why, I—I have nothing whatever to do with Mrs. MacKenzie. Let go, God damn you!"

The grip relaxed, and he sat breathing heavily. MacKenzie had pulled up a chair to face him and sat down.

Forbes smoothed the sleeve of his coat, avoiding MacKenzie's stare and thinking rapidly. How had they found out? Or had they? Perhaps they were only trying a venture, with no sure knowledge.

"I am grieved to hear that any misfortune might have befallen Mrs. MacKenzie," he said politely. "Am I to take it that you have somehow misplaced her?"

MacKenzie looked him up and down for a moment without answering, then made a small sound of contempt.

"I heard ye speak in Mecklenberg," he said, his tone conversational. "Very glib ye were. A great deal about justice, I heard, and protection of our wives and children. Such eloquence."

"Fine talk," Ian Murray put in, "for a man who would abduct a helpless woman." He was still crouching on the floor like a savage, but had moved round a little, so as to stare directly into Forbes's face. The lawyer found it slightly unnerving, and chose instead to meet MacKenzie's eyes, man to man.

"I regret your misfortune extremely, sir," he said, striving for a tone of concern. "I should be pleased to help, in any way possible, of course. But I do not—"

"Where is Stephen Bonnet?"

The question struck Forbes like a blow to the liver. He gaped for a moment, thinking that he had made a mistake in choosing MacKenzie to look at; that flat green gaze was like a snake's.

"Who is Stephen Bonnet?" he asked, licking his lips. His lips were dry, but the rest of him was heavily bedewed; he could feel sweat pooling in the creases of his neck, soaking the cambric of his shirt beneath his oxters.

"I heard ye, ken," Murray remarked pleasantly. "When ye made the bargain wi' Richard Brown. In your warehouse, it was."

Forbes's head snapped round. He was so shocked that it was a moment before he realized that Murray was holding a knife, laid casually across his knee.

"What? You say—what? I tell you, sir, you are mistaken—

mistaken!" He half-rose, stammering. MacKenzie shot to his feet and seized him by the shirtfront, twisting.

"No, sir," he said very softly, his face so close that Forbes felt the heat of his breath. "It is yourself has been mistaken. Most grievously mistaken, in choosing my wife to serve your wicked ends."

There was a ripping sound as the fine cambric tore. MacKenzie shoved him back violently into the chair, then leaned forward, seizing his neckcloth in a grip that threatened to choke him on the spot. His mouth opened, gasping, and black spots flickered in his vision—but not sufficiently as to obscure those brilliant, cold green eyes.

"Where has he taken her?"

Forbes gripped the arms of his chair, breathing heavily.

"I know nothing about your wife," he said, his voice pitched low and venomous. "And as for grievous error, sir, you are in the process of committing one. How dare you assault me? I shall prefer charges, I do assure you!"

"Oh, assault, forbye," Murray said, scoffing. "We havena done any such thing. Yet." He sat back on his haunches, tapping the knife thoughtfully against his thumbnail and regarding Forbes with an air of estimation, like one planning to carve a suckling pig on a platter.

Forbes set his jaw and glared up at MacKenzie, who was still standing, looming over him.

"This is a public place," he pointed out. "You cannot harm me without notice being taken." He glanced behind MacKenzie, hoping that someone would come into the parlor and interrupt this grossly uncomfortable tête-à-tête, but it was a quiet morning, and all the chambermaids and ostlers inconveniently about their duties elsewhere.

"Do we care if anyone notices, *a charaid*?" Murray inquired, glancing up at MacKenzie.

"Not really." Nonetheless, MacKenzie resumed his seat and resumed his stare. "We can wait a bit, though." He glanced at the case clock by the mantel, its pendulum moving with a serene tick-tock. "It won't be long."

Belatedly, it occurred to Forbes to wonder where Jamie Fraser was.

ELSPETH FORBES was rocking gently on the veranda of her sister's house, enjoying the coolness of the morning air, when a visitor was announced.

"Why, Mr. Fraser!" she exclaimed, sitting up. "What brings ye to Edenton? Is it Gerald ye're in search of? He's gone to—"

"Ah, no, Mistress Forbes." He swept her a low bow, the morning sun gleaming off his hair as though it were bronze metal. "It is yourself I've come for."

"Oh? Oh!" She sat up in her chair, hastily brushing away crumbs of toast on her sleeve, and hoping her cap was on straight. "Why, sir, what could ye possibly want with an old woman?"

He smiled—such a nice-looking lad he was, so fine in his gray coatie, and that look of mischief in his eyes—and leaned close to whisper in her ear.

"I've come to steal ye away, Mistress."

"Och, awa' with ye!" She flapped a hand at him, laughing, and he took it, kissing her knuckles.

"I shallna take 'no' for answer, now," he assured her, and gestured toward the edge of the porch, where he had left a large, promising-looking basket, covered with a checkered cloth. "I've a mind to eat my luncheon in the country, under a tree. I've the very tree in mind—a braw, fine tree—but it's a poor meal, taken without company."

"Surely to goodness ye could find better company than mine, lad," she said, thoroughly charmed. "And where's your dear wife, then?"

"Ah, she's left me," he said, affecting sorrow. "Here's me, with a wonderful picnic planned, and her off to a birthing. So I said to myself, well, Jamie, it's shame to waste such a feast—who might be at liberty to share it with ye? And what should I see next but your most elegant self, taking your ease. An answer to prayer, it was; surely ye wouldna go against heavenly guidance, Mistress Forbes?"

"Hmph," she said, trying not to laugh at him. "Och, well. If it's a matter of wasting . . ."

Before she could say more, he had stooped down and

plucked her from her chair, lifting her in his arms. She whooped with surprise.

"If it's a proper abduction, I must carry ye away, aye?" he said, smiling down at her.

To her mortification, the sound she made could be called nothing but a giggle. He seemed not to mind, though, and bending to sweep up the basket in one strong hand, carried her like a bit of thistledown out to his carriage.

"YOU CANNOT keep me prisoner here! Let me pass, or I will shout for help!"

They had, in fact, held him for more than an hour, blocking all attempts on his part to rise and leave. He was right, though, Roger thought; traffic was beginning to pick up in the street outside, and he could hear—as could Forbes—the noises of a maid setting out the tables for dinner in the next room.

He glanced at Ian. They had discussed it; if word hadn't come within an hour, they would have to try to remove Forbes from the inn, take him to a more private place. That could be a dicey business; the lawyer was intimidated, but stubborn as a ball bearing. And he *would* call for help.

Ian pursed his lips thoughtfully, and drew the knife he had been playing with down the side of his breeches, polishing the blade.

"Mr. MacKenzie?" A small boy had popped up beside him like a mushroom, dirt-smeared and round-faced.

"I am," he said, a wave of thankfulness washing through him. "Have ye got something for me?"

"Aye, sir." The urchin handed over a small twist of paper, accepted a coin in return, and was gone, in spite of Forbes's call of "Wait, boy!"

The lawyer had half-risen from his seat in agitation. Roger made a sharp move toward him, though, and he sank back at once, not waiting to be pushed. Good, Roger thought grimly, he was learning.

Undoing the twist of paper, he found himself holding a large brooch in the shape of a bunch of flowers, done in garnets and silver. It was a good piece of workmanship, but rather ugly. Its impression on Forbes, though, was substantial.

"You wouldn't. He wouldn't." The lawyer was staring at the brooch in Roger's hand, his heavy face gone pale.

"Oh, I expect he would, if ye mean Uncle Jamie," Ian Murray said. "He's fond of his daughter, aye?"

"Nonsense." The lawyer was making a game attempt to bluff it out, but he couldn't keep his eyes off the brooch. "Fraser is a gentleman."

"He's a Highlander," Roger said brutally. "Like your father, aye?" He'd heard stories about the elder Forbes, who by all accounts had escaped Scotland just ahead of the hangman.

Forbes chewed his lower lip.

"He would not harm an old woman," he said, with as much bravado as he could summon.

"Would he not?" Ian's sketchy brows lifted. "Aye, perhaps not. He might just send her awa', though—to Acadia, maybe? Ye seem to ken him fair weel, Mr. Forbes. What d'ye think?"

The lawyer drummed his fingers on the arm of the chair, breathing through his teeth, evidently reviewing what he knew of Jamie Fraser's character and reputation.

"All right," he said suddenly. "All right!"

Roger felt the tension running through him snap like a cut wire. He'd been strung like a puppet since Jamie had come to fetch him last night.

"Where?" he said, feeling breathless. "Where is she?"

"She's safe," Forbes said hoarsely. "I wouldn't have her harmed." He looked up, wild-eyed. "For God's sake, I wouldn't harm her!"

"Where?" Roger clamped the brooch tight, not caring that its edges cut into his hand. "Where is she?"

The lawyer sagged like a half-filled bag of meal.

"Aboard a ship called *Anemone*, Captain Bonnet." He swallowed hard, unable to keep his eyes away from the brooch. "She—I told—they are bound for England. But she is safe, I tell you!"

Shock tightened Roger's grip, and he felt the sudden slick of blood on his fingers. He flung the brooch onto the floor, wiping his hand on his breeches, struggling for words. The shock had tightened his throat, as well; he felt as though he were strangling.

Seeing his trouble, Ian stood abruptly and pressed his knife against the lawyer's throat.

"When did they sail?"

"I—I—" The lawyer's mouth opened and closed at random, and he looked helplessly from Ian to Roger, eyes bulging.

"Where?" Roger forced the word past the blockage in his throat, and Forbes flinched at the sound.

"She—she was put aboard here. In Edenton. Two—two days ago."

Roger nodded abruptly. Safe, he said. In Bonnet's hands. Two days, in Bonnet's hands. But he had sailed with Bonnet, he thought, trying to steady himself, keep a grip on his rationality. He knew how the man worked. Bonnet was a smuggler; he would not sail for England without a full cargo. He might—*might*—be going down the coast, picking up small shipments before turning to the open sea and the long voyage for England.

And if not—he might still be caught, with a fast ship.

No time to be lost; people on the docks might know where the *Anemone* was headed next. He turned and took a step toward the door. Then a red wave washed through him and he whirled back, smashing his fist into Forbes's face with the full weight of his body behind it.

The lawyer gave a high-pitched scream, and clutched both hands to his nose. All noises in the inn and in the street seemed to stop; the world hung suspended. Roger took a short, deep breath, rubbing his knuckles, and nodded once more.

"Come on," he said to Ian.

"Oh, aye."

Roger was halfway to the door when he realized that Ian was not with him. He looked back, and was just in time to see his cousin-by-marriage take Forbes gently by one ear and cut it off.

104

SLEEPING WITH A SHARK

STEPHEN BONNET WAS as good as his word—if that's how one would describe it. He made no sexual advances toward her, but did insist that she share his bed.

"I like a warm body in the night," he said. "And I think ye might prefer my bed to the cargo hold, sweetheart."

She would most emphatically have preferred the cargo hold, though her explorations—once free of land, she was allowed out of the cabin—had revealed the hold as a dark and comfortless hole, in which several hapless slaves were chained among a collection of boxes and barrels, in constant danger of being crushed should the cargo shift.

"Where are we going, miss? And what will happen when we get there?" Josh spoke in Gaelic, his handsome face small and frightened in the shadows of the hold.

"I think we're going to Ocracoke," she said in the same language. "Beyond that—I don't know. Do you still have your rosary?"

"Oh, yes, miss." He touched his chest, where the crucifix hung. "It's the only thing that keeps me from despair."

"Good. Keep praying." She glanced at the other slaves: two women, two men, all with slender bodies and delicate, fine-boned faces. She had brought food for Josh from her own supper, but had nothing to offer them, and was troubled.

"Do they feed you down here?"

"Yes, miss. Fairly well," he assured her.

"Do they"—she moved her chin a little, delicately indicating the other slaves—"know anything? About where we're going?"

"I don't know, miss. I can't talk to them. They're African—

Fulani, I can see that from the way they look, but that's all I know."

"I see. Well . . ." She hesitated, eager to be out of the dark, clammy hold, but reluctant to leave the young groom there.

"You go along, miss," he said quietly in English, seeing her doubt. "I be fine. We all be fine." He touched his rosary, and did his best to give her a smile, though it wavered round the edges. "Holy Mother see us safe."

Having no words of comfort to impart, she nodded, and climbed the ladder into the sunlight, feeling five sets of eyes upon her.

Bonnet, thank God, spent most of his time on deck during the day. She could see him now, coming down the rigging like a nimble ape.

She stood very still, no movement save the brush of windblown hair, of skirts against her frozen limbs. He was as sensitive to the movements of her body as was Roger—but in his own way. The way of a shark, signaled to and drawn by the flappings of its prey.

She had spent one night in his bed so far, sleepless. He had pulled her casually against himself, said, "Good night, darlin'," and fallen instantly asleep. Whenever she had tried to move, to extricate herself from his grip, though, he had shifted, moving with her, to keep her firmly by him.

She was obliged to an unwelcome intimacy with his body, an acquaintance that awoke memories she had with great difficulty put away—the feel of his knee pushing her thighs apart, the rough joviality of his touch between her legs, the sun-bleached blond hairs that curled crisply on his thighs and forearms, the unwashed, musky male smell of him. The mocking presence of LeRoi, rising at intervals during the night, pressed in firm and mindless hunger against her buttocks.

She had a moment of intense thankfulness, both for her present pregnancy—for she was in no doubt of it now—and for her certain knowledge that Stephen Bonnet had not fathered Jemmy.

He dropped from the rigging with a thud, saw her, and smiled. He said nothing, but squeezed her bottom familiarly as he passed, making her clench her teeth and cling to the rail.

Ocracoke, at the dark of the moon. She looked up into the brilliant sky, wheeling with clouds of terns and gulls; they could not be far offshore. How long, for God's sake, 'til the dark of the moon?

105

THE PRODIGAL

THEY HAD NO trouble in finding persons familiar with *Anemone* and her captain. Stephen Bonnet was well-known on the Edenton docks, though his reputation varied, depending on his associations. An honest captain was the usual opinion, but hard in his dealings. A blockade runner, a smuggler, said others—and whether that was good or bad depended on the politics of the person saying it. He'd get you anything, they said—for a price.

Pirate, said a few. But those few spoke in low tones, looking frequently over their shoulders, and strongly desired not to be quoted.

The *Anemone* had left quite openly, with a homely cargo of rice and fifty barrels of smoked fish. Roger had found one man who recalled seeing the young woman go aboard with one of Bonnet's hands: "Great huge doxy, with flaming hair a-loose, flowing down to her arse," the man had said, smacking his lips. "Mr. Bonnet's a good-size man himself, though; expect he can handle her."

Only Ian's hand on his arm had stopped him hitting the man.

What they had not yet found was anyone who knew for sure where *Anemone* was headed.

"London, I think," said the harbormaster, dubious. "But not directly; he's not yet got a full cargo. Likely he'll be going down the coast, trading here and there—perhaps sail for Europe from Charlestown. But then again," the man added, rubbing his chin, "could be he's bound for New England. Terrible risky business, getting anything into Boston these days—but well worth it if you do. Rice and smoked fish like to be worth their weight in gold up there, if you can get it ashore without the navy's warships blowing you out of the water."

Jamie, looking a little pale, thanked the man. Roger, unable to speak for the knot in his throat, merely nodded, and followed his father-in-law out of the harbormaster's office, back into the sun of the docks.

"Now what?" Ian asked, stifling a belch. He had been trawling through the dockside taverns, buying beer for casual laborers who might have helped load *Anemone,* or who might have spoken with her hands regarding her destination.

"The best I can think of is maybe for you and Roger Mac to take ship down the coast," Jamie said, frowning at the masts of the sloops and packet boats rocking at anchor. "Claire and I could go up, toward Boston."

Roger nodded, still unable to speak. It was far from being a good plan, particularly in light of the disruption the undeclared war was having on shipping—but the need of doing *something* was acute. He felt as though the marrow of his bones was burning; only movement would quench it.

To hire a small ship—even a fishing smack—or take passage on a packet boat, though, was expensive business.

"Aye, well." Jamie curled his hand in his pocket, where the black diamond still lay. "I'll go and see Judge Iredell; he can maybe put me in touch with an honest banker who'll advance me money against the sale of the stone. Let's go and tell Claire what's to do, first."

As they turned off the docks, though, a voice hailed Roger.

"Mr. MacKenzie!"

He turned, to find the Reverend Doctor McCorkle, his secretary, and the Reverend McMillan, carrying bags, all staring at him.

There was a brief scuffle of introduction—they had of course met Jamie when he came to fetch Roger, but not Ian—and then a slightly awkward pause.

"You—" Roger cleared his throat, addressing the elder. "You are leaving, then, sir? For the Indies?"

McCorkle nodded, his large, kindly face set in concern.

"I am, sir. I regret so much that I must go—and that you were not able to—well." Both McCorkle and the Reverend McMillan had tried to persuade him to return to them the day before, to take his place at the service of ordination. But he could not. Could not spare hours to such a thing, could not possibly engage himself to undertake the commitment with anything less than a single mind—and while his mind was in fact single just now, it was not toward God. There was room in his heart just now for only one thing—Brianna.

"Well, doubtless it is God's will," McCorkle said with a sigh. "Your wife, Mr. MacKenzie? There is no word of her?"

He shook his head, and muttered acknowledgment of their concern, their promises to pray for him and for the safe return of his wife. He was too much worried to find this much solace, yet still, he was touched by their kindness, and parted from them with many good wishes in both directions.

Roger, Jamie, and Ian walked silently back toward the inn where they had left Claire.

"Just by way of curiosity, Ian, what did ye do with Forbes's ear?" Jamie asked, breaking the silence as they turned into the wide street where the inn was.

"Oh, I have it safe, Uncle," Ian assured him, patting the small leather pouch at his belt.

"What in the name of G—" Roger stopped abruptly, then resumed. "What d'ye mean to do with it?"

"Keep it with me until we find my cousin," Ian said, seeming surprised that this was not obvious. "It will help."

"It will?"

Ian nodded, serious.

"When ye set about a difficult quest—if ye're Kahnyen'kehaka, I mean—ye generally go aside for a time, to fast and pray for guidance. We havena time to be doing that now, of course. But often, while ye're doing that, ye choose a talisman—or to be right about it, it chooses you—" He sounded completely matter-of-fact about this procedure, Roger noted.

"And ye carry it with ye through the quest, to keep the attention of the spirits upon your desire and ensure your success."

"I see." Jamie rubbed the bridge of his nose. He appeared—

like Roger—to be wondering what the Mohawk spirits might make of Gerald Forbes's ear. It would, probably, ensure their attention, at least. "The ear . . . did ye pack it in salt, I hope?"

Ian shook his head.

"Nay, I smoked it over the kitchen fire at the inn last night. Dinna fash yourself, Uncle Jamie; it will keep."

Roger found a perverse sort of comfort in this conversation. Between the prayers of the Presbyterian clergy and the support of the Mohawk spirits, perhaps they had a chance—but it was the presence of his two kinsmen, stalwart and determined on either side of him, that kept him in hope. They would not give up until Brianna was found, no matter what it took.

He swallowed the lump in his throat for the thousandth time since hearing the news, thinking of Jemmy. The little boy was safe at River Run—but how could he tell Jem that his mother was gone? Well . . . he wouldn't, that was all. They'd find her.

In this mood of resolution, he led the way through the door of the Brewster, only to be hailed again.

"Roger!"

This time, it was Claire's voice, sharp with excitement. He turned at once, to see her rising from a bench in the taproom. Seated across the table from her were a plump young woman and a slightly built young man with a cap of tightly curled black hair. Manfred McGillivray.

"I SAW YE before, sir, two days ago." Manfred bobbed his head apologetically toward Jamie. "I . . . er . . . well, I hid myself, sir, and I do regret it. But of course, I'd no way of knowing, until Eppie came back from Roanoke and showed me the ring. . . ."

The ring lay on the table, its cabochon ruby casting a tiny, calm pool of ruddy light on the boards. Roger picked it up and turned it in his fingers. He barely heard the explanations—that Manfred lived with the whore, who made periodic expeditions to the ports near Edenton, and upon seeing the ring had overcome his sense of shame and come to find Jamie—

too much overcome by this small, hard, tangible evidence of Brianna.

Roger closed his fingers over it, finding the warmth of it a comfort, and came to himself in time to hear Hepzibah say earnestly, "Ocracoke, sir. At the dark of the moon." She coughed modestly, ducking her head. "The lady did say, sir, as you might feel some gratitude for the news of her whereabouts. . . ."

"Ye'll be paid, and paid well," Jamie assured her, though he was clearly giving her no more than a fraction of his attention. "The dark of the moon," he said, turning to Ian. "Ten days?"

Ian nodded, his face shining with excitement.

"Aye, about that. She didna ken whereabouts on Ocracoke Island this was?" he asked the whore.

Eppie shook her head.

"Nay, sir. I ken Stephen's got a house there, a large one, hidden in the trees, but that's all."

"We'll find it." Roger's own voice surprised him; he hadn't meant to speak aloud.

Manfred had been looking uneasy throughout. He leaned forward, putting his hand on top of Eppie's.

"Sir—when ye do find it . . . ye'll not say to anybody, will ye, about Eppie telling ye? Mr. Bonnet's a dangerous man, and I wouldna have her imperiled from him." He glanced at the young woman, who blushed and smiled at him.

"No, we won't say anything about her," Claire assured him. She had been scrutinizing both Manfred and Hepzibah carefully while they talked, and now leaned across the table to touch Manfred's forehead, which showed a stippling of some sort of rash. "Speaking of peril . . . she's in a great deal more danger from *you,* young man, than from Stephen Bonnet. Did you tell her?"

Manfred went a little paler, and for the first time, Roger noticed that the young man looked truly ill, his face thin and deeply lined.

"I did, *Frau* Fraser. From the first."

"Oh, about the pox?" Hepzibah affected nonchalance, though Roger could see her hand tighten on Manfred's. "Aye, he did tell me. But I says to him as it makes no difference. I daresay I've had a few men what are poxed before, not knowing. If I should get it . . . well. God's will, innit?"

"No," Roger said to her quite gently. "It isn't. But you'll go with Mrs. Claire, you and Manfred both, and do exactly what she tells you. Ye'll be all right, and so will he. Won't they?" he asked, turning to Claire, suddenly a little uncertain.

"Yes, they will," she said dryly. "Fortunately, I have quite a bit of penicillin with me."

Manfred's face was a study in confusion.

"But—do ye mean, *meine Frau,* that ye can—can *cure* it?"

"That is exactly what I mean," Claire assured him, "as I tried to tell you before you ran away."

His mouth hung open, and he blinked. Then he turned to Hepzibah, who was staring at him in puzzlement.

"*Liebchen!* I can go home! *We* can go home," he amended quickly, seeing her face change. "We will be married. We will go home," he repeated, in the tones of one seeing a beatific vision but not quite trusting in its reality yet.

Eppie was frowning in uncertainty.

"I'm a whore, Freddie," she pointed out. "And from the stories you tell about your mother . . ."

"I rather think that *Frau* Ute will be so happy to have Manfred back that she won't be disposed to ask too many questions," Claire said, with a glance at Jamie. "The Prodigal Son, you know?"

"Ye won't need to be a whore any longer," Manfred assured her. "I'm a gunsmith; I'll earn a good living. Now that I know I *shall* be living!" His thin face was suddenly suffused with joy, and he flung his arms around Eppie and kissed her.

"Oh," she said, flustered, but looking pleased. "Well. Hm. This . . . er . . . this penny—?" She looked inquiringly at Claire.

"The sooner, the better," Claire said, standing up. "Come with me." Her own face was a little flushed, Roger saw, and she put out a quick hand to Jamie, who took it and pressed it hard.

"We'll go and see to things," he said, glancing at Ian and Roger in turn. "With luck, we'll sail this evening."

"Oh!" Eppie had already stood up to follow Claire, but at

this reminder of their business, she turned to Jamie, a hand to her mouth. "Oh. I've thought of the one more thing." Her pleasant round face was puckered in concentration. "There are wild horses that run near the house. On Ocracoke. I heard Stephen speak o' them once." She looked from one man to the other. "Might that help?"

"It might," Roger said. "Thank you—and God bless you."

It wasn't until they were outside, heading for the docks again, that he realized the ring was still clutched tight in his hand. What was it Ian had said?

"Ye choose a talisman—or to be right about it, it chooses you."

His hands were slightly bigger than Brianna's, but he pushed the ring onto his finger, and closed his hand around it.

SHE WOKE FROM a damp and restless sleep, mother-sense at once aroused. She was halfway out of bed, moving by instinct toward Jemmy's trundle, when a hand grabbed her wrist, a convulsive grip like the bite of a crocodile.

She jerked back, groggy and alarmed. The sound of footsteps came to her from the deck overhead and she realized belatedly that the sound of distress that had wakened her had not come from Jemmy, but from the darkness at her side.

"Don't go," he whispered, and the fingers dug deep into the soft flesh of her inner wrist.

Unable to wrench free, she reached out with the other hand, to push him away. She touched damp hair, hot skin—and a trickle of wetness, cool and surprising on her fingers.

"What is it?" she whispered back, and leaned toward him by instinct. She reached again, touched his head, smoothed his hair—all the things she had waked prepared to do. She felt her hand rest on him and thought to stop, but did not. It was as though the spurt of maternal comfort, once called forth, could not be pressed back into her, no more than the spurt of breast milk summoned by an infant's cry could be recalled to its source.

"Are you all right?" She kept her voice low, and as impersonal as the words allowed. She lifted her hand, and he moved, rolling toward her, pressing his head hard against the curve of her thigh.

"Don't go," he said again, and caught his breath in what might have been a sob. His voice was low and rough, but not as she had ever heard it before.

"I'm here." Her trapped wrist was growing numb. She laid her free hand on his shoulder, hoping he would let go if she seemed willing to stay.

He did relax his grip, but only to reach out and seize her by the waist, pulling her back into bed. She went, because there was no choice, and lay in silence, Bonnet's breathing harsh and warm on the back of her neck.

At length, he let go and rolled onto his back with a sigh, allowing her to move. She rolled onto her own back, cautious, trying to keep a few inches between them. Moonlight came through the stern windows in a silver flood, and she could see the silhouette of his face, catch the glint of light from forehead and cheek as he turned his head.

"Bad dream?" she ventured. She'd meant to sound sarcastic, but her own heart was still tripping fast from the alarm of the awakening, and the words had a tentative sound.

"Aye, aye," he said with a shuddering sigh. "The same. It comes to me over and over again, see? Ye'd think I'd know what it was about and wake, but I never do. Not 'til the waters close over my head." He rubbed a hand under his nose, sniffing like a child.

"Oh." She didn't want to ask for details, didn't want to encourage any further sense of intimacy. What she wanted, though, had nothing much to do with things anymore.

"Since I was a lad, I've dreamed of drowning," he said, and his voice, normally so assured, was unsteady. "The sea comes in, and I cannot move—not at all. The tide's risin', and I know it will kill me, but there's no way to move." His hand clutched the sheet convulsively, pulling it away from her.

"It's gray water, full of mud, and there are blind things swimmin' in it. They're waitin' on the sea to finish its business wit' me, see—and then they've business of their own."

She could hear the horror of it in his voice, and was torn between wanting to edge farther away from him and the ingrained habit of offering comfort.

"It was only a dream," she said at last, staring up at the boards of the deck, no more than three feet above her head. If only *this* were a dream!

"Ah, no," he said, and his voice had dropped to little more than a whisper in the darkness beside her. "Ah, no. It's the sea herself. Callin' me, see?"

Quite suddenly, he rolled toward her, seizing her and pressing her hard against him. She gasped, stiffening, and he pressed harder, responding, sharklike, to her struggles.

To her own horror, she felt LeRoi rising, and forced herself to be still. Panic and the need to escape his dream might all too easily make him forget his aversion to having sex with pregnant women, and that was the very last thing, the *very* last thing . . .

"Sshh," she said firmly, and clutched him round the head, forcing his face down into her shoulder, patting him, stroking his back. "Shh. It will be all right. It was only a dream. I won't let it hurt you—I won't let anything hurt you. Hush, hush now."

She went on patting him, her eyes closed, trying to imagine herself holding Jemmy after such a nightmare, quiet in their cabin, the hearth fire low, Jem's little body relaxing in trust, the sweet little-boy smell of his hair near her face. . . .

"I won't let you drown," she whispered. "I promise. I won't let you drown."

She said it over and over, and slowly, slowly, his breathing eased, and his grip on her slackened as sleep overcame him. Still she repeated it, a soft, hypnotic murmur, her words half-lost in the sound of water, hissing past the side of the ship, and she spoke no longer to the man beside her, but to the slumbering child within.

"I won't let anything hurt you. *Nothing* will hurt you. I promise."

106

RENDEZVOUS

ROGER PAUSED TO WIPE the sweat out of his eyes. He'd tied a folded kerchief round his head, but the humidity in the thick growth of the tidal forest was so high that sweat formed in his eye sockets, stinging and blurring his vision.

From a taproom in Edenton, the knowledge that Bonnet was—or would be—on Ocracoke had seemed all heady conviction; the search narrowed suddenly to one tiny sandbar, versus the millions of other places the pirate could have been; how difficult could it be? Once *on* the bloody sandbar, the perspective had altered. The frigging island was narrow, but several miles long, with large patches of scrub forest, and most of its coastline fraught with hidden bars and dangerous eddies.

The skipper of the fishing boat they'd hired had got them there in good time; then they'd spent two days sailing up and down the length of the damn thing, looking for possible landing spots, likely pirate hideouts, and herds of wild horses. So far, none of these had appeared.

Having spent long enough retching over the side—Claire hadn't brought her acupuncture needles, having not foreseen the need of them—Jamie had insisted upon being put ashore. He would walk the length of the island, he said, keeping an eye out for anything untoward. They could pick him up at sundown.

"And what if you run smack into Stephen Bonnet, all on your own?" Claire had demanded, when he refused to allow her to accompany him.

"I'd rather be run through than puke to death," was Jamie's elegant reply, "and besides, Sassenach, I need ye to stay here and make sure yon misbegotten son of a—of a captain doesna sail away without us, aye?"

So they had rowed him ashore and left him, watching as he strode away, staggering only slightly, into the thicket of scrub pines and palmetto.

Another day of frustration, spent sailing slowly up and down the coast, seeing nothing but the occasional ramshackle fishing shack, and Roger and Ian had begun to see the wisdom of Jamie's approach, as well.

"See yon houses?" Ian pointed at a tiny cluster of shacks on the shore.

"If ye want to call them that, yes." Roger shaded his hand over his eyes to look, but the shacks looked deserted.

"If they can get boats off there, we can get one on. Let's go ashore and see will the folk there tell us anything."

Leaving Claire glowering behind them, they had rowed ashore to make inquiries—to no avail. The only inhabitants of the tiny settlement were a few women and children, all of whom heard the name "Bonnet" and scuttled into their homes like clams digging into the sand.

Still, having felt solid ground under their feet, they were less than eager to admit defeat and go back to the fishing shack. "Let's have a look, then," Ian had said, gazing thoughtfully into the sun-striped forest. "We'll crisscross, aye?" He drew a quick series of X's in the sand in illustration. "We'll cover more ground, and meet up every so often. Whoever reaches the shore first each time will wait on the other."

Roger had nodded agreement, and with a cheery wave at the fishing boat and the small, indignant figure on its bow, had turned inland.

It was hot and still under the pines, and his progress was impaired by all sorts of low bushes, creepers, patches of sandburs and other stickery things. The going was a little easier near the shore, as the forest thinned and gave way to stretches of coarse sea oats, with dozens of tiny crabs that scuttled out of his way—or occasionally crunched under his feet.

Still, it was a relief to move, to feel that somehow he was doing something, was making progress toward finding Bree—though he admitted to himself that he wasn't sure exactly what they were looking for. Was she here? Had Bonnet arrived on the island already? Or would he be coming in a day or two, at the dark of the moon, as Hepzibah had said?

Despite the worry, the heat, and the millions of gnats and mosquitoes—they didn't bite, for the most part, but insisted upon crawling into his ears, eyes, nose, and mouth—he smiled at the thought of Manfred. He'd been praying for the boy ever since his disappearance from the Ridge, that he might be restored to his family. Granted, to find him firmly attached to an ex-prostitute was likely not quite the answer to prayer that Ute McGillivray had been hoping for, but he'd learned before that God had His own methods.

Lord, let her be safe. He didn't care how that prayer was answered, provided only that it was. *Let me have her back, please.*

It was well past mid-afternoon, and his clothes stuck to him with sweat, when he came to one of the dozens of small tidal inlets that cut into the island like the holes in Swiss cheese. It was too wide to leap across, so he made his way down the sandy bank and into the water. It was deeper than he'd thought—he was up to his neck by mid-channel, and had to swim a few strokes before he found solid footing on the other side.

The water pulled at him, rushing toward the sea; the tide had begun to turn. Likely the inlet would be much shallower when the tide was out—but he thought a boat could make it up the inlet easily, with the tide coming in.

That was promising. Encouraged, he crawled out on the far side and began to follow the channel inland. Within minutes, he heard a sound in the distance and stopped dead, listening.

Horses. He would swear it was the sound of neighing, though so far away he couldn't be sure of it. He turned in a circle, trying to locate it, but the sound had vanished. Still, it seemed a sign, and he pushed on with renewed vigor, frightening a family of raccoons washing their meal in the water of the channel.

But then the inlet began to narrow, the water level dropping to no more than a foot—and then less, only a few inches of water running clear over dusky sand. He was loath to give up, though, and shoved his way under a low canopy of pine and twisted scrub oak. Then he stopped dead, skin tingling from scalp to sole.

Four of them. Crude stone pillars, pale in the shadow of the trees. One stood actually in the channel itself, tilted drunkenly by the action of the water. Another, on the bank, had carvings on its face, abstract symbols that he didn't recognize. He stood frozen, as though they were live things that might see him if he moved.

It seemed abnormally silent; even the insects seemed temporarily to have deserted him. He had no doubt that this was the circle the man Donner had described to Brianna. Here, the five men had chanted, walked their pattern, and turned, passing to the left of the inscribed stone. And here at least one of them had died. A profound shiver ran through him, despite the oppressive heat.

He moved at last, very carefully, backing away, as though the stones might wake, but did not turn his back on them until he was a good distance away—so far away that the stones were lost to sight, buried in the heavy growth. Then he turned and walked back toward the sea, fast, and then faster, 'til the breath burned in his throat, feeling as though invisible eyes bored into his back.

I SAT IN the shade of the forecastle, sipping cool beer and watching the shore. Just like bloody men, I thought, frowning at the tranquil stretch of sand. Charge in pigheaded, leaving the women to mind the store. Still . . . I wasn't so sure that I would have wanted to slog the length of the beastly island on foot myself. By repute, Blackbeard and a number of his confederates had used the place as a lair, and the reason why was obvious. A less hospitable shore I'd seldom seen.

The chance of finding anything in that secretive, wooded place by randomly poking into holes was low. Still, sitting on my bum in a boat while Brianna was dealing with Stephen Bonnet was making me twitch with anxiety and the urgent desire to *do* something.

But there was nothing *to* do, and the afternoon wore slowly away. I watched the shore steadily; now and then, I would see Roger or Ian pop out of the undergrowth, then the two of them would confer briefly before popping back in. Now and then, I looked to the north—but there was no sign of Jamie.

Captain Roarke, who *was* in fact a misbegotten son of a poxed whore, as he cheerfully admitted himself, sat down with me for a time and accepted a bottle of beer. I congratulated myself on my forethought in having brought a few dozen, a few of which I'd put over the side in a net to keep cool; the beer was doing a lot to soothe my impatience, though my stomach was still knotted with worry.

"None o' your men are what ye might call sailing men, are they?" Captain Roarke observed, after a thoughtful silence.

"Well, Mr. MacKenzie's spent a bit of time on fishing boats in Scotland," I said, dropping an empty bottle into the net. "But I wouldn't say he's an able seaman, no."

"Ah." He drank a bit more.

"All right," I said finally. "Why?"

He lowered his bottle and belched loudly, then blinked.

"Oh. Well, ma'am—I believe I did hear one o' the young men say as how there was a rondayvooz to occur, at dark o' moon?"

"Yes," I said a little guardedly. We had told the captain as little as possible, not knowing whether he might have some association with Bonnet. "The dark of the moon is tomorrow night, isn't it?"

"It is," he agreed. "But what I mean to say is—when one says 'dark o' moon,' most likely one *does* mean nighttime, aye?" He peered into the empty neck of his bottle, then lifted it and blew thoughtfully across it, making a deep *wooooog* sound.

I took the hint and handed him another.

"Thank you kindly, ma'am," he said, looking happy. "See, the tide turns about half-eleven, this time o' month—and it's going *out,*" he added with emphasis.

I gave him a blank look.

"Well, if you look careful, ma'am, you'll see the tide is half out now"—he pointed toward the south—"yet there's middling deep water close to shore all along o' here. Come the nighttime, though, it won't be."

"Yes?" I was still missing his point, but he was patient.

"Well, with the tide out, it's easier to see the bars and inlets, sure—and were you coming in with a boat with a shallow draft, that would be the time to choose. But was the rondayvooz to be with something bigger, maybe anything that draws more than four feet . . . well, then." He took a gulp, and pointed the bottom of his bottle toward a spot far down the shore. "The water there is deep, ma'am—see the color of it? Was I a ship of any size, that would be the safest place to anchor, when the tide is on the ebb."

I regarded the spot he'd indicated. The water *was* distinctly darker there, a deeper blue-gray than the waves surrounding it.

"You could have told us that earlier," I said with a certain note of reproach.

"So I could, ma'am," he agreed cordially, "save for not knowin' as you'd like to hear it." He got up then and wandered toward the stern, an empty bottle in hand, absently going *woog-woog-woog,* like a distant foghorn.

As the sun sank into the sea, Roger and Ian appeared on the shore, and Captain Roarke's hand, Moses, rowed ashore to fetch them off. Then we hoisted sail and made our way slowly up the coast of Ocracoke, until we found Jamie, waving from a tiny spit of sand.

Anchored offshore for the night, we exchanged notes of our findings—or lack of them. All the men were drained, exhausted from heat and searching and with little appetite for supper, despite their exertions. Roger, in particular, looked drawn and pale, and said almost nothing.

The last sliver of the waning moon rose in the sky. With a minimum of conversation, the men took their blankets and lay down on deck, asleep within minutes.

Quantities of beer notwithstanding, I was wide awake. I sat beside Jamie, my own blanket wrapped about my shoulders against the coolness of the night wind, watching the low black mystery of the island. The anchorage Captain Roarke had pointed out to me was invisible in the darkness. Would we know, I wondered, if a ship were to come tomorrow night?

IN FACT, it came that night. I woke in the very early morning, dreaming of corpses. I sat up, heart pounding, to see Roarke and Moses at the rail, and a dreadful smell in the air. It wasn't a smell one would ever forget, and when I got to my feet and went to the rail to look, I was not at all surprised to hear Roarke murmur, "Slaver," nodding toward the south.

The ship was anchored half a mile or so away, its masts black against the paling sky. Not a huge ship, but definitely too big to make its way into the small channels of the island. I watched a long time, joined by Jamie, Roger, and Ian as they woke—but no boats were lowered.

"What d'ye suppose it's doing there?" Ian said. He spoke in a low voice; the slave ship made everyone nervous.

Roarke shook his head; he didn't like it, either.

"Damned if I know," he said. "Wouldn't expect such a thing in such a place. Not at all."

Jamie rubbed a hand across his unshaven chin. He hadn't shaved in days, and, green-faced and hollow-eyed beneath the stubble—he'd vomited over the rail within minutes of rising, though the swell was very gentle—looked even more disreputable than Roarke himself.

"Can ye lay us alongside her, Mr. Roarke?" he said, eyes on the slave ship. Roger glanced at him sharply.

"Ye don't suppose Brianna's aboard?"

"If she is, we'll find out. If she's not—we'll maybe find out who yon ship has come to see."

It was full daylight by the time we came along the ship, and there were a number of hands on deck, all of whom peered curiously down over the rail at us.

Roarke hallooed up, asking permission to come aboard. There was no immediate response to this, but after a few minutes, a large man with an air of authority and an ill-tempered face appeared.

"What d'ye want?" he called down.

"To come aboard," Roarke bellowed back.

"No. Shove off."

"We are in search of a young woman!" Roger called up. "We should like to ask you a few questions!"

"Any young women on this ship are mine," the captain—if that's what he was—said definitely. "Bugger off, I said." He turned and gestured to his hands, who scattered at once, reappearing in moments with muskets.

Roger cupped his hands to his mouth.

"BRIANNA!" he bellowed. "BRIANNAAAA!"

One man raised his gun and fired, the ball whistling safely over our heads, and ripping through the mainsail.

"Oi!" shouted Roarke, incensed. "What's the matter of you?"

The only answer to this was a fusillade of further shots, followed by the opening of the port lids nearest us, and the sudden appearance of the long black noses of several cannon, along with a more intense gust of stink.

"Jesus God," said Roarke, astonished. "Well, if that's how you feel about—well, God damn you!" he shouted, brandishing a fist. "God damn you, I say!"

Moses, less interested in rhetoric, had made sail with the first shot and was already at the tiller; we slid past the slave ship and into clean water within moments.

"Well, *something's* going on," I remarked, looking back at the ship. "Whether it's to do with Bonnet or not."

Roger was clinging to the rail, his knuckles white.

"It is," Jamie said. He wiped a hand across his mouth, and grimaced. "Can ye keep in sight of her, but out of range, Mr. Roarke?" A fresh wave of the smell of sewage, corruption, and hopelessness hit us, and he turned the color of rancid suet. "And maybe upwind, too?"

We were obliged to sail well out into the ocean and tack to and fro in order to meet these various conditions, but at length had beaten our way back and anchored a safe distance away, the slave ship barely visible. Here we lay through the rest of the day, taking it in turns to keep an eye on the strange ship through Captain Roarke's telescope.

Nothing happened, though; no boats came from the ship, nor from the shore. And as we all sat silent on deck, watching the stars come out in a moonless sky, the ship was swallowed by the dark.

107

THE DARK OF THE MOON

THEY ANCHORED LONG before dawn, and a small boat took them ashore.

"Where is *this*?" she asked, voice rusty with disuse—Bonnet had wakened her in the dark. They had made three stops along the way, at nameless coves where mysterious men came out of the shrubbery, rolling barrels or carrying bales, but she had not been taken off at any of them. This was a long, low island, thick with scrub forest and hazy with mist, looking haunted under a dying moon.

"Ocracoke," he answered, leaning forward to peer into the fog. "A bit farther to port, Denys." The seaman at the oars leaned harder to the side, and the nose of the boat turned slowly, drawing nearer to the shore.

It was cold on the water; she was grateful for the thick cloak he had wrapped around her before handing her into the boat. Even so, the chill of the night and the open sea had little to do with the small, constant shiver that made her hands tremble and numbed her feet and fingers.

Soft murmurs between the pirates, further direction. Bonnet jumped off into waist-deep, muddy water, and waded into the shadows, pushing aside the heavy growth so that the water of the hidden inlet showed suddenly, a smooth dark gleam before them. The boat nosed its way under the overhanging trees, then paused, so that Bonnet could pull himself over the gunwales, splashing and dripping.

A shattering cry sounded near them, so close that she jerked, heart pounding, before realizing that it was only a bird somewhere in the swamp around them. Otherwise, the night was quiet, save for the muted, regular splash of the oars.

They had put Josh and the Fulani men into the boat, too;

Josh sat at her feet, a hunched black form. He was shivering; she could feel it. Disengaging a fold of the cloak, she put it over him, and put a hand on his shoulder under it, meaning to give him what encouragement she could. A hand rose and settled softly over hers, squeezing, and thus linked, they sailed slowly into the dark unknown beneath the dripping trees.

The sky was lightening by the time the boat reached a small landing, and streaks of rose-tinted cloud reached across the horizon. Bonnet hopped out, and reached down to take her hand. Reluctantly, she let go of Josh, and stood up.

There was a house, half-hidden in the trees. Made of gray clapboards, it seemed to sink into the remnants of fog, as though it weren't quite real and might disappear at any moment.

The wind-borne stink, though, was real enough. She'd never smelled it before herself, but had heard her mother's vivid description of it, and recognized it instantly—the smell of a slaver, anchored offshore. Josh recognized it, too; she heard his sudden gasp, and then a hasty murmur—he was saying the Hail Mary in Gaelic, as fast as he could.

"Take these to the barracoon," Bonnet said to the seaman, pushing Josh in his direction and waving at the Fulani. "Then go back to the ship. Tell Mr. Orden we sail for England in four days' time; he'll see to the rest of the provisioning. Come for me Saturday, an hour before high tide."

"Josh!" She called after him, and he looked back, eyes white with fear, but the seaman hustled him along, and Bonnet dragged her in the other direction, up the path toward the house.

"Wait! Where is he taking him? What are you going to do with him?" She dug her feet into the mud, and grabbed hold of a mangrove, refusing to move.

"Sell him, what else?" Bonnet was matter-of-fact about that, and also about her refusal to move. "Come along, darlin'. Ye know I can make ye, and ye know ye won't like it if I do." He reached out, flipped back the edge of her cloak, and pinched her nipple, hard, in illustration.

Burning with anger, she snatched the cloak back and wrapped it tight around her, as though that might soothe the pain. He had already turned, and was making his way up the path, quite certain that she would follow. To her everlasting shame, she did.

THE DOOR WAS opened by a black man, nearly as tall as Bonnet himself, and even wider through the chest and shoulder. A thick vertical scar between his eyes ran nearly from his hairline to the bridge of his nose, but it had the clean look of a deliberate tribal scar, not the result of accident.

"Emmanuel, me man!" Bonnet greeted the man cheerfully, and pushed Brianna ahead of him into the house. "Look what the cat dragged in, will ya?"

The black man looked her up and down with an expression of doubt.

"She damn tall," he said, in a voice that held an African lilt. He took her by the shoulder and turned her round, running a hand down her back and cupping her buttocks briefly through the cloak. "Nice fat arse, though," he admitted grudgingly.

"Isn't it, though? Well, be seeing to her, then come tell me how it is here. The hold's near full—oh, and I've picked up four—no, five—more blacks. The men can go to Captain Jackson, but the women—ah, now, those are somethin' special." He winked at Emmanuel. "Twins."

The black man's face went rigid.

"Twins?" he said in a tone of horror. "You bring them in the house?"

"I will," Bonnet said firmly. "Fulani, and gorgeous things they are, too. No English, no training—but they'll go for fancies, sure. Speakin' of which, have we word from *Signor* Ricasoli?"

Emmanuel nodded, though his brow was furrowed; the scar pulled the frown lines into a deep "V."

"He be here on Thursday. *Monsieur* Houvener comes then, too. Mister Howard be here tomorrow, though."

"Splendid. I'm wanting me breakfast now—and I imagine you're hungry as well, aren't ye, darlin'?" he asked, turning to Brianna.

She nodded, torn between fear, outrage, and morning sickness. She had to eat something, and fast.

"Fine, then. Take her somewhere"—he flipped a hand toward the ceiling, indicating rooms upstairs—"and feed her. I'll eat in me office; come find me there."

Without acknowledgment of the order, Emmanuel clamped a hand like a vise on the back of her neck, and shoved her toward the stairs.

THE BUTLER—if one could describe something like Emmanuel with such a domestic term—pushed her into a small room and shut the door behind her. It was furnished, but sparsely: a bed frame with a bare mattress, one woolen blanket, and a chamber pot. She made use of the latter object with relief, then made a rapid reconnaissance of the room itself.

There was only one window, a small one, set with metal bars. There was no glass, only inside shutters, and the breath of sea and scrub forest filled the room, vying with dust and the stale smell of the stained mattress. Emmanuel might be a factotum, but he wasn't much of a housekeeper, she thought, trying to keep her spirits up.

A familiar sound came to her, and she craned her neck to see. Not much was visible from the window—only the white crushed shells and sandy mud that surrounded the house, and the tops of stunted pines. If she pressed her face to the side of the window, though, she could see a small slice of a distant beach, with white breakers rolling in. As she watched, three horses galloped across it, vanishing out of her view—but with the wind-borne sound of neighing, then came five more, and then another group of seven or eight. Wild horses, the descendants of Spanish ponies left here a century ago.

The sight of them charmed her, and she watched for a long time, hoping they would come back, but they didn't; only a flight of pelicans passed by, and a few gulls, diving for fish.

The sight of the horses had made her feel less alone for a few moments, but no less empty. She had been in the room for half an hour, at least, and there were no sounds of footsteps in the hall outside, bringing food. Cautiously, she tried the door, and was surprised to find it unlocked.

There *were* sounds downstairs; someone was here. And the warm, grainy aromas of porridge and baking bread were faint in the air.

Swallowing to keep her stomach down, she moved soft-footed through the house and down the stairs. There were male voices in a room at the front of the house—Bonnet and Emmanuel. The sound of them made her diaphragm tighten, but the door was closed, and she tiptoed past.

The kitchen was a cookshack, a separate small building outside, connected to the house by a short breezeway and surrounded by a fenced yard that also enclosed the back of the house. She gave the fence—very tall, and spiked—a glance, but first things first: she had to have food.

There was someone in the kitchen; she could hear the movements of pots, and a woman's voice, muttering something. The smell of food was strong enough to lean against. She pushed open the door and went in, pausing to let the cook see her. Then she saw the cook.

She was so battered by circumstance at this point that she only blinked, certain she was seeing things.

"Phaedre?" she said uncertainly.

The girl swung around, wide-eyed and open-mouthed with shock.

"Oh, sweet Jesus!" She glanced wildly behind Brianna, then, seeing that she was alone, grabbed Brianna's arm and pulled her out into the yard.

"What you doing here?" she demanded, sounding fierce. "How do you come to be *here*?"

"Stephen Bonnet," Brianna said briefly. "How on earth did you—did he kidnap you? From River Run?" She couldn't think how—or why—but everything from the moment she had learned she was pregnant had had the surreal feel of hallucination, and how much of this was due to pregnancy alone she had no real idea.

Phaedre was shaking her head, though.

"No, miss. That Bonnet, he got me a month ago. From a man name Butler," she added, mouth twisting in an expression that made clear her loathing of Butler.

The name seemed vaguely familiar to Brianna. She thought it was the name of a smuggler; she had never met him, but had heard the name now and then. He wasn't the smuggler who provided her aunt with tea and other contraband luxuries, though—she *had* met that man, a disconcertingly effete and dainty gentleman named Wilbraham Jones.

"I don't understand. But—wait, is there anything to eat?" she asked, the floor of her stomach dropping suddenly.

"Oh. Surely. You wait here." Phaedre vanished back into the kitchen, light-footed, and was back in an instant with half a loaf of bread and a crock of butter.

"Thank you." She grabbed the bread and ate some hastily, not bothering to butter it, then put down her head between her knees and breathed for a few minutes, until the nausea subsided.

"Sorry," she said, raising her head at last. "I'm pregnant."

Phaedre nodded, plainly unsurprised.

"Who by?" she asked.

"My husband," Brianna answered. She'd spoken tartly, but then realized, with a small lurch of her unsettled innards, that it could so easily be otherwise. Phaedre had been gone from River Run for months—God only knew what had happened to her in that span of time.

"He's not had you long, then." Phaedre glanced at the house.

"No. You said a month—have you tried to get away?"

"Once." The girl's mouth twisted again. "You see that man Emmanuel?"

Brianna nodded.

"He an Ibo. Track a haunt through a cypress swamp, and make it sorry when he catch it." She wrapped her arms around herself, though the day was warm.

The yard was fenced with eight-foot pointed pine stakes, laced with rope. She might get over them, with a foot up from Phaedre . . . but then she saw the shadow of a man pass by on the other side, a gun across his shoulder.

She would have guessed as much, had she been capable of organized thought. This was Bonnet's hideaway—and judging from the piles of boxes, bundles, and casks stacked haphazardly in the yard, it was also where he kept valuable cargo before selling it. Naturally, it would be guarded.

A faint breeze wafted through the pickets of the fence, carrying the same vile stench she had smelled when they came ashore. She took another quick bite of bread, forcing it down as ballast for her queasy stomach.

Phaedre's nostrils flared, then pinched at the reek.

"Be a slave ship, anchored past the breakers," she said very quietly, and swallowed. "Captain come in yesterday, see if Mr. Bonnet have something for him, but he ain't back yet. Captain Jackson say he come again tomorrow."

Brianna could feel Phaedre's fear, like a pale yellow miasma wavering over her skin, and took another bite of bread.

"He won't—he wouldn't sell you to this Jackson?" She wouldn't put anything at all past Bonnet. But she did by now understand things about slavery. Phaedre was a prime item: light-skinned, young, and pretty—and trained as a body servant. Bonnet could get a very good price for her almost anywhere, and from what little she knew of slavers, they dealt in raw slaves from Africa.

Phaedre shook her head, her lips gone pale.

"I don't think so. He say I'm what he call a 'fancy.' That's why he's kept me so long; he got some men he know, come up from the Indies this week. Planters." She swallowed again, looking ill. "They buy pretty women."

The bread Brianna had eaten melted suddenly into a soggy, slimy mass in her stomach, and with a certain feeling of fatality, she got up and took a few steps away before throwing up over a bale of raw cotton.

Stephen Bonnet's voice echoed in her head, cheerfully jovial.

"Why bother takin' ye all the way to London, where ye'd be of no particular use to anyone? Besides, it rains quite a bit in London; I'm sure ye wouldn't like it."

"They buy pretty women," she whispered, leaning against the palisades, waiting for the sense of clamminess to fade. But *white* women?

Why not? said the coldly logical part of her brain. Women are property, black or white. If you can be owned, you can be sold. She herself had owned Lizzie, for a time.

She wiped her sleeve over her mouth, and went back to Phaedre, who was sitting on a roll of copper, her fine-boned face thin and drawn with worry.

"Josh—he took Josh, too. When we came ashore, he told them to take Josh to the barracoon."

"Joshua?" Phaedre sat up straight, eyes huge. "Joshua, Miss Jo's groom? He's *here*?"

"Yes. Where's the barracoon, do you know?"

Phaedre had hopped to her feet and was striding to and fro, agitated.

"I ain't knowing for sure. I cook up food for the slaves there, but be one of the seamen takes it. Can't be far from the house, though."

"Is it a big one?"

Phaedre shook her head emphatically at that.

"No'm. Mr. Bonnet, he ain't really in the slaving business. He pick up a few, here and there—and then he got his 'fancies'"—she grimaced at that—"but can't be more'n a dozen here, amount of food they eat. Three girls in the house—five, counting they Fulani he say he's bringing."

Feeling better, Brianna began to cast about the yard, searching for anything that might be of use. It was a hodgepodge of valuable things—everything from bolts of Chinese silk, wrapped in linen and oiled cloth, and crates of porcelain dishes, to rolls of copper, casks of brandy, bottles of wine packed in straw, and chests of tea. She opened one of these, breathing in the soft perfume of the leaves and finding it wonderfully soothing to her internal distress. She'd give almost anything for a hot cup of tea just now.

Even more interesting, though, were a number of small barrels, thick-walled and tightly sealed, containing gunpowder.

"If only I had a few matches," she muttered to herself, looking at them longingly. "Or even a striker." But fire was fire, and there was certainly one in the kitchen. She looked at the house carefully, thinking exactly where to place the barrels—but she couldn't blow the place up, not with the other slaves inside, and not without knowing what she'd do next.

The sound of the door opening galvanized her; by the time Emmanuel looked out, she had jumped away from the gunpowder, and was examining an enormous box enclosing a grandfather clock, the gilded face—decorated with three animated sailing ships on a sea of silver—peeping out behind the protective laths nailed over it.

"You, girl," he said to Brianna, and jerked his chin. "You come wash yourself." He gave Phaedre a hard look—Brianna saw that she wouldn't meet his eyes, but hastily began to pick up sticks of kindling from the ground.

The hand clamped hard on her neck again, and she was marched ignominiously back into the house.

THIS TIME, Emmanuel *did* lock the door. He brought her a basin and ewer, a towel, and a clean shift. Much, much later, he came back, bringing a tray of food. But he ignored all questions, and locked the door again upon leaving.

She pulled the bed over to the window and knelt on it, elbows wedged between the bars. There was nothing to do but think—and that was something she would as soon put off a little longer. She watched the forest and the distant beach, the shadows of the scrub pines creeping over the sand, the oldest of sundials, marking the snaillike progress of the hours.

After a long time, her knees grew numb and her elbows hurt, and she spread the cloak over the nasty mattress, trying not to consider the various stains on it, nor the smell. Lying on her side, she watched the sky through the window, the infinitesimal changes of the light from one moment to the next, and considered in detail the specific pigments and the exact brushstrokes she would use to paint it. Then she got up and began pacing to and fro, counting her steps, estimating distance.

The room was about eight feet by ten; 5,280 feet in a mile. Five hundred and twenty-eight laps. She really hoped Bonnet's office was underneath her.

Nothing, though, was enough, and as the room darkened and she reached two miles, she found Roger in her mind—where he had been all along, unacknowledged.

She sank down on the bed, hot from the exercise, and watched the last of the flaming color fade from the sky.

Had he been ordained, as he wanted so much? He had been worried about the question of predestination, not sure that he could take the Holy Orders he desired, if he were not able to subscribe wholeheartedly to that notion—well, *she* called it a notion; to Presbyterians, it was dogma. She smiled wryly, thinking of Hiram Crombie.

Ian had told her about Crombie earnestly attempting to explain the doctrine of predestination to the Cherokee. Most of them had listened politely, then ignored him. Bird's wife, Penstemon, though, had been interested by the argument, and followed Crombie about during the day, playfully pushing him, then crying out, 'Did your God know I would do *that*? How could he know that—*I* didn't know I would do that!', or in a more thoughtful mood, trying to get him to explain how the idea of predestination might work in terms of gambling—like most of the Indians, Penstemon would bet on almost anything.

She thought Penstemon had probably had a lot to do with the shortness of Crombie's initial visit to the Indians. She had to give him credit, though: he'd gone back. And back again. He believed in what he was doing.

As did Roger. Damn, she thought wearily, there he was again, those soft moss-green eyes of his dark with thought, running a finger slowly down the bridge of his nose.

"Does it really matter?" she'd said at last, tiring of the discussion of predestination, and privately pleased that Catholics weren't required to believe any such thing and were content to let God work in mysterious ways. "Doesn't it matter more that you can help people, that you can offer comfort?"

They'd been in bed, the candle extinguished, talking by the glow of the hearth. She could feel the shift of his body as he moved, his hand playing with a strand of her hair as he considered.

"I don't know," he'd said at last. He'd smiled a little then, looking up at her.

"Do ye not think any time-traveler must be a bit of a theologian, though?"

She'd taken a deep, martyred breath, and he'd laughed then, and let it go, kissing her instead and descending to far earthier matters.

He'd been right, though. No one who had traveled through the stones could help asking it: why me? And who would answer that question, if not God?

Why me? And the ones who didn't make it—why them? She felt a small chill, thinking of those. The anonymous bodies, listed in Geillis Duncan's notebook; Donner's companions, dead on arrival. And speaking of Geillis Duncan . . . the thought came to her suddenly; the witch had died *here,* out of her own time.

Putting metaphysics aside and looking at the matter purely in terms of science—and it *must* have a scientific basis, she argued stubbornly, it wasn't magic, no matter what Geillis Duncan had thought—the laws of thermodynamics held that neither mass nor energy could be created nor destroyed. Only changed.

Changed how, though? Did movement through time constitute change? A mosquito whined past her ear, and she flapped her hand to drive it away.

You could go both ways; they knew that for a fact. The obvious implication—which neither Roger nor her mother had mentioned, so perhaps they hadn't seen it—was that one could go into the future from a starting point, rather than only into the past and back.

So perhaps if someone traveled to the past and died there, as Geillis Duncan and Otter-Tooth had both demonstrably done . . . perhaps that must be balanced by someone traveling to the future and dying *there*?

She closed her eyes, unable—or unwilling—to follow that train of thought any further. Far in the distance, she heard the sound of the surf, pounding on the sand, and thought of the slave ship. Then she realized that the smell of it was *here,* and rising suddenly, went to the window. She could just see the far end of the path that led to the house; as she watched, a big man in a dark-blue coat and hat stumped rapidly out of the trees, followed by two others, shabbily dressed. *Sailors,* she thought, seeing the roll of their gait.

This must be Captain Jackson, then, come to conduct his business with Bonnet.

"Oh, Josh," she said out loud, and had to sit down on the bed, a wave of faintness washing over her.

Who had it been? One of the Saint Theresas—Theresa of Avila? Who'd said in exasperation to God, *"Well, if this is how You treat Your friends, no wonder You have so few of them!"*

SHE HAD FALLEN asleep thinking of Roger. She waked in the morning thinking of the baby.

For once, the nausea and the odd sense of dislocation were absent. All she felt was a deep peace, and a sense of . . . curiosity?

Are you there? she thought, hands across her womb. Nothing so definite as an answer; but knowledge was there, as sure as the beating of her own heart.

Good, she thought, and fell asleep again.

Noises from below awakened her sometime later. She sat up suddenly, hearing loud voices raised, then swayed, feeling faint, and lay down again. The nausea had returned, but if she closed her eyes and kept very still, it lay dormant, like a sleeping snake.

The voices continued, rising and falling, with the occasional loud thud for punctuation, as though a fist had struck a wall or table. After a few minutes, though, the voices ceased, and she heard nothing further until light footsteps came to her door. The lock rattled, and Phaedre came in, with a tray of food.

She sat up, trying not to breathe; the smell of anything fried . . .

"What's going on down there?" she asked.

Phaedre pulled a face.

"That Emmanuel, he's not best pleased with they Fulani women. Ibo, they think twins are bad, bad luck—any woman bear twins, she take them out in the forest, leave them there to die. Emmanuel want to send the Fulani off with Captain Jackson first thing, get them out the house, but Mr. Bonnet, he say he waiting on the gentlemen from the Indies, get a lots better price."

"Gentlemen from the Indies—what gentlemen?"

Phaedre lifted her shoulders.

"I ain't knowing. Gentlemen he think he sell things to. Sugar planters, I reckon. You eat that; I be back later."

Phaedre turned to go, but Brianna suddenly called after her.

"Wait! You didn't tell me yesterday—who took you from River Run?"

The girl turned back, looking reluctant.

"Mr. Ulysses."

"Ulysses?" Brianna said, disbelieving. Phaedre heard the doubt in her voice, and gave her a flat, angry look.

"What, you don't believe me?"

"No, no," Brianna hastily assured her. "I do believe you. Only—why?"

Phaedre breathed in deeply through her nose.

"Because I am one damn stupid nigger," she said bitterly. "My mama told me, she say never, ever cross Ulysses. But did I listen?"

"Cross him," Brianna said warily. "How did you cross him?" She gestured to the bed, inviting Phaedre to sit down. The girl hesitated for a moment, but then did, smoothing a hand over the white cloth tied round her head, over and over, while she searched for words.

"Mr. Duncan," she said at last, and her face softened a little. "He a nice, nice man. You know he never been with a woman? He got kicked by a horse when he young, hurt his balls, think he can't do nothing that way."

Brianna nodded; she'd heard something of Duncan's trouble from her mother.

"Well," Phaedre said with a sigh. "He wrong about that." She glanced at Brianna, to see how she might take this admission. "He wasn't meaning no harm, and nor was I. It just—happened." She shrugged. "But Ulysses, he find it out; he find out every single thing goes on at River Run, sooner or later. Maybe one of the girls told him, maybe some other way, but he knew. And he told me that ain't right, I put a stop to it this minute."

"But you didn't?" Brianna guessed.

Phaedre shook her head slowly, lips pushed out.

"Told him I'd stop when Mr. Duncan didn't want to no more—not *his* business. See, I thought Mr. Duncan, he the master. Ain't true, though; Ulysses be the master at River Run."

"So he—he took you away—sold you?—to stop you sleeping with Duncan?" Why would he care? she wondered. Was he afraid Jocasta would discover the affair and be hurt?

"No, he sell me because I told him if he don't leave me and Mr. Duncan be, then I tell about him and Miss Jo."

"Him and . . ." Brianna blinked, not believing what she was hearing. Phaedre looked at her, and gave a small, ironic smile.

"He share Miss Jo's bed these twenty years and more. Since before Old Master die, my mama said. Every slave there knows it; ain't one stupid enough to say so to his face, 'cept me."

Brianna knew she was gaping like a goldfish, but couldn't help it. A hundred tiny things she'd seen at River Run, myriad small intimacies between her aunt and the butler, suddenly took on new significance. No wonder her aunt had gone to such lengths to get him back after the death of Lieutenant Wolff. And no wonder, either, that Ulysses had taken instant action. Phaedre might have been believed, or not; the mere accusation would have destroyed him.

Phaedre sighed, and rubbed a hand over her face.

"He ain't waste no time. That very night, he and Mr. Jones come take me from my bed, wrap me up tight in a blanket, and carry me away in a wagon. Mr. Jones, he say he ain't no slaver, but he do it as a favor for Mr. Ulysses. So he don't keep me; he take me way downriver, though, sell me in Wilmington to a man what owns an ordinary. That's not too bad, but then a couple months later, Mr. Jones comes and takes me back—Wilmington's not far enough away to suit Ulysses. So he give me to Mr. Butler, and Mr. Butler, he take me to Edenton."

She looked down, pleating the quilt between long, graceful fingers. Her lips were tight, and her face slightly flushed. Brianna forbore to ask what she had done for Butler in Edenton, thinking that she had likely been employed in a brothel.

"And . . . er . . . Stephen Bonnet found you there?" she hazarded.

Phaedre nodded, not looking up.

"Won me in a card game," she said succinctly. She stood up. "I got to go; I had me enough of crossing black men—ain't risking no more beatings from that Emmanuel."

Brianna was beginning to emerge from the shock of hearing about Ulysses and her aunt. A sudden thought occurred to her, and she jumped out of bed, hurrying to catch Phaedre before she reached the door.

"Wait, wait! Just one more thing—do you—do the slaves at River Run—know anything about the gold?"

"What, in Old Master's tomb? Surely." Phaedre's face expressed a cynical surprise that there could be any doubt about it. "Ain't nobody touch it, though. Everybody know there a curse on it."

"Do you know anything about its disappearing?"

Phaedre's face went blank.

"Disappearing?"

"Oh, wait—no, you wouldn't know; you . . . left, long before it disappeared. I just wondered, you know, whether maybe Ulysses had something to do with that."

Phaedre shook her head.

"I don't know nothing about that. But I ain't put one thing past Ulysses, curse or no." There was a sound of heavy footsteps on the stair, and she paled. Without a word or gesture of farewell, she slipped out the door and closed it; Brianna heard the frantic fumbling of the key on the other side, and then the click of the closing lock.

EMMANUEL, silent as a lizard, brought her a dress in the afternoon. It was too short by a good bit, and too tight in the bosom, but a heavy blue watered silk, and well-made. It had plainly been worn before; there were sweat stains on it and it smelled—of fear, she thought, repressing a shudder as she struggled into it.

She was sweating herself as Emmanuel led her downstairs, though a pleasant breeze swept through the open windows, stirring the curtains. The house was very simple, for the most part, with bare wooden floors and little more than stools and bed frames by way of furniture. The room downstairs to which Emmanuel showed her was such a contrast that it might have belonged to a different house entirely.

Rich Turkey rugs covered the floor in a overlapping riot of color, and the furniture, while of several different styles, was all heavy and elaborate, carved wood and silk upholstery. Silver and crystal glittered from every available surface, and a chandelier—much too large for the room—hung with crystal pendants sprayed the room with tiny rainbows. It was a pirate's idea of a rich man's room—lavish abundance, displayed with no sense of style or taste.

The rich man seated by the window appeared not to mind his surroundings, though. A thin man in a wig, with a prominent Adam's apple, he looked to be in his thirties, though his skin was lined and yellowed by some tropical disease. He glanced sharply at the door as she entered, then rose to his feet.

Bonnet had been entertaining his guest; there were glasses and a decanter on the table, and the smell of brandy was sweet and heavy in the air. Brianna felt her stomach shift queasily, and wondered what they'd do if she were to vomit on the Turkey rug.

"There ye are, darlin'," Bonnet said, coming to take her by the hand. She pulled it away from him, but he affected not to notice, and instead pushed her toward the thin man, a hand in the small of her back. "Come and make your bob to Mr. Howard, sweetheart."

She drew herself to her full height—she was a good four inches taller than Mr. Howard, whose eyes widened at sight of her—and glowered down at him.

"I am being held against my will, Mr. Howard. My husband and my father will—ow!" Bonnet had gripped her wrist and twisted it, hard.

"Lovely, is she not?" he said conversationally, as though she had not spoken.

"Oh, yes. Yes, indeed. Very *tall,* though . . ." Howard walked round her, examining her dubiously. "And red hair, Mr. Bonnet? I do really prefer blond."

"Oh, do you indeed, you little pissant!" she snapped, in spite of Bonnet's grip on her arm. "Where do you get off, preferring things?" With a wrench, she pulled away from Bonnet and rounded on Howard.

"Now, look," she said, trying to sound reasonable—he was blinking at her in a faintly bewildered fashion— "I am a woman of good—of *excellent*—family, and I have been kidnapped. My father's name is James Fraser, my husband is Roger MacKenzie, and my aunt is Mrs. Hector Cameron, of River Run Plantation."

"Is she really of good family?" Howard addressed this question to Bonnet, appearing to be more interested.

Bonnet bowed slightly in affirmation.

"Oh, indeed she is, sir. The finest blood!"

"Hmmm. And good health, I see." Howard had resumed his examination, leaning close to peer at her. "Has she bred before?"

"Aye, sir, a healthy son."

"Good teeth?" Howard rose on his toes, looking inquisitive, and Bonnet obligingly yanked one arm behind her back to hold her still, then took a handful of her hair and jerked her head back, making her gasp.

Howard took her chin in one hand and pried at the corner of her mouth with the other, poking experimentally at her molars.

"Very nice," he said approvingly. "And I will say the skin is very fine. But—"

She jerked her chin out of his grasp, and bit down as hard as she could on Howard's thumb, feeling the meat of it shift and tear between her molars with a sudden copper taste of blood.

He shrieked and struck at her; she let go and dodged, enough so his hand glanced off her cheek. Bonnet let go, and she took two fast steps back and fetched up hard against the wall.

"She's bitten me thumb off, the bitch!" Eyes watering in agony, Mr. Howard swayed to and fro, cradling his wounded hand against his chest. Fury flooded his face and he lunged toward her, free hand drawn back, but Bonnet seized him by the wrist and pulled him aside.

"Now then, sir," he said. "I cannot allow ye to damage her, sure. She's not yours yet, is she?"

"I don't care if she's mine or not," Howard cried, face suffused with blood. "I'll beat her to death!"

"Oh, no, surely ye don't mean that, Mr. Howard," Bonnet said, his voice jovially soothing. "A cruel waste that would be. Leave her to me, will ye, then?" Not waiting for an answer, he pulled Brianna after him, dragging her stumbling across the room, and thrust her toward the silent factotum, who had waited motionless by the door through the conversation.

"Take her out, Manny, and teach her her manners, will ye? And gag her before ye bring her back."

Emmanuel didn't smile, but a faint light seemed to burn in the black depths of his pupilless eyes. His fingers dug between the bones of her wrist and she gasped with pain, jerking in a vain attempt to free herself. With a single quick movement, the Ibo whirled her round and twisted up her arm behind her back, bending her half forward. Sharp pain shot up her arm as she felt her shoulder tendons begin to part. He pulled harder and a dark wave passed over her vision. Through it, she heard Bonnet's voice calling out behind them as Emmanuel propelled her through the door.

"Not in the face, mind, Manny, and no permanent marks."

HOWARD'S VOICE had quite lost its choked note of fury. It was still choked, but with something more like awe.

"My God," he said. "Oh, my God."

"A charmin' sight, is it not?" Bonnet agreed cordially.

"Charming," Howard echoed. "Oh—the most charming thing I believe I have ever seen. Such a shade! Might I—" The hunger in his voice was evident, and Brianna felt the vibration of his footstep on the carpet, a split second before his hands clamped tight on her buttocks. She screamed behind the gag, but she was bent hard across the table, with the edge cutting into her diaphragm, and the sound came out as no more than a grunt. Howard laughed joyfully, and let go.

"Oh, look," he said, sounding enchanted. "Look, do you see? The most perfect print of my hands—so white on the crimson . . . she is so *hot* . . . oh, it's fading. Let me just—"

She clenched her legs tight together and stiffened as he fondled her naked privates, but then his touch was gone, and Bonnet had taken his hand off her neck, and was pulling his customer away from her.

"Ah, now, that's enough, sir. After all, she's not your property—not yet." Bonnet's tone was jovial, but firm. Howard's response was immediately to offer a sum that made her gasp behind the gag, but Bonnet only laughed.

"That's generous, sir, so it is, but 'twouldn't be fair on my other customers, would it, to be takin' your offer without letting them make their own? No, sir, I do appreciate it, but I mean to auction this one; I'm afraid ye'll needs be waiting on the day."

Howard was disposed to protest, to offer more—he was most urgently in earnest, he protested that he could not wait, was ravished by desire, a great deal too warm to abide delay . . . but Bonnet only demurred, and in a few moments had ushered him out of the room. Brianna heard his voice protesting, dying away as Emmanuel removed him.

She had stood up as soon as Bonnet took his hand off her neck, wriggling madly to shake her skirts down. Emmanuel had tied her hands behind her back, as well as gagging her. If he hadn't, she would have tried to kill Stephen Bonnet with her bare hands.

This thought must have been visible on her face, for Bonnet glanced at her, looked again, and laughed.

"Ye did amazing well, darlin'," he said, and leaning over, negligently pulled the gag down from her mouth. "That man will empty his purse for the chance to get his hands on your arse again."

"You God damn . . . you—" She shook with rage, and with the futility of finding any epithet that came close to being strong enough. "I will fucking *kill* you!"

He laughed again.

"Oh, now, sweetheart. For a sore arse? Consider it a repayment—in part—for my left ball." He chucked her under the chin, and went toward the table where the tray with the decanters stood. "Ye've earned a drink. Brandy or porter?"

She ignored the offer, trying to keep her rage in check. Her cheeks flamed with furious blood, and so did her outraged bottom.

"What do you mean, 'auction'?" she demanded.

"I should think that clear enough, sweetheart. Ye've heard the word, sure." Bonnet gave her a glance of mild amusement, and pouring himself a tot of brandy, drank it off in two swallows. "Hah." He exhaled, blinking, and shook his head.

"Hoo. I've two more customers in the market for someone like you, darlin'. They'll be here tomorrow or next day to be having a look. Then I'll ask for bids, and ye'll be off to the Indies by Friday, I expect."

He spoke casually, without the slightest hint of jeering. That, more than anything, made her insides waver. She was a matter of business, a piece of merchandise. To him, and to his goddamned bloody customers, too—Mr. Howard had made that clear. It didn't matter what she said; they weren't at all interested in who she was or what she might want.

Bonnet was watching her face, his pale green eyes assessing. *He* was interested, she realized, and her insides curled up into a knot.

"What did ye use on her, Manny?" he asked.

"A wooden spoon," the manservant said indifferently. "You said no marks."

Bonnet nodded, thoughtful.

"Nothing permanent, I said," he corrected. "We'll leave her as she is for Mr. Ricasoli, I think, but Mr. Houvener . . . well, we'll wait and see."

Emmanuel merely nodded, but his eyes rested on Brianna with sudden interest. Her stomach everted itself neatly and she vomited, absolutely ruining the fine silk dress.

THE SOUND OF high-pitched whinnying reached her; wild horses, rioting down the beach. If this were a romance novel, she thought grimly, she'd make a rope from the bedclothes, let herself down from the window, find the horse herd, and, by exercising her mystical skills with horses, persuade one of them to carry her to safety.

As it was, there were no bedclothes—only a ratty mattress made of ticking stuffed with sea grass—and as for getting within a mile of wild horses . . . She would have given a lot for Gideon, and felt tears prickle at thought of him.

"Oh, now you *are* losing your mind," she said aloud, wiping her eyes. "Crying over a horse." Especially *that* horse. That was so much better than thinking of Roger, though—or Jem. No, she absolutely could *not* think about Jemmy, nor the possibility of his growing up without her, without knowing why she had abandoned him. Or the new one . . . and what life might be like for the child of a slave.

But she was thinking of them, and the thought was enough to overcome her momentary despair.

All right, then. She was getting out of here. Preferably before Mr. Ricasoli and Mr. Houvener, whoever they were, turned up. For the thousandth time, she moved restlessly around the room, forcing herself to move slowly, look at what was there.

Damn little, and what there was, stoutly built, was the discouraging answer. She'd been given food, water for washing, a linen towel, and a hairbrush with which to tidy herself. She picked it up, assessing its potential as a weapon, then threw it down again.

The chimney stack rose through this room, but there was no open hearth. She thumped the bricks experimentally, and pried at the mortar with the end of the spoon they'd given her to eat with. She found one place where the mortar was cracked enough to pry, but a quarter of an hour's trying managed to dislodge only a few inches of mortar; the brick itself stayed firmly in place. Given a month or so, that might be worth a try—though the chances of someone her size managing to squeeze up an eighteenth-century flue . . .

It was getting up to rain; she heard the excited rattle of the palmetto leaves as the wind came through, sharp with the smell of rain. It was not quite sunset, but the clouds had darkened the sky so the room seemed dim. She had no candle; no one expected her to read or sew.

She threw her weight against the bars of the window for the dozenth time, and for the dozenth time found them solidly set and unyielding. Again, in a month, she might contrive to sharpen the spoon's end by grinding it against the chimney bricks, then use it as a chisel to chip away enough of the frame to dislodge one or two bars. But she didn't have a month.

They'd taken away the fouled dress, and left her in shift and stays. Well, that was something. She pulled off the stays, and by picking at the ends of the stitching, extracted the busk—a flat, twelve-inch strip of ivory that ran from sternum to navel. A better weapon than a hairbrush, she thought. She took it over to the chimney, and began to rasp the end against the brick, sharpening its point.

Could she stab someone with it? *Oh, yes,* she thought fiercely. *And please let it be Emmanuel.*

108

DAMN TALL

ROGER WAITED IN the cover of the thick bayberry bushes near the shore; a little way beyond, Ian and Jamie lay likewise in wait.

The second ship had arrived in the morning, coming to anchor a fastidious distance beyond the slaver. Sloshing nets over the side of Roarke's ship in the guise of fishermen, they had been able to watch as first the captain of the slaver went ashore, and then, an hour later, a boat from the second ship was lowered and rowed ashore, with two men—and a small chest—in it.

"A gentleman," Claire had reported, scanning them through the telescope. "Wig, nicely dressed. The other man's a servant of some kind—is the gentleman one of Bonnet's customers, do you think?"

"I do," Jamie had said, watching the boat pull to the shore. "Take us a bit to the north, if ye please, Mr. Roarke; we'll go ashore."

The three of them had landed half a mile from the beach and worked their way down through the wood, then took up their positions in the shrubbery and settled down to wait. The sun was hot, but so close to the shore, there was a fresh breeze, and it was not uncomfortable in the shade, bar the insects. For the hundredth time, Roger brushed away something crawling on his neck.

The waiting was making him jumpy. His skin itched with salt, and the scent of the tidal forest, with its peculiar mix of aromatic pine and distant seaweed, the crunch of shell and needle beneath his feet, brought back to him in vivid detail the day he had killed Lillywhite.

He had gone then—as now—with the intent of killing

Stephen Bonnet. But the elusive pirate had been warned, and an ambush laid. It had been by the will of God—and the skill of Jamie Fraser—that he hadn't left his own carcass in a similar forest, bones scattered by wild pigs, bleaching among the gleam of dry needles and the white of empty shells.

His throat was tight again, but he couldn't shout or sing to loosen it.

He should pray, he thought, but could not. Even the constant litany that had echoed through his heart since the night he had learned she was gone—*Lord, that she might be safe*—even that small petition had somehow dried up. His present thought—*Lord, that I might kill him*—he couldn't voice that, even to himself.

The deliberate intent and desire to murder—surely he couldn't expect such a prayer to be heard.

For a moment, he envied Jamie and Ian their faith in gods of wrath and vengeance. While Roarke and Moses had brought the fishing boat in, he had heard Jamie murmur to Claire and take her hands in his. And heard her then bless him in the Gaelic, with the invocation to Michael of the red domain, the blessing of a warrior on his way to battle.

Ian had merely sat, cross-legged and silent, watching the shore draw nearer, his face remote. If he prayed, there was no telling to whom. When they landed, though, he had paused on the bank of one of the myriad inlets, and scooping up mud in his fingers, had carefully painted his face, drawing a line from forehead to chin, then four parallel streaks across his left cheek, a thick dark circle around his right eye. It was remarkably unsettling.

Quite obviously, neither of them had the slightest qualms about the business, nor the least hesitation in asking God to aid their efforts. He envied them.

And sat in stubborn silence, the gates of heaven closed against him, his hand on the hilt of his knife and a loaded pistol in his belt, planning murder.

A little past noon, the burly captain of the slaver came back, footsteps crunching indifferently on the layer of dried pine needles. They let him pass, waiting.

Late in the afternoon, it began to rain.

SHE HAD DOZED off again, from sheer boredom. It began to rain; the sound roused her briefly, then drove her more deeply into slumber, drops pattering softly on the palmetto thatch above. She woke abruptly when one of the drops fell cold on her face, followed quickly by a few of its fellows.

She jerked upright, blinking with momentary disorientation. She rubbed a hand over her face and looked up; there was a small wet patch on the plaster ceiling, surrounded by a much larger stain from previous leaks, and drops were forming in its center like magic, each perfect bead falling one after another after another to splat on the mattress ticking.

She got up to push the bed out from under the leak, and then stopped. Slowly she straightened up, and put up a hand to the wet patch. The ceiling was a normal one for the time, less than seven feet; she could reach it easily.

"She damn tall," she said aloud. "Damn right she is."

She put her hand flat on the wet patch and pushed as hard as she could. The wet plaster gave way at once, and so did the rotten laths behind it. She jerked back her hand, scratching her arm on the jagged edges of lath, and a small cascade of dirty water, centipedes, mouse droppings, and fragments of palmetto leaf poured in through the hole she'd made.

She wiped her hand on her shift, reached up, seized the edge of the hole, and pulled, ripping down chunks of lath and plaster, until she'd made a hole that would accommodate her head and shoulders.

"Okay," she whispered to the baby, or herself. She glanced around the room, put on her stays over her shift, then tucked the sharpened busk down the front.

Then, standing on the bed, she took a deep breath, shoved her steepled hands upward as though about to dive, and grabbed for anything solid enough to provide leverage. Little by little, she hauled herself, sweating and grunting, up into the steaming thatch of sharp-edged leaves, teeth gritted and eyes closed against the dirt and dead insects.

Her head thrust into moist open air and she gasped for breath. She had an elbow hooked over a beam and, using that for leverage, pulled farther up. Her legs kicked vainly in empty air, trying to propel her upward, and she felt the wrench of shoulder muscles, but sheer desperation propelled her upward—that, and the nightmare vision of Emmanuel coming into the room and seeing the bottom half of her hanging out of the ceiling.

With a rending shower of leaves, she hauled herself out, to lie flat on the rain-wet thatch of the roof. The rain was still coming down heavily, and she was soaked in moments. A little way away, she saw some sort of structure sticking up amid the palmetto leaves of the thatch, and wriggled her way cautiously toward it, constantly fearful lest the roof give way beneath her weight, probing with hands and elbows for the firmness of the roof beams below the thatched leaves.

The structure proved to be a small platform, firmly set on the beams, with a railing on one side. She scrambled onto this and crouched, panting. It was still raining onshore, but out to sea, the sky was mostly clear, and the setting sun behind her spilled a burnt, bloody orange over sky and water through black streaks of shattered cloud. It looked like the end of the world, she thought, her ribs heaving against the lacing of her stays.

From the vantage point of the roof, she could see over the scrub forest; the slice of beach she had glimpsed from her window was clearly visible—and beyond it, two ships, lying close offshore.

Two boats were pulled up on shore, though well separated from each other—probably one from each ship, she thought. One of the ships must be the slaver, the other likely Howard's. A wash of humiliated rage ran over her—she was surprised that the rain didn't steam off her skin. There was no time to dwell on that, though.

Voices came faintly through the patter of rain, and she ducked down, then realized that no one was likely to look up and see her. Raising her head to peer through the railing, she saw figures come out of the trees onto the beach—a single file of chained men, with two or three guards.

"Josh!" She strained her eyes to see, but in the eerie twilight, the figures were no more than silhouettes. She thought she made out the tall, slender figures of the two Fulani men—perhaps the shorter one behind them was Josh, but she couldn't tell.

Her fingers curled tight around the railing, impotent. She couldn't help, she knew it, but to be obliged simply to watch . . . As she watched, a thin scream came from the beach, and a smaller figure ran out of the wood, skirts flying. The guards turned, startled; one of them seized Phaedre—it had to be her; Brianna could hear her screaming "Josh! Josh!", the sound of it harsh as the cry of a distant gull.

She was struggling with the guard—some of the chained men turned abruptly, lunging at the other. A struggling knot of men fell to the sand. Someone was running toward them from the boat, something in his hand . . .

The vibration in her feet jerked her attention from the scene on the beach.

"Crap!" she said involuntarily. Emmanuel's head poked up over the edge of the roof, staring in disbelief. Then his face contorted, and he heaved himself up—there must be a ladder attached to the side of the house, she thought, well, of course there would be, you wouldn't have a lookout platform and no way to get up to it. . . .

While her mind was busying itself with *that* nonsense, her body was taking more concrete steps. She had drawn the sharpened busk and was crouched against the platform, hand low as Ian had taught her.

Emmanuel made a derisive face at the thing in her hand and grabbed at her.

THEY COULD HEAR the gentleman coming well before they saw him. He was singing softly to himself, a French air of some kind. He was alone; the servant must have gone back to the ship while they were making their way through the woods.

Roger got softly to his feet, crouched behind his chosen bush. His limbs were stiff, and he stretched inconspicuously.

As the gentleman drew even with him, Jamie stepped out into the path in front of him. The man—a small, foppish-looking sort—uttered a girlish shriek of alarm. Before he could flee, though, Jamie had stepped forward and grasped his arm, smiling pleasantly.

"Your servant, sir," he said courteously. "Have ye been calling upon Mr. Bonnet, by chance?"

The man blinked at him, confused.

"Bonnet? Why, why . . . yes."

Roger felt a tightness in his chest ease suddenly. *Thank God.* They'd found the right place.

"Who are you, sir?" the small man was demanding, trying to draw his forearm out of Jamie's grip, to no avail.

There was no need to keep hidden now; Roger and Ian stepped out of the bushes, and the gentleman gasped at sight of Ian in his war paint, then glanced wildly back and forth between Jamie and Roger.

Evidently settling on Roger as the most civilized-looking person present, the gentleman appealed to him.

"I beg you, sir—who are you, and what do you want?"

"We are in search of an abducted young woman," Roger said. "A very tall young woman with red hair. Have you—" Before he could finish, he saw the man's eyes dilate with panic. Jamie saw it, too, and twisted the man's wrist, sending him to his knees, mouth awry with pain.

"I think, sir," Jamie said, with impeccable courtesy, holding tight, "we must oblige you to tell us what ye know."

SHE COULDN'T LET him get hold of her. That was her only conscious thought. He grabbed at her weaponless arm and she yanked free, skin slippery with rain, and struck at him in the same motion. The point of the busk skidded up his arm, leaving a reddening furrow, but he ignored this and lunged at her. She fell backward over the railing, landing awkwardly on her hands and knees in the leaves, but he hadn't got her; he'd fallen on his own knees on the platform, with a thud that shook the whole roof.

She scrabbled madly to the edge of the roof, hands and knees poking randomly through the thatch, and threw her legs over the edge into space, kicking frantically for the rungs of the ladder.

He was after her, had her wrist in a grip like an eel's bite, was hauling her back onto the roof. She drew back her free hand and lashed him hard across the face with the busk. He roared and his grip loosened; she wrenched free and dropped.

She hit the sand flat on her back with a bone-shaking *thump!* and lay paralyzed, unable to breathe, the rain pelting down on her face. A hoot of triumph came from the roof, and then a growl of exasperated dismay. He thought he'd killed her.

Great, she thought muzzily. *Keep thinking that.* The shock of impact was beginning to wear off, her diaphragm lurched into motion, and glorious air rushed into her lungs. Could she move?

She didn't know, and didn't dare to try. Through rain-clotted lashes, she saw Emmanuel's bulk ease over the edge of the roof, foot groping for the crude ladder rungs she could now see, nailed to the wall.

She'd lost the busk when she fell, but saw it gleaming dully, a foot from her head. With Emmanuel's back momentarily turned, she whipped her hand up and grabbed it, then lay still, playing possum.

THEY HAD NEARLY reached the house when sounds from the nearby forest stopped them. Roger froze, then ducked off the path. Jamie and Ian had already melted into the wood. The sounds weren't coming from the path, though, but from somewhere off to the left—voices, men's voices, shouting orders, and the shuffling of feet, the clink of chains.

A thrill of panic shot through him. Were they taking her away? He was already soaked with rain, but felt the bloom of cold sweat over his body, colder than the rain.

Howard, the man they'd apprehended in the wood, had assured them Brianna was safe in the house, but what would he know? He listened, straining his ears for the sound of a woman's voice, and heard it, a high, thin scream.

He jerked toward it, only to find Jamie beside him, gripping his arm.

"That's not Brianna," his father-in-law said urgently. "Ian will go. You and I—for the house!"

There was no time for argument. The sounds of violence on the beach came faintly—shouts and cries—but Jamie was right, that voice wasn't Brianna's. Ian was running toward the beach, making no effort now to be silent.

An instant's hesitation, instinct urging him to go after Ian, then Roger was on the path, following Jamie toward the house at the run.

EMMANUEL BENT OVER HER; she felt his bulk and lunged upward like a striking snake, sharpened busk like a fang. She'd aimed for his head, hoping for eye or throat, but counting at least on his jerking reflexively back, putting him at a disadvantage.

He jerked, all right, up and away, but was much faster than she'd thought. She struck with all her force, and the sharpened busk drove under his arm with a rubbery shock. He froze for a moment, mouth open in incredulity, looking at the ivory rod that stuck out of his armpit. Then he wrenched it out, and lunged for her with an outraged bellow.

She was already on her feet, though, and running for the woods. From somewhere ahead, she heard more yelling—and a bloodcurdling scream. Another, and then more, these coming from the front of the house.

Dazed and terrified, she kept running, her mind only slowly grasping that some of the screams had words.

"Casteal DHUUUUUUUIN!"

Da, she thought, in absolute astonishment, then tripped over a branch on the ground and fell arse over teakettle, landing in a disheveled heap.

She struggled to her feet, thinking absurdly, *This* can't *be good for the baby,* and groping for another weapon.

Her fingers were trembling, wouldn't work. She scrabbled the ground, vainly. Then Emmanuel popped up beside her like the Demon King, grabbing her arm with a gloating, *"HA!"*

The shock made her sway, her vision going gray at the edges. She could still hear bloodcurdling screams on the distant beach, but no more yelling at the house. Emmanuel was saying something, full of satisfaction and threat, but she wasn't listening.

There seemed to be something wrong with his face; it

went in and out of focus, and she blinked hard, shaking her head to clear her sight. It wasn't her eyes, though—it was him. His face melted slowly from bare-toothed menace to a look of faint astonishment. He frowned, lips pursing so she saw the pink lining of his mouth, and blinked two or three times. Then he made a small choked noise, put a hand to his chest, and dropped to his knees, still gripping her arm.

He fell over, and she landed on top of him. She pulled away—his fingers came away easily, all their strength suddenly gone—and stumbled to her feet, panting and shaking.

Emmanuel was lying on his back, legs bent under him at what would have been an excruciating angle, had he been alive. She gulped for air, trembling, afraid to believe it. But he *was* dead; there was no mistaking the look of it.

Her breath was coming better now, and she began to be conscious of the cuts and bruises on her bare feet. She still felt stunned, unable to decide what to do next.

The decision was made for her in the next instant, as Stephen Bonnet came dashing toward her through the wood.

SHE JERKED TO instant alertness, and spun on her heel to flee. She made it no more than six paces before he had an arm about her throat, dragging her off her feet.

"Hush, now, darlin'," he said in her ear, sounding breathless. He was hot, and his stubble rasped her cheek. "I mean ye no harm. I'll leave ye safe on the shore. But ye're the only thing I've got right now will keep your men from killin' me."

He ignored the body of Emmanuel entirely. The heavy forearm left her throat and he grabbed her arm, trying to drag her in the direction away from the beach—evidently, he meant to make for the hidden inlet on the opposite side of the island, where they had landed the day before. "Move, darlin'. Now."

"Let go!" She dug her feet in hard, yanking on her trapped arm. "I'm not going anywhere with you. HELP!" she shrieked as loudly as she could. "HELP! ROGER!"

He looked startled, and raised his free arm to wipe the streaming rain out of his eyes. There was something in his hand; the last of the light gleamed orange on glass. Holy Lord, he'd brought his testicle.

"Bree! Brianna! Where are you?" Roger's voice, frantic, and a jolt of adrenaline shot through her at the sound, giving her the strength to jerk her arm from Bonnet's grasp.

"Here! Here I am! Roger!" she shouted at the top of her voice.

Bonnet glanced over his shoulder; the bushes were shaking, two men at least coming through them. He wasted no time, but darted into the forest, bending low to avoid a branch, and was gone.

In the next instant, Roger crashed out of the brush and seized her, crushing her against him.

"You're all right? Has he hurt you?" He'd dropped his knife, and held her by the arms, eyes trying to look everywhere at once—her face, her body, into her eyes. . . .

"I'm fine," she said, feeling dizzy. "Roger, I'm—"

"Where has he gone?" It was her father, soaking wet and grim as death, dirk in his hand.

"That—" She turned to point, but he was already gone, running wolflike. She saw the marks of Bonnet's passage now, the scuffed footmarks clear in the muddy sand. Before she could turn round again, Roger was after him.

"Wait!" she shrieked, but no answer came save the rapidly receding rustle of brush as heavy bodies flung themselves heedlessly through.

She stood still for a moment, head hanging as she breathed. The rain was pooling in the sockets of Emmanuel's open eyes; the orange light glowed in them, making them look like the eyes of a Japanese movie monster.

That random thought passed across her mind, then vanished, leaving her blank and numb. She wasn't sure what to do at this point. There were no sounds from the beach anymore; the noises of Bonnet's flight had long since faded.

The rain was still falling, but the last of the sun shone through the wood, the long rays nearly horizontal, filling the space between the shadows with an odd, shifting light that seemed to waver as she watched, as though the world around her were about to disappear.

In the midst of it, dreamlike, she saw the women appear,

the Fulani twins. They turned the identical faces of fawns to her, huge eyes black with fear, and ran into the wood. She called out to them, but they disappeared. Feeling unutterably tired, she trudged after them.

She didn't find them. Nor was there a sign of anyone else. The light began to die, and she turned back, limping, toward the house. She ached everywhere, and began to suffer from the illusion that there was no one left in the world but her. Nothing but the burning light, fading to ashes moment by moment.

Then she remembered the baby in her womb, and felt better. No matter what, she wasn't alone. Nonetheless, she gave a wide berth to the place where she thought Emmanuel's body lay. She had meant to circle back toward the house, but went too far. As she turned to go back, she caught a glimpse of them, standing together in the shelter of the trees on the other side of a stream.

The wild horses, tranquil as the trees around them, flanks gleaming bay and chestnut and black with the wet. They raised their heads, scenting her, but didn't run, only stood regarding her with big, gentle eyes.

THE RAIN HAD stopped when she reached the house. Ian sat on the stoop, wringing water out of his long hair.

"You have mud on your face, Ian," she said, sinking down beside him.

"Oh, have I?" he said, giving her a half-smile. "How is it, then, coz?"

"Oh. I'm . . . I think I'm fine. What—?" She gestured at his shirt, stained with watery blood. Something seemed to have hit him in the face; besides the smudges of mud, his nose was puffed, there was a swelling just above his brow, and his clothes were torn, as well as wet.

He drew a deep, deep breath and sighed, as though he were as tired as she was.

"I got back the wee black lass," he said. "Phaedre."

That pierced the dreamlike fugue that filled her mind, but only a little.

"Phaedre," she said, the name feeling like that of someone she had once known, long ago. "Is she all right? Where—"

"In there." Ian nodded back toward the house, and she became aware that what she had thought the sound of the sea was in fact someone weeping, the small sobs of someone who has already wept herself to exhaustion, but cannot stop.

"Nay, leave her to herself, coz." Ian's hand on her arm stopped her from rising. "Ye canna help."

"But—"

He stopped her, reaching into his shirt. From around his neck, he took a battered wooden rosary, and handed it to her.

"She'll maybe want this—later. I picked it up from the sand, after the ship . . . left."

For the first time since her escape, the nausea was back, a sense of vertigo that threatened to pull her down into blackness.

"Josh," she whispered. Ian nodded silently, though it hadn't been a question.

"I'm sorry, coz," he said very softly.

IT WAS NEARLY dark when Roger appeared at the edge of the wood. She hadn't been worrying, only because she was in a state of shock too deep even to think of what was happening. At sight of him, though, she was on her feet and flying toward him, all the fears she had suppressed erupting at last into tears, running down her face like the rain.

"Da," she said, choking and sniffling into his wet shirt. "He's—is he—"

"He's all right. Bree—can ye come with me? Are ye strong enough—just for a bit?"

Gulping and wiping her nose on the soggy arm of her shift, she nodded, and leaning on his arm, limped into the darkness under the trees.

Bonnet was lying against a tree, head lolling to one side. There was blood on his face, running down onto his shirt. She felt no sense of victory at sight of him, only an infinitely weary distaste.

Her father was standing silently under the same tree.

When he saw her, he stepped forward and folded her wordlessly into his arms. She closed her eyes for one blissful moment, wanting nothing more than to abandon everything, let him pick her up like a child and carry her home. But they had brought her here for a reason; with immense effort, she lifted her head and looked at Bonnet.

Did they want congratulations? she wondered fuzzily. But then she remembered what Roger had told her, describing her father leading her mother through the scene of butchery, making her look, so that she would know her tormentors were dead.

"Okay," she said, swaying a little. "All right, I mean. I—I see. He's dead."

"Well . . . no. Actually, he isn't." Roger's voice held an odd note of strain, and he coughed, with a look that shot daggers at her father.

"D'ye want him dead, lass?" Her father touched her shoulder, gently. "It is your right."

"Do I—" She looked wildly from one to the other of the grave, shadowed faces, then at Bonnet, realizing for the first time that blood *was* running down his face. Dead men, as her mother had often explained, don't bleed.

They had found Bonnet, Jamie said, run him to earth like a fox, and set about him. It had been an ugly fight, close-to, with knives, as their pistols were useless in the wet. Knowing that he fought for his life, Bonnet had struck viciously—there was a red-stained gash in the shoulder of Jamie's coat, a scratch high on Roger's throat, where a knife blade had passed within a fraction of slashing his jugular. But Bonnet had fought to escape, and not to kill—retreating into a space between trees where only one could come at him, he had grappled with Jamie, thrown him off, then bolted.

Roger had given chase, and boiling with adrenaline, had thrown himself at Bonnet bodily, knocking the pirate headfirst into the tree he now lay against.

"So there he lies," Jamie said, giving Bonnet a bleak eye. "I had hoped he'd broken his neck, but no such luck, alas."

"But he is unconscious," Roger said, and swallowed.

She understood, and in her present mood, this particular male quirk of honor seemed reasonable. To kill a man in fair fight—or even an unfair fight—was one thing; to cut his throat while he lay unconscious at your feet was another.

But she hadn't understood at all. Her father wiped his dirk on his breeches and handed it to her, hilt first.

"What . . . me?" She was too shocked even to feel astonishment. The knife was heavy in her hand.

"If ye wish it," her father said, with grave courtesy. "If not, Roger Mac or I will do it. But it is your choice, *a nighean*."

Now she understood Roger's look—they had been arguing about it, before he had come to fetch her. And she understood exactly why her father offered her the choice. Whether it was vengeance or forgiveness, she held the man's life in her hand. She took a deep breath, the awareness that it would not be vengeance coming over her with something like relief.

"Brianna," Roger said softly, touching her arm. "Say the word if ye'll have him dead; I'll do it."

She nodded, and took a deep breath. She could hear the savage longing in his voice—he would. She could hear the choked sound of his voice in memory, too, when he had told her of killing Boble—when he woke from dreams of it, drenched in sweat.

She glanced at her father's face, nearly drowned in shadow. Her mother had said only a little of the violent dreams that haunted him since Culloden—but that little was enough. She could hardly ask her father to do this—to spare Roger what he suffered himself.

Jamie raised his head, feeling her eyes on him, and met her gaze, straight on. Jamie Fraser had never turned from a fight he saw as his—but this was not his fight, and he knew it. She had a sudden flash of awareness; it wasn't Roger's fight, either, though he would take the weight of it from her shoulders, and gladly.

"If you—if *we*—if we don't kill him here and now—" Her chest was tight, and she stopped for breath. "What will we do with him?"

"Take him to Wilmington," her father said matter-of-factly. "The Committee of Safety there is strong, and they know him for a pirate; they'll deal with him by law—or what passes for it now."

They'd hang him; he would be just as dead—but his blood wouldn't be on Roger's hands, or in his heart.

The light was gone. Bonnet was no more than a lumpen shape, dark against the sandy ground. He might die of his wounds, she thought, and dimly hoped so—it would save trouble. But if they took him to her mother, Claire would be compelled to try to save him. *She* never turned from a fight that was hers, either, Brianna thought wryly, and was surprised to feel a small lightening of spirit at the thought.

"Let him live to be hanged, then," she said quietly, and touched Roger's arm. "Not for his sake. For yours and mine. For your baby."

For an instant, she was sorry that she'd told him now, in the night-dark wood. She would so much have liked to see his face.

109

ALL THE NEWS THAT'S FIT TO PRINT

FROM *L'OIGNON–INTELLIGENCER, SEPTEMBER 25, 1775*

A ROYAL PROCLAMATION—

A Proclamation was issued in London upon the 23rd of August, in which His Majesty George III proclaims the American Colonies to be "in a State of open and avowed Rebellion."

"NOTHING BUT OUR OWN EXERTIONS MAY DEFEAT THE MINISTERIAL SENTENCE OF DEATH OR ABJECT SUBMISSION"—The Continental Congress in Philadelphia

has now rejected the Objectionable Proposals put forth by Lord North, intended to promote the Object of Reconciliation. The Delegates to this Congress state unequivocally the Right of the American Colonies to raise Appropriations and to have a say in the Disbursement of Same. The Statement of the Delegates reads in Part: "As the British Ministry has pursued its Ends and prosecuted Hostilities with great Armaments and Cruelty, can the World be deceived into an Opinion that we are Unreasonable, or can it hesitate to believe with us that Nothing but our own Exertions may defeat the Ministerial Sentence of Death or Abject Submission?"

A FALCON STOOPS BUT IS DEPRIVED OF HER PREY—Upon the 9th of August, HMS Falcon, *commanded by Captain John Linzee, gave Chase to two American Schooners, returning from the West Indies to Salem, Massachusetts. One Schooner was captured by Captain Linzee, who then pursued the other into Gloucester Harbor. Troops upon the Shore fired upon the* Falcon, *which did return this Fire, but was then forced to withdraw, losing both Schooners, two Barges, and Thirty-Five Men.*

A NOTORIOUS PIRATE CONDEM'D—One Stephen Bonnet, known as a Pirate and Infamous Smuggler, was tryed before the Wilmington Committee of Safety, and upon Testimony of his Crimes having been presented by a Number of Persons, was convicted of them and sentenced to Death by Drowning.

AN ALARM is raised regarding prowling Bands of Negroes, who have despoiled a number of Farms near Wilmington and Brunswick. Unarmed save for Clubs, the Ruffians have stolen Livestock, Food, and four Hogsheads of Rum.

CONGRESS CONCEIVES A PLAN FOR CURRENCY REDEMPTION—Two Million Spanish Dollars in Bills of Credit now issue forth from the Presses, with One Million Dollars more authorized by Congress, which now announces a Plan for the Redemption of this Currency, viz., *that each Colony must assume Responsibility for its Portion of the Debt and must redeem the Same in four Installments, these to be paid upon the last Day of November in the Years 1779, 1780, 1781, and 1782. . . .*

110

THE SMELL OF LIGHT

October 2, 1775

IT WAS NOT thinkable to return Phaedre to River Run, even though she technically remained the property of Duncan Innes. We had discussed the matter at some length, and finally decided not to tell Jocasta that her slave had been recovered, though we did send brief word with Ian, when he went to collect Jemmy, telling of Brianna's safe return and regretting the loss of Joshua—omitting a good bit of detail regarding the whole affair.

"Should we tell them about Gerald Forbes?" I'd asked, but Jamie had shaken his head.

"Forbes willna trouble any member of my family again," he said definitely. "And to tell my aunt or Duncan about it . . . I think Duncan has sufficient trouble on his hands; he'd feel obliged to take issue wi' Forbes, and that's a stramash he doesna need to start just now. As for my aunt . . ." He didn't complete the statement, but the bleakness of his countenance spoke well enough. The MacKenzies of Leoch were a vengeful lot, and neither he nor I would put it past Jocasta to invite Gerald Forbes to dinner and poison him.

"Always assuming that Mr. Forbes is accepting dinner invitations these days," I joked uneasily. "Do you know what Ian did with the . . . er . . ."

"He said he was going to feed it to his dog," Jamie replied thoughtfully. "But I dinna ken was he serious or not."

Phaedre had been a good deal shocked, both by her experiences and by the loss of Josh, and Brianna insisted that we bring her back to the Ridge with us to recover, until we could find a reasonable place for her.

"We have to get Aunt Jocasta to free her," Bree had argued.

"I think that willna be difficult," Jamie had assured her

with a certain grimness. "Not knowing what we know. But wait a bit, until we find a place for the lass—then I'll see to it."

As it was, that particular matter took care of itself with stunning abruptness.

I opened the door to a knock one afternoon in October, to find three weary horses and a pack mule in the dooryard, and Jocasta, Duncan, and the black butler Ulysses standing on the stoop.

The sight of them was so utterly incongruous that I merely stood there gaping at them, until Jocasta said acerbically, "Weel, lass, d'ye mean us to stand here until we're melted away like sugar in a dish o' tea?"

It was in fact raining quite hard, and I stepped back so quickly to let them in that I trod on Adso's paw. He uttered a piercing yowl, which brought Jamie out of his study, Mrs. Bug and Amy from the kitchen—and Phaedre out of the surgery, where she had been grinding herbs for me.

"Phaedre!" Duncan's jaw dropped, and he took two steps toward her. He stopped abruptly, just before taking her into his arms, but his face suffused with joy.

"Phaedre?" said Jocasta, sounding utterly astounded. Her face had gone quite blank with shock.

Ulysses said nothing, but the look on *his* face was one of unalloyed horror. Within a second, it was gone, replaced by his usual austere expression of dignity, but I'd seen it—and kept a narrow eye on him during the ensuing confusion of exclamations and embarrassments.

Finally, I got them all out of the front hall. Jocasta suffered a diplomatic headache—though seeing her drawn face, I thought it wasn't entirely feigned—and was escorted upstairs by Amy, who put her to bed with a cold compress. Mrs. Bug went back to the kitchen, excitedly revising the supper menu. Phaedre, looking frightened, disappeared, doubtless to take refuge in Brianna's cabin and tell her all about the unexpected arrival—which meant there would be another three for supper.

Ulysses went to deal with the horses, leaving Duncan at last alone to explain matters to Jamie in the study.

"We are emigrating to Acadia," he said, closing his eyes and inhaling the aroma of the glass of whisky in his hand as though it were smelling salts. He looked like he needed them; he was gaunt, and his face was nearly as gray as his hair.

"Acadia?" Jamie said, as surprised as I was. "For God's sake, Duncan, what have ye been doing?"

Duncan smiled wearily, opening his eyes.

"More what I didna do, *Mac Dubh,*" he said. Brianna had told us about the disappearance of the secret hoard of gold, and had mentioned something about Duncan's dealings with Lord Dunsmore in Virginia, but had been vague about it—understandably so, as she had been kidnapped a few hours afterward, and had no details.

"I should never ha' believed matters could come to such a pass—nor sae quickly," he said, shaking his head. Loyalists had gone suddenly from being a majority in the piedmont to being a threatened and frightened minority. Some folk had been literally chased from their homes, to take refuge skulking in swamps and woods; others had been beaten and badly injured.

"Even Farquard Campbell," Duncan said, and rubbed a hand tiredly over his face. "The Committee of Safety called him before them, on charges of being loyal to the Crown, and threatened to confiscate his plantation. He put up a great deal of money, pledged as surety for his good behavior, and they let him go—but it was a near thing."

Near enough to have frightened Duncan badly. The debacle of the promised guns and powder had deprived him of any influence with the local Loyalists and left him completely isolated, vulnerable to the next wave of hostilities—which any fool could see would not be long in coming.

He had therefore moved swiftly to sell River Run at a decent price, before it was seized. He had kept one or two warehouses on the river and a few other assets, but had disposed of the plantation, slaves, and livestock, and proposed to remove at once with his wife to Acadia, as many other Loyalists were doing.

"Hamish MacKenzie is there, ken," he explained. "He and some others from Leoch settled in Nova Scotia, when they left Scotland in the wake of Culloden. He's Jocasta's nephew, and we've money enough—" He glanced vaguely toward the hall, where Ulysses had dumped the saddlebags. "He'll help us to find a place."

He smiled crookedly.

"And if things shouldna turn out well . . . they do say the fishing's good."

Jamie smiled at the feeble joke, and poured him more whisky, but he shook his head when he came to join me in the surgery, before dinner.

"They mean to travel overland to Virginia, and with luck take ship there for Nova Scotia. They can perhaps get out of Newport News; it's a small port, and the British blockade isna tight there—or so Duncan hopes."

"Oh, dear." It would be a grueling journey—and Jocasta was not a young woman. And the state of her eye . . . I was not fond of Jocasta, in light of what we had learned about her recently, but to think of her ripped from her home, forced to emigrate while suffering excruciating pain—well, it caused one to think there might be such a thing as divine retribution, after all.

I lowered my voice, looking over my shoulder to be sure Duncan had in fact gone upstairs. "What about Ulysses? And Phaedre?"

Jamie's lips pressed tight.

"Ah. Well, as to the lass—I asked Duncan to sell her to me. I shall set her free as quickly as I can; perhaps send her to Fergus, in New Bern. He agreed at once, and wrote out a bill of sale on the spot." He nodded toward his office. "As for Ulysses . . ." His face was grim. "I think that matter will adjust itself, Sassenach."

Mrs. Bug came bustling down the hall to announce that the supper was served, and I had no chance to ask him what he meant by that remark.

I SQUEEZED OUT the poultice of witch hazel and Carolina allspice, and laid it gently over Jocasta's eyes. I'd already given her willow-bark tea for the pain, and the poultice would do nothing for the underlying glaucoma—but it would be soothing, at least, and it was a relief to both patient and physician to be able to offer something, even though that might be the merest palliative.

"Will ye have a keek in my saddlebags, lass?" she asked,

stretching a little to ease herself on the bed. "There's a bittie parcel in there of an herb ye might find of interest."

I found it immediately—by smell.

"Where on earth did you get that?" I asked, halfway amused.

"Farquard Campbell," she replied matter-of-factly. "When ye told me what the difficulty was with my eyes, I asked Fentiman if he kent anything that might be of help, and he told me that he'd heard somewhere that hemp might be of use. Farquard Campbell has a field of it under cultivation, so I thought I might as well try it. It does seem to help. Would ye put it in my hand, please, niece?"

Fascinated, I put the parcel of hemp and the little stack of papers down on the table beside her, and guided her hand to it. Rolling carefully onto her side to prevent the poultice falling off, she took a good pinch of aromatic herb, sprinkled it down the center of the paper, and rolled as tidy a joint as I had ever seen in Boston.

Without comment, I held the candle flame for her to light it, and she eased herself back on the pillow, nostrils flaring as she took a deep lungful of smoke.

She smoked in silence for some time, and I busied myself in putting things away, not wanting to leave her lest she fall asleep and set the bed on fire—she was clearly exhausted, and relaxing further by the moment.

The pungent, heady smell of the smoke brought back instant, though fragmentary, memories. Several of the younger medical students had smoked it on weekends, and would come to the hospital with the scent of it in their clothes. Some of the people brought into the emergency room had reeked of it. Now and then, I'd smelled the faintest hint of it on Brianna—but never inquired.

I hadn't ever tried it, myself, but now found the smell of the fragrant smoke rather soothing. Rather *too* soothing, and I went and sat down by the window, open a crack to admit fresh air.

It had been raining off and on all day, and the air was sharp with ozone and tree resins, welcomely cold against my face.

"Ye know, don't you?" Jocasta's voice came softly from behind me. I looked round; she hadn't moved, but lay like a tomb figure on the bed, straight as a die. The poultice bandage over her eyes made her look like the image of Justice—ironic, that, I thought.

"I know," I said, matching her own calm tone. "Not very fair to Duncan, was it?"

"No." The word drifted out with the smoke, almost soundless. She lifted the cigarette lazily and drew air through it, making the end glow red. I kept a narrow eye, but she seemed to have a feel for the ash, tapping it now and then into the saucer base of the candlestick.

"He knows, too," she said, almost casually. "About Phaedre. I told him, finally, to stop him searching for her. I am sure he knows about Ulysses, too—but he doesna speak of it."

She reached out, unerring, and tapped the ash neatly from the joint.

"I told him I wouldna blame him if he left me, ken." Her voice was very soft, nearly without emotion. "He wept, but then he stopped, and said to me that he had said, 'For better or for worse'—and so had I, had I not? I said I had, and he said, 'Well, then.' And here we are." She shrugged a little, settling herself more comfortably, and fell silent, smoking.

I turned my face again to the window and leaned my forehead against the frame. Below, I saw a sudden spill of light as the door opened, and a dark figure came quickly out. The door closed, and I lost sight of him in the darkness for an instant; then my eyes adapted and I saw him again, just before he vanished on the path to the barn.

"He's gone, isn't he?" Startled, I turned round to look at her, realizing that she must have heard the closing of the door below.

"Ulysses? Yes, I think so."

She was still for quite a while, the cigarette burning unregarded in her hand. Just before I thought I must rise and take it from her, she lifted it again to her lips.

"His true name was Joseph," she said softly, releasing the smoke. Wisps of it swirled slowly in a cloud around her head. "So appropriate, I always thought—for he was sold into slavery by his own people."

"Have you ever seen his face?" I asked suddenly. She shook her head, and ground out the last of the cigarette.

"Nay, but I kent him always," she said very softly. "He smelled of light."

JAMIE FRASER sat patiently in the darkness of his barn. It was a small one, with stallage for only half a dozen animals, but soundly built. Rain beat solidly on the roof, and wind whined like a *ban-sidhe* round the corners, but not a drip came through the shingled roof, and the air inside was warm with the heat of somnolent beasts. Even Gideon was a-nod over his manger, half-chewed hay hanging from the corner of his mouth.

It was past midnight now, and he had been waiting for more than two hours, the pistol loaded and primed, resting on his knee.

There it was; above the rain, he heard the soft grunt of someone pushing at the door, and the rumble as it slid open, admitting a breath of cold rain to mingle with the warmer scents of hay and manure.

He sat still, not moving.

He could see a tall form pause against the lighter black of the rain-drenched night, waiting for his eyes to adapt to the dark within, then throw his weight against the heavy door to open it enough to slip inside.

The man had brought a dark-lantern, not trusting that he could find the necessary bits of harness and apply them in the dark. He drew back the slide and turned the lantern slowly, letting the shaft of light travel over the stalls, one by one. The three horses Jocasta had brought were here, but done in. Jamie heard the man click his tongue softly in consideration, turning the light back and forth between the mare, Jerusha, and Gideon.

Making up his mind, Ulysses set the lantern on the floor, and made to pull the pin fastening the door to Gideon's stall.

"It would serve ye right, and I let ye take him," Jamie said conversationally.

The butler let out a sharp yelp and whirled round, glaring, his fists clenched. He couldn't see Jamie in the dark, but the evidence of his ears caught up with him a second later, and he breathed deeply and lowered his fists, realizing who it was.

"Mr. Fraser," he said. His eyes were live in the lantern light, and watchful. "You took me by surprise."

"Well, I did intend to," Jamie replied equably. "Ye mean to be off, I suppose."

He could see thoughts flit through the butler's eyes, quick as dragonflies, wondering, calculating. But Ulysses was no fool, and came to the correct conclusion.

"The girl's told you, then," he said, quite calmly. "Shall you kill me—for your aunt's honor?" Had that last been said with any trace of a sneer, Jamie might have killed him indeed—he'd been of two minds on the matter while he waited. But it was said simply, and Jamie's finger eased on the trigger.

"If I were a younger man, I would," he said, matching Ulysses's tone. *And if I did not have a wife and daughter who once called a black man friend.*

"As it is," he went on, lowering the pistol, "I try not to kill these days unless I must." *Or until I must.* "Do ye offer me denial? For I think there can be nay defense."

The butler shook his head slightly. The light gleamed on his skin, dark, with a reddish undertone that made him look as though carved from aged cinnabar.

"I loved her," he said softly, and spread his hands. "Kill me." He was dressed for traveling, in cloak and hat, with a pouch and canteen hung at his belt, but no knife. Slaves, even trusted ones, dared not go armed.

Curiosity warred with distaste, and—as usual in such warfare—curiosity won.

"Phaedre said ye lay with my aunt, even before her husband died. Is that true?"

"It is," Ulysses said softly, his expression unreadable. "I do not justify it. I cannot. But I loved her, and if I must die for that . . ."

Jamie believed the man; his sincerity was evident in voice and gesture. And knowing his aunt as he did, he was less inclined to blame Ulysses than the world at large would be. At the same time, he was not letting down his guard; Ulysses was good-sized, and quick. And a man who thought he had nothing to lose was very dangerous indeed.

"Where did ye mean to go?" he asked with a nod toward the horses.

"Virginia," the black man replied with a barely perceptible hesitation. "Lord Dunsmore has offered freedom to any slave who will join his army."

He hadn't meant to ask, though it was a question that had raised itself in his mind from the moment he heard Phaedre's story. With this opening, though, he could not resist.

"Why did she not free you?" he asked. "After Hector Cameron died?"

"She did," was the surprising answer. The butler touched the breast of his coat. "She wrote the papers of manumission nearly twenty years ago—she said she could not bear to think that I came to her bed only because I must. But a request for manumission must be approved by the Assembly, you know. And if I had been openly freed, I could not have stayed to serve her as I did." That was true enough; a freed slave was compelled to leave the colony within ten days or risk being enslaved again, by anyone who chose to take him; the vision of large gangs of free Negroes roaming the countryside was one that made the Council and Assembly shit themselves with fear.

The butler looked down for a moment, eyes hooded against the light.

"I could choose Jo—or freedom. I chose her."

"Aye, verra romantic," Jamie said with extreme dryness—though in fact, he was not unaffected by the statement. Jocasta MacKenzie had married for duty, and duty again—and he thought she had had little happiness in any of her marriages until finding some measure of contentment with Duncan. He was shocked at her choice, disapproving of her adultery, and very angry indeed at her deception of Duncan, but some part of him—the MacKenzie part, doubtless—could not but admire her boldness in taking happiness where she could.

He sighed deeply. The rain was easing now; the thundering on the roof had dwindled to a soft pattering.

"Well, then. I have one question more."

Ulysses inclined his head gravely, in a gesture Jamie had seen a thousand times. *At your service, sir,* it said—and *that* was done with more irony than there was in anything the man had said.

"Where is the gold?"

Ulysses's head jerked up, eyes wide with startlement. For the first time, Jamie felt a shred of doubt.

"You think *I* took it?" the butler said incredulously. But then his mouth twisted to one side. "I suppose you would, after all." He rubbed a hand under his nose, looking worried and unhappy—as well he might, Jamie reflected.

They stood regarding each other in silence for some time, at an impasse. Jamie did not have the feeling that the other was attempting to deceive him—and God knew the man was good at *that,* he thought cynically.

At last, Ulysses heaved his wide shoulders, and let them drop in helplessness.

"I cannot prove that I did not," he said. "I can offer nothing save my word of honor—and I am not entitled to have such a thing." For the first time, bitterness rang in his voice.

Jamie suddenly felt very tired. The horses and mules had long since gone back to their drowse, and he wanted nothing so much as his own bed, and his wife beside him. He also wanted Ulysses to be gone, long before Duncan discovered his perfidy. And while Ulysses was patently the most obvious person to have taken the gold, the fact remained that he could have taken it anytime in the last twenty years, with a good deal less danger. Why now?

"Will ye swear on my aunt's head?" he asked abruptly. Ulysses's eyes were sharp, shining in the lantern light, but steady.

"Yes," he said at last, quietly. "I do so swear."

Jamie was about to dismiss him, when one last thought occurred to him.

"Do you have children?" he asked.

Indecision crossed the chiseled face; surprise and wariness, mingled with something else.

"None I would claim," he said at last, and Jamie saw what it was—scorn, mixed with shame. His jaw tensed, and his chin rose slightly. "Why do you ask me that?"

Jamie met his gaze for a moment, thinking of Brianna growing heavy with child.

"Because," he said at last, "it is only the hope of betterment for my children, and theirs, that gives me the courage to do what must be done here." Ulysses's face had gone blank; it gleamed black and impassive in the light.

"If you have no stake in the future, you have no reason to suffer for it. Such children as you may have—"

"They are slaves, born of slave women. What can they be, to me?" Ulysses's hands were clenched, pressed against his thighs.

"Then go," Jamie said softly, and stood aside, gesturing toward the door with the barrel of his pistol. "Die free, at least."

111

JANUARY TWENTY-FIRST

January 21, 1776

JANUARY 21 WAS THE coldest day of the year. Snow had fallen a few days before, but now the air was like cut crystal, the dawn sky so pale it looked white, and the packed snow chirped like crickets under our boots. Snow, snow-shrouded trees, the icicles that hung from the eaves of the house—the whole world seemed blue with cold. All of the stock had been put up the night before in stable or barn, with the exception of the white sow, who appeared to be hibernating under the house.

I peered dubiously at the small, melted hole in the crust of snow that marked the sow's entrance; long, stertorous snores were audible inside, and a faint warmth emanated from the hole.

"Come along, *mo nighean.* Yon creature wouldna notice if the house fell down atop her." Jamie had come down from feeding the animals in the stable, and was hovering impatiently behind me, chafing his hands in the big blue mittens Bree had knitted for him.

"What, not even if it was on fire?" I said, thinking of Lamb's "Essay on Roast Pork." But I turned obligingly to follow him down the trampled path past the side of the house, then slowly, slipping on the icy patches, across the wide clearing toward Bree and Roger's cabin.

"Ye're sure the hearth fire's out?" Jamie asked, for the third time. His breath wreathed round his head like a veil as he looked over his shoulder at me. He had lost his woolen cap hunting, and instead had a woolly white muffler wrapped around his ears and tied on top of his head, the long ends flopping, which made him look absurdly like an enormous rabbit.

"It is," I assured him, suppressing an urge to laugh at sight of him. His long nose was pink with cold, and twitched suspiciously, and I buried my face in my own muffler, making small snorting noises that emerged as puffs of white, like a steam engine.

"And the bedroom candle? The wee lamp in your surgery?"

"Yes," I assured him, emerging from the depths of the muffler. My eyes were watering and I would have liked to wipe them, but I had a huge bundle in one arm and a covered basket hung on the other. This contained Adso, who had been forcibly removed from the house, and wasn't pleased about it; small growls emerged from the basket, and it swayed and thumped against my leg.

"And the rush dip in the pantry, and the candle in the wall sconce in the hall, and the brazier in your office, and the fish-oil lantern you use in the stables. I went over the whole house with a nit comb. Not a spark anywhere."

"Well enough, then," he said—but couldn't help an uneasy glance backward at the house. I looked, too; it looked cold and forlorn, the white of its boards rather grimy against the pristine snow.

"It won't be an accident," I said. "Not unless the white sow is playing with matches in her den."

That made him smile, in spite of the circumstances. Frankly, at the moment, the circumstances struck me as slightly absurd; the whole world seemed deserted, frozen solid and immobile under a winter sky. Nothing seemed less likely than that cataclysm could descend to destroy the house by fire. Still . . . better safe than sorry. And as Jamie had remarked more than once during the years since Roger and Bree had brought word of that sinister newspaper clipping, "If ye ken the house is meant to burn down on a certain day, why would ye be standing in it?"

So we weren't standing in it. Mrs. Bug had been told to stay at home, and Amy McCallum and her two little boys were already at Brianna's cabin—puzzled, but obliging. If Himself said that no one was to set foot in the house until dawn tomorrow . . . well, then, there was nothing more to be said, was there?

Ian had been up since before dawn, chopping kindling and hauling in firewood from the shed; everyone would be snug and warm.

Jamie himself had been up all night, tending stock, dispersing his armory—there was not a grain of gunpowder anywhere in the house, either—and prowling restlessly upstairs and down, alert to every cracking ember on a hearth, every burning candle flame, any faint noise without that might portend the approach of an enemy. The only thing he hadn't done was to sit on the roof with a wet sack, keeping a suspicious eye out for lightning—and that, only because it had been a cloudless night, the stars immense and bright overhead, burning in the frozen void.

I hadn't slept a great deal, either, disturbed equally by Jamie's prowling and by vivid dreams of conflagration.

The only conflagration visible, though, was the one sending a welcome shower of smoke and sparks from Brianna's chimney, and we opened the door to the grateful warmth of a roaring hearth and a number of bodies.

Aidan and Orrie, roused in the dark and dragged through the cold, had promptly crawled into Jemmy's trundle, and the three little boys were sound asleep, curled up like hedgehogs beneath their quilt. Amy was helping Bree with the breakfast; savory smells of porridge and bacon rose from the hearth.

"Is all well, ma'am?" Amy hurried over to take the big bundle I had brought—this contained my medical chest, the more scarce and valuable herbs from my surgery—and the sealed jar with the latest shipment of white phosphorus that Lord John had sent as a farewell present to Brianna.

"It is," I assured her, setting Adso's basket on the floor. I yawned, and eyed the bed wistfully, but set about to stow my chest in the lean-to pantry, where the children wouldn't get into it. I put the phosphorus on the highest shelf, well back from the edge, and moved a large cheese in front of it, just in case.

Jamie had divested himself of cloak and rabbit ears, and handing Roger the fowling piece, shot pouch, and powder horn he'd carried, was stamping snow from his boots. I saw him glance round the cabin, counting heads, then, at last, draw a small breath, nodding to himself. All safe, so far.

The morning passed peacefully. Breakfast eaten and cleared away, Amy, Bree, and I settled down by the fire with an enormous heap of mending. Adso, tail still twitching with indignation, had taken up a place on a high shelf, from whence he glared at Rollo, who had taken over the trundle bed when the boys got out of it.

Aidan and Jemmy, each now the proud possessor of *two* vrooms, drove them over hearthstones, under the bed, and through our feet, but for the most part, refrained from punching each other or stepping on Orrie, who was sitting placidly under the table gnawing on a piece of toast. Jamie, Roger, and Ian took turns going outside to pace back and forth and stare at the Big House, deserted in the shelter of the snow-dusted spruce.

As Roger came back from one of these expeditions, Brianna looked up suddenly from the sock she was darning.

"What?" he said, seeing her face.

"Oh." She had paused, needle halfway through the sock, and now looked down, completing her stitch. "Nothing. Just a—just a thought."

The tone of her voice made Jamie, who had been frowning his way through a battered copy of *Evelina,* look up.

"What sort of thought was that, *a nighean*?" he asked, his radar quite as good as Roger's.

"Er . . . well." She bit her lower lip, but then blurted, "What if it's *this* house?"

That froze everyone except the little boys, who continued crawling industriously around the room and over bed and table, screeching and vrooming.

"It could be, couldn't it?" Bree looked round, from rooftree to hearth. "All the—the prophecy said"—with an awkward nod toward Amy McCallum—"was *the home of James Fraser* would burn. But this was your home, to start with. And it's not like there's a street address. It just said, *on Fraser's Ridge.*"

Everyone stared at her, and she flushed deeply, dropping her eyes to the sock.

"I mean . . . it's not like they—er, prophecies—like they're always accurate, is it? They might have got the details wrong."

Amy nodded seriously; evidently, vagueness in the matter of detail was an accepted characteristic of prophecies.

Roger cleared his throat explosively; Jamie and Ian exchanged glances, then looked at the fire, leaping on the hearth and the towering stack of bone-dry firewood next to it, the overflowing kindling basket . . . Everyone's eyes turned expectantly to Jamie, whose face was a study in conflicting emotions.

"I suppose," he said slowly, "we could remove to Arch's place."

I began to count on my fingers: "You, me, Roger, Bree, Ian, Amy, Aidan, Orrie, Jemmy—plus Mr. and Mrs. Bug—is eleven people. In a one-room cabin that measures eight feet by ten?" I closed my fists and stared at him. "No one would have to set the place on fire; half of us would be sitting in the hearth already, well alight."

"Mmphm. Well, then . . . the Christie place is empty."

Amy's eyes went round with horror, and everyone looked automatically away from everyone else. Jamie took a deep breath and let it out, audibly.

"Perhaps we'll just be . . . very careful," I suggested. Everyone exhaled slightly, and we resumed our occupations, though without our former sense of snug safety.

Dinner passed without incident, but in midafternoon, a knock came on the door. Amy screamed, and Brianna dropped the shirt she was mending into the fire. Ian leaped to his feet and jerked the door open, and Rollo, jerked out of a doze, charged past him, roaring.

Jamie and Roger struck the doorway—and each other—simultaneously, stuck for an instant, and fell through. All the little boys shrieked and ran to their respective mothers, who were frantically beating at the smoldering shirt as though it were a live snake.

I had leaped to my feet, but was pressed against the wall, unable to get past Bree and Amy. Adso, startled by the racket and by my popping up beside him, hissed and took a swipe at me, narrowly missing my eye.

A number of oaths in a mixture of languages were coming from the dooryard, accompanied by a series of sharp barks from Rollo. Everyone sounded thoroughly annoyed, but there were no sounds of conflict. I edged my way delicately past the knot of mothers and sons, and peered out.

Major MacDonald, wet to the eyebrows and covered in clumps of snow and dirty slush, was gesticulating with some energy at Jamie, while Ian rebuked Rollo, and Roger—from the look on his face—was trying very hard not to burst out laughing.

Jamie, compelled by his own sense of propriety, but eyeing the Major with deep suspicion, invited him in. The inside of the cabin smelled of burned fabric, but at least the riot had calmed down, and the Major greeted us all with a fair assumption of cordiality. There was a lot of fuss, getting him stripped of his soaking-wet clothes, dried off, and—for lack of any better alternative—temporarily swathed in Roger's spare shirt and breeches, in which he appeared to be drowning, as he was a good six inches shorter than Roger.

Food and whisky having been ceremonially offered and accepted, the household fixed the Major with a collective eye and waited to hear what had brought him to the mountains in the dead of winter.

Jamie exchanged a brief glance with me, indicating that he could hazard a guess. So could I.

"I have come, sir," MacDonald said formally, hitching up the shirt to keep it from sliding off his shoulder, "to offer ye command of a company of militia, under the orders of General Hugh MacDonald. The General's troops are gathering, even as we speak, and will undertake their march to Wilmington at the end of the month."

I felt a deep qualm of apprehension at that. I was accustomed to MacDonald's chronic optimism and tendency to overstatement, but there was nothing of exaggeration in this statement. Did that mean that the help Governor Martin had requested, the troops from Ireland, would be landing soon, to meet General MacDonald's troops at the coast?

"The General's troops," Jamie said, poking up the fire. He and MacDonald had taken over the fireside, with Roger and Ian ranged on either side of them, like firedogs. Bree, Amy, and I repaired to the bed, where we perched like a row of roosting hens, watching the conversation with a mingling of interest and alarm, while the little boys retired under the table.

"How many men does he have, would ye say, Donald?"

I saw MacDonald hesitate, torn between truth and desire. He coughed, though, and said matter-of-factly, "He had a few more than a thousand when I left him. Ye ken weel, though—once we begin to move, others will come to join us. Many others. The more particularly," he added pointedly, "if such gentlemen as yourself are in command."

Jamie didn't reply to that at once. Meditatively, he shoved a burning wood fragment back into the fire with his foot.

"Powder and shot?" he asked. "Arms?"

"Aye, well; we'd a bit of a disappointment there." MacDonald took a sip of his whisky. "Duncan Innes had promised us a great deal in that way—but in the end, he was obliged to renege upon his promise." The Major's lips pressed tight, and I thought from the expression on his face that perhaps Duncan had not been overreacting in his decision to move to Acadia.

"Still," MacDonald continued more cheerfully, "we are not destitute in that regard. And those gallant gentlemen who have flocked to our cause—and who *will* come to join us—bring with them both their own weapons and their courage. You, of all people, must appreciate the force of the Hieland charge!"

Jamie looked up at that, and regarded MacDonald for a long moment before replying.

"Aye, well. Ye were behind the cannon at Culloden, Donald. I was in front of them. With a sword in my hand." He took up his own glass and drained it, then got up and moved to pour another, leaving MacDonald to recover his countenance.

"*Touché,* Major," Brianna murmured under her breath. I didn't think Jamie had ever before referred to the fact that the

Major had fought with the government forces during the Rising—but I wasn't surprised that he hadn't forgotten.

With a brief nod to the company, Jamie stepped outside—ostensibly to visit the privy, more likely to check on the well-being of the house. Still more likely to give MacDonald a little breathing room.

Roger, with the courtesy of a host—and the suppressed keenness of a historian—was asking MacDonald questions regarding the General and his activities. Ian, impassive and watchful, sat by his feet, one hand toying with Rollo's ruff.

"The General's rather elderly for such a campaign, surely?" Roger took another stick of wood and pushed it into the fire. "Especially a winter campaign."

"He has the odd wee spell of catarrh," MacDonald admitted, offhand. "But who doesna, in this climate? And Donald McLeod, his lieutenant, is a man of vigor. I assure ye, sir, should the General be at any point indisposed, Colonel McLeod is more than capable of leading the troops to victory!"

He went on at some length about the virtues—both personal and military—of Donald McLeod. I ceased listening, my attention distracted by a stealthy movement on the shelf above his head. Adso.

MacDonald's red coat was spread over the back of a chair to dry, steaming in the heat. His wig, damp and disheveled from Rollo's attack, hung on the cloak peg above it. I got up hastily and possessed myself of the wig, receiving a look of puzzlement from the Major, and one of green-eyed hostility from Adso, who plainly considered it low of me to hog this desirable prey for myself.

"Er . . . I'll just . . . um . . . put it somewhere safe, shall I?" Clutching the damp mass of horsehair to my bosom, I sidled outside and round to the pantry, where I tucked the wig safely away behind the cheese with the phosphorus.

Coming out, I met Jamie, red-nosed with cold, coming back from a reconnaissance of the Big House.

"All's well," he assured me. He glanced up at the chimney above us, spuming clouds of thick gray smoke. "Ye dinna suppose the lass might be right, do ye?" He sounded as though he were joking, but he wasn't.

"God knows. *How* long 'til tomorrow's dawn?" The shadows were already falling long, violet and chill across the snow.

"Too long." He had violet shadows in his face, too, from one sleepless night; this would be another. He hugged me against himself for a moment, though, warm in spite of the fact that he wore nothing over his shirt but the rough jacket in which he did chores.

"Ye dinna suppose MacDonald will come back and fire the house, if I refuse him, do ye?" he asked, releasing me with a fair attempt at a smile.

"What do you mean *'if'*?" I demanded, but he was already on his way back in.

MacDonald stood up in respect when Jamie came in, waiting until he was seated again before taking his own stool.

"Have ye had a moment, then, to think on my offer, Mr. Fraser?" he asked formally. "Your presence would be of the greatest value—and valued greatly by General MacDonald and the Governor, as well as myself."

Jamie sat silent for a moment, looking into the fire.

"It grieves me, Donald, that we should find ourselves so opposed," he said at last, looking up. "Ye canna be in ignorance, though, of my position in this matter. I have declared myself."

MacDonald nodded, lips tightening a little.

"I ken what ye've done. But it is not too late for remedy. Ye've done nothing yet that is irrevocable—and a man may surely admit mistake."

Jamie's mouth twitched a little.

"Oh, aye, Donald. Might you admit your own mistake, then, and join the cause of liberty?"

MacDonald drew himself up.

"It may please ye to tease, Mr. Fraser," he said, obviously keeping a grip on his temper, "but my offer is made in earnest."

"I know that, Major. My apologies for undue levity. And also for the fact that I must make ye a poor reward of your efforts, coming so far in bitter weather."

"Ye refuse, then?" Red smudges burned on MacDonald's cheeks, and his pale blue eyes had gone the color of the winter sky. "Ye will abandon your kin, your ain folk? Ye would betray your blood, as well as your oath?"

Jamie had opened his mouth to reply, but stopped at this. I could feel something going on inside him. Shock, at this blunt—and very accurate—accusation? Hesitation? He had never discussed the situation in those terms, but he must have grasped them. Most of the Highlanders in the colony either had joined the Loyalist side already—like Duncan and Jocasta—or likely would.

His declaration had cut him off from a great many friends—and might well cut him off from the remnants of his family in the New World, as well. Now MacDonald was holding out the apple of temptation, the call of clan and blood.

But he had had years to think of it, to ready himself.

"I have said what I must, Donald," he said quietly. "I have pledged myself and my house to what I believe is right. I cannot do otherwise."

MacDonald sat for a moment, looking at him narrowly. Then, without a word, he stood and pulled Roger's shirt off over his head. His torso was pale and lean, but with a slight middle-aged softness round the waist, and bore several white scars, the marks of bullet wounds and sabre cuts.

"You don't mean to go, surely, Major? It's freezing out, and nearly dark!" I came to stand by Jamie, and Roger and Bree rose, too, adding their protestations to mine. MacDonald, though, was obdurate, merely shaking his head as he pulled on his own damp clothing, fastening his coat with difficulty, as the buttonholes were stiff with damp.

"I will not take hospitality from the hand of a traitor, mum," he said very quietly, and bowed to me. He straightened then, and met Jamie's eye, man to man.

"We shall not meet again as friends, Mr. Fraser," he said. "I regret it."

"Then let us hope we do not meet again at all, Major," Jamie said. "I too regret it."

MacDonald bowed again, to the rest of the company, and clapped his hat on his head. His expression changed as he did so and felt the damp coldness of it on his bare head.

"Oh, your wig! Just a moment, Major—I'll fetch it." I rushed out and round to the pantry—just in time to hear a crash as something fell inside. I jerked open the door, left ajar from my last visit, and Adso streaked past me, the Major's wig in his mouth. Inside, the lean-to was in brilliant blue flames.

I HAD INITIALLY wondered how I would keep awake all night. In the event, it wasn't difficult at all. In the aftermath of the blaze, I wasn't sure I'd ever sleep again.

It could have been much worse; Major MacDonald, in spite of now being a sworn enemy, had come nobly to our aid, rushing out and flinging his still-wet cloak over the blaze, thus preventing the total destruction of the pantry—and, doubtless, the cabin. The cloak had not put out the fire entirely, though, and quenching the flames that sprang up here and there had entailed a great deal of excitement and rushing about, in the course of which Orrie McCallum was misplaced, toddled off, and fell into the groundhog kiln, where he was found—many frantic minutes later—by Rollo.

He was fished out undamaged, but the hullabaloo caused Brianna to have what she thought was premature labor. Fortunately, this proved to be merely a bad case of hiccups, caused by the combination of nervous strain and eating excessive quantities of sauerkraut and dried-apple pie, for which she had conceived a recent craving.

"Flammable, she said." Jamie looked at the charred remains of the pantry floor, then at Brianna, who had, in spite of my recommendation that she lie down, come out to see what could be salvaged from the smoking remains. He shook his head. "It's a miracle that ye've not burnt the place to ashes long since, lass."

She emitted a smothered "hic!" and glowered at him, one hand on her bulging stomach.

"*Me?* You'd better not be try—hic!—ing to make out that this is *my*—hic!—fault. Did *I* put the Major's—hic!—wig next to the—"

"BOO!" Roger bellowed, darting a hand at her face.

She shrieked, and hit him. Jemmy and Aidan, running out to see what the commotion was about, started dancing round her, ecstatically shouting, "Boo! Boo!" like a gang of miniature lunatic ghosts.

Bree, her eyes gleaming dangerously, bent and scooped up a handful of snow. In an instant, she had molded it into a ball, which she flung at her husband's head with deadly accuracy. It struck him right between the eyes, exploding in a shower that left white granules clinging to his eyebrows and melting globs of snow running down his cheeks.

"What?" he said incredulously. "What's that for? I was only trying to—hey!" He ducked the next one, only to be pelted round the knees and waist by handsful of snow lobbed at short range by Jemmy and Aidan, quite berserk by now.

Modestly accepting thanks for his action earlier, the Major had been persuaded—not least by the fact that it was now full dark and beginning to snow again—to accept the hospitality of the cabin, with the understanding that it was Roger, not Jamie, who was offering it. Watching his hosts whooping and hiccing as they plastered one another with snow, he looked as though he might be having second thoughts about being so fine as to refuse to dine with a traitor, but he rather stiffly bowed in response when Jamie and I bade him farewell, then trudged into the cabin, the muddy shreds that Adso had left of his wig clasped in his hand.

It seemed extremely—and most gratefully—quiet as we made our way through the falling snow toward our own house, alone. The sky had gone a pinkish lavender, and the flakes floated down around us, supernatural in their silence.

The house loomed before us, its quiet bulk somehow welcoming, in spite of the darkened windows. Snow was swirling across the porch in little eddies, piling in drifts on the sills.

"I suppose it would be harder for a fire to start if it's snowing—wouldn't you think?"

Jamie bent to unlock the front door.

"I dinna much mind if the place bursts into flame by spontaneous combustion, Sassenach, provided I have my supper first."

"A cold supper, were you thinking?" I asked dubiously.

"I was not," he said firmly. "I mean to light a roaring fire in the kitchen hearth, fry up a dozen eggs in butter, and eat them all, then lay ye down on the hearth rug and roger ye 'til you—is that all right?" he inquired, noticing my look.

"'Til I what?" I asked, fascinated by his description of the evening's program.

"'Til ye burst into flame and take me with ye, I suppose," he said, and stooping, swooped me up into his arms and carried me across the darkened threshold.

112

OATHBREAKER

February 2, 1776

HE CALLED THEM all together, and they came. The Jacobites of Ardsmuir, the fishermen from Thurso, the outcasts and opportunists who had come to settle on the Ridge over the last six years. He had called for the men, and most came alone, making their way through the dripping woods, slipping on mossy rocks and muddy trails. Some of the wives came, as well, though, curious, wary, though they hung modestly back and allowed Claire to shepherd them into the house one by one.

The men stood in the dooryard, and he regretted that; the memory of the last time they had gathered here was much too fresh in everyone's mind. But there was no choice about it; there were too many to fit in the house. And it was broad day, now, not night—though he saw more than one man turn his head sharply to glance at the chestnut trees, as though he saw the ghost of Thomas Christie there, poised once more to walk through the crowd.

He crossed himself, and said a hasty prayer, as he always did when he thought of Tom Christie, then stepped out on the porch. They had been talking together—awkwardly, but with a fair assumption of ease—but the talk died abruptly when he appeared.

"I have received word summoning me to Wilmington," he said to them without preamble. "I go to join the militias there, and I will take with me such men as will come willingly."

They gaped at him like sheep disturbed at grazing. He had a moment's unsettling impulse to laugh, but it passed at once.

"We will go as militia, but I do not command your service." Privately, he doubted that he *could* command more than a handful of them now, but as well to put a good face on it.

Most were still blinking at him, but one or two had got a grip on themselves.

"You declare yourself a rebel, *Mac Dubh*?" That was Murdo, bless him. Loyal as a dog, but slow of thought. He needed things to be put in the simplest of terms, but once grasped, he would deal with them tenaciously.

"Aye, Murdo, I do. I am a rebel. So will any man be who marches with me."

That caused a fair degree of murmuring, glances of doubt. Here and there in the crowd, he heard the word "oath," and steeled himself for the obvious question.

He was taken aback by the man who asked it, though. Arch Bug drew himself up, tall and stern.

"Ye swore an oath to the King, *Seaumais mac Brian,*" he said, his voice unexpectedly sharp. "So did we all."

There was a murmur of agreement at this, and faces turned to him, frowning, uneasy. He took a deep breath, and felt his stomach knot. Even now, knowing what he knew, and knowing too the immorality of a forced oath, to break his sworn word openly made him feel that he had stepped on a step that wasn't there.

"So did we all," he agreed. "But it was an oath forced upon us as captives, not one given as men of honor."

This was patently true; still, it was an oath, and Highlanders did not take any oath lightly. *May I die and be buried far from my kin . . .* Oath or no, he thought grimly, that fate would likely be theirs.

"But an oath nonetheless, sir," said Hiram Crombie, lips drawn tight. "We have sworn before God. Do you ask us to put aside such a thing?" Several of the Presbyterians murmured acquiescence, drawing closer to Crombie in show of support.

He took another deep breath, feeling his belly tighten.

"I ask nothing." And knowing full well what he did, despising himself in a way for doing it—he fell back upon the ancient weapons of rhetoric and idealism.

"I said that the oath of loyalty to the King was an oath extorted, not given. Such an oath is without power, for no man swears freely, save he is free himself."

No one shouted disagreement, so he went on, voice pitched to carry, but not shouting.

"Ye'll ken the Declaration of Arbroath, will ye? Four hundred years since, it was our sires, our grandsires, who put their hands to these words: . . . *for as long as but a hundred of us remain alive, never will we on any conditions be brought under English rule."* He stopped to steady his voice, then went on. *"It is in truth not for glory, nor riches, nor honours that we are fighting, but for freedom—for that alone, which no honest man gives up but with life itself."*

He stopped dead then. Not for its effect on the men to whom he spoke, but because of the words themselves—for in speaking them, he had found himself unexpectedly face to face with his own conscience.

To this point, he had been dubious about the justifications of the revolution, and more so of its ends; he had been compelled to the rebel stand because of what Claire, Brianna, and Roger Mac had told him. But in the speaking of the ancient words, he found the conviction he thought he pretended—and was stricken by the thought that he did indeed go to fight for something more than the welfare of his own people.

And ye'll end up just as dead in the end, he thought, resigned. *I dinna expect it hurts less, to ken it's for good cause—but maybe so.*

"I shall leave in a week," he said quietly, and left them staring after him.

HE HAD EXPECTED his Ardsmuir men to come: the three Lindsay brothers, Hugh Abernathy, Padraic MacNeill, and the rest. Not expected, but gladly welcomed, were Robin McGillivray and his son, Manfred.

Ute McGillivray had forgiven him, he saw, with a certain sense of amusement. Besides Robin and Freddie, fifteen men from near Salem had come, all relatives of the redoubtable *frau.*

A great surprise, though, was Hiram Crombie, who alone of the fisher-folk had decided to join him.

"I have prayed on the matter," Hiram informed him, managing to look more piously sour than usual, "and I believe ye're right about the oath. I expect ye'll have us all hangit and burned oot of our homes—but I'll come, nonetheless."

The rest—with great mutterings and agitated debate—had not. He didn't blame them. Having survived the aftermath of Culloden, the perilous voyage to the Colonies, and the hardship of exile, the very last thing a sensible person could wish was to take up arms against the King.

The greatest surprise, though, awaited him as his small company rode out of Cooperville and turned into the road that led south.

A company of men, some forty strong, was waiting at the crossroad. He drew near warily, and a single man spurred out of the crowd and drew up with him—Richard Brown, pale-faced and grim.

"I hear you go to Wilmington," Brown said without preamble. "If so be as it's agreeable, my men and I will ride with you." He coughed, and added, "Under your command, to be sure."

Behind him, he heard a small "hmph!" from Claire, and suppressed a smile. He was quite aware of the phalanx of narrowed eyes at his back. He caught Roger Mac's eye, and his son-in-law gave a small nod. War made strange bedfellows; Roger Mac knew that as well as he did—and for himself, he had fought with worse than Brown, during the Rising.

"Be welcome, then," he said, and bowed from his saddle. "You and your men."

WE MET ANOTHER militia company near a place called Moore's Creek, and camped with them under the longleaf pines. There had been a bad ice storm the day before, and the ground was thick with fallen branches, some as large around as my waist. It made the going more difficult, but had its advantages, so far as making campfires went.

I was throwing a hastily assembled bucket of ingredients into the kettle for stew—scraps of ham, with bones, beans, rice, onions, carrots, crumbled stale biscuit—and listening to the other militia commander, Robert Borthy, who was telling Jamie—with considerable levity—about the state of the Emigrant Highland Regiment, as our opponents were formally known.

"There can't be more than five or six hundred, all told," he was saying with amused derision. "Old MacDonald and his aides have been tryin' to scoop 'em up from the countryside for months, and I gather the effort has been akin to scoopin' water with a sieve."

On one occasion, Alexander McLean, one of the general's aides, had set up a rendezvous point, calling upon all the Highlanders and Scotch–Irish in the neighborhood to assemble—cannily providing a hogshead of liquor as inducement. Some five hundred men had in fact shown up—but as soon as the liquor was drunk, they had melted away again, leaving McLean alone, and completely lost.

"The poor man wandered about for nearly two days, lookin' for the road, before someone took pity on him and led him back to civilization." Borthy, a hearty backwoods soul with a thick brown beard, grinned widely at the tale, and accepted a cup of ale with due thanks before going on.

"God knows where the rest of 'em are now. I hear tell that what troops Old MacDonald has are mostly brand-new emigrants—the Governor made 'em swear to take up arms to defend the colony before he'd grant them land. Most of them poor sods are fresh off the boat from Scotland—they don't know north from south, let alone just where they are."

"Oh, I ken where they are, even if they don't." Ian came into the firelight, grubby but cheerful. He had been riding dispatches back and forth among the various militia companies converging on Wilmington, and his statement caused a rush of general interest.

"Where?" Richard Brown leaned forward into the firelight, narrow face keen and foxy.

"They're comin' down Negro Head Point Road, marching like a proper regiment," Ian said, sinking onto a hastily offered log with a small groan. "Is there anything hot to drink, Auntie? I'm frozen and parched, both."

There was a nasty sort of dark liquid, called "coffee" for courtesy's sake, and made from boiling burned acorns. I rather dubiously poured him a cup, but he consumed it with every evidence of enjoyment, meanwhile recounting the results of his expeditions.

"They meant to circle round to the west, but Colonel Howe's men got there first, and cut them off. So then they went across, meaning to take the ford—but Colonel Moore put his men to the quick-step and marched all night to forestall them."

"They made no move to engage either Howe or Moore?" Jamie asked, frowning. Ian shook his head, and gulped the rest of his acorn coffee.

"Wouldna come close. Colonel Moore says they dinna mean to engage until they reach Wilmington—they're expecting reinforcement there."

I exchanged a glance with Jamie. The expected reinforcement was presumably the British regular troops, promised by General Gage. But a rider from Brunswick we had met the day before had told us that no ships had arrived when *he* left the coast, four days before. If there was reinforcement awaiting them, it would have to come from the local Loyalists—and from the various rumors and reports we'd heard so far, the local Loyalists were a weak reed on which to lean.

"Well, so. They're cut off on either side, aye? Straight down the road is where they're headed—they might reach the bridge late tomorrow."

"How far is it, Ian?" Jamie asked, squinting through the vista of longleaf pines. The trees were very tall, and the grassland under them wide open—very reasonable for riding.

"Maybe half a day on horseback."

"Aye, then." Jamie relaxed a little, and reached for his own cup of the vile brew. "We've time to sleep first, then."

WE REACHED the bridge at Moore's Creek by midday the next day, and joined the company commanded by Richard Caswell, who greeted Jamie with pleasure.

The Highland regiment was nowhere in sight—but dispatch riders arrived regularly, reporting their steady movement down Negro Head Point Road—a wide wagon thoroughfare that led directly to the solid plank bridge that crossed the Widow Moore's creek.

Jamie, Caswell, and several of the other commanders were walking up and down the bank, pointing at the bridge and up and down the shore. The creek ran through a stretch of treacherous, swampy ground, with cypress trees stretching up from water and mud. The creek itself deepened as it narrowed, though—a plumb line that some curious soul dropped into the water off the bridge said it was fifteen feet deep at that point—and the bridge was the only feasible place for an army of any size to cross.

Which did a great deal to explain Jamie's silence over supper. He had helped to throw up a small earthwork on the far side of the creek, and his hands were smeared with dirt—and grease.

"They've cannon," he said quietly, seeing me eye the smudges on his hands. He wiped them absently on his breeks, much the worse for wear. "Two small guns from the town—but cannon, nonetheless." He looked toward the bridge, and grimaced slightly.

I knew what he was thinking—and why.

Ye were behind the cannon at Culloden, Donald, he had said to the Major. *I was in front of them. With a sword in my hand.* Swords were the Highlanders' natural weapons—and for most, likely their only weapons. From all we had heard, General MacDonald had managed to assemble only a small quantity of muskets and powder; most of his troops were armed with broadswords and targes. And they were marching straight into ambush.

"Oh, Christ," Jamie said, so softly I could barely hear him. "The poor wee fools. The poor gallant wee fools."

MATTERS BECAME still worse—or much better, depending on your viewpoint—as dusk fell. The temperature had risen since the ice storm, but the ground was sodden; moisture rose from it during the day, but then as night came on, condensed into a fog so thick that even the campfires were barely visible, each one glowing like a sullen coal in the mist.

Excitement was passing through the militia like a mosquito-borne fever, as the new conditions gave rise to new plans.

"Now," Ian said softly, appearing like a ghost out of the fog beside Jamie. "Caswell's ready."

Such supplies as we had were already packed; carrying guns, powder, and food, eight hundred men, together with an uncounted quantity of camp-followers like myself, stole quietly through the mist toward the bridge, leaving the campfires burning behind us.

I wasn't sure exactly where MacDonald's troops were just now—they might be still on the wagon road, or might have cautiously detoured, coming down to the edge of the swamp to reconnoiter. Good luck to them in *that* case, I thought. My own insides were tight with tension as I stepped carefully across the bridge; it was silly to tiptoe, but I felt a reluctance to put my feet down firmly—the fog and silence compelled a sense of secrecy and furtiveness.

I stubbed a toe against an uneven plank and lurched forward, but Roger, walking beside me, caught me by the arm and set me upright. I squeezed his arm, and he smiled a little, his face barely visible through the mist, though he was no more than a foot away.

He knew quite as well as Jamie and the rest did what was coming. Nonetheless, I sensed a strong excitement in him, mingled with dread. It was, after all, to be his first battle.

On the other side, we dispersed to make fresh camps on the hill above the circular earthwork the men had thrown up a hundred yards from the creek. I passed close enough to the guns to see their elongated snouts, poking inquisitively through the mist: Mother Covington and her daughter, the men called the two cannon—I wondered idly which was which, and who the original Mother Covington might have been. A redoubtable lady, I assumed—or possibly the proprietor of the local brothel.

Firewood was easy to find; the ice storm had extended to the pines near the creek, too. It was, however, bloody damp, and damned if I was going to spend an hour on my knees with a tinderbox. Luckily, no one could see *what* I was doing in this pea-soup fog, and I stealthily removed a small tin of Brianna's matches from my pocket.

As I was blowing on the kindling, I heard a series of odd, rending screeches from the direction of the bridge, and knelt upright, staring down the hill. I couldn't see anything, of course, but realized almost at once that it was the sound of nails giving way as planks were pried up—they were dismantling the bridge.

It seemed a long time before Jamie came to find me. He refused food, but sat against a tree and beckoned to me. I sat down between his knees and leaned back against him, grateful for his warmth; the night was cold, with a damp that crept into every crevice and chilled the marrow.

"Surely they'll see that the bridge is out?" I said, after a long silence filled with the myriad noises of the men working below.

"Not if the fog lasts 'til morning—and it will." Jamie sounded resigned, but he seemed more peaceful than he had earlier. We sat quietly together for some time, watching the play of flames on the fog—an eerie sight, as the fire seemed to shimmer and merge with the mist, the flames stretching strangely up and up, disappearing into the swirl of white.

"D'ye believe in ghosts, Sassenach?" Jamie asked suddenly.

"Er . . . well, not to put too fine a point on it, yes," I said. He knew I did, because I'd told him about my meeting with the Indian whose face was painted black. I knew he did, too—he was a Highlander. "Why, have you seen one?"

He shook his head, wrapping his arms more securely around me.

"Not to say 'seen,'" he said, sounding thoughtful. "But I will be damned if he's no there."

"Who?" I said, rather startled at this.

"Murtagh," he said, surprising me further. He shifted more

comfortably, resettling me against him. "Ever since the fog came in, I've had the most peculiar sense of him, just by me."

"Really?" This was fascinating, but made me thoroughly uneasy. Murtagh, Jamie's godfather, had died at Culloden, and—so far as I knew—hadn't been going about manifesting himself since. I didn't doubt his presence; Murtagh's had been an extremely strong—if dour—personality, and if Jamie said he was there, he very likely was. What made me uneasy was the contemplation of just *why* he might be there.

I concentrated for a time, but got no sense of the tough little Scotsman myself. Evidently, he was only interested in Jamie. *That* frightened me.

While the conclusion of the morrow's battle was a foregone one, a battle was a battle, and men might be killed on the winning side, as well. Murtagh had been Jamie's godfather, and took his duty to Jamie seriously. I sincerely hoped he hadn't had word that Jamie was about to be killed, and shown up to conduct him to heaven—visions on the eve of battle were a fairly common occurrence in Highland lore, but Jamie did say he hadn't *seen* Murtagh. That was something, I supposed.

"He, um, hasn't *said* anything to you, has he?"

Jamie shook his head, seeming unfazed by this ghostly visitation.

"Nay, he's just . . . there." He seemed, in fact, to find this "thereness" a comfort, and so I didn't voice my own doubts and fears. I had them, nonetheless, and spent the rest of the short night pressed close against my husband, as though daring Murtagh or anyone else to take him from me.

113

THE GHOSTS OF CULLODEN

COME DAWN, ROGER stood behind the low earthwork by his father-in-law, musket in hand, straining his eyes to peer into the mist. The sounds of an army came to him clearly; sound carried through fog. The measured tramp of feet, though they were not marching in any sort of unison. The clank of metal and rustle of cloth. Voices—the shouts of officers, he thought, beginning to rally their troops.

They would by now have found the deserted campfires; they'd know that the enemy now lay across the creek.

The smell of tallow was strong in the air; Alexander Lillington's men had greased the support timbers, after the planks had been removed. He'd been grasping his gun for hours, it seemed, and yet the metal was still cold in his hand—his fingers were stiff.

"D'ye hear the shouting?" Jamie nodded toward the mist that hid the far bank. The wind had changed; no more than disconnected Gaelic phrases came from beyond the ghostly cypress trunks, and I made no sense of them. Jamie did.

"Whoever's leading them—I think it's McLeod, by the voice—he means to charge the creek," he said.

"But that's suicide!" Roger blurted. "Surely they know—surely someone's seen the bridge?"

"They are Highlanders," Jamie said, still softly, eyes on the ramrod he pulled from its rest. "They will follow the man to whom they vow loyalty, even though he leads them to their death."

Ian was nearby; he glanced quickly toward Roger, then over his shoulder, where Kenny and Murdo Lindsay stood with Ronnie Sinclair and the McGillivrays. They stood in a casual knot, but every hand touched a musket or rifle, and their eyes darted toward Jamie every few seconds.

They had joined Colonel Lillywhite's men on this side of the creek; Lillington was passing to and fro through the men, assessing readiness.

Lillington stopped abruptly at sight of Jamie, and Roger felt a nervous qualm in the pit of his stomach. Randall Lillington had been a second cousin of the Colonel's.

Alexander Lillington wasn't a man to hide his thoughts; it had quite evidently dawned on him that his own men were forty feet away and that Jamie's men stood between him and them. His eyes darted toward the mist, where Donald McLeod's bellowing was being answered by increasing roars from the Highlanders with him, then back at Jamie.

"What does he say?" Lillington demanded, rising on his toes and frowning toward the far bank, as though concentration might yield him meaning.

"He says to them that courage will carry the day." Jamie glanced toward the crest of the rise behind them. Mother Covington's long black snout was just visible through the mist. *"Would that it could,"* he added quietly in Gaelic.

Alexander Lillington reached out suddenly and grabbed Jamie's wrist.

"And you, sir?" he said, suspicion open in eyes and voice. "Are you not a Highlander, as well?"

Lillington's other hand was on the pistol in his belt. Roger felt the casual talk among the men behind him stop, and glanced back. All Jamie's men were watching, with expressions of great interest but no particular alarm. Evidently, they felt Jamie could deal with Lillington by himself.

"I ask you, sir—to whom is your loyalty?"

"Where do I stand, sir?" Jamie said with elaborate politeness. "On this side of the creek, or on that?"

A few men grinned at that, but forbore to laugh; the question of loyalty was a raw one still, and no man would risk it unnecessarily.

Lillington's grip on his wrist relaxed, but did not yet let go, though he acknowledged Jamie's statement with a nod.

"Well enough. But how are we to know that you do not

mean to turn and fall upon us in battle? For you *are* a Highlander, are you not? And your men?"

"I am a Highlander," Jamie said bleakly. He glanced once more at the far bank, where occasional glimpses of tartan showed through the mist, and then back. The shouting echoed from the fog. "And I am the sire of Americans." He pulled his wrist from Lillington's grasp.

"And I give ye leave, sir," he continued evenly, lifting his rifle and standing it on its butt, "to stand behind me and thrust your sword through my heart if I fire amiss."

With that, he turned his back on Lillington and loaded his gun, ramming ball, powder, and patch with great precision.

A voice bellowed from the fog, and a hundred other throats took up the cry in Gaelic. *"KING GEORGE AND BROADSWORDS!"*

The last Highland charge had begun.

THEY BURST OUT OF the mist a hundred feet from the bridge, howling, and his heart jumped in his chest. For an instant—an instant only—he felt he ran with them, and the wind of it snapped in his shirt, cold on his body.

But he stood stock-still, Murtagh beside him, looking cynically on. Roger Mac coughed, and Jamie raised the rifle to his shoulder, waiting.

"Fire!" The volley struck them just before they reached the gutted bridge; half a dozen fell in the road, but the others came on. Then the cannon fired from the hill above, one and then the other, and the concussion of their discharge was like a shove against his back.

He had fired with the volley, aiming above their heads. Now swung the rifle down and pulled the ramrod. There was screaming on both sides, the shriek of wounded and the stronger bellowing of battle.

"A righ! A righ!" The King! The King!

McLeod was at the bridge; he'd been hit, there was blood on his coat, but he brandished sword and targe, and ran onto the bridge, stabbing his sword into the wood to anchor himself.

The cannon spoke again, but were aimed too high; most of

the Highlanders had crowded down to the banks of the creek—some were in the water, clinging to the bridge supports, inching across. More were on the timbers, slipping, using their swords like McLeod to keep their balance.

"Fire!" and he fired, powder smoke blending with the fog. The cannon had the range, they spoke one-two, and he felt the blast push against him, felt as though the shot had torn through him. Most of those on the bridge were in the water now, more threw themselves flat upon the timbers, trying to wriggle their way across, only to be picked off by the muskets, every man firing at will from the redoubt.

He loaded, and fired.

There he is, said a voice, dispassionate; he had no notion was it his, or Murtagh's.

McLeod was dead, his body floating in the creek for an instant before the weight of the black water pulled him down. Many men were struggling in that water—the creek was deep here, and mortal cold. Few Highlanders could swim.

He glimpsed Allan MacDonald, Flora's husband, pale and staring in the crowd on the shore.

Major Donald MacDonald floundered, rising halfway in the water. His wig was gone and his head showed bare and wounded, blood running from his scalp down over his face. His teeth were bared, clenched in agony or ferocity, there was no telling which. Another shot struck him and he fell with a splash—but rose again, slow, slow, and then pitched forward into water too deep to stand, but rose yet again, splashing frantically, spraying blood from his shattered mouth in the effort to breathe.

Let it be you, then, lad, said the dispassionate voice. He raised his rifle and shot MacDonald cleanly through the throat. He fell backward and sank at once.

IT WAS OVER in minutes, the fog thick with powder smoke, the black creek choked with the dying and dead.

"King George and broadswords, eh?" said Caswell, bleakly surveying the damage. "Broadswords against cannon. Poor buggers."

On the other side, all was confusion. Those who had not fallen at the bridge were in flight. Already, men on this side of the creek were carrying the timbers down to repair the bridge. Those who were running wouldn't get far.

He should go, too, summon his men to help in pursuit. But he stood as though turned to stone, the cold wind singing in his ears.

JACK RANDALL *stood still. His sword was in his hand, but he made no effort to raise it. Only stood there, that odd smile on his lips, dark eyes burning in Jamie's own.*

If he had been able to break that gaze . . . but he couldn't, and so caught the blur of movement behind Randall. Murtagh, running, bounding tussocks like a sheep. And the glint of his godfather's blade—had he seen that, or only imagined it? No matter; he'd known without doubt from the cock of Murtagh's arm, and seen before it happened the murderous strike come upward toward the Captain's red-clad back.

But Randall spun, warned maybe by some change in his eyes, the sob of Murtagh's breath—or only by a soldier's instinct. Too late to avoid the thrust, but soon enough that the dirk missed its fatal aim into the kidney. Randall had grunted with the blow—Christ, he could hear it—and jerked aside staggering, but turning as he fell, grasping Murtagh's wrist, dragging him down in a shower of spray from the wet gorse they fell through.

They had rolled away into a hollow, locked together, struggling, and he had flung himself through the clinging plants in pursuit, some weapon—what, what had he held?—in his fist.

But the feel of it faded against his skin; he felt the weight of the thing in his hand, but there was no shape of hilt or trigger to remind him, and it was gone again.

Leaving him with that one image: Murtagh. Murtagh, teeth clenched and bared as he struck. Murtagh, running, coming to save him.

HE BECAME SLOWLY aware again of where he was. There was a hand on his arm—Roger Mac, white-faced, but steady.

"I am going to see to them," Roger Mac said, with a brief nod toward the creek. "You're all right, yourself?"

"Aye, of course," he said, though with the feeling he so often had in waking from a dream—as though he were not in fact quite real.

Roger Mac nodded and turned to walk away. Then suddenly turned back, and laying his hand once more on Jamie's arm, said very quietly, *"Ego te absolvo."* Then turned again and went resolutely to tend the dying and bless the dead.

Part Twelve

Time Will Not Be Ours Forever

114

AMANDA

FROM *L'OIGNON–INTELLIGENCER, MAY 15, 1776*

INDEPENDENCE!!

In the Wake of the famous Victory at Moore's Creek Bridge, the Fourth Provincial Congress of North Carolina has voted to adopt the Halifax Resolves. These Resolutions authorize Delegates to the Continental Congress to concur with the other Delegates of the other Colonies in declaring Independency and forming foreign Alliances, reserving to this Colony the sole and exclusive Right of forming a Constitution and Laws for this Colony, and by Passage of the Halifax Resolves, North Carolina thus becomes the first Colony officially to indorse Independency.

THE FIRST SHIP of a Fleet commanded by Sir Peter Parker has arrived at the Mouth of the Cape Fear River, upon the eighteenth of April. The Fleet consists of nine Ships in total, and is bringing British Troops to pacify and unite the Colony, by the Word of Governor Josiah Martin.

STOLEN: Goods amounting to twenty-six Pounds, ten Shillings and Fourpence in Total, abstracted from the Warehouse of Mr. Gerald Forbes on Water Street. Thieves broke a Hole in the Back of the Warehouse during the Night of May twelfth, and carried the Goods away by means of a Wagon. Two Men, one White, one Black, were seen driving a Wagon away with a Team of bay Mules. Any Word pertaining to this atrocious Crime will be generously Rewarded. Apply to W. Jones, in care of the Gull and Oyster on the Market Square.

BORN, to Captain Roger MacKenzie of Fraser's Ridge and his lady, a girl, on the twenty-first of April. Child and Mother are reported in good Health, the Child's name given as Amanda Claire Hope MacKenzie.

Roger had never felt so terrified as he did when his newborn daughter was placed in his arms for the first time. Minutes old, skin tender and perfect as an orchid's, she was so delicate he feared he would leave fingerprints on her—but so alluring that he had to touch her, drawing the back of his knuckle gently, so gently, down the perfect curve of her fat little cheek, stroking the black cobweb silk of her hair with an unbelieving forefinger.

"She looks like you." Brianna, sweaty, disheveled, deflated—and so beautiful he could scarcely bear to look at her—lay back against the pillows with a grin that came and went like the Cheshire Cat's—never entirely absent, even though it faded now and then from tiredness.

"Does she?" He studied the tiny face with complete absorption. Not for any sign of himself—only because he couldn't take his eyes off her.

He had come to know her intimately, through the months of being roused suddenly by pokes and kicks, of watching the liquid heave of Brianna's belly, of feeling the little one swell and retreat under his hands as he lay behind his wife, cupping her stomach and making jokes.

But he'd known her as Little Otto, the private name they'd used for the unborn child. Otto had had a distinct personality—and for a moment, he felt a ridiculous pang of loss, realizing that Otto was gone. This tiny, exquisite being was someone entirely new.

"Is she Marjorie, do you think?" Bree was lifting her head, peering at the blanket-wrapped bundle. They'd discussed names for months, making lists, arguing, making fun of each other's choices, choosing ridiculous things like Montgomery or Agatha.

At last, tentatively, they'd decided that if it was a boy, the name might be Michael; if a girl, Marjorie, after Roger's mother.

His daughter opened her eyes quite suddenly and looked at him. Her eyes were slanted; he wondered if they would stay that way, like her mother's. A sort of soft, middle blue, like the sky in mid-morning—nothing remarkable, at a glance, but when you looked straight into it . . . vast, illimitable.

"No," he said softly, staring into those eyes. Could she see him yet? he wondered.

"No," he said again. "Her name's Amanda."

I HADN'T SAID anything to begin with. It was a common thing in newborns—especially babies born a bit early, as Amanda had been—nothing to worry about.

The ductus arteriosus is a small blood vessel that in the fetus joins the aorta to the pulmonary artery. Babies have lungs, of course, but prior to birth don't use them; all their oxygen comes from the placenta, via the umbilical cord. Ergo, no need for blood to be circulated to the lungs, save to nourish the developing tissue—and so the ductus arteriosus bypasses the pulmonary circulation.

At birth, though, the baby takes its first breath, and oxygen sensors in this small vessel cause it to contract—and close permanently. With the ductus arteriosus closed, blood heads out from the heart to the lungs, picks up oxygen, and comes back to be pumped out to the rest of the body. A neat and elegant system—save that it doesn't always work properly.

The ductus arteriosus doesn't always close. If it doesn't, blood still does go to the lungs, of course—but the bypass is still there. Too much blood goes to the lungs, in some cases, and floods them. The lungs swell, become congested, and with diverted blood flow to the body, there are problems with oxygenation—which can become acute.

I moved my stethoscope over the tiny chest, ear pressed to it, listening intently. It was my best stethoscope, a model from the nineteenth century called a Pinard—a bell with a flattened disc at one end, to which I pressed my ear. I had one carved of wood; this one was made of pewter; Brianna had sand-cast it for me.

In fact, though, the murmur was so distinct that I felt as though I barely needed a stethoscope. Not a click or a misplaced beat, not a too-long pause or a leaky swish—there were any number of unusual sounds a heart could make, and auscultation was the first step of diagnosis. Atrial defects, ventral defects, malformed valves—all have specific murmurs, some occurring between beats, some blending with the heart sounds.

When the ductus arteriosus fails to close, it's said to be "patent"—open. A patent ductus arteriosus makes a continuous shushing murmur, soft, but audible with a little concentration, particularly in the supraclavicular and cervical regions.

For the hundredth time in two days, I bent close, ear pressed to the Pinard as I moved it over Amanda's neck and chest, hoping against hope that the sound would have disappeared.

It hadn't.

"Turn your head, lovey, yes, that's right. . . ." I breathed, delicately turning her head away from me, Pinard pressed to the side of her neck. It was hard to get the stethoscope close to her fat little neck . . . there. The murmur increased. Amanda made a little breathy noise that sounded like a giggle. I brought her head back the other way—the sound decreased.

"Oh, bloody hell," I said softly, so as not to scare her. I put down the Pinard and picked her up, cradling her against my shoulder. We were alone; Brianna had gone up to my room for a nap, and everyone else was out.

I carried her to the surgery window and looked out; it was a beautiful day in the mountain spring. The wrens were nesting under the eaves again; I could hear them above me, rustling round with sticks, conversing in small, clear chirps.

"Bird," I said, my lips close to her tiny seashell of an ear. "Noisy bird." She squirmed lazily, and farted in reply.

"Right," I said, smiling despite myself. I held her out a little, so I could look into her face—lovely, perfect—but not as fat as it had been when she was born a week before.

It was perfectly normal for babies to lose a little weight at first, I told myself. It was.

A patent ductus arteriosus may have no symptoms, beyond that odd, continuous murmur. But it may. A bad one deprives the child of needed oxygen; the main symptoms are pulmonary—wheezing; rapid, shallow breathing; bad color—and failure to thrive, because of the energy burned up in the effort to get enough oxygen.

"Just let Grannie have a little listen again," I said, laying her down on the quilt I'd spread over the surgery table. She gurgled and kicked as I picked up the Pinard and placed it on her chest again, moving it over neck, shoulder, arm . . .

"Oh, Jesus," I whispered, closing my eyes. "Don't let it be bad." But the sound of the murmur seemed to grow louder, drowning my prayers.

I opened my eyes to see Brianna, standing in the doorway.

"I KNEW THERE was *something* wrong," she said steadily, wiping Mandy's bottom with a damp rag before rediapering her. "She doesn't nurse like Jemmy did. She acts hungry, but she'll only nurse for a few minutes before she falls asleep. Then she wakes up and fusses again a few minutes later."

She sat down and offered Mandy a breast, as though in illustration of the difficulty. Sure enough, the baby latched on with every evidence of starvation. As she nursed, I picked up one of the tiny fists, unfolding her fingers. The minute nails were faintly tinged with blue.

"So," Brianna said calmly, "what happens now?"

"I don't know." This was the usual answer in most cases, truth be told—but it was always unsatisfactory, and clearly not less so now. "Sometimes there are no symptoms, or only very minor ones," I said, trying for amendment. "If the opening is very large, and you have pulmonary symptoms—and we have—then . . . she *might* be all right, only not thriving—not growing properly, because of the feeding difficulties. Or"—I took a deep breath, steeling myself—"she could develop heart failure. Or pulmonary hypertension—that's a very high blood pressure in the lungs—"

"I know what it is," Bree said, her voice tight. "Or?"

"Or infective endocarditis. Or—not."

"Will she die?" she asked bluntly, looking up at me. Her

jaw was set, but I saw the way she held Amanda closer, waiting for an answer. I could give her nothing but the truth.

"Probably." The word hung in the air between us, hideous. "I can't say for sure, but—"

"Probably," Brianna echoed, and I nodded, turning away, unable to look at her face. Without such modern assistances as an echocardiogram, I of course couldn't judge the extent of the problem. But I had not only the evidence of my eyes and ears, but what I had felt passing from her skin to mine—that sense of not-rightness, that eerie conviction that comes now and then.

"Can you fix it?" I heard the tremor in Brianna's voice, and went at once to put my arms around her. Her head was bent over Amanda, and I saw the tears fall, one, then another, darkening the wispy curls on top of the baby's head.

"No," I whispered, holding them both. Despair washed over me, but I tightened my hold, as though I could keep time and blood both at bay. "No, I can't."

"WELL, THERE'S NO choice, is there?" Roger felt preternaturally calm, recognizing it as the artificial calm produced by shock but wishing to cling to it as long as possible. "You've got to go."

Brianna leveled a look at him, but didn't reply. Her hand roamed over the baby, sleeping in her lap, smoothing the woolly blanket over and over again.

Claire had explained it all to him, more than once, patiently, seeing that he could not take it in. He still did not believe it—but the sight of those tiny fingernails, turning blue as Amanda strove to suck, had sunk into him like an owl's talons.

It was, she had said, a simple operation—in a modern operating room.

"You can't . . . ?" he'd asked, with a vague motion toward her surgery. "With the ether?"

She'd closed her eyes and shaken her head, looking nearly as ill as he felt.

"No. I can do very simple things—hernias, appendixes, tonsils—and even those are a risk. But something so invasive, on such a tiny body . . . no," she repeated, and he saw resignation in her face when she met his eyes. "No. If she's to live—you have to take her back."

And so they had begun to discuss the unthinkable. Because there *were* choices—and decisions to be made. But the unalterable basic fact was clear. Amanda must go through the stones—if she could.

JAMIE FRASER took his father's ruby ring, and held it over the face of his granddaughter. Amanda's eyes fixed on it at once, and she stuck out her tongue with interest. He smiled, despite the heaviness of his heart, and lowered the ring for her to grab at.

"She likes that well enough," he said, skillfully removing it from her grip before she could get it into her mouth. "Let's try the other."

The other was Claire's amulet—the tiny, battered leather pouch given to her by an Indian wisewoman years before. It contained assorted bits and bobs, herbs, he thought, and feathers, perhaps the tiny bones of a bat. But in among them was a lump of stone—nothing much to look at, but a true gemstone, a raw sapphire.

Amanda turned her head at once, more interested in the pouch than she had been in the shiny ring. She made cooing noises and batted wildly with both hands, trying to reach it.

Brianna took a deep, half-strangled breath.

"Maybe," she said, in the voice of one who fears as much as hopes. "But we can't tell for sure. What if I—take her, and I go through, but she can't?"

They all looked at one another in silence, envisioning the possibility.

"You'd come back," Roger said gruffly, and put a hand on Bree's shoulder. "You'd come right back."

The tension in her body eased a little at his touch. "I'd try," she said, and attempted a smile.

Jamie cleared his throat.

"Is wee Jem about?"

Of course he was; he never went far from home or Brianna

these days, seeming to sense that something was wrong. He was retrieved from Jamie's study, where he had been spelling out words in—

"Jesus Christ on a piece of toast!" his grandmother blurted, snatching the book from him. "Jamie! How *could* you?"

Jamie felt a deep blush rise over him. How could he, indeed? He'd taken the battered copy of *Fanny Hill* in trade, part of a parcel of used books bought from a tinker. He hadn't looked at the books before buying them, and when he did come to look them over . . . Well, it was quite against his instincts to throw away a book—any book.

"What's P-H-A-L-L-U-S?" Jemmy was asking his father.

"Another word for prick," Roger said briefly. "Don't bloody use it. Listen—can ye hear anything, when ye listen to that stone?" He indicated Jamie's ring lying on the table. Jem's face lighted at sight of it.

"Sure," he said.

"What, from there?" Brianna said, incredulous. Jem looked around the circle of parents and grandparents, surprised at their interest. "Sure," he repeated. "It sings."

"Do ye think wee Mandy can hear it sing, too?" Jamie asked carefully. His heart was beating heavily, afraid to know, either way.

Jemmy picked up the ring and leaned over Mandy's basket, holding it directly over her face. She kicked energetically and made noises—but whether because of the ring, or merely at the sight of her brother . . .

"She can hear it," Jem said, smiling into his sister's face.

"How do you know?" Claire asked, curious. Jem looked up at her, surprised.

"She says so."

NOTHING WAS SETTLED. At the same time, everything was settled. I was in no doubt as to what my ears and my fingers told me—Amanda's condition was slowly worsening. Very slowly—it might take a year, two years, before serious damage began to show—but it was coming.

Jem might be right; he might not be. But we had to proceed on the assumption that he was.

There were arguments, discussions—tears. Not yet any decision as to who should attempt the journey through the stones. Brianna and Amanda must go; that was certain. But ought Roger to go with them? Or Jemmy?

"I will not let you go without me," Roger said through his teeth.

"I don't *want* to go without you!" Bree cried, looking exasperated. "But how can we leave Jemmy here, without us? And how can we make him go? A baby—we think that can work, because of the legends, but Jem—how will he make it? We can't let him risk being killed!"

I looked at the stones on the table—Jamie's ring, my pouch with the sapphire.

"I think," I said carefully, "that we need to find two more stones. Just in case."

And so, in late June, we came down from the mountain, into turmoil.

115

NOSEPICKER

July 4, 1776

IT WAS CLOSE and hot in the inn room, but I couldn't go out; little Amanda had finally fussed herself to sleep—she had a rash on her bottom, poor thing—and was curled in her basket, tiny thumb in her mouth and a frown on her face.

I unfolded the gauze mosquito netting and draped it carefully over the basket, then opened the window. The air outside was hot, too, but fresh, and moving. I pulled off my cap—

without it, Mandy was fond of clutching my hair in both her hands and yanking; she had an amazing amount of strength, for a child with a heart defect. For the millionth time, I wondered whether I could have been wrong.

But I wasn't. She was asleep now, with the delicate rose bloom of a healthy baby on her cheeks; awake and kicking, that soft flush faded, and an equally beautiful but unearthly blue tinge showed now and then in her lips, in the beds of her tiny nails. She was still lively—but tiny. Bree and Roger were both large people; Jemmy had put on weight like a small hippopotamus through his first several years of life. Mandy weighed scarcely more than she had at birth.

No, I wasn't wrong. I moved her basket to the table, where the warm breeze could play over her, and sat down beside it, laying my fingers gently on her chest.

I could feel it. Just as I had in the beginning, but stronger now that I knew what it was. If I had had a proper operating suite, the blood transfusions, the calibrated and carefully administered anesthesia, the oxygen mask, the swift, trained nurses . . . No surgery on the heart is a minor thing, and surgery on an infant is always a great risk—but I could have done it. Could feel in the tips of my fingers exactly what needed to be done, could see in the back of my eyes the heart, smaller than my fist, the slippery, pumping, rubbery muscle and the blood washing through the ductus arteriosus, a small vessel, no bigger than an eighth of an inch in circumference. A small nick in the axillary vessel, a quick ligation of the ductus itself with a number-8 silk ligature. Done.

I knew. But knowledge is not, alas, always power. Nor is desire. It wouldn't be me who would save this precious granddaughter.

Would anyone? I wondered, giving way momentarily to the dark thoughts I fought to keep at bay when anyone else was near. Jemmy might not be right. Any baby might grab at a brightly colored shiny thing like a ruby ring—but then I remembered her cooing, batting at my decrepit leather amulet pouch with the raw sapphire inside.

Perhaps. I didn't want to think about the dangers of the passage—or the certainty of permanent separation, no matter whether the journey through the stones was successful or not.

There were noises outside; I looked toward the harbor, and saw the masts of a large ship, far out to sea. Another, still farther out. My heart skipped a beat.

They were oceangoing ships, not the little packet boats and fishing smacks that sailed up and down the coast. Could they be part of the fleet, sent in answer to Governor Martin's plea for help to suppress, subdue, and reclaim the colony? The first ship of that fleet had arrived at Cape Fear in late April—but the troops it carried had been lying low, waiting for the rest.

I watched for some time, but the ships didn't come in closer. Perhaps they were hanging off, waiting for the rest of the fleet? Perhaps they weren't British ships at all, but Americans, escaping the British blockade of New England by sailing south.

I was distracted from my thoughts by the clumping of male feet on the stairs, accompanied by snorts and that peculiarly Scottish sort of giggling usually depicted in print—but by no means adequately—as "Heuch, heuch, heuch!"

It was clearly Jamie and Ian, though I couldn't understand what was giving rise to so much hilarity, since when last seen they had been bound for the docks, charged with dispatching a shipment of tobacco leaves, obtaining pepper, salt, sugar, cinnamon—if findable—and pins—somewhat rarer than cinnamon—for Mrs. Bug, and procuring a large fish of some edible sort for our supper.

They'd got the fish, at least: a large king mackerel. Jamie was carrying it by the tail, whatever it had been wrapped in having evidently been lost in some accident. His queue had come undone, so that long red strands frayed out over the shoulder of his coat, which in turn had a sleeve half wrenched off, a fold of white shirt protruding through the torn seam. He was covered with dust, as was the fish, and while the latter's eyes both bulged accusingly, one of his own was swollen nearly shut.

"Oh, God," I said, burying my face in one hand. I looked up at him through splayed fingers. "Don't tell me. Gerald Forbes?"

"Ach, no," he said, dropping the fish with a splat on the

table in front of me. "A wee difference of opinion wi' the Wilmington Chowder and Marching Society."

"A difference of opinion," I repeated.

"Aye, they thought they'd throw us in the harbor, and we thought they wouldn't." He slung a chair round with his boot and sat down on it backward, arms crossed on its back. He looked indecently cheerful, face flushed with sun and laughter.

"I don't want to know," I said, though of course I did. I glanced at Ian, who was still sniggering quietly to himself, and observed that while he was slightly less battered than Jamie, he had one forefinger lodged in his nose up to the knuckle.

"Have you got a bloody nose, Ian?"

He shook his head, still giggling. "No, Auntie. Some o' the Society do, though."

"Well, why have you got your finger up your nose, then? Have you picked up a tick or something?"

"No, he's keepin' his brains from falling out," Jamie said, and went off into another fit. I glanced at the basket, but Mandy slept peacefully on, quite used to racket.

"Well, maybe you'd best stick both your own fingers up your nose, then," I suggested. "Keep you out of trouble for a moment or two, at least." I tilted up Jamie's chin to get a better look at the eye. "You hit someone with that fish, didn't you?"

The giggling had died down to a subterranean vibration between them, but threatened at this to break out anew.

"Gilbert Butler," Jamie said with a masterful effort at self-control. "Smack across the face. Sent him straight across the quay and into the water."

Ian's shoulders shook with remembered ecstasy.

"Bride, what a splash! Oh, it was a braw fight, Auntie! I thought I'd broke my hand on a fellow's jaw, but it's all right now the deadness has worn off. Just a bit numb and tingly." He wiggled the free fingers of his hand at me in illustration, wincing only slightly as he did so.

"Do take your finger out of your nose, Ian," I said, anxiety over their condition fading into annoyance at how they'd got that way. "You look like a half-wit."

For some reason, they both found that hysterically funny

and laughed like loons. Ian did, however, eventually withdraw the finger, with an expression of wary cautiousness, as though he truly expected his brains to follow in its wake. Nothing did emerge, though, not even the ordinary bits of unsavory excreta one might expect from such a maneuver.

Ian looked puzzled, then mildly alarmed. He sniffed, prodding experimentally at his nose, then stuck the finger back into his nostril, rooting vigorously.

Jamie went on grinning, but his amusement began to fade as Ian's explorations became more frantic.

"What? Ye've not lost it, have ye, lad?"

Ian shook his head, frowning.

"Nay, I feel it. It's . . ." He stopped, giving Jamie a panic-stricken look over the embedded finger. "It's stuck, Uncle Jamie! I canna get it out!"

Jamie was on his feet at once. He pulled the finger from its resting-place with a moist, sucking noise, then tilted back Ian's head, peering urgently up his nose with his one good eye.

"Bring a light, Sassenach, will ye?"

There was a candlestick on the table, but I knew from experience that the only likely effect of using a candle to look up someone's nose was to set their nose hairs on fire. Instead, I bent and pulled my medical kit out from under the settle where I had stowed it.

"I'll get it," I said, with the confidence of one who has removed everything from cherry pits to live insects from the nasal cavities of small children. I drew out my longest pair of thin forceps, and clicked the slender blades together in token of assurance. "Whatever it is. Just keep quite still, Ian."

The whites of Ian's eyes showed briefly in alarm as he looked at the shining metal of the forceps, and he looked pleadingly at Jamie.

"Wait. I've a better idea." Jamie laid a quelling hand on my arm for an instant, then disappeared out the door. He thundered downstairs, and I heard a sudden burst of laughter from below, as the door to the taproom opened. The sound was as suddenly cut off as the door closed, like the valve on a faucet.

"Are you all right, Ian?" There was a smear of red on his upper lip; his nose *was* beginning to bleed, aggravated by his jabbings and pokings.

"Well, I do hope so, Auntie." His original jubilation was beginning to be replaced by a certain expression of worry. "Ye dinna think I can have pushed it into my brain, do ye?"

"I think it very unlikely. What on earth—"

But the door below had opened and closed again, spilling another brief spurt of talk and laughter into the stairwell. Jamie took the stairs two at a time and popped back into the room, smelling of hot bread and ale, and holding a small, battered snuffbox in his hand.

Ian seized on this with gratitude and, sprinkling a quick pinch of black, dusty grains on the back of his hand, hastily inhaled it.

For an instant, all three of us held breathless—and then it came, a sneeze of gargantuan proportions that rocked Ian's body back on its stool, even as his head flew forward—and a small, hard object struck the table with a *ping!* and bounced off into the hearth.

Ian went on sneezing, in a fusillade of hapless snorts and explosions, but Jamie and I were both on our knees, scrabbling in the ashes, heedless of filth.

"I've got it! I think," I added, sitting back on my heels and peering at the handful of ashes I held, in the midst of which was a small, round, dust-covered object.

"Aye, that's it." Jamie seized my neglected forceps from the table, plucked the object delicately from my hand, and dropped it into my glass of water. A delicate plume of ash and soot floated up through the water to form a dusty gray film on the surface. Below, the object glittered up at us, serene and glowing, its beauty at last revealed. A faceted clear stone, the color of golden sherry, half the size of my thumbnail.

"Chrysoberyl," Jamie said softly, a hand on my back. He looked at Mandy's basket, the silky black curls lifting gently in the breeze. "D'ye think it will serve?"

Ian, still wheezing and watery-eyed, and with a red-stained handkerchief pressed to his much-abused proboscis, came to look over my other shoulder.

"Half-wit, is it?" he said in tones of deep satisfaction. "Ha!"

"Wherever did you get that? Or rather," I corrected myself, "who did you steal it from?"

"Gerald Forbes." Jamie picked the gem up, turning it gently

over in his fingers. "There were a good deal more o' the Chowder Society than there were of us, so we ran down the street and round the corner, down between the warehouses there."

"I kent Forbes's place, aye, because I'd been there before," Ian put in. One of Mandy's feet was sticking up out of the basket; he touched the sole of it with a fingertip, and smiled to see her toes extend in reflex. "There was a great hole in the back where someone had broken down the wall, just covered over with a sheet of canvas, nailed over it, like. So we pulled it loose and ducked inside."

Where they had found themselves standing next to the small enclosed space Forbes used for an office—and for the moment, deserted.

"It was sitting in a bittie wee box on the desk," Ian said, coming to look proprietorially at the chrysoberyl. "Just sitting there! I'd just picked it up to look at, when we hear the watchman coming. So—" He shrugged and smiled at me, happiness momentarily transforming his homely features.

"And you think the watchman won't tell him you were there?" I asked skeptically. The two of them could scarcely be more conspicuous.

"Oh, I imagine he will." Jamie bent over Mandy's basket, holding the chrysoberyl between thumb and forefinger. "Look what Grandda and Uncle Ian have brought ye, *a muirninn,*" he said softly.

"We decided that it was a small enough ransom to pay for what he did to Brianna," Ian said, sobering somewhat. "I expect Mr. Forbes may feel it reasonable, too. And if not—" He smiled again, though not with happiness, and put his hand to his knife. "He's got another ear, after all."

Very slowly, a tiny fist rose through the netting, fingers flexing as they grasped at the stone.

"Is she still asleep?" I whispered. Jamie nodded, and gently withdrew the stone.

On the far side of the table, the fish stared austerely at the ceiling, ignoring everything.

116

THE NINTH EARL OF ELLESMERE

July 9, 1776

"THE WATER WILL BE COLD."

She'd spoken automatically, without thinking.

"I shouldn't think that will matter much." A nerve jumped in Roger's cheek, and he turned away abruptly. She reached out, touching him delicately, as though he were a bomb that might explode if jarred. He glanced at her, hesitated, then took the hand she offered him, with a small, crooked smile.

"Sorry," he said.

"I'm sorry, too," she said softly. They stood close together, fingers knotted, watching the tide recede across the narrow beach, a fraction of an inch uncovered with each lap of the tiny waves.

The flats were gray and bleak in the evening light, pebble-strewn and rust-stained from the peaty waters of the river. With the tide going out, the harbor water was brown and feculent, the stain reaching past the ships at anchor, nearly to the open sea. When it turned, the clear gray water of the ocean would flow in, sweeping up the Cape Fear, obliterating the mudflats and everything on them.

"Over there," she said, still softly, though there was no one near enough to hear them. She tilted her head, indicating a group of weathered mooring posts driven deep into the mud. A skiff was tied to one; two of the pirettas, the four-oared "dragonflies" that plied the harbor, to another.

"You're sure?" He shifted his weight, glancing up and down the shore.

The narrow beach fell away into cold pebbles, exposed and gleaming with the leaving of the tide. Small crabs skittered hastily among them, not to waste a moment's gleaning.

"I'm sure. People in the Blue Boar were talking about it. A traveler asked where, and Mrs. Smoots said it was the old mooring posts, near the warehouses." A torn flounder lay dead among the rocks, white flesh washed clean and bloodless. The small busy claws picked and shredded, tiny maws gaped and gulped, pinching at morsels. She felt her gorge rise at the sight, and swallowed hard. It wouldn't matter what came after; she knew that. But still . . .

Roger nodded absently. His eyes narrowed against the harbor wind, calculating distances.

"There'll be quite a crowd, I expect."

There already was one; the turn of the tide wouldn't be for an hour or more, but people were drifting down to the harbor in twos and threes and fours, standing in the lee of the chandlery to smoke their pipes, sitting on the barrels of salt fish to talk and gesture. Mrs. Smoots had been right; several were pointing out the mooring posts to their less knowledgeable companions.

Roger shook his head.

"It'll have to be from that side; the best view is from there." He nodded across the inner arc of the harbor toward the three ships that rocked at the main quay. "From one of the ships? What do you think?"

Brianna fumbled in the pocket tied at her waist, and pulled out her small brass telescope. She frowned in concentration, lips pursed as she surveyed the ships—a fishing ketch, Mr. Chester's brig, and a larger ship, part of the British fleet, that had come in in the early afternoon.

"Whoa, Nellie," she murmured, arresting the sweep of her gaze as the pale blotch of a head filled the lens. "Is that who I think . . . hot dog, it is!" A tiny flame of delight flared in her bosom, warming her.

"Is who?" Roger squinted, straining to see unaided.

"It's John! Lord John!"

"Lord John Grey? You're sure?"

"Yes! On the brig—he must have come down from Virginia. Woops, he's gone now—but he's there, I saw him!" She turned to Roger, excited, folding her telescope as she gripped him by the arm.

"Come on! Let's go and find him. He'll help."

Roger followed, though with considerably less enthusiasm. "You're going to tell him? Do you think that's wise?"

"No, but it doesn't matter. He knows me."

Roger looked sharply at her, but the dark look on his face thawed into a reluctant smile.

"You mean he knows better than to try stopping you doing whatever you've made up your bloody-minded mind to do?"

She smiled back at him, thanking him with her eyes. He didn't like it—in fact, he hated it, and she didn't blame him—but he wouldn't try to stop her, either. He knew her, too.

"Yes. Come on, before he disappears!"

It was a slow slog round the curve of the harbor, pushing through the knots of gathering sightseers. Outside The Breakers, the crowd grew abruptly thicker. A cluster of red-coated soldiers stood and sat in disarray on the pavement, seabags and chests scattered round them, their number too great to fit inside the tavern. Ale pots and pints of cider were being passed from hand to hand from the interior of the public house, slopping freely on the heads of those over whom they passed.

A sergeant, harassed but competent, was leaning against the timbered wall of the inn, riffling through a sheaf of papers, issuing orders and eating a meat pie, simultaneously. Brianna wrinkled her nose as they stepped carefully through the obstacle course of scattered men and luggage; a reek of seasickness and unclean flesh rose from the serried ranks.

A few onlookers muttered under their breath at sight of the soldiers; several more cheered and waved as they passed, to receive genial shouts in return. Newly liberated from the bowels of the *Scorpion,* the soldiers were too thrilled with their freedom and the taste of fresh food and drink to care who did or said anything whatever.

Roger stepped in front of her, thrusting a way through the crowd with shoulders and elbows. Appreciative shouts and whistles rose from the soldiers as they saw her, but she kept her head down, eyes fixed on Roger's feet as he shoved ahead.

She heaved a sigh of relief as they emerged from the press at the head of the quay. The soldiers' equipment was being unloaded from the *Scorpion* at the far side of the dock, but there was little foot traffic near the brig. She paused, looking to and fro for a glimpse of Lord John's distinctive fair head.

"There he is!" Roger tugged at her arm, and she swung in the direction he was pointing, only to collide heavily with him as he stepped abruptly back.

"What—" she began crossly, but then stopped, feeling as though she had been punched in the chest.

"Who in God's holy name is *that*?" Roger spoke softly, echoing her thoughts.

Lord John Grey stood near the far end of the quay, in animated conversation with one of the red-coated soldiers. An officer; gold braid gleamed on his shoulder and he carried a laced tricorne beneath one arm. It wasn't the man's uniform that caught her attention, though.

"Jesus H. Roosevelt Christ," she whispered, feeling numb around the lips.

He was tall—very tall—with a breadth of shoulder and a stretch of white-stockinged calf that were attracting admiring glances from a cluster of oyster girls. It was something more than height or build that made gooseflesh ripple down the length of her spine, though; it was the fact of his carriage, his outline, a cock of the head and an air of physical self-confidence that drew eyes like a magnet.

"It's Da," she said, knowing even as she spoke that this was ridiculous. Even had Jamie Fraser for some unimaginable reason chosen to disguise himself in a soldier's uniform and come down to the docks, this man was different. As he turned to look at something across the harbor, she saw that he *was* different—lean, like her father, and muscular, but still with the slenderness of boyishness. Graceful—like Jamie—but with the slight hesitancy of teenaged awkwardness not long past.

He turned further, backlit by the glow of light off the water, and she felt her knees go weak. A long, straight nose, rising to a high forehead . . . the sudden curve of a broad Viking cheekbone . . . Roger gripped her tightly by the arm, but his attention was as riveted on the young man as hers was.

"I . . . will . . . be . . . damned," he said.

She gulped air, trying to get enough breath.

"You and me both. *And* him."

"Him?"

"Him, him, *and* him!" Lord John, the mysterious young soldier—and most of all, her father. "Come on." She pulled free and strode down the quay, feeling oddly disembodied, as though she watched herself from a distance.

It was like watching herself come toward a fun-house mirror, seeing herself—her face, her height, her gestures—suddenly transposed inside a red coat and doeskin breeches. His hair was dark, chestnut-brown, not red, but it was thick like hers, with the same slight wave to it, the same cowlick that lifted it off his brow.

Lord John turned his head slightly, and caught sight of her. His eyes bulged and a look of absolute horror blanched his features. He made a feeble flapping motion with one hand, trying to stop her coming nearer, but he might as well have tried to stop the Cornish Express.

"Hello there!" she said brightly. "Fancy meeting *you* here, Lord John!"

Lord John made a faint quacking noise, like a stepped-on duck, but she wasn't paying attention. The young man turned to face her, smiling cordially.

Holy God, he had her father's eyes, too. Dark-lashed, and so young the skin near them was fresh and clear, completely unlined—but the same slanted blue Fraser cat eyes. Just like hers.

Her heart was hammering so hard in her chest she was sure they could hear it. The young man seemed to find nothing amiss, though; he bowed to her, smiling, but very correct.

"Your servant, ma'am," he said. He glanced at Lord John, plainly expecting an introduction.

Lord John pulled himself together with an obvious effort, and made her a leg.

"My dear. How . . . delightful to encounter you again. I had no idea. . . ."

Yeah, I bet you didn't, she thought, but went on smiling pleasantly. She could feel Roger beside her, nodding and saying something in response to his Lordship's greeting, trying his best not to stare.

"My son," Lord John was saying. "William, Lord Ellesmere." He eyed her narrowly, as though daring her to say anything. "Might I present Mr. Roger MacKenzie, William? And his wife."

"Sir. Mrs. MacKenzie." The young man took her hand before she realized what he meant to do, and bowed low over it, planting a small formal kiss upon her knuckles.

She nearly gasped at the unexpected touch of his breath on her skin, but instead gripped his hand, much harder than she'd meant to. He looked momentarily disconcerted, but extricated himself with reasonable grace. He was much younger than she'd thought at first glance; it was the uniform and the air of self-possession that made him seem older. He was looking at her with a slight frown on his clear-cut features, as though trying to place her.

"I think . . ." he began, hesitant. "Have we met, Mrs. MacKenzie?"

"No," she said, astonished to hear her voice emerge sounding normal. "No, I'm afraid not. I would have remembered." She darted a daggerlike glance at Lord John, who had gone slightly green around the gills.

Lord John had been a soldier, too, though. He pulled himself together with a visible effort, putting a hand on William's arm.

"You'd best go and see to your men, William," he said. "Shall we dine together later?"

"I am engaged to the Colonel for supper, Father," William said. "But I am sure he would not object, was you to join us. It may be quite late, though," he added. "I understand there is to be an execution in the morning, and my troops are asked to be at the ready, in case of disturbance in the town. It will take some time to settle and organize everything."

"Disturbance." Lord John was eyeing her over William's shoulder. "Is a disturbance expected, then?"

William shrugged.

"I cannot say, Papa. Apparently it is not a political matter, though, but only a pirate. I shouldn't think there would be any trouble."

"These days everything is a political matter, Willie," his father said, rather sharply. "Never forget that. And it's always wiser to expect trouble than to meet it unprepared."

The young man flushed slightly, but kept his countenance.

"Quite," he said in clipped tones. "I am sure you have a familiarity with the local conditions which I lack. I am obliged to you for your advice, Father." He relaxed slightly, and turned to bow to Brianna.

"Pleased to have your acquaintance, Mrs. MacKenzie. Your servant, sir." He nodded to Roger, turned, and strode off down the quay, adjusting his tricorne to the proper angle of authority.

Brianna inhaled deeply, hoping that by the time she let her breath out, she would have words to go with it. Lord John beat her to it.

"Yes," he said simply. "Of course he is."

Amid the logjam of thoughts, reactions, and emotions that clogged her brain, she seized on the one that seemed momentarily most important.

"Does my mother know?"

"Does Jamie know?" Roger asked at the same instant. She looked at him in surprise, and he raised one eyebrow at her. Yes, a man could certainly father a child without realizing it. He had.

Lord John sighed. With William's departure, he had relaxed somewhat, and the natural color was coming back to his face. He had been a soldier long enough to recognize the inevitable when he saw it.

"They both know, yes."

"How old is he?" Roger asked abruptly. Lord John shot him a sharp glance.

"Eighteen. And to save your counting backward, it was 1758. In a place called Helwater, in the Lake District."

Brianna took another breath, finding this one came a little easier.

"Okay. So it—he—it was before my mother . . . came back."

"Yes. From France, supposedly. Where, I gather, you were born and raised." He gave her a gimlet look; he knew she spoke no more than bastard French.

She could feel the blood rushing to her face.

"This is no time for secrets," she said. "If you want to know about my mother and me, I'll tell you—but *you're* going to tell me about *him*." She jerked her head angrily backward, toward the tavern. "About my brother!"

Lord John pursed his lips, regarding her through narrowed eyes as he thought. Finally he nodded.

"I see no help for it. One thing, though—are your parents here, in Wilmington?"

"Yes. In fact . . ." She looked upward, trying to make out the position of the sun through the thin coastal haze. It hung just above the horizon, a disc of burning gold. "We were going to meet them for supper."

"Here?"

"Yes."

Lord John swung round to Roger.

"Mr. MacKenzie. You will very much oblige me, sir, if you will go at once to find your father-in-law, and apprise him of the presence of the ninth Earl of Ellesmere. Tell him that I trust his good judgment will dictate an immediate removal from Wilmington upon receipt of this news."

Roger stared at him for a moment, brows quirked in interest.

"The Earl of Ellesmere? How the hell did he manage that?"

Lord John had recovered all his natural color, and a bit more. He was distinctly pink in the face.

"Never mind! Will you go? Jamie must leave the town, at once, before they meet by inadvertence—or before someone sees the two of them separately and begins to speculate aloud."

"I doubt Jamie will leave," Roger said, looking at Lord John with a certain degree of speculation himself. "Not before tomorrow, in any case."

"Why not?" Lord John demanded, looking from one to the other. "Why are you all here in the first place? It isn't the exe—oh, good Lord, don't tell me." He clapped a hand to his face, and dragged it slowly down, glaring through his fingers with the expression of a man tried beyond bearing.

Brianna bit her lower lip. When she spotted Lord John, she had been not only pleased but relieved of a small bit of her burden of worry, counting on him to help in her plan. With this new complication, though, she felt torn in two, unable to cope with either situation, or even to think about them coherently. She looked over at Roger, seeking advice.

He met her eyes in one of those long, unspoken marital exchanges. Then he nodded, making the decision for her.

"I'll go find Jamie. You have a bit of a chat with his Lordship, eh?"

He bent and kissed her, hard, then turned and strode away down the dock, walking in a way that made people draw unconsciously aside, avoiding the touch of his garments.

Lord John had closed his eyes, and appeared to be praying—presumably for strength. She gripped him by the arm and his eyes sprang open, startled as though he had been bitten by a horse.

"Is it as striking as I think?" she said. "Him and me?" The word felt funny on her tongue. *Him.*

Lord John looked at her, fair brow furrowed in troubled concentration as he searched her face, feature by feature.

"I think so," he said slowly. "To me, certainly. To a casual observer, perhaps much less so. There is the difference of coloring, to be sure, and of sex; his uniform . . . but, my dear, you know that your own appearance is so striking—" So freakish, he meant. She sighed, taking his meaning.

"People stare at me anyway," she finished for him. She pulled down the brim of her hat, drawing it far enough forward to hide not only hair but face, as well, and glowered at him from its shadow. "Then we'd better go where no one who knows him will see me, hadn't we?"

THE QUAY and the market streets were thronged. Every public house in town—and not a few private ones—would soon be full of quartered soldiers. Her father and Jem were with Alexander Lillington, her mother and Mandy at Dr. Fentiman's, both places centers of business and gossip, and she had declared that she possessed no intention of going near either parent in any case—not until she knew all there was to know. Lord John thought that might be rather more than he was himself prepared to tell her, but this was not a time for quibbles.

Still, the exigencies of privacy left them a choice of graveyard or the deserted racetrack, and Brianna said—a marked edge in her voice—that under the circumstances, she wanted no heavy-handed reminders of mortality.

"These mortal circumstances," he said carefully, leading her around a large puddle. "You refer to tomorrow's execution? It *is* Stephen Bonnet, I collect?"

"Yes," she said, distracted. "That can wait, though. You aren't engaged for supper, are you?"

"No. But—"

"William," she said, eyes on her shoes as they paced slowly round the sandy oval. "William, ninth Earl of Ellesmere, you said?"

"William Clarence Henry George," Lord John agreed. "Viscount Ashness, Master of Helwater, Baron Derwent, and, yes, ninth Earl of Ellesmere."

She pursed her lips.

"Which would sort of indicate that the world at large thinks his father is somebody else. Not Jamie Fraser, I mean."

"*Was* somebody else," he corrected. "One Ludovic, eighth Earl of Ellesmere, to be precise. I understand that the eighth earl unfortunately died on the day his . . . er . . . his heir was born."

"Died of what? Shock?" She was clearly in a dangerous mood; he was interested to note both her father's manner of controlled ferocity and her mother's sharp tongue at work—the combination was both fascinating and alarming. He hadn't any intention of allowing her to run this interview on her own terms, though.

"Gunshot," he said with affected cheerfulness. "Your father shot him."

She made a small choking noise and stopped dead.

"That is not, by the way, common knowledge," he said, affecting not to notice her reaction. "The coroner's court returned a verdict of death by misadventure—which was not incorrect, I believe."

"Not incorrect," she murmured, sounding a trifle dazed. "I guess being shot is pretty misadventurous, all right."

"Of course there was talk," he said, offhanded, taking her arm and urging her forward again. "But the only witness, aside from William's grandparents, was an Irish coachman, who was rather quickly pensioned off to County Sligo, following the incident. The child's mother having also died that day, gossip was inclined to consider his lordship's death as—"

"His mother's dead, too?" She didn't stop this time, but turned to give him a penetrating glance from those deep blue eyes. Lord John had had sufficient practice in withstanding Fraser cat looks, though, and was not discomposed.

"Her name was Geneva Dunsany. She died shortly after William's birth—of an entirely natural hemorrhage," he assured her.

"Entirely natural," she muttered, half under her breath. She shot him another look. "This Geneva—she was married to the earl? When she and Da . . ." The words seemed to stick in her throat; he could see doubt and repugnance struggling with her memories of William's undeniable face—and her knowledge of her father's character.

"He has not told me, and I would in no circumstance ask him," he said firmly. She gave him another of those looks, which he returned with interest. "Whatever the nature of Jamie's relations with Geneva Dunsany, I cannot conceive of his committing an act of such dishonor as to deceive another man in his marriage."

She relaxed fractionally, though her grip on his arm remained.

"Neither can I," she said, rather grudgingly. "But—" Her lips compressed, relaxed. "Was he in love with her, do you think?" she blurted.

What startled him was not the question, but the realization that it had never once occurred to him to ask it—certainly not of Jamie, but not even of himself. Why not? he wondered. He had no right to jealousy, and if he was fool enough to suffer it, it would have been considerably *ex post facto* in the case of Geneva Dunsany; he had had no inkling of William's origins until several years after the girl's death.

"I have no idea," he said shortly.

Brianna's fingers drummed restlessly on his arm; she would have pulled free, but he put a hand on hers to still her.

"Damn," she muttered, but ceased fidgeting, and walked on, matching the length of his shorter stride. Weeds had sprung up in the oval, were sprouting through the sand of the track. She kicked at a clump of wild rye grass, sending a spray of dry seeds flying.

"If they were in love, why didn't he marry her?" she asked at last.

He laughed, in sheer incredulity at the notion.

"Marry her! My dear girl, he was the family groom!"

A look of puzzlement flashed in her eye—he would have sworn that if she had spoken, the word would have been *"So?"*

"Where in the name of God were you raised?" he demanded, stopping dead.

He could see things moving in her eyes; she had Jamie's trick of keeping her face a mask, but her mother's transparency still shone from within. He saw the decision in her eyes, a moment before the slow smile touched her lips.

"Boston," she said. "I'm an American. But you knew I was a barbarian already, didn't you?"

He grunted in response.

"That does go some distance toward explaining your remarkably republican attitudes," he replied very dryly. "Though I would strongly suggest that you disguise these dangerous sentiments, for the sake of your family. Your father is in sufficient trouble on his own account. However, you may accept my assurance that it would not be possible for the daughter of a baronet to marry a groom, no matter how exigent the nature of their emotions."

Her turn to grunt at that; a highly expressive, if totally unfeminine sound. He sighed, and took her hand again, tucking it in the curve of his elbow for safekeeping.

"He was a paroled prisoner, too—a Jacobite, a traitor. Believe me, marriage would not have occurred to either of them."

The damp air was misting on her skin, clinging to the down hairs on her cheeks.

"But that was in another country," she quoted softly. *"And besides, the wench is dead."*

"Very true," he said quietly.

They scuffed silently through the damp sand for a few moments, each alone in thought. At last Brianna heaved a sigh, deep enough that he felt as well as heard it.

"Well, she's dead, anyway, and the earl—do you know *why* Da killed him? Did he tell you that?"

"Your father has never spoken of the matter—of Geneva,

of the earl, or even directly of William's parentage—to me." He spoke precisely, eyes fixed on a pair of gulls probing the sand near a clump of saw grass. "But I know, yes."

He glanced at her.

"William is *my* son, after all. In the sense of common usage, at least." In a great deal more than that, but that was not a matter he chose to discuss with Jamie's daughter.

Her eyebrows rose.

"Yes. How did that happen?"

"As I told you, both of William's parents—his putative parents—died on the day of his birth. His father—the earl, I mean—had no close kin, so the boy was left to the guardianship of his grandfather, Lord Dunsany. Geneva's sister, Isobel, became William's mother in all but fact. And I—" He shrugged, nonchalant. "I married Isobel. I became William's guardian, with Dunsany's consent, and he has regarded me as his stepfather since he was six years old—he is my son."

"You? You *married*?" She was goggling down at him, with an air of incredulity that he found offensive.

"You have the most peculiar notions concerning marriage," he said crossly. "It was an eminently suitable match."

One red eyebrow went up in a gesture that was Jamie to the life.

"Did your wife think so?" she asked, in an uncanny echo of her mother's voice, asking the same question. When her mother had asked it, he had been nonplussed. This time, he was prepared.

"That," he said tersely, "was in another country. And Isobel . . ." As he had hoped, that silenced her.

A fire was burning at the far end of the sandy oval, where travelers had made a rough camp. People come downriver to see the execution, he wondered? Men seeking to enlist in the rebel militias? A figure moved, dimly seen through the haze of smoke, and he turned, leading Brianna back along the way they had come. This conversation was sufficiently awkward, without the risk of interruption.

"You asked about Ellesmere," he said, taking control of the conversation once more. "The story given to the coroner's court by Lord Dunsany was that Ellesmere had been showing him a new pistol, which discharged by accident. It was the sort of story that is told in order to be disbelieved—giving the impression that in reality the earl had shot himself, doubtless from grief at the death of his wife, but that the Dunsanys wished to avoid the stigma of suicide, for the sake of the child. The coroner naturally perceived both the falsity of the story and the wisdom of allowing it to stand."

"That's not what I asked," she said, a noticeable edge in her voice. "I asked why my father shot him."

He sighed. She could have found gainful employment with the Spanish Inquisition, he thought ruefully; no chance of escape or evasion.

"I understand that his Lordship, apprehending that the newborn infant was in fact not of his blood, intended to expunge the stain upon his honor by dropping the child out of the window, onto the slates in the courtyard thirty feet below," he said bluntly.

Her face had paled perceptibly.

"How did he find out?" she demanded. "And if Da was a groom, why was he there? Did the earl know he was—responsible?" She shuddered, plainly envisioning a scene in which Jamie was summoned to the earl's presence, to witness the death of his illegitimate offspring before facing a similar fate himself. John had no difficulty in discerning her imagination; he had envisioned such a scene himself, more than once.

"An acute choice of words," he replied dryly. "Jamie Fraser is 'responsible' for more than any man I know. As to the rest, I have no idea. I know the essentials of what happened, because Isobel knew; her mother was present and presumably told her only the briefest outline of the incident."

"Huh." She kicked a small stone, deliberately. It skittered across the packed sand in front of her, ending a few feet away. "And you never asked Da about it?"

The stone lay in his line of march; he kicked it neatly as he walked, rolling it back into her path.

"I have never spoken to your father regarding Geneva, Ellesmere, or William himself—save to inform him of my marriage to Isobel and to assure him that I would fulfill my responsibilities as William's guardian to the best of my ability."

She set her foot on the stone, driving it into the soft sand, and stopped.

"You never said *anything* to him? What did he say to you?" she demanded.

"Nothing." He returned her stare.

"Why did you marry Isobel?"

He sighed, but there was no point in evasion.

"In order to take care of William."

The thick red brows nearly touched her hairline.

"So you got married, in spite of—I mean, you turned your whole life upside down, just to take care of Jamie Fraser's illegitimate son? And neither one of you ever *talked* about it?"

"No," he said, baffled. "Of course not."

Slowly, the brows came down again, and she shook her head.

"Men," she said cryptically. She glanced back toward the town. The air was calm, and a haze from the chimneys of Wilmington lay heavy above the trees. No roofs showed; it might have been a dragon that lay sleeping on the shore, for all that could be seen. The low, rumbling noise was not a reptilian snore, though; a small but constant stream of people had been passing by the track, headed for the town, and the reverberations of an increasing crowd were clearly audible, whenever the wind was right.

"It's nearly dark. I have to go back." She turned toward the lane that led into town, and he followed, relieved for the moment, but under no illusion that the inquisition was over.

She had only one more question, though.

"When are you going to tell him?" she asked, turning to look at him as she reached the edge of the trees.

"Tell who what?" he replied, startled.

"Him." She frowned at him, irritated. "William. My brother." The irritation faded as she tasted the word. She was still pale, but a sort of excitement had begun to glow beneath her skin. Lord John felt as though he had eaten something that violently disagreed with him. A cold sweat broke out along his jaw, and his guts clenched into fistlike knots. His knees turned to water.

"Are you quite mad?" He grasped at her arm, as much to keep from stumbling as to prevent her going off.

"I gather he doesn't know who his father really is," she said with a bit of asperity. "Given that you and Da never talked to each other about it, you probably didn't see any point talking to *him,* either. But he's grown up now—he has a right to know, surely."

Lord John closed his eyes with a low moan.

"Are you all right?" she asked. He felt her bending close to inspect him. "You don't look very good."

"Sit." He sat himself, back to a tree, and pulled her down beside him on the ground. He breathed deeply, keeping his eyes closed while his mind raced. Surely she was joking? Surely not, his cynically observant self assured him. She had a marked sense of humor, but it wasn't in evidence at the moment.

She couldn't. He couldn't let her. It was inconceivable that she—but how could he stop her? If she wouldn't listen to him, perhaps Jamie or her mother . . .

A hand touched his shoulder.

"I'm sorry," she said softly. "I didn't stop to think."

Relief filled him. He felt his bowels begin to uncramp, and opened his eyes to see her gazing at him with a peculiar sort of limpid sympathy that he didn't understand at all. His bowels promptly convulsed again, making him fear that he was about to suffer an embarrassing attack of flatulence on the spot.

His bowels had read her better than he had.

"I should have thought," she reproached herself. "I should have known how you'd feel about it. You said it yourself—he's *your* son. You've raised him all this time, I can see how much you love him. It must make you feel terrible to think of William finding out about Da and maybe blaming you for not telling him sooner." Her hand was massaging his collarbone in what he assumed was meant to be a soothing gesture. If that was her intent, the movement had singularly failed.

"But—" he began, but she had taken his hand in both hers and was squeezing it earnestly, her blue eyes shimmering with tears.

"He won't," she assured him. "William would never stop loving you. Believe me. It was the same for me—when I found out about Da. I didn't want to believe it at first; I *had* a father, and I loved him, and I didn't want another one. But then I met

Da, and it was—he was . . . who he is—" She shrugged slightly, and lifted one hand to wipe her eyes on the lace at her wrist.

"But I haven't forgotten my other father," she said very softly. "I never will. Never."

Touched despite the general seriousness of the situation, Lord John cleared his throat.

"Yes. Well. I am sure your sentiments do you great credit, my dear. And while I hope that I likewise enjoy William's affectionate regard at present and will continue to do so in future, that is really not the point I was endeavoring to make."

"It's not?" She looked up, wide-eyed, tears clumping her lashes into dark spikes. She was really a lovely young woman, and he felt a small twinge of tenderness.

"No," he said, quite gently under the circumstances. "Look, my love. I told you who William is—or who he thinks he is."

"Viscount Whatnot, you mean?"

He sighed deeply.

"Quite. The five people who know of his true parentage have expended considerable effort for the last eighteeen years, to the end that no one—William included—should ever have cause to doubt that he *is* the ninth Earl of Ellesmere."

She looked down at that, her thick brows knitted, lips compressed. Christ, he hoped that her husband had succeeded in locating Jamie Fraser in time. Jamie Fraser was the only person who had a hope of being more effectually stubborn than his daughter.

"You don't understand," she said finally. She looked up, and he saw that she had come to some decision.

"We're leaving," she said abruptly. "Roger and I and the—the children."

"Oh?" he said cautiously. This might be good news—on several counts. "Where do you propose to go? Will you remove to England? Or Scotland? If England or Acadia, I have several social connexions who might be of—"

"No. Not there. Not anywhere you have 'connexions.'" She smiled painfully at him, then swallowed before continuing.

"But you see—we'll be gone. For—for good. I won't—I don't think I'll ever see you again." That realization had just dawned on her; he saw it on her face, and despite the strength of the pang it gave him, he was deeply moved by her obvious distress at the thought.

"I will miss you very much, Brianna," he said gently. He had been a soldier most of his life, and then a diplomat. He had learned to live with separation and absence, with the occasional death of friends left behind. But the notion of never seeing this odd girl again caused him a most unexpected degree of grief. Almost, he thought with surprise, as though she were his own daughter.

But he had a son, as well, and her next words snapped him back to full alertness.

"So you see," she said, leaning toward him with an intentness that he would otherwise have found charming, "I have to talk to William, and tell him. We'll never have another chance." Then her face changed, and she put a hand to her bosom.

"I have to go," she said abruptly. "Mandy—Amanda, my daughter—she needs to be fed."

And with that, she was up and gone, scudding across the sand of the racetrack like a storm cloud, leaving the threat of destruction and upheaval in her wake.

117

SURELY JUSTICE AND MERCY SHALL FOLLOW ME

July 10, 1776

THE TIDE TURNED FROM THE EBB just before five o'clock in the morning. The sky was fully light, a clear pale color without clouds, and the mudflats beyond the quay stretched gray and shining, their smoothness marred here and there by weed and stubborn sea grass, sprouting from the mud like clumps of hair.

Everyone rose with the dawn; there were plenty of people on the quay to see the small procession go out, two officers from the Wilmington Committee of Safety, a representative from the Merchants Association, a minister carrying a Bible, and the prisoner, a tall, wide-shouldered figure, walking bareheaded across the stinking mud. Behind them all came a slave, carrying the ropes.

"I don't want to watch this," Brianna said under her breath. She was very pale, her arms folded over her middle as though she had a stomachache.

"Let's go, then." Roger took her arm, but she pulled back.

"No. I have to."

She dropped her arms and stood straight, watching. People around them were jostling for a better view, jeering and catcalling so loudly that whatever was said out there was inaudible. It didn't take long. The slave, a big man, grabbed the mooring post and shook it, testing for steadfastness. Then stood back, while the two officers backed Stephen Bonnet up to the stake and wrapped his body with rope from chest to knees. The bastard wasn't going anywhere.

Roger thought he should be searching his heart for compassion, praying for the man. He couldn't. Tried to ask forgiveness, and couldn't do that, either. Something like a ball of worms churned in his belly. He felt as though he were himself tied to a stake, waiting to drown.

The black-coated minister leaned close, his hair whipping in the early morning breeze, mouth moving. Roger didn't think that Bonnet made any reply, but couldn't tell for sure. After a few moments, the men doffed their hats, stood while the minister prayed, then put them on again and headed back toward shore, their boots squelching, ankle-deep in the sandy mud.

The moment the officials had disappeared, a stream of people poured out onto the mud: sightseers, hopping children—and a man with a notebook and pencil, who Roger recognized as Amos Crupp, the current proprietor of the *Wilmington Gazette.*

"Well, that'll be a scoop, won't it?" Roger muttered. No matter what Bonnet actually said—or didn't—there would undoubtedly be a broadsheet hawked through the streets tomorrow, containing either a lurid confession or mawkish reports of remorse—perhaps both.

"Okay, I *really* can't watch this." Abruptly, Brianna turned, taking his arm.

She made it past the row of warehouses before turning abruptly to him, burying her face in his chest and bursting into tears.

"Ssh. It's okay—it's going to be all right." He patted her, tried to infuse some conviction into the words, but his own throat had a lump in it the size of a lemon. He finally took her by the shoulders and held her away from him, so that he could look into her eyes.

"Ye don't have to do it," he said.

She stopped crying and sniffed, wiping her nose on her sleeve like Jemmy—but wouldn't meet his eyes.

"It's—I'm okay It's not even *him.* It's just—just everything. M-Mandy"—her voice wavered on the word—"and meeting my brother—Oh, Roger, if I can't tell him, he'll never know, and I'll never see him or Lord John again. Or Mama—" Fresh tears overwhelmed her, welling up in her eyes, but she gulped and swallowed, forcing them back.

"It's not him," she said in a choked, exhausted voice.

"Maybe it's not," he said softly. "But ye still don't have to do it." His stomach still churned, and his hands felt shaky, but resolution filled him.

"I should have killed him on Ocracoke," she said, closing her eyes and brushing back strands of loosened hair. The sun was higher now, and bright. "I was a coward. I th-thought it would be easier to let—let the law do it." She opened her eyes, and now did meet his gaze, her eyes reddened but clear. "I can't let it happen this way, even if I hadn't given my word."

Roger understood that; he felt the terror of the tide coming in, that inexorable creep of water, rising in his bones. It would be nearly nine hours before the water reached Bonnet's chin; he was a tall man.

"I'll do it," he said very firmly.

She made a small attempt at a smile, but abandoned it.

"No," she said. "You won't." She looked—and sounded—absolutely drained; neither of them had slept much the night before. But she also sounded determined, and he recognized Jamie Fraser's stubborn blood.

Well, what the hell—he had some of that blood, too.

"I told ye," he said. "What your father said, that time. *'It is myself who kills for her.'* If it has to be done"—and he was obliged to agree with her; he couldn't stand it, either—"then I'll do it."

She was getting a grip on herself. She wiped her face with a fold of her skirt, and took a deep breath before meeting his eyes again. Hers were deep and vivid blue, much darker than the sky.

"You told me. And you told me why he said that, too—what he said to Arch Bug: *'There is a vow upon her.'* She's a doctor; she doesn't kill people."

The hell she doesn't, Roger thought, but better judgment prevented his saying so. Before he could think of something more tactful, she went on, placing her hands flat on his chest.

"You have one, too," she said. That stopped him cold.

"No, I haven't."

"Oh, yes, you do." She was quietly emphatic. "Maybe it isn't official yet—but it doesn't need to be. Maybe it doesn't even have words, the vow that you took—but you did it, and I know it."

He couldn't deny it, and was moved that she *did* know it.

"Aye, well . . ." He put his hands over hers, clasping her long, strong fingers. "And I made one to you, too, when I told ye. I said I would never put God before my—my love for you." Love. He couldn't believe that he was discussing such a thing in terms of love. And yet, he had the queerest feeling that that was exactly how she saw it.

"I don't have that sort of vow," she said firmly, and pulled her hands out of his. "And I gave my word."

She had gone with Jamie after dark the night before, to the place where the pirate was being held. Roger had no idea what sort of bribery or force of personality had been employed, but they had been admitted. Jamie had brought her back to their room very late, white-faced, with a sheaf of papers that she handed over to her father. Affidavits, she said; sworn statements of Stephen Bonnet's business dealings with various merchants up and down the coast.

Roger had given Jamie a murderous look, and got the same back, with interest. *This is war,* Fraser's narrowed eyes had said. *And I will use any weapon I can.* But all he had said was, "Good night, then, *a nighean,*" and touched her hair with tenderness before departing.

Brianna had sat down with Mandy and nursed her, eyes closed, refusing to speak. After a time, her face eased from its white, strained lines, and she burped the baby and laid her sleeping in her basket. Then she came to bed, and made love to him with a silent fierceness that surprised him. But not as much as she surprised him now.

"And there's one other thing," she said, sober and slightly sad. "I'm the only person in the world for whom this isn't murder."

With that, she turned and walked away fast, toward the inn where Mandy waited to be fed. Out on the mudflats, he could still hear the sound of excited voices, raucous as gulls.

AT NINE O'CLOCK in the morning, Roger helped his wife into a small rowboat, tied to the quay near the row of warehouses. The tide had been coming in all day; the water was more than five feet deep. Out in the midst of the shining gray stood the cluster of mooring posts—and the small dark head of the pirate.

Brianna was remote as a pagan statue, her face expressionless. She lifted her skirts to step into the boat, and sat down, the weight in her pocket clunking against the wooden slat as she did so.

Roger took up the oars and rowed, heading toward the posts. They would arouse no particular interest; boats had been going out ever since dawn, carrying sightseers who wished to look upon the condemned man's face, shout taunts, or clip a strand of his hair for a souvenir.

He couldn't see where he was going; Brianna directed him left or right with a silent tilt of her head. She could see; she sat straight and tall, her right hand hidden in her skirt.

Then she lifted her left hand suddenly, and Roger lay on the oars, digging with one to slew the tiny craft around.

Bonnet's lips were cracked, his face chapped and crusted with salt, his lids so reddened that he could barely open his eyes. But his head lifted as they drew near, and Roger saw a man ravished, helpless and dreading a coming embrace—so much that he half welcomes its seductive touch, yielding his flesh to cold fingers and the overwhelming kiss that steals his breath.

"Ye've left it late enough, darlin'," he said to Brianna, and the cracked lips parted in a grin that split them and left blood on his teeth. "I knew ye'd come, though."

Roger paddled with one oar, working the boat close, then closer. He was looking over his shoulder when Brianna drew the gilt-handled pistol from her pocket, and put the barrel to Stephen Bonnet's ear.

"Go with God, Stephen," she said clearly, in Gaelic, and pulled the trigger. Then she dropped the gun into the water and turned round to face her husband.

"Take us home," she said.

118

REGRET

LORD JOHN STEPPED into his room at the inn, and was surprised—astonished, in fact—to discover that he had a visitor.

"John." Jamie Fraser turned from the window, and gave him a small smile.

"Jamie." He returned it, trying to control the sudden sense of elation he felt. He had used Jamie Fraser's Christian name perhaps three times in the last twenty-five years; the intimacy of it was exhilarating, but he mustn't let it show.

"Will I order us refreshment?" he asked politely. Jamie had

not moved from the window; he glanced out, then back at John and shook his head, still smiling faintly.

"I thank ye, no. We are enemies, are we not?"

"We find ourselves regrettably upon opposing sides of what I trust will be a short-lived conflict," Lord John corrected.

Fraser looked down at him, with an odd, regretful sort of expression.

"Not short," he said. "But regrettable, aye."

"Indeed." Lord John cleared his throat, and moved to the window, careful not to brush against his visitor. He looked out, and saw the likely reason for Fraser's visit.

"Ah," he said, seeing Brianna Fraser MacKenzie on the wooden sidewalk below. "Oh!" he said, in a different tone. For William Clarence Henry George Ransom, ninth Earl of Ellesmere, had just come out of the inn and bowed to her.

"Sweet Jesus," he said, apprehension making his scalp prickle. "Will she tell him?"

Fraser shook his head, his eyes on the two young people below.

"She will not," he said quietly. "She gave me her word."

Relief coursed through his veins like water.

"Thank you," he said. Fraser shrugged slightly, dismissing it. It was, after all, what he desired, as well—or so Lord John assumed.

The two of them were talking together—William said something and Brianna laughed, throwing back her hair. Jamie watched in fascination. Dear God, they were alike! The small tricks of expression, of posture, of gesture . . . It must be apparent to the most casual observer. In fact, he saw a couple pass them and the woman smile, pleased at the sight of the handsome matched pair.

"She will not tell him," Lord John repeated, somewhat dismayed by the sight. "But she displays herself to him. Will he not—but no. I don't suppose he will."

"I hope not," Jamie said, eyes still fixed on them. "But if he does—he still will not *know.* And she insisted she must see him once more—that was the price of her silence."

John nodded, silent. Brianna's husband was coming now, their little boy held by one hand, the boy's hair as vivid as his mother's in the bright summer sun. MacKenzie held a baby in the crook of his arm—Brianna took it from him, turning back the blanket to display the child to William, who inspected it with every indication of politeness.

He realized suddenly that every fragment of Fraser's being was focused on the scene outside. Of course; he had not seen Willie since the boy was twelve. And to see the two together—his daughter and the son he could never speak to or acknowledge. He would have touched Fraser, put a hand on his arm in sympathy, but knowing the probable effect of his touch, forbore to do it.

"I have come," Fraser said suddenly, "to ask a favor of you."

"I am your servant, sir," Lord John said, terribly pleased, but taking refuge in formality.

"Not for myself," Fraser said with a glance at him. "For Brianna."

"My pleasure will be the greater," John assured him. "I am exceeding fond of your daughter, her temperamental resemblances to her sire notwithstanding."

The corner of Fraser's mouth lifted, and he returned his gaze to the scene below.

"Indeed," he said. "Well, then. I canna tell ye why I require this—but I need a jewel."

"A jewel?" Lord John's voice sounded blank, even to his own ears. "What sort of jewel?"

"Any sort." Fraser shrugged, impatient. "It doesna matter—so long as it should be some precious gem. I once gave ye such a stone—" His mouth twitched at that; he had handed over the stone, a sapphire, under duress, as a prisoner of the Crown. "Though I dinna suppose ye'd have that by ye, still."

In point of fact, he did. That particular sapphire had traveled with him for the last twenty-five years, and was at this moment in the pocket of his waistcoat.

He glanced at his left hand, which bore a broad gold band, set with a brilliant, faceted sapphire. Hector's ring. Given to him by his first lover at the age of sixteen. Hector had died at Culloden—soon after John had met James Fraser, in the dark of a Scottish mountain pass.

Without hesitation, but with some difficulty—the ring had been worn a long time, and had sunk a little way into the flesh of his finger—he twisted it off and dropped it into Jamie's hand.

Fraser's brows rose in astonishment.

"This? Are ye sur—"

"Take it." He reached out then, and closed Jamie's fingers around it with his own. The contact was fleeting, but his hand tingled, and he closed his own fist, hoping to keep the sensation.

"Thank you," Jamie said again, quietly.

"It is—my very great pleasure." The party below was breaking up—Brianna was taking her leave, the baby held in her arms, her husband and son already halfway down the walk. William bowed, hat off, the shape of his chestnut head so perfectly echoing that of the red—

Suddenly, Lord John could not bear to see them part. He wished to keep that, too—the sight of them together. He closed his eyes and stood, hands on the sill, feeling the movement of the breeze past his face. Something touched his shoulder, very briefly, and he felt a sense of movement in the air beside him.

When he opened his eyes again, all three of them were gone.

119

LOTH TO DEPART

September 1776

ROGER WAS LAYING the last of the water pipes when Aidan and Jemmy popped up beside him, sudden as a pair of jack-in-the-boxes.

"Daddy, Daddy, Bobby's here!"

"What, Bobby Higgins?" Roger straightened up, feeling

his back muscles protest, and looked toward the Big House, but saw no sign of a horse. "Where is he?"

"He went up to the graveyard," Aidan said, looking important. "D'ye think he's gone to look for the ghost?"

"I doubt it," Roger said calmly. "What ghost?"

"Malva Christie's," Aidan said promptly. "She walks. Everybody says so." He spoke bravely, but wrapped his arms about himself. Jemmy, who plainly hadn't heard that bit of news before, looked wide-eyed.

"Why does she walk? Where's she going?"

"Because she was murrrrderrred, silly," Aidan said. "Folk what are murdered always walk. They're lookin' for the one who killed them."

"Nonsense," Roger said firmly, seeing the uneasy look on Jemmy's face. Jem had known Malva Christie was dead, of course; he'd gone to her funeral, along with all the other children on the Ridge. But he and Brianna had simply told the boy that Malva had died, not that she had been murdered.

Well, Roger thought grimly, little hope of keeping something like that secret. He hoped Jem wouldn't have nightmares.

"Malva's not walking about looking for anyone," he said, with as much conviction as he could infuse into his voice. "Her soul is in heaven with Jesus, where she's happy and peaceful—and her body . . . well, when people die, they don't need their bodies anymore, and so we bury them, and there they stay, all tidy in their graves, until the Last Day."

Aidan looked patently unconvinced by this.

"Joey McLaughlin saw her, two weeks ago Friday," he said, bobbing up and down on his toes. "A-flittin' through the wood, he said, all dressed in black—and howlin' most mournful!"

Jemmy was beginning to look truly upset. Roger laid down the spade, and picked Jem up in his arms.

"I expect Joey McLaughlin was a bit the worse for a dram too much," he said. Both boys were entirely familiar with the concept of drunkenness. "If it was flitting through the wood howling, it was most likely Rollo he saw. Come on, though, we'll go find Bobby, and ye'll see Malva's grave for yourselves."

He put out a hand to Aidan, who took it happily and chattered like a magpie all the way up the hill.

And what was Aidan going to do, when he left? he wondered. The idea of leaving, at first so abrupt as to seem completely unreal, unthinkable, had been filtering into his consciousness, day by day. As he worked at the chores, dug the trenches for Brianna's water pipes, carried hay, chopped wood, he would try to think: "Not much longer." And yet it seemed impossible that one day he would not be on the Ridge, would not push open the door to the cabin and find Brianna involved in some fiendish experiment on the kitchen table, Jem and Aidan madly vrooming around her feet.

The feeling of unreality was even more pronounced when he preached of a Sunday or went round as minister—if yet without portfolio—to visit the sick or counsel the troubled. Looking into all those faces—attentive, excited, bored, dour, or preoccupied—he simply couldn't believe that he meant to go, callously to abandon them all. How would he tell them? he wondered, with a sort of anguish at the thought. Especially the ones he felt most responsible for—Aidan and his mother.

He'd prayed about it, looking for strength, for guidance.

And yet . . . and yet the vision of Amanda's tiny blue fingernails, the faint wheeze of her breathing, never left him. And the looming stones by the creek on Ocracoke seemed to grow nearer, more solid, day by day.

Bobby Higgins was indeed in the graveyard, his horse tethered under the pines. He was sitting by Malva's grave, head bowed in contemplation, though he looked up at once when Roger and the boys appeared. He looked pale and somber, but scrambled to his feet and shook Roger's hand.

"I'm glad to see ye back, Bobby. Here, you lot go and play, aye?" He set Jemmy down, and was pleased to see that after one suspicious glance at Malva's grave—adorned with a wilted bunch of wildflowers—Jemmy went off quite happily with Aidan to hunt for squirrels and chipmunks in the wood.

"I—er—wasn't expecting to see you again," he added a little awkwardly. Bobby looked down, slowly dusting pine needles from his breeches.

"Well, zur . . . the fact of the matter is, I've come to stay. If so be as that's agreeable," he added hastily.

"To stay? But—of course it's fine," Roger said, recovering from his surprise. "Have you—that is—you've not had a falling-out with his Lordship, I hope?"

Bobby looked astonished at the thought, and shook his head decidedly.

"Oh, no, zur! His Lordship's been proper kind to me, ever since he took me on." He hesitated, biting his lower lip. "It's only—well, ye see, zur, there's a deal of folk what come to stay with his Lordship these days. Politicals, and—and army folk."

Despite himself, he touched the brand on his cheek, which had faded now to a pinkish scar but was still apparent—and always would be. Roger understood.

"You weren't comfortable there any longer, I suppose?"

"That's it, zur." Bobby gave him a grateful look. "Time was, 'twas just his Lordship and me and Manoke the cook. Sometimes a guest would come for dinner or to stay a few days, but 'twas all easy and what ye might call simple. When I went for to run messages or errands for his Lordship, folk would stare, but only for the first time or two; after that, they'd be used to this"—he touched his face again—"and it was all right. But now . . ." He trailed off unhappily, leaving Roger to imagine the probable response of British army officers, starched, polished, and either openly disapproving of this blot on the service—or painfully polite.

"His Lordship saw the difficulty; he's good that way. And he said as how he would miss me, but if I chose to seek my fortune elsewhere, he would give me ten pounds and his best wishes."

Roger whistled respectfully. Ten pounds was a very respectable sum. Not a fortune, but quite enough to set Bobby on his road.

"Very nice," he said. "Did he know ye meant to come here?"

Bobby shook his head.

"I wasn't sure myself," he admitted. "Once, I should—" He cut himself off abruptly, with a glance at Malva's grave, then turned back to Roger, clearing his throat.

"I thought I best talk to Mr. Fraser, before I was to make up my mind. Could be there's naught for me here any longer, either." This was phrased as a statement, but the question was clear. Everyone on the Ridge knew Bobby and accepted him; that wasn't the difficulty. But with Lizzie married and Malva gone . . . Bobby wanted a wife.

"Oh . . . I think ye might find yourself welcome," Roger said with a thoughtful look at Aidan, hanging upside down by his knees from a tree branch, while Jemmy pegged pinecones at him. A most peculiar feeling went through him—something between gratitude and jealousy—but he pushed the latter feeling firmly down.

"Aidan!" he shouted. "Jem! Time to go!" And turned casually back to Bobby, saying, "I think ye'll maybe not have met Aidan's mother, Amy McCallum—a young widow, aye, with a house and a bit of land. She's come to work at the Big House; if ye'll come sit down to supper there . . ."

"I'VE THOUGHT OF it now and then," Jamie admitted. "Wondered, ye ken? What if I could? How would it be?"

He glanced at Brianna, smiling, but a little helpless, and shrugged.

"What d'ye think, lass? What should I do there? How would it be?"

"Well, it—" she began, and stopped, trying to envision him in that world—behind the wheel of a car? Going to an office, in a three-piece suit? That idea was so ludicrous, she laughed. Or sitting in a darkened theater, watching Godzilla films with Jem and Roger?

"What's Jamie spelled backward?" she asked.

"Eimaj, I suppose," he replied, bewildered. "Why?"

"I think you'd do fine," she said, smiling. "Never mind. You'd—well, I suppose you could . . . publish newspapers. The printing presses are bigger and faster, and it takes a lot more people to gather the news, but otherwise—I don't think it's so different then from what it is now. You know how to do that."

He nodded, a crease of concentration forming between the thick brows that were so like hers.

"I suppose so," he said a little dubiously. "Could I be a

farmer, d'ye think? Surely folk still eat; someone must feed them."

"You could." She looked round, taking fresh note of all the homely details of the place: the chickens scratching peaceably in the dirt; the soft, weathered boards of the stable; the thrown-up dirt near the foundation of the house where the white pig had burrowed in. "There are people then who still farm just this way; small places, way up in the mountains. It's a hard life—" She saw him smile, and laughed in return. "All right, it's not any harder than it is now—but it's a lot easier in the cities."

She paused, thinking.

"You wouldn't have to fight," she said finally.

He seemed surprised at that.

"No? But ye did say there are wars."

"There certainly are," she said, needles of ice piercing her belly, as the images pierced her mind: fields of poppies, fields of white crosses—a man on fire, a naked child running with burned skin, the contorted face of a man in the instant before the bullet entered his brain. "But—but then it's only the young men who fight. And not all of them; only some."

"Mmphm." He thought for a bit, his brow furrowed, then looked up searching her face.

"This world of yours, this America," he said finally, matter-of-factly. "The freedom that ye go to. There will be a fearful price to be paid. Will it be worth it, do ye think?"

It was her turn then to be silent and think. At last she put her hand on his arm—solid, warm, steady as iron.

"Almost nothing would be worth losing you," she whispered. "But maybe that comes close."

AS THE WORLD turns toward winter and the nights grow long, people begin to wake in the dark. Lying in bed too long cramps the limbs, and dreams dreamt too long turn inward on themselves, grotesque as a Mandarin's fingernails. By and large, the human body isn't adapted for more than seven or eight hours' sleep—but what happens when the nights are longer than that?

What happens is the second sleep. You fall asleep from tiredness, soon after dark—but then wake again, rising toward the surface of your dreams like a trout coming up to feed. And should your sleeping partner also wake then—and people who have slept together for a good many years know at once when each other wakes—you have a small, private place to share, deep in the night. A place in which to rise, to stretch, to bring a juicy apple back to bed, to share slice by slice, fingers brushing lips. To have the luxury of conversation, uninterrupted by the business of the day. To make love slowly in the light of an autumn moon.

And then, to lie close, and let a lover's dreams caress your skin as you begin to sink once more beneath the waves of consciousness, blissful in the knowledge that dawn is far off—that's second sleep.

I came very slowly to the surface of my first sleep, to find that the highly erotic dream I had been having had some basis in reality.

"I'd never thought myself the sort who'd molest a corpse, Sassenach." Jamie's voice tickled the tender flesh below my ear, murmuring. "But I will say the notion has more appeal than I'd thought."

I wasn't sufficiently coherent as to respond to this, but thrust my hips back toward him in a fashion that he seemed to find as eloquent an invitation as one written in calligraphy on parchment. He took a deep breath, a firm grip on my buttocks, and brought me to an awakening that could be called rude in several senses of the word.

I squirmed like a worm impaled on a fish-hook, making small urgent noises that he interpreted correctly, rolling me onto my face and proceeding to leave me in no doubt that I was not merely alive and awake, but functioning.

I emerged at length from a nest of flattened pillows, damp, gasping, quivering in every engorged and slippery nerve-ending, and thoroughly awake.

"What brought that on?" I inquired. He hadn't pulled away; we lay still joined, washed in the light of a big golden half-moon, riding low in the sky above the chestnut trees. He made a small sound, partly amusement, partly dismay.

"I canna look at ye asleep without wanting to wake ye,

Sassenach." His hand cupped my breast, gently now. "I suppose I find myself lonely without ye."

There was an odd note in his voice, and I turned my head toward him, but couldn't see him in the dark behind me. Instead, I put back a hand and touched the leg still wrapped halfway over mine. Even relaxed, it was hard, the long groove of the muscle graceful under my fingers.

"I'm here," I said, and his arm tightened suddenly round me.

I HEARD the breath catch in his throat, and my hand tightened on his thigh.

"What is it?" I said.

He drew breath, but didn't answer at once. I felt him draw back a little, and fumble under the pillow. Then his hand came round me again, but this time seeking the hand that lay on his leg. His fingers curled into mine, and I felt a small, hard, roundish object thrust into my hand.

I heard him swallow.

The stone, whatever it was, seemed slightly warm to the touch. I ran a thumb slowly over it; a raw stone of some kind, but big, the size of one of my finger-joints.

"Jamie . . ." I said, feeling my throat close.

"I love you," he said, so softly that I barely heard him, close as we were.

I lay still for a moment, feeling the stone grow warmer in the palm of my hand. Surely it was imagination that made it seem to throb in time with my heart. Where on earth had he gotten it?

Then I moved—not suddenly, but with deliberation, my body sliding slowly free of his. I rose, feeling light-headed, and crossed the room. Pushed open the window to feel the sharp touch of the autumn wind on my naked bed-warm skin, and drawing back my arm, hurled the tiny object into the night.

Then I came back to bed, saw his hair a dark mass on the pillow, and the shine of his eyes in the moonlight.

"I love you," I whispered, and slid under the sheet beside him, putting my arms around him, hugging him close, warmer than the stone—so much warmer—and his heart beat with mine.

"I'm none so brave as I was before, ken?" he said very softly. "Not brave enough to live without ye anymore."

But brave enough to try.

I drew his head down to me, stroking the tumble of his hair, coarse and smooth at once, live beneath my fingers.

"Lay your head, man," I said softly. "It's a long time 'til dawn."

120

IF ONLY FOR MYSELF

THE SKY WAS A flat, leaden color, threatening rain, and the wind gusted through the palmettos, rattling the leaves like sabers. Down in the depths of the tidal forest, the four stones loomed beside the creek.

"I am the wife of the laird of Balnain," Brianna whispered, next to me. "The faeries have stolen me over again." She was white to the lips, Amanda clutched close to her breast.

We had made our farewells—we had been saying farewell, I thought, since the day I pressed the stethoscope to Mandy's heart. But Brianna turned and flung herself—baby and all—at Jamie, who pressed her so tight against his heart, I thought one of them must break.

Then she was flying at me, a cloud of cloak and loosened hair, and her face was cold against mine, her tears and mine mingling on my skin.

"I love you, Mama! I love you!" she said in desperation, then turned and, without looking back, began to walk the pattern Donner had described, quietly chanting under her breath. A circle right, between two stones, a circle left, and back through the center—and then to the left of the largest stone.

I had been expecting it; when she began to walk the pattern, I had run away from the stones, stopping at what I thought a safe distance. It wasn't. The sound of them—a roar, this time, instead of a shriek—thundered through me, stopping my breath and nearly my heart. Pain froze in a band round my chest and I dropped to my knees, swaying and helpless.

They were gone. I could see Jamie and Roger running to check—terrified of finding bodies, at once desolate and elated to find none. I couldn't see well—my vision swam, flickering in and out—but didn't need to. I knew they were gone, from the hole in my heart.

"TWO DOWN," Roger whispered. His voice was no more than a faint rasp, and he cleared his throat, hard. "Jeremiah." He looked down at Jem, who blinked and sniffed, and drew himself up tall at the sound of his formal name.

"Ye ken what we're about now, aye?" Jemmy nodded, though he flicked a scared glance toward the towering stone where his mother and his baby sister had just vanished. He swallowed hard, and wiped the tears off his cheeks.

"Well, then." Roger reached out a hand and rested it gently on Jemmy's head. "Know this, *mo mac*—I shall love ye all my life, and never forget ye. But this is a terrible thing we're doing, and ye need not come with me. Ye can stay with your grandda and grannie Claire; it will be all right."

"Won't I—won't I see Mama again?" Jemmy's eyes were huge, and he couldn't keep from looking at the stone.

"I don't know," Roger said, and I could see the tears he was fighting himself, and hear them in his thickened voice. He didn't know whether he would ever see Brianna again himself, or baby Mandy. "Probably . . . probably not."

Jamie looked down at Jem, who was clinging to his hand, looking back and forth between father and grandfather, confusion, fright, and longing in his face.

"If one day, *a bhailach,*" Jamie said conversationally, "ye should meet a verra large mouse named Michael—ye'll tell him your grandsire sends his regards." He opened his hand, then, letting go, and nodded toward Roger.

Jem stood staring for a moment, then dug in his feet and sprinted toward Roger, sand spurting from under his shoes. He leaped into his father's arms, clutching him around the neck, and with a final glance backward, Roger turned and stepped behind the stone, and the inside of my head exploded in fire.

Unimaginable time later, I came slowly back, coming down from the clouds in fragments, like hailstones. And found myself lying with my head in Jamie's lap. And heard him saying softly, to himself or to me, "For your sake, I will continue—though for mine alone . . . I would not."

121

ACROSS THE ABYSS

THREE NIGHTS LATER, I woke from a restless sleep in an inn in Wilmington, my throat parched as the salt bacon I had eaten in the dinner stew. Sitting up to find water, I found that I was alone—the moonlight through the window shone white on the vacant pillow beside me.

I found Jamie outside, behind the inn, his nightshirt a pale blotch in the darkness of the innyard. He was sitting on the ground with his back against a chopping block, arms wrapped about his knees.

He didn't speak as I came toward him, but turned his head, body shifting in a silent welcome. I sat down on the chopping block behind him, and he leaned his head back against my thigh, with a long, deep sigh.

"Couldn't sleep?" I touched him gently, smoothing back the hair from his face. He slept with it unbound, and it fell thick and wild about his shoulders, tangled from bed.

"Nay, I slept," he said quietly. His eyes were open, looking up at the great gold moon, three-quarters full over the aspens near the inn. "I had a dream."

"A nightmare?" He had them seldom anymore, but they did come sometimes: the bloody memories of Culloden, of futile death and slaughter; prison dreams of hunger and confinement—and sometimes, very rarely, Jack Randall returned to him in sleep, with loving cruelty. Such dreams would always drive him from his bed to walk to and fro for hours, until exhaustion cleansed him of their visions. But he had not dreamed that way since Moore's Creek Bridge.

"No," he said, sounding half-surprised. "Not at all. I dreamed of her—of our lassie—and the bairns."

My heart gave an odd little hop, the consequence of startlement and what might almost have been envy.

"You dreamed about Brianna and the children? What happened?"

He smiled, face tranquil and abstracted in the moonlight, as though he still saw some part of the dream before him.

"It is all right," he said. "They are safe. I saw them in a town—it seemed like Inverness, but it was different, somehow. They walked up the step of a house—Roger Mac was with them," he added, offhand. "They knocked at the door, and a wee brown-haired woman opened to them. She laughed wi' joy to see them, and brought them in, and they went down a hallway, wi' strange things like bowls hanging from the ceiling.

"Then they were in a room, wi' sofas and chairs, and the room had great windows all down one wall, from the floor to the ceiling, and the afternoon sun was streaming in, setting Brianna's hair to fire, and makin' wee Mandy cry when it got in her eyes."

"Did . . . did any of them call the brown-haired woman by name?" I asked, my heart beating in a queer, fast way.

He frowned, moonlight making a cross of light over nose and brows.

"Aye, they did," he said. "I canna just—oh, aye; Roger Mac called her Fiona."

"Did he?" I said. My hands rested on his shoulder, and my mouth was a hundred times drier than it had been when I woke up. The night was chilly, but not enough to account for the temperature of my hands.

I had told Jamie any amount of things about my own time over the years of our marriage. About trains and planes and automobiles and wars and indoor plumbing. But I was nearly sure that I had never told him what the study looked like in the manse where Roger had grown up with his adoptive father.

The room with the window wall, made to accommodate the Reverend's painting hobby. The manse with its long hallway, furnished with old-fashioned light fixtures, shaped like hanging bowls. And I knew I had never told him about the Reverend's last housekeeper, a girl with dark, curly hair, called Fiona.

"Were they happy?" I asked at last, very quietly.

"Aye. Brianna and the lad—they had some shadows to their faces, but I could see they were glad nonetheless. They all sat down to eat—Brianna and her lad close together, leaning on each other—and wee Jem stuffed his face wi' cakes and cream." He smiled at the picture, teeth a brief gleam in the darkness.

"Oh—at the last, just before I woke . . . wee Jem was messin' about, picking things up and putting them down as he does. There was a . . . thing . . on the table. I couldna say what it was; I've never seen the like."

He held his hands about six inches apart, frowning at them. "It was maybe this wide, and just a bit longer—something like a box, maybe, only sort of . . . humped."

"Humped?" I said, puzzled as to what this could be.

"Aye, and it had a thing on top like a wee club, only wi' a knob to each end, and the club was tied to the box wi' a sort of black cord, curled up on itself like a piggie's tail. Jem saw it, and he reached out his hand, and said, 'I want to talk to Grandda.' And then I woke."

He leaned his head back farther, so as to look up into my face.

"Would ye ken what a thing like that might be, Sassenach? It was like nothing I've ever seen."

The autumn wind came rustling down from the hill, dry leaves hurrying in its wake, quick and light as the footsteps of a ghost, and I felt the hair rise on nape and forearms.

"Yes," I said. "I've told you about them, I know." I didn't think, though, that I had ever described one to him, in more than general terms. I cleared my throat.

"It's called a telephone."

122

THE GUARDIAN

IT WAS NOVEMBER; there were no flowers. But the holly bushes gleamed dark green, and the berries had begun to ripen. I cut a small bunch, careful of the prickles, added a tender branch of spruce for fragrance, and climbed the steep trail to the tiny graveyard.

I went every week, to leave some small token on Malva's grave, and say a prayer. She and her child had not been buried with a cairn—her father hadn't wanted such a pagan custom—but people came and left pebbles there by way of remembrance. It gave me some small comfort to see them; there were others who remembered her.

I stopped abruptly at the head of the trail; someone was kneeling by her grave—a young man. I caught the murmur of his voice, low and conversational, and would have turned about to go, save that he raised his head, and the wind caught his hair, short and tufted, like an owl's feathers. Allan Christie.

He saw me, too, and stiffened. There was nothing to do but go and speak to him, though, and so I went.

"Mr. Christie," I said, the words feeling strange in my mouth. That was what I had called his father. "I'm sorry for your loss."

He stared up at me blankly; then some sort of awareness seemed to stir in his eyes. Gray eyes, rimmed with black lashes, so much like those of his father and sister. Bloodshot with weeping and lack of sleep, judging from the shocking smudges under them.

"Aye," he said. "My loss. Aye."

I stepped around him to lay down my evergreen bouquet, and with a small spurt of alarm, saw that there was a pistol on the ground beside him, cocked and primed.

"Where have you been?" I said as casually as possible, under the circumstances. "We've missed you."

He shrugged, as though it really didn't matter where he'd been—perhaps it didn't. He wasn't looking at me anymore, but at the stone we'd placed at the head of her grave.

"Places," he said vaguely. "But I had to come back." He turned away a little, plainly indicating that he wanted me to leave. Instead, I pulled up my skirts and knelt gingerly beside him. I didn't *think* he'd blow his brains out in front of me. I had no idea what to do, other than to try to make him talk to me and hope that someone else would come along.

"We're glad to have you home," I said, trying for an easy, conversational note.

"Aye," he said vaguely. And again, his eyes going to the headstone, "I had to come back." His hand wandered toward the pistol, and I seized it, startling him.

"I know you loved your sister very much," I said. "It—it was a terrible shock to you, I know." What, what did one say? There were things one might say to a person contemplating suicide, I knew, but what?

"Your life has value." I'd said that to Tom Christie, who had only replied, *"If it did not, this would not matter."* But how should I convince his son of that?

"Your father loved you both," I said, wondering as I said it whether he knew what his father had done. His fingers were very cold, and I wrapped both my hands round his, trying to offer him a little warmth, hoping that the human contact would help.

"Not as I loved her," he said softly, not looking at me. "I loved her all her life, from the time she was born and they gave her me to hold. There was nay other, for either of us. Faither was gone to prison, and then my mither—ah, Mither." His lips pulled back, as though to laugh, but there was no sound.

"I know about your mother," I said. "Your father told me."

"Did he?" His head jerked up to look at me, eyes clear and hard. "Did he tell ye they took me and Malva to her execution?"

"I—no. I don't think he knew, did he?" My stomach clenched.

"He did. I told him, later, when he sent for us, brought us here. He said that was good, we'd seen with our own eyes the ends of wickedness. He bade me remember the lesson—and so I did," he added more quietly.

"How—how old were you?" I asked, horrified.

"Ten. Malva was nay more than two; she'd no idea what was happening. She cried out for her Mam when they brought Mither out to the hangsman, and kicked and screamed, reaching out for her."

He swallowed, and turned his head away.

"I tried to take her, to push her head into my bosom, so she shouldna see—but they wouldna let me have her. They held her wee head and made her watch, and Auntie Darla saying in her ear that this was what happened to witches, and pinching her legs 'til she shrieked. We lived with Auntie Darla for six years after that," he said, his face remote.

"She wasna best pleased about it, but she said she kent her Christian duty. The auld besom barely fed us, and 'twas me took care of Malva."

He was silent for a bit, and so was I, thinking the best—the only—thing I could offer him now was the chance to speak. He pulled his hand from mine, leaned over, and touched the gravestone. It was no more than a lump of granite, but someone had gone to the trouble to carve her name on it—only the one word, MALVA, in crude block letters. It reminded me of the memorials that dotted Culloden, the clanstones, each with a single name.

"She was perfect," he whispered. His finger traced its way over the stone, delicate, as though he touched her flesh. "So perfect. Her wee privates looked like a flower's bud, and her skin sae fresh and soft. . . ."

A sense of coldness grew in the pit of my stomach. Did he mean . . . yes, of course he did. A sense of inevitable despair began to grow within me.

"She was mine," he said, and looking up to see my eye upon him, repeated it more loudly. "She was mine!"

He looked down, then, at the grave, and his mouth turned in upon itself, in grief and anger.

"The auld man never knew—never guessed what we were to each other."

Didn't he? I thought. Tom Christie might have confessed to the crime to save one he loved—but he loved more than one. Having lost a daughter—or rather, a niece—would he not do all he could to save the son who was the last remnant of his blood?

"You killed her," I said quietly. I was in no doubt, and he showed no surprise.

"He would ha' sold her away, given her to some clod of a farmer." Allan's fist clenched on his thigh. "I thought of that, as she grew older, and sometimes when I would lie with her, I couldna bear the thought, and would slap her face, only from the rage of thinking of it."

He drew a deep, ragged breath.

"It wasna her fault, none of it. But I thought it was. And then I caught her wi' that soldier, and again, wi' filthy wee Henderson. I beat her for it, but she cried out that she couldna help it—she was with child."

"Yours?"

He nodded, slowly.

"I never thought of it. I should, of course. But I never did. She was always wee Malva, see, a bittie wee lass. I saw her breasts swell, aye, and the hair come out to mar her sweet flesh—but I just never thought . . .

He shook his head, unable to deal with the thought, even now.

"She said she must marry—and there must be reason for her husband to think the child his, whoever she wed. If she couldna make the soldier wed her, then it must be another. So she took as many lovers as she might, quickly.

"I put a stop to that, though," he assured me, a faintly nauseating tone of self-righteousness in his voice. "I told her I wouldna have it—I would think of another way."

"And so you put her up to saying the child was Jamie's." My horror at the story and my anger at what he had done to us was subsumed by a flood of sorrow. *Oh, Malva,* I thought in despair. *Oh, my darling Malva. Why didn't you tell me?* But of course she wouldn't have told me. Her only confidant was Allan.

He nodded, and reached out to touch the stone again. A gust of wind quivered through the holly, stirring the stiff leaves.

"It would explain the bairn, see, but she wouldna have to wed anyone. I thought—Himself would give her money to go away, and I would go with her. We could go to Nova Scotia, perhaps, or to the Indies." His voice sounded dreamy, as though he envisioned some idyllic life, where no one knew.

"But why did you kill her?" I burst out. "What made you *do* that?" The sorrow and the senselessness were overwhelming; I clenched my hands in my apron, not to batter him.

"I had to," he said heavily. "She said she couldna go through with it." He blinked, looking down, and I saw that his eyes were heavy with tears.

"She said—she loved you," he said, low-voiced and thick. "She couldna hurt ye so. She meant to tell the truth. No matter what I said to her, she just kept saying that—she loved ye, and she'd tell."

He closed his eyes, shoulders slumping. Two tears ran down his cheeks.

"Why, hinny?" he cried, crossing his arms over his belly in a spasm of grief. "Why did ye make me do it? Ye shouldna have loved anyone but me."

He sobbed then, like a child, and curled into himself, weeping. I was weeping, too, for the loss and the pointlessness, for the utter, terrible *waste* of it all. But I reached out and took the gun from the ground. Hands shaking, I dumped out the priming pan, and shook the ball from the barrel, then put the pistol in the pocket of my apron.

"Leave," I said, my voice half-choked. "Go away again, Allan. There are too many people dead."

He was too grief-stricken to hear me; I shook him by the shoulder and said it again, more strongly.

"You can't kill yourself. I forbid it, do you hear?"

"And who are you to say?" he cried, turning on me. His face was contorted with anguish. "I cannot live, I cannot!"

But Tom Christie had given up his life for his son, as well as for me; I couldn't let that sacrifice go for naught.

"You must," I said, and stood up, feeling light-headed, unsure whether my knees would hold me. "Do you hear me? You must!"

He looked up, eyes burning through the tears, but didn't speak. There was a keening whine like the hum of a mosquito, and a soft, sudden thump. He didn't change expression, but his eyes slowly died. He stayed on his knees for a moment, but bowed then forward, like a flower nodding on its stem, so I saw the arrow protruding from the center of his back. He coughed, once, sputtering blood, and fell sideways, curled on his sister's grave. His legs jerked spasmodically, grotesquely froglike. Then he lay still.

I stood stupidly staring at him for some immeasurable span of time, becoming only gradually aware that Ian had walked out of the wood and stood beside me, bow over his shoulder. Rollo nosed curiously at the body, whining.

"He's right, Auntie," Ian said quietly. "He can't."

123

RETURN OF THE NATIVE

OLD GRANNIE ABERNATHY looked at least a hundred and two. She admitted—under pressure—to ninety-one. She was nearly blind and nearly deaf, curled up like a pretzel from osteoporosis, and with skin gone so fragile that the merest scrape tore it like paper.

"I'm nay more than a bag o' bones," she said every time I saw her, shaking a head that trembled with palsy. "But at least I've still got maist o' my teeth!"

For a wonder, she had; I thought that was the only reason she had made it this far—unlike many people half her age, she wasn't reduced to living on porridge, but could still stomach meat and greens. Perhaps it was improved nutrition that kept her going—perhaps it was mere stubbornness. Her married name was Abernathy, but she had, she confided, been born a Fraser.

Smiling at the thought, I finished wrapping the bandage about her sticklike shin. Her legs and feet had almost no flesh upon them, and felt hard and cold as wood. She'd knocked her shin against the leg of the table and taken off a strip of skin the width of a finger; such a minor injury that a younger person would think nothing of it—but her family worried over her, and had sent for me.

"It will be slow healing, but if you keep it clean—for God's sake, do *not* let her put hog fat on it!—I think it will be all right." The younger Mrs. Abernathy, known as Young Grannie—herself about seventy—gave me a sharp eye at that; like her mother-in-law, she put a good deal of faith in hog fat and turpentine as cure-alls, but nodded grudgingly. Her daughter, whose high-flown name of Arabella had been shortened to the cozier Grannie Belly, grinned at me behind Young Grannie's back. She had been less fortunate in the way of teeth—her smile showed significant gaps—but was cheerful and good-natured.

"Willie B.," she instructed a teenaged grandson, "just be steppin' doon to the root cellar, and bringing up a wee sack of turnips for Herself."

I made the usual protestations, but all parties concerned were comfortably aware of the proper protocol in such matters, and within a few minutes, I was on my way home, the richer by five pounds of turnips.

They were welcome. I had forced myself to go back to my garden in the spring after Malva's death—I had to; sentiment was all very well, but we had to eat. The subsequent disturbances of life and my prolonged absences, though, had resulted in dreadful neglect of the autumn crop. Despite Mrs. Bug's best efforts, the turnips had all succumbed to thrips and black rot.

Our supplies in general were sadly depleted. With Jamie and Ian gone so frequently, not there to harvest or hunt, and without Bree and Roger, the grain crops had been half of their usual yield, and only a pitiful single haunch of venison hung in the smoking shed. We needed nearly all the grain for our own use; there was none to trade or sell, and only a scant few bags of barleycorn sat under canvas near the malting shed—where they were likely to rot, I thought grimly, as no one had had time to see to the malting of a fresh batch before the cold weather set in.

Mrs. Bug was slowly rebuilding her flock of chickens, after a disastrous attack by a fox that got into the henhouse—but it was slow going, and we got only the occasional egg for breakfast, grudgingly spared.

On the other hand, I reflected more cheerfully, we *did* have ham. Lots of ham. Likewise, immense quantities of bacon, headcheese, pork chops, tenderloin . . . to say nothing of suet and rendered fat.

The thought led me back to hog fat, and to the crowded, overflowingly familiar coziness of the Abernathys' cluster of cabins—and by contrast, to the thought of the dreadful emptiness at the Big House.

In a place with so many people, how could the loss of only four be so important? I had to stop and lean against a tree, let the sorrow wash through me, making no attempt to stop it. I'd learned. *"Ye canna hold a ghost at bay,"* Jamie had told me. *"Let them in."*

I let them in—I could never keep them out. And took what small comfort I could in hoping—no, I didn't hope, I told myself fiercely, I *knew*—that they were not ghosts in fact. Not dead, but only . . . elsewhere.

After a few moments, the overwhelming grief began to recede, going slowly as the ebbing tide. Sometimes it uncovered treasure: small forgotten images of Jemmy's face, smeared with honey, Brianna's laughter, Roger's hands, deft with a knife, carving one of the little cars—the house was still littered with them—then leaning to spear a muffin from a passing plate. And if to look at these caused fresh pain, at least I had them, and could keep them in my heart, knowing that in the fullness of time, they would bring consolation.

I breathed, and felt the tightness in my chest and throat ease. Amanda was not the only one who might benefit from modern surgery, I thought. I couldn't tell what might be done for Roger's vocal cords, but maybe . . . and yet, his voice now was good. Full and resonant, if rough. Perhaps he would choose to keep it as it was—he'd fought for it, and earned it.

The tree I leaned against was a pine; the needles swayed softly above me, then settled, as though in agreement. I had to go; it was late in the day and the air was growing colder.

Wiping my eyes, I settled the hood of my cloak and went on. It was a long walk from the Abernathys'—I should really have ridden Clarence, but he'd come up lame the day before, and I'd let him rest. I'd have to hurry, though, if I was to reach home before dark.

I cast a wary eye upward, judging the clouds, which had that soft, uniform gray of coming snow. The air was cold and thick with moisture; when the temperature dropped at nightfall, snow would fall.

The sky was still light, but only just, as I came down past the springhouse and into the backyard. Light enough to tell me that something was wrong, though—the back door stood open.

That set off alarm bells, and I turned to run back into the woods. I turned, and ran smack into a man who had come out of the trees behind me.

"Who the hell are you?" I demanded, stepping hastily back.

"Don't worry about that, Mrs.," he said, and grabbing me by the arm, yelled toward the house, "Hey, Donner! I got her!"

WHATEVER WENDIGO Donner been doing for the last year, it hadn't been profitable, by the looks of him. Never a natty dresser at the best of times, he was now so ragged that his coat was literally falling apart, and a slice of stringy buttock showed through a rent in his breeches. His mane of hair was greasy and matted, and he stank.

"Where are they?" he demanded hoarsely.

"Where are what?" I swung round to face his companion, who seemed in slightly better condition. "And where are my housemaid and her sons?" We were standing in the kitchen, and the hearth fire was out; Mrs. Bug hadn't come that morning, and wherever Amy and the boys were, they'd been gone for some time.

"Dunno." The man shrugged, indifferent. "Wasn't nobody to home when we came."

"Where are the jewels?" Donner grabbed at my arm, jerking me round to face him. His eyes were sunk in his head, and his grip was hot; he was burning with fever.

"I haven't got any," I said shortly. "You're ill. You should—"

"You do! I know you do! Everybody knows!"

That gave me momentary pause. Gossip being what it was, everybody likely *thought* they knew that Jamie had a small cache of jewels. Small wonder if word of this hypothetical treasure had reached Donner—and little likelihood that I could convince him otherwise. I had no choice but to try, though.

"They're gone," I said simply.

Something flickered in his eyes at that.

"How?" he said.

I raised an eyebrow in the direction of his accomplice. Did he want the man to know?

"Go find Richie and Jed," Donner said briefly to the thug, who shrugged and went out. Richie and Jed? How on earth many people had he brought? Past the first shock of seeing him, I now became aware that there were thumping feet upstairs, and the sound of cupboard doors being banged impatiently down the hall.

"My surgery! Get them out of there!" I dove for the door to the hallway, intending to perform this office myself, but Donner grabbed at my cloak to stop me.

I was bloody tired of being manhandled, and I wasn't afraid of this miserable excuse for a human being.

"Let go!" I snapped, and kicked him briskly in the kneecap to emphasize the point. He yelped, but let go; I could hear him cursing behind me as I rushed through the door and down the hall.

Papers and books had been flung out into the hallway from Jamie's office, and a puddle of ink had been poured over them. The explanation of the ink was apparent when I saw the thug rifling my surgery—he had a big blot of ink on the front of his shirt, where he had apparently sequestered the stolen pewter inkwell.

"What are you *doing,* you nitwit?" I said. The thug, a boy of sixteen or so, blinked at me, mouth open. He had one of Mr. Blogweather's perfect glass globes in his hand; at this, he grinned maliciously and let it drop to the floor, where it shattered into a spray of fragments. One of the flying shards lanced through his cheek, slicing it open; he didn't feel it, until the blood began to well. Then he put a hand to the wound, frowning in puzzlement, and bellowed in fright at the blood on his hand.

"Crap," said Donner, behind me. He put his arms around me, and dragged me after him back to the kitchen.

"Look," he said urgently, releasing me. "All I want is two. You can keep the rest. I gotta have one to pay these guys, and one to—to travel with."

"But it's true," I insisted, knowing that he wouldn't believe me. "We haven't got any. My daughter and her family—they've gone. Gone back. They used all we had. There aren't any more."

He stared at me, disbelief plain in his burning eyes.

"Yes, there are," he said positively. "There have to be. I gotta get out of here!"

"Why?"

"Never you mind. I gotta go, and quick." He swallowed, eyes darting around the kitchen, as though the gems might be sitting casually on the sideboard. "Where are they?"

A hideous crash from the surgery, followed by an outbreak of shouted curses, prevented any reply I might have made. I moved by reflex toward the door, but Donner moved in front of me.

I was infuriated at this invasion, and beginning to be alarmed. While I'd never seen any indication of violence from Donner, I wasn't so sure about the men he'd brought with him. They *might* eventually give up and leave, when it became apparent that there were in fact no gems on the premises—or they might try to beat the location of said gems out of me.

I pulled my cloak more tightly around myself and sat down on a bench, trying to think calmly.

"Look," I said to Donner. "You've taken the house apart—" A crash from upstairs shook the house, and I jumped. My God, it sounded as though they'd tipped over the wardrobe. "You've taken the house apart," I repeated, through gritted teeth, "and you haven't found anything. Wouldn't I give them to you, if I had any, to save you wrecking the place?"

"No, I don't reckon you would. I wouldn't, if I was you." He rubbed a hand across his mouth. "*You* know what's going on—the war and all." He shook his head in confusion. "I didn't know it would be this way. Swear to God, half the people I meet don't know which way is up anymore. I thought it'd be like, you know, redcoats and all, and you just keep away from anybody in a uniform, keep away from the battles, and it'd be fine. But I haven't seen a redcoat *anywhere,* and people—you know, just plain old *people*—they're shooting each other and running around burning up each other's houses. . . ."

He closed his eyes for a minute. His cheeks went from red one moment to white the next; I could see he was very ill. I could hear him, too; the breath rattled wetly in his chest, and he wheezed faintly. If he fainted, how would I get rid of his companions?

"Anyway," he said, opening his eyes. "I'm going. Going back. I don't care what things are like then; it's a hell of a lot better'n here."

"What about the Indians?" I inquired, with no more than a touch of sarcasm. "Leaving them to their own devices, are you?"

"Yeah," he said, missing the sarcasm. "Tell you the truth, I'm not so keen on Indians anymore, either." He rubbed absently at his upper chest, and I saw a large, puckered scar through a rent in his shirt.

"Man," he said, longing clear in his voice, "what I wouldn't give for a cold Bud and a baseball game on TV." Then his wandering attention snapped back to me. "So," he said in a halfway reasonable tone, "I need those diamonds. Or whatever. Hand 'em over and we'll leave."

I had been turning over various schemes for getting rid of them, to no particular avail, and was getting more uneasy by the moment. We had very little worth stealing, and from the looks of the rifled sideboard, they'd already got what there was—including, I realized, with a fresh stab of alarm, the pistols and powder. Before too much longer, they'd grow impatient.

Someone might come—Amy and the boys were likely at Brianna's cabin, which they were in the process of moving into; they could come back at any moment. Someone could come looking for Jamie or myself—though the chances of that receded by the moment, with the dying light. Even if someone did, though, the effect was likely to be disastrous.

Then I heard voices on the front porch, and the stamping of feet, and leapt to my own feet, my heart in my mouth.

"Would you quit doin' that?" Donner said irritably. "You're the jumpiest twat I ever saw."

I ignored him, having recognized one of the voices. Sure enough, in the next moment, two of the thugs, brandishing pistols, shoved Jamie into the kitchen.

He was wary and disheveled, but his eyes went immediately to me, running up and down my body to assure himself that I was all right.

"I'm fine," I said briefly. "These idiots think we have gemstones, and they want them."

"So they said." He straightened himself, shrugging to settle the coat on his shoulders, and glanced at the cupboards, hanging open, and the despoiled sideboard. Even the pie hutch had been overturned, and the remains of a raisin pie lay squashed on the floor, marked with a large heelprint. "I gather they've looked."

"Look, mate," said one of the thugs, reasonably, "all we want's the swag. Just tell us where it is, and we go, no 'arm done, eh?"

Jamie rubbed the bridge of his nose, eyeing the man who'd spoken.

"I imagine my wife has told ye that we have no gems?"

"Well, she would, wouldn't she?" the thug said tolerantly. "Women, you know." He seemed to feel that now Jamie had showed up, they could get on with things in a more businesslike fashion, man-to-man.

Jamie sighed and sat down.

"Why d'ye think I've got any?" he inquired, rather mildly. "I have had, I admit—but no longer. They've been sold."

"Where's the money, then?" The second thug was obviously quite willing to settle for that, no matter what Donner thought.

"Spent," Jamie said briefly. "I'm a colonel of militia—surely ye ken that much? It's an expensive business, provisioning a militia company. Food, guns, powder, shoes—it adds up, aye? Why, the cost in shoe leather alone—and then, to say nothing of shoon for the horses! Wagons, too; ye wouldna believe the scandalous cost of wagons. . . ."

One of the thugs was frowning, but half-nodding, following this reasonable exegesis. Donner and his other companion were noticeably agitated, though.

"Shut up about the damn wagons," Donner said rudely, and bending, he snatched up one of Mrs. Bug's butcher knives from the floor. "Now, look," he said, scowling and trying to look menacing. "I've *had* it with the stalling around. You tell me where they are, or—or I'll—I'll cut her! Yeah, I'll cut her throat. Swear I will." With this, he clutched me by the shoulder and put the knife to my throat.

It had become clear to me some little time ago that Jamie *was* stalling for time, which meant that he expected something to happen. Which in turn meant he was expecting someone to come. That was reassuring, but I did think the apparent nonchalance of his demeanor in the face of my theoretically impending demise was perhaps carrying things a trifle too far.

"Oh," he said, scratching at the side of his neck. "Well, I wouldna do that, if I were you. She's the one who kens where the gems are, aye?"

"I *what*?" I cried indignantly.

"She is?" One of the other thugs brightened at that.

"Oh, aye," Jamie assured him. "Last time I went out wi' the militia, she hid them. Wouldna tell me where she'd put them."

"Wait—I thought you said you sold 'em and spent the money," Donner said, plainly confused.

"I was lying," Jamie explained, patient.

"Oh."

"But if ye're going to kill my wife, well, then, of course that alters the case."

"Oh," said Donner, looking somewhat happier. "Yeah. Exactly!"

"I believe we havena been introduced, sir," Jamie said politely, extending a hand. "I am James Fraser. And you are . . . ?"

Donner hesitated for a minute, unsure what to do with the knife in his right hand, but then shifted it awkwardly to his left and leaned forward to shake Jamie's hand briefly.

"Wendigo Donner," he said. "Okay, now we're getting somewhere."

I made a rude noise, but it was drowned by a series of crashes and the sound of breaking glass from the surgery. The lout in there must be clearing the shelves wholesale, flinging bottles and jars on the floor. I grasped Donner's hand and pulled the knife away from my throat, then sprang to my feet, in much the same state of insane fury in which I had once torched a field full of grasshoppers.

This time, it was Jamie who seized me around the middle as I darted toward the door, swinging me half off my feet.

"Let go! I'll frigging *kill* him!" I said, kicking madly.

"Well, wait just a bit about that, Sassenach," he said, low-voiced, and lugged me back to the table, where he sat down with his arms wrapped around me, holding me firmly pinned on his lap. Further sounds of depredation came down the hall—the splintering of wood and crunch of glass under a bootheel. Evidently, the young lout had given up searching for anything and was simply destroying for the fun of it.

I took a deep breath, preparatory to emitting a scream of frustration, but stopped.

"Jeez," Donner said, wrinkling his nose. "What's that smell? Somebody cut one?" He looked accusingly at me, but I paid no attention. It was ether, heavy and sickly sweet.

Jamie stiffened slightly. He knew what it was, too, and essentially what it did.

Then he took a deep breath and carefully moved me off his lap, setting me on the bench beside him. I saw his eyes go to the knife sagging in Donner's hand, and heard what his keener ears had already picked up. Someone was coming.

He moved a little forward, getting his feet under him to spring, and flicked his eyes toward the cold hearth, where a heavy Dutch oven was sitting in the ashes. I nodded, very briefly, and as the back door opened, made a lunge across the kitchen.

Donner, with unexpected swiftness, stuck out a leg and tripped me. I fell headlong and slid, fetching up against the settle with a head-ringing thump. I groaned and lay still for a few moments, eyes closed, feeling all at once that I was much too old for this sort of carry-on. I opened my eyes reluctantly, and very stiffly got to my feet, to find the kitchen now full of people.

Donner's original sidekick had returned with two others, presumably Richie and Jed, and with them, the Bugs, Murdina looking alarmed, and Arch, coldly furious.

"A leannan!" Mrs. Bug cried, rushing toward me. "Are ye hurt, then?"

"No, no," I said, still rather dazed. "Just let me . . . sit down for a moment." I looked at Donner, but he no longer held his knife. He had been frowning at the floor—evidently he had dropped it when he tripped me—but his head jerked up at sight of the newcomers.

"What? Did you find anything?" he asked eagerly, for both Richie and Jed were beaming with self-importance.

"Sure did," one of them assured him. "Looka here!" He was holding Mrs. Bug's workbag, and at this, he upended it and shook the contents out onto the table, where a mass of woolly knitting landed with a massive *thunk!* Eager hands pawed the wool away, revealing an eight-inch-long ingot of gold, the metal shaved away at one end, and stamped in the center with the royal French fleur-de-lis.

Stunned silence followed the appearance of this apparition. Even Jamie looked completely nonplussed.

Mrs. Bug had been pale when they came in; now she had gone the color of chalk, and her lips had disappeared. Arch's eyes went straight to Jamie's, dark and defiant.

The only person unimpressed by sight of the glowing metal was Donner.

"Well, neato-mosquito," he said. "What about the jewels? Keep your eye on the goal here, people!"

His accomplices, however, had lost interest in theoretical jewels, with solid gold actually in hand, and were simultaneously discussing the possibility of more and squabbling over who should have custody of the present ingot.

My own head was spinning: from the blow, from the sudden appearance of the ingot and its revelations regarding the Bugs—and particularly from the fumes of ether, which were getting notably stronger. No one in the kitchen had noticed, but all sound from the surgery had ceased; the young lout in there had undoubtedly passed out.

The bottle of ether had been nearly full; enough to anesthetize a dozen elephants, I thought dizzily—or a houseful of people. Already, I could see Donner struggling to keep his head upright. A few minutes more, and all the thugs would likely have subsided into a state of innocuous desuetude—but so would we.

Ether is heavier than air; the stuff would sink to the floor, where it would gradually rise in a pool around our knees. I stood up, taking a quick breath from the presumably purer air higher up. I had to get the window open.

Jamie and Arch were speaking Gaelic to each other, much too fast for me to follow, even had my head been in normal working order. Donner was frowning at them, mouth open as though he meant to tell them to stop but couldn't quite find the words.

I fumbled with the catch of the inside shutters, having to concentrate very hard in order to make my fingers work. Finally, the latch flipped free and I swung the shutter open—revealing the leering face of an unfamiliar Indian in the twilight outside the window.

I shrieked and staggered back. Next thing, the back door sprang open and a squat bearded figure rushed in, bellowing in some incomprehensible tongue, followed by Ian, who was followed by yet another strange Indian, screaming and laying about himself with something—tomahawk? club? I couldn't get my eyes to focus well enough to tell.

All was pandemonium, seen through glazed eyes. I clutched the windowsill to keep from sinking to the floor, but couldn't summon the presence of mind to open the damn window. Everyone was struggling and fighting, but the inhabitants of the kitchen were doing it in slow motion, yelling and staggering like drunks. As I watched, my mouth hanging unbecomingly open, Jamie painstakingly drew Donner's knife out from under his buttocks, brought it up in a slow, graceful arc, and buried it under Donner's breastbone.

Something flew past my ear and crashed through the window, destroying what was probably the only intact pane of glass left in the house.

I breathed in deep gulps of fresh air, trying to clear my head, and made frantic waving motions with my hands, shouting—or trying to shout—"Get out! Get out!"

Mrs. Bug was trying to do just that, crawling on hands and knees toward the half-open door. Arch hit the wall and slid slowly down beside her, face gone blank. Donner had fallen face forward over the table, his blood dripping nastily onto the floorboards, and another thug was lying in the extinct hearth, his skull crushed. Jamie was still upright, swaying, and the squat bearded figure was standing beside him, shaking his head and looking confused as the fumes began to affect him.

"What's going on?" I heard him ask.

The kitchen was nearly dark now, the figures swaying like fronds of kelp in some underwater forest.

I closed my eyes for a second. When I opened them again, Ian was saying, "Wait, I'll light a candle." He had one of Brianna's matches in his hand, the tin in the other.

"IAN!" I shrieked, and then he struck the match.

There was a soft *whoof!* noise, then a louder *whoomp!* as the ether in the surgery ignited, and suddenly we were standing in a pool of fire. For a fraction of a second, I felt nothing, and then a burst of searing heat. Jamie seized my arm and hurled me toward the door; I staggered out, fell into the blackberry bushes, and rolled through them, thrashing and flailing at my smoking skirts.

Panicked and still uncoordinated from the ether, I struggled with the strings of my apron, finally managing to rip loose the strings and wriggle out of it. My linen petticoats were singed, but not charred. I crouched panting in the dead weeds of the dooryard, unable to do anything for the moment but breathe. The smell of smoke was strong and pungent.

Mrs. Bug was on the back porch on her knees, jerking off her cap, which was on fire.

Men erupted through the back door, beating at their clothes and hair. Rollo was in the yard, barking hysterically, and on the other side of the house, I could hear the screams of frightened horses. Someone had got Arch Bug out—he was stretched at full length in the dead grass, most of his hair and eyebrows gone, but evidently still alive.

My legs were red and blistered, but I wasn't badly burned—thank God for layers of linen and cotton, which burn slowly, I thought groggily. Had I been wearing something modern like rayon, I should have gone up like a torch.

The thought made me look back toward the house. It was full dark by now, and all the windows on the lower floor were alight. Flame danced in the open door. The place looked like an immense jack-o'-lantern.

"Ye're Mistress Fraser, I suppose?" The squat, bearded person bent over me, speaking in a soft Scottish burr.

"Yes," I said, coming gradually to myself. "Who are you, and where's Jamie?"

"Here, Sassenach." Jamie stumbled out of the dark and sat down heavily beside me. He waved a hand at the Scotsman. "May I present Mr. Alexander Cameron, known more generally as Scotchee?"

"Your servant, ma'am," he said politely.

I was feeling gingerly at my hair. Clumps of it had been singed to crispy thread, but at least I still had some.

I felt, rather than saw, Jamie look up at the house. I followed the direction of his glance, and saw a dark figure at the window upstairs, framed in the dim glow from the burning downstairs. He shouted something in the incomprehensible tongue, and began throwing things out of the window.

"Who's *that*?" I asked, feeling more than slightly surreal.

"Oh." Jamie rubbed at his face. "That would be Goose."

"Of course it would," I said, nodding. "He'll be a cooked goose, if he stays in there." This struck me as wildly hilarious, and I doubled up in laughter.

Evidently, it wasn't quite as witty as I'd thought; no one else seemed to think it funny. Jamie stood up and shouted something at the dark figure, who waved nonchalantly and turned back into the room.

"There's a ladder in the barn," Jamie said calmly to Scotchee, and they moved off into the darkness.

The house burned fairly slowly for a while; there weren't a lot of easily flammable objects down below, bar the books and papers in Jamie's study. A tall figure belted out of the back door, shirt pulled up over his nose with one hand, the tail of his shirt held up with the other to form a bag.

Ian came to a stop beside me, dropped to his knees, gasping, and let down his shirttail, releasing a pile of small objects.

"That's all I could get, I'm afraid, Auntie." He coughed a few times, waving his hand in front of his face. "D'ye ken what happened?"

"It's not important," I said. The heat was becoming more intense, and I struggled to my knees. "Come on; we'll need to get Arch further away."

The effects of the ether had mostly worn off, but I was still conscious of a strong sense of unreality. I hadn't anything but cold well water with which to treat burns, but bathed Arch's neck and hands, which had been badly blistered. Mrs. Bug's hair had been singed, but she, like me, had been largely protected by her heavy skirts.

Neither she nor Arch said a word.

Amy McCallum came running up, face pale in the fiery glow; I told her to take the Bugs to Brianna's cabin—hers now—and for God's sake, keep the little boys safe away. She nodded and went, she and Mrs. Bug supporting Arch's tall form between them.

No one made any effort to bring out the bodies of Donner and his companions.

I could see when the fire took hold in the stairwell; there was a sudden strong glow in the upstairs windows, and shortly thereafter, I could see flames in the heart of the house.

Snow began to fall, in thick, heavy, silent flakes. Within half an hour, the ground, trees, and bushes were dusted with white. The flames glowed red and gold, and the white snow reflected a soft reddish glow; the whole clearing seemed filled with the light of the fire.

Somewhere around midnight, the roof fell in, with a crash of glowing timbers and a tremendous shower of sparks that fountained high into the night. The sight was so beautiful that everyone watching went "Oooooh!" in involuntary awe.

Jamie's arm tightened round me. We could not look away.

"What's the date today?" I asked suddenly.

He frowned for a moment, thinking, then said, "December twenty-first."

"And we aren't dead, either. Bloody newspapers," I said. "They never get *anything* right."

For some reason, he thought *that* was very funny indeed, and laughed until he had to sit down on the ground.

124

PROPERTY OF THE KING

WE SPENT THE remainder of the night sleeping—or at least horizontal—on the floor of the cabin, with the Bugs, Goose and his brother, Light—who confused me initially by referring to themselves as Jamie's "sons"—Scotchee, and Ian. On their way to visit Bird's village, the Indians—for Alexander Cameron was as much an Indian as the others, I thought—had met Jamie and Ian, hunting, and accepted Jamie's hospitality.

"Though it was a warmer welcome than we expected, Bear-Killer!" Goose said, laughing.

They did not ask who Donner was, nor make any reference to the men whose bodies burned in the funeral pyre of the house—only asked awed questions about the ether, and shook their heads in amazement, watching the fire.

For Jamie's part, I noticed that he did not ask why they were going to Bird's village—and concluded that he did not want to hear that some of the Cherokee had decided to support the King. He listened to the talk, but said little, spending his time fingering through the pile of objects saved from the fire. There was little of value there—a few scorched, loose pages from my casebook, some pewter spoons, a bullet mold. But when he fell asleep at last next to me, I saw that his fist was closed around something, and peering closely in the dark, made out the protruding head of the little cherrywood snake.

I woke just past dawn to find Aidan peering down at me, Adso in his arms.

"I found your wee cheetie in my bed," Aidan whispered. "D'ye want him?"

I was about to refuse, but then saw the look in Adso's eye. He was very tolerant of small children normally, but Aidan was holding him round the middle like a bag of laundry, his back legs dangling ludicrously.

"Yes," I said, my voice hoarse from smoke. "Here—I'll take him."

I sat up, but having accepted the cat, saw that most of the household was still asleep, rolled in blankets on the floor. Two notable exceptions: Jamie and Arch Bug were missing. I got up, and borrowing Amy's cloak from beside the door, went out.

The snow had stopped during the night, but there were two or three inches on the ground. I put Adso down under the eaves, where the ground was clear, and then—with a deep breath to steady myself—turned to look at the house.

Steam rose from the charred remains, which stood inkblot black and stark against the white-furred trees behind them. Only about half the house had burned completely; the west wall was still standing, as were the stone chimney stacks. The rest was a mass of charred timbers and mounded ash, already turning gray. The upper story was completely gone, and as for my surgery . . .

I turned away, hearing voices behind the house. Jamie and Arch were in the woodshed, but the door was open; I could see them inside, face to face. Jamie saw me hovering, and beckoned me in with a nod.

"Good morning, Arch," I said, peering at our erstwhile factor. "How are you?"

"I've been better, *a nighean,* thank ye kindly," he said, and coughed. His voice was little more than a harsh whisper, damaged by smoke, and there were enormous, fluid-filled blisters on both hands and face. Bar the loss of his hair and eyebrows, though, I thought he was otherwise all right.

"Arch was just about to explain this to me, Sassenach." Jamie pointed a toe at the gleaming metal of the gold ingot lying in the sawdust and wood chips at his feet. "Were ye not, Arch?"

His voice was outwardly pleasant, but I heard the steel in it as clearly as Arch did. Arch Bug was no pushover, though, eyebrows or no eyebrows.

"I owe ye nay explanations of anything, *Seaumais mac Brian,*" he said with equal pleasantness.

"I give ye the chance of explanation, man, not the choice." He'd dropped the pleasant tone. Jamie was smudged with soot, and scorched round the edges, but his eyebrows were intact and being put to good use. He turned to me, gesturing to the gold.

"Ye've seen it before, aye?"

"Of course." The last time I'd seen it, it had been gleaming in the lantern light, packed solid with its fellows in the bottom of a coffin in Hector Cameron's mausoleum, but the shape of the ingots and the fleur-de-lis stamp were unmistakable. "Unless Louis of France has been sending someone else vast quantities of gold, it's part of Jocasta's hoard."

"That it is not, and never was," Arch corrected me firmly.

"Aye?" Jamie cocked a thick brow at him. "To whom does it belong, then, if not to Jocasta Cameron? D'ye claim it as your own?"

"I do not." He hesitated, but the urge to speak was powerful. "It is the property of the King," he said, and his old mouth closed tight on the last word.

"What, the King of—oh," I said, realizing at long last. "*That* king."

"Le roi, c'est mort," Jamie said softly, as though to himself, but Arch turned fiercely to him.

"Is Scotland dead?"

Jamie drew breath, but didn't speak at once. Instead, he gestured me to a seat on the stack of chopped cordwood, and nodded at Arch to take another, before sitting down beside me.

"Scotland will die when her last son does, *a charaid,*" he said, and waved a hand toward the door, taking in the mountains and hollows around us—and all the people therein. "How many are here? How many will be? Scotland lives—but not in Italy." In Rome, he meant, where Charles Stuart eked out what remained to him of a life, drowning his disappointed dreams of a crown in drink.

Arch narrowed his eyes at this, but kept a stubborn silence.

"Ye were the third man, were ye not?" Jamie asked, disregarding this. "When the gold was brought ashore from France. Dougal MacKenzie took one-third, and Hector Cameron another. I couldna say what Dougal did with his—gave it to Charles Stuart, most likely, and may God have mercy on his soul for that. You were tacksman to Malcolm Grant; he sent ye, did he not? You took one-third of the gold on his behalf. Did ye give it to him?"

Arch nodded, slowly.

"It was given in trust," he said, and his voice cracked. He cleared his throat and spat, the mucus tinged with black. "To me, and then to the Grant—who should have given it in turn to the King's son."

"Did he?" Jamie asked, interested. "Or did he think, like Hector Cameron, that it was too late?"

It had been; the cause was already lost at that point—no gold could have made a difference. Arch's lips pressed so tightly together as almost to be invisible.

"He did what he did," he said shortly. "What he thought right. That money was spent for the welfare of the clan. But Hector Cameron was a traitor, and his wife with him."

"It was you who spoke to Jocasta in her tent," I said suddenly, realizing. "At the Gathering where you met Jamie. You'd come there to find her, hadn't you?"

Arch seemed surprised that I had spoken, but inclined his head an inch or so in acknowledgment. I wondered whether he had accepted—had sought?—a place with Jamie on account of his relationship with Jocasta.

"And that"—I poked a toe at the shaved ingot—"you found in Jocasta's house, when you went with Roger and Duncan to bring back the fisher-folk." Proof—if he had needed it—that Jocasta did indeed still have Hector's share of the French gold.

"What I am wondering, myself," Jamie said, rubbing a finger down the long, straight bridge of his nose, "is how the devil ye found the rest of it, and then got it away."

Arch's lips pursed for a moment, then reluctantly unsealed themselves.

"'Twas no great feat. I saw the salt at Hector's tomb—the way the black slaves kept awa'. If he didna rest easy, it was nay wonder—but where would the gold better be, save wi' him?" A wintry light shone in his faded eyes. "I kent Hector Cameron, a bit. He wasna the man to give up anything, only by reason of bein' dead."

Arch made frequent trips to Cross Creek as factor, to buy and trade. He was not usually a guest at River Run, but had been there often enough to be familiar with the property. If anyone saw a figure near the mausoleum at night—well, everyone knew that Hector Cameron's ghost "walked," confined to one spot only by the lines of salt; no one would ever go close enough to investigate.

And so he had simply abstracted one ingot on each trip—and not on every trip—eventually removing the whole hoard, before Duncan Innes discovered the loss.

"I shouldna have kept out that first ingot, I see that," he said, ruefully nodding at it. "At the first, though, I thought we might have need of it—Murdina and I. And then, when she was obliged to kill yon Brown—"

Jamie's head jerked up, and we both stared at him. He coughed.

"The wicked creature grew well enough to poke about the cabin when she was oot; he found that"—he nodded again at the ingot—"in her workbag, where she'd hidden it. He couldna ken, of course, what it was—but he kent well enough that ragged folk such as we ought not to have such a thing." His thin mouth pressed tight again, and I remembered that he had been chief tacksman for the Grant of clan Grant—a man of worth. Once.

"He asked about it, and she wouldna tell him anything, of course. But then, when he made his way to your house, she feared he would tell what he'd seen. And so she made an end to him."

It was said calmly; after all, what else could she do? Not for the first time, I wondered just what other things the Bugs had done—or been forced to do—in the years after Culloden.

"Well, ye kept the gold out of King George's hands, at

least," Jamie said, a certain note of bleakness in his voice. I thought he was thinking of the battle at Moore's Creek Bridge. If Hugh MacDonald had had that gold, with which to buy powder and arms, the victory there would not have been so easily won. Nor would the Highlanders have been slaughtered—again—charging sword in hand into the mouths of cannon.

"Arch," I said, when the silence threatened to become oppressive, "*what,* exactly, did you plan to do with it?"

He blinked at that, and looked down at the ingot.

"I . . . I meant at first only to see if it was true what I'd heard—that Hector Cameron had taken his part of the gold away with him, used it for his own ends. Then I found Hector dead, but 'twas clear from the way his wife lived that he had indeed taken it. So I wondered—was there any left?"

One hand crept up, massaging his withered throat.

"To tell ye the truth, mistress—I wished mostly to take it back from Jocasta Cameron. Having done that, though . . ." His voice died away, but then he shook himself.

"I am a man of my word, *Seaumais mac Brian.* I swore an oath to my chief—and kept it, 'til he died. I swore my oath to the King across the water"—James Stuart, he meant—"but he is dead, now, too. And then—I swore loyalty to George of England when I came upon this shore. So tell me now where my duty lies?"

"Ye swore an oath to me, too, *Archibald mac Donagh,*" Jamie said.

Arch smiled at that, a wry expression, but a smile nonetheless.

"And by reason of that oath, ye're still alive, *Seaumais mac Brian,*" he said. "I could have killed ye last night in your sleep and been well awa'."

Jamie's mouth twisted in a look that expressed considerable doubt of this statement, but he forbore to contradict.

"You are free of your oath to me," he said formally in Gaelic. "Take your life from my hand." And inclining his head toward the ingot, said, "Take that—and go."

Arch regarded him for a moment, unblinking. Then stooped, picked up the ingot, and went.

"You didn't ask him where the gold is now," I observed,

watching the tall old man make his way round the cabin to rouse his wife.

"Ye think he would ha' told me?" He stood up then, and stretched himself. Then he shook himself like a dog, and went to stand in the doorway of the shed, arms braced in the door frame, looking out. It was beginning to snow again.

"I see it's not only the Frasers who are stubborn as rocks," I said, coming to stand beside him. "Scotland lives, all right." That made him laugh.

He put one arm around me, and I rested my head on his shoulder.

"Your hair smells of smoke, Sassenach," he said softly.

"Everything smells of smoke," I replied just as softly.

The burned ruins of the house were still too warm for snow to stick, but that would pass. If it went on snowing, by tomorrow the house would be obliterated, white as the rocks and trees. We, too—eventually.

I thought of Jocasta and Duncan, gone to the safety of Acadia, the welcome of kinfolk. Where would the Bugs go—back to Scotland? For an instant, I longed to go, too. Away from loss and desolation. Home.

But then I remembered.

"So long as one hundred of us remain alive . . . ," I quoted.

Jamie tilted his head against mine for a moment, then raised it and turned to look down at me.

"And when ye go to a sick man's bed, Sassenach—to a wounding or a birth—how is it, then, that ye can rise from your own bed, even from mortal weariness, and go in the dark, alone? Why is it that ye willna wait, that ye dinna say no, ever? Why is it that ye willna forbear, even when ye know the case to be hopeless?"

"I can't." I kept my gaze on the ruin of the house, its ashes growing cold before my eyes. I knew what he meant, the unwelcome truth he would force me to speak—but the truth lay between us, and must be told. "I cannot . . . can *not* . . . admit . . . that there is anything to do but win."

He cupped my chin and tilted my face upward, so that I was obliged to meet his eyes. His own face was worn with tiredness, the lines cut deep by eyes and mouth, but the eyes themselves were clear, cool, and fathomless as the waters of a hidden spring.

"Nor can I," he said.

"I know."

"Ye can at least promise me the victory," he said, but his voice held the whisper of a question.

"Yes," I said, and touched his face. I sounded choked, and my vision blurred. "Yes, I can promise that. This time." No mention made of what that promise spared, of the things I could not guarantee. Not life, not safety. Not home, nor family; not law nor legacy. Just the one thing—or maybe two.

"The victory," I said. "And that I will be with you 'til the end."

He closed his eyes for a moment. Snowflakes pelted down, melting as they struck his face, sticking for an instant, white on his lashes. Then he opened his eyes and looked at me.

"That is enough," he said softly. "I ask no more."

He reached forward then and took me in his arms, held me close for a moment, the breath of snow and ashes cold around us. Then he kissed me, released me, and I took a deep breath of cold air, harsh with the scent of burning. I brushed a floating smut off my arm.

"Well . . . good. *Bloody* good. Er . . ." I hesitated. "What do you suggest we do next?"

He stood looking at the charred ruin, eyes narrowed, then lifted his shoulders and let them fall.

"I think," he said slowly, "we shall go—" He stopped suddenly, frowning. "What in God's name . . . ?"

Something was moving at the side of the house. I blinked away the snowflakes, standing on tiptoe to see better.

"Oh, it *can't* be!" I said—but it was. With a tremendous upheaval of snow, dirt, and charred wood, the white sow thrust her way into daylight. Fully emerged, she shook her massive shoulders, then, pink snout twitching irritably, moved purposefully off toward the wood. A moment later, a smaller version likewise emerged—and another, and another . . . and eight half-grown piglets, some white, some spotted, and one as black as the timbers of the house, trotted off in a line, following their mother.

"Scotland lives," I said again, giggling uncontrollably. "Er—where did you say we were going?"

"To Scotland," he said as though this were obvious. "To fetch my printing press."

He was still looking at the house, but his eyes were fixed somewhere beyond the ashes, far beyond the present moment. An owl hooted deep in the distant wood, startled from its sleep. He stood silent for a bit, then shook off his reverie, and smiled at me, snow melting in his hair.

"And then," he said simply, "we shall come back to fight."

He took my hand and turned away from the house, toward the barn where the horses stood waiting, patient in the cold.

EPILOGUE I
LALLYBROCH

THE PENLIGHT'S BEAM moved slowly across the heavy oak rafter, paused at a suspicious hole, then passed on. The heavyset man wore a frown of scrupulous concentration, lips pursed like one momentarily expecting some unpleasant surprise.

Brianna stood beside him, looking up at the shadowed recesses of the ceiling in the entry hall, wearing a similar frown of concentration. She would not recognize woodworm or termites unless a rafter actually fell on her, she thought, but it seemed polite to behave as though she were paying attention.

In fact, only half her attention was focused on the heavyset gentleman's murmured remarks to his helot, a small young woman in an overall too big for her, with pink streaks in her hair. The other half was focused on the noises from upstairs, where the children were theoretically playing hide 'n seek among the jumble of packing boxes. Fiona had brought over her brood of three small fiends, and then craftily abandoned them, running off to do an errand of some sort, promising to return by teatime.

Brianna glanced at her wristwatch, still surprised at seeing it there. Half an hour yet to go. If they could avoid bloodshed until—

A piercing scream from upstairs made her grimace. The helot, less hardened, dropped her clipboard with a yelp.

"MAMA!" Jem, in tattling mode.

"WHAT?" she roared in answer. "I'm BUSY!"

"But Mama! Mandy *hit* me!" came an indignant report from the top of the stairs. Looking up, she could see the top of his head, the light from the window glowing on his hair.

"She did? Well—"

"With a *stick*!"

"What sort of—"

"On *purpose*!"

"Well, I don't think—"

"AND . . ."—a pause before the damning denouement—"SHE DIDN'T SAY SHE WAS SORRY!"

The builder and his helot had given up looking for woodworm, in favor of following this gripping narrative, and now both of them looked at Brianna, doubtless in expectation of some Solomonic decree.

Brianna closed her eyes momentarily.

"MANDY," she bellowed. "Say you're sorry!"

"Non't!" came a high-pitched refusal from above.

"Aye, ye will!" came Jem's voice, followed by scuffling. Brianna headed for the stair, blood in her eye. Just as she set her foot on the tread, Jem uttered a piercing squeal.

"She BIT me!"

"Jeremiah MacKenzie, don't you *dare* bite her back!" she shouted. "Both of you stop it this instant!"

Jem thrust a disheveled head through the banister, hair sticking up on end. He was wearing bright blue eye shadow, and someone had applied pink lipstick in a crude mouth-shape from one ear to the other.

"She's a feisty wee baggage," he ferociously informed the fascinated spectators below. "My grandda said so."

Brianna wasn't sure whether to laugh, cry, or utter a loud shriek, but with a hasty wave at the builder and his assistant, she ran up the stairs to sort them out.

The sorting took rather more time than expected, since she discovered in the process that Fiona's three little girls, so notably quiet during the latest squabble, had been quiet because—having decorated Jem, Mandy, and themselves—they were busily engaged in painting faces on the bathroom walls with Brianna's new makeup.

Coming back down a quarter of an hour later, she discovered the builder sitting peaceably on an upturned coal scuttle, having his tea break, while the helot wandered open-mouthed about the entry hall, a half-eaten scone in one hand.

"All those kids yours?" she asked Brianna, with a sympathetic quirk of one pierced brow.

"No, thank God. Does everything look all right down here?"

"Touch o' damp," the builder said cheerfully. "Only to be expected, though, old place like this. When's it built, then, hen, d'ye know?"

"1720, thickie," the helot said, with comfortable scorn. "Did ye not see it carved in the lintel, there, where we came in?"

"Nah, then, is it?" The builder looked interested, but not enough to get up and look for himself. "Cost a fortune to put back in shape, won't it?" He nodded at the wall, where one of the oak panels showed the damage of boots and sabers, crisscrossed with slashes whose rawness had darkened with the years, but still showed clear.

"No, we won't fix that," Brianna said, a lump in her throat. "That was done right after the '45. It'll stay that way." *We keep it so,* her uncle had told her, *to remember always what the English are.*

"Oh, historic-like. Right you are, then," the builder said, nodding wisely. "Americans don't often mind about the history so much, do they? Wanting all mod cons, electric cookers, effing automatic thisses and thats. Central heating!"

"I'll settle for toilets that flush," she assured him. "That, and hot water. Speaking of which, will you have a look at the boiler? It's in a shed in the yard, and it's fifty years old if it's a day. And we'll want to replace the geyser in the upstairs bath, too."

"Oh, aye." The builder brushed crumbs from his shirt, corked his Thermos flask, and rose ponderously to his feet. "Come on, Angie, let's have a look, then."

Brianna hovered suspiciously at the foot of the stair, listening for any sounds of riot before following, but all was well above; she could hear the crash of building blocks, evidently being thrown at the walls, but no yells of outrage. She turned to follow, just in time to see the builder, who had paused to look up at the lintel.

"The '45, eh? Ever think what it'd be like?" he was saying. "If Bonnie Prince Charlie had won, I mean."

"Oh, in your dreams, Stan! He'd never a chance, bloody Eyetalian ponce."

"Naw, naw, he'd have done it, sure, was it no for the effing Campbells. Traitors, aye? To a man. And a woman, too, I expect," he added, laughing—from which Brianna gathered that the helot's last name was very likely Campbell.

They passed on toward the shed, their argument growing more heated, but she stopped, not wanting to go after them until she had herself under control.

Oh, God, she prayed passionately, *oh, God—that they might be safe! Please, please, let them be safe.* It didn't matter how ridiculous it might be to pray for the safety of people who had been—who had to be—dead for more than two hundred years. It was the only thing she could do, and did it several times each day, whenever she thought of them. Much more often, now that they had come to Lallybroch.

She blinked back tears, and saw Roger's Mini Cooper come down the winding drive. The backseat was piled high with boxes; he was finally clearing out the last bits of rubbish from the Reverend's garage, salvaging those items that might have value to someone—a dismayingly high proportion of the contents.

"Just in time," she said, a little shaky, as he came up the walk smiling, a large box under his arm. She still found him startling with short hair. "Ten minutes more, and I'd kill somebody, for sure. Probably Fiona, for starters."

"Oh, aye?" He bent and kissed her with particular enthusiasm, indicating that he probably hadn't heard what she'd said. "I've got something."

"So I see. What—"

"Damned if I know."

The box he laid on the ancient dining table was wood, as well; a sizable casket made of maple, darkened by years, soot, and handling, but with the workmanship still apparent to her practiced eye. It was beautifully made, the joints perfectly dovetailed, with a sliding top—but the top didn't slide, having been at some point sealed with a thick bead of what looked like melted beeswax, gone black with age.

The most striking thing about it, though, was the top.

Burned into the wood was a name: *Jeremiah Alexander Ian Fraser MacKenzie.*

She felt a clenching in her lower belly at the sight of it, and glanced up at Roger, who was tense with some suppressed feeling; she could feel it vibrating through him.

"What?" she whispered. "Who *is* that?"

Roger shook his head, and pulled a filthy envelope from his pocket.

"This was with it, taped to the side. It's the Reverend's handwriting, one of the little notes he'd sometimes put with something to explain its significance, just in case. But I can't say this is an explanation, exactly."

The note was brief, stating merely that the box had come from a defunct banking house in Edinburgh. Instructions had been stored with the box, stating that it was not to be opened, save by the person whose name was inscribed thereon. The original instructions had perished, but were passed on verbally by the person from whom he obtained the box.

"And who was *that*?" she asked.

"No idea. Do you have a knife?"

"Do I have a knife," she muttered, digging in the pocket of her jeans. "Do I ever *not* have a knife?"

"That was a rhetorical question," he said, kissing her hand and taking the bright red Swiss Army knife she offered him.

The beeswax cracked and split away easily; the lid of the box, though, was unwilling to yield after so many years. It took both of them—one clutching the box, the other pushing and pulling on the lid—but finally, it came free with a small squealing noise.

The ghost of a scent floated out; something indistinguishable, but plantlike in origin.

"Mama," she said involuntarily. Roger glanced at her, startled, but she gestured at him urgently to go on. He reached carefully into the box and removed its contents: a stack of letters, folded and sealed with wax, two books—and a small snake made of cherrywood, heavily polished by long handling.

She made a small, inarticulate sound and seized the top letter, pressing it so hard against her chest that the paper crackled and the wax seal split and fell away. The thick, soft paper, whose fibers showed the faint stains of what had once been flowers.

Tears were falling down her face, and Roger was saying something, but she didn't attend the words, and the children were making an uproar upstairs, the builders were still arguing outside, and the only thing in the world she could see were the faded words on the page, written in a sprawling, difficult hand.

December 31, 1776

My dear daughter,

As you will see if ever you receive this, we are alive. . . .

EPILOGUE II

THE DEVIL IS IN THE DETAILS

"WHAT'S THIS, THEN?" Amos Crupp squinted at the page laid out in the bed of the press, reading it backward with the ease of long experience.

"It is with grief that the news is received of the deaths by fire . . . Where'd that come from?"

"Note from a subscriber," said Sampson, his new printer's devil, shrugging as he inked the plate. "Good for a bit of filler, there, I thought; General Washington's address to the troops run short of the page."

"Hmph. I s'pose. Very old news, though," Crupp said, glancing at the date. "January?"

"Well, no," the devil admitted, heaving on the lever that lowered the page onto the plate of inked type. The press sprang up again, the letters wet and black on the paper, and he picked the sheet off with nimble fingertips, hanging it up to dry. " 'Twas December, by the notice. But I'd set the page already in the Caslon small pica, with the date in long primer, and someone"—he glanced accusingly at the dog dozing on the hearth—"seems to have mislaid the long primer's capital 'D.' So I thought January's close enough, aye?"

"To be sure," said Amos, losing interest in the matter, as he perused the last paragraphs of Washington's speech. "Scarcely signifies, anyway. After all, they're all dead, aren't they?"

Be sure to read the next installment of the acclaimed OUTLANDER series . . .

DIANA GABALDON'S

AN ECHO IN THE BONE

Available now from Dell Books!

Read on for a preview. . . .

AN ECHO IN THE BONE

On Sale Now!

Fraser's Ridge, colony of North Carolina
March 1777

ONE THING ABOUT a devastating fire, I reflected. It did make packing easier. At present, I owned one gown, one shift, three petticoats—one woolen, two muslin—two pairs of stockings (I'd been wearing one pair when the house burned; the other had been carelessly left drying on a bush a few weeks before the fire and was discovered later, weathered but still wearable), a shawl, and a pair of shoes. Jamie had procured a horrible cloak for me somewhere—I didn't know where, and didn't want to ask. Made of thick wool the color of leprosy, it smelled as though someone had died in it and lain undiscovered for a couple of days. I'd boiled it with lye soap, but the ghost of its previous occupant lingered.

Still, I wouldn't freeze.

My medical kit was nearly as simple to pack. With a regretful sigh for the ashes of my beautiful apothecary's chest, with its elegant tools and numerous bottles, I turned over the pile of salvaged remnants from my surgery. The dented barrel of my microscope. Three singed ceramic jars, one missing its lid, one cracked. A large tin of goose grease mixed with camphor—now nearly empty after a winter of catarrhs and coughs. A handful of singed pages, ripped from the casebook started by Daniel Rawlings and continued by myself—though my spirits were lifted a bit by the discovery that the salvaged pages included one bearing Dr. Rawlings's special receipt for Bowel-Bind.

It was the only one of his receipts I'd found effective, and while I'd long since committed the actual formula to memory, having it to hand kept my sense of him alive. I'd never met Daniel Rawlings in life, but he'd been my friend since the day Jamie gave me his chest and casebook. I folded the paper carefully and tucked it into my pocket.

Most of my herbs and compounded medications had perished in the flames, along with the earthenware jars, the glass vials, the large bowls in which I incubated penicillin broth, and my surgical saws. I still had one scalpel and the darkened blade of a small amputation saw; the handle had been charred, but Jamie could make me a new one.

The residents of the Ridge had been generous—as generous as people who had virtually nothing themselves could be at the tail end of winter. We had food for the journey, and many of the women had brought me bits of their household simples; I had small jars of lavender, rosemary, comfrey, and mustard seed, two precious steel needles, a small skein of silk thread to use for sutures and dental floss (though I didn't mention that last use to the ladies, who would have been deeply affronted by the notion), and a very small stock of bandages and gauze for dressings.

One thing I had in abundance, though, was alcohol. The corncrib had been spared from the flames, and so had the still. Since there was more than enough grain for both animals and household, Jamie had thriftily transformed the rest into a very raw—but potent—liquor, which we would take along to trade for necessary goods along the way. One small cask had been kept for my especial use, though; I'd carefully painted the legend *Sauerkraut* on the side, to discourage theft on the road.

"And what if we should be set upon by illiterate banditti?" Jamie had asked, amused by this.

"Thought of that," I informed him, displaying a small corked bottle full of cloudy liquid. "*Eau de sauerkraut.* I'll pour it on the cask at first sight of anyone suspicious."

"I suppose we'd best hope they're not German bandits, then."

"Have you ever met a German bandit?" I asked. With the exception of the occasional drunkard or wife-beater, almost all the Germans we knew were honest, hardworking, and virtuous to a fault. Not all that surprising, given that so many of them had come to the colony as part of a religious movement.

"Not as such," he admitted. "But ye mind the Muellers, aye? And what they did to your friends. They wouldna have called themselves bandits, but the Tuscarora likely didna make the same distinction."

That was no more than the truth, and a cold thumb pressed the base of my skull. The Muellers, German neighbors, had had a beloved daughter and her newborn child die of measles, and had blamed the nearby Indians for the infection. Deranged by grief, old *Herr* Mueller had led a party of his sons and sons-in-law to take revenge—and scalps. My viscera still remembered the shock of seeing my friend Nayawenne's white-streaked hair spill out of a bundle into my lap.

"Is my hair turning white, do you think?" I said abruptly. He raised his eyebrows, but bent forward and peered at the top of my head, fingering gently through my hair.

"There's maybe one hair in fifty that's gone white. One in five-and-twenty is silver. Why?"

"I suppose I have a little time, then. Nayawenne . . ." I hadn't spoken her name aloud in several years, and found an odd comfort in the speaking, as though it had conjured her. "She told me that I'd come into my full power when my hair turned white."

"Now there's a fearsome thought," he said, grinning.

"No doubt. Since it hasn't happened yet, though, I suppose if we stumble into a nest of sauerkraut thieves on the road, I'll have to defend my cask with my scalpel," I said.

He gave me a slightly queer look at this, but then laughed and shook his head.

His own packing was a little more involved. He and Young Ian had removed the gold from the house's foundation the night after Mrs. Bug's funeral—a delicate process preceded by my putting out a large slop basin of stale bread soaked in corn liquor, then calling "Sooo-eeee!" at the top of my lungs from the head of the garden path.

A moment of silence, and then the white sow emerged from her den, a pale blotch against the smoke-stained rocks of the foundation. I knew exactly what she was, but the sight of that white, rapidly moving form still made the hairs stand up on the back of my neck. It had come on to snow—one of the reasons for Jamie's decision to act at once—and she came through the whirl of big, soft flakes with a velocity that made her seem like the spirit of the storm itself, leading the wind.

For an instant, I thought she was going to charge me; I saw her head swing toward me and caught the loud snuff as she took my scent—but she scented the food as well, and swerved away. An instant later, the ungodly sounds of a pig in ecstasy floated through the hush of the snow, and Jamie and Ian hurried out of the trees to begin their work.

It took more than two weeks to move the gold; they worked only at night, and only when fresh snow was either falling or about to fall, to cover their tracks. Meantime, they took it in turn to guard the remains of the Big House, keeping an eye peeled for any sign of Arch Bug.

"Do you think he still cares about the gold?" I'd asked Jamie in the midst of this endeavor, chafing his hands to get enough heat into them for him to hold his spoon. He'd come in for breakfast, frozen and exhausted after a long night spent walking round and round the burnt house to keep his blood flowing.

"He's no much else left to care about, has he?" He spoke softly, to avoid waking the Higgins family. "Other than Ian."

I shivered, as much from thought of old Arch, living wraithlike in the forest, surviving on the heat of his hatred, as from the cold that had come in with Jamie. He'd let his beard grow for warmth—all the men did in winter, on the mountain—and ice glimmered in his whiskers and frosted his brows.

"You look like Old Man Winter himself," I whispered, bringing him a bowl of hot porridge.

"I feel like it," he replied hoarsely. He passed the bowl under his nose, inhaling the steam and closing his eyes beatifically. "Pass the whisky, aye?"

"You're proposing to pour it on your porridge? It's got butter and salt on, already." Nonetheless, I passed him the bottle from its shelf over the hearth.

"Nay, I'm going to thaw my wame enough to eat it. I'm solid ice from the neck down."

No one had seen hide nor hair of Arch Bug—not even an errant track in the snow—since his appearance at the funeral. He might be denned up for the winter, snug in some refuge. He might have gone away to the Indian villages. He might be dead, and I rather hoped he was, uncharitable as the thought might be.

I mentioned this, and Jamie shook his head. The ice in his hair had melted now, and the firelight glimmered like diamonds on the water droplets in his beard.

"If he's dead, and we never learn of it, Ian willna have a moment's peace—ever. D'ye want him to be looking over his shoulder at his wedding, afraid of a bullet through his wife's heart as she speaks her vows? Or wed with a family, fearing each day to leave his house and his bairns, for fear of what he might come back to?"

"I'm impressed at the scope and morbidity of your imagination—but you're right. All right, I don't hope he's dead—not unless we find his body."

But no one did find his body, and the gold was moved, bit by bit, to its new hiding place.

That had taken a bit of thought and considerable private discussion between Jamie and Ian. Not the whisky cave. Very few people knew about that—but some did. Joseph Wemyss, his daughter, Lizzie, and her two husbands—I marveled, rather, that I'd got to the point where I could think about Lizzie and the Beardsleys without boggling—all knew, of necessity, and Bobby and Amy Higgins would need to be shown its location before we left, as they would be making whisky themselves in our absence. Arch Bug had not been told of the cave's location—but very likely knew it.

Jamie was adamant that no one should know even of the gold's existence on the Ridge, let alone its location.

"Let even a rumor of it get out, and everyone here is in danger," he'd said. "Ye ken what happened when yon Donner told folk we had jewels here."

I kent, all right. I still woke up in the midst of nightmares, hearing the muffled *whumph!* of exploding ether fumes, hearing the crash of glass and smashing wood as the raiders wrecked the house.

In some of these dreams, I ran fruitlessly to and fro, trying to rescue someone—who?—but met always by locked doors, blank walls, or rooms engulfed in flame. In others, I stood rooted, unable to move a muscle, as fire crawled up the walls, fed with delicate greed on the clothes of bodies at my feet, burst through a corpse's hair, caught in my skirts and swarmed upward, wrapping my legs in a blazing web.

I still felt overpowering sadness—and a deep, cleansing rage—when I looked at the sooty smudge in the clearing that had once been my home, but I always had to go out in the morning after one of these dreams and look at it nonetheless: walk round the cold ruins and smell the taint of dead ash, in order to quench the flames that burned behind my eyes.

"Right," I said, and pulled my shawl tighter round me. We were standing by the springhouse, looking down on the ruins as we talked, and the chill was seeping into my bones. "So . . . where, then?"

"The Spaniard's Cave," he said, and I blinked at him.

"The what?"

"I'll show ye, *a nighean*," he said, grinning at me. "When the snow melts."

SPRING HAD SPRUNG, and the creek was rising. Swelled by melting snow and fed by hundreds of tiny waterfalls that trickled and leapt down the mountain's face, it roared past my feet, exuberant with spray. I could feel it cold on my face, and knew that I'd be wet to the knees within minutes, but it didn't matter. The fresh green of arrowhead and pickerelweed rimmed the banks, some plants dragged out of the soil by the rising water and whirled downstream, more hanging on by their roots for dear life, leaves trailing in the racing wash. Dark mats of cress swirled under the water, close by the sheltering banks. And fresh greens were what I wanted.

My gathering basket was half full of fiddleheads and ramp shoots. A nice big lot of tender new cress, crisp and cold from the stream, would top off the winter's vitamin C deficiency very well. I took off my shoes and stockings, and after a moment's hesitation, took off my gown and shawl as well and hung them over a tree branch. The air was chilly in the shade of the silver birches that overhung the creek here, and I shivered a bit but ignored the cold, kirtling up my shift before wading into the stream.

That cold was harder to ignore. I gasped, and nearly dropped the basket, but found my footing among the slippery rocks and made my way toward the nearest mat of tempting dark green. Within seconds, my legs were numb, and I'd lost any sense of cold in the enthusiasm of forager's frenzy and salad hunger.

A good deal of our stored food had been saved from the fire, as it was kept in the outbuildings: the springhouse, corncrib, and smoking shed. The root cellar had been destroyed, though, and with it not only the carrots, onions, garlic, and potatoes but most of my carefully gathered stock of dried apples and wild yams, and the big hanging clusters of raisins, all meant to keep us from the ravages of scurvy. The herbs, of course, had gone up in smoke, along with the rest of my surgery. True, a large quantity of pumpkins and squashes had escaped, these having been piled in the barn, but one grows tired of squash pie and succotash after a couple of months—well, after a couple of days, speaking personally.

Not for the first time, I mourned Mrs. Bug's abilities as a cook, though of course I did miss her for her own sake. Amy McCallum Higgins had been raised in a crofter's cottage in the Highlands of Scotland and was, as she put it, "a good plain cook." Essentially, that meant she could bake bannocks, boil porridge, and fry fish simultaneously, without burning any of it. No mean feat, but a trifle monotonous, in terms of diet.

My own pièce de résistance was stew—which, lacking onions, garlic, carrots, and potatoes, had devolved into a sort of pottage consisting of venison or turkey stewed with cracked corn, barley, and possibly chunks of stale bread. Ian, surprisingly, had turned out to be a passable cook; the succotash and squash pie were his contributions to the communal menu. I did wonder who had taught him to make them, but thought it wiser not to ask.

So far no one had starved, nor yet lost any teeth, but by mid-March, I would have been willing to wade neck-deep in freezing torrents in order to acquire something both edible and green.

Ian had, thank goodness, gone on breathing. And after a week or so had ceased acting quite so shell-shocked, eventually regaining something like his normal manner. But I noticed Jamie's eyes follow him now and then, and Rollo had taken to sleeping with his head on Ian's chest, a new habit. I wondered whether he really sensed the pain in Ian's heart, or whether it was simply a response to the cramped sleeping conditions in the cabin.

I stretched my back, hearing the small pops between my vertebrae. Now that the snowmelt had come, I could hardly wait for our departure. I would miss the Ridge and everyone on it—well, almost everyone. Possibly not Hiram Crombie, so much. Or the Chisholms, or—I short-circuited this list before it became uncharitable.

"On the *other* hand," I said firmly to myself, "think of beds."

Granted, we would be spending a good many nights on the road, sleeping rough—but eventually we would reach civilization. Inns. With food. And beds. I closed my eyes momentarily, envisioning the absolute bliss of a mattress. I didn't even aspire to a feather bed; anything that promised more than an inch of padding between myself and the floor would be paradise. And, of course, if it came with a modicum of privacy—even better.

Jamie and I had not been completely celibate since December. Lust aside—and it wasn't—we needed the comfort and warmth of each other's body. Still, covert congress under a quilt, with Rollo's yellow eyes fixed upon us from two feet away, was less than ideal, even assuming that Young Ian was invariably asleep, which I didn't think he was, though he was sufficiently tactful as to pretend.

A hideous shriek split the air, and I jerked, dropping the basket. I flung myself after it, barely snatching the handle before it was whirled away on the flood, and stood up dripping and trembling, heart hammering as I waited to see whether the scream would be repeated.

It was—followed in short order by an equally piercing screech, but one deeper in timbre and recognizable to my well-trained ears as the sort of noise made by a Scottish Highlander suddenly immersed in freezing water. Fainter, higher-pitched shrieks, and a breathless "Fook!" spoken in a Dorset accent indicated that the gentlemen of the household were taking their spring bath.

I wrang out the hem of my shift and, snatching my shawl from the branch where I'd left it, slipped on my shoes and made my way in the direction of the bellowing.

There are few things more enjoyable than sitting in relative warmth and comfort while watching fellow human beings soused in cold water. If said human beings present a complete review of the nude male form, so much the better. I threaded my way through a small growth of fresh-budding river willows, found a conveniently screened rock in the sun, and spread out the damp skirt of my shift, enjoying the warmth on my shoulders, the sharp scent of the fuzzy catkins, and the sight before me.

Jamie was standing in the pool, nearly shoulder-deep, his hair slicked back like a russet seal. Bobby stood on the bank, and picking up Aidan with a grunt, threw him to Jamie in a pinwheel of flailing limbs and piercing shrieks of delighted fright.

"Me-me-me-*me*!" Orrie was dancing around his stepfather's legs, his chubby bottom bouncing up and down among the reeds like a little pink balloon.

Bobby laughed, bent, and hoisted him up, holding him for a moment high overhead as he squealed like a seared pig, then flung him in a shallow arc out over the pool.

He hit the water with a tremendous splash and Jamie grabbed him, laughing, and pulled him to the surface, whence he emerged with a look of open-mouthed stupefaction that made them all hoot like gibbons. Aidan and Rollo were both dog-paddling round in circles by now, shouting and barking.

I looked across to the opposite side of the pool and saw Ian rush naked down the small hill and leap like a salmon into the pool, uttering one of his best Mohawk war cries. This was cut off abruptly by the cold water, and he vanished with scarcely a splash.

I waited—as did the others—for him to pop back up, but he didn't. Jamie looked suspiciously behind him, in case of a sneak attack, but an instant later Ian shot out of the water directly in front of Bobby with a bloodcurdling yell, grabbed him by the leg, and yanked him in.

Matters thereafter became generally chaotic, with a great deal of promiscuous splashing, yelling, hooting, and jumping off of rocks, which gave me the opportunity to reflect on just how delightful naked men are. Not that I hadn't seen a good many of them in my time, but aside from Frank and Jamie, most men I'd seen undressed usually had been either ill or injured, and were encountered in such circumstances as to prevent a leisurely appreciation of their finer attributes.

From Orrie's chubbiness and Aidan's spidery winter-white limbs to Bobby's skinny, pale torso and neat little flat behind, the McCallum-Higginses were as entertaining to watch as a cageful of monkeys.

Ian and Jamie were something different—baboons, perhaps, or mandrills. They didn't really resemble each other in any attribute other than height, and yet were plainly cut from the same cloth. Watching Jamie squatting on a rock above the pool, thighs tensing for a leap, I could easily see him preparing to attack a leopard, while Ian stretched himself glistening in the sun, warming his dangly bits while keeping an alert watch for intruders. All they needed were purple bottoms, and they could have walked straight onto the African veldt, no questions asked.

They were all lovely, in their wildly various ways, but it was Jamie my gaze returned to, over and over again. He was battered and scarred, his muscles roped and knotted, and age had grooved the hollows between them. The thick welt of the bayonet scar writhed up his thigh, wide and ugly, while the thinner white line of the scar left by a rattlesnake's bite was nearly invisible, clouded by the thick fuzz of his body hair, this beginning to dry now and stand out from his skin in a cloud of reddish-gold. The scimitar-shaped sword cut across his ribs had healed well, too, no more than a hair-thin white line by now.

He turned round and bent to pick up a cake of soap from the rock, and my insides turned over. It wasn't purple but could not otherwise have been improved on, being high, round, delicately dusted with red-gold, and with a delightful muscular concavity to the sides. His balls, just visible from behind, *were* purple with the cold, and gave me a strong urge to creep up behind him and cup them in my rock-warmed hands.

I wondered whether the resultant standing broad-jump would enable him to clear the pool.

I had not, in fact, seen him naked—or even substantially undressed—in several months.

But now . . . I threw back my head, closing my eyes against the brilliant spring sun, enjoying the tickle of my own fresh-washed hair against my shoulder blades. The snow was gone, the weather was good—and the whole outdoors beckoned invitingly, filled with places where privacy could be assured, bar the odd skunk.

I LEFT THE MEN dripping and sunning themselves on the rocks, and went to retrieve my clothes. I didn't put these on, though. Instead, I went quickly up to the springhouse, where I submerged my basket of greens in the cool water—if I took it to the cabin, Amy would seize them and boil them into submission—and left my gown, stays, and stockings rolled up on the shelf where the cheeses were stacked. Then I went back toward the stream.

The splashing and shouting had ceased. Instead, I heard low-voiced singing, coming along the trail. It was Bobby, carrying Orrie, sound asleep after his exertions. Aidan, groggy with cleanliness and warmth, ambled slowly beside his stepfather, dark head tilting to and fro to the rhythm of the song.

It was a lovely Gaelic lullaby; Amy must have taught it to Bobby. I did wonder if she'd told him what the words meant.

S'iomadh oidhche fhliuch is thioram
Sìde nan seachd sian
Gheibheadh Griogal dhomhsa creagan
Ris an gabhainn dìon.

(Many a night, wet and dry
Even in the worst of weather
Gregor would find a little rock for me
Beside which I could shelter.)

Òbhan, òbhan òbhan ìri
Òbhan ìri ò!
Òbhan, òbhan òbhan ìri
'S mòr mo mhulad 's mòr.

(Woe is me, woe is me
Woe is me, great indeed is my sorrow.)

I smiled to see them, though with a catch in my throat. I remembered Jamie carrying Jem back from swimming, the summer before, and Roger singing to Mandy in the night, his harsh, cracked voice little more than a whisper—but music, all the same.

I nodded to Bobby, who smiled and nodded back, though without interrupting his song. He raised his brows and jerked a thumb over his shoulder and uphill, presumably indicating where Jamie had gone. He betrayed no surprise at seeing me in shift and shawl—doubtless he thought I was bound for the stream to wash, as well, inspired by the singular warmth of the day.

Eudail mhòir a shluagh an domhain
Dhòirt iad d' fhuil an dè
'S chuir iad do cheann air stob daraich
Tacan beag bhod chrè.

(Great sweetheart of all people of the world
They poured your blood yesterday
And they put your head on an oak stick
A short distance from your body.)

Òbhan, òbhan òbhan ìri
Òbhan ìri ò!
Òbhan, òbhan òbhan ìri
'S mòr mo mhulad 's mòr.

(Woe is me, woe is me
Woe is me, great indeed is my sorrow.)

I waved briefly and turned up the side trail that led to the upper clearing. "New House," everyone called it, though the only indications that there might someday *be* a house there were a stack of felled logs and a number of pegs driven into the ground, with strings tied between them. These were meant to mark the placement and dimensions of the house Jamie intended to build in replacement of the Big House—when we came back.

He'd been moving the pegs, I saw. The wide front room was now wider, and the back room intended for my surgery had developed a growth of some sort, perhaps a separate stillroom.

The architect was sitting on a log, surveying his kingdom, stark naked.

"Expecting me, were you?" I asked, taking off my shawl and hanging it on a convenient branch.

"I was." He smiled, and scratched his chest. "I thought the sight of my naked backside would likely inflame ye. Or was it maybe Bobby's?"

"Bobby hasn't got one. Do you know, you haven't got a single gray hair below the neck? Why is that, I wonder?"

He glanced down, inspecting himself, but it was true. There were only a few strands of silver among the fiery mass of his hair, though his beard—the winter growth tediously and painfully removed a few days before—was heavily frosted with white. But the hair on his chest was still a dark auburn, and that below a fluffy mass of vivid ginger.

He combed his fingers thoughtfully through the exuberant foliage, looking down.

"I think it's hiding," he remarked, and glanced up at me, one eyebrow raised. "Want to come and help me hunt for it?"

I came round in front of him and obligingly knelt down. The object in question was in fact quite visible, though admittedly looking rather shell-shocked by the recent immersion, and a most interesting shade of pale blue.

"Well," I said, after a moment's contemplation. "Great oaks from tiny acorns grow. Or so I'm told."

A shiver ran through him at the warmth of my mouth and I lifted my hands involuntarily, cradling his balls.

"Holy God," he said, and his hands rested lightly on my head in benediction.

"What did ye say?" he asked, a moment later.

"I said," I said, coming up momentarily for air, "I find the gooseflesh rather erotic."

"There's more where that came from," he assured me. "Take your shift off, Sassenach. I havena seen ye naked in nearly four months."

"Well . . . no, you haven't," I agreed, hesitating. "And I'm not sure I want you to."

One eyebrow went up.

"Whyever not?"

"Because I've been indoors for weeks on end without sun or exercise to speak of. I probably look like one of those grubs you find under rocks—fat, white, and squidgy."

"Squidgy?" he repeated, breaking into a grin.

"Squidgy," I said with dignity, wrapping my arms around myself.

He pursed his lips and exhaled slowly, eyeing me with his head on one side.

"I like it when ye're fat, but I ken quite well that ye're not," he said, "because I've felt your ribs when I put my arms about you, each night since the end of January. As for white—ye've been white all the time I've known ye; it's no likely to come a great shock to me. As for the squidgy part"—he extended one hand and wiggled the fingers beckoningly at me—"I think I might enjoy that."

"Hmm," I said, still hesitant. He sighed.

"Sassenach," he said, "I said I havena seen ye naked in four months. That means if ye take your shift off now, ye'll be the best thing I've seen in four months. And at my age, I dinna think I remember farther back than that."

I laughed, and without further ado, stood up and pulled the ribbon tie at the neck of my shift. Wriggling, I let it fall in a puddle round my feet.

He closed his eyes. Then breathed deep and opened them again.

"I'm blinded," he said softly, and held out a hand to me.

"Blinded as in sun bouncing off a vast expanse of snow?" I asked dubiously. "Or as in coming face to face with a gorgon?"

"Seeing a gorgon turns ye to stone, not strikes ye blind," he informed me. "Though come to think"—he prodded himself with an experimental forefinger—"I may turn to stone yet. Will ye come here, for God's sake?"

I came.

I FELL ASLEEP IN the warmth of Jamie's body, and woke some time later, snugly wrapped in his plaid. I stretched, alarming a squirrel overhead, who ran out on a limb to get a better view. Evidently he didn't like what he saw, and began scolding and chattering.

"Oh, hush," I said, yawning, and sat up. The squirrel took exception to this gesture and began having hysterics, but I ignored him. To my surprise, Jamie was gone.

I thought he'd likely just stepped into the wood to relieve himself, but a quick glance round didn't discover him, and when I scrambled to my feet, the plaid clutched to me, I saw no sign of him.

I hadn't heard anything; surely if someone had come, I would have wakened—or Jamie would have wakened me. I listened carefully, but—the squirrel having now gone about its own business—heard nothing beyond the normal sounds of a forest waking to spring: the murmur and rush of wind through new-leafed trees, punctuated by the occasional crack of a falling branch, or the rattle of last year's pinecones and chestnut hulls bouncing through the canopy; the call of a distant jay, the conversation of a gang of pygmy nuthatches foraging in the long grass nearby, the rustle of a hungry vole in the winter's dead leaves.

The jay was still calling; another had joined it now, shrill with alarm. Perhaps that was where Jamie had gone.

I unwound myself from the plaid and pulled on my shift and shoes. It was getting on for evening; we—or I, at least—had slept a long time. It was still warm in the sun, but the shadows under the trees were cold, and I put on my shawl and bundled up Jamie's plaid into my arms—likely he'd want it.

I followed the calling of the jays uphill, away from the clearing. There was a pair nesting near the White Spring; I'd seen them building the nest only two days before.

It wasn't far from the house site at all, though that particular spring always had the air of being remote from everything. It lay in the center of a small grove of white ash and hemlock, and was shielded on the east by a jagged outcropping of lichen-covered rock. All water has a sense of life about it, and a mountain spring carries a particular sense of quiet joy, rising pure from the heart of the earth. The White Spring, so called for the big pale boulder that stood guardian over its pool, had something more—a sense of inviolate peace.

The closer I came to it, the surer I was that that was where I'd find Jamie.

"There's something there that listens," he'd told Brianna once, quite casually. "Ye see such pools in the Highlands; they're called saints' pools—folk say the saint lives by the pool and listens to their prayers."

"And what saint lives by the White Spring?" she'd asked, cynical. "Saint Killian?"

"Why him?"

"Patron saint of gout, rheumatism, and whitewashers."

He'd laughed at that, shaking his head.

"Whatever it is that lives in such water is older than the notion of saints," he assured her. "But it listens."

I walked softly, approaching the spring. The jays had fallen silent now.

He was there, sitting on a rock by the water, wearing only his shirt. I saw why the jays had gone about their business—he was still as the white boulder itself, his eyes closed, hands turned upward on his knees, loosely cupped, inviting grace.

I stopped at once when I saw him. I had seen him pray here once before—when he'd asked Dougal MacKenzie for help in battle. I didn't know who he was talking to just now, but it wasn't a conversation I wished to intrude upon.

I ought to leave, I supposed—but aside from the fear that I might disturb him by an inadvertent noise, I didn't want to go. Most of the spring lay in shadow, but fingers of light came down through the trees, stroking him. The air was thick with pollen, and the light was filled with motes of gold. It struck answering glints from the crown of his head, the smooth high arch of his foot, the blade of his nose, the bones of his face. He might have grown there, part of earth and stone and water, might have been himself the spirit of the spring.

I didn't feel unwelcome. The peace of the place reached out to touch me gently, slow my heart.

Was that what he sought here, I wondered? Was he drawing the peace of the mountain into himself, to remember, to sustain him during the months—the years, perhaps—of coming exile?

I would remember.

The light began to go, brightness falling from the air. He stirred, finally, lifting his head a little.

"Let me be enough," he said quietly.

I started at the sound of his voice, but he hadn't been speaking to me.

He opened his eyes and rose then, quiet as he'd sat, and came past the stream, long feet bare and silent on the layers of damp leaves. As he came past the outcropping of rock, he saw me and smiled, reaching out to take the plaid I held out to him, wordless. He said nothing, but took my cold hand in his large warm one and we turned toward home, walking together in the mountain's peace.

A FEW DAYS LATER, he came to find me. I was foraging along the creek bank for leeches, which had begun to emerge from their winter's hibernation, ravenous for blood. They were simple to catch; I merely waded slowly through the water near shore.

At first, the thought of acting as live bait for the leeches was repellent, but after all, that was how I usually obtained leeches—by letting Jamie, Ian, Bobby, or any of a dozen young males wade through the streams and pick them off. And once you got used to the sight of the creatures, slowly engorging with your blood, it wasn't all that bad.

"I have to let them have enough blood to sustain themselves," I explained, grimacing as I eased a thumbnail under the sucker of a leech in order to dislodge it, "but not enough that they'll be comatose, or they won't be of any use."

"A matter of nice judgment," Jamie agreed, as I dropped the leech into a jar filled with water and duckweed. "When ye've done feeding your wee pets, then, come along and I'll show ye the Spaniard's Cave."

It was no little distance. Perhaps four miles from the Ridge, through cold, muddy creeks and up steep slopes, then through a crack in a granite cliff face that made me feel as though I were being entombed alive, only to emerge into a wilderness of jutting boulders, smothered in nets of wild grape.

"We found it, Jem and I, out hunting one day," Jamie explained, lifting a curtain of leaves for me to pass beneath. The vines snaked over the rocks, thick as a man's forearm and knotted with age, the rusty-green leaves of spring not yet quite covering them. "It was a secret between us. We agreed we'd tell no one else—not even his parents."

"Nor me," I said, but wasn't offended. I heard the loss in his voice at the mention of Jem.

The entrance to the cave was a crack in the ground, over which Jamie had pushed a large, flat rock. He slid this back with some effort, and I bent over cautiously, experiencing a brief clench of the innards at the faint sound of moving air through the fissure. The surface air was warm, though; the cave was drawing, not blowing.

I remembered all too well the cave at Abandawe, that had seemed to breathe around us, and it took some force of will to follow Jamie as he disappeared into the earth. There was a rough wooden ladder—new, I saw, but replacing a much older one that had fallen to pieces; some bits of rotted wood were still in place, dangling from the rock on rusted iron spikes.

It could have been no more than ten or twelve feet to the bottom, but the neck of the cave was narrow, and the descent seemed endless. At last I reached the bottom, though, and saw that the cave had opened out, like the bottom of a flask. Jamie was crouched to one side; I saw him draw out a small bottle and smelled the sharp scent of turpentine.

He'd brought a torch, a pine knot with a head dipped in tar and wrapped with a rag. He soaked the rag with turpentine, then drew the fire-starter Bree had made for him. A shower of sparks lit his face, intent and ruddy. Twice more, and the torch caught, the flame bursting through the flammable cloth and catching the tar.

He lifted the torch, and gestured toward the floor behind me. I turned and nearly jumped out of my skin.

The Spaniard leaned against the wall, bony legs stretched out, skull fallen forward as if in a doze. Tufts of reddish, faded hair still clung here and there, but the skin had gone entirely. His hands and feet were mostly gone, too, the small bones carried away by rodents. No large animals had been able to get at him, though, and while the torso and long bones showed signs of nibbling, they were largely intact; the swell of the rib cage poked through a tissue of cloth so faded that there was no telling what color it had ever been.

He *was* a Spaniard, too. A crested metal helmet, red with rust, lay by him, along with an iron breastplate and a knife.

"Jesus H. Roosevelt Christ," I whispered. Jamie crossed himself, and knelt by the skeleton.

"I've no notion how long he's been here," he said,

also low-voiced. "We didna find anything with him save the armor and that." He pointed to the gravel just in front of the pelvis. I leaned closer to look; a small crucifix, probably silver, now tarnished black, and a few inches away, a tiny triangular shape, also black.

"A rosary?" I asked, and Jamie nodded.

"I expect he was wearing it about his neck. It must have been made of wood and string, and when it rotted, the metal bits fell. That"—his finger gently touched the little triangle—"says *Nr. Sra. Ang.* on the one side—*Nuestra Señora de los Angeles,* I think it means, 'Our Lady of the Angels.' There's a wee picture of the Blessed Virgin on the other side."

I crossed myself by reflex.

"Was Jemmy scared?" I asked, after a moment's respectful silence.

"I was," Jamie said dryly. "It was dark when I came down the shaft, and I nearly stepped on this fellow. I thought he was alive, and the shock of it liked to stop my heart."

He'd cried out in alarm, and Jemmy, left aboveground with strict instructions not to move from the spot, had promptly scrambled into the hole, losing his grip of the broken ladder halfway down and landing feetfirst on his grandfather.

"I heard him scrabbling and looked up, just in time to have him plunge out of the heavens and strike me in the breast like a cannonball." Jamie rubbed the left side of his chest with rueful amusement. "If I hadn't looked up, he'd have broken my neck—and he'd never have got out, by himself."

And we'd never have known what happened to either one of you. I swallowed, dry-mouthed at the thought. And yet . . . on any given day, something just as random might happen. To anyone.

"A wonder neither one of you broke anything," I said instead, and gestured toward the skeleton. "What do you think happened to this gentleman?" *His people never knew.*

Jamie shook his head.

"I dinna ken. He wasna expecting an enemy, because he wasna wearing his armor."

"You don't think he fell in and couldn't get out?" I squatted by the skeleton, tracing the tibia of the left leg. The bone was dried and cracked, gnawed at the end by small sharp teeth—but I could see what might be a greenstick fracture of the bone. Or might just be the cracking of age.

Jamie shrugged, glancing up.

"I shouldna think so. He was a good bit shorter than I am, but I think the original ladder must have been here when he died—for if someone built the ladder later, why would they leave this gentleman here at the bottom of it? And even with a broken leg, he should have been able to climb it."

"Hmm. He might have died of a fever, I suppose. That would account for his taking off his breastplate and helmet." Though I personally would have taken them off at the first opportunity; depending on the season, he must either have been boiled alive or suffered severely from mildew, semi-enclosed in metal.

"Mmphm."

I glanced up at this sound, which indicated dubious acceptance of my reasoning but disagreement with my conclusion.

"You think he was killed?"

He shrugged.

"He has armor—but nay weapon save a wee knife. And ye can see he was right-handed, but the knife's lying to his left."

The skeleton *had* been right-handed; the bones of the right arm were noticeably thicker, even by the flicker of torchlight. Possibly a swordsman? I wondered.

"I kent a good many Spanish soldiers in the Indies, Sassenach. All of them fair bristled wi' swords and spears and pistols. If this man died of a fever, his companions might take his arms—but they'd take the armor, too, *and* the knife. Why leave it?"

"But by that token," I objected, "why did whoever killed him—if he was killed—leave the armor and the knife?"

"As for the armor—they didna want it. It wouldna be particularly useful to anyone other than a soldier. As for the knife—because it was sticking in him?" Jamie suggested. "And it's no a very good knife to begin with."

"Very logical," I said, swallowing again. "Putting aside the question of how he died—what in God's name was he doing in the mountains of North Carolina in the first place?"

"The Spanish sent explorers up as far as Virginia, fifty or sixty years ago," he informed me. "The swamps discouraged them, though."

"I can see why. But why . . . *this*?" I stood up, waving a hand to encompass the cave and its ladder. He didn't reply, but took my arm and lifted his torch, turning me to the side of the cave opposite the ladder. Well above my head, I saw another small fissure in the rock, black in the torchlight, barely wide enough for a man to wriggle through.

"There's a smaller cave through there," he said, nodding upward. "And when I put Jem up to look, he told me there were marks in the dust—square marks, as though heavy boxes had sat there."

Which is why, when the need to hide treasure had occurred to him, so had thought of the Spaniard's Cave.

"We'll bring the last of the gold tonight," he said, "and pile rocks to hide the opening up there. Then we'll leave the *señor* here to his rest."

I was obliged to admit that the cave made as suitable a resting place as any. And the Spanish soldier's presence would likely discourage anyone who stumbled on the cave from further investigation, both Indians and settlers having a distinct aversion to ghosts. For that matter, so did Highlanders, and I turned curiously to Jamie.

"You and Jem—you weren't troubled about being haunted by him?"

"Nay, we said the proper prayer for the repose of his soul, when I sealed the cave, and scattered salt around it."

That made me smile.

"You know the proper prayer for every occasion, don't you?"

He smiled faintly in return, and rubbed the head of the torch in the damp gravel to extinguish it. A faint shaft of light from above glowed on the crown of his head.

"There's always a prayer, *a nighean*, even if it's only *A Dhia, cuidich mi.*" *Oh, God—help me.*

Also by Diana Gabaldon

THE **OUTLANDER** SERIES

DianaGabaldon.com

AuthorDianaGabaldon   @Writer_DG

RANDOM HOUSE   BALLANTINE • BANTAM • DELL

Also by Diana Gabaldon

THE COMPANION VOLUME

THE OUTLANDER GRAPHIC NOVEL

THE LORD JOHN SERIES

Lord John and the Private Matter
Lord John and the Brotherhood of the Blade
Lord John and the Hand of Devils
The Scottish Prisoner

Continue the saga with original eNovellas, engrossing tales to complement the Outlander series.

A Plague of Zombies

The Custom of the Army

A Leaf on the Wind of All Hallows

The Space Between

DianaGabaldon.com
AuthorDianaGabaldon @Writer_DG

Random House Bantam • Dell • Delacorte

A STARZ ORIGINAL SERIES
OUTLANDER
STARZ

PRAISE FOR THE OUTLANDER NOVELS

AN ECHO IN THE BONE

"Adventure, history, romance, fantasy and sex, all you've come to expect from Gabaldon." —*The Arizona Republic*

"Diana Gabaldon gives her legion of fans excellent value in *An Echo in the Bone.* . . . Pages fly by and leave readers hungering to know what comes next for a set of engagingly colorful characters who by now feel like old friends."
—BookLoons.com

"*An Echo in the Bone* is a wonderful, adventure-filled, emotion-packed reunion with the Frasers. . . . Meticulous research of historical events, facts, and people, flora and fauna, geography, food, clothing, and weaponry brings the eighteenth century to vivid life. . . . Don't miss the long-awaited continuation of this fabulous series. It will keep you up late for a few nights!" —*Romance Reviews Today*

A BREATH OF SNOW AND ASHES

"Time travelers revolutionize colonial America with . . . cliff-hangers galore, in Gabaldon's sixth Outlander epic."
—*Kirkus Reviews*

"This compulsively readable mix of authentically set historical fiction and completely satisfying romance maps both violent loss and strong family ties. . . . The large scope of the novel allows Gabaldon to do what she does best, paint in exquisite detail the lives of her characters." —*Booklist*

"Essential for every fiction collection." —*Library Journal*

THE FIERY CROSS

"Each and every one of its 979 pages abounds with Ms. Gabaldon's sexy combination of humor, wild adventure and, underlying it all, the redemptive power of true love."
—*The Dallas Morning News*

"Fans of the series will be delighted with this novel and there are threads left dangling for another mega epic from the great author." —*Midwest Book Review*

"It is a grand adventure written on a canvas that probes the heart, weighs the soul and measures the human spirit across ten generations." —CNN

OUTLANDER

"Marvelously entertaining . . . a page-turner of the highest order and a good read from start to finish."
—*Chattanooga Times*

"Absorbing and heartwarming . . . lavishly evokes the land and lore of Scotland." —*Publishers Weekly*

"History comes deliciously alive on the page."
—New York *Daily News*

DRAGONFLY IN AMBER

"A triumph! A powerful tale layered in history and myth. I loved every page." —NORA ROBERTS

"Compulsively readable." —*Publishers Weekly*

"Diana Gabaldon is a born storyteller . . . the pages practically turn themselves." —*Arizona Republic*

VOYAGER

"Triumphant . . . Her use of historical detail and a truly adult love story confirm Gabaldon as a superior writer."
—*Publishers Weekly*

"An amazing read." —*Arizona Tribune*

"Memorable storytelling." —*The Seattle Times*

DRUMS OF AUTUMN

"Unforgettable characters . . . richly embroidered with historical detail . . . I just can't put it down." —*The Cincinnati Post*

"Wonderful . . . This is escapist historical fiction at its best."
—*San Antonio Express-News*

By Diana Gabaldon

(in chronological order)
Outlander
Dragonfly in Amber
Voyager
Drums of Autumn
The Fiery Cross
A Breath of Snow and Ashes
An Echo in the Bone
Written in My Own Heart's Blood

The Outlandish Companion
Vols. 1 & 2
(nonfiction)

The Exile
(graphic novel)

(in chronological order)
Lord John and the Hellfire Club (novella)
Lord John and the Private Matter
Lord John and the Succubus
Lord John and the Brotherhood of the Blade
Lord John and the Haunted Soldier (novella)
Custom of the Army (novella)
Lord John and the Hand of Devils (collected novellas)
The Scottish Prisoner
A Plague of Zombies (novella)

Other Outlander-related novellas
A Leaf on the Wind of All Hallows
The Space Between
Virgins

DIANA GABALDON

AN ECHO IN THE BONE

A NOVEL

DELL
NEW YORK

2011 Dell Mass Market Edition

Published in the United States by Dell, an imprint of The Random House Publishing Group, a division of Random House, Inc., New York.

DELL is a registered trademark of Random House, Inc., and the colophon is a trademark of Random House, Inc.

Originally published in hardcover in the United States by Delacorte, an imprint of The Random House Publishing Group, a division of Random House, Inc., in 2009.

This book contains an excerpt from the forthcoming book *Written in My Own Heart's Blood* by Diana Gabaldon. This excerpt has been set for this edition only and may not reflect the final content of the forthcoming edition.

ISBN 978-0-440-24568-1
ebook ISBN: 978-0-440-33887-1

Cover design: Marietta Anastassatos
Cover illustration: © Robert Hunt

Printed in the United States of America

randomhousebooks.com

28 27 26 25 24 23 22

Dell mass market edition: June 2011

To all my good dogs:

Penny Louise
Tipper John
John
Flip
Archie and Ed
Tippy
Spots
Emily
Ajax
Molly
Gus
Homer and JJ

ACKNOWLEDGMENTS

It takes me a good three years to write one of these books, during which time I constantly ask people questions, and during which time helpful people offer me fascinating bits of information that I didn't think to ask for. I'll never remember them all, but think of them all with enormous gratitude.

In addition, I wish to offer grateful thanks to . . .

. . . John Flicker and Bill Massey, my editors, both gentlemen of gall and kidney, who coped nobly with a book written in pieces (lots of pieces), and an author who lives dangerously.

. . . Danny Baror and Russell Galen, my literary agents, two gentlemen literally worth their weight in gold—which is saying something in these recessionary days.

. . . Kathy Lord, heroic copy editor, and Virginia Norey, book designer (aka "the book goddess"), who are jointly responsible for the beauty and readability of this book.

. . . Vincent La Scala and the other cruelly used members of the production crew, who succeeded in getting this book into print on time against looooong odds.

. . . Steven Lopata for his vivid description of being chased overland by a cottonmouth—as well as the poetic description of what they smell like ("A combination of that snake-house smell from the zoo and rotten cucumbers").

. . . Catherine MacGregor and Catherine-Ann MacPhee for *Gàidhlig* translations and help in the subtleties of Gaelic usage. Also Katie Beggs and various unsung but much appreciated members of the International Gaelic Mafia.

. . . Tess Jones the nurse, Dr. Amarilis Iscold, Sarah Meir (Certified Nurse Midwife), and a number of other helpful medical professionals, for advice on matters medical, picturesque maladies, and horrifying surgical details.

. . . Janet McConnaughey for *OEDILF* (Omnificent English Dictionary in Limerick Form) entries, being the Muse of Bloody Axes, and drawing my attention to exploding cypress trees.

. . . Larry Tuohy (and others) for telling me what a Spitfire pilot's flight jacket looked like.

. . . Ron Parker, Helen, Esmé and Lesley, for 'elp with the 'airy ape.

. . . Beth and Matthew Shope and Jo Bourne for useful information regarding the Religious Society of Friends. Any inaccuracies are definitely my fault.

. . . Jari Backman, for his detailed time lines and excerpt listings, and for help with the night sky and which stars are visible in Inverness and Fraser's Ridge.

. . . Katrina Stibohar for her exquisitely detailed lists of who was born when and What Happened to Everybody then. Also to the hordes of kindly trivia freaks who are always on hand to tell me how old someone is, or whether Lord John met Fergus when he had the measles.

. . . Pamela Patchet Hamilton (and Buddy) for a nose-wrenchingly vivid description of a close-range skunking.

. . . Karen Henry, Czarina of Traffic, who keeps my folder in the Compuserve Books and Writers Community tidy and the inhabitants diplomatically herded.
(http://community.compuserve.com/n/pfx/forum.aspx?nav=start&webtag=ws-books)

. . . Nikki Rowe and her daughter Caitlin, for the wonderful YouTube channel they created for me.
(http://www.youtube.com/user/voyagesoftheartemis—for those who want to see whether I really do sound like Donald Duck when I talk).

. . . Rosana Madrid Gatti, my web-mistress, for prompt and faithful updates and imaginative design.

. . . Susan Butler, for constant logistic support, dog sleep-overs, keeping me supplied with black-ink cartridges, and for her brilliant suggestion regarding Jem.

. . . Allene Edwards, Catherine MacGregor, and Susan Butler, for proofreading and Extremely Helpful (if eyeball-numbing) nitpicking.

. . . Shirley Williams for the Moravian cookies and vistas of New Bern.

. . . Becky Morgan for the historical cookbooks.

. . . my great-grandfather, Stanley Sykes, for Jamie's line about marksmanship.

. . . Bev LaFrance, Carol Krenz, and many others for help with French. Also Florence the translator, Peter Berndt, and Gilbert Sureau for the nice distinctions between the French Lord's Prayer of 1966 (*accorde-lui*) versus the earlier, more formal version (*accordez-lui*).

. . . John S. Kruszka, for the proper spelling and pronunciation of "Kościuszko" (it's "kohs-CHOOSH-koh," in case you wondered; nobody in the Revolution could pronounce it, either—they really did all call him "Kos").

. . . the Ladies of Lallybroch, for continuous support and Really Interesting Gifts.

. . . my husband, because he knows fine what a man is for, too.

. . . Alex Krislov, Janet McConnaughey, and Margaret Campbell, sysops of the Compuserve Books and Writers Community, and the many, many, many helpful people who roam through the site daily, offering observations, information, and general entertainment.

. . . Alfred Publishing for permission to quote from the lyrics to "Tighten Up," by Archie Bell and the Drells.

"The White Swan," taken from *Carmina Gadelica,* is reproduced by kind permission of Floris Books.

"The Hippopotamus Song" (referenced briefly in Claire's thoughts on pages 160–61) was written (1959) by Michael Flanders, of the famous comedy duo Flanders and Swann.

CONTENTS

PART THREE

Privateer

PART FOUR

Conjunction

PART FIVE

To the Precipice

PART SEVEN

Reap the Whirlwind

AN ECHO IN THE BONE

PROLOGUE

THE BODY IS amazingly plastic. The spirit, even more so. But there are some things you don't come back from.

Say ye so, *a nighean*? True, the body's easily maimed, and the spirit can be crippled—yet there's that in a man that is never destroyed.

Part One

A Troubling of the Waters

1

SOMETIMES THEY'RE REALLY DEAD

Wilmington, colony of North Carolina
July 1776

THE PIRATE'S HEAD had disappeared. William heard the speculations from a group of idlers on the quay nearby, wondering whether it would be seen again.

"Na, him be gone for good," said a ragged man of mixed blood, shaking his head. "De ally-gator don' take him, de water will."

A backwoodsman shifted his tobacco and spat into the water in disagreement.

"No, he's good for another day—two, maybe. Them gristly bits what holds the head on, they dry out in the sun. Tighten up like iron. Seen it many a time with deer carcasses."

William saw Mrs. MacKenzie glance quickly at the harbor, then away. She looked pale, he thought, and maneuvered himself slightly so as to block her view of the men and the brown flood of high tide, though since it *was* high, the corpse tied to its stake was naturally not visible. The stake was, though—a stark reminder of the price of crime. The pirate had been staked to drown on the mudflats several days before, the persistence of his decaying corpse an ongoing topic of public conversation.

"Jem!" Mr. MacKenzie called sharply, and lunged past William in pursuit of his son. The little boy, red-haired like his mother, had wandered away to listen to the men's talk, and was now leaning perilously out over the water, clinging to a bollard in an attempt to see the dead pirate.

Mr. MacKenzie snatched the boy by the collar, pulled him in, and swept him up in his arms, though the boy struggled, craning back toward the swampish harbor.

"I want to see the wallygator eat the pirate, Daddy!"

The idlers laughed, and even MacKenzie smiled a little, though the smile disappeared when he glanced at his wife. He was at her side in an instant, one hand beneath her elbow.

"I think we must be going," MacKenzie said, shifting his son's weight in order better to support his wife, whose distress was apparent. "Lieutenant Ransom—Lord Ellesmere, I mean"—he corrected with an apologetic smile at William—"will have other engagements, I'm sure."

This was true; William was engaged to meet his father for supper. Still, his father had arranged to meet him at the tavern just across the quay; there was no risk of missing him. William said as much, and urged them to stay, for he was enjoying their company—Mrs. MacKenzie's, particularly—but she smiled regretfully, though her color was better, and patted the capped head of the baby in her arms.

"No, we do have to be going." She glanced at her son, still struggling to get down, and William saw her eyes flicker toward the harbor and the stark pole that stood above the flood. She resolutely looked away, fixing her eyes upon William's face instead. "The baby's waking up; she'll be wanting food. It was so lovely to meet you, though. I wish we might talk longer." She said this with the greatest sincerity, and touched his arm lightly, giving him a pleasant sensation in the pit of the stomach.

The idlers were now placing wagers on the reappearance of the drowned pirate, though by the looks of things, none of them had two groats to rub together.

"Two to one he's still there when the tide goes out."

"Five to one the body's still there, but the head's gone. I don't care what you say about the gristly bits, Lem, that there head was just a-hangin' by a thread when this last tide come in. Next un'll take it, sure."

Hoping to drown this conversation out, William embarked on an elaborate farewell, going so far as to kiss Mrs. MacKenzie's hand with his best court manner—and, seized by inspiration, kissed the baby girl's hand, too, making them all laugh. Mr. MacKenzie gave him rather an odd look, but didn't seem offended, and shook his hand in a most republican manner—playing out the joke by setting down his son and making the little boy shake hands as well.

"Have you kilt anybody?" the boy inquired with interest, looking at William's dress sword.

"No, not yet," William replied, smiling.

"My grandsire's kilt two dozen men!"

"Jemmy!" Both parents spoke at once, and the little boy's shoulders went up around his ears.

"Well, he *has*!"

"I'm sure he is a bold and bloody man, your grandsire," William assured the little boy gravely. "The King always has need of such men."

"My grandda says the King can kiss his arse," the boy replied matter-of-factly.

"JEMMY!"

Mr. MacKenzie clapped a hand over his outspoken offspring's mouth.

"You *know* your grandda didn't say that!" Mrs. MacKenzie said. The little boy nodded agreeably, and his father removed the muffling hand.

"No. Grannie did, though."

"Well, that's somewhat more likely," Mr. MacKenzie murmured, obviously trying not to laugh. "But we still don't say things like that to soldiers—they work for the King."

"Oh," said Jemmy, clearly losing interest. "Is the tide going out now?" he asked hopefully, craning his neck toward the harbor once more.

"No," Mr. MacKenzie said firmly. "Not for hours. You'll be in bed."

Mrs. MacKenzie smiled at William in apology, her cheeks charmingly flushed with embarrassment, and the family took its leave with some haste, leaving William struggling between laughter and dismay.

"Oy, Ransom!"

He turned at his name, to find Harry Dobson and Colin Osborn, two second lieutenants from his regiment, evidently escaped from duty and eager to sample the fleshpots of Wilmington—such as they were.

"Who's that?" Dobson looked after the departing group, interested.

"A Mr. and Mrs. MacKenzie. Friends of my father's."

"Oh, married, is she?" Dobson sucked in his cheeks, still watching the woman. "Well, make it a bit harder, I suppose, but what's life without a challenge?"

"Challenge?" William gave his diminutive friend a jaundiced look. "Her husband's roughly three times your size, if you hadn't noticed."

Osborn laughed, going red in the face.

"She's *twice* his size! She'd crush you, Dobby."

"And what makes you think I mean to be on the bottom?" Dobson inquired with dignity. Osborn hooted.

"What's this obsession of yours with giantesses?" William demanded. He glanced at the little family, now nearly out of sight at the end of the street. "That woman's nearly as tall as I am!"

"Oh, rub it in, why don't you?" Osborn, who was taller than Dobson's five feet, but still a head shorter than William, aimed a mock kick at his knee. William dodged it and cuffed Osborn, who ducked and shoved him into Dobson.

"Gennelmen!" The menacing cockney tones of Sergeant Cutter brought them up sharp. They might outrank the sergeant, but not one of them would have the nerve to point this out. The entire battalion went in fear of Sergeant Cutter, who was older than God and approximately Dobson's height, but who contained within his diminutive physique the sheer fury of a full-sized volcano on the boil.

"Sergeant!" Lieutenant William Ransom, Earl of Ellesmere and senior of the group, drew himself up straight, chin pressed back into his stock. Osborn and Dobson hastily followed his lead, quaking in their boots.

Cutter strode back and forth in front of them, in the manner of a stalking leopard. You could just see the lashing tail and the preliminary licking of chops, William thought. Waiting for the bite was almost worse than getting it in the arse.

"And where's your troops, then?" Cutter snarled. *"Sirs?"*

Osborn and Dobson at once began sputtering explanations, but Lieutenant Ransom—for once—walked on the side of the angels.

"My men are guarding the Governor's Palace, under Lieutenant Colson. I'm given leave, Sergeant, to dine with my father," he said respectfully. "By Sir Peter."

Sir Peter Packer's was a name to conjure with, and Cutter abated in mid-spew. Rather to William's surprise, though, it wasn't Sir Peter's name that had produced this reaction.

"Your father?" Cutter said, squinting. "That's Lord John Grey, is it?"

"Er . . . yes," William replied cautiously. "Do you . . . know him?"

Before Cutter could reply, the door of a nearby tavern opened, and William's father came out. William smiled in delight at this timely appearance, but quickly erased the smile as the sergeant's gimlet gaze fixed on him.

"Don't you be a-grinnin' at *me* like an 'airy ape," the sergeant began, in dangerous tones, but was interrupted by Lord John's clapping him familiarly on the shoulder—something none of the three young lieutenants would have done if offered significant money.

"Cutter!" Lord John said, smiling warmly. "I heard those dulcet tones and said to myself, why damn me if it isn't Sergeant Aloysius Cutter! There can't be another man alive who sounds so much like a bulldog that's swallowed a cat and lived to tell about it."

"Aloysius?" Dobson mouthed at William, but William merely grunted briefly in response, unable to shrug, as his father had now turned his attention in his direction.

"William," he said, with a cordial nod. "How very punctual you are. My apologies for being so late; I was detained." Before William could say anything or introduce the others, though, Lord John had embarked upon a lengthy reminiscence with Sergeant Cutter, reliving high old times on the Plains of Abraham with General Wolfe.

This allowed the three young officers to relax slightly, which, in Dobson's case, meant a return to his earlier train of thought.

"You said that red-haired poppet's a friend of your father's?" he whispered to William. "Find out from him where she's staying, eh?"

"Idiot," hissed Osborn. "She isn't even pretty! She's long-nosed as—as—as Willie!"

"Didn't see as high as her face," Dobson said, smirking. "Her tits were right at eye-level, though, and *those* . . ."

"Ass!"

"Shh!" Osborn stamped on Dobson's foot to shut him up as Lord John turned back to the young men.

"Will you introduce me to your friends, William?" Lord John inquired politely. Rather red in the face—he had reason to know that his father had acute hearing, despite his artillery experiences—William did so, and Osborn and Dobson both bowed, looking rather awed. They hadn't realized who his father was, and William was at once proud that they were impressed, and mildly dismayed that they'd discovered Lord John's identity—it would be all over the battalion before supper tomorrow. Not that Sir Peter didn't know, of course, but—

He gathered his wits, realizing that his father was taking leave for them both, and returned Sergeant Cutter's salute, hastily but in good form, before hurrying after his father, leaving Dobby and Osborn to their fate.

"I saw you speaking to Mr. and Mrs. MacKenzie," Lord John said casually. "I trust they are well?" He glanced down the quay, but the MacKenzies had long since disappeared from view.

"Seemed so," Willie said. He was *not* going to ask where they stayed, but the impression the young woman had made on him lingered. He couldn't say if she was pretty or not; her eyes had struck him, though—a wonderful deep blue with long auburn lashes, and fixed on him with a flattering intensity that had warmed the cockles of his heart. Grotesquely tall, of course, but—what was he thinking? The woman was married—with children! And red-haired, to boot.

"You've—er—known them long?" he asked, thinking of the startlingly perverse political sentiments that evidently flourished in the family.

"Quite some time. She is the daughter of one of my oldest friends, Mr. James Fraser. Do you recall him, by chance?"

William frowned, not placing the name—his father had thousands of friends, how should he . . .

"Oh!" he said. "Not an English friend, you don't mean. Was it not a Mr. Fraser that we visited in the mountains, that time when you fell sick of the—of the measle?" The bottom of his stomach dropped a little, remembering the sheer terror of that time. He had traveled through the mountains in a daze of misery; his mother had died only a month before. Then Lord John had caught the measle, and William had been sure that his father was about to die likewise, leaving him completely alone in the wilderness. There hadn't been room for anything in his mind but fear and grief, and he retained only a jumble of confused impressions from the visit. He had some dim recollection that Mr. Fraser had taken him fishing and been kind to him.

"Yes," his father said, with a sidelong smile. "I'm touched, Willie. I should have thought you might recall that visit more because of your own misadventure than mine."

"Mis—" Memory rushed over him, succeeded by a flood of heat, hotter than the humid summer air. "Thanks very much! I'd managed to expunge that from my memory, until you mentioned it!"

His father was laughing, and making no attempt to hide it. In fact, he was convulsed.

"I'm sorry, Willie," he said, gasping and wiping his eyes with a corner of his handkerchief. "I can't help it; it was the most—the most—oh, God, I'll never forget what you looked like when we pulled you out of that privy!"

"You *know* it was an accident," William said stiffly. His cheeks burned with remembered mortification. At least Fraser's daughter hadn't been present to witness his humiliation at the time.

"Yes, of course. But—" His father pressed the handkerchief to his mouth, his shoulders shaking silently.

"Feel free to stop cackling at any point," William said coldly. "Where the devil are we going, anyway?" They'd reached the end of the quay, and his father was leading them—still snorting like a grampus—into one of the quiet, tree-lined streets, away from the taverns and inns near the harbor.

"We're dining with a Captain Richardson," his father said, controlling himself with an obvious effort. He coughed, blew his nose, and put away the handkerchief. "At the house of a Mr. Bell."

Mr. Bell's house was whitewashed, neat, and prosperous, without being ostentatious. Captain Richardson gave much the same sort of impression: of middle age, well-groomed and well-tailored, but without any notable style, and with a face you couldn't pick out of a crowd two minutes after seeing it.

The two Misses Bell made a much stronger impression, particularly the younger, Miriam, who had honey-colored curls peeping out of her cap, and big, round eyes that remained fixed on William throughout dinner. She was seated too far away for him to be able to converse with her directly, but he fancied that the language of the eyes was sufficient to indicate to her that the fascination was mutual, and if an opportunity for more personal communication should offer later . . . ? A smile, and a demure lowering of honey-colored lashes, followed by a quick glance toward a door that stood open to the side porch, for air. He smiled back.

"Do you think so, William?" his father said, loudly enough to indicate that it was the second time of asking.

"Oh, certainly. Um . . . think what?" he asked, since it was after all Papa, and not his commander. His father gave him the look that meant he would have rolled his eyes had they not been in public, but replied patiently.

"Mr. Bell was asking whether Sir Peter intends to remain long in Wilmington." Mr. Bell, at the head of the table, bowed graciously—though William observed a certain narrowing of his eyes in Miriam's direction. Perhaps he'd best come back to call tomorrow, he thought, when Mr. Bell might be at his place of business.

"Oh. I believe we'll remain here for only a short time, sir," he said respectfully to Mr. Bell. "I collect that the chief trouble is in the backcountry, and so we will no doubt move to suppress it without delay."

Mr. Bell looked pleased, though from the corner of his eye, William saw Miriam pout prettily at the suggestion of his imminent departure.

"Good, good," Bell said jovially. "No doubt hundreds of Loyalists will flock to join you along your march."

"Doubtless so, sir," William murmured, taking another spoonful of soup. He doubted that Mr. Bell would be among them. Not really the marching type, to look at. And not that the assistance of a lot of untrained provincials armed with shovels would be helpful in any case, but he could hardly say so.

William, trying to see Miriam without looking directly at her, instead intercepted the flicker of a glance that traveled between his father and Captain Richardson, and for the first time, began to wonder. His father had distinctly said they were dining with Captain Richardson—meaning that a meeting with the captain was the point of the evening. Why?

Then he caught a look from Miss Lillian Bell, who was seated across from him, next his father, and ceased thinking about Captain Richardson. Dark-eyed, taller and more slender than her sister—but really quite a handsome girl, now he noticed.

Still, when Mrs. Bell and her daughters rose and the men retired to the porch after dinner, William was not surprised to find himself at one end with Captain Richardson, while his father engaged Mr. Bell at the other in a spirited discussion of tar prices. Papa could talk to anyone about anything.

"I have a proposition to put before you, Lieutenant," Richardson said, after the usual cordialities had been exchanged.

"Yes, sir," William said respectfully. His curiosity had begun to rise. Richardson was a captain of light dragoons, but not presently with his regiment; that much he had revealed over dinner, saying casually that he was on detached duty. Detached to do what?

"I do not know how much your father has told you regarding my mission?"

"Nothing, sir."

"Ah. I am charged with the gathering of intelligence in the Southern Department. Not that I am in command of such operations, you understand"—the captain smiled modestly—"but a small part of them."

"I . . . appreciate the great value of such operations, sir," William said, groping for diplomacy, "but I—for myself, that is to say—"

"You have no interest in spying. No, of course not." It was dark on the porch, but the dryness of the captain's tone was evident. "Few men who regard themselves as soldiers do."

"I meant no offense, sir."

"None taken. I am not, however, recruiting you as a spy—that is a delicate occupation, and one involving some danger—but rather as a messenger. Though should you find opportunity to act the intelligencer along your way . . . well, that would be an additional contribution, and much appreciated."

William felt the blood rise in his face at the implication that he was capable neither of delicacy nor danger, but kept his temper, saying only, "Oh?"

The captain, it seemed, had gathered significant information regarding local conditions in the Carolinas, and now required to send this to the commander of the Northern Department—General Howe, presently in Halifax.

"I will of course be sending more than one messenger," Richardson said. "It is naturally somewhat quicker by ship—but I desire to have at least one messenger travel overland, both for safety's sake and for the sake of making observations *en route.* Your father speaks very highly of your abilities, Lieutenant"—did he detect a hint of amusement in that dry-as-sawdust voice?—"and I collect that you have traveled extensively in North Carolina and Virginia. That is a valuable attribute. You will appreciate that I do not wish my messenger to disappear into the Dismal Swamp, never to be seen again."

"Ha-ha," said William, politely, perceiving this to be meant as a jest. Clearly, Captain Richardson had never been near the Great Dismal; William had, though he didn't think anyone in his right mind would go that way a-purpose, save to hunt.

He also had severe doubts regarding Richardson's suggestion—though even as he told himself that he shouldn't consider leaving his men, his regiment . . . he was already seeing a romantic vision of himself, alone in the vast wilderness, bearing important news through storm and danger.

More of a consideration, though, was what he might expect at the other end of the journey.

Richardson anticipated his question, answering before he could speak.

"Once in the north, you would—it being agreeable—join General Howe's staff."

Well, now, he thought. Here was the apple, and a juicy red one, too. He was aware that Richardson meant "it being agreeable" to General Howe, rather than to William—but he had some confidence in his own capabilities, and rather thought he might prove himself useful.

He had been in North Carolina only a few days, but that was quite long enough for him to have made an accurate assessment of the relative chances for advancement between the Northern Department and the Southern. The entire Continental army was with Washington in the north; the southern rebellion appeared to consist of troublesome pockets of backwoodsmen and impromptu militia—hardly a threat. And as for the relative status of Sir Peter and General Howe as commanders . . .

"I would like to think on your offer, if I might, Captain," he said, hoping eagerness didn't show in his voice. "May I give my answer tomorrow?"

"Certainly. I imagine you will wish to discuss the prospects with your father—you may do so."

The captain then deliberately changed the subject, and within a few moments, Lord John and Mr. Bell had joined them, the conversation becoming general.

William paid little heed to what was said, his own attention distracted by the sight of two slender white figures that hovered ghostlike among the bushes at the outer edge of the yard. Two capped white heads drew together, then apart. Now and then, one turned briefly toward the porch in what looked like speculation.

" 'And for his vesture, they cast lots,' " his father murmured, shaking his head.

"Eh?"

"Never mind." His father smiled, and turned toward Captain Richardson, who had just said something about the weather.

Fireflies lit the yard, drifting like green sparks among the damp, lush growth of plants. It was good to see fireflies again; he had missed them, in England—and that peculiar softness of the southern air that molded his linen to his body and made the blood throb in his fingertips. Crickets were chirping all around them, and for an instant, their song seemed to drown out everything save the sound of his pulse.

"Coffee's ready, gen'mun." The soft voice of the Bells' slave cut through the small ferment of his blood, though, and he went in with the other men, with no more than a glance toward the yard. The white figures had disappeared, but a sense of promise lingered in the soft, warm air.

An hour later, he found himself walking back toward his billet, thoughts in a pleasant muddle, his father strolling silent by his side.

Miss Lillian Bell had granted him a kiss among the fireflies at the end of the evening, chaste and fleeting, but upon the lips, and the thick summer air seemed to taste of coffee and ripe strawberries, despite the pervasive dank smell of the harbor.

"Captain Richardson told me of the proposal he made to you," Lord John said casually. "Are you inclined?"

"Don't know," William replied, with equal casualness. "I should miss my men, of course, but . . ." Mrs. Bell had pressed him to come to tea, later in the week.

"Little permanence in a military life," his father said, with a brief shake of the head. "I did warn you."

William gave a brief grunt of assent, not really listening.

"A good opportunity for advancement," his father was saying, adding offhandedly, "though of course there is some danger to the proposition."

"What?" William scoffed, hearing this. "Riding from Wilmington to take ship at New York? There's a road, nearly all the way!"

"And quite a number of Continentals on it," Lord John pointed out. "General Washington's entire army lies this side of Philadelphia, if the news I hear be correct."

William shrugged.

"Richardson said he wanted me because I knew the country. I can make my way well enough without roads."

"Are you sure? You have not been in Virginia for nearly four years."

The dubious tone of this annoyed William.

"Do you think me incapable of finding my way?"

"No, not at all," his father said, still with that note of doubt in his voice. "But there is no little *risk* to this proposition; I should not like to see you undertake it without due thought."

"Well, I *have* thought," said William, stung. "I'll do it."

Lord John walked in silence for a few steps, then nodded, reluctantly.

"It's your decision, Willie," he said softly. "I should be personally obliged if you would take care, though."

William's annoyance melted at once.

"Course I will," he said gruffly. They walked on beneath the dark canopy of maple and hickory, not talking, close enough that their shoulders brushed now and then.

At the inn, William bade Lord John good night, but didn't return at once to his own lodgings. Instead, he wandered out along the quay, restless, unready for sleep.

The tide had turned and was well out, he saw; the smell of dead fish and decaying seaweed was stronger, though a smooth sheet of water still covered the mudflats, quiet in the light of a quarter-moon.

It took a moment to locate the stake. For an instant, he thought it had gone, but no—there it was, a thin dark line against the glimmer of the water. Empty.

The stake no longer stood upright, but leaned sharply, as though about to fall, and a thin loop of rope trailed from it, floating like a hangman's noose on the waning tide. William was conscious of some visceral uneasiness; the tide alone would not have taken the whole body. Some said there were crocodiles or alligators here, though he had not yet seen one himself. He glanced down involuntarily, as though one of these reptiles might suddenly lunge from the water at his feet. The air was still warm, but a small shiver went through him.

He shook this off, and turned away toward his lodgings. There would be a day or two before he must go, he thought, and wondered whether he might see the blue-eyed Mrs. MacKenzie again before he left.

LORD JOHN LINGERED for a moment on the porch of the inn, watching his son vanish into the shadows under the trees. He had some qualms; the matter had been arranged with more haste than he would have liked—but he did have confidence in William's abilities. And while the arrangement clearly had its risks, that was the nature of a soldier's life. Some situations were riskier than others, though.

He hesitated, hearing the buzz of talk from the taproom inside, but he had had enough of company for the night, and the thought of tossing to and fro under the low ceiling of his room, stifling in the day's trapped heat, determined him to walk about until bodily exhaustion should ensure sleep.

It wasn't just the heat, he reflected, stepping off the porch and setting off in the opposite direction to the one Willie had taken. He knew himself well enough to realize that even the apparent success of his plan would not prevent his lying awake, worrying at it like a dog with a bone, testing for weaknesses, seeking for ways of improvement. After all, William would not depart immediately; there was a little time to consider, to make alterations, should that be necessary.

General Howe, for instance. Had that been the best choice? Perhaps Clinton . . . but no. Henry Clinton was a fussy old woman, unwilling to stir a foot without orders in triplicate.

The Howe brothers—one a general, one an admiral—were famously uncouth, both having the manners, aspect, and general aroma of boars in rut. Neither of them was stupid, though—God knew they weren't timid—and Grey thought Willie fully capable of surviving rough manners and harsh words. And a commander given to spitting on the floor—Richard Howe had once spat on Grey himself, though this was largely accidental, the wind having changed unexpectedly—was possibly easier for a young subaltern to deal with than the quirks of some other military gentlemen of Grey's acquaintance.

Though even the most peculiar of the brotherhood of the blade was preferable to the diplomats. He wondered idly what the term of venery might be for a collection of diplomats. If writers formed the brotherhood of the quill, and a group of foxes be termed a skulk . . . a stab of diplomats, perhaps? Brothers of the stiletto? No, he decided. Much too direct. An opiate of diplomats, more like. Brotherhood of the boring. Though the ones who were not boring could be dangerous, on occasion.

Sir George Germain was one of the rarer sorts: boring *and* dangerous.

He walked up and down the streets of the town for some time, in hopes of exhausting himself before going back to his small, stuffy room. The sky was low and sullen, with heat lightning flickering among the clouds, and the atmosphere was damp as a bath sponge. He should have been in Albany by now—no less humid and bug-ridden, but somewhat cooler, and near the sweet dark forests of the Adirondacks.

Still, he didn't regret his hasty journey to Wilmington. Willie was sorted; that was the important thing. And Willie's sister, Brianna—he stopped dead for a moment, eyes closed, reliving the moment of transcendence and heartbreak he had experienced that afternoon, seeing the two of them together for what would be their only meeting, ever. He'd scarcely been able to breathe, his eyes fixed on the two tall figures, those handsome, bold faces, so alike—and both so like the man who had stood beside him, unmoving, but by contrast with Grey, taking in great tearing gulps of air, as though he feared he might never breathe again.

Grey rubbed idly at his left ring finger, not yet accustomed to finding it bare. He and Jamie Fraser had done the best they could to safeguard those they loved, and despite his melancholy, he was comforted at the thought that they were united in that kinship of responsibility.

Would he ever meet Brianna Fraser MacKenzie again? he wondered. She had said not—and seemed as saddened by that fact as he was.

"God bless you, child," he murmured, shaking his head as he turned back toward the harbor. He would miss her very much—but as with Willie, his relief that she would soon be out of Wilmington and out of danger overwhelmed his personal sense of loss.

He glanced involuntarily at the water as he came out onto the quay, and drew a deep sigh of relief at seeing the empty stake, aslant in the tide. He hadn't understood her reasons for doing what she'd done, but he'd known her father—and her brother, for that matter—far too long to mistake the stubborn conviction he'd seen in those catlike blue eyes. So he'd got her the small boat she'd asked for, and stood on the quay with his heart in his throat, ready to create a distraction if needed, as her husband had rowed her out toward the bound pirate.

He'd seen men die in great numbers, usually unwillingly, occasionally with resignation. He'd never seen one go with such passionate gratitude in his eyes. Grey had no more than a passing acquaintance with Roger MacKenzie, but suspected him to be a remarkable man, having not only survived marriage to that fabulous and dangerous creature but actually having sired children upon her.

He shook his head and turned, heading back toward the

inn. He could safely wait another two weeks, he thought, before replying to Germain's letter—which he had deftly magicked out of the diplomatic pouch when he'd seen William's name upon it—at which time he could truthfully say that, alas, by the time the letter had been received, Lord Ellesmere was somewhere in the wilderness between North Carolina and New York, and thus could not be informed that he was recalled to England, though he (Grey) was positive that Ellesmere would greatly regret the loss of his opportunity to join Sir George's staff, when he learned of it—several months hence. Too bad.

He began to whistle "Lillibulero," and strode back to the inn in good spirits.

He paused in the taproom, and asked for a bottle of wine to be sent up—only to be informed by the barmaid that "the gentleman" had already taken a bottle upstairs with him.

"And two glasses," she added, dimpling at him. "So I don't s'pose he meant to drink it all himself."

Grey felt something like a centipede skitter up his spine.

"I beg your pardon," he said. "Did you say that there is a gentleman in my room?"

"Yes, sir," she assured him. "He said as he's an old friend of yours. . . . Now, he did tell me his name . . ." Her brow furrowed for an instant, then cleared. "Bow-shaw, he said, or summat of the kind. Frenchy kind of name," she clarified. "And a Frenchy kind of gentleman, too. Will you be wanting food at all, sir?"

"No, I thank you." He waved her off, and went up the stairs, thinking rapidly whether he had left anything in his room that he shouldn't have.

A Frenchman, named Bow-shaw . . . *Beauchamp.* The name flashed in his mind like the flicker of heat lightning. He stopped dead for an instant in the middle of the staircase, then resumed his climb, more slowly.

Surely not . . . but who else might it be? When he had ceased active service, some years before, he had begun diplomatic life as a member of England's Black Chamber, that shadowy organization of persons charged with the interception and decoding of official diplomatic mail—and much less official messages—that flowed between the governments of Europe. Every one of those governments possessed its own

Black Chamber, and it was not unusual for the inhabitants of one such chamber to be aware of their opposite numbers—never met, but known by their signatures, their initials, their unsigned marginal notes.

Beauchamp had been one of the most active French agents; Grey had run across his trail several times in the intervening years, even though his own days in the Black Chamber were well behind him. If he knew Beauchamp by name, it was entirely reasonable that the man knew him as well—but their invisible association had been years ago. They had never met in person, and for such a meeting to occur *here* . . . He touched the secret pocket in his coat, and was reassured by the muffled crackle of paper.

He hesitated at the top of the stair, but there was no point in furtiveness; clearly, he was expected. With a firm step, he walked down the hall and turned the white china knob of his door, the porcelain smooth and cool beneath his fingers.

A wave of heat engulfed him and he gasped for air, involuntarily. Just as well, as it prevented his uttering the blasphemy that had sprung to his lips.

The gentleman occupying the room's only chair was indeed "Frenchy"—his very well-cut suit set off by cascades of snowy lace at throat and cuff, his shoes buckled with a silver that matched the hair at his temples.

"Mr. Beauchamp," Grey said, and slowly closed the door behind him. His damp linen clung to him, and he could feel his pulse thumping in his own temples. "I fear you take me at something of a disadvantage."

Perseverance Wainwright smiled, very slightly.

"I'm glad to see you, John," he said.

GREY BIT HIS tongue to forestall anything injudicious—which description covered just about anything he might say, he thought, with the exception of "Good evening."

"Good evening," he said. He lifted an eyebrow in question. "*Monsieur* Beauchamp?"

"Oh, yes." Percy got his feet under him, making to rise, but Grey waved him back and turned to fetch a stool, hoping the seconds gained by the movement would allow him to regain his composure. Finding that they didn't, he took another moment to open the window, and stood for a couple of lungfuls of the thick, dank air, before turning back and taking his own seat.

"How did that happen?" he asked, affecting casualness. "Beauchamp, I mean. Or is it merely a *nom de guerre*?"

"Oh, no." Percy took up his lace-trimmed handkerchief and dabbed sweat delicately from his hairline—which was beginning to recede, Grey noted. "I married one of the sisters of the Baron Amandine. The family name is Beauchamp; I adopted it. The relationship provided a certain *entrée* to political circles, from which . . ." He shrugged charmingly and made a graceful gesture that encompassed his career in the Black Chamber—and doubtless elsewhere, Grey thought grimly.

"My congratulations on your marriage," Grey said, not bothering to keep the irony out of his voice. "Which one are you sleeping with, the baron or his sister?"

Percy looked amused.

"Both, on occasion."

"Together?"

The smile widened. His teeth were still good, Grey saw, though somewhat stained by wine.

"Occasionally. Though Cecile—my wife—really prefers the attentions of her cousin Lucianne, and I myself prefer the attentions of the sub-gardener. Lovely man named Emile; he reminds me of you . . . in your younger years. Slender, blond, muscular, and brutal."

To his dismay, Grey found that he wanted to laugh.

"It sounds extremely French," he said dryly, instead. "I'm sure it suits you. What do you want?"

"More a matter of what *you* want, I think." Percy had not yet drunk any of the wine; he took up the bottle and poured carefully, red liquid purling dark against the glasses. "Or perhaps I should say—what England wants." He held out a glass to Grey, smiling. "For one can hardly separate your interests from those of your country, can one? In fact, I confess that you have always seemed to me to *be* England, John."

Grey wished to forbid him the use of his Christian name, but to do so would merely emphasize the memory of their intimacy—which was, of course, what Percy intended. He chose to ignore it, and took a sip of his wine, which was good. He wondered whether he was paying for it—and if so, how.

"What England wants," he repeated, skeptical. "And what is your impression of what England wants?"

Percy took a swallow of the wine and held it in his mouth, evidently savoring it, before finally swallowing.

"Hardly a secret, my dear, is it?"

Grey sighed, and stared pointedly at him.

"You've seen this 'Declaration of Independency' issued by the so-called Continental Congress?" Percy asked. He turned and, reaching into a leather bag he had slung over the back of the chair, withdrew a folded sheaf of papers, which he handed to Grey.

Grey had not in fact seen the document in question, though he'd certainly heard about it. It had been printed only two weeks previous, in Philadelphia, yet copies had spread like wind-borne weeds through the Colonies. Raising a brow at Percy, he unfolded the paper and skimmed it rapidly.

"The King is a tyrant?" he said, half-laughing at the outrageousness of some of the document's more extreme sentiments. He folded the sheets back together and tossed them on the table.

"And if I am England, I suppose you are the embodiment of France, for the purposes of this conversation?"

"I represent certain interests there," Percy replied blandly. "And in Canada."

That rang small alarm bells. Grey had fought in Canada with Wolfe, and was well aware that while the French had lost much of their North American holdings in that war, they remained ferociously entrenched in the northern regions, from the Ohio Valley to Quebec. Close enough to cause trouble now? He thought not—but wouldn't put anything past the French. Or Percy.

"England wants a quick end to this nonsense, plainly." A long, knob-jointed hand waved toward the paper. "The Continental army—so-called—is a flimsy association of men with no experience and conflicting notions. What if I were prepared to provide you with information that might be used to . . . separate one of Washington's chief officers from his allegiance?"

"What if you were?" Grey replied, making no effort to

conceal the skepticism in his voice. "How would this benefit France—or your own interests, which I take leave to think are possibly not entirely identical?"

"I see that time has not softened your natural cynicism, John. One of your less attractive traits—I don't know whether I ever mentioned that to you."

Grey widened his stare slightly, and Percy sighed.

"Land, then," he said. "The Northwest Territory. We want it back."

Grey uttered a short laugh.

"I daresay you do." The territory in question, a large tract northwest of the Ohio River Valley, had been ceded to Great Britain from France at the end of the French and Indian War. Britain had not occupied the territory, though, and had prevented the colonists' expansion into it, owing to armed resistance from the natives and the ongoing negotiation of treaties with them. The colonists weren't pleased about it, he understood. Grey had encountered some of said natives himself, and was inclined to think the British government's position both reasonable and honorable.

"French traders had extensive ties with the aboriginals in that area; you have none."

"The fur-trading merchants being some of the . . . interests . . . you represent?"

Percy smiled openly at that.

"Not the major interests. But some."

Grey didn't bother asking why Percy was approaching him—an ostensibly retired diplomat of no particular influence—in the matter. Percy knew the power of Grey's family and connections from the days of their personal association—and "Monsieur Beauchamp" knew a great deal more about his present personal connections from the nexus of information that fed the Black Chambers of Europe. Grey could not act in the matter, of course. But he was well placed to bring the offer quietly to the attention of those who could.

He felt as though every hair on his body was standing on end like an insect's antennae, alert for danger.

"We would require something more than the suggestion, of course," he said, very cool. "The name of the officer in question, for example."

"Not mine to share, at the moment. But once a negotiation in good faith is opened . . ."

Grey was already wondering to whom he should take this offer. *Not* Sir George Germain. Lord North's office? That could wait, though.

"And your personal interests?" he asked, with an edge. He knew Percy Wainwright well enough to know that there would be some aspect of the affair to Percy's personal benefit.

"Ah, that." Percy sipped at his wine, then lowered the glass and gazed limpidly at Grey across it. "Very simple, really. I am commissioned to find a man. Do you know a Scottish gentleman named James Fraser?"

Grey felt the stem of his glass crack. He went on holding it, though, and sipped the wine carefully, thanking God, firstly, that he had never told Percy Jamie Fraser's name and, secondly, that Fraser had left Wilmington that afternoon.

"No," he said calmly. "What do you want with this Mr. Fraser?"

Percy shrugged, and smiled.

"Only a question or two."

Grey could feel blood seeping from his lacerated palm. Holding the cracked glass carefully together, he drank the rest of his wine. Percy was quiet, drinking with him.

"My condolences upon the loss of your wife," Percy said quietly. "I know that she—"

"You know nothing," Grey said roughly. He leaned over and set the broken glass on the table; the bowl rolled crazily, the lees of wine washing the glass. "Not one thing. About my wife, *or* about me."

Percy lifted his shoulders in the faintest of Gallic shrugs. *As you like,* it said. And yet his eyes—they were still beautiful, damn him, dark and soft—rested on Grey with what seemed a genuine sympathy.

Grey sighed. Doubtless it *was* genuine. Percy could not be trusted—not ever—but what he'd done had been done from weakness, not from malice, or even lack of feeling.

"What do you want?" he repeated.

"Your son—" Percy began, and Grey turned suddenly on him. He gripped Percy's shoulder, hard enough that the man gave a little gasp and stiffened. Grey leaned down, looking into Wainwright's—sorry, *Beauchamp's*—face, so close that he felt the warmth of the man's breath on his cheek and smelled his cologne. He was getting blood on Wainwright's coat.

"The last time I saw you," Grey said, very quietly, "I came within an inch of putting a bullet through your head. Don't give me cause to regret my restraint."

He let go and stood up.

"Stay away from my son—stay away from me. And if you will take a well-meant bit of advice—go back to France. Quickly."

Turning on his heel, he went out, shutting the door firmly behind him. He was halfway down the street before he realized that he had left Percy in his own room.

"The devil with it," he muttered, and stamped off to beg a billet for the night from Sergeant Cutter. In the morning, he would make sure that the Fraser family and William were all safely out of Wilmington.

2

AND SOMETIMES THEY AREN'T

Lallybroch
Inverness-shire, Scotland
September 1980

"WE ARE ALIVE," Brianna MacKenzie repeated, her voice tremulous. She looked up at Roger, the paper pressed to her chest with both hands. Her face streamed with tears, but a glorious light glowed in her blue eyes. "Alive!"

"Let me see." His heart was hammering so hard in his chest that he could barely hear his own words. He reached out a hand, and reluctantly she surrendered the paper to him, coming at once to press herself against him, clinging to his arm as he read, unable to take her eyes off the bit of ancient paper.

It was pleasantly rough under his fingers, handmade paper with the ghosts of leaves and flowers pressed into its fibers. Yellowed with age, but still tough and surprisingly flexible. Bree had made it herself—more than two hundred years before.

Roger became aware that his hands were trembling, the paper shaking so that the sprawling, difficult hand was hard to read, faded as the ink was.

December 31, 1776

My dear daughter,

As you will see if ever you receive this, we are alive . . .

His own eyes blurred, and he wiped the back of his hand across them, even as he told himself that it didn't matter, for they were surely dead now, Jamie Fraser and his wife, Claire—but he felt such joy at those words on the page that it was as though the two of them stood smiling before him.

It *was* the two of them, too, he discovered. While the letter began in Jamie's hand—and voice—the second page took up in Claire's crisply slanted writing.

Your father's hand won't stand much more. And it's a bloody long story. He's been chopping wood all day, and can barely uncurl his fingers—but he insisted on telling you himself that we haven't—yet—been burnt to ashes. Not but what we may be at any moment; there are fourteen people crammed into the old cabin, and I'm writing this more or less sitting in the hearth, with old Grannie MacLeod wheezing away on her pallet by my feet so that if she suddenly begins to die, I can pour more whisky down her throat.

"My God, I can *hear* her," he said, amazed.

"So can I." Tears were still coursing down Bree's face, but it was a sun-shower; she wiped at them, laughing and sniffing. "Read more. Why are they in our cabin? What's happened to the Big House?"

Roger ran his finger down the page to find his place and resumed reading.

"Oh, Jesus!" he said.

You recall that idiot, Donner?

Gooseflesh ran up his arms at the name. A time-traveler, Donner. And one of the most feckless individuals he'd ever met or heard of—but nonetheless dangerous for that.

Well, he surpassed himself by getting together a gang of thugs from Brownsville to come and steal the treasure in gems he'd convinced them we had. Only we hadn't, of course.

They hadn't—because he, Brianna, Jemmy, and Amanda had taken the small hoard of remaining gemstones to safeguard their flight through the stones.

They held us hostage and rubbished the house, damn them—breaking, amongst other things, the carboy of ether in my surgery. The fumes nearly gassed all of us on the spot . . .

He read rapidly through the rest of the letter, Brianna peering over his shoulder and making small squeaks of alarm and dismay. Finished, he laid the pages down and turned to her, his insides quivering.

"So *you* did it," he said, aware that he shouldn't say it, but unable not to, unable not to snort with laughter. "You and your bloody matches—*you* burned the house down!"

Her face was a study, features shifting between horror, indignation—and, yes, a hysterical hilarity that matched his own.

"Oh, it was not! It was Mama's ether. Any kind of spark could have set off the explosion—"

"But it wasn't any kind of spark," Roger pointed out. "Your cousin Ian lit one of your matches."

"Well, so it was Ian's fault, then!"

"No, it was you and your mother. Scientific women," Roger said, shaking his head. "The eighteenth century is lucky to have survived you."

She huffed a little.

"Well, the whole thing would never have happened if it weren't for that bozo Donner!"

"True," Roger conceded. "But he was a troublemaker from the future, too, wasn't he? Though admittedly neither a woman nor very scientific."

"Hmph." She took the letter, handling it gently, but unable to forbear rubbing the pages between her fingers. "Well, *he* didn't survive the eighteenth century, did he?" Her eyes were downcast, their lids still reddened.

"You aren't feeling *sorry* for him, are you?" Roger demanded, incredulous.

She shook her head, but her fingers still moved lightly over the thick, soft page.

"Not . . . *him,* so much. It's just—the idea of anybody dying like that. Alone, I mean. So far from home."

No, it wasn't Donner she was thinking of. He put an arm round her and laid his head against her own. She smelled of Prell shampoo and fresh cabbages; she'd been in the kailyard. The words on the page faded and strengthened with the dip of the pen that had written them, but nonetheless were sharp and clear—a surgeon's writing.

"She isn't alone," he whispered, and putting out a finger, traced the postscript, again in Jamie's sprawling hand. "Neither of them is. And whether they've a roof above their heads or not—both of them are home."

I PUT BY THE LETTER. Time enough to finish it later, I thought. I'd been working on it as time allowed over the last few days; not as though there was any rush to catch the outgoing mail, after all. I smiled a little at that, and folded the sheets carefully, putting them in my new workbag for safekeeping. I wiped the quill and put it aside, then rubbed my aching fingers, savoring for a little longer the sweet sense of connection the writing gave me. I could write much more easily than Jamie could, but flesh and blood had its limits, and it had been a very long day.

I looked over at the pallet on the far side of the fire, as I had been doing every few minutes, but she was still quiet. I could hear her breath, a wheezing gurgle that came at intervals so long that I could swear she had died between each one. She hadn't, though, and from my estimation wouldn't for a while. I was hoping that she would, before my limited supply of laudanum gave out.

I didn't know how old she was; she looked a hundred or so, but might be younger than I. Her two grandsons, boys in their teens, had brought her in two days before. They had been traveling down from the mountains, meaning to take their grandmother to relatives in Cross Creek before heading to Wilmington to join the militia there, but the grandmother had "been took bad," as they put it, and someone had told them there was a conjure-woman on the Ridge nearby. So they had brought her to me.

Grannie MacLeod—I had no other name for her; the boys had not thought to tell me before departing, and she was in no condition to do so herself—almost certainly was in the terminal stages of a cancer of some kind. Her flesh had wasted, her face pinched with pain even while unconscious, and I could see it in the grayness of her skin.

The fire was burning low; I should stir it, and add another stick of pine. Jamie's head was resting against my knee, though. Could I reach the woodpile without disturbing him? I put a light hand on his shoulder for balance and stretched, just getting my fingers on the end of a small log. I wiggled this gently free, teeth set in my lower lip, and managed by leaning to poke it into the hearth, breaking up the drifts of red-black embers and raising clouds of sparks.

Jamie stirred under my hand and murmured something unintelligible, but when I thrust the log into the freshened fire and sat back in my chair, he sighed, resettled himself, and fell back into sleep.

I glanced at the door, listening, but heard nothing save the rustle of trees in the wind. Of course, I thought, I *would* hear nothing, given that it was Young Ian I was waiting for.

He and Jamie had been taking it in turns to watch, hiding in the trees above the burnt ruins of the Big House. Ian had been out for more than two hours; it was nearly time for him to come in for food and a turn at the fire.

"Someone's been trying to kill the white sow," he'd announced at breakfast three days ago, looking bemused.

"What?" I handed him a bowl of porridge, garnished with a lump of melting butter and a drizzle of honey—luckily my kegs of honey and boxes of honeycomb had been in the springhouse when the fire happened. "Are you sure?"

He nodded, taking the bowl and inhaling its steam in beatific fashion.

"Aye, she's got a slash in her flank. Not deep, and it's healing, Auntie," he added, with a nod in my direction, evidently feeling that I would regard the sow's medical well-being with the same interest as that of any other resident of the Ridge.

"Oh? Good," I said—though there was precious little I could have done if she weren't healing. I could—and did—doctor horses, cows, goats, stoats, and even the occasional non-laying chicken, but that particular pig was on her own.

Amy Higgins crossed herself at mention of the sow.

"Likely 'twas a bear," she said. "Nothing else would dare. Aidan, mind what Mr. Ian says, here! Dinna be wandering far from the place, and mind your brother outside."

"Bears sleep in winter, Mam," Aidan said absently. His attention was fixed on a new top that Bobby, his new stepfather, had carved for him, and which he hadn't yet got to spin properly. Giving it a cross-eyed glare, he set it gingerly on the table, held the string for a breathless moment, and yanked. The top shot across the table, ricocheted off the honey jar with a sharp *crack!,* and headed for the milk at a high rate of speed.

Ian reached out and snatched the top in the nick of time. Chewing toast, he motioned to Aidan for the string, rewound it, and with a practiced flick of the wrist, sent the top whizzing straight down the center of the table. Aidan watched it, open-mouthed, then dived under the table as the top fell off the end.

"No, it wasna an animal," Ian said, finally succeeding in swallowing. "It was a clean slash. Someone went for her wi' a knife or a sword."

Jamie looked up from the burnt piece of toast he had been examining.

"Did ye find his body?"

Ian grinned briefly, but shook his head.

"Nay, if she killed him, she ate him—and I didna find any leavings."

"Pigs are messy eaters," Jamie observed. He essayed a cautious bite of the burnt toast, grimaced, and ate it anyway.

"An Indian, d'ye think?" Bobby asked. Little Orrie was struggling to get down from Bobby's lap; his new stepfather obligingly set him down in his favorite spot under the table.

Jamie and Ian exchanged glances, and I felt a slight stirring of the hair at the back of my neck.

"No," Ian answered. "The Cherokee near here all ken her weel, and wouldna touch her with a ten-foot pole. They think she's a demon, aye?"

"And traveling Indians from the north would have arrows or tomahawks," Jamie finished.

"Ye're sure it wasna a panther?" Amy asked, dubious. "They hunt in the winter, no?"

"They do," Jamie assured her. "I saw pug-marks up by the Green Spring yesterday. D'ye hear me there?" he said, bending to speak to the boys under the table. "Go canny, aye?

"But no," he added, straightening up. "Ian kens the difference between claw marks and a knife slash, I think." He gave Ian a grin. Ian politely refrained from rolling his eyes, and merely nodded, eyes fixed dubiously on the toast basket.

No one suggested that any resident of the Ridge or from Brownsville might have been hunting the white sow. The local Presbyterians would not have seen eye-to-eye with the Cherokee on any other spiritual matter you might name, but they were in decided agreement on the sow's demonic character.

Personally, I wasn't sure they weren't right. The thing had survived even the burning of the Big House unscathed, emerging from her den beneath its foundations amid a shower of burnt wood, followed by her latest litter of half-grown piglets.

"Moby Dick!" I now said aloud, inspired.

Rollo raised his head with a startled "Wuff?," gave me a yellow-eyed look and laid it down again, sighing.

"Dick who?" said Jamie, drowsy. He sat up, stretching and groaning, then rubbed a hand over his face and blinked at me.

"I just thought what it is that sow reminds me of," I explained. "Long story. About a whale. I'll tell you tomorrow."

"If I live that long," he said, with a yawn that nearly dislocated his jaw. "Where's the whisky—or d'ye need it for yon poor woman?" He nodded at Grannie MacLeod's blanket-wrapped form.

"Not yet. Here." I bent and rummaged in the basket beneath my chair, coming up with a corked bottle.

He pulled the cork and drank, the color gradually coming back to his face. Between spending his days hunting or chopping wood and half the nights lurking in a freezing forest, even Jamie's great vitality was showing signs of flagging.

"How long will you keep this up?" I asked, low-voiced so as not to rouse the Higginses—Bobby, Amy, the two little boys, and Amy's two sisters-in-law from her first marriage, who had come for the wedding held a few days before, accompanied by a total of five children under the age of ten—all asleep in the small bedroom. The departure of the MacLeod boys had eased the congestion in the cabin slightly, but with Jamie, me, Ian, Ian's dog, Rollo, and the old woman sleeping on the floor of the main room, and such possessions as we had managed to salvage from the fire stacked round the walls, I sometimes felt a distinct surge of claustrophobia. Little wonder if Jamie and Ian were patrolling the woods, as much to get a breath of air as from a conviction that there was something out there.

"No much longer," he assured me, shuddering slightly as a large swallow of whisky went down. "If we dinna see anything tonight, we'll—" He broke off, his head turning abruptly toward the door.

I hadn't heard anything, but saw the latch move, and an instant later, a freezing gust of air rolled into the room, poking frigid fingers under my skirts and stirring up a shower of sparks from the fire.

I hastily seized a rag and beat these out before they could set Grannie MacLeod's hair or bedding on fire. By the time I had the fire back under control, Jamie was putting pistol, shot bag, and powder horn on his belt, talking low-voiced with Ian by the door. Ian himself was red-cheeked with cold and clearly excited about something. Rollo was up, too, nosing at Ian's legs, tail wagging in anticipation of an icy adventure.

"Best ye stay, *a choin,*" Ian told him, rubbing his ears with cold fingers. *"Sheas."*

Rollo made a disgruntled noise in his throat and tried to push past Ian, but was deftly blocked by a leg. Jamie turned, shrugging on his coat, bent, and kissed me hastily.

"Bolt the door, *a nighean,*" he whispered. "Dinna open to anyone save me or Ian."

"What—" I began, but they were gone.

THE NIGHT WAS COLD and pure. Jamie breathed deep and shivered, letting the cold enter him, strip away the warmth of wife, the smoke and smell of his hearth. Ice crystals shimmered in his lungs, sharp in his blood. He turned his head to and fro like a wolf scenting, breathing the night. There was little wind, but the air moved from the east, bringing the bitter smell of ashes from the ruins of the Big House . . . and a faint tang he thought was blood.

He looked to his nephew, question in the cock of his head, and saw Ian nod, dark against the lavender glow of the sky.

"There's a dead pig, just beyond Auntie's garden," the lad said, low-voiced.

"Oh, aye? Not the white sow, ye don't mean?" His heart misgave him for an instant at the thought, and he wondered whether he'd mourn the thing or dance on its bones. But no. Ian shook his head, the movement felt rather than seen.

"Nay, not that wily beast. A young one, maybe last year's farrowing. Someone's butchered it, but taken nay more than a collop or two from the haunch. And a good bit of what they *did* take, they scattered in chunks down the trail."

Jamie glanced round, surprised.

"What?"

Ian shrugged.

"Aye. One more thing, Uncle. 'Twas killed and butchered with an ax."

The ice crystals in his blood solidified with a suddenness that nearly stopped his heart.

"Jesus," he said, but it was not so much shock as it was unwilling admission of something he had known for a long time. "It's him, then."

"Aye." Both of them had known it, though neither one had been willing to speak of it. Without consultation, they moved away from the cabin, into the trees.

"Aye, well." Jamie took a long, deep breath and sighed, the mist of it white in the darkness. He'd hoped the man had taken his gold and his wife and left the Ridge—but it had never been more than a hope. Arch Bug was a Grant by blood, and clan Grant were a vengeful lot.

The Frasers of Glenhelm had caught Arch Bug on their lands some fifty years before, and given him the choice: lose an eye or the first two fingers of his right hand. The man had come to terms with his crippled hand, turning from the bow he could no longer draw to the use of an ax, which he wielded and threw with a skill equal to any Mohawk's, despite his age.

What he had not come to terms with was the loss of the Stuart cause and the loss of the Jacobite gold, sent too late from France, rescued—or stolen, depending on your view of things—by Hector Cameron, who had brought one third of it to North Carolina, this share then stolen—or retrieved—from Cameron's widow in turn by Arch Bug.

Nor had Arch Bug come to terms with Jamie Fraser.

"Is it threat, d'ye think?" Ian asked. They had moved away from the cabin, but kept to the trees, circling the large clearing where the Big House had been. The chimney and half a wall still stood, charred and bleak against the dirty snow.

"I canna think so. If it was threat he meant, why wait until now?" Still, he gave silent thanks that his daughter and her weans were safely gone. There were worse threats than a dead pig, and he thought Arch Bug would not hesitate to make them.

"Perhaps he left," Ian suggested. "To see his wife settled, and he's only now come back."

It was a reasonable thought—if there was one thing in the world Arch Bug loved, it was his wife, Murdina, his helpmate of more than fifty years.

"Perhaps," Jamie said. *And yet . . .* And yet he'd felt eyes on his back more than once in the weeks since the Bugs had left. Felt silence in the forest that was not the silence of the trees and rocks.

He didn't ask whether Ian had looked for the ax-wielder's track; if one could be found, Ian would have found it. But it hadn't snowed in more than a week, and what was left on the ground was patchy and trodden by the feet of innumerable people. He looked up at the sky; snow again, and soon.

He made his way up a small outcrop, careful among the ice; the snow was melting in the day, but the water froze again at night, hanging from the cabin's eaves and from every branch in glittering icicles that filled the forest with the light of blue dawn, then dripped gold and diamonds in the rising sun. Now they were colorless, tinkling like glass as his sleeve brushed the twigs of an ice-covered bush. He stopped, crouching at the top of the outcrop, looking down across the clearing.

All right. The certainty that Arch Bug was here had set off a chain of half-conscious deductions, the conclusion of which now floated to the top of his mind.

"He'd come again for one of two reasons," he said to Ian. "To do me harm—or to get the gold. All of it."

He'd given Bug a chunk of gold when he'd sent the man and his wife away, upon the discovery of the Bugs' treachery. Half a French ingot, it would have allowed an elderly couple to live the rest of their lives in modest comfort. But Arch Bug was not a modest man. He'd once been tacksman to the Grant of Grant, and while he'd hidden his pride for a time, it was not the nature of pride to stay buried.

Ian glanced at him, interested.

"All of it," he repeated. "So ye think he hid it here—but somewhere he couldna get it easily when ye made him go."

Jamie lifted one shoulder, watching the clearing. With the house now gone, he could see the steep trail that led up behind it, toward the place where his wife's garden had once stood, safe behind its deer-proof palisades. Some of the palisades still stood, black against the patchy snow. He would make her a new garden one day, God willing.

"If his purpose was only harm, he's had the chance." He could see the butchered pig from here, a dark shape on the path, shadowed by a wide pool of blood.

He pushed away a sudden thought of Malva Christie, and forced himself back to his reasoning.

"Aye, he's hidden it here," he repeated, more confident

now. "If he had it all, he'd be long gone. He's been waiting, trying for a way to get to it. But he hasna been able to do it secretly—so now he's trying something else."

"Aye, but what? That—" Ian nodded toward the amorphous shape on the path. "I thought it might be a snare or a trap of some kind, but it's not. I looked."

"A lure, maybe?" The smell of blood was evident even to him; it would be a plain call to any predator. Even as he thought this, his eye caught movement near the pig, and he put a hand on Ian's arm.

A tentative flicker of movement, then a small, sinuous shape darted in, disappearing behind the pig's body.

"Fox," both men said together, then laughed, quietly.

"There's that panther in the wood above the Green Spring," Ian said dubiously. "I saw the tracks yesterday. Can he mean to draw it wi' the pig, in hopes that we should rush out to deal with it and he could reach the gold whilst we were occupied?"

Jamie frowned at that, and glanced toward the cabin. True, a panther might draw the men out—but not the women and children. And where might he have put the gold in such a densely inhabited space? His eye fell on the long, humped shape of Brianna's kiln, lying some way from the cabin, unused since her departure, and a spurt of excitement drew him upright. That would be—but no; Arch had stolen the gold from Jocasta Cameron one bar at a time, conveying it secretly to the Ridge, and had begun his theft long before Brianna had gone. But maybe . . .

Ian stiffened suddenly, and Jamie turned his head sharp to see what the matter was. He couldn't see anything, but then caught the sound that Ian had heard. A deep, piggish grunt, a rustle, a crack. Then there was a visible stirring among the blackened timbers of the ruined house, and a great light dawned.

"Jesus!" he said, and gripped Ian's arm so tightly that his nephew yelped, startled. "It's under the Big House!"

The white sow emerged from her den beneath the ruins, a massive cream-colored blotch upon the night, and stood swaying her head to and fro, scenting the air. Then she began to move, a ponderous menace surging purposefully up the hill.

Jamie wanted to laugh at the sheer beauty of it.

Arch Bug had cannily hidden his gold beneath the foundations of the Big House, choosing his times when the sow was out about her business. No one would have dreamed of invading the sow's domain; she was the perfect guardian—and doubtless he'd meant to retrieve the gold in the same way when he was ready to go: carefully, one ingot at a time.

But then the house had burned, the timbers collapsing into the foundation, rendering the gold unreachable without a great deal of work and trouble—which would certainly draw attention. It was only now, when the men had cleared away most of the rubble—and spread soot and charcoal all over the clearing in the process—that anyone might be able to reach something hidden under it without attracting notice.

But it was winter, and the white sow, while not hibernating like a bear, kept strictly to her cozy den—save when there was something to eat.

Ian made a small exclamation of disgust, hearing slobbering and crunching from the path.

"Pigs havena got much delicacy of feeling," Jamie murmured. "If it's dead, they'll eat it."

"Aye, but it's likely her own offspring!"

"She eats her young alive now and then; I doubt she'd boggle at eating them dead."

"Hst!"

He hushed at once, eyes fixed on the blackened smear that had once been the finest house in the county. Sure enough, a dark figure emerged from behind the springhouse, sidling cautiously on the slippery path. The pig, busy with her grisly feast, ignored the man, who seemed to be clad in a dark cloak and carrying something like a sack.

I DIDN'T BOLT THE door at once, but stepped out to breathe fresh air for a moment, shutting Rollo in behind me. Within moments, Jamie and Ian had vanished into the trees. I glanced uneasily round the clearing, looked across to the black mass of the forest, but could see nothing amiss. Nothing moved, and the night was soundless; I wondered what Ian might have found. Unfamiliar tracks, perhaps? That would account for his sense of urgency; it was clearly about to snow.

No moon was visible, but the sky was a deep pinkish gray, and the ground, though trodden and patchy, was still covered with old snow. The result was a strange, milky glow in which objects seemed to float as though painted on glass, dimensionless and dim. The burnt remains of the Big House stood at the far side of the clearing, no more at this distance than a smudge, as though a giant, sooty thumb had pressed down there. I could feel the heaviness of impending snow in the air, hear it in the muffled sough of the pines.

The MacLeod boys had come over the mountain with their grandmother; they'd said it was very hard going through the high passes. Another big storm would likely seal us in until March or even April.

Thus reminded of my patient, I took one last look round the clearing and set my hand on the latch. Rollo was whining, scratching at the door, and I pushed a knee unceremoniously into his face as I opened it.

"Stay, dog," I said. "Don't worry, they'll be back soon." He made a high, anxious noise in his throat, and cast to and fro, nudging at my legs, seeking to get out.

"No," I said, pushing him away in order to bolt the door. The bolt dropped into place with a reassuring *thunk,* and I turned toward the fire, rubbing my hands. Rollo put back his head and gave a low, mournful howl that raised the hair on the back of my neck.

"What?" I said, alarmed. "Hush!" The noise had made one of the small children in the bedroom wake and cry; I heard rustling bedclothes and sleepy maternal murmurs, and I knelt quickly and grabbed Rollo's muzzle before he could howl again.

"Shhhhh," I said, and looked to see whether the sound had disturbed Grannie MacLeod. She lay still, waxen-faced, her eyes closed. I waited, automatically counting the seconds before the next shallow rise of her chest.

. . . *six* . . . *seven* . . . "Oh, bloody hell," I said, realizing.

Hastily crossing myself, I shuffled over to her on my knees, but closer inspection told me nothing I hadn't seen already. Self-effacing to the last, she had seized my moment of distraction to die inconspicuously.

Rollo was shifting to and fro, no longer howling, but uneasy. I laid a hand gently on the sunken chest. Not seeking diagnosis or offering aid, not any longer. Just . . . a necessary acknowledgment of the passing of a woman whose first name I didn't know.

"Well . . . God rest your soul, poor thing," I said softly, and sat back on my heels, trying to think what to do next.

Proper Highland protocol held that the door must be opened at once after a death, to allow the soul to leave. I rubbed a knuckle dubiously over my lips; might the soul have made a quick dash when I opened the door to come in? Probably not.

One would think that in a climate as inhospitable as Scotland's, there would be a bit of climatological leeway in such matters, but I knew that wasn't the case. Rain, snow, sleet, wind—Highlanders always *did* open the door and leave it open for hours, both eager to free the departing soul and anxious lest the spirit, impeded in its exit, might turn and take up permanent residence as a ghost. Most crofts were too small to make that a tolerable prospect.

Little Orrie was awake now; I could hear him singing happily to himself, a song consisting of his stepfather's name.

"Baaaaah-by, baaah-by, BAAAH-by . . ."

I heard a low, sleepy chuckle, and Bobby's murmur in reply.

"There's my wee man. You need the pot, *acooshla*?" The Gaelic endearment—*a chuisle,* "my heart's blood"—made me smile, both at the word and at the oddness of it in Bobby's Dorset accent. Rollo made an uneasy noise in his throat, though, bringing back to me the need for some action.

If the Higginses and in-laws rose in a few hours to discover a corpse on the floor, they'd all be disturbed, their sense of rightness affronted—and agitated at thought of a dead stranger possibly clinging to their hearth. A very bad omen for the new marriage and the new year. At the same time, her presence was undeniably agitating Rollo, and the prospect of his rousing them all in the next few moments was agitating me.

"Right," I said under my breath. "Come on, dog." There were, as always, bits of harness needing mending on a peg near the door. I disentangled a sound length of rein and fashioned a makeshift come-along with which I lassoed Rollo. He was more than happy to go outside with me, lunging ahead as I opened the door, though somewhat less delighted to be dragged to the lean-to pantry, where I wrapped the makeshift leash hastily round a shelf upright, before returning to the cabin for Grannie MacLeod's body.

I looked about carefully before venturing out again, Jamie's admonitions in mind, but the night was as still as a church; even the trees had fallen silent.

The poor woman couldn't weigh more than seventy pounds, I thought; her collarbones poked through her skin, and her fingers were frail as dried twigs. Still, seventy pounds of literal dead weight was a bit more than I could manage to lift, and I was obliged to unfold the blanket wrapped round her and use it as an impromptu sledge, on which I dragged her outside, murmuring mingled prayers and apologies under my breath.

Despite the cold, I was panting and damp with sweat by the time I'd got her into the pantry.

"Well, at least your soul's had plenty of time to make a getaway," I muttered, kneeling to check the body before resettling it in its hasty shroud. "And I shouldn't imagine you want to hang about haunting a pantry, in any case."

Her eyelids were not quite closed, a sliver of white showing, as though she had tried to open them for one last glimpse of the world—or perhaps in search of a familiar face.

"Benedicite," I whispered, and gently shut her eyes, wondering as I did so whether one day some stranger might do the same for me. The odds of it were good. Unless . . .

Jamie had declared his intention to return to Scotland, fetch his printing press, and then come back to fight. *But what,* said a small, cowardly voice inside me, *if we didn't come back?* What if we went to Lallybroch and stayed there?

Even as I thought of that prospect—with its rosy visions of being enfolded by family, able to live in peace, to grow slowly old without the constant fear of disruption, starvation, and violence—I knew it wouldn't work.

I didn't know whether Thomas Wolfe had been right about not being able to go home again—well, I *wouldn't* know about that, I thought, a little bitterly; I hadn't had one to go back to—but I did know Jamie. Idealism quite aside—and he did have some, though of a very pragmatic sort—the simple fact was that he was a proper man, and thus required to have proper work. Not just labor; not just making a living. Work. I understood the difference.

And while I was sure that Jamie's family would receive him with joy—the nature of my own reception was in somewhat more doubt, but I supposed they wouldn't actually call the priest and try to have me exorcised—the fact was that Jamie was no longer laird of Lallybroch, and never would be.

" '. . . and his place shall know him no more,' " I murmured, wiping the old woman's intimate parts—surprisingly unwithered; perhaps she had been younger than I thought—with a damp cloth. She hadn't eaten anything in days; even the relaxation of death hadn't had much effect—but anyone deserved to go clean to their grave.

I paused. That was a thought. Would we be able to bury her? Or might she just rest peacefully under the huckleberry jam and the sacks of dried beans until spring?

I tidied her clothes, breathing out, openmouthed, trying to judge the temperature from the steam of my breath. This would be only the second major snowfall of the winter, and we had not yet had a really hard freeze; that usually happened in mid to late January. If the ground had not yet frozen, we could probably bury her—provided the men were willing to shovel away the snow.

Rollo had lain down, resigned, while I went about my business, but at this point, his head jerked upright, ears pointed.

"What?" I said, startled, and turned round on my knees to look out the open pantry door. "What's happening?"

"SHALL WE TAKE HIM now?" Ian murmured. He had his bow over one shoulder; he let his arm fall, and the bow dropped silently into his hand, ready.

"No. Let him find it first." Jamie spoke slowly, trying to make up his mind what was right to do with the man, so suddenly reappeared before him.

Not kill him; he and his wife had made a good deal of trouble with their treachery, aye, but hadn't intended harm to his family—not to start, at least. Was Arch Bug even truly a thief, by his own lights? Surely Jamie's aunt Jocasta had no greater—if no lesser—claim to the gold than he did.

He sighed and put a hand to his belt, where his dirk and pistol hung. Still, he couldn't allow Bug to make off with the gold, nor could he merely drive him off and leave him free to make more trouble. As to what in God's name to do with him once caught . . . it would be like having a snake in a sack. But naught to do now save catch him, and worry later what to do with the sack. Perhaps some bargain might be struck . . .

The figure had reached the black smear of the foundations and was climbing awkwardly among the stones and the charred timbers that remained, the dark cloak lifting and billowing as the air shifted.

Snow began to fall, sudden and silent, big, lazy flakes that seemed not so much to fall from the sky as simply to appear, whirling out of the air. They brushed his face and stuck thick in his lashes; he wiped them away, and motioned to Ian.

"Go behind," he whispered. "If he runs, send a shaft past his nose to stop him. And keep well back, aye?"

"*You* keep well back, Uncle," Ian whispered back. "If ye get within decent pistol shot o' the man, he can brain ye with his ax. And I'm no going to explain *that* to Auntie Claire."

Jamie snorted briefly and nudged Ian away. He loaded and primed his pistol, then walked firmly out through the falling snow toward the ruin of his house.

He'd seen Arch fell a turkey with his ax at twenty feet. And it was true that most pistols weren't accurate at much more than that. But he didn't mean to shoot the man, after all. He drew the pistol, holding it clear in his hand.

"Arch!" he called. The figure had its back to him, bent over as it rooted about in the ashes. At his call, it seemed to stiffen, still crouched.

"Arch Bug!" he shouted. "Come out o' there, man. I'd speak with ye!"

In answer, the figure drew itself up abruptly, turned, and a spurt of flame lit the falling snow. In the same instant, the flame seared his thigh, and he staggered.

He was conscious mostly of surprise; he'd never known Arch Bug to use a pistol, and was impressed that he could aim so well with his left—

He'd gone to one knee in the snow, but even as he brought

his own weapon up to bear, he realized two things: the black figure was aiming a second pistol at him—but not with the left hand. Which meant—

"Jesus! Ian!" But Ian had seen him fall, and seen the second pistol, too. Jamie didn't hear the arrow's flight, above the rush of wind and snow; it appeared as though by magic, stuck in the figure's back. The figure went straight and stiff, then fell in a heap. Almost before it hit the ground, he was running, hobbling, his right leg buckling under him with every step.

"God, no, God, no," he was saying, and it sounded like someone else's voice.

A voice came through snow and night, calling out in desperation. Then Rollo was bounding past him, a blur—who had let him out?—and a rifle cracked from the trees. Ian bellowed, somewhere near, calling the dog, but Jamie had no time to look, was scrambling heedless over the blackened stones, slipping on the skim of fresh snow, stumbling, his leg was cold and hot at once, but no matter, oh, *God,* please, no . . .

He reached the black figure and flung himself on his knees beside it, grappling. He knew at once; he'd known from the moment he realized the pistol had been held in her right hand. Arch, with his missing fingers, couldn't fire a pistol right-handed. But, oh, God, no . . .

He'd got her over, feeling the short, heavy body limp and unwieldy as a fresh-killed deer. Pushed back the hood of the cloak, and passed his hand, gentle, helpless, over the soft round face of Murdina Bug. She breathed against his hand—perhaps . . . but he felt the shaft of the arrow, too, against his hand. It had come through her neck, and her breath bubbled wet; his hand was wet, too, and warm.

"Arch?" she said hoarsely. "I want Arch." And died.

3

LIFE FOR LIFE

I TOOK JAMIE into the pantry. It was dark, and cold, particularly for a man with no breeches on, but I didn't want to risk any of the Higginses being wakened. God, not now. They'd all erupt from their sanctum like a flight of panicked quail—and I quailed myself at thought of having to deal with them before I had to. It would be sufficiently horrible to tell them what had happened by daylight; I couldn't face the prospect now.

For lack of any better alternative, Jamie and Ian had laid Mrs. Bug in the pantry alongside Grannie MacLeod, tucked under the lowest shelf, her cloak drawn up over her face. I could see her feet sticking out, with their cracked, worn boots and striped stockings. I had a sudden vision of the Wicked Witch of the West, and clapped a hand to my mouth before anything truly hysterical could escape.

Jamie turned his head toward me, but his gaze was inward, his face haggard, deep-lined in the glow of the candle he carried.

"Eh?" he said vaguely.

"Nothing," I said, my voice trembling. "Nothing at all. Sit—sit down." I put down the stool and my medical kit, took the candle and tin of hot water from him, and tried to think of absolutely nothing but the job before me. Not feet. Not, for God's sake, Arch Bug.

Jamie had a blanket wrapped round his shoulders, but his legs were necessarily bare, and I could feel the hairs bristling with gooseflesh as my hand brushed them. The bottom of his shirt was soaked with half-dried blood; it stuck to his leg, but he made no sound when I pulled it loose and nudged his legs apart.

He had been moving like a man in a bad dream, but the approach of a lighted candle to his balls roused him.

"Ye'll take care wi' that candle, Sassenach, aye?" he said, putting a protective hand over his genitals.

Seeing his point, I gave him the candle to hold, and with a brief admonition to beware of dripping hot wax, returned to my inspection.

The wound was oozing blood, but plainly minor, and I plunged a cloth into the hot water and began to work. His flesh was chilled, and the cold damped even the pungent odors of the pantry, but I could still smell him, his usual dry musk tainted with blood and frantic sweat.

It was a deep gouge that ran four inches through the flesh of his thigh, high up. Clean, though.

"A John Wayne special," I said, trying for a light, dry tone. Jamie's eyes, which had been fixed on the candle flame, changed focus and fixed on me.

"What?" he said hoarsely.

"Nothing serious," I said. "The ball just grazed you. You may walk a little oddly for a day or two, but the hero lives to fight another day." The ball had in fact gone between his legs, deeply creasing the inside of his thigh, near both to his testicles and his femoral artery. One inch to the right, and he'd be dead. One inch higher . . .

"Not a great help, Sassenach," he said, but the ghost of a smile touched his eyes.

"No," I agreed. "But some?"

"Some," he said, and briefly touched my face. His hand was very cold, and trembled; hot wax ran over the knuckles of his other hand, but he didn't seem to feel it. I took the candlestick gently from him and set it on the shelf.

I could feel the grief and self-reproach coming off him in waves, and fought to keep it at bay. I couldn't help him if I gave in to the enormity of the situation. I wasn't sure I could help him in any case, but I'd try.

"Oh, Jesus," he said, so softly I barely heard him. "Why did I not let him take it? What did it matter?" He struck a fist on his knee, soundless. "*God,* why did I not just let him take it!?"

"You didn't know who it was, or what they meant to do," I said, just as softly, putting a hand on his shoulder. "It was an accident." His muscles were bunched, hard with anguish. I felt it, too, a hard knot of protest and denial—*No, it* can't *be true, it can't have happened!*—in my throat, but there was work to be done. I'd deal with the inescapable later.

He put a hand over his face, shaking his head slowly to and fro, and neither spoke nor moved while I finished the cleaning and bandaging of the wound.

"Can ye do aught for Ian?" he said, when I'd finished. He took his hand away and looked up at me as I stood, his face drawn in exhausted misery, but calm again. "He's . . ." He swallowed, and glanced at the door. "He's badly, Sassenach."

I glanced at the whisky I'd brought: a quarter of a bottle. Jamie followed the direction of my gaze and shook his head.

"Not enough."

"You drink it, then." He shook his head, but I put the bottle in his hand and pressed his fingers round it.

"Orders," I said, soft but very firm. "Shock." He resisted, made to put the bottle back, and I tightened my hand on his.

"I *know,*" I said. "Jamie—I know. But you can't give in. Not now."

He looked up at me for a moment, but then he nodded, accepting it because he had to, the muscles of his arm relaxing. My own fingers were stiff, chilled from water and frigid air, but still warmer than his. I folded both hands round his free one, and held it, hard.

"There's a reason why the hero never dies, you know," I said, and attempted a smile, though my face felt stiff and false. "When the worst happens, someone still has to decide what to do. Go into the house now, and get warm." I glanced out at the night, lavender-skied and wild with swirling snow. "I'll . . . find Ian."

WHERE WOULD HE have gone? Not far, not in this weather. Given his state of mind when he and Jamie had come back with Mrs. Bug's body, he *might,* I thought, simply have walked off into the woods, not caring where he went or what happened to him—but he'd had the dog with him. No matter what he felt like, he wouldn't take Rollo off into a howling blizzard.

And a blizzard was what it was shaping up to be. I made my way slowly uphill toward the outbuildings, sheltering my lantern under a fold of my cloak. It came to me suddenly to wonder whether Arch Bug might have taken shelter in the springhouse or the smoke shed. And . . . oh, God—did he *know*? I stopped dead on the path for an instant, letting the thickly falling snow settle like a veil on my head and shoulders.

I had been so shocked by what had happened that I hadn't thought to wonder whether Arch Bug knew that his wife was dead. Jamie said that he had called out, called for Arch to come, as soon as he realized—but there had been no answer. Perhaps Arch had suspected a trick; perhaps he had simply fled, seeing Jamie and Ian and assuming that they would certainly not harm his wife. In which case . . .

"Oh, *bloody* hell," I said under my breath, appalled. But there was nothing I could do about that. I hoped there was something I could do about Ian. I rubbed a forearm over my face, blinked snow from my lashes, and went on, slowly, the light from the lantern swallowed in the vortex of whirling snow. Were I to find Arch . . . My fingers clenched on the lantern's handle. I'd have to tell him, bring him back to the cabin, let him see . . . Oh, dear. If I came back with Arch, could Jamie and Ian occupy him long enough for me to remove Mrs. Bug from the pantry and display her in more seemly fashion? I hadn't had time to remove the jutting arrow or lay out the body decently. I dug the fingernails of my free hand into the palm, trying to get a grip of myself.

"Jesus, don't let me find him," I said under my breath. "Please don't let me find him."

But springhouse, smoke shed, and corncrib were all—thank God—empty, and no one could have hidden in the chicken coop without the chickens making a fuss about it; they were silent, sleeping out the storm. The sight of the coop brought Mrs. Bug suddenly to mind, though—the vision of her scattering corn from her apron, crooning to the silly things. She'd named them all. I didn't bloody care whether we were eating Isobeail or Alasdair for supper, but just at the moment, the fact that no one now would ever be able to tell one from another, or rejoice in the fact that Elspeth had hatched ten chicks, seemed unspeakably heartrending.

I found Ian at last in the barn, a dark form huddled in the straw by the feet of Clarence the mule, whose ears pricked up at my appearance. He brayed ecstatically at the prospect of more company, and the goats blatted hysterically, thinking I was a wolf. The horses, surprised, tossed their heads, snorting and nickering in question. Rollo, nestled in the hay next to his master, gave a short, sharp bark of displeasure at the racket.

"Ruddy Noah's Ark in here," I remarked, shaking snow off my cloak and hanging the lantern on a hook. "All we need is a pair of elephants. Hush, Clarence!"

Ian turned his face toward me, but I could see from his blank expression that he hadn't taken in what I'd said.

I squatted next to him and cupped a hand round his cheek; it was cold, bristled with young beard.

"It wasn't your fault," I said gently.

"I know," he said, and swallowed. "But I dinna see how I can live." He wasn't dramatic about it at all; his voice was simply bewildered. Rollo licked his hand, and his fingers sank into the dog's ruff, as though for support.

"What can I do, Auntie?" He looked at me, helpless. "There's nothing, is there? I canna take it back, or undo it. And yet I keep looking for some way that I can. Something I can do to make things right. But there's . . . nothing."

I sat down in the hay next to him and put an arm round his shoulder, pressing his head toward me. He came, reluctantly, though I felt small constant shudders of exhaustion and grief running through him like a chill.

"I loved her," he said, so low I could barely hear him. "She was like my grandmother. And I—"

"She loved you," I whispered. "She wouldn't blame you." I had been holding on to my own emotions like grim death, in order to do what had to be done. But now . . . Ian was right. There was nothing, and in sheer helplessness, tears began to roll down my face. I wasn't crying. Grief and shock simply overflowed; I could not contain them.

Whether he felt the tears on his skin or only the vibrations of my grief, I couldn't tell, but quite suddenly Ian gave way as well, and he wept in my arms, shaking.

I wished with all my heart that he was a small boy, and that the storm of grief could wash away his guilt and leave him cleansed, at peace. But he was far beyond such simple things;

all I could do was hold him, and stroke his back, making small, helpless noises myself. Then Clarence offered his own support, breathing heavily on Ian's head and nibbling thoughtfully on a lock of his hair. Ian jerked away, slapping at the mule's nose.

"Och, awa' wi' ye!"

He choked, laughed in a shocked way, wept a little more, and then straightened up and wiped his nose on his sleeve. He sat still for a little while, gathering the pieces of himself, and I let him be.

"When I killed that man in Edinburgh," he said at last, his voice thick but controlled, "Uncle Jamie took me to confession, and told me the prayer that ye say when ye've killed someone. To commend them to God. Will ye say it with me, Auntie?"

I hadn't thought of—let alone said—"Soul Leading" in many years, and stumbled awkwardly through the words. Ian spoke it without hesitation, though, and I wondered how often he had used it through those years.

The words seemed puny and powerless, swallowed among the sounds of hay rustling and beasts chewing. But I felt a tiny bit of comfort for having said them. Perhaps it was only that the sense of reaching out to something larger than yourself gives you some feeling that there *is* something larger—and there really has to be, because plainly *you* aren't sufficient to the situation. I surely wasn't.

Ian sat for a time, eyes closed. Finally, he opened them and looked at me, his eyes black with knowledge, face very pale under the stubble of his beard.

"And then, he said, ye live with it," he said softly.

He rubbed a hand across his face.

"But I dinna think I can." It was a simple statement of fact, and scared me badly. I had no more tears, but felt as though I looked into a black, bottomless hole—and couldn't look away.

I drew a deep breath, trying to think of something to say, then pulled a handkerchief from my pocket and gave it to him.

"Are you breathing, Ian?"

His mouth twitched a little.

"Aye, I think so."

"That's all you have to do, for now." I got up, brushed hay from my skirts, and held out a hand to him. "Come along. We need to go back to the cabin before we're snowed in here."

The snow was thicker now, and a gust of wind put out the candle in my lantern. It didn't matter; I could have found the cabin blindfolded. Ian went ahead of me without comment, breaking a trail through the fresh-fallen snow. His head was bent against the storm, his narrow shoulders hunched.

I hoped the prayer had helped him, at least a little, and wondered whether the Mohawk had any better means of dealing with unjust death than did the Catholic Church.

Then I realized that I knew exactly what the Mohawk would do in such a case. So did Ian; he'd done it. I pulled the cloak tighter round me, feeling as though I had swallowed a large ball of ice.

4

NOT YET AWHILE

AFTER A GOOD deal of discussion, the two corpses were carried gently outside and laid at the edge of the porch. There simply was no room to lay them out properly inside, and given the circumstances . . .

"We canna let auld Arch be in doubt any longer than he must," Jamie had said, putting an end to the arguments. "If the body's in plain sight, maybe he'll come out and maybe he'll not—but he'll ken his wife's dead."

"He will," Bobby Higgins said, with an uneasy look toward the trees. "And what d'ye think he'll do then?"

Jamie stood for a moment, looking toward the wood, then shook his head.

"Grieve," he said quietly. "And in the morning, we'll see what's to do."

It wasn't the normal sort of wake, but it was conducted with what ceremony we could manage. Amy had donated her own shroud—made after her first wedding, and carefully kept by—for Mrs. Bug, and Grannie MacLeod was clad in the remnants of my spare chemise and a couple of aprons, hastily stitched up into respectability. They were laid one on either side of the porch, foot to foot, with a small saucer of salt and a slice of bread on the chest of each corpse, though no sin-eater was available. I had packed a small clay firepot with coals and set this near the bodies, and it was agreed that we would all take it in turns through the night to sit over the deceased, as the porch would hold no more than two or three people.

"The moon on the breast of the new-fallen snow/Gave the lustre of mid-day to objects below," I said softly. It did; the storm had blown over and the three-quarter moon cast a pure, cold light that made each snow-covered tree stand out, stark and delicate as a painting in Japanese ink. And in the distant ruins of the Big House, the jackstraw of charred timbers hid whatever lay below.

Jamie and I were taking the first watch. No one had argued when Jamie announced this. No one spoke of it, but the image of Arch Bug, lurking alone in the forest, was in everyone's mind.

"You think he's there?" I asked Jamie, low-voiced. I nodded toward the dark trees, peaceful in their own soft shrouds.

"If it were you lying here, *a nighean,*" Jamie said, looking down at the still white figures at the edge of the porch, "I should be beside ye, alive or dead. Come sit down."

I sat down beside him, the firepot close to our cloak-wrapped knees.

"Poor things," I said, after a bit. "It's a long way from Scotland."

"It is," he said, and took my hand. His fingers were no warmer than my own, but the size and strength of them were a comfort, nonetheless. "But they'll be buried amongst folk who ken their ways, if not among their own kin."

"True." Should Grannie MacLeod's grandsons ever come back, at least they would find a marker for her grave and know she had been treated with kindness. Mrs. Bug hadn't any kin, save Arch—no one to come and look for the grave marker. But she would be among people who'd known and loved her. What about Arch, though? If he had kin in Scotland, he'd never mentioned it. His wife had been everything to him, as he to her.

"You, um, don't think that Arch might . . . do away with himself?" I asked delicately. "Once he knows?"

Jamie shook his head, definite.

"No," he said. "It's not in him."

On one level, I was relieved to hear this. On a lower and less compassionate level, I couldn't help wondering uneasily just what a man of Arch's passions might do, stricken by this mortal blow, now bereft of the woman who had been his anchor and safe harbor for most of his life.

What *would* such a man do? I wondered. Run before the wind until he hit a reef and sank? Or tie his life to the makeshift anchor of fury, and take revenge as his new compass? I'd seen the guilt Jamie and Ian were bearing; how much more was Arch carrying? Could any man bear such guilt? Or must he turn it outward, as a matter of simple survival?

Jamie had said nothing about his own speculations, but I'd noticed that he had both pistol and dirk in his belt—and the pistol was loaded and primed; I could smell the whiff of black powder under the resinous breath of spruce and fir. Of course, it *might* be for driving off a roving wolf or foxes . . .

We sat in silence for a little while, watching the shifting glow of the coals in the firepot and the flicker of light in the folds of the shrouds.

"Ought we to pray, do you think?" I whispered.

"I havena given over praying since it happened, Sassenach."

"I know what you mean." I did—the passionate prayer that it might not be, and the desperate prayer for guidance thereafter; the need to do something, when nothing, really, could be done. And, of course, prayer for the repose of the recently departed. At least Grannie MacLeod had expected death—and welcomed it, I thought. Mrs. Bug, on the other hand, must have been terribly startled at being so suddenly dead. I had a disconcerting vision of her standing in the snow just off the porch, glaring at her corpse, hands on stout hips, lips pursed in annoyance at having been so rudely disembodied.

"It *was* rather a shock," I said apologetically to her shade.

"Aye, it was that."

Jamie reached into his cloak and drew out his flask. Uncorking this, he leaned forward and carefully poured a few drops of whisky on the head of each of the dead women, then lifted the flask in silent toast to Grannie MacLeod, then to Mrs. Bug.

"Murdina, wife of Archibald, ye were a great cook," he said simply. "I'll recall your biscuits all my life, and think of ye wi' my morning parritch."

"Amen," I said, my voice trembling between laughter and tears. I accepted the flask and took a sip; the whisky burned through the thickness in my throat, and I coughed.

"I know her receipt for piccalilli. That shouldn't be lost; I'll write it down."

The thought of writing reminded me quite suddenly of the unfinished letter, still folded up in my workbag. Jamie felt the slight stiffening of my posture and turned his head toward me in question.

"I was only thinking of that letter," I said, clearing my throat. "I mean, in spite of Roger and Bree knowing the house has burnt down, they'll be happy to hear that we're still alive—always supposing they do eventually get it."

Aware both of the precarious times and of the uncertain survival of historical documents, Jamie and Roger had worked out several schemes for the passage of information, ranging from the publication of coded messages in various newspapers to something elaborate involving the Church of Scotland and the Bank of England. All of these, of course, relied upon the basic fact of the MacKenzie family having made the passage through the stones safely and arrived in more or less the right time—but I was obliged for my own peace of mind to assume that they had.

"But I don't want to end it by having to tell them—about this." I nodded toward the shrouded figures. "They loved Mrs. Bug—and Bree would be so upset for Ian."

"Aye, ye're right," Jamie said thoughtfully. "And chances are that Roger Mac would think it all through and realize about Arch. Knowing, and not able to do anything about it . . . aye, they'd be worrit, 'til they found another letter telling them how it's all come out—and God knows how long it may be before it *has* all come out."

"And if they didn't *get* the next letter . . ." *Or if we didn't survive long enough to write it,* I thought.

"Aye, best not tell them. Not yet awhile."

I moved closer, leaning against him, and he put his arm round me. We sat quiet for a bit, still troubled and sorrowful, but comforted at thought of Roger, Bree, and the children.

I could hear sounds from the cabin behind me; everyone had been quiet, shocked—but normality was fast reasserting itself. Children couldn't be kept quiet long, and I could hear high-pitched questions, demands for food, the chatter of little ones excited at being up so late, their voices threading through the clanging and thumps of food preparation. There would be bannocks and pasties for the next part of the wake; Mrs. Bug would be pleased. A sudden shower of sparks flew from the chimney and fell all round the porch like falling stars, brilliant against the dark night and the white, fresh snow.

Jamie's arm tightened round me, and he made a small sound of pleasure at the sight.

"That—what ye said about the breast o' the new-fallen snow"—the word emerged as "breest" in his soft Highland lilt—"that's a poem, is it?"

"It is. Not really appropriate to a wake—it's a comic Christmas poem called 'A Visit from Saint Nicholas.' "

Jamie snorted, his breath white.

"I dinna think the word 'appropriate' has much to do wi' a proper wake, Sassenach. Give the mourners enough drink, and they'll be singing '*O thoir a-nall am Botul*' and the weans dancing ring-a-round-a-rosy in the dooryard by moonlight."

I didn't quite laugh, but could envision it, all too easily. There *was* enough to drink, too; there was a fresh tub of beer just brewed in the pantry, and Bobby had fetched down the emergency keg of whisky from its hiding place in the barn. I lifted Jamie's hand and kissed the cold knuckles. The shock and sense of dislocation had begun to fade with the growing awareness of the pulse of life behind us. The cabin was a small, vibrant island of life, afloat in the cold of the black-and-white night.

"No man is an island, entire of itself," Jamie said softly, picking up my unspoken thought.

"Now, that one *is* appropriate," I said, a little dryly. "Maybe too appropriate."

"Aye? How so?"

"*Never send to know for whom the bell tolls, it tolls for thee*? I never hear *No man is an island* without that last line tolling right behind it."

"Mmphm. Ken the whole of it, do ye?" Not waiting for my reply, he leaned forward and stirred the coals with a stick, sending up a tiny drift of silent sparks. "It isna really a poem, ken—or the man didna mean it to be one."

"No?" I said, surprised. "What is it? Or was it?"

"A meditation—something atwixt a sermon and a prayer. John Donne wrote it as part of his 'Devotions upon Emergent Occasions.' That's sufficiently appropriate, no?" he added, with a hint of wry humor.

"They don't get much more emergent than this, no. What am I missing, then?"

"Mmm." He pulled me closer, and bent his head to rest on mine. "Let me call what I can to mind. I'll not have all of it, but there are bits that struck me, so I remember those." I could hear his breathing, slow and easy, concentrating.

"All mankind is of one author," he said slowly, "*and is one volume. When one man dies, one chapter is not torn out of the book, but translated into a better language; and every chapter must be so translated.* Then there are bits I havena got by heart, but I liked this one: *The bell doth toll for him that thinks it doth*"—and his hand squeezed mine gently—"*and though it intermit again, yet from that minute that that occasion wrought upon him, he is united to God.*"

"Hmm." I thought about that for a bit. "You're right; that's less poetic, but a bit more . . . hopeful?"

I felt him smile.

"I've always found it so, aye."

"Where did you get that?"

"John Grey lent me a wee book of Donne's writing, when I was prisoner at Helwater. That was in it."

"A very literate gentleman," I said, somewhat piqued at this reminder of the substantial chunk of Jamie's life that John Grey had shared and I had not—but grudgingly glad that he had had a friend through that time of trial. How often, I wondered suddenly, had Jamie heard that tolling bell?

I sat up, reached for the flask, and took a cleansing swallow. The smell of baking, of onion and simmered meat, was seeping through the door, and my stomach rumbled in an unseemly manner. Jamie didn't notice; he was squinting thoughtfully off toward the west, where the bulk of the mountain lay hidden by cloud.

"The MacLeod lads said the passes were already hip-deep in snow when they came down," he said. "If there's a foot of new snow on the ground here, there are three in the high passes. We're going nowhere 'til the spring thaw, Sassenach. Time enough to carve proper grave markers, at least," he added, with a glance at our quiet guests.

"You do still mean to go to Scotland, then?" He'd said so, after the Big House burned, but hadn't mentioned it since then. I wasn't sure whether he'd meant it or had merely been reacting to the pressure of events at the time.

"Aye, I do. We canna be staying here, I think," he said, with some regret. "Come the spring, the backcountry will be boiling again. We've come close enough to the fire." He lifted his chin in the direction of the Big House's charred remains. "I've no mind to be roasted, next time."

"Well . . . yes." He was right, I knew. We could build another house—but it was unlikely we would be allowed to live peaceably in it. Among other things, Jamie was—or at least had been—a colonel of militia. Short of physical incapacity or simple absence, he couldn't relinquish that responsibility. And sentiment in the mountains was by no means all in favor of rebellion. I knew a number of people who had been beaten, burnt out, and driven into the woods or swamps, or killed outright as the direct result of injudiciously expressed political sentiments.

The weather prevented our leaving, but it also put a stopper on the movement of militias—or roving bands of brigands. The thought of that sent a sudden bolt of cold through me, and I shivered.

"Shall ye go in, *a nighean*?" Jamie asked, noticing. "I can bear watch alone for a bit."

"Right. And we'll come out with the bannocks and honey and find you stretched out beside the old ladies with an ax in your head. I'm fine." I took another sip of whisky, and handed him the flask.

"We wouldn't necessarily have to go to Scotland, though," I said, watching him drink. "We could go to New Bern. You could join Fergus in the printing business there." That's what he'd said he meant to do: go to Scotland, fetch the printing press he had left in Edinburgh, then come back to join the fight, armed with lead in the form of type slugs, rather than musket balls. I wasn't sure which method might be the more dangerous.

"Ye dinna suppose your presence would stop Arch trying to brain me, if that's what he's got in mind?" Jamie smiled briefly at that, slanted eyes creasing into triangles. "No—Fergus has a right to put himself in danger, and he wants to. But I've no right to drag him and his family into my own."

"Which tells me all I need to know about what sort of printing you have in mind to do. And my presence might not stop Arch going for you, but I could at least shout 'Look out!' if I saw him creeping up behind you."

"I should always want ye at my back, Sassenach," he assured me gravely. "Ye kent already what I mean to do, surely?"

"Yes," I said with a sigh. "Occasionally I have the vain hope that I'm wrong about you—but I never am."

That made him laugh outright.

"No, ye're not," he agreed. "But ye're still here, aye?" He lifted the flask in salute to me, and drank from it. "Good to know someone will miss me, when I fall."

"I did not miss that 'when,' rather than 'if,' " I said coldly.

"It's always been 'when,' Sassenach," he said gently. "*Every chapter must be so translated.* Aye?"

I took a deep breath and watched it drift out in a plume of mist.

"I sincerely hope I'm not going to have to do it," I said, "but should the question arise—would you want to be buried here? Or taken back to Scotland?" I was thinking of a granite marriage stone in the graveyard at St. Kilda, with his name on it, and mine, too. The bloody thing had nearly given me heart failure when I saw it, and I wasn't sure I had forgiven Frank for it, even though it had accomplished what he'd meant it to.

Jamie made a small snorting noise, not quite a laugh.

"I shall be lucky to be buried at all, Sassenach. Much more likely I shall be drowned, burnt, or left to rot on some battlefield. Dinna fash yourself. If ye've got to dispose of my carcass, just leave it out for the crows."

"I'll make a note of that," I said.

"Will ye mind going to Scotland?" he asked, eyebrows raised.

I sighed. Despite my knowing that he wasn't going to lie under that particular gravestone, I couldn't quite rid myself of the notion that he would at some point die there.

"No. I'll mind leaving the mountains. I'll mind watching you turn green and puke your guts out on the ship, and I may well mind whatever happens on the way *to* said ship, but . . . Edinburgh and printing presses aside, you want to go to Lallybroch, don't you?"

He nodded, eyes on the glowing coals. The light from the firepot was faint but warm on the ruddy arch of his brows, a line of gilding down the long, straight bridge of his nose.

"I promised, aye?" he said simply. "I said I'd bring Young Ian back to his mother. And after this . . . best he goes."

I nodded silently. Three thousand miles of ocean might not be enough for Ian to escape his memories—but it couldn't hurt. And perhaps the joy of seeing his parents, his brothers and sisters, the Highlands . . . perhaps it would help heal him.

Jamie coughed, and rubbed a knuckle over his lips.

"There's the one other thing," he said, a little shy. "Another promise, ye might say."

"What's that?"

He turned his head then, and met my eyes, his own dark and serious.

"I've sworn to myself," he said, "that I shallna ever face my son across the barrel of a gun."

I took a deep breath and nodded. After a moment's silence, I looked up from my contemplation of the shrouded women.

"You didn't ask what I want done with *my* body." I'd meant it at least half in jest, to lighten his mood, but his fingers curled so abruptly over mine that I gasped.

"No," he said softly. "And I never will." He wasn't looking at me but at the whiteness before us. "I canna think of ye dead, Claire. Anything else—but not that. I can't."

He stood abruptly. The rattle of wood, the clang of a falling pewter dish, and voices raised in adjuration inside saved me from reply. I simply nodded and let him lift me to my feet, as the door opened, spilling light.

THE MORNING dawned clear and bright, with a scant foot of fresh snow on the ground. By noon, the icicles that hung from the cabin's eaves had begun to loose their hold, dropping like random daggers with muffled, intermittent *thunks.* Jamie and Ian had gone up the hill to the small burying ground, with spades, to see whether the ground might be dug deep enough for two decent graves.

"Take Aidan and one or two of the other boys with you," I'd said at breakfast. "They need to be gotten out from underfoot." Jamie had given me a sharp glance, but nodded. He knew very well what I was thinking. If Arch Bug *didn't* yet know that his wife was dead, he'd certainly start drawing conclusions if he saw a grave being dug.

"Best if he'll come and speak to me," Jamie had said quietly to me, under cover of the noise made by the boys readying themselves to go, their mothers packing lunch to be taken up the hill, and the smaller children playing ring-a-round-a-rosy in the back room.

"Yes," I said, "and the boys won't stop him doing that. But if he *doesn't* choose to come out and speak to you . . ." Ian had told me that he'd heard a rifle fired during the encounter the night before; Arch Bug was no particular marksman, though, and would presumably hesitate to fire on a group that included young children.

Jamie had nodded, silent, and sent Aidan to fetch his two eldest cousins.

Bobby and Clarence the mule had gone up with the grave-digging party. There was a stock of freshly sawn pine boards at the site higher up on the mountainside, where Jamie had declared our new house would one day rise; if graves could be dug, Bobby would bring back some of the boards to make coffins.

From my viewpoint on the front porch, I could see Clarence now, heavily laden, but mincing downhill with ballerina grace, ears pointed delicately to either side as though to aid his balance. I caught a glimpse of Bobby walking on the far side of the mule, reaching up now and then to keep the load from slipping; he saw me and waved, smiling. The M branded on his cheek was visible even at this distance, livid against the cold-chapped ruddiness of his skin.

I waved back and turned in to the house, to tell the women that we would indeed have a funeral.

WE MADE OUR WAY up the winding trail to the small graveyard next morning. The two old ladies, unlikely companions in death, lay side by side in their coffins on a sledge, pulled by Clarence and one of the McCallum women's mules, a little black jenny called Puddin'.

We were not dressed in our best; no one *had* a "best," with the exception of Amy McCallum Higgins, who had worn her lace-trimmed wedding kerchief as a sign of respect. We were mostly clean, though, and the adults at least were sober in aspect, and watchful. Very watchful.

"Which will be the new guardian, Mam?" Aidan asked his mother, eyeing the two coffins as the sledge creaked slowly uphill ahead of us. "Which died first?"

"Why . . . I dinna ken, Aidan," Amy replied, looking mildly taken aback. She frowned at the coffins, then glanced at me. "D'ye know that, Mrs. Fraser?"

The question hit me like a thrown pebble, and I blinked. I did know, of course, but—with some effort, I refrained from glancing into the trees that lined the trail. I had no idea exactly where Arch Bug was, but he was near; I had no doubt of that at all. And if he were near enough to overhear this conversation . . .

Highland superstition held that the last person to be buried in a graveyard became the guardian and must defend the souls who rested there from any evil, until another should die and take the guardian's place—whereupon the earlier guardian was released and might go on to heaven. I didn't think Arch would be at all happy about the notion of his wife trapped on earth to guard the graves of Presbyterians and sinners like Malva Christie.

I felt a small chill in the heart at thought of Malva—who

was, now I thought of it, presumably the graveyard's present guardian. "Presumably," because while other people had died on the Ridge since her own death, she was the last to have been buried in the graveyard proper. Her brother, Allan, was buried nearby, a little way into the forest, in a secret, unmarked grave; I didn't know whether that was near enough to count. And her father . . .

I coughed into my fist, and clearing my throat said, "Oh, Mrs. MacLeod. She was dead when we came back to the cabin with Mrs. Bug." Which was strictly true; the fact that she'd been dead when I *left* the cabin seemed better suppressed.

I had been looking at Amy when I spoke. I turned my head back to the trail, and there he was, right in front of me. Arch Bug, in his rusty black cloak, white head bared and bent, following the sledge through the snow, slow as an earthbound raven. A faint shudder ran through the mourners.

He turned his head then, and saw me.

"Will ye sing, Mrs. Fraser?" he asked, his voice quiet and courtly. "I'd have her taken to her rest wi' the proper observances."

"I—yes, of course." Enormously flustered, I groped for something suitable. I simply wasn't up to the challenge of composing a proper *caithris,* a lament for the dead—let alone providing the formal wailing that a truly first-class Highland funeral would have.

I settled hastily for a Gaelic psalm that Roger had taught me, *"Is e Dia fèin a's buachaill dhomh."* It was a line chant, each line meant to be sung by a precentor, then echoed line by line by the congregation. It was simple, though, and while my voice seemed thin and insubstantial on the mountainside, those around me were able to take it up, and by the time we reached the burying ground, we had achieved a respectable level of fervor and volume.

The sledge stopped at the edge of the pine-circled clearing. A few wooden crosses and cairns were visible through the half-melted snow, and the two fresh graves gaped in the center, muddy and brutal. The sight of them stopped the singing as abruptly as a pail of cold water.

The sun shone pale and bright through the trees, and there was a gang of nuthatches conversing in the branches at the edge of the clearing, incongruously cheerful. Jamie had been leading the mules, and had not glanced back at Arch's appearance. Now, though, he turned to Arch and with a small gesture at the nearer coffin, asked in a low voice, "Will ye look upon your wife once more?"

It was only as Arch nodded and moved to the side of the sledge, that I realized that while the men had nailed down the lid of Mrs. MacLeod's coffin, they had left Mrs. Bug's lying loose. Bobby and Ian lifted it off, their eyes on the ground.

Arch had unbound his hair as a sign of grief; I had never seen it loose before. It was thin, pure white, and wavered about his face like wisps of smoke as he bent and gently lifted the shroud from Murdina's face.

I swallowed hard, clenching my hands. I'd removed the arrow—not a pleasant business—and had then wrapped her throat carefully in a clean bandage before combing her hair. She looked all right, though terribly unfamiliar; I didn't think I'd ever seen her without her cap, and the bandage across her full throat gave her the sternly formal air of a Presbyterian minister. I saw Arch flinch, just slightly, and his own throat move. He got control of his face almost at once, but I saw the lines that ran from nose to chin like gullies through wet clay, and the way in which he opened and closed his hands, over and over, seeking a grip on something that wasn't there.

He gazed into the coffin for a long moment, then reached into his sporran and drew out something. I saw when he put back his cloak that his belt was empty; he had come without weapons.

The thing in his hand was small and glittering. He leaned down and tried to fix it to the shroud, but could not, with his missing fingers. He fumbled, said something under his breath in Gaelic, then looked up at me, with something near panic in his eyes. I went at once to him, and took the thing from his hand.

It was a brooch, a small, beautifully made thing in the shape of a flying swallow. Made of gold, and very new-looking. I took it from him and, turning back the shroud, pinned it to Mrs. Bug's kerchief. I'd never seen the brooch before, either on Mrs. Bug or among her things, and it came to me that Arch had likely had it made from the gold he had taken from Jocasta Cameron—perhaps when he began to take the ingots, one by one; perhaps later. A promise made to his wife—that their years of penury and dependence were over. Well . . . indeed they were. I glanced at Arch, and at his nod, pulled the shroud gently up over his wife's cold face.

I put out a hand impulsively to touch him, take his arm, but he drew away and stood back, watching impassively as Bobby nailed down the lid. At one point, his gaze rose and passed slowly over Jamie, then Ian, in turn.

I pressed my lips tight, glancing at Jamie as I came back to his side, seeing the trouble etched so plainly on his face. So much guilt! Not that there wasn't enough and to spare—and plainly enough, Arch felt his own. Did it not occur to any of them that Mrs. Bug had had something to do with this, herself? Had she not fired at Jamie . . . but people didn't always behave intelligently, or well, and did the fact that someone had contributed to their own demise lessen the tragedy of it?

I caught sight of the small boulder that marked the grave of Malva and her son, only the top of it visible through the snow—rounded, wet, and dark, like the crowning of a baby's head at birth.

Rest in peace, I thought, and felt a small easing of the tension I'd been under for the last two days. *You can go now.*

It occurred to me that whatever I'd told Amy and Aidan, it didn't alter the truth of which woman really *had* died first. Still, considering Mrs. Bug's personality, I rather thought she might enjoy being in charge, clucking and fussing after the resident souls like her flock of much-loved chickens, banishing evil spirits with a sharp word and a brandished sausage.

That thought got me through the brief reading from the Bible, the prayers, the tears—from the women and the children, most of whom had no idea why they were crying—the removal of the coffins from the sledge, and a rather disjoint recitation of the Lord's Prayer. I missed Roger very much—his sense of calm order and genuine compassion in the conducting of a funeral. And he would, perhaps, have known what to say in eulogy of Murdina Bug. As it was, no one spoke when the prayer concluded, and there was a long, awkward pause, people shifting uneasily from foot to foot—we were standing in a foot of snow, and the women's petticoats were wet to the knee.

I saw Jamie shift his shoulders, as though his coat was too tight, and glance at the sledge, where the shovels lay under a blanket. Before he could signal Ian and Bobby, though, Ian drew a deep, gasping breath and stepped forward.

He came to the side of Mrs. Bug's waiting coffin, opposite the bereaved husband, and stopped, plainly wanting to speak. Arch ignored him for a long moment, staring down into the hole, but finally raised his face, impassive. Waiting.

"It was by my hand that this"—Ian swallowed—"that this woman of great worth has died. I didna take her life by malice, or of purpose, and it is sorrow to me. But she died by my hand."

Rollo whined softly by Ian's side, feeling his master's distress, but Ian laid a hand on his head, and he stilled. Ian drew the knife from his belt and laid it on the coffin in front of Arch Bug, then straightened and looked him in the eye.

"Ye swore once to my uncle, in a time of great wrong, and offered life for life, for this woman. I swear by my iron, and I offer the same." His lips pressed together for an instant, and his throat moved, his eyes dark and sober. "I think ye maybe didna mean it, sir—but I do."

I found that I was holding my breath, and forced myself to breathe. Was this Jamie's plan? I wondered. Ian plainly meant what he said. Still, the chances of Arch accepting that offer on the spot and cutting Ian's throat in front of a dozen witnesses were slim, no matter how exigent his feelings. But if he publicly declined the offer—then the possibility of a more formal and less bloody recompense was opened, yet young Ian would be relieved of at least a measure of his guilt. Bloody Highlander, I thought, glancing up at Jamie—not without a certain admiration.

I could feel small jolts of energy running through him, though, every few seconds, each one suppressed. He wouldn't interfere with Ian's attempt at atonement—but neither would he see him injured, if by chance old Arch *did* opt for blood. And evidently he thought it a possibility. I glanced at Arch, and thought so, too.

The old man looked at Ian for a moment, heavy brows wild with curling iron-gray old-man hairs—and the eyes beneath them iron-gray, too, and cold as steel.

"Too easy, boy," he said at last, in a voice like rusty iron.

He looked down at Rollo, who was standing next to Ian, ears pricked and wolf eyes wary.

"Will ye give me your hound to kill?"

Ian's mask broke in an instant, shock and horror making him suddenly young. I heard him gulp air and steady himself, but his voice was cracked in reply.

"No," he said. "He's done nothing. It's my—my crime, not his."

Arch smiled then, very slightly, though it did not touch his eyes.

"Aye. Ye see, then. And he's no but a flea-ridden beast. Not a wife." "Wife" was spoken in barely a whisper. His throat worked as he cleared it. Then he looked carefully from Ian to Jamie, and then at me.

"Not a wife," he said softly. I'd thought my blood ran cold already; that froze my heart.

In no hurry, Arch turned his gaze deliberately upon each man in turn; Jamie, then Ian, whom he regarded for an instant that seemed a lifetime.

"When you've something worth taking, boy—you'll see me again," he said quietly, then turned upon his heel and walked into the trees.

5

MORALITY FOR TIME-TRAVELERS

THERE WAS AN electric desk lamp in his study, but Roger often preferred to work by candlelight in the evening. He took a match from the box, and struck it with one soft scratch. After Claire's letter, he didn't think he'd ever light a match again without thinking of her story of the burning of the Big House. God, he wished he'd been there.

The match flame shrank as he touched it to the wick, and the translucent wax of the candle went a dim, unearthly blue for an instant, then brightened into its normal glow. He glanced at Mandy, singing to a collection of stuffed toys on the sofa; she'd had her bath and was meant to be keeping out of trouble while Jem had his. Keeping one eye on her, he sat down at his desk and opened his notebook.

He'd begun it half as a joke. The other half as the only thing he could think of to combat paralyzing fear.

"You can teach kids not to cross the street alone," Bree had pointed out. "Surely you can teach them to stay the heck away from standing stones."

He'd agreed, but with substantial mental reservations. Small kids, yes; you could brainwash them into not sticking forks in the electric outlets. But as they became teenagers, with all that inchoate yearning for self-discovery and things unknown? He recalled his own teenaged self much too vividly. Tell a teenaged boy not to stick forks in the outlet, and he'd be off rifling the silverware drawer the minute your back was turned. Girls might be different, but he doubted it.

He glanced again at the sofa, where Amanda was now lying on her back, legs thrust into the air and a large, ratty-looking stuffed bear balanced on her feet, to which she was singing "Frère Jacques." Mandy had been so young that she wouldn't remember. Jem would. He did; Roger could tell, when the little boy woke up from nightmares, eyes huge and staring at nothing, and could not describe his dream. Thank God, it didn't happen often.

He still broke out in a cold sweat whenever he remembered it himself. That last passage. He'd clutched Jemmy to his chest and stepped into . . . God, there was no name for it, because humanity at large had never experienced it, and lucky for them they hadn't. It wasn't even *like* anything to which it could be compared.

None of the senses worked there—and at the same time, all of them did, in such a state of hypersensitivity that you'd die of it if it lasted any longer than it did. A howling void, where sound seemed to batter you, pulsing through your body, trying to separate each cell from the next. Absolute blindness, but the blindness of looking into the sun. And the impact of . . . bodies? Ghosts? Unseen others who brushed past like moth wings or seemed to hurtle right through you in a colliding thump of entangling bones. A constant sense of screaming.

Did it smell? He paused, frowning, trying to remember. Yes, it damned well did. And oddly enough, it was a describable smell: the scent of air burnt by lightning—ozone.

It smells strongly of ozone, he wrote, feeling remarkably relieved to have even this small foothold of reference to the normal world.

This relief disappeared in the next instant, as he returned to the struggle of memory.

He'd felt as though nothing save his own will held them together, nothing but raw determination to survive held *him* together. Knowing what to expect hadn't helped in the slightest; it was different—and much worse—than his previous experiences.

He did know not to look at them. The ghosts, if that's what they were. "Look" wasn't the right word . . . pay attention to them? Again, there wasn't a word, and he sighed in exasperation.

"Sonnez les matines, sonnez les matines . . ."

"Din dan don," he sang softly with her chorus. *"Din dan don."*

He tapped the pen on the paper for a minute, thinking, then shook his head and bent over the paper again, trying to explain his first attempt, the occasion on which he'd come within . . . moments? inches? Some unthinkably small degree of separation of meeting his father—and destruction.

I think you cannot cross your own lifeline, he wrote slowly. Both Bree and Claire—the scientific women—had assured him that two objects cannot exist in the same space, whether said objects were subatomic particles or elephants. That being true, it would explain why one couldn't exist twice in the same time period, he supposed.

He assumed it was that phenomenon that had come so close to killing him on his first attempt. He had been thinking of his father when he entered the stones, and—presumably—of his father as he, Roger, had known him. Which was, of course, during the period of his own life.

He tapped the pen on the page again, thinking, but could not bring himself just now to write about that encounter. Later. Instead, he flipped back to the rudimentary outline in the front of the book.

A Practical Guide for Time-Travelers

I. Physical Phenomena

A. Known Locations (Ley Lines?)

B. Genetic Inheritance

C. Mortality

D. The Influence and Properties of Gemstones

E. Blood?

He'd scratched through that last one, but hesitated, looking at it. Did he have an obligation to tell everything he knew, believed, or suspected? Claire thought that the notion of a blood sacrifice being required or useful was nonsense—a pagan superstition without real validity. She might be right; she was the scientist, after all. But he had the uneasy memory of the night Geillis Duncan had gone through the stones.

Long blond hair, flying in the rising wind of a fire, the whipping locks silhouetted for an instant against the face of a standing stone. The gagging scent of petrol mingled with roasting flesh, and the log that was not a log lying charred in the center of the circle. And Geillis Duncan had gone too far.

"It's always two hundred years, in the old fairy tales," Claire had told him. Literal fairy tales; stories of people stolen by the fairies, "taken through the stones" of faerie hills. *It was a time, two hundred years ago,* such tales often began. Or the people were returned to their own place—but two hundred years past the time they had left. Two hundred years.

Claire, Bree, himself—each time they had traveled, the span of time was the same: two hundred and two years, close enough to the two hundred years of the ancient tales. But Geillis Duncan had gone too far.

With great reluctance, he slowly wrote *Blood* again, and added a parenthetical *(Fire??),* but nothing beneath it. Not now; later.

For reassurance, he glanced at the spot on the bookshelf where the letter lay, weighted down by a small snake carved of cherrywood. *We are alive. . . .*

He wanted suddenly to go and fetch the wooden box, pull out the other letters, rip them open and read. Curiosity, sure, but something more—wanting to touch them, Claire and Jamie, press the evidence of their lives against his face, his heart, erase the space and time between them.

He forced back the impulse, though. They'd decided—or rather, Bree had, and they were her parents.

"I don't want to read them all at once," she'd said, turning over the contents of the box with long, gentle fingers. "It's . . . it's like once I've read them all, then they'll be . . . *really* gone."

He'd understood. As long as one letter remained unread, they *were* alive. In spite of his historian's curiosity, he shared her sentiment. Besides . . .

Brianna's parents had not written those letters as journal entries, meant for the eventual eyes of a vaguely imagined posterity. They'd been written with the definite and specific intent of communication—with Bree, with *him*. Which meant that they might well contain unsettling things; both his in-laws had a talent for such revelation.

Despite himself, he rose, took down the letter and unfolded it, and read the postscript once more, just to assure himself he hadn't been imagining it.

He hadn't. With the word "blood" ringing faintly in his ears, he sat back down. *An Italian gentleman.* That was Charles Stuart; couldn't be anyone else. Christ. After staring off into space for a bit—Mandy had now started in on "Jingle Bells"—he shook himself, flipped over a few pages and started in again, doggedly.

II. Morality

A. Murder and Wrongful Death

Naturally, we assume that the killing of someone for any reason short of self-defense, the protection of another, or the legitimate use of force in wartime is completely indefensible.

He looked at that for a moment, muttered, "Pompous ass," and ripped the page out of the notebook, crumpling it.

Ignoring Mandy's warbling rendition of *"Gingle bells, Bamman smells, Wobin waid enegg!"* he scooped up the notebook and stomped across the hall to Brianna's study.

"Who am I to be gassing on about morality?" he demanded. She looked up from a sheet showing the disassembled components of a hydroelectric turbine, with the rather blank look that indicated she was aware of being spoken to, but had not detached her mind sufficiently from the subject matter as to realize who was speaking or what they were saying. Familiar with this phenomenon, he waited with mild impatience for her mind to let go of the turbine and focus on him.

" . . . gassing on . . . ?" she said, frowning. She blinked at him and her gaze sharpened. "Who are you gassing on to?"

"Well . . ." He lifted the scribbled notebook, feeling suddenly shy. "The kids, sort of."

"You're supposed to gas on to your kids about morality," she said reasonably. "You're their father; it's your job."

"Oh," he said, rather at a loss. "But—I've *done* a lot of the things I'm telling them not to." *Blood.* Yeah, maybe it was protection of another. Maybe it wasn't.

She raised a thick, ruddy brow at him.

"You never heard of benign hypocrisy? I thought they teach you stuff like that when you go to minister school. Since you mention gassing away about morality. That's a minister's job, too, isn't it?"

She stared at him, blue-eyed and waiting. He took a good, deep breath. Trust Bree, he thought wryly, to walk straight up to the elephant in the room and grab it by the trunk. She hadn't said a word since their return about his near-ordination, or what he proposed to do now about his calling. Not a word, during their year in America, Mandy's surgery, their decision to move to Scotland, the months of renovation after they'd bought Lallybroch—not until he'd opened the door. Once opened, of course, she'd walked straight through it, knocked him over, and planted a foot on his chest.

"Yeah," he said evenly. "It is," and stared back.

"Okay." She smiled, very gently, at him. "So what's the problem?"

"Bree," he said, and felt his heart stick in his scarred throat. "If I knew, I'd tell you."

She stood up then and put her hand on his arm, but before either of them could say more, the thump of small, bare feet came hop-skipping down the hall, and Jem's voice came from the door of Roger's study, saying, "Daddy?"

"Here, pal," he called back, but Brianna was already moving toward the door. Following, he found Jem—in his blue Superman pajamas, wet hair standing up in spikes—standing by his desk, examining the letter with interest.

"What's this?" he asked.

"Wassis?" Mandy echoed faithfully, rushing over and scrambling up on the chair to see.

"It's a letter from your grandda," Brianna replied, not missing a beat. She put a hand casually on the letter, obscuring most of the postscript, and pointed with the other at the last paragraph. "He sent you a kiss. See there?"

A huge smile lighted Jem's face.

"He said he wouldn't forget," he said, contented.

"Kissy, Grandda," Mandy exclaimed, and bending forward so her mass of black curls fell over her face, planted a loud "MWAH!" on the letter.

Caught between horror and laughter, Bree snatched it up and wiped the moisture off it—but the paper, old as it was, was tough. "No harm done," she said, and handed the letter casually to Roger. "Come on, what story are we reading tonight?"

"Aminal Nursy Tales!"

"An-i-mal," Jem said, bending down to speak distinctly into his sister's face. "An-i-mal Nur-ser-y Tales."

"Okay," she said amiably. "Me first!" and scampered madly out the door, giggling, followed by her brother in hot pursuit. Brianna took three seconds to seize Roger by the ears and kiss him firmly on the mouth, then released him and set off after their offspring.

Feeling happier, he sat down, listening to the uproar of toothbrushing and face-washing above. Sighing, he put the notebook back in the drawer. Plenty of time, he thought. Years before it might be needed. Years and years.

He folded up the letter with care, and standing on tiptoe, put it on the highest shelf of the bookcase, moving the little snake to guard it. He blew out the candle then, and went to join his family.

Postscriptum: I see I am to have the last Word—a rare Treat to a Man living in a House that contains (at last count) eight Women. We propose to leave the Ridge so soon as the Climate thaws, and to go to Scotland, there to procure my printing Press, and return with it. Travel in these times is uncertain, and I cannot predict when—or if—it will be possible to write again. (Nor do I know whether you will receive this Letter at all, but I proceed in necessary Faith that you will.)

I wished to tell you of the Disposition of the Property which was once held in trust by the Camerons for an Italian Gentleman. I think it unwise to carry this with us, and have therefore removed it to a Place of safety. Jem knows the Place. If you should at some Time have need of this Property, tell him the Spaniard guards it. If so, be sure to have it blessed by a Priest; there is Blood upon it.

Sometimes I wish that I might see the Future; much more often, I give thanks to God that I cannot. But I will always see your Faces. Kiss the Children for me.

Your loving father,
JF

THE CHILDREN washed, toothbrushed, kissed, and put to bed, their parents returned to the library, a dram of whisky, and the letter.

"An Italian gentleman?" Bree looked at Roger, one brow raised in a way that brought Jamie Fraser so immediately to mind that Roger glanced involuntarily at the sheet of paper. "Does he mean—"

"Charles Stuart? He can't mean anyone else."

She picked the letter up and read the postscript for perhaps the dozenth time.

"And if he *does* mean Charles Stuart, then the property . . ."

"He's found the gold. And Jem knows where it is?" Roger couldn't help this last taking on the tone of a question, as he cast his eyes toward the ceiling, above which his children were presumably asleep, wrapped in virtue and cartoon pajamas.

Bree frowned.

"Does he? That isn't exactly what Da said—and if he *did* know . . . that's an awfully big secret to ask an eight-year-old boy to keep."

"True." Eight or not, Jem was very good at keeping secrets, Roger thought. But Bree was right—her father would never burden anyone with dangerous information, let alone his beloved grandson. Certainly not without a good reason, and his postscript made it clear that this information was provided only as a contingency in case of need.

"You're right. Jem doesn't know anything about the gold—just about this Spaniard, whatever that may be. He's never mentioned anything like that to you?"

She shook her head, then turned as a sudden puff of wind from the open window blew through the curtains, breathing immanent rain. Bree got up and went hastily to close it, then trotted upstairs to close the windows there, waving at Roger to see to those on the ground floor. Lallybroch was a large house, and unusually well provided with windows—the children kept trying to count them, but never came up with the same number twice.

Roger supposed he could go and count them himself one day and settle the matter, but was reluctant to do this. The house, like most old houses, had a distinct personality. Lallybroch was welcoming, all right; large and gracious, comfortably rather than grandly built, with the echoes of generations murmuring in its walls. But it was a place that had its secrets, too, no doubt of that. And hiding the number of its windows was quite in keeping with the sense he had of the house as being rather playful.

The windows in the kitchen—now equipped with modern refrigerator, Aga cooker, and decent plumbing, but still with its ancient granite counters stained with the juice of currants, the blood of game and poultry—were all closed, but he went through it nonetheless, and through the scullery. The light in the back hall was off, but he could see the grating in the floor near the wall that gave air to the priest's hole below.

His father-in-law had hidden there briefly, during the days after the Rising, before being imprisoned at Ardsmuir. Roger had gone down there once—also briefly—when they had bought the house, and had come up out of the dank, fetid little space with a complete understanding of why Jamie Fraser had chosen to live in a wilderness on a remote mountaintop, where there was no constraint in any direction.

Years of hiding, of duress, of imprisonment . . . Jamie Fraser was not a political creature, and he knew better than most what the true cost of war was, whatever its presumed purpose. But Roger had seen his father-in-law now and then rub absently at his wrists, where the marks of fetters had long since faded—but the memory of their weight had not. Roger had not the slightest doubt that Jamie Fraser would live free, or die. And wished for an instant, with a longing that gnawed his bones, that he might be there, to fight by his father-in-law's side.

The rain had started; he could hear the patter of it on the slate roofs of the outbuildings, then the rush as it came on in earnest, wrapping the house in mist and water.

"For ourselves . . . and our posterity," he said aloud, but quietly.

It was a bargain made between men—unspoken, but understood completely. Nothing mattered but that the family be preserved, the children protected. And whether the cost of it was paid in blood, sweat, or soul—it would be paid.

"Oidche mhath," he said, with a brief nod in the direction of the priest's hole. Good night, then.

He stood a moment longer in the old kitchen, though, feeling the embrace of the house, its solid protection against the storm. The kitchen had always been the heart of the house, he thought, and found the warmth of the cooker as much a comfort as the fire on the now-empty hearth had once been.

He met Brianna at the foot of the stairs; she'd changed for bed—as opposed to sleep. The air in the house was always cool, and the temperature had dropped several degrees with the onset of rain. She wasn't wearing her woolies, though; rather, a thin nightgown of white cotton, deceptively innocent-looking, with a small red ribbon threaded through it. The white cloth clung to the shape of her breasts like cloud to a mountain peak.

He said as much, and she laughed—but made no objection when he cupped his hands around them, her nipples against his palms round as beach pebbles through the thin cloth.

"Upstairs?" she whispered, and leaning in, ran the tip of her tongue along his lower lip.

"No," he said, and kissed her solidly, quelling the tickle of the touch. "In the kitchen. We haven't done it there, yet."

He had her, bent over the ancient counter with its mysterious stains, the sound of her small grunts a punctuation to the rush of wind and rain on the ancient shutters. Felt her shiver and liquefy and let go, too, his knees trembling with it, so he fell slowly forward, clutched her by the shoulders, his face pressed into the shampoo-fragrant waves of her hair, the old granite smooth and cool beneath his cheek. His heart was beating slow and hard, steady as a bass drum.

He was naked, and a cold draft from somewhere raised gooseflesh down his back and legs. Brianna felt him shiver and turned her face to his.

"Cold?" she whispered. She wasn't; she glowed like a live coal, and he wanted nothing more than to slide into bed beside her and ride out the storm in snug warmth.

"I'm fine." He bent and scooped up the clothes he had thrown on the floor. "Let's go to bed."

The rain was louder upstairs.

"Oh, the animals went in two by two," Bree sang softly, as they climbed the stairs, *"the elephants and the kangaroos . . ."*

Roger smiled. You *could* imagine the house an ark, floating on a roaring world of water—but all snug within. Two by two—two parents, two kids . . . maybe more, someday. There was plenty of room, after all.

With the lamp put out and the beating of rain on the shutters, Roger lingered on the edge of sleep, reluctant to surrender the pleasure of the moment.

"We won't ask him, will we?" Bree whispered. Her voice

was drowsy, her soft weight warm all down the side of his body. "Jem?"

"Oh? No. Of course not. No need."

He felt the prick of curiosity—who was the Spaniard? And the notion of buried treasure was always a lure—but they didn't need it; they had enough money for the present. Always assuming the gold was still wherever Jamie had put it, which was a long shot in itself.

Nor had he forgotten the last injunction of Jamie's postscript.

Have it blessed by a priest; there is blood upon it. The words melted as he thought them, and what he saw on the inside of his eyelids was not gold ingots but the old granite counter in the kitchen, dark stains sunk so far into the stone as to have become part of it, ineradicable by the most vigorous scrubbing, let alone an invocation.

But it didn't matter. The Spaniard, whoever he was, could keep his gold. The family was safe.

Part Two

Blood, Sweat, and Pickles

6

LONG ISLAND

ON JULY 4, 1776, the Declaration of Independence was signed in Philadelphia.

ON JULY 24, Lieutenant General Sir William Howe arrived on Staten Island, where he set up field headquarters at the Rose and Crown Tavern in New Dorp.

ON AUGUST 13, Lieutenant General George Washington arrived in New York to reinforce the fortifications of the city, which the Americans held.

ON AUGUST 21, William Ransom, Lieutenant Lord Ellesmere, arrived at the Rose and Crown in New Dorp, reporting—somewhat late—for duty as the newest and most junior member of General Howe's staff.

ON AUGUST 22 . . .

LIEUTENANT Edward Markham, Marquis of Clarewell, peered searchingly into William's face, offering him an unappetizingly close view of a juicy pimple—just ready to burst—on the former's forehead.

"You all right, Ellesmere?"

"Fine." William managed the word between clenched teeth.

"Only, you look rather . . . green." Clarewell, looking concerned, reached into his pocket. "Want a suck of my pickle?"

William just about made it to the rail in time. There was a certain amount of jocularity going on behind him regarding Clarewell's pickle, who might suck it, and how much its owner would be obliged to pay for said service. This, interspersed with Clarewell's protestations that his aged grandmother swore by a sour pickle for the prevention of seasickness, and plainly it worked, for look at him, solid as a rock . . .

William blinked watering eyes and fixed his vision on the approaching shore. The water wasn't particularly rough, though the weather was brewing, no doubt about it. It didn't matter, though; even the gentlest of up-and-down motions on water, the briefest of journeys, and his stomach promptly tried to turn itself inside out. Every damned time!

It was still trying, but as there was nothing left in it, he could pretend it wasn't. He wiped his mouth, feeling clammy despite the heat of the day, and straightened his shoulders.

They would drop anchor any minute; time he was going below and badgering the companies under his command into some kind of order before they went into the boats. He risked a brief glance over the rail, and saw the *River* and the *Phoenix* just astern. The *Phoenix* was Admiral Howe's flagship, and his brother the general was aboard. Would they have to wait, bobbing like corks on the increasingly choppy waves, until General Howe and Captain Pickering, his aide-de-camp, got ashore? God, he hoped not.

In the event, the men were allowed to disembark at once. "With ALL POSSIBLE SPEED, gennelmun!" Sergeant Cutter informed them at the top of his voice. "We're going to catch the rebel whoresons on the 'op, so we are! And WOE BETIDE any man what I see lollygaggin'! YOU, there . . . !" He strode off, forceful as a plug of black tobacco, to apply the spurs to a delinquent second lieutenant, leaving William feeling somewhat better. Surely nothing truly terrible could happen in a world containing Sergeant Cutter.

He followed his men down the ladder and into the boats, forgetting his stomach entirely in the rush of excitement. His first real battle was waiting to be fought, somewhere on the plains of Long Island.

EIGHTY-EIGHT frigates. That's what he'd heard Admiral Howe had brought, and he didn't doubt it. A forest of sails filled Gravesend Bay, and the water was choked with small boats, ferrying troops ashore. William was half choked himself, with anticipation. He could feel it gathering among the men, as the corporals collected their companies from the boats and marched off in good order, making room for the next wave of arrivals.

The officers' horses were being swum ashore, rather than rowed, the distance not being great. William ducked aside as one big bay surged up out of the surf nearby and shook himself in a shower of salt spray that drenched everyone within ten feet. The stable-lad clinging to his bridle looked like a drowned rat, but shook himself off likewise and grinned at William, his face blanched with cold but vivid with excitement.

William had a horse, too—somewhere. Captain Griswold, a senior member of Howe's staff, was lending him a mount, there having been no time to organize anything else. He supposed whoever was minding the horse would find him, though he didn't see how.

Organized confusion reigned. The shore here was a tidal flat, and coveys of redcoats swarmed amongst the sea wrack like flocks of shorebirds, the bellowing of sergeants a counterpoint to the shrieking of gulls overhead.

With some difficulty, as he'd been introduced to the corporals only that morning and did not have their faces firmly fixed in memory yet, William located his four companies and marched them up the shore into sand dunes thick with some sort of wiry grass. It was a hot day, sweltering in heavy uniform and full equipment, and he let the men take their ease, drink water or beer from their canteens, eat a bit of cheese and biscuit. They'd be on the move soon.

Where? That was the question preying on his mind at the moment. A hasty staff meeting the night before—his first—had reiterated the basics of the invasion plan. From Gravesend Bay, half the army would march inland, turning north toward the Brooklyn Heights, where the rebel forces were thought to be entrenched. The remainder of the troops would spread outward along the shore to Montauk, forming a line of defense that could move inward across Long Island, forcing the rebels back into a net, if necessary.

William wanted, with an intensity that knotted his spine, to be in the vanguard, attacking. Realistically, he knew it wasn't likely. He was completely unfamiliar with his troops, and not impressed with their looks. No sensible commander would put such companies in the front line—unless to serve as cannon fodder. That thought gave him pause for a moment, but only a moment.

Howe wasn't a waster of men; he was known to be cautious, sometimes to a fault. His father had told him that. Lord John hadn't mentioned that that consideration was the major reason for his consent to William's joining Howe's staff, but William knew it anyway. He didn't care; he'd calculated that his chances of seeing significant action were still a great deal better with Howe than fiddling about in the North Carolina swamps with Sir Peter Packer.

And after all . . . he turned slowly, side to side. The sea was a mass of British ships, the land before him crawling with soldiers. He would never have admitted aloud to being impressed by the sight—but his stock was tight across his throat. He realized he was holding his breath and consciously let it go.

The artillery was coming ashore, floating perilously on flat-bottomed barges, manned by swearing soldiers. The limbers, the caissons, and the draft horses and oxen needed to drag them were splashing up the beach in a thrashing, sand-spattered herd, neighing and lowing in protest, having come ashore farther south. It was the biggest army he had ever seen.

"Sir, sir!" He looked down to see a short private soldier, perhaps no older than William himself, plump-cheeked and anxious.

"Yes?"

"Your spontoon, sir. And your horse has come," the private added, gesturing at the rangy light bay gelding whose reins he held. "Captain Griswold's compliments, sir."

William took the spontoon, seven feet long, its burnished steel head gleaming dully even under the clouded sky, and felt the weight of it thrill through his arm.

"Thank you. And you are . . . ?"

"Oh. Perkins, sir." The private hastily knuckled his brow in salute. "Third company, sir; the Hackers, they call us."

"Do they? Well, we will hope to give you plenty of opportunity to justify your name." Perkins looked blank.

"Thank you, Perkins," William said, gesturing the private off.

He took the bridle of the horse, joy rising in his heart. It was the biggest army he'd ever seen. And he was part of it.

HE WAS LUCKIER THAN he'd thought he might be, if not as lucky as he'd hoped. His companies were to be in the second wave, following up the vanguard of foot, guarding the artillery. Not a guarantee of action, but a good chance nonetheless, if the Americans were half the fighters they were reputed to be.

It was past noon before he lifted his spontoon into the air and shouted, "Forward, march!" The brewing weather had broken in a spattering rain, a welcome relief from the heat.

Beyond the shore, a fringe of woods gave way to a broad and beautiful plain. Waving grasses lay before them, flecked with wildflowers, the colors rich in the dim, rainy light. Far ahead, he could see flights of birds—doves? quail? too far to see—rising into the air despite the rain, as the marching soldiers drove them from their cover.

His own companies marched close to the center of the advancing line, snaking in orderly columns behind him, and he directed a grateful thought toward General Howe. As a junior staff officer, he should by rights have been delegated to messenger duty, scampering to and fro among the companies on the field, relaying orders from Howe's headquarters, carrying information to and from the two other generals, Sir Henry Clinton and Lord Cornwallis.

Given his late arrival, though, he knew none of the other officers or the army's disposition; he was completely ignorant of who was who, let alone where they should be at any moment. He would be useless as a messenger. General Howe, somehow finding a moment in the bustle of the oncoming invasion, had not only welcomed him with great courtesy but had offered him the choice: accompany Captain Griswold, serving in such manner as the captain might direct—or take command of a few companies orphaned of their own lieutenant, who had fallen ill of the ague.

He had jumped at the chance, and now sat proud in his saddle, his spontoon resting in its loop, leading men to war. He shifted a little, enjoying the feel of the new red wool coat on his shoulders, the orderly club of the queued pigtail on his neck, the stiff leather stock about his throat, and the small weight of his officer's gorget, that tiny silver remnant of Roman armor. He'd not worn uniform for nearly two months and, rain-damp or not, felt its resumption to be a glorious apotheosis.

A company of light horse traveled near them; he heard the shout of their officer and saw them draw ahead and turn toward a distant copse of wood. Had they seen something?

No. A tremendous cloud of blackbirds exploded from the copse, in a chatter so great that many of the horses shied and spooked. The horse soldiers foraged about, weaving through the trees with sabers drawn, slashing at branches, but just for show. If anyone had been hiding there, they had gone, and the light horse rode back to rejoin the advance, catcalling each other.

He relaxed back into his saddle, releasing his grip on the spontoon.

No Americans in sight—but they wouldn't be. He'd seen and heard enough in his intelligencing to know that only real Continentals were likely to fight in an organized fashion. He'd seen militia drilling in village squares, shared food with men who belonged to such militias. None of them were soldiers—seen in groups drilling, they were laughable, barely able to march in a line, let alone in step—but nearly all were skilled hunters, and he'd seen too many of them shoot wild geese and turkey on the fly to share the common contempt of most British soldiers.

No, if there were Americans nearby, the first warning of it was likely to be men falling dead. He signaled to Perkins, had him convey orders to the corporals, to keep the men alert, weapons loaded and primed. He saw one corporal's shoulders stiffen at receipt of this message, which he plainly considered an insult—but the man did it nonetheless, and William's sense of tension eased a bit.

His thoughts returned to his recent journey, and he wondered when—and where—he might meet with Captain Richardson, to turn over the results of his intelligencing.

He had committed most of his observations to memory while on the road, writing down only what he must, and that coded in a small copy of the New Testament that his grandmother had given him. It was still in the pocket of his civilian coat, back on Staten Island. Now that he was safely returned to the bosom of the army, perhaps he ought to write up his observations, in proper reports? He could—

Something raised him in his stirrups, just in time to catch the flash and crack of musket fire from the woods on the left.

"Hold!" he shouted, seeing his men start to lower their weapons. "Wait!"

It was too far, and there was another column of infantry, closer to the wood. These swung into firing order and loosed a volley into the woods; the first rank knelt and the second fired over their heads. Return fire came from the wood; he saw one or two men fall, others stagger, but the line pulled together.

Another two volleys, the sparks of returning fire, but more sporadic—from the corner of his eye, he saw movement and whirled in his saddle, to see a gang of woodsmen in hunting shirts running from the far side of the copse.

The company in front of him saw them, too. A shout from their sergeant, and they fixed bayonets and ran, though it was plain to William that they'd never catch the fleeing woodsmen.

This sort of random skirmishing kept up all afternoon, as the army pressed on. The fallen were picked up and carried to the rear, but they were few. One of William's companies was fired upon at one point, and he felt godlike as he gave the order to attack and they poured into the wood like a stream of angry hornets, bayonets fixed, managing to kill one rebel, whose body they dragged out onto the plain. The corporal suggested hanging it from a tree as discouragement to the other rebels, but William firmly declined this suggestion as not honorable and made them lay the man at the edge of the wood, where he could be found by his friends.

Toward evening, orders came along the line of march, from General Clinton. They would not stop to make camp. A brief pause for cold rations, and then press on.

There were murmurs of surprise in the ranks, but no grumbling. They'd come to fight, and the march resumed with a greater sense of urgency.

It was raining sporadically, and the harassment from skirmishers faded with the sullen light. It was not cold, and despite the growing soddenness of his garments, William preferred the chill and damp to the sultry oppression of the day before. At least the rain dampened the spirits of his horse, which was a good thing; it was a nervous, skittish creature, and he had cause to doubt Captain Griswold's goodwill in lending it to him. Worn down by the long day, though, the gelding ceased shying at windblown branches and jerking at the reins, and plodded onward with its ears falling sideways in tired resignation.

It wasn't bad for the first several hours of the night march. After midnight, though, the strain of exertion and sleeplessness began to tell on the men. Soldiers began to stumble and slow, and a sense of the vast expanse of dark and effort between themselves and dawn settled upon them.

William called Perkins up beside him. The soft-cheeked private showed up yawning and blinking, and paced beside him, a hand on William's stirrup leather as William explained what he wanted.

"Sing?" Perkins said doubtfully. "Well, I s'pose I can sing, yes, sir. Nobbut hymns, though."

"Not quite what I had in mind," William said. "Go and ask Sergeant . . . Millikin, is it? The Irishman? Anything he likes, so long as it's loud and lively." After all, they weren't trying to hide their presence; the Americans knew exactly where they were.

"Yes, sir," Perkins said dubiously, and let go the stirrup, fading at once into the night. William rode for some minutes, then heard Patrick Millikin's very loud Irish voice lifted in a very bawdy song. There was a ripple of laughter through the men, and by the time he reached the first chorus, a few had joined in. Two more verses and they were all roaring lustily along, William included.

They couldn't keep it up for hours while marching at

speed with full equipment, of course, but by the time they had exhausted their favorite songs and grown breathless, everyone was awake and optimistic once more.

Just before dawn, William smelled the sea and the rank mud scent of a marsh in the rain. The men, already wet, began to splash through a number of tiny tidal inlets and creeks.

A few minutes later, the boom of cannon broke the night, and marsh birds rose into the lightening sky with shrieks of alarm.

OVER THE COURSE of the next two days, William never had any idea where he was. Names such as "Jamaica Pass," "Flatbush," and "Gowanus Creek" occurred now and then in the dispatches and hasty messages that passed through the army, but they might as well have said "Jupiter" or "the backside of the moon" for all the meaning they had.

He did see Continentals, at last. Hordes of them, swarming out of the marshes. The first few clashes were fierce, but William's companies were held to the rear, supporting; only once were they close enough to fire, in order to repulse an oncoming group of Americans.

Nonetheless, he was in a constant state of excitement, trying to hear and see everything at once, intoxicated by the smell of powder smoke, even as his flesh quivered at the report of cannon. When the firing ceased at sunset, he took a little biscuit and cheese, but without tasting it, and slept only briefly, from sheer exhaustion.

In late afternoon of the second day, they found themselves some little way behind a large stone farmhouse that the British and some Hessian troops had taken over as an artillery emplacement; the barrels of cannon protruded from the upper windows, shining wet with the constant rain.

Wet powder was a problem now; the cartridges were all right, but if the powder poured into priming pans was left more than a few minutes, it began to cake and go dead. The order to load, then, had to be delayed until the last possible moment before firing; William found himself grinding his teeth in anxiety as to when the order should be given.

On the other hand, sometimes there was no doubt at all.

With hoarse shouts, a number of Americans charged out of the trees near the front of the house and made for the doors and windows. Musket fire from the troops inside got several of them, but some made it as far as the house itself, where they began to clamber into the shattered windows. William automatically reined up and rode to the right, far enough to get a look at the rear of the house. Sure enough, a larger group was already at it, a number of them climbing the wall by means of the ivy that covered the back of the house.

"That way!" he bellowed, wheeling his horse around and waving his spontoon. "Olson, Jeffries, the back! Load and fire as soon as you're in range!"

Two of his companies ran, ripping the ends of cartridges with their teeth, but a party of green-coated Hessians was there before him, seizing Americans by the legs and pulling them from the ivy to club them on the ground.

He reined round and dashed the other way, to see what was happening in front, and came in sight just in time to see a British artilleryman fly out of one of the open upper windows. The man landed on the ground, one leg bent under him, and lay screaming. One of William's men, close enough, darted forward and grabbed the man's shoulders, only to be shot by someone within the house. He crumpled and fell, his hat rolling off into the bushes.

They spent the rest of that day at the stone farmhouse; four times, the Americans made forays—twice, they succeeded in overcoming the inhabitants and briefly seizing the guns, but both times were overrun by fresh waves of British troops and evicted or killed. William never got closer than two hundred yards or so to the house itself, but once managed to interpose one of his companies between the house and a surge of desperate Americans dressed like Indians and yelling like banshees. One of them raised a long rifle and fired directly at him, but missed. He drew his sword, intending to ride the man down, but a shot from somewhere struck the man and sent him rolling down the face of a small hillock.

William urged his mount closer, to see whether the man was dead or not—the man's companions had already fled round the far corner of the house, pursued by British troops. The gelding wasn't having any; trained to the sound of musket fire, it found artillery unnerving, and the cannon happening to speak at this particular moment, the gelding laid its ears flat back and bolted.

William had his sword still in hand, the reins loosely wrapped round his other hand; the sudden jolt unseated him, and the horse whipped to the left, jerking his right foot from the stirrup and pitching him off. He had barely presence of mind to let go of the sword as he fell, and landed on one shoulder, rolling.

Simultaneously thanking God that his left foot hadn't been trapped in its stirrup and cursing the horse, he scrambled up onto hands and knees, smeared with grass and mud, heart in his mouth.

The guns in the house had stopped; the Americans must be in there again, engaged in hand-to-hand fighting with the gun crews. He spat out mud, and began to make a cautious withdrawal; he thought he was in range of the upper windows.

To his left, though, he caught sight of the American who had tried to shoot him, still lying in the wet grass. With a wary glance at the house, he crawled to the man, who was lying on his face, unmoving. He wanted to see the man's face, for what reason he couldn't have said. He rose on his knees and took the man by both shoulders, pulling him over.

The man was clearly dead, shot through the head. Mouth and eyes sagged half open and his body felt strange, heavy and flopping. He wore a militia uniform of sorts; William saw the wooden buttons, with "PUT" burnt into them. That meant something, but his dazed mind made no sense of it. Gently laying the man back in the grass, he rose and went to fetch his sword. His knees felt peculiar.

Halfway to the spot where his sword lay, he stopped, turned round, and came back. Kneeling down, cold-fingered and hollow-bellied, he closed the man's dead eyes against the rain.

THEY MADE CAMP that night, to the pleasure of the men. Camp kitchens were dug, the cook wagons brought up, and the scent of roasting meat and fresh bread filled the damp air. William had just sat down to eat when Perkins, that harbinger of doom, appeared apologetically at his side with a message: report to General Howe's field headquarters at once. Snatching a loaf of bread and a steaming chunk of roast pork to put in it, he went, chewing.

He found the three generals and all of their staff officers gathered together, deep in a discussion of the day's results. The generals sat at a small table thick with dispatches and hastily drawn maps. William found a place among the staff officers, standing respectfully back against the walls of the big tent.

Sir Henry was arguing for an attack on the Brooklyn Heights, come morning.

"We could dislodge them easily," Clinton said, waving a hand at the dispatches. "They've lost half their men, if not more—and weren't such a lot of 'em to start with."

"Not easily," said my lord Cornwallis, pursing fat lips. "You saw them fight. Yes, we could get them out of there—but at some cost. What say you, sir?" he added, turning deferentially to Howe.

Howe's lips all but disappeared, only a white line marking their former existence.

"I can't afford another victory like the last one," he snapped. "Or if I could, I don't want it." His eyes left the table and passed over the juniors standing against the wall. "I lost every man on my staff at that damned hill in Boston," he said, more quietly. "Twenty-eight of them. Every one." His eyes lingered on William, the youngest of the junior officers present, and he shook his head, as though to himself, and turned back to Sir Henry.

"Stop the fighting," he said.

Sir Henry wasn't pleased, William could see that, but he merely nodded.

"Offer them terms?"

"No," Howe said shortly. "They've lost nearly half their men, as you said. No one but a madman would go on fighting without cause. They—you, sir. Did you have an observation to make?"

With a start, William realized that Howe was addressing this remark to him; those round eyes were boring into his chest like bird shot.

"I—" he began, but then caught himself and drew up straight. "Yes, sir. It's General Putnam in command. There at the creek. He's . . . perhaps not a madman, sir," he added carefully, "but he has the name of a stubborn man."

Howe paused, eyes narrowed.

"A stubborn man," he repeated. "Yes. I should say he is."

"He was one of the commanders at Breed's Hill, wasn't he?" objected Lord Cornwallis. "The Americans ran fast enough away from *there*."

"Yes, but—" William stopped dead, paralyzed by the fixed joint stares of three generals. Howe motioned him impatiently to go on.

"With respect, my lord," he said, and was glad that his voice didn't shake, "I . . . hear that the Americans did not run in Boston until they had exhausted every scrap of ammunition. I think . . . that is not the case, here. And with regard to General Putnam—there was no one behind him at Breed's Hill."

"And you think that there is now." It wasn't a question.

"Yes, sir." William tried not to look pointedly at the stack of dispatches on Sir William's table. "I'm sure of it, sir. I think nearly all of the Continentals are on the island, sir." He tried not to make that sound like a question; he'd heard as much from a passing major the day before, but it might not be true. "If Putnam's in command here—"

"How do you know it's Putnam, Lieutenant?" Clinton interrupted, giving William the fish-eye.

"I am lately come from an—an intelligencing expedition, sir, which took me through Connecticut. I heard there, from many people, that militia were gathering to accompany General Putnam, who was to join with General Washington's forces near New York. And I saw a button on one of the rebel dead near the creek this afternoon, sir, with 'PUT' carved on it. That's what they call him, sir—General Putnam: 'Old Put.' "

General Howe straightened himself before Clinton or Cornwallis could interject anything further.

"A stubborn man," he repeated. "Well, perhaps he is. Nonetheless . . . suspend the fighting. He is in an untenable position, and must know it. Give him a chance to think it over—to consult with Washington if he likes. Washington is perhaps a more sensible commander. And if we might gain the surrender of the whole Continental army without further bloodshed . . . I think it worth the risk, gentlemen. But we will not offer terms."

Which meant that if the Americans saw sense, it would be an unconditional surrender. And if they didn't? William had heard stories about the fight at Breed's Hill—granted, stories told by Americans, and therefore he took them with several grains of salt. But by account, the rebels there had taken the nails from the fencing of their fortifications—from the very heels of their shoes—and fired them at the British when their shot ran out. They had retreated only when reduced to throwing stones.

"But if Putnam's expecting reinforcement from Washington, he'll only sit and wait," Clinton said, frowning. "And then we'll have the whole boiling of them. Had we best not—"

"That's not what he meant," Howe interruputed. "Was it, Ellesmere? When you said there was no one behind him at Breed's Hill?"

"No, sir," William said, grateful. "I meant . . . he has something to protect. Behind him. I don't think he's waiting for the rest of the army to come to his aid. I think he's covering their retreat."

Lord Cornwallis's hooped brows shot up at that. Clinton scowled at William, who recalled too late that Clinton had been the field commander at the Pyrrhic victory of Breed's Hill and was likely sensitive on the subject of Israel Putnam.

"And why are we soliciting the advice of a boy still wet behind the—have you ever even seen combat, sir?" he demanded of William, who flushed hotly.

"I'd be fighting now, sir," he said, "were I not detained here!"

Lord Cornwallis laughed, and a brief smile flitted across Howe's face.

"We shall make certain to have you properly blooded, Lieutenant," he said dryly. "But not today. Captain Ramsay?" He motioned to one of the senior staff, a short man with very square shoulders, who stepped forward and saluted. "Take Ellesmere here and have him tell you the results of his . . . intelligencing. Convey to me anything which strikes you as being of interest. In the meantime"—he turned back to his two generals—"suspend hostilities until further notice."

WILLIAM HEARD NO more of the generals' deliberations, he being led away by Captain Ramsay.

Had he spoken too much out of turn? he wondered. Granted, General Howe had asked him a direct question; he had had to answer. But to put forward his paltry month's intelligencing, against the combined knowledge of so many experienced senior officers . . .

He said something of his doubts to Captain Ramsay, who seemed a quiet sort but friendly enough.

"Oh, you hadn't any choice but to speak up," Ramsay assured him. "Still . . ."

William dodged round a pile of mule droppings in order to keep up with Ramsay.

"Still?" he asked.

Ramsay didn't answer for a bit, but led the way through the encampment, down neat aisles of canvas tents, waving now and then at men round a fire who called out to him.

At last, they arrived at Ramsay's own tent, and he held back the flap for William, gesturing him in.

"Heard of a lady called Cassandra?" Ramsay said at last. "Some sort of Greek, I think. Not very popular."

THE ARMY SLEPT soundly after its exertions, and so did William.

"Your tea, sir?"

He blinked, disoriented and still wrapped in dreams of walking through the Duke of Devonshire's private zoo, hand in hand with an orangutan. But it was Private Perkins's round and anxious face, rather than the orangutan's, that greeted him.

"What?" he said stupidly. Perkins seemed to swim in a sort of haze, but this was not dispelled by blinking, and when he sat up to take the steaming cup, he discovered the cause of it was that the air itself was permeated with a heavy mist.

All sound was muffled; while the normal noises of a camp rising were to be heard, they sounded far away, subdued. No surprise, then, when he poked his head out of his tent a few minutes later, to find the ground blanketed with a drifting fog that had crept in from the marshes.

It didn't matter much. The army was going nowhere. A dispatch from Howe's headquarters had made the suspension of hostilities official; there was nothing to do but wait for the Americans to see sense and surrender.

The army stretched, yawned, and sought distraction. William was engaged in a hot game of hazard with Corporals Yarnell and Jeffries when Perkins came up again, breathless.

"Colonel Spencer's compliments, sir, and you're to report to General Clinton."

"Yes? What for?" William demanded. Perkins looked baffled; it hadn't occurred to him to ask the messenger what for.

"Just . . . I suppose he wants you," he said, in an effort to be helpful.

"Thank you very much, Private Perkins," William said, with a sarcasm wasted on Perkins, who beamed in relief and retired without being dismissed.

"Perkins!" he bellowed, and the private turned, round face startled. "Which way?"

"What? Er . . . what, sir, I mean?"

"In which direction does General Clinton's headquarters lie?" William asked, with elaborate patience.

"Oh! The hussar . . . he came from . . ." Perkins rotated slowly, like a weather vane, frowning in concentration. "That way!" He pointed. "I could see that bit of hillock behind him." The fog was still thick near the ground, but the crests of hills and tall trees were now and then visible, and William had no difficulty in spotting the hillock to which Perkins referred; it had an odd lumpy look to it.

"Thank you, Perkins. Dismissed," he added quickly, before Perkins could make off again. He watched the private disappear into the shifting mass of fog and bodies, then shook his head and went to hand command over to Corporal Evans.

The gelding didn't like the fog. William didn't like it, either. Fog gave him an uneasy feeling, as though someone was breathing on the back of his neck.

This was a sea fog, though: heavy, dank, and cold, but not smothering. It thinned and thickened, with a sense of movement to it. He could see a few feet before him, and could just make out the dim shape of the hillock Perkins had indicated, though the top kept appearing and disappearing like some fantastic conjuration in a fairy tale.

What might Sir Henry want with him? he wondered. And was it only he who'd been sent for, or was this a meeting called to apprise the line officers of some change of strategy?

Maybe Putnam's men had surrendered. They should, certainly; they had no hope of victory in the circumstances, and that must be plain to them.

But he supposed Putnam would need, perhaps, to consult with Washington. During the fighting at the old stone farmhouse, he'd seen a small group of horsemen on the crest of a distant hill, an unfamiliar flag fluttering amongst them; someone at the time had pointed at it and said, "That's him there, Washington. Shame we've not got a twenty-four in place—teach him to gawk!" and laughed.

Sense said they'd surrender. But he had an uneasy feeling that had nothing to do with the fog. During his month on the road, he'd had occasion to listen to a good many Americans. Most were uneasy themselves, not wanting conflict with England, particularly not wanting to be anywhere near armed strife—a very sensible conclusion. But the ones who *were* decided on revolt . . . were very decided indeed.

Maybe Ramsay had conveyed some of this to the generals; he hadn't seemed at all impressed by any of William's information, let alone his opinions, but perhaps—

The horse stumbled, and he lurched in his saddle, accidentally jerking the reins. The horse, annoyed, whipped round its head and bit him, big teeth scraping on his boot.

"Bastard!" He smacked the horse across the nose with the ends of the reins, and hauled the gelding's head round forcibly, until the rolling eyes and curled lip were nearly in his lap. Then, his point made, he slowly released the pressure. The horse snorted and shook his mane violently, but resumed progress without further argument.

He seemed to have been riding for some time. But time as well as distance was deceiving in fog. He glanced up at the hillock that was his goal, only to discover that it had vanished again. Well, doubtless it would come back.

Only it didn't.

The fog continued to shift around him, and he heard the

dripping of moisture from the leaves of the trees that seemed to come suddenly out of the mist at him and as suddenly retreat again. But the hillock stayed stubbornly invisible.

It occurred to him that he hadn't heard any sounds of men for some time now.

He should have.

If he were approaching Clinton's headquarters, he should not only be hearing all the normal camp sounds, he should have encountered any number of men, horses, campfires, wagons, tents . . .

There was no noise anywhere near him, save the rushing of water. He'd bloody bypassed the camp.

"Damn you, Perkins," he said under his breath.

He drew up for a moment and checked the priming of his pistol, sniffing at the powder in the pan; it smelled different when the damp got at it. Still all right, he thought; it smelled hot and nose-prickling, not so much of the rotten-egg scent of sulfur as wet powder had.

He kept the pistol in his hand, though so far he'd seen nothing threatening. The fog was too heavy to see more than a few feet in front of him, though; someone could come out of it suddenly, and he'd have to decide on the instant whether to shoot them or not.

It was quiet; their own artillery was silent; there was no random musket fire like the day before. The enemy was in retreat; no doubt about that. But if he should stumble across a stray Continental, lost in the fog like himself, ought he to shoot? The thought made his hands sweat, but he thought he must; the Continental would likely have no hesitation about shooting *him,* the instant he saw the red uniform.

He was somewhat more worried about the humiliation of being shot by his own troops than about the actual prospect of death, but was not entirely oblivious to the risk of that, either.

The bloody fog had got thicker, if anything. He looked in vain for the sun, to give some sense of direction, but the sky was invisible.

He fought back the small quiver of panic that tickled his tailbone. Right, there were 34,000 British troops on this bloody island; he had to be within pistol shot of any number of them at this moment. *And you only need be in pistol shot of one American,* he reminded himself, grimly pushing through a growth of larches.

He heard rustlings and the cracking of branches nearby; the wood was inhabited, no doubt about it. But by whom?

The British troops wouldn't be moving in this fog, that was one thing. Curse Perkins! If he heard movement, then, as of a body of men, he'd stop and stay hidden. And otherwise . . . all he could hope to do was to run across a body of troops, or to hear something unmistakably military in nature—shouted orders, perhaps . . .

He rode on slowly for some time, and finally put the pistol away, finding the weight of it wearisome. God, how long had he been out? An hour? Two? Ought he to turn around? But he had no way of knowing what "around" was—he might be traveling in circles; the ground all looked the same, a gray blur of trees and rocks and grasses. Yesterday, he'd spent every minute keyed to fever pitch, ready for the attack. Today, his enthusiasm for fighting had ebbed substantially.

Someone stepped out in front of him and the horse reared, so abruptly that William had only the vaguest impression of the man. Enough to know he wasn't wearing a British uniform, though, and he would have snatched his pistol out, were both hands not occupied in trying to control the horse.

The horse, having given way to hysteria, crow-hopped in mad circles, jarring William to the spine with each landing. His surroundings spun past in a blur of gray and green, but he was half conscious of voices, whooping in what might be either derision or encouragement.

After what seemed an age, but must be only half a minute or so, William succeeded in bringing the bloody creature to a standstill, panting and blowing, still flinging its head around, the whites of its eyes showing, gleaming wet.

"You fucking piece of cat's meat!" William said to it, hauling its head round. The horse's breath sank damp and hot through the doeskin of his breeches, and its sides heaved under him.

"Not the best-tempered horse I ever seen," a voice agreed, and a hand came up, seizing the bridle. "Healthy-looking, though."

William got a glimpse of a man in hunting dress, stout and

swarthy—and then someone else seized him round the waist from behind and hauled him bodily off the horse.

He hit the ground hard and flat on his back, knocking out his wind, but tried valiantly to get to his pistol. A knee pressed into his chest, and a large hand wrestled the pistol out of his grip. A bearded face grinned down at him.

"Not very sociable," the man said, reproving. "Thought you-all was meant to be civilized, you British."

"You let him get up and at you, Harry, I imagine he'd civilize you, all right." This was another man, shorter and slightly built, with a soft, educated voice like a schoolmaster, who peered over the shoulder of the man kneeling on William's chest. "You could let him breathe, though, I suppose."

The pressure on William's chest relaxed, and he got a whisper of air into his lungs. This was promptly driven out again when the man who had held him down punched him in the stomach. Hands promptly began to rifle his pockets, and his gorget was jerked off over his head, painfully scraping the underside of his nose. Someone reached round him and unbuckled his belt, neatly removing it with a whistle of pleasure at the equipment attached.

"Very nice," said the second man, approving. He glanced down at William, lying on the ground and gasping like a landed fish. "I thank you, sir; we're much obliged. All right, Allan?" he called, turning toward the man holding the horse.

"Aye, I've got 'im," said a nasal Scottish voice. "Let's be off!"

The men moved away, and for an instant, William thought they had left. Then a meaty hand seized his shoulder and flipped him over. He writhed up onto his knees by sheer will, and the same hand seized his pigtail and jerked his head back, exposing his throat. He caught the gleam of a knife, and the man's broad grin, but had neither breath nor time for prayers or curses.

The knife slashed down, and he felt a yank at the back of his head that brought water to his eyes. The man grunted, displeased, and hacked twice more, finally coming away triumphant, William's pigtail held up in a ham-sized hand.

"Souvenir," he said to William, grinning, and whirling on his heel, made off after his friends. The horse's whinny drifted back to William through the fog, mocking.

HE WISHED, URGENTLY, that he had managed to kill at least one of them. But they'd taken him as easily as a child, plucked him like a goose and left him lying on the ground like a fucking turd! His rage was so overwhelming that he had to stop and punch a tree trunk. The pain of that left him gasping, still murderous but breathless.

He clutched the injured hand between his thighs, hissing between his teeth until the pain abated. Shock was mingling with fury; he felt more disoriented than ever, his head spinning. Chest heaving, he reached behind his head with his sound hand, feeling the bristly stumpage left there—and overcome with fresh rage, kicked the tree with all his strength.

He limped round in circles, swearing, then finally collapsed onto a rock and put his head down on his knees, panting.

Gradually, his breath slowed, and his ability to think rationally began to return.

Right. He was still lost in the wilds of Long Island, only now minus horse, food, or weapons. Or hair. *That* made him sit up straight, fists clenched, and he fought back the fury, with some difficulty. Right. He hadn't time to be angry now. If he ever laid eyes on Harry, Allan, or the little man with the educated voice . . . well, time enough for that when it happened.

For now, the important thing was to locate some part of the army. His impulse was to desert on the spot, take ship to France, and never come back, leaving the army to presume that he'd been killed. But he couldn't do that for assorted reasons, not least his father—who'd probably prefer that he *was* killed than run cravenly away.

No help for it. He rose resignedly to his feet, trying to feel grateful that the bandits had at least left him his coat. The fog was lifting a little here and there, but still lay damp and chilly on the ground. Not that he was troubled by that; his own blood was still boiling.

He glared round at the shadowy shapes of rocks and trees.

They looked just like all the other fucking rocks and trees he'd encountered in the course of this misbegotten day.

"Right," he said aloud, and stabbed a finger into the air, turning as he did so. "Eeny-meeny-miney-mo, catch a Frenchy by the toe, if he's squealing—oh, the hell with it."

Limping slightly, he set off. He had no idea where he was going, but he had to move, or burst.

He entertained himself for some little time in reimagining the recent encounter, with satisfying visions of himself seizing the fat man named Harry and wringing his nose into bloody pulp before smashing his head on a rock. Grabbing the knife away from him and gutting that supercilious little bastard . . . ripping his lungs out . . . there was a thing called the "blood eagle" that the savage German tribes used to do, slitting a man's back and dragging out his lungs through the slits, so they flapped like wings as he died . . .

Gradually, he grew calmer, only because it was impossible to sustain such a level of fury.

His foot felt better; his knuckles were skinned, but not throbbing as much, and his fantasies of revenge began to seem faintly absurd to him. Was that what the fury of battle was like? he wondered. Did you want not just to shoot and stab because it was your duty to kill, but did you *like* it? Want it like wanting a woman? And did you feel like a fool after doing it?

He'd thought about killing in battle. Not all the time, but on and off. He'd made a great effort to visualize it when he'd made up his mind to join the army. And he did realize that there might be regret attached to the act.

His father had told him, baldly and with no effort at self-justification, about the circumstances under which he had killed his first man. Not in battle, but following one. The point-blank execution of a Scot, wounded and left on the field at Culloden.

"Under orders," his father had said. "No quarter to be given; those were our written orders, signed by Cumberland." His father's eyes had been fixed on his bookshelves during the telling, but at this point he'd looked at William directly.

"Orders," he repeated. "You follow orders, of course; you have to. But there will be times when you have no orders, or find yourself in a situation which has changed suddenly. And there will be times—there *will* be times, William—when your own honor dictates that you cannot follow an order. In such circumstances, you must follow your own judgment, and be prepared to live with the consequences."

William had nodded, solemn. He'd just brought his commission papers for his father to look over, Lord John's signature being required as his guardian. He'd regarded the signing as a mere formality, though; he hadn't been expecting either a confession or a sermon—if that's what this was.

"I shouldn't have done it," his father had said abruptly. "I shouldn't have shot him."

"But—your orders—"

"They didn't affect me, not directly. I hadn't yet got my commission; I'd gone with my brother on campaign, but I wasn't a soldier yet; I wasn't under the army's authority. I could have refused."

"If you had, wouldn't someone else have shot him?" William asked practically.

His father smiled, but without humor.

"Yes, they would. But that's not the point. And it's true that it never occurred to me that I had a choice in the matter—but that *is* the point. You always have a choice, William. Do remember that, will you?"

Without waiting for an answer, he'd leaned forward and plucked a quill from the blue-and-white Chinese jar on his desk, and flipped open his rock-crystal inkwell.

"You're sure?" he'd said, looking seriously at William, and at the latter's nod, signed his name with a flourish. Then had looked up and smiled.

"I'm proud of you, William," he'd said quietly. "I always will be."

William sighed. He didn't doubt that his father would always love him, but as for making him proud . . . this particular expedition did not seem likely to cover him in glory. He'd be lucky to get back to his own troops before someone noticed how long he'd been gone and raised the alarm. God, how ignominious, to get lost and robbed, as his first notable act!

Still, better than having his first notable act being killed by bandits.

He continued to make his way cautiously through the fog-draped woods. The footing wasn't bad, though there were boggy places where the rain had pooled in low spots. Once, he heard the ragged crack of musket fire and hurried toward it, but it stopped before he came in sight of whoever had been firing.

He trudged grimly along, wondering just how long it might take to traverse the whole of the bloody island on foot, and how close he was to having done so? The ground had risen sharply; he was climbing now, sweat running freely down his face. He fancied the fog was thinning as he climbed, and sure enough, at one point he emerged onto a small rocky promontory and had a brief glimpse of the ground below—completely covered in swirling gray fog. The sight gave him vertigo, and he was obliged to sit down on a rock for a few moments with his eyes closed before continuing.

Twice, he heard the sound of men and horses, but the sound was subtly wrong; the voices didn't have the rhythms of the army, and he turned away, edging cautiously in the opposite direction.

He found the ground change abruptly, becoming a sort of scrub forest, full of stunted trees poking from a light-colored soil that scrunched under his boots. Then he heard water—waves lapping on a beach. The sea! Well, thank God for that, he thought, and hastened his steps toward the sound.

As he made his way toward the sound of the waves, though, he suddenly perceived other sounds.

Boats. The grating of hulls—more than one—on gravel, the clank of oarlocks, splashing. And voices. Hushed voices, but agitated. Bloody hell! He ducked under the limb of a runty pine, hoping for a break in the drifting fog.

A sudden movement sent him lunging sideways, hand reaching for his pistol. He barely remembered that the pistol was gone, before realizing that his adversary was a great blue heron, which eyed him with a yellow glare before launching itself skyward in a clatter of affront. A cry of alarm came from the bushes, no more than ten feet away, together with the boom of a musket, and the heron exploded in a shower of feathers, directly over his head. He felt drops of the bird's blood, much warmer than the cold sweat on his face, and sat down very suddenly, black spots dizzy before his eyes.

He didn't dare move, let alone call out. There was a whisper of voices from the bushes, but not loud enough that he could make out any words. After a few moments, though, he heard a stealthy rustling that moved gradually away. Making as little noise as possible, he rolled onto hands and knees and crawled for some distance in the other direction, until he felt it safe to rise to his feet again.

He thought he still heard voices. He crept closer, moving slowly, his heart thumping. He smelled tobacco, and froze.

Nothing moved near him, though—he could still hear the voices, but they were a good way distant. He sniffed, cautiously, but the scent had vanished; perhaps he was imagining things. He moved on, toward the sounds.

He could hear them clearly now. Urgent, low-voiced calls, the rattle of oarlocks and the splash of feet in the surf. The shuffle and murmur of men, blending—almost—with the susurrus of sea and grass. He cast one last desperate glance at the sky, but the sun was still invisible. He *had* to be on the western side of the island; he was sure of it. Almost sure of it. And if he was . . .

If he was, the sounds he was hearing had to be those of American troops, fleeing the island for Manhattan.

"Don't. Stir." The whisper behind him coincided exactly with the pressure of a gun's barrel, jammed hard enough into his kidney as to freeze him where he stood. It withdrew for an instant and returned, rammed home with a force that blurred his eyes. He made a guttural sound and arched his back, but before he could speak, someone with horny hands had seized his wrists and jerked them back.

"No need," said the voice, deep, cracked, and querulous. "Stand aside and I'll shoot him."

"No, 'ee won't," said another, just as deep but less annoyed. " 'e's nobbut a youngun. And pretty, too." One of the horny hands stroked his cheek and he stiffened, but whoever it was had already bound his hands tight.

"And if 'ee meant to shoot 'im, you'm 've done it already, sister," the voice added. "Turn y'self, boy."

Slowly, he turned round, to see that he had been captured by a pair of old women, short and squat as trolls. One of them, the one with the gun, was smoking a pipe; it was her tobacco he'd smelled. Seeing the shock and disgust on his features, she lifted one corner of a seamed mouth while keeping a firm grip on the pipestem with the stumps of brown-stained teeth.

" 'Andsome is as 'andsome does," she observed, looking him up and down. "Still, no need to waste shot."

"Madam," he said, collecting himself and trying for charm. "I believe you mistake me. I am a soldier of the King, and—"

Both of them burst into laughter, creaking like a pair of rusty hinges.

"Wouldn't never've guessed," the pipe-smoker said, grinning round the stem of her pipe. "Thought 'ee was a jakesman, sure!"

"Hush up, sonny," her sister interrupted his further attempt to speak. "We bain't going to harm 'ee, so long as 'ee stands still and keeps mum." She eyed him, taking in the damage.

"Been in the wars, have 'ee?" she said, not without sympathy. Not waiting for an answer, she pushed him down onto a rock, this liberally crusted with mussels and dripping weed, from which he deduced his closeness to the shore.

He didn't speak. Not for fear of the old women, but because there was nothing to say.

He sat, listening to the sounds of the exodus. No idea how many men might be involved, as he had no notion how long it had been going on. Nothing useful was said; there were only the breathless half-heard exchanges of men working, the mutter of waiting, here and there the sort of muffled laughter born of nervousness.

The fog was lifting off the water. He could see them now—not more than a hundred yards away, a tiny fleet of rowboats, dories, here and there a fishing ketch, moving slowly to and fro across water smooth as glass—and a steadily dwindling crowd of men on shore, keeping their hands on their guns, glancing continually over their shoulders, alert for pursuit.

Little did they know, he reflected bitterly.

At the moment, he had no concern for his own future; the humiliation of being an impotent witness as the entire American army escaped under his nose—and the further thought of being obliged to return and recount this occurrence to General Howe—was so galling that he didn't care whether the old women had it in mind to cook and eat him.

Focused as he was on the scene on the beach, it didn't occur to him at once that if he could now see the Americans, he was himself visible to them. In fact, so intent were the Continentals and militiamen on their retreat that none of them *did* notice him, until one man turned away from the retreat, seeming to search the upper reaches of the shore for something.

The man stiffened, then, with a brief glance back at his oblivious companions, came purposefully up across the shingle, eyes fixed on William.

"What's this, Mother?" he asked. He was dressed in the uniform of a Continental officer, built short and wide, much like the two women, but a good deal bigger, and while his face was outwardly calm, there were calculations going on behind his bloodshot eyes.

"Been fishing," said the pipe-smoker. "Caught this wee redfish, but we think we'll throw 'im back."

"Aye? Maybe not just yet."

William had stiffened with the man's appearance, and stared up at him, keeping his own face as grim as possible.

The man glanced up at the shredding fog behind William. "More like you at home, are there, boy?"

William sat silent. The man sighed, drew back his fist, and hit William in the stomach. He doubled up, fell off the rock, and lay retching on the sand. The man grasped him by the collar and hauled him up, as though he weighed nothing.

"Answer me, lad. I haven't much time, and 'ee don't want me to be hasty in my asking." He spoke mildly, but touched the knife at his belt.

William wiped his mouth, as well as he could, on his shoulder and faced the man, eyes burning. *All right,* he thought, and felt a certain calmness descend on him. *If this is where I die, at least I'll die for something.* The thought was almost a relief.

The pipe-smoker's sister put paid to the dramatics, though, poking his interrogator in the ribs with her musket.

"If there was more, sister and I'd'a heard 'em long since," she said, mildly disgusted. "They ain't quiet, sojers."

"True, that," the pipe-smoker agreed, and paused to remove her pipe long enough to spit. "This 'un's only lost, 'ee can see as much. 'Ee can see he won't talk to 'ee, either." She grinned familiarly at William, displaying one remaining yellow dogtooth. "Rather die than speak, eh, lad?"

William inclined his head a stiff inch, and the women giggled. No other word for it: they *giggled* at him.

"Get on with 'ee," the aunt told the man, waving a hand at the beach behind him. "They'll leave without 'ee."

The man didn't look at her—didn't take his eyes off William's. After a moment, though, he nodded briefly and turned on his heel.

William felt one of the women behind him; something sharp touched his wrist, and the twine they'd bound him with parted. He wanted to rub his wrists, but didn't.

"Go, boy," the pipe-smoker said, almost gently. "Before someun else sees 'ee and gets ideas."

He left.

At the top of the beach, he paused and looked back. The old women had vanished, but the man was sitting in the stern of a rowboat, drawing rapidly away from the shore, now nearly empty. The man was staring at him.

William turned away. The sun was finally visible, a pale orange circle burning through the haze. It was coming down the sky now, early afternoon. He turned inland and struck southwest, but felt eyes on his back for a long time after the shore had fallen out of sight behind him.

His stomach was sore, and the only thought in his mind was what Captain Ramsay had said to him. *Heard of a lady called Cassandra?*

7

AN UNCERTAIN FUTURE

Lallybroch Inverness-shire, Scotland
September 1980

NOT ALL OF the letters were dated, but some were. Bree sorted gingerly through the half-dozen on top, and with a sense of being poised at the top of a roller coaster, chose one with *2 March, A.D. 1777* written across the flap.

"I think this one's next." She had trouble taking a full breath. "It's—thin. Short."

It was, no more than a page and a half, but the reason for its brevity was clear; her father had written the whole of it. His awkward, determined writing wrung her heart.

"We are never letting a teacher try to make Jemmy write with his right hand," she said fiercely to Roger. "Never!"

"Right," he said, surprised and a little amused at her outburst. "Or left, if you prefer."

2 March, Anno Domini 1777
Fraser's Ridge, colony of
North Carolina

My dearest daughter—

We prepare now to remove to Scotland. Not forever, or even for long. My Life—our Lives—lie here in America. And in all Honesty, I should greatly prefer to be stung to Death by Hornets than set foot on board another Ship; I try not to dwell upon the

Prospect. But there are two chief Concerns which compel me to this Decision.

Had I not the Gift of Knowledge that you and your Mother and Roger Mac have brought me, I would likely think—as the great Majority of People in the Colony do think—that the Continental Congress will not last six Months, and Washington's Army less than that. I have spoken myself with a man from Cross Creek, who was discharged (honourably) from the Continental army on account of a festering Wound in the Arm—your Mother has of course dealt with this; he screamed a great Deal and I was pressed into service to sit upon him—who tells me that Washington has no more than a few thousand regular Soldiers, all very poor in Equipment, Clothes, and Arms, and all owed Money, which they are unlikely to receive. Most of his men are Militia, enlisted on short Contracts of two or three Months, and already melting away, needing to return Home for the Planting.

But I do know. At the same Time, I cannot be sure how the Things that I know will come about. Am I meant to be in some Way Part of this? Should I hold back, will that somehow damage or prevent the Success of our Desires? I often wish I could discuss these Questions with your Husband, though Presbyterian that he is, I think he would find them even more unsettling than I do. And in the end, it does not matter. I am what God has made me, and must deal with the Times in which He has placed me.

While I have not yet lost the Faculties of Sight or Hearing, nor even Control of my Bowels, I am not a young Man. I have a Sword, and a Rifle, and can use them both—but I also have a printing Press, and can use that to much greater Effect; it does not escape me that one can wield Sword or Musket only upon one Enemy at a time, while Words may be employed upon any Number.

Your Mother—doubtless contemplating the Prospect of my being seasick for several Weeks in her immediate Vicinity—suggests that I might enter

Business with Fergus, making use of L'Oignon*'s Press, rather than travel to Scotland to retrieve my own.*

I considered this, but I cannot in Conscience expose Fergus and his Family to Danger by making use of their Press for such Purposes as I intend. Theirs is one of only a few Presses in operation between Charleston and Norfolk; even were I to do my Printing with the utmost Secrecy, Suspicion would focus upon them in short order—New Bern is a Hotbed of Loyalist Sentiment, and the Origins of my pamphleteering would become known almost immediately.

Beyond Consideration for Fergus and his Family, I think there may be some Benefit in visiting Edinburgh in order to retrieve my own Press. I had a varied Acquaintance there; some may have escaped Prison or the Noose.

The second—and most important—Consideration that compels me to Scotland, though, is your Cousin Ian. Years ago, I swore to his Mother—upon the Memory of our own Mother—that I would bring him Home to her, and this I mean to do, though the Man I bring back to Lallybroch is not the Lad who left there. God alone knows what they will make of each other, Ian and Lallybroch—and God has a most peculiar Sense of Humor. But if he is to go back at all, it must be now.

The Snow is melting; Water drips from the Eaves all Day, and Icicles reach from the Roof of the Cabin nearly to the Ground by Morning. Within a few Weeks, the Roads will be clear enough for Travel. It seems strange to ask that you pray for the Safety of a Voyage which will have been long completed by the Time you learn of it—for good or ill—but I ask it, nonetheless. Tell Roger Mac that I think God takes no account of Time. And kiss the Children for me.

Your most affectionate Father,
JF

Roger sat back a little, eyebrows raised, and glanced at her. "The French Connection, you think?"

"The *what*?" She frowned over his shoulder, saw where his finger marked the text. "Where he's talking about his friends in Edinburgh?"

"Aye. Were not a good many of his Edinburgh acquaintances smugglers?"

"That's what Mama said."

"Hence the remark about nooses. And where were they smuggling things *from,* mostly?"

Her stomach gave a small hop.

"Oh, you're kidding. You think he's planning to mess with French smugglers?"

"Well, not smugglers, necessarily; he apparently knew a good many seditionists, thieves, and prostitutes, too." Roger smiled briefly, but then grew serious again.

"But I told him as much as I knew about the shape of the Revolution—admittedly, not a lot of detail, it not being my period—and I certainly told him how important France would be to the Americans. I'm just thinking"—he paused, a little awkwardly, then looked up at her—"he isn't going to Scotland to avoid the fighting; he's pretty clear about that."

"So you think he might be looking for political connections?" she asked slowly. "Not just grabbing his printing press, dropping Ian off at Lallybroch, and beating it back to America?"

She found the idea something of a relief. The notion of her parents intriguing in Edinburgh and Paris was much less hair-raising than her visions of them in the midst of explosions and battlefields. And it *would* be both of them, she realized. Where her father went, her mother would be, too.

Roger shrugged.

"That offhand remark about being what God made him. Ye ken what he means by that?"

"A bloody man," she said softly, and moved closer to Roger, putting a hand on his shoulder as though to ensure that he wouldn't suddenly vanish. "He told me he was a bloody man. That he'd seldom chosen to fight, but knew he was born to do it."

"Aye, that," Roger said, just as softly. "But he's no longer the young laird who took up his sword and led thirty crofters to a doomed battle—and took them home again. He knows a lot more now, about what one man can do. I think he means to do it."

"I think so, too." Her throat felt tight, but as much with pride as fear.

Roger reached up and put his hand over hers, squeezing.

"I remember . . ." he said slowly. "A thing your mother said, telling us about—about when she came back, and how she became a doctor. A thing your—Frank—that he said to her. Something about it being bloody inconvenient to the people round her, but a great blessing that she knew what it was she was meant to be. He was right about that, I think. And Jamie does know."

She nodded. She probably shouldn't say it, she thought. But she couldn't hold the words back any longer.

"Do *you* know?"

He was silent for a long time, looking at the pages on the table, but at last shook his head, the motion so small that she felt rather than saw it.

"I used to," he said quietly, and let go of her hand.

HER FIRST IMPULSE was to punch him in the back of the neck; her second was to seize him by the shoulders, bend down with her eyeballs an inch from his, and say—calmly, but distinctly—"What the hell do you mean by *that*?"

She refrained from doing either, only because both were likely to lead to a prolonged conversation of a sort deeply inappropriate for children, and both the kids were in the hall a few feet from the study door; she could hear them talking.

"See that?" Jemmy was saying.

"Un-huh."

"Bad people came here, a long time ago, looking for Grandda. Bad *English* people. They did that."

Roger's head turned as he caught what Jemmy was saying, and he caught Brianna's eye, with a half smile.

"Bad Engwish!" Mandy repeated obligingly. "Make 'em cwean it up!"

In spite of her annoyance, Brianna couldn't help sharing Roger's smile, though she felt a small shimmer in the pit of her stomach, recalling her uncle Ian—so calm, so kind a man—showing her the saber slashes in the wooden paneling of the hall and telling her, "We keep it so, to show the children—and tell them, this is what the English are." There had been steel in his voice—and hearing a faint, absurdly childish echo of it in Jemmy's voice, she had her first doubts regarding the wisdom of keeping this particular family tradition.

"Did you tell him about it?" she asked Roger, as the children's voices moved away toward the kitchen. "I didn't."

"Annie'd told him part of it; I thought I'd best tell him the rest." He raised his eyebrows. "Should I have told him to ask you?"

"Oh. No. No," she repeated, dubiously. "But—should we be teaching him to hate English people?"

Roger smiled at that.

" 'Hate' might be pitching it a bit strong. And he did say *bad* English people. They *were* bad English people who did that. Besides, if he's going to grow up in the Highlands, he'll likely hear a few barbed remarks regarding Sassenachs—he'll balance those against his memories of your mother; your da always called her 'Sassenach,' after all."

He glanced at the letter on the table, caught a glimpse of the wall clock, and rose abruptly.

"Christ, I'm late. I'll stop at the bank whilst I'm in town—need anything from the Farm and Household?"

"Yes," she said dryly, "a new pump for the milk separator."

"Right," he said, and kissing her hastily, went out, one arm already into his jacket.

She opened her mouth to call after him that she'd been joking, but on second thought closed it. The Farm and Household Stores just *might* have a pump for a milk separator. A large, bewilderingly crowded building on the edge of Inverness, the Farm and Household supplied just about anything a farm might need, including pitchforks, rubber fire buckets, baling wire, and washing machines, as well as crockery, jars for canning, and not a few mysterious implements whose use she could only guess at.

She stuck her head into the corridor, but the kids were in the kitchen with Annie MacDonald, the hired girl; laughter and the wire *clong!* of the ancient toaster—it had come with the house—floated past the ratty green baize door, along with the enticing scent of hot buttered toast. The smell and the laughter drew her like a magnet, and the warmth of home flowed over her, golden as honey.

She paused to fold up the letter, though, before going to join them, and the memory of Roger's last remark tightened her mouth.

"I used to."

Snorting ferociously, she tucked the letter back into the box and went out into the hall, only to be arrested by sight of a large envelope on the table near the door, where the daily mail—and the contents of Roger's and Jemmy's pockets—were daily unloaded. She grabbed the envelope out of the pile of circulars, pebbles, pencil stubs, links of bicycle chain, and . . . was that a dead mouse? It was; flattened and dried, but adorned with a stiff loop of pink tail. She picked it up gingerly and, with the envelope clasped against her breast, made her way toward tea and toast.

In all honesty, she thought, Roger wasn't the only one keeping things to himself. The difference was, she planned to tell him what she was thinking—once it was settled.

8

SPRING THAW

Fraser's Ridge, colony of North Carolina
March 1777

ONE THING about a devastating fire, I reflected. It did make packing easier. At present, I owned one gown, one shift, three petticoats—one woolen, two muslin—two pairs of stockings (I'd been wearing one pair when the house burned; the other had been carelessly left drying on a bush a few weeks before the fire and was discovered later, weathered but still wearable), a shawl, and a pair of shoes. Jamie had procured a horrible cloak for me somewhere—I didn't know where, and didn't want to ask. Made of thick wool the color of leprosy, it smelled as though someone had died in it and lain undiscovered for a couple of days. I'd boiled it with lye soap, but the ghost of its previous occupant lingered.

Still, I wouldn't freeze.

My medical kit was nearly as simple to pack. With a regretful sigh for the ashes of my beautiful apothecary's chest, with its elegant tools and numerous bottles, I turned over the pile of salvaged remnants from my surgery. The dented barrel of my microscope. Three singed ceramic jars, one missing its lid, one cracked. A large tin of goose grease mixed with camphor—now nearly empty after a winter of catarrhs and coughs. A handful of singed pages, ripped from the casebook started by Daniel Rawlings and continued by myself—though my spirits were lifted a bit by the discovery that the salvaged pages included one bearing Dr. Rawlings's special receipt for Bowel-Bind.

It was the only one of his receipts I'd found effective, and while I'd long since committed the actual formula to memory, having it to hand kept my sense of him alive. I'd never met Daniel Rawlings in life, but he'd been my friend since the day Jamie gave me his chest and casebook. I folded the paper carefully and tucked it into my pocket.

Most of my herbs and compounded medications had perished in the flames, along with the earthenware jars, the glass vials, the large bowls in which I incubated penicillin broth, and my surgical saws. I still had one scalpel and the darkened blade of a small amputation saw; the handle had been charred, but Jamie could make me a new one.

The residents of the Ridge had been generous—as generous as people who had virtually nothing themselves could be at the tail end of winter. We had food for the journey, and many of the women had brought me bits of their household simples; I had small jars of lavender, rosemary, comfrey, and mustard seed, two precious steel needles, a small skein of silk thread to use for sutures and dental floss (though I didn't mention that last use to the ladies, who would have been deeply affronted by the notion), and a very small stock of bandages and gauze for dressings.

One thing I had in abundance, though, was alcohol. The corncrib had been spared from the flames, and so had the still. Since there was more than enough grain for both animals and household, Jamie had thriftily transformed the rest into a very raw—but potent—liquor, which we would take along to trade for necessary goods along the way. One small cask had been kept for my especial use, though; I'd carefully painted the legend *Sauerkraut* on the side, to discourage theft on the road.

"And what if we should be set upon by illiterate banditti?" Jamie had asked, amused by this.

"Thought of that," I informed him, displaying a small corked bottle full of cloudy liquid. "*Eau de sauerkraut.* I'll pour it on the cask at first sight of anyone suspicious."

"I suppose we'd best hope they're not German bandits, then."

"Have you ever met a German bandit?" I asked. With the exception of the occasional drunkard or wife-beater, almost all the Germans we knew were honest, hardworking, and virtuous to a fault. Not all that surprising, given that so many of them had come to the colony as part of a religious movement.

"Not as such," he admitted. "But ye mind the Muellers, aye? And what they did to your friends. They wouldna have called themselves bandits, but the Tuscarora likely didna make the same distinction."

That was no more than the truth, and a cold thumb pressed the base of my skull. The Muellers, German neighbors, had had a beloved daughter and her newborn child die of measles, and had blamed the nearby Indians for the infection. Deranged by grief, old *Herr* Mueller had led a party of his sons and sons-in-law to take revenge—and scalps. My viscera still remembered the shock of seeing my friend Nayawenne's white-streaked hair spill out of a bundle into my lap.

"Is my hair turning white, do you think?" I said abruptly. He raised his eyebrows, but bent forward and peered at the top of my head, fingering gently through my hair.

"There's maybe one hair in fifty that's gone white. One in five-and-twenty is silver. Why?"

"I suppose I have a little time, then. Nayawenne . . ." I hadn't spoken her name aloud in several years, and found an odd comfort in the speaking, as though it had conjured her. "She told me that I'd come into my full power when my hair turned white."

"Now there's a fearsome thought," he said, grinning.

"No doubt. Since it hasn't happened yet, though, I suppose if we stumble into a nest of sauerkraut thieves on the road, I'll have to defend my cask with my scalpel," I said.

He gave me a slightly queer look at this, but then laughed and shook his head.

His own packing was a little more involved. He and Young Ian had removed the gold from the house's foundation the night after Mrs. Bug's funeral—a delicate process preceded by my putting out a large slop basin of stale bread soaked in corn liquor, then calling "Sooo-eeee!" at the top of my lungs from the head of the garden path.

A moment of silence, and then the white sow emerged from her den, a pale blotch against the smoke-stained rocks of the foundation. I knew exactly what she was, but the sight of that white, rapidly moving form still made the hairs stand up on the back of my neck. It had come on to snow—one of the reasons for Jamie's decision to act at once—and she came through the whirl of big, soft flakes with a velocity that made her seem like the spirit of the storm itself, leading the wind.

For an instant, I thought she was going to charge me; I saw her head swing toward me and caught the loud snuff as she took my scent—but she scented the food as well, and swerved away. An instant later, the ungodly sounds of a pig in ecstasy floated through the hush of the snow, and Jamie and Ian hurried out of the trees to begin their work.

It took more than two weeks to move the gold; they worked only at night, and only when fresh snow was either falling or about to fall, to cover their tracks. Meantime, they took it in turn to guard the remains of the Big House, keeping an eye peeled for any sign of Arch Bug.

"Do you think he still cares about the gold?" I'd asked Jamie in the midst of this endeavor, chafing his hands to get enough heat into them for him to hold his spoon. He'd come in for breakfast, frozen and exhausted after a long night spent walking round and round the burnt house to keep his blood flowing.

"He's no much else left to care about, has he?" He spoke softly, to avoid waking the Higgins family. "Other than Ian."

I shivered, as much from thought of old Arch, living wraithlike in the forest, surviving on the heat of his hatred, as from the cold that had come in with Jamie. He'd let his beard grow for warmth—all the men did in winter, on the mountain—and ice glimmered in his whiskers and frosted his brows.

"You look like Old Man Winter himself," I whispered, bringing him a bowl of hot porridge.

"I feel like it," he replied hoarsely. He passed the bowl under his nose, inhaling the steam and closing his eyes beatifically. "Pass the whisky, aye?"

"You're proposing to pour it on your porridge? It's got butter and salt on, already." Nonetheless, I passed him the bottle from its shelf over the hearth.

"Nay, I'm going to thaw my wame enough to eat it. I'm solid ice from the neck down."

No one had seen hide nor hair of Arch Bug—not even an errant track in the snow—since his appearance at the funeral. He might be denned up for the winter, snug in some refuge. He might have gone away to the Indian villages. He might be dead, and I rather hoped he was, uncharitable as the thought might be.

I mentioned this, and Jamie shook his head. The ice in his hair had melted now, and the firelight glimmered like diamonds on the water droplets in his beard.

"If he's dead, and we never learn of it, Ian willna have a moment's peace—ever. D'ye want him to be looking over his shoulder at his wedding, afraid of a bullet through his wife's heart as she speaks her vows? Or wed with a family, fearing each day to leave his house and his bairns, for fear of what he might come back to?"

"I'm impressed at the scope and morbidity of your imagination—but you're right. All right, I don't hope he's dead—not unless we find his body."

But no one did find his body, and the gold was moved, bit by bit, to its new hiding place.

That had taken a bit of thought and considerable private discussion between Jamie and Ian. Not the whisky cave. Very few people knew about that—but some did. Joseph Wemyss, his daughter, Lizzie, and her two husbands—I marveled, rather, that I'd got to the point where I could think about Lizzie and the Beardsleys without boggling—all knew, of necessity, and Bobby and Amy Higgins would need to be shown its location before we left, as they would be making whisky themselves in our absence. Arch Bug had not been told of the cave's location—but very likely knew it.

Jamie was adamant that no one should know even of the gold's existence on the Ridge, let alone its location.

"Let even a rumor of it get out, and everyone here is in danger," he'd said. "Ye ken what happened when yon Donner told folk we had jewels here."

I kent, all right. I still woke up in the midst of nightmares, hearing the muffled *whumph!* of exploding ether fumes, hearing the crash of glass and smashing wood as the raiders wrecked the house.

In some of these dreams, I ran fruitlessly to and fro, trying to rescue someone—who?—but met always by locked doors, blank walls, or rooms engulfed in flame. In others, I stood rooted, unable to move a muscle, as fire crawled up the walls, fed with delicate greed on the clothes of bodies at my feet, burst through a corpse's hair, caught in my skirts and swarmed upward, wrapping my legs in a blazing web.

I still felt overpowering sadness—and a deep, cleansing rage—when I looked at the sooty smudge in the clearing that had once been my home, but I always had to go out in the morning after one of these dreams and look at it nonetheless: walk round the cold ruins and smell the taint of dead ash, in order to quench the flames that burned behind my eyes.

"Right," I said, and pulled my shawl tighter round me. We were standing by the springhouse, looking down on the ruins as we talked, and the chill was seeping into my bones. "So . . . where, then?"

"The Spaniard's Cave," he said, and I blinked at him.

"The what?"

"I'll show ye, *a nighean,*" he said, grinning at me. "When the snow melts."

SPRING HAD SPRUNG, and the creek was rising. Swelled by melting snow and fed by hundreds of tiny waterfalls that trickled and leapt down the mountain's face, it roared past my feet, exuberant with spray. I could feel it cold on my face, and knew that I'd be wet to the knees within minutes, but it didn't matter. The fresh green of arrowhead and pickerelweed rimmed the banks, some plants dragged out of the soil by the rising water and whirled downstream, more hanging on by their roots for dear life, leaves trailing in the racing wash. Dark mats of cress swirled under the water, close by the sheltering banks. And fresh greens were what I wanted.

My gathering basket was half full of fiddleheads and ramp shoots. A nice big lot of tender new cress, crisp and cold from the stream, would top off the winter's vitamin C deficiency very well. I took off my shoes and stockings, and after a moment's hesitation, took off my gown and shawl as well and hung them over a tree branch. The air was chilly in the shade of the silver birches that overhung the creek here, and I shivered a bit but ignored the cold, kirtling up my shift before wading into the stream.

That cold was harder to ignore. I gasped, and nearly dropped the basket, but found my footing among the slippery rocks and made my way toward the nearest mat of tempting dark green. Within seconds, my legs were numb, and I'd lost any sense of cold in the enthusiasm of forager's frenzy and salad hunger.

A good deal of our stored food had been saved from the fire, as it was kept in the outbuildings: the springhouse, corncrib, and smoking shed. The root cellar had been destroyed, though, and with it not only the carrots, onions, garlic, and potatoes but most of my carefully gathered stock of dried apples and wild yams, and the big hanging clusters of raisins, all meant to keep us from the ravages of scurvy. The herbs, of course, had gone up in smoke, along with the rest of my surgery. True, a large quantity of pumpkins and squashes had escaped, these having been piled in the barn, but one grows tired of squash pie and succotash after a couple of months—well, after a couple of days, speaking personally.

Not for the first time, I mourned Mrs. Bug's abilities as a cook, though of course I did miss her for her own sake. Amy McCallum Higgins had been raised in a crofter's cottage in the Highlands of Scotland and was, as she put it, "a good plain cook." Essentially, that meant she could bake bannocks, boil porridge, and fry fish simultaneously, without burning any of it. No mean feat, but a trifle monotonous, in terms of diet.

My own pièce de résistance was stew—which, lacking onions, garlic, carrots, and potatoes, had devolved into a sort of pottage consisting of venison or turkey stewed with cracked corn, barley, and possibly chunks of stale bread. Ian, surprisingly, had turned out to be a passable cook; the succotash and squash pie were his contributions to the communal menu. I did wonder who had taught him to make them, but thought it wiser not to ask.

So far no one had starved, nor yet lost any teeth, but by mid-March, I would have been willing to wade neck-deep in freezing torrents in order to acquire something both edible and green.

Ian had, thank goodness, gone on breathing. And after a week or so had ceased acting quite so shell-shocked, eventually regaining something like his normal manner. But I noticed Jamie's eyes follow him now and then, and Rollo had taken to sleeping with his head on Ian's chest, a new habit. I wondered whether he really sensed the pain in Ian's heart, or whether it was simply a response to the cramped sleeping conditions in the cabin.

I stretched my back, hearing the small pops between my vertebrae. Now that the snowmelt had come, I could hardly wait for our departure. I would miss the Ridge and everyone on it—well, almost everyone. Possibly not Hiram Crombie, so much. Or the Chisholms, or—I short-circuited this list before it became uncharitable.

"On the *other* hand," I said firmly to myself, "think of beds."

Granted, we would be spending a good many nights on the road, sleeping rough—but eventually we would reach civilization. Inns. With food. And beds. I closed my eyes momentarily, envisioning the absolute bliss of a mattress. I didn't even aspire to a feather bed; anything that promised more than an inch of padding between myself and the floor would be paradise. And, of course, if it came with a modicum of privacy—even better.

Jamie and I had not been completely celibate since December. Lust aside—and it wasn't—we needed the comfort and warmth of each other's body. Still, covert congress under a quilt, with Rollo's yellow eyes fixed upon us from two feet away, was less than ideal, even assuming that Young Ian was invariably asleep, which I didn't think he was, though he was sufficiently tactful as to pretend.

A hideous shriek split the air, and I jerked, dropping the basket. I flung myself after it, barely snatching the handle before it was whirled away on the flood, and stood up dripping and trembling, heart hammering as I waited to see whether the scream would be repeated.

It was—followed in short order by an equally piercing screech, but one deeper in timbre and recognizable to my well-trained ears as the sort of noise made by a Scottish Highlander suddenly immersed in freezing water. Fainter, higher-pitched shrieks, and a breathless "Fook!" spoken in a Dorset accent indicated that the gentlemen of the household were taking their spring bath.

I wrang out the hem of my shift and, snatching my shawl from the branch where I'd left it, slipped on my shoes and made my way in the direction of the bellowing.

There are few things more enjoyable than sitting in relative warmth and comfort while watching fellow human beings soused in cold water. If said human beings present a complete review of the nude male form, so much the better. I threaded my way through a small growth of fresh-budding river willows, found a conveniently screened rock in the sun, and spread out the damp skirt of my shift, enjoying the warmth on my shoulders, the sharp scent of the fuzzy catkins, and the sight before me.

Jamie was standing in the pool, nearly shoulder-deep, his hair slicked back like a russet seal. Bobby stood on the bank, and picking up Aidan with a grunt, threw him to Jamie in a pinwheel of flailing limbs and piercing shrieks of delighted fright.

"Me-me-me-*me*!" Orrie was dancing around his stepfather's legs, his chubby bottom bouncing up and down among the reeds like a little pink balloon.

Bobby laughed, bent, and hoisted him up, holding him for a moment high overhead as he squealed like a seared pig, then flung him in a shallow arc out over the pool.

He hit the water with a tremendous splash and Jamie grabbed him, laughing, and pulled him to the surface, whence he emerged with a look of open-mouthed stupefaction that made them all hoot like gibbons. Aidan and Rollo were both dog-paddling round in circles by now, shouting and barking.

I looked across to the opposite side of the pool and saw Ian rush naked down the small hill and leap like a salmon into the pool, uttering one of his best Mohawk war cries. This was cut off abruptly by the cold water, and he vanished with scarcely a splash.

I waited—as did the others—for him to pop back up, but he didn't. Jamie looked suspiciously behind him, in case of a sneak attack, but an instant later Ian shot out of the water directly in front of Bobby with a bloodcurdling yell, grabbed him by the leg, and yanked him in.

Matters thereafter became generally chaotic, with a great deal of promiscuous splashing, yelling, hooting, and jumping off of rocks, which gave me the opportunity to reflect on just how delightful naked men are. Not that I hadn't seen a good many of them in my time, but aside from Frank and Jamie, most men I'd seen undressed usually had been either ill or injured, and were encountered in such circumstances as to prevent a leisurely appreciation of their finer attributes.

From Orrie's chubbiness and Aidan's spidery winter-white limbs to Bobby's skinny, pale torso and neat little flat behind, the McCallum-Higginses were as entertaining to watch as a cageful of monkeys.

Ian and Jamie were something different—baboons, perhaps, or mandrills. They didn't really resemble each other in any attribute other than height, and yet were plainly cut from the same cloth. Watching Jamie squatting on a rock above the pool, thighs tensing for a leap, I could easily see him preparing to attack a leopard, while Ian stretched himself glistening in the sun, warming his dangly bits while keeping an alert watch for intruders. All they needed were purple bottoms, and they could have walked straight onto the African veldt, no questions asked.

They were all lovely, in their wildly various ways, but it was Jamie my gaze returned to, over and over again. He was battered and scarred, his muscles roped and knotted, and age had grooved the hollows between them. The thick welt of the bayonet scar writhed up his thigh, wide and ugly, while the thinner white line of the scar left by a rattlesnake's bite was nearly invisible, clouded by the thick fuzz of his body hair, this beginning to dry now and stand out from his skin in a cloud of reddish-gold. The scimitar-shaped sword cut across his ribs had healed well, too, no more than a hair-thin white line by now.

He turned round and bent to pick up a cake of soap from the rock, and my insides turned over. It wasn't purple but could not otherwise have been improved on, being high, round, delicately dusted with red-gold, and with a delightful muscular concavity to the sides. His balls, just visible from behind, *were* purple with the cold, and gave me a strong urge to creep up behind him and cup them in my rock-warmed hands.

I wondered whether the resultant standing broad-jump would enable him to clear the pool.

I had not, in fact, seen him naked—or even substantially undressed—in several months.

But now . . . I threw back my head, closing my eyes against the brilliant spring sun, enjoying the tickle of my own fresh-washed hair against my shoulder blades. The snow was gone, the weather was good—and the whole outdoors beckoned invitingly, filled with places where privacy could be assured, bar the odd skunk.

I LEFT THE MEN dripping and sunning themselves on the rocks, and went to retrieve my clothes. I didn't put these on, though. Instead, I went quickly up to the springhouse, where I submerged my basket of greens in the cool water—if I took it to the cabin, Amy would seize them and boil them into submission—and left my gown, stays, and stockings rolled up on the shelf where the cheeses were stacked. Then I went back toward the stream.

The splashing and shouting had ceased. Instead, I heard low-voiced singing, coming along the trail. It was Bobby, carrying Orrie, sound asleep after his exertions. Aidan, groggy with cleanliness and warmth, ambled slowly beside his stepfather, dark head tilting to and fro to the rhythm of the song.

It was a lovely Gaelic lullaby; Amy must have taught it to Bobby. I did wonder if she'd told him what the words meant.

S'iomadh oidhche fhliuch is thioram
Sìde nan seachd sian
Gheibheadh Griogal dhomhsa creagan
Ris an gabhainn dìon.

(Many a night, wet and dry
Even in the worst of weather
Gregor would find a little rock for me
Beside which I could shelter.)

Òbhan, òbhan òbhan ìri
Òbhan ìri ò!
Òbhan, òbhan òbhan ìri
'S mòr mo mhulad 's mòr.

(Woe is me, woe is me
Woe is me, great indeed is my sorrow.)

I smiled to see them, though with a catch in my throat. I remembered Jamie carrying Jem back from swimming, the summer before, and Roger singing to Mandy in the night, his harsh, cracked voice little more than a whisper—but music, all the same.

I nodded to Bobby, who smiled and nodded back, though without interrupting his song. He raised his brows and jerked a thumb over his shoulder and uphill, presumably indicating where Jamie had gone. He betrayed no surprise at seeing me in shift and shawl—doubtless he thought I was bound for the stream to wash, as well, inspired by the singular warmth of the day.

Eudail mhòir a shluagh an domhain
Dhòirt iad d'fhuil an dè
'S chuir iad do cheann air stob daraich
Tacan beag bhod chrè.

(Great sweetheart of all people of the world
They poured your blood yesterday
And they put your head on an oak stick
A short distance from your body.)

Òbhan, òbhan òbhan ìri
Òbhan ìri ò!
Òbhan, òbhan òbhan ìri
'S mòr mo mhulad 's mòr.

(Woe is me, woe is me
Woe is me, great indeed is my sorrow.)

I waved briefly and turned up the side trail that led to the upper clearing. "New House," everyone called it, though the only indications that there might someday *be* a house there were a stack of felled logs and a number of pegs driven into the ground, with strings tied between them. These were meant to mark the placement and dimensions of the house Jamie intended to build in replacement of the Big House—when we came back.

He'd been moving the pegs, I saw. The wide front room was now wider, and the back room intended for my surgery had developed a growth of some sort, perhaps a separate stillroom.

The architect was sitting on a log, surveying his kingdom, stark naked.

"Expecting me, were you?" I asked, taking off my shawl and hanging it on a convenient branch.

"I was." He smiled, and scratched his chest. "I thought the sight of my naked backside would likely inflame ye. Or was it maybe Bobby's?"

"Bobby hasn't got one. Do you know, you haven't got a single gray hair below the neck? Why is that, I wonder?"

He glanced down, inspecting himself, but it was true. There were only a few strands of silver among the fiery mass of his hair, though his beard—the winter growth tediously and painfully removed a few days before—was heavily frosted with white. But the hair on his chest was still a dark auburn, and that below a fluffy mass of vivid ginger.

He combed his fingers thoughtfully through the exuberant foliage, looking down.

"I think it's hiding," he remarked, and glanced up at me, one eyebrow raised. "Want to come and help me hunt for it?"

I came round in front of him and obligingly knelt down. The object in question was in fact quite visible, though admittedly looking rather shell-shocked by the recent immersion, and a most interesting shade of pale blue.

"Well," I said, after a moment's contemplation. "Great oaks from tiny acorns grow. Or so I'm told."

A shiver ran through him at the warmth of my mouth and I lifted my hands involuntarily, cradling his balls.

"Holy God," he said, and his hands rested lightly on my head in benediction.

"What did ye say?" he asked, a moment later.

"I said," I said, coming up momentarily for air, "I find the gooseflesh rather erotic."

"There's more where that came from," he assured me. "Take your shift off, Sassenach. I havena seen ye naked in nearly four months."

"Well . . . no, you haven't," I agreed, hesitating. "And I'm not sure I want you to."

One eyebrow went up.

"Whyever not?"

"Because I've been indoors for weeks on end without sun or exercise to speak of. I probably look like one of those grubs you find under rocks—fat, white, and squidgy."

"Squidgy?" he repeated, breaking into a grin.

"Squidgy," I said with dignity, wrapping my arms around myself.

He pursed his lips and exhaled slowly, eyeing me with his head on one side.

"I like it when ye're fat, but I ken quite well that ye're not," he said, "because I've felt your ribs when I put my arms about you, each night since the end of January. As for white—ye've been white all the time I've known ye; it's no likely to come a great shock to me. As for the squidgy part"—he extended one hand and wiggled the fingers beckoningly at me—"I think I might enjoy that."

"Hmm," I said, still hesitant. He sighed.

"Sassenach," he said, "I said I havena seen ye naked in four months. That means if ye take your shift off now, ye'll be the best thing I've seen in four months. And at my age, I dinna think I remember farther back than that."

I laughed, and without further ado, stood up and pulled the ribbon tie at the neck of my shift. Wriggling, I let it fall in a puddle round my feet.

He closed his eyes. Then breathed deep and opened them again.

"I'm blinded," he said softly, and held out a hand to me.

"Blinded as in sun bouncing off a vast expanse of snow?" I asked dubiously. "Or as in coming face to face with a gorgon?"

"Seeing a gorgon turns ye to stone, not strikes ye blind," he informed me. "Though come to think"—he prodded himself with an experimental forefinger—"I may turn to stone yet. Will ye come here, for God's sake?"

I came.

I FELL ASLEEP IN the warmth of Jamie's body, and woke some time later, snugly wrapped in his plaid. I stretched, alarming a squirrel overhead, who ran out on a limb to get a better view. Evidently he didn't like what he saw, and began scolding and chattering.

"Oh, hush," I said, yawning, and sat up. The squirrel took exception to this gesture and began having hysterics, but I ignored him. To my surprise, Jamie was gone.

I thought he'd likely just stepped into the wood to relieve himself, but a quick glance round didn't discover him, and when I scrambled to my feet, the plaid clutched to me, I saw no sign of him.

I hadn't heard anything; surely if someone had come, I would have wakened—or Jamie would have wakened me. I listened carefully, but—the squirrel having now gone about its own business—heard nothing beyond the normal sounds of a forest waking to spring: the murmur and rush of wind through new-leafed trees, punctuated by the occasional crack of a falling branch, or the rattle of last year's pinecones and chestnut hulls bouncing through the canopy; the call of a distant jay, the conversation of a gang of pygmy nuthatches foraging in the long grass nearby, the rustle of a hungry vole in the winter's dead leaves.

The jay was still calling; another had joined it now, shrill with alarm. Perhaps that was where Jamie had gone.

I unwound myself from the plaid and pulled on my shift and shoes. It was getting on for evening; we—or I, at least—

had slept a long time. It was still warm in the sun, but the shadows under the trees were cold, and I put on my shawl and bundled up Jamie's plaid into my arms—likely he'd want it.

I followed the calling of the jays uphill, away from the clearing. There was a pair nesting near the White Spring; I'd seen them building the nest only two days before.

It wasn't far from the house site at all, though that particular spring always had the air of being remote from everything. It lay in the center of a small grove of white ash and hemlock, and was shielded on the east by a jagged outcropping of lichen-covered rock. All water has a sense of life about it, and a mountain spring carries a particular sense of quiet joy, rising pure from the heart of the earth. The White Spring, so called for the big pale boulder that stood guardian over its pool, had something more—a sense of inviolate peace.

The closer I came to it, the surer I was that that was where I'd find Jamie.

"There's something there that listens," he'd told Brianna once, quite casually. "Ye see such pools in the Highlands; they're called saints' pools—folk say the saint lives by the pool and listens to their prayers."

"And what saint lives by the White Spring?" she'd asked, cynical. "Saint Killian?"

"Why him?"

"Patron saint of gout, rheumatism, and whitewashers."

He'd laughed at that, shaking his head.

"Whatever it is that lives in such water is older than the notion of saints," he assured her. "But it listens."

I walked softly, approaching the spring. The jays had fallen silent now.

He was there, sitting on a rock by the water, wearing only his shirt. I saw why the jays had gone about their business—he was still as the white boulder itself, his eyes closed, hands turned upward on his knees, loosely cupped, inviting grace.

I stopped at once when I saw him. I had seen him pray here once before—when he'd asked Dougal MacKenzie for help in battle. I didn't know who he was talking to just now, but it wasn't a conversation I wished to intrude upon.

I ought to leave, I supposed—but aside from the fear that I might disturb him by an inadvertent noise, I didn't want to go.

Most of the spring lay in shadow, but fingers of light came down through the trees, stroking him. The air was thick with pollen, and the light was filled with motes of gold. It struck answering glints from the crown of his head, the smooth high arch of his foot, the blade of his nose, the bones of his face. He might have grown there, part of earth and stone and water, might have been himself the spirit of the spring.

I didn't feel unwelcome. The peace of the place reached out to touch me gently, slow my heart.

Was that what he sought here, I wondered? Was he drawing the peace of the mountain into himself, to remember, to sustain him during the months—the years, perhaps—of coming exile?

I would remember.

The light began to go, brightness falling from the air. He stirred, finally, lifting his head a little.

"Let me be enough," he said quietly.

I started at the sound of his voice, but he hadn't been speaking to me.

He opened his eyes and rose then, quiet as he'd sat, and came past the stream, long feet bare and silent on the layers of damp leaves. As he came past the outcropping of rock, he saw me and smiled, reaching out to take the plaid I held out to him, wordless. He said nothing, but took my cold hand in his large warm one and we turned toward home, walking together in the mountain's peace.

A FEW DAYS LATER, he came to find me. I was foraging along the creek bank for leeches, which had begun to emerge from their winter's hibernation, ravenous for blood. They were simple to catch; I merely waded slowly through the water near shore.

At first, the thought of acting as live bait for the leeches was repellent, but after all, that was how I usually obtained leeches—by letting Jamie, Ian, Bobby, or any of a dozen young males wade through the streams and pick them off. And once you got used to the sight of the creatures, slowly engorging with your blood, it wasn't all that bad.

"I have to let them have enough blood to sustain themselves," I explained, grimacing as I eased a thumbnail under the sucker of a leech in order to dislodge it, "but not enough that they'll be comatose, or they won't be of any use."

"A matter of nice judgment," Jamie agreed, as I dropped the leech into a jar filled with water and duckweed. "When ye've done feeding your wee pets, then, come along and I'll show ye the Spaniard's Cave."

It was no little distance. Perhaps four miles from the Ridge, through cold, muddy creeks and up steep slopes, then through a crack in a granite cliff face that made me feel as though I were being entombed alive, only to emerge into a wilderness of jutting boulders, smothered in nets of wild grape.

"We found it, Jem and I, out hunting one day," Jamie explained, lifting a curtain of leaves for me to pass beneath. The vines snaked over the rocks, thick as a man's forearm and knotted with age, the rusty-green leaves of spring not yet quite covering them. "It was a secret between us. We agreed we'd tell no one else—not even his parents."

"Nor me," I said, but wasn't offended. I heard the loss in his voice at the mention of Jem.

The entrance to the cave was a crack in the ground, over which Jamie had pushed a large, flat rock. He slid this back with some effort, and I bent over cautiously, experiencing a brief clench of the innards at the faint sound of moving air through the fissure. The surface air was warm, though; the cave was drawing, not blowing.

I remembered all too well the cave at Abandawe, that had seemed to breathe around us, and it took some force of will to follow Jamie as he disappeared into the earth. There was a rough wooden ladder—new, I saw, but replacing a much older one that had fallen to pieces; some bits of rotted wood were still in place, dangling from the rock on rusted iron spikes.

It could have been no more than ten or twelve feet to the bottom, but the neck of the cave was narrow, and the descent seemed endless. At last I reached the bottom, though, and saw that the cave had opened out, like the bottom of a flask. Jamie was crouched to one side; I saw him draw out a small bottle and smelled the sharp scent of turpentine.

He'd brought a torch, a pine knot with a head dipped in tar and wrapped with a rag. He soaked the rag with turpentine, then drew the fire-starter Bree had made for him. A shower of sparks lit his face, intent and ruddy. Twice more, and the torch caught, the flame bursting through the flammable cloth and catching the tar.

He lifted the torch, and gestured toward the floor behind me. I turned and nearly jumped out of my skin.

The Spaniard leaned against the wall, bony legs stretched out, skull fallen forward as if in a doze. Tufts of reddish, faded hair still clung here and there, but the skin had gone entirely. His hands and feet were mostly gone, too, the small bones carried away by rodents. No large animals had been able to get at him, though, and while the torso and long bones showed signs of nibbling, they were largely intact; the swell of the rib cage poked through a tissue of cloth so faded that there was no telling what color it had ever been.

He *was* a Spaniard, too. A crested metal helmet, red with rust, lay by him, along with an iron breastplate and a knife.

"Jesus H. Roosevelt Christ," I whispered. Jamie crossed himself, and knelt by the skeleton.

"I've no notion how long he's been here," he said, also low-voiced. "We didna find anything with him save the armor and that." He pointed to the gravel just in front of the pelvis. I leaned closer to look; a small crucifix, probably silver, now tarnished black, and a few inches away, a tiny triangular shape, also black.

"A rosary?" I asked, and Jamie nodded.

"I expect he was wearing it about his neck. It must have been made of wood and string, and when it rotted, the metal bits fell. That"—his finger gently touched the little triangle—"says *Nr. Sra. Ang.* on the one side—*Nuestra Señora de los Angeles,* I think it means, 'Our Lady of the Angels.' There's a wee picture of the Blessed Virgin on the other side."

I crossed myself by reflex.

"Was Jemmy scared?" I asked, after a moment's respectful silence.

"I was," Jamie said dryly. "It was dark when I came down the shaft, and I nearly stepped on this fellow. I thought he was alive, and the shock of it liked to stop my heart."

He'd cried out in alarm, and Jemmy, left aboveground with strict instructions not to move from the spot, had promptly scrambled into the hole, losing his grip of the broken ladder halfway down and landing feetfirst on his grandfather.

"I heard him scrabbling and looked up, just in time to have him plunge out of the heavens and strike me in the breast like a cannonball." Jamie rubbed the left side of his chest with rueful amusement. "If I hadn't looked up, he'd have broken my neck—and he'd never have got out, by himself."

And we'd never have known what happened to either one of you. I swallowed, dry-mouthed at the thought. And yet . . . on any given day, something just as random might happen. To anyone.

"A wonder neither one of you broke anything," I said instead, and gestured toward the skeleton. "What do you think happened to this gentleman?" *His people never knew.*

Jamie shook his head.

"I dinna ken. He wasna expecting an enemy, because he wasna wearing his armor."

"You don't think he fell in and couldn't get out?" I squatted by the skeleton, tracing the tibia of the left leg. The bone was dried and cracked, gnawed at the end by small sharp teeth—but I could see what might be a greenstick fracture of the bone. Or might just be the cracking of age.

Jamie shrugged, glancing up.

"I shouldna think so. He was a good bit shorter than I am, but I think the original ladder must have been here when he died—for if someone built the ladder later, why would they leave this gentleman here at the bottom of it? And even with a broken leg, he should have been able to climb it."

"Hmm. He might have died of a fever, I suppose. That would account for his taking off his breastplate and helmet." Though I personally would have taken them off at the first opportunity; depending on the season, he must either have been boiled alive or suffered severely from mildew, semi-enclosed in metal.

"Mmphm."

I glanced up at this sound, which indicated dubious acceptance of my reasoning but disagreement with my conclusion.

"You think he was killed?"

He shrugged.

"He has armor—but nay weapon save a wee knife. And ye can see he was right-handed, but the knife's lying to his left."

The skeleton *had* been right-handed; the bones of the right arm were noticeably thicker, even by the flicker of torchlight. Possibly a swordsman? I wondered.

"I kent a good many Spanish soldiers in the Indies, Sassenach. All of them fair bristled wi' swords and spears and pistols. If this man died of a fever, his companions might take his arms—but they'd take the armor, too, *and* the knife. Why leave it?"

"But by that token," I objected, "why did whoever killed him—if he was killed—leave the armor and the knife?"

"As for the armor—they didna want it. It wouldna be particularly useful to anyone other than a soldier. As for the knife—because it was sticking in him?" Jamie suggested. "And it's no a very good knife to begin with."

"Very logical," I said, swallowing again. "Putting aside the question of how he died—what in God's name was he doing in the mountains of North Carolina in the first place?"

"The Spanish sent explorers up as far as Virginia, fifty or sixty years ago," he informed me. "The swamps discouraged them, though."

"I can see why. But why . . . *this*?" I stood up, waving a hand to encompass the cave and its ladder. He didn't reply, but took my arm and lifted his torch, turning me to the side of the cave opposite the ladder. Well above my head, I saw another small fissure in the rock, black in the torchlight, barely wide enough for a man to wriggle through.

"There's a smaller cave through there," he said, nodding upward. "And when I put Jem up to look, he told me there were marks in the dust—square marks, as though heavy boxes had sat there."

Which is why, when the need to hide treasure had occurred to him, he had thought of the Spaniard's Cave.

"We'll bring the last of the gold tonight," he said, "and pile rocks to hide the opening up there. Then we'll leave the *señor* here to his rest."

I was obliged to admit that the cave made as suitable a resting place as any. And the Spanish soldier's presence would likely discourage anyone who stumbled on the cave from further investigation, both Indians and settlers having a distinct aversion to ghosts. For that matter, so did Highlanders, and I turned curiously to Jamie.

"You and Jem—you weren't troubled about being haunted by him?"

"Nay, we said the proper prayer for the repose of his soul, when I sealed the cave, and scattered salt around it."

That made me smile.

"You know the proper prayer for every occasion, don't you?"

He smiled faintly in return, and rubbed the head of the torch in the damp gravel to extinguish it. A faint shaft of light from above glowed on the crown of his head.

"There's always a prayer, *a nighean,* even if it's only *A Dhia, cuidich mi.*" *Oh, God—help me.*

9

A KNIFE THAT KNOWS MY HAND

NOT ALL THE GOLD rested with the Spaniard. Two of my petticoats had an extra turnup in the hem, with shavings of gold evenly distributed in tiny pockets, and my large pocket itself had several ounces of gold stitched into the seam at the bottom. Jamie and Ian each carried a small amount in his sporran. And each of them would carry two substantial shot pouches on his belt. We had retired, the three of us, to the New House clearing, to make the shot in private.

"Now, ye'll no forget which side to load from, aye?" Jamie dropped a fresh musket ball out of the mold, glowing like a miniature sunrise, into the pot of grease and soot.

"As long as ye dinna take my shot bag in mistake, no," Ian said caustically. He was making lead shot, dropping the hot fresh balls into a hollow lined with moist leaves, where they smoked and steamed in the crisp spring evening.

Rollo, lying nearby, sneezed as a wisp of smoke drifted past his nose, and snorted explosively. Ian glanced at him with a smile.

"Will ye like chasing the red deer through the heather, *a choin*?" he asked. "Ye'll need to keep off the sheep, though, or someone's like to shoot ye for a wolf."

Rollo sighed and let his eyes go to drowsy slits.

"Thinking what ye'll say to your mam when ye see her?" Jamie asked, squinting against the smoke of the fire as he held the ladle of gold shavings over the flame.

"Tryin' not to think too much," Ian replied frankly. "I get a queer feeling in my wame when I think of Lallybroch."

"Good queer or bad queer?" I asked, gingerly scooping the cooled gold balls out of the grease with a wooden spoon and dropping them into the shot pouches.

Ian frowned, eyes fixed on his ladle as the lead went suddenly from crumpled blobs to a quivering puddle.

"Both, I think. Brianna told me once about a book she'd read in school that said ye can't go home again. I think that's maybe true—but I want to," he added softly, eyes still on his work. The melted lead hissed into the mold.

I looked away from the wistfulness in his face, and found Jamie looking at me, his gaze quizzical, eyes soft with sympathy. I looked away from him, too, and rose to my feet, groaning slightly as my knee joint cracked.

"Yes, well," I said briskly. "I suppose it depends on what you think home is, doesn't it? It isn't always a place, you know."

"Aye, that's true." Ian held the bullet mold for an instant, letting it cool. "But even when it's a person—ye can't always go back, aye? Or maybe ye can," he added, his mouth quirking a little as he glanced up at Jamie, and then at me.

"I think ye'll find your parents much as ye left them," Jamie said dryly, choosing to ignore Ian's reference. "You may come as a greater shock to them."

Ian glanced down at himself and smiled.

"Got a bit taller," he said.

I gave a brief snort of amusement. He'd been fifteen when he'd left Scotland—a tall, scrawny gowk of a boy. He *was* a couple of inches taller now. He was also lean and hard as a strip of dried rawhide, and normally tanned to much the same color, though the winter had bleached him, making the tattooed dots that ran in semicircles across his cheekbones stand out more vividly.

"You remember that other line I told you?" I asked him. "When we came back to Lallybroch from Edinburgh, after I . . . found Jamie again. *Home is where, when you have to go there, they have to take you in.*"

Ian raised a brow, looked from me to Jamie, and shook his head.

"Nay wonder ye're sae fond of her, Uncle. She must be a rare comfort to ye."

"Well," Jamie said, his eyes fixed on his work, "she keeps takin' me in—so I suppose she must be home."

THE WORK FINISHED, Ian and Rollo took the filled shot pouches back to the cabin, while Jamie stamped out the fire and I packed up the paraphernalia of bullet-making. It was growing late, and the air—already so fresh it tickled the lungs—acquired that extra edge of cool liveliness that caressed the skin as well, the breath of spring moving restless over the earth.

I stood for a moment, enjoying it. The work had been close, and hot, despite being done in the open, and the cold breeze that lifted the hair off my neck was delightful.

"Have ye got a penny, *a nighean*?" said Jamie, next to me.

"A what?"

"Well, any sort of money will do."

"I don't *think* so, but . . ." I rummaged in the pocket tied at my waist, which by this point in our preparations held nearly as large a collection of improbabilities as did Jamie's sporran. Among hanks of thread, twists of paper containing seeds or dried herbs, needles stuck through bits of leather, a small jar full of sutures, a woodpecker's black-and-white-spotted feather, a chunk of white chalk, and half a biscuit, which I had evidently been interrupted while eating, I did in fact discover a grubby half-shilling, covered in lint and biscuit crumbs.

"That do you?" I asked, wiping it off and handing it over.

"It will," he said, and held out something toward me. My

hand closed automatically over what turned out to be the handle of a knife, and I nearly dropped it in surprise.

"Ye must always give money for a new blade," he explained, half smiling. "So it kens ye for its owner, and willna turn on ye."

"Its owner?" The sun was touching the edge of the Ridge, but there was still plenty of light, and I looked at my new acquisition. It was a slender blade, but sturdy, single-edged and beautifully honed; the cutting edge shone silver in the dying sun. The hilt was made from a deer's antler, smooth and warm in my hand—and had been carved with two small depressions, these just fitting my grip. Plainly it was my knife.

"Thank you," I said, admiring it. "But—"

"Ye'll feel safer if ye have it by you," he said, matter-of-fact. "Oh—just the one more thing. Give it here."

I handed it back, puzzled, and was startled to see him draw the blade lightly across the ball of his thumb. Blood welled up from the shallow cut, and he wiped it on his breeches and stuck his thumb in his mouth, handing me back the knife.

"Ye blood a blade, so it knows its purpose," he explained, taking the wounded digit out of his mouth.

The hilt of the knife was still warm in my hand, but a small chill went through me. With rare exceptions, Jamie wasn't given to purely romantic gestures. If he gave me a knife, he thought I'd need it. And not for digging up roots and hacking tree bark, either. Know its purpose, indeed.

"It fits my hand," I said, looking down and stroking the small groove that fit my thumb. "How did you know to make it so exactly?"

He laughed at that.

"I've had your hand round my cock often enough to know the measure of your grip, Sassenach," he assured me.

I snorted briefly in response to this, but turned the blade and pricked the end of my own thumb with the point. It was amazingly sharp; I scarcely felt it, but a bead of dark-red blood welled up at once. I put the knife into my belt, took his hand, and pressed my thumb to his.

"Blood of my blood," I said.

I didn't make romantic gestures, either.

10

FIRESHIP

New York
August 1776

IN FACT, WILLIAM'S news of the Americans' escape was received much better than he had expected. With the intoxicating feeling that they had the enemy cornered, Howe's army moved with remarkable speed. The admiral's fleet was still in Gravesend Bay; within a day, thousands of men were marched hastily to the shore and reembarked for the quick crossing to Manhattan; by sunset of the next day, armed companies began the attack upon New York—only to discover the trenches empty, the fortifications abandoned.

While something of a disappointment to William, who had hoped for a chance of direct and physical revenge, this development pleased General Howe inordinately. He moved, with his staff, into a large mansion called Beekman House and set about solidifying his hold upon the colony. There was a certain amount of chafing among senior officers in favor of running the Americans to ground—certainly William favored that notion—but General Howe was of the opinion that defeat and attrition would shred Washington's remaining forces, and the winter would finish them off.

"And meanwhile," said Lieutenant Anthony Fortnum, looking round the stifling attic to which the three most junior staff officers had been consigned, "we are an army of occupation. Which means, I think, that we are entitled to the pleasures of the post, are we not?"

"And what would those be?" William inquired, looking in vain for a spot in which to put the weathered portmanteau that presently contained most of his worldly goods.

"Well, women," Fortnum said consideringly. "Certainly women. And surely New York has fleshpots?"

"I didn't see any on the way in," Ralph Jocelyn said dubiously. "And I looked!"

"Not hard enough," Fortnum said firmly. "I feel sure there must be fleshpots."

"There's beer," William suggested. "Decent public house called Fraunces Tavern, just off Water Street. I had a good pint there on the way in."

"Has to be something closer than that," Jocelyn objected. "I'm not walking miles in this heat!" Beekman House had a pleasant situation, with spacious grounds and clean air—but was a good way outside the city.

"Seek and ye shall find, my brothers." Fortnum twisted a side-curl into place and slung his coat over one shoulder. "Coming, Ellesmere?"

"No, not just now. I've letters to write. If you find any fleshpots, I shall expect a written report. In triplicate, mind."

Left momentarily to his own devices, he dropped his bag on the floor and took out the small sheaf of letters Captain Griswold had handed him.

There were five of them; three with his stepfather's smiling half-moon seal—Lord John wrote to him promptly on the fifteenth of every month, though at other times, as well—one from his uncle Hal, and he grinned at sight of that; Uncle Hal's missives were occasionally confusing, but invariably entertaining—and one in an unfamiliar but feminine-looking hand, with a plain seal.

Curious, he broke the seal and opened the letter to discover two closely written sheets from his cousin Dottie. His eyebrows went up at that; Dottie had never written to him before.

They stayed up as he perused the letter.

"I will be damned," he said aloud.

"Why?" asked Fortnum, who had come back to retrieve his hat. "Bad news from home?"

"What? Oh. No. No," he repeated, returning to the first page of the letter. "Just . . . interesting."

Folding up the letter, he put it inside his coat, safely away from Fortnum's interested gaze, and took up Uncle Hal's note, with its crested ducal seal. Fortnum's eyes widened at sight of that, but he said nothing.

William coughed and broke the seal. As usual, the note occupied less than a page and included neither salutation nor closing, Uncle Hal's opinion being that since the letter had a direction upon it, the intended recipient was obvious, the seal indicated plainly who had written it, and he did not waste his time in writing to fools.

Adam is posted to New York under Sir Henry Clinton. Minnie has given him some obnoxiously cumbersome Things for you. Dottie sends her Love, which takes up much less room.

John says you are doing something for Captain Richardson. I know Richardson and I think you shouldn't.

Give Colonel Spencer my regards, and don't play Cards with him.

Uncle Hal, William reflected, could cram more information—cryptic as it often was—into fewer words than anyone he knew. He did wonder whether Colonel Spencer cheated at cards or was simply very good or very lucky. Uncle Hal had doubtless omitted purposely to say, because if it had been one of the latter alternatives, William would have been tempted to try his skill—dangerous as he knew it was to win consistently against a superior officer. Once or twice, though . . . No, Uncle Hal was a very good cardsman himself, and if he was warning William off, prudence suggested he take the warning. Perhaps Colonel Spencer was both honest and an indifferent player but a man to take offense—and revenge—if beaten too often.

Uncle Hal was a cunning old devil, William thought, not without admiration.

Which was what worried him, rather, about that second paragraph. *I know Richardson* . . . In this instance, he understood quite well why Uncle Hal had omitted the particulars; mail might be read by anyone, and a letter with the Duke of Pardloe's crest might attract attention. Granted, the seal didn't seem to have been tampered with, but he'd seen his own father remove and replace seals with the greatest dexterity and a hot knife, and was under no illusions on that score.

That didn't stop him from wondering just *what* Uncle Hal knew about Captain Richardson and why he was suggesting that William stop his intelligencing—for evidently Papa had told Uncle Hal what he was doing.

Further food for thought—if Papa had told his brother what William was doing, then Uncle Hal would have told Papa what he knew about Captain Richardson, if there was anything to the captain's discredit. And if he had done that—

He put by Uncle Hal's note and ripped open the first of his father's letters. No, nothing about Richardson. . . . The second? Again no. In the third, a veiled reference to intelligencing, but only a wish for his safety and an oblique remark about his posture.

A tall man is always notable in company; the more so if his glance be direct and his dress neat.

William smiled at that. Westminster, where he'd gone to school, held its classes in one large room, this divided by a hanging curtain into the upper and lower classes, but there were boys of all ages being taught together, and William had quickly learned when—and how—to be either inconspicuous or outstanding, depending upon the immediate company.

Well, then. Whatever Uncle Hal knew about Richardson, it wasn't something that troubled Papa. Of course, he reminded himself, it needn't be anything discreditable. The Duke of Pardloe was fearless on his own behalf, but tended to excessive caution with regard to his family. Perhaps he only thought Richardson reckless; if that was the case, Papa would presumably trust to William's own good sense, and thus not mention it.

The attic was stifling; sweat was running down William's face and wilting his shirt. Fortnum had gone out again, leaving the end of his cot tilted up at an absurd angle over his protruding trunk. It did leave just enough floor space vacant as to allow William to stand up and walk to the door, though, and he made his escape into the outer air with a sense of relief. The air outside was hot and humid, but at least it was moving. He put his hat on his head and set off to find out just where his cousin Adam was billeted. *Obnoxiously cumbersome* sounded promising.

As he pressed through a crowd of farm wives headed for the market square, though, he felt the crackle of the letter in his coat, and remembered Adam's sister.

Dottie sends her love, which takes up much less room. Uncle Hal was cunning, William thought, but the cunningest of devils has the occasional blind spot.

OBNOXIOUSLY *cumbersome* fulfilled its promise: a book, a bottle of excellent Spanish sherry, a quart of olives to accompany it, and three pairs of new silk stockings.

"I am awash in stockings," his cousin Adam assured William, when the latter tried to share this bounty. "Mother buys them by the gross and dispatches them by every carrier, I think. You're lucky she didn't think to send you fresh drawers; I get a pair in every diplomatic pouch, and if you don't think *that's* an awkward thing to explain to Sir Henry . . . Wouldn't say no to a glass of your sherry, though."

William was not entirely sure his cousin was joking about the drawers; Adam had a grave mien that served him well in relations with senior officers, and had also the Grey family trick of saying the most outrageous things with a perfectly straight face. William laughed, nonetheless, and called downstairs for a pair of glasses.

One of Adam's friends brought three, helpfully staying to assist with disposal of the sherry. Another friend appeared, apparently out of the woodwork—it was very good sherry—and produced a half bottle of porter from his chest to add to the festivities. With the inevitability of such gatherings, both bottles and friends multiplied, until every surface in Adam's room—admittedly a small one—was occupied by one or the other.

William had generously made free with his olives, as well as the sherry, and toward the bottom of the bottle raised a glass to his aunt for her generous gifts, not omitting to mention the silk stockings.

"Though I rather think your mother was not responsible for the book?" he said to Adam, lowering his empty glass with an explosion of breath.

Adam broke into a fit of the giggles, his usual gravity quite dissolved in a quart of rum punch.

"No," he said, "nor Papa, neither. That was my own contribution to the cause of cutlural, culshural, I mean, advanshment in the colonies."

"A signal service to the sensibilities of civilized man," William assured him gravely, showing off his own ability to hold his liquor and manage his tongue, no matter how many slippery esses might throw themselves in his way.

A general cry of "What book? What book? Let us see this famous book!" resulting, he was obliged to produce the prize of his collection of gifts—a copy of Mr. Harris's famous *List of Covent Garden Ladies,* this being a lavishly descriptive catalog of the charms, specialties, price, and availability of the best whores to be found in London.

Its appearance was greeted with cries of rapture, and following a brief struggle over possession of the volume, William rescued it before it should be torn to pieces, but allowed himself to be induced to read some of the passages aloud, his dramatic rendering being greeted by wolflike howls of enthusiasm and hails of olive pits.

Reading is of course dry work, and further refreshment was called for and consumed. He could not have said who first suggested that the party should constitute itself an expeditionary force for the purpose of compiling a similar list for New York. Whoever first bruited the suggestion, though, was roundly seconded and hailed in bumpers of rum punch—the bottles having all been drained by now.

And so it fell out that he found himself wandering in a spirituous haze through narrow streets whose darkness was punctuated by the pinpricks of candlelit windows and the occasional hanging lantern at a crossroad. No one appeared to have any direction in mind, and yet the whole body advanced insensibly as one, drawn by some subtle emanation.

"Like dogs following a bitch in heat," he observed, and was surprised to receive a buffet and shout of approbation from one of Adam's friends—he hadn't realized that he'd spoken aloud. And yet he had been correct, for eventually they came to an alley down which two or three lanterns hung, sheathed in red muslin so the light spilled in a bloody glow across the doorways—all welcomingly ajar. Whoops greeted the sight, and the body of would-be investigators advanced a-purpose, pausing only for a brief argument in the center of the street regarding the choice of establishment in which to begin their researches.

William himself took little part in the argument; the air was close, muggy, and fetid with the stench of cattle and sewage, and he was suddenly aware that one of the olives he had consumed had quite possibly been a wrong 'un. He was sweating heavily and unctuously, and his wet linen clung to him with a clasping insistence that terrified him with the thought that he might not be able to get his breeches down in time, should his inward disturbance move suddenly southward.

He forced a smile, and with a vague swing of the arm, indicated to Adam that he might proceed as he liked—William would venture a bit farther.

This he did, leaving the moil of riotous young officers behind him, and staggered past the last of the red lanterns. He was looking rather desperately for some semblance of seclusion in which to be sick, but finding nothing to his purpose, at length stumbled to a halt and vomited profusely in a doorway—whereupon, to his horror, the door swung open, revealing a highly indignant householder, who did not wait for explanations, apologies, or offers of recompense, but seized a cudgel of some kind from behind his door and, bellowing incomprehensible oaths in what might be German, chased William down the alleyway.

What with one thing and another, it was some time of wandering through pig yards, shacks, and ill-smelling wharves before he found his way back to the proper district, there to find his cousin Adam going up and down the street, banging on doors and hallooing loudly in search of him.

"Don't knock on that one!" he said in alarm, seeing Adam about to attack the door of the cudgel-wielding German. Adam swung about in relieved surprise.

"There you are! All right, old man?"

"Oh, yes. Fine." He felt somewhat pale and clammy, despite the sweltering heat of the summer night, but the acute inner distress had purged itself, and had the salutary side effect of sobering him in the process.

"Thought you'd been robbed or murdered in an alleyway. I'd never be able to look Uncle John in the face, was I to have to tell him I'd got you done in."

They were walking down the alley, back toward the red lanterns. All of the young men had disappeared into one or another of the establishments, though the sounds of revelry and banging from within suggested that their high spirits had not abated, but merely been relocated.

"Did you find yourself decently accommodated?" Adam asked. He jerked his chin in the direction from which William had come.

"Oh, fine. You?"

"Well, she wouldn't rate more nor a paragraph in Harris, but not bad for a sinkhole like New York," Adam said judiciously. His stock was hanging loose round his neck, and as they passed the faint glow of a window, William saw that one of the silver buttons of his cousin's coat was missing. "Swear I've seen a couple of these whores in camp, though."

"Sir Henry send you out to make a census, did he? Or do you just spend so much time with the camp followers you know them all by—"

He was interrupted by a change in the noise coming from one of the houses down the street. Shouting, but not of the genially drunken sort evident heretofore. This was ugly shouting, a male voice in a rage and the shrieks of a woman.

The cousins exchanged glances, then started as one toward the racket.

This had increased as they hurried toward its source, and as they came even with the farthest house, a number of half-dressed soldiers spilled out into the alleyway, followed by a burly lieutenant to whom William had been introduced during the party in Adam's room, but whose name he did not recall, dragging a half-naked whore by one arm.

The lieutenant had lost both coat and wig; his dark hair was polled close and grew low on his brow, which, together with his thick-shouldered build, gave him the look of a bull about to charge. In fact, he did, turning and ramming a shoulder into the woman he'd dragged out, slamming her into the wall of the house. He was roaring drunk, and bellowing incoherent profanities.

"Fireship."

William didn't see who'd spoken the word, but it was taken up in excited murmurs, and something ugly ran through the men in the alley.

"Fireship! She's a fireship!"

Several women had gathered in the doorway. The light behind them was too dim to show their faces, but they were clearly frightened, huddling together. One called out, tentative, stretching out an arm, but the others pulled her back. The black-haired lieutenant took no notice; he was battering the whore, punching her repeatedly in the stomach and breasts.

"Hoy, fellow!"

William started forward, shouting, but several hands grasped his arms, preventing him.

"Fireship!" The men were beginning to chant it, with each blow of the lieutenant's fists.

A fireship was a poxed whore, and as the lieutenant left off his bashing and hauled the woman under the light of the red lantern, William could see that indeed she was; the rash across her face was plain.

"Rodham! Rodham!" Adam was shouting the lieutenant's name, trying to break through the crush of men, but they moved together, pushing him back, and the chant of "Fireship!" got louder.

Shrieks came from the whores in the doorway, and they crammed back as Rodham flung the woman down on the doorstep. William lunged and succeeded in breaking through the press, but before he could reach the lieutenant, Rodham had seized the lantern and, dashing it against the front of the house, flung blazing oil over the whore.

He fell back then, panting, eyes wide and staring as though in disbelief, as the woman leapt to her feet, arms windmilling in panic as the flames caught her hair, her gauzy shift. Within seconds, she was wrapped in fire, screaming in a high, thin voice that cut through the confusion of noise in the street and ran straight into William's brain.

The men fell back as she staggered toward them, lurching, hands reaching—whether in a futile plea for help or in the desire to immolate them as well, he couldn't tell. He stood rooted to the spot, his body clenched with the need to do something, the impossibility of doing anything, the overwhelming sense of disaster. An insistent pain in his arm made him glance mechanically aside, to find Adam beside him, fingers digging hard into the muscle of his forearm.

"Let's go," Adam whispered, his face white and sweating. "For God's sake, let's go!"

The door of the whorehouse had slammed shut. The burning woman fell against it, hands pressed against the wood. The appetizing smell of roasting meat filled the close, hot confines of the alley, and William felt his gorge rise once more.

"God curse you! May your goddamned pricks all rot and fall off!" The scream came from a window above; William's head jerked up and he saw a woman shaking a fist at the men below. There was a rumble from the men, and one shouted something foul in reply; another bent and seized a cobblestone and, rising, flung it hard. It bounced against the front of the house below the window, and fell back, striking one of the soldiers, who cursed and shoved the man who'd thrown it.

The burning woman had sunk down by the door; the flames had made a charred spot on it. She was still making a faint keening noise, but had ceased to move.

Suddenly William lost his mind and, grabbing the man who had thrown the stone, took him by the neck and cracked his head against the doorpost of the house. The man stiffened and slumped, his knees giving way, and sat in the street, moaning.

"Get out!" William bellowed. "All of you! Leave!" Fists clenched, he turned on the black-haired lieutenant, who, his rage all vanished, was standing motionless, staring at the woman on the stoop. Her skirts had vanished; a pair of blackened legs twitched feebly in the shadow.

William reached the man in one stride and took him by the front of his shirt, yanking him round.

"Go," he said, in a dangerous voice. "Leave. Now!"

He released the man, who blinked, swallowed, and, turning, walked like an automaton into the dark.

Panting, William turned on the rest of them, but they had lost the thirst for violence as quickly as it had come upon them. There were a few glances toward the woman—she had gone still now—and shufflings, incoherent murmurs. None of them would meet another's eye.

He was vaguely conscious of Adam by his side, trembling with shock but solidly beside him. He put a hand on his smaller cousin's shoulder and held on, trembling himself, as the men melted away. The man sitting in the street got slowly to his hands and feet, half-rose, and lurched after his companions, caroming off the fronts of houses as he made his way into the dark.

The alley fell quiet. The fire had gone out. The other red lanterns in the street had been extinguished. He felt as though he had grown to the spot, would stand in this hateful place forever—but Adam moved a little, and his hand fell from his cousin's shoulder and he found that his feet would carry him.

They turned away, and walked in silence back through the dark streets. They came by a sentry point, where soldiers on guard were standing round a fire, keeping casual watch. They were to keep order in the occupied city, the guards. The sentries glanced at them, but did not stop them.

In the light of the fire, he saw the tracks of wetness on Adam's face and realized that his cousin was crying.

So was he.

11

TRANSVERSE LIE

Fraser's Ridge
March 1777

THE WORLD WAS dripping. Freshets leapt down the mountain, grass and leaves were wet with dew, and the shingles steamed in the morning sun. Our preparations were made and the passes were clear. There remained only one more thing to do before we could leave.

"Today, d'ye think?" Jamie asked hopefully. He was not a man made for peaceful contemplation; once a course of action was decided upon, he wanted to be acting. Babies, unfortunately, are completely indifferent to both convenience and impatience.

"Maybe," I said, trying to keep a grip on my own patience. "Maybe not."

"I saw her last week, and she looked then as though she was goin' to explode any minute, Auntie," Ian remarked, handing Rollo the last bite of his muffin. "Ken those mushrooms? The big round ones? Ye touch one and *poof!*" He flicked his fingers, scattering muffin crumbs. "Like that."

"She's only having the one, no?" Jamie asked me, frowning.

"I told you—six times so far—I think so. I bloody *hope* so," I added, repressing an urge to cross myself. "But you can't always tell."

"Twins run in families," Ian put in helpfully.

Jamie did cross himself.

"I've heard only one heartbeat," I said, keeping a grip on my temper, "and I've been listening for months."

"Can ye not count the bits that stick out?" Ian inquired. "If it seemed to have six legs, I mean . . ."

"Easier said than done." I could, of course, make out the general aspect of the child—a head was reasonably easy to feel, and so were buttocks; arms and legs a bit more problematical. That was what was disturbing me at the moment.

I'd been checking Lizzie once a week for the past month—and had been going up to her cabin every other day for the last week, though it was a long walk. The child—and I did *think* there was only one—seemed very large; the fundus of the uterus was a good bit higher than I thought it should be. And while babies frequently changed position in the weeks prior to birth, this one had remained in a transverse lie—wedged sideways—for a worryingly long time.

The fact was that without a hospital, operating facilities, or anesthesia, my ability to deal with an unorthodox delivery was severely limited. *Sans* surgical intervention, with a transverse lie, a midwife had four alternatives: let the woman die after days of agonizing labor; let the woman die after doing a cesarean section without benefit of anesthesia or asepsis—but possibly save the baby; possibly save the mother by killing the child in the womb and then removing it in bits (Daniel Rawlings had had several pages in his book—

illustrated—describing this procedure) or attempt an internal inversion, trying to turn the baby into a position in which it might be delivered.

While superficially the most attractive option, that last one could easily be as dangerous as the others, resulting in the deaths of mother *and* child.

I'd tried an external version the week before, and managed—with difficulty—to induce the child to turn head-down. Two days later, it had turned right back, evidently liking its supine position. It might turn again by itself before labor started—and it might not.

Experience being what it was, I normally managed to distinguish between intelligent planning for contingencies and useless worrying over things that might not happen, thus allowing myself to sleep at night. I'd lain awake into the small hours every night for the last week, though, envisioning the possibility that the child wouldn't turn in time, and running through that short, grim list of alternatives in futile search for one more choice.

If I had ether . . . but what I'd had had gone when the house burned.

Kill Lizzie, in order to save the new child? No. If it came to that, better to kill the child *in utero,* and leave Rodney with a mother, Jo and Kezzie with their wife. But the thought of crushing the skull of a full-term child, healthy, ready to be born . . . or decapitating it with a loop of sharp wire—

"Are ye no hungry this morning, Auntie?"

"Er . . . no. Thank you, Ian."

"Ye look a bit pale, Sassenach. Are ye sickening for something?"

"No!" I got up hastily before they could ask any more questions—there was absolutely no point in anyone but me being terrorized by what I was thinking—and went out to fetch a bucket of water from the well.

Amy was outside; she had started a fire going under the big laundry kettle, and was chivying Aidan and Orrie, who were scrambling round to fetch wood, pausing periodically to throw mud at each other.

"Are ye wanting water, *a bhana-mhaighstir*?" she asked, seeing the bucket in my hand. "Aidan will fetch it down for ye."

"No, that's all right," I assured her. "I wanted a bit of air. It's so nice out in the mornings now." It was; still chilly until the sun got high, but fresh, and dizzy with the scents of grass, resin-fat buds, and early catkins.

I took my bucket up to the well, filled it, and made my way down the path again, slowly, looking at things as you do when you know you might not see them again for a long time. If ever.

Things had changed drastically on the Ridge already, with the coming of violence, the disruptions of the war, the destruction of the Big House. They'd change a great deal more, with Jamie and me both gone.

Who would be the natural leader? Hiram Crombie was the *de facto* head of the Presbyterian fisher-folk who had come from Thurso—but he was a rigid, humorless man, much more likely to cause friction with the rest of the community than to maintain order and foster cooperation.

Bobby? After considerable thought, Jamie had appointed him factor, with the responsibility of overseeing our property—or what was left of it. But aside from his natural capabilities or lack thereof, Bobby was a young man. He—along with many of the other men on the Ridge—could so easily be swept up in the coming storm, taken away and obliged to serve in one of the militias. Not the Crown's forces, though; he had been a British soldier, stationed in Boston seven years before, where he and several of his fellows had been menaced by a mob of several hundred irate Bostonians. In fear for their lives, the soldiers had loaded their muskets and leveled them at the crowd. Stones and clubs were thrown, shots were fired—by whom, no one could establish; I had never asked Bobby—and men had died.

Bobby's life had been spared at the subsequent trial, but he bore a brand on his cheek—"M," for "Murder." I had no idea of his politics—he never spoke of such things—but he would never fight with the British army again.

I pushed open the door to the cabin, my equanimity somewhat restored.

Jamie and Ian were now arguing as to whether the new child would be a sister or brother to little Rodney or a half sibling.

"Well, no way of telling, is there?" Ian said. "Nobody kens

whether Jo or Kezzie fathered wee Rodney, and the same for this bairn. If Jo is Rodney's father, and Kezzie this one's—"

"It doesn't really matter," I interrupted, pouring water from the bucket into the cauldron. "Jo and Kezzie are identical twins. That means their . . . er . . . their sperm is identical, as well." That was oversimplifying matters, but it was much too early in the day to try to explain reproductive meiosis and recombinant DNA. "If the mother is the same—and she is—and the father is genetically the same—and they are—any children born would be full sisters or brothers to each other."

"Their spunk's the same, too?" Ian demanded, incredulous. "How can ye tell? Did ye *look*?" he added, giving me a look of horrified curiosity.

"I did not," I said severely. "I didn't have to. I know these things."

"Oh, aye," he said, nodding with respect. "Of course ye would. I forget sometimes what ye are, Auntie Claire."

I wasn't sure what he meant by that, exactly, but it didn't seem necessary either to inquire or to explain that my knowledge of the Beardsleys' intimate processes was academic, rather than supernatural.

"But it *is* Kezzie that's this one's father, no?" Jamie put in, frowning. "I sent Jo away; it's Kezzie she's been living with this past year."

Ian gave him a pitying look.

"Ye think he went? Jo?"

"I've not seen him," Jamie said, but the thick red brows drew together.

"Well, ye wouldn't," Ian conceded. "They'll ha' been gey careful about it, not wantin' to cross ye. Ye never do see more than one of them—at a time," he added, offhanded.

We both stared at him. He looked up from the chunk of bacon in his hand and raised his brows.

"I ken these things, aye?" he said blandly.

AFTER SUPPER, the household shifted and settled for the night. All the Higginses retired to the back bedroom, where they shared the single bedstead.

Obsessively, I opened my midwifery bundle and laid out

the kit, checking everything over once more. Scissors, white thread for the cord. Clean cloths, rinsed many times to remove all trace of lye soap, scalded and dried. A large square of waxed canvas, to waterproof the mattress. A small bottle of alcohol, diluted fifty percent with sterile water. A small bag containing several twists of washed—but not boiled—wool. A rolled-up sheet of parchment, to serve in lieu of my stethoscope, which had perished in the fire. A knife. And a length of thin wire, sharpened at one end, coiled up like a snake.

I hadn't eaten much at dinner—or all day—but had a constant sense of rising bile at the back of my throat. I swallowed and wrapped the kit up again, tying the twine firmly round it.

I felt Jamie's eyes on me and looked up. He said nothing, but smiled a little, warmth in his eyes, and I felt a momentary easing—then a fresh clenching, as I wondered what he would think, if worst came to worst, and I had to—but he'd seen that twist of fear in my face. With his eyes still on mine, he quietly took his rosary from his sporran, and began silently to tell the beads, the worn wood sliding slowly through his fingers.

TWO NIGHTS LATER, I came instantly awake at the sound of feet on the path outside and was on my own feet, pulling on my clothes, before Jo's knock sounded on the door. Jamie let him in; I heard them murmuring together as I burrowed under the settle for my kit. Jo sounded excited, a little worried—but not panicked. That was good; if Lizzie had been frightened or in serious trouble, he would have sensed it at once—the twins were nearly as sensitive to her moods and welfare as they were to each other's.

"Shall I come?" Jamie whispered, looming up beside me.

"No," I whispered back, touching him for strength. "Go back to sleep. I'll send, if I need you."

He was tousled from sleep, the embers of the fire making shadows in his hair, but his eyes were alert. He nodded and kissed my forehead, but instead of stepping back, he laid his hand on my head and whispered, "O blessed Michael of the Red Domain . . ." in Gaelic, then touched my cheek in farewell.

"I'll see ye in the morning then, Sassenach," he said, and pushed me gently toward the door.

To my surprise, it was snowing outside. The sky was gray and full of light and the air alive with huge, whirling flakes that brushed my face, melting instantly on my skin. It was a spring storm; I could see the flakes settle briefly on the grass stems, then vanish. There would likely be no trace of snow by morning, but the night was filled with its mystery. I turned to look back, but could not see the cabin behind us—only the shapes of trees half shrouded, uncertain in the pearl-gray light. The path before us looked likewise unreal, the trace disappearing into strange trees and unknown shadows.

I felt weirdly disembodied, caught between past and future, nothing visible save the whirling white silence that surrounded me. And yet I felt calmer than I had in many days. I felt the weight of Jamie's hand on my head, with its whispered blessing. *O blessed Michael of the Red Domain . . .*

It was the blessing given to a warrior going out to battle. I had given it to him, more than once. He'd never done such a thing before, and I had no idea what had made him do it now—but the words glowed in my heart, a small shield against the dangers ahead.

The snow covered the ground now in a thin blanket that hid dark earth and sprouting growth. Jo's feet left crisp black prints that I followed upward, the needles of fir and balsam brushing cold and fragrant against my skirt, as I listened to a vibrant silence that rang like a bell.

If ever there were a night when angels walked, I prayed it might be this one.

IT WAS NEARLY an hour's walk to the Beardsley cabin, in daylight and good weather. Fear hastened my footsteps, though, and Jo—I thought it was Jo, by his voice—was hard-pressed to keep up with me.

"How long has she been at it?" I asked. You could never tell, but Lizzie's first labor had been fast; she'd delivered little Rodney quite alone and without incident. I didn't think we were going to be that lucky tonight, though my mind couldn't help hopefully envisioning an arrival at the cabin to find

Lizzie already holding the new baby, safely popped out without difficulty.

"Not long," he panted. "Her waters came all of a sudden, when we were all abed, and she said I best come fetch you at once."

I tried not to notice that "all abed"—after all, he and/or Kezzie might have slept on the floor—but the Beardsley *ménage* was the literal personification of double entendre; nobody who knew the truth could think of them without thinking of . . .

I didn't bother asking how long he and Kezzie had both been living at the cabin; from what Ian had said, they'd likely both been there all the time. Given the normal conditions of life in the backcountry, no one would have blinked at the notion of a man and his wife living with his brother. And so far as the general population of the Ridge was aware, Lizzie was married to Kezzie. She was. She was also married to Jo, as the result of a set of machinations that still caused me to marvel, but the Bearsdley household kept that fact quiet, on Jamie's orders.

"Her pap'll be there," Jo said, breath pluming white as he pulled alongside me where the trail opened out. "And Auntie Monika. Kezzie went to fetch 'em."

"You left Lizzie *alone*?"

His shoulders hunched defensively, uncomfortable.

"She said to," he said simply.

I didn't bother replying, but hastened my step, until a stitch in my side made me slow a little. If Lizzie hadn't already given birth and hemorrhaged or had some other disaster while alone, it might be a help to have "Auntie Monika"—Mr. Wemyss's second wife—to hand. Monika Berrisch Wemyss was a German lady, of limited and eccentric English but boundless courage and common sense.

Mr. Wemyss had his share of courage, too, though it was a quiet sort. He was waiting for us on the porch, with Kezzie, and it was clear that Mr. Wemyss was supporting his son-in-law, rather than the reverse. Kezzie was openly wringing his hands and jigging from foot to foot, while Mr. Wemyss's slight figure bent consolingly toward him, a hand on his arm. I caught low murmurs, and then they saw us and turned toward us, sudden hope in the straightening of their bodies.

A long, low howl came from the cabin, and all the men stiffened as though it had been a wolf springing out of the dark at them.

"Well, she sounds all right," I said mildly, and all of them exhaled at once, audibly. I wanted to laugh, but thought better not, and pushed open the door.

"Ugh," said Lizzie, looking up from the bed. "Oh, it's you, ma'am. Thank the Lord!"

"*Gott bedanket,* aye," agreed Auntie Monika, tranquilly. She was on her hands and knees, sponging the floor with a wad of cloth. "Not so long now, I hope."

"I hope not, too," said Lizzie, grimacing. "GAAAAAR-RRRRGH!" Her face convulsed into a rictus and went bright red, and her swollen body arched backward. She looked more like someone in the grip of tetanus than an expectant mother, but luckily the spasm was short-lived, and she collapsed into a limp heap, panting.

"It wasna like this, last time," she complained, opening one eye as I palpated her abdomen.

"It's never the same," I said absently. One quick glance had made my heart leap; the child was no longer sideways. On the other hand . . . it wasn't neatly head-down, either. It wasn't moving—babies generally didn't, during labor—and while I thought I had located the head up under Lizzie's ribs, I wasn't at all sure of the disposition of the rest.

"Let me just have a look here . . ." She was naked, wrapped in a quilt. Her wet shift was hanging over the back of a chair, steaming in front of the fire. The bed wasn't soaked, though, and I deduced that she'd felt the rupturing of her membranes and made it to a standing position before her water broke.

I'd been afraid to look, and let my breath out in audible relief. The chief fear with a breech presentation was that part of the umbilical cord would prolapse when the membranes ruptured, the loop then being squeezed between the pelvis and some part of the fetus. All clear, though, and a quick feel indicated that the cervix was very nearly effaced.

The only thing to do now was to wait and see what came out first. I undid my bundle, and—shoving the coil of sharpened wire hastily under a packet of cloths—spread out the waxed canvas, hoicking Lizzie onto it with Auntie Monika's help.

Monika blinked and glanced at the trundle where little Rodney was snoring when Lizzie let out another of those unearthly howls. She looked to me for reassurance that nothing was wrong, then took hold of Lizzie's hands, murmuring softly to her in German while she grunted and wheezed.

The door creaked gently, and I looked round to see one of the Beardsleys peering in, his face showing a mixture of fear and hope.

"Is it here?" he whispered hoarsely.

"NO!" bellowed Lizzie, sitting bolt upright. "Get your neb out of my sight, or I'll twist your wee ballocks off! All four o' them!"

The door promptly closed, and Lizzie subsided, puffing.

"I hate them," she said through clenched teeth. "I want them to die!"

"Mmm-hmm," I said sympathetically. "Well, I'm sure they're suffering, at least."

"Good." She went from fury to pathos in a split second, tears welling in her eyes. "Am I going to die?"

"No," I said, as reassuringly as possible.

"EEEAAAAARRRRRRGGGGG!"

"Großer Gott," Auntie Monika said, crossing herself. *"Ist das gut?"*

"Ja," I said, still reassuring. "I don't suppose there are any scissors . . . ?"

"Oh, *ja,*" she replied, reaching for her bag. She produced a tiny pair of very worn but once-gilded embroidery scissors. "Dese you need?"

"Danke."

"BLOOOOOORRRRRGGGG!"

Monika and I both looked at Lizzie.

"Don't overdo it," I said. "They're frightened, but they aren't idiots. Besides, you'll scare your father. *And* Rodney," I added, with a glance at the little heap of bedclothes in the trundle bed.

She subsided, panting, but managed a nod and the ghost of a smile.

Matters proceeded fairly rapidly thereafter; she *was* fast. I checked her pulse, then her cervix, and felt my own heart rate double as I touched what was plainly a tiny foot, on its way out. Could I get the other one?

I glanced at Monika, with an eye to size and strength. She was tough as whipcord, I knew, but not that large. Lizzie, on the other hand, was the size of—well, Ian had not been exaggerating when he thought it might be twins.

The creeping thought that it still *might* be twins made the hair on the back of my neck stand up, despite the humid warmth of the cabin.

No, I said firmly to myself. *It isn't; you know it isn't. One is going to be bad enough.*

"We're going to need one of the men, to help hold her shoulders up," I said to Monika. "Get one of the twins, will you?"

"Both," Lizzie gasped, as Monika turned toward the door.

"One will be—"

"Both! Nnnnnngggg . . ."

"Both," I said to Monika, who nodded in a matter-of-fact manner.

The twins came in on a rush of cold air, their faces identical ruddy masks of alarm and excitement. Without my saying anything to them, they came at once to Lizzie, like a pair of iron filings to a magnet. She had struggled into a sitting position, and one of them knelt behind her, his hands gently kneading her shoulders as they relaxed from the last spasm. His brother sat beside her, a supportive arm round what used to be her waist, his other hand smoothing back the sweat-soaked hair from her brow.

I tried to arrange the quilt round her, over her protruding belly, but she pushed it away, hot and fretful. The cabin was filled with moist heat, from the steaming cauldron and the sweat of effort. Well, presumably the twins were somewhat more familiar with her anatomy than I was, I reflected, and handed the wadded quilt to Auntie Monika. Modesty had no place in childbirth.

I knelt in front of her, scissors in hand, and snipped the episiotomy quickly, feeling a tiny spray of warm blood across my hand. I seldom needed to do one for a routine birth, but for this, I was going to need room to maneuver. I pressed one of my clean cloths to the cut, but the amount of bleeding was negligible, and the insides of her thighs were streaked with bloody show in any case.

It *was* a foot; I could see the toes, long ones, like a frog's, and glanced automatically at Lizzie's bare feet, planted solidly on the floor to either side of me. No, hers were short and compact; it must be the twins' influence.

The humid, swampish scent of birth waters, sweat, and blood rose like fog from Lizzie's body, and I felt my own sweat running down my sides. I groped upward, hooked a finger round the heel, and brought the foot down, feeling the life in the child move in its flesh, though the baby itself was not moving, helpless in the grip of birth.

The other one, I needed the other one. Feeling urgently through the belly wall between one contraction and the next, I slid my other hand up the emergent leg, found the tiny curve of the buttock. Switched hands hastily and, with my eyes closed, found the curve of the flexed thigh. Bloody hell, it seemed to have its knee tucked up under its chin . . . felt the yielding stiffness of tiny, cartilaginous bones, solid in the squish of fluid, the stretch of muscle . . . got a finger, two fingers, circling the other ankle, and—snarling, "Brace her! Hold her!" as Lizzie's back arched and her bottom scooted toward me—brought the second foot down.

I sat back, eyes open and breathing hard, though it hadn't been a physical strain. The little froggy feet twitched once, then drooped, as the legs came into view with the next push.

"Once more, sweetheart," I whispered, a hand on Lizzie's straining thigh. "Give us one more like that."

A growl from the depths of the earth as Lizzie reached that point where a woman no longer cares whether she lives, dies, or splits apart, and the child's lower body slid slowly into view, the umbilicus pulsing like a thick purple worm looped across the belly. My eyes were fixed on that, thinking, *Thank God, thank God,* when I became aware of Auntie Monika, peering intently over my shoulder.

"*Sind das* balls?" she said, puzzled, pointing at the child's genitals.

I hadn't spared time to look, concerned as I was with the cord, but I glanced down and smiled.

"No. *Es ist ein Mädchen,*" I said. The baby's sex was edematous; it did look much like a little boy's equipment, the clitoris protruding from swollen labia, but wasn't.

"What? What is it?" One of the Beardsleys was asking, leaning down to look.

"You haff a leedle girl," Auntie Monika told him, beaming up.

"A girl?" the other Beardsley gasped. "Lizzie, we have a daughter!"

"Will you fucking *shut up*?!?" Lizzie snarled. "NNNNNNNGGGGG!"

At this point, Rodney woke up and sat bolt upright, open-mouthed and wide-eyed. Auntie Monika was on her feet at once, scooping him out of his bed before he could start to scream.

Rodney's sister was inching reluctantly into the world, shoved by each contraction. I was counting in my head, *One hippopotamus, two hippopotamus* . . . From the appearance of the umbilicus to successful delivery of the mouth and the first breath, we could afford no more than four minutes before brain damage from lack of oxygen began to occur. But I couldn't pull and risk damage to the neck and head.

"Push, sweetheart," I said, bracing my hands on both Lizzie's knees, my voice calm. "Hard, now."

Thirty-four hippopotamus, thirty-five . . .

All we needed now was for the chin to hang up on the pelvic bone. When the contraction eased, I slid my fingers hastily up onto the child's face, and got two fingers over the upper maxilla. I felt the next contraction coming, and gritted my teeth as the force of it crushed my hand between the bones of the pelvis and the baby's skull, but didn't pull back, fearful of losing my traction.

Sixty-two hippopotamus . . .

Relaxation, and I drew down, slowly, slowly, pulling the child's head forward, easing the chin past the rim of the pelvis . . .

Eighty-nine hippopotamus, ninety hippopotamus . . .

The child was hanging from Lizzie's body, bloody-blue and shining in the firelight, swaying in the shadow of her thighs like the clapper of a bell—or a body from a gibbet, and I pushed that thought away . . .

"Should not we take . . . ?" Auntie Monika whispered to me, Rodney clutched to her breast.

One hundred.

"No," I said. "Don't touch it—her. Not yet." Gravity was slowly helping the delivery. Pulling would injure the neck, and if the head were to stick . . .

One hundred ten hippo—that was a lot of hippopotami, I thought, abstractedly envisaging herds of them marching down to the hollow, there they will wallow, in mud, glooooorious . . .

"Now," I said, poised to swab the mouth and nose as they emerged—but Lizzie hadn't waited for prompting, and with a long deep sigh and an audible *pop!,* the head delivered all at once, and the baby fell into my hands like a ripe fruit.

I DIPPED A LITTLE more water from the steaming cauldron into the washing bowl and added cold water from the bucket. The warmth of it stung my hands; the skin between my knuckles was cracked from the long winter and the constant use of dilute alcohol for sterilization. I'd just finished stitching Lizzie up and cleaning her, and the blood floated away from my hands, dark swirls in the water.

Behind me, Lizzie was tucked up neatly in bed, clad in one of the twins' shirts, her own shift being not yet dried. She was laughing with the euphoria of birth and survival, the twins on either side of her, fussing over her, murmuring admiration and relief, one tucking back her loose, damp fair hair, the other softly kissing her neck.

"Are you fevered, my lover?" one asked, a tinge of concern in his voice. That made me turn round to look; Lizzie suffered from malaria, and while she hadn't had an attack in some time, perhaps the stress of birth . . .

"No," she said, and kissed Jo or Kezzie on the forehead. "I'm only flushed from bein' happy." Kezzie or Jo beamed at her in adoration, while his brother took up the neck-kissing duties on the other side.

Auntie Monika coughed. She'd wiped down the baby with a damp cloth and some wisps of the wool I'd brought—soft and oily with lanolin—and had it now swaddled in a blanket. Rodney had got bored with the proceedings long since and gone to sleep on the floor by the wood-basket, a thumb in his mouth.

"Your *Vater,* Lizzie," she said, a slight hint of reproof in her voice. "He vill cold begetting. *Und die Kleine* he vant see, *mit* you, but maybe not so much *mit den beiden . . .*" She managed to incline her head toward the bed, while simultaneously modestly averting her eyes from the frolicsome trio on it. Mr. Wemyss and his sons-in-law had had a gingerly reconciliation after the birth of Rodney, but best not to press things.

Her words galvanized the twins, who hopped to their feet, one stooping to scoop up Rodney, whom he handled with casual affection, the other rushing for the door to retrieve Mr. Wemyss, forgotten on the porch in the excitement.

While slightly blue round the edges, relief made his thin face glow as though lit from within. He smiled with heartfelt joy at Monika, sparing a brief glance and a ginger pat for the swaddled bundle—but his attention was all for Lizzie, and hers for him.

"Your hands are frozen, Da," she said, giggling a little, but tightening her grip as he made to pull away. "No, stay; I'm warm enough. Come sit by me and say good e'en to your wee granddaughter." Her voice rang with a shy pride, as she reached out a hand to Auntie Monika.

Monika set the baby gently in Lizzie's arms, and stood with a hand on Mr. Wemyss's shoulder, her own weathered face soft with something much deeper than affection. Not for the first time, I was surprised—and vaguely abashed that I should be surprised—by the depth of her love for the frail, quiet little man.

"Oh," Mr. Wemyss said softly. His finger touched the baby's cheek; I could hear her making small smacking noises. She'd been shocked by the trauma of birth and not interested in the breast at first, but plainly was beginning to change her mind.

"She'll be hungry." A rustle of bedclothes as Lizzie took up the baby and put her to the breast with practiced hands.

"What will ye call her, *a leannan*?" Mr. Wemyss asked.

"I hadna really thought of a girl's name," Lizzie answered. "She was so big, I thought sure she was a—ow!" She laughed, a low, sweet sound. "I'd forgot how greedy a newborn wean is. Ooh! There, *a chuisle,* aye, that's better . . ."

I reached for the sack of wool, to rub my own raw hands with one of the soft, oily wisps, and happened to see the twins, standing back out of the way, side by side, their eyes fixed on Lizzie and their daughter, and each wearing a look that echoed Auntie Monika's. Not taking his eyes away, the Beardsley holding little Rodney bent his head and kissed the top of the little boy's round head.

So much love in one small place. I turned away, my own eyes misty. Did it matter, really, how unorthodox the marriage at the center of this odd family was? Well, it would to Hiram Crombie, I reflected. The leader of the rock-ribbed Presbyterian immigrants from Thurso, he'd want Lizzie, Jo, and Kezzie stoned, at the least—together with the sinful fruit of their loins.

No chance of that happening, so long as Jamie was on the Ridge—but with him gone? I slowly cleaned blood from under my nails, hoping that Ian was right about the Beardsleys' capacity for discretion—and deception.

Distracted by these musings, I hadn't noticed Auntie Monika, who had come quietly up beside me.

"Danke," she said softly, laying a gnarled hand on my arm.

"Gern geschehen." I put my hand over hers and squeezed gently. "You were a great help—thank you."

She still smiled, but a line of worry bisected her forehead. "Not so much. But I am afraid, *ja?*" She glanced over her shoulder at the bed, then back at me. "What happens, next time, you are not *hier*? Dey don't stop, you know," she added, discreetly making a circle of thumb and forefinger and running the middle finger of the other hand into it in a most indiscreet illustration of exactly what she meant.

I converted a laugh hastily into a coughing fit, which fortunately went ignored by the relevant parties, though Mr. Wemyss glanced over his shoulder in mild concern.

"You'll be here," I told her, recovering. She looked horrified.

"Me? *Nein,*" she said, shaking her head. "*Das reicht nicht.* Me—" She poked herself in her meager chest, seeing that I hadn't understood. "I . . . am not enough."

I took a deep breath, knowing that she was right. And yet . . .

"You'll have to be," I said, very softly.

She blinked once, her large, wise brown eyes fixed on mine. Then slowly nodded, accepting.

"Mein Gott, hilf mir," she said.

JAMIE HADN'T BEEN able to go back to sleep. He had trouble sleeping these days, in any case, and often lay awake late, watching the fading glow of embers in the hearth and turning things over in his mind, or seeking wisdom in the shadows of the rafters overhead. If he did fall asleep easily, he often came awake later, sudden and sweating. He knew what caused that, though, and what to do about it.

Most of his strategies for reaching slumber involved Claire—talking to her, making love to her—or only looking at her while she slept, finding solace in the solid long curve of her collarbone, or the heartbreaking shape of her closed eyelids, letting sleep steal upon him from her peaceful warmth.

But Claire, of course, was gone.

Half an hour of saying the rosary convinced him that he had done as much in that direction as was necessary or desirable for the sake of Lizzie and her impending child. Saying the rosary for penance—aye, he saw the point of that, particularly if you had to say it on your knees. Or to quiet one's mind, fortify the soul, or seek the insight of meditation on sacred topics, aye, that, too. But not for petition. If he were God, or even the Blessed Virgin, who was renowned for patience, he thought he would find it tedious to listen to more than a decade or so of someone saying please about something over and over, and surely there was no point to boring a person whose aid you sought?

Now, the Gaelic prayers seemed much more useful to the purpose, being as they were concentrated upon a specific request or blessing, and more pleasing both in rhythm and variety. If you asked him, not that anyone was likely to.

Moire gheal is Bhride;
Mar a rug Anna Moire,
Mar a rug Moire Criosda,
Mar a rug Eile Eoin Baistidh
Gun mhar-bhith dha dhi,

Cuidich i na 'h asaid,
Cuidich i a Bhride!

Mar a gheineadh Criosd am Moire
Comhliont air gach laimh,
Cobhair mise, mhoime,
An gein a thoir bho 'n chnaimh;
'S mar a chomhn thu Oigh an t-solais,
Gun or, gun odh, gun ni,
Comhn i 's mor a th' othrais,
Comhn i a Bhride!

he murmured as he climbed.

Mary fair and Bride;
As Anna bore Mary,
As Mary bore Christ,
As Eile bore John the Baptist
Without flaw in him,
Aid thou her in her unbearing,
Aid her, O Bride!

As Christ was conceived of Mary
Full perfect on every hand,
Assist thou me, foster mother,
The conception to bring from the bone;
And as thou didst aid the Virgin of joy,
Without gold, without corn, without kine,
Aid thou her, great is her sickness,
Aid her, O Bride!

He'd left the cabin, unable to bear its smothering confines, and wandered in a contemplative fashion through the Ridge in the falling snow, ticking through mental lists. But the fact was that all his preparation was done, bar the packing of the horses and mules, and without really thinking about it, he found that he was making his way up the trail toward the Beardsley place. The snow had ceased to fall now, but the sky stretched gray and gentle overhead, and cold white lay calm upon the trees and stilled the rush of wind.

Sanctuary, he thought. It wasn't, of course—there was no

safe place in time of war—but the feel of the mountain night reminded him of the feel of churches: a great peace, waiting.

Notre Dame in Paris . . . St. Giles' in Edinburgh. Tiny stone churches in the Highlands, where he'd sometimes gone in his years of hiding, when he thought it safe. He crossed himself, remembering that; the plain stones, often nothing more than a wooden altar inside—and yet the relief of entering, sitting on the floor if there was no bench, just sitting, and knowing himself to be not alone. Sanctuary.

Whether the thought of churches or of Claire reminded him, he remembered another church—the one they had married in, and he grinned to himself at the memory of that. Not a peaceful waiting, no. He could still feel the thunder of his heart against his ribs as he'd stepped inside, the reek of his sweat—he'd smelled like a rutting goat, and hoped she didn't notice—the inability to draw a full breath. And the feel of her hand in his, her fingers small and freezing cold, clutching at him for support.

Sanctuary. They'd been that for each other then—and were so now. *Blood of my blood.* The tiny cut had healed, but he rubbed the ball of his thumb, smiling at the matter-of-fact way she'd said it.

He came in sight of the cabin, and saw Joseph Wemyss waiting on the porch, hunched and stamping his feet against the cold. He was about to hail Joseph, when the door suddenly opened and one of the Beardsley twins—Christ, what were *they* doing in there?—reached out and seized his father-in-law by the arm, nearly pulling him off his feet in his excitement.

It *was* excitement, too, not grief or alarm; he'd seen the boy's face clearly in the glow of the firelight. He let out the breath he hadn't realized he was holding, white in the dark. The child was come, then, and both it and Lizzie had survived.

He relaxed against a tree, touching the rosary around his neck.

"Moran taing," he said softly, in brief but heartfelt thanks. Someone in the cabin had put more wood on the fire; a shower of sparks flew up from the chimney, lighting the snow in red and gold and hissing black where cinders fell.

Yet man is born to trouble, as the sparks fly upward. He'd read that line of Job many times in prison, and made no great sense of it. Upward-flying sparks caused no trouble, by and large, unless you had very dry shingles; it was the ones that spat straight out of the hearth that might set your house on fire. Or if the writer had meant only that it was the nature of man to be in trouble—as plainly it was, if his own experience was aught to go by—then he was making a comparison of inevitability, saying that sparks always flew upward—which anyone who'd ever watched a fire for long could tell you they didn't.

Still, who was he to be criticizing the Bible's logic, when he ought to be repeating psalms of praise and gratitude? He tried to think of one, but was too content to think of more than odd bits and pieces.

He realized with a small shock that he was entirely happy. The safe birth of the child was a great thing in itself, to be sure—but it also meant that Claire had come safe through her trial, and that he and she were now free. They might leave the Ridge, knowing they had done all that could be done for the folk who remained.

Aye, there was always a sadness in leaving home—but in this case, it might be argued that their home had left *them,* when the house burned, and in any case, it was overbalanced by his rising sense of anticipation. Free and away, Claire by his side, no daily chores to do, no petty squabbles to settle, no widows and orphans to provide for—well, that was an unworthy thought, doubtless, and yet . . .

War was a terrible thing, and this one would be, too—but it was undeniably exciting, and the blood stirred in him from scalp to soles.

"Moran taing," he said again, in heartfelt gratitude.

A short time later, the door of the cabin opened again, spilling light, and Claire came out, pulling up the hood of her cloak, her basket over her arm. Voices followed her, and bodies crowded the door. She turned to wave farewell to them, and he heard her laugh; the sound of it sent a small thrill of pleasure through him.

The door closed and she came down the path in the gray-lit dark; he could see that she staggered just a little, from weariness, and yet there was an air of something about her—he thought it might be the same euphoria that lifted him.

"Like the sparks that fly upward," he murmured to himself, and smiling, stepped out to greet her.

She wasn't startled, but turned at once and came toward him, seeming almost to float on the snow.

"It's well, then," he said, and she sighed and came into his arms, solid and warm within the cold folds of her cloak. He reached inside it, drew her close, inside the wool of his own big cloak.

"I need you, please," she whispered, her mouth against his, and without reply he took her up in his arms—Christ, she was right, that cloak stank of dead meat; had the man who sold it to him used it to haul a butchered deer in from the forest?—and kissed her deep, then put her down and led her down the hill, the light snow seeming to melt away from their feet as they walked.

It seemed to take no time at all to reach the barn; they spoke a little on the trail, but he could not have said what they talked about. It only mattered to be with each other.

It wasn't precisely cozy inside the barn, but not freezing, either. Welcoming, he thought, with the pleasant warm smell of the beasts in the dark. The weird gray light of the sky filtered in, just a bit, so you could see the hunched shapes of horses and mules dozing in their stalls. And there was dry straw to lie on, for all it was old and a trifle musty.

It was too cold to undress, but he laid his cloak in the straw, her upon it, and lay upon her, both of them shivering as they kissed, so their teeth clacked together and they drew back, snorting.

"This is silly," she said, "I can see my breath—*and* yours. It's cold enough to blow smoke rings. We'll freeze."

"No, we won't. Ken the way the Indians make fire?"

"What, rubbing a dry stick on a . . ."

"Aye, friction." He'd got her petticoats up; her thigh was smooth and cold under his hand. "I see it's no going to be dry, though—Christ, Sassenach, what have ye been about?" He had her firmly in the palm of his hand, warm and soft and juicy, and she squealed at the chill of his touch, loud enough that one of the mules let out a startled wheeze. She wriggled, just enough to make him take his hand out from between her legs and insert something else, quick.

"Ye're going to rouse the whole barn," he observed,

breathless. God, the enveloping shock of the heat of her made him giddy.

She ran her cold hands up under his shirt and pinched both his nipples, hard, and he yelped, then laughed.

"Do that again," he said, and bending, stuck his tongue in her cold ear for the pleasure of hearing her shriek. She wriggled and arched her back, but didn't—he noticed—actually turn her head away. He took her earlobe gently between his teeth and began to worry it, rogering her slowly and laughing to himself at the noises she made.

It had been a long time of making silent love.

Her hands were busy at his back; he'd only let down the flap of his breeks and pulled his shirttail up out of the way, but she'd got the shirt out at the back now, and shoved both hands down his breeks and got his hurdies in a good two-handed grip. She pulled him in tight, digging in her nails, and he took her meaning. He let go her ear, rose on his hands, and rode her solid, the straw a-rustle round them like the crackle of burning.

He wanted simply to let go at once, spill himself and fall on her, hold her to his body and smell her hair in a doze of warmth and joy. A dim sense of obligation reminded him that she'd asked him for this; she'd needed it. He couldn't go and leave her wanting.

He closed his eyes and slowed himself, lowered himself onto her so her body strained and rose along his length, the cloth of their clothes rasping and bunching up between them. He got a hand down under her, cupped her bare bum, and slid his fingers into the straining warm crease of her buttocks. Slid one a little farther, and she gasped. Her hips rose, trying to get away, but he laughed deep in his throat and didn't let her. Wiggled the finger.

"Do that again," he whispered in her ear. "Make that noise again for me."

She made a better one, one he'd never heard before, and jerked under him, quivering and whimpering.

He pulled out the finger and guddled her, light and quick, all along the slick deep parts, feeling his own cock under his fingers, big and slippery, stretching her . . .

He made a terrible noise himself—like a dying cow—but was too happy to be shamed.

"Ye're no verra peaceful, Sassenach," he murmured a moment later, breathing in the smell of musk and new life. "But I like ye fine."

12

ENOUGH

I TOOK MY LEAVE, starting from the springhouse. Stood inside for a moment, listening to the trickle of the water in its stone channel, breathing the cold, fresh smell of the place, with its faint sweet scents of milk and butter. Coming out, I turned left, passing the weathered palisades of my garden, covered with the tattered, rattling remnants of gourd vines. I paused, hesitating; I hadn't set foot in the garden since the day that Malva and her child had died there. I set my hands on two of the wooden stakes, leaning to look between them.

I was glad I hadn't looked before; I couldn't have borne to see it in its winter desolation, the ragged stems blackened and stiff, the rags of leaves rotted into the ground. It was still a sight to strike a pang to a gardener's heart, but no longer desolate. Fresh green sprouted everywhere, spangled with tiny flowers; the kindness of spring laying garlands over winter's bones. Granted, half the green things growing were grass and weeds; by summer, the woods would have reclaimed the garden, smothering the stunted sproutings of cabbages and onions. Amy had made a new vegetable patch near the old cabin; neither she nor anyone else on the Ridge would set foot here.

Something stirred in the grass, and I saw a small gopher snake slide through, hunting. The sight of something live comforted me, little as I cared for snakes, and I smiled as I lifted my eyes and saw that bees were humming to and fro from one of the old bee gums that still stood at the foot of the garden.

I looked last at the spot where I had planted salad greens; that's where she had died. In memory, I'd always seen the spreading blood, imagined it still there, a permanent stain soaked dark into the earth among the churned wreckage of uprooted lettuces and wilting leaves. But it was gone; nothing marked the spot save a fairy ring of mushrooms, tiny white heads poking out of the wild grass.

"I will arise and go now," I said softly, *"and go to Innisfree, and a small cabin build there, of clay and wattles made; nine bean rows will I have there, a hive for the honeybee, and live alone in the bee-loud glade."* I paused for a moment, and as I turned away, added in a whisper, *"And I shall have some peace there, for peace comes dropping slow."*

I made my way briskly down the path then; no need to apostrophize the ruins of the house, nor yet the white sow. I'd remember *them* without effort. As for the corncrib and hen coop—if you've seen one, you've seen them all.

I could see the little gathering of horses, mules, and people moving in the slow chaos of imminent departure in front of the cabin. I wasn't quite ready yet for goodbyes, though, and stepped into the wood to pull myself together.

The grass was long beside the trail, soft and feathery against the hem of my weighted skirts. Something heavier than grass brushed them, and I looked down to see Adso. I'd been looking for him most of yesterday; typical of him to show up at the last minute.

"So there you are," I said, accusing. He looked at me with his huge calm eyes of celadon green, and licked a paw. On impulse, I scooped him up and held him against me, feeling the rumble of his purr and the soft, thick fur of his silvery belly.

He'd be all right; I knew that. The woods were his private game preserve, and Amy Higgins liked him and had promised me to see him right for milk and a warm spot by the fire in bad weather. I knew that.

"Go on, then," I said, and set him on the ground. He stood for a moment, tail waving slowly, head raised in search of food or interesting smells, then stepped into the grass and vanished.

I bent, very slowly, arms crossed, and shook, weeping silently, violently.

I cried until my throat hurt and I couldn't breathe, then sat in the grass, curled into myself like a dried leaf, tears that I couldn't stop dropping on my knees like the first fat drops of a coming storm. Oh, God. It was only the beginning.

I rubbed my hands hard over my eyes, smearing the wetness, trying to scrub away grief. A soft cloth touched my face, and I looked up, sniffing, to find Jamie kneeling in front of me, handkerchief in hand.

"I'm sorry," he said, very softly.

"It's not—don't worry, I'm . . . He's only a cat," I said, and a small fresh grief tightened like a band round my chest.

"Aye, I know." He moved beside me and put an arm round my shoulders, pulling my head to his chest, while he gently wiped my face. "But ye couldna weep for the bairns. Or the house. Or your wee garden. Or the poor dead lass and her bairn. But if ye weep for your cheetie, ye know ye can stop."

"How do you know that?" My voice was thick, but the band round my chest was not quite so tight.

He made a small, rueful sound.

"Because I canna weep for those things, either, Sassenach. And I havena got a cat."

I sniffled, wiped my face one last time, and blew my nose before giving him back the handkerchief, which he stuffed into his sporran without grimace or thought.

Lord, he'd said. *Let me be enough.* That prayer had lodged in my heart like an arrow when I'd heard it and thought he asked for help in doing what had to be done. But that wasn't what he'd meant at all—and the realization of what he *had* meant split my heart in two.

I took his face between my hands, and wished so much that I had his own gift, the ability to say what lay in my heart, in such a way that he would know. But I hadn't.

"Jamie," I said at last. "Oh, Jamie. You're . . . everything. Always."

An hour later, we left the Ridge.

13

UNREST

IAN LAY DOWN with a sack of rice under his head for a pillow. It was hard, but he liked the whisper of the small grains when he turned his head and the faint starched smell of it. Rollo rooted under the plaid with his snout, snorting as he worked his way close against Ian's body, ending with his nose cozily buried in Ian's armpit. Ian scratched the dog's ears gently, then lay back, watching the stars.

It was a sliver moon, thin as a nail paring, and the stars were big and brilliant in the purple-black of the sky. He traced the constellations overhead. Would he see the same stars in Scotland? he wondered. He'd not paid much mind to the stars when he was home in the Highlands, and you couldn't see stars at all in Edinburgh, for the smoke of the reeking lums.

His aunt and uncle lay on the other side of the smoored fire, close enough together as to look like one log, sharing warmth. He saw the blankets twitch, settle, twitch again, and then a stillness, waiting. He heard a whisper, too low to make out the words but the intent behind them clear enough.

He kept his breathing regular, a little louder than usual. A moment, and then the stealthy movements began again. It was hard to fool Uncle Jamie, but there are times when a man wants to be fooled.

His hand rested gently on the dog's head, and Rollo sighed, the huge body going limp, warm and heavy against him. If not for the dog, he would never be able to sleep out of doors. Not that he ever slept soundly, or for long—but at least he could surrender now and then to bodily need, trusting that Rollo would hear any footstep long before he did.

"Ye're safe enough," his uncle Jamie had told him, their first night on the road. He'd been unable to fall asleep then for nerviness, even with Rollo's head on his chest, and had got up to sit by the fire, poking sticks into the embers until the flames rose up into the night, pure and vivid.

He was well aware that he was perfectly visible to anyone who might be watching, but there was nothing to be done about that. And if he had a target painted on his chest, lighting it up wouldn't make a deal of difference.

Rollo, lying watchful beside the growing fire, had lifted his big head suddenly, but only turned it toward a faint sound in the dark. That meant someone familiar, and Ian wasn't bothered, nor yet surprised when his uncle came out of the wood where he'd gone to relieve himself and sat down beside him.

"He doesna want ye dead, ken," Uncle Jamie had said without preamble. "You're safe enough."

"I dinna ken if I want to be safe," he'd blurted, and his uncle had glanced at him, his face troubled—but not surprised. Uncle Jamie had only nodded, though.

He knew what his uncle meant; Arch Bug didn't want him to die, because that would end his guilt, and thus his suffering. Ian had looked into those ancient eyes, the whites of them yellowed and threaded with red, watering with cold and grief, and seen something there that had frozen the core of his soul. No, Arch Bug wouldn't kill him—yet.

His uncle was staring into the fire, the light of it warm on the broad bones of his face, and the sight gave Ian both comfort and panic.

Does it not occur to you? he'd thought, anguished, but did not say. *He said he'd take what I love. And there ye sit beside me, clear as day.*

The first time the thought had come to him, he'd pushed it away; old Arch owed Uncle Jamie, for what he'd done for the Bugs, and he was a man to acknowledge a debt—though perhaps more ready to claim one. And he had nay doubt Bug respected his uncle as a man, too. For a time, that had seemed to settle the matter.

But other thoughts had come to him, uneasy, many-legged things that crept out of the sleepless nights since he'd killed Murdina Bug.

Arch was an old man. Tough as a fire-hardened spear, and twice as dangerous—but old. He'd fought at Sheriffmuir; he had to be rising eighty. Revenge might keep him alive for a time, but all flesh came to an end. He might well think that he hadn't time to wait for Ian to acquire "something worth taking." If he meant to keep his threat, he'd need to act soon.

Ian could hear the subtle shifts and rustlings from the other side of the fire, and swallowed, his mouth dry. Old Arch might try to take his aunt, for surely Ian loved her, and she would be much easier to kill than Uncle Jamie. But no—Arch might be half crazed with grief and rage, but he wasn't insane. He'd know that to touch Auntie Claire—without killing Uncle Jamie at the same time—would be suicide.

Maybe he wouldn't care. That was another thought that walked over his belly with small, cold feet.

He should leave them; he knew that. He'd meant to—he still meant to. Wait 'til they'd fallen asleep, then rise and steal away. They'd be safe then.

But his heart had failed him, that first night. He'd been trying to gather his courage, there by the fire, to go—but his uncle had forestalled him, coming out of the wood and sitting by him, silent but companionable, until Ian had felt able to lie down again.

Tomorrow, he'd thought. After all, there was no sign of Arch Bug; hadn't been, since his wife's funeral. *And maybe he's dead.* He *was* an old man, and alone.

And there was the consideration that if he left without a word, Uncle Jamie would come after him. He'd made it clear that Ian was going back to Scotland, whether he did it willingly or tied in a sack. Ian grinned, despite his thoughts, and Rollo made a small grunt as the chest under him moved in a silent laugh.

He'd barely spared a thought for Scotland and what might await him there.

Perhaps it was the noises from the other side of the fire that made him think it—a sudden high-pitched intake of breath and the deep twin sighs that followed it, his familiarity providing a vivid physical memory of the action that had caused that sigh—but he wondered suddenly whether he might find a wife in Scotland.

He couldn't. Could he? Would Bug be able to follow him so far? *Maybe he's already dead,* he thought again, and shifted a bit. Rollo grumbled in his throat but, recognizing the signs, shuffled off him and curled up a little distance away.

His family would be there. Surrounded by the Murrays, surely he—and a wife—would be safe. It was simple to lurk and steal through the dense woods here in the mountains—not nearly so simple in the Highlands, where every eye was sharp and no stranger passed unnoticed.

He didn't know quite what his mother would do when she saw him—but once she got used to it, maybe she could think of a girl who wouldn't be too frightened of him.

A suck of breath and a sound not quite a moan from his uncle—he did that when she put her mouth on his nipple; Ian had seen her do it once or twice, by the glow of embers from the cabin's hearth, her eyes closed, a quick wet gleam of teeth, and her hair falling back from naked shoulders in a cloud of light and shadow.

He put a hand on his cock, tempted. He had a private collection of images that he cherished for the purpose—and not a few of them were of his cousin, though it shamed him a little. She was Roger Mac's wife, after all. But he'd thought at one point that he'd need to marry her himself, and while terrified at the prospect—he'd been only seventeen and she considerably older—had been emboldened at the thought of having her to bed.

He'd watched her close for several days, seeing her arse round and solid, the dark shadow of her red-haired quim under the thin muslin of her shift when she went to bathe, imagining the thrill of seeing it plain on the night when she'd lie down and open her legs for him.

What was he doing? He couldn't be thinking of Brianna like that, not lying a dozen feet from her father!

He grimaced and squinched his eyes tight shut, hand slowing as he summoned up a different image from his private library. Not the witch—not tonight. Her memory aroused him with great urgency, often painfully, but was tinged with a sense of helplessness. Malva . . . No, he was afraid to summon her; he often thought her spirit was not yet so very far away.

Wee Mary. Aye, her. His hand settled at once into its rhythm and he sighed, escaping with relief to the small pink breasts and encouraging smile of the first lass he'd ever lain with.

Hovering moments later on the edge of a dream of a wee blond girl who was his wife, he thought drowsily, *Aye, maybe he's already dead.*

Rollo made a deep, dissentient noise in his throat, and rolled over with his paws in the air.

14

DELICATE MATTERS

London
November 1776

THERE WERE MANY compensations to growing older, Lord John thought. Wisdom, perspective, position in life, the sense of accomplishment, of time well spent, a richness of affection for friends and family . . . and the fact that he needn't keep his back pressed against a wall when talking to Lord George Germain. While both his looking glass and his valet assured him that he continued to be presentable, he was at least twenty years too old to appeal to the secretary of state, who liked them young and tender-skinned.

The clerk who had shown him in met this description, being equipped also with long dark lashes and a soft pout. Grey spared him no more than a glance; his own tastes were harder-edged.

It was not early—knowing Germain's habits, he had waited until one o'clock—but the man still showed the effects of a long night. Deep blue pouches cupped eyes like soft-boiled eggs, which surveyed Grey with a distinct lack of enthusiasm. Still, Germain made an effort at courtesy, bidding

Grey sit and sending the doe-eyed clerk for brandy and biscuits.

Grey seldom took strong drink before teatime, and wanted a clear head now. He therefore barely sipped his own brandy, excellent though it was, but Germain dipped the famous Sackville nose—sharply protrusive as a letter opener—into his glass, inhaled deeply, then drained it and poured another. The liquid appeared to have some restorative effect, for he emerged from his second glass looking somewhat happier and inquired of Grey how he did.

"Very well, I thank you," Grey said politely. "I have recently returned from America, and have brought you several letters from mutual acquaintances there."

"Oh, have you?" Germain brightened a bit. "Kind of you, Grey. Decent voyage, was it?"

"Tolerable." In fact, it had been miserable; they had run a gauntlet of storms across the Atlantic, pitching and yawing without cease for days on end, to the point that Grey had wished fervently for the ship to sink, just to put an end to it all. But he did not want to waste time on trivial chat.

"I had a rather remarkable encounter, just before leaving the colony of North Carolina," he said, judging that Germain was now sufficiently alert as to listen. "Allow me to tell you about it."

Germain was both vain and petty, and had brought the art of political vagueness to a fine point—but could apply himself to a matter when he wished, which was largely when he perceived some benefit to himself in a situation. The mention of the Northwest Territory focused his attention admirably.

"You did not speak to this Beauchamp further?" A third glass of brandy sat by Germain's elbow, half drunk.

"No. He had delivered his message; there was nothing to be gained by further conversation, as plainly he has no power to act upon his own. And had he intended to divulge the identity of his principals, he would have done so."

Germain picked up his glass, but did not drink, instead turning it in his hands as an aid to thought. It was plain, not faceted, and smeared with fingerprints and the smudges of Germain's mouth.

"Is the man familiar to you? Why did he seek you out, in particular?" *No, not stupid,* Grey thought.

"I had encountered him many years ago," he replied equably. "In the course of my work with Colonel Bowles."

Nothing on earth would compel Grey to reveal Percy's true identity to Germain; Percy had been—well, still *was*—stepbrother to himself and Hal, and only good fortune and Grey's own determination had prevented an almighty scandal at the time of Percy's presumed death. Some scandals dimmed with time—that one wouldn't.

Germain's plucked eyebrow flickered at mention of Bowles, who had headed England's Black Chamber for many years.

"A spy?" Mild distaste showed in his voice; spies were vulgar necessities; not something a gentleman would touch with his bare hands.

"At one time, perhaps. Apparently he has risen in the world." He picked up his own glass, took a healthy mouthful—it was very good brandy, after all—then set it down and stood up to take his leave. He knew better than to prod Germain. Leave the matter in the secretary's lap, and trust to his own self-interest to pursue it.

Grey left Germain sitting back in his chair, staring contemplatively into his empty glass, and took his cloak from the soft-lipped clerk, whose hand brushed his in passing.

NOT, HE REFLECTED, pulling the cloak around him and tugging down his hat against the rising wind, that he proposed to leave the matter to Germain's capricious sense of responsibility. Germain was secretary of state for America, true—but this was not a matter that concerned only America. There were two other secretaries of state in Lord North's cabinet—one for the Northern Department, that being all of Europe, and another for the Southern Department, this constituting the rest of the world. He would have preferred not to deal with Lord Germain at all. However, both protocol and politics prevented him from going straight to Lord North, which had been his first impulse. He'd give Germain a day's head start, then call upon the Southern secretary, Thomas Thynne, Viscount Weymouth, with the invidious Mr. Beauchamp's proposal. The Southern secretary was charged with dealing with the Catholic countries of Europe, thus matters with a French connection were his concern as well.

If both men chose to take up the matter, it would certainly come to Lord North's attention—and North, or one of his ministers, would come to Grey.

A storm was rolling up the Thames; he could see billows of black cloud, fuming as though to unleash their fury directly upon the Houses of Parliament.

"A bit of thunder and lightning would do them good," he murmured balefully, and hailed a cab, as the first thick drops began to fall.

The rain was pelting down in sheets by the time he arrived at the Beefsteak, and he was nearly drenched in the three paces from curb to doorway.

Mr. Bodley, the elderly steward, received him as though he had come in the day before, rather than some eighteen months.

"Turtle soup with sherry tonight, my lord," he informed Grey, gesturing to a minion to take Grey's damp hat and cloak. "Very warming to the stomach. Followed by a nice lamb cutlet with new potatoes?"

"The very thing, Mr. Bodley," Grey replied, smiling. He took his place in the dining room, soothed by its good fire and cool white napery. As he leaned back to allow Mr. Bodley to tuck the napkin under his chin, though, he noted a new addition to the room's decoration.

"Who is that?" he asked, startled. The painting, prominently displayed upon the wall opposite, showed a stately Indian, festooned in ostrich plumes and embroidered draperies. It looked distinctly odd, set as it was among the staid portraits of several distinguished—and mostly deceased—members.

"Oh, that is Mr. Brant, of course," Mr. Bodley said, with an air of mild reproof. "Mr. Joseph Brant. Mr. Pitt brought him to dine last year, when he was in London."

"Brant?"

Mr. Bodley's brows rose. Like most Londoners, he assumed that everyone who had been in America must of necessity know every other person there.

"He is a Mohawk chief, I believe," he said, pronouncing the word "Mohawk" carefully. "He has been to visit the King, you know!"

"Indeed," Grey murmured. He wondered whether the King or the Indian had been more impressed.

Mr. Bodley withdrew, presumably to fetch the soup, but returned within moments to lay a letter upon the cloth before Grey.

"This was sent for you in care of the secretary, sir."

"Oh? Thank you, Mr. Bodley." Grey took it up, recognizing his son's hand immediately, and suffering a mild drop of the stomach in consequence. What had Willie not wanted to send in care either of his grandmother or of Hal?

Something he didn't want to risk either of them reading. His mind supplied the logical answer at once, and he took up his fish knife to open the letter with due trepidation.

Was it Richardson? Hal disliked the man, and hadn't approved at all of William's working for him, though he had nothing concrete to adduce against him. Perhaps he should have been more cautious about setting William on that particular path, knowing what he did about the black world of intelligencing. Still, it had been imperative to get Willie away from North Carolina, before he came face-to-face with either Jamie Fraser or Percy so-called Beauchamp.

And you did have to let a son go, to make his own way in the world, no matter what it cost you; Hal had told him that, more than once. Three times, to be exact, he thought with a smile—every time one of Hal's boys had taken up his commission.

He unfolded the letter with caution, as though it might explode. It was penned with a care that he found instantly sinister; Willie was normally legible, but not above the odd blot.

To Lord John Grey
The Society for Appreciation of the English Beefsteak
From Lieutenant William Lord Ellesmere
7 September, 1776
Long Island
The Royal Colony of New York

Dear Father,
I have a Matter of some delicacy to confide.

Well, there was a sentence to chill the blood of any parent, Grey thought. Had Willie got a young woman with child, gambled and lost substantial property, contracted a venereal complaint, challenged someone or been challenged to a duel? Or—had he encountered something sinister in the course of his intelligencing, on his way to General Howe? He reached for the wine, and took a prophylactic swallow before returning, thus braced, to the letter. Nothing could have prepared him for the next sentence, though.

I am in love with Lady Dorothea.

Grey choked, spluttering wine over his hand, but waved off the steward hastening toward him with a towel, instead wiping his hand on his breeches as he hastily scanned the rest of the page.

We have both been conscious of a growing Attraction for some time, but I hesitated to make any Declaration, knowing that I was soon to depart for America. However, we discovered ourselves unexpectedly alone in the Garden at Lady Belvedere's Ball, the Week before I left, and the beauty of the Setting, the romantic sense of the Evening, and the intoxicating nearness of the Lady overpowered my Judgment.

"Oh, Jesus," Lord John said aloud. "Tell me you didn't deflower her under a bush, for God's sake!"

He caught the interested gaze of a nearby diner, and with a brief cough, returned to the letter.

I blush with Shame to admit that my Feelings overcame me, to an Extent that I hesitate to commit to Paper. I apologized, of course, not that there could be any sufficient Apology for such dishonourable Conduct. Lady Dorothea was both generous in her Forgiveness and vehement in her Insistence that I must not—as I was at first inclined—to go at once to her Father.

"Very sensible of you, Dottie," Grey murmured, envisioning all too well the response of his brother to any such revelation. He could only hope that Willie was blushing over some indiscretion a good deal short of . . .

I intended to ask you to speak to Uncle Hal for me next Year, when I should return Home and be able to formally request Lady Dorothea's Hand in Marriage. However, I have just learned that she has received another Offer, from Viscount Maxwell, and that Uncle Hal is seriously considering this.

I would not besmirch the lady's Honour in any Way, but under the Circumstances, clearly she cannot marry Maxwell.

You mean Maxwell would discover that she's not a virgin, Grey thought grimly, *and come barreling round the morning after the wedding night to tell Hal so.* He rubbed a hand hard over his face and went on.

Words cannot convey my Remorse at my actions, Father, and I cannot bring myself to ask a Forgiveness I do not deserve, for so grievously disappointing you. Not for my Sake, but for hers, I beg that you will speak to the Duke. I hope that he can be persuaded to entertain my Suit and allow us to be affianced, without the Necessity of making such explicit Discoveries to him as might distress the Lady.

Your most humble Prodigal,
William

He sank back in the chair and closed his eyes. The first shock was beginning to dissipate, and his mind come to grips with the problem.

It should be possible. There would be no bar to a marriage between William and Dottie. While titularly cousins, there were no blood ties between them; William was his son in all ways that mattered, but not by blood. And while Maxwell was young, wealthy, and very suitable, William was an earl in his own right, as well as heir to Dunsany's baronetcy, and far from poor.

No, that part was all right. And Minnie liked William very much. Hal and the boys . . . well, provided they never got wind of William's behavior, they should be agreeable. On the other hand, should any of them discover it, William would be lucky to escape with being horsewhipped and having every bone in his body broken. So would Grey.

Hal would be very much surprised, of course—the cousins had seen a good deal of each other during Willie's time in London, but William had never spoken of Dottie in a way that would have indicated . . .

He picked up the letter and read it over again. And again. Set it down and gazed at it for several minutes with narrowed eyes, thinking.

"I'm damned if I believe it," he said aloud, at last. "What the devil are you up to, Willie?"

He crumpled the letter, and taking a candlestick from a nearby table with a nod of apology, set fire to the missive. The steward, observing this, instantly produced a small china dish, into which Grey dropped the flaming paper, and together they watched the writing blacken into ash.

"Your soup, my lord," said Mr. Bodley, and waving the smoke of conflagration gently away with a napkin, placed a steaming plate before him.

WILLIAM BEING OUT of reach, the obvious course of action must be to go and confront his partner in crime—whatever sort of crime it was. The more he considered, the more convinced he became that whatever complicity lay between William, Ninth Earl of Ellesmere, and Lady Dorothea Jacqueline Benedicta Grey, it was not the complicity either of love or guilty passion.

How was he to speak to Dottie, though, without exciting the notice of either of her parents? He could not hang about in the street until both Hal and Minnie went somewhere, hopefully leaving Dottie alone. Even if he managed to catch her somehow alone at home and interview her privately, the servants would certainly mention that he had done so, and Hal—

who had a sense of protective alertness regarding his daughter akin to that of a large mastiff regarding its favorite bone—would be round promptly to find out why.

He declined the doorman's offer to secure him a carriage, and walked back to his mother's house, pondering ways and means. He could invite Dottie to dine with him . . . but it would be very unusual for such an invitation not to include Minnie. Likewise, were he to invite her to a play or opera; he often escorted the women, as Hal could not sit still long enough to hear an entire opera, and considered most plays to be tedious twaddle.

His way lay through Covent Garden, and he skipped nimbly out of the way of a swash of water, flung from a bucket to wash the slimy cabbage leaves and rotten apples from the cobbles by a fruiterer's stall. In summer, wilted blooms littered the pavement; before dawn, the fresh flowers would come in by cart from the countryside, and fill the square with scent and freshness. In autumn, the place held a ripely decadent smell of squashed fruit, decaying meat, and broken vegetables that was the signature to the changing of the guard in Covent Garden.

During the day, vendors shouted their wares, haggled, fought pitched battles with one another, fought off thieves and pickpockets, and shambled off at nightfall to spend half their profits in the taverns in Tavistock and Brydges streets. With the shades of evening drawing nigh, the whores claimed the Garden for their own.

The sight of a couple of these, arrived early and trolling hopefully for customers among the home-going vendors, distracted him momentarily from his familial quandary and returned his thoughts to the earlier events of his day.

The entrance to Brydges Street lay before him; he could just see the genteel house that stood near the far end, set back a little in elegant discretion. That was a thought; whores knew a great deal—and could find out more, with suitable inducement. He was tempted to go and call upon Nessie now, if only for the pleasure her company gave him. But no—not yet.

He needed to find out what was already known about Percy Beauchamp in more official circles, before he started his own hounds in pursuit of that rabbit. And before he saw Hal.

It was too late in the day to make official calls. He'd send a note, though, making an appointment—and in the morning, would visit the Black Chamber.

15

THE BLACK CHAMBER

GREY WONDERED what romantic soul had originally christened the Black Chamber—or whether it was in fact a romantic designation. Perhaps the spies of an earlier day had been consigned to a windowless hole under the stairs at Whitehall, and the name was purely descriptive. These days, the Black Chamber designated a class of employment rather than a specific location.

All the capitals of Europe—and not a few lesser cities—had Black Chambers, these being the centers wherein mail intercepted *en route* or by spies or simply removed from diplomatic pouches was inspected, decoded with varying degrees of success, and then sent to whichever person or agency had need of the information thus derived. England's Black Chamber had employed four gentlemen—not counting clerks and office boys—when Grey had labored there. There were more of them now, distributed in random holes and corners in the buildings down Pall Mall, but the main center of such operations was still in Buckingham Palace.

Not in any of the beautifully equipped areas that served the Royal Family or their secretaries, ladies' maids, housekeepers, butlers, or other upper servants—but still, within the palace precincts.

Grey passed the guard at the back gate with a nod—he'd worn his uniform, with the lieutenant-colonel's insignia, to facilitate entry—and made his way down a shabby, ill-lit corridor whose scent of ancient floor polish and ghosts of boiled cabbage and burnt tea cake gave him a pleasant *frisson* of nostalgia. The third door on the left stood ajar, and he entered without knocking.

He was expected. Arthur Norrington greeted him without rising, and motioned him to a chair.

He'd known Norrington for years, though they were not particular friends, and found it comforting that the man seemed not to have changed at all in the years since their last meeting. Arthur was a large, soft man, whose large, slightly protruding eyes and thick lips gave him the mien of a turbot on ice: dignified and faintly reproachful.

"I appreciate your help, Arthur," Grey said, and as he sat, deposited on the corner of the desk a small wrapped parcel. "A small token of that appreciation," he added, waving a hand at it.

Norrington raised one thin brow and took the package, which he unwrapped with greedy fingers.

"Oh!" he said, with unfeigned delight. He turned the tiny ivory carving over gently in his large, soft hands, bringing it close to his face to see the details, entranced. "Tsuji?"

Grey shrugged, pleased with the effect of his gift. He knew nothing of *netsuke* himself, but knew a man who dealt in ivory miniatures from China and Japan. He had been surprised at the delicacy and artistry of the tiny thing, which showed a half-clothed woman engaged in a very athletic form of sexual congress with a naked obese gentleman with his hair in a topknot.

"I'm afraid it has no provenance," he said apologetically, but Norrington waved that aside, eyes still fixed on the new treasure. After a moment, he sighed happily, then tucked the thing away in the inner pocket of his coat.

"Thank you, my lord," he said. "As for the subject of your own inquiry, I am afraid that we have relatively little material available regarding your mysterious Mr. Beauchamp." He nodded at the desk, where a battered, anonymous leather folder reposed. Grey could see that there was something bulky inside—something not paper; the folder was pierced, and a small piece of twine ran through it, fastening the object in place.

"You surprise me, Mr. Norrington," he said politely, and

reached for the folder. "Still, let me see what you do have, and perhaps—"

Norrington pressed his fingers flat against the file and frowned for a moment, trying to convey the impression that official secrets could not be imparted to just *anyone.* Grey smiled at him.

"Come off it, Arthur," he said. "If you want to know what *I* know about our mysterious Mr. Beauchamp—and I assure you, you do—you'll show me every word you have about him."

Norrington relaxed a little, letting his fingers slide back—though still with a show of reluctance. Cocking one eyebrow, Grey picked up the leather folder and opened it. The bulky object was revealed to be a small cloth bag; beyond that, there were only a few sheets of paper. Grey sighed.

"Poor protocol, Arthur," he said reprovingly. "There are snowdrifts of paper involving Beauchamp—cross-referenced to that name, too. Granted, he hasn't been active in years, but someone ought to have looked."

"We did," Norrington said, an odd note in his voice that made Grey look sharply up. "Old Crabbot remembered the name, and we looked. The files are gone."

The skin across Grey's shoulders tightened, as though he'd been struck with a lash.

"That *is* odd," he said calmly. "Well, then . . ." He bent his head over the folder, though it took a moment to subdue his racing thoughts enough to see what he was looking at. No sooner had his eyes focused on the page than the name "Fraser" leapt out of it, nearly stopping his heart.

Not Jamie Fraser, though. He breathed slowly, turned the page, read the next, turned back. There were four letters in all, only one completely decoded, though another had been started; it bore someone's tentative notes in the margin. His lips tightened; he had been a good decoder in his day, but had been absent from the field of battle far too long to have any notion of the current common idioms in use by the French, let alone the idiosyncratic terms an individual spy might use—and these letters were the work of at least two different hands; so much was clear.

"I've looked them over," Norrington said, and Grey looked up to find Arthur's protruding hazel eyes fixed on him like a toad eyeing a juicy fly. "I haven't *officially* decoded them yet, but I've a good general idea what they say."

Well, he'd already decided that it had to be done, and he'd come prepared to tell Arthur, who was the most discreet of his old Black Chamber contacts.

"Beauchamp is one Percival Wainwright," he said bluntly, wondering even as he said it, why he kept the secret of Percival's real name. "He's a British subject—was an army officer, arrested for the crime of sodomy but never tried. It was thought that he'd died in Newgate awaiting trial, but"—he smoothed the letters and closed the folder over them—"evidently not."

Arthur's plump lips rounded in a soundless "O."

Grey wondered for an instant if he could leave it there—but no. Arthur was persistent as a dachshund digging into a badger sett, and if he discovered the rest of it on his own, he would at once suspect Grey of withholding much more.

"He's also my stepbrother," Grey said, as casually as possible, and laid the folder on Arthur's desk. "I saw him in North Carolina."

Arthur's mouth sagged for an instant. He firmed it up at once, blinking.

"I see," he said. "Well, then . . . I see."

"Yes, you do," Grey said dryly. "You see exactly why I must know the contents of these letters"—he nodded at the folder—"as soon as possible."

Arthur nodded, compressing his lips, and settled himself, taking the letters into his hands. Once determined to be serious, there was no nonsense about him.

"Most of what I could decode seems to deal with matters of shipping," he said. "Contacts in the West Indies, cargoes to be delivered—simple smuggling, though on a fairly large scale. One reference to a banker in Edinburgh; I couldn't make out his connection exactly. But three of the letters mentioned the same name *en clair*—you will have seen that, of course."

Grey didn't bother denying it.

"Someone in France wants very much to find a man named Claudel Fraser," Arthur said, and raised one brow. "Any idea who that is?"

"No," Grey said, though he certainly had the glimmer of an idea. "Any idea *who* it is that wants to find him—or why?"

Norrington shook his head.

"No idea why," he said frankly. "As to who, though—I think it may be a French nobleman." He opened the folder again and, from the little bag attached to it, carefully removed two wax seals, one cracked almost in half, the other largely intact. Both showed a martlet against a rising sun.

"Haven't found anyone yet who recognized it," Norrington said, poking one of the seals gently with a podgy forefinger. "Do you, by chance?"

"No," Grey said, his throat gone suddenly dry. "But you might look into one Baron Amandine. Wainwright mentioned that name to me as—a personal connexion of his."

"Amandine?" Norrington looked puzzled. "Never heard of him."

"Neither has anyone else." Grey sighed and rose to his feet. "I begin to wonder whether he exists."

HE WAS STILL wondering, as he made his way to Hal's house. The Baron Amandine might or might not exist; if he did, he might be only a front, disguising the interest of someone much more prominent. If he didn't . . . matters became simultaneously more confusing and simpler of approach; with no way of knowing who was behind the matter, Percy Wainwright was the only possible avenue of approach.

None of Norrington's letters had mentioned the Northwest Territory nor held any hint of the proposition Percy had put before him. That was not surprising, though; it would have been extremely dangerous to put such information on paper, though he had certainly known spies do such things before. If Amandine did exist, and was directly involved, apparently he was both sensible and cautious.

Well, Hal would have to be told about Percy, in any case. Perhaps he would know something regarding Amandine, or could find out; Hal had a number of friends in France.

The thought of what Hal must be told reminded him abruptly of William's letter, which he had nearly forgotten in the intrigues of the morning. He breathed strongly through his nose at the thought. No. He wasn't mentioning *that* to his brother until he'd had a chance to speak to Dottie, alone. Perhaps he could contrive a private word with her, arrange to meet later.

Dottie proved not to be at home, though, when Grey arrived at Argus House.

"She's at one of Miss Brierley's musical afternoons," his sister-in-law Minnie informed him, when he inquired politely how his niece and goddaughter did. "She's very sociable these days. She'll be sorry to have missed you, though." She stood on tiptoe and kissed him, beaming. "It's good to see you again, John."

"And you, Minnie," he said, meaning it. "Is Hal at home?"

She rolled her eyes expressively at the ceiling.

"He's been at home for a week, with the gout. Another week, and I shall put poison in his soup."

"Ah." That reinforced his decision not to speak to Hal of William's letter. Hal in good spirits was a prospect that daunted hardened soldiers and lifetime politicians; Hal in ill health . . . Presumably that was why Dottie had had the good sense to absent herself.

Well, it wasn't as though his news would improve Hal's mood in any case, he thought. He pushed open the door to Hal's study with due caution, though; his brother had been known to throw things when peevish—and nothing peeved him more than bodily indisposition.

As it was, Hal was asleep, slumped in his chair before the fire, his bandaged foot on a stool. The smell of some strong and acrid medicine floated in the air, overlying the scents of burning wood, melted tallow, and stale bread. A congealed plate of soup sat upon a tray at Hal's side, untasted. Perhaps Minnie had made her threat explicit, Grey thought with a smile. Aside from himself and their mother, Minnie was likely the only other person in the world who was never afraid of Hal.

He sat down quietly, wondering whether to wake his brother. Hal looked ill and tired, much thinner than usual—and Hal was normally lean to start with. He could not look less than elegant, even clad in breeches and a worn linen shirt, bare-legged, and with a ratty shawl draped about his shoulders, but the lines of a life spent fighting were eloquent in his face.

Grey's heart contracted with a sudden, unexpected tenderness, and he wondered whether, after all, he should trouble Hal with his news. But he couldn't risk Hal being confronted unexpectedly with the tidings of Percy's untimely resurrection; he would have to be warned.

Before he could make up his mind whether to go away and come back, though, Hal's eyes opened abruptly. They were clear and alert, the same light blue as Grey's own, with no sign of drowsiness or distraction.

"You're back," Hal said, and smiled with great affection. "Pour me a brandy."

"Minnie says you have the gout," Grey said, with a glance at Hal's foot. "Don't the quacks say you ought not to take strong drink, with the gout?" Nonetheless, he rose to his feet.

"They do," Hal said, pulling himself upright in his chair and grimacing as the movement jarred his foot. "But from the look of you, you're about to tell me something that means I'll need it. Best bring the decanter."

IT WAS SEVERAL hours before he left Argus House—declining Minnie's invitation to stay for supper—and the weather had deteriorated substantially. There was autumn chill in the air; a gusty wind was getting up, and he could taste salt in the air—the traces of sea fog drifting toward shore. It would be a good night to stay indoors.

Minnie had apologized for not being able to offer her coach, as Dottie had gone off to her afternoon *salon* in it. He had assured her that walking suited him, assisting him to think. It did, but the whoosh of wind flapping the skirts of his coat and threatening to carry away his hat was a distraction, and he was beginning to regret the coach, when he suddenly saw the equipage itself, waiting in the drive of one of the big houses near the Alexandra Gate, the horses blanketed against the wind.

He turned in at the gate and, hearing a cry of "Uncle John!" looked toward the house and was in time to see his niece, Dottie, bearing down on him like a ship under full sail—literally. She wore a plum silk mantua and a rose-pink cloak and, with the wind behind her, billowed alarmingly. In fact, she scudded toward him with such velocity that he was obliged to catch her in his arms in order to halt her forward progress.

"Are you a virgin?" he demanded without preamble.

Her eyes widened, and without the least hesitation, she wrested one arm free and slapped his cheek.

"What?" she said.

"My apologies. That was a trifle abrupt, wasn't it?" He glanced at her waiting coach—and the driver, looking rigidly ahead—and, calling to the driver to wait, took her by the arm and turned her in the direction of the park.

"Where are we going?"

"Just for a little walk. I have a few questions to ask you, and they aren't the sort that I wish to have overheard—nor do you, I assure you."

Her eyes widened still further, but she didn't argue; merely clapped a hand to her saucy little hat and came with him, her skirts foaming in the wind.

Weather and passersby prevented his asking any of the questions he had in mind until after they had made their way well into the park and found themselves in a more or less deserted path that led through a small topiary garden, where evergreen bushes and trees had been clipped into fanciful shapes.

The wind had dropped momentarily, though the sky was darkening. Dottie pulled to a halt in the shelter of a topiary lion and said, "Uncle John. *What* is this taradiddle about?"

Dottie had her mother's autumn-leaf coloring, with hair the color of ripened wheat and cheeks with the perpetual faint flush of rose hips. But where Minnie's face was pretty and gently appealing, Dottie's was underlain by Hal's fine bones and embroidered with his dark lashes; her beauty had a dangerous edge to it.

The edge was uppermost in the look she turned on her uncle, and he thought that, in fact, if Willie *was* enamored of her, it was perhaps not surprising. *If* he was.

"I had a letter from William, intimating that he had—if not actually forced his attentions upon you—behaved in a manner unbecoming a gentleman. Is it true?"

Her mouth fell open in undissimulated horror.

"He told you *what?*"

Well, that relieved his mind of one burden. She was likely still a virgin, and he needn't have William shipped off to China to avoid her brothers.

"It was, as I say, an intimation. He didn't provide me with details. Come, let us walk before we freeze." He took her by the arm and guided her up one of the paths that led to a small oratory. Here they took shelter in the vestibule, overlooked only by a stained-glass window of St. Barbara, carrying her severed breasts on a platter. Grey affected to study this elevating image, allowing Dottie a moment to settle her wind-flustered garments—and decide what she was going to tell him.

"Well," she began, turning to him with her chin raised, "it's true that we—well, that I let him kiss me."

"Oh? Where? I mean"—he added hastily, seeing the momentary shock in her eye—and *that* was interesting, for would a completely inexperienced young lady realize that it was possible to be kissed elsewhere than on lips or hand?—"in what geographical location?"

The flush in her cheeks deepened, for she realized as well as he what she had just given away, but she met his eye directly.

"In Lady Windermere's garden. We'd both come to her musicale, and the supper wasn't ready, so William invited me to walk outside with him for a bit, and—I did. It was *such* a beautiful evening," she added ingenuously.

"Yes, he noted that, as well. I had not previously realized the intoxicant properties of good weather."

She gave him a slight glare.

"Well, anyway, we're in love! Did he say *that,* at least?"

"Yes, he did," Grey replied. "He began with a statement to that effect, in fact, before going on to make his scandalous confessions regarding your virtue."

Her eyes widened.

"He—what, exactly, did he say?" she demanded.

"Enough to persuade me—he hoped—to go at once to your father and put before him the desirability of William's suit for your hand."

"Oh." She drew a deep breath at that, as though relieved,

and looked away for a moment. "Well. Are you going to, then?" she asked, swiveling big blue eyes back in his direction. "Or have you already?" she added, with an air of hopefulness.

"No, I have said nothing to your father regarding William's letter. For one thing, I thought I had best speak to *you* first, and see whether you were in such agreement with William's sentiments as he appears to think."

She blinked, then gave him one of her radiant smiles.

"That was *very* considerate of you, Uncle John. Many men wouldn't bother with the woman's opinion of the situation—but you've always been *so* thoughtful. Mother cannot say enough good things about your kindness."

"Don't over-egg the pudding, Dottie," he said tolerantly. "So you say that you are willing to marry William?"

"Willing?" she cried. "Why, I desire it more than anything!"

He gave her a long, level look, and while she continued to meet his eye, the blood rose precipitously in her throat and cheeks.

"Oh, yes?" he said, allowing all the skepticism he felt to show in his voice. "Why?"

She blinked twice, very fast.

"Why?"

"Why?" he repeated patiently. "What is there in William's character—or appearance, I suppose," he added fairly, for young women had no great reputation as judges of character, "that so attracts you as to desire marriage to him? And hasty marriage at that."

He could just about see one or both of them developing an attraction—but what was the hurry? Even if William feared Hal's deciding to allow Viscount Maxwell's suit, Dottie herself could not possibly be under the illusion that her doting father would force her to marry anyone she did not want to.

"Well, we are in love, of course!" she said, though with a rather uncertain note in her voice for such a theoretically fervent declaration. "As for his—his *character* . . . why, Uncle, you are his own father; surely you cannot be in ignorance of his . . . his . . . intelligence!" She came up with the word triumphantly. "His kindness, his good humor . . ." she was picking up speed now, ". . . his gentleness . . ."

Now it was Lord John's turn to blink. William was undoubtedly intelligent, good-humored, and reasonably kind, but "gentle" was not the word that sprang immediately to mind with regard to him. On the other hand, the hole in the paneling of his mother's dining room, through which William had inadvertently thrown a companion during a tea party, had still not been repaired, and this image was fresh in Grey's mind. Probably Willie behaved more circumspectly in Dottie's company, but still . . .

"He is the very model of a gentleman!" she declaimed with enthusiasm, having now got the bit well between her teeth. "And his appearance—well, of course he is admired by every woman I know! So tall, so imposing a figure . . ."

He noticed, with an air of clinical detachment, that while she touched on several of William's notable characteristics, she did not at any point mention his eyes. Aside from his height—which could scarcely escape notice—his eyes were probably his most striking feature, being a deep and brilliant blue, and unusually shaped, with a catlike slant. They were, in fact, Jamie Fraser's eyes, and they gave John a faint, passing clench of the heart whenever Willie looked at him with a certain expression.

Willie knew the effect his eyes had on young women excellently well—and had no hesitation in making the most of it. Had he been gazing longingly into Dottie's own eyes, she would have been transfixed, whether she loved him or not. And that touching account of rapture in the garden . . . Following a musicale, or during a ball, and at Lady Belvedere's or at Lady Windermere's . . .

He had been so occupied by his own thoughts that he did not realize for a moment that she had stopped talking.

"I beg your pardon," he said, with great courtesy. "And I thank you for the encomia regarding William's character, which cannot fail to warm a father's heart. Still—what is the urgency in arranging a marriage? William will be sent home in a year or two, surely."

"He might be killed!" she said, and there was in her voice a sudden note of real fear, so real that his attention sharpened. She swallowed visibly, a hand going to her throat.

"I couldn't bear it," she said, her voice suddenly small. "If he were killed, and we'd never . . . never had a chance to . . ."

She looked up at him, her eyes brilliant with emotion, and put her hand pleadingly on his arm.

"I have to," she said. "Really, Uncle John. I must, and I cannot wait. I want to go to America and be married."

His mouth fell open. Wanting to be married was one thing, but *this* . . . !

"You cannot possibly be serious," he said. "You cannot think that your parents—your father, in particular—would ever countenance such a thing."

"He would," she countered. "If *you* put the matter to him properly. He values your opinion more than anyone's," she went on persuasively, squeezing a little. "And you, of all people, must understand the horror I feel at the thought that something might . . . happen to William before I see him again."

Indeed, he thought, the only thing weighing in her favor was the feeling of desolation that the mention of William's possible death caused in his own heart. Yes, he *could* be killed. Any man might be, in time of war, and most particularly a soldier. That was one of the risks you took—and he could not in conscience have prevented William taking it, even though the mere thought of William blown to pieces by cannon fire or shot through the head or dying in agony of the flux . . .

He swallowed, dry-mouthed, and with some effort shoved those pusillanimous images firmly back into the locked mental closet in which he normally kept them confined.

He took a long breath.

"Dorothea," he said firmly. "I *will* discover what you're up to."

She looked at him for a long, thoughtful moment, as though estimating the chances. The corner of her mouth rose insensibly as her eyes narrowed, and he saw the response on her face, as clearly as if she'd said it aloud.

No. I don't think so.

The expression was no more than a flicker, though, and her face resumed its air of indignation mingled with pleading.

"Uncle John! How dare you accuse me and William—your own son!—of, of . . . what *are* you accusing us of?"

"I don't know," he admitted.

"Well, then! *Will* you speak to Papa for us? For me? Please? Today?"

Dottie was a born flirt; as she spoke, she leaned toward him, so that he could smell the fragrance of violets in her hair, and twined her fingers charmingly in the lapels of his coat.

"I can't," he said, striving to extricate himself. "Not just now. I've already given him one bad shock today; another might finish him off."

"Tomorrow, then," she coaxed.

"Dottie." He took her hands in his, and was rather touched to find them cold and trembling. She *did* mean it—or mean something, at least.

"Dottie," he repeated, more gently. "Even if your father were disposed to send you to America to be married—and I cannot think that anything less exigent than your being with child would compel it—there is no possibility of sailing before April. There is therefore no need to harry Hal into an early grave by telling him any of this, at least not until he has recovered from his current indisposition."

She wasn't pleased, but was obliged to admit the force of his reasoning.

"Besides," he added, letting go of her hands, "campaigning ceases in winter; you know that. The fighting will stop soon, and William will be relatively safe. You need have no fears for him." *Other than accident, flux, ague, blood poisoning, griping belly, tavern brawls, and ten or fifteen other life-threatening possibilities,* he added privately to himself.

"But—" she began, but stopped, and sighed. "Yes, I suppose you're right. But . . . you *will* speak to Papa soon, won't you, Uncle John?"

He sighed in turn, but smiled at her nonetheless.

"I will, if that is what you truly desire." A gust of wind hit the oratory and the stained-glass image of St. Barbara shivered in its leaded frame. A rush of sudden rain rattled across the roof slates, and he drew his cloak around him.

"Stay here," he advised his niece. "I'll fetch the coach round to the road."

As he made his way against the wind, one hand on his hat to prevent it taking flight, he recalled with some unease his own words to her: *I cannot think that anything less exigent than your being with child would compel it.*

She wouldn't. Would she? No, he assured himself. Become pregnant by someone in order to convince her father to allow her to marry someone else? Fat chance; Hal would have her married to the guilty party before she could say "cat." Unless, of course, she chose someone impossible to do the deed: a married man, say, or—But this was nonsense! What would William say, were she to arrive in America, pregnant by another man?

No. Not even Brianna Fraser MacKenzie—the most hair-raisingly pragmatic woman he had ever known—would have done something like that. He smiled a little to himself at thought of the formidable Mrs. MacKenzie, recalling her attempt at blackmailing *him* into marriage—while pregnant by someone who was definitely not him. He'd always wondered if the child was in fact her husband's. Perhaps *she* would. But not Dottie.

Surely not.

16

UNARMED CONFLICT

Inverness, Scotland
October 1980

THE OLD HIGH Church of St. Stephen's stood serene on the bank of the Ness, the weathered stones in its kirkyard a testament to righteous peace. Roger was aware of the serenity—but none of it was for him.

His blood was still throbbing in his temples, and the collar of his shirt was damp from exertion, chilly though the day was. He'd walked from the High Street car park, at a ferocious pace that seemed to eat the distance in seconds.

She'd called him a coward, by God. She'd called him a lot

of other things, too, but that was the one that stung—and she knew it.

The fight had started after supper the day before, when she'd put a crusted pot into the old stone sink, turned to him, drawn a deep breath, and informed him that she had an interview for a job at the North of Scotland Hydro Electric Board.

"Job?" he'd said stupidly.

"Job," she'd repeated, narrowing her eyes at him.

He *had* been swift enough to suppress the automatic "But you've got a job" that had sprung to his lips, substituting a rather mild—he thought—"Why?"

Never one for quiet diplomacy, she'd fixed him with a stare and said, "Because one of us needs to work, and if it isn't going to be you, it'll have to be me."

"What do you mean, 'needs to work'?" he'd asked—damn it, she was right, he *was* a coward, because he knew goddamned well what she meant by it. "We've money enough for a time."

"For a time," she agreed. "A year or two—maybe more, if we're careful. And you think we should just sit on our asses until the money runs out, and then what? *Then* you start thinking about what you ought to be doing?"

"I've been thinking," he said through his teeth. True, that; he'd been doing little else for months. There was the book, of course; he was writing down all the songs he'd committed to memory in the eighteenth century with commentary—but that was hardly a job in itself, nor would it earn much money. Mostly thinking.

"Yeah? So have I." She turned her back on him, turning on the tap, either to drown out whatever he might say next, or just in order to get a grip on herself. The water ceased, and she turned round again.

"Look," she said, trying to sound reasonable. "I can't wait much longer. I can't stay out of the field for years and years and just walk back into it anytime. It's been nearly a year since the last consulting job I did—I can't wait any longer."

"You never said you meant to go back to work full-time." She'd done a couple of small jobs in Boston—brief consulting projects, once Mandy was out of the hospital and all right. Joe Abernathy had got them for her.

"Look, man," Joe had said confidentially to Roger, "she's

antsy. I know that girl; she needs to *move.* She's been focused on the baby day and night, probably since she was born, been cooped up with doctors, hospitals, clingy kids for weeks now. She's gotta get out of her own head."

And I don't? Roger had thought—but couldn't say so.

An elderly man in a flat cap was weeding round one of the gravestones, a limp mass of uprooted greenery lying on the ground beside him. He'd been watching Roger as he hesitated near the wall, and nodded to him in a friendly way, but didn't speak.

She was a mother, he'd wanted to say. Wanted to say something about the closeness between her and the kids, the way they needed her, like they needed air and food and water. He was now and then jealous over not being needed in the same primal way; how could she deny that gift?

Well, he'd *tried* to say something of the kind. The result had been what might be expected by lighting a match in a mine filled with gas.

He turned abruptly and walked out of the kirkyard. He couldn't speak to the rector right this minute—couldn't speak at all, come to that; he'd have to cool down first, get his voice back.

He turned left and went down along Huntly Street, seeing the facade of St. Mary's across the river from the corner of his eye; the only Catholic church in Inverness.

During one of the earlier, more rational parts of the fight, she'd made an effort. Asked if it was her fault.

"Is it me?" she'd asked seriously. "Being a Catholic, I mean. I know—I know that makes it more complicated." Her lips twitched. "Jem told me about Mrs. Ogilvy."

He hadn't felt at all like laughing, but couldn't help a brief smile at the memory. He'd been out by the barn, shoveling well-rotted manure into a wheelbarrow to spread on the kailyard, Jem assisting with his own small spade.

"Sixteen tons and what do you get?" Roger had sung—if the sort of hoarse croaking he produced could be called that.

"Another day older and deeper in shit!" Jem bellowed, doing his best to pitch his voice down into Tennessee Ernie Ford range, but then losing control in a glissando of giggles.

It was at this unfortunate moment that he'd turned round to find that they had visitors: Mrs. Ogilvy and Mrs. MacNeil, pillars of the Ladies' Altar and Tea Society at the Free North Church in Inverness. He knew them—and he knew just what they were doing here, too.

"We've come to call upon your good wife, Mr. MacKenzie," Mrs. MacNeil said, smiling with pursed lips. He wasn't sure whether the expression was meant to indicate inner reservations, or whether it was merely that she feared her ill-fitting false teeth might fall out if she opened her mouth more than a quarter of an inch.

"Ah. She'll be away to the town just now, I'm afraid." He'd wiped his hand on his jeans, thinking to offer it, but looked at it, thought better of it, and nodded to them instead. "But please to come in. Will I have the girl make tea?"

They shook their heads in unison.

"We havena seen your wife in kirk as yet, Mr. MacKenzie." Mrs. Ogilvy fixed him with a fishy eye.

Well, he'd been expecting that one. He could buy a little time by saying, ach, the baby'd been ailing—but no point; the nettle would have to be grasped sooner or later.

"No," he said pleasantly, though his shoulders stiffened by reflex. "She's a Catholic. She'll be to the Mass at St. Mary's of a Sunday."

Mrs. Ogilvy's square face sagged into a momentary oval of astonishment.

"Your wife's a Papist?" she said, giving him a chance to correct the clearly insane thing he'd just said.

"She is, aye. Born one." He shrugged lightly.

There had been relatively little conversation following this revelation. Just a glance at Jem, a sharp question about whether he went to Sunday school, an intake of breath at the answer, and a gimlet-eyed stare at Roger before they took their leave.

Do you want me to convert? Bree had demanded, in the course of the argument. And it had been a demand, not an offer.

He'd wanted suddenly and fiercely to ask her to do just that—only to see if she would, for love of him. But religious conscience would never let him do such a thing; still less, his conscience as her lover. Her husband.

Huntly Street turned suddenly into Bank Street, and the foot traffic of the shopping precinct disappeared. He passed the small memorial garden, put up to commemorate the service of nurses during World War II, and thought—as he always did—of Claire, though this time with less than the usual admiration he had for her.

And what would you *say?* he thought. He knew damned well what she'd say—or at least, whose side she'd be on, in this. *She* hadn't hung about being a full-time mum, had she? She'd gone to medical school when Bree was seven. And Bree's dad, Frank Randall, had taken up the slack, whether he wanted to or not. He slowed his step briefly, realizing. No wonder, then, if Bree was thinking . . .

He passed the Free North Church and half-smiled at it, thinking of Mrs. Ogilvy and Mrs. MacNeil. They'd be back, he knew, if he didn't do something about it. He knew their brand of determined kindliness. Dear God, if they heard that Bree had gone to work and—to their way of thinking—abandoned him with two small children, they'd be running shepherd's pies and hot stovies out to him in relays. That mightn't be such a bad thing, he thought, meditatively licking his lips—save that they'd stay to poke their noses into the workings of his household, and letting them into Brianna's kitchen would be not merely playing with dynamite but deliberately throwing a bottle of nitroglycerin into the midst of his marriage.

"Catholics don't believe in divorce," Bree had informed him once. "We *do* believe in murder. There's always Confession, after all."

On the far shore was the only Anglican church in Inverness, St. Andrew's. One Catholic church, one Anglican church—and no fewer than six Presbyterian churches, all standing foursquare by the river, in the space of less than a quarter mile. Tell you all you needed to know, he thought, about the basic character of Inverness. And he *had* told Bree—though without, he admitted, mentioning his own crisis of faith.

She hadn't asked. He'd give her that. He'd come within a hair of ordination in North Carolina—and in the traumatic aftermath of that interruption, with Mandy's birth, the disintegration of the Ridge's community, the decision to risk the passage through the stones . . . no one had mentioned it. Likewise, when they'd come back, the immediate demands of taking care of Mandy's heart and then assembling some kind of life . . . the question of his ministry had been ignored.

He thought Brianna hadn't mentioned it because she wasn't sure how he meant to handle it and didn't want to seem to push him in either direction—if her being a Catholic made his being a Presbyterian minister in Inverness more complicated, he couldn't ignore the fact that his being a minister would cause major complications in her life, and she'd know that.

The upshot was that neither of them had talked about it when working out the details of their return.

They'd worked out the practicalities as best they could. He couldn't go back to Oxford—not without a truly elaborate cover story.

"You just can't drop in and out of academia," he'd explained to Bree and to Joe Abernathy, the doctor who had been Claire's longtime friend before her own departure to the past. "You can go on a sabbatical, true—or even an extended leave. But you have to have a stated purpose and something to show for your absence when you come back, in terms of published research."

"You could write a killer book about the Regulation, though," Joe Abernathy had observed. "Or the run-up to the Revolution in the South."

"I could," he admitted. "But not a respectable scholarly one." He'd smiled wryly, feeling a slight itch in the joints of his fingers. He *could* write a book—one that no one else could write. But not as a historian.

"No sources," he'd explained, with a nod at the shelves in Joe's study, where they were holding the first of several councils of war. "If I wrote a book as a historian, I'd need to provide sources for all the information—and for most of the unique situations I could describe, I'm sure nothing was ever recorded. 'Eyewitness testimony of author' wouldn't go over well with a university press, I assure you. I'd have to do it as a novel." That idea actually held some small appeal—but wouldn't impress the colleges of Oxford.

Scotland, though . . .

People didn't appear in Inverness—or anywhere else in the Highlands—unremarked. But Roger wasn't an "incomer." He'd grown up in the manse in Inverness, and there were still a good many people who had known him as an adult. And with an American wife and children to explain his absence . . .

"See, folk there don't really care what it is you were doing when you were away," he explained. "They only care about what you do when you're there."

He'd reached the Islands of the Ness by now. A small, quiet park set on small islets that lay only a few feet off the river's bank, it had packed-dirt paths, big trees, and little traffic at this time of day. He wandered the paths, trying to empty his mind, let it be filled only with the sound of the rushing water, the quietness of the overcast sky.

He reached the end of the island and stood for a time, half-seeing the debris left in the branches of the bushes that edged the water—wodges of dead leaves, birds' feathers, fish bones, the odd cigarette packet, deposited by the passage of high water.

He had, of course, been thinking of himself. What *he'd* be doing, what folk would think about *him*. Why had it never occurred to him to wonder what Brianna intended doing, if they went to Scotland?

Well, that was obvious—if stupid—in retrospect. On the Ridge, Bree had done . . . well, a bit more than the usual woman there did, true—one couldn't overlook the buffalo-hunting, turkey-shooting, goddess–huntress, pirate-killing side of her—but also what the usual woman did. Mind her family, feed, clothe, comfort—or occasionally smack—them. And with Mandy sick, and Brianna grieving the loss of her parents, the question of working at anything had been irrelevant. Nothing could have separated her from her daughter.

But Mandy was well now—hair-raisingly healthy, as the trail of destruction that followed her testified. The painstaking details of reestablishing their identities in the twentieth century had been accomplished, the purchase of Lallybroch made from the bank that owned it, the physical removal to Scotland accomplished, Jem settled—more or less—into the village school nearby, and a nice girl from the same village engaged to come clear up and help look after Mandy.

And now Brianna was going to work.

Roger was going to hell. Metaphorically, if not literally.

BRIANNA COULDN'T say she hadn't been warned. It was a man's world she was walking into.

A rough job it had been, a tough undertaking—the toughest, digging the tunnels that carried the miles of cable from the turbines of the hydroelectric plants. "Tunnel tigers," they'd called the men who dug them, many of them Polish and Irish immigrants who'd come for a job in the 1950s.

She'd read about them, seen pictures of them, grimy-faced and white-eyed as coal miners, in the Hydro Electric authority office—the walls were covered with them, documentation of Scotland's proudest modern achievement. *What had been Scotland's proudest ancient achievement?* she wondered. *The kilt?* She'd suppressed a laugh at the thought, but evidently it made her look pleasant, because Mr. Campbell, the personnel manager, had smiled kindly at her.

"You're in luck, lass; we've an opening at Pitlochry, starting in a month," he'd said.

"That's wonderful." She had a folder in her lap, containing her credentials. He didn't ask to see it, which rather surprised her, but she set it on the desk before him, flipping it open. "Here are my . . . er . . . ?" He was staring at the curriculum vitae on top, his mouth hanging open far enough for her to see the steel fillings in his back teeth.

He shut his mouth, glanced up at her in astonishment, then looked back at the folder, slowly lifting the CV as though afraid there might be something even more shocking underneath.

"I think I have all the qualifications," she said, restraining the nervous urge to clench her fingers in the fabric of her skirt. "To be a plant inspector, I mean." She knew damned well she did. She had the qualifications to *build* a freaking hydroelectric station, let alone inspect one.

"Inspector . . ." he said faintly. Then he coughed, and flushed a bit. Heavy smoker; she could smell the fug of tobacco that clung to his clothes.

"I'm afraid there's been a bit of a misunderstanding, my dear," he said. "It's a secretary we're needing at Pitlochry."

"Perhaps you do," she said, giving in to the cloth-clenching urge. "But the advertisement I replied to was for plant inspector, and that's the position I'm applying for."

"But . . . my dear . . ." He was shaking his head, clearly appalled. "You're a woman!"

"I am," she said, and any of a hundred men who'd known her father would have picked up the ring of steel in her voice and given in on the spot. Mr. Campbell unfortunately hadn't known Jamie Fraser—but was about to be enlightened. "Would you care to explain to me exactly which aspects of plant inspection require a penis?"

His eyes bulged and he turned the shade of a turkey's wattles in courting season.

"That—you—that is—" With evident effort, he mastered himself enough to speak courteously, though the shock was still plain on his blunt features.

"Mrs. MacKenzie. I'm not unfamiliar with the notion of women's liberation, aye? I've daughters of my own." *And none of them would have said something like* that *to me,* his raised brow said. "It's not that I think ye'd be incompetent." He glanced at the open folder, raised both brows briefly, then shut it firmly. "It's the—the work environment. It wouldn't be suitable for a woman."

"Why not?"

He was recovering his aplomb by now.

"The conditions are often physically rough—and to be honest, Mrs. MacKenzie, so are the men you would encounter. The company cannot in good conscience—or as a matter of good business—risk your safety."

"You employ men who would be likely to assault a woman?"

"No! We—"

"You have plants that are physically dangerous? Then you *do* need an inspector, don't you?"

"The legalities—"

"I'm well up on the regulations pertaining to hydroelectric plants," she said firmly, and reaching into her bag, produced the printed booklet of regulations—obviously well thumbed—supplied by the Highlands and Islands Development Board. "I can spot problems, and I can tell you how to rectify them promptly—and as economically as possible."

Mr. Campbell was looking deeply unhappy.

"And I hear that you haven't had many applicants for this position," she finished. "None, to be exact."

"The men . . ."

"Men?" she said, and allowed the smallest edge of amusement to tinge the word. "I've worked with men before. I get on with them well."

She looked at him, not saying anything. *I know what it's like to kill a man,* she thought. *I know just how easy it is. And you don't.* She was not aware of having changed expression, but Campbell lost a bit of his high color and looked away. She wondered for a split second whether Roger would look away, if he saw that knowledge in her eyes. But this was no time to think of things like that.

"Why don't you show me one of the work sites?" she said gently. "Then we'll talk some more."

IN THE EIGHTEENTH century, St. Stephen's had been used as a temporary prison for captured Jacobites. Two of them had been executed in the graveyard, by some accounts. It wasn't the worst thing to have as your last sight of earth, he supposed: the wide river and the vast sky, both flowing to the sea. They carried an abiding sense of peace, wind and cloud and water did, despite their constant movement.

"If ever you find yourself in the midst of paradox, you can be sure you stand on the edge of truth," his adoptive father had told him once. *"You may not know what it* is, *mind,"* he'd added with a smile. *"But it's there."*

The rector at St. Stephen's, Dr. Weatherspoon, had had a few aphorisms to share, too.

"When God closes a door, he opens a window." Yeah. The problem was that this particular window opened off the tenth story, and he wasn't so sure God supplied parachutes.

"Do You?" he asked, looking up at the drifting sky over Inverness.

"Beg pardon?" said the startled sexton, popping up from the gravestone behind which he'd been working.

"Sorry." Roger flapped a hand, embarrassed. "Just . . . talking to myself."

The elderly man nodded understandingly. "Aye, aye. Nay

bother, then. It's when ye start getting answers ye should worry." Chuckling hoarsely, he descended back out of sight.

Roger made his way down from the high graveyard to street level, walking slowly back to the car park. Well, he'd taken the first step. Well past the time he should have done—Bree was right, to a degree; he *had* been a coward—but he had done it.

The difficulty wasn't resolved as yet, but it had been a great comfort, only being able to lay it out for someone who understood and sympathized.

"I'll pray for you," Dr. Weatherspoon had said, shaking his hand in parting. That was a comfort, too.

He started up the dank concrete steps of the car park, fumbling in his pocket for the keys. Couldn't say he was entirely at peace with himself, just yet—but he felt a lot more peaceable toward Bree. Now he could go home and tell her . . .

No, damn it. He couldn't, not yet. He had to check.

He didn't have to check; he knew he was right. But he had to have it in his hands, had to be able to show Bree.

Turning abruptly on his heel, he strode past a puzzled car-park attendant coming up behind him, took the stairs two at a time, and walked up Huntly Street as though he trod on red-hot coals. He stopped briefly at the Fox, digging in his pocket for coins, and rang through from the call box to Lallybroch. Annie answered the phone with her customary rudeness, saying "Yiss?" with such abruptness that it emerged as little more than an interrogatory hiss.

He didn't bother rebuking her phone manners.

"It's Roger. Tell the Missus I'm going down to Oxford to look something up. I'll spend the night."

"Mmphm," she said, and hung up.

SHE WANTED TO HIT Roger over the head with a blunt object. Something like a champagne bottle, maybe.

"He went *where?*" she asked, though she'd heard Annie MacDonald clearly. Annie lifted both narrow shoulders to the level of her ears, indicating that she understood the rhetorical nature of the question.

"To Oxford," she said. "To *England.*" The tone of her

voice underlined the sheer outrageousness of Roger's action. He hadn't simply gone to look up something in an old book—which would have been strange enough, though to be sure himself was a scholar and they'd do anything—but had abandoned his wife and children without notice and hied away to a foreign country!

"Himself did say as he'd come home tomorrow," Annie added, with great dubiousness. She picked up the bottle of champagne in its carrier bag, gingerly, as though it might explode. "Ought I put this to the ice, d'ye think?"

"To the—oh, no, don't put it in the freezer. Just in the fridge. Thank you, Annie."

Annie disappeared into the kitchen, and Brianna stood in the drafty hall for a moment, trying to get her feelings firmly under control before going to find Jem and Mandy. Kids being kids, they had ultra-sensitive radar concerning their parents. They already knew something was the matter between her and Roger; having their father suddenly disappear was *not* calculated to give them a feeling of cozy security. Had he even said goodbye to them? Assured *them* he'd be back? No, of course not.

"Bloody selfish, self-centered . . ." she muttered. Unable to find a satisfying noun with which to complete this, she said, "rat-fink *bastard!*" and then snorted with reluctant laughter. Not merely at the silliness of the insult, but with a wry acknowledgment that she'd got what she wanted. Both ways.

Granted, he couldn't have stopped her going for the job—and once he got past the dislocations involved, she thought he'd be all right with it.

"Men hate things to change," her mother had once casually told her. *"Unless it's their idea, of course. But you can make them think it* is *their idea, sometimes."*

Maybe she should have been less direct about it; tried to get Roger to feel that at least he had something to say about her going to work, even if not to think it was his idea—*that* would have been pushing it. She'd been in no mood to be devious, though. Or even diplomatic.

As for what she'd done to *him* . . . well, she'd put up with his immobility for as long as she could, and then she'd pushed him off a cliff. Deliberately.

"And I don't feel the least bit guilty about it!" she said to the coatrack.

She hung up her coat slowly, taking a little extra time to check the pockets for used tissues and crumpled receipts.

So, had he gone off out of pique—to get back at her for going back to work? Or out of anger at her having called him a coward? He hadn't liked that one bit; his eyes had gone dark and he'd nearly lost his voice—strong emotion choked him, quite literally, freezing his larynx. She'd done it on purpose, though. She knew where Roger's soft spots were—just as he knew hers.

Her lips tightened at that, just as her fingers closed on something hard in the inner pocket of her jacket. A weathered shell, turreted and smooth, worn white by sun and water. Roger had picked it up on the shingle by Loch Ness and handed it to her.

"To live in," he'd said, smiling, but given away by the gruffness of his damaged voice. "When ye need a hiding place."

She closed her fingers gently over the shell, and sighed.

Roger wasn't petty. Ever. He wouldn't go off to Oxford—a reluctant bubble of amusement floated up at the thought of Annie's shocked description: *to England!*—just to worry her.

So he'd gone for some specific reason, doubtless something jarred loose by their fight—and *that* worried her a bit.

He'd been wrestling with things since they came back. So had she, of course: Mandy's illness, decisions about where to live, all the petty details of relocating a family in both space and time—they'd done all that together. But there were things he wrestled with alone.

She'd grown up an only child, just as he had; she knew how it was, how you live in your own head a lot. But damn him, whatever he was living with in his head was eating him up before her eyes, and if he wouldn't tell her what it was, it was either something he considered too private to share—which bugged her, but she could live with it—or it was something he thought too disturbing or too dangerous to share, and she wasn't bloody *having* that.

Her fingers had clenched round the shell, and she deliberately loosened them, trying to calm down.

She could hear the kids upstairs, in Jem's room. He was reading something to Mandy—*The Gingerbread Man,* she thought. She couldn't hear the words, but could tell by the rhythm, counterpointed by Mandy's excited shouts of "Wun! Wun!"

No point in interrupting them. Time enough later to tell them Daddy'd be away overnight. Maybe they wouldn't be bothered, if she was matter-of-fact about it; he'd never left them since they'd come back, but when they lived on the Ridge, he was often gone with Jamie or Ian, hunting. Mandy wouldn't remember that, but Jem . . .

She'd meant to go into her study, but found herself drifting across the hall, through the open door to Roger's. It was the old speak-a-word room of the house; the room where her uncle Ian had run the affairs of the estate for years—her father for a short time before that, and her grandfather before him.

And now it was Roger's. He'd asked if she wanted the room, but she'd said no. She liked the little sitting room across the hall, with its sunny window and the shadows of the ancient yellow rose that flagged that side of the house with its color and scent. Aside from that, though, she just felt that this room was a man's place, with its clean, scuffed wooden floor and comfortably battered shelves.

Roger had managed to find one of the old farm ledgers, from 1776; it sat on an upper shelf, its worn cloth binding sheltering the patient, careful minutiae of life on a Highland farm: *one-quarter pound of silver fir seed, a he-goat for breeding, six rabbits, thirty-weight of seed potatoes* . . . had her uncle written it? She didn't know, had never seen a sample of his writing.

She wondered, with an odd little quiver of the insides, if her parents had made it back to Scotland—back *here.* Had seen Ian and Jenny again; if her father had sat—*would* sit?—here in this room, at home once more, talking over the matters of Lallybroch with Ian. And her mother? From the little Claire had said about it, she hadn't parted from Jenny on the best of terms, and Brianna knew her mother felt sad about that; once, they had been close friends. Maybe things could be mended—maybe they *had* been mended.

She glanced at the wooden box, safe on its high shelf beside the ledger, the little cherrywood snake curved in front of it. On impulse, she took the snake down, finding some comfort in the sleek curve of the body and the comical look of its face, peering back over its nonexistent shoulder. She smiled back at it, involuntarily.

"Thanks, Uncle Willie," she said softly, out loud, and felt an extraordinary shiver run through her. Not fear, or cold—a kind of delight, but a quiet kind. Recognition.

She'd seen that snake so often—on the Ridge, and now here, where it had first been made—that she never thought of its maker, her father's older brother, dead at the age of eleven. But he was here, too, in the work of his hands, in the rooms that had known him. When she'd visited Lallybroch before—in the eighteenth century—there had been a painting of him on the upstairs landing, a small, sturdy red-haired boy, standing with a hand on the shoulder of his baby brother, blue-eyed and serious.

Where is that now? she wondered. And the other paintings done by her grandmother? There was the one self-portrait, which had made it somehow to the National Portrait Gallery—she must be sure to take the kids down to London to see it, when they were a little older—but the others? There had been one of a very young Jenny Murray feeding a tame pheasant who had her uncle Ian's soft brown eyes, and she smiled at the memory.

It had been the right thing. Coming here, bringing the kids . . . home. It didn't matter if it took a little doing for her and Roger to find their places. Though maybe she shouldn't speak for Roger, she thought with a grimace.

She looked up at the box again. She wished her parents were here—either of them—so she could tell them about Roger, ask their opinion. Not that she wanted advice, so much. . . . What she wanted, if she was honest, she thought, was a reassurance that she'd done the right thing.

With a heightened flush in her cheeks, she reached up with both hands and brought down the box, feeling guilty for not waiting to share the next letter with Roger. But . . . she wanted her mother just now. She took the first letter on top that bore her mother's writing on the outside.

Offices of L'Oignon, New Bern, North Carolina
April 12, 1777

Dear Bree (and Roger and Jem and Mandy, of course),

We've made it to New Bern, without major incident. Yes, I hear you thinking, Major? *And it is true that we were held up by a pair of would-be bandits on the road south of Boone. Given that they were probably nine and eleven respectively, and armed solely with an ancient wheel-lock musket that would have blown them both to bits had they been able to fire it, though, we weren't in any marked danger.*

Rollo leapt out of the wagon and knocked one of them flat, whereupon his brother dropped the gun and legged it. Your cousin Ian ran him down, though, hauling him back by the scruff of the neck.

It took your father some time to get anything sensible out of them, but a little food worked wonders. They said their names are Herman and—no, really—Vermin. Their parents died during the winter—their father went hunting and didn't come back, the mother died giving birth, and the baby died a day later, as the two boys had no way to feed it. They know of no people on their father's side, but they said their mother's family name was Kuykendall. Luckily, your father knows a Kuykendall family, near Bailey Camp, and so Ian took the little vagabonds off to find the Kuykendalls and see if they could be settled. If not, I suppose he'll bring them along to New Bern, and we'll try to apprentice them somewhere, or perhaps take them with us to Wilmington and find them a berth as cabin boys.

Fergus and Marsali and the children seem all to be doing very well, both physically—bar a family tendency to enlarged adenoids and the biggest wart I've ever seen *on Germain's left elbow—and financially.*

Aside from the Wilmington Gazette, L'Oignon *is*

the only regular newspaper in the colony, and Fergus thus gets a great deal of business. Add in the printing and sale of books and pamphlets, and he's doing very well indeed. The family now owns two milch goats, a flock of chickens, a pig, and three *mules, counting Clarence, whom we are bequeathing to them on our way to Scotland.*

Conditions and uncertainties being what they are [meaning, *Brianna thought,* that you don't know who might read this letter, or when] *I'd better not be specific about* what *he's printing, besides newspapers.* L'Oignon *itself is carefully evenhanded, printing rabid denunciations by both Loyalists and those less loyal, and publishing satirical poetry by our good friend "Anonymous," lampooning both sides of the present political conflict. I've seldom seen Fergus so happy.*

War agrees with some men, and Fergus, rather oddly, is one of them. Your cousin Ian is another, though in his case, I think perhaps it keeps him from thinking too much.

I do wonder what his mother will make of him. But knowing her as I do, my guess is that after the first shock has passed, she'll begin the work of finding him a wife. Jenny is a very perceptive woman, all things said—and just as stubborn as your father. I do hope he remembers that.

Speaking of your father, he's out and about a good deal with Fergus, doing bits of "business" (unspecified, which means he's probably doing something that would turn my hair white—or whiter—to know about) and inquiring among the merchants for a possible ship—though I think our chances of finding one will be better in Wilmington, where we'll go as soon as Ian joins us.

Meanwhile, I've set up my shingle—literally. It's tacked to the front of Fergus's printshop, and says, TEETH PULLED, RASHES, PHLEGM, AND THE AGUE CURED, this being Marsali's work. She wanted to add a line about the pox, but both Fergus and I dissuaded her—he from a fear that it would lower the tone of his establishment, self from a certain morbid attachment to truth in advertising, as there is in fact nothing I can presently do about any condition they call the pox. Phlegm . . . well, there's always something you can do about phlegm, even if it's nothing more than a cup of hot tea (these days, that's hot water over sassafras root, catnip, or lemon balm) with a dram in it.

I called on Dr. Fentiman in Cross Creek on our way, and was able to buy several necessary instruments and a few medicines from him to refurbish my kit (this at the cost of a bottle of whisky and of being forced to admire the latest addition to his ghastly collection of pickled curiosities—no, you don't want to know; you really *don't. A good thing he can't see Germain's wart, or he'd be down to New Bern in a flash, sneaking round the printshop with an amputation saw).*

I still lack a pair of good surgical scissors, but Fergus knows a silversmith called Stephen Moray in Wilmington who he says could make a pair to my specifications. For the moment, I occupy myself largely in the pulling of teeth, as the barber who used to do it was drowned last November, having fallen into the harbor while drunk.

With all my love,
Mama

P.S. Speaking of the Wilmington Gazette, *your father has it in mind to call there and see if he can find out just who left that blasted notice about the fire. Though I suppose I oughtn't to complain; if you hadn't found it, you might never have come back. And while there are a lot of things I wish hadn't happened as a result of your coming—I can't ever regret that you know your father, and he you.*

17

WEE DEMONS

IT WASN'T MUCH different than any of the deer trails they'd come across; in fact, it had doubtless begun as one of them. But there was something about this particular trace that said "people" to Ian, and he'd been so long accustomed to such judgments that he seldom registered them consciously. He didn't now, but gave Clarence's leading rein a twitch, turning his own horse's head aside.

"Why're we stoppin'?" Herman asked suspiciously. "Ain't nothin' here."

"There's someone living up there." Ian jerked his chin toward the wooded slope. "The trail's not wide enough for horses; we'll tie up here, and walk."

Herman and Vermin exchanged a wordless glance of deep skepticism, but slid off the mule and trudged after Ian, up the trail.

He was beginning to have his doubts; no one he'd spoken to in the last week knew of any Kuykendalls in the area, and he couldn't take too much more time about the matter. He might have to bring the wee savages down to New Bern with him, after all, and he had no notion how they'd take to the suggestion.

He had no notion how they took much of anything, come to that. They were not so much shy as secretive, whispering together behind him as they rode, then shutting up like clams the minute he looked at them, regarding him with carefully bland faces, behind which he plainly saw any amount of reckoning going on. What the devil were they plotting?

If they meant to run from him, he thought he might not make any monstrous great effort to chase them down. If, on the other hand, they meant to steal Clarence and the horse while he slept, that was another matter.

The cabin was there, a curl of smoke coming from its chimney; Herman turned a look of surprise on him, and he smiled at the boy.

"Told ye," he said, and hallooed.

The door creaked open, and the barrel of a musket poked out of it. This was not an uncommon response to strangers in the far backcountry, and Ian was not put off by it. He raised his voice and stated his business, pushing Herman and Vermin in front of him as evidence of his *bona fides*.

The gun wasn't withdrawn, but lifted in a significant manner. Obeying instinct, Ian flung himself flat, yanking the boys down with him, as the shot roared overhead. A woman's voice yelled something strident in a foreign tongue. He didn't understand the words, but took the meaning clearly, and pulling the little boys to their feet, ushered them hastily back down the trail.

"Ain't gonna live with *her*," Vermin informed him, focusing a narrow glare of dislike over his shoulder. "Tell you that for free."

"No, ye're not," Ian agreed. "Keep moving, aye?" For Vermin had stopped dead.

"Gotta shit."

"Oh, aye? Well, be quick about it." He turned away, having discovered early on that the boys had an exaggerated requirement for privacy in such matters.

Herman had gone on already; the tangled mess of his dirty-blond hair was just visible, some twenty yards down the slope. Ian had suggested that the boys might cut, if not comb, their hair, and maybe wash their faces, as a gesture of civility toward any relations who might be faced with the prospect of taking them in, but this suggestion had been rejected with vehemence. Fortunately he was not responsible for forcing the wee buggers to wash—and to be fair, he thought washing would make little difference to their smell, given the state of their clothes, which they had plainly been living in for some months. He did make them sleep on the other side of the fire from himself and Rollo at night, in hopes of limiting his exposure to the lice both of them crawled with.

Could the notable infestation he sported possibly be where

the younger boy's parents had acquired his name? he wondered. Or had they no notion of its meaning and had only picked it to rhyme with his elder brother's?

Clarence's earsplitting bray pulled him abruptly from his thoughts. He lengthened his stride, berating himself for having left his own gun in its saddle loop. He hadn't wanted to approach the house armed, but—

A shriek from below sent him dodging off the path, into the trees. Another shriek was cut off suddenly, and he scrambled down the slope, as quickly as he might without making a racket. Panther? A bear? Nay, Clarence would be bellowing like a grampus, if it was that; instead, he was gurgling and wheezing like he did when he spotted—

Someone he knew.

Ian stopped dead, behind a screen of poplars, his heart cold in his chest.

Arch Bug turned his head, hearing the noise, faint as it was.

"Come on out, lad," he called. "I see ye there."

Plainly he did; the ancient eyes were looking straight at him, and Ian came slowly out of the trees.

Arch had taken the gun from the horse; it was slung across his shoulder. He had an arm crooked round Herman's throat, and the little boy's face was bright red from the choking; his feet kicked like a dying rabbit's, a few inches off the ground.

"Where's the gold?" Arch said, without preamble. His white hair was neatly bound up, and he seemed, so far as Ian could see, to have taken no harm from the winter. Must have found folk to bide with. *Where?* he wondered. *Brownsville, maybe?* Bloody dangerous, if he'd told the Browns about the gold—but he thought old Arch was too downy a bird to talk in such company.

"Where ye'll never find it," Ian said bluntly. He was thinking furiously. He'd a knife in his belt—but it was a good deal too far to throw it, and if he missed . . .

"What d'ye want wi' that wean?" he asked, moving a little closer. "He's naught to do wi' you."

"No, but he seems somewhat to do wi' *you*." Herman was making rasping squeaks, and his feet, while still kicking, were slowing.

"No, he's naught to me, either," Ian said, striving for casualness. "I'm only helping him to find his people. Ye plan to cut his throat if I dinna tell ye where the gold is? Go ahead; I'm no telling ye."

He didn't see Arch pull the knife, but it was there, suddenly, in his right hand, held awkwardly because of the missing fingers, but doubtless useful enough.

"All right," Arch said calmly, and put the point of the knife under Herman's chin.

A scream burst from behind Ian, and Vermin half-ran, half-fell down the last few feet of the trail. Arch Bug looked up, startled, and Ian crouched to rush him, but was forestalled by Vermin.

The little boy rushed at Arch Bug and gave him a tremendous kick in the shin, shouting, "You bad old man! You let her go right now!"

Arch seemed as startled by the speech as by the kick, but didn't let go.

"Her?" he said, and looked down at the child in his grasp, who promptly turned her—her?—head and bit him fiercely in the wrist. Ian, seizing the moment, lunged at him, but was impeded by Vermin, who had now seized Arch by the thigh and was clinging like grim death, trying to punch the old man in the balls with one small clenched fist.

With a ferocious grunt, Arch jerked the little girl—if that's what she was—up and flung her staggering into Ian. He then brought one big fist down on top of Vermin's head, stunning him. He shook the child off his leg, kicked the boy in the ribs as he staggered back, then turned and ran.

"Trudy, Trudy!" Herman ran for his—no, her—brother, who was lying in the leaf mold, mouth opening and closing like a landed trout.

Ian hesitated, wanting to pursue Arch, worried that Vermin might be badly hurt—but Arch was already gone, vanished into the wood. Gritting his teeth, he crouched and passed his hands rapidly over Vermin. No blood, and the wean was getting back his breath now, gulping and wheezing like a leaky bellows.

"Trudy?" Ian said to Herman, who was clinging tightly to Vermin's neck. Not waiting for an answer, he pulled up Vermin's ragged shirt, pulled out the waistband of his too-big breeches, and peeked inside. He let go hastily.

Herman leapt up, eyes bugged and hands clasped protectively over her—yes, her!—crotch.

"No!" she said. "I won't let you stick your nasty prick in me!"

"Ye couldna pay me to," Ian assured her. "If this is Trudy"—he nodded at Vermin, who had rolled up onto his—no, her—hands and knees and was vomiting into the grass—"what the devil's *your* name?"

"Hermione," the lassie said, sullen. "She's Ermintrude."

Ian ran a hand over his face, trying to adjust to this information. Now he looked . . . well, no, they still looked like filthy wee demons rather than little girls, their slitted eyes burning through the greasy, matted underbrush of their hair. They'd have to have their heads shaved, he supposed, and hoped he was nowhere in the neighborhood when it was done.

"Aye," he said, for lack of anything sensible. "Well, then."

"You've got gold?" said Ermintrude, having stopped her retching. She sat up, wiped a small hand over her mouth, and spat expertly. "Where?"

"If I wouldna tell him, why would I tell you? And ye can just forget *that* notion right now," he assured her, seeing her eyes dart to the knife in his belt.

Damn. What was he to do now? He pushed away the shock of Arch Bug's appearance—time to think of that later—and ran a hand slowly through his hair, considering. The fact that they were girls didn't change anything, really, but the fact that they knew he had gold hidden did. He didn't dare leave them with anyone now, because if he did . . .

"If you leave us, we'll tell about the gold," Hermione said promptly. "We don't want to live in a stinky cabin. We want to go to London."

"What?" He stared at her, incredulous. "What d'ye ken of London, for God's sake?"

"Our mam came from there," Herman—no, Hermione—said, and bit her lip to stop it trembling at mention of her mother. It was the first time she *had* spoken of her mother, Ian noted with interest. Let alone displayed any sign of vulnerability. "She told us about it."

"Mmphm. And why would I no just kill ye myself?" he demanded, exasperated. To his astonishment, Herman smiled at him, the first halfway-pleasant expression he'd ever seen on her face.

"The dog likes you," she said. "He wouldn't like you if you killed people."

"That's all you know," he muttered, and stood up. Rollo, who had been off about his own business, chose this opportune moment to saunter out of the underbrush, sniffing busily.

"And where were *you* when I needed ye?" Ian demanded. Rollo smelled carefully round the spot where Arch Bug had stood, then lifted his leg and urinated on a bush.

"Would that bad old man have killed Hermie?" the little one asked suddenly, as he boosted her onto the mule behind her sister.

"No," he said, with certainty. But as he swung up into his own saddle, he wondered. He had the very uncomfortable feeling that Arch Bug understood the nature of guilt much too well. Enough to kill an innocent child, only because her death would make Ian feel guilty for it? And Ian would; Arch knew that.

"No," he repeated more strongly. Arch Bug was both vengeful and vindictive—and had a right to be, he'd admit that. But Ian had nay grounds to think the man a monster.

Still, he made the little girls ride in front of him, until they made camp that night.

THERE WAS NO further sign of Arch Bug, though Ian felt now and then the crawling sensation of being watched, when they camped. Was the man following him? Very likely he was, Ian thought—for surely it wasn't accident that had made him appear so suddenly.

So. He'd gone back to the ruins of the Big House, then, thinking to retrieve the gold after Uncle Jamie had left, only to find it gone. He wondered briefly whether Arch had managed to kill the white sow, but dismissed that notion; his uncle said the creature was plainly from the infernal regions and thus indestructible, and he was himself inclined to believe it.

He glanced at Rollo, who was dozing by his feet, but the dog gave no sign that anyone was near, though his ears were half cocked. Ian relaxed a little, though he kept the knife on his person, even while sleeping.

Not entirely in respect of Arch Bug, marauders, or wild beasts, either. He looked across the fire, to where Hermione and Trudy lay rolled up together in his blank—only they weren't. The blanket was cunningly wadded so as to appear to contain bodies, but a gust of wind had pulled a corner loose, and he could see that it lay flat.

He closed his eyes in exasperation, then opened them and glanced down at the dog.

"Why did ye no say something?" he demanded. "Surely ye saw them leave!"

"We ain't gone," said a gruff, small voice behind him, and he whirled to find the two of them crouched on either side of his open saddlebag, busily rifling it for food.

"We 'uz hungry," said Trudy, matter-of-factly stuffing the remains of a journeycake into her face.

"I fed ye!" He'd shot a few quail and baked them in mud. Granted, it wasn't a feast, but—

"We's *still* hungry," Hermione said, with impeccable logic. She licked her fingers and burped.

"Have ye drunk all the beer?" he demanded, snatching up a stone bottle rolling near her feet.

"Mmm-hmm," she said dreamily, and sat down, quite suddenly.

"Ye canna be thieving food," he said severely, taking the depleted saddlebag from Trudy. "If ye eat it all now, we'll be starving before I get ye to—wherever we're going," he ended, rather weakly.

"If we don't eat it, we'll starve now," Trudy said logically. "Best starve later."

"Where *are* we going?" Hermione was swaying gently to and fro, like a small filthy flower in the wind.

"To Cross Creek," he said. "It's the first good-sized town we'll come to, and I ken folk there." Whether he knew anyone who might be of help in this present circumstance . . . too bad about his great-auntie Jocasta. Were she still at River Run, he could easily have left the girls there, but as it was, Jocasta and her husband, Duncan, had emigrated to Nova Scotia. There was Jocasta's body slave, Phaedre . . . He thought she was employed as a barmaid in Wilmington. But, no, she couldn't—

"Is it as big as London?" Hermione collapsed gently onto her back and lay with her arms spread out. Rollo got up and came and sniffed her; she giggled—the first innocent sound he'd heard from her.

"You all right, Hermie?" Trudy scampered over to her sister and squatted next to her in concern. Rollo, having smelled Hermione thoroughly, turned his attention to Trudy, who merely pushed aside his inquisitive nose. Hermione was now humming tunelessly to herself.

"She's fine," Ian said, after a quick glance. "She's no but a bit drunk. It'll pass."

"Oh." Reassured, Trudy sat down next to her sister, hugging her knees. "Pap used to get drunk. He hollered and broke things, though."

"Did he?"

"Uh-huh. He broke my mam's nose once."

"Oh," Ian said, having no idea how to answer this. "Too bad."

"You think he's dead?"

"I hope so."

"Me, too," she said, satisfied. She yawned hugely—he could smell her rotting teeth from where he sat—and then curled herself on the ground, cuddling close to Hermione.

Sighing, Ian got up and fetched the blanket, and covered them both, tucking it gently round their small, limp bodies.

Now what? He wondered. The recent exchange was the closest thing he'd had yet to an actual conversation with the girls, and he was under no illusions that their brief foray into amiability would last past daylight. Where would he find someone willing and able to deal with them?

A tiny snore, like the buzzing of a bee's wings, came from the blanket, and he smiled involuntarily. Wee Mandy, Bree's daughter, had made a noise like that when she slept.

He'd held Mandy, sleeping, now and then—once for more than an hour, not wanting to surrender the tiny, warm weight, watching the flicker of the pulse in her throat. Imagining, with longing and a pain tempered by distance, his own daughter. Stillborn, her face a mystery to him. Yeksa'a, the Mohawk had called her—"little girl," too young to have a name. But she did have a name. Iseabaìl. That's what he'd called her.

He wrapped himself in the ragged plaid Uncle Jamie had given him when he'd chosen to be a Mohawk and lay down by the fire.

Pray. That's what his uncle, his parents, would have advised. He was unsure who to pray to, really, or what to say. Should he speak to Christ, or His mother, or perhaps one of the saints? The spirit of the red cedar that stood sentinel beyond the fire, or the life that moved in the wood, whispering on the night breeze?

"A Dhia," he whispered at last to the open sky, *"cuidich mi,"* and slept.

Whether it was God or the night itself who answered him, at dawn he woke with a notion.

HE'D BEEN EXPECTING the walleyed maid, but Mrs. Sylvie came to the door herself. She recalled him; he saw a flicker of recognition and—he thought—pleasure in her eyes, though it didn't go so far as a smile, of course.

"Mr. Murray," she said, cool and calm. She looked down then, and lost a trifle of her composure. She pushed the wire-rimmed spectacles up on her nose for a better look at what accompanied him, then raised her head and fixed him with suspicion.

"What's this?"

He'd been expecting this reaction and was ready for it. Without answering, he held up the fat wee pouch he'd made ready and shook it, so she could hear the metal clink inside.

Her face changed at that, and she stood back to let them in, though she went on looking wary.

Not so wary as the little heathens—he still had trouble thinking of them as girls—who hung back until he took them each by a scrawny neck and propelled them firmly into Mrs. Sylvie's parlor. They sat—under compulsion—but looked as though they had something in mind, and he kept a beady gaze on them, even as he talked with the proprietor of the establishment.

"Maids?" she said, in open disbelief, looking at the girls.

He'd washed them *in* their clothes—forcibly, and had several bites to show for it, though luckily none had festered yet—but there had been nothing to do about their hair save chop it off, and he wasn't about to come near either one with a knife, for fear of injuring them or himself in the subsequent struggle. They sat and glared through the mats of their hair like gargoyles, red-eyed and malignant.

"Well, they dinna want to be whores," he said mildly. "And I dinna want them to be, either. Not that I've any objection to the profession personally," he added for the sake of politeness.

A muscle twitched by her mouth and she shot him a sharp glance—tinged with amusement—through her spectacles.

"I'm glad to hear it," she said dryly. And dropped her eyes to his feet and raised them slowly, almost appraisingly, up the length of his body in a way that made him feel suddenly as though he'd been dipped in hot water. The eyes came to rest on his face again, and the look of amusement had intensified considerably.

He coughed, recollecting—with a mixture of embarrassment and lust—a number of interesting images from their encounter more than two years before. Outwardly, she was a plain woman past thirty, her face and manner much more those of an autocratic nun than a whore. Beneath the unassuming calico gown and muslin apron, though . . . she gave fair value, did Mistress Sylvie.

"I'm no asking as a favor, aye?" he said, and nodded at the pouch, which he had put down on the table by his chair. "I had it in mind to apprentice them, maybe?"

"Apprentice girls. In a brothel." She didn't make it a question, but her mouth twitched again.

"Ye could start them as maids—surely ye've cleaning to be done? Chamber pots to be emptied, and the like? And then if they should be clever enough"—he shot them a narrow glance of his own, and Hermione stuck out her tongue at him—"ye could maybe train them up to be cooks. Or sempstresses. Ye must need a deal of mending done, aye? Torn sheets and the like?"

"Torn shifts, more like," she said, very dryly. Her eyes flickered toward the ceiling, where a sound of rhythmic squeaking indicated the presence of a paying customer.

The girls had sidled off their stools and were prowling the parlor like wild cats, nosing things and bristling with caution. He realized suddenly that they'd never seen a town, let alone a civilized person's house.

Mrs. Sylvie leaned forward and picked up the pouch, her eyes widening in surprise at the weight of it. She opened it and poured a handful of greasy black shot into her hand, glancing sharply up from it to him. He didn't speak, but smiled and, reaching forward, took one of the balls from the palm of her hand, dug his thumbnail hard into it, and dropped it back into her hand, the scored line glinting bright gold amid the darkness.

She pursed her lips, weighing the bag again.

"All of it?" It was, he'd estimated, more than fifty pounds' worth of gold: half what he'd been carrying.

He made a long reach and took a china ornament out of Hermione's hands.

"It'll no be an easy job," he said. "Ye'll earn it, I think."

"I think so, too," she said, watching Trudy, who—with extreme nonchalance—had lowered her breeches and was relieving herself in a corner of the hearth. The secret of their sex revealed, the girls had quite abandoned their requirements of privacy.

Mrs. Sylvie rang her silver bell, and both girls turned toward the sound in surprise.

"Why me?" she asked.

"I couldna think of anyone else who might be able to deal with them," Ian said simply.

"I'm *very* flattered."

"Ye should be," he said, smiling. "Have we a bargain, then?"

She drew a deep breath, eyeing the girls, who had their heads together, whispering, as they viewed her with the deepest suspicion. She let it out again, shaking her head.

"I think it's likely a bad bargain—but times are hard."

"What, in your business? I should think the demand must be fairly constant." He'd meant to joke, but she rounded on him, eyes narrowing.

"Oh, the customers are ready enough to knock on my door, no matter what," she said. "But they've no money these days—no one does. I'll take a chicken or a flitch of bacon—

but half of them haven't got so much as that. They'll pay with proclamation money, or Continentals, or scrip from a militia unit—want to guess how much any of those are worth in the market?"

"Aye, I—" But she was steaming like a kettle, and turned on him, hissing.

"Or they don't pay at all. When times are fair, so are men, mostly. But pinch them a bit, and they stop seeing just why they need to pay for their pleasure—after all, what does it cost *me*? And I cannot refuse, or they will simply take what they want and then burn my house or hurt us for my temerity. You see that, I suppose?"

The bitterness in her voice stung like a nettle, and he abruptly abandoned a half-formed impulse to propose that they seal their bargain in a personal way.

"I see that," he replied, as evenly as he could. "Is such a thing not always a risk of your profession, though? And ye've prospered so far, aye?"

Her mouth compressed for an instant.

"I had a . . . patron. A gentleman who offered me protection."

"In return for . . . ?"

A hot flush rose in her thin cheeks.

"None of your business, sir."

"Is it not?" He nodded at the pouch in her hand. "If I'm placing my—these—well, them"—he gestured at the girls, now fingering the fabric of a curtain—"with you, surely I am entitled to ask whether I might be placing them in danger by doing so?"

"They're girls," she replied briefly. "They were born in danger and will live their lives in that condition, regardless of circumstance." But her hand had tightened on the pouch, knuckles white. He was that bit impressed that she was so honest, given that she plainly did need the money badly. In spite of her bitterness, though, he was rather enjoying the joust.

"D'ye think life's no dangerous for a man, then?" he asked, and without pausing, "What happened to your pimp?"

The blood washed abruptly from her face, leaving it white as bleached bone. Her eyes flashed in it like sparks.

"He was my brother," she said, and her voice dropped to a

furious whisper. "The Sons of Liberty tarred and feathered him and left him on my doorstep to die. Now, sir—have you any further questions regarding my affairs, or is our business *done*?"

Before he could make shift to find any response at all to this, the door opened and a young woman came in. He felt a visceral shock at seeing her, and the edges of his vision went white. Then the room steadied round him and he found he could draw breath again.

It wasn't Emily. The young woman—looking curiously from him to the little savages wrapped in the curtains—was part-Indian, small and gracefully built, with Emily's long, thick, raven's-wing hair flowing loose down her back. With Emily's broad cheekbones and delicate round chin. But she wasn't Emily.

Thank God, he thought, but at the same time suffered a hollowness of the wame. He felt as though the sight of her had been a cannonball that had struck him and, having passed straight through his body, left a gaping hole in its wake.

Mrs. Sylvie was giving the Indian girl brisk instructions, pointing at Hermione and Trudy. The girl's black brows rose briefly, but she nodded, and smiling at the girls, invited them to accompany her to the kitchen for some food.

The little girls promptly disentangled themselves from the curtains; it had been a long time since breakfast, and he'd had nothing for them then save a bit of drammach and some jerked bear meat, hard as shoe leather.

They followed the Indian girl to the door of the room, sparing him not a glance. At the door, though, Hermione turned, and hitching up her baggy-seated breeches, fixed him with a glare and pointed a long, skinny finger of accusation at him.

"If we turns out to be whores after all, you fucker, I'm gonna hunt you down, cut your balls off, and stuff 'em up your arse."

He took his leave with what dignity he could, the peals of Mrs. Sylvie's laughter ringing in his ears.

18

PULLING TEETH

New Bern, colony of North Carolina
April 1777

I HATED PULLING teeth. The figure of speech that likens something of extreme difficulty to pulling teeth is not hyperbole. Even in the best of situations—a large person with a big mouth and a placid temperament, the affected tooth one of those toward the front of the mouth and in the upper jaw (less in the way of roots and much easier of access)—it was a messy, slippery, bone-crack business. And underlying the sheer physical unpleasantness of the job was usually an inescapable feeling of depression at the probable outcome.

It was necessary—beyond the pain of an abscessed tooth, a bad abscess could release bacteria into the bloodstream, causing septicemia and even death—but to remove a tooth, with no good means of replacing it, was to compromise not merely the patient's appearance but also the function and structure of the mouth. A missing tooth allowed all those near it to shift out of place, altering the bite and making chewing much less efficient. Which in turn affected the patient's nutrition, general health, and prospects for a long and happy life.

Not, I reflected grimly, changing position yet again in hopes of gaining a view of the tooth I was after, that even the removal of several teeth would greatly damage the dentition of the poor little girl whose mouth I was working on.

She couldn't be more than eight or nine, with a narrow jaw and a pronounced overbite. Her canine baby teeth had not fallen out on time, and the permanent ones had come in behind them, giving her a sinister double-fanged appearance.

This was aggravated by the unusual narrowness of her upper jaw, which had forced the two emergent front incisors to buckle inward, turning toward each other in such a way that the front surfaces of each tooth almost touched each other.

I touched the abscessed upper molar and she jerked against the straps that bound her to the chair, letting out a shriek that ran under my fingernails like a bamboo splinter.

"Give her a bit more, please, Ian." I straightened up, feeling as though my lower back had been squeezed in a vise; I'd been working for several hours in the front room of Fergus's printshop, and had a small bowl full of bloodstained teeth at my elbow and a rapt crowd outside the window to show for it.

Ian made a dubious Scottish noise, but picked up the bottle of whisky and made an encouraging clucking noise toward the little girl, who screamed again at sight of his tattooed face and clamped her mouth shut. The girl's mother, out of patience, slapped her briskly, snatched the bottle from Ian's hand, and inserting it into her daughter's mouth, upended it, pinching the girl's nose shut with the other hand.

The child's eyes went round as pennies and an explosion of whisky droplets sprayed from the corners of her mouth—but her scrawny little neck bobbed convulsively as she swallowed, nonetheless.

"I really think that's enough," I said, rather alarmed at the quantity of whisky the child was swallowing. It was very bad whisky, acquired locally, and while Jamie and Ian had both tasted it and, after some discussion, decided that it probably wouldn't make anyone go blind, I had reservations about using it in any great amount.

"Hmm," said the mother, examining her daughter critically, but not removing the bottle. "That'll do it, I suppose."

The child's eyes had rolled back in her head, and the straining little body suddenly relaxed, falling limp against the chair. The mother removed the whisky bottle, wiped the mouth of it tidily on her apron, and handed it back to Ian with a nod.

I hastily examined her pulse and breathing, but she seemed in reasonably good shape—so far, at least.

"Carpe diem," I muttered, grabbing my tooth pliers. "Or perhaps I mean *carpe vinorum*? Watch to see she keeps breathing, Ian."

Ian laughed and tilted the bottle, wetting a tiny swab of clean cloth with whisky for the mopping up.

"I think ye'll have time to take more than the one tooth, Auntie, if ye want. Ye could likely pull every tooth in the poor lassie's head and she wouldna twitch."

"It's a thought," I said, turning the child's head. "Can you bring the mirror, Ian?"

I had a tiny square of looking glass which could, with luck, be used to direct sunlight into a patient's mouth. And there was sunlight streaming through the window in abundance, warm and bright. Unfortunately, there were any number of curious heads pressed against the window, too, which kept moving into the path of the sun, frustrating Ian's attempts to beam sunlight where I needed it.

"Marsali!" I called, a thumb on the girl's pulse, just in case.

"Aye?" She came through from the back room where she'd been cleaning—or, rather, dirtying—type, wiping inky hands on a rag. "D'ye need Henri-Christian again?"

"If you—or he—don't mind."

"Not him," she assured me. "Likes nothing better, the wee praise-hog. Joanie! Félicité! Come fetch the wean, will ye? He's wanted out front."

Félicité and Joan—aka the hell-kittens, as Jamie called them—came eagerly; they enjoyed Henri-Christian's performances nearly as much as he did.

"Come on, Bubbles!" Joanie called, holding open the door to the kitchen. Henri-Christian came scampering out, rolling from side to side on short, bowed legs, ruddy face beaming.

"Hoopla, hoopla, hoopla!" he shouted, making for the door.

"Put his hat on him!" Marsali called. "The wind will get in his ears."

It was a bright day, but *was* windy, and Henri-Christian had a tendency to ear infection. He had a woolen hat that tied under the chin, though, knitted in blue and white stripes and decorated with a row of red bobbles—Brianna had made it for him, and the sight of it squeezed my heart a little, warmth and pain together.

The girls each took him by a hand—Félicité stretching up at the last moment to grab an old slouch hat of her father's from the peg, to put out for coins—and went out, to cheers and whistles from the crowd. Through the window, I could see Joanie clearing the books displayed on the table outside, and Félicité hoisting Henri-Christian up in their stead. He spread his stubby, powerful arms, beaming, and bowed in accomplished fashion to one side and the other. Then he bent, put his hands on the tabletop, and, with a remarkable degree of controlled grace, stood on his head.

I didn't wait to watch the rest of his show—it was mostly simple dancing and kicks, interspersed with somersaults and headstands, but made enchanting by his dwarfed stature and vivid personality. He had shifted the crowd away from the window momentarily, though, which was what I wanted.

"Now, Ian," I said, and went back to work. With the flickering light from the mirror, it was a little easier to see what I was doing, and I got to grips with the tooth almost at once. This was the tricky part, though; the tooth was badly cracked, and there was a good chance that it might fracture when I twisted it, rather than draw cleanly. And if that should happen . . .

But it didn't. There was a small, muffled *crack!* as the roots of the tooth parted from the jawbone, and I was holding the tiny white thing, intact.

The child's mother, who had been watching intently, sighed and relaxed a little. The little girl sighed, too, and settled in the chair. I checked again, but her pulse was fine, though her breathing was shallow. She'd likely sleep for—

A thought struck me.

"You know," I said to the mother, a little hesitantly, "I *could* draw one or two more teeth without hurting her. See . . ." I moved aside, motioning her to look. "These"—I touched the overdue baby canines—"ought to be drawn at once, to let the teeth behind take their places. And you see these front teeth, of course. . . . Well, I've taken the upper bicuspid molar on the left; if I were to take the same tooth on the right, I *think* that perhaps her teeth would shift a bit, to fill the empty space. And if you could persuade her to press with her tongue against those front teeth, whenever she thought of it . . ." It wasn't orthodontia by any means, and it did carry some increased risk of infection, but I was sorely tempted. The poor child looked like a cannibal bat.

"Hmmmm," said the mother, frowning into her daughter's mouth. "How much will you give me for them?"

"How much . . . you want me to pay *you*?"

"They're fine, sound teeth," the mother replied promptly. "The tooth-drawer down to the harbor 'ud give me a shilling apiece. And Glory'll need the money for her dowry."

"Her dowry?" I repeated, surprised. The mother shrugged.

"No one's likely to take the poor creature for her looks, now, are they?"

I was obliged to admit that this was likely true; her deplorable dentition quite aside, calling the child homely would be a compliment.

"Marsali," I called. "Have you got four shillings?" The gold in my hem swung heavily round my feet, but I couldn't make use of it in this situation.

Marsali turned from the window, where she'd been keeping an eye on Henri-Christian and the girls, startled.

"Not cash money, no."

"It's all right, Auntie. I've some money." Ian put down the mirror and dug in his sporran, emerging with a handful of coins. "Mind," he said, fixing the woman with a hard eye, "ye'd no get more nor thruppence each for sound teeth—and likely no but a penny for a child's."

The woman, nothing daunted, looked down her nose at him.

"There speaks a grasping Scotchman," she said. "For all you're tattooed like a savage. Sixpence each, then, you penny-pinching miser!"

Ian grinned at her, displaying his own fine teeth, which, if not entirely straight, were in excellent condition.

"Going to carry the wean down to the quay and let yon butcher rip her mouth to shreds?" he inquired pleasantly. "She'll be awake by then, ken. And screaming. Three."

"Ian!" I said.

"Well, I'm no going to let her cheat ye, Auntie. Bad enough she's wantin' ye to draw the lassie's teeth for nothing, let alone pay for the honor!"

Emboldened by my intervention, the woman stuck out her chin and repeated, "Sixpence!"

Marsali, attracted by the altercation, came to peer into the girl's mouth.

"Ye'll not find that one a husband for less than ten pound," she informed the woman bluntly. "Not lookin' like that. A man would be feart of bein' bitten when he kissed her. Ian's right. In fact, ye should be payin' double for it."

"Ye agreed to pay when ye came in, no?" Ian pressed. "Tuppence to have the tooth drawn—and my aunt made ye a bargain at that, out of pity for the wean."

"Bloodsuckers!" the woman exclaimed. "It's true what they say—you Scots 'ud take the pennies from a dead man's eyes!"

Plainly this wasn't going to be settled in a hurry; I could feel both Ian and Marsali settling down to an enjoyable session of tag-team haggling. I sighed and took the mirror out of Ian's hand. I wouldn't need it for the canines, and perhaps by the time I got to the other bicuspid, he'd be paying attention again.

In fact, the canines were simple; baby teeth, almost without roots, and ready to fall—I could probably have tweaked them out with my fingers. One quick twist each and they were out, the gums barely bleeding. Pleased, I dabbed the sites with a whisky-soaked swab, then considered the bicuspid.

It was on the other side of the mouth, which meant that by tilting the girl's head back, I could get a bit of light without using the mirror. I took Ian's hand—he was so engaged in argument that he barely noticed—and put it on the girl's head to hold it back and steady, then carefully insinuated my pliers.

A shadow crossed my light, vanished—then came back, blocking it utterly. I turned in annoyance, to find a rather elegant-looking gentleman peering through the window, a look of interest on his face.

I scowled at him and motioned him aside. He blinked at me, but then nodded apology and stepped aside. Not waiting for any further interruption, I crouched, got hold of the tooth, and twisted it free with a lucky wrench.

Humming with satisfaction, I dribbled whisky over the bleeding hole, then tilted her head to the other side and pressed a swab gently over the gum, to help drain the abscess. Felt a sudden extra slackness in the wobbly little neck and froze.

Ian felt it, too; he broke off in the middle of a sentence and shot me a startled look.

"Untie her," I said. "Quick."

He had her loosed in an instant, and I seized her under the arms and laid her on the floor, her head flopping like a rag doll's. Ignoring startled exclamations from Marsali and the girl's mother, I tilted back her head, swiped the swab out of her mouth, and, pinching shut her nose with my fingers, sealed my mouth to hers and started resuscitation.

It was like blowing up a small, tough balloon: reluctance, resistance, then, finally, a rise of the chest. But chests don't yield like rubber; the blowing didn't get easier.

I had the fingers of my other hand on her neck, feeling desperately for a carotid pulse. There . . . Was it? . . . Yes, it was! Her heart was still beating, though faintly.

Breathe. Pause. Breathe. Pause . . . I felt the tiny gush of exhalation, and then the narrow chest moved by itself. I waited, blood pounding in my ears, but it didn't move again. Breathe. Pause. Breathe . . .

Again the chest moved, and this time continued to rise and fall under its own power. I sat up on my heels, my own breath coming fast and a cold sweat misting my face.

The girl's mother was staring down at me, her mouth half open. I noted dimly that her own dentition wasn't bad; God knew what her husband looked like.

"She's—is she . . . ?" the woman asked, blinking and glancing back and forth between me and her daughter.

"She's fine," I said flatly. I stood up slowly, feeling lightheaded. "She can't go until the whisky's worn off, though; I think she'll be all right, but she might stop breathing again. Someone needs to watch her 'til she wakes. Marsali . . . ?"

"Aye, I'll put her in the trundle," Marsali said, coming to look. "Oh, there ye are, Joanie—will ye come and keep an eye on this poor wean for a bit? She needs to lie down on your bed."

The children had come in, red-cheeked and giggling, with a hatful of small coins and buttons, but seeing the girl on the floor, hurried over to look, too.

"Hoopla," Henri-Christian remarked, impressed.

"Is she deid?" Félicité asked, more practically.

"If she was, *Maman* wouldna be asking me to watch her," Joanie pointed out. "She's no going to sick up in my bed, is she?"

"I'll put a towel down," Marsali promised, squatting to scoop the little girl up. Ian beat her to it, lifting the child gently.

"We'll just charge ye tuppence, then," he said to the mother. "But we'll give ye all the teeth for free, aye?"

Looking stunned, she nodded, then followed the crowd into the back of the house. I heard the thunder of multiple feet going up the stairs, but didn't follow; my own legs had gone to water, and I sat down quite suddenly.

"Are you all right, *madame*?" I looked up to find the elegant stranger inside the shop, looking curiously at me.

I picked up the half-empty bottle of whisky and took a substantial swallow. It burned like brimstone and tasted like charred bones. I made wheezing noises and my eyes watered, but I didn't actually cough.

"Fine," I said hoarsely. "Perfectly fine." I cleared my throat and wiped my eyes on my sleeve. "Can I help you?"

A faint look of amusement crossed his features.

"I do not require to have a tooth drawn, which is probably good luck for both of us. However—may I?" He withdrew a slim silver flask from his pocket and handed it to me, then sat down. "I think it's perhaps a little more fortifying than . . . that." He nodded at the uncorked whisky bottle, his nose wrinkling a little.

I uncorked the flask, and the full-bodied scent of very good brandy floated out like a genie.

"Thank you," I said briefly, and drank, closing my eyes. "Very much indeed," I added a moment later, opening them. Fortifying, indeed. Warmth collected in my center and purled like smoke through my limbs.

"My pleasure, *madame,*" he said, and smiled. He was undeniably a dandy, and a rich one, too, with a good deal of lace about his person, gilt buttons on his waistcoat, a powdered wig, and two black silk beauty patches on his face—a star beside his left brow, and a rearing horse on his right cheek. Not a getup one saw often in North Carolina, especially not these days.

Despite the encrustations, he was a handsome man, I thought, perhaps forty or so, with soft dark eyes that glinted with humor, and a delicate, sensitive face. His English was very good, though it carried a distinct Parisian accent.

"Have I the honor of addressing Mrs. Fraser?" he asked. I saw his eyes pass over my scandalously bare head, but he politely made no comment.

"Well, you have," I said dubiously. "But I may not be the one you want. My daughter-in-law is Mrs. Fraser, too; she and her husband own this shop. So if you were wanting something printed—"

"Mrs. James Fraser?"

I paused instinctively, but there wasn't much alternative to answering.

"I am, yes. Is it my husband you want?" I asked warily. People wanted Jamie for a lot of things, and it wasn't always desirable that they find him.

He smiled, eyes crinkling pleasantly.

"It is indeed, Mrs. Fraser. The captain of my ship said that Mr. Fraser had come to speak with him this morning, seeking passage."

My heart gave a sharp leap at this.

"Oh! You have a ship, Mr. . . . ?"

"Beauchamp," he said, and, picking up my hand, kissed it gracefully. "Percival Beauchamp, at your service, *madame.* I do—she is called *Huntress.*"

I actually thought my heart had stopped for a moment, but it hadn't, and resumed beating with a noticeable thump.

"Beauchamp," I said. "Beechum?" He'd pronounced it in the French way, but at this, he nodded, smile growing wider.

"Yes, the English say it that way. You said your daughter-in-law . . . so the Mr. Fraser who owns this shop is your husband's son?"

"Yes," I said again, but automatically. *Don't be silly,* I scolded myself. *It isn't an uncommon name. Likely he hasn't anything at all to do with your family!* And yet—a French–English connection. I knew my father's family had come from France to England sometime in the eighteenth century—but that was all I knew about them. I stared at him in fascination. Was there anything familiar about his face, anything I could match with my faint recollections of my parents, the stronger ones of my uncle?

He had pale skin, like mine, but then, most upper-class people did, they taking great pains to shelter their faces from the sun. His eyes were much darker than mine, and beautiful, but shaped differently, rounder. The brows—had my uncle Lamb's brows had that shape, heavy near the nose, trailing off in a graceful arch . . . ?

Absorbed in this tantalizing puzzle, I'd missed what he was saying.

"I beg your pardon?"

"The little boy," he repeated, with a nod toward the door through which the children had disappeared. "He was shouting, 'Hoopla!' As French street performers do. Has the family a French connection of some kind?"

Belated alarms began to go off, and unease rippled the hairs on my forearms.

"No," I said, trying to iron my face into a politely quizzical expression. "Likely he's just heard it from someone. There was a small troupe of French acrobats who passed through the Carolinas last year."

"Ah, doubtless that's it." He leaned forward a little, dark eyes intent. "Did you see them yourself?"

"No. My husband and I . . . don't live here," I ended hurriedly. I'd been about to tell him where we *did* live, but I didn't know how much—if anything—he knew about Fergus's circumstances. He sat back, pursing his lips a little in disappointment.

"Ah, too bad. I thought perhaps the gentleman I am in search of might have belonged to this troupe. Though I suppose you would not have known their names, even had you seen them," he added as an afterthought.

"You're looking for someone? A Frenchman?" I lifted the bowl of bloodstained teeth and began to pick through it, affecting nonchalance.

"A man named Claudel. He was born in Paris—in a brothel," he added, with a faint air of apology for using such an indelicate term in my presence. "He would be in his early forties now—forty-one or -two, perhaps."

"Paris," I repeated, listening for Marsali's footfalls on the stair. "What leads you to suppose that he's in North Carolina?"

He lifted one shoulder in a graceful shrug.

"He may well not be. I do know that roughly thirty years ago, he was taken from the brothel by a Scotsman, and that this man was described as of striking appearance, very tall, with brilliant red hair. Beyond that, I encountered a morass of possibilities . . ." He smiled wryly. "Fraser was described to me variously as a wine merchant, a Jacobite, a Loyalist, a traitor, a spy, an aristocrat, a farmer, an importer—or a smuggler; the terms are interchangeable—with connections reaching from a convent to the Royal court."

Which was, I thought, an extremely accurate portrait of Jamie. Though I could see why it hadn't been much help in finding him. On the other hand . . . here Beauchamp was.

"I did discover a wine merchant named Michael Murray, who, upon hearing this description, told me that it resembled his uncle, one James Fraser, who had emigrated to America more than ten years ago." The dark eyes were less humorous now, fixed intently upon me.

"When I inquired about the child Claudel, though, Monsieur Murray professed complete ignorance of such a person. In rather vehement terms."

"Oh?" I said, and picked up a large molar with serious caries, squinting at it. Jesus H. Roosevelt Christ. I knew Michael only by name; one of Young Ian's elder brothers, he had been born after my departure and had already gone to France by the time I returned to Lallybroch—there to be educated and taken into the wine business with Jared Fraser, an elderly and childless cousin of Jamie's. Michael had, of course, grown up with Fergus at Lallybroch and knew bloody well what his original name was. And apparently had detected or suspected something in this stranger's demeanor that had alarmed him.

"Do you mean to say that you came all the way to America, knowing nothing except a man's name and that he has red hair?" I asked, trying to seem mildly incredulous. "Goodness—you must have considerable interest in finding this Claudel!"

"Oh, I do, *madame*." He looked at me, smiling faintly, head on one side. "Tell me, Mrs. Fraser—has your husband red hair?"

"Yes," I said. There was no point in denying it, since anyone in New Bern would tell him so—and likely had already, I reflected. "So do any number of his relations—and about half the population of the Scottish Highlands." This was a wild overstatement, but I was reasonably sure that Mr. Beauchamp hadn't been combing the Highlands personally, either.

I could hear voices upstairs; Marsali might be coming down any minute, and I didn't want her walking into the midst of this particular conversation.

"Well," I said, and got to my feet in a decided manner. "I'm sure you'll be wanting to talk to my husband—and he to you. He's gone on an errand, though, and won't be back until sometime tomorrow. Are you staying somewhere in the town?"

"The King's Inn," he said, rising, as well. "If you will tell your husband to find me there, *madame*? I thank you." Bending low, he took my hand and kissed it again, then smiled at me and backed out of the shop, leaving a scent of bergamot and hyssop mingled with the ghost of good brandy.

A GOOD MANY merchants and businessmen had left New Bern, owing to the chaotic state of politics; with no civil authority, public life had come to a standstill, bar the simplest of market transactions, and many people—of both Loyalist and rebel sympathies—had left the colony out of fear of violence. There were only two good inns in New Bern these days; the King's Inn was one, and the Wilsey Arms the other. Luckily, Jamie and I had a room in the latter.

"Will you go and talk to him?" I had just finished telling Jamie about the visit of Monsieur Beauchamp—an account that had left him with a deep crease of concern between his brows.

"Christ. How did he find out all that?"

"He must have begun with a knowledge that Fergus was at that brothel, and started his inquiries there. I imagine it wouldn't have been difficult to find someone who'd seen you there, or heard about the incident. You're rather memorable, after all." Despite my own agitation, I smiled at the memory of Jamie, aged twenty-five, who had taken temporary refuge in the brothel in question armed—quite coincidentally—with a large sausage, and then escaped through a window, accompanied by a ten-year-old pickpocket and sometime child-whore named Claudel.

He shrugged, looking mildly embarrassed.

"Well, aye, perhaps. But to discover quite so much . . ." He scratched his head, thinking. "As to speaking with him—not before I speak to Fergus. I think we might want to know a bit more about this Monsieur Beauchamp, before we make him a present of ourselves."

"I'd like to know a bit more about him, too," I said. "I did wonder whether . . . Well, it's a remote possibility, the name isn't all that uncommon—but I did wonder whether he might be connected in some way with a branch of my family. They *were* in France in the eighteenth century, I know that much. But not much more."

He smiled at me.

"And what would ye do, Sassnenach, if I discover that he's really your six-times-great-grandfather?"

"I—" I stopped abruptly because, in fact, I didn't know *what* I'd do in such a circumstance. "Well . . . probably nothing," I admitted. "And we probably can't find that out for sure in any case, since I don't recall—if I ever knew—what my six-times-great-grandfather's first name was. I just—would be interested to know more, that's all," I finished, feeling mildly defensive.

"Well, of course ye would," he said, matter-of-fact. "But not if my asking might put Fergus in any danger, would ye?"

"Oh, no! Of course not. But do you—"

I was interrupted by a soft knock on the door that struck me dumb. I raised my brows at Jamie, who hesitated a moment, but then shrugged and went to open it.

Small as the room was, I could see the door from where I sat; to my surprise, it was filled with what appeared to be a deputation of women—the corridor was a sea of white caps, floating in the dimness like jellyfish.

"Mr. Fraser?" One of the caps bobbed briefly. "I am—my name is Abigail Bell. My daughters"—she turned, and I caught a glimpse of a strained white face—"Lillian and Miriam." The other two caps—yes, there were only three, after all—bobbed in turn. "May we speak with you?"

Jamie bowed and ushered them into the room, raising his eyebrows at me as he followed them in.

"My wife," he said, nodding as I rose, murmuring pleasantries. There was only the bed and one stool, so we all remained standing, awkwardly smiling and bobbing at one another.

Mrs. Bell was short and rather stout, and had probably once been as pretty as her daughters. Her once-plump cheeks now sagged, though, as though she had lost weight suddenly, and her skin was creased with worry. Her daughters looked worried, too; one was twisting her hands in her apron, and the other kept stealing glances at Jamie from downcast eyes, as though afraid he might do something violent if gazed at too directly.

"I beg your pardon, sir, for coming to you in this bold way." Mrs. Bell's lips were trembling; she had to stop and compress them briefly before continuing. "I—I hear that you are looking for a ship bound to Scotland."

Jamie nodded warily, plainly wondering where this woman had learned of it. He'd said everyone in the town would know within a day or two—evidently he'd been right about that.

"Do ye ken someone with such a voyage in view?" he asked politely.

"No. Not exactly. I . . . that is . . . perhaps—it is my husband," she blurted, but the speaking of the word made her voice break, and she clapped a handful of apron to her mouth. One of the daughters, a dark-haired girl, took her mother gently by the elbow and drew her aside, standing up bravely to face the fearsome Mr. Fraser herself.

"My father is in Scotland, Mr. Fraser," she said. "My mother is in hopes that you might find him, when you go there, and assist him to return to us."

"Ah," Jamie said. "And your father would be . . . ?"

"Oh! Mr. Richard Bell, sir, of Wilmington." She curtsied hastily, as though further politeness would help to make her case. "He is—he *was*—"

"He *is*!" her sister hissed, low-voiced but emphatic, and the first sister, the dark one, gave her a glare.

"My father was a merchant in Wilmington, Mr. Fraser. He had considerable business interests, and in the course of his business he . . . had reason to have contact with various British officers, who came to him for supplies. It was entirely a matter of business!" she assured him.

"But business in these dreadful times is never only business." Mrs. Bell had got hold of herself, and came to stand shoulder to shoulder with her daughter. "They said—my husband's enemies—they put it about that he was a Loyalist."

"Only because he was," put in the second sister. This one—fair-haired and blue-eyed—wasn't trembling; she faced Jamie with a lifted chin and blazing eyes. "My father was true to his King! I for one do not think that is something to be excused and apologized for! Nor do I think it right to pretend otherwise, only to get the help of a man who has broken every oath—"

"Oh, *Miriam*!" said her sister, exasperated. "Could you not keep quiet for one *second*? Now you've spoilt everything!"

"I haven't," Miriam snapped. "Or if I have, it wasn't ever going to work in the first place! Why should someone like him hel—"

"Yes, it would! Mr. Forbes said—"

"Oh, bother Mr. Forbes! What would *he* know?"

Mrs. Bell moaned softly into her apron.

"Why did your father go to Scotland?" Jamie asked, cutting through the confusion.

Taken by surprise, Miriam Bell actually answered him.

"He didn't *go* to Scotland. He was abducted in the street and thrust onto a ship bound for Southampton."

"By whom?" I asked, wiggling my way through the obstructing forest of skirts on my way to the door. "And why?"

I stuck my head out into the corridor and gestured to the boy cleaning boots on the landing that he should go down to the taproom and bring up a jug of wine. Given the apparent state of the Bells, I thought something to restore the social amenities might be a good idea.

I popped back inside in time to hear Miss Lillian Bell explaining that they didn't actually know who had abducted her father.

"Or not by name, at least," she said, face flushed with fury at the telling. "The villains wore hoods over their heads. But it was the Sons of Liberty, I know it!"

"Yes, it was," Miss Miriam said decidedly. "Father had had threats from them—notes pinned to the door, a dead fish wrapped in a bit of red flannel and left upon the porch to make a stink. That sort of thing."

The matter had gone beyond threats at the end of the previous August. Mr. Bell had been on his way to his warehouse, when a group of hooded men had rushed out from an alleyway, seized him, and carried him down the quay, then flung him bodily aboard a ship that had just cast off its hawser, sails filling as it drew slowly away.

I had heard of troublesome Loyalists being summarily "deported" in this manner, but hadn't run into an actual occurrence of the practice before.

"If the ship was bound for England," I inquired, "how did he end up in Scotland?"

There was a certain amount of confusion as all three Bells tried to explain at once what had happened, but Miriam won out once again.

"He arrived in England penniless, of course, with no more than the clothes on his back, and owing money for food and passage on the ship. But the ship's captain had befriended him, and took him from Southampton to London, where my father knew some men with whom he had done business in the past. One of these advanced him a sum to cover his indebtedness to the captain, and promised him passage to Georgia, if he would oversee the cargo on a voyage from Edinburgh to the Indies, thence to America.

"So he traveled to Edinburgh under the auspices of his patron, only to discover there that the intended cargo to be picked up in the Indies was a shipload of Negroes."

"My husband is an abolitionist, Mr. Fraser," Mrs. Bell put in, with timid pride. "He said he could not countenance slavery, nor assist in its practice, no matter what the cost to himself."

"And Mr. Forbes told us what you had done for that woman—Mrs. Cameron's body slave," Lillian put in, anxious-faced. "So we thought . . . even if you were . . ." She trailed off, embarrassed.

"An oath-breaking rebel, aye," Jamie said dryly. "I see. Mr. Forbes—this would be . . . Neil Forbes, the lawyer?" He sounded faintly incredulous, and with good reason.

Some years before, Forbes had been a suitor for Brianna's hand—encouraged by Jocasta Cameron, Jamie's aunt. Bree had rejected him, none too gently, and he had taken his revenge some time later by having her abducted by a notorious pirate. A very messy state of affairs had ensued, involving

Jamie's reciprocal abduction of Forbes's elderly mother—the old lady had loved the adventure—and the cutting off of Forbes's ear by Young Ian. Time might have healed his external wounds, but I couldn't imagine anyone less likely to have been singing Jamie's praises.

"Yes," said Miriam, but I didn't miss the uncertain look that passed between Mrs. Bell and Lillian.

"What, exactly, did Mr. Forbes say about me?" Jamie asked. All three of them went pale, and his eyebrows went up.

"What?" he repeated, with a definite edge. He said it directly to Mrs. Bell, whom he had instantly identified as the weakest link in the family chain.

"He said what a good thing it was that you were dead," that lady replied faintly. Whereupon her eyes rolled up into her head and she slumped to the floor like a bag of barleycorn.

FORTUNATELY, I HAD got a bottle of spirits of ammonia from Dr. Fentiman. This roused Mrs. Bell promptly into a sneezing fit, and her daughters helped her, gasping and choking, onto the bed. The wine fortunately arriving at this juncture, I served liberal helpings to everyone in sight, reserving a sizable mugful for myself.

"Now, then," Jamie said, giving the women the sort of slow, penetrating look intended to cause miscreants to go weak in the knees and confess everything, "tell me where ye heard Mr. Forbes say about my being dead."

Miss Lillian, settled on the bed with a protective hand on her mother's shoulder, spoke up.

"I heard him. In Symond's ordinary. While we were still in Wilmington—before we came here to live with Aunt Burton. I'd gone to get a pitcher of hot cider—it was sometime in February; it was still very cold out. Anyway, the woman—Faydree, she's called—she works there, and went to draw and heat the cider for me. Mr. Forbes came in while I was there, and spoke to me. He knew about Father, and was sympathetic, asking how we were managing . . . then Faydree came out with the pitcher, and he saw her."

Forbes had, of course, recognized Phaedre, whom he'd seen many times at River Run, Jocasta's plantation. Expressing great surprise at her presence, he had inquired for an explanation and received a suitably modified version of the truth—in which Phaedre had apparently made much of Jamie's kindness in securing her freedom.

I gurgled briefly in my mug at this. Phaedre knew exactly what had happened to Neil Forbes's ear. She was a very quiet, soft-spoken person, Phaedre, but not above sticking pins in people she didn't like—and I knew she didn't like Neil Forbes.

"Mr. Forbes was rather flushed—perhaps it was from the cold," Lillian said tactfully, "and he said, yes, he understood that Mr. Fraser had always had a great regard for Negroes. . . . I'm afraid he said that rather nastily," she added, with an apologetic look at Jamie. "And then he laughed, though he tried to pretend he was coughing, and said what a pity it was that you and your family had all been burnt to cinders, and no doubt there would be great lamentations in the slave quarter."

Jamie, who had been taking a swallow of wine, choked.

"Why did he think that?" I demanded. "Did he say?"

Lillian nodded earnestly.

"Yes, ma'am. Faydree asked him that, too—I think she thought he was only saying it to upset her—and he said he'd read it in the newspaper."

"The *Wilmington Gazette,*" Miriam put in, plainly not liking her sister to be hogging the limelight. "We don't read newspapers, of course, and since Daddy . . . well, we seldom have callers anymore." She glanced down involuntarily, her hand automatically pulling her neat apron straight, to hide a large patch on her skirt. The Bells were tidy and well-groomed, and their clothes had originally been of good quality but were growing noticeably threadbare round the hems and sleeves. I imagined that Mr. Bell's business affairs must have been substantially impaired, both by his absence and by the interference of war.

"My daughter had told me about the meeting." Mrs. Bell had recovered herself so far as to sit up, her cup of wine clasped carefully in both hands. "So when my neighbor told me last night that he had met you by the docks . . . well, I didn't know quite what to think, but supposed there had been a stupid mistake of some kind—really, you cannot believe anything you read these days, the newspapers are grown quite wild. And my neighbor mentioned that you were seeking passage to Scotland. So we began to think . . ." Her voice trailed off, and she dipped her face toward her wine cup, embarrassed.

Jamie rubbed a finger down his nose, thinking.

"Aye, well," he said slowly. "It's true that I mean to go to Scotland. And of course I should be pleased to inquire after your husband and assist him if I can. But I've no immediate prospect of obtaining passage. The blockade—"

"But we can get you a ship!" Lillian interrupted eagerly. "That's the point!"

"We think we can get you *to* a ship," Miriam corrected. She gave Jamie a considering, narrow-eyed sort of look, judging his character. He smiled faintly at her, acknowledging the scrutiny, and after a moment she returned the smile, grudging.

"You remind me of someone," she said. Evidently, whoever it was, it was someone she liked, though, for she nodded to her mother, giving permission. Mrs. Bell sighed, her shoulders slumping a little in relief.

"I do still have friends," she said, with a tinge of defiance. "In spite of . . . everything."

Among these friends was a man named DeLancey Hall, who owned a fishing ketch, and—like half the town, probably—augmented his income with the odd bit of smuggling.

Hall had told Mrs. Bell that he expected the arrival of a ship from England, coming into Wilmington sometime within the next week or so—always assuming that it hadn't been seized or sunk *en route.* As both ship and cargo were the property of one of the local Sons of Liberty, it could not venture into the Wilmington harbor, where two British warships were still crouched. It would, therefore, lurk just outside the harbor, where assorted small local craft would make rendezvous with it, unloading the cargo for surreptitious transport to shore. After which, the ship would sail north to New Haven, there to retrieve a cargo.

"And then will sail for Edinburgh!" Lillian put in, her face bright with hope.

"My father's kinsman there is named Andrew Bell,"

Miriam put in, lifting her chin a little. "He is very well known, I believe. He is a printer, and—"

"Wee Andy Bell?" Jamie's face had lighted up. "Him who printed the great encyclopedia?"

"The very man," Mrs. Bell said, surprised. "You do not mean to say you know him, Mr. Fraser?"

Jamie actually laughed, startling the Bells.

"Many's the evening I've passed in a tavern wi' Andy Bell," he assured them. "In fact, he's the man I mean to see in Scotland, for he's got my printing press, safe in his shop. Or at least I hope he does," he added, though his cheerfulness was unimpaired.

This news—along with a fresh round of wine—heartened the Bell women to an amazing extent, and when they left us at last, they were flushed with animation and chattering amongst themselves like a flock of amiable magpies. I glanced out the window and saw them making their way down the street, clustered together in hopeful excitement, staggering into the street occasionally from the effects of wine and emotion.

"We don't only sing but we dance just as good as we walk," I murmured, watching them go.

Jamie gave me a startled look.

"Archie Bell and the Drells," I explained. "Never mind. Do you think it's safe? This ship?"

"God, no." He shuddered, and kissed the top of my head. "Put aside the question of storms, woodworm, bad caulking, warped timbers, and the like, there's the English warships in the harbor, privateers outside the harbor—"

"I didn't mean that," I interrupted. "That's more or less par for the course, isn't it? I meant the owner—and this DeLancey Hall. Mrs. Bell thinks she knows what their politics are, but . . ." But the thought of delivering ourselves—and our gold—so completely into the hands of unknown persons was unsettling.

"But," he agreed. "Aye, I mean to go and speak to Mr. Hall first thing tomorrow morning. And maybe Monsieur Beauchamp, as well. For now, though—" He ran a hand lightly down my back and cupped my bottom. "Ian and the dog willna be back for an hour, at least. Will ye have another glass of wine?"

HE LOOKED LIKE a Frenchman, Jamie thought. Which was to say, thoroughly out of place in New Bern. Beauchamp had just come out of Thorogood Northrup's warehouse and stood in casual conversation with Northrup himself, the breeze off the water fluttering the silk ribbon that tied back his dark hair. Elegant, Claire had described him as, and he was that: not—not quite—foppish, but dressed with taste and expense. A good deal of expense, he thought.

"He looks like a Frenchman," Fergus observed, echoing his thoughts. They were seated next to the window in the Whinbush, a middling tavern that catered to the needs of fishermen and warehouse laborers, and whose atmosphere was composed of equal parts beer, sweat, tobacco, tar, and aged fish guts.

"Is that his ship?" Fergus asked, a frown creasing his brow as he nodded toward the very trim black-and-yellow sloop that rocked gently at anchor, some distance out.

"It's the ship he travels in. Couldna say whether he owns it. Ye dinna ken his face, though?"

Fergus leaned into the window, nearly flattening his own face against the wavery panes in an attempt to get a better look at Monsieur Beauchamp.

Jamie, beer in hand, studied Fergus's face in turn. Despite having lived in Scotland since the age of ten, and in America for the last ten years or more, Fergus himself still looked French, he thought. It was something more than a matter of feature; something in the bone itself, perhaps.

The bones of Fergus's face were pronounced, with a jaw sharp enough to cut paper, an imperiously beaked nose, and eye sockets set deep under the ridges of a high brow. The thick dark hair brushed back from that brow was threaded with gray, and it gave Jamie a queer moment to see that; he carried within himself a permanent image of Fergus as the ten-year-old orphaned pickpocket he had rescued from a Paris brothel, and that image sat oddly on the gaunt, handsome face before him.

"No," Fergus said at last, sitting back on the bench and shaking his head. "I have never seen him."

Fergus's deep-set dark eyes were alive with interest and

speculation. "No one else in the town knows him, either. Though I *have* heard that he had made inquiries for this Claudel Fraser"—his nostrils flared with amusement; Claudel was his own birth name, and the only one he had, though Jamie thought likely no one had ever used it outside Paris or anytime in the last thirty years—"in Halifax and Edenton, as well."

Jamie opened his mouth to observe that he hoped Fergus had been careful in his inquiries, but thought better of it, and drank his beer instead. Fergus hadn't been surviving as a printer in these troublous times by having a lack of discretion.

"Does he remind ye of anyone?" he asked instead. Fergus gave him a brief look of surprise, but returned to his neck-craning before settling back, shaking his head.

"No. Should he?"

"I dinna think so." He didn't, but was glad of Fergus's corroboration. Claire had told him her thought—that the man might be some relation of hers, perhaps a direct ancestor. She had tried to be casual about it, dismiss the idea even as she spoke it, but he'd seen the eager light in her eyes and been touched. The fact that she had no family or close kin in her own time had always struck him as a dreadful thing, even while he realized that it had much to do with her devotion to him.

He'd looked as carefully as he could, with that in mind, but saw nothing in Beauchamp's face or carriage that reminded him much of Claire—let alone Fergus.

He didn't think *that* thought—that Beauchamp might be some actual relation to himself—had crossed Fergus's mind. Jamie was reasonably sure that Fergus thought of the Frasers of Lallybroch as his only family, other than Marsali and the children, whom he loved with all the fervor of his passionate nature.

Beauchamp was taking his leave of Northrup now, with a very Parisian bow, accompanied by a graceful flutter of his silk handkerchief. Fortuitous that the man had happened to step out of the warehouse just in front of them, Jamie thought. They'd planned to go and have a keek at him later in the day, but his timely appearance saved them having to go and look for him.

"It's a good ship," Fergus observed, his attention deflected to the sloop called *Huntress.* He glanced back at Jamie, considering. "You're sure you do not wish to investigate the possibility of passage with Monsieur Beauchamp?"

"Aye, I'm sure," Jamie said dryly. "Put myself and my wife in the power of a man I dinna ken and whose motives are suspect, in a wee boat on a wide sea? Even a man who didna suffer from seasickness might boggle at that prospect, no?"

Fergus's face split in a grin.

"Milady proposes to stick you full of needles again?"

"She does," Jamie replied, rather crossly. He hated being stabbed repeatedly, and disliked being obliged to appear in public—even within the limited confines of a ship—bristling with spines like some outlandish porcupine. The only thing that would make him do it was the sure knowledge that if he didn't, he'd be puking his guts out for days on end.

Fergus didn't notice his discontent, though; he was leaning into the window again.

"Nom d'nom . . ." he said softly, with such an expression of apprehension that Jamie turned on the bench at once to look.

Beauchamp had proceeded some way down the street, but was still in sight. He had come to a stop, though, and appeared to be executing a sort of ungainly jig. This was sufficiently odd, but what was more disturbing was that Fergus's son Germain was crouched in the street directly in front of the man, and seemed to be hopping to and fro in the manner of an agitated toad.

These peculiar gyrations continued for a few seconds longer and then came to an end, Beauchamp now standing still, but waving his arms in expostulation, while Germain seemed to be groveling in front of the man. The boy stood up, though, tucking something into his shirt, and after a few moments' conversation, Beauchamp laughed and put out his hand. They exchanged a brief bow and handshake, and Germain came down the street toward the Whinbush while Beauchamp continued on his course.

Germain came in and, spotting them, slid onto the bench beside his father, looking pleased with himself.

"I've met that man," he said without preamble. "The man who wants Papa."

"Aye, we saw," Jamie said, brows raised. "What the devil were ye doing with him?"

"Well, I saw him coming, but I did not think he would stop and talk to me if I only shouted at him. So I tossed Simon and Peter into his path."

"Who—" Jamie began, but Germain was already groping within the depths of his shirt. Before Jamie could finish the sentence, the boy had produced two sizable frogs, one green and one a sort of vile yellow color, who huddled together on the bare boards of the table, goggling in a nervous manner.

Fergus cuffed Germain round the ear.

"Take those accursed creatures off the table, before we are thrown out of here. No wonder you are covered in warts, consorting with *les grenouilles*!"

"*Grandmère* told me to," Germain protested, nonetheless scooping up his pets and returning them to captivity.

"She did?" Jamie was not usually startled anymore by his wife's cures, but this seemed odd, even by her standards.

"Well, she said there was nothing to do for the wart on my elbow except rub it with a dead frog and bury it—the frog, I mean—at a crossroads at midnight."

"Oh. I think she might possibly have been being facetious. What did the Frenchman say to ye, then?"

Germain looked up, wide-eyed and interested.

"Oh, he's not a Frenchman, *Grandpère.*"

A brief pulse of astonishment went through him.

"He's not? Ye're sure?"

"Oh, aye. He cursed most blasphemous when Simon landed on his shoe—but not the way Papa does." Germain aimed a bland look at his father, who looked disposed to cuff him again, but desisted at Jamie's gesture. "He is an Englishman. I'm sure."

"He cursed *in* English?" Jamie asked. It was true; Frenchmen often invoked vegetables when cursing, not infrequently mingled with sacred references. English cursing generally had nothing to do with saints, sacraments, or cucumbers, but dealt with God, whores, or excrement.

"He did. But I cannot say *what* he said, or Papa will be offended. He has very pure ears, Papa," Germain added, with a smirk at his father.

"Leave off deviling your father and tell me what else the man said."

"Aye, well," Germain said obligingly. "When he saw it was no but a pair o' wee froggies, he laughed and asked me was I taking them home for my dinner. I said no, they were my pets, and asked him was it his ship out there, because everyone said so and it was a bonny thing, no? I was making out to be simple, aye?" he explained, in case his grandfather might not have grasped the stratagem.

Jamie suppressed a smile.

"Verra clever," he said dryly. "What else?"

"He said no, the ship is not his but belongs to a great nobleman in France. And I of course said, oh, who was that? And he said it is the Baron Amandine."

Jamie exchanged looks with Fergus, who looked surprised and raised one shoulder in a shrug.

"I asked then how long he might remain, for I should like to bring my brother down to see the ship. And he says he will sail tomorrow on the evening tide, and asked me—but he was joking, I could tell—if I wished to come and be a cabin boy on the voyage. I told him no, my frogs suffer from seasickness—like my grandfather." He turned the smirk on Jamie, who eyed him severely.

"Has your father taught ye *'Ne petez pas plus haute que votre cul'*?"

"Mama will wash your mouth out with soap if you say things like that," Germain informed him virtuously. "Do you want me to pick his pocket? I saw him go into the inn on Cherry Street. I could—"

"You could not," Fergus said hastily. "And do not say such things where people can hear. Your mother will assassinate both of us."

Jamie felt a cold prickle at the back of his neck, and glanced hastily round to make sure that no one *had* heard.

"Ye've been teaching him to—"

Fergus looked mildly shifty.

"I thought it a pity that the skills should be lost. It is a family legacy, you might say. I do not let him steal things, of course. We put them back."

"We'll have a word in private later, I think," Jamie said, giving the pair of them a look full of menace. Christ, if Germain had been caught at it . . . He'd best put the fear of God into the two of them before they both ended up pilloried, if not hanged from a tree outright for theft.

"What about the man you were actually *sent* to find?" Fergus asked his son, seizing the chance of deflecting Jamie's ire.

"I found him," Germain said, and nodded toward the door. "There he is."

DELANCEY HALL WAS a small, neat man, with the quiet, nose-twitching manner of a church mouse. Anything less like a smuggler to look at could scarcely have been imagined—which, Jamie thought, was likely a valuable attribute in that line of business.

"A shipper of dry goods" was the way Hall discreetly described his business. "I facilitate the finding of ships for specific cargoes. Which is no easy matter these days, gentlemen, as you may well suppose."

"I do indeed." Jamie smiled at the man. "I have nay cargo to ship, but I am in hopes that ye might know of a situation that would suit. Myself, my wife, and my nephew seek passage to Edinburgh." His hand was under the table, in his sporran. He had taken some of the gold spheres and flattened them with a hammer, into irregular disks. He took three of these and, moving only slightly, placed them on Hall's lap.

The man didn't change expression in the slightest, but Jamie felt the hand dart out and seize the disks, weigh them for an instant, and then vanish into his pocket.

"I think that might be possible," he said blandly. "I know a captain departing from Wilmington in about two weeks' time, who might be induced to carry passengers—for a consideration."

Sometime later, they walked back toward the printshop, Jamie and Fergus together, discussing the probabilities of Hall's being able to produce a ship. Germain wandered dreamily in front of them, zigzagging to and fro in response to whatever was going on inside his remarkably fertile brain.

Jamie's own brain was more than occupied. Baron Amandine. He knew the name, but had no face to go with it, nor did he recall the context in *which* he knew it. Only that he had encountered it at some point, in Paris. But when? When he had attended the *université* there . . . or later, when he and Claire—yes. That was it; he'd heard the name at court. But no matter how he cudgeled his brain, it would give up no further information.

"D'ye want me to speak to this Beauchamp?" Jamie asked abruptly. "I could perhaps find out what he means toward you."

Fergus's mouth drew in a bit, then relaxed as he shook his head.

"No," he said. "I said I had heard this man had made inquiries concerning me in Edenton?"

"Ye're sure it *is* you?" Not that the ground in North Carolina crawled with Claudels, but still . . .

"I think so, yes." Fergus spoke very softly, with an eye on Germain, who had started emitting soft croaks, evidently conversing with the frogs in his shirt. "The person who told me of this said that man had not only a name, but a small information, of sorts. That the Claudel Fraser he sought had been taken from Paris by a tall red-haired Scotsman. Named James Fraser. So I think you cannot speak to him, no."

"Not without exciting his attention, no," Jamie agreed. "But . . . we dinna ken what his purpose is, but it may be something of great advantage to ye, aye? How likely is it that someone in France would go to the trouble and expense of sending someone like him to do ye harm, when they could be content just to leave ye be in America?" He hesitated. "Perhaps . . . the Baron Amandine is some relation to ye?"

The notion seemed the stuff of romances, and likely the sheerest moonshine. But at the same time, Jamie was at a loss to think of some sensible reason for a French nobleman to be hunting a brothel-born bastard across two continents.

Fergus nodded, but didn't reply at once. He was wearing his hook today, rather than the bran-stuffed glove he wore for formal occasions, and delicately scratched his nose with the tip before answering.

"For a long time," he said at last, "when I was small, I pretended to myself that I was the bastard of some great man. All orphans do this, I think," he added dispassionately. "It makes life easier to bear, to pretend that it will not always be as it is, that someone will come and restore you to your rightful place in the world."

He shrugged.

"Then I grew older, and knew this was not true. No one would come to rescue me. But then—" He turned his head and gave Jamie a smile of surpassing sweetness.

"Then I grew older still, and discovered that, after all, it was true. I *am* the son of a great man."

The hook touched Jamie's hand, hard and capable.

"I wish for nothing more."

19

AE FOND KISS

Wilmington, colony of North Carolina
April 18, 1777

THE HEADQUARTERS of the *Wilmington Gazette* were easy to find. The embers had cooled, but the all-too-familiar reek of burning was still thick in the air. A roughly dressed gentleman in a slouch hat was poking through the charred timbers in a dubious way, but left off at Jamie's hailing him and made his way out of the wreckage, lifting his feet high in ginger avoidance.

"Are ye the proprietor of the newspaper, sir?" Jamie asked, extending a hand to help him over a pile of half-burnt books that sprawled over the threshold. "My sympathies, if so."

"Oh, no," the man replied, wiping smudges of soot from his fingers onto a large, filthy handkerchief, which he then passed to Jamie. "Amos Crupp, he'd be the printer. He's gone, though—lit out when they burnt the shop. I'm Herbert Longfield; I own the land. Did own the shop," he added, with a rueful glance behind him. "You wouldn't be a salvor, would you? Got a nice lump of iron, there."

Fergus and Marsali's printing press was now evidently the sole press in operation between Charleston and Newport. The *Gazette*'s press stood twisted and blackened amid the wreckage: still recognizable, but beyond salvage as anything save scrap.

"How long ago did it happen?" I asked.

"Night before last. Just after midnight. It was well a-gone before the bucket brigade could get started."

"An accident with the furnace?" Jamie asked. He bent and picked up one of the scattered pamphlets.

Longfield laughed cynically.

"Not from around here, are you? You said you were looking for Amos?" He glanced warily from Jamie to me and back again. He wasn't likely to confide anything to strangers of unknown political affiliations.

"James Fraser," Jamie said, reaching out to shake his hand firmly. "My wife, Claire. Who was it? The Sons of Liberty?"

Longfield's eyebrows arched high.

"You really aren't from around here." He smiled, but not happily. "Amos was with the Sons. Not quite one of 'em, maybe, but of their mind. I told him to walk a narrow road with what he wrote and what he printed in the paper, and he mostly tried. But these days, it doesn't take much. A whisper of treason, and a man's beaten half to death in the street, tarred and feathered, burnt out—killed, even."

He eyed Jamie consideringly.

"So you didn't know Amos. May I ask what your business with him was?"

"I had a question regarding a bit of news that was published in the *Gazette.* Ye say Crupp's gone. D'ye ken where I might find him? I mean him nay ill," he added.

Mr. Longfield glanced thoughtfully at me, apparently gauging the prospects that a man bound on political violence would bring his wife along. I smiled, trying to look as respectably charming as possible, and he smiled uncertainly back. He had a long upper lip that gave him the aspect of a rather worried camel, this being substantially enhanced by his eccentric dentition.

"No, I don't," he said, turning back to Jamie with the air of a man making up his mind. "He did have a business partner, though, and a devil. Might be that one of them would know what you're looking for?"

Now it was Jamie's turn to size up Longfield. He made his own mind up in an instant, and handed the pamphlet to me.

"It might be. A small item of news regarding a house fire in the mountains was published last year. I wish to discover who might have given that item to the newspaper."

Longfield frowned, puzzled, and scratched at his long upper lip, leaving a smudge of soot.

"I don't recall that, myself. But then—well, I tell you what, sir. I was bound to see George Humphries—that's Amos's business partner—after looking over the premises . . ." He looked over his shoulder, grimacing. "Why don't you come along with me and ask your question?"

"That's most obliging of ye, sir." Jamie flicked an eyebrow at me, as a signal that I was no longer required for window dressing and thus might go about my own business. I wished Mr. Longfield good day, accordingly, and went to forage in the fleshpots of Wilmington.

Business here was somewhat better than it was in New Bern. Wilmington had a deepwater harbor, and while the English blockade had of necessity affected importing and exporting, local boats and coastal packets still came into the port. Wilmington also was substantially larger and still boasted a thriving market in the town square, where I spent a pleasant hour collecting herbs and picking up local gossip, before acquiring a cheese roll for my lunch, whereupon I wandered down to the harbor to eat it.

I strolled casually along, hoping to spot the vessel that might be carrying us to Scotland, but saw nothing at anchor that looked in any way large enough for such a voyage. But of course—DeLancey Hall had said that we would need to embark on a small ship, perhaps his own fishing ketch, and slip out of the harbor to rendezvous with the larger ship at sea.

I sat down on a bollard to eat, drawing a small crowd of interested seagulls, who floated down like overweight snowflakes to surround me.

"Think again, mate," I said, pointing a monitory finger at one particularly intransigent specimen, who was sidling toward my feet, eyeing my basket. "It's *my* lunch." I still had the half-burnt pamphlet Jamie had handed me; I flapped it vigorously at the gulls, who whirled up in a screech of alarm but then resettled round me, at a slightly more respectful distance, beady eyes all focused on the roll in my hand.

"Ha," I said to them, and moved the basket behind my feet, just in case. I kept a good grip on my roll and one eye on the gulls. The other was free to survey the harbor. A British man-of-war was anchored a little way out, and the sight of the Union Jack flying from its bow gave me a peculiarly paradoxical feeling of pride and unease.

The pride was reflexive. I'd been an Englishwoman all my life. I'd served Great Britain in hospitals, on battlefields—in duty and with honor—and I'd seen many of my countrymen and women fall in that same service. While the Union Jack I saw now was slightly different in design to the one I'd lived with, it was identifiably the same flag, and I felt the same instinctive lift of the heart at sight of it.

At the same time, I was all too aware of the menace that that flag now posed to me and mine. The ship's upper gunports were open; evidently some drill was being conducted, for I saw the cannon rolled rapidly in and out, in succession, blunt snouts poking out, then drawing in, like the heads of pugnacious gophers. There had been *two* men-of-war in the harbor the day before; the other had gone . . . where? On a particular mission—or merely cruising restlessly up and down outside the harbor mouth, ready to board, seize, fire upon, or sink any ship that looked suspicious?

I couldn't think of anything that would look more suspicious than the ship belonging to Mr. Hall's smuggling friend.

I thought again of the mysterious Mr. Beauchamp. France was still neutral; we would be a good deal safer in a ship flying French colors. Safer from the depredations of the British Navy, at least. As for Beauchamp's own motives . . . I reluctantly accepted Fergus's desire to have nothing to do with the man, but still wondered what on earth Beauchamp's interest in Fergus could be.

I also still wondered whether he might have any connection to my own family of Beauchamps, but there was no way of knowing; Uncle Lamb had done a rudimentary family genealogy, I knew—mostly for my sake—but I'd paid no attention to it. Where was it now? I wondered. He'd given it to me and Frank when we married, neatly typed up and put in a manila folder.

Perhaps I'd mention Mr. Beauchamp in my next letter to Brianna. She'd have all our old family records—the boxes of ancient income-tax forms, the collections of her own schoolwork and art projects. . . . I smiled at the memory of the clay dinosaur she'd made at the age of eight, a toothy creature leaning drunkenly to one side, a small cylindrical object hanging from its jaws.

"That's a mammal he's eating," she had informed me.

"What happened to the mammal's legs?" I'd asked.

"They fell off when the dinosaur stepped on it."

The memory had distracted me for a moment, and a bold gull swooped low and struck my hand, knocking the last remnant of my roll to the ground, where it was instantly engulfed by a shrieking crowd of its fellows.

I said a bad word—the gull had left a bleeding scratch across the back of my hand—and, picking up the pamphlet, flung it into the midst of the scrabbling birds. It hit one of them in the head, and the bird rolled over in a mad flutter of wings and pages that dispersed the mob, who all flapped off, yelling gull curses, leaving not a crumb behind.

"Ha," I said again, with a certain grim satisfaction. With some obscure twentieth-century inhibition against littering—certainly no such notions existed here—I retrieved the pamphlet, which had come apart into several pieces, and tidied them back into a rough rectangle.

An Examination of Mercy, it was titled, with a subtitle reading, *Thoughts upon the Nature of Divine Compassion, its Manifestation within the Human Bosom, and the Instruction of its Inspiration to the Improvement of the Individual and Mankind.* Possibly not one of Mr. Crupp's bestselling titles, I thought, stuffing it into the end of my basket.

Which led me to another thought. I wondered whether Roger would see it in an archive someday. I rather thought he might.

Did that mean that we—or I—ought to be doing things on purpose to ensure our appearance in said record? Given that most of the things that made the press in any era were war, crime, tragedy, and other hideous disasters, I rather thought not. My few brushes with notoriety had not been pleasant, and the last thing I wanted Roger to find was a report of my being hanged for bank robbery, executed for witchcraft, or having been pecked to death by vengeful gulls.

No, I concluded. I'd best just tell Bree about Mr. Beauchamp and the Beauchamp family genealogy, and if Roger wanted to poke about in *that,* well and good. Granted, I'd never know if he found Mr. Percival in the list, but if so, Jem and Mandy would have a little further knowledge of their family tree.

Now, where was it, that folder? The last time I'd seen it, it had been in Frank's office, sitting on his filing cabinet. I remembered it distinctly, because Uncle Lamb had rather whimsically drawn what I assumed to be the family coat of—

"I beg your pardon, madam," a deep voice said respectfully behind me. "I see that you—"

Jarred abruptly from my memory, I turned blankly toward the voice, thinking vaguely that I knew—

"Jesus H. Roosevelt Christ!" I blurted, leaping to my feet. "You!"

I took a step backward, stumbled over the basket, and nearly fell into the harbor, saved only by Tom Christie's instinctive grab for my arm.

He jerked me away from the edge of the quay and I fell against his chest. He recoiled as though I were made of molten metal, then seized me in his arms, pressed me hard against himself, and kissed me with passionate abandon.

He broke off, peered into my face, and gasped, "You're dead!"

"Well, no," I said, stunned into apology.

"I beg—I beg your pardon," he managed, letting his arms drop. "I—I—I—" He looked white as a ghost, and I rather thought *he* might fall into the harbor. I doubted that I looked much better, but I did at least have my feet under me.

"You'd better sit down," I said.

"I—not here," he said abruptly.

He was right. The quay was a *very* public place, and our little *rencontre* had attracted considerable notice. A couple of idlers were staring openly, nudging each other, and we were collecting slightly less-obvious glances from the traffic of merchants, seamen, and dock laborers going about their business. I was beginning to recover from the shock, enough to think.

"You have a room? Oh, no—that won't do, will it?" I could imagine all too well what sorts of stories would be flying round town within minutes of our leaving the docks; if we left and repaired to Mr. Christie's—I couldn't think of him presently as anything but "Mr. Christie"—room . . .

"The ordinary," I said firmly. "Come on."

IT WAS ONLY A FEW minutes' walk to Symonds' ordinary, and we passed those minutes in total silence. I stole occasional glances at him, though, both to assure myself that he *wasn't* a ghost and to assess his current situation.

The latter seemed tolerable; he was decently dressed in a dark gray suit, with clean linen, and if he was not fashionable—I bit my lip at the thought of Tom Christie being fashionable—he was at least not shabby.

Otherwise, he looked very much as I'd last seen him—well, no, I corrected myself. He actually looked much better. I'd last seen him in the extremity of exhausted grief, shredded by the tragedy of his daughter's death and its subsequent complications. My last sight of him had been on the *Cruizer,* the British ship on which Governor Martin had taken refuge when he was driven out of the colony, almost two years ago.

At that point, Mr. Christie had declared, first, his intent to confess to the murder of his daughter—of which I was accused—secondly, his love for me, and thirdly, his intent to be executed in my place. All of which made his sudden resurrection not merely surprising but more than slightly awkward.

Adding to the awkwardness was the question as to what—if anything—he knew about the fate of his son, Allan, who *had* been responsible for Malva Christie's death. The circumstances were nothing that any father ought to have to hear, and panic gripped me at the thought that I might have to tell him.

I glanced at him again. His face was deeply lined, but he was neither gaunt nor overtly haunted. He wore no wig, though his wiry salt-and-pepper hair was close-clipped as always, matching his neatly trimmed beard. My face tingled, and I barely kept myself from scrubbing my hand across my mouth to erase the feeling. He was clearly disturbed—well, so was I—but had got himself back under control, and opened the door of the ordinary for me with impeccable courtesy. Only the twitch of a muscle beside his left eye betrayed him.

I felt as though my entire body was twitching, but Phaedre, serving in the taproom, glanced at me with no more than mild interest and a cordial nod. Of course, she'd never met Thomas Christie, and while she'd doubtless heard about the scandal following my arrest, she wouldn't connect the gentleman accompanying me with it.

We found a table by the window in the dining room, and sat down.

"I thought you were dead," I said abruptly. "What did you mean, you thought *I* was dead?"

He opened his mouth to answer but was interrupted by Phaedre, who came to serve us, smiling pleasantly.

"I get you something, sir, ma'am? You wanting food? We've a nice ham today, roast taters, and Mrs. Symonds's special mustard 'n raisin sauce to go along of it."

"No," Mr. Christie said. "I—just a cup of cider, if ye please."

"Whisky," I said. "A lot of it."

Mr. Christie looked scandalized, but Phaedre only laughed and whisked off, the grace of her movement attracting the quiet admiration of most of the male patrons.

"Ye haven't changed," he observed. His eyes traveled over me, intense, taking in every detail of my appearance. "I ought to have known ye by your hair."

His voice was disapproving, but tinged with a reluctant amusement; he had always been vociferous in his disapproval of my refusal to wear a cap or otherwise restrain my hair. "Wanton," he'd called it.

"Yes, you should," I said, reaching up to smooth the hair in question, which was considerably the worse for recent encounters. "You didn't recognize me 'til I turned round, though, did you? What made you speak to me?"

He hesitated, but then nodded toward my basket, which I'd set on the floor beside my chair.

"I saw that ye had one of my tracts."

"What?" I said blankly, but looked where he was looking and saw the singed pamphlet on *Divine Compassion* sticking out from under a cabbage. I reached down and pulled it out, only now noticing the author: *by Mr. T. W. Christie, MA, University of Edinburgh.*

"What does the 'W' stand for?" I asked, laying it down.

He blinked.

"Warren," he replied rather gruffly. "Where in God's name did ye come from?"

"My father always claimed he'd found me under a cabbage leaf in the garden," I replied flippantly. "Or did you mean today? If so—the King's Arms."

He was beginning to look a little less shocked, his normal irritation at my lack of womanly decorum drawing his face back into its usual stern lines.

"Don't be facetious. I was told that ye were dead," he said, accusingly. "You and your entire family were burnt up in a fire."

Phaedre, delivering the drinks, glanced at me, eyebrows raised.

"She ain't looking too crispy round the edges, sir, if you pardon my mention of it."

"Thank ye for the observation," he said between his teeth. Phaedre exchanged a glance of amusement with me, and went off again, shaking her head.

"Who told you that?"

"A man named McCreary."

I must have looked blank, for he added, "from Brownsville. I met him here—in Wilmington, I mean—in late January. He had just come down from the mountain, he said, and told me of the fire. *Was* there a fire?"

"Well, yes, there was," I said slowly, wondering whether—and how much—to tell him of the truth of *that.* Very little, in a public place, I decided. "Maybe it was Mr. McCreary, then, who placed the notice of the fire in the newspaper—but he can't have." The original notice had appeared in 1776, Roger had said—nearly a year before the fire.

"I placed it," Christie said. Now it was my turn to blink.

"You what? When?" I took a good-sized mouthful of whisky, feeling that I needed it more than ever.

"Directly I heard of it. Or—well, no," he corrected. "A few days thereafter. I . . . was very much distressed at the news," he added, lowering his eyes and looking away from me for the first time since we'd sat down.

"Ah. I'm sorry," I said, lowering my own voice, and feeling rather apologetic—though why I should feel apologetic for not having been burnt up . . .

He cleared his throat.

"Yes. Well. It, er, seemed to me that some . . . something should be done. Some formal observance of your—your passing." He looked up then, gray eyes direct. "I could not abide the thought that you—all of you," he added, but it was clearly an afterthought, "should simply vanish from the earth, with no formal marking of the—the event."

He took a deep breath, and a tentative sip of the cider.

"Even if a proper funeral had been held, there would be no point in my returning to Fraser's Ridge, even if I—well. I could not. So I thought I would at least make a record of the event here. After all," he added more softly, looking away again, "I could not lay flowers on your grave."

The whisky had steadied me a bit, but also rasped my throat and made it difficult to talk when hampered by emotion. I reached out and touched his hand briefly, then cleared my throat, finding momentarily neutral ground.

"Your hand," I said. "How is it?"

He looked up, surprised, but the taut lines of his face relaxed a bit.

"Very well, I thank you. See?" He turned over his right hand, displaying a large Z-shaped scar upon the palm, well healed but still pink.

"Let me see."

His hand was cold. With an assumption of casualness, I took it in mine, turning it, bending the fingers to assess their flexibility and degree of movement. He was right: it *was* doing well; the movement was nearly normal.

"I—did the exercises you set me," he blurted. "I do them every day."

I looked up to find him regarding me with a sort of anguished solemnity, his cheeks now flushed above his beard, and realized that this ground was not nearly so neutral as I'd thought. Before I could let go his hand, it turned in mine, covering my fingers—not tightly, but sufficiently that I couldn't free myself without a noticeable effort.

"Your husband." He stopped dead, having obviously not thought of Jamie at all to this point. "He is alive, too?"

"Er, yes."

To his credit, he didn't grimace at this news, but nodded, exhaling.

"I am—glad to hear it."

He sat in silence for a moment, looking at his undrunk cider. He was still holding my hand. Without looking up, he said in a low voice, "Does he . . . know? What I—how I—I did not tell him the reason for my confession. Did you?"

"You mean your"—I groped for some suitable way of putting it—"your, um, very gallant feelings toward me? Well, yes, he does; he was very sympathetic toward you. He knowing from experience what it's like to be in love with me, I mean," I added tartly.

He almost laughed at that, which gave me an opportunity to extricate my fingers. He did not, I noticed, inform me that he *wasn't* in love with me any longer. Oh, dear.

"Well, anyway, we aren't dead," I said, clearing my throat again. "What about you? Last time I saw you . . ."

"Ah." He looked less than happy, but gathered himself, changing gears, and nodded. "Your rather hasty departure from the *Cruizer* left Governor Martin without an amanuensis. Discovering that I was to some degree literate"—his mouth twisted a little—"and could write a fair hand, thanks to your ministrations, he had me removed from the brig."

I wasn't surprised at that. Driven completely out of his colony, Governor Martin was obliged to conduct his business from the tiny captain's cabin of the British ship on which he had taken refuge. Such business perforce consisted entirely of letters—all of which must be not only composed, drafted, and fair-copied but then reproduced several times each. A copy was required first for the governor's own official correspondence files, then for each person or entity having some interest in the subject of the letter, and, finally, several additional copies of any letters going to England or Europe must be made, because they would be sent by different ships, in hopes that at least one copy would make it through, should the others be sunk, seized by pirates or privateers, or otherwise lost in transit.

My hand ached at the mere memory of it. The exigencies of bureaucracy in a time before the magic of Xerox had kept me from rotting in a cell; no wonder they had freed Tom Christie from durance vile as well.

"You see?" I said, rather pleased. "If I hadn't fixed your hand, he'd likely have had you either executed on the spot or at least sent back to shore and immured in some dungeon."

"I am duly grateful," he said, with extreme dryness. "I was not, at the time."

Christie had spent several months as *de facto* secretary to the governor. In late November, though, a ship had arrived from England, bearing orders to the governor—essentially ordering him to subdue the colony, though offering no troops, armament, or useful suggestions as to how this might be managed—and an official secretary.

"At this point, the governor was faced with the prospect of disposing of me. We had . . . become acquainted, working in such close quarters . . ."

"And as you were no longer quite an anonymous murderer, he didn't want to yank the quill out of your hand and hang you from the yardarm," I finished for him. "Yes, he's actually rather a kind man."

"He is," Christie said thoughtfully. "He has not had an easy time of it, poor fellow."

I nodded. "He told you about his little boys?"

"Aye, he did." His lips compressed—not out of anger, but to control his own emotion. Martin and his wife had lost three small sons, one after another, to the plagues and fevers of the colony; small wonder if hearing of the governor's pain had reopened Tom Christie's own wounds. He shook his head a little, though, and returned to the subject of his deliverance.

"I had . . . told him a bit about . . . about my daughter." He picked up the barely touched cup of cider and drank half of it off at a swallow, as if dying of thirst. "I admitted privately to him that my confession had been false—though I stated also that I was certain of your innocence," he assured me. "And if you should ever be arrested again for the crime, my confession would stand."

"Thank you for that," I said, and wondered with still

greater uneasiness whether he knew who *had* killed Malva. He had to have suspected, I thought—but that was a long way from having to know, let alone having to know why. And no one knew where Allan was now—save me, Jamie, and Young Ian.

Governor Martin had received this admission with some relief, and decided that the only thing to do in the circumstances was to put Christie ashore, there to be dealt with by the civil authorities.

"There *aren't* any civil authorities anymore," I said. "Are there?"

He shook his head.

"None capable of dealing with such a matter. There are still gaols and sheriffs, but neither courts nor magistrates. Under the circumstances"—he almost smiled, dour though the expression was—"I thought it a waste of time to try to find someone to whom to surrender myself."

"But you said you had sent a copy of your confession to the newspaper," I said. "Weren't you, er, received coldly by the people in New Bern?"

"By the grace of divine Providence, the newspaper there had ceased its operations before my confession was received by them, the printer being a Loyalist. I believe Mr. Ashe and his friends called upon him, and he wisely decided to find another mode of business."

"Very wise," I said dryly. John Ashe was a friend of Jamie's, a leading light of the local Sons of Liberty, and the man who had instigated the burning of Fort Johnston and effectively driven Governor Martin into the sea.

"There was some gossip," he said, looking away again, "but it was overwhelmed by the rush of public events. No one quite knew what had happened on Fraser's Ridge, and after a time it became fixed in everyone's mind simply that some personal tragedy had befallen me. People came to regard me with a sort of . . . sympathy." His mouth twisted; he wasn't the sort to receive sympathy with any graciousness.

"You seem to be thriving," I said, with a nod at his suit. "Or at least you aren't sleeping in the gutter and living off discarded fish heads from the docks. I had no idea that the tract-writing business was profitable."

He'd gone back to his normal color during the previous

conversation, but flushed up again at this—with annoyance, this time.

"It isn't," he snapped. "I take pupils. And I—I preach of a Sunday."

"I can't imagine anyone better for the job," I said, amused. "You've always had a talent for telling everyone what's wrong with them in Biblical terms. Have you become a clergyman, then?"

His color grew deeper, but he choked down his choler and answered me evenly.

"I was nearly destitute upon my arrival here. Fish heads, as you say—and the occasional bit of bread or soup given by a New Light congregation. I came in order to eat, but remained for the service out of courtesy. I thus heard a sermon given by the Reverend Peterson. It—remained with me. I sought him out, and we . . . spoke. One thing led to another." He glanced up at me, his eyes fierce. "The Lord does answer prayer, ye know."

"What had you prayed for?" I asked, intrigued.

That took him back a bit, though it had been an innocent question, asked from simple curiosity.

"I—I—" He broke off and stared at me, frowning. "You are a most uncomfortable woman!"

"You wouldn't be the first person to think so," I assured him. "And I don't mean to pry. I just . . . wondered."

I could see the urge to get up and leave warring with the compulsion to bear witness to whatever had happened to him. But he was a stubborn man, and he stayed put.

"I . . . asked why," he said at last, very evenly. "That's all."

"Well, it worked for Job," I observed. He looked startled, and I nearly laughed; he was always startled at the revelation that anyone other than himself had read the Bible. He got a grip, though, and glowered at me in something more like his usual fashion.

"And now you are here," he said, making it sound like an accusation. "I suppose your husband has formed a militia—or joined one. I have had enough of war. I am surprised that your husband has not."

"I don't think it's precisely a taste for war," I said. I spoke with an edge, but something in him compelled me to add, "It's that he feels he was born to it."

Something flickered deep in Tom Christie's eyes—surprise? Acknowledgment?

"He is," he said quietly. "But surely—" He didn't finish the thought, but instead asked abruptly, "What are you doing here, though? In Wilmington?"

"Looking for a ship," I said. "We're going to Scotland."

I'd always had a talent for startling him, but this one took the biscuit. He had lifted his mug to drink, but upon hearing my declaration, abruptly spewed cider across the table. The subsequent choking and wheezing attracted a good bit of attention, and I sat back, trying to look less conspicuous.

"Er . . . we'll be going to Edinburgh, for my husband's printing press," I said. "Is there anyone you'd like me to see for you? Deliver a message, I mean? You have a brother there, I think you said."

His head shot up and he glared at me, eyes streaming. I felt a spasm of horror at the sudden recollection and could have bitten my tongue off at the root. His brother had had an affair with Tom's wife while Tom was imprisoned in the Highlands after the Rising, and his wife had then poisoned his brother and subsequently been executed for witchcraft.

"I'm so sorry," I said, low-voiced. "Forgive me, please. I didn't—"

He seized my hand in both of his, so hard and so abruptly that I gasped, and a few heads turned curiously in our direction. He paid no attention, but leaned toward me across the table.

"Listen to me," he said, low and fierce. "I have loved three women. One was a witch and a whore, the second only a whore. Ye well may be a witch yourself, but it makes nay whit o' difference. The love of you has led me to my salvation, and to what I thought was my peace, once I thought ye dead."

He stared at me and shook his head slowly, his mouth going tight for a moment in the seam of his beard.

"And here you are."

"Er . . . yes." I felt once more as though I should apologize for not being dead, but didn't.

He drew a deep breath and let it out in a sigh.

"I shall have no peace while ye live, woman."

Then he lifted my hand and kissed it, stood up, and walked away.

"Mind," he said, turning at the door to look back at me over his shoulder, "I dinna say I regret it."

I picked up the glass of whisky and drained it.

I WENT ABOUT THE rest of my errands in a daze—not entirely induced by whisky. I hadn't any idea what to think of the resurrection of Tom Christie, but was thoroughly unsettled by it. Still, there seemed nothing, really, to *do* about him, and so I went on to the shop of Stephen Moray, a silversmith from Fife, to commission a pair of surgical scissors. Luckily, he proved an intelligent man, who appeared to understand both my specifications and the purpose behind them, and promised to have the scissors made within three days. Heartened by this, I ventured a slightly more problematic commission.

"Needles?" Moray knit his white brows in puzzlement. "Ye dinna require a silversmith for—"

"Not sewing needles. These are longer, quite thin, and without an eye. They have a medical purpose. And I should like you to make them from this."

His eyes went wide as I laid what appeared to be a gold nugget the size of a walnut on the counter. It was in fact a bit of one of the French ingots, hacked off and hammered into a lump, then rubbed with dirt by way of disguise.

"My husband won it in a card game," I said, with the tone of mingled pride and apology that seemed appropriate to such an admission. I didn't want anyone thinking that there was gold on Fraser's Ridge—in any form. Boosting Jamie's reputation as a card player wasn't likely to do any harm; he was already well known—if not quite notorious—for his abilities in that line.

Moray frowned a bit over the written specifications for the acupuncture needles, but agreed to make them. Luckily, he appeared never to have heard of voodoo dolls, or I might have had a bit more trouble.

With the visit to the silversmith and a quick trip through the market square for spring onions, cheese, peppermint leaves, and anything else available in the herbal line, it was late afternoon before I came back to the King's Arms.

Jamie was playing cards in the taproom, with Young Ian watching over his shoulder, but he saw me come in and, giving over his hand to Ian, came to take my basket, following me up the stairs to our room.

I turned round inside the door, but before I could speak, he said, "I know Tom Christie's alive. I met him in the street."

"He kissed me," I blurted.

"Aye, I heard," he said, eyeing me with what might have been amusement. For some reason, I found that very annoying. He saw *that,* and the amusement deepened.

"Like it, did ye?"

"It wasn't funny!"

The amusement didn't go away, but it retreated a bit.

"*Did* ye like it?" he repeated, but now there was curiosity in his voice, rather than teasing.

"No." I turned away abruptly. "That—I hadn't time to . . . to think about it."

Without warning, he put a hand behind my neck and kissed me briefly. And by simple reflex, I slapped him. Not hard—I'd tried to pull back even as I struck—and clearly I hadn't hurt him. I was as surprised and discomfited as though I'd knocked him flat.

"Doesna take much thought, does it?" he said lightly, and stepped back, surveying me with interest.

"I'm sorry," I said, feeling simultaneously mortified and angry—and angrier still in that I didn't understand why I *was* angry in the slightest. "I didn't mean to—I'm sorry."

He tilted his head to one side, eyeing me.

"Had I better go and kill him?"

"Oh, don't be ridiculous." I fidgeted, untying my pocket, not wanting to meet his eyes. I was prickly, discomfited, irritated—and the more discomfited by not really knowing *why.*

"It was an honest question, Sassenach," he said quietly. "Not a serious one, maybe—but honest. I think ye maybe owe me an honest answer."

"Of course I don't want you to kill him!"

"D'ye want me to tell you why ye slapped me, instead?"

"Why—" I stood with my mouth open for a second, then closed it. "Yes. I do."

"I touched ye against your will," he said, his eyes intent on mine. "Didn't I?"

"You did," I said, and breathed a little easier. "And so did Tom Christie. And, no, I *didn't* like it."

"But not on Tom's account," he finished. "Poor fellow."

"He wouldn't want your sympathy," I said tartly, and he smiled.

"He would not. But he's got it, nonetheless. Still, I'm glad of it," he added.

"Glad of what? That he's alive—or—surely not that he thinks he's in love with me?" I said, incredulous.

"Dinna belittle his feelings, Sassenach," he said, more quietly. "He's laid down his life for ye once. I'd trust him to do it again."

"I didn't want him to do it the first time!"

"You're bothered," he said, in a tone of clinical interest.

"Yes, I am bloody bothered!" I said. "And"—the thought struck me and I gave him a hard look—"so are you." I recalled suddenly that he'd said he'd met Tom Christie in the street. What had Tom said to him?

He tilted his head in mild negation, but didn't deny it.

"I willna say I *like* Thomas Christie," he said consideringly, "but I respect him. And I *am* verra much pleased to find him alive. Ye didna do wrong to grieve him, Sassenach," he said gently. "I did, too."

"I hadn't even thought of that." In the shock of seeing him, I hadn't remembered, but I'd wept for him—and for his children. "I don't regret it, though."

"Good. The thing about Tom Christie," he went on, "is that he wants ye. Badly. But he doesna ken a thing about you."

"And you do." I left it somewhere between question and challenge, and he smiled. He turned and shot the bolt on the door, then crossed the room and drew the calico curtain on the one small window, casting the room into a pleasant blue dimness.

"Oh, I've need and want in plenty—but I've knowing, too." He was standing very close, close enough that I had to look up to him. "I've never kissed ye without knowing who ye were—and that's a thing poor Tom will never know." God, what *had* Tom told him?

My pulse, which had been jumping up and down, settled down to a quick, light thump, discernible in my fingertips.

"You didn't know a thing about me when you married me."

His hand closed gently on my behind.

"No?"

"Besides that, I mean!"

He made a small Scottish sound in his throat, not quite a chuckle.

"Aye, well, it's a wise man who kens what he doesna know—and I learn fast, *a nighean.*"

He drew me gently close then, and kissed me—with thought and tenderness, with knowing—and with my full consent. It didn't obliterate my memory of Tom Christie's impassioned, blundering embrace, and I thought it wasn't meant to; it was meant to show me the difference.

"You *can't* be jealous," I said, a moment later.

"I can," he said, not joking.

"You can't possibly think—"

"I don't."

"Well, then—"

"Well, then." His eyes were dark as seawater in the dimness, but the expression in them was entirely readable, and my heart beat faster. "I ken what ye feel for Tom Christie—and he told me plain what he feels for you. Surely ye ken that love's nothing to do wi' logic, Sassenach?"

Knowing a rhetorical question when I heard one, I didn't bother answering that, but instead reached out and tidily unbuttoned his shirt. There was nothing I could reasonably say about Tom Christie's feelings, but I had another language in which to express my own. His heart was beating fast; I could feel it as though I held it in my hand. Mine was, too, but I breathed deep and took comfort in the warm familiarity of his body, the soft crispness of the cinnamon-colored hairs of his chest, and the gooseflesh that raised them under my fingers. While I was thus engaged, he slid his fingers into my hair, separating a lock which he viewed appraisingly.

"It's not gone white yet. I suppose I've a little time, then, before ye get too dangerous for me to bed."

"Dangerous, forsooth," I said, setting to work on the buttons of his breeks. I wished he had on his kilt. "Exactly what do you think I might do to you in bed?"

He scratched his chest consideringly, and rubbed absently at the tiny knot of scar tissue where he'd cut Jack Randall's brand from his flesh.

"Well, so far, ye've clawed me, bitten me, stabbed me—more than once—and—"

"I have not stabbed you!"

"Ye did, too," he informed me. "Ye stabbed me in the backside wi' your nasty wee needle spikes—fifteen times! I counted—and then a dozen times or more in the leg with a rattlesnake's fang."

"I was saving your bloody life!"

"I didna say otherwise, did I? Ye're no going to deny ye enjoyed it, though, are ye?"

"Well . . . not the rattlesnake fang, so much. As for the hypodermic . . ." My mouth twitched, despite myself. "You deserved it."

He gave me a look of profound cynicism.

"Do nay harm, is it?"

"Besides, you were counting what I'd done to you in bed," I said, neatly returning to the point. "You can't count the shots."

"I was in bed!"

"I wasn't!"

"Aye, ye took unfair advantage," he said, nodding. "I wouldna hold that against ye, though."

He'd got my jacket off and was busily untying my laces, head bent in absorption.

"How'd you like it if *I* were jealous?" I asked the crown of his head.

"I'd like that fine," he replied, breath warm on my exposed flesh. "And ye were. Of Laoghaire." He looked up, grinning, eyebrow raised. "Maybe ye still are?"

I slapped him again, and this time I meant it. He could have stopped me but didn't.

"Aye, that's what I thought," he said, wiping a watering eye. "Will ye come to bed wi' me, then? It'll be just us," he added.

IT WAS LATE WHEN I woke; the room was dark, though a slice of fading sky showed at the top of the curtain. The fire hadn't yet been lit and the room was chilly, but it was warm and cozy under the quilts, snug against Jamie's body. He had turned onto his side, and I curled spoonlike against his back and put my arm over him, feeling the gentle rise and fall of his breath.

It *had* been just us. I'd worried, at the start, that the memory of Tom Christie and his awkward passion might fall between us—but Jamie, evidently thinking the same thing and determined to avoid any echo of Tom's embrace that might remind me, had started at the other end, kissing my toes.

Given the size of the room and the fact that the bed was jammed tightly into one end of it, he had been obliged to straddle me in order to do this, and the combination of having my feet nibbled and the view from directly behind and beneath a naked Scotsman had been sufficient to remove anything else from my head.

Warm, safe, and calm now, I could think about the earlier encounter without feeling threatened, though. And I *had* felt threatened. Jamie had seen that. *D'ye want me to tell you why ye slapped me? . . . I touched ye against your will.*

He was right; it was one of the minor aftereffects of what had happened to me when I had been abducted. Crowds of men made me nervous with no cause, and being grabbed unexpectedly made me recoil and jerk away in panic. Why hadn't I seen that?

Because I didn't want to think about it, that's why. I still didn't. What good would thinking do? Let things heal on their own, if they would.

But even things that heal leave scars. The evidence of that was literally in front of my face—pressed against it, in fact.

The scars on Jamie's back had faded into a pale spiderweb, with only a slight raised bit here or there, ridged under my fingers when we made love, like barbed wire beneath his skin. I remembered Tom Christie taunting him about them once, and my jaw tightened.

I laid a hand softly on his back, tracing one pale loop with my thumb. He twitched in his sleep and I stilled, hand flat.

What might be coming? I wondered. For him. For me. I

heard Tom Christie's sarcastic voice: *I have had enough of war. I am surprised that your husband has not.*

"Well enough for *you,*" I muttered under my breath. "Coward." Tom Christie had been imprisoned as a Jacobite—which he was, but not a soldier. He'd been a commissary supply officer in Charles Stuart's army. He'd risked his wealth and his position—and lost both—but not his life or body.

Still, Jamie did respect him—which meant something, Jamie being no mean judge of character. And I knew enough from watching Roger to realize that becoming a clergyman was not the easy path that some people thought it. Roger was not a coward, either, and I wondered how he would find his path in the future?

I turned over, restless. Supper was being prepared; I could smell the rich, saltwater smell of fried oysters from the kitchen below, borne on a wave of woodsmoke and roasting potatoes.

Jamie stirred a little and rolled onto his back, but didn't wake. Time enough. He was dreaming; I could see the movement of his eyes, twitching beneath sealed lids, and the momentary tightening of his lips.

His body tightened, too, suddenly hard beside me, and I jerked back, startled. He growled low in his throat, and his body arched with effort. He was making strangled noises, whether shouting or screaming in his dream I didn't know, and didn't wait to find out.

"Jamie—wake up!" I said sharply. I didn't touch him—I knew better than to do that while he was in the grip of a violent dream; he'd nearly broken my nose once or twice. "Wake up!"

He gasped, caught his breath, and opened unfocused eyes. Plainly he didn't know where he was, and I spoke to him more gently, repeating his name, reassuring him that he was all right. He blinked, swallowed heavily, then turned his head and saw me.

"Claire," I said helpfully, seeing him groping for my name.

"Good," he said hoarsely. He closed his eyes, shook his head, and then opened them again. "All right, Sassenach?"

"Yes. You?"

He nodded, closing his eyes again briefly.

"Aye, fine. I was dreaming about the house burning. Fighting." He sniffed. "Is something burning?"

"Supper, at a guess." The savory smells from below had in fact been interrupted by the acrid stench of smoke and scorched food. "I think the stewpot boiled over."

"Perhaps we'll eat elsewhere tonight."

"Phaedre said Mrs. Symonds had baked ham with mustard and raisin sauce at noon. There might be some left. Are you all right?" I asked again. The room was cold, but his face and breast were sheened with sweat.

"Oh, aye," he replied, sitting up and rubbing his hands vigorously through his hair. "That sort of dream, I can live with." He shoved his hair out of his face and smiled at me. "Ye look like a milkweed puff, Sassenach. Were ye sleeping restless, too?"

"No," I told him, getting up and pulling my shift on before groping for my hairbrush. "It was the restless part *before* we fell asleep. Or do you not remember that bit?"

He laughed, wiped his face, and got up to use the chamber pot, then pulled his shirt on.

"What about the other dreams?" I asked abruptly.

"What?" He emerged from the shirt, looking quizzical.

"You said, 'That sort of dream, I can live with.' What about the ones you can't live with?"

I saw the lines of his face shiver like the surface of water when you've thrown a pebble into it, and on impulse, reached out and clutched his wrist.

"Don't hide," I said softly. I held his eyes with mine, keeping him from raising his mask. "Trust me."

He did look away then, but only to gather himself; he didn't hide. When he glanced back at me, it was all still there in his eyes—confusion, embarrassment, humiliation, and the vestiges of a pain long suppressed.

"I dream . . . sometimes . . ." he said haltingly, "about things that were done to me against my will." He breathed through his nose, deep, exasperated. "And I wake from it with a cockstand and my balls throbbing and I want to go and kill someone, starting with myself," he ended in a rush, grimacing.

"It doesna happen often," he added, giving me a brief, direct look. "And I never . . . I would never turn to you in the wake of such a thing. Ye should know that."

I tightened my grip on his wrist. I wanted to say, "*You could—I wouldn't mind,*" for that was the truth, and once I would have said it without hesitation. But I knew a great deal more now, and had it been me, had I ever dreamed of Harley Boble or the heavy, soft-bodied man and wakened from it aroused—and thank *God* I never had—no, the last thing I would ever have done would be to take that feeling and turn to Jamie, or use his body to purge it.

"Thank you," I said instead, quietly. "For telling me," I added. "And for the knife."

He nodded, and turned to pick up his breeks.

"I like ham," he said.

20

I REGRET . . .

Long Island, colony of New York
September 1776

WILLIAM WISHED he could speak to his father. It wasn't, he assured himself, that he wanted Lord John to exert any influence; certainly not. He just wanted a bit of practical advice. Lord John had returned to England, though, and William was on his own.

Well, not precisely on his own. He was at the moment in charge of a detachment of soldiers guarding a customs checkpoint on the edge of Long Island. He slapped viciously at a mosquito that lighted on his wrist, and, for once, obliterated it. He wished he could do the same to Clarewell.

Lieutenant Edward Markham, Marquis of Clarewell. Otherwise known—to William and a couple of his more intimate friends—as Chinless Ned, or the Ponce. William swatted at a crawling sensation on his own prominent jaw, noticed that two of his men had momentarily disappeared, and stalked toward the wagon they had been inspecting, bellowing their names.

Private Welch appeared from behind the wagon like a jack-in-the-box, looking startled and wiping his mouth. William leaned forward, sniffed his breath, and said briefly, "Charges. Where's Launfal?"

In the wagon, hastily concluding a bargain with the wagon's owner for three bottles of the contraband brandywine that gentleman was seeking to illicitly import. William, grimly slapping at the man-eating hordes of mosquitoes that swarmed out of the nearby marshes, arrested the wagoneer, summoned the other three men of his detail, and told them off to escort the smuggler, Welch, and Launfal to the sergeant. He took up a musket then and stood in the middle of the road, alone and ferocious, his attitude daring anyone to try to pass.

Ironically, though the road had been busy all morning, no one did try for some time, giving him opportunity to refocus his bad temper on the thought of Clarewell.

Heir of a *very* influential family, and one with intimate ties to Lord North, Chinless Ned had arrived in New York a week before William and likewise been placed on Howe's staff, where he had nestled cozily into the woodwork, smarming round General Howe—who, to his credit, tended to blink and stare hard at the Ponce, as though trying to remember who the devil he was—and Captain Pickering, the general's chief aide-de-camp, a vain man, and one much more susceptible to Ned's enthusiastic arse-creeping.

As a result, Chinless had been routinely bagging the choicer assignments, riding with the general on short exploratory expeditions, attending him in meetings with Indian dignitaries and the like, while William and several other junior officers were left to shuffle papers and kick their heels. Hard cheese, after the freedoms and excitements of intelligencing.

He could have stood the constraints of life in quarters and army bureaucracy. His father had schooled him thoroughly in the necessity of restraint in trying circumstances, the withstanding of boredom, the handling of dolts, and the art of icy politeness as a weapon. Someone lacking William's strength of character, though, had snapped one day and, unable to resist the possibilities for caricature conjured up by a contemplation of Ned's profile, had drawn a cartoon of Captain Pickering with his breeches round his ankles, engaged in lecturing the junior staff and apparently ignorant of the Ponce, emergent headfirst and smirking from Pickering's arse.

William had not drawn this bit of diversion—though he rather wished he had—but had been discovered laughing at it by Ned himself, who—in a rare show of manliness—had punched William in the nose. The resultant brawl had cleared the junior officers' quarters, broken a few inconsequent items of furniture, and resulted in William, dripping blood onto his shirtfront, standing to attention in front of a cold-eyed Captain Pickering, the scurrilous cartoon laid out in evidence on the desk.

William had, of course, denied authorship of the thing but declined to identify the artist. He'd used the icy-politeness thing, which had worked to the extent that Pickering had not in fact sent William to the stockade. Merely to Long Island.

"Frigging fart-catcher," he muttered, glaring at an approaching milkmaid with such ferocity that she stopped dead, then edged past him, eyeing him with a wide-eyed alarm that suggested she thought he might explode. He bared his teeth at her, and she emitted a startled squeak and scuttled off so fast that some of her milk slopped out of the buckets she carried on a yoke across her shoulders.

That made him repentant; he wished he could follow her and apologize. But he couldn't; a pair of drovers were coming down the road toward him, bringing in a herd of pigs. William took one look at the oncoming mass of heaving, squealing, spotted hog flesh, tatter-eared and mud-besmeared, and hopped nimbly up onto the bucket that served as his command post. The drovers waved gaily at him, shouting what might be either greetings or insults—he wasn't sure they were even speaking English, and didn't care to find out.

The pigs passed, leaving him amid a sea of hoof-churned mud, liberally scattered with fresh droppings. He slapped at the cloud of mosquitoes that had regathered inquisitively round his head, and thought that he'd had just about enough. He'd been on Long Island for two weeks—which was thirteen and a half days too long. Not quite long enough yet to make him apologize to either Chinless or the captain, though.

"Lickspittle," he muttered.

He did have an alternative. And the longer he spent out here with the mosquitoes, the more attractive it began to look.

It was far too long a ride from his customs outpost to headquarters to make the journey twice each day. In consequence, he'd been temporarily billeted on a man called Culper and his two sisters. Culper wasn't best pleased; his left eye began to twitch whenever he saw William, but the two elderly ladies made much of him, and he returned the favor when he could, bringing them the odd confiscated ham or flask of cambric. He'd come in the night before with a flitch of good bacon, to have Miss Abigail Culper inform him in a whisper that he had a visitor.

"Out a-smoking in the yard," she'd said, inclining her bonneted head toward the side of the house. "Sister wouldn't let him smoke in the house, I'm afraid."

He'd expected to find one of his friends, come to bear him company or perhaps with news of an official pardon that would bring him back from exile on Long Island. Instead, he'd found Captain Richardson, pipe in hand, meditatively watching the Culpers' rooster tread a hen.

"Pleasures of a bucolic life," the captain remarked, as the rooster fell off backward. The cock staggered to his feet and crowed in disheveled triumph, while the hen shook her feathers into order and resumed pecking as though nothing had happened. "Very quiet out here, is it not?"

"Oh, yes," William said. "Your servant, sir."

In fact, it was not. Miss Beulah Culper kept a half-dozen goats, who blatted day and night, though Miss Beulah assured William that they served to keep thieves out of the corncrib. One of the creatures at this point gave a wild braying laugh from its pen, causing Captain Richardson to drop his tobacco pouch. Several more of the goats commenced to utter loud *mehs*, as though jeering.

William bent and picked the pouch up, keeping his face tactfully blank, though his heart was pounding. Richardson hadn't come all the way out to Long Island simply to pass the time.

"Christ," Richardson muttered, with a look at the goats. He

shook his head, and gestured toward the road. "Will you walk a bit with me, Lieutenant?"

William would, gladly.

"I heard a bit regarding your present situation." Richardson smiled. "I'll have a word with Captain Pickering, if you like."

"That's very kind of you, sir," William said. "But I'm afraid I can't apologize for something I haven't done."

Richardson waved his pipe, dismissing it. "Pickering's got a short temper, but he doesn't hold a grudge. I'll see to it."

"Thank you, sir." *And what do you want in return?* William thought.

"There is a Captain Randall-Isaacs," Richardson said casually, "who is traveling within the month to Canada, where he has some military business to transact. While there, though, it is possible that he will meet with . . . a certain person who may provide the army with valuable information. I have some reason to suppose that this person has little English, though—and Captain Randall-Isaacs, alas, has no French. A traveling companion fluent in that language might be . . . useful."

William nodded, but asked no questions. Time enough for that, if he decided to accept Richardson's commission.

They exchanged commonplaces for the remainder of the walk back, whereupon Richardson politely declined Miss Beulah's invitation to take supper, and left with a reiterated promise to speak to Captain Pickering.

Should he do it? William wondered later, listening to Abel Culper's wheezing snores below. The moon was full, and while the loft had no windows, he could feel its pull; he never could sleep when the moon was full.

Ought he to hang on in New York, in hopes either of improving his position, or at least of eventually seeing some action? Or cut his losses and take Richardson's new commission?

His father would doubtless advise the former course of action; an officer's best chance of advancement and notice lay in distinguishing himself in battle, not in the shady—and vaguely disreputable—realm of intelligencing. Still . . . the routine and constraints of the army chafed, rather, after his weeks of freedom. And he *had* been useful, he knew.

What difference could one lieutenant make, buried under the crushing weight of the ranks above him, perhaps given command of his own companies but still obliged to follow orders, never allowed to act according to his own judgment. . . . He grinned up at the rafters, dimly visible a foot above his face, thinking what his uncle Hal might have to say regarding the judgment of junior officers.

But Uncle Hal was much more than simply a career soldier; he cared passionately for his regiment: its welfare, its honor, the men under his command. William had not really thought beyond the immediate future in terms of his own career with the army. The American campaign wouldn't last long; what next?

He was rich—or would be, when he achieved his majority, and that wasn't far off, though it seemed like one of those pictures his father was fond of, with a vanishing perspective that led the eye into an impossible infinity. But when he *did* have his money, he could buy a better commission where he liked—perhaps a captaincy in the Lancers. . . . It wouldn't matter whether he'd done anything to distinguish himself in New York.

His father—William could hear him now, and put the pillow over his face to drown him out—would tell him that reputation depended often on the smallest of actions, the daily decisions made with honor and responsibility, not the huge drama of heroic battles. William was not interested in daily responsibility.

It was, however, much too hot to stay under the pillow, and he threw it off onto the floor with an irritable grunt.

"No," he said aloud to Lord John. "I'm going to Canada," and flopped back into his damp and lumpy bed, shutting eyes and ears against any further wise counsel.

A WEEK LATER, the nights had grown chilly enough to make William welcome Miss Beulah's hearth and her oyster stew—and, thank God, cold enough to discourage the damned mosquitoes. The days were still very warm, though, and William found it almost a pleasure when his detail was told off to comb the shore in search of a supposed smuggler's cache that Captain Hanks had caught wind of.

"A cache of what?" Perkins asked, mouth hanging half open as usual.

"Lobsters," William answered flippantly, but relented at Perkins's look of confusion. "I don't know, but you'll probably recognize it if you find it. Don't drink it, though—come fetch me."

Smugglers' boats brought almost everything into Long Island, but the odds of the current rumor concerning a cache of bed linens or boxes of Dutch platters were low. Might be brandy, might be ale, but almost certainly something drinkable; liquor was by far the most profitable contraband. William sorted the men into pairs and sent them off, watching until they were a decent distance away before heaving a deep sigh and leaning back against a tree.

Such trees as grew near the shore here were runty twisted pines, but the sea wind moved pleasantly among their needles, soughing in his ears with a soothing rush. He sighed again, this time in pleasure, remembering just how much he liked solitude; he hadn't had any in a month. If he took Richardson's offer, though . . . Well, there'd be Randall-Isaacs, of course, but still—weeks on the road, free of the army constraints of duty and routine. Silence in which to think. No more Perkins!

He wondered idly whether he might be able to sneak into the junior officers' quarters and pound Chinless to a pulp before vanishing into the wilderness like a red Indian. Need he wear a disguise? Not if he waited 'til after dark, he decided. Ned might suspect, but couldn't prove anything if he couldn't see William's face. Was it cowardly to attack Ned in his sleep, though? Well, that was all right; he'd douse Chinless with the contents of his chamber pot to wake him up before setting in.

A tern swept by within inches of his head, startling him out of these enjoyable cogitations. His movement in turn startled the bird, which let out an indignant shriek at finding him not edible after all and sailed off over the water. He scooped up a pinecone and flung it at the bird, missing by a mile, but not caring. He'd send a note to Richardson this very evening, saying yes. The thought of it made his heart beat faster, and a sense of exhilaration filled him, buoyant as the tern's drift upon the air.

He rubbed sand off his fingers onto his breeches, then stiffened, seeing movement on the water. A sloop was tacking to and fro, just offshore. Then he relaxed, recognizing it—that villain Rogers.

"And what are *you* after, I should like to know?" he muttered. He stepped out onto the sandy edge of the shore and stood amid the marram grass, fists on his hips, letting his uniform be seen—just in case Rogers had somehow missed the sight of William's men strung all down the shore, reddish dots crawling over the sandy dunes like bedbugs. If Rogers had heard about the smuggler's cache, too, William meant to make sure Rogers knew that William's soldiers had rights over it.

Robert Rogers was a shady character who'd come slinking into New York a few months before and somehow wangled a major's commission from General Howe and a sloop from his brother, the admiral. Said he was an Indian fighter, and was fond of dressing up as an Indian himself. Effective, though: he'd recruited men enough to form ten companies of nattily uniformed rangers, but Rogers continued to prowl the coastline in his sloop with a small company of men as disreputable-looking as he was, looking for recruits, spies, smugglers, and—William was convinced—anything that wasn't nailed down.

The sloop came in a little closer, and he saw Rogers on deck: a dark-skinned man in his late forties, seamed and battered-looking, with an evil cast to his brow. He spotted William, though, and waved genially. William raised a civil hand in reply; if his men found anything, he might need Rogers to carry the booty back to the New York side—accompanied by a guard to keep it from disappearing *en route.*

There were a lot of stories about Rogers—some plainly put about by Rogers himself. But so far as William knew, the man's chief qualification was that he had at one point attempted to pay his respects to General Washington, who not only declined to receive him but had him slung unceremoniously out of the Continentals' camp and refused further entry.

William considered this evidence of good judgment on the part of the Virginian.

Now what? The sloop had dropped her sails, and was putting out a small boat. It was Rogers, rowing over on his own. William's wariness was roused at once. Still, he waded in and grabbed the gunwale, helping Rogers to drag the boat up onto the sand.

"Well met, Lieutenant!" Rogers grinned at him, gap-toothed but self-confident. William saluted him briefly and formally.

"Major."

"Your fellows looking for a cache of French wine, by chance?"

Damn, he'd already found it!

"We had word of smuggling activities taking place in this vicinity," William said stiffly. "We are investigating."

"'Course you are," Rogers agreed amiably. "Save you a bit of time? Try up the other way . . ." He turned, lifting his chin toward a cluster of dilapidated fishing shacks a quarter mile in the distance. "It's—"

"We did," William interrupted.

"It's buried in the sand behind the shacks," Rogers finished, ignoring the interruption.

"Much obliged, Major," William said, with as much cordiality as he could manage.

"Saw two fellows a-burying it last evening," Rogers explained. "But I don't think they've come back for it yet."

"You're keeping an eye on this stretch of shore, I see," William observed. "Anything in particular you're looking for? Sir," he added.

Rogers smiled.

"Since you mention it, *sir,* I am. There's a fellow walking round asking questions of a damnable inquisitive sort, and I should very much like to talk to him. If might be as you or your men should spot the man . . . ?"

"Certainly, sir. Do you know his name, or his appearance?"

"Both, as it happens," Rogers replied promptly. "Tall fellow, with scars upon his face from a gunpowder explosion. You'd know him if you saw him. A rebel, from a rebel family in Connecticut—Hale is his name."

William experienced a sharp jolt to the midsection.

"Oh, you *have* seen him?" Rogers spoke mildly, but his dark eyes had sharpened. William felt a stab of annoyance that his face should be so readable, but inclined his head.

"He passed the customs point yesterday. Very voluble fellow," he added, trying to recall the details of the man. He'd noticed the scars: faded welts that mottled the man's cheeks and forehead. "Nervous; he was sweating and his voice shook—the private who stopped him thought he had tobacco or something else concealed, and made him turn out his pockets, but he hadn't any contraband." William closed his eyes, frowning in the effort of recall. "He had papers. . . . I saw them." He'd seen them, all right, but had not had the chance to examine them himself, as he'd been concerned with a merchant bringing in a cartload of cheeses, bound—he said—for the British commissary. By the time he'd done with that, the man had been waved on.

"The man who spoke with him . . ." Rogers was peering down the shore toward the desultory searchers in the distance. "Which is he?"

"A private soldier named Hudson. I'll call him for you if you like," William offered. "But I doubt he can tell you much about the papers; he can't read."

Rogers looked vexed at this, but nodded for William to call Hudson anyway. Thus summoned, Hudson verified William's account of the matter, but could recall nothing regarding the papers, save that one of the sheets had had some numbers written upon it. "And a drawing, I think," he added. "Didn't notice what it was, though, sir, I'm afraid."

"Numbers, eh? Good, good," Rogers said, all but rubbing his hands together. "And did he say whence he was bound?"

"To visit a friend, sir, as lived near Flushing." Hudson was respectful, but looked curiously at the ranger; Rogers was barefoot and dressed in a pair of ratty linen breeches with a short waistcoat made of muskrat fur. "I didn't ask the friend's name, sir. Didn't know as it might be important."

"Oh, I doubt it is, Private. Doubt the friend exists at all." Rogers chuckled, seeming delighted at the news. He stared into the hazy distance, eyes narrowed as though he might distinguish the spy among the dunes, and nodded slowly in satisfaction.

"Very good," he said softly, as though to himself, and was turning to go when William stopped him with a word.

"My thanks for the information regarding the smuggler's cache, sir." Perkins had overseen the digging whilst William and Rogers were interviewing Hudson, and was now chivying a small group of soldiers along, several sand-caked casks rolling bumpily down the dunes before them. One of the casks hit a hard spot in the sand, bounced into the air, and landed hard, rolling off at a crazy angle, pursued with whoops by the soldiers.

William flinched slightly, seeing this. If the wine survived its rescue, it wouldn't be drinkable for a fortnight. Not that that was likely to stop anyone trying.

"I should like to request permission to bring the seized contraband aboard your sloop for transport," he said formally to Rogers. "I will accompany and deliver it myself, of course."

"Oh, of course." Rogers seemed amused, but nodded agreement. He scratched his nose, considering something. "We shan't be sailing back until tomorrow—d'you want to come along of us tonight? You might be of help, as you've actually seen the fellow we're after."

William's heart leapt with excitement. Miss Beulah's stew paled in comparison with the prospect of hunting a dangerous spy. And being in at the capture could do nothing but good to his reputation, even if the major share of the credit was Rogers's.

"I should be more than pleased to assist you in any way, sir!"

Rogers grinned, then eyed him up and down.

"Good. But you can't go spy-catching like that, Lieutenant. Come aboard, and we'll fit you out proper."

WILLIAM PROVED TO be six inches taller than the tallest of Rogers's crew, and thus ended up awkwardly attired in a flapping shirt of rough linen—the tails left out by necessity, to disguise the fact that the top buttons of his flies were left undone—and canvas breeches that threatened to emasculate him should he make any sudden moves. These could not be buckled, of course, and William elected to emulate Rogers and go barefoot, rather than suffer the indignity of striped stockings that left his knees and four inches of hairy shin exposed between stocking-top and breeches.

The sloop had sailed to Flushing, where Rogers, William, and four men disembarked. Rogers maintained an informal recruiting office here, in the back room of a merchant's shop in the high road of the village. He vanished into this establishment momentarily, returning with the satisfactory news that Hale had not been seen in Flushing and was likely therefore stopping at one of the two taverns to be found at Elmsford, two or three miles from the village.

The men accordingly walked in that direction, dividing for the sake of caution into smaller groups, so that William found himself walking with Rogers, a ragged shawl slung round his shoulders against the evening chill. He had not shaved, of course, and fancied that he looked a proper companion for the ranger, who had added a slouch hat with a dried flying fish stuck through the brim to his costume.

"Do we pose as oystermen, or carters, perhaps?" William asked. Rogers grunted in brief amusement and shook his head.

"You'd not pass for either, should anyone hear you talk. Nay, lad, keep your mouth shut, save to put something in it. The boys and I 'ull manage the business. All you need do is nod, if you spot Hale."

The wind had come onshore and blew the scent of cold marshes toward them, spiced with a distant hint of chimney smoke. No habitation was yet in sight, and the fading landscape was desolate around them. The cold, sandy dirt of the road was soothing to his bare feet, though, and he did not find the bleakness of their surroundings depressing in the least; he was too eager at thought of what lay ahead.

Rogers was silent for the most part, pacing with his head down against the cold breeze. After a bit, though, he said casually, "I carried Captain Richardson over from New York. And back."

William thought momentarily of saying, *"Captain Richardson?"* in tones of polite ignorance, but realized in time that this wouldn't do.

"Did you?" he said instead, and kept his own silence. Rogers laughed.

"Fly cove, aren't you? Perhaps he's right, then, choosing you."

"He told you that he had chosen me for . . . something?"

"Good lad. Never give anything away for free—but sometimes it pays to oil the wheels a bit. Nay, Richardson's a downy bird—he said not a word about you. But I know who he is, and what he does. And I know where I left him. He wasn't calling upon the Culpers, I'll warrant that."

William made an indeterminate sound of interest in his throat. Plainly, Rogers meant to say something. Let him say, then.

"How old are you, lad?"

"Nineteen," William said, with an edge. "Why?"

Rogers shrugged, his outline little more than a shadow among many in the gathering dusk.

"Old enough to risk your neck on purpose, then. But you might want to think twice before saying yes to whatever Richardson's suggesting to you."

"Assuming that he did indeed suggest something—again, why?"

Rogers touched his back, urging him forward.

"You're about to see that for yourself, lad. Come on."

THE WARM SMOKY light of the tavern and the smell of food embraced William. He had not been really conscious of cold, dark, or hunger, his mind intent on the adventure at hand. Now, though, he drew a long, lingering breath, filled with the scent of fresh bread and roast chicken, and felt like an insensible corpse, newly roused from the grave and restored to full life upon the day of Resurrection.

The next breath stopped dead in his throat, though, and his heart gave a tremendous squeeze that sent a surge of blood through his body. Rogers, next to him, made a low warning hum in his throat, and glanced casually round the room as he led the way to a table.

The man, the spy, was sitting near the fire, eating chicken and chatting with a couple of farmers. Most of the men in the tavern had glanced at the door when the newcomers appeared—more than one of them blinked at William—but the spy was so absorbed in his food and conversation that he didn't even look up.

William had taken little notice of the man when first seen, but would have known him again at once. He was not so tall as William himself, but several inches more than the average, and striking in appearance, with flax-blond hair and a high forehead, this displaying the flash-mark scars of the gunpowder accident Rogers had mentioned. He had a round, broad-brimmed hat, which lay on the table beside his plate, and wore an unremarkable plain brown suit.

Not in uniform . . . William swallowed heavily, not entirely in respect of his hunger and the smell of food.

Rogers sat down at the next table, motioning William to a stool across from him, and raised his brows in question. William nodded silently, but didn't look again in Hale's direction.

The landlord brought them food and beer, and William devoted himself to eating, glad that he was not required to join in conversation. Hale himself was relaxed and voluble, telling his companions that he was a Dutch schoolmaster from New York.

"Conditions there are so unsettled, though," he said, shaking his head, "that the majority of my students have gone—fled with their families to relatives in Connecticut or New Jersey. I might suppose similar—or perhaps worse—conditions obtain here?"

One of the men at his table merely grunted, but the other blew out his lips with a derisive sound.

"You might say so. Goddam lobsterbacks seize everything as hasn't been buried. Tory, Whig, or rebel, makes no goddam difference to those greedy bastards. Speak a word of protest, and you're like to be struck over the head or dragged off to the goddam stockade, so as to make it easier for 'em. Why, one hulking brute stopped me at the customs point last week, and took my whole load of apple cider and the goddam wagon to boot! He—"

William choked on a bite of bread, but didn't dare cough. Christ, he hadn't recognized the man—the man's back was to him—but he recalled the apple cider well enough. Hulking brute?

He reached for his beer and gulped, trying to dislodge the chunk of bread; it didn't work and he coughed silently, feeling his face go purple and seeing Rogers frowning at him in consternation. He gestured feebly at the cider farmer, struck himself in the chest, and, rising, made his way out of the room as quietly as possible. His disguise, excellent as it was, would in no way conceal his essential hulkingness, and if the man were to recognize him as a British soldier, bang went the whole enterprise.

He managed not to breathe until he was safely outside, where he coughed until he thought the bottom of his stomach might force its way out of his mouth. At last he stopped, though, and leaned against the side of the tavern, taking long, gasping breaths. He wished he'd had the presence of mind to bring some beer with him, instead of the chicken leg he held.

The last of Rogers's men had come along the road, and with a baffled glance at William, went inside. He wiped his mouth with the back of his hand and, straightening up, crept round the side of the building until he reached a window.

The new arrivals were taking up their own spot, near to Hale's table. Standing carefully to one side to save being spotted, he saw that Rogers had now insinuated himself into conversation with Hale and the two farmers, and appeared to be telling them a joke. The apple-cider fellow hooted and pounded the table at the end; Hale made an attempt at a grin, but looked frankly shocked; the jest must have been indelicate.

Rogers leaned back, casually including the whole table with the sweep of a hand, and said something that had them nodding and murmuring agreement. Then he leaned forward, intent, to ask Hale something.

William could catch only snatches of the conversation, above the general noise of the tavern and the whistling of the cold wind past his ears. So far as he could gather, Rogers was professing to be a rebel, his own men nodding agreement from their table, gathering closer to form a secretive knot of conversation about Hale. Hale looked intent, excited, and very earnest. He might easily have been a schoolmaster, William thought—though Rogers had said he was a captain in the Continental army. William shook his head; Hale didn't look any sort of a soldier.

At the same time, he hardly looked the part of a spy, either. He was noticeable, with his fair good looks, his flash-scarred face, his . . . height.

William felt a small, cold lump in the pit of his stomach. Christ. Was that what Rogers had meant? Saying that there was something William should be warned of, with regard to Captain Richardson's errands, and that he would see for himself, tonight?

William was quite accustomed both to his own height and to people's automatic responses to it; he quite liked being looked up to. But on his first errand for Captain Richardson, it had never struck him for a moment that folk might recall him on account of it—or that they could describe him with the greatest of ease. Hulking brute was no compliment, but it *was* unmistakable.

With a sense of incredulity, he heard Hale not only reveal his own name and the fact that he held rebel sympathies, but also confide that he was making observations regarding the strength of the British presence—this followed by an earnest inquiry as to whether the fellows he spoke with might have noticed any redcoated soldiers in the vicinity?

William was so shocked by this recklessness that he put his eye to the edge of the window frame, in time to see Rogers glance round the room in exaggerated caution before leaning in confidentially, tapping Hale upon the forearm, and saying, "Why, now, sir, I have, indeed I have, but you must be more wary of what you say in a public place. Why, anyone at all might hear you!"

"Pshaw," said Hale, laughing. "I am among friends here. Have we not all just drunk to General Washington and to the King's confusion?" Sobering, but still eager, he pushed his hat aside and waved to the landlord for more beer. "Come, have another, sir, and tell me what you have seen."

William had a sudden overwhelming impulse to shout, *"Shut your mouth, you ninnyhammer!"* or to throw something at Hale through the window. But it was far too late, even could he actually have done it. The chicken leg he had been eating was still in his hand; noticing, he tossed it away. His stomach was knotted, and there was a taste of sick at the back of his throat, though his blood still boiled with excitement.

Hale was making still more damaging admissions, to the admiring encouragements and patriotic shouts of Rogers's men, all of whom were playing out their parts admirably, he had to admit. How long would Rogers let it go on? Would they take him here, in the tavern? Probably not—some others of those present were doubtless rebel sympathizers, who might be moved to intervene on Hale's behalf, did Rogers go to arrest him in their midst.

Rogers appeared in no hurry. Nearly half an hour of tedious raillery followed, Rogers giving what appeared to be small admissions, Hale making much larger ones in return, his slab-sided cheeks glowing with beer and excitement over the information he was gaining. William's legs, feet, hands, and face were numb, and his shoulders ached with tension. A crunching sound nearby distracted him from his close attendance on the scene within, and he glanced down, suddenly aware of a penetrating aroma that had somehow insinuated itself without his cognizance.

"Christ!" He jerked back, nearly putting his elbow through the window, and fell into the wall of the tavern with a heavy thump. The skunk, disturbed in its enjoyment of the discarded chicken leg, instantly elevated its tail, the white stripe making the movement clearly visible. William froze.

"What was that?" someone said inside, and he heard the scrape of a bench being pushed back. Holding his breath, he edged one foot to the side, only to be frozen in place again by a faint thumping noise and the quivering of the white stripe. Damn, the thing was stamping its feet. An indication of imminent attack, he'd been told—and told by people whose sorry condition made it apparent that they spoke from experience.

Feet were coming toward the door, someone coming to investigate. Christ, if they found him eavesdropping outside . . . He gritted his teeth, nerving himself to what duty told him must be a self-sacrificial lunge out of sight—but if he did, what then? He could not rejoin Rogers and the others, reeking of skunk. But if—

The opening of the door put paid to all speculations. William lunged for the corner of the building by simple reflex. The skunk also acted by reflex—but, startled by the opening of the door, apparently adjusted its aim in consequence. William tripped over a branch and sprawled at full length into a heap of discarded rubbish, hearing a full-throated shriek behind him as the night was made hideous.

William coughed, choked, and tried to stop breathing long enough to get out of range. He gasped from necessity, though, and his lungs were filled with a substance that went so far beyond the concept of smell as to require a completely new sensory description. Gagging and spluttering, eyes burning and watering from the assault, he stumbled into the darkness on the other side of the road, from which vantage point he witnessed the skunk making off in a huff and the skunk's victim collapsed in a heap on the tavern's step, making noises of extreme distress.

William hoped it wasn't Hale. Beyond the practical difficulties involved in arresting and transporting a man who had suffered such an assault, simple humanity compelled one to think that hanging the victim would be adding insult to injury.

It wasn't Hale. He saw the flaxen hair shining in the torchlight among the heads that were thrust out in inquiry, only to be drawn hastily back again.

Voices reached him, discussing how best to proceed. Vinegar, it was agreed, was needed, and in quantity. The victim had by now sufficiently recovered himself as to crawl off into the weeds, from which the sounds of violent retching proceeded. This, added to the mephitis still tainting the atmosphere, caused a number of other gentlemen to vomit, as well, and William felt his own gorge rise, but controlled it by vicious nose-pinching.

He was nearly chilled through, though thankfully aired out, by the time the victim's friends saw him off—driving him like a cow along the road, as no one would touch him—and the tavern emptied, no one having further appetite for either food or drink in such an atmosphere. He could hear the landlord cursing to himself as he leaned out to take down the torch that burned beside the hanging sign and plunge it, sizzling, into the rain barrel.

Hale bade a general good night, his educated voice distinctive in the dark, and set off along the road toward Flushing, where doubtless he meant to seek a bed. Rogers—

William knew him by the fur waistcoat, identifiable even by starlight—lingered near the road, silently collecting his men about him as the crowd departed. Only when everyone was out of sight did William venture to join them.

"Yes?" Rogers said, seeing him. "All present, then. Let's go." And they moved off, a silent pack coursing down the road, intent upon the track of their unknowing prey.

THEY SAW THE FLAMES from the water. The city was burning, mostly the district near the East River, but the wind was up, and the fire was spreading. There was much excited speculation among Rogers's men; had rebel sympathizers fired the city?

"Just as likely drunken soldiers," Rogers said, his voice grimly dispassionate. William felt queasy, seeing the red glow in the sky. The prisoner was silent.

They found General Howe—eventually—in his headquarters at Beekman House outside the city, red-eyed from smoke, lack of sleep, and a rage that was buried bone-deep. It stayed buried, though, for the moment. He summoned Rogers and the prisoner into the library where he had his office, and—after one brief, astonished look at William's attire—sent him to his bed.

Fortnum was in the attic, watching the city burn from the window. There was nothing to be done about it. William came to stand beside him. He felt strangely empty, somehow unreal. Chilled, though the floor was warm under his bare feet.

An occasional fountain of sparks shot up now and then, as the flames struck something particularly flammable, but from such a distance there was really little to be seen but the bloody glow against the sky.

"They'll blame us, you know," Fortnum said after a bit.

THE AIR WAS STILL thick with smoke at noon the next day.

He couldn't take his eyes off Hale's hands. They had clenched involuntarily as a private soldier tied them, though he had put them behind his back with no protest. Now his fingers were clasped tight together, so hard that the knuckles had gone white.

Surely the flesh protested, William thought, even if the mind had resigned itself. His own flesh was protesting simply being here, his skin twitching like a horse plagued by flies, his bowels cramping and loosening in horrid sympathy—they said a hanged man's bowels gave way; would Hale's? Blood washed through his face at the thought, and he looked at the ground.

Voices made him look up again. Captain Moore had just asked Hale whether he wished to make any remarks. Hale nodded; evidently he had been prepared for this.

William felt that he should himself have been prepared by now; Hale had spent the last two hours in Captain Moore's tent, writing notes to be delivered to his family, while the men assembled for the hasty execution shifted their weight from foot to foot, waiting. He wasn't prepared at all.

Why was it different? He'd seen men die, some horribly. But this preliminary courtesy, this formality, this . . . obscene *civility,* all conducted with the certain knowledge of imminent and shameful death. Deliberation. The awful deliberation, that was it.

"At last!" Clarewell muttered in his ear. "Bloody get on with it; I'm starving."

A young black man named Billy Richmond, a private soldier whom William knew casually, was sent up the ladder to tie the rope to the tree. He came down now, nodding to the officer.

Now Hale was mounting the ladder, the sergeant major steadying him. The noose was round his neck, a thick rope, new-looking. Didn't they say new ropes stretched? But it was a high ladder . . .

William was sweating like a pig, though the day was mild. He mustn't close his eyes or look away. Not with Clarewell watching.

He tightened the muscles of his throat and concentrated again on Hale's hands. The fingers were twisting, helplessly, though the man's face was calm. They were leaving faint damp marks on the skirt of his coat.

A grunt of effort and a grating noise; the ladder was pulled away, and there was a startled *whoof!* from Hale as he dropped. Whether it was the newness of the rope or something else, his neck did not break cleanly.

He'd refused the hood, and so the spectators were obliged to watch his face for the quarter of an hour it took him to die. William stifled a horrific urge to laugh from pure nerves, seeing the pale blue eyes bulge to bursting point, the tongue thrust out. So surprised. He looked so surprised.

There was only a small group of men assembled for the execution. He saw Richardson a little way away, watching with a look of remote abstraction. As though aware of his glance, Richardson looked sharply up at him. William looked away.

21

THE MINISTER'S CAT

Lallybroch
October 1980

SHE WAS UP EARLY, before the children, though she knew this was foolish—whatever Roger had gone to Oxford for, it would take him a good seven or eight hours to drive there, and the same back. Even if he had left at dawn—and he might not be able to, if he hadn't arrived in time to do whatever it was the day before—he couldn't be home before midday at the earliest. But she'd slept restlessly, dreaming one of those monotonous and inescapably unpleasant dreams, this one featuring the sight and sound of the tide coming in, lapping wave by lapping wave by lapping . . . and wakened at first light feeling dizzy and unwell.

It had occurred to her for one nightmare instant that she might be pregnant—but she'd sat up abruptly in bed, and the world had settled at once into place around her. None of that sense of having shoved one foot through the looking glass that early pregnancy entails. She set one foot cautiously out of bed, and the world—and her stomach—stayed steady. Good, then.

Still, the feeling of unease—whether from the dream, Roger's absence, or the specter of pregnancy—stayed with her, and she went about the daily business of the household with a distracted mind.

She was sorting socks toward midday when she became aware that things were quiet. Quiet in a way that made the hair rise on the back of her neck.

"Jem?" she called. "Mandy?"

Total silence. She stepped out of the laundry, listening for the usual thumps, bangings, and screeches from above, but there was not the slightest sound of trampling feet, toppling blocks, or the high-pitched voices of sibling warfare.

"Jem!" she shouted. "Where are you?"

No reply. The last time this had happened, two days before, she'd discovered her alarm clock in the bottom of the bathtub, neatly disassembled into its component parts, and both children at the far end of the garden, glowing with unnatural innocence.

"*I* didn't do it!" Jem had declared virtuously, hauled into the house and faced with the evidence. "And Mandy's too little."

"Too widdle," Mandy had agreed, nodding her mop of black curls so ferociously as to obscure her face.

"Well, I don't think Daddy did it," Bree said, raising a stern brow. "And I'm sure it wasn't Annie Mac. Which doesn't leave very many suspects, does it?"

"Shussspects, shussspects," Mandy said happily, enchanted by the new word.

Jem shook his head in resigned fashion, viewing the scattered gears and dismembered hands.

"We must have got piskies, Mama."

"Pishkies, pishkies," Mandy chirped, pulling her skirt up over her head and yanking at her frilly underpants. "Needa go pishkie, Mama!"

In the midst of the urgency occasioned by this statement, Jem had faded artfully, not to be seen again until dinner, by which time the affair of the alarm clock had been superseded by the usual fierce rush of daily events, not to be recalled until bedtime, when Roger remarked the absence of the alarm clock.

"Jem doesn't usually lie," Roger had said thoughtfully, having been shown the small pottery bowl now containing the clock's remains.

Bree, brushing out her hair for bed, gave him a jaundiced look.

"Oh, you think we have pixies, too?"

"Piskies," he said absently, stirring the small pile of gears in the bowl with a finger.

"What? You mean they really are called 'piskies' here? I thought Jem was just mispronouncing it."

"Well, no—'pisky' is Cornish; they're called pixies in other parts of the West Country, though."

"What are they called in Scotland?"

"We haven't really got any. Scotland's got its fair share of the fairy folk," he said, scooping up a handful of clock innards and letting them tinkle musically back into the bowl. "But Scots tend toward the grimmer manifestations of the supernatural—water horses, *ban-sidhe,* blue hags, and the Nuckelavee, aye? Piskies are a wee bit frivolous for Scotland. We have got brownies, mind," he added, taking the brush from her hand, "but they're more of a household help, not mischief-makers like piskies. Can ye put the clock back together?"

"Sure—if the piskies didn't lose any of the parts. What on earth is a Nuckelavee?"

"It's from the Orkneys. Nothing ye want to hear about just before bed," he assured her. And, bending, breathed very softly on her neck, just below the earlobe.

The faint tingle engendered by the memory of what had happened after that momentarily overlaid her suspicions of what the children might be up to, but the sensation faded, to be replaced by increasing worry.

There was no sign of either Jem or Mandy anywhere in the house. Annie MacDonald didn't come on Saturdays, and the kitchen . . . At first glance, it seemed undisturbed, but she was familiar with Jem's methods.

Sure enough, the packet of chocolate biscuits was missing,

as was a bottle of lemon squash, though everything else in the cupboard was in perfect order—and the cupboard was six feet off the ground. Jem showed great promise as a cat burglar, she thought. At least he'd have a career if he got chucked out of school for good one of these days after telling his classmates something especially picturesque he'd picked up in the eighteenth century.

The missing food allayed her uneasiness. If they'd taken a picnic, they were outside, and while they might be anywhere within a half mile of the house—Mandy wouldn't walk farther than that—chances were they wouldn't have gone far before sitting down to eat biscuits.

It was a beautiful fall day, and despite the need to track down her miscreants, she was glad to be out in the sun and breeze. Socks could wait. And so could turning the vegetable beds. And speaking to the plumber about the geyser in the upstairs bath. And . . .

"It doesna matter how many things ye do on a farm, there's always more than ye can *do. A wonder the place doesna rise up about my ears and swallow me, like Jonah and the whale."*

For an instant, she heard her father's voice, full of exasperated resignation at encountering another unexpected chore. She glanced round at him, smiling, then stopped, realization and longing sweeping over her in waves.

"Oh, Da," she said softly. She walked on, more slowly, suddenly seeing not the albatross of a big, semi-decayed house, but the living organism that was Lallybroch, and all those of her blood who had been part of it—who still were.

The Frasers and Murrays who had put their own sweat and blood and tears into its buildings and soil, woven their lives into its land. Uncle Ian, Aunt Jenny—the swarm of cousins she had known so briefly. Young Ian. All of them dead now . . . but, curiously enough, not gone.

"Not gone at all," she said aloud, and found comfort in the words. She'd reached the back gate of the kailyard and paused, glancing up the hill toward the ancient broch that gave the place its name; the burying ground was up on that same hill, most of its stones so weathered that the names and their dates were indecipherable, the stones themselves mostly obliterated by creeping gorse and heather. And amidst the splashes of gray, black-green, and deep purple were two small moving splotches of red and blue.

The pathway was badly overgrown; brambles ripped at her jeans. She found the children on hands and knees, following a trail of ants—who were in turn following a trail of cookie crumbs, carefully placed so as to lead the ants through an obstacle course of sticks and pebbles.

"Look, Mama!" Jem barely glanced up at her, absorbed in the sight before him. He pointed at the ground, where he had sunk an old teacup into the dirt and filled it with water. A black glob of ants, lured to their doom by chocolate crumbs, were struggling in the midst of it.

"Jem! That's mean! You mustn't drown ants—unless they're in the house," she added, with vivid memories of a recent infestation in the pantry.

"They're not drowning, Mama. Look—see what they do?"

She crouched beside him, looking closer, and saw that, in fact, the ants weren't drowning. Single ants that had fallen in struggled madly toward the center, where a large mass of ants clung together, making a ball that floated, barely denting the surface. The ants in the ball were moving, slowly, so that they changed places constantly, and while one or two near the edge of the mass were motionless, possibly dead, the majority were clearly in no immediate danger of drowning, supported by the bodies of their fellows. And the mass itself was gradually drawing closer to the rim of the cup, propelled by the movements of the ants in it.

"That's really cool," she said, fascinated, and sat beside him for some time, watching the ants, before finally decreeing mercy and making him scoop the ball of ants out on a leaf, where once laid on the ground, they scattered and at once went back to their business.

"Do you think they do it on purpose?" she asked Jem. "Cluster together like that, I mean. Or are they just looking for anything to hang on to?"

"Dinna ken," he said, shrugging. "I'll look in my ant book and see does it say."

She gathered up the remnants of the picnic, leaving one or two biscuit fragments for the ants, who had, she felt, earned them. Mandy had wandered off while she and Jem watched the ants in the teacup, and was presently squatting in the shade of a bush some way uphill, engaged in animated conversation with an invisible companion.

"Mandy wanted to talk to Grandda," Jem said matter-of-factly. "That's why we came up here."

"Oh?" she said slowly. "Why is here a good place to talk to him?"

Jem looked surprised, and glanced toward the weathered, tipsy stones of the burying ground.

"Isn't he here?"

Something much too powerful to be called a shiver shot up her spine. It was as much Jem's matter-of-factness as the possibility that it might be true that took her breath away.

"I—don't know," she said. "I suppose he could be." While she tried not to think too much about the fact that her parents were now dead, she had somehow vaguely assumed that they would have been buried in North Carolina—or somewhere else in the Colonies, if war had taken them away from the Ridge.

But she remembered the letters suddenly. He'd said he meant to come back to Scotland. And Jamie Fraser being a determined man, more than likely he'd done just that. Had he never left again? And if he hadn't—was her mother here, too?

Without really meaning to, she found herself making her way upward, past the foot of the old broch and through the stones of the burying ground. She'd come up here once, with her aunt Jenny. It had been early evening, with a breeze whispering in the grass, and an air of peace upon the hillside. Jenny had shown her the graves of her grandparents, Brian and Ellen, together under a marriage stone; yes, she could still make out the curve of it, overgrown and mossy as it was, the names weathered away. And the child who had died with Ellen was buried with her—her third son. Robert, Jenny said; her father, Brian, had insisted he be baptized, and her wee dead brother's name was Robert.

She was standing among the stones now; so many of them. A good many of the later ones were still readable, these with dates in the late 1800s. Murrays and McLachlans and McLeans, for the most part. Here and there the odd Fraser or MacKenzie.

The earlier ones, though, were all too weathered to read, no more than the shadows of letters showing through the black stains of lichen and the soft, obliterating moss. There, next to Ellen's grave, was the tiny square stone for Caitlin Maisri Murray, Jenny and Ian's sixth child, who had lived only a day or so. Jenny had shown Brianna the stone, stooping to run a gentle hand across the letters and laying a yellow rose from the path beside it. There had been a small cairn there, too—pebbles left by those who visited the grave. The cairn had been scattered long since, but Brianna stooped and found a pebble now and placed it by the little stone.

There was another, she saw, beside it. Another small stone, as for a child. Not quite as weathered, but plainly almost as old. Only two words on it, she thought, and, closing her eyes, ran her fingers slowly over the stone, feeling out the shallow, broken lines. There was an "E" in the first line. A "Y," she thought, in the second. And maybe a "K."

What sort of Highland name begins with "Y"? she thought, puzzled. *There's McKay, but that's in the wrong order . . .*

"You—er—don't know which grave might be Grandda's, do you?" she asked Jem hesitantly. She was almost afraid to hear the answer.

"No." He looked surprised, and glanced where she was looking, toward the assemblage of stones. Obviously he hadn't connected their presence with his grandfather. "He just said he'd like to be buried here, and if I came here, I should leave him a stane. So I did." His accent slid naturally into the word, and she heard her father's voice again, distinctly, but this time smiled a little.

"Where?"

"Up there. He likes to be up high, ken? Where he can see," Jem said casually, pointing up the hill. Just beyond the shadow of the broch, she could see the traces of something not quite a trail through a mass of gorse, heather, and broken rock. And poking out of the mass at the crest of the hill, a big, lumpy boulder, on whose shoulder sat a tiny pyramid of pebbles, barely visible.

"Did you leave all those today?"

"No, I put one whenever I come. That's what ye're meant to do, aye?"

There was a small lump in her throat, but she swallowed it and smiled. "Aye, it is. I'll go up and leave one, too."

Mandy was now sitting on one of the fallen gravestones, laying out burdock leaves as plates around the dirty teacup, which she had unearthed and set in the middle. She was chatting to the guests at her invisible tea party, politely animated. There was no need to disturb her, Brianna decided, and followed Jem up the rocky trail—the last of the journey accomplished on hands and knees, owing to the steepness.

It was windy, so near the crest of the hill. Damp with perspiration, she added her own pebble ceremoniously to the wee cairn, and sat down for a moment to enjoy the view. Most of Lallybroch was visible from here, as was the road that led to the highway. She looked that way, but no sign yet of Roger's bright-orange Morris Mini. She sighed and looked away.

It was nice, up so high. Quiet, with just the sigh of the cool wind and the buzz of bees busy working in the yellow blossoms. No wonder her father liked—

"Jem." He was slumped comfortably against the rock, looking out over the surrounding hills.

"Aye?"

She hesitated, but had to ask.

"You . . . can't *see* your grandda, can you?"

He shot her a startled blue look.

"No. He's dead."

"Oh," she said, at once relieved and slightly disappointed. "I know. I . . . just wondered."

"I think maybe Mandy can," Jem said, nodding toward his sister, a bright red blot on the landscape below. "But ye can't really tell. Babies talk to lots of people ye can't see," he added tolerantly. "Grannie says so."

She didn't know whether to wish he would stop referring to his grandparents in the present tense or not. It was more than slightly unnerving, but he had said he couldn't see Jamie. She didn't want to ask whether he could see Claire—she supposed not—but she felt her parents close, whenever Jem or Mandy mentioned them, and she certainly wanted Jem and Mandy to feel close to them, as well.

She and Roger had explained things to the kids as well as such things could be explained. And evidently her father had had his own private talk with Jem; a good thing, she thought. Jamie's blend of devout Catholicism and matter-of-fact Highland acceptance of life, death, and things not seen was probably a lot better suited to explaining things like how you could be dead on one side of the stones, but—

"He said he'd look after us. Grandda," he added, turning to look at her.

She bit her tongue. No, he was not reading her mind, she told herself firmly. They'd just been talking of Jamie, after all, and Jem had chosen this particular place in which to pay his respects. So it was only natural that his grandfather would be still in his mind.

"Of course he will," she said, and put a hand on his square shoulder, massaging the knobby bones at the base of his neck with her thumb. He giggled and ducked out from under her hand, then hopped suddenly down the trail, sliding on his bottom partway, to the detriment of his jeans.

She paused for a last look round before following him, and noticed the jumble of rock on top of a hill a quarter mile or so away. A jumble of rock was exactly what one might expect to see on any Highland hilltop—but there was something slightly different about this particular assortment of stones. She shaded her eyes with her hand, squinting. She might be wrong—but she was an engineer; she knew the look of a thing built by men.

An Iron Age fortress, maybe? she thought, intrigued. There were layered stones at the bottom of that heap, she'd swear it. A foundation, perhaps. She'd have to climb up there one of these days for a closer look—maybe tomorrow, if Roger . . . Again, she glanced at the road, and again found it empty.

Mandy had grown tired of her tea party and was ready to go home. Holding her daughter firmly by one hand and the teacup in the other, Brianna made her way down the hill toward the big white-harled house, its windows fresh-washed and glinting companionably.

Had Annie done that? she wondered. She hadn't noticed, and surely window-washing on that scale would have entailed a good bit of fuss and bother. But then, she'd been distracted, what with the anticipations and apprehensions of the new job. Her heart gave a small hop at the thought that on Monday she would fit back one more piece of who she'd once been, one more stone in the foundation of who she now was.

"Maybe the piskies did it," she said aloud, and laughed.

"Pishkies diddit," Mandy echoed happily.

Jem had nearly reached the bottom, and turned, impatient, waiting for them.

"Jem," she said, the thought occurring as they came even with him. "Do you know what a Nuckelavee is?"

Jem's eyes went huge, and he clapped his hands over Mandy's ears. Something with a hundred cold tiny feet skittered up Brianna's back.

"Aye," he said, his voice small and breathless.

"Who told you about it?" she asked, keeping her voice calm. She'd *kill* Annie MacDonald, she thought.

But Jem's eyes slid sideways, as he glanced involuntarily over her shoulder, up at the broch.

"He did," he whispered.

"He?" she said sharply, and grabbed Mandy by the arm as the little girl wiggled free and turned furiously on her brother. "*Don't* kick your brother, Mandy! Who do you mean, Jemmy?"

Jem's lower teeth caught his lip.

"Him," he blurted. "The Nuckelavee."

"THE CREATURE'S home was in the sea, but it ventured upon land to feast upon humans. The Nuckelavee rode a horse on land, and its horse was sometimes indistinguishable from its own body. Its head was ten times larger than that of a man, and its mouth thrust out like a pig's, with a wide, gaping maw. The creature had no skin, and its yellow veins, muscle structure, and sinews could clearly be seen, covered in a red slimy film. The creature was armed with venomous breath and great strength. It did, however, have one weakness: an aversion to freshwater. The horse on which it rode is described as having one red eye, a mouth the size of a whale's, and flappers like fins around its forelegs."

"Ick!" Brianna put down the book—one of Roger's collection of Scottish folklore—and stared at Jem. "You saw one of these? Up by the broch?"

Her son shifted from foot to foot. "Well, he said he was. He said if I didna clear straight off, he'd change into himself, and I didna want to see *that,* so I cleared."

"Neither would I." Brianna's heart began to slow down a little. All right. He'd met a man, then, not a monster. Not that she'd actually believed . . . but the fact that someone had been hanging around the broch was worrying enough.

"What did he look like, this man?"

"Well . . . big," Jem said dubiously. Given that Jem was not quite nine, most men would be.

"As big as Daddy?"

"Maybe."

Further catechism elicited relatively few details; Jem knew what a Nuckelavee was—he'd read most of the more sensational items in Roger's collection—and had been so terrified at meeting someone who might at any moment shed his skin and eat him that his impressions of the man were sparse. Tall, with a short beard, hair that wasn't very dark, and clothes "like Mr. MacNeil wears." Working clothes, then, like a farmer.

"Why didn't you tell me or Daddy about him?"

Jem looked about to cry.

"He said he'd come back and eat Mandy if I did."

"Oh." She put an arm around him and pulled him to her. "I see. Don't be afraid, honey. It's all right." He was trembling now, as much with relief as with memory, and she stroked his bright hair, soothing him. A tramp, most likely. Camping in the broch? Likely he was gone by now—so far as she could tell from Jem's story, it had been more than a week since he had seen the man—but . . .

"Jem," she said slowly. "Why did you and Mandy go up there today? Weren't you afraid the man would be there?"

He looked up at her, surprised, and shook his head, red hair flying.

"Nay, I cleared, but I hid and watched him. He went away to the west. That's where he lives."

"He said so?"

"No. But things like that all live in the west." He pointed at the book. "When they go away to the west, they dinna come back. And I've not seen him again; I watched, to be sure."

She nearly laughed, but was still too worried. It was true; a good many Highland fairy tales did end with some supernatural creature going away to the west, or into the rocks or the water where they lived. And of course they didn't come back, since the story was over.

"He was just a nasty tramp," she said firmly, and patted Jem's back before releasing him. "Don't worry about him."

"Sure?" he said, obviously wanting to believe her, but not quite ready to relax into security.

"Sure," she said firmly.

"Okay." He heaved a deep sigh and pushed away from her. "Besides," he added, looking happier, "Grandda wouldn't let him eat Mandy or me. I should have thought o' that."

IT WAS NEARLY SUNSET by the time she heard the chugging of Roger's car on the farm road. She rushed outside, and he'd barely got out of the car before she flung herself into his arms.

He didn't waste time with questions. He embraced her passionately and kissed her in a way that made it clear that their argument was over; the details of mutual apology could wait. For an instant, she allowed herself to let go of everything, feeling weightless in his arms, breathing the scents of petrol and dust and libraries full of old books that overlay his natural smell, that indefinable faint musk of sun-warmed skin, even when he hadn't been in the sun.

"They say women can't really identify their husbands by smell," she remarked, reluctantly coming back to earth. "I don't believe it. I could pick you out of King's Cross tube station in the pitch-dark."

"I did have a bath this morning, aye?"

"Yes, and you stayed in college, because I can smell the horrible industrial-strength soap they use there," she said, wrinkling her nose. "I'm surprised it doesn't take your skin off. And you had black pudding for your breakfast. With fried tomato."

"Right, Lassie," he said, smiling. "Or do I mean Rin-Tin-Tin? Saved any small children or tracked any robbers to their lairs today, have ye?"

"Well, yes. Sort of." She glanced up at the hill behind the house, where the broch's shadow had grown long and black.

"But I thought I'd better wait until the sheriff came back from town before I went any further."

ARMED WITH A STOUT blackthorn walking stick and an electric torch, Roger approached the broch, angry but cautious. It wasn't likely the man was armed, if he was still there, but Brianna was at the kitchen door, the telephone—at the full stretch of its long cord—beside her, and two nines already dialed. She'd wanted to come with him, but he'd convinced her that one of them had to stay with the kids. Still, it would have been a comfort to have her at his back; she was a tall, muscular woman, and not one to shrink from physical violence.

The door of the broch hung askew; the ancient leather hinges had long since rotted away and been replaced with cheap iron, which had rusted in turn. The door was still attached to its frame, but barely. He lifted the latch and maneuvered the heavy, splintering wood inward, pulling it away from the floor so it swung without scraping.

There was still plenty of light outside; it wouldn't be full dark for half an hour yet. Inside the broch, though, it was black as a well. He shone his torch on the floor and saw fresh drag marks in the dirt that crusted the stone floor. Aye, someone had been here, then. Jem might be able to move the door, but the kids weren't allowed to go in the broch without an adult, and Jem swore he hadn't.

"Halloooo!" he shouted, and was answered by a startled movement somewhere far above. He gripped his stick in reflex, but recognized the flutter and rustle for what it was almost at once. Bats, hanging up under the conical roof. He flashed his light round the ground floor and saw a few stained and crumpled newspapers by the wall. He picked one up and smelled it: old, but the scent of fish and vinegar was still discernible.

He hadn't thought Jem was making up the Nuckelavee story, but this evidence of recent human occupation renewed his anger. That someone should not only come and lurk on his property, but threaten his son . . . He almost hoped the fellow was still here. He wanted a word.

He wasn't, though. No one with sense would have gone to the upper floors of the broch; the boards were half rotted, and as his eyes adjusted, he could see the gaping holes, a faint light coming through them from the slit windows higher up. Roger heard nothing, but an urge to be certain propelled him up the narrow stone stair that spiraled round the inside of the tower, testing each step for loose stones before trusting his weight to it.

He disturbed a quantity of pigeons on the top floor, who panicked and whirled round the inside of the tower like a feathery tornado, shedding down feathers and droppings, before finding their way out of the windows. He pressed himself against the wall, heart pounding as they battered blindly past his face. Something—a rat, a mouse, a vole—ran over his foot, and he jerked convulsively, nearly losing his torch.

The broch was alive, all right; the bats up above were shifting around, uneasy at all the racket below. But no sign of an intruder, human or not.

Coming down, he put his head out to signal to Bree that all was well, then closed the door and made his way down to the house, brushing dirt and pigeon feathers off his clothes.

"I'll put a new hasp and a padlock on that door," he told Brianna, lounging against the old stone sink as she started the supper. "Though I doubt he'll be back. Likely just a traveler."

"From the Orkneys, do you think?" She was reassured, he could tell, but there was still a line of worry between her brows. "You said that's where they have stories about the Nuckelavee."

He shrugged.

"Possible. But ye find the stories written down; the Nuckelavee's not so popular as kelpies or fairies, but anyone might come across him in print. What's that?" She had opened the refrigerator to get the butter out, and he'd glimpsed the bottle of champagne on the shelf, its foiled label gleaming.

"Oh, that." She looked at him, ready to smile, but with a certain apprehension in her eyes. "I, um, got the job. I thought we might . . . celebrate?" The tentative question smote him to the heart, and he smacked himself on the forehead.

"Christ, I forgot to ask! That's great, Bree! I knew ye would, mind," he said, smiling with every bit of warmth and conviction he could muster. "Never a doubt."

He could see the tension leave her body as her face lit up, and felt a certain peace descend on him, as well. This pleasant feeling lasted through the rib-cracking hug she gave him and the very nice kiss that followed, but was obliterated when she stepped back and, taking up a saucepan, asked with elaborate casualness, "So . . . did you find what you were looking for in Oxford?"

"Yeah." It came out in a gruff croak; he cleared his throat and tried again. "Yeah, more or less. Look—can the supper wait a bit, d'ye think? I think I'd have more appetite if I tell ye first."

"Sure," she said slowly, putting down the saucepan. Her eyes were fixed on him, interested, maybe a bit fearful. "I fed the kids before you got home. If you're not starving . . ."

He was; he hadn't stopped for lunch on the way back and his stomach was flapping, but it didn't matter. He reached out a hand to her.

"Come on out. The evening's fine." And if she took it badly, there were no saucepans out of doors.

"I WENT ROUND to Old St. Stephen's," he said abruptly, as soon as they'd left the house. "To talk to Dr. Weatherspoon; he's rector there. He was a friend of the Reverend's—he's known me since I was a lad."

Her hand had tightened on his arm as he spoke. He risked a glance at her and saw her looking anxious but hopeful.

"And . . . ?" she said, tentative.

"Well . . . the upshot of it is I've got a job, too." He smiled, self-conscious. "Assistant choirmaster."

That, of course, hadn't been what she was expecting at all, and she blinked. Then her eyes went to his throat. He knew fine what she was thinking.

"*Are you going to wear* that*?*" she had asked, hesitant, the first time they prepared to go into Inverness for shopping.

"I was, aye. Why, have I got a spot?" He'd craned to look over the shoulder of his white shirt. No surprise if he had. Mandy had rushed in from her play to greet him, plastering his legs with sandy hugs. He'd dusted her off a bit before lifting her for a proper kiss, but . . .

"Not that," Bree had said, her lips compressing for a minute. *"It's just . . . What will you say about . . ."* She made a throat-cutting gesture.

His hand had gone to the open collar of his shirt, where the rope scar made a curving line, distinct to the touch, like a chain of tiny pebbles under the skin. It had faded somewhat, but was still very visible.

"Nothing."

Her brows rose, and he'd given her a lopsided smile.

"But what will they be thinking?"

"I suppose they'll just assume I'm into autoerotic asphyxiation and went a bit too far one day."

Familiar as he was with the rural Highlands, he imagined that was the least of what they would think. Externally proper his putative congregation might be—but no one could imagine more lurid depravity than a devout Scottish Presbyterian.

"Did . . . er . . . did you tell Dr. Weatherspoon . . . What *did* you tell him?" she asked now, after a moment's consideration. "I mean—he had to have noticed."

"Oh, aye. He noticed. I didn't say anything, though, and neither did he."

"Look, Bree," he'd told her on that first day, *"it's a straight choice. We tell everyone the absolute truth, or we tell them nothing—or as close to nothing as possible—and let them think what they like. Concocting a story won't work, will it? Too many ways to trip up."*

She hadn't liked it; he could still see the way her eyes had drawn down at the corners. But he was right, and she knew it. Decision had spread across her face, and she'd nodded, her shoulders squaring.

They'd had to do a certain amount of lying, of course, in order to legalize the existence of Jem and Mandy. But it was the late seventies; communes abounded in the States, and impromptu bands of "travelers," as they called themselves, drifted to and fro across Europe in cavalcades of rusted buses and clapped-out vans. They had brought very little through the stones with them, bar the children themselves—but among the tiny hoard Brianna had tucked into her pockets and down her stays were two handwritten birth certificates, attested by one Claire Beauchamp Randall, MD, attending physician.

"It's the proper form for a home birth," Claire had said, making the loops of her signature with care. *"And I* am*—or I was,"* she'd corrected, with a wry twist of the mouth, *"a registered physician, licensed by the Commonwealth of Massachusetts."*

"Assistant choirmaster," Bree said now, eyeing him.

He drew a deep breath; the evening air *was* fine, clear and soft, if beginning to be populated by midgies. He waved a cloud of them away from his face, and grasped the nettle.

"I didn't go for a job, mind. I went to . . . to get my mind clear. About being a minister."

She stopped dead at that.

"And . . . ?" she prompted.

"Come on." He pulled her gently into motion once more. "We'll be eaten alive if we stand here."

They strolled through the kailyard and out past the barn, walking along the path that led by the back pasture. He'd already milked the two cows, Milly and Blossom, and they'd settled for the night, big humped dark shapes in the grass, peacefully chewing their cuds.

"I told you about the Westminster Confession, aye?" This was the Presbyterian equivalent to the Catholics' Nicene Creed—their statement of officially accepted doctrine.

"Uh-huh."

"Well, see, to be a Presbyterian minister, I'd need to be able to swear that I accepted everything in the Westminster Confession. I did, when I—well, before." He'd come so close, he thought. He'd been on the eve of ordination as a minister when fate had intervened, in the person of Stephen Bonnet. Roger had been compelled to drop everything, to find and rescue Brianna from the pirate's lair on Ocracoke. Not that he regretted doing it, mind. . . . She paced beside him, red and long-limbed, graceful as a tiger, and the thought that she might so easily have vanished from his life forever—and that he'd never have known his daughter . . .

He coughed and cleared his throat, abstractedly touching the scar.

"Maybe I still do. But I'm not sure. And I have to be."

"What changed?" she asked curiously. "What could you accept then that you can't now?"

What changed? he thought wryly. *Good question.*

"Predestination," he said. "In a manner of speaking." There was still enough light that he saw a look of mildly derisive amusement flicker across her face, though whether simply from the ironic juxtaposition of question and answer or from the concept itself, he didn't know. They'd never argued questions of faith—they were more than cautious with each other on *those* grounds—but they were at least familiar with the general shape of each other's beliefs.

He'd explained the idea of predestination in simple terms: not some inescapable fate ordained by God, nor yet the notion that God had laid out each person's life in great detail before his or her birth—though not a few Presbyterians saw it just that way. It had to do with salvation and the notion that God chose a pathway that led to that salvation.

"For some people," she'd said skeptically. "And He chooses to damn the rest?"

A lot of people thought *that,* too, and it had taken better minds than his to argue their way past that impression.

"There are whole books written about it, but the basic idea is that salvation's not just the result of our choice—God acts first. Extending the invitation, ye might say, and giving us an opportunity to respond. But we've still got free choice. And really," he added quickly, "the only thing that's not optional—to be a Presbyterian—is a belief in Jesus Christ. I've still got that."

"Good," she said. "But to be a minister . . . ?"

"Yeah, probably. And—well, here." He reached abruptly into his pocket and handed her the folded photocopy.

"I thought I'd best not steal the book," he said, trying for levity. "In case I *do* decide to be minister, I mean. Bad example for the flock."

"Ho-ho," she said absently, reading. She looked up, one eyebrow quirked.

"It's different, isn't it?" he said, the breathless feeling back beneath his diaphragm.

"It's . . ." Her eyes shot back to the document, and a frown creased her brow. She looked up at him a moment later, pale and swallowing. "Different. The date's different."

He felt a slight easing of the tension that had wound him up for the last twenty-four hours. He wasn't losing his mind, then. He put out a hand, and she gave him back the copy of the clipping from the *Wilmington Gazette*—the death notice for the Frasers of the Ridge.

"It's only the date," he said, running a thumb beneath the blurred type of the words. "The text—I think that's the same. Is it what you remember?" She'd found the same information, looking for her family in the past—it was what had propelled her through the stones, and him after her. *And that,* he thought, *has made all the difference. Thank you, Robert Frost.*

She'd pressed against him, to read it over again. Once, and twice, and once more for good measure, before she nodded.

"Only the date," she said, and he heard the same breathlessness in her voice. "It . . . changed."

"Good," he said, his voice sounding queer and gruff. "When I started wondering . . . I had to go and see, before I talked to you about it. Just to check—because the clipping I'd seen in a book, that couldn't be right."

She nodded, still a little pale.

"If I . . . if I went back to the archive in Boston where I found that newspaper—would it have changed, too, do you think?"

"Yeah, I do."

She was silent for a long moment, looking at the paper in his hand. Then she looked at him, intent.

"You said, when you started wondering. What made you start wondering?"

"Your mother."

IT HAD BEEN a couple of months before they left the Ridge. Unable to sleep one night, he'd gone out into the woods and, roaming restlessly to and fro, had encountered Claire, kneeling in a hollow full of white flowers, their shapes like a mist around her.

He'd just sat down then and watched her at her gathering, as she broke stems and stripped leaves into her basket. She wasn't touching the flowers, he saw, but pulling up something that grew beneath them.

"You need to gather these at night," she remarked to him after a little. "Preferably at the dark of the moon."

"I shouldn't have expected—" he began, but broke off abruptly.

She laughed, a small fizzing sound of amusement.

"You wouldn't have expected that I should put stock in such superstitions?" she asked. "Wait, young Roger. When you've lived as long as I, you may begin to regard superstitions yourself. As for this one . . ." Her hand moved, a pale blur in the darkness, and broke a stem with a soft, juicy snap. A pungent aroma suddenly filled the air, sharp and plangent through the softer aroma of the flowers.

"Insects come and lay their eggs on the leaves of some plants, do you see? The plants secrete certain rather strong-smelling substances in order to repel the bugs, and the concentration of these substances is highest when the need is greatest. As it happens, those insecticidal substances happen also to have quite powerful medicinal properties, and the chief thing that troubles this particular sort of plant"—she brushed a feathery stem under his nose, fresh and damp—"is the larvae of moths."

"Ergo, it has more of the substance late at night, because that's when the caterpillars feed?"

"Got it." The stem was withdrawn, the plant thrust into her bag with a rustle of muslin, and her head bent as she felt about for more. "And some plants are fertilized by moths. Those, of course . . ."

"Bloom at night."

"Most plants, though, are troubled by daylight insects, and so they begin to secrete their useful compounds at dawn; the concentration rises as the day waxes—but then, when the sun gets too hot, some of the oils will begin to vaporize from the leaves, and the plant will stop producing them. So most of the very aromatic plants, you pick in late morning. And so the shamans and the herbalists tell their apprentices to take one plant in the dark of the moon and another at midday—thus making it a superstition, hmm?" Her voice was rather dry, but still amused.

Roger sat back on his heels, watching her grope about. Now that his eyes were accustomed, he could make out her shape with ease, though the details of her face were still hidden.

She worked for a time, and then sat back on her heels and stretched; he heard the creak of her back.

"I saw him once, you know." Her voice was muffled; she had turned away from him, probing under the drooping branches of a rhododendron.

"Saw him? Who?"

"The King." She found something; he heard the rustle of leaves as she tugged at it, and the snap of the breaking stem.

"He came to Pembroke Hospital, to visit the soldiers there. He came and spoke separately to us—the nurses and doctors. He was a quiet man, very dignified, but warm in his manner. I couldn't tell you a thing that he said. But it was . . . remarkably inspiring. Just that he was there, you know."

"Mmphm." Was it the onset of war, he wondered, making her recall such things?

"A journalist asked the Queen if she would be taking her children and evacuating to the country—so many were, you know."

"I know." Roger saw suddenly in his mind's eye a pair of children: a boy and a girl, thin-faced and silent, huddling near each other beside a familiar hearth. "We had two of them—at our house in Inverness. How odd, I hadn't remembered them at all until just now."

She wasn't paying attention, though.

"She said—and I may not have the quote exactly right, but this is the gist of it—'Well, the children can't leave me, and I can't leave the King—and of course the king won't leave.' When was your father killed, Roger?"

Whatever he'd been expecting her to say, it wasn't that. For an instant, the question seemed so incongruous as not to be comprehensible.

"What?" But he *had* heard her, and shaking his head to dispel a feeling of surreality, he answered, "October 1941. I'm not sure I remember the exact date—no, I do, the Reverend had it written on his genealogy. The thirty-first of October, 1941. Why?" *"Why in God's name,"* he wanted to say, but he'd been trying to control the impulse toward casual blasphemy. He choked off the stronger impulse to escape into random thought and repeated, very calmly, "Why?"

"You said he'd been shot down in Germany, didn't you?"

"Over the Channel on his way to Germany. So I was told."

He could just make out her features in the moonlight, but couldn't read her expression.

"Who told you? Do you remember?"

"The Reverend, I suppose. Or I suppose it might have been my mother." The sense of unreality was wearing off, and he was beginning to feel angry. "Does it matter?"

"Probably not. When we first met you—Frank and I, in Inverness—the Reverend said then that your father had been shot down over the Channel."

"Yes? Well . . ." *So what?* was unspoken, but she plainly picked it up, for there was a small snort of not-quite laughter from the rhododendrons.

"You're right, it doesn't matter. But—both you and the Reverend mentioned that he was a Spitfire pilot. Is that correct?"

"Yes." Roger wasn't sure why, but he was beginning to have an uneasy sense at the back of his neck, as though something might be standing behind him. He coughed, making an excuse to turn his head, but glimpsed nothing behind him but the black-and-white forest, smudged by moonlight.

"I do know that for sure," he said, feeling oddly defensive. "My mother had a photograph of him with his plane. *Rag Doll,* the plane was called; the name was painted on the nose, with a crude picture of a dolly in a red dress, with black curls." He did know that for sure. He'd slept with the picture under his pillow for a long time after his mother was killed—the studio portrait of his mother was too big, and he worried that someone would notice it missing.

"Rag Doll," he repeated, suddenly struck by something.

"What? What is it?"

He waved a hand, awkward.

"It—nothing. I—I just realized that 'Rag Doll' was probably what my father called my mother. A nickname, you know? I saw a few of his letters to her; they were usually addressed to *Dolly.* And just now, thinking of the black curls—my mother's portrait . . . Mandy. Mandy's got my mother's hair."

"Oh, good," Claire said dryly. "I'd hate to think I was entirely responsible for it. Do tell her that, when she's older, will you? Girls with very curly hair invariably hate it—at least in the early years, when they want to look like everyone else."

Despite his preoccupation, he heard the small note of desolation in her voice, and reached for her hand, disregarding the fact that she still held a plant in it.

"I'll tell her," he said softly. "I'll tell her everything. Don't ever think we'd let the kids forget you."

She squeezed his hand, hard, and the fragrant white flowers spilled over the darkness of her skirt.

"Thank you," she whispered. He heard her sniff a little, and she wiped the back of her other hand swiftly across her eyes.

"Thanks," she said again, more strongly, and straightened herself. "It *is* important. To remember. If I didn't know that, I wouldn't tell you."

"Tell me . . . what?"

Her hands, small and hard and smelling of medicine, wrapped his.

"I don't know what happened to your father," she said. "But it wasn't what they told you."

"I WAS *THERE*, ROGER," she repeated, patient. "I read the papers—I nursed airmen; I talked to them. I saw the planes. Spitfires were small, light planes, meant for defense. They never crossed the Channel; they hadn't the range to go from England into Europe and back, though they were used there later."

"But . . ." Whatever argument he'd meant to make—blown off course, miscalculation—faded. The hairs had risen on his forearms without his noticing.

"Of course, things happen," she said, as though able to read his thoughts. "Accounts get garbled, too, over time and distance. Whoever told your mother might have been mistaken; she might have said something that the Reverend misconstrued. All those things are possible. But during the War, I had letters from Frank—he wrote as often as he could, up until they recruited him into MI6. After that, I often wouldn't hear anything for months. But just before that, he wrote to me, and mentioned—just as casual chat, you know—that he'd run into something strange in the reports he was handling. A Spitfire had gone down, crashed—not shot down, they thought it must have been an engine failure—in Northumbria, and while it hadn't burned, for a wonder—there was no sign of the pilot. None. And he did mention the name of the pilot, because he thought Jeremiah rather an appropriately doomed sort of name."

"Jerry," Roger said, his lips feeling numb. "My mother always called him Jerry."

"Yes," she said softly. "And there are circles of standing stones scattered all over Northumbria."

"Near where the plane—"

"I don't know. " He saw the slight movement as she shrugged, helpless.

He closed his eyes and breathed deep, the air thick with the scent from the broken stems.

"And you're telling me now because we're going back," he said, very calmly.

"I've been arguing with myself for weeks," she said, sounding apologetic. "It was only a month or so ago that I remembered. I don't often think about the—my—past, but what with everything . . ." She waved a hand, encompassing their imminent departure and the intense discussions surrounding it. "I was just thinking of the War—I wonder if anyone who was in it ever thinks of it without a capital 'W'—and telling Jamie about it."

It was Jamie who had asked her about Frank. Wanted to know what role he had played in the war.

"He's curious about Frank," she said abruptly.

"I would be, too, under the circumstances," Roger had replied dryly. "Was Frank not curious about him?"

That seemed to unsettle her, and she'd not replied directly but had pulled the conversation firmly back on track—if you could use such a word for such a conversation, he thought.

"Anyway," she said, "it was that that reminded me of Frank's letters. And I was trying to recall the things he'd written me about, when suddenly I remembered that one phrase—about Jeremiah being a name with a certain doom about it." He heard her sigh.

"I wasn't sure . . . but I talked to Jamie, and he said I should tell you. He says he thinks you've a right to know—and that you'd do the right thing with the knowledge."

"I'm flattered," he said. More like flattened.

"SO THAT'S IT." The evening stars had begun to come out, faint over the mountains. Not as brilliant as the stars had been on the Ridge, where the mountain night came down like black velvet. They'd come back to the house by now, but lingered in the dooryard, talking.

"I'd thought about it, now and again: how does the time-traveling fit into God's plan? Can things be changed? *Ought* they be changed? Your parents—they tried to change history, tried damned hard, and couldn't do it. I'd thought that was all there was to it—and from a Presbyterian point of view." He let a little humor show in his voice. "It was a comfort, almost, to think that it *couldn't* change. It shouldn't be able to be changed. Ye know: *God's in His heaven, all's right with the world* sort of thing."

"But." Bree was holding the folded photocopy; she waved it at a passing moth, a tiny white blur.

"But," he agreed. "Proof that things *can* be changed."

"I talked to Mama a little bit about it," Bree said, after a moment's thought. "She laughed."

"Did she?" Roger said dryly, and got the breath of a laugh from Bree in answer.

"Not like she thought it was funny," she assured him. "I'd asked her if she thought it was possible for a traveler to change things, change the future, and she told me it was, obviously—because she changed the future every time she kept someone from dying who would have died if she hadn't been there. Some of them went on to have children they wouldn't have had, and who knew what those children would do, that they wouldn't have done if they hadn't . . . and *that* was when she laughed and said it was a good thing Catholics believed in Mystery and didn't insist on trying to figure out exactly *how* God worked, like Protestants do."

"Well, I don't know that I'd say—oh, was she talking about me?"

"Probably. I didn't ask."

Now it was his turn to laugh, though it hurt his throat to do it.

"Proof," she said thoughtfully. She was sitting on the

bench near the front door, folding the photocopy in long, nervously deft fingers. "I don't know. *Is* it proof?"

"Maybe not up to your rigorous engineering standards," he said. "But I do remember—and so do you. If it was only me, then, yeah, I'd think it was just my mind going. But I've got a little more faith in *your* mental processes. Are you making a paper airplane out of that?"

"No, it's—whoa. Mandy." She was up and moving before he'd quite registered the wail from the nursery upstairs, and had vanished into the house a moment later, leaving him to lock up below. They didn't usually bother locking the doors—no one did, in the Highlands—but tonight . . .

His heart rate surged as a long gray shadow shot out across the path in front of him. Then dropped as he smiled. Wee Adso, out for a prowl. A neighbor boy had come round with a basket of kittens a few months before, looking for homes for them, and Bree had taken the gray one, a green-eyed ringer for her mother's cat, and given it the same name. If they got a watchdog, would they name it Rollo? he wondered.

"Cat a Mhinister . . ." he said. *The minister's cat is a hunting cat.*

"Good hunting, then," he added to the tail disappearing under the hydrangea bush, and bent to retrieve the half-folded paper from the path where Brianna had dropped it.

No, it wasn't a paper airplane. What was it? A paper hat? No telling, and he tucked it into his shirt pocket and went in.

He found Bree and Mandy in the front parlor, in front of a freshly made fire. Mandy, comforted and given milk, had half-dozed off again already in Bree's arms; she blinked sleepily at him, sucking on a thumb.

"Aye, what's the trouble, then, *a leannan*?" he asked her softly, pushing tumbled curls out of her eyes.

"Bad dream," Bree said, her voice carefully casual. "A naughty thing outside, trying to get in her window."

He and Brianna had been sitting below that very window at the time, but he glanced reflexively at the window beside him, which reflected only the domestic scene of which he was a part. The man in the glass looked wary, shoulders hunched in readiness to lunge at something. He got up and drew the curtains.

"Here," he said abruptly, sitting down and reaching for

Mandy. She came into his arms with the slow amiability of a tree sloth, sticking her wet thumb in his ear in the process.

Bree went to fetch them cups of cocoa, returning with a rattle of crockery, the scent of hot milk and chocolate, and the look of someone who's been thinking what to say about a difficult matter.

"Did you . . . I mean, given the nature of the, er, difficulty . . . did you maybe think of asking God?" she said, diffident. "Directly?"

"Yeah, I did think of that," he assured her, torn between annoyance and amusement at the question. "And yes, I did ask—a number of times. Especially on the way to Oxford. Where I found that." He nodded at the bit of paper. "What is it, by the way? The shape, I mean."

"Oh." She picked it up and made the last few folds, quick and sure, then held it out on the palm of her hand. He frowned at it for a moment, then realized what it was. A Chinese fortune-teller, kids called them; there were four pockets showing, and you put your fingers in them and could open the thing in different combinations as questions were asked, so as to show the different answers—*Yes, No, Sometimes, Always*—written on the flaps inside.

"Very appropriate," he said.

They fell silent for a moment, drinking cocoa in a silence that balanced precariously on the edge of question.

"The Westminster Confession also says, *God alone is Lord of the conscience.* I'll make my peace with it," he said quietly, at last, "or I won't. I said to Dr. Weatherspoon that it seemed a bit odd, having an assistant choirmaster who couldn't sing—he just smiled and said he was wanting me to take the job so as to keep me in the fold while I thought things over, as he put it. Probably afraid I'd jump ship else, and go over to Rome," he added, as a feeble joke.

"That's good," she said softly, not looking up from the depths of the cocoa she wasn't drinking.

More silence. And the shade of Jerry MacKenzie, RAF, came and sat down by the fire in his fleece-lined leather flight jacket, watching the play of light in his granddaughter's ink-black hair.

"So you—" He could hear the little pop as her tongue parted from her dry mouth. "You're going to look? See if you can find out where your father went? Where he might . . . be?"

Where he might be. Here, there, then, now? His heart gave a sudden convulsive lurch, thinking of the tramp who'd stayed in the broch. God . . . no. It couldn't be. No reason to think it, none. Only wanting.

He'd thought about it a lot, on the way to Oxford, between the praying. What he'd say, what he'd ask, if he had the chance. He wanted to ask everything, say everything—but there really was only the one thing to say to his father, and that thing was snoring in his arms like a drunken bumblebee.

"No." Mandy squirmed in her sleep, emitted a small burp, and settled back against his chest. He didn't look up, but kept his eyes fixed in the dark labyrinth of her curls. "I couldn't risk my own kids losing their father." His voice had nearly disappeared; he felt his vocal cords grinding like gears to force the words out.

"It's too important. You don't forget having a dad."

Bree's eyes slid sideways, the blue of them no more than a spark in the firelight.

"I thought . . . you were so young. You do remember your father?"

Roger shook his head, the chambers of his heart clenching hard, grasping emptiness.

"No," he said softly, and bent his head, breathing in the scent of his daughter's hair. "I remember yours."

22

FLUTTERBY

Wilmington, colony of North Carolina
May 3, 1777

I COULD SEE AT once that Jamie had been dreaming again. His face had an unfocused, inward look, as though he were seeing something other than the fried black pudding on his plate.

Seeing him like this gave me an urgent desire to ask what he had seen—quelled at once, for fear that if I asked too soon, he might lose some part of the dream. It also, truth be told, knotted me with envy. I would have given anything to see what he saw, whether it was real or not. That hardly mattered—it was connection, and the severed nerve ends that had joined me to my vanished family sparked and burned like shorted-out electrical cables when I saw that look on his face.

I couldn't stand not to know what he had dreamed, though in the usual manner of dreams, it was seldom straightforward.

"You've been dreaming of them, haven't you?" I said, when the serving maid had gone out. We'd risen late, tired from the long ride to Wilmington the day before, and were the only diners in the inn's small front room.

He glanced at me and nodded slowly, a small frown between his brows. *That* made me uneasy; the occasional dreams he had of Bree or the children normally left him peaceful and happy.

"What?" I demanded. "What happened?"

He shrugged, still frowning.

"Nothing, Sassenach. I saw Jem and the wee lass—" A smile came over his face at that. "God, she's a feisty wee baggage! She minds me o' you, Sassenach."

This was a dubious compliment as phrased, but I felt a deep glow at the thought. I'd spent hours looking at Mandy and Jem, memorizing every small feature and gesture, trying to extrapolate, imagine what they would look like as they grew—and I was almost sure that Mandy had my mouth. I knew for a fact that she had the shape of my eyes—and my hair, poor child, for all it was inky black.

"What were they doing?"

He rubbed a finger between his brows as though his forehead itched.

"They were outside," he said slowly. "Jem told her to do something and she kicked him in the shin and ran away from him, so he chased her. I think it was spring." He smiled, eyes fixed on whatever he'd seen in his dream. "I mind the wee flowers, caught in her hair, and lying in drifts across the stones."

"What stones?" I asked sharply.

"Oh. The gravestones," he answered, readily enough. "That's it—they were playing among the stones on the hill behind Lallybroch."

I sighed happily. This was the third dream that he'd had, seeing them at Lallybroch. It might be only wishful thinking, but I knew it made him as happy as it made me, to feel that they had made a home there.

"They could be," I said. "Roger went there—when we were looking for you. He said the place was standing vacant, for sale. Bree would have money; they might have bought it. They *could* be there!" I'd told him that before, but he nodded, pleased.

"Aye, they could be," he said, his eyes still soft with his memory of the children on the hill, chasing through the long grass and the worn gray stones that marked his family's rest.

"A flutterby came with them," he said suddenly. "I'd forgot that. A blue one."

"Blue? Are there blue butterflies in Scotland?" I frowned, trying to remember. Such butterflies as I'd ever noticed had tended to be white or yellow, I thought.

Jamie gave me a look of mild exasperation.

"It's a dream, Sassenach. I could have flutterbys wi' tartan wings, and I liked."

I laughed, but refused to be distracted.

"Right. What was it that bothered you, though?"

He glanced curiously at me.

"How did ye ken I was troubled?"

I looked at him down my nose—or as much down my nose as was possible, given the disparity of height.

"You may not have a glass face, but I *have* been married to you for thirty-odd years."

He let the fact that I hadn't actually been *with* him for twenty of those years pass without comment, and only smiled.

"Aye. Well, it wasna anything, really. Only that they went into the broch."

"The broch?" I said uncertainly. The ancient tower for which Lallybroch was named did stand on the hill behind the house, its shadow passing daily through the burying ground like the stately march of a giant sundial. Jamie and I had gone up there often of an evening in our early days at Lallybroch, to sit on the bench that stood against the broch's wall and be away from the hubbub of the house, enjoying the peaceful sight of the estate and its grounds spread white and green below us, soft with twilight.

The small frown was back between his brows.

"The broch," he repeated, and looked at me, helpless. "I dinna ken what it was. Only that I didna want them to go in. It . . . felt as though there was something inside. Waiting. And I didna like it at all."

PART THREE

Privateer

23

CORRESPONDENCE FROM THE FRONT

October 3, 1776
Ellesmere
to Lady Dorothea Grey

Dear Coz—

I write in haste to catch the Courier. I am embarked upon a brief Journey in company with another Officer, on behalf of Captain Richardson, and do not know for certain what my Whereabouts may be for the immediate Future. You may write to me in care of your Brother Adam; I will endeavor to keep in Correspondence with him.

I have executed your Commission to the best of my Ability, and will persevere in your Service. Give my Father and yours my best Regards and Respects, as well as my continuing Affection, and do not omit to keep a large Part of this last Quantity for yourself.

Your most obedient,
William

October 3, 1776
Ellesmere to Lord John Grey

Dear Father,

After due Thought, I have decided to accept

Captain Richardson's Proposal that I accompany a senior Officer on a Mission to Quebec, acting as Interpreter for him, my French being thought adequate to the Purpose. General Howe is agreeable.

I have not yet met Captain Randall-Isaacs, but will join him in Albany next Week. I do not know when we may return, and cannot say what Opportunities there may be to write, but I will do so when I can, and in the meantime beg that you will think fondly of

Your son,
William

Late October 1776
Quebec

WILLIAM WASN'T sure quite what to make of Captain Denys Randall-Isaacs. On the surface, he was just the sort of genial, unremarkable fellow you found in any regiment: about thirty, decent with cards, ready with a joke, good-looking in a dark sort of way, open-faced, and reliable. He was a very pleasant traveling companion, too, with a fund of entertaining stories for the road and a thoroughgoing knowledge of bawdy songs and poems of the lower sort.

What he didn't do was talk about himself. Which, in William's experience, was what most people did best—or at least most frequently.

He'd tried a little tentative prodding, offering the rather dramatic story of his own birth, and receiving in turn a few spare facts: Randall-Isaacs's own father, an officer of dragoons, had died in the Highlands campaign before Denys's birth, and his mother had remarried a year later.

"My stepfather is a Jew," he'd told William. "A rich one," he'd added, with a wry smile.

William had nodded, amiable.

"Better than a poor one," he'd said, and left it at that. It wasn't much, as facts went, but it did go some way to explain why Randall-Isaacs was working for Richardson rather than pursuing fame and glory with the Lancers or the Welch Fusiliers. Money would buy a commission, but it would not ensure a warm reception in a regiment nor the sorts of opportunity that family connections and the influence spoken of delicately as "interest" would.

It occurred—fleetingly—to William to wonder just why he was turning his back on his own substantial connections and opportunities in order to engage in Captain Richardson's shadowy ventures, but he dismissed that consideration as a matter for later contemplation.

"Amazing," Denys murmured, looking up. They had reined in their horses on the road that led up from the bank of the St. Lawrence to the citadel of Quebec; from here, they could see the steep cliff face that Wolfe's troops had climbed, seventeen years before, to capture the citadel—and Quebec—from the French.

"My father made that climb," William said, trying to sound casual.

Randall-Isaacs's head swiveled toward him in astonishment. "He did? Lord John, you mean—he fought on the Plains of Abraham with Wolfe?"

"Yes." William eyed the cliff with respect. It was thick with saplings, but the underlying rock was crumbling shale; he could see the jagged dark fissures and quadrangular cracks through the leaves. The notion of scaling that height in the dark, and not only climbing it, but hauling all the artillery up the cliffside with them . . . !

"He said the battle was over almost as soon as it started—only the one great volley—but the climb to the battlefield was the worst thing he'd ever done."

Randall-Isaacs grunted respectfully, and paused for a moment before gathering his reins.

"You said your father knows Sir Guy?" he said. "Doubtless he'll appreciate hearing the story."

William glanced at his companion. Actually, he *hadn't* said that Lord John knew Sir Guy Carleton, the commander in chief for North America—though he did. His father knew everyone. And with that simple thought, he realized suddenly what his true function on this expedition was. He was Randall-Isaacs's calling card.

It was true that he spoke French very well—languages came easy to him—and that Randall-Isaacs's French was rudimentary. Richardson had likely been telling the truth about that bit; always best to have an interpreter you can trust. But while Randall-Isaacs had exhibited a flattering interest in William, William became aware *ex post facto* that Randall-Isaacs was much more specifically interested in Lord John: the highlights of his military career, where he had been posted, whom he had served with or under, who he knew.

It had happened twice already. They'd called upon the commanders of Fort Saint-Jean and Fort Chambly, and in both instances Randall-Isaacs had presented their credentials, mentioning casually that William was the son of Lord John Grey. Whereupon the official welcome had warmed at once into a long, late evening of reminiscence and conversation, fueled by good brandy. During which—William now realized—he and the commanders had done all the talking. And Randall-Isaacs had sat listening, his handsome, high-colored face aglow with a flattering interest.

Huh, William thought to himself. Having worked it out, he wasn't sure how he felt about it. On the one hand, he was pleased with himself for having smoked what was going on. On the other, he was less pleased to think that he was desirable mainly for his connections, rather than his own virtues.

Well, it was useful, if humbling, to know. What he *didn't* know was exactly what Randall-Isaacs's role was. Was he only gathering information for Richardson? Or had he other business, unspoken? Often enough, Randall-Isaacs had left him to his own devices, saying casually that he had a private errand for which he thought his own French adequate.

They were—according to the very limited instruction Captain Richardson had given him—assessing the sentiments of the French *habitants* and English settlers in Quebec, with an eye to future support in case of incursion by the American rebels or attempted threats and seductions by the Continental Congress.

These sentiments so far seemed clear, if not what he might have expected. The French settlers in the area were in sympathy with Sir Guy, who—as governor general of North America—had passed the Quebec Act, which legalized Catholicism and protected the French Catholics' trade. The

English were disgruntled by the same act, for obvious reasons, and had declined *en masse* to answer Sir Guy's calls for militia assistance during the American attack on the city during the previous winter.

"They must have been insane," he remarked to Randall-Isaacs, as they crossed the open plain before the citadel. "The Americans who tried it on here last year, I mean."

They'd reached the top of the cliff now, and the citadel rose from the plain before them, peaceful and solid—very solid—in the autumn sun. The day was warm and beautiful, and the air was alive with the rich, earthy smells of the river and forest. He'd never seen such a forest. The trees that edged the plain and grew all along the banks of the St. Lawrence grew impenetrably thick, now blazing with gold and crimson. Seen against the darkness of the water and the impossible deep blue of the vast October sky, the whole of it gave him the dreamlike feeling of riding through a medieval painting, glowing with gold leaf and burning with a sense of otherworldly fervor.

But beyond the beauty of it, he felt the savagery of the place. Felt it with a clarity that made his bones feel transparent. The days were still warm, but the chill of winter was a sharp tooth that bit harder with each day's twilight, and it took very little imagination for him to see this plain as it would be a few weeks from now, cloaked in bitter ice, whitely inhospitable to all life. With a ride of two hundred miles behind him, and an immediate understanding of the problems of supply for two riders on the rugged journey north in *good* weather, combined with what he knew of the rigors of supplying an army in bad weather . . .

"If they weren't insane, they wouldn't be doing what they *are* doing." Randall-Isaacs interrupted his thoughts, he, too, drawing up for a moment to look over the prospect with a soldier's eye. "It was Colonel Arnold who led them here, though. That man is certainly insane. But a damned good soldier." Admiration showed in his voice, and William glanced curiously at him.

"Know him, do you?" he asked casually, and Randall-Isaacs laughed.

"Not to speak to," he replied. "Come on." He spurred up, and they turned toward the citadel gate. He wore an amused, half-contemptuous expression, though, as if dwelling on a memory, and after a few moments, he spoke again.

"He might have done it. Arnold, I mean; taken the city. Sir Guy hadn't any troops to speak of, and had Arnold got here when he planned to, and with the powder and shot he needed . . . well, it would have been a different story. But he chose the wrong man to ask directions of."

"What do you mean by that?"

Randall-Isaacs looked suddenly wary, but then seemed to shrug internally, as though to say, *"What does it matter?"* He was in good humor, already looking forward to a hot dinner, a soft bed, and clean linen, after weeks of camping in the dark forests.

"He couldn't make it overland," he said. "Seeking a way to carry an army and its necessities north by water, Arnold had gone looking for someone who had made the hazardous trip and knew the rivers and portages," Randall-Isaacs said. "He'd found one, too—Samuel Goodwin."

"But it never occurred to him that Goodwin might be a Loyalist." Randall-Isaacs shook his head at this naïveté. "Goodwin came to me and asked what he should do. So I told him, and he gave Arnold his maps—carefully rewritten to serve their purpose."

And serve their purpose they had. By misstating distances, removing landmarks, indicating passages where there were none, and providing maps that were pure figments of imagination, Mr. Goodwin's guidance succeeded in luring Arnold's force deep into the wilderness, obliging them to carry their ships and supplies overland for days on end, and eventually delaying them so badly that the winter caught them, well short of Quebec City.

Randall-Isaacs laughed, though there was a tinge of regret about it, William thought.

"I was amazed when they told me he'd made it after all. Aside from everything else, he'd been swindled by the carpenters who made his ships—I do believe that was sheer incompetence, not politics, though these days it's sometimes hard to tell. Made with green timbers and badly fitted. More than half of them came apart and sank within days of launching.

"It had to have been sheer hell," Randall-Isaacs said, as though to himself. He pulled himself up straight then, shaking his head.

"But they followed him. All his men. Only one company turned back. Starving, half naked, freezing . . . they followed him," he repeated, marveling. He glanced sideways at William, smiling. "Think your men would follow you, Lieutenant? In such conditions?"

"I hope I should have better sense than to lead them into such conditions," William replied dryly. "What happened to Arnold in the end? Was he captured?"

"No," Randall-Isaacs said thoughtfully, lifting a hand to wave at the guards by the citadel gate. "No, he wasn't. As to what's happened to him now, God only knows. Or God and Sir Guy. I'm hoping the latter can tell us."

24

JOYEUX NOËL

London
December 24, 1776

MOST PROSPEROUS madams were stout creatures, Lord John reflected. Whether it was only the satisfaction of appetites denied in their early years, or was a shield against the possibility of a return to the lower stations of their trade, almost all of them were well armored in flesh.

Not Nessie. He could see the shadow of her body through the thin muslin of her shift—he had inadvertently roused her from her bed—as she stood before the fire to pull on her bedsacque. She bore not an ounce more upon her scrawny frame than she had when he'd first met her, then aged—she'd said—

fourteen, though he'd suspected at the time that she might be eleven.

That would make her thirty-odd. She still looked fourteen.

He smiled at the notion, and she smiled back, tying her gown. The smile aged her a bit, for there were gaps among her teeth, and the remainder showed black at the root. If she was not stout, it was because she lacked the capacity to become so; she adored sugar, and would eat an entire box of candied violets or Turkish Delight in minutes, compensating for the starvation of her youth in the Scottish Highlands. He'd brought her a pound of sugarplums.

"Think I'm that cheap, do ye?" she said, raising a brow as she took the prettily wrapped box from him.

"Never," he assured her. "That is merely by way of apology for having disturbed your rest." That was improvisation; he had in fact expected to find her at work, it being past ten o'clock at night.

"Aye, well, it *is* Christmas Eve," she said, answering his unasked question. "Any man wi' a home to go to's in it." She yawned, pulled off her nightcap, and fluffed her fingers through the wild mass of curly dark hair.

"Yet you seem to have some custom," he observed. Distant singing came from two floors below, and the parlor had seemed well populated when he passed.

"Och, aye. The desperate ones. I leave them to Maybelle to deal with; dinna like to see them, poor creatures. Pitiful. They dinna really want a woman, the ones who come on Christmas Eve—only a fire to sit by, and folk to sit with." She waved a hand and sat down, greedily pulling the bow from her present.

"Let me wish you a happy Christmas, then," he said, watching her with amused affection. She popped one of the sweetmeats into her mouth, closed her eyes, and sighed in ecstasy.

"Mmp," she said, not pausing to swallow before inserting and masticating another. From the cordial intonation of this remark, he assumed her to be returning the sentiment.

He'd known it was Christmas Eve, of course, but had somehow put the knowledge of it out of his head during the long, cold hours of the day. It had poured all day, driving needles of freezing rain, augmented now and then by irritable bursts of hail, and he'd been chilled through since just before dawn, when Minnie's footman had roused him with the summons to Argus House.

Nessie's room was small but elegant, and smelled comfortably of sleep. Her bed was vast, hung with woolen bed curtains done in the very fashionable pink and black "Queen Charlotte" checks. Tired, cold, and hungry as he was, he felt the pull of that warm, inviting cavern, with its mounds of goose-down pillows, quilts, and clean, soft sheets. What would she think, he wondered, if he asked to share her bed for the night?

"A fire to sit by, and folk to sit with." Well, he had that, at least for the moment.

Grey became aware of a low buzzing noise, something like a trapped bluebottle flinging itself against a windowpane. Glancing toward the sound, he perceived that what he had thought to be merely a heap of rumpled bedclothes in fact contained a body; the elaborately passementeried tassel of a nightcap trailed across the pillow.

"That's no but Rab," said an amused Scottish voice, and he turned to find her grinning at him. "Fancy it three ways, do ye?"

He realized, even as he blushed, that he liked her not only for herself, or for her skill as an intelligence agent, but because she had an unexcelled ability to disconcert him. He thought she did not know the shape of his own desires exactly, but she'd been a whore since childhood and likely had a shrewd apprehension of almost anyone's desires, whether conscious or not.

"Oh, I think not," he said politely. "I shouldn't wish to disturb your husband." He tried not to think of Rab MacNab's brutal hands and solid thighs; Rab had been a chairman, before his marriage to Nessie and the success of the brothel they owned. Surely he didn't also . . . ?

"Ye couldna wake yon wee oaf wi' cannon fire," she said, with an affectionate glance into the bed. She got up, though, and pulled the curtains across, muffling the snoring.

"Speak o' cannon," she added, bending to peer at Grey as she returned to her seat, "ye look as though ye've been in the wars yourself. Here, have a dram, and I'll ring for a bit of hot supper." She nodded at the decanter and glasses that stood on the elbow table and reached for the bell rope.

"No, I thank you. I haven't much time. But I will take a drop to keep the cold out, thank you."

The whisky—she drank nothing else, scorning gin as a beggar's drink and regarding wine as good but insufficient to its purpose—warmed him, and his wet coat had begun to steam in the fire's heat.

"Ye've not much time," she said. "Why's that, then?"

"I'm bound for France," he said. "In the morning."

Her eyebrows shot up, and she put another comfit in her mouth.

" 'Oo 'don me tkp Kismus wi yrfmily?"

"Don't talk with your mouth full, my dear," he said, smiling nonetheless. "My brother suffered a bad attack last night. His heart, the quack says, but I doubt he really knows. The usual Christmas dinner is likely to be somewhat less of an occasion than usual, though."

"I'm that sorry to hear," Nessie said, more clearly. She wiped sugar from the corner of her mouth, brow puckered with a troubled frown. "His lordship's a fine man."

"Yes, he—" He stopped, staring at her. "You've *met* my brother?"

Nessie dimpled demurely at him.

"Discretion is a madam's most val-u-able stock in trade," she chanted, clearly parroting the wisdom of a former employer.

"Says the woman who's spying for me." He was trying to envision Hal . . . or perhaps *not* to envision Hal . . . for surely he wouldn't . . . to spare Minnie his demands, perhaps? But he'd thought . . .

"Aye, well, spying's no the same as idle gossip, now, is it? I want tea, even if you don't. Talking's thirsty work." She rang the bell for the porter, then turned back, one eyebrow raised. "Your brother's dying, and ye're goin' to France? Must be summat urgent, then."

"He's not dying," Grey said sharply. The thought of it split the carpet at his feet, a grinning abyss waiting to pull him in. He looked determinedly away from it.

"He . . . had a shock. Word was brought that his youngest son was wounded in America and has been captured."

Her eyes widened at that, and she clutched the dressing gown closer to her nonexistent breasts.

"The youngest. That would be . . . Henry, no?"

"It would. And how the *devil* do you know that?" he demanded, agitation making his voice harsh. A gap-toothed smile glimmered at him, but then went away as she saw the depth of his distress.

"One of his lordship's footmen is a regular," she said simply. "Thursdays; it's his night off."

"Oh." He sat still, hands on his knees, trying to bring his thoughts—and his feelings—under some kind of control. "It—I see."

"It's late in the year to be getting messages from America, no?" She glanced at the window, which was covered in layers of red velvet and lace that were unable to keep out the sound of lashing rain. "Did a late ship come in?"

"Yes. Blown off course and limped in to Brest with a wounded mainmast. The message was brought overland."

"And is it Brest ye're going to, then?"

"It is not."

A soft scratching came at the door before she could ask anything further, and she went to let in the porter, who had—without being asked, Grey noted—brought up a tray laden with tea things, including a thickly iced cake.

He turned it over in his mind. Could he tell her? But she hadn't been joking about discretion, he knew. In her own way, she kept secrets as much—and as well—as he did.

"It's about William," he said, as she shut the door and turned back to him.

HE KNEW DAWN WAS near, from the ache in his bones and the faint chime of his pocket watch. There was no sign of it in the sky. Clouds the color of chimney sweepings brushed the rooves of London, and the streets were blacker than they had been at midnight, all lanterns having been long since extinguished, all hearth fires burnt low.

He'd been up all night. There were things he must do; he ought to go home and sleep for a few hours before catching the Dover coach. He couldn't go without seeing Hal once more, though. Just to assure himself.

There were lights in the windows of Argus House. Even

with the drapes drawn, a faint gleam showed on the wet cobbles outside. It was snowing thickly, but wasn't yet sticking to the ground. There was a good chance that the coach would be detained—was sure to be slow, bogged down on the miry roads.

Speaking of coaches—his heart gave a sickly leap at the sight of a battered-looking carriage standing in the porte cochere, which he thought belonged to the doctor.

His thump at the door was answered at once by a half-dressed footman, nightshirt tucked hastily into his breeches. The man's anxious face relaxed a little when he recognized Grey.

"The duke—"

"Took bad in the night, my lord, but easier now," the man—Arthur, that was his name—interrupted him, stepping back to let him in and taking the cloak from his shoulders, shaking off the snow.

He nodded and made for the stair, not waiting to be shown up. He met the doctor coming down—a thin gray man, marked by his black ill-smelling coat and the bag in his hand.

"How is he?" he demanded, seizing the man by the sleeve as he reached the landing. The doctor drew back, affronted, but then saw his face in the glow from the sconce and, recognizing his resemblance to Hal, settled his ruffled feathers.

"Somewhat better, my lord. I have let him blood, three ounces, and his breathing is grown easier."

Grey let go the sleeve and bounded up the stairs, his own chest tight. The door to Hal's suite of rooms stood open and he went in at once, startling a maid who was carrying out a chamber pot, lidded and then delicately draped with a cloth handsomely embroidered with large, brilliant flowers. He brushed past her with a nod of apology and went into Hal's bedroom.

Hal was sitting up against the bolster, pillows wedged behind him; he looked nearly dead. Minnie was beside him, her pleasant round face gaunt with anxiety and sleeplessness.

"I see you even shit with style, Your Grace," Grey remarked, sitting down on the other side of the bed.

Hal opened one gray lid and eyed him. The face might be that of a skeleton, but the pale, sharp eye was the living Hal, and Grey felt his chest flood with relief.

"Oh, the cloth?" Hal said, weakly but clearly. "That's Dottie. She will not go out, even though I assured her that if I thought I was going to die, I should certainly wait for her return to do it." He paused to breathe, with a faint wheezing note, then coughed and went on: "She is not the sort, thank God, to indulge in pieties, she has no musical talent, and her vitality is such that she is a menace to the kitchen staff. So Minnie set her to needlework, as some outlet for her formidable energies. She takes after Mother, you know."

"I *am* sorry, John," Minnie said apologetically to him. "I sent her to bed, but I saw that her candle is still lit. I believe she is at work this moment on a pair of carpet slippers for you."

Grey thought carpet slippers were likely innocuous, whatever motif she had chosen, and said so.

"So long as she isn't embroidering a pair of drawers for me. The knotwork, you know . . ."

That made Hal laugh, which in turn made him cough alarmingly, though it brought a little color back into his face.

"So you aren't dying?" Grey asked.

"No," Hal said shortly.

"Good," said Grey, smiling at his brother. "Don't."

Hal blinked, and then, recalling the occasion on which he had said exactly that to Grey, smiled back.

"Do my best," he said dryly, and then, turning, laid an affectionate hand on Minnie's. "My dear . . ."

"I'll have some tea brought up," she said, rising at once. "And a good hot breakfast," she added, after a scrutinizing look at Grey. She closed the door delicately behind her.

"What is it?" Hal hitched himself higher on the pillow, disregarding the bloodstained cloth wrapped round one forearm. "You have news?"

"Very little. But a great number of alarming questions."

The news of Henry's capture had been enclosed as a note for Hal inside a letter to himself, from one of his contacts in the intelligencing world, and carried an answer to his inquiries regarding the known French connections of one Percival Beauchamp. He hadn't wanted to discuss that with Hal until he'd seen Nessie, though—and Hal had been in no condition for such discussions, anyway.

"No known connections between Beauchamp and Vergennes"—naming the French foreign minister—"but he has been seen often in company with Beaumarchais."

That provoked another coughing fit.

"Little fucking wonder," Hal observed hoarsely, upon his recovery. "A mutual interest in hunting, no doubt?" That last was a sarcastic reference, both to Percy's disinclination for blood sports and to Beaumarchais's title of "Lieutenant General of Hunting," bestowed upon him some years previous by the late king.

"*And,*" Grey went on, ignoring this, "with one Silas Deane."

Hal frowned. "Who?"

"An American merchant. In Paris on behalf of the American Congress. He skulks round Beaumarchais, rather. And *he's* been seen speaking with Vergennes."

"Oh, him." Hal flapped a hand. "Heard of him. Vaguely."

"Have you heard of a business called *Rodrigue Hortalez et Cie*?"

"No. Sounds Spanish, doesn't it?"

"Or Portuguese. My informant had nothing but the name and a rumor that Beaumarchais has something to do with it."

Hal grunted and lay back.

"Beaumarchais has his fingers in any number of pies. Makes watches, for God's sake, as though writing plays weren't bad enough. Has Beauchamp anything to do with this company?"

"Not known. It's all vague associations at this point, nothing more. I asked for everything that could be turned up that had anything—anything not generally known, I mean—to do with Beauchamp or the Americans; this is what came back."

Hal's slender fingers played restless scales on the coverlet.

"Does your informant know what this Spanish company does?"

"Trade, what else?" Grey replied ironically, and Hal snorted.

"If they were bankers, as well, I'd think you might have something."

"I might, at that. But the only way to find out, I think, is to go and poke at things with a sharp stick. I'm taking the coach to Dover in"—he squinted at the carriage clock on the mantel, obscured by the gloom—"three hours."

"Ah."

The voice was noncommittal, but Grey knew his brother very well indeed.

"I'll be back from France by the end of March at the latest," he said, adding gently, "I shall be on the first ship that sails for the Colonies in the new year, Hal. And I'll bring Henry back." *Alive or dead.* Neither of them spoke the words; they didn't need to.

"I'll be here when you do," Hal said at last, quietly.

Grey put his hand over his brother's, which turned at once to take his. It might look frail, but he was heartened at the determined strength in Hal's grasp. They sat in silence, hands linked, until the door opened and Arthur—now fully dressed—sidled in with a tray the size of a card table, laden with bacon, sausages, kidneys, kippers, shirred eggs in butter, grilled mushrooms and tomatoes, toast, jam, marmalade, a huge pot of fragrantly steaming tea, bowls of sugar and milk—and a covered dish which he set ceremoniously before Hal, this proving to be filled with a sort of nasty thin gruel.

Arthur bowed and went out, leaving Grey wondering whether he was the footman who went to Nessie's house on Thursdays. He turned back to find Hal helping himself liberally to Grey's kidneys.

"Aren't you meant to be eating your slop?" Grey inquired.

"Don't tell me *you're* determined to hasten me into my grave, too," Hal said, closing his eyes in brief rapture as he chewed. "How the devil anyone expects me to recover, fed on things like rusks and gruel . . ." Huffing, he speared another kidney.

"Is it really your heart, do you think?" Grey asked.

Hal shook his head.

"I really don't think so," he said, his tone detached. "I listened to it, you know, after the first attack. Whanging away just as usual." He paused to prod himself experimentally in the chest, fork suspended in the air. "It doesn't hurt there. Surely it would, wouldn't it?"

Grey shrugged.

"What sort of attack was it, then?"

Hal swallowed the last of the kidney and reached for a slice of buttered toast, taking up the marmalade knife in his other hand.

"Couldn't breathe," he said casually. "Turned blue, that kind of thing."

"Oh. Well, then."

"I feel quite well, just now," Hal said, sounding mildly surprised.

"Do you?" Grey said, smiling. He had a moment's reservation, but after all . . . he was going abroad, and unexpected things not only could happen but often did. Best not leave the matter hanging, just in case something untoward befell either one of them before they met again.

"Well, then . . . if you're sure that a minor shock will not shuffle off your mortal coil, allow me to tell you something."

His news regarding the *tendresse* existing between Dottie and William made Hal blink and stop eating momentarily, but after a moment's contemplation he nodded and resumed chewing.

"All right," he said.

"All *right*?" Grey echoed. "You have no objections?"

"Hardly sit well with you if I did, would it?"

"If you expect me to believe that a concern for my feelings would in any way affect your own actions, your illness *has* severely damaged you."

Hal grinned briefly, and drank tea.

"No," he said, setting down the empty cup. "Not that. It's just—" He leaned back, hands clasped over his—very slightly—protruding belly, and gave Grey a straight look. "I *could* die. Don't mean to; don't think I will. But I could. I'd die easier if I knew she was settled with someone who'd protect her and look after her properly."

"I'm flattered that you think William would," Grey said dryly, though he was in fact immensely pleased.

"Of course he would," Hal said, matter-of-fact. "He's your son, isn't he?"

A church bell began to ring, somewhere in the distance, reminding Grey.

"Oh!" he said. "Happy Christmas!"

Hal looked equally surprised, but then smiled.

"The same to you."

GREY WAS STILL filled with Christmas feeling when he set off for Dover—literally, as the pockets of his greatcoat were jammed with sweetmeats and small gifts and he carried under his arm a wrapped parcel containing the infamous carpet slippers, these lavishly embellished with lily pads and green frogs done in crewelwork. He had hugged Dottie when she gave them to him, managing to whisper in her ear that her job was done. She had kissed him with such vigor that he could still feel it on his cheek and rubbed absently at the spot.

He must write to William at once—though in fact there was no particular hurry, as a letter could not be carried any faster than he would go himself. He'd meant what he'd told Hal; as soon as a ship could set sail in the spring, he'd be on it. He only hoped he'd be in time.

And not only for Henry.

The roads were quite as bad as he'd expected, and the Calais ferry was worse, but he was oblivious to the cold and discomfort of the journey. With his anxiety for Hal somewhat allayed, he was free to think about what Nessie had told him—a bit of information he'd thought of mentioning to Hal but hadn't, not wanting to burden his brother's mind, in case it might hamper his recovery.

"Your Frenchman didn't come *here,*" Nessie had told him, licking sugar off her fingers. "But he went to Jackson's regular, when he was in town. He's gone off now, though; back to France, they say."

"Jackson's," he'd said slowly, wondering. He didn't patronize bawdy houses himself—bar Nessie's establishment—but he certainly knew about Jackson's and had been there once or twice with friends. A flash house, offering music on the ground floor, gaming on the first floor, and more private diversions higher up. Very popular with mid-echelon army officers. But not, he was certain, a place catering to Percy Beauchamp's particular tastes.

"I see," he'd said, calmly drinking tea, feeling his heart beat in his ears. "And have you ever come across an officer named Randall-Isaacs?" That was the part of his letter he hadn't told Hal; Denys Randall-Isaacs was an army officer known to frequent Beauchamp's company, both in France and in London, his informant had said—and the name had gone straight through Grey's heart like an icicle.

It *might* be no more than coincidence that a man known to associate with Percy Beauchamp had taken William on an intelligencing expedition to Quebec—but damned if he thought it was.

Nessie had lifted her head abruptly at the name "Randall-Isaacs," like a dog hearing the rustle of something in the brush.

"Aye, I have," she said slowly. There was a blob of fine sugar on her lower lip; he wished to wipe it off for her, and in other circumstances would have. "Or heard of him. He's a Jew, they say."

"A Jew?" That startled him. "Surely not." A Jew would never be allowed to take a commission in the army or navy, no more than a Catholic.

Nessie arched a dark brow at him.

"Perhaps he doesna want anyone to know," she said, and, licking her lips like a cat, tidied away the blob of sugar. "But if not, he ought to stay awa' from kittle-hoosies, that's all I can say!" She laughed heartily, then sobered, hunching her bed-sacque over her shoulders and staring at him, dark-eyed in the firelight.

"He's got summat to do wi' your wee lad, the Frenchie, too," she said. "For it was a girl from Jackson's told me about the Jewish cove and what a shock it was to her when he took his breeches off. She said she wouldn't've, only his friend the Frenchie was there, too, wanting to watch, and when he—the Frenchie, I mean—saw she was put off, he offered her double, so she did it. She said when ye came right down to it"—and here she grinned lewdly at him, the tip of her tongue resting against the front teeth she still had—"it was nicer than some."

"Nicer than some," he muttered distractedly to himself, only half-noticing the wary glance cast toward him by the only other ferry passenger hardy enough to stay abovedecks. "Bloody *hell*!"

The snow was falling thickly over the Channel, and now swept nearly horizontal as the howling wind changed direction and the ship gave a sickening lurch. The other man shook himself and went below, leaving Grey to eat brandied peaches with his fingers from a jar in his pocket and stare bleakly at the oncoming coast of France, visible only in glimpses through low-lying clouds.

December 24, 1776
Quebec City

Dear Papa—

I write you from a Convent. Not, I hasten to explain, one of the Covent Garden variety, but a real Roman Convent, run by Ursuline Nuns.

Captain Randall-Isaacs and I arrived at the Citadel in late October, intending to call upon Sir Guy and discover his Opinion of the local Sympathies regarding the American Insurrection, only to be told that Sir Guy had marched to Fort Saint-Jean, to deal personally with an Outbreak of said Insurrection, this being a Sea Battle (or so I suppose I must call it), which took place upon Lake Champlain, this a narrow Body connecting with Lake George, which perhaps you will know from your own Time here.

I was much in favor of going to join Sir Guy, but Captain Randall-Isaacs was reluctant in consideration of the Distance involved and the Time of Year. In Fact his Judgment was proved sound, as the next Day brought freezing Rain, this giving way shortly to a howling Blizzard, so fierce as to darken the Sky so that you could not tell Day from Night, and which buried the World in Snow and Ice within Hours. Seeing this Spectacle of Nature, I will admit that my Disappointment at missing an Opportunity to join Sir Guy was substantially allayed.

As it was, I should have been too late in any Case, as the Engagement had already taken place, upon the 1st October. We did not learn the Particulars until mid-November, when some Hessian Officers from Baron von Riedesel's Regiment arrived at the Citadel with News of it. Most likely you will have heard more official and direct Descriptions of the Engagement by the Time you receive this Letter, but there may be some Details of interest omitted from the official Versions—and to be frank, the Composition of such an Account is the only Employment available to me at present, as I have declined a kind Invitation from the Mother Superior to attend the Mass they hold at midnight tonight in observance of Christmas. (The Bells of the city's Churches ring every quarter Hour, marking time through the Day and Night. The convent's Chapel lies directly beyond the Wall of the Guesthouse in which I am lodged upon the highest Floor, and the Bell is perhaps twenty Feet from my Head when I lie in Bed. I can thus inform you faithfully that it is now 9:15 p.m.)

To particulars, then: Sir Guy was alarmed by the attempted Invasion of Quebec last Year, even though it ended in abject Failure, and had thus determined to increase his Hold upon the upper Hudson, this being the only possible Avenue by which further Trouble could come, the Difficulties of land Travel being so exigent as to prevent any but the most determined (I have a small Jar of spirits of Wine with which to present you, this containing a Deerfly measuring nearly two Inches in Length, as well as a Quantity of very large Ticks, these removed from my Person with the assistance of Honey, which smothers them if applied liberally, causing them to loose their Grip).

While the Invasion of last Winter did not succeed, Colonel Arnold's Men determined to deny Sir Guy Access to the Lakes, and thus sank or burned all the Ships at Fort Saint-Jean as they withdrew, as well as burning the Sawmill and the Fort itself.

Sir Guy had therefore requisitioned collapsible Ships to be sent to him from England (I wish I had seen these!) and, ten of them arriving, went down to St. John to oversee their assembly upon the upper Richelieu River. Meanwhile, Colonel Arnold (who seems an amazing, industrious Fellow, if half what I hear of him is true) had been madly building his own Fleet of ramshackle Galleys and hog-beamed Sloops.

Not content with his Prodigies of collapsibility, Sir Guy also had the Indefatigable, *a Frigate of some 180 tonnes (some Argument between my informants as to the number of Guns she carries; after a second Bottle of the convent's Claret [the Nuns make it themselves, and from the Shade of the priest's Nose, no little of it gets consumed here, too], Consensus was reached, with "a bloody Lot, mate," always allowing for Errors of Translation, being the final Number), taken apart, hauled to the River, and there reassembled.*

Colonel Arnold apparently decided that to wait any longer was to lose what Advantage of Initiative he might possess, and sallied out from his Hiding place at Valcour Island on 30 September. By Report, he had fifteen Craft, to Sir Guy's twenty-five, these former all hastily built, unseaworthy, and manned by Landsmen who did not know a Binnacle from a Bunion—the American Navy, in all its glory!

Still, I must not laugh too much. The more I hear of Colonel Arnold (and I hear a great Deal about him, here in Quebec), the more I think he must be a Gentleman of Gall and Kidney, as Grandpapa Sir George is wont to say; I should like to meet him one day.

There is Singing outside; the habitants *are coming to the Cathedral nearby. I don't know the Music, and it's too far to make out the Words, but I can see the Glow of Torches from my Eyrie. The Bells say it is ten o'clock.*

*(The Mother Superior says that she knows you, by the way—*Soeur *Immaculata is her Name. I should scarcely have been startled by this; told her that you know the Archbishop of Canterbury* and *the Pope, by which she professed to be much impressed, and begs you will convey her most humble Obeisance to His Holiness when next you see him. She kindly asked me to Dinner, and told me Stories of the taking of the Citadel in '59, and how you quartered a number of Highlanders upon the Convent. How shocked the Sisters all were by their bare Legs, and sought a*

Requisition of Canvas that they might make the men Trousers. My Uniform has suffered noticeably through the last few Weeks of Travel, but I am still decently covered below the Waist, I am relieved to say. So was Mother Superior, no doubt!)

*I return to my Account of the Battle: Sir Guy's Fleet sailed south, intending to reach and recapture Crown Point, then Ticonderoga. As they passed Valcour Island, though, two of Arnold's Ships sprang out upon them, firing in challenge. These then attempted to withdraw, but one (*Royal Savage, *they said) could not make Way against the Headwinds, and ran aground. Several British Gunboats swarmed her and captured a few Men, but were forced to withdraw under heavy Fire from the Americans—though not omitting to set Fire to the* Royal Savage *as they did so.*

A great deal of Maneuvering then ensued in the Strait, and the Battle began in earnest about Midday, the Carleton *and* Inflexible *bearing most of the Brunt of the Action, along with the Gunboats. Arnold's* Revenge *and* Philadelphia *were badly hit by Broadsides, and the* Philadelphia *sank near Evening.*

The Carleton *continued firing until a fortunate Shot from the Americans severed the Line to her Anchor, causing her to drift. She was heavily attacked and a number of her Men killed or injured, the Butcher's Bill including her Captain, a Lieutenant James Dacres (I have an uneasy feeling that I have met him, perhaps at a Dance last Season) and the senior Officers. One of her Midshipmen took Command and carried her to Safety. They said it was Edward Pellew—and I* know *I have met him, once or twice, at Boodles with Uncle Harry.*

To resume: Another lucky Shot struck the Magazine of a Gunboat and blew it up, but meanwhile, the Inflexible *was finally brought into play and battered the American Boats with her heavy Guns. The smaller of Sir Guy's Craft landed Indians meanwhile upon the Shores of Valcour Island and the Shore of the Lake, thus cutting off this Avenue of*

Escape, and the Remnants of Arnold's Fleet were thus obliged to retreat down the Lake.

They succeeded in slipping past Sir Guy, the Night being foggy, and took Refuge at Schuyler Island, some miles south. Sir Guy's Fleet pursued them, though, and was able to draw within Sight of them the next Day, Arnold's Boats being much hampered by Leakage, Damage, and the Weather, which had turned to heavy Rain and high Wind. The Washington *was caught, attacked, and forced to strike her Colors, her Crew of more than a hundred Men being captured. The rest of Arnold's Fleet, though, managed to get through to Buttonmold Bay, where, I understand, the Waters are too shallow to allow Sir Guy's Ships to follow.*

There Arnold beached, stripped, and set afire most of his Craft—their Flags still flying, as a Mark of Defiance, the Germans said; they were amused by this, but admired it. Colonel Arnold (or must we now call him Admiral Arnold?) personally set Fire to the Congress, *this being his Flagship, and set off Overland, narrowly escaping the Indians who had been set to prevent him. His troops did reach Crown Point, but did not linger there, pausing only to destroy the Fort before withdrawing to Ticonderoga.*

Sir Guy did not march his Prisoners back to Quebec, but returned them to Ticonderoga under a Flag of Truce—a very pretty Gesture, much admired by my Informants.

10:30. Did you see the aurora borealis *when you were here, or was it too early in the Year? It is a most remarkable Sight. Snow has fallen all Day, but ceased near Sunset and the Sky has cleared. From my Window, I see a northern Exposure, and there is presently an amazing shimmer that fills the whole Sky, waves of pale blue and some green—though I have seen it to be red sometimes—that swirl like Drops of Ink spilt in Water and stirred. I cannot hear it at present, because of the Singing—someone is Playing a Fiddle in the Distance; it is a very sweet and piercing Tune—but when I have seen the*

Phenomenon outside the City, in the Woods, there is often a most peculiar Sound, or Sounds, that accompany it. Sometimes a sort of faint Whistling, as of Wind around a Building, though there is no Movement of the Air; sometimes a strange, high, hissing Noise, interrupted now and then by a Fusillade of Clicks and Cracklings, as though a Horde of Crickets were advancing upon the Listener through dry Leaves—though by the time the Aurora begins to be seen, the Cold has long since killed all Insects (and good riddance! We applied an Ointment used by the local Indians, which was of some help against stinging Flies and Mosquitoes, but does nothing to discourage the inquisitiveness of Earwigs, Roaches, and Spiders).

We had a Guide for our Journey between St. John and Quebec, a Man of mixed Blood (he had a most remarkable Head of Hair, thick and curly as Sheep's Wool and the color of Cinnamon Bark) who told us that some of the native People think that the Sky is a Dome, separating Earth from Heaven, but that there are Holes in the Dome, and that the Lights of the Aurora are the Torches of Heaven, sent out to guide the Spirits of the Dead through the Holes.

But I see I have yet to finish my Account, though it is only to add that following the Battle, Sir Guy withdrew to winter Quarters in St. John, and likely will not return to Quebec until the Spring.

So now I come to the true Point of my letter. I rose Yesterday to discover Captain Randall-Isaacs had decamped during the Night, leaving me with a brief Note stating that he had urgent Business, had enjoyed my Company and valuable Assistance, and that I was to remain here until either his Return or the arrival of new Orders.

The Snow is deep, more may come at any Moment, and Business must be urgent indeed which could compel a man to venture any Distance. I am of course somewhat disturbed at Captain Randall-Isaacs's abrupt Departure, curious as to what might have happened to cause it, and somewhat anxious as to his Welfare. This does not seem a Situation in which I would be justified in ignoring my Orders, however, and so . . . I wait.

11:30. I stopped writing for some little time, to stand and watch the Sky. The Lights of the Aurora come and go, but I think they have gone altogether now; the Sky is black, the Stars bright but tiny by contrast with the vanished brilliance of the Lights. There is a vast Emptiness in the Sky that one seldom senses in a City. Despite the Clangor of the Bells, the Bonfires in the Square, and the Singing of People—there is a Procession of some kind going on—I can feel the great Silence beyond it.

The Nuns are going in to their Chapel. I leaned out of my Window just now to watch them hurrying along, two by two like a marching Column, their dark Gowns and Cloaks making them look like small Pieces of the Night, drifting among the Stars of their Torches. (I have been writing a long Time, you must forgive the Fancies of an exhausted Brain.)

This is the first Christmas I have spent with no Sight of Home or Family. The First of many, no doubt.

I think of you often, Papa, and hope you are well and looking forward to roast Goose tomorrow with Grandmama and Grandpapa Sir George. Give my Love to them, please, and to Uncle Hal and his family. (And to my Dottie, especially.)

A very merry Christmas from your Son,
William

PostScriptum: 2:00 a.m. I went down after all, and stood at the Back of the Chapel. It was somewhat Popish, and there was a great Deal of Incense, but I said a Prayer for Mother Geneva and for Mama Isobel. When I emerged from the Chapel, I saw that the Lights have come back. Now they are blue.

25

THE BOSOM OF THE DEEP

May 15, 1777

My dears,

I hate Boats. I despise them with the utmost Fiber of my Being. And yet I find myself once more launched upon the dreadful Bosom of the Sea, aboard a Craft known as the Tranquil Teal, *from which Absurdity you may deduce the grim Whimsy of her Captain. This Gentleman is a Smuggler of mixed Race, evil Countenance, and low Humor, who tells me, straight-faced, that his name is Trustworthy Roberts.*

JAMIE PAUSED to dip his quill, glanced at the receding shore of North Carolina, and, observing it to rise and fall in an unsettling manner, fixed his eyes at once upon the page he had tacked to his lap desk to prevent its being borne away by the stiff breeze that filled the sails above his head.

We are in good Health, he wrote slowly. Putting aside the notion of seasickness, upon which he did not propose to dwell. Ought he to tell them about Fergus? he wondered.

"Feeling all right?"

He looked up to see Claire, bending to peer at him with that look of intent but cautious curiosity she reserved for people who might at any moment vomit, spurt blood, or die. He'd already done the first two, as a result of her having accidentally put one of her needles into a small blood vessel in his scalp, but hoped she didn't distinguish any further signs of his impending demise.

"Well enough." He didn't want even to think about his stomach, for fear of inciting it, and changed the subject in order to avoid further discussion. "Shall I tell Brianna and Roger Mac about Fergus?"

"How much ink have you got?" she asked, with a sidelong smile. "Yes, of course you should. They'll be very interested. And it will distract you," she added, squinting slightly at him. "You're still rather green."

"Aye, thanks."

She laughed with the cheerful callousness of the good sailor, kissed the top of his head—avoiding the four needles protruding from his forehead—and went to stand by the rail, watching the wavering land recede from view.

He averted his gaze from this distressing prospect, and returned to his letter.

> *Fergus and his family are also well, but I must tell you of a puzzling occurrence. A man who calls himself Percival Beauchamp . . .*

It took him most of a page to describe Beauchamp and his baffling interest. He glanced up at Claire, wondering whether he should also include the possibility of Beauchamp's relationship to her family, but decided against it. His daughter certainly knew her mother's maiden name and would notice it at once. He had no further useful information to provide in that respect—and his hand was beginning to ache.

Claire was still at the rail, one hand on it for balance, her face dreaming.

She had tied back the mass of her hair with ribbon, but the wind was whipping strands of it out, and with hair and skirts and shawl streaming back, the cloth of her gown molded to what was still a very fine bosom, he thought she looked like a ship's figurehead, graceful and fierce, a protective spirit against the dangers of the deep.

He found that thought obscurely comforting, and returned to his composition in better heart, despite the disturbing content he had now to confide.

Fergus elected not to speak with Monsieur Beauchamp, which I thought wise, and so we presumed this to be the end of the Matter.

While we were in Wilmington, though, I went down to the Docks one Evening to meet Mr. DeLancey Hall, our Liaison with Captain Roberts. Owing to the Presence of an English Man-of-war in the Harbor, the Arrangement was that we should repair discreetly aboard Mr. Hall's fishing Ketch, which would transport us outwith the Harbor, whence we should rendezvous with the Teal, *Captain Roberts disliking close Proximity to the British navy. (This is a fairly universal Response on the part of private and merchant Captains, owing both to the prevalence of Contraband aboard most Ships and to the Navy's rapacious Attitude toward the Ships' Crews, who are routinely abducted—pressed, they call it—and to all Intents and Purposes, enslaved for Life, save they are willing to risk Hanging for Desertion.)*

I had brought with me some minor Items of Luggage, intending under the Pretext of taking these aboard to inspect both the Ketch and Mr. Hall more closely before entrusting our Lives to either. The Ketch was not at Anchor, though, and Mr. Hall did not appear for some Time, so that I began to worry lest I had mistaken his Instructions or that he had run afoul either of His Majesty's Navy or some fellow Rapscallion or Privateer.

I waited until it had grown Dark, and was on the point of returning to our Inn, when I saw a small Boat come into the Harbor with a blue Lantern at its Tail. This was Mr. Hall's Signal, and the Boat was his Ketch, which I assisted him to tie up to the Quay. He told me that he had some News, and we repaired to a local Tavern, where he said that he had been in New Bern the Day before, and there found the Town in an Uproar, owing to an infamous Assault upon the Printer, Mr. Fraser.

By report, he—Fergus—was making his Rounds of Delivery, and had just got down from the Mule Cart when someone sprang upon him from behind, thrusting a Sack over his Head, and someone else attempted at the same Time to seize his Hands, presumably with the Intent of binding them. Fergus naturally resisted these Attempts with some Vigor, and according to Mr. Hall's Story, succeeded in wounding one Assailant with his Hook, there being a certain Amount of Blood to substantiate this Assumption. The wounded Man fell back with a Scream and uttered loud Oaths (I should have been interested to know the content of said Oaths, in order to know whether the Speaker might be French or English, but this Information was not included), whereupon Clarence (who you will remember, I think) became excited and apparently bit the second Assailant, this Man and Fergus having fallen against the Mule in their Struggle. The second Man was discouraged by this vigorous Intervention, but the first returned to the Fray at this Point, and Fergus—still blinded by the Sack but bellowing for Help—grappled with him, striking at him again with his Hook. Some Reports (says Mr. Hall) claim that the Villain wrenched the Hook from Fergus's Wrist, while others claim that Fergus succeeded in striking him again but that the Hook became entangled in the Villain's Clothing and was pulled off in the Struggle.

In any Event, people in Thompson's Ordinary heard the Stramash and rushed out, whereupon the Villains fled, leaving Fergus somewhat bruised and most indignant at the loss of his Hook, but otherwise unharmed, for which God and St. Dismas (he being Fergus's particular Patron) be thanked.

I questioned Mr. Hall as closely as I could, but there was little more to be learned. He said that public Opinion was divided, with many saying that this was an attempted Deportation and the Sons of Liberty were to blame for the attack, while some members of the Sons of Liberty indignantly denied this Accusation, claiming that it was the work of Loyalists incensed over Fergus's printing of a particularly inflammatory Speech by Patrick Henry, and the Abduction was a Prelude to Tar and Feathers. Apparently Fergus has been so successful in avoiding the Appearance of taking Sides in the Conflict that both Sides are equally likely to have taken Offense and decided to eliminate his Influence.

This is, of course, possible. But with the Presence and Behavior of Monsieur Beauchamp in Mind, I think a third Explanation is more likely. Fergus declined to speak with him, but it would not have required a great deal of further Inquiry for him to learn that despite his Name and Scottish Wife, Fergus is a Frenchman. Surely most of the Inhabitants of New Bern know this, and someone could easily have told him.

I confess myself to be at a Loss as to why Beauchamp should wish to abduct Fergus, rather than simply come and confront him in Person to inquire whether he might be the Person for whom the Gentleman claimed to be searching. I must assume that he does not mean Fergus immediate Harm, for if he did, it would be a fairly simple Matter to have arranged to have him killed; there are a great many Men of no Attachment and mean Character drifting through the Colony these Days.

The Occurrence is worrying, but there is little I can do about it in my present abject Position. I have sent Fergus a Letter—ostensibly regarding the Specifications of a printing Job—which lets him know that I have placed a Sum with a Goldsmith in Wilmington, which he may draw upon in case of Need. I had discussed with him the Dangers of his present Position, not knowing at the Time how dangerous they might actually be, and he agreed that there might be some Advantage to his Family's Safety in his moving to a City where public Opinion is more strongly aligned with his own Inclinations. This latest Incident may compel his Decision, the more particularly as Proximity to ourselves is no longer a Consideration.

He had to stop again, as pain was radiating through his hand and up his wrist. He stretched the fingers, stifling a groan; a hot wire seemed to stab from his fourth finger up his forearm in brief electric jolts.

He was more than worried for Fergus and his family. If Beauchamp had tried once, he would try again. But why?

Perhaps the fact of Fergus's being French was not sufficient evidence that he was the Claudel Fraser that Beauchamp sought, and he proposed to satisfy himself upon this point in privacy, by whatever means came to hand? Possible, but that argued a coldness of purpose that disturbed Jamie more than he had wished to say in his letter.

And in fairness, he must admit that the notion of the attack having been executed by persons of inflamed political sensibility was a distinct possibility, and perhaps of a higher probability than the sinister designs of Monsieur Beauchamp, which were both romantical and theoretical to a high degree.

"But I havena lived this long without knowing the smell of a rat when I see one," he muttered, still rubbing his hand.

"Jesus H. Roosevelt Christ!" said his personal figurehead, appearing suddenly beside him with an expression of marked concern. "Your hand!"

"Aye?" He looked down at it, cross with discomfort. "What's amiss? All my fingers are still attached to it."

"That's the most that could be said for it. It looks like the Gordian knot." She knelt down beside him and took the hand into hers, massaging it in a forceful way that was doubtless helpful but so immediately painful that it made his eyes water. He closed them, breathing slowly through clenched teeth.

She was scolding him for writing too much at once. What was the hurry, after all?

"It will be days before we reach Connecticut, and then *months* on the way to Scotland. You could write one sentence per day and quote the whole Book of Psalms along the way."

"I wanted to," he said.

She said something derogatory under her breath, in which the words "Scot" and "pigheaded" featured, but he chose to take no notice. He *had* wanted to; it clarified his thoughts to put them down in black and white, and it was to some degree a relief to express them on paper, rather than to have the worry clogged up in his head like mud in mangrove roots.

And beyond that—not that he required an excuse, he thought, narrowing his eyes at the top of his wife's bent head—seeing the shore of North Carolina drop away had made him lonely for his daughter and Roger Mac, and he'd wanted the sense of connection that writing to them gave him.

"Do you think you will see them?" Fergus had asked him that, soon before they took leave of each other. *"Perhaps you will go to France."* So far as Fergus and Marsali and the folk on the Ridge were concerned, Brianna and Roger Mac had gone to France to escape the oncoming war.

"No," he'd said, hoping the bleakness of his heart didn't show in his voice. "I doubt we shall ever see them again."

Fergus's strong right hand had tightened on his forearm, then relaxed.

"Life is long," he said quietly.

"Aye," he'd answered, but thought, *No one's life is that long.*

His hand was growing easier now; while she still massaged it, the motion no longer hurt so much.

"I miss them, too," she said quietly, and kissed his knuckles. "Give me the letter; I'll finish it."

Your father's hand won't stand any more today. There is one notable thing about this ship, beyond the captain's name. I was down in the hold earlier in the day, and saw a good number of boxes, all stenciled with the name "Arnold" and "New Haven, Connecticut." I said to the hand (whose name is a very pedestrian John Smith, though no doubt to make up for this distressing lack of distinction he has three gold earrings in one ear and two in the other. He told me that each one represents his survival from the sinking of a ship. I am hoping that your father doesn't know this) that Mr. Arnold must be a very successful merchant. Mr. Smith laughed and said that, in fact, Mr. Benedict Arnold is a colonel in the Continental army, and a very gallant officer he is, too. The boxes are bound for delivery to his sister, Miss Hannah Arnold, who minds both his three small sons and his importing and dry-goods store in Connecticut, while he is about the business of the war.

I must say that a goose walked across my grave when I heard that. I've met men whose history I knew before—and at least one of those I knew to carry a doom with him. You don't get used to the feeling, though. I looked at those boxes and wondered—ought I to write to Miss Hannah? Get off the ship in New Haven and go to see her? And tell her what, exactly?

All our experience to date suggests that there is absolutely nothing I could do to alter what's going to happen. And looking at the situation objectively, I don't see any way . . . and yet. And yet*!*

And yet, I've come close to so many people whose actions have a noticeable effect, whether or not they end up making history as such. How can it not be so? your father says. Everyone's actions have some effect upon the future. And plainly he's right. And yet, to brush so close to a name like Benedict Arnold gives one a right turn, as Captain Roberts is fond of saying. (No doubt a situation that gave one a left turn would be very shocking indeed.)

Well. Returning tangentially to the original subject of this letter, the mysterious Monsieur Beauchamp. If your father's—Frank's, I mean—if you still have the boxes of papers and books from his home office, and a free moment, you might go through them and see if you find an old manila folder in there, with a coat of arms drawn on it in colored pencil. I think that it's azure and gold, and I recall that it has martlets on it. With luck, it still contains the Beauchamp family genealogy that my uncle Lamb wrote up for me, lo these many years ago.

You might just have a look and see whether the incumbent of the name in 1777 was perhaps a Percival. For the sake of curiosity.

The wind's come up a bit, and the water's getting

rough. Your father has gone rather pale and clammy, like fish bait; I'll close and take him down below for a nice quiet vomit and a nap, I think.

All my love,
Mama

26

STAG AT BAY

ROGER BLEW thoughtfully across the mouth of an empty stout bottle, making a low, throaty moan. Close. A little deeper, though . . . and of course it lacked that hungry sound, that growling note. But the pitch . . . He got up and rummaged in the refrigerator, finding what he was looking for behind a heel of cheese and six margarine tubs full of God knew what; he'd lay odds it wasn't margarine.

There was no more than an inch or so of champagne left in the bottle—a remnant of their celebratory dinner the week before, in honor of Bree's new job. Someone had thriftily covered the neck of the bottle with tinfoil, but the wine had of course gone flat. He went to pour it out in the sink, but a lifetime of Scottish thrift was not so easily dismissed. With no more than an instant's hesitation, he drank the rest of the champagne, lowering the empty bottle to see Annie MacDonald holding Amanda by the hand and staring at him.

"Well, at least ye're no puttin' it on your cornflakes yet," she said, edging past him. "Here, pet, up ye go." She hoisted Mandy into her booster seat and went out, shaking her head over her employer's low moral character.

"Gimme, Daddy!" Mandy reached for the bottle, attracted by the shiny label. With the statutory parental pause as he mentally ran through potential scenarios of destruction, he instead gave her his glass of milk and hooted across the champagne bottle's fluted lip, producing a deep, melodious tone. Yes, that was it—something close to the F below middle C.

"Do again, Daddy!" Mandy was charmed. Feeling mildly self-conscious, he hooted again, making her fall about in a cascade of giggles. He picked up the stout bottle and blew across that one, then alternated, working up a two-note variation to the rhythm of "Mary Had a Little Lamb."

Attracted by the hooting and Mandy's ecstatic shrieks, Brianna appeared in the doorway, a bright blue plastic hard hat in her hand.

"Planning to start your own jug band?" she asked.

"Already got one," he replied, and having decided that the worst thing Mandy could do with the champagne bottle was drop it onto the rug, handed it to her and stepped out into the hall with Brianna, where he pulled her close and kissed her deeply, the baize door swinging shut with a cushioned *foosh.*

"Champagne for breakfast?" she broke the kiss long enough to ask, then returned for more, tasting him.

"Needed the bottle," he mumbled, tasting back. She'd had porridge with butter and honey for breakfast, and her mouth was sweet, turning the champagne bitter on the edges of his tongue. The hall was chilly, but she was warm as toast under her fleece jumper. His fingers lingered just under the edge of it, on the bare soft skin at the small of her back.

"Ye'll have a good day, aye?" he whispered. He fought the urge to slide his fingers down the back of her jeans; not respectful to be fingering the arse of a brand-new inspector of the North of Scotland Hydro Electric Board. "You're bringing the hat home, after?"

"Sure. Why?"

"Thought ye might wear it in bed." He took it from her hand and set it gently on her head. It made her eyes go navy blue. "Wear it, and I'll tell ye what I wanted with the champagne bottle."

"Oh, now there's an offer I can't re—" The navy-blue eyes slid suddenly sideways, and Roger glanced in that direction, to see Annie at the end of the hall, broom and dustpan in hand and an expression of deep interest on her narrow face.

"Yeah. Ah . . . have a good day," Roger said, letting go hastily.

"You, too." Face twitching, Brianna took him firmly by the shoulders and kissed him, before striding down the hall and past a round-eyed Annie, whom she airily wished good day in the Gaelic.

A sudden crash came from the kitchen. He turned automatically toward the baize door, though less than half his attention was on the incipient disaster. The greater part was focused on the sudden realization that his wife appeared to have departed for work wearing no knickers.

MANDY HAD, God knew how, managed to throw the champagne bottle through the window and was standing on the table, reaching for the jagged edge of the pane, when Roger rushed in.

"Mandy!" He grabbed her, swung her off the table, and in the same motion smacked her bottom once. She emitted an ear-piercing howl, and he carried her out under his arm, passing Annie Mac, who stood in the doorway with mouth and eyes all round as "O"s.

"See to the glass, aye?" he said.

He felt guilty as hell; what had he been thinking, handing her the bottle? Let alone leaving her by herself with it!

He also felt a certain irritation with Annie Mac—after all, she was employed to watch the children—but fairness made him admit that he ought to have made sure she'd come back to watch Mandy before he left. The irritation extended to Bree, as well, prancing off to her new job, expecting him to mind the household.

He recognized that the irritation was only his attempt to escape the guilt, though, and did his best to put it aside while soothing Mandy, having a wee chat about not standing on tables, not throwing things in the house, not touching sharp things, calling for a grown-up if she needed help—fat chance, he thought, with a wry inward smile; Mandy was the most independent three-year-old he'd ever seen. Which was saying something, considering that he'd also seen Jem at that age.

One thing about Amanda: she didn't hold a grudge. Five

minutes after being smacked and scolded, she was giggling and begging him to play dollies with her.

"Daddy's got to work this morning," he said, but bent so she could scramble onto his shoulders. "Come on, we'll find Annie Mac; you and the dollies can maybe help her get the pantry sorted."

Leaving Mandy and Annie Mac happily working in the pantry, supervised by an assortment of scabby-looking dolls and grubby stuffed animals, he went back to his office and got out the notebook into which he was transcribing the songs he'd so painstakingly committed to memory. He had an appointment later in the week to talk with Siegfried MacLeod, the choirmaster at St. Stephen's, and had it in mind to present him with a copy of some of the rarer songs, by way of creating goodwill.

He thought he might need it. Dr. Weatherspoon had been reassuring, saying that MacLeod would be delighted to have help, especially with the children's choir, but Roger had spent enough time in academic circles, Masonic lodges, and eighteenth-century taverns to know how local politics worked. MacLeod might well resent having an outsider—so to speak—foisted on him without warning.

And there was the delicate issue of a choirmaster who couldn't sing. He touched his throat, with its pebbled scar.

He'd seen two specialists, one in Boston, another in London. Both of them had said the same thing. There was a possibility that surgery might improve his voice, by removing some of the scarring in his larynx. There was an equal possibility that the surgery might further damage—or completely destroy—his voice.

"Surgery on the vocal cords is a delicate business," one of the doctors had said to him, shaking his head. "Normally, we don't risk it unless there's a dire necessity, such as a cancerous growth, a congenital malformation that's preventing any useful speech—or a strong professional reason. A well-known singer with nodules, for instance; in that case, the desire to restore the voice might be sufficient motive to risk surgery—though in such cases, there usually isn't a major risk of rendering the person permanently mute. In your case . . ."

He pressed two fingers against his throat and hummed, feeling the reassuring vibration. No. He remembered all too well what it felt like to be unable to speak. He'd been convinced at the time that he'd never speak—let alone sing—again; the memory of that despair made him sweat. Never speak to his children, to Bree? No, he wasn't risking that.

Dr. Weatherspoon's eyes had lingered on his throat with interest, but he hadn't said anything. MacLeod might be less tactful.

Whom the Lord loveth, he chasteneth. Weatherspoon—to his credit—hadn't said that in the course of their discussion. It had, however, been the quotation chosen for that week's Bible group; it had been printed on their flyer, which was sitting on the rector's desk. And in Roger's hypersensitive frame of mind at the time, everything looked like a message.

"Well, if that's what Ye've got in mind, I appreciate the compliment," he said out loud. "Be all right with me if I wasn't Your favorite just this week, though."

It was said half jokingly, but there was no denying the anger behind it. Resentment at having to prove himself—*to* himself—one more time. He'd had to do it physically last time. Now to do it again, spiritually, in this slippery, less straightforward world? He'd been willing, hadn't he?

"You asked. Since when do Ye not take yes for an answer? Am I missing something here?"

Bree had thought so; the height of their quarrel came back to him now, making him flush with shame.

"You had—I *thought* you had," she'd corrected, "a vocation. Maybe that's not what Protestants call it, but that's what it *is,* isn't it? You told me that God spoke to you." Her eyes were intent on his, unswerving, and so penetrating that he wanted to look away—but didn't.

"Do you think God changes His mind?" she asked more quietly, and laid her hand on his arm, squeezing. "Or do you think you were mistaken?"

"No," he'd said, in instant reflex. "No, when something like that happens . . . well, when it *did* happen, I wasn't in any doubt."

"Are you now?"

"You sound like your mother. Making a diagnosis." He'd meant it as a joke, but it wasn't. Bree resembled her father physically to such a degree that he seldom saw Claire in her, but the calm ruthlessness in her questions was Claire Beauchamp to the life. So was the slight arch of one brow, waiting for an answer. He took a deep breath. "I don't know."

"Yes, you do."

Anger bubbled up, sudden and bright, and he'd jerked his arm away from her grasp.

"Where in hell do you get off telling me what I know?"

She widened her stare. "I'm *married* to you."

"You think that entitles you to try to read my mind?"

"I think that entitles me to worry about you!"

"Well, don't!"

They'd made it up, of course. Kissed—well, a bit more than that—and forgiven each other. Forgiving, of course, didn't mean forgetting.

"Yes, you do."

Did he know?

"Yes," he said defiantly to the broch, visible from his window. "Yes, I damned well do!" What to do about it: that was the difficulty.

Was he perhaps meant to be a minister but not a Presbyterian? Become a nondenominational, an evangelical . . . a *Catholic*? The thought was so disturbing, he was obliged to get up and walk to and fro for a bit. It wasn't that he had anything against Catholics—well, bar the reflexes inbred by a life spent as a Protestant in the Highlands—but he just couldn't see it. "Going over to Rome" was how Mrs. Ogilvy and Mrs. MacNeil and all the rest of them would see it ("Going straight to the Bad Place" being the unspoken implication); his defection would be discussed in tones of low horror for . . . well, for years. He grinned reluctantly at the thought.

Well, and besides, he couldn't be a Catholic priest, now, could he? Not with Bree and the kids. That made him feel a little calmer, and he sat down again. No. He'd have to trust that God—through the agency of Dr. Weatherspoon—proposed to show him the way through this particular thorny passage of his life. And if He did . . . well, was that not evidence of predestination in itself?

Roger groaned, thrust the whole thing out of his head, and immersed himself doggedly in his notebook.

Some of the songs and poems he'd written down were well-known: selections from his previous life, traditional songs he'd sung as a performer. Many of the rare ones, he'd acquired during the eighteenth century, from Scottish immigrants, travelers, peddlers, and seamen. And some he'd unearthed from the trove of boxes the Reverend had left behind. The garage of the old manse had been filled with them, and he and Bree had made no more than a dent in it. Pure luck that he'd run across the wooden box of letters so soon after their return.

He glanced up at it, tempted. He couldn't read the letters without Bree; that wouldn't be right. But the two books—they'd looked briefly at the books when they found the box, but had been concerned mostly with the letters and with finding out what had happened to Claire and Jamie. Feeling like Jem absconding with a packet of chocolate biscuits, he brought the box down carefully—it was very heavy—and set it on the desk, rummaging carefully down under the letters.

The books were small, the largest what was called a crown octavo volume, about five by seven inches. It was a common size, from a time when paper was expensive and difficult to get. The smaller was likely a crown sixteenmo, only about four by five inches. He smiled briefly, thinking of Ian Murray; Brianna had told him her cousin's scandalized response to her description of toilet paper. He might never wipe his arse again without a feeling of extravagance.

The small one was carefully bound in blue-dyed calfskin, with gilt-edged pages; an expensive, beautiful book. *Pocket Principles of Health,* it was entitled, by *C. E. B. R. Fraser, M.D.* A limited edition, produced by *A. Bell, Printer, Edinburgh.*

That gave him a small thrill. So they'd made it to Scotland, under the care of Captain Trustworthy Roberts. Or at least he supposed they must—though the scholar in him cautioned that this wasn't proof; it was always possible that the manuscript had somehow made it to Scotland, without necessarily being carried in person by the author.

Had they come here? he wondered. He looked around the worn, comfortable room, easily envisioning Jamie at the big old desk by the window, going through the farm ledgers with his brother-in-law. If the kitchen was the heart of the house—and it was—this room had likely always been its brain.

Moved by impulse, he opened the book and nearly choked. The frontispiece, in customary eighteenth-century style, showed an engraving of the author. A medical man, in a neat tiewig and black coat, with a high black stock. From above which his mother-in-law's face looked serenely out at him.

He laughed out loud, causing Annie Mac to peer cautiously in at him, in case he might be having a fit of some kind, as well as talking to himself. He waved her off and shut the door before returning to the book.

It was her, all right. The wide-spaced eyes under dark brows, the graceful firm bones of cheek, temple, and jaw. Whoever had done the engraving had not got her mouth quite right; it had a sterner shape here, and a good thing, too—no man had lips like hers.

How old . . . ? He checked the date of printing: MDCCLXXVIII. 1778. Not much older than when he'd last seen her, then—and looking still a good deal younger than he knew her to be.

Was there a picture of Jamie in the other . . . ? He seized it and flipped it open. Sure enough, another steel-point engraving, though this was a more homely drawing. His father-in-law sat in a wing chair, his hair tied simply back, a plaid draped over the chair behind him, and a book open upon his knee. He was reading to a small child sitting upon his other knee—a little girl with dark curly hair. She was turned away, absorbed in the story. Of course—the engraver couldn't have known what Mandy's face would look like.

Grandfather Tales, the book was titled, with the subtitle, "Stories from the Highlands of Scotland and the Backcountry of the Carolinas," by *James Alexander Malcolm MacKenzie Fraser.* Again, printed by *A. Bell, Edinburgh,* in the same year. The dedication said simply, *For my grandchildren.*

Claire's portrait had made him laugh; this one moved him almost to tears, and he closed the book gently.

Such faith they had had. To create, to hoard, to send these things, these fragile documents, down through the years, with only the hope that they would survive and reach those for whom they were intended. Faith that Mandy would be here to read them one day. He swallowed, the lump in his throat painful.

How had they managed it? Well, they did say faith moved mountains, even if his own seemed presently not adequate to flatten a molehill.

"Jesus," he muttered, not sure if this was simple frustration or a prayer for assistance.

A flicker of motion through the window distracted him from the paper, and he glanced up to see Jem coming out of the kitchen door at the far end of the house. He was red in the face, small shoulders hunched, and had a large string bag in one hand, through which Roger could see a bottle of lemon squash, a loaf of bread, and a few other foodlike bulges. Startled, Roger looked at the clock on the mantel, thinking he had lost complete track of time—but he hadn't. It was just on one o'clock.

"What the—" Shoving the paper aside, he got up and made for the back of the house, emerging just in time to see Jem's small figure, clad in wind-cheater and jeans—he wasn't allowed to wear jeans to school—making its way across the hayfield.

Roger could have caught him up easily, but instead slowed his pace, following at a distance.

Plainly Jem wasn't ill—so likely something drastic had happened at school. Had the school sent him home, or had he simply left on his own? No one had called, but it was just past the school's dinner hour; if Jem had seized the opportunity to run for it, it was possible they hadn't yet missed him. It was nearly two miles to walk, but that was nothing to Jem.

Jem had got to the stile in the drystone dyke that walled the field, hopped over, and was making determinedly across a pasture full of sheep. Where was he heading?

"And what the bloody hell did you do this time?" Roger muttered to himself.

Jem had been in the village school at Broch Mordha for only a couple of months—his first experience with twentieth-century education. After their return, Roger had tutored Jem at home in Boston, while Bree was with Mandy during her recovery from the surgery that had saved her life. With Mandy safe home again, they'd had to decide what to do next.

It was mostly Jem that had made them go to Scotland rather than stay in Boston, though Bree had wanted that anyway.

"It's their heritage," she'd argued. "Jem and Mandy are Scots on both sides, after all. I want to keep that for them."

And the connection with their grandfather; that went without saying.

He'd agreed, and agreed also that Jem would likely be less conspicuous in Scotland—despite exposure to television and months in the United States, he still spoke with a strong Highland lilt that would make him a marked man in a Boston elementary school. On the other hand, as Roger observed privately, Jem was the sort of person who drew attention, no matter what.

Still, there was no question that life on Lallybroch and in a small Highland school were a great deal more like what Jem had been accustomed to in North Carolina—though given the natural flexibility of kids, he thought he'd adapt pretty well to wherever he found himself.

As to his own prospects in Scotland . . . he'd kept quiet about that.

Jem had reached the end of the pasture and shooed off a group of sheep that were blocking the gate that led to the road. A black ram lowered its head and menaced him, but Jem wasn't bothered about sheep; he shouted and swung his bag, and the ram, startled, backed up sharply, making Roger smile.

He had no qualms about Jem's intelligence—well, he did, but not about its lack. Much more about what kind of trouble it could lead him into. School wasn't simple for anyone, let alone a new school. And a school in which one stuck out, for any reason . . . Roger remembered his own school in Inverness, where he was peculiar first for having no real parents, and then as the minister's adopted son. After a few miserable weeks of being poked, taunted, and having his lunch stolen, he'd started hitting back. And while that had led to a certain amount of difficulty with the teachers, it had eventually taken care of the problem.

Had Jem been fighting? He hadn't seen any blood, but he might not have been close enough. He'd be surprised if it was that, though.

There'd been an incident the week before, when Jem had noticed a large rat scurrying into a hole under the school's foundation. He had brought a bit of twine with him next day, set a snare just before going in to the first lesson, and gone out at the recess to retrieve his prey, which he had then proceeded to skin in a businesslike manner, to the admiration of his male classmates and the horror of the girls. His teacher hadn't been best pleased, either; Miss Glendenning was a city woman from Aberdeen.

Still, it was a Highland village school, and most of the students came from the nearby farms and crofts. Their fathers fished and hunted—and they certainly understood about rats. The principal, Mr. Menzies, had congratulated Jem on his cunning, but told him not to do it again at school. He had let Jem keep the skin, though; Roger had nailed it ceremoniously to the door of the toolshed.

Jem didn't trouble opening the pasture gate; just ducked between the bars, dragging the bag after him.

Was he making for the main road, planning to hitchhike? Roger put on a bit of speed, dodging black sheep droppings and kneeing his way through a cluster of grazing ewes, who gave way in indignation, uttering sharp *baah*s.

No, Jem had turned the other way. Where the devil could he be going? The dirt lane that led to the main road in one direction led absolutely nowhere in the other—it petered out where the land rose into steep, rocky hills.

And that, evidently, was where Jem was headed—for the hills. He turned out of the lane and began climbing, his small form almost obscured by the luxuriant growth of bracken and the drooping branches of rowan trees on the lower slopes. Evidently he was taking to the heather, in the time-honored manner of Highland outlaws.

It was the thought of Highland outlaws that made the penny drop. Jem was heading for the Dunbonnet's cave.

Jamie Fraser had lived there for seven years after the catastrophe of Culloden, almost within sight of his home but hidden from Cumberland's soldiers—and protected by his tenants, who never used his name aloud but called him "the Dunbonnet," for the color of the knitted Highland bonnet he wore to conceal his fiery hair.

That same hair flashed like a beacon, halfway up the slope, before disappearing again behind a rock.

Realizing that, red hair or no, he could easily lose Jem in the rugged landscape, Roger lengthened his stride. Ought he to call out? He knew approximately where the cave was—Brianna had described its location to him—but he hadn't yet been up there himself. It occurred to him to wonder how Jem knew where it was. Perhaps he didn't and was searching for it.

Still, he didn't call, but started up the hill himself. Now he came to look, he could see the narrow path of a deer trail through the growth and the partial print of a small sneaker in the mud of it. He relaxed a little at the sight, and slowed down. He wouldn't lose Jem now.

It was quiet on the hillside, but the air was moving, restless in the rowan trees.

The heather was a haze of rich purple in the hollows of the soaring rock above him. He caught the tang of something on the wind and turned after it, curious. Another flash of red: a stag, splendidly antlered and reeking of rut, ten paces from him on the slope below. He froze, but the deer's head came up, wide black nostrils flaring to scent the air.

He realized suddenly that his hand was pressed against his belt, where he'd once carried a skinning knife, and his muscles were tensed, ready to rush down and cut the deer's throat, once the hunter's shot took it down. He could all but feel the tough hairy skin, the pop of the windpipe, and the gush of hot, reeking blood over his hands, see the long yellow teeth exposed, slimed with the green of the deer's last meal.

The stag belled, a guttural, echoing roar, his challenge to any other stag within hearing. For the space of a breath, Roger expected one of Ian's arrows to whir out of the rowans behind the deer or the echo of Jamie's rifle to crack the air. Then he shook himself back into his skin and, bending, picked up a stone to throw—but the deer had heard him and was off, with a crash that took it rattling into the dry bracken.

He stood still, smelling his own sweat, still dislocated. But it wasn't the North Carolina mountains, and the knife in his pocket was meant for cutting twine and opening beer bottles.

His heart was pounding, but he turned back to the trail, still fitting himself back into time and place. Surely it got easier with practice? They'd been back well more than a year now, and still he woke sometimes at night with no notion where or when he was—or, worse, stepped through some momentary wormhole into the past while still awake.

The kids, being kids, hadn't seemed to suffer much from that sense of being . . . otherwhere. Mandy, of course, had been too young and too sick to remember anything, either of her life in North Carolina or the trip through the stones. Jem remembered. But Jem—he'd taken one look at the automobiles on the road they'd reached half an hour after their emergence from the stones on Ocracoke and stood transfixed, a huge grin spreading across his face as the cars whizzed past him.

"Vroom," he'd said contentedly to himself, the trauma of separation and time travel—Roger had himself barely been able to walk, feeling that he had left a major and irretrievable piece of himself trapped in the stones—apparently forgotten.

A kindly motorist had stopped for them, sympathized with their story of a boating accident, and driven them to the village, where a collect phone call to Joe Abernathy had sorted out the immediate contingencies of money, clothes, a room, and food. Jem had sat on Roger's knee, gazing openmouthed out the window as they drove up the narrow road, the wind from the open window fluttering his soft, bright hair.

Couldn't wait to do it again. And once they'd got settled at Lallybroch, had pestered Roger into letting him drive the Morris Mini round the farm tracks, sitting in Roger's lap, small hands clenching the steering wheel in glee.

Roger smiled wryly to himself; he supposed he was lucky Jem had decided to abscond on foot this time—another year or two, and he'd likely be tall enough to reach the pedals. He'd best start hiding the car keys.

He was high above the farm now, and slowed to look up the slope. Brianna had said the cave was on the south face of the hill, about forty feet above a large whitish boulder known locally as "Leap o' the Cask." So known because the Dunbonnet's servant, bringing ale to the hidden laird, had encountered a group of British soldiers and, refusing to give them the cask he carried, had had his hand cut off—

"Oh, Jesus," Roger whispered. "Fergus. Oh, God, Fergus." Could see at once the laughing, fine-boned face, dark eyes snapping with amusement as he lifted a flapping fish with the hook he wore in place of his missing left hand—and the vision of a small, limp hand, lying bloody on the path before him.

Because it was here. Right here. Turning, he saw the rock, big and rough, bearing silent, stolid witness to horror and despair—and to the sudden grip of the past that took him by the throat, fierce as the bite of a noose.

He coughed hard, trying to open his throat, and heard the hoarse eerie bell of another stag, close above him on the slope but still invisible.

He ducked off the trail, flattening himself against the rock. Surely to God he hadn't sounded bad enough that the stag had taken him for a rival? No—more likely it was coming down in challenge to the one he'd seen a few moments before.

Sure enough; an instant later a big stag came down from above, picking its way almost daintily through heather and rocks. It was a fine animal, but was already showing the strain of rutting season, its ribs shadowed under the thick coat and the flesh of its face sunk in, eyes red with sleeplessness and lust.

It saw him; the big head swiveled in his direction, and he saw the rolling, bloodshot eyes fix on him. It wasn't afraid of him, though; likely had no room in its brain for anything save fighting and copulation. It stretched its neck in his direction and belled at him, eyes showing white with the effort.

"Look, mate, you want her, you can have her." He backed slowly away, but the deer followed him, menacing him with lowered antlers. Alarmed, he spread his arms, waved and shouted at the deer; normally that would have sent it bounding away. Red deer in rut weren't normal; the thing lowered its head and charged him.

Roger dodged aside and threw himself flat at the base of the rock. He was wedged as tightly next to the rock's face as he could get, in hopes of keeping the maddened stag from trampling him. It stumbled to a stop a few feet from him, thrashing at the heather with its antlers and breathing like a bellows—but then it heard the blatting of the challenger below, and jerked its head up.

Another roar from below, and the new stag turned on its haunches and bounded clear over the trail, the sound of its hell-bent passage down the slope marked by the crunch of breaking heather and the rattle of stones spurned by its hooves.

Roger scrambled to his feet, adrenaline running through his veins like quicksilver. He hadn't realized the red deer were at it up here, or he'd not have been wasting time strolling along maundering about the past. He needed to find Jem *now,* before the boy ran afoul of one of the things.

He could hear the roars and clashing of the two below, fighting it out for control of a harem of hinds, though they were out of sight from where he stood.

"Jem!" he bellowed, not caring whether he sounded like a rutting deer or a bull elephant. "Jem! Where are you? Answer me this minute!"

"I'm up here, Da." Jemmy's voice came from above him, a little tremulous, and he whirled to see Jem sitting on the Leap o' the Cask, string bag clutched to his chest.

"Right, you. Down. Now." Relief fought with annoyance but edged it out. He reached up, and Jem slid down the rock, landing heavily in his father's arms.

Roger grunted and set him down, then leaned down to pick up the string bag, which had fallen to the ground. In addition to bread and lemon squash, he saw, it held several apples, a large chunk of cheese, and a packet of chocolate biscuits.

"Planning to stay for a while, were ye?" he asked. Jemmy flushed and looked away.

Roger turned and looked up the slope.

"Up there, is it? Your grandda's cave?" He couldn't see a thing; the slope was a jumble of rock and heather, liberally splotched with scrubby gorse bushes and the odd sprout of rowan and alder.

"Aye. Just there." Jemmy pointed up the slope. "See, where that witch tree's leaning?"

He saw the rowan—a full-grown tree, gnarled with age; surely it couldn't have been there since Jamie's time, could it?—but still saw no sign of the cave's opening. The sounds of combat from below had ceased; he glanced round in case the loser should be coming back this way, but evidently not.

"Show me," he said.

Jem, who had been looking deeply uneasy, relaxed a little at this and, turning, scrambled up the slope, Roger at his heels.

You could be right next to the cave's opening and never see it. It was screened by an outcrop of rock and a heavy growth of gorse; you couldn't see the narrow opening at all unless you were standing in front of it.

A cool breath came out of the cave, moist on his face. He

knelt down to peer in; couldn't see more than a few feet inside, but it wasn't inviting.

"Be cold to sleep in there," he said. He glanced at Jem, and motioned to a nearby rock.

"Want to sit down and tell me what happened at school?"

Jem swallowed and shifted from foot to foot.

"No."

"Sit down." He didn't raise his voice, but made it evident he expected to be obeyed. Jem didn't quite sit down but edged backward, leaning against the rocky outcrop that hid the cave mouth. He wouldn't look up.

"I got the strap," Jem muttered, chin buried in his chest.

"Oh?" Roger kept his voice casual. "Well, that's a bugger. I got it once or twice, when I was at school. Didn't like it."

Jem's head jerked up, eyes wide.

"Aye? What for, then?"

"Fighting, mostly," Roger said. He supposed he oughtn't to be telling the boy that—bad example—but it was the truth. And if fighting was Jem's problem . . .

"That what happened today?" He'd looked Jem over briefly when he sat down, and gave him a closer look now. Jem seemed undamaged, but when he turned his head away, Roger could see that something had happened to his ear. It was a deep crimson, the lobe of it nearly purple. He suppressed an exclamation at sight of it and merely repeated, "What happened?"

"Jacky McEnroe said if ye heard I'd got the strap, ye'd give me another whipping when I got home." Jem swallowed, but now looked at his father directly. "Will you?"

"I don't know. I hope I won't have to."

He'd tawsed Jemmy once—he'd had to—and neither of them wanted to repeat the experience. He reached out and touched Jem's flaming ear gently.

"Tell me what happened, son."

Jem took a deep breath, blowing out his cheeks, then deflated into resignation.

"Aye. Well, it started when Jimmy Glasscock said Mam and me and Mandy were all goin' to burn in hell."

"Yeah?" Roger wasn't all that surprised; Scottish Presbyterians weren't known for their religious flexibility, and the breed hadn't altered all that much in two hundred years. Manners might keep most of them from telling their papist acquaintance they were going straight to hell—but most of them likely thought it.

"Well, ye know what to do about that, though, don't you?" Jem had heard similar sentiments expressed on the Ridge—though generally more quietly, Jamie Fraser being who he was. Still, they'd talked about it, and Jem was well prepared to answer that particular conversational gambit.

"Oh, aye." Jem shrugged, looking down at his shoes again. "Just say, 'Aye, fine, I'll see ye there, then.' I did."

"And?"

Deep sigh.

"I said it in the *Gàidhlig.*"

Roger scratched behind his ear, puzzled. Gaelic was disappearing in the Highlands, but was still common enough that you heard it once in a while in the pub or the post office. No doubt a few of Jem's classmates had heard it from their grans, but even if they didn't understand what he'd said . . . ?

"And?" he repeated.

"And Miss Glendenning grabbed me by the ear and like to tore it off." A flush was rising in Jemmy's cheeks at the memory. "She shook me, Da!"

"By the ear?" Roger felt an answering flush in his own cheeks.

"Yes!" Tears of humiliation and anger were welling in Jem's eyes, but he dashed them away with a sleeve and pounded his fist on his leg. "She said, 'We—do—not—speak—like—THAT! We—speak—ENGLISH!' " His voice was some octaves higher than the redoubtable Miss Glendenning's, but his mimicry made the ferocity of her attack more than evident.

"And then she took a strap to you?" Roger asked incredulously.

Jem shook his head, and wiped his nose on his sleeve.

"No," he said. "That was Mr. Menzies."

"What? Why? Here." He handed Jem a crumpled paper handkerchief from his pocket, and waited while the boy blew his nose.

"Well . . . I was already fussed wi' Jimmy, and when she grabbed me like that, it hurt bad. And . . . well, my dander got up," he said, giving Roger a blue-eyed look of burning righteousness that was so much his grandfather that Roger nearly smiled, despite the situation.

"And ye said something else to her, did ye?"

"Aye." Jem dropped his eyes, rubbing the toe of his sneaker in the dirt. "Miss Glendenning doesna like the *Gàidhlig,* but she doesn't know any, either. Mr. Menzies does."

"Oh, God."

Drawn by the shouting, Mr. Menzies had emerged onto the play yard just in time to hear Jem giving Miss Glendenning the benefit of some of his grandfather's best Gaelic curses, at the top of his lungs.

"So he made me bend over a chair and gave me three good ones, then sent me to the cloakroom to stay 'til school was out."

"Only you didn't stay there."

Jem shook his head, bright hair flying.

Roger bent and picked up the string bag, fighting back outrage, dismay, laughter, and a throat-clutching sympathy. On second thought, he let a bit of the sympathy show.

"Running away from home, were ye?"

"No." Jem looked up at him, surprised. "I didna want to go to school tomorrow, though. Not and have Jimmy laugh at me. So I thought to stay up here 'til the weekend, and maybe by Monday, things would get sorted. Miss Glendenning might die," he added hopefully.

"And maybe your mam and I would be so worried by the time ye came down, ye'd get off without a second whipping?"

Jem's deep-blue eyes widened in surprise.

"Och, no. Mam would give me laldy if I just went off wi' no word. I put a note on my bed. Said I was living rough a day or two." He said this with perfect matter-of-factness. Then he wiggled his shoulders and stood up, sighing.

"Can we get it over and go home?" he asked, his voice trembling only a little. "I'm hungry."

"I'm not going to whip you," Roger assured him. He reached out an arm and gathered Jemmy to him. "Come here, pal."

Jemmy's brave facade gave way at that, and he melted into Roger's arms, crying a little in relief but letting himself be comforted, cuddling like a puppy against his father's shoulder, trusting Da to make it all right. *And his da bloody would,* Roger promised silently. No matter if he had to strangle Miss Glendenning with his bare hands.

"Why is it bad to speak *Gàidhlig,* Da?" he murmured, worn out by so much emotion. "I didna mean to do anything bad."

"It's not," Roger whispered, smoothing the silky hair behind Jem's ear. "Dinna fash yourself. Mam and I will get it sorted. I promise. And ye haven't got to go to school tomorrow."

Jem sighed at that, going inert as a bag of grain. Then he lifted his head and gave a small giggle.

"D'ye think Mam will give Mr. Menzies laldy?"

27

TUNNEL TIGERS

BRIANNA'S FIRST intimation of disaster was the slice of light on the track, shrinking to nothing in the split second it took for the enormous doors to swing shut, echoing behind her with a boom that seemed to shiver the air in the tunnel.

She said something that she would have washed Jem's mouth out for saying, and said it with heartfelt fury—but said it also under her breath, having realized in the instant that it took the doors to close what was happening.

She couldn't see a thing save the swirls of color that were her retinas' response to sudden dark, but she was only ten feet or so inside the tunnel and could still hear the sound of the bolts sliding home; they were worked by big wheels on the outside of the steel doors and made a grinding sound like bones being chewed. She turned carefully, took five steps, and put out her hands. Yes, there were the doors; big, solid, made of steel, and now solidly locked. She could hear the sound of laughter outside.

Giggling, she thought with furious contempt. *Like little boys!*

Little boys, indeed. She took a few deep breaths, fighting off both anger and panic. Now that the dazzle of the darkness had faded, she could see the thin line of light that bisected the fifteen-foot doors. A man-height shadow interrupted the light but was jerked away, to the accompaniment of whispers and more giggling. Someone trying to peek in, the idiot. Good luck to him, seeing anything in *here.* Aside from the hair of light between the doors, the hydroelectric tunnel under Loch Errochty was dark as the pits of hell.

At least she could use that hair of light for orientation. Still breathing with deliberation, she made her way—stepping carefully; she didn't want to amuse the baboons outside any more than necessary by stumbling and falling noisily—to the metal box on the left wall where the power switches that controlled the tunnel lighting were located.

She found the box and was momentarily panicked to find it locked, before recalling that she had the key; it was on the big jangle of grubby keys that Mr. Campbell had given her, each one dangling a worn paper tag with its function written on. Of course, she couldn't *read* the bloody tags—and frigging Andy Davies had casually borrowed the flashlight that should have been in her belt, on the pretext of looking under the truck for an oil leak.

They'd planned it pretty well, she thought grimly, trying one key, then the next, fumbling and scratching to insert the tip in the tiny invisible slot. All three of them were clearly in on it: Andy, Craig McCarty, and Rob Cameron.

She was of an orderly mind, and when she'd tried each key in careful turn with no result, didn't try them again. She knew they'd thought of that one, too; Craig had taken the keys from her to unlock the toolbox in the panel truck, and returned them with a bow of exaggerated gallantry.

They'd stared at her—naturally—when she was introduced to them as the new safety inspector, though she supposed they'd already been informed she was that shocking thing, a woman. Rob Cameron, a handsome young man who clearly fancied himself, had looked her frankly up and down before extending his hand with a smile. She'd returned the slow up-and-down before taking it, and the other two had laughed. So had Rob, to his credit.

She hadn't sensed any hostility from them on the drive to Loch Errochty, and she thought she'd have seen it if it had been there. This was just a stupid joke. Probably.

In all honesty, the doors closing behind her had *not* been her first intimation that something was up, she thought grimly. She'd been a mother much too long to miss the looks of secretive delight or preternatural innocence that marked the face of a male up to mischief, and such looks had been all over the faces of her maintenance and repair team, if she'd spared the attention to look at them. Her mind had been only half on her job, though; the other half had been in the eighteenth century, worried for Fergus and Marsali, but encouraged by the vision of her parents and Ian safely bound at last for Scotland.

But whatever was going on—*had* gone on, she corrected herself firmly—in the past, she had other things to worry about in the here and now.

What did they expect her to do? she wondered. Scream? Cry? Beat on the doors and beg to be let out?

She walked quietly back to the door and pressed her ear to the crack, in time to hear the roar of the truck's engine starting up and the spurt of gravel from its wheels as it turned up the service road.

"You bloody *bastards*!" she said out loud. What did they mean by this? Since she hadn't satisfied them by shrieking and crying, they'd decided simply to leave her entombed for a while? Come back later in hopes of finding her in shards—or, better yet, red-faced with fury? Or—more-sinister thought—did they mean to go back to the Hydro Electric Board office, innocent looks on their faces, and tell Mr. Campbell that his new inspector simply hadn't shown up for work this morning?

She breathed out through her nose, slow, deliberate.

Right. She'd eviscerate them when the opportunity offered. But what to do just now?

She turned away from the power box, looking into the utter black. She hadn't been in this particular tunnel before, though she'd seen one like it during her tour with Mr. Campbell. It was one of the original tunnels of the hydroelectric project, dug by hand with pick and shovel by the "hydro boys" back in the 1950s. It ran nearly a mile through the mountain and under part of the flooded valley that now held the greatly expanded Loch Errochty, and a toylike electric train ran on its track down the center of the tunnel.

Originally, the train had carried the workmen, the "tunnel tigers," to the work face and back; now reduced to only an engine, it served the occasional hydroelectric workers checking the huge cables that ran along the tunnel's walls or servicing the tremendous turbines at the foot of the dam, far off at the other end of the tunnel.

Which was, it occurred to her, what Rob, Andy, and Craig were meant to be doing. Lifting one of the massive turbines and replacing its damaged blade.

She pressed her back against the tunnel wall, hands flat on the rough rock, and thought. That's where they'd gone, then. It made no difference, but she closed her eyes to improve her concentration and summoned up the pages of the massive binder—presently on the seat of the vanished truck—that contained the structural and engineering details of all the hydroelectric stations under her purview.

She'd looked at the diagrams for this one last night and again, hastily, while brushing her teeth this morning. The tunnel led *to* the dam, and had obviously been used in the construction of the lower levels of that dam. How low? If the tunnel joined at the level of the turbine chamber itself, it would have been walled off. But if it joined at the level of the servicing chamber above—a huge room equipped with the multi-ton ceiling cranes needed to lift the turbines from their nests—then there would still be a door; there would have been no need to seal it off, with no water on the other side.

Try as she might, she couldn't bring the diagrams to mind in sufficient detail to be sure there was an opening into the dam at the far end of the tunnel—but it would be simple enough to find out.

SHE'D SEEN THE TRAIN, in that brief moment before the doors closed; it didn't take much fumbling round to get into the open cab of the tiny engine. Now, had those clowns taken the key to the engine, too? Ha. There was no key; it worked by a switch on the console. She flipped it, and a red button glowed with sudden triumph as she felt the hum of electricity run through the track beneath.

The train couldn't have been simpler to run. It had a single lever, which you pushed forward or back, depending on which direction you meant to go. She shoved it gently forward, and felt air move past her face as the train moved silently off into the bowels of the earth.

She had to go slowly. The tiny red button shed a comforting glow over her hands, but did nothing to pierce the darkness ahead, and she had no idea where or how much the track curved. Neither did she want to hit the end of the track at a high rate of speed and derail the engine. It felt as though she was inching through the dark, but it was much better than walking, feeling her way over a mile of tunnel lined with high-voltage cables.

It hit her in the dark. For a split second, she thought someone had laid a live cable on the track. In the next instant, a sound that wasn't a sound thrummed through her, plucking every nerve in her body, making her vision go white. And then her hand brushed rock and she realized that she had fallen across the console, was hanging halfway out of the tiny, trundling engine, was about to fall out into darkness.

Head spinning, she managed to grab the edge of the console and pull herself back into the cab. Flipped the switch with one shaking hand and half-fell to the floor, where she curled up, gripping her knees, her breath a whimpering in the dark.

"Holy God," she whispered. "Oh, Blessed Mother. Oh, Jesus."

She could feel it out there. Still feel it. It didn't make a sound now, but she felt its nearness and couldn't stop trembling.

She sat still for a long time, head on her knees, until rational thought began to come back.

She couldn't be mistaken. She'd passed through time twice, and *knew* the feeling. But this hadn't been nearly so shocking. Her skin still prickled and her nerves jumped and her inner ears rang as though she'd thrust her head into a hive of hornets—but she felt solid. She felt as though a red-hot wire had sliced her in two, but she hadn't had the horrible sense of being disassembled, turned physically inside out.

A terrible thought sent her surging to her feet, clinging to the console. Had she jumped? Was she somewhere—some*when*—else? But the metal console was cool and solid under her hands, the smell of damp rock and cable insulation unchanged.

"No," she whispered, and flicked the power light for reassurance. It came on, and the train, still in gear, gave a sudden lurch. Hastily, she throttled back the speed to less than a crawl.

She couldn't have jumped into the past. Small objects in direct contact with a traveler's person seemed to move with them, but an entire train and its track was surely pushing it. "Besides," she said out loud, "if you'd gone more than twenty-five years or so into the past, the tunnel wouldn't *be* here. You'd be inside . . . solid rock." Her gorge rose suddenly, and she threw up.

The sense of . . . it . . . was receding, though. It—whatever it was—was behind her. Well, that settled it, she thought, wiping her mouth with the back of her hand. There bloody well *had* to be a door at the far end, because there was no way she was going back the way she'd come.

There was a door. A plain, ordinary, industrial metal door. And a padlock, unlocked, hanging from an open hasp. She could smell WD-40; someone had oiled the hinges, very recently, and the door swung open easily when she turned the knob. She felt suddenly like Alice, after falling down the White Rabbit's hole. A really mad Alice.

A steep flight of steps lay on the other side of the door, dimly lit—and at the top was another metal door, edged with light. She could hear the rumble and the metallic whine of a ceiling crane in operation.

Her breath was coming fast, and not from the effort of climbing the stairs. What would she find on the other side? It was the servicing chamber inside the dam; she knew that much. But would she find Thursday on the other side? The *same* Thursday she'd had when the tunnel doors had closed behind her?

She gritted her teeth and opened the door. Rob Cameron was waiting, lounging back against the wall, lit cigarette in hand. He broke into an enormous grin at sight of her, dropped the butt, and stepped on it.

"Knew ye'd make it, hen," he said. Across the room, Andy and Craig turned from their work and applauded.

"Buy ye a pint after work, then, lass," Andy called.

"Two!" shouted Craig.

She could still taste bile at the back of her throat. She gave Rob Cameron the sort of look she'd given Mr. Campbell.

"Don't," she said evenly, "call me hen."

His good-looking face twitched and he tugged at his forelock with mock subservience.

"Anything you say, boss," he said.

28

HILLTOPS

IT WAS NEARLY seven by the time he heard Brianna's car in the drive. The kids had had their supper, but came swarming out to her, clinging to her legs as though she'd just come back from darkest Africa or the North Pole.

It was some time before the kids were settled for the night and Bree had time to give her undivided attention to him. He didn't mind.

"Are you starving?" she said. "I can fix—"

He interrupted her, taking her by the hand and drawing her into his office, where he carefully closed and locked the door. She was standing there, hair half matted from her hard hat, grimy from spending the day in the bowels of the earth. She smelled of earth. Also engine grease, cigarette smoke, sweat, and . . . beer?

"I've a lot to tell you," he said. "And I know ye've a lot to tell me. But first . . . could ye just slip off your jeans, maybe, sit on the desk, and spread your legs?"

Her eyes went perfectly round.

"Yes," she said mildly. "I could do that."

ROGER HAD OFTEN wondered whether it was true what they said about redheaded people being more volatile than the usual—or whether it was just that their emotions showed so suddenly and alarmingly on their skins. Both, he thought.

Maybe he should have waited 'til she'd got her clothes on before telling her about Miss Glendenning. If he had, though, he'd have missed the remarkable sight of his wife, naked and flushed with fury from the navel upward.

"That bloody old besom! If she thinks she can get away with—"

"She can't," he interrupted firmly. "Of course she can't."

"You bet she can't! I'll go down there first thing tomorrow and—"

"Well, maybe not."

She stopped and looked at him, one eye narrowed.

"Maybe not *what*?"

"Maybe not you." He fastened his own jeans, and picked hers up. "I was thinking it might be best if I go."

She frowned, turning that one over.

"Not that I think ye'd lose your temper and set about the old bitch," he added, smiling, "but you have got your job to go to, aye?"

"Hmmm," she said, seeming skeptical of his ability to adequately impress Miss Glendenning with the magnitude of her crime.

"And if ye *did* lose the heid and nut the woman, I'd hate to have to explain to the kids why we were visiting Mummy in jail."

That made her laugh, and he relaxed a little. He really didn't *think* she'd resort to physical violence, but then, she hadn't seen Jemmy's ear right after he'd come home. He'd had a strong urge himself to go straight down to the school and show the woman what it felt like, but he was in better command of himself now.

"So what *do* you mean to say to her?" She fished her brassiere out from under the desk, giving him a succulent view of her rear aspect, as she hadn't put the jeans on yet.

"Nothing. I'll speak to the principal. *He* can have a word with her."

"Well, that might be better," she said slowly. "We don't want Miss Glendenning to take it out on Jemmy."

"Right." The beautiful flush was fading. Her hard hat had rolled off under the chair; he picked it up and set it on her head again. "So—how was work today? And why don't ye wear knickers to work?" he asked, suddenly remembering.

To his startlement, the flush roared back like a brushfire.

"I got out of the habit in the eighteenth century," she snapped, plainly taking the huff. "I only wear knickers for ceremonial purposes anymore. What did you think, I was planning to seduce Mr. Campbell?"

"Well, not if he's anything like you described him, no," he said mildly. "I just noticed when ye left this morning, and wondered."

"Oh." She was still ruffled, he could see that and wondered why. He was about to ask again about her day when she took the hat off and eyed him speculatively.

"You said if I wore the hat, you'd tell me what you were doing with that champagne bottle. Other than giving it to Mandy to throw through the window," she added, with a tinge of wifely censoriousness. "What were you *thinking,* Roger?"

"Well, in all honesty, I was thinking about your arse," he said. "But it never occurred to me that she'd throw the thing. Or that she *could* throw it like that."

"Did you ask her why she did it?"

He stopped, nonplused.

"It hadn't occurred to me that she'd have a reason," he confessed. "I snatched her off the table as she was about to pitch face-first into the broken window, and I was so frightened that I just picked her up and smacked her bum."

"I don't think she'd do something like that for no reason," Bree said meditatively. She'd put aside the hard hat and was scooping herself into her brassiere, a spectacle Roger found diverting under just about any circumstances.

It wasn't until they'd gone back to the kitchen for their own late supper that he remembered to ask again how her workday had gone.

"Not bad," she said, with a good assumption of casualness. Not so good as to convince him, but good enough that he thought better of prodding, and instead asked, "Ceremonial purposes?"

A broad grin spread across her face.

"You know. For you."

"Me?"

"Yes, you and your fetish for women's lacy underthings."

"What—you mean you only wear knickers for—"

"For you to take off, of course."

There was no telling where the conversation might have gone from this point, but it was interrupted by a loud wail from above, and Bree disappeared hastily in the direction of the stairs, leaving Roger to contemplate this latest revelation.

He'd got the bacon fried and the tinned beans simmering by the time she reappeared, a small frown between her brows.

"Bad dream," she said, in answer to his lifted brow. "The same one."

"The bad thing trying to get in her window again?"

She nodded and took the saucepan of beans he handed her, though she didn't move immediately to serve out the food.

"I asked her why she threw the bottle."

"Aye?"

Brianna took the bean spoon, holding it like a weapon.

"She said she saw him outside the window."

"Him? The—"

"The Nuckelavee."

IN THE MORNING, the broch was just as it had been the last time he'd looked. Dark. Quiet, save for the rustling of the doves overhead. He'd taken away the rubbish; no new fish papers had come. *Swept and garnished,* he thought. Waiting for the occupation of whatever roaming spirit might happen by?

He shook that thought off and closed the door firmly. He'd

get new hinges and a padlock for it, next time he passed by the Farm and Household Stores.

Had Mandy really seen someone? And if she had, was it the same tramp who had frightened Jem? The idea of someone hanging round, spying on his family, made something hard and black curl through his chest, like a sharp-pointed iron spring. He stood for a moment, narrowly surveying the house, the grounds, for any trace of an intruder. Anywhere a man might hide. He'd already searched the barn and the other outbuildings.

The Dunbonnet's cave? The thought—with his memory of Jem standing right by the mouth of the cave—chilled him. Well, he'd soon find out, he thought grimly, and with a last glance at Annie MacDonald and Mandy, peacefully hanging out the family washing in the yard below, he set off.

He kept a sharp ear out today. He heard the echo of the red stags belling, still hard at it, and once saw a small herd of hinds in the distance, but luckily met no lust-crazed males. No lurking tramps, either.

It took him some time of casting about to find the cave's entrance, even though he'd been there only the day before. He made a good bit of noise, approaching, but stood outside and called, "Hallo, the cave!" just in case. No answer.

He approached the entrance from the side, pressing back the covering gorse with a forearm, ready in case the tramp might be lurking inside—but he could tell as soon as the damp breath of the place touched his face that it was unoccupied.

Nonetheless, he poked his head in, then swung himself down into the cave itself. It was dry, for a cave in the Highlands, which was not saying all that much. Cold as a tomb, though. It was no wonder Highlanders had a reputation for toughness; anyone who wasn't would have succumbed to starvation or pneumonia in short order.

Despite the chill of the place, he stood for a minute, imagining his father-in-law here. It was empty and cold, but oddly peaceful, he thought. No sense of foreboding. In fact, he felt . . . welcomed, and the notion made the hairs prickle on his arms.

"Grant, Lord, that they may be safe," he said quietly, his

hand resting on the stone at the entrance. Then he climbed out, into the sun's warm benediction.

That strange sense of welcome, of having been somehow acknowledged, remained with him.

"Well, what now, *athair-céile*?" he said aloud, half joking. "Anyplace else I should look?"

Even as he said it, he realized that he *was* looking. On the top of the next small hill was the heap of stones Brianna had told him about. Human-made, she'd said, and thought it might be an Iron Age fort. There didn't look to be enough of whatever it was standing to offer shelter to anyone, but out of sheer restlessness, he made his way down through the tumble of rock and heather, splashed through a tiny burn that gurgled through the rock at the foot of the hill, and toiled his way up to the heap of ancient rubble.

It *was* ancient—but not as old as the Iron Age. What he found looked like the ruins of a small chapel; a stone on the ground had a cross chiseled crudely into it, and he saw what looked like the weathered fragments of a stone statue, scattered by the entrance. There was more of it than he'd thought from a distance; one wall still reached as high as his waist, and there were parts of two more. The roof had long since fallen in and disappeared, but a length of the rooftree was still there, the wood gone hard as metal.

Wiping sweat from the back of his neck, he stooped and picked up the statue's head. Very old. Celtic, Pictish? Not enough left to tell even the statue's intended gender.

He passed a thumb gently over the statue's sightless eyes, then set the head carefully atop the half wall; there was a depression there, as though there might once have been a niche in the wall.

"Okay," he said, feeling awkward. "See you later, then." And, turning, made his way down the rough hill toward home, still with that odd sense of being accompanied on his way.

The Bible says, "Seek, and ye shall find," he thought. And said aloud to the vibrant air, "But there's no guarantee about *what* you'll find, is there?"

29

CONVERSATION WITH A HEADMASTER

AFTER A PEACEFUL lunch with Mandy, who seemed to have forgotten all about her nightmares, he dressed with some care for his interview with the headmaster of Jem's school.

Mr. Menzies was a surprise; Roger hadn't thought to ask Bree what the man was like, and had been expecting something squat, middle-aged, and authoritarian, along the lines of his own headmaster at school. Instead, Menzies was close to Roger's own age, a slender, pale-skinned man with spectacles and what looked like a humorous eye behind them. Roger didn't miss the firm set of the mouth, though, and thought he'd been right to keep Bree from coming.

"Lionel Menzies," the headmaster said, smiling. He had a solid handshake and a friendly air, and Roger found himself revising his strategy.

"Roger MacKenzie." He let go and took the proffered seat, across the desk from Menzies. "Jem's—Jeremiah's—dad."

"Oh, aye, of course. I rather thought I might see you or your wife, when Jem didn't turn up at school this morning." Menzies leaned back a little, folding his hands. "Before we go very far . . . could I just ask exactly what Jem told ye about what happened?"

Roger's opinion of the man rose a grudging notch.

"He said that his teacher heard him say something to another lad in the Gaelic, whereupon she grabbed him by the ear and shook him. That made him mad and he called her names—also in Gaelic—for which you belted him." He'd spotted the strap itself, hung up inconspicuously—but still quite visible—on the wall beside a filing cabinet.

Menzies's eyebrows rose behind his spectacles.

"Is that not what happened?" Roger asked, wondering for the first time whether Jem had lied or omitted something even more horrible from his account.

"No, that's what happened," Menzies said. "I've just never heard a parent give such a concise account. Generally speaking, it's a half hour of prologue, dissociated trivia, contumely, and contradiction—that's if both parents come—and personal attacks before I can make out precisely what the trouble is. Thank you." He smiled, and quite involuntarily, Roger smiled back.

"I was sorry to have to do it," Menzies went on, not pausing for reply. "I like Jem. He's clever, hardworking—and really funny."

"He is that," Roger said. "But—"

"But I hadn't a choice, really," Menzies interrupted firmly. "If none of the other students had known what he was saying, we might have done with a simple apology. But—did he tell ye what it was he said?"

"Not in detail, no." Roger hadn't inquired; he'd heard Jamie Fraser curse someone in Gaelic only three or four times—but it was a memorable experience, and Jem had an excellent memory.

"Well, I won't, either, then, unless you insist. But the thing is, while only a few of the kids on the play yard likely understood him, they would tell—well, they have told, in fact—all their friends exactly what he said. And they know I understood it, too. I've got to support the authority of my teachers; if there's no respect for the staff, the whole place goes to hell. . . . Did your wife tell me ye'd taught yourself? At Oxford, I think she said? That's very impressive."

"That was some years ago, and I was only a junior don, but yes. And I hear what you're saying, though I unfortunately had to keep order and respect without the threat of physical force." Not that he wouldn't have loved to be able to punch one or two of his Oxford second-year students in the nose . . .

Menzies eyed him with a slight twinkle.

"I'd say your presence was likely adequate," he said. "And given that you're twice my size, I'm pleased to hear that you're not inclined to use force."

"Some of your other parents are?" Roger asked, raising his own brows.

"Well, none of the fathers has actually struck me, no, though it's been threatened once or twice. Did have one mother come in with the family shotgun, though." Menzies inclined his head at the wall behind him, and looking up, Roger saw a spray of black pockmarks in the plaster, mostly—but not entirely—covered by a framed map of Africa.

"Fired over your head, at least," Roger said dryly, and Menzies laughed.

"Well, no," he said, deprecating. "I asked her please to set it down carefully, and she did, but not carefully enough. Caught the trigger somehow and *blam!* The poor woman was really unnerved—though not quite as much as I was."

"You're bloody good, mate," Roger said, smiling in acknowledgment of Menzies's skill in handling difficult parents—including Roger—but leaning forward a little to indicate that he meant to take control of the conversation. "But I'm not—not yet, anyway—complaining about your belting Jem. It's what led to that."

Menzies drew breath and nodded, setting his elbows on the desk and steepling his hands.

"Aye, right."

"I understand the need to support your teachers," Roger said, and set his own hands on the desk. "But that woman nearly tore my son's ear off, and evidently for no crime greater than saying a few words—not cursing, just words—in the *Gàidhlig*."

Menzies eyes sharpened, catching the accent.

"Ah, you've got it, then. Wondered, ken, was it you or your wife had it."

"You make it sound like a disease. My wife's an American—surely ye noticed?"

Menzies gave him an amused look—no one failed to notice Brianna—but said only, "Aye, I noticed. She told me her da was Scots, though, and a Highlander. You speak it at home?"

"No, not much. Jem got it from his grandda. He's . . . no longer with us," he added.

Menzies nodded.

"Ah," he said softly. "Aye, I had it from my grandparents,

as well—my mam's folk. Dead, too, now. They were from Skye." The usual implied question hovered, and Roger answered it.

"I was born in Kyle of Lochalsh, but I grew up mostly in Inverness. Picked up most of my own Gaelic on the fishing boats in the Minch." And in the mountains of North Carolina.

Menzies nodded again, for the first time looking down at his hands rather than at Roger.

"Been on a fishing boat in the last twenty years?"

"No, thank God."

Menzies smiled briefly, but didn't look up.

"No. You won't find much of the Gaelic there these days. Spanish, Polish, Estonian . . . quite a bit of those, but not the Gaelic. Your wife said ye'd spent a number of years in America, so you'll maybe not have noticed, but it's not much spoken in public anymore."

"To be honest, I hadn't paid it much mind—not 'til now."

Menzies nodded again, as though to himself, then took off his spectacles and rubbed at the marks they'd left on the bridge of his nose. His eyes were pale blue and seemed suddenly vulnerable, without the protection of his glasses.

"It's been on the decline for a number of years. Much more so for the last ten, fifteen years. The Highlands are suddenly part of the UK—or at least the rest of the UK says so—in a way they've never been before, and keeping a separate language is seen as not only old-fashioned but outright destructive.

"It's no what you'd call a written policy, to stamp it out, but the use of Gaelic is strongly . . . discouraged . . . in schools. Mind"—he raised a hand to forestall Roger's response—"they couldn't get away with that if the parents protested, but they don't. Most of them are eager for their kids to be part of the modern world, speak good English, get good jobs, fit in elsewhere, be able to leave the Highlands . . . Not so much for them here, is there, save the North Sea?"

"The parents . . ."

"If they've learnt the Gaelic from their own parents, they deliberately don't teach it to their kids. And if they haven't got it, they certainly make no effort to learn. It's seen as backward, ignorant. Very much a mark of the lower classes."

"Barbarous, in fact," Roger said, with an edge. "The barbarous Erse?"

Menzies recognized Samuel Johnson's dismissive description of the tongue spoken by his eighteenth-century Highland hosts, and the brief, rueful smile lit his face again.

"Exactly. There's a great deal of prejudice—much of it outspoken—against . . ."

"Teuchters?" "Teuchter" was a Lowland Scots term for someone in the Gaeltacht, the Gaelic-speaking Highlands, and in cultural terms the general equivalent of "hillbilly" or "trailer trash."

"Oh, ye do know, then."

"Something." It was true; even as recently as the sixties, Gaelic speakers had been viewed with a certain derision and public dismissiveness, but this . . . Roger cleared his throat.

"Regardless, Mr. Menzies," he said, coming down a bit on the "Mr.," "I object very much to my son's teacher not only disciplining him for speaking Gaelic but actually assaulting him for doing so."

"I share your concern, Mr. MacKenzie," Menzies said, looking up and meeting his eyes in a way that made it seem as though he truly did. "I've had a wee word with Miss Glendenning, and I think it won't happen again."

Roger held his gaze for moment, wanting to say all sorts of things but realizing that Menzies was not responsible for most of them.

"If it does," he said evenly, "I won't come back with a shotgun—but I will come back with the sheriff. And a newspaper photographer, to document Miss Glendenning being taken off in handcuffs."

Menzies blinked once and put his spectacles back on.

"You're sure ye wouldn't rather send your wife round with the family shotgun?" he asked wistfully, and Roger laughed, despite himself.

"Fine, then." Menzies pushed back his chair and stood up. "I'll see ye out; I've got to lock up. We'll see Jem on the Monday, then, will we?"

"He'll be here. With or without handcuffs."

Menzies laughed.

"Well, he needn't worry about his reception. Since the Gaelic-speaking kids *did* tell their friends what it was he said, and he took his belting without a squeak, I think his entire form now regards him as Robin Hood or Billy Jack."

"Oh, God."

30

SHIPS THAT PASS IN THE NIGHT

May 19, 1777

THE SHARK WAS easily twelve feet long, a dark, sinuous shape keeping pace with the ship, barely visible through the storm-stirred gray waters. It had appeared abruptly just before noon, startling me badly when I looked over the rail and saw its fin cut the surface.

"What's amiss with its head?" Jamie, appearing in response to my startled cry, frowned into the dark water. "It has a growth of some sort."

"I think it's what they call a hammerhead." I clung tight to the railing, slippery with spray. The head *did* look misshapen: a queer, clumsy, blunt thing at the end of such a sinisterly graceful body. As we watched, though, the shark came closer to the surface and rolled, bringing one fleshy stalk and its distant cold eye momentarily clear of the water.

Jamie made a sound of horrified disgust.

"They normally look like that," I informed him.

"Why?"

"I suppose God was feeling bored one day." That made him laugh, and I viewed him with approval. His color was high and healthy, and he'd eaten breakfast with such appetite that I'd felt I could dispense with the acupuncture needles.

"What's the strangest thing you've ever seen? An animal, I mean. A nonhuman animal," I added, thinking of Dr. Fentiman's ghastly collection of pickled deformities and "natural curiosities."

"Strange by itself? Not deformed, I mean, but as God meant it to be?" He squinted into the sea, thinking, then grinned. "The mandrill in Louis of France's zoo. Or . . . well, no. Maybe a rhinoceros, though I havena seen one of those in the flesh. Does that count?"

"Let's say something you've seen in the flesh," I said, thinking of a few pictorial animals I'd seen in this time that appeared to have been deeply affected by the artist's imagination. "You thought the mandrill was stranger than the orangutan?" I recalled his fascination with the orangutan, a solemn-faced young animal who had seemed equally fascinated by *him,* this leading to a number of jokes regarding the origins of red hair on the part of the Duc d'Orleans, who'd been present.

"Nay, I've seen a good many people who looked stranger than the orangutan," he said. The wind had shifted, yanking auburn lashings of hair out of his ribbon. He turned to face into the breeze and smoothed them back, sobering a little. "I felt sorry for the creature; it seemed to ken it was alone and might never see another of its kind again."

"Maybe it *did* think you were one of its kind," I suggested. "It seemed to like you."

"It was a sweet wee thing," he agreed. "When I gave it an orange, it took the fruit from my hand like a Christian, verra mannerly. Do ye suppose . . ." His voice died away, his eyes going vague.

"Do I suppose . . . ?"

"Oh. I was only thinking"—he glanced quickly over his shoulder, but we were out of earshot of the sailors—"what Roger Mac said about France being important to the Revolution. I thought I should ask about, when we're in Edinburgh. See whether there might be any of the folk I knew who had fingers in France . . ." He lifted one shoulder.

"You aren't actually thinking of *going* to France, are you?" I asked, suddenly wary.

"No, no," he said hurriedly. "I only happened to think—if by some chance we did, might the orangutan still be there? It's been a great while, but I dinna ken how long they live."

"Not quite as long as people, I don't think, but they *can*

live to a great age, if they're well cared for," I said dubiously. The doubt was not all on the orangutan's account. Go back to the French court? The mere thought made my stomach flip-flop.

"He's dead, ken," Jamie said quietly. He turned his head to look at me, eyes steady. "Louis."

"Is he?" I said blankly. "I . . . when?"

He ducked his head and made a small noise that might have been a laugh.

"He died three years ago, Sassenach," he said dryly. "It *was* in the papers. Though I grant ye, the *Wilmington Gazette* didna make a great deal of the matter."

"I didn't notice." I glanced down at the shark, still patiently keeping company with the ship. My heart, after the initial leap of surprise, had relaxed. My general reaction, in fact, was thankfulness—and that in itself surprised me, rather.

I'd come to terms with my memory of sharing Louis's bed—for the ten minutes it had taken—long since, and Jamie and I had long since come to terms with each other, turning to each other in the wake of the loss of our first daughter, Faith, and all the terrible things that had happened in France before the Rising.

It wasn't that hearing of Louis's death made any real difference at all—but still, I had a feeling of relief, as though some tiresome bit of music that had been playing in the far distance had finally come to a graceful end, and now the silence of peace sang to me in the wind.

"God rest his soul," I said, rather belatedly. Jamie smiled, and laid his hand over mine.

"*Fois shìorruidh thoir dha,*" he echoed. God rest his soul. "Makes ye wonder, ken? How it might be for a king, to come before God and answer for your life. Might it be a great deal worse, I mean, having to answer for all the folk under your care?"

"Do you think he would?" I asked, intrigued—and rather uneasy at the thought. I hadn't known Louis in any intimate way—bar the obvious, and that seemed less intimate than a handshake; he'd never even met my eyes—but he hadn't seemed like a man consumed by care for his subjects. "Can a person really be held to account for the welfare of a whole kingdom? Not just his own peccadilloes, you think?"

He considered that seriously, the stiff fingers of his right hand tapping slowly on the slippery rail.

"I think so," he said. "Ye'd answer for what ye'd done to your family, no? Say ye'd done ill by your children, abandoned them or left them to starve. Surely that would weigh against your soul, for you're responsible for them. If you're born a king, then ye're given responsibility for your subjects. If ye do ill by them, then—"

"Well, but where does that stop?" I protested. "Suppose you do well by one person and badly by another? Suppose you have people under your care—so to speak—and their needs are in opposition to one another? What do you say to that?"

He broke into a smile.

"I'd say I'm verra glad I'm not God and havena got to try to reckon such things."

I was silent for a moment, imagining Louis standing before God, trying to explain those ten minutes with me. I was sure he'd thought he had a right—kings, after all, were kings—but on the other hand, both the seventh and the ninth commandments were fairly explicit and didn't seem to have any clauses exempting royalty.

"If you were there," I said impulsively, "in heaven, watching that judgment—would you forgive him? I would."

"Who?" he said, surprised. "Louis?" I nodded, and he frowned, rubbing a finger slowly down the bridge of his nose. Then he sighed and nodded.

"Aye, I would. Wouldna mind watching him squirm a bit first, mind," he added, darkly. "A wee pitchfork in the arse would be fine."

I laughed at that, but before I could say anything further, we were interrupted by a shout of "Sail, ho!" from above. While we'd been alone the instant before, this advice caused sailors to pop out of hatches and companionways like weevils out of a ship's biscuit, swarming up into the rigging to see what was up.

I strained my eyes, but nothing was immediately visible. Young Ian, though, had gone aloft with the others, and now landed on the deck beside us with a thump. He was flushed with wind and excitement.

"A smallish ship, but she's got guns," he told Jamie. "And she's flying the Union flag."

"She's a naval cutter," said Captain Roberts, who had appeared on my other side and was peering grimly through his telescope. "Shit."

Jamie's hand went to his dirk, unconsciously checking, and he looked over the captain's shoulder, eyes narrowed against the wind. I could see the sail now, coming up rapidly to starboard.

"Can we outrun her, Cap'n?" The first mate had joined the crowd at the rail, watching the oncoming ship. She did have guns; six, that I could see—and there were men behind them.

The captain pondered, absently clicking his glass open and shut, then glanced up into the rigging, presumably estimating the chances of our putting on enough sail to outdistance the pursuer. The mainmast was cracked; he'd been intending to replace it in New Haven.

"No," he said gloomily. "The main'll be away, if there's any strain put on her." He shut the telescope with a decisive *click* and stowed it away in his pocket. "Have to brass it out, best we can."

I wondered just how much of Captain Roberts's cargo was contraband. His taciturn face didn't give anything away, but there was a distinct air of uneasiness among the hands, which grew noticeably as the cutter drew alongside, hailing.

Roberts gave the terse order to heave to, and the sails loosened, the ship slowing. I could see seamen at the guns and rail of the cutter; glancing sideways at Jamie, I saw that he was counting them and glanced back.

"I make it sixteen," Ian said, low-voiced.

"Undermanned, God damn it," said the captain. He looked at Ian, estimating his size, and shook his head. "They'll likely mean to press what they can out of us. Sorry, lad."

The rather formless alarm I'd felt at the cutter's approach sharpened abruptly at this—and sharpened still further as I saw Roberts glance appraisingly at Jamie.

"You don't think they—" I began.

"Shame you shaved this morning, Mr. Fraser," Roberts observed to Jamie, ignoring me. "Takes twenty years off your age. And you look a damned sight healthier than men half your age."

"I'm obliged to ye for the compliment, sir," Jamie replied dryly, one eye on the railing, where the cocked hat of the cutter's captain had suddenly poked up like an ill-omened mushroom. He unbuckled his belt, slid the dirk's scabbard free, and handed it to me.

"Keep that for me, Sassenach," he said under his breath, buckling his belt again.

The cutter's captain, a squat middle-aged man with a sullen brow and a pair of much-mended breeches, took a quick, piercing look around the deck when he came aboard, nodded to himself as though his worst suspicions had been confirmed, then shouted back over his shoulder for six men to follow.

"Search the hold," he said to his minions. "You know what to look for."

"What sort of way is this to carry on?" Captain Roberts demanded angrily. "You've no right to search my ship! What do you lot think you are, a raft of bloody pirates?"

"Do I look like a pirate?" The cutter's captain looked more pleased than insulted by the idea.

"Well, you can't be a naval captain, I'm sure," Roberts said coldly. "A nice, gentlemanlike set of individuals, I've always found His Majesty's navy. Not the sort to board a respectable merchant without leave, let alone without proper introduction."

The cutter's captain appeared to find this funny. He took off his hat and bowed—to me.

"Allow me, mum," he said. "Captain Worth Stebbings, your most humble." He straightened up, clapping on his hat, and nodded to his lieutenant. "Go through the holds like a dose of salts. And you—" He tapped Roberts on the chest with a forefinger. "Get all your men on deck, front and center, cully. *All* of them, mind. If I have to drag them up here, I won't be best pleased, I warn you."

Tremendous bangings and rumblings from below ensued, with seamen popping up periodically to relay news of their findings to Captain Stebbings, who lounged by the rail, watching as the men of the *Teal* were rounded up and herded together on deck—Ian and Jamie among them.

"Here, now!" Captain Roberts was game, I'd give him that. "Mr. Fraser and his nephew aren't crew; they're paying passengers! You've no call to molest free men, about their lawful business. And no right to press my crew, either!"

"They're British subjects," Stebbings informed him briefly. "I've every right. Or do you all claim to be *Americans*?" He leered briefly at that; if the ship could be considered a rebel vessel, he could simply take the whole thing as a prize, crew and all.

A mutter at this ran through the men on deck, and I saw more than one of the hands' eyes dart to the belaying pins along the rail. Stebbings saw it, too, and called over the rail for four more men to be brought aboard—with arms.

Sixteen minus six minus four is six, I thought, and edged a little closer to the rail to peer into the cutter rocking in the swell a little way below and tethered by a line to the *Teal*. *If the sixteen doesn't include Captain Stebbings. If it does . . .*

One man was at the helm, this being not a wheel but a sort of sticklike arrangement poking up through the deck. Two more were manning a gun, a long brass thing on the bow, pointed at the *Teal*'s side. Where were the others? Two on deck. The others perhaps below.

Captain Roberts was still haranguing Stebbings behind me, but the cutter's crew were bumping barrels and bundles over the deck, calling for a rope to lower away to the cutter. I looked back to find Stebbings walking along the row of crewmen, indicating his choices to four burly men who followed him. These jerked his choices out of line and set about tying them together, a line running from ankle to ankle. Three men had already been chosen, John Smith among them, looking white-faced and tense. My heart jumped at sight of him, then nearly stopped altogether as Stebbings came to Ian, who looked down at him impassively.

"Likely, likely," Stebbings said with approval. "A cross-grained son of a bitch, by the looks of you, but we'll soon knock sense into you. Take him!"

I saw the muscles swell in Ian's forearms as his fists clenched, but the press-gang was armed, two with pistols drawn, and he stepped forward, though with an evil look that would have given a wiser man pause. I had already observed that Captain Stebbings was not a wise man.

Stebbings took two more, then paused at Jamie, looking him up and down. Jamie's face was carefully blank. And slightly green; the wind was still up, and with no forward way on the ship, she was rising and falling heavily, with a lurch that would have disconcerted a much better sailor than he was.

"Nice big 'un, sir," said one of the press-gang, with approval.

"Trifle elderly," Stebbings said dubiously. "And I don't much like the look on his face."

"I dinna care much for the look of yours," Jamie said pleasantly. He straightened, squaring his shoulders, and looked down his long, straight nose at Stebbings. "If I didna ken ye for an arrant coward by your actions, sir, I should know ye for a fig-licker and a fopdoodle by your foolish wee face."

Stebbings's maligned face went blank with astonishment, then darkened with rage. One or two of the press-gang grinned behind his back, though hastily erasing these expressions as he whirled round.

"Take him," he growled to the press-gang, shouldering his way toward the booty collected by the rail. "And see that you drop him a few times on the way."

I was frozen in shock. Clearly Jamie couldn't let them press Ian and take him away, but surely he couldn't mean to abandon me in the middle of the Atlantic Ocean, either.

Not even with his dirk thrust into the pocket tied beneath my skirt, and my own knife in its sheath around my thigh.

Captain Roberts had watched this little performance open-mouthed, though whether with respect or astonishment, I couldn't tell. He was a short man, rather tubby, and clearly not constructed for physical confrontation, but he set his jaw and stamped up to Stebbings, seizing him by the sleeve.

The crew ushered their captives over the rail.

There wasn't time to think of anything better.

I seized the rail and more or less rolled over it, skirts flying. I hung by my hands for a terrifying instant, feeling my fingers slide across the wet wood, groping with my toes for the rope ladder the cutter's crew had thrown over the rail. A roll of the ship threw me hard against the side, I lost my grip, plunged several feet, and caught the ladder, just above the cutter's deck.

The rope had burned through my right hand, and it felt as though I'd lost all the skin off my palm, but there was no time to trouble about that now. Any minute, one of the cutter's crew would see me, and—

Timing my jump to the next heave of the cutter's deck, I let go and landed like a bag of rocks. A sharp pain shot up the inside of my right knee, but I staggered to my feet, lurching to and fro with the roll of the deck, and lunged toward the companionway.

"Here! You! What you doing?" One of the gunners had seen me and was gaping at me, clearly unable to decide whether to come down and deal with me or stay with his gun. His partner looked over his shoulder at me and bellowed at the first man to stay put, it wasn't but monkey business of some sort, he said. *"Stay put, God damn your eyes!"*

I ignored them, my heart pounding so hard I could scarcely breathe. What now? What next? Jamie and Ian had disappeared.

"Jamie!" I shouted, as loudly as I could. "I'm here!" And then ran toward the line that held the cutter to the *Teal,* jerking up my skirt as I ran. I did this only because my skirts had twisted in my undignified descent, and I couldn't find the slit to reach through in order to get at the knife in its sheath on my thigh, but the action itself seemed to disconcert the helmsman, who had turned at my shout.

He gawped like a goldfish, but had sufficient presence of mind as to keep his hand on the tiller. I got my own hands on the line and dug my knife into the knot, using it to pry the tight coils loose.

Roberts and his crew, bless them, were making a terrible racket on the *Teal* above, quite drowning out the shouts of the helm and gunners. One of these, with a desperate glance toward the deck of the *Teal* above, finally made up his mind and came toward me, jumping down from the bow.

What wouldn't I give for a pistol just now? I thought grimly. But a knife was what I had, and I jerked it out of the half-loosened knot and drove it into the man's chest as hard as I could. His eyes went round, and I felt the knife strike bone and twist in my hand, skipping through the flesh. He shrieked and fell backward, landing on deck in a thump and nearly—but not quite—taking my knife with him.

"Sorry," I gasped, and, panting, resumed work on the knot, the fractious rope now smeared with blood. There were noises coming from the companionway now. Jamie and Ian might not be armed, but my guess was that that wouldn't matter a lot, in close quarters.

The rope slid reluctantly free. I jerked the last coil loose and it fell, slapping against the *Teal*'s side. At once, the current began to carry the boats apart, the smaller cutter sliding past the big sloop. We weren't moving quickly at all, but the optical illusion of speed made me stagger, gripping at the rail for balance.

The wounded gunner had got onto his feet and was advancing on me, staggering but furious. He was bleeding, but not heavily, and was by no means disabled. I stepped quickly sideways and glancing at the companionway, was relieved beyond measure to see Jamie coming out of it.

He reached me in three strides.

"Quick, my dirk!"

I stared blankly at him for a moment, but then remembered, and with no more than minimum fumbling, managed to get at my pocket. I jerked at the hilt of the dirk, but it was tangled in the fabric. Jamie seized it, ripped it free—tearing both the pocket and the waistband of my skirt in the process—whirled, and charged back into the bowels of the ship. Leaving me facing a wounded gunner, an unwounded gunner now making his way cautiously down from his station, and the helmsman, who was yelling hysterically for someone to do something to some sort of sail.

I swallowed and took a good hold on the knife.

"Stand back," I said, in as loud and commanding a voice as I could manage. Given my shortness of breath, the wind, and the prevailing noise, I doubt they heard me. On the other hand, I doubted that it would have made a difference if they had. I yanked my sagging skirt up with one hand, crouched, and lifted the knife in a determined manner, meant to indicate that I knew what to do with it. I did.

Waves of heat were going over my skin and I felt perspiration prickle my scalp, drying at once in the cold wind. The panic had gone, though; my mind felt very clear and very remote.

You aren't going to touch me was the only thing in my mind. The man I had wounded was cautious, hanging back. The other gunner saw nothing but a woman and didn't bother to arm himself, simply reaching for me with angry contempt. I saw the knife move upward, fast, and arc as though moving by itself, the shimmer of it dulled with blood as I slashed him across the forehead.

Blood poured down over his face, blinding him, and he gave a strangled yell of hurt and astonishment and backed away, both hands pressed to his face.

I hesitated for a moment, not quite sure what to do next, the blood still pounding through my temples. The ship was drifting, rising and falling on the waves; I felt the gold-laden hem of my skirt scrape across the boards, and jerked the torn waistband up again, feeling irritated.

Then I saw a belaying pin stuck into its hole in the railing, a line wrapped round it. I walked over and, poking the knife down the bodkin of my stays for lack of any better place to put it, took hold of the pin with both hands and jerked it free. Holding it like a short baseball bat, I shifted back on one heel and brought it down with as much force as I could on the head of the man whose face I'd slashed. The wooden pin bounced off his skull with a hollow ringing noise, and he staggered away, caroming off the mast.

The helmsman at this point had had enough. Leaving his helm to mind itself, he scrambled up out of his station and made for me like an angry monkey, all reaching limbs and bared teeth. I tried to hit him with the pin, but I'd lost my grip when I struck the gunner, and it slipped out of my hand, rolling away down the heaving deck as the helmsman flung himself on me.

He was small and thin, but his weight bore me back and we lurched together toward the rail; my back struck it and all my breath rushed out in a whoosh, the impact a solid bar of shock across my kidneys. This transformed within seconds to live agony, and I writhed under him, sliding downward. He came with me, grappling for my throat with a single-minded purpose. I flailed at him, my arms, my hands striking windmill-like at his head, the bones of his skull bruising me.

The wind was roaring in my ears; I heard nothing but breathless cursing, harsh gasps that might be mine or his, and then he knocked my hands away and grabbed me by the neck, one-handed, his thumb digging hard up under my jaw.

It hurt and I tried to knee him, but my legs were swaddled in my skirt and pinned beneath his weight. My vision went dark, with little bursts of gold light going off in the blackness, tiny fireworks heralding my death. Someone was making little mewling noises, and I realized dimly that it must be me. The grip on my neck tightened, and the flashing lights faded into black.

I WOKE WITH A confused sense of being simultaneously terrified and rocked in a cradle. My throat hurt, and when I tried to swallow, the resultant pain made me choke.

"Ye're all right, Sassenach." Jamie's soft voice came out of the surrounding gloom—where *was* I?—and his hand squeezed my forearm, reassuring.

"I'll . . . take your . . . word for it," I croaked, the effort making my eyes water. I coughed. It hurt, but seemed to help a little. "What . . . ?"

"Have a bit of water, *a nighean.*" A big hand cradled my head, lifting it a bit, and the mouth of a canteen pressed against my lip. Swallowing the water hurt, too, but I didn't care; my lips and throat were parched, and tasted of salt.

My eyes were beginning to accustom themselves to the darkness. I could see Jamie's form, hunched under a low ceiling, and the shape of rafters—no, timbers—overhead. A strong smell of tar and bilges. Ship. Of course, we were in a ship. But *which* ship?

"Where . . . ?" I whispered, waving a hand.

"I havena got the slightest idea," he said, sounding rather irritable. "The *Teal*'s people are managing the sails—I hope—and Ian's holding a pistol on one o' the naval folk to make him steer, but for all I ken, the man's taking us straight out to sea."

"I meant . . . what . . . ship." Though his remarks had made that clear enough; we must be on the naval cutter.

"They said the name of it's the *Pitt.*"

"How very appropriate." I looked glassily around the murky surroundings, and my sense of reality suffered another jolt as I saw a huge mottled bundle of some kind, apparently hanging in the dim air a few feet beyond Jamie. I sat up abruptly—or tried to, only at this point realizing that I was in a hammock.

Jamie seized me by the waist with a cry of alarm, in time to save me pitching out on my head, and as I steadied, clutching him, I realized that the thing I had taken as an enormous cocoon was in fact a man, lying in another hammock suspended from the rafters, but trussed up in it like a spider's dinner and gagged. His face pressed against the mesh, glaring at me.

"Jesus H. Roosevelt . . . ," I croaked, and lay back, breathing heavily.

"D'ye want to rest a bit, Sassenach, or shall I set ye on your feet?" Jamie asked, clearly edgy. "I dinna want to leave Ian on his own too long."

"No," I said, struggling upright once more. "Help me out, please." The room—cabin, whatever it was—spun round me, as well as heaving up and down, and I was obliged to cling to Jamie with my eyes closed for a moment, until my internal gyroscope took hold.

"Captain Roberts?" I asked. "The *Teal*?"

"God knows," Jamie said tersely. "We ran for it as quick as I could set the men to sailing this thing. For all I ken, they're on our tail, but I couldna see anything when I looked astern."

I was beginning to feel steadier, though the blood still throbbed painfully in my throat and temples with each heartbeat, and I could feel the tender patches of bruising on my elbows and shoulders, and a vivid band across my back, where I'd fallen against the rail.

"We've shut most of the crew up in the hold," Jamie said, with a nod at the man in the hammock, "save this fellow. I didna ken whether ye might want to look at him first. In the medical way, I mean," he added, seeing my momentary incomprehension. "Though I dinna think he's hurt badly."

I approached the fellow in the hammock and saw that it was the helmsman who had tried to throttle me. There was a large lump visible on his forehead, and he had the beginnings of a monstrous black eye, but from what I could see, leaning close in the dim light, his pupils were the same size and—allowing for the rag stuffed into his mouth—his breath was coming regularly. Probably not badly hurt, then. I stood for a moment staring at him. It was difficult to tell—the only light belowdecks came from a prism embedded in the deck above—but I thought that perhaps what I had taken for a glare was really just a look of desperation.

"Do you need to have a pee?" I inquired politely.

The man and Jamie made nearly identical noises, though in the first case it was a groan of need, and in Jamie's, of exasperation.

"For God's sake!" he said, grabbing my arm as I started to reach for the man. "I'll deal with him. Go upstairs." It was apparent from his much-tried tone that he had just about reached the last-straw stage, and there was no point in arguing with him. I left, making my ginger way up the companionway ladder to the accompaniment of a lot of Gaelic muttering that I didn't try to translate.

The belting wind above was enough to make me sway alarmingly as it caught my skirts, but I seized a line and held on, letting the fresh air clear my head before I felt steady enough to go aft. There I found Ian, as advertised, sitting on a barrel, a loaded pistol held negligently atop one knee, evidently engaged in amiable discourse with the sailor at the helm.

"Auntie Claire! All right, are ye?" he asked, jumping up and gesturing me toward his barrel.

"Fine," I said, taking it. I didn't think I had torn anything in my knee, but it felt a little wobbly. "Claire Fraser," I said, nodding politely to the gentleman at the helm, who was black and bore facial tattoos of an elaborate sort, though from the neck down he was dressed in ordinary sailor's slops.

"Guinea Dick," he said, with a broad grin that displayed—no doubt about it—filed teeth. "Youah sahvint, Mum!"

I regarded him openmouthed for a moment, but then regained some semblance of self-possession and smiled at him.

"I see His Majesty takes his seamen where he can get them," I murmured to Ian.

"He does for a fact. Mr. Dick here was pressed out of a Guinea pirate, who took him from a slave ship, who in turn took him from a barracoon on the Guinea coast. I'm not so sure whether he thinks His Majesty's accommodations are an improvement—but he says he's got nay particular reservation about going along of us."

"Is your trust upon him?" I asked, in halting Gaelic.

Ian gave me a mildly scandalized look.

"Of course not," he replied in the same language. "And you will oblige me by not going too close to him, wife of my mother's brother. He says to me that he does not eat human flesh, but this is no surety that he is safe."

"Right," I said, returning to English. "What happened to—"

Before I could complete my question, a loud thump on deck made me turn, to see John Smith—he of the five gold earrings—who had dropped out of the rigging. He, too, smiled when he saw me, though his face was strained.

"Well enough so far," he said to Ian, and touched his forelock to me. "You all right, ma'am?"

"Yes." I looked aft, but saw nothing save tumbling waves. The same in all the other directions, as well. "Er . . . do you happen to know where we're going, Mr. Smith?"

He looked a trifle surprised at that.

"Why, no, ma'am. The captain hasn't said."

"The cap—"

"That would be Uncle Jamie," Ian said, sounding amused. "Puking his guts out below, is he?"

"Not when last seen." I began to have an uneasy feeling at the base of my spine. "Do you mean to tell me that *no* one aboard this ship has any idea where—or even which way—we're heading?"

An eloquent silence greeted this question.

I coughed.

"The, um, gunner. Not the one with the slashed forehead—the other one. Where is he, do you know?"

Ian turned and looked at the water.

"Oh," I said. There was a large splotch of blood on the deck where the man had fallen when I stabbed him. "Oh," I said again.

"Och, which reminds me, Auntie. I found this lyin' on the deck." Ian took my knife from his belt and handed it to me. It had been cleaned, I saw.

"Thank you." I slipped it back through the slit of my petticoats and found the scabbard, still fastened round my thigh, though someone had removed my torn skirt and pocket. With thought for the gold in the hem, I hoped it was Jamie. I felt rather peculiar, as though my bones were filled with air. I coughed and swallowed again, massaging my bruised throat, then returned to my earlier point.

"So *no* one knows which way we're heading?"

John Smith smiled a little.

"Well, we're not a-heading out to sea, ma'am, if that's what you were fearing."

"I was, actually. How do you know?"

All three of them smiled at that.

"Him sun over dere," Mr. Dick said, shrugging a shoulder at the object in question. He nodded in the same direction. "So him land over dere, too."

"Ah." Well, that was comforting, to be sure. And in fact, since "him sun" *was* over there—that is, sinking rapidly in the west—that meant we were in fact headed north.

Jamie joined the party at this point, looking pale.

"Captain Fraser," Smith said respectfully.

"Mister Smith."

"Orders, Cap'n?"

Jamie stared at him bleakly.

"I'll be pleased if we don't sink. Can ye manage that?"

Mr. Smith didn't bother hiding his grin.

"If we don't hit another ship or a whale, sir, I think we'll stay afloat."

"Good. Kindly don't." Jamie wiped the back of his hand across his mouth and straightened up. "Is there a port we might reach within the next day or so? The helmsman says there's food and water enough for three days, but the less of it we need, the happier I'll be."

Smith turned to squint toward the invisible land, the setting sun glinting off his earrings.

"Well, we're past Norfolk," he said, thoughtful. "The next big regular port would be New York."

Jamie gave him a jaundiced look.

"Is the British navy not anchored in New York?"

Mr. Smith coughed.

"I b'lieve they were, last I heard. 'Course, they might have moved."

"I was more in mind of a small port," Jamie said. "Verra small."

"Where the arrival of a royal naval cutter will make the maximum impression on the citizenry?" I inquired. I sympathized with his strong desire to set foot on land as soon as possible, but the question was—what then?

The enormity of our position was only now beginning to dawn on me. We had gone in the space of an hour from passengers on the way to Scotland to fugitives, on the way to God knew where.

Jamie closed his eyes and drew a long, deep breath. There was a heavy swell, and he was looking green again, I saw. And, with a pang of uneasiness, realized that I had lost my acupuncture needles, left behind in my hasty exodus from the *Teal*.

"What about Rhode Island, or New Haven, Connecticut?" I asked. "New Haven is where the *Teal* was going, anyway—and I think we're much less likely to run into Loyalists or British troops in either of those ports."

Jamie nodded, eyes still closed, grimacing at the movement.

"Aye, maybe."

"Not Rhode Island," Smith objected. "The British sailed into Newport in December, and the American navy—what there is of it—is blockaded inside Providence. They might not fire on us, if we come a-sailing into Newport with the British colors flying"—he gestured at the mast, where the Union Jack still fluttered—"but the reception once ashore might be warmer than we might find comfortable."

Jamie had cracked one eye open and was regarding Smith consideringly.

"I take it ye've no Loyalist leanings yourself, Mr. Smith? For if ye had, nothing simpler than to tell me to land at Newport; I'd not have known any better."

"No, sir." Smith tugged at one of his earrings. "Mind, I'm not a Separatist, neither. But I have got a marked disinclination to be sunk again. Reckon I've just about used up my luck in that direction."

Jamie nodded, looking ill.

"New Haven, then," he said, and I felt a small thump of uneasy excitement. Might I meet with Hannah Arnold, after all?

Or—and there was an uneasier notion still—Colonel Arnold himself? I supposed he must visit his family once in a while.

A certain amount of technical discussion, involving a lot of shouting to and fro between deck and rigging, ensued, regarding navigation: Jamie knew how to use both a sextant and an astrolabe—the former was actually available—but had no idea how to apply the results to the sailing of a ship. The impressed hands from the *Teal* were more or less agreeable to sailing the ship wherever we cared to take her, as their only immediate alternative was being arrested, tried, and executed for involuntary piracy, but while all were good able seamen, none of them possessed anything in the way of navigational skills.

This left us with the alternative strategies of interviewing the captive seamen in the hold, discovering whether any of them could sail the ship, and if so, offering such inducements in the way of violence or gold as might compel him to do so, or sailing within sight of land and hugging the coast, which was slower, much more dangerous in terms of encountering either sandbanks or British men of war, and uncertain, insofar as none of the *Teal* hands presently with us had ever seen the port of New Haven before.

Having nothing useful to contribute to this discussion, I went to stand by the rail, watching the sun come down the sky and wondering how likely we were to run aground in the dark, without the sun to steer by?

The thought was cold, but the wind was colder. I had been wearing only a light jacket when I made my abrupt exit from the *Teal,* and without my woolen overskirt, the sea wind was cutting through my clothes like a knife. That unfortunate imagery reminded me of the dead gunner, and, steeling myself, I glanced over my shoulder toward the dark bloodstain on deck.

As I did so, my eye caught the flicker of a movement from the helm, and I opened my mouth to call out. I hadn't managed a sound, but Jamie happened to be looking in my direction and whatever was showing on my face was enough. He turned and threw himself without hesitation at Guinea Dick, who had produced a knife from somewhere about his person and was preparing to plunge it into Ian's negligently turned back.

Ian whirled round at the noise, saw what was up, and, thrusting the pistol into Mr. Smith's surprised hands, flung himself on the thrashing ball of humanity rolling round under the swinging helm. Fallen off her steerage, the ship slowed, her sails slackening, and she began to roll alarmingly.

I took two steps across the slanting deck and plucked the pistol neatly out of Mr. Smith's hand. He looked at me, blinking in bewilderment.

"It's not that I don't trust you," I said apologetically. "It's just that I can't take the chance. All things considered." Calmly—all things considered—I checked the pistol's priming—it was primed and cocked; a wonder it hadn't gone off by itself, with all this rough handling—and aimed it at the center of the melee, waiting to see who might emerge from it.

Mr. Smith looked back and forth, from me to the fight, and then backed slowly away, hands delicately raised.

"I'll . . . just . . . be up top," he said. "If wanted."

The outcome had been a foregone conclusion, but Mr. Dick had acquitted himself nobly as a British seaman. Ian rose slowly, swearing and pressing his forearm against his shirt, where a jagged wound left red blotches.

"The treacherous bugger *bit* me!" he said, furious. "Goddamned cannibal heathen!" He kicked his erstwhile foe, who grunted at the impact but remained inert, and then seized the swinging helm with an angry oath. He moved this slowly to and fro, seeking direction, and the ship steadied, her head turning into the wind as her sails filled again.

Jamie rolled off the supine body of Mr. Dick and sat on the deck beside him, head hanging, panting for breath. I lowered the gun and uncocked it.

"All right?" I asked him, for form's sake. I felt very calm, in a remote, strange sort of way.

"Tryin' to recall how many lives I've got left," he said, between gasps.

"Four, I think. Or five. Surely you don't consider this a near-miss, do you?" I glanced at Mr. Dick, whose face was considerably the worse for wear. Jamie himself had a large red patch down the side of his face that would undoubtedly be black and blue within hours, and was holding his middle, but seemed otherwise undamaged.

"Does nearly dyin' of seasickness count?"

"No." With a wary eye on the fallen helmsman, I squatted beside Jamie and peered at him. The red light of the sinking sun bathed the deck, making it impossible to judge his color, even had the color of his skin made this easy. Jamie held out a hand, and I gave him the pistol, which he tucked into his belt. Where, I saw, he had restored his dirk and its scabbard.

"Did you not have time to draw that?" I asked, nodding at it.

"Didna want to kill him. He's no dead, is he?" With a noticeable effort, he rolled onto hands and knees and breathed for a moment before thrusting himself to his feet.

"No. He'll come round in a minute or two." I looked toward Ian, whose face was averted but whose body language was eloquent. His stiff shoulders, suffused back of neck, and bulging forearms conveyed fury and shame, which were understandable, but there was a droop to his spine that spoke of desolation. I wondered at that last, until a thought occurred to me, and that odd sense of calm vanished abruptly in a burst of horror as I realized what must have made him drop his guard.

"Rollo!" I whispered, clutching Jamie's arm. He looked up, startled, saw Ian, and exchanged appalled glances with me.

"Oh, God," he said softly.

The acupuncture needles were not the only things of value left behind aboard the *Teal*.

Rollo had been Ian's closest companion for years. The immense by-product of a casual encounter between an Irish wolfhound and a wolf, he terrified the hands on the *Teal* to such an extent that Ian had shut him in the cabin; otherwise, chances were that he would have taken the throat out of Captain Stebbings when the sailors seized Ian. What would he do when he realized that Ian was gone? And what would Captain Stebbings, his men, or the crew of the *Teal* do to him in response?

"Jesus. They'll shoot the dog and drop him overboard," Jamie said, voicing my thought, and crossed himself.

I thought of the hammerhead again, and a violent shudder ran through me. Jamie squeezed my hand tightly.

"Oh, God," he said again, very quietly. He stood thinking for a moment, then shook himself, rather like Rollo shaking water from his fur, and let go my hand.

"I'll have to speak to the crew, and we must feed them—and the sailors in the hold. Will ye go below, Sassenach, and see what ye can do wi' the galley? I'll just . . . have a word with Ian first." I saw his throat move as he glanced at Ian, standing stiff as a wooden Indian at the helm, the dying light harsh on his tearless face.

I nodded, and made my way unsteadily to the black, gaping hole of the companionway, and the descent into darkness.

THE GALLEY WAS NO more than a four-by-four space belowdecks at the end of the mess, with a sort of low brick altar containing the fire, several cupboards on the bulkhead, and a hanging rack of coppers, pot-lifters, rags, and other bits of kitchen impedimenta. No problem in spotting it; there was still a sullen red glow from the galley fire, where—thank God!—a few embers still lived.

There was a sandbox, a coal box, and a basket of kindling, tidied under the tiny countertop, and I set at once to coaxing the fire back into life. A cauldron hung over the fire; some of the contents had slopped over the side as a result of the ship's rolling, partially extinguishing the fire and leaving gummy streaks down the side of the cauldron. Luck again, I thought. Had the slop not put the fire mostly out, the contents of the pot would long since have boiled dry and burned, leaving me with the job of starting some kind of supper from scratch.

Perhaps literally from scratch. There were several stacked cages of chickens near the galley; they'd been dozing in the warm darkness but roused at my movement, fluttering, muttering, and jerking their silly heads to and fro in agitated inquiry, beady eyes blinking redly at me through the wooden lattice.

I wondered whether there might be other livestock aboard, but if there was, it wasn't living in the galley, thank goodness. I stirred the pot, which seemed to contain a glutinous sort of stew, and then began to look for bread. There would be some sort of farinaceous substance, I knew; sailors lived on either hardtack—the very aptly named unleavened ship's biscuit—or soft tack, this being any kind of leavened bread, though the term "soft" was often relative. Still, they would have bread. Where . . . ?

I found it at last: hard round brown loaves in a netting bag hung from a hook in a dark corner. To keep it from rats, I supposed, and glanced narrowly around the floor, just in case. There should be flour, as well, I thought—oh, of course. It would be in the hold, along with the other ship's stores. And the disgruntled remnants of the original crew. Well, we'd worry about them later. There was enough here to feed everyone aboard supper. I'd worry about breakfast later, too.

The exertion of building up the fire and searching the galley and mess warmed me and distracted me from my bruises. The sense of chilled disbelief that had attended me ever since I went over the *Teal*'s rail began to dissipate.

This wasn't entirely a good thing. As I began to emerge from my state of stunned shock, I also began to apprehend the true dimensions of the current situation. We were no longer headed for Scotland and the dangers of the Atlantic, but were under way to an unknown destination in an unfamiliar craft with an inexperienced, panic-stricken crew. And we had, in fact, just committed piracy on the high seas, as well as whatever crimes were involved in resisting impressment and assaulting His Majesty's navy. And murder. I swallowed, my throat still tender, and my skin prickled despite the warmth of the fire.

The jar of the knife hitting bone still reverberated in the bones of my own hand and forearm. How could I have killed him? I knew I hadn't penetrated his chest cavity, couldn't possibly have struck the large vessels of the neck. . . . Shock, of course . . . but could shock alone . . . ?

I couldn't think about the dead gunner just now, and pushed the thought of him firmly away. Later, I told myself. I would come to terms with it—it had been self-defense, after all—and I would pray for his soul, but later. Not now.

Not that the other things presenting themselves to me as I worked were much more appealing. Ian and Rollo—no, I couldn't think about that, either.

I scraped the bottom of the pot determinedly with a big wooden spoon. The stew was a little scorched at the bottom, but still edible. There were bones in it, and it was thick and gummy, with lumps. Gagging slightly, I filled a smaller pot from a water butt and hung it to boil.

Navigation. I settled on that as a topic for worry, on grounds that while it was deeply concerning, it lacked the emotional aspects of some of the other things on my mental agenda. How full was the moon? I tried to recall what it had looked like the night before, from the deck of the *Teal.* I hadn't really noticed, so it wasn't near the full; the full moon rising out of the sea is breathtaking, with that shining path across the water that makes you feel how simple it would be to step over the rail and walk straight on, into that peaceful radiance.

No, no peaceful radiance last night. I'd gone up to the ship's head, though, quite late, instead of using a chamber pot, because I'd wanted air. It had been dark on deck, and I'd paused for a moment by the rail, because there was phosphorescence in the long, rolling waves, a beautiful eerie glimmer of green light under the water, and the wake of the ship plowed a glowing furrow through the sea.

Dark moon, then, I decided, or a sliver, which would amount to the same thing. We couldn't come close into shore by night, then. I didn't know how far north we were—maybe John Smith did?—but was aware that the coastline of the Chesapeake involved all kinds of channels, sandbars, tide flats, and ship traffic. Wait, though, Smith had said we'd passed Norfolk . . .

"Well, bloody hell!" I said exasperated. "Where *is* Norfolk?" I knew where it was in relation to Highway I-64, but had no notion whatever what the blasted place looked like from the ocean.

And if we were obliged to stand far out from land during the night, what was to keep us from drifting *very* far out to sea?

"Well, on the good side, we needn't trouble about running out of gas," I said encouragingly to myself. Food and water . . . well, not yet, at least.

I seemed to be running out of good impersonal worrying material. What about Jamie's seasickness? Or any other medical catastrophe that might occur aboard? Yes, that was a good one. I had no herbs, no needles, no sutures, no bandages, no instruments—I was for the moment completely without any practical medicine at all, save boiling water and what skill might be contained in my two hands.

"I suppose I could reduce a dislocation or put my thumb on a spurting artery," I said aloud, "but that's about it."

"Uhh . . ." said a deeply uncertain voice behind me, and I spun round, inadvertently spattering stew from my ladle.

"Oh. Mr. Smith."

"Didn't mean to take you unawares, ma'am." He sidled into the light like a wary spider, keeping a cautious distance from me. " 'Specially not as I saw your nephew hand you back that knife of yours." He smiled a little, to indicate that this was a joke, but he was plainly uneasy. "You . . . um . . . were right handy with it, I must say."

"Yes," I said flatly, picking up a rag to mop the splatters. "I've had practice."

This led to a marked silence. After a moment or two, he coughed.

"Mr. Fraser sent me to ask—in a gingerly sort of way—whether there might be anything to eat soon?"

I gave a grudging snort of laughter at that.

"Was the 'gingerly' his idea or yours?"

"His," he replied promptly.

"You can tell him the food is ready, whenever anyone likes to come and eat it. Oh—Mr. Smith?"

He turned back at once, earrings swinging.

"I only wondered—what do the men . . . well, they must be very upset, of course, but what do the hands from the *Teal* feel about . . . er . . . recent developments? If you happen to know, that is," I added.

"I know. Mr. Fraser asked me that, not ten minutes ago," he said, looking mildly amused. "We been a-talking, up in the tops, as you may imagine, ma'am."

"Oh, I do."

"Well, we're much relieved not to be pressed, of course. Was that to happen, likely none of us would see home nor family again for years. To say nothing of being forced maybe to fight our own countrymen." He scratched at his chin; like all the men, he was becoming bristly and piratical-looking. "On t'other hand, though . . . well, you must allow of our situation at the moment being not all our friends might wish.

Perilous, I mean to say, and us now minus our pay and our clothes, to boot."

"Yes, I can see that. From your point of view, what might be the most desirable outcome of our situation?"

"Make land as near to New Haven as we can get, but not in the harbor. Run her aground on a gravel bar and set her afire," he replied promptly. "Take her boat ashore, then run like the dickens."

"Would you burn the ship with the sailors in the hold?" I asked, as a matter of curiosity. To my relief, he appeared shocked at the suggestion.

"Oh, no, ma'am! Might be as Mr. Fraser would want to turn them over to the Continentals to use for exchange, maybe, but we wouldn't mind was they to be set free, either."

"That's very magnanimous of you," I assured him gravely. "And I'm sure Mr. Fraser is very grateful for your recommendations. Do you, er, know where the Continental army *is* just now?"

"Somewhere in New Jersey is what I heard," he replied, with a brief smile. "I don't suppose they'd be that hard to find, though, if you wanted 'em."

Aside from the royal navy, the last thing I personally wanted to see was the Continental army, even at a distance. New Jersey seemed safely remote, though.

I sent him to rummage the crew's quarters for utensils—each man would have his own mess kid and spoon—and set about the tricky task of lighting the two lamps that hung over the mess table, in hopes that we might see what we were eating.

Having got a closer look at the stew, I changed my mind about the desirability of more illumination, but considering how much trouble it had been to light the lamps, wasn't disposed to blow them out, either.

All in all, the meal wasn't bad. Though it likely wouldn't have mattered if I'd fed them raw grits and fish heads; the men were famished. They devoured the food like a horde of cheerful locusts, their spirits remarkably high, considering our situation. Not for the first time, I marveled at the ability of men to function capably in the midst of uncertainty and danger.

Part of it, of course, was Jamie. One couldn't overlook the

irony of someone who hated the sea and ships as he did suddenly becoming the *de facto* captain of a naval cutter, but while he might loathe ships, he did in fact know more or less how one was run—and he had the knack of calm in the face of chaos, as well as a natural sense of command.

If you can keep your head when all about you are losing theirs and blaming it on you . . . I thought, watching him talk calmly and sensibly to the men.

Pure adrenaline had kept me going until now, but, now out of immediate danger, it was fading fast. Between fatigue, worry, and a bruised throat, I was able to eat only a bite or two of the stew. My other bruises had begun to throb, and my knee still felt tender. I was taking a morbid inventory of physical damage when I saw Jamie's eyes fixed on me.

"Ye need food, Sassenach," he said mildly. "Eat." I opened my mouth to say that I wasn't hungry, but thought better of it. The last thing he needed was to worry about me.

"Aye, aye, Captain," I said, and resignedly picked up my spoon.

31

A GUIDED TOUR THROUGH THE CHAMBERS OF THE HEART

I SHOULD BE GOING to sleep. God knew I needed sleep. And there would be precious little of it until we reached New Haven. *If we ever do,* the back of my mind commented skeptically, but I ignored this remark as unhelpful to the current situation.

I longed to plunge into sleep, as much to escape the fears and uncertainties of my mind as to restore my much abused flesh. I was so tired, though, that mind and body had begun to separate.

It was a familiar phenomenon. Doctors, soldiers, and mothers encounter it routinely; I had, any number of times. Unable to respond to an immediate emergency while clouded by fatigue, the mind simply withdraws a little, separating itself fastidiously from the body's overwhelming self-centered needs. From this clinical distance, it can direct things, bypassing emotions, pain, and tiredness, making necessary decisions, cold-bloodedly overruling the mindless body's needs for food, water, sleep, love, grief, pushing it past its fail-safe points.

Why emotions? I wondered dimly. Surely emotion was a function of the mind. And yet it seemed so deeply rooted in the flesh that this abdication of the mind always suppressed emotion, too.

The body resents this abdication, I think. Ignored and abused, it will not easily let the mind return. Often, the separation persists until one is finally allowed to sleep. With the body absorbed in its quiet intensities of regeneration, the mind settles cautiously back into the turbulent flesh, feeling its delicate way through the twisting passages of dreams, making peace. And you wake once more whole.

But not yet. I had the feeling that something remained to be done but no idea what. I had fed the men, sent food to the prisoners, checked the wounded . . . reloaded all the pistols . . . cleaned the stewpot . . . My slowing mind went blank.

I set my hands on the table, fingertips feeling out the grain of the wood as though the tiny ridges, worn smooth by years of service, might be the map that would enable me to find my way to sleep.

I could see myself in the eye of the mind, sitting there. Slender, nearly scrawny; the edge of my radius showed sharp against the skin of my forearm. I'd got thinner than I realized, over the last few weeks of traveling. Round-shouldered with fatigue. Hair a bushy, tangled mass of writhing strands, streaked with silver and white, a dozen shades of dark and light. It reminded me of something Jamie had told me, some expression the Cherokee had . . . combing snakes from the hair, that was it. To relieve the mind of worry, anger, fear, possession by demons—that was to comb the snakes from your hair. Very apt.

I did not, of course, possess a comb at the moment. I'd had one in my pocket, but had lost it in the struggle.

My mind felt like a balloon, tugging stubbornly at its tether. I wouldn't let it go, though; I was suddenly and irrationally afraid that it might not come back at all.

Instead, I focused my attention fiercely on small physical details: the weight of the chicken stew and bread in my belly; the smell of the oil in the lamps, hot and fishy. The thump of feet on the deck above, and the song of the wind. The hiss of water down the sides of the ship.

The feel of a blade in flesh. Not the power of purpose, the guided destruction of surgery, damage done in order to heal. A panicked stab, the jump and stutter of a blade striking bone unexpected, the wild careen of an uncontrolled knife. And the wide dark stain on the deck, fresh-wet and smelling of iron.

"I didn't mean it," I whispered aloud. "Oh, God. I didn't mean it."

Quite without warning, I began to cry. No sobbing, no throat-gripping spasms. Water simply welled in my eyes and flowed down my cheeks, slow as cold honey. A quiet acknowledgment of despair as things spiraled slowly out of control.

"What is it, lass?" Jamie's voice came softly from the door.

"I'm so tired," I said thickly. "So tired."

The bench creaked under his weight as he sat beside me, and a filthy handkerchief dabbed gently at my cheeks. He put an arm round me and whispered to me in Gaelic, the soothing endearments one makes to a startled animal. I turned my cheek into his shirt and closed my eyes. The tears were still running down my face, but I was beginning to feel better; still weary unto death, but not utterly destroyed.

"I wish I hadn't killed that man," I whispered. His fingers had been smoothing the hair behind my ear; they paused for a moment, then resumed.

"Ye didna kill anyone," he said, sounding surprised. "Was that what's been troubling ye, Sassenach?"

"Among other things, yes." I sat up, wiping my nose on my

sleeve, and stared at him. "I didn't kill the gunner? Are you sure?"

His mouth drew up in what might have been a smile, if it were a shade less grim.

"I'm sure. I killed him, *a nighean.*"

"You—oh." I sniffed, and looked at him closely. "You aren't saying that to make me feel better."

"I am not." The smile faded. "I wish I hadna killed him, either. No much choice about it, though." He reached out and pushed a lock of hair behind my ear with a forefinger. "Dinna fash yourself about it, Sassenach. I can stand it."

I was crying again—but this time with feeling. I wept with pain and with sorrow, certainly with fear. But the pain and sorrow were for Jamie and the man he had no choice but to kill, and that made all the difference.

After a bit, the storm subsided, leaving me limp but whole. The buzzing sense of detachment had gone. Jamie had turned round on the bench, his back against the table as he held me on his lap, and we sat in peaceful silence for a bit, watching the glow of the fading coals in the galley fire and the wisps of steam rising from the cauldron of hot water. *I should put something on to cook through the night,* I thought drowsily. I glanced at the cages, where the chickens had settled themselves to sleep, with no more than an occasional brief cluck of startlement as one roused from whatever chickens dream about.

No, I couldn't bring myself to kill a hen tonight. The men would have to do with whatever came to hand in the morning.

Jamie had also noticed the chickens, though to different effect.

"D'ye recall Mrs. Bug's chickens?" he said, with a rueful humor. "Wee Jem and Roger Mac?"

"Oh, God. Poor Mrs. Bug."

Jem, aged five or so, had been entrusted with the daily chore of counting the hens to be sure they had all returned to their coop at night. After which, of course, the door was fastened securely, to keep out foxes, badgers, or other chicken-loving predators. Only Jem had forgotten. Just once, but once was enough. A fox had got into the hen coop, and the carnage had been terrible.

It's all rot to say that man is the only creature who kills for pleasure. Possibly they learned it from men, but all the dog family do it, too—foxes, wolves, and theoretically domesticated dogs, as well. The walls of the hen coop had been plastered with blood and feathers.

"Oh, my bairnies!" Mrs. Bug kept saying, tears rolling down her cheeks like beads. "Oh, my puir wee bairnies!"

Jem, called into the kitchen, couldn't look.

"I'm sorry," he whispered, eyes on the floor. "I'm really sorry."

"Well, and so ye should be," Roger had said to him. "But sorry's no going to help much, is it?"

Jemmy shook his head, mute, and tears welled in his eyes.

Roger cleared his throat, with a noise of gruff menace.

"Well, here it is, then. If ye're old enough to be trusted with a job, ye're old enough to take the consequences of breaking that trust. D'ye understand me?"

It was rather obvious that he didn't, but he bobbed his head earnestly, sniffling.

Roger took in a deep breath through his nose.

"I mean," he said, "I'm going to whip you."

Jem's small, round face went quite blank. He blinked and looked at his mother, openmouthed.

Brianna made a small movement toward him, but Jamie's hand closed on her arm, stopping her.

Without looking at Bree, Roger put a hand on Jem's shoulder and turned him firmly toward the door.

"Right, mate. Out." He pointed toward the door. "Up to the stable and wait for me."

Jemmy gulped audibly. He'd gone a sickly gray when Mrs. Bug brought in the first feathery corpse, and subsequent events had not improved his color.

I thought he might throw up, but he didn't. He'd stopped crying and didn't start again, but seemed to shrink into himself, shoulders hunching.

"Go," said Roger, and he went.

As Jemmy trudged out, head hanging, he looked so exactly like a prisoner headed for execution that I wasn't sure whether to laugh or cry. I caught Brianna's eye and saw that she was struggling with a similar feeling; she looked distressed, but her mouth twitched at the corner, and she looked hastily away.

Roger heaved an explosive sigh and made to follow, squaring his shoulders.

"Christ," he muttered.

Jamie had been standing silent in the corner, watching the exchange, though not without sympathy. He moved just slightly, and Roger glanced at him. He coughed.

"Mmphm. I ken it's the first time—but I think ye'd best make it hard," he said softly. "The poor wee lad feels terrible."

Brianna cut her eyes at him, surprised, but Roger nodded, the grim line of his mouth relaxing a little. He followed Jem out, unbuckling his belt as he left.

The four of us stood awkwardly round the kitchen, not quite sure what to do next. Brianna drew herself up with a sigh rather like Roger's, shook herself like a dog, and reached for one of the dead chickens.

"Can we eat them?"

I prodded one of the hens experimentally; the flesh moved under the skin, limp and wobbly, but the skin hadn't yet begun to separate. I picked the rooster up and sniffed; there was a sharp tang of dried blood and the musty scent of dribbled feces, but no sweet smell of rot.

"I think so, if they're thoroughly cooked. The feathers won't be much good, but we can stew some, and boil the rest for broth and fricassee."

Jamie went to fetch onions, garlic, and carrots from the root cellar, while Mrs. Bug retired to lie down and Brianna and I began the messy job of plucking and gutting the victims. We didn't say much, beyond brief murmured queries and answers about the job at hand. When Jamie came back, though, Bree looked up at him as he set the basket of vegetables on the table beside her.

"It will help?" she asked seriously. "Really?"

He'd nodded. "Ye feel badly when ye've done something wrong, and want to put it right, aye? But there's no means to put something like that right again." He gestured toward the pile of dead chickens. Flies were beginning to gather, crawling over the soft feathers.

"The best ye can do is feel ye've paid for it."

A faint shriek reached us through the window. Brianna had started instinctively at the sound, but then shook her head slightly and reached for a chicken, waving away the flies.

"I remember," I now said softly. "So does Jemmy, I'm sure."

Jamie made a small sound of amusement, then lapsed into silence. I could feel his heart beating against my back, slow and steady.

WE KEPT WATCH AT two-hour intervals all night, making sure that either Jamie, Ian, or myself was awake. John Smith seemed solid—but there was always the possibility that someone from the *Teal* might take it into his head to liberate the sailors in the hold, thinking that might save them from being hanged as pirates later.

I managed the midnight watch well enough, but rousing at dawn was a struggle. I fought my way up out of a deep well lined with soft black wool, an aching fatigue clinging to my bruised and creaking limbs.

Jamie had promptly fallen into the blanket-lined hammock, directly I was out of it, and despite the urgent reflexive desire to tip him out and climb back in myself, I smiled a little. Either he had complete trust in my ability to keep watch, or he was about to die from fatigue and seasickness. Or both, I reflected, picking up the sea officer's cloak he'd just discarded. That was one thing gained from the present situation: I'd left the horrid dead leper's cloak aboard the *Teal*. This one was a vast improvement, being made of new dark-blue thick wool, lined with scarlet silk, and still holding a good deal of Jamie's body heat.

I pulled it close around me, stroked his head to see if he would smile in his sleep—he did, just a twitch of the mouth—and made my way to the galley, yawning.

Another small benefit: a canister of good Darjeeling tea in the cupboard. I'd built up the fire under the cauldron of water when I came to bed; it was hot clear through now, and I dipped out a cup, using what was obviously the captain's private china, painted with violets.

I carried this above, and after an official stroll round the decks, eyeing the two hands on duty—Mr. Smith had the helm—I stood by the rail to drink my fragrant booty, watching the dawn come up out of the sea.

If one were in the mood to count blessings—and, oddly enough, I seemed to be—here was another one. I had seen dawnings in warm seas that came like the bloom of some tremendous flower, a great, slow unfurling of heat and light. This was a northern sunrise, like the slow opening of a bivalve's shell—cold and delicate, the sky shimmering nacre over a soft gray sea. There was something intimate about it, I thought, as though it presaged a day of secrets.

Just as I was getting well stuck into the poetic thoughts, they were interrupted by a shout of "Sail, ho!" from directly above me. Captain Stebbings's violet-painted china cup shattered on the deck, and I whirled to see the tip of a white triangle on the horizon behind us, growing larger by the second.

THE NEXT FEW moments were filled with low comedy, as I rushed into the captain's cabin so flustered and out of breath that I was unable to do more than gasp, "Ho! . . . s'l . . . Ho!" like a demented Santa Claus. Jamie, who could spring to instant wakefulness out of a deep sleep, did so. He also attempted to spring out of bed, forgetting in the stress of the moment that he was in a hammock. By the time he picked himself up, swearing, from the floor, feet were thundering on the deck as the rest of the *Teal*'s hands sprang more adroitly from their own hammocks and ran to see what was up.

"Is it the *Teal*?" I asked John Smith, straining my eyes to see. "Can you tell?"

"Yes," he said absently, squinting at the sail. "Or no, rather. I can tell, and she isn't. She's got three masts."

"I'll take your word for it." At this distance, the approaching ship looked like a wavering cloud scudding toward us over the water; I couldn't make out her hull at all yet.

"We don't need to run from her, do we?" I asked Jamie, who had rooted out a spyglass from Stebbings's desk and was examining our pursuer with a deep frown. He lowered the glass at this, shaking his head.

"It doesna matter whether we need to or not; we'd no stand a chance." He passed the glass to Smith, who clapped it to his eye, muttering, "Colors . . . she's got no colors flying—"

Jamie's head jerked sharply up and around at that, and I realized abruptly that the *Pitt* was still flying the Union Jack.

"That's good, don't you think?" I asked. "They won't trouble a naval ship, surely."

Jamie and John Smith both looked exceedingly dubious at this piece of logic.

"If they come within hailing distance, they'll likely notice something's fishy and it ain't a whale," Smith said. He glanced sideways at Jamie. "Still . . . would you maybe think of puttin' on the captain's coat? It might help—at a distance."

"If they get close enough for it to matter, it willna matter anyway," Jamie said, looking grim.

Still, he disappeared, pausing briefly to retch over the rail, and returned moments later looking splendid—if you stood well back and squinted—in Captain Stebbings's uniform. As Stebbings was perhaps a foot shorter than Jamie and a good deal larger round the middle, the coat strained across the shoulders and flapped around the waist, both sleeves and breeches showed a much greater expanse of shirtsleeve and stocking than was usual, and the breeches had been cinched up in folds with Jamie's sword belt in order not to fall off. He was now sporting the captain's sword, I saw, *and* a pair of loaded pistols, as well as his own dirk.

Ian's brows went up at sight of his uncle thus attired, but Jamie glared at him, and Ian said nothing, though his expression lightened for the first time since we had met the *Pitt.*

"Not so bad," Mr. Smith said, encouraging. "Might's well try to brass it out, eh? Nothing to be lost, after all."

"Mmphm."

"*The boy stood on the burning deck, whence all but he had fled,*" I said, causing Jamie to switch the glare to me.

Having seen Guinea Dick, I wasn't worried about Ian's passing muster as a hand in the royal navy, tattoos and all. The rest of the *Teal*'s hands were fairly unexceptionable. We might just get away with it.

The oncoming ship was close enough now for me to see her figurehead, a black-haired female who seemed to be clutching a—

"Is that really a snake she's holding?" I asked dubiously. Ian leaned forward, squinting over my shoulder.

"It's got fangs."

"So's the ship, lad." John Smith nodded at the vessel, and at this point I saw that indeed it did: the long snouts of two small brass guns protruded from the bow, and as the wind drove her toward us at a slight angle, I could also see that she had gunports. They might or might not be real; merchantmen sometimes painted their sides with false gunports, to discourage interference.

The bow chasers were real, though. One of them fired, a puff of white smoke and a small ball that splashed into the water near us.

"Is that courteous?" Jamie asked dubiously. "Does he mean to signal us?"

Evidently not; both bow chasers spoke together, and a ball tore through one of the sails overhead, leaving a large hole with singed edges. We gaped at it.

"What does he think he's about, firing on a King's ship?" Smith demanded indignantly.

"He thinks he's a bloody privateer, and he means to take us, is what," Jamie said, recovering from his shock and hastily disrobing. "Strike the colors, for God's sake!"

Smith glanced uneasily between Jamie and the oncoming ship. Men were visible at the railings. Armed men.

"They have cannon and muskets, Mr. Smith," Jamie said, throwing his coat overboard with a heave that sent it spiraling out onto the waves. "I'm no going to try to fight them for His Majesty's ship. Run down that flag!"

Mr. Smith bolted, and began rooting among the myriad lines for the one connected to the Union Jack. Another boom came from the bow chasers, though this time a lucky roll of the sea carried us into a trough and both balls passed over us.

The colors came rattling down, to land in an ignominious heap on the deck. I had a moment's scandalized, reflexive impulse to rush over and pick them up, but stopped myself.

"Now what?" I asked, an uneasy eye on the ship. It was near enough that I could make out the shapes of the gunners, who were definitely reloading the brass bow chasers and re-aiming them. And the men at the railings behind them were indeed bristling with armament; I thought I made out swords and cutlasses, as well as muskets and pistols.

The gunners had paused; someone was pointing over the railing, turning to call to someone behind him. Shading my eyes with my hand, I saw the captain's coat, afloat on the rising swell. That appeared to have baffled the privateer; I saw a man hop up onto the bow and stare toward us.

What now? I wondered. Privateers could be anything from professional captains sailing under a letter of marque from one government or another to out-and-out pirates. If the vessel on our tail was the former, chances were that we would fare all right as passengers. If the latter, they could easily cut our throats and throw us into the sea.

The man in the bow shouted something to his men and hopped down. The ship had hauled her wind for a moment; now the bow turned and the sails filled with an audible thump of wind.

"She's going to ram us," Smith said, his tone one of blank disbelief.

I was sure he was right. The figurehead was close enough that I could see the snake grasped in the woman's hand, pressed against her bare breast. Such is the nature of shock that I was conscious of my mind idly considering whether the ship was more likely named *Cleopatra* or *Asp,* when it passed us in a foaming rush and the air shattered in a crash of searing metal.

The world dissolved and I was lying flat, my face pressed into ground that smelled of butchery, deafened and straining for my life to hear the scream of the next mortar round, the one that would strike us dead center.

Something heavy had fallen on me, and I struggled mindlessly to get out from under it, to get to my feet and run, run anywhere, anywhere away . . . away . . .

I gradually realized from the feel of my throat that I was making whimpering noises and that the surface under my flattened cheek was salt-sticky board, not blood-soaked mud. The weight on my back moved suddenly of its own volition, as Jamie rolled off, rising to his knees.

"Jesus *Christ*!" he shouted in fury. "What's *wrong* wi' you!?"

The only answer to this was a single boom, this coming evidently from a gun at the stern of the other ship, which had passed us.

I stood up, trembling, but so far past simple fright that I noticed with a purely detached sort of interest that there was a leg lying on the deck a few feet away. It was barefooted, clad in the torn-off leg of a pair of canvas breeches. There was a good deal of blood spattered here and there.

"Holy God, holy GOD," someone kept saying. I glanced incuriously to the side and saw Mr. Smith, staring upward with a look of horror.

I looked, too. The top of the single mast was gone, and the remains of sails and rigging sagged in a tattered, smoking mass over half the deck. Evidently the privateer's gunports were *not* just for show.

Dazed as I was, I hadn't even begun to ask myself why they'd done this. Jamie wasn't wasting any time asking questions, either. He seized Mr. Smith by the arm.

"Bloody hell! The wicked *nàmhaid* are comin' back!"

They were. The other ship had been moving too fast, I belatedly realized. She'd shot past as she unleashed her broadside, but likely only one of the heavy cannonballs had actually hit us, taking out the mast and the unfortunate Teal who'd been in the rigging.

The rest of the Teals were now on deck, shouting questions. The only answer was dealt by the privateer, who was now describing a wide circle, only too clearly meaning to come back and finish what she'd started.

I saw Ian glance sharply at the *Pitt*'s cannon—but that was plainly futile. Even if the *Teal*'s men included some with gunnery experience, there was no possibility of them being able to man the guns on the spur of the moment.

The privateer had completed her circle. She was coming back. All over the *Pitt*'s deck, men were shouting, waving their arms, crashing into one another as they stumbled toward the rail.

"We surrender, you filthy buggers!" one of them screamed. "Are you *deaf*?!"

Evidently so; a stray waft of wind brought me the sulfurous smell of slow match, and I could see muskets being brought to bear on us. A few of the men near me lost their heads and rushed belowdecks. I found myself thinking that perhaps that was not such a bad idea.

Jamie had been waving and shouting beside me. Suddenly he was gone, though, and I turned to see him running across the deck. He whipped his shirt off over his head and leapt up onto our bow chaser, a gleaming brass gun called a long nine.

He waved the shirt in a huge, fluttering white arc, his free hand clamped on Ian's shoulder for balance. That caused confusion for a moment; the crackle of firing stopped, though the sloop continued her deadly circle. Jamie waved the shirt again, to and fro. Surely they must see him!

The wind was toward us; I could hear the rumble of the guns running out again, and the blood froze in my chest.

"They're going to sink us!" Mr. Smith shrieked, and this was echoed in cries of terror from some of the other men.

The smell of black powder came to us on the wind, sharp and acrid. There were shouts from the men in the rigging, half of them now desperately waving their shirts, as well. I saw Jamie pause for an instant, swallow, then bend down and say something to Ian. He squeezed Ian's shoulder hard, then lowered himself on hands and knees to the gun.

Ian shot past me, nearly knocking me over in his haste.

"Where are you going?" I cried.

"To let the prisoners out! They'll drown if we sink!" he called over his shoulder, disappearing into the companionway.

I turned back to the oncoming ship, to find that Jamie had not come down off the gun, as I'd thought. Instead, he had scrambled round so his back was to the oncoming sloop.

Braced against the wind, arms spread for balance, and knees gripping the brass of the gun for all he was worth, he stretched to his full height, arms out, displaying his bare back—and the web of scars on it, these gone red with the blanching of his skin in the cold wind.

The oncoming ship had slowed, maneuvering to slide alongside us and blast us out of the water with a final broadside. I could see the heads of men poking up over her rail, leaning out from her rigging, all craning in curiosity. But not firing.

I suddenly felt my heart beating with huge, painful thumps, as though it had actually stopped for a minute and now, reminded of its duty, was trying to make up for lost time.

The side of the sloop loomed above us, and the deck fell into deep, cold shadow. So close, I could hear the talk of the gun crews, puzzled, questioning; hear the deep clink and rattle of shot in its racks, the creak of the gun carriages. I couldn't look up, didn't dare to move.

"Who *are* you?" said a nasal, very American voice from above. It sounded deeply suspicious and very annoyed.

"If ye mean the ship, she's called the *Pitt.*" Jamie had got down from the gun and stood beside me, half naked and so pebbled with gooseflesh that the hairs stood out from his body like copper wires. He was shaking, though whether from terror, rage, or simply from cold, I didn't know. His voice didn't shake, though; it was filled with fury.

"If ye mean me, I am Colonel James Fraser, of the North Carolina militia."

A momentary silence, as the master of the privateer digested that.

"Where's Captain Stebbings?" the voice asked. The suspicion in it was undiminished, but the annoyance had waned a bit.

"It's a bloody long story," Jamie said, sounding cross. "But he's no aboard. If ye want to come over and look for him, do so. D'ye mind if I put my shirt back on?"

A pause, a murmur, and the clicks of hammers being eased. At this point, I unfroze enough to look up. The rail was a-bristle with the barrels of muskets and pistols, but most of these had been withdrawn and were now pointing harmlessly upward, while their owners pressed forward to gawk over the rail.

"Just a minute. Turn about," the voice said.

Jamie drew a deep breath in through his nose, but did so. He glanced at me, briefly, then stood with his head up, jaw clenched, and eyes fixed on the mast, around which the prisoners from the hold were now assembled, under Ian's eye. They looked completely baffled, gaping up at the privateer, then looking wildly round the deck before spotting Jamie, half naked and glaring like a basilisk. Had I not begun to worry that I was having a heart attack, I would have found it funny.

"Deserter from the British army, were you?" said the voice from the sloop, sounding interested. Jamie turned round, preserving the glare.

"I am not," he said shortly. "I am a free man—and always have been."

"Have you, then?" The voice was beginning to sound amused. "All right. Put your shirt on, and come aboard."

I could barely breathe and was bathed in cold sweat, but my heart began to beat more reasonably.

Jamie, now clothed, took my arm.

"My wife and nephew are coming with me," he called, and without waiting for assent from the sloop, seized me by the waist and lifted me to stand on the *Pitt*'s rail, from where I could grab the rope ladder that the sloop's crew had thrown down. He was taking no chances on being separated from either me or Ian again.

The ship was rolling in the swell, and I had to cling tightly to the ladder with my eyes closed for a moment, as dizziness swept over me. I felt nauseated as well as dizzy, but surely that was only a reaction to shock. With my eyes closed, my stomach settled a little, and I was able to set my foot on the next rung.

"Sail, ho!"

Tilting my head far back, I could just see the waving arm of the man above. I turned to look, the ladder twisting under me, and saw the sail approaching. On the deck above, the nasal voice was shouting orders, and bare feet drummed on the wood as the crew ran for their stations.

Jamie was on the rail of the *Pitt,* gripping me by the waist to save me falling.

"Jesus H. Roosevelt Christ," he said, in tones of utter astonishment, and I looked over my shoulder to see him turned to watch the oncoming ship. "It's the bloody *Teal.*"

A TALL, VERY THIN man with gray hair, a prominent Adam's apple, and piercing ice-blue eyes met us at the top of the ladder.

"Captain Asa Hickman," he barked at me, and then instantly switched his attention to Jamie. "What's that ship? And where's Stebbings?"

Ian scrambled over the rail behind me, looking anxiously back over his shoulder.

"I'd pull that ladder up if I were you," he said briefly to one of the sailors.

I glanced down at the deck of the *Pitt,* where a milling confusion of men was swarming toward the rail, pushing and shoving. There was a good deal of arm-waving and shouting, the naval seamen and the pressed men trying to put their cases, but Captain Hickman wasn't in the mood.

"Pull it up," he said to the sailor, and, "Come with me," to Jamie. He stalked off along the deck, not waiting for an answer and not turning to see whether he was followed. Jamie gave the sailors surrounding us a narrow look but apparently decided they were safe enough, and, with a terse "Look after your auntie" to Ian, went off after Hickman.

Ian was not paying attention to anything save the oncoming *Teal.*

"Jesus," he whispered, eyes fixed on the sail. "D'ye think he's all right?"

"Rollo? I certainly hope so." My face was cold; colder than just from the ocean spray; my lips had gone numb. And there were small flashing lights at the edges of my sight. "Ian," I said, as calmly as possible. "I think I'm going to faint."

The pressure in my chest seemed to rise, choking me. I forced a cough and felt a momentary easing. Dear God, *was* I having a heart attack? Pain in left arm? No. Pain in jaw? Yes, but I was clenching my teeth, no wonder. . . . I didn't feel myself fall, but felt the pressure of hands as someone caught and lowered me to the deck. My eyes were open, I thought, but I couldn't see anything. Dimly, it occurred to me that I might be dying, but I rejected that notion out of hand. No, I bloody *wasn't.* I couldn't. But there was an odd sort of gray swirling mist approaching me.

"Ian," I said—or thought I said. I felt very calm. "Ian, just in case—tell Jamie that I love him." Everything did not go black, rather to my surprise, but the mist reached me, and I felt gently enveloped in a peaceful gray cloud. All the pressure, the choking, the pain had eased. I could have floated, happily mindless, in the gray mist, save that I could not be sure I'd really spoken, and the need to convey the message niggled like a cocklebur in the sole of a foot.

"Tell Jamie," I kept saying to a misty Ian. "Tell Jamie that I love him."

"Open your eyes and tell me yourself, Sassenach," said a deep, urgent voice somewhere close.

I tried opening my eyes and found that I could. Apparently I had not died after all. I essayed a cautious breath and found that my chest moved easily. My hair was damp, and I was lying on something hard, covered by a blanket. Jamie's face swam above me, then steadied as I blinked.

"Tell me," he repeated, smiling a little, though anxiety creased the skin beside his eyes.

"Tell you . . . oh! I love you. Where . . . ?" Memory of recent events flooded in upon me, and I sat up abruptly. "The *Teal*? What—"

"I havena got the slightest idea. When did ye last have anything to eat, Sassenach?"

"I don't remember. Last night. What do you mean, you haven't the slightest idea? Is it still *there*?"

"Oh, aye," he said, with a certain grimness. "It is. It fired two shots at us a few minutes gone—though I suppose ye couldna hear them."

"It fired shots at—" I rubbed a hand over my face, pleased to find that I could now feel my lips, and that normal warmth had returned to my skin. "Do I look gray and sweaty?" I asked Jamie. "Are my lips blue?"

He looked startled at that, but bent to peer closely at my mouth.

"No," he said positively, straightening up after a thorough inspection. Then he bent and quickly kissed them, putting a seal on my state of pinkness. "I love ye, too," he whispered. "I'm glad ye're no dead. Yet," he added in a normal tone of voice, straightening up as an unmistakable cannon shot came from somewhere at a distance.

"I assume Captain Stebbings has taken over the *Teal*?" I asked. "Captain Roberts wouldn't be going around taking potshots at strange ships, I don't think. But why is Stebbings firing at us, I wonder? Why isn't he trying to board the *Pitt* and take her back? It's his for the taking now."

My symptoms had all but disappeared by now, and I felt quite clearheaded. Sitting up, I discovered that I had been laid out on a pair of large, flat-topped chests in what appeared to be a small hold; there was a latticed hatch cover overhead, through which I caught the fluttering shadows of moving sails, and the walls were stacked with a miscellaneous assortment of barrels, bundles, and boxes. The air was thick with the smells of tar, copper, cloth, gunpowder, and . . . coffee? I sniffed more deeply, feeling stronger by the moment. Yes, coffee!

The sound of another muffled cannon-shot came through the walls, muffled by distance, and a small visceral quiver ran through me. The notion of being trapped in the hold of a ship that might at any moment be sunk was enough to overcome even the smell of coffee.

Jamie had turned in response to the shot, too, half rising. Before I could stand and suggest that we go above, and quickly, there was a shift in the light, and a round, bristly head poked through the hatchway.

"Is the lady summat recovered?" a young boy asked politely. "Cap'n says if she's dead, you're no longer needed here, and he desires you to come above and speak to him prompt, sir."

"And if I'm not dead?" I inquired, trying to straighten out my petticoats, which were wet round the hems, damp through, and hopelessly rumpled. Drat. Now I had left my gold-weighted skirt and pocket aboard the *Pitt.* At this rate, I'd be lucky to arrive on dry land in my chemise and stays.

The boy—at second glance, he was likely twelve or so, though he looked much younger—smiled at this.

"In that case, he offered to come and drop you overboard himself, ma'am, in hopes of concentrating your husband's mind. Cap'n Hickman's a bit hasty in his speech," he added, with an apologetic grimace. "He doesn't mean much by it. Usually."

"I'll come with you." I stood up without losing my balance, but did accept Jamie's arm. We made our way through the ship, led by our new acquaintance, who helpfully informed me that his name was Abram Zenn ("My pa being a reading man, and much taken by Mr. Johnson's Dictionary, he was tickled by the thought of me being A through Zed, you see"), that he was the ship's boy (the ship's name *was* in fact *Asp,* which pleased me), and that the reason for Captain Hickman's present agitation was a long-standing grievance against the navy's Captain Stebbings: "which there's been more than one run-in betwixt the two, and Cap'n Hickman's sworn that there won't be but one more."

"I gather Captain Stebbings is of like mind?" Jamie asked dryly, to which Abram nodded vigorous assent.

"Fellow in a tavern in Roanoke told me Cap'n Stebbings was drinking there and said to the assembled as how he meant to hang Cap'n Hickman from his own yardarm, and leave him for the gulls to peck his eyes. They would, too," he added darkly, with a glance at the seabirds wheeling over the ocean nearby. "They're wicked buggers, gulls."

Further interesting tidbits were curtailed by our arrival in Captain Hickman's inner sanctum, a cramped stern cabin, as crammed with cargo as the hold had been. Ian was there, doing his impression of a captured Mohawk about to be burned at the stake, from which I deduced that he hadn't taken to Captain Hickman. The feeling seemed to be mutual, judging from the hectic patches of color burning in the latter's rawboned cheeks.

"Ah," Hickman said shortly, seeing us. "Glad to see you've not departed this life yet, ma'am. Be a sad loss to your husband, such a devoted woman." There was a sarcastic intonation to this last that made me wonder uncomfortably just how many times I'd told Ian to relay my love to Jamie and just how many people had heard me doing it, but Jamie simply ignored the comment, showing me to a seat on the captain's unmade bed before turning to deal with the man himself.

"I'm told that the *Teal* is firing at us," he observed mildly. "Does this occasion ye no concern, sir?"

"Not yet it doesn't." Hickman spared a negligent glance at his stern windows, half of them covered with deadlights, presumably because of broken glass; a good many of the panes were shattered. "He's just firing in hopes of a lucky shot. We've got the weather gauge on him, and will likely keep it for the next couple of hours."

"I see," said Jamie, with a convincing attitude of knowing what this meant.

"Captain Hickman is debating in his mind whether to engage the *Teal* in action, Uncle," Ian put in tactfully, "or whether to run. Having the weather gauge is a matter of maneuverability, and thus gives him somewhat more latitude in the matter than the *Teal* has presently, I think."

"Heard the one about *He who fights and runs away, lives to fight another day?*" Hickman said, giving Ian a glare. "If I can sink him, I will. If I can shoot him on his own quarterdeck and take the ship, I'll like that better, but I'll settle for sending him to the bottom if I have to. But I won't let him sink *me,* not today."

"Why not today?" I asked. "Rather than any other day, I mean?"

Hickman looked surprised; he had obviously assumed I was purely ornamental.

"Because I have an important cargo to deliver, ma'am. One that I daren't risk. Not unless I could get my hands on that rat Stebbings without taking any great chances," he added broodingly.

"I gather that your assumption that Captain Stebbings was aboard accounts for your most determined attempt to sink the *Pitt*?" Jamie asked. The ceiling of the cabin was so low that he, Ian, and Hickman were all obliged to converse in a crouching position, like a convention of chimpanzees. There was really nowhere to sit other than the bed, and kneeling on the floor would of course lack the requisite dignity for a meeting of gentlemen.

"It was, sir, and I'm obliged to you for stopping me in time. Perhaps we may share a jar, when there's more leisure, and you can tell me what happened to your back."

"Perhaps not," Jamie said politely. "I gather further that we are under sail. Where is the *Pitt* presently?"

"Adrift, about two miles off the larboard quarter. If I *can* deal with Stebbings," and Hickman's eyes fairly glowed red at the prospect, "I'll come back and take her, too."

"If there's anyone left alive on board to sail her," Ian said. "There was a fair-sized riot on her deck, when last I saw it. What might predispose ye to take on the *Teal,* sir?" he asked, raising his voice. "My uncle and I can give ye information regarding her guns and crew—and even if Stebbings has taken the ship, I doubt but he'll have a job to fight her. He's got no more than ten men of his own, and Captain Roberts and his crew will want nay part of an engagement, I'm sure."

Jamie gave Ian a narrow look.

"Ye ken they've likely killed him already."

Ian didn't resemble Jamie at all, but the look of implacable stubbornness on his face was one I knew intimately.

"Aye, maybe. Would ye leave *me* behind, if ye only thought I *might* be dead?"

I could see Jamie open his mouth to say, "*He's a dog.*" But he didn't. He closed his eyes and sighed, obviously contemplating the prospect of instigating a sea battle—and incidentally risking all of our lives six ways from Sunday, to say nothing of the lives of the men aboard the *Teal*—for the sake of an aging dog, who might be already dead, if not devoured by a shark. Then he opened them and nodded.

"Aye, all right." He straightened, as much as was possible in the cramped cabin, and turned to Hickman. "My nephew's particular friend is aboard the *Teal* and likely in danger. I ken that's no concern of yours, but it explains our own interest. As for yours . . . in addition to Captain Stebbings, there is a cargo aboard the *Teal* in which ye may have an interest, as well—six cases of rifles."

Ian and I both gasped. Hickman straightened up abruptly, cracking his head on a timber.

"Ow! Holy Moses. You're sure of that?"

"I am. And I imagine the Continental army might make use of them?"

I thought that was treading on dangerous ground; after all, the fact that Hickman had a strong animus toward Captain Stebbings didn't necessarily mean he was an American patriot. From the little I'd seen of him, Captain Stebbings looked entirely capable of inspiring purely personal animus, quite separate from any political considerations.

But Hickman made no denial; in fact, he'd barely noticed Jamie's remark, inflamed by mention of the rifles. Was it true? I wondered. But Jamie had spoken with complete certainty. I cast my mind back over the contents of the *Teal*'s hold, looking for anything . . .

"Jesus H. Roosevelt Christ," I said. "The boxes bound for New Haven?" I barely kept myself from blurting out Hannah Arnold's name, realizing just in time that *if* Hickman was indeed a patriot—for it did occur to me that he might merely be a businessman, as willing to sell to either side—he might well recognize the name and realize that these rifles were almost certainly already intended to reach the Continentals via Colonel Arnold.

Jamie nodded, watching Hickman, who was gazing at a

small barometer on the wall as though it were a crystal ball. Whatever it told him seemed to be favorable, for Hickman nodded once, then dashed out of the cabin as though his breeches were on fire.

"Where's he gone?" Ian demanded, staring after him.

"To check the wind, I imagine," I said, proud of knowing something. "To make certain he still has the weather gauge."

Jamie was rifling Hickman's desk, and emerged at this point with a rather wizened apple, which he tossed into my lap. "Eat that, Sassenach. What the devil *is* a weather gauge?"

"Ah. Well, there you have me," I admitted. "But it has to do with wind, and it seems to be important." I sniffed the apple; it had plainly seen better days, but still held a faint, sweet smell that suddenly raised the ghost of my vanished appetite. I took a cautious bite and felt saliva flood my mouth. I ate it in two more bites, ravenous.

Captain Hickman's high nasal voice came piercingly from the deck. I couldn't hear what he said, but the response was immediate; feet thumped to and fro on deck, and the ship shifted suddenly, turning as her sails were adjusted. The chime and grunt of shot being lifted and the rumble of gun carriages echoed through the ship. Apparently, the weather gauge was still ours.

I could see a fierce excitement light Ian's face and rejoiced to see it, but couldn't help voicing a qualm or two.

"You haven't any hesitation about this?" I said to Jamie. "I mean—after all, he *is* a dog."

He gave me an eye and a moody shrug.

"Aye, well. I've known battles fought for worse reasons. And since this time yesterday, I've committed piracy, mutiny, and murder. I may as well add treason and make a day of it."

"Besides, Auntie," Ian said reprovingly, "he's a *good* dog."

WEATHER GAUGE OR no, it took an endless time of cautious maneuvering before the ships drew within what seemed a dangerous distance of each other. The sun was no more than a handsbreadth above the horizon by now, the sails were beginning to glow a baleful red, and my chastely pristine dawn looked like ending in a wallowing sea of blood.

The *Teal* was cruising gently, no more than half her canvas set, less than half a mile away. Captain Hickman stood on the *Asp*'s deck, hands clenched on the rail as though it were Stebbings's throat, wearing the look of a greyhound just before the rabbit is released.

"Time you went below, ma'am," Hickman said, not looking at me. "Matters will be hotting up directly here." His hands flexed once in anticipation.

I didn't argue. The tension on deck was so thick I could smell it, testosterone spiced with brimstone and black powder. Men being the remarkable creatures that they are, everyone seemed cheerful.

I paused to kiss Jamie—a gesture he returned with a gusto that left my lower lip throbbing slightly—resolutely ignoring the possibility that the next time I saw him, it might be in separate pieces. I'd faced that possibility a number of times before, and while it didn't get less daunting with practice, I had got better at ignoring it.

Or at least I thought I had. Sitting in the main hold in near-total darkness, smelling the low-tide reek of the bilges and listening to what I was sure were rats rustling in the chains, I had a harder time ignoring the sounds from above: the rumbling of gun carriages. The *Asp* had only four guns to a side, but they were twelve-pounders: heavy armament for a coastal schooner. The *Teal,* equipped as an oceangoing merchantman who might have to fight off all manner of menace, fought eight to a side, sixteen-pounders, with two carronades on the upper deck, plus two bow chasers and a stern gun.

"She'd run from a man-o'-war," Abram explained to me, he having asked me to describe the *Teal*'s armament. "And she wouldn't be likely to try to seize or sink another vessel, so she wouldn't ship tremendous hardware, even was she built for it, and I doubt she is. Now, I doubt as well that Captain Stebbings can man even a whole side to good effect, though, so we mustn't be downhearted." He spoke with great confidence, which I found amusing and also oddly reassuring. He seemed to realize this, for he leaned forward and patted my hand gently.

"Now, you needn't fret, ma'am," he said. "Mr. Fraser said to me I must be sure to let no harm come to you, and I shall not—be sure of that."

"Thank you," I said gravely. Not wanting either to laugh or to cry, I cleared my throat instead and asked, "Do you know what caused the trouble between Captain Hickman and Captain Stebbings?"

"Oh, yes, ma'am," he replied promptly. "Captain Stebbings has been a plague on the district for some years, stopping ships what he hasn't any right to search, taking off legal goods what he says are contraband—and we take leave to doubt that any of it ever sees the inside of a Customs warehouse!" he added, obviously quoting something he'd heard more than once. "But it was what happened with the *Annabelle,* really."

The *Annabelle* was a large ketch, owned by Captain Hickman's brother. The *Pitt* had stopped her and attempted to press men from her crew. Theo Hickman had protested, resistance had broken out, and Stebbings had ordered his men to fire into the *Annabelle,* killing three crewmen—Theo Hickman among them.

There had been considerable public outcry over this, and an effort was made to bring Captain Stebbings to justice for his deeds. The captain had insisted that no local court had the right to try him for anything, though; if anyone wished to bring an action against him, it must be done in an English court. And the local justices had agreed with this.

"Was this before war was declared last year?" I asked curiously. "For if after—"

"Well before," young Zenn admitted. "Still," he added with righteous indignation, "they are cowardly dogs and ought be tarred and feathered, the lot of them, and Stebbings, too!"

"No doubt," I said. "Do you think—"

But I had no opportunity to explore his opinions further, for at this point the ship gave a violent lurch, throwing us both onto the damp floorboards, and the sound of a violent and prolonged explosion shattered the air around us.

I couldn't at first tell which ship had fired—but an instant later, the *Asp*'s guns spoke overhead, and I knew the first broadside had been from the *Teal.*

The *Asp*'s reply was ragged, the guns along her starboard side going off at more or less random intervals overhead, punctuated by the flat bangs of small-arms fire.

I resisted Abram's gallant attempts to throw his meager body protectively on top of mine and, rolling over, got up onto my hands and knees, listening intently. There was a lot of shouting, none of it comprehensible, though the shooting had stopped. We appeared not to be leaking water, so far as I could tell, so presumably we had not been struck below the waterline.

"They can't have given up, surely?" Abram said, scrambling to his feet. He sounded disappointed.

"I doubt it." I got to my own feet, bracing a hand against a large barrel. The main hold was quite as crowded as the forward one, though with bulkier items; there was barely room for Abram and me to worm our way between the netted bulk of crates and tiers of casks—some of which smelled strongly of beer. The ship was heeling to one side now. We must be coming about—probably to try again. The wheels of the gun carriages ground on the deck above; yes, they were reloading. Had anyone yet been hurt? I wondered. And what the devil was I going to do about it if they had?

The sound of a single cannon-shot came from overhead.

"The dog must be fleeing," Abram whispered. "We're chasing him down."

There was a long period of relative silence, during which I thought the ship was tacking but couldn't really tell. Maybe Hickman *was* pursuing the *Teal.*

Sudden yelling from overhead, with a sound of surprised alarm, and the ship heaved violently, flinging us to the floor once again. This time I landed on top. I delicately removed my knee from Abram's stomach and helped him to sit up, gasping like a landed fish.

"What—" he wheezed, but got no further. There was a hideous jolt that knocked us both flat again, followed at once by a grinding, rending noise of squealing timbers. It sounded as though the ship was coming apart around us, and I had no doubt that it was.

Shrieking like banshees and the thunder of feet on deck.

"We're being boarded!" I could hear Abram swallow, and my hand went to the slit in my petticoat, touching my knife for courage. If—

"No," I whispered, straining my eyes up into darkness as

though that would help me hear better. "No. We're boarding *them.*" For the pounding feet above had vanished.

THE YELLING HADN'T; even muffled by distance, I could hear the note of insanity in it, the clear joy of the berserker. I thought I could make out Jamie's Highland screech, but that was likely imagination; they all sounded equally demented.

"Our Father, who art in heaven . . . Our Father, who art in heaven . . ." Abram was whispering to himself in the dark, but had stuck on the first line.

I clenched my fists and closed my eyes in reflex, screwing up my face as though by sheer force of will I could help.

Neither of us could.

It was an age of muffled noises, occasional shots, thuds and bangs, grunting and shouting. And then silence.

I could just see Abram's head turn toward me, questioning. I squeezed his hand.

And then a ship's gun went off with a crash that echoed across the deck above, and a shock wave thrummed through the air of the hold, hard enough that my ears popped. Another followed, I felt rather than heard a *thunk,* and then the floor heaved and tilted, and the ship's timbers reverberated with an odd, deep *bwong.* I shook my head hard, swallowing, trying to force air through my Eustachian tubes. They popped again, finally, and I heard feet on the side of the ship. More than one pair. Moving slowly.

I leapt to my feet, grabbed Abram, and hauled him bodily up, propelling him toward the ladder. I could hear water. Not racing along the ship's sides; a gushing noise, as of water gurgling into the hold.

The hatchway had been closed overhead but not battened down, and I knocked it loose with a desperate bang of both hands, nearly losing my balance and plunging into darkness but luckily sustained by Abram Zenn, who planted a small but solid shoulder under my buttocks by way of support.

"Thank you, Mr. Zenn," I said, and, reaching behind me, pulled him up the ladder into the light.

There was blood on the deck; that was the first thing I saw.

Wounded men, too—but not Jamie. He was the second thing I saw, leaning heavily over the remains of a shattered rail with several other men. I hurried to see what they were looking at, and saw the *Teal* a few hundred yards away.

Her sails were fluttering wildly, and her masts seemed oddly tilted. Then I realized that the ship herself was tilted, the bow raised half out of the water.

"Rot me," said Abram, in tones of amazement. "She's run onto rocks."

"So have we, son, but not so bad," said Hickman, glancing aside at the cabin boy's voice. "Is there water in the hold, Abram?"

"There is," I replied before Abram, lost in contemplation of the wounded *Teal,* could gather his wits to answer. "Have you any medical instruments aboard, Captain Hickman?"

"Have I what?" he blinked at me, distracted. "This is no time for—why?"

"I'm a surgeon, sir," I said, "and you need me."

WITHIN A QUARTER hour, I found myself back in the small forward cargo hold where I had roused from my fainting spell a few hours earlier, this being now designated as the sick bay.

The *Asp* did not travel with a surgeon, but had a small store of medicinals: a half-full bottle of laudanum, a fleam and bleeding bowl, a large pair of tweezers, a jar of dead and desiccated leeches, two rusty amputation saws, a broken tenaculum, a bag of lint for packing wounds, and a huge jar of camphorated grease.

I was strongly tempted to drink the laudanum myself, but duty called. I tied back my hair and began poking about among the cargo, in search of anything useful. Mr. Smith and Ian had rowed across to the *Teal* in hopes of retrieving my own kit, but given the amount of damage I could see in the area where our cabin had been, I didn't have much hope. A lucky shot from the *Asp* had holed the *Teal* below the waterline; had she not run aground, she would likely have sunk sooner or later.

I'd done a rapid triage on deck; one man killed outright,

several minor injuries, three serious but not instantly life-threatening. There were likely more on the *Teal;* from what the men said, the ships had exchanged broadsides at a distance of no more than a few yards. A quick and bloody little action.

A few minutes after the conclusion, the *Pitt* had limped into sight, her contentiously mixed crew having evidently come to a sufficient accommodation as to allow her to sail, and she was now occupied in ferrying the wounded. I heard the faint shout of her bosun's hail over the whine of the wind above.

"Incoming," I murmured, and, picking up the smaller of the amputation saws, prepared for my own quick and bloody action.

"YOU HAVE GUNS," I pointed out to Abram Zenn, who was rigging a couple of hanging lanterns for me, the sun having now almost set. "Presumably this means that Captain Hickman was prepared to use them. Didn't he think there might be a possibility of casualties?"

Abram shrugged apologetically.

"It's our first voyage as a letter of marque, ma'am. We'll do better next time, I'm sure."

"Your first? What sort of—how long has Captain Hickman been sailing?" I demanded. I was ruthlessly rummaging the cargo by now, and was pleased to find a chest that held lengths of printed calico.

Abram frowned at the wick he was trimming, thinking.

"Well," he said slowly, "he had a fishing boat for some time, out of Marblehead. Him—he, I mean—and his brother owned it together. But after his brother ran afoul of Captain Stebbings, he went to work for Emmanuel Bailey, as first mate on one of his—Mr. Bailey's, I mean—ships. Mr. Bailey's a Jew," he explained, seeing my raised eyebrow. "Owns a bank in Philadelphia and three ships as sail regularly to the West Indies. He owns this ship, too, and it's him who got the letter of marque from the Congress for Captain Hickman, when the war was announced."

"I see," I said, more than slightly taken aback. "But this is Captain Hickman's first cruise as captain of a sloop?"

"Yes, ma'am. But privateers don't usually have a supercargo, do you see," he said earnestly. "It would be the supercargo's job to provision the ship and see to such things as the medical supplies."

"And you know this because—how long have *you* been sailing?" I asked curiously, liberating a bottle of what looked like very expensive brandy, to use as antiseptic.

"Oh, since I was eight years old, ma'am," he said. He stood a-tiptoe to hang the lantern, which cast a warm, reassuring glow over my impromptu operating theater. "I've six elder brothers, and the oldest runs the farm, with his sons. The others . . . well, one's a shipwright in Newport News, and he got to talking with a captain one day and mentioned me, and next thing I know, I'm one of the cabin boys on the *Antioch,* her being an Indiaman. I went back with the captain to London, and we sailed to Calcutta the very day after." He came down onto his heels and smiled at me. "I've been a-sea ever since, ma'am. I find it suits me."

"That's very good," I said. "Your parents—are they still alive?"

"Oh, no, ma'am. My mother died birthing me, and my pa when I was seven." He seemed untroubled by this. But after all, I reflected, ripping calico into bandage lengths, that was half his lifetime ago.

"Well, I hope the sea will continue to suit you," I said. "Do you have any doubts, though—after today?"

He thought about that, his earnest young face furrowed in the lantern shadows.

"No," he said slowly, and looked up at me, his eyes serious—and not nearly so young as they had been a few hours ago. "I knew when I signed on with Captain Hickman that there might be fighting." His lips tightened, perhaps to keep them from quivering. "I don't mind killing a man, if I have to."

"Not now . . . you don't," said one of the wounded men, very softly. He was lying in the shadows, stretched across two crates of English china, breathing slowly.

"No, not now, you don't," I agreed dryly. "You might want

to speak to my nephew or my husband about it, though, when things have settled a bit."

I thought that would be the end of it, but Abram followed me as I laid out my rudimentary tools and set about such sterilization as could be managed, splashing out brandy with abandon, 'til the hold smelled like a distillery—this to the scandalization of the wounded men, who thought it waste to use good drink so. The galley fire had been put out during the battle, though; it would be some time before I had hot water.

"Are you a patriot, ma'am? If you don't mind me asking," he added, blushing with awkwardness.

The question took me back a bit. The straightforward answer would be "Yes, of course." Jamie was, after all, a rebel, so declared by his own hand. And while he had made the original declaration out of simple necessity, I thought necessity had now become conviction. But me? Certainly I had been, once.

"Yes," I said—I couldn't very well say anything else. "Plainly you are, Abram. Why?"

"Why?" He seemed staggered that I would ask, and stood blinking at me over the top of the lantern he held.

"Tell me later," I suggested, taking the lantern. I'd done what I could on deck; the wounded who needed further attention were being brought down. It was no time for political discussion. Or so I thought.

Abram bravely settled down to help me and did fairly well, though he had to stop now and then to vomit into a bucket. After the second occurrence of this, he took to asking questions of the wounded—those in any condition to answer. I didn't know whether this was simple curiosity or an attempt to distract himself from what I was doing.

"What do you think of the Revolution, sir?" he earnestly asked one grizzled seaman from the *Pitt* with a crushed foot. The man gave him a distinctly jaundiced look but replied, probably in order to distract himself.

"Bloody waste of time," he said gruffly, digging his fingers into the edge of the chest he sat on. "Better to be fighting the frogs than Englishmen. What's to be gained by it? Dear Lord," he said under his breath, going pale.

"Give him something to bite on, Abram, will you?" I said, busy picking shattered bits of bone out of the wreckage and wondering whether he might do better with a swift amputation. Perhaps less risk of infection, and he would always walk with a painful limp in any case, but still, I hated to . . .

"No, that's all right, mum," he said, sucking in a breath. "What do *you* think of it, then, youngster?"

"I think it is right and necessary, sir," Abram replied stoutly. "The King is a tyrant, and tyranny must be resisted by all proper men."

"What?" said the seaman, shocked. "The King, a tyrant? Who says such a naughty thing?"

"Why . . . Mr. Jefferson. And—and all of us! We all think so," Abram said, taken aback at such vehement disagreement.

"Well, then, you're all a pack of bleedin' fools—saving your presence, mum," he added, with a nod to me. He got a look at his foot and swayed a bit, closing his eyes, but asked, "You don't think such a silly thing, do you, mum? You ought to talk sense into your boy here."

"Talk sense?" cried Abram, roused. "You think it sense that we may not speak or write as we wish?"

The seaman opened one eye.

"Of course that's sense," he said, with an evident attempt to be reasonable. "You get silly buggers—your pardon, mum—a-saying all kinds of things regardless, stirrin' folk up to no good end, and what's it lead to? Riot, that's what, and what you may call disorderliness, with folk having their houses burnt and being knocked down in the street. Ever hear of the Cutter riots, boy?"

Abram rather obviously had not, but countered with a vigorous denunciation of the Intolerable Acts, which caused Mr. Ormiston—we had got onto personal terms by now—to scoff loudly and recount the privations Londoners endured by comparison with the luxury enjoyed by the ungrateful colonists.

"Ungrateful!" Abram said, his face congested. "And what should we be grateful for, then? For having soldiers foisted upon us?"

"Oh, foisted, is it?" cried Mr. Ormiston in righteous indignation. "Such a word! And if it means what I think it does, young man, you should get down on your knees and thank God for such foistingness! Who do you think saved you all from being scalped by red Indians or overrun by the French? And who do you think paid for it all, eh?"

This shrewd riposte drew cheers—and not a few jeers—from the waiting men, who had all been drawn into the discussion by now.

"That is absolute . . . desolute . . . *stultiloquy,*" began Abram, puffing up his insignificant chest like a scrawny pigeon, but he was interrupted by the entrance of Mr. Smith, a canvas bag in hand and an apologetic look on his face.

"I'm afraid your cabin was all ahoo, ma'am," he said. "But I picked up what bits was scattered on the floor, in case they—"

"Jonah Marsden!" Mr. Ormiston, on the verge of standing up, plumped back onto the chest, openmouthed. "Bless me if it isn't!"

"Who?" I asked, startled.

"Jonah—well, 'tisn't his real name, what was it . . . oh, Bill, I think it was, but we took to calling him Jonah, owing to him being sunk so many times."

"Now, Joe." Mr. Smith—or Mr. Marsden—was backing toward the door, smiling nervously. "That was all a long time ago, and—"

"Not so long as all that." Mr. Ormiston got ponderously to his feet, balancing with one hand on a stack of herring barrels so as not to put weight on his bandaged foot. "Not so long as would make the navy forget you, you filthy deserter!"

Mr. Smith disappeared abruptly up the ladder, pushing past two seamen attempting to come down these, handling a third like a side of beef between them. Muttering curses, they dropped him on the deck in front of me with a thud and stood back, gasping. It was Captain Stebbings.

" 'E's not dead," one of them informed me helpfully.

"Oh, good," I said. My tone of voice might have left something to be desired, for the captain opened one eye and glared at me.

"You're leaving me . . . to be butchered . . . by this bitch?" he said hoarsely, between labored gasps. "I'd ra-rather die hon-honorablblbl . . ." The sentiment gurgled off into a bubbling noise that made me rip open his smoke-stained, blood-soaked second-best coat and shirt. Sure enough, there was a neat round hole in his right breast and the nasty wet slurp of a sucking chest wound coming from it.

I said a very bad word, and the two men who had brought

him to me shuffled and muttered. I said it again, louder, and, seizing Stebbings's hand, slapped it over the hole.

"Hold that there, if you want a chance at an honorable death," I said to him. "You!" I shouted at one of the men trying to edge away. "Bring me some oil from the galley. Now! And *you*—" My voice caught the other, who jerked guiltily to a halt. "Sailcloth and tar. Fast as you can!"

"Don't talk," I advised Stebbings, who seemed inclined to make remarks. "You have a collapsed lung, and either I get it reinflated or you die like a dog, right here."

"Hg," he said, which I took for assent. His hand was a nice meaty one, and doing a reasonably good job of sealing the hole for the moment. The trouble was that he undoubtedly had not only a hole in his chest but a hole in the lung, too. I had to provide a seal for the external hole so air couldn't get into the chest and keep the lung compressed, but had also to make sure there was a way for air from the pleural space around the lung to make an exit. As it was, every time he exhaled, air from the injured lung went straight into that space, making the problem worse.

He might also be drowning in his own blood, but there wasn't a hell of a lot I could do about that, so I wouldn't worry about it.

"On the good side," I told him, "it was a bullet, and not shrapnel or a splinter. One thing about red-hot iron: it sterilizes the wound. Lift your hand for a moment, please. Breathe out." I grabbed his hand myself and lifted it for the count of two while he exhaled, then slapped it back over the wound. It made a squelching sound, owing to the blood. It was a lot of blood for a hole like that, but he wasn't coughing or spitting blood. . . . Where—oh.

"Is this blood yours or someone else's?" I demanded, pointing at it.

His eyes were half shut, but at this he turned his head and bared his bad teeth at me in a wolf's grin.

"Your . . . husband's," he said in a hoarse whisper.

"Wanker," I said crossly, lifting his hand again. "Breathe out." The men had seen me dealing with Stebbings; there were other casualties from the *Teal* coming or being carried along, but most of them seemed ambulatory. I gave cursory directions to the able-bodied with them, regarding the application of pressure to wounds or the placement of broken limbs so as to avoid further injury.

It seemed an age before the oil and cloth arrived, and I had sufficient time to wonder where Jamie and Ian were, but the first-aid supplies came at last. I ripped off a patch of sailcloth with my knife, tore a longish strip of calico to use as field dressing, then pushed Stebbings's hand away, wiped off the blood with a fold of my petticoat, sloshed lamp oil over his chest and the sailcloth patch, then pressed the cloth down to form a rudimentary seal, putting his hand back over it in such a way that one end of the patch remained free, while I wound the improvised field dressing round his torso.

"All right," I said. "I'll need to stick the patch down with tar for a better seal, but it will take a little time to warm that. You can go and be doing that now," I advised the sailor who had brought the oil, who was once again trying to execute a quiet sneak. I scooted round to view the casualties squatting or sprawling on the deck. "Right. Who's dying?"

For a wonder, only two of the men brought in from the *Teal* were dead, one with hideous head wounds from flying splinters and grapeshot, the other exsanguinated as a result of losing half his left leg, probably to a cannonball.

Might have saved that one, I thought, but the moment's regret was subsumed in the needs of the next moment.

Not all that bad, I thought, working my way quickly down the line on my knees, doing a hasty triage and issuing instructions to my unwilling assistants. Splinter wounds, two grazed by musket balls, one with half an ear torn off, one with an embedded ball in the thigh, but nowhere near the femoral artery, thank God . . .

Bangings and shufflings were coming from the lower hold, where repairs were being effected. As I worked, I pieced together the actions of the battle from the remarks passed by the wounded men awaiting my attention.

Following a ragged exchange of broadsides, which had brought down the *Teal*'s cracked mainmast and holed the *Asp* above the waterline, the *Teal*—opinions differed on whether Captain Roberts had done it a-purpose or not—had veered sharply toward the *Asp,* scraping the side of the ship and bringing the two vessels railing to railing.

It seemed inconceivable that Stebbings had intended to

board the *Asp,* with so few dependable men as he had; if it had been deliberate, he might have meant to ram us. I glanced down, but the captain's eyes were closed, and he was a nasty color. I lifted his hand and heard a small hiss of air, then placed it back on his chest and went on with my work. Plainly he was in no shape to set the record straight regarding his intentions.

Whatever they had been, Captain Hickman had forestalled them, leaping over the *Teal*'s rail with a shriek, followed by a swarm of Asps. They had cut their way across the deck without much resistance, though the men from the *Pitt* had gathered together around Stebbings near the helm and fought ferociously. It was clear that the Asps must win the day, though—and then the *Teal* had struck heavily aground, throwing everyone flat on deck.

Convinced that the ship was about to sink, everyone who could move did, boarders and defenders together going back over the rail onto the *Asp*—which sheered abruptly away, with some benighted defender who remained on the *Teal* sending a last shot or two after her, only to scrape her own bottom on a gravel bar.

"Not to worry, ma'am," one of the men assured me. "She'll swim directly the tide comes in."

The noises from below began to diminish, and I looked over my shoulder every few moments, in hopes of seeing Jamie or Ian.

I was examining one poor fellow who'd taken a splinter in one eyeball, when his other eye suddenly widened in horror, and I turned to find Rollo panting and dripping by my side, enormous teeth exposed in a grin that put Stebbings's feeble attempt to shame.

"Dog!" I cried, delighted. I couldn't hug him—well, I wouldn't, really—but looked quickly round for Ian, who was limping in my direction, sopping wet, too, but with a matching grin.

"We fell into the water," he said hoarsely, squatting on the deck beside me. A small puddle formed under him.

"So I see. Breathe deeply for me," I said to the man with the splinter in his eye. "One . . . yes, that's right . . . two . . . yes . . ." As he exhaled, I took hold of the splinter and pulled, hard. It slid free, followed by a gush of vitreous humor and blood that made me grit my teeth and made Ian retch. Not a lot of blood, though. *If it hasn't gone through the orbit, I might be able to stave off infection by removing the eyeball and packing the socket. That'll have to wait, though.* I slashed a ribbon of cloth from the man's shirttail, folded it hastily into a wad, soaked it in brandy, pressed it to the ruined eye, and made him hold it firmly in place. He did, though he groaned and swayed alarmingly, and I feared he might fall over.

"Where's your uncle?" I asked Ian, with a gnawing sense that I didn't want to hear the answer.

"Right there," Ian said, nodding to one side. I swung round, one hand still bracing the shoulder of the one-eyed man, to see Jamie coming down the ladder, in heated argument with Captain Hickman, who was following him. Jamie's shirt was soaked with blood, and he was holding a wad of something likewise blood-soaked against his shoulder with one hand. Possibly Stebbings hadn't been merely trying to aggravate me. Jamie wasn't falling down, though, and while he was white, he was also furious. I was reasonably sure he wouldn't die while angry and seized another strip of sailcloth to stabilize a compound fracture of the arm.

"Dog!" said Hickman, coming to a stop beside the supine Stebbings. He didn't say it with the same intonation I had used, though, and Stebbings opened one eye.

"Dog, yourself," he said thickly.

"Dog, dog, dog! Fucking dog!" Hickman added for good measure, and aimed a kick at Stebbings's side. I grabbed for his foot and managed to shove him off balance, so that he lurched sideways. Jamie caught him, grunting with pain, but Hickman struggled upright, pushing Jamie away.

"Ye canna murder the man in cold blood!"

"Can, too," Hickman replied promptly. "Watch me!" He drew an enormous horse pistol out of a ratty leather holster and cocked it. Jamie took it by the barrel and plucked it neatly out of his hand, leaving him flexing his fingers and looking surprised.

"Surely, sir," Jamie said, striving for reasonableness, "ye canna mean to kill a wounded enemy—one in uniform, taken under his own flag, and a man who has surrendered himself to ye. That couldna be condoned by any honorable man."

Hickman drew himself up, going puce.

"Are you impugning my honor, sir?"

I saw the muscles in Jamie's neck and shoulders tense, but before he could speak, Ian stepped up beside him, shoulder to shoulder.

"Aye, he is. So am I."

Rollo, his fur still sticking up in wet spikes, growled and rolled back his black lips, showing most of his teeth in token of his support of this opinion.

Hickman glanced from Ian's scowling, tattooed visage, to Rollo's impressive carnassials, and back to Jamie, who had uncocked the pistol and put it in his own belt. He breathed heavily.

"On your head be it, then," he said abruptly, and turned away.

Captain Stebbings was breathing heavily, too, a wet, nasty sound. He was white to the lips, and the lips themselves were blue. Still, he was conscious. His eyes had been fixed on Hickman throughout the conversation and followed him now as he left the cabin. When the door had closed behind Hickman, Stebbings relaxed a little, shifting his gaze to Jamie.

"Might've . . . saved yourself . . . the trouble," he wheezed. "But you have . . . my thanks. For what . . ." He gave a strangled cough, pressed a hand hard against his chest, and shook his head, grimacing. " . . . what they're worth," he managed.

He closed his eyes, breathing slowly and painfully—but still, breathing. I rose stiffly to my feet and at last had a moment to look at my husband.

"No but a wee cut," he assured me, in answer to my look of suspicious inquiry. "I'll do for now."

"Is all of that blood yours?" He glanced down at the shirt pasted to his ribs and lifted the non-wounded shoulder dismissively.

"I've enough left to be going on with." He smiled at me, then glanced around the deck. "I see ye've got matters well in hand here. I'll have Smith bring ye a bit of food, aye? It's going to rain soon."

It was; the smell of the oncoming storm swept through the hold, fresh and tingling with ozone, lifting the hair off my damp neck.

"Possibly not Smith," I said. "And where are you going?" I asked, seeing him turn away.

"I need to speak wi' Captain Hickman and Captain Roberts," he said, with a certain grimness. He glanced upward, and the matted hair behind his ears stirred in the breeze. "I dinna think we're going to Scotland in the *Teal,* but damned if I ken where we *are* going."

THE SHIP EVENTUALLY grew quiet—or as quiet as a large object composed of creaking boards, flapping canvas, and that eerie hum made by taut rigging can get. The tide had come in, and the ship did swim; we were moving north again, under light sail.

I had seen off the last of the casualties; only Captain Stebbings remained, laid on a crude pallet behind a chest of smuggled tea. He was still breathing, and not in terrible discomfort, I thought, but his condition was much too precarious for me to let him out of my sight.

By some miracle, the bullet seemed to have seared its way into his lung, rather than simply severing blood vessels in its wake. That didn't mean he wasn't bleeding into his lung, but if so, it was a slow seep; I would long since have known about it, otherwise. He must have been shot at close range, I thought sleepily. The ball had still been red-hot when it struck him.

I had sent Abram to bed. I should lie down myself, for tiredness dragged at my shoulders and had settled in aching lumps at the base of my spine. Not yet, though.

Jamie had not yet come back. I knew he would come to find me when he'd finished his summit meeting with Hickman and Roberts. And there were a few preparations still to be made, just in case.

In the course of Jamie's earlier rummaging through Hickman's desk in search of food, I'd noticed a bundle of fresh goose quills. I'd sent Abram to beg a couple of these and to bring me the largest sailmaker's needle to be found—and a couple of wing bones discarded from the chicken stew aboard the *Pitt.*

I chopped off the ends of a slender bone, looked to be sure the marrow had all been leached out by cooking, then shaped one end into a careful point, using the ship's carpenter's small sharpening stone for the purpose. The quill was easier; the tip had already been cut to a point for writing; all I had to do was to cut off the barbs, then submerge quill, bone, and needle in a shallow dish of brandy. That would do, then.

The smell of the brandy rose sweet and heavy in the air, competing with the tar, turpentine, tobacco, and the salt-soaked old timbers of the ship. It did at least partially obliterate the scents of blood and fecal matter left by my patients.

I'd discovered a case of bottled Meursault wine in the cargo, and now thoughtfully extracted a bottle, adding it to the half bottle of brandy and a stack of clean calico bandages and dressings. Sitting down on a keg of tar, I leaned back against a big hogshead of tobacco, yawning and wondering idly why it was called that. It did not appear to be shaped like a hog's head, certainly not like the head of any hog *I* knew.

I dismissed that thought and closed my eyes. I could feel my pulse throbbing in fingertips and eyelids. I didn't sleep, but I slowly descended into a sort of half consciousness, dimly aware of the sough of water past the ship's sides, the louder sigh of Stebbings's breath, the unhurried bellows of my own lungs, and the slow, placid thumping of my heart.

It seemed years since the terrors and uproar of the afternoon, and from the distance imposed by fatigue and intensity, my worry that I might have been having a heart attack seemed ridiculous. Was it, though? It wasn't impossible. Surely it had been nothing more than panic and hyperventilation—ridiculous in themselves, but not threatening. Still . . .

I put two fingers on my chest and waited for the pulsing in my fingertips to equalize with the pulsing of my heart. Slowly, almost dreaming, I began to pass through my body, from crown to toes, feeling my way through the long quiet passages of veins, the deep violet color of the sky just before night. Nearby I saw the brightness of arteries, wide and fierce with crimson life. Entered into the chambers of my heart and felt enclosed, the thick walls moving in a solid, comforting, unending, uninterrupted rhythm. No, no damage, not to the heart nor to its valves.

I felt my digestive tract, tightly knotted up under my diaphragm for hours, relax and settle with a grateful gurgle, and a sense of well-being flowed down like warm honey through limbs and spine.

"I dinna ken what ye're doing, Sassenach," a soft voice said nearby. "But ye look well content."

I opened my eyes and sat up. Jamie came down the ladder, moving carefully, and sat down.

He was very pale, and his shoulders were slumped with exhaustion. He smiled faintly at me, though, and his eyes were clear. My heart, solid and reliable as I just proved it to be, warmed and softened as though it had been made of butter.

"How do you—" I began, but he raised a hand, stopping me.

"I'll do," he said, with a glance at the pallet where the recumbent Stebbings lay, breathing shallowly and audibly. "Is he asleep?"

"I hope so. And you *should* be," I observed. "Let me tend you so you can lie down."

"It's no verra bad," he said, gingerly picking at the wad of crusty fabric tucked inside his shirt. "But it could use a stitch or two, I suppose."

"I suppose so, too," I said, eyeing the brown stains down the right side of his shirt. Given his customary inclination to understatement, he likely had a gaping slash down his breast. At least it would be easy to get at, unlike the awkward wound suffered by one of the *Pitt*'s sailors, who had somehow been struck just behind the scrotum by a pellet of grapeshot. I thought it must have struck something else first and bounced upward, for it luckily hadn't penetrated deeply, but was flattened as a sixpence when I got it out. I'd given it to him as a souvenir.

Abram had brought a can of fresh hot water just before he left. I put a finger into it and was pleased to find it still warm.

"Right," I said, with a nod at the bottles on the chest. "Do you want brandy, or wine, before we start?"

The corner of his mouth twitched, and he reached for the wine bottle.

"Let me keep the illusion of civilization for a wee bit longer."

"Oh, I think that's reasonably civilized stuff," I said. "I haven't a corkscrew, though."

He read the label, and his eyebrows rose.

"No matter. Is there something to pour it into?"

"Just here." I pulled a small, elegant wooden box out of a nest of straw inside a packing case and opened it triumphantly to display a Chinese porcelain tea set, gilt-edged and decorated with tiny red and blue turtles, all looking inscrutably Asiatic, swimming through a forest of gold chrysanthemums.

Jamie laughed—no more than a breath, but definitely laughter—and, scoring the neck of the bottle with the point of his dirk, knocked it neatly off against the rim of a tobacco hogshead. He poured the wine carefully into the two cups I'd set out, nodding at the vivid turtles.

"The wee blue one there reminds me of Mr. Willoughby, aye?"

I laughed myself, then glanced guiltily at Stebbings's feet—all that was showing of him at the moment. I'd taken his boots off, and the loose toes of his grimy stockings drooped comically over his feet. The feet didn't twitch, though, and the slow, labored breathing went on as before.

"I haven't thought of Mr. Willoughby in years," I observed, lifting my cup in toast. "Here's to absent friends."

Jamie replied briefly in Chinese and touched the rim of his own cup to mine with a faint *tink!*

"You remember how to speak Chinese?" I asked, intrigued, but he shook his head.

"No much. I havena had occasion to speak it since I last saw him." He breathed in the bouquet of the wine, closing his eyes. "That seems a verra long time ago."

"Long ago and far away." The wine smelled warmly of almonds and apples, and was dry but full-bodied, clinging richly to the palate. Jamaica, to be exact, and more than ten years ago. "Time flies when you're having fun. Do you think he's still alive—Mr. Willoughby?"

He considered that, sipping.

"Aye, I do. A man who escaped from a Chinese emperor and sailed halfway round the world to keep his balls is one wi' a good deal of determination."

He seemed disinclined to reminisce further about auld acquaintance, though, and I let him drink in silence, feeling the night settle comfortably around us with the gentle rise and fall of the ship. After his second cup of wine, I peeled his crusty shirt off and gingerly lifted the blood-caked wad of handkerchief that he'd used to stanch the wound.

Rather to my surprise, he was right: the wound was small, and wouldn't need more than two or three stitches to put right. A blade had gone in deep, just under his collarbone, and ripped a triangular flap of flesh coming out.

"Is this all your blood?" I asked, puzzled, lifting the discarded shirt.

"Nay, I've got a bit left," he said, eyes creasing at me over the teacup. "Not much, mind."

"You know quite well what I mean," I said severely.

"Aye, it's mine." He drained his cup and reached for the bottle.

"But from such a small . . . oh, dear God." I felt slightly faint. I could see the tender blue line of his subclavian vein, passing just under the collarbone and running directly above the clotted gape of the wound.

"Aye, I was surprised," he said casually, cradling the delicate china in both big hands. "When he jerked the blade out, the blood sprayed out like a fountain and soaked us both. I've never seen it do like that before."

"You have probably not had anyone nick your subclavian artery before," I said, with what attempt at calm I could muster. I cast a sideways glance at the wound. It *had* clotted; the edges of the flap had turned blue and the sliced flesh beneath was nearly black with dried blood. No oozing, let alone an arterial spray. The blade had thrust up from below, missing the vein and just piercing the artery behind it.

I took a long, deep breath, trying with no success whatever not to imagine what would have happened had the blade gone the barest fraction of an inch deeper, or what might have happened, had Jamie not had a handkerchief and the knowledge and opportunity to use pressure on the wound.

Belatedly, I realized what he'd said: "*The blood sprayed out like a fountain and soaked us both.*" And when I'd asked Stebbings whether it was his own blood soaking his shirt, he'd leered and said, "*Your husband's.*" I'd thought he was only being unpleasant, but—

"Was it Captain Stebbings who stabbed you?"

"Mmphm." He made a brief affirmative noise as he shifted his weight, leaning back to let me get at the wound. He drained the cup again and set it down, looking resigned. "I was surprised he managed it. I thought I'd dropped him, but he hit the floor and came up wi' a knife in his hand, the wee bugger."

"*You* shot him?"

He blinked at my tone of voice.

"Aye, of course."

I couldn't think of any bad words sufficient as to encompass the situation and, muttering "Jesus H. Roosevelt *Christ*!" under my breath, set about swabbing and suturing.

"Now, listen to me," I said, in my best military surgeon's voice. "So far as I can tell, it was a very small nick, and you managed to stop the bleeding long enough for a clot to form. But that clot is *all* that is keeping you from bleeding to death. Do you understand me?" This was not completely true—or it wouldn't be, once I'd stitched the supporting flesh back into place—but this was no time to give him a loophole.

He looked at me for a long moment, quite expressionless.

"I do."

"That means," I emphasized, stabbing the needle into his flesh with sufficient force that he yelped, "you must *not* use your right arm for at least the next forty-eight hours. You must not haul on ropes, you must not climb rigging, you must not punch people, you must not so much as scratch your arse with your right hand, do you hear me?"

"I expect the whole ship hears ye," he muttered, but glanced down his cheek, trying to see his collarbone. "I generally scratch my arse wi' my left hand, anyway."

Captain Stebbings had definitely heard us; a low chuckle came from behind the tea chest, followed by a rumbling cough and a faint wheeze of amusement.

"And," I continued, drawing the thread through the skin, "you may *not* get angry."

His breath drew in with a hiss.

"Why not?"

"Because it will make your heart beat harder, thus raising your blood pressure, which will—"

"Blow me up like a bottle of beer that's been corked too long?"

"Much the same. Now—"

Whatever I had been going to say vanished from my mind

in the next instant as Stebbings's breathing suddenly changed. I dropped the needle and, turning, seized the dish. I shoved the tea chest aside, putting the dish on it, and fell to my knees next to Stebbings's body.

His lips and eyelids were blue, and the rest of his face was the color of putty. He was making a horrid gasping noise, his mouth gaping wide, gulping air that wasn't helping.

There were luckily well-known bad words for *this* situation, and I used a few of them, swiftly turning back the blanket and digging my fingers into his pudgy side in search of ribs. He squirmed and emitted a high, ludicrous *heeheehee,* which made Jamie—the needle still swinging by its thread from his collarbone—give a nervous laugh in response.

"This is no time to be ticklish," I said crossly. "Jamie—take one of those quills and slide the needle inside." While he did this, I rapidly swabbed Stebbings's skin with a brandy-soaked wad of cloth, then took the quill-and-needle in one hand, the brandy bottle in the other, and drove the quill point-first into the second intercostal space, like hammering in a nail. I felt the subterranean *pop* as it went through the cartilage into the pleural space.

He made a high *eeeeee* sound at that, but it wasn't laughter. I'd cut the quill a little shorter than the needle, but the needle had sunk in when I'd hit it. I had a moment of panic, trying to get hold of the needle with my fingernails to pull it out, but finally managed. Stale-smelling blood and fluid sprayed out through the hollow quill, but only for a moment, then diminished to a faint hiss of air.

"Breathe slowly," I said more quietly. "*Both* of you."

I was watching the quill anxiously, looking for any further drainage of blood—plainly, if he was bleeding heavily into the lung, there was almost nothing I could do—but I was seeing only the light seepage from the puncture wound, a red smear on the outside of the quill.

"Sit down," I said to Jamie, who did, ending cross-legged on the floor beside me.

Stebbings was looking better; the lung had at least partially inflated, and he was white now, his lips pale, but pale pink. The hissing from the hollow quill died to a sigh, and I put my finger over the open end of it.

"Ideally," I said in a conversational tone, "I'd be able to run a length of tubing from your chest into a jar of water. That way the air around your lung could escape, but air couldn't get back in. As I haven't got anything tubelike that's longer than a few inches, that's not going to work." I rose up on my knees, motioning to Jamie.

"Come here and put your finger over the end of this quill. If he starts suffocating again, take it off for a moment, until the air stops hissing out."

He couldn't conveniently reach Stebbings with his left hand; with a sidelong glance at me, he reached slowly out with his right and stoppered the quill with his thumb.

I got to my feet, groaning, and went to rummage the cargo again. It might have to be tar. I'd tacked the oiled patch to his chest on three sides with warm tar, and there was plenty left. Not ideal; I likely couldn't get it out again in a hurry. Would a small plug of wet fabric be better?

In one of Hannah Arnold's chests, though, I found treasure: a small collection of dried herbs in jars—including one of powdered gum arabic. The herbs were interesting and useful in themselves, being plainly imported: cinchona bark—I must try to send that back to North Carolina for Lizzie, if we ever got off this horrible tub—mandrake, and ginger, things that never grew in the Colonies. Having them to hand made me feel suddenly rich. Stebbings groaned behind me, and I heard the scuff of fabric and a soft hiss as Jamie took his thumb away for a moment.

Not even the riches of the fabled East would do Stebbings much good. I opened the jar of gum arabic and, scooping out a bit into the palm of my hand, dribbled water into it and set about fashioning the resultant gooey ball into a roughly cylindrical plug, which I wrapped in a scrap of yellow calico printed with honeybees, finishing it off with a neat twist at the top. This accomplished to my satisfaction, I came back and, without comment, pulled the hollow quill—already showing signs of cracking from the working of Stebbings's rib muscles—out of its hole and wriggled the sturdier—and larger—hollow chicken bone into its place.

He didn't laugh this time, either. I plugged the end of the bone neatly and, kneeling in front of Jamie, resumed my stitching on his collarbone.

I felt perfectly clearheaded—but in that oddly surreal way

that is an indication of total exhaustion. I'd done what had to be done, but I knew I couldn't stay upright much longer.

"What does Captain Hickman have to say?" I asked, much more by way of distracting both of us than because I really wanted to know.

"A great number of things, as ye might imagine." He took a deep breath and fixed his eyes on a huge turtle shell that had been wedged in among the boxes. "Discarding the purely personal opinions and a certain amount of excessive language, though . . . we're bound up the Hudson. For Fort Ticonderoga."

"We . . . what?" I frowned at the needle pushed halfway through the skin. "Why?"

His hands were braced on the deck, fingers pressing into the boards so hard the nails were white.

"That's where he was bound when the complications occurred, and that's where he means to go. He's a gentleman of verra fixed views, I find."

A loud snort came from behind the tea chest.

"I did notice something of the sort." I tied the last suture and clipped the thread neatly with my knife. "Did you say something, Captain Stebbings?"

The snort was repeated, more loudly, but without emendation.

"Can't he be convinced to put us ashore?"

Jamie's fingers hovered over the fresh stitching, obviously wanting to rub the stinging site, but I pushed them away.

"Aye, well . . . there are further complications, Sassenach."

"Do tell," I murmured, standing up and stretching. "Oh, God, my back. What *sort* of complications? Do you want some tea?"

"Only if there's a good deal of whisky in it." He leaned his head back against the bulkhead, closing his eyes. There was a hint of color in his cheeks, though his forehead shone with sweat.

"Brandy do you?" I needed tea—minus alcohol—badly myself, and headed for the ladder, not waiting for his nod. I saw him reach for the wine bottle as I set foot on the lowest rung.

There was a brisk wind blowing up above; it swirled the long cloak out around me as I emerged from the depths, and whooshed up my petticoats in a most revivifying fashion. It revivified Mr. Smith—or, rather, Mr. Marsden—too, who blinked and looked hastily away.

"Evening, ma'am," he said politely, when I'd got my assorted garments back under control. "The colonel doing well, I hope?"

"Yes, he's—" I broke off and gave him a sharp look. "The colonel?" I had a slight sinking sensation.

"Yes'm. He's a militia colonel, isn't he?"

"He *was,*" I said with emphasis.

Smith's face broke into a smile.

"No *was* about it, ma'am," he said. "He's done us the honor to take command of a company—Fraser's Irregulars, we're to be called."

"How apt," I said. "What the devil—how did this happen?"

He tugged nervously at one of his earrings, seeing that I perhaps wasn't as pleased by the news as might be hoped.

"Ah. Well, to tell the truth, ma'am, I'm afraid it was my fault." He ducked his head, abashed. "One of the hands aboard the *Pitt* recognized me, and when he told the captain who I was . . ."

The revelation of Mr. Marsden's real name—in combination with his adornments—had caused considerable uproar among the motley crew presently on board the *Asp.* Sufficiently so that he had been in some danger of being thrown overboard or set adrift in a boat. After a certain amount of acrimonious discussion, Jamie had suggested that perhaps Mr. Marsden could be persuaded to change his profession and become a soldier—for a number of the hands aboard the *Asp* had already proposed to leave her and join the Continental forces at Ticonderoga, portaging the goods and weapons across to Lake Champlain and then remaining as militia volunteers.

This found general approbation—though a few disgruntled persons were still heard to mutter that a Jonah was a Jonah, didn't matter if he was a sailor or not. "That being why I thought I best make myself scarce below, if you see what I mean, ma'am," Mr. Marsden concluded.

It also solved the problem of what to do with the imprisoned hands from the *Pitt* and the displaced seamen from the

Teal; those who preferred joining the American militia would be allowed to do so, while those British seamen who preferred the prospect of life as prisoners of war could be accommodated in this desire at Fort Ticonderoga. About half the men from the *Teal* had expressed a decided preference for employment on land, after their recent seagoing adventures, and they also would join the Irregulars.

"I see," I said, rubbing two fingers between my brows. "Well, if you'll excuse me, Mr. . . . Marsden, I must be going and making a cup of tea. With a lot of brandy in it."

THE TEA HEARTENED me, sufficiently to send Abram—found drowsing by the galley fire in spite of having been ordered to bed—to take some to Jamie and Captain Stebbings while I made the rounds of my other patients. They were mostly as comfortable as might be expected—that is, not very, but stoic about it, and in no need of exigent medical intervention.

The temporary strength lent me by tea and brandy had mostly ebbed by the time I made my way back down the ladder into the hold, though, and my foot slipped off the final rung, causing me to drop heavily onto the deck, with a thump that elicited a startled cry from Stebbings, followed by a groan. Waving away Jamie's raised brow, I hurried over to check the patient.

He was very hot to the touch, his full face flushed, and a nearly full cup of tea lay discarded near him.

"I tried to make him drink, but he said he couldna swallow more than a mouthful." Jamie had followed me, and spoke softly behind me.

I bent and placed my ear near Stebbings's chest, auscultating as best I could through the layer of blubber covering it. The chicken-bone tube, momentarily unplugged, gave only a modest hiss of air and no more than a trace of blood.

"So far as I can tell, the lung's expanded at least partially," I said, addressing Stebbings for form's sake, though he merely stared at me, glassy-eyed. "And I think the bullet must have cauterized a good deal of the damage; otherwise, I think we'd be seeing much more alarming symptoms." Otherwise, he'd be dead by now, but I thought it more tactful not to say so. He might easily be dead soon, in any case, from fever, but I didn't say that, either.

I persuaded him to drink some water and sponged his head and torso with more of it. The hatch cover had been left off, and it was reasonably cool in the hold, though the air didn't move much down below. Still, I saw no benefit in taking him into the wind on deck, and the less he was moved, the better.

"Is that . . . my . . . cloak?" he asked suddenly, opening one eye.

"Er . . . probably," I replied, disconcerted. "Do you want it back?"

He made a brief grimace and shook his head, then lay back, eyes closed, breathing shallowly.

Jamie was propped against the tea chest, head back, eyes closed, and breathing heavily. Feeling me sit down beside him, though, he raised his head and opened his eyes.

"Ye look as though ye're about to fall over, Sassenach," he said softly. "Lie down, aye? I'll mind the captain."

I saw his point. In fact, I saw two of them—and him. I blinked and shook my head, momentarily reuniting the two Jamies, but there was no denying that he was right. I'd lost touch with my body again, but my mind, instead of sticking to the job, had simply wandered off somewhere in a daze. I rubbed my hands hard over my face, but it didn't help appreciably.

"I'll have to sleep," I explained to the men, all four of them now watching me with the perfect wide-eyed attention of barn owls. "If you feel the pressure building up again—and I think it will," I said to Stebbings, "pull the plug out of the tube until it eases, then put it back. If either of you think you're dying, wake me up."

With no further ado, and feeling as though I were watching myself doing it, I eased down onto the planking, put my head on a fold of Stebbings's cloak, and fell asleep.

I WOKE an unaccountable time later and lay for some minutes lacking coherent thought, my mind rising and falling with the movement of the deck beneath me. At some point, I began to distinguish the murmur of men's voices from the shush and bang of seagoing noises.

I had fallen so deeply into oblivion that the events prior to my falling asleep took a moment to recall, but the voices brought them back. Wounds, the reek of brandy, the rip of sailcloth tearing, rough in my hands, and the smell of the dye in the bright, wet calico. Jamie's bloody shirt. The sucking sound of the hole in Stebbings's chest. The memory of that would have brought me upright at once, but I had stiffened from lying on the boards. A sharp twinge of agony lanced from my right knee to my groin, and the muscles of my back and arms hurt amazingly. Before I could stretch them enough to struggle to my feet, I heard the captain's voice.

"Call Hickman." Stebbings's voice was hoarse and low, but definite. "I'd rather be shot than do this anymore."

I didn't think he was joking. Neither did Jamie.

"I dinna blame ye," he said. His voice was soft but serious, as definite as Stebbings's.

My eyes were beginning to focus again, as the paralyzing ache in my muscles eased a little. From where I lay, I could see Stebbings from the knees down and most of Jamie, sitting beside him, head bowed on his own knees, tall form slumped against the tea chest.

There was a pause, and then Stebbings said, "You don't, eh? Good. Go get Hickman."

"Why?" Jamie asked, after what seemed an equal pause for thought—or perhaps only to gather strength to answer. He didn't lift his head; he sounded almost drugged with fatigue. "Nay need to rouse the man from his bed, is there? If ye want to die, just pull that thing out of your chest."

Stebbings made some sort of noise. It might have started as a laugh, a groan, or an angry retort, but ended in a hiss of air between clenched teeth. My body tensed. Had he actually tried to pull it out?

No. I heard the heavy movement of his body, saw his feet curl briefly as he sought a more comfortable position, and heard Jamie's grunt as he leaned over to help.

"Someone . . . might as well get . . . satisfaction from me . . . dying," he wheezed.

"I put yon hole in ye," Jamie pointed out. He straightened up and stretched with painful care. "It wouldna please me overmuch to watch ye die from it." I thought he must be well past the point of exhaustion, and plainly he was as stiff as I was. I must get up, make him go lie down. But he was still talking to Stebbings, sounding unconcerned, like a man discussing an abstruse point of natural philosophy.

"As for satisfying Captain Hickman—d'ye feel some sense of obligation toward him?"

"I don't." That one came out short and sharp, though succeeded by a deep gasp for air.

"It's a clean death," Stebbings managed after a few more breaths. "Quick."

"Aye, that's what I thought," Jamie said, sounding drowsy. "When it was me."

Stebbings gave a grunt that might have been interrogative. Jamie sighed. After a moment, I heard the rustle of cloth and saw him move his left leg, groaning as he did so, and turn back the cloth of his kilt.

"See that?" His finger ran slowly up the length of his thigh, from just above the knee, almost to the groin.

Stebbings gave a slightly more interested grunt, this one definitely questioning. The drooping toes of his socks moved as his feet twitched.

"Bayonet," Jamie said, casually flipping his kilt back over the twisting, runneled scar. "I lay for two days after, wi' the fever eating me alive. My leg swelled, and it stank. And when the English officer came to blow our brains out, I was pleased enough."

A brief silence.

"Culloden?" Stebbings asked. His voice was still hoarse, and I could hear the fever in it, but there was interest there now, too. "Heard . . . about it."

Jamie said nothing in response but yawned suddenly, not bothering to smother it, and rubbed his hands slowly over his face. I could hear the soft rasp of beard stubble.

Silence, but the quality of it had changed. I could feel Stebbings's anger, his pain and fright—but there was a faint sense of amusement in his labored breath.

"Going to . . . make me . . . ask?"

Jamie shook his head.

"Too long a story, and one I dinna care to tell. Leave it that

I wanted him to shoot me, verra badly, and the bastard wouldna do it."

The air in the little hold was stale but uneasy, filled with the shifting scents of blood and luxury, of industry and illness. I breathed in, gently, deep, and could smell the tang of the men's bodies, a sharp copper savage smell, bitter with effort and exhaustion. Women never smelled like that, I thought, even in extremity.

"Revenge, then, is it?" Stebbings asked after a bit. His restless feet had stilled. His dirty stockings drooped and his voice was tired.

Jamie's shoulders moved, slowly, as he sighed, and his own voice was nearly as tired as Stebbings's.

"No," he said, very softly. "Call it payment of a debt."

A debt? I thought. To whom? To the Lord Melton who had declined to kill him, out of honor, who had instead sent him home from Culloden, hidden in a wagon filled with hay? To his sister, who had refused to let him die, who had dragged him back to life by sheer strength of will? Or to those who had died when he had not?

I had stretched myself enough now to be able to rise, but didn't, yet. There was no urgency. The men were silent, their breathing part of the breathing of the ship, the sigh of the sea outside.

It came to me, quiet but sure, that I knew. I had glimpsed the abyss often, over someone's shoulder as they stood on the edge, looking down. But I had looked once, too. I knew the vastness and the lure of it, the offer of surcease.

I knew they were standing now, side by side and each alone, looking down.

Part Four

Conjunction

32

A FLURRY OF SUSPICION

Lord John Grey to Mr. Arthur Norrington
4 February 1777
(Cipher 158)

My dear Norrington,

Pursuant to our conversation, I have made certain discoveries which I think it prudent to confide.

I paid a visit to France at the end of the year and, while there, visited the Baron Amandine. I stayed with the baron for several days, in fact, and had conversation of him on a number of occasions. I have reason to believe that Beauchamp is indeed concerned in the matter we discussed and has formed an attachment to Beaumarchais, who is thus likely similarly involved. I think Amandine is not himself concerned but that Beauchamp may use him as a front of some kind.

I requested an audience with Beaumarchais, but was denied. As he would normally have received me, I think I have poked a stick into some nest. It would be useful to watch that quarter.

Be also alert to any mention in the French correspondence of a company called Rodrigue Hortalez et Cie *(I beg you will speak with the person handling the Spanish correspondence, as well). I cannot discover anything amiss, but neither can I discover anything solid regarding them, such as the names of the directors, and that in itself strikes me as suspicious.*

If your duty allow, I should be pleased to hear of anything you learn concerning these matters.

Your servant, sir,
Lord John Grey

Postscriptum: If you can tell me, who is presently in charge of the American Department, with regard to correspondence?

Lord John Grey to Harold, Duke of Pardloe
4 February 1777
(family cipher)

Hal—

I saw Amandine. Wainwright does live at the manor house—a place called Trois Flèches*—and does maintain an unwholesome relationship with the baron. I met the baron's sister, Wainwright's wife. She certainly knows of the link between her brother and her husband, but does not admit it openly. Beyond that, she appears to know nothing whatever. I have seldom met a more stupid woman. She is openly lewd in manner and a very bad cardplayer. So is the baron, by which token I am convinced that he* does *know something of Wainwright's political machinations; he behaved shiftily when I steered the conversation in that direction, and I am sure he is not schooled in the art of misdirection. He is not stupid, though. Even if he were, he will certainly have told Wainwright of my visit. I have alerted Norrington to watch for any activity on that front.*

Knowing what I do of Wainwright's abilities and connexions (or rather, the lack of them), I cannot quite fathom his involvement. Granted, if the French government does have such schemes in mind as he indicated, they would hardly make open communication regarding them, and sending someone like Wainwright to speak to someone like me might be considered sufficiently sub rosa. *Certainly such an approach has the benefit of being deniable. And yet something seems wrong in this, in a way I cannot yet define.*

I will be with you soon, and hope by then to be in possession of some definite information regarding one Captain Ezekiel Richardson, likewise one Captain Denys Randall-Isaacs. Should you be able to investigate either of these names through your own connexions, you would greatly oblige

Your most affectionate brother,
John

Postscriptum: I trust your health is mending.

Harold, Duke of Pardloe, to Lord John Grey
6 March 1777
Bath
(family cipher)

I'm not dead. Wish I were. Bath is vile. I am daily wrapped in canvas and carried off like a parcel to be sunk in boiling water that smells of rotten eggs, then hauled out and forced to drink *it, but Minnie says she will divorce me by petition in the House of Lords on the grounds of insanity caused by immoral acts if I don't submit. I doubt this, but here I am.*

Denys Randall-Isaacs is the son of a Englishwoman named Mary Hawkins and a British army officer: one Jonathan Wolverton Randall, captain of dragoons, deceased, killed at Culloden. The mother is still alive and married to a Jew named Robert Isaacs, a merchant in Bristol. He's still alive, too, and has a half interest in a warehouse in Brest. Denys is one of your damned politicals, got ties to

Germain, but I can't find out more than that without being too overt for your tastes. Can't find out anything in bloody Bath.

Don't know much about Richardson, but will find out directly. Sent letters to some people in America. Yes, I am discreet, thank you, and so are they.

John Burgoyne is here, taking the cure. Very cock-a-hoop, as Germain has approved his scheme to invade from Canada. I have mentioned William to him, as his French and German are good and Burgoyne is to have a number of Brunswickers. Still, tell Willie to be careful; Burgoyne seems to think he is to be commander-in-chief of the army in America—a notion that I daresay will come as rather a surprise both to Guy Carleton and Dick Howe.

Trois Flèches. *Three arrows. Who is the third?*

London
March 26, 1777
The Society for the Appreciation of the English Beefsteak, a Gentleman's Club

"WHO IS the third?" Grey repeated in astonishment, staring at the note he had just opened.

"The third what?" Harry Quarry handed his sopping cloak to the steward and sank heavily into the chair beside Grey's, sighing with relief as he held his hands out to the fire. "God's teeth, I'm frozen solid. You're going to Southampton in *this*?" He flung one big cold-blanched hand at the window, which framed a dismal prospect of icy sleet, driven almost horizontal by the wind.

"Not 'til tomorrow. It may have cleared by then."

Harry gave the window a look of deep suspicion and shook his head. "Not a chance. Steward!"

Mr. Bodley was already tottering toward them under the weight of a tea tray laden with seedcake, sponge cake, strawberry jam, marmalade, hot buttered crumpets in a basket wrapped in white linen, scones, clotted cream, almond biscuits, sardines on toast, a pot of beans baked with bacon and onion, a plate of sliced ham with gherkins, a bottle of brandy with two glasses, and—perhaps as an afterthought—a steaming teapot with two china cups and saucers alongside.

"Ah!" said Harry, looking happier. "I see you expected me."

Grey smiled. If not on campaign or called away by duty, Harry Quarry invariably entered the Beefsteak at four-thirty on a Wednesday.

"I thought you'd need sustenance, with Hal on the sick list." Harry was one of the two regimental colonels—as distinct from Hal, who was Colonel of the Regiment, it being his own regiment. Not all colonels took an active hand in the operations of their regiments, but Hal did.

"Malingering bugger," Harry said, reaching for the brandy. "How is he?"

"Quite his usual self, to judge from his correspondence." Grey handed Quarry the unfolded letter, which the latter read with a burgeoning grin.

"Aye, Minnie will have him sorted like a hand of whist." He put down the letter, nodding at it as he raised his glass. "Who's Richardson and why do you want to know about him?"

"Ezekiel Richardson, Captain. Lancers, but detached for intelligence work."

"Oh, intelligence laddie, eh? One of your Black Chamber lot?" Quarry wrinkled his nose, though it was not clear whether this was a response to the notion of intelligence laddies or the presence of a dish of grated horseradish accompanying the sardines.

"No, I don't know the man well personally," Grey admitted, and felt the same pang of deep unease that had been afflicting him with increased frequency ever since his receipt of William's letter from Quebec a week before. "I had been introduced to him by Sir George, who knew his father, but we didn't talk much on that occasion. I had heard a few things to his credit—in a quiet sort of way—"

"That being, I suppose, the only way one wants to hear anything about a man in that line of business. Huuuuuh!" Harry drew a tremendous gasp of air through his open mouth and up into his sinuses, by the sound of it, then coughed once or twice, eyes watering, and shook his head in admiration.

"Fresh horseradish," he croaked, taking another large spoonful. "Very . . . huuuuuuh . . . fresh."

"Quite. Anyway, I met him again in North Carolina, we talked a bit more, and he asked my permission to approach William with a proposition regarding intelligencing."

Quarry stopped, a slice of sardine-laden toast halfway to his mouth.

"You don't mean to say you've let him lure Willie off into the weeds?"

"That was certainly not my intent," Grey said, nettled. "I had some reason to feel that the suggestion would be good for Willie; for one thing, it would get him out of North Carolina and end with him attached to Howe's staff."

Quarry nodded, masticating with care, and swallowed thickly.

"Aye, right. But now you have doubts?"

"I do. The more so because I can find very few people who actually know Richardson well. Everyone who recommended him to me in the first place did so by reason of someone else's recommendation, it seems. Except for Sir George Stanley, who is presently in Spain with my mother, and old Nigel Bruce, who's rather inconveniently died in the meantime."

"Thoughtless."

"Yes. I imagine I could root out more information, had I time, but I haven't. Dottie and I sail day after tomorrow. Weather permitting," he added, with a glance at the window.

"Ah, this would be where I come in," Harry observed, without animus. "What shall I do with any information I find? Tell Hal, or send it to you?"

"Tell Hal," Grey said with a sigh. "God knows what the post may be like in America, even with the Congress sitting in Philadelphia. If anything seems urgent, Hal can expedite matters here far more easily than I can there."

Quarry nodded and refilled Grey's glass. "You're not eating," he observed.

"I lunched late." Quite late. In fact, he hadn't had luncheon yet. He took a scone and spread it desultorily with jam.

"And Denys Wossname?" Quarry asked, flicking the letter with a pickle fork. "Shall I inquire about him, too?"

"By all means. Though I may make better progress with him on the American end of the matter. That's at least where he was last seen." He took a bite of scone, observing that it had achieved that delicate balance between crumbliness and half-set mortar that is the ideal of every scone, and felt some stirrings of appetite return. He wondered whether he should put Harry onto the worthy Jew with the warehouse in Brest, but decided not. The question of French connections was more than delicate, and while Harry was thorough, he was not subtle.

"Right, then." Harry selected a slice of sponge cake, topped it with two almond biscuits and a dollop of clotted cream, and inserted the whole into his mouth. Where did he put it? Grey wondered. Harry was thickset and burly, but never stout. No doubt he sweated it off during energetic exercise in brothels, that being his favorite sport despite advancing age.

How old was Harry? he wondered suddenly. A few years older than Grey, a few years younger than Hal. He'd never thought about it, no more than he had with reference to Hal. The two of them had always seemed immortal; he had never once contemplated a future lacking either one of them. But the skull beneath Harry's wig was nearly hairless now—he had, in his usual way, removed it to scratch his head at some point and set it casually back without regard to straightness—and the joints of his fingers were swollen, though he handled his teacup with his usual delicacy.

Grey felt of a sudden his own mortality, in the stiffening of a thumb, the twinge of a knee. Most of all, in the fear that he might not be there to protect William, while he was still needed.

"Eh?" said Harry, raising a brow at whatever showed on Grey's face. "What?"

Grey smiled and shook his head, taking up his brandy glass once more.

"*Timor mortis conturbat me,*" he said.

"Ah," said Quarry thoughtfully, and raised his own. "I'll drink to that."

33

THE PLOT THICKENS

28 February, A.D. 1777
London

Major General John Burgoyne,
to Sir George Germain
. . . I do not conceive any expedition from the sea can be so formidable to the enemy, or so effectual to close the war, as an invasion from Canada by Ticonderoga.

April 4, 1777
on board HMS Tartar

HE'D TOLD Dottie that the *Tartar* was only a twenty-eight-gun frigate and that she must therefore be modest in her packing. Even so, he was surprised to see the single trunk—granted, a large one—two portmanteaux, and a bag of needlework that comprised her entire luggage.

"What, not a single flowered mantua?" he teased. "William won't know you."

"Bosh," she replied with her father's talent for succinct clarity. But she smiled a little—she was very pale, and he hoped it wasn't incipient seasickness—and he squeezed her hand and went on holding it all the time until the last dark sliver of England sank into the sea.

He was still amazed that she'd managed it. Hal must be more frail than he'd let on, to be bamboozled into allowing his daughter to take ship for America, even under Grey's protection and for the laudable purpose of nursing her wounded brother. Minnie, of course, would not be parted from Hal for a moment, though naturally worried sick for her son. But that she had uttered no word of protest at this adventure . . .

"Your mother's in on it, is she?" he asked casually, provoking a startled look through a veil of windblown hair.

"On what?" Dottie pawed at the blond spiderweb of her hair, escaped *en masse* from the inconsequent snood in which she'd bound it and dancing over her head like flames. "Oh, help!"

He captured her hair, smoothing it tight to her head with both hands, then gathering it at her neck, where he plaited it expertly, to the admiration of a passing seaman, clubbed it, and tied it up with the velvet ribbon that was all that remained from the wreck of her snood.

"On what, forsooth," he told the back of her head, as he finished the job. "On whatever the dreadful enterprise is on which you've embarked."

She turned round and faced him, her stare direct.

"If you want to describe rescuing Henry as a dreadful enterprise, I agree entirely," she said with dignity. "But my mother would naturally do anything she could to get him back. So would you, presumably, or you wouldn't be here." And without waiting for a reply, she turned smartly on her heel and made for the companionway, leaving him speechless.

One of the first ships of the spring had brought a letter with further word of Henry. He was still alive, thank God, but had been badly wounded: shot in the abdomen, and very ill in consequence through the brutal winter. He had survived, though, and been moved to Philadelphia with a number of other British prisoners. The letter had been written by a fellow officer there, another prisoner, but Henry had managed to scribble a few words of love to his family at the bottom and sign his name; the memory of that straggling scrawl ate at John's heart.

He was encouraged somewhat by the fact that it *was* Philadelphia, though. He had met a prominent Philadelphian while he was in France and had formed an immediate liking for him that he thought was returned; there might be something of use in the acquaintance. He grinned involuntarily, recalling the instant of his meeting with the American gentleman.

He hadn't paused long in Paris, only long enough to make inquiries after Percival Beauchamp, who was not there. Retired to his home in the country for the winter, he was told. The Beauchamp family's main estate, a place called *Trois Flèches,* near Compiègne. And so he had bought a fur-lined hat and a pair of seaboots, wrapped himself in his warmest cloak, hired a horse, and set grimly off into the teeth of a howling gale.

Arriving mud-caked and frozen, he had been greeted with suspicion, but the quality of his accoutrements and his title had gained him entrance, and he had been shown to a well-appointed parlor—with, thank God, an excellent fire—to await the baron's pleasure.

He'd formed an expectation of the Baron Amandine on the basis of Percy's remarks, though he thought Percy had likely been practicing upon him. He also knew how futile it was to theorize in advance of observation, but it was inhuman not to imagine.

In terms of imagining, he'd done a good job of not thinking of Percy during the last . . . was it eighteen years, nineteen? But once it became obvious that thinking of him was now a professional as well as a personal necessity, he was both surprised and disconcerted to find just how much he remembered. He knew what Percy liked and therefore had evolved a mental picture of Amandine in accordance.

The reality was different. The baron was an older man, perhaps a few years Grey's senior, short and rather plump, with an open, pleasant face. Well dressed, but without ostentation. He greeted Grey with great courtesy. But then he took Grey's hand, and a small electric shock ran through the Englishman. The baron's expression was civil, no more—but the eyes held a look of interest and avidity, and despite the baron's unprepossessing appearance, Grey's flesh answered the look.

Of course. Percy had told Amandine about him.

Surprised and wary, he gave the brief explanation he had prepared, only to be informed that, *hélas,* Monsieur Beauchamp was not at home but had gone with Monsieur Beaumarchais to hunt wolves in Alsace. Well, there was one supposition confirmed, Grey thought. But surely his lordship would condescend to accept the hospitality of *Trois Flèches,* for the night at least?

He accepted this invitation with many expressions of unworthy thanks, and having doffed his outer clothes and replaced his seaboots with Dottie's garish carpet slippers—which made Amandine blink, though he at once praised them exceedingly—he was propelled down a long corridor lined with portraits.

"We will take some refreshment in the library," Amandine was saying. "Plainly, you are perishing of cold and inanition. But if you do not mind, allow me to introduce you *en route* to my other guest; we will invite him to join us."

Grey had murmured acquiescence, distracted by the light pressure of Amandine's hand, which rested on his back—slightly lower than was usual.

"He is an American," the baron was saying, as they reached a door toward the end of the corridor, and his voice conveyed considerable in the way of amusement in that word. He had a most unusual voice—soft, warm, and somehow smoky, like oolong tea with a lot of sugar.

"He enjoys to spend some time each day in the solar," the baron went on, pushing open the door and gesturing Grey ahead of him. "He says it keeps him in a state of robust health."

Grey had been looking politely at the baron during this introduction, but now turned to speak to the American guest and so was introduced to Dr. Franklin, reclining comfortably in a padded chair, lit by a flood of sunlight, stark naked.

In the subsequent conversation—conducted with the greatest aplomb on the part of all parties—he learned that it was Dr. Franklin's invariant practice to bathe in air every day when possible, as skin breathed quite as much as did lungs, taking in air and releasing impurities; thus the ability of the body to defend itself from infection was substantially impaired if the skin were constantly suffocated in insanitary clothing.

Throughout the introductions and conversation, Grey was acutely aware of Amandine's eyes upon him, full of speculation and amusement, and of the cumbersome feel of his own insanitary clothing upon his doubtless suffocating skin.

It was an odd feeling, to meet a stranger and know that said stranger was already privy to his deepest secret, that he in fact—if Percy were not altogether lying, and Grey didn't think he had been—shared it. It gave him a feeling of danger and vertigo, as though he leaned out from some sharp precipice. It also bloody excited him, and *that* alarmed him very much.

The American (now speaking pleasantly about an unusual geological formation he had seen on his journey from Paris; had his lordship noticed it?) was an elderly man, and his body, while in fair condition aside from patches of some purplish eczema about the lower limbs, was not an object of sexual consideration. Nonetheless, Grey's flesh was tight on his bones, and not enough of his blood was in his head. He could feel Amandine's eyes on him, frankly evaluating him, and recalled all too clearly the exchange with Percy regarding Percy's wife and his brother-in-law the baron: *Both, on occasion. Together?* Had the baron's sister accompanied her husband, or was she perhaps at home? For one of the few times in his life, Grey wondered seriously whether he might be a pervert.

"Shall we join the good doctor in his beneficial practice, my lord?"

Grey jerked his eyes away from Franklin, to see the baron beginning to peel off his coat. Fortunately, before he could think of anything to say, Franklin rose, remarking that he felt he had had sufficient benefit for the day. "Though of course," he said, meeting Grey's eyes directly, with an expression of the deepest interest—and not a little amusement, too, "you must not allow my departure to prevent your own indulgence, *messieurs.*"

The baron, impeccably polite, at once resumed his coat, and saying he would join them for *un apéritif* in the library, disappeared into the corridor.

Franklin had a silk dressing gown; Grey held it for him, watching the white, slightly sagging—but remarkably firm and unwrinkled—buttocks disappear as the American slowly worked his arms into the sleeves, remarking as he did so upon a touch of arthritis in his shoulder joints.

Turning and tying the sash, he fixed an open gray gaze upon Grey.

"Thank you, my lord," he said. "I take it you were not previously acquainted with Amandine?"

"No. I knew his . . . brother-in-law, Monsieur Beauchamp, some years ago. In England," he added, for no particular reason.

Something flickered in Franklin's eyes at the name "Beauchamp," causing Grey to ask, "You know him?"

"I know the name," Franklin replied equably. "Is Beauchamp an Englishman, then?"

A number of astonishing possibilities had flashed through Grey's mind at that simple remark "*I know the name,*" but an equally rapid evaluation of them decided him upon the truth as safest, and he merely said, "Yes," in a tone indicating that this was simple fact, no more.

Over the next few days, he and Franklin had had a number of interesting conversations, in which the name of Percy Beauchamp was conspicuous by its absence. When Franklin returned to Paris, though, Grey was left both with a genuine liking for the elderly gentleman—who upon learning that Grey was bound for the Colonies in the spring had insisted upon giving him letters of introduction to several friends there—and a conviction that Dr. Franklin knew precisely what Percy Beauchamp was and had been.

"Beg pardon, sir," said one of the *Tartar*'s hands, elbowing Grey ungently out of the way and breaking his reverie. He blinked, coming back to find that his ungloved hands had turned to ice in the wind and his cheeks were numb. Leaving the sailors to their freezing task, he went below, feeling a peculiar small and shameful warmth at the memory of his visit to *Trois Flèches*.

3 May, 1777
New York

Dear Papa,

I have just received your Letter about Cousin Henry, and hope very much that you will be able to discover his Whereabouts and obtain his Release. If I can hear Anything of him, I will do my best to let you know. Is there anyone to whom I should address

Letters to you in the Colonies? (If I hear of no Alternative, I shall send them in care of Mr. Sanders in Philadelphia, with a Copy for Safety to Judge O'Keefe in Richmond.)

I hope you will excuse my own sad Delinquency in corresponding. It does not—alas—stem from any press of urgent Activity on my Part, but rather from ennui *and lack of anything of Interest about which to write. After a tedious Winter immured in Quebec (though I did considerable Hunting, and shot a very vicious Thing called a Glutton), I finally received my new orders from General Howe's Aide-de-camp in late March, when some of Sir Guy's people came back to the Citadel, and I returned to New York in consequence of them.*

I never received any Word from Captain Randall-Isaacs, nor have I been able to hear anything of him since my Return. I fear very much that he may have been lost in the Blizzard. If you know his people, perhaps you would send them a Note with my Hopes for his Survival? I would do so myself, save that I am not sure where to find them, nor how to phrase my Sentiments delicately, in case they are also in Doubt of his Fate, or worse, are not in Doubt. You will know what to say, though; you always do.

I was somewhat luckier in my own Travels, having suffered only minor Shipwreck on my way downriver (we came to Grief during the Portage at Ticonderoga, being fired upon by a Party of American Sharp-shooters from the Fort. No one was harmed, but the Canoes were peppered with Shot and some Holes were unfortunately not discovered before we put back into the Water, whereupon two of them sank abruptly), this followed by waist-deep Mud and the reemergence of carnivorous Insects when I took to the Roads. Since my Return, though, we have done little of interest, though there are constant rumors of what we may *do. Finding that Inactivity chafes more in what you may call a civilized Setting (though none of the Girls in New York can dance at all), I volunteered to ride Dispatches, and have found some Relief in that.*

Yesterday, however, I received Orders sending me back to Canada, there to join General Burgoyne's Staff. Do I detect your fine Italian Hand in this, Papa? If so, thank you!

Also, I have seen Captain Richardson again; he came to my Rooms last Night. I had not seen him for nearly a Year, and was much surprised. He did not ask for an Account of our Journey into Quebec (not surprising, as the Information would be sadly out-of-date by now), and when I asked after Randall-Isaacs, only shook his Head and said he did not know.

He had heard I had an Errand to carry special Dispatches to Virginia, before going to Canada, and while of course Nothing must delay me in that Errand, had thought of asking me to do a small Service for him as I returned northward. Somewhat wary as a Result of my long Sojourn in the frozen North, I asked what this might be, and was told that it was no more than the Delivery of a cipher Message to a group of Loyalist gentlemen in Virginia, something that would be simple for me, owing to my Familiarity with the Terrain; the job would not delay me more than a Day or two, he assured me.

I said I would do it, but more because I should like to see some Parts of Virginia that I remember with fondness than because I should like to oblige Captain Richardson. I am somewhat wary of him.

Godspeed your travels, Papa, and please give my Love to my precious Dottie, whom I long to see. (Tell her I trapped forty-two Ermine in Canada; she shall have a Cloak made of the Skins!)

Your most affectionate Reprobate,
William

34

PSALMS, 30

October 6, 1980
Lallybroch

BRIANNA'S arrangement with the Hydro Electric Board provided for her working three days a week doing site inspections, overseeing maintenance and repair operations as required, but allowed her to stay at home doing reports, forms, and other paperwork the other two days. She was trying to decipher Rob Cameron's notes regarding the power feed from the second turbine at Loch Errochty, which appeared to have been written with grease pencil on the remains of the bag that had held his lunch, when she became aware of sounds in the laird's study across the hall.

She'd been vaguely conscious of a low humming for some time, but insofar as she'd noticed the sound had put it down to a fly trapped by the window. The hum had now acquired words, though, and a fly would not have been singing "*The King of Love my Shepherd is,*" to the tune of "St. Columba."

She froze, realizing that she'd *recognized* the tune. The voice was rough as coarse-grit sandpaper, and it cracked now and then . . . but it went up and it went down, and it was, it *really* was, a song.

The song stopped abruptly in a fit of coughing, but after some heavy-duty throat-clearing and cautious humming, the voice started up again, this time using an old Scottish tune she thought was called "Crimond."

"The Lord's my Shepherd, I'll not want.
He makes me down to lie

In pastures green; He leadeth me
The quiet waters by."

"*The quiet waters by*" was repeated once or twice in different keys, and then, with increased vigor, the hymn went on:

"My soul He doth restore again:
And me to walk doth make
Within the paths of righteousness,
Even for His Name's own sake."

She sat at her desk, shaking, tears running down her cheeks and a handkerchief pressed to her mouth so he wouldn't hear. "Thank you," she whispered into its folds. "Oh, thank you!"

The singing stopped, but the humming resumed, deep and contented. She got herself back under control and wiped the tears hastily away; it was nearly noon—he'd be coming in any time to ask if she was ready for lunch.

Roger had had considerable doubt about the assistant choirmaster's position—doubt he'd tried not to let her see, and doubt she'd shared until he came home to tell her he'd been given the Children's Choir as his main responsibility. Her own doubt had flown then; children were at once totally uninhibited about voicing the sorts of remarks regarding social oddity that their elders never would, and entirely accepting of such oddity, once they got used to it.

"How long did it take them to ask about your scar?" she'd asked, when he'd come home smiling from his first solo practice with the kids.

"I didn't time it, but maybe thirty seconds." He rubbed two fingers lightly over the ragged mark across his throat, but didn't stop smiling. *"Please, Mr. MacKenzie, what's happened to your neck? Was ye hangit?"*

"And what did you tell them?"

"Told them aye, I was hangit in America, but I lived, praise God. And a couple of them had elder siblings who'd seen *High Plains Drifter* and told them about it, so that raised my stock a good bit. I think they expect me to wear my six-guns to the next practice, though, now the secret's out." He gave her a Clint Eastwood one-eyed squint, which had made her burst out laughing.

She laughed now, remembering it, and just in time, for Roger stuck his head in, saying, "How many different versions of the Twenty-third Psalm would ye say there are, set to music?"

"Twenty-three?" she guessed, rising.

"Only six in the Presbyterian hymnal," he admitted, "but there are metrical settings for it—in English, I mean—that go back to 1546. There's one in the *Bay Psalm Book* and another in the old *Scottish Psalter,* and any number of others here and there. I've seen the Hebrew version, too, but I think I'd best not try that one on the St. Stephen's congregation. Do the Catholics have a musical setting?"

"Catholics have a musical setting for everything," she told him, lifting her nose to sniff for indications of lunch from the kitchen. "But psalms we usually sing to a chant setting. I know four different Gregorian chant forms," she informed him loftily, "but there are lots more."

"Yeah? Chant it for me," he demanded, and stopped dead in the corridor, while she hastily tried to recall the words to the Twenty-third Psalm. The simplest chant form came back automatically—she'd sung it so often in childhood that it was part of her bones.

"That's really something," he said, appreciative, when she'd finished. "Go through it a time or two with me later? I'd like to do it for the kids, just for them to hear. I think they could do Gregorian chant really well."

The kitchen door burst open and Mandy scampered out, clutching Mr. Polly, a stuffed creature who had started out life as a bird of some kind, but now resembled a grubby terry-cloth bag with wings.

"Soup, Mama!" she shouted. "Come eat soup!"

And soup they ate, Campbell's Chicken Noodle made from the can, and cheese sandwiches and pickles to fill the cracks. Annie MacDonald was not a fancy cook, but everything she made was edible, and that was saying a good deal, Brianna thought, with memories of other meals eaten around dying fires on soggy mountaintops or scraped as burnt offerings out of an ashy hearth. She cast a glance of deep affection at the gas-fired Aga cooker that kept the kitchen the coziest room in the house.

"Sing me, Daddy!" Mandy, teeth coated in cheese and mustard round her mouth, gave Roger an entreating grin.

Roger coughed on a crumb and cleared his throat.

"Oh, aye? Sing what?"

" 'Free Bly Mice'!"

"All right. Ye'll need to sing with me, though—keep me from getting off." He smiled at Mandy and beat time softly on the table with the handle of his spoon.

"Three blind mice . . ." he sang, and pointed the handle at Mandy, who drew a heroic breath and echoed, "Free, Bly, MICE!" at the top of her lungs—but with perfect rhythm. Roger raised his eyebrows at Bree and continued the song, in the same counterpoint fashion. After five or six rousing repetitions, Mandy tired of it, and, with a brief "M'scuse me," rose from the table and took off like a low-flying bumblebee, caroming off the doorjamb on her way out.

"Well, she's got a definite sense of rhythm," Roger said, wincing as a loud thud echoed back from the corridor, "if not of coordination. Be a little while before we know if she's got any pitch, though. Your da had a great sense of rhythm, but he couldn't hit the same note twice."

"That reminded me a bit of what you used to do on the Ridge," she said, on impulse. "Singing a line of a psalm and having the people answer it back."

His face changed a little at mention of that time. He'd come newly to his vocation then, and the certainty of it had transformed him. She'd never seen him so happy before—or since, and her heart turned over at the flash of longing she saw in his eyes.

He smiled, though, and, reaching out a napkin-covered finger, wiped a smear of mustard from beside her own mouth.

"Old-fashioned," he said. "Though they still do it that way—the line-singing in kirk—on the Isles, and maybe in the remoter bits of the Gaeltacht. The American Presbyterians won't have it, though."

"They won't?"

"*It is proper to sing without parceling out the psalm line by line,*" he quoted. "*The practice of reading the psalm, line by line, was introduced in times of ignorance, when many in the congregation could not read; therefore, it is recommended that it be laid aside, so far as convenient.* That's from the Constitution of the American Presbyterian Church."

Oh, so you did think about being ordained while we were in Boston, she thought but didn't say aloud.

"Times of ignorance," she repeated, instead. "I'd like to know what Hiram Crombie would have had to say to that!"

He laughed, but shook his head.

"Well, it's true enough; most of the folk on the Ridge couldn't read. But I'd disagree with the notion that ye'd only sing the psalms that way because of ignorance, or a lack of books." He paused for thought, idly scraping up a stray noodle and eating it.

"Singing all together, that's grand, no doubt about it. But to do it in that back-and-forth way—I think there's maybe something about it that draws the people closer, makes them feel more involved in what they're singing, what's truly happening. Maybe it's only because they've got to concentrate harder to remember each line." He smiled briefly, and looked away.

Please! she thought passionately, whether to God, the Blessed Virgin, Roger's guardian angel, or all three. *You've got to let him find a way!*

"I . . . meant to ask ye something," he said, suddenly diffident.

"What's that?"

"Well . . . Jemmy. He *can* sing. Would ye—of course he'd go to Mass with you still—but would ye mind if he was to come along with me, as well? Only if he liked," he added hastily. "But I think he might enjoy being in the choir. And I'd . . . like him to see I have a job, too, I suppose," he added, with a half-rueful smile.

"He'd love that," Brianna said, remarking mentally to the heavenly host, *Well, that was fast!* Because she saw at once—and wondered whether Roger had, but she didn't think so—that this offered a graceful way by which she and Mandy could attend the Presbyterian services, as well, without any overt conflict between their two faiths.

"Would you come with us to the early Mass at St. Mary's?" she asked. "Because then we could all just go across to St. Stephen's together and see you and Jem sing."

"Yes, of course."

He stopped, the sandwich halfway to his mouth, and smiled at her, his eyes green as moss.

"It's better, isn't it?" he said.

"Lots," she said.

LATER IN THE afternoon, Roger called her across to the study. There was a map of Scotland laid on his desk, next to the open notebook in which he was compiling the thing they had taken to calling—with a jokiness that barely covered the aversion they felt in even talking about it—"The Hitchhiker's Guide," after the BBC radio comedy.

"Sorry to interrupt," he said. "But I thought we'd best do it before Jem comes home. If ye're going back to Loch Errochty tomorrow . . ." He put the point of his pencil on the blue blotch labeled *L.Errochty.* "You could maybe get an accurate bearing for the tunnel, if ye're not quite sure where it is. Or are you?"

She swallowed, feeling the remains of her cheese sandwich stir uneasily at the memory of the dark tunnel, the rocking of the little train, of passing through . . . it.

"I don't, but I have something better. Wait." She stepped across to her own office and brought back the binder of Loch Errochty's specs.

"Here are the drawings for the tunnel construction," she said, flipping the binder open and laying it on the desk. "I have the blueprints, too, but they're at the main office."

"No, this is great," he assured her, poring over the drawing. "All I really wanted is the compass orientation of the tunnel to the dam." He glanced up at her. "Speaking of that—have ye been all across the dam itself?"

"Not all across," she said slowly. "Just the east side of the servicing bay. But I don't think—I mean, look." She put a finger on the drawing. "I hit it somewhere in the middle of the tunnel, and the tunnel is nearly in a straight line with the dam. If it runs in a line—is that what you think it does?" she added, looking at him curiously. He shrugged.

"It's a place to start. Though I suppose engineers would have a better-sounding word than 'guess'?"

"Working hypothesis," she said dryly. "Anyway, if it *does*

run in a line, rather than just existing in random spots, I'd probably have felt it in the dam if it was there at all. But I could go back and check." Even she could hear the reluctance in her voice; he certainly did, and ran a light hand down her back in reassurance.

"No. I'll do it."

"What?"

"I'll do it," he repeated mildly. "We'll see if I feel it, too."

"No!" She straightened up abruptly. "You can't. You don't—I mean, what if something . . . happens? You can't take that kind of risk!"

He looked at her thoughtfully for a moment, and nodded.

"Aye, I suppose there's something of a risk. But small. I've been all over the Highlands, ken, in my younger years. And now and again I've felt something queer pass through me. So have most folk who live here," he added with a smile. "Queerness is part of the place, aye?"

"Yes," she said, with a brief shudder at thought of water horses, *ban-sidhe,* and Nuckelavees. "But you know what sort of queerness this is—and you know damned well it can kill you, Roger!"

"Didn't kill you," he pointed out. "Didn't kill us on Ocracoke." He spoke lightly, but she could see the shadow of that journey on his face with the speaking. It hadn't killed them—but it had come close.

"No. But—" She looked at him and had a deep, wrenching instant in which she experienced at once the feel of his long, warm body next to hers in bed, the sound of his deep, corncrake voice—and the cold silence of his absence. "No," she said, and made it apparent by her tone that she was prepared to be as stubborn as necessary about it. He heard that and gave a mild snort.

"All right," he said. "Let me just put it down, then." Comparing drawing and map, he chose a spot on the map that might correspond roughly with the center of the tunnel and raised one dark eyebrow in question. She nodded, and he made a light pencil mark in the shape of a star.

There was a large, definite star, made in black ink, over the site of the stone circle on Craigh na Dun. Smaller ones in light pencil at the sites of other stone circles. Someday, they might have to visit those circles. But not yet. Not now.

"Ever been to Lewis?" Roger asked—casually, but not as though it were an idle question.

"No, why?" she said warily.

"The Outer Hebrides are part of the Gaeltacht," he said. "They do the line-singing in the *Gàidhlig* on Lewis, and on Harris, too. Don't know about Uist and Barra—they're mostly Catholic—but maybe. I'm thinking I'd like to go and see what it's like these days."

She could see the Isle of Lewis on the map, shaped like a pancreas, off the west coast of Scotland. It was a large map. Large enough for her to see the small legend *Callanish Stones,* on the Isle of Lewis.

She exhaled slowly.

"Fine," she said. "I'll go with you."

"Ye've got work, haven't you?"

"I'll take time off."

They looked at each other in silence for a moment. Brianna broke away first, glancing at the clock on the shelf.

"Jem'll be home soon," she said, the prosaic nature of daily life asserting itself. "I'd better start something for supper. Annie brought us a nice salmon that her husband took. Shall I marinate it and bake it, or would you like it grilled?"

He shook his head and, rising, began to fold the map away. "I won't be in to supper tonight. It's lodge night."

THE PROVINCIAL grand Masonic Lodge of Inverness-shire included a number of local lodges, two of them in Inverness. Roger had joined Number 6, the Old Inverness Lodge, in his early twenties, but had not set foot inside the building in fifteen years, and did so now with a mingled sense of wariness and anticipation.

It was, though, the Highlands—and home. The first person he saw upon walking in was Barney Gaugh, who had been the burly, smiling station agent when Roger had come to Inverness on the train, aged five, to live with his great-uncle. Mr. Gaugh had shrunk considerably, and his tobacco-stained teeth had long since been replaced by equally tobacco-stained dentures, but he recognized Roger at once and beamed in delight, seizing him by the arm and towing him into a group of other old men, half of whom likewise exclaimed over his return.

It was weird, he thought a bit later, as they settled to the business of the lodge, doing the routine rituals of the Scottish Rite. *Like a time warp,* he thought, and nearly laughed out loud.

There were differences, aye, but they were slight—and the *feeling* of it . . . He could close his eyes and, if he imagined the haze of stubbed-out cigarettes to be the smoke of a hearth, it could be the Crombies' cabin on the Ridge, where the lodge there had met. The close murmur of voices, line and response, and then the relaxation, the shifting of bodies, fetching of tea and coffee, as the evening became purely social.

There were a good many present—many more than he was used to—and he didn't at first notice Lionel Menzies. The headmaster was across the room, frowning in concentration, listening to something a tall bloke in shirtsleeves was saying to him, leaning close. Roger hesitated, not wanting to break in upon their conversation, but the man talking to Menzies glanced up, saw Roger, returned to his conversation—but then stopped abruptly, gaze jerking back to Roger. To his throat, specifically.

Everyone in lodge had stared at the scar, whether openly or covertly. He'd worn an open-collared shirt under his jacket; there was no point in trying to hide it. Better to get it over with. The stranger stared at the scar so openly, though, as almost to be offensive.

Menzies noticed his companion's inattention—he could hardly not—and, turning, saw Roger and broke into a smile.

"Mr. MacKenzie," he said.

"Roger," Roger said, smiling; first names were usual in lodge, when they weren't being formally "brother so-and-so." Menzies nodded and tilted his head, drawing his companion into introduction. "Rob Cameron, Roger MacKenzie. Rob's my cousin—Roger's one of my parents."

"I thought so," Cameron said, shaking him warmly by the hand. "Thought you must be the new choirmaster, I mean. My wee nephew's in your infants' choir—that'll be Bobby Hurragh. He told us all about ye over supper last week."

Roger had seen the private glance exchanged between the men as Menzies introduced him and thought that the headmaster must also have mentioned him to Cameron, likely telling him about his visit to the school following Jem's Gaelic incident. That didn't concern him at the moment, though.

"Rob Cameron," he repeated, giving the man's hand a slightly stronger squeeze than usual before releasing it, this causing him to look startled. "You work for the Hydro, do you?"

"Aye. What—"

"Ye'll ken my wife, I think." Roger bared his teeth in what might—or might not—be taken for a genial smile. "Brianna MacKenzie?"

Cameron's mouth opened, but no sound came out. He realized this and closed it abruptly, coughing.

"I—uh. Yeah. Sure."

Roger had sized the man up automatically as he'd grasped his hand, and knew if it came to a fight it'd be a short one. Evidently, Cameron knew it, too.

"She, uh . . ."

"She told me, aye."

"Hey, it was no but a wee joke, right?" Cameron eyed him warily, in case Roger meant to invite him to step outside.

"Rob?" said Menzies curiously. "What—"

"What's this, what's this?" cried old Barney, bustling up to them. "Nay politics in lodge, lad! Ye want to talk your SNP shite to brother Roger, take it roond to the pub later." Seizing Cameron by the elbow, Barney towed him off to another group across the room, where Cameron at once settled into conversation, with no more than a brief glance back at Roger.

"SNP shite?" Roger asked, brows raised at Menzies. The headmaster lifted one shoulder, smiling.

"Ken what auld Barney said. Nay politics in lodge!" It was a Masonic rule, one of the most basic—no discussion of religion or politics in lodge—and probably the reason Freemasonry had lasted as long as it had, Roger thought. He didn't care much about the Scottish National Party, but he did want to know about Cameron.

"Wouldn't dream of it," Roger said. "Our Rob's a political, though, is he?"

"My apologies, brother Roger," Menzies said. The look of humorous good nature hadn't deserted him, but he did look somewhat apologetic. "I didn't mean to expose your family's business, but I did tell my wife about Jem and Mrs. Glendenning, and women being what they are, and my wife's sister living next door to Rob, Rob got to hear about it. He was interested because of the *Gàidhlig,* aye? And he does get carried away a bit. But I'm sure he didn't mean to be seeming too familiar with your wife."

It dawned on Roger that Menzies had hold of the wrong end of the stick regarding Rob Cameron and Brianna, but he didn't mean to enlighten him. It wasn't only the women; gossip was a way of life in the Highlands, and if word got round about the trick Rob and his mates had played on Bree, it might cause more trouble for her at her work.

"Ah," he said, seeking for a way to steer the conversation away from Brianna. "Of course. The SNP's all for resurrecting the *Gàidhlig,* aren't they? Does Cameron have it himself?"

Menzies shook his head. "His parents were among those who didn't want their kids to speak it. Now, of course, he's keen to learn. Speak of that—" He broke off abruptly, eyeing Roger with his head to one side. "I had a thought. After we spoke the other day."

"Aye?"

"I wondered, just. Would ye maybe think of doing a wee class now and then? Maybe only for Jem's form, maybe a presentation for the school as a whole, if you felt comfortable about it."

"A class? What, in the *Gàidhlig*?"

"Yes. You know, very basic stuff, but maybe with a word or two about the history, maybe a bit of a song—Rob said ye're choirmaster at St. Stephen's?"

"Assistant," Roger corrected. "And I don't know about the singing. But the *Gàidhlig* . . . aye, maybe. I'll think about it."

HE FOUND BRIANNA waiting up, in his study, a letter from her parents' box in her hand, unopened.

"We don't have to read it tonight," she said, putting it down, rising, and coming to kiss him. "I just felt like I wanted to be close to them. How was lodge?"

"Odd." The business of the lodge was secret, of course, but he could tell her about Menzies and Cameron, and did.

"What's the SNP?" she asked, frowning.

"The Scottish National Party." He skinned out of his coat, and shivered. It was cold, and there was no fire in the study. "Came in during the late thirties, but didn't get really going until quite recently. Elected eleven members to Parliament by 1974, though—respectable. As ye might gather from the name, their goal is Scottish independence."

"Respectable," she repeated, sounding dubious.

"Well, moderately. Like any party, they have their lunatic elements. For what it's worth," he added, "I don't think Rob Cameron's one of them. Just your average arsehole."

That made her laugh, and the sound of it warmed him. So did her body, which she pressed against his, arms round his shoulders.

"That would be Rob," she agreed.

"Menzies says he's interested in the Gaelic, though. If I teach a class, I hope he doesn't turn up in the front row."

"Wait—what? Now you're teaching Gaelic classes?"

"Well, maybe. We'll see about it." He found himself reluctant to think too much about Menzies's suggestion. Maybe it was only the mention of singing. Croaking out a tune to guide the kids was one thing; singing alone in public—even if it was only schoolkids—was something else again.

"That can wait," he said, and kissed her. "Let's read your letter."

June 2, 1777
Fort Ticonderoga

"Fort Ticonderoga?" Bree's voice rose in astonishment, and she all but jerked the letter from Roger's hands. "What on earth are they doing in Fort Ticonderoga?"

"I don't know, but if ye'll settle for a moment, we'll maybe find out."

She didn't reply but came round the desk and leaned over, her chin propped on his shoulder, her hair brushing his cheek as she focused anxiously on the page.

"It's okay," he said, turning to kiss her cheek. "It's your mum, and she's in an especially parenthetical mood. She doesn't normally do that unless she's feeling happy."

"Well, yes," Bree murmured, frowning at the page, "but . . . Fort Ticonderoga?"

Dear Bree, et al—

As you've doubtless gathered from the heading of this letter, we are not (yet) in Scotland. We had a certain amount of difficulty on our voyage, involving a) the Royal navy, in the person of one Captain Stebbings, who attempted to press your father and your cousin Ian (it didn't work); b) an American privateer (though her captain, one—and one of him is more than enough—Asa Hickman insists upon the more dignified "letter of marque" as the designation of his ship's mission, which is essentially piracy but executed under the authority of the Continental Congress); c) Rollo; and d) the gentleman I mentioned to you earlier, named (I thought) John Smith, but who turns out to be a deserter from the Royal navy named Bill (aka "Jonah," and I begin to think they are right) Marsden.

Without going into the details of the whole blood-soaked farce, I will merely report that Jamie, Ian, the damned dog, and I are all fine. So far. I'm hoping this state of affairs continues for the next forty-two days, that being when your father's short-term militia contract expires. (Don't ask. Essentially, he was saving Mr. Marsden's neck, as well as providing for the welfare of a couple of dozen seamen inadvertently forced into piracy.) Once it does, we propose to leave promptly on whatever transport might be headed in the general direction of Europe, provided only that said transport is not captained by Asa Hickman. We may have to travel overland to Boston in order to do this, but so be it. (I suppose it would be interesting to see what Boston looks like these days. The Back Bay still being water and all, I mean. At least the Common will still be there, if sporting rather more cows than we were used to.)

The fort is under the command of one General Anthony Wayne, and I have the uncomfortable feeling that I have heard Roger mention this man, using the nickname "Mad Anthony." I'm hoping this designation either does or will refer to his conduct in battle, rather than in administration. So far he seems rational, if harried.

Being harried is *rational, as he is expecting the more or less imminent arrival of the British army. Meanwhile, his chief engineer, a Mr. Jeduthan Baldwin (you'd like him, I think. Very energetic fellow!), is building a Great Bridge, to connect the fort with the hill they call Mount Independence. Your father is commanding a crew of laborers at work on this bridge; I can see him just now, from my perch on one of the fort's demilune batteries. He stands out, rather, being not only twice the size of most of the men but one of the few wearing a shirt. Most of them in fact work naked, or wearing only a clout, because of the heat and wet. Given the mosquitoes, I think this is a mistake, but no one asked me.*

No one asked my opinion of the hygienic protocols involved in maintaining a proper sick bay and prisoner accommodations, either (we brought several British prisoners with us, including the aforementioned Captain Stebbings who should by all rights be dead, but somehow isn't), but I told them anyway. I am thus persona non grata *with Lieutenant Stactoe, who thinks he is a surgeon but isn't, and therefore am prevented from treating the men under his care, most of whom will be dead within a month. Fortunately, no one cares if I treat the women, children, or prisoners, and so I am usefully occupied, there being a lot of them.*

I have a distinct notion that Ticonderoga changed hands at some point, probably more than once, but have no idea who took it from whom, or when. This last point rather weighs upon my mind.

General Wayne has almost no regular troops.

Jamie says the fort is seriously undermanned—and even I can see this; half the barracks are vacant—and while the occasional militia company comes in from New Hampshire or Connecticut, these normally enroll for only two or three months, as we did. Even so, the men often don't stay their full term; there is a constant melting away, and General Wayne complains—publicly—that he is reduced to (and I quote) "Negroes, Indians, and women." I told him that he could do worse.

Jamie says also that the fort lacks half its guns, these having been abstracted by a fat bookseller named Henry Knox, who took them two years ago and managed by some feat of persistence and engineering to get them all the way to Boston (Mr. Knox himself having to be conveyed in a cart along with them, he weighing in excess of three hundred pounds. One of the officers here, who accompanied that expedition, described it, to general hilarity), where they proved very useful indeed in getting rid of the British.

What's somewhat more worrying than these points is the existence of a small hill, directly across the water from us, and no great distance away. The Americans named it Mount Defiance when they took Ticonderoga away from the British in '75 (you remember Ethan Allen? "Surrender in the name of the Great Jehovah and the Continental Congress!" I hear that poor Mr. Allen is presently in England, being tried for treason, he having rather overreached himself by trying to take Montreal on the same terms), and that's rather apt—or would be, if the fort was capable of putting men and artillery on top of it. They aren't, and I think the fact that Mount Defiance commands the fort and is within cannon-shot of it probably will not be lost on the British army, if and when they get here.

On the good side, it is almost summer. The fish are jumping, and if there was any cotton, it would probably reach my waist. It rains frequently, and I've never seen so much vegetation in one place. (The air is so rich with oxygen, I occasionally think I will pass out, and am obliged to nip into the barracks for a restorative whiff of dirty laundry and chamber pots (though the local usage is "thunder-mug," and for good reason). Your cousin Ian takes foraging parties out every few days, Jamie and a number of the other men are accomplished fishermen, and we eat extremely well in consequence.

I won't go on at great length here, as I'm not sure when or where I'll be able to dispatch this letter via one or more of Jamie's several routes (we copy each letter, if there's time, and send multiple copies, since even normal correspondence is chancy these days). With luck, it will go with us to Edinburgh. In the meantime, we send you all our love. Jamie dreams now and then of the children; I wish I did.

Mama

Roger sat in silence for a moment, to be sure Bree had had time to finish reading the letter—though in fact she read much faster than he did; he thought she must be reading it twice. After a moment, she sighed through her nose in a troubled fashion and straightened up. He put up a hand and rested it on her waist, and she covered it with her own. Not mechanically; she gripped his fingers tightly—but absently. She was looking across at the bookshelves.

"Those are new, aren't they?" she asked quietly, lifting her chin toward the right-hand bay.

"Yeah. I sent to Boston for them. They came in a couple of days ago." The spines were new and shiny. History texts, dealing with the American Revolution. *Encyclopedia of the American Revolution,* by Mark M. Boatner III. *A Narrative of a Revolutionary Soldier,* by Joseph Plumb Martin.

"Do you want to know?" he asked. He nodded at the open box on the table before them, where a thick sheaf of letters still remained unopened, on top of the books. He hadn't yet brought himself to admit to Bree that he'd looked at the books. "I mean—we know they probably made it out of Ticonderoga all right. There are a lot more letters."

"We know one of them probably did," Bree said, eyeing the letters. "Unless . . . Ian knows, I mean. He could have . . ."

Roger pulled his hand back and reached with determination into the box. Bree drew in her breath, but he ignored it, taking a handful of letters from the box and flipping through them.

"Claire, Claire, Claire, Jamie, Claire, Jamie, Jamie, Claire, Jamie"—he stopped, blinking at a letter addressed in an unfamiliar hand—"maybe you're right about Ian; do you know what his handwriting looks like?"

She shook her head.

"I don't think I ever saw him write anything—though I suppose he *can* write," she added, dubious.

"Well . . ." Roger put down the folded sheet, and looked from the scatter of letters to the bookshelf and thence to her. She was slightly flushed. "What do you want to do?"

She considered, her eyes flicking to and from the bookshelves and the wooden box.

"The books," she said, decided, and strode across to the shelves. "Which one of these will tell us when Ticonderoga fell?"

George III, Rex Britanniae
to Lord George Germain

. . . Burgoyne may command the corps to be sent from Canada to Albany . . .

As sickness and other contingencies must be expected, I should think not above 7,000 effectives can be spared over Lake Champlain, for it would be highly imprudent to run any risk in Canada . . . Indians must be employed.

35

TICONDEROGA

June 1, 1777
Fort Ticonderoga

I FOUND JAMIE asleep, lying naked on the pallet in the tiny chamber that had been allotted to us. It was at the top of one of the stone-built barracks buildings, and thus hot as Hades by mid-afternoon. Still, we were rarely in it during the day, Jamie being out on the lake with the bridge builders, and I being in the hospital building or the family quarters—all of those being equally hot, of course.

By the same token, though, the stones held enough heat to keep us warm in the cool evenings—there was no fireplace—and it did have a small window. There was a good breeze off the water toward sunset, and for a few hours between, say, ten p.m. and two a.m., it was very pleasant. It was about eight now—still light out and still toasty in; sweat shone on Jamie's shoulders and darkened the hair at his temples to a deep bronze.

On the good side, our tiny attic was the only room at the top of the building and thus had some modicum of privacy. On the other hand, there were forty-eight stone steps up to our aerie, and water must be carried up and slops carried down them. I'd just hauled up a large bucket of water, and the half of it that hadn't spilled down the front of my dress weighed a ton. I put it down with a clunk that brought Jamie upright in an instant, blinking in the gloom.

"Oh, sorry," I said. "I didn't mean to wake you."

"No matter, Sassenach," he said, and yawned immensely. He sat up, stretched, then scrubbed his hands through his damp, loose hair. "Have ye had supper?"

"Yes, I ate with the women. Have you?" He normally ate with his crew of laborers when they stopped work, but sometimes was summoned to dine with General St. Clair or the other militia officers, and these quasi-formal occasions took place much later.

"Mmm-hmm." He lay back on the pallet and watched as I poured water into a tin washing bowl and dug out a tiny lump of lye soap. I stripped to my shift and began meticulously scrubbing, though the strong soap stung my already raw skin and the fumes of it were enough to make my eyes water.

I rinsed my hands and arms, tossed the water out the window—pausing briefly to shout, "Gardy-loo!" before doing so—and started over.

"Why are ye doing that?" Jamie asked curiously.

"Mrs. Wellman's little boy has what I'm almost sure is the mumps. Or ought that to be *are* the mumps? I've never been sure whether it's plural or not. In any case, I'm taking no chance on transmitting it to you."

"Is it a terrible thing, mumps? I thought only weans got it."

"Well, normally it *is* a child's disease," I said, wincing at the touch of the soap. "But when an adult gets it—particularly an adult male—it's a more serious matter. It tends to settle in the testicles. And unless you *want* to have balls the size of muskmelons—"

"Are ye sure ye have enough soap there, Sassenach? I could go and find more." He grinned at me, then sat up again and reached for the limp strip of linen that served us as a towel. "Here, *a nighean,* let me dry your hands."

"In a minute." I wriggled out of my stays, dropped my shift, and hung it on the hook by the door, then pulled my "home" shift over my head. It wasn't quite as sanitary as having surgical scrubs to wear to work, but the fort absolutely crawled with diseases, and I'd do whatever I could to avoid bringing them back to Jamie. He'd run into enough of them in the open.

I splashed the last of the water over my face and arms, then sat down on the pallet beside Jamie, giving a small cry as my knee cracked painfully.

"God, your poor hands," he murmured, gently patting them with the towel, then swabbing my face. "And your nose is sunburnt, too, the wee thing."

"What about yours?" Callused as they normally were, his hands were still a mass of nicks, scraped knuckles, splinters, and blisters, but he dismissed that with a brief flick of one hand and lay back down again with a luxurious groan.

"Does your knee still hurt, Sassenach?" he asked, seeing me rub it. It hadn't ever quite recovered from being strained during our adventures on the *Pitt,* and climbing stairs provoked it.

"Oh, just part of the general decline," I said, trying to make a joke of it. I flexed my right arm, gingerly, feeling a twinge in the elbow. "Things don't bend quite so easily as they used to. And other things hurt. Sometimes I think I'm falling apart."

Jamie closed one eye and regarded me.

"I've felt like that since I was about twenty," he observed. "Ye get used to it." He stretched, making his spine give off a series of muffled pops, and held out a hand. "Come to bed, *a nighean.* Nothing hurts when ye love me."

He was right; nothing did.

I FELL BRIEFLY ASLEEP, but woke by instinct a couple of hours later to go and check the few patients who needed an eye kept on them. These included Captain Stebbings, who had—to my surprise—stoutly refused either to die or to be doctored by anyone but me. That hadn't gone over well with Lieutenant Stactoe or the other surgeons, but as Captain Stebbings's demand was backed up by the intimidating presence of Guinea Dick—pointed teeth, tattoos, and all—I remained his personal surgeon.

I found the captain mildly feverish and wheezing audibly, but asleep. Guinea Dick rose from his own pallet at the sound of my step, looking like a particularly fearsome manifestation of someone's nightmare.

"Has he eaten?" I asked softly, laying my hand lightly on Stebbings's wrist. The captain's tubby form had shrunk considerably; even in the gloom, I could easily see the ribs I'd once had to grope for.

"Him has little soup, ma'am," the African whispered, and moved a hand toward a bowl on the floor, covered with a handkerchief to keep out the roaches. "Like you say. I give him more when he wake to piss."

"Good." Stebbings's pulse was a little fast, but not alarming, and when I leaned over him and inhaled deeply, I detected no scent of gangrene. I'd been able to withdraw the tube from his chest two days before, and while there was a slight exudation of pus from the site, I thought it a local infection that would likely clear without assistance. It would have to; I had nothing to assist it.

There was almost no light in the hospital barracks, only a rush-dip near the door and what little illumination came from the fires in the courtyard. I couldn't judge of Stebbings's color, but I saw the flash of white as he half-opened his eyes. He grunted when he saw me, and closed them again.

"Good," I said again, and left him in the tender charge of Mr. Dick.

The Guinea man had been offered the chance to enlist in the Continental army but had refused, choosing to become a prisoner of war with Captain Stebbings, the wounded Mr. Ormiston, and a few other seamen from the *Pitt.*

"I am English, free man," he had said simply. "Prisoner maybe for a little, but free man. Seaman, but free man. American, maybe not free man."

Maybe not.

I left the hospital barracks, called in at the Wellmans' quarters to check on my case of mumps—uncomfortable, but not dangerous—and then strolled slowly across the courtyard under a rising moon. The evening breeze had died down, but the night air had some coolness in it, and moved by impulse, I climbed to the demilune battery that looked across the narrow end of Lake Champlain to Mount Defiance.

There were two guards, but both were fast asleep, reeking of liquor. It wasn't unusual. Morale at the fort was not high, and alcohol was easily available.

I stood by the wall, a hand on one of the guns, its metal still faintly warm from the day's heat. Would we get away, I wondered, before it was hot from being fired? Thirty-two days to go, and they couldn't go fast enough to suit me. Aside from the menace of the British, the fort festered and stank; it was like living in a cesspool, and I could only hope that Jamie, Ian, and I would leave it without having contracted some vile disease or having been assaulted by some drunken idiot.

I heard a faint step behind me and turned to see Ian himself, tall and slender in the glow of the fires below.

"Can I speak to ye, Auntie?"

"Of course," I said, wondering at this unaccustomed formality. I stood aside a little, and he came to stand beside me, looking down.

"Cousin Brianna would have a thing or two to say about that," he said, with a nod through the half-built bridge below. "So has Uncle Jamie."

"I know." Jamie had been saying it for the last two weeks—to the fort's new commander, Arthur St. Clair, to the other militia colonels, to the engineers, to anyone who would listen, and not a few who wouldn't. The folly of expending vast amounts of labor and material in building a bridge that could be easily destroyed by artillery on Mount Defiance was clear to everyone except those in command.

I sighed. It wasn't the first time I'd seen military blindness, and I was very much afraid it wouldn't be the last.

"Well, leaving that aside . . . what did you want to speak to me about, Ian?"

He took a deep breath and turned toward the moonlit vista over the lake.

"D'ye ken the Huron who came to the fort a wee while past?"

I did. Two weeks before, a party of Huron had visited the fort, and Ian had spent an evening smoking with them, listening to their stories. Some of these concerned the English General Burgoyne, whose hospitality they had previously enjoyed.

Burgoyne was actively soliciting the Indians of the Iroquois League, they said, spending a great deal of time and money in wooing them.

"He says his Indians are his secret weapon," one of the Huron had said, laughing. "He will unleash them upon the Americans, to burn like lightning, and strike them all dead."

Knowing what I did of Indians in general, I thought Burgoyne might be a trifle overoptimistic. Still, I preferred not to think what might happen if he *did* succeed in persuading any number of Indians to fight for him.

Ian was still staring at the distant hump of Mount Defiance, lost in thought.

"Be that as it may," I said, calling the meeting to order. "Why are you telling me this, Ian? You should tell Jamie and St. Clair."

"I did." The cry of a loon came across the lake, surprisingly loud and eerie. They sounded like yodeling ghosts, particularly when more than one of them was at it.

"Yes? Well, then," I said, slightly impatient. "What did you want to talk to me about?"

"Babies," he said abruptly, straightening up and turning to face me.

"What?" I said, startled. He'd been quiet and moody ever since the Hurons' visit, and I assumed that something they'd told him had caused it—but I couldn't imagine what they might have said to him regarding babies.

"How they're made," he said doggedly, though his eyes slid away from mine. Had there been more light, I was sure I could have seen him blushing.

"Ian," I said, after a brief pause. "I decline to believe that you don't know how babies are made. What do you *really* want to know?"

He sighed, but at last he looked at me. His lips compressed for a moment, then he blurted, "I want to know why I canna make one."

I rubbed a knuckle across my lips, disconcerted. I knew—Bree had told me—that he had had a stillborn daughter with his Mohawk wife, Emily, and that she had then miscarried at least twice. Also that it was this failure that had led to Ian's leaving the Mohawk at Snaketown and returning to us.

"Why do you think it might be you?" I asked bluntly. "Most men blame the woman when a child is stillborn or miscarried. So do most women, for that matter."

I had blamed both myself and Jamie.

He made a small Scottish noise in his throat, impatient.

"The Mohawk don't. They say when a man lies wi' a woman, his spirit does battle with hers. If he overcomes her, then the child is planted; if not, it doesna happen."

"Hmm," I said. "Well, that's one way of putting it. And I wouldn't say they're wrong, either. It *can* be something to do with either the man or the woman—or it may be something about them together."

"Aye." I heard him swallow before he went on. "One of the women wi' the Huron was Kahnyen'kehaka—a woman from Snaketown, and she kent me, from when I was there. And she said to me that Emily has a child. A live child."

He had been moving restlessly from foot to foot as he talked, cracking his knuckles. Now he stilled. The moon was well up and shone on his face, making hollows of his eyes.

"I've been thinking, Auntie," he said softly. "I've been thinking for a verra long time. About her. Emily. About Yeksa'a. The—my wee bairn." He stopped, big knuckles pressed hard into his thighs, but he gathered himself again and went on, more steadily.

"And just lately I have been thinking something else. If—*when,*" he corrected, with a glance over one shoulder, as though expecting Jamie to pop up through a trap, glaring, "we go to Scotland, I dinna ken how things might be. But if I—if I was to wed again, maybe, either there or here . . ." He looked up at me suddenly, his face old with sorrow but heartbreakingly young with hope and doubt.

"I couldna take a lass to wife if I kent that I should never give her live bairns."

He swallowed again, looking down.

"Could ye maybe . . . look at my parts, Auntie? To see if maybe there's aught amiss?" His hand went to his breechclout, and I stopped him with a hasty gesture.

"Perhaps that can wait a bit, Ian. Let me take a history first; then we'll see if I need to do an examination."

"Are ye sure?" He sounded surprised. "Uncle Jamie told me about the sperm ye showed him. I thought maybe mine might not be quite right in some way."

"Well, I'd need a microscope to see, in any case. And while there *are* such things as abnormal sperm, usually when that's the case, conception doesn't take place at all. And as I understand it, that wasn't the difficulty. Tell me—" I didn't want to ask, but there was no way round it. "Your daughter. Did you see her?"

The nuns had given me my stillborn daughter. "*It's better if you see,*" they had said, gently insistent.

He shook his head.

"Not to say so. I mean—I saw the wee bundle they'd made of her, wrapped in rabbit skin. They put it up high in the fork of a red cedar. I went there at night, for some time, just to . . . well. I did think of taking the bundle down, of unwrapping her, just to see her face. But it would ha' troubled Emily, so I didn't."

"I'm sure you're right. But did . . . oh, hell, Ian, I'm so sorry—but did your wife or any of the other women ever say that there was anything visibly wrong with the child? Was she . . . deformed in any way?"

He glanced at me, eyes wide with shock, and his lips moved soundlessly for a moment.

"No," he said at last, and there was both pain and relief in his voice. "No. I asked. Emily didna want to talk about her, about Iseabail—that's what I would ha' named her, Iseabail—" he explained, "but I asked and wouldna stop until she told me what the baby looked like.

"She was perfect," he said softly, looking down at the bridge, where a chain of lanterns glowed, reflected in the water. "Perfect."

So had Faith been. Perfect.

I put a hand on his forearm, ropy with hard muscle.

"That's good," I said quietly. "Very good. Tell me as much as you can, then, about what happened during the pregnancy. Did your wife have any bleeding between the time you knew she was pregnant and when she gave birth?"

Slowly I led him through the hope and fear, the desolation of each loss, such symptoms as he could remember, and what he knew of Emily's family; had there been stillbirths among her relations? Miscarriages?

The moon passed overhead and started down the sky. At last I stretched and shook myself.

"I can't be positive," I said. "But I think it's at least possible that the trouble was what we call an Rh problem."

"A what?" He was leaning against one of the big guns, and lifted his head at this.

There was no point in trying to explain blood groups, antigens, and antibodies. And it wasn't actually all that different from the Mohawk explanation of the problem, I thought.

"If a woman's blood is Rh-negative, and her husband's blood is Rh-positive," I explained, "then the child will be Rh-positive, because that's dominant—never mind what that means, but the child will be positive like the father. Sometimes the first pregnancy is all right, and you don't see a problem until the next time—sometimes it happens with the first. Essentially, the mother's body produces a substance that kills the child. *But,* if an Rh-negative woman should have a child by an Rh-negative man, then the fetus is always Rh-negative, too, and there's no problem. Since you say Emily has had a live birth, then it's possible that her new husband is Rh-negative, too." I knew absolutely nothing about the prevalence of Rhesus-negative blood type in Native Americans, but the theory did fit the evidence.

"And if that's so," I finished, "then you shouldn't have that problem with another woman—most European women are Rh-positive, though not all."

He stared at me for so long that I wondered whether he had understood what I'd said.

"Call it fate," I said gently, "or call it bad luck. But it wasn't your fault. Or hers." Not mine. Nor Jamie's.

He nodded, slowly, and leaning forward, laid his head on my shoulder for a moment.

"Thank ye, Auntie," he whispered, and lifting his head, kissed my cheek.

The next day, he was gone.

36

THE GREAT DISMAL

June 21, 1777

WILLIAM MARVELED at the road. True, there were only a few miles of it, but the miracle of being able to ride straight into the Great Dismal, through a place where he vividly recalled having had to swim his horse on a previous visit, all the while dodging snapping turtles and venomous snakes—the convenience of it was astonishing. The horse seemed of similar mind, picking up its feet in a lighthearted way, outpacing the clouds of tiny yellow horseflies that tried to swarm them, the insects' eyes glinting like tiny rainbows when they drew close.

"Enjoy it while you can," William advised the gelding, with a brief scratch of the mane. "Muddy going up ahead."

The road itself, while clear of the sweet gum saplings and straggling pines that crowded its edge, was muddy enough, in all truth. Nothing like the treacherous bogs and unexpected pools that lurked beyond the scrim of trees, though. He rose a little in the stirrups, peering ahead.

How far? he wondered. Dismal Town stood on the shore of Lake Drummond, which lay in the middle of the swamp. He had never come so far into the Great Dismal as he was now, though, and had no notion of its actual size.

The road didn't go so far as the lake, he knew that. But surely there was a trace to follow; those inhabitants of Dismal Town must come and go on occasion.

"Washington," he repeated under his breath. "Washington, Cartwright, Harrington, Carver." Those were the names he'd been given by Captain Richardson, of the Loyalist gentlemen from Dismal Town; he'd committed them to memory and punctiliously burned the sheet of paper containing them. Having done so, though, he was seized by irrational panic lest he forget the names, and had been repeating them to himself at intervals throughout the morning.

It was well past noon now, and the wispy clouds of the morning had been knitting themselves up into a low sky the color of dirty wool. He breathed in slowly, but the air didn't have that prickling scent of impending downpour—yet. Besides the ripe reek of the swamp, rich with mud and rotting plants, he could smell his own skin, salty and rank. He'd washed his hands and head as he could but hadn't changed nor washed his clothes in two weeks, and the rough hunting shirt and homespun breeches were beginning to itch considerably.

Though perhaps it wasn't just dried sweat and dirt. He clawed viciously at a certain crawling sensation in his breeches. He'd swear he'd picked up a louse in the last tavern.

The louse, if there was one, wisely desisted, and the itch died. Relieved, William breathed deep and noticed that the swamp's scents had grown more pungent, the sap of resinous trees rising in answer to the oncoming rain. The air had suddenly assumed a muffled quality that deadened sound. No birds sang now; it was as though he and the horse rode alone through a world wrapped in cotton wool.

William didn't mind being alone. He'd grown up essentially alone, without brothers or sisters, and was content in his own company. Besides, solitude, he told himself, was good for thinking.

"Washington, Cartwright, Harrington, and Carver," he chanted softly. But beyond the names, there was little to think of with regard to his present errand, and he found his thoughts turn in a more familiar direction.

What he thought of most frequently on the road was women, and he touched the pocket under the tail of his coat, reflective. The pocket would hold one small book; it had been a choice on this journey between the New Testament his grandmother had given him or his treasured copy of *Harris's List of Covent Garden Ladies*. No great contest.

When William was sixteen, his father had caught him and a friend engrossed in the pages of his friend's father's copy of Mr. Harris's notorious guide to the splendors of London's women of pleasure. Lord John had raised an eyebrow and flipped slowly through the book, pausing now and then to raise the other eyebrow. He had then closed the book, taken a deep breath, administered a brief lecture on the necessary respect due to the female sex, then told the boys to fetch their hats.

At a discreet and elegant house at the end of Brydges Street, they took tea with a beautifully gowned Scottish lady, a Mrs. McNab, who appeared to be on the friendliest of terms with his father. At the conclusion of the refreshment, Mrs. McNab had rung a small brass bell, and . . .

William shifted in his saddle, sighing. Her name had been Margery, and he had written a perfervid panegyric to her. Had been madly in love with her.

He'd gone back, after a fevered week of reckoning his accounts, with the fixed intent of proposing marriage. Mrs. McNab had greeted him kindly, listened to his stumbling professions with the most sympathetic attention, then told him that Margery would, she was sure, be pleased with his good opinion but was, alas, occupied just this minute. However, there was a sweet young lass named Peggy, just come from Devonshire, who seemed lonely and would doubtless be so pleased to have a bit of conversation whilst he was waiting to speak with Margery . . .

The realization that Margery was just that minute doing with someone else what she'd done with *him* was such a staggering blow that he'd sat staring openmouthed at Mrs. McNab, rousing only when Peggy came in, fresh-faced, blond, and smiling, and with the most remarkable—

"Ah!" William slapped at the back of his neck, stung by a horsefly, and swore.

The horse had slowed without his noticing, and now that he *did* notice . . .

He swore again, louder. The road had disappeared.

"How the bloody hell did *that* happen?" He'd spoken loudly, but his voice seemed small, muted by the staggered trees. The flies had followed him; one bit the horse, who snorted and shook his head violently.

"Come on, then," William said, more quietly. "Can't be far off, can it? We'll find it."

He reined the horse's head around, riding slowly in what

he hoped was a wide semicircle that might cut the road. The ground was damp here, rumpled with tussocks of long, tangled grass, but not boggy. The horse's feet left deep curves where they struck in the mud, and thick flecks of matted mud and grass flew up, sticking to the horse's hocks and sides and William's boots.

He had been heading north–northwest. . . . He glanced instinctively at the sky, but no help to be found there. The uniform soft gray was altering, here and there a heavy-bellied cloud bulging through the muffling layer, sullen and murmurous. A faint rumble of thunder reached him, and he swore again.

His watch chimed softly, the sound strangely reassuring. He reined up for a moment, not wanting to risk dropping it in the mud, and fumbled it out of his watch pocket. Three o'clock.

"Not so bad," he said to the horse, encouraged. "Plenty of daylight left." Of course, this was a mere technicality, given the atmospheric conditions. It might as well have been the far side of twilight.

He looked up at the gathering clouds, calculating. No doubt about it: it was going to rain, and soon. Well, it wouldn't be the first time he and the horse had gotten wet. He sighed, dismounted, and unrolled his canvas bed-sack, part of his army equipment. He got up again and, with the canvas draped round his shoulders, his hat unlaced and pulled well down, resumed a dogged search for the road.

The first drops came pattering down, and a remarkable smell rose from the swamp in response. Earthy, rich, green, and . . . fecund, somehow, as though the swamp stretched itself, opening its body in lazy pleasure to the sky, releasing its scent like the perfume that wafts from an expensive whore's tumbling hair.

William reached by reflex for the book in his pocket, meaning to write down that poetic thought in the margins, but then shook his head, muttering, "Idiot," to himself.

He wasn't really worried. He had, as he'd told Captain Richardson, been in and out of the Great Dismal many times. Granted, he'd not been here by himself; he and his father had come now and then with a hunting party or with some of his father's Indian friends. And some years before. But—

"Shit!" he said. He'd pressed the horse through what he'd hoped was the thicket edging the road, only to find more thicket—dark clumps of hairy-barked juniper, aromatic as a glass of Holland gin in the rain. No room to turn. Muttering, he kneed the horse and pulled back, clicking his tongue.

Uneasily, he saw that the imprints of the horse's hooves were filling slowly with water. Not from the rain; the ground was wet. Very wet. He heard the sucking noise as the horse's back hooves struck bog, and by reflex he leaned forward, urgently kneeing the horse in the ribs.

Caught wrong-footed, the horse stumbled, caught himself—and then the horse's hind legs gave way suddenly, slipping in the mud, and he flung up his head, whinnying in surprise. William, taken equally unaware, bounced over his rolled bed-sack and fell off, landing with a splash.

He rose up like a scalded cat, panicked at the thought of being sucked down into one of the quaking bogs that lurked in the Great Dismal. He'd seen the skeleton of a deer caught in one once, nothing still visible save the antlered skull, half sunk and twisted to one side, its long yellow teeth showing in what he'd imagined to be a scream.

He splashed hastily toward a tussock, sprang atop it, and crouched there like the toad-king, heart hammering. His horse—was it trapped, had the bog got it?

The gelding was down, thrashing in the mud, whinnying in panic, muddy water flying in sheets from its struggles.

"Jesus." He clutched handsful of the rough grass, balanced precariously. Was it bog? Or only a slough?

Gritting his teeth, he stretched one long leg out, gingerly setting foot on the agitated surface. His boot pressed down . . . down . . . He pulled it hastily back, but it came readily, with a *ploop!* of mud and water. Again . . . yes, there was a bottom! All right, now the other . . . He stood up, arms waving storklike for balance, and . . .

"All right!" he said, breathless. A slough—no more, thank God!

He splashed toward the horse and snatched up the canvas bed-sack, loosened in the fall. Flinging it over the horse's head, he wrapped it hastily round the animal's eyes. It was what you did for a horse too panicked to leave a burning barn;

his father had shown him how when the barn at Mount Josiah had been struck by lightning one year.

Rather to his astonishment, it seemed to help. The horse was shaking its head to and fro but had quit churning its legs. He seized the bridle and blew into the horse's nostrils, talking calming nonsense.

The horse snorted, spraying him with droplets, but seemed to collect itself. He pulled its head up, and it rolled onto its chest with a great swash of muddy water, and in almost the same motion, surged heavily to its feet. It shook itself from head to tail, the canvas flapping loose and mud showering everything within ten feet of the animal.

William was much too happy to care. He seized the end of the canvas and pulled it off, then took hold of the bridle.

"Right," he said, breathless. "Let's get out of this."

The horse was not paying attention; its dish-faced head lifted suddenly, turned to the side.

"What—"

The huge nostrils flared red, and with an explosive grunt, the horse charged past him, jerking the reins from his hands and knocking him flat in the water—again.

"You frigging *bastard*! What the devil—" William stopped short, crouched in the mud. Something long, drab, and extremely fast passed less than two paces from him. Something big.

His head jerked round, but it was already gone, silent in pursuit of the blundering horse, whose panicked flight he could hear receding in the distance, punctuated by the crashing of broken brush and the occasional clang of shed equipment.

He swallowed. They hunted now and then together, he'd heard. Catamounts. In pairs.

The back of his neck prickled, and he turned his head as far as he could manage, afraid to move more for fear of drawing the attention of anything that might be lurking in the dark tangle of gum trees and underbrush behind him. No sound, save the increasing patter of raindrops on the swamp.

An egret burst white from the trees on the far side of the slough, nearly stopping his heart. He froze, breath held until he thought he'd suffocate in the effort to hear, but nothing happened, and at last he breathed and rose to his feet, the skirts of his coat plastered to his thighs, dripping.

He was standing in a peat bog; there was spongy vegetation under his feet, but the water rose up over the tops of his boots. He wasn't sinking, but he couldn't pull the boots out with his feet still in them and was obliged to draw his feet out one at a time, then wrench the boots free and squelch toward higher ground in his stockings, boots in his hands.

The sanctuary of a rotted log reached, he sat down to empty the water out of his boots, grimly reckoning his situation as he put them on again.

He was lost. In a swamp known to have devoured any number of people, both Indian and white. On foot, without food, fire, or any shelter beyond the flimsy protection offered by the canvas bed-sack—this the standard army issue, a literal sack made of canvas with a slit in it, meant to be stuffed with straw or dry grass—both these substances conspicuously lacking in his present circumstances. All he possessed otherwise was the contents of his pockets, this consisting of a clasp knife, a lead pencil, a very soggy bit of bread and cheese, a filthy handkerchief, a few coins, his watch, and his book, also doubtless soaked. He reached to check, discovered that the watch had stopped and the book was gone, and swore, loudly.

That seemed to help a bit, so he did it again. The rain was falling heavily now, not that it mattered in the slightest, given his state. The louse in his breeches, evidently waking to discover its habitat flooded, set off on a determined march to discover drier quarters.

Muttering blasphemies, he stood up, draped the empty canvas over his head, and limped off in the direction in which his horse had departed, scratching.

HE NEVER FOUND THE horse. Either the catamount had killed it, somewhere out of sight, or it had escaped to wander alone through the swamp. He did find two items shed from its saddle: a small waxed packet containing tobacco, and a frying pan. Neither of these seemed immediately useful, but he was loath to part with any remnant of civilization.

Soaked to the skin and shivering under the scanty shelter

of his canvas, he crouched among the roots of a sweet gum tree, watching lightning split the night sky. Each blue-white flash was blinding, even through closed eyelids, each jolt of thunder shaking air gone sharp as a knife with the acrid smell of lightning and burnt things.

He had grown almost accustomed to the cannonade when a tremendous blast knocked him flat and swept him skidding sideways through mud and rotted leaves. Choking and gasping, he sat up, swiping mud off his face. What the *devil* had happened? A sharp pain in his arm penetrated his confusion, and, looking down, he saw by the light of the lightning's flash that a splinter of wood, perhaps six inches long, was embedded in the flesh of his right forearm.

Glaring wildly round, he saw that the swamp near him was suddenly studded with splinters and chunks of fresh wood, and the smell of sap and heartwood rose, piercing amid the hot, dancing scent of electricity.

There. Another flash, and he saw it. A hundred feet away, he had noted a huge bald cypress, thinking to use it as a landmark come dawn; it was by far the tallest tree within sight. No longer: the lightning showed him empty air where the towering trunk had been, another flash, the ragged spike of what was left.

Quivering and half deafened by the thunder, he pulled the splinter out of his arm and pressed the fabric of his shirt to the wound to stop it bleeding. It wasn't deep, but the shock of the explosion made his hand shake. He pulled his canvas tight round his shoulders against the driving rain, and curled up again among the sweet gum's roots.

Sometime in the night, the storm moved off, and with the cessation of the noise, he lapsed into an uneasy doze, from which he woke to find himself staring into the white nothingness of fog.

A coldness beyond the bone chill of dawn went through him. His childhood had been spent in the Lake District of England, and he'd known from his earliest memories that the coming of fog on the fells was a danger. Sheep were often lost in the fog, falling to their deaths, parted from the flock and killed by dogs or foxes, freezing, or simply disappearing. Men were sometimes lost in the fog, as well.

The dead came down with the fog, Nanny Elspeth said. He

could see her, a spare old woman, straight-backed and fearless, standing at the nursery window, looking out at the drifting white. She'd said it quietly, as though to herself; he didn't think she'd realized he was there. When she did, she drew the curtain with a brisk snap and came to make his tea, saying nothing more.

He could do with a cup of hot tea, he thought, preferably with a great deal of whisky in it. Hot tea, hot buttered toast, jam sandwiches, and cake . . .

The thought of nursery teas recalled his wodge of soggy bread and cheese, and he drew this carefully out of his pocket, immeasurably heartened by its presence. He ate it slowly, savoring the tasteless mass as though it were a brandied peach, and felt very much better, despite the clammy touch of the fog on his face, the dripping of water from the ends of his hair, and the fact that he was still wet to the skin; his muscles ached from shivering all night.

He *had* had the presence of mind to set the frying pan out in the rain the night before, and thus had fresh water to drink, tasting deliciously of bacon fat.

"Not so bad," he said aloud, wiping his mouth. "Yet."

His voice sounded strange. Voices always did, in a fog.

He'd been lost in fog twice before, and he had no desire to repeat that experience, though repeat it he did, now and then, in nightmares. Stumbling blind through a white so thick he couldn't see his own feet, hearing the voices of the dead.

He closed his eyes, preferring momentary darkness to the swirl of white, but could still feel its fingers, cold on his face.

He'd heard the voices then. He tried not to listen now.

He got to his feet, determined. He had to move. At the same time, to go wandering blind through bogs and clinging growth would be madness.

He tied the frying pan to his belt and, slinging the wet canvas over his shoulder, put out a hand and began to grope. Juniper wouldn't do; the wood shredded under a knife, and the trees grew in such fashion that no branch ran straight for more than a few inches. Sweet gum or tupelo was better, but an alder would be best.

He found a small stand of alder saplings after an age of sidling cautiously through the mist, planting one foot at a time and waiting to see the effect, pausing whenever he hit a tree to press its leaves to his mouth and nose by way of identification.

Feeling about among the slender trunks, he picked one an inch or so in diameter and, planting his feet solidly, grasped the sapling with both hands and wrenched it up. It came, with a groan of yielding earth and a shower of leaves—and a heavy body slithered suddenly across his boot. He let out a cry and smashed the root end of his sapling down, but the snake had long since fled.

Sweating despite the chill, he undid the frying pan and used it to prod gingerly at the unseen ground. Eliciting no movement, and finding the surface relatively firm, he turned the pan over and sat upon it.

By bringing the wood close to his face, he could make out the movements of his hands sufficiently as to avoid cutting himself and, with a good deal of labor, managed to strip the sapling and trim it to a handy six-foot length. He then set about whittling the end to a sharpened point.

The Great Dismal was dangerous, but it teemed with game. That was the lure that drew hunters into its mysterious depths. William wasn't about to try to kill a bear, or even a deer, with a homemade spear. He was, however, reasonably adept at gigging frogs, or had been. A groom on his grandfather's estate had taught him long ago, he'd done it often with his father in Virginia, and while it wasn't a skill he'd found occasion to practice in the last few years in London, he felt sure that he hadn't forgotten.

He could hear the frogs all round him, cheerfully unimpressed by the fog.

"Brek-ek-ek-ex, co-ax, co-ax," he murmured. "Brek-ek-ek-ex co-ax!" The frogs seemed likewise unimpressed with quotations from Aristophanes.

"Right, you. Just wait," he said to them, testing his point with a thumb. Adequate. A gigging spear ideally would be trident-shaped. . . . Well, why not? He had time.

Biting his tongue with concentration, he set about to carve two additional sharpened twigs and notch them to join the main spear. He briefly considered twisting bits of juniper bark to make a binding, but rejected that notion in favor of unraveling a length of thread from the fringe of his shirt.

The swamp was sodden in the wake of the storm. He'd lost

his tinderbox, but he doubted that even one of Jehovah's thunderbolts, such as he'd witnessed the night before, would ignite a fire here. On the other hand, by the time the sun came out and he eventually succeeded in catching a frog, he'd probably be desperate enough to eat it raw.

He paradoxically found this thought comforting. He wasn't going to starve, then, nor would he die of thirst—being in this swamp was like living in a sponge.

He had nothing so definite as a plan. Only the knowledge that the swamp was large but finite. That being so, once he had the sun to guide him and could be assured of not wandering in circles, he proposed to make his way in a straight line until he reached solid ground or the lake. If he found the lake . . . well, Dismal Town was built on its edge. He had only to walk round the circumference, and eventually he would find it.

So, provided that he took care with the quaking bogs, didn't fall prey to some large animal, wasn't bitten by a venomous snake, and didn't take a fever from putrid water or the swamp's miasma, everything would be all right.

He tested the binding, jabbing the spear gently into the mud, and found it secure. Nothing to do but wait, then, for the fog to lift.

The fog showed no disposition to lift. If anything, it was thicker; he could barely make out his fingers, held a few inches from his eyes. Sighing, he gathered his damp coat round him, settled the gig by his side, and wriggled his spine into a precarious rest against the remaining alders. He put his arms round his knees to hoard what little heat his body still held, and closed his eyes to block the whiteness.

The frogs were still at it. Now without distraction, though, he began to hear the other noises of the swamp. Most of the birds were silent, waiting out the fog as he was, but now and then the deep, startling boom of a bittern echoed through the fog. There were scurrying noises and splashings now and then—muskrat? he wondered.

A loud *plunk!* betokened a turtle dropping off a log into water. He preferred those sounds, because he knew what they were. More unnerving were the faint rustlings, which might be the rubbing of branches—though the air was too still, surely, for wind?—or the movement of something hunting.

The shrill cry of something small, cut off abruptly. And the creakings and groanings of the swamp itself.

He'd heard the rocks talking to themselves on the fells at Helwater. The Lake District, his maternal grandparents' home. In the fog. He hadn't told anyone that.

He moved a little and felt something just below his jaw. Clapping a hand to the spot, he discovered a leech that had attached itself to his neck. Revolted, he ripped it loose and flung it as hard as he could into the fog. Patting himself all over with trembling hands, he settled back into his crouch, trying to repel the memories that came flooding in with the swirling mist. He'd heard his mother—his real mother—whisper to him, too. That was why he'd gone into the fog. They'd been picnicking on the fells, his grandparents and Mama Isobel and some friends, with a few servants. When the fog came down, sudden as it sometimes did, there was a general scurry to pack up the luncheon things, and he had been left by himself, watching the inexorable white wall roll silently toward him.

And he'd swear he'd heard a woman's whisper, too low to make out words but holding somehow a sense of longing, and he had known she spoke to him.

And he'd walked into the fog. For a few moments, he was fascinated by the movement of the water vapor near the ground, the way it flickered and shimmered and seemed alive. But then the fog grew thicker, and in moments he'd known he was lost.

He'd called out. First to the woman he thought must be his mother. *The dead come down in the fog.* That was nearly all he knew about his mother—that she was dead. She'd been no older than he was now when she died. He'd seen three paintings of her. They said he had her hair and her hand with a horse.

She'd answered him, he'd swear she'd answered him—but in a voice with no words. He'd felt the caress of cool fingers on his face, and he'd wandered on, entranced.

Then he fell, badly, tumbling over rocks into a small hollow, bruising himself and knocking out all his wind. The fog had billowed over him, marching past, urgent in its hurry to engulf things, as he lay stunned and breathless in the bottom of his small declivity. Then he began to hear the rocks murmur all around him, and he'd crawled, then run, as fast as he could, screaming. Fell again, got up and went on running.

Fell down, finally unable to go further, and huddled terrified and blind on the rough grass, surrounded by vast emptiness. Then he heard them calling out for him, voices he knew, and he tried to cry out in reply, but his throat was raw from screaming, and he made no more than desperate rasping noises, running toward where he thought the voices were. But sound moves in a fog, and nothing is as it seems: not sound, not time nor place.

Again and again and again, he ran toward the voices but fell over something, tripped and rolled down a slope, stumbled into rocky outcrops, found himself clinging to the edge of a scarp, the voices now behind him, fading into the fog, leaving him.

Mac had found him. A big hand had suddenly reached down and grabbed him, and the next minute he was lifted up, bruised and scraped and bleeding but clutched tight against the Scottish groom's rough shirt, strong arms holding him as though they'd never let him go.

He swallowed. When he had the nightmare, sometimes he woke with Mac holding him. Sometimes he didn't and woke in a cold sweat, unable to go back to sleep for fear of the waiting fog and the voices.

He froze now, hearing footsteps. Breathed cautiously—and smelled the unmistakable ripe smell of pig shit. He didn't move; wild pigs were dangerous if you startled them.

Snuffling noises, more footsteps, the rustle and shower of water drops as heavy bodies brushed the leaves of holly and yaupon bushes. Several of them, moving slowly but moving nonetheless. He sat up sharp, turning his head to and fro, trying to locate the sound exactly. Nothing could move with purpose in this fog—unless they were following a path.

The swamp was crisscrossed with game paths, made by the deer and used by everything from possums to black bears. These paths wound aimlessly, only two things certain about them: one, that they did lead to drinkable water, and two, that they did not lead into a quaking bog. Which, under the circumstances, was enough for William.

They'd said one other thing about his mother. "*Reckless,*" his grandmother had said sadly, shaking her head. *"She was always so reckless, so impulsive.*" And her eyes had rested then on him, apprehensive. *And you're just like her,* said those anxious eyes. *God help us all.*

"Maybe I am," he said out loud, and, gripping his frog spear, stood up, defiant. "But *I'm* not dead. Not yet."

He knew that much. And that to stand still when lost was a good idea only if someone was looking for you.

37

PURGATORY

AT MIDDAY on the third day, he found the lake. He'd come to it through a cathedral of towering bald cypress, theirgreat buttressed trunks rising like pillars from the flooded ground. Half starved, light-headed from a rising fever, he walked slowly through calf-deep water.

The air was still; so was the water. The only movement was the slow drag of his feet and the buzzing insects that plagued him. His eyes were swollen from the bites of mosquitoes, and the louse had company in the form of chiggers and sand fleas. The darning needles that darted to and fro didn't bite like the hundreds of swarming tiny flies, but had their own form of torment—they made him glance at them, sunlight glinting gold and blue and red from their gauzy wings and shining bodies, dizzying in the light.

The smooth surface of the water reflected the trees standing in it so perfectly that he could not be sure quite where he himself was, balanced precariously between two looking-glass worlds. He kept losing his sense of up and down, the dizzying sight through the branches of the towering cypress above the same as that below. The trees loomed more than eighty feet over him, and the sight of drifting clouds seeming to sail straight through the gently stirring branches below gave him the constant queer sense that he was about to fall—up or down, he couldn't tell.

He'd pulled the cypress splinter from his arm and done his best to bleed the wound, but there were smaller slivers of wood left behind, trapped under the skin, and his arm was hot and throbbing. So was his head. The chill and fog had disappeared as though they had never existed, and he walked slowly through a world of heat and stillness that shimmered round the edges. The backs of his eyes burned.

If he kept his eyes fixed on the purling of water away from his boots, the V-shaped waves broke the disturbing reflection and kept him upright. But watching the dragonflies . . . That made him sway and lose his bearings, as they seemed not fixed in either air or water, but part of both.

A strange depression appeared in the water, a few inches from his right calf. He blinked, then saw the shadow, sensed the weight of the heavy body undulating through the water. An evil, pointed, triangular head.

He gulped air and stopped dead. The moccasin, by great good fortune, did not.

He watched it swim away, and wondered whether it might be fit to eat. No matter; he'd broken his frog spear, though he'd caught three frogs before the fragile binding gave way. Small ones. They hadn't tasted bad, despite the rubbery feel of the raw flesh. His stomach clenched, gnawing, and he fought the insane impulse to dive after the snake, seize it, and rip the flesh from its bones with his teeth.

Maybe he could catch a fish.

He stood still for several minutes, to be sure the snake had left. Then swallowed and took another step. And walked on, eyes fixed on the small waves his moving feet made, breaking the looking-glass water into fragments around him.

A short time later, though, the surface began to move, hundreds of tiny wavelets lapping against the gray-brown wood of the cypress trees, shimmering so that the dizzy swirl of trees and clouds disappeared. He lifted his head and saw the lake before him.

It was vast. Much bigger than he had thought it would be. Giant bald cypresses stood in the water, the stumps and carcasses of earlier progenitors bleaching in the sun among them. The far shore was dark, thick with tupelo, alder, and hobblebush. And the water itself seemed to stretch for miles before him, brown as tea with the infusions of the trees that grew in it.

Licking his lips, he bent and scooped up a handful of the brown water and drank, then drank again. It was fresh, a little bitter.

He wiped a wet hand across his face; the cool wetness made him shiver with a sudden chill.

"Right, then," he said, feeling breathless. He pushed ahead, the ground sloping away gradually beneath him, until he stood in the open water, the dense growth of the swamp behind him. Chills still swept him, but he ignored them.

Lake Drummond had been named for an early governor of North Carolina. A hunting party, including Governor William Drummond, had gone into the swamp. A week later, Drummond, the sole survivor, had staggered out, half dead from hunger and fever but with news of a huge, unsuspected lake in the midst of the Great Dismal.

William drew a long, shuddering breath. Well, nothing had eaten him yet. And he'd reached the lake. Which way was Dismal Town?

He scanned the shore slowly, looking for any trace of chimney smoke, any break in the dense growth that might betoken a settlement. Nothing.

With a sigh, he reached into his pocket and found a sixpence. He flipped it into the air and nearly missed catching it, fumbling wildly as it bounced off his slow fingers. *Got it, got it!* Tails. Left, then. He turned resolutely and set off.

His leg knocked against something in the water, and he glanced down, just in time to see the white flash of the moccasin's mouth as it rose up in the water and struck at his leg. Reflex alone jerked his foot up, and the snake's fangs stuck briefly in the leather of his boot top.

He yelled and shook his leg violently, dislodging the reptile, which flew off and landed with a splash. Nothing daunted, the thing turned round upon itself almost instantly and arrowed toward him through the water.

William ripped the frying pan from his belt and swung it with all his strength, scooping the snake from the water and lofting it into the air. He didn't wait to see where it landed, but turned and ran, splashing wildly toward the shore.

He rushed up into the growth of gum and juniper and paused, gasping for breath, relieved. The relief was short-lived. He did turn then, to look, and saw the snake, its brown skin gleaming like copper, slither its way up onto the bank in his wake and come undulating determinedly after him across the matted ground.

He let out a yelp and fled.

He ran blindly, feet squelching at every step, ricocheting off trees and through slapping branches, his legs seized by hobblebush and holly, through which he fought his way in a shower of leaves and torn-off twigs. He didn't look back, but wasn't really looking forward, either, and thus ran without warning slap into a man standing in his path.

The man let out a cry and went over backward, William atop him. He pushed himself up and found himself looking down into the face of an astonished Indian. Before he could apologize, someone else grabbed him by the arm and pulled him roughly upright.

It was another Indian, who said something to him, angry and interrogative.

He groped for any stray bit of trade talk, found nothing, and, pointing in the direction of the lake, gasped, "Snake!" The Indians evidently understood the word, though, for their faces changed at once to wariness, and they looked where he was pointing. In support of his story, the annoyed moccasin shot into sight, wriggling through the roots of a sweet gum.

The Indians both let out exclamations, and one of them seized a club from a sling at his back and struck at the snake. He missed, and the snake writhed up at once into a tight coil and struck at him. The snake missed, too, but not by much, and the Indian jerked back, dropping his club.

The other Indian said something in disgust. Taking his own club in hand, he began warily to circle the moccasin. The snake, further enraged by this persecution, spun upon its own contortious coils with a loud hiss and launched itself, spear-like, at the second Indian's foot. He let out a cry and leapt back, though he did keep hold of his club.

William, meanwhile, delighted not to be the focus of the snake's annoyance, had backed out of the way. Seeing the snake momentarily off balance, though—if snakes could be said to have any in the first place—he gripped his frying pan, swung it high, and brought it down, edge-on, with all his force.

Brought it down again, and again and again, his strength driven by panic. At last he stopped, breathing like a blacksmith's bellows, sweat pouring down his face and body. Swallowing, he lifted the frying pan gingerly, expecting to find the snake a bloody mince on the riven ground.

Nothing. He could smell the reptile—a low stench, like that of rotten cucumbers—but could see nothing. He squinted, trying to make sense of the mass of cut-up mud and leaves, then looked up at the Indians.

One of them shrugged. The other pointed off toward the lake and said something. Evidently, the snake had prudently decided that it was outnumbered and returned to its own pursuits.

William stood up awkwardly, frying pan in hand. The men all exchanged nervous smiles.

He was comfortable with Indians, generally; many of them crossed his land, and his father always made them welcome, smoking with them on the veranda, taking supper with them. He couldn't tell which people these two claimed—the faces had the look of some one of the Algonkian tribes, high-cheeked and bold, but surely this was far south of their usual hunting grounds?

The Indians were examining him in turn, and exchanged a glance that set something tingling at the base of his spine. One of them said something to the other, watching him sidelong to see whether he understood. The other smiled broadly at him, showing brown-stained teeth.

"Tobacco?" the Indian asked, extending a hand, palm upward.

William nodded, trying to slow his breathing, and reached slowly into his coat, right-handed, so as not to have to set down the frying pan in his left.

Likely these two knew the way out of the swamp; he should establish friendly relations, and then . . . He was trying to think logically, but his lower faculties were interfering. His lower faculties thought he should get the devil away from here, and now.

Coming out with the waxed parcel of tobacco, he threw it

as hard as he could at the foremost Indian, who had started toward him, and ran.

A startled exclamation behind him, and then the sound of grunts and thumping feet. His lower faculties, thoroughly justified in their apprehensions, spurred him on, but he knew he couldn't keep it up for long; being chased by the snake had consumed most of what strength he had—and being obliged to run with an iron frying pan in one hand wasn't helping.

His best chance lay in outdistancing them sufficiently as to find a hiding place. With this thought in mind, he drove himself to greater exertions, dashing over open ground beneath a growth of gum trees, then swerving into a thicket of juniper, popping out again almost immediately onto a game trail. He hesitated for an instant—hide in the thicket?—but the urge to run was overwhelming, and he pounded down the narrow trail, vines and branches snatching at his clothes.

He heard the pigs in time, thank God. Startled snorts and grunts, and a great rustling of brush and sucking sounds, as a number of heavy bodies scrambled to their feet. He smelled warm mud and the reek of pig flesh; there must be a wallow round the curve of the path.

"Shit," he said under his breath, and leapt into the brush off the path. Jupiter, now what? Climb a tree? He was breathing hard, sweat running in his eyes.

All the trees nearby were juniper, some very large but dense and twisted, impossible to climb. He dodged round one and crouched behind it, trying to still his breathing.

His heart was hammering in his ears; he'd never hear pursuit. Something touched his hand, and he swung the frying pan by reflex, leaping to his feet.

The dog let out a surprised yelp as the pan glanced off its shoulder, then bared its teeth and growled at him.

"What the devil are you doing here?" William hissed at it. Bloody hell, the thing was the size of a small horse!

The dog's hackles rose, making it look exactly like a wolf—Jesus, it couldn't *be* a wolf, surely?—and it began to bark.

"Shut up, for God's sake!" But it was too late; he could hear Indian voices, excited and quite near. "Stay," he whispered, putting out a palm toward the dog as he edged backward. "Stay. Good dog."

The dog did not stay, but followed him, continuing to growl and bark. The sound of this further disturbed the pigs; there was a thunder of hooves along the path and a surprised whoop from one of the Indians.

William caught a flicker of movement from the corner of his eye and whirled, weapon at the ready. A very tall Indian blinked at him. Hell, more of them.

"Leave off, dog," said the Indian mildly, in a distinct Scots accent. William blinked in turn.

The dog did cease barking, though it continued to circle him, unnervingly close and growling all the time.

"Who—" William began, but was interrupted by the two original Indians, who at this point appeared suddenly out of the undergrowth. They came to an abrupt halt at sight of the newcomer—and cast a wary eye at the dog, who turned its attention on them, wrinkling back its muzzle and displaying an impressive array of gleaming teeth.

One of the original Indians said something sharp to the newcomer—thank God, they weren't together. The tall Indian replied, in a distinctly unfriendly tone. William had no idea what he'd said, but it didn't sit well with the other two. Their faces darkened, and one put a hand impulsively to his club. The dog made a sort of gurgling noise in its throat, and the hand fell at once.

The original Indians seemed disposed to argue, but the tall Indian cut them off, saying something peremptory and flipped a hand in an unmistakable "Be off with you" gesture. The other two exchanged glances, and William, straightening up, moved to stand by the side of the tall Indian and glowered at them. One of them gave him back the evil look, but his friend looked thoughtfully from the tall Indian to the dog and shook his head, the movement almost imperceptible. Without a further word, the two turned and left.

William's legs were shaking, waves of fever heat passing over him. Despite a disinclination to get any closer to the dog's level than necessary, he sat down on the ground. His fingers had gone stiff, he'd clutched the handle of the frying pan so hard. With some difficulty, he unbent them and set the thing down beside him.

"Thank you," he said, and wiped a sleeve across his sweating jaw. "You—speak English?"

"I've met Englishmen who'd say no, but I think ye'll maybe understand me, at least." The Indian sat down beside him, looking at him curiously.

"Christ," William said, "you aren't an Indian." *That* certainly wasn't an Algonkian face. Seen clearly now, the man was much younger than he'd thought, perhaps only a little older than himself, and plainly white, though his skin was sun-browned and he bore facial tattoos, a double line of dots that looped across his cheekbones. He was dressed in leather shirt and leggings, and wore a most incongruous red-and-black Scotchman's plaid over one shoulder.

"Aye, I am," the man said dryly. He raised his chin, indicating the direction taken by the departing Indians. "Where did ye meet wi' that lot?"

"By the lake. They asked for tobacco, and I—gave it to them. But then they chased me; I don't know why."

The man shrugged.

"They thought to take ye west and sell ye as a slave in the Shawnee lands." He smiled briefly. "They offered me half your price."

William took a deep breath.

"I thank you, then. That is—I suppose you haven't any intention of doing the same thing?"

The man didn't laugh aloud, but gave off a distinct sense of amusement.

"No. I'm no going west."

William began to feel a little easier, though the heat of his endeavors was beginning to give way to chills again. He wrapped his arms about his knees. His right arm was beginning to hurt again.

"You don't—do you suppose they might come back?"

"No," the man said, casually indifferent. "I told them to be gone."

William stared at him.

"And why do you think they'll do as you say?"

"Because they're Mingo," the man replied patiently, "and I'm Kahnyen'kehaka—a Mohawk. They're afraid of me."

William gave him a narrow look, but the man was not practicing upon him. He was nearly as tall as William himself, but thin as a coach whip, his dark-brown hair slicked back with bear grease. He looked competent, but not a person to inspire fear.

The man was studying him with an interest equal to his own. William coughed and cleared his throat, then extended a hand. "Your servant, sir. I'm William Ransom."

"Oh, I ken ye well enough," the man said, a rather odd note in his voice. He put out his own hand and shook William's firmly. "Ian Murray. We've met." His eyes traveled over William's torn, disheveled clothes, his scratched, sweating face, and his mud-caked boots. "Ye look a bit better than the last time I saw ye—but not much."

MURRAY LIFTED the camp kettle off the fire and set it on the ground. He laid the knife in the embers for a moment, then dipped the hot blade into the frying pan, now filled with water. The hot metal hissed and gave off clouds of steam.

"Ready?" he said.

"Yes."

William knelt down by a big poplar log and laid his injured arm flat on the wood. It was visibly swollen, the bulge of a large remnant splinter dark under his skin, the skin around it stretched and transparent with pus, painfully inflamed.

The Mohawk—he couldn't yet think of him as anything else, despite the name and accent—glanced at him across the log, eyebrows raised quizzically.

"Was that you I heard? Screamin', earlier?" He took hold of William's wrist.

"I shouted, yes," William said stiffly. "A snake struck at me."

"Oh." Murray's mouth twitched a little. "Ye scream like a lassie," he said, eyes returning to his work. The knife pressed down.

William made a deeply visceral noise.

"Aye, better," said Murray. He smiled briefly, as though to himself, and with a firm grip on William's wrist sliced cleanly through the skin beside the splinter, laying it open for six inches or so. Turning back the skin with the point of the knife, he flicked out the large splinter, then picked delicately at the smaller slivers the cypress shard had left behind.

Having removed as much as he could, he then wrapped a fold of his ragged plaid round the handle of the camp kettle, picked it up, and poured the steaming water into the open wound.

William made a much more visceral sound, this one accompanied by words.

Murray shook his head, and clicked his tongue in reproof.

"Aye, well. I suppose I'll have to keep ye from dying, because if ye do die, ye're bound to go to hell, usin' language like that."

"I don't propose to die," William said shortly. He was breathing hard, and mopped his brow with his free arm. He lifted the other gingerly and shook blood-tinged water from his fingertips, though the resulting sensation made him lightheaded. He sat down on the log, rather suddenly.

"Put your heid atween your knees, if ye're giddy," Murray suggested.

"I am not giddy."

There was no response to this save the sound of chewing. While waiting for the kettle to boil, Murray had waded into the water and pulled several handsful of some strong-smelling herb that grew on the verge. He was in process now of chewing the leaves, spitting the resultant green wads into a square of cloth. Extracting a rather shriveled onion from the haversack he carried, he cut a generous slice from this and eyed it critically, but seemed to think it would pass without mastication. He added it to his packet, folding the cloth neatly over the contents.

This he placed over the wound and wrapped it in place with strips of cloth torn from William's shirttail.

Murray glanced up at him thoughtfully.

"I suppose ye're verra stubborn?"

William stared at the Scot, put out at this remark, though in fact he had been told repeatedly, by friends, relatives, and military superiors, that his intransigence would one day kill him. Surely it didn't show on his face!

"What the devil do you mean by that?"

"It wasna meant as an insult," Murray said mildly, and bent to tighten the knot of the impromptu bandage with his teeth. He turned away and spat out a few threads. "I hope ye are—because it'll be a good distance to find ye help, and if you're sufficiently stubborn as not to die on me, that would be good, I think."

"I said I don't propose to die," William assured him. "And I don't need help. Where—are we anywhere near Dismal Town?"

Murray pursed his lips.

"No," he said, and raised one brow. "Were ye bound there?"

William considered for an instant, but nodded. No harm in telling him that, surely.

Murray raised an eyebrow.

"Why?"

"I—have business with some gentlemen there." As he said this, William's heart gave a lurch. Christ, the book! He'd been so confounded by his various trials and adventures that the true importance of his loss had not even struck him.

Beyond its general entertainment value and its usefulness as palimpsest for his own meditations, the book was vital to his mission. It contained several carefully marked passages whose code gave him the names and locations of those men he was to visit—and, more importantly, what he was to tell them. He could recall a good many of the names, he thought, but for the rest . . .

His dismay was so great that it overshadowed the throbbing in his arm, and he stood up abruptly, seized by the urge to rush back into the Great Dismal and begin combing it, inch by inch, until he should recover the book.

"Are ye all right, man?" Murray had risen, too, and was looking at him with a combination of curiosity and concern.

"I—yes. Just—I thought of something, that's all."

"Well, think about it sitting down, aye? Ye're about to fall into the fire."

In fact, William's vision had gone bright, and pulsating dots of dark and light obscured most of Murray's face, though the look of alarm was still visible.

"I—yes, I will." He sat down even more abruptly than he'd risen, a heavy cold sweat sudden on his face. A hand on his good arm urged him to lie down, and he did, feeling dimly that it was preferable to fainting.

Murray made a Scottish noise of consternation and muttered something incomprehensible. William could feel the other man hovering over him, uncertain.

"I'm fine," he said—without opening his eyes. "I just . . . need to rest a bit."

"Mmphm."

William couldn't tell whether this particular noise was meant as acceptance or dismay, but Murray went away, coming back a moment later with a blanket, with which he covered William without comment. William made a feeble gesture of thanks, unable to speak, as his teeth had begun to chatter with a sudden chill.

His limbs had been aching for some time, but he had ignored it in the need to push on. Now the burden of it fell full on him, a bone-deep ache that made him want to moan aloud. To keep from it, he waited until the chill relaxed enough to let him speak, then called to Murray.

"You are familiar with Dismal Town yourself, sir? You've been there?"

"Now and again, aye." He could see Murray, a dark silhouette crouched by the fire, and hear the chink of metal on stone. "It's verra aptly named."

"Ha," William said weakly. "I daresay. And h-h-have you met a Mr. Washington, by chance?"

"Five or six of them. The general's got a good many cousins, aye?"

"The g-g—"

"General Washington. Ye've heard of him, maybe?" There was a distinct hint of amusement in the Scottish Mohawk's voice.

"I have, yes. But—surely that . . ." This made no sense. His voice trailed off, and he rallied, forcing his drifting thoughts back into coherence. "It is a Mr. Henry Washington. He is kin to the general, too?"

"So far as I ken, anyone named Washington within three hundred miles is kin to the general." Murray stooped to his bag, coming out with a large furry mass, a long, naked tail dangling from it. "Why?"

"I—nothing." The chill had eased, and he drew a grateful breath, the knotted muscles of his belly relaxing. But the faint threads of wariness were making themselves felt through puzzlement and the gathering fog of fever. "Someone told me that Mr. Henry Washington was a prominent Loyalist."

Murray turned toward him in astonishment.

"Who in Bride's name would tell ye that?"

"Plainly someone grossly mistaken." William pressed the heels of his hands against his eyes. His wounded arm hurt. "What is that thing? Possum?"

"Muskrat. Dinna fash; it's fresh. I killed it just before I met ye."

"Oh. Good." He felt obscurely comforted and couldn't think why. Not the muskrat; he'd eaten muskrat often enough and found it tasty, though the fever had stolen his appetite. He felt weak with hunger, but had no desire to eat. Oh. No, it was the "dinna fash." Spoken with just that kindly, matter-of-fact intonation—Mac the groom had used to say that to him, often, whether the trouble was being thrown from his pony or not being allowed to ride into the town with his grandfather. *"Dinna fash; it will be all right."*

The ripping sound of skin parting from the underlying muscle made him momentarily dizzy and he closed his eyes.

"Ye've got a red beard."

Murray's voice came to him, filled with surprise.

"You've only just now noticed that?" William said crossly, and opened his eyes. The color of his beard was an embarrassment to him; while the hair on his head, chest, and limbs was a decent sort of dark chestnut, that on his chin and privates was an unexpectedly vivid shade that mortified him. He shaved fastidiously, even on shipboard or on the road—but his razor, of course, had departed with the horse.

"Well, aye," Murray said mildly. "I expect I was distracted earlier." He fell silent, concentrating on his work, and William tried to relax his mind, hoping to sleep for a time. He was tired enough. Repeated images of the swamp played themselves out before his closed eyes, though, wearying him with visions that he could neither ignore nor dismiss.

Roots like the loops of snares, mud, rank brown dollops of cold pig shit, the turds uneasily humanlike . . . churned dead leaves . . .

Dead leaves floating on water like brown glass, reflections shattering around his shins . . . words in the water, the pages of his book, faint, mocking as they sank away . . .

Looking up, the sky as vertiginous as the lake, feeling that he might fall up as easily as down and drown in the water-clogged air . . . drowning in his sweat . . . a young woman licked the sweat from his cheek, tickling, her body heavy, hot, and cloying, so that he turned and twisted, but could not escape her oppressive attentions . . .

. . . sweat collecting behind his ears, thick and greasy in his hair . . . growing like fat slow pearls in the stubble of his vulgar beard . . . chilling on his skin, his clothes a dripping shroud . . . the woman was still there, dead now, dead weight on his chest, pinning him to the icy ground . . .

Fog and the creeping cold . . . white fingers prying into his eyes, his ears. He must keep his mouth shut or it would reach inside him . . . All white.

He curled into a ball, shaking.

William did at last fall deeper into a fitful sleep, from which he roused some time later, to the rich smell of roasted muskrat, and found the enormous dog lying pressed against him, snoring.

"Jesus," he said, with disconcerting recollections of the young woman in his dreams. He pushed feebly at the dog. "Where did *that* come from?"

"That's Rollo," Murray said reprovingly. "I made him lie wi' ye for a bit of heat; ye've got a shaking ague, if ye hadn't noticed."

"I had noticed that, yes." William struggled upright and made himself eat but was happy to lie down again, at a safe distance from the dog, who was now lying on his back, paws drooping, looking like nothing so much as a giant hairy dead insect. William passed a hand downward over his clammy face, trying to remove *that* disturbing image from his mind before it made its way into his fever dreams.

Night had come well on, and the sky opened overhead, clear and empty and vast, moonless but brilliant with distant stars. He thought of his father's father, dead long before his own birth, but a noted amateur astronomer. His father had often taken him—and sometimes his mother—to lie on the lawns at Helwater, to look up at the stars and name the constellations. It was a cold sight, that blue-black emptiness, and made his fevered blood tremble, but the stars were a comfort, nonetheless.

Murray was looking upward too, a look of distance on his tattooed face.

William lay back, half-propped against the log, trying to think. What was he to do next? He was still trying to absorb the news that Henry Washington and thus, presumably, the rest of his Dismal Town contacts were rebels. Was this odd Scottish Mohawk right in what he'd said? Or did he seek to mislead him, for some purpose of his own?

What would that be, though? Murray could have no notion who William was, beyond his name and his father's name. And Lord John had been a private citizen when they had met years before, on Fraser's Ridge. Murray could not tell, surely, that William was a soldier, let alone an intelligencer, and could not possibly know his mission.

And if he did not wish to mislead him and was correct in what he said . . . William swallowed, his mouth sticky and dry. Then he had had a narrow escape. What might have happened, had he walked into a nest of rebels, in such a remote place as Dismal Town, and blithely revealed himself and his purpose? *They'd hang you from the nearest tree,* his brain said coldly, *and toss your body into the swamp. What else?*

Which led to an even more uncomfortable thought: how could Captain Richardson have been so mistaken in his information?

He shook his head violently, trying to shake his thoughts into order, but the only result was to make him dizzy again. Murray's attention had been attracted by the motion, though; he looked in William's direction, and William spoke, on impulse.

"You are a Mohawk, you said."

"I am."

Seeing that tattooed face, the eyes dark in their sockets, William didn't doubt it.

"How did that come to be?" he asked hurriedly, lest Murray think he was casting aspersions on the other's truthfulness. Murray hesitated visibly, but did answer.

"I married a woman of the Kahnyen'kehaka. I was adopted into the Wolf clan of the people of Snaketown."

"Ah. Your . . . wife is . . . ?"

"I am no longer wed." It wasn't said with any tone of hostility, but with a sort of bleak finality that put paid to any further conversation.

"I'm sorry," William said formally, and fell silent. The chills were coming back, and despite his reluctance, he slid down, drawing the blanket up around his ears, and huddled against the dog, who sighed deeply and released a burst of flatulence but didn't stir.

When the ague finally eased again, he lapsed back into dreams, these now violent and dreadful. His mind had taken hold somehow of Indians, and he was pursued by savages who turned into snakes, snakes who became tree roots that writhed through the crevices of his brain, bursting his skull, liberating further nests of snakes who coiled themselves into nooses . . .

He woke again, drenched in sweat and aching to the bones. He tried to rise but found his arms would not support him. Someone knelt by him—it was the Scot, the Mohawk . . . Murray. He located the name with something like relief, and with even more relief, realized that Murray was holding a canteen to his lips.

It was water from the lake; he recognized its odd, fresh-tasting bitterness, and drank thirstily.

"Thank you," he said hoarsely, and gave back the empty canteen. The water had given him strength enough to sit up. His head still swam with fever, but the dreams had retreated, at least for the moment. He imagined that they lurked just beyond the small ring of light cast by the fire, waiting, and determined that he would not sleep again—not at once.

The pain in his arm was worse: a hot, stretched feeling, and a throbbing that ran from fingertips to the middle of his upper arm. Anxious to keep both the pain and the night at bay, he had another try at conversation.

"I have heard that the Mohawk think it unmanly to show fear—that if captured and tortured by an enemy, they will not show any sign of distress. Is that true?"

"Ye try not to be in that position," Murray said, very dry. "Should it happen, though . . . ye must show your courage, that's all. Ye sing your death song and hope to die well. Is it different for a British soldier, then? Ye dinna want to die as a coward, do ye?"

William watched the flickering patterns behind his closed eyelids, hot and ever-changing, shifting with the fire.

"No," he admitted. "And it's not so different—the hoping to die well if you have to, I mean. But it's more likely to be a matter of just being shot or knocked on the head, isn't it, if you're a soldier—rather than being tortured to death by inches. Save you run afoul of a savage, I suppose. What—have you ever seen someone die like that?" he asked curiously, opening his eyes.

Murray reached out one long arm to turn the spit, not answering at once. The firelight showed his face, unreadable.

"Aye, I have," he said quietly, at last.

"What did they do to him?" He wasn't sure why he'd asked; perhaps only for distraction from the throbbing in his arm.

"Ye dinna want to know." This was said very definitely; Murray was not by any means teasing him into further inquiry. Nonetheless, it had the same effect; William's vague interest sharpened at once.

"Yes, I do."

Murray's lips tightened, but William knew a few things about extracting information by this time and was wise enough to preserve silence, merely keeping his eyes fixed on the other man.

"Skinned him," Murray said at last, and poked at the fire with a stick. "One of them. In bitty pieces. Thrust burning slivers of pitch pine into the raw places. Cut away his privates. Then built up the fire about his feet, to burn him before he could die of the shock. It . . . took some time."

"I daresay." William tried to conjure a picture of the proceedings—and succeeded much too well, turning away his eyes from the blackened muskrat carcass, stripped to bones.

He shut his eyes. His arm continued to throb with each beat of his heart, and he tried not to imagine the sensation of burning slivers being forced into his flesh.

Murray was silent; William couldn't even hear his breathing. But he knew, as surely as if he were inside the other's head, that he, too, was imagining the scene—though in his case, imagination was not necessary. He would be reliving it.

William shifted a little, sending a hot blaze of pain through his arm, and clenched his teeth, not to make any noise.

"Do the men—did *you,* I should say—think how you would do, yourself?" he asked quietly. "If you could stand it?"

"Every man thinks that." Murray got up abruptly and went to the far edge of the clearing. William heard him make water, but it was some minutes longer before he came back.

The dog wakened suddenly, head lifting, and wagged its huge tail slowly to and fro at sight of its master. Murray laughed softly and said something in an odd tongue—Mohawk? Erse?—to the dog, then bent and ripped a haunch from the muskrat's remains, tossing it to the beast. The animal rose like lightning, its teeth snapping shut on the carcass, then trotted happily to the far side of the fire and lay down, licking its prize.

Bereft of his bed companion, William lay down gingerly, head pillowed on his good arm, and watched as Murray cleaned his knife, scrubbing blood and grease from it with handfuls of grass.

"You said you sing your death song. What sort of song is that?"

Murray looked nonplused at that.

"I mean," William fumbled for clearer meaning, "what sort of thing would you—would one—say in a death song?"

"Oh." The Scotsman looked down at his hands, the long knobbed fingers rubbing slowly down the length of the blade. "I've only heard the one, mind. The other two I saw die that way—they were white men and didna have death songs, as such. The Indian—he was an Onondaga—he . . . well, there was a good deal in the beginning about who he was: a warrior of what people, I mean, and his clan, his family. Then quite a bit about how much he despised u—the folk who were about to kill him." Murray cleared his throat.

"A bit about what he'd done: his victories, valiant warriors he'd killed, and how they'd welcome him in death. Then . . . how he proposed to cross the . . ." He groped for a word. " . . . the—it—the way between here and what lies after death. The divide, I suppose ye'd say, though the word means something more like a chasm."

He was quiet for a moment, but not as though he had finished—more as though trying to recall something exactly. He straightened himself suddenly, took a deep breath, and with his eyes closed, began to recite something in what William supposed to be the Mohawk tongue. It was fascinating—a tattoo of "n"s and "r"s and "t"s, steady as a drumbeat.

"Then there was a bit where he went on about the nasty creatures he'd encounter on his way to paradise," Murray said, breaking off abruptly. "Things like flying heads, wi' teeth."

"Ew," said William, and Murray laughed, taken by surprise.

"Aye. I wouldna like to see one, myself."

William considered this for a moment.

"Do you compose your own death song ahead of time—in case of need, I mean? Or just trust to the, um, inspiration of the moment?"

Murray looked a little taken back by that. He blinked and looked aside.

"I . . . well . . . it's no usually talked about, ken? But aye—I did have a friend or two who told me a bit about what they'd thought of, should there ever be need."

"Hmm." William turned on his back, looking up at the stars. "Do you sing a death song only if you're being tortured to death? What if you're only ill but think you might die?"

Murray stopped what he was doing and peered toward him, suspicious.

"Ye're no dying, are ye?"

"No, just wondering," William assured him. He didn't *think* he was dying.

"Mmphm," the Scot said dubiously. "Aye, well. No, ye sing your death song if ye're sure ye're about to die; it doesna matter why."

"The more credit to you, though," William suggested, "if you do it whilst having burning splinters stuck into you?"

The Scot laughed out loud, and suddenly looked much less like an Indian. He rubbed his knuckles across his mouth.

"To be honest . . . the Onondaga . . . I didna think he did it so verra well," Murray blurted. "It doesna seem right to criticize, though. I mean, I canna say I'd do better—in the circumstances."

William laughed, too, but both men fell silent then. William supposed that Murray was, as he was, imagining himself in such case, tied to a stake, about to suffer appalling torture. He gazed up into the void above, tentatively composing a few lines: *I am William Clarence Henry George Ransom, Earl of* . . . No, he'd never liked his string of names. *I am William* . . . he thought muzzily. *William* . . . *James* . . . James was his secret name; he hadn't thought of it in years. Better than Clarence, though. *I am William.* What else was there to say? Not much, as yet. No, he'd better not die, not until he'd done something worth a proper death song.

Murray was silent, the fire reflected in his somber eyes. Watching him, William thought the Scottish Mohawk had had his own death song ready for some time. Shortly he fell asleep to the crackle of fire and the quiet crunching of bones, burning, but brave.

HE WAS WANDERING through a haze of tortured dreams involving being chased by black serpents across an endless wobbling bridge over a bottomless chasm. Flying yellow heads with rainbow eyes attacked him in swarms, their tiny teeth, sharp as a mouse's, piercing his flesh. He waved an arm to beat them off, and the pain that shot through the arm at the motion roused him.

It was still dark, though the cool, live feel of the air told him the dawn was not far off. The touch of it on his face made him shiver, prompting another chill.

Someone said something that he didn't understand, and still entangled in the miasma of fever dreams, he thought it must be one of the serpents he'd been talking to earlier, before they started chasing him.

A hand touched his forehead, and a large thumb pried up one of his eyelids. An Indian's face floated in his sleep-bleared vision, looking quizzical.

He made an irritable noise and jerked his head away, blinking. The Indian said something, questioning, and a familiar voice replied. Who . . . Murray. The name seemed to have been floating by his elbow, and he recalled dimly that Murray himself had accompanied him in his dream, rebuking the serpents in a stern Scotch burr.

He wasn't speaking English now, though, nor even the peculiar Scotch tongue from the Highlands. William forced his head to turn, though his body was still convulsed with chill.

A number of Indians were crouched round the fire, squatting to keep their backsides from the dew-wet grass. One, two, three . . . six of them. Murray was sitting on the log with one of them, engaged in conversation.

No, seven. Another man, the one who had touched him, leaned over him, peering into his face.

"Think you're going to die?" the man asked, with a faint air of curiosity.

"No," William said between clenched teeth. "Who the devil are you?"

The Indian seemed to think this an amusing question and called to his fellows, apparently repeating it. They all laughed, and Murray glanced in his direction, rising as he saw that William was awake.

"Kahnyen'kehaka," the man looming over him said, and grinned. "Who the devil are *you*?"

"My kinsman," Murray said shortly, before William could reply. He nudged the Indian aside and squatted beside William. "Still alive, then?"

"Evidently." He scowled up at Murray. "Care to introduce me to your . . . friends?"

The first Indian went off into gales of laughter at this and apparently translated it to the two or three others who had come to peer interestedly at him. They thought it funny, too.

Murray seemed substantially less amused.

"My kinsmen," he said dryly. "Some of them. D'ye need water?"

"You have a lot of kinsmen . . . cousin. Yes, if you please."

He struggled upright, one-armed, reluctant to leave the clammy comfort of his dew-wet blanket but obeying an innate urge that told him he wanted to be on his feet. Murray seemed to know these Indians well, but kin or not, there was a certain tenseness to Murray's mouth and shoulders. And it was plain enough that Murray had told them that William was his kinsman because if he hadn't . . .

"Kahnyen'kehaka." That's what the Indian had said when asked who he was. It wasn't his name, William realized suddenly. It was what he was. Murray had used the word yesterday, when he'd sent away the two Mingos.

"*I'm Kahnyen'kehaka,*" he'd said. "*A Mohawk. They're afraid of me.*" He'd said it as a simple statement of fact, and William had not chosen to make an issue of it, circumstances being as they were. Seeing a number of what were plainly Mohawk together, he could appreciate the Mingos' prudence. The Mohawk gave off an air of genial ferocity, this overlying a casual confidence entirely proper to men who were prepared to sing—however badly—whilst being emasculated and burnt alive.

Murray handed him a canteen, and he drank thirstily, then splashed a little water over his face. Feeling a bit better, he went for a piss, then walked to the fire and squatted between two of the braves, who eyed him with open curiosity.

Only the man who had pried his eyelid open seemed to speak English, but the rest nodded to him, reserved but friendly enough. William glanced across the fire and started back, nearly losing his balance. A long, tawny shape lay in the grass beyond the fire, the light gleaming on its flanks.

"It's dead," Murray said dryly, seeing his startlement. The Mohawk all laughed.

"Gathered that," he replied, just as dryly, though his heart was still pounding from the shock. "Serve it right, if it's the one that took my horse." Now he came to look, he perceived other shapes beyond the fire. A small deer, a pig, a spotted cat, and two or three egrets, small white mounds in the dark grass. Well, that explained the Mohawks' presence in the swamp: they'd come for the hunting, like everyone else.

Dawn was coming; the faint wind stirred the damp hair on his neck and brought him the tang of blood and musk from the animals. Both his mind and his tongue felt thick and slow, but he managed a few words of praise for the success of the hunters; he knew how to be polite. Murray, translating for him, looked surprised, though pleased, to discover that William had manners. William didn't feel well enough to take offense.

Conversation became general then, accomplished for the most part in Mohawk. The Indians showed no particular interest in William, though the man beside him handed him a chunk of cold meat in a companionable fashion. He nodded thanks and made himself eat it, though he would as soon have forced down one of his shoe soles. He felt unwell and clammy, and when he had finished the meat, nodded politely to the Indian next him and went to lie down again, hoping he wouldn't vomit.

Seeing this, Murray lifted his chin in William's direction and said something to his friends in Mohawk, ending with a question of some kind.

The English-speaker, a short, thickset fellow in a checked wool shirt and buckskin trousers, shrugged in reply, then got up and came to bend over him again.

"Show me this arm," he said, and without waiting for William to comply, picked up his wrist and pulled up the sleeve of his shirt. William nearly passed out.

When the black spots stopped whirling in front of his eyes, he saw that Murray and two more Indians had come to join the first. All of them were looking at his exposed arm in open consternation. He didn't want to look, but risked a glance. His forearm was grotesquely swollen, nearly twice its normal size, and dark reddish streaks ran from under the tightly bandaged poultice, down his arm toward the wrist.

The English-speaker—what had Murray called him? *Glutton,* he thought, but why?—drew his knife and cut the bandage. Only with the removal of its constriction did William realize how uncomfortable the binding had been. He repressed the urge to rub his arm, feeling the pins and needles of returning circulation. Pins and needles, bloody hell. It felt as though his arm were engulfed by a mass of fire ants, all stinging.

"Shit," he said, through his teeth. All the Indians knew that word, evidently, for they all laughed, save Glutton and Murray, who were squinting at his arm.

Glutton—he didn't look fat, why was he called that?—poked gingerly at the arm, shook his head, and said something to Murray, then pointed off toward the west.

Murray rubbed a hand over his face, then shook his head violently, in the manner of a man shaking off fatigue or worry. Then he shrugged and asked something of the group at large. Nods and shrugs, and several of the men got up and went into the wood.

A number of questions revolved slowly through William's brain, round and bright like the metal globes of his grandfather's orrery in the library of the London house at Jermyn Street.

What are they doing?

What's happening?

Am I dying?

Am I dying like a British soldier?

Why did he . . . British soldier . . . His mind caught the tail of that one as it passed, pulling it down to look at more carefully. "*British soldier*"—who had said that? The answer spun slowly into view. Murray. When they'd talked in the night . . . what had Murray said?

"Is it different for a British soldier, then? Ye dinna want to die as a coward, do ye?"

"Not going to die at all," he muttered, but his mind ignored him, intent on tracking this small mystery. What had Murray meant by that? Had he been speaking theoretically? Or had he in fact recognized William *as* a British soldier?

Not possible, surely.

And what the devil had he said in reply? The sun was coming up, the dawning light bright enough to hurt his eyes, soft as it was. He squinted, concentrating.

"*It's not so different—the hoping to die well if you have to,*" he'd said. So he'd answered as though he *was* a British soldier, damn him.

At the moment, he didn't really care whether he died well or like a dog. . . . Where was the—oh, there. Rollo sniffed at his arm, making a small whining noise in the back of his throat, then nosed at the wound and began to lick it. It felt most peculiar: painful, but weirdly soothing, and he made no move to drive the dog away.

What . . . oh, yes. He had simply replied, not noticing what Murray had said. But what if Murray *did* know who—or what—he was? A small stab of alarm pierced the muddle of his slowing thoughts. Had Murray been following him, before he came into the swamp? Seen him speaking to the man at the wilderness farm near the edge of the swamp, perhaps, and followed, ready to intercept him when the opportunity should offer? But if that were true . . .

What Murray had said about Henry Washington, about Dismal Town—was it a lie?

The stocky Indian knelt down beside him, nudging the dog

away. William couldn't ask any of the questions clogging his brain.

"Why do they call you Glutton?" he asked instead, through the haze of hot pain.

The man grinned and pulled open the neck of his shirt, to display a mass of welted scars that covered neck and chest.

"Killed one," he said. "With my hands. My spirit animal now. You have one?"

"No."

The Indian looked reproving at this.

"You need one, you going to live through this. Pick one. Pick a strong one."

Muzzily obedient, William groped through random images of animals: pig . . . snake . . . deer . . . catamount . . . no, too rank, foul-smelling.

"Bear," he said, settling on that with a sense of certainty. Didn't get any stronger than a bear, did it?

"Bear," the Indian repeated, nodding. "Yes, that's good." He slit William's sleeve with his knife; the fabric would no longer fit easily over the swollen arm. Sunlight washed suddenly over him, glanced silver from the blade of his knife. He looked at William then and laughed.

"You got one red beard, Bear Cub, you know that?"

"I know that," William said, and shut his eyes against the spears of morning's light.

GLUTTON WANTED the catamount's skin, but Murray, alarmed by William's condition, refused to wait for him to skin it. The upshot of the resulting argument was that William found himself occupying a hastily constructed travois, cheek by jowl with the dead cat, being dragged over rough terrain behind Murray's horse. Their destination, he was given to understand, was a small settlement some ten miles distant, which boasted a doctor.

Glutton and two of the other Mohawk came with them in order to show the way, leaving their other companions to continue hunting.

The catamount had been gutted, which William supposed might be better than not—the day was warm, and getting hot—but the scent of blood drew masses of flies, which feasted at their leisure, as the horse, burdened with the travois, could not go fast enough to outpace them. The flies hummed and buzzed and shrilled about his ears, setting his nerves on edge, and while most were interested in the cat, enough of them cared to try William for taste as sufficed to keep his mind off his arm.

When the Indians paused for urination and water, they hauled William to his feet—a relief, even wobbly as he was. Murray glanced at his fly-bitten, sunburned features, and reaching into a skin bag slung at his waist, pulled out a battered tin, which turned out to contain a highly malodorous ointment, with which he anointed William liberally.

"It's no but another five or six miles," he assured William, who hadn't asked.

"Oh, good," William said, with what vigor he could muster. "It's not hell after all, then—only purgatory. What's another thousand years?"

That made Murray laugh, though Glutton regarded him in puzzlement.

"Ye'll do," Murray said, clapping him on the shoulder. "Want to walk for a bit?"

"God, yes."

His head swam, his feet refused to point forward, and his knees seemed to bend in unwonted directions, but anything was better than another hour of communing with the flies that blanketed the catamount's glazed eyes and drying tongue. Provided with a stout stick cut from an oak sapling, he plodded doggedly behind the horse, alternately drenched with sweat and shaking with clammy chills, but determined to stay upright until and unless he actually fell down.

The ointment did keep the flies at bay—all the Indians were likewise smeared with it—and when not fighting the shaking, he lapsed into a sort of trance, concerned only with putting one foot before the other.

The Indians and Murray kept an eye on him for a time, but then, satisfied that he could remain upright, returned to their own conversations. He could not understand the two Mohawk-speakers, but Glutton appeared to be catechizing Murray closely concerning the nature of purgatory.

Murray was having some difficulty in explaining the concept, apparently owing to the Mohawk having no notion of sin, or of a God concerned with the wickedness of man.

"You're lucky you became Kahnyen'kehaka," Glutton said at last, shaking his head. "A spirit not satisfied with an evil man being dead but that wants to torture him after death? And Christians think we're cruel!"

"Aye, well," Murray replied, "but think. Say a man is a coward and hasna died well. Purgatory gives him a chance to prove his courage after all, no? And once he is proved a proper man, then the bridge is open to him, and he can pass through the clouds of terrible things unhindered to paradise."

"Hmm!" Glutton said, though he seemed still dubious. "I suppose if a man can stand to be tortured for hundreds of years . . . but how does he do this, if no body?"

"D'ye think a man needs a body to be tortured?" Murray asked this with a certain dryness, and Glutton grunted in what might be either agreement or amusement and dropped the subject.

They all walked in silence for some time, surrounded by birdcalls and the loud buzzing of flies. Preoccupied with the effort of remaining upright, William had fixed his attention on the back of Murray's head as a means of not veering off the trail and thus noticed when the Scot, who was leading the horse, slowed his pace a little.

He thought at first that this was on his account and was about to protest that he could keep up—for a little while, at least—but then saw Murray glance swiftly at the other Mohawk, who had drawn ahead, then turn to Glutton and ask something, in a voice too low for William to make out the words.

Glutton hunched his shoulders in reluctance, then let them fall, resigned. "Oh, I see," he said. "She's your purgatory, eh?"

Murray made a sound of reluctant amusement. "Does it matter? I asked if she's well."

Glutton sighed, shrugging one shoulder.

"Yes, well. She has a son. A daughter, too, I think. Her husband . . ."

"Aye?" Murray's voice had hardened in some fashion.

"You know Thayendanegea?"

"I do." Now Murray sounded curious. William was curious himself, in a vague, unfocused sort of way, and waited to hear who Thayendanegea might be and what he had to do with the woman who was—who had been—Murray's paramour? Oh, no.

"I am no longer wed." His wife, then. William felt a faint pang of sympathy, thinking of Margery. He had thought of her only casually, if at all, in the past four years, but suddenly her betrayal seemed tragedy. Images of her swam about him, fractured by a sense of grief. He felt moisture running down his face, didn't know if it was sweat or tears. The thought came to him, slowly, as from a great distance, that he must be off his head, but he had no notion what to do about it.

The flies weren't biting but were still buzzing in his ears. He listened to the hum with great concentration, convinced that the flies were trying to tell him something important. He listened with great attention, but could make out only nonsense syllables. "Shosha." "Nik." "Osonni." No, that was a word, he knew that one! White man, it meant white man—were they talking about him?

He pawed clumsily at his ear, brushing at the flies, and caught that word again: "purgatory."

For a time, he could not place the meaning of the word; it hung in front of him, covered with flies. Dimly, he perceived the horse's hindquarters, gleaming in the sun, the twin lines made in the dust by the—what was it? A thing made of—bed—no, canvas; he shook his head. It was his bedsack, wrapped about two trailing saplings, trailing . . . "travois," that was the word—yes. And the cat, there was a cat there, looking at him with eyes like rough amber, its head turned over its shoulder, openmouthed, its fangs showing.

Now the cat was talking to him, too.

"You mad, you know that?"

"I know that," he murmured. He didn't catch the cat's reply, growled in a Scottish accent.

He leaned closer, to hear. Felt as though he floated down, through air thick as water, toward that open mouth. Suddenly all sense of effort ceased; he was no longer moving but was supported somehow. Couldn't see the cat . . . oh. He was lying facedown on the ground, grass and dirt beneath his cheek.

The cat's voice floated back to him, angry but resigned.

"This purgatory of yours? You think you can get out walking backward?"

Well, no, William thought, feeling peaceful. That made no sense at all.

38

PLAIN SPEECH

THE YOUNG woman snicked the blades of her scissors in thoughtful fashion.

"Thee is sure?" she asked. "It seems shame, Friend William. Such a striking color!"

"I should think you'd consider it unseemly, Miss Hunter," William said, smiling. "I had always heard that Quakers think bright colors to be worldly." The only color in her own dress was a small bronzy-colored brooch that held her kerchief together. Everything else was shades of cream and butternut—though he thought these suited her.

She looked reprovingly at him.

"Immodest ornament in dress is hardly the same as grateful acceptance of the gifts God hath given. Do bluebirds pluck out their feathers, or roses fling away their petals?"

"I doubt that roses itch," he said, scratching at his chin. The notion of his beard as a gift of God was novel, but not sufficiently persuasive as to convince him to go about as a whiskeranto. Beyond its unfortunate color, it grew with vigor, but sparsely. He looked disapprovingly at the modest square of looking glass in his hand. He could do nothing about the peeling sunburn that patched his nose and cheeks, or the scabbed scrapes and scratches left by his adventures in the swamp—but the hideous copper curls that sprouted jauntily from his chin and plastered themselves like a disfiguring moss along his jaw—that, at least, could be amended at once.

"If you please?"

Her lips twitched, and she knelt down beside his stool, turning his head with a hand beneath his chin so as to take best advantage of the light from the window.

"Well, then," she said, and laid the scissors cool against his face. "I'll ask Denny to come and shave thee. I daresay I can cut thy beard without wounding thee, but"—her eyes narrowed and she leaned closer, snipping delicately round the curve of his chin—"I've not shaved anything more lively than a dead pig, myself."

"Barber, barber," he murmured, trying not to move his lips, "shave a pig. How ma—"

Her fingers pressed up under his chin, firmly shutting his mouth, but she made the small snorting sound that passed with her for laughter. *Snip, snip, snip.* The blades tickled pleasantly against his face, and the wiry hairs brushed his hands as they fell into the worn linen towel she'd placed across his lap.

He'd had no opportunity to study her face at such close range and took full advantage of the brief opportunity. Her eyes were almost brown and not quite green. He wished suddenly to kiss the end of her nose. He shut his eyes, instead, and breathed. She'd been milking a goat, he could tell.

"I can shave myself," he said, when she lowered the scissors.

She raised her brows and glanced downward at his arm. "I should be surprised if thee can feed thyself yet, let alone shave."

In all truth, he could barely lift his right arm, and she had been feeding him for the last two days. That being so, he thought better of telling her that he was in fact left-handed.

"It's healing well," he said, instead, and turned his arm so the light shone upon it. Dr. Hunter had removed the dressing only that morning, expressing gratification at the results. The wound was still red and puckered, the skin around it unpleasantly white and moist. It was, however, undoubtedly healing; the arm was no longer swollen, and the ominous red streaks had disappeared.

"Well," she said consideringly, "it's a fine scar, I think. Well knit, and rather pretty."

"Pretty?" William echoed, looking skeptically at his arm.

He'd heard men now and then describe a scar as "pretty," but most commonly they meant one that had healed straight and clean and did not disfigure the bearer by passing through some significant feature. This one was jagged and sprawling, with a long tail leading toward his wrist. He had—he was told sometime after the fact—narrowly escaped loss of the arm: Dr. Hunter had grasped it and placed his amputation saw just above the wound, only to have the abscess that had formed below it burst in his hand. Seeing this, the doctor had hastily drained the wound, packed it with garlic and comfrey, and prayed—to good effect.

"It looks like an enormous star," Rachel Hunter said approvingly. "One of significance. A great comet, perhaps. Or the Star of Bethlehem, which led the Wise Men to the manger of Christ."

William turned his arm, considering. He thought it looked rather more like a bursting mortar shell, himself, but said merely, "Hmm!" in an encouraging manner. He wished to continue the conversation—she seldom lingered when she fed him, having much other work to do—and so lifted his newly shorn chin and gestured at the brooch she wore.

"That's pretty," he said. "Not too worldly?"

"No," she said tartly, putting a hand to the brooch. "It's made of my mother's hair. She died when I was born."

"Ah. I'm sorry," he said, and with a moment's hesitation added, "So did mine."

She stopped then and looked at him, and for a moment, he saw a flicker of something in her eyes that was more than the matter-of-fact attention she would give to a cow in calf or a dog that had eaten something that disagreed with it.

"I'm sorry, too," she said softly, then turned with decision. "I'll fetch my brother."

Her footsteps went down the narrow stair, quick and light. He picked up the ends of the towel and shook it out the window, scattering the ruddy hair clippings to the four winds, and good riddance. He might have grown a beard as a rudimentary disguise, had it been a decently sober brown. As it was, a full beard of that garish color would rivet the eye of everyone who saw him.

What to do now? he wondered. Surely he would be fit to leave by tomorrow.

His clothes were still wearable, if worse for wear; Miss Hunter had patched the tears in his breeches and coat. But he had no horse, no money save two sixpences that had been in his pocket, and had lost the book with the list of his contacts and their messages. He might recall a few of their names, but without the proper code words and signs . . .

He thought quite suddenly of Henry Washington, and that hazy half-remembered conversation with Ian Murray by the fire, before they had begun to speak of death songs. Washington, Cartwright, Harrington, and Carver. The chanted list returned to him, together with Murray's puzzled reply to his mention of Washington and Dismal Town.

He could not think of any reason why Murray should seek to mislead him on the matter. But if he was correct—was Captain Richardson grossly mistaken in his intelligence? That was possible, certainly. Even in as short a time as he had been in the Colonies, he had learned just how quickly loyalties could shift, with changing news of threat or opportunity.

But . . . said the small, cold voice of reason, and he felt its chilly touch on his neck. *If Captain Richardson was not mistaken . . . then he meant to send you to death or imprisonment.*

The sheer enormity of the idea dried his mouth, and he reached for the cup of herbal tea that Miss Hunter had brought him earlier. It tasted foul, but he scarcely noticed, clutching it as though it might be a talisman against the prospect he imagined.

No, he assured himself. It wasn't possible. His father knew Richardson. Surely if the captain were a traitor—what was he thinking? He gulped the tea, grimacing as he swallowed.

"No," he said aloud, "not possible. Or not likely," he added fairly. "Occam's razor."

The thought calmed him a little. He had learned the basic principles of logic at an early age and had found William of Occam a sound guide before. Was it more likely that Captain Richardson was a hidden traitor who had deliberately sent William into danger—or that the captain had been misinformed or had simply made a mistake?

Come to that—what would be the point of it? William was under no delusions concerning his own importance in the scheme of things. Where would be the benefit to Richardson—or anyone else—in destroying a junior officer engaged in minor intelligencing?

Well, then. He relaxed a bit, and taking an unwary mouthful of the ghastly tea, choked on it and coughed, spraying tea everywhere. He was still wiping up the residue with his towel when Dr. Hunter came trotting briskly up the stair. Denzell Hunter was perhaps ten years his sister's senior, somewhere in his late twenties, small-boned and cheerful as a cock sparrow. He beamed at sight of William, plainly so delighted at his patient's recovery that William smiled warmly back.

"Sissy tells me thee requires to shave," the doctor said, setting down the shaving mug and brush he had brought. "Plainly, thee must be feeling well enough to contemplate a return to society—for the first thing any man does when free of social constraint is to let his beard grow. Has thee moved thy bowels as yet?"

"No, but I propose to do so almost at once," William assured him. "I am not, however, of a mind to venture out in public looking like a bandit—not even to the privy. I shouldn't wish to scandalize your neighbors."

Dr. Hunter laughed, and withdrawing a razor from one pocket and his silver-rimmed spectacles from another, set the latter firmly on his nose and picked up the shaving brush.

"Oh, Sissy and I are already a hissing and a byword," he assured William, leaning close to apply the lather. "Seeing banditti emerging from our privy would merely confirm the neighbors in their opinions."

"Really?" William spoke carefully, twisting his mouth so as to avoid having it inadvertently filled with soap. "Why?" He was surprised to hear this; once regaining his senses, he had asked where he was and learned that Oak Grove was a small Quaker settlement. He had thought Quakers in general to be most united in their religious sentiments—but then, he did not really know any Quakers.

Hunter heaved a deep sigh, and laying down the shaving brush, took up the razor in its stead.

"Oh, politics," he said, in an offhand tone, as of one wishing to dismiss a tiresome but trivial subject. "Tell me, Friend Ransom, is there someone to whom I might send, to tell them of thy mishap and delivery?" He paused in the shaving, to allow William to reply.

"No, I thank you, sir—I shall tell them myself," William said, smiling. "I am sure I will be able to leave by tomorrow—though I assure you that I will not forget your kindness and hospitality when I reach my . . . friends."

Denzell Hunter's brow furrowed a little, and his mouth compressed as he resumed the shaving, but he made no argument.

"I trust thee will forgive my inquisitiveness," he said after a moment, "but where does thee intend to go from here?"

William hesitated, not sure what to reply. He had in fact not decided exactly where to go, given the lamentable state of his finances. The best notion that had occurred to him was that he might head for Mount Josiah, his own plantation. He was not positive but thought he must be within forty or fifty miles of it—if the Hunters might give him a little food, he thought he could reach it within a few days, a week at most. And once there, he could reequip himself with clothes, a decent horse, arms, and money, and thus resume his journey.

It was a tempting prospect. To do that, though, was to reveal his presence in Virginia—and to cause considerable comment, as everyone in the county not only knew him but knew that he was a soldier. To turn up in the neighborhood dressed as he was . . .

"There are a few Catholics at Rosemount," Dr. Hunter observed with diffidence, wiping the razor on the much-abused towel. William glanced at him in surprise.

"Oh?" he said warily. Why the devil was Hunter telling him about Catholics?

"I beg pardon, Friend," the doctor apologized, seeing his reaction. "Thee had mentioned thy friends—I thought . . ."

"You thought I was—" Puzzlement was succeeded by a jolt of realization, and William slapped a hand in reflex against his chest, naturally finding nothing but the much-worn nightshirt he was wearing.

"Here it is." The doctor bent swiftly to open the blanket box at the foot of the bed and stood up, the wooden rosary swinging from one hand. "We had to remove it, of course, when we undressed thee, but Sissy put it safe away to keep for thee."

"We?" William said, seizing on this as a means of delaying inquiry. "You—and Miss Hunter—undressed me?"

"Well, there was no one else," the doctor said apologetically. "We were obliged to lay thee naked in the creek, in hopes of quelling thy fever—thee does not recall?"

He did—vaguely—but had assumed the memory of overwhelming cold and a sense of drowning to be more remnants of his fever dreams. Miss Hunter's presence had fortunately—or perhaps unfortunately—not formed part of those memories.

"I could not carry thee alone," the doctor was explaining earnestly. "And the neighbors—I did provide a towel for the preservation of thy modesty," he assured William hastily.

"What quarrel do your neighbors have with you?" William inquired curiously, reaching out to take the rosary from Hunter's hand. "I am not a Papist myself," he added offhandedly. "It is a . . . memento, given me by a friend."

"Oh." The doctor rubbed a finger across his lip, plainly disconcerted. "I see. I had thought—"

"The neighbors . . . ?" William asked, and suppressing his embarrassment, hung the rosary once more around his neck. Perhaps the mistake over his religion was the basis of the neighbors' animus?

"Well, I daresay they would have helped to carry thee," Dr. Hunter admitted, "had there been time to go and fetch someone. The matter was urgent, though, and the nearest house is a goodly distance."

This left the question of the neighbors' attitude toward the Hunters unanswered, but it seemed unmannerly to press further. William merely nodded and stood up.

The floor tilted abruptly under him and white light flickered at the edge of his vision. He grabbed at the windowsill to keep from falling and came to his senses a moment later, bathed in sweat, with Dr. Hunter's surprisingly strong grip of his arm preventing his tumbling headfirst into the yard below.

"Not quite so fast, Friend Ransom," the doctor said gently, and, hauling him in, turned him back toward the bed. "Another day, perhaps, before thee stands alone. Thee has more phlegm than is useful to thee, I fear."

Mildly nauseated, William sat on the bed and allowed Dr. Hunter to wipe his face with the towel. Evidently he had a bit more time in which to decide where to go.

"How long, do you think, before I can walk a full day?"

Denzell Hunter gave him a considering look.

"Five days, perhaps—four, at the least," he said. "Thee is robust and full-blooded, else I would say a week."

William, feeling puny and pallid, nodded and lay down. The doctor stood frowning at him for a moment, though it did not seem that the frown was directed at him; it seemed rather an expression of some inner concern.

"How . . . far will thy travels take thee?" the doctor asked, choosing his words with apparent care.

"Quite some distance," William replied, with equal wariness. "I am headed . . . toward Canada," he said, suddenly realizing that to say more might imply more than he wished to give away regarding his reasons for travel. True, a man might have business in Canada without necessarily having dealings with the British army who occupied Quebec, but as the doctor had mentioned politics . . . best to be politic about the matter. And certainly he would not mention Mount Josiah. Whatever the Hunters' strained relations with their neighbors, news concerning their visitor might easily spread.

"Canada," the doctor repeated, as though to himself. Then his gaze returned to William. "Yes, that is some considerable distance. Luckily, I have killed a goat this morning; we will have meat. That will help to restore thy strength. I will bleed thee tomorrow, to restore some balance to thy humors, and then we shall see. For the moment . . ." He smiled and extended a hand. "Come. I'll see thee safe to the privy."

39

A MATTER OF CONSCIENCE

THERE WAS A storm coming; William could feel it in the shifting of the air, see it in the racing cloud shadows that scudded across the worn floorboards. The heat and damp oppression of the summer day had lifted, and the restlessness of the air seemed to stir him, as well. Though still weak, he could not remain abed, and managed to get up, clinging to the washstand until the initial giddiness left him.

Left to himself, he then passed some time in walking from one side of the room to the other—a distance of ten feet or so—one hand pressed against the wall for balance. The effort drained and dizzied him, and now and then he was obliged to sit down on the floor, head hung between his knees, until the spots ceased to dance before his eyes.

It was on one of these occasions, while seated beneath the window, that he heard voices from the yard below. Miss Rachel Hunter's voice, surprised and questioning—a man's reply, low-voiced and husky. A familiar voice—Ian Murray!

He shot to his feet and just as quickly subsided back onto the floor, vision black and head swimming. He clenched his fists and panted, trying to will the blood to return to his head.

"He will live, then?" The voices were distant, half buried in the murmur of the chestnut trees near the house, but he caught that. He struggled up onto his knees and caught hold of the sill, blinking into the cloud-shattered brightness of the day.

Murray's tall figure was visible at the edge of the dooryard, gaunt in buckskins, the huge dog at his side. There was no sign of Glutton or the other Indians, but two horses were cropping grass in the lane behind Murray, reins dangling. Rachel Hunter was gesturing to the house, plainly inviting Murray to come in, but he shook his head. He reached into the bag at his waist and withdrew a small package of some sort, which he handed to the girl.

"Hoy!" William shouted—or tried to shout; he hadn't much breath—and waved his arms. The wind was rising with a shivering rush through the chestnut leaves, but the motion must have caught Murray's eye, for he glanced up, and seeing William in the window, smiled and lifted his own hand in greeting.

He made no move to enter the house, though. Instead, he picked up the reins of one horse and put them into Rachel Hunter's hand. Then, with a wave of farewell toward William's window, he swung himself up onto the other horse with an economical grace and rode away.

William's hands tightened on the sill, disappointment surging through him at seeing Murray vanish into the trees. Wait, though—Murray had left a horse. Rachel Hunter was leading it around the house, her apron and petticoats aswirl in the rising wind, one hand on her cap to keep it in place.

It must be for him, surely! Did Murray mean to come back for him, then? Or was he to follow? Heart thumping in his ears, William pulled on his patched breeches and the new stockings Rachel had knitted for him, and after a short struggle got his water-stiffened boots on over them. The effort left him trembling, but he stubbornly made his way downstairs, lurching, sweating, and slipping but arriving in the kitchen at the bottom in one piece.

The back door opened with a blast of wind and light, then slammed abruptly, jerked out of Rachel's hand. She turned, saw him, and yelped in startlement.

"Lord save us! What is thee doing down here?" She was panting with exertion and fright, and glared at him, tucking wisps of dark hair back under her cap.

"Didn't mean to startle you," William said in apology. "I wanted—I saw Mr. Murray leaving. I thought I might catch him up. Did he say where I was to meet him?"

"He did not. Sit, for heaven's sake, before thee falls down."

He didn't want to. The desire to be out, to go, was overwhelming. But his knees were shaking, and if he didn't sit down shortly . . . Reluctantly, he sat.

"What did he say?" he asked, and realizing suddenly that he was sitting in a lady's presence, gestured at the other stool. "Sit, please. Tell me what he said."

Rachel eyed him but sat, smoothing her windblown clothing back into place. The storm was rising; cloud shadows raced across the floor, across her face, and the air seemed to waver, as though the room were underwater.

"He asked after thy health, and when I told him thee was mending, he gave me the horse, saying it was for thee." She hesitated for an instant, and William pushed.

"He gave you something else, did he not? I saw him give you a package of some kind."

Her lips pressed together for an instant, but she nodded, and reaching into her pocket, handed him a small bundle, loosely wrapped in cloth.

He was eager to see what the packet contained—but not so eager that he did not notice the marks in the cloth, deep lines where string had once been tied round it. And tied very recently. He glanced up at Rachel Hunter, who looked away, chin high, but with color rising in her cheeks. He cocked an eyebrow at her, then bent his attention to the packet.

Opened, it contained a small sheaf of paper continentals; a worn pouch containing the sum of one guinea, three shillings, and tuppence in coin; a much-folded—and refolded, if he was any judge—letter; and another, smaller, bundle, this one still tied. Setting aside this and the money, he opened the letter.

Cousin,

I hope to find you in better health than when last seen. If so, I will leave a horse and some funds to assist your travels. If not, I will leave the money, to pay either for medicine or your burial. The other thing is a gift from a friend whom the Indians call Bear-Killer. He hopes that you will wear it in good health. I wish you luck in your ventures.

Your ob't. serv.,
Ian Murray

"Hmm!" William was baffled by this. Evidently Murray had business of his own and could not or did not wish to stay until William was able to travel. Though somewhat disappointed—he would have liked to talk further with Murray, now that his mind was clear again—he could see that it might be better that Murray did not mean them to travel together.

It dawned upon him that his immediate problem was solved; he now had the means to resume his mission—or as much of it as he could. He could at least reach General Howe's headquarters, make a report, and get new instructions.

It was remarkably generous of Murray; the horse had looked sound, and the money was more than enough to see him comfortably fed and lodged all the way to New York. He wondered where on earth Murray had got it; by his looks, the man hadn't a pot to piss in—though he had a good rifle, William reminded himself—and he was plainly educated, for he made a decent fist of writing. What could have caused the odd Scottish Indian to take such interest in him, though?

Bemused, he reached for the smaller bundle and untied the string. Unwrapped, the contents proved to be the claw of a large bear, pierced and strung on a leather thong. It was old; the edges were worn, and the knot in the leather had hardened so far that it would plainly never be untied again.

He stroked the claw with a thumb, tested the point. Well, the bear spirit had stood him in good stead so far. Smiling to himself, he put the thong over his head, leaving the claw to hang outside his shirt. Rachel Hunter stared at it, her face unreadable.

"You read my letter, Miss Hunter," William said reprovingly. "Very naughty of you!"

The flush rose higher in her cheeks, but she met his eye with a directness he was unaccustomed to find in a woman—with the marked exception of his paternal grandmother.

"Thy speech is far superior to thy clothes, Friend William—even were they new. And while thee has been in thy right mind for some days now, thee has not chosen to say what brought thee to the Great Dismal. It is not a place frequented by gentlemen."

"Oh, indeed it is, Miss Hunter. Many gentlemen of my acquaintance go there for the hunting, which is unexcelled. But naturally, one does not hunt wild boar or catamounts in one's best linen."

"Neither does one go hunting armed only with a frying pan, Friend William," she riposted. "And if thee is a gentleman in truth—where is thy home, pray?"

He fumbled for an instant, unable to recall at once his alter ego's particulars, and seized instead on the first city to come to his mind.

"Ah—Savannah. In the Carolinas," he added helpfully.

"I know where it is," she snapped. "And have heard men speak who come from there. Thee doesn't."

"Are you calling me a liar?" he said, amazed.

"I am."

"Oh." They sat gazing at each other in the half light of the gathering storm, each calculating. For an instant, he had the illusion that he was playing chess with his grandmother Benedicta.

"I am sorry for reading thy letter," she said abruptly. "It was not vulgar curiosity, I assure thee."

"What, then?" He smiled a little, to indicate that he bore no animus for her trespass. She didn't smile back, but looked at him narrowly—not in suspicion, but as though gauging him in some way. At last she sighed, though, and her shoulders slumped.

"I wished to know a little of thee, and of thy character. The companions who brought thee to us seem dangerous men. And thy cousin? If thee is one like them, then—" Her teeth fixed briefly in her upper lip, but she shook her head, as though to herself, and continued more firmly.

"We must leave here within a few days—my brother and myself. Thee told Denny that thee travels north; I wish that we may travel with thee, at least for a time."

Whatever he'd been expecting, it wasn't that. He blinked and said the first thing that came to his mind.

"Leave here? Why? The . . . er . . . the neighbors?"

She looked surprised at that.

"What?"

"I beg your pardon, ma'am. Your brother seemed to indicate that relations between your family and those who dwell nearby were . . . somewhat strained?"

"Oh." One corner of her mouth tucked back; he could not

tell if this betokened distress or amusement—but rather thought it was the latter.

"I see," she said, and drummed her fingers thoughtfully on the table. "Yes, that's true, though it was not what I—well, and yet it has to do with the matter. I see I must tell thee everything, then. What does thee know about the Society of Friends?"

He knew only one family of Quakers, the Unwins. Mr. Unwin was a wealthy merchant who knew his father, and he had met the two daughters at a musicale once, but the conversation had not touched upon philosophy or religion.

"They—er, you—dislike conflict, I believe?" he answered cautiously.

That surprisingly made her laugh, and he felt pleasure at having removed the tiny furrow between her brows, if only temporarily.

"Violence," she corrected. "We thrive upon conflict, if it be verbal. And given the form of our worship—Denny says thee is not a Papist after all, yet I venture to suppose that thee have never attended a Quaker meeting?"

"The opportunity has not so far occurred, no."

"I thought not. Well, then." She eyed him consideringly. "We have preachers who will come to speak at meeting—but anyone may speak at meeting, upon any subject, if the spirit moves him or her to do so."

"Her? Women speak in public, too?"

She gave him a withering look.

"I have a tongue, just as thee does."

"I'd noticed," he said, and smiled at her. "Continue, please."

She leaned forward a little to do so but was interrupted by the crash of a shutter swinging back against the house, this followed by a spatter of rain, dashed hard across the window. Rachel sprang to her feet with a brief exclamation.

"I must get the chickens in! Close the shutters," she ordered him, and dashed out.

Taken aback but amused, he did so, moving slowly. Going upstairs to fasten the upper shutters made him dizzy again, and he paused on the threshold of the bedroom, holding the doorjamb until his balance returned. There were two rooms upstairs: the bedroom at the front of the house, where they had put him, and a smaller room in the rear. The Hunters now shared this room; there was a truckle bed, a washstand with a silver candlestick upon it, and little else, save a row of pegs upon which hung the doctor's spare shirt and breeches, a woolen shawl, and what must be Rachel Hunter's go-to-meeting gown, a sober-looking garment dyed with indigo.

With rain and wind muffled by the shutters, the dim room seemed still now, and peaceful, a harbor from the storm. His heart had slowed from the exertion of climbing the stair, and he stood for a moment, enjoying the slightly illicit sense of trespass. No sound from below; Rachel must be still in pursuit of the chickens.

There was something faintly odd about the room, and it took him only a moment to decide what it was. The shabbiness and sparsity of the Hunters' personal possessions argued poverty—yet these contrasted with the small signs of prosperity evident in the furnishings: the candlestick was silver, not plate or pewter, and the ewer and basin were not earthenware but good china, painted with sprawling blue chrysanthemums.

He lifted the skirt of the blue dress hanging on the peg, examining it curiously. Modesty was one thing; threadbareness was another. The hem was worn nearly white, the indigo faded so that the folds of the skirt showed a fan-shaped pattern of light and dark. The Misses Unwin had dressed quietly, but their clothes were of the highest quality.

On sudden impulse, he brought the cloth to his face, breathing in. It smelled faintly still of indigo, and of grass and live things—and very perceptibly of a woman's body. The musk of it ran through him like the pleasure of good wine.

The sound of the door closing below made him drop the dress as though it had burst into flame, and he made for the stairs, heart hammering.

Rachel Hunter was shaking herself on the hearth, shedding drops of water from her apron, her cap wilted and soggy on her head. Not seeing him, she took this off, wrung it out with a mutter of impatience, and hung it on a nail hammered into the chimney breast.

Her hair fell down her back, wet-tailed and shining, dark against the pale cloth of her jacket.

"The chickens are all safe, I trust?" He spoke, because to

watch her unawares with her hair down, the smell of her still vivid in his nose, seemed suddenly to be an unwarrantable intimacy.

She turned round, eyes wary, but made no immediate move to cover her hair.

"All but the one my brother calls the Great Whore of Babylon. No chicken possesses anything resembling intelligence, but that one is perverse beyond the usual."

"Perverse?" Evidently she perceived that he was contemplating the possibilities inherent in this description and finding them entertaining, for she snorted through her nose and bent to open the blanket chest.

"The creature is sitting twenty feet up in a pine tree, in the midst of a rainstorm. Perverse." She pulled out a linen towel and began to dry her hair with it.

The sound of the rain altered suddenly, hail rattling like tossed gravel against the shutters.

"Hmmph," said Rachel, with a dark look at the window. "I expect she will be knocked senseless by the hail and devoured by the first passing fox, and serve her right." She resumed drying her hair. "No great matter. I shall be pleased never to see any of those chickens again."

Seeing him still standing, she sat down, gesturing him to another stool.

"You did say that you and your brother proposed to leave this place and travel north," he reminded her, sitting down. "I collect the chickens will not make the journey with you?"

"No, and the Lord be praised. They are already sold, along with the house." Laying the crumpled towel aside, she groped in her pocket and withdrew a small comb carved from horn. "I did say I would tell thee why."

"I believe we had reached the point of learning that the matter has something to do with your meeting?"

She breathed deeply through her nose and nodded.

"I said that when a person is moved of the spirit, he speaks in meeting? Well, the spirit moved my brother. That is how we came to leave Philadelphia."

A meeting might be formed, she explained, wherever there were sufficient Friends of like mind. But in addition to these small local meetings, there were larger bodies, the Quarterly and Yearly Meetings, at which weighty matters of principle were discussed and actions affecting Quakers in general were decided upon.

"Philadelphia Yearly Meeting is the largest and most influential," she said. "Thee is right: the Friends eschew violence, and seek either to avoid it or to end it. And in this question of rebellion, Philadelphia Yearly Meeting thought and prayed upon the matter, and advised that the path of wisdom and peace plainly lay in reconciliation with the mother country."

"Indeed." William was interested. "So all of the Quakers in the Colonies are now Loyalists, do you mean?"

Her lips compressed for an instant.

"That is the advice of the Yearly Meeting. As I said, though, Friends are led of the spirit, and one must do as one is led to do."

"And your brother was led to speak in favor of rebellion?" William was amused, though wary; Dr. Hunter seemed an unlikely firebrand.

She dipped her head, not quite a nod.

"In favor of independency," she corrected.

"Surely there is something lacking in the logic of that distinction," William observed, raising one brow. "How might independency be achieved without the exercise of violence?"

"If thee thinks the spirit of God is necessarily logical, thee know Him better than I do." She ran a hand through the damp hair, flicking it over her shoulders with impatience.

"Denny said that it was made clear to him that liberty, whether that of the individual or of countries, is a gift of God, and that it was laid upon him that he must join in the fight to gain and preserve it. So we were put out of meeting," she ended abruptly.

It was dark in the room, with the shutters closed, but he could see her face by the dim glow from the smothered hearth. That last statement had moved her strongly; her mouth was pinched, and there was a brightness to her eyes that suggested she might weep, were she not determined not to.

"I collect this is a serious thing, to be put out of meeting?" he asked cautiously.

She nodded, looking away. She picked up the discarded damp towel, smoothed it slowly, and folded it, plainly choosing her words.

"I told thee that my mother died when I was born. My father died three years later—drowned in a flood. We were left with nothing, my brother and I. But the local meeting saw to it that we did not starve, that there was a roof—if one with holes—over our heads. There was a question in meeting, how Denny might be 'prenticed. I know he feared that he must become a drover or a cobbler—he lacks somewhat to be a blacksmith," she added, smiling a little despite her seriousness. "He would have done it, though—to keep me fed."

Luck had intervened, however. One of the Friends had taken it upon himself to try to trace any relatives of the orphaned Hunter children, and after a number of letters to and fro, had discovered a distant cousin, originally from Scotland but presently in London.

"John Hunter, bless his name. He is a famous physician, he and his elder brother, who is *accoucheur* to the Queen herself." Despite her egalitarian principles, Miss Hunter looked somewhat awed, and William nodded respectfully. "He inquired as to Denny's abilities, and hearing good report, made provision for Denny to remove to Philadelphia, to board there with a Quaker family and to go to the new medical college. And then he went so far as to have Denny go to London, to study there with himself!"

"Very good luck, indeed," William observed. "But what about you?"

"Oh. I—was taken in by a woman in the village," she said, with a quick casualness that did not deceive him. "But Denzell came back, and so of course I came to keep his house until he might wed."

She was pleating the towel between her fingers, looking down into her lap. There were small lights in her hair where the fire caught it, a hint of bronze in the dark brown locks.

"The woman—she was a goodly woman. She took care I should learn to keep a house, to cook, to sew. That I should . . . know what is needful for a woman to know." She glanced at him with that odd directness, her face sober.

"I think thee cannot understand," she said, "what it means to be put out of meeting."

"Something like being drummed out of one's regiment, I expect. Disgraceful and distressing."

Her eyes narrowed for a moment, but he had spoken seriously, and she saw that.

"A Friends' meeting is not only a fellowship of worship. It is . . . a community of mind, of heart. A larger family, in a way."

And for a young woman bereft of her own family?

"And to be put out, then . . . yes, I see," he said quietly.

There was a brief silence in the room then, broken only by the sound of the rain. He thought he heard a rooster crow, somewhere far off.

"Thy mother is dead, too, thee said." Rachel looked at him, dark eyes soft. "Does thy father live?"

He shook his head.

"You will think I am exceeding dramatic," he said. "It is the truth, though—my father also died upon the day of my birth."

She blinked at that.

"Truly. He was a good fifty years my mother's senior. When he heard that she was dead in ch—in childbirth, he suffered an apoplexy and died upon the spot." He was annoyed; he seldom stuttered anymore. She had not noticed, though.

"So thee is orphaned, too. I am sorry for thee," she said quietly.

He shrugged, feeling awkward.

"Well. I knew neither of my parents. And in fact, I did have parents. My mother's sister became my mother, in all respects—she's dead now, too—and her husband . . . I have always thought of him as my father, though he is not related to me by blood." It occurred to him that he was treading on dangerous ground here, talking too much about himself. He cleared his throat and endeavored to guide the conversation back to less personal matters.

"Your brother. How does he propose to . . . er . . . to implement this revelation of his?"

She sighed.

"This house—it belonged to a cousin of our mother's. He was a widower, and childless. He had willed the house to Denzell, though when he heard about our being put out of meeting, he wrote to say that he meant to alter his will. By happenstance, though, he caught a bad ague and died before he could do so. But all his neighbors knew, of course—about Denny—which is why . . ."

"I see." It seemed to William that while God might not be logical, He seemed to be taking a most particular interest in Denzell Hunter. He thought it might not be mannerly to say so, though, and inquired in a different direction.

"You said the house was sold. So your brother—"

"He has gone in to the town, to the courthouse, to sign the papers for the sale of the house and make arrangement for the goats, pigs, and chickens. As soon as that is done, we will . . . leave." She swallowed visibly. "Denny means to join the Continental army as a surgeon."

"And you will go with him? As a camp follower?" William spoke with some disapproval; many soldiers' wives—or concubines—did "follow the drum," essentially joining the army with their husbands. He had not seen much of camp followers yet himself, as there had been none on the Long Island campaign—but he'd heard his father speak of such women now and then, mostly with pity. It wasn't a life for a woman of refinement.

She lifted her chin, hearing his disapproval.

"Certainly."

A long wooden pin lay on the table; she must have taken it from her hair when she removed her cap. Now she twisted her damp hair up into a knot and stabbed the pin decisively through it.

"So," she said. "Will thee travel with us? Only so far as thee may be comfortable in doing so," she added quickly.

He had been turning the notion over in the back of his mind all the while they had talked. Plainly, such an arrangement would have advantages for the Hunters—a larger group was always safer, and it was apparent to William that, his revelation notwithstanding, the doctor was not a natural warrior. It would, he thought, have some advantage to himself, as well. The Hunters knew something of the immediate countryside, which he did not, and a man traveling in a group—particularly a group including a woman—was much less noticeable, and much less suspicious, than one alone.

It dawned on him suddenly that if Hunter meant to join the Continental army, there might be excellent opportunity of getting close enough to Washington's forces to gain valuable intelligence of them—something that would go a long way toward compensating for the loss of his book of contacts.

"Yes, certainly," he said, and smiled at Miss Hunter. "An admirable suggestion!"

A flash of lightning stabbed suddenly through the slits of the shutters, and a clap of thunder crashed overhead, almost simultaneously. Both of them started violently at the noise.

William swallowed, feeling his ears still ring. The sharp scent of lightning burned the air.

"I do hope," he said, "that that was a signal of approval."

She didn't laugh.

40

THE BLESSING OF BRIDE AND OF MICHAEL

THE MOHAWK knew him as Thayendanegea—Two Wagers. To the English, he was Joseph Brant. Ian had heard much of the man when he dwelt among the Mohawk, by both his names, and had wondered more than once just how well Thayendanegea managed the treacherous ground between two worlds. Was it like the bridge? he thought suddenly. The slender bridge that lay between this world and the next, the air around it assailed by flying heads with rending teeth? Sometime he would like to sit by a fire with Joseph Brant and ask him.

He was going to Brant's house now—but not to speak with Brant. Glutton had told him that Sun Elk had left Snaketown to join Brant and that his wife had gone with him.

"They are in Unadilla," Glutton had said. "Probably still there. Thayendanegea fights with the English, you know. He's talking to the Loyalists up there, trying to get them to join him and his men. He calls them 'Brant's Volunteers.' " He spoke casually; Glutton was not interested in politics, though he would fight now and then, when the spirit moved him.

"Does he?" Ian said, just as casually. "Well, then."

He had no particular idea where Unadilla was, save that it was in the colony of New York, but that was no great difficulty. He set out next day at dawn, heading north.

He had no company save the dog and his thoughts, most of the time. At one point, though, he came to a summer camp of Mohawk and was welcomed there.

He sat with the men, talking. After a time, a young woman brought him a bowl of stew, and he ate it, barely noticing what was in it, though his belly seemed grateful for the warmth and stopped clenching itself.

He couldn't say what drew his eye, but he looked up from the men's talk to see the young woman who had brought him the stew sitting in the shadow just outside the fire, looking at him. She smiled, very slightly.

He chewed more slowly, the taste of the stew suddenly a savor in his mouth. Bear meat, rich with fat. Corn and beans, spiced with onions and garlic. Delicious. She tilted her head to one side; one dark brow rose, elegant, then she rose, too, as though lifted by her question.

Ian set down his bowl and belched politely, then got up and went outside, paying no attention to the knowing looks of the men with whom he'd been eating.

She was waiting, a pale blur in the shadow of a birch. They talked—he felt his mouth form words, felt the tickle of her speech in his ears, but was not really aware of what they said. He held the glow of his anger like a live coal in the palm of his hand, an ember smoking in his heart. He had no thought of her as water to his scorching, nor did he think to kindle her. There were flames behind his eyes, and he was mindless as fire is, devouring where there was fuel, dying where there was not.

He kissed her. She smelled of food, worked skins, and sun-warmed earth. No hint of wood, no tinge of blood. She was tall; he felt her breasts soft and pushing, dropped his hands to the curve of her hips.

She moved against him, solid, willing. Drew back, letting cool air touch his skin where she had been, and took him by the hand to lead him to her longhouse. No one glanced at them as she took him into her bed and, in the half-dark warmth, turned to him, naked.

He'd thought it would be better if he couldn't see her face. Anonymous, quick, some pleasure for her, perhaps. Surcease, for him. For the few moments when he lost himself, at least.

But in the dark, she was Emily, and he fled from her bed in shame and anger, leaving astonishment behind.

FOR THE NEXT TWELVE days he walked, the dog by his side, and spoke to no one.

THAYENDANEGEA'S house stood by itself in large grounds, but near enough the village to be still part of it. The village was much as any other, save that many of the houses had two or three grindstones by the step; each woman ground meal for her family, rather than take it to a mill.

There were dogs in the street, dozing in the shadows of wagons and walls. Every one sat up, startled, when Rollo came within scenting distance. A few growled or barked, but none offered to fight.

The men were another matter. There were several men leaning on a fence, watching another with a horse in a field. All of them cast glances at him, half curious, half wary. He didn't know most of them. One of them, though, was a man named Eats Turtles, whom he had known in Snaketown. Another was Sun Elk.

Sun Elk blinked at him, startled as any of the dogs, and then stepped out into the road to face him.

"What are you doing here?"

He considered for a split second telling the truth—but it wasn't a truth that could be told quickly, if at all, and certainly not before strangers.

"None of your business," he answered calmly.

Sun Elk had spoken to him in Mohawk, and he'd answered in the same language. He saw eyebrows rise, and Turtle made to greet him, clearly hoping to avert whatever storm was in the offing by making it clear that Ian was Kahnyen'kehaka himself. He returned Turtle's greeting, and the others drew back a little, puzzled—and interested—but not hostile.

Sun Elk, on the other hand . . . Well, Ian hadn't expected the man to fall on his neck, after all. He'd hoped—insofar as he'd thought about Sun Elk, which was very little—that he'd be elsewhere, but here he was, and Ian smiled wryly to himself, thinking of old Grannie Wilson, who had once described her son-in-law, Hiram, as looking "*like he wouldn't give the road to a bear.*"

It was an apt description, and Sun Elk's disposition was not improved either by Ian's reply nor by the subsequent smile.

"What do you want?" Sun Elk demanded.

"Nothing that's yours," Ian replied, as mildly as possible.

Sun Elk's eyes narrowed, but before he could say anything else, Turtle intervened, inviting Ian to come into his house, to eat, to drink.

He should. It wasn't polite to refuse. And he could ask, later, privately, where Emily was. But the need that had brought him over three hundred miles of wilderness acknowledged no requirements of civility. Neither would it brook delay.

Besides, he reflected, readying himself, he'd known it would come to this. No point in putting it off.

"I wish to speak with her who was once my wife," he said. "Where is she?"

Several of the men blinked at that, interested or taken back—but he saw Turtle's eyes flick toward the gates of the large house at the end of the road.

Sun Elk, to his credit, merely drew himself up and planted himself more solidly in the road, ready to defy *two* bears, if necessary. Rollo didn't care for this and lifted his lip in a growl that made one or two of the men step back sharply. Sun Elk, who had better reason than most of them to know just what Rollo was capable of, didn't move an inch.

"Do you mean to set your demon on me?" he asked.

"Of course not. *Sheas, a choin,*" he said quietly to Rollo. The dog stood his ground for a moment longer—just long enough to indicate that it was *his* idea—and then turned aside and lay down, though he kept up a low grumble, like distant thunder.

"I have not come to take her from you," Ian said to Sun Elk. He'd meant to be conciliatory, but he hadn't really expected it to work, and it didn't.

"You think you *could*?"

"If I dinna want to, does it matter?" Ian said testily, lapsing into English.

"She wouldn't go with you, even if you killed me!"

"How many times must I say that I dinna want to take her away from ye?"

Sun Elk stared at him for a minute, his eyes quite black.

"Often enough for your face to say the same thing," he whispered, and clenched his fists.

An interested murmur rose from the other men, but there was an intangible drawing away. They wouldn't interfere in a fight over a woman. That was a blessing, Ian thought vaguely, watching Sun Elk's hands. The man was right-handed, he remembered that. There was a knife on his belt, but his hand wasn't hovering near it.

Ian spread his own hands peaceably.

"I wish only to talk with her."

"Why?" Sun Elk barked. He was close enough for Ian to feel the spray of spittle on his face, but he didn't wipe it away. He didn't back away, either, and dropped his hands.

"That's between me and her," he said quietly. "I daresay she'll tell ye later." The thought of it gave him a pang. The statement didn't seem to reassure Sun Elk, who without warning hit him in the nose.

The crunch echoed through his upper teeth, and Sun Elk's other fist struck him a glancing blow on the cheekbone. He shook his head to clear it, saw the blur of movement through watering eyes, and—more by good fortune than intent—kicked Sun Elk solidly in the crotch.

He stood breathing heavily, dripping blood on the roadway. Six pairs of eyes went from him to Sun Elk, curled in the dust and making small, urgent noises. Rollo got up, walked over to the fallen man, and smelled him with interest. All the eyes came back to Ian.

He made a small motion of the hand that brought Rollo to

heel and walked up the road toward Brant's house, six pairs of eyes fixed on his back.

WHEN THE DOOR opened, the young white woman who stood there gaped at him, eyes round as pennies. He'd been in the act of wiping his bloody nose with his shirttail. He completed this action and inclined his head civilly.

"Will ye be so good as to ask Wakyo'teyehsnonhsa if she will be pleased to speak wi' Ian Murray?"

The young woman blinked, twice. Then she nodded and swung the door to—pausing with it halfway shut, in order to look at him once more and assure herself that she'd really seen him.

Feeling strange, he stepped down into the garden. It was a formal English garden, with rosebushes and lavender and stone-flagged paths. The smell of it reminded him of Auntie Claire, and he wondered briefly whether Thayendanegea had brought back an English gardener from London.

There were two women at work in the garden, some distance away; one was a white woman, by the color of the hair beneath her cap, and in her middle years by the stoop of her shoulders—perhaps Brant's wife? he wondered. Was the young woman who had answered the door their daughter? The other woman was Indian, with her hair in a plait down her back but streaked with white. Neither one turned to look at him.

When he heard the click of the door latch behind him, he waited a moment before turning around, steeling himself against the disappointment of being told that she was not here—or, worse, that she had refused to see him.

But she was there. Emily. Small and straight, with her breasts showing round in the neck of a blue calico gown, her long hair bound up behind but uncovered. And her face fearful—but eager. Her eyes lit with joy at the sight of him, and she took a step toward him.

He would have crushed her to him had she come to him, made any gesture inviting it. *And what then?* he wondered dimly, but it didn't matter; after that first impulsive movement toward him, she stopped and stood, her hands fluttering for an instant as though they would shape the air between them, but then folding tight before her, hidden in the folds of her skirt.

"Wolf's Brother," she said softly, in Mohawk. "My heart is warm to see you."

"Mine, too," he said in the same language.

"Have you come to speak with Thayendanegea?" she asked, tilting her head back toward the house.

"Perhaps later." Neither of them mentioned his nose, though from the throbbing, it was likely twice its normal size and there was blood all down the front of his shirt. He glanced around; there was a path that led away from the house, and he nodded at that. "Will you walk with me?"

She hesitated for a moment. The flame in her eyes had not gone out, but it burned lower now; there were other things there—caution, mild distress, and what he thought was pride. He was surprised that he should see them so clearly. It was as though she were made of glass.

"I—the children," she blurted, half turning toward the house.

"It doesna matter," he said. "I only—" A dribble of blood from one nostril stopped him, and he paused to wipe the back of his hand across his upper lip. He took the two steps necessary to bring them within touching distance, though he was careful not to touch her.

"I wished to say to you that I am sorry," he said formally, in Mohawk. "That I could not give you children. And that I am glad you have them."

A lovely warm flush rose in her cheeks, and he saw the pride in her overcome the distress.

"May I see them?" he asked, surprising himself as much as her.

She wavered for an instant, but then turned and went into the house. He sat on a stone wall, waiting, and she returned a few moments later with a small boy, maybe five years old, and a girl of three or so in short plaits, who looked gravely at him and sucked her fist.

Blood had run down the back of his throat; it felt raw and tasted of iron.

Now and then on his journey, he'd gone carefully over the explanation Auntie Claire had given him. Not with any notion of telling it to Emily; it could mean nothing to her—he barely understood it himself. Only, maybe, as some shield against this moment, seeing her with the children he could not give her.

"*Call it fate,*" Claire had said, looking at him with a hawk's eye, the one that sees from far above, so far above, maybe, that what seems mercilessness is truly compassion. *"Or call it bad luck. But it wasn't your fault. Or hers."*

"Come here," he said in Mohawk, putting out a hand to the little boy. The boy glanced at his mother, but then came to him, looking up in curiosity to his face.

"I see you in his face," he said softly to her, speaking English. "And in his hands," he added in Mohawk, taking the child's hands—so amazingly small—in his own. It was true: the boy had her hands, fine-boned and supple; they curled up like sleeping mice in his palms, then the fingers sprang out like a spider's legs and the boy giggled. He laughed, too, closed his own hands swiftly on the boy's, like a bear gulping a pair of trout, making the child shriek, then let go.

"Are you happy?" he asked her.

"Yes," she said softly. She looked down, not meeting his eyes, and he knew it was because she would answer honestly but did not wish to see if her answer hurt him. He put a hand under her chin—her skin was so soft!—and lifted her face to him.

"Are you happy?" he asked again, and smiled a little as he said it.

"Yes," she said again. But then gave a small sigh, and her own hand touched his face at last, light as a moth's wing. "But sometimes I miss you, Ian." There was nothing wrong with her accent, but his Scots name sounded impossibly exotic on her tongue—it always had.

He felt a lump in his throat, but kept the faint smile on his face.

"I see you dinna ask me whether *I'm* happy," he said, and could have kicked himself.

She gave him a quick look, direct as a knife point.

"I have eyes," she said, very simply.

There was a silence between them. He looked away but could feel her there, breathing. Ripe. Soft. He felt her softening further, opening. She had been wise not to go into the garden with him. Here, with her son playing in the dirt near her feet, it was safe. For her, at least.

"Do you mean to stay?" she asked at last, and he shook his head.

"I am going to Scotland," he said.

"You will take a wife among your own people." There was relief in that, but regret, too.

"Are your people no longer my own?" he asked, with a flash of fierceness. "They washed the white blood from my body in the river—you were there."

"I was there."

She looked at him for a long time, searching his face. Likely enough that she would never see him again; did she seek to remember him, or was she looking for something in his features, he wondered?

The latter. She turned abruptly, raising a hand to him to wait, and disappeared into the house.

The little girl ran after her, not wanting to stay with the stranger, but the little boy lingered, interested.

"Are you Wolf's Brother?"

"I am, aye. And you?"

"They call me Digger." It was a child's sort of name, used for convenience until the person's real name should declare itself in some way. Ian nodded, and they remained a few minutes, looking each other over with interest, but with no sense of awkwardness between them.

"She who is mother's mother to my mother," Digger said quite suddenly. "She talked about you. To me."

"She did?" said Ian, startled. That would be Tewaktenyonh. A great woman, head of the Women's Council at Snaketown—and the person who had sent him away.

"Does Tewaktenyonh still live?" he asked, curious.

"Oh, yes. She's older than the mountains," the little boy answered seriously. "She has only two teeth left, but she still eats."

Ian smiled at that.

"Good. What did she say to you of me?"

The boy screwed up his face, recollecting the words.

"She said I was the child of your spirit but I should not say so to my father."

Ian felt the blow of that, harder than any the child's father had dealt him, and couldn't speak for a moment.

"Aye, I dinna think ye should say so, either," he said, when words returned to him. He repeated the sentiment in Mohawk, in case the boy might not have understood English, and the child nodded, tranquil.

"Will I be with you, sometime?" he asked, only vaguely interested in the answer. A lizard had come out onto the stone wall to bask, and his eyes were fixed on it.

Ian forced his own words to be casual.

"If I live."

The boy's eyes were narrowed, watching the lizard, and the tiny right hand twitched, just a little. The distance was too far, though; he knew it, and glanced at Ian, who was closer. Ian cut his eyes at the lizard without moving, then looked back at the boy and agreement sprang up between them. *Don't move,* his eyes warned, and the boy seemed to cease breathing.

It didn't do to think in such situations. Without pausing to draw breath, he snatched, and the lizard was in his hand, astonished and thrashing.

The little boy chortled and hopped up and down, clapping his hands with glee, then held them out for the lizard, which he received with the greatest concentration, folding his hands about it so that it might not escape.

"And what will ye do with him?" Ian asked, smiling.

The boy held the lizard up to his face, peering at it intently, and his brow furrowed in thought.

"I will name him," he said at last. "Then he will be mine and bless me when I see him again." He brought the lizard up, eyeball to eyeball, and each stared unblinking at the other.

"Your name is Bob," the boy declared at last in English, and with great ceremony set the lizard on the ground. Bob leapt from his hands and disappeared under a log.

"A verra good name," Ian said gravely. His bruised ribs hurt with the need not to laugh, but the urge vanished in the next moment, as the distant door opened and Emily came out, a bundle in her arms.

She came up to him and presented him with a child, swaddled and bound to a cradleboard, in much the same way he had presented the lizard to Digger.

"This is my second daughter," she said, shyly proud. "Will you choose her name?"

He was moved, and touched Emily's hand, very lightly, before taking the cradleboard onto his knee and looking searchingly into the tiny face. She could not have given him greater honor, this permanent mark of the feeling she had once held for him—still might hold for him.

But as he looked at the little girl—she regarded him with round, serious eyes, taking in this new manifestation of her personal landscape—a conviction took root in him. He didn't question it; it was simply there, and undeniable.

"Thank you," he said, and smiled at Emily with great affection. He laid his hand—huge, and rough with callus and the nicks of living—on the tiny, perfect, soft-haired head. "I will bless all your children wi' the blessings of Bride and of Michael." He lifted his hand then, and reaching out, drew Digger to him. "But this one is mine to name."

Her face went quite blank with astonishment, and she looked quickly from him to her son and back. She swallowed visibly, unsure—but it didn't matter; *he* was sure.

"Your name is Swiftest of Lizards," he said, in Mohawk. The Swiftest of Lizards thought for a minute, then nodded, pleased, and with a laugh of pure delight, darted away.

41

SHELTER FROM THE STORM

NOT FOR THE first time, William was startled to realize the breadth of his father's acquaintance. In casual conversation as they rode, he had mentioned to Denzell Hunter that his father had once known a Dr. John Hunter—in fact, the association, involving an electric eel, an impromptu duel, and the implications of body-snatching, was part of the situation that had sent Lord John to Canada and the Plains of Abraham. Might this John Hunter perhaps be the beneficent relative that Miss Rachel had mentioned?

Denny Hunter had brightened at once.

"How remarkable! Yes, it must be the same. Particularly since thee mentions body-snatching in connection with him." He coughed, seeming a little embarrassed.

"It was a most . . . educational association," Hunter said. "Though a disturbing one, upon occasion." He glanced back at his sister, but Rachel was well behind them, her mule ambling and Rachel herself half asleep in the saddle, her head nodding like a sunflower's.

"Thee understands, Friend William," Hunter said, lowering his voice, "that in order to become skilled in the arts of surgery, it is necessary to learn how the human body is constructed and to understand its workings. Only so much can be learned from texts—and the texts upon which most medical men rely are . . . well, to be blunt about it, they are wrong."

"Oh, yes?" William was only half attending to the conversation. The other half of his mind was evenly divided among his assessment of the road, a hope that they might reach somewhere habitable in time to procure supper, and an appreciation of the slenderness of Rachel Hunter's neck on the rare occasions when she rode in front of him. He wanted to turn round and look at her again, but couldn't do it so soon, in all decency. Another few minutes . . .

" . . . Galen and Aesculapius. The common conception is—and has been for a very long time—that the ancient Greeks had written down everything known regarding the human body; there was no need to doubt these texts or to create mystery where there was none."

William grunted. "You should hear my uncle go on about ancient military texts. He's all for Caesar, who he says was a very decent general, but he takes leave to doubt that Herodotus ever saw a battlefield."

Hunter glanced at him in surprised interest. "Exactly what John Hunter said—in different terms—regarding Avicenna! 'The man's never seen a pregnant uterus in his life.'" He smacked a fist upon his pommel to emphasize the point, and his horse jerked its head, startled.

"Whoa, whoa," said Hunter, alarmed, sawing on the reins in a way calculated to have the horse rearing and pawing in moments. William leaned over and neatly took the reins out of Denzell's hands, giving them slack.

He was rather glad of the brief distraction, as it kept Hunter from discoursing further about uteruses. William was not at all sure what a uterus was, but if it got pregnant, it must have to do with a woman's privates, and that was not something he wished to discuss within the hearing of Miss Hunter.

"But you said your association with Dr. John Hunter was disturbing," he said, handing Hunter back the reins and hastening to change the subject before the doctor could think of something more embarrassing to mention. "Why was that?"

"Well . . . we—his students—learned the mysteries of the human body from . . . the human body."

William felt a slight clench of the belly.

"Dissection, you mean?"

"Yes." Hunter glanced at him, concerned. "It is a distasteful prospect, I know—and yet, to see the marvelous fashion in which God has ordered things! The intricacies of a kidney, the amazing interior of a lung—William, I cannot tell thee what revelation it is!"

"Well . . . yes, I see it must be," William said guardedly. Now he could reasonably glance back, and did so. Rachel had straightened, stretching her back, head tilted so that her straw hat fell back, the sun on her face, and he smiled. "You . . . er . . . where did you get the bodies to dissect?"

Dr. Hunter sighed.

"That was the disturbing aspect. Many were paupers from the workhouse or the street, and their deaths were most pitiable. But many were the bodies of executed criminals. And while I must be pleased that some good came of their deaths, I could not but be appalled at those deaths."

"Why?" William asked, interested.

"Why?" Hunter blinked at him behind his spectacles, but then shook his head, as though shaking off flies. "But I forget thee is not one of us—your pardon. We do not condone violence, Friend William, and surely not killing."

"Not even criminals? Murderers?"

Denzell's lips compressed, and he looked unhappy, but shook his head.

"No. Let them be imprisoned or put to some useful labor. But for the state to commit murder in its turn is a dreadful violation of God's commandment; it implicates all of us in the commission of this sin. Does thee not see?"

"I see that the state, as you call it, has responsibility for its subjects," William said, rather nettled. "You expect constables and judges to see that you and your property are secure, don't you? If the state has that responsibility, surely it must have the means of carrying it out."

"I do not contest that—imprison criminals, if necessary, as I say. But the state has no right to kill people on my behalf!"

"Has it not?" William said dryly. "Have you any idea of the nature of some of the criminals who are executed? Of their crimes?"

"Has thee?" Hunter gave him a raised brow.

"I have, yes. The Governor of Newgate Prison is an acquaintance—another acquaintance—of my father's; I have sat at table with him and heard stories that would take the curl out of your wig, Dr. Hunter. If you wore one," he added.

Hunter responded to the jest with a fleeting smile.

"Call me by my name," he said. "Thee knows we do not hold by titles. And I admit the truth of what thee says. I have heard—and seen—more terrible things than you have likely heard at your father's table. But justice lies in God's hand. To do violence—to take a life—is to violate God's command and do grievous sin."

"And if you are attacked, injured, you may not fight back?" William demanded. "You may not defend yourselves? Your families?"

"We rely upon the goodness and mercy of God," Denzell said firmly. "And if we are killed, then we die in the firm expectation of God's life and resurrection."

They rode in silence for a moment before William said conversationally, "Or you rely upon the willingness of someone else to commit violence for you."

Denzell drew a deep, instinctive breath, but thought better of whatever he had meant to say. They rode in silence for some time, and when they spoke again, it was of birds.

IT WAS RAINING WHEN they woke next day. Not a quick thundershower, here and gone, but a heavy, remorseless sort of rain that looked set to pour steadily all day. There was no point in staying where they were; the rocky overhang under which they had sheltered for the night lay directly exposed to the wind, and the rain had already dampened the firewood sufficiently as to cause their breakfast fire to yield much more smoke than heat.

Still coughing intermittently, William and Denny loaded the pack mule while Rachel bound up a bundle of the least-damp sticks in canvas. If they found shelter by nightfall, they might at least be able to start a fire to cook their supper, even if the rain continued.

There was little conversation. Even had they been so inclined, the rain beat so heavily upon trees and ground and upon their hats that anything said had to be half shouted to be heard.

In a state of sodden but dogged determination, they rode slowly north by northeast, Denny anxiously consulting his compass when they reached a crossroad.

"What think thee, Friend William?" Denny took off his spectacles and wiped them—to little effect—on the skirt of his coat. "Neither road runs precisely as we might wish, and Friend Lockett did not mention this crossroad in his instruction. That one"—he pointed at the road that crossed the one they were set upon—"appears to run north, while this one is due east. At the moment." He glanced at William, his face oddly naked without his spectacles.

A farmer named Lockett and his wife had been their last contact with humanity, three days before. She had given them supper, sold them bread, eggs, and cheese, and her husband had set them on the road—toward Albany, he said; they should run across an indication of the Continental army somewhere between here and there. But he *hadn't* mentioned a crossroad.

William gave the muddy ground a glance, but the crossroad itself lay in a low spot and was nothing more now than a small lake. No clues to traffic—but the road they were on seemed substantially wider than the smaller one crossing it.

"This one," he said firmly, and nudged his horse squelching through the lake to the other side.

Now it was late afternoon, and he was beginning to be worried about his decision. Had they been upon the right road, they should—said Mr. Lockett—encounter a small hamlet called Johnson's Ford by the end of the day. Of course, the rain had slowed them, he told himself. And while the countryside looked as vacant and writhingly verdant as ever, villages and farmsteads *did* pop up as suddenly as mushrooms after a heavy rain. In which case, they might encounter Johnson's Ford at any moment.

"Maybe the place has dissolved." Rachel leaned out from her saddle to call to him. Rachel had nearly dissolved herself, and he grinned, in spite of his worry. The rain had beaten the brim of her straw hat down, so that it hung limp as a duster around her head; she was obliged to lift the front of it in order to peer out, like a suspicious toad under a harrow. Her clothes were soaked through, as well, and as she was wearing three layers of everything, she resembled nothing so much as a large, untidy bale of wet laundry, forked steaming from the kettle.

Before he could reply to her, though, her brother sat up straight in his saddle, showering water in all directions, and pointed dramatically down the road.

"Look!"

William jerked his head round, assuming that their destination was in sight. It wasn't, but the road was no longer empty. A man was walking briskly toward them through the mud, a split burlap sack shielding his head and shoulders from the rain. In the current state of desolation, anything human was a sight to gladden the eyes, and William spurred up a little to hail the fellow.

"Well met, young sir," said the man, peering up at William from his burlap refuge. "Where ye bound, this dismal day?" He lifted a lip in ingratiation, showing a broken dogtooth, stained with tobacco.

"Johnson's Ford. Are we headed aright?"

The man reared back, as though astonished.

"Johnson's Ford, you say?"

"I do, yes," William said, with a certain amount of testiness. He sympathized with the lack of company in rural parts and the subsequent impulse of the inhabitants to detain travelers as long as possible, but this was not the day for it. "Where is it?"

The man shook his head back and forth in slow dismay.

" 'Fraid ye've missed your turn, sir. Ought to've gone left at the crossroads."

Rachel made a small, pitiable sound at this. The light was already failing, shadow beginning to pool round the horses' feet. It was several hours' ride back to the crossroad; they could not hope to reach it before nightfall, let alone make their way to Johnson's Ford.

The man plainly realized this, as well. He smiled happily at William, revealing a wide expanse of brown gum.

"If so be as you gennelmen'll help me cotch my cow and drive 'er home, the wife'd be pleased to offer ye supper and a bed."

There being no reasonable alternative, William accepted this suggestion with what grace he could, and leaving Rachel sheltering under a tree with the animals, he and Denny Hunter went to assist with the cow-cotching.

The cow in question, a rawboned shaggy beast with a wild eye, proved both elusive and obdurate, and it took the combined talents of all three men to capture it and drag it to the road. Soaked to the skin and thickly plastered with mud, the bedraggled party then followed Mr. Antioch Johnson—for so their host had introduced himself—through the gathering shades of night to a small ramshackle farmhouse.

The rain was still pelting down, though, and any roof was welcome, leaky or not.

Mrs. Johnson proved to be a ragged slattern of uncertain age, with even fewer teeth than her husband and a sullen disposition. She glared at the dripping guests and turned her back rudely upon them, but did produce wooden bowls of a vile, congealed stew—and there was fresh milk from the cow. William noticed that Rachel took but a single bite of the stew, turned pale, removed something from her mouth, and set down her spoon, after which she confined herself to the milk.

He himself was much too hungry either to taste the stew or care what was in it—and, fortunately, it was too dark to examine the contents of his bowl.

Denny was making an effort to be sociable, though he was swaying with weariness, answering Mr. Johnson's unending questions about their origins, journey, destination, connections, news of the road, and opinions and news regarding the war. Rachel attempted a smile now and then, but her eyes kept passing uneasily around their surroundings, returning again and again to their hostess, who sat in the corner, her own eyes hooded, brooding over a fuming clay pipe that hung from a slack lower lip.

Belly full and with dry stockings, William felt the labors of the day begin to catch up to him. There was a decent fire in the hearth, and the leaping flames lulled him into a sort of trance, the voices of Denny and Mr. Johnson fading into a pleasant murmur. He might have fallen asleep right there, had the rustle of Rachel rising to her feet to visit the privy not broken the trance, reminding him that he should check the horses and mules. He'd rubbed them dry as well as he could and paid Mr. Johnson for hay, but there was no real barn to shelter them, only a crude roof of branches perched on spindly poles. He didn't want them standing all night in mud should the shelter be flooded.

It was still raining, but the air outside was clean and fresh, filled with the night scent of trees, grasses, and rushing water. After the fug indoors, William felt nearly light-headed with the fragrance. He ducked through the rain to the shelter, doing his best to keep the small torch he had brought alight, enjoying every breath.

The torch sputtered but kept burning, and he was glad to see that the shelter had not flooded; the horses and mules—and the wild-eyed cow—were all standing on damp straw, but not hock-deep in mud. The privy door creaked, and he saw Rachel's slender dark shape emerge. She saw the torch and came to join him, drawing her shawl about her against the rain.

"Are the beasts all right?" Raindrops sparkled in her damp hair, and he smiled at her.

"I expect their supper was better than ours."

She shuddered in recollection.

"I should much prefer to have eaten hay. Did thee *see* what was in—"

"No," he interrupted, "and I shall be much happier if you don't tell me."

She snorted, but desisted. He had no desire to go back into

the fetid house at once, and Rachel seemed similarly disinclined, moving to scratch her mule's drooping ears.

"I do not like the way that woman looks at us," Rachel said after a moment, not looking at him. "She keeps staring at my shoes. As though she wonders whether they would fit her."

William glanced at Rachel's feet himself; her shoes were not in any way fashionable but were sturdy and well made, though also well worn and smeared with dried mud.

Rachel glanced uneasily at the house. "I will be pleased to leave here, even if it should still be raining in the morning."

"We'll leave," he assured her. "Without waiting for breakfast, if you prefer." He leaned against one of the upright poles that supported the shelter, feeling the mist of rain cool on his neck. The drowsiness had left him, though the tiredness had not, and he realized that he shared her sense of unease.

Mr. Johnson seemed amiable, if uncouth, but there was something almost too eager in his manner. He leaned forward avidly in conversation, eyes agleam, and his dirty hands were restless on his knees.

It might be only the natural loneliness of a man who lacked company—for surely the presence of the sullen Mrs. Johnson would be little consolation—but William's father had taught him to pay attention to his instincts, and he therefore did not try to argue himself out of them. Without comment or apology, he rummaged in the saddlebag hanging from the post and found the small dagger that he carried in his boot while riding.

Rachel's eyes followed it as he tucked it into the waist of his breeches and pulled his shirt loose to cover it. Her chin was puckered, but she didn't protest.

The torch was beginning to gutter, almost burned out. He held out his arm, and Rachel took it without protest, drawing close to him. He wanted to put his arm around her but contented himself with drawing in his elbow, finding the distant warmth of her body a comfort.

The bulk of the farmhouse was darker than the night, lacking either door or window at the back. They circled it in silence, rain thumping on their skulls, feet squelching on the sodden ground. Only a flicker of light showed through the shutters, the faintest indication of human tenancy. He heard

Rachel swallow, and touched her hand lightly as he opened the door for her.

"Sleep well," he whispered to her. "The dawn will come before you know it."

IT WAS THE STEW that saved his life. He slept almost at once, overcome by weariness, but found his sleep troubled by obnoxious dreams. He was walking down a hallway with a figured Turkey carpet, but realized after a time that what he had taken for twining patterns in the rug were in fact snakes, which raised their heads, swaying, at his approach. The snakes were slow-moving, and he was able to skip over them but lurched from side to side as a result, hitting the walls of the corridor, which seemed to be closing in upon him, narrowing the way.

Then he was enclosed so tightly that he must proceed sideways, the wall behind him scraping his back, the plaster surface before him so close that he could not bend his head to look down. He was worried about the snakes in the carpet, but couldn't see them, and kicked out to the side with his feet, now and then hitting something heavy. Panicked, he felt one twine about his leg, then glide upward, wrapping round his body and burrowing its head through the front of his shirt, prodding him hard and painfully in the abdomen, looking for somewhere to bite.

He woke suddenly, panting and sweating, aware that the pain in his guts was real. It bit with a sharp cramp, and he pulled up his legs and rolled onto his side an instant before the ax struck the floorboards where his head had just been.

He let out a tremendous fart and rolled in blind panic toward the dark figure struggling to free the ax from the wood. He struck Johnson's legs, grabbed them, and yanked. The man fell on him with a curse and grabbed him by the throat. William punched and thrashed at his opponent, but the hands on his throat clung like grim death, and his vision darkened and flashed with colored lights.

There was screaming going on somewhere nearby. More by instinct than plan, William suddenly lunged forward, striking Johnson in the face with his forehead. It hurt, but the death grip on his throat relaxed, and he wrenched loose and rolled over, scrambling to his feet.

The fire had died to embers, and there was no more than a faint glow of light in the room. A heaving mass of bodies in the corner was the source of the screaming, but nothing he could do about that.

Johnson had kicked the ax loose; William saw the dull gleam of its blade in the split second before Johnson seized it and swung it at his head. He ducked, rushed in, and managed to grab Johnson's wrist, pulling hard. The cheek of the falling ax blade struck his knee a paralyzing blow, and he crumpled, pulling Johnson down with him, but got the other knee up in time to keep from being flattened beneath the other man's body.

He jerked to the side, felt sudden heat at his back and the ping of sparks; they had rolled into the edge of the hearth. He reached back and seized a handful of hot embers, which he ground into Johnson's face, ignoring the searing pain in his palm.

Johnson fell back, clutching his face and making short *ah! ah!* noises, as though he had not breath to scream. The ax was dangling from one hand; he sensed William rise and swung it blindly, one-handed.

William grabbed the ax handle, jerked it from Johnson's grasp, took a good two-handed hold upon the throat of the handle, and brought the bit down on Johnson's head with a *choonk* like a kicked pumpkin. The impact vibrated through his hands and arms; he let go and stumbled backward.

His mouth was full of bile; saliva overflowed and he wiped a sleeve across his mouth. He was breathing like a bellows but could not seem to get any air in his lungs.

Johnson reeled toward him, arms outstretched, the ax sticking in his head. The handle quivered, turning to and fro like an insect's feeler. Slowly, horribly, Johnson's hands reached up to take hold of it.

William wanted to scream but didn't have the breath for it. Backing away in panic, he brushed a hand against his breeches and felt wetness there. He glanced down, fearing the worst, but saw instead the cloth dark with blood, and at the same time realized that there was a slight stinging sensation at the top of his thigh.

"Bloody . . . hell," he muttered, fumbling at his waist. He'd managed to stab himself with his own dagger, but it was still there, thank God. The feel of the hilt steadied him, and he pulled it out, still backing away as Johnson came toward him, making a sort of yowling noise, yanking at the ax handle.

The ax came loose, releasing a gush of blood that rolled down Johnson's face and splattered William's face and arms and chest. Johnson swung the ax with a huff of effort, but his movements were slow and clumsy. William ducked aside, farting with the movement but regaining his nerve.

He tightened his grip on the dagger and looked for a place to stick it. Round the back, his mind suggested. Johnson was dashing one forearm uselessly across his face, trying to clear his eyes, the ax held in the other hand, sweeping to and fro in wide, trembling swaths.

"William!" Surprised by the voice, he glanced aside and was nearly struck by the wavering blade.

"Shut up," he said crossly. "I'm busy."

"Yes, I see that," said Denny Hunter. "Let me help thee." He was white-faced and shaking nearly as much as Johnson, but stepped forward and, with a sudden lunge, seized the ax handle and pulled the implement out of Johnson's grasp. He stepped back and dropped it on the floor with a *thunk,* looking as though he might be sick at any moment.

"Thank you," said William. He stepped forward and drove the dagger upward under Johnson's ribs, into his heart. Johnson's eyes opened wide with the shock and stared directly into William's. They were gray-blue, with a scattering of gold and yellow flecks near the dark iris. William had never seen anything more beautiful and stood transfixed for an instant, until the feel of the pumping blood over his hand returned him to himself.

He jerked the knife free and stood back, letting the body fall. He was trembling all over and about to shit himself. He turned blindly and headed for the door, brushing past Denny, who said something that he didn't quite hear.

Shuddering and gasping in the privy, though, he thought the doctor had said, "Thee did not have to do that."

Yes, he thought, *I did,* and bowed his head upon his knees, waiting for everything to abate.

WILLIAM EMERGED at last from the privy, feeling clammy and rubber-limbed but less internally volatile. Denny Hunter rushed past him and into the structure, from which explosive noises and loud groans were immediately heard. Moving hastily away, he made his way through a spatter of rain toward the house.

Dawn was some way off, but the air had begun to stir, and the farmhouse stood out against the paling sky, black and skeletal. He entered, feeling very uncertain, to find Rachel, white as bone, standing guard with a broom over Mrs. Johnson, who was wrapped tightly in a filthy sheet, thrashing a bit and making peculiar hissing and spitting noises.

Her husband's remains lay facedown by the hearth in a pool of congealing blood. He didn't want to look at the body, but felt it would be somehow wrong not to, and went and stood by it for a moment, looking down. One of the Hunters had poked up the fire and added wood; there was warmth in the room, but he couldn't feel it.

"He's dead," Rachel said, her voice colorless.

"Yes." He didn't know how he was meant to feel in such a situation and had no real idea how he *did* feel. He turned away, though, with a slight sense of relief, and came to look at the prisoner.

"Did she . . . ?"

"She tried to cut Denny's throat, but she stepped on my hand and woke me. I saw the knife and screamed, and he seized her, and . . ." She pulled a hand through her hair, and he saw that she had lost her cap, and the hair was loose and tangled.

"I sat on her," she said, "and Denny rolled her up in the sheet. I don't think she can speak," Rachel added, as he stooped to look at the woman. "Her tongue is split."

Mrs. Johnson, hearing this, thrust out her tongue in vindictive fashion and waggled the two halves of it independently at him. With the memory of the dream snakes vivid in his mind, he flinched in instinctive revulsion, but saw the look of satisfaction that crossed her face.

"If she can do that with her nasty tongue, she can talk," he said, and, reaching down, took hold of the woman's scrawny throat. "Tell me why I shouldn't kill you, too."

"Iss not my fault!" she said promptly, in such a rasping hiss that he nearly let go of her in shock. "He makess me help him."

William glanced over his shoulder at the body on the hearth.

"Not anymore." He tightened his grip, feeling the beat of her pulse against his thumb. "How many travelers have you killed, the two of you?"

She didn't answer but stroked her upper lip lasciviously with her tongue, first one half and then the other. He let go her throat and slapped her hard across the face. Rachel gasped.

"Thee must not—"

"Oh, yes, I must." He rubbed his hand against the side of his breeches, trying to get rid of the feel of the woman's sweat, her slack skin, her bony throat. His other hand was beginning to throb painfully. He wanted suddenly to pick up the ax and smash her with it, over and over—crush her head, hack her to bits. His body trembled with the urge; she saw it in his eyes and stared back at him, eyes black and glittering.

"You don't want me to kill her?" he asked Rachel.

"Thee must not," she whispered. Very slowly, she reached for his burned hand, and, when he did not pull away, took it into hers. There was a roaring in his ears, and he felt dizzy.

"Thee is hurt," she said softly. "Come outside. I will wash it."

She led him out, half blind and stumbling, and made him sit on the chopping block while she brought a bucket of water from the trough. It had stopped raining, though the world dripped and the dawn air was moist and fresh in his chest.

Rachel bathed his hand in the cold water, and the burning eased a little. She touched his thigh, where the blood had dried in a long patch down his breeches, but let it go when he shook his head.

"I'll bring thee whisky; there is some in Denny's bag." She stood up, but he grabbed her wrist with his good hand, holding hard.

"Rachel." His own voice sounded odd to him, remote, as though someone else was speaking. "I've never killed anyone before. I don't—I don't quite know what to do about it." He looked up at her, searching her face for understanding. “If it had been—I expected it to be in battle. That—I think I’d know how. How to feel, I mean. If it had been like that.”

She met his eyes, her face drawn in troubled thought. The light touched her, a pink softer than the sheen of pearls, and after a long time she touched his face, very gently.

“No,” she said. “Thee wouldn’t.”

Part Five

To the Precipice

42

CROSSROAD

WILLIAM PARTED from the Hunters at a nameless crossroad somewhere in New Jersey. It was not politic for him to go further; their inquiries regarding the position of the Continental army were being greeted with increasing hostility, indicating that they were getting close. Neither rebel sympathizers nor Loyalists who feared reprisal from an army on their doorstep wished to say anything to mysterious travelers who might be spies or worse.

The Quakers would have an easier time of it without him. They were so plainly what they were and Denzell's intent to enlist as a surgeon both so simple and so admirable that, if they were alone, people would help them, he thought. Or at least receive their inquiries more kindly. With William, though . . .

Saying that he was a friend of the Hunters had been sufficient, earlier in the journey. Folk were curious about the little group, but not suspicious. As they drew farther into New Jersey, though, the agitation of the countryside increased markedly. Farms had been raided by foraging parties, both by Hessians from Howe's army, trying to lure Washington into open battle from his lurking place in the Watchung Mountains, and from the Continental army, desperate for supplies.

Farmhouses that would normally have welcomed strangers for the news they bore now repelled them with muskets and harsh words. Food was growing harder to find. Rachel's presence sometimes helped them get close enough to offer money—and William's small store of gold and silver was certainly helpful; Denzell had put most of the money from the sale of their house with a bank in Philadelphia to secure Rachel's future safety, and the paper money issued by the Congress was almost universally rejected.

There was no means by which William could masquerade as a Quaker, though. Beyond his inability to master plain speech, his size and bearing made people nervous—the more so as he, with the memories of Captain Nathan Hale vivid in his mind, would not say that he meant to enlist in the Continental army nor ask any questions that might later be presented as evidence of spying. His silence—perceived as menacing—also made people nervous.

He hadn't spoken to the Hunters regarding their parting, and both Denzell and Rachel had been careful not to ask about his own plans. Everyone knew the time had come, though; he could feel it in the air when he woke that morning. When Rachel handed him a chunk of bread for breakfast, her hand brushed his, and he nearly seized her fingers. She felt the strength of his stifled impulse and looked up, startled, directly into his eyes. More green than brown today, and he would have sent discretion to the devil and kissed her—he thought she would not have objected—had her brother not just then emerged from the bushes, buttoning his flies.

He chose the place, all of a sudden. Naught to be gained by delay, and maybe better to do it without thinking too much. He pulled his horse to a stop in the middle of the crossroad, startling Denzell, whose mare bridled and danced at the jerk on her reins.

"I will leave you here," William said abruptly, and more harshly than he had intended. "My way lies north"—he nodded in that direction, and thank God the sun was up so he could tell which way north was—"while I think that if you continue to the east, you will encounter some representatives of Mr. Washington's army. If . . ." He hesitated, but they should be warned. From what the farmers had said, it was plain that Howe had sent troops into the area.

"If you meet with British troops or Hessian mercenaries—do you speak German, by chance?"

Denzell shook his head, eyes wide behind his spectacles. "Only a little French."

"That's good. Most Hessian officers have good French. If you meet with Hessians who don't and they offer to molest you, say to them, '*Ich verlange, Euren Vorgesetzten zu sehen; ich bin mit seinem Freund bekannt.*' That means, 'I demand to see your officer; I know his friend.' Say the same thing if you meet with British troops. In English, of course," he added awkwardly.

A faint smile crossed Denzell's face.

"I thank thee," he said. "But if they do take us to an officer, and he demands to know the name of this theoretical friend?"

William smiled back.

"It won't really matter. Once you're in front of an officer, you will be safe. But as for a name—Harold Grey, Duke of Pardloe, Colonel of the Forty-sixth Foot." Uncle Hal didn't know everyone, as his own father did, but anyone in the military world would know *him*—or of him, at least.

He could see Denzell's lips move silently, committing this to memory.

"And who is Friend Harold to thee, William?" Rachel had been regarding him narrowly beneath the sagging brim of her hat, and now pushed this back on her head to view him more directly.

He hesitated again, but after all, what did it matter now? He would never see the Hunters again. And while he knew that Quakers would not be impressed by worldly shows of rank and family, he still sat straighter in his saddle.

"Some kin to me," he said casually, and, digging in his pocket, brought out the small purse the Scotsman Murray had given him. "Here. You will need this."

"We will do well enough," Denzell said, waving it away.

"So will I," William said, and tossed the purse toward Rachel, who put up her hands in reflex and caught it, looking as much surprised by the fact that she had done so as by his own action. He smiled at her, too, his heart full.

"Fare thee well," he said gruffly, then wheeled his horse and set off at a brisk trot, not looking back.

"THEE KNOWS HE is a British soldier?" Denny Hunter said quietly to his sister, watching William ride away. "Likely a deserter."

"And if he is?"

"Violence follows such a man. Thee knows it. To remain long with such a man is a danger—not only to the body. But to the soul, as well."

Rachel sat her mule in silence for a moment, watching the empty road. Insects buzzed loud in the trees.

"I think thee may be a hypocrite, Denzell Hunter," she said evenly, and pulled her mule's head around. "He saved my life *and* thine. Would thee prefer him to have held his hand and see me dead and butchered in that dreadful place?" She shuddered slightly in spite of the heat of the day.

"I would not," her brother said soberly. "And I thank God that he was there to save thee. I am sinner enough to prefer thy life to the welfare of that young man's soul—but not hypocrite enough to deny it, no."

She snorted and, taking off her hat, waved away a gathering cloud of flies.

"I am honored. But as for thy talk of violent men and the danger of being in the vicinity of such men—is thee not taking me to join an army?"

He laughed ruefully.

"I am. Perhaps thee is right and I am a hypocrite. But, Rachel—" He leaned out and caught her mule's bridle, keeping her from turning away. "Thee knows I would have no harm befall thee, either of body or soul. Say the word and I will find thee a place with Friends, where you may stay in safety. I am sure that the Lord has spoken to me, and I must follow my conscience. But there is no need for thee to follow it, too."

She gave him a long, level look.

"And how does thee know that the Lord has not spoken to me, as well?"

His eyes twinkled behind his spectacles.

"I am happy for thee. What did He say?"

"He said, 'Keep thy fat-headed brother from committing suicide, for I will require his blood at thy hand,'" she snapped, slapping his hand away from the bridle. "If we are going to join the army, Denny, let us go and find it."

She kicked the mule viciously in the ribs. Its ears sprang straight up, and with a startled whoop from its rider, it shot down the road as though fired from a cannon.

WILLIAM RODE FOR some way, back particularly straight, showing excellent form in his horsemanship. After the road curved out of sight of the crossroad, he slowed and relaxed a bit. He was sorry to leave the Hunters, but already beginning to turn his thoughts ahead.

Burgoyne. He'd met General Burgoyne once, at a play. A play written by the general, no less. He didn't recall anything about the play itself, as he'd been engaged in a flirtation of the eyes with a girl in the next box, but afterward he'd gone down with his father to congratulate the successful playwright, who was flushed and handsome with triumph and champagne.

"Gentleman Johnny" they called him in London. A light in London society's firmament, in spite of the fact that he and his wife had some years before been obliged to flee to France to escape arrest for debt. No one held debt against a man, though; it was too common.

William was more puzzled by the fact that his uncle Hal seemed to like John Burgoyne. Uncle Hal had no time for plays, nor for the people who wrote them—though, come to think, he had the complete works of Aphra Behn on his shelves, and William's father had once told him, in deepest secrecy, that his brother Hal had conceived a passionate attachment for Mrs. Behn following the death of his first wife and before his marriage to Aunt Minnie.

"Mrs. Behn was dead, you see," his father had explained. "Safe."

William had nodded, wishing to seem worldly and understanding, though in fact he had no real notion what his father meant by this. Safe? How, safe?

He shook his head. He didn't expect ever to understand Uncle Hal, and chances were that was best for both of them. His grandmother Benedicta was probably the only person who did. Thought of his uncle, though, led him to think of his cousin Henry, and his mouth tightened a little.

Word would have reached Adam, of course, but he likely could do nothing for his brother. Neither could William, whose duty called him north. Between his father and Uncle Hal, though, surely . . .

The horse threw up his head, snorting a little, and William looked ahead to see a man standing by the road, one arm raised to hail him.

He rode slowly, a sharp eye on the wood, lest the man have confederates hidden to waylay unwary travelers. The verge was open here, though, with a thick but spindly growth of saplings behind it; no one could hide in there.

"Good day to you, sir," he said, reining up a safe distance from the old man. For old he was; his face was seamed like a tin mine's slag heap, he leaned on a tall staff, and his hair was pure white, tied back in a plait.

"Well met," the old gentleman said. Gentleman for he stood proud, and his clothes were decent, and now William came to look, there was a good horse, too, hobbled and cropping grass some distance away. William relaxed a little.

"Where do you fare, sir?" he asked politely. The old man shrugged a little, easy.

"That may depend upon what you can tell me, young man." The old man was a Scot, though his English was good. "I am in search of a man called Ian Murray, whom I think you know?"

William was disconcerted by this; how did the old man know that? But he knew Murray; perhaps Murray had mentioned William to him. He replied cautiously, "I know him. But I am afraid I have no idea where he is."

"No?" The old man looked keenly at him. *As though he thinks I might lie to him,* William thought. *Suspicious old sod!*

"No," he repeated firmly. "I met him in the Great Dismal, some weeks ago, in company with some Mohawk. But I do not know where he might have gone since then."

"Mohawk," the old man repeated thoughtfully, and William saw the sunken eyes fasten on his chest, where the great bear claw rested outside his shirt. "Did you get that wee bawbee from the Mohawk, then?"

"No," William replied stiffly, not knowing what a bawbee was, but thinking that it sounded in some way disparaging. "Mr. Murray brought it to me, from a—friend."

"A friend." The old man was frankly studying his face, in a way that made William uncomfortable and therefore angry. "What is your name, young man?"

"None of your business, sir," William said, as courteously as possible, and gathered his reins. "Good day to you!"

The old man's face tightened, as did his hand on the staff, and William turned sharply, lest the old bugger mean to try to strike him with it. He didn't, but William noticed, with a small sense of shock, that two fingers of the hand that grasped the staff were missing.

He thought for a moment that the old man might mount and come after him, but when he glanced back, the man was still standing by the road, looking after him.

It made no real difference, but, moved by some obscure notion of avoiding notice, William put the bear's claw inside his shirt, where it hung safely concealed next to his rosary.

43

COUNTDOWN

Fort Ticonderoga
June 18, 1777

Dear Bree and Roger,

Twenty-three days and counting. I hope *we'll be able to leave on schedule. Your cousin Ian left the fort a month ago, saying that he had a wee bit of business to take care of but would be back by the time Jamie's militia enlistment was up. Ian himself declined to enlist, being instead a volunteer forager, so he's not technically AWOL. Not that the fort's commander is really in a position to do anything about deserters, save hang them if they're silly enough to come back, and none of them do. I'm not sure what Ian's doing, but I have some hope that it may be good for him.*

Speaking of the fort's commander, we have a new one. Great excitement! Colonel Wayne left a few weeks ago—doubtless sweating with relief as much as with the humidity—but we have come up in the world. The new commander is a major general, no less: one Arthur St. Clair, a genial and very handsome Scot, whose attractiveness is considerably enhanced by the pink sash he affects on formal occasions. (The nice thing about belonging to an ad hoc *army is that one apparently gets to design one's own uniform. None of this stuffy old British convention about regimentals.)*

General St. Clair comes with outriders: no fewer than three *lesser generals, one of them French (your father says General Fermoy is rather fishy, militarily speaking), and about three thousand new recruits. This has substantially heartened everyone (though placing an ungodly strain on the latrine facilities. The lines are fifteen deep in the mornings at the pits, and there is a severe shortage of thunder mugs), and St. Clair made a nice speech, assuring us that the fort cannot possibly be taken now. Your father, who was standing next to the general at the time, said something under his breath in Gaelic at this point, but not very far under, and while I understand the general was born in Thurso, he conveniently affected not to understand.*

The bridge-building between the fort and Mount Independence continues apace . . . and Mount Defiance continues to sit there across the water. An inoffensive little hill, to look at—but a good bit higher than the fort. Jamie had Mr. Marsden row across with a target—a four-foot square of wood, painted white—and set it up near the top of the hill, where it was plainly visible from the fort's batteries. He invited General Fermoy (he does not *get a pink sash, despite being French) to come and try his hand at shooting with one of the new rifles (Jamie having thoughtfully abstracted several of these from the cargo of the* Teal *before patriotically donating the rest to the American cause). They blasted the target to bits, an act whose significance was not lost on General St. Clair, who came along to watch. I think General St. Clair will be almost as pleased as I will be when your father's enlistment is up.*

The new influx has made things busier, of course. Most of the new recruits are reasonably healthy, for a wonder, but there are the usual minor accidents, cases of venereal disease, and summer ague—enough that Major Thacher—he's the chief medical officer—has taken to turning a blind eye when I surreptitiously bind up a wound, though he draws the line at allowing me access to sharp instruments. Fortunately, I have a small knife with which to lance boils.

I am also growing very short of useful herbs, since Ian's defection. He used to bring me things from his foraging expeditions, but it really isn't safe to venture out of the fort save in large bodies. Two men who went out hunting a few days ago were found murdered and scalped.

While my medical kit thus remains a little sparse, I have as some compensation acquired a ghoul. This is a Mrs. Raven from New Hampshire, whose husband is a militia officer. She's relatively young, in her thirties, but has never had children and thus has a lot of emotional energy to expend. She battens on the sick and dying, though I'm sure she considers herself to be sympathetic in the extreme. She revels in ghastly detail, which, while mildly repulsive in itself, does make her a competent aide, since she can be counted on not to faint while I set a compound fracture or amputate (quickly, before Major Thacher or his henchman, Lieutenant Stactoe, notices) a gangrenous digit, for fear of missing something. Granted, she does wail and carry on a bit, and is much given to clutching her rather flat chest and allowing her eyes to bulge while describing these adventures to other people afterward (she nearly prostrated herself from hyperventilation when they brought in the men who were scalped), but one takes what one can get in the way of help.

At the other end of the scale in terms of medical competence, though, the new influx of recruits has brought with it a young Quaker doctor named Denzell Hunter and his sister, Rachel. I haven't yet spoken to him personally, but from what I see, Dr. Hunter really is *a doctor, and seems even to have some vague notion of germ theory, owing to his having trained with John Hunter, one of the great men of medicine (on the chance that Roger will be reading this, I will refrain from telling you the manner in which John Hunter discovered how gonorrhea is transmitted—well, no, actually I won't: he stabbed himself in the penis with a lancet covered in pus from an infected victim and was deeply gratified with the results, according to Denny Hunter, who recounted this interesting incident to your father while bandaging his thumb, which got squashed between two rolling logs—don't worry, it isn't broken; just badly bruised). I'd love to see how Mrs. Raven would take this story, but I suppose propriety would prevent young Dr. Hunter telling her.*

You are, of course, minding the children's vaccination schedule.

With all my love,
Mama

BRIANNA HAD CLOSED the book, but her hand kept returning involuntarily to the cover, as though she wished to open it again, in case it might say something different.

"What's twenty-three days past June eighteenth?" She should be able to reckon that—she could do things like that in her head—but nervousness had deprived her of the ability to compute.

"Thirty days hath September," Roger chanted quickly under his breath, rolling up his eyes to the ceiling, "April, June—right, June's got thirty days, so twelve days from the eighteenth to the thirtieth, and ten more makes it the tenth of July."

"Oh, dear Lord."

She'd read it three times, looking again wouldn't make a difference; still, she opened the book once more, to the page with John Burgoyne's portrait. A handsome man—"And doesn't he just know it, too!" she said aloud, making Roger frown at her in consternation—as painted by Sir Joshua Reynolds, he was in uniform, his hand resting on the hilt of his sword, standing against a dramatic backdrop of gathering storm clouds. And there it was on the next page, plain in black and white.

On the sixth of July, General Burgoyne attacked Fort Ticonderoga with a force of some 8,000 regulars, plus several German regiments under the Baron von Riedesel, and a number of Indians.

WILLIAM FOUND General Burgoyne and his army somewhat more easily than the Hunters had discovered General Washington's whereabouts. On the other hand, General Burgoyne was making no attempt to hide.

It was a lavish camp, by army standards. Neatly arranged rows of white canvas tents covered three fields and ran off into the woods. Making his way to the commander's tent to report, he spotted a pile of empty wine bottles near the general's tent that rose nearly to his knee. As he had not heard that the general was a notable souse, he assumed this largesse to be the result of an open-handed hospitality and a liking for company. A good sign in a commander, he thought.

A yawning servant was picking off the remnants of the lead seals, tossing the metal into a can, presumably to be melted for bullets. He gave William a sleepy, inquiring eye.

"I've come to report to General Burgoyne," William said, drawing himself up. The servant's eye traveled slowly up the length of his body, lingering with vague curiosity on his face and making him doubt the thoroughness of his morning shave.

"Dinner party with the brigadier and Colonel St. Leger last night," the servant said at last, and belched slightly.

"Come back this afternoon. Meanwhile"—he stood slowly, wincing as though the movement hurt his head, and pointed—"the mess tent's over there."

44

FRIENDS

Fort Ticonderoga
June 22, 1777

MUCH TO MY surprise, I found Captain Stebbings sitting up. White-faced, bathed in sweat, and swaying like a pendulum—but upright. Mr. Dick hovered over him, clucking with the tender anxiety of a hen with one chick.

"I see you're feeling better, Captain," I said, smiling at him. "Have you on your feet any day now, won't we?"

"Been . . . on my feet," he wheezed. "Think I might die."

"What?"

"Him be *walking*!" Mr. Dick assured me, torn between pride and dismay. "On my arm, but him walk, sure!"

I was on my knees, listening to lungs and heart through the wooden stethoscope Jamie had made for me. A pulse fit for an eight-cylinder race car, and a good bit of gurgling and wheezing, but nothing horribly alarming.

"Congratulations, Captain Stebbings!" I said, lowering the stethoscope and smiling at him. He still looked dreadful, but his breathing was beginning to slow. "You probably won't die today. What brought on this burst of ambition?"

"My . . . bosun," he managed, before a fit of coughing intervened.

"Joe Ormiston," Mr. Dick clarified, with a nod in my direction. "Him foot stink. The captain go see him."

"Mr. Ormiston. His foot stinks?" That sounded all sorts of alarm bells. For a wound in this particular setting to smell so notably as to draw attention was a very bad indication. I rose to my feet but was detained by Stebbings, who had taken a firm grip of my skirt.

"You—" he said, laboring for air. "You take care of him."

He bared stained teeth at me in a grin.

" 'S an order," he wheezed. "Ma'am."

"Aye, aye, Cap'n," I said tartly, and made off for the hospital building, where the majority of the sick and wounded were housed.

"Mrs. Fraser! What's amiss?" The eager cry came from Mrs. Raven, who was coming out of the commissary as I passed. She was tall and lean, with dark hair that perpetually straggled out from under her cap, which it was doing at the moment.

"I don't know yet," I said briefly, not stopping. "But it might be serious."

"Oh!" she said, barely refraining from adding, "Goody!" Tucking her basket under her arm, she fell in beside me, firmly set to Do Good.

Invalid British prisoners were housed alongside the American sick in a long stone building lit by narrow, glassless windows and either freezing or stifling, depending on the weather. It was presently hot and humid outdoors—it was mid-afternoon—and entering the building was like being struck in the face with a hot, wet towel. A *dirty* hot, wet towel.

It wasn't hard to find Mr. Ormiston; there was a knot of men standing round his cot. Lieutentant Stactoe was among them—that was bad—arguing with little Dr. Hunter—that was good—with a couple of other surgeons trying to put in their own opinions.

I knew without looking what they were arguing about; clearly Mr. Ormiston's foot had taken a turn for the worse, and they intended to amputate it. In all probability, they were right. The argument would likely be about *where* to amputate, or who was to do it.

Mrs. Raven hung back, nervous at sight of the surgeons.

"Do you really think . . ." she began, but I paid her no attention. There are times for thinking, but this wasn't one of them. Only action, and fast, decisive action at that, would serve. I took in a lungful of the thick air and stepped forward.

"Good afternoon, Dr. Hunter," I said, elbowing my way between the two militia surgeons and smiling at the young Quaker doctor. "Lieutenant Stactoe," I added as an afterthought, not to be overtly rude. I knelt beside the patient's cot, wiped my sweaty hand on my skirt, and took his.

"How are you, Mr. Ormiston? Captain Stebbings has sent me to take care of your foot."

"He *what*?" Lieutenant Stactoe began, in a peeved sort of voice. "Really, Mrs. Fraser, what can you possibly—"

"That's good, ma'am," Mr. Ormiston interrupted. "The captain said as how he'd send you; I was just a-telling these gentlemen here as they needn't be concerned, as I was sure *you'd* know the best way to do it."

And I'm sure they were pleased to hear that, I thought, but smiled at him and squeezed his hand. His pulse was fast and a little light, but regular. His hand, though, was very hot, and I wasn't even faintly surprised to see the reddish streaks of septicemia rising up his leg from the mangled foot.

They had unwrapped the foot, and Mr. Dick had unquestionably been right: him stank.

"Oh, my *God,*" said Mrs. Raven behind me, in complete sincerity.

Gangrene had set in; if the smell and tissue crepitation were not enough, the toes had begun to blacken already. I didn't waste time in being angry at Stactoe; given the original condition of the foot, and the treatment available, I might not have been able to save it, either. And the fact that gangrene was so clearly present was actually a help; there couldn't be any question that amputation was necessary. But in that case, I wondered, why were they arguing?

"I take it you agree that amputation is necessary, Mrs. Fraser?" the lieutenant said, with sarcastic courtesy. "As the patient's *physician*?" He had his instruments already laid out on cloth, I saw. Decently kept; not disgustingly filthy—but plainly not sterilized.

"Certainly," I said mildly. "I'm very sorry about it, Mr. Ormiston, but he's right. And you will feel much better with it off. Mrs. Raven, will you go and bring me a pan of boiling water?" I turned to Denzell Hunter, who, I saw, was holding Mr. Ormiston's other hand, plainly counting his pulse.

"Do you not agree, Dr. Hunter?"

"I do, yes," he said mildly. "We are in disagreement regarding the degree of amputation required, not its necessity. What is the boiling water for, Friend . . . Fraser, he said?"

"Claire," I said briefly. "Sterilization of the instruments. To prevent postoperative infection. As much as possible," I added honestly. Stactoe made a very disrespectful noise at this, but I ignored it. "What do you recommend, Dr. Hunter?"

"Denzell," he said, with a fleeting smile. "Friend Stactoe wishes to amputate below the knee—"

"Of course I do!" Stactoe said, furious. "I wish to preserve the knee joint, and there is no need to do it higher!"

"Oddly enough, I'm inclined to agree with you," I told him, but turned back to Denzell Hunter. "But you don't?"

He shook his head and pushed his spectacles up the bridge of his nose.

"We must do a mid-femoral amputation. The man has a popliteal aneurysm. That means—"

"I know what it means." I did, and was already feeling behind Mr. Ormiston's knee. He emitted a high-pitched giggle, stopped abruptly, and went red in the face with embarrassment. I smiled at him.

"Sorry, Mr. Ormiston," I said. "I won't tickle you again."

I wouldn't need to. I could feel the aneurysm plainly; it throbbed gently against my fingers, a big, hard swelling right in the hollow of the joint. He must have had it for some time; a wonder it hadn't burst during the sea battle or the arduous portage to Ticonderoga. In a modern operating room, it might be possible to do the lesser amputation and repair the aneurysm—but not here.

"You're right, Friend Denzell," I said, straightening up. "As soon as Mrs. Raven brings the hot water, we'll—" But the men weren't listening to me. They were staring at something behind me, and I turned to see Guinea Dick, stripped to a breechclout because of the heat and glistening with sweat, *all* his tattoos on display, advancing upon us with a black glass bottle held ceremoniously between his hands.

"Him captain send you grog, Joe," he said to Mr. Ormiston.

"Well, God bless the captain for a good un!" Mr. Ormiston said in heartfelt thanks. He took the bottle of rum, drew the cork with his teeth, and began to swallow with a single-minded determination.

Sloshing and splashing heralded Mrs. Raven's return with the water. Nearly every fire had a kettle on; finding boiling water was no difficulty. She had, bless her, also brought a bucket of cold water so that I could wash my hands without burning myself.

I took one of the short-bladed, brutal amputation knives, preparing to plunge it into the hot water, only to have it snatched from my hand by an outraged Lieutenant Stactoe.

"What are you doing, madam!" he exclaimed. "That is my best blade!"

"Yes, that's why I propose to use it," I said. "*After* I wash it."

Stactoe was a small man with close-cropped, bristly gray hair; he was also two or three inches shorter than I, as I discovered when I stood up and faced him, eyeball to eyeball. His face went a shade or two redder.

"You will ruin the temper of the metal, subjecting it to boiling water!"

"No," I said, keeping my own temper—for the moment. "Hot water will do nothing but clean it. And I will not use a dirty blade on this man."

"Oh, won't you?" Something like satisfaction glimmered in his eyes, and he clutched the blade protectively to his bosom. "Well, then. I suppose you'll have to leave the work to those who can do it, won't you?"

Guinea Dick, who had remained to watch after delivery of the bottle, had been following the progress of the argument with interest and, at this point, leaned over and plucked the knife from Stactoe's hand.

"Him captain says her does for Joe," he said calmly. "Her does."

Stactoe's mouth fell open in outrage at this gross insult to his rank, and he lunged at Dick, grabbing for the blade. Dick, with reflexes honed by tribal warfare and years of British seamanship, swung the blade at Stactoe with the obvious intent of removing his head. He would likely have succeeded, save for Denzell Hunter's equally good reflexes, which sent him leaping for Dick's arm. He missed but succeeded in knocking the big Guineaman into Stactoe. They clutched each other—Dick dropping the knife—and staggered to and fro for an instant before both overbalanced and crashed into Ormiston's cot, sending patient, rum bottle, hot water, Denzell Hunter, and the rest of the instruments sprawling across the stone floor with a clatter that stopped every conversation in the building.

"Oooh!" said Mrs. Raven, deliciously shocked. This was turning out even better than she had expected.

"Denny!" said an equally shocked voice behind me. "What does thee think thee is doing?"

"I am . . . assisting Friend Claire in her surgery," Denzell said with some dignity, sitting up and patting round the floor in search of his spectacles.

Rachel Hunter bent and picked up the errant spectacles, which had slid across the stones, and restored these firmly to her brother's face, while keeping a wary eye on Lieutenant Stactoe, who was slowly rising from the floor, much in the manner of a hot-air balloon, visibly swelling with rage.

"You," he said in a hoarse voice, and pointed a small, trembling finger at Dick. "I shall have you hanged for assaulting an officer. I shall have *you,* sir"—swinging the accusatory digit toward Denzell Hunter—"court-martialed and broke! As for you, *madam*—" He spat the word, but then stopped dead, momentarily unable to think of anything sufficiently terrible with which to threaten me. Then, "I shall ask your husband to beat you!" he said.

"Come 'n' tickle me, darlin'," a slurred voice said from the floor. I looked down, to see a leering Mr. Ormiston. He had kept hold of the rum bottle during the wreck, continued to employ it afterward, and, face suffused with rum, was now making random pawing motions in the vicinity of my knee.

Lieutenant Stactoe made a noise indicating that this was the frozen limit, if not well beyond, and, hastily bundling up his fallen instruments, he marched off, bristling with knives and saws, dropping occasional small objects in his wake.

"Did thee want me, Sissy?" Denzell Hunter had got to his feet by this time and was righting the fallen cot.

"Not so much me as Mrs. Brown," his sister said, a dry

note in her voice. "She says it is her time, and she wants thee. Right. Now."

He snorted briefly, and glanced at me.

"Mrs. Brown is an hysteric, in the literal meaning of the term," he said apologetically. "I think she cannot deliver for another month yet, but she suffers false labor on a regular basis."

"I know her," I said, suppressing a smile. "Better you than me, mate." Mrs. Brown *was* an hysteric. Also the wife of a colonel of militia and therefore—she thought—well above the services of a mere midwife. Hearing that Dr. Denzell Hunter had worked with Dr. John Hunter, who was *accoucheur* to the *Queen*!—obviously, my services could be dispensed with.

"She is not bleeding, nor her water broke?" Denzell was asking his sister in a resigned voice. Guinea Dick, totally unperturbed by the recent conflict, had restored the bedding to the cot and now squatted, lifted all fifteen stone of Mr. Ormiston as if he were a feather bed, and deposited him and his bottle gently thereon.

"I think him ready," he announced, after scrutinizing the patient, who was now lying back, eyes closed, happily murmuring, "Just a little lower, dear, aye, that's it, tha's it . . ."

Denzell looked helplessly from Mr. Ormiston to his sister to me.

"I will have to go to Mrs. Brown, though I think it not pressingly urgent. Can thee wait a little while and I will do this for thee?"

"Her does it," said Dick, glowering.

"Yes, her does," I assured him, tying back my hair. "But what her is going to do it *with* is another question. Have you any instruments that I might borrow, Dr.—er, Friend Denzell?"

He rubbed his forehead, thinking.

"I have a decent saw." He smiled briefly. "And I do not mind if thee wishes to boil it. But no heavy blade. Shall I send Rachel to ask one of the other surgeons?"

Rachel's face closed a bit at this suggestion, and I thought that perhaps Dr. Hunter was not all that popular with the other surgeons.

I eyed Mr. Ormiston's very solid leg, estimating the thickness of flesh to be cut, and put a hand through the slit in my skirt to the sheath of my knife. It was a good, sturdy knife, and Jamie had just sharpened it for me. A curved blade would be better, but I thought the length was sufficient . . .

"No, don't trouble. I think this will work. If you would find your brother's saw, Miss—er, Rachel." I smiled at her. "And, Mrs. Raven, I'm afraid the water's gone, would you—"

"Oh, yes!" she cried, and seizing the pan, clattered off, kicking one of Lieutenant Stactoe's oddments on the way.

A number of people had been watching the drama of Mr. Ormiston's foot, fascinated. Now that the lieutenant was gone, they began to sidle nearer, looking fearfully at Guinea Dick, who grinned genially at them.

"Can Mrs. Brown wait a quarter of an hour?" I asked Denzell. "It will be a little easier if I have someone who knows what they're doing to support the leg while I cut. Dick can restrain the patient."

"A quarter of an hour?"

"Well, the actual amputation will take a little less than a minute, if I don't encounter any difficulties. But I'll need a bit of time to prepare, and I could use your help in ligating the severed blood vessels afterward. Where has the rum bottle gone, by the way?"

Denzell's dark brows were almost touching his hairline, but he gestured to Mr. Ormiston, who had gone to sleep and was now snoring loudly, the rum bottle cradled in his arm.

"I don't propose to drink it," I said dryly, answering his expression. I pulled the bottle free and poured a little onto a clean rag, with which I began to swab Mr. Ormiston's hairy thigh. The lieutenant had fortunately left his jar of sutures, and the oddment Mrs. Raven had kicked was a tenaculum. I would need it to seize the ends of severed arteries, which had an annoying tendency to pop back into the flesh and hide, squirting blood all the while.

"Ah," said Denzell, still at a loss but game. "I see. Can I . . . help?"

"If I might borrow your belt for a ligature?"

"Oh, yes," he murmured, and unbuckled it without hesitation, looking interested. "I collect thee has done this before."

"Many times, unfortunately." I bent to check Mr. Ormiston's breathing, which was stertorous but not labored. He'd downed nearly half the bottle within five minutes. That was a dose that would likely kill someone less inured to rum than a British seaman, but his vital signs were reasonably good, fever notwithstanding. Drunkenness was not by any means the equivalent of anesthesia; the patient was stunned, not unconscious, and would certainly come to when I began cutting. It did allay fear, though, and might dull the immediate pain slightly. I wondered whether—and when—I might ever be able to make ether again.

There were two or three small tables in the long room, these heaped with bandages, lint, and other dressing materials. I chose a good supply of relatively clean materials and returned with them to the bedside just as Mrs. Raven—panting and red-faced, anxious lest she had missed anything—arrived, water bucket sloshing. A moment later, Rachel Hunter returned, similarly panting from her hurry, with her brother's saw.

"If you would not mind dousing the saw blade, Friend Denzell?" I said, tying a burlap sack round my waist to serve as an apron. Sweat was running down my back, tickling between my buttocks, and I tied a length of bandaging round my head bandanna-style, to keep the sweat from running into my eyes as I worked. "And scrub the stains there near the handle? Then my knife and that tenaculum, if you don't mind."

Looking bemused, he did, to interested murmurs from the crowd, who had plainly never witnessed such an outlandish proceeding, though Mr. Dick's savage presence was keeping them at a safe distance.

"Does thee suppose the lieutenant would indeed have our friend here hanged?" Denzell whispered to me, with a nod at Dick. "Or could, come to that?"

"I'm sure he'd love to, but I really don't think he can, no. Mr. Dick is an English prisoner. Can he have you court-martialed, do you think?"

"I suppose he might try," Denzell said, seeming not perturbed at the prospect. "I enlisted, after all."

"Did you?" That seemed odd, but he wasn't the only Quaker I'd met on a battlefield, so to speak.

"Oh, yes. I think the army does not have so many surgeons that it can afford to hang one, though. And I doubt that being reduced in rank would much affect my expertise." He smiled cheerfully at me. "Thee has no rank at all, if I am not mistaken, and yet I trust thee will manage."

"God willing," I said, and he nodded gravely.

"God willing," he repeated, and handed me the knife, still hot from the boiling water.

"You might want to stand back a bit," I said to the spectators. "It's going to be messy."

"Oh, dear, oh, dear," said Mrs. Raven, with a tremulous gasp of anticipation. "How perfectly *ghastly*!"

45

THREE ARROWS

Mottville, Pennsylvania
June 10, 1777

GREY SAT UP suddenly, narrowly avoiding cracking his head on the low beam that passed above his bed. His heart was pounding, his neck and temples wet with sweat, and he had no notion for a moment where he was.

"The third arrow," he said aloud, and shook his head, trying to match the words to the extraordinarily vivid dream from which he had so abruptly emerged.

Was it dream, memory, or something partaking of the nature of both? He had been standing in the main salon of *Trois Flèches,* looking at the very fine Stubbs hanging to the right of the baroque mantelpiece. The walls were crowded with pictures—hung above, below, crammed in without regard to subject or merit.

Was that how it had been? He remembered vaguely a sense of oppression at the abundance of ornament, but had the paintings truly crowded in so, portraits leering from above, below, faces in every direction?

In the dream, the Baron Amandine had stood to one side of him, the solid shoulder touching his; they were much of a height. The Baron was speaking of one of the paintings, but Grey could not remember what he was saying—something about the technique employed by the painter, perhaps.

On his other side stood Cecile Beauchamp, the baron's sister, standing equally close, a bare shoulder brushing Grey's. She wore powder in her hair and a perfume of jasmine; the baron, a feral cologne of bergamot and civet. He remembered—for surely dreams had no smell?—the mingling of the thick fragrances with the bitterness of wood ash in the stifling warmth of the room, and the faint feeling of nausea this mingling induced. Someone's hand had cupped one of his buttocks, squeezed it familiarly, and then commenced to stroke it in an insinuating fashion. He didn't know whose hand it was.

That hadn't been part of the dream.

He lay back slowly on his pillow, eyes closed, trying to recapture the images from his sleeping mind. The dream had changed after that to something erotic, someone's mouth on his highly responsive flesh; it was the sensations associated with this, in fact, that wakened him. He didn't know whose mouth it was, either. Dr. Franklin had been somewhere in this dream, as well; Grey recalled the white buttocks, slightly sagging, still firm, as the man walked down a corridor in front of him, long gray hair straggling down a bony back, loose rolls of skin around the waist, talking with complete unconcern about the pictures, which lined the walls of the corridor, as well. It was a vivid recollection, charged with feeling. Surely he hadn't—not with Franklin, even in a dream. But it was something to do with the paintings . . .

He tried to recall some of the paintings but was no longer sure what was real, what emerged from the bourne of dreams. There were landscapes . . . a thing purporting to be an Egyptian scene, though he took leave to doubt that the painter had ever set foot south of the Breton coast. The usual family portraits—

"Yes!" he sat up abruptly and this time *did* smack the

crown of his head on the beam, hard enough that he saw stars and emitted a grunt of pain.

"Uncle John?" Dottie's voice came clearly from the other bed, startled, and a rustling of bedclothes from the floor indicated that her maid had likewise wakened. "What's happened?"

"Nothing, nothing. Go back to sleep." He swung his legs out of bed. "Just . . . going to the privy."

"Oh." Flouncings and mutterings from the floor, a sternly rebuking *shush!* from Dottie. He found the chamber door by feel, for the shutters had been put up and the room was black as sin, and made his way downstairs by the dim light from the banked fire in the inn's main room.

The air outside was fresh and cool, scented with something he didn't recognize but that tugged at his memory. It was a relief to let go the struggle with his obstinate dream and submerge himself in this purely sensory remembrance. It brought back long rides in Virginia, muddy roads, fresh leaves, the sense of a horse beneath him, the kick of a gun, the feel of a deer's blood spilling hot over his hand . . . of course, hunting with William.

He felt the immediacy of the wilderness wash over him, that strong, strange sense so peculiar to America: the sense of something waiting among the trees—not inimical, but not welcoming, either. He had loved those few years in Virginia, away from the intrigues of Europe, the constant sociality of London. Valued them mostly, though, for the closeness that had grown between him and his son in those years in the wilderness.

He had not yet seen fireflies on this journey. He glanced into the thick grass as he walked, but it was probably too late; fireflies came out mostly in the early evening. He looked forward to showing them to Dottie. William had been enchanted by his first sight of them when they came to live in Virginia—had caught them in his hand, cupping one gently and exclaiming as it lit the darkened hollow of his palm. Had greeted their return each summer with joy.

Relieved in body and at least superficially soothed in mind, he sat slowly down on the chopping block in the innyard, unwilling to return yet to the frowsy darkness above.

Where was Henry? he wondered. Where did he sleep

tonight? Housed in some dungeon? No, the Colonies really had no such thing. Even common houses were remarkably comfortable and airy. Perhaps his nephew was held in a gaol, a barn, some cellar—and yet he had, so far as they knew, survived the winter in spite of what must be a serious wound. He would have had money, though; perhaps he had been able to pay for better housing, perhaps a doctor's care.

God willing, they would find him soon. They were no more than two days' ride from Philadelphia. And he had the letters of introduction Franklin had given him—Franklin again! Damn the man and his air-bathing. Though Grey had joined him in this process once, from curiosity, and found it oddly pleasant, if a little unnerving, to be sitting mother-naked in a room equipped with elegant furniture, potted plants in the corners, paintings on the—

No. No, there were no paintings in the solar at *Trois Flèches,* of course not.

There it was. The tail of his elusive dream, twitching tantalizingly at him from under a rock. He closed his eyes, filled his lungs with the scent of the summer night, and purposely forced his mind to go blank.

Trois Flèches. Three arrows. Who is the third? The words of Hal's letter appeared on the inside of his eyelids, sufficiently startling that he opened his eyes. Used as he was to Hal's oblique thought processes, he hadn't made much of this at the time. Evidently it had taken root in his mind, though, only to emerge in the middle of the night in the middle of nowhere, out of the depths of an absurd dream. Why?

He rubbed gently at the crown of his head, which was sore from his collision with the beam, but not broken. His fingers unconsciously moved down, fingering the spot where Jamie Fraser's wife had covered the trephine hole in his skull with a silver sixpence hammered flat. She had stitched the skin over it quite cleverly and the hair had grown again, but it was easy to feel the small hard curve under it. He seldom noticed or thought of it save in cold weather, when the metal grew markedly cold and sometimes caused headache and made his nose run.

It had been cold, very cold, when he visited *Trois Flèches.* The thought floated through his head like a moth.

There were sounds behind the inn. The clop of hooves on packed dirt, the murmur of voices. He sat very still.

The moon was halfway down; it was late, but hours yet 'til dawn. No one should have business at this hour, save it was a dark business. The sort of business he had no desire to witness—let alone to be seen witnessing.

They were coming, though; he couldn't move without being seen, and instead stilled even his breathing to the barest wisp of air.

Three men, quiet, purposeful, on horseback, one leading a laden mule. They passed no more than two paces from him, but he didn't move, and the horses, if they sensed him, found him no threat. They turned onto the road that led to Philadelphia. Why this secrecy? he wondered—but didn't waste time in much wondering. He had noticed it at once upon his return to North Carolina the year before: a morbid excitement, an uneasiness in the air itself. It was more pronounced here; he had been aware of it since they had landed.

People were wary in a way that they hadn't been. *They don't know who to trust,* he thought. *And so they trust no one.*

The thought of trust conjured an immediate and vivid recollection of Percy Wainwright. *If there is anyone in the world I trust less . . .*

And just like that, he had it. The picture of Percy, dark-eyed and smiling, thumb running over the surface of his wineglass as though he stroked Grey's prick, saying casually, "*I married one of the sisters of the Baron Amandine . . .*"

"*One* of the sisters," Grey whispered aloud, and the dream crystallized in his mind, the sense of cold from the stones of *Trois Flèches* so vivid that he shivered, though the night was not cold at all. Felt the warmth of those two lascivious, vicious bodies pressing on him from either side. And on the wall to one side, disregarded among the careless profusion, a small painting of three children, two girls, one boy, posed with a dog, and the outer wall of *Trois Flèches* recognizable behind them.

The second sister. The third arrow, whom Hal, with his unerring sense of oddity, had never seen but had noticed nonetheless.

The Beauchamps were a noble, ancient family—and like most such families, they referred often, if casually, to themselves. He had heard during his visit of the doings of cousins, uncles, aunts, distant connections . . . but never of the second sister.

She might have died in childhood, of course; such things were common. But in that case, why would Percy have said . . . ?

Now his head *was* beginning to ache. With a sigh, he rose and went inside. He had no notion where or when—but he was going to have to speak to Percy again. He was appalled to find that the prospect did not alarm him.

46

LEY LINES

BRIANNA PAUSED by the fish-viewing chamber. It wasn't yet the breeding season, when—she'd been told—the great salmon swarmed through the chutes of the fish ladder that allowed them to climb the dam at Pitlochry, but now and then a silvery flash shot into view with heart-stopping suddenness, fighting strongly against the current for a moment before shooting up into the tube that led to the next stage of the ladder. The chamber itself was a small white housing let into the side of the fish ladder, with an algae-clouded window. She'd paused there to gather her thoughts—or, rather, to suppress some of them—before going in to the dam.

It was nonsense to worry about something that had already happened. And she did know that her parents were all right. Or at least, she amended, had made it out of Fort Ticonderoga; there were a good many letters left.

And she could at any moment *read* those letters, too, and find out. That was what made it so ridiculous. She supposed she wasn't really *worried.* Just . . . preoccupied. The letters were wonderful. But at the same time, she was only too aware of how much even the most complete letter must leave out. And according to Roger's book, General Burgoyne had left Canada in early June, his plan being to march south and join General Howe's troops, cutting the Colonies essentially in half. And on July 6, 1777, he had paused to attack Fort Ticonderoga. What—

"Coimhead air sin!" said a voice behind her. She jerked round, startled, to find Rob Cameron standing there, gesturing excitedly at the fish-viewing window. She turned back just in time to see a tremendous silver fish, spotted dark over the back, give a great heave against the current before disappearing up the chute.

"Nach e sin an rud as brèagha a chunnaic thu riamh?" he said, the wonder of it still showing on his face. Is that not the most beautiful thing you've ever seen?

"Cha mhór!" she replied, wary, but unable not to smile in return. Almost.

His own smile remained but became more personal as he focused on her. "Ah, ye do have the *Gàidhlig*! My cousin said, but I didna quite believe it—you with your prah-pah Bah-ston accent," he said, drawling the syllables in what he plainly thought *was* a Boston accent.

"Yeah, pahk yah cah in Hah-vahd Yahd," she said, in a real—but exaggerated—one. He burst out laughing.

"How d'ye do that? Ye don't speak *Gàidhlig* with that sort of accent. I mean—ye've got one, but it's . . . different. More like ye'd hear on the Isles—Barra, maybe, or Uist."

"My da was Scots," she said. "I got it from him."

That made him look at her afresh, as though she were a novel sort of fish he'd just pulled up on his hook.

"Yeah? From around here? What's his name?"

"James Fraser," she replied. Safe enough; there were dozens. "And was. He's . . . gone."

"Ach, too bad," he said sympathetically, and briefly touched her arm. "Lost my dad last year. Tough, eh?"

"Yes," she said briefly, and made to go past him. He turned at once and fell into step beside her.

"Ye've got wee ones, too, Roger said?" He felt her start of surprise, and smiled sideways at her. "Met him in lodge. Nice guy."

"Yes, he is," she said, guarded. Clearly Roger had talked with Rob long enough for Rob to know that Roger was her husband and that they had children. Rob didn't pursue the reference any further, though, instead stretching and throwing back his head.

"Gahhh . . . too nice a day to spend in a dam. Wish I could be on the water." He nodded toward the tumbling river, where half a dozen be-wadered anglers stood among the waves with the predatory intentness of herons. "You or Roger fly-fish at all?"

"I have," she said, and felt the memory of a casting rod whipping in her hands, sending a small thrill up the nerve endings. "You fish, then?"

"Aye, I've got a permission for Rothiemurchus." He looked proud, as though this was something special, so she made approving noises. He glanced sideways at her, caramel-eyed and smiling. "If ever ye want to come out with your rod, just say the word. Boss." He grinned suddenly at her, careless and charming, and went ahead of her into the dam office, whistling.

A ley line is an observed alignment between two geographical features of interest, usually an ancient monument or megalith. There are a number of theories about ley lines and considerable controversy as to whether they actually exist as a phenomenon, and not only as an artifact.

By that I mean that if you choose any two points that have interest for humans, there's very likely to be a path that leads between them, no matter what those points are. There is a major roadway between London and Edinburgh, for instance, because people frequently want to go from one to the other, but this is not normally called a ley line. What people usually have in mind when using this term is an ancient pathway that leads, say, from a standing stone to an ancient abbey, which is itself likely built on a spot of much older worship.

Since there isn't much objective evidence beyond the obvious existence of such lines, there's a lot of guff talked about them. Some people think the lines have a magical or mystical significance. I don't see any grounds for this myself, and neither does your mother, who is a scientist. On the other hand, science changes its mind now and then, and what looks like magic may really have a scientific explanation (NB—put in footnote about Claire and the plant-harvesting).

However, among the theories regarding ley lines, there is one that appears to have at least a possible physical basis. Perhaps you will already know what dowsers are, by the time you come to read this; I will take you out with one as soon as the opportunity occurs. Just in case, though—a dowser is a person who can detect the presence of water or sometimes bodies of metal underground, like the ore in mines. Some of them use a Y-forked stick, a metal rod, or some other object with which to "divine" the water; some merely sense it. The actual basis of this skill is not known; your mother says that Occam's razor would say that such people just recognize the type of geology that is most likely to harbor underground water. I've seen dowsers work, though, and am pretty sure there is more to it than that—especially in view of the theories I'm telling you here.

One theory of how dowsing works is that the water or metal has a magnetic current, to which the dowser is sensitive. Your mother says that the first part of this is true and that, furthermore, there are large bands of geomagnetic force in the earth's crust, which run in opposing directions all round the globe. Further, she tells me that these bands are detectible by objective measures but are not necessarily permanent; indeed, the earth undergoes occasional (every umpty-million years, I think; she didn't know the exact frequency) reversals of its geomagnetic force—nobody knows why, but the usual suspect is sunspots—with the poles exchanging places.

Another interesting bit of information is that homing pigeons (and quite possibly other sorts of birds) demonstrably do *sense these geomagnetic lines, and use them to navigate by, though no one yet has figured out quite how they do it.*

What we suspect—your mother and I—and I must emphasize that we may easily be wrong in this supposition—is that ley lines do exist, that they are (or correlate with) lines of geomagnetic force, and that where they cross or converge you get a spot where this magnetic force is . . . different, for lack of a better word. We think these convergences—or some of them—may be the places where it is possible for people who are sensitive to such forces (like pigeons, I suppose) to go from one time to another (that would be your mother and me, and you, Jem, and Mandy). If the person reading this is a child (or grandchildren) not yet born, then I don't know whether you will have this sensitivity, ability, what-you-may-call-it, but I assure you that it is real. Your grandmother speculated that it is a genetic trait, much like the ability to roll one's tongue; if you haven't got it, the "how" of it is simply incomprehensible, even though you can observe it in someone who does have the trait. If that's the case for you, I don't know whether to apologize or congratulate you, though I suppose it's no worse than the other things parents give their children, all unknowing, like crooked teeth or shortsightedness. We didn't do it on purpose, either way, please believe that.

Sorry, I've got off the track here. The basic point is that the ability to time-travel may be dependent on a genetic sensitivity to these . . . convergences? vortices? . . . of ley lines.

Owing to the peculiar geological history of the British Isles, you find a lot of ley lines here and, likewise, a great number of archaeological sites that seem to be linked by those lines. Your mother and I intend to note, so far as can be done without danger—and make no mistake about this; it is very *dangerous—the occurrence of such sites as might be portals. Obviously, there's no way of knowing for sure whether a specific site is a portal or not.**

The observation that sites seem to be "open" on the dates that correspond to the sun feasts and fire feasts of the ancient world (or at least more open than at other times) may—if this hypothesis is right—have something to do with the gravitational pull of the sun and moon. This seems reasonable, given that those bodies really do affect the behavior of the earth with respect to tides, weather, and the like—why not time vortices, too, after all?

**Footnote: Your mother says—well, she said quite a bit, in which I picked out the words "Unified Field Theory," which I gather is something that doesn't yet exist, but if it did, it would explain a hell of a lot of things, and among these might be an answer to why a convergence of geomagnetic lines might affect time in the spot where the convergence occurs. All I personally got from this explanation is the notion that space and time are occasionally the same thing, and gravity is somehow involved. This makes as much sense to me as anything else regarding this phenomenon.*

Footnote 2:

"Does that make sense?" Roger asked. "So far, at least?"

"Insofar as anything about it makes sense, yes." Despite the uneasiness that came over her whenever they discussed it, she couldn't help smiling at him; he looked so earnest. There was a blotch of ink on his cheek, and his black hair was ruffled up on one side.

"Professoring must be in the blood," she said, pulling a tissue out of her pocket, licking it in mother-cat fashion, and applying it to his face. "You know, there's this wonderful modern invention called a ballpoint . . ."

"Hate them," he said, closing his eyes and suffering himself to be tidied. "Besides, a fountain pen is a great luxury, compared to a quill."

"Well, that's true. Da always looked like an explosion in an ink factory when he'd been writing letters." Her eyes returned to the page, and she snorted briefly at the first footnote, making Roger smile.

"Is that a decent explanation?"

"Considering that this is meant for the kids, more than adequate," she assured him, lowering the page. "What goes in Footnote Two?"

"Ah." He leaned back in his chair, hands linked, looking uneasy. "That."

"Yes, that," she said, instantly alerted. "Is there something like an Exhibit A that's meant to go there?"

"Well, yes," he said reluctantly, and met her eyes. "Geillis Duncan's notebooks. Mrs. Graham's book would be Exhibit B. Your mother's explanation of planting superstitions is Footnote Four."

Brianna could feel the blood draining from her head and sat down, just in case.

"You're sure that's a good idea?" she asked, tentative. She didn't herself know where Geillis Duncan's notebooks *were*—and didn't want to. The little book that Fiona Graham, Mrs. Graham's granddaughter, had given them was safely tucked away in a safe-deposit box in the Royal Bank of Scotland in Edinburgh.

Roger blew out his breath and shook his head.

"No, I'm not," he said frankly. "But look. We don't know how old the kids will be when they read this. Which reminds me—we need to make some kind of provision about it. Just in case something happens to us before they're old enough to be told . . . everything."

She felt as though a melting ice cube were sliding slowly down her back. He was right, though. They might both be killed in a car crash, like her mother's parents. Or the house might burn—

"Well, no," she said aloud, looking at the window behind Roger, which was set into a stone wall some eighteen inches thick. "I don't suppose *this* house will burn down."

That made him smile.

"No, not too worried about that. But the notebooks—aye, I know what ye mean. And I did think of maybe just going through them myself and sort of straining out the information—she did have quite a bit about which stone circles seemed to be active, and that's useful. Because reading the rest of it is . . ." He waved a hand in search of the right word.

"Creepy," she supplied.

"I was going to say like watching someone go slowly mad in front of you, but 'creepy' will do." He took the pages from her and tapped them together. "It's just an academic tic, I suppose. I don't feel right in suppressing an original source."

She gave a different snort, one indicating what she thought of Geillis Duncan as an original source of anything bar trouble. Still . . .

"I suppose you're right," she said reluctantly. "Maybe you could do a summary, though, and just mention where the notebooks are, in case someone down the line is *really* curious."

"Not a bad thought." He put the papers inside the notebook and rose, closing it as he did so. "I'll go down and get them, then, maybe when school's out. I could take Jem and show him the city; he's old enough to walk the Royal Mile, and he'd love the castle."

"Do *not* take him to the Edinburgh Dungeon!" she said at once, and he broke into a broad grin.

"What, ye don't think wax figures of people being tortured are educational? It's all historical, aye?"

"It would be a lot less horrible if it wasn't," she said, and, turning, caught sight of the wall clock. "Roger! Aren't you supposed to be doing your Gaelic class at the school at two o'clock?"

He glanced at the clock in disbelief, snatched up the pile of books and papers on his desk, and shot out of the room in a flurry of very eloquent Gaelic.

She went out into the hall to see him hastily kiss Mandy and charge for the door. Mandy stood in the open doorway, waving enthusiastically.

"Bye-bye, Daddy!" she cried. "Bwing me ice cweam!"

"If he forgets, we'll go into the village after supper and get some," Brianna promised, bending down to pick her daughter up. She stood there holding Mandy, watching Roger's ancient orange Morris cough, choke, shudder, and start up with a brief belch of blue smoke. She frowned slightly at the sight, thinking she must get him a set of new spark plugs, but waved as he leaned out at the corner of the drive, smiling back at them.

Mandy snuggled close, murmuring one of Roger's more picturesque Gaelic phrases, which she was obviously committing to memory, and Bree bent her head, inhaling the sweet scent of Johnson's baby shampoo and grubby child. No doubt it was the mention of Geillis Duncan that was making her feel still uneasy. The woman was well and truly dead, but after all . . . she was Roger's multiple great-grandmother. And perhaps the ability to travel through stone circles was not the only thing to be passed down through the blood.

Though surely some things were diluted by time. Roger, for instance, had nothing in common with William Buccleigh MacKenzie, Geillis's son by Dougal MacKenzie—and the man responsible for Roger's being hanged.

"Son of a witch," she said, under her breath. "I hope you rot in hell."

"'At's a bad word, Mummy," Mandy said reprovingly.

IT WENT BETTER than he could have hoped. The schoolroom was crowded, with lots of kids, a number of parents, and even a few grandparents crammed in round the walls. He had that moment of light-headedness—not quite panic or stage fright, but a sense of looking into some vast canyon that he couldn't see the bottom of—that he was used to from his days as a performer. He took a deep breath, put down his stack of books and papers, smiled at them, and said, *"Feasgar math!"*

That's all it ever took; the first words spoken—or sung—and it was like taking hold of a live wire. A current sprang up between him and the audience, and the next words seemed to come from nowhere, flowing through him like the crash of water through one of Bree's giant turbines.

After a word or two of introduction, he started with the notion of Gaelic cursing, knowing why most of the kids had come. A few parents' brows shot up, but small, knowing smiles appeared on the faces of the grandparents.

"We haven't got bad words in the *Gàidhlig,* like there are in the English," he said, and grinned at the feisty-looking towhead in the second row, who had to be the wee Glasscock bugger who'd told Jemmy he was going to hell. "Sorry, Jimmy.

"Which is not to say ye can't give a good, strong opinion of someone," he went on, as soon as the laughter subsided. "But *Gàidhlig* cursing is a matter of art, not crudeness." That got a ripple of laughter from the old people, too, and several of the kids' heads turned toward their grandparents, amazed.

"For example, I once heard a farmer whose pig got into the mash tell her that he hoped her intestines would burst through her belly and be eaten by crows."

An impressed "Oo!" from the kids, and he smiled and went on, giving carefully edited versions of some of the more creative things he'd heard his father-in-law say on occasion. No need to add that, lack of bad words notwithstanding, it is indeed possible to call someone a "daughter of a bitch" when wishing to be seriously nasty. If the kids wanted to know what Jem had really said to Miss Glendenning, they'd have to ask him. If they hadn't already.

From there, he went to a more serious—but quick—description of the Gaeltacht, that area of Scotland where Gaelic was traditionally spoken, and told a few anecdotes of learning the Gaelic on herring boats in the Minch as a teenager—including the entire speech given by a particular Captain Taylor when a storm scoured out his favorite lobster hole and made away with all his pots (this piece of eloquence having been addressed, with shaken fist, to the sea, the heavens, the crew, and the lobsters). That one had them rolling again, and a couple of the old buggers in the back were grinning and muttering to one another, they having obviously encountered similar situations.

"But the *Gàidhlig* is a language," he said, when the laughter had died down once more. "And that means its primary use is for communication—people talking to one another. How many of you have ever heard line singing? Waulking songs?"

Murmurs of interest; some had, some hadn't. So he explained what waulking was: "The women all working together, pushing and pulling and kneading the wet wool cloth to make it tight and waterproof—because they didn't have macs or wellies in the auld days, and folk would need to be out of doors day and night, in all kinds of weather, tending their animals or their crofts." His voice was well warmed by now; he thought he could make it through a brief waulking song and, flipping open the folder, sang them the first verse and refrain, then got them to do it, as well. They got four verses, and then he could feel the strain starting to tell and brought it to a close.

"My gran used to sing that one," one of the mothers blurted impulsively, then blushed red as a beet as everyone looked at her.

"Is your gran still alive?" Roger asked, and at her abashed nod, said, "Well, then, have her teach it to you, and you can teach it to your kids. That kind of thing shouldn't be lost, aye?"

A small murmur of half-surprised agreement, and he smiled again and lifted the battered hymnbook he'd brought.

"Right. I mentioned the line singing, too. Ye'll still hear this of a Sunday in kirk out on the Isles. Go to Stornoway, for instance, and ye'll hear it. It's a way of singing the psalms that goes back to when folk hadn't many books—or maybe not so many of the congregation could read. So there'd be a precentor, whose job it was to sing the psalm, one line at a time, and then the congregation would sing it back to him. This book"—and he raised the hymnal—"belonged to my own father, the Reverend Wakefield; some of you might recall him. But originally it belonged to another clergyman, the Reverend Alexander Carmichael. Now he . . ." And he went on to tell them about the Reverend Carmichael, who had combed the Highlands and the Isles in the nineteenth century, talking with people, urging them to sing him their songs and tell him their ways, collecting "hymns, charms, and incantations" from the oral tradition wherever he could find them, and had published this great work of scholarship in several volumes, called the *Carmina Gadelica.*

He'd brought one volume of the *Gadelica* with him, and while he passed the ancient hymnal round the room, along with a booklet of waulking songs he'd put together, he read them one of the charms of the new moon, the Cud Chewing Charm, the Indigestion Spell, the Poem of the Beetle, and some bits from "The Speech of Birds."

Columba went out
An early mild morning;
He saw a white swan,
"Guile, guile,"
Down on the strand,

"Guile, guile,"
With a dirge of death,
"Guile, guile."

A white swan and she wounded, wounded,
A white swan and she bruised, bruised,
The white swan of the two visions,
"Guile, guile,"
The white swan of the two omens,
"Guile, guile,"
Life and death,
"Guile, guile,"
"Guile, guile."

When thy journey,
Swan of mourning?
Said Columba of love,
"Guile, guile,"
From Erin my swimming,
"Guile, guile,"
From the Fiann my wounding,
"Guile, guile,"
The sharp wound of my death,
"Guile, guile,"
"Guile, guile."

White swan of Erin,
A friend am I to the needy;
The eye of Christ be on thy wound,
"Guile, guile,"
The eye of affection and of mercy,
"Guile, guile,"
The eye of kindness and of love,
"Guile, guile,"
Making thee whole,
"Guile, guile,"
"Guile, guile."

Swan of Erin,
"Guile, guile,"
No harm shall touch thee,

"Guile, guile,"
Whole be thy wounds,
"Guile, guile."

Lady of the wave,
"Guile, guile,"
Lady of the dirge,
"Guile, guile,"
Lady of the melody,
"Guile, guile."

To Christ the glory,
"Guile, guile,"
To the Son of the Virgin,
"Guile, guile,"
To the great High-King,
"Guile, guile,"
To Him be thy song,
"Guile, guile,"
To Him be thy song,
"Guile, guile,"
"Guile guile!"

His throat hurt almost unbearably from doing the swan calls, from the soft moan of the wounded swan to the triumphant cry of the final words, and his voice cracked with it at the last, but triumphant it was, nonetheless, and the room erupted in applause.

Between soreness and emotion, he couldn't actually speak for a few moments, and instead bowed and smiled and bowed again, mutely handing the stack of books and folders to Jimmy Glasscock to be passed round, while the audience swarmed up to congratulate him.

"Man, that was *great*!" said a half-familiar voice, and he looked up to find that it was Rob Cameron wringing his hand, shining-eyed with enthusiasm. Roger's surprise must have shown on his face, for Rob bobbed his head toward the little boy at his side: Bobby Hurragh, whom Roger knew well from the choir. A heartbreakingly pure soprano, and a wee fiend if not carefully watched.

"I brought wee Bobby," Rob said, keeping—Roger

noticed—a tight grip on the kid's hand. "My sister's had to work today and couldn't get off. She's a widow," he added, by way of explanation, both of the mother's absence and his own stepping in.

"Thanks," Roger managed to croak, but Cameron just wrung his hand again, and then gave way to the next well-wisher.

Among the mob was a middle-aged woman whom he didn't know but who recognized him.

"My husband and I saw you sing once, at the Inverness Games," she said, in an educated accent, "though you went by your late father's name then, did you not?"

"I did," he said, in the bullfrog croak that was as far as his voice was prepared to go just now. "Your—you have—a grandchild?" He waved vaguely at the buzzing swarm of kids milling round an elderly lady who, pink with pleasure, was explaining the pronunciation of some of the odd-looking Gaelic words in the storybook.

"Yes," the woman said, but wouldn't be distracted from her focus, which was the scar across his throat. "What happened?" she asked sympathetically. "Is it permanent?"

"Accident," he said. " 'Fraid so."

Distress creased the corners of her eyes and she shook her head.

"Oh, *such* a loss," she said. "Your voice was beautiful. I am so sorry."

"Thanks," he said, because it was all he could say, and she let him go then, to receive the praise of people who'd never heard him sing. Before.

Afterward, he thanked Lionel Menzies, who stood by the door to see people out, beaming like the ringmaster of a successful circus.

"It was wonderful," Menzies said, clasping him warmly by the hand. "Even better than I'd hoped. Tell me, would ye think of doing it again?"

"Again?" He laughed, but broke off coughing in the middle. "I barely made it through this one."

"Ach." Menzies waved that off. "A dram'll see your throat right. Come down the pub with me, why don't you?"

Roger was about to refuse, but Menzies's face shone with such pleasure that he changed his mind. The fact that he was wringing with sweat—performing always raised his body temperature by several degrees—and had a thirst fit for the Gobi Desert had nothing to do with it, of course.

"Just the one, then," he said, and smiled.

As they crossed the parking lot, a battered small blue panel truck pulled up and Rob Cameron leaned out of the window, calling to them.

"Like it, did ye, Rob?" Menzies asked, still beaming.

"Loved it," Cameron said, with every evidence of sincerity. "Two things, Rog—I wanted to ask, maybe, if ye'd let me see some of the old songs ye have; Siegfried MacLeod showed me the ones you did for him."

Roger was a little taken aback, but pleased.

"Aye, sure," he said. "Didn't know you were a fan," he joked.

"I love all the old stuff," Cameron said, serious for once. "Really, I'd appreciate it."

"Okay, then. Come on out to the house, maybe, next weekend?"

Rob grinned and saluted briefly.

"Wait—two things, ye said?" Menzies asked.

"Oh, aye." Cameron reached over and picked up something from the seat between Bobby and him. "This was in with the Gaelic bits ye were handing round. It looked as though it was in there by mistake, though, so I took it out. Writing a novel, are ye?"

He handed out the black notebook, "The Hitchhiker's Guide," and Roger's throat clenched as though he'd been garroted. He took the notebook, nodding speechlessly.

"Maybe ye'll let me read it when it's done," Cameron said casually, putting his truck in gear. "I'm a great one for the science fiction."

The truck pulled away, then stopped suddenly and reversed. Roger took a firmer grip on the notebook, but Rob didn't look at it.

"Hey," he said. "Forgot. Brianna said ye've got an old stone fort or some such on your place?"

Roger nodded, clearing his throat.

"I've got a friend, an archaeologist. Would ye mind, maybe, if he was to come and have a look at it sometime?"

"No," Roger croaked, then cleared his throat again and said more firmly, "No, that'd be fine. Thanks."

Rob grinned cheerfully at him and revved the engine.

"Nay bother, mate," he said.

47

HIGH PLACES

ROB'S ARCHAEOLOGIST friend, Michael Callahan, turned out to be a genial bloke in his fifties with thinning sandy hair, sunburned so badly and so often that his face looked like patchwork, dark freckles blotched among patches of raw pink skin. He ferreted about among the collapsed stones of the old church with every sign of interest, asking Roger's permission to dig a trench along the outside of one wall.

Rob, Brianna, and the kids all came up briefly to watch, but archaeological work is not a spectator sport, and when Jem and Mandy got bored, the lot of them went down to the house to make lunch, leaving Roger and Mike to their poking.

"I don't need you," Callahan said, glancing up at Roger after a bit. "If you've things to do."

There were always things to do—it was a farm, after all, if a small one—but Roger shook his head.

"I'm interested," he said. "If I won't be in your way . . . ?"

"Not a bit of it," Callahan said cheerfully. "Come and help me lift this, then."

Callahan whistled through his teeth as he worked, occasionally muttering to himself, but for the most part made no comment on whatever he was looking at. Roger was called on now and then to help clear away rubble or hold an unstable stone while Callahan peered underneath it with a small torch, but for the most part Roger sat on the bit of uncollapsed wall, listening to the wind.

It was quiet on the hilltop, in the way that wild places are quiet, with a constant sense of unobtrusive movement, and it struck him odd that this should be so. Normally you didn't get that feeling in places where people had lived, and plainly people had been mucking about on this hilltop for a good long time, judging from the depth of Callahan's trench and the small whistles of interest he gave off now and then, like a marmoset.

Brianna brought them up sandwiches and lemonade and sat down beside Roger on the wall to eat.

"Rob gone off, then?" Roger asked, noticing that the truck was gone from the dooryard.

"Just to run some errands, he said. He said it didn't look as though Mike would be finished anytime soon," she said, with a glance at Callahan's trouser seat, this sticking out from a bush as he burrowed happily beneath it.

"Maybe not," Roger said, smiling, and leaning forward, kissed her lightly. She made a low, contented noise in her throat and stepped back, but kept hold of his hand for a moment.

"Rob asked about the old songs you did up for Sig MacLeod," she said, with a sideways glance down toward the house. "Did you tell him he could see them?"

"Oh, aye, I'd forgot that. Sure. If I'm not down when he comes back, you can show him them. The originals are in my bottom file drawer, in a folder labeled *Cèolas.*"

She nodded and went down, long sneakered feet sure as a deer's on the stony path, and her hair down her back in a tail the color of the same deer's pelt.

As the afternoon wore on, he found himself dropping into a state not far off trance, his mind moving sluggishly and his body not much faster, coming in leisurely fashion to lend a hand where wanted, exchanging the barest of words with Callahan, who seemed similarly bemused. The drifting haze of the morning had thickened, and the cool shadows amid the stones faded with the light. The air was cool with water on his skin, but there was no hint of rain. You could almost feel the stones rising up around you, he thought, coming back to what they once were.

There were comings and goings at the house below: the slam of doors, Brianna hanging out the family wash, the kids and a couple of wee lads from the next farm over who'd come to spend the night with Jem all racing through the kailyard and outbuildings, playing some kind of tag that involved a good deal of noise, their shrieks high and sharp as the cries of fishing ospreys. Once he glanced down and saw the Farm and Household truck, presumably come to deliver the pump for the cream separator, for Roger saw Brianna shepherding the driver into the barn, he unable to see around the large carton in his arms.

Around five, a fresh strong breeze came up, and the haze began to dissipate. As though this was a signal waking Callahan from his dream, the archaeologist straightened, stood a moment looking down at something, then nodded.

"Well, it may be an ancient site," he said, climbing out of his trench and groaning as he leaned to and fro, stretching his back. "The structure's not, though. Likely built sometime in the last couple of hundred years, though whoever built it used much older stones in the construction. Probably brought them from somewhere else, though some may be from an earlier structure built on the spot." He smiled at Roger. "Folk are thrifty in the Highlands; last week I saw a barn with an ancient Pictish stone used in the foundation and a floor made with bricks from a demolished public lavatory in Dornoch."

Callahan looked out to the west, shading his eyes, where the haze now hung low over the distant shore.

"High places," he said, matter-of-factly. "They always chose the high places, the old ones. Whether it was a fort or a place of worship, they always went up."

"The old ones?" Roger asked, and felt a brief prickle of the hair on his nape. "Which old ones?"

Callahan laughed, shaking his head.

"Don't know. Picts, maybe—all we know about them is the bits of stonework they left here and there—or the folk who came before them. Sometimes you see a bit of something that you know was made—or at least placed—by men, but can't fit it into a known culture. The megaliths, for instance—the standing stones. Nobody knows who set those up or what for."

"Don't they," Roger murmured. "Can you tell what sort of ancient site this was? For war or worship, I mean?"

Callahan shook his head.

"Not from what's apparent on the surface, no. Maybe if we excavated the underlying site—but to be honest, I don't see anything that would make anyone really want to do that. There are hundreds of sites like this on high places, all through the British Isles and Brittany, too—old Celtic, many of them, Iron Age, lots much older." He picked up the battered saint's head, stroking it with a sort of affection.

"This lady's much more recent; maybe the thirteenth, fourteenth century. Maybe the family's patron saint, handed down over the years." He gave the head a brief, unself-conscious kiss and handed it gently to Roger.

"For what it's worth, though—and this isn't scientific, just what I think myself, having seen more than a few such places—if the modern structure was a chapel, then the ancient site beneath it was likely a place of worship, too. Folk in the Highlands are set in their ways. They may build a new barn every two or three hundred years—but chances are it'll be right where the last one stood."

Roger laughed.

"True enough. Our barn's still the original one—built in the early 1700s, along with the house. But I found the stones of an earlier croft buried when I dug up the stable floor to put in a new drain."

"The 1700s? Well, you'll not be needing a new roof for at least another hundred years, then."

It was nearly six but still full daylight. The haze had vanished in that mysterious way it sometimes did, and a pale sun had come out. Roger traced a small cross with his thumb on the statue's forehead and set the head gently in the niche that seemed made for it. They'd finished, but neither man made a move to leave just yet. There was a sense of comfort in each other's company, a sharing of the spell of the high place.

Down below, he saw Rob Cameron's battered truck parked in the dooryard and Rob himself sitting on the back stoop, Mandy, Jem, and Jem's friends leaning in on either side of him, evidently absorbed in the pages he held. What the devil was he doing?

"Is that singing I hear?" Callahan, who had been looking

off to the north, turned half round, and as he did so, Roger heard it, too. Faint and sweet, no more than a thread of sound, but enough to pick up the tune of "Crimond."

The strength of the stab of jealousy that went through him took his breath, and he felt his throat close as though some strong hand choked him.

Jealousy is cruel as the grave: the coals thereof are coals of fire.

He closed his eyes for an instant, breathing slow and deep, and with a little effort, dredged up the first bit of that quotation: *Love is strong as death.*

He felt the choking sensation begin to ease and reason return. Of course Rob Cameron could sing; he was in the men's choir. Only make sense that if he saw the rudimentary musical settings Roger had noted for some of the old songs, he'd try to sing them. And kids—especially his kids—were attracted to music.

"Have you known Rob for long, then?" he asked, and was pleased to hear his voice sound normal.

"Oh, Rob?" Callahan considered. "Fifteen years, maybe . . . No, I tell a lie, more like twenty. He came along as a volunteer on a dig I had going on Shapinsay—that's one of the Orkneys—and he wasn't but a lad then, in his late teens, maybe." He gave Roger a mild, shrewd look. "Why?"

Roger shrugged.

"He works with my wife, for the Hydro Board. I don't know him much myself. Only met him recently, in lodge."

"Ah." Callahan watched the scene below for a moment, silent, then said, not looking at Roger, "He was married, to a French girl. Wife divorced him a couple of years ago, took their son back to France. He's not been happy."

"Ah." That explained Rob's attachment to his widowed sister's family, then, and his enjoyment of Jem and Mandy's company. He breathed once more, freely, and the small flame of jealousy flickered out.

As though this brief exchange had put a period to the day, they picked up the leavings from their lunch and Callahan's rucksack and came down the hill, companionable in silence.

"WHAT'S THIS?" There were two wineglasses set on the counter. "Are we celebrating something?"

"We are," Bree said firmly. "The children going to bed, for one thing."

"Oh, bad, were they?" He felt a small twinge of guilt—not very severe—for having spent the afternoon in the high, cool peace of the ruined chapel with Callahan rather than chivvying small mad things out of the kailyard.

"Just really energetic." She cast a suspicious glance toward the door to the hall, through which the muted roar of a television came from the big front parlor. "I *hope* they'll be too worn out to spend the night jumping on the beds. They've had enough pizza to put six grown men into a coma for a week."

He laughed at that—he'd eaten most of a full-sized pepperoni himself and was beginning to feel comfortably stuporous.

"What else?"

"Oh, what else are we celebrating?" She gave him a cat-in-the-cream look. "Well, as for me . . ."

"Yes?" he said, obliging.

"I've passed the provisional employment period; now I'm permanent, and they can't get rid of me, even if I wear perfume to work. And *you,*" she added, reaching into the drawer and placing an envelope in front of him, "are formally invited by the school board to do a reprise of your *Gàidhlig* triumph at five different schools next month!"

He felt a moment's shock, then a warm flood of something he couldn't quite identify, and realized with a greater shock that he was blushing.

"Really?"

"You don't think I'd tease you about something like that?" Not waiting for an answer, she poured the wine, purple-rich and aromatic, and handed him a glass. He clinked it ceremoniously against her own.

"Here's tae us. Wha's like us?"

"Damned few," she replied in broad Scots, "and they're all deid."

THERE WAS A certain amount of crashing upstairs after the children were sent to bed, but a brief appearance by Roger in the persona of Heavy Father put a stop to that, and the slumber party simmered down into storytelling and stifled giggles.

"Are they telling dirty jokes?" Bree asked, when he came back down.

"Very likely. Ought I make Mandy come down, do you think?"

She shook her head.

"She's probably asleep already. And if not, the sort of jokes nine-year-old boys tell won't warp her. She isn't old enough to remember the punch lines."

"That's true." Roger took up his refilled glass and sipped, the wine soft on his tongue and dense with the scents of black currant and black tea. "How old was Jem when he finally learned to tell jokes? You remember how he got the form of jokes but didn't really understand the idea of content?"

"What's the difference between a . . . a . . . a button and a sock?" she mimicked, catching Jem's breathless excitement to a T. "A . . . BUFFALO! HAHAHAHAHA!"

Roger burst out laughing.

"Why are you laughing?" she demanded. Her eyes were growing heavy-lidded, and her lips were stained dark.

"Must be the way you tell it," he said, and lifted his glass to her. "Cheers."

"Slàinte."

He closed his eyes, breathing the wine as much as drinking it. He was beginning to have the pleasant illusion that he could feel the heat of his wife's body, though she sat a few feet away. She seemed to emanate warmth, in slow, pulsing waves.

"What do they call it, how you find distant stars?"

"A telescope," she said. "You can't be drunk on half a bottle of wine, good as it is."

"No, that's not what I mean. There's a term for it—heat signature? Does that sound right?"

She closed one eye, considering, then shrugged.

"Maybe. Why?"

"You've got one."

She looked down at herself, squinting.

"Nope. Two. Definitely two."

He *wasn't* quite drunk, and neither was she, but whatever they were was a lot of fun.

"A heat signature," he said, and, reaching out, took hold of her hand. It was markedly warmer than his, and he was positive he could feel the heat of her fingers throb slowly, increasing and diminishing with her pulse. "I could pick you out of a crowd blindfolded; you glow in the dark."

She put aside her glass and slid out of her chair, coming to a stop kneeling between his knees, her body not quite touching his. She *did* glow. If he closed his eyes, he could just about see it through the white shirt she wore.

He tipped up his glass and drained it.

"Great wine. Where did ye get it?"

"I didn't. Rob brought it—a thank-you, he said, for letting him copy the songs."

"Nice guy," he said generously. At the moment, he actually thought so.

Brianna reached for the wine bottle and poured the last of it into Roger's glass. Then she sat back on her heels and looked at him owl-eyed, the empty bottle clutched to her chest.

"Hey. You owe me."

"Big-time," he assured her gravely, making her giggle.

"No," she said, recovering. "You said if I brought my hard hat home, you'd tell me what you were doing with that champagne bottle. All that hooting, I mean."

"Ah." He considered for a moment—there was a distinct possibility she'd hit him with the wine bottle if he told her, but then, a bargain was a bargain, after all—and the vision of her naked save for the hard hat, radiating heat in all directions, was enough to make a man cast caution to the winds.

"I was trying to see if I could get the exact pitch of the sounds ye make when we're making love and you're just about to . . . er . . . to . . . it's something between a growl and a really deep hum."

Her mouth opened slightly, and her eyes slightly more. The tip of her tongue was a dark, dark red.

"I think it's the F below middle C," he concluded hurriedly. She blinked.

"You're kidding."

"I am not." He picked up his half-full glass and tilted it gently, so the rim touched her lip. She closed her eyes and drank, slowly. He smoothed her hair behind her ear, his finger moving slowly down the length of her neck, watching her throat move as she swallowed, moved his fingertip along the strong arch of her collarbone.

"You're getting warmer," she whispered, not opening her eyes. "The second law of thermodynamics."

"What's that?" he said, his voice dropping, too.

"The entropy of an isolated system that is not in equilibrium tends to increase, reaching a maximum at equilibrium."

"Oh, aye?"

"Mmm-hmm. That's why a warm body loses heat to a colder one, until they're the same temperature."

"I knew there had to be a reason why that happened." All sounds from upstairs had ceased, and his voice sounded loud, even though he was whispering.

Her eyes opened suddenly, an inch from his, and her black-currant breath on his cheek was as warm as his skin. The bottle hit the parlor carpet with a soft thud.

"Want to try for E flat?"

48

HENRY

June 14, 1777

HE HAD forbidden Dottie to accompany him. He wasn't sure what he might find. In the event, though, he was surprised. The address to which he had been directed was in a modest street in Germantown, but the house was commodious and well kept, though not large.

He knocked at the door and was greeted by a pleasant-faced young African woman in neat calico, whose eyes widened at sight of him. He had thought best not to wear his uniform, though there were men in British uniform here and there in the streets—paroled prisoners, perhaps, or soldiers bearing official communications. Instead, he had put on a good suit of bottle-green, with his best waistcoat, this being gold China silk, embroidered with a number of fanciful butterflies. He smiled, and the woman smiled in turn and put a hand over her mouth to hide it.

"May I help you, sir?"

"Is your master at home?"

She laughed. Softly, and with real amusement.

"Bless you, sir, I have no master. The house is mine."

He blinked, disconcerted.

"Perhaps I have been misdirected. I am in search of a British soldier, Captain Viscount Asher—Henry Grey is his name. A British prisoner of war?"

She lowered her hand and stared at him, eyes wide. Then her smile returned, broad enough to show two gold-stuffed teeth at the back.

"Henry! Well, why didn't you say so, sir? Come in, come in!"

And before he could put down his stick, he was whisked inside, up a narrow staircase, and into a neat small bedroom, where he discovered his nephew Henry, sprawled on his back and naked from the waist up, with a small, beaky-looking man in black poking at his belly—this crisscrossed with a number of violent-looking scars.

"I beg your pardon?" He peered over the beaky man's shoulder and waved gingerly. "How do you do, Henry?"

Henry, whose eyes had been fastened on the ceiling in a tense sort of way, glanced at him, away, back, then sat up abruptly, this movement resulting in an exclamation of protest from the little beaky person and a cry of pain from Henry.

"Oh, God, oh, God, oh, God." Henry doubled over, arms clutching his belly and his face clenched in pain. Grey seized him by the shoulders, seeking to ease him back.

"Henry, my dear. Do forgive me. I didn't mean—"

"And who are you, sir?" the beaky man cried angrily, springing to his feet and facing Grey with clenched fists.

"I am his uncle," Grey informed him shortly. "Who are you, sir? A doctor?"

The little man drew himself up with dignity.

"Why, no, sir. I am a dowser. Joseph Hunnicutt, sir, professional dowser."

Henry was still bent double, gasping, but seemed to be getting a little of his breath back. Grey touched his bare back gently. The flesh was warm, a little sweaty, but didn't seem fevered.

"I am sorry, Henry," he said. "Will you survive, do you think?"

Henry, to his credit, managed a breathless grunt of laughter.

"It'll do," he got out. "Just . . . it takes . . . a minute."

The pleasant-faced black woman was hovering at the door, a sharp eye on Grey.

"This man says he's your uncle, Henry. Is that so?"

Henry nodded, panting a little. "Lord John . . . Grey. May I pre . . . sent Mrs. Mercy Wood . . . cock?"

Grey bowed punctiliously, feeling slightly ridiculous.

"Your servant, madam. And yours, Mr. Hunnicutt," he added politely, bowing again.

"Might I ask," he said, straightening up, "*why* there is a dowser poking you in the abdomen, Henry?"

"Why, to find the bit o' metal what's a-troubling the poor young man, o' course," said Mr. Hunnicutt, looking up his long nose—for he was shorter than Grey by several inches.

"I called for him, sir—your lordship, I mean." Mrs. Woodcock had come into the room by this time, and was looking at him with a faint air of apology. "It's only that the surgeons hadn't any luck, and I was so afraid that they'd kill him next time."

Henry had by now managed to unbend. Grey eased him slowly back until he lay against the pillow, pale and sweating.

"I couldn't bear it again," he said, closing his eyes briefly. "I can't."

With Henry's stomach exposed to view and an opportunity to examine it at leisure, Grey could see the puckered scars of two bullet wounds and the longer, clean-edged scars made by a surgeon digging for metal. Three of them. Grey had five such scars himself, crisscrossing the left side of his chest, and he touched his nephew's hand in sympathy.

"Is it truly necessary to remove the ball—or balls?" he asked, looking up at Mrs. Woodcock. "If he has survived so far, perhaps the ball is lodged in a place where—"

But Mrs. Woodcock shook her head decidedly.

"He can't eat," she said bluntly. "He can't swallow a thing but soup, and none so much of that. He wasn't but skin and bones when they brought him to me," she said, gesturing at Henry. "And you can see, he's not that much more now."

He wasn't. Henry took after his mother rather than Hal, being normally ruddy-cheeked and of a rather stocky build. There was no evidence of either trait at the moment; every rib showed plain, his belly was so sunken that the points of his hip bones poked up sharp through the linen sheet, and his face was approximately the same hue as said sheet, bar deep violet circles under the eyes.

"I see," Grey said slowly. He glanced at Mr. Hunnicutt. "Have you managed to locate anything?"

"Well, I have," the dowser said, and, leaning over Henry's body, laid a long, thin finger gently on the young man's belly. "One, at least. T'other, I'm not so sure of, just yet."

"I told you, Mercy, it's no good." Henry's eyes were still closed, but his hand rose a little and Mrs. Woodcock took it, with a naturalness that made Grey blink. "Even if he was sure—I can't do it again. I'd rather die." Weak as he was, he spoke with an absolute conviction, and Grey recognized the family stubbornness.

Mrs. Woodcock's pretty face was creased in a worried frown. She seemed to feel Grey's eyes upon her, for she looked briefly up at him. He didn't change expression, and she lifted her chin a little, meeting his eyes with something not far from fierceness, still holding Henry's hand.

Oh, like that, is it? Grey thought. *Well, well.*

He coughed, and Henry opened his eyes.

"Be that as it may, Henry," he said, "you will oblige me by not dying before I can bring your sister to bid you farewell."

49

RESERVATIONS

July 1, 1777

THE INDIANS worried him. General Burgoyne found them enchanting. But General Burgoyne wrote plays.

It is not, William wrote slowly in the letter to his father that he was composing, struggling to find form in words for his reservations, *that I think him a fantasist or suspect that he does not appreciate the essential nature of the Indians he deals with. He appreciates it very much. But I remember talking with Mr. Garrick once in London, and his reference to the playwright as a little god who directs the actions of his creations, exerting absolute control upon them. Mrs. Cowley argued with this, saying that it is delusion to assume that the creator controls his creations and that an attempt to exert such control while ignoring the true nature of those creations is doomed to failure.*

He stopped, biting his quill, feeling that he had come close to the heart of the matter but perhaps not quite reached it.

I think General Burgoyne does not quite apprehend the independence of mind and purpose that . . . No, that wasn't quite it. He drew a line through the sentence and dipped his quill for a fresh try. He turned a phrase over in his mind, rejected it, did the same with another, and at last abandoned the search for eloquence in favor of a simple unburdening of his mind. It was late, he'd walked nearly twenty miles in the course of the day, and he was sleepy.

He believes he can use the Indians as a tool, and I think he is wrong. He stared at the sentence for a bit, shook his head at its bluntness, but could think of nothing better and could waste no more time on the effort; the stub of his candle had almost burned out. Comforting himself with the idea that, after all, his father knew Indians—and probably General Burgoyne—much better than he did, he briskly signed, sanded, blotted, and sealed the letter, then fell into his bed and a dreamless sleep.

The sense of uneasiness regarding the Indians remained with him, though. He had no dislike of Indians; in fact, he enjoyed their company, and hunted now and again with some of them, or shared a companionable evening drinking beer and telling stories round their fires.

"The thing is," he said to Balcarres one evening, as they walked back from a particularly bibulous dinner that the general had held for his staff officers, "they don't read the Bible."

"Who don't? Hold up." Major Alexander Lindsay, Sixth Earl of Balcarres, put out a hand to ward off a passing tree and, clutching it one-handed to keep his balance, groped for his flies.

"Indians."

It was dark, but Sandy turned his head and William could just about see one eye shut slowly in the effort to fix the other on him. There had been a great deal of wine with dinner, and a number of ladies present, which added to the conviviality.

Balcarres concentrated on his pissing, then exhaled with relief and closed both eyes.

"No," he said. "They mostly don't." He seemed content to leave the matter there, but it had occurred to William—himself a little less organized in thought than usual—that perhaps he had failed to express himself completely.

"I mean," he said, swaying just a little as a gust of wind boomed down through the trees, "the centurion. You know, he says go and the fellow goeth. You tell an Indian go and maybe he goeth and maybe he damned well goeth not, depending how the prospect strikes him."

Balcarres was now concentrating on the effort of doing up his flies and didn't answer.

"I mean," William amplified, "they don't take orders."

"Oh. No. They don't."

"You give your Indians orders, though?" He'd meant to make it a statement, but it didn't quite come out that way. Balcarres led a regiment of light infantry but also kept a large group of rangers, many of them Indians; he not infrequently dressed like one himself.

"But then, you're a Scot."

Balcarres had succeeded in doing up his flies and now stood in the center of the path, squinting at William.

"You're drunk, Willie." This was said with no tone of accusation; more with the pleased sense of one who has made a useful deduction.

"Yes. But I'll be sober in the morning and you'll *still* be a Scot." This struck them both as hilarious and they staggered some distance together, repeating the jest at intervals and bumping into each other. By simple chance, they stumbled upon William's tent first, and he invited Balcarres to join him in a glass of negus before bed.

"Sett . . . les the stomach," he said, narrowly avoiding falling headfirst into his campaign chest as he groped for cups and bottles. "Makes you sleep better."

Balcarres had succeeded in lighting the candle and sat holding it, blinking owl-eyed in its glow. He sipped the negus William handed to him carefully, eyes closed as though to savor it, then suddenly opened them.

"What's being a Scot have to do with reading the Bible?" he demanded, this remark having evidently returned suddenly to his cognizance. "You calling me a heathen? My grandmother's Scots and she reads the Bible all the time. I've read it myself. Bits of it," he added, and gulped the rest of his glass.

William frowned, trying to remember what on earth . . .

"Oh," he said. "Not the Bible. Indians. Stubborn buggers. Don't goeth. Scots don't goeth either when you tell them, or not all the time. I thought maybe that was why. Why they listen to you," he added as an afterthought. "Your Indians."

Balcarres thought that funny, too, but when he had at length stopped laughing, he shook his head slowly to and fro.

"It's . . . you know a horse?"

"I know a lot of horses. Which one?"

Balcarres spit a small quantity of negus down his chin, but wiped it away.

"A horse," he repeated, drying his hand on his breeches. "You can't make a horse do anything. You see what he's going to do and then you tell him to do that, and he thinks it's your idea, so next time you tell him something, he's more likely to do what you tell him."

"Oh." William considered this carefully. "Yes." They drank for a bit in silence, mulling over this profundity. At last Balcarres looked up from a long contemplation of his glass.

"Who do you think has better tits?" he asked seriously. "Mrs. Lind or the baroness?"

50

EXODUS

Fort Ticonderoga
June 27, 1777

MRS. RAVEN WAS beginning to worry me. I found her waiting outside the barracks at dawn, looking as though she had slept in her clothes, eyes hollow but gleaming with intensity. She clung to me, close on my heels through the day, talking constantly, and her conversation, usually focused at least nominally on the patients we were seeing and the inescapable logistics of daily life in a fort, began to deviate from the narrow confines of the present.

At first, it was no more than an occasional reminiscence of her early married life in Boston; her first husband had been a fisherman, and she had kept two goats whose milk she sold in the streets. I didn't mind hearing about the goats, named Patsy and Petunia; I had known a few memorable goats myself, noticeably a billy goat named Hiram, whose broken leg I had set.

It wasn't that I was uninterested in her randomly dropped remarks about her first husband; they were, if anything, too interesting. The late Mr. Evans appeared to have been a violent drunkard on shore—which was far from unusual—with a penchant for cutting off the ears or noses of people who displeased him, which was a trifle more individualistic.

"He nailed the ears to the lintel of my goat shed," she said, in the tone one might use to describe one's breakfast. "Up high, so the goats couldn't get at them. They shrivel up in the sun, you know, like dried mushrooms."

"Ah," I said. I thought of remarking that smoking a severed ear prevented that little problem, but thought better of it. I didn't know whether Ian was still carrying a lawyer's ear in his sporran, but I was reasonably sure he wouldn't welcome Mrs. Raven's eager interest in it, if so. Both he and Jamie made off when they saw her coming, as though she had the plague.

"They say the Indians cut pieces off their captives," she said, her voice going low, as one imparting a secret. "The fingers first, one joint at a time."

"How very revolting," I said. "Do please go to the dispensary and get me a bag of fresh lint, would you?"

She went off obediently—she always did—but I thought I heard her talking to herself under her breath as she did so. As the days crept on and tension mounted in the fort, I became convinced of it.

Her conversational swings were getting wider—and wilder. Now she ranged from the distant past of her idealized childhood in Maryland to an equally distant future—a rather grisly one, in which we had all been either killed by the British army or captured by Indians, with consequences ranging from rape to dismemberment—these procedures often accomplished simultaneously, though I told her that most men had neither the necessary concentration nor yet the coordination for it. She was still capable of focusing on something directly in front of her, but not for long.

"Could you speak to her husband, do you think?" I asked Jamie, who had just come in at sunset to tell me that he'd seen her trudging in circles round and round the big cistern near the parade ground, counting under her breath.

"D'ye think he hasn't noticed that his wife's going mad?" he replied. "If he hasn't, I think he'll no appreciate being told. And if he has," he added logically, "what d'ye expect him to do about it?"

There was in fact not much anyone could do about it, bar

keep an eye on her and try to soothe her more vivid fancies—or at least keep her from talking about them to the more impressionable patients.

As the days went on, though, Mrs. Raven's eccentricities seemed not much more pronounced than the anxieties of most of the fort's inhabitants, particularly the women, who could do nothing but tend their children, wash the laundry—under heavy guard on the lakeshore, or in small mobs round the steaming cauldrons—and wait.

The woods were not safe; a few days before, two picket guards had been found no more than a mile from the fort, murdered and scalped. This grisly discovery had had the worst effect on Mrs. Raven, but I couldn't say that it did much for my own fortitude. I couldn't look out from the batteries with my earlier sense of pleasure in the endless miles of thick green; the very vigor of the forest itself seemed a threat now. I still wanted clean linen, but my skin tingled and crept whenever I left the fort.

"Thirteen days," I said, running a thumb down the doorpost of our sanctum. Jamie had, with no comment, cut a notch for each day of the enlistment period, slashing through each notch when he came to bed at night. "Did you notch the posts when you were in prison?"

"Not in Fort William or the Bastille," he said, considering. "Ardsmuir . . . aye, we did then. There wasna any sentence to keep track of, but . . . ye lose so much, so fast. It seemed important to keep a hold on something, even if it was only the day of the week."

He came to stand beside me, looking at the doorpost and its long line of neat notches.

"I think I might have been tempted to run," he said, very quietly. "If it weren't for Ian being gone."

It wasn't anything I hadn't thought—or been aware of him thinking. It was becoming more obvious by the second that the fort couldn't stand attack by the size of the force that was—indubitably—on its way. Scouts were coming in more frequently with reports on Burgoyne's army, and while they were whisked instantly into the commandant's office and just as hastily trundled out of the fort again, everyone knew within an hour what news they had brought—precious little so far, but that little, alarming. And yet Arthur St. Clair could not bring himself to order the evacuation of the fort.

"A blot on his record," Jamie said, with an evenness that betrayed his anger. "He canna bear to have it said that he lost Ticonderoga."

"But he will lose it," I said. "He must, mustn't he?"

"He will. But if he fights and loses it, that's one thing. To fight and lose it to a superior force is honorable. To abandon it to the enemy without a fight? He canna reconcile himself to it. Though he's no a wicked man," he added thoughtfully. "I'll talk to him again. We all will."

"All" being the militia officers, who could afford to be outspoken. A number of the regular army officers shared the militia's feelings, but discipline prevented most of them from speaking bluntly to St. Clair.

I didn't think Arthur St. Clair was a wicked man, either—nor yet a stupid one. He knew—must know—what the cost of fighting would be. Or the cost of surrender.

"He's waiting for Whitcomb, ken," Jamie said conversationally. "Hoping he'll tell him Burgoyne hasna got any artillery to speak of." The fort could indeed hold out against standard siege tactics; forage and provisions had been coming in from the surrounding countryside in abundance, and Ticonderoga still had some artillery defenses and the small wooden fort on Mount Independence, as well as a substantial garrison decently supplied with muskets and powder. It could not hold out against major artillery placed on Mount Defiance, though. Jamie had been up there, and told me that the entire interior of the fort was visible—and thus subject to enfiladement at the enemy's discretion.

"He can't really think that, surely?"

"No, but until he knows for sure, he hasna got to make up his mind for sure, either. And none of the scouts has yet brought him anything certain."

I sighed and pressed a hand to my bosom, blotting a tickle of sweat.

"I can't sleep in there," I said abruptly. "It's like sleeping in hell."

That took him by surprise and made him laugh.

"All right for you," I said, rather cross. "You get to go sleep under canvas tomorrow." Half the garrison was being moved to tents outside the fort, the better to be out and maneuverable, ready in case of Burgoyne's approach.

The British were coming; how close they were, how many men they had, and how well armed they were was unknown.

Benjamin Whitcomb had gone to find out. Whitcomb was a lanky, pockmarked man in his thirties, one of the men known as the Long Hunters, men who could—and did—spend weeks in the wilderness, living off the land. Such men were not sociable, having no use for civilization, but they were valuable. Whitcomb was the best of St. Clair's scouts; he had taken five men to go and find Burgoyne's main force. I hoped they would return before the enlistment period was up; Jamie wanted to be gone—so did I, badly—but plainly we couldn't go without Ian.

Jamie moved abruptly, turning and going back into our room.

"What do you need?" He was digging in the small blanket chest that contained our few spare clothes and the other oddments we'd picked up since coming to the fort.

"My kilt. If I'm going to make representations to St. Clair, I'd best be formal about it."

I helped him to dress and brushed and plaited his hair for him. He had no proper coat, but he had clean linen, at least, and his dirk, and even in shirtsleeves he looked impressive.

"I haven't seen you in your kilt in weeks," I said, admiring him. "I'm sure you'll make an impression on the general, even without a pink sash."

He smiled and kissed me.

"It'll do no good," he said, "but it wouldna be right not to try."

I walked with him across the parade ground to St. Clair's house. There were thunderheads rising out on the lake, charcoal black against the blazing sky, and I could smell ozone in the air. It seemed a suitable portent.

SOON. EVERYTHING said, *Soon.* The fragmentary reports and rumors that flew like pigeons through the fort, the closeness of the sultry air, the occasional boom of cannon in the distance, fired for practice—we hoped it was only practice—from the distant picket position called the Old French Lines.

Everyone was restless, unable to sleep in the heat unless drunk. I wasn't drunk, and I was restless. Jamie had been gone for more than two hours, and I wanted him. Not because I cared what St. Clair had had to say to the militia. But between heat and exhaustion, we hadn't made love in more than a week, and I was beginning to suspect that time was growing short. If we were obliged either to fight or to flee in the next few days, heaven only knew how long it might be before we had a private moment again.

I had been strolling round the parade ground, keeping an eye on St. Clair's house, and when at last I saw him come out, I made my way toward him, walking slowly to allow him to take leave of the other officers who had come out with him. They stood for a moment close together, the slump of shoulders and angry tilt of heads telling me that the effect of their protests had been exactly what Jamie had predicted.

He walked slowly away, hands behind him, head bent in thought. I came quietly alongside and tucked my hand into the crook of his elbow, and he looked down at me, surprised but smiling.

"Ye're out late, Sassenach. Is aught amiss?"

"Not at all," I said. "It just seemed like a nice evening for a walk in a garden."

"In a garden," he repeated, giving me a sideways glance.

"The commandant's garden, to be exact," I said, and touched the pocket of my apron. "I, um, have the key." There were a number of small gardens inside the fort, most of them practical plots meant for the production of vegetables. The formal garden behind the commandant's quarters had been designed by the French many years before, though, and while it had since been neglected and overrun by the seeds of airborne weeds, it had one rather interesting aspect—a high wall surrounding it, with a gate that locked. I'd thoughtfully abstracted the key earlier in the day from General St. Clair's cook, who had come to me for a throat wash. I would put it back when I called on him the next day to check his sore throat.

"Ah," said Jamie thoughtfully, and turned obligingly back toward the commandant's house.

The gate was round the back, out of view, and we slipped hastily down the alley that led past the garden wall, while the guard outside St. Clair's house was talking to a passerby. I closed the gate quietly behind us, locked it, and pocketed the key, then went to Jamie's arms.

He kissed me slowly, then raised his head, eyeing me.

"I might need a bit of help, mind."

"That can be arranged," I assured him. I laid a hand on his knee, where the kilt had folded up, exposing flesh. I moved a thumb lightly, liking the soft, wiry feel of the hairs on his leg. "Um . . . did you have any particular sort of help in mind?"

I could smell him in spite of his careful washing, the dried sweat of his labor on his skin spiced with dust and wood chips. He'd taste of it, too, sweet and salt and musk.

I slid my hand up his thigh beneath the kilt, feeling him shift and flex, the sudden groove of muscle smooth beneath my fingers. To my surprise, though, he stopped me, grasping my hand through the fabric.

"Thought you wanted help," I said.

"Touch yourself, *a nighean,*" he said softly.

That was a trifle disconcerting, particularly given that we were standing in an overgrown garden no more than twenty feet from an alleyway much patronized by militiamen looking for a place to get quietly drunk. Still . . . I leaned back against the wall and obligingly pulled the shift above my knee. I held it there, gently stroking the skin of my inner thigh—which was, in fact, very soft. I drew the other hand up the line of my stays, to the top, where my breasts swelled out against the thin, damp cotton.

His eyes were heavy; he was still half drunk with fatigue but becoming more alert by the moment. He made a small interrogative sound.

"Ever hear the one about sauce for the gander?" I said, twiddling thoughtfully with the string that held the neckline of my shift.

"What?" That had brought him out of the haze; he was starkly awake, bloodshot eyes wide open.

"You heard me."

"Ye want me to . . . to—"

"I do."

"I couldna do that! In front of you?"

"If I can do it in front of *you,* you can certainly return the favor. Of course, if you'd rather I stopped . . ." I let my hand fall—slowly—from the string. Paused, thumb very lightly ticking to and fro, to and fro, over my breast like the hand of a metronome. I could feel my nipple, round and hard as a musket ball; it must be visible through the fabric, even in this light.

He swallowed; I heard it.

I smiled and let my hand fall farther, taking hold of the hem of my skirt. And paused, one eyebrow raised.

As though hypnotized, he reached down and took hold of the hem of his kilt.

"That's a good lad," I murmured, leaning back on one hand. I raised one knee and set my foot on the wall, letting the skirt fall away, baring my thigh. Reached down.

He said something under his breath in Gaelic. I couldn't tell if it was an observation on the imminent prospect before him or whether he was commending his soul to God. In either case, he lifted his kilt.

"What do you mean, you need help?" I asked, eyeing him.

He made a small, urgent noise indicating that I should continue, so I did.

"What are you thinking?" I asked after a moment, fascinated.

"I'm not thinking."

"Yes, you are; I can see it on your face."

"Ye don't want to know." Sweat was beginning to gleam across his cheekbones, and his eyes had gone to slits.

"Oh, yes, I do—oh, wait. If you're thinking about someone other than me, I *don't* want to know."

He opened his eyes at that, and fixed me with a look that ran straight up between my quivering legs. He didn't stop.

"Oh," I said, a little breathless myself. "Well . . . when you can talk again, I *do* want to know, then."

He went on looking at me, with a gaze that now struck me as markedly akin to that of a wolf eyeing a fat sheep. I shifted a little against the wall and waved away a cloud of gnats. He was breathing fast, and I could smell his sweat, musky and acrid.

"You," he said, and I saw his throat move as he swallowed. He crooked the index finger of his free hand at me.

"Come here."

"I—"

"Now."

Mesmerized, I slid away from the wall and took two steps toward him. Before I could say or do anything else, there was a flurry of kilt and a large, hot hand was gripping me by the scruff of the neck. Then I was lying on my back in long grass and wild tobacco, Jamie solidly inside me, and the hand was over my mouth—a good thing, I realized dimly, as there were voices coming toward us along the alley on the other side of the garden wall.

"Play wi' fire and ye may get singed, Sassenach," he whispered in my ear. He had me pinned like a butterfly and, with a solid grip on my wrists, kept me from moving, even though I was jerking and writhing under him, slippery and desperate. Very slowly, he lowered himself so his full weight rested on me.

"Ye want to know what I was thinking, do ye?" he murmured in my ear.

"Mmp!"

"Well, I'll tell ye, *a nighean,* but—" He paused in order to lick my earlobe.

"NNG!"

The hand tightened warningly over my mouth. The voices were near enough to make out words now: a small party of young militiamen, half drunk and in search of whores. Jamie's teeth closed delicately on my ear, and he began to nibble thoughtfully, his breath warm and tickling. I wriggled madly, but he wasn't budging.

He gave the same thorough treatment to the other ear before the men had moved out of earshot, then kissed the end of my nose, taking his hand off my mouth at last.

"Ah. Now, where was I? Oh, aye—ye wanted to hear what I was thinking of."

"I've changed my mind." I was panting shallowly, as much from the weight on my chest as from desire. Both were considerable.

He made a Scottish noise indicating deep amusement and tightened his grip on my wrists.

"You started it, Sassenach—but I'll finish it." Whereupon he put his lips to my wet ear and told me in a slow whisper *ex-*

actly what he'd been thinking. Not moving an inch while he did so, save to put his hand back over my mouth when I began to call him names.

Every muscle in my body was jumping like a snapped rubber band when he finally moved. In one sudden motion, he raised himself and slid back, then forward hard.

When I could see and hear again, I realized that he was laughing, still balanced above me.

"Put ye out of your misery, did I, Sassenach?"

"You . . ." I croaked. Words failed me, but two could play at this game. He hadn't moved, in part to torture me—but in equal part because he couldn't; not without ending it at once. I flexed my soft, slick muscles once around him, slowly, gently—then did it three times, fast. He made a gratifying noise and lost it, jerking and groaning, the pulse of it exciting an echo in my own flesh. Very slowly, he lowered himself, sighing like a deflated bladder, and lay beside me, breathing slowly, eyes closed.

"*Now* you can sleep," I said, stroking his hair. He smiled without opening his eyes, breathed deep, and his body relaxed, settling into the earth.

"And next time, you bloody Scot," I whispered in his ear, "I'll tell you what *I* was thinking."

"Oh, God," he said, and laughed without making a sound. "D'ye remember the first time I kissed ye, Sassenach?"

I lay there for some time, feeling the bloom of sweat on my skin and the reassuring weight of him curled asleep in the grass beside me, before I finally remembered.

"I said I was a virgin, not a monk. If I find I need help . . . I'll ask."

IAN MURRAY WOKE from a deep and dreamless sleep to the sound of a bugle. Rollo, lying close beside him, lurched upright with a startled, deep *WOOF!,* and glared round for the threat, hackles raised.

Ian scrambled up, as well, one hand on his knife, the other on the dog.

"Hush," he said under his breath, and the dog relaxed fractionally, though he kept up a low, rolling growl, just below the range of human hearing—Ian felt it, a constant vibration in the huge body under his hand.

Now he was awake, he heard them easily. A subterranean stirring through the wood, as submerged—but quite as vibrant—as Rollo's growl. A very large body of men, a camp, beginning to wake at no very great distance. How had he managed not to perceive them the night before? He sniffed, but the wind was wrong; he picked up no scent of smoke—though now he *saw* smoke, thin threads of it rising against the pale dawn sky. A lot of campfires. A very big camp.

He had been rolling up his blanket as he listened. There was nothing more to his own camp, and within seconds he had faded into the brush, blanket tied to his back and his rifle in hand, the dog huge and silent at his heel.

51

THE BRITISH ARE COMING

Three Mile Point, New York Colony
July 3, 1777

THE DARK PATCH of sweat between Brigadier Fraser's broad shoulders had the shape of the Isle of Man on the map in the old schoolroom at home. Lieutenant Greenleaf's coat was entirely soaked with sweat, the body almost black, and only the faded sleeves showing red.

William's own coat was less faded—shamefully new and bright, in fact—but likewise clung to his back and shoulders, heavy with the humid exhalations of his body. His shirt was wringing; it had been stiff with salt when he put it on a few hours before, the constant sweating of the previous days' exertion crystallized in the linen, but the stiffness had washed away as the sun rose, borne on a flood of fresh sweat.

Looking up at the hill the brigadier proposed to climb, he had had some hope of coolness at the summit, but the exertion of the climb had canceled out any benefit of altitude. They had left camp just after dawn, the air then so delicious in its freshness that he'd longed to run naked through the woods like an Indian, catch fish from the lake, and eat a dozen of them for his breakfast, fried in cornmeal, fresh and hot.

This was Three Mile Point, so called because it was three miles south of the fort at Ticonderoga. The brigadier, leading the advance force, had staged his troops here and proposed to climb to a height with Lieutenant Greenleaf, an engineer, to survey the terrain before moving further.

William had been assigned to the brigadier a week earlier, to his pleasure. The brigadier was a friendly, sociable commander, but not in the same way as General Burgoyne. Though William would not have cared had the man been a tartar—he would be in the forward lines; that was all that mattered.

He was carrying some of the engineer's equipment, as well as a couple of canteens of water and the brigadier's dispatch box. He helped to set up the surveying tripod and obligingly held measuring rods at intervals, but at length it was done, everything recorded, and the brigadier, having conferred with Greenleaf at some length, sent the engineer back to camp.

The immediate business concluded, the brigadier seemed disinclined to descend at once, instead walking slowly about, appearing to enjoy the slight breeze, and then settling on a rock, uncorking his canteen with a sigh of pleasure.

"Sit, William," he said, motioning William to his own rock. They sat in silence for a bit, listening to the sounds of the forest.

"I know your father," the brigadier said suddenly, then smiled, a charming smile. "Everyone tells you that, I suppose."

"Well, yes, they do," William admitted. "Or if not him, my uncle."

General Fraser laughed. "A considerable burden of family history to be borne," he commiserated. "But I'm sure you bear it nobly."

William didn't know what to say and made a politely indeterminate noise in response. The brigadier laughed again and passed him the canteen. The water was so warm that he barely felt it pass down his throat, but it smelled fresh and he could feel it slake his thirst.

"We were together at the Plains of Abraham. Your father and I, I mean. Did he ever tell you about that night?"

"Not a great deal," William said, wondering if he was doomed to meet every soldier who had fought on that field with James Wolfe.

"We came down the river at night, you know. All of us petrified. Especially me." The brigadier looked out over the lake, shaking his head a little at the memory. "Such a river, the St. Lawrence. General Burgoyne mentioned that you had been in Canada. Did you see it?"

"Not a great deal, sir. I traveled overland for the most part on the way to Quebec, and then came down the Richelieu. My father told me about the St. Lawrence, though," he felt obliged to add. "He said it was a noble river."

"Did he tell you that I nearly broke his hand? He was next to me in the boat, and as I leaned out to call to the French sentry, hoping that my voice would not break, he gripped my hand to steady me. I felt his bones grinding, but under the circumstances didn't really notice until I let go and heard him gasp."

William saw the brigadier's eyes drift to his own hands and the small ripple across his wide brow, not quite puzzlement but the look of someone trying unconsciously to fit memory to present circumstance. His father had long, slender, elegant hands with fine bones. William's fingers were long, but his hands were vulgarly large, broad of palm and brute-knuckled.

"He—Lord John—he is my stepfather," he blurted, then blushed painfully, embarrassed both by the admission and by whatever freak of mind had made him say it.

"Oh? Oh, yes," the brigadier said vaguely. "Yes, of course."

Had the brigadier thought he spoke from pride, pointing out the ancientness of his own bloodline?

The only comfort was that his face—the brigadier's face, too—was so red from exertion that the blush could not show. The brigadier, as though responding to the thought of heat, struggled out of his coat, then unbuttoned his waistcoat and flapped it, nodding to William that he might do likewise—which he did, sighing with relief.

The conversation turned casually to other campaigns: those the brigadier had fought in, those William had (mostly) heard of. He became gradually aware that the brigadier was gauging him, weighing his experience and his manner. He was uncomfortably aware that the former was inglorious; was General Fraser aware of what had happened during the Battle of Long Island? Word did travel fast in the service.

Eventually, there was a pause in the conversation and they sat companionably in their shirtsleeves for a bit, listening to the soughing of the trees overhead. William wished to say something in his own defense but could think of no way to approach the matter gracefully. But if he did not speak, explain what had happened . . . well, there was no good explanation. He'd been a booby, that was all.

"General Howe speaks well of your intelligence and boldness, William," the brigadier said, as though continuing their earlier conversation, "though he said he thought you had not had opportunity as yet to show your talent for command."

"Ah . . . no, sir," William replied, sweating.

The brigadier smiled.

"Well, we must be sure to remedy that lack, must we not?" He stood up, groaning slightly as he stretched and shrugged his way back into his coat. "You'll dine with me later. We shall discuss it with Sir Francis."

52

CONFLAGRATION

Fort Ticonderoga
July 1, 1777

WHITCOMB had come back. With several British scalps, according to popular rumor. Having met Benjamin Whitcomb and one or two of the other Long Hunters, I was prepared to believe this. They spoke civilly enough, and they were far from the only men at the fort who dressed in rough leather and ragged homespun or whose skin shrank tight to raw bones. But they were the only men with the eyes of animals.

The next day, Jamie was called to the commandant's house and didn't come back until after dark.

A man was singing by one of the courtyard fires near St. Clair's quarters, and I was sitting on an empty salt-pork barrel listening, when I saw Jamie pass by on the far side of the fire, heading for our barracks. I rose quickly and caught him up.

"Come away," he said softly, and led me toward the commandant's garden. There was no echo of our last encounter in this garden, though I was terribly aware of his body, of the tension in it and the beating of his heart. Bad news, then.

"What's happened?" I asked, my voice low.

"Whitcomb caught a British regular and brought him in. He wouldna say anything, of course—but St. Clair was canny enough to put Andy Tracy in a cell with the man, saying he was accused of being a spy—that Tracy was a spy, I mean."

"That was bright," I said with approval. Lieutenant Andrew Hodges Tracy was an Irishman, bluff and charming, a born liar—and if anyone could winkle information out of someone without the use of force, Tracy would have been my own first choice. "I take it he found out something?"

"He did. We also had in three British deserters—Germans. St. Clair wanted me to talk to them."

Which he had. The information brought by the deserters might be suspect—save that it correlated with the information tricked from the captured British soldier. The solid information for which St. Clair had been waiting for the last three weeks.

General Carleton had remained in Canada with a small force; it was indeed General John Burgoyne, in charge of a large invasion army, who was heading toward the fort. He was reinforced by General von Riedesel, himself in command of seven Brunswick regiments, *plus* a light infantry battalion and four companies of dragoons. And his vanguard was less than four days' march away.

"Not too good," I observed, taking a deep breath.

"It is not," he agreed. "Worse, Burgoyne has Simon Fraser as brigadier under him. He has the forward command."

"A relative of yours?" That was a rhetorical question; no one with that name could possibly be anything else, and I saw the shadow of a smile cross Jamie's face.

"He is," he said dryly. "A second cousin, I think. And a verra bonny fighter."

"Well, he would be, wouldn't he? Is that the last of the bad news?"

He shook his head.

"Nay. The deserters said Burgoyne's army is short of supplies. The dragoons are on foot, because they canna get fresh horses. Though I dinna ken whether they've eaten them or not."

It was a hot, muggy night, but a shiver raised the hairs on my arms. I touched Jamie's wrist and found the hairs there bristling, as well. *He'll dream of Culloden tonight,* I thought abruptly. I dismissed that for the moment, though.

"I should think that would be good news. Why isn't it?"

His wrist turned and his hand took mine, lacing our fingers tight together.

"Because they havena supplies enough to mount a siege. They'll need to overrun us and take us by force. And they verra likely can."

THREE DAYS LATER, the first British lookouts appeared on Mount Defiance.

THE NEXT DAY, anyone could see—and everyone *did* see—the beginnings of an artillery emplacement being built on Mount Defiance. Arthur St. Clair, bowing at last to the inevitable, gave word to begin the evacuation of Fort Ticonderoga.

Most of the garrison was to move to Mount Independence, taking with them all the most valuable supplies and ordnance. Some of the sheep and cattle must be slaughtered, the rest driven off into the woods. Some militia units were to leave through the woods and find the road to Hubbardton, where they would wait as reinforcements. Women, children, and invalids were to be dispatched down the lake by boat, with a light guard. It began in an orderly manner, with word sent out to bring everything that would float up to the lakeshore after dark, men collecting and checking their equipment, and orders sent out for the systematic destruction of everything that could not be carried away.

This was the usual procedure, to deny the enemy any use of supplies. In this instance, the matter was somewhat more pressing: the deserters had said that Burgoyne's army was running short of supplies already; denying him the facilities of Ticonderoga might bring him to a halt—or at least slow him down perceptibly, as his men would be obliged to forage and live off the country while they waited for supplies from Canada to follow him.

All of this—the packing, the loading, the slaughtering and livestock-driving, the destruction—must be accomplished clandestinely, under the very noses of the British. For if they saw that a retreat was imminent, they would fall on us like wolves, destroying the garrison as they left the safety of the fort.

Tremendous thunderheads boiled up over the lake in the afternoons, towering black things that rose miles high and full of lightning. Sometimes they broke after nightfall, pounding the lake, the mounts, the picket lines, and the fort with water that fell as though dumped from a bottomless bucket. Sometimes they only drifted past, grumbling and ominous.

Tonight the clouds were low and fierce, veined with lightning and blanketing the sky. Heat lightning throbbed through their bodies and crackled between them in bursts of sudden, silent conversation. And now and then a sudden fork shot blue-white and vivid to the ground with a crack of thunder that made everyone jump.

There was very little to pack. Just as well, as there was very little time in which to pack it. I could hear the flurry all through the barracks as I worked: people calling out in search of lost objects, mothers bellowing for lost children, and the shuffle and thunder of feet, steady as echoing rain in the wooden stairwells.

Outside, I could hear the agitated baaing of a number of sheep, disturbed at being turned out of their pens, and a sudden racket of shouting and mooing, as a panicked cow made a break for it. Not surprising; there was a strong smell of fresh blood in the air, from the slaughtering.

I had seen the garrison on parade, of course; I knew how many men there were. But to see three or four thousand people pushing and shoving, trying to accomplish unaccustomed tasks in a tearing hurry, was like watching a kicked-over anthill. I made my own way through the seething mass, clutching a flour sack with spare clothes, my few medical supplies, and a large chunk of ham I had acquired from a grateful patient, wrapped in my extra petticoat.

I would evacuate with the boat brigade, minding a group of invalids—but I didn't mean to go without seeing Jamie.

My heart had been in my mouth for so long that I could barely speak. Not for the first time, I thought how convenient it was to have married a very tall man. It was always easy to pick Jamie out of a crowd, and I saw him within moments, standing on one of the demilune batteries. Some of his militiamen were with him, all looking downward. I assumed that the boat brigade must be forming below; that was heartening.

The prospect, once I reached the edge of the battery and could see, was considerably less heartening. The lakeshore below the fort looked like the return of a particularly disastrous fishing fleet. There *were* boats. All kinds of boats, from canoes and rowboats to dories and crude rafts. Some were dragged up onto the shore, others were evidently floating away, unmanned—I caught sight during a brief lightning flash of a few heads bobbing in the water as men and boys swam after them to fetch them back. There were few lights on the shore, for fear of giving away the plan of retreat, but here and there a torch burned, showing arguments and fistfights, and beyond the reach of torchlight, the ground seemed to heave and ripple in the dark, like a swarming carcass.

Jamie was shaking hands with Mr. Anderson, one of the *Teal*'s original hands, who had become his *de facto* corporal.

"Go with God," he said. Mr. Anderson nodded and turned away, leading the small knot of militiamen. They passed me as I came up, and one or two nodded to me, their faces invisible in the shadow of their hats.

"Where are they going?" I asked Jamie.

"Toward Hubbardton," he replied, his eyes still on the lakeshore below. "I told them it was their own choice, but I thought best they went sooner rather than later." He lifted his chin toward the humped black shape of Mount Defiance, where the sparks of campfires glowed near the summit. "If they dinna ken what's happening, it's gross incompetence. Were I Simon Fraser, I should be on the march before first light."

"You don't mean to go with your men?" A spark of hope sprang up in my heart.

There was little light on the battery, only the reflected glow from the torches on the stairs and the bigger fires inside the fort. This was enough for me to see his face clearly, though, when he turned to look at me. It was somber, but there was an eagerness in the set of his mouth, and I recognized the look of a soldier ready to surge into action.

"No," he said. "I mean to go with you." He smiled suddenly, and I gripped his hand. "Ye dinna think I mean to leave ye to wander in the wilderness with a parcel o' diseased half-wits? Even if it does mean getting into a boat," he added with a touch of distaste.

I laughed despite myself.

"Not very kind," I said. "But not inaccurate, either, if you mean Mrs. Raven. You haven't seen her anywhere, have you?"

He shook his head. The wind had pulled half his hair loose from its thong, and he removed this now and placed it between his teeth, gathering up his hair in a heavy tail to rebind it.

Someone down the battery said something, sounding startled, and both Jamie and I jerked round to look. Mount Independence was on fire.

"FIRE! FIRE!"

The screams brought people—already flustered and upset—rushing out of the barracks like coveys of flushed quail. The fire was just beneath the summit of Mount Independence, where General Fermoy had established an outpost with his men. A tongue of flame soared upward, steady as a candle taking breath. Then a gust of wind flattened it, and the flame squatted for a moment, as though someone had turned down the gas on a stove, before bursting out again in a much wider conflagration that lit up the mount, showing the tiny black shapes of what looked like hundreds of people in the act of striking tents and loading baggage, all silhouetted against the fire.

"It's Fermoy's quarters on fire," a soldier said beside me, disbelieving. "Isn't it?"

"It is," said Jamie on my other side, sounding grim. "And if we can see the retreat starting from here, Burgoyne's lookouts must surely see it, too."

And as simply as that, the rout began.

Had I ever doubted the existence of something like telepathy, this would have been enough to quell any reservations. The soldiers were already at breaking point from St. Clair's delay and the constant drum of rumors beating on stretched nerves. As the fire on Mount Independence spread, the conviction that the redcoats and the Indians would be upon us at once spread from mind to mind without the necessity for speech. Panic was loose, spreading its broad black wings over the fort, and the confusion at the water's edge was disintegrating into chaos before our eyes.

"Come, then," Jamie said. And before I knew it, I was

being hustled down the narrow steps of the battery. A few wooden huts had been set on fire—these on purpose, to deprive the invaders of useful matériel—and the light from the flames lit up a scene from hell. Women dragging half-dressed children, screaming and trailing bedclothes, men throwing furniture from windows. A thunder mug crashed on the stones, sending shards of sharp pottery slicing across the legs of the people nearby.

A voice came breathless behind me. "A golden guinea says the silly French bugger set the house on fire himself."

"I'll gie ye nay odds on that one," Jamie replied briefly. "I only hope he went up with it."

A tremendous flash of lightning lit up the fort like day and screams rose from every part of it, only to be drowned almost instantly by the explosion of thunder. Predictably, half the people thought the wrath of God was about to be visited upon us—this, in spite of the fact that we had been having thunderstorms of similar ferocity for days, I thought crossly—while those of secular mind were still more panicked because the militia units on the outer lines were being lit up as they withdrew, in full sight of the British on Mount Defiance. Either way, it didn't help matters.

"I have to fetch my invalids!" I shouted into Jamie's ear. "You go and get the things from the barracks."

He shook his head. His flying loose hair was lit up by another lightning flash, and he looked like one of the principal demons himself.

"I'm no leaving you," he said, taking a firm clasp of my arm. "I might never find ye again."

"But—" My objection died as I looked. He was right. There were thousands of people running, pushing, or simply standing in place, too stunned to think what to do. If we were separated, he might *not* find me, and the thought of being alone in the woods below the fort—these infested with bloodthirsty Indians as well as redcoats—was not something I wanted to contemplate for more than ten seconds.

"Right," I said. "Come on, then."

The scene inside the hospital barracks was less frantic only because most of the patients were less capable of movement. They were, if anything, more agitated than the people outside, as they'd gleaned only the most fragmentary intelligence from people rushing in and out. Those with families were being dragged bodily from the building with barely enough time to seize their clothes; those without were in the spaces between cots, hopping on one foot to get into their breeches or staggering toward the door.

Captain Stebbings, of course, was not doing any of these things. He lay placidly on his cot, hands folded on his chest, observing the chaos with interest, a rush dip burning placidly on the wall above him.

"Mrs. Fraser!" He greeted me cheerfully. "I suppose I shall be a free man again shortly. Hope the army brings me some food; I think there's not much chance of supper here tonight."

"I suppose you will," I said, unable not to smile back at him. "You'll take care of the other British prisoners, will you? General St. Clair is leaving them behind."

He looked mildly offended at this.

"They're my men," he said.

"So they are." In fact, Guinea Dick, almost invisible against the stone wall in the dim light, was crouching beside the captain's bed, a stout walking stick in his hand—in order to fend off would-be looters, I supposed. Mr. Ormiston was sitting up on his own cot, pale-faced but excited, picking at the binding on his stump.

"They're really coming, are they, ma'am? The army?"

"Yes, they are. Now, you must take good care of your wound and keep it clean. It's healing well, but you mustn't put any strain at all on it for another month at least—and wait at least two months before you have a peg fitted. *Don't* let the army surgeons bleed you—you need all your strength."

He nodded, though I knew he'd be lining up for a fleam and a bleeding-bowl the moment a British surgeon showed up; he believed deeply in the virtues of being let blood and had been slightly mollified only by my having leeched his stump now and then.

I clasped his hand in farewell, and was turning to go when his own grip tightened.

"A moment, ma'am?" He let go my hand, fumbling at his neck, and withdrew something on a string. I could barely see it in the gloom, but he put it into my hand and I felt a metal disc, warm from his body.

"If happen you might see that boy Abram again, ma'am, I should take it kind if you'd give him that. That's my lucky piece, what I've carried for thirty-two years; you tell him it will keep him safe in time o' danger."

Jamie was looming up in the dark beside me, radiating impatience and agitation. He had a small group of invalids in tow, all clutching random possessions. I could hear Mrs. Raven's distinctive high-pitched voice in the distance, wailing. I thought she was calling my name. I ducked my head and put Mr. Ormiston's lucky piece around my neck.

"I'll tell him, Mr. Ormiston. Thank you."

SOMEONE HAD SET fire to Jeduthan Baldwin's elegant bridge. A pile of rubbish smoldered near one end, and I saw black devil shapes running to and fro along the span with chisels and pry bars, ripping up the planks and throwing them into the water.

Jamie shouldered a way through the mob, me behind him and our little band of women, children, and invalids scurrying at my heels like goslings, honking in agitation.

"Fraser! Colonel Fraser!" I turned at the shout, to see Jonah—Bill, I mean—Marsden running down the shore.

"I'll come with you," he said, breathless. "You'll need someone can steer a boat."

Jamie didn't hesitate for more than a fraction of a second. He nodded, jerking his head toward the shore.

"Aye, run. I'll bring them along as fast as I can."

Mr. Marsden vanished into the dark.

"The rest of your men?" I said, coughing from the smoke.

He shrugged, a broad-shouldered silhouette against the black shimmer of the water.

"Gone."

Hysterical screams came from the direction of the Old French Lines. These spread like wildfire through the woods and down the lakeshore, people shouting that the British were coming. Panic beating its wings. It was so strong a thing, that panic, that I felt a scream rise in my own throat. I throttled it and felt irrational anger in its place, displaced from myself to the fools behind me who were shrieking and would have scattered, had they been able to. But we were close upon the shore now, and people were pressing toward the boats in such numbers that they were capsizing some of the craft as they piled in, higgledy-piggledy.

I didn't *think* the British were at hand—but I didn't know. I knew that there had been more than one battle at Fort Ticonderoga . . . but when had they occurred? Was one of them going to be tonight? I didn't know, and the sense of urgency propelled me to the shore, helping to support Mr. Wellman, who had contracted the mumps from his son, poor man, and was doing very badly in consequence.

Mr. Marsden, bless him, had commandeered a large canoe, which he had paddled a little way out from shore to prevent its being overrun. When he saw Jamie approaching, he came in, and we succeeded in getting a total of eighteen people—these including the Wellmans and Mrs. Raven, pale and staring as Ophelia—into it.

Jamie glanced quickly back at the fort. The main gates hung wide, and firelight shone out of them. Then he glanced up at the battery where he and I had stood a little while before.

"There are four men by the cannon trained on the bridge," he said, his eyes still fixed on the red-bellied billows of smoke rising from the interior of the fort. "Volunteers. They'll stay behind. The British—or some of them—will certainly come across the bridge. They can destroy almost everyone on the boom, and then flee—if they can."

He turned away then, and his shoulders bunched and flexed as he dug the paddle hard.

53

MOUNT INDEPENDENCE

Mid-afternoon, July 6

BRIGADIER Fraser's men advanced upon the picket fort at the top of the mount, the one the Americans ironically called "Independence." William led one of the forward parties and had his men fix their bayonets as they drew close. There was a deep silence, broken only by the snap of branches and shuffle of boots in the thick leaf mold, the stray clack of a cartridge box against musket butt. Was it a waiting silence, though?

The Americans could not fail to know they were coming. Did the rebels lie in ambush, ready to fire upon them from the crude but very solid fortification he could see through the trees?

He motioned to his men to stop some two hundred yards short of the summit, hoping to pick up some indication of the defenders, if defenders there were. His own company halted obediently, but there were men behind, and they began to push into and through his own company without regard, eager to storm the fort.

"Halt!" he shouted, aware as he did so that the sound of his voice presented almost as good a target to an American rifleman as would the sight of his red coat. Some of the men did halt but were at once dislodged by more behind them, and within seconds the whole of the hillside was a mass of red. They could not stop longer; they would be trampled. And if the defenders had meant to fire, they could not ask for a better opportunity—and yet the fort stayed silent.

"On!" William roared, throwing up his arm, and the men burst from the trees in a splendid charge, bayonets held ready.

The gates hung ajar, and the men charged straight in, heedless of danger—but danger there was none. William came in with his men, to find the place deserted. Not only abandoned, but evidently abandoned in an amazing hurry.

The defenders' personal belongings were strewn everywhere, as though dropped in flight: not only heavy things like cooking utensils, but clothes, shoes, books, blankets . . . even money, seemingly cast aside or dropped in panic. Much more to the point, so far as William was concerned, was the fact that the defenders had made no effort to blow up ammunition or powder that could not be carried away; there must be two hundredweight, stacked in kegs! Provisions, too, had been left behind, a welcome sight.

"Why did they not set fire to the place?" Lieutenant Hammond asked him, looking goggle-eyed round at the barracks, still fully furnished with beds, bedding, chamber pots—ready for the conquerors to move straight in to.

"God knows," William replied briefly, then lunged forward as he saw a private soldier come out of one of the rooms, festooned in a lacy shawl and with his arms full of shoes. "You, there! We'll have no looting, none! Do you hear me, sir?"

The private did and, dropping his armful of shoes, made off precipitately, lacy fringes flapping. A good many others were at it, too, though, and it was clear to William that he and Hammond would be unable to stop it. He shouted above the increasing din for an ensign and, seizing the man's dispatch box, scribbled a hasty note.

"Take that to General Fraser," he said thrusting it back at the ensign. "Fast as ever you can go!"

Dawn
July 7, 1777

"I WILL NOT HAVE these horrid irregularities!" General Fraser's face was deeply creased, as much with rage as with fatigue. The small traveling clock in the general's tent showed just before five o'clock in the morning, and William had the oddly dreamy feeling that his head was floating somewhere over his left shoulder. "Looting, theft, rampant undiscipline—I will not have it, I say. Am I understood? All of you?"

The small, tired group of officers gave assent in a chorus of grunts. They had been up all night, chivvying their troops into some form of rough order, keeping back the rank and file from the worst excesses of looting, hurriedly surveying the abandoned outposts at the Old French Lines, and tallying the unexpected bounty of provisions and ammunition left for them by the fort's defenders—four of whom had been found when the fort was stormed, dead drunk by the side of a primed cannon, trained on the bridge below.

"Those men, the ones who were taken. Has anyone been able to talk with them as yet?"

"No, sir," Captain Hayes said, stifling a yawn. "Still dead to the world—very nearly dead for good, the surgeon said, though he thinks they'll survive."

"Shit themselves with fear," Hammond said softly to William. "Waiting all that time for us to come."

"More likely boredom," William murmured back without moving his mouth. Even so, he caught the brigadier's bloodshot eye and straightened up unconsciously.

"Well, it's not as though we need them to tell us much." General Fraser waved a hand to dispel a cloud of smoke that had drifted in, and coughed. William inhaled gently. There was a succulent scent embodied in that smoke, and his stomach coiled in anticipation. Ham? Sausage?

"I've sent word back to General Burgoyne that Ticonderoga is ours—again," the brigadier added, breaking into a grin at the hoarse cheer from the officers. "And to Colonel St. Leger. We shall leave a small garrison to take stock and tidy things up here, but the rest of us . . . Well, there are rebels to be caught, gentlemen. I cannot offer you much respite, but certainly there is time for a hearty breakfast. *Bon appétit!*"

54

RETURN OF THE NATIVE

Night, July 7

IAN MURRAY passed into the fort without difficulty. There were rangers and Indians aplenty, mostly lounging against the buildings, many of them drunk, others poking through the deserted barracks, occasionally chased away by harassed-looking soldiers set to guard the fort's unexpected bounty.

There was no sign of slaughter, and he breathed easier. That had been his first fear, but while there was mess—and to spare—there was no blood and no smell of powder smoke. No shot had been fired here in the last day or so.

He had a thought and went toward the hospital barracks, largely ignored, as it held nothing anyone would want. The smells of urine, shit, and old blood had decreased; most of the patients must have gone with the retreating troops. There were a few people there, one in a green coat who he thought must be a surgeon, some plainly orderlies. As he watched, a pair of stretcher-bearers came out through the door, boots scraping as they negotiated the shallow stone steps. He leaned back into the concealment of the doorway, for following the stretcher was the tall form of Guinea Dick, his face split in a cannibal's grin.

Ian smiled himself, seeing it; Captain Stebbings still lived, then—and Guinea Dick was a free man. And here, Jesus, Mary, and Bride be thanked, came Mr. Ormiston behind him, stumping slowly on a pair of crutches, tenderly supported on either side by a pair of orderlies, the puny wee creatures dwarfed by the seaman's bulk. He could tell Auntie Claire, then—she'd be pleased to hear they were all right.

If he found Auntie Claire again—but he wasn't much worried, really. Uncle Jamie would see her safe, come hell, wildfire, or the entire British army. When or where he'd see them again was another matter, but he and Rollo moved much faster than any army could; he'd catch them up soon enough.

He waited, curious to see whether there was anyone else left in the hospital, but either there was not or they were to be left there for the nonce. Had the Hunters gone with St. Clair's troops? In a way, he hoped they had—even knowing that they would likely fare better with the British than on the run down the Hudson Valley with the refugees from Ticonderoga. As Quakers, he thought they would do well enough; the British probably woudn't molest them. But he thought he would like to see Rachel Hunter again sometime, and his chance of that was much better if she and her brother had gone with the rebels.

A little more poking about convinced him of two things: that the Hunters had indeed gone, and that the leaving of Ticonderoga had been accomplished in the midst of panic and disorder. Someone had set fire to the bridge below, but it had only partially burned, perhaps put out by a rainstorm. There was a great deal of debris on the lakeshore, suggesting a massive embarkation—automatically he glanced toward the lake, where he could plainly see two large ships, both flying the Union flag. From his current perch on the battery, he could see redcoats swarming over both Mount Defiance and Mount Independence, and knew a small, surprising flare of resentment against them.

"Well, you'll not keep it long," he said under his breath. He spoke in Gaelic, and a good thing, too, for a passing soldier glanced casually at him, as though feeling the stress of his regard. He looked away himself, turning his back on the fort.

There was nothing to do here, no one to wait for. He'd eat and pick up some provisions, then go fetch Rollo and be off. He could—

A shattering *whoom!* close at hand made him jerk round. To his right, one of the cannon was trained downward toward the bridge, and just behind it, openmouthed with shock, was a Huron man, swaying with drink.

There was a lot of shouting from below; the troops thought they were being fired on from the fort, though the shot had gone high, splashing harmlessly into the lake.

The Huron giggled.

"What did you do?" Ian asked, in an Algonkian tongue he thought the man would most likely know. Whether he understood or not, the man simply laughed harder, tears beginning to run down his face. He gestured to a smoking tub nearby; good Christ, the defenders had gone so fast, they had left a tub of slow match burning.

"Boom," said the Huron, and gestured at a length of slow match, pulled from the tub and left draped on the stones like a glowing snake. "Boom," he said again, nodding at the cannon, and laughed until he had to sit down.

Soldiers were running up to the battery, and the shouting from outside was equaled by that inside the fort. It was probably a good time to go.

55

RETREAT

. . . we are pursuing the rebels, a great number of whom have taken to the lake in boats. The two sloops on the lake are following, but I am sending four companies down to the portage point, where I think the chance of capture is good.

—Brigadier General Simon Fraser,
to Major General J. Burgoyne

July 8, 1777

WILLIAM WISHED he hadn't accepted the brigadier's invitation to breakfast. If he had contented himself with the lean rations that were a lieutenant's lot, he would have been hungry, but happy. As it was, he was on the spot—blissfully filled to the eyes with fried sausage, buttered toast, and grits with honey, for which the brigadier had developed a fondness—when the message had come from General Burgoyne. He didn't even know what it had said; the brigadier had read it while sipping coffee, frowning slightly, then sighed and called for ink and quill.

"Want a ride this morning, William?" he'd asked, smiling across the table.

Which is how he'd come to be at General Burgoyne's field headquarters when the Indians had come in. Wyandot, one of the soldiers said; he wasn't familiar with them, though he had heard that they had a chief called Leatherlips, and he did wonder how that had come about. Perhaps the man was an indefatigable talker?

There were five of them, lean, wolfish-looking rascals. He couldn't have said what they wore or how they were armed; all his attention was focused on the pole that one of them carried, this decorated with scalps. Fresh scalps. White scalps. A musky smell of blood hung in the air, unpleasantly ripe, and flies moved with the Indians, buzzing loudly. The remains of William's lavish breakfast coagulated in a hard ball just under his ribs.

The Indians were looking for the paymaster; one of them was asking, in a surprisingly melodious English, where the paymaster was. So it was true, then. General Burgoyne had unleashed his Indians, sent them coursing through the woods like hunting dogs to fall upon the rebels and spread terror among them.

He did *not* want to look at the scalps but couldn't help it; his eyes followed them as the pole bobbed through a growing crowd of curious soldiers—some mildly horrified, some cheering. Jesus. Was that a *woman's* scalp? It had to be; a flowing mass of honey-colored hair, longer than any man would wear his hair, and shining as though its owner brushed it a hundred strokes every night, like his cousin Dottie said she did. It was not unlike Dottie's hair, though a little darker—

He turned away abruptly, hoping that he wouldn't be sick, but turned just as abruptly back when he heard the cry. He'd never heard a sound like that before—a shriek of such horror, such grief, that his heart froze in his chest.

"Jane! Jane!" A Welsh lieutenant he knew slightly, called David Jones, was forcing his way through the crowd, beating at the men with fists and elbows, lunging toward the surprised Indians, his face contorted with emotion.

"Oh, God," breathed a soldier near him. "His fiancée's called Jane. He can't mean—"

Jones threw himself at the pole, snatching at the fall of honey-colored hair, shrieking "JANE!" at the top of his lungs. The Indians, looking disconcerted, jerked the pole away. Jones flung himself on one of them, knocking the surprised Indian to the ground and hammering him with the strength of insanity.

Men were pushing forward, grabbing at Jones—but not doing so with any great heart. Appalled looks were being shot at the Indians, who clustered together, eyes narrowed and hands at their tomahawks. The whole sense of the gathering had changed in an instant from approval to outrage, and the Indians plainly sensed it.

An officer William didn't know strode forward, daring the Indians with a hard eye, and tore the blond scalp from the pole. Then stood holding it, disconcerted, the mass of hair seeming alive in his hands, the long strands stirring, waving up around his fingers.

They had finally pulled Jones off the Indian; his friends were patting his shoulders, trying to urge him away, but he stood stock-still, tears rolling down his face and dripping from his chin. "Jane," he mouthed silently. He held out his hands, cupped and begging, and the officer who held the scalp placed it gently into them.

56

WHILE STILL ALIVE

LIEUTENANT Stactoe was standing by one corpse, arrested. Very slowly, he squatted down, his eyes fixed on something, and as though by reflex covered his mouth with one hand.

I really didn't want to look.

He'd heard my footsteps, though, and took his hand away from his mouth. I could see the sweat trickling down his neck, the band of his shirt pasted to his skin, dark with it.

"Do you suppose that was done while he was still alive?" he asked, in an ordinary tone of voice.

Reluctantly, I looked over his shoulder.

"Yes," I said, my voice as unemotional as his. "It was."

"Oh," he said. He stood, contemplated the corpse for a moment, then walked away a few steps and threw up.

"Never mind," I said gently, and took him by the sleeve. "He's dead now. Come and help."

Many of the boats had gone astray, been captured before they reached the end of the lake; many more had been taken by British troops waiting at the portage point. Our canoe and several more had escaped, and we had made our way through the woods for a day and a night and most of another day before meeting with the main body of troops fleeing overland from the fort. I was beginning to think that those who were captured were the lucky ones.

I didn't know how long it had been since the small group we had just discovered was attacked by Indians. The bodies were not fresh.

GUARDS WERE POSTED at night. Those not on watch slept as though poleaxed, exhausted by a day of flight—if anything so cumbrous and labored could be described by such a graceful word. I woke just past dawn from dreams of Snow White trees, gape-mouthed and grasping, to find Jamie crouched beside me, a hand on my arm.

"Ye'd best come, *a nighean,*" he said softly.

Mrs. Raven had cut her throat with a penknife.

There wasn't time to dig a grave. I straightened her limbs and closed her eyes, and we piled rocks and branches over her before staggering back to the rut that passed for a road through the wilderness.

AS DARKNESS CAME up through the trees, we began to hear them. High ululating shrieks. Hunting wolves.

"March on, march on! Indians!" one of the militiamen shouted.

As if summoned by the shout, a bloodcurdling shriek wavered through the darkness nearby, and the stumbling retreat turned at once to headlong panic, men dropping their bundles and pushing one another out of the way in their haste to flee.

There were shrieks from the refugees, too, though these were quickly stifled.

"Off the road," Jamie said, low and fierce, and began pushing the slow and bewildered into the woods. "They may not know where we are. Yet."

And then again, they might.

"D'ye have your death song ready, Uncle?" Ian whispered. He had caught us up the day before, and now he and Jamie were pressed close on either side of me, where we had taken cover behind a huge fallen trunk.

"Oh, I'll sing them a death song, if it comes to that," Jamie muttered, half under his breath, and took out one of the pistols from his belt.

"You can't sing," I said. I hadn't meant to be funny—I was so frightened that I said it by reflex, the first thing that came into my mind—and he didn't laugh.

"That's true," he said. "Well, then."

He primed the pistol, closed the pan and thrust it into his belt.

"Dinna be afraid, *a nighean,*" Jamie whispered, and I saw his throat work as he swallowed. "I'll not let them take ye. Not alive." He touched the pistol at his belt.

I stared at him, then at the pistol. I hadn't thought it possible to be more afraid.

I felt suddenly as though my spinal cord had snapped; my limbs wouldn't move, and my bowels very literally turned to water. I understood in that moment exactly what had led Mrs. Raven to slash her own throat.

Ian whispered something to Jamie and slid away, silent as a shadow.

It occurred to me, belatedly, that by taking time to shoot me if we should be overrun, Jamie was very likely to fall alive into the hands of the Indians himself. And I was sufficiently terrorized that I couldn't tell him not to do it.

I took hold of my courage with both hands and swallowed hard.

"Go!" I said. "They won't—they probably won't harm women." My outer skirt hung in tatters, as did my jacket, and the whole ensemble was covered in mud, leaves, and the small bloody splotches of slow-moving mosquitoes—but I was still identifiably female.

"The devil I will," he said briefly.

"Uncle." Ian's voice came softly out of the darkness. "It's not Indians."

"What?" I made no sense of this, but Jamie straightened abruptly.

"It's a redcoat, running alongside us, shrieking like an Indian. Driving us."

Jamie swore under his breath. It was almost completely dark by now; I could see only a few vague shapes, presumably those of the people with us. I heard a whimper, almost underfoot, but when I looked, could see no one.

The shrieks came again, now from the other side. If the man was driving us—did he know we were there? If so, where did he mean to drive us? I could feel Jamie's indecision—which way? A second, perhaps two, and he took me by the arm, pulling me deeper into the wood.

We ran slap into a large group of refugees within minutes;

they had stopped dead, too terrified to move in any direction. They huddled together, the women clutching their children, hands clasped tight over the little ones' mouths, breathing "Hush!" like the wind.

"Leave them," Jamie said in my ear, and tightened his grip on my arm. I turned to go with him, and suddenly a hand seized my other arm. I screamed, and everyone near erupted in screams by sheer reflex. Suddenly the wood around us was alive with moving forms and shouts.

The soldier—it was a British soldier; from so close I could see the buttons on his uniform and felt the thump of his cartridge box as it swung, striking me in the hip—leaned down to peer at me and grinned, his breath stale and scented with decay.

"Stand still, love," he said. "You're going nowhere now."

My heart was pounding so hard in my ears that it was a full minute before I realized that the grip on my other arm was gone. Jamie had vanished.

WE WERE MARCHED back up the road in a tight group, moving slowly through the night. They let us drink at a stream at daylight but kept us moving until the early afternoon, by which time even the most able-bodied were ready to drop.

We were herded, none too gently, into a field. Farmer's wife that I was, I winced to see the stalks—only weeks away from harvest—being trampled underfoot, the fragile gold of the wheat cut and mangled into black mud. There was a cabin among the trees at the far end of the field; I saw a girl run out onto the porch, clap a hand to her mouth in horror, and disappear back inside.

Three British officers came across the field, heading for the cabin, ignoring the seething mass of invalids, women, and children, all of whom were milling to and fro, with no idea what to do next. I wiped the sweat out of my eyes with the end of my kerchief, tucked it back into my bodice, and looked round for anyone who might be nominally in charge.

None of our own officers or able-bodied men seemed to have been captured; there had been only a couple of surgeons superintending the removal of the invalids, and I hadn't seen either one in two days. Neither one was here. *All right, then,* I thought grimly, and walked up to the nearest British soldier, who was surveying the chaos through narrowed eyes, musket in hand.

"We need water," I said to him without preamble. "There's a stream just beyond those trees. May I take three or four women to fetch back water for the sick and wounded?"

He was sweating, too; the faded red wool of his coat was black under the arms, and melted rice powder from his hair was rimed in the creases of his forehead. He grimaced, indicating that he didn't want to deal with me, but I simply stared at him, as close as I could get. He glanced around, in hopes of finding someone to send me to, but the three officers had disappeared into the cabin. He raised one shoulder in surrender, looking away.

"Aye, go on, then," he muttered, and turned his back, stalwartly guarding the road, along which new prisoners were still being herded.

A quick traverse of the field turned up three buckets and a like number of sensible women, worried but not hysterical. I sent them to the stream and began to quarter the field, making a quick assessment of the situation—as much in order to keep my own worry at bay as because there was no one else to do it.

Would we be kept here long? I wondered. If we would be held here for more than a few hours, sanitation trenches must be dug—but the soldiers would have the same need. I'd leave that for the army to deal with, then. Water was coming; we'd need to run relays to the stream nonstop for a bit. Shelter . . . I glanced at the sky; it was hazy but clear. Those who could move on their own were already helping to drag the desperately sick or wounded into the shade of the trees along one side of the field.

Where was Jamie? Had he got away safe?

Above the calls and anxious conversations, I heard now and then the whisper of distant thunder. The air clung to my skin, thick with humidity. They would have to move us somewhere—to the nearest settlement, wherever that might be—but it might take several days. I had no idea where we were.

Had he been captured, too? If so, would they take him to the same place they'd take the invalids?

Chances were that they would release the women, not wishing to feed them. The women would stay with their sick men, though—or most of them would—sharing whatever food was available.

I was walking slowly across the field, conducting a mental triage—the man on the stretcher there was going to die, probably before nightfall; I could hear the rales of his breathing from six feet away—when I caught sight of movement on the cabin's porch.

The family—two adult women, two teenagers, three children, and a baby in arms—was leaving, clutching baskets, blankets, and such bits of their household as could be carried. One of the officers was with them; he took them across the field and spoke with one of the guards, evidently instructing him to let the women pass. One of the women paused at the edge of the road and looked back—just once. The others went straight on, without a backward glance. Where were their men?

Where are mine?

"Hallo," I said, smiling at a man with a recently amputated leg. I didn't know his name but recognized his face; he was one of the few black men at Ticonderoga, a carpenter. I knelt down beside him. His bandages were awry, and the stump was leaking badly. "Bar the leg, how do you feel?" His skin was pale gray and clammy as a wet sheet, but he gave me a feeble grin in return.

"My left hand doesn't hurt much right now." He lifted it in illustration, but dropped it like a chunk of lead, lacking strength to hold it up.

"That's good," I said, sliding my fingers under his thigh to lift it. "Let me fix this for you—we'll have you some water in a minute."

"That'd be nice," he murmured, and shut his eyes against the sun.

The flapping end of the loose bandage was twisted up like a snake's tongue, stiff with dried blood, and the dressing awry. The dressing itself, a poultice of flaxseed and turpentine, was soggy, pink with leaking blood and lymph. No choice but to reuse it, though.

"What's your name?"

"Walter." His eyes were still closed, his breath coming in shallow gasps. So was mine; the thick, hot air was like a pressure bandage round my chest. "Walter . . . Woodcock."

"Pleased to know you, Walter. My name's Claire Fraser."

"Know you," he murmured. "You're Big Red's lady. He make it out of the fort?"

"Yes," I said, and blotted my face against my shoulder to keep the sweat out of my eyes. "He's all right."

Dear God, let him be all right.

The English officer was coming back toward the cabin, passing within a few feet of me. I glanced up, and my hands froze.

He was tall, slender but broad-shouldered, and I would have known that long stride, that unself-conscious grace, and that arrogant tilt of the head anywhere. He paused, frowning, and turned his head to survey the littered field. His nose was straight as a knife blade, just that tiny bit too long. I closed my eyes for an instant, dizzy, sure I was hallucinating—but opened them again at once, knowing that I wasn't.

"William Ransom?" I blurted, and his head jerked toward me, surprised. Blue eyes, dark blue, Fraser cat-eyes, narrowed to a slant against the sun.

"I, er, beg your pardon." *God, what did you speak to him for?* But I couldn't have helped it. My fingers were pressed against Walter's leg, holding the bandage; I could feel his femoral pulse against my fingertips, bumping as erratically as my own.

"Do I know you, ma'am?" William asked, with the shadow of a bow.

"Well, yes, you do," I said, rather apologetically. "You stayed for a little time with my family, some years ago. A place called Fraser's Ridge."

His face changed at once at the name, and his gaze sharpened, focusing on me with interest.

"Why, yes," he said slowly. "I recall. You are Mrs. Fraser, are you not?" I could see his thoughts working, and was fascinated; he hadn't got Jamie's way of hiding what he thought—or if he did, wasn't using it. I could see him wondering—nice, well-mannered boy that he was—what the proper social response to this awkward situation might be, and—a quick glance over his shoulder at the cabin—how the demands of his duty might conflict with it.

His shoulders stiffened with decision, but before he could say anything, I leapt in.

"Do you think it might be possible to find some buckets for water? And bandages?" Most of the women had already torn strips from their petticoats to serve this function; much longer, and we'd all be half naked.

"Yes," he said slowly, and glanced down at Walter, then toward the road. "Buckets, yes. There's a surgeon with the division behind us; when I have a moment, I'll send someone back with a request for bandages."

"And food?" I asked hopefully. I hadn't eaten more than a handful of half-ripe berries in nearly two days. I wasn't suffering hunger pangs—my stomach was in knots—but I was having bouts of light-headedness, spots passing before my eyes. No one else was in much better case; we were going to lose a number of the invalids to the heat and simple weakness, if we weren't given food and shelter soon.

He hesitated, and I saw his eyes flit over the field, obviously estimating numbers.

"That may be . . . our supply train is—" His lips firmed, and he shook his head. "I'll see what can be done. Your servant, ma'am." He bowed politely and turned away, striding toward the road. I watched him go, fascinated, the soggy dressing limp in my hand.

He was dark-haired, though the sun struck a gleam of red from the crown of his head; he wore no powder. His voice had deepened—well, of course it had; he'd been no more than twelve the last time I met him—and the sheer oddness of hearing Jamie speaking in a cultured English accent made me want to laugh, despite our precarious situation and my worry for Jamie and Ian. I shook my head and returned to the task at hand.

A British private arrived an hour after my conversation with Lieutenant Ransom, bearing four buckets, which he dropped unceremoniously at my side without remark before heading back to the road. Two hours later, a sweating orderly came trundling through the trampled wheat with two large haversacks filled with bandages. Interestingly enough, he headed directly for me, which made me wonder just how William had described me.

"Thank you." I took the sacks of bandages with gratitude. "Do you—do you think we might get some food soon?"

The orderly was looking over the field, grimacing. Of course—the invalids were likely about to become his responsibility. He turned back to me, though, civil but obviously very tired.

"I doubt it, ma'am. The supply train is two days behind us, and the troops are living off what they're carrying or what they find as they go." He nodded toward the road; on the other side, I could see a number of English soldiers making camp. "I'm sorry," he added formally, and turned to go.

"Oh." He stopped, and taking the strap of his canteen off, handed it to me. It was heavy and gurgled enticingly. "Lieutenant Ellesmere said I was to give you this." He smiled briefly, the lines of tiredness easing. "He said you looked hot."

"Lieutenant Ellesmere." That must be William's title, I realized. "Thank you. And please thank the lieutenant, if you see him." He was clearly on the point of departure, but I couldn't help asking, "How did you know who I was?"

His smile deepened as he glanced at my head.

"The lieutenant said you'd be the curly-wig giving orders like a sergeant-major." He looked round the field once more, shaking his head. "Good luck, ma'am."

THREE MEN DIED before sunset. Walter Woodcock was still alive, but barely. We'd moved as many men as we could into the shade of the trees along the edge of the field, and I'd divided the seriously wounded into small groups, each allocated a bucket and two or three women or walking invalids to tend them. I'd also designated a latrine area and done my best to separate the infectious cases from those who were fevered from wounds or malaria. There were three suffering from what I hoped was only "summer ague," and one who I feared might have diphtheria. I sat beside him—a young wheelwright from New Jersey—checking the membranes of his throat at intervals, giving him as much water as he would take. Not from my canteen, though.

William Ransom, bless his soul, had filled his canteen with brandy.

I uncorked it and took a sparing sip. I'd poured out small cupfuls for each small group, adding each cupful to a bucket of water—but had kept a bit for my own use. It wasn't selfishness; for better or worse, I was in charge of the captives for the moment. I had to stay on my feet.

Or my bottom, as the case might be, I thought, leaning back against the bole of an oak tree. My feet ached all the way to my knees, my back and ribs twinged with each breath, and I had to close my eyes now and then to control the dizziness. But I was sitting still, for what seemed like the first time in several days.

The soldiers across the road were cooking their meager rations; my mouth watered and my stomach contracted painfully at the scent of roasting meat and flour. Mrs. Wellman's little boy was whining with hunger, his head laid on his mother's lap. She was stroking his hair mechanically, her eyes fixed on her husband's body, which lay a little way away. We had no sheet or blanket with which to shroud him, but someone had given her a handkerchief to cover his face. The flies were very bad.

The air had cooled, thank God, but was still heavy with the threat of rain; thunder was a constant faint rumble over the horizon and it would probably pour sometime during the night. I plucked the sweat-soaked fabric away from my chest; I doubted it would have time to dry before we were drenched with rain. I eyed the encampment across the road, with its lines of small tents and brush shelters, with envy. There was a slightly larger officers' tent as well, though several officers had taken up temporary quarters in the commandeered cabin.

I ought to go there, I thought. See the most senior officer present, and beg for food for the children, at least. When the shadow of that tall pine sapling touched my foot, I decided. Then I'd go. In the meantime, I uncorked the canteen and took another small swallow.

Movement caught my eye, and I looked up. The unmistakable figure of Lieutenant Ransom stalked out of the tents and came across the road. It lifted my heart a little to see him, though the sight of him renewed my worry for Jamie—and reminded me, with a small sharp pang, of Brianna. At least *she* was safe, I thought. Roger and Jemmy and Amanda, too. I repeated their names to myself as a small refrain of comfort, counting them like coins. Four of them safe.

William had undone his stock, and his hair was untidy, his coat stained with sweat and dirt. Evidently the pursuit was wearing on the British army, too.

He glanced round the field, spotted me, and turned purposefully in my direction. I got my feet under me, struggling upward against the press of gravity like a hippopotamus rising from a swamp.

I'd barely got to my feet and raised a hand to smooth my hair when someone else's hand poked me in the back. I started violently but luckily didn't scream.

"It's me, Auntie," Young Ian whispered from the shadows behind me. "Come with—oh, Jesus."

William had come within ten paces of me and, raising his head, had spied Ian. He leapt forward and grabbed me by the arm, yanking me away from the trees. I yelped, as Ian had an equally firm grip on the other arm and was yanking lustily in that direction.

"Let her go!" William barked.

"The devil I will," Ian replied hotly. "*You* let go!"

Mrs. Wellman's little son was on his feet, staring round-eyed and openmouthed into the forest.

"Mama, Mama! *Indians!*"

Shrieks rose from the women near us, and everyone began a mad scramble away from the forest, leaving the wounded to their own devices.

"Ah, bugger!" Ian said, letting go in disgust. William didn't, jerking me with such force that I crashed into him, whereupon he promptly wrapped his arms about my waist and dragged me a little way into the field.

"Will ye bloody leave go of my auntie?" Ian said crossly, emerging from the trees.

"You!" said William. "What are you—well, never mind that. Your aunt, you say?" He looked down at me. "Are you? His aunt? Wait—no, of course you are."

"I am," I agreed, pushing at his arms. "Let go."

His grasp loosened a little, but he didn't release me.

"How many others are in there?" he demanded, lifting his chin toward the forest.

"If there were any others, ye'd be deid," Ian informed him. "It's just me. Give her to me."

"I can't do that." But there was an uncertain note in William's voice, and I felt his head turn, glancing toward the cabin. So far, no one had come out, but I could see some of the sentries near the road shifting to and fro, wondering what the matter was. The other captives had stopped running, but were quivering with incipient panic, eyes frantically searching the shadows among the trees.

I rapped William sharply on the wrist with my knuckles and he let go and took a step back. My head was spinning again—not least from the very peculiar sensation of being embraced by a total stranger whose body felt so familiar to me. He was thinner than Jamie, but—

"D'ye owe me a life or not?" Not waiting for an answer, Ian jerked a thumb at me. "Aye, then—it's hers."

"Hardly a question of her life," William said, rather crossly, with an awkward nod in my direction, acknowledging that I might have a possible interest in this discussion. "Surely you don't suppose we kill women?"

"No," Ian said evenly. "I dinna suppose it at all. I ken verra well that ye do."

"We do?" William echoed. He looked surprised, but a sudden flush burned in his cheeks.

"You do," I assured him. "General Howe hanged three women at the head of his army in New Jersey, as an example."

He seemed completely nonplused by this.

"Well . . . but—they were spies!"

"You think I don't look like a spy?" I inquired. "I'm much obliged for your good opinion, but I don't know that General Burgoyne would share it." There were, of course, a good many other women who'd died at the hands of the British army, if less officially, but this didn't seem the moment to make an account of them.

"General Burgoyne is a gentleman," William said stiffly. "So am I."

"Good," Ian said briefly. "Turn your back for thirty seconds, and we'll trouble ye nay more."

I don't know whether he would have done it or not, but

just then, Indian cries tore the air, coming from the far side of the road. Further frantic screams came from the captives, and I bit my own tongue in order not to scream, too. A tongue of fire shot up into the lavender sky from the top of the officers' tent. As I gaped, two more flaming comets shot across the sky. It looked like the descent of the Holy Ghost, but before I could mention this interesting observation, Ian had seized my arm and jerked me nearly off my feet.

I managed to snatch up the canteen as we passed, on a dead run for the forest. Ian grabbed it from me, almost dragging me in his haste. Gunfire and screams were breaking out behind us, and the skin all down my back contracted in fear.

"This way." I followed him without heed for anything underfoot, stumbling and twisting my ankles in the dusk as we threw ourselves headlong into the brush, expecting every moment to be shot in the back.

Such is the brain's capacity for self-amusement, I was able to imagine in vivid detail my wounding, capture, descent into infection and sepsis, and eventual lingering death—but not before being obliged to witness the capture and execution of both Jamie—I had recognized the source of the Indian screams and flaming arrows without difficulty—and Ian.

It was only as we slowed—perforce; I had such a stitch in my side that I could barely breathe—that I thought of other things. The sick and wounded I had left behind. The young wheelwright with the bright red throat. Walter Woodcock, teetering over the abyss.

You couldn't give any of them more than a hand to hold, I told myself fiercely, limping as I stumbled after Ian. It was true; I knew it was true. But I also knew that now and then a hand in the dark gave a sick man something to cling to, against the rushing wind of the dark angel. Sometimes it was enough; sometimes it wasn't. But the ache of those left behind dragged at me like a sea anchor, and I wasn't sure whether the wetness streaming down my cheeks was sweat or tears.

It was full dark now, and the boiling clouds covered the moon, allowing only fitful glimpses of its brilliant light. Ian had slowed still more, to let me keep up with him, and took my arm now and then to help me over rocks or across creeks.

"How . . . far?" I gasped, stopping once more for breath.

"Not much," Jamie's voice replied softly beside me. "Are ye all right, Sassenach?"

My heart gave a tremendous bump, then settled back in my chest as he groped for my hand, then gathered me briefly against himself. I had a moment of relief so profound that I thought my bones had dissolved.

"Yes," I said, into his chest, and with great effort lifted my head. "You?"

"Well enough now," he said, passing a hand over my head, touching my cheek. "Can ye walk just a bit further?"

I straightened, swaying a little. It had begun to rain; heavy drops plopped into my hair, cold and startling on my scalp.

"Ian—have you got that canteen?"

There was a soft *pop!* and Ian set the canteen in my hand. Very carefully, I tilted it into my mouth.

"Is that brandy?" Jamie said, sounding astonished.

"Mmm-hmm." I swallowed, as slowly as I could, and handed the canteen to him. There were a couple of swallows left.

"Where did ye get it?"

"Your son gave it to me," I said. "Where are we going?"

There was a long pause from the darkness, and then the sound of brandy being drunk.

"South," he said at last, and taking my hand, led me on into the wood, the rain whispering on the leaves all round us.

SOAKED AND SHIVERING, we caught up to a militia unit just before dawn, and were nearly shot in mistake by a nervous sentry. By that point, I didn't really care. Being dead was immensely preferable to the prospect of taking one more step.

Our *bona fides* being established, Jamie disappeared briefly and came back with a blanket and three fresh corn dodgers. I inhaled my share of this ambrosia in four seconds flat, wrapped myself in the blanket, and lay down under a tree where the ground was damp but not soggy and so thick with dead leaves that it gave spongily beneath me.

"I'll be back in a bit, Sassenach," Jamie whispered, squatting beside me. "Dinna go anywhere, aye?"

"Don't worry—I'll be here. If I move a muscle before Christmas, it will be too soon." A faint warmth was already returning to my shivering muscles, and sleep was pulling me down with the inexorability of quicksand.

He gave the breath of a laugh, and reached out a hand, tucking the blanket in around my shoulders. The dawn light showed the deep lines that the night had carved in his face, the smudges of dirt and exhaustion that stained the strong bones. The wide mouth, compressed for so long, had relaxed now in the relief of momentary safety, looking oddly young and vulnerable.

"He looks like you," I whispered. His hand stopped moving, still on my shoulder, and he looked down, long lashes hiding his eyes.

"I know," he said, very softly. "Tell me of him. Later, when there's time."

I heard his footsteps, a rustle in damp leaves, and fell asleep, a prayer for Walter Woodcock half finished in my mind.

57

THE DESERTER GAME

THE WHORE grunted through the rag clenched in her teeth.

"Nearly done," I murmured, and ran the backs of my knuckles gently down her calf by way of reassurance before returning to the debridement of the nasty wound in her foot. An officer's horse had stepped on her as they—and a number of other people and animals—had jostled to drink at a creek during the retreat. I could clearly see the print of the horseshoe nails, black in the red puffy flesh of her instep. The edge of the shoe itself, worn paper-thin and sharp as a knife, had made a deep, curved gash that ran across the metatarsals, vanishing between the fourth and fifth toes.

I'd been afraid I was going to have to remove the little toe—it seemed to be dangling by no more than a shred of skin—but when I examined the foot more closely, I discovered that all the bones were miraculously intact—as nearly as I could tell, without access to an X-ray machine.

The horse's hoof had driven her foot into the mud of the stream bank, she'd told me; that had likely saved the bones from being crushed. Now if I could manage to stem the infection and didn't have to amputate the foot, she might just be able to walk again normally. Maybe.

With a degree of cautious hope, I put down the scalpel and reached for a bottle of what I hoped was a penicillin-containing liquid brought with me from the fort. I'd salvaged the barrel optic of Dr. Rawlings's microscope from the house fire and found it very useful indeed for starting fires—but without the eyepiece, staging mechanism, or mirror, it was of limited use in determining the genus of microorganisms. I could be sure that what I'd grown and filtered was bread mold, all right—but beyond that . . .

Suppressing a sigh, I poured the liquid generously over the raw flesh I'd just exposed. It wasn't alcoholic, but the flesh *was* raw. The whore made a high-pitched noise through the cloth and breathed through her nose like a steam engine, but by the time I'd made a compress of lavender and comfrey and bound up the foot, she was calm, if flushed.

"There," I said, with a small pat to her leg. "I think that will do nicely now." I started to say automatically, "Keep it clean," but bit my tongue. She hadn't any shoes or stockings and was either walking daily through a wilderness of rocks, dirt, and streams, or living in a filthy camp littered with piles of dung, both human and animal. The bottoms of her feet were hard as horn and black as sin.

"Come and find me in a day or two," I said instead. *If you can,* I thought. "I'll check it and change the dressing." *If I can,* I thought, with a glance at the knapsack in the corner where I kept my dwindling stocks of medicaments.

"Thank 'ee kindly," the whore said, sitting up and putting her foot gingerly to the ground. Judging from the skin of her legs and feet, she was young, though you couldn't tell from her face. Her skin was weathered, lined with hunger and strain. Her cheekbones were sharp with hunger, and her mouth was drawn in on one side where the teeth were missing—lost to decay or knocked out by a customer or another whore.

"Will 'ee be here for a bit, think?" she asked. "I've a friend, like, got the itch."

"I'll be here for the night, at least," I assured her, suppressing a groan as I rose to my feet. "Send your friend; I'll see what I can do."

Our group of militia had met with others, forming a large body, and within a few days we began to cross paths with other rebel groups. We were running into fragments of General Schuyler's and General Arnold's armies, these also moving south down the Hudson Valley.

We were still moving all day but began to feel secure enough to sleep at night, and with food provided—irregularly, but still food—by the army, my strength began to return. The rain usually came at night, but today it had been raining at dawn, and we had been trudging through mud for hours before some shelter came in sight.

General Arnold's troops had stripped the farmstead and burnt the house. The barn was heavily charred down one side, but the fire had gone out before consuming the building.

A gust of wind blew through the barn, raising eddies of decayed straw and dirt, whipping our petticoats round our legs. The barn had originally had a plank floor; I could see the lines of the boards, embedded in the dirt. The foragers had taken them for firewood, but it had been too much trouble for them to knock down the barn, thank God.

Some of the refugees fleeing Ticonderoga had sought shelter here; more would be along before nightfall. A mother with two small, exhausted children slept curled by the far wall; her husband had settled them here and gone to look for food.

Pray ye that your flight be not in the winter, nor on the Sabbath day . . .

I followed the whore to the door and stood looking after her. The sun was touching the horizon now; perhaps an hour of light left, but the sunset breeze was already moving in the treetops, night's skirts rustling as she came. I shivered reflexively, though the day was still warm enough. The old barn was chilly.

And what then? said the small, apprehensive voice that lived in the pit of my stomach. *What would it be like when the weather turned truly cold?*

"Then I'll put on another pair of stockings," I muttered to it. "Hush up!"

A truly Christian person would doubtless have given the spare stockings to the barefoot whore, remarked the sanctimonious voice of my conscience.

"You hush up, too," I said. "Plenty of opportunity to be Christian later, if the urge should strike me." Half the people fleeing needed stockings, I dared say.

I wondered what I might be able to do for the whore's friend, if she did come. "The itch" might be anything from eczema or cowpox to gonorrhea—though given the woman's profession, something venereal was the best bet. Back in Boston, it would likely have been a simple yeast infection—oddly enough, I almost never saw those here, and speculated idly that it might be owing to the nearly universal lack of underclothes. So much for the advances of modernity!

I glanced at my knapsack again, calculating what I had left and how I might use it. A fair amount of bandages and lint. A pot of gentian ointment, good for scrapes and minor wounds, which occurred in abundance. A small stock of the most useful herbs for tincture and compress: lavender, comfrey, peppermint, mustard seed. By some miracle, I still had the box of cinchona bark I had acquired in New Bern—I thought of Tom Christie and crossed myself, but dismissed him from mind; there was nothing I could do about him and much too much to think of here. Two scalpels I had taken from Lieutenant Stactoe's body—he had succumbed to a fever on the road—and my silver surgical scissors. Jamie's gold acupuncture needles; those might be used to treat others, save that I had no idea how to place them for anything other than seasickness.

I could hear voices, parties of foragers moving through the trees, here and there someone calling out a name, searching for a friend or family member lost in transit. The refugees were beginning to settle for the night.

Sticks cracked near at hand, and a man came out of the woods. I didn't recognize him. One of the "greasy-stockinged knaves" from one of the militias, no doubt; he had a musket in one hand and a powder horn at his belt. Not much else. And yes, he was barefoot, though his feet were much too big to wear my stockings—a fact that I pointed out to my conscience, in case it should feel compelled to try to prod me into charitable behavior again.

He saw me in the door and raised a hand.

"You the conjure-woman?" he called.

"Yes." I'd given up trying to make people call me a doctor, let alone a physician.

"Met a whore with a mighty fine new bandage on her foot," the man said, giving me a smile. "She said as there's a conjure-woman up to the barn, has some medicines."

"Yes," I said again, giving him a quick once-over. I saw no obvious wound, and he wasn't sick—I could tell that from his color and the upright way he walked. Perhaps he had a wife or child, or a sick comrade.

"Hand 'em over to me now," he said, still smiling, and pointed the muzzle of the musket at me.

"What?" I said, surprised.

"Give me the medicines you've got." He made a small jabbing motion with the gun. "Could just shoot you and take 'em, but I ain't wanting to waste the powder."

I stood still and stared at him for a moment.

"What the devil do you want them for?" I'd been held up once before for drugs—in a Boston emergency room. A young addict, sweating and glassy-eyed, with a gun. I'd handed them over instantly. At the moment, I wasn't inclined.

He snorted and cocked his gun. Before I could even think about being scared, there was a sharp bang and the scent of powder smoke. The man looked terribly surprised, the musket sagging in his hands. Then he fell at my feet.

"Hold that, Sassenach." Jamie thrust the just-fired pistol into my hand, stooped, and took the body by the feet. He dragged it out of the barn into the rain. I swallowed, reached into my bag, and took out the extra stockings. I dropped these in the woman's lap, then went to set down the pistol and my sack by the wall. I was conscious of the eyes of the mother and her children on me—and saw them shift suddenly to the open door. I turned to see Jamie come in, soaked to the skin, his face drawn and set with fatigue.

He crossed the barn and sat down by me, laid his head on his knees, and closed his eyes.

"Thank you, sir," said the woman, very softly. "Ma'am."

I thought for a moment that he had fallen instantly asleep, for he didn't stir. After a moment, though, he said, in an equally soft voice, "Ye're welcome, ma'am."

I WAS MORE THAN pleased to find the Hunters when we reached the next village; they had been in one of the barges that had been captured early, but had succeeded in escaping by the simple expedient of walking into the woods after dark. As the soldiers who had captured them had not bothered to count their captives, no one noticed they had gone.

Overall, things were looking up somewhat. Food was becoming more abundant, and we were among regular Continentals. We were still only a few miles in front of Burgoyne's army, though, and the strain of the long retreat was telling. Desertion was frequent—though no one knew quite how frequent. Organization, discipline, and military structure were being restored as we came under the sway of the Continental army, but there were still men who could melt away unobtrusively.

It was Jamie who thought of the deserter game. Deserters would be welcomed into the British camps, fed, given clothes, and interrogated for information.

"So we'll give it to them, aye?" he said. "And it's only fair we take the same in return, is it not?"

Smiles began to grow on the faces of the officers to whom he was propounding this idea. And within a few days, carefully chosen "deserters" were making their way surreptitiously to the enemy camps and being taken before British officers, where they poured out the stories with which they'd been carefully prepared. And after a good supper, they would take the first opportunity to re-desert back to the American side—bringing with them useful information about the British forces pursuing us.

Ian dropped in to Indian camps now and then if it seemed safe, but didn't play this particular game; he was memorable.

I thought Jamie would have liked to masquerade as a deserter—it would appeal to his sense of drama, as well as his sense of adventure, which was acute. His size and striking appearance put this notion out of consideration, though; the deserters must all be ordinary-looking men who were unlikely to be recognized later.

"Because sooner or later, the British are going to realize what's afoot. They're not fools. And they willna take it kindly when they do realize."

We had found shelter for the night in another barn—this one unburnt and still equipped with a few piles of musty hay, though the stock had long since vanished. We were alone, but probably wouldn't be for long. The interlude in the commandant's garden seemed as though it had taken place in someone else's life, but I laid my head on Jamie's shoulder, relaxing against his solid warmth.

"Do ye think maybe—"

Jamie stopped abruptly, his hand tightening on my leg. An instant later, I heard the stealthy rustling that had alerted him, and my mouth went dry. It might be anything from a prowling wolf to an Indian ambush—but whatever it was was sizable, and I fumbled—as silently as possible—for the pocket in which I had stowed the knife he'd given me.

Not a wolf; something passed the open door, a shadow the height of a man, and vanished. Jamie squeezed my thigh and then was gone, moving crouched through the empty barn without a sound. For an instant, I couldn't see him in the dark, but my eyes were well adapted, and I found him seconds later, a long dark shadow pressed against the wall, just inside the door.

The shadow outside had come back; I saw the brief silhouette of a head against the paler black of the night outside. I got my feet under me, skin prickling with fear. The door was the only egress; perhaps I should throw myself on the floor and roll up against the base of a wall. I might escape detection—or, with luck, be able to grab the ankles of an intruder, or stab him through the foot.

I was just about to implement this strategy when a tremulous whisper came out of the dark.

"Friend—Friend James?" it said, and I let out the breath I had been holding in a gasp.

"Is that you, Denzell?" I said, trying to sound normal.

"Claire!" He burst through the door in relief, promptly tripped over something, and fell headlong with a crash.

"Welcome back, Friend Hunter," Jamie said, the nervous urge to laugh evident in his voice. "Are ye hurt?" The long shadow detached itself from the wall and bent to help our visitor up.

"No. No, I don't think so. Though in fact I scarcely know . . . James, I did it!"

There was a momentary silence.

"How close, *a charaid*?" Jamie asked quietly. "And do they move?"

"No, thank the Lord." Denzell sat down abruptly beside me, and I could feel his trembling. "They're waiting for their wagons to come up. They daren't outrun their supply line too far, and they're having terrible trouble; we've made such a mess of the roads"—the pride in his voice was palpable—"and the rain's helped a great deal, too."

"D'ye ken how long it might be?"

I saw Denzell nod, eager.

"One of the sergeants said it might be two, even three days. He was telling some of the soldiers to be mindful of their flour and beer, as they wouldn't get any more until the wagons came."

Jamie exhaled, and I felt some of the tension leave him. Mine did, too, and I felt a passionate wave of thankfulness. There would be time to sleep. I had just begun to relax a little; now the tension flowed out of me like water, to such an extent that I barely noticed what else Denzell had to confide. I heard Jamie's voice, murmuring congratulations; he clapped Denzell on the shoulder, and slid out of the barn, no doubt to go pass on the information.

Denzell sat still, breathing audibly. I gathered what was left of my concentration and made an effort to be amiable.

"Did they feed you, Denzell?"

"Oh." Denzell's voice changed, and he began to fumble in his pocket. "Here. I brought this away for thee." He pushed something into my hands: a small squashed loaf, rather burnt about the edges—I could tell from the hard crust and the smell of ashes. My mouth began to water uncontrollably.

"Oh, no," I managed to say, trying to give it back. "You should—"

"They fed me," he assured me. "Stew, of a sort. I ate all I could. And I've another loaf in my pocket for my sister. They gave me the food," he assured me earnestly. "I didn't steal it."

"Thank you," I managed to say, and with the greatest self-control, tore the loaf in half and tucked one half in my pocket for Jamie. Then I crammed the remainder in my mouth and ripped at it like a wolf wrenching bloody mouthfuls from a carcass.

Denny's stomach echoed mine, rumbling with a series of great borborygmi.

"I thought you said you ate!" I said, accusing.

"I did. But the stew seems not inclined to lie quiet," he said, with a small, pained laugh. He bent forward, arms folded over his stomach. "I—um, don't s'pose that thee might have a bit of barley water or peppermint to hand, Friend Claire?"

"I do," I said, unspeakably relieved that I still had the remnants in my sack. I hadn't much left, but I did have peppermint. There was no hot water; I gave him a handful to chew, washed down with water from a canteen. He drank thirstily, burped, and then stopped, breathing in a way that told me just what was happening. I guided him hastily to the side and held his head while he vomited, losing peppermint and stew together.

"Food poisoning?" I asked, trying to feel his forehead, but he slid away from me, collapsing onto a heap of straw, his head on his knees.

"He said he'd hang me," he whispered suddenly.

"Who?"

"The English officer. A Captain Bradbury, I think his name was. Said he thought I was a-playing at spies and soldiers, and if I didn't confess at once, he'd hang me."

"But he didn't," I said softly, and put a hand on his arm.

He was trembling all over, and I saw a drop of sweat hanging from the tip of his chin, translucent in the dimness.

"I told him—told him he could, I s'posed. If he pleased. And I truly thought he would. But he didn't." His breath came thick, and I realized that he was crying, silently.

I put my arms around him, held him, making hushing

noises, and after a little he stopped. He was quiet for a few minutes.

"I thought—I would be prepared to die," he said softly. "That I would go happy to the Lord, whenever He chose to call me. I am ashamed to find it untrue. I was so much afraid."

I took a long, deep breath, and sat back beside him.

"I always wondered about martyrs," I said. "No one ever said they weren't afraid. It's only that they were willing to go and do whatever they did in spite of it. You went."

"I did not set up to be a martyr," he said after a moment. He sounded so meek, I nearly laughed.

"I doubt very much that many people do," I said. "And I think a person who did would be very obnoxious indeed. It's late, Denzell, and your sister will be worried. And hungry."

IT WAS AN HOUR or more before Jamie came back. I was lying in the hay, my shawl pulled over me, but wasn't asleep. He crawled in beside me and lay down, sighing, putting an arm over me.

"Why him?" I asked after a moment, trying to keep my voice calm. It didn't work; Jamie was acutely sensitive to tones of voice—anyone's, but particularly mine. I saw his head turn sharply toward me, but he paused a moment in turn before answering.

"He wished to go," he said, doing much better with the approximation of calmness than I had. "And I thought he'd do well with it."

"Do *well*? He's no actor! You know he can't lie; he must have been stammering and tripping over his tongue! I'm astonished that they believed him—if they did," I added.

"Oh, they did, aye. D'ye think a real deserter wouldna be terrified, Sassenach?" he said, sounding faintly amused. "I meant him to go in sweating and stammering. Had I tried to give him lines to speak, they'd ha' shot him on the spot."

The thought of it made the bolus of bread rise in my throat. I forced it back down.

"Yes," I said, and took a few breaths, feeling cold sweat prickle over my own face, seeing little Denny Hunter, sweating and stammering before the cold eyes of a British officer.

"Yes," I said again. "But . . . couldn't someone else have done it? It's not just that Denny Hunter is a friend—he's a doctor. He's needed."

Jamie's head turned toward me again. The sky outside was beginning to lighten; I could see the outline of his face.

"Did ye not hear me say he wished to do it, Sassenach?" he asked. "I didna ask him. In fact, I tried to dissuade him—for the very reason ye said. But he wouldna hear it and only asked me to look after his sister, should he not come back."

Rachel. My stomach clenched afresh at mention of her.

"What can he have been *thinking*?"

Jamie sighed deeply and turned onto his back.

"He's a Quaker, Sassenach. But he's a man. If he was the sort of man who'd not fight for what he believes, he'd ha' stayed in his wee village and poulticed horses and looked after his sister. But he's not." He shook his head and looked at me.

"Would ye have had me stay at home, Sassenach? Turn back from the fight?"

"I would," I said, agitation fading into crossness. "In a heartbeat. I just know you aren't bloody *going* to, so what's the point?"

That made him laugh.

"So ye do understand," he said, and took my hand. "It's the same for Denzell Hunter, aye? If he's bound to risk his life, then it's my job to see he gets the most return from his gambling."

"Bearing in mind that the return of most gambling is a big, fat zero," I remarked, trying to repossess the hand. "Hasn't anyone ever told you that the house always wins?" He wasn't letting go, but had begun to run the ball of his thumb gently back and forth over the tips of my fingers.

"Aye, well. Ye reckon the odds and cut the cards, Sassenach. And it's not *all* luck, ken?" The light had grown, in that imperceptible predawn way. Nothing so blatant as a sunbeam; just a gradual emergence of objects as the shadows round them went from black to gray to blue.

His thumb slipped inside my hand, and I curled my fingers involuntarily over it.

"Why isn't there a word that means the opposite of 'fade'?" I asked, watching the lines of his face emerge from night's shadow. I traced the shape of one rough brow with my thumb and felt the springy mat of his short beard against the palm of my hand, changing as I watched it from amorphous smudge to a distinction of tiny curls and wiry springs, a glowing mass of auburn, gold, and silver, vigorous against his weathered skin.

"I dinna suppose ye need one," he said. "If ye mean the light." He looked at me and smiled as I saw his eyes trace the outlines of my face. "If the light is fading, the night's coming on—and when the light grows again, it's the night that's fading, aye?"

It was, too. We should sleep, but the army would be astir around us shortly.

"Why is it that women don't make war, I wonder?"

"Ye're no made for it, Sassenach." His hand cupped my cheek, hard and rough. "And it wouldna be right; you women take so much more with ye, when ye go."

"What do you mean by that?"

He made the small shrugging movement that meant he was looking for a word or a notion, an unconscious movement, as though his coat was too tight, though he wasn't wearing one at the moment.

"When a man dies, it's only him," he said. "And one is much like another. Aye, a family needs a man, to feed them, protect them. But any decent man can do it. A woman . . ." His lips moved against my fingertips, a faint smile. "A woman takes life with her when she goes. A woman is . . . infinite possibility."

"Idiot," I said, very softly. "If you think one man is just like any other."

We lay for a bit, watching the light grow.

"How many times have ye done it, Sassenach?" he asked suddenly. "Sat betwixt the dark and the dawn, and held a man's fear in the palms of your hands?"

"Too many," I said, but it wasn't the truth, and he knew it. I heard his breath come, the faintest sound of humor, and he turned my hand palm up, his big thumb tracing the hills and valleys, joints and calluses, lifeline and heartline, and the smooth fleshy swell of the mount of Venus, where the faint scar of the letter "J" was still barely visible. I'd held him in my hand for the best part of my life.

"Part of the job," I said, meaning no flippancy, and he did not take it that way.

"D'ye think I'm not afraid?" he asked quietly. "When I do my job?"

"Oh, you're afraid," I said. "But you do it anyway. You're a frigging gambler—and the biggest gamble of all is a life, isn't it? Maybe yours—maybe someone else's."

"Aye, well," he said softly. "Ye'd know about that, I suppose.

"I'm the less bothered for myself," he said thoughtfully. "Looking at it all in all, I mean, I've done the odd useful thing here and there. My children are grown; my grandchildren are thriving—that's the most important thing, no?"

"It is," I said. The sun was up; I heard a rooster crow, somewhere in the distance.

"Well, so. I canna say I'm so verra much afraid as I used to be. I shouldna like dying, of course—but there'd maybe be less regret in it. On the other hand"—one side of his mouth turned up as he looked at me—"while I'm maybe less afraid for myself, I'm that wee bit more reluctant to kill young men who've not yet lived their lives." And that, I thought, was as close as I'd get to an apology for Denny Hunter.

"Going to assess the age of the people shooting at you, are you?" I asked, sitting up and beginning to brush hay out of my hair.

"Difficult," he admitted.

"And I sincerely hope that you don't propose to let some whippersnapper kill you, merely because they haven't had such a full life as yours yet."

He sat up, too, and faced me, serious, ends of hay bristling from hair and clothes.

"No," he said. "I'll kill them. I'll just mind it more."

58

INDEPENDENCE DAY

Philadelphia
July 4, 1777

GREY HAD NEVER been to Philadelphia before. Bar the streets, which were execrable, it seemed a pleasant city. Summer had graced the city's trees with huge verdant crowns, and a walk left him lightly dusted with leaf fragments and the soles of his boots sticky with fallen sap. Perhaps it was the febrile temperature of the air that was responsible for Henry's apparent state of mind, he thought darkly.

Not that he blamed his nephew. Mrs. Woodcock was lissome but rounded, with a lovely face and a warm character. *And* she had nursed him away from death's door when the local prison officer had brought him to her, worried lest a potentially lucrative prisoner die before yielding a full harvest. That sort of thing formed a bond, he knew—though he had never, thank God, felt any sort of *tendresse* for any of the women who had attended him in ill health. Except for . . .

"Shit," he said involuntarily, causing a clerical-looking gentleman to glare at him in passing.

He had clapped a mental teacup over the thought that had buzzed through his head like a meddlesome fly. Unable not to look at it, though, he cautiously lifted the cup and found Claire Fraser under it. He relaxed a little.

Certainly not a *tendresse.* On the other hand, he was damned if he could have said what it had been. A most peculiar sort of unsettling intimacy, at least—no doubt the result of her being Jamie Fraser's wife and her knowing what his own feelings for Jamie were. He dismissed Claire Fraser, and went back to worrying about his nephew.

Pleasant Mrs. Woodcock undeniably was, and just as undeniably rather too fond of Henry for a married woman—though her husband was a rebel, Henry had told him, and God knew when or whether he might return. Well enough; there was no danger of Henry losing his head and marrying her, at least. He could imagine the scandal, should Henry bring home a carpenter's widow, and she a sable enchantress, to boot. He grinned at the thought and felt more charitable toward Mercy Woodcock. She had, after all, saved Henry's life.

For now. The unwelcome thought buzzed in before he could clap the teacup over it. He couldn't avoid it for long; it kept coming back.

He understood Henry's reluctance to undergo another surgery. And there was the lingering fear that he might be too weak to withstand it. But at the same time, he could not be allowed to remain in his present state; he would simply dwindle and die, once illness and pain had drained the last of his vitality. Not even the fleshly attractions of Mrs. Woodcock would hold him, once that happened.

No, the surgery must be done, and soon. In Grey's conversations with Dr. Franklin, the old gentleman had made him acquainted with a friend, Dr. Benjamin Rush, who he claimed was a most prodigious medical man. Dr. Franklin urged Grey to visit him, should he ever find himself in the city—had given Grey a letter of introduction, in fact. He was on his way to present this, in hopes that Dr. Rush might either be practiced in surgery or be able to refer him to someone who was. Because, whether Henry wanted it or not, it had to be done. Grey could not take Henry home to England in his present state, and he had promised both Minnie and his brother that he would bring their youngest son back, were he still alive.

His foot slipped on a muddy cobble, and he let out a whoop and pitched sideways, arms pinwheeling for balance. He caught himself and shook his clothes back into order with a good assumption of dignity, ignoring the giggles of two milkmaids who had been watching.

Damn it all, she was back. Claire Fraser. Why? . . . Of

course. The ether, as she called it. She'd asked him for a carboy of some sort of acid and had told him that she required it to make ether. Not as in the ethereal realm but a chemical substance that rendered people unconscious, so as to make surgery . . . painless.

He stopped dead in the middle of the street. Jamie had told him about his wife's experiments with the substance, with a full account of the amazing operation she had performed on a young boy, he rendered completely senseless as she opened his abdomen, removed an offending organ, and sewed him back together. After which the child was right as a grig, apparently.

He walked on more slowly, thinking furiously. Would she come? It was a laborious journey to almost anywhere from Fraser's Ridge. Not such a terrible trip from the mountain to the shore, though. It was summer, the weather was good; the journey could be made in less than two weeks. And if she would come to Wilmington, he could arrange for her to be brought to Philadelphia on whatever naval vessel was available—he knew people in the navy.

How long? How long might it take her—if she would come? More sobering thought: how long did Henry have?

He was pulled from these troubling reflections by what appeared to be a small riot proceeding down the street in his direction. A number of people, most of them drunken to judge by their behavior, which involved a good deal of shouting and pushing and waving of handkerchiefs. A young man was beating a drum, with much enthusiasm and no skill, and two children bore between them an outlandish banner, striped red and white but with no legend upon it.

He pressed back against a house, to give them room to pass. They did not pass, however, but instead hauled up before a house on the opposite side of the street and stood there shouting slogans in English and German. He caught the shout of "Liberty," and someone blew a cavalry charge upon a trumpet. And then he caught the shout of "Rush! Rush! Rush!"

Good God, it must be the house he was seeking, that of Dr. Rush. The mob seemed good-humored; he supposed they did not mean to drag the doctor out for a dose of tar and feathers, this being a notable form of public entertainment, or so he had been told. Cautiously, he approached and tapped a young woman on the shoulder.

"I beg your pardon." He had to lean close and shout into her ear to be heard; she whirled and blinked in surprise, then caught sight of his butterfly waistcoat and broke into a broad smile. He smiled back.

"I am seeking Dr. Benjamin Rush," he shouted. "Is this his house?"

"Yes, it is." A young man beside the young woman heard him and turned, his eyebrows shooting up at sight of Grey. "You have business with Dr. Rush?"

"I have a letter of introduction to the doctor from a Dr. Franklin, a mutual—"

The young man's face broke into a huge grin. Before he could say anything, though, the door of the house opened and a slender, well-dressed man in his thirties came out onto the stoop. There was a roar from the crowd, and the man, who must surely be Dr. Rush himself, held out his hands to them, laughing. The noise quieted for a moment, the man leaning out to talk with someone in the crowd. Then he ducked into the house, came out again with his coat on, came down the steps to a roar of applause, and the whole mob moved off again, banging and bugling with renewed fervor.

"Come along!" the young man bellowed in his ear. "There'll be free beer!"

Which is how Lord John Grey found himself in the taproom of a prosperous tavern, celebrating the first anniversary of the publication of the Declaration of Independence. There were political speeches of an impassioned, if not very eloquent, variety, and it was in the course of these that Grey learned that Dr. Rush was not only a wealthy and influential rebel sympathizer but a prominent rebel himself; in fact, as he learned from his newfound friends, both Rush *and* Dr. Franklin turned out to have signed the seditious document in the first place.

Word spread through the people round them that Grey was a friend of Franklin's, and he was much hailed in consequence, eventually being conveyed by insensible degrees through the crowd until he found himself face-to-face with Benjamin Rush.

It wasn't the first time Grey had been in close proximity to a criminal, and he kept his composure. This was plainly not the time to lay his nephew's situation before Rush, and Grey contented himself with shaking the young doctor by the hand and mentioning his connection with Franklin. Rush was most cordial, and shouted over the noise that Grey must come to call at his house when they both should be at leisure, perhaps in the morning.

Grey expressed his great willingness to do so and retired gracefully through the crowd, hoping that the Crown would not manage to hang Rush before he had a chance to examine Henry.

A racket in the street outside put a momentary stop to the festivities. There was considerable shouting and the thump of projectiles striking the front of the building. One of these—which proved to be a large, muddy rock—struck and shattered a pane of the establishment's window, allowing the bellows of "Traitors! Renegados!" to be heard more clearly.

"Shut your face, lickspittle!" shouted someone inside the tavern. Globs of mud and more rocks were hurled, some of these coming through the open door and broken window, along with patriotic shouts of "God Save the King!"

"Geld the Royal Brute!" shouted Grey's earlier acquaintance in reply, and half the tavern rushed out into the street, some pausing to break legs from stools to assist in the political discussion which then ensued.

Grey was somewhat concerned lest Rush be set upon by the Loyalists in the street and attacked before he could be of use to Henry, but Rush and a few others whom he took to be prominent rebels, as well, hung back from the fray and, after taking brief counsel, elected to leave through the tavern's kitchen.

Grey found himself left in the company of a man from Norfolk named Paine, a malnourished, ill-dressed wretch, large of nose and vivid of personality, possessed of strong opinions on the subjects of liberty and democracy and a most remarkable command of epithet regarding the King. Finding conversation difficult, as he could not reasonably express any of his own contrary opinions on these subjects, Grey excused himself with the intention of following Rush and his friends out the back way.

The riot outside, having reached a brief crescendo, had

proceeded to its natural conclusion with the flight of the Loyalists, and people now had begun to flow back into the tavern, borne on a tide of righteous indignation and self-congratulation. Among these was a tall, slender, dark man, who looked round from his conversation, met Grey's eye, and stopped dead.

Grey walked up to him, hoping that the beating of his heart was not audible above the fading noise in the street.

"Mr. Beauchamp," he said, and took Perseverance Wainwright by hand and wrist, in what might be taken for cordial greeting but was in reality firm detention. "A private word with you, sir?"

HE WOULD NOT bring Percy to the house he had taken for himself and Dottie. Dottie would not recognize him, for she had not even been born when Percy vanished from Grey's life; it was merely the operation of the instinct which would have prevented him giving a small child a venomous snake to play with.

Percy, whatever his motive, did not suggest taking Grey to *his* lodgings, probably didn't want Grey knowing where he was staying, in case he thought to abscond quietly. After a moment's indecision—for Grey did not yet know the city—Grey agreed to Percy's suggestion that they walk to the common called Southeast Square.

"It's a potter's field," Percy said, leading the way. "Where they bury strangers to the city."

"How appropriate," Grey said, but Percy either didn't hear or affected not to. It was some way, and they didn't talk much, the streets being full of people. Despite the holiday aspects and the striped banners hung here and there—they all seemed to have a field of stars, though he hadn't seen the same arrangement twice, and the stripes varied in size and color, some having red, white, and blue stripes, some only red and white—there was a frenetic air to the gaiety, and an edged sense of danger in the streets. Philadelphia might be the rebels' capital, but it was far from being a stronghold.

The common was quieter, as might be expected of a graveyard. At that, it was surprisingly pleasant. There were only a few wooden grave markers here and there, giving such details as were known about the person interred beneath them; no one would have gone to the expense of placing gravestones, though some charitable soul had erected a large stone cross upon a plinth in the center of the field. Without conference, they headed for this object, following the course of a small creek that ran through the common.

It had occurred to Grey that Percy might have suggested their destination in order to give himself time to think on the way. Well enough—he'd been thinking, too. So when Percy sat down upon the base of the plinth and turned to him with an air of expectation, he didn't bother with observations on the weather.

"Tell me about the Baron Amandine's second sister," he said, standing before Percy.

Percy blinked, startled, but then smiled.

"Really, John, you amaze me. Claude didn't tell you about Amelie, I'm sure."

Grey didn't reply to that, but folded his hands beneath the tail of his coat and waited. Percy thought for a moment, then shrugged.

"All right. She was Claude's older sister; my wife, Cecile, is the younger."

" 'Was,' " Grey repeated. "So she's dead."

"She's been dead for some forty years. Why are you interested in her?" Percy pulled a handkerchief from his sleeve to dab at his temples; the day was hot, and it had been a long walk; Grey's own shirt was damp.

"Where did she die?"

"In a brothel in Paris." That stopped Grey in his tracks. Percy saw it and gave a wry smile. "If you must know, John, I am looking for her son."

Grey stared at him for a moment, then slowly sat down beside him. The gray stone of the plinth was warm under his buttocks.

"All right," he said, after a moment. "Tell me, if you would be so good."

Percy gave him a sideways glance of amusement—full of wariness, but still amused.

"There are things I cannot tell you, John, as you must surely appreciate. By the way, I hear that there is a rather heated discussion taking place between the British secretaries of state as to which of them shall make an approach regarding my previous offer—and to whom, exactly, to make it. I suppose this is your doing? I thank you."

"Don't change the subject. I'm not asking you about your previous offer." *Not yet, anyway.* "I'm asking you about Amelie Beauchamp and her son. I cannot see how they may be connected with the other matter, so I assume they have some personal significance to you. Naturally, there are things you cannot tell me regarding the larger matter"—he bowed slightly—"but this mystery about the baron's sister seems somewhat more personal."

"It is." Percy was turning something over in his mind; Grey could see it working behind his eyes. The eyes were lined and a little pouched but the same as ever; a warm, lively brown, the color of sherry-sack. His fingers drummed briefly on the stone, then stopped, and he turned to Grey with an air of decision.

"Very well. Bulldog that you are, if I *don't* tell you, you will doubtless be following me all over Philadelphia, in an effort to discover my purpose in being here."

This was precisely what Grey intended doing in any case, but he made an indeterminate noise that might be taken as encouragement before asking, "What *is* your purpose in being here?"

"I'm looking for a printer named Fergus Fraser." Grey blinked at that; he hadn't been expecting any concrete answer.

"Who is . . . ?"

Percy held up a hand, folding down the fingers as he spoke.

"He is, first, the son of one James Fraser, a notable ex-Jacobite and current rebel. He is, secondly, a printer, as indicated—and, I suspect, a rebel like his father. And, thirdly, I strongly suspect that he is the son of Amelie Beauchamp."

There were blue and red dragonflies hovering over the creek; Grey felt as though one of these insects had flown suddenly up his nose.

"You are telling me that James Fraser had an illegitimate son by a French whore? Who happened also to be the daughter of an ancient noble family?" Shock did not begin to describe his feelings, but he kept his tone light, and Percy laughed.

"No. The printer *is* Fraser's son, but is adopted. He took the boy from a brothel in Paris more than thirty years ago." A trickle of sweat ran down the side of Percy's neck, and he wiped it away. The warmth of the day had made his cologne blossom on his skin; Grey caught the hint of ambergris and carnation, spice and musk together.

"Amelie was, as I said, Claude's older sister. In her teens she was seduced by a much older man, a married nobleman, and got with child. The normal thing would have been for her simply to be married hastily off to a complaisant husband, but the nobleman's wife died quite suddenly, and Amelie made a fuss, insisting that since he was now free, he must marry *her.*"

"He was not so inclined?"

"No. Claude's father was, though. I suppose he thought such a marriage would improve the family fortunes; the comte was a very wealthy man, and while not political, did have a certain . . . standing."

The old Baron Amandine had been willing to keep things quiet in the beginning, but as he began to see the possibilities of the situation, he became bolder and threatened all kinds of things, from a complaint to the King—for old Amandine was active at court, unlike his son—to a lawsuit for damages and an application to the Church for excommunication.

"Could he actually have done that?" Grey asked, fascinated despite his reservations about Percy's veracity. Percy smiled briefly.

"He could have complained to the King. In any case, he didn't get the chance. Amelie disappeared."

The girl had vanished from her home in the middle of one night, taking her jewels. It was thought that perhaps she had intended to run away to her lover, in the hope that he would give in and marry her, but the comte professed complete ignorance of the matter, and no one came forward to say that they had seen her, either leaving *Trois Flèches* or entering the Paris mansion of the Comte St. Germain.

"And you think she somehow ended in a Paris brothel?" Grey said incredulously. "How? And if so, how did you discover this?"

"I found her marriage lines."

"What?"

"A contract of marriage, between Amélie Élise LeVigne

Beauchamp and Robert-François Quesnay de St. Germain. Signed by both parties. And a priest. It was in the library at *Trois Flèches,* inside the family Bible. Claude and Cecile are not very religiously inclined, I'm afraid," Percy said, shaking his head.

"And you are?" That made Percy laugh; he knew that Grey knew precisely what his feelings regarding religion were.

"I was bored," he said without apology.

"Life at *Trois Flèches* must have been tedious indeed, if it forced you to read the Bible. Did the sub-gardener quit?"

"Did—oh, Emile." Percy grinned. "No, but he had a terrible bout of *la grippe* that month. Couldn't breathe through his nose at all, poor man."

Grey felt again a treacherous impulse to laugh, but restrained it, and Percy went on without a pause.

"I actually wasn't *reading* it; I have all of the most excessive damnations memorized, after all. I was interested in the cover."

"Heavily bejeweled, was it?" Grey asked dryly, and Percy gave him a look of mild offense.

"It has not *always* got to do with money, John, even for those of us not blessed with such substance as yourself."

"My apologies," said Grey. "Why the Bible, then?"

"I will have you know that I am a bookbinder of no mean repute," Percy said, preening a little. "I took it up in Italy as a means of making a living. After you so gallantly saved my life. Thank you for that, by the way," he said, with a direct look whose sudden seriousness made Grey look down to avoid his eyes.

"You're welcome," he said gruffly, and, bending, carefully induced a small green caterpillar that was inching its way across the polished toe of his boot to inch onto his finger.

"Anyway," Percy went on, not losing a beat, "I discovered this curious document. I had heard of the family scandal, of course, and recognized the names at once."

"You asked the present baron about it?"

"I did. What did you think of Claude, by the way?" Percy had always been like quicksilver, Grey thought, and he hadn't lost any of his mutability with age.

"Bad cardplayer. A wonderful voice, though—does he sing?"

"Indeed he does. And you're right about the cards. He can keep a secret, if he likes, but he can't lie at all. You'd be amazed at how powerful a thing perfect honesty is, in some circumstances," Percy added reflectively. "It almost makes me think there might be something in the Eighth Commandment."

Grey muttered something about "more honored in the breach," but then coughed and begged that Percy might continue.

"He didn't know about the marriage contract, I'm sure of it. He was genuinely staggered. And after a certain amount of hesitation—'bloody, bold, and resolute' may be your watchwords, John, but they are not his—he gave his consent for me to dig into the matter."

Grey ignored the implied flattery—if that's what it was, and he thought it was—and carefully deposited the caterpillar onto the leaves of what looked like an edible bush.

"You looked for the priest," he said with certainty.

Percy laughed with what sounded like genuine pleasure, and it occurred to Grey with a small shock that of course he knew Percy's mind, and Percy his; they had been conversing, through the veils of statecraft and secrecy, for many years. Of course, Percy had likely known to whom he was talking, and Grey hadn't.

"Yes, I did. He was dead—murdered. Killed in the street at night while hurrying to give the last rites to a dying parishioner, such a terrible thing. A week after the disappearance of Amelie Beauchamp."

This was beginning to rouse Grey's professional interest, though the private side of him was still more than wary.

"The next thing would have been the comte—but if he was capable of killing a priest to keep his secrets, it would have been dangerous to approach him directly," Grey said. "His servants, then?"

Percy nodded, mouth quirked at one corner in appreciation of Grey's acuity.

"The comte was dead, too—or he disappeared, at least; he had a reputation as a sorceror, oddly enough—and he died a good ten years after Amelie. But I looked for his old servants, yes. I found a few of them. For some people, it really *is* always about money, and the assistant coachman was one of those. Two days after Amelie disappeared, he delivered a carpet to a brothel near the Rue Fauborg. A very heavy carpet that had about it a smell of opium—which he recognized, because he had at one point transported a troupe of Chinese acrobats who came to entertain at a fete at the mansion."

"And so you went to the brothel. Where money . . ."

"They say water is the universal solvent," Percy said, shaking his head, "but it isn't. You could plunge a man into a barrel of freezing water and leave him for a week, and you would accomplish much less than you might with a modest quantity of gold."

Grey silently noted the adjective "freezing," and nodded to Percy to continue.

"It took some time, repeated visits, different attempts—the madam was a true professional, meaning that whoever had paid her predecessor had done so on a staggering scale, and her doorkeeper, while old enough, had had his tongue torn out at an early age; no help there. And of course none of the whores had been there when the infamous carpet was delivered, that being so long before."

He had, however, patiently traced the families of the present whores—for some occupations run in families—and managed after months of work to discover an old woman who had been employed at the brothel and who recognized the miniature of Amelie that he had brought from *Trois Flèches.*

The girl had indeed been brought to the brothel, in the middle stages of pregnancy. That had not mattered particularly; there were patrons with such tastes. A few months later, she had been delivered of a son. She had survived childbirth but died a year later, during a plague of influenza.

"And I could not *begin* to tell you the difficulties of finding out anything about a child born in a Paris brothel forty-odd years ago, my dear." Percy sighed, employing his handkerchief again.

"But your name is Perseverance," Grey noted with extreme dryness, and Percy glanced sharply at him.

"Do you know," he said lightly, "I believe you are the only person in the world who knows that?" And from the expression in his eyes, that was one too many.

"Your secret is safe with me," Grey said. "That one, at least. What about Denys Randall-Isaacs?"

It worked. Percy's face shimmered like a pool of quicksilver in the sun. In half a heartbeat, he had the perfect blankness back in place—but it was too late.

Grey laughed, though without humor, and stood up.

"Thank you, Perseverance," he said, and walked away through the grassy graves of the nameless poor.

That night, when his household was asleep, he took pen and ink to write to Arthur Norrington, to Harry Quarry, and to his brother. Toward dawn, he began, for the first time in two years, to write to Jamie Fraser.

59

BATTLE OF BENNINGTON

General Burgoyne's camp
August 11, 1777

THE SMOKE OF burnt and burning fields hung over the camp, had done so for days. The Americans were still withdrawing, destroying the countryside in their wake.

William was with Sandy Lindsay, talking about the best way to cook a turkey—one of Lindsay's scouts having just brought him one—when the letter arrived. It was likely William's imagination that a dreadful silence fell upon the camp, the earth shook, and the veil of the temple was rent in twain. But it was very shortly apparent that something had happened, nonetheless.

There was a definite change in the air, something amiss in the rhythms of speech and movement among the men surrounding them. Balcarres felt it, too, and stopped in his examination of the turkey's outspread wing, looking at William with eyebrows raised.

"What?" said William.

"I don't know, but it isn't good." Balcarres thrust the limp turkey into his orderly's hands and, snatching up his hat, made for Burgoyne's tent, William on his heels.

They found Burgoyne tight-lipped and white with anger, his senior officers in clusters round him, speaking to one another in low, shocked voices.

Captain Sir Francis Clerke, the general's aide-de-camp, emerged from the press, head down and face shadowed. Balcarres caught at his elbow as he passed.

"Francis—what's happened?"

Captain Clerke was looking noticeably agitated. He glanced behind him into the tent, then stepped aside and moved out of earshot, taking Balcarres and William with him.

"Howe," he said. "He's not coming."

"Not coming?" William said stupidly. "But—is he not leaving New York after all?"

"He's leaving," Clerke said, his lips so tight it was a wonder he could speak at all. "To invade Pennsylvania."

"But—" Balcarres darted an appalled look toward the entrance to the tent, then back at Clerke.

"Exactly."

The true proportions of the disaster were revealing themselves to William. General Howe was not merely cocking a snook at General Burgoyne by ignoring his plan, which would be bad enough from Burgoyne's point of view. By choosing to march on Philadelphia rather than coming up the Hudson to join Burgoyne's troops, Howe had left Burgoyne essentially to his own devices, in terms of supply and reinforcement.

In other words, they were on their own, separated from their supply trains, with the disagreeable choice of continuing to pursue the retreating Americans through a wilderness from which all sustenance had been stripped—or turning round and marching ignominiously back to Canada, through a wilderness from which all sustenance had been stripped.

Balcarres had been expostulating along these lines to Sir Francis, who rubbed a hand over his face in frustration, shaking his head.

"I know," he said. "If you'll excuse me, my lords—"

"Where are you going?" William asked, and Clerke glanced at him.

"To tell Mrs. Lind," Clerke said. "I thought I'd best warn her." Mrs. Lind was the wife of the chief commissary officer. She was also General Burgoyne's mistress.

WHETHER MRS. LIND had exerted her undeniable gifts to good effect, or whether the general's natural resiliency of character had asserted itself, the blow of Howe's letter was swiftly encompassed. *Whatever you want to say about him,* William wrote in his weekly letter to Lord John, *he knows the benefit of certain decision and swift action. We have resumed our pursuit of the Americans' chief body of troops with redoubled effort. Most of our horses have been abandoned, stolen, or eaten. I have quite worn through the soles of one pair of boots.*

In the meantime, we receive intelligence from one of the scouts to the effect that the town of Bennington, which is not too far distant, is being used as a gathering place for the American commissary. By report, it is lightly guarded, and so the General is sending Colonel Baum, one of the Hessians, with five hundred troops to capture these much-needed supplies. We leave in the morning.

Whether his drunken conversation with Balcarres was in part responsible, William never knew, but he had discovered that he was now spoken of as being "good with Indians." And whether it was owing to this dubious capacity or to the fact that he could speak basic German, he found himself on the morning of August 12 deputed to accompany Colonel Baum's foraging expedition, this including a number of dismounted Brunswick cavalry, two three-pounder artillery pieces, and a hundred Indians.

By report, the Americans were receiving cattle, funneled out of New England, these being collected in quantity in Bennington, as well as a considerable number of wagons, these full of corn, flour, and other necessaries.

It was, for a wonder, not raining when they set out, and that alone gave the expedition a feeling of optimism. Anticipation of food increased this sense significantly. Rations had been short for what seemed a very long time, though in fact it had been only a week or so. Still, more than a day spent marching without adequate food seems a long time, as William had good cause to know.

Many of the Indians were still mounted; they circled the main body of soldiers, riding ahead a little way to scout the road, coming back to offer guidance through or around places where the road—no more than a trace at the best of times—had given up the fight and been absorbed by the forest or drowned by one of the rain-swollen streams that leapt unexpectedly out of the hills. Bennington was near a river called the Walloomsac, and as they walked, William was discussing in a desultory way with one of the Hessian lieutenants whether it might be possible to load the stores onto rafts for transport to a rendezvous downstream.

This discussion was entirely theoretical, since neither of them knew where the Walloomsac went nor whether it was navigable to any extent, but it gave both men a chance to practice the other's language and so passed the time on a long, hot march.

"My father spent much time in Germany," William told Ober-Leftenant Gruenwald, in his careful, slow German. "He is of the food of Hanover very fond."

Gruenwald, from Hesse-Cassel, allowed himself a derisive twitch of the mustache at mention of Hanover, but contented himself with the observation that even a Hanoverian could roast a cow and perhaps boil some potatoes to accompany it. But his own mother made a dish from the flesh of swine and apples, beswimming in red wine and spiced with nutmeg and cinnamon, that made his mouth water only to remember.

Water was running down Gruenwald's face, sweat making tracks in the dust and dampening the collar of his light-blue coat. He took off his tall grenadier's headdress and wiped his head with a giant spotted kerchief, sodden from many earlier employments.

"I think we will maybe not find cinnamon today," Willie said. "Maybe a pig, though."

"If we do, I will him roast for you," Gruenwald assured him. "As for apples . . ." he tucked a hand into his tunic and withdrew a handful of small red crab apples, which he shared out with William. "I haff a bushel of these. I haff–"

Excited yips from an Indian riding back down the column

interrupted him, and William looked up to see the rider throw back an arm, gesturing behind him and shouting, "River!"

The word enlivened the sagging columns, and William saw the cavalry—who had insisted upon wearing their high boots and their broadswords, in spite of their lack of horses, and had suffered in consequence—draw themselves up, clanking loudly with anticipation.

Another shout came from the forward line.

"Cow turds!"

That caused a general cheer and much laughter among the men, who hastened on with a quicker step. William saw Colonel Baum, who did still have a horse, turn out of the column and wait on the roadside, leaning down to speak briefly with the officers as they came past. William saw his aide lean close, pointing up a small hill opposite.

"What do you think—" he said, turning to Gruenwald, and was startled to find the ober-leftenant staring at him blank-faced, his jaw hanging open. The man's hand loosened and fell to his side, and the mitred helmet fell and rolled away in the dust. William blinked and saw a thick worm of red snake its way slowly down from under Gruenwald's dark hair.

Gruenwald sat down quite suddenly and fell backward in the road, his face gone a muddy white.

"Shit!" said William, and jerked suddenly to an awareness of what had just happened. "*Ambush!*" he bellowed at the top of his lungs. *"Das ist ein Überfall!!"*

There were shouts of alarm rising from the column, and the crack of sporadic firing from the woods. William grabbed Gruenwald under the arms and dragged him hastily into the shelter of a group of pine trees. The ober-leftenant was still alive, though his coat was wet with sweat and blood. William made sure the German's pistol was loaded and in his hand before taking his own pistol and dashing toward Baum, who was standing in his stirrups, shrieking directions in high, shrill German.

He caught only a word here and there and looked urgently round, to see whether he could tell what the colonel's orders were from the actions of the Hessians. He caught sight of a little group of scouts, running down the road toward him, and ran to meet them.

"Goddamned lot of rebels," one scout gasped, out of breath, pointing behind him. "Coming."

"Where? How far?" He felt as though he were about to run out of his skin, but forced himself to stand still, speak calmly, breathe.

A mile, maybe two. He did breathe then, and managed to ask how many there were. Maybe two hundred, maybe more. Armed with muskets, but no artillery.

"Right. Go back and keep an eye on them." He turned back toward Colonel Baum, feeling the surface of the road strange under his feet, as though it wasn't quite where he expected it to be.

THEY DUG IN, hastily but efficiently, entrenching themselves behind shallow earthworks and makeshift barricades of fallen trees. The guns were dragged up the small hill and aimed to cover the road. The rebels, of course, ignored the road, and swarmed in from both sides.

There might have been two hundred men in the first wave; it was impossible to count them as they darted through the heavy wood. William could see the flicker of movement and fired at it, but without any great hope of hitting anyone. The wave hesitated, but only for a moment.

Then a strong voice bellowed, somewhere behind the rebel front, "We take them now, or Molly Stark's a widow tonight!"

"What?" said William, disbelieving. Whatever the man shouting had meant, his exhortation had a marked effect, for an enormous number of rebels came boiling out of the trees, headed at a mad run for the guns. The soldiers minding the guns promptly fled, and so did a good many of the others.

The rebels were making short work of the rest, and William had just settled down grimly to do what he could before they got him, when two Indians came springing over the rolling ground, seized him under the arms, and, yanking him to his feet, propelled him rapidly away.

Which was how Lieutenant Ellesmere found himself once more cast in the role of Cassandra, reporting the debacle at Bennington to General Burgoyne. Men killed and wounded, guns lost—and not a single cow to be shown for it.

And I haven't yet killed a single rebel, either, he thought tiredly, making his way slowly back to his tent afterward. He thought he should regret that, but wasn't sure he did.

60

DESERTER GAME, ROUND II

JAMIE HAD BEEN bathing in the river, sluicing sweat and grime from his body, when he heard remarkably odd swearing in French. The words were French, but the sentiments expressed were definitely not. Curious, he clambered out of the water, dressed, and went down the bank a little way, where he discovered a young man waving his arms and gesturing in an agitated attempt to make himself understood to a bemused party of workmen. As half of them were Germans and the rest Americans from Virginia, his efforts to communicate with them in French had so far succeeded only in entertaining them.

Jamie had introduced himself and offered his services as interpreter. Which is how he had come to spend a good bit of each day with the young Polish engineer whose unpronounceable last name had quickly been shortened to "Kos."

He found Kos both intelligent and rather touching in his enthusiasm—and was himself interested in the fortifications Kościuszko (for he prided himself on being able to say it correctly) was building. Kos, for his part, was both grateful for the linguistic assistance and interested in the occasional observations and suggestions that Jamie was able to make, as the result of his conversations with Brianna.

Talking about vectors and stresses made him miss her almost unbearably but at the same time brought her somehow nearer to him, and he found himself spending more and more time with the young Pole, learning bits of his language and allowing Kos to practice what he fondly imagined to be English.

"What is it that brought ye here?" Jamie asked one day. In spite of the lack of pay, a remarkable number of European officers had come to join—or tried to join—the Continental army, evidently feeling that even if the prospects of plunder were limited, they could bamboozle the Congress into granting them rank as generals, which they could then parlay into further occupation back in Europe. Some of these dubious volunteers were actually of use, but he'd heard a good bit of muttering about those who weren't. Thinking of Matthias Fermoy, he was inclined to mutter a bit himself.

Kos wasn't one of these, though.

"Well, first, money," he said frankly, when asked how he had come to be in America. "My brother the manor in Poland has, but family no money, nothing for me. No girl look at me without money." He shrugged. "No place in Polish army, but I know how to build things, I come where things to build." He grinned. "Maybe girls, too. Girls with good family, good money."

"If ye came for money and girls, man, ye joined the wrong army," Jamie said dryly, and Kościuszko laughed.

"I say *first* money," he corrected. "I come to Philadelphia, read there *La Declaration*." He pronounced it in French, and bared his head in reverence at the name, clasping his sweat-stained hat to his breast. "This thing, this writing . . . I am ravish."

So ravished was he by the sentiments expressed in that noble document that he had at once sought out its author. While probably surprised by the sudden advent of a passionate young Pole in his midst, Thomas Jefferson had made him welcome, and the two men had spent most of a day deeply involved in the discussion of philosophy (in French), from which they had emerged fast friends.

"Great man," Kos assured Jamie solemnly, crossing himself before putting his hat back on. "God keep him safe."

"*Dieu accorde-lui la sagesse,*" Jamie replied. *God grant him wisdom.* He thought that Jefferson would certainly be safe, as he was no soldier.

Kos had wiped a strand of stringy dark hair out of his mouth and shaken his head.

"Maybe wife, one day, if God wills. This—what we do here—more important than wife."

They returned to work, but Jamie found his mind dwelling with interest on the conversation. The notion that it was better to spend one's life in pursuit of a noble goal than merely to seek safety—he agreed with that entirely. But surely such purity of purpose was the province of men without families? A paradox there: a man who sought his own safety was a coward; a man who risked his family's safety was a poltroon, if not worse.

That led on to more rambling paths of thought and further interesting paradoxes: Do women hold back the evolution of such things as freedom and other social ideals, out of fear for themselves or their children? Or do they in fact inspire such things—and the risks required to reach them—by providing the things worth fighting for? Not merely fighting to defend, either, but to propel forward, for a man wanted more for his children than he would ever have.

He would have to ask Claire what she thought of this, though he smiled to think of some of the things she *might* think of it, particularly the part about whether women hindered social evolution by their nature. She'd told him something of her own experiences in the Great War—he couldn't think of it by any other name, though she told him there was another, earlier one by that name. She said disparaging things about heroes now and then, but only when he'd hurt himself; she knew fine what men were for.

Would he be here, in fact, if it weren't for her? Would he do this anyway, only for the sake of the ideals of the Revolution, if he were not assured of victory? He had to admit that only a madman, an idealist, or a truly desperate man would be here now. Any sane person who knew anything about armies would have shaken his head and turned away, appalled. He often felt appalled, himself.

But he would, in fact, do it—were he alone. A man's life had to have more purpose than only to feed himself each day. And this was a grand purpose—grander, maybe, than anyone else fighting for it knew. And if it took his own life in the doing . . . he wouldn't enjoy it, but he'd be comforted in the dying, knowing he'd helped. After all, it wasn't as though he would be leaving his wife helpless; unlike most wives, Claire would have a place to go if something befell him.

He was once more in the river, floating on his back and thinking along these lines, when he heard the gasp. It was a feminine gasp, and he put his feet down at once and stood up, wet hair streaming over his face. He shoved it back to find Rachel Hunter standing on the bank, both hands pressed over her eyes and every line of her body strained in an eloquence of distress.

"Did ye want me, Rachel?" he asked, wiping water out of his eyes in an effort to locate just where on the riverbank he had left his clothes. She gasped again and turned her face in his direction, hands still over her eyes.

"Friend James! Thy wife said I would find thee here. I beg pardon for—please! Come out at once!" Her anguish broke out and her hands dropped, though she kept her eyes tight shut as she reached out to him, pleading.

"What—"

"Denny! The British have him!"

Cold shot through his veins, much colder than the wind on his exposed wet skin.

"Where? How? Ye can look now," he added, hastily buttoning his breeches.

"He went with another man, posing as deserters." He was up the bank beside her, shirt over his arm, and saw that she had her brother's spectacles in the pocket of her apron; her hand kept going to them, clutching them. "I told him not to, I did!"

"I told him, too," Jamie said grimly. "Are ye sure, lass?"

She nodded, pale as a sheet and her eyes huge in her face, but not—not yet—weeping.

"The other man—he came back, just now, and ran to find me. He—it was ill-luck, he said; they were brought before a major, and it was the same man who had threatened to hang Denny when he did it last time! The other man ran for it and escaped, but they caught Denny, and this time, this time . . ." She was gasping for breath and could barely speak for dread, he saw. He put a hand on her arm.

"Find the other man and send him to my tent, so he can tell me exactly where your brother is. I'll go to fetch Ian and we'll get him back." He squeezed her arm gently to make her look at him, and she did, though so distracted he thought she barely saw him.

"Dinna fash yourself. We'll get him back for ye," he repeated gently. "I swear it, by Christ and His Mother."

"Thee must not swear—oh, the devil with it!" she cried, then clapped a hand over her mouth. She shut her eyes, swallowed, and took it away again.

"Thank you," she said.

"Ye're welcome," he said, with an eye to the sinking sun. Did the British prefer to hang people at sunset or at dawn? "We'll get him back," he said once more, firmly. *Dead or alive.*

THE CAMP'S commanding officer had built a gibbet in the center of the camp. It was a crude affair of unbarked logs and rough timber, and from the holes and gouges round its nails, had been disassembled and moved several times. It looked effective, though, and the dangling noose gave Jamie a feeling of ice in his water.

"We've played the deserter game once too often," Jamie whispered to his nephew. "Or maybe three."

"D'ye think he's ever used it?" Ian murmured back, peering down at the sinister thing through their screen of oak saplings.

"He wouldna go to that much work only to scare someone."

It scared *him,* badly. He didn't point out to Ian the spot near the bottom of the main upright, where someone's—or someones'—desperately flailing feet had kicked away chunks of the bark. The makeshift gibbet wasn't high enough for the drop to break a man's neck; a man hanged on it would strangle slowly.

He touched his own neck in reflexive aversion, Roger Mac's mangled throat and its ugly raw scar clear in his mind. Even clearer was the memory of the grief that had overwhelmed him, coming to take down Roger Mac from the tree they'd hanged him on, knowing him dead and the world changed forever. It had been, too, though he hadn't died.

Well, it wasn't going to change for Rachel Hunter. They weren't too late, that was the important thing. He said as much to Ian, who didn't reply but gave him a brief glance of surprise.

How do you know? it said, plain as words. He lifted a shoulder and inclined his head toward a spot a little farther down the hill, where an outcrop of rock covered in moss and bearberry would give them cover. They moved off silently, keeping low, making their movements in the same slow rhythm to which the wood was moving. It was twilight and the world was full of shadows; it was no trick to be two more.

He knew they hadn't hanged Denny Hunter yet, because he'd seen men hanged. Execution left a stain upon the air and marked the souls of those who saw it.

The camp was quiet. Not literally—the soldiers were making considerable racket, and a good thing, too—but in terms of its spirit. There was neither a sense of dread oppression nor the sick excitement that sprang from the same source; you could feel such things. So Denny Hunter was either here, alive—or had been sent elsewhere. If he was here, where would he be?

Confined somehow, and under guard. This wasn't a permanent camp; there was no stockade. It was a big camp, though, and it took them some time to circle it, checking to see whether Hunter might be somewhere in the open, tied to a tree or shackled to a wagon. He was nowhere in sight, though. That left the tents.

There were four large ones, and one of these plainly housed the commissary; it stood apart and had a small cluster of wagons near it. It had also a constant stream of men going in and out, emerging with sacks of flour or dried peas. No meat, though he could smell cooking rabbit and squirrel from some of the campfires. The German deserters had been right, then; the army was living off the land, as well as it could.

"The commander's tent?" Ian whispered softly to him. It was plain to see, with its pennants and the knot of men who stood about just outside its entrance.

"I hope not." Plainly they'd have taken Denny Hunter *to* the commander for interrogation. And if he were still in doubt as to Hunter's *bona fides,* he might have kept the man close at hand for further questioning.

Had he already made up his mind on the matter, though—and Rachel had been convinced of it—he wouldn't keep him. He would have been sent somewhere under guard to await his reckoning. Under guard and out of sight, though Jamie doubted the British commander feared a rescue attempt.

"Eeny-meeny-miney-mo," he muttered under his breath, twitching a finger back and forth between the two remaining tents. A guard with a musket was standing more or less between them; no telling which he was set to guard. "That one." He lifted his chin to the one on the right, but even as he did so felt Ian stiffen beside him.

"Nay," Ian said softly, eyes riveted. "The other."

There was something strange in Ian's voice, and Jamie glanced at him in surprise, then down at the tent.

At first, his only thought was a fleeting sense of confusion. Then the world changed.

It was twilight, but they were by now no more than fifty yards away; there was no mistaking it. He hadn't seen the boy since he was close to twelve, but he had memorized every moment they'd spent in each other's presence: the way he carried himself, the quick, graceful movement—*that's from his mother,* he thought in a daze of shock, seeing the tall young officer make a gesture of the hand that was Geneva Dunsany to the life—the shape of his back, his head and ears, though the slender shoulders had thickened to a man's. *Mine,* he thought, with a surge of pride that shocked him nearly as much as William's sudden appearance had. *They're mine.*

Jarring as they were, these thoughts took less than half a second to dash through his head and out again. He breathed in, very slowly, and out again. Had Ian remembered William from their meeting seven years earlier? Or was the resemblance so instantly visible to a casual eye?

It didn't matter now. The camp was beginning its supper preparations; within minutes everyone would be engrossed in the meal. It was better to move then, even without the cover of darkness.

"It has to be me, aye?" Ian gripped his wrist, compelling his attention. "D'ye want to make the diversion before or after?"

"After." He'd been thinking, in the back of his mind, all the time they were creeping toward the camp, and now the decision lay ready, as though someone else had made it. "Best if we can get him away quiet. Try, and if things go wrong, screech."

Ian nodded and, with no further conversation, dropped to his belly and began a stealthy worming through the brush. The evening was cool and pleasant after the heat of the day, but Jamie's hands felt cold and he cupped them round the clay belly of the little firepot. He'd carried it from their own camp, feeding it bits of dry stick along the way. It was hissing softly to itself as it fed on a chunk of dried hickory, both the sight and the smell of it safely hidden in the haze of campfire smoke that drifted through the trees, dispelling the gnats and the bloodthirsty mosquitoes, thank God and His mother.

Wondering at his own twitching—it wasn't like him—he touched his sporran, checking yet again that the cork had not come loose from the bottle of turpentine, even though he knew well it hadn't; he'd smell it.

The arrows in his quiver shifted as he shifted his weight, the fletchings rustling. He was in easy bowshot of the commander's tent, could have the canvas well alight in seconds if Ian screeched. If he didn't . . .

He began to move again, eyes flitting over the ground, searching for a patch that would do. Dry grass there was in plenty, but it would go up too fast if that was all there was. He wanted a fast flame but a big one.

The soldiers would have already scavenged the nearby forest for firewood, but he spotted a fallen fir snag, too heavy to carry away. Foragers had snapped the lower branches off, but there were plenty left, thick with dried needles that the wind hadn't taken yet. He moved back slowly, far enough out of sight that he could move quickly again, gathering armfuls of dry grass, bark scraped hasty from a log, anything that would kindle.

Flaming arrows in the commander's tent would compel instant attention, to be sure, but they would also cause widespread alarm; soldiers would boil out of the camp like hornets, looking for attackers. A grass fire, no. Such things were common, and while it would certainly create diversion, no one would be looking further once they'd seen it was nothing.

A few minutes and he had his diverson ready. So busy he'd been, he hadn't even taken thought to look again at his son.

"God damn ye for a liar, Jamie Fraser," he said under his breath, and looked.

William was gone.

THE SOLDIERS WERE at their supper; cheerful talk and the sounds of eating covered any small noises Ian made as he walked softly round the side of the left-hand tent. If someone saw him, he'd speak to them in Mohawk, claim to be a scout from Burgoyne's camp, come with information. By the time they got him in front of the commander, he'd either have thought of some good, picturesque information, or he'd scream and reckon to fight his way out while they were distracted by flaming arrows.

That wouldn't help Denny Hunter, though, and he was careful. There were pickets posted, but he and Uncle Jamie had watched long enough to see the pattern of them and spy the dead spot where a picket's vision was obstructed by the trees. He knew he couldn't be seen behind the tent, save someone heading for the woods for a piss stumbled over him.

There was a gap at the bottom of the tent and a candlestick lit inside; a spot in the canvas glowed dim in the twilight. He watched the gap and saw no shadow move. Right, then.

He lay down and inserted a cautious hand, feeling along the dirt floor, hoping no one inside stamped on his hand. If he could find a cot, he could squirm in and lie under it. If—something touched his hand and he bit his tongue, hard.

"Is thee a friend?" whispered Denny's voice. Ian could see the Quaker's shadow on the canvas, a squatting blur, and Denny's hand held his hard.

"Aye, it's me," he whispered back. "Keep quiet. Stand back."

Denny moved, and Ian heard the clink of metal. Dammit, the buggers had him in fetters. He compressed his lips and slid under the edge of the tent.

Denny greeted him silently, his face alight with hope and alarm. The little Quaker lifted his hands, nodded to his feet. Full irons. Christ, they *did* mean to hang him.

Ian leaned in close to whisper in Denny's ear.

"I go out before ye. Lie down there, easy as ye can, close as ye can." He jerked his chin at the back wall of the tent. "Dinna move yourself; I'll pull ye through." Then get Denny onto his shoulders like a dead fawn and head for the woods, hooting like an owl to let Uncle Jamie know it was time to set the fire.

It wasn't possible to move a man in chains in total silence, but with any luck at all, the scraping of spoons on mess kits and the soldiers' conversation would cover any stray clinking. He pulled the canvas out as far as he could, reached under, and took firm hold of Denny's shoulders. The wee bugger was heavier than he looked, but Ian got Denny's upper body mostly clear of the tent without too much trouble. Sweating, he scuttled to the side and reached in to take hold of Denny's ankles, wrapping the chain round his own wrist to take up the slack.

There was no sound, but Ian's head jerked up before his mind even told him that the air near him had moved in a way that meant someone was standing there.

"Hush!" he said by reflex, not knowing whether he was talking to Denny or to the tall soldier who had stepped out of the wood behind him.

"What the devil—" the soldier began, sounding startled. He didn't finish the question, but took three paces fast and grabbed Ian by the wrist.

"Who are you and what are you—Good God, where did *you* come from?" William the soldier stared into Ian's face, and Ian thanked God briefly for the fact that his other wrist was immobilized by Denny's chain, for otherwise William would be already dead. And he didn't want to have to tell Uncle Jamie *that.*

"He has come to help me escape, Friend William," Denny Hunter said mildly from the shadows on the ground behind Ian. "I would take it kindly if thee did not hinder him, though I will understand if thy duty compels thee."

William's head jerked, looked wildly round, then down. Had the circumstances been less dire, Ian would have laughed at the expressions—for there were a great number of them, run through in the course of a heartbeat—on it. William closed his eyes for an instant, then opened them again.

"Don't tell me," he said shortly. "I don't want to know." He squatted beside Ian and, between them, they had Denny out in a matter of seconds. Ian took a deep breath, put his hands to his mouth, and hooted, then paused a moment and did it once again. William stared at him in mingled puzzlement and anger. Then Ian ducked the point of his shoulder into Denny's midriff and, with William heaving, got the doctor onto his shoulders with little more than a startled grunt and a slight clanking of fetters.

William's hand closed on Ian's forearm, and his head, a dark oval in the last traces of light, jerked toward the woods.

"Left," he whispered. "There are latrine trenches on the right. Two pickets, a hundred yards out." He squeezed hard and let go.

"May you be held in God's light, Friend William." Denny's whisper came breathless by Ian's ear, but Ian was already going and didn't know whether William had heard. He supposed it didn't matter.

A few moments later, he heard the first shouts of "Fire!" behind him in the camp.

61

NO BETTER COMPANION THAN THE RIFLE

September 15, 1777

BY EARLY SEPTEMBER, we had reached the main army, encamped on the Hudson near the village of Saratoga. General Horatio Gates was in command, and received the ragtag and bobtail refugees and random militia with pleasure. For once, the army was tolerably well supplied, and we were equipped with clothes, decent food—and the remarkable luxury of a small tent, in honor of Jamie's status as a colonel of militia, in spite of the fact that he had no men.

Knowing Jamie as I did, I was reasonably sure this would be a temporary state of affairs. For my part, I was delighted to have an actual cot to sleep on, a tiny table to eat from—and food to put on it on a fairly regular basis.

"I've brought ye a present, Sassenach." Jamie plumped the bag down on the table with a pleasantly meaty-sounding thump and a waft of fresh blood. My mouth began to water.

"What is it? Birds?" It wasn't ducks or geese; those had a distinctive scent about them, a musk of body oils, feathers, and decaying waterweeds. But partridges, say, or grouse . . . I swallowed heavily at the thought of pigeon pie.

"No, a book." He pulled a small package wrapped in tattered oilcloth from the bulging sack and proudly set it in my hands.

"A book?" I said blankly.

He nodded encouragingly.

"Aye. Words printed on paper, ye'll recall the sort of thing? I ken it's been a long time."

I gave him an eye and, attempting to ignore the rumbling of my stomach, opened the package. It was a well-worn pocket-sized copy of *The Life and Opinions of Tristram Shandy, Gentleman—Vol. I,* and despite my disgruntlement at being presented with literature instead of food, I was interested. It *had* been a long time since I'd had a good book in my hands, and this was a story I'd heard of but never read.

"The owner must have been fond of it," I said, turning the little volume over gently. The spine was nearly worn through, and the edges of the leather cover were rubbed shiny. A rather nasty thought struck me.

"Jamie . . . you didn't . . . take this from a, er, a *body,* did you?" Stripping weapons, equipment, and usable clothing from fallen enemies was not considered looting; it was an unpleasant necessity. Still . . .

He shook his head, though, still rummaging in the bag.

"Nay, I found it at the edge of a wee creek. Dropped in flight, I expect."

Well, that was better, though I was sure the man who had dropped it would regret the loss of this treasured companion. I opened the book at random and squinted at the small type.

"Sassenach."

"Hmm?" I glanced up, jerked out of the text, to see Jamie regarding me with a mixture of sympathy and amusement.

"Ye need spectacles, don't ye?" he said. "I hadna realized."

"Nonsense!" I said, though my heart gave a small jump. "I see perfectly well."

"Oh, aye?" He moved beside me and took the book out of my hand. Opening it to the middle, he held it in front of me. "Read that."

I leaned backward, and he advanced in front of me.

"Stop that!" I said. "How do you expect me to read anything that close?"

"Stand still, then," he said, and moved the book away from my face. "Can ye see the letters clear yet?"

"No," I said crossly. "Farther. Farther. No, bloody farther!"

And at last was obliged to admit that I could not bring the letters into focus at a distance of nearer than about eighteen inches.

"Well, it's *very* small type!" I said, flustered and discomfited. I had, of course, been aware that my eyesight was not so keen as it once had been, but to be so rudely confronted with the evidence that I was, if not blind as a bat, definitely in competition with moles was a trifle upsetting.

"Twelve-point Caslon," Jamie said, giving the text a professional glance. "I will say the leading's terrible," he added critically. "And the gutters are half what they should be. Even so—" He flipped the book shut and looked at me, one eyebrow raised. "Ye need spectacles, *a nighean,*" he repeated gently.

"Hmph!" I said. And on impulse picked up the book, opened it, and handed it to him. "So—read it yourself, why don't you?"

Looking surprised and a little wary, he took the book and looked into it. Then extended his arm a little. And a little more. I watched, experiencing that same odd mix of amusement and sympathy, as he finally held the book nearly at arm's length, and read, *"So that the life of a writer, whatever he might fancy to the contrary, was not so much a state of composition, as a state of warfare; and his probation in it, precisely that of any other man militant upon earth—both depending alike, not half so much upon the degrees of his WIT—as his RESISTANCE."*

He closed it and looked at me, the edge of his mouth tucked back.

"Aye, well," he said. "I can still shoot, at least."

"And I can tell one herb from another by smell, I suppose," I said, and laughed. "Just as well. I don't suppose there's a spectacle-maker this side of Philadelphia."

"No, I suppose not," he said ruefully. "When we get to Edinburgh, though, I ken just the man. I'll buy ye a tortoiseshell pair for everyday, Sassenach, and a pair wi' gold rims for Sundays."

"Expect me to read the Bible with them, do you?" I inquired.

"Ah, no," he said, "that's just for show. After all"—he picked up my hand, which smelled of dill weed and coriander, and, lifting it to his mouth, ran the point of his tongue delicately down the lifeline in my palm—"the important things ye do by touch, aye?"

WE WERE INTERRUPTED by a cough from the door of the tent, and I turned to see a large, bearlike man with long gray hair loose upon his shoulders. He had an amiable face with a scar through the upper lip and a mild but keen eye, which went at once to the bag on the table.

I stiffened a little; there were strict prohibitions against the looting of farms, and while Jamie had taken these particular hens scratching in the wild, there was no way of proving that, and this gentleman, while dressed in casual homespun and hunting shirt, bore himself with the unmistakable authority of an officer.

"You'd be Colonel Fraser?" he said, with a nod toward Jamie, and extended a hand. "Daniel Morgan."

I recognized the name, though the only thing I knew about Daniel Morgan—a footnote in Brianna's eighth-grade history book—was that he was a famous rifleman. This wasn't particularly useful; everyone knew that, and the camp had buzzed with interest when he had arrived at the end of August with a number of men.

He now glanced with interest at *me,* and then at the bag of chickens, flecked with incriminating tufts of feather.

"By your leave, ma'am," he said, and without waiting for my leave, picked up the sack and pulled out a dead chicken. The neck flopped limp, showing the large, bloody hole through its head where an eye—well, two eyes—had once been. His scarred mouth pursed in a soundless whistle and he looked sharply up at Jamie.

"You do that a-purpose?" he asked.

"I always shoot them through the eye," Jamie replied politely. "Dinna want to spoil the meat."

A slow grin spread over Colonel Morgan's face, and he nodded. "Come with me, Mr. Fraser. Bring your rifle."

WE ATE THAT night at Daniel Morgan's fire, and the company—filled with chicken stew—raised cups of beer and hooted to toast the addition of a new member to their elite corps. I hadn't had a chance of private conversation with Jamie since Morgan's abduction of him that afternoon, and rather wondered what he made of his apotheosis. But he seemed comfortable with the riflemen, though he glanced now and then at Morgan, with the look that meant he was still making up his mind.

For my part, I was extremely pleased. By their nature, riflemen fought from a distance—and often a distance much greater than a musket's range. They were also valuable, and commanders were not likely to risk them in close combat. No soldier was safe, but some occupations had a much higher rate of mortality—and while I accepted the fact that Jamie was a born gambler, I liked him to have the best odds possible.

Many of the riflemen were Long Hunters, others what they called "over-mountain men," and thus had no wives with them here. Some did, and I made instant acquaintance with the women by the simple expedient of admiring one young woman's baby.

"Mrs. Fraser?" one older lady said, coming to plump down on the log beside me. "Are you the conjure-woman?"

"I am," I said pleasantly. "They call me the White Witch."

That reared them back a bit, but the forbidden has its own strong appeal—and after all, what could I do in the middle of military camp, surrounded by their husbands and sons, all armed to the teeth?

Within minutes, I was dispensing advice on everything from menstrual cramps to colic. I caught a glimpse of Jamie, grinning at sight of my popularity, and gave him a discreet wave before turning back to my audience.

The men, of course, continued drinking, with outbreaks of raucous laughter, then the fall of voices as one man took over a story, only to have the cycle repeat. At one point, though, the atmosphere changed, so abruptly that I broke off an intense discussion of diaper rash and looked over toward the fire.

Daniel Morgan was rising laboriously to his feet, and there was a distinct air of anticipation among the watching men. Was he about to make a speech, welcoming Jamie?

"Oh, dear Lord," said Mrs. Graham under her breath beside me. "He's a-doing it again."

I hadn't time to ask her *what* he was a-doing, before he a-did it.

He shambled to the center of the gathering, where he stood swaying like an old bear, his long gray hair wafting in the wind of the fire and his eyes creased with amiability. They were focused on Jamie, though, I saw.

"Got something to show you, Mr. Fraser," he said, loudly enough that the women who had still been talking stopped, every eye going to him. He took hold of the hem of his long woolen hunting shirt and pulled it off over his head. He dropped it on the ground, spread his arms like a ballet dancer, and stumped slowly round.

Everyone gasped, though from Mrs. Graham's remark, most of them must have seen it before. His back was ridged with scars from neck to waist. Old scars, to be sure—but there wasn't a square inch of unmarked skin on his back, massive as it was. Even I was shocked.

"The British did that," he said conversationally, turning back and dropping his arms. "Give me four hundred and ninety-nine lashes. I counted." The gathering erupted in laughter, and he grinned. "Was supposed to give me five hundred, but he missed one. I didn't point it out to him."

More laughter. Obviously, this was a frequent performance, but one that his audience loved. There were cheers and more toasts when he finished and went to sit beside Jamie, still naked to the waist, his shirt wadded casually in his hand.

Jamie's face gave nothing away—but I saw that his shoulders had relaxed. Evidently he had made up his mind about Dan Morgan.

JAMIE LIFTED THE LID of my small iron pot, with an expression somewhere between caution and hope.

"Not food," I informed him, rather unnecessarily, as he was wheezing in the manner of one who has inadvertently inhaled horseradish into the sinuses.

"I should hope not," he said, coughing and wiping his eyes. "Christ, Sassenach, that's worse than usual. D'ye mean to poison someone?"

"Yes, *Plasmodium vivax.* Put the lid back on." I was simmering a decoction of cinchona bark and gallberries, for the treatment of malarial cases.

"Have we *got* any food?" he asked plaintively, dropping the lid back in place.

"In fact we have." I reached into the cloth-covered pail at my feet and triumphantly pulled out a meat pie, its crust golden and shimmering with lard.

His face assumed the expression of an Israelite beholding the promised land, and he held out his hands, receiving the pie with the reverence due a precious object, though this impression was dispelled in the next instant as he took a large bite out of it.

"Where did ye get it?" he asked, after a few moments of blissful mastication. "Are there more?"

"There are. A nice prostitute named Daisy brought them for me."

He paused, examined the pie critically for signs of its provenance, then shrugged and took another bite.

"Do I want to know what it was ye did for her, Sassenach?"

"Well, probably not while you're eating, no. Have you seen Ian?"

"No." The response might have been abbreviated by the exigencies of eating pie, but I caught the slightest shiftiness in his manner and stopped, staring at him.

"Do you *know* where Ian is?"

"More or less." He kept his eyes fixed firmly on the meat pie, thus confirming my suspicions.

"Do I want to know what he's doing?"

"No, ye don't," he said definitely.

"Oh, God."

IAN MURRAY, having carefully dressed his hair with bear grease and a pair of turkey feathers, removed his shirt, leaving this rolled up with his tattered plaid under a log, and told Rollo to guard it, then walked across a small stretch of open ground toward the British camp.

"Hold!"

He turned a face of bored impassivity toward the sentry who had hailed him. The sentry, a boy of fifteen or so, was holding a musket whose barrel shook noticeably. Ian hoped the numpty wouldn't shoot him by accident.

"Scout," he said succinctly, and walked past the sentry without a backward glance, though he felt a spider strolling to and fro between his shoulder blades. *Scout,* he thought, and felt a small bubble of laughter rise up. Well, it was the truth, after all.

He strolled through the camp in the same manner, ignoring the occasional stare—though most of those who noticed him merely glanced at him and then away.

Burgoyne's headquarters was easy to spot, a large tent of green canvas that sprouted like a toadstool among the neat aisles of small white tents that housed the soldiers. It was some distance away—and he didn't mean to get any closer just now—but he could glimpse the comings and goings of staff officers, messengers . . . and the occasional scout, though none of these was Indian.

The Indian camps were on the far side of the army encampment, scattered in the forest outside the neat military grid. He was not sure whether he might meet some of Thayendanegea's people, who might in turn recognize him. This wouldn't be a difficulty, as he had said nothing regarding politics during his ill-fated visit to Joseph Brant's house; they would likely accept him on sight without any awkward questions.

If he were to encounter some of the Huron and Oneida that Burgoyne employed to harass the Continentals, that might be a wee bit touchier. He had complete confidence in his ability to impress them with his identity as a Mohawk—but if they were either too suspicious or too impressed, he wouldn't learn much.

He had learned a few things simply from his walk through the camp. Morale was not high; there was rubbish between some of the tents, and most of the washerwomen among the camp followers were sitting in the grass drinking gin, their kettles cold and empty. Still, the atmosphere in general seemed subdued but resolute; some men were dicing and drinking, but more were melting lead and making musket balls, repairing or polishing their weapons.

Food was short; he could sense hunger in the air, even without seeing the line of men waiting outside the baker's tent. None of them looked at him; they were focused on the loaves that emerged—these broken in half before being handed out. Half rations, then; that was good.

None of this was important, though, and as for troop numbers and armament—these were well established by now. Uncle Jamie and Colonel Morgan and General Gates would like to know about the stores of powder and ammunition, but the artillery park and powder magazine would be well guarded, with no conceivable reason for an Indian scout to be nosing round there.

Something tugged at the corner of his vision and he glanced cautiously round, then hastily jerked his eyes forward, forcing himself to walk at the same pace. Jesus, it was the Englishman he'd saved from the swamp—the man who'd helped him get wee Denny free. And—

He clamped down on that thought. He kent it well enough; no one could look like that and *not* be. But he felt it dangerous even to acknowledge the thought to himself, lest it show somehow on his face.

He forced himself to breathe as usual and walk without concern, because a Mohawk scout would have none. Damn. He'd meant to spend the remaining hours of daylight with some of the Indians, picking up what information he could, and then after dark come quietly back into camp, stealing up within earshot of Burgoyne's tent. If yon wee lieutenant was wuthering round, though, it might be too dangerous to try. The last thing he wanted was to meet the man face-to-face.

"Hey!" The shout ran into his flesh like a sharp splinter. He recognized the voice, knew it was aimed at him, but didn't turn round. Six paces, five, four, three . . . He reached the end of an alley of tents and sheared off to the right, out of sight.

"Hey!" The voice was closer, almost behind him, and he broke into a run, heading for the cover of the trees. Only one or two soldiers saw him; one started to his feet but then stood, uncertain what to do, and he pushed past the man and dived into the trees.

"Well, that's torn it," he muttered, crouched behind a brush shelter. The tall lieutenant was questioning the man he'd shoved past. Both of them were looking toward the wood, the soldier shaking his head and shrugging helplessly.

Christ, the wee loon was coming toward him! He turned and stepped silently through the trees, working his way deeper into the wood. He could hear the Englishman behind him, crashing and rustling like a bear just out of its den in the spring.

"Murray!" he was shouting. "Murray—is that you? Wait!"

"Wolf's Brother! Is that you?"

Ian said something very blasphemous under his breath in Gaelic, and turned to see who had addressed him in Mohawk.

"It *is* you! Where's your demon wolf? Did something finally eat it?" His old friend Glutton was beaming at him, adjusting his breechclout after having a piss.

"I hope something eats you," Ian said to his friend, keeping his voice low. "I need to get away. There is an Englishman following me."

Glutton's face changed at once, though it didn't lose either its smile or its eager expression. The wide grin widened further, and he jerked his head behind him, indicating the opening to a trail. Then his face went suddenly slack, and he staggered from one side to the other, lurching in the direction Ian had come.

Ian barely made it out of sight before the Englishman called William came rushing into the clearing, only to run slap into Glutton, who clutched him by the lapels of his coat, gazed up soulfully into his eyes, and said, "Whisky?"

"I haven't any whisky," William said, brusque but not impolite, and tried to detach Glutton. This proved a difficult proposition; Glutton was much more agile than his squat appearance suggested, and the instant a hand was removed from one spot, it clung limpetlike to another. To add to the performance, Glutton began to tell the lieutenant—in Mohawk—the story of the famous hunt that had given him his name, pausing periodically to shout, "WHISHKEE!" and fling his arms about the Englishman's body.

Ian spared no time to admire the Englishman's own facility with language, which was considerable, but made off as fast as possible, circling to the west. He couldn't go back through the camp. He might take refuge in one of the Indian camps, but it was possible that William would look for him there, once he'd escaped from Glutton.

"What the hell does he want with me?" he muttered, no longer bothering with silence but cleaving the brush with a minimum of breakage. William the lieutenant had to know he was a Continental, because of Denny Hunter and the deserter game. Yet he had not raised a general alarm upon seeing him—only called out in surprise, and then as one wanting conversation.

Well, maybe that was a trick. Wee William might be young, but he was not stupid. Couldn't be, considering who his fath—and the man *was* chasing him.

He could hear voices fading behind him—he thought that William had perhaps now recognized Glutton, in spite of the fact that he had been half dead with fever when they met. If so, he would know Glutton was his, Ian's, friend—and instantly detect the ruse. But it didn't matter; he was well into the wood by now. William would never catch him.

The smell of smoke and fresh meat caught his nose, and he turned, going downhill toward the bank of a small stream. There was a Mohawk camp there; he knew it at once.

He paused, though. The scent of it, the knowledge of it,

had drawn him like a moth—but he mustn't enter. Not now. If William *had* recognized Glutton, the first place he would look for Ian was the Mohawks' camp. And if she should be there . . .

"You, *again*?" said an unpleasant Mohawk voice. "You don't learn, do you?"

Actually, he did. He'd learned enough to hit first. He turned on his heel and swung from somewhere behind his knees, continuing up with all the power in his body. "*Aim to hit* through *the bugger's face,*" Uncle Jamie had instructed him when he began to go about in Edinburgh alone. It was, as usual, good advice.

His knuckles burst with a crunch that shot blue lightning straight up his arm and into his neck and jaw—but Sun Elk flew backward two paces and crashed into a tree.

Ian stood panting and gently touching his knuckles, recalling too late that Uncle Jamie's advice had begun with, "*Hit them in the soft parts if ye can.*" It didn't matter; it was worth it. Sun Elk was moaning softly, his eyelids fluttering. Ian was debating the merits of saying something of a dismissive nature and walking grandly away, versus kicking him in the balls again before he could get up, when William the Englishman walked out from the trees.

He looked from Ian, still breathing as though he'd run a mile, to Sun Elk, who had rolled onto his hands and knees but didn't seem to want to get up. Blood was dripping from his face onto the dead leaves. *Splat. Splat.*

"I have no wish to intrude upon a private affair," William said politely. "But I would appreciate a word with you, Mr. Murray." He turned, not waiting to see if Ian would come, and walked back into the trees.

Ian nodded, having no notion what to say, and followed the Englishman, cherishing in his heart the last faint *splat!* of Sun Elk's blood.

The Englishman was leaning against a tree, watching the Mohawk camp by the stream below. A woman was stripping meat from a fresh deer's carcass, hanging it to dry on a frame. She wasn't Works With Her Hands.

William switched his dark-blue gaze to Ian, giving him an odd feeling. Ian already felt odd, though, so it didn't really matter.

"I am not going to ask what you were doing in the camp."

"Oh, aye?"

"No. I wished to thank you for the horse and money and to ask you whether you have seen Miss Hunter, since you so kindly left me in the keeping of her and her brother."

"I have, aye." The knuckles on his right hand were already puffed to twice their size and starting to throb. He'd go and see Rachel; she'd bandage them for him. The thought was so intoxicating that he didn't at first realize that William was waiting—not all that patiently—for him to expound on his statement.

"Ah. Aye, the . . . er . . . the Hunters are wi' the army. The . . . um . . . *other* army," he said, a little awkwardly. "Her brother's an army surgeon."

William's face didn't change but seemed somehow to solidify. Ian watched it in fascination. He'd seen Uncle Jamie's face do the exact same thing, many times, and knew what it meant.

"Here?" William said.

"Aye, here." He inclined his head toward the American camp. "There, I mean."

"I see," William said calmly. "When you see her again, will you give her my kindest regards, then? And her brother, too, of course."

"Oh . . . aye," Ian said, thinking, *Like that, is it? Well, ye're no going to see her yourself, and she'd have nothing to do wi' a soldier anyway, so think again!* "Certainly," he added, belatedly aware that his only value to William at this point lay in his supposed role as messenger to Rachel Hunter, and wondering just how much that was worth.

"Thank you." William's face had lost that look of iron; he was examining Ian carefully, and at last nodded.

"A life for a life, Mr. Murray," he said quietly. "We're quits. Don't let me see you next time. I may not have a choice."

He turned and left, the red of his uniform visible for some time through the trees.

62

ONE JUST MAN

September 19, 1777

THE SUN ROSE invisible, to the sound of drums. Drums on both sides; we could hear the British reveille, and by the same token they must hear ours. The riflemen had had a brief skirmish with British troops two days before, and owing to the work of Ian and the other scouts, General Gates knew very well the size and disposition of Burgoyne's army. Kościuszko had chosen Bemis Heights for a defensive position; it was a high river bluff, with numerous small ravines down to the river, and his crews had labored like madmen for the last week with shovels and axes. The Americans were ready. More or less.

The women were not, of course, admitted to the councils of the generals. Jamie was, though, and thus I heard all about the argument between General Gates, who was in command, and General Arnold, who thought he should be. General Gates, who wanted to sit tight on Bemis Heights and wait for the British attack, versus General Arnold, who argued vehemently that the Americans must make the first move, forcing the British regulars to fight through the thickly wooded ravines, ruining their formations and making them vulnerable to the riflemen's sniper fire, falling back—if necessary—to the breastworks and entrenchments on the Heights.

"Arnold's won," Ian reported, popping briefly up out of the fog to snag a piece of toasted bread. "Uncle Jamie's away wi' the riflemen already. He says he'll see ye this evening, and in the meantime . . ." He bent and gently kissed my cheek, then grinned impudently and vanished.

My own stomach was knotted, though with the pervasive

excitement as much as with fear. The Americans were a ragged, motley lot, but they had had time to prepare, they knew what was coming, and they knew what was at stake. This battle would decide the campaign in the north. Either Burgoyne would overcome and march on, trapping George Washington's army near Philadelphia between his forces and General Howe's—or his army of invasion would be brought to a halt and knocked out of the war, in which case Gates's army could move south to reinforce Washington. The men all knew it, and the fog seemed electric with their anticipation.

By the sun, it was near ten o'clock when the fog lifted. The shots had begun some time earlier, brief, distant pings of rifle fire. Daniel Morgan's men were taking out the pickets, I thought—and knew from what Jamie had said the night before that they were meant to aim for the officers, to kill those soldiers wearing silver gorgets. I hadn't slept the night before, envisioning Lieutenant Ransom and the silver gorget at his throat. In fog, in the dust of battle, at a distance . . . I swallowed, but my throat stayed stubbornly closed; I couldn't even drink water.

Jamie had slept, with the stubborn concentration of a soldier, but had waked in the deep hours of the night, his shirt soaked with sweat in spite of the chill, trembling. I didn't ask what he had been dreaming about; I knew. I had got him a dry shirt and made him lie down again with his head in my lap, then stroked his head until he closed his eyes—but I thought he hadn't slept again.

It wasn't chilly now; the fog had burned away, and we heard sustained rattles of gunfire, patchy, but repeated volleys. Faint, distant shouting, but impossible to make out who was shouting what at whom. Then the sudden crash of a British fieldpiece, a resounding boom that struck the camp silent. A lull, and then full-scale battle broke out, shooting and screaming and the intermittent thud of cannon. Women huddled together or set about grimly packing up their belongings, in case we should have to flee.

About midday, a relative silence fell. Was it over? We waited. After a little, children began whining to be fed and a sort of tense normality descended—but nothing happened. We could hear moaning and calls for help from men wounded—but no wounded were brought in.

I was ready. I had a small mule-drawn wagon, equipped with bandages and medical equipment, and a small tent as well, which I could set up in case I needed to perform surgery in the rain. The mule was staked nearby, grazing placidly and ignoring both the tension and the occasional burst of musketry.

In the middle of the afternoon, hostilities broke out again, and this time the camp followers and cook wagons actually began to retreat. There was artillery on both sides, enough of it that the continuous cannonading rolled like thunder, and I saw a huge cloud of black powder smoke rise up from the bluff. It was not quite mushroom-shaped, but made me think nonetheless of Nagasaki and Hiroshima. I sharpened my knife and scalpels for the dozenth time.

IT WAS NEAR evening; the sun sank invisibly, staining the fog with a dull and sullen orange. The evening wind off the river was rising, lifting the fog from the ground and sending it scudding in billows and swirls.

Clouds of black powder smoke lay heavy in the hollows, lifting more slowly than the lighter shreds of mist and lending a suitable stink of brimstone to a scene that was—if not hellish—at least bloody eerie.

Here and there a space would suddenly be cleared, like a curtain pulled back to show the aftermath of battle. Small dark figures moved in the distance, darting and stooping, stopping suddenly, heads uplifted like baboons keeping watch for a leopard. Camp followers; the wives and whores of the soldiers, come like crows to scavenge the dead.

Children, too. Under a bush, a boy of nine or ten straddled the body of a red-coated soldier, smashing at the face with a heavy rock. I stopped, paralyzed at the sight, and saw the boy reach into the gaping, bloodied mouth and wrench out a tooth. He slipped the bloody prize into a bag that hung by his side, groped farther, tugging, and, finding no more teeth loose, picked up his rock in a businesslike way and went back to work.

I felt bile rise in my throat and hurried on, swallowing. I was no stranger to war, to death and wounds. But I had never been so near a battle before; I had never before come on a battlefield where the dead and wounded still lay, before the ministrations of medics and burial details.

There were calls for help and occasional moans or screams, ringing disembodied out of the mist, reminding me uncomfortably of Highland stories of the *urisge,* the doomed spirits of the glen. Like the heroes of such stories, I didn't stop to heed their call but pressed on, stumbling over small rises, slipping on damp grass.

I had seen photographs of the great battlefields, from the American Civil War to the beaches of Normandy. This was nothing like that—no churned earth, no heaps of tangled limbs. It was still, save for the noises of the scattered wounded and the voices of those calling, like me, for a missing friend or husband.

Shattered trees lay toppled by artillery; in this light, I might have thought the bodies turned into logs themselves, dark shapes lying long in the grass—save for the fact that some of them still moved. Here and there, a form stirred feebly, victim of war's sorcery, struggling against the enchantment of death.

I paused and shouted into the mist, calling his name. I heard answering calls, but none in his voice. Ahead of me lay a young man, arms outflung, a look of blank astonishment on his face, blood pooled round his upper body like a great halo. His lower half lay six feet away. I walked between the pieces, keeping my skirts close, nostrils pinched tight against the thick iron smell of blood.

The light was fading now, but I saw Jamie as soon as I came over the edge of the next rise. He was lying on his face in the hollow, one arm flung out, the other curled beneath him. The shoulders of his dark blue coat were nearly black with damp, and his legs thrown wide, booted heels askew.

The breath caught in my throat, and I ran down the slope toward him, heedless of grass clumps, mud, and brambles. As I got close, though, I saw a scuttling figure dart out from behind a nearby bush and dash toward him. It fell to its knees beside him and, without hesitation, grasped his hair and yanked his head to one side. Something glinted in the figure's hand, bright even in the dull light.

"Stop!" I shouted. "Drop it, you bastard!"

Startled, the figure looked up as I flung myself over the last yards of space. Narrow red-rimmed eyes glared up at me out of a round face streaked with soot and grime.

"Get off!" she snarled. "I found 'im first!" It was a knife in her hand; she made little jabbing motions at me, in an effort to drive me away.

I was too furious—and too afraid for Jamie—to be scared for myself.

"Let go of him! Touch him and I'll kill you!" I said. My fists were clenched, and I must have looked as though I meant it, for the woman flinched back, loosing her hold on Jamie's hair.

"He's mine," she said, thrusting her chin pugnaciously at me. "Go find yourself another."

Another form slipped out of the mist and materialized by her side. It was the boy I had seen earlier, filthy and scruffy as the woman herself. He had no knife but clutched a crude metal strip, cut from a canteen. The edge of it was dark, with rust or blood.

He glared at me. "He's ours, Mum said! Get on wi' yer! Scat!"

Not waiting to see whether I would or not, he flung a leg over Jamie's back, sat on him, and began to grope in the side pockets of his coat.

" 'E's still alive, Mum," he advised. "I can feel 'is 'eart beatin'. Best slit his throat quick; I don't think 'e's bad hurt."

I grabbed the boy by the collar and jerked him off Jamie's body, making him drop his weapon. He squealed and flailed at me with arms and elbows, but I kneed him in the rump, hard enough to jar his backbone, then got my elbow locked about his neck in a stranglehold, his skinny wrist vised in my other hand.

"Leave him go!" The woman's eyes narrowed like a weasel's, and her eyeteeth shone in a snarl.

I didn't dare take my eyes away from the woman's long enough to look at Jamie. I could see him, though, at the edge of my vision, head turned to the side, his neck gleaming white, exposed and vulnerable.

"Stand up and step back," I said, "or I'll choke him to death, I swear I will!"

She crouched over Jamie's body, knife in hand, as she measured me, trying to make up her mind whether I meant it. I did.

The boy struggled and twisted in my grasp, his feet hammering against my shins. He was small for his age, and thin as a stick, but strong nonetheless; it was like wrestling an eel. I tightened my hold on his neck; he gurgled and quit struggling. His hair was thick with rancid grease and dirt, the smell of it rank in my nostrils.

Slowly, the woman stood up. She was much smaller than I, and scrawny with it—bony wrists stuck out of the ragged sleeves. I couldn't guess her age—under the filth and the puffiness of malnutrition, she might have been anything from twenty to fifty.

"My man lies yonder, dead on the ground," she said, jerking her head at the fog behind her. " 'E hadn't nothing but his musket, and the sergeant'll take that back."

Her eyes slid toward the distant wood, where the British troops had retreated. "I'll find a man soon, but I've children to feed in the meantime—two besides the boy." She licked her lips, and a coaxing note entered her voice. "You're alone; you can manage better than we can. Let me have this one—there's more over there." She pointed with her chin toward the slope behind me, where the rebel dead and wounded lay.

My grasp must have loosened slightly as I listened, for the boy, who had hung quiescent in my grasp, made a sudden lunge and burst free, diving over Jamie's body to roll at his mother's feet.

He got up beside her, watching me with rat's eyes, beady-bright and watchful. He bent and groped about in the grass, coming up with the makeshift dagger.

"Hold 'er off, Mum," he said, his voice raspy from the choking. "I'll take 'im."

From the corner of my eye, I had caught the gleam of metal, half buried in the grass.

"Wait!" I said, and took a step back. "Don't kill him. Don't." A step to the side, another back. "I'll go, I'll let you have him, but . . ." I lunged to the side and got my hand on the cold metal hilt.

I had picked up Jamie's sword before. It was a cavalry sword, larger and heavier than the usual, but I didn't notice now.

I snatched it up and swung it in a two-handed arc that ripped the air and left the metal ringing in my hands.

Mother and son jumped back, identical looks of ludicrous surprise on their round, grimy faces.

"Get away!" I said.

Her mouth opened, but she didn't say anything.

"I'm sorry for your man," I said. "But my man lies here. Get away, I said!" I raised the sword, and the woman stepped back hastily, dragging the boy by the arm.

She turned and went, muttering curses at me over her shoulder, but I paid no attention to what she said. The boy's eyes stayed fixed on me as he went, dark coals in the dim light. He would know me again—and I him.

They vanished in the mist, and I lowered the sword, which suddenly weighed too much to hold. I dropped it on the grass and fell to my knees beside Jamie.

My own heart was pounding in my ears and my hands were shaking with reaction, as I groped for the pulse in his neck. I turned his head and could see it, throbbing steadily just below his jaw.

"Thank God!" I whispered to myself. "Oh, thank God!"

I ran my hands over him quickly, searching for injury before I moved him. I didn't think the scavengers would come back; I could hear the voices of a group of men, distant on the ridge behind me—a rebel detail coming to fetch the wounded.

There was a large knot on his brow, already turning purple. Nothing else that I could see. The boy had been right, I thought, with gratitude; he wasn't badly hurt. Then I rolled him onto his back and saw his hand.

Highlanders were accustomed to fight with sword in one hand, targe in the other, the small leather shield used to deflect an opponent's blow. He hadn't had a targe.

The blade had struck him between the third and fourth fingers of his right hand and sliced through the hand itself, a deep, ugly wound that split his palm and the body of his hand, halfway to the wrist.

Despite the horrid look of the wound, there wasn't much blood; the hand had been curled under him, his weight acting as a pressure bandage. The front of his shirt was smeared with red, deeply stained over his heart. I ripped open his shirt and felt inside, to be sure that the blood was from his hand, but it was. His chest was cool and damp from the grass but unscathed, his nipples shrunken and stiff with chill.

"That . . . tickles," he said in a drowsy voice. He pawed awkwardly at his chest with his left hand, trying to brush my hand away.

"Sorry," I said, repressing the urge to laugh with the joy of seeing him alive and conscious. I got an arm behind his shoulders and helped him to sit up. He looked drunk, with one eye swollen half shut and grass in his hair. He acted drunk, too, swaying alarmingly from side to side.

"How do you feel?" I asked.

"Sick," he said succinctly. He leaned to the side and threw up.

I eased him back on the grass and wiped his mouth, then set about bandaging his hand.

"Someone will be here soon," I assured him. "We'll get you back to the wagon, and I can take care of this."

"Mmphm." He grunted slightly as I pulled the bandage tight. "What happened?"

"What happened?" I stopped what I was doing and stared at him. "*You're* asking *me*?"

"What happened in the battle, I mean," he said patiently, regarding me with his one good eye. "I know what happened to me—roughly," he added, wincing as he touched his forehead.

"Yes, roughly," I said rudely. "You got yourself chopped like a butchered hog, and your head half caved in. Being a sodding bloody hero again, that's what happened to you!"

"I wasna—" he began, but I interrupted, my relief over seeing him alive being rapidly succeeded by rage.

"You didn't have to go to Ticonderoga! You *shouldn't* have gone! Stick to the writing and the printing, you said. You weren't going to fight unless you had to, you said. Well, you *didn't* have to, but you did it anyway, you vainglorious, pigheaded, grandstanding Scot!"

"Grandstanding?" he inquired.

"You know just what I mean, because it's just what you did! You might have been killed!"

"Aye," he agreed ruefully. "I thought I was, when the dragoon came down on me. I screeched and scairt his horse, though," he added more cheerfully. "It reared up and got me in the face with its knee."

"Don't change the subject!" I snapped.

"Is the subject not that I'm not killed?" he asked, trying to raise one brow and failing, with another wince.

"No! The subject is your stupidity, your bloody selfish stubbornness!"

"Oh, that."

"Yes, that! You—you—oaf! How dare you do that to me? You think I haven't got anything better to do with my life than trot round after you, sticking pieces back on?" I was frankly shrieking at him by this time.

To my increased fury, he grinned at me, his expression made the more rakish by the half-closed eye.

"Ye'd have been a good fishwife, Sassenach," he observed. "Ye've the tongue for it."

"You shut up, you fucking bloody—"

"They'll hear you," he said mildly, with a wave toward the party of Continental soldiers making their way down the slope toward us.

"I don't care who hears me! If you weren't already hurt, I'd—I'd—"

"Be careful, Sassenach," he said, still grinning. "Ye dinna want to knock off any more pieces; ye'll only have to stick them back on, aye?"

"Don't bloody tempt me," I said through my teeth, with a glance at the sword I had dropped.

He saw it and reached for it, but couldn't quite manage. With an explosive snort, I leaned across his body and grabbed the hilt, putting it in his hand. I heard a shout from the men coming down the hill and turned to wave at them.

"Anyone hearing ye just now would likely think ye didna care for me owermuch, Sassenach," he said, behind me.

I turned to look down at him. The impudent grin was gone, but he was still smiling.

"Ye've the tongue of a venemous shrew," he said, "but you're a bonnie wee swordsman, Sassenach."

My mouth opened, but the words that had been so abundant a moment before had all evaporated like the rising mist.

He laid his good hand on my arm. "For now, *a nighean donn*—thank ye for my life."

I closed my mouth. The men had nearly reached us, rustling through the grass, their exclamations and chatter drowning out the ever-fainter moans of the wounded.

"You're welcome," I said.

"HAMBURGER," I SAID under my breath, but not far enough under. He raised an eyebrow at me.

"Chopped meat," I elaborated, and the eyebrow fell.

"Oh, aye, it is. Stopped a sword stroke wi' my hand. Too bad I didna have a targe; I could have turned the stroke, easy."

"Right." I swallowed. It wasn't the worst injury I'd seen, by a long shot, but it still made me slightly sick. The tip of his fourth finger had been sheared off cleanly, at an angle just below the nail. The stroke had sliced a strip of flesh from the inside of the finger and ripped down between the third and fourth fingers.

"You must have caught it near the hilt," I said, trying for calm. "Or it would have taken off the outside half of your hand."

"Mmphm." The hand didn't move as I prodded and poked, but there was sweat on his upper lip, and he couldn't keep back a brief grunt of pain.

"Sorry," I murmured automatically.

"It's all right," he said, just as automatically. He closed his eyes, then opened them.

"Take it off," he said suddenly.

"What?" I drew back and looked at him, startled.

He nodded at his hand.

"The finger. Take it off, Sassenach."

"I can't do that!" Even as I spoke, though, I knew that he was right. Aside from the injuries to the finger itself, the tendon was badly damaged; the chances of his ever being able to move the finger, let alone move it without pain, were infinitesimal.

"It's done me little good in the last twenty years," he said, looking at the mangled stump dispassionately, "and likely to do no better now. I've broken the damned thing half a dozen times, from its sticking out like it does. If ye take it off, it willna trouble me anymore, at least."

I wanted to argue, but there was no time; wounded men were beginning to drift up the slope toward the wagon. The men were militia, not regular army; if there was a regiment near, there might be a surgeon with them, but I was closer.

"Once a frigging hero, always a frigging hero," I muttered under my breath. I thrust a wad of lint into Jamie's bloody palm and wrapped a linen bandage swiftly around the hand. "Yes, I'll have to take it off, but later. Hold still."

"Ouch," he said mildly. "I did say I wasna a hero."

"If you aren't, it isn't for lack of trying," I said, yanking the linen knot tight with my teeth. "There, that will have to do for now; I'll see to it when I have time." I grabbed the wrapped hand and plunged it into the small basin of alcohol and water.

He went white as the alcohol seeped through the cloth and struck raw flesh. He inhaled sharply through his teeth, but didn't say anything more. I pointed peremptorily at the blanket I had spread on the ground, and he lay back obediently, curling up under the shelter of the wagon, bandaged fist cradled against his breast.

I rose from my knees, but hesitated for a moment. Then I knelt again and hastily kissed the back of his neck, brushing aside the queue of his hair, matted with half-dried mud and dead leaves. I could just see the curve of his cheek; it tightened briefly as he smiled and then relaxed.

Word had spread that the hospital wagon was there; there was already a straggling group of walking wounded awaiting attention, and I could see men carrying or half-dragging their injured companions toward the light of my lantern. It was going to be a busy evening.

Colonel Everett had promised me two assistants, but God knew where the colonel was at the moment. I took a moment to survey the gathering crowd and picked out a young man who had just deposited a wounded friend beneath a tree.

"You," I said, tugging on his sleeve. "Are you afraid of blood?"

He looked momentarily startled, then grinned at me through a mask of mud and powder smoke. He was about my height, broad-shouldered and stocky, with a face that might have been called cherubic had it been less filthy.

"Only if it's mine, ma'am, and so far it ain't, Lord be praised."

"Then come with me," I said, smiling back. "You're now a triage aide."

"Say what? Hey, Harry!" he yelled to his friend. "I been promoted. Tell your mama next time you write, Lester done amounted to something, after all!" He swaggered after me, still grinning.

The grin rapidly faded into a look of frowning absorption as I led him quickly among the wounded, pointing out degrees of severity.

"Men pouring blood are the first priority," I told him. I thrust an armful of linen bandages and a sack of lint into his hands. "Give them these—tell their friends to press the lint hard on the wounds or put a tourniquet round the limb above the wound. You know what a tourniquet is?"

"Oh, yes, ma'am," he assured me. "Put one on, too, when a panther clawed up my cousin Jess, down to Caroline County."

"Good. Don't spend time doing it yourself here unless you have to, though—let their friends do it. Now, broken bones can wait a bit—put them over there under that big beech tree. Head injuries and internal injuries that aren't bleeding, back there, by the chestnut tree, if they can be moved. If not, I'll go to them." I pointed behind me, then turned in a half circle, surveying the ground.

"If you see a couple of whole men, send them up to put up the hospital tent; it's to go in that flattish spot, there. And then a couple more, to dig a latrine trench . . . over there, I think."

"Yes, sir! Ma'am, I mean!" Lester bobbed his head and took a firm grip on his sack of lint. "I be right after it, ma'am. Though I wouldn't worry none about the latrines for a while," he added. "Most of these boys already done had the shit scairt out of 'em." He grinned and bobbed once more, then set out on his rounds.

He was right; the faint stink of feces hung in the air as it always did on battlefields, a low note amid the pungencies of blood and smoke.

With Lester sorting the wounded, I settled down to the work of repair, with my medicine box, suture bag, and bowl of alcohol set on the wagon's tailboard and a keg of alcohol for the patients to sit on—provided they could sit.

The worst of the casualties were bayonet wounds; luckily

there had been no grapeshot, and the men hit by cannonballs were long past the point where I could help them. As I worked, I listened with half an ear to the conversation of the men awaiting attention.

"Wasn't that the damnedest thing ye ever saw? How many o' the buggers were there?" one man was asking his neighbor.

"Damned if I know," his friend replied, shaking his head. "For a space there, ever'thing I saw was red, and nothin' but. Then a cannon went off right close, and I didn't see nothin' but smoke for a good long time." He rubbed at his face; tears from watering eyes had made long streaks in the black soot that covered him from chest to forehead.

I glanced back at the wagon but couldn't see under it. I hoped shock and fatigue had enabled Jamie to sleep, in spite of his hand, but I doubted it.

Despite the fact that nearly everyone near me was wounded in some fashion, their spirits were high and the general mood was one of exuberant relief and exultation. Farther down the hill, in the mists near the river, I could hear whoops and shouts of victory and the undisciplined racket of fifes and drums, rattling and screeching in random exhilaration.

Among the noise, a nearer voice called out: a uniformed officer, on a bay horse.

"Anybody seen that big redheaded bastard who broke the charge?"

There was a murmur and a general looking around, but no one answered. The horseman dismounted and, wrapping his reins over a branch, made his way through the throng of wounded toward me.

"Whoever he is, I tell you, he's got balls the size of ten-pound shot," remarked the man whose cheek I was stitching.

"And a head of the same consistency," I murmured.

"Eh?" He glanced sideways at me in bewilderment.

"Nothing," I said. "Hold still just a moment longer; I'm nearly done."

IT WAS A HELLISH night. Some of the wounded still lay in the ravines and hollows, as did all the dead. The wolves that came silently out of the wood did not distinguish between them, judging from the distant screams.

It was nearly dawn before I came back to the tent where Jamie lay. I lifted the flap quietly, so as not to disturb him, but he was already awake, lying curled on his side facing the flap, head resting on a folded blanket.

He smiled faintly when he saw me.

"A hard night, Sassenach?" he asked, his voice slightly hoarse from cold air and disuse. Mist seeped under the edge of the flap, tinted yellow by the lantern light.

"I've had worse." I smoothed the hair off his face, looking him over carefully. He was pale but not clammy. His face was drawn with pain, but his skin was cool to the touch—no trace of fever. "You haven't slept, have you? How do you feel?"

"A bit scairt," he said. "And a bit sick. But better now you're here." He gave me a one-sided grimace that was almost a smile.

I put a hand under his jaw, fingers pressed against the pulse in his neck. His heart bumped steadily under my fingertips, and I shivered briefly, remembering the woman in the field.

"You're chilled, Sassenach," he said, feeling it. "And tired, too. Go and sleep, aye? I'll do a bit longer."

I *was* tired. The adrenaline of the battle and the night's work was fading fast; fatigue was creeping down my spine and loosening my joints. But I had a good idea of what the hours of waiting had cost him already.

"It won't take long," I reassured him. "And it will be better to have it over. Then you can sleep easy."

He nodded, though he didn't look noticeably reassured. I unfolded the small worktable I had carried in from the operating tent and set it up in easy reach. Then I took out the precious bottle of laudanum and poured an inch of the dark, odorous liquid into a cup.

"Sip it slowly," I said, putting it into his left hand. I began to lay out the instruments I would need, making sure that everything lay orderly and to hand. I had thought of asking Lester to come and assist me, but he had been asleep on his feet, swaying drunkenly under the dim lanterns in the operating tent, and I had sent him off to find a blanket and a spot by the fire.

A small scalpel, freshly sharpened. The jar of alcohol,

with the wet ligatures coiled inside like a nest of tiny vipers, each toothed with a small, curved needle. Another with the waxed dry ligatures for arterial compression. A bouquet of probes, their ends soaking in alcohol. Forceps. Long-handled retractors. The hooked tenaculum, for catching the ends of severed arteries.

The surgical scissors with their short, curved blades and the handles shaped to fit my grasp, made to my order by the silversmith Stephen Moray. Or almost to my order. I had insisted that the scissors be as plain as possible, to make them easy to clean and disinfect. Stephen had obliged with a chaste and elegant design, but had not been able to resist one small flourish—one handle boasted a hooklike extension against which I could brace my little finger in order to exert more force, and this extrusion formed a smooth, lithe curve, flowering at the tip into a slender rosebud against a spray of leaves. The contrast between the heavy, vicious blades at one end and this delicate conceit at the other always made me smile when I lifted the scissors from their case.

Strips of cotton gauze and heavy linen, pads of lint, adhesive plasters stained red with the dragon's-blood juice that made them sticky. An open bowl of alcohol for disinfection as I worked, and the jars of cinchona bark, mashed garlic paste, and yarrow for dressing.

"There we are," I said with satisfaction, checking the array one last time. Everything must be ready, since I was working by myself; if I forgot something, no one would be at hand to fetch it for me.

"It seems a great deal o' preparation, for one measly finger," Jamie observed behind me.

I swung around to find him leaning on one elbow, watching, the cup of laudanum undrunk in his hand.

"Could ye not just whack it off wi' a wee knife and seal the wound with hot iron, like the regimental surgeons do?"

"I could, yes," I said dryly. "But fortunately I don't have to; we have enough time to do the job properly. That's why I made you wait."

"Mmphm." He surveyed the row of gleaming instruments without enthusiasm, and it was clear that he would much rather have had the business over and done with as quickly as possible. I realized that to him this looked like slow and ritualized torture, rather than sophisticated surgery.

"I mean to leave you with a working hand," I told him firmly. "No infection, no suppurating stump, no clumsy mutilation, and—God willing—no pain, once it heals."

His eyebrows went up at that. He had never mentioned it, but I was well aware that his right hand and its troublesome fourth finger had caused him intermittent pain for years, ever since it had been crushed at Wentworth Prison, when he was held prisoner there in the days before the Stuart Rising.

"A bargain's a bargain," I said, with a nod at the cup in his hand. "Drink it."

He lifted the cup and poked a long nose reluctantly over the rim, nostrils twitching at the sickly-sweet scent. He let the dark liquid touch the end of his tongue and made a face.

"It will make me sick."

"It will make you sleep."

"It gives me terrible dreams."

"As long as you don't chase rabbits in your sleep, it won't matter," I assured him. He laughed despite himself, but had one final try.

"It tastes like the stuff ye scrape out of horses' hooves."

"And when was the last time you licked a horse's hoof?" I demanded, hands on my hips. I gave him a medium-intensity glare, suitable for the intimidation of petty bureaucrats and low-level army officials.

He sighed.

"Ye mean it, aye?"

"I do."

"All right, then." With a reproachful look of long-suffering resignation, he threw back his head and tossed the contents of the cup down in one gulp.

A convulsive shudder racked him, and he made small choking noises.

"I did say to sip it," I observed mildly. "Vomit, and I'll make you lick it up off the floor."

Given the scuffled dirt and trampled grass underfoot, this was plainly an idle threat, but he pressed his lips and eyes tight shut and lay back on the pillow, breathing heavily and swallowing convulsively every few seconds. I brought up a low stool and sat down by the camp bed to wait.

"How do you feel?" I asked, a few minutes later.

"Dizzy," he replied. He cracked one eye open and viewed me through the narrow blue slit, then groaned and closed it. "As if I'm falling off a cliff. It's a verra unpleasant sensation, Sassenach."

"Try to think of something else for a minute," I suggested. "Something pleasant, to take your mind off it."

His brow furrowed for a moment, then relaxed.

"Stand up a moment, will ye?" he said. I obligingly stood, wondering what he wanted. He opened his eyes, reached out with his good hand, and took a firm grip of my buttock.

"There," he said. "That's the best thing I can think of. Having a good hold on your arse always makes me feel steady."

I laughed and moved a few inches closer to him, so his forehead pressed against my thighs.

"Well, it's a portable remedy, at least."

He closed his eyes then and held on tight, breathing slowly and deeply. The harsh lines of pain and exhaustion in his face began to soften as the drug took effect.

"Jamie," I said softly, after a minute. "I'm sorry about it."

He opened his eyes, looked upward, and smiled, giving me a slight squeeze.

"Aye, well," he said. His pupils had begun to shrink; his eyes were sea-deep and fathomless, as though he looked into a great distance.

"Tell me, Sassenach," he said, a moment later. "If someone stood a man before ye and told ye that if ye were to cut off your finger, the man would live, and if ye did not, he would die—would ye do it?"

"I don't know," I said, slightly startled. "If that was the choice, and no doubt about it, and he was a good man . . . yes, I suppose I would. I wouldn't like it a bit, though," I added practically, and his mouth curved in a smile.

"No," he said. His expression was growing soft and dreamy. "Did ye know," he said after a moment, "a colonel came to see me, whilst ye were at work wi' the wounded? Colonel Johnson; Micah Johnson, his name was."

"No; what did he say?"

His grip on my bottom was beginning to slacken; I put my own hand over his, to hold it in place.

"It was his company—in the fight. Part of Morgan's, and

the rest of the regiment just over the hill, in the path of the British. If the charge had gone through, they'd ha' lost the company surely, he said, and God knows what might have become o' the rest." His soft Highland burr was growing broader, his eyes fixed on my skirt.

"So you saved them," I said gently. "How many men are there in a company?"

"Fifty," he said. "Though they wouldna all have been killed, I dinna suppose." His hand slipped; he caught it and took a fresh grip, chuckling slightly. I could feel his breath through my skirt, warm on my thighs.

"I was thinking it was like the Bible, aye?"

"Yes?" I pressed his hand against the curve of my hip, keeping it in place.

"That bit where Abraham is bargaining wi' the Lord for the Cities of the Plain. 'Wilt thou not destroy the city,' " he quoted, " 'for the sake of fifty just men?' And then Abraham does Him down, a bit at a time, from fifty to forty, and then to thirty, and twenty and ten."

His eyes were half closed, and his voice peaceful and unconcerned.

"I didna have time to inquire into the moral state of any o' the men in that company. But ye'd think there might be ten just men among them—good men?"

"I'm sure there are." His hand was heavy, his arm gone nearly limp.

"Or five. Or even one. One would be enough."

"I'm sure there's one."

"The apple-faced laddie that helped ye wi' the wounded—he's one?"

"Yes, he's one."

He sighed deeply, his eyes nearly shut.

"Tell him I dinna grudge him the finger, then," he said.

I held his good hand tightly for a minute. He was breathing slowly and deeply, his mouth gone slack in utter relaxation. I rolled him gently onto his back and laid the hand across his chest.

"Bloody man," I whispered. "I knew you'd make me cry."

THE CAMP OUTSIDE lay quiet, in the last moments of slumber before the rising sun should stir the men to movement. I could hear the occasional call of a picket and the murmur of conversation as two foragers passed close by my tent, bound for the woods to hunt. The campfires outside had burned to embers, but I had three lanterns, arranged to cast light without shadow.

I laid a thin square of soft pine across my lap as a working surface. Jamie lay facedown on the camp bed, head turned toward me so I could keep an eye on his color. He was solidly asleep; his breath came slow and he didn't flinch when I pressed the sharp tip of a probe against the back of his hand. All ready.

The hand was swollen, puffy, and discolored, the sword wound a thick black line against the sun-gold skin. I closed my eyes for a moment, holding his wrist, counting his pulse. *One-and-two-and-three-and-four . . .*

I seldom prayed consciously when preparing for surgery, but I did look for something—something I could not describe but always recognized: a certain quietness of soul, the detachment of mind in which I could balance on that knife-edge between ruthlessness and compassion, at once engaged in utmost intimacy with the body under my hands and capable of destroying what I touched in the name of healing.

One-and-two-and-three-and-four . . .

I realized with a start that my own heartbeat had slowed; the pulse in my fingertip matched that in Jamie's wrist, beat for beat, slow and strong. If I was waiting for a sign, I supposed that would do. *Ready, steady, go,* I thought, and picked up the scalpel.

A short horizontal incision over the fourth and fifth knuckles, then down, cutting the skin nearly to the wrist. I undermined the skin carefully with the scissors' tips, then pinned back the loose flap of skin with one of the long steel probes, digging it into the soft wood of the board.

I had a small bulb atomizer filled with a solution of distilled water and alcohol; sterility being impossible, I used this to lay a fine mist over the operating field and wash away the first welling of blood. Not too much; the vasoconstrictor I had given him was working, but the effect wouldn't last long.

I gently nudged apart the muscle fibers—those that were

still whole—to expose the bone and its overlying tendon, gleaming silver among the vivid colors of the body. The sword had cut the tendon nearly through, an inch above the carpal bones. I severed the few remaining fibers, and the hand twitched disconcertingly in reflex.

I bit my lip, but it was all right; aside from the hand, he hadn't moved. He felt different; his flesh had more life than that of a man under ether or Pentothal. He was not anesthetized but only drugged into stupor; the feel of his flesh was resilient, not the pliant flaccidity I had been accustomed to in my days at the hospital in my own time. Still, it was a far cry—and an immeasurable relief—from the live and panicked convulsions that I had felt under my hands in the surgeon's tent.

I brushed the cut tendon aside with the forceps. There was the deep branch of the ulnar nerve, a delicate thread of white myelin, with its tiny branches spreading into invisibility, deep in the tissues. Good, it was far enough toward the fifth finger that I could work without damage to the main nerve trunk.

You never knew; textbook illustrations were one thing, but the first thing any surgeon learned was that bodies were unnervingly unique. A stomach would be roughly where you expected it to be, but the nerves and blood vessels that supplied it might be anywhere in the general vicinity, and quite possibly varying in shape and number, as well.

But now I knew the secrets of this hand. I could see the engineering of it, the structures that gave it form and movement. There was the beautiful strong arch of the third metacarpal, and the delicacy of the web of blood vessels that supplied it. Blood welled, slow and vivid: deep red in the tiny pool of the open field; brilliant scarlet where it stained the chopped bone; a dark and royal blue in the tiny vein that pulsed below the joint; a crusty black at the edge of the original wound, where it had clotted.

I had known, without asking myself how, that the fourth metacarpal was shattered. It was; the blade had struck near the proximal end of the bone, splintering its tiny head near the center of the hand.

I would take that, too, then; the free chunks of bone would have to be removed in any case, to prevent them irritating the adjoining tissues. Removing the metacarpal would let the third and fifth fingers lie close together, in effect narrowing the hand and eliminating the awkward gap that would be left by the missing finger.

I pulled hard on the mangled finger, to open the articular space between the joints, then used the tip of the scalpel to sever the ligament. The cartilages separated with a tiny but audible *pop!* and Jamie jerked and groaned, his hand twisting in my grasp.

"Hush," I whispered to him, holding tight. "Hush, it's all right. I'm here, it's all right."

I could do nothing for the boys dying on the field, but here, for him, I could offer magic and know the spell would hold. He heard me, deep in troubled opium dreams; he frowned and muttered something unintelligible, then sighed deeply and relaxed, his wrist going once more limp under my hand.

Somewhere near at hand, a rooster crowed, and I glanced at the wall of the tent. It was noticeably lighter, and a faint dawn wind drifted through the slit behind me, cool on the back of my neck.

Detach the underlying muscle with as little damage as could be managed. Tie off the small digital artery and two other vessels that seemed large enough to bother with, sever the last few fibers and shreds of skin that held the finger, then lift it free, the dangling metacarpal surprisingly white and naked, like a rat's tail.

It was a clean, neat job, but I felt a brief sense of sadness as I set the mangled piece of flesh aside. I had a fleeting vision of him holding newly born Jemmy, counting the tiny fingers and toes, delight and wonder on his face. His father had counted his fingers, too.

"It's all right," I whispered, as much to myself as to him. "It's all right. It will heal."

The rest was quick. Forceps to pluck out the tiny pieces of shattered bone. I debrided the wound as best I could, removing bits of grass and dirt, even a tiny swatch of fabric that had been driven into the flesh. Then no more than a matter of cleaning the ragged edge of the wound, snipping a small excess of skin, and suturing the incisions. A paste of garlic and white-oak leaves, mixed with alcohol and spread thickly over the hand, a padding of lint and gauze, and a tight bandage of linen and adhesive plasters, to reduce the swelling and encourage the third and fifth fingers to draw close together.

The sun was nearly up; the lantern overhead seemed dim and feeble. My eyes were burning from the close work and the smoke of fires. There were voices outside, the voices of officers moving among the men, rousing them to face the day—and the enemy?

I laid Jamie's hand on the cot, near his face. He was pale, but not excessively so, and his lips were a light rosy color, not blue. I dropped the instruments into a bucket of alcohol and water, suddenly too tired to clean them properly. I wrapped the discarded finger in a linen bandage, not quite sure what to do with it, and left it on the table.

"Rise and shine! Rise and shine!" came the sergeants' rhythmic cry from outside, punctuated by witty variations and crude responses from reluctant risers.

I didn't bother to undress; if there was fighting today, I would be roused soon enough. Not Jamie, though. I had nothing to worry about; no matter what happened, he wouldn't fight today.

I unpinned my hair and shook it down over my shoulders, sighing with relief at its looseness. Then I lay down on the cot beside him, close against him. He lay on his stomach; I could see the small, muscular swell of his buttocks, smooth under the blanket that covered him. On impulse, I laid my hand on his rump and squeezed.

"Sweet dreams," I said, and let the tiredness take me.

63

SEPARATED FOREVER FROM MY FRIENDS AND KIN

LIEUTENANT Lord Ellesmere had finally killed a rebel. Several, he thought, though he could not be sure of those he'd shot at; some of them fell but might be only wounded. He was sure of the man who had attacked one of the British cannon, with a party of other rebels. He'd hacked that man half through the body with a cavalry saber, and he felt a strange numbness in his sword arm for several days after, this making him flex his left hand every few minutes to be sure he could still use it.

The numbness was not limited to his arm.

The days after the battle in the British camp were spent partially in the orderly retrieval of the wounded, the burial of the dead, and in regathering their forces. What forces remained to be gathered. Desertion was rife; there was a constant small stream of furtive departures—one day a whole company of Brunswickers defected.

He oversaw more than one burial detail, watching with set face as men—and boys—he knew were consigned to the earth. On the first couple of days, they hadn't buried the bodies deep enough, and were obliged to listen all night to the howling and snarling of wolves fighting over the carcasses they had dragged from the shallow graves. They reburied what was left the next day, deeper.

Fires burned every hundred yards around the camp at night, for American sharpshooters came close in the dark, taking out the pickets.

The days were blazingly hot, the nights miserably cold—

and no one rested. Burgoyne had issued an order that *no officer nor soldier should ever sleep without his cloaths,* and William had not changed his linen in more than a week. It didn't matter what he smelled like; his own reek was undetectable. The men were obliged to be in the lines, with their arms, an hour before dawn, and to remain there until the sun had burned away the fog, to be sure the fog did not hide Americans ready to attack.

The daily bread allowance was cut. Salt pork and flour were running out, and the sutlers lacked tobacco and brandy, to the disgruntlement of the German troops. On the good side, the British defenses were in splendid order, with two large redoubts built and a thousand men sent out to cut trees to open fields of fire for the artillery. And Burgoyne had announced that General Clinton was expected within ten days, with a supporting force—and food, it was to be hoped. All they had to do was wait.

"The Jews wait the Messiah not more than we wait General Clinton," joked Ober-Leftenant Gruenwald, who had by some miracle survived his wound at Bennington.

"Ha-ha," said William.

THE AMERICAN CAMP was in good spirits, more than ready to finish the job they had started. Unfortunately, while the British camp was short of rations, the Americans were short of ammunition and powder. The result was a period of restless stasis, during which the Americans picked constantly at the periphery of the British camp but could make no real progress.

Ian Murray found this tedious in the extreme, and after a token foray in the fog had resulted in a careless companion's stepping on a discarded gun spike and puncturing his foot, he decided this was adequate excuse to pay a visit to the hospital tent where Rachel Hunter was assisting her brother.

The prospect so animated him, though, that he paid inadequate attention to his own footing in the fog and plunged headfirst into a ravine, striking his head a glancing blow on a rock. Thus it was that the two men limped into camp, supporting each other, and made their halting way to the hospital tent.

It was busy in the tent; this was not where the battle-wounded lay but where those with trivial afflictions came for treatment. Ian's head was not broken, but he was seeing two of everything, and closed one eye in hopes that this might help him spot Rachel.

"Ho ro," someone behind him said in open approval, *"mo nighean donn bhoideach!"* For one head-spinning instant, he thought it was his uncle speaking and blinked stupidly, wondering why Uncle Jamie should be making flirtatious remarks to his aunt while she was working—but Auntie Claire wasn't here at all, his slow wits reminded him, so what . . .

One hand over his eye to keep it from falling out of his head, he turned carefully and saw a man in the opening of the tent.

The morning sun struck sparks from the man's hair, and Ian's mouth fell open, feeling that he had been struck in the pit of the stomach.

It wasn't Uncle Jamie, he could see that at once as the man came in, also helping a limping comrade. The face was wrong: red and weather-beaten, with cheerful, snub features; the hair was ginger, not rufous, and receded sharply from the man's temples. He was solidly built, not terribly tall, but the way he moved . . . like a catamount, even burdened with his friend, and for some reason Ian could not remove the lingering impression of Jamie Fraser.

The red-haired man was kilted; they both were. *Highlanders,* he thought, thoroughly fuddled. But he'd known that from the moment the man spoke.

"Có thu?" Ian asked abruptly. *Who are you?*

Hearing the Gaelic, the man looked at him, startled. He gave Ian a quick up-and-down, taking in his Mohawk dress, before answering.

"Is mise Seaumais Mac Choinnich à Boisdale," he answered, courteously enough. *"Có tha faighneachd?" I am Hamish MacKenzie, of Boisdale. Who asks?*

"Ian Murray," he replied, trying to focus his addled wits. The name sounded faintly familiar—but why would it not? He knew hundreds of MacKenzies. "My grandmother was a

MacKenzie," he offered, in the usual way of establishing relations among strangers. "Ellen MacKenzie, of Leoch."

The man's eyes sprang wide

"Ellen, of Leoch?" cried the man, very excited. "Daughter of him they called Jacob Ruaidh?"

In his excitement, Hamish's grip had tightened on his friend, and the man gave a yelp. This attracted the attention of the young woman—the one Hamish had greeted as "O, beautiful nut-brown maiden"—and she came hurrying to see the matter.

She *was* nut brown, Ian saw; Rachel Hunter, tanned by the sun to the exact soft shade of a hickory nut, what showed of her hair beneath her kerchief the shade of walnut hulls, and he smiled at the thought. She saw him and narrowed her eyes.

"Well, and if thee is able to grin like an ape, thee is not much hurt. Why—" She stopped, astonished at the sight of Ian Murray locked in embrace with a kilted Highlander, who was weeping with joy. Ian was not weeping, but was undeniably pleased.

"Ye'll want to meet my uncle Jamie," he said, adroitly disentangling himself. "*Seaumais Ruaidh,* I think ye called him."

JAMIE FRASER HAD his eyes shut, cautiously exploring the pain in his hand. It was sharp-edged, strong enough to make him queasy, but with that deep, grinding ache common to broken bones. Still, it was a healing ache. Claire spoke of bones knitting—and he'd often thought this was more than a metaphor; it sometimes felt that someone was indeed stabbing steel needles into the bone and forcing the shattered ends back into some pattern, heedless of how the flesh around them felt about it.

He should look at his hand, he knew that. He had to get used to it, after all. He'd had the one quick glance, and it had left him dizzy and on the point of vomiting out of sheer confoundment. He could not reconcile the sight, the feel of it, with the strong memory of how his hand *ought* to be.

He'd done it before, though, he reminded himself. He'd got used to the scars and the stiffness. And yet . . . he could remember how his young hand had felt, had looked, so easy, limber and painless, folded round the handle of a hoe, the hilt of a sword. Clutching a quill—well, no. He smiled ruefully to himself. That hadn't been either easy or limber, even with his fingers at their unmarred best.

Would he be able to write at all with his hand now? he wondered suddenly, and in curiosity flexed his hand a little. The pain made him gasp, but . . . his eyes were open, fixed on his hand. The disconcerting sight of his little finger pressed close to the middle one did make his belly clench, but . . . his fingers curled. It hurt like Christ crucified, but it was just pain; there was no pull, no stubborn hindrance from the frozen finger. It . . . worked.

"I mean to leave you with a working hand." He could hear Claire's voice, breathless but sure.

He smiled a little. It didn't do to argue with the woman over any matter medical.

I CAME INTO the tent to fetch my small cautery iron and found Jamie sitting on the cot, slowly flexing his injured hand and contemplating his severed finger, which lay on a box beside him. I had wrapped it hastily in a plaster bandage, and it looked like a mummified worm.

"Er," I said delicately. "I'll, um, dispose of that, shall I?"

"How?" He put out a tentative forefinger, touched it, then snatched back his hand as though the detached finger had moved suddenly. He made a small, nervous sound that wasn't quite a laugh.

"Burn it?" I suggested. That was the usual method for disposing of amputated limbs on battlefields, though I had never personally done it. The notion of building a funeral pyre for the cremation of a single finger seemed suddenly absurd—though no more so than the idea of simply tossing it into one of the cookfires and hoping no one noticed.

Jamie made a dubious noise in his throat, indicating that he wasn't keen on the idea.

"Well . . . I suppose you could smoke it," I said, with equal dubiety. "And keep it in your sporran as a souvenir. Like

Young Ian did with Neil Forbes's ear. Has he still got that, do you know?"

"Aye, he does." Jamie's color was beginning to come back, as he regained his self-possession. "But, no, I dinna think I want to do that."

"I could pickle it in spirits of wine," I offered. That got the ghost of a smile.

"Ten to one, someone would drink it before the day was out, Sassenach." I thought that was generous odds, myself. More like a thousand to one. I managed to keep my medicinal alcohol mostly intact only by virtue of having one of Ian's more ferocious Indian acquaintances guard it, when I wasn't using it—and sleeping with the keg next to me at night.

"Well, I think that leaves burial as the only other option."

"Mmphm." That sound indicated agreement, but with reservations, and I glanced up at him.

"What?"

"Aye, well," he said, rather diffidently. "When wee Fergus lost his hand, we . . . well, it was Jenny's notion. But we held a bit of a funeral, ken?"

I bit my lip. "Well, why not? Will it be a family affair, or shall we invite everyone?"

Before he could answer this, I heard Ian's voice outside, talking to someone, and an instant later his disheveled head pushed through the flap. One of his eyes was black and swollen and there was a sizable lump on his head, but he was grinning from ear to ear.

"Uncle Jamie?" he said. "There's someone here to see ye."

"HOW IS IT that ye come to be here, *a charaid*?" Jamie asked, somewhere after the third bottle. We had had supper long since, and the campfire was burning low.

Hamish wiped his mouth and handed the new bottle back.

"Here," he repeated. "Here in the wilderness, d'ye mean? Or here, fighting against the King?" He gave Jamie a direct blue look, so like one of Jamie's own that Jamie smiled, recognizing it.

"Is the second of those questions the answer to the first?" he said, and Hamish gave him the shadow of a smile in return.

"Aye, that would be it. Ye were always quick as the hummingbird, *a Sheaumais*. In body *and* mind." Seeing from my expression that I was perhaps not quite so swift in my perceptions, he turned to me.

"It was the King's troops who killed my uncle, the King's soldiers who killed the fighting men of the clan, who destroyed the land, who left the women and the bairns to starve—who battered down my home and exiled me, who killed half the people left to me with cold and hunger and the plagues of the wilderness." He spoke quietly, but with a passion that burned in his eyes.

"I was eleven years old when they came to the castle and put us out. I turned twelve on the day that they made me swear my oath to the King—they said I was a man. And by the time we reached Nova Scotia . . . I was."

He turned to Jamie.

"They made ye swear, too, *a Sheaumais*?"

"They did," Jamie said softly. "A forced oath canna bind a man, though, or keep him from his knowledge of right."

Hamish put out a hand, and Jamie gripped it, though they did not look at each other.

"No," he said, with certainty. "That it cannot."

Perhaps not; but I knew they were both thinking, as I was, of the language of that oath: *May I lie in an unconsecrated grave, separated forever from my friends and kin.* And both thinking—as I was—how great the odds were that that fate was exactly what would happen to them.

And to me.

I cleared my throat.

"But the others," I said, impelled by the memory of so many I had known in North Carolina, and knowing the same was true of many in Canada. "The Highlanders who are Loyalists?"

"Aye, well," Hamish said softly, and looked into the fire, the lines of his face cut deep by its glow. "They fought bravely, but the heart of them was killed. They want only peace now and to be left alone. But war doesna leave any alone, does it?" He looked suddenly at me, and for a startling instant I saw Dougal MacKenzie looking out of his eyes, that impatient, violent man who had hungered for war. Not waiting for an answer, he shrugged and went on.

"War's found them again; they've nay choice but to fight. But anyone can see what a pitiful rabble the Continental army is—or was." He lifted his head, nodding a little, as though to himself, at sight of the campfires, the tents, the vast cloud of starlit haze that hung above us, full of smoke and dust and the scent of guns and ordure. "They thought the rebels would be crushed, and quickly. Oath notwithstanding, who but a fool would join such risky business?"

A man who had had no chance to fight before, I thought.

He smiled crookedly at Jamie.

"I am surprised we were not crushed," he said, sounding in fact faintly surprised. "Are ye not surprised as well, *a Sheaumais*?"

"Amazed," Jamie said, a faint smile on his own face. "Glad of it, though. And glad of you . . . *a Sheaumais.*"

They talked through most of the night. When they lapsed into Gaelic, I got up, put a hand on Jamie's shoulder in token of good night, and crawled into my blankets. Exhausted by the day's work, I drifted into sleep at once, soothed by the sound of their quiet talk, like the sound of bees in the heather. The last thing I saw before sleep took me was Young Ian's face across the fire, rapt at hearing of the Scotland that had vanished just as he himself was born.

64

A GENTLEMAN CALLER

"MRS. FRASER?" A pleasant masculine voice spoke behind me, and I turned to see a stocky, broad-shouldered officer in the doorway of my tent, in shirtsleeves and waistcoat, a box cradled in one arm.

"I am. May I help you?"

He didn't look sick; in fact, he was healthier-looking than

most of the army, his face very weathered but well-fleshed and ruddy. He smiled, a sudden, charming smile that quite transformed his big beaky nose and heavy brows.

"I was in hopes that we might transact a little business, Mrs. Fraser." He raised one of the bushy brows and, at my gesture of invitation, came into the tent, ducking only a little.

"I suppose that depends what you're looking for," I said, with a curious look at his box. "If it's whisky, I can't give you that, I'm afraid." There was in fact a small keg of this valuable substance hidden under the table at the moment, along with a larger keg of my raw medicinal alcohol—and the smell of the latter was strong in the air, as I was steeping herbs in it. This gentleman was not the first to have been drawn by the scent—it attracted soldiers of all ranks like flies.

"Oh, no," he assured me, though casting an interested look at the table behind me, where I had several large jars in which I was growing what I hoped was penicillin. "I'm told, though, that you possess a stock of cinchona bark. Is that so?"

"Well, yes. Please, sit." I waved him to my patient stool and sat down myself, knee to knee. "Do you suffer from malaria?" I didn't think so—the whites of his eyes were clear; he wasn't jaundiced.

"No, may the Lord be thanked for His mercy. I have a gentleman in my command—a particular friend—who does, though, very badly, and our surgeon has no Jesuit bark. I hoped that you might be induced, perhaps, to make a trade . . . ?"

He had laid the box on the table beside us, and at this flipped it open. It was divided into small compartments and contained a remarkable assortment of things: lace edging, silk ribbon, a pair of tortoiseshell hair combs, a small bag of salt, a pepperbox, an enameled snuffbox, a pewter brooch in the shape of a lily, several bright hanks of embroidery silk, a bundle of cinnamon sticks, and a number of small jars filled apparently with herbs. And a glass bottle, whose label read . . .

"Laudanum!" I exclaimed, reaching for it involuntarily. I stopped myself, but the officer gestured to me to go ahead, and I pulled it carefully from its resting place, drew the cork, and moved the bottle warily past my nose. The pungent, sickly-sweet scent of opium drifted out, a genie in a bottle. I cleared my throat and put the cork back in.

He was watching me with interest.

"I was not sure what might best suit you," he said, waving at the box's contents. "I used to run a store, you see—a great deal of apothecary's stuff, but luxurious dry goods in general. I learnt in the course of my business that it is always best to give the ladies a good deal of choice; they tend to be much more discriminating than do the gentlemen."

I gave him a sharp glance, but it wasn't flummery; he smiled at me again, and I thought that he was one of those unusual men—like Jamie—who actually liked women, beyond the obvious.

"I imagine we can accommodate each other, then," I said, returning the smile. "I ought not to ask, I suppose—I don't intend to hold you up; I'll give you what you need for your friend—but with thought of possible future trade, have you got more laudanum?"

He continued to smile, but his gaze sharpened—he had rather unusual eyes, that pale gray often described as "spit-colored."

"Why, yes," he said slowly. "I have quite a bit. Do you . . . require it regularly?"

It occurred to me that he was wondering whether I was an addict; it wasn't at all uncommon, in circles where laudanum was easily obtainable.

"I don't use it myself, no," I replied equably. "And I administer it to those in need with considerable caution. But relief of pain is one of the more important things I can offer some of the people who come to me—God knows I can't offer many of them cure."

His brows went up at that. "That's a rather remarkable statement. Most persons in your profession seem to promise cure to nearly everyone."

"How does that saying go? 'If wishes were horses, beggars might ride'?" I smiled, but without much humor. "Everyone wants a cure, and certainly there's no physician who doesn't want to give them one. But there are a lot of things beyond the power of any physician, and while you might not tell a patient that, it's as well to know your own limits."

"You think so?" He tilted his head, regarding me curiously. "Do you not think that the admission of such limits, *a priori*—and I do not mean only in the medical way, but in any arena of endeavor—that such an admission in itself *establishes* limits? That is, might that expectation prevent one from accomplishing all that is possible, because one assumes that something is *not* possible and therefore does not strive with all one's power to achieve it?"

I blinked at him, rather surprised.

"Well . . . yes," I said slowly. "If you put it that way, I rather think I agree with you. After all"—I waved a hand toward the tent flap, indicating the surrounding army—"if I didn't—*we* didn't—believe that one can accomplish things beyond all reasonable expectation, would my husband and I be *here*?"

He laughed at that.

"Brava, ma'am! Yes, an impartial observer would, I think, call this venture sheer madness. And they might be right," he added, with a rueful tilt of the head. "But they'll have to defeat us, nonetheless. We shan't give up."

I heard voices outside: Jamie, talking casually with someone, and in the next moment he had ducked inside the tent.

"Sassenach," he began, "can ye come and—" He stopped dead, seeing my visitor, and drew up a bit, with a formal bow. "Sir."

I glanced back at the visitor, surprised; Jamie's manner made it clear that this was a superior officer of some sort; I'd thought him perhaps a captain or a major. As for the officer himself, he nodded, friendly but reserved.

"Colonel. Your wife and I have been discussing the philosophy of endeavor. What do you say—does a wise man know his limits, or a bold one deny them? And which way do you declare yourself?"

Jamie looked mildly startled and glanced at me; I lifted one shoulder an inch.

"Ah, well," he said, switching his attention back to my visitor. "I've heard it said that a man's reach must exceed his grasp—or what's a heaven for?"

The officer stared at him for an instant, mouth open, then laughed with delight and slapped his knee.

"You and your wife are two of a kind, sir! *My* kind. That's splendid; do you recall where you heard it?"

Jamie did; he'd heard it from me, more than once over the years. He merely smiled and shrugged, though.

"A poet, I believe, but I've forgot the name."

"Well, a perfectly expressed sentiment, nonetheless, and I mean to go and try it on Granny directly—though I imagine he'll just blink stupidly at me through his spectacles and bleat about supplies. *There's* a man who knows his limits," he remarked to me, still good-humored but with a distinct edge in his voice. "Knows his own damnably low limits and won't let anyone else exceed them. A heaven's not for the likes of him."

That last remark went beyond edgy; the smile had faded from his face, and I glimpsed a hot anger at the back of his pale eyes. I had a moment of disquiet; "Granny" could only be General Gates, and this man was plainly a disaffected member of the high command. I sincerely hoped Robert Browning and I hadn't just landed Jamie in the middle of something.

"Well," I said, trying to make light of it, "they can't defeat you if you won't give up."

The shadow that had rested on his brow cleared and he smiled at me, merry-eyed once more.

"Oh, they'll never defeat me, Mrs. Fraser. Trust me!"

"I will," I assured him, turning to open one of my boxes. "Let me get the Jesuit bark for you . . . er . . ." I hesitated, not knowing his rank, and he noticed, clapping a hand to his forehead in apology.

"My apologies, Mrs. Fraser! What can you think of a man who bursts into your presence, rudely demanding medicaments and failing even to introduce himself properly?"

He took the small package of shredded bark from my hand, retaining the hand itself, and bowed low over it, gently kissing my knuckles.

"Major General Benedict Arnold. Your servant, ma'am."

JAMIE LOOKED AFTER the departing general, a slight frown on his face. Then he glanced back at me and the frown disappeared instantly.

"Are ye all right, Sassenach? Ye look as though you're about to fall over."

"I might, at that," I said rather faintly, and groped for my stool. I sat on it and discovered the new bottle of laudanum on the table beside me. I picked it up, finding the solid weight of it a reassurance that I hadn't imagined the gentleman who'd just left us.

"I was mentally prepared to run into George Washington or Benjamin Franklin in person at some point," I said. "Even John Adams. But I didn't really expect *him* . . . and I *liked* him," I added ruefully.

Jamie's brows were still up, and he glanced at the bottle in my lap as though wondering whether I'd been having a nip.

"Why should ye not like—oh." His face changed. "Ye know something about him?"

"Yes, I do. And it's not something I want to know." I swallowed, feeling a little ill. "He's not a traitor yet—but he will be."

Jamie glanced back over his shoulder, to be sure we were not overheard, then came and sat on the patient's stool, taking my hands in his.

"Tell me," he said, low-voiced.

There were limits to what I *could* tell him—and, not for the first time, I regretted not having paid more attention to Bree's history homework, as that formed the nucleus of my specific knowledge regarding the American Revolution.

"He fought on our—on the American side for some time, and was a brilliant soldier, though I don't know any of the details of that. But at some point, he became disillusioned, decided to switch sides, and began making overtures to the British, using a man called John André as his go-between—André was captured and hanged, I know that much. But I think Arnold got away to England. For an American *general* to turn his coat . . . it was such a spectacular act of treason that the name 'Benedict Arnold' became a synonym for traitor. *Will* become, I mean. If someone commits some horrible act of betrayal, you call them 'a Benedict Arnold.' "

The sick feeling hadn't gone away. Somewhere—right this minute—one Major John André was happily going about his business, presumably without the slightest notion of what lay in his future.

"When?" Jamie's fingers pressing mine drew my attention away from Major André's impending doom and back to the more urgent matter.

"That's the problem," I said helplessly. "I don't know. Not yet—I *think* not yet."

Jamie thought for a moment, brows drawn down.

"I'll watch him, then," he said quietly.

"Don't," I said, by reflex. We stared at each other for a long moment, recalling Charles Stuart. It hadn't escaped either of us that attempting to interfere with history could have serious unintended consequences—if in fact it could be done at all. We had no notion what it was that might turn Arnold from patriot—which he certainly was at the moment—to the traitor he would be. Was his fight with Gates the niggling grain of sand that would form the heart of a treacherous pearl?

"You don't know what small thing might affect someone's mind," I pointed out. "Look at Robert the Bruce and that spider."

That made him smile.

"I'll gang warily, Sassenach," he said. "But I'll watch him."

65

HAT TRICK

October 7, 1777

. . . Well, then, order on Morgan to begin the Game.

General Horatio Gates

ON A QUIET autumn morning, crisp and golden, a British deserter entered the American camp. Burgoyne was sending out a reconnaissance force, he said. Two thousand men, to test the strength of the American right wing.

"Granny Gates's eyes nearly popped through his spectacles," Jamie told me, hastily reloading his cartridge box. "And nay wonder."

General Arnold, present when the news came, urged Gates to send out a strong force against this foray. Gates, true to form, had been cautious, and when Arnold requested permission to go out and see for himself what the British were about, had given his subordinate a cold look and said, "I am afraid to trust you, Arnold."

"Matters rather went downhill from there," Jamie said, grimacing slightly. "The end of it all was that Gates said to him—and I quote ye exactly, Sassenach—'General Arnold, I have nothing for you to do. You have no business here.' "

I felt a chill that had nothing to do with the temperature of the morning air. Was this the moment? The thing that had—or would—turn Benedict Arnold against the cause he had fought for? Jamie saw what I was thinking, for he lifted one shoulder and said simply, "At least it's nothing to do wi' us this time."

"That *is* a comfort," I said, and meant it. "Take care, will you?"

"I will," he said, taking up his rifle.

This time, he was able to kiss me goodbye in person.

THE BRITISH reconnaissance had a double purpose: not only to see exactly where the Americans were—for General Burgoyne had no real idea; American deserters had stopped coming in long since—but also to acquire much-needed forage for the remaining animals. Consequently, the leading companies stopped in a promising wheat field.

William sent his infantrymen to sit down in double rows among the standing grain, while the foragers began cutting the grain and loading it on horses. A lieutenant of dragoons, a black-headed Cornishman named Absolute, waved from the other side of the field and called him to a game of hazard in his tent in the evening. He had just taken breath to call back when the man beside him let out a gasp and crumpled to the ground. He never heard the bullet, but ducked to the ground, calling out to his men.

Nothing further happened, though, and after a few moments they rose cautiously and went about their work. They began to see small parties of rebels, though, stealing through the trees, and William became conscious of a growing conviction that they were being surrounded. When he spoke of this to another officer, though, the man assured him that the rebels had decided to remain behind their defenses to be attacked.

They were soon undeceived on this point when, in mid-afternoon, a large body of Americans appeared in the woods on their left and heavy cannon opened up, slamming six- and twelve-pound balls that would have done great damage, were it not for the intervening trees.

The infantrymen scattered like quail, despite the calls of their officers. William caught sight of Absolute, pelting down the field through the wheat after a group of his men, and, turning, seized a corporal of one of his own companies.

"Gather them!" he said, and, not waiting for an answer, grabbed the bridle of one of the foragers' horses, a surprised-looking bay gelding. It was his intent to ride for the main camp for reinforcements, for plainly the Americans were out in force.

He never got there, for as he pulled the horse's head around, the brigadier rode onto the field.

JAMIE FRASER crouched in the grove at the base of the wheat field with a group of Morgan's men, taking aim as he could. It was as hot a battle as he'd seen, and the smoke from the cannon in the wood drifted through the field in heavy, choking clouds. He saw the man on the horse, a high-ranking British officer, to judge from his braid. Two or three others, juniors, were near him, also on horseback, but he had eyes only for the one.

Grasshoppers flew out of the field like hailstones, panicked by the trampling feet; one struck him in the cheek, buzzing, and he slapped at it, heart thumping as though it had been a musket ball.

He knew the man, though only by his general's uniform. He had met Simon Fraser of Balnain two or three times, but when they both were lads in the Highlands—Simon was a few years younger, and Jamie's vague memories of a small, round, cheerful wee lad who trotted after the older boys, waving a shinty stick taller than himself, had nothing in common with the stout, solid man who rose now in his stirrups, calling out and brandishing his sword, attempting to rally his panicked troops by sheer force of personality.

The aides were urging their mounts round his, trying to shield him, plainly urging him to come away, but he ignored them. Jamie caught a white glimpse of a face turned toward the wood, then away—plainly they knew the trees were full of riflemen, or could be, and were trying to keep out of range.

"There he is!" It was Arnold, crashing his small brown mare regardless through the heavy brush, his face alight with savage glee. "The generals!" he bellowed, rising in his own stirrups and throwing out an arm. "Shoot the generals, boys! Five dollars to the man who shoots yon fat bastard from his saddle!"

The random crack of rifle fire answered him at once. Jamie

saw Daniel Morgan's head turn sharp, eyes fierce at Arnold's voice, and the rifleman started toward him, moving as fast as his rheumatism-crippled limbs would let him.

"Again! Try again!" Arnold smote a fist on his thigh, caught sight of Jamie watching him. "You—shoot him, can't you?"

Jamie shrugged and, lifting the rifle to his shoulder, aimed deliberately high and wide. The wind had turned and the smoke of the shot stung his eyes, but he saw one of the junior officers near Simon jump and clap a hand to his head, twisting in the saddle to see his hat roll away into the wheat.

He wanted to laugh, though his wame curled a bit, realizing that he had nearly shot the man through the head, entirely by accident. The young man—yes, he was young, tall, and thin—rose in his stirrups and shook a fist at the wood.

"You owe me a hat, sir!" he shouted.

Arnold's high, piercing laugh echoed through the wood, clear over the shouting, and the men with him hooted and screamed like crows.

"Come over here, younker, and I'll buy you two!" Arnold shouted back, then reined his horse in a restless circle, bellowing at the riflemen. "Damn your eyes for a crew of blind men, will nobody kill me that frigging general?"

One or two shots spattered through the branches, but most of the men had seen Daniel Morgan stumping toward Arnold like an animated tree, gnarled and implacable, and held their fire.

Arnold must have seen him, too, but ignored him. He jerked a pistol from his belt and fired sideways across his body at Fraser, though he could not hope to hit anything at that distance, and his horse startled at the noise, ears flat back. Morgan, who had nearly reached him, was obliged to jerk back to avoid being trampled; he stumbled, and fell flat.

Without an instant's hesitation, Arnold leapt off his horse and bent to raise the older man, apologizing with a completely sincere solicitude. Which, Jamie saw, was unappreciated by Morgan. He thought old Dan might just give Arnold one in the stones, rank and rheumatism notwithstanding.

The general's horse was trained to stand, but the unexpected shot over her ears had spooked her; she was dancing nervously, feet a-rattle in the drifts of dead leaves and eyes showing white.

Jamie seized the reins and pulled the mare's nose down, blowing into her nostrils to distract her. She whuffed and shook her head, but ceased to dance. He stroked her neck, clicking his tongue, and her ears rose a bit; his hand was bleeding again, he saw, but it was a slow seep through the bandage, not important. Over the solid curve of the mare's neck, he could see Morgan, upright now and violently rejecting Arnold's efforts to dust the leaf mold from his clothes.

"You are relieved of command, sir! How dare you to order my men?"

"Oh, fuck that for a game of soldiers!" Arnold said, impatient. "I'm a general. He's a general"—he jerked his head toward the distant figure on horseback—"and I want him dead. Time enough for politics when it's over—this is a fight, dammit!" Jamie caught a sudden strong whiff of rum, sweet and fierce under the smell of smoke and trampled wheat. Aye, well, perhaps that had somewhat to do with it—though from what he knew of Arnold, there was little enough to choose between the man stone sober and another raving with drink.

The wind came in gusts, hot past his ears, thick with smoke and random sounds: the rattle of muskets punctuated by the crash of artillery to the left, and through it the shouting of Simon Fraser and his juniors, calling the Hessians and English to rally, the grunts of impact and shrieks of pain from farther away, where the Hessians fought to break through General Enoch Poor's advancing men.

General Ebenezer Learned's column was pressing the Hessians from above; Jamie could see the knot of green German uniforms, struggling amid a surge of Continentals but being forced back from the edge of the field. Some were trying to break away, to head downfield toward General Fraser. A glimpse of motion drew his eye; the young man he had deprived of a hat was galloping up the field, bent low over his horse's neck, saber drawn.

The general had moved a little, away from the wood. He was nearly out of range for most of Morgan's men—but Jamie was well placed; he had a clear shot from here. He glanced down. He had dropped his rifle when he took the horse, but the gun was loaded; he had reloaded by reflex after his first shot. The half-empty cartridge was still folded in the hand that held the reins; priming would take but an instant.

"*Sheas, a nighean,*" he murmured to the horse, and took a deep breath, trying to will himself to calm, will that calmness into the mare, though his hand was throbbing with the rush of his blood. *"Cha chluinn thu an còrr a chuireas eagal ort,"* he said, under his breath. *No more. Ye'll hear nay more to fright ye.*

He had not even thought about it when he'd fired to miss Fraser. He would kill any other man on the field—but not that one. Then he caught sight of the young soldier on the horse, coat bright red among the thrashing sea of green and blue and homespun, laying about him with his saber, and felt his mouth twitch. Not that one, either.

It seemed the young man was having a lucky day. He had cut through Learned's column at the gallop, taking most of the Continentals unaware, and those who saw him were too much occupied with fighting or unable to shoot him because they had discharged their weapons and were fixing bayonets.

Jamie stroked the horse absently, whistling gently through his teeth and watching. The young officer had reached the Hessians, had got the attention of some, and was now fighting his way back down the field, a stream of dark green coats in his wake, Hessians at the trot, making for the narrowing gap as Poor's men rushed in from the left.

Jamie was so much occupied by this entertaining spectacle that he had ignored the shouting match taking place between Dan Morgan and General Arnold. The sound of a whoop from overhead interrupted both.

"I got him, by Jaysus!"

Jamie looked up, startled, and saw Tim Murphy perched in the branches of an oak, grinning like a goblin, the barrel of his rifle snug in a fork. Jamie jerked his head round and saw Simon Fraser, slumped and swaying in his saddle, arms folded round his body.

Arnold let out a matching whoop, and Morgan glanced up at Murphy, nodding grudging approval.

"Good shot," he called.

Simon Fraser was wobbling, about to fall—one of his aides reached for him, shouting desperately for help, another reined his horse to and fro, undecided where to go, what to do. Jamie clenched his fist, felt a jolt of pain shoot through his maimed hand, and stopped, palm flat on the saddle. Was Simon dead?

He couldn't tell. The aides had overcome their panic; two of them rode close on either side, supporting the slumping figure, fighting to keep him in the saddle, heedless of the cheering from the wood.

He glanced up the field, searching for the young man with the saber. He couldn't find him and felt a small stab of loss—then picked him up, engaged in a hand-to-hand with a mounted militia captain. No kind of finesse in that sort of fight; it was as much the horse as the man, and as he watched, the horses were forced apart by the crush of bodies round them. The British officer didn't try to force his mount back; he had a goal in mind and shouted and gestured, urging on the small company of Hessians he had extracted from the melee above. Then he turned back toward the wood and saw what was happening, General Fraser's horse being urged away, the general's swaying body a splotch of red against the trampled wheat.

The young man stood in his stirrups for an instant, dropped, and spurred his horse toward the general, leaving his Hessians to follow as they might.

Jamie was close enough to see the darker crimson of the blood that soaked the middle of Simon Fraser's body. If Simon wasn't dead already, he thought, it wouldn't be long. Grief and fury at the waste of it burned in his throat. Tears from the smoke were already running down his cheeks; he blinked and shook his head violently to clear his eyes.

A hand jerked the reins unceremoniously from his fingers, and Arnold's stocky body brushed him away from the mare in a gust of rum. Arnold swung up into the saddle, face red as the scarlet maple leaves with excitement and victory.

"Follow me, boys!" he shouted, and Jamie saw that the wood was aswarm with militia, companies Arnold had collected on his mad dash for the battlefield. "To the redoubt!"

The men cheered and rushed after him, breaking branches and stumbling in their eagerness.

"Follow that goddamned fool," Morgan said shortly, and Jamie glanced at him in surprise. Morgan scowled at Arnold's back.

"He'll be court-martialed, mark my words," the old rifleman said. "He'd best have a good witness. You're it, James. Go!"

Without a word, Jamie seized his rifle from the ground and set off at a run, leaving the wood with its gentle rain of gold and brown. Following Arnold's broad-shouldered whooping form, his waving hat. Into the wheat.

THEY DID FOLLOW him. A bellowing horde, an armed rabble. Arnold was mounted, but his horse found it heavy going, and the men were not hard-pressed to keep up. Jamie saw the back of Arnold's blue coat blotched black with sweat, molded like a rind to the burly shoulders. One shot from the rear, the confusion of battle . . . But it was no more than a passing thought, gone in an instant.

Arnold was gone, too, with a whoop, spurring his mare up and around, past the redoubt. Jamie assumed he must be meaning to ride in from the rear—suicide, as the place was crawling with German grenadiers; he could see their mitred hats poking up above the walls of the redoubt. Perhaps Arnold meant to commit suicide—perhaps only to create a diversion for the men attacking the redoubt from the front, with his own death an acceptable price to be paid for it.

The redoubt itself stood fifteen feet high, a packed earthen wall with a palisade of logs built atop it—and between earth and palisade were abatis, logs sharpened to a point and flung down pointing outward.

Balls were spattering the field before the redoubt, and Jamie ran, dodging bullets he couldn't see.

He scrabbled with his feet, clawing for purchase on the logs of the abatis, got one hand through a gap and onto a log, but lost his grip on the flaking bark and fell back, landing bruisingly on his rifle and knocking out his wind. The man beside him fired up through the gap, and white smoke spurted over him, hiding him momentarily from the Hessian he'd glimpsed above. He rolled over and crawled fast away before the smoke could drift off or the fellow decide to drop a grenade through it.

"Get clear!" he shouted over his shoulder, but the man

who'd fired was trying his own luck with a running jump. The grenade fell through the gap just as the man leapt upward. It caught him in the chest and went off.

Jamie rubbed his hand on his shirt, swallowing bile. The skin of his palm stung, scraped and full of bark splinters. Shards of metal and wood chips had exploded outward; something had struck Jamie in the face, and he felt the sting of his sweat and the warmth of blood running down his cheek. He could see the grenadier, a glimpse of green coat through the gap in the abatis. Quick, before he moved.

He grabbed a cartridge from his bag and ripped it with his teeth, counting. He could load a rifle in twelve seconds, he knew it, had timed it. *Nine . . . eight . . .* What was it Bree taught the weans, counting seconds? Hippopotami, aye. *Six hippopotami . . . five hippopotami . . .* He had an insane urge to laugh, seeing in his mind's eye a group of several hippopotami solemnly watching him and making critical remarks regarding his progress. *Two hippopotami . . .* He wasn't dead yet, so he pressed himself close up under the abatis, aimed the barrel through the gap, and fired at the smear of green that might be a fir tree but wasn't, since it screamed.

He slung the rifle onto his back and once more leaped, fingers digging desperately into the unpeeled log. They slipped, splinters running up under his nails, and pain shot through his hand like lightning but now he had his other hand up, grabbed his right wrist with his sound left hand, and locked his grip round the log. His feet slid on the loose-packed dirt, and for an instant he swung free, like a squirrel hanging from a tree branch. He pulled upward against his weight and felt something tear in his shoulder, but couldn't stop to favor it. A foot, he had his foot braced on the underside of the log now. A wild swing with his free leg and he was clinging like a sloth. Something chunked into the log he clung to; he felt the shiver through the wood.

"Hold on, Red!" someone screamed below him, and he froze. Another chunking sound and something came down on the wood an inch from his fingers—an ax? He didn't have time to be scared; the man below fired past his shoulder—he heard the ball whiz past, buzzing like an angry hornet—and he pulled himself toward the base of the log in a rush, hand over hand as fast as he could, worming his way between the logs, clothes ripping, and his joints, too.

There were two Hessians lying just above his gap, dead or wounded. Another, ten feet away, saw his head pop through and reached into his sack, teeth bared beneath a waxed mustache. A bloodcurdling yell came from behind the Hessian, though, and one of Morgan's men brought down a tomahawk on his skull.

He heard a noise and turned in time to see a corporal step on one of the Hessian bodies, which abruptly came to life, rolling up with musket in hand. The Hessian struck up with all his force, the blade of the bayonet ripping up through the corporal's breeches as he stumbled, tearing free in a spray of blood.

By reflex, Jamie seized his rifle by the barrel and swung it, the motion snapping through his shoulders, arms, and wrists as he tried to drive the butt through the man's head. The jolt of collision wrenched his arms, and he felt the bones of his neck pop and his sight go white. He shook his head to clear it and smeared sweat and blood from his eye sockets with the heel of his hand. Shit, he'd bent the rifle.

The Hessian was dead for good, a look of surprise on what was left of his face. The wounded corporal was crawling away, one leg of his breeches soaked with blood, his musket slung onto his back, his own bayonet blade in his hand. He glanced over his shoulder and, seeing Jamie, shouted, "Rifleman! Your back!"

He didn't turn to see what it was but dived headlong and to the side, rolling into leaves and trampled earth. Several bodies rolled over him in a grunting tangle and crashed against the palisades. He got up slowly, took one of the pistols from his belt, cocked it, and blew out the brains of a grenadier poised to throw one of his grenades over the edge.

A few more shots, groans, and thumps, and as quickly as that, the fight died down. The redoubt was littered with bodies—most of them green-clad. He caught a glimpse of Arnold's little mare, white-eyed and limping, riderless. Arnold was on the ground, struggling to stand.

Jamie felt nearly unable to stand himself; his knees had gone to water and his right hand was paralyzed, but he wobbled over to Arnold and half-fell down beside him. The general had been shot; his leg was all-over blood, and his face was white and clammy, his eyes half-closing from the shock. Jamie reached out and gripped Arnold's hand, calling his name to pull him back, thinking even as he did so that this was madness; he should slip his dirk into the man's ribs and spare both him and the victims of his treachery. But the choice was made and past before he had time to think about it. Arnold's hand tightened on his.

"Where?" Arnold whispered. His lips were blanched. "Where am I hit?"

"It's your leg, sir," Jamie said. "The same where ye were hit before."

Arnold's eyes opened and fixed upon his face.

"I wish it had been my heart," he whispered, and closed them again.

66

DEATHBED

A BRITISH ENSIGN came just after nightfall, under a flag of truce. General Gates sent him to our tent; Brigadier Simon Fraser had learned of Jamie's presence and wished to see him.

"Before it's too late, sir," the ensign said, low-voiced. He was very young and looked shattered. "Will you come?"

Jamie was already rising, though it took him two tries to get up. He wasn't hurt, beyond a number of spectacular bruises and a sprained shoulder, but he hadn't had the strength even to eat when he staggered back after the battle. I'd washed his face for him and given him a glass of beer. He was still holding it, undrunk, and now set it down.

"My wife and I will come," he said hoarsely.

I reached for my cloak—and, just in case, my kit.

I NEEDN'T HAVE bothered with the kit. General Fraser lay on a long dining table in the main room of a large log cabin—the Baroness von Riedesel's house, the little ensign had murmured—and it was apparent from a glance that he was beyond any aid I could offer. His broad face was almost bloodless in the candlelight, and his body was wrapped in bandages, these soaked with blood. Fresh blood, too; I saw the wet patches slowly spreading, darker than the patches of dried blood already there.

Absorbed by the dying man, I'd only dimly registered the presence of several other people in the room and had consciously noticed only two: the surgeons who stood near the bed, bloodstained and white-faced with fatigue. One of them darted a glance at me, then stiffened a little. His eyes narrowed, and he nudged his fellow, who looked up from his contemplation of General Fraser, frowning. He looked at me with no particular comprehension and went back to his fruitless meditation.

I gave the first surgeon a straight look, but without any hint of confrontation. I did not mean to intrude on his territory. There was nothing I could do here, nothing anyone could do, as the surgeons' exhausted attitudes clearly showed. The second man hadn't given up, and I admired him for it, but the scent of putrefaction in the air was unmistakable, and I could hear the general's breathing—long, stertorous sighs, with a nerve-wringing silence between them.

There was nothing I could do for General Fraser as a doctor, and there were people here who could offer better comfort than I could. Jamie, perhaps, among them.

"He hasn't long," I whispered to Jamie. "If there's anything you want to say to him . . ."

He nodded, swallowing, and went forward. A British colonel at the side of the impromptu deathbed narrowed his eyes but, at a murmur from another officer, stepped back a little so that Jamie could approach.

The room was small and very crowded. I kept back, trying to stay out of the way.

Jamie and the British officer murmured together for a moment. A young officer, no doubt the general's aide, knelt in the shadow on the far side of the table, holding the general's hand, his own head bowed in obvious distress. I pushed the cloak back over my shoulders. Cold as it was outside, the air inside was beastly hot, unhealthy and suffocating, as though the fever that was devouring General Fraser before our eyes had risen from the bed and spread through the cabin, unsatisfied with its meager prey. It was a miasma, thick with decaying bowels, stale sweat, and the taste of black powder that hung in the men's clothes.

Jamie bent, then knelt himself, to come closer to Fraser's ear. The general's eyes were closed, but he was conscious; I saw his face twitch at the sound of Jamie's voice. His head turned and his eyes opened, the dullness in them brightening momentarily in recognition.

"Ciamar a tha thu, a charaid?" Jamie asked softly. *How are you, cousin?*

The general's mouth twitched a little.

"Tha ana-cnàmhadh an Diabhail orm," he replied hoarsely. *"Feumaidh gun do dh'ìth mi rudegin nach robh dol leam." I have the devil of an indigestion. I must have eaten something that disagreed with me.*

The British officers stirred a little, hearing the Gaelic, and the young officer on the far side of the bed looked up, startled.

Not nearly as startled as I was.

The shadowed room seemed to shift around me, and I half-fell against the wall, pressing my hands against the wood in hopes of finding something solid to hold on to.

Sleeplessness and grief lined his face, and it was still grimed with smoke and blood, smeared racoonlike across his brow and cheekbones by a careless sleeve. None of that made the slightest difference. His hair was dark, his face narrower, but I would have known that long, straight nose and those slanted blue cat-eyes anywhere. He and Jamie knelt on either side of the general's deathbed, no more than five feet apart. Surely, no one could fail to see the resemblance, if . . .

"Ellesmere." A captain of infantry stepped forward and

touched the young man's shoulder with a murmured word and a small jerk of the head, plainly telling him to leave the general's side, in order to give General Fraser a moment's privacy, should he desire it.

Don't look up! I thought as fiercely as I could in Jamie's direction. *For God's sake, don't look up!*

He didn't. Whether he had recognized the name or had caught a glimpse of that soot-smeared face across the bed, he kept his own head bent, his features hid in shadow, and leaned nearer, speaking very low to his cousin Simon.

The young man rose to his feet, slow as Dan Morgan on a cold morning. His shadow wavered on the rough-cut logs behind him, tall and spindly. He was paying no attention to Jamie; every fiber of his being was focused on the dying general.

"It is gladness to be seeing you once more on earth, *Seaumais mac Brian,*" Fraser whispered, bringing both his hands across with an effort to clasp Jamie's. "I am content to die among my comrades, whom I love. But you will tell this to those of our blood in Scotland? Tell them . . ."

One of the other officers spoke to William, and he turned reluctantly away from the bedside, answering low-voiced. My fingers were damp with sweat, and I could feel beads of perspiration running down my neck. I wanted desperately to take off my cloak but feared to make any movement that might draw William's attention to me and thus toward Jamie.

Jamie was still as a rabbit under a bush. I could see his shoulders tight under the damp-dark coat, his hands gripping the general's, and only the flicker of the firelight on the ruddy crown of his head gave any illusion of movement.

"It shall be as you say, *Shimi mac Shimi.*" I could barely hear his whisper. "Lay your wish upon me; I will bear it."

I heard a loud sniff beside me and glanced aside to see a small woman, dainty as a porcelain doll despite the hour and the circumstance. Her eyes shone with unshed tears; she turned her head to dab at them, saw me watching, and gave me a tremulous attempt at a smile.

"I am so glad that your husband is come, madam," she whispered to me in a soft German accent. "It—it is a comfort, perhaps. That our dear friend shall have the solace of a kinsman by his side."

Two of them, I thought, biting my tongue, and by an effort of will didn't look in William's direction. The awful thought came suddenly to me that William might recognize *me,* and make some effort to come and speak with me. Which might well mean disaster, if . . .

The baroness—for she must be von Riedesel's wife—seemed to sway a little, though it might be only an effect of the shifting firelight and the press of bodies. I touched her arm.

"I need air," I whispered to her. "Come outside with me."

The surgeons were drifting back toward the bed, intent as vultures, and the Gaelic murmurings were broken suddenly by a terrible groan from Simon Fraser.

"Bring a candle!" one of the surgeons said sharply, moving quickly toward the bedside.

The baroness's eyes shut tight, and I saw her throat move as she swallowed. I took her hand and led her quickly out.

IT WASN'T LONG but seemed an age before the men came out, heads bowed.

There was a short, sharp argument outside the cabin, conducted in low voices by reason of respect for the dead, but nonetheless heated. Jamie kept to one side, with his hat on, pulled well down, but one of the British officers turned to him now and then, obviously requesting his opinion.

Lieutenant William Ransom, aka Lord Ellesmere, kept to himself, too, as befitted his relatively lowly rank in this company. He didn't join in the argument, seeming too much shocked by the death. I wondered whether he had seen anyone he knew die before—and then realized how idiotic that thought was.

But battlefield deaths, however violent, are not the same as the death of a friend. And from the looks of young William, Simon Fraser had been friend as well as commander to him.

Occupied by these surreptitious observations, I hadn't been paying more than the most cursory attention to the main point of argument—that being the immediate disposition of General Fraser's body—and none at all to the two medical men, who had come out of the cabin and now stood a little apart, murmuring to each other. From the corner of my eye, I saw one reach into his pocket and hand the other a twist of tobacco, wave off the other's thanks, then turn away. What he said, though, seized my attention as effectively as though his head had burst into flame.

"*See you a bit later, then, Dr. Rawlings,*" he'd said.

"Dr. Rawlings?" I said by reflex, and the second doctor turned.

"Yes, ma'am?" he said politely, but with the air of an exhausted man struggling against an overwhelming urge to tell the world to go to hell. I recognized the impulse and sympathized—but having spoken, had no choice but to continue.

"I beg your pardon," I said, flushing a little. "I just caught your name and was struck by it—I used to know a Dr. Rawlings."

The effect of this casual remark was unexpected. His shoulders drew back abuptly and his dull gaze sharpened into eagerness.

"You did? Where?"

"Er . . ." I floundered for a moment, as in fact I had never actually met Daniel Rawlings—though I certainly felt I knew him—and temporized by saying, "His name was Daniel Rawlings. Would that perhaps be a relative of yours?"

His face lighted up and he seized me by the arm.

"Yes! Yes, he is my brother. Pray tell me, ma'am, do you know where he is?"

I had a nasty sinking feeling in the pit of my stomach. I did in fact know exactly where Daniel Rawlings was, but the news wasn't going to be welcome to his brother. There was no choice, though; I had to tell him.

"I'm terribly sorry to have to tell you that he's dead," I said, as gently as I could. I put my own hand over his and squeezed, my throat constricting again as the light in his eyes died.

He stood unmoving for the space of several breaths, his eyes focused somewhere beyond me. Slowly, they refocused on me and he took one more deep breath and firmed his mouth.

"I see. I . . . had feared that. How did he—how did it happen, do you know?"

"I do," I said hurriedly, seeing Colonel Grant shift his

weight in a manner indicating imminent departure. "But it's—a long story."

"Ah." He caught the direction of my glance and turned his head. All the men were moving now, straightening their coats, putting on their hats as they exchanged a few final words.

"I'll find you," he said abruptly, turning back to me. "Your husband—he is the tall Scottish rebel, I think they said he is kin to the general?"

I saw his gaze flick momentarily toward something beyond me, and alarm pricked like needles in my skin. Rawlings's brows were slightly knitted, and I knew, as clearly as if he had spoken, that the word "kin" had triggered some connection in his mind—and that he was looking at William.

"Yes. Colonel Fraser," I said hurriedly, grasping him by the sleeve before he could look at Jamie and complete the thought that was forming.

I had been groping in my kit as we spoke and at this point found the folded square of paper I'd been looking for. I pulled it out and, unfolding it quickly, handed it to him. There was still room for doubt, after all.

"Is this your brother's hand?"

He seized the paper from me and devoured the small, neat script with an expression in which eagerness, hope, and despair were mingled. He closed his eyes for an instant, then opened them, reading and rereading the receipt for Bowel-Bind as if it were Holy Writ.

"The page is burnt," he said, touching the singed edge. His voice was husky. "Did Daniel . . . die in a fire?"

"No," I said. There was no time; one of the British officers stood impatiently behind him, waiting. I touched the hand that held the page. "Keep that, please. And if you can manage to cross the lines—I suppose you can now—you'll find me most easily in my tent, near the artillery park. They . . . er . . . they call me the White Witch," I added diffidently. "Ask anyone."

His bloodshot eyes widened at that, then narrowed as he examined me closely. But there was no time for further questions; the officer stepped forward and muttered something in Rawlings's ear, with no more than a cursory glance in my direction.

"Yes," Rawlings said. "Yes, certainly." He bowed to me,

deeply. "Your servant, madam. I am very much obliged to you. May I . . . ?" He lifted the paper, and I nodded.

"Yes, of course, please keep it."

The officer had turned, obviously intent on chivvying another errant member of his party, and with a brief glance at his back, Dr. Rawlings stepped close and touched my hand.

"I'll come," he said, low-voiced. "As soon as I may. Thank you." He looked up then at someone behind me, and I realized that Jamie had finished his business and come to fetch me.

He stepped forward and, with a brief nod to the doctor, took my hand.

"Where is your hat, Lieutenant Ransom?" The colonel spoke behind me, quietly reproving, and for the second time in five minutes I felt the hair stand up on the back of my neck. Not at the colonel's words but at the murmured reply.

" . . . rebel whoreson shot it off my head," said a voice. It was an English voice, young, hoarse with suppressed grief, and tinged with anger. Other than that—it was Jamie's voice, and Jamie's hand tightened so abruptly on mine that he nearly crushed my fingers.

We were at the trailhead that led upward from the river; two more steps would see us safely into the shelter of the fog-veiled trees. Instead of taking those two steps, Jamie stopped dead for the space of a heartbeat, then dropped my hand, turned on his heel, and, taking the hat off his head, strode over and thrust it into Lieutenant Ransom's hands.

"I believe I owe ye a hat, sir," he said politely, and turned away at once, leaving the young man blinking at the battered tricorne in his hands. Glancing back, I caught a glimpse of William's baffled face as he looked after Jamie, but Jamie was propelling me up the path as though Red Indians were at our heels, and a stand of fir saplings hid the lieutenant from view within seconds.

I could feel Jamie vibrating like a plucked violin string, and his breath was coming fast.

"Have you quite lost your mind?" I inquired conversationally.

"Very likely."

"What on earth—" I began, but he only shook his head and pulled me along, until we were well out of both sight and hearing of the cabin. A fallen log that had so far escaped the woodcutters lay half across the path, and Jamie sat down suddenly on this and put a shaking hand to his face.

"Are you all right? What on earth is the matter?" I sat beside him and put a hand on his back, beginning to be worried.

"I dinna ken whether to laugh or to weep, Sassenach," he said. He took his hand away from his face, and I saw that, in fact, he appeared to be doing both. His lashes were wet, but the corners of his mouth were twitching.

"I've lost a kinsman and found one, all in the same moment—and a moment later realize that for the second time in his life, I've come within an inch of shooting my son." He looked at me and shook his head, quite helpless between laughter and dismay.

"I shouldna have done it, I ken that. It's only—I thought all at once, *What if I dinna miss, a third time?* And—and I thought I must just . . . speak to him. As a man. In case it should be the only time, aye?"

COLONEL GRANT cast a curious look at the trailhead, where a trembling branch marked the passage of the rebel and his wife, then turned his gaze on the hat in William's hands.

"What the devil was that about?"

William cleared his throat. "Evidently, Colonel Fraser was the, um, rebel whoreson who deprived me of my hat during the battle yesterday," he said, hoping for a tone of dry detachment. "He has . . . recompensed me."

A hint of humor came into Grant's strained face.

"Really? Decent of him." He peered dubiously at the object in question. "Has it got lice, do you think?"

In another man, at another time, this might have been interpreted as calumny. But Grant, while more than ready to denigrate the Colonials' courage, abilities, and dispositions, clearly intended the question only as a practical discovery of fact; most of the English and Hessian troops were crawling with lice, and so were the officers.

William tilted the hat, scrutinizing it as well as the dim light allowed. The thing was warm in his hands, but nothing moved along the seams.

"Don't think so."

"Well, put it on, then, Captain Ransom. We must show a good example to the men, you know."

William had in fact assumed the object, feeling slightly queer at the warmth of it on his head, before properly hearing what Grant had said.

"Captain . . . ?" he said faintly.

"Congratulations," Grant said, the ghost of a smile lightening the exhaustion on his face. "The brigadier . . ." He glanced back at the reeking, silent cabin, and the smile faded. "He wanted you made captain after Ticonderoga—should have been done then, but . . . well." His lips thinned, but then relaxed. "General Burgoyne signed the order last night, after hearing several accounts of the battle. I gather that you distinguished yourself."

William ducked his head awkwardly. His throat was thick and his eyes burned. He couldn't remember what he'd done—only that he'd failed to save the brigadier.

"Thank you," he managed, and could not keep from glancing back himself. They had left the door open. "Do you know—did he—no, it doesn't matter."

"Did he know?" Grant said gently. "I told him. I brought the order."

Unable to speak, William bobbed his head. The hat, for a wonder, fit him, and stayed in place.

"God, it's cold," Grant said softly. He tugged his coat closer, glancing round at the dripping trees and the fog that lay thick among them. The others had gone back to their duties, leaving them alone. "What a desolate place. Terrible time of day, too."

"Yes." William felt a momentary relief at being able to admit his own sense of desolation—though the hour and the place had little to do with it. He swallowed, glancing back at the cabin. The open door bothered him; while the fog lay heavy as a feather bed on the forest, the mist near the cabin was rising, drifting around the windows, and he had the uneasy fancy that it was somehow . . . *coming* for the brigadier.

"I'll just . . . close that door, shall I?" He'd started for the cabin, but was arrested by Grant's gesture.

"No, don't."

William glanced at him in surprise, and the colonel shrugged, trying to make light of it.

"The donor of your hat said we must leave it open. Some Highland fancy—something about the, um, soul requiring an exit," he said delicately. "And at least it's too bloody cold for the flies," he added, with no delicacy at all.

William's shriveled stomach clenched, and he swallowed the bitterness that rose in the back of his throat at the vision of swarming maggots.

"But surely we can't . . . How long?" he demanded.

"Not long," Grant assured him. "We're only waiting for a burial detail."

William stifled the protest that rose to his lips. Of course. What else could be done? And yet the memory of the trenches they had dug by the Heights, the dirt freckling his corporal's cold round cheeks . . . After the last ten days, he would have thought himself beyond sensitivity to such things. But the sounds of the wolves that came to eat the dying and the dead echoed suddenly in the hollow pit of his stomach.

With a muttered excuse, he stepped aside into the wet shrubbery and threw up, as quietly as he could. Wept a little, silent, then wiped his face with a handful of wet leaves and came back.

Grant tactfully affected to believe William had simply gone to relieve himself, and made no inquiries.

"An impressive gentleman," he remarked casually. "The general's kinsman, I mean. Wouldn't think they were related to look at, would you?"

Caught up in dying hope and tearing grief, William had barely noticed Colonel Fraser before the latter had so suddenly given him the hat—and been too startled to notice much about him then. He shook his head in agreement, though, having a vague recollection of a tall figure kneeling down by the bed, the firelight touching the crown of his head briefly with red.

"Looks more like you than like the brigadier," Grant added offhandedly, then laughed, a painful creak. "Sure you haven't a Scottish branch in your family?"

"No, Yorkshiremen back to the Flood on both sides, save one French great-grandmother," William replied, grateful for the momentary distraction of light conversation. "My stepfather's mother is half Scotch—that count, do you think?"

Whatever Grant might have said in reply was lost, as the sound of a doomed soul came down to them through the gloom. Both men froze, listening. The brigadier's piper was coming, with Balcarres and some of his rangers. The burial detail.

The sun had risen but was invisible, blocked by cloud and the canopy of trees. Grant's face was the same color as the fog, pale, sheened with moisture.

The sound seemed to come from a great distance and yet from the forest itself. Then wails and ululating shrieks joined the piper's lament—Balcarres and his Indians. Despite the chilling sounds, William was a little comforted; it would not be just a hasty field burial, undertaken without regard or respect.

"Sound like howling wolves, don't they?" muttered Grant. He ran a hand down his face, then fastidiously wiped his wet palm on his thigh.

"Yes, they do," said William. He took a firm stance and waited to receive the mourners, conscious all the time of the cabin at his back, its door standing silent, open to the mist.

67

GREASIER THAN GREASE

I HAD ALWAYS assumed that surrender was a fairly simple thing. Hand over your sword, shake hands, and march off—to parole, prison, or the next battle. I was disabused of this simpleminded assumption by Dr. Rawlings, who did indeed make his way across the lines two days later to speak to me about his brother. I'd told him everything I could, expressing my particular attachment to his brother's casebook, through which I felt I'd known Daniel Rawlings. The second Dr. Rawlings—his name was David, he said—was easy to talk to and lingered for a while, the conversation moving on to other subjects.

"Gracious, no," he said, when I'd mentioned my surprise that the ceremony of surrender had not occurred at once. "The terms of surrender must be negotiated first, you know—and that's a prickly business."

"Negotiated?" I said. "Does General Burgoyne have a *choice* in the matter?"

He seemed to find that funny.

"Oh, indeed he does," he assured me. "I happen to have seen the proposals which Major Kingston brought over this morning for General Gates's perusal. They begin with the rather firm statement, that having fought Gates twice, General Burgoyne is quite prepared to do it a third time. He's not, of course," the doctor added, "but it saves his face by allowing him to then note that he has of course noticed the rebels' superiority in numbers and thus feels justified in accepting surrender in order to save the lives of brave men upon honorable terms. By the way, the battle is not officially over yet," he added, with a faint air of apology. "General Burgoyne proposes a cessation of hostilities while negotiations are under way."

"Oh, really," I said, amused. "I wonder if General Gates is disposed to accept this at face value."

"No, he's not," said a dry Scottish voice, and Jamie ducked his head and came into the tent, followed by his cousin Hamish. "He read Burgoyne's proposal, then reached into his pocket and whipped out his own. He demands an unconditional surrender and requires both British and German troops to ground their arms in camp and march out as prisoners. The truce will last 'til sunset, at which time Burgoyne must make his reply. I thought Major Kingston would have an apoplexy on the spot."

"Is he bluffing, do you think?" I asked. Jamie made a small Scottish noise in his throat and cut his eyes at Dr. Rawlings, indicating that he thought this an improper thing to be discussing in front of the enemy. And given Dr. Rawlings's evident access to the British high command, perhaps he was right.

David Rawlings tactfully changed the subject, opening the lid of the case he had brought with him.

"Is this the same as the case you had, Mrs. Fraser?"

"Yes, it is." I had noticed it immediately but hadn't liked to stare at it. It was somewhat more battered than my case, and had a small brass nameplate attached to it, but was otherwise just the same.

"Well, I was in no real doubt as to my brother's fate," he said, with a small sigh, "but that settles the matter entirely. The cases were given to us by our father, himself a physician, when we entered practice."

I glanced at him, startled.

"You don't mean to tell me—were you twins?"

"We were, yes." He looked surprised that I hadn't known that.

"Identical?"

He smiled.

"Our mother could invariably tell us apart, but few other people could."

I stared at him, feeling an unusual warmth—almost embarrassment. I had, of course, built up a mental picture of Daniel Rawlings as I read his casebook entries. Suddenly meeting him face-to-face, as it were, gave me something of a turn.

Jamie was staring at me in bemusement, eyebrows raised. I coughed, blushing, and he shook his head slightly and, with another Scottish noise, picked up the deck of cards he'd come for and led Hamish out.

"I wonder—are you in need of anything particular in the medical line?" David Rawlings asked, blushing in turn. "I am quite short of medicinals, but I do have duplicates of some instruments—and quite a good selection of scalpels. I should be most honored if you would . . ."

"Oh." That was a gallant offer, and my embarrassment was at once submerged in a tide of acquisitiveness. "Would you perhaps have an extra pair of tweezers? Small forceps, I mean?"

"Oh, yes, of course." He pulled out the lower drawer, pushing a clutter of small instruments aside in search of the tweezers. As he did so, I caught sight of something unusual and pointed at it.

"What on earth is that?"

"It is called a jugum penis," Dr. Rawlings explained to me, his color increasing noticeably.

"It looks like a bear trap. What is it—it can't be a device for performing circumcision, surely?" I picked up the object, which caused Dr. Rawlings to gasp, and I eyed him curiously.

"It—er, please, dear lady . . ." He almost snatched the thing out of my hands, thrusting it back into his chest.

"What on earth is it for?" I asked, more amused than offended by his reaction. "Given the name, obviously—"

"It prevents nocturnal . . . er . . . tumescence." His face by this time was a dark, unhealthy sort of red, and he wouldn't meet my eye.

"Yes, I imagine it would do that." The object in question consisted of two concentric circles of metal, the outer one flexible, with overlapping ends, and a sort of key mechanism that enabled it to be tightened. The inner one was sawtoothed—much like a bear trap, as I'd said. Rather obviously, it was meant to be fastened round a limp penis—which would stay in that condition, if it knew what was good for it.

I coughed. "Um . . . *why,* precisely, is that desirable?"

His embarrassment faded slightly into shock.

"Why . . . it . . . the . . . the loss of the male essence is most debilitating. It drains the vitality and exposes a man to all manner of sickness, as well as grossly impairing his mental and spiritual faculties."

"Just as well no one's thought of mentioning that to my husband," I said.

Rawlings gave me a completely scandalized look, but before the discussion could assume even more improper proportions, we were fortunately interrupted by a stir outside, and he took the opportunity to shut his case and tuck it hastily back under his arm before coming to join me at the tent's entrance.

There was a small parade crossing the camp, a hundred feet away. A British major in dress uniform, blindfolded, and so red in the face I thought he might pop. He was being led by two Continental soldiers, and a fife player was following them at a semi-discreet distance, playing "Yankee Doodle." Bearing in mind what Jamie had said about an apoplexy, I was in no doubt that this was the unfortunate Major Kingston who had been selected to deliver Burgoyne's surrender proposals.

"Dear me," murmured Dr. Rawlings, shaking his head at the sight. "I am afraid this process could take some time."

IT DID. A week later, we were all still sitting there, as letters made their stately way once or twice a day between the two camps. There was a general air of relaxation in the American camp; I thought things were probably still a little tense across the way, but Dr. Rawlings had not come back, so general gossip was the only way of judging the progress—or lack of it—of the surrender negotiations. Evidently General Gates *had* been bluffing, and Burgoyne had been astute enough to realize it.

I was pleased to be in one place long enough to wash my clothes without risk of being shot, scalped, or otherwise molested. Beyond that, there were a good many casualties from the two battles who still required nursing.

I had been aware, in a vague sort of way, of a man lurking round the edges of our encampment. I'd seen him several times, but he had never come close enough to speak to me, and I'd put him down as likely suffering from some embarrassing ailment like clap or piles. It often took such men a good while to muster either the courage or the desperation to ask for help, and once they did, they'd still wait to speak to me privately.

The third or fourth time I noticed him, I tried to catch his eye, to induce him to come close enough so that I could arrange to examine him privately, but each time he slid away, eyes downcast, and disappeared into the anthill of seething militia, Continentals, and camp followers.

He reappeared quite suddenly toward sunset of the next day, while I was making a sort of pottage, using a bone—unidentifiable as to animal, but reasonably fresh, and with shreds of meat still clinging to it—given me by a patient, two wizened yams, a handful of grain, another handful of beans, and some stale bread.

"You are Mrs. Fraser?" he asked, in a surprisingly educated Lowland Scottish accent. Edinburgh, I thought, and had a faint pang at the memory of Tom Christie's similar speech. He had always insisted upon calling me "Mrs. Fraser," spoken in just that clipped, formal way.

Thoughts of Tom Christie vanished in the next instant, though.

"They call you the White Witch, do they not?" the man said, and smiled. It wasn't in any way a pleasant expression.

"Some do. What of it?" I said, taking a good grip on my spurtle and staring him down. He was tall and thin, narrow-faced and dark, dressed in the uniform of a Continental. Why had he not gone to his regimental surgeon, in preference to a witch? I wondered. Did he want a love philter? He scarcely seemed the type.

He laughed a little, and bowed.

"I wished only to be sure I had come to the right place, madam," he said. "I intended no offense."

"None taken." He was not doing anything noticeably threatening, other than perhaps standing too close to me, but I didn't like him. And my heart was beating faster than it ought.

"You evidently know my name," I said, striving for coolness. "What's yours, then?"

He smiled again, looking me over with a careful air that struck me as one inch short of insolence—and a short inch, at that.

"My name doesn't matter. Your husband is James Fraser?"

I had a sudden strong urge to dot him one with the spurtle but didn't; it might annoy him but wouldn't get rid of him. I didn't want to admit to Jamie's name and didn't bother asking myself why not. I simply said, "Excuse me," and, taking the camp kettle off the fire, set it on the ground and walked off.

He hadn't expected that and didn't follow me at once. I walked away fast, whisked round behind a small tent belonging to the New Hampshire militia and into a group of people gathered round another fire—militiamen, some with their wives. One or two looked surprised by my abrupt appearance, but all of them knew me and cordially made room, nodding and murmuring greetings.

I looked back from this refuge and could see the man, silhouetted by the sinking sun, standing by my own abandoned fire, the evening wind lifting wisps of his hair. It was no doubt my imagination that made me think he looked sinister.

"Who's that, Auntie? One of your rejected suitors?" Young Ian spoke by my ear, a grin in his voice.

"Certainly rejected," I said, keeping an eye on the man. I'd thought he might follow me, but he remained where he was, face turned in my direction. His face was a black oval, but I knew he was staring at me. "Where's your uncle, do you know?"

"Oh, aye. He and Cousin Hamish are takin' Colonel Martin's money at loo, over there." He jerked his chin in the direction of the Vermont militia encampment, where Colonel Martin's tent rose, recognizable by a large tear in the top, which had been patched with a piece of yellow calico.

"Is Hamish good at cards?" I asked curiously, glancing toward the tent.

"No, but Uncle Jamie is, and he kens when Hamish will do the wrong thing, which is almost as good as him doing the right thing, aye?"

"I'll take your word for it. Do you know who that man is? The one standing by my fire?"

Ian squinted against the low sun, then suddenly frowned.

"No, but he's just spat in your soup."

"He *what*?!" I spun on my heel, in time to see the anonymous gentleman stalk away, back stiff. "Why, that bloody filthy *arsehole*!"

Ian cleared his throat and nudged me, indicating one of the militia wives, who was viewing me with considerable disapproval. I cleared my own throat, swallowed my further remarks on the subject, and gave her what I hoped was an apologetic smile. We were, after all, probably going to be obliged to beg her hospitality, if we were to get any supper now.

When I looked back at our own fire, the man was gone.

"Shall I tell ye something, Auntie?" Ian said, frowning thoughtfully at the empty shadows lengthening beneath the trees. "He'll be back."

JAMIE AND HAMISH did not return for supper, leading me to suppose that the loo must be going well for them. Things were going reasonably well for me, too; Mrs. Kebbits, the militia wife, did feed Ian and myself, and very hospitably, with fresh corn dodgers and rabbit stew with onions. Best of all, my sinister visitor didn't return.

Ian had gone off about his own business, Rollo at heel, so I banked the fire and prepared to set off for the hospital tents for evening rounds. Most of the severely injured had died within the first two or three days after the battle; of the rest, those who had wives, friends, or relatives to care for them had been taken off to their own camps. There were three dozen or so left, men on their own, with lingering but not immediately life-threatening injuries or illnesses.

I put on a second pair of stockings, wrapped my thick wool cloak around myself, and thanked God for the cold weather. A chill had struck in late September, setting the woods afire with a glory of red and gold, but also helpfully killing off the insects. The relief of camp life without flies was marvelous in itself—no surprise to me that flies had been one of the Ten Plagues of Egypt. The lice, alas, were still with us, but without flies, fleas, and mosquitoes, the threat of epidemic illness was tremendously decreased.

Still, every time I came near the hospital tent, I found myself sniffing the air, alert for the telltale fecal stench that might portend a sudden irruption of cholera, typhus, or the lesser evils of a salmonella outbreak. Tonight, though, I smelled nothing beyond the usual cesspit smell of the latrines, overlaid by the funk of unwashed bodies, filthy linens, and a lingering tang of old blood. Reassuringly familiar.

Three orderlies were playing cards under a canvas lean-to next to the biggest tent, their game lit by a rush dip whose flame rose and flickered in the evening wind. Their shadows swelled and shrank on the pale canvas, and I caught the sound of their laughter as I passed. That meant none of the regimental surgeons was about; just as well.

Most of them were simply grateful for whatever help was offered and thus left me to do what I would. There were always one or two who'd stand on their dignity and insist on their authority, though. Usually no more than a nuisance, but very dangerous in case of emergency.

No emergencies tonight, thank God. There were a number of tin candlesticks and stubs of varying lengths in a bowl outside the tent; I lit a candle from the fire and, ducking inside, made my way through the two large tents, checking vital signs, chatting with the men who were awake, and evaluating their condition.

Nothing very bad, but I had some concern for Corporal Jebediah Shoreditch, who had suffered three separate bayonet wounds during the storming of the great redoubt. By some miracle, none had hit any vital organs, and while the corporal was rather uncomfortable—one thrust having plowed upward through his left buttock—he wasn't displaying any major signs of fever. There was some sign of infection in the buttock wound, though.

"I'm going to irrigate this," I told him, eyeing my half-full bottle of tincture of gentian. This was nearly the last of it, but with luck, there shouldn't be great need again until I was in a position to make more. "Wash it out, I mean, to rid you of the pus. How did it happen?" The irrigation wasn't going to be comfortable; better if he could be distracted a little by telling me the details.

"Wasn't retreatin', ma'am, and don't you think it," he assured me, taking a good grip on the edge of his pallet as I turned back the blanket and peeled away the crusty bits of a tar-and-turpentine dressing. "One o' them sneaky Hessian sons of bitches was a-playin' dead, and when I went to step over him, he come to life and reared up like a copperhead, bay'net in hand."

"Bayonet in *your* hand, you mean, Jeb," joked a friend who lay nearby.

"Nah, that was another un." Shoreditch shrugged off the joke with a casual glance at his right hand, wrapped in bandages. One of the Hessians had pinned his hand to the ground with a bayonet blade, he told me—whereupon Shoreditch had snatched up his fallen knife with his left hand and swiped it murderously across the Hessian's calves, felling him, and then had cut the Hessian's throat—disregarding a third attacker, whose thrust had removed the top part of his left ear.

"Somebody shot that un, Lord be praised, afore he could improve his aim. Speak of hands, Ma'am, is the colonel's hand a-doing well?" His forehead shone with sweat in the lantern light, and the tendons stood out in his forearms, but he spoke courteously.

"I think it must be," I said, pressing slowly on the plunger of my irrigating syringe. "He's been at cards with Colonel Martin since this afternoon—and if his hand was poor, he'd have come back by now."

Shoreditch and his friend both chuckled at this feeble pun, but he let go a long sigh when I took my hands away from the new dressing, and rested his forehead on the pallet for a moment before rolling painfully onto his good side.

"Thank you kindly, ma'am," he said. His eyes passed with apparent casualness over the figures that moved to and fro in the darkness. "If you was to see Friend Hunter or Doc Tolliver, might you ask 'em to stop a moment?"

I raised a brow at this, but nodded and poured him a cup of ale; there was plenty now that the supply lines from the south had caught up, and it would do him no harm.

I did the same for his friend, a man from Pennsylvania named Neph Brewster, who was suffering from dysentery, though I added a small handful of Dr. Rawling's Bowel-Bind mixture before handing over the cup.

"Jeb ain't meanin' no disrespect to you, ma'am," Neph whispered, leaning confidentially close as he took the drink. "It's only as he can't shit 'thout help, and that ain't somethin' he wants to ask a lady. Mr. Denzell or the Doc don't come by soon, I'll help him, though."

"Shall I fetch one of the orderlies?" I asked, surprised. "They're just outside."

"Oh, no, ma'am. Once the sun goes down, they figure as how they're off duty. Won't come in, save there's a fight or the tent catches fire."

"Hmm," I said. Plainly attitudes among medical orderlies weren't that different from one time to another.

"I'll find one of the surgeons," I assured him; Mr. Brewster was thin and yellow, and his hand shook so badly that I had to put my own fingers round his to help him drink. I doubted he could stand long enough to manage his own necessities, let alone help Corporal Shoreditch with his. Mr. Brewster was game, though.

"Shittin' is somethin' I can claim to have some skill at by now," he said, grinning at me. He wiped his face with a trembling hand and paused between swallows to breathe heavily. "Ah . . . might you have a bit o' cooking grease to hand, ma'am? My arsehole's raw as a fresh-skinned rabbit. I can put it on myself—unless you'd *like* to help, o' course."

"I'll mention it to Dr. Hunter," I replied dryly. "I'm sure he'd be delighted."

I finished my rounds quickly—most of the men were asleep—and went in search of Denny Hunter, who I found outside his own tent, bundled up against the cold with a muffler round his neck, dreamily listening to a ballad being sung at a nearby campfire.

"Who?" He came out of his trance at my appearance, though it took him a moment to return fully to earth. "Oh, Friend Jebediah, to be sure. Of course—I'll go at once."

"Have you got any goose or bear grease?"

Denny settled his spectacles more firmly on his nose, giving me a quizzical look.

"Friend Jebediah is not constipated, is he? I understood his difficulty to be more one of engineering than of physiology."

I laughed, and explained.

"Oh. Well. I do *have* some ointment," he said doubtfully. "But it is mentholated—for the treatment of grippe and pleurisy, thee knows. I fear that will do Friend Brewster's arse no favors."

"I fear not," I agreed. "Why don't you go and help Mr. Shoreditch, and I'll find a bit of plain grease and bring it along?"

Grease—any kind of grease—was a staple of cooking, and it took only two inquiries at campfires to procure a cup of it. It was, the donor informed me, rendered possum fat. "Greasier than grease," the lady assured me. "Tasty, too." This last characteristic was unlikely to be of much interest to Mr. Brewster—or at least I hoped not—but I thanked her effusively and set off through the darkness, back toward the small hospital tent.

At least I *intended* to head in that direction. The moon had not yet risen, though, and within a few minutes I found myself on a thickly wooded hillside that I didn't remember, stumbling over roots and fallen branches.

Muttering to myself, I turned left—surely that was . . . No, it wasn't. I stopped, cursing silently. I couldn't be lost; I was in the middle of a campground containing at least half the Continental army, to say nothing of dozens of militia companies. Exactly where I was on said campground, though . . . I could see the glimmer of several fires through the trees, but the configuration of them seemed unfamiliar. Disoriented, I turned the other way, straining my eyes in search of the patched roof of Colonel Martin's large tent, that being the biggest landmark likely to be visible in the darkness.

Something ran over my foot, and I jerked in reflex, slopping liquefied possum fat over my hand. I gritted my teeth and wiped it gingerly on my apron. Possum fat *is* extremely greasy, its major drawback as a general-purpose lubricant being that it smells like dead possum.

My heart was beating fast from the shock and gave a convulsive leap when an owl came out of the copse to my right, a piece of the night taking sudden silent flight a few feet from my face. Then a branch cracked suddenly, and I heard the movements of several men, murmuring together as they pushed through the undergrowth nearby.

I stood quite still, teeth set in my lower lip, and felt a wave of sudden, irrational terror.

It's all right! I told myself, furious. *It's only soldiers looking for a shortcut. No threat, no threat at all!*

Tell that *to the Marines,* my nervous system replied, at the sound of a muffled curse, the scuffle and crunch of dry leaves and breaking branches, and the sudden kicked-melon thump of a solid object meeting someone's head. A cry, the crash of a falling body, and hurried rustling as the thieves rifled their victim's pockets.

I couldn't move. I wanted desperately to run but was rooted to the spot; my legs simply wouldn't respond. It was exactly like a nightmare, with something terrible coming my way but no ability to move.

My mouth was open, and I was exerting all my strength to keep from screaming, while at the same time terrified that I *couldn't* scream. My own breathing was loud, echoing inside my head, and all of a sudden I felt my throat harsh with swallowed blood, my breath labored, nostrils blocked. And the weight on me, heavy, amorphous, crushing me into ground rough with stones and fallen pinecones. I felt hot breath in my ear.

There, now. I'm sorry, Martha, but you got to take it. I got to give it to you. Yeah, there . . . oh, Christ, there . . . there . . .

I didn't remember falling to the ground. I was curled into a ball, face pressed to my knees, shaking with rage and terror. Crashing in the brush nearby, several men passed within a few feet of me, laughing and joking.

And then some small fragment of my sanity spoke up in the recesses of my brain, cool as dammit, dispassionately remarking, *Oh, so* that's *a flashback. How interesting.*

"I'll show you interesting," I whispered—or thought I did. I don't believe I made a sound. I was fully dressed—swaddled against the cold—I could *feel* the cold on my face, but it made no difference. I was naked, felt cool air on my breasts, my thighs—between my thighs . . .

I clamped my legs together as tightly as I could and bit my lip as hard as I could. Now I really did taste blood. But the next thing didn't happen. I remembered it vividly. But it *was* a memory. It didn't happen again.

Very slowly, I came back. My lip hurt, and I was drooling blood; I could feel the gouge, a loose flap of flesh in my inner lip, and taste silver and copper, as though my mouth was filled with pennies.

I was breathing as though I'd run a mile, but I *could* breathe; my nose was clear, my throat soft and open, not bruised, not abraded. I was drenched in sweat, and my muscles hurt from being clenched so hard.

I could hear moaning in the brush to my left. *They didn't kill him, then,* I thought dimly. I supposed I should go and see, help him. I didn't want to, didn't want to touch a man, see a man, be anywhere near one. It didn't matter, though; I couldn't move.

I was no longer frozen in the grip of terror; I knew where I was, that I was safe—safe enough. But I couldn't move. I stayed crouched, sweating and trembling, and listened.

The man groaned a few times, then rolled slowly over, branches rustling.

"Oh, shit," he mumbled. He lay still, breathing heavily, then sat up abruptly, exclaiming, "Oh, *shit*!"—whether at the pain of the movement or the memory of the robbery, I didn't know. There was mumbled cursing, a sigh, silence . . . then a shriek of pure terror that hit my spinal cord like a jolt of electricity.

Mad scrambling sounds as the man scuffled to his feet—why, why, what was going on? Crashing and rattling of flight. Terror was infectious; I wanted to run, too, was on my feet, my heart in my mouth, but didn't know where to go. I couldn't hear anything above that idiot's crashing. What was bloody out there?

A faint rustle of dry leaves made me jerk my head round—and saved me by a split second from having a heart attack when Rollo thrust his wet nose into my hand.

"Jesus H. Roosevelt Christ!" I exclaimed, relieved at the sound of my own voice. The sound of rustling footsteps came toward me through the leaves.

"Oh, there ye are, Auntie." A tall presence loomed up, no more than a shadow in the dark, and Young Ian touched my arm. "Are ye all right, Auntie?" There was an anxious tone in his voice, bless him.

"Yes," I said rather faintly, then with more conviction, "Yes. I am. I got turned about, in the dark."

"Oh." The tall figure relaxed. "I thought ye must have lost your way. Denny Hunter came and said ye'd gone off to find some grease but ye'd no come back, and he was worrit for ye. So Rollo and I came to find ye. Who was yon fellow that Rollo scared the bejesus out of?"

"I don't know." The mention of grease made me look for the cup of possum grease. It was on the ground, empty and clean. From the lapping noises, I deduced that Rollo, having finished off what was in the cup, was now tidily licking the dead leaves on which grease had spilled when I dropped it. Under the circumstances, I didn't feel I could really complain.

Ian bent and scooped up the cup.

"Come back to the fire, Auntie. I'll find some more grease."

I made no demur at this and followed him down off the hillside, paying no real attention to my surroundings. I was too occupied in rearranging my mental state, settling my feelings, and trying to regain some kind of equilibrium.

I'd heard the word "flashback" only briefly, in Boston in the sixties. We didn't call it flashback earlier, but I'd heard about it. And I'd seen it. Shell shock, they said in the First World War. Battle fatigue, in the Second. It's what happens when you live through things you shouldn't have been able to live through and can't reconcile that knowledge with the fact that you did.

Well, I did, I said defiantly to myself. *So you can just get used to it.* I wondered for an instant who I was talking to and—quite seriously—whether I was losing my mind.

I certainly remembered what had happened to me during my abduction years before. I'd have strongly preferred not to but knew enough about psychology not to try to suppress the memories. When they showed up, I looked carefully at them, doing deep-breathing exercises, then stuffed them back where they'd come from and went to find Jamie. After a time, I found that only certain details showed up vividly: the cup of a dead ear, purple in the dawn light, looking like an exotic fungus; the brilliant burst of light I'd seen when Harley Boble had broken my nose; the smell of corn on the breath of the teenaged idiot who'd tried to rape me. The soft, heavy weight of the man who did. The rest was a merciful blur.

I had nightmares, too, though Jamie generally woke at once when I began to make whimpering noises and grabbed me hard enough to shatter the dream, holding me against him and stroking my hair, my back, humming to me, half asleep himself, until I sank back into his peace and slept again.

This was different.

IAN WENT FROM fire to fire in search of grease and at length obtained a small tin containing half an inch of goose grease mixed with comfrey. It was more than a bit rancid, but Denny Hunter had told him what it was for, and he didn't suppose the state of it mattered so much.

The state of his aunt concerned him somewhat more. He knew fine well why she sometimes twitched like a wee cricket or moaned in her sleep. He'd seen the state of her when they'd got her back from the bastards, and he knew the sort of things they'd done to her. Blood rose in him and the vessels at his temples swelled at memory of the fight when they'd taken her back.

She hadn't wished to take her own revenge, when they'd rescued her; he thought perhaps that had been a mistake, though he understood the part about her being a healer and sworn not to kill. The thing was, some men needed killing. The Church didn't admit that, save it was war. The Mohawk understood it fine. So did Uncle Jamie.

And the Quakers . . .

He groaned.

Out of the frying pan, into the fire. The instant he'd got the grease, his steps had turned, not toward the hospital tent where Denny almost surely was—but toward the Hunters' tent. He could pretend he was going to the hospital tent; the two were near enough together. But he'd never seen any point in lying to himself.

Not for the first time, he missed Brianna. He could say anything to her, and she to him—more, he thought, than she could sometimes say to Roger Mac.

Mechanically, he crossed himself, muttering, *"Gum biodh iad sabhailte, a Dhìa." That they might be safe, O God.*

For that matter, he wondered what Roger Mac might have counseled were he here. He was a quiet man, and a godly one, if a Presbyterian. But he'd been on that night's ride and joined in the work, and not a word said about it after.

Ian spared a moment's contemplation of Roger Mac's future congregation and what they'd think of that picture of their minister, but shook his head and went on. All these wonderings were only means to keep him from thinking what he'd say when he saw her, and that was pointless. He wanted only to say one thing to her, and that was the one thing he couldn't say, ever.

The tent flap was closed, but there was a candle burning within. He coughed politely outside, and Rollo, seeing where they were, wagged his tail and uttered a cordial *woof!*

The flap was thrust back at once, and Rachel stood there, mending in one hand, squinting into the dark but already smiling; she'd heard the dog. She'd taken off her cap, and her hair was messed, coming down from its pins.

"Rollo!" she said, bending down to scratch his ears. "And I see thee've brought thy friend along, too."

Ian smiled, lifting the little tin.

"I brought some grease. My aunt said your brother needed

it for his arsehole." An instant too late, he re-collected himself. "I mean—for *an* arsehole." Mortification flamed up his chest, but he was speaking to perhaps the only woman in camp who might take arseholes as a common topic of conversation. Well, the only one save his auntie, he amended. Or the whores, maybe.

"Oh, he'll be pleased; I thank thee."

She reached to take the tin from him, and her fingers brushed his. The tin box was smeared with the grease and slippery; it fell and both of them bent to retrieve it. She straightened first; her hair brushed his cheek, warm and smelling of her.

Without even thinking, he put both hands on her face and bent to her. Saw the flash and darkening of her eyes, and had one heartbeat, two, of perfect warm happiness, as his lips rested on hers, as his heart rested in her hands.

Then one of those hands cracked against his cheek, and he staggered back like a drunkard startled out of sleep.

"What does thee do?" she whispered. Her eyes wide as saucers, she had backed away, was pressed against the wall of the tent as though to fall through it. "Thee must not!"

He couldn't find the words to say. His languages boiled in his mind like stew, and he was mute. The first word to surface through the moil in his mind was the *Gàidhlig,* though.

"*Mo chridhe,*" he said, and breathed for the first time since he'd touched her. Mohawk came next, deep and visceral. *I need you.* And tagging belatedly, English, the one best suited to apology. "I—I'm sorry."

She nodded, jerky as a puppet.

"Yes. I—yes."

He should leave; she was afraid. He knew that. But he knew something else, too. It wasn't him she was afraid of. Slowly, slowly, he put out a hand to her, the fingers moving without his will, slowly, as though to guddle a trout.

And by an expected miracle, but miracle nonetheless, her hand stole out toward his, trembling. He touched the tips of her fingers, found them cold. His own were warm, he would warm her. . . . In his mind, he felt the chill of her flesh against his own, noted the nipples hard against the cloth of her dress and felt the small round weight of her breasts, cold in his hands, the press of her thighs, chill and hard against his heat.

He was gripping her hand, drawing her back. And she was coming, boneless, helpless, drawn to his heat.

"Thee must not," she whispered, barely audible. "We must not."

It came to him dimly that of course he could not simply draw her to him, sink to the earth, push her garments out of the way, and have her, though every fiber of his being demanded that he do just that. Some faint memory of civilization asserted itself, though, and he grabbed for it. At the same time, with a terrible reluctance, he released her hand.

"No, of course," he said, in perfect English. "Of course we mustn't."

"I—thee—" She swallowed and ran the back of her hand across her lips. Not as though to wipe away his kiss, but in astonishment, he thought. "Does thee know—" She stopped dead, helpless, and stared at him.

"I'm not worried about whether ye love me," he said, and knew he spoke the truth. "Not now. I'm worried about whether ye might die because ye do."

"Thee has a cheek! I didn't say I loved thee."

He looked at her then, and something moved in his chest. It might have been laughter. It might not.

"A great deal better ye don't," he said softly. "I'm no a fool, and neither are you."

She made an impulsive gesture toward him, and he drew back, just a hair.

"I think ye'd best not touch me, lass," he said, still staring intently into her eyes, the color of cress under rushing water. "Because if ye do, I'll take ye, here and now. And then it's too late for us both, isn't it?"

Her hand hung in the air, and while he could see her willing it, she could not draw it back.

He turned from her then and went out into the night, his skin so hot that the night air turned to steam as it touched him.

RACHEL STOOD stock-still for a moment, listening to the pounding of her heart. Another regular sound began to intrude, a soft lapping noise, and she looked down, blinking, to see that Rollo had tidily polished off the last of the goose grease from the tin she had dropped and was now licking the empty tin.

"Oh, Lord," she said, and put a hand over her mouth, afraid that if she laughed, it would erupt into hysterics. The dog looked up at her, his eyes yellow in the candlelight. He licked his lips, long tail waving gently.

"What am I to do?" she asked him. "Well enough for thee; thee can chase about after him all day, and share his bed at night, and not a word said."

She sat down on the stool, her knees feeling weak, and took a grip of the thick fur that ruffed the dog's neck.

"What does he mean?" she asked him. " 'I'm worried about whether ye might die because ye do?' Does he think me one of those fools who pines and swoons and looks pale for love, like Abigail Miller? Not that she'd think of actually dying for anyone's sake, let alone her poor husband's." She looked down at the dog and shook his ruff. "And what does he mean, kissing that chit—forgive my lack of charity, Lord, but there's no good to be done by ignoring the truth—and not three hours later kissing me? Tell me that! What does he *mean* by it?"

She let go of the dog then. He licked her hand politely, then vanished silently through the tent flap, no doubt to convey her question to his annoying master.

She ought to be putting coffee on to boil and getting up some supper; Denny would be back soon from the hospital tent, hungry and cold. She continued to sit, though, staring at the candle flame, wondering whether she would feel it were she to pass her hand through it.

She doubted it. Her whole body had ignited when he'd touched her, sudden as a torch soaked in turpentine, and she was still afire. A wonder her shift did not burst into flames.

She knew what he was. He'd made no secret of it. A man who lived by violence, who carried it within him.

"And I used that when it suited me, didn't I?" she asked the candle. Not the act of a Friend. She had not been content to trust in God's mercy, not willing to accept His will. She'd not only connived at and encouraged violence, she'd put Ian Murray in gross danger of both soul and body. No, no good to be done by ignoring the truth.

"Though if it's truth we're speaking here," she said to the candle, still feeling defiant, "I bear witness that he did it for Denny, as much as for me."

"Who did what?" Her brother's bent head poked into the tent, and he straightened up, blinking at her.

"Will thee pray for me?" she asked abruptly. "I am in great danger."

Her brother stared at her, eyes unblinking behind his spectacles.

"Indeed thee is," he said slowly. "Though I am in doubt that prayer will aid thee much."

"What, has thee no faith left in God?" She spoke sharp, made still more anxious by the thought that her brother might have been overcome by the things he had seen in the last month. She feared they had shaken her own faith considerable but depended upon her brother's faith as she would on shield and buckler. If that were gone . . .

"Oh, endless faith in God," he said, and smiled. "In thee? Not quite so much." He took off his hat and hung it on the nail he had driven into the tent pole, and checked to be sure that the flap was closed and tied fast behind him.

"I heard wolves howling on my walk back," he remarked. "Closer than was comfortable." He sat down and looked directly at her.

"Ian Murray?" he asked bluntly.

"How did thee know that?" Her hands were trembling, and she wiped them irritably on her apron.

"I met his dog just now." He eyed her with interest. "What did he say to thee?"

"I—nothing."

Denny cocked one brow in disbelief, and she relented.

"Not much. He said—I was in love with him."

"Is thee?" Denny asked, sounding not at all surprised.

"How can I be in love with such a man?"

"If thee were not, I do not suppose thee would be asking me to pray for thee," he pointed out logically. "Thee would simply send him away. 'How' is probably not a question I am qualified to answer—though I imagine thee means it rhetorical, in any case."

She laughed, in spite of her agitation.

"No," she said, smoothing the apron over her knees. "I do

not mean it rhetorical. More . . . well, would thee say that Job was being rhetorical when he asked the Lord what He was thinking? I mean it in that way."

"Questioning the Lord is an awkward business," her brother said thoughtfully. "Thee does get answers, but they are inclined to lead thee to strange places." He smiled at her again, but gently and with a depth of sympathy in his eyes that made her look away.

She sat pleating the cloth of the apron between her fingers, hearing the shouts and drunken singing that marked every night in camp. She wished to say that places didn't get much stranger than this—two Friends, in the midst of an army, and part of it—but it was indeed Denny's questioning of the Lord that had got them here, and she did not wish him to feel that she blamed him for it.

Instead, she looked up and asked earnestly, "Has thee ever been in love, Denny?"

"Oh," he said, and looked at his own hands, cupped on his knees. He still smiled, but it had altered, become inward, as though he saw something inside his head. "Yes. I suppose so."

"In England?"

He nodded. "Yes. It—would not do, though."

"She . . . was not a Friend?"

"No," he said softly. "She was not."

In a way, that was a relief; she had been fearing that he had fallen in love with a woman who would not leave England, but had felt obliged himself to return to America—for her sake. Insofar as her own feelings for Ian Murray were concerned, though, this did not augur well.

"I'm sorry about the grease," she said abruptly.

He blinked.

"Grease?"

"For someone's arsehole, Friend Murray said. The dog ate it."

"The dog ate . . . oh, the dog ate the grease." His mouth twitched, and he rubbed the thumb of his right hand slowly over his fingers. "That's all right; I found some."

"You're hungry," she said abruptly, and stood up. "Wash thy hands and I'll put the coffee on."

"That would be good. I thank thee, Rachel. Rachel . . ." He hesitated, but was not a man to avoid things. "Friend Murray said to thee that thee loves him—but not that he loves thee? That seems—a peculiar way of expression, does it not?"

"It does," she said, in a tone indicating that she didn't wish to discuss Ian Murray's peculiarities. She was not about to try to explain to Denny that Ian Murray had not declared himself to her in words because he hadn't needed to. The air around her still shimmered with the heat of his declaration. Though . . .

"Perhaps he did," she said slowly. "He said *something* to me, but it wasn't in English, and I didn't understand. Does thee know what '*mo cree-ga*' might mean?"

Denny frowned for a moment, then his brow cleared.

"That would be the Highlander's tongue, what they call the *Gàidhlig,* I think. No, I don't know what it means—but I have heard Friend Jamie say that to his wife, in such circumstances as to make it evident that it is a term of deep . . . affection." He coughed.

"Rachel—does thee wish me to speak to him?"

Her skin still burned, and her face felt as though it glowed with fever, but at this, a deep shard of ice seemed to pierce her heart.

"Speak to him," she repeated, and swallowed. "And say . . . what?" She had found the coffeepot and the pouch of roasted acorns and chicory. She poured a handful of the blackened mixture into her mortar and commenced to pound it as though the cup were full of snakes.

Denny shrugged, watching her with interest.

"Thee will break that mortar," he observed. "As to what I should say—why, thee must tell me, Rachel." His eyes were still intent upon her, but serious now, with no hint of humor. "I will tell him to stay away and never to speak to thee again, if thee wishes it. Or if thee prefers, I can assure him that thy affection for him is only that of a friend and that he must refrain from further awkward declarations."

She poured the grounds into the pot and then added water from the canteen she kept hanging on the tent pole.

"Are those the only alternatives you see?" she asked, trying to keep her voice steady.

"Sissy," he said, very gently, "thee cannot wed such a man and remain a Friend. No meeting would accept such a union.

Thee knows that." He waited a moment and added, "Thee did ask me to pray for thee."

She didn't answer or look at him but untied the tent flap and went out to put the coffeepot among the coals, pausing to poke up the fire and add more wood. The air glowed near the ground, lit by the smoke and fiery haze of thousands of small fires like hers. But the night above stretched black and clear and infinite, the stars burning with their own cold fire.

When she went back in, he was half under the bed, muttering.

"What?" she demanded, and he backed out, bringing with him the small crate that held their foodstuffs—save that it didn't. Only a scattering of raw acorns and an apple, half-gnawed by mice, remained.

"*What?*" she repeated, shocked. "What has happened to the food?"

Denny was flushed and plainly angry, and rubbed his knuckles hard across his lips before replying.

"Some misbegotten son of a—of Belial . . . has slit the tent and taken it."

The resultant flood of fury at this news was almost welcome, for the distraction that it offered.

"Why, that—that—"

"Doubtless," Denny said, taking a deep breath and seeking to regain control of himself, "he was hungry. Poor soul," he added, with a distinct lack of charitable intonation.

"If so, he might have asked to be fed," she snapped. "He is a thief, plain and simple." She tapped a foot, fuming. "Well. I will go and beg some food myself, then. Watch the coffee."

"Thee need not go on my account," he protested, but it was a halfhearted protest; she knew he had not eaten since morning and was starved, and she said as much to him with a wide-eyed stare in his direction.

"The wolves . . ." he said, but she was already wrapping up her cloak and pulling on her cap.

"I'll take a torch," she assured him. "And it would be an unlucky wolf who made the mistake of crossing me in my present mood, I assure thee!" She seized her gathering bag and went out quickly, before he could ask her where she proposed to go.

SHE MIGHT HAVE gone to a dozen different tents nearby. Puzzlement and suspicion of the Hunters had faded after Denny's adventures as a deserter, and Rachel herself had cordial relations with a number of the militia wives who camped near them.

She might have told herself that she hesitated to disturb these worthy women so late. Or that she wished to hear the latest news regarding the surrender—Friend Jamie was always privy to the negotiations and would tell her what he could. Or that she thought to consult Claire Fraser regarding a small but painful wart upon her great toe and might as well do this while seeking food, for the sake of convenience.

But she was an honest woman and told herself none of these things. She was walking toward the Frasers' camp as though drawn by a magnet, and the magnet's name was Ian Murray. She saw this clearly, thought her own behavior insane—and could no more do otherwise than she could change the color of her eyes.

What she meant to do, say, or even think if she *did* see him was unimaginable, but she walked on nonetheless, steady as though she went to market, the light of her torch a beacon upon the trampled dirt of her path, her own shadow following, huge and strange upon the pale canvas of the tents she passed.

68

DESPOILER

I WAS TENDING the fire when I heard the sound of slow footsteps approaching. I turned, to see a massive shape between me and the moon, coming fast. I tried to run but couldn't make my legs obey me. As in all the best nightmares, I tried to scream, only to find it trapped in my throat. I choked, and it came out as a small, strangled "*eep.*"

The monstrous shape—manlike, but humped and headless, grunting—stopped before me, and there was a short whoosh and a loud thump of something hitting the ground that sent the cold air rushing up under my skirt.

"I brought ye a present, Sassenach," Jamie said, grinning and wiping sweat from his jaw.

"A . . . present," I said faintly, looking at the enormous heap of . . . what? . . . he had dropped on the ground at my feet. Then the smell reached me.

"A buffalo robe!" I exclaimed. "Oh, Jamie! A real buffalo robe?"

Not much doubt of that. It was not—thank God—a fresh one, but the scent of its original owner was still perceptible, even in the cold. I fell to my knees, running my hands over it. It was well-cured, flexible, and relatively clean, the wool of it rough under my hands but free of mud, burrs, clumps of dung, and the other impedimenta that normally attended live buffalo. It was enormous. And warm. Wonderfully warm.

I sank my freezing hands into the depths of it, which still held Jamie's body heat.

"Oh," I breathed. "You won it?"

"I did," he said proudly. "From one of the British officers. A decent man at cards," he added fairly, "but no luck."

"You've been playing with British officers?" I cast an uneasy look in the direction of the British camp, though it wasn't visible from here.

"Just one. A Captain Mansel. He came wi' the latest reply from Burgoyne and was obliged to wait while Granny chews it over. He'll be lucky if he's not skinned to the bone before he goes back," he added callously. "Worse luck wi' cards I never saw."

I paid no attention, engrossed in examining the robe. "This is marvelous, Jamie! It's huge!"

It was. A good eight feet long, and wide enough that two people could lie cradled in its warmth—provided they didn't mind sleeping close. The thought of crawling into that enveloping shelter, warm and cozy, after so many nights shivering under threadbare blankets . . .

Jamie appeared to have been thinking along similar lines.

"Big enough for the two of us," he said, and touched my breast, very delicately.

"Oh, really?"

He leaned closer, and I caught his own scent above the gamy pong of the buffalo robe—dry leaves, and the bitterness of acorn coffee, laced with sweet brandy, top notes to the deep male scent of his skin.

"I could pick you out of a dozen men in a dark room," I said, closing my eyes and inhaling enjoyably.

"I daresay ye could; I havena bathed in a week." He put his hands on my shoulders and bent his head until our foreheads touched.

"I want to unlace the neck o' your shift," he whispered, "and suckle your breasts until ye curl up like a wee shrimp, wi' your knees in my balls. Then take ye fast and hard, and fall asleep wi' my head pillowed on your naked breasts. Really," he added, straightening up.

"Oh," I said. "What a good idea."

IN FAVOR AS I WAS of the suggested program, I could see that Jamie required nourishment before executing anything of a further strenuous nature; I could hear his stomach rumbling from a yard away.

"Playing cards takes it out of you, does it?" I observed, watching him demolish three apples in six bites.

"Aye, it does," he said briefly. "Have we any bread?"

"No, but there's beer."

As though the word had evoked him, Young Ian materialized out of the gloom.

"Beer?" he said hopefully.

"Bread?" Jamie and I said together, sniffing like dogs. Wafting from Ian's clothes was a yeasty, half-burned fragrance, which proved to come from two small loaves in his pockets.

"Where did you get these, Ian?" I asked, handing him a canteen of beer.

He drank deep, then lowered the canteen and stared vacantly at me for a moment.

"Ah?" he said vaguely.

"Are you all right, Ian?" I peered at him in some concern, but he blinked, and intelligence returned momentarily to his face.

"Aye, Auntie, fine. I'll just . . . ah . . . oh, thank ye for the beer." He handed back the empty canteen, smiled at me as though I were a stranger, and wandered off into the darkness.

"Did you see that?" I turned to find Jamie absorbed in dabbing up bread crumbs from his lap with a moistened finger.

"No, what? Here, Sassenach." He handed me the second loaf.

"Ian acting like a half-wit. Here, you have half; you need it more than I do."

He didn't argue.

"He wasna bleeding or staggering, was he? Well, then, I suppose he's fallen in love wi' some poor lass."

"Oh? Well, that would fit the symptoms. But . . ." I nibbled the bread slowly, to make it last; it was crusty and fresh, clearly just out of the ashes. I'd seen young men in love, certainly, and Ian's behavior *did* fit the symptomology. But I hadn't seen it in Ian, not since . . . "I wonder who?"

"God knows. I hope it's no one of the whores." Jamie sighed and rubbed a hand over his face. "Though maybe better that than someone else's wife."

"Oh, he wouldn't—" I began, but then saw the wry look on his face. "Oh, he *didn't*?"

"No, he didn't," Jamie said, "but a near thing—and no credit to the lady involved."

"Who?"

"Colonel Miller's lady."

"Dear me." Abigail Miller was a sprightly young blonde of twenty or so, and twenty or so years younger than her rather stout—and distinctly humorless—husband. "Just . . . *how* near a thing?"

"Near enough," Jamie said grimly. "She had him up against a tree, rubbing up to him like a wee cat in heat. Though I imagine her husband will ha' put a stop to her antics by now."

"He *saw* them?"

"Aye. He and I were walking together, came round a bush, and there they were. It was clear enough to me that it wasna the lad's idea—but he wasna resisting all that much, either."

Colonel Miller had frozen for an instant, then strode forward, gripped his startled wife by the arm, and with a murmured "Good day, sir" to Jamie, had dragged her off, squealing, in the direction of his camp.

"Jesus H. . . . when did this happen?" I demanded.

Jamie glanced at the rising moon, estimating.

"Oh, maybe five or six hours ago."

"And he's already managed to fall in love with someone *else*?"

He smiled at me.

"Ever heard of *coup de foudre,* Sassenach? It didna take me more than one good look at you."

"Hmm," I said, pleased.

WITH SOME EFFORT, I heaved the heavy buffalo robe over the stack of cut fir branches that formed the foundation of our bed, spread our two blankets over the robe, then folded the whole thing over like a dumpling, creating a large, weatherproof, cozy pocket into which I inserted myself, shivering in my shift.

I left the tent flap open, watching Jamie as he drank coffee and talked with two militiamen who had come by to gossip.

As my feet thawed for the first time in a month, I relaxed

into untrammeled bliss. Like most people obliged to live outdoors in the autumn, I normally slept in everything I owned. Women moving with the army would occasionally remove their stays—if it wasn't raining, you saw them hung to air from tree branches in the mornings sometimes, like huge, malodorous birds poised for flight—but most simply loosened the ties and lay down regardless. Stays are quite comfortable to wear while standing up, but leave a lot to be desired in terms of nightwear.

Tonight, with the prospect of warm, waterproof shelter at hand, I had actually gone so far as to take off not only my stays—rolled up under my head as a pillow—but also skirt, blouse, jacket, and kerchief, crawling into bed in nothing save my shift and stockings. I felt absolutely depraved.

I stretched luxuriously and ran my hands down the length of my body, then thoughtfully cupped my breasts, contemplating Jamie's proposed plan of action.

The warmth of the buffalo robe was making me deliciously drowsy. I thought I needn't struggle to stay awake; I could tell that Jamie wasn't in any mood to forbear waking me out of chivalrous regard for my rest.

Had the fortuitous acquisition of the buffalo robe inspired him? I wondered, thumb dreamily circling one nipple. Or had sexual desperation inspired him to bet on the thing? What with his injured hand, it had been . . . how many days? I was absently totting up the total in my mind when I heard the low murmur of a new voice by the fire, and sighed.

Ian. Not that I wasn't pleased to see him, but . . . oh, well. At least he hadn't turned up just as we were . . .

He was sitting on one of the stones near the fire, head bent. He took something from his sporran and rubbed it thoughtfully between his fingers as he talked. His long, homely face was worried—but bore an odd sort of glow.

How peculiar, I thought. I'd seen it before, that look. A sort of intent concentration on something wonderful, a marvelous secret held to himself.

It was a girl, I thought, both amused and touched. He'd looked just that way at Mary, the young prostitute who had been his first. And Emily?

Well, yes . . . I thought so, though in that instance his joy in her had been terribly shadowed by the knowledge of his impending separation from everyone and everything else he loved.

Cuimhnich, Jamie had said to him, laying his own plaid over Ian's shoulders in farewell. *"Remember."* I had thought my heart would break, to leave him—I knew Jamie's had.

He was still wearing the same ragged plaid, pinned to the shoulder of his buckskins.

"Rachel *Hunter*?" Jamie said, loud enough for me to hear, and I jerked upright, startled.

"Rachel *Hunter*?" I echoed. "You're in love with Rachel?"

Ian looked at me, startled by my jack-in-the-box appearance.

"Oh, there ye are, Auntie. I wondered where ye'd got to," he said mildly.

"Rachel Hunter?" I repeated, not intending to let him elude the question.

"Well . . . aye. At least, I . . . well, aye. I am." The admission made the blood rise in his cheeks; I could see it even by firelight.

"The lad is thinking we'd maybe have a word wi' Denzell, Sassenach," Jamie explained. He looked amused, but slightly worried, as well.

"A word? What for?"

Ian looked up and glanced from one to the other of us. "It's only . . . Denny Hunter's no going to like it. But he thinks the world of Auntie Claire, and he respects you, of course, Uncle Jamie."

"Why would he not like it?" I asked. I had by now extracted myself from the robe and, wrapping my shawl round my shoulders, sat down on a rock beside him. My mind was racing. I liked Rachel Hunter very much. And I was *very* pleased—to say nothing of relieved—if Ian had at last found a decent woman to love. But . . .

Ian gave me a look.

"Surely ye've noticed that they're Quaker, Auntie?"

"I did, yes," I said, giving him back the look. "But—"

"And I'm not."

"Yes, I'd noticed that, too. But—"

"She'd be put out of meeting, if she weds me. Most likely they both would. They've been put out once already for Denny's going wi' the army, and that was hard for her."

"Oh," said Jamie, pausing in the act of tearing off a bit of bread. He held it for a moment, frowning. "Aye, I suppose they would." He put the bread into his mouth and chewed slowly, considering.

"Do you think she loves you, too, Ian?" I asked, as gently as possible.

Ian's face was a study, torn between worry, alarm, and that inner glow that kept breaking through the clouds of distress.

"I—well . . . I think so. I hope so."

"You haven't *asked* her?"

"I . . . not exactly. I mean—we didna really *talk,* ken?"

Jamie swallowed his bread and coughed.

"Ian," he said. "Tell me ye havena bedded Rachel Hunter."

Ian gave him a look of affront. Jamie stared at him, brows raised. Ian dropped his gaze back to the object in his hands, rolling it between his palms like a ball of dough.

"No," he muttered. "I wish I had, though."

"What?"

"Well . . . if I had, then she'd have to wed me, no? I wish I'd thought of that—but no, I couldna; she said stop, and I did." He swallowed, hard.

"Very gentlemanly of you," I murmured, though in fact I rather saw his point. "And very intelligent of her."

He sighed. "What am I to do, Uncle Jamie?"

"I don't suppose you could become a Quaker yourself?" I asked hesitantly.

Both Jamie and Ian looked at me. They didn't resemble each other in the slightest, but the look of ironic amusement on both faces was identical.

"I dinna ken very much about myself, Auntie," Ian said, with a painful half smile, "but I think I wasna born to be a Quaker."

"And I suppose you couldn't—no, of course not." The thought of professing a conversion that he didn't mean had plainly never entered his mind.

It struck me quite suddenly that, of all people, Ian would understand exactly what the cost to Rachel would be if her love for him severed her from her people. No wonder he hesitated at the thought of her paying such a price.

Always assuming, I reminded myself, that she *did* love him. I had better have a talk with Rachel first.

Ian was still turning something over in his hands. Looking closer, I saw that it was a small, darkened, leathery-looking object. Surely it wasn't—

"That isn't Neil Forbes's ear, is it?" I blurted.

"Mr. Fraser?"

The voice brought me up standing, hairs prickling at the back of my neck. Bloody hell, not *him* again? Sure enough, it was the Continental soldier, the despoiler of my soup. He came slowly into the circle of firelight, deep-set eyes fixed on Jamie.

"I am James Fraser, aye," Jamie said, setting down his cup and gesturing politely toward a vacant rock. "Will ye take a cup of coffee, sir? Or what passes for it?"

The man shook his head, not speaking. He was looking Jamie over appraisingly, like one about to buy a horse and not sure of its temper.

"Perhaps ye'd prefer a warm cup o' spittle?" Ian said, in an unfriendly tone. Jamie glanced at him, startled.

"Seo mac na muice a thàinig na bu thràithe gad shiubhal," Ian added. He didn't take his eyes off the stranger. *"Chan eil e ag iarraidh math dhut idir 'uncle.'* This is the misbegotten son of a pig who came earlier in search of you. He means you no good, Uncle."

"Tapadh leat Iain. Cha robh fios air a bhith agam," Jamie answered in the same language, keeping his voice pleasantly relaxed. "Thank you, Ian. I should never have guessed. Have ye business with me, sir?" he asked, changing to English.

"I would speak with you, yes. In privacy," the man added, with a dismissive glance at Ian. Apparently I didn't count.

"This is my nephew," Jamie said, still courteous but wary. "Ye may speak in front of him."

"I fear ye may think differently, Mr. Fraser, when you hear what I've to say. And once said, such things cannot be unsaid. Leave, young man," he said, not bothering to look at Ian. "Or you will both regret it."

Both Jamie and Ian stiffened visibly. Then they moved, at nearly the same instant, bodies shifting subtly, their feet coming under them, shoulders squaring. Jamie gazed thoughtfully at the man for a moment, then inclined his head an inch toward Ian. Ian rose without a word and disappeared into the darkness.

The man stood waiting, until the sound of Ian's footsteps

had faded and the night settled into silence around the tiny fire. Then he moved round the fire and sat down slowly, opposite Jamie, still maintaining that unnerving air of scrutiny. Well, it unnerved *me;* Jamie merely picked up his cup and drained it, calm as though he were sitting at his own kitchen table.

"If ye've aught to say to me, sir, say it. It's late, and I'm for my bed."

"A bed with your lovely wife in it, I daresay. Lucky man." I was beginning to dislike this gentleman intensely. Jamie ignored both the comment and the mocking tone in which it was spoken, leaning forward to pour the last of the coffee into his cup. I could smell the bitter tang of it, even over the scent the buffalo robe had left on my shift.

"Does the name of Willie Coulter recall itself to you?" the man asked abruptly.

"I've kent several men of that name and that ilk," Jamie replied. "Mostly in Scotland."

"Aye, it was in Scotland. On the day before the great slaughter at Culloden. But you had your own wee slaughter on that day, no?"

I had been racking my memory for any notion of a Willie Coulter. The mention of Culloden struck me like a fist in the stomach.

Jamie had been obliged to kill his uncle Dougal MacKenzie on that day. And there had been one witness to the deed besides me: a MacKenzie clansman named Willie Coulter. I had assumed him long dead, either at Culloden or in the difficulties that followed—and I was sure Jamie had thought likewise.

Our visitor rocked back a little on his rock, smiling sardonically.

"I was once overseer on a sugar plantation of some size, you see, on the island of Jamaica. We'd a dozen black slaves from Africa, but blacks of decent quality grow ever more expensive. And so the master sent me to market one day with a purse of silver, to look over a new crop of indentures—transported criminals, the most of them. From Scotland."

And among the two dozen men the overseer had culled from the ragged, scrawny, lice-ridden ranks was Willie Coulter. Captured after the battle, tried and condemned in quick order, and loaded onto a ship for the Indies within a month, never to see Scotland again.

I could just see the side of Jamie's face and saw a muscle jump in his jaw. Most of his Ardsmuir men had been similarly transported; only the interest of John Grey had saved him from the same fate, and he had distinctly mixed feelings about it, even so many years after the fact. He merely nodded, though, vaguely interested, as though listening to some traveler's tale in an inn.

"They all died within two weeks," the stranger said, his mouth twisting. "And so did the blacks. Bloody pricks brought some filthy fever with them from the ship. Lost me my position. But I did get one thing of value to take away with me. Willie Coulter's last words."

JAMIE HADN'T MOVED appreciably since Mr. X had sat down, but I could sense the tension thrumming through him; he was strung like a bow with the arrow nocked.

"What is it ye want?" he asked calmly, and leaned forward to pick up the tin mug of coffee, wrapped in rags.

"Mmphm." The man made a pleased sound in his throat and sat back a little, nodding.

"I kent ye for a sensible gentleman. I'm a modest man, sir—shall we say a hundred dollars? To show your good faith," he added, with a grin that displayed snaggled teeth discolored by snuff. "And to save ye the trouble of protest, I'll just mention that I ken ye've got it in your pocket. I happened to speak wi' the gentleman ye won it from this afternoon, aye?"

I blinked at that; evidently Jamie had had an extraordinary run of luck. At cards, at least.

"To show good faith," Jamie repeated. He looked at the cup in his hand, then at the Lowlander's grinning face, but evidently decided that the distance was too great to throw it at him. "And to be going on with . . . ?"

"Ah, well. We can be discussing that later. I hear ye're a man of considerable substance, Colonel Fraser."

"And ye propose to batten on me like a leech, do ye?"

"Why, a bit of leeching does a man good, Colonel. Keeps

the humors in balance." He leered at me. "I'm sure your good wife kens the wisdom of it."

"And what do you mean by *that,* you slimy little worm?" I said, standing up. Jamie might have decided against throwing a cup of coffee at him, but I was willing to have a try with the pot.

"Manners, woman," he said, giving me a censorious glance before shifting his gaze back to Jamie. "Do ye not beat her, man?"

I could see the tautness in Jamie's body subtly shifting; the bow was being drawn.

"Don't—" I began, turning to Jamie, but never got to finish. I saw the expression change on Jamie's face, saw him leap toward the man—and whirled just in time to see Ian materialize out of the darkness behind the blackmailer and put a sinewy arm round his throat.

I didn't see the knife. I didn't have to; I saw Ian's face, so intent as almost to be expressionless—and I saw the ex-overseer's face. His jaw dropped and the whites of his eyes showed, his back arching up in a futile attempt at escape.

Then Ian let go, and Jamie caught the man as he began to fall, his body gone suddenly and horribly limp.

"Jesus God!"

The exclamation came from directly behind me, and I whirled again, this time to see Colonel Martin and two of his aides, as drop-jawed as Mr. X had been a moment before.

Jamie glanced up at them, startled. Then in the next breath, he turned and said quietly over his shoulder, *"Ruith." Run.*

"Hi! Murder!" one of the aides shouted, springing forward. "Stop, villain!"

Ian had lost no time in taking Jamie's advice; I could see him darting toward the edge of the distant wood, but there was enough light from the many campfires to reveal his flight, and the shouts of Martin and his aides were rousing everyone in hearing; people were jumping up from their firesides, peering into the dark, shouting questions. Jamie dropped the overseer's body by the fire and ran after Ian.

The younger of the aides hurtled past me, legs churning in furious pursuit. Colonel Martin dashed after him, and I managed to stick out a foot and trip him. He went sprawling through the fire, sending a fountain of sparks and ashes into the night.

Leaving the second aide to beat out the flames, I picked up my shift and ran as fast as I could in the direction Ian and Jamie had taken.

The encampment looked like something from Dante's *Inferno,* black figures shouting against the glow of flames, pushing one another amid smoke and confusion, shouts of "Murder! Murder!" ringing from different directions as more people heard and took it up.

I had a stitch in my side but kept running, stumbling over rocks and hollows and trampled ground. Louder shouts from the left—I paused, panting, hand to my side, and saw Jamie's tall form jerking free of a couple of pursuers. He must mean to draw pursuit away from Ian—which meant . . . I turned and ran the other way.

Sure enough, I saw Ian, who had sensibly stopped running as soon as he saw Jamie take off, now walking at a good clip toward the wood.

"Murderer!" a voice shrieked behind me. It was Martin, blast him, somewhat scorched but undaunted. "Stop, Murray! Stop, I say!"

Hearing his name shouted, Ian began to run again, zigzagging around a campfire. As he passed in front of it, I saw the shadow at his heels—Rollo was with him.

Colonel Martin had drawn up even with me, and I saw with alarm that he had his pistol in hand.

"St—" I began, but before the word was out, I crashed headlong into someone and fell flat with them.

It was Rachel Hunter, wide-eyed and openmouthed. She scrambled to her feet and ran toward Ian, who had frozen when he saw her. Colonel Martin cocked his pistol and pointed it at Ian, and a second later Rollo leapt through the air and seized the colonel's arm in his jaws.

The pandemonium grew worse. There were bangs from two or three pistols, and Rollo dropped writhing to the ground with a yelp. Colonel Martin jerked back, cursing and clutching his injured wrist, and Jamie drew back and punched him in the belly. Ian was already rushing toward Rollo; Jamie grabbed the dog by two legs, and, between them, they made off into the darkness, followed by Rachel and me.

We made it to the edge of the wood, heaving and gasping, and I fell at once to my knees beside Rollo, feeling frantically over the huge shaggy body, hunting for the wound, for damage.

"He's not dead," I panted. "Shoulder . . . broken."

"Oh, God," Ian said, and I felt him turn to glance in the direction from which pursuit was surely headed. "Oh, Jesus." I heard tears in his voice, and he reached to his belt for his knife.

"What are you *doing*?!" I exclaimed. "He can be healed!"

"They'll kill him," he said, savage. "If I'm no there to stop them, they'll kill him! Better I do it."

"I—" Jamie began, but Rachel Hunter forestalled him, falling to her knees and grabbing Rollo by the scruff.

"I'll mind thy dog for thee," she said, breathless but certain. "Run!"

He took one last despairing look at her, then at Rollo. And he ran.

69

TERMS OF SURRENDER

WHEN THE message came from General Gates in the morning, Jamie knew what it must be about. Ian had got clean away, and little surprise. He'd be in the wood or perhaps in an Indian camp; either way, no one would find him until he wished to be found.

The lad had been right, too; they *did* want to kill the dog, particularly Colonel Martin, and it had taken not only all Jamie's resources but the young Quaker lass's prostrating herself upon the hound's hairy carcass and declaring that they must kill her first.

That had taken Martin back a bit, but there was still considerable public opinion in favor of dragging her away and doing the dog in. Jamie had prepared himself to step in—but then Rachel's brother had come out of the dark like an avenging angel. Denny stood in front of her and denounced the crowd as cowards, recreants, and inhuman monsters who would seek to revenge themselves upon an innocent animal, to say nothing of their damnable injustice—yes, he'd really said "damnable," with the greatest spirit, and the memory of it made Jamie smile, even in the face of the upcoming interview—in driving a young man to exile and perdition out of their own suspicion and iniquity, and could they not seek to find within their own bowels the slightest spark of the divine compassion that was the God-given life of every man . . .

Jamie's arrival at Gates's headquarters cut short these enjoyable reminiscences, and he straightened himself, assuming the grim demeanor suitable to trying occasions.

Gates looked as though he had been severely tried himself—which he had, in all justice. The bland, round face never looked as though it had any bones, but now it sagged like a soft-boiled egg, and the small eyes behind the wire-rimmed spectacles were huge and bloodshot when they looked at Jamie.

"Sit down, Colonel," Gates said, and pushed a glass and decanter toward him.

Jamie was dumbfounded. He'd had enough grim interviews with high-ranking officers to know that you didn't start them out with a cordial dram. He accepted the drink, though, and sipped it cautiously.

Gates drained his own, much less cautiously, set it down, and sighed heavily.

"I require a favor of you, Colonel."

"I shall be pleased, sir," he replied, with still more caution. What could the fat bugger possibly want of him? If it was Ian's whereabouts or an explanation of the murder, he could whistle for that and must know it. If not . . .

"The surrender negotiations are almost complete." Gates gave a bleak glance to a thick stack of handwritten papers, perhaps drafts of the thing.

"Burgoyne's troops are to march out of camp with the honors of war and ground arms at the bank of the Hudson at the command of their own officers. All officers will retain their swords and equipment, the soldiers, their knapsacks. The army is to march to Boston, where they will be properly fed and sheltered before embarking for England. The only condition imposed is that they are not to serve in North America again during the present war. Generous terms, I think you will agree, Colonel?"

"Verra generous, indeed, sir." Surprisingly so. What had made a general who undeniably held the whip hand to the extent that Gates did offer such extraordinary terms?

Gates smiled sourly.

"I see you are surprised, Colonel. Perhaps you will be less so if I tell you that Sir Henry Clinton is heading north." And Gates was in a rush to conclude the surrender and get rid of Burgoyne in order to have time to prepare for an attack from the south.

"Aye, sir, I see."

"Yes, well." Gates closed his eyes for an instant and sighed again, seeming exhausted. "There is one additional request from Burgoyne before he will accept this arrangement."

"Yes, sir?"

Gates's eyes were open again and passed slowly over him.

"They tell me you are a cousin to Brigadier General Simon Fraser."

"I am."

"Good. Then I am sure you will have no objection to performing a small service for your country."

A small service pertaining to Simon? Surely . . .

"He had at one time expressed a desire to several of his aides that, should he die abroad, they might bury him at once—which they did, in fact; they buried him in the Great Redoubt—but that when convenient, he wished to be taken back to Scotland, that he might lie at peace there."

"Ye want me to take his body to Scotland?" Jamie blurted. He could not have been more astonished had Gates suddenly got up and danced a hornpipe on his desk. The general nodded, his amiability increasing.

"You are very quick, Colonel. Yes. That is Burgoyne's final request. He says that the brigadier was much beloved by his men and that knowing his wish is fulfilled will reconcile them to marching away, as they will not feel they are abandoning his grave."

This sounded thoroughly romantic, and quite like something Burgoyne might do, Jamie reflected. He had a reputation for dramatic gesture. And he was probably not wrong in his estimation of the feelings of the men who had served under Simon—he was a good fellow, Simon.

Only belatedly did it dawn on him that the final result of this request . . .

"Is . . . there some provision to be made for my reaching Scotland with the body, sir?" he asked delicately. "There is a blockade."

"You will be transported—with your wife and servants, if you like—on one of His Majesty's ships, and a sum will be provided you for transporting the coffin once it has come ashore in Scotland. Have I your agreement, Colonel Fraser?"

He was so stunned, he scarcely knew what he said in response, but evidently it was sufficient, for Gates smiled tiredly and dismissed him. He made his way back to his tent with his head in a whirl, wondering whether he could disguise Young Ian as his wife's maid, in the manner of Charles Stuart.

OCTOBER 17, like all the days that had gone before it, dawned dark and foggy. In his tent, General Burgoyne dressed with particular care, in a gorgeous scarlet coat with gold braid and a hat decorated with plumes. William saw him, when he went with the other officers to Burgoyne's tent for their last, anguished meeting.

Baron von Riedesel spoke to them, too; he took all the regimental flags. He would give them to his wife, he said, to be sewn inside a pillow and taken secretly back to Brunswick.

William cared for none of this. He was conscious of deep sorrow, for he had never before left comrades on a battlefield and marched away. Some shame, but not much—the general was right in saying that they could not have mounted another attack without losing most of the army, so wretched was their condition.

They looked wretched now, lining up in silence, and yet when fife and drum began to play, each regiment in its turn followed the flying colors, heads high in their tattered uniforms—or whatever clothing they could find. The enemy had withdrawn on Gates's order, the general said. That was delicate, William thought numbly; the Americans would not be present to witness their humiliation.

Redcoats first, and then the German regiments: dragoons and grenadiers in blue, the green-clad infantry and artillery from Hesse-Cassel.

On the river flats, scores of horses lay dead, the stench adding to the somber horror of the occasion. The artillery parked their cannon here, and the infantry, rank by rank by unending rank, poured out their cartridge boxes and stacked their muskets. Some men were sufficiently furious as to smash the butts of their guns before throwing them on the piles; William saw a drummer put his foot through his drum before turning away. He was not furious, or horrified.

All he wanted now was to see his father again.

THE CONTINENTAL troops and the militia marched to the meetinghouse at Saratoga and from there lined up along both sides of the river road. Some women came, watching from a distance. I could have stayed in camp, to see the historic ceremony of surrender between the two generals, but I followed the troops instead.

The sun had risen and the fog had fled, just as it had done every day for the last few weeks. There was a smell of smoke in the air, and the sky was the infinite deep blue of October.

Artillery and infantry stood along the road, evenly spaced, but that spacing was the only uniform thing about them. There was no common dress, and each man's equipment was distinctively his own, in form and how he held it—but each man held his musket, or his rifle, or stood beside his cannon.

They were a motley crew in every sense of the word, festooned with powder horns and shot bags, some wearing outlandish old-fashioned wigs. And they stood in grave silence, each man with his right foot forward, right hands on their guns, to watch the enemy march out, with the honors of war.

I stood in the wood, a little way behind Jamie, and I saw his shoulders stiffen a little. William walked past, tall and straight, his face the face of a man who is not really there. Jamie didn't dip his head or make any effort not to be seen—

but I saw his head turn just slightly, following William out of sight in the company of his men. And then his shoulders dropped just a little, as though a burden dropped from them.

Safe, that gesture said, though he still stood straight as the rifle beside him. *Thank God. He is safe.*

70

SANCTUARY

Lallybroch

ROGER COULD not have said quite what impelled him to do it, other than the sense of peace that hung about the place, but he had begun to rebuild the old chapel. By hand, and alone, one stone upon another.

He'd tried to explain it to Bree; she'd asked.

"It's *them,*" he said at last, helpless. "It's a sort of . . . I feel as though I need to connect with them, back there."

She took one of his hands in her own, spreading his fingers, and ran the ball of her thumb gently over his knuckles, down the length of his fingers, touching the scabs and grazes, the blackened nail where a stone had slipped and bruised it.

"Them," she repeated carefully. "You mean my parents."

"Yes, among other things." Not only with Jamie and Claire but with the life their family had built. With his own sense of himself as a man—protector, provider. And yet it was his bone-deep urge to protect that had led him to abandon all his Christian principles—on the eve of ordination, no less—and set out in pursuit of Stephen Bonnet.

"I suppose I'm hoping I can make sense of . . . things," he'd said, with a wry smile. "How to reconcile what I thought I knew then with what I think I am now."

"It's not Christian to want to save your wife from being

raped and sold into slavery?" she inquired, a distinct edge in her voice. "Because if it's not, I'm taking the kids and converting to Judaism or Shinto or something."

His smile had grown more genuine.

"I found something there." He fumbled for words.

"You lost a few things, too," she whispered. Not taking her eyes from his, she reached out, the tips of her fingers cool on his throat. The rope scar had faded somewhat but was still darkly visible; he made no effort to hide it. Sometimes when he spoke with people, he could see their eyes fix on it; given his height, it was not unusual for men to seem to be speaking directly *to* the scar, rather than to himself.

Found a sense of himself as a man, found what he thought was his calling. And that, he supposed, was what he was looking for under those piles of fallen stone, under the eyes of a blind saint.

Was God opening a door, showing him that he should be a teacher now? Was this, the Gaelic thing, what he was meant to do? He had plenty of room to ask questions, room and time and silence. Answers were scarce. He'd been at it most of the aftenoon; he was hot, exhausted, and ready for a beer.

Now his eye caught the edge of a shadow in the doorway, and he turned—Jem or maybe Brianna, come to fetch him home to tea. It was neither of them.

For a moment, he stared at the newcomer, searching his memory. Ragged jeans and sweatshirt, dirty-blond hair hacked off and tousled. Surely he knew the man; the broad-boned, handsome face was familiar, even under a thick layer of light-brown stubble.

"Can I help you?" Roger asked, taking a grip on the shovel he'd been using. The man wasn't threatening but was roughly dressed and dirty—a tramp, perhaps—and there was something indefinable about him that made Roger uneasy.

"It's a church, aye?" the man said, and grinned, though no hint of warmth touched his eyes. "Suppose I've come to claim sanctuary, then." He moved suddenly into the light, and Roger saw his eyes more clearly. Cold, and a deep, striking green.

"Sanctuary," William Buccleigh MacKenzie repeated. "And then, Minister dear, I want ye to tell me who ye are, who *I* am—and what in the name of God almighty *are* we?"

Part Six

Coming Home

71

A STATE OF CONFLICT

September 10, 1777

JOHN GREY FOUND himself wondering how many horns a dilemma could have. Two, he believed, was the standard number, but supposed that it was theoretically possible to encounter a more exotic form of dilemma—something like the four-horned sheep he had once seen in Spain.

The most pressing of the horns arrayed under him at present concerned Henry.

He'd written to Jamie Fraser, explaining Henry's state and asking whether Mrs. Fraser might see her way to come. He had, as delicately as possible, assured her of his willingness to bear all expenses of the journey, to expedite her travel in both directions by ship (with protection from the exigencies of warfare insofar as the royal navy could provide it), and to provide her with whatever materials and instruments she might require. Had even gone so far as to procure a quantity of vitriol, which he recalled her needing for the composition of her ether.

He had spent a good deal of time with quill suspended over the page, wondering whether to add anything regarding Fergus Fraser, the printer, and the incredible story Percy had told him. On the one hand, this might bring Jamie Fraser belting up from North Carolina to look into the matter, thus improving the chances of Mrs. Fraser coming, as well. On the other . . . he was more than reluctant to expose any matter having to do with Percy Beauchamp to Jamie Fraser, for assorted reasons, both personal and professional. In the end, he had said nothing of it and made his appeal solely on behalf of Henry.

Grey had waited through an anxious month, watching his nephew suffer from heat and inanition. At the end of the month, the courier he had sent to take his letter to North Carolina returned, sweat-soaked, caked with mud, and with two bullet holes in his coat, to report that the Frasers had left Fraser's Ridge with the declared intent of removing to Scotland, though adding helpfully that this removal was presumed to be only in the nature of a visit, rather than a permanent emigration.

He had fetched a physician to visit Henry, of course, not waiting for Mrs. Fraser's reply. He had succeeded in introducing himself to Benjamin Rush and had that gentleman examine his nephew. Dr. Rush had been grave but encouraging, saying that he believed one of the musket balls, at least, had created scarring, this partially obstructing Henry's intestines and encouraging a localized pocket of sepsis, which caused his persistent fever. He had bled Henry and prescribed a febrifuge, but made the strongest representations to Grey that the situation was delicate and might worsen abruptly; only surgical intervention might effect a cure.

At the same time, he said that he did believe Henry to be strong enough to survive such surgery—though there was, of course, no certainty of a happy outcome. Grey had thanked Dr. Rush but had chosen to wait just a little while, in hopes of hearing from Mrs. Fraser.

He looked out the window of his rented house on Chestnut Street, watching brown and yellow leaves scour to and fro among the cobbles, driven by a random wind.

It was mid-September. The last ships would depart for England at the end of October, just ahead of the Atlantic gales. Ought he to try to get Henry on one of them?

He had made the acquaintance of the local American officer in charge of prisoners of war billeted in Philadelphia and made an application for parole. This had been granted without difficulty; captured officers were normally paroled, save there was something unusual or dangerous about them, and Henry plainly was unlikely to attempt escape, foment rebellion, or support insurrection in his present state.

But he had not yet managed to arrange to have Henry exchanged, which status would permit Grey to move him back to England. Always assuming that Henry's health would stand the journey, and that Henry himself would be willing to go. Which it likely wouldn't, and Henry wasn't, he being so much attached to Mrs. Woodcock. Grey was quite willing to take her to England, too, but she wouldn't consider leaving, as she had heard that her husband had been taken prisoner in New York.

Grey rubbed two fingers between his brows, sighing. Could he force Henry aboard a naval vessel against his will—drugged, perhaps?—thus breaking his parole, ruining his career, and endangering his life, on the supposition that Grey could find a surgeon in England more capable than Dr. Rush of dealing with the situation? The best that could be hoped from such a course of action was that Henry would survive the journey long enough to say goodbye to his parents.

But if he did *not* undertake this drastic step, he was left with the choice of forcing Henry to submit to a horrifying surgery that he feared desperately and which was very likely to kill him—or watching the boy die by inches. Because he *was* dying; Grey saw it plainly. Sheer stubbornness and Mrs. Woodcock's nursing were all that was keeping him alive.

The thought of having to write to Hal and Minnie and tell them . . . No. He stood up abruptly, unable to bear more indecision. He would call upon Dr. Rush at once and make arrangements—

The front door slammed open, admitting a blast of wind, dead leaves, and his niece, pale-faced and round-eyed.

"Dottie!" His first, heart-stopping fear was that she had rushed home to tell him that Henry had died, for she had gone to visit her brother as she usually did every afternoon.

"Soldiers!" she gasped, clutching him by the arm. "There are soldiers in the street. Riders. Someone said Howe's army is coming! Advancing on Philadelphia!"

HOWE MET Washington's army at Brandywine Creek on September 11, some distance south of the city. Washington's troops were driven back, but rallied to make a stand a few days later. A tremendous rainstorm arose in the midst of the battle, though, putting an end to hostilities and allowing Washington's army to escape to Reading Furnace, leaving a small force behind under General Anthony Wayne at Paoli.

One of Howe's commanders, Major General Lord Charles Grey—a distant cousin of Grey's—attacked the Americans at Paoli at night, with orders to his troops to remove the flints from their muskets. This prevented discovery from the accidental discharge of a weapon, but also obliged the men to use bayonets. A number of Americans were bayoneted in their beds, their tents burned, a hundred or so made captive—and Howe marched into the city of Philadelphia, triumphant, on September 21.

Grey watched them, rank upon rank of redcoats, marching to drum music, from the porch of Mrs. Woodcock's house. Dottie had feared that the rebels, forced to abandon the city, might fire the houses or kill their British prisoners outright.

"Nonsense," Grey had said to this. "They are rebel Englishmen, not barbarians." Nonetheless, he had put on his own uniform and his sword, tucked two pistols into his belt, and spent twenty-four hours sitting on the porch of Mrs. Woodcock's house—with a lantern by night—coming down now and then to speak to any officer he knew who passed by, both to glean news of the situation and to ensure that the house remained unmolested.

The next day he returned to his own house, through streets of shuttered windows. Philadelphia was hostile, and so was the surrounding countryside. Still, the occupation of the city was peaceful—or as peaceful as a military occupation well can be. Congress had fled as Howe approached, and so had many of the more prominent rebels, including Dr. Benjamin Rush.

So had Percy Beauchamp.

72

THE FEAST OF ALL SAINTS

Lallybroch
October 20, 1980

BRIANNA PRESSED the letter to her nose and inhaled deeply. So long after, she was sure it was imagination rather than odor, but still she sensed the faint aromas of smoke in the pages. Maybe it was memory as much as imagination; she knew what the air was like in an ordinary, full of the scents of hearthfire, roasting meat, and tobacco, with a mellow smell of beer beneath it all.

She felt silly smelling the letters in front of Roger but had developed the habit of sniffing them privately, when she read them over by herself. They'd opened this one the night before and had read it several times together, discussing it—but she'd got it out again now, wanting just to hold it privately and be alone with her parents for a bit.

Maybe the scent was really there. She'd noticed that you don't actually remember smells, not the same way you remember something you've seen. It's just that when you smell that smell again, you know what it is—and often it brings back a lot of other memories with it. And she was sitting here on a fall day, surrounded by the ripeness of apples and heather, the dust of ancient wood paneling, and the hollow smell of wet stone—Annie MacDonald had just mopped the hall—but she was seeing the front room of an eighteenth-century ordinary, and smelling smoke.

November 1, 1777
New York

Dear Bree, et al—

Do you remember the high school field trip when your economics class went to Wall Street? I am at the moment sitting in an ordinary at the foot of Wall Street, and neither a bull nor a bear to be seen, let alone a ticker-tape machine. No wall, either. A few goats, though, and a small cluster of men under a big leafless buttonwood tree, smoking pipes and conferring head-to-head. I can't tell whether they're Loyalists complaining, rebels plotting in public (which is, by the way, very much safer than doing it in private, though I do hope you won't need to make use of that bit of special knowledge), or simply merchants and traders—business is being done, I can tell that; hands shaken, bits of paper scribbled and exchanged. It's amazing how business thrives in wartime; I think it's because the normal rules—whatever they normally are—are suspended.

That's true of most human transactions, by the way. Hence the flowering of wartime romances and the founding of great fortunes in the wake of wars. It seems rather paradoxical—though maybe it's only logic (ask Roger whether there is such a thing as a logical paradox, will you?)—that a process so wasteful of lives and substance should then result in an explosion of babies and business.

Since I speak of war—we are all alive, and mostly intact. Your father was slightly wounded during the first battle at Saratoga (there were two, both very bloody), and I was obliged to remove the fourth finger of his right hand—the stiff one; you'll recall it. This was traumatic, of course (as much to me as to him, I think), but not altogether a disaster. It's healed very well, and while the hand is still giving him a good bit of pain, it's much more flexible and I think will be more useful to him overall.

We are—belatedly—about to take ship to Scotland,

under rather peculiar circumstances. We are to sail tomorrow, on HMS Ariadne, *accompanying the body of Brigadier General Simon Fraser. I met the brigadier very briefly before his death—he was dying at the time—but he was evidently a very good soldier and much beloved by his men. The British commander at Saratoga, John Burgoyne, asked as a sort of footnote to the surrender agreement that your father (he being a kinsman of the brigadier's and knowing where his family place in the Highlands is) take the body to Scotland, in accordance with the brigadier's wishes. This was unexpected, but rather fortuitous, to say the least. I can't think how we should have managed it otherwise, though your father says he would have thought of something.*

The logistics of this expedition are a trifle delicate, as you might suppose. Mr. Kościuszko (known as "Kos" to his intimates, which includes your father—well, actually, he's known as "Kos" to everybody, because no one (other than your father) can pronounce his name, or cares to try. Your father's very fond of him and vice versa) offered his services, and with the aid of General Burgoyne's butler (doesn't everyone take their butler to war with them?), who supplied him with a great deal of lead foil from wine bottles (well, you really can't blame General Burgoyne if he's taken to drink, in the circumstances, though my general impression is that everyone on both sides drinks like a fish all of the time, regardless of the military situation of the moment), has produced a miracle of engineering: a lead-lined coffin (very necessary) on detachable wheels (also very necessary; the thing must weigh close to a ton—your father says no, it's only seven or eight hundredweight, but as he hasn't tried to lift it, I don't see how he would know).

General Fraser had been buried for a week or so and had to be exhumed for transport. It wasn't pleasant, but could have been worse. He had a number of Indian rangers, many of whom also esteemed him; some of these came to the unburying with a medicine person (I think it was a man but couldn't be sure; it was short and round and wore a bird mask), who incensed the remains heavily with burning sage and sweetgrass (not much help in terms of olfaction, but the smoke did draw a gentle veil over the more horrid aspects of the situation) and sang over him at some length. I should have liked to ask Ian what was being sung, but owing to an unpleasant set of circumstances that I won't go into here, he wasn't present.

I'll explain it all in a later letter; it's very complicated, and I must finish this before the sailing. The important points, in re Ian, are that he is in love with Rachel Hunter (who is a lovely young woman, and a Quaker, which presents some difficulties) and that he is technically a murderer and thus unable to appear in public in the vicinity of the Continental army. As a side result of the technical murder (a very unpleasant person, and no great loss to humanity, I assure you), Rollo was shot and injured (beyond the superficial bullet wound, he has a broken scapula; he should recover but can't be moved easily. Rachel is keeping him for Ian while we go to Scotland).

As the brigadier was known to be revered by his Indian associates, the Ariadne*'s captain was startled, but not overly disturbed, to be informed that the body is being accompanied not only by his close kinsman (and wife) but by a Mohawk who speaks little English (I should be more than surprised if anyone in the royal navy can tell the difference between Gaelic and Mohawk, come to that).*

I hope this attempt is rather less eventful than our first voyage. If so, the next letter should be written in Scotland. Keep your fingers crossed.

All my love,
Mama

P.S. Your father insists upon adding a few words to this. This will be his first try at writing with his altered hand, and I would like to watch to see how it's working, but he instructs me firmly that he requires privacy. I don't know whether this is to do with his subject matter or simply with the fact that he doesn't want anyone to see him struggle. Both, probably.

The third page of the letter was markedly different. The writing was much larger than usual, and more sprawling. Still identifiably her father's hand, but the letters seemed looser, less jagged somehow. She felt her heart twist, not only from the thought of her father's mutilated hand, slowly drawing each letter—but for what he had thought it worth so much effort to write:

My Dearest,

Your Brother is alive, and unwounded. I saw him march out from Saratoga with his Troops, bound for Boston and eventually England. He will not fight again in this War. Deo gratias.

Your most loving Father,
JF

Postscriptum: It is the Feast of All Saints. Pray for me.

The nuns had always told them—and she'd told him. By saying an Our Father, a Hail Mary, and a Glory Be on the Feast of All Saints, you can obtain the release of a soul from purgatory.

"You bloody man," she muttered, sniffing ferociously and fumbling in her desk for a tissue. "I knew you'd make me cry. *Again.*"

"BRIANNA?"

Roger's voice came from the kitchen, surprising her. She hadn't expected him to come down from the chapel ruins for another hour or two, and she blew her nose hastily, calling, "Coming!" and hoping that the recent tears didn't show in her voice. It was only as she hit the corridor and saw him holding the green baize door to the kitchen half open that it occurred to her that there had been something odd about his voice, as well.

"What is it?" she said, hastening her step. "The kids—"

"They're fine," he interrupted. "I told Annie to take them down to the post office in the village for an ice cream." He stepped away from the door then and beckoned her to enter.

She stopped dead, just inside the door. A man was leaning back against the old stone sink, arms folded. He straightened up when he saw her and bowed, in a way that struck her as terribly odd and yet familiar. Before she could think why that should be, he straightened again and said, "Your servant, ma'am," in a soft Scottish voice.

She looked straight into eyes that were the twins of Roger's, then glanced wildly *at* Roger, just to be sure. Yes, they were.

"Who—"

"Allow me to introduce William Buccleigh MacKenzie," Roger said, a distinct edge in his voice. "Also known as the Nuckelavee."

For an instant, none of this made any sense whatever. Then things—astonishment, fury, disbelief—came flooding into her mind at such a rate that none of them could make it to her mouth, and she simply gaped at the man.

"I'll ask your pardon, ma'am, for frightening your weans," the man said. "I'd nay notion they were yours, for the one thing. I ken what weans are like, though, and I didna wish to be discovered before I'd made some sense of it all."

"All . . . *what*?" Brianna finally found a couple of words. The man smiled, very slightly.

"Aye, well. As to that, I think you and your husband may know better than I."

Brianna pulled out a chair and sat down rather abruptly, motioning to the man to do the same. As he came forward into the light from the window, she saw that there was a graze on his cheekbone—a prominent cheekbone, and one that with the modeling of his temple and eye socket seemed terribly familiar; the man himself seemed familiar. But of course he was, she thought dazedly.

"Does he know who he is?" she asked, turning to Roger.

Who, now that she noticed, was nursing his right hand, which appeared to have blood on the knuckles. He nodded.

"I told him. Not sure he believes me, though."

The kitchen was its usual solid, homely place, peaceful with the autumn sun coming in and the blue-checkered dish towels hung on the Aga. But now it felt like the backside of Jupiter, and when she reached for the sugar bowl, she would not have been at all surprised to see her hand pass through it.

"I should be inclined to believe a good deal more today than I should have been three months ago," the man said, with a dry intonation that held some faint echo of her father's voice.

She shook her head violently, in hopes of clearing it, and said, "Would you like some coffee?" in a polite voice that could have belonged to a sitcom housewife.

His face lightened at that, and he smiled. His teeth were stained and a little crooked. *Well, of course they are,* she thought with remarkable lucidity. *No dentists to speak of in the eighteenth century.* The thought of the eighteenth century sent her surging to her feet.

"You!" she exclaimed. "*You* got Roger hanged!"

"I did," he said, not looking very perturbed. "Not that I meant to. And if he likes to strike me again for it, I'll let him. But—"

"That was for scaring the kids," Roger said with equal dryness. "The hanging . . . we'll maybe talk about that a bit later."

"Fine talk for a minister," the man said, looking faintly amused. "Not that most ministers go about interfering wi' a man's wife."

"I—" Roger began, but she interrupted him.

"*I'll* bloody hit you," Brianna said, glaring at the man. Who, to her annoyance, squinched his eyes shut and leaned forward, features clenched.

"All right," he said, through compressed lips. "Go ahead."

"Not in the face," Roger advised, surveying a bruised knuckle. "Make him stand up and go for his balls."

William Buccleigh's eyes popped open, and he looked reproachfully at Roger.

"D'ye think she needs advice?"

"I think *you* need a fat lip," she told him, but sat slowly down again, eyeing him. She took a breath down to her toenails and let it out.

"Right," she said, more or less calmly. "Start talking."

He nodded cautiously and touched the bruise on his cheekbone, wincing a little.

Son of a witch, she thought suddenly. *Does he know* that?

"Did ye not mention coffee?" he asked, sounding a little wistful. "I havena had real coffee in years."

HE WAS FASCINATED by the Aga and pressed his backside against it, fairly shivering with delight.

"Oh, sweet Virgin," he breathed, eyes closed as he reveled in the heat. "Is it not the lovely thing."

The coffee he pronounced good in itself but rather feeble—reasonable, Brianna thought, knowing that such coffee as he was used to was boiled over a fire, often for several hours, rather than gently perked. He apologized for his manners, which were actually fine, saying that he hadn't eaten in some little while.

"How have ye been feeding yourself?" Roger asked, eyeing the steadily diminishing pile of peanut-butter-and-jelly sandwiches.

"Stole from cottages, to begin with," Buccleigh admitted frankly. "After a bit, I found my way to Inverness and was sittin' on the curb of the street, quite dazed by the huge great roaring things goin' by me—I'd seen the cars on the road north, of course, but it's different when they're whizzin' past your shins. Anyway, I'd sat down outside the High Street Church, for I knew that place, at least, and thought I'd go and ask the minister for a bite of bread when I'd got myself a bit more in hand. I was that wee bit rattled, ken," he said, leaning confidentially toward Brianna.

"I suppose so," she murmured, and lifted an eyebrow at Roger. "Old High St. Stephen's?"

"Aye, it was the High Church—meaning on the High Street, not Anglican—before it was Old, or joined congregations with St. Stephen's." He switched his attention to William Buccleigh. "Did ye, then? Speak to the minister? Dr. Weatherspoon?"

Buccleigh nodded, mouth full.

"He saw me sitting there and came out to me, the kind man. Asked was I in need, and when I assured him I was, he told me where to go for food and a bed, and I went there. An aid society, they called it, a charity, and it surely was."

The people who ran the aid society had given him clothes—"for what I had on was little more than rags"—and helped him to find a job doing rough labor for a dairy farm outside the town.

"So why are ye not on the dairy farm?" Roger asked, at the same moment that Brianna asked, "But how did you come to Scotland?" Their words colliding, they stopped, gesturing to each other to continue, but William Buccleigh waved a hand at them both and chewed rapidly for a moment, then swallowed several times and gulped more coffee.

"Mother of God, that stuff's tasty, but it sticks in your craw. Aye, ye want to know why I'm here in your kitchen eating your food and not dead in a creek in North Carolina."

"Since you mention it, yes," said Roger, leaning back in his chair. "Start with North Carolina, why don't you?"

Buccleigh nodded once more, leaned back in turn with his hands linked comfortably over his stomach, and began.

HE'D BEEN STARVED out of Scotland, like so many folk after Culloden, and had scraped together the money to emigrate with his wife and infant son.

"I know," Roger said. "It was me you asked to save them, on the ship. The night the captain put the sick ones over the rail."

Buccleigh looked up, startled, green eyes wide.

"Was it, then? I didna see ye at all, in the dark and me desperate. If I'd kent that . . ." He trailed off, then shook his head. "Well, what's done is done."

"It is," Roger said. "I couldn't see you in the dark, either. I only kent ye later, because of your wife and son, when I met them again at Alaman-k." To his intense annoyance, the last sound caught in his throat with a glottal click. He cleared it and repeated evenly, "At Alamance."

Buccleigh nodded slowly, eyes fastened with interest on

Roger's throat. Was that regret in his eyes? Probably not, Roger thought. He hadn't thanked him for saving his wife and child, either.

"Aye. Well, I'd thought to take land and farm it, but . . . well, the long and the short of it was, I wasna much of a farmer. Nor a builder. Didna ken the first thing about the wilderness, not much more about crops. Not a hunter, either. We would ha' starved, surely, had I not taken Morag and Jem—that's my son's name, too, is that not strange?—back down to the piedmont and scraped a little work on a wee turpentine plantation there."

"Stranger than you know," Bree said, half under her breath. And a little louder, "So?"

"So the fellow I worked for turned out for the Regulation, and those of us on the place went, too. I should have left Morag behind, but there was a fellow on the place who had a hot eye for her—he was the blacksmith and had but one leg, so he'd not be coming with us to the fight. I couldna leave her to him, so she and the wean came with me. Where the next fellow she meets is *you,*" he said pointedly.

"Did she not tell ye who I was?" Roger asked testily.

"Well, she did, then," Buccleigh admitted. "She'd said about the ship and all, and said that was you. Even so," he added, giving Roger a hard eye, "d'ye go about makin' love to other men's wives regular, or was it just Morag took your fancy?"

"Morag is my five—or maybe only four—times great-grandmother," Roger said evenly. He fixed Buccleigh with a stare equal to the other man's. "And since you asked me who ye are—you're my grandda. Five or six times back. My son's named Jeremiah after my da, who was named for his grandda—who was named for *your* son. I think," he added. "I might be missing one or two Jeremiahs along the way."

Buccleigh stared at him, stubbled face gone quite blank. He blinked once or twice, glanced at Brianna, who nodded, then returned his stare to Roger, carefully scrutinizing his face.

"Look at his eyes," Brianna said helpfully. "Shall I bring you a mirror?"

Buccleigh's mouth opened as though to answer, but he found no words and shook his head as though dislodging flies. He picked up his cup, stared into it for a moment as though astonished to find it empty, and set it down. Then looked at Brianna.

"Ye wouldna have anything in the house stronger than coffee, would ye, *a bhana-mhaighstir*?"

IT TOOK ROGER a little rummaging in his study to find the genealogical table the Reverend had drawn up years before. While he was gone, Bree found the bottle of Oban and poured William Buccleigh a generous glass. With no hesitation, she poured for herself and Roger, as well, and put a jug of water on the table.

"Do you take a little water?" she asked politely. "Or do you like it neat?"

Rather to her surprise, he reached at once for the water and splashed a little into the whisky. He saw her expression and smiled.

"If it was the rotgut, I'd throw it down. Whisky worth drinking, a little water opens the flavor. But ye ken that, don't ye? Ye're no Scots, though."

"Yes, I am," she said. "On my father's side. His name is—was—James Fraser, of Lallybroch. They called him the Dunbonnet."

He blinked, looked round the kitchen, then back at her.

"Are you . . . another, then?" he said. "Like your husband and me. Another of—whatever it is?"

"Whatever it is," she agreed. "And yes. You knew my father?"

He shook his head, closing his eyes as he sipped, and took a moment to reply while the whisky made its way down.

"Dear Lord, that's good," he breathed, and opened his eyes. "Nay, I was born only a year or so before Culloden. I heard of the Dunbonnet, though, when I was a lad."

"You said you weren't much of a farmer," Bree said curiously. "What did you do in Scotland, before you left?"

He took a deep breath and let it out through his nose, in just the way her father did. *A MacKenzie thing,* she thought, entertained.

"I was a lawyer," he said abruptly, and picked up his glass.

"Well, there's a useful profession," Roger said, coming in in time to hear this. He eyed Buccleigh contemplatively, then shook his head and spread out the MacKenzie family tree on the tabletop.

"There you are," he said, putting a finger on the relevant entry, then moved a finger down the page. "And there I am."

Buccleigh blinked at it, then bent closer to study it in silence. Brianna saw his throat move as he swallowed once or twice. His face was pale beneath the stubble when he looked up.

"Aye, those are my parents, my grandparents. And there's wee Jem—my Jem—where he should be, right enough. I've another child, though," he said suddenly, turning to Bree. "Or I think I have. Morag was breeding when I—when I—went."

Roger sat down. His face had lost a little of the angry wariness, and he regarded William Buccleigh with what might be sympathy.

"Tell us that bit," he suggested. "How you went."

Buccleigh pushed across his empty whisky glass but didn't wait for it to be refilled.

The owner of the plantation he'd worked on had been ruined in the wake of Alamance, gaoled for taking part in the Regulation and his property confiscated. The MacKenzies had drifted for a time, having no money and no home, no close kin who might help them.

Brianna exchanged a quick glance with Roger. Had Buccleigh known it, he was within a short distance of close kin—and wealthy kin, at that. Jocasta Cameron was Dougal MacKenzie's sister—this man's aunt. If he knew it.

She raised her brows in silent question to Roger, but he shook his head slightly. Let that wait.

At last, Buccleigh said, they'd made the decision to go back to Scotland. Morag had family there, a brother in Inverness who'd done well for himself, was a prosperous corn chandler. Morag had written to him, and he had urged them to come back, saying he would find a place for William in his business.

"At that point, I should ha' been glad of a place shoveling dung out of the holds of cattle ships," Buccleigh admitted with a sigh. "Ephraim—that's Morag's brother, Ephraim Gunn—said he thought he might have use for a clerk, though. And I *can* write a fair hand and do sums."

The lure of work—work that he was well equipped to do—and a place to live was strong enough to make the little family willing to embark once more on the perilous Atlantic voyage. Ephraim had sent a draft on his bank for their passage, and so they had come back, landing in Edinburgh, and from there had made their slow way north.

"By wagon, for the most part." Buccleigh was on his third glass of whisky, Brianna and Roger not so far behind. He poured a little water into his empty glass and swished it round his mouth before swallowing, to clear his throat, then coughed and went on.

"The wagon broke down—again—near the place they call Craigh na Dun. I'm thinking the two of ye will know it?" He glanced back and forth between them, and they nodded. "Aye. Well, Morag wasna feeling all that peart, and the bairn was peely-wally, too, so they lay down in the grass to sleep a bit whilst the wheel was mending. The drover had a mate and didna need my help, so I set off to stretch my legs."

"And you climbed the hill, to the stones," Brianna said, her own chest feeling tight at the thought.

"Do you know what date it was?" Roger broke in.

"Summer," William Buccleigh said slowly. "Near Midsummer Day, but I couldna swear to the day exactly. Why?"

"The summer solstice," Brianna said, and hiccuped slightly. "It's—we think it's open. The—whatever it is—on the sun feasts and the fire feasts."

The sound of a car coming down the drive came faintly to them, and all three looked up as though surprised in some furtive business.

"Annie and the kids. What are we going to do with him?" she asked Roger.

He glanced with narrowed eyes at Buccleigh for an instant, then made up his mind. "We'll need a bit of thought to explain ye," Roger said, rising. "Just for the moment, though—come with me, aye?"

Buccleigh stood at once and followed Roger into the scullery. She heard Buccleigh's voice rise in momentary astonishment, a brief mutter of explanation from Roger, then the grating noise as they moved the bench that hid the access panel covering the priest's hole.

Moving as if in a trance, Brianna rose hastily to clear and

wash the three glasses, to put away the whisky and water. Hearing the knocker go against the front door, she jumped a little. Not the kids, after all. Who could that be?

She swept the family tree off the table and hurried down the hall, pausing to toss it onto Roger's desk as she made her way to the door.

How old is he? she thought abruptly, as she reached for the handle. *He looks to be in his late thirties, maybe, but—*

"Hi," said Rob Cameron, looking faintly alarmed at the look on her face. "Have I come at a bad time, then?"

ROB HAD COME to bring back a book Roger had lent him and to deliver an invitation: would Jem like to come to the pictures with Bobby on the Friday, then have a nice fish supper and spend the night?

"I'm sure he would," Brianna said. "But he's not—oh, there he is." Annie had just driven up, with a clashing of gears that made the engine die in the driveway. Brianna shuddered slightly, pleased that Annie hadn't taken *her* car.

By the time the kids had been extracted from the car, wiped off, and made to shake hands politely with Mr. Cameron, Roger had come out from the back of the house and was at once drawn into a conversation about his efforts on the chapel, which went on to such an extent that it became obvious that it was supper-time, and it would have been rude not to ask him to stay . . .

And so Brianna found herself scrambling eggs and heating beans and frying potatoes in a sort of daze, thinking of their uninvited guest under the scullery floor, who must be smelling the cooking and dying of hunger—and *what* on earth were they going to do with him?

All the time they ate, making pleasant conversation, herding the kids off to bed while Roger and Rob talked Pictish stones and archaeological excavations in the Orkneys, she found her mind dwelling on William Buccleigh MacKenzie.

The Orkneys, she thought. *Roger said the Nuckelavee is an Orkney ghoulie. Has he been in the Orkneys? When? And why the bloody hell was he hanging round our broch all this time?*

When he found what had happened, why didn't he just go right back? What is he doing *here?*

By the time Rob took his leave—and another book—with profuse thanks for the food and a reminder of the movie date on Friday, she was prepared to haul William Buccleigh out of the priest's hole by the scruff of the neck, drive him straight to Craigh na Dun herself, and stuff him bodily into a stone.

But when he finally clambered out, moving slowly, white-faced and clearly hungry, she found her agitation lessening. Just a little. She made fresh eggs for him, quickly, and sat with him while Roger went round the house, checking doors and windows.

"Though I suppose we needn't worry so much about that," she observed caustically, "since you're *inside* now."

He looked up, tired but wary.

"I did say I was sorry," he said softly. "D'ye want me to go?"

"And where *would* you go, if I said yes?" she asked unkindly.

He turned his face toward the window over the kitchen sink. In the daylight, it looked out on peace, on the kailyard with its worn wooden gate and the pasture beyond. Now there was nothing out there but the black of a moonless Highland night. The sort of night when Christians stayed indoors and put holy water on the doorposts, because the things that walked the moors and the high places were not always holy.

He didn't say anything but swallowed, and she saw the fair hairs on his forearms rise.

"You don't have to go," she said, gruff. "We'll find you a bed. But tomorrow . . ."

He bobbed his head, not looking at her, and made to rise. She stopped him with a hand on his arm and he looked at her, startled, his eyes dark in the quiet light.

"Just tell me one thing now," she said. "Do you want to go back?"

"Oh, God, yes," he said, and turned his head away, but his voice was thick. "I want Morag. I want my wee lad."

She let go of his wrist and stood up, but another thought had occurred to her.

"How old are you?" she asked abruptly, and he shrugged, brushing the back of his wrist across his eyes.

"Eight and thirty," he said. "Why?"

"Just . . . curious," she said, and moved to turn the Aga's heat down to its nighttime setting. "Come with me; I'll make you a bed in the parlor. Tomorrow we'll—we'll see."

She led him down the hall past Roger's study, and in her stomach was a ball of ice. The light was on, and the family tree Roger had taken out to show William Buccleigh was still where she'd tossed it, on the desk. Had he seen the date? She thought not—or if he had, he hadn't noticed. The dates of birth and death weren't listed for everyone on that table—but they were for him. William Buccleigh MacKenzie had died, according to that table, at age thirty-eight.

He won't get back, she thought, and the ice rose up around her heart.

LOCH ERROCHTY LAY dull as pewter under a lowering sky. They were standing on the footbridge across Alt Ruighe nan Saorach, the river that fed the loch, looking down to where the man-made loch spread itself between the smooth hills. Buck—he'd said that was what folk called him in America, and he'd got used to it—looked and looked, his face a study in amazement and dismay.

"Down there," he said softly, pointing. "See where that wee burn comes down into it? That's where my auntie Ross's house stood. About a hundred feet below the burn."

About thirty feet below the surface of the loch now.

"I imagine it's something of a wrench," Brianna said, not without sympathy. "To see things so changed."

"It is that." He glanced at her, those eyes, so unsettlingly like Roger's, quick in his face. "It's maybe more that so much *hasna* changed. Up there, aye?" He lifted his chin toward the distant mountains. "Just like they always were. And the wee birds in the grass, and the salmon jumping in the river. I could set foot on yon shore"—he nodded toward the end of the footbridge—"and feel as though I had walked there yesterday. I *did* walk there yesterday! And yet . . . all the people are gone.

"All of them," he ended softly. "Morag. My children. They're all dead. Unless I can go back."

She hadn't planned to ask him anything; better to wait

until she and Roger could talk to him together in the evening after the kids were down. But the opportunity offered itself. Roger had driven Buck around the Highlands near Lallybroch, down the Great Glen along Loch Ness, and finally dropped him off at the Loch Errochty dam, where she was working today; she'd drive him back with her for supper.

They'd argued—in whispers—about it the night before. Not about what to say about him; he'd be Daddy's relative, come for a short visit. That was the truth, after all. But whether to take him into the tunnel. Roger had been in favor of this, she very much against, remembering the shock of the . . . timeline? . . . cutting through her like a sharpened wire. She still hadn't decided.

But now he'd brought up the subject of going back, on his own.

"When you came to yourself after you . . . came through, and realized what had happened," she asked curiously, "why didn't you go back into the circle right then?"

He shrugged.

"I did. Though I canna say that I realized straight off what *had* happened. I didna come to that for some days. But I kent something terrible had happened and the stones were to do wi' it. So I was wary of them, as I imagine ye can understand." He quirked an eyebrow at her, and she nodded reluctantly.

She *could* understand. She wouldn't go within a mile of a standing stone herself, unless it was to save some member of her family from a horrible fate. And even then she might think twice. She dismissed the thought, though, and returned to her interrogation.

"But you did go back, you said. What happened?"

He looked helplessly at her, spreading his hands.

"I dinna ken how to describe it to ye. Nothing like that's ever happened to me before."

"Try," she suggested, hardening her voice, and he sighed.

"Aye. Well, I walked up to the circle, and this time I could hear them—the stones. Talking to themselves, like, buzzing like a hive of bees, and with a sound in it made the hairs stand up on my nape."

He'd wanted to turn and run then, but with thought of

Morag and Jemmy in his mind, had determined to push on. He'd walked into the center of the circle, where the sound assailed him from all sides.

"I thought I'd lose my mind from it," he said frankly. "Putting my fingers in my ears did nay good at all; it was inside me, like as if 'twas comin' from my bones. Was it like that for you?" he asked suddenly, peering at her curiously.

"Yes, it was," she answered shortly. "Or close enough. Go on. What did you do then?"

He'd seen the big cleft stone he'd gone through the first time and, taking as deep a breath as he could hold, had lunged through it.

"And ye can skin me for a liar if ye like," he assured her. "I canna for the life of me tell ye what happened next, but after it did, I was lyin' on the grass in the midst of the stones, and I was on fire."

She looked at him, startled.

"Literally? I mean, were your clothes burning, or was it just—"

"I ken what 'literally' means," he said, with an edge in his voice. "I may not be what you are, but I *was* educated."

"Sorry." She made a small apologetic nod and gestured to him to go on.

"Anyway, aye, I was *literally* on fire. My shirt was in flames. Here—" He unzipped his wind-cheater and fumbled with the buttons of Roger's blue cambric shirt, pulling the edges apart to show her the sprawling reddish mark of a healing burn on his chest. He would have buttoned it again at once, but she motioned him not to and bent to look closer. It seemed to be centered on his heart. Was that significant? she wondered.

"Thank you," she said, straightening up. "What—what were you thinking about when you went through?"

He stared at her.

"I was thinking I wanted to get back, what else?"

"Yes, of course. But were you thinking of someone in particular? Of Morag, I mean, or your Jem?"

The most extraordinary expression—shame? embarrassment?—crossed his face, and he looked away.

"I was," he said briefly, and she knew he lied but couldn't think why. He coughed and went on hurriedly.

"Well, so. I rolled upon the grass to put it out, and then I was sick. I lay there for a good while, not having the strength to rise. I dinna ken how long, but a long time. Ye ken what it's like here, close to Midsummer Day? That milky light when ye canna see the sun, but it's not really set?"

"The summer dim," she murmured. "Aye—I mean, yes, I know. So did you try again?"

It *was* shame now. The sun was low and the clouds glowed a dull orange that washed loch and hills and bridge in a sullen flush, but it was still possible to make out the darker flush that spread across his broad cheekbones.

"No," he muttered. "I was afraid."

Despite her distrust of him and her lingering anger over what he'd done to Roger, she felt an involuntary spurt of sympathy at the admission. After all, both she and Roger had *known,* more or less, what they were getting into. He hadn't expected what happened at all and still knew almost nothing.

"I would have been, too," she said. "Did you—"

A shout from behind interrupted her, and she turned to see Rob Cameron bounding along the riverbank. He waved and came up onto the bridge, puffing a little from the run.

"Hi, boss," he said, grinning at her. "Saw ye on my way out. If ye're off the clock, I thought would ye fancy a drink on the way home? And your friend, too, of course," he added, with a friendly nod toward William Buccleigh.

With that, of course, she had no alternative but to introduce them, passing Buck off with their agreed-on story: Roger's relative, staying with them, just in town briefly. She politely declined the offer of a drink, saying that she must get home for the kids' supper.

"Another time, then," Rob said lightly. "Nice to meet ye, pal." He bounded off again, light-footed as a gazelle, and she turned to find William Buccleigh looking after him with narrowed eye.

"What?" she demanded.

"Yon man's got a hot eye for you," he said abruptly, turning to her. "Does your husband know?"

"Don't be ridiculous," she said, just as abruptly. Her heart had sped up at his words, and she didn't like it. "I work with him. He's in the lodge with Roger, and they talk about old songs. That's all."

He made one of those Scottish noises that can convey all manner of indelicate meaning and shook his head.

"I may not be what you are," he repeated, smiling unpleasantly. "But I'm no a fool, either."

73

ONE EWE LAMB RETURNS TO THE FOLD

November 24, 1777
Philadelphia

LORD JOHN GREY desperately needed a valet. He had employed a person so described but found the man worse than useless, and a thief to boot. He had discovered the erstwhile valet slipping teaspoons down his breeches and had—after forcibly extracting the spoons—dismissed him. He should, he supposed, have had the man arrested, but really was not sure what the local constable would do if summoned by a British officer.

Most of the British prisoners of war had been taken out of the city as Howe's army advanced, the Americans wishing to keep them for exchange. Henry had not.

He brushed his own uniform, grimly considering. He wore it daily now, as protection for Dottie and Henry. He had not been an actively serving officer for years but, unlike most men in that position, had not resigned his lieutenant-colonel's commission, either. He wasn't sure what Hal would have done had he *tried* to resign, but since it was a commission in Hal's own regiment and Grey didn't need to sell it, the point was moot.

One of the buttons was loose. He took the hussif out of his kit, threaded a needle without squinting, and whipped the button tightly to the coat. The action gave him a small feeling of satisfaction, though acknowledging it made him admit just how little he felt he could control these days—so little that sewing on a button should seem cause for satisfaction.

He frowned at himself in the glass and twitched irritably at the gold lace on his coat, which was tarnished in places. He did know what to do about that, but damned if he was going to sit polishing it up with a lump of urine-soaked bread. Knowing General Sir William Howe as he did, he doubted that his own appearance would affect his reception, even should he roll up to Howe's headquarters in a sedan chair with his head wrapped in a Turkish turban. Howe frequently didn't bathe or change his linen for a month or more—and not only when in the field.

Still. It would have to be an army surgeon, and Grey wanted his pick of them. He grimaced at the thought. He had known too many army surgeons, some of them at unpleasantly close range. But Howe's army had come into the city in late September. It was mid-November now, the occupation was well established, and with it a general animus among the citizenry.

Those physicians of a rebellious bent had either left the city or would have nothing to do with a British officer. Those with Loyalist sympathies would have been more than happy to oblige him—he was invited to many parties given by the wealthy Loyalists of the city and had been introduced to two or three physicians there—but he had found none with any reputation for surgery. One dealt mostly with cases of venereal disease, another was an *accoucheur,* and the third was plainly a quacksalver of the worst sort.

So he was bound for Howe's headquarters, to beg assistance. He couldn't wait any longer; Henry had held his own and even seemed to gain a bit of strength with the cooling of the weather. Better it was done now, to give him a chance to heal a little before the winter came with its chill and the fetid squalor of closed houses.

Ready, he buckled on his sword and stepped out into the street. There was a soldier, half bowed under a heavy rucksack, walking slowly along the street toward him, looking at the houses. He barely glanced at the man as he came down the steps—but a glance was enough. He looked again, incredulous, and then ran down the street, heedless of hat, gold lace, sword, or dignity, and seized the tall young soldier in his arms.

"Willie!"

"Papa!"

His heart overflowed in a most remarkable way; he could seldom remember being so happy but did his best to contain it, not wanting to embarrass Willie with unmanly excesses of emotion. He didn't let go of his son but stood back a little, looking him up and down.

"You're . . . dirty," he said, unable to repress a large, foolish grin. "Very dirty indeed." He was. Also tattered and threadbare. He still wore his officer's gorget, but his stock was missing, as were several buttons, and one cuff of his coat was torn quite away.

"I have lice, too," Willie assured him, scratching. "Is there any food?"

"Yes, of course. Come in, come in." He took the rucksack off Willie's shoulder and beckoned him to follow. "Dottie!" he shouted up the stairs as he pushed open the door. "Dottie! Come down!"

"I *am* down," his niece said behind him, coming out of the day parlor, where she was accustomed to breakfast. She had a piece of buttered toast in her hand. "What do you—oh, *Willie*!"

Disregarding questions of filth and lice, William swept her up in his arms, and she dropped the toast on the carpet and squeezed him round the body, laughing and crying, until he protested that she had cracked all his ribs and he should never breathe easy again.

Grey stood watching this with the utmost benevolence, even though they had quite trampled the buttered toast into the rented carpet. They really *did* appear to love each other, he reflected. Maybe he'd been wrong. He coughed politely, which did not disentangle them but did at least make Dottie look blankly over her shoulder at him.

"I'll go and order some breakfast for William, shall I?" he said. "Take him into the parlor, why don't you, my dear, and give him a dish of tea."

"Tea," Willie breathed, his face assuming the beatific air of one beholding—or being told about—some prodigious miracle. "I haven't had tea in weeks. Months!"

Grey went out to the cookhouse, this standing at a little distance behind the house proper so that the latter should not be destroyed when—not if—something caught fire and burned the cookhouse to the ground. Appetizing smells of fried meat and stewed fruit and fresh bread floated out of this ramshackle structure.

He had employed Mrs. Figg, a nearly spherical black woman, as cook, on the assumption that she could not have gained such a figure without having both an appreciation of good food and the ability to cook it. In this assumption he had been proved right, and not even that lady's uncertain temperament and taste for foul language made him regret his decision, though it did make him approach her warily. Hearing his news, though, she obligingly put aside the game pie she was making in order to assemble a tea tray.

He waited to take this back himself, meaning to give William and Dottie a little time alone together. He wanted to hear everything—for of course everyone in Philadelphia knew about Burgoyne's disastrous meeting at Saratoga, but he particularly wanted to find out from William what John Burgoyne had known or understood beforehand. According to some of his military acquaintances, Sir George Germain had assured Burgoyne that his plan had been accepted and that Howe would march north to meet him, cutting the American colonies in half. According to others—several of Howe's staff among them—Howe had never been apprised of this plan in the first place, let alone consented to it.

Was this arrogance and presumptuousness on Burgoyne's part, obstinacy and pride on Howe's, idiocy and incompetence on Germain's—or some combination of all three? If pressed, he'd place his wager on this last possibility, but was curious to know how deeply Germain's office might have been involved. With Percy Beauchamp vanished from Philadelphia, leaving not a wrack behind, his further movements would have to be observed by someone else, and Arthur Norrington was likely to communicate his own findings to Germain rather than to Grey.

He carried the loaded tray carefully back, to find William

on the sofa in his shirtsleeves drinking tea, his hair unbound and loose on his shoulders.

Dottie was sitting in the wing chair before the fire, holding her silver comb on her knee, and with a look on her face that nearly made Grey drop the tray. She turned a startled face on him as he came in, so blank that it was clear she barely saw him. Then something changed and her face altered, like one coming back in a twinkling from somewhere leagues away.

"Here," she said, rising at once and reaching for the tray. "Let me have that."

He did, covertly glancing between the two young people. Sure enough, Willie looked odd, too. Why? he wondered. They had been excited, thrilled, exuberantly affectionate with each other a few moments before. Now she was pale but trembling with an inner excitement that made the cups rattle in their saucers as she began to pour out tea. *He* was flushed where she was pale, but not—Grey was almost sure—with any sort of sexual excitement. He had the look of a man who . . . well, no. It *was* sexual excitement, he thought, intrigued—he had, after all, seen it often and was a keen observer of it in men—but it wasn't focused on Dottie. Not at all.

What the devil are they up to? he thought. He affected to ignore their distraction, though, and sat down to drink tea and hear Willie's experiences.

The telling calmed William a little. Grey watched William's face change as he talked, sometimes haltingly, and felt a deep pang at seeing it. Pride, yes, great pride; William was a man now, a soldier, and a good one. But Grey had also a lurking regret for the disappearance of the last traces of Willie's innocence; the briefest look at his eyes proved that had gone.

The accounts of battle, politics, Indians, all had the opposite effect on Dottie, he saw. Far from being calmed or happy, she grew more visibly agitated by the moment.

"I was about to go to visit Sir William, but I think I'll go see Henry first," Grey said at last, rising and brushing toast crumbs from the skirts of his coat. "Do you want to come with me, Willie? Or the both of you, for that matter? Or would you rather rest?"

They exchanged a look in which complicity and plotting were so evident that he blinked. Willie coughed and stood up, too.

"Yes, Papa. I do want to see Henry, of course. But Dottie has just been telling me how grave his state is—and about your intent to get an army surgeon to deal with it. I was . . . thinking . . . I know an army surgeon. A most excellent fellow. Very knowing, and wonderfully gentle in his manner—but quick as a snake with his blade," he hastened to add. His color had risen remarkably, saying this, and Grey viewed him with fascination.

"Really," Grey said slowly. "He sounds an answer to prayer. What is his name? I could ask Sir William—"

"Oh, he's not with Sir William," Willie said hastily.

"Oh, one of Burgoyne's men?" The paroled soldiers of Burgoyne's defeated army had all—with exceptions like William—marched to Boston, there to embark for England. "Well, I would of course like to have him, but I doubt we can send to Boston for him and have him come in a timely fashion, given the time of year and the likelihood—"

"No, he's not in Boston." Willie exchanged another of those looks with Dottie. She caught Grey watching them this time, went red as the roses on the teacups, and looked sedulously at her toes. Willie cleared his throat.

"In fact, he is a Continental surgeon. But Washington's army has gone into winter quarters at Valley Forge—that's no more than a day's ride. He will come if I go in person to ask him, I am sure of it."

"I see," Grey said, thinking rapidly. He was sure that he didn't see the half of it—whatever "it" was—but on the face of things, this did seem an answer to prayer. It would be a simple matter to ask Howe to arrange an escort and a flag of truce for Willie, as well as a guarantee of safe passage for the surgeon.

"All right," he said, making up his mind on the moment. "I'll speak to Sir William about it this afternoon."

Dottie and Willie gave identical sighs—of relief? *What the devil?* he thought yet again.

"Right, then," he said briskly. "Come to think, you'll wish to wash and change, Willie. I'll go to Howe's headquarters now, and we'll see Henry this afternoon. What is the name of this famous Continental surgeon, that I may have Sir William write a pass for him?"

"Hunter," said Willie, and his sunburned face seemed to glow. "Denzell Hunter. Be sure to tell Sir William to write the pass for two; Dr. Hunter's sister is his nurse—he'll need her to come along and help."

74

TWENTY-TWENTY

December 20, 1777
Edinburgh

THE PRINT ON the page sprang into focus, clear and black, and I exclaimed in startlement.

"Ah, close, then?" Mr. Lewis, the spectacle-maker, twinkled at me over his own spectacles. "Try these." He gently removed the trial spectacles from my nose and handed me another pair. I put them on, examined the page of the book before me, then looked up.

"I had no idea," I said, amazed and delighted. It was like being reborn; everything was fresh, new, crisp, and vivid. I had suddenly reentered the half-forgotten world of fine print.

Jamie stood by the shop's window, book in hand and a handsome pair of steel-rimmed square spectacles on his long nose. They gave him a most unaccustomed scholarly air, and he looked for a moment like a distinguished stranger, until he turned to look at me, his eyes slightly magnified behind the lenses. He shifted his gaze over the top of them and smiled at sight of me.

"I like those," he said with approval. "The round ones suit your face, Sassenach."

I had been so taken with the new detail of the world around me that it hadn't even occurred to me to wonder what *I* looked like. Curious, I got up and came to peer into the small looking glass hung on the wall.

"Goodness," I said, recoiling slightly. Jamie laughed, and Mr. Lewis smiled indulgently.

"They are most becoming to you, ma'am," he said.

"Well, possibly," I said, warily examining the stranger's reflection in the glass. "It's just rather a shock." It wasn't really that I'd forgotten what I looked like. It was just that I hadn't thought about it in months, beyond putting on clean linen and not wearing gray, which tended to make me look as though I'd been inexpertly embalmed.

I had on brown today, an open jacket of brown velvet the color of ripe cattails, with a narrow grosgrain ribbon in gold down the edges, over my new gown—this a heavy coffee-colored silk with a close-fitted bodice and three lace-edged petticoats to show at the ankle. We would not be long in Edinburgh, owing to the exigencies of getting the brigadier to his final resting place and Jamie's eagerness to be away to the Highlands—but we did have business to conduct here. Jamie had said firmly that we could not appear as ragamuffins and had sent for a dressmaker and a tailor as soon as we reached our lodgings.

I stood back a little, preening. In all honesty, I was surprised to find how well I looked. During the long months of traveling, of retreat and battle with the Continental army, I had been reduced to my basic essence: survival and function. What I looked like would have been entirely irrelevant, even had I had a mirror.

In fact, I'd subconsciously expected to find a witch in the glass, a worn-looking woman with wild gray hair and a fierce expression. Possibly a long hair or two sprouting from the chin.

Instead . . . well, it was still recognizably me. My hair—uncapped but covered by a small, flat straw hat with a dainty bunch of cloth daisies on it—was tied up behind. But flattering small wisps curled round my temples, and my eyes were a bright clear amber behind the new spectacles, with a surprising look of guileless expectancy.

I had the lines and creases of my age, of course, but on the whole, my face had settled peaceably on my bones, rather than running away in jowls and wattles down my neck. And the bosom, with just a discreet shadow showing the swell of my breasts—the royal navy had fed us lavishly on the sea journey, and I had regained some of the weight I had lost during the long retreat from Ticonderoga.

"Well, not all that bad, really," I said, sounding so surprised that Jamie and Mr. Lewis both laughed. I took off the spectacles with considerable regret—Jamie's spectacles were simple steel-rimmed reading glasses, so could be taken at once, but my own pair would be ready, complete with gold rims, by the next afternoon, Mr. Lewis promised—and we left the shop to embark upon our next errand: Jamie's printing press.

"WHERE'S IAN this morning?" I asked, as we made our way to Princes Street. He'd been gone when I awoke, leaving not a wrack behind, let alone any word of his whereabouts. "You don't suppose he's decided to run for it rather than go home?"

"If he has, I'll track him down and beat him to a pudding, and he kens that perfectly well," Jamie said absently, looking up across the park to the great bulk of the castle on its rock, then putting on his glasses—futilely—to see whether they made a difference. "Nay, I think he's likely gone to the brothel."

"At eleven o'clock in the morning?" I blurted.

"Well, there's nay rule about it," Jamie said mildly, taking off the glasses, wrapping them in his handkerchief, and putting them into his sporran. "I've been known to do it in the morning now and then. Though I doubt he's bent on carnal knowledge just this minute," he added. "I told him to go and see whether Madame Jeanne still owns the place, for if so, she'll be able to tell me more, in a shorter space of time, than anyone else in Edinburgh. If she's there, I'll go and see her in the afternoon."

"Ah," I said, not really liking the notion of his going round for a cozy tête-à-tête with the elegant Frenchwoman who had once been his partner in the whisky-smuggling business but admitting the economy of the proposal. "And where would Andy Bell be at eleven o'clock in the morning, do you suppose?"

"In bed," Jamie said promptly. "Sleeping," he added with a grin, seeing the look on my face. "Printers are sociable creatures, as a rule, and they congregate in taverns of an evening. I've never known one to rise wi' the lark, save he's got bairns wi' the colic."

"You're proposing to roust him out of bed?" I asked, stretching my step to keep up with him.

"No, we'll find him at Mowbray's at dinnertime," he said. "He's a graver—he needs *some* light to work by, so he rises by noon. And he eats at Mowbray's most days. I only want to see whether his shop's burnt down or not. And whether the wee bugger's been using my press."

"You make it sound as though he's been using your wife," I said, amused at the grim tone of this last.

He made a small Scottish noise acknowledging the presumed humor of this remark while simultaneously declining to share in it. I hadn't realized that he felt so strongly about his printing press, but after all, he'd been separated from it for nearly twelve years. Little wonder if his lover's heart was beginning to beat at thought of being reunited with it at last, I thought, privately entertained.

Then again, perhaps he *was* afraid Andy Bell's shop had burned down. It wasn't an idle fear. His own printer's shop *had* burned down twelve years before; such establishments were particularly vulnerable to fire, owing both to the presence of a small open forge for melting and recasting type and to the quantities of paper, ink, and similar flammable substances kept on the premises.

My stomach growled softly at thought of a midday dinner at Mowbray's; I had very pleasant memories of our last—and only—visit there, which had involved some excellent oyster stew and an even better chilled white wine, among other pleasures of the flesh.

It would be a little time 'til dinner, though; laborers might open their dinner pails at noon, but fashionable Edinburgh dined at the civilized hour of three o'clock. Possibly we could acquire a fresh bridie from a street vendor, I thought, hastening in Jamie's wake. Just to tide us over.

Andrew Bell's shop was, luckily, still standing. The door was closed against the draft, but a small bell rang over it to announce our presence, and a middle-aged gentleman in shirtsleeves and apron looked up from a basket of slugs he was sorting.

"A good morning to you, sir. Ma'am," he said cordially, nodding to us, and I saw at once that he was not a Scot. Or, rather, not born in Scotland, for his accent was the soft, slightly drawling English of the Southern colonies. Jamie heard it and smiled.

"Mr. Richard Bell?" he asked.

"I am," said the man, looking rather surprised.

"James Fraser, your servant, sir," Jamie said politely, bowing. "And may I present my wife, Claire."

"Your servant, sir." Mr. Bell bowed in return, looking rather bewildered but with perfect manners.

Jamie reached into the breast of his coat and withdrew a small bundle of letters, tied with a pink ribbon.

"I've brought ye word from your wife and daughters," he said simply, handing them over. "And I've come to see about sending ye home to them."

Mr. Bell's face went blank, and then all the blood drained out of it. I thought he was going to faint for a moment, but he didn't, merely grasping the edge of the counter for support.

"You-you—home?" he gasped. He had clutched the letters to his breast, and now brought them down, looking at them, his eyes welling. "How—how did she . . . My wife. Is she well?" he asked abruptly, jerking up his head to look at Jamie, sudden fear in his eyes. "Are they all right?"

"They were all bonny as doves when I saw them in Wilmingon," Jamie assured him. "Verra much desolated by your absence from them, but well in themselves."

Mr. Bell was trying desperately to control his face and his voice, and the effort reduced him to speechlessness. Jamie leaned over the counter and touched him gently on the arm.

"Go and read your letters, man," he suggested. "Our other business will wait."

Mr. Bell's mouth opened once or twice, soundless, then he nodded abruptly and, whirling round, blundered through the door that led to the back room.

I sighed, and Jamie glanced down at me, smiling.

"It's good when something comes right, isn't it?" I said.

"It's no made right yet," he said, "but it will be." He then pulled his new spectacles out of his sporran and, clapping them onto his nose, flipped up the counter flap and strode purposefully through.

"It *is* my press!" he exclaimed accusingly, circling the enormous thing like a hawk hovering over its prey.

"I'll take your word for it, but how can you tell?" I came cautiously after him, keeping back my skirts from the ink-stained press.

"Well, it's got my name on it, for the one thing," he said, stooping and pointing up at something under it. "Some of them, anyway." Leaning upside down and squinting, I made out *Alex. Malcolm* carved on the underside of a small beam.

"Apparently it still works all right," I observed, straightening up and looking round the room at the posters, ballads, and other examples of the printing and engraving arts displayed there.

"Mmphm." He tried the moving parts and examined the press minutely before reluctantly admitting that, in fact, it seemed in good condition. He still glowered, though.

"And I've been *paying* the wee bugger all these years, to keep it for me!" he muttered. He straightened up, looking balefully at the press. I had in the meantime been poking about the tables near the front wall, which held books and pamphlets for sale, and picked up one of the latter, which was titled at the top *Encyclopedia Britannica,* and below this, "Laudanum."

Tincture of opium, or liquid laudanum, otherwise called the thebaic tincture, is made as follows: take of prepared opium two ounces, of cinnamon and cloves, each one drachm, of white wine one pint, infuse them a week without heat, and then filter it through paper.

Opium at present is in great esteem, and is one of the most valuable of all the simple medicines. Applied externally, it is emollient, relaxing, and discutient, and greatly promotes suppuration: if long kept upon the skin, it takes off hair, and always occasions an itching; sometimes it exulcerates it, and raises little blisters, if applied to a tender part: sometimes, on external application, it allays pain, and even occasions sleep: but it must by no means be applied to the head, espe-

cially to the sutures of the skull; for it has been known to have the most terrible effects in this application, and even bring death itself. Opium taken internally removes melancholy, eases pain, and disposes of sleep; in many cases removes hemorrhages, provokes sweating.

A moderate dose is commonly under a grain . . .

"Do you know what 'discutient' means?" I asked Jamie, who was reading the type set up in the form on the press, frowning as he did so.

"I do. It means whatever ye're talking about can dissolve something. Why?"

"Ah. Perhaps that's why applying laudanum to the sutures of the skull is a bad idea."

He gave me a baffled look.

"Why would ye do that?"

"I haven't the faintest idea." I returned to the pamphlets, fascinated. One of them, titled "The Womb," had some very good engravings of a dissected female pelvis and internal organs, done from varying angles, as well as depictions of the fetus in various stages of development. If this was Mr. Bell's work, I thought, he was both a superb craftsman and a very diligent observer.

"Have you got a penny? I'd like to buy this."

Jamie dug into his sporran and laid a penny on the counter, glanced at the pamphlet in my hand, and recoiled.

"Mother of God," he said, crossing himself.

"Well, probably not," I said mildly. "Certainly *a* mother, though." Before he could reply to this, Richard Bell came out of the back room, red-eyed but composed, and seized Jamie by the hand.

"You cannot know what you have done for me, Mr. Fraser," he said earnestly. "If you can indeed help me to return to my family, I—I—well, in fact, I do not know what I could possibly do to show my gratitude, but be assured that I will bless your soul forever!"

"I'm much obliged to ye for the thought, sir," Jamie said to him, smiling. "It may be that ye can do me a small service, but if not, I shall still be most thankful for your blessings."

"If there is anything I can do, sir, anything at all!" Bell assured him fervently. Then a faint hesitation came over his face—possibly a recollection of whatever his wife had had to say about Jamie in her letter. "Anything short of . . . of treason, I should say."

"Och, no. Well short of treason," Jamie assured him, and we took our leave.

I TOOK A SPOONFUL of the oyster stew and closed my eyes in ecstasy. We had come a little early, in order to get a seat by the window overlooking the street, but Mowbray's had filled up fast, and the clishmaclaver of cutlery and conversation was almost deafening.

"You're sure he's not here?" I said, leaning across the table to make myself heard. Jamie shook his head, rolling a sip of the cold Moselle around his mouth with an expression of bliss.

"Ye'll ken well enough when he is," he said, swallowing it.

"All right. What sort of not-quite-treasonous thing are you planning to make poor Mr. Bell do in return for passage home?"

"I mean to send him home in charge of my printing press," he replied.

"What, entrust your precious darling to a virtual stranger?" I asked, amused. He gave me a mildly dirty look in return, but finished his bite of buttered roll before answering.

"I dinna expect him to be abusing her. He's no going to print a thousand-run of *Clarissa* on her aboard ship, after all."

"Oh, it's a her, is it?" I said, vastly entertained. "And what, may I ask, is her name?"

He flushed a little and looked away, taking particular care to coax a specially succulent oyster into his spoon, but finally muttered, "Bonnie," before gulping it.

I laughed, but before I could make further inquiries, a new noise intruded on the racket, and people began to put down their spoons and stand up, craning to see out of the windows.

"*That* will be Andy," Jamie told me.

I looked down into the street and saw a small knot of boys and idlers, clapping and cheering. Looking up the street to see what was coming, I beheld one of the biggest horses I had ever seen. It wasn't a draft horse but an enormously tall gelding, close to seventeen hands, so far as my inexpert eye could judge.

On top of it was a very small man, sitting up straight and regally ignoring the cheers of the crowd. He came to a stop directly below us and, turning round, removed a wooden square from the saddle behind him. He shook this out, revealing it to be a folding wooden ladder, and one of the street children ran forward to hold the foot of it while Mr. Bell—for it couldn't be anyone else—descended to the plaudits of passersby. He tossed a coin to the child who'd held the ladder, another to a lad who'd taken his horse's head, and disappeared from view.

A few moments later, he came through the door into the main dining room, taking off his cocked hat and bowing graciously to the calls of greeting from the diners. Jamie raised a hand, calling "Andy Bell!" in a resonant voice that cut through the thrum of talk, and the little man's head jerked in our direction, surprised. I watched with fascination as he came toward us, a slow grin spreading over his face.

I couldn't tell whether he had some form of dwarfism or had merely suffered badly from malnutrition and scoliosis in his youth, but his legs were short in proportion to his upper body, and his shoulders crooked; he barely topped four feet, and only the crown of his head—this covered by a very fashionable wig—showed as he passed between the tables.

These aspects of appearance faded into insignificance, though, as he drew close and I perceived his most striking attribute. Andrew Bell had the biggest nose I had ever seen, and in the course of an eventful life, I had seen a number of prize specimens. It began between his eyebrows, and curved gently down for a short distance as though nature had intended him to have the profile of a Roman emperor. Something had gone amiss in the execution, though, and to this promising beginning, something that looked like a small potato had been affixed. Knobbly and red, it took the eye.

It took quite a few eyes; as he drew close to our table, a young lady nearby saw him, gasped audibly, and then clapped a hand over her mouth, this precaution being quite insufficient to quell her giggles.

Mr. Bell heard her, and without breaking his stride, he reached into his pocket, withdrew an immense papier-mâché nose decorated with purple stars, which he clapped over his own, and, fixing the young woman with an icy stare, passed by.

"My dear," Jamie said to me, grinning as he rose to his feet and extending a hand to the little engraver, "may I name my friend, Mr. Andrew Bell? My wife, Andy. Claire is her name."

"Charmed, madam," he said, removing the false nose and bowing low over my hand. "When did you acquire this rare creature, Jamie? And whatever would such a lovely lass want with a great, vulgar lout such as you, I wonder?"

"I lured her into marriage wi' descriptions of the beauties of my printing press," Jamie said dryly, sitting down and motioning to Andy Bell to join us.

"Ah," said Andy, with a sharp look at Jamie, who raised his brows and widened his eyes. "Hmm. I see ye've been by the shop, then." He nodded at my reticule, from which the top of the pamphlet I'd bought was protruding.

"We have," I said hastily, pulling out the pamphlet. I didn't *think* Jamie proposed to squash Andy Bell like a bug for having made free with his printing press, but his relationship with "Bonnie" was news to me, and I wasn't sure quite how deep his sense of affronted proprietorship went.

"This is remarkably fine work," I said to Mr. Bell, with complete sincerity. "Tell me, how many different specimens did you use?"

He blinked a little but answered readily, and we had a pleasant—if rather gruesome—conversation regarding the difficulties of dissection in warm weather and the effect of saline solution versus alcohol for preservation. This caused the people at the next table to end their meal rather hurriedly, casting veiled looks of horror as they left. Jamie leaned back in his chair, looking pleasant but fixing Andy Bell with an unwavering gaze.

The little engraver betrayed no particular discomfort under this basilisk stare and went on telling me about the response when he had published the bound edition of the *Encyclopedia*—the King had somehow happened to see the plates of the "Womb" section and had ordered those pages to be torn out of the book, the ignorant German blatherskite!—but when the waiter came to take his order, he ordered both a very expensive wine and a large bottle of good whisky.

"What, whisky wi' the stew?" blurted the waiter, astonished.

"No," he said with a sigh, pushing back his wig. "Concubinage. If that's what ye call it when ye rent the services of a man's beloved."

The waiter shifted his look of astonishment to me, then went bright red and, choking slightly, backed away.

Jamie fixed a narrow eye on his friend, now buttering a roll with aplomb.

"It'll take more than whisky, Andy."

Andy Bell sighed and scratched his nose.

"Aye, then," he said. "Say on."

WE FOUND IAN waiting at the small hotel, chatting with a couple of draymen in the street. Seeing us, he took his leave—and a small package, thrust surreptitiously under his coat—and came in with us. It was teatime, and Jamie ordered it to be brought up to our rooms, for the sake of discretion.

We had lashed out, rather, in the matter of accommodations, and had taken a suite of rooms. The tea was now laid out in the parlor, an appetizing array of grilled finnan haddie, Scotch eggs, toast with marmalade, and scones with jam and clotted cream, accompanying an enormous pot of strong black tea. I inhaled the fragrant steam from the table and sighed with pleasure.

"It's going to be rather a wrench, going back to no tea," I observed, pouring out for everyone. "I don't suppose we'll get any in America for another, what—three or four years?"

"Oh, I wouldna say that," Jamie said judiciously. "Depends where we go back to, aye? Ye can get tea fine in places like Philadelphia or Charleston. Ye only need to ken a good smuggler or two, and if Captain Hickman's no been sunk or hanged by the time we go back . . ."

I put down my cup and stared at him.

"You don't mean you aren't planning to go ho—to go back to the Ridge?" I had a sudden empty feeling in the pit of my stomach, remembering our plans for the New House, the smell of balsam fir, and the quiet of the mountains. Did he really mean to move to Boston or Philadelphia?

"No," he said, surprised. "Of course we shall go back there. But if I mean to be in the printing trade, Sassenach, we shall need to be in a city for a time, no? Only 'til the war is over," he said, encouraging.

"Oh," I said in a small voice. "Yes. Of course." I drank tea, not tasting it. How could I have been so stupid? I had never once thought that, of course, a printing press would be pointless on Fraser's Ridge. In part, I supposed, I simply hadn't really believed he *would* get his press back, let alone thought ahead to the logical conclusion if he did.

But now he had his Bonnie back, and the future had suddenly acquired a disagreeable solidity. Not that cities didn't have considerable advantages, I told myself stoutly. I could finally acquire a decent set of medical instruments, replenish my medicines—why, I could even make penicillin and ether again! With a little better appetite, I took a Scotch egg.

"Speaking of smugglers," Jamie was saying to Ian, "what is it ye have in your coat? A present for one of the ladies at Madame Jeanne's?"

Ian gave his uncle a cold look and removed the small package from his pocket.

"A wee bit o' French lace. For my mam."

"Good lad," Jamie said with approval.

"What a sweet thought, Ian," I said. "Did you—I mean, was Madame Jeanne still *in situ*?"

He nodded, putting the package back into his coat.

"She is. And verra eager to renew her acquaintance wi' *you,* Uncle," he added, with a slightly malicious grin. "She asked would ye care to come round this evening for a bit of entertainment."

Jamie's nose twitched as he glanced at me.

"Oh, I think not, Ian. I'll send a note saying we shall wait upon her tomorrow morning at eleven. Though ye're free to take up her invitation yourself, of course." It was clear that he was only teasing, but Ian shook his head.

"Nay, I wouldna go wi' a whore. Not 'til it's settled between Rachel and me," he said seriously. "One way or the other. But I shallna take another woman to my bed until she tells me that I must."

We both looked at him in some surprise across the teacups.

"You *do* mean it, then," I said. "You feel . . . er . . . betrothed to her?"

"Well, of course he does, Sassenach," Jamie said, reaching for another slice of toast. "He left her his dog."

I ROSE LATE and leisurely next morning, and as Jamie and Ian were likely to be some time about their business, I dressed and went shopping. Edinburgh being a city of commerce, Jamie had been able to convert our stock of gold—still quite a lot of it left—to bank drafts and cash, as well as to make arrangements for deposition of the cache of letters we had accumulated since Fort Ticonderoga. He had left a fat purse for my use, and I proposed to spend the day shopping, as well as collecting my new spectacles.

It was with these perched proudly on my nose and a bag containing a selection of the best of the herbs and medicines available from Haugh's Apothecary that I returned to Howard's hotel at teatime, with a rare appetite.

My appetite received a slight check, though, when the hotel's majordomo stepped out of his sanctum, wearing a slightly pained expression, and asked if he might have a word, madam?

"We do appreciate the honor of General Fraser's . . . presence," he said apologetically, conducting me to a small, cramped stairwell leading to the basement. "A great man, and a very fine warrior, and of course we are cognizant of the heroic nature of the . . . er . . . the manner of his death. It's only that . . . well, I hesitate to mention it, madam, but a coalman this morning mentioned a . . . *smell.*"

This last word was so discreet that he fairly hissed it into my ear as he ushered me off the stair and into the Howard's coal cellar, where we had made arrangements for the general to repose in dignity until we left for the Highlands. The smell itself was not nearly so discreet, and I snatched a handkerchief from my pocket and clapped it to my nose. There was a small window high up in one wall, from which a dim, smeary light seeped into the basement. Beneath this was a wide chute, under which stood a small mountain of coal.

In solitary dignity, draped with a canvas, the general's coffin stood well apart, lit by a solemn beam from the tiny window. A beam that gleamed from the small puddle beneath the coffin. The general was leaking.

"AND SAW THE skull beneath the skin," I quoted, tying a turpentine-soaked rag about my head, just under my nose, *"and breastless creatures under ground leaned backward with a lipless grin."*

"Apt," said Andy Bell, giving me a sideways glance. "Your own, is it?"

"No, a gentleman named Eliot," I told him. "As you say, though—apt."

Given the agitation of the hotel staff, I thought I had better take steps without waiting for Jamie and Ian to return, and after a moment's thought, had sent the bootboy on the run to inquire if Mr. Bell might like to come and observe something interesting in the medical line?

"The light's wretched," Bell said, standing on tiptoe to peer down into the coffin.

"I've called for a couple of lanterns," I assured him. "And buckets."

"Aye, buckets," he agreed, looking thoughtful. "What d'ye think, though, for what ye might call the longer term? It'll be some days to get him intae the Highlands—maybe weeks, this time o' year."

"If we tidy things up a bit, I thought perhaps you would know a discreet blacksmith who might be able to come and patch the lining." A seam in the lead foil lining the coffin had come apart, probably from the jostling involved in getting it from the ship, but it looked like a fairly simple repair—granted a blacksmith with a strong stomach and a low level of superstition regarding corpses.

"Mmm." He had taken out a sketching block and was making preliminary drawings, light notwithstanding. He scratched his potatolike nose with the end of his silver pencil, thinking. "Could do that, aye. But there are other ways."

"Well, we could boil him down to the bones, yes," I said, a little testily. "Though I hate to think what the hotel would say if I asked for the lend of their laundry cauldrons."

He laughed at that, to the undisguised horror of the footman who had appeared on the stairway, holding two lanterns.

"Ah, dinna fash yoursel', sonny," Andy Bell told him, taking the lanterns. "Naebody here but us ghouls."

He grinned broadly at the sound of the footman taking the stairs three at a time, but then turned and eyed me speculatively.

"It's a thought, aye? I could take him back tae my shop. Get him aff your hands, and naebody the wiser, sae heavy as your box there is. Mean to say, like, no one's going to want to gaze upon the dear departed's face once ye get him where he's going, are they?"

I didn't take offense at the suggestion, but shook my head.

"Putting aside the possibility of one or both of us being taken up as body snatchers, the poor man *is* my husband's kinsman. And he didn't want to be here in the first place."

"Well, nae one does, surely?" Bell said, blinking. "No much help for it, though. *The skull beneath the skin,* as your man Eliot so movingly puts it."

"I meant Edinburgh, not a coffin," I clarified. Fortunately, my purchases from Haugh's had included a large bottle of denatured alcohol, which I had brought down, discreetly wrapped in a rough apron procured from one of the housemaids. "He wanted to be buried in America."

"Really," Bell murmured. "Quaint notion. Ah, well. Two things I can think of, then. Repair the leak, and fill up the box wi' a gallon or twa o' cheap gin—well, it's cheaper than what ye've got there," he said, seeing my look. "Or . . . how long can ye stay in Edinburgh, do ye think?"

"We hadn't meant to stay longer than a week—but we might stretch it a day or two," I said cautiously, unbundling the bale of rags the majordomo had given me. "Why?"

He tilted his head back and forth, contemplating the remains by lantern light. An apt word, "remains."

"Maggots," he said succinctly. "They'll do a nice, clean job of it, but they do take time. Still, if we can take most o' the flesh off—hmm. Got a knife of any sort?" he asked.

I nodded, reaching into my pocket. Jamie had, after all, given me the knife because he thought I'd need it.

"Got maggots?" I said.

I DROPPED THE misshapen ball of lead into a saucer. It clinked and rolled to a stop, and we all looked at it in silence.

"That's what killed him," I said at last. Jamie crossed himself and murmured something in Gaelic, and Ian nodded soberly. "God rest him."

I hadn't eaten much of the excellent tea; the smell of corruption lingered at the back of my throat, in spite of the turpentine and the virtual bath I had taken in alcohol, followed by a real bath in the hotel's tub with soap and water as hot as I could stand.

"So," I said, clearing my throat. "How was Madame Jeanne?"

Jamie looked up from the bullet, his face lightening.

"Oh, verra bonnie," he said, grinning. "She had a good bit to say about the state of things in France. And a certain amount to say about one Percival Beauchamp."

I sat up a little straighter.

"She *knows* him?"

"She does indeed. He calls at her establishment now and then—though not in the way of business. Or rather," he added, with a sidelong glance at Ian, "not in the way of her usual business."

"Smuggling?" I asked. "Or spying?"

"Possibly both, but if it's the latter, she wasna telling me about it. He brings in quite a bit of stuff from France, though. I was thinking that maybe Ian and I would go across, whilst the general's doing whatever he's doing—how long did wee Andy think it would take to make him decent?"

"Anything from three or four days to a week, depending on how, um, active the maggots are." Ian and Jamie both shuddered reflexively. "It's just the same thing that happens underground," I pointed out. "It will happen to all of *us*, eventually."

"Well, aye, it is," Jamie admitted, taking another scone and ladling quantities of cream onto it. "But it's generally done in decent privacy so ye havena got to think about it."

"The general is quite private," I assured him, with a shade

of acerbity. "He's covered in a good layer of bran. No one will see a thing, unless they go poking about."

"Well, that's a thought, isn't it?" Ian chipped in, sticking a finger in the jam. "This is Edinburgh. The place has a terrible reputation for body snatching, because of all the doctors wanting them to cut up for study. Had ye best not put a guard on the general, just to be sure he makes it to the Highlands wi' all his pieces?" He stuck the finger in his mouth and raised his brows at me.

"Well, in fact, there *is* a guard," I admitted. "Andy Bell suggested it, for just that reason." I didn't add that Andy had made a bid for the general's body himself—nor that I had told Mr. Bell in no uncertain terms what would happen to him if the general turned up missing.

"Ye said Andy helped ye with the job?" Jamie asked curiously.

"He did. We got on extremely well. In fact . . ." I hadn't been going to mention the subject of our conversation until Jamie had had a pint or so of whisky, but the moment seemed opportune, so I plumped in.

"I was describing various things to him while we worked—interesting surgeries and medical trivia, you'll know the sort of things."

Ian murmured something under his breath about ghoulies of a feather, but I ignored him.

"Aye, so?" Jamie was looking wary; he knew something was coming but not what it was.

"Well," I said, taking a breath, "the long and the short of it is that he suggested I write a book. A medical book."

Jamie's eyebrows had risen slowly, but he nodded at me to go on.

"A sort of manual for regular people, not for doctors. With principles of proper hygiene and nutrition, and guides to the common sorts of illness, how to make up simple medicines, what to do for wounds and bad teeth—that sort of thing."

The brows were still up, but he kept nodding, finishing the last bite of scone. He swallowed.

"Aye, well, it sounds a good sort of book—and surely ye'd be the person to write it. Did he happen to 'suggest' how much he thought it might cost to have such a thing printed and bound?"

"Ah." I let out the breath I'd been holding. "He'll do three hundred copies, a maximum of a hundred fifty pages, buckram binding, *and* distribute them through his shop, in exchange for the twelve years' rent he owes you for your printing press."

Jamie's eyes bulged and his face went red.

"And he's throwing in the maggots for free. *And* the guard," I added hastily, shoving the port in front of him before he could speak. He seized the glass and downed it in a gulp.

"That wee grasper!" he said, when he could speak. "Ye didna sign anything, did ye?" he asked anxiously. I shook my head.

"I did tell him I thought you'd maybe want to bargain with him," I offered meekly.

"Oh." His color began to recede toward normal levels.

"I do want to," I said, looking down at my hands, clasped together in my lap.

"Ye'd never said anything about wanting to write a book before, Auntie," Ian said, curious.

"Well, I hadn't really thought about it," I said defensively. "And it would have been terribly difficult and expensive to do while we were living on the Ridge."

Jamie muttered, "Expensive," and poured another glass of port, which he drank more slowly, making occasional faces at the taste as he thought.

"Ye really want this, Sassenach?" he said at last, and at my nod, set down the glass with a sigh.

"All right," he said with resignation. "But ye're having a leather-bound special edition, too, wi' gilded end pages. And five hundred copies. I mean, ye'll want some to take back to America, won't you?" he added, seeing my stunned look.

"Oh. Yes. I would like that."

"Well, then." He picked up the bell and rang for the maid. "Tell the young woman to take away this wretched stuff and bring some decent whisky. We'll toast your book. And then I'll go and speak to the wicked wee man."

I HAD A FRESH QUIRE of good-quality paper. I had half a dozen sturdy goose quills, a silver penknife with which to sharpen them, and an inkwell provided by the hotel—rather battered but filled, the majordomo had assured me, with the very best iron-gall ink. Jamie and Ian had gone to France for a week, to look into various interesting leads given them by Madame Jeanne, leaving me to mind the general and commence my book. I had all the time and leisure I required.

I took a sheet of paper, pristine and creamy, placed it just so, and dipped my quill, excitement thrumming in my fingers.

I closed my eyes in reflex, then opened them again. Where ought I to begin?

Begin at the beginning and go on till you come to the end: then stop. The line from *Alice's Adventures in Wonderland* drifted through my mind, and I smiled. Good advice, I supposed—but only if you happened to know where the beginning was, and I didn't quite.

I twiddled the quill a bit, thinking.

Perhaps I should have an outline? That seemed sensible—and a little less daunting than starting straight in to write. I lowered the quill and held it poised above the paper for a moment, then picked it up again. An outline would have a beginning, too, wouldn't it?

The ink was beginning to dry on the point. Rather crossly, I wiped it and was just about to dip it again, when the maid scratched discreetly at the door.

"Mrs. Fraser? There's a gentleman downstairs, askin' to see ye," she said. From her air of respect, I supposed it couldn't be Andy Bell. Besides, she likely would have said so if it was; everyone in Edinburgh knew Andy Bell.

"I'll come down," I said, rising. Perhaps my subconscious would come to some kind of conclusion regarding beginnings while I dealt with this gentleman, whomever he was.

Whomever he was, he *was* a gentleman, I saw that at once. He was also Percival Beauchamp.

"Mrs. Fraser," he said, his face lighting with a smile as he turned at the sound of my step. "Your servant, *madame.*"

"Mr. Beauchamp," I said, allowing him to take my hand and raise it to his lips. An elegant person of the time would doubtless have said something like, "*I fear you take me at a disadvantage, sir,*" with anything between haughtiness and flirtation. Not being an elegant person of the time, I merely said, "What are *you* doing here?"

Mr. Beauchamp, on the other hand, had any amount of elegance.

"Looking for you, dear lady," he replied, and gave my hand a slight squeeze before releasing it. I repressed a reflexive urge to wipe it on my dress and nodded toward a pair of armchairs arranged by the window.

"Not that I'm not flattered," I said, arranging my skirts. "But don't you want my husband? Oh!" I said, another thought occurring. "Or did you want to consult me medically?"

His lips twitched as though he thought this an amusing notion, but he shook his head respectfully. "Your husband is in France—or so Jeanne LeGrand tells me. I came to speak to you."

"Why?"

He lifted his smooth dark brows at that but didn't answer at once, instead lifting a finger in a gesture to the hotel clerk to summon refreshment. I didn't know if he was merely being polite or wanted the time to formulate his address, now that he'd seen me again. In any case, he took his time.

"I have a proposition for your husband, *madame.* I would have spoken with him," he said, forestalling my question, "but he had left for France already when I learned he was in Edinburgh, and I, alas, must leave myself before he will return. I thought it better to speak directly with you, though, rather than to explain myself in a letter. There are things it's wiser not to commit to writing, you know," he added, with a sudden smile that made him very appealing.

"All right," I said, settling myself. "Say on."

I LIFTED THE GLASS of brandy and took a sip, then raised it and looked critically through it.

"No, it's just brandy," I said. "Not opium."

"I beg your pardon?" He looked involuntarily into his own glass, just in case, and I laughed.

"I mean," I clarified, "that good as it is, it's not nearly good enough to make me believe a story like that."

He didn't take offense but tilted his head to one side.

"Can you think of any reason why I should invent such a tale?"

"No," I admitted, "but that doesn't mean there isn't one, does it?"

"What I have told you is not impossible, is it?"

I considered that one for a moment.

"Not *technically* impossible," I conceded. "But certainly implausible."

"Have you ever seen an ostrich?" he asked, and, without inquiring, poured more brandy into my glass.

"Yes. Why?"

"You must admit that ostriches are frankly implausible," he said. "But clearly not impossible."

"One to you," I conceded. "But I do think that Fergus being the lost heir to the Comte St. Germain's fortune is slightly more implausible than an ostrich. Particularly if you consider the part about the marriage license. I mean . . . a lost *legitimate* heir? It is France we're talking about, isn't it?"

He laughed at that. His face had flushed with brandy and amusement, and I could see how very attractive he must have been in his youth. He wasn't by any means bad-looking now, come to that.

"Do you mind my asking what you do for a living?" I asked curiously.

He was disconcerted by that and rubbed a hand over his jaw before answering, but met my eyes.

"I sleep with rich women," he said, and his voice held a faint but disturbing trace of bitterness.

"Well, I do hope you aren't regarding me in the light of a business opportunity. The gold-rimmed spectacles notwithstanding, I really haven't got any money."

He smiled and hid it in his brandy glass.

"No, but you would be a great deal more entertaining than the usual woman who does."

"I'm flattered," I said politely. We sipped brandy in silence for a bit, both thinking how to proceed. It was raining—naturally—and the patter of it on the street outside and the hiss of the fire beside us was soothing in the extreme. I felt oddly comfortable with him, but after all, I couldn't spend all day here; I had a book to write.

"All right," I said. "*Why* have you told me this story?

Wait—there are two parts to that. One, why tell me rather than Fergus himself? And two, what is your personal interest in the situation, assuming it *is* true?"

"I did try to tell Mr. Fraser—Fergus Fraser, that is," he said slowly. "He declined to speak with me."

"Oh!" I said, recalling something. "Was it you who tried to abduct him, in North Carolina?"

"No, it wasn't," he said promptly, and with every evidence of sincerity. "I did hear about the occasion, but I don't know who his assailant was. More than likely, it was someone he had annoyed with his work." He shrugged that off and continued. "As for my personal interest . . . that runs along with the reason for my telling your husband—because I'm telling *you* only as your husband is unavailable."

"And that would be?"

He glanced quickly round to see that we were not overheard. No one was near us, but he still lowered his voice.

"I—and the interests I represent in France—wish the rebellion in America to succeed."

I didn't know what I'd been expecting, but it wasn't that, and I gawked at him.

"You expect me to believe you're an American patriot?"

"Not at all," he said. "I don't care about politics in the slightest. I'm a man of business." He eyed me assessingly. "Have you ever heard of a company called *Hortalez et Cie*?"

"No."

"It is ostensibly an importing and exporting business, run out of Spain. What it actually is is a facade for the purpose of funneling money to the Americans, without visibly involving the French government. We have so far moved many thousands through it, mostly to buy arms and ammunition. *Madame* LeGrand mentioned the company to your husband but without telling him what it was. She left it to me to decide whether to reveal the true nature of *Hortalez* to him."

"You're a French intelligence agent—is that what you're telling me?" I said, the penny dropping at last.

He bowed.

"But you aren't French, I don't think," I added, looking hard at him. "You're English."

"I was." He looked away. "I am a citizen of France now."

He fell silent, and I leaned back a little in my chair, watching him—and wondering. Wondering both how much of this was true and, in a more distant way, whether he might conceivably be an ancestor of mine. Beauchamp was not an uncommon name, and there was no great physical resemblance between us. His hands were long-fingered and graceful, like mine, but the fingers were shaped differently. The ears? His were somewhat large, though delicately shaped. I really had no idea what my own ears looked like, but assumed that if they were noticeably large, Jamie would have mentioned it at some point.

"What is it that you want?" I asked quietly at last, and he looked up.

"Tell your husband what I have told you, if you please, *madame,*" he said, quite serious for once. "And suggest to him that it is not only in the best interests of his foster son to pursue this matter—but very much in the interests of America."

"How is that?"

He lifted one shoulder, slim and elegant.

"The Comte St. Germain had extensive land holdings in a part of America that is currently held by Great Britain. The French part of his estate—currently being squabbled over by a number of claimants—is extremely valuable. If Fergus Fraser can be proved to be Claudel Rakoczy—Rakoczy is the family name, you understand—and the heir to this fortune, he would be able to use it to help in financing the revolution. From what I know of him and his activities—and I know a good deal, by this time—I think he would be amenable to these aims. If the revolution is successful, then those who backed it would have substantial influence over whatever government is formed."

"And you could stop sleeping with rich women for money?"

A wry smile spread over his face.

"Precisely." He rose and bowed deeply to me. "A great pleasure to speak with you, *madame.*"

He had almost reached the door when I called after him.

"*Monsieur* Beauchamp!"

"Yes?" He turned and looked back, a dark, slender man whose face was marked with humor—and with pain, I thought.

"Have you any children?"

He looked completely startled at that.

"I really don't think so."

"Oh," I said. "I only wondered. Good day to you, sir."

75

SIC TRANSIT GLORIA MUNDI

The Scottish Highlands

IT WAS A LONG walk from the farmhouse at Balnain. As it was early January in Scotland, it was also wet and cold. Very wet. And *very* cold. No snow—and I rather wished there had been, as it might have discouraged Hugh Fraser's insane notion—but it had been raining for days, in that dismal way that makes hearths smoke, and even clothes that have not been outside grow damp, and drives the chill so far into your bones that you think you'll never be warm again.

I'd come to this conviction myself some hours ago, but the only alternative to continuing to slog through the rain and mud was to lie down and die, and I hadn't quite reached that extremity. Yet.

The creaking of the wheels stopped abruptly, with that slushing sound that indicated they had sunk once more in the mud. Under his breath, Jamie said something grossly inappropriate to a funeral, and Ian smothered a laugh with a cough—which became real and went hoarsely on and on, sounding like the bark of a large, tired dog.

I took the flask of whisky out from under my cloak—I didn't think something with that kind of alcohol content would freeze, but I wasn't taking any chances—and handed it to Ian. He gulped, wheezed as though he'd been hit by a truck, coughed some more, and then handed the flask back, breathing hard, and nodded thanks. His nose was red and running.

So were all the noses around me. Some of them possibly from grief, though I suspected that either the weather or the catarrh was responsible for most of them. The men had all gathered without comment—they'd had practice—around the coffin and, with concerted heaving, managed to get it out of the ruts and onto a firmer section of road, this covered mostly in rocks.

"How long do you think it's been since Simon Fraser last came home?" I whispered to Jamie, as he came back to take his place beside me toward the end of the funeral procession. He shrugged and wiped his nose with a soggy handkerchief.

"Years. He wouldna really have had cause, would he?"

I supposed not. As a result of the wake held the night before at the farmhouse—a place a little smaller than Lallybroch but constructed on much the same lines—I now knew a great deal more about Simon Fraser's military career and exploits than I had before, but the eulogy hadn't included a timetable. If he'd fought everywhere they said he had, though, he would hardly have had time to change his socks between campaigns, let alone come home to Scotland. And the estate wasn't his, after all; he was the second youngest of nine children. His wife, the tiny *bainisq* trudging at the head of the procession on her brother-in-law Hugh's arm, had no household of her own, I gathered, and lived with Hugh's family, she having no children alive—or nearby, at least—to care for her.

I did wonder whether she was pleased that we'd brought him home. Would it not have been better just to know that he'd died abroad, doing his duty and doing it well, than to be presented with the dismayingly pitiful detritus of her husband, no matter how professionally packaged?

But she had seemed, if not happy, at least somewhat gratified at being the center of such a fuss. Her crumpled face had flushed and seemed to unfold a little during the festivities of the night, and now she walked on with no sign of flagging, doggedly stepping over the ruts made by her husband's coffin.

It was Hugh's fault. Simon's much elder brother and the owner of Balnain, he was a spindly little old man, barely taller than his widowed sister-in-law, and with romantic notions. It was his pronouncement that, instead of planting Simon decently in the family burying ground, the family's most gallant warrior should be interred in a place more suited to his honor and the reverence due him.

Bainisq, pronounced "bann-eeshg," meant a little old lady; was a little old man merely an "eeshg"? I wondered, looking at Hugh's back. I thought I wouldn't ask until we were back at the house—assuming we made it there by nightfall.

At long last, Corrimony hove into sight. According to Jamie, the name meant "a hollow in the moor," and it was. Within the cup-shaped hollow in the grass and heather rose a low dome; as we grew closer, I saw that it was made from thousands and thousands of small river rocks, most the size of a fist, some the size of a person's head. And around this dark gray rain-slicked cairn was a circle of standing stones.

I clutched Jamie's arm by reflex. He glanced at me in surprise, then realized what I was looking at and frowned.

"D'ye hear anything, Sassenach?" he murmured.

"Only the wind." This had been moaning along with the funeral procession, mostly drowning out the old man chanting the *coronach* before the coffin, but as we came out onto the open moor, it picked up speed and rose several tones in pitch, sending cloaks and coats and skirts flapping like ravens' wings.

I kept a cautious eye on the stones but sensed nothing as we drew to a halt before the cairn. It was a passage tomb, of the general kind they called a *clava* cairn; I had no notion what that signified, but Uncle Lamb had had photographs of many such sites. The passage was meant to orient with some astronomical object on some significant date. I glanced up at the leaden, weeping sky and decided that today was probably not the day, anyway.

"We dinna ken who was buried there," Hugh had explained to us the day before. "But clearly a great chieftain of some sort. Must ha' been, the terrible trouble it is to build a cairn like that!"

"Aye, to be sure," Jamie had said, adding delicately. "The great chieftain: he's no buried there anymore?"

"Oh, no," Hugh assured us. "The earth took him, long since. There's no but a wee stain of his bones there now. And ye needna be worrit about there being a curse upon the place, either."

"Oh, good," I murmured, but he paid no attention.

"Some lang nebbit opened the tomb a hundred years ago or more, so if there *was* to be a curse on it, it surely went off attached to him."

This was comforting, and in fact none of the people now standing about the cairn seemed at all put off or bothered by its proximity. Though it might just be that they had lived near it for so long that it had become no more than a feature of the landscape.

There was a certain amount of practical discussion, the men looking at the cairn and shaking their heads dubiously, gesturing in turn toward the open passage that led to the burial chamber, then toward the top of the cairn, where the stones had either been removed or had simply fallen in and been cleared away below. The women gravitated closer together, waiting. We had arrived in a fog of fatigue the day before, and while I had been introduced to all of them, I had trouble keeping the proper name attached to the proper face. In truth, their faces all looked similar—thin, worn, and pale, with a sense of chronic exhaustion about them, a tiredness much deeper than waking the dead would account for.

I had a sudden recollection of Mrs. Bug's funeral. Makeshift and hasty—and yet carried out with dignity and genuine sorrow on the part of the mourners. I thought these people had barely known Simon Fraser.

How much better to have regarded his own last wish as stated and left him on the battlefield with his fallen comrades, I thought. But whoever said funerals were for the benefit of the living had had the right of it.

The sense of failure and futility that had followed the defeat at Saratoga had made his own officers determined to accomplish *something,* to make a proper gesture toward a man they had loved and a warrior they honored. Perhaps they had wanted to send him home, too, because of their desire for their own homes.

The same sense of failure—plus a deadly streak of romanticism—had doubtless made General Burgoyne insist upon the gesture; I thought he likely felt his own honor required it. And then Hugh Fraser, reduced to a hand-to-mouth existence in the wake of Culloden and faced with the unexpected homecoming of his younger brother, unable to produce much in the way of a funeral, but deeply romantic himself . . . and the end of it this strange procession, bringing Simon Fraser to a home no longer his and a wife who was a stranger to him.

And his place will know him no more. The line came to mind as the men made their decision and began to dismount the coffin from its wheels. I had drawn closer, along with the other women, and found I was now standing within a foot or two of one of the standing stones that ringed the cairn. These were smaller than the stones on Craigh na Dun—no more than two or three feet high. Moved by sudden impulse, I reached out and touched it.

I hadn't expected anything to happen, and it very luckily didn't. Though had I suddenly vanished in the midst of the burial, it would have substantially enlivened the event.

No buzzing, no screaming, no sensation at all. It was just a rock. After all, I thought, there was no reason why *all* standing stones should be assumed to mark time portals. Presumably the ancient builders had used stones to mark any place of significance—and surely a cairn like this one must have been significant. I wondered what sort of man—or woman, perhaps?—had lain here, leaving no more than an echo of their bones, so much more fragile than the enduring rocks that sheltered them.

The coffin was lowered to the ground and—with much grunting and puffing—shoved through the passage into the burial chamber in the center of the tomb. There was a large flat slab of stone that lay against the cairn, this incised with strange cup-shaped marks, presumably made by the original builders. Four of the stronger men took hold of this and maneuvered it slowly over the top of the cairn, sealing the hole above the chamber.

It fell with a muffled thud that sent a few small rocks rolling down the sides of the cairn. The men came down then, and we all stood rather awkwardly round it, wondering what to do next.

There was no priest here. The funeral Mass for Simon had been said earlier, in a small, bare stone church, before the procession to this thoroughly pagan burial. Evidently, Hugh's researches hadn't discovered anything regarding rites for such things.

Just when it seemed that we would be obliged simply to turn round and slog our way back to the farmhouse, Ian coughed explosively and stepped forward.

The funeral procession was drab in the extreme, none of the bright tartans that had graced Highland ceremonies in the past. Even Jamie's appearance was subdued, cloaked, and his hair covered with a black slouch hat. The sole exception to the general somberness was Ian.

He had provoked stares when he'd come downstairs this morning, and the staring hadn't stopped. With good reason. He'd shaved most of his head and greased the remaining strip of hair into a stiff ridge down the middle of his scalp, to which he had attached a dangling ornament of turkey feathers with a pierced silver sixpence. He *was* wearing a cloak, but under it had put on his worn buckskins, with the blue-and-white wampum armlet his wife, Emily, had made for him.

Jamie had looked him slowly up and down when he appeared and nodded, one corner of his mouth turning up.

"It willna make a difference, aye?" he'd said quietly to Ian as we headed for the door. "They'll still ken ye for who ye are."

"Will they?" Ian had said, but then ducked out into the downpour without waiting for an answer.

Jamie had undoubtedly been right; the Indian finery was a dress rehearsal in preparation for his arrival at Lallybroch, for we were bound there directly, once Simon's body was decently disposed of and the farewell whisky had been drunk.

It had its uses now, though. Ian slowly removed his cloak and handed it to Jamie, then walked to the entrance of the passage and turned to face the mourners—who watched this apparition, bug-eyed. He spread his hands, palms upward, closed his eyes, put back his head so the rain ran down his face, and began to chant something in Mohawk. He was no singer, and his voice was so hoarse from his cold that many words broke or disappeared, but I caught Simon's name in the beginning. The general's death song. It didn't go on for long, but when he dropped his hands, the congregation uttered a deep, collective sigh.

Ian walked away, not looking back, and without a word the mourners followed. It was finished.

76

BY THE WIND GRIEVED

THE WEATHER continued to be terrible, with fitful gusts of snow now added to the rain, and Hugh pressed us to stay, at least for another few days, until the sky should clear.

"It might well be Michaelmas before that happens," Jamie said to him, smiling. "Nay, cousin, we'll be off."

And so we were, bundled in all the clothes we possessed. It took more than two days to reach Lallybroch, and we were obliged to shelter overnight in an abandoned croft, putting the horses in the cow byre next to us. There was no furniture nor peat for the hearth, and half the roof had gone, but the stone walls broke the wind.

"I miss my dog," Ian grumbled, huddling under his cloak and pulling a blanket over his goose-pimpled head.

"Would he sit on your heid?" Jamie inquired, taking a firmer hold on me as the wind roared past our shelter and threatened to rip away the rest of the threadbare thatch overhead. "Ye should have thought about it being January, before ye shaved your scalp."

"Well enough for you," Ian replied, peering balefully out from under his blanket. "Ye've got Auntie Claire to keep warm with."

"Well, ye might get a wife yourself one of these days. Is Rollo going to sleep with the both of ye when ye do?" Jamie inquired.

"Mmphm," Ian said, and pulled the blanket down over his face, shivering.

I shivered, too, in spite of Jamie's warmth, our combined cloaks, three woolen petticoats, and two pairs of stockings. I had been in a number of cold places in my life, but there's something remarkably *penetrating* about the Scottish cold. In spite of my longing for a warm fire and the remembered coziness of Lallybroch, though, I was almost as uneasy about our approaching homecoming as Ian was—and Ian had been growing more like a cat on hot bricks, the farther we got into the Highlands. He twitched and muttered to himself now, thrashing in his blankets in the darkened confines of the shed.

I had wondered when we landed in Edinburgh whether we ought to send word of our arrival to Lallybroch. When I'd suggested this, though, Jamie laughed.

"D'ye think we stand the slightest chance of getting within ten miles o' the place without everyone hearing of it? Never fear, Sassenach," he'd assured me. "The minute we set foot in the Highlands, everyone from Loch Lomond to Inverness will know that Jamie Fraser's comin' home with his English witch, and a red Indian with him, to boot."

"English witch?" I said, not sure whether to be entertained or offended. "Did they call me that? When we were at Lallybroch?"

"Frequently to your face, Sassenach," he said dryly. "But ye didna have enough Gaelic then to know it. They didna mean it as an insult, *a nighean,*" he added more gently. "Nor will they now. It's only that Highlanders call a thing as they see it."

"Hmm," I said, a trifle taken back.

"They'll no be wrong, now, will they?" he'd asked, grinning.

"Are you implying that I *look* like a witch?"

"Well, not sae much just this minute," he said, narrowing one eye judiciously. "First thing in the morning, maybe—aye, that's a more fearsome prospect."

I hadn't a looking glass, not having thought to acquire one in Edinburgh. I did still have a comb, though, and snuggling now with my head beneath Jamie's chin, resolved to stop some way short of Lallybroch and employ it thoroughly, rain or no rain. Not, I thought, that it would likely make much difference whether I arrived looking like the Queen of England or like a dandelion gone to seed. It was Ian's homecoming that was important.

On the other hand . . . I wasn't sure quite what my own

welcome might be. There was unfinished business, to put it mildly, between myself and Jenny Murray.

We had been good friends once. I hoped we might be again. But she had been the chief engineer of Jamie's marriage to Laoghaire MacKenzie. From the best of motives, no doubt; she'd worried for him, lonely and rootless on his return from captivity in England. And in all justice, she'd thought me dead.

What had she thought, I wondered, when I'd suddenly appeared again? That I had abandoned Jamie before Culloden and then had second thoughts? There hadn't been time for explanations and rapprochement—and there *had* been that very awkward moment when Laoghaire, summoned by Jenny, had showed up at Lallybroch, accompanied by her daughters, taking Jamie and me very much by surprise.

A bubble of laughter rose in my chest at thought of that encounter, though I certainly hadn't laughed at the time. Well, perhaps there would be time to talk now, once Jenny and Ian had recovered from the shock of their youngest son's homecoming.

I became aware, from subtle shiftings behind me, that while the horses were breathing heavily and peacefully in their byre and Ian had finally subsided into phlegm-rattling snores, I wasn't the only one still lying awake thinking of what might await us.

"You aren't asleep, either, are you?" I whispered to Jamie.

"No," he said softly, and shifted his weight again, gathering me more closely against him. "Thinking about the last time I came home. I had such fear—and a verra wee bit of hope. I imagine it's maybe like that for the lad now."

"And for you now?" I asked, folding my own hands over the arm that encircled me, feeling the solid, graceful bones of wrist and forearm, gently touching his maimed right hand. He sighed deeply.

"Dinna ken," he said. "But it'll be all right. You're with me, this time."

THE WIND DROPPED sometime in the night, and the day, by some miracle, dawned clear and bright. Still cold as a polar bear's bottom, but not raining. I thought that a good omen.

Nobody spoke as we cleared the last high pass that led to Lallybroch and saw the house below. I felt a loosening in my chest and only then realized how long I'd been holding my breath.

"It hasn't changed, has it?" I said, my breath white on the cold air.

"There's a new roof on the dovecote," Ian said. "And Mam's sheep pen is bigger." He was doing his best to sound nonchalant, but there was no mistaking the eagerness in his voice. He nudged his horse and pulled a little in front of us, the turkey feathers in his hair lifting on the breeze.

It was early afternoon, and the place was quiet; the morning chores had been done, the evening milking and supper-making not yet started. I didn't see anyone outside save a couple of big, shaggy Highland cattle munching hay in the near pasture, but the chimneys were smoking and the big white-harled farmhouse had its usual hospitable, settled air.

Would Bree and Roger ever go back here? I wondered suddenly. She'd mentioned it, when the notion of their leaving became fact and they had begun to plan.

"It's vacant," she'd said, eyes fixed on the twentieth-century-style shirt she was making. "For sale. Or it was, when Roger went there a few years—ago?" She looked up with a wry smile; it wasn't really possible to discuss time in any customary way. "I'd like the kids to live there, maybe. But we'll just have to see how . . . things work out."

She'd glanced then at Mandy, asleep in her cradle, faintly blue around the lips.

"It will work out fine," I'd said firmly. "Everything will be just fine."

Lord, I prayed now silently, *that they might be safe!*

Ian had swung off his horse and was waiting impatiently for us. As we dismounted, he headed for the door, but our arrival had been noted, and it swung wide before he could touch it.

Jenny stopped dead in the doorway. She blinked, once, and her head tilted slowly back as her eyes traveled up the long, buckskin-covered body, with its roped muscles and small scars, to the crested, feathered head with its tattooed face, so carefully expressionless—save for the eyes, whose hope and fear he could not hide, Mohawk or no.

Jenny's mouth twitched. Once . . . twice . . . then her face broke and she began to utter small, hysterical whoops that turned into unmistakable laughter. She gulped, whooped again, and laughed so hard that she staggered backward into the house and had to sit down on the bench in the hall, where she bent double with her arms wrapped round her middle and laughed until the sound gave out and her breath came in faint, wheezing gasps.

"Ian," she said at last, shaking her head. "Oh, God, Ian. My wee lad."

Ian looked entirely taken aback. He looked at Jamie, who shrugged, his own mouth twitching, then back at his mother.

She gulped for air, her chest heaving, then stood up, went to him, and wrapped her arms about him, her tear-streaked face pressed to his side. His arms went slowly, carefully around her, and he held her to him like something fragile, of immense value.

"Ian," she said again, and I saw her small, taut shoulders suddenly slump. "Oh, Ian. Thank God ye've come in time."

SHE WAS SMALLER than I had remembered, and thinner, her hair with a little more gray in it though still darkly vibrant—but the deep-blue cat-eyes were just the same, as was the natural air of command she shared with her brother.

"Leave the horses," she said briskly, wiping her eyes on the corner of her apron. "I'll have one o' the lads take care of them. Ye'll be frozen and starving—take off your things and come into the parlor." She glanced at me, with a brief look of curiosity and something else that I couldn't interpret—but didn't meet my eyes directly or say more than "Come," as she led the way to the parlor.

The house smelled familiar but strange, steeped in peat smoke and the scent of cooking; someone had just baked bread, and the yeasty smell floated down the hall from the kitchen. The hall itself was nearly as cold as the outdoors; all the rooms had their doors closed tight to keep in the heat from their fires, and a welcome wave of warmth eddied out when she opened the door to the parlor, turning to pull Ian in first.

"Ian," she said, in a tone I'd never heard her use before. "Ian, they've come. Your son's come home."

Ian the elder was sitting in a large armchair close to the fire, a warm rug over his legs. He struggled to his feet at once, a little unsteady on the wooden peg he wore in replacement of a leg lost in battle, and took a few steps toward us.

"Ian," Jamie said, his voice soft with shock. "God, Ian."

"Oh, aye," Ian said, his own voice wry. "Dinna fash; it's still me."

Phthisis, they called it. Or doctors did. It meant "wasting," in the Greek. Laymen called it by the blunter name "consumption," and the reason why was all too apparent. It consumed its victims, ate them alive. A wasting disease, and waste it did. Ate flesh and squandered life, profligate and cannibal.

I'd seen it many times in England of the thirties and forties, much more here in the past. But I'd never seen it carve the living flesh from the bones of someone I loved, and my heart went to water and drained from my chest.

Ian had always been whipcord thin, even in times of plenty. Sinewy and tough, his bones always near the surface of his skin, just as Young Ian's were. Now . . .

"I may cough, but I won't break," he assured Jamie, and, stepping forward, put his arms round Jamie's neck. Jamie enfolded him very gently, the gingerness of the embrace growing firmer as he found that Ian didn't break—and closed his eyes to keep the tears in check. His arms tightened, trying involuntarily to keep Ian from the abyss that all too plainly yawned at his feet.

I can count all my bones. The Biblical quote came unbidden to my mind. I quite literally *could;* the cloth of his shirt lay over ribs that showed so clearly that I could see the articulations where each one joined the protruding knobs of his backbone.

"How long?" I blurted, turning to Jenny, who was watching the men, her own eyes bright with unshed tears. "How long has he had it?"

She blinked once and swallowed.

"Years," she said, steadily enough. "He came back from

the Tolbooth in Edinburgh with the cough, and it never left. It's got worse over the last year, though."

I nodded. A chronic case, then; that was something. The acute form—"galloping consumption," they called it—would have taken him in months.

She gave me back the question I had asked her, but with a different meaning.

"How long?" she said, so softly that I barely heard her.

"I don't know," I said, with equal softness. "But . . . not long."

She nodded; she had known this for a long time.

"Just as well ye came in time, then," she said, matter-of-fact.

Young Ian's eyes had been fixed on his father from the moment we entered the room. The shock showed plainly on his face, but he kept himself in hand.

"Da," he said, and his voice was so hoarse that the word emerged in a strangled croak. He cleared it viciously and repeated, "Da," coming forward. The elder Ian looked at his son, and his face lit with a joy so profound that it eclipsed the marks of illness and suffering.

"Oh, Ian," he said, holding out his arms. "My wee lad!"

IT WAS THE Highlands. And it was Ian and Jenny. Which meant that matters that might have been avoided out of confusion or delicacy were instead addressed forthrightly.

"I may die tomorrow, or not for a year," Ian said frankly, over jam bread and tea, hastily magicked out of the kitchen to sustain the weary travelers until supper should be ready. "I'm betting on three months, myself. Five to two, if anyone fancies a wager. Though I dinna ken how I'll collect my winnings." He grinned, the old Ian showing suddenly through his death's-head face.

There was a murmur of something not quite laughter among the adults. There were a great many people crammed into the parlor, for the announcement that had brought forth bread and jam had also caused every inhabitant of Lallybroch to come boiling out of its rooms and recesses, thundering down the stairs in their anxiety to greet and reclaim their prodigal. Young Ian had nearly been knocked flat and trampled by his family's affection, and this, coming on the heels of the shock of seeing his father, had stunned him into muteness, though he kept smiling, quite helpless in the face of a thousand questions and exclamations.

Jenny had rescued him at last from the maelstrom, taking him by the hand and pushing him firmly into the parlor with the elder Ian, then popping back out herself to quell the riot with a flashing eye and a firm word before ushering the rest of them in an orderly fashion.

Young Jamie—Ian and Jenny's eldest, and Jamie's namesake—now lived at Lallybroch with his wife and children, as did his sister, Maggie, and her two children, her husband being a soldier. Young Jamie was out on the estate, but the women came to sit with me. All of the children were clustered round Young Ian, staring and asking so many questions that they collided with one another, and pushed and shoved, arguing as to who asked what and who should be answered first.

The children had paid no attention to the elder Ian's remark. They already knew Grandda was dying, and the fact was of no interest by comparison with the fact of their fascinating new uncle. A tiny girl with her hair in stubby plaits sat in Young Ian's lap, tracing the lines of his tattoos with her fingers, now and then sticking one inadvertently in his mouth as he smiled and made hesitant answers to his inquisitive nieces and nephews.

"Ye could have written," Jamie said to Jenny, with an edge of reproach in his voice.

"I did," she said, with her own edge. "A year ago, when his flesh began to melt away and we kent it was more than a cough. I asked ye to send Young Ian then, if ye could."

"Ah," Jamie said, discomfited. "We must ha' left the Ridge before it came. But did I not write last April, to tell ye we were coming? I sent the letter from New Bern."

"If ye did, I never got it. Nay wonder, with the blockade; we see no more than half what we used to that's sent from America. And if ye left last March, it's been a long voyage, no?"

"A bit longer than I expected, aye," Jamie said dryly. "Things happened along the way."

"So I see." Without the least hesitation, she picked up his

right hand and examined the scar and the close-set fingers with interest. She glanced at me, one eyebrow quirked, and I nodded.

"It—he was wounded, at Saratoga," I said, feeling oddly defensive. "I had to."

"It's a good job," she said, gently flexing his fingers. "Does it pain ye much, Jamie?"

"It aches in the cold. Nay bother otherwise, though."

"Whisky!" she exclaimed, sitting bolt upright. "Here ye are, frozen to the bone, and I've not thought—Robbie! Run and fetch down the special bottle from the shelf above the coppers." A gangling boy who had been hovering on the edge of the crowd round Young Ian gave his grandmother a reluctant glance, but then, catching the depth charge of her eye, shot out of the room to do her bidding.

The room was more than warm; with a peat fire simmering on the hearth and so many people talking, laughing, and exuding body heat, it was on the verge of tropical. But there was a deep chill around my heart whenever I looked at Ian.

He lay back in his chair now, still smiling. But exhaustion was evident in the slump of his bony shoulders, the droop of his eyelids, the clear effort it took to keep smiling.

I looked away and found Jenny looking at me. She glanced away at once, but I had seen speculation in her eyes, and doubt. Yes, we'd have to talk.

THEY SLEPT WARM that first night, tired to the point of collapse, close together and enfolded by Lallybroch. But Jamie heard the wind on the edge of waking. It had come back in the night, a cold moan around the eaves of the house.

He sat up in bed in the dark, hands wrapped around his knees, listening. The storm would be coming; he could hear snow in the wind.

Claire lay beside him, half curled in sleep, her hair a dark smudge across the white pillow. He listened to her breathe, thanking God for the sound, feeling guilt at the soft, unhindered flow of it. He'd been hearing Ian's cough all evening and gone to sleep with the sound of that labored breathing in his mind, if not his ears.

He'd managed from sheer exhaustion to put aside the matter of Ian's illness, but it was there with the waking, heavy as a stone in his chest.

Claire shifted in her sleep, turning half onto her back, and desire for her welled up in him like water. He hesitated, aching for Ian, guilty for what Ian had already lost and he still had, reluctant to wake her.

"I feel maybe like you did," he whispered to her, too low to wake her. "When ye came through the stones. Like the world is still there—but it's no the world ye had."

He'd swear she hadn't wakened, but a hand came out from the sheets, groping, and he took it. She sighed, long and sleep-laden, and pulled him down beside her. Took him in her arms and cradled him, warm on her soft breasts.

"You're the world I have," she murmured, and then her breathing changed, and she took him down with her into safety.

77

MEMORARAE

THEY'D BEEN eating breakfast in the kitchen, just the two Ians, for his father had waked coughing before dawn and fallen back into such a deep sleep afterward that his mother hadn't wanted to waken him, and he himself had been hunting over the hills with his brother and nephews all night. They had stopped on the way back at Kitty's house, and Young Jamie had declared they would stay to eat and sleep a bit, but Ian had been restless, wanting to come home, though he couldn't have said why.

Perhaps for this, he thought, watching his father shake salt over his porridge in the same way he'd seen him do it for fifteen years, before he'd left Scotland. He'd never once thought of it, in all his time away, but now that he saw it again, it was as though he'd never left, as though he'd spent every morning of his life here at this table, watching his father eat porridge.

He was possessed of a sudden desire to memorize this moment, to know and to sense every last thing about it, from the worn-smooth wood under his elbows to the stained granite of the countertop and the way the light fell through the tattered curtains at the window, lighting the bulge of muscle at the corner of his father's jaw as he chewed a bit of sausage.

The elder Ian glanced up suddenly, as though feeling his son's eyes on him.

"Shall we go out on the moor?" he said. "I've a fancy to see if the red deer are calving yet."

He was surprised at his father's strength. They walked for several miles, talking of nothing—and everything. He knew it was so they could grow easy with each other again and say the things that had to be said—but he dreaded the saying.

They stopped at last far up on a high stretch of moorland, where they could see the roll of the great smooth mountains and a few wee lochs, glittering like fish under a pale high sun. They found a saint's spring, a tiny pool with an ancient stone cross, and drank from the water, saying the prayer of respect for the saint, and then sat down to rest a little way beyond.

"It was a place like this where I died the first time," his father said casually, running a wet hand over his sweating face. He looked rosy and healthy, though so thin. That bothered Young Ian, knowing he was dying yet seeing him like this.

"Aye?" he said. "When was that, then?"

"Oh, in France. When I lost my leg." The elder Ian glanced down at his wooden peg, indifferent. "One minute I was standing up to fire my musket, and the next I was lyin' on my back. I didna even ken I'd been hit. Ye'd think ye'd notice being hit by a six-pound iron ball, wouldn't ye?"

His father grinned at him, and he smiled grudgingly back.

"I would. Surely ye thought *something* must ha' happened, though."

"Oh, aye, I did. And after a moment or two, it came to me that I must ha' been shot. But I couldna feel any pain at all."

"Well, that was good," Young Ian said encouragingly.

"I kent then I was dying, aye?" His father's eyes were on him but looked beyond him, at that far-off battlefield. "I wasna really bothered, though. And I wasna alone." His gaze focused then on his son, and he smiled a little. Reaching out, he took hold of Ian's hand—his own wasted to the bone, the joints of it swollen and knobbled, but the span of his grasp still as big as his son's.

"Ian," he said, and paused, his eyes crinkling. "D'ye ken how odd it is, to say someone's name when it's yours, as well? Ian," he repeated, more gently, "dinna fash. I wasna afraid then. I'm not afraid now."

I am, Ian thought, but he couldn't say that.

"Tell me about the dog," his father said then, smiling. And so he told his father about Rollo. About the sea battle where he'd thought Rollo drowned or dead, how it had all come about that they'd gone to Ticonderoga and been at the terrible battles of Saratoga.

And told him, without thinking about it, for thinking would have frozen the words in his throat, about Emily. About Iseabail. And about the Swiftest of Lizards.

"I—havena told anyone else about that," he said, suddenly shy. "About the wee lad, I mean."

His father breathed deep, looking happy. Then coughed, whipped out a handkerchief, and coughed some more, but eventually stopped. Ian tried not to look at the handkerchief, in case it should be stained with blood.

"Ye should—" the elder Ian croaked, then cleared his throat and spat into the handkerchief with a muffled grunt. "Ye should tell your mother," he said, his voice clear again. "She'd be happy to ken ye've got a son, no matter the circumstances."

"Aye, well. Maybe I will."

It was early for bugs, but the moor birds were out, poking about, taking flight past their heads and calling out in alarm. He listened to the sounds of home for a bit and then said, "Da. I've got to tell ye something bad."

And sitting by a saint's pool, in the peace of the early spring day, Ian told him what had happened to Murdina Bug.

His father listened with a grave attention, head bowed. Young Ian could see the heavy streaks of gray in his hair and found the sight both moving and paradoxically comforting. *At least he's lived a good life,* he thought. *But maybe Mrs. Bug did, too. Would I feel worse about it if she'd been a young girl?* He thought he would, but he felt badly enough as it was. A little better for the telling, though.

The elder Ian rocked back on his haunches, arms clasped about his good knee, thinking.

"It wasna your fault, of course," he said, with a sidelong look at his son. "D'ye ken that, in your heart?"

"No," Ian admitted. "But I'm trying."

His father smiled at that, but then grew grave again.

"Ye'll manage. If ye've lived with it this long, ye'll be all right in the end. But this matter of old Arch Bug, now. He must be as old as the hills, if he's the same one I kent—a tacksman for Malcolm Grant, he was."

"That's the man. I keep thinking that—he's old, he'll die—but what if he dies and I dinna ken he's dead?" He made a gesture of frustration. "I dinna want to kill the man, but how can I not, and him wandering about, set to do harm to Ra—to my—well, if I should ever have a wife . . ." He was floundering, and his father put a stop to it, grasping his arm.

"Who is she?" he asked, interest bright in his face. "Tell me about her."

And so he told about Rachel. He was surprised that there was so much to tell, in fact, considering that he'd known her only a few weeks and kissed her just the once.

His father sighed—he sighed all the time, it was the only way he got enough breath, but this one was a sigh of happiness.

"Ah, Ian," he said fondly. "I'm happy for ye. I canna say how happy. It's what your mother and I have prayed for, these many years, that ye'd have a good woman to love and a family by her."

"Well, it's soon to be speaking of my family," Young Ian pointed out. "Considering she's a Quaker and likely won't wed me. And considering I'm in Scotland and she's wi' the Continental army in America, probably bein' shot at or infected wi' plague right this minute."

He'd meant it seriously and was somewhat offended when his father laughed. But then the elder Ian leaned forward and said with utter seriousness, "Ye needna wait for me to die. Ye need to go and find your young woman."

"I canna—"

"Aye, ye can. Young Jamie's got Lallybroch, the girls are

well wed, and Michael—" He grinned at the thought of Michael. "Michael will do well enough, I think. A man needs a wife, and a good one is the greatest gift God has for a man. I'd go much easier, *a bhailach,* if I kent ye were well fettled in that way."

"Aye, well," Young Ian murmured. "Maybe so. But I'll not go just yet."

78

OLD DEBTS

JAMIE SWALLOWED the last bite of porridge and took a deep breath, laying down his spoon.

"Jenny?"

"O' course there's more," she said, reaching for his bowl. Then she caught sight of his face and stopped, eyes narrowing. "Or is that not what ye had need of?"

"I wouldna say it's a need, precisely. But . . ." He glanced up at the ceiling to avoid her gaze and commended his soul to God. "What d'ye ken of Laoghaire MacKenzie?"

He risked a quick glance at his sister and saw that her eyes had gone round, bright with interest.

"Laoghaire, is it?" She sat back down and began to tap her fingers thoughtfully on the tabletop. Her hands were good for her age, he thought: work-worn, but the fingers still slim and lively.

"She's not wed," Jenny said. "But ye'll ken that, I imagine."

He nodded shortly.

"What is it ye want to know about her?"

"Well . . . how she fares, I suppose. And . . ."

"And who's sharing her bed?"

He gave his sister a look.

"Ye're a lewd woman, Janet Murray."

"Oh, aye? Well, awa' wi' ye, then, and ask the cat." Blue eyes just like his own glittered at him for an instant, and the dimple showed in her cheek. He knew that look and yielded with what grace was possible.

"D'ye know?"

"No," she said promptly.

He raised one brow in disbelief. "Oh, aye. Pull the other one."

She shook her head and ran a finger round the edge of the honey jar, wiping off a golden bead. "I swear on St. Fouthad's toenails."

He hadn't heard that one since he was ten and laughed out loud, despite the situation.

"Well, then, no more to be said, is there?" He leaned back in his chair, affecting indifference. She made a small huffing noise, got up, and began busily to clear the table. He watched her with narrowed eyes, not sure whether she was messing him about only for the sake of mischief—in which case, she'd yield in a moment—or whether there was something more to it.

"Why is it ye want to know?" she asked suddenly, eyes on the stack of sticky bowls. That brought him up short.

"I didna say I *did* want to know," he pointed out. "But since ye mentioned it—anyone would be curious, no?"

"They would," she agreed. She straightened up and looked at him, a long, searching sort of look that made him wonder whether he'd washed behind his ears.

"I *don't* know," she said at last. "And that's the truth. I only heard from her that once that I wrote ye."

Aye, and just why did ye write me about it? he wondered, but didn't say so out loud.

"Mmphm," he said. "And ye expect me to believe that ye left it there?"

HE REMEMBERED IT. Standing here in his old room at Lallybroch, the one he'd had as a boy, on the morning of his wedding to Laoghaire.

He'd had a new shirt for the occasion. There wasn't money

for much beyond the barest essentials, and sometimes not that—but Jenny had contrived him a shirt; he suspected she'd sacrificed the best of her two shifts for it. He remembered shaving in the reflection in his washbasin, seeing the gaunt, stern face of a stranger emerge beneath his razor, thinking that he must remember to smile when he met Laoghaire. He didn't want to frighten her, and what he saw in the water was enough to frighten *him.*

He thought suddenly of sharing her bed. He resolutely put aside the thought of Claire's body—he had a great deal of practice in that—which caused him instead to think suddenly that it had been years—aye, years! He'd lain with a woman only twice in the last fifteen years, and it was five, six, maybe seven years since the last time. . . .

He'd suffered a moment's panic at the thought that he might find himself unable and touched his member gingerly through his kilt, only to find that it had already begun to stiffen at the mere thought of bedding.

He drew a deep breath, somewhat relieved. One less thing to worry over, then.

A brief sound from the door jerked his head round to see Jenny standing there, wearing an unreadable expression. He coughed and took his hand off his cock.

"Ye haven't got to do it, Jamie," she said quietly, eyes fixed on his. "If ye've thought better of it, tell me."

He'd nearly done it. But he could hear the house. There was a sense of bustle in it, a purpose and a happiness it had lacked for a very long time. It wasn't only his own happiness at stake here—it never had been.

"No," he'd said abruptly. "I'm fine." And smiled reassuringly at her.

As he went downstairs to meet Ian at the foot, though, he heard the rain on the windows and felt a sudden sense of drowning—an unwelcome recollection of his first wedding day and how they'd held each other up, he and Claire, both bleeding, both terrified.

"All right, then?" Ian had said to him, leaning in, low-voiced.

"Aye, fine," he replied, and was pleased at how calm his voice was.

Jenny's face appeared briefly round the door to the parlor. She looked worried, but relaxed when she saw him.

"It's all right, *mo nighean,*" Ian had assured her, grinning. "I've got a grip on him, in case he takes it into his head to bolt." Ian was in fact gripping his arm, rather to Jamie's surprise, but he didn't protest.

"Well, drag him in, then," his sister had said, very dry. "The priest's come."

He'd gone in with Ian, taken up his place beside Laoghaire in front of old Father McCarthy. She glanced up at him briefly, then away. Was she frightened? Her hand was cool in his but didn't shake. He squeezed her fingers gently and she turned her head, looking up at him then, directly. No, not fright, and not candle glow or starshine. There was gratitude in her gaze—and trust.

That trust had entered his heart, a small, soft weight that steadied him, restored at least a few of the severed roots that had held him to his place. He'd been grateful, too.

He turned at the sound of footsteps now and saw Claire coming along the hall. He smiled—noting that he'd done so without the slightest thought—and she came to him, taking his hand as she peered into the room.

"Yours, wasn't it? When you were young, I mean."

"Aye, it was."

"I thought Jenny told me so—when we came here the first time, I mean." Her mouth twisted a little. She and Jenny did speak now, of course, but it was a stilted kind of speaking, both of them overcareful, shy of saying too much or the wrong thing. Aye, well, he was afraid of saying too much or the wrong thing himself, but damned if he'd be a woman about it.

"I need to go and see Laoghaire," he said abruptly. "Will ye kill me if I do?"

She looked surprised. And then, damn her, amused.

"Are you asking my permission?"

"I am not," he said, feeling stiff and awkward. "I only—well, I thought I should tell ye, is all."

"Very considerate of you." She was still smiling, but the smile had taken on a certain wariness. "Would you . . . care to tell me *why* you want to go and see her?"

"I didna say I *want* to see her," he said, a noticeable edge in his voice. "I said I need to."

"Would it be presumptuous of me to ask why you need to see her?" Her eyes were just that bit wider and yellower than usual; he'd roused the hawk in her. He hadn't meant to, at all, but he wavered for an instant, suddenly wanting to seek refuge from his own confusion in an almighty row. But he couldn't in conscience do that. Still less could he explain the memory of Laoghaire's face on their wedding day, the look of trust in her eyes, and the nagging feeling that he had betrayed that trust.

"Ye can ask me anything, Sassenach—and ye have," he added pointedly. "I'd answer if I thought I could make sense."

She made a small sniffing noise, not quite "Hmph!" but he took her meaning clear enough.

"If you only want to know who she's sleeping with, there are probably less direct ways of finding out," she said. Her voice was carefully level, but her pupils had dilated.

"I dinna care who she's sleeping with!"

"Oh, yes, you do," she said promptly.

"I don't!"

"Liar, liar, pants on fire," she said, and on the verge of an explosion, he burst out laughing instead. She looked momentarily taken back but then joined him, snorting with it and her nose going pink.

They stopped in seconds, abashed at being hilarious in a house that hadn't known open laughter for too long—but were still smiling at each other.

"Come here," he said softly, and held out a hand to her. She took it at once, her fingers warm and strong on his, and came to put her arms around him.

Her hair smelled different. Still fresh, and full of the scent of live green things, but different. Like the Highlands. Like heather, maybe.

"You do want to know who it is, you know," she said, her voice warm and tickling through the fabric of his shirt. "Do you want me to tell you why?"

"Aye, I do, and no, I don't," he said, tightening his hold. "I ken well enough why, and I'm sure you and Jenny and every other woman in fifty miles think they do, too. But that's not why I need to see her."

She pushed a little way back then and brushed the falling curls out of her eyes to look up at him. She searched his face thoughtfully and nodded.

"Well, do give her my very best regards, then, won't you?"

"Why, ye vengeful wee creature. I'd never ha' thought it of ye!"

"Wouldn't you, indeed?" she said, dry as toast. He smiled down at her and ran a thumb gently down the side of her cheek.

"No," he said. "I wouldn't. Ye're no one to hold a grudge, Sassenach; ye never have been."

"Well, I'm not a Scot," she observed, smoothing back her hair. "It's not a matter of national pride, I mean." She put a hand on his chest before he could answer, and said, quite seriously, "She never made you laugh, did she?"

"I may have smiled once or twice," he said gravely. "But no."

"Well, just you remember that," she said, and with a swish of skirts, was off. He grinned like a fool and followed her.

When he reached the stairs, she was waiting, halfway down.

"One thing," she said, lifting a finger at him.

"Aye?"

"If you find out who she's sleeping with and don't tell me, I *will* kill you."

BALRIGGAN WAS A small place, little more than ten acres, plus the house and outbuildings. Still, it was bonnie, a large gray stone cottage tucked into the curve of a hill, a bittie wee loch glimmering like a looking glass at its foot. The English had burned the fields and the barn during the Rising, but fields came back. Much more easily than the men who tilled them.

He rode slowly past the loch, thinking that this visit was a mistake. It was possible to leave things behind—places, people, memories—at least for a time. But places held tight to the things that had happened in them, and to come again to a place you had once lived was to be brought face-to-face with what you had done there and who you had been.

Balriggan, though . . . it hadn't been a bad place; he had loved the wee loch and the way it mirrored the sky, so still some mornings that you felt you might walk down into the clouds you saw reflected there, feeling their cold mist rise up about you, to wrap you in their drifting peace. Or in the summer evenings, when the surface glimmered in hundreds of overlapping rings as the hatch rose, the rhythm of it broken now and then by the sudden splash of a leaping salmon.

The road took him closer, and he saw the stony shallows where he'd shown wee Joan and Marsali how to guddle fish, all three of them so intent on their business they'd paid no heed to the midgies biting, and gone home wet to the waist and red with bites and sunburn, the wee maids skipping and swinging from his hands, gleeful in the sunset. He smiled just a little—then turned his horse's head away, up the hill to the house.

The place was shabby but in decent repair, he grudgingly noted. There was a saddle mule browsing in the paddock behind the house, elderly but sound-looking. Well enough. Laoghaire wasn't spending his money on follies or a coach-and-four, at least.

He set his hand on the gate and felt a twist go through his wame. The feel of the wood under his hand was eerily familiar; he'd lifted it without thinking, at the spot where it was always inclined to drag on the path. That twist corkscrewed its way up to his mouth as he recalled his last meeting with Ned Gowan, Laoghaire's lawyer. "*What does the bloody woman want, then?*" he'd demanded, exasperated. To which Ned had replied cheerfully, "*Your head, mounted above her gate.*"

With a brief snort, he went through, closing the gate a bit harder than necessary, and glanced up at the house.

Movement took his eye. A man was sitting on the bench outside the cottage, staring at him over a bit of broken harness on his knee.

An ill-favored wee lad, Jamie thought, scrawny and narrow-faced as a ferret, with a walleye and a mouth that hung open as though in astonishment. Still, Jamie greeted the man pleasantly, asking was his mistress to home the day?

The lad—seen closer to, he must be in his thirties—blinked at him, then turned his head to bring his good eye to bear.

"Who're you, then?" he asked, sounding unfriendly.

"Fraser of Broch Tuarach," Jamie replied. It was a formal occasion, after all. "Is Mrs.—" He hesitated, not knowing how to refer to Laoghaire. His sister had said she persisted in calling herself "Mrs. Fraser," despite the scandal. He hadn't felt he could object—the fault of it being his and he being in America in any case—but damned if he'd call her that himself, even to her servant.

"Fetch your mistress, if ye please," he said shortly.

"What d'ye want wi' her?" The straight eye narrowed in suspicion.

He hadn't expected obstruction and was inclined to reply sharply, but reined himself in. The man clearly kent something of him, and it was as well if Laoghaire's servant was concerned for her welfare, even if the man's manner was crude.

"I wish to speak with her, if ye've no great objection," he said, with extreme politeness. "D'ye think ye might make shift to go and tell her so?"

The man made a rude sound in his throat but put aside the harness and stood up. Too late, Jamie saw that his spine was badly twisted and one leg shorter than the other. There was no way to apologize that would not make matters worse, though, and so he only nodded shortly and let the man lurch his way off into the house, thinking that it was just like Laoghaire to keep a lame servant for the express purpose of embarrassing him.

Then he shook himself in irritation, ashamed of his thought. What was it about him that a hapless woman such as Laoghaire MacKenzie should bring out every wicked, shameful trait he possessed? Not that his sister couldn't do it, too, he reflected ruefully. But Jenny would evoke some bit of bad temper or hasty language from him, fan the flames 'til he was roaring, and then extinguish him neatly with a word, as though she'd doused him with cold water.

"*Go see her,*" Jenny had said.

"All right, then," he said belligerently. "I'm here."

"I see that," said a light, dry voice. "Why?"

He swung round to face Laoghaire, who was standing in the doorway, broom in hand, giving him a cool look.

He snatched off his hat and bowed to her.

"Good day to ye. I hope I see ye well the day." Apparently so; her face was slightly flushed beneath a starched white kerch, blue eyes clear.

She looked him over, expressionless save for fair brows arched high.

"I heard ye were come home. Why are ye here?"

"To see how ye fare."

Her brows rose that wee bit higher.

"Well enough. What d'ye want?"

He'd gone through it in his mind a hundred times but should have known that for the waste of effort it was. There were things that could be planned for, but none of them involved women.

"I've come to say sorry to ye," he said bluntly. "I said it before, and ye shot me. D'ye want to listen this time?"

The brows came down. She glanced from him to the broom in her hand, as though estimating its usefulness as a weapon, then looked back at him and shrugged.

"Suit yourself. Will ye come in, then?" She jerked her head toward the house.

"It's a fine day. Shall we walk in the garden?" He had no wish to enter the house, with its memories of tears and silences.

She regarded him for a moment or two, then nodded and turned toward the garden path, leaving him to follow if he would. He noticed that she kept a grip on the broom, though, and was not sure whether to be amused or offended.

They walked in silence through the kailyard and through a gate into the garden. It was a kitchen garden, made for utility, but it had a small orchard at the end of it, and there were flowers growing between the pea vines and onion beds. She'd always liked flowers; he remembered that with a small twist of the heart.

She'd put the broom over her shoulder, like a soldier carrying a rifle, and strolled beside him—in no hurry but not offering him an opening, either. He cleared his throat.

"I said I'd come to apologize."

"So ye did." She didn't turn to look at him but stopped and poked her toe at a curling potato vine.

"When we . . . wed," he said, trying to retrieve the careful speech he'd thought of. "I should not have asked ye. My heart was cold. I'd no right to offer ye a dead thing."

Her nostrils flared briefly, but she didn't look up. Just went on frowning at the potato vine, as though she suspected it might have bugs.

"I knew that," she said at last. "I did hope—" She broke off, lips pressing tight as she swallowed. "I did hope I might be of help to ye, though. Everyone could see ye needed a woman. Just not *me,* I suppose," she added bitterly.

Stung, he said the first thing that came to his tongue.

"I thought ye needed *me.*"

She looked up then, her eyes gone bright. Christ, she was going to weep, he knew it. But she didn't.

"I'd weans to feed." Her voice was hard and flat and hit him like a slap on the cheek.

"So ye did," he said, keeping his temper. It was honest, at least. "They've grown now, though." *And* he'd found dowries for both Marsali and Joan, too, but he didn't suppose he'd be given any credit for that.

"So that's it," she said, her voice growing colder. "Ye think ye can talk your way out of paying me now, is that it?"

"No, that is *not* it, for God's sake!"

"Because," she said, ignoring his denial and swinging round to face him, bright-eyed, "ye can't. Ye shamed me before the whole parish, Jamie Fraser, luring me into a sinful match wi' you and then betraying me, laughin' at me behind your hand wi' your Sassenach whore!"

"I didna—"

"And now ye come back from America, fardeled up like an English popinjay"—her lip curled in scorn at his good ruffled shirt, which he'd worn to show her respect, God damn it!—"flauntin' your wealth and playin' the great yin wi' your ancient hussy foamin' in her silks and satins on your arm, is it? Well, I'll tell ye—" She swung the broom down from her shoulder and drove the handle of it violently into the ground. "Ye dinna understand one thing about me, and ye think ye can awe me into crawlin' away like a dyin' dog and troubling ye no more! Think again, that's all I'll say to ye—just think again!"

He snatched the purse out of his pocket and flung it at the door of the garden shed, where it struck with a boom and bounced off. He had just a moment to regret having brought a chunk of gold, and not coins that would jingle, before his temper flared.

"Aye, ye're right about *that,* at least! I dinna understand one thing about ye! I never have, try as I might!"

"Oh, try as ye might, is it?" she cried, ignoring the purse. "Ye never tried for an instant, Jamie Fraser! In fact—" Her face clenched up like a fist as she fought to keep her voice under control. "Ye never truly *looked* at me. Never—well, no, I suppose ye looked once. When I was sixteen." Her voice trembled on the word, and she looked away, jaw clamped tight. Then she looked back at him, eyes bright and tearless.

"Ye took a beating for me. At Leoch. D'ye recall that?"

For an instant, he didn't. Then he stopped, breathing heavily. His hand went instinctively to his jaw, and against his will he felt the ghost of a smile rise against the anger.

"Oh. Aye. Aye, I do." Angus Mhor had given him an easier time than he might have—but it was a fair beating, nonetheless. His ribs had ached for days.

She nodded, watching him. Her cheeks were splotched with red, but she'd calmed herself.

"I thought ye'd done it because ye loved me. I went on thinking that, ken, until well after we'd wed. But I was wrong, wasn't I?"

Bafflement must have showed on his face, for she made that small "Mph!" in her nose that meant she was aggravated. He knew her well enough to know *that,* at least.

"Ye pitied me," she said flatly. "I didna see that then. Ye pitied me at Leoch, not only later, when ye took me to wife. I thought ye loved me," she repeated, spacing the words as though speaking to a simpleton. "When Dougal made ye wed the Sassenach whore, I thought I'd die. But I thought maybe *you* felt like dyin', too—and it wasna like that at all, was it?"

"Ah . . . no," he said, feeling awkward and foolish. He'd seen nothing of her feelings then. Hadn't seen a thing but Claire. But of course Laoghaire had thought he loved her; she was sixteen. And would have known that his marriage to Claire was a forced one, never realizing that he was willing. Of course she'd thought she and he were star-crossed lovers. Except that he'd never looked at her again. He rubbed a hand over his face, feeling complete helplessness.

"Ye never told me that," he said finally, letting his hand drop.

"What good would it ha' done?" she said.

So there it was. She'd known—she must have known—by the time he married her what the truth of it was. But still, she must have hoped . . . Unable to find anything to say in reply, his mind took refuge in the irrelevant.

"Who was it?" he asked.

"Who?" Her brow furrowed in puzzlement.

"The lad. Your father wanted ye punished for wantonness, no? Who did ye play the loon with, then, when I took the beating for ye? I never thought to ask."

The red splotches on her cheeks grew deeper.

"No, ye never would, would ye?"

A barbed silence of accusation fell between them. He hadn't asked, then; he hadn't cared.

"I'm sorry," he said softly, at last. "Tell me, though. Who was it?" He hadn't cared then in the least but found himself curious now, if only as a way of not thinking of other things—or not saying them. They hadn't had the past she'd thought, but the past lay still between them, forming a tenuous connection.

Her lips thinned and he thought she wouldn't say, but then they parted, reluctant.

"John Robert MacLeod."

He frowned, at a loss for a moment, and then the name dropped into its proper place in memory and he stared at her.

"John Robert? What, him from Killiecrankie?"

"Aye," she said. "Him." Her mouth snapped shut on the word.

He hadn't known the man well at all, but John Robert MacLeod's reputation among young women had been the subject of a good deal of talk among the men-at-arms at Leoch in his brief time there. A sly, good-looking slink of a man, handsome and lean-jawed—and the fact that he'd a wife and weans at home in Killiecrankie seemed to hamper him not at all.

"Jesus!" he said, unable to stop himself. "Ye're lucky ye kept your maidenheid!"

An ugly flush washed darkly over her from stays to cap, and his jaw dropped.

"Laoghaire MacKenzie! Ye werena such a wanton fool to let him take ye virgin to his bed!?"

"I didna ken he was marrit!" she cried, stamping her foot. "And it was after ye wed the Sassenach. I went to him for comfort."

"Oh, and he gave it ye, I'm sure!"

"Hush your gob!" she shrieked, and, picking up a stone watering pot from the bench by the shed, hurled it at his head. He hadn't expected that—Claire threw things at him frequently, but Laoghaire never had—and was nearly brained; it struck him in the shoulder as he ducked aside.

The watering pot was followed by a hail of other objects from the bench and a storm of incoherent language, all manner of unwomanly swearing, punctuated by shrieks like a teakettle. A pan of buttermilk hurtled toward him, missed its aim, but soaked him from chest to knees with curds and whey.

He was half laughing—from shock—when she suddenly seized a mattock from the shed wall and made for him. Seriously alarmed, he ducked and grabbed her wrist, twisting so she dropped the heavy tool with a thump. She let out a screech like a *ban-sidhe* and whipped her other hand across his face, half-blinding him with her nails. He snatched that wrist, too, and pressed her back into the wall of the shed, her still kicking at his shins, struggling and writhing against him like a snake.

"I'm sorry!" He was shouting in her ear to be heard above the noise she was making. "Sorry! D'ye hear me—I'm *sorry*!" The clishmaclaver stopped him hearing anything behind, though, and he had not the slightest warning when something monstrous struck him behind the ear and sent him staggering, lights flashing in his head.

He kept his grip on her wrists as he stumbled and fell, dragging her down atop him. He wrapped his arms tight round her, to keep her from clawing him again, and blinked, trying to clear his watering eyes.

"Free her, *MacIfrinn*!" The mattock chunked into the earth beside his head.

He flung himself over, Laoghaire still clutched to him, rolling madly through the beds. The sound of panting and uneven steps, and the mattock came down again, pinning his sleeve to the ground and scraping the flesh of his arm.

He jerked free, heedless of tearing skin and cloth, rolled away from Laoghaire, and sprang to his feet, then launched himself without pause at the weazened figure of Laoghaire's servant, who was in the act of raising the mattock above his head, narrow face contorted with effort.

He butted the man in the face with a crunch and bore him flat, punching him in the belly before they hit the ground. He scrambled atop the man and went on punching him, the violence some relief. The man was grunting, whimpering, and gurgling, and he'd drawn back his knee to give the bugger one in the balls to settle the matter when he became dimly aware of Laoghaire, screeching and beating at his head.

"Leave him alone!" she was shrieking, crying and slapping at him with her hands. "Leave him, leave him, for the love of Bride, don't hurt him!"

He stopped then, panting, feeling suddenly a terrible fool. Beating a scrawny cripple who meant only to protect his mistress from obvious attack, manhandling a woman like a street ruffian—*Christ,* what was the matter with him? He slid off the man, repressing an impulse to apologize, and got awkwardly to his feet, meaning to give the poor bugger a hand up, at least.

Before he could manage, though, Laoghaire fell to her knees beside the man, weeping and grappling at him, finally getting him partway sitting, his narrow head pressed to her soft round bosom, she heedless of the blood gushing from his smashed nose, petting and stroking him, murmuring his name. Joey, it seemed to be.

Jamie stood swaying a bit, staring at this demonstration. Blood was dripping from his fingers, and his arm was beginning to burn where the mattock had skinned it. He felt something stinging run into his eyes and, wiping it away, found that his forehead was bleeding; Joey the openmouthed had evidently inadvertently bitten him when he'd butted the man. He grimaced with disgust, feeling the tooth marks in his forehead, and groped for a handkerchief with which to stanch the blood.

Meanwhile, foggy as his head felt, matters on the ground in front of him were becoming clearer by the moment. A good mistress might try to comfort a wounded servant, but he'd yet to hear a woman call a servant *mo chridhe.* Let alone kiss him passionately on the mouth, getting her own face smeared with blood and snot in the process.

"Mmphm," he said.

Startled, Laoghaire turned a blood-smeared, tearstained face to him. She'd never looked lovelier.

"*Him?*" Jamie said incredulously, nodding toward the crumpled Joey. "Why, for God's sake?"

Laoghaire glared at him slit-eyed, crouched like a cat about to spring. She considered him for a moment, then slowly straightened her back, gathering Joey's head once more against her breast.

"Because he needs me," she said evenly. "And you, ye bastard, never did."

HE LEFT THE HORSE to graze along the edge of the loch and, stripping off his clothes, walked into the water. The sky was overcast, and the loch was full of clouds.

The rocky bottom fell away and he let the gray cold water take him, his legs trailing loose behind, his small injuries chilling into numbness. He put his face under the water, eyes closed, to wash the cut on his head, and felt the bubbles of his breath soft and tickling over his shoulders.

He raised his head and began to swim, slowly, with no thought at all.

He lay on his back among the clouds, hair afloat like kelp, and stared up into the sky. A spatter of rain dimpled the water around him, then thickened. It was a soft rain, though; no feel of the drops striking him, only a sense of the loch and its clouds bathing his face, his body, washing away the blood and fret of the last little while.

Would he ever come back? he wondered.

The water filled his ears with its own rush, and he was comforted by the realization that, in fact, he had never left.

He turned at last and struck out for the shore, cutting smooth through the water. It was still raining, harder now, the drops a constant tapping on his bare shoulders as he swam. Still, the sinking sun shone under the clouds and lit Balriggan and its hill with a gentle glow.

He felt the bottom rise and put his feet down, then stood for a moment, waist-deep, looking at it for a bit.

"No," he said softly, and felt remorse soften into regret and, at last, the absolution of resignation. "Ye're right—I never did. I'm sorry."

He walked out of the water then, and with a whistle to the horse, pulled the wet plaid over his shoulders and turned his face toward Lallybroch.

79

THE CAVE

USEFUL HERBS, I wrote, and paused—as usual—to consider. Writing with a quill caused one to be both more deliberate and more economical in writing than doing it with ballpoint or typewriter. Still, I thought, I'd best just make a list here and jot down notes regarding each herb as they came to me, then make a clean draft when I'd got it all straight and made sure to include everything, rather than try to do it all in a single run.

Lavender, peppermint, comfrey, I wrote without hesitation. *Calendula, feverfew, foxglove, meadow-sweet.* Then went back to add a large asterisk beside *foxglove* to remind me to add strong cautions about the use, as all parts of the plant were extremely poisonous in any but very small doses. I twiddled the quill, biting my lip in indecision. Ought it to mention that one at all, given that this was meant to be a useful medical guide for the common man, not for medical practitioners with experience in various medicaments? Because, really, you ought not dose *anyone* with foxglove unless you'd been trained . . . Best not. I crossed it out but then had second thoughts. Perhaps I'd better mention it, with a drawing, but also with a severe warning that it should be used *only* by a physician, in case someone had the bright idea of remedying Uncle Tophiger's dropsy permanently. . . .

A shadow fell across the floor in front of me and I looked up. Jamie was standing there with a most peculiar look on his face.

"What?" I said, startled. "Has something happened?"

"No," he said, and advancing into the study, leaned down and put his hands on the desk, bringing his face within a foot of mine.

"Have ye ever been in the slightest doubt that I need ye?" he demanded.

It took roughly half a second of thought to answer this.

"No," I replied promptly. "To the best of my knowledge, you needed me urgently the moment I saw you. And I haven't had reason to think you've got any more self-sufficient since. What on *earth* happened to your forehead? Those look like tooth—" He lunged across the desk and kissed me before I could finish the observation.

"Thank ye," he said fervently, and, un-lunging, whirled and went out, evidently in the highest of spirits.

"What's amiss wi' Uncle Jamie?" Ian demanded, coming in on Jamie's heels. He glanced back toward the open door into the hall, from the depths of which a loud, tuneless humming was coming, like that of a trapped bumblebee. "Is he drunk?"

"I don't think so," I said dubiously, running my tongue across my lips. "He didn't taste of anything alcoholic."

"Aye, well." Ian lifted a shoulder, dismissing his uncle's eccentricities. "I was just up beyond Broch Mordha, and Mr. MacAllister said to me that his wife's mother was taken bad in the night, and would ye maybe think of coming by, if it wasn't a trouble to ye?"

"No trouble at all," I assured him, rising with alacrity. "Just let me get my bag."

FOR ALL IT was spring, a cold, treacherous season, the tenants and neighbors seemed remarkably healthy. With some caution, I had resumed my doctoring, tentatively offering advice and medicine where it might be accepted. After all, I was no longer the lady of Lallybroch, and many of the folk who'd known me before were now dead. Those who weren't seemed generally glad to see me, but there was a wariness in their eyes that hadn't been there before. It saddened me to see it, but I understood it, all too well.

I had left Lallybroch, left Himself. Left *them.* And while they affected to believe the story Jamie put about, about my having thought him dead and fled to France, they couldn't help but feel I had betrayed them by going. *I* felt I had betrayed them.

The easiness that had once existed between us was gone, and so I didn't routinely visit as I once had; I waited to be called. And in the meantime, when I *had* to get out of the house, I went foraging on my own or walked with Jamie—who also had to get out of the house now and then.

One day, when the weather was windy but fine, he took me farther than usual, saying that he would show me his cave, if I liked.

"I would, very much," I said. I put my hand above my eyes to shield them from the sun as I looked up a steep hill. "Is it up there?"

"Aye. Can ye see it?"

I shook my head. Aside from the big white rock the people called Leap o' the Cask, it could have been any Highland hillside, clustered with gorse, broom, and heather, what ground showed in between only rocks.

"Come on, then," Jamie said, and setting foot on an invisible foothold, smiled and reached a hand to help me up.

It was a hard climb, and I was panting and damp with perspiration by the time he pushed aside a screen of gorse to show me the narrow mouth of the cave.

"I WANT TO go in."

"No, ye don't," he assured her. "It's cold and it's dirty."

She gave him an odd look and half a smile.

"I'd never have guessed," she said, very dry. "I still want to go in."

There was no point in arguing with her. He shrugged and took off his coat to save its getting filthy, hanging it on a rowan sapling that had sprouted near the entrance. He put up his hands to the stones on either side of the entrance, but then was unsure; was it there he had always grasped the stone, or not? *Christ, does it matter?* he chided himself, and, taking firm hold of the rock, stepped in and swung down.

It was just as cold as he'd known it would be. It was out of the wind, at least—not a biting cold, but a dank chill that sank through the skin and gnawed at the bone ends.

He turned and reached up his hands, and she leaned to him, tried to climb down, but lost her footing and half-fell, landing in his arms in a fluster of clothes and loose hair. He laughed and turned her round to look, but kept his arms around her. He was loath to surrender the warmth of her and held her like a shield against cold memory.

She was still, leaning back against him, only her head moving as she looked from one end of the cave to the other. It was barely eight feet long, but the far end was lost in shadow. She lifted her chin, seeing the soft black stains that coated the rock to one side by the entrance.

"That's where my fire was—when I dared have one." His voice sounded strange, small and muffled, and he cleared his throat.

"Where was your bed?"

"Just there by your left foot."

"Did you sleep with your head at this end?" She tapped her foot on the graveled dirt of the floor.

"Aye. I could see the stars, if the night was clear. I turned the other way if it rained." She heard the smile in his voice and put her hand along his thigh, squeezing.

"I hoped that," she said, her own voice a little choked. "When we learned about the Dunbonnet, and the cave . . . I thought about you, alone here—and I hoped you could see the stars at night."

"I could," he whispered, and bent his head to put his lips to her hair. The shawl she'd pulled over her head had slipped off, and her hair smelled of lemon balm and what she said was catmint.

She made a small *hmp* noise in her throat and folded her own arms over his, warming him through his shirt.

"I feel as though I've seen it before," she said, sounding a little surprised. "Though I suppose one cave probably looks a good deal like any other cave, unless you have stalactites hanging from the ceiling or mammoths painted on the walls."

"I've never had a talent for decoration," he said, and she *hmp*'ed again, amused. "As for being here . . . ye've been here many nights wi' me, Sassenach. You and the wee lass, both." *Though I didna ken then she was a lassie,* he added silently, remembering with a small odd pang that now and then he had sat there on the flat rock by the entrance, imagining sometimes a daughter warm in his arms, but now and then feeling a tiny son on his knee and pointing out the stars to travel by, explaining to him how the hunting was done and the prayer ye must say when ye killed for food.

But he'd told those things to Brianna later—and to Jem. The knowledge wouldn't be lost. Would it be of use, though? he wondered suddenly.

"Do folk still hunt?" he asked. "Then?"

"Oh, yes," she assured him. "Every fall, we'd have a rash of hunters coming in to the hospital—mostly idiots who'd got drunk and shot each other by mistake, though once I had a gentleman who'd been badly trampled by a deer he thought was dead."

He laughed, both shocked and comforted. The notion of hunting while drunken . . . though he'd seen fools do it. But at least men still did hunt. Jem would hunt.

"I'm sure Roger Mac wouldna let Jem take too much drink before hunting," he said. "Even if the other lads do."

Her head tilted a little to and fro, in the way it did when she was wondering whether to tell him something, and he tightened his arms a little.

"What?"

"I was just imagining a gang of second-graders having a tot of whisky all round before setting off home from school in the rain," she said, snorting briefly. "Children don't drink alcohol then—at all. Or at least they aren't meant to, and it's scandalous child neglect if they're allowed."

"Aye?" That seemed odd; he'd been given ale or beer with his food since . . . well, as far back as he recalled. And certainly a dram of whisky against the cold, or if his liver were chilled or he had the earache or . . . It was true, though, that Brianna made Jem drink milk, even after he was out of smocks.

The rattle of stones on the hillside below startled him, and he let go of Claire, turning toward the entrance. He doubted it was trouble but nonetheless motioned to her to stay, hoisting himself out of the cave mouth and reaching for his coat and the knife in its pocket even before he looked to see who had come.

There was a woman some way below, a tall figure in cloak and shawl, down by the big rock where Fergus had lost his hand. She was looking up, though, and saw him come out of the cave. She waved to him and beckoned, and with a quick glance round that assured him she was alone, he made his way half-sliding down the slope to the trail where she stood.

"Feasgar math," he greeted her, shrugging into the coat. She was fairly young, perhaps in her early twenties, but he didn't know her. Or thought he didn't, until she spoke.

"*Ciamar a tha thu, mo athair,*" she said formally. *How do you do, Father*?

He blinked, startled, but then leaned forward, peering at her.

"Joanie?" he said, incredulous. "Wee Joanie?" Her long, rather solemn face broke into a smile at that, but it was brief.

"Ye know me, then?"

"Aye, I do, now I come to see—" He put out a hand, wanting to embrace her, but she stood a bit away from him, stiff, and he let the hand drop, clearing his throat to cover the moment. "It's been some time, lass. Ye've grown," he added lamely.

"Bairns mostly do," she said, dry. "Is it your wife ye've got with you? The first one, I mean."

"It is," he replied, the shock of her appearance replaced by wariness. He gave her a quick look-over, in case she might be armed, but couldn't tell; her cloak was wrapped round her against the wind.

"Perhaps ye'd summon her down," Joan suggested. "I should like to meet her."

He rather doubted that. Still, she seemed composed, and he could scarcely refuse to let her meet Claire, if she wished it. Claire would be watching; he turned and gestured toward the cave, beckoning her, then turned back to Joan.

"How d'ye come to be here, lass?" he asked, turning back

to her. It was a good eight miles to Balriggan from here, and there was nothing near the cave to draw anyone.

"I was coming to Lallybroch to see ye—I missed your visit when ye came to the house," she added, with a brief flash of what might have been amusement. "But I saw you and . . . your wife . . . walking, so I came after ye."

It warmed him, to think she'd wanted to see him. At the same time, he was cautious. It had been twelve years, and she'd been a child when he left. And she'd spent those years with Laoghaire, doubtless hearing no good opinions of him in that time.

He looked searchingly into her face, seeing only the vaguest memory of the childish features he recalled. She was not beautiful, or even pretty, but had a certain dignity about her that was attractive; she met his gaze straight on, not seeming to care what he thought of what he saw. She had the shape of Laoghaire's eyes and nose, though little else from her mother, being tall, dark, and rawboned, heavy-browed, with a long, thin face and a mouth that was not much used to smiling, he thought.

He heard Claire making her way down the slope behind him and turned to help her, though keeping one eye on Joanie, just in case.

"Dinna fash," Joan said calmly behind him. "I dinna mean to shoot her."

"Och? Well, that's good." Discomposed, he tried to remember—had she been in the house when Laoghaire shot him? He thought not, though he'd been in no condition to notice. She'd certainly known about it, though.

Claire took his hand and hopped down onto the trail, not pausing to settle herself but coming forward at once and taking Joan's hands in both her own, smiling.

"I'm happy to meet you," she said, sounding as though she meant it. "Marsali said I was to give you this." And, leaning forward, she kissed Joan on the cheek.

For the first time, he saw the girl taken aback. She flushed and pulled her hands away, turning aside and rubbing a fold of her cloak under her nose as though taken by an itch, lest anyone see her eyes well up.

"I—thank you," she said, with a hasty dab at her eyes. "You—my sister's written of you." She cleared her throat and blinked hard, then stared at Claire with open interest—an interest that was being returned in full.

"Félicité looks like you," Claire said. "So does Henri-Christian, just a bit—but Félicité very much."

"Poor child," Joan murmured, but couldn't repress the smile that had lit her face at this.

Jamie coughed.

"Will ye not come down to the house, Joanie? Ye'd be welcome."

She shook her head.

"Later, maybe. I wanted to speak to ye, *a athair,* where no one could hear. Save your wife," she added, with a glance at Claire. "As she's doubtless something to say on the matter."

That sounded mildly sinister, but then she added, "It's about my dowry."

"Oh, aye? Well, come away out o' the wind, at least." He led them toward the lee of the big rock, wondering what was afoot. Was the lass wanting to wed someone unsuitable and her mother was refusing to give her her dowry? Had something happened to the money? He doubted that; old Ned Gowan had devised the documents, and the money was safe in a bank in Inverness. And whatever he thought of Laoghaire, he was sure she'd never do anything to the hurt of her daughters.

A huge gust of wind came up the track, whirling up the women's petticoats like flying leaves and pelting them all with clouds of dust and dry heather. They darted into the shelter of the rock and stood smiling and laughing a little with the intoxication of the weather, brushing off the dirt and settling their clothes.

"So, then," Jamie said, before the good mood should have a chance to curdle on them, "who is it ye mean to wed?"

"Jesus Christ," Joan replied promptly.

He stared at her for a moment, until he became aware that his mouth was hanging open and closed it.

"You want to be a nun?" Claire's brows were raised with interest. "Really?"

"I do. I've kent for a long time that I've a vocation, but . . ." She hesitated. " . . . it's . . . complicated."

"I daresay it is," Jamie said, recovering himself somewhat.

"Have ye spoken to anyone about it, lass? The priest? Your mother?"

Joan's lips pressed into a thin line.

"Both of them," she said shortly.

"And what did they say?" Claire asked. She was plainly fascinated, leaning back against the rock, combing back her hair with her fingers.

Joan snorted. "My mother says," she said precisely, "that I've lost my mind from reading books—and that's all *your* fault," she added pointedly to Jamie, "for giving me the taste for it. She wants me to wed auld Geordie McCann, but I said I'd rather be dead in the ditch."

"How old *is* auld Geordie McCann?" Claire inquired, and Joan blinked at her.

"Five-and-twenty or so," she said. "What's that to do with it?"

"Just curious," Claire murmured, looking entertained. "There's a young Geordie McCann, then?"

"Aye, his nephew. He's three," Joan added, in the interests of strict accuracy. "I dinna want to wed him, either."

"And the priest?" Jamie intervened, before Claire could derail the discussion entirely.

Joan drew breath, seeming to grow taller and sterner with it.

"*He* says that it's my duty to stay to hame and tend to my aged mother."

"Who's swiving Joey the hired man in the goat shed," Jamie added helpfully. "Ye ken that, I suppose?" From the corner of his eye, he saw Claire's face, which entertained him so much that he was obliged to turn away and not look at her. He lifted a hand behind his back, indicating that he'd tell her later.

"Not while I'm in the house, she doesn't," Joan said coldly. "Which is the only reason I *am* in the house, still. D'ye think my conscience will let me leave, knowing what they'll be up to? This is the first time I've gone further than the kail-yard in three months, and if it wasna sinful to place wagers, I'd bet ye my best shift they're at it this minute, damning both their souls to hell."

Jamie cleared his throat, trying—and failing—not to think

of Joey and Laoghaire, wrapped in passionate embrace on her bed with the blue-and-gray quilt.

"Aye, well." He could feel Claire's eyes boring into the back of his neck and felt the blood rise there. "So. Ye want to go for a nun, but the priest says ye mustn't, your mother willna give ye your dowry for it, and your conscience willna let ye do it anyway. Is that the state o' things, would ye say?"

"Aye, it is," Joan said, pleased with his concise summary.

"And, um, what is it that you'd like Jamie to do about it?" Claire inquired, coming round to stand by him. "Kill Joey?" She shot Jamie a sidelong yellow-eyed glance, full of wicked enjoyment at his discomfiture. He gave her a narrow look, and she grinned at him.

"Of course not!" Joan's heavy brow drew down. "I want them to wed. Then they'd no be in a state of mortal sin every time I turned my back, *and* the priest couldna say I've to stay at home, not if my mother's got a husband to care for her."

Jamie rubbed a finger slowly up and down the bridge of his nose, trying to make out just how he was meant to induce two middle-aged reprobates to wed. By force? Hold a fowling piece on them? He could, he supposed, but . . . well, the more he thought of it, the better he liked the notion . . .

"Does he *want* to marry her, do you think?" Claire asked, surprising him. It hadn't occurred to him to wonder that.

"Aye, he does," Joan said, with obvious disapproval. "He's always moaning on about it to me, how much he looooves her . . ." She rolled her eyes. "Not that I think he shouldna love her," she hastened to add, seeing Jamie's expression. "But he shouldna be telling *me* about it, now, should he?"

"Ah . . . no," he said, feeling mildly dazed. The wind was booming past the rock, and the whine of it in his ears was eating at him, making him feel suddenly as he used to in the cave, living in solitude for weeks, with no voice but the wind's to hear. He shook his head violently to clear it, forcing himself to focus on Joan's face, hear her words above the wind.

"She's willing, I think," Joan was saying, still frowning. "Though she doesna talk to me about it, thank Bride. She's fond of him, though; feeds him the choice bits and that."

"Well, then . . ." He brushed a flying strand of hair out of his mouth, feeling dizzy. "Why do they not marry?"

"Because of you," Claire said, sounding a trifle less amused. "And that's where I come into this, I suppose?"

"Because of—"

"The agreement you made with Laoghaire, when I . . . came back." Her attention was focused on Joan, but she came closer and touched his hand lightly, not looking at him. "You promised to support her—and find dowries for Joan and Marsali—but the support was to stop if she married again. That's it, isn't it?" she said to Joan, who nodded.

"She and Joey might make shift to scrape along," she said. "He does what he can, but . . . ye've seen him. If ye were to stop the money, though, she'd likely have to sell Balriggan to live—and that would break her heart," she added quietly, dropping her eyes for the first time.

An odd pain seized his heart—odd because it was not his own but he recognized it. It was sometime in the first weeks of their marriage, when he'd been digging new beds in the garden. Laoghaire had brought him out a mug of cool beer and stood while he drank it, then thanked him for the digging. He'd been surprised and laughed, saying why should she think to thank him for that?

"Because ye take care for my place," she'd said simply, "but ye don't try to take it from me." Then she'd taken the empty mug from him and gone back to the house.

And once, in bed—and he flushed at the thought, with Claire standing right by him—he'd asked her why she liked Balriggan so much; it wasna a family place, after all, nor remarkable in any way. And she'd sighed a little, pulled the quilt up to her chin, and said, "It's the first place I've felt safe." She wouldn't say more when he asked her, but only turned over and pretended to fall asleep.

"She'd rather lose Joey than Balriggan," Joan was saying to Claire. "But she doesna mean to lose *him,* either. So ye see the difficulty, aye?"

"I do, yes." Claire was looking sympathetic but shot him a glance indicating that this was—naturally—*his* problem. Of course it was, he thought, exasperated.

"I'll . . . do something," he said, having not the slightest notion what, but how could he refuse? God would probably strike him down for interfering with Joan's vocation, if his own sense of guilt didn't finish him off first.

"Oh, Da! *Thank* you!"

Joan's face broke into a sudden, dazzling smile, and she threw herself into his arms—he barely got them up in time to catch her; she was a very solid young woman. But he folded her into the embrace he'd wanted to give her on meeting and felt the odd pain ease, as this strange daughter fitted herself tidily into an empty spot in his heart he hadn't known was there.

The wind was still whipping by, and it might have been a speck of dust that made Claire's eyes glisten as she looked at him, smiling.

"Just the one thing," he said sternly, when Joan had released him and stood back.

"Anything," she said fervently.

"Ye'll pray for me, aye? When ye're a nun?"

"Every day," she assured him, "and twice on Sundays."

THE SUN WAS starting down the sky by now, but there was still some time to supper. I should, I supposed, be there to offer to help with the meal preparations; these were both enormous and laborious, with so many people coming and going, and Lallybroch could no longer afford the luxury of a cook. But even if Jenny was taken up with nursing Ian, Maggie and her young daughters and the two housemaids were more than capable of managing. I would only be in the way. Or so I told myself, well aware that there was always work for a spare pair of hands.

But I clambered down the stony hill behind Jamie and said nothing when he turned away from the trail to Lallybroch. We wandered down toward the little loch, well content.

"Perhaps I *did* have something to do wi' the books, aye?" Jamie said, after a bit. "I mean, I read to the wee maids in the evenings now and again. They'd sit on the settle with me, one on each side, wi' their heads against me, and it was—" He broke off with a glance at me and coughed, evidently worried that I might be offended at the idea that he'd ever enjoyed a moment in Laoghaire's house. I smiled and took his arm.

"I'm sure they loved it. But I really doubt that you read anything to Joan that made her want to become a nun."

"Aye, well," he said dubiously. "I did read to them out of the *Lives of the Saints.* Oh, and *Fox's Book of the Martyrs,* too, even though there's a good deal of it to do wi' Protestants, and Laoghaire said Protestants couldna be martyrs because they were wicked heretics, and I said bein' a heretic didna preclude being a martyr, and—" He grinned suddenly. "I think that might ha' been the closest thing we had to a decent conversation."

"Poor Laoghaire!" I said. "But putting her aside—and do let's—what do you think of Joan's quandary?"

He shook his head dubiously.

"Well, I can maybe bribe Laoghaire to marry yon wee cripple, but it would take a deal of money, since she'd want more than she gets from me now. I havena got that much left of the gold we brought, so it would need to wait until I can get back to the Ridge and extract some more, take that to a bank, arrange for a draft . . . I hate to think of Joan having to spend a year at home, trying to keep yon lust-crazed weasels apart."

"Lust-crazed weasels?" I said, entertained. "No, really. Did you see them at it?"

"Not exactly," he said, coughing. "Ye could see there was an attraction atween them, though. Here, let's go along the shore; I saw a curlew's nest the other day."

The wind had quieted and the sun was bright and warm—for the moment. I could see clouds lurking over the horizon, and doubtless it would be raining again by nightfall, but for the moment it was a lovely spring day, and we were both disposed to enjoy it. By unspoken consent, we put aside all disagreeable matters and talked of nothing in particular, only enjoying each other's company, until we reached a shallow, grass-covered mound where we could perch and enjoy the sun.

Jamie's mind seemed to return now and then to Laoghaire, though—I supposed he couldn't help it. I didn't really mind, as such comparisons as he made were entirely to my benefit.

"Had she been my first," he said thoughtfully at one point, "I think I might have a much different opinion of women in general."

"Well, you can't define all women in terms of what they're like—or what one of them is like—in bed," I objected. "I've known men who, well . . ."

"Men? Was Frank not your first?" he demanded, surprised.

I put a hand behind my head and regarded him.

"Would it matter if he wasn't?"

"Well . . ." Clearly taken aback by the possibility, he groped for an answer. "I suppose—" He broke off and eyed me, meditatively stroking one finger down the bridge of his nose. One corner of his mouth turned up. "I don't know."

I didn't know, myself. On the one hand, I rather enjoyed his shock at the notion—and at my age, I was not at all averse to feeling mildly wanton, if only in retrospect. On the other hand . . .

"Well, where do you get off, anyway, casting stones?"

"Ye were *my* first," he pointed out, with considerable asperity.

"So you *said,*" I said, teasing. To my amusement, he flushed up like the rosy dawn.

"Ye didna believe me?" he said, his voice rising in spite of himself.

"Well, you did seem rather well informed, for a so-called virgin. To say nothing of . . . imaginative."

"For God's sake, Sassenach, I grew up on a farm! It's a verra straightforward business, after all." He looked me closely up and down, his gaze lingering at certain points of particular interest. "And as for imagining things . . . Christ, I'd spent months—years!—imagining!" A certain light filled his eyes, and I had the distinct impression that he hadn't stopped imagining in the intervening years, not by any means.

"What are you thinking?" I asked, intrigued.

"I'm thinking that the water in the loch's that wee bit chilly, but if it didna shrink my cock straight off, the feel of the heat when I plunged into ye . . . Of course," he added practically, eyeing me as though estimating the effort involved in forcing me into the loch, "we wouldna need to do it *in* the water, unless ye liked; I could just dunk ye a few times, drag ye onto the shore, and—God, your arse looks fine, wi' the wet linen of your shift clinging to it. It goes all transparent, and I can see the weight of your buttocks, like great smooth round melons—"

"I take it back—I don't want to know what you're thinking!"

"You asked," he pointed out logically. "And I can see the sweet wee crease of your arse, too—and once I've got ye pinned under me and ye canna get away . . . d'ye want it lying on your back, Sassenach, or bent over on your knees, wi' me behind? I could take a good hold either way, and—"

"I am not going into a freezing loch in order to gratify your perverted desires!"

"All right," he said, grinning. Stretching himself out beside me, he reached round behind and took a generous handful. "Ye can gratify them here, if ye like, where it's warm."

80

OENOMANCY

LALLYBROCH WAS A working farm. Nothing on a farm can stop for very long, even for grief. Which is how it came to be that I was the only person in the front of the house when the door opened in the middle of the afternoon.

I heard the sound and poked my head out of Ian's study to see who had come in. A strange young man was standing in the foyer, gazing round appraisingly. He heard my step and turned, looking at me curiously.

"Who are *you*?" we said simultaneously, and laughed.

"I'm Michael," he said, in a soft, husky voice with the trace of a French accent. "And ye'll be Uncle Jamie's faery-woman, I suppose."

He was examining me with frank interest, and I felt therefore free to do the same.

"Is that what the family's been calling me?" I asked, looking him over.

He was a slight man, lacking either Young Jamie's burly strength or Young Ian's wiry height. Michael was Janet's twin but did not resemble her at all, either. This was the son who had gone to France, to become a junior partner in Jared Fraser's wine business, Fraser *et Cie.* As he took off his traveling cloak, I saw that he was dressed very fashionably for the Highlands, though his suit was sober in both color and cut—and he wore a black crepe band around his upper arm.

"That, or the witch," he said, smiling faintly. "Depending whether it's Da or Mam who's talking."

"Indeed," I said, with an edge—but couldn't help smiling back. He was quiet but an engaging young man—well, relatively young. He must be near thirty, I thought.

"I'm sorry for your . . . loss," I said, with a nod toward the crepe band. "May I ask—"

"My wife," he said simply. "She died two weeks ago. I should have come sooner, else."

That took me aback considerably.

"Oh. I . . . see. But your parents, your brothers and sisters—they don't know this yet?"

He shook his head and came forward a little, so the light from the fan-shaped window above the door fell on his face, and I saw the dark circles under his eyes and the marks of the bone-deep exhaustion that is grief's only consolation.

"I am so sorry," I said, and, moved by impulse, put my arms around him. He leaned toward me, under the same impulse. His body yielded for an instant to my touch, and there was an extraordinary moment in which I sensed the deep numbness within him, the unacknowledged war of acknowledgment and denial. He knew what had happened, what was happening—but could not feel it. Not yet.

"Oh, dear," I said, stepping back from the brief embrace. I touched his cheek lightly, and he stared at me, blinking.

"I will be damned," he said mildly. "They're right."

A DOOR OPENED and closed above, I heard a foot on the stair—and an instant later, Lallybroch awoke to the knowledge that the last child had come home.

The swirl of women and children wafted us into the kitchen, where the men appeared, by ones and twos through the back door to embrace Michael or clap him on the shoulder.

There were outpourings of sympathy, the same questions and answers repeated several times—how had Michael's wife, Lillie, died? She had died of the influenza; so had her grandmother; no, he himself had not caught it; her father sent his prayers and concerns for Michael's father—and eventually the preparations for washing and supper and the putting of children to bed began, and Michael slipped out of the maelstrom.

Coming out of the kitchen myself to fetch my shawl from the study, I saw him at the foot of the stair with Jenny, talking quietly. She touched his face, just as I had, asking him something in a low voice. He half-smiled, shook his head, and, squaring his shoulders, went upstairs alone to see Ian, who was feeling too poorly to come down to supper.

ALONE AMONG THE Murrays, Michael had inherited the fugitive gene for red hair, and burned among his darker siblings like a coal. He had inherited an exact copy of his father's soft brown eyes, though. "And a good thing, too," Jenny said to me privately, "else his da would likely be sure I'd been at it wi' the goatherd, for God knows, he doesna look like anyone else in the family."

I'd mentioned this to Jamie, who looked surprised but then smiled.

"Aye. She wouldna ken it, for she never met Colum MacKenzie face-to-face."

"Colum? Are you sure?" I looked over my shoulder.

"Oh, aye. The coloring's different—but allowing for age and good health . . . There was a painting at Leoch, done of Colum when he was maybe fifteen, before his first fall. Recall it, do ye? It hung in the solar on the third floor."

I closed my eyes, frowning in concentration, trying to reconstruct the floor plan of the castle.

"Walk me there," I said. He made a small amused noise in his throat but took my hand, tracing a delicate line on my palm.

"Aye, here's the entrance, wi' the big double door. Ye'd cross the courtyard, once inside, and then . . ."

He walked me unerringly to the exact spot in my mind, and sure enough, there was a painting there of a young man with a thin, clever face and look of far-seeing in his eyes.

"Yes, I think you're right," I said, opening my eyes. "If he *is* as intelligent as Colum, then . . . I have to tell him."

Jamie's eyes, dark with thought, searched my face.

"We couldna change things, earlier," he said, a note of warning in his voice. "Ye likely canna change what's to come in France."

"Maybe not," I said. "But what I knew—what I told you, before Culloden. It didn't stop Charles Stuart, but *you* lived."

"Not on purpose," he said dryly.

"No, but your men lived, too—and that *was* on purpose. So maybe—just maybe—it *might* help. And I can't live with myself if I don't."

He nodded, sober.

"Aye, then. I'll call them."

THE CORK EASED free with a soft *pop!,* and Michael's face eased, too. He sniffed the darkened cork, then passed the bottle delicately under his nose, eyes half closing in appreciation.

"Well, what d'ye say, lad?" his father asked. "Will it poison us or no?"

He opened his eyes and gave his father a mildly dirty look.

"You said it was important, aye? So we'll have the negroamaro. From Apulia," he added, with a note of satisfaction, and turned to me. "Will that do, Aunt?"

"Er . . . certainly," I said, taken back somewhat. "Why ask me? You're the wine expert."

Michael glanced at me, surprised.

"Ian said—" he began, but stopped and smiled at me. "My apologies, Aunt. I must have misunderstood."

Everyone turned and looked at Young Ian, who reddened at this scrutiny.

"What exactly did ye say, Ian?" Young Jamie asked. Young

Ian narrowed his eyes at his brother, who seemed to be finding something funny in the situation.

"I said," Young Ian replied, straightening himself defiantly, "that Auntie Claire had something of importance to say to Michael, and that he must listen, because she's a . . . a . . ."

"*Ban-sidhe,* he said," Michael ended helpfully. He didn't grin at me, but a deep humor glowed in his eyes, and for the first time I saw what Jamie had meant by comparing him to Colum MacKenzie. "I wasn't sure whether he meant that, Auntie, or if it's only you're a conjure-woman—or a witch."

Jenny gasped at the word, and even the elder Ian blinked. Both of them turned and looked at Young Ian, who hunched his shoulders defensively.

"Well, I dinna ken *exactly* what she is," he said. "But she's an Auld One, isn't she, Uncle Jamie?"

Something odd seemed to pass through the air of the room; a sudden live, fresh wind moaned down the chimney, exploding the banked fire and showering sparks and embers onto the hearth. Jenny got up with a small exclamation and beat them out with the broom.

Jamie was sitting beside me; he took my hand and fixed Michael with a firm sort of look.

"There's no real word for what she is—but she has knowledge of things that will come to pass. Listen to her."

That settled them all to attention, and I cleared my throat, deeply embarrassed by my role as prophet but obliged to speak nonetheless. For the first time, I had a sudden sense of kinship with some of the more reluctant Old Testament prophets. I thought I knew *just* what Jeremiah felt like when told to go and prophesy the destruction of Nineveh. I just hoped I'd get a better reception; I seemed to recall that the inhabitants of Nineveh had thrown him into a well.

"You'll know more than I do about the politics in France," I said, looking directly at Michael. "I can't tell you anything in terms of specific events for the next ten or fifteen years. But after that . . . things are going to go downhill fast. There's going to be a revolution. Inspired by the one that's happening now in America, but not the same. The King and Queen will be imprisoned with their family, and both of them will be beheaded."

A general gasp went up from the table, and Michael blinked.

"There will be a movement called the Terror, and people will be pulled out of their homes and denounced, all the aristocrats will either be killed or have to flee the country, and it won't be too good for rich people in general. Jared may be dead by then, but you won't be. And if you're half as talented as I think, you *will* be rich."

He snorted a little at that, and there was a breath of laughter in the room, but it didn't last long.

"They'll build a machine called the guillotine—perhaps it already exists, I don't know. It was originally made as a humane method of execution, I think, but it will be used so often that it will be a symbol of the Terror, and of the revolution in general. You *don't* want to be in France when that happens."

"I—how do ye know this?" Michael demanded. He looked pale and half belligerent. Well, here was the rub. I took a firm grip of Jamie's hand under the table and told them how I knew.

There was a dead silence. Only Young Ian didn't look dumbfounded—but he knew already, and more or less believed me. I could tell that most of those around the table didn't. At the same time, they couldn't really call me a liar.

"That's what I know," I said, speaking straight to Michael. "And that's how I know it. You have a few years to get ready. Move the business to Spain, or Portugal. Sell out and emigrate to America. Do anything you like—but don't stay in France for more than ten years more. That's all," I said abruptly. I got up and went out, leaving utter silence in my wake.

I SHOULDN'T HAVE been surprised, but I was. I was in the hen coop, collecting eggs, when I heard the excited squawk and flutter of the hens outside that announced someone had come into their yard. I fixed the last hen with a steely glare that dared her to peck me, snatched an egg out from under her, and came out to see who was there.

It was Jenny, with an apronful of corn. That was odd; I knew the hens had already been fed, for I'd seen one of Maggie's daughters doing it an hour earlier.

She nodded to me and tossed the corn in handfuls. I tucked the last warm egg into my basket and waited. Obviously she wanted to talk to me and had made an excuse to do so in private. I had a deep feeling of foreboding.

Entirely justified, too, for she dropped the last handful of cracked corn and, with it, all pretense.

"I want to beg a favor," she said to me, but she avoided my eye, and I could see the pulse in her temple going like a ticking clock.

"Jenny," I said, helpless either to stop her or to answer her. "I know—"

"Will ye cure Ian?" she blurted, lifting her eyes to mine. I'd been right about what she meant to ask, but wrong about her emotion. Worry and fear lay behind her eyes, but there was no shyness, no embarrassment; she had the eyes of a hawk, and I knew she would rip my flesh like one if I denied her.

"Jenny," I said again. "I can't."

"Ye can't, or ye won't?" she said sharply.

"I *can't*. For God's sake, do you think I wouldn't have done it already if I had the power?"

"Ye might not, for the sake of the grudge ye hold against me. If that's it—I'll say I'm sorry, and I do mean it, though I meant what I did for the best."

"You . . . what?" I was honestly confused, but this seemed to anger her.

"Dinna pretend ye've no notion what I mean! When ye came back before, and I sent for Laoghaire!"

"Oh." I hadn't quite *forgotten* that, but it hadn't seemed important, in light of everything else. "That's . . . all right. I don't hold it against you. Why *did* you send for her, though?" I asked, both out of curiosity and in hopes of diffusing the intensity of her emotion a little. I'd seen a great number of people on the ragged edge of exhaustion, grief, and terror, and she was firmly in the grip of all three.

She made a jerky, impatient motion and seemed as though she would turn away but didn't.

"Jamie hadn't told ye about her, nor her about you. I could see why, maybe, but I kent if I brought her here, he'd have nay choice then but to take the bull by the horns and clear up the matter."

"She nearly cleared *him* up," I said, beginning to get somewhat hot myself. "She *shot* him, for God's sake!"

"Well, I didna give her the gun, did I?" she snapped. "I didna mean him to say whatever he said to her, nor her to take up a pistol and put a ball in him."

"No, but you told me to go away!"

"Why wouldn't I? Ye'd broken his heart once already, and I thought ye'd do it again! And you wi' the nerve to come prancing back here, fine and blooming, when we'd been . . . we'd been—it was that that gave Ian the cough!"

"That—"

"When they took him away and put him in the Tolbooth. But you werena here when that happened! Ye werena here when we starved and froze and feared for the lives of our men and our bairns! Not for any of it! You were in France, warm and safe!"

"I was in Boston, two hundred years from now, thinking Jamie was dead," I said coldly. "And I *can't* help Ian." I struggled to subdue my own feelings, uncorked with a rush by this ripping of scabs off the past, and found compassion in the look of her, her fine-boned face gaunt and harrowed with worry, her hands clenched so hard that the nails bit into the flesh.

"Jenny," I said more quietly. "Please believe me. If I could do anything for Ian, I'd give my soul to do it. But I'm not magic; I haven't any power. Only a little knowledge, and not enough. I'd give my *soul* to do it," I repeated, more strongly, leaning toward her. "But I can't. Jenny . . . I can't."

She stared at me in silence. A silence that lengthened past bearing, and finally I stepped around her and walked toward the house. She didn't turn around, and I didn't look back. But behind me, I heard her whisper.

"You have nay soul."

81

PURGATORY II

WHEN IAN FELT well enough, he came out walking with Jamie. Sometimes only as far as the yard or the barn, to lean on the fence and make remarks to Jenny's sheep. Sometimes he felt well enough to walk miles, which amazed—and alarmed—Jamie. Still, he thought, it was good to walk side by side through the moors and the forest and down beside the loch, not talking much but side by side. It didn't matter that they walked slowly; they always had, since Ian had come back from France with a wooden leg.

"I'm lookin' forward to having back my leg," Ian had remarked casually once, when they sat in the shelter of the big rock where Fergus had lost his hand, looking out over the small burn that ran down at the foot of the hill, watching for the stray flash of a leaping trout.

"Aye, that'll be good," Jamie had said, smiling a little—and a little wry about it, too, recalling when he'd waked after Culloden and thought his own leg missing. He'd been upset and tried to comfort himself with the thought that he'd get it back eventually, if he made it out of purgatory and into heaven. Of course, he'd thought he was dead, too, but that hadn't seemed nearly as bad as the imagined loss of his leg.

"I dinna suppose ye'll have to wait," he said idly, and Ian blinked at him.

"Wait for what?"

"Your leg." He realized suddenly that Ian had no notion what he'd been thinking, and hastened to explain.

"So I was only thinking, ye wouldna spend much time in purgatory—if at all—so ye'll have it back soon."

Ian grinned at him. "What makes ye sae sure I willna

spend a thousand years in purgatory? I might be a terrible sinner, aye?"

"Well, aye, ye might be," Jamie admitted. "Though if so, ye must think the devil of a lot of wicked thoughts, because if ye'd been *doing* anything, I'd know about it."

"Oh, ye think so?" Ian seemed to find this funny. "Ye havena seen me in years. I might ha' been doing anything, and ye'd never ken a thing about it!"

"Of course I would," Jamie said logically. "Jenny would tell me. And ye dinna mean to suggest she wouldna ken if ye had a mistress and six bastard bairns, or ye'd taken to the highways and been robbing folk in a black silk mask?"

"Well, possibly she would," Ian admitted. "Though come on, man, there's nothing ye could call a highway within a hundred miles. And I'd freeze to death long before I came across anyone worth robbin' in one o' the passes." He paused, eyes narrowed against the wind, contemplating the criminal possibilities open to him.

"I could ha' been stealing cattle," he offered. "Though there're sae few beasts these days, the whole parish would ken it at once should one go missing. And I doubt I could hide it amongst Jenny's sheep wi' any hope of its not bein' noticed."

He thought further, chin in hand, then reluctantly shook his head.

"The sad truth is, Jamie, no one's had a thing worth stealin' in the Highlands these twenty years past. Nay, theft's right out, I'm afraid. So is fornication, because Jenny would ha' killed me already. What does that leave? There's no really anything to covet. . . . I suppose lying and murder is all that's left, and while I've met the odd man I would ha' *liked* to kill, I never did." He shook his head regretfully, and Jamie laughed.

"Oh, aye? Ye told me ye killed men in France."

"Well, aye, I did, but that was a matter of war—or business," he added fairly. "I was bein' paid to kill them; I didna do it out o' spite."

"Well, then, I'm right," Jamie pointed out. "Ye'll sail straight through purgatory like a rising cloud, for I canna think of a single lie ye've ever told me."

Ian smiled with great affection.

"Aye, well, I may ha' told lies now and then, Jamie—but no, not to you."

He looked down at the worn wooden peg stretched before him and scratched at the knee on that side.

"I wonder, will it feel different?"

"How could it not?"

"Well, the thing is," Ian said, wiggling his sound foot to and fro, "I can still feel my missing foot. Always have been able to, ever since it went. Not all the time, mind," he added, looking up. "But I do feel it. A verra strange thing. Do ye feel your finger?" he asked curiously, raising his chin at Jamie's right hand.

"Well . . . aye, I do. Not all the time, but now and then—and the nasty thing is that even though it's gone, it still *hurts* like damnation, which doesna seem really fair."

He could have bitten his tongue at that, for here Ian was dying, and him complaining that the loss of his finger wasn't fair. Ian wheezed with amusement, though, and leaned back, shaking his head.

"If life was fair, then what?"

They sat in companionable silence for a while, watching the wind move through the pines on the hillside opposite. Then Jamie reached into his sporran and brought out the tiny white-wrapped package. It was a bit grubby from being in his sporran but had been tidily preserved and tightly wrapped.

Ian eyed the little bundle in his palm.

"What's this?"

"My finger," Jamie said. "I—well . . . I wondered whether ye'd maybe not mind to have it buried with ye."

Ian looked at him for a moment. Then his shoulders started to shake.

"God, don't laugh!" Jamie said, alarmed. "I didna mean to make ye laugh! Christ, Jenny will kill me if ye cough up a lung and die out here!"

Ian *was* coughing, fits of it interspersed with long-drawn-out wheezes of laughter. Tears of mirth stood in his eyes, and he pressed both fists into his chest, struggling to breathe. At last, though, he left off and straightened slowly up, making a sound like a bellows. He sniffed deep and casually spat a glob of horrifying scarlet into the rocks.

"I'd rather die out here laughin' at you than in my bed wi'

six priests sayin' prayers," he said. "Doubt I'll get the chance, though." He put out a hand, palm up. "Aye, give it here."

Jamie laid the little white-wrapped cylinder in his hand, and Ian tucked the finger casually into his own sporran.

"I'll keep it safe 'til ye catch me up."

HE CAME DOWN through the trees and made his way toward the edge of the moorland that lay below the cave. It was sharply cold, with a stiff breeze blowing, and the light changed over the land like the flicker of a bird's wings as the clouds slid overhead, long and fleeting. He'd picked up a deer trail through the heather earlier in the morning, but it had disappeared in a stony fall near a brae, and now he was coming back toward the house; he was behind the hill on which the broch stood, this side of it thick with a little wood of beech and pine. He'd not seen a deer or even a coney this morning, but wasn't bothered.

With so many in the house, they could use a deer, to be sure—but he was happy only to be out of the house, even if he came back with nothing.

He couldn't look at Ian without wanting to stare at his face, to commit him to memory, to impress these last bits of his brother-in-law upon his mind in the way that he recalled special vivid moments, there to be taken out and lived through again at need. But at the same time, he didn't *want* to remember Ian as he was now; much better to keep what he had of him: firelight on the side of Ian's face, laughing fit to burst as he'd forced Jamie's arm over in a wrestling match, his own wiry strength surprising them both. Ian's long, knob-jointed hands on the gralloch knife, the wrench and the hot metal smell of the blood that smeared his fingers, the look of his brown hair ruffling in the wind off the loch, the narrow back, bent and springy as a bow as he stooped to snatch one of his toddling bairns or grandchildren off their feet and throw them up giggling into the air.

It was good they'd come, he thought. Better than good that they'd brought the lad back in time to speak to his father as a man, to comfort Ian's mind and take his leave properly. But to live in the same house with a beloved brother dying by inches under your nose wore sadly on the nerves.

With so many women in the house, squabbling was inevitable. With so many of the women Frasers, it was like walking through a gunpowder mill with a lit candle. Everyone tried so hard to manage, to keep in countenance, to accommodate—but that only made it worse when some spark finally set the powder keg off. He wasn't only out hunting because they needed meat.

He spared a sympathetic thought for Claire. After Jenny's anguished request, Claire had taken to hiding in their room or in Ian's study—he had invited her to use it, and Jamie thought that aggravated Jenny still more—writing busily, making the book Andy Bell had put in her mind. She had great powers of concentration and could stay inside her mind for hours—but she had to come out to eat. And it was always there, the knowledge that Ian was dying, grinding like a quern, slow but relentless, wearing away the nerves.

Ian's nerves, too.

He and Ian had been walking—slowly—by the side of the loch two days before, when Ian stopped suddenly, curling in on himself like an autumn leaf. Jamie hurried to take him by the arm before he could fall, and he lowered him to the ground, finding a boulder to brace his back, pulling the shawl high around the wasted shoulders, looking for anything, anything at all he could do.

"What is it, *a charaid*?" he said, anxious, crouching beside his brother-in-law, his friend.

Ian was coughing, almost silently, his body shaking with the force of it. At last the spasm eased and he could draw breath, his face bright with the consumptive flush, that terrible illusion of health.

"It hurts, Jamie." The words were spoken simply, but Ian's eyelids were closed, as though he didn't want to look at Jamie while he spoke.

"I'll carry ye back. We'll get ye a bit of laudanum, maybe, and—"

Ian waved a hand, quelling his anxious promises. He breathed shallowly for a moment before shaking his head.

"Aye, my chest feels like there's a knife in it," he said finally. "But that's no what I meant. I'm no bothered so much about dying—but Christ, the slowness of it is killing me." He did open his eyes then, meeting Jamie's, and laughed as silently as he'd coughed, the barest breath of sound as his body shook with it.

"This dying hurts me, Dougal. I'd have it over." The words came into his mind as clearly as if they'd been spoken just now in front of him, rather than thirty years before in a dark church, ruined by cannon fire. Rupert had said that, dying slow. *"You're my chief, man,"* he'd said to Dougal, imploring. *"It's your job."* And Dougal MacKenzie had done what love and duty called for.

He had been holding Ian's hand, clasping hard, trying to force some notion of well-being from his own callused palm into Ian's thin gray skin. His thumb slid upward now, pressing on the wrist where he had seen Claire grip, searching out the truth of a patient's health.

He felt the skin give, sliding across the bones of Ian's wrist. He thought suddenly of the blood vow given at his marriage, the sting of the blade and Claire's cold wrist pressed to his and the blood slick between them. Ian's wrist was cold, too, but not from fear.

He glanced at his own wrist, but there was no trace of a scar, either from vows or fetters; those wounds were fleeting, long-healed.

"D'ye remember when we gave each other blood for blood?" Ian's eyes were closed, but he smiled. Jamie's hand tightened on the bony wrist, a little startled but not truly surprised that Ian had reached into his mind and caught the echo of his thoughts.

"Aye, of course." He couldn't help a small smile of his own, a painful one.

They'd been eight years old, the two of them. Jamie's mother and her bairn had died the day before. The house had been full of mourners, his father dazed with shock. They had slipped out, he and Ian, scrambling up the hill behind the house, trying not to look at the fresh-dug grave by the broch. Into the wood, safe under the trees.

Had slowed then, wandering, come to a stop at last at the top of the high hill, where some old stone building that they called the fort had fallen down long ago. They'd sat on the rubble, wrapped in their plaids against the wind, not talking much.

"I thought I'd have a new brother," he'd said suddenly. "But I don't. It's just Jenny and me, still." In the years since, he'd succeeded in forgetting that small pain, the loss of his hoped-for brother, the boy who might have given him back a little of his love for his older brother, Willie, dead of the smallpox. He'd cherished that pain for a little, a flimsy shield against the enormity of knowing his mother gone forever.

Ian had sat thinking for a bit, then reached into his sporran and got out the wee knife his father had given him on his last birthday.

"I'll be your brother," he'd said, matter-of-fact, and cut across his thumb, hissing a little through his teeth.

He'd handed the knife to Jamie, who'd cut himself, surprised that it hurt so much, and then they'd pressed their thumbs together and sworn to be brothers always. And had been.

He took a deep breath, bracing himself against the nearness of death, the black finality.

"Ian. Shall I . . ." Ian's eyelids lifted, the soft brown of his gaze sharpening into clarity at what he heard in the thickness of Jamie's voice. Jamie cleared his throat hard and looked away, then looked back, feeling obscurely that to look away was cowardly.

"Will ye have me hasten ye?" he asked, very softly. Even as he spoke, the cold part of his mind sought the way. Not by the blade, no; it was quick and clean, a proper man's departure, but it would cause his sister and the weans grief; neither he nor Ian had the right to leave a final memory stained with blood.

Ian's grip neither slackened nor clung, but of a sudden Jamie felt the pulse he had looked for in vain, a small, steady throb against his own palm.

He hadn't looked away, but his eyes blurred, and he bent his head to hide the tears.

Claire . . . She would know how, but he couldn't ask her to do it. Her own vow kept her from it.

"No," Ian said. "Not yet, anyway." He'd smiled, eyes soft. "But I'm glad to ken ye'll do it if I need ye to, *mo brathair.*"

The flicker of a movement stopped him in his tracks and jerked him instantly from his thoughts.

It hadn't seen him, though he was in sight. The wind was toward him, though, and the deer was busy, nibbling among the crusts of dry heather for sheltered bits of grass and softer moor plants. He waited, listening to the wind. Only the deer's head and shoulders were visible behind a gorse bush, though he thought from the size of the neck that it was a male.

He waited, feeling the way of it seep back into him. Hunting red deer on the moor was different from hunting in the forests of North Carolina. A slower thing altogether. The deer moved out a little from behind the gorse bush, intent on its feeding, and he began, by imperceptible degrees, to raise his rifle. He'd had a gunsmith in Edinburgh straighten the barrel for him but hadn't used it since; he hoped it would aim true.

Hadn't used it since he'd clouted the Hessian with it in the redoubt. He had a sudden, vivid recollection of Claire dropping the misshapen bullet that had killed Simon into the china plate, felt the chink and roll of it in his blood.

Another step, two; the deer had found something tasty and was tugging and chewing with great concentration. Like a thing completing itself, the muzzle of the rifle settled gently on its target. A big buck deer, and no more than a hundred yards. He could feel the big solid heart, pumping under his own ribs, pulsing in the tips of his fingers on the metal. The stock snugged hard into the hollow of his shoulder.

He was just beginning to squeeze the trigger when he heard the screams from the wood behind him. The gun went off, the shot went wild, the deer vanished with a crash of breaking heather, and the screams stopped.

He turned and strode fast into the woods, in the direction where he'd heard them, his heart pounding. Who? A woman, but who?

He found Jenny without much difficulty, standing frozen in the small clearing where he and she and Ian came when they were young, to share out stolen treats and play at knights and soldiers.

She'd been a good soldier.

Maybe she'd been waiting for him, having heard his gun. Maybe she just couldn't move. She stood straight-backed but empty-eyed and watched him come, her shawls wrapped like rusty armor round her.

"Are ye all right, lass?" he asked, setting down his rifle by the big pine where she'd read to him and Ian in the long summer nights when the sun barely set from dusk to dawn.

"Aye, fine," she said, her voice colorless.

"Aye, right," he said, sighing. Coming close, he insisted upon taking her hands in his; she didn't give them to him but didn't resist. "I heard ye scream."

"I didna mean anyone to hear."

"Of course ye didn't." He hesitated, wanting to ask again was she all right, but that was foolish. He knew fine well what the trouble was and why she needed to come and scream in the wood, where no one would hear her and ask stupidly was she all right.

"D'ye want me to go away?" he asked instead, and she grimaced, pulling at her hand, but he didn't let go.

"No. What difference does it make? What difference does anything make?" He heard the note of hysteria in her voice.

"At least . . . we brought the lad home in time," he said, for lack of anything else to offer her.

"Aye, ye did," she said, with an effort at self-control that shredded like old silk. "And ye brought your wife back, too."

"Ye blame me for bringing my wife?" he said, shocked. "Why, for God's sake? Should ye no be happy she's come back? Or d'ye—" He choked off the next words fast; he'd been about to demand whether she resented him still having a wife when she was about to lose her husband, and he couldn't say *that.*

But that wasn't what Jenny had meant, at all.

"Aye, she's come back. But for what?" she cried. "What good is a faery-woman too coldhearted to lift a finger to save Ian?"

He was so staggered by this that he couldn't do anything but repeat "Coldhearted? Claire?" in a dazed fashion.

"I asked, and she denied me." His sister's eyes were tearless, frantic with grief and urgency. "Can ye not make her help me, Jamie?"

The life in his sister, always bright and pulsing, thrummed under his fingers like chained lightning now. Better if she let it loose on him, he thought. She couldn't hurt him.

"*A piuthar,* she'd heal him if she could," he said, as gently as possible without letting go of her. "She told me ye'd asked—and she wept in the telling. She loves Ian as much—"

"Don't ye *dare* be telling me she loves my husband as much as I do!" she shouted, jerking her hands out of his with such violence that he was sure she meant to strike him. She did, slapping his face so hard that his eye watered on that side.

"I wasna going to tell ye that at all," he said, keeping his temper. He touched the side of his face gingerly. "I was *going* to say that she loves him as much—"

He'd intended to say, "*as she loves me,*" but didn't get that far. She kicked him in the shin hard enough to buckle his leg, and he stumbled, flailing to keep his balance, which gave her the opportunity to turn and fly down the hill like a witch on a broomstick, her skirts and shawls whirling out like a storm around her.

82

DISPOSITIONS

CLEANSING OF *wounds,* I wrote carefully, and paused, marshaling my thoughts. Boiling water, clean rags, removal of foreign matter. Use of maggots on dead flesh (with a note of caution regarding blowfly and screwworm larvae? No, pointless; no one would be able to tell the difference without a magnifying glass). The stitching of wounds (sterilization of needle and thread). Useful poultices. Ought I to put in a separate section on the production and uses of penicillin?

I tapped the quill on the blotter, making tiny stars of ink, but finally decided against it. This was meant to be a useful guide for the common person. The common person was not equipped for the painstaking process of making penicillin, nor yet likely to have an injection apparatus—though I did think briefly of the penis syringe Dr. Fentiman had shown me, with a faint twinge of amusement.

That in turn made me think—briefly but vividly—of David Rawlings and his jugum penis. Did he really use it himself? I wondered, but hastily dismissed the vision conjured up by the thought and flipped over a few sheets, looking for my list of main topics.

Masturbation, I wrote thoughtfully. If some doctors discussed it in a negative light—and they most certainly did—I supposed there was no reason why I shouldn't give the opposing view—discreetly.

I found myself still making inky stars a few moments later, thoroughly distracted by the problem of talking discreetly about the benefits of masturbation. God, what if I said in print that women did it?

"They'd burn the whole printing, and likely Andy Bell's shop, too," I said aloud.

There was a sharp intake of breath, and I glanced up to see a woman standing in the door of the study.

"Oh, are you looking for Ian Murray?" I said, pushing back from the desk. "He's—"

"No, it's you I was looking for." There was a very odd tone to her voice, and I stood up, feeling suddenly defensive without knowing why.

"Ah," I said. "And you are . . . ?"

She stepped out of the shadowed hall into the light.

"Ye'll not know me, then?" Her mouth twitched in an angry half smile. "Laoghaire MacKenzie . . . Fraser," she added, almost reluctantly.

"Oh," I said.

I would have recognized her at once, I thought, save for the incongruity of context. This was the last place I would have expected her to be, and the fact that she was here . . . A recollection of what had happened the last time she had come to Lallybroch made me reach inconspicuously for the letter opener on the desk.

"You were looking for me," I repeated warily. "Not Jamie?"

She made a contemptuous gesture, pushing the thought of Jamie aside, and reached into the pocket at her waist, bringing out a folded letter.

"I've come to ask ye a favor," she said, and for the first time I heard the tremor in her voice. "Read that. If ye will," she added, and pressed her lips tight together.

I looked warily at her pocket, but it was flat; if she'd brought a pistol, she wasn't carrying it there. I picked up the letter and motioned her to the chair on the other side of the desk. If she took it into her head to attack me, I'd have a little warning.

Still, I wasn't really afraid of her. She was upset; that was clear. But very much in control of herself.

I opened the letter, and, with the occasional glance to be sure she stayed where she was, began to read.

15 February 1778
Philadelphia

"Philadelphia?" I said, startled, and looked up at Laoghaire. She nodded.

"They went there in the summer last year, himself thinking 'twould be safer." Her lips twisted a little. "Two months later, the British army came a-marching into the city, and there they've been since."

"Himself," I supposed, was Fergus. I noted the usage with interest; evidently Laoghaire had become reconciled to her older daughter's husband, for she used the word without irony.

Dear Mam,

I must ask you to do something for love of me and my children. The trouble is with Henri-Christian. Because of his oddness of form, he has always had some trouble in breathing, particularly when suffering from the catarrh, and has snored like a grampus since he was born. Now he has taken to stopping breathing altogether when he sleeps, save he is propped up with cushions in a particular position. Mother Claire had looked in his throat when she and Da saw us in New Bern and said then that his adenoids—this being something in his throat—were overlarge and might give trouble in future. (Germain has these, also, and breathes with his mouth open a good deal of the time, but it is not a danger to him as it is to Henri-Christian.)

I am in mortal terror that Henri-Christian will stop breathing one night and no one will know in time to save him. We take it in turns to sit up with him, to keep his head just right and to wake him when he stops breathing, but I do not know how long we can contrive to keep it up. Fergus is worn out with the work of the shop and I with the work of the house (I help in the shop, as well, and so of course does Germain. The little girls are great help to me in the house, bless them, and so willing to care for their little brother—but they cannot be left to sit up with him by night alone).

I have had a physician to look at Henri-Christian. He agrees that the adenoids are likely to blame for the obstruction of breathing, and he bled the wee lad and gave me medicine to shrink them, but this was of no use at all and only made Henri-Christian cry and vomit. Mother Claire—forgive me for speaking of her to you, for I know your feelings, but I must—had said that it might be necessary to remove Henri-Christian's tonsils and adenoids at some point, to ease his breathing, and plainly this point has been reached. She did this for the Beardsley twins some time ago on the Ridge, and I would trust no one else to attempt such an operation on Henri-Christian.

Will you go to see her, Mam? I think she must be at Lallybroch now, and I will write to her there, begging her to come to Philadelphia as soon as possible. But I fear my inability to communicate the horror of our situation.

As you love me, Mam, please go to her and ask her to come as quickly as may be.

Your most affectionate daughter,
Marsali

I set down the letter. *I fear my inability to communicate the horror of our situation.* No, she'd done that, all right.

Sleep apnea, they called it; the tendency to stop breathing

suddenly when asleep. It was common—and much more common in some sorts of dwarfism, where the respiratory airways were constricted by the skeletal abnormalities. Most people who had it would wake themselves, thrashing and snorting as they breathed again. But the enlarged adenoids and tonsils obstructing his throat—probably a hereditary problem, I thought distractedly, for I'd noted them in Germain and to a lesser extent in the girls, as well—would aggravate the difficulty, since even if the reflex that causes a person short of oxygen to breathe kicked in belatedly, Henri-Christian likely couldn't draw the immediate deep breath that would waken him.

The vision of Marsali and Fergus—and probably Germain—taking it in turns to sit up in a dark house, watching the little boy sleep, perhaps nodding off themselves in the cold and quiet, jerking awake in terror lest he have shifted in his sleep and stopped breathing . . . A sick knot of fear had formed under my ribs, reading the letter.

Laoghaire was watching me, blue eyes direct under her cap. For once, the anger, hysteria, and suspicion with which she had always regarded me was gone.

"If ye'll go," she said, and swallowed, "I'll give up the money."

I stared at her.

"You think that I—" I began incredulously, but stopped. Well, yes, she plainly *did* believe I would require to be bribed. She thought that I had abandoned Jamie after Culloden, returning only when he had become prosperous again. I struggled with the urge to try to tell her . . . but that was pointless, and quite beside the point now, too. The situation was clear and sharp as broken glass.

She leaned forward abruptly, her hands on the desk, pressed down so hard that her fingernails were white.

"Please," she said. *"Please."*

I was conscious of strong, conflicting urges: on the one hand, to smack her, and on the other, to put a sympathetic hand over hers. I fought down both and forced myself to think calmly for a moment.

I would go, of course; I'd have to. It had nothing to do with Laoghaire, or with what lay between us. If I did not go, and Henri-Christian died—he well *might*—I'd never be able to live with myself. If I came in time, I could save him; no one else could. It was as simple as that.

My heart sank precipitously at the thought of leaving Lallybroch now. How horrible; how could I, knowing that I left Ian for the last time, perhaps leaving them all and the place itself for the last time. But even as I thought these things, the part of my mind that was a surgeon had already grasped the necessity and was setting about the business of planning the quickest way to Philadelphia, contemplating how I should acquire what I needed once there, the possible obstructions and complications that might arise—all the practical analysis of how I should do what had so suddenly been asked of me.

And as my mind clicked through these things, the ruthless logic overwhelming shock, subduing emotion, it began to dawn upon me that this sudden disaster might have other aspects.

Laoghaire was waiting, eyes fixed on me, her mouth firm, willing me to do it.

"All right," I said, leaning back in my chair and fixing her in turn with a level look. "Let's come to terms, then, shall we?"

"SO," I SAID, eyes fixed on the flight of a gray heron as it crossed the loch, "we made a bargain. I'll go to Philadelphia as quickly as I can to take care of Henri-Christian. She'll marry Joey, give up the alimony—and give her permission for Joan to go to the convent. Though I suppose we'd best get it in writing, just in case."

Jamie stared at me, speechless. We were sitting in the long rough grass at the side of the loch, where I'd brought him to tell him what had happened—and what was going to happen.

"She—Laoghaire—has kept Joan's dowry intact; Joan will have that, for traveling and for her entry to the convent," I added. I took a deep breath, hoping to keep my voice steady. "I'm thinking that—well, Michael will be leaving in a few days. Joan and I could go with him to France; I could sail from there on a French ship, and he could see her safely to her convent."

"You—" he began, and I reached to squeeze his hand, to stop him speaking.

"You can't go now, Jamie," I said softly. "I know you can't."

He closed his eyes, grimacing, and his hand tightened on mine in instinctive denial of the obvious. I clung to his fingers just as tightly, in spite of the fact that it was his tender right hand I held. The thought of being parted from him for any amount of time or space—let alone the Atlantic Ocean and the months it might take before we saw each other again—made the bottom of my stomach fall away and filled me with desolation and a sense of vague terror.

He would go with me if I asked—if I even gave him room for doubt about what he must do. I must not.

He needed this so much. Needed what small time remained with Ian; needed even more to be here for Jenny when Ian died, for he could be her comfort in a way that not even her children could be. And if he had needed to go and see Laoghaire out of guilt over the failure of their marriage—how much more acute would be his guilt at abandoning his sister, yet again, and in her most desperate time of need.

"You can't leave," I whispered, urgent. "I *know,* Jamie."

He opened his eyes then and looked at me, eyes dark with anguish.

"I canna let ye go. Not without me."

"It . . . won't be long," I said, forcing the words past the lump in my throat—a lump that acknowledged both my sorrow in parting from him and the greater sorrow for the reason why our separation wouldn't be a long one.

"I've gone farther by myself, after all," I said, trying to smile. His mouth moved, wanting to respond, but the trouble in his eyes didn't change.

I lifted his crippled hand to my lips and kissed it, pressed my cheek against it, my head turned away—but a tear ran down my cheek and I knew he felt the wetness of it on his hand, for his other hand reached for me and drew me into him, and we sat pressed together for a long, long time, listening to the wind that stirred the grass and touched the water. The heron had set down at the far side of the loch and stood on one leg, waiting patiently amid the tiny ripples.

"We'll need a lawyer," I said at last, not moving. "Is Ned Gowan still alive?"

MUCH TO MY astonishment, Ned Gowan *was* still alive. How old could he possibly be? I wondered, looking at him. Eighty-five? Ninety? He was toothless and wrinkled as a crumpled paper bag, but still jaunty as a cricket, and with his lawyer's bloodlust quite intact.

He had drawn up the agreement of annulment for the marriage between Jamie and Laoghaire, cheerfully arranging the annual payments to Laoghaire, the dowries for Marsali and Joan. He set himself now just as cheerfully to dismantling it.

"Now, the question of Mistress Joan's dowry," he said, thoughtfully licking the point of his quill. "You specified, sir, in the original document, that this amount—may I say, this very *generous* amount—was to be endowed upon the young woman upon the occasion of her marriage and to remain her sole property thereafter, not passing to her husband."

"Aye, that's right," Jamie said, not very patiently. He'd told me privately that he would prefer to be staked out naked on an anthill than to have to deal with a lawyer for more than five minutes, and we had been dealing with the complications of this agreement for a good hour. "So?"

"So she is not marrying," Mr. Gowan explained, with the indulgence due to someone not very bright but still worthy of respect by reason of the fact that he was paying the lawyer's fee. "The question of whether she can receive the dowry under this contract—"

"She *is* marrying," Jamie said. "She's becoming a Bride o' Christ, ye ignorant Protestant."

I glanced at Ned in some surprise, having never heard that he *was* a Protestant, but he made no demur at this. Mr. Gowan, sharp as ever, noticed my surprise and smiled at me, eyes twinkling.

"I have no religion save the law, ma'am," he said. "Observance of one form of ritual over another is irrelevant; God to me is the personification of Justice, and I serve Him in that guise."

Jamie made a Scottish noise deep in his throat in response to this sentiment.

"Aye, and a fat lot o' good that will do ye, and your clients here ever realize ye're no a papist."

Mr. Gowan's small dark eyes did not cease to twinkle as he turned them on Jamie.

"I am sure ye dinna suggest such a low thing as blackmail, sir? Why, I hesitate even to name that honorable Scottish institution, knowing as I do the nobility of your character—and the fact that ye're no going to get this bloody contract done without me."

Jamie sighed deeply and settled into his chair.

"Aye, get on with it. What's to do about the dowry, then?"

"Ah." Mr. Gowan turned with alacrity to the matter at hand. "I have spoken with the young woman regarding her own wishes in the matter. As the original maker of the contract, you may—with the consent of the other signatory, which, I understand, has been given"—he uttered a dry little cough at this oblique mention of Laoghaire—"alter the terms of the original document. *Since,* as I say, Mistress Joan does not propose to wed, do you wish to rescind the dowry altogether, to keep the existing terms, or to alter them in some way?"

"I want to give the money to Joan," Jamie said, with an air of relief at finally being asked something concrete.

"Absolutely?" Mr. Gowan inquired, pen poised. "The word 'absolutely' having a meaning in law other than—"

"Ye said ye talked to Joan. What the devil does *she* want, then?"

Mr. Gowan looked happy, as he usually did upon perceiving a new complication.

"She wishes to accept only a small portion of the original dowry, this to be used to provide for her reception into a convent; such a donation is customary, I believe."

"Aye?" Jamie raised one eyebrow. "And what about the rest?"

"She wishes the residue to be given to her mother, Laoghaire MacKenzie Fraser, but not given absolutely, if you follow me. Given with conditions."

Jamie and I exchanged looks.

"*What* conditions?" he asked carefully.

Mr. Gowan held up a withered hand, folding down the fingers as he enumerated the conditions.

"One, that the money shall *not* be released until a proper record of the marriage of Laoghaire MacKenzie Fraser and Joseph Boswell Murray shall be written in the parish register of Broch Mordha, witnessed and attested by a priest. Two, that a contract be signed, reserving and guaranteeing the estate of Balriggan and all its inclusive goods as the sole property of Laoghaire MacKenzie Fraser until her death, thereafter being willed as the aforesaid Laoghaire MacKenzie Fraser shall so dispose in a proper will. Thirdly, the money shall not be given absolutely, but shall be retained by a trustee and disbursed in the amount of twenty pounds per annum, paid jointly to the aforesaid Laoghaire MacKenzie Fraser and Joseph Boswell Murray. Fourth, that these annual payments shall be used only for matters pertaining to the upkeep and improvement of the estate of Balriggan. Fifth, that payment of each year's disbursement shall be contingent upon the receipt of proper documentation regarding the use of the previous year's disbursement." He folded down his thumb and lowered his closed fist, and held up one finger of his other hand.

"Sixth—and lastly—that one James Alexander Gordon Fraser Murray, of Lallybroch, shall be trustee for these funds. Are these conditions agreeable, sir?"

"They are," Jamie said firmly, rising to his feet. "Make it so, if ye please, Mr. Gowan—and now, if no one minds, I am going away and having a wee dram. Possibly two."

Mr. Gowan capped his inkwell, tidied his notes into a neat pile, and likewise rose, though more slowly.

"I'll join ye in that dram, Jamie. I want to hear about this war of yours in America. It sounds the grandest of adventures!"

83

COUNTING SHEEP

AS THE TIME grew shorter, Ian found it impossible to sleep. The need to go, to find Rachel, burned in him so that he felt hot coals in the pit of his stomach all of the time. Auntie Claire called it heartburn, and it was. She said it was from bolting his food, though, and it wasn't that—he could barely eat.

He spent his days with his father, as much as he could. Sitting in the corner of the speak-a-word room, watching his father and his elder brother go about the business of Lallybroch, he couldn't understand how it would be possible to stand up and walk away, to leave them behind. To leave his father forever behind.

During the days, there were things to be done, folk to be visited, to talk to, and the land to be walked over, the stark beauty of it soothing when his feelings grew too heated to bear. At night, though, the house lay quiet, the creaking silence punctuated by his father's distant cough and his two young nephews' heavy breathing in the room beside him. He began to feel the house itself breathe around him, drawing one ragged, heavy-chested gasp after another, and to feel the weight of it on his own chest, so he sat up in bed, gulping air only to be sure he could. And finally he would slide out of bed, steal downstairs with his boots in his hands, and let himself out of the kitchen door to walk the night under clouds or stars, the clean wind fanning the coals of his heart to open flame, until he should find his tears and peace in which to shed them.

One night he found the door unbolted already. He went out cautiously, looking round, but saw no one. Likely Young Jamie gone to the barn; one of the two cows was due to calf any day. He should go and help, maybe . . . but the burning under his ribs was painful, he needed to walk a bit first. Jamie would have fetched him in any case, had he thought he needed help.

He turned away from the house and its outbuildings and headed up the hill, past the sheep pen, where the sheep lay in somnolent mounds, pale under the moon, now and then emitting a soft, sudden *bah!*, as though startled by some sheep dream.

Such a dream took shape before him suddenly, a dark form moving against the fence, and he uttered a brief cry that made the nearer sheep start and rustle in a chorus of low-pitched *bah*s.

"Hush, *a bhailach*," his mother said softly. "Get this lot started, and ye'll wake the dead."

He could make her out now, a small, slender form, with her unbound hair a soft mass against the paleness of her shift.

"Speak o' the dead," he said rather crossly, forcing his heart down out of his throat. "I thought ye were a ghost. What are ye doing out here, Mam?"

"Counting sheep," she said, a thread of humor in her voice. "That's what ye're meant to do when ye canna sleep, aye?"

"Aye." He came and stood beside her, leaning on the fence. "Does it work?"

"Sometimes."

They stood still for a bit, watching the sheep stir and settle. They smelled sweetly filthy, of chewed grass and sheep shit and greasy wool, and Ian found that it was oddly comforting just to be with them.

"Does it work to count them, when ye ken already how many there are?" he asked, after a short silence. His mother shook her head.

"No, I say their names over. It's like saying the rosary, only ye dinna feel the need to be asking. It wears ye down, asking."

Especially when ye ken the answer's going to be no, Ian thought, and moved by sudden impulse, put his arm around her shoulders. She made a small sound of amused surprise, but then relaxed, laying her head against him. He could feel the small bones of her, light as a bird's, and thought his heart might break.

They stood for a while that way, and then she freed herself, gently, moving away a little and turning to him.

"Sleepy yet?"

"No."

"Aye, well. Come on, then." Not waiting for an answer, she turned and made her way through the dark, away from the house.

There was a moon, half full, and he'd been out more than long enough for his eyes to adjust; it was simple to follow, even through the jumbled grass and stones and heather that grew on the hill behind the house.

Where was she taking him? Or rather, why? For they were heading uphill, toward the old broch—and the burying ground that lay nearby. He felt a chill round his heart—did she mean to show him the site of his father's grave?

But she stopped abruptly and stooped, so he nearly tripped over her. Straightening up, she turned and put a pebble into his hand.

"Over here," she said softly, and led him to a small square stone set in the earth. He thought it was Caitlin's grave—the child who'd come before Young Jenny, the sister who'd lived but one day—but then saw that Caitlin's stone lay a few feet away. This one was the same size and shape, but—he squatted by it, and running his fingers over the shadows of its carving, made out the name.

Yeksa'a.

"Mam," he said, and his voice sounded strange to his own ears.

"Is that right, Ian?" she said, a little anxious. "Your da said he wasna quite certain of the spelling of the Indian name. I had the stone carver put both, though. I thought that was right."

"Both?" But his hand had already moved down and found the other name.

Iseabaìl.

He swallowed hard.

"That was right," he said very softly. His hand rested flat on the stone, cool under his palm.

She squatted down beside him, and reaching, put her own pebble on the stone. It was what you did, he thought, stunned, when you came to visit the dead. You left a pebble to say you'd been there; that you hadn't forgotten.

His own pebble was still in his other hand; he couldn't quite bring himself to lay it down. Tears were running down his face, and his mother's hand was on his arm.

"It's all right, *a duine*," she said softly. "Go to your young woman. Ye'll always be here wi' us."

The steam of his tears rose like the smoke of incense from his heart, and he laid the pebble gently on his daughter's grave. Safe among his family.

It wasn't until many days later, in the middle of the ocean, that he realized his mother had called him a man.

84

THE RIGHT OF IT

IAN DIED JUST after dawn. The night had been hellish; a dozen times, Ian had come close to drowning in his own blood, choking, eyes bulging, then rising up in convulsion, spewing up bits of his lungs. The bed looked like some slaughter had taken place, and the room reeked of the sweat of a desperate, futile struggle, the smell of Death's presence.

In the end, though, he had lain quiet, thin chest barely moving, the sound of his breathing a faint rattle like the scratch of the rose briers at the window.

Jamie had stood back, to give Young Jamie the place at Ian's side as eldest son; Jenny had sat all night on his other side, wiping away the blood, the evil sweat, all the foul liquids that oozed from Ian, dissolving his body before their eyes. But near the end, in the dark, Ian had raised his right hand and whispered, "Jamie." He hadn't opened his eyes to look, but all of them knew which Jamie it was that he wanted, and Young

Jamie had made way, stumbling, so that his uncle could come and grasp that seeking hand.

Ian's bony fingers had closed round his with surprising strength. Ian had murmured something, too low to hear, and then let go—not in the involuntary relaxation of death; simply let go, that business done, and let his hand fall back, open, to his children.

He did not speak again but seemed to settle, his body diminishing as life and breath fled from it. When his last breath came, they waited in dull misery, expecting another, and only after a full minute of silence did they begin to look at one another covertly, steal glances at the ravaged bed, the stillness in Ian's face—and realize slowly that it was over at last.

DID JENNY MIND? he wondered. That Ian's last words had been to him? But he thought not; the one mercy to a going such as his brother-in-law's had been was that there was time to take leave. He had made a time to speak alone with each of his children, Jamie knew. Comfort them as he could, maybe leave them with a bit of advice, at the least the reassurance that he loved them.

He had been standing next to Jenny when Ian died. She had sighed and seemed to slump beside him, as though the iron rod that had run up her back for the last year had suddenly been pulled out through her head. Her face had showed no sorrow, though he knew it was there; for that moment, though, she had only been glad it was over—for Ian's sake, for all their sakes.

So surely they had found time, she and Ian, to say what had to be said between them, in the months since they knew.

What would he say to Claire in such circumstances? he wondered suddenly. Probably what he *had* said to her, in parting. *"I love you. I'll see you again."* He didn't see any way of improving on the sentiment, after all.

He couldn't stay in the house. The women had washed Ian and laid him out in the parlor and were now embarked on an orgy of furious cooking and cleaning, for word had gone out and people were already beginning to come for the wake.

The day had dawned spitting rain, but for the moment,

none was falling. He went out through the kailyard and climbed the little slope to the arbor. Jenny was sitting there, and he hesitated for a moment, but then came and sat down beside her. She could send him away if she wanted solitude.

She didn't; she reached up for his hand and he took it, engulfing hers, thinking how fine-boned she was, how frail.

"I want to leave," she said calmly.

"I dinna blame ye," he said, with a glance at the house. The arbor was covered with new leaves, the green of them fresh and soft from the rain, but someone would find them soon. "Shall we walk down by the loch for a bit?"

"No, I mean I want to leave here. Lallybroch. For good."

That took him aback more than a bit.

"Ye dinna mean that, I think," he said at last, cautious. "It's been a shock, after all. Ye shouldna—"

She shook her head and put a hand to her breast.

"Something's broken in me, Jamie," she said softly. "Whatever it was that bound me . . . it binds me nay more."

He didn't know what to say. He'd avoided the sight of the broch and the burying ground at its foot when he came out of the house, unable to bear the dark wet patch of raw ground there—but now he turned his head deliberately and raised his chin to point at it.

"And ye'd leave Ian?" he asked.

She made a small noise in her throat. Her hand lay against her breast still, and at this she pressed it flat, fierce against her heart.

"Ian's with me," she said, and her back straightened in defiance of the fresh-dug grave. "He'll never leave me, nor I him." She turned her head and looked at him then; her eyes were red, but dry.

"He'll never leave ye, either, Jamie," she said. "Ye ken that, as well as I do."

Tears welled in his own eyes then, unexpected, and he turned his head away.

"I ken that, aye," he muttered, and hoped it was true. Just now the place inside him where he was accustomed to find Ian was empty, hollow and echoing as a *bodhran.* Would he come back? Jamie wondered. Or had Ian only moved a bit, to a different part of his heart, a place he hadn't yet looked? He hoped—but he wouldn't go looking just yet awhile and kent it was for fear of finding nothing.

He wanted to change the subject, give her time and space to think. But it was difficult to find anything to say that didn't have to do with Ian being dead. Or with death in general. All loss is one, and one loss becomes all, a single death the key to the gate that bars memory.

"When Da died," he said suddenly, surprising himself as much as her. "Tell me what happened."

He felt her turn to look at him but kept his own eyes on his hands, the fingers of his left hand rubbing slowly over the thick red scar that ran down the back of his right.

"They brought him home," she said at last. "Lying in a wagon. It was Dougal MacKenzie with them. He told me Da had seen ye being whipped, and all of a sudden he'd fallen down, and when they picked him up, one side of his face was drawn up in anguish but the other was slack. He couldna speak, or walk, and so they took him away and brought him home."

She paused, swallowing, her eyes fixed on the broch and the burying ground.

"I had a doctor to him. He bled Da, more than once, and burned things in a wee burner and wafted the smoke under his nose. He tried to give him medicine, but Da couldna really swallow. I put drops of water on his tongue, but that was all." She sighed deeply. "He died the next day, about noon."

"Ah. He . . . never spoke?"

She shook her head. "He couldna speak at all. Only moved his mouth now and then and made wee gurgling sounds." Her chin puckered a little at the memory, but she firmed her lips. "I could see, though, near the end, he was trying to speak. His mouth was trying to shape the words, and his eyes were on mine, trying to make me understand." She glanced at him.

"He did say, 'Jamie,' the once. I ken that much for sure. For I thought he was trying to ask for you, and I told him Dougal said ye were alive and promised that ye'd be all right. That seemed to comfort him a bit, and he died soon after."

He swallowed thickly, the sound of it loud in his ears. It had begun to rain again, lightly, drops pattering on the leaves overhead.

"*Taing,*" he said softly at last. "I wondered. I wish I could have said 'Sorry' to him."

"Ye didna need to," she said just as softly. "He'd ha' known it."

He nodded, unable to speak for a moment. Getting himself under control, though, he took her hand again and turned to her.

"I can say 'Sorry' to you, though, *a pìuthar,* and I do."

"For what?" she said, surprised.

"For believing Dougal when he told me . . . well, when he said ye'd become an English soldier's whore. I was a fool." He looked at his maimed hand, not wanting to meet her eyes.

"Aye, well," she said, and laid her hand on his, light and cool as the new leaves that fluttered round them. "Ye needed him. I didn't."

They sat awhile longer, feeling peaceful, holding hands.

"Where d'ye think he is now?" Jenny said suddenly. "Ian, I mean."

He glanced at the house, then at the new grave waiting, but of course that wasn't Ian anymore. He was panicked for a moment, his earlier emptiness returning—but then it came to him, and, without surprise, he knew what it was Ian had said to him.

"On your right, man." On his right. Guarding his weak side.

"He's just here," he said to Jenny, nodding to the spot between them. "Where he belongs."

Part Seven

Reap the Whirlwind

85

SON OF A WITCH

WHEN ROGER and Buccleigh drove up to the house, Amanda rushed out to meet them and returned to her mother, waving a blue plastic pinwheel on a stick.

"Mama! Look what I got, look what *I* got!"

"Oh, how pretty!" Brianna bent to admire it and, blowing, made the toy spin round.

"I do it, I do it!" Amanda grabbed it back, puffing and blowing with great determination but making little headway.

"From the side, *a leannan,* from the side." William Buccleigh came round the car and picked Amanda up, gently turning her hand so the pinwheel was perpendicular to her face. "Now blow." He put his face close to hers and helped blow, and the pinwheel whirred like a June bug.

"Aye, that's fine, isn't it? You have a go, then, on your own." He gave Bree a half-apologetic shrug and carried Amanda up the path, she industriously puffing and blowing. They passed Jem, who stopped to admire the pinwheel. Roger got out of the car with a couple of carrier bags and paused for a private word with Brianna.

"If we had a dog, I wonder if it would like him, too?" she murmured, nodding after their guest, who was now engaged in animated conversation with both children.

"A man may smile, and smile, and be a villain," Roger replied, watching with a narrowed eye. "And the claims of instinct quite aside, I don't think either dogs or children are necessarily good judges of character."

"Mm. Did he tell you anything else while you were out

today?" Roger had taken William Buccleigh into Inverness to replenish his wardrobe, as he possessed nothing more than the jeans, T-shirt, and charity-store jacket in which he'd arrived.

"A few things. I asked him how he'd come here—to Lallybroch, I mean—and what was he doing hanging about. He said he'd seen me on the street in Inverness and recognized me, but I'd got in my car and gone before he could make up his mind to talk to me. He saw me once or twice more, though, and asked cautiously round to find out where I lived. He—" He stopped and looked at her, with a half smile. "Bear in mind what he is and when he came from. He thought—and I don't think he was telling me a tale—that I must be an Old One."

"Really?"

"Aye, really. And on the face of it . . . well, I did survive being hanged, which most people don't." His mouth twisted a little as he touched the scar on his throat. "And I—we—did, obviously, travel safely through the stones. I mean . . . I could see his point."

Despite her disquiet, she sniffed with amusement.

"Well, yes. You mean he was afraid of you?"

Roger shrugged, helpless. "He was. And I think I believe him—though I will say that if that's the case, he puts up a good front."

"Would you *act* afraid if you were going to confront a powerful supernatural being? Or would you try to play it cool? Being a male of the species, as Mama puts it. Or a proper man, as Da says. You and Da both act like John Wayne if there's anything fishy going on, and this guy is related to both of you."

"Good point," he said, though his mouth twitched at the "powerful supernatural being." Or possibly the "John Wayne" part. "And he admitted that he was reeling a bit at the shock of everything. I could sympathize with *that.*"

"Mm. And we *knew* what we were doing. Sort of. He told me what happened when he came through—did he tell you that, too?"

They had been walking slowly but had nearly reached the door; she could hear Annie's voice in the hall, asking something, exclaiming among the children's chatter, and the lower rumble of William Buccleigh's voice in reply.

"Aye, he did. He wanted—wants, and wants badly—to get back to his own time. Clearly I knew how, and he'd have to come and talk to me to find out. But only a fool would walk straight up to a stranger's door, let alone a stranger you'd come close to killing, much less a stranger who might strike you dead on the spot or turn you into a crow." He shrugged again.

"So he left his job and took to lurking about the place, watching. To see if we were tossing human bones out the back door, I suppose. Jem ran into him out by the broch one day, and he told him he was a Nuckelavee—partly to scare him away, but also because if he came back and told me there was a Nuckelavee up the hill, I might come out and do something magical about it. And if I did . . ." He lifted his hands, palms up.

"If you did, you might be dangerous, but he'd also know you had the power to send him back. Like the Wizard of Oz."

He looked at her for a moment.

"Anyone less like Judy Garland than *him*—" he began, but was interrupted by Annie MacDonald demanding to know what they were hanging about being eaten by midgies for, when there was supper on the table? Apologizing, they went inside.

BRIANNA ATE SUPPER without really noticing what was on her plate. Jem was going to spend the night with Bobby again and go out fishing on Saturday with Rob on the Rothiemurchus estate. She felt a small twinge at that; she remembered her father patiently teaching Jem to cast, with the homemade rod and thread line that was all they had. Would he remember?

Still, it was just as well to have him out of the house. She and Roger were going to have to sit down with William Buccleigh and decide how best to get him back to his own time, and best if Jem wasn't lurking around the edges of such a discussion with his ears flapping. Should they consult Fiona? she wondered suddenly.

Fiona Graham was the granddaughter of old Mrs. Graham, who had kept house for Roger's adoptive father, the Reverend Wakefield. The very proper and elderly Mrs. Graham had also been the "caller"—the holder of a very old tradition indeed. On the fire feast of Beltane, the women whose families had passed the tradition down to them met at dawn and, clothed in white, performed a dance that Roger said was an ancient Norse circle dance. And at the end of it, the caller sang out in words that none of them understood anymore, bringing up the sun, so that as it rose above the horizon, the beam of light shot straight through the cleft of the split stone.

Mrs. Graham had died peacefully in her sleep years before—but had left her knowledge, and her role as caller, to her granddaughter, Fiona.

Fiona had helped Roger when he came through the stones to find Brianna—even contributing her own diamond engagement ring to help him, after his first attempt had ended much as William Buccleigh described his own: in flames in the center of the circle.

They could get a gemstone without much trouble, she thought, automatically passing the bowl of salad to Roger. From what they knew so far, it didn't have to be a terribly expensive stone, or even a large one. The garnets in Roger's mother's locket had apparently been enough to keep him from being killed during his first, abortive try.

She thought suddenly of the burn mark on William Buccleigh's chest and, as she did so, realized that she was staring at him—and he was staring back at her. She choked on a chunk of cucumber, and the subsequent hubbub of back-thumping and arm-raising and coughing and water-fetching luckily explained the redness of her face.

Everyone settled back to their food, but she was aware of Roger looking sideways at her. She shot him a brief look under her lashes, with a faint tilt of the head that said, *"Later. Upstairs,"* and he relaxed, resuming a three-way conversation with "Uncle Buck" and Jemmy about trout flies.

She wanted to talk to him about what Buccleigh had said, and decide what to do about him, as soon as possible. She was *not* going to tell him what William Buccleigh had said about Rob Cameron.

ROGER LAY IN BED, watching the moonlight on Brianna's sleeping face. It was quite late, but he found himself wakeful. Odd, for he usually fell asleep in seconds after making love to her. Fortunately, she did, too; she had tonight, curling into him like a large, affectionate shrimp before lapsing into naked, warm inertness in his arms.

It had been wonderful—but that wee bit different. She was almost always willing, even eager, and that had been no different, though she'd made a particular point of dead-bolting the bedroom door. He'd installed the dead bolt because Jem had learned to pick locks at the age of seven. It was still bolted, in fact, and seeing that, he slid carefully out from under the covers to unfasten it. Jem was spending the night with his new best friend, Bobby, but if Mandy needed them in the night, he didn't want the door locked.

The room was cool, but pleasantly so; they'd put in baseboard heaters, which would be barely adequate to the winter temperatures of the Highlands but fine for late autumn.

Bree slept hot; he'd swear her body temperature rose two or three degrees when she slept, and she often threw off the covers. She lay now, bare to the waist, arms flung over her head and snoring faintly. He cupped a hand absently under his balls, wondering idly whether they might have another go. He thought she wouldn't mind, but . . .

But maybe he shouldn't. When he made love to her, he often took his time and, at the last, was filled with a barbarous delight when she yielded her red-thatched quim—willingly, to be sure, but with an instant always of hesitation, just one final breath of something that was not quite resistance. He thought it was a means of assuring herself—if not him—that she had the right to refuse. A stronghold once breached and repaired has stouter defenses. He didn't think she realized consciously that she did this; he'd never mentioned it to her, wanting no ghost to rise between them.

It had been a little different tonight. She'd balked more noticeably, then yielded with something like ferocity, pulling him in and raking her nails down his back. And he . . .

He'd paused for that one instant, but once safely mounted

had had the insane urge to pillage ruthlessly, to show himself—if not her—that she was indeed his, and not her own, inviolate.

And she'd egged him on.

He noticed that he hadn't taken his hand away and was now eyeing his wife like a Roman soldier sizing up one of the Sabine women for weight and portabililty. *Raptio* was the Latin word, usually translated as "rape," though in fact it meant kidnapping, or seizing. *Raptio,* raptor, the seizing of prey. He could see it both ways, and noticed at this point that he *still* hadn't actually removed his hand from his genitals, which in the meantime had decided unilaterally that, no, she wouldn't mind at all.

His cerebral cortex, rapidly being overpowered by something a lot older and much lower down, hazarded a last faint notion that it was to do with having a stranger in the house—especially one like William Buccleigh MacKenzie.

"Well, he'll be gone by Samhain," Roger muttered, approaching the bed. The portal in the stones should be wide open then, and with some sort of gem in hand, the bugger ought to be back to his wife in . . .

He slid beneath the sheets, gathered his own wife up with a firm hand on her very warm bottom, and hissed in her ear, "I'll get you—and your little dog, too."

Her body quivered in a soundless subterranean laugh and, eyes closed, she reached down and drew a delicate fingernail up his very sensitive flesh.

"I'm meeeeeeeellllllllting," she murmured.

HE DID FALL ASLEEP after that. But waked again, somewhere in the wee hours, and found himself annoyingly alert.

It must be him, he thought, slithering out of bed again. *I'll not sleep sound until we get rid of him.* He didn't bother being careful; he could tell from the faint rasp of Brianna's snore that she was dead to the world. He pulled his pajamas over his nakedness and stepped out into the upstairs corridor, listening.

Lallybroch talked to itself at night, as all old houses do. He was used to the sudden startling cracks, as wooden beams in the room cooled at night, and even the creaking of the second-floor hallway, as though someone was walking rapidly up and down it. The rattle of windows when the wind was in the west, reminding him comfortably of Brianna's irregular snoring. It was remarkably quiet now, though, wrapped in the somnolence of deep night.

They'd put William Buccleigh at the far end of the hall, having decided without speaking of it that they didn't want him above, on the same floor with the kids. Keep him close; keep an eye on him.

Roger walked quietly down the hall, listening. The crack under Buccleigh's door was dark, and from inside the room, he heard a deep, regular snore, interrupted once as the sleeper turned in bed, muttered something incomprehensible, and dropped back into slumber.

"That's all right, then," Roger muttered to himself, and turned away. His cerebral cortex, interrupted earlier, now patiently resumed its train of thought. Of course it was to do with having a stranger in the house—and such a stranger. Both he and Brianna felt obscurely threatened by his presence.

In his own case, there was a solid substratum of anger under the wariness, and a good bit of confusion, too. He had, from sheer necessity as well as religious conviction, forgiven William Buccleigh for his role in the hanging that had taken his voice. After all, the man had not tried to kill him personally and couldn't have known what would happen.

But it was a damned sight easier to forgive somebody you knew had been dead for two hundred years than it was to maintain that forgiveness with the bastard living under your nose, eating your food, and being charming to your wife and children.

And let us not forget he is *a bastard, too,* Roger thought savagely, making his way down the stairs in the dark. The family tree he'd shown William Buccleigh MacKenzie revealed him as all correct, pinned down on paper, neatly bracketed by parents and son. The chart was a lie, though. William Buccleigh MacKenzie was a changeling: the illegitimate offspring of Dougal MacKenzie, war chief of Clan MacKenzie, and Geillis Duncan, witch. And Roger thought William Buccleigh didn't know it.

Safely at the bottom of the stair, he turned on the light in the lower hall and went to the kitchen to check that the back door was locked.

They'd discussed that one, he and Brianna, but hadn't come to an agreement yet. He was for letting sleeping dogs lie; what good could it do the man to know the truth of his origins? The Highlands that had spawned those two wild souls was gone, both now and in William Buccleigh's rightful time.

Bree had insisted that Buccleigh had some right to know the truth—though, challenged, could not say quite what right that was.

"*You* are who you think you are, and you always have been," she'd said at last, frustrated but trying to explain. "I wasn't. Do you think it would have been better if I'd never *known* who my real father was?"

In all honesty, it might have been, he thought. The knowledge, once revealed, had torn both their lives apart, exposed them both to terrible things. It had taken his voice. Almost taken his life. Had put her in danger, gotten her raped, been responsible for her having killed a man—he hadn't spoken to her about that; he should. He saw the weight of it in her eyes sometimes and knew it for what it was. He carried the same weight.

And yet . . . would he choose *not* to have known what he now knew? Never to have lived in the past, met Jamie Fraser, seen the side of Claire that existed only in Jamie's company?

It wasn't the tree of good and evil in the Garden of Eden, after all; it was the tree of the *knowledge* of good and evil. Knowledge might be a poisoned gift—but it was still a gift, and few people would voluntarily give it back. Which was just as well, he supposed, since they *couldn't* give it back. And that had been *his* point in the discussion.

"We don't know what harm it could do," he'd argued. "But we don't know it *couldn't* do harm, and serious harm. And what would be the benefit to the man, to know his mother was insane, a sorceress, or both, certainly a multiple murderess, and his father an adulterer and at the least an attempted murderer? It was enough of a shock to *me* when your mother told me about Geillis Duncan, and she's seven generations removed from me. And before you ask, yes, I could have lived without knowing that."

She'd bitten her lip at that and nodded, reluctant.

"It's just—I keep thinking about Willie," Bree had said at last, giving up. "Not William Buccleigh, I don't mean—my brother." She flushed a little, as she always did, self-conscious at speaking the word. "I really wanted him to *know.* But Da and Lord John . . . they so *didn't* want him to know, and maybe they were right. He has a life, a good one. And they said he couldn't keep on having that life if I told him."

"They were right," Roger had said bluntly. "To tell him—if he believed it—would force him to live in a state of deceit and denial, which would eat him alive, or to openly acknowledge that he's the bastard son of a Scottish criminal. Which is Just. Not. On. Not in eighteenth-century culture."

"They wouldn't take his title away," Bree had argued. "Da said that by British law, a child born in wedlock is the legal offspring of the husband, no matter whether the husband was the real father or not."

"No, but imagine living with a title ye don't think you're entitled *to,* knowing the blood in your veins isn't the blue ye've always thought it was. Having people call ye 'Lord So-and-So' and knowing what they'd call ye if they knew the truth." He'd shaken her gently, trying to make her see.

"Either way, it would destroy the life he has, as surely as if you'd set him on a keg of gunpowder and lit the fuse. You wouldn't know when the bang would come, but come it would."

"Mmphm," she'd said, and the argument ended there. But it hadn't been a sound of agreement, and he knew the argument wasn't over.

By now he had checked all the doors and windows on the ground floor, ending in his study.

He flipped on the light and came into the room. He was wide awake, nerves on edge. *Why?* he wondered. Was the house trying to tell him something? He snorted a little. Hard not to have fancies, in the middle of the night in an old house, with the wind rattling the windowpanes. And yet he usually felt very comfortable in this room, felt it was his place. What was wrong?

He glanced quickly over the desk, the deep windowsill with the small pot of yellow chrysanthemums that Bree had put there, the shelves—

He stopped dead, heart thumping in his chest. The snake wasn't there. No, no, it was—his roving eye fixed on it. It was in the wrong place, though. It wasn't in front of the wooden box that held Claire and Jamie's letters but sitting in front of the books two shelves below it.

He picked it up, automatically stroking the old polished cherrywood with his thumb. Perhaps Annie MacDonald had moved it? No. She did dust and sweep in the study, but she never moved anything from its place. Never moved anything anywhere, for that matter; he'd seen her pick up a pair of galoshes carelessly left in the middle of the mudroom, sweep carefully under them, and set them back in the same place, mud splashes and all. She would never have moved the snake.

Still less would Brianna have moved it. He knew—without knowing how he knew it—that she felt as he did about it; Willie Fraser's snake guarded his brother's treasure.

He was lifting down the box before his train of conscious thought had reached its logical conclusion.

Alarm bells were going off right and left. The contents of the box had been disturbed; the little books were on top of the letters at one end of the box, not underneath. He took out the letters, cursing himself for never having counted them. How would he know if one was missing?

He sorted them quickly, read and unread, and *thought* the unread pile was about the same; whoever had been in the box hadn't opened them, that was something. But whoever it was had probably wanted to avoid detection, too.

He thumbed hastily through the opened letters and became aware at once that one was missing: the one written on Brianna's handmade paper with the embedded flowers. The first one. Jesus, what had it said? *We are alive.* He remembered that much. And then Claire had told all about the explosion and the burning of the Big House. Had she said in that one they were going to Scotland? Maybe so. But why in bloody hell should—

Two floors above, Mandy sat up in bed and screamed like a *ban-sidhe.*

HE MADE IT TO Amanda's room a half step before Brianna and scooped the child out of her bed, cradling her against his pounding heart.

"Jemmy, Jemmy!" she sobbed. "He's gone, he's gone. He's *GONE*!!" This last was shrieked as she stiffened in Roger's arms, digging her feet hard into his belly.

"Hey, hey," he soothed, trying to rearrange her and pet her into calm. "It's okay, Jemmy's fine. He's *fine,* he's only gone to visit Bobby overnight. He'll be home tomorrow."

"He's *GONE*!" She squirmed like an eel, not trying to get away but merely possessed by a paroxysm of frantic grief. "He's not here, he's not here!"

"Aye, like I said, he's at Bobby's house, he—"

"Not *here,*" she said urgently, and thumped the palm of her hand repeatedly on the top of her head. "Not here wif me!"

"Here, baby, come here," Bree said urgently, taking the tear-streaked child from him.

"Mama, Mama! Jemmy's *GONE*!" She clung to Bree, staring desperately, still thumping her head. "He's not wif me!"

Bree frowned at Mandy, puzzled, a hand running over her, checking for temperature, swollen glands, tender tummy . . .

"Not with you," she repeated, speaking intently, trying to get Mandy out of her panic. "Tell Mummy what you mean, sweetheart."

"Not *here*!" In utter desperation, Mandy lowered her head and butted her mother in the chest.

"Oof!"

The door at the end of the hall opened, and William Buccleigh came out, wearing Roger's woolen dressing gown.

"What in the name of the Blessed Virgin's all this riot?" he inquired.

"He took him, he took him!" Mandy shrieked, and buried her head in Brianna's shoulder.

Despite himself, Roger was feeling infected by Amanda's fear, irrationally convinced that something terrible had happened.

"Do you know where Jem is?" he snapped at Buccleigh.

"I do not." Buccleigh frowned at him. "Is he not in his bed?"

"No, he isn't!" Brianna snapped. "You saw him leave, for heaven's sake." She forced her way between the men. "Quit it right now, both of you! Roger, take Mandy. I'm going to phone Martina Hurragh." She thrust Amanda, moaning around the thumb in her mouth, into his arms and hurried for the stairs, her hastily acquired nightclothes rustling like leaves.

He rocked Amanda, distracted, alarmed, nearly overcome by her sense of panic. She emitted fright and grief like a radio broadcasting tower, and his own breath came short and his hands were wet with sweat where he clutched her Winnie-the-Pooh nightie.

"Hush, *a chuisle,*" he said, pitching his voice as calmly as he could. "Hush, now. We'll fix it. You tell Daddy what waked you up, and I'll fix it, promise."

She obediently tried to stifle her sobs, rubbing chubby fists into her eyes.

"Jemmy," she moaned. "I want Jemmy!"

"We'll get him back straightaway," Roger promised. "Tell me, what made you wake up? Did you have a bad dream?"

"Uh-huh." She clutched him tighter, her face full of fear. "Was big wocks, *big* wocks. They scweamed at me!"

Ice water ran straight through his veins. Jesus, oh, Jesus. Maybe she *did* remember her trip through the stones.

"Aye, I see," he said, patting her as soothingly as he could, for the ferment in his own breast. He *did* see. In memory he saw those stones, felt and heard them again. And, turning a little, saw the pallor of William Buccleigh's face and knew he heard the ring of truth in Mandy's voice, too.

"What happened then, *a leannan*? Did you go close to the big rocks?"

"Not me; Jem! That man took him and the wocks *ate* him!" At this, she collapsed in tears again, sobbing inconsolably.

"That man," Roger said slowly, and turned a little more, so that William Buccleigh was in her field of view. "Do you mean *this* man, sweetheart? Uncle Buck?"

"No, nonononononono, a *other* man!" She straightened up, staring into his face with huge, tear-filled eyes, straining to make him understand. "Bobby's daddy!"

He heard Brianna coming upstairs. Fast, but unevenly; it sounded as though she was bumping against the walls of the staircase, losing her balance as she hurried.

She stumbled into view at the top of the stair, and Roger felt every hair on his body stand up at the sight of her white, staring face.

"He's gone," she said, hoarse. "Martina says he's not with Bobby, she didn't expect him tonight at all. I made her go outside and look—Rob lives three houses down. She says his truck is gone."

ROGER'S HANDS were numb with cold, and the steering wheel was slippery with their sweat. He took the turn off the highway at such speed that the off-wheels lifted slightly and the car tilted. William Buccleigh's head thumped the window.

"Sorry," Roger muttered mechanically, and received a grunt of acceptance in reply.

"Mind yourself," Buccleigh said, rubbing his temple. "Ye'll have us over in a ditch, and then what?"

Then what, indeed. With great effort, he eased his foot back on the gas. It was near moonset, and a wan quarter moon did little to light the landscape, black as pitch around them. The headlights of the little Morris barely dented the darkness, and the frail beams swung to and fro as they bounced crazily on the dirt road that led near Craigh na Dun.

"Why the devil should this *trusdair* take your son?" Buccleigh rolled down his window and stuck his head out, vainly trying to see farther than the view through the dust-coated windshield. "And why, for the sake of all holy, bring him *here*?"

"How do I know?" Roger said through his teeth. "Maybe he thinks he needs blood to open the stones. *Christ,* why did I write that?" He pounded a fist on the wheel in frustration.

Buccleigh blinked, very startled, but his gaze sharpened at once.

"Is that it?" he said, urgent. "*Is* that how ye do it? Blood?"

"No, dammit!" Roger said. "It's the time of year, and gemstones. We think."

"But ye wrote down blood, with a query mark next it."

"Yes, but—what do you mean? Did you read my notebook, too, you cunt?"

"Language, son," said William Buccleigh, grim but cool.

"Of course I did. I read everything in your study I could get my hands on—and so would you, in my place."

Roger throttled back the panic that gripped him, enough to manage a curt nod.

"Aye, maybe I would. And if *you'd* taken Jem—I'd kill ye once I found you, but I'd maybe understand why. But *this* fucker! What does he think he's *doing,* for God's sake?"

"Calm yourself," Buccleigh advised him briefly. "Ye'll do your wean no good if ye lose the heid. This Cameron—is he one like us?"

"I don't know. I don't bloody *know.*"

"There are others, though? It's not just in the family?"

"I don't know—I think there are others, but I don't know for sure." Roger struggled to think, struggled to keep the car rolling at a low enough speed to handle the curves of the road, half overgrown with creeping gorse.

He was trying to pray but managing nothing but a terror-stricken, incoherent *Lord, please!* He wished Bree was with him, but they couldn't have brought Mandy anywhere near the rocks, and if they should be in time to catch Cameron . . . if Cameron was even here . . . Buccleigh would help him, he was fairly sure of that.

The back of his mind harbored a forlorn hope that there was some misunderstanding, that Cameron had mistaken the night and, realizing it, was bringing Jem back home, even as Roger and his bloody five times great-grandfather tore over a rocky moor in the dark, headed straight for the most terrible thing either of them knew.

"Cameron—he read the notebook, too," Roger blurted, unable to bear his own thoughts. "By accident. He pretended to think it was all a—a—fiction, something I'd made up for fun. Jesus, what have I *done*?"

"Look out!" Buccleigh threw his arms over his face and Roger stood on the brake, swerving off the road and into a large rock—barely missing the old blue truck that stood on the road, dark and empty.

HE SCRAMBLED UP the hill, scrabbling for handholds in the dark, rocks rolling under his feet, gorse prickles piercing his palms, now and then stabbing under his nails, making him swear. Far below, he could hear William Buccleigh following. Slowly—but following.

He began to hear them long before he reached the crest. It was three days before Samhain, and the stones knew it. The sound that wasn't a sound at all vibrated through the marrow of his bones, made his skull ring and his teeth ache. He gritted his teeth together and kept on. By the time he reached the stones, he was on hands and knees, unable to stand upright.

Dear God, he thought, *God, preserve me! Keep me alive long enough to find him!*

He could barely form thoughts but recalled the flashlight. He'd brought it from the car and now fumbled it out of his pocket, dropping it, having to grope frantically over the short grass in the circle, finding it at last and squeezing the button with a finger that slipped off four times before finally achieving the strength to make the connection.

The beam of light sprang out, and he heard a muffled exclamation of amazement from the dark behind him. Of course, he thought dazedly, William Buccleigh hadn't yet seen a flashlight. The wavering beam passed slowly round the circle, back. What was he looking for? Footprints? Something Jem had dropped, that would show he'd come this way?

There was nothing.

Nothing but the stones. It was getting worse, and he dropped the flashlight, clutching his head with both hands. He had to move . . . had to go . . . go get Jem . . .

He was dragging himself over the grass, white-blind with the pain and nearly mindless, when strong hands grabbed him by the ankles and hauled him backward. He thought there might have been a voice, but if so, it was lost in the piercing scream that echoed inside his head, inside his soul, and he cried out his son's name as loud as he could to hear something besides that noise, felt his throat tear from the effort, but heard nothing.

Then the earth moved beneath him and the world fell away.

FELL AWAY QUITE literally. When he came to some time later, he found that he and William Buccleigh were resting in a shallow declivity in the side of the hill, forty feet below the stone circle. They'd fallen and rolled; he could tell that from the way he felt and the way Buccleigh looked. There was a hint of dawn in the sky, and he could see Buccleigh, scratched and torn, sitting hunched beside him, curled into himself as though his belly hurt.

"What . . . ?" Roger whispered. He cleared his throat and tried again to ask what had happened, but couldn't manage more than a whisper—and even that made his throat burn like fire.

William Buccleigh muttered something under his breath, and Roger realized that he was praying. He tried to sit up and made it, though his head spun.

"Did ye drag me free?" he demanded in his harsh whisper. Buccleigh's eyes were closed and stayed that way until he had finished his prayer. Then he opened them and glanced from Roger to the top of the hill, where the unseen stones still quired their ghastly song of time undone—no more from here, thank goodness, than an eerie whine that set his teeth on edge.

"I did," Buccleigh said. "I didna think ye were going to make it out on your own."

"I wasn't." Roger lowered himself back onto the ground, dizzy and aching. "Thanks," he added a moment later. There was a great void inside him, vast as the fading sky.

"Aye, well. Maybe it'll help to make up for getting ye hanged," Buccleigh said, in an offhand way. "What now?"

Roger stared up at the sky, rotating slowly overhead. It made him dizzier, so he closed his eyes and reached out a hand.

"Now we go home," he croaked. "And think again. Help me up."

86

VALLEY FORGE

WILLIAM WORE his uniform. It was necessary, he told his father.

"Denzell Hunter is a man of great conscience and principle. I cannot engage to winkle him out of the American camp without proper leave of his officer. I think he would not come. But if I can obtain permission—and I think I can—then I believe he will."

But to obtain formal permission for the services of a Continental surgeon, obviously he had to ask formally. Which meant riding into Washington's new winter quarters at Valley Forge in a red coat, no matter what happened next.

Lord John had closed his eyes for a moment, plainly envisioning just what sort of thing *might* happen next, but then opened them and said briskly, "All right, then. Will you take a servant with you?"

"No," William said, surprised. "Why would I need one?"

"To care for the horses, to manage your goods—and to be the eyes in the back of your head," his father said, giving him a look indicating that he should already have been aware of some of this. He therefore did *not* say, *"Horses?"* or *"What goods?"* but merely nodded and said, "Thank you, Papa. Can you find me someone suitable?"

"Suitable" turned out to be one Colenso Baragwanath, a stunted youth from Cornwall who had come with Howe's troops as a stable-boy. He did know horses, William would give him that.

There were four horses and a pack mule, this last laden with sides of pork, four or five fat turkeys, a bag of rough-skinned potatoes, another of turnips, and a large keg of cider.

"If conditions there are half as bad as I think they are," his father had told him, while overseeing the loading of the mule, "the commander would lend you the services of half a battalion in exchange for this, let alone a surgeon."

"Thank you, Papa," he said again, and swung into his saddle, his new captain's gorget about his neck and a white flag of truce folded neatly into his saddlebag.

Valley Forge looked like a gigantic encampment of doomed charcoal-burners. The place was essentially a wood lot, or had been before Washington's soldiers began felling everything in sight. Hacked stumps were everywhere, and the ground was strewn with broken branches. Huge bonfires burned in random spots, and piles of logs were stacked everywhere. They were building huts as fast as possible—and none too soon, for snow had begun falling three or four hours before, and the camp was already blanketed with white.

William hoped they'd be able to *see* the flag of truce.

"Right, up you go and ride ahead of me," he told Colenso, handing the boy the long stick to which he'd tied the flag. The youth's eyes widened in horror.

"What, me?"

"Yes, you," said Willie impatiently. "Up, or I'll kick your arse."

William's back itched between the shoulder blades as they entered the camp, Colenso crouched like a monkey on his horse's back, holding the flag as low as he dared and muttering strange oaths in Cornish. William's left hand itched, too, wanting to go for the hilt of his sword, the handle of his pistol. But he'd come unarmed. If they meant to shoot him, they'd shoot him, armed or not, and to come unarmed was a sign of good faith. So he put back his cloak, in spite of the snow, to show his lack of weapons, and rode slowly into the storm.

THE PRELIMINARIES went well. No one shot him, and he was directed to a Colonel Preston, a tall, ragged man in the remnants of a Continental uniform, who had eyed him askance but listened with surprising courtesy to his request. Permission was granted—but this being the *American* army, the permission granted was not license to take the surgeon away but rather license to *ask* the surgeon if he would go.

Willie left Colenso with the horses and mule, with strict instructions to keep his eyes open, and made his way up the little hill where he had been told Denzell Hunter likely was. His heart was beating fast, and not only from the exertion. In Philadelphia, he had been sure Hunter would come at his request. Now he wasn't quite so sure.

He had fought Americans, knew a great many of them who were in no respect different from the Englishmen they'd been two years previous. But he'd never walked through an American army camp before.

It seemed chaotic, but all camps did in their early stages, and he was able to perceive the rough order that did in fact exist among the piles of debris and butchered tree stumps. But there was something very different about the feel of this camp, something almost exuberant. The men he passed were ragged in the extreme; not one in ten had shoes, despite the weather, and groups of them huddled like beggars around the bonfires, wrapped in blankets, shawls, the remnants of canvas tents and burlap sacks. And yet they didn't huddle in miserable silence. They talked.

Conversed amiably, telling jokes, arguing, getting up to piss in the snow, to stamp round in circles to get the blood going. He'd seen a demoralized camp before, and this one *wasn't.* Which was, all things considered, amazing. He assumed Denzell Hunter must share this spirit. That being so, would he consent to leave his fellows? No way to tell, save by asking.

There was no door to knock on. He came round a stand of leafless oak saplings that had so far escaped the ax and found Hunter crouched on the ground, sewing up a gash in the leg of a man who lay before him on a blanket. Rachel Hunter held the man's shoulders, her capped head bent over him as she spoke encouragingly to him.

"Did I not tell thee he was quick?" she was saying. "No more than thirty seconds, I said, and so it has been. I counted it out, did I not?"

"Thee counts in a most leisurely fashion, Rachel," the doctor said, smiling as he reached for his scissors and clipped the thread. “A man might walk three times around St. Paul’s in one of your minutes.”

“Stuff,” she said mildly. “’Tis done, in any case. Here, sit thee up and take some water. Thee does not—” She had turned toward the bucket that sat beside her and, as she did so, perceived William standing there. Her mouth opened in shock, and then she was up and flying across the clearing to embrace him.

He hadn’t expected *that,* but was delighted and returned the embrace with great feeling. She smelled of herself and of smoke, and it made his blood run faster.

“Friend William! I thought never to see thee again,” she said, stepping back with glowing face. “What does thee here? For I think thee has not come to enlist,” she added, looking him up and down.

“No,” he said, rather gruffly. “I have come to beg a favor. From your brother,” he added, a little belatedly.

“Oh? Come, then, he is nearly finished.” She led him to Denny, still looking up at him in great interest.

“So thee is indeed a British soldier,” she remarked. “We thought thee must be but feared thee might be a deserter. I am pleased thee is not.”

“Are you?” he asked, smiling. “But surely you would prefer that I abjure my military service and seek peace?”

“Of course I would that thee should seek peace—and find it, too,” she said matter-of-factly. “But thee cannot find peace in oath-breaking and illegal flight, knowing thy soul steeped in deceit and fearing for thy life. Denny, look who has come!”

“Yes, I saw. Friend William, well met!” Dr. Hunter helped his freshly bandaged patient to his feet and came toward William, smiling. “Did I hear thee would ask a favor of me? If it is my power to grant it, it is thine.”

“I won’t hold you to that,” William said, smiling and feeling a knot relax at the base of his neck. “But hear me out, and I hope you will see fit to come.”

As he had half-expected, Hunter was at first hesitant to leave the camp. There were not many surgeons, and with so much illness due to the cold and the crowded conditions . . . it might be a week or more before he could return to camp . . . but William wisely kept silence, only glancing once at Rachel and then meeting Denzell’s eyes straight on.

Would you have her stay here through the winter?

"Thee wishes Rachel to come with me?" Hunter asked, instantly divining his meaning.

"I will come with thee whether he wishes it or not," Rachel pointed out. "And both of you know it perfectly well."

"Yes," said Denzell mildly, "but it seemed mannerly to ask. Besides, it is not only a matter of thy coming. It—"

William didn't hear the end of his sentence, for a large object was thrust suddenly between his legs from behind, and he emitted an unmanly yelp and leaped forward, whirling round to see who had assaulted him in this cowardly fashion.

"Yes, I was forgetting the dog," Rachel said, still composed. "He can walk now, but I doubt he can manage the journey to Philadelphia on foot. Can thee make shift to transport him, does thee think?"

He recognized the dog at once. There couldn't possibly be two like him.

"Surely this is Ian Murray's dog?" he asked, putting out a tentative fist for the enormous beast to sniff. "Where is his master?"

The Hunters exchanged a brief glance, but Rachel answered readily enough.

"Scotland. He has gone to Scotland on an urgent errand, with his uncle, James Fraser. Does thee know Mr. Fraser?" It seemed to William that both Hunters were staring at him rather intently, but he merely nodded and said, "I met him once, many years ago. Why did the dog not go to Scotland with his master?"

Again that glance between them. What was it about Murray? he wondered.

"The dog was injured, just before they took ship. Friend Ian was kind enough to leave his companion in my care," Rachel said calmly. "Can thee procure a wagon, perhaps? I think thy horse may not like Rollo."

LORD JOHN FITTED the leather strap between Henry's teeth. The boy was half unconscious from a dose of laudanum but knew enough still of his surroundings to give his uncle the bare attempt at a grin. Grey could feel the fright pulsing through Henry—and shared it. There was a ball of venomous snakes in his belly, a constant slithering sensation, punctuated by sudden stabs of panic.

Hunter had insisted upon binding Henry's arms and legs to the bed, that there should be no movement during the operation. The day was brilliant; sun coruscated from the frozen snow that rimmed the windows, and the bed had been moved to take best advantage of it.

Dr. Hunter had been told of the dowser but declined courteously to have the man come again, saying that this smacked of divination, and if he were to ask God's help in this endeavor, he thought he could not do so sincerely were there anything of witchcraft about the process. That had rather affronted Mercy Woodcock, who puffed up a bit, but she kept silence, too glad—and too anxious—to argue.

Grey was not superstitious but *was* of a practical turn of mind and had taken a careful note of the dowser's location of the ball he had found. He explained this, and with Hunter's reluctant assent, took out a small ruler and triangulated the spot on Henry's sunken belly, dabbing a bit of candle black on the place to mark it.

"I think we are in readiness," Denzell said, and, coming close to the bed, put his hands on Henry's head and prayed briefly for guidance and support for himself, for endurance and healing for Henry, and ended in acknowledging the presence of God among them. Despite his purely rational sentiments, Grey felt a small lessening of the tension in the room and sat down opposite the surgeon, with the snakes in his belly calmed for the moment.

He took his nephew's limp hand in his and said calmly, "Just hold on, Henry. I won't let go."

IT *WAS* QUICK. Grey had seen army surgeons at work and knew their dispatch, but even by those standards, Denzell Hunter's speed and dexterity were remarkable. Grey had lost all sense of time, absorbed in the erratic clenching of Henry's fingers, the shrill keen of his screaming through the leather gag, and the doctor's movements, quickly brutal, then finicking as he picked delicately, swabbed, and stitched.

As the last stitches went in, Grey breathed, for what seemed the first time in hours, and saw by the carriage clock on the mantel that barely a quarter of an hour had elapsed. William and Rachel Hunter stood by the mantelpiece, out of the way, and he saw with some interest that they were holding hands, their knuckles as white as their faces.

Hunter was checking Henry's breathing, lifting his eyelids to peer at his pupils, wiping the tears and snot from his face, touching the pulse under his jaw—Grey could see this, weak and irregular but still pumping, a tiny blue thread beneath the waxen skin.

"Well enough, well enough, and thanks be to the Lord who has strengthened me," Hunter was murmuring. "Rachel, will thee bring me the dressings?"

Rachel at once detached herself from William and fetched the neat stack of folded gauze pads and torn linen strips, together with a glutinous mass of some sort, soaking green through the cloth that bound it.

"What is *that*?" Grey asked, pointing at it.

"A poultice recommended to me by a colleague, a Mrs. Fraser. I have seen it to have laudable effects upon wounds of all kinds," the doctor assured him.

"Mrs. Fraser?" Grey said, surprised. "Mrs. *James* Fraser? Where the de—I mean, where did you happen to encounter the lady?"

"At Fort Ticonderoga" was the surprising answer. "She and her husband were with the Continental army through the battles at Saratoga."

The snakes in Grey's belly roused abruptly.

"Do you mean to tell me that Mrs. Fraser is now at Valley Forge?"

"Oh, no." Hunter shook his head, concentrated on his dressing. "If thee will please lift him a little, Friend Grey? I require to pass this bandage underneath—ah, yes, exactly right, I thank thee. No," he resumed, straightening up and wiping his forehead, for it was very warm in the room, with so many people and a blazing fire built up in the hearth. "No, the Frasers have gone to Scotland. Though Mr. Fraser's nephew was sufficiently kind as to leave us his dog," he added, as Rollo, made curious by the smell of blood, now rose from his spot in the corner and poked his nose under Grey's elbow. He sniffed interestedly at the splattered sheets, up and down Henry's naked body. He then sneezed explosively, shook his head, and padded back to lie down, where he promptly rolled onto his back and relaxed, paws in the air.

"Someone must remain with him for the next day or so," Hunter was saying, wiping his hands on a rag. "He must not be left alone, lest he cease breathing. Friend William," he said, turning to Willie, "might it be possible to find a place for us to stay? I should be near for several days, so that I may call regularly to see how he progresses."

William assured him that this had already been taken care of: a most respectable inn, and—here he glanced at Rachel—quite near at hand. Might he convey the Hunters there? Or take Miss Rachel, if her brother should be not quite finished?

It was apparent to Grey that Willie would like nothing better than a ride through the snow-sparkling city alone with this comely Quaker, but Mrs. Woodcock put a spoke in that wheel by observing that, in fact, it was Christmas; she had not had time or opportunity to make much of a meal, but would the gentlemen and lady not honor her house and the day by taking a glass of wine, to drink to Lieutenant Grey's recovery?

This was generally agreed to as a capital idea, and Grey volunteered to sit with his nephew while the wine and glasses were being fetched.

With so many people suddenly gone, the room felt much cooler. Nearly cold, in fact, and Grey drew both sheet and coverlet gently up over Henry's bandaged stomach.

"You'll be all right, Henry," he whispered, though his nephew's eyes were closed, and he thought the young man might be asleep—hoped he was.

But he wasn't. Henry's eyes slowly opened, his pupils showing the effect of the opium; his creased lids showed the pain that the opium could not touch.

"No, I won't," he said, in a weak, clear voice. "He got only one. The second ball will kill me."

His eyes closed again, as the sound of Christmas cheer came up the stairs. The dog sighed.

RACHEL HUNTER PUT one hand to her stomach, another to her mouth, and stifled a rising eructation.

"Gluttony is a sin," she said. "But one that carries its own punishment. I think I may vomit."

"All sins do," her brother replied absently, dipping his pen. "But thee is not a glutton. I saw thee eat."

"But I am like to burst!" she protested. "And, besides, I cannot help but think of the poor Christmas those we left at Valley Forge will make, by comparison with the . . . *the* . . . *decadence* of our meal tonight."

"Well, that is guilt, not gluttony, and false guilt at that. Thee ate no more than would constitute a normal meal; it is only that thee hasn't had one in months. And I think roast goose is perhaps not the uttermost word in decadence, even when stuffed with oysters and chestnuts. Now, had it been a pheasant stuffed with truffles, or a wild boar with a gilded apple in its mouth . . ." He smiled at her over his papers.

"Thee has seen such things?" she asked curiously.

"I have, yes. When I worked in London with John Hunter. He was much in society and would now and then take me with him to attend a case and sometimes to accompany him and his wife to some grand occasion—most kind of him. But we must not judge, thee knows, most particularly by appearance. Even one who seems most frivolous, spendthrift, or light-minded yet has a soul and is valuable before God."

"Yes," she said vaguely, not really attending. She pulled back the curtain from the window, seeing the street outside as a white blur. There was a lantern hung by the inn's door that cast a small circle of light, but the snow was still falling. Her own face floated in the dark glass of the window, thin and big-eyed, and she frowned at it, pushing a straggle of dark hair back under her cap.

"Does thee think he knows?" she asked abruptly. "Friend William?"

"Does he know what?"

"His very striking resemblance to James Fraser," she said, letting the curtain fall. "Surely thee does not think this coincidence?"

"I think it is not our business." Denny resumed scratching with his quill.

She heaved an exasperated sigh. He was right, but that

didn't mean she was forbidden to observe and to wonder. She had been happy—more than happy—to see William again, and while his being a British soldier was no less than she had suspected, she had been extremely surprised to find him an officer of high rank. Much more than surprised to learn from his villainous-looking Cornish orderly that he was a lord, though the little creature had been uncertain what kind.

Yet surely no two men could look so alike who did not share blood in some close degree. She had seen James Fraser many times and admired him for his tall, straight dignity, thrilling a bit at the fierceness in his face, always feeling that niggle of recognition when she saw him—but it wasn't until William suddenly stepped out before her at the camp that she realized *why*. Yet how could an English lord be in any way related to a Scottish Jacobite, a pardoned criminal? For Ian had told her something of his own family history—though not enough; not nearly enough.

"Thee is thinking of Ian Murray again," her brother observed, not looking up from his paper. He sounded resigned.

"I thought thee abjured witchcraft," she said tartly. "Or does thee not include mind reading among the arts of divination?"

"I notice thee does not deny it." He looked up then, pushing his spectacles up his nose with a finger, the better to look through them at her.

"No, I don't deny it," she said, lifting her chin at him. "How did thee know, then?"

"Thee looked at the dog and sighed in a manner betokening an emotion not usually shared between a woman and a dog."

"Hmph!" she said, disconcerted. "Well, what if I *do* think of him? Is that not my business, either? To wonder how he does, what his family in Scotland makes of him? Whether he feels he has come home there?"

"Whether he will come back?" Denny took off his spectacles and rubbed a hand over his face. He was tired; she could see the day in his features.

"He will come back," she said evenly. "He would not abandon his dog."

That made her brother laugh, which annoyed her very much.

"Yes, he will likely come back for the dog," he agreed. "And if he comes back with a wife, Sissy?" His voice was gentle now, and she swung round to the window again, to keep him from seeing that the question disturbed her. Not that he needed to see to know that.

"It might be best for thee and for him if he did, Rachel." Denny's voice was still gentle but held a warning note. "Thee knows he is a man of blood."

"What would thee have me do, then?" she snapped, not turning round. "Marry William?"

There was a brief silence from the direction of the desk.

"William?" Denny said, sounding mildly startled. "Does thee feel for him?"

"I—of course I feel friendship for him. And gratitude," she added hastily.

"So do I," her brother observed, "yet the thought of marrying him had not crossed my mind."

"Thee is a most annoying person," she said crossly, turning round and glaring at him. "Can thee not refrain from making fun of me for one day, at least?"

He opened his mouth to answer, but a sound from outside took her attention, and she turned again to the window, pulling back the heavy curtain. Her breath misted the dark glass, and she rubbed it impatiently with her sleeve in time to see a sedan chair below. The door of it opened and a woman stepped out into the swirling snow. She was clad in furs and in a hurry; she handed a purse to one of the chair-bearers and rushed into the inn.

"Well, that is odd," Rachel said, turning to look first at her brother, and then at the small clock that graced their rooms. "Who goes a-visiting at nine o'clock on Christmas night? It cannot be a Friend, surely?" For Friends did not keep Christmas and would find the feast no bar to travel, but the Hunters had no connections—not yet—with the Friends of any Philadelphia meeting.

A thump of footsteps on the staircase prevented Denzell's reply, and an instant later the door of the room burst open. The fur-clad woman stood on the threshold, white as her furs.

"Denny?" she said in a strangled voice.

Her brother stood up as though someone had applied a hot coal to the seat of his breeches, upsetting the ink.

"Dorothea!" he cried, and in one bound had crossed the room and was locked in passionate embrace with the fur-clad woman.

Rachel stood transfixed. The ink was dripping off the table onto the painted canvas rug, and she thought she ought to do something about that, but didn't. Her mouth was hanging open. She thought she ought to close it, and did.

Quite suddenly she understood the impulse that caused men to engage in casual blasphemy.

RACHEL PICKED UP her brother's spectacles from the floor and stood holding them, waiting for him to disentangle himself. *Dorothea,* she thought to herself. *So this is the woman—but surely this is William's cousin?* For William had mentioned his cousin to her as they rode in from Valley Forge. Indeed, the woman had been in the house when Denny performed the operation on—but then, Henry Grey must be this woman's brother! She had hidden in the kitchen when Rachel and Denny came to the house this afternoon. Why . . . Of course: it was not squeamishness or fear but a wish not to come face-to-face with Denny, and him on his way to perform a dangerous operation.

She thought somewhat better of the woman for that, though she was not yet disposed to clasp her to her own bosom and call her sister. She doubted the woman felt so toward her, either—though in fact, she might not even have noticed Rachel yet, let alone have conclusions about her.

Denny let go of the woman and stood back, though from the look on his glowing face, he could hardly bear not to touch her.

"Dorothea," he said. "Whatever does thee—"

But he was forestalled; the young woman—she was very pretty, Rachel saw now—stepped back and dropped her elegant ermine cloak on the floor with a soft thud. Rachel blinked. The young woman was wearing a sack. No other word for it, though now that she looked, she perceived that it had sleeves. It was made of some coarse gray fabric, though, and hung from the young woman's shoulders, barely touching her body elsewhere.

"I will be a Quaker, Denny," she said, lifting her chin a little. "I have made up my mind."

Denny's face twitched, and Rachel thought he could not make up his own mind whether to laugh, cry, or cover his beloved with her cloak again. Not liking to see the lovely thing lie disregarded on the floor, Rachel bent and picked it up herself.

"Thee—Dorothea," he said again, helpless. "Is thee sure of this? I think thee knows nothing of Friends."

"Certainly I do. You—thee, I mean—see God in all men, seek peace in God, abjure violence, and wear dull clothes so as not to distract your minds with the vain things of the world. Is that not right?" Dorothea inquired anxiously. *Lady* Dorothea, Rachel corrected herself. William had said his uncle was a duke.

"Well . . . more or less, yes," Denny said, his lips twitching as he looked her up and down. "Did thee . . . make that garment?"

"Yes, of course. Is something wrong with it?"

"Oh, no," he said, sounding somewhat strangled. Dorothea looked sharply at him, then at Rachel, suddenly seeming to notice her.

"What's wrong with it?" she appealed to Rachel, and Rachel saw the pulse beating in her round white throat.

"Nothing," she said, fighting her own urge to laugh. "Friends are allowed to wear clothes that fit, though. Thee need not purposefully uglify thyself, I mean."

"Oh, I see." Lady Dorothea gazed thoughtfully at Rachel's tidy skirt and jacket, which might be of butternut homespun but most assuredly fit well, and became her, too, if she did say so.

"Well, that's good, then," Lady Dorothea said. "I'll just take it in a bit here and there." Dismissing this, she stepped forward again and took Denny's hands in her own.

"Denny," she said softly. "Oh, Denny. I thought I should never see you again."

"I thought so, too," he said, and Rachel saw a new struggle taking place in his face—one between duty and desire, and her heart ached for him. "Dorothea . . . thee cannot stay here. Thy uncle—"

"He doesn't know I've gone out. I'll go back," Dorothea assured him. "Once we've settled things between us."

"Settled things," he repeated, and, with a noticeable effort, withdrew his hands from hers. "Thee means—"

"Will thee take a little wine?" Rachel broke in, reaching for the decanter the servant had left for them.

"Yes, thank you. He'll have some, too," Dorothea said, smiling at Rachel.

"I expect he will need it," Rachel murmured, with a glance at her brother.

"Dorothea . . ." Denny said helplessly, running a hand through his hair. "I know what thee means. But it is not only a matter of thee becoming a Friend—always assuming that to be . . . to be . . . possible."

She drew herself up, proud as a duchess.

"Do you doubt my conviction, Denzell Hunter?"

"Er . . . not exactly. I just think that perhaps thee has not given the matter sufficient thought."

"That's what you think!" A flush rose in Lady Dorothea's cheeks, and she glared at Denny. "I'll have you—thee, I mean—know that I've done nothing *but* think, ever since you left London. How the devil do you—thee—think I bloody got here?"

"Thee conspired to have thy brother shot in the abdomen?" Denny inquired. "That seems somewhat ruthless, and perhaps not certain of success."

Lady Dorothea drew two or three long breaths in through her nose, eyeing him.

"Now, you see," she said, in a reasonable tone of voice, "was I not quite the perfect Quaker, I would strike you. Thee. But I have not, have I? Thank you, my dear," she said to Rachel, taking a glass of wine. "You are his sister, I collect?"

"Thee has not," Denny admitted warily, ignoring Rachel. "But even allowing, for the sake of argument," he added, with a glimmer of his usual self, "that God has indeed spoken to thee and said that thee must join us, that still leaves the small matter of thy family."

"There is nothing in your principles of faith that requires me to have my father's permission to marry," she snapped. "I asked."

Denny blinked.

"Who?"

"Priscilla Unwin. She's a Quaker I know in London. You know her, too, I think; she said you'd—thee'd? That can't be right—that you'd lanced a boil on her little brother's bum."

At this point, Denny became aware—perhaps because his eyes were sticking out of his head looking at Lady Dorothea, Rachel thought, not altogether amused—that his spectacles were missing. He put out a finger to push them up the bridge of his nose, then stopped and looked about, squinting. With a sigh, Rachel stepped forward and settled them onto his nose. Then she picked up the second glass of wine and handed it to him.

"She's right," she told him. "Thee needs it."

"PLAINLY," LADY DOROTHEA said, "we are getting nowhere." She did not look like a woman accustomed to getting nowhere, Rachel thought, but was keeping a fair grip on her temper. On the other hand, she was not even close to giving in to Denny's urging that she must go back to her uncle's house.

"I'm not going back," she said, in a reasonable tone of voice, "because if I do, you'll sneak off to the Continental army in Valley Forge, where you think I won't follow you."

"Thee would not, surely?" Denny said, and Rachel thought she divined a thread of hope in the question, but she wasn't sure what kind of hope it was.

Lady Dorothea fixed him with a wide blue stare.

"I have followed thee across an entire bloody ocean. You—thee—think a damned army can stop me?"

Denny rubbed a knuckle down the bridge of his nose.

"No," he admitted. "I don't. That is why I have not left. I do not wish thee to follow me."

Lady Dorothea swallowed audibly but bravely kept her chin up.

"Why?" she said, and her voice shook only a little. "Why do you not wish me to follow you?"

"Dorothea," he said, as gently as possible. "Putting aside the fact that thy going with me would put thee in rebellion and in conflict with thy family—it is an army. Moreover, it is a very poor army, and one lacking every conceivable comfort, including clothing, bedding, shoes, and food. Beyond that, it is an army on the verge of disaster and defeat. It is no fit place for you."

"And it is a fit place for your sister?"

"Indeed it is not," he said. "But—" He stopped short, obviously realizing that he was on the verge of stepping into a trap.

"But thee can't stop me coming with thee." Rachel sprang it for him, sweetly. She was not quite sure she should help this strange woman, but she did admire the Lady Dorothea's spirit.

"And you can't stop me, either," Dorothea said firmly.

Denny rubbed three fingers hard between his brows, closing his eyes as though in pain.

"Dorothea," he said, dropping his hand and drawing himself up. "I am called to do what I do, and it is the Lord's business and mine. Rachel comes with me not only because she is pigheaded but also because she is my responsibility; she has no other place to go."

"I do, too!" Rachel said hotly. "Thee said thee would find me a place of safety with Friends, if I wanted. I didn't, and I don't."

Before Denny could come back with anything else, Lady Dorothea held out her hand in a dramatic gesture of command, stopping him dead.

"I have an idea," she said.

"I greatly fear to ask what it is," Denny said, sounding entirely sincere.

"I don't," Rachel said. "What?"

Dorothea looked from one to the other. "I have been to a Quaker meeting. Two, in fact. I know how it's done. Let us hold a meeting and ask the Lord to guide us."

Denny's mouth fell open, greatly entertaining Rachel, who was seldom able to dumbfound her brother but was beginning to enjoy seeing Dorothea do it.

"That—" he began, sounding stunned.

"Is an excellent idea," Rachel said, already dragging another chair near to the fire.

Denny could hardly argue. Looking remarkably discombobulated, he sat, though Rachel noticed that he put her between Dorothea and himself. She wasn't sure whether he was afraid to be too close to Dorothea, lest the power of her presence overwhelm him, or whether it was only that sitting across the hearth from her gave him the best view.

They all settled slowly, shifting a bit for comfort, and lapsed into silence. Rachel closed her eyes, seeing the warm redness of the fire inside her lids, feeling the comfort of it on her hands and feet. She gave silent thanks for it, remembering the constant griping of cold in the camp, the nails of her fingers and toes on fire with it, and the continual shivering that lessened but did not stop when she huddled into her blankets at night and left her muscles fatigued and sore. It was no wonder Denny didn't want Dorothea to go with them. She didn't want to go back, would give almost anything not to go—anything but Denny's well-being. She hated being cold and hungry, but it would be much worse to be warm and well-fed and know that he suffered alone.

Did Lady Dorothea have any idea what it would be like? she wondered, and opened her eyes. Dorothea sat quiet but upright, graceful hands folded in her lap. She supposed Denny was imagining, as Rachel was, those hands reddened and marred by chilblains, that lovely face gaunt with hunger and blotched with dirt and cold.

Dorothea's eyes were shadowed by her lids, but Rachel was sure she was looking at Denny. This was a considerable gamble on Dorothea's part, she thought. For what if the Lord spoke to Denny and said it was impossible, that he must send her away? What if the Lord spoke to Dorothea now, she thought suddenly, or what if He had already? Rachel was quite taken back at the thought. It wasn't that Friends thought that the Lord spoke only to them; it was only that they weren't sure other folk listened very often.

Had she been listening herself? In all honesty, she was forced to admit that she had not. And she knew why: out of a disinclination to hear what she was afraid she must—that she must turn away from Ian Murray and abandon the thoughts of him that warmed her body and heated her dreams in the freezing forest, so she woke sometimes sure that if she put out her hand to the falling snow, it would hiss and vanish from her palm.

She swallowed hard and closed her eyes, trying to open herself to the truth but trembling in fear of hearing it.

All she heard, though, was a steady panting noise, and an instant later Rollo's wet nose nudged her hand. Disconcerted, she scratched his ears. Surely it wasn't seemly to be doing that in meeting, but he would keep nudging her until she complied, she knew. He half-closed his yellow eyes in pleasure and rested his heavy head upon her knee.

The dog loves him, she thought, rubbing gently through the thick, coarse fur. *Can he be a bad man, if that is so?* It wasn't God she heard in reply but her brother, who would certainly say, *"While dogs are worthy creatures, I think they are perhaps no judge of character."*

But I am, she thought to herself. *I know what he is—and I know him for what he might be, too.* She looked at Dorothea, motionless in her gray bag of a dress. Lady Dorothea Grey was prepared to abandon her former life, and very likely her family, to become a Friend, for Denny's sake. Might it not be, she wondered, that Ian Murray could turn from violence for hers?

Well, there is a proud thought, she scolded herself. *What sort of power does thee think thee has, Rachel Mary Hunter? No one has that sort of power, save the Lord.*

But the Lord did have it. And if the Lord should be so inclined, anything was possible. Rollo's tail moved gently, thumping thrice upon the floor.

Denzell Hunter straightened a little on his stool. It was the slightest movement, but coming as it did out of utter stillness, it surprised both the women, who lifted their heads like startled birds.

"I love thee, Dorothea," he said. He spoke very quietly, but his soft eyes burned behind his spectacles, and Rachel felt her chest ache. "Will thee marry me?"

87

SEVERANCE AND REUNION

April 20, 1778

AS TRANSATLANTIC voyages went—and after our adventures with Captains Roberts, Hickman, and Stebbings, I considered myself something of a connoisseur of seagoing disaster—the trip to America was quite dull. We did have a slight brush with an English man-of-war but fortunately outran her, did run into two squalls and a major storm but luckily didn't sink, and while the food was execrable, I was much too distracted to do more than knock weevils out of the biscuit before eating it.

Half my mind was on the future: Marsali and Fergus's precarious situation, the danger of Henri-Christian's condition, and the logistics of dealing with it. The other half—well, to be fair, seven-eighths—was still at Lallybroch with Jamie.

I felt raw and bruised. Severed in some vital part, as always when parted from Jamie for very long, but also as though I had been violently ejected from my home, like a barnacle ripped from its rock and heedlessly tossed into boiling surf.

The greater part of that, I thought, was Ian's impending death. Ian was so much a part of Lallybroch, his presence there so much a constant and a comfort to Jamie all these years, that the sense of his loss was in a way the loss of Lallybroch itself. Oddly enough, Jenny's words, hurtful as they might have been, didn't really trouble me; I knew only too well the frantic grief, the desperation that one turned to rage because it was the only way to stay alive. And in truth, I understood her feelings, too, because I shared them: irrational or not, I felt that I should have been able to help Ian. What good was all my knowledge, all my skill, if I couldn't help when help was truly vital?

But there was a further sense of loss—and a further nagging guilt—in the fact that I could not be there when Ian died, that I had had to leave him for the last time knowing that I would not see him again, unable to offer comfort to him, or to be with Jamie or his family when the blow fell, or even simply to bear witness to his passing.

Young Ian felt this, too, to an even greater degree. I often found him sitting near the stern, staring into the ship's wake with troubled eyes.

"D'ye think he's gone yet?" he asked me abruptly on one occasion when I'd come to sit beside him there. "Da?"

"I don't know," I told him honestly. "I'd think so, on the basis of how ill he was—but people do sometimes hang on amazingly. When is his birthday, do you know?"

He stared at me in bafflement. "It's in May sometime, near Uncle Jamie's. Why?"

I shrugged and pulled my shawl tighter against the chill of the wind.

"Often people who are very ill, but are near their birthday, seem to wait until it's passed before dying. I read a study of it once. For some reason, it's more likely if the person is famous or well known."

That made him laugh, though painfully.

"Da's never been that." He sighed. "Right now I wish I'd stayed for him. I know he said to go—and I wanted to go," he added fairly. "But I feel bad that I did."

I sighed, too. "So do I."

"But you had to go," he protested. "Ye couldna let poor wee Henri-Christian choke. Da would understand that. I know he did."

I smiled at his earnest attempt to make me feel better.

"He understood why you needed to go, too."

"Aye, I know." He was silent for a bit, watching the furrow of the wake; it was a brisk day and the ship was traveling well, though the sea was choppy, dotted with whitecaps. "I wish—" he said suddenly, then stopped and swallowed. "I wish Da could ha' met Rachel," he said, low-voiced. "I wish she could meet him."

I made a sympathetic sound. I remembered all too vividly the years during which I had watched Brianna grow, aching because she would never know her father. And then a miracle had happened—but it wouldn't happen for Ian.

"I know you told your da about Rachel—he told me you had and was so happy to know about her." That made him smile a little. "Did you tell Rachel about your father? Your family?"

"No." He sounded startled. "No, I never did."

"Well, you'll just have to—what's wrong?" His brow had furrowed, and his mouth turned down.

"I—nothing, really. It's only, I just thought—I never told her anything. I mean, we—didna really talk, aye? I mean, I said things to her now and then, and her me, but just in the ordinary way of things. And then we—I kissed her, and . . . well, that was all about it." He made a helpless gesture. "But I never asked her. I was just sure."

"And now you're not?"

He shook his head, brown hair flying in the wind.

"Oh, no, Auntie; I'm as sure of what's between us as I am of . . . of . . ." He looked about in search of some symbol of solidity on the heaving deck, but then gave up. "Well, I'm surer of how I feel than I am that the sun will come up tomorrow."

"I'm sure she knows that."

"Aye, she does," he said, in a softer voice. "I know she does."

We sat for a bit in silence. Then I stood up and said, "Well, in that case—perhaps you ought to say a prayer for your father and then go and sit near the bow."

I HAD BEEN in Philadelphia once or twice in the twentieth century, for medical conferences. I hadn't liked the place then, finding it grubby and unwelcoming. It was different now, but not much more attractive. The roads that weren't cobbled were seas of mud, and streets that would eventually be lined with run-down row houses with yards full of rubbish, broken plastic toys, and motorcycle parts were now edged with ramshackle shanties with yards full of rubbish, discarded oyster shells, and tethered goats. Granted, there were no black-suited feral policemen visible, but the petty criminals were still the same, and still visible, despite the very obvious presence of the British army; redcoats swarmed near the taverns, and marching columns went past the wagon, muskets on their shoulders.

It was spring. I'd give it that much. There were trees everywhere, thanks to William Penn's dictum that one acre in five should be left in trees—even the avaricious politicians of the twentieth century hadn't quite succeeded in deforesting the place, though probably only because they couldn't figure out how to make a profit at it without being caught—and many of the trees were in bloom, a confetti of white petals drifting over the horses' backs as the wagon turned into the city proper.

An army patrol was set up on the main road into the city; they had stopped us, demanding passes from the driver and his two male passengers. I had put on a proper cap, didn't meet anyone's eye, and murmured that I was coming in from the country to tend my daughter, who was about to give birth. The soldiers glanced briefly into the large basket of food I had on my lap, but didn't even look at my face before waving the wagon on. Respectability had its uses. I wondered idly how many spymasters had thought of using elderly ladies? You didn't hear about old women as spies—but then again, that might merely indicate how good they were at it.

Fergus's printshop was not in the most fashionable district but not far off, and I was pleased to see that it was a substantial red-brick building, standing in a row of solid, pleasant-looking houses like it. We had not written ahead to say I was coming; I would have arrived as soon as the letter. With a rising heart, I opened the door.

Marsali was standing at the counter, sorting stacks of paper. She glanced up as the bell above the door rang, blinked, then gaped at me.

"How are you, dear?" I said, and, putting down the basket, hurried to put up the flap of the counter and take her in my arms.

She looked like death warmed over, though her eyes lit with a passionate relief upon seeing me. She nearly fell into my arms and burst into uncharacteristic sobs. I patted her back, making soothing sounds and feeling somewhat alarmed. Her clothes hung limp on her bones, and she smelled stale, her hair unwashed for too long.

"It will be all right," I repeated firmly for the dozenth time, and she stopped sobbing and stood back a bit, groping in her pocket for a grubby handkerchief. To my shock, I saw that she was pregnant again.

"Where's Fergus?" I asked.

"I dinna ken."

"He's left you?!" I blurted, horrified. "Why, that wretched little—"

"No, no," she said hurriedly, almost laughing through her tears. "He's not left me, not at all. It's only he's in hiding—he changes his place every few days, and I dinna ken just which one he's in right now. The weans will find him."

"Why is he in hiding? Not that I need to ask, I suppose," I said, with a glance at the squat black printing press that stood behind the counter. "Anything specific, though?"

"Aye, a wee pamphlet for Mr. Paine. He's got a series of them going, ken, called 'The American Crisis.' "

"Mr. Paine—the Common Sense fellow?"

"Aye, that's him," she said, sniffing and dabbing. "He's a nice man, but ye dinna want to drink with him, Fergus says. Ken how some men are sweet and loving when they're drunk, but some get fou' and it's up wi' the bonnets o' bonnie Dundee and them not even Scots for an excuse?"

"Oh, that sort. Yes, I know it well. How far along are you?" I asked, changing the subject back to one of general interest. "Shouldn't you sit down? You oughtn't to be on your feet for a long time."

"How far . . . ?" She looked surprised and put a hand involuntarily where I was looking, to her slightly swollen stomach. Then she laughed. "Oh, that." She burrowed under her apron and removed a bulging leather sack she had tied around her waist.

"For escaping," she explained. "In case they fire the house and I have to make a run for it wi' the weans."

The sack was surprisingly heavy when I took it from her, and I heard a muffled clicking down at the bottom, beneath the layer of papers and children's small toys.

"The Caslon Italic 24?" I asked, and she smiled, shedding at least ten years on the spot.

"All except 'X.' I had to hammer that one back into a lump and trade it to a goldsmith for enough money for food, after Fergus left. There's still an 'X' in there, mind," she said, taking back the bag, "but that one's real lead."

"Did you have to use the Goudy Bold 10?" Jamie and Fergus had cast two full sets of type from gold, these rubbed in soot and covered with ink until they were indistinguishable from the many sets of genuine lead type in the type case that stood demurely against the wall behind the press.

She shook her head and reached to take the bag back again.

"Fergus took that wi' him. He meant to bury it somewhere safe, just in case. Ye look fair fashed wi' travel, Mother Claire," she went on, leaning forward to peer at me. "Will I send Joanie down to the ordinary for a jug o' cider?"

"That would be wonderful," I said, still reeling a little from the revelations of the last few minutes. "Henri-Christian, though—how is he? Is he here?"

"Out back wi' his friend, I think," she said, rising. "I'll call him in. He's that wee bit tired, poor mite, from not sleepin' well, and he's got such a throat he sounds like a costive bullfrog. Doesna dampen him much, though, I'll tell ye that." She smiled, despite her tiredness, and went through the door into the living quarters, calling "Henri-Christian!" as she went.

"In case they fire the house." Who? I wondered, feeling a chill. The British army? Loyalists? And however was she managing, running a business and a family alone, with a husband in hiding and a sick child who couldn't be left alone while he slept? *The horror of our situation,* she'd said in her letter to Laoghaire. And that had been months ago, when Fergus was still at home.

Well, she wasn't alone now. For the first time since I'd left Jamie in Scotland, I felt something more than the pull of grim necessity in my situation. I'd write to him this evening, I decided. He might—I hoped he would—leave Lallybroch before my letter reached him there, but if so, Jenny and the rest of the family would be glad to know what was going on here. And if by chance Ian was still alive . . . but I didn't want to think of that; knowing that his death meant Jamie's release to come to me made me feel like a ghoul, as though I wished for his death to come sooner. Though in all honesty, I thought Ian himself might wish it to be sooner rather than later.

These morbid thoughts were interrupted by Marsali's return, Henri-Christian scampering beside her.

"Grandmère!" he shouted, seeing me, and leapt into my arms, nearly knocking me over. He was a very solid little boy.

He nuzzled me affectionately, and I felt a remarkable rush of warm joy at seeing him. I kissed and hugged him fiercely, feeling the hole left in my heart by Mandy and Jem's departure fill up a bit. Isolated from Marsali's family in Scotland, I had nearly forgotten that I still had four lovely grandchildren left and was grateful to be reminded of it.

"Want to see a trick, *Grandmère*?" Henri-Christian croaked eagerly. Marsali was right; he did sound like a constipated bullfrog. I nodded, though, and, hopping off my lap, he pulled three small leather bags stuffed with bran out of his pocket and began at once to juggle them with amazing dexterity.

"His da taught him," Marsali said, with a certain amount of pride.

"When I'm big like Germain, Da will teach me to pick pockets, too!"

Marsali gasped and clapped a hand over his mouth.

"Henri-Christian, we dinna ever speak o' that," she said sternly. "Not to anybody. D'ye hear?"

He glanced at me, bewildered, but nodded obediently.

The chill I had felt earlier returned. Was Germain picking pockets professionally, so to speak? I looked at Marsali, but she shook her head slightly; we'd talk about it later.

"Open your mouth and stick out your tongue, sweetheart," I suggested to Henri-Christian. "Let Grannie see your sore throat—it sounds very ouchy."

"Owg-owg-owg," he said, grinning widely, but obligingly opened up. A faint putrid smell wafted out of his wide-open mouth, and even lacking a lighted scope, I could see that the swollen tonsils nearly obstructed his throat altogether.

"Goodness gracious," I said, turning his head to and fro to get a better view. "I'm amazed that he can eat, let alone sleep."

"Sometimes he can't," Marsali said, and I heard the strain

in her voice. "Often enough, he canna manage to swallow anything but a bit o' milk, and even that's like knives in his throat, poor bairn." She crouched beside me, smoothing the fine dark hair off Henri-Christian's flushed face. "Can ye help, d'ye think, Mother Claire?"

"Oh, yes," I said, with much more confidence than I actually felt. "Absolutely."

I felt the tension drain out of her like water, and, as though it were a literal draining, tears began to run quietly down her face. She pulled Henri-Christian's head into her bosom so he couldn't see her cry, and I reached out to embrace both of them, laying my cheek against her capped head, smelling the stale musky tang of her terror and exhaustion.

"It's all right now," I said softly, rubbing her thin back. "I'm here. You can sleep."

MARSALI SLEPT the rest of the day and all through the night. I was tired from the journey but managed to doze in the big chair by the kitchen fire, Henri-Christian cradled in my lap, snoring heavily. He did stop breathing twice during the night, and while I got him started again with no difficulty, I could see that something had to be done at once. Consequently, I had a brief nap in the morning and, having washed my face and eaten a bit, went out in search of what I'd need.

I had the most rudimentary of medical instruments with me, but the fact was, tonsillectomy and adenoidectomy didn't really require anything complex in that line.

I wished that Ian had come into the city with me; I could have used his help, and so could Marsali. But it was dangerous for a man of his age; he couldn't enter the city openly without being stopped and questioned by British patrols, likely arrested as a suspicious character—which he most assuredly was. Beyond that . . . he'd been afire to look for Rachel Hunter.

The task of finding two people—and a dog—who might be almost anywhere between Canada and Charleston, with no means of communication other than the foot and the spoken word, would have daunted anyone less stubborn than a person of Fraser blood. Agreeable as he might be, though, Ian was as capable as Jamie of pursuing a chosen course, come hell, high water, or reasonable suggestions.

He did, as he'd pointed out, have one advantage. Denny Hunter was presumably still an army surgeon. If so, he was obviously with the Continental army—some part of the Continental army. So Ian's notion was to discover where the closest part of the army might be just now and begin his inquiries there. To which end he proposed to skulk round the edges of Philadelphia, creeping into taverns and shebeens on the outskirts, and, by means of local gossip, discover where some part of the army presently was.

The most I had been able to persuade him to do was to send word to Fergus's printshop telling us where he was bound, once he'd discovered anything that gave him a possible destination.

In the meantime, all I could do was say a quick prayer to his guardian angel—a most overworked being—then have a word with my own (whom I envisioned as a sort of grandmotherly shape with an anxious expression) and set about doing what I'd come to do.

I now walked through the muddy streets, pondering the procedure. I had done a tonsillectomy only once—well, twice, if you counted the Beardsley twins separately—in the last ten years. It was normally a straightforward, quick procedure, but then again, it wasn't normally performed in a gloomy printshop on a dwarf with a constricted airway, a sinus infection, and a peritonsillar abscess.

Still . . . I needn't do it in the printshop, if I could find a better-lighted place. Where would that be? I wondered. A rich person's house, most likely; one where candle wax was squandered profligately. I'd been in many such houses, particularly during our time in Paris, but knew no one even moderately well-to-do in Philadelphia. Neither did Marsali; I'd asked.

Well, one thing at a time. Before I worried any more about an operating theater, I needed to find a blacksmith capable of fine work, to make the wire-loop instrument I required. I could, in a pinch, cut the tonsils with a scalpel, but it would be more than difficult to remove the adenoids, located above the soft palate, that way. And the last thing I wanted was to be slicing and poking round in Henri-Christian's severely inflamed throat in the dark with a sharp instrument. The wire loop would be sharp enough but was unlikely to damage anything it bumped into; only the edge surrounding the tissue to be removed would cut, and then only when I made the forceful scooping motion that would sever a tonsil or adenoid neatly.

I wondered uneasily whether he had a strep infection. His throat was bright red, but other infections could cause that.

No, we'd have to take our chances with the strep, I thought. I *had* set some penicillin bowls to brew, almost the moment I arrived. There was no way of telling whether the extract I might get from them in a few days was active or not—nor, if it was, just *how* active. But it was better than nothing, and so was I.

I did have one undeniably useful thing—or would, if this afternoon's quest was successful. Nearly five years ago, Lord John Grey had sent me a glass bottle of vitriol and the pelican glassware necessary to distill ether using it. He'd procured those items from an apothecary in Philadelphia, I thought, though I couldn't recall the name. But there couldn't *be* many apothecaries in Philadelphia, and I proposed to visit all of them until I found what I was looking for.

Marsali had said there were two large apothecary's shops in town, and only a large one would have what I needed to make ether. What was the name of the gentleman from whom Lord John Grey had acquired my pelican apparatus? Was he in Philadelphia at all? My mind was a blank, either from fatigue or from simple forgetfulness; the time when I had made ether in my surgery on Fraser's Ridge seemed as distant and mythical as Noah's Flood.

I found the first apothecary and got from him some useful items, including a jar of leeches—though I boggled a little at the thought of putting one inside Henri-Christian's mouth; what if he managed to swallow the thing?

On the other hand, I reflected, he was a four-year-old boy with a very imaginative elder brother. He'd probably swallowed much worse things than a leech. With luck, though, I wouldn't need them. I had also got two cautery irons, very small ones. It was a primitive and painful way of stopping bleeding—but, in fact, very effective.

The apothecary had not had any vitriol, though. He had

apologized for the lack, saying that such things must be imported from England, and with the war . . . I thanked him and went on to the second place. Where I was informed that they had had some vitriol but had sold it some time previous, to an English lord, though what he wanted with such a thing, the man behind the counter couldn't begin to imagine.

"An English lord?" I said, surprised. Surely it couldn't be Lord John. Though, come to that, it wasn't as though the English aristocracy was flocking to Philadelphia these days, save those members who were soldiers. And the man had said "a lord," not a major or a captain.

Nothing ventured, nothing gained; I asked and was obligingly told that it was a Lord John Grey, and that he had requested the vitriol be delivered to his house on Chestnut Street.

Feeling a little like Alice down the rabbit hole—I was still a bit light-headed from lack of sleep and the fatigues of the journey from Scotland—I asked the way to Chestnut Street.

The door to the house was opened by an extraordinarily beautiful young woman, dressed in a fashion that made it clear she was no servant. We blinked at each other in surprise; she plainly hadn't been expecting me, either, but when I inquired for Lord John, saying I was an old acquaintance, she readily invited me in, saying that her uncle would be back directly, he had only taken a horse to be shod.

"You would think he'd send the boy," the young woman—who gave her name as Lady Dorothea Grey—said apologetically. "Or my cousin. But Uncle John is most particular about his horses."

"Your cousin?" I asked, my slow mind tracing the possible family connections. "You don't mean William Ransom, do you?"

"Ellesmere, yes," she said, looking surprised but pleased. "Do you know him?"

"We've met once or twice," I said. "If you don't mind my asking—how does he come to be in Philadelphia? I . . . er . . . had understood that he was paroled with the rest of Burgoyne's army and had gone to Boston in order to sail home to England."

"Oh, he is!" she said. "Paroled, I mean. He came here, though, first, to see his father—that's Uncle John—and my brother." Her large blue eyes clouded a little at the mention. "Henry's very ill, I'm afraid."

"I'm so sorry to hear it," I said, sincerely but briefly. I was much more interested in William's presence here, but before I could ask anything further, there was a quick, light step on the porch and the front door opened.

"Dottie?" said a familiar voice. "Have you any idea where—oh, I beg your pardon." Lord John Grey had come into the parlor and stopped, seeing me. Then he actually saw me, and his jaw dropped.

"How nice to see you again," I said pleasantly. "But I'm sorry to hear that your nephew is ill."

"Thank you," he said, and, eyeing me rather warily, bowed low over my hand, kissing it gracefully. "I am delighted to see you again, Mrs. Fraser," he added, sounding as though he actually meant it. He hesitated for a moment, but of course couldn't help asking, "Your husband . . . ?"

"He's in Scotland," I said, feeling rather mean at disappointing him. It flickered across his face but was promptly erased—he was a gentleman, and a soldier. In fact, he was wearing an army uniform, which rather surprised me.

"You've returned to active duty, then?" I asked, raising my brows at him.

"Not exactly. Dottie, have you not called for Mrs. Figg yet? I'm sure Mrs. Fraser would like some refreshment."

"I'd only just come," I said hastily, as Dottie leapt up and went out.

"Indeed," he said, courteously repressing the *why?* that showed plainly on his face. He motioned me to a chair and sat down himself, wearing a rather odd expression, as though trying to think how to say something awkward.

"I am delighted to see you," he said again, slowly. "Did you—I do not wish to sound in any way ungracious, Mrs. Fraser, you must excuse me—but . . . did you come to bring me a message from your husband, perhaps?"

He couldn't help the small light that sprang up in his eyes, and I felt almost apologetic as I shook my head.

"I'm sorry," I said, and was surprised to find that I meant it. "I've come to beg a favor. Not on my own behalf—for my grandson."

He blinked at that.

"Your grandson," he repeated blankly. "I thought that your daughter . . . oh! Of course, I was forgetting that your husband's foster son—his family is here? It is one of his children?"

"Yes, that's right." Without more ado, I explained the situation, describing Henri-Christian's state and reminding him of his generosity in sending me the vitriol and glass apparatus more than four years before.

"Mr. Sholto—the apothecary on Walnut Street?—told me that he had sold you a large bottle of vitriol some months ago. I wondered—do you by any chance still have it?" I made no effort to keep the eagerness out of my voice, and his expression softened.

"Yes, I do," he said, and, to my surprise, smiled like the sun coming out from behind a cloud. "I bought it for you, Mrs. Fraser."

A BARGAIN WAS struck at once. He would not only give me the vitriol but also purchase any other medical supplies I might require, if I would consent to perform surgery on his nephew.

"Dr. Hunter removed one of the balls at Christmas," he said, "and that improved Henry's condition somewhat. The other remains embedded, though, and—"

"Dr. Hunter?" I interrupted him. "Not Denzell Hunter, you don't mean?"

"I do mean that," he said, surprised and frowning a little. "He says he knows you."

"Yes, indeed," I said, smiling. "We worked together often, both at Ticonderoga and at Saratoga with Gates's army. But what is he doing in Philadelphia?"

"He—" he began, but was interrupted by the sound of light footsteps coming down the stair. I had been vaguely conscious of footsteps overhead as we talked but had paid no attention. I looked toward the doorway now, though, and my heart leapt at the sight of Rachel Hunter, who was standing in it, staring at me with her mouth in a perfect "O" of astonishment.

The next moment she was in my arms, hugging me fit to break my ribs.

"Friend Claire!" she said, letting go at last. "I never thought to see—that is, I am so pleased—oh, Claire! Ian. Has he come back with thee?" Her face was alive with eagerness and fear, hope and wariness chasing each other like racing clouds across her features.

"He has," I assured her. "He's not here, though." Her face fell.

"Oh," she said in a small voice. "Where—"

"He's gone to look for you," I said gently, taking her hands.

Joy blazed up in her eyes like a forest fire.

"Oh!" she said, in a completely different voice. "Oh!"

Lord John coughed politely.

"Perhaps it would be unwise for me to know exactly where your nephew is, Mrs. Fraser," he observed. "As I assume he shares your husband's principles? Just so. If you will excuse me, then, I will go and tell Henry of your arrival. I suppose you wish to examine him?"

"Oh," I said, recalled suddenly to the matter at hand. "Yes. Yes, of course. If you wouldn't mind . . ."

He smiled, glancing at Rachel, whose face had gone white at seeing me but who was now the shade of a russet apple with excitement.

"Not at all," he said. "Come upstairs when you are at leisure, Mrs. Fraser. I'll wait for you there."

88

RATHER MESSY

I MISSED BRIANNA all the time, in greater or lesser degree depending upon the circumstance. But I missed her most particularly now. She could, I was sure, have solved the problem of getting light down Henri-Christian's throat.

I had him laid on a table at the front of the printshop now, taking every advantage of such light as came in there. But this was Philadelphia, not New Bern. If the sky wasn't overcast with clouds, it was hazed with smoke from the city's chimneys. And the street was narrow; the buildings opposite blocked most of what light there was.

Not that it mattered that much, I told myself. The room could have been blazing with sun, and I still couldn't have seen a thing in the inner reaches of Henri-Christian's throat. Marsali had a small mirror with which to direct light, and that would perhaps help with the tonsils—the adenoids would have to be done by touch.

I could feel the soft, spongy edge of one adenoid, just behind the soft palate; it took shape in my mind as I carefully fitted the wire loop around it, handling it with great delicacy so as not to let the edge cut either my fingertips or the body of the swollen adenoid. There was going to be a gush of blood when I sliced through it.

I had Henri-Christian braced at an angle, Marsali holding his inert body almost on his side. Denzell Hunter kept his head steady, clamping the pad soaked in ether firmly over his nose. I had no means of suction other than my own mouth; I'd have to turn him quickly after I made the cut and let the blood run out of his mouth before it ran down his throat and choked him. The tiny cautery iron was heating, its spade-shaped tip thrust into a pan of hot coals. That might be the trickiest part, I thought, pausing to steady myself and steady Marsali with a nod. I didn't want to burn his tongue or the inside of his mouth, and it would be slippery. . . .

I twisted the handle sharply and the little body jerked under my hand.

"Hold him tight," I said calmly. "A little more ether, please."

Marsali's breath was coming hard, and her knuckles were white as her face. I felt the adenoid separate cleanly, come adrift, and scooped it between my fingers, pulling it out of his throat before it could slip down into his esophagus. Tilted his head quickly to the side, smelling the sheared-metal smell of hot blood. I dropped the severed bit of tissue into a pan and nodded to Rachel, who pulled the cautery iron from its coals and put it carefully into my hand.

I still had my other hand in his mouth, keeping the tongue and uvula out of the way, a finger on the site of the ex-adenoid, marking my place. The cautery iron seared a white line of pain down my finger as I slid it down his throat, and I let out a small hiss but didn't move my finger. The scorched scent of burning blood and tissue came hot and thick, and Marsali made a small, frantic noise but didn't loosen her hold on her son's body.

"It is well, Friend Marsali," Rachel whispered to her, clasping her shoulder. "He breathes well; he is not in pain. He is held in the light, he will do well."

"Yes, he will," I said. "Take the iron now, Rachel, if you will? Dip the loop in the whisky please, and give me that again. One down, three to go."

"I HAVE NEVER seen anything like it," Denzell Hunter said, for perhaps the fifth time. He looked from the pad of fabric in his hand to Henri-Christian, who was beginning to stir and whimper in his mother's arms. "I should not have believed it, Claire, had I not seen it with my own eyes!"

"Well, I thought you'd better see it," I said, wiping sweat from my face with a handkerchief. A sense of profound well-being filled me. The surgery had been fast, no more than five or six minutes, and Henri-Christian was already coughing and crying, coming out of the ether. Germain, Joanie, and Félicité all watched wide-eyed from the doorway into the kitchen, Germain keeping tight hold of his sisters' hands. "I'll teach you to make it, if you like."

His face, already shining with happiness at the successful surgery, lit up at this.

"Oh, Claire! Such a gift! To be able to cut without giving pain, to keep a patient quite still without restraint. It—it is unimaginable."

"Well, it's a long way from perfect," I warned him. "And it is very dangerous—both to make and to use." I'd distilled the ether the day before, out in the woodshed; it was a very volatile compound, and there was a better than even chance that it would explode and burn the shed down, killing me in the process. All had gone well, though the thought of doing it again made me feel rather hollow and sweaty-palmed.

I lifted the dropping bottle and shook it gently; more than three-quarters full, and I had another, slightly larger bottle as well.

"Will it be enough, does thee think?" Denny asked, realizing what I was thinking.

"It depends what we find." Henri-Christian's surgery, despite the technical difficulties, had been very simple. Henry Grey's wouldn't be. I had examined him, Denzell beside me to explain what he had seen and done during the earlier surgery, which had removed a ball lodged just under the pancreas. It had caused local irritation and scarring but had not actually damaged a vital organ very badly. He hadn't been able to find the other ball, as it was lodged very deeply in the body, somewhere under the liver. He feared that it might lie near the hepatic portal vein and thus hadn't dared to probe hard for it, as a hemorrhage would almost certainly have been fatal.

I was reasonably sure that the ball hadn't damaged the gallbladder or bile duct, though, and given Henry's general state and symptomology, I suspected that the ball had perforated the small intestine but had seared the internal entrance wound shut in its wake; otherwise, the boy would almost surely have died within days, of peritonitis.

It might be encysted in the wall of the intestine; that would be the best situation. It might be lodged actually within the intestine itself, and that wouldn't be good at all, but I couldn't say how bad it might be until I got there.

But we did have ether. And the sharpest scalpels Lord John's money could buy.

THE WINDOW, after what seemed to John Grey to be an excruciatingly prolonged discussion between the two physicians, remained partly open. Dr. Hunter insisted on the benefit of fresh air, and Mrs. Fraser agreed with this because of the ether fumes but kept talking about something she called germs, worrying that these would come in through the window and contaminate her "surgical field." *She speaks as though she views it as a battleground,* he thought, but then looked closely at her face and realized that indeed she did.

He had never seen a woman look like that, he thought, fascinated despite his worry for Henry. She had tied back her outrageous hair and wrapped her head carefully in a cloth like a Negro slave woman. With her face so exposed, the delicate bones made stark, the intentness of her expression—with those yellow eyes darting like a hawk's from one thing to another—was the most unwomanly thing he had ever seen. It was the look of a general marshaling his troops for battle, and seeing it, he felt the ball of snakes in his belly relax a little.

She knows what she's doing, he thought.

She looked at him then, and he straightened his shoulders, instinctively awaiting orders—to his utter amazement.

"Do you want to stay?" she asked.

"Yes, of course." He felt a little breathless, but there was no doubt in his voice. She'd told him frankly what Henry's chances were—not good, but there *was* a chance—and he was determined to be with his nephew, no matter what happened. If Henry died, he would at least die with someone who loved him there. Though, in fact, he was quite determined that Henry would not die. Grey would not let him.

"Sit over there, then." She nodded him to a stool on the far side of the bed, and he sat down, giving Henry a reassuring smile as he did so. Henry looked terrified but determined.

"I can't live like this anymore," he'd said the night before, finally making up his mind to allow the operation. *"I just can't."*

Mrs. Woodcock had insisted upon being present, too, and after a close catechism, Mrs. Fraser had declared that she might administer the ether. This mysterious substance sat in a dropping bottle on the bureau, a faint sickly odor drifting from it.

Mrs. Fraser gave Dr. Hunter something that looked like a handkerchief, and raised another to her face. It *was* a handkerchief, Grey saw, but one with strings affixed to its corners. She tied these behind her head, so the cloth covered her nose and mouth, and Hunter obediently followed suit.

Used as Grey was to the swift brutality of army surgeons, Mrs. Fraser's preparations seemed laborious in the extreme: she swabbed Henry's belly repeatedly with an alcoholic solution she had concocted, talking to him through her highwayman's mask in a low, soothing voice. She rinsed her hands—and made Hunter and Mrs. Woodcock do the same—and her instruments, so that the whole room reeked like a distillery of low quality.

Her motions were in fact quite brisk, he realized after a moment. But her hands moved with such sureness and . . . yes, grace, that was the only word . . . that they gave the illusion of gliding like a pair of gulls upon the air. No frantic flapping, only a sure, serene, and almost mystic movement. He found himself quieting as he watched them, becoming entranced and half forgetting the ultimate purpose of this quiet dance of hands.

She moved to the head of the bed, bending low to speak to Henry, smooth the hair away from his brow, and Grey saw the hawk's eyes soften momentarily into gold. Henry's body relaxed slowly under her touch; Grey saw his clenched, rigid hands uncurl. She had yet another mask, he saw, this one a stiff thing made of basket withes lined with layers of soft cotton cloth. She fitted this gently to Henry's face and, saying something inaudible to him, took up her dropping bottle.

The air filled at once with a pungent, sweet aroma that clung to the back of Grey's throat and made his head swim slightly. He blinked, shaking his head to dispel the giddiness, and realized that Mrs. Fraser had said something to him.

"I beg your pardon?" He looked up at her, a great white bird with yellow eyes—and a gleaming talon that sprouted suddenly from her hand.

"I said," she repeated calmly through her mask, "you might want to sit back a little farther. It's going to be rather messy."

WILLIAM, RACHEL, and Dorothea sat on the edge of the porch like birds on a fence rail, Rollo sprawled on the brick walk at their feet, enjoying the spring sun.

"It's bloody quiet up there," William said, glancing uneasily at the window above, where Henry's room lay. "D'you think they've started yet?" He thought, but didn't say, that he would have expected to hear Henry making a certain amount of noise if they had, despite Rachel's description of her brother's account of the marvels of Mrs. Fraser's ether. A man lie quietly asleep while someone cut open his belly with a knife? All stuff, he would have said. But Denzell Hunter wasn't a man who could be easily beguiled—though he supposed Dottie had somehow managed it. He gave his cousin a sideways glance.

"Have you written Uncle Hal yet? About you and Denny, I mean?" He knew she hadn't—she'd told Lord John, perforce, but persuaded him to let her break the news to her father—but wanted to distract her if he could. She was white to the lips, and her hands had bunched the fabric over her knees into nests of creases. He still hadn't got used to seeing her in dove and cream instead of her usual brilliant plumage—though he thought in fact that the quiet colors suited her, particularly as Rachel had assured her that she might still wear silk and muslin if she liked, rather than sacking material.

"No," Dottie said, giving him a look that thanked him for the distraction, even while acknowledging that she knew what he was doing. "Or, yes, but I haven't sent it yet. If all's well with Henry, I'll write at once with the news and add the bit about Denny and me at the bottom, as a postscript. They'll be so overjoyed about Henry that perhaps they won't notice—or at least won't be as upset about it."

"I rather think they'll notice," William said thoughtfully. "Papa did." Lord John had gone quite dangerously quiet when told and had given Denzell Hunter a look suggesting swords at dawn. But the fact was that Denny had saved Henry's life once and was now helping—with luck and Mrs. Fraser—to save it again. And Lord John was, above all, a man of honor. Besides, William thought that his father was actually relieved to finally know what it was that Dottie had been up to. He hadn't said anything directly to William regarding William's own role in her adventure—yet. He would.

"May the Lord hold thy brother in his hand," Rachel said, ignoring William's remark. "And mine and Mrs. Fraser, as well. But what if all should not go as we wish? Thee will still have to tell thy parents, and they may see news of thy impending marriage as adding insult to injury."

"You are the most tactless plain-spoken creature," William told her, rather irritably, seeing Dottie go whiter still at the reminder that Henry might die in the next minutes, hours, or days. "Henry will be fine. I know it. Denny is a great physician, and Mrs. Fraser . . . she's . . . er . . ." In all honesty, he wasn't sure what Mrs. Fraser was, but she scared him a little. "Denny says she knows what she's doing," he ended lamely.

"If Henry dies, nothing will matter," Dottie said softly, looking at the toes of her shoes. "Not to any of us."

Rachel made a small, sympathetic sound and reached to put her arm round Dottie's shoulder. William added his own gruff clearing of the throat and for an instant thought the dog had done the same.

Rollo's intent, though, was not sympathetic. He had lifted his head suddenly, and the hackles half-rose at his neck, a low growl rumbling through his chest. William glanced automatically in the direction the dog was looking and felt a sudden tightening of his muscles.

"Miss Hunter," he said casually. "Do you know that man? The one down there, near the end of the street, talking to the butter-and-egg woman?"

Rachel shaded her eyes with her hand, looking where he nodded, but shook her head.

"No. Why? Is he what's troubling the dog, does thee think?" She prodded Rollo in the side with her toe. "What's amiss, then, Friend Rollo?"

"I don't know," William said honestly. "It might be the cat; one ran across the road just behind the woman. But I've seen that man before; I'm sure of it. I saw him by the roadside, somewhere in New Jersey. He asked me if I knew Ian Murray—and where he might be."

Rachel gave a little gasp at that, making William look sideways at her in surprise.

"What?" he said. "Do you know where Murray is?"

"No," she said sharply. "I have not seen him since the autumn, at Saratoga, and I have no notion where he is. Does thee know this man's name?" she added, frowning. The man had disappeared now, walking off down a side street. "For that matter, is thee sure he is the same?"

"No," William admitted. "But I think so. He had a staff with him, and so did this man. And there's something about the way he stands—a little stooped. The man I met in New Jersey was very old, and this one walks the same way." He didn't mention the missing fingers; no need to remind Dottie of violence and mutilation just this minute, and he couldn't see the man's hand at this distance anyway.

Rollo had left off growling and settled himself with a brief grunt, but his yellow eyes were still watchful.

"When do you mean to be married, Dottie?" William asked, wishing to keep her mind occupied. A strange smell was coming from the window above them; the dog was wrinkling his nose, shaking his head in a confused sort of way, and William didn't blame him. It was a nasty, sickly kind of thing—but he could distinctly smell blood, as well, and the faint stink of shit. It was a battlefield smell, and it made his insides shift uneasily.

"I want to be married before the fighting starts again in earnest," his cousin answered seriously, turning to face him, "so that I can go with Denny—and Rachel," she added, taking her prospective sister-in-law's hand with a smile.

Rachel returned the smile, but briefly.

"What a strange thing," she said to both of them, but her hazel eyes were fixed on William, soft and troubled. "In only a little while we shall be enemies again."

"I have never felt myself your enemy, Miss Hunter," he replied, just as softly. "And I shall always be your friend."

A smile touched her lips, but the trouble stayed in her eyes.

"Thee knows what I mean." Her eyes slid from William to Dottie, on her other side, and it occurred to William with a jolt that his cousin was about to wed a rebel—to become one herself, in fact. That he must in fact soon be directly at war with a part of his own family. The fact that Denny Hunter would not take up arms would not protect him—or Dottie. Or Rachel. All three of them were guilty of treason. Any of them might be killed, captured, imprisoned. What would he do, he thought suddenly, appalled, if he had to see Denny hanged one day? Or even Dottie?

"I know what you mean," he said quietly. But he took Rachel's hand, and she gave it him, and the three of them sat in silence, linked, awaiting the verdict of the future.

89

INK-STAINED WRETCH

I MADE MY WAY TO the printshop, dead tired and in that state of mind in which one feels drunk—euphoric and uncoordinated. I was in truth somewhat physically drunk, too; Lord John had insisted upon plying both Denzell Hunter and myself with his best brandy, seeing how done up we both were in the wake of the surgery. I hadn't said no.

It was one of the most hair-raising pieces of surgery I'd done in the eighteenth century. I'd done only two other abdominal surgeries: the successful removal of Aidan McCallum's appendix, under the influence of ether—and the very unsuccessful cesarean I'd performed with a garden knife upon the murdered body of Malva Christie. The thought of that gave me the usual pang of sadness and regret, but it was oddly tempered. What I remembered now, walking home in the cool evening, was the feeling of the life I'd held in my hands—so brief, so fleeting—but *there,* unmistakable and intoxicant, a brief blue flame.

I'd held Henry Grey's life in my hands two hours before

and felt that blaze again. Once more I'd willed all my strength into the burning of that flame—but this time had felt it steady and rise in my palms, like a candle taking hold.

The bullet had entered his intestine but had not encysted. Instead, it remained embedded but mobile, not able to leave the body but moving enough to irritate the lining of the intestine, which was badly ulcerated. After a quick discussion with Denzell Hunter—who was so fascinated with the novelty of examining a person's working insides while they lay unconscious that he could barely keep his mind on the business at hand, exclaiming in awe at the vivid colors and pulsating throb of live organs—I had decided that the ulceration was too extensive. To excise it would narrow the small intestine dramatically and risk scarring—constricting it further and perhaps obstructing it altogether.

We'd done a modest resection instead, and I felt a twinge of something between laughter and dismay at the recollection of Lord John's face when I severed the ulcerated segment of intestine and dropped it with a *splat* on the floor at his feet. I hadn't done it on purpose; I'd simply needed both my hands and Denzell's to control the bleeding, and we'd lacked a nurse to help.

The boy wasn't out of the woods, not by a long chalk. I didn't know whether my penicillin would be effective, or whether he might develop some hideous infection despite it. But he *was* awake, and his vital signs were surprisingly strong—perhaps, I thought, because of Mrs. Woodcock, who had gripped his hand and stroked his face, urging him to wake with a fierce tenderness that left her feelings for him in no doubt whatever.

I did wonder briefly what the future held for her. Struck by her unusual name, I'd inquired cautiously about her husband and was sure that it was he whose amputated leg I'd tended on the retreat from Ticonderoga. I thought it very likely he was dead; if so, what might happen between Mercy Woodcock and Henry Grey? She was a free woman, not a slave. Marriage wasn't unthinkable—not even as unthinkable as such a relationship would be in the United States two hundred years in the future: marriages involving black and mulatto women of good family to white men were, if not common in the Indies, not a matter of public scandal, either. Philadelphia was not the Indies, though, and from what Dottie had told me of her father . . .

I was simply too tired to think about it, and I needn't—Denny Hunter had volunteered to stay with Henry through the night. I dismissed that particular pair from my mind as I wandered down the street, weaving slightly. I hadn't eaten anything since breakfast, and it was nearly dark; the brandy had sunk directly through the walls of my empty stomach and entered my bloodstream, and I hummed gently to myself as I walked. It was the twilight hour, when things float on the air, when curved cobblestones seem insubstantial and the leaves of trees hang heavy as emeralds, glowing with a green whose fragrance enters the blood.

I should walk faster; there was a curfew. Still, who would arrest me? I was too old for patrolling soldiers to molest me, as they would a young girl, and of the wrong sex to be suspicious. Should I meet a patrol, they wouldn't do more than abuse me and tell me to go home—which I was doing, in any case.

It struck me quite suddenly that I could move the things Marsali described circumspectly as "Mr. Smith's job": the written letters circulated by the Sons of Liberty that passed between villages, between towns, that whirled through the colonies like leaves driven by a spring storm, were copied and sent on, sometimes printed and distributed within the towns, if a bold printer could be found to do the work.

There was a loose network through which these things moved, but it was always prone to discovery, with people arrested and imprisoned frequently. Germain carried such papers often, and my heart was in my throat when I thought of it. An agile boy was less noticeable than a young man or a tradesman going about his business—but the British were not fools and would certainly stop him if he looked at all suspicious. Whereas I . . .

Turning the possibilities over in my mind, I reached the shop and went in, to the smell of a savory supper, the greetings of excited children, and something that drove all thought of my potential new career as a spy from my mind: two letters from Jamie.

20 March, A.D. 1778
Lallybroch

My dearest Claire;

Ian is dead. It has been ten days since the Event, and I thought I should now be able to write calmly. Yet to see those Words written on the Page just now smote me with the most unexpected Grief; Tears are running down the sides of my Nose, and I was forced to stop to mop my Face with a Handkerchief before continuing. It was not an easy Death and I should be relieved that Ian is now at Peace, and glad for his Translation into Heaven. So I am. But I am also desolate, in a Way that I have never been before. Only the Thought of being able to confide in you, my Soul, gives me Comfort.

Young Jamie has the Estate, as he should; Ian's Will has been read out, and Mr. Gowan will see it executed. There is not much beyond the Land and Buildings; only the smallest Bequests to the other Children, these largely of personal Items. My Sister he has confided to my Care (he having inquired before his Death whether I was willing. I told him he knew better than to ask. He said he did, but thought to inquire whether I felt myself also equal to the Task, and laughed like a Loon. Dear God, I shall miss him).

There were some trifling Debts to be paid; I have discharged them, as we agreed I should.

Jenny worries me. I know she grieves Ian with all her Heart, but she does not weep much, but only sits for long Periods, looking at Something that only she sees. There is a Calmness about her that is almost eerie, as though her Soul has flown with Ian, leaving only the Shell of her Body behind. Though since I mention Shells, it occurs to me that perhaps she is like a Chambered Nautilus, like the one that Lawrence Sterne showed us in the Indies. A large, beautiful Shell, made of many Chambers, but all empty, save the innermost one, in which the small Animal hides itself in safety.

Since I speak of her, though—she bids me tell you of her Remorse regarding Things said to you. I told her we had spoken of it between us, and that your Compassion would not hold it against her, realizing the desperate Circumstances in which she spoke.

On the Morning of Ian's Death, she spoke to me with apparent Rationality, and said she thought she would leave Lallybroch, that with his Death, nothing holds her here. I was, as you may suppose, much astonished to hear this, but did not try to question or dissuade her, assuming this to be only the Counsel of a Mind deranged by Sleeplessness and Grief.

She has since repeated this Sentiment to me, though, with firm Assurance that she is indeed in her right Mind. I am going to France for a short Time—both to accomplish some private Transactions that I will not write of here, and to assure myself before departing for America that both Michael and Joan are settled, they having left together, the Day following Ian's Burial. I said to Jenny that she must think carefully whilst I am absent—but that if she is in Fact convinced that this is what she wants, I will bring her to America. Not to stay with us (I smile, imagining your Face, which is transparent, even in my Mind).

She would have a Place, though, with Fergus and Marsali, where she would be of Use, and yet would not be reminded daily of her Loss—and where she would be in a Position to help and support Young Ian, should he require such Help (or at least to know how he does, if he does not).

(It also occurs to me—as it surely has to her—that Young Jamie's Wife will now be the Lady of Lallybroch, and that there is not Room for Two such. She is wise enough to know what the Difficulties of such a Situation would be, and kind enough to wish to avoid them, for the Sake of her Son and his Wife.)

In any Case, I propose to depart for America by the End of this Month, or as near to that as Passage may be obtained. The Prospect of being Reunited with you lightens my Heart and I remain forever

Your Devoted Husband,
Jamie

Paris
1 April

My dearest Wife;

I am returned very late to my new Lodging in Paris tonight. In fact, I found the Door bolted against me on my Return, and was obliged to shout for the Landlady, who was somewhat ill-tempered at being roused from her Bed. I was the more ill-tempered in my Turn, at finding no Fire laid, no Supper kept, and Nothing upon the Bedframe save a moldy Tick and threadbare Blanket which would not serve to shelter the meanest Beggar.

Further Shouts earned me Nothing save Abuse (from behind a safely lock'd Door), and my Pride would not suffer me to offer Bribes even would my Purse do so. I remain thus in my barren Garret, frozen and starving (this pitiful Picture is here drawn for the craven Purpose of soliciting your Sympathy, and to convince you of how poorly I Fare without you).

I am determined to depart this Place as soon as it be Light, and seek whether better Lodging can be found without excessive Damage to my Purse. Meanwhile, I shall endeavor to forget both Cold and Hunger in pleasant Converse with you, hoping that the Effort of writing will summon your Image before me and lend me the Illusion of your Company.

(I have possessed myself of adequate Light by stealing Downstairs in my Stockings and snatching two silver Candlesticks from the front Parlor, whose deceitful Grandeur seduced me into assuming

Residence here. I shall return the Candlesticks tomorrow—when Madame returns the extortionate Fee for this miserable Accommodation.)

To more pleasant Subjects: I have seen Joan, now secure in her Convent, and apparently content (why, no, since you ask; I did not attend the Wedding of her Mother to Joseph Murray—who is, it turns out, a second Cousin to Ian. I sent a handsome Present and my good Wishes, which are sincere). I will visit Michael tomorrow; I look forward to seeing Jared again and will give him your kindest Regards.

In the Meantime, I sought Sustenance this Morning in a Coffee-house in Montmartre, and was there fortunate to encounter Mr. Lyle, whom I had met in Edinburgh. He greeted me most kindly, inquired after my Fortunes, and after some small Conversation of a personal Nature, invited me to attend the Meeting of a certain Society, whose Members include Voltaire, Diderot, and others whose Opinions are heard in the Circles I seek to influence.

I went thus by Appointment at two o'clock to a House, where I was admitted and found all within most grandly appointed, it being the Paris Residence of Monsieur Beaumarchais.

The Company there gathered was mixt indeed; it ran the Gamut from the shabbiest of Coffee-house Philosophers to the most elegant Ornaments of Parisian Society, the Character common to them all being only a love of Talk. Some Pretentions to Reason and Intellect were made, to be sure, but not insisted on. I could not ask a fairer Wind for my maiden Voyage as a political Provocateur—and Wind, you will see, is a most apt Image in considering the Events of the Day.

After some inconsequent Babble over the refreshment Tables (had I been forewarned of Conditions here, I should have taken Care to stuff my Pockets surreptitiously with Cakes, as I saw more than one of my fellow Guests doing), the Company withdrew into a large Room and took Seats, for the

Purpose of witnessing a formal Debate between two Parties.

The Matter under Debate was that popular Thesis, Resolved: that the Pen be mightier than the Sword, with Mr. Lyle and his Adherents defending the Proposition, M. Beaumarchais and his friends stoutly averring the Counter. The Talk was lively, with much Allusion to the Works of Rousseau and Montaigne (and not a little personal Disparagement of the Former, owing to his immoral Views on Marriage), but eventually Mr. Lyle's Party prevailed in their arguments. I thought of showing the Society my Right Hand, as Evidence for the Counter-proposition (a Sample of my Penmanship must have proved the Case to the Satisfaction of All), but Forbore, being but an Observer.

I found Opportunity later to approach Monsieur Beaumarchais, and made such an Observation to him in Jest, by way of fixing his Attention. He was most imprest by sight of my missing Digit, and inform'd of the Occasion of it (or rather, what I chose to tell him), became most animated and insistent that I accompany his Party to the house of the Duchess de Chaulnes, whence he was obliged for Supper, as the Duke is known to have a great Interest in Matters pertaining to the Aboriginal Inhabitants of the Colonies.

You will be wondering, no doubt, what Connexion exists between Aboriginal Savages and your most elegant Surgery? Have Patience for a few Lines longer.

The ducal Residence is placed in a Street with a sweeping Drive upon which I perceived several fine Carriages ahead of M. Beaumarchais's. Imagine my Delight upon being informed that the Gentleman who descended just before us was none other than M. Vergennes, the Foreign Minister.

I congratulated myself upon my good Fortune in so soon encountering so many Persons suited to my Purpose, and did my best to ingratiate myself with them—to this End, telling Tales of my Travels in

America, and borrowing in the Process not a few Stories from our Good Friend Myers.

The Company was most gratifyingly astonished, being particularly attentive to the Story of our Meeting with the Bear and with Nacognaweto and his Fellows. I made much of your valiant Efforts with the Fish, which much amused the Party, though the Ladies appeared most Shocked at my Description of your Indian Attire. Mr. Lyle, to the Contrary, was agog to hear more of your Appearance in leather Trouserings—I judged him by this a confirm'd Lecher and a Reprobate, a Judgement verified later in the Evening by a Passage I observ'd in the Hallway between Mr. Lyle and Mademoiselle Erlande, who I perceive to be most wanton in her own Conduct.

In any Case, this Story led Mr. Lyle to draw the Attention of the Company to my Hand, and urge me to tell them the Story which I had unfolded to him in the Afternoon, of how I came to lose my Finger.

Seeing that the Company had reached such a Pitch of Enjoyment—being well lubricated with Champagne, Holland Gin, and large quantities of Hock—that they hung upon my Words, I spared no Pains in weaving them a Tale of Horror calculated to leave them shivering in their Beds.

I had (I said) been taken Captive by the dreadful Iroquois while journeying from Trenton to Albany. I described in great Detail the frightful Appearance and bloodthirsty Habit of these Savages—which required no great Exaggeration, to be sure—and dwelt at Length upon the fearful Tortures which the Iroquois are wont to inflict upon their hapless Victims. La Comtesse Poutoude swooned at my recounting of the grisly Death of Father Alexandre, and the rest of the Party was much affected.

I told them of Two Spears, who I trust will not object to my Slandering his Character in a good Cause, the more so as he will never hear of it. This Chief, I said, being determined to put me to the Torture, caused me to be stripped naked, and most cruelly whip'd. With Thought of our good Friend

Daniel, who has turned the same Misfortune to his Advantage, I raised my Shirt and Displayed my Scars. (I felt somewhat the Whore, but it has been my Observation that most Whores pursue this Profession from Necessity, and I comfort myself that it is much the same.) The reaction of my Audience was all that could be hoped, and I continued my Narrative, secure in the Knowledge that from this Point, they would believe Anything.

Thereafter (I said), two of the Indian Braves brought me fainting into the Chief's Presence, and secured me extended flat upon a large Stone, whose Surface bore sinister Witness to previous Sacrifice conducted thereon.

A heathen Priest or Shaman then approached me, uttering hideous Cries and shaking a Stick decorated by many waving Scalps, which caused me to fear that my own Hair might prove of such Attraction by Virtue of its unusual Colour as shortly to be added to his Collection (I had not powder'd my Hair, tho' from lack of Powder, rather than Forethought). This Fear was much enhanced when the Shaman drew forth a large Knife and advanced upon me, Eyes glittering with Malice.

At this Point, the Eyes of my Hearers were glittering as well, being enlarged to the size of Saucers by Reason of their Attention to my Story. Many of the Ladies cried out in Pity for my desperate Situation, and the Gentlemen uttered fierce Execrations of the foul Savages responsible for my Plight.

I told them then how the Shaman had driven his Knife straight through my Hand, causing me to lose Consciousness by Reason of Fear and Pain. I awoke (I continued) to find my fourth Finger sever'd completely, and Blood pouring from my wounded Hand.

But most horrifying of all was the sight of the Iroquois Chief, seated upon the carved Trunk of a giant Tree, tearing the Flesh from the severed Digit with his Teeth, as one might gobble the Meat of a Chicken's Leg.

At this point in my narrative, La Comtesse swooned again, and—not to be outdone—the Honorable Miss Elliott launched into a full-fledg'd fit of the Hysterics, which fortunately saved me from having to invent the Means of my Escape from the Savages. Professing myself undone by the Memories of my Trials, I accepted a Glass of Wine (I was sweating pretty freely by this time), and escaped from the Party instead, assailed by Invitations on all Sides.

I am much pleased by the Effects of my first Foray. I am further uplifted by Reflection that should Age or Injury prevent my making a Livelihood by means of Sword, Plow, or Printing Press, I might still find useful Employment as a scribbler of Romances.

I expect Marsali will wish to know in great Detail the Appearance of the Gowns worn by the Ladies present, but I must beg her Forbearance for the Moment. I do not pretend not to have observ'd the Matter (though I might so protest, if I thought by so doing to relieve your Mind of Apprehensions concerning any supposed Vulnerability to the Wiles of Femininity. Knowing your suspicious and irrational Nature, my Sassenach, I make no such Protestations), but my Hand will not bear the Strain of recounting such Descriptions now. For the Moment, suffice it to say that the Gowns were of very rich Stuff, and the Charms of the Ladies inside them made most apparent by the Style.

My pilfered Candles are burning low, and both my Hand and my Eyes are so fatigued that I have Difficulty in deciphering my own Words, let alone in forming them—I can only hope you will be able to read the last Part of this illegible Epistle. Still, I retire to my inhospitable Bed in good Spirits, encouraged by the day's Events.

Thus I bid you goodnight, with Assurance of my most tender Thoughts, in trust that you will have patience with and abiding Affection for

Your Ink-stain'd Wretch and Most Devoted Husband,
James Fraser

Postscriptum: Ink-stained Wretch, indeed, as I see that I have contriv'd to cover both my Paper and my Person with unsightly Blots. I flatter myself that the Paper is the more disfigured.

Postscriptum 2: I have been so absorbed in Composition as to forget my original Intent in writing: to say that I have booked Passage on the Euterpe, *sailing from Brest in two Weeks' Time. Should anything transpire to prevent this, I will write again.*

Postscriptum 3: I yearn to lie beside you again, and know your Body complicit with mine.

90

ARMED WITH DIAMONDS AND WITH STEEL

BRIANNA CUT THE brooch apart with a steady hand and a pair of kitchen shears. It was an antique but not a valuable one—an ugly Victorian thing in the shape of a sprawling silver flower surrounded by writhing vines. Its only worth lay in the scatter of small diamonds that decorated the leaves like dewdrops.

"I hope they're big enough," she said, and was surprised at how calm her own voice sounded. She had been screaming inside her own head for the last thirty-six hours, which was how long it had taken them to make their plans and preparations.

"I think they'll be fine," Roger said, and she felt the tension under the calm of his own words. He was standing behind her, his hand on her shoulder, and the warmth of it was comfort and torment. Another hour, and he would be gone. Perhaps forever.

But there was no choice about it, and she went about the necessary things dry-eyed and steady.

Amanda, very weirdly, had fallen asleep quite suddenly after Roger and William Buccleigh had left in pursuit of Rob Cameron. Brianna had laid her in her bed and sat there watching her sleep and worrying until the men had returned near dawn with their horrifying news. But Amanda had waked as usual, sunny as the day, and apparently with no memory of her dream of screaming rocks. Neither was she bothered about Jem's absence; she had asked once, casually, when he would be home and, receiving a noncommittal "Soon," had gone back to her play, apparently contented.

She was with Annie now; they'd gone into Inverness to do a big shopping, with the promise of a toy. They wouldn't be home until mid-afternoon, and by then the men would be gone.

"Why?" William Buccleigh had asked. "Why would he take your lad?"

That was the same question she and Roger had been asking themselves since the moment they discovered Jem's loss—not that the answer was likely to help.

"Only two things it might be," Roger had answered, his voice thick and cracked. "Time travel—or gold."

"Gold?" Buccleigh's dark green eyes had turned to Brianna, puzzled. "What gold?"

"The missing letter," she'd explained, too tired to worry whether it was safe to tell him. Nothing was safe anymore, and nothing mattered. "The postscript my father wrote. Roger said you'd read the letters. *The property of an Italian gentleman*—you remember that?"

"I took no great notice," Buccleigh admitted. "That's gold, is it? Who's the Italian gentleman, then?"

"Charles Stuart." And so they'd explained, in disjoint fashion, about the gold that had come ashore in the last days of the Jacobite Rising—Buccleigh himself would have been about Mandy's age then, Brianna thought, startled by the notion—to be divided for safety among three Scottish gentlemen, trusted tacksmen of their clans: Dougal MacKenzie, Hector Cameron, and Arch Bug, of clan Grant. She watched carefully, but he gave no sign of recognition at the name of Dougal MacKenzie. No, she thought, he doesn't know. But that was not important now, either.

No one knew what had become of the two-thirds of the French gold held by the MacKenzies or the Grants—but Hector Cameron had fled Scotland in the last days of the Rising, the chest of gold under the seat of his carriage, and had brought it with him to the New World, where part of it had bought his plantation, River Run. The rest . . .

"The Spaniard guards it?" Buccleigh said, heavy fair brows knitted. "What the devil does that mean?"

"We don't know," Roger said. He was sitting at the table, head sunk in his hands, staring down at the wood. "Only Jem knows." Then he had raised his head suddenly, looking at Brianna.

"The Orkneys," he said. "Callahan."

"What?"

"Rob Cameron," he'd said urgently. "How old d'ye think he is?"

"I don't know," she'd said, confused. "Mid, late thirties, maybe. Why?"

"Callahan said Cameron went on archaeological digs with him in his early twenties. Is that far enough back—I mean, I only just now thought—" He had to stop to clear his throat and did so angrily before going on. "If he was into the ancient stuff fifteen, eighteen years ago—might he have known Geilie Duncan? Or Gillian Edgars, I suppose she still was then."

"Oh, no," Brianna said, but in denial, not disbelief. "Oh, no. Not another Jacobite nut!"

Roger had almost smiled at that one.

"I doubt it," he'd said dryly. "I don't think the man's insane, let alone a political idealist. But he does belong to the SNP. They aren't insane, either—but what's the odds that Gillian Edgars would have been involved with them?"

There was no telling, not without digging into Cameron's connections and history, and there was no time for that. But it was possible. Gillian—who'd later taken the name of a famous Scottish witch—had certainly been deeply interested both in Scottish antiquity and in Scottish politics. She might have crossed paths with Rob Cameron, easily. And if so . . .

"If so," Roger said grimly, "God only knows what she might have told him, might have left him with." A few of Geillis's notebooks were in his study; if Rob had known her, he would have recognized them.

"And we bloody well know he read your da's postscript," he added. He rubbed his forehead—there was a dark bruise along his hairline—and sighed. "It doesn't matter, does it? The only thing that matters now is Jem."

And so Brianna gave each of them a chunk of silver studded with small diamonds and two peanut butter sandwiches. "For the road," she said, with a ghastly attempt at humor. Warm clothes and stout shoes. She gave Roger her Swiss army knife; Buccleigh took a stainless-steel steak knife from the kitchen, admiring its serrated edge. There wasn't time for much more.

The sun was still high when the blue Mustang bumped along the dirt road that led near the base of Craigh na Dun; she had to be back before Mandy came home. Rob Cameron's blue truck was still there; a shudder went through her at the sight of it.

"Go ahead," Roger said roughly to Buccleigh when she stopped. "I'll be along directly."

William Buccleigh had given Brianna a quick look, direct and disconcerting, with those eyes, so like Roger's, touched her hand briefly, and got out. Roger didn't hesitate; he'd had time on the way to decide what to say—and there was only one thing to say, in any case.

"I love you," he said softly, and took her by the shoulders, holding her together long enough to say the rest. "I'll bring him back. Believe me, Bree—I'll see you again. In *this* world."

"I love you," she'd said, or tried to. It came out as a soundless whisper against his mouth, but he took it, along with her breath, smiled, gripped her shoulders so hard that she would find bruises there later—and opened the door.

She'd watched them—she couldn't help watching them—as they climbed toward the top of the hill, toward the invisible stones, until they disappeared, out of her sight. Perhaps it was imagination; perhaps she really could hear the stones up there: a weird buzzing song that lived in her bones, a memory that would live there forever. Trembling and tear-blinded, she drove home. Carefully, carefully. Because now she was all that Mandy had.

91

FOOTSTEPS

LATE THAT NIGHT, she made her way to Roger's study. She felt dull and heavy, the horror of the day blunted by fatigue. She sat at his desk, trying to feel his presence, but the room was empty.

Mandy was asleep, surprisingly unworried by the chaos of her parents' feelings. Of course, she was used to Roger's occasional absences, gone to London or to Oxford, lodge nights in Inverness. Would she remember him if he never came back? Brianna thought with a pang.

Unable to bear that thought, she got up and prowled restlessly round the office, seeking the unfindable. She hadn't been able to eat anything and was feeling light-headed and friable.

She took up the little snake, finding a minimal comfort in its smooth sinuosity, its pleasant face. She glanced up at the box, wondering whether she should seek solace in her parents' company—but the thought of reading letters that Roger might never read with her . . . She put the snake down and stared blindly at the books on the lower shelves.

Beside the books on the American Revolution that Roger had ordered were her father's books, the ones from his old office. *Franklin W. Randall,* the neat spines said, and she took one out and sat down, holding it to her chest.

She'd asked him once before for help—to look after Ian's lost daughter. Surely he would look after Jem.

She thumbed the pages, feeling a little soothed by the friction of the paper.

Daddy, she thought, finding no words beyond that, and needing no more. The folded sheet of paper tucked among the leaves came as no surprise at all.

The letter was a draft—she could see that at once from the crossings-out, the marginal additions, words circled with question marks. And being a draft, it had neither date nor salutation but was plainly intended for her.

You've just left me, dearest deadeye, after our wonderful afternoon at Sherman's (the clay pigeon place—will she remember the name?). My ears are still ringing. Whenever we shoot, I'm torn between immense pride in your ability, envy of it, and fear. I don't know quite when you will read this, or if you will. Maybe I'll have the courage to tell you before I die (or I'll do something so unforgivable that your mother will—no, she won't. I've never met anyone so honorable as Claire, notwithstanding. She'll keep her word).

What a queer feeling it is, writing this. I know that you'll eventually learn who—and perhaps what—you are. But I have no idea how you'll come to that knowledge. Am I about to reveal you to yourself, or will this be old news when you find it? I can only hope that I've succeeded in saving your life, either way. And that you <u>will</u> find it, sooner or later.

I'm sorry, sweetheart, that's terribly melodramatic. And the last thing I want to do is alarm you. I have all the confidence in the world in you. But I am your father and thus prey to the fears that afflict all parents—that something dreadful and unpreventable will happen to your child, and you powerless to protect them. And the truth is that through no fault of your own, you are . . .

Here he had changed his mind several times, writing *a dangerous person,* amending that to *always in some danger,* then crossing that out in turn, adding *in a dangerous position,* crossing *that* out, and circling *a dangerous person,* though with a question mark.

"I get the point, Daddy," she muttered. "What are you *talking* about? I—"

A sound froze the words in her throat. Footsteps were coming down the hall. Slow, confident steps. A man's. Every hair on her body rose.

The light was on in the hall; it darkened briefly as a shape took form in the door to the study.

She stared at him, dumbfounded.

"What are *you* doing here?" Even as she spoke, she was rising from the chair, groping for something that might be used as a weapon, her mind lagging far behind her body, not yet able to penetrate the fog of horror that gripped her.

"I came for you, hen," he said, smiling. "And for the gold." He laid something on the desk: her parents' first letter. *"Tell Jem the Spaniard guards it,"* Rob Cameron quoted, tapping it. "I thought maybe it's best you tell Jem that. And tell him to show me where this Spaniard is. If ye'd like to keep him alive, I mean. Up to you, though." The smile widened. "Boss."

92

INDEPENDENCE DAY, II

Brest

SEEING JENNY DEAL with it all was disturbing his own presence of mind considerably. He could see her heart in her throat the first time she spoke French to a real Frenchman; her pulse fluttered in the hollow of her neck like a trapped hummingbird. But the *boulanger* understood her—Brest was full of foreigners, and her peculiar accent roused no particular interest—and the sheer delight on her face when the man took her penny and handed her a baguette filled with cheese and olives made Jamie want to laugh and cry at the same time.

"He understood me!" she said, clutching him by the arm as they left. "Jamie, he understood me! I spoke *French* to him, and he kent what I said, clear as day!"

"Much more clearly than he would have had ye spoken to him in the *Gaidhlig*," he assured her. He smiled at her excitement, patting her hand. "Well done, *a nighean.*"

She was not listening. Her head turned to and fro, taking in the vast array of shops and vendors that filled the crooked street, assessing the possibilities now open to her. Butter, cheese, beans, sausage, cloth, shoes, buttons . . . Her fingers dug into his arm.

"Jamie! I can buy anything! By myself!"

He couldn't help sharing her joy at thus rediscovering her independence, even though it gave him a small twinge. He'd been enjoying the novel sensation of having her rely on him.

"Well, so ye can," he agreed, taking the baguette from her. "Best not to buy a trained squirrel or a longcase clock, though. Be difficult to manage on the ship."

"Ship," she repeated, and swallowed. The pulse in her throat, which had subsided momentarily, resumed its fluttering. "When will we . . . go on the ship?"

"Not yet, *a nighean,*" he said gently. "We'll go and ha' a bite to eat first, aye?"

THE *EUTERPE* WAS meant to sail on the evening tide, and they went down to the docks in mid-afternoon to go aboard and settle their things. But the slip at the dock where the *Euterpe* had floated the day before was empty.

"Where the devil is the ship that was here yesterday?" he demanded, seizing a passing boy by one arm.

"What, the *Euterpe?*" The boy looked casually where he was pointing, and shrugged. "Sailed, I suppose."

"You *suppose*?" His tone alarmed the boy, who pulled his arm free and backed off, defensive.

"How would I know, *Monsieur*?" Seeing Jamie's face, he

hastily added, "Her master went into the district a few hours ago; probably he is still there."

Jamie saw his sister's chin dimple slightly and realized that she was near to panic. He wasn't so far off it himself, he thought.

"Oh, is he?" he said, very calm. "Aye, well, I'll just be going to fetch him, then. Which house does he go to?"

The boy shrugged helplessly. "All of them, *Monsieur*."

Leaving Jenny on the dock to guard their baggage, he went back into the streets that adjoined the quay. A broad copper halfpenny secured him the services of one of the urchins who hung about the stalls, hoping for a half-rotten apple or an unguarded purse, and he followed his guide grimly into the filthy alleys, one hand on his purse, the other on the hilt of his dirk.

Brest was a port city, and a bustling port, at that. Which meant, he calculated, that roughly one in three of its female citizenry was a prostitute. Several of the independent sort hailed him as he passed.

It took three hours and several shillings, but he found the master of the *Euterpe* at last, dead drunk. He pushed the whore sleeping with him unceremoniously aside and roused the man roughly, slapping him into semiconsciousness.

"The ship?" The man stared at him blearily, wiping a hand across his stubbled face. "Fuck. Who cares?"

"I do," Jamie said between clenched teeth. "And so will you, ye wee arsewipe. Where is she, and why are ye not on her?"

"The captain threw me off," the man said sullenly. "We had a disagreement. Where is she? On her way to Boston, I suppose." He grinned unpleasantly. "If you swim fast enough, maybe you can catch her."

IT TOOK THE last of his gold and a well-calculated mixture of threats and persuasion, but he found another ship. This one was headed south, to Charleston, but at the moment he would settle for being on the right continent. Once in America, he'd think again.

His sense of grim fury began finally to abate as the *Philo-*

mene reached the open sea. Jenny stood beside him, small and silent, hands braced on the rail.

"What, *a piuthar*?" He put his hand in the small of her back, rubbing gently with his knuckles. "You're grieving Ian?"

She closed her eyes for a moment, pressing back into his touch, then opened them and turned her face up to him, frowning.

"No, I'm troubled, thinkin' of your wife. She'll be peeved wi' me—about Laoghaire."

He couldn't help a wry smile at thought of Laoghaire.

"Laoghaire? Why?"

"What I did—when ye brought Claire home again to Lallybroch, from Edinburgh. I've never said sorry to ye for that," she added, looking up earnestly into his face.

He laughed.

"I've never said sorry to *you,* have I? For bringing Claire home and being coward enough not to tell her about Laoghaire before we got there."

The frown between her brows eased, and a flicker of light came back into her eyes.

"Well, no," she said. "Ye haven't told me sorry. So we're square, are we?"

He hadn't heard her say that to him since he'd left home at fourteen to foster at Leoch.

"We're square," he said. He put an arm round her shoulders and she slipped her own around his waist, and they stood close together, watching the last of France sink into the sea.

93

A SERIES OF SHORT, SHARP SHOCKS

I WAS IN MARSALI'S kitchen, plaiting Félicité's hair while keeping one eye on the porridge over the fire, when the bell over the printshop door rang. I whipped a ribbon round the end of the plait and, with a quick admonition to the girls to watch the porridge, went out to attend to the customer.

To my surprise, it was Lord John. But a Lord John I had never seen before. He was not so much disheveled as shattered, everything in order save his face.

"What?" I said, deeply alarmed. "What's happened? Is Henry—"

"Not Henry," he said hoarsely. He put a hand flat on the counter, as though to steady himself. "I have—bad news."

"I can see that," I said, a little tartly. "Sit down, for God's sake, before you fall down."

He shook his head like a horse shaking off flies and looked at me. His face was ghastly, shocked and white, and the rims of his eyes showed red. But if it wasn't Henry . . .

"Oh, God," I said, a fist clenching deep in my chest. "Dottie. What's happened to her?"

"Euterpe," he blurted, and I stopped dead, jarred to the backbone.

"What?" I whispered. *"What?"*

"Lost," he said, in a voice that wasn't his own. "Lost. With all hands."

"No," I said, trying for reason. "No, it's not."

He looked at me directly then, for the first time, and seized me by the forearm.

"Listen to me," he said, and the pressure of his fingers terrified me. I tried to jerk away but couldn't.

"Listen," he said again. "I heard it this morning from a naval captain I know. I met him at the coffeehouse, and he was recounting the tragedy. He saw it." His voice trembled, and he stopped for a moment, firming his jaw. "A storm. He had been chasing the ship, meaning to stop and board her, when the storm came upon them both. His own ship survived and limped in, badly damaged, but he saw the *Euterpe* swamped by a broaching wave, he said—I have no notion what that is—" He waved away his own digression, annoyed. "She went down before his eyes. The *Roberts*—his ship—hung about in hopes of picking up survivors." He swallowed. "There were none."

"None," I said blankly. I heard what he said but took no meaning from the words.

"He is dead," Lord John said softly, and let go of my arm. "He is gone."

From the kitchen came the smell of burning porridge.

JOHN GREY STOPPED walking because he had come to the end of the street. He had been walking up and down the length of State Street since sometime before dawn. The sun was high now, and sweat-damp grit irritated the back of his neck, mud and dung splashed his stockings, and each step seemed to drive the nails in his shoe sole into the sole of his foot. He didn't care.

The Delaware River flowed across his view, muddy and fish-smelling, and people jostled past him, crowding toward the end of the dock in hopes of getting on the ferry making its slow way toward them from the other side. Wavelets rose and lapped against the pier with an agitated sound that seemed to provoke the people waiting, for they began to push and shove, and one of the soldiers on the dock took down his musket from his shoulder and used it to shove a woman back.

She stumbled, shrieking, and her husband, a bantam-rooster of a man, bounced forward, fists clenched. The soldier said something, bared his teeth and made a shooing motion with the gun, his fellow, attracted by the disturbance, turned to see, and with no more incitement than that, there was suddenly a heaving knot of people at the end of the dock and shouts and screams ran through the rest, as people toward the rear tried to get away from the violence, men in the crowd tried to press toward it, and someone was pushed into the water.

Grey took three steps back and watched as two little boys rushed out of the crowd, their faces bloated with fright, and ran off up the street. Somewhere in the crowd, he heard a woman's high call, distraught: "Ethan! Johnny! *Joooooohnnny!*"

Some dim instinct said he should step forward, raise his own voice, assert his authority, sort this. He turned and walked away.

He wasn't in uniform, he told himself. They wouldn't listen, would be confused, he might do more harm than good. But he wasn't in the habit of lying to himself, and dropped that line of argument at once.

He'd lost people before. Some of them dearly loved, more than life itself. But now he'd lost himself.

He walked slowly back toward his house in a numb daze. He hadn't slept since the news had come, save in the snatches of complete physical exhaustion, slumped in the chair on Mercy Woodcock's porch, waking disoriented, sticky with sap from the sycamores in her yard and covered with the tiny green caterpillars that swung down from the leaves on invisible strands of silk.

"Lord John." He became aware of an insistent voice, and with it, the realization that whoever was speaking had called his name several times already. He stopped, and turned to find himself facing Captain Richardson. His mind went quite blank. Possibly his face had, too, for Richardson took him by the arm in a most familiar manner and drew him into an ordinary.

"Come with me," Richardson said in a low voice, releasing his arm, but jerking his head toward the stair. Faint stirrings of curiosity and wariness made themselves felt through the haze that wrapped him, but he followed, the sound of his shoes hollow in the wooden stairwell.

Richardson closed the door of the room behind him and began speaking before Grey could gather his wits to begin questioning him regarding the very peculiar circumstances William had recounted.

"Mrs. Fraser," Richardson said without preamble. "How well do you know her?"

Grey was so taken aback by this that he answered.

"She is the wife—the widow"—he corrected himself, feeling as though he had stuck a pin into a raw wound—"of a good friend."

"A good friend," Richardson repeated, with no particular emphasis. The man could scarcely look more nondescript, Grey thought, and had a sudden creeping vision of Hubert Bowles. The most dangerous spies were men whom no one would look at twice.

"A good friend," Grey repeated firmly. "His political loyalties are no longer an issue, are they?"

"Not if he's truly dead, no," Richardson agreed. "You think he is?"

"I am quite sure of it. What is it you wish to know, sir? I have business."

Richardson smiled a little at this patently false statement.

"I propose to arrest the lady as a spy, Lord John, and wished to be certain that there was no . . . personal attachment on your part, before I did so."

Grey sat down, rather abruptly, and braced his hands on the table.

"I—she—what the devil for?" he demanded.

Richardson courteously sat down opposite him.

"She has been passing seditious materials to and fro all over Philadelphia for the last three months—possibly longer. And before you ask, yes, I'm sure. One of my men intercepted some of the material; have a look, if you like." He reached into his coat and withdrew an untidy wad of papers, these looking to have passed through several hands. Grey didn't think Richardson was practicing upon him, but took his time in deliberate examination. He put down the papers, feeling bloodless.

"I heard that the lady had been received at your house, and that she is often at the house where your nephew abides," Richardson said. His eyes rested on Grey's face, intent. "But she is not a . . . friend?"

"She is a physician," Grey said, and had the small satisfaction of seeing Richardson's brows shoot up. "She has been of—of the greatest service to me and my nephew." It occurred to him that it was likely better that Richardson did not know how much esteem he might hold for Mrs. Fraser, as if he thought there *was* a personal interest, he would immediately cease to give Grey information. "That is ended, though," he added, speaking as casually as possible. "I respect the lady, of course, but there is no attachment, no." He rose then, in a decided manner, and took his leave, for to ask more questions would compromise the impression of indifference.

He set off toward Walnut Street, no longer numb. He felt once more himself, strong and determined. There was, after all, one more service he might perform for Jamie Fraser.

"YOU MUST MARRY me," he repeated.

I'd heard him the first time, but it made no more sense upon repetition. I stuck a finger in one ear and wiggled it, then repeated the process with the other.

"You can't possibly have said what I think you said."

"Indeed I did," he said, his normal dry edge returning.

The numbness of shock was beginning to wear off, and something horrible was beginning to crawl out of a small hole in my heart. I couldn't look at that and took refuge in staring at Lord John.

"I know I'm shocked," I told him, "but I'm sure I'm neither delusional nor hearing things. Why the bloody hell are you *saying* that, for God's sake?!" I rose abruptly, wanting to strike him. He saw it and took a smart step back.

"You are going to marry me," he said, a fierce edge in his voice. "Are you aware that you are about to be arrested as a spy?"

"I—no." I sat down again, as abruptly as I'd stood up. "What . . . why?"

"You would know that better than I would," he said coldly.

In fact, I would. I repressed the sudden flutter of panic that threatened to overwhelm me, thinking of the papers I had conveyed secretly from one pair of hands to another in the cover of my basket, feeding the secret network of the Sons of Liberty.

"Even if that were true," I said, struggling to keep my own voice level, "why the bloody hell would I marry you? Let alone why you would want to marry *me,* which I don't believe for an instant."

"Believe it," he advised me briefly. "I will do it because it is the last service I can render Jamie Fraser. I can protect you; as my wife, no one can touch you. And *you* will do it because . . ." He cast a bleak glance behind me, raising his chin, and I looked around to see all four of Fergus's children huddled in the doorway, the girls and Henri-Christian watching me with huge, round eyes. Germain was looking straight at Lord John, fear and defiance plain on his long, handsome face.

"Them, too?" I asked, taking a deep breath and turning to meet his gaze. "You can protect them, too?"

"Yes."

"I—yes. All right." I rested both hands flat on the counter, as though that somehow could keep me from spinning off into space. "When?"

"Now," he said, and took my elbow. "There is no time to lose."

I HAD NO MEMORY whatever of the brief ceremony, conducted in the parlor of Lord John's house. The only memory I retained of the entire day was the sight of William, standing soberly beside his father—his stepfather—as best man. Tall, straight, long-nosed, his slanted cat-eyes resting on me with uncertain compassion.

He can't be dead, I remembered thinking, with unusual lucidity. *There he is.*

I said what I was told to say and then was escorted upstairs to lie down. I fell asleep at once and didn't wake until the next afternoon.

Unfortunately, it was still real when I did.

DOROTHEA WAS there, hovering near me with concern. She stayed with me through the day, trying to coax me to eat something, offering me sips of whisky and brandy. Her presence was not exactly a comfort—nothing could be that—but she was at least an innocuous distraction, and I let her talk, the words washing over me like the sound of rushing water.

Toward evening, the men came back—Lord John and Willie. I heard them downstairs. Dottie went down and I heard her talking to them, a slight rise of interest in her voice, and then her steps on the stairs, quick and light.

"Aunt," she said, breathless. "Are you well enough to come down, do you think?"

"I—yes, I suppose so." Slightly taken aback at being called "Aunt," I rose and made vague tidying motions. She took the brush from my hand, twisted up my hair, and, whipping out a ribboned cap, tucked my hair tenderly under it. I let her, and let her convey me gently downstairs, where I found Lord John and William in the parlor, both of them a little flushed.

"Mother Claire." Willie took my hand and gently kissed it. "Come and look. Papa has found something he thinks you will like. Come and see it," he repeated, drawing me gently toward the table.

"It" was a large wooden chest, made of some expensive wood, banded in gold. I blinked at it and put out a hand to touch it. It looked rather like a cutlery safe but much bigger.

"What . . . ?" I looked up to find Lord John standing beside me, looking somewhat abashed.

"A, um, present," he said, deprived for once of his smooth manners. "I thought—I mean, I perceived that you lacked somewhat in the way of . . . equipment. I do not wish you to abandon your profession," he added gently.

"My profession." A chill was beginning to spread up my spine, along the edges of my jaw. Fumbling a little, I tried to raise the lid of the chest, but my fingers were sweating; they slipped, leaving a slick of moisture gleaming on the wood.

"No, no, this way." Lord John bent to show me, turning the chest toward himself. He slipped the hidden catch, lifted the lid, and swung the hinged doors open, then stood back with something of the air of a conjurer.

My scalp prickled with cold sweat, and black spots began to flicker at the corners of my eyes.

Two dozen empty gold-topped bottles. Two shallow drawers below. And above, gleaming in its velvet bed, the pieces of a brass-bound microscope. A medical chest.

My knees gave way and I fainted, welcoming the cool wood of the floor against my cheek.

94

THE PATHS OF DEATH

LYING IN THE tangled hell of my bed at night, I searched for the way to death. I longed with every fiber of my being to pass from this present existence. Whether what lay on the other side of life was undreamed glory or only merciful oblivion, mystery was infinitely preferable to my present inescapable misery.

I cannot say what it was that kept me from a simple and violent escape. The means, after all, were always to hand. I had my choice of pistol ball or blade, of poisons ranging from swiftness to stupor.

I rummaged through the jars and bottles of the medicine chest like a madwoman, leaving the little drawers ajar, the doors hanging open, seeking, scrabbling in my haste, ransacking knowledge and memory as I did the chest, knocking jars and bottles and bits of the past to the floor in a jumble.

At last I thought I had them all and, with a shaking hand, laid them one by one by one on the tabletop before me.

Aconite. Arsenic . . .

So many kinds of death to choose from. How, then?

The ether. That would be the easiest, if not quite the surest. Lie down, soak a thick pad of cloth in the stuff, put the mask over my nose and mouth, and drift painlessly away. But there was always the chance that someone would find me. Or that, losing consciousness, my head might fall to one side or I'd suffer convulsions that would dislodge the rag, and I would simply wake again to this aching void of existence.

I sat still for a moment, and then, feeling dreamlike, reached out to pick up the knife that lay on the table, where I had carelessly left it after using it to cut flax stems. The knife Jamie had given me. It was sharp; the edge gleamed raw and silver.

It would be sure, and it would be fast.

JAMIE FRASER STOOD on the deck of the *Philomene,* watching the water slide endlessly away, thinking about death. He had at least stopped thinking about it in a personal manner, since the seasickness had—at long, long last—abated. His thoughts now were more abstract.

To Claire, he thought, death was always the Enemy. Something always to be fought, never yielded to. He was as well acquainted with death as she was but had perforce made his peace with it. Or thought he had. Like forgiveness, it was not a thing once learned and then comfortably put aside but a matter of constant practice—to accept the notion of one's own mortality, and yet live fully, was a paradox worthy of Socrates. And that worthy Athenian had embraced exactly that paradox, he reflected, with the ghost of a smile.

He'd come face-to-face with death often enough—and remembered those encounters with sufficient vividness—to realize that there were indeed worse things. Much better to die than be left to mourn.

He had still a dreadful feeling of something worse than sorrow when he looked at his sister, small and solitary, and heard the word "widow" in his mind. It was wrong. She could not be that, couldn't be severed in that brutal way. It was like watching her be cut in pieces, and he helpless to do anything.

He turned from that thought to his memories of Claire, his longing for her, the flame of her his candle in the dark. Her touch a comfort and a warmth beyond that of the body. He remembered the last evening before she'd left, holding hands on the bench outside the broch, feeling her heartbeat in her fingers, his own steadying to that warm, quick pulse.

Odd how the presence of death seemed to bring with it so

many attendants, shades long-forgotten, glimpsed briefly in the gathering shadow. The thought of Claire, and how he had sworn to protect her from the first time he held her, brought back to him the nameless girl.

She'd died in France, on the far side of the void in his head that had been made by the blow of an ax. He hadn't thought of her in years, but suddenly she was there again. She'd been in his mind when he'd held Claire at Leoch, and he'd felt that his marriage might be some small atonement. He'd learned—slowly—to forgive himself for what had not been his fault and, in loving Claire, gave the girl's shade some peace, he hoped.

He had felt obscurely that he owed God a life and had paid that debt by taking Claire to wife—though God knew he would have taken her in any case, he thought, and smiled wryly. But he'd kept faith with the promise to protect her. *The protection of my name, my clan—and the protection of my body,* he'd said.

The protection of my body. There was an irony in that that made him squirm, as he glimpsed another face among the shades. Narrow, mocking, long-eyed—so young.

Geneva. One more young woman dead as the result of his lust. Not his fault, precisely—he'd fought that through, in the long days and nights following her death, alone in his cold bed above the stables, taking what comfort he could in the solid, voiceless presence of the horses shifting and champing in their stalls below. But had he not lain with her, she would not have died; that was inescapable.

Did he owe God another life? he wondered. He had thought it was Willie, the life he'd been given to protect with his own, in exchange for Geneva's. But that trust had had to be handed to another.

Well, he had his sister now and assured Ian silently that he would keep her safe. *As long as I live,* he thought. And that should be some time yet. He thought he'd used only five of the deaths the fortune-teller in Paris had promised him.

"You'll die nine times before you rest in your grave," she'd said. Did it take so many tries to get it right? he wondered.

I LET MY HAND fall back, exposing my wrist, and placed the tip of the knife midway up my forearm. I'd seen many unsuccessful suicides, those who slashed their wrists from side to side, the wounds small mouths that cried for help. I'd seen those who meant it. The proper way was to slit the veins lengthwise, deep, sure cuts that would drain me of blood in minutes, assure unconsciousness in seconds.

The mark was still visible on the mound at the base of my thumb. A faint white "J," the mark he'd left on me on the eve of Culloden, when we first faced the stark knowledge of death and separation.

I traced the thin white line with the tip of the knife and felt the seductive whisper of metal on my skin. I'd wanted to die with him then, and he had sent me on with a firm hand. I carried his child; I could not die.

I carried her no longer—but she was still there. Perhaps reachable. I sat motionless for what seemed a long time, then sighed and put the knife back on the table carefully.

Perhaps it was the habit of years, a bent of mind that held life sacred for its own sake, or a superstitious awe of extinguishing a spark kindled by a hand not my own. Perhaps it was obligation. There were those who needed me—or at least to whom I could be useful. Perhaps it was the stubbornness of the body, with its inexorable insistence on never-ending process.

I could slow my heart, slow enough to count the beats . . . slow the flowing of my blood 'til my heart echoed in my ears with the doom of distant drums.

There were pathways in the dark. I knew; I had seen people die. Despite physical decay, there was no dying until the pathway was found. I couldn't—yet—find mine.

95

NUMBNESS

THE NEW MEDICAL chest sat on the table in my room, gleaming softly in the candlelight. Beside it were the gauze bags of dried herbs I had bought during the morning, the fresh bottles of the tinctures I had brewed in the afternoon, much to Mrs. Figg's displeasure at having her kitchen's purity so perverted. Her slitted eyes said that she knew me for a rebel and thought me likely a witch; she'd retreated to the doorway of the cookhouse while I worked but wouldn't leave altogether, instead keeping silent suspicious watch over me and my cauldron.

A large decanter of plum brandy was keeping me company. Over the course of the last week, I had found that a glass of it at night would let me find surcease in sleep, at least for a little. It wasn't working tonight. I heard the clock on the mantelpiece downstairs chime softly, once.

I stooped to pick up a box of dried chamomile that had spilled, sweeping the scattered leaves carefully back into their container. A bottle of syrup of poppies had fallen over, too, lying on its side, the aromatic liquid oozing round the cork. I set it upright, wiped the golden droplets from its neck with my kerchief, blotted up the tiny puddle from the floor. A root, a stone, a leaf. One by one, I picked them up, set them straight, put them away, the accoutrements of my calling, the pieces of my destiny.

The cool glass seemed somehow remote, the gleaming wood an illusion. Heart beating slowly, erratically, I put a hand flat on the box, trying to steady myself, to fix myself in space and time. It was becoming more difficult by the day.

I remembered, with sudden, painful vividness, a day on the retreat from Ticonderoga. We had reached a village, found momentary refuge in a barn. I'd worked all day then, doing what could be done with no supplies, no medicines, no instruments, no bandages save what I made from the sweat-sodden, filthy clothes of the wounded. Feeling the world recede further and further as I worked, hearing my voice as though it belonged to someone else. Seeing the bodies under my hands, only bodies. Limbs. Wounds. Losing touch.

Darkness fell. Someone came, pulled me to my feet, and sent me out of the barn, into the little tavern. It was crowded, overwhelmed with people. Someone—Ian?—said that Jamie had food for me outside.

He was alone there, in the empty woodshed, dimly lit by a distant lantern.

I'd stood in the doorway, swaying. Or perhaps it was the room that swayed.

I could see my fingers dug into the wood of the doorjamb, nails gone white.

A movement in the dimness. He rose fast, seeing me, came toward me. What was his—

"Jamie." I'd felt a distant sense of relief at finding his name.

He'd seized me, drawn me into the shed, and I wondered for an instant whether I was walking or whether he was carrying me; I heard the scrape of the dirt floor under my feet but didn't feel my weight or the shift of it.

He was talking to me, the sound of it soothing. It seemed a dreadful effort to distinguish words. I knew what he must be saying, though, and managed to say, "All right. Just . . . tired," wondering even as I spoke them whether these sounds were words at all, let alone the right ones.

"Will ye sleep, then, lass?" he'd said, worried eyes fixed on me. "Or can ye eat a bit first?" He let go of me, to reach for the bread, and I put out a hand to the wall to support myself, surprised to find it solid.

The sense of cold numbness had returned.

"Bed," I said. My lips felt blue and bloodless. "With you. Right now."

He'd cupped my cheek, calloused palm warm on my skin. Big hand. Solid. Above all, solid.

"Are ye sure, *a nighean*?" he'd said, a note of surprise in his voice. "Ye look as though—"

I'd laid a hand on his arm, half fearing that it would go through his flesh.

"Hard," I'd whispered. "Bruise me."

My glass was empty, the decanter halfway full. I poured another and took hold of the glass carefully, not wanting to spill it, determined to find oblivion, no matter how temporary.

Could I separate entirely? I wondered. Could my soul actually leave my body without my dying first? Or had it done so already?

I drank the glass slowly, one sip at a time. Another. One sip at a time.

There must have been some sound that made me look up, but I wasn't aware of having raised my head. John Grey was standing in the doorway of my room. His neckcloth was missing and his shirt hung limp on his shoulders, wine spilled down the front of it. His hair was loose and tangled, and his eyes as red as mine.

I stood up, slow, as though I were underwater.

"I will not mourn him alone tonight," he said roughly, and closed the door.

I WAS SURPRISED to wake up. I hadn't really expected to and lay for a bit trying to fit reality back into place around me. I had only a slight headache, which was almost more surprising than the fact that I was still alive.

Both those things paled in significance beside the fact of the man in bed beside me.

"How long has it been since you last slept with a woman, if you don't mind my asking?"

He didn't appear to mind. He frowned a little and scratched his chest thoughtfully.

"Oh . . . fifteen years? At least that." He glanced at me, his expression altering to one of concern. "Oh. I do apologize."

"You do? For what?" I arched one brow. I could think of a number of things he *might* apologize for, but probably none of those was what he had in mind.

"I am afraid I was perhaps not . . ." he hesitated. "Very gentlemanly."

"Oh, you weren't," I said, rather tartly. "But I assure you that I wasn't being at all ladylike myself."

He looked at me, and his mouth worked a bit, as though trying to frame some response to that, but after a moment or two he shook his head and gave it up.

"Besides, it wasn't me you were making love to," I said, "and both of us know it."

He looked up, startled, his eyes very blue. Then the shadow of a smile crossed his face, and he looked down at the quilted coverlet.

"No," he said softly. "Nor were you, I think, making love to *me.* Were you?"

"No," I said. The grief of the night before had softened, but the weight of it was still there. My voice was low and husky, because my throat was halfway closed, where the hand of sorrow clutched me unawares.

John sat up and reached to the table, where a carafe stood along with a bottle and a glass. He poured something out of the bottle and handed it to me.

"Thank you," I said, and lifted it to my lips. "Good grief, is that *beer*?"

"Yes, and very good beer, too," he said, tilting back the bottle. He took several hearty gulps, eyes half closed, then lowered it with a sigh of satisfaction. "Clears the palate, freshens the breath, and prepares the stomach for digestion."

Despite myself, I was amused—and shocked.

"Do you mean to tell me that you are in the habit of drinking beer for breakfast every day?"

"Of course not. I have food with it."

"I am amazed that you have a single tooth in your head," I said severely—but risked a small sip. It *was* good beer: heavy-bodied and sweet, with just the right sour edge.

At this point, I noticed a certain tenseness in his posture, which the content of the conversation didn't account for. Slow-witted as I was, it took a moment for me to realize what was amiss.

"Oh. If you need to fart," I said, "don't trouble on my account. Go ahead."

He was sufficiently startled by my observation that he did.

"I do beg your pardon, madam!" he said, his fair skin flushing up to the hairline.

I tried not to laugh, but suppressed amusement jiggled the bed, and he went redder still.

"Would you have any hesitation about it were you in bed with a man?" I asked, out of idle curiosity.

He rubbed his knuckles against his mouth, the color fading a bit from his cheeks.

"Ah. Well, that would depend upon the man. By and large, though, no."

The man. I knew that Jamie was the man in his mind—just as he was in mine. At the moment, I wasn't disposed to resent it.

He knew what I was thinking, too.

"He offered me his body once. You knew that?" His voice was dry.

"I take it you didn't accept." I knew he hadn't but was more than curious to hear his side of that encounter.

"No. What I wanted from him was not that—or not entirely that," he added, with honesty. "I wanted all of it—and was young and proud enough to think that if I could not have that, then I would accept no less. And that, of course, he couldn't give me."

I was silent for a time, thinking. The window was open, and the long muslin curtains moved in the breeze.

"Did you regret it?" I asked. "Not taking him up on his offer, I mean?"

"Ten thousand times, at the very least," he assured me, breaking into a rueful grin. "At the same time . . . refusing him was one of the few acts of true nobility to which I would lay claim for myself. It's true, you know," he added, "selflessness does carry its own reward—for if I *had* taken him, that would have destroyed forever what did exist between us.

"To have given him instead the gift of my understanding, hard come by as it was," he added ironically, "left me with his friendship. So I am left with momentary regret on the one hand, but satisfaction on the other. And in the end it was the friendship that I valued most."

After a moment's silence, he turned to me.

"May I . . . You will think me odd."

"Well, you *are* a bit odd, aren't you?" I said tolerantly. "I don't really mind, though. What is it?"

He gave me a look, strongly suggesting that if one of us

was indeed odd, he didn't think it was himself. Gentlemanly instincts suppressed any remark he might have made to this effect, though.

"Will you allow me to see you? Ah . . . naked?"

I closed one eye and looked at him.

"This certainly isn't the first time you've slept—I do mean *slept* with—a woman, is it?" I asked. He *had* been married, though I seemed to recall that he had spent much of his married life living separately from his wife.

He pursed his lips thoughtfully, as though trying to recall.

"Well, no. I do think it may be the first time I've done it entirely voluntarily, though."

"Oh, I *am* flattered!"

He glanced at me, smiling slightly.

"So you should be," he said quietly.

I was of an age, after all, where . . . Well, on the other hand, he presumably didn't have the same instinctive reactions that the majority of men did, in terms of feminine attractions. Which rather left open the question . . .

"Why?"

A shy smile touched the corner of his mouth, and he hitched himself up against the pillow.

"I . . . am not quite sure, to tell you the truth. Perhaps it is only an effort to reconcile my memories of last night with the . . . er . . . actuality of the experience?"

I felt a sharp jolt, as though he had punched me in the chest. He couldn't have known my first thoughts on waking and seeing him—that sharp, disorienting flash when I had thought he was Jamie, remembering so acutely Jamie's flesh and weight and ardor, and so urgently wanted him to be Jamie that I had succeeded for an instant in thinking that he was, only to be crushed like a grape at the realization that he wasn't, all my soft insides spurting out.

Had he felt or thought the same things, waking to find me there beside him?

"Or perhaps it is curiosity," he said, smiling a little more broadly. "I have not seen a naked woman in some time, bar Negro slaves at the docks in Charleston."

"How long is some time? Fifteen years, you said?"

"Oh, a good deal longer than that. Isobel—" He stopped

abruptly, the smile vanishing. He hadn't mentioned his dead wife before.

"You never saw her naked?" I asked, with more than idle curiosity. He turned his face away a little, eyes cast down.

"Ah . . . no. It wasn't . . . She did not . . . No." He cleared his throat, then raised his eyes, looking into mine with an honesty raw enough to make me want to look away.

"I am naked to you," he said simply, and drew back the sheet.

Thus invited, I could hardly not look at him. And in all truth, I wanted to, out of simple curiosity. He was trim and lightly built, but muscular and solid. A little softness at the waist, but no fat—and softly furred with vigorous blond hair, darkening to brown at his crutch. It was a warrior's body; I was well acquainted with those. One side of his chest was heavily marked with crisscrossing scars, and there were others—a deep one across the top of one thigh, a jagged thing like a lightning bolt down his left forearm.

At least my own scars weren't visible, I thought, and before I could hesitate further, I pulled the sheet away from my own body. He looked at it with deep curiosity, smiling a little.

"You are very lovely," he said politely.

"For a woman of my age?"

His gaze passed over me dispassionately, not with any sense of judgment but rather with the air of a man of educated tastes evaluating what he saw in the light of years of seeing.

"No," he said finally. "Not for a woman of your age; not for a woman at all, I think."

"As what, then?" I asked, fascinated. "An object? A sculpture?" In a way, I could see that. Something like museum sculptures, perhaps: weathered statues, fragments of vanished culture, holding within them some remnant of the original inspiration, this remnant in some odd way magnified by the lens of age, sanctified by antiquity. I had never regarded myself in such a light, but I couldn't think what else he might mean.

"As my friend," he said simply.

"Oh," I said, very touched. "Thank you."

I waited, then drew the sheet up over both of us.

"Since we're friends . . ." I said, somewhat emboldened.

"Yes?"

"I only wondered . . . have you . . . been quite alone all this time? Since your wife died?"

He sighed, but smiled to let me know he didn't mind the question.

"If you really must know, I have for many years enjoyed a physical relationship with my cook."

"With . . . your cook?"

"Not with Mrs. Figg, no," he said hastily, hearing the horror in my voice. "I meant with my cook at Mount Josiah, in Virginia. His name is Manoke."

"Ma—oh!" I recalled Bobby Higgins telling me that Lord John retained an Indian named Manoke to cook for him.

"It is not merely the relief of necessary urges," he added pointedly, turning his head to meet my eyes. "There is true liking between us."

"I'm pleased to hear that," I murmured. "He, er, he's . . ."

"I have no idea whether his preference is solely for men. I rather doubt it—I was somewhat surprised when he made his desires known in re myself—but I am in no position to complain, whatever his tastes may be."

I rubbed a knuckle over my lips, not wanting to seem vulgarly curious—but vulgarly curious, all the same.

"You don't mind, if he . . . takes other lovers? Or he you, come to that?" I had a sudden uneasy apprehension. I did not intend that what had happened the night before should *ever* happen again. In fact, I was still trying to convince myself that it hadn't happened this time. Nor did I mean to go to Virginia with him. But what if I should and Lord John's household then assumed . . . I had visions of a jealous Indian cook poisoning my soup or lying in wait behind the necessary house with a tomahawk.

John himself seemed to be considering the matter, lips pursed. He had a heavy beard, I saw; the blond stubble softened his features and at the same time gave me an odd feeling of strangeness—I had so seldom seen him less than perfectly shaved and groomed.

"No. There is . . . no sense of possession in it," he said finally.

I gave him a look of patent disbelief.

"I assure you," he said, smiling a little. "It—well. Perhaps I can describe it best by analogy. At my plantation—it belongs to William, of course; I refer to it as mine only in the sense of habitation—"

I made a small polite sound in my throat, indicating that he might curtail his inclinations toward complete accuracy in the interests of getting on with it.

"At the plantation," he said, ignoring me, "there is a large open space at the rear of the house. It was a small clearing at first, and over the years I have enlarged it and finally made a lawn of it, but the edge of the clearing runs up to the trees. In the evenings, quite often, deer come out of the forest to feed at the edges of the lawn. Now and then, though, I see a particular deer. It's white, I suppose, but it looks as though it's made of silver. I don't know whether it comes only in the moonlight or whether it's only that I cannot see it save by moonlight—but it is a sight of rare beauty."

His eyes had softened, and I could see that he wasn't looking at the plaster ceiling overhead but at the white deer, coat shining in the moonlight.

"It comes for two nights, three—rarely, four—and then it's gone, and I don't see it again for weeks, sometimes months. And then it comes again, and I am enchanted once more."

He rolled onto his side in a rustle of bedclothes, regarding me.

"Do you see? I do not own this creature—would not, if I could. Its coming is a gift, which I accept with gratitude, but when it's gone, there is no sense of abandonment or deprivation. I'm only glad to have had it for so long as it chose to remain."

"And you're saying that your relationship with Manoke is the same. Does he feel that way about you, do you think?" I asked, fascinated. He glanced at me, clearly startled.

"I have no idea."

"You, um, don't . . . talk in bed?" I said, striving for delicacy.

His mouth twitched, and he looked away.

"No."

We lay in silence for a few moments, examining the ceiling.

"Have you ever?" I blurted.

"Have I what?"

"Had a lover that you talked to."

He cut his eyes at me.

"Yes. Perhaps not quite so frankly as I find myself talking to *you,* but, yes." He opened his mouth as though to say or ask something further, but instead breathed in, shut his mouth firmly, and let the air out slowly through his nose.

I knew—I couldn't not know—that he wanted very much to know what Jamie was like in bed, beyond what I had inadvertently shown him the night before. And I was obliged to admit to myself that I was very tempted to tell him, only in order to bring Jamie back to life for the brief moments while we talked. But I knew that such revelations would have a price: not only a later sense of betrayal of Jamie but a sense of shame at using John—whether he wished such usage or not. But if the memories of what had passed between Jamie and myself in our intimacy were no longer shared—still, they belonged only to that intimacy and were not mine to give away.

It occurred to me—belatedly, as so many things did these days—that John's intimate memories belonged to him, as well.

"I didn't mean to pry," I said apologetically.

He smiled faintly, but with real humor.

"I am flattered, madam, that you should entertain an interest in me. I know many more . . . conventional marriages in which the partners remain by preference in complete ignorance of each other's thoughts and histories."

With considerable startlement, I realized that there was now an intimacy between myself and John—unexpected and uninvited on both our parts, but . . . there it was.

The realization made me shy, and with that realization came a more practical one: to wit, that a person with functional kidneys cannot lie in bed drinking beer forever.

He noticed my slight shifting and rose at once himself, donning his banyan before fetching my own dressing gown—which, I saw with a sense of unease, some kindly hand had hung over a chair to warm before the fire.

"Where did that come from?" I asked, nodding at the silk robe he held for me.

"From your bedroom, I assume." He frowned at me for a moment before discerning what I meant. "Oh. Mrs. Figg brought it in when she built the fire."

"Oh," I said faintly. The thought of Mrs. Figg seeing me in

Lord John's bed—doubtless out cold, disheveled, and snoring, if not actually drooling—was hideously mortifying. For that matter, the mere fact of my *being* in his bed was deeply embarrassing, no matter what I had looked like.

"We *are* married," he pointed out, with a slight edge to his voice.

"Er . . . yes. But . . ." A further thought came to me: perhaps this was not so unusual an occurrence for Mrs. Figg as I thought—had he entertained other women in his bed from time to time?

"Do you sleep with women? Er . . . not sleep, I mean, but . . ."

He stared at me, stopped in the act of untangling his hair.

"Not willingly," he said. He paused, then laid down his silver comb. "Is there anything else you would like to ask me," he inquired, with exquisite politeness, "before I allow the bootboy to come in?"

Despite the fire, the room was chilly, but my cheeks bloomed with heat. I drew the silk dressing gown tighter.

"Since you offer . . . I know Brianna told you what—what we are. Do you believe it?"

He considered me for a time without speaking. He didn't have Jamie's ability to mask his feelings, and I could see his mild irritation at my previous question fade into amusement. He gave me a small bow.

"No," he said, "but I give you my word that I will of course behave in all respects as if I did."

I stared at him until I became aware that my mouth was hanging unattractively open. I closed it.

"Fair enough," I said.

The odd little bubble of intimacy in which we had spent the last half hour had burst, and despite the fact that I had been the one asking nosy questions, I felt like a snail suddenly deprived of its shell—not merely naked but fatally exposed, emotionally as well as physically. Thoroughly rattled, I murmured a farewell and made for the door.

"Claire?" he said, a question in his voice.

I stopped, hand on the doorknob, feeling quite queer; he'd never called me by my name before. It took a small effort to look over my shoulder at him, but when I did, I found him smiling.

"Think of the deer," he said gently. "My dear."

I nodded, wordless, and made my escape. Only later, after I had washed—vigorously—dressed, and had a restorative cup of tea with brandy in it, did I make sense of this last remark.

Its coming is a gift, he'd said of the white deer, *which I accept with gratitude.*

I breathed the fragrant steam and watched the tiny curls of tea leaf drift to the bottom of the cup. For the first time in weeks, I wondered just what the future might hold.

"Fair enough," I whispered, and drained the cup, the shreds of tea leaf strong and bitter on my tongue.

96

FIREFLY

IT WAS DARK. Darker than any place he'd ever been. Night outside wasn't really ever dark, even when the sky was cloudy, but this was darker than the back of Mandy's closet when they played hide 'n seek. There was a crack between the doors, he could feel it with his fingers, but no light came through it at all. It must still be night. Maybe there'd be light through the crack when it got morning.

But maybe Mr. Cameron would come back when it got morning, too. Jem moved a little away from the door, thinking that. He didn't think Mr. Cameron wanted to hurt him, exactly—he *said* he didn't, at least—but he might try to take him back up to the rocks and Jem wasn't going *there*, not for anything.

Thinking about the rocks hurt. Not as much as when Mr. Cameron pushed him against one and it . . . started, but it hurt. There was a scrape on his elbow where he banged it, fighting back, and he rubbed at it now, because it was lots better to feel that than to think about the rocks. No, he told himself, Mr. Cameron *wouldn't* hurt him, because he'd pulled him back out of the rock when it tried to . . . He swallowed hard, and tried to think about something else.

He sort of thought he knew where he was, only because he remembered Mam telling Da about the joke Mr. Cameron played on her, locking her in the tunnel, and she said the wheels that locked the doors sounded like bones being chewed, and that's *just* what it sounded like when Mr. Cameron shoved him in here and shut the doors.

He was kind of shaking. It was cold in here, even with his jacket on. Not as cold as when he and Grandda got up before dawn and waited in the snow for the deer to come down and drink, but still pretty cold.

The air felt weird. He sniffed, trying to smell what was going on, like Grandda and Uncle Ian could. He could smell rock—but it was just plain old rock, not . . . *them*. Metal, too, and an oily sort of smell, kind of like a gas station. A hot kind of smell he thought was electricity. There was something in the air that wasn't a smell at all, but a kind of hum. That was power, he recognized that. Not quite the same as the big chamber Mam had showed him and Jimmy Glasscock, where the turbines lived, but sort of the same. Machines, then. He felt a little better. Machines felt friendly to him.

Thinking about machines reminded him that Mam said there was a train in here, a little train, and that made him feel lots better. If there was a train in here, it wasn't all just empty dark space. That hum maybe belonged to the train.

He put out his hands and shuffled along until he bumped into a wall. Then he felt around and walked along with one hand on the wall, found out he was going the wrong way when he walked face first into the doors and said, "Ow!"

His own voice made him laugh, but the laughter sounded funny in the big space and he quit and turned around to walk the other way, with his other hand on the wall to steer by.

Where was Mr. Cameron now? He hadn't said where he was going. Just told Jem to wait and he'd come back with some food.

His hand touched something round and smooth, and he jerked it back. It didn't move, though, and he put his hand on it. Power cables, running along the wall. Big ones. He could feel a little hum in them, same as he could when Da turned on the car's motor. It made him think of Mandy. She had that kind of quiet hum when she was sleeping, and a louder one when she was awake.

He wondered suddenly whether Mr. Cameron might have gone to take Mandy, and the thought made him feel scared. Mr. Cameron wanted to know how you got through the stones, and Jem couldn't tell him—but Mandy for sure couldn't be telling him, she was only a baby. The thought made him feel hollow, though, and he reached out, panicked.

There she was, though. Something like a little warm light in his head, and he took a breath. Mandy was OK, then. He was interested to find he could tell that with her far away. He'd never thought to try before, usually she was just right *there*, being a pain in the arse, and when him and his friends went off without her, he wasn't thinking about her.

His foot struck something and he stopped, reaching out with one hand. He didn't find anything and after a minute got up his nerve to let go of the wall and reach out further, then to edge out into the dark. His heart thumped and he started to sweat, even though he was still cold. His fingers stubbed metal and his heart leaped in his chest. The train!

He found the opening, and felt his way in on his hands and knees, and cracked his head on the thing where the controls were, standing up. That made him see colored stars and he said *"Ifrinn!"* out loud. It sounded funny, not so echoey now he was inside the train, and he giggled.

He felt around over the controls. They were like Mam said, just a switch and a little lever, and he pushed the switch. A red light popped into life, and made him jump. It made him feel lots better, though, just to see it. He could feel the electricity coming through the train, and that made him feel better, too. He pushed the lever, just a little, and was thrilled to feel the train move.

Where did it go? He pushed the lever a little more, and air moved past his face. He sniffed at it, but it didn't tell him anything. He was going away from the big doors, though—away from Mr. Cameron.

Maybe Mr. Cameron would go and try to find out about the stones from Mam or Da? Jem hoped he *would*. Da would settle Mr. Cameron's hash, he kent that for sure, and the thought warmed him. Then they'd come and find him and it would be OK. He wondered if Mandy could tell them where he was. She kent him the same way he kent her, and he looked at the little red light on the train. It glowed like Mandy, steady and warm-looking, and he felt good looking at it. He pushed the lever a little farther, and the train went faster into the dark.

97

NEXUS

RACHEL POKED suspiciously at the end of a loaf. The bread-seller, catching sight, turned on her with a growl.

"Here, don't you be touching that! You want it, it's a penny. You don't, go away."

"How old is this bread?" Rachel said, ignoring the young woman's glower. "It smells stale, and if it is as stale as it looks, I would not give thee more than half a penny for a loaf."

"It's no more than a day old!" The young woman pulled back the tray of loaves, indignant. "There'll be no fresh bread 'til Wednesday; my master can't get flour 'til then. Now, d'you want bread or not?"

"Hmm," said Rachel, feigning skepticism. Denny would have fits if he thought she was trying to cheat the woman, but there was a difference between paying a fair price and being robbed, and it was no more fair to allow the woman to cheat her than it was the other way about.

Were those crumbs on the tray? And were those tooth marks in the end of that loaf? She bent close, frowning, and Rollo whined suddenly.

"Does thee think the mice have been at these, dog?" she said to him. "So do I."

Rollo wasn't interested in mice, though. Ignoring both Rachel's question and the bread-seller's indignant reply, he was sniffing the ground with great industry, making an odd, high-pitched noise in his throat.

"Whatever ails thee, dog?" Rachel said, staring at this performance in consternation. She put a hand on his ruff and was startled at the vibration running through the great hairy frame.

Rollo ignored her touch as well as her voice. He was moving—almost running—in small circles, whining, nose to the ground.

"That dog's not gone mad, has he?" the baker's assistant asked, watching this.

"Of course not," Rachel said absently. "Rollo . . . *Rollo!*"

The dog had suddenly shot out of the shop, nose to the ground, and was heading down the street, half-trotting in his eagerness.

Muttering under her breath, Rachel seized her marketing basket and went after him.

To her alarm, he was already at the next street and vanished round the corner as she watched. She ran, calling after him, the basket bumping against her leg as she went and threatening to spill out the goods she'd already bought.

What was the matter with him? He'd never acted thus before. She ran faster, trying to keep him in sight.

"Wicked dog," she panted. "Serve thee right if I let thee go!" And yet she ran after him, calling. It was one thing for Rollo to leave the inn on his own hunting expeditions—he always returned. But she was well away from the inn and feared his being lost.

"Though if thy sense of smell is so acute as it seems, doubtless you could follow me back!" she panted, and then stopped dead, struck by a thought.

He was following a scent, so much was clear. But what kind of scent would make the dog do that? Surely no cat, no squirrel . . .

"Ian," she whispered to herself. "Ian."

She picked up her skirts and ran flat out in pursuit of the dog, heart hammering in her ears, even as she tried to restrain the wild hope she felt. The dog was still in sight, nose to the ground and tail held low, intent on his trail. He went into a narrow alley and she followed without hesitation, hopping and lurching in an effort to avoid stepping on the various squashy, nasty things in her path.

Any of these would normally have fascinated any dog, including Rollo—and yet he ignored them all, following his trail.

Seeing this, she realized suddenly what "dogged" really meant, and smiled to herself at the thought.

Could it be Ian? It was surely folly to think so; her hope would be dashed, and yet she could not conquer the conviction that had sprung up in her breast with the possibility. Rollo's tail flicked round the corner, and she dashed after, breathless.

If it was Ian, what could he be doing? The trail was leading them toward the edge of the town—not along the main road but quite out of the settled, prosperous part of the city, into an area of ramshackle houses and the informal camps of the British camp followers. A flock of chickens squawked and scattered at Rollo's approach, but he didn't pause. Now he was circling back, coming round the far side of a shed and out into a narrow street of packed dirt, curling like a tongue between rows of close-packed, ill-built houses.

She had a pain in her side and sweat was pouring down her face, but she, too, knew the meaning of "dogged" and kept on. The dog was drawing away from her, though; she would lose sight of him at any moment—her right shoe had rubbed the skin from her heel, and she felt as though her shoe was filling with blood, though likely this was imagination. She'd seen men with shoes filled with blood . . .

Rollo vanished at the end of the street, and she dashed madly after him, her stockings falling down and her petticoat drooping so she stepped on the hem and tore it. If she did find Ian, she'd have a thing to say to him, she thought. If she could speak by then.

There was no sign of the dog at the end of the street. She looked round wildly. She was at the back of a tavern; she could smell the hops from the brew tubs, and the stink of the midden, and voices came from the street on the other side of the building. Soldiers' voices—there was no mistaking the way soldiers talked, even if she couldn't make out the words—and she halted, heart in her throat.

But they hadn't caught someone; it was only the usual way men talked, casual, getting ready to do something. She caught the clink and jingle of equipment, the sound of boots on the pavement—

A hand seized her arm, and she swallowed the shriek before it could tear out of her throat, terrified of giving Ian away. But it wasn't Ian who had grabbed her. Hard fingers dug into her upper arm, and a tall, white-haired old man looked down at her with burning eyes.

IAN WAS FAMISHED. He had not eaten in more than twenty-four hours, unwilling to take time either to hunt or to find a farmhouse that might give him food. He had covered the twenty miles from Valley Forge in a daze, hardly noticing the distance.

Rachel was here. By some miracle, *here,* in Philadelphia. It had taken him some time to overcome the suspicion of Washington's soldiers, but at last a rather stout German officer with a big nose and a peering, friendly way had come along and expressed curiosity regarding Ian's bow. A brief demonstration of archery and a conversation in French—for the German officer had only the most rudimentary English—and he was at last able to inquire as to the whereabouts of a surgeon named Hunter.

This at first produced only blank looks, but von Steuben had taken a liking to Ian and sent someone to ask while he found a little bread. At long last, the someone had come back and said that there *was* a surgeon named Hunter, who was usually in camp, but who went now and then to Philadelphia to tend a private patient. Hunter's sister? The someone had shrugged.

But Ian knew the Hunters: where Denzell was, Rachel was. Granted, no one knew *where* in Philadelphia Dr. Hunter's private patient might be—there was some reserve about it, some hostility that Ian didn't understand but was much too impatient to unravel—but they were at least in Philadelphia.

And now so was Ian. He'd crept into the city just before dawn, threading his way silently through the camps that ringed the city, past the sleeping, blanket-wrapped forms and smothered, reeking campfires.

There was food in the city, food in abundance, and he paused for a moment of anticipatory bliss on the edge of the market square, deciding between fish fried in batter or a Cornish pasty. He had just stepped forward, money in hand, to the pasty-seller's stall, when he saw the woman look over his shoulder and her face change to a look of horror.

He whirled round and was knocked flat. There were screams and shouts, but these were lost in the mad slobber of Rollo's tongue licking every inch of his face, including the inside of his nose.

He whooped at that and half-sat up, fending off the ecstatic dog.

"A cú!" he said, and hugged the huge, wriggling creature in delight. He seized the dog's ruff in both hands then, laughing at the lolling tongue.

"Aye, I'm glad to see ye, too," he told Rollo. "But what have ye done wi' Rachel?"

FERGUS'S MISSING hand itched. It hadn't done that for some time, and he wished it didn't now. He was wearing a bran-stuffed glove pinned to his sleeve rather than his useful hook—he was much too memorable with that—and it was impossible to rub his stump for relief.

Seeking distraction, he came out of the barn where he'd been sleeping and slouched casually toward a nearby campfire. Mrs. Hempstead nodded at him and picked up a tin mug, into which she ladled thin porridge and passed it over. Aye, well, he thought, there was some advantage to the glove, after all—he couldn't grasp the mug with it but could use it to cradle the hot cup against his chest without burning himself. And, he was pleased to discover, the heat killed the itch.

"Bonjour, madame," he said, with a polite bow, and Mrs. Hempstead smiled, despite her bedraggled tiredness. Her husband had been killed at Paoli, and she eked out a bare living for her three children by doing laundry for English officers. Fergus augmented her income in return for food and shelter. Her house had been taken by her husband's brother,

but he had graciously allowed her and her family to sleep in the barn—one of three or four such bolt-holes Fergus employed in turn.

"There was a man looking out for you, sir," she said in a low voice, coming to give him a cup of water.

"Aye?" He kept himself from glancing round; if the man was still here, she would have told him. "Did you see this man?"

She shook her head.

"No, sir. 'Twas Mr. Jessop he spoke to, and Jessop told Mrs. Wilkins's youngest, who came by and said to my Mary. Jessop said he was a Scotchman, very tall, a fine-looking man. Thought he might have been a soldier once."

Excitement sprang up in Fergus's breast, hot as the porridge.

"Had he red hair?" he asked, and Mrs. Hempstead looked surprised.

"Well, I don't know as how the young'un said. Let me ask Mary, though."

"Do not trouble yourself, madame. I will ask myself." He swallowed the rest of the porridge, nearly scalding his throat, and handed back the cup.

Small Mary, carefully questioned, did not know whether the tall Scotchman had red hair; she hadn't seen him, and Tommy Wilkins didn't say. He had, however, told her where Mr. Jessop had seen the man, and Fergus, thanking Mary with his best Gallic courtesy—which made her blush—made his way into the city, heart beating fast.

RACHEL JERKED HER arm, but the old man merely tightened his grip, his thumb digging hard into the muscle below her shoulder.

"Let me go, Friend," she said calmly. "Thee has mistaken me for someone else."

"Oh, I think not," he said politely, and she perceived him to be a Scot. "Yon dog is yours, is he not?"

"No," she said, puzzled and beginning to be vaguely alarmed. "I am but minding him for a friend. Why? Has he eaten one of thy chickens? I will be pleased to pay thee for it. . . ." She leaned away, groping with her free hand for her purse, gauging the possibilities of escape.

"Ian Murray is the name of your friend," he said, and she was now genuinely alarmed to see he did not phrase this as a question.

"Let me go," she said, more strongly. "Thee has no right to detain me."

He paid no attention to this but looked intently into her face. His eyes were ancient, red-rimmed, and rheumy—but sharp as razors.

"Where is he?"

"In Scotland," she told him, and saw him blink with surprise. He bent a little to peer directly into her eyes.

"Do you love him?" the old man asked softly—but there was nothing soft about his tone.

"Let go!" She kicked at his shin, but he stepped aside with an adroitness that surprised her. His cloak swung aside as he moved, and she caught the gleam of metal in his belt. It was a small ax, and with the sudden memory of the dreadful house in New Jersey, she jerked back and shrieked out loud.

"Hush!" the old man snapped. "Come with me, lass." He put a large, dirty hand over her mouth and tried to pull her off her feet, but she struggled and kicked and got her mouth free long enough to scream again, as loudly as she could.

Startled exclamations, as well as the sound of heavy boots, came rapidly toward her.

"Rachel!" A familiar bellow reached her ears, and her heart bounded at the sound.

"William! Help me!"

William was running toward her, and some distance behind him were three or four British soldiers, muskets in hand. The old man said something in Gaelic, in tones of absolute amazement, and let go of her so suddenly that she staggered back, tripped on the torn hem of her petticoat, and sat down hard in the road.

The old man was backing away, but William was roused; he charged the old man, ducking his shoulder, clearly meaning to knock him off his feet. The old man had his ax in his hand, though, and Rachel screamed, "William!" at the top of her voice. But it was no good. There was a flash of light on metal and a sickening thud, and William lurched sideways, took two ungainly steps, and fell.

"William, William! Oh, Lord, oh, Lord . . ." She couldn't get to her feet but crawled to him as fast as she could, moaning. The soldiers were shouting, roaring, running after the old man, but she had no attention to spare for them. All she saw was William's face, ghastly pale, his eyes rolled up in his head so the whites of them showed, and the blood running dark, soaking his hair.

I TUCKED WILLIAM up in bed, despite his protests, and bade him stay there. I was reasonably sure the protests were for Rachel's sake, since as soon as I had shooed her out the door, he allowed me to ease him back onto his pillow, his face pale and clammy under the bandage wrapped around his forehead.

"Sleep," I said. "You'll feel perfectly bloody in the morning, but you won't die."

"Thank you, Mother Claire," he murmured, with the faintest of smiles. "You're always such a comfort. Before you go, though . . ." Despite how ill he plainly felt, his hand on my arm was solid and firm.

"What?" I asked warily.

"The man who attacked Rachel. Do you have any idea who he might be?"

"Yes," I said reluctantly. "From her description, he's a man named Arch Bug. He used to live near us in North Carolina."

"Ah." His face was pale and clammy, but the deep blue eyes brightened a little with interest. "Is he mad?"

"Yes, I think so. He . . . lost his wife under very tragic circumstances, and I do believe it turned his wits to some degree." I did in fact think this was true, and the months and months since that winter night on the Ridge, spent alone in the woods, walking endless roads, listening for the vanished voice of his dead wife . . . If he had not been mad to start with, I thought he would be now. At the same time, I wasn't about to tell William the whole story. Not now, and possibly not ever.

"I'll speak to someone," he said, and suddenly gave a massive yawn. "Sorry. I'm . . . awfully sleepy."

"You have a concussion," I told him. "I'll come and wake you every hour. Speak to whom?"

"Officer," he said indistinctly, his eyes already closing. "Have men look for him. Can't let him . . . Rachel." Her name came out on a sigh as the big young body went slowly limp. I watched him for a moment to be sure he was soundly asleep. Then I kissed his forehead gently, thinking—with the same wrench of the heart with which I had kissed his sister at the same age—*God, you are so like him.*

Rachel herself was waiting on the landing, anxious and disheveled, though she'd made some effort to tidy her hair and cap.

"Will he be all right?"

"Yes, I think so. He has a mild concussion—you know what that is? Yes, of course you do. That, and I've put three stitches into his head. He'll have an ungodly headache tomorrow, but it was a glancing wound, nothing serious."

She sighed, slender shoulders drooping suddenly as the tension went out of them.

"Thank the Lord," she said, then glanced at me and smiled. "And thee, too, Friend Claire."

"My pleasure," I said sincerely. "Are you sure that you're all right? You should sit down and have something to drink." She wasn't hurt, but the shock of the experience had plainly marked her. I knew she wouldn't drink tea, as a matter of principle, but a little brandy, or even water . . .

"I'm fine. Better than fine." Relieved of her worry about William, she looked at me now, her face aglow. "Claire—he's here! Ian!"

"What? Where?"

"I don't know!" She glanced at the door to William's room and drew me a little way away, lowering her voice. "The dog—Rollo. He smelled something and went off after it like a shot. I ran after him, and that's when I ran into the poor madman. I know, thee will tell me he might chase anything, and he might—but, Claire, he has not come back! If he had not found Ian, he would have come back."

I caught her sense of excitement, though I was afraid to hope as much as she did. There were other things that could prevent the dog coming back, and none of them was good. One of them was Arch Bug.

Her description of him just now had taken me aback—and yet she was right, I realized. Ever since Mrs. Bug's funeral at Fraser's Ridge, I had seen Arch Bug only as a threat to Ian—and yet, with Rachel's words, I also saw the maimed, arthritic hands fumbling to pin a bird-shaped brooch to his loved wife's shroud. Poor madman, indeed.

And a bloody dangerous one.

"Come downstairs," I said to her, with another glance at William's door. "I need to tell you about Mr. Bug."

"OH, IAN," SHE whispered, when I had finished my account. "Oh, poor man." I didn't know whether this last referred to Mr. Bug or Ian, but she was right, either way. She didn't weep, but her face had gone pale and still.

"Both of them," I agreed. "All three, if you count Mrs. Bug."

She shook her head, in dismay rather than disagreement.

"Then that is why—" she said, but stopped.

"Why what?"

She grimaced a little, but glanced at me and gave a small shrug.

"Why he said to me that he was afraid I might die because I loved him."

"Yes, I expect so."

We sat for a moment over our steaming cups of lemon balm tea, contemplating the situation. At last, she looked up and swallowed.

"Does thee think Ian means to kill him?"

"I—well, I don't know," I said. "Certainly not to begin with; he felt terrible about what happened to Mrs. Bug—"

"About the fact that he killed her, thee means." She gave me a direct look; not one for easy evasions, Rachel Hunter.

"I do. But if he realizes that Arch Bug knows who you are, knows what you mean to Ian, and means you harm—and make no mistake about it, Rachel, he *does* mean you harm"—I took a swallow of hot tea and a deep breath—"yes, I think Ian would try to kill him."

She went absolutely still, the steam from her cup the only movement.

"He must not," she said.

"How do you mean to stop him?" I asked, out of curiosity.

She let out a long, slow breath, eyes fixed on the gently swirling surface of her tea.

"Pray," she said.

98

MISCHIANZA

May 18, 1778
Walnut Grove, Pennsylvania

IT HAD BEEN quite a long time since I'd seen a gilded roast peacock, and I hadn't really expected to see another. Certainly not in Philadelphia. Not that I should have been surprised, I thought, leaning closer to look—yes, it *did* have eyes made of diamonds. Not after the regatta on the Delaware, the three bands of musicians carried on barges, and the seventeen-gun salute from the warships on the river. The evening had been billed as a "mischianza." The word means "medley" in Italian—I was told—and in the current instance appeared to have been interpreted so as to allow the more creative souls in the British army and the Loyalist community free rein in the production of a gala celebration to honor General Howe, who had resigned as commander in chief, to be replaced by Sir Henry Clinton.

"I am sorry, my dear," John murmured at my side.

"For what?" I asked, surprised.

He was surprised in turn; his fair brows went up.

"Why, knowing your loyalties, I must suppose that it would be painful to you, to see so much . . ." He made a discreet motion of the wrist, indicating the lavish displays around us, which were certainly not limited to the peacock. "... so much pomp and extravagant expense devoted to—to—"

"Gloating?" I ended dryly. "I might—but I don't. I know what will happen."

He blinked at that, very much taken aback.

"What will happen? To whom?"

The sort of prophecy I possessed was seldom a welcome gift; in these circumstances, though, I took a rather grim pleasure in telling him.

"To you. The British army, I mean, not you personally. They'll lose the war, in three years' time. What price gilded peacocks then, eh?"

His face twitched, and he hid a smile.

"Indeed."

"Yes, indeed," I replied amiably. *"Fuirich agus chi thu."*

"What?" He stared at me.

"Gaelic," I said, with a small, deep twinge. "It means 'Wait and see.'"

"Oh, I shall," he assured me. "In the meantime, allow me to make known Lieutenant-Colonel Banastre Tarleton, of the British Legion." He bowed to a short, wiry young gentleman who had approached us, an officer of dragoons in a bottle-green uniform. "Colonel Tarleton, my wife."

"Lady John." The young man bowed low over my hand, brushing it with very red, very sensual lips. I wanted to wipe my hand on my skirt, but didn't. "Are you enjoying the festivities?"

"I'm looking forward to the fireworks." He had foxy, clever eyes that missed nothing, and his ripe red mouth twisted at this, but he smiled and left it, turning to Lord John. "My cousin Richard bids me give you his best regards, sir."

John's air of pleasant cordiality warmed into genuine pleasure at that.

"Richard Tarleton was my ensign at Crefeld," he explained to me before switching his attention back to the green dragoon. "How does he do these days, sir?"

They lapsed at once into a detailed conversation of commissions, promotions, campaigns, troop movements, and parliamentary politics, and I moved away. Not out of boredom, but rather out of tact. I had not promised John that I would refrain from passing on useful information; he hadn't asked it. But delicacy and a certain sense of obligation required that I at least not acquire such information through him, or directly under his nose.

I drifted slowly through the crowd in the ballroom, admiring the ladies' dresses, many of them imported from Europe, most of the rest modeled on such imports with such materials as could be obtained locally. The brilliant silks and sparkling embroidery were such a contrast to the homespuns and muslins I was accustomed to see that it seemed surreal—as though I'd found myself in a sudden dream. This impression was heightened by the presence among the crowd of a number of knights, dressed in surcoats and tabards, some with helms tucked under their arms—the afternoon's entertainment had included a mock jousting tournament—and a number of people in fantastic masks and extravagant costume, whom I assumed would later be part of some theatrical presentation.

My attention drifted back over the table where the gaudier viands were displayed: the peacock, tail feathers spread in a huge fan, occupied pride of place in the center of the table, but it was flanked by an entire roast boar on a bed of cabbage—this emitting a smell that made my stomach growl—and three enormous game pies, decorated with stuffed songbirds. Those reminded me suddenly of the King of France's dinner with the stuffed nightingales, and my appetite vanished at once in a puff of nausea and grief recalled.

I shifted my gaze hastily back to the peacock, swallowing. I wondered idly how difficult it might be to abstract those diamond eyes and whether someone was keeping an eye on them. Almost certainly so, and I looked to see if I could spot him. Yes, there he was, a uniformed soldier standing in a nook between the table and the huge mantelpiece, eyes alert.

I didn't need to steal diamonds, though, I thought, and my stomach curled a little. I had them. John had given me a pair of diamond earrings. When the time came for me to leave . . .

"Mother Claire!"

I had been feeling pleasantly invisible and, startled out of this delusion, now glanced across the room to see Willie, his disheveled head sticking out from the red-crossed tabard of a Knight Templar, waving enthusiastically.

"I do wish you could think of something else to call me," I said, reaching his side. "I feel as though I ought to be swishing round in a habit with a rosary at my waist."

He laughed at that, introduced the young lady making goo-goo eyes at him as Miss Chew, and offered to get us both an ice. The temperature in the ballroom was rising eighty, at least, and sweat darkened not a few of the bright silks.

"What an elegant gown," Miss Chew said politely. "Is it from England?"

"Oh," I said, rather taken aback. "I don't know. But thank you," I added, looking down at myself for the first time. I hadn't really noticed the gown, beyond the mechanical necessities of getting into it; dressing was no more than a daily nuisance, and so long as nothing was too tight or chafed, I didn't care what I wore.

John had presented me with the gown this morning, as well as summoning a hairdresser to deal with me from the neck up. I'd shut my eyes, rather shocked at how enjoyable the man's fingers felt in my hair—but still more shocked when he handed me a looking glass and I saw a towering confection of curls and powder, with a tiny ship perched in it. Full-rigged.

I'd waited 'til he left, then hurriedly brushed it all out and pinned it up as simply as I could. John had given me a look, but said nothing. Concerned with my head, though, I hadn't taken any time to look at myself below the neck, and was vaguely pleased now to see how well the cocoa-colored silk fit me. Dark enough that it might not show sweat stains, I thought.

Miss Chew was watching William like a cat eyeing up a fat, handsome mouse, frowning a little as he stopped to flirt with two other young ladies.

"Will Lord Ellesmere be remaining long in Philadelphia?" she asked, eyes still on him. "I believe someone told me that he is not to go with General Howe. I do hope that is the case!"

"That's right," I said. "He surrendered with General Burgoyne; those troops are all on parole and are meant to go back to England, but there's some administrative reason why they can't embark just yet." I knew William was hoping to be exchanged, so that he could fight again, but didn't mention it.

"Really," she said, brightening. "What splendid news! Perhaps he will be here for my ball next month. Naturally, it will not be quite so good as this one"—she arched her neck a little, tilting her head toward the musicians who had begun to play at the far end of the room—"but Major André says he will lend his skill to paint the backdrops so we may have tableaux, so it will be—"

"I'm sorry," I interrupted, "did you say Major André? Major . . . John André?"

She glanced at me in surprise, half-annoyed at my interruption. "Of course. He designed the costumes for the joust today and has written the play they will do later. Look, there he is, speaking with Lady Clinton."

I looked where she pointed with her fan, feeling a sudden chill wash through me, despite the heat in the room.

Major André was the center of a group, men and women both, laughing and gesturing, plainly the focus of everyone's attention. He was a handsome young man in his late twenties, his uniform tailored to perfection and his face vivid, flushed with heat and pleasure.

"He seems . . . very charming," I murmured, wanting to look away from him, but unable to do so.

"Oh, yes!" Miss Chew was enthusiastic. "He and I and Peggy Shippen did almost all of the work for the mischianza together—he's a marvel, always with such good ideas, and he plays the flute just delightful. So sad that Peggy's father would not let her come tonight—quite unfair!" I thought there was an underlying tone of satisfaction to her voice, though; she was quite pleased not to have to share the limelight with her friend.

"Do let me present him to you," she said suddenly, and folding her fan, slipped her arm through mine. I was taken entirely by surprise and couldn't think of a way to extricate myself before I found myself towed into the group around André, with Miss Chew chattering brightly to him, laughing up at him, her hand familiarly on his arm. He smiled at her, then switched his gaze to me, his eyes warm and lively.

"I am enchanted, Lady John," he said, in a soft, husky voice. "Your servant, madame."

"I—yes," I said abruptly, quite forgetting the usual form. "You—yes. Glad to meet you!" I pulled my hand out of his before he could kiss it, disconcerting him, and backed away. He blinked, but Miss Chew reclaimed his attention at once, and I turned away, going to stand near the door where there was at least a little air. I was covered in cold sweat and vibrating in every limb.

"Oh, there you are, Mother Claire!" Willie popped up beside me, two half-melted ices in his hands, sweating freely. "Here."

"Thank you." I took one, noting absently that my fingers were nearly as cold as the misted silver cup.

"Are you quite all right, Mother Claire?" He bent down to look at me, concerned. "You look quite pale. As though you'd seen a ghost." He winced in brief apology at this clumsy reference to death, but I made an effort to smile back. Not a terribly successful effort, because he was right. I had just seen a ghost.

Major John André was the British officer with whom Benedict Arnold—hero of Saratoga and still a legendary patriot—would eventually conspire. And the man who would go to the gallows for his part in that conspiracy, sometime in the next three years.

"Had you better sit down for a bit?" Willie was frowning in concern, and I made an effort to shake off my cold horror. I didn't want him offering to leave the ball to see me home; he was plainly having a good time. I smiled at him, barely feeling my lips.

"No, that's all right," I said. "I think . . . I'll just step outside for some air."

99

A BUTTERFLY IN A BUTCHER'S YARD

ROLLO LAY UNDER a bush, noisily devouring the remains of a squirrel he'd caught. Ian sat on a rock, contemplating him.

The city of Philadelphia lay just out of sight; he could smell the haze of fire, the stink of thousands of people living cheek by jowl. Could hear the clop and rattle of people going there, on the road that lay only a few hundred yards away. And somewhere, within a mile of him, hidden in that mass of buildings and people, was Rachel Hunter.

He wanted to step out on the road, stride down it into the heart of Philadelphia, and begin taking the place apart, brick by brick, until he found her.

"Where do we begin, *a cú*?" he said to Rollo. "The print-shop, I suppose."

He'd not been there, but supposed it would not be hard to find. Fergus and Marsali would give him shelter—and food, he thought, feeling his stomach growl—and perhaps Germain and the girls could help him hunt for Rachel. Perhaps Auntie Claire could . . . Well, he knew she wasn't a witch or a fairy, but there was no doubt at all in his mind that she was something, and perhaps she would be able to find Rachel for him.

He waited for Rollo to finish his meal, then rose, an extraordinary sense of warmth suffusing him, though the day was overcast and cool. Could he find her that way? he wondered. Walk through the streets, playing the children's game of "warmer, colder," growing steadily warmer as he approached her more closely, coming to her at last just before he burst into flame?

"You could help, ye know," he said reproachfully to Rollo. He'd tried getting Rollo to backtrack to her at once when the dog had found him, but the dog had been so berserk with joy at Ian's return that there was no speaking to him. That was a thought, though—if they somehow ran across her trail, Rollo might take it up, now that he was more sober-minded.

He smiled crookedly at that thought; the bulk of the British army was encamped at Germantown, but there were thousands of soldiers quartered in Philadelphia itself. As well ask the dog to follow the scent of a butterfly through a butcher's yard.

"Well, we won't find her, sitting here," he said to Rollo, and stood up. "Come on, dog."

100

LADY IN WAITING

I WAS WAITING for things to make sense. Nothing did. I had lived in John Grey's house, with its gracious stair and crystal chandelier, its Turkey rugs and fine china, for nearly a month, and yet I woke each day with no idea where I was, reaching across an empty bed for Jamie.

I could not believe he was dead. *Could* not. I shut my eyes at night and heard him breathing slow and soft in the night beside me. Felt his eyes on me, humorous, lusting, annoyed, alight with love. Turned half a dozen times a day, imagining I heard his step behind me. Opened my mouth to say something to him—and more than once really *had* spoken to him, realizing only when I heard the words dwindle on the empty air that he was not there.

Each realization crushed me anew. And yet none reconciled me to his loss. I had, with shrinking mind, envisioned his death. He would so have hated drowning. Of all ways to die! I could only hope that the sinking of the ship had been violent, and that he had gone unconscious into the water. Because otherwise . . . he couldn't give up, he wouldn't have. He would have swum and kept swimming, endless miles from any shores, alone in the empty deep, swum stubbornly because he could not give up and let himself sink. Swum until that powerful frame was exhausted, until he could not lift a hand again, and then . . .

I rolled over and pressed my face hard into my pillow, heart squeezing with horror.

"What a bloody, bloody *waste*!" I said into the feathers, clenching handfuls of pillow in my fists as hard as I could. If he'd died in battle, at least . . . I rolled back over and shut my eyes, biting my lip until the blood came.

At last my breathing slowed, and I opened my eyes on darkness again, and resumed waiting. Waiting for Jamie.

Some time later, the door opened, and a slice of light from the hallway fell into the room. Lord John came in, setting a candle on the table by the door, and approached the bed. I didn't look at him, but knew he was looking down at me.

I lay on my bed, staring at the ceiling. Or, rather, looking through it to the sky. Dark, full of stars and emptiness. I hadn't bothered to light a candle, but I didn't curse the darkness, either. Only looked into it. Waiting.

"You are very lonely, my dear," he said, with great gentleness, "and I know it. Will you not let me bear you company, for a little time at least?"

I said nothing, but did move over a little and did not resist when he lay down beside me and gathered me carefully into his arms.

I rested my head on his shoulder, grateful for the comfort of simple touch and human warmth, though it didn't reach the depths of my desolation.

Try not to think. Accept what there is; don't think about what there is not.

I lay still, listening to John breathe. He breathed differently than Jamie, shallower, faster. A very slight catch in his breath.

It dawned on me, slowly, that I was not alone in my desolation or my loneliness. And that I knew all too well what had happened last time this state of affairs had become obvious to both of us. Granted, we were not drunk, but I thought he couldn't help but remember it, as well.

"Do you . . . wish me to . . . comfort you?" he said quietly. "I do know how, you know." And, reaching down, he moved a finger very slowly, in such a place and with such exquisite delicacy that I gasped and jerked away.

"I know you do." I did have a moment's curiosity as to how exactly he had learned, but was not about to ask. "It's not that I don't appreciate the thought—I do," I assured him, and felt my cheeks flush hotter. "It's—it's only—"

"That you would feel unfaithful?" he guessed. He smiled a little sadly. "I understand."

There was a long silence then. And a sense of growing awareness.

"You wouldn't?" I asked. He lay quite still, as if asleep, but wasn't.

"A standing cock is quite blind, my dear," he said at last, eyes still shut. "Surely you know that, physician that you are."

"Yes," I said, "I do know that." And taking him gently but firmly in hand, I dealt with him in tender silence, avoiding any thought of whom he might see in his mind's eye.

COLENSO BARAGWANATH ran as though his boot heels were on fire. He burst into the Fox tavern near the foot of State Street, and barreled through the taproom into the cardroom at the back.

"They found him," he panted. "The ol' man. Ax. With the ax."

Captain Lord Ellesmere was already rising to his feet. To Colenso, he looked some eight feet tall, and awful in aspect. The place where the doctor had stitched his head was bristly with new hair, but the black stitching still showed. His eyes might have been shooting flames, but Colenso was afraid to look too closely. His chest heaved from running and he was out of breath, but he couldn't have thought of a thing to say, even so.

"Where?" said the captain. He spoke very softly, but Colenso heard him and backed toward the door, pointing. The captain picked up the pair of pistols he had laid aside, and putting them in his belt, came toward him.

"Show me," he said.

RACHEL SAT ON the tall stool behind the printshop's counter, head on her hand. She'd wakened with a sense of pressure in her head, probably from the impending storm, and it had ripened into a throbbing headache. She would rather have gone back to Friend John's house, to see if Claire might have a tea that would help, but she'd promised Marsali that she would come and mind the shop while her friend took the children to the cobbler to have their shoes mended and Henri-Christian fitted for a pair of boots, for his feet were too short and wide to fit his sisters' outgrown shoes.

At least the shop was quiet. Only one or two folk had come in, and only one of those had spoken to her—asking the way to Slip Alley. She rubbed her stiff neck, sighing, and let her eyes close. Marsali would be back soon. Then she could go and lie down with a wet rag on her head, and—

The bell above the printshop door went *ting!* and she straightened up, a welcoming smile forming on her face. She saw the visitor and the smile died.

"Leave," she said, scrambling off the stool, measuring the distance between her and the door into the house. "Leave this minute." If she could get through, and out the back—

"Stand still," said Arch Bug, in a voice like rusty iron.

"I know what thee means to do," she said, backing up a step. "And I do not blame thee for thy grief, thy rage. But thee must know it is not right what thee intend, the Lord cannot wish thee to—"

"Be quiet, lass," he said, and his eyes rested on her with an odd sort of gentleness. "Not yet. We'll wait for him."

"For . . . him?"

"Aye, him." With that, he lunged across the counter and seized her arm. She screamed and struggled but could not get loose, and he flipped up the flap in the counter and dragged her through, pushing her hard against the table of books so that the stacks wobbled and fell with papery thumps.

"Thee cannot hope to—"

"I have nay hope," he interrupted, quite calm. The ax was in his belt; she saw it, bare and silver. "I need none."

"Thee will surely die," she said, and made no effort to keep her voice from trembling. "The soldiers will take thee."

"Oh, aye, they will." His face softened a little then, surprisingly. "I shall see my wife again."

"I could not counsel suicide," she said, edging as far away as she could get. "But if thee does intend to die in any case, why does thee insist upon—upon staining thy death, thy soul, with violence?"

"Ye think vengeance a stain?" The beetling white brows lifted. "It is a glory, lass. My glory, my duty to my wife."

"Well, certainly not mine," she said heatedly. "Why should I be forced to serve thy beastly vengeance? I have done nothing to thee or thine!"

He wasn't listening. Not to her, at least. He had turned a little, his hand going to his ax, and smiled at the sound of racing footsteps.

"Ian!" she shrieked. "Don't come in!!"

He came in, of course. She grasped a book and flung it at the old man's head, but he dodged it easily and grabbed her by the wrist once more, his ax in hand.

"Let her go," said Ian, hoarse with running. His chest heaved and sweat was running down his face; she could smell him, even above the old man's musty reek. She jerked her hand out of Arch Bug's clasp, speechless with horror.

"Don't kill him," she said, to both of them. Neither of them listened.

"I told ye, did I not?" Arch said to Ian. He sounded reasonable, a teacher pointing out the proof of a theorem. *Quod erat demonstrandum. Q.E.D.*

"Get away from her," Ian said.

His hand hovered above his knife, and Rachel, choking on the words, said, "Ian! Don't. Thee must not. Please!"

Ian gave her a look of furious confusion, but she held his eyes, and his hand dropped away. He took a deep breath and then a quick step to the side. Bug whirled to keep him in range of the ax, and Ian slid fast in front of Rachel, screening her with his body.

"Kill me, then," he said deliberately to Bug. "Do it."

"No!" Rachel said. "That is not what I—no!"

"Come here, lass," Arch said, and put out his good hand, beckoning. "Dinna be afraid. I'll make it fast."

Ian shoved her hard, so she slammed into the wall and knocked her head, and braced himself before her, crouched and waiting. Unarmed, because she'd asked it.

"Ye'll fucking kill me first," he said, in a conversational tone.

"No," said Arch Bug. "Ye'll wait your turn." The old eyes measured him, cold and clever, and the ax moved a little, eager.

Rachel shut her eyes and prayed, finding no words but praying all the same, in a frenzy of fear. She heard a sound and opened them.

A long gray blur shot through the air, and in an instant, Arch Bug was on the ground, Rollo on top of him, snarling and snapping at the old man's throat. Old he might be but still hale, and he had the strength of desperation. His good hand seized the dog's throat, pushing back, holding off the slavering jaws, and a long, sinewy arm flung out, ax gripped in a maimed fist, and rose.

"No!" Ian dove forward, knocking Rollo aside, grappling for the hand that held the ax, but it was too late; the blade came down with a *chunk!* that made Rachel's vision go white, and Ian screamed.

She was moving before she could see, and screamed herself when a hand suddenly seized her shoulder and hurled her backward. She hit the wall and slid down it, landing winded and openmouthed. There was a writhing ball of limbs, fur, clothes, and blood on the floor before her. A random shoe cracked against her ankle and she scuttled away crabwise, staring.

There seemed to be blood everywhere. Spattered against the counter and the wall, smeared on the floor, and the back of Ian's shirt was soaked with red and clinging so she saw the muscles of his back straining beneath it. He was kneeling half atop a struggling Arch Bug, grappling one-handed for the ax, his left arm hanging limp, and Arch was stabbing at his face with stiffened fingers, trying to blind him, while Rollo darted eellike and bristling into the mass of straining limbs, growling and snapping. Fixed on this spectacle, she was only dimly aware of someone standing behind her but looked up, uncomprehending, when his foot touched her bum.

"Is there something about you that attracts men with axes?" William asked crossly. He sighted carefully along his pistol's barrel, and fired.

101

REDIVIVUS

I WAS PINNING up my hair for tea when there was a scratch at the bedroom door.

"Come," John called, in the act of pulling on his boots. The door opened cautiously, revealing the odd little Cornish boy who sometimes served as William's orderly. He said something to John, in what I assumed to be English, and handed him a note. John nodded kindly and dismissed him.

"Could you understand what he said?" I asked curiously, as he broke the seal with his thumb.

"Who? Oh, Colenso? No, not a word," he said absently, and pursed his lips in a soundless whistle at whatever he was reading.

"What is it?" I asked.

"A note from Colonel Graves," he said, carefully refolding it. "I wonder if—"

There was another knock at the door, and John frowned at it.

"Not now," he said. "Come back later."

"Well, I would," said a polite voice in a Scottish accent. "But there's some urgency, ken?"

The door opened, and Jamie stepped in, closing it behind him. He saw me, stood stock-still for an instant, and then I was in his arms, the overwhelming warmth and size of him blotting out in an instant everything around me.

I didn't know where my blood had gone. Every drop had left my head, and flickering lights danced before my eyes—but none of it was supplying my legs, which had abruptly dissolved under me.

Jamie was holding me up and kissing me, tasting of beer and his beard stubble rasping my face, his fingers buried in my hair, and my breasts warmed and swelled against his chest.

"Oh, there it is," I murmured.

"What?" he asked, breaking off for a moment.

"My blood." I touched my tingling lips. "Do that again."

"Oh, I will," he assured me. "But there are a number of English soldiers in the neighborhood, and I think—"

The sound of pounding came from below, and reality snapped back into place like a rubber band. I stared at him and sat down very suddenly, my heart pounding like a drum.

"Why the bloody hell aren't you dead?"

He lifted one shoulder in a brief shrug, the corner of his mouth turning up. He was very thin, brown-faced, and dirty; I could smell his sweat and the grime of long-worn clothes. And the faint whiff of vomit—he'd not been long off a boat.

"Delay for a few seconds longer, Mr. Fraser, and you may well go back to being dead." John had gone to the window, peering down into the street. He turned, and I saw that his face was pale but glowing like a candle.

"Aye? They were a bit faster than I thought, then," Jamie said ruefully, going to look out. He turned from the window and smiled. "It's good to see ye, John—if only for the moment."

John's answering smile lit his eyes. He reached out a hand and touched Jamie's arm, very briefly, as though wishing to assure himself that he was in fact solid.

"Yes," he said, reaching then for the door. "But come. Down the back stair. Or there's a hatchway to the attic—if you can get onto the roof—"

Jamie looked at me, his heart in his eyes.

"I'll come back," he said. "When I can." He lifted a hand toward me but stopped with a grimace, turned abruptly to follow John, and they were gone, the sound of their footsteps nearly drowned by the noises from downstairs. I heard the door open below and a rough male voice demanding entrance. Mrs. Figg, bless her intransigent little heart, was having none of it.

I'd been sitting like Lot's wife, shocked into immobility, but at the sound of Mrs. Figg's rich expletives was galvanized into action.

My mind was so stunned by the events of the last five minutes that it was, paradoxically, quite clear. There was simply no room in it for thoughts, speculations, relief, joy, or even worry—the only mental faculty I still possessed, apparently, was the ability to respond to an emergency. I snatched my cap, crammed it on my head, and started for the door, stuffing my hair up into it as I went. Mrs. Figg and I together could surely delay the soldiers long enough . . .

This scheme would probably have worked, save that, as I rushed out onto the landing, I ran into Willie—literally, as he came bounding up the stair and collided heavily with me.

"Mother Claire! Where's Papa? There are—" He had seized me by the arms as I reeled backward, but his concern for me was superseded by a sound from the hall beyond the landing. He glanced toward the sound—then let go of me, his eyes bulging.

Jamie stood at the end of the hall, some ten feet away; John stood beside him, white as a sheet, and his eyes bulging as much as Willie's were. This resemblance to Willie, striking as it was, was completely overwhelmed by Jamie's own resemblance to the Ninth Earl of Ellesmere. William's face had hardened and matured, losing all trace of childish softness, and from both ends of the short hall, deep blue Fraser cat-eyes stared out of the bold, solid bones of the MacKenzies. And Willie was old enough to shave on a daily basis; he *knew* what he looked like.

Willie's mouth worked, soundless with shock. He looked wildly at me, back at Jamie, back at me—and saw the truth in my face.

"Who are you?" he said hoarsely, wheeling on Jamie.

I saw Jamie draw himself slowly upright, ignoring the noise below.

"James Fraser," he said. His eyes were fixed on William with a burning intensity, as though to absorb every vestige of a sight he would not see again. "Ye kent me once as Alex MacKenzie. At Helwater."

William blinked, blinked again, and his gaze shifted momentarily to John.

"And who—who the *bloody* hell am *I*?" he demanded, the end of the question rising in a squeak.

John opened his mouth, but it was Jamie who answered.

"You are a stinking Papist," he said, very precisely, "and your baptismal name is James." The ghost of regret crossed his face and then was gone. "It was the only name I had a right to give ye," he said quietly, eyes on his son. "I'm sorry."

Willie's left hand slapped at his hip, reflexively looking for a sword. Finding nothing, he slapped at his chest. His hands were shaking so badly that he couldn't manage buttons; he simply seized the fabric and ripped open his shirt, reached in and fumbled for something. He pulled it over his head and, in the same motion, hurled the object at Jamie.

Jamie's reflexes brought his hand up automatically, and the wooden rosary smacked into it, the beads swinging, tangled in his fingers.

"God damn you, sir," Willie said, voice trembling. "God damn you to hell!" He half-turned blindly, then spun on his heel to face John. "And you! You *knew,* didn't you? God damn you, too!"

"William—" John reached out a hand to him, helpless, but before he could say anything more, there was a sound of voices in the hall below and heavy feet on the stair.

"Sassenach—keep him back!" Jamie's voice reached me through the hubbub, sharp and clear. By sheer reflex, I obeyed and seized Willie by the arm. He glanced at me, mouth open, completely nonplused.

"What—" His voice was drowned by the thunder of feet on the stairs and a triumphant whoop from the redcoat in front.

"There he is!"

Suddenly the landing was thronged with bodies pushing and shoving, trying to get past Willie and me into the hallway. I clung like grim death, despite the jostling and despite Willie's own belated efforts to free himself.

All at once the shouting stopped, and the press of bodies relaxed just a bit. My cap had been knocked over my eyes in the struggle, and I let go of Willie's arm with one hand in order to pull it off. I dropped it on the floor. I had a feeling that my status as a respectable woman wasn't going to be important for much longer.

Brushing disheveled hair out of my eyes with a forearm, I resumed my grip on Willie, though this was largely unnecessary, as he seemed turned to stone. The redcoats were shifting on their feet, clearly ready to charge but inhibited by something. I turned a little and saw Jamie, one arm wrapped around John Grey's throat, holding a pistol to John's temple.

"One step more," he said, calmly but loud enough to be easily heard, "and I put a ball through his brain. D'ye think I've anything to lose?"

Actually, given that Willie and myself were standing right in front of him, I rather thought he did—but the soldiers didn't know that, and judging from the expression on Willie's face, he would have torn his tongue out by the roots rather than blurt out the truth. I also thought he didn't particularly care at the moment if Jamie *did* kill John and then die in a fusillade of bullets. His arm was like iron under my grip; he'd have killed them both himself, if he could.

There was a murmur of menace from the men around me and a shifting of bodies, men readying themselves—but no one moved.

Jamie glanced once at me, face unreadable, then moved toward the back stair, half-dragging John with him. They vanished from view, and the corporal next to me sprang into action, turning and gesturing to his men on the stair.

"Round back! Hurry!"

"Hold!" Willie had come abruptly to life. Jerking his arm away from my slackened grip, he turned on the corporal. "Have you men posted at the back of the house?"

The corporal, noticing Willie's uniform for the first time, straightened himself and saluted.

"No, sir. I didn't think—"

"Idiot," Willie said shortly.

"Yes, sir. But we can catch them if we hurry, sir." He was rocking up onto his toes as he spoke, in an agony to be gone.

Willie's fists were clenched, and so were his teeth. I could see the thoughts crossing his face, as clearly as if they'd been printed on his forehead in movable type.

He didn't *think* Jamie would shoot Lord John but wasn't sure of it. If he sent men after them, there was a decent chance that the soldiers would catch up to them—which in turn meant some chance that one or both would die. And if neither died but Jamie was captured—there was no telling what he might say or to whom. Too much risk.

With a faint sense of déjà vu, I saw him make these calculations, then turn to the corporal.

"Return to your commander," he said calmly. "Let him know that Colonel Grey has been taken hostage by . . . by the rebels, and ask him to notify all guard posts. I am to be informed at once of any news."

There was a displeased murmur from the soldiers on the landing but nothing that could actually be called insubordination, and even this died away in the face of William's glare. The corporal's teeth set briefly in his lip, but he saluted.

"Yes, sir." He turned smartly on his heel, with a peremptory gesture that sent the soldiers clumping heavily down the stair.

Willie watched them go. Then, as though suddenly noticing it, he bent and picked up my cap from the floor. Kneading it between his hands, he gave me a long, speculative look. The next little while was going to be interesting, I saw.

I didn't care. While I was quite sure that Jamie wouldn't shoot John under any circumstances, I was under no misapprehensions about the danger to either of them. I could smell it; the scent of sweat and gunpowder hung thick in the air on the landing, and the soles of my feet still vibrated from the slam of the heavy door below. None of it mattered.

He was alive.

So was I.

GREY WAS STILL IN his shirtsleeves; the rain had cut through the cloth to his flesh.

Jamie went to the shed's wall and put his eye to a crack between the boards. He raised a hand, adjuring silence, and John stood waiting, shivering, as the sound of hooves and voices went past. Who might it be? Not soldiers; there was no sound of brass, no jingling spurs or arms. The sounds faded, and Jamie turned back. He frowned, noticing for the first time that Grey was wet through, and, taking the cloak from his shoulders, wrapped it round him.

The cloak was damp, too, but made of wool, and Jamie's body heat lingered in it. Grey closed his eyes for an instant, embraced.

"May I know what it is that you've been doing?" Grey inquired, opening them.

"When?" Jamie gave him a half smile. "Just now, or since I saw ye last?"

"Just now."

"Ah." Jamie sat down on a barrel and leaned back—gingerly—against the wall.

Grey noted with interest that the sound was nearly "ach," and deduced that Fraser had spent much of his time of late with Scots. He also observed that Fraser's lips were pursed in thought. The slanted blue eyes cut in his direction.

"Ye're sure ye want to know? It's likely better if ye don't."

"I put considerable trust in your judgment and discretion, Mr. Fraser," Grey said politely, "but somewhat more in my own. I'm sure you will forgive me."

Fraser appeared to find that funny; the wide mouth twitched, but he nodded and produced a small packet, sewn in oilskin, from inside his shirt.

"I was observed in the act of accepting this from my foster son," he said. "The person who saw me followed me to an ordinary, then went to fetch the nearest company of soldiers whilst I was refreshing myself. Or so I assume. I saw them coming down the street, supposed that it might be myself they sought, and . . . left."

"You are familiar, I suppose, with the trope regarding the guilty who flee when no man pursues? How do you know they were after you to begin with and not merely interested by your abrupt departure?"

The half smile flickered again, this time tinged with rue.

"Call it the instinct of the hunted."

"Indeed. I am surprised that you allowed yourself to be cornered, as it were, your instincts being what they are."

"Aye, well, even foxes grow old, do they not?" Fraser said dryly.

"Why the devil did you come to my house?" Grey demanded, suddenly irritable. "Why did you not run for the edge of town?"

Fraser looked surprised.

"My wife," he said simply, and it occurred to Grey, with a pang, that it had not been inadvertence or lack of caution that had impelled Jamie Fraser to come to his house, even with soldiers on his heels. He'd come for her. For Claire.

Jesus! He thought with sudden panic. *Claire!*

But there was no time to say anything, even could he have thought what to say. Jamie rose and, taking the pistol from his belt, beckoned him to come.

They went down an alleyway, then through the backyard of a pub, squeezing past the open brew tub, its surface pocked by falling rain. Smelling faintly of hops, they emerged into a street and slowed down. Jamie had gripped his wrist throughout this journey, and Lord John felt his hand beginning to go numb but said nothing. They passed two or three groups of soldiers, but he walked with Jamie, matching him stride for stride, keeping his eyes front. There was no conflict of heart and duty here: to shout for help might result in Jamie's death; it almost surely would result in the death of at least one soldier.

Jamie kept his pistol out of sight, half hidden in his coat but in his hand, putting it back into his belt only when they reached the place where he had left his horse. It was a private house; he left Grey by himself on the porch for a moment with a muttered "Stay here," while he disappeared inside.

A strong sense of self-preservation urged Lord John to run, but he didn't and was rewarded when Jamie emerged again and smiled a little, seeing him. *So you weren't sure I'd stay? Fair enough,* Grey thought. He hadn't been sure, either.

"Come on, then," Jamie said, and with a jerk of his head beckoned Grey to follow him to the stable, where he quickly saddled and bridled a second horse, handing the reins to Grey before mounting his own.

"Pro forma," he said politely to Grey, and, drawing the pistol, pointed it at him. "Should anyone ask later. Ye'll come with me, and I *will* shoot you, should ye make any move to give me away before we're out of the city. We are understood, I hope?"

"We are," Grey replied briefly, and swung up into the saddle.

He rode a little ahead of Jamie, conscious of the small round spot between his shoulder blades. *Pro forma* or not, he'd meant it.

He wondered whether Jamie would shoot him in the chest or simply break his neck when he found out. Likely bare hands, he thought. It was a visceral sort of thing, sex.

The idea of concealing the truth hadn't seriously occurred to him. He didn't know Claire Fraser nearly as well as Jamie did—but he knew beyond the shadow of a doubt that she couldn't keep secrets. Not from anyone. And certainly not from Jamie, restored to her from the dead.

Of course, it might be some time before Jamie was able to speak to her again. But he knew Jamie Fraser infinitely better than he knew Claire—and the one thing he was certain of was that nothing whatever would stand long between Jamie and his wife.

The rain had passed, and the sun shone on the puddles as they splashed through the streets. There was a sense of movement all around, agitation in the air. The army was quartered in Germantown, but there were always soldiers in the city, and their knowledge of imminent departure, anticipation of the return to campaigning, infected the city like a plague, a fever passing invisibly from man to man.

A patrol on the road out of the city stopped them but waved them on when Grey gave his name and rank. His companion he introduced as Mr. Alexander MacKenzie and thought he felt a vibration of humor from said companion. Alex MacKenzie was the name Jamie had used at Helwater—as Grey's prisoner.

Oh, God, Grey thought suddenly, leading the way out of sight of the patrol. *William.* In the shock of the confrontation and their abrupt departure, he hadn't had time to think. If Grey were dead, what would William do?

His thoughts buzzed like a swarm of hiving bees, crawling over one another in a seething mass; impossible to focus on one for more than an instant before it was lost in the deafening hum. Denys Randall-Isaacs. Richardson. With Grey gone, he would almost certainly move to arrest Claire. William would try to stop him, if he knew. But William didn't know what

Richardson was. . . . Grey didn't know, either, not for sure. Henry and his Negro lover—Grey knew they were lovers now, had seen it in both their faces—Dottie and her Quaker: if the twin shocks didn't kill Hal, he'd be on a ship bound for America in nothing flat, and *that* would certainly kill him. Percy. Oh, Jesus, Percy.

Jamie was in front of him now, leading the way. There were little groups of people on the road: mostly farmers coming in with wagonloads of supplies for the army. They looked curiously at Jamie, much more so at Grey. But no one stopped or challenged them, and an hour later Jamie led them down a trace off the main road and into a small woodland dripping and steaming from the recent rain. There was a stream; Jamie swung down off his horse and left it to drink, and Grey did likewise, feeling strangely unreal, as though the leather of saddle and reins was foreign to his skin, as though rain-chilled air passed through him, body and bones, rather than around him.

Jamie crouched by the stream and drank, then splashed water over his head and face and stood up, shaking himself like a dog.

"Thank ye, John," he said. "I hadna time to say it earlier. I'm verra grateful to ye."

"Thank me? It was hardly my choice. You abducted me at gunpoint."

Jamie smiled; the tension of the last hour had eased, and with it the lines of his face.

"Not that. For taking care of Claire, I mean."

"Claire," he repeated. "Ah. Yes. That."

"Aye, that," Jamie said patiently, and bent a little to peer at him in concern. "Are ye quite well, John? Ye look a wee bit peaked."

"Peaked," Grey muttered. His heart was beating very erratically; perhaps it would conveniently stop. He waited for a moment to allow it to do this if it liked, but it went on cheerfully thumping away. No help, then. Jamie was still looking quizzically at him. Best to get it over quickly.

He took a deep breath, shut his eyes, and commended his soul to God.

"I have had carnal knowledge of your wife," he blurted.

He had expected to die more or less instantaneously upon

this utterance, but everything continued just as usual. Birds continued chirping in the trees, and the rip and slobber of the horses champing grass was the only sound above that of the rushing water. He opened one eye to find Jamie Fraser standing there regarding him, head to one side.

"Oh?" said Jamie curiously. "Why?"

102

BRED IN THE BONE

I . . . UH . . . IF you'll excuse me for a moment . . ." I backed slowly to the door of my room and, seizing the knob, whipped inside and shut the door, leaving Willie to recover himself in decent privacy. And not only Willie.

I pressed myself against the door as though pursued by werewolves, my blood thundering in my ears.

"Jesus H. Roosevelt Christ," I whispered. Something like a geyser rose up inside me and burst in my head, the spray of it sparkling with sunlight and diamonds. I was dimly aware that it had come on to rain outside, and dirty gray water was streaking the windowpanes, but that didn't matter a bit to the effervescence inside me.

I stood still for several minutes, eyes closed, not thinking anything, just murmuring, "Thank you, God," over and over, soundlessly.

A tentative rap on the door jarred me out of this trance, and I turned to open it. William stood on the landing.

His shirt still hung open where he'd torn it, and I could see the pulse beat fast in the hollow of his throat. He bowed awkwardly to me, trying to achieve a smile but notably failing in the attempt. He gave it up.

"I am not sure what to call you," he said. "Under the—the circumstances."

"Oh," I said, mildly disconcerted. "Well. I don't think—at least I *hope* that the relationship between you and me hasn't changed." I realized, with a sudden dampening of my euphoria, that it very well might now, and the thought gave me a deep pang. I was very fond of him, for his own sake, as well as for his father's—or fathers', as the case might be.

"Could you bring yourself to go on calling me 'Mother Claire,' do you think? Just until we can think of something more . . . appropriate," I added hastily, seeing reluctance narrow his eyes. "After all, I suppose I am still your stepmother. Regardless of the . . . er . . . the situation."

He turned that over for a moment, then nodded briefly.

"May I come in? I wish to talk to you."

"Yes, I suppose you do."

If I hadn't known both his fathers, I would have marveled at his ability to suppress the rage and confusion he had so clearly exhibited a quarter of a hour ago. Jamie did it by instinct, John by long experience—but both of them had an iron power of will, and whether William's was bred in the bone or acquired by example, he most assuredly had one.

"Shall I send for something?" I asked. "A little brandy? It's good for shock."

He shook his head. He wouldn't sit—I didn't think he could—but leaned against the wall.

"I suppose that you knew? You could scarcely help but notice the resemblance, I suppose," he added bitterly.

"It *is* rather striking," I agreed, with caution. "Yes, I knew. My husband told me"—I groped for some delicate way of putting it—"the, um, circumstances of your birth some years ago."

And just how was *I* going to describe those circumstances?

It hadn't exactly escaped me that there were a few awkward explanations to be made—but caught up in the alarms of Jamie's sudden reappearance and escape and the giddiness of my own subsequent euphoria, it somehow hadn't occurred to me that I would be the person making them.

I'd seen the little shrine he kept in his room, the double portrait of his two mothers—both so heartbreakingly young. If age was good for anything, surely it should have given me the wisdom to deal with this?

How could I tell him that he was the result of an impulsive, self-willed young girl's blackmail? Let alone tell him that he had been the cause of both his legal parents' deaths? And if anyone was going to tell him what his birth had meant to Jamie, it was going to have to *be* Jamie.

"Your mother . . ." I began, and hesitated. Jamie would have taken the blame solely upon himself rather than blacken Geneva's memory to her son, I knew. I wasn't having that.

"She was reckless," William said, watching me closely. "Everybody says she was reckless. Was it—I suppose I only want to know, was it rape?"

"God, no!" I said, horrified, and saw his fists uncurl a little.

"That's good," he said, and let out the breath he'd been holding. "You're sure he didn't lie to you?"

"I'm sure." He and his father might be able to hide their feelings; I certainly couldn't, and while I would never be able to make a living playing cards, having a glass face was occasionally a good thing. I stood still and let him see that I told the truth.

"Do you think—did he say—" He stopped and swallowed, hard. "Did they love each other, do you think?"

"As much as they could, I think," I said softly. "They hadn't much time, only the one night." I ached for him and would have liked so much to take him in my arms and comfort him. But he was a man, and a young one, fierce about his pain. He'd deal with it as he could, and I thought it would be some years—if ever—before he learned to share it.

"Yes," he said, and pressed his lips together, as though he'd been going to say something else and thought better of it. "Yes, I—I see." It was quite clear from his tone that he didn't but, reeling under the impact of realization, had no idea what to ask next, let alone what to do with the information he had.

"I was born almost exactly nine months after my parents' marriage," he said, giving me a hard look. "Did they deceive my father? Or did my mother play the whore with her groom before she wed?"

"That might be a bit harsh," I began.

"No, it isn't," he snapped. "Which was it?"

"Your fa—Jamie. He'd never deceive another man in his marriage." *Except Frank,* I thought, a little wildly. But, of course, he hadn't known at first that he was doing it . . .

"My father," he said abruptly. "Pa—Lord John, I mean. He knew—knows?"

"Yes." Thin ice again. I didn't think he had any idea that Lord John had married Isobel principally for his sake—and Jamie's—but didn't want him going anywhere near the question of Lord John's motives.

"All of them," I said firmly, "all four of them; they wanted what was best for you."

"Best for me," he repeated bleakly. "Right." His knuckles had gone white again, and he gave me a look through narrowed eyes that I recognized all too well: a Fraser about to go off with a bang. I also knew perfectly well that there was no way of stopping one from detonating but had a try anyway, putting out a hand to him.

"William," I began. "Believe me—"

"I do," he said. "Don't bloody tell me any more. God *damn* it!" And, whirling on his heel, he drove his fist through the paneling with a thud that shook the room, wrenched his hand out of the hole he'd made, and stormed out. I heard crunching and rending as he paused to kick out several of the balusters on the landing and rip a length of the stair railing off, and I made it to the door in time to see him draw back a four-foot chunk of wood over his shoulder, swing, and strike the crystal chandelier that hung over the stairwell in an explosion of shattering glass. For a moment, he teetered on the open edge of the landing and I thought he would fall, or hurl himself off, but he staggered back from the edge and threw the chunk of wood like a javelin at the remnant of the chandelier with a burst of breath that might have been a grunt or a sob.

Then he rushed headlong down the stairs, thumping his wounded fist at intervals against the wall, where it left bloody smudges. He hit the front door with his shoulder, rebounded, jerked it open, and went out like a locomotive.

I stood frozen on the landing in the midst of chaos and destruction, gripping the edge of the broken balustrade. Tiny rainbows danced on walls and ceiling like multicolored dragonflies sprung out of the shattered crystal that littered the floor.

Something moved; a shadow fell across the floor of the hall below. A small, dark figure walked slowly in through the open doorway. Putting back the hood of her cloak, Jenny

Fraser Murray looked round at the devastation, then up at me, her face a pale oval glimmering with humor.

"Like father, like son, I see," she remarked. "God help us all."

103

THE HOUR OF THE WOLF

THE BRITISH ARMY was leaving Philadelphia. The Delaware was choked with ships, and the ferries ran nonstop from the end of State Street across to Cooper's Point. Three thousand Tories were leaving the city, too, afraid to stay without the army's protection; General Clinton had promised them passage, though their baggage made a dreadful mess—stacked on the docks, crammed into the ferries—and occupied a good deal of space on board the ships. Ian and Rachel sat on the riverbank below Philadelphia, under the shade of a drooping sycamore, and watched an artillery emplacement being disassembled, a hundred yards away.

The artillerymen worked in shirtsleeves, their blue coats folded on the grass nearby, removing the guns that had defended the city, preparing them for shipping. They were in no hurry and took no particular notice of spectators; it didn't matter now.

"Does thee know where they are going?" Rachel asked.

"Aye, I do. Fergus says they're going north, to reinforce New York."

"Thee has seen him?" She turned her head, interested, and the leaf shadows flickered over her face.

"Aye, he came home last night; he'll be safe now, wi' the Tories and the army gone."

"Safe," she said, with a skeptical intonation. "As safe as

anyone may be, in times like these, thee means." She'd taken off her cap because of the heat and brushed the damp, dark hair back from her cheeks.

He smiled, but said nothing. She knew as well as he did what the illusions of safety were.

"Fergus says the British mean to cut the colonies in half," he remarked. "Separate north from south and deal with them separately."

"Does he? And how does he know this?" she asked, surprised.

"A British officer named Randall-Isaacs; he talks to Fergus."

"He is a spy, thee means? For which side?" Her lips compressed a little. He wasn't sure where spying fell, in terms of Quaker philosophy, but didn't care to ask just now. It was a tender subject, Quaker philosophy.

"I shouldna like to have to guess," he said. "He passes himself off as an American agent, but that may be all moonshine. Ye canna trust anyone in wartime, aye?"

She turned round to look at him at that, hands behind her back as she leaned against the sycamore.

"Can thee not?"

"I trust you," he said. "And your brother."

"And thy dog," she said, with a glance at Rollo, writhing on the ground to scratch his back. "Thy aunt and uncle, too, and Fergus and his wife? That seems a fair number of friends." She leaned toward him, squinting in concern. "Does thy arm pain thee?"

"Och, it's well enough." He shrugged with his good shoulder, smiling. His arm did hurt, but the sling helped. The ax blow had nearly severed his left arm, cutting through the flesh and breaking the bone. His aunt said he had been lucky, in that it had not damaged the tendons. The body is plastic, she said. Muscle would heal, and so would bone.

Rollo's had; there was no trace of stiffness from the gunshot wound, and while his muzzle was growing white, he slid through the bushes like an eel, sniffing industriously.

Rachel sighed and gave him a direct look under dark, level brows.

"Ian, thee is thinking something painful, and I would

much prefer thee tells me what it is. Has something happened?"

A great many things had happened, were happening all around them, would continue to happen. How could he tell her . . . ? And yet he couldn't not.

"The world is turning upside down," he blurted. "And you are the only constant thing. The only thing I—that binds me to the earth."

Her eyes softened.

"Am I?"

"Ye ken verra well that you are," he said gruffly. He looked away, his heart pounding. Too late, he thought, with a mixture of dismay and elation. He'd begun to speak; he couldn't stop now, no matter what might come of it.

"I know what I am," he said, awkward but determined. "I would turn Quaker for your sake, Rachel, but I ken I'm not one in my heart; I think I never could be. And I think ye wouldna want me to say words I dinna mean or pretend to be something I canna be."

"No," she said softly. "I would not want that."

He opened his mouth but couldn't find more words to say. He swallowed, dry-mouthed, waiting. She swallowed, too; he saw the slight movement of her throat, soft and brown; the sun had begun to touch her again, the nut-brown maiden ripening from winter's pale bloom.

The artillerymen loaded the last of the cannon into a wagon, hitched their limbers to teams of oxen, and with laughter and raucous talk moved up the road toward the ferry point. When they were gone at last, a silence fell. There were still noises—the sound of the river, the rustle of the sycamore, and far beyond, the bellowings and crashings of an army on the move, the sound of violence impending. But between them, there was silence.

I've lost, he thought, but her head was still bent in thought. Is she maybe praying? Or only trying to think how to send me away?

Whichever it was, she lifted her head and stood up, away from the tree. She pointed at Rollo, who was lying couchant now, motionless but alert, yellow eyes following every movement of a fat robin foraging in the grass.

"That dog is a wolf, is he not?"

"Aye, well, mostly."

A small flash of hazel told him not to quibble.

"And yet he is thy boon companion, a creature of rare courage and affection, and altogether a worthy being?"

"Oh, aye," he said with more confidence. "He is."

She gave him an even look.

"Thee is a wolf, too, and I know it. But thee is my wolf, and best thee know that."

He'd started to burn when she spoke, an ignition swift and fierce as the lighting of one of his cousin's matches. He put out his hand, palm forward, to her, still cautious lest she, too, burst into flame.

"What I said to ye, before . . . that I kent ye loved me—"

She stepped forward and pressed her palm to his, her small, cool fingers linking tight.

"What I say to thee now is that I do love thee. And if thee hunts at night, thee will come home."

Under the sycamore, the dog yawned and laid his muzzle on his paws.

"And sleep at thy feet," Ian whispered, and gathered her in with his one good arm, both of them blazing bright as day.

AUTHOR'S NOTES

Brigadier General Simon Fraser

There are, as anyone who's read my books will already realize, a *lot* of Simon Frasers running around the eighteenth century. The Brigadier who fought gallantly and was killed at Saratoga is not one of the Frasers of Lovat, but a Fraser of Balnain. That is, not a direct descendant of the Old Fox but certainly a relation of the family. He had an illustrious military career, including the famous taking of Quebec with James Wolfe in 1759 (which battle forms a part of a novella entitled "The Custom of the Army," a Lord John Grey story which was published in March of 2010 as part of an anthology titled *Warriors*—in case you want more details).

My reason for mentioning the Brigadier particularly, though, is the interesting matter of his grave. Most accounts of Saratoga that mention Simon Fraser of Balnain report that he was buried in the evening of the day he died, within the boundaries of the Great Redoubt (not Breymann's Redoubt, which Jamie stormed with Benedict Arnold, but the larger one on the field), at his own request. Some accounts add details, such as the attendance of Balcarres's rangers, or of the Americans firing a minute gun in Fraser's honor when they realized what was taking place, while other accounts consider these romantic but probably apocryphal details and say that he was attended only by the close members of his staff.

Now, it isn't always possible to go in person to a place you're writing about, nor is it always necessary. It *is* usually desirable, though, and luckily, Saratoga is pretty accessible, and the battlefield there is well preserved and curated. I've walked the field there three times over the course of several years since I first decided that I wanted to use this particular battle as a centerpiece of a book, if not the book I happened to be writing at the time. On one of these occasions, I was there alone, there were no other tourists, and I got into conversation with one of the park employees (dressed in period costume and posted at the rebuilt site of the Bemis farm). After he patiently answered a lot of intrusive questions ("Are you wearing underwear?" being one of them, and "No," being the answer. "Long shirttails," being the further explanation for how one avoids chafing while wearing homespun breeches), allowed me to handle his Brown Bess musket and explained the loading and firing of it, we got into a discussion of the battle and its personalities—since I did, at this point, know quite a lot about it.

General Fraser's grave was at that point noted on the Park Service map—but it wasn't in the Great Redoubt; it was located near the river. I'd been down there but found no marker for it, and so inquired where it was—and why wasn't it in the Great Redoubt? I was informed that the Park Service had at one point—I don't know when, but fairly recently—done an archaeological excavation of the Great Redoubt, including the supposed gravesite. To everyone's surprise, General Fraser was *not* buried there, nor was anyone else. There were signs that a grave had once been dug, and a uniform button was found there, but no signs whatever of a body. (And while the body itself would be long since decomposed, you would expect still to see some signs.) There was (the employee told me) an account that said that General Fraser's grave had been moved to a site near the river, and that that was why the map was so marked—but no one knew where the specific place was, or, in fact, whether the General was in *that* one, either, which was why there was no marker there.

Well, novelists are a conscienceless lot. Those of us who deal with history tend to be fairly respectful of such facts as are recorded (always bearing in mind the proviso that just because it's in print, it isn't necessarily *true*). But give us a hole to slide through, an omission in the historic record, one of those mysterious lacunae that occur in even the best-documented life . . . so all in all, I rather thought that perhaps General Fraser had been sent home to Scotland. (Yes, they did send bodies to and fro in the eighteenth century, on occasion. Someone exhumed poor old Tom Paine from his grave in

France, intending to ship him back to America so he could be interred there with honor as a prophet of the Revolution. His body was lost in transit, and no one's ever found it. Speaking of interesting lacunae . . .)

Anyway, as it happened, I went to Scotland last year, and while wandering round the countryside in search of a logical place near Balnain in which to plant General Fraser, stumbled over (literally) the large chambered cairn at Corrimony. Such sites are always evocative, and when I read on the sign posted there that there had once been a body in the central chamber, but it had evidently decayed into the soil (there *were* traces of bones left in the earth, even after a thousand years or more), *and* that the tomb had been broken into sometime in the nineteenth century (thus explaining why you won't find anything in the cairn if you happen to go there now) . . . well, hey. (People always ask novelists where they get their ideas. Everywhere!)

Quaker Plain Speech

The Religious Society of Friends was founded around 1647 by George Fox. As part of the Society's belief in the equality of all men before God, they did not use honorific titles (such as "Mr./Mrs.," "General/Colonel," etc.), and used "plain speech" in addressing everyone.

Now, as any of you who know a second language with Latin roots (Spanish, French, etc.) realize, these languages have both a familiar and a formal version of "you." So did English, once upon a time. The "thee" and "thou" forms that most of us recognize as Elizabethan or biblical are in fact the English familiar forms of "you"—with "you" used as both the plural familiar form ("all y'all"), and the formal pronoun (both singular and plural). As English evolved, the familiar forms were dropped, leaving us with the utilitarian "you" to cover all contingencies.

Quakers retained the familiar forms, though, as part of their "plain speech," until the twentieth century. Over the years, though, plain speech also evolved, and while "thee/thy" remained, "thou/thine" largely disappeared, and the verb forms associated with "thee/thy" changed. From about the mid-eighteenth century onward, plain speech used "thee" as the singular form of "you" (the plural form remained "you," even in plain speech), with the same verb forms normally used for third-person singular. For example, "He knows that/Thee knows that." The older verb endings—"knowest," "doth," etc.—were no longer used.

Scots/Scotch/Scottish

As noted elsewhere (*Lord John and the Brotherhood of the Blade,* see Author's Notes), in the eighteenth century (and indeed, well into the mid-twentieth century), the word "Scotch" and its variants (e.g., "Scotchman") were commonly used (by both English people *and* Scots) to describe an inhabitant of Scotland. The terms "Scottish" and "Scots" were also occasionally used, though less common.

Typos and Terminology

There may be an impulse to regard the term "mess-kid" (as used in Part Three of this book) as a typographical error. It's not. A mess-kid was a shallow, circular bucket in which sailors of the eighteenth and nineteenth centuries were served their food. A mess-*kit*, on the other hand, referred to the utensils carried and used by a soldier.

By the same token, while "crotch" is the usual American English term, the older form, "crutch," would have been used in eighteenth-century English-English usage. Which is not to say there aren't any typographical errors in this book (despite the heroic efforts of Ms. Kathy Lord, the copy editor; the alerts of various friends and translators who read the manuscript in chunks; and a fair amount of diligence by myself, these things happen) but these particular terms aren't.

Saratoga

A tremendous amount of historical research goes into a book like this (I am often bemused by letters from people telling me they'd visited a museum, seen some eighteenth-century artifacts, and been struck all a-heap by discovering that I hadn't just made it all up!), and while there isn't room to acknowledge or list even a fraction of the sources I've used, I did want to mention one specific book.

The two battles of Saratoga were historically important, remarkably dramatic, and very complex, both in the logistics of the battles and in the troop movements and politics that led up to them. I was fortunate to find, early on in my researches, Richard M. Ketchum's *Saratoga,* which is an amazingly well-done portrait of the battles, the background, and the plethora of colorful individuals who took part. I just wanted to recommend this book to those of you with a deeper interest in the historical aspects, as these could only be touched on lightly in the context of a novel.

Loch Errochty and Tunnel Tigers

During the 1950s and '60s, a great hydroelectric scheme was implemented in the Scottish Highlands. The work of a great many "tunnel tigers" (also known as "the Hydro boys")—laborers, many of them from Ireland and Poland—went into digging tunnels through the mountains and building dams for the creation of man-made lochs. Loch Errochty is in fact one of these man-made lochs. The tunnel I've drawn as being associated with it (complete with miniature train) is like those common to the hydroelectric scheme as a whole, but I don't know that there actually *is* one at Loch Errochty. On the other hand, the dam, turbine service chamber, and fish-viewing chamber at Pitlochry are indeed all there. So are the anglers.

And don't miss the next installment of the acclaimed OUTLANDER series . . .

DIANA GABALDON'S

WRITTEN IN MY OWN HEART'S BLOOD

Coming soon
from Delacorte Press!

Read on for a preview. . . .

CHAPTER ONE

A HUNDREDWEIGHT OF STONES

June 16, 1778
The forest between Philadelphia and Valley Forge

IAN MURRAY STOOD WITH a stone in his hand, eyeing the ground he'd chosen. A small clearing, out of the way, up among a scatter of great lichened boulders, under the shadow of firs, and at the foot of a big red cedar; a place where no casual passerby would go, but not inaccessible. He meant to bring them up here—the family.

Fergus, to begin with. Maybe just Fergus, by himself. Mam had raised Fergus from the time he was ten, and he'd had no mother before that. Ian himself had been born about that same time, so Fergus had known Mam as long as he had, and loved her as much. *Maybe more,* he thought, his grief aggravated by guilt. Fergus had stayed with her at Lallybroch, helped to take care of her and the place; he hadn't. He swallowed hard and, walking into the small clear space, set his stone in the middle, then stood back to look.

Even as he did so, he found himself shaking his head. No, it had to be two cairns. His mam and Uncle Jamie were brother and sister, and the family could mourn them here together—but there were others he might bring, maybe, to remember and pay their respects. And those were the folk who would have known Jamie Fraser and loved him well but wouldn't ken Jenny Murray from a hole in the—

The image of his mother *in* a hole in the ground stabbed him like a fork, retreated with the recollection that she wasn't after all in a grave, and stabbed again all the harder for that. He really couldn't bear the vision of them drowning, maybe clinging to each other, struggling to keep—

"A Dhia!" he said violently, and dropped the stone, turning back at once to find more. He'd seen people drown.

Tears ran down his face with the sweat of the summer day; he didn't mind it, only stopping now and then to wipe his nose on his sleeve. He'd tied a rolled kerchief round his head to keep the hair and the stinging sweat out of his eyes; it was sopping before he'd added more than twenty stones to each of the cairns.

He and his brothers had built a fine cairn for their father, at the head of the carved stone that bore his name—all his names, in spite of the expense—in the burying ground at Lallybroch. And all the family, followed by the tenants and then at the funeral later, the servants would have come one by one to add a stone each to the weight of remembrance.

Fergus, then. Or . . . no, what was he thinking? Auntie Claire must be the first he brought here. She wasn't Scots herself, but she kent fine what a cairn was and would maybe be comforted a bit to see Uncle Jamie's. Aye, right. Auntie Claire, then Fergus. Uncle Jamie was Fergus's foster father; he had a right. And then maybe Marsali and the children. But maybe Germain was old enough to come with Fergus? He was almost eleven, near enough to being a man to understand, to be treated like a man. And Uncle Jamie was his grandsire; it was proper.

He stepped back again and wiped his face, breathing heavily. Bugs whined and buzzed past his ears and hovered over him, wanting his blood, but he'd stripped to a loincloth and rubbed himself with bear grease and mint in the Mohawk way; they didn't touch him.

"Look over them, O spirit of red cedar," he said softly in Mohawk, looking up into the fragrant branches of the tree. "Guard their souls and keep their presence here, fresh as thy branches."

He crossed himself and bent to dig about in the soft leaf mold. A few more rocks, he thought. In case they might be scattered by some passing animal. Scattered like his thoughts, which roamed restless to and fro among the faces of his family, the folk of the Ridge—God, might he ever go back there? Brianna. Oh, Jesus, Brianna . . .

He bit his lip and tasted salt, licked it away and moved on, foraging. She was safe with Roger Mac and the weans. But, Jesus, he could have used her advice—even more, Roger Mac's.

Who was left for him to ask, if he needed help in taking care of them all?

Thought of Rachel came to him, and the tightness in his chest eased a little. Aye, if he had Rachel . . . She was younger than him, nay more than nineteen, and, being a Quaker, had very strange notions of how things should be, but if he had her, he'd have solid rock under his feet. He hoped he *would* have her, but there were still things he must say to her, and the thought of that conversation made the tightness in his chest come back.

The picture of his cousin Brianna came back, too, and lingered in his mind: tall, long-nosed, and strong-boned as her father . . . and with it rose the image of his other cousin, Bree's half brother. Holy God, William. And what ought he to do about William? He doubted the man kent the truth, kent that he was Jamie Fraser's son—was it Ian's responsibility to tell him so? To bring him here and explain what he'd lost?

He must have groaned at the thought, for his dog, Rollo, lifted his massive head and looked at him in concern.

"No, I dinna ken that, either," Ian told him. "Let it bide, aye?" Rollo laid his head back on his paws, shivered his shaggy hide against the flies, and relaxed in boneless peace.

Ian worked awhile longer and let the thoughts drain away with his sweat and his tears. He finally stopped when the sinking sun touched the tops of his cairns, feeling tired but more at peace. The cairns rose knee-high, side by side, small but solid.

He stood still for a bit, not thinking anymore, just listening to the fussing of wee birds in the grass and the breathing of the wind among the trees. Then he sighed deeply, squatted, and touched one of the cairns.

"Tha gaol agam oirbh, a Mhàthair," he said softly. *My love is upon you, Mother.* Closed his eyes and laid a scuffed hand on the other heap of stones. The dirt ground into his skin made his fingers feel strange, as though he could maybe reach straight through the earth and touch what he needed.

He stayed still, breathing, then opened his eyes.

"Help me wi' this, Uncle Jamie," he said. "I dinna think I can manage, alone."

CHAPTER TWO

SCHMUTZIGER BASTARD

WILLIAM RANSOM, NINTH EARL of Ellesmere, Viscount Ashness, and Baron Derwent, shoved his way through the crowds on Market Street, oblivious to the complaints of those rebounding from his impact.

He didn't know where he was going, or what he might do when he got there. All he knew was that he'd burst if he stood still.

His head throbbed like an inflamed boil. Everything throbbed. His hand—he'd probably broken something, but he didn't care. His heart, pounding and sore inside his chest. His foot, for God's sake—what, had he kicked something? He lashed out viciously at a loose cobblestone and sent it rocketing through a crowd of geese, who set up a huge cackle and lunged at him, hissing and beating at his shins with their wings.

Feathers and goose shit flew wide, and the crowd scattered in all directions.

"Bastard!" shrieked the goose-girl, and struck at him with her crook, catching him a shrewd thump on the ear. "Devil take you, *schmutziger Bastard*!"

This sentiment was echoed by a number of other angry voices, and he veered into an alley, pursued by shouts and honks of agitation.

He rubbed his throbbing ear, lurching into buildings as he

passed, oblivious to everything but the one word throbbing ever louder in his head. *Bastard.*

"Bastard!" he said out loud, and shouted, "Bastard, bastard, *bastard!!"* at the top of his lungs, hammering at the brick wall next to him with a clenched fist.

"Who's a bastard?" said a curious voice behind him. He swung round to see a young woman looking at him with some interest. Her eyes moved slowly down his frame, taking note of the heaving chest, the bloodstains on the facings of his uniform coat, and the green smears of goose shit on his breeches. Her gaze reached his silver-buckled shoes and returned to his face with more interest.

"I am," he said, hoarse and bitter.

"Oh, really?" She left the shelter of the doorway in which she'd been standing and came across the alley to stand right in front of him. She was tall and slim and had a very fine pair of high young breasts—which were clearly visible under the thin muslin of her shift, because, while she had a silk petticoat, she wore no stays. No cap, either—her hair fell loose over her shoulders. A whore.

"I'm partial to bastards myself," she said, and touched him lightly on the arm. "What kind of bastard are you? A wicked one? An evil one?"

"A sorry one," he said, and scowled when she laughed. She saw the scowl, but didn't pull back.

"Come in," she said, and took his hand. "You look as though you could do with a drink." He saw her glance at his knuckles, burst and bleeding, and she caught her lower lip behind small white teeth. She didn't seem afraid, though, and he found himself drawn, unprotesting, into the shadowed doorway after her.

What did it matter? he thought, with a sudden savage weariness. *What did anything matter?*

CHAPTER THREE

IN WHICH THE WOMEN, AS USUAL, PICK UP THE PIECES

No. 17 Chestnut Street, Philadelphia
The residence of Lord and Lady John Grey

WILLIAM HAD LEFT THE house like a thunderclap, and the place looked as though it had been struck by lightning. I certainly felt like the survivor of a massive electrical storm, hairs and nerve endings all standing up straight on end, waving in agitation.

Jenny Murray had entered the house on the heels of William's departure, and while the sight of her was a lesser shock than any of the others so far, it still left me speechless. I goggled at my erstwhile sister-in-law—though, come to think, she still was my sister-in-law . . . because Jamie was alive. *Alive.*

He'd been in my arms not ten minutes before, and the memory of his touch flickered through me like lightning in a bottle. I was dimly aware that I was smiling like a loon, despite massive destruction, horrific scenes, William's distress—if you could call an explosion like that "distress"—Jamie's danger, and a faint wonder as to what either Jenny or Mrs. Figg, Lord John's cook and housekeeper, might be about to say.

Mrs. Figg was smoothly spherical, gleamingly black, and inclined to glide silently up behind one like a menacing ball bearing.

"What's *this*?" she barked, manifesting herself suddenly behind Jenny.

"Holy Mother of God!" Jenny whirled, eyes round and hand pressed to her chest. "Who in God's name are you?"

“This is Mrs. Figg,” I said, feeling a surreal urge to laugh, despite—or maybe because of—recent events. “Lord John Grey’s cook. And Mrs. Figg, this is Mrs. Murray. My, um . . . my . . .”

“Your good-sister,” Jenny said firmly. She raised one black eyebrow. “If ye’ll have me still?” Her look was straight and open, and the urge to laugh changed abruptly into an equally strong urge to burst into tears. Of all the unlikely sources of succor I could have imagined . . . I took a deep breath and put out my hand.

“I’ll have you.” We hadn’t parted on good terms in Scotland, but I had loved her very much, once, and wasn’t about to pass up any opportunity to mend things.

Her small firm fingers wove through mine, squeezed hard, and, as simply as that, it was done. No need for apologies or spoken forgiveness. She’d never had to wear the mask that Jamie did. What she thought and felt was there in her eyes, those slanted blue cat-eyes she shared with her brother. She knew the truth now of what I was, and she knew I loved and always had loved her brother with all my heart and soul—despite the minor complications of my being presently married to someone else.

She heaved a sigh, eyes closing for an instant, then opened them and smiled at me, mouth trembling only a little.

“Well, fine and dandy,” said Mrs. Figg shortly. She narrowed her eyes and rotated smoothly on her axis, taking in the panorama of destruction. The railing at the top of the stair had been ripped off, and cracked banisters, dented walls, and bloody smudges marked the path of William’s descent. Shattered crystals from the chandelier littered the floor, glinting festively in the light from the open front door, the door itself cracked through and hanging drunkenly from one hinge.

“Merde on toast,” Mrs. Figg murmured. She turned abruptly to me, her small black-currant eyes still narrowed. “Where’s his lordship?”

“Ah,” I said. This was going to be rather sticky, I saw. While deeply disapproving of most people, Mrs. Figg was devoted to John. She wasn’t going to be at all pleased to hear that he’d been abducted by—

“For that matter, where’s my brother?” Jenny inquired,

glancing round as though expecting Jamie to appear suddenly out from under the settee.

"Oh," I said. "Hmm. Well . . ." Possibly worse than sticky. Because . . .

"And where's my sweet William?" Mrs. Figg demanded, sniffing the air. "He's been here; I smell that stinky cologne he puts on his linen." She nudged a dislodged chunk of plaster disapprovingly with the toe of her shoe.

I took another long, deep breath and a tight grip on what remained of my sanity.

"Mrs. Figg," I said, "perhaps you would be so kind as to make us all a cup of tea?"

We sat in the parlor, while Mrs. Figg came and went to the cookhouse, keeping an eye on her terrapin stew.

"You don't want to scorch turtle, no, you don't," she said severely to us, setting down the teapot in its padded yellow cozy on her return. "Not with so much sherry as his lordship likes in it. Almost a full bottle—terrible waste of good liquor, that would be."

My insides turned over promptly. Turtle soup—with a lot of sherry—had certain strong and private associations for me, these being connected with Jamie, feverish delirium, and the way in which a heaving ship assists sexual intercourse. Contemplation of which would *not* assist the impending discussion in the slightest. I rubbed a finger between my brows, in hopes of dispelling the buzzing cloud of confusion gathering there. The air in the house still felt electric.

"Speaking of sherry," I said, "or any other sort of strong spirits you might have convenient, Mrs. Figg . . ."

She looked thoughtfully at me, nodded, and reached for the decanter on the sideboard.

"Brandy is stronger," she said, and set it in front of me.

Jenny looked at me with the same thoughtfulness and, reaching out, poured a good-sized slug of the brandy into my cup, then a similar one into her own.

"Just in case," she said, raising one brow, and we drank for a few moments. I thought it might take something stronger than brandy-laced tea to deal with the effect of recent events on my nerves—laudanum, say, or a large slug of straight Scotch whisky—but the tea undeniably helped, hot and aromatic, settling in a soft trickling warmth amidships.

"So, then. We're fettled, are we?" Jenny set down her own cup and looked expectant.

"It's a start." I took a deep breath and gave her a précis of recent events.

Jenny's eyes were disturbingly like Jamie's. She blinked at me once, then twice, and shook her head as though to clear it, accepting what I'd just told her.

"So Jamie's gone off wi' your Lord John, the British army is after them, the tall lad I met on the stoop wi' steam comin' out of his ears is Jamie's son—well, of course he is; a blind man could see that—and the town's aboil wi' British soldiers. Is that it, then?"

"He's not exactly *my* Lord John," I said. "But, yes, that's essentially the position. I take it Jamie told you about William?"

"Aye, he did." She grinned at me over the rim of her teacup. "I'm that happy for him. But what's troubling his lad, then? He looked like he wouldna give the road to a bear."

"What did you say?" Mrs. Figg's voice cut in abruptly. She set down the tray she had just brought in, the silver milk jug and sugar basin rattling like castanets. "William is *whose* son?"

I took a fortifying gulp of tea. Mrs. Figg did know that I'd been married to—and theoretically widowed from—one James Fraser. But that was all she knew.

"Well," I said, and paused to clear my throat. "The, um, tall gentleman with the red hair who was just here—you saw him?"

"I did." Mrs. Figg eyed me narrowly.

"Did you get a good look at him?"

"Didn't pay much heed to his face when he came to the door and asked where you were, but I saw his backside pretty plain when he pushed past me and ran up the stairs."

"Possibly the resemblance is less marked from that angle." I took another mouthful of tea. "Um . . . that gentleman is James Fraser, my . . . er . . . my—" "First husband" wasn't accurate, and neither was "last husband"—or even, unfortunately, "most recent husband." I settled for the simplest alternative. "My husband. And, er . . . William's father."

Mrs. Figg's mouth opened, soundless for an instant. She

backed up slowly and sat down on a needlework ottoman with a soft phumph.

"William know that?" she asked, after a moment's contemplation.

"He does *now,"* I said, with a brief gesture toward the devastation in the stairwell, clearly visible through the door of the parlor where we were sitting.

"Merde on—I mean, Holy Lamb of God preserve us." Mrs. Figg's second husband was a Methodist preacher, and she strove to be a credit to him, but her first had been a French gambler. Her eyes fixed on me like gun-sights.

"You his mother?"

I choked on my tea.

"No," I said, wiping my chin with a linen napkin. "It isn't quite *that* complicated." In fact, it was more so, but I wasn't going to explain just how Willie had come about, either to Mrs. Figg or to Jenny. Jamie had to have told Jenny who William's mother was, but I doubted that he'd told his sister that William's mother, Geneva Dunsany, had forced him into her bed by threatening Jenny's family. No man of spirit likes to admit that he's been effectively blackmailed by an eighteen-year-old girl.

"Lord John became William's legal guardian when William's grandfather died, and at that point, Lord John also married Lady Isobel Dunsany, Willie's mother's sister. She'd looked after Willie since his mother's death in childbirth, and she and Lord John were essentially Willie's parents since he was quite young. Isobel died when he was eleven or so."

Mrs. Figg took this explanation in stride, but wasn't about to be distracted from the main point at issue.

"James Fraser," she said, tapping a couple of broad fingers on her knee and looking accusingly at Jenny. "How comes he not to be dead? News was he drowned." She cut her eyes at me. "I thought his lordship was like to throw himself in the harbor, too, when he heard it."

I closed my own eyes with a sudden shudder, the salt-cold horror of that news washing over me in a wave of memory. Even with Jamie's touch still joyful on my skin and the knowledge of him glowing in my heart, I relived the crushing pain of hearing that he was dead.

"Well, I can enlighten ye on that point, at least."

I opened my eyes to see Jenny drop a lump of sugar into her fresh tea and nod at Mrs. Figg. "We were to take passage on a ship called *Euterpe*—my brother and myself—out o' Brest. But the blackhearted thief of a captain sailed without us. Much good it did him," she added, frowning.

Much good, indeed. The *Euterpe* had sunk in a storm in the Atlantic, lost with all hands. As I—and John Grey—had been told.

"Jamie found us another ship, but it landed us in Virginia, and we'd to make our way up the coast, partly by wagon, partly by packet boat, keepin' out of the way of the soldiers. Those wee needles ye gave Jamie against the seasickness work most o' the time," she added, turning approvingly to me. "He showed me how to put them in for him. But when we came to Philadelphia yesterday," she went on, returning to her tale, "we stole into the city by night, like a pair o' thieves, and made our way to Fergus's printshop. Lord, I thought my heart would stop a dozen times!"

She smiled at the memory, and I was struck by the change in her. The shadow of sorrow still lay on her face, and she was thin and worn by travel, but the terrible strain of her husband Ian's long dying had lifted. There was color in her cheeks again, and a brightness in her eyes that I had not seen since I had first known her thirty years before. She had found her peace, I thought, and felt a thankfulness that eased my own soul.

". . . so Jamie taps on the door at the back, and there's no answer, though we can see the light of a fire comin' through the shutters. He knocks again, makin' a wee tune of it—" She rapped her knuckles lightly on the table, *bump-ba-da-bump-ba-da-bump-bump-bump,* and my heart turned over, recognizing the theme from *The Lone Ranger,* which Brianna had taught him.

"And after a moment," Jenny went on, "a woman's voice calls out fierce, 'Who's there?' And Jamie says in the *Gaidhlig,* 'It is your father, my daughter, and a cold, wet, and hungry man he is, too.' For it was rainin' hammer handles and pitchforks, and we were both soaked to the skin."

She rocked back a little, enjoying the telling.

"The door opens then, just a crack, and there's Marsali wi' a horse pistol in her hand, and her two wee lasses behind her, fierce as archangels, each with a billet of wood, ready to crack a thief across his shins. They see the firelight shine on Jamie's face then, and all three of them let out skellochs like to wake the dead and fall upon him and drag him inside and all talkin' at once and greetin', askin' was he a ghost and why was he not drowned, and that was the first we learned that the *Euterpe* had sunk." She crossed herself. "God rest them, poor souls," she said, shaking her head.

I crossed myself, too, and saw Mrs. Figg look sideways at me; she hadn't realized I was a Papist.

"I've come in, too, of course," Jenny went on, "but everyone's talkin' at once and rushin' to and fro in search of dry clothes and hot drinks and I'm just lookin' about the place, for I've never been inside a printshop before, and the smell of the ink and the paper and lead is a wonder to me, and, sudden-like, there's a tug at my skirt and this sweet-faced wee mannie says to me, 'And who are you, madame? Would you like some cider?'"

"Henri-Christian," I murmured, smiling at the thought of Marsali's youngest, and Jenny nodded.

"'Why, I'm your grannie Janet, son,' says I, and his eyes go round, and he lets out a shriek and grabs me round the legs and gives me such a hug as to make me lose my balance and fall down on the settle. I've a bruise on my bum the size of your hand," she added out of the corner of her mouth to me.

I felt a small knot of tension that I hadn't realized was there. Jenny did of course know that Henri-Christian had been born a dwarf—but knowing and seeing are sometimes different things. Clearly they hadn't been, for Jenny.

Mrs. Figg had been following this account with interest, but maintained her reserve. At mention of the printshop, though, this reserve hardened a bit.

"These folk—Marsali is your daughter, then, ma'am?" I could tell what she was thinking. The entire town of Philadelphia knew that Jamie was a rebel—and, by extension, so was I. It was the threat of my imminent arrest that had caused John to insist upon my marrying him in the wake of the tumult following Jamie's presumed death. The mention of printing in British-occupied Philadelphia was bound to raise questions as to just what was being printed, and by whom.

"No, her husband is my brother's adopted son," Jenny explained. "But I raised Fergus from a wee lad myself, so he's my foster son, as well, by the Highland way of reckoning."

Mrs. Figg blinked. She had been gamely trying to keep the cast of characters in some sort of order to this point, but now gave it up with a shake of her head that made the pink ribbons on her cap wave like antennae.

"Well, where the devil—I mean, where on earth has your brother gone with his lordship?" she demanded. "To this printshop, you think?"

Jenny and I exchanged glances.

"I doubt it," I said. "More likely he's gone outside the city, using John—er, his lordship, I mean—as a hostage to get past the pickets, if necessary. Probably he'll let him go as soon as they're far enough away for safety."

Mrs. Figg made a deep humming noise of disapproval.

"And maybe he'll make for Valley Forge and turn him over to the rebels instead."

"Oh, I shouldna think so," Jenny said soothingly. "What would they want with him, after all?"

Mrs. Figg blinked again, taken aback at the notion that anyone might not value his lordship to the same degree that she did, but after a moment's lip-pursing allowed as this might be so.

"He wasn't in his uniform, was he, ma'am?" she asked me, brow furrowed. I shook my head. John didn't hold an active commission. He was a diplomat, though technically still lieutenant-colonel of his brother's regiment, and therefore wore his uniform for purposes of ceremony or intimidation, but he was officially retired from the army, not a combatant, and in plain clothes he would be taken as citizen rather than soldier—thus of no particular interest to General Washington's troops at Valley Forge.

I didn't think Jamie was headed for Valley Forge in any case. I knew, with absolute certainty, that he would come back. Here. For me.

The thought bloomed low in my belly and spread upward in a wave of warmth that made me bury my nose in my teacup to hide the resulting flush.

Alive. I caressed the word, cradling it in the center of my heart. Jamie was alive. Glad as I was to see Jenny—and gladder still to see her extend an olive branch in my direction—I really wanted to go up to my room, close the door, and lean against the wall with my eyes shut tight, reliving the seconds after he'd entered the room, when he'd taken me in his arms and kissed me, the simple, solid, warm fact of his presence so overwhelming that I might have collapsed onto the floor without his arms' support.

Alive, I repeated silently to myself. *He's alive.*

Nothing else mattered. Though I did wonder briefly what he'd done with John.

Also by Diana Gabaldon

THE **OUTLANDER** SERIES

DianaGabaldon.com

AuthorDianaGabaldon @Writer_DG

RANDOM HOUSE BALLANTINE • BANTAM • DELL

Also by DIANA GABALDON

THE COMPANION VOLUME

THE OUTLANDER GRAPHIC NOVEL

THE LORD JOHN SERIES

Lord John and the Private Matter
Lord John and the Brotherhood of the Blade
Lord John and the Hand of Devils
The Scottish Prisoner

Continue the saga with original eNovellas, engrossing tales to complement the Outlander series.

A Plague of Zombies

The Custom of the Army

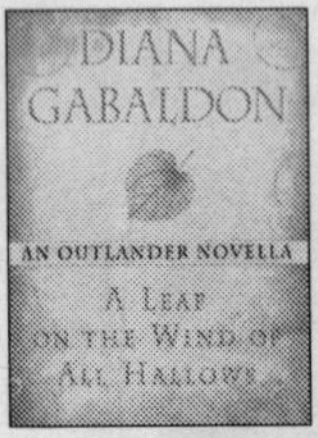

A Leaf on the Wind of All Hallows

The Space Between

DianaGabaldon.com
AuthorDianaGabaldon @Writer_DG

Random House Bantam • Dell • Delacorte • Del Rey

PRAISE FOR THE OUTLANDER NOVELS

OUTLANDER

"Marvelously entertaining . . . a page-turner of the highest order and a good read from start to finish."
—*Chattanooga Times*

"Absorbing and heartwarming . . . lavishly evokes the land and lore of Scotland."
—*Publishers Weekly*

"History comes deliciously alive on the page."
—*Daily News* (N.Y.)

DRAGONFLY IN AMBER

"A triumph! A powerful tale layered in history and myth. I loved every page."—Nora Roberts

"Compulsively readable."—*Publishers Weekly*

"Diana Gabaldon is a born storyteller . . . the pages practically turn themselves."
—*Arizona Republic*

Please turn the page for more extraordinary acclaim. . . .

VOYAGER

"Triumphant . . . Her use of historical detail and a truly adult love story confirm Gabaldon as a superior writer."

—*Publishers Weekly*

"An amazing read."

—*Arizona Tribune*

"Memorable storytelling."

—*The Seattle Times*

DRUMS OF AUTUMN

"Unforgettable characters . . . richly embroidered with historical detail . . . I just can't put it down."

—*The Cincinnati Post*

"Passionate . . . remarkable—a mix of history, fantasy, romance and unabashedly ribald storytelling."

—*The Arizona Republic*

"Wonderful . . . This is escapist historical fiction at its best."

—*San Antonio Express-News*

By Diana Gabaldon

(in chronological order)
Outlander
Dragonfly in Amber
Voyager
Drums of Autumn
The Fiery Cross
A Breath of Snow and Ashes
An Echo in the Bone
Written in My Own Heart's Blood

The Outlandish Companion
(nonfiction)

The Exile
(graphic novel)

(in chronological order)
Lord John and the Hellfire Club (novella)
Lord John and the Private Matter
Lord John and the Succubus
Lord John and the Brotherhood of the Blade
Lord John and the Haunted Soldier (novella)
Custom of the Army (novella)
Lord John and the Hand of Devils (collected novellas)
The Scottish Prisoner
Plague of Zombies (novella)

Other Outlander-related novellas
A Leaf on the Wind of All Hallows
The Space Between
Virgins

DIANA GABALDON

THE FIERY CROSS

A DELL BOOK

THE FIERY CROSS
A Dell Book

PUBLISHING HISTORY
Delacorte hardcover edition published November 2001
Delta trade paperback edition / August 2004
Dell mass market edition / September 2005

Published by
Bantam Dell
A Division of Random House, Inc.
New York, New York

This is a work of fiction. Names, characters, places, and incidents either are the product of the author's imagination or are used fictitiously. Any resemblance to actual persons, living or dead, events, or locales is entirely coincidental.

Cover illustration courtesy of Diana Gabaldon and Running Changes, Inc.
Cover design by Marietta Anastassatos

Library of Congress Catalog Card Number: 2001047063

ISBN 978-0-440-22166-1

Printed in the United States of America

www.bantamdell.com

OPM 30 29 28 27 26 25

This book is for my Sister, Theresa Gabaldon,
with whom I told the first Stories.

ACKNOWLEDGMENTS

The author's profound thanks to . . .

. . . my editor, Jackie Cantor, always the book's champion above all.

. . . my agent, Russ Galen, who's always on my side, with shield and lance.

. . . Stacey Sakal, Tom Leddy, and the other wonderful Production people who have sacrificed their time, talent, and mental health to the production of this book.

. . . Kathy Lord, that rarest and most delightful of creatures, an excellent copy editor.

. . . Virginia Norey, the book's designer *(aka Book Goddess)*, who somehow managed to fit the Whole Thing between two covers and make it look great.

. . . Irwyn Applebaum and Nita Taublib, publisher and deputy publisher, who came to the party, and brought their stuff.

. . . Rob Hunter and Rosemary Tolman, for unpublished information on the War of the Regulation and their very colorful and interesting ancestors, James Hunter and Hermon Husband. *(No, I don't make all these people up; just some of them.)*

. . . Beth and Matthew Shope, and Liz Gaspar, for information on North Carolina Quaker history and beliefs. *(And we do note as a matter of strict accuracy that Hermon Husband was not technically a Quaker at the time of this story, having been put out of the local Meeting for being too inflammatory.)*

. . . Bev LaFlamme, Carol Krenz, and their *(respectively)* French and French-Canadian husbands *(who no doubt wonder just what sort of friends their wives have, anyway),* for expert opinions on the subtleties of French bowel movements, and help with Very Picturesque French idioms.

. . . Julie Giroux, for Roger's music, and the marvelous "Culloden Symphony," Roy Williamson for "The Flower of Scotland" (words and music) copyright © The Corries (music) Ltd.

. . . Roger H.P. Coleman, R.W. Odlin, Ron Parker, Ann Chapman, Dick Lodge, Olan Watkins, and many members of the Compuserve Masonic Forum for information on Freemasonry and Irregular Lodges, circa 1755 *(which was a good bit prior to the establishment of the Scottish Rite, so let's not bother writing me about that, shall we?)*

. . . Karen Watson and Ron Parker, for advice on WWII London Tube Stations—with which I proceeded to take minor technical liberties.

. . . Steven Lopata, Hall Elliott, Arnold Wagner, R.G. Schmidt, and Mike Jones, honorable warriors all, for useful discussions of how men think and behave, before, during, and after battle.

. . . R.G. Schmidt and several other nice persons whose names I unfortunately forgot to write down, who contributed bits and pieces of helpful information regarding Cherokee belief, language, and custom. *(The bear-hunting chant ending with "Yoho!" is a matter of historical record. There are lots of things I couldn't make up if I tried.)*

. . . the Chemodurow family, for generously allowing me to take liberties with their personae, in portraying them as Russian swineherds. *(Russian boars really were imported into North Carolina for hunting in the 18th century. This may have something to do with the popularity of barbecue in the South.)*

. . . Laura Bailey, for invaluable advice and commentary on 18th century costume and customs—most of which I paid careful attention to.

. . . Susan Martin, Beth Shope, and Margaret Campbell, for expert opinions on the flora, fauna, geography, weather, and mental climate of North Carolina *(and all of whom wish to note that only a barbarian would put tomatoes in barbecue sauce)*. Aberrations in these aspects of the story are a result of inadvertence, literary license, and/or pigheadedness on the part of the author.

. . . Janet McConnaughey, Varda Amir-Orrel, Kim Laird, Elise Skidmore, Bill Williams, Arlene McCrea, Lynne Sears Williams, Babs Whelton, Joyce McGowan, and the dozens of other kind and helpful people of the Compuserve Writers Forum, who will answer any silly question at the drop of a hat, especially if it has anything to do with maiming, murder, disease, quilting, or sex.

. . . Dr. Ellen Mandell, for technical advice on how to hang someone, then cut his throat, and not kill him in the process. Any errors in the execution of this advice are mine.

. . . Piper Fahrney, for his excellent descriptions of what it feels like to be taught to fight with a sword.

. . . David Cheifetz, for dragon-slaying.

. . . Iain MacKinnon Taylor, for his invaluable help with Gaelic translations, and his lovely suggestions for Jamie's bonfire speech.

. . . Karl Hagen, for advice on Latin grammar, and to Barbara Schnell, for Latin and German bits, to say nothing of her stunning translations of the novels into German.

. . . Julie Weathers, my late father-in-law, Max Watkins, and Lucas, for help with the horses.

. . . the Ladies of Lallybroch, for their enthusiastic and continuing moral support, including the thoughtful international assortment of toilet paper.

. . . the several hundred people who have kindly and voluntarily sent me interesting information on everything from the development and uses of penicillin to the playing of bodhrans, the distribution of red spruce, and the way possum tastes *(I'm told it's greasy, in case you were wondering)*.

. . . and to my husband, Doug Watkins, for the last line of the book.

—Diana Gabaldon
www.dianagabaldon.com

I have lived through war, and lost much. I know what's worth the fight, and what is not.

Honor and courage are matters of the bone, and what a man will kill for, he will sometimes die for, too.

And that, O kinsman, is why a woman has broad hips; that bony basin will harbor a man and his child alike. A man's life springs from his woman's bones, and in her blood is his honor christened.

For the sake of love alone, would I walk through fire again.

PART ONE

In Medias Res

1

HAPPY THE BRIDE THE SUN SHINES ON

Mount Helicon
The Royal Colony of North Carolina
Late October, 1770

I WOKE TO THE PATTER OF RAIN on canvas, with the feel of my first husband's kiss on my lips. I blinked, disoriented, and by reflex put my fingers to my mouth. To keep the feeling, or to hide it? I wondered, even as I did so.

Jamie stirred and murmured in his sleep next to me, his movement rousing a fresh wave of scent from the cedar branches under our bottom quilt. Perhaps the ghost's passing had disturbed him. I frowned at the empty air outside our lean-to.

Go away, Frank, I thought sternly.

It was still dark outside, but the mist that rose from the damp earth was a pearly gray; dawn wasn't far off. Nothing stirred, inside or out, but I had the distinct sense of an ironic amusement that lay on my skin like the lightest of touches.

Shouldn't I come to see her married?

I couldn't tell whether the words had formed themselves in my thoughts, or whether they—and that kiss—were merely the product of my own subconscious. I had fallen asleep with my mind still busy with wedding preparations; little wonder that I should wake from dreams of weddings. And wedding nights.

I smoothed the rumpled muslin of my shift, uneasily aware that it was rucked up around my waist and that my skin was flushed with more than sleep. I didn't remember anything concrete about the dream that had wakened me; only a confused jumble of image and sensation. I thought perhaps that was a good thing.

I turned over on the rustling branches, nudging close to Jamie. He was warm and smelled pleasantly of woodsmoke and whisky, with a faint tang of sleepy maleness under it, like the deep note of a lingering chord. I stretched myself, very slowly, arching my back so that my pelvis nudged his hip. If he were sound asleep or disinclined, the gesture was slight enough to pass unnoticed; if he were not . . .

He wasn't. He smiled faintly, eyes still closed, and a big hand ran slowly down my back, settling with a firm grip on my bottom.

"Mmm?" he said. "Hmmmm." He sighed, and relaxed back into sleep, holding on.

I nestled close, reassured. The immediate physicality of Jamie was more than enough to banish the touch of lingering dreams. And Frank—if that *was* Frank—was right, so far as that went. I was sure that if such a thing were possible, Bree would want both her fathers at her wedding.

I was wide awake now, but much too comfortable to move. It was raining outside; a light rain, but the air was cold and damp enough to make the cozy nest of quilts more inviting than the distant prospect of hot coffee. Particularly since the getting of coffee would involve a trip to the stream for water, making up the campfire—oh, God, the wood would be damp, even if the fire hadn't gone completely out—grinding the coffee in a stone quern and brewing it, while wet leaves blew round my ankles and drips from overhanging tree branches slithered down my neck.

Shivering at the thought, I pulled the top quilt up over my bare shoulder and instead resumed the mental catalogue of preparations with which I had fallen asleep.

Food, drink . . . luckily I needn't trouble about that. Jamie's aunt Jocasta would deal with the arrangements; or rather, her black butler, Ulysses, would. Wedding guests—no difficulties there. We were in the middle of the largest Gathering of Scottish Highlanders in the Colonies, and food and drink were being provided. Engraved invitations would not be necessary.

Bree would have a new dress, at least; Jocasta's gift as well. Dark blue wool—silk was both too expensive and too impractical for life in the backwoods. It was a far cry from the white satin and orange blossom I had once envisioned her wearing to be married in—but then, this was scarcely the marriage anyone might have imagined in the 1960s.

I wondered what Frank might have thought of Brianna's husband. He likely would have approved; Roger was a historian—or once had been—like Frank himself. He was intelligent and humorous, a talented musician and a gentle man, thoroughly devoted to Brianna and little Jemmy.

Which is very admirable indeed, I thought in the direction of the mist, *under the circumstances.*

You admit that, do you? The words formed in my inner ear as though he had spoken them, ironic, mocking both himself and me.

Jamie frowned and tightened his grasp on my buttock, making small whuffling noises in his sleep.

You know I do, I said silently. *I always did, and you know it, so just bugger off, will you?!*

I turned my back firmly on the outer air and laid my head on Jamie's shoulder, seeking refuge in the feel of the soft, crumpled linen of his shirt.

I rather thought Jamie was less inclined than I—or perhaps Frank—to give Roger credit for accepting Jemmy as his own. To Jamie, it was a simple matter of obligation; an honorable man could not do otherwise. And I knew he had his doubts as to Roger's ability to support and protect a family in the Carolina wilderness. Roger was tall, well-built, and capable—but "bonnet, belt, and swordie" were the stuff of songs to Roger; to Jamie, they were the tools of his trade.

The hand on my bottom squeezed suddenly, and I started.

"Sassenach," Jamie said drowsily, "you're squirming like a toadling in a wee lad's fist. D'ye need to get up and go to the privy?"

"Oh, you're awake," I said, feeling mildly foolish.

"I am *now*," he said. The hand fell away, and he stretched, groaning. His bare feet popped out at the far end of the quilt, long toes spread wide.

"Sorry. I didn't mean to wake you."

"Och, dinna fash yourself," he assured me. He cleared his throat and rubbed a hand through the ruddy waves of his loosened hair, blinking. "I was dreaming like a fiend; I always do when I sleep cold." He lifted his head and peered down across the quilt, wiggling his exposed toes with disfavor. "Why did I not sleep wi' my stockings on?"

"Really? What were you dreaming about?" I asked, with a small stab of uneasiness. I rather hoped he hadn't been dreaming the same sort of thing I had.

"Horses," he said, to my immediate relief. I laughed.

"What sort of fiendish dreams could you be having about horses?"

"Oh, God, it was terrible." He rubbed his eyes with both fists and shook his head, trying to clear the dream from his mind. "All to do wi' the Irish kings. Ye ken what MacKenzie was sayin' about it, at the fire last night?"

"Irish ki—oh!" I remembered, and laughed again at the recollection. "Yes, I do."

Roger, flushed with the triumph of his new engagement, had regaled the company around the fireside the night before with songs, poems, and entertaining historical anecdotes—one of which concerned the rites with which the ancient Irish kings were said to have been crowned. One of these involved the successful candidate copulating with a white mare before the assembled multitudes, presumably to prove his virility—though I thought it would be a better proof of the gentleman's *sangfroid*, myself.

"I was in charge o' the horse," Jamie informed me. "And *everything* went wrong. The man was too short, and I had to find something for him to stand on. I found a rock, but I couldna lift it. Then a stool, but the leg came off in my hand. Then I tried to pile up bricks to make a platform, but they crumbled to sand. Finally they said it was all right, they would just cut the legs off the mare, and I was trying to stop them doing that, and the man who would be king was jerkin' at his breeks and complaining that his fly buttons wouldna come loose, and then someone noticed that it was a *black* mare, and that wouldna do at all."

I snorted, muffling my laughter in a fold of his shirt for fear of wakening someone camped near us.

"Is that when you woke up?"

"No. For some reason, I was verra much affronted at that. I said it *would* do, in fact the black was a much better horse, for everyone knows that white horses have weak een, and I said the offspring would be blind. And they said no, no, the black was ill luck, and I was insisting it was not, and . . ." He stopped, clearing his throat.

"And?"

He shrugged and glanced sideways at me, a faint flush creeping up his neck.

"Aye, well. I said it would do fine, I'd show them. And I had just grasped the mare's rump to stop her moving, and was getting ready to . . . ah . . . make myself king of Ireland. *That's* when I woke."

I snorted and wheezed, and felt his side vibrate with his own suppressed laughter.

"Oh, now I'm *really* sorry to have wakened you!" I wiped my eyes on the corner of the quilt. "I'm sure it was a great loss to the Irish. Though I do wonder how the queens of Ireland felt about that particular ceremony," I added as an afterthought.

"I canna think the ladies would suffer even slightly by comparison," Jamie assured me. "Though I have heard of men who prefer—"

"I wasn't thinking of *that*," I said. "It was more the hygienic implications, if you see what I mean. Putting the cart before the horse is one thing, but putting the horse before the queen . . ."

"The—oh, aye." He was flushed with amusement, but his skin darkened further at that. "Say what ye may about the Irish, Sassenach, but I do believe they wash now and then. And under the circumstances, the king might possibly even have found a bit of soap useful, in . . . in . . ."

"*In medias res*?" I suggested. "Surely not. I mean, after all, a horse is quite large, relatively speaking . . ."

"It's a matter of readiness, Sassenach, as much as room," he said, with a repressive glance in my direction. "And I can see that a man might require a bit of encouragement, under the circumstances. Though it's *in medias res*, in any case," he added. "Have ye never read Horace? Or Aristotle?"

"No. We can't all be educated. And I've never had much time for Aristotle, after hearing that he ranked women somewhere below worms in his classification of the natural world."

"The man can't have been married." Jamie's hand moved slowly up my back, fingering the knobs of my spine through my shift. "Surely he would ha' noticed the bones, else."

I smiled and lifted a hand to his own cheekbone, rising stark and clean above a tide of auburn stubble.

As I did so, I saw that the sky outside had lightened into dawn; his head was silhouetted by the pale canvas of our shelter, but I could see his face clearly. The expression on it reminded me exactly why he had taken off his stockings the night before. Unfortunately, we had both been so tired after the prolonged festivities that we had fallen asleep in mid-embrace.

I found that belated memory rather reassuring, offering as it did some explanation both for the state of my shift and for the dreams from which I had awakened. At the same time, I felt a chilly draft slide its fingers under the quilt, and shivered. Frank and Jamie were very different men, and there was no doubt in my mind as to who had kissed me, just before waking.

"Kiss me," I said suddenly to Jamie. Neither of us had yet brushed our teeth, but he obligingly skimmed my lips with his, then, when I caught the back of his head and pressed him closer, shifted his weight to one hand, the better to adjust the tangle of bedclothes round our lower limbs.

"Oh?" he said, when I released him. He smiled, blue eyes creasing into dark triangles in the dimness. "Well, to be sure, Sassenach. I must just step outside for a moment first, though."

He flung back the quilt and rose. From my position on the ground, I had a rather unorthodox view which provided me with engaging glimpses under the hem of his long linen shirt.

I did hope that what I was looking at was not the lingering result of his nightmare, but thought it better not to ask.

"You'd better hurry," I said. "It's getting light; people will be up and about soon."

He nodded and ducked outside. I lay still, listening. A few birds cheeped faintly in the distance, but this was autumn; not even full light would provoke the raucous choruses of spring and summer. The mountain and its many camps still lay slumbering, but I could feel small stirrings all around, just below the edge of hearing.

I ran my fingers through my hair, fluffing it out round my shoulders, and rolled over, looking for the water bottle. Feeling cool air on my back, I glanced over my shoulder, but dawn had come and the mist had fled; the air outside was gray but still.

I touched the gold ring on my left hand, restored to me the night before, and still unfamiliar after its long absence. Perhaps it was his ring that had summoned Frank to my dreams. Perhaps tonight at the wedding ceremony, I would touch it again, deliberately, and hope that he could see his daughter's happiness somehow through my eyes. For now, though, he was gone, and I was glad.

A small sound, no louder than the distant birdcalls, drifted through the air. The brief cry of a baby waking.

I had once thought that no matter the circumstances, there ought really to be no more than two people in a marriage bed. I still thought so. However, a baby was more difficult to banish than the ghost of a former love; Brianna and Roger's bed must perforce accommodate three.

The edge of the canvas lifted, and Jamie's face appeared, looking excited and alarmed.

"Ye'd best get up and dress, Claire," he said. "The soldiers are drawn up by the creek. Where are my stockings?"

I sat bolt upright, and far down the mountainside the drums began to roll.

COLD FOG LAY like smoke in the hollows all round; a cloud had settled on Mount Helicon like a broody hen on a single egg, and the air was thick with damp. I blinked blearily across a stretch of rough grass, to where a detachment of the 67th Highland regiment was drawn up in full splendor by the creek, drums rumbling and the company piper tootling away, grandly impervious to the rain.

I was very cold, and more than slightly cross. I'd gone to bed in the expectation of waking to hot coffee and a nourishing breakfast, this to be followed by two weddings, three christenings, two tooth extractions, the removal of an infected toenail, and other entertaining forms of wholesome social intercourse requiring whisky.

Instead, I'd been wakened by unsettling dreams, led into amorous dalliance, and then dragged out into a cold drizzle *in medias* bloody *res*, apparently to hear a proclamation of some sort. No coffee yet, either.

It had taken some time for the Highlanders in their camps to rouse themselves and stagger down the hillside, and the piper had gone quite purple in the face before he at last blew the final blast and left off with a discordant wheeze. The echoes were still ringing off the mountainside, as Lieutenant Archibald Hayes stepped out before his men.

Lieutenant Hayes's nasal Fife accent carried well, and the wind was with him. Still, I was sure the people farther up the mountain could hear very little. Standing as we did at the foot of the slope, though, we were no more than twenty yards from the Lieutenant and I could hear every word, in spite of the chattering of my teeth.

"By his EXCELLENCY, WILLIAM TRYON, Esquire, His Majesty's Captain-General, Governor, and Commander-in-Chief, in and over the said Province," Hayes read, lifting his voice in a bellow to carry above the noises of wind and water, and the premonitory murmurs of the crowd.

The moisture shrouded trees and rocks with dripping mist, the clouds spat intermittent sleet and freezing rain, and erratic winds had lowered the temperature by some thirty degrees. My left shin, sensitive to cold, throbbed at the spot where I had broken the bone two years before. A person given to portents and metaphors might have been tempted to draw comparisons between the nasty weather and the reading of the Governor's Proclamation, I thought—the prospects were similarly chill and foreboding.

"Whereas," Hayes boomed, glowering at the crowd over his paper, *"I have received information that a great Number of outrageous and disorderly Persons did tumultuously assemble themselves together in the Town of Hillsborough, on the 24th and 25th of last Month, during the sitting of the Superior Court of Justice of that District to oppose the Just Measures of Government and in open Violation of the Laws of their Country, audaciously attacking his Majesty's Associate Justice in the Execution of his Office, and barbarously beating and wounding several Persons in and during the sitting of said Court, and offering other enormous Indignities and Insults to his Majesty's Government, committing the most violent Outrages on the Persons and properties of the Inhabitants of the said Town, drinking Damnation to their lawful Sovereign King George and Success to the Pretender—"*

Hayes paused, gulping air with which to accomplish the next clause. Inflating his chest with an audible whoosh, he read on:

"To the End therefore, that the Persons concerned in the said outrageous Acts may be brought to Justice, I do, by the Advice and Consent of his Majesty's Council, issue this my Proclamation, hereby requiring and strictly enjoining all his Majesty's Justices of the Peace in this Government to make diligent Inquiry into the above recited Crimes, and to receive the Deposition of such Person or Persons as shall appear before them to make Information of and concerning the same; which Depositions are to be transmitted to me, in Order to be laid before the General Assembly, at New Bern, on the 30th day of November next, to which time it stands Prorogued for the immediate Dispatch of Public Business."

A final inhalation; Hayes's face was nearly as purple as the piper's by now.

"Given under my Hand, and the Great Seal of the Province, at New Bern, the 18th Day of October, in the 10th Year of his Majesty's Reign, Anno Domini 1770.

"Signed, William Tryon," Hayes concluded, with a final puff of steamy breath.

"Do you know," I remarked to Jamie, "I believe that was all one single sentence, bar the closing. Amazing, even for a politician."

"Hush, Sassenach," he said, his eyes still fixed on Archie Hayes. There was a subdued rumble from the crowd behind me, of interest and consternation—touched with a certain amount of amusement at the phrases regarding treasonous toasts.

This was a Gathering of Highlanders, many of them exiled to the Colonies in the wake of the Stuart Rising, and had Archie Hayes chosen to take official notice of what was said over the cups of ale and whisky passed round the fires the night before . . . but then, he had but forty soldiers with him, and whatever his own opinions of King George and that monarch's possible damnation, he kept them wisely to himself.

Some four hundred Highlanders surrounded Hayes's small beachhead on the creekbank, summoned by the tattoo of drums. Men and women sheltered among the trees above the clearing, plaids and arisaids pulled tight against the rising wind. They too were keeping their own counsel, judging from the array of stony faces visible under the flutter of scarves and bonnets. Of course, their expressions might derive from cold as much as from natural caution; my own cheeks were stiff, the end of my nose had gone numb, and I hadn't felt my feet anytime since daybreak.

"Any person wishing to make declaration concerning these most serious matters may entrust such statements safely to my care," Hayes announced, his round face an official blank. "I will remain in my tent with my clerk for the rest of the day. God save the King!"

He handed the Proclamation to his corporal, bowed to the crowd in dismissal, and turned smartly toward a large canvas tent that had been erected near the trees, regimental banners flapping wildly from a standard next to it.

Shivering, I slid a hand into the slit of Jamie's cloak and over the crook of his arm, my cold fingers comforted by the warmth of his body. Jamie pressed his elbow briefly to his side in acknowledgment of my frozen grasp, but didn't look down at me; he was studying Archie Hayes's retreating back, eyes narrowed against the sting of the wind.

A compact and solid man, of inconsequent height but considerable presence, the Lieutenant moved with great deliberation, as though oblivious of the crowd on the hillside above. He vanished into his tent, leaving the flap invitingly tied up.

Not for the first time, I reluctantly admired Governor Tryon's political instincts. This Proclamation was clearly being read in towns and villages throughout the colony; he could have relied on a local magistrate or sheriff to carry his message of official fury to this Gathering. Instead, he had taken the trouble to send Hayes.

Archibald Hayes had taken the field at Culloden by his father's side, at the age of twelve. Wounded in the fight, he had been captured and sent south. Presented with a choice of transportation or joining the army, he had taken the King's shilling and made the best of it. The fact that he had risen to be an officer in his mid-thirties, in a time when most commissions were bought rather than earned, was sufficient testimony to his abilities.

He was as personable as he was professional; invited to share our food and fire the day before, he had spent half the night talking with Jamie—and the other half moving from fire to fire under the aegis of Jamie's presence, being introduced to the heads of all the important families present.

And whose notion had that been? I wondered, looking up at Jamie. His long, straight nose was reddened by the cold, his eyes hooded from the wind, but his face gave no inkling of what he was thinking. And that, I thought, was a bloody good indication that he was thinking something rather dangerous. Had he known about this Proclamation?

No English officer, with an English troop, could have brought such news into a Gathering like this, with any hope of cooperation. But Hayes and his Highlanders, stalwart in their tartan . . . I didn't miss the fact that Hayes had had his tent erected with its back to a thick grove of pines; anyone who wished to speak to the Lieutenant in secret could approach through the woods, unseen.

"Does Hayes expect someone to pop out of the crowd, rush into his tent, and surrender on the spot?" I murmured to Jamie. I personally knew of at least a dozen men among those present who had taken part in the Hillsborough riots; three of them were standing within arm's length of us.

Jamie saw the direction of my glance and put his hand over mine, squeezing it in a silent adjuration of discretion. I lowered my brows at him; surely he didn't think I would give anyone away by inadvertence? He gave me a faint smile and one of those annoying marital looks that said, more plainly than words, *You know how ye are, Sassenach. Anyone who sees your face kens just what ye think.*

I sidled in a little closer, and kicked him discreetly in the ankle. I might have a glass face, but it certainly wouldn't arouse comment in a crowd like this! He didn't wince, but the smile spread a little wider. He slid one arm inside my cloak, and drew me closer, his hand on my back.

Hobson, MacLennan, and Fowles stood together just in front of us, talking quietly among themselves. All three came from a tiny settlement called Drunkard's Creek, some fifteen miles from our own place on Fraser's Ridge. Hugh Fowles was Joe Hobson's son-in-law, and very young, no more than twenty. He was doing his best to keep his composure, but his face had gone white and clammy as the Proclamation was read.

I didn't know what Tryon intended to do to anyone who could be proved to have had a part in the riot, but I could feel the currents of unrest created by the Governor's Proclamation passing through the crowd like the eddies of water rushing over rocks in the nearby creek.

Several buildings had been destroyed in Hillsborough, and a number of public officials dragged out and assaulted in the street. Gossip had it that one ironically titled justice of the peace had lost an eye to a vicious blow aimed with a horsewhip. No doubt taking this demonstration of civil disobedience to heart, Chief Justice Henderson had escaped out of a window and fled the town, thus effectively preventing the Court from sitting. It was clear that the Governor was *very* annoyed about what had happened in Hillsborough.

Joe Hobson glanced back at Jamie, then away. Lieutenant Hayes's presence at our fire the previous evening had not gone unremarked.

If Jamie saw the glance, he didn't return it. He lifted one shoulder in a shrug, tilting his head down to speak to me.

"I shouldna think Hayes expects anyone to give themselves up, no. It may be his duty to ask for information; I thank God it isna mine to answer." He hadn't spoken loudly, but loudly enough to reach the ears of Joe Hobson.

Hobson turned his head and gave Jamie a small nod of wry acknowledgment. He touched his son-in-law's arm, and they turned away, scrambling up the slope toward the scattered campsites above, where their womenfolk were tending the fires and the younger children.

This was the last day of the Gathering; tonight there would be marryings and christenings, the formal blessing of love and its riotous fruits, sprung from the loins of the unchurched multitude during the year before. Then the last songs would be sung, the last stories told, and dancing done amid the leaping flames of many fires—rain or no rain. Come morning, the Scots and their households would all disperse back to their homes, scattered from the settled banks of the Cape Fear River to the wild mountains of the west—carrying news of the Governor's Proclamation and the doings at Hillsborough.

I wiggled my toes inside my damp shoes and wondered uneasily who among the crowd might think it their duty to answer Hayes's invitation to confession or incrimination. Not Jamie, no. But others might. There had been a good deal of boasting about the riots in Hillsborough during the week of the Gathering, but not all the listeners were disposed to view the rioters as heroes, by any means.

I could feel as well as hear the mutter of conversation breaking out in the wake of the Proclamation; heads turning, families drawing close together, men moving from group to group, as the content of Hayes's speech was relayed up the hill, repeated to those who stood too far away to have heard it.

"Shall we go? There's a lot to do yet before the weddings."

"Aye?" Jamie glanced down at me. "I thought Jocasta's slaves were managing the food and drink. I gave Ulysses the barrels of whisky—he'll be *soghan.*"

"Ulysses? Did he bring his wig?" I smiled at the thought. The *soghan* was the man who managed the dispensing of drink and refreshment at a Highland wedding; the term actually meant something like "hearty, jovial fellow." Ulysses was possibly the most dignified person I had ever seen—even without his livery and powdered horsehair wig.

"If he did, it's like to be stuck to his head by the evening." Jamie glanced up at the lowering sky and shook his head. "Happy the bride the sun shines on," he quoted. "Happy the corpse the rain falls on."

"That's what I like about Scots," I said dryly. "An appropriate proverb for all occasions. Don't you dare say that in front of Bree."

"What d'ye take me for, Sassenach?" he demanded, with a half-smile down at me. "I'm her father, no?"

"Definitely yes." I suppressed the sudden thought of Brianna's other father, and glanced over my shoulder, to be sure she wasn't in hearing.

There was no sign of her blazing head among those nearby. Certainly her father's daughter, she stood six feet tall in her stocking feet; nearly as easy as Jamie himself to pick out of a crowd.

"It's not the wedding feast I need to deal with, anyway," I said, turning back to Jamie. "I've got to manage breakfast, then do the morning clinic with Murray MacLeod."

"Oh, aye? I thought ye said wee Murray was a charlatan."

"I said he was ignorant, stubborn, and a menace to the public health," I corrected. "That's not the same thing—quite."

"Quite," said Jamie, grinning. "Ye mean to educate him, then—or poison him?"

"Whichever seems most effective. If nothing else, I might accidentally step on his fleam and break it; that's probably the only way I'll stop him bleeding people. Let's go, though, I'm freezing!"

"Aye, we'll away, then," Jamie agreed, with a glance at the soldiers, still drawn up along the creekbank at parade rest.

"No doubt wee Archie means to keep his lads there 'til the crowd's gone; they're going a wee bit blue round the edges."

Though fully armed and uniformed, the row of Highlanders was relaxed; imposing, to be sure, but no longer threatening. Small boys—and not a few wee girls—scampered to and fro among them, impudently flicking the hems of the soldiers' kilts or dashing in, greatly daring, to touch the gleaming muskets, dangling canteens, and the hilts of dirks and swords.

"Abel, *a charaid*!" Jamie had paused to greet the last of the men from Drunkard's Creek. "Will ye ha' eaten yet the day?"

MacLennan had not brought his wife to the Gathering, and thus ate where luck took him. The crowd was dispersing around us, but he stood stolidly in place, holding the ends of a red flannel handkerchief pulled over his balding head against the spatter of rain. Probably hoping to cadge an invitation to breakfast, I thought cynically.

I eyed his stocky form, mentally estimating his possible consumption of eggs, parritch, and toasted bread against the dwindling supplies in our hampers. Not that simple shortage of food would stop any Highlander from offering hospitality—certainly not Jamie, who was inviting MacLennan to join us, even as I mentally divided eighteen eggs by nine people instead of eight. Not fried, then; made into fritters with grated potatoes, and I'd best borrow more coffee from Jocasta's campsite on the way up the mountain.

We turned to go, and Jamie's hand slid suddenly downward over my backside. I made an undignified sound, and Abel MacLennan turned round to gawk at me. I smiled brightly at him, resisting the urge to kick Jamie again, less discreetly.

MacLennan turned away, and scrambled up the slope in front of us with alacrity, coattails bouncing in anticipation over worn breeks. Jamie put a hand under my elbow to help me over the rocks, bending down as he did so to mutter in my ear.

"Why the devil are ye not wearing a petticoat, Sassenach?" he hissed. "Ye've nothing at all on under your skirt—you'll catch your death of cold!"

"You're not wrong there," I said, shivering in spite of my cloak. I did in fact have on a linen shift under my gown, but it was a thin, ragged thing, suitable for rough camping-out in summertime, but quite insufficient to stem the wintry blasts that blew through my skirt as though it were cheesecloth.

"Ye had a fine woolen petticoat yesterday. What's become of it?"

"You don't want to know," I assured him.

His eyebrows went up at this, but before he could ask further questions, a scream rang out behind us.

"Germain!"

I turned to see a small blond head, hair flying as the owner streaked down the slope below the rocks. Two-year-old Germain had taken advantage of his mother's preoccupation with his newborn sister to escape custody and make a dash for the row of soldiers. Eluding capture, he charged headlong down the slope, picking up speed like a rolling stone.

"Fergus!" Marsali screamed. Germain's father, hearing his name, turned round from his conversation, just in time to see his son trip over a rock and fly headlong. A born acrobat, the little boy made no move to save himself, but collapsed gracefully, rolling into a ball like a hedgehog as he struck the grassy slope on one shoulder. He rolled like a cannonball through the ranks of soldiers, shot off the edge of a rocky shelf, and plopped with a splash into the creek.

There was a general gasp of consternation, and a number of people ran down the hill to help, but one of the soldiers had already hurried to the bank. Kneeling, he thrust the tip of his bayonet through the child's floating clothes and towed the soggy bundle to the shore.

Fergus charged into the icy shallows, reaching out to clasp his waterlogged son.

"Merci, mon ami, merci beaucoup," he said to the young soldier. *"Et toi, garnement,"* he said, addressing his spluttering offspring with a small shake. *"Comment vas-tu,* ye wee chowderheid?"

The soldier looked startled, but I couldn't tell whether the cause was Fergus's unique patois, or the sight of the gleaming hook he wore in place of his missing left hand.

"That's all right then, sir," he said, with a shy smile. "He'll no be damaged, I think."

Brianna appeared suddenly from behind a chinkapin tree, six-month-old Jemmy on one shoulder, and scooped baby Joan neatly out of Marsali's arms.

"Here, give Joanie to me," she said. "You go take care of Germain."

Jamie swung the heavy cloak from his shoulders and laid it in Marsali's arms in place of the baby.

"Aye, and tell the soldier laddie who saved him to come and share our fire," he told her. "We can feed another, Sassenach?"

"Of course," I said, swiftly readjusting my mental calculations. Eighteen eggs, four loaves of stale bread for toast—no, I should keep back one for the trip home tomorrow—three dozen oatcakes if Jamie and Roger hadn't eaten them already, half a jar of honey . . .

Marsali's thin face lighted with a rueful smile, shared among the three of us, then she was gone, hastening to the aid of her drenched and shivering menfolk.

Jamie looked after her with a sigh of resignation, as the wind caught the full sleeves of his shirt and belled them out with a muffled *whoomp*. He crossed his arms across his chest, hunching his shoulders against the wind, and smiled down at me, sidelong.

"Ah, well. I suppose we shall both freeze together, Sassenach. That's all right, though. I wouldna want to live without ye, anyway."

"Ha," I said amiably. "You could live naked on an ice floe, Jamie Fraser, and melt it. What have you done with your coat and plaid?" He wore nothing besides his kilt and sark save shoes and stockings, and his high cheekbones were reddened with cold, like the tips of his ears. When I slipped a hand back inside the crook of his arm, though, he was warm as ever.

"Ye dinna want to know," he said, grinning. He covered my hand with one large, callused palm. "Let's go; I'm starved for my breakfast."

"Wait," I said, detaching myself. Jemmy was indisposed

to share his mother's embrace with the newcomer, and howled and squirmed in protest, his small round face going red with annoyance under a blue knitted cap. I reached out and took him from Brianna, as he wriggled and fussed in his wrappings.

"Thanks, Mama." Brianna smiled briefly, boosting tiny Joan into a more secure position against her shoulder. "Are you sure you want that one, though? This one's quieter—and weighs half as much."

"No, he's all right. Hush, sweetie, come see Grannie." I smiled as I said it, with thc still-new feeling of mingled surprise and delight that I could actually be someone's grandmother. Recognizing me, Jemmy abandoned his fuss and went promptly into his mussel-clinging-to-a-rock routine, chubby fists gripped tight in my hair. Disentangling his fingers, I peered over his head, but things below seemed under control.

Fergus, breeches and stockings soaking wet, Jamie's cloak draped round his shoulders, was wringing out his shirtfront one-handed, saying something to the soldier who had rescued Germain. Marsali had whipped off her arisaid and wrapped the little boy in it, her loosened blond hair flying out from under her kerch like cobwebs in the wind.

Lieutenant Hayes, attracted by the noise, was peering out from the flap of his tent like a whelk from its shell. He looked up, and caught my eye; I waved briefly, then turned to follow my own family back to our campsite.

Jamie was saying something to Brianna in Gaelic, as he helped her over a rocky patch in the trail ahead of me.

"Yes, I'm ready," she said, replying in English. "Where's your coat, Da?"

"I lent it to your husband," he said. "We dinna want him to look a beggar at your wedding, aye?"

Bree laughed, wiping a flying strand of red hair out of her mouth with her free hand.

"Better a beggar than an attempted suicide."

"A what?" I caught up with them as we emerged from the shelter of the rocks. The wind barreled across the open space, pelting us with sleet and bits of stinging gravel, and I pulled the knitted cap further down over Jemmy's ears, then pulled the blanket up over his head.

"Whoof!" Brianna hunched over the swaddled baby girl she carried, sheltering her from the blast. "Roger was shaving when the drums started up; he nearly cut his throat. The front of his coat is covered with bloodstains." She glanced at Jamie, eyes watering with the wind. "So you've seen him this morning. Where is he now, do you know?"

"The lad's in one piece," he assured her. "I told him to go and talk wi' Father Donahue, while Hayes was about his business." He gave her a sharp look. "Ye might have told me the lad was no a Catholic."

"I might," she said, unperturbed. "But I didn't. It's no big deal to me."

"If ye mean by that peculiar expression, that it's of no consequence—" Jamie began with a distinct edge in his voice, but was interrupted by the appearance of Roger himself, resplendent in a kilt of green-and-white MacKenzie tartan, with the matching plaid draped over Jamie's good coat and waistcoat. The coat fit decently—both men were of a size, long-limbed and broad-shouldered, though Jamie was an inch or two the taller—and the gray wool was quite as becoming to Roger's dark hair and olive skin as it was to Jamie's burnished auburn coloring.

"You look very nice, Roger," I said. "Where did you cut yourself?" His face was pink, with the raw look common to just-shaved skin, but otherwise unmarked.

Roger was carrying Jamie's plaid under his arm, a bundle of red and black tartan. He handed it over and tilted his head to one side, showing me the deep gash just under his jawbone.

"Just there. Not so bad, but it bled like the dickens. They don't call them cutthroat razors for nothing, aye?"

The gash had already crusted into a neat dark line, a cut some three inches long, angled down from the corner of his jaw across the side of his throat. I touched the skin near it briefly. Not bad; the blade of the razor had cut straight in, no flap of skin needing suture. No wonder it had bled a lot, though; it did look as though he had tried to cut his throat.

"A bit nervous this morning?" I teased. "Not having second thoughts, are you?"

"A little late for that," Brianna said dryly, coming up beside me. "Got a kid who needs a name, after all."

"He'll have more names than he knows what to do with," Roger assured her. "So will you—Mrs. MacKenzie."

A small flush lit Brianna's face at the name, and she smiled at him. He leaned over and kissed her on the forehead, taking the cocooned baby from her as he did so. A look of sudden shock crossed his face as he felt the weight of the bundle in his arms, and he gawked down at it.

"That's not ours," Bree said, grinning at his look of consternation. "It's Marsali's Joan. Mama has Jemmy."

"Thank God," he said, holding the bundle with a good deal more caution. "I thought he'd evaporated or something." He lifted the blanket slightly, exposing tiny Joan's sleeping face, and smiled—as people always did—at sight of her comical quiff of brown hair, which came to a point like a Kewpie doll's.

"Not a chance," I said, grunting as I hoisted a well-nourished Jemmy, now peacefully comatose in his own wrappings, into a more comfortable position. "I think he's gained a pound or two on the way uphill." I was flushed from exertion, and held the baby a little away from myself, as a sudden wave of heat flushed my cheeks and perspiration broke out under the waves of my disheveled hair.

Jamie took Jemmy from me, and tucked him expertly under one arm like a football, one hand cupping the baby's head.

"Ye've spoken wi' the priest, then?" he said, eyeing Roger skeptically.

"I have," Roger said dryly, answering the look as much as the question. "He's satisfied I'm no the Anti-Christ. So long as I'm willing the lad should be baptized Catholic, there's no bar to the wedding. I've said I'm willing."

Jamie grunted in reply, and I repressed a smile. While Jamie had no great religious prejudices—he had dealt with, fought with, and commanded far too many men, of every possible background—the revelation that his son-in-law was a Presbyterian—and had no intention of converting—had occasioned some small comment.

Bree caught my eye and gave me a sidelong smile, her own eyes creasing into blue triangles of catlike amusement.

"Very wise of you not to mention religion ahead of time," I murmured, careful not to speak loudly enough for Jamie to hear me. Both men were walking ahead of us, still rather stiff in their attitudes, though the formality of their demeanor was rather impaired by the trailing draperies of the babies they carried.

Jemmy let out a sudden squawk, but his grandfather swung him up without breaking stride, and he subsided, round eyes fixed on us over Jamie's shoulder, sheltered under the hooding of his blanket. I made a face at him, and he broke into a huge, gummy smile.

"Roger wanted to say something, but I told him to keep quiet." Bree stuck out her tongue and wiggled it at Jemmy, then fixed a wifely look on Roger's back. "I knew Da wouldn't make a stramash about it, if we waited 'til just before the wedding."

I noted both her astute evaluation of her father's behavior, and her easy use of Scots. She resembled Jamie in a good deal more than the obvious matter of looks and coloring; she had his talent for human judgment and his glibness with language. Still, there was something niggling at my mind, something to do with Roger and religion . . .

We had come up close enough behind the men to hear their conversation.

". . . about Hillsborough," Jamie was saying, leaning toward Roger so as to be heard over the wind. "Calling for information about the rioters."

"Oh, aye?" Roger sounded both interested and wary. "Duncan Innes will be interested to hear that. He was in Hillsborough during the troubles, did you know?"

"No." Jamie sounded more than interested. "I've barely seen Duncan to speak to this week. I'll ask him, maybe, after the wedding—if he lives through it." Duncan was to marry Jamie's aunt, Jocasta Cameron, in the evening, and was nervous to the point of prostration over the prospect.

Roger turned, shielding Joan from the wind with his body as he spoke to Brianna.

"Your aunt's told Father Donahue he can hold the weddings in her tent. That'll be a help."

"Brrrr!" Bree hunched her shoulders, shivering. "Thank goodness. It's no day to be getting married under the greenwood tree."

A huge chestnut overhead sent down a damp shower of yellow leaves, as though in agreement. Roger looked a little uneasy.

"I don't imagine it's quite the wedding you maybe thought of," he said. "When ye were a wee girl."

Brianna looked up at Roger and a slow, wide smile spread across her face. "Neither was the first one," she said. "But I liked it fine."

Roger's complexion wasn't given to blushing, and his ears were red with cold in any case. He opened his mouth as though to reply, caught Jamie's gimlet eye, and shut it again, looking embarrassed but undeniably pleased.

"Mr. Fraser!"

I turned to see one of the soldiers making his way up the hill toward us, his eyes fixed on Jamie.

"Corporal MacNair, your servant, sir," he said, breathing hard as he reached us. He gave a sharp inclination of the head. "The Lieutenant's compliments, and would ye be so good as to attend him in his tent?" He caught sight of me, and bowed again, less abruptly. "Mrs. Fraser. My compliments, ma'am."

"Your servant, sir." Jamie returned the Corporal's bow. "My apologies to the Lieutenant, but I have duties that require my attendance elsewhere." He spoke politely, but the Corporal glanced sharply up at him. MacNair was young, but not callow; a quick look of understanding crossed his lean, dark face. The last thing any man would want was to be seen going into Hayes's tent by himself, immediately following that Proclamation.

"The Lieutenant bids me request the attendance upon him of Mr. Farquard Campbell, Mr. Andrew MacNeill, Mr. Gerald Forbes, Mr. Duncan Innes, and Mr. Randall Lillywhite, as well as yourself, sir."

A certain amount of tension left Jamie's shoulders.

"Does he," he said dryly. So Hayes meant to consult the powerful men of the area: Farquard Campbell and Andrew MacNeill were large landowners and local magistrates; Gerald Forbes a prominent solicitor from Cross Creek, and a justice of the peace; Lillywhite a magistrate of the circuit court. And Duncan Innes was about to become the largest plantation owner in the western half of the colony, by virtue of his impending marriage to Jamie's widowed aunt. Jamie himself was neither rich nor an official of the Crown—but he *was* the proprietor of a large, if still largely vacant, land grant in the backcountry.

He gave a slight shrug and shifted the baby to his other shoulder, settling himself.

"Aye. Well, then. Tell the Lieutenant I shall attend him as soon as may be convenient."

Nothing daunted, MacNair bowed and went off, presumably in search of the other gentlemen on his list.

"And what's all that about?" I asked Jamie. "Oops." I reached up and skimmed a glistening strand of saliva from Jemmy's chin before it could reach Jamie's shirt. "Starting a new tooth, are we?"

"I've plenty of teeth," Jamie assured me, "and so have you, so far as I can see. As to what Hayes may want with me, I canna say for sure. And I dinna mean to find out before I must, either." He cocked one ruddy eyebrow at me, and I laughed.

"Oh, a certain flexibility in that word 'convenient,' is there?"

"I didna say it would be convenient for *him*," Jamie pointed out. "Now, about your petticoat, Sassenach, and why you're scampering about the forest bare-arsed—Duncan, *a charaid*!" The wry look on his face melted into genuine pleasure at sight of Duncan Innes, making his way toward us through a small growth of bare-limbed dogwood.

Duncan clambered over a fallen log, the process made rather awkward by his missing left arm, and arrived on the path beside us, shaking water droplets from his hair. He was already dressed for his wedding, in a clean ruffled shirt and starched linen stock above his kilt, and a coat of scarlet broadcloth trimmed in gold lace, the empty sleeve pinned up with a brooch. I had never seen Duncan look so elegant, and said so.

"Och, well," he said diffidently. "Miss Jo did wish it." He shrugged off the compliment along with the rain, carefully brushing away dead needles and bits of bark that had adhered to his coat in the passage through the pines.

"Brrr! A gruesome day, *Mac Dubh*, and no mistake." He looked up at the sky and shook his head. "Happy the bride the sun shines on; happy the corpse the rain falls on."

"I do wonder just how delighted you can expect the average corpse to be," I said, "whatever the meteorological conditions. But I'm sure Jocasta will be quite happy regardless," I added hastily, seeing a look of bewilderment spread itself across Duncan's features. "And you too, of course!"

"Oh . . . aye," he said, a little uncertainly. "Aye, of course. I thank ye, ma'am."

"When I saw ye coming through the wood, I thought perhaps Corporal MacNair was nippin' at your heels," Jamie said. "You're no on your way to see Archie Hayes, are you?"

Duncan looked quite startled.

"Hayes? No, what would the Lieutenant want wi' me?"

"You were in Hillsborough in September, aye? Here, Sassenach, take this wee squirrel away." Jamie interrupted himself to hand me Jemmy, who had decided to take a more active interest in the proceedings and was attempting to climb his grandfather's torso, digging in his toes and making loud grunting noises. The sudden activity, however, was not Jamie's chief motive for relieving himself of the burden, as I discovered when I accepted Jemmy.

"Thanks a lot," I said, wrinkling my nose. Jamie grinned at me, and turned Duncan up the path, resuming their conversation.

"Hmm," I said, sniffing cautiously. "Finished, are you? No, I thought not." Jemmy closed his eyes, went bright red, and emitted a popping noise like muffled machine-gun fire. I undid his wrappings sufficiently to peek down his back.

"Whoops," I said, and hastily unwound the blanket, just in time. "*What* has your mother been feeding you?"

Thrilled to have escaped his swaddling bands, Jemmy

churned his legs like a windmill, causing a noxious yellowish substance to ooze from the baggy legs of his diaper.

"Pew," I said succinctly, and holding him at arm's length, headed off the path toward one of the tiny rivulets that meandered down the mountainside, thinking that while I could perhaps do without such amenities as indoor plumbing and motorcars, there were times when I sincerely missed things like rubber pants with elasticated legs. To say nothing of toilet rolls.

I found a good spot on the edge of the little stream, with a thick coating of dead leaves. I knelt, laid out a fold of my cloak, and parked Jemmy on it on his hands and knees, pulling the soggy clout off without bothering to unpin it.

"Weee!" he said, sounding surprised as the cold air struck him. He clenched his fat little buttocks and hunched like a small pink toad.

"Ha," I told him. "If you think a cold wind up the bum is bad, just wait." I scooped up a handful of damp yellow-brown leaves, and cleaned him off briskly. A fairly stoic child, he wiggled and squirmed, but didn't screech, instead making high-pitched "Eeeeee" noises as I excavated his crevices.

I flipped him over, and with a hand held prophylactically over the danger zone, administered a similar treatment to his private parts, this eliciting a wide, gummy grin.

"Oh, you *are* a Hieland man, aren't you?" I said, smiling back.

"And just what d'ye mean by that remark, Sassenach?" I looked up to find Jamie leaning against a tree on the other side of the streamlet. The bold colors of his dress tartan and white linen sark stood out bright against the faded autumn foliage; face and hair, though, made him look like some denizen of the wood, all bronze and auburn, with the wind stirring his hair so the free ends danced like the scarlet maple leaves above.

"Well, he's apparently impervious to cold and damp," I said, concluding my labors and discarding the final handful of soiled leaves. "Beyond that . . . well, I've not had much to do with male infants before, but isn't this rather precocious?"

One corner of Jamie's mouth curled up, as he peered at

the prospect revealed under my hand. The tiny appendage stood up stiff as my thumb, and roughly the same size.

"Ah, no," he said. "I've seen a many wee lads in the raw. They all do that now and again." He shrugged, and the smile grew wider. "Now, whether it's only *Scottish* lads, I couldna be saying . . ."

"A talent that improves with age, I daresay," I said dryly. I tossed the dirty clout across the streamlet, where it landed at his feet with a splat. "Get the pins and rinse that out, will you?"

His long, straight nose wrinkled slightly, but he knelt without demur and picked the filthy thing up gingerly between two fingers.

"Oh, so *that's* what ye've done wi' your petticoat," he said. I had opened the large pocket I wore slung at my waist and extracted a clean, folded rectangle of cloth. Not the unbleached linen of the clout he held, but a thick, soft, often-washed wool flannel, dyed a pale red with the juice of currants.

I shrugged, checked Jemmy for the prospect of fresh explosions, and popped him onto the new diaper.

"With three babies all in clouts, and the weather too damp to dry anything properly, we were rather short of clean bits." The bushes around the clearing where we had made our family camp were all festooned with flapping laundry, most of it still wet, owing to the inopportune weather.

"Here." Jamie stretched across the foot-wide span of rock-strewn water to hand me the pins extracted from the old diaper. I took them, careful not to drop them in the stream. My fingers were stiff and chilly, but the pins were valuable; Bree had made them of heated wire, and Roger had carved the capped heads from wood, in accordance with her drawings. Honest-to-goodness safety pins, if a bit larger and cruder than the modern version. The only real defect was the glue used to hold the wooden heads to the wire; made from boiled milk and hoof parings, it was not entirely waterproof, and the heads had to be reglued periodically.

I folded the diaper snugly about Jemmy's loins and thrust a pin through the cloth, smiling at sight of the wooden cap.

Bree had taken one set and carved a small, comical frog—each with a wide, toothless grin—onto each one.

"All right, Froggie, here you go, then." Diaper securely fastened, I sat down and boosted him into my lap, smoothing down his smock and attempting to rewrap his blanket.

"Where did Duncan go?" I asked. "Down to see the Lieutenant?"

Jamie shook his head, bent over his task.

"I told him not to go yet. He *was* in Hillsborough during the troubles there. Best he should wait a bit; then if Hayes should ask, he can swear honestly there's no man here who took part in the riots." He looked up and smiled, without humor. "There won't be, come nightfall."

I watched his hands, large and capable, wringing out the rinsed clout. The scars on his right hand were usually almost invisible, but they stood out now, ragged white lines against his cold-reddened skin. The whole business made me mildly uneasy, though there seemed no direct connection with us.

For the most part, I could think of Governor Tryon with no more than a faint sense of edginess; he was, after all, safely tucked away in his nice new palace in New Bern, separated from our tiny settlement on Fraser's Ridge by three hundred miles of coastal towns, inland plantations, pine forest, piedmont, trackless mountains, and sheer howling wilderness. With all the other things he had to worry about, such as the self-styled "Regulators" who had terrorized Hillsborough, and the corrupt sheriffs and judges who had provoked the terror, I hardly thought he would have time to spare a thought for us. I hoped not.

The uncomfortable fact remained that Jamie held title to a large grant of land in the North Carolina mountains as the gift of Governor Tryon—and Tryon in turn held one small but important fact tucked away in his vest pocket: Jamie was a Catholic. And Royal grants of land could be made only to Protestants, by law.

Given the tiny number of Catholics in the colony, and the lack of organization among them, the question of religion was rarely an issue. There were no Catholic churches, no resident Catholic priests; Father Donahue had made the arduous journey down from Baltimore, at Jocasta's request. Jamie's aunt Jocasta and her late husband, Hector Cameron, had been influential among the Scottish community here for so long that no one would have thought of questioning their religious background, and I thought it likely that few of the Scots with whom we had been celebrating all week knew that we were Papists.

They were, however, likely to notice quite soon. Bree and Roger, who had been handfasted for a year, were to be married by the priest this evening, along with two other Catholic couples from Bremerton—and with Jocasta and Duncan Innes.

"Archie Hayes," I said suddenly. "Is he a Catholic?"

Jamie hung the wet clout from a nearby branch and shook water from his hands.

"I havena asked him," he said, "but I shouldna think so. That is, his father was not; I should be surprised if he was—and him an officer."

"True." The disadvantages of Scottish birth, poverty, and being an ex-Jacobite were sufficiently staggering; amazing enough that Hayes had overcome these to rise to his present position, without the additional burden of the taint of Papistry.

What was troubling me, though, was not the thought of Lieutenant Hayes and his men; it was Jamie. Outwardly, he was calm and assured as ever, with that faint smile always hiding in the corner of his mouth. But I knew him very well; I had seen the two stiff fingers of his right hand—maimed in an English prison—twitch against the side of his leg as he traded jokes and stories with Hayes the night before. Even now, I could see the thin line that formed between his brows when he was troubled, and it wasn't concern over what he was doing.

Was it simply worry over the Proclamation? I couldn't see why that should be, given that none of our folk had been involved in the Hillsborough riots.

". . . a Presbyterian," he was saying. He glanced over at me with a wry smile. "Like wee Roger."

The memory that had niggled at me earlier dropped suddenly into place.

"You knew that," I said. "You *knew* Roger wasn't a Catholic. You saw him baptize that child in Snaketown, when we . . . took him from the Indians." Too late, I saw the shadow cross his face, and bit my tongue. When we took Roger—and left in his place Jamie's dearly loved nephew Ian.

A shadow crossed his face momentarily, but he smiled, pushing away the thought of Ian.

"Aye, I did," he said.

"But Bree—"

"She'd marry the lad if he were a Hottentot," Jamie interrupted. "Anyone can see that. And I canna say I'd object overmuch to wee Roger if he *were* a Hottentot," he added, rather to my surprise.

"You wouldn't?"

Jamie shrugged, and stepped over the tiny creek to my side, wiping wet hands on the end of his plaid.

"He's a braw lad, and he's kind. He's taken the wean as his own and said no word to the lass about it. It's no more than a man should do—but not every man would."

I glanced down involuntarily at Jemmy, curled up cozily in my arms. I tried not to think of it myself, but could not help now and then searching his bluntly amiable features for any trace that might reveal his true paternity.

Brianna had been handfast with Roger, lain with him for one night—and then been raped two days later, by Stephen Bonnet. There was no way to tell for sure who the father had been, and so far Jemmy gave no indication of resembling either man in the slightest. He was gnawing his fist at the moment, with a ferocious scowl of concentration, and with his soft fuzz of red-gold plush, he looked like no one so much as Jamie himself.

"Mm. So why all the insistence on having Roger vetted by a priest?"

"Well, they'll be married in any case," he said logically. "I want the wee lad baptized a Catholic, though." He laid a large hand gently on Jemmy's head, thumb smoothing the tiny red brows. "So if I made a bit of a fuss about MacKenzie, I thought they'd be pleased to agree about *an gille ruaidh* here, aye?"

I laughed, and pulled a fold of blanket up around Jemmy's ears.

"And I thought Brianna had *you* figured out!"

"So does she," he said, with a grin. He bent suddenly and kissed me.

His mouth was soft and very warm. He tasted of bread and butter, and he smelled strongly of fresh leaves and unwashed male, with just the faintest trace of effluvium of diaper.

"Oh, that's nice," I said with approval. "Do it again."

The wood around us was still, in the way of woods. No bird, no beast, just the sough of leaves above and the rush of water underfoot. Constant movement, constant sound—and at the center of it all, a perfect peace. There were a good many people on the mountain, and most of them not that far away—yet just here, just now, we might have been alone on Jupiter.

I opened my eyes and sighed, tasting honey. Jamie smiled at me, and brushed a fallen yellow leaf from my hair. The baby lay in my arms, a heavy, warm weight, the center of the universe.

Neither of us spoke, not wishing to disturb the stillness. It was like being at the tip of a spinning top, I thought—a whirl of events and people going on all round, and a step in one direction or another would plunge us back into that spinning frenzy, but here at the very center—there was peace.

I reached up and brushed a scatter of maple seeds from his shoulder. He seized my hand, and brought it to his mouth with a sudden fierceness that startled me. And yet his lips were tender, the tip of his tongue warm on the fleshy mound at the base of my thumb—the mount of Venus, it's called, love's seat.

He raised his head, and I felt the sudden chill on my hand, where the ancient scar showed white as bone. A letter "J," cut in the skin, his mark on me.

He laid his hand against my face, and I pressed it there with my own, as though I could feel the faded "C" he bore on his own palm, against the cold skin of my cheek. Neither of us spoke, but the pledge was made, as we had made it once before, in a place of sanctuary, our feet on a scrap of bedrock in the shifting sands of threatened war.

It was not near; not yet. But I heard it coming, in the sound of drums and proclamation, saw it in the glint of steel, knew the fear of it in heart and bone when I looked in Jamie's eyes.

The chill had gone, and hot blood throbbed in my hand as though to split the ancient scar and spill my heart's blood for him once again. It would come, and I could not stop it.

But this time, I wouldn't leave him.

I FOLLOWED JAMIE out of the trees, across a scrabble of rocks and sand and tufted grass, to the well-trampled trail that led upward to our campsite. I was counting in my head, readjusting the breakfast requirements yet again, in light of Jamie's revelation that he had invited two more families to join us for the meal.

"Robin McGillivray and Geordie Chisholm," he said, holding back a branch for me to pass. "I thought we should make them welcome; they mean to come and settle on the Ridge."

"Do they," I said, ducking as the branch slapped back behind me. "When? And how many of them are there?"

These were loaded questions. It was close to winter—much too close to count on building even the crudest cabin for shelter. Anyone who came to the mountains now would likely have to live in the big house with us, or crowd into one of the small settlers' cabins that dotted the Ridge. Highlanders could, did, and would live ten to a room when necessary. With my less strongly developed sense of English hospitality, I rather hoped it wouldn't be necessary.

"Six McGillivrays and eight Chisholms," Jamie said, smiling. "The McGillivrays will come in the spring, though. Robin's a gunsmith—he'll have work in Cross Creek for the winter—and his family will bide with kin in Salem—his wife's German—until the weather warms."

"Oh, that's good." Fourteen more for breakfast, then, plus

me and Jamie, Roger and Bree, Marsali and Fergus, Lizzie and her father—Abel MacLennan, mustn't forget him—oh, and the soldier lad who'd rescued Germain, that made twenty-four . . .

"I'll go and borrow some coffee and rice from my aunt, shall I?" Jamie had been reading the growing look of dismay on my features. He grinned, and held out his arms for the baby. "Give me the laddie; we'll go visiting, and leave your hands free for the cooking."

I watched them go with a small sense of relief. Alone, if only for a few moments. I drew a long, deep breath of damp air, becoming aware of the soft patter of the rain on my hood.

I loved Gatherings and social occasions, but was obliged to admit to myself that the strain of unrelieved company for days on end rather got on my nerves. After a week of visiting, gossip, daily medical clinics, and the small but constant crises that attend living rough with a large family group, I was ready to dig a small hole under a log and climb in, just for the sake of a quarter hour's solitude.

Just at the moment, though, it looked as though I might be saved the effort. There were shouts, calls, and snatches of pipe music from higher up the mountain; disturbed by the Governor's Proclamation, the Gathering was reestablishing its normal rhythm, and everyone was going back to their family hearths, to the clearing where the competitions were held, to the livestock pens beyond the creek, or to the wagons set up to sell everything from ribbons and churns to powdered mortar and fresh—well, relatively fresh—lemons. No one needed me for the moment.

It was going to be a very busy day, and this might be my only chance of solitude for a week or more—the trip back would take at least that long, moving slowly with a large party, including babies and wagons. Most of the new tenants had neither horses nor mules, and would make the journey on foot.

I needed a moment to myself, to gather my strength and focus my mind. What focus I had, though, was not on the logistics of breakfast or weddings, nor even on the impending surgery I was contemplating. I was looking farther forward, past the journey, longing for home.

Fraser's Ridge was high in the western mountains, far beyond any town—or even any established roads. Remote and isolated, we had few visitors. Few inhabitants, too, though the population of the Ridge was growing; more than thirty families had come to take up homesteads on Jamie's granted land, under his sponsorship. Most of these were men he had known in prison, at Ardsmuir. I thought Chisholm and McGillivray must be ex-prisoners, too; Jamie had put out a standing invitation for such men, and would hold to it, no matter the expense involved in helping them—or whether we could afford it.

A raven flew silently past, slow and heavy, its feathers burdened by the rain. Ravens were birds of omen; I wondered whether this one meant us good or ill. Rare for any bird to fly in such weather—that must mean it was a special omen.

I knocked the heel of my hand against my head, trying to smack the superstition out of it. Live with Highlanders long enough, and every damn rock and tree meant something!

Perhaps it did, though. There were people all round me on the mountain—I knew that—and yet I felt quite alone, shielded by the rain and fog. The weather was still cold, but I was not. The blood thrummed near the surface of my skin, and I felt heat rise in my palms. I reached a hand out to the pine that stood by me, drops of water trembling on each needle, its bark black with wet. I breathed its scent and let the water touch my skin, cool as vapor. The rain fell in shushing stillness all around me, dampening my clothes 'til they clung to me softly, like clouds upon the mountain.

Jamie had told me once that he must live on a mountain, and I knew now why this was so—though I could in no wise have put the notion into words. All my scattered thoughts receded, as I listened for the voice of rocks and trees—and heard the bell of the mountain strike once, somewhere deep beneath my feet.

I might have stood thus enchanted for some time, all thought of breakfast forgotten, but the voices of rocks and trees hushed and vanished with the clatter of feet on the nearby path.

"Mrs. Fraser."

It was Archie Hayes himself, resplendent in bonnet and sword despite the wet. If he was surprised to see me standing by the path alone, he didn't show it, but inclined his head in courteous greeting.

"Lieutenant." I bowed back, feeling my cheeks flush as though he had caught me in the midst of bathing.

"Will your husband be about, ma'am?" he asked, voice casual. Despite my discomfiture, I felt a stab of wariness. Young Corporal MacNair had come to fetch Jamie, and failed. If the mountain had come to Mohammed now, the matter wasn't casual. Was Hayes intending to drag Jamie into some sort of witch-hunt for Regulators?

"I suppose so. I don't really know *where* he is," I said, consciously not looking up the hill to the spot where Jocasta's big tent showed its canvas peak among a stand of chestnut trees.

"Ah, I expect he'll be that busy," Hayes said comfortably. "A great deal to do for a man like himself, and this the last day of the Gathering."

"Yes. I expect . . . er . . . yes."

The conversation died, and I was left in a state of increasing discomfort, wondering how on earth I was to escape without inviting the Lieutenant to breakfast. Even an Englishwoman couldn't get away with the rudeness of not offering food without exciting remark.

"Er . . . Corporal MacNair said you wanted to see Farquard Campbell as well," I said, seizing the bull by the horns. "Perhaps Jamie's gone to talk with him. Mr. Campbell, I mean." I waved helpfully toward the Campbells' family campsite, which lay on the far side of the slope, nearly a quarter mile from Jocasta's.

Hayes blinked, drops running from his lashes down his cheeks.

"Aye," he said. "Perhaps that's so." He stood a moment longer, then tipped his cap to me. "Good day to ye, mum." He turned away up the path—toward Jocasta's tent. I stood watching him go, all sense of peace destroyed.

"Damn," I said under my breath, and set off to see about breakfast.

2

LOAVES AND FISHES

WE HAD CHOSEN A SITE well off the main path, but situated in a small, rocky clearing with a good view of the wide creekbank below. Glancing downward through a scrim of holly bushes, I could see the flash of green-and-black tartans as the last of the soldiers dispersed; Archie Hayes encouraged his men to mingle with the people at the Gathering, and most were only too glad to obey.

I wasn't sure whether this policy of Archie's was dictated by guile, penury, or simply humanitarianism. Many of his soldiers were young, separated from home and family; they were glad of the chance to hear Scottish voices again, to be welcomed at a homely fireside, offered brose and parritch, and to bask in the momentary warmth of familiarity.

As I came out of the trees, I saw that Marsali and Lizzie were making a small fuss of the bashful young soldier who had fished Germain out of the creek. Fergus stood close to the fire, wisps of steam rising from his wet garments, muttering in French as he rubbed Germain's head briskly with a towel, one-handed. His hook was braced against the little boy's shoulder to keep him steady, and the blond head wobbled back and forth, Germain's face quite tranquil, in complete disregard of his father's scolding.

Neither Roger nor Brianna were anywhere in sight, but I was rather alarmed to see Abel MacLennan sitting on the far side of the clearing, nibbling a bit of toasted bread on a stick. Jamie was already back with the borrowed supplies, which he was unpacking on the ground next to the fire. He was frowning to himself, but the frown melted into a smile at sight of me.

"There ye are, Sassenach!" he said, rising to his feet. "What kept ye?"

"Oh . . . I met an acquaintance on the trail," I said, with a significant look toward the young soldier. It was evidently not significant enough, since Jamie knitted his brows in puzzlement.

"The Lieutenant is looking for you," I hissed, leaning close to him.

"Well, I kent *that*, Sassenach," he said, in a normal tone of voice. "He'll find me soon enough."

"Yes, but . . . ahem." I cleared my throat and raised my brows, glancing pointedly from Abel MacLennan to the young soldier. Jamie's notions of hospitality wouldn't countenance having his guests dragged away from under his rooftree, and I would have supposed that the same principle applied to his campfire as well. The young soldier might find it awkward to arrest MacLennan, but I was sure the Lieutenant would have no such hesitation.

Jamie looked rather amused. Raising his own brows, he took my arm, and led me over to the young man.

"My dear," he said formally, "may I present Private Andrew Ogilvie, late of the village of Kilburnie? Private Ogilvie, my wife."

Private Ogilvie, a ruddy-faced boy with dark curly hair, blushed and bowed.

"Your servant, mum!"

Jamie squeezed my arm lightly.

"Private Ogilvie was just telling me that the regiment is bound for Portsmouth, in Virginia—there to take ship for Scotland. Ye'll be glad to see home, I expect, lad?"

"Oh, aye, sir!" the lad said fervently. "The regiment will disband in Aberdeen, and then I'm off home, so fast as my legs will carry me!"

"The regiment is disbanding?" Fergus asked, coming to join the conversation, a towel draped round his neck and Germain in his arms.

"Aye, sir. With the Frenchies settled—er, beggin' your

pardon, sir—and the Indians safe, there's naught for us to do here, and the Crown willna pay us to sit at home," the lad said ruefully. "Peace may be a guid thing, all in all, and I'm glad of it, surely. But there's no denying as it's hard on a soldier."

"Almost as hard as war, aye?" Jamie said dryly. The boy flushed darkly; young as he was, he couldn't have seen much in the way of actual fighting. The Seven Years War had been over for nearly ten years—at which time Private Ogilvie would likely still have been a barefoot lad in Kilburnie.

Ignoring the boy's embarrassment, Jamie turned to me.

"The lad tells me," he added, "that the Sixty-seventh is the last regiment left in the Colonies."

"The last Highland regiment?" I asked.

"No, mum, the last of the Crown's regular troops. There are the garrisons here and there, I suppose, but all of the standing regiments have been recalled to England or Scotland. We're the last—and behind our time, too. We meant to sail from Charleston, but things went agley there, and so we're bound for Portsmouth now, so fast as we can make speed. It's late in the year, but the Lieutenant's had word of a ship that may risk passage to take us. If not—" He shrugged, glumly philosophic. "Then we shall winter in Portsmouth, I suppose, and make shift as we can."

"So England means to leave us unprotected?" Marsali looked rather shocked at the thought.

"Oh, I shouldna think there's any great danger, mum," Private Ogilvie assured her. "We've dealt wi' the Frenchies for good and all, and the Indians willna be up to much without the frogs to stir them up. Everything's been quite peaceful for a good time now, and doubtless it'll stay so." I made a small noise in the back of my throat, and Jamie squeezed my elbow lightly.

"Have ye not thought perhaps to stay, then?" Lizzie had been peeling and grating potatoes while listening to this; she put down the bowl of glistening white shreds by the fire and began to smear grease on the griddle. "Stay in the Colonies, I mean. There's plenty of land still to be had, to the west."

"Oh." Private Ogilvie glanced down at her, her white

kerch modestly bent over her work, and his color deepened again. "Well, I will say I've heard worse prospects, miss. But I am bound to go wi' my regiment, I'm afraid."

Lizzie picked up two eggs and cracked them neatly against the side of the bowl. Her own face, usually pale as whey, bore a faint pink echo of the Private's rich blush.

"Ah. Well, it's a great pity that ye should go awa so soon," she said. Her pale blond lashes swept down against her cheeks. "Still, we'll not send ye away on an empty stomach."

Private Ogilvie went slightly pinker round the ears.

"That's . . . verra kind of ye, miss. Verra kind indeed."

Lizzie glanced up shyly, and blushed more deeply.

Jamie coughed gently and excused himself, leading me away from the fire.

"Christ," he said in an undertone, bending down so I could hear him. "And she's been a woman less than a full day, too! Have ye been givin' her lessons, Sassenach, or are women just born wi' it?"

"Natural talent, I expect," I said circumspectly.

The unexpected advent of Lizzie's menarche after supper last night had in fact been the straw that broke the camel's back, with regard to clean clouts, and the precipitating event that had caused me to sacrifice my petticoat. Lizzie naturally had no menstrual cloths with her, and I didn't want to oblige her to share the children's diapers.

"Mmphm. I suppose I'd best begin looking for a husband for her, then," Jamie said in resignation.

"A husband! Why, she's scarcely fifteen!"

"Aye, so?" He glanced at Marsali, who was rubbing Fergus's dark hair dry with the towel, and then back at Lizzie and her soldier, and raised a cynical brow at me.

"Aye, so, yourself," I said, a little crossly. All right, Marsali *had* been only fifteen when she married Fergus. That didn't mean—

"The point being," Jamie went on, dismissing Lizzie for the moment, "that the regiment leaves for Portsmouth tomorrow; they havena got either time nor disposition to trouble with this business in Hillsborough—that's Tryon's concern."

"But what Hayes said—"

"Oh, if anyone tells him anything, I'm sure he'll send the

depositions along to New Bern—but as for himself, I imagine he'd not much care if the Regulators set fire to the Governor's Palace, so long as it doesna delay his sailing."

I heaved a deep sigh, reassured. If Jamie was right, the last thing Hayes would do was take prisoners, no matter what the evidence to hand. MacLennan was safe, then.

"But what do you suppose Hayes wants with you and the others, then?" I asked, bending to rummage in one of the wicker hampers for another loaf of bread. "He *is* hunting you—in person."

Jamie glanced back over his shoulder, as though expecting the Lieutenant to appear at any moment through the holly bushes. As the screen of prickly green remained intact, he turned back to me, frowning slightly.

"I dinna ken," he said, shaking his head, "but it's naught to do with this business of Tryon's. If it was that, he might have told me last night—for that matter, if he cared himself about the matter, he *would* have told me last night," he added. "No, Sassenach, depend upon it, the rioters are no more than a matter of duty to wee Archie Hayes.

"As for what he wants wi' me—" He leaned over my shoulder to swipe a finger round the top of the honey pot. "I dinna mean to trouble about it until I must. I've three kegs of whisky left, and I mean to turn them into a plowshare, a scythe blade, three ax-heids, ten pound of sugar, a horse, and an astrolabe before this evening. Which is a conjuring trick that might take some attention, aye?" He drew the sticky tip of his finger gently across my lips, then turned my head toward him and bent to kiss me.

"An astrolabe?" I said, tasting honey. I kissed him back. "Whatever for?"

"And then I want to go home," he whispered, ignoring the question. His forehead was pressed against mine, and his eyes very blue.

"I want to take ye to bed—*in* my bed. And I mean to spend the rest of the day thinking what to do to ye once I've got ye there. So wee Archie can just go and play at marbles with his ballocks, aye?"

"An excellent thought," I whispered back. "Care to tell him that yourself?"

My eye had caught the flash of a green-and-black tartan on the other side of the clearing, but when Jamie straightened up and whirled round, I saw that the visitor was in fact not Lieutenant Hayes but rather John Quincy Myers, who was sporting a soldier's plaid wrapped round his waist, the ends fluttering gaily in the breeze.

This added a further touch of color to Myers's already striking sartorial splendor. Extremely tall, and decorated from the top down with a slouch hat stuck through with several needles and a turkey quill, two ragged pheasant feathers knotted into his long black hair, a vest of dyed porcupine quills worn over a beaded shirt, his usual breechclout, and leggings wrapped with strings of small bells, the mountain man was hard to miss.

"Friend James!" John Quincy smiled broadly at sight of Jamie, and hastened forward, hand extended and bells chiming. "Thought I should find you at your breakfast!"

Jamie blinked slightly at this vision, but gamely returned the mountain man's encompassing handshake.

"Aye, John. Will ye join us?"

"Er . . . yes," I chimed in, with a surreptitious look into the food hamper. "Please do!"

John Quincy bowed ceremoniously to me, sweeping off his hat.

"Your servant, ma'am, and I'm much obliged. Maybe later. Right now, I come to fetch away Mr. Fraser, though. He's wanted, urgent-like."

"By whom?" Jamie asked warily.

"Robbie McGillivray, he says his name is. You know the man?"

"Aye, I do." Whatever Jamie knew about McGillivray, it was causing him to delve into the small chest where he kept his pistols. "What's the trouble?"

"Well." John Quincy scratched meditatively at his bushy black beard. " 'Twas his wife as asked me to come find you, and she don't speak what you'd call right good English, so may be as I've muddled the account of it a bit. But what I *think* she said to me was as how there was a thief-taker who'd grabbed holt of her son, sayin' as how the boy was one o' the ruffians who broke up Hillsborough, and meanin' to take him to the gaol in New Bern. Only Robbie, he says no one's takin' a son of his anywhere, and—well, after that, the poor woman got right flustered and I couldn't make out but one word to the dozen. But I do believe Robbie would 'preciate it if you'd come by and lend a hand with the proceedings."

Jamie grabbed Roger's bloodstained green coat, which was hung on a bush waiting to be cleaned. Shrugging into it, he thrust the newly loaded pistol through his belt.

"Where?" he said.

Myers gestured economically with one large thumb, and pushed off into the holly bushes, Jamie at his heels.

Fergus, who had been listening to this exchange, Germain in his arms, set the boy down at Marsali's feet.

"I must go help *Grand-père*," he told Germain. He picked up a stick of firewood and put it into the little boy's hands. "You stay; protect *Maman* and little Joan from bad people."

"Oui, Papa." Germain scowled fiercely under his blond fringe and took a firm grip on his stick, settling himself to defend the camp.

Marsali, MacLennan, Lizzie, and Private Ogilvie had been watching the byplay with rather glazed looks. As Fergus picked up another length of firewood and plunged purposefully into the holly bushes, Private Ogilvie came to life, stirring uneasily.

"Er . . ." he said. "Perhaps I . . . should I go for my sergeant, do ye think, ma'am? If there's like to be any trouble . . ."

"No, no," I said hurriedly. The last thing we needed was for Archie Hayes and his regiment to show up en masse. This struck me as the sort of situation which would benefit strongly from being kept unofficial.

"I'm sure everything will be quite all right. It's sure to be nothing but a misunderstanding. Mr. Fraser will sort it directly, never fear." Even as I spoke, I was sidling round the fire toward the spot where my medical supplies lay, sheltered from the drizzle under a sheet of canvas. Reaching under the edge, I grabbed my small emergency kit.

"Lizzie, why don't you give Private Ogilvie some of the strawberry preserves for his toast? And Mr. MacLennan would like a bit of honey in his coffee, I'm sure. Do excuse me, won't you, Mr. MacLennan, I must just go and . . . er . . ." Smiling inanely, I sidled through the holly leaves. As the branches swished and crackled behind me, I paused to take my bearings. A faint chime of bells reached me on the rainy wind; I turned toward the sound, and broke into a run.

IT WAS SOME WAY; I was out of breath and sweating from the exercise by the time I caught them up near the competition field. Things were just getting under way; I could hear the buzz of talk from the crowd of men gathering, but no shouts of encouragement or howls of disappointment as yet. A few brawny specimens stamped to and fro, stripped to the waist and swinging their arms to limber up; the local "strongmen" of various settlements.

The drizzle had started up again; the wetness gleamed on curving shoulders and plastered swirls of dark body hair flat against the pale skins of chests and forearms. I had no time to appreciate the spectacle, though; John Quincy threaded his way adroitly through the knots of spectators and competitors, waving cordially to this and that acquaintance as we passed. On the far side of the crowd, a small man detached himself from the mass and came hurrying to meet us.

"*Mac Dubh!* Ye've come, then—that's good."

"Nay bother, Robbie," Jamie assured him. "What's to do, then?"

McGillivray, who looked distinctly harried, glanced at the strongmen and their supporters, then jerked his head toward the nearby trees. We followed him, unnoticed by the crowd gathering round two large stones wrapped with rope, which I assumed some of the strongmen present were about to prove their prowess by lifting.

"It's your son, is it, Rob?" Jamie asked, dodging a water-filled pine branch.

"Aye," Robbie answered, "or it was."

That sounded sinister. I saw Jamie's hand brush the butt of his pistol; mine went to my medical kit.

"What's happened?" I asked. "Is he hurt?"

"Not him," McGillivray replied cryptically, and ducked ahead, beneath a drooping chestnut bough hung with scarlet creeper.

Just beyond was a small open space, not really big enough to be called a clearing, tufted with dead grass and studded with pine saplings. As Fergus and I ducked under the creeper after Jamie, a large woman in homespun whirled toward us, shoulders hunching as she raised the broken tree limb she clutched in one hand. She saw McGillivray, though, and relaxed fractionally.

"Wer ist das?" she asked suspiciously, eyeing us. Then John Quincy appeared from under the creeper, and she lowered the club, her solidly handsome features relaxing further.

"Ha, Myers! You brung me den Jamie, *oder*?" She cast me a curious look, but was too busy glancing between Fergus and Jamie to inspect me closely.

"Aye, love, this is Jamie Roy—*Sheumais Mac Dubh*." McGillivray hastened to take credit for Jamie's appearance, putting a respectful hand on his sleeve. "My wife, Ute, *Mac Dubh*. And *Mac Dubh*'s son," he added, waving vaguely at Fergus.

Ute McGillivray looked like a Valkyrie on a starchy diet; tall, very blond, and broadly powerful.

"Your servant, ma'am," Jamie said, bowing.

"Madame," Fergus echoed, making her a courtly leg.

Mrs. McGillivray dropped them a low curtsy in return, eyes fixed on the prominent bloodstains streaking the front of Jamie's—or rather, Roger's—coat.

"Mein Herr," she murmured, looking impressed. She turned and beckoned to a young man of seventeen or eighteen, who had been lurking in the background. He bore such a marked resemblance to his small, wiry, dark-haired father that his identity could scarcely be in doubt.

"Manfred," his mother announced proudly. "*Mein* laddie."

Jamie inclined his head in grave acknowledgment.

"Mr. McGillivray."

"Ah . . . your s-servant, sir?" The boy sounded rather dubious about it, but put out his hand to be shaken.

"A pleasure to make your acquaintance, sir," Jamie

assured him, shaking it. The courtesies duly observed, he looked briefly round at the quiet surroundings, raising one eyebrow.

"I had heard that you were suffering some inconvenience wi' regard to a thief-taker. Do I take it that the matter has been resolved?" He glanced in question from McGillivray Junior to McGillivray Senior.

The three McGillivrays exchanged assorted glances among themselves. Robin McGillivray gave an apologetic cough.

"Well, not to say *resolved*, quite, *Mac Dubh*. That is to say . . ." He trailed off, the harried look returning to his eyes.

Mrs. McGillivray gave him a stern look, then turned to Jamie.

"*Ist kein* bother," she told him. "*Ich haf den* wee ball of shite safe put. But only we want to know, how we best *den Korpus* hide?"

"The . . . body?" I said, rather faintly.

Even Jamie looked a bit disturbed at that.

"Ye've killed him, Rob?"

"Me?" McGillivray looked shocked. "Christ's sake, *Mac Dubh*, what d'ye take me for?"

Jamie raised the eyebrow again; evidently the thought of McGillivray committing violence was scarcely far-fetched. McGillivray had the grace to look abashed.

"Aye, well. I suppose I might have—and I did—well, but, *Mac Dubh*! That business at Ardsmuir was all long ago and done wi', aye?"

"Aye," Jamie said. "It was. What about this business wi' the thief-taker, though? Where is he?"

I heard a muffled giggle behind me, and swung round to see that the rest of the family McGillivray, silent 'til now, was nonetheless present. Three teenaged girls sat in a row on a dead log behind a screen of saplings, all immaculately attired in clean white caps and aprons, only slightly wilted with the rain.

"*Meine* lassies," Mrs. McGillivray announced, with a wave in their direction—unnecessarily, since all three of the girls looked like smaller versions of herself. "Hilda, Inga, *und* Senga."

Fergus bowed elegantly to the three.

"Enchanté, Mesdemoiselles."

The girls giggled and bobbed their heads in response, but without rising, which struck me as odd. Then I noticed some disturbance taking place under the skirt of the oldest girl; a sort of heaving flutter, accompanied by a muffled grunt. Hilda swung her heel sharply into whatever it was, all the time smiling brightly at me.

There was another grunt—much louder this time—from under the skirt, which caused Jamie to start and turn in her direction.

Still smiling brightly, Hilda bent and delicately picked up the edge of her skirt, under which I could see a frantic face, bisected by a dark strip of cloth tied round his mouth.

"That's him," said Robbie, sharing his wife's talent for stating the obvious.

"I see." Jamie's fingers twitched slightly against the side of his kilt. "Ah . . . perhaps we could have him out, then?"

Robbie motioned to the girls, who all stood up together and stepped aside, revealing a small man who lay against the base of the dead log, bound hand and foot with an assortment of what looked like women's stockings, and gagged with someone's kerchief. He was wet, muddy, and slightly battered round the edges.

Myers bent and hoisted the man to his feet, holding him by the collar.

"Well, he ain't much to look at," the mountain man said critically, squinting at the man as though evaluating a substandard beaver skin. "I guess thief-takin' don't pay so well as ye might think."

The man was in fact skinny and rather ragged, as well as disheveled, furious—and frightened. Ute sniffed contemptuously.

"Saukerl!" she said, and spat neatly on the thief-taker's boots. Then she turned to Jamie, full of charm.

"So, *mein Herr*. How we are to kill him best?"

The thief-taker's eyes bulged, and he writhed in Myers's

grip. He bucked and twisted, making frantic gargling noises behind the gag. Jamie looked him over, rubbing a knuckle across his mouth, then glanced at Robbie, who gave a slight shrug, with an apologetic glance at his wife.

Jamie cleared his throat.

"Mmphm. Ye had something in mind, perhaps, ma'am?"

Ute beamed at this evidence of sympathy with her intentions, and drew a long dagger from her belt.

"I thought maybe to butcher, *wie ein Schwein, ja?* But see . . ." She poked the thief-taker gingerly between the ribs; he yelped behind the gag, and a small spot of blood bloomed on his ragged shirt.

"Too much *Blut*," she explained, with a moue of disappointment. She waved at the screen of trees, behind which the stone-lifting seemed to be proceeding well. "*Die Leute* will schmell."

"Schmell?" I glanced at Jamie, thinking this some unfamiliar German expression. He coughed, and brushed a hand under his nose. "Oh, *smell*!" I said, enlightened. "Er, yes, I think they might."

"I dinna suppose we'd better shoot him, then," Jamie said thoughtfully. "If ye're wanting to avoid attention, I mean."

"I say we break his neck," Robbie McGillivray said, squinting judiciously at the trussed thief-taker. "That's easy enough."

"You think?" Fergus squinted in concentration. "I say a knife. If you stab in the right spot, the blood is not so much. The kidney, just beneath the ribs in back . . . eh?"

The captive appeared to take exception to these suggestions, judging from the urgent sounds proceeding from behind the gag, and Jamie rubbed his chin dubiously.

"Well, that's no verra difficult," he agreed. "Or strangle him. But he *will* lose his bowels. If it were to be a question of the smell, even crushing his skull . . . but tell me, Robbie, how does the man come to be here?"

"Eh?" Robbie looked blank.

"You're no camped nearby?" Jamie waved a hand briefly at the tiny clearing, making his meaning clear. There was no trace of hearthfire; in fact, no one had camped on this side of the creek. And yet all the McGillivrays were here.

"Oh, no," Robbie said, comprehension blossoming on his spare features. "Nay, we're camped some distance up. Only, we came to have a wee keek at the heavies"—he jerked his head toward the competition field—"and the friggin' vulture spied our Freddie and took hold of him, so as to drag him off." He cast an unfriendly look at the thief-taker, and I saw that a coil of rope dangled snakelike from the man's belt. A pair of iron manacles lay on the ground nearby, the dark metal already laced with orange rust from the damp.

"We saw him grab aholt of Brother," Hilda put in at this point. "So we grabbed aholt of *him* and pushed him through here, where nobody could see. When he said he meant to take Brother away to the sheriff, me and my sisters knocked him down and sat on him, and Mama kicked him a few times."

Ute patted her daughter fondly on one sturdy shoulder.

"They are *gut*, strong *Mädchen*, *meine* lasses," she told Jamie. "Ve *komm* see *hier die Wettkämpfer*, maybe choose husband for Inga or Senga. Hilda *hat einen Mann* already promised," she added, with an air of satisfaction.

She looked Jamie over frankly, her eye dwelling approvingly on his height, the breadth of his shoulders, and the general prosperity of his appearance.

"He is fine, big, your *Mann*," she said to me. "You haf sons, maybe?"

"No, I'm afraid not," I said apologetically. "Er . . . Fergus is married to my husband's daughter," I added, seeing her gaze shift appraisingly to Fergus.

The thief-taker appeared to feel that the subject was drifting somewhat afield, and summoned attention back to himself with an indignant squeal behind his gag. His face, which had gone pale at the discussion of his theoretical demise, had grown quite red again, and his hair was matted down across his forehead in spikes.

"Oh, aye," Jamie said, noticing. "Perhaps we should let the gentleman have a word?"

Robbie narrowed his eyes at this, but reluctantly nodded. The competitions had got well under way by now, and there was a considerable racket emanating from the field; no one would notice the odd shout over here.

"Don't let 'em kill me, sir! You know it ain't right!" Hoarse from his ordeal, the man fixed his appeal on Jamie as soon as the gag was removed. "I'm only doin' as I ought, delivering a criminal to justice!"

"Ha!" all the McGillivrays said at once. Unanimous as their sentiment appeared to be, the expression of it immediately disintegrated into a confusion of expletives, opinions, and a random volley of kicks aimed at the gentleman's shins by Inga and Senga.

"Stop that!" Jamie said, raising his voice enough to be heard over the uproar. As this had no result, he grabbed McGillivray Junior by the scruff of the neck and roared, *"Ruhe!"* at the top of his lungs, which startled them into momentary silence, with guilty looks over their shoulders in the direction of the competition field.

"Now, then," Jamie said firmly. "Myers, bring the gentleman, if ye will. Rob, Fergus, come along with ye. *Bitte*, Madame?" He bowed to Mrs. McGillivray, who blinked at him, but then nodded in slow acquiescence. Jamie rolled an eye at me, then, still holding Manfred by the neck, he marched the male contingent off toward the creek, leaving me in charge of the ladies.

"Your *Mann*—he will save my son?" Ute turned to me, fair brows knitted in concern.

"He'll try." I glanced at the girls, who were huddled together behind their mother. "Do you know whether your brother *was* at Hillsborough?"

The girls looked at one another, and silently elected Inga to speak.

"Well, *ja*, he was, then," she said, a little defiantly. "But he wasna riotin', not a bit of it. He'd only gone for to have a bit of harness mended, and was caught up in the mob."

I caught a quick glance exchanged between Hilda and Senga, and deduced that this was perhaps not the entire story. Still, it wasn't my place to judge, thank goodness.

Mrs. McGillivray's eyes were fixed on the men, who stood murmuring together some distance away. The thief-taker had been untied, save for his hands, which remained bound. He stood with his back against a tree, looking like a cornered rat, eyeteeth showing in a snarl of defiance. Jamie and Myers were both looming over him, while Fergus stood by, frowning attentively, his chin propped on his hook. Rob McGillivray had taken out a knife, with which he was contemplatively flicking small chips of wood from a pine twig, glancing now and then at the thief-taker with an air of dark intent.

"I'm sure Jamie will be able to . . . er . . . do something," I said, privately hoping that the something wouldn't involve too much violence. The unwelcome thought occurred to me that the diminutive thief-taker would probably fit tidily in one of the empty food hampers.

"Gut." Ute McGillivray nodded slowly, still watching. "Better that I do not kill him." Her eyes turned suddenly back to me, light blue and very bright. "But I vill do it, if I must."

I believed her.

"I see," I said carefully. "But—I do beg your pardon—but even if that man took your son, could you not go to the sheriff too, and explain . . ."

More glances among the girls. This time it was Hilda who spoke.

"*Nein*, ma'am. See, it wouldna have been sae bad, had the thief-taker come on us at the camp. But down here—" She widened her eyes, nodding toward the competition field, where a muffled thud and a roar of approval marked some successful effort.

The difficulty, apparently, was Hilda's fiancé, one Davey Morrison, from Hunter's Point. Mr. Morrison was a farmer of some substance, and a man of worth, as well as an athlete skilled in the arcana of stone-throwing and caber-tossing. He had family, too—parents, uncles, aunts, cousins—all of the most upright character and—I gathered—rather judgmental attitudes.

Had Manfred been taken by a thief-taker in front of such a crowd, filled with Davey Morrison's relations, word would have spread at the speed of light, and the scandal would result in the prompt rupture of Hilda's engagement—a prospect that clearly perturbed Ute McGillivray much more than the notion of cutting the thief-taker's throat.

"Bad, too, I kill him and someone see," she said frankly, waving at the thin scrim of trees shielding us from the competition field. "*Die* Morrisons would not like."

"I suppose they might not," I murmured, wondering whether Davey Morrison had any idea what he was getting into. "But you—"

"I vill haf *meine* lassies well wed," she said firmly, nodding several times in reinforcement. "I find *gut* men *für Sie*, fine big men, *mit* land, *mit* money." She put an arm round Senga's shoulders and hugged her tight. *"Nicht wahr, Liebchen?"*

"*Ja*, Mama," Senga murmured, and laid her neat capped head affectionately on Mrs. McGillivray's broad bosom.

Something was happening on the men's side of things; the thief-taker's hands had been untied, and he stood rubbing his wrists, no longer scowling, but listening to whatever Jamie was saying with an expression of wariness. He glanced at us, then at Robin McGillivray, who said something to him and nodded emphatically. The thief-taker's jaw worked, as though he were chewing over an idea.

"So you all came down to watch the competitions this morning and look for suitable prospects? Yes, I see."

Jamie reached into his sporran and drew out something, which he held under the thief-taker's nose, as though inviting him to smell it. I couldn't make out what it was at this distance, but the thief-taker's face suddenly changed, going from wariness to alarmed disgust.

"*Ja*, only to look." Mrs. McGillivray was not watching; she patted Senga and let her go. "Ve go now to Salem, where *ist meine Familie.* Maybe ve find there a good *Mann*, too."

Myers had stepped back from the confrontation now, his shoulders drooping in relaxation. He inserted a finger under the edge of his breechclout, scratched his buttocks comfortably, and glanced around, evidently no longer interested in the proceedings. Seeing me looking in his direction, he ambled back through the sapling grove.

"No need to worry more, ma'am," he assured Mrs. McGillivray. "I knew Jamie Roy would take care of it, and so he has. Your lad's safe."

"Ja?" she said. She looked doubtfully toward the sapling grove, but it was true; the attitudes of all the men had relaxed now, and Jamie was handing the thief-taker back his set of

manacles. I saw the way he handled them, with brusque distaste. He had worn irons, at Ardsmuir.

"Gott sei dank," Mrs. McGillivray said, with an explosive sigh. Her massive form seemed suddenly to diminish as the breath went out of her.

The little man was leaving, making his way away from us, toward the creek. The sound of the swinging irons at his belt reached us in a faint chime of metal, heard between the shouts of the crowd behind us. Jamie and Rob McGillivray stood close together, talking, while Fergus watched the thief-taker's departure, frowning slightly.

"Exactly what did Jamie tell him?" I asked Myers.

"Oh. Well." The mountain man gave me a broad, gap-toothed grin. "Jamie Roy told him serious-like that it was surely luck for the thief-taker—his name's Boble, by the way, Harley Boble—that we done come upon y'all when we did. He give him to understand that if we hadn't, then this lady here"—he bowed toward Ute—"would likely have taken him home in her wagon, and slaughtered him like a hog, safe out of sight."

Myers rubbed a knuckle under his red-veined nose and chortled softly in his beard.

"Boble said as how he didn't believe it, he thought she was only a-tryin' to scare him with that knife. But then Jamie Roy leaned down close, confidential-like, and said he mighta thought the same—only that he'd heard so much about Frau McGillivray's reputation as a famous sausage-maker, and had had the privilege of bein' served some of it to his breakfast this morning. Right about then, Boble started to lose the color in his face, and when Jamie Roy pulled out a bit of sausage to show him—"

"Oh, dear," I said, with a vivid memory of exactly what that sausage smelled like. I had bought it the day before from a vendor on the mountain, only to discover that it had been improperly cured, and once sliced, smelled so strongly of rotting blood that no one had been able to stomach it at supper. Jamie had wrapped the offending remainder in his handkerchief and put it in his sporran, intending either to procure a refund or to shove it down the vendor's throat. "I see."

Myers nodded, turning to Ute.

"And your husband, ma'am—bless his soul, Rob McGillivray's a real born liar—chimes in solemn-like, agreeing to it all, shakin' his head and sayin' as how he's got his work cut out to shoot enough meat for you."

The girls tittered.

"Da can't kill anything," Inga said softly to me. "He willna even wring a chicken's neck."

Myers raised his shoulders in a good-humored shrug, as Jamie and Rob made their way toward us through the wet grass.

"So Jamie promised on his word as a gentleman to protect Boble from you, and Boble promised on *his* word as a . . . well, he said as he'd keep clear of young Manfred."

"Hmp," said Ute, looking rather disconcerted. She didn't mind at all being considered an habitual murderess, and was quite pleased that Manfred was out of danger—but was rather put out at having her reputation as a sausage-maker maligned.

"As though I vould effer make such shite," she said, wrinkling her nose in disdain at the odorous lump of meat Jamie offered for her inspection. "Pfaugh. *Ratzfleisch*." She waved it away with a fastidious gesture, then turned to her husband and said something softly in German.

Then she took a deep breath and expanded once more, gathering all her children like a hen clucking after chicks, urging them to thank Jamie properly for his help. He flushed slightly at the chorus of thanks, bowing to her.

"Gern geschehen," he said. *"Euer ergebener Diener, Frau Ute."*

She beamed at him, composure restored, as he turned to say something in parting to Rob.

"Such a fine, big *Mann*," she murmured, shaking her head slightly as she looked him up and down. Then she turned, and caught my glance from Jamie to Rob—for while the gunsmith was a handsome man, with close-clipped, dark curly hair and a chiseled face, he was also fine-boned as a sparrow, and some inches shorter than his wife, reaching approximately to the level of her brawny shoulder. I couldn't help wondering, given her apparent admiration for large men . . .

"Oh, vell," she said, and shrugged apologetically. "Luff, you know." She sounded as though love were an unfortunate but unavoidable condition.

I glanced at Jamie, who was carefully swaddling his sausage before tucking it back into his sporran. "Well, yes," I said. "I do."

BY THE TIME we returned to our own campsite, the Chisholms were just departing, having been capably fed by the girls. Fortunately, Jamie had brought plenty of food from Jocasta's camp, and I sat down at last to a pleasant meal of potato fritters, buttered bannocks, fried ham, and—at last!—coffee, wondering just what *else* might happen today. There was plenty of time; the sun was barely above the trees, almost invisible behind the drifting rain clouds.

A little later, pleasantly full of breakfast, and with a third cup of coffee to hand, I went and threw back the canvas covering what I thought of as my medical supply dump. It was time to begin the business of organizing for the morning's surgery; looking at jars of sutures, restocking the herb jars in my chest, refilling the large alcohol bottle, and brewing up the medicines that must be made fresh.

Somewhat depleted of the commoner herbs I had brought with me, my stock had been augmented by the good offices of Myers, who had brought me several rare and useful things from the Indian villages to the north, and by judicious trading with Murray MacLeod, an ambitious young apothecary who had made his way inland and set up shop in Cross Creek.

I bit the inside of my cheek, considering young Murray. He harbored the usual sort of nasty notions that passed for medical wisdom nowadays—and was not shy about asserting the superiority of such scientific methods as bleeding and blistering over the old-fashioned herbcraft that such ignorant crones as myself were prone to practice!

Still, he was a Scot, and thus possessed of a strong streak of pragmatism. He had given Jamie's powerful frame one look and hastily swallowed the more insulting of his opinions. I had six ounces of wormwood and a jar of wild ginger root, and he wanted them. He was also shrewd enough to have observed that many more of the folk on the mountain who ailed with anything came to me than to him—and that most who accepted my cures were improved. If I had secrets, he wanted those, too—and I was more than happy to oblige.

Good, I had plenty of willow bark still left. I hesitated over the small rank of bottles in the upper right tray of the chest. I had several very strong emmenagogues—blue cohosh, ergot, and pennyroyal—but picked instead the gentler tansy and rue, setting a handful into a bowl and pouring boiling water on them to steep. Beyond its effects in easing menstruation, tansy had a reputation for calming nerves—and a more naturally nervous person than Lizzie Wemyss it would be difficult to imagine.

I glanced back at the fire, where Lizzie was shoveling the last of the strawberry preserves into Private Ogilvie, who appeared to be dividing his attention among Lizzie, Jamie, and his slice of toast—the greater proportion going to the toast.

Rue was quite a good anthelmintic, to boot. I didn't *know* that Lizzie suffered from worms, but a good many people in the mountains did, and a dose would certainly do her no harm.

I eyed Abel MacLennan covertly, wondering whether to slip a quick slug of hellbrew into his coffee as well—he had the pinched, anemic look of one with intestinal parasites, in spite of his stocky build. Perhaps, though, the look of pale disquiet on his features was due more to his knowledge of thief-takers in the vicinity.

Baby Joan was wailing with hunger again. Marsali sat down, reached under her arisaid to unfasten her bodice, and set the baby to her breast, her lip clenched between her teeth with trepidation. She winced, gasped in pain, then relaxed a little, as the milk began to flow.

Cracked nipples. I frowned and returned to a perusal of the medicine chest. Had I brought any sheep's-wool ointment? Drat, no. I didn't want to use bear grease, with Joan suckling; perhaps sunflower oil . . .

"A bit of coffee, my dear?" Mr. MacLennan, who had been watching Marsali with troubled sympathy, extended his fresh cup toward her. "My own wife did say as hot coffee eased the pangs of nursing a wean. Whisky in it's better"—his mournful jowls lifted a bit—"but all the same . . ."

"Taing." Marsali took the cup with a grateful smile. "I'm chilled right through this morning." She sipped the steaming liquid cautiously, and a small flush crept into her cheeks.

"Will you be going back to Drunkard's Creek tomorrow, Mr. MacLennan?" she asked politely, handing back the empty cup. "Or are ye traveling to New Bern wi' Mr. Hobson?"

Jamie looked up sharply, breaking off his conversation with Private Ogilvie.

"Hobson is going to New Bern? How d'ye ken that?"

"Mrs. Fowles says so," Marsali replied promptly. "She told me when I went to borrow a dry shirt for Germain—she's got a lad his size. She's worrit for Hugh—that's her husband—because her father—that's Mr. Hobson—wishes him to go along, but he's scairt."

"Why is Joe Hobson going to New Bern?" I asked, peering over the top of my medicine chest.

"To present a petition to the Governor," Abel MacLennan said. "Much good it will do." He smiled at Marsali, a little sadly. "No, lassie. I dinna ken where I'm bound, tell ye the truth. 'Twon't be to New Bern, though."

"Nor back to your wife at Drunkard's Creek?" Marsali looked at him in concern.

"My wife's dead, lass," MacLennan said softly. He smoothed the red kerchief across his knee, easing out the wrinkles. "Dead two months past."

"Oh, Mr. Abel." Marsali leaned forward and clasped his hand, her blue eyes full of pain. "I'm that sorry!"

He patted her hand, not looking up. Tiny drops of rain gleamed in the sparse strands of his hair, and a trickle of moisture ran down behind one large red ear, but he made no move to wipe it away.

Jamie had stood up while questioning Marsali. Now he sat down on the log beside MacLennan, and laid a hand gently on the smaller man's back.

"I hadna heard, *a charaid,*" he said quietly.

"No." MacLennan looked blindly into the transparent flames. "I—well, the truth of it is, I'd not told anyone. Not 'til now."

Jamie and I exchanged looks across the fire. Drunkard's Creek couldn't possibly harbor more than two dozen souls, in a scatter of cabins spread along the banks. Yet neither the Hobsons nor the Fowleses had mentioned Abel's loss—evidently he really hadn't told anyone.

"What was it happened, Mr. Abel?" Marsali still clasped his hand, though it lay quite limp, palm-down on the red kerchief.

MacLennan looked up then, blinking.

"Oh," he said vaguely. "So much happened. And yet . . . not really very much, after all. Abby—Abigail, my wife—she died of a fever. She got cold, and . . . she died." He sounded faintly surprised.

Jamie poured a bit of whisky into an empty cup, picked up one of MacLennan's unresisting hands, and folded it around the cup, holding the fingers in place with his own, until MacLennan's hand tightened its grasp.

"Drink it, man," he said.

Everyone was silent, watching as MacLennan obediently tasted the whisky, sipped, sipped again. Young Private Ogilvie shifted uneasily on his stone, looking as though he should like to return to his regiment, but he too stayed put, as though fearing an abrupt departure might somehow injure MacLennan further.

MacLennan's very stillness drew every eye, froze all talk. My hand hovered uneasily over the bottles in my chest, but I had no remedy for this.

"I had enough," he said suddenly. "I did." He looked up from his cup and glanced round the fire, as though challenging anyone to dispute him. "For the taxes, aye? It was no so good a year as it might have been, but I was careful. I'd ten bushels of corn put aside, and four good deer hides. It was worth more than the six shillings of the tax."

But the taxes must be paid in hard currency; not in corn and hides and blocks of indigo, as the farmers did their business. Barter was the common means of trade—I knew that well enough, I thought, glancing down at the bag of odd things folk had brought me in payment for my herbs and simples. No one ever paid for anything in money—save the taxes.

"Well, that's only reasonable," said MacLennan, blinking earnestly at Private Ogilvie, as though the young man had protested. "His Majesty canna well be doing wi' a herd of pigs, or a brace of turkeys, now, can he? No, I see quite well why it must be hard money, anyone could. And I had the corn; it would ha' brought six shillings, easy."

The only difficulty, of course, lay in turning ten bushels of corn into six shillings of tax. There were those in Drunkard's Creek who might have bought Abel's corn, and were willing—but no one in Drunkard's Creek had money, either. No, the corn must be taken to market in Salem; that was the closest place where hard coin might be obtained. But Salem lay nearly forty miles from Drunkard's Creek—a week's journey, there and back.

"I'd five acres in late barley," Abel explained. "Ripe and yellochtie, achin' for the scythe. I couldna leave it to be spoilt, and my Abby—she was a wee, slight woman, she couldna be scything and threshing."

Unable to spare a week from his harvest, Abel had instead sought help from his neighbors.

"They're guid folk," he insisted. "One or two could spare me the odd penny—but they'd their ain taxes to pay, hadn't they?" Still hoping somehow to scrape up the necessary coin without undertaking the arduous trip to Salem, Abel had delayed—and delayed too long.

"Howard Travers is Sheriff," he said, and wiped unconsciously at the drop of moisture that formed at the end of his nose. "He came with a paper, and said he mun' put us oot, and the taxes not paid."

Faced with necessity, Abel had left his wife in their cabin, and gone posthaste to Salem. But by the time he returned, six shillings in hand, his property had been seized and sold—to Howard Travers's father-in-law—and his cabin was inhabited by strangers, his wife gone.

"I kent she'd no go far," he explained. "She'd not leave the bairns."

And that in fact was where he found her, wrapped in a threadbare quilt and shivering under the big spruce tree on the hill that sheltered the graves of the four MacLennan children, all dead in their first year of life. In spite of his entreaties, Abigail would not go down to the cabin that had been theirs, would seek no aid from those who had dispossessed her. If it was madness from the fever that gripped her, or only stubbornness, he could not tell; she had clung to the branches of the tree with demented strength, crying out the names of her children—and there had died in the night.

His whisky cup was empty. He set it carefully on the ground by his feet, ignoring Jamie's gesture toward the bottle.

"They'd given her leave to carry awa what she could. She'd a bundle with her, and her grave-claes in it. I ken weel her sitting down the day after we were wed, to spin her winding-sheet. It had wee flowers all along one edge, that she'd made; she was a good hand wi' a needle."

He had wrapped Abigail in her embroidered shroud, buried her by the side of their youngest child, and then walked two miles down the road, intending, he thought, to tell the Hobsons what had happened.

"But I came to the house, and found them all abuzzing like hornets—Hugh Fowles had had a visit from Travers, come for the tax, and no money to pay. Travers grinned like an ape and said it was all one to him—and sure enough, ten days later he came along wi' a paper and three men, and put them oot."

Hobson had scraped up the money to pay his own taxes, and the Fowleses were crowded in safely enough with the rest of the family—but Joe Hobson was foaming with wrath over the treatment of his son-in-law.

"He was a-rantin', Joe, bleezin' mad wi' fury. Janet Hobson bid me come and sit, and offered me supper, and there was Joe shoutin' that he'd take the price of the land out of Howard Travers's hide, and Hugh slumped down like a trampled dog, and his wife greetin', and the weans all squealin' for their dinners like a brood o' piglets, and . . . well, I thought of telling them, but then . . ." He shook his head, as though confused anew.

Sitting half-forgotten in the chimney-corner, he had been overcome by a strange sort of fatigue, one that made him so tired that his head nodded on his neck, lethargy stealing over him. It was warm, and he was overcome with a sense of unreality. If the crowded confines of the Hobsons' one-roomed cabin were not real, neither was the quiet hillside and its fresh grave beneath the spruce tree.

He slept under the table, and woke before dawn, to find that the sense of unreality persisted. Everything around him seemed no more than a waking dream. MacLennan himself seemed to have ceased to exist; his body rose, washed itself, and ate, nodded and spoke without his cognizance. None of the outer world existed any longer. And so it was that when Joe Hobson had risen and announced that he and Hugh would go to Hillsborough, there to seek redress from the Court, that Abel MacLennan had found himself marching down the road along with them, nodding and speaking when spoken to, with no more will than a dead man.

"It did come to me, walkin' doon the road, as we were all dead," he said dreamily. "Me and Joe and Hugh and the rest. I might sae well be one place as anither; it was only moving 'til the time came to lay my bones beside Abby. I didna mind it."

When they reached Hillsborough, he had paid no great mind to what Joe intended; only followed, obedient and unthinking. Followed, and walked the muddy streets sparkling with broken glass from shattered windows, seen the torchlight and mobs, heard the shouts and screams—all quite unmoved.

"It was no but dead men, a-rattling their bones against one anither," he said with a shrug. He was still for a moment, then turned his face to Jamie, and looked long and earnestly up into his face.

"Is it so? Are ye dead, too?" One limp, callused hand floated up from the red kerchief, and rested lightly against the bone of Jamie's cheek.

Jamie didn't recoil from the touch, but took MacLennan's hand and brought it down again, held tight between his own.

"No, *a charaid*," he said softly. "Not yet."

MacLennan nodded slowly.

"Aye. Give it time," he said. He pulled his hands free and sat for a moment, smoothing his kerchief. His head kept bobbing, nodding slightly, as though the spring of his neck had stretched too far.

"Give it time," he repeated. "It's none sae bad." He stood up then, and put the square of red cloth on his head. He turned to me and nodded politely, his eyes vague and troubled.

"I thank ye for the breakfast, ma'am," he said, and walked away.

3

BILIOUS HUMOURS

ABEL MACLENNAN'S DEPARTURE put an abrupt end to breakfast. Private Ogilvie excused himself with thanks, Jamie and Fergus went off in search of scythes and astrolabes, and Lizzie, wilting in the absence of Private Ogilvie, declared that she felt unwell and subsided palely into one of the lean-to shelters, fortified with a large cup of tansy and rue decoction.

Fortunately, Brianna chose to reappear just then, sans Jemmy. She and Roger had breakfasted with Jocasta, she assured me. Jemmy had fallen asleep in Jocasta's arms, and since both parties appeared content with that arrangement, she had left him there, and come back to help me with the morning's clinic.

"Are you sure you want to help me this morning?" I eyed Bree dubiously. "It's your wedding day, after all. I'm sure Lizzie or maybe Mrs. Martin could—"

"No, I'll do it," she assured me, swiping a cloth across the seat of the tall stool I used for my morning surgery. "Lizzie's feeling better, but I don't think she's up to festering feet and putrid stomachs." She gave a small shudder, closing her eyes at the memory of the elderly gentleman whose ulcerated heel I had debrided the day before. The pain had caused him to vomit copiously on his tattered breeches, which in turn had caused several of the people waiting for my attention to throw up too, in sympathetic reflex.

I felt a trifle queasy at the memory myself, but drowned it with a final gulp of bitter coffee.

"No, I suppose not," I agreed reluctantly. "Still, your gown isn't quite finished, is it? Perhaps you should go—"

"It's fine," she assured me. "Phaedre's hemming my dress, and Ulysses is ordering all the servants around up there like a drill sergeant. I'd just be in the way."

I gave way without further demur, though I wondered a little at her alacrity. While Bree wasn't squeamish about the exigencies of normal life, like skinning animals and cleaning fish, I knew the proximity of people with disfiguring conditions or obvious illness bothered her, though she did her best to disguise it. It wasn't distaste, I thought, but rather a crippling empathy.

I lifted the kettle and poured freshly boiled water into a large, half-full jar of distilled alcohol, narrowing my eyes against hot clouds of alcoholic steam.

It *was* difficult to see so many people suffering from things that could have been easily treated in a time of antiseptics, antibiotics, and anesthesia—but I had learned detachment in the field hospitals of a time when such medical innovations were not only new but rare, and I knew both the necessity and the value of it.

I could not help anyone, if my own feelings got in the way. And I must help. It was as simple as that. But Brianna had no such knowledge to use as a shield. Not yet.

She had finished wiping down the stools, boxes, and other impedimenta for the morning surgery, and straightened up, a small frown between her brows.

"Do you remember the woman you saw yesterday? The one with the retarded little boy?"

"Not something you'd forget," I said, as lightly as possible.

"Why? Here, can you deal with this?" I gestured at the folding table I used, which was stubbornly declining to fold up properly, its joints having swollen with the damp.

Brianna frowned slightly, studying it, then struck the offending joint sharply with the side of her hand. It gave way and collapsed obediently at once, recognizing superior force.

"There." She rubbed the side of her hand absently, still frowning. "You were making a big thing of telling her to try not to have any more children. The little boy—was it an inheritable condition, then?"

"You might say that," I replied dryly. "Congenital syphilis."

She looked up, blanching.

"Syphilis? You're sure?"

I nodded, rolling up a length of boiled linen for bandaging. It was still very damp, but no help for it.

"The mother wasn't showing overt signs of the late stages—yet—but it's quite unmistakable in a child."

The mother had come simply to have a gumboil lanced, the little boy clinging to her skirts. He'd had the characteristic "saddle nose," with its pushed-in bridge, as well as a jaw so malformed that I wasn't surprised at his poor nutrition; he could barely chew. I couldn't tell how much of his evident backwardness was due to brain damage and how much to deafness; he appeared to have both, but I hadn't tested their extent—there being exactly nothing I could do to remedy either condition. I had advised the mother to give him pot liquor, which might help with the malnutrition, but there was little else to be done for him, poor mite.

"I don't see it so often here as I did in Paris or Edinburgh, where there were a lot of prostitutes," I told Bree, tossing the ball of bandages into the canvas bag she held open. "Now and then, though. Why? You don't think Roger has syphilis, do you?"

She looked at me, openmouthed. Her look of shock was obliterated by an instant flood of angry red.

"I do *not*!" she said. "Mother!"

"Well, I didn't really think so," I said mildly. "Happens in the best of families, though—and you *were* asking."

She snorted heavily.

"I was *asking* about contraception," she said, through her teeth. "Or at least I meant to, before you started in with the *Physician's Guide to Venereal Disease*."

"Oh, that." I eyed her thoughtfully, taking in the dried milk stains on her bodice. "Well, breast-feeding is reasonably effective. Not absolute, by any means, but fairly effective. Less so, after the first six months"—Jemmy was now six months old—"but still effective."

"Mmphm," she said, sounding so like Jamie that I had to bite my lower lip in order not to laugh. "And exactly what *else* is effective?"

I hadn't really discussed contraception—eighteenth-century style—with her. It hadn't seemed necessary when she first appeared at Fraser's Ridge, and then it *really* wasn't necessary, she being already pregnant. So she thought it was now?

I frowned, slowly putting rolls of bandage and bundles of herbs into my bag.

"The most common thing is some sort of barrier. A piece of silk or a sponge, soaked with anything from vinegar to brandy—though if you have it, tansy oil or oil of cedar is supposed to work the best. I *have* heard of women in the Indies using half a lemon, but that's obviously not a suitable alternative here."

She uttered a short laugh.

"No, I wouldn't think so. I don't think the tansy oil works all that well, either—that's what Marsali was using when she got pregnant with Joan."

"Oh, she *was* using it? I thought perhaps she'd just not bothered once—and once is enough."

I felt, rather than saw her stiffen, and bit my lip again, this time in chagrin. Once *had* been enough—we just didn't know *which* once. She hunched her shoulders, though, then let them fall, deliberately dismissing whatever memories my thoughtless remark had conjured.

"She said she'd been using it—but she might have forgotten. It doesn't work all the time, though, does it?"

I slung the bag of surgical linens and dried herbs over my shoulder and picked up the medical chest by the leather strap Jamie had made for it.

"The only thing that always works is celibacy," I said. "I suppose that isn't a satisfactory option in the present case?"

She shook her head, her eyes fixed broodingly on a cluster of young men visible through the trees below, taking turns at pitching stones across the creek.

"That's what I was afraid of," she said, and bent to pick up the folding table and a pair of stools.

I looked round the clearing, considering. Anything else? No worry about leaving the campfire, even if Lizzie fell asleep; nothing on the mountainside would burn in this weather; even the kindling and firewood we had stored at the end of our lean-to the day before were damp. Something was missing, though . . . what? Oh, yes. I put down the box for a moment and knelt to crawl into the lean-to. I dug about in the jumble of quilts, coming out finally with my tiny leather medicine pouch.

I said a brief prayer to St. Bride and slipped it round my neck and down inside the bodice of my dress. I was so much in the habit of wearing the amulet when I set out to practice medicine that I had almost ceased to feel ridiculous about this small ritual—almost. Bree was watching me, a rather odd look on her face, but she said nothing.

I didn't, either; merely picked up my things and followed her across the clearing, stepping carefully round the boggiest spots. It wasn't raining now, but the clouds sat on the tops of the trees, promising more at any moment, and wisps of mist rose from fallen logs and dripping bushes.

Why was Bree worrying about contraception? I wondered. Not that I didn't think it sensible—but why now? Perhaps it was to do with the imminence of her wedding to Roger. Even if they had been living as man and wife for the last several months—and they had—the formality of vows spoken before God and man was enough to bring a new sobriety to even the giddiest of young people. And neither Bree nor Roger was giddy.

"There is another possibility," I said to the back of her neck, as she led the way down the slippery trail. "I haven't tried it on anyone yet, so I can't say how reliable it may be. Nayawenne—the old Tuscaroran lady who gave me my medicine bag—she said there were 'women's herbs.' Different mixtures for different things—but one plant in particular for that; she said the seeds of it would keep a man's spirit from overwhelming a woman's."

Bree paused, half-turning as I came up beside her.

"Is that how the Indians see pregnancy?" One corner of her mouth curled wryly. "The man wins?"

I laughed.

"Well, in a way. If the woman's spirit is too strong for the man's, or won't yield to it, she can't conceive. So if a woman wants a child and can't have one, most often the shaman will treat her husband, or both of them, rather than just her."

She made a small throaty noise, partly amusement—but only partly.

"What's the plant—the women's herb?" she asked. "Do you know it?"

"I'm not positive," I admitted. "Or not sure of the name, I should say. She did show it to me, both the growing plant and the dried seeds, and I'm sure I'd know it again—but it wasn't a plant I knew by an English name. One of the Umbelliferae, though," I added helpfully.

She gave me an austere look that reminded me once more of Jamie, then turned to the side to let a small stream of Campbell women go by, clattering with empty kettles and pails, each one bobbing or bowing politely to us as they passed on their way down to the creek.

"Good day to ye, Mistress Fraser," said one, a neat young woman that I recognized as one of Farquard Campbell's younger daughters. "Is your man about? My faither would be glad of a word, he says."

"No, he's gone off, I'm afraid." I gestured vaguely; Jamie could be anywhere. "I'll tell him if I see him, though."

She nodded and went on, each of the women behind her pausing to wish Brianna happiness on her wedding day, their woolen skirts and cloaks brushing small showers of rainwater from the bayberry bushes that lined the path here.

Brianna accepted their good wishes with gracious politeness, but I saw the small line that formed between her thick red brows. Something was definitely bothering her.

"What?" I said bluntly, as soon as the Campbells were out of earshot.

"What's what?" she said, startled.

"What's troubling you?" I asked. "And don't say 'nothing,' because I see there is. Is it to do with Roger? Are you having second thoughts about the wedding?"

"Not exactly," she replied, looking wary. "I want to marry Roger, I mean—*that's* all right. It's just . . . I just . . . thought of something . . ." She trailed off, and a slow flush rose in her cheeks.

"Oh?" I asked, feeling rather alarmed. "What's that?"

"Venereal disease," she blurted. "What if I have it? Not Roger, not him, but—from Stephen Bonnet?"

Her face was flaming so hotly that I was surprised not to see the raindrops sizzle into steam when they struck her skin. My own face felt cold, my heart tight in my chest. The possibility had occurred to me—vividly—at the time, but I hadn't wanted even to suggest such a thing, if she hadn't thought of it herself. I remembered the weeks of watching her covertly for any hint of malaise—but women often showed no symptoms of early infection. Jemmy's healthy birth had been a relief in more ways than one.

"Oh," I said softly. I reached out and squeezed her arm. "Don't worry, lovey. You haven't."

She took a deep breath, and let it out in a pale misty cloud, some of the tension leaving her shoulders.

"You're sure?" she said. "You can tell? I feel all right, but I thought—women don't always have symptoms."

"They don't," I said, "but men most certainly do. And if Roger had contracted anything nasty from *you*, I'd have heard about it long since."

Her face had faded somewhat, but the pinkness came back at that. She coughed, mist rising from her breath.

"Well, that's a relief. So Jemmy's all right? You're sure?"

"Absolutely," I assured her. I had put drops of silver nitrate—procured at considerable cost and difficulty—in his eyes at birth, just in case, but I was indeed sure. Aside from the lack of any specific signs of illness, Jemmy had an air of robust health about him that made the mere thought of infection incredible. He radiated well-being like a potful of stew.

"Is that why you asked about contraception?" I asked,

waving a greeting as we passed the MacRaes' campsite. "You were worried about having more children, in case . . ."

"Oh. No. I mean—I hadn't even thought about venereal disease until you mentioned syphilis, and then it just struck me as a horrible realization—that he might have—" She stopped and cleared her throat. "Er, no. I just wanted to know."

A slippery patch of trail put paid to the conversation at that point, but not to my speculations.

It wasn't that a young bride's mind might not turn lightly to thoughts of contraception—but under the circumstances . . . what was it? I wondered. Fear for herself, or for a new baby? Childbirth could be dangerous, of course—and anyone who had seen the attendees at my surgery or heard the women's conversations round the campfires in the evening could be in no doubt as to the dangers to infants and children; it was the rare family that had not lost at least one infant to fever, morbid sore throat, or "the squitters"—uncontrolled diarrhea. Many women had lost three, four, or more babies. I remembered Abel MacLennan's story, and a small shiver ran down my spine.

Still, Brianna was very healthy, and while we did lack important things like antibiotics and sophisticated medical facilities, I had told her not to underestimate the power of simple hygiene and good nutrition.

No, I thought, watching the strong curve of her back as she lifted the heavy equipment over an entangling root that hunched across the trail. It wasn't that. She might have reason to be concerned, but she wasn't basically a fearful person.

Roger? On the face of it, it would seem that the best thing to do was to become pregnant again quickly, with a child that was definitely Roger's. That would certainly help to cement their new marriage. On the other hand . . . what if she did? Roger would be more than pleased—but what about Jemmy?

Roger had sworn a blood oath, taking Jemmy as his own. But human nature was human nature, and while I was sure that Roger would never abandon or neglect Jemmy, it was quite possible that he would feel differently—and obviously differently—for a child he knew was his. Would Bree risk that?

On due consideration, I rather thought she was wise to wait—if she could. Give Roger time to feel a close bond with Jemmy, before complicating the family situation with another child. Yes, very sensible—and Bree *was* an eminently sensible person.

It wasn't until we had arrived, finally, at the clearing where the morning surgeries were held that another possibility occurred to me.

"Can we be helpin' ye at all, Missus Fraser?"

Two of the younger Chisholm boys hurried forward to help, relieving me and Brianna of our heavy loads, and without being told, started in at once to unfold tables, fetch clean water, kindle a fire, and generally make themselves useful. They were no more than eight and ten, and watching them work, I realized afresh that in this time, a lad of twelve or fourteen could be essentially a grown man.

Brianna knew that, too. She would never leave Jemmy, I knew—not while he needed her. But . . . later? What might happen when he left *her*?

I opened my chest and began slowly to lay out the necessary supplies for the morning's work: scissors, probe, forceps, alcohol, scalpel, bandages, tooth pliers, suture needles, ointments, salves, washes, purges . . .

Brianna was twenty-three. She might be no more than in her mid-thirties by the time Jem was fully independent. And if he no longer needed her care—she and Roger might possibly go back. Back to her own time, to safety—to the interrupted life that had been hers by birth.

But only if she had no further children, whose helplessness would keep her here.

"Good morn to ye, ma'am." A short, middle-aged gentleman stood before me, the morning's first patient. He was bristling with a week's worth of whiskers, but noticeably pallid round the gills, with a clammy look and bloodshot eyes so raw with smoke and whisky that his malady was instantly discernible. Hangover was endemic at the morning surgery.

"I've a wee gripin' in my guts, ma'am," he said, swallowing unhappily. "Would ye have anything like to settle 'em, maybe?"

"Just the thing," I assured him, reaching for a cup. "Raw egg and a bit of ipecac. Have you a good vomit, and you'll be a new man."

THE SURGERY was held at the edge of the big clearing at the foot of the hill, where the great fire of the Gathering burned at night. The damp air smelled of soot and the acrid scent of wet ashes, but the blackened patch of earth—some ten feet across, at least—was already disappearing under a crisscross of fresh branches and kindling. They'd have a time starting it tonight, I thought, if the drizzle kept up.

The gentleman with the hangover disposed of, there was a short lull, and I was able to give my attention to Murray MacLeod, who had set up shop a short distance away.

Murray had gotten an early start, I saw; the ground by his feet was dark, the scattered ashes sodden and squishy with blood. He had an early patient in hand, too—a stout gentleman whose red, spongy nose and flabby jowls gave testimony to a life of alcoholic excess. He had the man stripped to his shirt despite the rain and cold, sleeve turned up and tourniquet in place, the bleeding bowl held across the patient's knees.

I was a good ten feet from the stool where Murray plied his trade, but could see the man's eyes, yellow as mustard even in the dim morning light.

"Liver disease," I said to Brianna, taking no particular pains to lower my voice. "You can see the jaundice from here, can't you?"

"Bilious humors," MacLeod said loudly, snapping open his fleam. "An excess of the humors, clear as day." Small, dark, and neat in his dress, Murray was not personally impressive, but he *was* opinionated.

"Cirrhosis due to drink, I daresay," I said, coming closer and looking the patient over dispassionately.

"An impaction of the bile, owing to an imbalance of the

phlegm!" Murray glowered at me, clearly thinking I intended to steal his thunder, if not his patient.

I ignored him and bent down to examine the patient, who looked alarmed at my scrutiny.

"You have a hard mass just under the ribs on the right, don't you?" I said, kindly. "Your piss is dark, and when you shit, it's black and bloody, am I right?"

The man nodded, mouth hanging open. We were beginning to attract attention.

"Mo-therr." Brianna was standing behind me. She gave Murray a nod and bent to mutter in my ear. "What can you do for cirrhosis, Mother? Nothing!"

I stopped, biting my lip. She was right. In my urge to show off by making the diagnosis—and keep Murray from using his stained, rusty-looking fleam on the man—I had overlooked the minor point that I had no alternative treatment to offer.

The patient was glancing back and forth between us, plainly uneasy. With an effort, I smiled at him, and nodded to Murray.

"Mr. MacLeod has the right of it," I said, forcing the words past my teeth. "Liver disease, surely—caused by an excess of humors." I supposed one could consider alcohol a humor, after all; the folk drinking Jamie's whisky last night had evidently found it hilarious.

Murray's face had been tense with suspicion; at my capitulation, it went quite comically blank with astonishment. Stepping in front of me, Brianna seized advantage of the moment.

"There's a charm," she said, smiling charmingly at him. "It . . . er . . . sharpens the blade, and eases the flow of the humors. Let me show you." Before he could tighten his grip, she snatched the fleam from his hand and turned to our small surgery fire, where a pot of water hung steaming from a tripod.

"In the name of Michael, wielder of swords, defender of souls," she intoned. I trusted that taking the name of St. Michael in vain was not actual blasphemy—or if it was, that Michael would not object in a good cause. The men laying the fire had stopped to watch, as had a few people coming to the surgery.

She raised the fleam and made a large, slow sign of the cross with it, looking from side to side, to be sure she had the attention of all the onlookers. She did; they were agog. Towering over most of the gawkers, blue eyes narrowed in concentration, she reminded me strongly of Jamie in some of his more bravura performances. I could only hope she was as good at it as he was.

"Bless this blade, for the healing of your servant," she said, casting her eyes up to heaven, and holding the fleam above the fire in the manner of a priest offering the Eucharist. Bubbles were rising through the water, but it hadn't quite reached the boil.

"Bless its edge, for the drawing of blood, for the spilling of blood, for the . . . er . . . the letting of poison from the body of your most humble petitioner. Bless the blade . . . bless the blade . . . bless the blade in the hand of your humble servant. . . . Thanks be to God for the brightness of the metal." Thanks be to God for the repetitious nature of Gaelic prayers, I thought cynically.

Thanks be to God, the water was boiling. She lowered the short, curved blade to the surface of the water, glowered significantly at the crowd, and declaimed, "Let the cleansing of the waters from the side of our Lord Jesus be upon this blade!"

She plunged the metal into the water and held it until the steam rising over the wooden casing reddened her fingers. She lifted the fleam and transferred it hastily to her other hand, raising it into the air as she surreptitiously waggled the scalded hand behind her.

"May the blessing of Michael, defender from demons, be on this blade and on the hand of its wielder, to the health of the body, to the health of the soul. Amen!"

She stepped forward and presented the fleam ceremoniously to Murray, handle first. Murray, no fool, gave me a look in which keen suspicion was mingled with a reluctant appreciation for my daughter's theatrical abilities.

"Don't touch the blade," I said, smiling graciously. "It will break the charm. Oh—and you repeat the charm, each time you use the blade. It has to be done with the water *boiling*, mind."

"Mmphm," he said, but took the fleam carefully by the handle. With a short nod to Brianna, he turned away to his patient, and I to mine—a young girl with nettle rash. Brianna followed, wiping her hands on her skirt and looking pleased with herself. I heard the patient's soft grunt behind me, and the ringing patter of blood running into the metal bowl.

I felt rather guilty about MacLeod's patient, but Brianna had been quite right; there was absolutely nothing I could do for him under the circumstances. Careful long-term nursing, coupled with excellent nutrition and a complete abstinence from alcohol, might prolong his life; the chances of the first two were low, the third, nonexistent.

Brianna had brilliantly saved him from a potentially nasty blood infection—and seized the opportunity to provide a similar protection for all MacLeod's future patients—but I couldn't help a nagging sense of guilt that I could not do more myself. Still, the first medical principle I had learned as a nurse on the battlefields of France still held: treat the patient in front of you.

"Use this ointment," I said sternly to the girl with nettle rash, "and *don't scratch*."

4

WEDDING GIFTS

THE DAY HADN'T CLEARED, but the rain had ceased for the moment. Fires smoked like smudge pots, as people hastened to take advantage of the momentary cessation to feed their carefully hoarded coals, pushing damp wood into the kindling blazes in a hasty effort to dry damp clothes and blankets. The air was still restless, though, and clouds of woodsmoke billowed ghostlike through the trees.

One such plume surged across the trail before him, and Roger turned to skirt it, making his way through tussocks of wet grass that soaked his stockings, and hanging boughs of pine that left dark patches of wetness on the shoulders of his coat as he passed. He paid the damp no mind, intent on his mental list of errands for the day.

To the tinkers' wagons first, to buy some small token as a wedding present for Brianna. What would she like? he wondered. A bit of jewelry, a ribbon? He had very little money, but felt the need to mark the occasion with a gift of some sort.

He would have liked to put his own ring on her finger when they made their vows, but she had insisted that the cabochon ruby that had belonged to her grandfather would do fine; it fit her hand perfectly, and there was no need to spend money on another ring. She was a pragmatic person, Bree was—sometimes dismayingly so, in contrast to his own romantic streak.

Something practical but ornamental, then—like a painted chamber pot? He smiled to himself at the idea, but the notion of practicality lingered, tinged with doubt.

He had a vivid memory of Mrs. Abercrombie, a staid and practical matron of Reverend Wakefield's congregation, who had arrived at the manse in hysterics one evening in the midst of supper, saying that she had killed her husband, and whatever should she do? The Reverend had left Mrs. Abercrombie in the temporary care of his housekeeper, while he and Roger, then a teenager, had hastened to the Abercrombie residence to see what had happened.

They had found Mr. Abercrombie on the floor of his kitchen, fortunately still alive, though groggy and bleeding profusely from a minor scalp wound occasioned by his having been struck by the new electric steam iron which he had presented to his wife on the occasion of their twenty-third wedding anniversary.

"But she said the old one scorched the tea towels!" Mr.

Abercrombie had repeated at plaintive intervals, as the Reverend skillfully taped up his head with Elastoplast, and Roger mopped up the kitchen.

It was the vivid memory of the gory splotches on the worn lino of the Abercrombies' kitchen that decided him. Pragmatic Bree might be, but this was their wedding. Better, worse, death do us part. He'd go for romantic—or as romantic as could be managed on one shilling, threepence.

There was a flash of red among the spruce needles nearby, like the glimpse of a cardinal. Bigger than the average bird, though; he stopped, bending to peer through an opening in the branches.

"Duncan?" he said. "Is that you?"

Duncan Innes came out of the trees, nodding shyly. He still wore the scarlet Cameron tartan, but had left off his splendid coat, instead wrapping the end of his plaid shawl-like round his shoulders in the cozy old style of the Highlands.

"A word, *a Smeòraich*?" he said.

"Aye, sure. I'm just off to the tinkers'—walk with me." He turned back to the trail—now clear of smoke—and they made their way companionably across the mountain, side by side.

Roger said nothing, waiting courteously for Duncan to choose his way into the conversation. Duncan was diffident and retiring by temperament, but observant, perceptive, and stubborn in a very quiet way. If he had something to say, he'd say it—given time. At last he drew breath and started in.

"*Mac Dubh* did say to me as how your Da was a minister—that's true, is it?"

"Aye," Roger said, rather startled at the subject. "Or at least—my real father was killed, and my mother's uncle adopted me; it was him was the minister." Even as he spoke, Roger wondered why he should feel it necessary to explain. For most of his life, he had thought and spoken of the Reverend as his father; and surely it made no difference to Duncan.

Duncan nodded, clicking his tongue in sympathy.

"But ye will have been Presbyterian yourself, then? I did hear *Mac Dubh* speak of it." Despite Duncan's normal good manners, a brief grin showed beneath the edge of his ragged mustache.

"I expect ye did, aye," Roger replied dryly. He'd be surprised if the whole Gathering hadn't heard *Mac Dubh* speak of it.

"Well, the thing about it is, so am I," Duncan said, sounding rather apologetic.

Roger looked at him in astonishment.

"You? I thought you were Catholic!"

Duncan made a small embarrassed noise, lifting the shoulder of his amputated arm in a shrug.

"No. My great-grandda on my mother's side was a Covenanter—verra fierce in his beliefs, aye?" He smiled, a little shyly. "That was watered down a good bit before it came to me; my Mam was godly, but Da wasna much of a one for the kirk, nor was I. And when I met up wi' *Mac Dubh* . . . well, it wasna as though he'd asked me to go to Mass with him of a Sunday, was it?"

Roger nodded, with a brief grunt of comprehension. Duncan had met with Jamie in Ardsmuir Prison, after the Rising. While most of the Jacobite troops had been Catholic, he knew there had been Protestants of different stripes among them, too—and most would likely have kept quiet about it, outnumbered by the Catholics in close quarters. And it was true enough that Jamie's and Duncan's later career in smuggling would have offered few occasions for religious discourse.

"Aye, so. And your wedding to Mrs. Cameron tonight . . ."

Duncan nodded, and sucked in a corner of his mouth, gnawing contemplatively at the edge of his mustache.

"That's it. Am I bound, d'ye think, to say anything?"

"Mrs. Cameron doesn't know? Nor Jamie?"

Duncan shook his head silently, eyes on the trampled mud of the trail.

Roger realized that it was, of course, Jamie whose opinion was important here, rather than Jocasta Cameron's. The issue of differing religion had evidently not seemed important to Duncan—and Roger had never heard that Jocasta was in any way devout—but hearing about Jamie's response to Roger's Presbyterianism, Duncan had now taken alarm.

"Ye went to see the priest, *Mac Dubh* said." Duncan glanced at him sidelong. "Did he—" He cleared his throat, flushing. "I mean, did he oblige ye to be . . . baptized Romish?"

An atrocious prospect to a devout Protestant, and plainly an uncomfortable one to Duncan. It was, Roger realized, an uncomfortable thought to him, too. Would he have done it, if he had to, to wed Bree? He supposed he would have, in the end, but he admitted to having felt a deep relief that the priest hadn't insisted on any sort of formal conversion.

"Ah . . . no," Roger said, and coughed as another fan of smoke washed suddenly over them. "No," he repeated, wiping streaming eyes. "But they don't baptize you, ye know, if ye've been christened already. You have been, aye?"

"Oh, aye." Duncan seemed heartened by that. "Aye, when I—that is—" A faint shadow crossed his face, but whatever thought had caused it was dismissed with another shrug. "Yes."

"Well, then. Let me think a bit, aye?"

The tinkers' wagons were already in sight, huddled like oxen, their merchandise shrouded in canvas and blankets against the rain, but Duncan stopped, clearly wanting the matter settled before going on to anything else.

Roger rubbed a hand over the back of his neck, thinking.

"No," he said finally. "No, I think ye needna say anything. See, it'll not be a Mass, only the marriage service—and that's just the same. Do ye take this woman, do ye take this man, richer, poorer, all that."

Duncan nodded, attentive.

"I can say that, aye," he said. "Though it did take a bit of coming to, the richer, poorer bit. Ye'll ken that, though, yourself."

He spoke quite without any sense of irony, merely as one stating an obvious fact, and was plainly taken aback at his glimpse of Roger's face in response to the remark.

"I didna mean anything amiss," Duncan said hastily. "That is, I only meant—"

Roger waved a hand, trying to brush it off.

"No harm done," he said, his voice as dry as Duncan's had been. "Speak the truth and shame auld Hornie, aye?"

It *was* the truth, too, though he had somehow managed to overlook it until this moment. In fact, he realized with a sinking sensation, his situation was a precise parallel with Duncan's: a penniless man without property, marrying a rich—or potentially rich—woman.

He had never thought of Jamie Fraser as being rich, perhaps because of the man's natural modesty, perhaps simply because he wasn't—yet. The fact remained that Fraser was the proprietor of ten thousand acres of land. If a good bit of that land was still wilderness, it didn't mean it would stay that way. There were tenants on that property now; there would be more soon. And when those tenancies began to pay rents, when there were sawmills and gristmills on the streams, when there were settlements and stores and taverns, when the handful of cows and pigs and horses had multiplied into fat herds of thriving stock under Jamie's careful stewardship . . . Jamie Fraser might be a very rich man indeed. And Brianna was Jamie's only natural child.

Then there was Jocasta Cameron, demonstrably already a very rich woman, who had stated her intention to make Brianna her heiress. Bree had exigently refused to countenance the notion—but Jocasta was as naturally stubborn as her niece, and had had more practice at it. Besides, no matter what Brianna said or did, folk would suppose . . .

And that was what was truly sitting in the bottom of his stomach like a curling stone. Not just the realization that he was in fact marrying well above his means and position—but the realization that everyone in the entire colony had realized it long ago, and had probably been viewing him cynically—and gossiping about him—as a rare chancer, if not an outright adventurer.

The smoke had left a bitter taste of ashes at the back of his mouth. He swallowed it down, and gave Duncan a crooked smile.

"Aye," he said. "Well. Better or worse. I suppose they must see *something* in us, eh? The women?"

Duncan smiled, a little ruefully.

"Aye, something. So, ye think it will be all right, then, about the religion? I wouldna have either Miss Jo or *Mac*

Dubh think I meant aught amiss by not speaking. But I didna like to make a fizz about it, and it's no needed."

"No, of course not," Roger agreed. He took a deep breath and brushed damp hair off his face. "Nay, I think it's all right. When I spoke to the—the Father, the only condition he made was that I should let any children be baptized as Catholics. But since that's not a consideration for you and Mrs. Cameron, I suppose . . ." He trailed off delicately, but Duncan seemed relieved at the thought.

"Och, no," he said, and laughed, a little nervously. "No, I think I'm no bothered about that."

"Well, then." Roger forced a smile, and clapped Duncan on the back. "Here's luck to you."

Duncan brushed a finger beneath his mustache, nodding. "And you, *a Smeòraich*."

He had expected Duncan to go off about his business, once his question was answered, but the man instead came with him, wandering slowly along the row of wagons in Roger's wake, peering at the wares on display with a slight frown.

After a week's haggling and bartering, the wagons were as full as they had been to start with—or more so, heaped with sacks of grain and wool, casks of cider, bags of apples, stacks of hides and other sundries taken in trade. The stock of fancies had dwindled considerably, but there were still things to be bought, as evidenced by the crowd of folk clustering round the wagons, thick as aphids on a rosebush.

Roger was tall enough to peer over the heads of most customers, and made his way slowly along the rank of wagons, squinting at this or that, trying to envision Brianna's response to it.

She was a beautiful woman, but not inclined to fuss over her looks. In fact, he had narrowly stopped her cutting off most of her glorious red mane out of impatience at it dangling in the gravy and Jemmy yanking on it. Maybe a ribbon *was* practical. Or a decorated comb? More likely a pair of handcuffs for the wean.

He paused by a vendor of cloth goods, though, and bent to peer under the canvas, where caps and bright ribbons hung safely suspended out of the wet, stirring in the cool dimness like the tentacles of brilliant jellyfish. Duncan, plaid hitched up about his ears against the gusting breeze, came closer, to see what he was looking at.

"Looking for something in particular, are ye, sirs?" A peddler-woman leaned forward over her goods, bosom resting on her folded arms, and divided a professional smile between them.

"Aye," Duncan said, unexpectedly. "A yard of velvet. Would ye be having such a thing? Good quality, mind, but the color's not important."

The woman's eyebrows lifted—even in his best clothes, Duncan would strike no one as a dandy—but she turned without comment and began to rootle through her diminished stock.

"D'ye think Mrs. Claire would have some lavender left?" Duncan asked, turning to Roger.

"Aye, I know she has," Roger replied. His puzzlement must have shown on his face, for Duncan smiled and ducked his head diffidently.

" 'Twas a thought I had," he said. "Miss Jo suffers from the megrims, and doesna sleep sae well as she might. I mind, my mither had a lavender pillow, and said she fell asleep like a babe the moment she laid her head upon it. So I thought, perhaps a bit o' velvet—so as she could feel it against her cheek, aye?—and perhaps Mrs. Lizzie would stitch it up for me. . . ."

In sickness and in health . . .

Roger nodded his approval, feeling touched—and slightly shamed—by Duncan's thoughtfulness. He had had the impression that the marriage between Duncan and Jocasta Cameron was principally a matter of convenience and good business—and perhaps it was. But mad passion wasn't a necessary prerequisite for tenderness or consideration, was it?

Duncan, purchase concluded, took his leave and went off with the velvet safely sheltered under his plaid, leaving Roger to make a slow circuit of the remaining vendors, mentally selecting, weighing, and discarding, as he wracked his brain to think what item of this myriad would best please his bride. Earrings? No, the kid would pull them. Same for a necklace—*or* a hair ribbon, now he thought.

Still, his mind dwelled on jewelry. Normally, she wore very little. But she *had* worn her father's ruby ring—the one Jamie had given him, the one he had given her when she accepted him for good—all through the Gathering. Jem slobbered on it now and then, but couldn't really damage it.

He stopped suddenly, letting the crowd flow round him. He could see the gold in his mind's eye, and the deep pink-red of the cabochon ruby, vivid on her long pale finger. *Her father's ring*. Of course; why had he not seen that before?

True, Jamie had given him the ring, but that didn't make it his to give in turn. And he wanted, very suddenly and very badly, to give Brianna something truly of his own.

He turned with decision, and made his way back to a wagon whose metal wares gleamed and glinted, even in the rain. He knew from experiment that his little finger was just the size of her ring finger.

"This one," he said, holding up a ring. It was cheap; made of braided strands of copper and brass, it would undoubtedly turn her finger green in minutes. *So much the better*, he thought, handing over his money. Whether she wore it all the time or not, she would be marked as his.

For this reason shall a woman leave her father's house, and cleave unto her husband, and the two shall be one flesh.

5

RIOTOUS UNREST

BY THE END OF THE FIRST HOUR, I had a substantial crowd of patients waiting, despite the intermittent drizzle. It was the final day of the Gathering, and people who had stood the pain of a toothache or the doubt of a rash had suddenly decided that they must seize the chance of having it seen to.

I dismissed a young woman with incipient goiter, admonishing her to procure a quantity of dried fish, as she lived too far inland to be sure of getting fresh each day, and eat some daily for its iodine content.

"Next!" I called, brushing damp hair out of my eyes.

The crowd parted like the Red Sea, revealing a small, elderly man, so thin he might be a walking skeleton, clad in rags and carrying a bundle of fur in his arms. As he shambled toward me through the ranks of recoiling people, I discovered the reason for the crowd's deference; he stank like a dead raccoon.

For a moment, I thought the pile of grayish fur might *be* a dead raccoon—there was already a small pile of furs and hides near my feet, though my patients usually went to the trouble of separating these from their original possessors before presenting them to me—but then the fur stirred, and a pair of bright eyes peered out of the tangled mass.

"My dog's hurt," the man announced brusquely. He set the dog on my table, shoving the jumble of instruments aside, and pointed to a jagged tear in the animal's flank. "You'll tend him."

This wasn't phrased as a request, but it was, after all, the dog who was my patient, and *he* seemed fairly civil. Medium-sized and short-legged, with a bristly, mottled coat and ragged ears, he sat placidly panting, making no effort to get away.

"What happened to him?" I moved the tottering basin out of danger, and bent to rummage for my jar of sterile sutures. The dog licked my hand in passing.

"Fightin' with a she-coon."

"Hmm," I said, surveying the animal dubiously. Given its improbable parentage and evident friendliness, I thought any overtures made to a female raccoon were probably inspired by lust, rather than ferocity. As though to confirm this impression, the animal extruded a few inches of moist pink reproductive equipment in my direction.

"He likes you, Mama," Bree said, keeping a straight face.

"How flattering," I muttered, hoping that the dog's owner would not be moved to any similar demonstration of regard. Fortunately, the old man appeared not to like me in the slightest; he ignored me completely, sunken eyes fixed broodingly on the clearing below, where the soldiers were going through some drill.

"Scissors," I said, resigned, holding out my palm.

I clipped away the matted fur near the wound, and was pleased to find no great swelling or other signs of infection. The gash had clotted well; evidently it had been some time since the injury. I wondered whether the dog had met its nemesis on the mountain. I didn't recognize the old man, nor did he have the speech of a Scot. Had he been at the Gathering at all? I wondered.

"Er . . . would you hold his head, please?" The dog might be friendly; that didn't mean his good nature would remain unimpaired as I jabbed a needle through his hide. His owner stayed sunk in gloom, though, and made no move to oblige. I glanced around for Bree, looking for help, but she had suddenly disappeared.

"Here, *a bhalaich*, here, then," said a soothing voice beside me, and I turned in surprise to find the dog sniffing interestedly at the proffered knuckles of Murray MacLeod. Seeing my look of surprise, he shrugged, smiled, and leaned over the table, grabbing the astonished dog by scruff and muzzle.

"I should advise ye to be quick about it, Mrs. Fraser," he said.

I took a firm grip of the leg nearest me and started in. The dog responded exactly as most humans did in similar circumstances, wriggling madly and trying to escape, its claws scrabbling on the rough wood of the table. At one point, it succeeded in breaking free of Murray, whereupon it leaped off the table altogether and made for the wide-open spaces, sutures trailing. I flung myself bodily upon it, and rolled through leaves and mud, scattering onlookers in all directions until one or two of the bolder souls came to my assistance, pinning the mangy beast to the ground so that I might finish the job.

I tied the last knot, clipped the waxed thread with Murray's fleam—which had in fact been trampled underfoot in the struggle, though unfortunately not broken—and took my knee off the hound's side, panting nearly as heavily as the dog was.

The spectators applauded.

I bowed, a little dazed, and shoved masses of disheveled curls out of my face with both hands. Murray was in no better case, his queue come undone and a jagged rent in his coat, which was covered with mud. He bent, seized the dog under the belly, and swung it off its feet, heaving it up on the table beside its owner.

"Your dog, sir," he said, and stood wheezing gently.

The old man turned, laid a hand on the dog's head, and frowned, glancing back and forth between me and Murray, as though unsure what to make of this tag-team approach to surgery. He looked back over his shoulder toward the soldiers below, then turned toward me, his sparse brows knotted over a beak of a nose.

"Who're *they*?" he said, in tones of deep puzzlement. Not waiting for an answer, he shrugged, turned, and walked off. The dog, tongue lolling, hopped off the table and trotted off at its owner's side, in search of more adventure.

I took a deep breath, brushed mud off my apron, smiled thanks to Murray, and turned to wash my hands before dealing with the next patient.

"Ha," said Brianna, under her breath. "Got him!" She lifted her chin slightly, indicating something over my shoulder, and I turned to look.

The next patient was a gentleman. A real gentleman, that is, judging by his dress and bearing, both of which were a good deal superior to the general run. I had noticed him hovering near the edge of the clearing for some time, glancing back and forth between my center of operations and that of Murray, obviously in doubt as to which medico should have the privilege of his custom. Evidently the incident of the trapper's dog had tipped the balance in my favor.

I glanced at Murray, who was looking distinctly po-faced. A gentleman would likely pay in cash. I gave Murray a slight shrug of apology, then put on a pleasant professional smile, and gestured the new patient onto my stool.

"Do sit down, sir," I said, "and tell me where it hurts."

The gentleman was a Mr. Goodwin of Hillsborough, whose chief complaint, it seemed, was a pain in his arm. This was not his only trouble, I saw; a freshly healed scar zigzagged down the side of his face, the livid weal drawing down the corner of his eye and giving him a most ferocious squint. A faint discoloration over the cheek showed where some heavy object had hit him square above the jaw, as well, and his features had the blunt and swollen look of someone who had been badly beaten in the not-so-distant past.

Gentlemen were as likely to engage in brawls as anyone, given sufficient provocation, but this one seemed of rather advanced years for such entertainments, looking to be in his middle fifties, with a prosperous paunch pressing against the silver-buttoned waistcoat. Perhaps he had been set upon somewhere and robbed, I thought. Not on his way to the Gathering, though; these injuries were weeks old.

I felt my way carefully over his arm and shoulder, making him lift and move the arm slightly, asking brief questions as I palpated the limb. The trouble was obvious enough; he had dislocated the elbow, and while the dislocation had fortunately reduced itself, I thought he had torn a tendon, which was now caught between the olecranon process and the head of the ulna, the injury being thus aggravated by movement of the arm.

Not that that was all; palpating my way carefully down his arm, I discovered no fewer than three half-healed simple fractures to the bones of his forearm. The damage was not all internal; I could see the fading remnants of two large bruises on the forearm above the sites of fracture, each an irregular blotch of yellow-green with the darker red-black of deep hemorrhage at the center. Self-defense injuries, I thought, or I was a Chinaman.

"Bree, find me a decent splint, will you?" I asked. Bree nodded silently and vanished, leaving me to anoint Mr. Goodwin's lesser contusions with cajeput ointment.

"How did you come by these injuries, Mr. Goodwin?" I asked casually, sorting out a length of linen bandage. "You look as though you've been in quite a fight. I hope at least the other fellow looks worse!"

Mr. Goodwin smiled faintly at my attempted witticism.

" 'Twas a battle, indeed, Mrs. Fraser," he replied, "and yet no fight of my own. A matter of misfortune, rather—being in the wrong place at the wrong time, as you might say. Still . . ." He closed the squinting eye in reflex as I touched the scar. An artless job by whoever had stitched it, but cleanly healed.

"Really?" I said. "Whatever happened?"

He grunted, but seemed not displeased at the necessity of telling me.

"You heard the officer this morning, surely, ma'am—reading out the Governor's words regarding the atrocious behavior of the rioters?"

"I shouldn't think the Governor's words escaped anyone's attention," I murmured, pulling gently on the skin with my fingertips. "So you were at Hillsborough, is that what you're telling me?"

"Indeed it is." He sighed, but relaxed a little, finding that I wasn't hurting him with my probings. "I live within the town of Hillsborough, in point of fact. And if I had remained quietly at home—as my good wife begged me to do"—he gave a rueful half-smile—"doubtless I should have escaped."

"They do say that curiosity killed the cat." I had spotted something when he smiled, and pressed gently with my thumb over the discolored area on his cheek. "Someone struck you across the face here, with some force. Did they break any teeth?"

He looked mildly startled.

"Aye, ma'am. But it's nothing you can mend." He pulled up his upper lip, revealing a gap where two teeth were missing. One premolar had been knocked out clean, but the other had broken off at the root; I could see a jagged line of yellowed enamel, gleaming against the dark red of his gum.

Brianna, arriving at this juncture with the splint, made a slight gagging noise. Mr. Goodwin's other teeth, while essentially whole, were heavily crusted with yellow calculus, and quite brown with the stains of tobacco chewing.

"Oh, I think I can help a bit there," I assured him, ignoring Bree. "It's painful to bite there, isn't it? I can't mend it, but I can draw the remnants of the broken tooth, and treat the gum to prevent infection. Who hit you, though?"

He shrugged slightly, watching with a slightly apprehensive interest as I laid out the shiny pliers and straight-bladed scalpel for dentistry.

"To tell the truth, ma'am, I scarcely know. I had but ventured into the town to visit the courthouse. I am bringing suit against a party in Edenton," he explained, a frown forming on his face at the thought of it, "and I am required to file documents in support of this action. However, I was unable to transact my business, as I found the street before the courthouse quite choked with men, many armed with cudgels, whips, and rough implements of that sort."

Seeing the mob, he had thought to leave, but just then, someone threw a rock through a window of the courthouse. The crash of glass acted on the mob like a signal, and they had surged forward, breaking down the doors and shouting threats.

"I became concerned for my friend, Mr. Fanning, whom I knew to be within."

"Fanning . . . that would be Edmund Fanning?" I was only listening with half an ear, as I decided how best to approach the extraction, but I did recognize that name. Farquard Campbell had mentioned Fanning, while telling Jamie the gory details of the riots following in the wake of the Stamp Act a few years previous. Fanning had been appointed postmaster for the colony, a lucrative position that had likely cost him a pretty penny to acquire, and had cost him still more dearly when he had been obliged to resign it under force. Evidently, his unpopularity had escalated in the five years since.

Mr. Goodwin compressed his lips, tightening them to a seam of disapproval.

"Yes, ma'am, that is the gentleman. And whatever scandal folk do spread about him, he has ever been a friend to me and mine—so when I heard such grievous sentiments expressed, to the threat of his life, I determined that I must go to his aid."

In this gallant endeavor, Mr. Goodwin had been less than successful.

"I tried to force a path through the crowd," he said, his

eyes fixed on my hands as I laid his arm along the splint and arranged the linen bandage beneath it. "I could not make much way, though, and had barely gained the foot of the steps, when there came a great shout from within, and the crowd fell back, carrying me with it."

Struggling to keep his feet, Mr. Goodwin had been horrified to see Edmund Fanning dragged bodily through the courthouse door, knocked down, and then pulled feet first down the steps, his head striking each one in turn.

"Such a noise as it made," he said, shuddering. "I could hear it above the shouting, thumping like a melon being rolled downstairs."

"Dear me," I murmured. "But he wasn't killed, was he? I hadn't heard of any deaths at Hillsborough. Relax your arm, please, and take a deep breath."

Mr. Goodwin took a deep breath, but only in order to utter a loud snort. This was succeeded by a much deeper gasp, as I turned the arm, freeing the trapped tendon and bringing the joint into good alignment. He went quite pale, and a sheen of sweat broke out on his pendulous cheeks, but he blinked a few times, and recovered nobly.

"And if he wasn't, it was by no mercy of the rioters," he said. " 'Twas only that they thought to have better sport with the Chief Justice, and so left Fanning insensible in the dust, as they rushed inside the courthouse. Another friend and I made shift to raise the poor man, and sought to make off with him to a place of shelter nearby, when comes the halloo in our rear, and we were beset all at once by the mob. That was how I came by this"—he raised his freshly splinted arm—"and these." He touched the weal by his eye, and the shattered tooth.

He frowned at me, heavy brows drawn down.

"Believe me, ma'am, I hope some folk here are moved to give up the names of the rioters, that they may be justly punished for such barbarous work—but were I to see here the fellow who struck me, I shouldn't be inclined to surrender him to the Governor's justice. Indeed I should not!"

His fists closed slowly, and he glowered at me as though suspecting that I had the miscreant in question hidden under my table. Brianna shifted uneasily behind me. No doubt she was thinking, as I was, of Hobson and Fowles. Abel MacLennan I was inclined to consider an innocent bystander, no matter what he might have done in Hillsborough.

I murmured something sympathetically noncommittal, and brought out the bottle of raw whisky I used for disinfection and crude anesthesia. The sight of it seemed to hearten Mr. Goodwin considerably.

"Just a bit of this to . . . er . . . fortify your spirits," I suggested, pouring him out a healthy cupful. And disinfect the nasty environs of his mouth, too. "Hold it in your mouth for a moment before you swallow—it will help to numb your tooth."

I turned to Bree, as Mr. Goodwin obediently took a large gulp of the liquor and sat with his mouth full, cheeks puffed like a frog about to burst into song. She seemed a little pale, though I wasn't sure whether it was Mr. Goodwin's story or the view of his teeth that had affected her.

"I don't think I'll need you any longer this morning, darling," I said, patting her arm in reassurance. "Why don't you go and see whether Jocasta is ready for the weddings tonight?"

"You're sure, Mama?" Even as she asked, she was untying her blood-spotted apron and rolling it into a ball. Seeing her glance toward the trailhead, I looked in that direction and saw Roger lurking behind a bush, his eyes fixed on her. I saw his face light when she turned toward him, and felt a small warm glow at sight of it. Yes, they would be all right.

"Now then, Mr. Goodwin. Just you take a drop more of that, and we'll finish dealing with this little matter." I turned back to my patient, smiling, and picked up the pliers.

6

FOR AULD LANG SYNE

ROGER WAITED AT THE EDGE of the clearing, watching Brianna as she stood by Claire's side, pounding herbs, measuring off liquids into small bottles, and tearing bandages. She had rolled up her sleeves, in spite of the chill, and the effort of ripping the tough linen made the muscles of her bare arms flex and swell beneath the freckled skin.

Strong in the wrists, he thought, with a faintly disturbing memory of Estella in Dickens's *Great Expectations*. Noticeably strong all over; the wind flattened her skirt against the solid slope of hips and a long thigh pressed briefly against the fabric as she turned, smooth and round as an alder trunk.

He wasn't the only one noticing. Half the people waiting for the attention of the two physicians were watching Brianna; some—mostly women—with faint and puzzled frowns, some—all men—with a covert admiration tinged with earthy speculation that gave Roger an urge to step into the clearing and assert his rights to her on the spot.

Well, let them look, he thought, quelling the urge. *It only matters if she's looking back, aye?*

He moved out of the trees, just a little, and her head turned at once as she caught sight of him. The slight frown on her face melted at once, her face lighting. He smiled back, then jerked his head in invitation, and turned away down the path, not waiting.

Was he sufficiently petty to want to demonstrate to that gang of gawpers that his woman would drop everything and come at his beck? Well . . . yes, he was. Embarrassment at that realization was tempered by a pleasantly fierce sense of possession at the sound of her step on the path above; yes, she *would* come to him.

She had left her work behind, but carried something in her hand; a small packet, wrapped in paper and tied with thread. He put out a hand and led her off the path, down toward a small copse where a scrim of tattered red and yellow maple leaves offered a decent semblance of privacy.

"Sorry to take you from your work," he said, though he wasn't.

"It's okay. I was glad to get away. I'm afraid I'm not all that good at blood and guts." She made a rueful face at the admission.

"That's all right," he assured her. "It's not one of the things I was looking for in a wife."

"Maybe you should have been," she said, shooting him a brooding sort of glance. "Here in *this* place, you might need a wife who can pull your teeth when they go bad, and sew your fingers back on when you cut them off chopping wood."

The grayness of the day seemed to have affected her spirits—or perhaps it was the job she had been doing. A brief glance at the run of Claire's patients was enough to depress anyone—anyone but Claire—with their parade of deformities, mutilations, wounds, and ghastly illnesses.

At least what he meant to tell Brianna might take her mind off the more gruesome details of eighteenth-century life for a bit. He cupped her cheek, and smoothed one thick red brow with a chilly thumb. Her face was cold, too, but the flesh behind her ear, beneath her hair, was warm—like her other hidden places.

"I've got what I wanted," he said firmly. "What about you, though? You're sure ye don't want a man who can scalp Indians and put dinner on the table with his gun? Blood's not my main thing, either, aye?"

A spark of humor reappeared in her eyes, and her air of preoccupation lightened.

"No, I don't think I want a bloody man," she said. "That's what Mama calls Da—but only when she's mad at him."

He laughed.

"And what will you call me, when you're mad at me?" he teased. She looked at him speculatively, and the spark grew brighter.

"Oh, don't worry; Da won't teach me any bad words in Gaelic, but Marsali taught me a lot of really evil things to say in French. Do you know what *un soûlard* is? *Une grande gueule*?"

"*Oui, mon petit chou*—not that I've ever seen a cabbage with quite such a red nose." He flicked a finger at her nose, and she ducked, laughing.

"Maudit chien!"

"Save something for after the wedding," he advised. "Ye might need it." He took her hand, to draw her toward a convenient boulder, then noticed again the small package she held.

"What's that?"

"A wedding present," she said, and held it out to him with two fingers, distasteful as though it had been a dead mouse.

He took it gingerly, but felt no sinister shapes through the paper. He bounced it on his palm; it was light, almost weightless.

"Embroidery silk," she said, in answer to his questioning look. "From Mrs. Buchanan." The frown was back between her brows, and that look of . . . worry? No, something else, but damned if he could put a name to it.

"What's wrong with embroidery silk?"

"Nothing. It's what it's for." She took the package from him, and tucked it into the pocket she wore tied under her petticoat. She was looking down, rearranging her skirts, but he could see the tightness of her lips. "She said it's for our winding claes."

Spoken in Brianna's odd version of a Bostonian Scots accent, it took a moment for Roger to decipher this.

"Winding cl—oh, you mean shrouds?"

"Yes. Evidently, it's my wifely duty to sit down the morning after the wedding and start spinning cloth for my shroud." She bit the words off through clenched teeth. "That way, I'll have it woven and embroidered by the time I die in childbirth. And if I'm a fast worker, I'll have time to make one for you, too—otherwise, your *next* wife will have to finish it!"

He would have laughed, had it not been clear that she was really upset.

"Mrs. Buchanan is a great fool," he said, taking her hands. "You should not be letting her worry you with her nonsense." Brianna glanced at him under lowered brows.

"Mrs. Buchanan," she said precisely, "is ignorant, stupid, and tactless. The one thing she *isn't* is wrong."

"Of course she is," he said, with assumed certainty, feeling nonetheless a stab of apprehension.

"How many wives has Farquard Campbell buried?" she demanded. "Gideon Oliver? Andrew MacNeill?"

Nine, among the three of them. MacNeill would take a fourth wife this evening—an eighteen-year-old girl from Weaver's Gorge. The stab came again, deeper, but he ignored it.

"And Jenny ban Campbell's borne eight children and deviled two husbands into the ground," he countered firmly. "For that matter, Mrs. Buchanan herself has five bairns, and she's certainly still kicking. I've seen them; turnip-headed to a man, but all healthy."

That got him a reluctant twitch of the mouth, and he pressed on, encouraged.

"You've no need to fear, hen. You had no trouble with Jemmy, aye?"

"Yeah? Well, if you think it's no trouble, next time *you* can do it!" she snapped, but the corner of her mouth curled slightly up. She tugged at his hand, but he held on, and she didn't resist.

"So you're willing there should be a next time, are you? Mrs. Buchanan notwithstanding?" His tone was deliberately light, but he drew her close and held her, his face hidden in her hair, for fear she should see how much the question meant to him.

She wasn't fooled. She drew back a little, and her eyes, blue as water, searched his.

"You'd marry me, but live celibate?" she asked. "That's the only sure way. The tansy oil doesn't always work—look at Marsali!" The existence of baby Joan was eloquent testimony to the ineffectiveness of that particular method of birth control. Still . . .

"There are other ways, I expect," he said. "But if you want celibacy—then yes, you'll have it."

She laughed, because his hand had tightened possessively on her arse, even as his lips renounced it. Then the laughter faded, and the blue of her eyes grew darker, clouded.

"You mean it, don't you?"

"Yes," he said, and did, though the thought of it lay heavy in his chest, like a swallowed stone.

She sighed, and drew her hand down the side of his face, tracing the line of his neck, the hollow of his throat. Her thumb pressed against his hammering pulse, so he felt the beat of it, magnified in his blood.

He meant it, but he bent his head to hers and took her mouth, so short of breath he must have hers, needing so urgently to join with her that he would do it in whatever way he might—hands, breath, mouth, arms; his thigh pressed between hers, opening her legs. Her hand lay flat against his chest, as though to push him off—then tightened convulsively, grasping shirt and flesh together. Her fingers dug deep in the muscle of his breast, and then they were glued together, openmouthed and gasping, front teeth scraping painfully in the flurry of their wanting.

"I don't . . . we're not . . ." He broke free for a moment, his mind grasping dimly for the fragments of words. Then her hand found its way under his kilt, a cold, sure touch on his heated flesh, and he lost all power of speech.

"Once more before we quit," she said, and her breath wreathed him in heat and mist. "For old times' sake." She sank to her knees in the wet yellow leaves, pulling him down to her.

IT HAD STARTED raining again; her hair lay tumbled round her, streaked with damp. Her eyes were closed, her face upturned to the drizzling heavens, and raindrops struck her face, rolling down like tears. She wasn't sure whether to laugh or cry, in fact.

Roger lay with her, half on her, his weight a warm and solid comfort, his kilt spread over their tangled bare legs, protection from the rain. Her hand cupped the back of his head and stroked his hair, wet and sleek as a black seal's fur.

He stirred then, with a groan like a wounded bear, and lifted himself. A draft of cold air struck her newly exposed body, damp and heated where they had touched.

"I'm sorry," he muttered. "God, I'm sorry. I shouldn't have done that." She opened one eye to a slit; he rose to his knees above her, swaying, and bent to pull her crumpled skirt down into decency. He'd lost his stock, and the cut under his jaw had reopened. She'd torn his shirt, and his waistcoat hung open, half its buttons gone. He was streaked with mud and blood and there were dead leaves and acorn fragments in the waves of his loose black hair.

"It's all right," she said, and sat up. She was in no better case; her breasts were heavy with milk, and huge wet spots had soaked through the fabric of shift and bodice, chilling her skin. Roger saw, and picked up her fallen cloak, draping it gently around her shoulders.

"Sorry," he said again, and reached to brush the tangled hair from her face; his hand was cold against her cheek.

"It's okay," she said, trying to gather all the stray fragments of herself that seemed to be rolling round the tiny clearing like beads of mercury. "It's only six months, and I'm still nursing Jemmy. It's—I mean, I think it's still safe." But for how much longer? she wondered. Little jolts of desire still shot through her, mingled with spurts of dread.

She had to touch him. She picked up one corner of her cloak and pressed it to the seeping wound beneath his jaw. Celibacy? When the feel of him, the smell of him, the memory of the last few minutes, made her want to knock him flat in the leaves and do it all again? When tenderness for him welled up in her like the milk that rushed unbidden to her breasts?

Her breasts ached with unsatisfied desire, and she felt dribbles of milk run tickling down her ribs beneath the cloth. She touched one breast, heavy and swollen, her guarantee of safety—for a while.

Roger put away her hand, reaching up to touch the cut.

"It's all right," he said. "It's stopped bleeding." He wore the oddest expression—or expressions. Normally his face was pleasantly reserved, even a little stern. Now his features seemed unable to settle themselves, shifting from moment to moment between a look of undeniable satisfaction and one of just as undeniable dismay.

"What's the matter, Roger?"

He shot her a quick glance, then looked away, a slight flush rising in his cheeks.

"Oh," he said. "Well. It's only that we . . . er . . . we aren't actually married at the moment."

"Well, of course not. The wedding's not 'til tonight. Speaking of which . . ." She looked at Roger, and a bubble of laughter rose from the pit of her stomach. "Oh, dear," she said, fighting back a fit of giggles. "You look like somebody's had their will of you in the woods, Mr. MacKenzie."

"Very funny, Mrs. Mac," he said, eyeing her own bedraggled state. "Ye've been in a rare fight, too, by the looks of you. But what I meant was that we've been handfast for the last year—and that's legally binding, in Scotland at least. But the year and a day have been up for a bit—and we're not formally married 'til this evening."

She squinted at him, wiping rain out of her eyes with the back of one hand, and once more gave way to the urge to laugh.

"My God, you think it *matters*?"

He grinned back, a little reluctantly.

"Well, no. It's only I'm a preacher's lad; I know it's fine—but somewhere inside is an old Scotch Calvinist, muttering that it's just a wee bit wicked, to be carrying on so with a woman not really my wife."

"Ha," she said, and settled her arms comfortably on her drawn-up knees. She leaned to one side and nudged him gently.

"Old Scotch Calvinist, my ass. What is it, really?"

He wouldn't look directly at her, but kept his eyes down, looking at the ground. Droplets glittered on his strongly marked dark brows and lashes, gilding the skin of his cheekbones with silver. He drew a deep breath, and let it out slowly.

"I can't say you're not right to be afraid," he said quietly. "I hadn't realized—not really thought about it before today—just how dangerous marriage is for a woman." He looked up and smiled at her, though the look of worry stayed in his moss-green eyes.

"I want you, Bree—more than I can say. It's only that I was thinking of what we just did and how fine it was—and realizing that I'll maybe—no, I *will*—be risking your life if I keep on doing it. But damned if I want to stop!"

The small strands of dread had coalesced into a cold snake that ran down her backbone and coiled deep in her belly, twisting around her womb. She knew what he wanted, and it wasn't only the thing they'd just shared—powerful as that was. Knowing what he wanted, though—and why—how could she hesitate to give it to him?

"Yeah." She took a breath to match his, and blew it out in a plume of white. "Well, it's too late to worry about that, I think." She looked at him and touched his arm. "I want you, Roger." She pulled down his head and kissed him, taking comfort from her fears in the strength of his arm around her, the warmth of his body beside her.

"Oh, God, Bree," he murmured into her hair. "I want to tell you that I'll keep you safe, save you and Jemmy from anything that might threaten you—ever. It's a terrible thing, to think it might be me that would be the threat, that I could kill you with my love—but it's true."

His heart was beating under her ear, solid and steady. She felt the warmth return to her hands, clasped tight on the bones of his back, and the thaw reached deeper, uncoiling some of the frozen strands of fear inside her.

"It's all right," she said at last, wanting to offer him the comfort he could not quite give her. "I'm sure it'll be okay. I've got the hips for it, everybody says so. Jugbutt, that's me." She ran a hand ruefully down the lush swell of one hip, and he smiled, following her hand with his own.

"You know what Ronnie Sinclair said to me last night? He was watching you bend down to pick up a stick of wood for the fire, and he sighed and said, 'Ye ken how to pick a good lass, MacKenzie? Start at the bottom and work your way up!' Oof!" He recoiled, laughing, as she slugged him.

Then he bent and kissed her, very gently. The rain was still falling, pattering on the layer of dead leaves. Her fingers were sticky with the blood from his wound.

"You want a baby, don't you?" she asked softly. "One you know is yours?"

He kept his head bent for a moment, but at last looked up at her, letting her see the answer in his face; a great yearning, mingled with anxious concern.

"I don't mean—" he began, but she put a hand across his mouth to stop him.

"I know," she said. "I understand." She did—almost. She was an only child, as he was; she knew the yearning for connection and closeness—but hers had been gratified. She had had not one loving father but two. A mother who had loved her beyond the bounds of space and time. The Murrays of Lallybroch, that unexpected gift of family. And most of all, her son, her flesh, her blood, a small and trusting weight that anchored her firmly to the universe.

But Roger was an orphan, alone in the world for such a long time. His parents gone before he knew them, his old uncle dead—he had no one to claim him, no one to love him for the sake only of his flesh and bone—no one save her. Little wonder if he hungered for the certainty she held in her arms when she nursed her child.

He cleared his throat suddenly.

"I—ah—I was going to give ye this tonight. But maybe . . . well." He reached into the inner pocket of his coat and handed her a soft bundle, wrapped in cloth.

"Sort of a wedding present, aye?" He was smiling, but she could see the uncertainty in his eyes.

She opened the cloth, and a pair of black button eyes looked up at her. The doll wore a shapeless smock of green calico, and red-yarn hair exploded from its head. Her heart beat heavily in her chest, and her throat tightened.

"I thought the wean might like it—to chew on, perhaps."

She moved, and the pressure of the sodden fabric on her breasts made them tingle. She was afraid, all right; but there were things stronger than fear.

"There'll be a next time," she said, and laid a hand on his arm. "I can't say when—but there will."

He laid his hand on hers and squeezed it tight, not looking at her.

"Thanks, Jugbutt," he said at last, very softly.

THE RAIN WAS HEAVIER; it was pissing down now. Roger thumbed the wet hair out of his eyes and shook himself like a dog, scattering drops from the tight-woven wool of coat and plaid. There was a smear of mud down the front of the gray wool; he brushed at it, to no effect.

"Christ, I can't be getting married like this," he said, trying to lighten the mood between them. "I look like a beggar."

"It's not too late, you know," she said. She smiled, teasing a little tremulously. "You could still back out."

"It's been too late for me since the day I saw you," he said gruffly. "Besides," he added, lifting one brow, "your father would gut me like a hog if I said I'd had second thoughts on the matter."

"Ha," she said, but the hidden smile popped out, dimpling one cheek.

"Bloody woman! You like the idea!"

"Yes. No, I mean." She was laughing again now; that's what he'd wanted. "I don't want him to gut you. It's just nice to know he *would*. A father ought to be protective."

She smiled at him, touched him lightly. "Like you, Mr. MacKenzie."

That gave him an odd, tight feeling in the chest, as though his waistcoat had shrunk. Then a tinge of cold, as he recalled what he had to tell her. Fathers and their notions of protection varied, after all, and he wasn't sure how she would see this one.

He took her arm and drew her away, out of the rain and into the shelter of a clump of hemlocks, where the layers of needles lay dry and fragrant underfoot, protected by the wide-spreading branches overhead.

"Well, come and sit with me a moment, Mrs. Mac. It's not important, but there's a small thing I wanted to tell you about before the wedding." He drew her down to sit beside him on a rotting log, rusted with lichen. He cleared his throat, gathering the thread of his story.

"When I was in Inverness, before I followed you through the stones, I spent some time trolling through the Reverend's bumf, and I came across a letter to him, written by your father. By Frank Randall, I mean. It's no great matter—not now—but I thought . . . well, I thought perhaps there should be no secrets between us, before we marry. I told your father about it last night. So let me tell you now."

Her hand lay warm in his, but the fingers tightened as he talked, and a deep line grew between her brows as she listened.

"Again," she said, when he'd finished. "Tell me that again."

Obligingly, he repeated the letter—as he'd memorized it, word for word. As he'd told it the night before, to Jamie Fraser.

"That gravestone in Scotland with Da's name on it is a *fake*?" Her voice rose slightly with astonishment. "Dad—Frank—had the Reverend make it, and put it there, in the kirkyard at St. Kilda, but Da isn't—won't be, I mean—won't be under it?"

"Yes, he did, and no, he won't," Roger said, keeping careful track of the "he's" involved. "He—Frank Randall, that is—meant the stone as a sort of acknowledgment, I think; a debt owed to your father—your other father, I mean; Jamie."

Brianna's face was blotched with chill, the ends of nose and ears nipped red as the heat of their lovemaking faded.

"But he couldn't know we'd ever find it, Mama and me!"

"I don't know that he *wanted* you to find it," Roger said. "Perhaps he didn't know, either. But he felt he had to make the gesture. Besides," he added, struck by a memory, "didn't Claire say that he'd meant to bring you to England, just before he was killed? Perhaps he meant to take you there, make sure you found it—then leave it to you and Claire what to do."

She sat still, chewing that one over.

"He knew, then," she said slowly. "That he—that Jamie Fraser survived Culloden. He *knew* . . . but he didn't say?"

"I don't think you can blame him for not saying," Roger said gently. "It wasn't only selfish, you know."

"Wasn't it?" She was still shocked, but not yet angry. He could see her turning it over, trying to see it all before making up her mind what to think, how to feel.

"No. Think of it, hen," he urged. The spruce was cold at his back, the bark of the fallen log damp under his hand. "He loved your mother, aye, and didn't want to risk losing her again. That's maybe selfish, but she was his wife first, after all; no one could blame him for not wanting to give her up to another man. But that's not all of it."

"What's the rest, then?" Her voice was calm, blue eyes straight and level.

"Well—what if he *had* told her? There she was, with you, a young child—and remember, neither of them would have thought that you might cross through the stones as well."

The eyes were still straight, but clouded once more with trouble.

"She would have had to choose," she said softly, her gaze fixed on him. "To stay with us—or go to him. To Jamie."

"To leave you behind," Roger said, nodding, "or to stay, and live her life, knowing her Jamie was alive, maybe reachable—but out of reach. Break her vows—on purpose, this time—and abandon her child . . . or live with yearning. I can't think *that* would have done your family life much good."

"I see." She sighed, the steam of her exhaled breath disappearing like a ghost in cold air.

"Perhaps Frank was afraid to give her the choice," Roger said, "but he did save her—and you—from the pain of having to make it. At least then."

Her lips drew in, pushed out, relaxed.

"I wonder what her choice would have been, if he *had* told her," she said, a little bleakly. He laid his hand on hers, squeezed lightly.

"She would have stayed," he said, with certainty. "She made the choice once, did she not? Jamie sent her back, to keep you safe, and she went. She would have known he wanted that, and she would have stayed—so long as you needed her. She wouldn't have gone back, even when she did, save that you insisted. Ye ken that well enough, surely?"

Her face eased a bit, accepting this.

"I guess you're right. But still . . . to know he was alive, and not try to reach him . . ."

He bit the inside of his cheek, to keep from asking. *If it were your choice, Brianna? If it was the bairn or me?* For how could any man force a choice like that on a woman whom he loved, even hypothetically? Whether for her sake or his own . . . he would not ask.

"But he did put that gravestone there. Why did he do that?" The line between her brows was still deep, but no longer straight; it twisted with a growing perturbation.

He hadn't known Frank Randall, but he felt a certain empathy for the man—and not only a disinterested sympathy, either. He hadn't fully realized why he'd felt he must tell her about the letter now, before the wedding, but his own motives were becoming clearer—and more disturbing to him—by the moment.

"I think it was obligation, as I said. Not just to Jamie or your mother—to you. If it—" he started, then stopped and squeezed her hand, hard. "Look. Take wee Jemmy. He's mine, as much as you are—he always will be." He took a deep breath. "But if I were the other man . . ."

"If you were Stephen Bonnet," she said, and her lips were tight, gone white with chill.

"If I were Bonnet," he agreed, with a qualm of distaste at the notion, "if I knew the child was mine, and yet he was being raised by a stranger—would I not want the child to know the truth, sometime?"

Her fingers convulsed in his, and her eyes went dark.

"You mustn't tell him! Roger, for God's sake, promise me you won't tell him, ever!"

He stared at her in astonishment. Her nails were digging painfully into his hand, but he made no move to free himself.

"Bonnet? Christ, no! If I ever see the man again, I'll not waste time talking!"

"Not Bonnet." She shuddered, whether from cold or emotion, he couldn't tell. "God, keep away from that man! No, it's Jemmy I mean." She swallowed hard, and gripped both his hands. "Promise me, Roger. If you love me, promise that you'll never tell Jemmy about Bonnet, never. Even if something happens to me—"

"Nothing will happen to you!"

She looked at him, and a small, wry smile formed on her lips.

"Celibacy's not my thing, either. It might." She swallowed. "And if it does . . . promise me, Roger."

"Aye, I promise," he said, reluctantly. "If you're sure."

"I'm sure!"

"Would you not have wanted ever to know, then—about Jamie?"

She bit her lip at that, her teeth sinking deep enough to leave a purple mark in the soft pink flesh.

"Jamie Fraser is not Stephen Bonnet!"

"Agreed," he said dryly. "But I wasna speaking of Jemmy to start with. All I meant was that if I were Bonnet, I should want to know, and—"

"He does know." She pulled her hand from his, abruptly, and stood up, turning away.

"He *what*?" He caught up with her in two strides, and grabbed her by the shoulder, turning her back to face him. She flinched slightly, and he loosened his grip. He took a deep breath, fighting to keep his voice calm. "Bonnet knows about Jemmy?"

"Worse than that." Her lips were trembling; she pressed them tightly together to stop it, then opened them just enough to let the truth escape. "He thinks Jemmy is his."

She wouldn't sit down with him again, but he drew her arm tightly through his and made her walk with him, walk through the falling rain and tumbled stones, past the rush of the creek and the swaying trees, until the movement calmed her enough to talk, to tell him about her days left alone at River Run, a prisoner of her pregnancy. About Lord John Grey, her father's friend, and hers; how she had confided to Lord John her fears and struggles.

"I was afraid you were dead. All of you—Mama, Da, you." Her hood had fallen back and she made no effort to reclaim it. Her red hair hung in dripping rattails on her shoulders, and droplets clung to her thick red brows.

"The last thing Da said to me—he didn't say it, even, he wrote it—he had to write it, I wouldn't talk to him. . . ." She swallowed and ran a hand beneath her nose, wiping away a pendant drop. "He said—I had to find a way to . . . to forgive him. B-Bonnet."

"To do *what*?" She pulled her arm away slightly, and he realized how hard his fingers were digging into her flesh. He loosened his grip, with a small grunt of apology, and she tilted her head briefly toward him in acknowledgment.

"He knew," she said, and stopped. She turned to face him, her feelings now in hand. "You know what happened to him—at Wentworth."

Roger gave a short, awkward nod. In actuality, he had no clear notion what had been done to Jamie Fraser—and had no wish to know more than he did. He knew about the scars on Fraser's back, though, and knew from the few things Claire had said that these were but a faint reminder.

"He knew," she said steadily. "And he knew what had to be done. He told me—if I wanted to be . . . whole . . . again, I had to find a way to forgive Stephen Bonnet. So I did."

He had Brianna's hand in his, held so tight that he felt the small shift of her bones. She had not told him, he had not asked. The name of Stephen Bonnet had never been mentioned between them, not until now.

"You did." He spoke gruffly, and had to stop to clear his throat. "You found him, then? You spoke to him?"

She brushed wet hair back from her face, nodding. Grey had come to her, told her that Bonnet had been taken, condemned. Awaiting transport to Wilmington and execution, he was being held in the cellar beneath the Crown warehouse in Cross Creek. It was there that she had gone to him, bearing what she hoped was absolution—for Bonnet, for herself.

"I was huge." Her hand sketched the bulge of advanced pregnancy before her. "I told him the baby was his; he was going to die, maybe it would be some comfort to him, to think that there'd be . . . something left."

Roger felt jealousy grip his heart, so abrupt in its attack

that for a moment, he thought the pain was physical. *Something left*, he thought. *Something of him. And what of me? If I die tomorrow—and I might, girl! Life's chancy here for me as well as you—what will be left of me, tell me that?*

He oughtn't ask, he knew that. He'd vowed never to voice the thought that Jemmy was not his, ever. If there was a true marriage between them, then Jem was the child of it, no matter the circumstances of his birth. And yet he felt the words spill out, burning like acid.

"So you were sure the child was his?"

She stopped dead and turned to look at him, eyes wide with shock.

"No. No, of course not! If I knew that, I would have told you!"

The burning in his chest eased, just a little.

"Oh. But you told him it was—you didn't say to him that there was doubt about it?"

"He was going to die! I wanted to give him some comfort, not tell him my life story! It wasn't any of his goddamn business to hear about you, or our wedding night, or—damn you, Roger!" She kicked him in the shin.

He staggered with the force of it, but grabbed her arm, preventing her from running off.

"I'm sorry!" he said, before she could kick him again, or bite him, which she looked prepared to do. "I'm sorry. You're right, it wasn't his business—and it's not my business, either, to be making you think of it all again."

She drew in a deep breath through her nose, like a dragon preparing to sear him into ash. The spark of fury in her eyes lessened slightly, though her cheeks still blazed with it. She shook off his hand, but didn't run away.

"Yes, it is," she said. She gave him a dark, flat look. "You said there shouldn't be secrets between us, and you were right. But when you tell a secret, sometimes there's another one behind it, isn't there?"

"Yeah. But it's not— I don't mean—"

Before he could say more, the sound of feet and conversation interrupted him. Four men came out of the mist, speaking casually in Gaelic. They carried sharpened sticks and nets, and all were barefoot, wet to the knees. Strings of fresh-caught fish gleamed dully in the rain-light.

"A Smeòraich!" One man, peering out from under the sodden brim of his slouch hat, caught sight of them and broke into a broad grin, as shrewd eyes passed over their dishevelment. "It is yourself, Thrush! And the daughter of the Red One, too? What, can you not restrain yourselves until the darkness?"

"No doubt it is sweeter to taste stolen fruit than to wait on a blessing from a shriveled priest." Another man thrust back his bonnet on his head, and clasped himself briefly, making clear just what he meant by "shriveled."

"Ah, no," said the third, wiping drops from the end of his nose as he eyed Brianna, her cloak pulled tight around her. "He's no but after singing her a wee wedding song, is he not?"

"I know the words to that song, too," said his companion, his grin broadening enough to show a missing molar. "But I sing it still more sweetly!"

Brianna's cheeks had begun to blaze again; her Gaelic was less fluent than Roger's, but she was certainly able to gather the sense of crude teasing. Roger stepped in front of her, shielding her with his body. The men meant no harm, though; they winked and grinned appreciatively, but made no further comment. The first man pulled off his hat and beat it against his thigh, shedding water, then set to business.

"It's glad I am to be meeting you thus, *a Òranaiche*. My mother did hear your music at the fire last night, and told it to my aunts and my cousins, how your music was making the blood dance in her feet. So now they will hear nothing but that you must come and sing for the ceilidh at Spring Creek. It is my youngest cousin will be wed, and her the only child of my uncle, who owns the flour mill."

"It will be a great affair, surely!" put in one of the younger men, the son of the first speaker, by his resemblance to the former.

"Oh, it's a wedding?" said Roger, in slow, formal Gaelic. "We'll have an extra herring, then!"

The two older men burst into laughter at the joke, but their sons merely looked bewildered.

"Ah, the lads would not be knowing a herring, was it slapped wet against their cheeks," said the bonneted man, shaking his head. "Born here, the two of them."

"And where was your home in Scotland, sir?" The man jerked, surprised at the question, put in clear-voiced Gaelic. He stared at Brianna for a moment, then his face changed as he answered her.

"Skye," he said softly. "Skeabost, near the foot of the Cuillins. I am Angus MacLeod, and Skye is the land of my sires and my grandsires. But my sons were born here."

He spoke quietly, but there was a tone in his voice that quelled the hilarity in the younger men as though a damp blanket had been thrown over them. The man in the slouch hat looked at Brianna with interest.

"And were you born in Scotland, *a nighean*?"

She shook her head mutely, drawing the cloak higher on her shoulders.

"I was," said Roger, answering a look of inquiry. "In Kyle of Lochalsh."

"Ah," said MacLeod, satisfaction spreading itself across his weathered features. "It is so, then, that you know all the songs of the Highlands and the Isles?"

"Not all," said Roger, smiling. "But many—and I will learn more."

"Do that," said MacLeod, nodding slowly. "Do that, Singer—and teach them to your sons." His eye lighted on Brianna, and a faint smile curled on his lips. "Let them sing to my sons, that they will know the place they came from—though they will never see it."

One of the younger men stepped forward, bashfully holding out a string of fish, which he presented to Brianna.

"For you," he said. "A gift for your wedding."

Roger could see one corner of her mouth twitch slightly—with humor or incipient hysteria? he wondered—but she stretched out a hand and took the dripping string with grave dignity. She picked up the edge of her cloak with one hand, and swept them all a deep curtsy.

"Chaneil facal agam dhuibh ach taing," she said, in her slow, strangely accented Gaelic. I have no words to say to you but thanks.

The young men went pink, and the older men looked deeply pleased.

"It is good, *a nighean,*" said MacLeod. "Let your husband teach you, then—and teach the *Gaidhlig* to your sons. May you have many!" He swept off his bonnet and bowed extravagantly to her, bare toes squelching in the mud to keep his balance.

"Many sons, strong and healthy!" chimed in his companion, and the two lads smiled and nodded, murmuring shyly. "Many sons to you, mistress!"

Roger made the arrangements for the ceilidh automatically, not daring to look at Brianna. They stood in silence, a foot or two apart, as the men left, casting curious looks behind them. Brianna stared down into the mud and grass where they stood, arms crossed in front of her. The burning feeling was still in Roger's chest, but now it was different. He wanted to touch her, to apologize again, but he thought that would only make things worse.

In the end, she moved first. She came to him and laid her head on his chest, the coolness of her wet hair brushing the wound in his throat. Her breasts were huge, hard as rocks against his chest, pushing against him, pushing him away.

"I need Jemmy," she said softly. "I need my baby."

The words jammed in his throat, caught between apology and anger. He had not realized how much it would hurt to think of Jemmy as belonging to someone else—not his, but Bonnet's.

"I need him, too," he whispered at last, and kissed her briefly on the forehead before taking her hand to cross the meadow once again. The mountain above lay shrouded in mist, invisible, though shouts and murmurs, scraps of speech and music drifted down, like echoes from Olympus.

7

SHRAPNEL

THE DRIZZLE HAD STOPPED by mid-morning, and brief glimpses of pale blue sky showed through the clouds, giving me some hope that it might clear by evening. Proverbs and omens quite aside, I didn't want the wedding ceremonies dampened for Brianna's sake. It wouldn't be St. James's with rice and white satin, but it could at least be *dry*.

I rubbed my right hand, working out the cramp from the tooth-pulling pliers; Mr. Goodwin's broken tooth had been more troublesome to extract than I expected, but I had managed to get it out, roots and all, sending him away with a small bottle of raw whisky, and instructions to swish it round his mouth once an hour to prevent infection. Swallowing was optional.

I stretched, feeling the pocket under my skirt swing against my leg with a small but gratifying *chink*. Mr. Goodwin had indeed paid cash; I wondered whether it was enough for an astrolabe, and what on earth Jamie wanted with one. My speculations were disturbed, though, by a small but official-sounding cough behind me.

I turned around to find Archie Hayes, looking mildly quizzical.

"Oh!" I said. "Ah—can I help you, Lieutenant?"

"Weel, that's as may be, Mistress Fraser," he said, looking me over with a slight smile. "Farquard Campbell said his slaves are convinced that ye can raise the dead, so it might be as a bit of stray metal would pose no great trial to your skills as a surgeon?"

Murray MacLeod, overhearing, uttered a loud snort at this, and turned away to his own waiting patients.

"Oh," I said again, and rubbed a finger under my nose, embarrassed. One of Campbell's slaves had suffered an epileptic seizure four days before, happening to recover abruptly from it just as I laid an exploratory hand on his chest. In vain had I tried to explain what had happened; my fame had spread like wildfire over the mountain.

Even now, a small group of slaves squatted near the edge of the clearing, playing at knucklebones and waiting 'til the other patients should be attended to. I gave them a narrow eye, just in case; if one of them were dying or dangerously ill, I knew they would make no effort to tell me—both from deference to my white patients, and from their confident conviction that if anything drastic should happen while they were waiting, I would simply resurrect the corpse at my own convenience and deal with the problem then.

All of them seemed safely vertical at the moment, though, and likely to remain so for the immediate future. I turned back to Hayes, wiping muddy hands on my apron.

"Well . . . let me see the bit of metal, why don't you, and I'll see what can be done."

Nothing loath, Hayes stripped off bonnet, coat, waistcoat, stock, and shirt, together with the silver gorget of his office. He handed his garments to the aide who accompanied him, and sat down on my stool, his placid dignity quite unimpaired by partial nakedness, by the gooseflesh that stippled his back and shoulders, or by the murmur of awed surprise that went up from the waiting slaves at sight of him.

His torso was nearly hairless, with the pale, suety color of skin that had gone years with no exposure to sunlight, in sharp contrast to the weathered brown of his hands, face, and knees. The contrasts went further than that, though.

Over the milky skin of his left breast was a huge patch of bluish-black that covered him from ribs to clavicle. And while the nipple on the right was a normal brownish-pink, the one on the left was a startling white. I blinked at the sight, and heard a soft *"A Dhia!"* behind me.

"A Dhia, tha e 'tionndadh dubh!" said another voice, somewhat louder. By God, he is turning black!

Hayes appeared not to hear any of this, but sat back to let me make my examination. Close inspection revealed that the dark coloration was not natural pigmentation but a mottling caused by the presence of innumerable small dark granules embedded in the skin. The nipple was gone altogether, replaced by a patch of shiny white scar tissue the size of a sixpence.

"Gunpowder," I said, running my fingertips lightly over the darkened area. I'd seen such things before; caused by a misfire or shot at close range, which drove particles of powder—and often bits of wadding and cloth—into the deeper layers of the skin. Sure enough, there were small bumps beneath the skin, evident to my fingertips, dark fragments of whatever garment he had been wearing when shot.

"Is the ball still in you?" I could see where it had entered; I touched the white patch, trying to envision the path the bullet might have taken thereafter.

"Half of it is," he replied tranquilly. "It shattered. When the surgeon went to dig it out, he gave me the bits of it. When I fitted them together after, I couldna make but half a ball, so the rest of it must have stayed."

"Shattered? A wonder the pieces didn't go through your heart or your lung," I said, squatting down in order to squint more closely at the injury.

"Oh, it did," he informed me. "At least, I suppose that it must, for it came in at my breest as ye see—but it's keekin' out from my back just now."

To the astonishment of the multitudes—as well as my own—he was right. I could not only feel a small lump, just under the outer border of his left scapula, I could actually *see* it; a darkish swelling pressing against the soft white skin.

"I will be damned," I said, and he gave a small grunt of amusement, whether at my surprise or my language, I couldn't tell.

Odd as it was, the bit of shrapnel presented no surgical difficulty. I dipped a cloth into my bowl of distilled alcohol, wiped the area carefully, sterilized a scalpel, and cut quickly into the skin. Hayes sat quite still as I did it; he was a soldier and a Scot, and as the markings on his breast bore witness, he had endured much worse than this.

I spread two fingers and pressed them on either side of the incision; the lips of the small slit pouted, then a dark, jagged bit of metal suddenly protruded like a stuck-out tongue—far enough for me to grasp it with forceps and pull it free. I dropped the discolored lump into Hayes's hand, with a small exclamation of triumph, then clapped a pad soaked with alcohol against his back.

He expelled a long breath between pursed lips, and smiled over his shoulder at me.

"I thank ye, Mrs. Fraser. This wee fellow has been wi' me for some time now, but I canna say as I'm grieved to part company with him." He cupped his blood-smeared palm, peering at the bit of fractured metal in it with great interest.

"How long ago did it happen?" I asked curiously. I didn't think the bit of shrapnel had actually passed completely through his body, though it certainly gave the illusion of having done so. More likely, I thought, it had remained near the surface of the original wound, and traveled slowly round the torso, propelled between skin and muscle by Hayes's movements, until reaching its present location.

"Oh, twenty year and more, mistress," he said. He touched the patch of tough, numbed white that had once been one of the most sensitive spots on his body. "That happened at Culloden."

He spoke casually, but I felt gooseflesh ripple over my arms at the name. Twenty years and more . . . twenty-five, more like. At which point . . .

"You can't have been more than twelve!" I said.

"No," he replied, one eyebrow lifted. "Eleven. My birthday was the next day, though."

I choked back whatever I might have said in reply. I had thought I had lost my capacity to be shocked by the realities of the past, but evidently not. Someone had shot him—an eleven-year-old boy—at point-blank range. No chance of mistake, no shot gone awry in the heat of battle. The man who had shot him had known it was a child he meant to kill—and had fired, anyway.

My lips pressed tight as I examined my incision. No more than an inch long, and not deep; the fractured ball had lain just below the surface. Good, it wouldn't need stitching. I pressed a clean pad to the wound and moved in front of him, to fasten the linen strip that bound it in place.

"A miracle you survived," I said.

"It was that," he agreed. "I was lyin' on the ground, and Murchison's face over me, and I—"

"Murchison!" The exclamation popped out of me, and I saw a flicker of satisfaction cross Hayes's face. I had a brief premonitory qualm, remembering what Jamie had said about Hayes the night before. *He thinks more than he says, does wee Archie—and he talks quite a lot. Be careful of him, Sassenach.* Well, a little late for caution—but I doubted it could matter; even if it *had* been the same Murchison—

"You'll ken the name, I see," Hayes observed pleasantly. "I had heard in England that a Sergeant Murchison of the 26th was sent to North Carolina. But the garrison at Cross Creek was gone when we reached the town—a fire, was it?"

"Er, yes," I said, rather edgy at this reference. I was glad that Bree had left; only two people knew the whole truth of what had happened when the Crown's warehouse on Cross Creek burned, and she was one of them. As for the other—well, Stephen Bonnet was not likely to cross paths with the Lieutenant anytime soon—if Bonnet himself was still alive.

"And the men of the garrison," Hayes pursued, "Murchison and the rest—where have they gone, d'ye know?"

"Sergeant Murchison is dead," said a deep, soft voice behind me. "Alas."

Hayes looked beyond me and smiled.

"A Sheumais ruaidh," he said. "I did think ye might come to your wife, sooner or later. I've been seekin' ye the morn."

I was startled at the name, and so was Jamie; a look of surprise flashed across his features, then disappeared, replaced by wariness. No one had called him "Red Jamie" since the days of the Rising.

"I heard," he said dryly. He sat down on my extra stool, facing Hayes. "Let's have it, then. What is it?"

Hayes pulled up the sporran that dangled between his knees, rummaged for a moment, and pulled out a square of folded paper, secured with a red wax seal, marked with a crest I recognized. My heart skipped a beat at the sight; I somehow doubted that Governor Tryon was sending me a belated birthday wish.

Hayes turned it over, checked carefully to see that the name inscribed on the front was Jamie's, and handed it across. To my surprise, Jamie didn't open it at once, but sat holding it, eyes fixed on Hayes's face.

"What brought ye here?" he asked abruptly.

"Ah, duty, to be sure," Hayes answered, thin brows arched in innocent astonishment. "Does a soldier do aught for any other reason?"

"Duty," Jamie repeated. He tapped the missive idly against his leg. "Aye, well. Duty might take ye from Charleston to Virginia, but there are quicker ways to get there."

Hayes started to shrug, but desisted at once, as the movement jarred the shoulder I was bandaging.

"I had the Proclamation to bring, from Governor Tryon."

"The Governor's no authority over you or your men."

"True," Hayes agreed, "but why should I not do the man a service, and I could?"

"Aye, and did he ask ye to do him the service, or was it your own notion?" Jamie said, a distinct tone of cynicism in his voice.

"Ye've grown a bit suspicious in your auld age, *a Sheumais ruaidh*," Hayes said, shaking his head reprovingly.

"That's how I've lived to grow as auld as I have," Jamie replied, smiling slightly. He paused, eyeing Hayes. "Ye say it was a man named Murchison who shot ye on the field at Drumossie?"

I had finished the bandaging; Hayes moved his shoulder experimentally, testing for pain.

"Why, ye kent that, surely, *a Sheumais ruaidh*. D'ye not recall the day, man?"

Jamie's face changed subtly, and I felt a small tremor of unease. The fact was that Jamie had almost no memory of the last day of the clans, of the slaughter that had left so many bleeding in the rain—him among them. I knew that small scenes from that day came back to him now and again in his sleep, fragments of nightmare—but whether it was from trauma, injury, or simple force of will, the Battle of Culloden was lost to him—or had been, until now. I didn't think he wanted it back.

"A great deal happened then," he said. "I dinna remember everything, no." He bent his head abruptly, and thrust a thumb beneath the fold of the letter, opening it so roughly that the wax seal shattered into fragments.

"Your husband's a modest man, Mistress Fraser." Hayes nodded to me as he summoned his aide with a flip of the hand. "Has he never told ye what he did that day?"

"There was a good bit of gallantry on that field," Jamie muttered, head bent over the letter. "And quite a bit of the reverse." I didn't think he was reading; his eyes were fixed, as though he were seeing something else, beyond the paper that he held.

"Aye, there was," Hayes agreed. "But it does seem worth remark, when a man's saved your life, no?"

Jamie's head jerked up at that, startled. I moved across to stand behind him, a hand laid lightly on his shoulder. Hayes took the shirt from his aide and put it slowly on, smiling in an odd, half-watchful way.

"Ye dinna recall how ye struck Murchison across the head, just as he was set to bayonet me on the ground? And then ye picked me up and carried me from the field, awa to a bittie well nearby? One of the chiefs lay on the grass there, and his men were bathin' his heid in the water, but I could see he was deid, he lay so still. There was someone there to tend me; they wished ye to stay, too, for ye were wounded and bleeding, but ye would not. Ye wished me well, in the name of St. Michael—and went back then, to the field."

Hayes settled the chain of his gorget, adjusting the small silver crescent beneath his chin. Without his stock, his throat looked bare, defenseless.

"Ye looked fair wild, man, for there was blood runnin' doon your face and your hair was loose on the wind. Ye'd sheathed your sword to carry me, but ye pulled it again as ye turned away. I didna think I should see ye again, for if ever I saw a man set to meet his death . . ."

He shook his head, his eyes half-closed, as though he saw not the sober, stalwart man before him, not the Fraser of

Fraser's Ridge—but Red Jamie, the young warrior who had not gone back from gallantry, but because he sought to throw his life away, feeling it a burden—because he had lost me.

"Did I?" Jamie muttered. "I had . . . forgotten." I could feel the tension in him, singing like a stretched wire under my hand. A pulse beat quick in the artery beneath his ear. There were things he had forgotten, but not that. Neither had I.

Hayes bent his head, as his aide fastened the stock around his neck, then straightened and nodded to me.

"I thank ye, ma'am, 'twas most gracious of ye."

"Think nothing of it," I said, dry-mouthed. "My pleasure." It had come on to rain again; the cold drops struck my hands and face, and moisture glimmered on the strong bones of Jamie's face, caught trembling in his hair and thick lashes.

Hayes shrugged himself into his coat, and fastened the loop of his plaid with a small gilt brooch—the brooch his father had given him, before Culloden.

"So Murchison is dead," he said, as though to himself. "I did hear"—his fingers fumbled for a moment with the clasp of the brooch—"as how there were two brothers of that name, alike as peas in the pod."

"There were," Jamie said. He looked up then, and met Hayes's eyes. The Lieutenant's face showed no more than mild interest.

"Ah. And would ye know, then, which it was? . . ."

"No. But it is no matter; both are dead."

"Ah," Hayes said again. He stood a moment, as though thinking, then bowed to Jamie, formally, bonnet held against his chest.

"*Buidheachas dhut, a Sheumais mac Brian*. And may Blessed Michael defend you." He lifted the bonnet briefly to me, clapped it on his head, and turned to go, his aide following in silence.

A gust of wind blew through the clearing, with a chilly burst of rain upon it, so like the freezing April rain of Culloden. Jamie shivered suddenly beside me, with a deep, convulsive shudder that crumpled the letter he still held in his hand.

"How much do you remember?" I asked, looking after Hayes, as he picked his way across the blood-soaked ground.

"Almost nothing," he replied. He stood up and turned to look down at me, his eyes as dark as the clouded skies above. "And that is still too much."

He handed me the crumpled letter. The rain had blotted and smeared the ink here and there, but it was still quite readable. By contrast to the Proclamation, it contained *two* sentences—but the additional period didn't dilute its impact.

New Bern, 20 October

Colonel James Fraser

Whereas the Peace and good Order of this Government has been lately violated and much Injury done to the Persons and Properties of many Inhabitants of this Province by a Body of People who Stile themselves Regulators, I do by the Advice of his Majesty's Council Order and direct you forthwith to call a General Muster of so many Men as you Judge suitable to serve in a Regiment of Militia, and make Report to me as soon as possible of the Number of Volunteers that are willing to turn out in the Service of their King and Country, when called upon, and also what Number of effective Men belong to your Regiment who can be ordered out in case of an Emergency, and in case any further Violence should be attempted to be committed by the Insurgents. Your Diligent and punctual Obedience to these Orders will be well received by

Your Obed't. Servant,
William Tryon

I folded the rain-spotted letter neatly up, noticing remotely that my hands were shaking. Jamie took it from me, and held it between thumb and forefinger, as though it were some disagreeable object—as indeed it was. His mouth quirked wryly as he met my eyes.

"I had hoped for a little more time," he said.

8

THE FACTOR

AFTER BRIANNA LEFT TO RETRIEVE Jemmy from Jocasta's tent, Roger made his way slowly up the hill toward their own campsite. He exchanged greetings and accepted congratulations from people he passed, but scarcely heard what was said to him.

There'll be a next time, she'd said. He held the words close, turning them over in his mind like a handful of coins in his pocket. She hadn't been just saying it. She meant it, and it was a promise that at the moment meant even more to him than the ones she'd made on their first wedding night.

The thought of weddings reminded him, finally, that there was in fact another coming. He glanced down at himself, and saw that Bree hadn't been exaggerating about his appearance. Damn, and it was Jamie's coat, too.

He began to brush off the pine needles and streaks of mud, but was interrupted by a halloo from the path above. He looked up, to see Duncan Innes making his way carefully down the steep slope, body canted to compensate for his missing arm. Duncan had put on his splendid coat, scarlet with blue facings and gold buttons, and his hair was plaited tight under a stylish new black hat. The transformation from Highland fisherman to prosperous landowner was startling; even Duncan's attitude seemed changed, more confident by half.

Duncan was accompanied by a tall, thin, elderly gentleman, very neat but threadbare in appearance, his scanty white locks tied back from a high and balding brow. His mouth had collapsed from lack of teeth, but retained its humorous curve, and his eyes were blue and bright, set in a long face whose skin was stretched so tight across the bone as scarce to leave enough to wrinkle round the eyes, though deep lines carved the mouth and brow. With a long-beaked nose, and clad in rusty, tattered black, he looked like a genial vulture.

"A Smeòraich," Duncan hailed Roger, looking pleased. "The very man I hoped to find! And I trust you're weel-fettled against your marriage?" he added, his eyes falling quizzically on Roger's stained coat and leaf-strewn hair.

"Oh, aye." Roger cleared his throat, converting his coat-brushing to a brief thump of his chest, as though to loosen phlegm. "Damp weather for a wedding, though, eh?"

"Happy the corpse the rain falls on," Duncan agreed, and laughed, a little nervously. "Still, we'll hope not to die o' the pleurisy before we're wed, eh, lad?" He settled the fine crimson coat more snugly on his shoulders, flicking an imaginary speck of dust from the cuff.

"You're very fine, Duncan," Roger said, hoping to distract attention from his own disreputable state with a bit of raillery. "Quite like a bridegroom!"

Duncan flushed a little behind his drooping mustache, and his one hand twiddled with the crested buttons on his coat.

"Ah, well," he said, seeming mildly embarrassed. "Miss Jo did say as she didna wish to stand up wi' a scarecrow." He coughed, and turned abruptly to his companion, as though the word had suddenly reminded him of the man's presence.

"Mr. Bug, here's Himself's good-son, Roger Mac, him I tellt ye of." He turned back toward Roger, waving vaguely at his companion, who stepped forward, extending his hand with a stiff but cordial bow. "This will be Arch Bug, *a Smeòraich*."

"Your servant, Mr. Bug," Roger said politely, slightly startled to observe that the large bony hand gripping his was missing its first two fingers.

"Ump," Mr. Bug replied, his manner indicating that he reciprocated the sentiment sincerely. He might have intended to expand on the subject, but when he opened his mouth, a high-pitched feminine voice, a little cracked with age, seemed to emerge from it.

"It's that kind, sir, of Mr. Fraser, and I'm sure as he'll have nay reason to regret it, indeed he'll not, as I said to him myself. I canna tell ye what a blessing it is, and us not sure where our next bite was comin' from or how to keep a roof above our heads! I said to Arch, I said, now we must just trust in Christ and Our Lady, and if we mun starve, we shall do it in a state of grace, and Arch, he says to me . . ."

A small, round woman, threadbare and elderly as her husband, but likewise neatly mended, emerged into view, still talking. Short as she was, Roger hadn't seen her, hidden behind the voluminous skirts of her husband's ancient coat.

"Mistress Bug," Duncan whispered to him, unnecessarily.

". . . and no but a silver ha'penny to bless ourselves with, and me a-wondering whatever was to become of us, and then that Sally McBride was sayin' as how she'd heard that Jamie Fraser had need of a good—"

Mr. Bug smiled above his wife's head. She halted in midsentence, eyes widening in shock at the state of Roger's coat.

"Why, look at that! Whatever have ye been up to, lad? Have ye had an accident? It looks as though someone's knocked ye down and dragged ye by your heels through the dung heap!"

Not waiting for answers, she whipped a clean kerchief from the bulging pocket tied at her waist, spat liberally on it, and began industriously cleaning the muddy smears from the breast of his coat.

"Oh, you needn't . . . I mean . . . er . . . thanks." Roger felt as though he'd been caught in some kind of machinery. He glanced at Duncan, hoping for rescue.

"Jamie Roy's asked Mr. Bug to come and be factor at the Ridge." Duncan seized the momentary lull afforded by Mrs. Bug's preoccupation to give a word of explanation.

"Factor?" Roger felt a small jolt at the word, as though someone had punched him just beneath the breastbone.

"Aye, for times when Himself must be abroad or occupied with other business. For it's true enough—fields and tenants dinna tend themselves."

Duncan spoke with a certain note of ruefulness; once a simple fisherman from Coigach, he frequently found the responsibilities of running a large plantation onerous, and he glanced now at Mr. Bug with a small gleam of covetousness, as though he thought momentarily of tucking this useful person into his pocket and taking him home to River Run. Of course, Roger reflected, that would have meant taking Mrs. Bug, too.

"And just the thing it is, too, *such* good fortune, and me telling Arch just yesterday that the best we might hope for was to find work in Edenton or Cross Creek, with Arch maybe takin' to the boats, but that's such a perilous living, is it no? Wet to the skin half the time and deadly agues risin' up from the swamps like ghoulies and the air sae thick wi' the miasma as it's not fit to breathe, and me perhaps to be takin' in laundry in the toon whilst he was gone abroad on the water, though I'm sure I should hate that, for we havena been apart one night since we married, have we, my dearie?"

She cast a glance of devotion upward at her tall husband, who smiled gently down at her. Perhaps Mr. Bug was deaf, Roger thought. Or perhaps they had only been married a week?

Without his needing to inquire, though, he was informed that the Bugs had been husband and wife for more than forty years. Arch Bug had been a minor tacksman to Malcolm Grant of Glenmoriston, but the years after the Rising had been hard. The estate he had held for Grant having been confiscated by the English Crown, Bug had made do for some years as a crofter, but then had been obliged by hardship and starvation to take his wife and their little remaining money and seek a new life in America.

"We had thought to try in Edinburgh—" the old gentleman said, his speech slow and courtly, with a soft Highland lilt. So he *wasn't* deaf, Roger thought. Yet.

"—for I had a cousin there as was to do wi' one of the banking houses, and we thought that perhaps it would be that he could speak a word in someone's ear—"

"But I was far too ancient and lacked sufficient skill—"

"—and lucky they would have been to have him, too! But nay, such fools as they were, they wouldna think of it, and so we had to come awa and try if we might . . ."

Duncan met Roger's eye and hid a smile beneath his

drooping mustache as the tale of the Bugs' adventures poured out in this syncopated fashion. Roger returned the smile, trying privately to dismiss a niggling sense of discomfort.

Factor. Someone to oversee matters on the Ridge, to mind the planting, tend the harvest, deal with the concerns of tenants when Jamie Fraser was away or busy. An obvious necessity, with the recent influx of new tenants and the knowledge of what the next few years would bring.

It wasn't until this moment, though, that Roger realized that he had subconsciously assumed that *he* would be Jamie's right hand in such affairs. Or the left, at least.

Fergus assisted Jamie to some extent, riding on errands and fetching back information. Fergus's lack of a hand limited what he could do physically, though, and he couldn't be dealing with the paperwork or accounts; Jenny Murray had taught the French orphan her brother had adopted to read—after a fashion—but had failed utterly to give him a grasp of numbers.

Roger stole a glance at Mr. Bug's hand, resting now in affection on his wife's plump shoulder. It was broad, work-worn, and strong-looking despite the mutilation, but the remaining fingers were badly twisted with arthritis, the joints knobby and painful in appearance.

So Jamie thought that even an elderly, half-crippled man would be better equipped than Roger to handle the affairs of Fraser's Ridge? That was an unexpectedly bitter thought.

He knew his father-in-law had doubts of his ability, beyond any father's natural mistrust of the man bedding his daughter. Totally tone-deaf himself, Jamie would naturally not value Roger's musical gift. And while Roger was decently sized and hardworking, it was unfortunately true that he had little practical knowledge of animal husbandry, hunting, or the use of deadly weapons. And granted, he had no great experience in farming or in running a large estate—which Mr. Bug plainly did. Roger would be the first to admit these things.

But he was Jamie's son-in-law, or about to be. Damn it, Duncan had just introduced him that way! He might have been raised in another time—but he was a Highland Scot, for all that, and he was well aware that blood and kinship counted for more than anything.

The husband of an only daughter would normally be considered as the son of the house, coming only second to the head of the household in authority and respect. Unless there was something drastically wrong with him. If he were commonly known to be a drunkard, for instance—or criminally dissolute. Or feeble-minded . . . Christ, was that what Jamie thought of him? A hopeless numpty?

"Sit ye doon, young man, and I'll attend to *this* fine boorachie," Mrs. Bug interrupted these dark musings. She pulled on his sleeve, making clicking noises of disapproval as she viewed the leaves and twigs in his hair.

"Look at ye, all gluthered and blashed about! Fightin', was it? Och, weel, I hope the other fellow looks worse, that's all I can say."

Before he could protest, she had him seated on a rock, had whipped a wooden comb from her pocket and the thong from his hair, and was dealing with his disordered locks in a brisk manner that felt calculated to rip several strands from his scalp.

"Thrush, is it, they call ye?" Mrs. Bug paused in her tonsorial activity, holding up a strand of glossy black and squinting suspiciously at it, as though in search of vermin.

"Oh, aye, but it's no for the color of his bonnie black locks," Duncan put in, grinning at Roger's obvious discomfiture. "It's for the singin'. Honey-throated as a wee nightingale, is Roger Mac."

"Singing?" cried Mrs. Bug. She dropped the lock of hair, enchanted. "Was it you we heard last night, then? Singin' 'Ceann-ràra,' and 'Loch Ruadhainn'? And playin' on the bodhran with it?"

"Well, it might have been," Roger murmured modestly. The lady's unbounded admiration—expressed at great length—flattered him, and made him ashamed of his momentary resentment of her husband. After all, he thought, seeing the shabbiness of her much-mended apron, and the lines in her face, the old people had clearly had a hard time of it. Perhaps Jamie had hired them as much from charity as from his own need of help.

That made him feel somewhat better, and he thanked Mrs. Bug very graciously for her assistance.

"Will ye come along to our fire now?" he asked, with an inquiring glance at Mr. Bug. "Ye'll not have met Mrs. Fraser yet, I suppose, or—"

He was interrupted by a noise like a fire engine's siren, distant but obviously coming closer. Quite familiar with this particular racket, he was not surprised to see his father-in-law emerge from one of the trails that crisscrossed the mountain, Jem squirming and squalling like a scalded cat in his arms.

Jamie, looking mildly harried, handed the child across to Roger. Roger took him and—for lack of any other inspiration—stuck his thumb in the wide-open mouth. The noise ceased abruptly, and everyone relaxed.

"What a sweet laddie!" Mrs. Bug stood a-tiptoe to coo over Jem, while Jamie, looking highly relieved, turned to greet Mr. Bug and Duncan.

"Sweet" was not the adjective Roger himself would have chosen. "Berserk" seemed more like it. The baby was bright red in the face, the tracks of tears staining his cheeks, and he sucked furiously on the sustaining thumb, eyes squashed shut in an effort to escape a patently unsatisfactory world. What hair he had was sticking up in sweaty spikes and whorls, and he had come out of his wrappings, which hung in disreputable folds and draggles. He also smelled like a neglected privy, for reasons which were all too obvious.

An experienced father, Roger at once instituted emergency measures.

"Where's Bree?"

"God knows, and He's no telling," Jamie said briefly. "I've been searchin' the mountainside for her since the wean woke in my arms and decided he wasna satisfied wi' my company." He sniffed suspiciously at the hand which had been holding his grandson, then wiped it on the skirts of his coat.

"He's not so very pleased with mine, either, seems like." Jem was champing on the thumb, drool running down his chin and over Roger's wrist, uttering squeals of frustration. "Have ye seen Marsali, then?" He knew Brianna didn't like anyone to feed Jemmy but herself, but this was plainly an emergency. He cast an eye about, hoping to spot a nursing mother somewhere nearby who might take pity on the child, if not on him.

"Let me have the poor wee bairnie," said Mrs. Bug, reaching for the baby and immediately altering her status from chattering busybody to angel of light, so far as Roger was concerned.

"There, now, *a leannan,* there, there." Recognizing a higher authority when he saw it, Jemmy promptly shut up, his eyes rounded with awe as he regarded Mrs. Bug. She sat down with the little boy on her lap and began to deal with him in the same firm and efficient manner with which she had just dealt with his father. Roger thought that perhaps Jamie had hired the wrong Bug to be factor.

Arch, though, was exhibiting both intelligence and competence, asking sensible questions of Jamie regarding stock, crops, tenants, and so forth. *But I could do that*, Roger thought, following the conversation closely. *Some of it*, he amended honestly, as the talk suddenly veered into a discussion of bag-rot. Perhaps Jamie was right to seek someone more knowledgeable . . . but Roger could learn, after all. . . .

"And who's the bonnie laddie, noo?" Mrs. Bug had risen to her feet, cooing over Jemmy, now respectably transformed into a tightly swaddled cocoon. She traced the line of a round cheek with one stubby finger, then glanced at Roger. "Aye, aye, he's eyes just like his father, then, hasn't he?"

Roger flushed, forgetting about bag-rot.

"Oh? I should say he favors his mother, mostly."

Mrs. Bug pursed her lips, narrowing her eyes at Roger, then shook her head decidedly, and patted Jem on the top of his head.

"Not the hair, maybe, but the shape of him, aye, that's yours, lad. Those fine broad shoulders!" She gave Roger a brief nod of approval, and kissed Jem on the brow. "Why, I shouldna be surprised but what his een will turn green as he ages, either. Mark me, lad, he'll be the spit of you by the time he's grown! Won't ye, wee mannie?" She nuzzled Jemmy. "Ye'll be a big, braw lad like your Da, won't ye, then?"

It's the usual thing folk say, he reminded himself, trying to quell the absurd rush of pleasure he felt at her words. *The old wifies, they always say how a bairn resembles this one or that one*. He discovered suddenly that he was afraid even to admit the possibility that Jemmy could really be his—he wanted it so badly. He told himself firmly that it didn't matter; whether the boy was his by blood or not, he would love and care for him as his son. He would, of course. But it did matter, he found—oh, it did.

Before he could say anything further to Mrs. Bug, though, Mr. Bug turned toward him, to include him courteously in the men's conversation.

"MacKenzie, is it?" he asked. "And will ye be one of the MacKenzies of Torridon, then, or maybe from Kilmarnock?"

Roger had been fielding similar questions all through the Gathering; exploring a person's antecedents was the normal beginning of any Scottish conversation—something that wouldn't change a bit in the next two hundred years, he thought, wariness tempered by the comfortable familiarity of the process. Before he could answer, though, Jamie's hand squeezed his shoulder.

"Roger Mac's kin to me on my mother's side," he said casually. "It will be MacKenzie of Leoch, aye?"

"Oh, aye?" Arch Bug looked impressed. "You're far afield, then, lad!"

"Och, no more than yourself, sir, surely—or anyone here, for that matter." Roger waved briefly at the mountainside above, from which the sounds of Gaelic shouts and the music of bagpipes drifted on the damp air.

"No, no, lad!" Mrs. Bug, Jemmy propped against her shoulder, rejoined the conversation. "That's no what Arch is meanin'," she explained. "It's that you're a good long way from the others."

"Others?" Roger exchanged a look with Jamie, who shrugged, equally puzzled.

"From Leoch," Arch got in, before his wife seized the thread of talk between her teeth.

"We did hear it on the ship, aye? There were a gaggle of them, all MacKenzies, all from the lands south of the auld castle. They'd stayed on after the laird left, him and the first lot, but now they meant to go and join what was left o' the clan, and see could they mend their fortunes, because—"

"The laird?" Jamie interrupted her sharply. "That would be Hamish mac Callum?" Hamish, son of Colum, Roger translated to himself, and paused. Or rather, Hamish mac Dougal—but there were only five people in the world who knew that. Perhaps only four, now.

Mrs. Bug was nodding emphatically. "Aye, aye, it is himself they were calling so. Hamish mac Callum MacKenzie, laird of Leoch. The third laird. They said it, just so. And—"

Jamie had evidently caught the knack of dealing with Mrs. Bug; by dint of ruthless interruption, he succeeded in extracting the story in less time than Roger would have thought possible. Castle Leoch had been destroyed by the English, in the purge of the Highlands following Culloden. So much Jamie had known, but, imprisoned himself, had had no word of the fate of those who lived there.

"And no great heart to ask," he added, with a rueful tilt of the head. The Bugs glanced at each other and sighed in unison, the same hint of melancholy shadowing their eyes that shaded Jamie's voice. It was a look Roger was well accustomed to by now.

"But if Hamish mac Callum still lives . . ." Jamie had not taken his hand from Roger's shoulder, and at this it squeezed tight. "That's news to gladden the heart, no?" He smiled at Roger, with such obvious joy that Roger felt an unexpected grin break out on his own face in answer.

"Aye," he said, the weight on his heart lightening. "Aye, it is!" The fact that he would not know Hamish mac Callum MacKenzie from a hole in the ground was unimportant; the man was indeed kin to him—blood kin—and that *was* a glad thought.

"Where have they gone, then?" Jamie demanded, dropping his hand. "Hamish and his followers?"

To Acadia—to Canada, the Bugs agreed. To Nova Scotia? To Maine? No—to an island, they decided, after a convoluted conference. Or was it perhaps—

Jemmy interrupted the proceedings with a yowl indicating imminent starvation, and Mrs. Bug started as though poked with a stick.

"We mun be takin' this puir lad to his Mam," she said rebukingly, dividing a glare impartially among the four men, as though accusing them collectively of conspiracy to murder the child. "Where does your camp lie, Mr. Fraser?"

"I'll guide ye, ma'am," Duncan said hastily. "Come wi' me."

Roger started after the Bugs, but Jamie kept him with a hand on his arm.

"Nay, let Duncan take them," he said, dismissing the Bugs with a nod. "I'll speak wi' Arch later. I've a thing I must say to you, *a chliamhuinn*."

Roger felt himself tense a bit at the formal term of address. So, was this where Jamie told him just what defects of character and background made him unsuitable to take responsibility for things at Fraser's Ridge?

But no, Jamie was bringing out a crumpled paper from his sporran. He handed it to Roger with a slight grimace, as though the paper burned his hand. Roger scanned it quickly, then glanced up from the Governor's brief message.

"Militia. How soon?"

Jamie lifted one shoulder.

"No one can say, but sooner than any of us should like, I think." He gave Roger a faint, unhappy smile. "Ye'll have heard the talk round the fires?"

Roger nodded soberly. He had heard the talk in the intervals of the singing, around the edges of the stone-throwing contests, among the men drinking in small groups under the trees the day before. There had been a fistfight at the caber-tossing—quickly stopped, and with no damage done—but anger hung in the air of the Gathering, like a bad smell.

Jamie rubbed a hand over his face and through his hair, and shrugged, sighing.

" 'Twas luck I should have come across auld Arch Bug and his wife today. If it comes to the fighting—and it will, I suppose, later, if not now—then Claire will ride with us. I shouldna like to leave Brianna to manage on her own, and it can be helped."

Roger felt the small nagging weight of doubt drop away, as all became suddenly clear.

"On her own. You mean—ye want me to come? To help raise men for the militia?"

Jamie gave him a puzzled look.

"Aye, who else?"

He pulled the edges of his plaid higher about his shoulders, hunched against the rising wind. "Come along, then, Captain MacKenzie," he said, a wry note in his voice. "We've work to do before you're wed."

9

GERM OF DISSENT

I PEERED UP THE NOSE of one of Farquard Campbell's slaves, half my mind on the nasal polyp obstructing the nostril, the other half on Governor Tryon. Of the two, I felt more charitably toward the polyp, and I intended to cauterize *that* out of existence with a hot iron.

It seemed so bloody unfair, I thought, frowning as I sterilized my scalpel and set the smallest cauterizing iron in a dish of hot coals.

Was this the beginning? Or one of them? It was the end of 1770; in five years more, all of the thirteen Colonies would be at war. But each colony would come to that point by a different process. Having lived in Boston for so long, I knew from Bree's school lessons what the process had been—or would be—for Massachusetts. Tax, Boston Massacre, Harbor, Hancock, Adams, Tea Party, all that. But North Carolina? How had it happened—how *would* it happen—here?

It could be happening now. Dissension had been simmering for several years between the planters of the eastern seaboard and the hardscrabble homesteaders of the western backcountry. The Regulators were mostly drawn from the latter class; the former were wholeheartedly in Tryon's camp—on the side of the Crown, that was to say.

"All right now?" I had given the slave a good slug of medicinal whisky, by way of fortification. I smiled encouragingly, and he nodded, looking uncertain but resigned.

I had never heard of Regulators, but here they were, nonetheless—and I had seen enough by now to know just how much the history books left out. Were the seeds of revolution being sown directly under my own nose?

Murmuring soothingly, I wrapped a linen napkin round my left hand, took firm hold of the slave's chin with it, poked the scalpel up his nostril and severed the polyp with a deft flick of the blade. It bled profusely, of course, the blood gushing warmly through the cloth round my hand, but evidently was not very painful. The slave looked surprised, but not distressed.

The cautery iron was shaped like a tiny spade, a bit of square, flattened metal on the end of a slender rod with a wooden handle. The flat bit was smoking in the fire, the edges glowing red. I pressed the cloth hard against the man's nose to blot the blood, took it away, and in the split second before the blood spurted out again, pressed the hot iron up his nose against the septum, hoping against hope that I'd got the proper spot.

The slave made a strangled noise in his throat, but didn't move, though tears poured down his cheeks, wet and warm on my fingers. The smell of searing blood and flesh was just the same as the scent that rose from the barbecue pits. My stomach growled loudly; the slave's bulging, bloodshot eye met mine, astonished. My mouth twitched, and he giggled faintly through the tears and snot.

I took the iron away, cloth poised. No fresh blood flowed. I tilted the man's head far back, squinting to see, and was pleased to find the small, clean mark, high on the mucosa. The burn would be a vivid red, I knew, but without the light of a scope, it looked black, a small scab hidden like a tick in the hairy shadows of the nostril.

The man spoke no English; I smiled at him, but addressed his companion, a young woman who had clutched his hand throughout the ordeal.

"He'll be quite all right. Tell him, please, not to pick at the scab. If there should be swelling, pus or fever"—I paused, for the next line should be—"go to your doctor at once," and that was not an option.

"Go to your mistress," I said, instead, reluctantly. "Or find an herb-woman." The present Mrs. Campbell was young, and rather muddleheaded, from the little I knew of her. Still, any plantation mistress should have the knowledge and wherewithal to treat a fever. And if it should go past simple infection and into septicemia . . . well, there was not much anyone could do, in that case.

I patted the slave's shoulder and sent him off, beckoning to the next in line.

Infection. That was what was brewing. Things seemed quiet overall—after all, the Crown was withdrawing all its troops! But dozens, hundreds, thousands of tiny germs of dissent must linger, forming pockets of conflict throughout the Colonies. The Regulation was only one.

A small bucket of distilled alcohol stood by my feet, for disinfecting instruments. I dipped the cautery iron in this, then thrust it back in the fire; the alcohol ignited with a brief, lightless *piff!*

I had the unpleasant feeling that the note presently burning a hole in Jamie's sporran was a similar flame, touched to one of a million small fuses. Some might be stamped out, some would fizzle on their own—but enough would burn, and go on burning, searing their destructive way through homes and families. The end of it would be a clean excision, but a great deal of blood would flow before the hot iron of guns should sear the open wound.

Were we never to have a little peace, Jamie and I?

"THERE'S DUNCAN MACLEOD, he's got three hundred acres near the Yadkin River, but no one on it save himself and his brother." Jamie rubbed a sleeve over his face, wiping off the sheen of moisture that clung to his bones. He blinked to clear his vision, and shook himself like a dog, spattering drops that had condensed in his hair.

"But," he went on, gesturing toward the plume of smoke that marked MacLeod's fire, "he's kin to auld Rabbie Cochrane. Rabbie's not come to the Gathering—ill wi' the dropsy, I hear—but he's got eleven grown bairns, scattered over the mountains like seed corn. So, take your time wi' MacLeod, make sure he's pleased to come, then tell him to send word to Rabbie. We'll muster at Fraser's Ridge in a fortnight, tell him."

He hesitated, one hand on Roger's arm to prevent an abrupt departure. He squinted into the haze, reckoning up the possibilities. They'd visited three campsites together, and got the pledges of four men. How many more could be found at the Gathering?

"After Duncan, go across to the sheep pens. Angus Og will be there, surely—ye ken Angus Og?"

Roger nodded, hoping he recalled the correct Angus Og. He'd met at least four men of that name in the last week, but one of them had had a dog at heel, and reeked of raw wool.

"Campbell, aye? Bent like a fishhook, and a cast in one eye?"

"Aye, that's him." Jamie gave a nod of approbation, relaxing his grip. "He's too crabbit to fight himself, but he'll see his nephews come, and spread the word amongst the settlements near High Point. So, Duncan, Angus . . . oh, aye, Joanie Findlay."

"Joanie?"

Fraser grinned.

"Aye, auld Joan, they call her. Her camp's near my aunt, her and her brother, Iain Mhor."

Roger nodded, dubious.

"Aye. It's her I speak to, though, is it?"

"Ye'll have to," Fraser said. "Iain Mhor's got nay speech. She's two more brothers who have, though, and two sons old enough to fight. She'll see they come."

Jamie cast an eye upward; the day had warmed slightly

and it wasn't raining so much as misting—a mizzle, they'd call it in Scotland. The clouds had thinned enough to show the disk of the sun, a pale blurry wafer still high in the sky, but sinking lower. Another two hours of good light, maybe.

"That'll do," he decided, wiping his nose on his sleeve. "Come back to the fire when ye've done wi' auld Joan, and we'll have a bit of supper before your wedding, aye?" He gave Roger an up-cocked brow and a slight smile, then turned away. Before Roger could move off, he turned back.

"Say straight off as you're Captain MacKenzie," he advised. "They'll mind ye better." He turned again and strode off in search of the more recalcitrant prospects on his list.

MacLeod's fire burned like a smudge pot in the mist. Roger turned toward it, repeating the names under his breath like a mantra. "Duncan MacLeod, Rabbie Cochrane, Angus Og Campbell, Joanie Findlay . . . Duncan MacLeod, Rabbie Cochrane . . ." No bother; three times and he'd have it cold, no matter whether it was the words of a new song to be learned, facts in a textbook, or directions to the psychology of potential militia recruits.

He could see the sense of finding as many of the backcountry Scots as possible now, before they scattered away to their farms and cabins. And he was heartened by the fact that the men Fraser had approached so far had accepted the militia summons with no more than a mild glower and throat-clearings of resignation.

Captain MacKenzie. He felt a small sense of embarrassed pride at the title Fraser had casually bestowed on him. "Instant Soldier," he muttered derisively to himself, straightening the shoulders of his sodden coat. "Just add water."

At the same time, he'd admit to a faint tingle of excitement. It might amount to no more than playing soldiers, now, indeed—but the thought of marching with a militia regiment, muskets shouldered and the smell of gunpowder on their hands . . .

It was less than four years from now, he thought, and militiamen would stand on the green at Lexington. Men who were no more soldiers to start with than these men he spoke to in the rain—no more than him. Awareness shivered over his skin, settled in his belly with an odd weight of significance.

It was coming. Christ, it was really coming.

MACLEOD WAS NO TROUBLE, but it took longer than he'd thought to find Angus Og Campbell, up to his arse in sheep, and irascible at the distraction. "Captain MacKenzie" had had little effect on the old bastard; the invocation of "Colonel Fraser"—spoken with a degree of menace—had had more. Angus Og had chewed his long upper lip with moody concentration, nodded reluctantly, and gone back to his bargaining with a gruff, "Aye, I'll send word."

The mizzle had stopped and the clouds were beginning to break up by the time he climbed back up the slope to Joan Findlay's camp.

"Auld Joan," to his surprise, was an attractive woman in her mid-thirties, with sharp hazel eyes that regarded him with interest under the folds of her damp arisaid.

"So it's come to that, has it?" she said, in answer to his brief explanation of his presence. "I did wonder, when I heard what the soldier-laddie had to say this morning."

She tapped her lip thoughtfully with the handle of her wooden pudding-spoon.

"I've an aunt who lives in Hillsborough, ken. She's a room in the King's House, straight across the street from Edmund Fanning's house—or where it used to be." She gave a short laugh, though it held no real humor.

"She wrote to me. The mob came a-boilin' down the street, wavin' pitchforks like a flock o' demons, she said. They cut Fanning's house from its sills, and dragged the whole of it down wi' ropes, right before her eyes. So now we're meant to send our men to pull Fanning's chestnuts from the fire, are we?"

Roger was cautious; he'd heard a good deal of talk about Edmund Fanning, who was less than popular.

"I couldna say as to that, Mrs. Findlay," he said. "But the Governor—"

Joan Findlay snorted expressively.

"Governor," she said, and spat into the fire. "Pah. The Governor's friends, more like. But there—poor men mun bleed for the rich man's gold, and always will, eh?"

She turned to two small girls who had materialized behind her, silent as small shawled ghosts.

"Annie, fetch your brothers. Wee Joanie, you stir the pot. Mind ye scrape the bottom well so it doesna burn." Handing the spoon to the smallest girl, she turned away, beckoning Roger to follow.

It was a poor camp, with no more than a woolen blanket stretched between two bushes to provide a shelter of sorts. Joan Findlay squatted down before the cavelike recess so provided, and Roger followed, bending down to peer over her shoulder.

"*A bhràthair*, here's Captain MacKenzie," she said, reaching out a hand to the man that lay on a pallet of dry grass under the blanket's shelter. Roger felt a sudden shock at the man's appearance, but suppressed it.

A spastic, they would have called him in the Scotland of Roger's own time; what did they call such a condition now? Perhaps nothing in particular; Fraser had said only, *He has nay speech.*

No, nor proper movement, either. His limbs were bony and wasted, his body twisted into impossible angles. A tattered quilt had been laid over him, but his jerking movements had pulled it awry, so that the cloth was bunched, wrenched hard between his legs, and his upper body was left exposed, the worn shirt also rumpled and pulled half off by his struggles. The pale skin over shoulder and ribs gleamed cold and blue-toned in the shadows.

Joan Findlay cupped a hand about the man's cheek and turned his head so that he could look at Roger.

"This will be my brother Iain, Mr. MacKenzie," she said, her voice firm, daring him to react.

The face too was distorted, the mouth pulled askew and drooling, but a pair of beautiful—and intelligent—hazel eyes looked back at Roger from the ruin. He took firm grip of his feelings and his own features, and reached out, taking the man's clawed hand in his own. It felt terrible, the bones sharp and fragile under skin so cold it might have been a corpse's.

"Iain Mhor," he said softly. "I have heard your name. Jamie Fraser sends ye his regards."

The eyelids lowered in a graceful sweep of acknowledgment, and came up again, regarding Roger with calm brightness.

"The Captain's come to call for militiamen," Joan said from behind Roger's shoulder. "The Governor's sent orders, aye? Seems he's had enough o' riot and disorder, so he says; he'll put it down by force." Her voice held a strong tone of irony.

Iain Mhor's eyes shifted to his sister's face. His mouth moved, struggling for shape, and his narrow chest strained with effort. A few croaking syllables emerged, thick with spittle, and he fell back, breathing hard, eyes intent on Roger.

"Will there be bounty money paid, he says, Captain?" Joan translated.

Roger hesitated. Jamie had addressed that question, but there was no definite answer. He could feel the subdued eagerness, though, both in the woman behind him and the man who lay before him. The Findlays were grinding poor; that much was plain from the little girls' ragged frocks and bare feet, from the threadbare clothes and bedding that gave Iain Mhor scant shelter from the cold. But honesty compelled him to answer.

"I don't know. There is none advertised as yet—but there may be." The payment of bounty money depended on the response to the Governor's call; if a simple order produced insufficient troops, the Governor might see fit to provide further inducement for militiamen to answer the summons.

An expression of disappointment flickered in Iain Mhor's eyes, replaced almost at once by resignation. Any income would have been welcome, but it was not really expected.

"Well, then." Joan's voice held the same resignation. Roger felt her draw back and turn aside, but he was still held by the long-lashed hazel eyes. They met his, unflinching and curious. Roger hesitated, unsure whether to simply take his leave. He wanted to offer help—but God, what help was there?

He stretched out a hand toward the gaping shirt, the rumpled quilt. Little enough, but something.

"May I?"

The hazel eyes closed for a moment, opened in acquiescence, and he set about the chore of putting things straight. Iain Mhor's body was emaciated, but surprisingly heavy, and awkward to lift from such an angle.

Still, it took no more than a few moments, and the man lay decently covered, and warmer at least. Roger met the hazel eyes again, smiled, nodded awkwardly, and backed away from the grass-lined nest, wordless as Iain Mhor himself.

Joan Findlay's two sons had come; they stood by their mother, sturdy lads of sixteen and seventeen, regarding Roger with cautious curiosity.

"This will be Hugh," she said, reaching up to put a hand on one shoulder, then the other, "and Iain Og."

Roger inclined his head courteously.

"Your servant, gentlemen."

The boys exchanged glances with each other, then looked at their feet, smothering grins.

"So, *Captain* MacKenzie." Joan Findlay's voice came down hard on the word. "If I lend ye my sons, will ye promise me, then, to send them safe home?"

The woman's hazel eyes were as bright and intelligent as her brother's—and as unflinching. He braced himself not to look away.

"So far as it lies in my power, ma'am—I will see them safe."

The edge of her mouth lifted slightly; she knew quite well what was in his power and what was not. She nodded, though, and her hands dropped to her sides.

"They'll come."

He took his leave then, and walked away, the weight of her trust heavy on his shoulders.

10

GRANNIE BACON'S GIFTS

THE LAST OF MY PATIENTS seen to, I stood on my toes and stretched luxuriously, feeling a pleasant glow of accomplishment. For all the conditions that I couldn't really treat, all the illnesses I couldn't cure . . . still, I had done what I could, and had done it well.

I closed the lid of my medical chest and picked it up in my arms; Murray had graciously volunteered to bring back the rest of my impedimenta—in return for a bag of dried senna leaves and my spare pill-rolling tile. Murray himself was still attending his last patient, frowning as he prodded the abdomen of a little old lady in bonnet and shawl. I waved in farewell at him, and he gave me an abstracted nod, turning to pick up his fleam. At least he did remember to dip it into the boiling water; I saw his lips move as he spoke Brianna's charm under his breath.

My feet were numb from standing on the cold ground, and my back and shoulders ached, but I wasn't really tired. There were people who would sleep tonight, their pain relieved. Others who would heal well now, wounds dressed cleanly and limbs set straight. A few whom I could truthfully say I had saved from the possibility of serious infection or even death.

And I had given yet another version of my own Sermon on the Mount, preaching the gospel of nutrition and hygiene to the assembled multitudes.

"Blessed are those who eat greens, for they shall keep their teeth," I murmured to a red-cedar tree. I paused to pull off a few of the fragrant berries, and crushed one with my thumbnail, enjoying the sharp, clean scent.

"Blessed are those who wash their hands after wiping their arses," I added, pointing a monitory finger at a blue jay who had settled on a nearby branch. "For they shall not sicken."

The camp was in sight now, and with it, the delightful prospect of a cup of hot tea.

"Blessed are those who boil water," I said to the jay, seeing a plume of steam rising from the small kettle hung over our fire. "For they shall be called saviors of mankind."

"Mrs. Fraser, mum?" A small voice piped up beside me, breaking my reverie, and I looked down to see Eglantine Bacon, aged seven, and her younger sister, Pansy, a pair of round-faced, towheaded little girls, liberally sprinkled with freckles.

"Oh, hallo, dear. And how are you?" I asked, smiling down at them. Quite well, from the looks of them; illness in a child is generally visible at a glance, and both the small Bacons were obviously blooming.

"Very well, mum, thank ye kindly." Eglantine gave a short bob, then reached over and pushed on Pansy's head to make her curtsy, too. The courtesies observed—the Bacons were townspeople, from Edenton, and the girls had been raised to have nice manners—Eglantine reached into her pocket and handed me a large wad of fabric.

"Grannie Bacon's sent ye a present," she explained proudly, as I unfolded the material, which proved to be an enormous mobcap, liberally embellished with lace and trimmed with lavender ribbons. "She couldna come to the Gathering this year, but she said as we must bring ye this, and give ye her thanks for the medicine ye sent for her . . . roo-mah-tics." She pronounced the word carefully, her face screwed up in concentration, then relaxed, beaming in pride at having gotten it out properly.

"Why, thank you. How lovely!" I held the cap up to admire, privately thinking a few choice things about Grannie Bacon.

I had encountered that redoubtable lady a few months earlier, at Farquard Campbell's plantation, where she was visiting Farquard's aged and obnoxious mother. Mrs. Bacon was almost as old as the ancient Mrs. Campbell, and quite as capable of annoying her descendants, but also possessed of a lively sense of humor.

She had disapproved, audibly, repeatedly, and eventually to my face, of my habit of going about with my head uncovered, it being her opinion that it was unseemly for a woman of my age not to wear either cap or kerch, reprehensible for the wife of a man of my husband's position—and furthermore, that only "backcountry sluts and women of low character" wore their hair loose upon their shoulders. I had laughed, ignored her, and given her a bottle of Jamie's second-best whisky, with instructions to have a wee nip with her breakfast and another after supper.

A woman to acknowledge a debt, she had chosen to repay it in characteristic fashion.

"Will ye not put it on?" Eglantine and Pansy were looking trustfully up at me. "Grannie told us to be sure ye put it on, so as we could tell her how it suited ye."

"Did she, indeed." No help for it, I supposed. I shook the object out, twisted up my hair with one hand, and pulled the mobcap on. It drooped over my brow, almost reaching the bridge of my nose, and draped my cheeks in ribboned swathes, so that I felt like a chipmunk peering out from its burrow.

Eglantine and Patsy clapped their hands in paroxysms of delight. I thought I heard muffled sounds of amusement from somewhere behind me, but didn't turn to see.

"Do tell your grannie I said thank you for the lovely present, won't you?" I patted the girls gravely on their blond heads, offered them each a molasses toffee from my pocket, and sent them off to their mother. I was just reaching up to pull off the excrescence on my head, when I realized that their mother was present—had probably been there all along, in fact, lurking behind a persimmon tree.

"Oh!" I said, converting my reach into an adjustment of the floppy chapeau. I held the overhanging flap up with one finger, the better to peer out. "Mrs. Bacon! I didn't see you there."

"Mrs. Fraser." Polly Bacon's face was flushed a delicate rose color—no doubt from the chill of the day. She had her lips pressed tight together, but her eyes danced under the ruffle of her own very proper cap.

"The girls wanted to give ye the cap," she said, tactfully averting her gaze from it, "but my mother-in-law did send ye another wee gift. I thought perhaps I'd best bring that myself, though."

I wasn't sure I wanted anything to do with any more of Grannie Bacon's gifts, but took the proffered parcel with as much grace as I could manage. It was a small bag of oiled silk, plumply stuffed with something, with a faintly sweet, slightly oily botanical scent about it. A crude picture of a plant had been drawn on the front in brownish ink; something with an upright stalk and what looked like umbels. It looked faintly familiar, but I could put no name to it. I undid the string, and poured a small quantity of tiny dark-brown seeds out into my palm.

"What are these?" I asked, looking up at Polly in puzzlement.

"I don't know what they're called in English," she said. "The Indians call them *dauco*. Grannie Bacon's own grannie was a Catawba medicine woman, aye? That's where she learnt the use of them."

"Was she really?" I was more than interested now. No wonder the drawing seemed familiar; this must be the plant that Nayawenne had once shown me—the women's plant. To be sure of it, though, I asked.

"What is the use of them?"

The color rose higher in Polly's cheeks, and she glanced round the clearing to be sure no one was close enough to hear before leaning forward to whisper to me.

"They stop a woman from getting wi' child. Ye take a teaspoonful each day, in a glass of water. Each day, mind, and a man's seed canna take hold in the womb." Her eyes met mine, and while the light of amusement still lingered at the backs of them, something more serious was there as well.

"Grannie said ye were a conjure-woman, she could tell. And that bein' so, ye'd have cause often to help women. And when it is a matter of miscarriage, stillbirth, or childbed fever, let alone the misery of losing a live babe—she said I must tell ye that an ounce o' prevention is worth a pound o' cure."

"Tell your mother-in-law thank you," I said sincerely. The

average woman of Polly's age might have five or six children; she had the two girls, and lacked the drained look of a woman worn with ill-timed bearing. Evidently, the seeds worked.

Polly nodded, the smile breaking out on her face.

"Aye, I'll tell her. Oh—she said as how her grannie told her it was women's magic; ye dinna mention it to men."

I glanced thoughtfully across the clearing, to where Jamie stood in conversation with Archie Hayes, Jemmy blinking sleepily in the crook of his arm. Yes, I could well see that some men might take exception to old Grannie Bacon's medicine. Was Roger one of them?

Bidding farewell to Polly Bacon, I took my chest across to our lean-to, and tucked the bag of seeds carefully away in it. A very useful addition to my pharmacopeia, if Nayawenne and Mrs. Bacon's grannie were correct. It was also a singularly well-timed gift, considering my earlier conversation with Bree.

Even more valuable than the small heap of rabbit skins I had accumulated, though those were more than welcome. Where had I put them? I looked round the scattered rubble of the campsite, half-listening to the men's conversation behind me. There they were, just under the edge of the canvas. I lifted the lid of one of the empty food hampers to put them away for the journey home.

". . . Stephen Bonnet."

The name stung my ear like a spider's bite, and I dropped the lid with a bang. I glanced quickly round the campsite, but neither Brianna nor Roger was within hearing distance. Jamie's back was turned to me, but it was he who had spoken.

I pulled the mobcap off my head, hung it carefully from a dogwood branch, and went purposefully to join him.

WHATEVER THE MEN had been talking about, they stopped when they saw me. Lieutenant Hayes thanked me gracefully once more for my surgical assistance, and took his leave, his bland round face revealing nothing.

"What *about* Stephen Bonnet?" I said, as soon as the Lieutenant was out of earshot.

"That's what I was inquiring about, Sassenach. Is the tea brewed yet?" Jamie made a move toward the fire, but I stopped him with a hand on his arm.

"Why?" I demanded. I didn't let go my grip, and he reluctantly turned to face me.

"Because I wish to know where he is," he said evenly. He made no pretense of not understanding me, and a small, cold feeling flickered through my chest.

"Did Hayes know where he is? Has he heard anything of Bonnet?"

He shook his head, silent. He was telling me the truth. My fingers loosened with relief, and he moved his arm out of my grasp—not angrily, but with a sense of quiet and definite detachment.

"It *is* my business!" I said, answering the gesture. I kept my voice low, glancing round to be sure that neither Bree nor Roger was within hearing. I didn't see Roger; Bree was standing by the fire, absorbed in conversation with the Bugs, the elderly couple Jamie had engaged to help care for the farm. I turned back to Jamie.

"Why are you looking for that man?"

"Is it not sense to know where danger may lie?" He wasn't looking at me but over my shoulder, smiling and nodding at someone. I glanced back to see Fergus heading for the fire, rubbing a cold-reddened hand beneath his arm. He waved cheerfully with his hook, and Jamie lifted a hand halfway in acknowledgment, but turned away a little, still facing me, effectively preventing Fergus from coming to join us.

The cold feeling returned, sharp as though someone had pierced my lung with a sliver of ice.

"Oh, of course," I said, as coolly as I could. "You want to know where he is, so that you can take pains not to go there, is that it?"

Something that might have been a smile flickered across his face.

"Oh, aye," he said. "To be sure." Given the scarcity of

population in North Carolina in general, and the remoteness of Fraser's Ridge in particular, the chances of our stumbling over Stephen Bonnet by accident were roughly equivalent to walking out of the front door and stepping on a jellyfish—and Jamie bloody knew it.

I narrowed my eyes at him. The corner of his wide mouth drew in for a moment, then relaxed, his eyes gone back to seriousness. There was precisely one good reason for his wanting to locate Stephen Bonnet—and *I* bloody knew *that*.

"Jamie," I said, and put a hand on his arm again. "Leave him alone. Please."

He put his own hand over mine, squeezing, but I felt no reassurance from the gesture.

"Dinna fash yourself, Sassenach. I've asked throughout the Gathering, all through the week, inquiring of men from Halifax to Charleston. There's nay report of the man anywhere in the colony."

"Good," I said. It was, but the fact did not escape me that he had been hunting Bonnet with assiduity—and had told me nothing of it. Nor did it escape me that he had not promised to stop looking.

"Leave him alone," I repeated softly, my eyes holding his. "There's enough trouble coming; we don't need more." He had drawn close to me, the better to forestall interruption, and I could feel the power of him where he touched me, his arm beneath my hand, his thigh brushing mine. Strength of bone and fire of mind, all wrapped round a core of steel-hard purpose that would make him a deadly projectile, once set on any course.

"Ye say it is your business." His eyes were steady, the blue of them bleached pale with autumn light. "I know it is mine. Are ye with me, then?"

The ice blossomed in my blood, spicules of cold panic. Damn him! He meant it. There was one reason to seek out Stephen Bonnet, and one reason only.

I swung round on my heel, pulling him with me, so we stood pressed close together, arms linked, looking toward the fire. Brianna, Marsali, and the Bugs were now listening raptly to Fergus, who was recounting something, his face alight with cold and laughter. Jemmy's face was turned toward us over his mother's shoulder, round-eyed and curious.

"*They* are your business," I said, my voice pitched low and trembling with intensity. "And mine. Hasn't Stephen Bonnet done enough damage to them, to us?"

"Aye, more than enough."

He pulled me closer to him; I could feel the heat of him through his clothes, but his voice was cold as the rain. Fergus's glance flicked toward us; he smiled warmly at me and went on with his story. To him, no doubt we looked like a couple sharing a brief moment of affection, heads bent together in closeness.

"I let him go," Jamie said quietly. "And evil came of it. Can I let him wander free, knowing what he is, and that I have loosed him to spread ruin? It is like loosing a rabid dog, Sassenach—ye wouldna have me do that, surely."

His hand was hard, his fingers cold on mine.

"You let him go once; the Crown caught him again—if he's free now, it's not your fault!"

"Perhaps not my fault that he is free," he agreed, "but surely it is my duty to see he doesna stay so—if I can."

"You have a duty to your family!"

He took my chin in his hand and bent his head, his eyes boring into mine.

"Ye think I would risk them? Ever?"

I held myself stiff, resisting for a long moment, then let my shoulders slump, my eyelids drop in capitulation. I took a long, trembling breath. I wasn't giving in altogether.

"There's risk in hunting, Jamie," I said softly. "You know it."

His grip relaxed, but his hand still cupped my face, his thumb tracing the outline of my lips.

"I know it," he whispered. The mist of his breath touched my cheek. "But I have been a hunter for a verra long time, Claire. I willna bring danger to them—I swear it."

"Only to yourself? And just what do you think will happen to us, if you—"

I caught a glimpse of Brianna from the corner of my eye. She had half-turned, seeing us, and was now beaming tender approval on this scene of what she supposed to be parental fondness. Jamie saw her, too; I heard a faint snort of amusement.

"Nothing will happen to me," he said definitely, and gathering me firmly to him, stifled further argument with an encompassing kiss. A faint spatter of applause rose from the direction of the fire.

"Encore!" shouted Fergus.

"No," I said to him as he released me. I whispered, but spoke vehemently for all that. "Not *encore*. I don't want to hear the name of Stephen Bonnet ever bloody again!"

"It will be all right," he whispered back, and squeezed my hand. "Trust me, Sassenach."

11

PRIDE

ROGER DIDN'T LOOK BACK, but thoughts of the Findlays went with him as he made his way downhill from their camp, through clumps of brush and trodden grass.

The two boys were sandy-haired and fair, short—though taller than their mother—but broad-shouldered. The two younger children were dark, tall, and slender, with their mother's hazel eyes. Given the gap of years between the older boys and their younger siblings, Roger concluded from the evidence that Mrs. Findlay had likely had two husbands. And from the look of things now was a widow again.

Perhaps he should mention Joan Findlay to Brianna, he thought, as further evidence that marriage and childbirth were not necessarily mortal to women. Or perhaps it was better just to leave that subject lie quiet for a bit.

Beyond thoughts of Joan and her children, though, he was haunted by the soft, bright eyes of Iain Mhor. How old was he? Roger wondered, grasping the springy branch of a pine to keep from sliding down a patch of loose gravel. Impossible to tell from looking; the pale, twisted face was lined and worn—but with pain and struggle, not age. He was no larger than a boy of twelve or so, but Iain Mhor was older than his namesake, clearly—and Iain Og was sixteen.

He was likely younger than Joan; but perhaps not. She had treated him with deference, bringing Roger to him as a woman would naturally bring a visitor to the head of the family. Not greatly younger, then—say thirty or more?

Christ, he thought, how did a man like that survive so long in times like these? But as he had backed awkwardly away from Iain Mhor, one of the little girls had crawled into the crude shelter from the back, pushing a bowl of milk pudding before her, and had sat down matter-of-factly by her uncle's head, spoon in hand. Iain Mhor had limbs and fingers enough—he had a family.

That thought gave Roger a tight feeling in his chest, somewhere between pain and gladness—and a sinking feeling lower down, as he recalled Joan Findlay's words.

Send them safe home. Aye, and if he didn't, then Joan was left with two young girls and a helpless brother. Had she any property? he wondered.

He had heard a good deal of talk on the mountain about the Regulation since the morning's Proclamation. Given that the matter had plainly not been sufficiently important to make it into the history books, he thought this militia business was unlikely to come to anything. If it did, though, he vowed to himself that he would find some way of keeping Iain Og and Hugh Findlay well away from any danger. And if there was bounty money, they should have their share.

In the meantime . . . he hesitated. He had just passed Jocasta Cameron's camp, bustling like a small village, with its cluster of tents, wagons, and lean-tos. In anticipation of her wedding—now a double wedding—Jocasta had brought almost all of her house slaves, and not a few of the field hands as well. Beyond the livestock, tobacco, and goods brought for trade, there were trunks of clothes and bedding and dishes, trestles, tables, hogsheads of ale, and mountains of food intended for the celebration afterward. He and Bree had breakfasted with Mrs. Cameron in her tent this morning off china painted with roses: slices of succulent fried ham, studded with cloves, oatmeal porridge with cream and sugar, a compote of preserved fruit, fresh corn dodgers with honey, Jamaican coffee . . . his stomach contracted with a pleasant growl of recollection.

The contrasts between that lavishness and the recent poverty of the Findlay encampment were too much to be borne with complacence. He turned upon his heel with sudden decision, and began the short climb back to Jocasta's tent.

Jocasta Cameron was at home, so to speak; he saw her mud-soaked boots outside the tent. Sightless as she was, she still ventured out to call upon friends, escorted by Duncan or her black butler, Ulysses. More often, though, she allowed the Gathering to come to her, and her own tent seethed with company throughout the day, all the Scottish society of the Cape Fear and the colony coming to enjoy her renowned hospitality.

For the moment, though, she seemed fortunately alone. Roger caught a glimpse of her through the lifted flap, reclining in her cane-bottomed chair, feet in slippers, and her head fallen back in apparent repose. Her body servant, Phaedre, sat on a stool near the open tent flap, needle in hand, squinting in the hazy light over a spill of blue fabric that filled her lap.

Jocasta sensed him first; she sat up in her armchair, and her head turned sharply as he touched the tent flap. Phaedre glanced up belatedly, reacting to her mistress's movement rather than his presence.

"Mr. MacKenzie. It *is* the Thrush, is it no?" Mrs. Cameron said, smiling in his direction.

He laughed, and ducked his head to enter the tent, obeying her gesture.

"It is. And how did ye ken that, Mrs. Cameron? I've said not a word, let alone sung one. Have I a tuneful manner of breathing?" Brianna had told him of her aunt's uncanny ability to compensate for her blindness by means of other senses, but he was still surprised at her acuity.

"I heard your step, and then I smelt the blood on you," she said matter-of-factly. "The wound's come open again, has it not? Come, lad, sit. Will we fetch ye a dish of tea, or a dram? Phaedre—a cloth, if ye please."

His fingers went involuntarily to the gash in his throat. He'd forgotten it entirely in the rush of the day's events, but she was right; it had bled again, leaving a crusty stain down the side of his neck and over the collar of his shirt.

Phaedre was already up, assembling a tray from the array of cakes and biscuits on a small table by Jocasta's chair. Were it not for the earth and grass underfoot, Roger thought, he would scarcely know they were not in Mrs. Cameron's drawing room at River Run. She was wrapped in a woolen arisaid, but even that was fastened by a handsome cairngorm brooch.

"It's nothing," he said, self-conscious, but Jocasta took the cloth from her maid's hand and insisted on cleaning the cut herself. Her long fingers were cool on his skin, and surprisingly deft.

She smelled of woodsmoke, as everybody on the mountain did, and the tea she had been drinking, but there was none of the faintly camphorated musty odor he normally associated with elderly ladies.

"Tch, ye've got it on your shirt," she informed him, fingering the stiff fabric disapprovingly. "Will we launder it for ye? Though I dinna ken d'ye want to wear it sopping; it'll never dry by nightfall."

"Ah, no, ma'am. I thank ye, I've another. For the wedding, I mean."

"Well, then." Phaedre had produced a small pot of medicinal grease; he recognized it as one of Claire's, by the smell of lavender and goldenseal. Jocasta scooped up a thumbnail of the ointment and spread it carefully over his wound, her fingers steady on his jawbone.

Her skin was well-kept and soft, but it showed the effects not only of age but weather. There were ruddy patches in her cheeks, nets of tiny broken veins that from a slight distance lent her an air of health and vitality. Her hands showed no liver spots—of course, she was of a wealthy family; she would have worn gloves out-of-doors all her life—but the joints were knobbed and the palms slightly callused from the tug of reins. Not a hothouse flower, this daughter of Leoch, despite her surroundings.

Finished, she passed her hand lightly over his face and head, picked a dried leaf from his hair, then wiped his face with the damp cloth, surprising him. She dropped the cloth, then took his hand, wrapping her own fingers around his.

"There, now. Presentable once more! And now that ye're fit for company, Mr. MacKenzie—did ye come to speak to me, or were ye only passing by?"

Phaedre put down a dish of tea and a saucer of cake by his side, but Jocasta continued to hold his left hand. He found that odd, but the unexpected atmosphere of intimacy made it slightly easier to begin his request.

He put it simply; he had heard the Reverend make such requests for charity before, and knew it was best to let the situation speak for itself, leaving ultimate decision to the conscience of the hearer.

Jocasta listened carefully, a small furrow between her brows. He'd expected her to pause for thought when he'd finished, but instead she replied at once.

"Aye," she said, "I ken Joanie Findlay, and her brother, too. Ye're right, her husband was carried off by the consumption, two year gone. Jamie Roy spoke to me of her yesterday."

"Oh, he did?" Roger felt mildly foolish.

Jocasta nodded. She leaned back a little, pursing her lips in thought.

"It's no just a matter of offering help, ye ken," she explained. "I'm glad of the chance. But she's a proud woman, Joan Findlay—she willna take charity." Her voice held a slight note of reproval, as though Roger ought to have realized that.

Perhaps he should, he thought. But he had acted on the impulse of the moment, moved by the Findlays' poverty. It hadn't occurred to him that if she had little else, it would be that much more important to Joan Findlay to cling to her one valuable possession—her pride.

"I see," he said slowly. "But surely—there must be a way to help that wouldn't offer offense?"

Jocasta tilted her head slightly to one side, then the other, in a small mannerism that he found peculiarly familiar. Of course—Bree did that now and then, when she was considering something.

"There may be," she said. "The feast tonight—for the wedding, aye?—the Findlays will be there, of course, and well-fed. It wouldna be amiss for Ulysses to make up a wee parcel of food for them to take for the journey home—'twould save it spoiling, after all." She smiled briefly, then the look of concentration returned to her features.

"The priest," she said, with a sudden air of satisfaction.

"Priest? Ye mean Father Donahue?"

One thick, burnished brow lifted at him.

"Ye ken another priest on the mountain? Aye, of course I do." She lifted her free hand, and Phaedre, ever alert, came to her mistress's side.

"Miss Jo?"

"Look out some bits from the trunks, lass," Jocasta said, touching the maid's arm. "Blankets, caps, an apron or two; breeks and plain shirts—the grooms can spare them."

"Stockings," Roger put in quickly, thinking of the little girls' dirty bare feet.

"Stockings." Jocasta nodded. "Plain stuff, but good wool and well-mended. Ulysses has my purse. Tell him to give ye ten shillings—sterling—and wrap it in one o' the aprons. Then make a bundle of the things and take them to Father Donahue. Tell him they're for Joan Findlay, but he's no to say where they've come from. He'll know what to say." She nodded again, satisfied, and dropped her hand from the maid's arm, making a little shooing gesture.

"Off wi' ye, then—see to it now."

Phaedre murmured assent and left the tent, pausing only to shake out the blue thing she had been sewing and fold it carefully over her stool. It was a decorated stomacher for Brianna's wedding dress, he saw, done with an elegant lacing of ribbons. He had a sudden vision of Brianna's white breasts, swelling above a low neckline of dark indigo, and returned to the conversation at hand with some difficulty.

"I beg your pardon, ma'am?"

"I said—will that do?" Jocasta was smiling at him, with a slightly knowing expression, as though she had been able to read his thoughts. Her eyes were blue, like Jamie's and Bree's, but not so dark. They were fixed on him—or at least pointed at him. He knew she could not see his face, but she did give the eerie impression of being able to see *through* him.

"Yes, Mrs. Cameron. That's—it's most kind of ye." He brought his feet under him, to stand and take his leave. He expected her to let go of his hand at once, but instead, she tightened her grip, restraining him.

"None so fast. I've a thing or two to say to ye, young man."

He settled back on his chair, composing himself.

"Of course, Mrs. Cameron."

"I wasna sure whether to speak now or wait until it was done—but as ye're here alone now . . ." She bent toward him, intent.

"Did my niece tell ye, lad, that I meant to make her heiress to my property?"

"Aye, she did."

He was at once on guard. Brianna had told him, all right—making it clear in no uncertain terms what she thought of that particular proposal. He steeled himself to repeat her objections now, hoping to do it more tactfully than she might have done herself. He cleared his throat.

"I'm sure my wife is most conscious of the honor, Mrs. Cameron," he began cautiously, "but—"

"Is she?" Jocasta asked dryly. "I shouldna have thought so, to hear her talk. But doubtless ye ken her mind better than I do. Be that as it may, though, I mean to tell her that I've changed my own mind."

"Oh? Well, I'm sure she'll—"

"I've told Gerald Forbes to be drawing up a will, leaving River Run and all its contents to Jeremiah."

"To—" It took a moment for his brain to make the connection. "What, to wee Jemmy?"

She was still leaning forward a little, as though peering at his face. Now she sat back, nodding, still holding firmly to his hand. It came to him, finally, that, unable to see his face, she thought to read him by means of this physical connection.

She was welcome to anything his fingers might tell her, he thought. He was too stunned at this news to have any notion how to respond to it. Christ, what would Bree say about it?

"Aye," she said, and smiled pleasantly. "It came to me, ye see, as how a woman's property becomes her husband's when she weds. Not that there are no means of settling it upon her, but it's difficult, and I wouldna involve lawyers more than I must—I think it always a mistake to go to the law, do ye not agree, Mr. MacKenzie?"

With a sense of complete astonishment, he realized that he was being deliberately insulted. Not only insulted, but warned. She thought—she did! She thought he was after Brianna's presumed inheritance, and was warning him not to resort to any legal contortions to get it. Mingled shock and outrage sealed his tongue for a moment, but then he found words.

"Why, that is the most—so ye take thought for Joan Findlay's pride, but ye think I have none? Mrs. Cameron, how dare ye suggest that—"

"Ye're a handsome lad, Thrush," she said, holding tight to his hand. "I've felt your face. And you've the name of MacKenzie, which is a good one, to be sure. But there are MacKenzies aplenty in the Highlands, aren't there? Men of honor, and men without it. Jamie Roy calls ye kinsman—but perhaps that's because ye're handfast to his daughter. I dinna think *I* ken your family."

Shock was giving way to a nervous impulse to laugh. Ken his family? Not likely; and how should he explain that he was the grandson—six times over—of her own brother, Dougal? That he was, in fact, not only Jamie's nephew, but her own as well, if a bit further down the family tree than one might expect?

"Nor does anyone I've spoken to this week at the Gathering," she added, head tilted to one side like a hawk watching prey.

So that was it. She'd been asking about him among her company—and had failed to turn up anyone who knew anything of his antecedents, for obvious reasons. A suspicious circumstance, to be sure.

He wondered whether she supposed he was a confidence trickster who had taken Jamie in, or whether perhaps he was meant to be involved in some scheme *with* Jamie? No, hardly that; Bree had told him that Jocasta had originally wanted to leave her property to Jamie—who had refused, wary of close involvement with the old leg-trap. His opinion of Jamie's intelligence was reaffirmed.

Before he could think of some dignified retort, she patted his hand, still smiling.

"So, I thought to leave it all to the wee lad. That will be a tidy way of managing, won't it? Brianna will have the use of the money, of course, until wee Jeremiah should come of age—unless anything should happen to the child, that is."

Her voice held a definite note of warning, though her mouth continued to smile, her blank eyes still fixed wide on his face.

"What? What in the name of God d'ye mean by that?" He pushed his stool back, but she held tight to his hand. She was very strong, despite her age.

"Gerald Forbes will be executor of my will, and there are three trustees to manage the property," she explained. "If Jeremiah should come to any mischief, though, then everything will go to my nephew Hamish." Her face was quite serious now. "You'd not see a penny."

He twisted his fingers in hers and squeezed, hard enough that he felt her bony knuckles press together. Let her read what she liked in that, then! She gasped, but he didn't let go.

"Are ye saying to me that ye think I would harm that child?" His voice sounded hoarse to his own ears.

She had gone pale, but kept her dignity, teeth clenched and chin upraised.

"Have I said so?"

"Ye've said a great deal—and what ye've not said speaks louder than what ye have. How dare you imply such things to me?" He released her hand, all but flinging it back in her lap.

She rubbed her reddened fingers slowly with her other hand, lips pursed in thought. The canvas sides of the tent breathed in the wind with a crackling sound.

"Well, then," she said at last. "I'll offer ye my apology, Mr. MacKenzie, if I've wronged ye in any way. I thought it would be as well, though, for ye to know what was in my mind."

"As well? As well for whom?" He was on his feet, and turned toward the flap. With great difficulty, he kept himself from seizing the china plates of cakes and biscuits and smashing them on the ground as a parting gesture.

"For Jeremiah," she said levelly, behind him. "And Brianna. Perhaps, lad, even for you."

He swung round, staring at her.

"Me? What d'ye mean by that?"

She gave the ghost of a shrug.

"If ye canna love the lad for himself, I thought ye might treat him well for the sake of his prospects."

He stared at her, words jamming in his throat. His face felt hot, and the blood throbbed dully in his ears.

"Oh, I ken how it is," she assured him. "It's only to be understood that a man might not feel just so kindly toward a bairn his wife's borne to another. But if—"

He stepped forward then and gripped her hard by the shoulder, startling her. She jerked, blinking, and the candle flames flashed from the cairngorm brooch.

"Madam," he said, speaking very softly into her face. "I do not want your money. My wife does not want it. And *my son* will not have it. Cram it up your hole, aye?"

He let her go, turned, and strode out of the tent, brushing past Ulysses, who looked after him in puzzlement.

12

VIRTUE

PEOPLE MOVED THROUGH the gathering shadows of late afternoon, visiting from one fireside to another, as they had each day, but there was a different feeling on the mountain today.

In part it was the sweet sadness of leavetaking; the parting of friends, the severing of newfound loves, the knowledge that some faces would be seen tonight for the last time on earth. In part it was anticipation; the longing for home, the pleasures and dangers of the journey to come. In part, sheer weariness; cranky children, men harried by responsibility, women exhausted by the labor of cooking over open fires, maintaining a family's clothes and health and appetites from the sustenance of saddlebags and mule packs.

I could sympathize with all three attitudes myself. Beyond the sheer excitement of meeting new people and hearing new talk, I had had the pleasure—for pleasure it definitely was, despite its grimmer aspects—of new patients, seeing novel ailments and curing what could be cured, grappling with the need to find a way to treat what could not.

But the longing for home was strong: my spacious hearth, with its huge cauldron and its roasting jack, the light-filled peace of my surgery, with the fragrant bunches of nettle and dried lavender overhead, dusty gold in the afternoon sun. My feather bed, soft and clean, linen sheets smelling of rosemary and yarrow.

I closed my eyes for a moment, summoning up a wistful vision of this haven of delight, then opened them to reality: a crusted griddle, black with the remnants of scorched oatcake;

soggy shoes and frozen feet; damp clothes that chafed with grit and sand; hampers whose abundance had dwindled to a single loaf of bread—well-nibbled by mice—ten apples, and a heel of cheese; three screeching babies; one frazzled young mother with sore breasts and cracked nipples; one expectant bride with a case of incipient nerves; one white-faced serving-maid with menstrual cramps; four slightly inebriated Scotsmen—and one Frenchman in similar condition—who wandered in and out of camp like bears and were not going to be any help whatever in packing up this evening . . . and a deep, clenching ache in my lower belly that gave me the unwelcome news that my own monthly—which had grown thankfully much less frequent than monthly of late—had decided to keep Lizzie's company.

I gritted my teeth, plucked a cold, damp clout off a clump of brush, and made my way duck-footed down the trail toward the women's privy trench, thighs pressed together.

The first thing to greet me on my return was the hot stink of scorching metal. I said something very expressive in French—a useful bit of phraseology acquired at L'Hôpital des Anges, where strong language was often the best medical tool available.

Marsali's mouth fell open. Germain looked at me in admiration and repeated the expression, correctly and with a beautiful Parisian accent.

"Sorry," I said, looking to Marsali in apology. "Someone's let the teakettle boil dry."

"Nay matter, Mother Claire," she said with a sigh, juggling little Joanie, who'd started to scream again. "It's no worse than the things his father teaches him a-purpose. Is there a dry cloth?"

I was already hunting urgently for a dry cloth or a pot-lifter with which to grasp the wire handle, but nothing came to hand save soggy diapers and damp stockings. Kettles were hard to come by, though, and I wasn't sacrificing this one. I wrapped my hand in a fold of my skirt, seized the handle, and jerked the kettle away from the flames. The heat shot through the damp cloth like a bolt of lightning, and I dropped it.

"Merde!" said Germain, in happy echo.

"Yes, quite," I said, sucking a blistered thumb. The kettle hissed and smoked in the wet leaves, and I kicked at it, rolling it off onto a patch of mud.

"Merde, merde, merde, merde," sang Germain, with a fair approximation of the tune of "Rose, Rose"—a manifestation of precocious musical feeling that went lamentably unappreciated in the circumstances.

"Do hush, child," I said.

He didn't. Jemmy began to screech in unison with Joan, Lizzie—who had had a relapse owing to the reluctant departure of Private Ogilvie—began to moan under her bush, and it started in to hail, small white pellets of ice dancing on the ground and pinging sharply off my scalp. I pulled the soggy mobcap off a branch and clapped it on my head, feeling like an extremely put-upon toad beneath a particularly homely mushroom. All it wanted was warts, I thought.

The hail was short-lived. As the rush and clattering lessened, though, the crunching noise of muddy boots came up the path. Jamie, with Father Kenneth Donahue in tow, crusted hail on their hair and shoulders.

"I've brought the good Father for tea," he said, beaming round the clearing.

"No, you haven't," I said, rather ominously. And if he thought I'd forgotten about Stephen Bonnet, he was wrong about that, too.

Turning at the sound of my voice, he jerked in an exaggeration of startled shock at sight of me in my mobcap.

"Is that you, Sassenach?" he asked in mock alarm, pretending to lean forward and peek under the drooping frill of my cap. Owing to the presence of the priest, I refrained from kneeing Jamie in some sensitive spot, and contented myself instead with an attempt to turn him into stone with my eyes, à la Medusa.

He appeared not to notice, distracted by Germain, who was now dancing in little circles while singing theme and variations on my initial French expression, to the tune of "Row, Row, Row Your Boat." Father Donahue was going bright pink with the effort of pretending that he didn't understand any French.

"Tais toi, petit sot," Jamie said, reaching into his sporran.

He said it amiably enough, but with the tone of one whose expectation of being obeyed is so absolute as not to admit question. Germain stopped abruptly, mouth open, and Jamie promptly thumbed a sweetie into it. Germain shut his mouth and began concentrating on the matter at hand, songs forgotten.

I reached for the kettle, using a handful of my hem again as pot holder. Jamie bent, picked up a sturdy twig, and hooked the handle of the kettle neatly from my hand with it.

"Voilà!" he said, presenting it.

"Merci," I said, with a distinct lack of gratitude. Nonetheless, I accepted the stick and set off toward the nearest rivulet, smoking kettle borne before me like a lance.

Reaching a rock-studded pool, I dropped the kettle with a clang, ripped off the mobcap, flung it into a clump of sedge, and stamped on it, leaving a large, muddy footprint on the linen.

"I didna mean to say it wasna flattering, Sassenach," said an amused voice behind me.

I raised a cold brow in his direction.

"You didn't mean to say it *was* flattering, did you?"

"No. It makes ye look like a poisonous toadstool. Much better without," he assured me.

He pulled me toward him and bent to kiss me.

"It's not that I don't appreciate the thought," I said, and the tone of my voice stopped him, a fraction of an inch from my mouth. "But one inch farther and I think I might just bite a small piece out of your lip."

Moving like a man who has just realized that the stone he has casually picked up is in actuality a wasp's nest, he straightened up and very, very slowly took his hands off my waist.

"Oh," he said, and tilted his head to one side, lips pursed as he surveyed me.

"Ye do look a bit frazzled, at that, Sassenach."

No doubt this was true, but it made me feel like bursting into tears to hear it. Evidently the urge showed, because he took me—very gently—by the hand, and led me to a large rock.

"Sit," he said. "Close your eyes, *a nighean donn*. Rest yourself a moment."

I sat, eyes closed and shoulders slumped. Sloshing noises and a muted clang announced that he was cleaning and filling the kettle.

He set the filled kettle at my feet with a soft clunk, then eased himself down on the leaves beside it, where he sat quietly. I could hear the faint sigh of his breath, and the occasional sniff and rustle as he wiped a dripping nose on his sleeve.

"I'm sorry," I said at last, opening my eyes.

He turned, half-smiling, to look up at me.

"For what, Sassenach? It's not as though ye've refused my bed—or at least I hope it's not come to that yet."

The thought of making love just at the moment was absolutely at the bottom of my list, but I returned the half-smile.

"No," I said ruefully. "After two weeks of sleeping on the ground, I wouldn't refuse *anyone's* bed." His eyebrows went up at that, and I laughed, taken off-guard.

"No," I said again. "I'm just . . . frazzled." Something griped low in my belly, and proceeded to twist. I grimaced, and pressed my hands over the pain.

"Oh!" he said again, in sudden understanding. "That kind of frazzled."

"That kind of frazzled," I agreed. I poked at the kettle with one toe. "I'd better take that back; I need to boil water so I can steep some willow bark. It takes a long time." It did; it would take an hour or more, by which time the cramps would be considerably worse.

"The hell with willow bark," he said, producing a silver flask from the recesses of his shirt. "Try this. At least ye dinna need to boil it first."

I unscrewed the stopper and inhaled. Whisky, and very good whisky, too.

"I love you," I said sincerely, and he laughed.

"I love ye too, Sassenach," he said, and gently touched my foot.

I took a mouthful and let it trickle down the back of my

throat. It seeped pleasantly through my mucous membranes, hit bottom, and rose up in a puff of soothing, amber-colored smoke that filled all my crevices and began to extend warm, soothing tendrils round the source of my discomfort.

"Oooooo," I said, sighing, and taking another sip. I closed my eyes, the better to appreciate it. An Irishman of my acquaintance had once assured me that very good whisky could raise the dead. I wasn't disposed to argue the point.

"That's wonderful," I said, when I opened my eyes again. "Where did you get it?" This was twenty-year-old Scotch, if I knew anything about it—a far cry from the raw spirit that Jamie had been distilling on the ridge behind the house.

"Jocasta," he said. "It was meant to be a wedding gift for Brianna and her young man, but I thought ye needed it more."

"You're right about that."

We sat in a companionable silence, and I sipped slowly, the urge to run amok and slaughter everyone in sight gradually subsiding, along with the level of whisky in the flask.

The rain had moved off again, and the foliage dripped peacefully around us. There was a stand of fir trees near; I could smell the cool scent of their resin, pungent and clean above the heavier smell of wet, dead leaves, smoldering fires, and soggy fabrics.

"It's been three months since the last of your courses," Jamie observed casually. "I thought they'd maybe stopped."

I was always a trifle taken aback to realize how acutely he observed such things—but he was a farmer and a husbandman, after all. He was intimately acquainted with the gynecological history and estrus cycle of every female animal he owned; I supposed there was no reason to think he'd make an exception simply because I was not likely either to farrow or come in heat.

"It's not like a tap that just switches off, you know," I said, rather crossly. "Unfortunately. It just gets rather erratic and eventually it stops, but you haven't any idea when."

"Ah."

He leaned forward, arms folded across the tops of his knees, idly watching twigs and bits of leaf bobbing through the riffles of the stream.

"I'd think it would maybe be a relief to have done wi' it all. Less mess, aye?"

I repressed the urge to draw invidious sexual comparisons regarding bodily fluids.

"Maybe it will," I said. "I'll let you know, shall I?"

He smiled faintly, but was wise enough not to pursue the matter; he could hear the edge in my voice.

I sipped a bit more whisky. The sharp cry of a woodpecker—the kind Jamie called a yaffle—echoed deep in the woods and then fell silent. Few birds were out in this weather; most simply huddled under what shelter they could find, though I could hear the conversational quacking of a small flock of migratory ducks somewhere downstream. *They* weren't bothered by the rain.

Jamie stretched himself suddenly.

"Ah . . . Sassenach?" he said.

"What is it?" I asked, surprised.

He ducked his head, uncharacteristically shy.

"I dinna ken whether I've done wrong or no, Sassenach, but if I have, I must ask your forgiveness."

"Of course," I said, a little uncertainly. What was I forgiving him for? Probably not adultery, but it could be just about anything else, up to and including assault, arson, highway robbery, and blasphemy. God, I hoped it wasn't anything to do with Bonnet.

"What have you done?"

"Well, as to myself, nothing," he said, a little sheepishly. "It's only what I've said *you'd* do."

"Oh?" I said, with minor suspicion. "And what's that? If you told Farquard Campbell that I'd visit his horrible old mother again . . ."

"Oh, no," he assured me. "Nothing like that. I promised Josiah Beardsley that ye'd maybe take out his tonsils today, though."

"That I'd *what*?" I goggled at him. I'd met Josiah Beardsley, a youth with the worst-looking set of abscessed tonsils I'd ever seen, the day before. I'd been sufficiently impressed by the pustulated state of his adenoids, in fact, to have described them in detail to all and sundry over dinner—causing Lizzie to go green round the gills and give her second potato to Germain—and had mentioned at the time that surgery was really the only possible effective cure. I hadn't expected Jamie to go drumming up business, though.

"Why?" I asked.

Jamie rocked back a little, looking up at me.

"I want him, Sassenach."

"You do? What for?" Josiah was barely fourteen—or at least he thought he was fourteen; he wasn't really sure when he'd been born and his parents had died too long ago to say. He was undersized even for fourteen, and badly nourished, with legs slightly bowed from rickets. He also showed evidence of assorted parasitic infections, and wheezed with what might be tuberculosis, or merely a bad case of bronchitis.

"A tenant, of course."

"Oh? I'd have thought you had more applicants than you can handle, as it is."

I didn't just think so; I knew so. We had absolutely no money, though the trade Jamie had done at the Gathering had just about—not quite—cleared our indebtedness to several of the Cross Creek merchants for ironmongery, rice, tools, salt, and other small items. We had land in plenty—most of it forest—but no means to assist people to settle on it or farm it. The Chisholms and McGillivrays were stretching well past our limits, in terms of acquiring new tenantry.

Jamie merely nodded, dismissing these complications.

"Aye. Josiah's a likely lad, though."

"Hmm," I said dubiously. It was true that the boy seemed tough—which was likely what Jamie meant by "likely"; simply to have survived this long by himself was evidence of that. "Maybe so. So are lots of others. What's he got that makes you want him specially?"

"He's fourteen."

I looked at him, one brow raised in question, and his mouth twisted in a wry smile.

"Any man between sixteen and sixty must serve in the militia, Sassenach."

I felt a small, unpleasant contraction in the pit of my stomach. I hadn't forgotten the Governor's unwelcome summons, but what with one thing and another, I hadn't had the leisure to reflect on exactly what the practical consequences of it were likely to be.

Jamie sighed and stretched out his arms, flexing his knuckles until they cracked.

"So you'll do it?" I asked. "Form a militia company and go?"

"I must," he said simply. "Tryon's got my ballocks in his hand, and I'm no inclined to see whether he'll squeeze, aye?"

"I was afraid of that."

Jamie's picturesque assessment of the situation was unfortunately accurate. Looking for a loyal and competent man willing to undertake the settlement of a large section of wild backcountry, Governor Tryon had offered Jamie a Royal grant of land just east of the Treaty Line, with no requirement of quitrent for a period of ten years. A fair offer, though given the difficulties of settlement in the mountains, not quite so generous as it might have looked.

The catch was that holders of such grants were legally required to be white Protestant males of good character, above the age of thirty. And while Jamie met the other requirements, Tryon was well aware of his Catholicism.

Do as the Governor required, and . . . well, the Governor was a successful politician; he knew how to keep his mouth shut about inconvenient matters. Defy him, though, and it would take no more than a simple letter from New Bern to deprive Fraser's Ridge of its resident Frasers.

"Hmm. So you're thinking that if you take the available men from the Ridge—can't you leave out a few?"

"I havena got so many to start with, Sassenach," he pointed out. "I can leave Fergus, because of his hand, and Mr. Wemyss to look after our place. He's a bond servant, so far as anyone knows, and only freemen are obliged to join the militia."

"And only able-bodied men. That lets out Joanna Grant's husband; he's got a wooden foot."

He nodded.

"Aye, and old Arch Bug, who's seventy if he's a day. That's four men—and maybe eight boys under sixteen—to look after thirty homesteads and more than a hundred and fifty people."

"The women can probably manage fairly well by themselves," I said. "It's winter, after all; no crops to deal with. And there shouldn't be any difficulties with the Indians, not these days." My ribbon had come loose when I pulled off the cap. Hair was escaping from its undone plaits in every direction, straggling down my neck in damp, curly strands. I pulled the ribbon off and tried to comb my hair out with my fingers.

"What's so important about Josiah Beardsley, anyway?" I asked. "Surely one fourteen-year-old boy can't make so much difference."

"Beardsley's a hunter," Jamie answered, "and a good one. He brought in nearly two hundred weight of wolf, deer, and beaver skins to the Gathering—all taken by himself alone, he said. I couldna do better, myself."

That was a true encomium, and I pursed my lips in silent appreciation. Hides were the main—in fact, the only—winter crop of any value in the mountains. We had no money now—not even the paper Proclamation money, worth only a fraction of sterling—and without hides to sell in the spring, we were going to have difficulty getting the seed corn and wheat we needed. And if all the men were required to spend a good part of the winter tramping round the colony subduing Regulators instead of hunting . . .

Most women on the Ridge could handle a gun, but almost none could hunt effectively, as they were tethered to their homes by the needs of their children. Even Bree, who was a very good hunter, could venture no more than half a day's travel away from Jemmy—not nearly far enough for wolf and beaver.

I rubbed a hand through my damp locks, fluffing out the loosened strands.

"All right, I understand that part. Where do the tonsils come in, though?"

Jamie looked up at me and smiled. Without answering at once, he got to his feet and circled behind me. With a firm hand, he gathered in the fugitive strands, captured the flying bits, and braided it into a tight, thick plait at the base of my neck. He bent over my shoulder, plucked the ribbon from my lap, and tied it neatly in a bow.

"There." He sat down by my feet again. "Now, as to the tonsils. Ye told the lad he must have them out, or his throat would go from bad to worse."

"It will."

Josiah Beardsley had believed me. And, having come near death the winter before when an abscess in his throat had nearly suffocated him before bursting, he was not eager to risk another such occurrence.

"You're the only surgeon north of Cross Creek," Jamie pointed out. "Who else could do it?"

"Well, yes," I said uncertainly. "But—"

"So, I've made the lad an offer," Jamie interrupted. "One section of land—wee Roger and myself will help him to put up a cabin on it when the time comes—and he'll go halves with me in whatever he takes in the way of skins for the next three winters. He's willing—provided you'll take out his tonsils as part o' the bargain."

"But why today? I can't take someone's tonsils out here!" I gestured at the dripping forest.

"Why not?" Jamie raised one eyebrow. "Did ye not say last night it was a small matter—only a few wee cuts wi' your smallest knife?"

I rubbed a knuckle under my nose, sniffing with exasperation. "Look, just because it isn't a massive bloody job like amputating a leg doesn't mean it's a simple matter!" It was, in fact, a relatively simple operation—surgically speaking. It was the possibility of infection following the procedure, and the need for careful nursing—a poor substitute for antibiotics, but much better than neglect—that raised complications.

"I can't just whack out his tonsils and turn him loose," I said. "When we get back to the Ridge, though—"

"He doesna mean to come back with us directly," Jamie interrupted.

"Why not?" I demanded.

"He didna say; only that he had a bit of business to do, and would come to the Ridge by the first week of December. He can sleep in the loft above the herb shed," he added.

"So you—and he—expect me just to slash out his tonsils, put in a few stitches, and see him on his merry way?" I asked sardonically.

"Ye did nicely wi' the dog," he said, grinning.

"Oh, you heard about that."

"Oh, aye. And the lad who chopped his foot with an ax, and the bairns wi' milk rash, and Mrs. Buchanan's toothache, and your battle wi' Murray MacLeod over the gentleman's bile ducts . . ."

"It *was* rather a busy morning." I shuddered briefly in remembrance, and took another sip of whisky.

"The whole Gathering is talking of ye, Sassenach. I did think of the Bible, in fact, seeing all the crowd clamoring round ye this morning."

"The Bible?" I must have looked blank at the reference, because the grin got wider.

"And the whole multitude sought to touch him," Jamie quoted. "For there went virtue out of him, and healed them all."

I laughed ruefully, interrupting myself with a small hiccup. "Fresh out of virtue at the moment, I'm afraid."

"Dinna fash. There's plenty in the flask."

Thus reminded, I offered him the whisky, but he waved it away, brows drawn down in thought. Melting hail had left wet streaks in his hair, and it lay like ribbons of melted bronze across his shoulders—like the statue of some military hero, weathered and glistening in a public park.

"So ye'll do the lad's tonsils, once he comes to the Ridge?"

I thought a moment, then nodded, swallowing. There would still be dangers in it, and normally I wouldn't do purely elective surgery. But Josiah's condition was truly dreadful, and the continued infections might well kill him eventually, if I didn't take some steps to remedy it.

Jamie nodded, satisfied.

"I'll see to it, then."

My feet had thawed, even wet as they were, and I was beginning to feel warm and pliable. My belly still felt as though I'd swallowed a large volcanic rock, but I wasn't minding all that much.

"I was wondering something, Sassenach," he said.

"Yes?"

"Speakin' of the Bible, ye ken."

"Got Scripture on the brain today, have you?"

One corner of his mouth curled up as he glanced at me.

"Aye, well. It's only I was thinking. When the Angel of the Lord comes along to Sarah and tells her she'll have a bairn the next year, she laughs and says that's a rare jest, as it's ceased to be wi' her after the manner of women."

"Most women in that situation likely wouldn't think it at all a funny idea," I assured him. "I often think God's got a very peculiar sense of humor, though."

He looked down at the large maple leaf he was shredding between thumb and forefinger, but I caught the faint twitch of his mouth.

"I've thought that now and again myself, Sassenach," he said, rather dryly. "Be that as it may, she did have the bairn, aye?"

"The Bible says she did. *I'm* not going to call the book of Genesis a liar." I debated the wisdom of drinking more, but decided to save it for a rainy—well, a rainier—day, and put the stopper back in the flask. I could hear a certain amount of stirring in the direction of the campsite, and my ears caught a word of inquiry, borne on the chilly breeze.

"Someone's looking for Himself," I said. "Again."

Himself glanced over his shoulder and grimaced slightly, but made no immediate move to answer the call. He cleared his throat, and I saw a faint flush move up the side of his neck.

"Well, the point is," he said, carefully not looking at me, "that so far as I ken, if your name's not Mary and the Holy Ghost isna involved in the matter, there's only the one way of getting wi' child. Am I right?"

"So far as I know, yes." I put a hand over my mouth to stifle a rising hiccup.

"Aye. And if so . . . well, that must mean that Sarah was still bedding wi' Abraham at the time, no?"

He still wasn't looking at me, but his ears had gone pink, and I belatedly realized the point of this religious discussion. I reached out a toe and prodded him gently in the side.

"You were thinking perhaps I wouldn't want you anymore?"

"Ye dinna want me *now*," he pointed out logically, eyes on the crumbled remains of his leaf.

"I feel as though my belly is full of broken glass, I'm half-soaked and mud to the knees, and whoever's looking for you is about to burst through the shrubbery with a pack of bloodhounds at any moment," I said, with a certain amount of asperity. "Are you actually inviting me to participate in carnal revelry with you in that mound of soggy leaves? Because if you are—"

"No, no," he said hastily. "I didna mean now. I only meant—I was only wondering if—" The tips of his ears had gone a dull red. He stood up abruptly, brushing dead leaves from his kilt with exaggerated force.

"If," I said in measured tones, "you were to get me with child at this point in the proceedings, Jamie Fraser, I would have your balls *en brochette*." I rocked back, looking up at him. "As for bedding with you, though . . ."

He stopped what he was doing and looked at me. I smiled at him, letting what I thought show plainly on my face.

"Once you have a bed again," I said, "I promise I won't refuse it."

"Oh," he said. He drew a deep breath, looking suddenly quite happy. "Well, that's all right, then. It's only—I wondered, ye ken."

A sudden loud rustling in the shrubbery was followed by the appearance of Mr. Wemyss, whose thin, anxious face poked out of a nannyberry bush.

"Oh, it's yourself, sir," he said, in evident relief.

"I suppose it must be," Jamie said, in resignation. "Is there a difficulty, Mr. Wemyss?"

Mr. Wemyss was delayed in answering, having become inextricably entangled with the nannyberry bush, and I was obliged to go and help release him. A onetime bookkeeper who had been obliged to sell himself as an indentured servant, Mr. Wemyss was highly unsuited to life in the wilderness.

"I do apologize for troubling ye, sir," he said, rather red in the face. He picked nervously at a spiny twig that had caught in his fair, flyaway hair.

"It's only—well, she did say as she meant to cleave him from crown to crutch wi' her ax if he didna leave off, and he said no woman would speak to him in that manner, and she does *have* an ax . . ."

Accustomed to Mr. Wemyss's methods of communication, Jamie sighed, reached out for the whisky flask, uncorked it, and took a deep, sustaining swig. He lowered the flask and fixed Mr. Wemyss with a gimlet eye.

"Who?" he demanded.

"Oh! Er . . . did I not say? Rosamund Lindsay and Ronnie Sinclair."

"Mmphm."

Not good news; Rosamund Lindsay *did* have an ax; she was roasting several pigs in a pit near the creek, over hickory embers. She also weighed nearly two hundred pounds and, while normally good-humored, was possessed of a notable temper when roused. For his part, Ronnie Sinclair was entirely capable of irritating the Angel Gabriel, let alone a woman trying to cook in the rain.

Jamie sighed and handed the flask back to me. He squared his shoulders, shaking droplets from his plaid as he settled it.

"Go and tell them I'm coming, Mr. Wemyss," he said.

Mr. Wemyss's thin face expressed the liveliest apprehension at the thought of coming within speaking range of Rosamund Lindsay's ax, but his awe of Jamie was even greater. He bobbed a quick, neat bow, turned, and blundered straight into the nannyberry bush again.

A wail like an approaching ambulance betokened the appearance of Marsali, Joan in her arms. She plucked a clinging branch from Mr. Wemyss's coat sleeve, nodding to him as she stepped carefully round him.

"Da," she said, without preamble. "Ye've got to come. Father Kenneth's been arrested."

Jamie's eyebrows shot up.

"Arrested? Just now? By whom?"

"Aye, this minute! A nasty fat man who said he was sheriff o' the county. He came up wi' two men and they asked who was the priest, and when Father Kenneth said it was him, they seized him by the arms and marched him straight off, with none so much as a by your leave!"

The blood was rising in Jamie's face, and his two stiff fingers tapped briefly against his thigh.

"They've taken him from my hearth?" he said. *"A Dhia!"*

This was plainly a rhetorical question, and before Marsali could answer it, a crunching of footsteps came from the other direction, and Brianna popped into sight from behind a pine tree.

"What?" he barked at her. She blinked, taken aback.

"Ah . . . Geordie Chisholm says one of the soldiers stole a ham from his fire, and will you go and see Lieutenant Hayes about it?"

"Yes," he said promptly. "Later. Meanwhile, do you go back wi' Marsali and find out where they've taken Father Kenneth. And Mr. Wemyss—" But Mr. Wemyss had at last escaped the clinging embrace of the nannyberry bush. A distant crashing signaled his rush to fulfill his orders.

A quick look at Jamie's face convinced both girls that a swift retreat was the order of the day, and within seconds, we were alone again. He took a deep breath, and let it slowly out through his teeth.

I wanted to laugh, but didn't. Instead I moved closer; cold and damp as it was, I could feel the heat of his skin through his plaid.

"At least it's only the sick ones who want to touch me," I said. I held out the flask to him. "What do *you* do when all the virtue's gone out of you?"

He glanced down at me, and a slow smile spread across his face. Ignoring the flask, he stooped, cupped my face in his hands, and kissed me, very gently.

"That," he said.

Then he turned and strode downhill, presumably full of virtue once more.

13

BEANS AND BARBECUE

I TOOK THE KETTLE BACK to our camp, only to find the place momentarily deserted. Voices and laughter in the distance indicated that Lizzie, Marsali, and Mrs. Bug—presumably with children in tow—were on their way to the women's privy, a latrine trench dug behind a convenient screen of juniper, some way from the campsites. I hung the full kettle over the fire to boil, then stood still for a moment, wondering in which direction my efforts might be best directed.

While Father Kenneth's situation might be the most serious in the long run, it wasn't one where my presence would be likely to make a difference. But I *was* a doctor—and Rosamund Lindsay *did* have an ax. I patted my damp hair and garments into some sort of order, and started downhill toward the creek, abandoning the mobcap to its fate.

Jamie had evidently been of the same mind regarding the relative importance of the emergencies in progress. When I fought my way through the thicket of willow saplings edging the creek, I found him standing by the barbecue pit, in peaceful conversation with Ronnie Sinclair—meanwhile leaning casually on the handle of the ax, of which he had somehow managed to possess himself.

I relaxed a bit when I saw that, and took my time in joining the party. Unless Rosamund decided to strangle Ronnie with her bare hands or beat him to death with a ham—neither of these contingencies being at all unthinkable—my medical services might not be needed after all.

The pit was a broad one, a natural declivity bored out of

the clay creekbank by some distant flood and then deepened by judicious spadework in the years succeeding. Judging by the blackened rocks and drifts of scattered charcoal, it had been in use for some time. In fact, several different people were using it now; the mingled scents of fowl, pork, mutton, and possum rose up in a cloud of apple-wood and hickory smoke, a savory incense that made my mouth water.

The sight of the pit was somewhat less appetizing. Clouds of white smoke billowed up from the damp wood, half-obscuring a number of shapes that lay upon their smoldering pyres—many of these looking faintly and hair-raisingly human through the haze. It reminded me all too vividly of the charnel pits on Jamaica, where the bodies of slaves who had not survived the rigors of the Middle Passage were burned, and I swallowed heavily, trying not to recall the macabre roasting-meat smell of those funeral fires.

Rosamund was working down in the pit at the moment, her skirt kirtled well above plump knees and sleeves rolled back to bare her massive arms as she ladled a reddish sauce onto the exposed ribs of a huge hog's carcass. Around her lay five more gigantic shapes, shrouded in damp burlap, with the wisps of fragrant smoke curling up around them, vanishing into the soft drizzle.

"It's poison, is what it is!" Ronnie Sinclair was saying hotly, as I came up behind him. "She'll ruin it—it'll no be fit for pigs when she's done!"

"It *is* pigs, Ronnie," Jamie said, with considerable patience. He rolled an eye at me, then glanced at the pit, where sizzling fat dripped onto the biers of hickory coals below. "Myself, I shouldna think ye could do anything to a pig—in the way of cooking, that is—that would make it not worth the eating."

"Quite true," I put in helpfully, smiling at Ronnie. "Smoked bacon, grilled chops, roasted loin, baked ham, headcheese, sausage, sweetbreads, black pudding . . . somebody once said you could make use of everything in a pig but the squeal."

"Aye, well, but this is the barbecue, isn't it?" Ronnie said stubbornly, ignoring my feeble attempt at humor. "Anyone kens that ye sass a barbecued hog wi' vinegar—that's the proper way of it! After all, ye wouldna put gravel into your sausage meat, would ye? Or boil your bacon wi' sweepings from the henhouse? Tcha!" He jerked his chin toward the white pottery basin under Rosamund's arm, making it clear that its contents fell into the same class of inedible adulterants, in his opinion.

I caught a savory whiff as the wind changed. So far as I could tell from smell alone, Rosamund's sauce seemed to include tomatoes, onions, red pepper, and enough sugar to leave a thick blackish crust on the meat and a tantalizing caramel aroma in the air.

"I expect the meat will be very juicy, cooked like that," I said, feeling my stomach begin to knot and growl beneath my laced bodice.

"Aye, a wonderful fat lot of pigs they are, too," Jamie said ingratiatingly, as Rosamund glanced up, glowering. She was black to the knees and her square-jowled face was streaked with rain, sweat, and soot. "Will they have been wild hogs, ma'am, or gently reared?"

"Wild," she said, with a certain amount of pride, straightening up and wiping a strand of wet, graying hair off her brow. "Fattened on chestnut mast—nothin' like it to give a flavor to the meat!"

Ronnie Sinclair made a Scottish noise indicative of derision and contempt.

"Aye, the flavor's so good ye must hide it under a larding o' yon grisly sauce that makes it look as though the meat's no even cooked yet, but bleeding raw!"

Rosamund made a rather earthy comment regarding the supposed manhood of persons who felt themselves squeamish at the thought of blood, which Ronnie seemed disposed to take personally. Jamie skillfully maneuvered himself between the two, keeping the ax well out of reach.

"Oh, I'm sure it's verra well cooked indeed," he replied soothingly. "Why, Mistress Lindsay has been hard at work since dawn, at least."

"Long before that, Mr. Fraser," the lady replied, with a certain grim satisfaction. "You want decent barbecue, you start at least a day before, and tend it all through the night. I been a-minding of these hogs since yesterday afternoon."

She drew in a great sniff of the rising smoke, wearing a beatific expression.

"Ah, that's the stuff! Not but what a savory sass like this 'un is wasted on you bastardly Scots," Rosamund said, replacing the burlap and patting it tenderly into place. "You've pickled your tongues with that everlastin' vinegar you slop on your victuals. It's all I can do to stop Kenny a-puttin' it on his corn bread and porridge of a mornin'."

Jamie raised his voice, drowning out Ronnie's incensed response to this calumny.

"And was it Kenny that hunted the hogs for ye, mistress? Wild hogs have a chancy nature; surely it's a dangerous business to be stalking beasts of that size. Like the wild boar that we hunted in Scotland, aye?"

"Ha." Rosamund cast a look of good-natured scorn toward the slope above, where her husband—roughly half her size—presumably was engaged in less strenuous pursuits. "No, indeed, Mr. Fraser, I kilt this lot myself. With that ax," she added pointedly, nodding toward the instrument in question and narrowing her eyes in a sinister fashion at Ronnie. "Caved in their skulls with one blow, I did."

Ronnie, not the most perceptive of men, declined to take the hint.

"It's the tomato fruits she's using, *Mac Dubh*," he hissed, tugging at Jamie's sleeve and pointing at the red-crusted bowl. "Devil's apples! She'll poison us all!"

"Oh, I shouldna think so, Ronnie." Jamie took a firm grip on Ronnie's arm, and smiled engagingly at Rosamund. "Ye mean to sell the meat, I suppose, Mrs. Lindsay? It's a poor merchant that would kill her customers, aye?"

"I ain't yet lost a one, Mr. Fraser," Rosamund agreed, turning back another sheet of burlap and leaning over to dribble sauce from a wooden ladle over a steaming haunch. "Ain't never had but good words about the taste, neither," she said, "though a-course that would be in Boston, where I come from."

Where folk have sense, her tone clearly implied.

"I met a man from Boston, last time I went to Charlottesville," Ronnie said, his foxy brows drawn down in disapproval. He tugged, trying to free his arm from Jamie's grip, but to no avail. "He said to me as it was his custom to have beans at his breakfast, and oysters to his supper, and so he'd done every day since he was a wean. A wonder he hadna blown up like a pig's bladder, filled wi' such wretched stuff as that!"

"Beans, beans, they're good for your heart," I said cheerily, seizing the opening. "The more you eat, the more you fart. The more you fart, the better you feel—so let's have beans for every meal!"

Ronnie's mouth dropped open, as did Mrs. Lindsay's. Jamie whooped with laughter, and Mrs. Lindsay's look of astonishment dissolved into a booming laugh. After a moment, Ronnie rather reluctantly joined in, a small grin twisting up the corner of his mouth.

"I lived in Boston for a time," I said mildly, as the hilarity died down a bit. "Mrs. Lindsay, that smells wonderful!"

Rosamund nodded with dignity, gratified.

"Why, so it does, ma'am, and I say so." She leaned toward me, lowering her voice—slightly—from its normal stentorian range. "It's my private recipe what does it," she said, with a proprietorial pat of the pottery bowl. "Brings out the flavor, see?"

Ronnie's mouth opened, but only a small yelp emerged, the evident result of Jamie's hand tightening about his biceps. Rosamund ignored this, engaging in an amiable discussion with Jamie that terminated in her agreeing to reserve an entire carcass for use at the wedding feast.

I glanced at Jamie, hearing this. Given that Father Kenneth was probably at present en route either back to Baltimore or to the gaol in Edenton, I had my doubts as to whether any marriages would in fact take place tonight.

On the other hand, I had learned never to underestimate Jamie, either. With a final word of compliment to Mrs. Lindsay, he dragged Ronnie bodily away from the pit, pausing just long enough to thrust the ax into my hands.

"See that safe, aye, Sassenach?" he said, and kissed me briefly. He grinned down at me. "And where did ye learn so much about the natural history of beans, tell me?"

"Brianna brought it home from school when she was about six," I said, smiling back. "It's really a little song."

"Tell her to sing it to her man," Jamie advised. The grin widened. "He can write it down in his wee book."

He turned away, putting a companionable arm firmly about the shoulders of Ronnie Sinclair, who showed signs of trying to escape back in the direction of the barbecue pit.

"Come along wi' me, Ronnie," he said. "I must just have a wee word wi' the Lieutenant. He wishes to buy a ham of Mistress Lindsay, I think," he added, blinking at me in the owllike fashion that passed with him for winking. He turned back to Ronnie. "But I ken he'll want to hear whatever ye can tell him, about his Da. Ye were a great friend of Gavin Hayes, no?"

"Oh," said Ronnie, his scowl lightening somewhat. "Aye. Aye, Gavin was a proper man. A shame about it." He shook his head, obviously referring to Gavin's death a few years before. He glanced up at Jamie, lips pursed. "Does his lad ken what happened?"

A tender question, that. Gavin had in fact been hanged in Charleston, for theft—a shameful death, by anyone's standards.

"Aye," Jamie said quietly. "I had to tell him. But it will help, I think, if ye can tell him a bit about his Da earlier—tell him how it was for us, there in Ardsmuir." Something—not quite a smile—touched his face as he looked at Ronnie, and I saw an answering softness on Sinclair's face.

Jamie's hand tightened on Ronnie's shoulder, then dropped away, and they set off up the hill, side by side, the subtleties of barbecue forgotten.

How it was for us . . . I watched them go, linked by the conjuration of that one simple phrase. Five words that recalled the closeness forged by days and months and years of shared hardship; a kinship closed to anyone who had not likewise lived through it. Jamie seldom spoke of Ardsmuir; neither did any of the other men who had come out of it and lived to see the New World here.

Mist was rising from the hollows on the mountain now; within moments, they had disappeared from view. From the hazy forest above, the sound of Scottish male voices drifted down toward the smoking pit, chanting in amiable unison:

"Beans, beans, they're good for your heart . . ."

RETURNING TO THE CAMPSITE, I found that Roger had returned from his errands. He stood near the fire, talking with Brianna, a troubled look on his face.

"Don't worry," I told him, reaching past his hip to retrieve the rumbling teakettle. "I'm sure Jamie will sort it somehow. He's gone to deal with it."

"He has?" He looked slightly startled. "He knows already?"

"Yes, as soon as he finds the sheriff, I imagine it will all come right." I upended the chipped teapot I used in camp with one hand, shook the old leaves out onto the ground, and putting it on the table, tipped a little boiling water in from the kettle to warm the pot. It had been a long day, and likely to be a long evening as well. I was looking forward to the sustenance of a properly brewed cup of tea, accompanied by a slice of the fruitcake one of my patients had given me during the morning clinic.

"The sheriff?" Roger gave Brianna a baffled look, faintly tinged with alarm. "She hasn't set a sheriff on me, has she?"

"Set a sheriff on you? Who?" I said, joining in the chorus of bafflement. I hung the kettle back on its tripod, and reached for the tin of tea leaves. "Whatever have you been doing, Roger?"

A faint flush showed over his high cheekbones, but before he could answer, Brianna snorted briefly.

"Telling Auntie Jocasta where she gets off." She glanced at Roger, and her eyes narrowed into triangles of mildly malicious amusement as she envisioned the scene. "Boy, I wish I'd been there!"

"Whatever did you say to her, Roger?" I inquired, interested.

The flush deepened, and he looked away.

"I don't wish to repeat it," he said shortly. "It wasna the sort of thing one ought to say to a woman, let alone an elderly one, and particularly one about to be related to me by marriage. I was just asking Bree whether I maybe ought to go and apologize to Mrs. Cameron before the wedding."

"No," Bree said promptly. "The nerve of her! You had every right to say what you did."

"Well, I don't regret the substance of my remarks," Roger said to her, with a wry hint of a smile. "Only the form.

"See," he said, turning to me, "I'm only thinking that perhaps I should apologize, to keep it from being awkward tonight—I don't want Bree's wedding to be spoiled."

"Bree's wedding? You think I'm getting married by myself?" she asked, lowering thick red brows at him.

"Oh, well, no," he admitted, smiling a little. He touched her cheek, gently. "I'll stand up next ye, to be sure. But so long as we end up married, I'm not so much bothered about the ceremony. Ye'll want it to be nice, though, won't ye? Put a damper on the occasion, and your auntie crowns me with a stick of firewood before I can say 'I will.' "

I was by now consumed by curiosity to know just what he *had* said to Jocasta, but thought I had better address the more immediate issue, which was that at the moment of going to press, it appeared that there might be no wedding to be spoiled.

"And so Jamie's out looking for Father Kenneth now," I finished. "Marsali didn't recognize the sheriff who took him, though, which makes it difficult."

Roger's dark brows lifted, then drew together in concern.

"I wonder . . ." he said, and turned to me. "Do ye know, I think perhaps I saw him, just a few moments ago."

"Father Kenneth?" I asked, knife suspended over the fruitcake.

"No, the sheriff."

"What? Where?" Bree half-turned on one heel, glaring round. Her hand curled up into a fist, and I thought it rather fortunate that the sheriff wasn't in sight. Having Brianna arrested for assault really *would* have a dampening effect on the wedding.

"He went that way." Roger gestured downhill, toward the

creek—and Lieutenant Hayes's tent. As he did so, we heard the sound of footsteps squelching through mud, and a moment later, Jamie appeared, looking tired, worried, and highly annoyed. Obviously, he hadn't yet found the priest.

"Da!" Bree greeted him with excitement. "Roger thinks he's seen the sheriff who took Father Kenneth!"

"Oh, aye?" Jamie at once perked up. "Where?" His left hand curled up in anticipation, and I couldn't help smiling.

"What's funny?" he demanded, seeing it.

"Nothing," I assured him. "Here, have some fruitcake." I handed him a slice, which he promptly crammed into his mouth, returning his attention to Roger.

"Where?" he demanded, indistinctly.

"I don't know that it was the man you're looking for," Roger told him. "He was a raggedy wee man. But he had got a prisoner; he was taking one of the fellows from Drunkard's Creek off in handcuffs. MacLennan, I think."

Jamie choked and coughed, spewing small bits of masticated fruitcake into the fire.

"He arrested Mr. MacLennan? And you *let* him?" Bree was staring at Roger in consternation. Neither she nor Roger had been present when Abel MacLennan had told his story over breakfast, but both of them knew him.

"I couldna very well prevent him," Roger pointed out mildly. "I did call out to MacLennan to ask if he wanted help—I thought I'd fetch your Da or Farquard Campbell, if he did. But he just looked through me, as though I might have been a ghost, and then when I called again, he gave me an odd sort of smile and shook his head. I didna think I ought to go and beat up a sheriff, just on general principle. But if you—"

"Not a sheriff," Jamie said hoarsely. His eyes were watering, and he paused to cough explosively again.

"A thief-taker," I told Roger. "Something like a bounty hunter, I gather." The tea wasn't nearly brewed yet; I found a half-full stone bottle of ale and handed that to Jamie.

"Where will he be taking Abel?" I asked. "You said Hayes didn't want prisoners."

Jamie shook his head, swallowed, and lowered the bottle, breathing a little easier.

"He doesna. No, Mr. Boble—it must be him, aye?—will take Abel to the nearest magistrate. And if wee Roger saw him just the now . . ." He turned, thinking, brows furrowed as he surveyed the mountainside around us.

"It will be Farquard, most likely," he concluded, his shoulders relaxing a little. "I ken four justices of the peace and three magistrates here at the Gathering, and of the lot, Campbell's the only one camped on this side."

"Oh, that's good." I sighed in relief. Farquard Campbell was a fair man; a stickler for the law, but not without compassion—and more importantly, perhaps, a very old friend of Jocasta Cameron.

"Aye, we'll ask my aunt to have a word—perhaps we'd best do it before the weddings." He turned to Roger. "Will ye go, MacKenzie? I must be finding Father Kenneth, if there are to *be* any weddings."

Roger looked as though he, too, had just choked on a bit of fruitcake.

"Er . . . well," he said, awkwardly. "Perhaps I'm no the best man to be saying anything to Mrs. Cameron just now."

Jamie was staring at him in mingled interest and exasperation.

"Why not?"

Blushing fiercely, Roger recounted the substance of his conversation with Jocasta—lowering his voice nearly to the point of inaudibility at the conclusion.

We heard it clearly enough, nonetheless. Jamie looked at me. His mouth twitched. Then his shoulders began to shake. I felt the laughter bubble up under my ribs, but it was nothing to Jamie's hilarity. He laughed almost silently, but so hard that tears came to his eyes.

"Oh, Christ!" he gasped at last. He clutched his side, still wheezing faintly. "God, I've sprung a rib, I think." He reached out and took one of the half-dried clean clouts from a bush, carelessly wiping his face with it.

"All right," he said, recovering himself somewhat. "Go and see Farquard, then. If Abel's there, tell Campbell I'll stand surety for him. Bring him back with ye." He made a brief shooing gesture, and Roger—puce with mortification but stiff with dignity—departed at once. Bree followed him, casting a glance of reproof at her father, which merely had the effect of causing him to wheeze some more.

I drowned my own mirth with a gulp of steaming tea, blissfully fragrant. I offered the cup to Jamie, but he waved it away, content with the rest of the ale.

"My aunt," he observed, lowering the bottle at last, "kens verra well indeed what money will buy and what it will not."

"And she's just bought herself—and everyone else in the county—a good opinion of poor Roger, hasn't she?" I replied, rather dryly.

Jocasta Cameron was a MacKenzie of Leoch; a family Jamie had once described as "charming as the larks in the field—and sly as foxes, with it." Whether Jocasta had truly had any doubt herself of Roger's motives in marrying Bree, or merely thought to forestall idle gossip along the Cape Fear, her methods had been undeniably successful. She was probably up in her tent chortling over her cleverness, looking forward to spreading the story of her offer and Roger's response to it.

"Poor Roger," Jamie agreed, his mouth still twitching. "Poor but virtuous." He tipped up the bottle of ale, drained it, and set it down with a brief sigh of satisfaction. "Though come to that," he added, glancing at me, "she's bought the lad something of value as well, hasn't she?"

"My son," I quoted softly, nodding. "Do you think he realized it himself before he said it? That he really feels Jemmy is his son?"

Jamie made an indeterminate movement with his shoulders, not quite a shrug.

"I canna say. It's as well he should have that fixed in his mind, though, before the next bairn comes along—one he kens for sure is his."

I thought of my conversation that morning with Brianna, but decided it was wiser to say nothing—at least for now. It was, after all, a matter between Roger and Bree. I only nodded, and turned to tidy away the tea things.

I felt a small glow in the pit of my stomach that was only partly the result of the tea. Roger had sworn an oath to take Jemmy as his own, no matter what the little boy's true paternity might be; he was an honorable man, Roger, and he meant it. But the speech of the heart is louder than the words of any oath spoken by lips alone.

When I had gone back, pregnant, through the stones, Frank had sworn to me that he would keep me as his wife, would treat the coming child as his own—would love me as he had before. All three of those vows his lips and mind had done his best to keep, but his heart, in the end, had sworn only one. From the moment that he took Brianna in his arms, she was his daughter.

But what if there had been another child? I wondered suddenly. It had never been a possibility—but if it had? Slowly, I wiped the teapot dry and wrapped it in a towel, contemplating the vision of that mythical child; the one Frank and I might have had, but never did, and never would. I laid the wrapped teapot in the chest, gently, as though it were a sleeping baby.

When I turned back, Jamie was still standing there, looking at me with a rather odd expression—tender, yet somehow rueful.

"Did I ever think to thank ye, Sassenach?" he said, his voice a little husky.

"For what?" I said, puzzled. He took my hand, and drew me gently toward him. He smelled of ale and damp wool, and very faintly of the brandied sweetness of fruitcake.

"For my bairns," he said softly. "For the children that ye bore me."

"Oh," I said. I leaned slowly forward, and rested my forehead against the solid warmth of his chest. I cupped my hands at the small of his back beneath his coat, and sighed. "It was . . . my pleasure."

"MR. FRASER, MR. FRASER!" I lifted my head and turned to see a small boy churning down the steep slope behind us, arms waving to keep his balance and face bright red with cold and exertion.

"Oof!" Jamie got his hands up just in time to catch the boy as he hurtled down the last few feet, quite out of control. He boosted the little boy, whom I recognized as Farquard

Campbell's youngest, up in his arms and smiled at him. "Aye, Rabbie, what is it? Does your Da want me to come for Mr. MacLennan?"

Rabbie shook his head, shaggy hair flying like a sheepdog's coat.

"No, sir," he panted, gasping for breath. He gulped air and the small throat swelled like a frog's with the effort to breathe and speak at once. "No, sir. My Da says he's heard where the priest is and I should show ye the way, sir. Will ye come?"

Jamie's brows flicked up in momentary surprise. He glanced at me, then smiled at Rabbie, and nodded, bending down to set him on his feet.

"Aye, lad, I will. Lead on, then!"

"Delicate of Farquard," I said to Jamie under my breath, with a nod at Rabbie, who scampered ahead, looking back over his shoulder now and then, to be sure we were managing to keep up with him. No one would notice a small boy, among the swarms of children on the mountain. Everyone would most assuredly have noticed had Farquard Campbell come himself or sent one of his adult sons.

Jamie huffed a little, the mist of his breath a wisp of steam in the gathering chill.

"Well, it's no Farquard's concern, after all, even if he has got a great regard for my aunt. And I expect if he's sent the lad to tell me, it means he kens the man who's responsible, and doesna mean to choose up sides wi' me against him." He glanced at the setting sun, and gave me a rueful look.

"I did say I should find Father Kenneth by sunset, but still—I dinna think we shall see a wedding tonight, Sassenach."

Rabbie led us onward and upward, tracing the maze of footpaths and trampled dead grass without hesitation. The sun had finally broken through the clouds; it had sunk deep in the notch of the mountains, but was still high enough to wash the slope with a warm, ruddy light that momentarily belied the chill of the day. People were gathering to their family fires now, hungry for their suppers, and no one spared a glance for us among the bustle.

At last, Rabbie came to a stop, at the foot of a well-marked path that led up and to the right. I had crisscrossed the mountain's face several times during the week of the Gathering, but had never ventured up this high. Who was in custody of Father Kenneth, I wondered—and what did Jamie propose to do about it?

"Up there," Rabbie said unnecessarily, pointing to the peak of a large tent, just visible through a screen of longleaf pine.

Jamie made a Scottish noise in the back of his throat at sight of the tent.

"Oh," he said softly, "so that's how it is?"

"Is it? Never mind how it is; *whose* is it?" I looked dubiously at the tent, which was a large affair of waxed brown canvas, pale in the gloaming. It obviously belonged to someone fairly wealthy, but wasn't one I was familiar with myself.

"Mr. Lillywhite, of Hillsborough," Jamie said, and his brows drew down in thought. He patted Rabbie Campbell on the head, and handed him a penny from his sporran. "Thank ye, laddie. Run away to your Mam now; it'll be time for your supper." Rabbie took the coin and vanished without comment, pleased to be finished with his errand.

"Oh, really." I cocked a wary eye at the tent. That explained a few things, I supposed—though not everything. Mr. Lillywhite was a magistrate from Hillsborough, though I knew nothing else about him, save what he looked like. I had glimpsed him once or twice during the Gathering, a tall, rather drooping man, his figure made distinctive by a bottle-green coat with silver buttons, but had never formally met him.

Magistrates were responsible for appointing sheriffs, which explained the connection with the "nasty fat man" Marsali had described, and why Father Kenneth was incarcerated here—but that left open the question of whether it was the sheriff or Mr. Lillywhite who had wanted the priest removed from circulation in the first place.

Jamie put a hand on my arm, and drew me off the path, into the shelter of a small pine tree.

"Ye dinna ken Mr. Lillywhite, do you, Sassenach?"

"Only by sight. What do you want me to do?"

He smiled at me, a hint of mischief in his eyes, despite his worry for Father Kenneth.

"Game for it, are ye?"

"Unless you're proposing that I bat Mr. Lillywhite over the head and liberate Father Kenneth by force, I suppose so. That sort of thing is much more your line of country than mine."

He laughed at that, and gave the tent what appeared to be a wistful look.

"I should like nothing better," he said, confirming this impression. "It wouldna be difficult in the least," he went on, eyeing the tan canvas sides of the tent appraisingly as they flexed in the wind. "Look at the size of it; there canna be more than two or three men in there, besides the priest. I could wait until the full dark, and then take a lad or two and—"

"Yes, but what do you want me to do now?" I interrupted, thinking I had best put a stop to what sounded a distinctly criminal train of thought.

"Ah." He abandoned his machinations—for the moment—and squinted at me, appraising my appearance. I had taken off the bloodstained canvas apron I wore for surgery, had put up my hair neatly with pins, and was reasonably respectable in appearance, if a trifle mud-draggled round the hems.

"Ye dinna have any of your physician's kit about ye?" he asked, frowning dubiously. "A bottle of swill, a bittie knife?"

"Bottle of swill, indeed. No, I—oh, wait a moment. Yes, there are these; will they do?" Digging about in the pocket tied at my waist, I had come up with the small ivory box in which I kept my gold-tipped acupuncture needles.

Evidently satisfied, Jamie nodded, and pulled out the silver whisky flask from his sporran.

"Aye, they'll do," he said, handing me the flask. "Take this too, though, for looks. Go up to the tent, Sassenach, and tell whoever's guarding the priest that he's ailing."

"The guard?"

"The priest," he said, giving me a look of mild exasperation. "I daresay everyone will ken ye as a healer by now, and know ye on sight. Say that Father Kenneth has an illness that you've been treating, and he must have a dose of his medicine at once, lest he sicken and die on them. I dinna suppose they want that—and they'll not be afraid of you."

"I shouldn't imagine they need be," I agreed, a trifle caustically. "You don't mean me to stab the sheriff through the heart with my needles, then?"

He grinned at the thought, but shook his head.

"Nay, I only want ye to learn why they've taken the priest and what they mean to do with him. If I were to go and demand answers myself, it might put them on guard."

Meaning that he had not completely abandoned the notion of a later commando raid on Mr. Lillywhite's stronghold, should the answers prove unsatisfactory. I glanced at the tent and took a deep breath, settling my shawl about my shoulders.

"All right," I said. "And what are you intending to do while I'm about it?"

"I'm going to go and fetch the bairns," he said, and with a quick squeeze of my hand for luck, he was off down the trail.

I WAS STILL WONDERING exactly what he meant by *that* cryptic statement—which "bairns"? Why?—as I came within sight of the open tent flap, but all speculation was driven from my mind by the appearance of a gentleman therein who met Marsali's description of "a nasty, fat man" so exactly that I had no doubt of his identity. He was short and toadlike, with a receding hairline, a belly that strained the buttons of a food-stained linen vest, and small, beady eyes that watched me as though assessing my immediate prospects as a food item.

"Good day to you, ma'am," he said. He viewed me without enthusiasm, no doubt finding me less than toothsome, but inclined his head with formal respect.

"Good day," I replied cheerily, dropping him a brief curtsy. Never hurt to be polite—at least not to start with. "You'll be the sheriff, won't you? I'm afraid I haven't had the pleasure of a formal introduction. I'm Mrs. Fraser—Mrs. James Fraser, of Fraser's Ridge."

"David Anstruther, Sheriff of Orange County—your servant, ma'am," he said, bowing again, though with no real evidence of delight. He didn't show any surprise at hearing Jamie's name, either. Either he simply wasn't familiar with it—rather unlikely—or he had been expecting such an ambassage.

That being so, I saw no point in beating round the bush.

"I understand that you're entertaining Father Donahue," I said pleasantly. "I've come to see him; I'm his physician."

Whatever he'd been expecting, it wasn't that; his jaw dropped slightly, exposing a severe case of malocclusion, well-advanced gingivitis, and a missing bicuspid. Before he could close it, a tall gentleman in a bottle-green coat stepped out of the tent behind him.

"Mrs. Fraser?" he said, one eyebrow raised. He bowed punctiliously. "You say you wish to speak with the clerical gentleman under arrest?"

"Under arrest?" I affected great surprise at that. "A priest? Why, whatever can he have done?"

The Sheriff and the magistrate exchanged glances. Then the magistrate coughed.

"Perhaps you are unaware, madam, that it is illegal for anyone other than the clergy of the established Church—the Church of England, that is—to undertake his office within the colony of North Carolina?"

I was not unaware of that, though I also knew that the law was seldom put into effect, there being relatively few of any kind of clergy in the colony to start with, and no one bothering to take any official notice of the itinerant preachers—many of them free lances in the most basic sense of the word—who did appear from time to time.

"Gracious!" I said, affecting shocked surprise to the best of my ability. "No, I had no idea. Goodness me! How very strange!" Mr. Lillywhite blinked slightly, which I took as an indication that that would just about do, in terms of my creating an impression of well-bred shock. I cleared my throat, and brought out the silver flask and case of needles.

"Well. I do hope any difficulties will be soon resolved. However, I should very much like to see Father Donahue for a moment. As I said, I am his physician. He has an . . . indisposition"—I slid back the cover of the case, and delicately displayed the needles, letting them imagine something suitably virulent—"that requires regular treatment. Might I see him for a moment, to administer his medicine? I . . . ah . . . should not like to see any mischief result from a lack of care on my part, you know." I smiled, as charmingly as possible.

The Sheriff pulled his neck down into the collar of his coat and looked malevolently amphibious, but Mr. Lillywhite seemed better affected by the smile. He hesitated, looking me over.

"Well, I am not sure that . . ." he began, when the sound of footsteps came squelching up the path behind me. I turned, half-expecting to see Jamie, but instead beheld my recent patient, Mr. Goodwin, one cheek still puffed from my attentions, but sling intact.

He was quite as surprised to see me, but greeted me with great cordiality, and a cloud of alcoholic fumes. Evidently Mr. Goodwin had been taking my advice regarding disinfection very seriously.

"Mrs. Fraser! You have not come to minister to my friend Lillywhite, I trust? I expect Mr. Anstruther would benefit from a good purge, though—clear the bilious humors, eh, David? Haha!" He clapped the Sheriff on the back in affectionate camaraderie; a gesture Anstruther suffered with no more than a small grimace, giving me some idea of Mr. Goodwin's importance in the social scheme of Orange County.

"George, my dear," Mr. Lillywhite greeted him warmly. "You are acquainted with this charming lady, then?"

"Oh, indeed, indeed I am, sir!" Mr. Goodwin turned a beaming countenance upon me. "Why, Mrs. Fraser did me great service this morning, great service indeed! See here!" He brandished his bound and splinted arm, which, I was pleased to see, was evidently giving him no pain whatever at the moment, though that probably had more to do with his self-administered anesthesia than with my workmanship.

"She quite cured my arm, with no more than a touch here, a touch there—and drew a broken tooth so clean that I scarce felt a thing! 'Ook!" He stuck a finger into the side of his mouth and pulled back his cheek, exposing a tuft of bloodstained wadding protruding from the tooth socket and a neat line of black stitching on the gum.

"Really, I am most impressed, Mrs. Fraser." Lillywhite sniffed at the waft of cloves and whisky from Mr. Goodwin's mouth, looking interested, and I saw the bulge of his cheek as his own tongue tenderly probed a back tooth.

"But what brings you up here, Mrs. Fraser?" Mr. Goodwin turned the beam of his joviality on me. "So late in the day—perhaps you will do me the honor of taking a bit of supper at my fire?"

"Oh, thank you, but I can't, really," I said, smiling as charmingly as possible. "I've just come to see another patient—that is—"

"She wants to see the priest," Anstruther interrupted.

Goodwin blinked at that, taken only slightly aback.

"Priest. There is a priest here?"

"A Papist," Mr. Lillywhite amplified, lips curling back a bit from the unclean word. "It came to my attention that there was a Catholic priest concealed in the assembly, who proposed to celebrate a Mass during the festivities this evening. I sent Mr. Anstruther to arrest him, of course."

"Father Donahue is a friend of mine," I put in, as forcefully as possible. "And he was not concealed; he was invited quite openly, as the guest of Mrs. Cameron. He is also a patient, and requires treatment. I've come to see that he gets it."

"A friend of yours? Are you Catholic, Mrs. Fraser?" Mr. Goodwin looked startled; it obviously hadn't occurred to him that he was being treated by a Popish dentist, and his hand went to his swollen cheek in bemusement.

"I am," I said, hoping that merely being a Catholic wasn't also against Mr. Lillywhite's conception of the law.

Evidently not. Mr. Goodwin gave Mr. Lillywhite a nudge.

"Oh, come, Randall. Let Mrs. Fraser see the fellow, what harm can it do? And if he's truly Jocasta Cameron's guest . . ."

Mr. Lillywhite pursed his lips in thought for a moment, then stood aside, holding back the flap of canvas for me.

"I suppose there can be no harm in your seeing your . . . friend," he said slowly. "Come in, then, madam."

Sundown was at hand, and the tent was dark inside, though one canvas wall still glowed brightly with the sinking sun behind it. I shut my eyes for a moment, to accustom them to the change of light, then blinked and looked about to get my bearings.

The tent seemed cluttered but relatively luxurious, being equipped with a camp bed and other furniture, the air within scented not only by damp canvas and wool but with the perfume of Ceylon tea, expensive wine, and almond biscuits.

Father Donahue was silhouetted in front of the glowing canvas, sitting on a stool behind a small folding table, on which were arrayed a few sheets of paper, an inkstand, and a quill. They might as well have been thumbscrews, pincers, and a red-hot poker, judging from his militantly upright attitude, evocative of expectant martyrdom.

The clinking of flint and tinderbox came from behind me, and then the faint glow of a light. This swelled, and a black boy—Mr. Lillywhite's servant, I supposed—came forward and silently set a small oil lamp on the table.

Now that I got a clear look at the priest, the impression of martyrdom grew more pronounced. He looked like Saint Stephen after the first volley of stones, with a bruise on his chin and a first-rate black eye, empurpled from browridge to cheekbone and swollen quite shut.

The nonblackened eye widened at sight of me, and he started up with an exclamation of surprise.

"Father Kenneth." I gripped him by the hand and squeezed, smiling broadly for the benefit of whatever audience might be peeking through the flap. "I've brought your medicine. How are you feeling?" I raised my eyebrows and waggled them, indicating that he should play along with the deception. He stared at me in fascination for a moment, but then appeared to catch on. He coughed, then, encouraged by my nod, coughed again, with more enthusiasm.

"It's . . . very kind of ye to . . . think of me, Mrs. Fraser," he wheezed, between hacks.

I pulled off the top of the flask, and poured out a generous measure of whisky.

"Are you quite all right, Father?" I asked, low-voiced, as I leaned across to hand it to him. "Your face . . ."

"Oh, it's nothing, Mrs. Fraser dear, not at all," he assured me, his faint Irish accent coming out under the stress of the occasion. " 'Twas only that I made the mistake of resistin' when the Sheriff arrested me. Not but what in the shock of it all, I didn't do a small bit of damage to the poor man's ballocks, and him only doing of his duty, may God forgive me." Father Kenneth rolled his undamaged eye upward in a pious expression—quite spoiled by the unregenerate grin underneath.

Father Kenneth was no more than middle height, and looked older than his years by virtue of the hard wear imposed by long seasons spent in the saddle. Still, he was no more than thirty-five, and lean and tough as whipcord under his worn black coat and frayed linen. I began to understand the Sheriff's belligerence.

"Besides," he added, touching his black eye gingerly, "Mr. Lillywhite did tender me a most gracious apology for the hurt." He nodded toward the table, and I saw that an opened bottle of wine and a pewter cup stood among the writing materials—the cup still full, and the level of wine in the bottle not down by much.

The priest picked up the whisky I had poured and drained it, closing his eyes in dreamy benediction.

"And a finer medicine I hope never to benefit from," he said, opening them. "I do thank ye, Mistress Fraser. I'm that restored, I might walk on water meself." He remembered to cough, this one a delicate hack, fist held over his mouth.

"What's wrong with the wine?" I asked, with a glance toward the door.

"Oh, not a thing," he said, taking his hand away. "Only that I did not think it quite right to accept the magistrate's refreshments, under the circumstances. Call it conscience." He smiled at me again, but this time with a note of wryness in the grin.

"Why have they arrested you?" I asked, my voice low. I looked again at the tent's door, but it was empty, and I caught the murmur of voices outside. Evidently, Jamie had been right; they weren't suspicious of me.

"For sayin' of the Holy Mass," he replied, lowering his voice to match mine. "Or so they said. It's a wicked lie, though. I've not said Mass since last Sunday, and that was in Virginia." He was looking wistfully at the flask. I picked it up and poured another generous tot.

I frowned a bit, thinking, while he drank it, more slowly this time. Whatever were Mr. Lillywhite and company up to? They couldn't, surely, be meaning to bring the priest to trial on the charge of saying Mass. It would be no great matter to find false witnesses to say he had, of course—but what would be the point of it?

While Catholicism was certainly not popular in North Carolina, I could see no great purpose in the arrest of a priest who would be leaving in the morning in any case. Father Kenneth came from Baltimore and meant to return there; he had come to the Gathering only as a favor to Jocasta Cameron.

"Oh!" I said, and Father Kenneth looked at me inquiringly over the rim of his cup.

"Just a thought," I said, gesturing to him to continue. "Do you happen to know whether Mr. Lillywhite is personally acquainted with Mrs. Cameron?" Jocasta Cameron was a prominent and wealthy woman—and one of strong character, therefore not without enemies. I couldn't see why Mr. Lillywhite would go out of his way to disoblige her in such a peculiar fashion, even so, but . . .

"I am acquainted with Mrs. Cameron," said Mr. Lillywhite, speaking behind me. "Though alas, I can claim no intimate friendship with the lady." I whirled to find him standing just within the tent's entrance, followed by Sheriff Anstruther and Mr. Goodwin, with Jamie bringing up the rear. The latter flicked an eyebrow at me, but otherwise maintained an expression of solemn interest.

Mr. Lillywhite bowed to me in acknowledgment.

"I have just been explaining to your husband, Madame, that it is my regard for Mrs. Cameron's interests that led me to attempt to regularize Mr. Donahue's position, so as to allow his continued presence in the colony." Mr. Lillywhite nodded coldly at the priest. "However, I am afraid my suggestion was summarily rejected."

Father Kenneth put down his cup and straightened up, his working eye bright in the lamplight.

"They wish me to sign an oath, sir," he said to Jamie, with

a gesture at the paper and quill on the table before him. "To the effect that I do not subscribe to a belief in transubstantiation."

"Do they, indeed." Jamie's voice betrayed no more than polite interest, but I understood at once what the priest had meant by his remark regarding conscience.

"Well, he can't do that, can he?" I said, looking round the circle of men. "Catholics—I mean—*we*"—I spoke with some emphasis, looking at Mr. Goodwin—"*do* believe in transubstantiation. Don't we?" I asked, turning to the priest, who smiled slightly in response, and nodded.

Mr. Goodwin looked unhappy, but resigned, his alcoholic joviality substantially reduced by the social awkwardness.

"I'm sorry, Mrs. Fraser, but that is the law. The only circumstance under which a clergyman who does not belong to the established Church may remain in the colony—legally—is upon the signing of such an oath. Many do sign it. You know the Reverend Urmstone, the Methodist circuit rider? He has signed the oath, as has Mr. Calvert, the New Light minister who lives near Wadesboro."

The Sheriff looked smug. Repressing an urge to stamp on his foot, I turned to Mr. Lillywhite.

"Well, but Father Donahue can't sign it. So what do you propose to do with him? Throw the poor man in gaol? You can't do that—he's ill!" On cue, Father Kenneth coughed obligingly.

Mr. Lillywhite eyed me dubiously, but chose instead to address Jamie.

"I could by rights imprison the man, but out of regard for you, Mr. Fraser, and for your aunt, I shall not do so. He must, however, leave the colony tomorrow. I shall have him escorted into Virginia, where he will be released from custody. You may rest assured that all care will be taken to assure his welfare on the journey." He turned a cold gray eye on the Sheriff, who straightened up and tried to look reliable, with indifferent results.

"I see." Jamie spoke lightly, looking from one man to another, his eyes coming to rest on the Sheriff. "I trust that is true, sir—for if I should hear of any harm coming to the good Father, I should be . . . most distressed."

The Sheriff met his gaze, stone-faced, and held it until Mr. Lillywhite cleared his throat, frowning at the Sheriff.

"You have my word upon it, Mr. Fraser."

Jamie turned to him, bowing slightly.

"I could ask no more, sir. And yet if I may presume—might the Father not spend tonight in comfort among his friends, that they might take their leave of him? And that my wife might attend his injuries? I would stand surety for his safe delivery into your hand come morning."

Mr. Lillywhite pursed his lips and affected to consider this suggestion, but the magistrate was a poor actor. I realized with some interest that he had foreseen this request, and had his mind made up already to deny it.

"No, sir," he said, trying for a tone of reluctance. "I regret that I cannot grant your request. Though if the priest wishes to write letters to various of his acquaintance"—he gestured at the sheaf of papers—"I will undertake to see them promptly delivered."

Jamie cleared his own throat and drew himself up a bit.

"Well, then," he said. "I wonder whether I might make so bold as to ask . . ." He paused, seeming slightly embarrassed.

"Yes, sir?" Lillywhite looked at him curiously.

"I wonder whether the good Father might be allowed to hear my confession." Jamie's eyes were fixed on the tent pole, sedulously avoiding mine.

"Your confession?"

Lillywhite looked astonished at this, though the Sheriff made a noise that might charitably be called a snigger.

"Got something pressing on your conscience?" Anstruther asked rudely. "Or p'r'aps you have some premonition of impending death, eh?" He gave an evil smile at this, and Mr. Goodwin, looking shocked, rumbled a protest at him. Jamie ignored both of them, focusing his regard on Mr. Lillywhite.

"Yes, sir. It has been some time since I last had the opportunity of being shriven, ye see, and it may well be some time before such a chance occurs again. As it is—" At this point, he caught my eye, and made a slight but emphatic motion with his head toward the tent flap. "If ye will excuse us for a moment, gentlemen?"

Not waiting for a response, he seized me by the elbow and propelled me swiftly outside.

"Brianna and Marsali are up the path wi' the weans," he hissed in my ear, the moment we were clear of the tent. "Make sure Lillywhite and yon bastard of a sheriff are well away, then fetch them in."

Leaving me standing on the path, astonished, he ducked back into the tent.

"Your pardon, gentlemen," I heard him say. "I thought perhaps . . . there are some things a man shouldna quite like to be saying before his wife . . . you understand?"

There were male murmurs of understanding, and I caught the word "confession" repeated in dubious tones by Mr. Lillywhite. Jamie lowered his voice to a confidential rumble in response, interrupted by a rather loud, "You *what*?" from the Sheriff, and a peremptory shushing by Mr. Goodwin.

There was a bit of confused conversation, then a shuffle of movement, and I barely made it off the path and into the shelter of the pines before the tent flap lifted and the three Protestants emerged from the tent. The day had all but faded now, leaving burning embers of sunlit cloud in the sky, but close as they were, there was enough light for me to see the air of vague embarrassment that beset them.

They moved a few steps down the path, stopping no more than a few feet from my own hiding place. They stood in a cluster to confer, looking back at the tent, from which I could now hear Father Kenneth's voice, raised in a formal Latin blessing. The lamp in the tent went out, and the forms of Jamie and the priest, dim shadows on the canvas, disappeared into a confessional darkness.

Anstruther's bulk sidled closer to Mr. Goodwin.

"What in fuck's name is transubstantiation?" he muttered.

I saw Mr. Goodwin's shoulders straighten as he drew himself up, then hunch toward his ears in a shrug.

"In all honesty, sir, I am not positive of the meaning of the term," he said, rather primly, "though I perceive it to be some form of pernicious Papist doctrine. Perhaps Mr. Lillywhite could supply you with a more complete definition—Randall?"

"Indeed," the magistrate said. "It is the notion that by the priest's speaking particular words in the course of offering his Mass, bread and wine are transformed into the very substance of Our Savior's body and blood."

"What?" Anstruther sounded confused. "How can anyone do that?"

"Change bread and wine into flesh and blood?" Mr. Goodwin sounded quite taken aback. "But that is witchcraft, surely!"

"Well, it would be, if it happened," Mr. Lillywhite said, sounding a bit more human. "The Church very rightly holds that it does not."

"Are we sure of that?" Anstruther sounded suspicious. "Have you seen them do it?"

"Have I attended a Catholic Mass? Assuredly not!" Lillywhite's tall form drew up, austere in the gathering dusk. "What do you take me for, sir!"

"Now, Randall, I am sure the Sheriff means no offense." Goodwin put a placatory hand on his friend's arm. "His office deals with more earthly matters, after all."

"No, no, no offense meant, sir, none at all," Anstruther said hurriedly. "I was meaning more, like, has *anybody* seen this kind of goings-on, so as to be a decent witness, for the prosecution of it, I mean."

Mr. Lillywhite appeared still to be somewhat offended; his voice was cold in reply.

"It is scarcely necessary to have witnesses to the heresy, Sheriff, as the priests themselves willingly admit to it."

"No, no. Of course not." The Sheriff's squat form seemed to flatten obsequiously. "But if I'm right, sir, Papists do . . . er . . . *partake* of this—this transubwhatnot, aye?"

"Yes, so I am told."

"Well, then. That's frigging cannibalism, isn't it?" Anstruther's bulk popped up again, enthused. "I know *that's* against the law! Why not let this bugger do his bit of hocus-pocus, and we'll arrest the whole boiling lot of 'em, eh? Get shut of any number of the bastards at one blow, I daresay."

Mr. Goodwin emitted a low moan. He appeared to be massaging his face, no doubt to ease a recurrent ache from his tooth.

Mr. Lillywhite exhaled strongly through his nose.

"No," he said evenly. "I am afraid not, Sheriff. My instructions are that the priest is not to be allowed to perform any ceremonial, and shall be prevented from receiving visitors."

"Oh, aye? And what's he doing now, then?" Anstruther demanded, gesturing toward the darkened tent, where Jamie's voice had begun to speak, hesitant and barely audible. I thought perhaps he was speaking in Latin.

"That is quite different," Lillywhite said testily. "Mr. Fraser is a gentleman. And the prohibition against visitors is to insure that the priest shall perform no secret marriages; hardly a concern at present."

"Bless me, Father, for I have sinned." Jamie's voice spoke in English, suddenly louder, and Mr. Lillywhite started. Father Kenneth murmured interrogatively.

"I have been guilty of the sins of lust and impurity, both in thought and in my flesh," Jamie announced—with what I thought rather more volume than was quite discreet.

"Oh, to be sure," said Father Kenneth, suddenly louder too. He sounded interested. "Now, these sins of impurity—what form, precisely, did they take, my son, and upon how many occasions?"

"Aye, well. I've looked upon women with lust, to be starting with. How many occasions—oh, make it a hundred, at least, it's been a time since I was last to confession. Did ye need to know which women, Father, or only what it was I thought of doing to them?"

Mr. Lillywhite stiffened markedly.

"I think we'll not have time for the lot, Jamie dear," said the priest. "But if ye were to tell me about one or two of these occasions, just so as I could be formin' a notion as to the . . . er . . . severity of the offense . . . ?"

"Och, aye. Well, the worst was likely the time wi' the butter churn."

"Butter churn? Ah . . . the sort with the handle pokin' up?" Father Kenneth's tone encompassed a sad compassion for the lewd possibilities suggested by this.

"Oh, no, Father; it was a barrel churn. The sort that lies on its side, aye, with a wee handle to turn it? Well, it's only that she was workin' the churn with great vigor, and the laces of her bodice undone, so that her breasts wobbled to and fro, and the cloth clinging to her with the sweat of her work. Now, the churn was just the right height—and curved, aye?—so as make me think of bendin' her across it and lifting her skirts, and—"

My mouth opened involuntarily in shock. That was my bodice he was describing, my breasts, and my butter churn! To say nothing of my skirts. I remembered that particular occasion quite vividly, and if it had started with an impure thought, it certainly hadn't stopped there.

A rustling and murmuring drew my attention back to the men on the path. Mr. Lillywhite had grasped the Sheriff—still leaning avidly toward the tent, ears flapping—by the arm and was hissing at him as he forced him hastily down the path. Mr. Goodwin followed, though with an air of reluctance.

The noise of their departure had unfortunately drowned out the rest of Jamie's description of that particular occasion of sin, but had luckily also covered the leaf-rustling and twig-snapping behind me that announced the appearance of Brianna and Marsali, Jemmy and Joan swaddled in their arms and Germain clinging monkeylike to his mother's back.

"I thought they'd never go," Brianna whispered, peering over my shoulder toward the spot where Mr. Lillywhite and his companions had disappeared. "Is the coast clear?"

"Yes, come along." I reached for Germain, who leaned willingly into my arms.

"Ou qu'on va, Grand-mère?" he inquired in a sleepy voice, blond head nuzzling affectionately into my neck.

"Shh. To see *Grand-père* and Father Kenneth," I whispered to him. "We have to be very quiet, though."

"Oh. Like this?" he hissed, in a loud whisper, and began to sing a very vulgar French song, chanting half under his breath.

"Shh!" I clapped a hand across his mouth, moist and sticky with whatever he'd been eating. "Don't sing, sweetheart, we don't want to wake the babies."

I heard a small, stifled noise from Marsali, a strangled snort from Bree, and realized that Jamie was still confessing. He appeared to have hit his stride, and was now inventing freely—or at least I hoped so. He certainly hadn't been doing any of that with *me.*

I poked my head out, looking up and down the trail, but no one was near. I motioned to the girls, and we scuttled across the path and into the darkened tent.

Jamie stopped abruptly as we fumbled our way inside. Then I heard him say quickly, "And sins of anger, pride, and jealousy—oh, and the odd wee bit of lying as well, Father. Amen." He dropped to his knees, raced through an Act of Contrition in French, and was on his feet and taking Germain from me before Father Kenneth had finished saying the *"Ego te absolvo."*

My eyes were becoming adapted to the dark; I could make out the voluminous shapes of the girls, and Jamie's tall outline. He stood Germain on the table before the priest, saying, "Quickly, then, Father; we havena much time."

"We haven't any water, either," the priest observed. "Unless you ladies thought to bring any?" He had picked up the flint and tinderbox, and was attempting to relight the lamp.

Bree and Marsali exchanged appalled glances, then shook their heads in unison.

"Dinna fash, Father." Jamie spoke soothingly, and I saw him reach out a hand for something on the table. There was the brief squeak of a cork being drawn, and the hot, sweet smell of fine whisky filled the tent, as the light caught and grew from the wick, the wavering flame steadying to a small, clear light.

"Under the circumstances . . ." Jamie said, holding out the open flask to the priest.

Father Kenneth's lips pressed together, though I thought with suppressed amusement, rather than irritation.

"Under the circumstances, aye," he repeated. "And what should be more appropriate than the water of life, after all?" He reached up, undid his stock, and pulled up a leather string fastened round his neck, from which dangled a wooden cross and a small glass bottle, stoppered with a cork.

"The holy chrism," he explained, undoing the bottle and setting it on the table. "Thank the Virgin Mother that I had it on my person. The Sheriff took the box with my Mass things." He made a quick inventory of the objects on the table, counting them off on his fingers. "Fire, chrism, water—of a sort—and a child. Very well, then. You and your husband will stand as godparents to him, I suppose, ma'am?"

This was addressed to me, Jamie having gone to take up a station by the tent flap.

"For all of them, Father," I said, and took a firm grip on Germain, who seemed disposed to leap off the table. "Hold still, darling, just for a moment."

I heard a small *whish* behind me; metal drawn from oiled leather. I glanced back to see Jamie, dim in the shadows, standing guard by the door with his dirk in his hand. A qualm of apprehension curled through my belly, and I heard Bree draw in her breath beside me.

"Jamie, my son," said Father Kenneth, in a tone of mild reproval.

"Be going on with it, if ye please, Father," Jamie replied, very calmly. "I mean to have my grandchildren baptized this night, and no one shall prevent it."

The priest drew in his breath with a slight hiss, then shook his head.

"Aye. And if you kill someone, I hope there'll be time for me to shrive you again before they hang us both," he muttered, reaching for the oil. "If there's a choice about it, try for the Sheriff, will you, man dear?"

Switching abruptly to Latin, he pushed back Germain's heavy mop of blond hair and his thumb flicked deftly over forehead, lips, and then—diving under the boy's gown in a gesture that made Germain double up in giggles—heart, in the sign of the Cross.

"On-behalf-of-this-child-do-you-renounce-Satan-and-all-his-works?" he asked, speaking so fast that I scarcely realized he was speaking English again, and barely caught up in time to join with Jamie in the godparents' response, dutifully reciting, "I do renounce them."

I was on edge, keeping an ear out for any noises that might portend the return of Mr. Lillywhite and the Sheriff, envisioning just what sort of brouhaha might ensue if they did come back to discover Father Kenneth in the midst of what would surely be considered an illicit "ceremonial."

I glanced back at Jamie; he was looking at me, and gave

me a faint smile that I thought was likely meant for reassurance. If so, it failed utterly; I knew him too well. He wanted his grandchildren baptized, and he would see their souls safely given into God's care, if he died for it—or if we all went to gaol, Brianna, Marsali, and the children included. Of such stuff are martyrs made, and their families are obliged to lump it.

"Do-you-believe-in-one-God-the-Father-the-Son-and-the-Holy-Ghost?"

"Stubborn man," I mouthed at Jamie. His smile widened, and I turned back, hastily chiming in with his firm, "I do believe." Was that a footfall on the path outside, or only the evening wind, making the tree branches crack as it passed?

The questions and responses finished, and the priest grinned at me, looking like a gargoyle in the flickering lamplight. His good eye closed briefly in a wink.

"We'll take it that your answers will be the same for the others, shall we, ma'am? And what will be this sweet lad's baptismal name?"

Not breaking his rhythm, the priest took up the whisky flask, and dribbled a careful stream of spirit onto the little boy's head, repeating, "I baptize thee, Germain Alexander Claudel MacKenzie Fraser, in the Name of the Father, the Son, and the Holy Ghost, Amen."

Germain watched this operation with profound interest, round blue eyes crossing as the amber liquid ran down the shallow bridge of his nose and dripped from its stubby tip. He put out a tongue to catch the drops, then made a face at the taste.

"Ick," he said clearly. "Horse piss."

Marsali made a brief, shocked "Tst!" at him, but the priest merely chuckled, swung Germain off the table, and beckoned to Bree.

She held Jemmy over the table, cradled in her arms like a sacrifice. She was intent on the baby's face, but I saw her head twitch slightly, her attention drawn by something outside. There *were* sounds on the path below; I could hear voices. A group of men, I thought, talking together, voices genial but not drunken.

I tensed, trying not to look at Jamie. If they came in, I

decided, I had better grab Germain, scramble under the far edge of the tent, and run for it. I took a preparatory grip on the collar of his gown, just in case. Then I felt a gentle nudge as Bree shifted her weight against me.

"It's all right, Mama," she whispered. "It's Roger and Fergus." She nodded toward the dark, then returned her attention to Jemmy.

It was, I realized, and the skin of my temples prickled with relief. Now that I knew, I could make out the imperious, slightly nasal sound of Fergus's voice, raised in a lengthy oration of some kind, and a low Scottish rumble that I thought must be Roger's. A higher-pitched titter that I recognized as Mr. Goodwin's drifted through the night, followed by some remark in Mr. Lillywhite's aristocratic drawl.

I did glance at Jamie this time. He still held the dirk, but his hand had fallen to his side, and his shoulders had lost a little of their tension. He smiled at me again, and this time I returned it.

Jemmy was awake, but drowsy. He made no objection to the oil, but startled at the cold touch of the whisky on his forehead, eyes popping open and arms flinging wide. He uttered a high-pitched "Yeep!" of protest, then, as Bree gathered him hastily up into his blanket against her shoulder, screwed up his face and tried to decide whether he was sufficiently disturbed to cry about it.

Bree patted his back like a bongo drum and made little hooting noises in his ear, distracting him. He settled for plugging his mouth with a thumb and glowering suspiciously at the assemblage, but by that time, Father Kenneth was already pouring whisky on the sleeping Joan, held low in Marsali's arms.

"I baptize thee, Joan Laoghaire Claire Fraser," he said, following Marsali's lead, and I glanced at Marsali, startled. I knew she was called Joan for Marsali's younger sister, but I hadn't known what the baby's other names would be. I felt a small lump in my throat, watching Marsali's shawled head bent over the child. Both her sister and her mother, Laoghaire, were in Scotland; the chances of either ever seeing this tiny namesake were vanishingly small.

Suddenly, Joan's slanted eyes popped wide open and so

did her mouth. She let out a piercing shriek, and everyone started as though a bomb had exploded in our midst.

"Go in peace, to serve the Lord! And go fast!" Father Kenneth said, his fingers already nimbly corking up bottle and flask, frantically whisking away all traces of the ceremony. Down the path, I could hear voices raised in puzzled question.

Marsali was out the tent flap in a flash, the squalling Joan against her breast, a protesting Germain clutched by the hand. Bree paused just long enough to put a hand behind Father Kenneth's head and kiss him on the forehead.

"Thank you, Father," she whispered, and was gone in a flurry of skirts and petticoats.

Jamie had me by the arm and was hustling me out of the tent as well, but stopped for a half-second at the door, turning back.

"Father?" he called in a whisper. *"Pax vobiscum!"*

Father Kenneth had already seated himself behind the table, hands folded, the accusing sheets of blank paper spread out once more before him. He looked up, smiling slightly, and his face was perfectly at peace in the lamplight, black eye and all.

"*Et cum spiritu tuo*, man," he said, and raised three fingers in parting benediction.

"WHAT ON EARTH did you do that for?" Brianna's whisper floated back to me, loud with annoyance. She and Marsali were only a few feet in front of us, going slowly because of the children, but close as they were, the girls' shawled and bunchy shapes were scarcely distinguishable from the bushes overgrowing the path.

"Do what? Leave that, Germain; let's find Papa, shall we? No, don't put it in your mouth!"

"You pinched Joanie—I saw you! You could have got us all caught!"

"But I had to!" Marsali sounded surprised at the accusation. "And it wouldna have mattered, really—the christening was done by then. They couldna make Father Kenneth take it back, now, could they?" She giggled slightly at the thought, then broke off. "Germain, I said drop it!"

"What do you mean, you had to? Let go, Jem, that's my hair! Ow! Let go, I said!"

Jemmy was evidently now wide awake, interested in the novel surroundings, and wanting to explore them, judging from his repeated exclamations of "Argl!" punctuated by the occasional curious "Gleb?"

"Why, she was asleep!" Marsali said, sounding scandalized. "She didna wake when Father Kenneth poured the water—I mean the whisky—on her head—Germain, come back here! *Thig air ais a seo!*—and ye ken it's ill luck for a child not to make a wee skelloch when it's baptized; that's how ye ken as the original sin is leaving it! I couldna let the *diabhol* stay in my wee lassie. Could I, *mo mhaorine*?" There were small kissing noises, and a faint coo from Joanie, promptly drowned by Germain, who had started to sing again.

Bree gave a small snort of amusement, her irritation fading.

"Oh, I see. Well, as long as you had a good reason. Though I'm not so sure it worked on Jemmy and Germain. Look at the way they're acting—I'd swear they were possessed. Ow! Don't bite me, you little fiend, I'll feed you in a minute!"

"Och, well, they're boys, after all," Marsali said tolerantly, raising her voice slightly to be heard above the racket. "Everyone kens that boys are full o' the devil; I suppose it would take more than a bit of holy water to drown it all, even if it *was* ninety-proof. Germain! *Where* did ye hear such a filthy song, ye wee ratten?"

I smiled, and next to me, Jamie laughed quietly, listening to the girls' conversation. We were far enough from the scene of the crime by now not to worry about being heard, among the snatches of song, fiddle music, and laughter that flickered through the trees with the light of the campfires, bright against the growing dark.

The business of the day was largely done, and folk were settling down to the evening meal, before the calling, the singing, and the last round of visits started. The scents of smoke and supper trailed tantalizing fingers through the cold, dark air, and my stomach rumbled gently in answer to their summons. I hoped Lizzie was sufficiently restored as to have begun cooking.

"What's *mo mhaorine*?" I asked Jamie. "I haven't heard that one before."

"It means 'my wee potato,' I think," he said. "It's Irish, aye? She learnt it from the priest."

He sighed, sounding deeply satisfied with the evening's work so far.

"May Bride bless Father Kenneth for a nimble-fingered man; for a moment, I thought we wouldna manage it. Is that Roger and wee Fergus?"

A couple of dark shadows had come out of the wood to join the girls, and the sound of muffled laughter and murmured voices—punctuated by raucous shrieks from both little boys at sight of their daddies—drifted back to us from the little knot of young families.

"It is. And speaking of that, my little sweet potato," I said, taking a firm grip of his arm to slow him, "what do you mean by telling Father Kenneth all that about me and the butter churn?"

"Ye dinna mean to say ye minded, Sassenach?" he said, in tones of surprise.

"Of course I minded!" I said. The blood rose warm in my cheeks, though I wasn't sure whether this was due to the memory of his confession—or to the memory of the original occasion. My innards warmed slightly at that thought as well, and the last remnants of cramp began to subside as my womb clenched and relaxed, eased by the pleasant inward glow. It was scarcely a suitable time or place, but perhaps later in the evening, we might manage sufficient privacy—I pushed the thought hastily aside.

"Privacy quite aside, it wasn't a sin at all," I said primly. "We're married, for goodness' sake!"

"Well, I did confess to telling lies, Sassenach," he said. I couldn't see the smile on his face, but I could hear it well enough in his voice. I supposed he could hear mine, too.

"I had to think of a sin frightful enough to drive Lillywhite away—and I couldna confess to theft or buggery; I may have to do business with the man one day."

"Oh, so you think he'd be put off by sodomy, but he'd consider your attitude toward women in wet chemises just a minor flaw of character?" His arm was warm under the cloth of his shirt. I touched the underside of his wrist, that vulnerable place where the skin lay bare, and stroked the line of the vein that pulsed there, disappearing under the linen toward his heart.

"Keep your voice down, Sassenach," he murmured, touching my hand. "Ye dinna want the bairns to hear ye. Besides," he added, his voice dropping low enough that he was obliged to lean down and whisper in my ear, "it's not all women. Only the ones with lovely round arses." He let go my hand and patted my backside familiarly, showing remarkable accuracy in the darkness.

"I wouldna cross the road to see a scrawny woman, if she were stark naked and dripping wet. As for Lillywhite," he resumed, in a more normal tone of voice, but without removing his hand, which was molding the cloth of my skirt thoughtfully round one buttock, "he may be a Protestant, Sassenach, but he's still a man."

"I didn't realize the two states were incompatible," Roger's voice said dryly, coming out of the darkness nearby.

Jamie snatched his hand away as though my bottom were on fire. It wasn't—quite—but there was no denying that his flint had struck a spark or two among the kindling, damp as it was. It was a long time before bedtime, though.

Pausing just long enough to administer a brief, private squeeze to Jamie's anatomy that made him gasp sharply, I turned to find Roger clasping a large wriggling object in his arms, its nature obscured by the dark. Not a piglet, I surmised, despite the loud grunting noises it was making, but rather Jemmy, who seemed to be gnawing fiercely on his father's knuckles. A small pink fist shot out into a random patch of light, clenched in concentration, then disappeared, meeting Roger's ribs with a solid thump.

Jamie gave a small grunt of amusement himself, but wasn't discomposed in the slightest by having his opinion of Protestants overheard.

" 'All are gude lasses,' " he quoted in broad Scots, " 'but where do the ill wives come frae?' "

"Eh?" Roger said, sounding a bit bewildered.

"Protestants are *born* wi' pricks," Jamie explained, "the men, at least—but some let them wither from disuse. A man who spends his time pokin' his . . . nose into others' sinfulness has nay time to tend his own."

I converted a laugh into a more tactful cough.

"And some just become bigger pricks, what with the practice," Roger said, more dryly still. "Aye, well. I came to thank you . . . for managing about the baptism, I mean."

I noticed the slight hesitation; he still had not settled on any comfortable name by which to call Jamie to his face. Jamie addressed *him* impartially as "Wee Roger," "Roger Mac," or "MacKenzie"—more rarely, by the Gaelic nickname Ronnie Sinclair had given Roger, *a Smeòraich*, in honor of his voice. *Singing Thrush*, it meant.

"It's me should be thanking you, *a charaid*. We shouldna have managed there at the last, save for you and Fergus," Jamie said, laughter warming his own voice.

Roger was clearly visible in outline, tall and lean, with the glow of someone's fire behind him. One shoulder rose as he shrugged, and he shifted Jemmy to his other arm, wiping residual drool from his hand against the side of his breeches.

"No trouble," he said, a little gruffly. "Will the—the Father be all right, d'ye think? Brianna said he'd been roughly handled. I hope they'll not mistreat him, once he's away."

Jamie sobered at that. He shrugged a little as he straightened the coat on his shoulders.

"I think he'll be safe enough, aye—I had a word with the Sheriff." There was a certain grim emphasis on "word" that made his meaning clear. A substantial bribe might have been more effective, but I was well aware that we had exactly two shillings, threepence, and nine farthings in cash to our names at the moment. Better to save the money and rely on threats, I thought. Evidently Jamie was of the same mind.

"I shall speak to my aunt," he said, "and have her send a note tonight to Mr. Lillywhite, wi' her own opinion on the subject. That will be a better safeguard for Father Kenneth than anything I can say myself."

"I don't suppose she'll be at all pleased to hear that her

wedding is postponed," I observed. She wouldn't be. Daughter of a Highland laird and widow of a very rich planter, Jocasta Cameron was used to having her own way.

"No, she won't," Jamie agreed wryly, "though I suppose Duncan may be a bit relieved."

Roger laughed, not without sympathy, and fell in beside us as we started down the path. He shifted Jemmy, still grunting ferociously, under his arm like a football.

"Aye, he will. Poor Duncan. So the weddings are definitely off, are they?"

I couldn't see Jamie's frown, but I felt the movement as he shook his head doubtfully.

"Aye, I'm afraid so. They wouldna give the priest to me, even with my word to hand him over in the morning. We could maybe take him by force, but even so—"

"I doubt that would help," I interrupted, and told them what I had overheard while waiting outside the tent.

"So I can't see them standing round and letting Father Kenneth perform marriages," I finished. "Even if you got him away, they'd be combing the mountain for him, turning out tents and causing riots."

Sheriff Anstruther wouldn't be without aid; Jamie and his aunt might be held in good esteem among the Scottish community, but Catholics in general and priests in particular weren't.

"Instructions?" Jamie repeated, sounding astonished. "You're sure of it, Sassenach? It was Lillywhite who said he had 'instructions'?"

"It was," I said, realizing for the first time how peculiar that was. The Sheriff was plainly taking instructions from Mr. Lillywhite, that being his duty. But who could be giving instructions to the magistrate?

"There's another magistrate here, and a couple of justices of the peace, but surely . . ." Roger said slowly, shaking his head as he thought. A loud squawk interrupted his thoughts, and he glanced down, the light from a nearby fire shining off the bridge of his nose, outlining a faint smile as he spoke to his offspring. "What? You're hungry, laddie? Don't fret yourself, Mummy will be back soon."

"Where *is* Mummy?" I said, peering into the shifting mass of shadows ahead. A light wind had risen, and the bare branches of oak and hickory rattled like sabers overhead. Still, Jemmy was more than loud enough for Brianna to hear him. I caught Marsali's voice faintly up ahead, engaged in what appeared to be amiable conversation with Germain and Fergus regarding supper, but there was no sound of Bree's lower, huskier Boston-bred tones.

"Why?" Jamie said to Roger, raising his voice to be heard over the wind.

"Why what? Here, Jem, see that? Want it? Aye, of course ye do. Yes, good lad, gnaw on that for a bit." A spark of light caught something shiny in Roger's free hand; then the object disappeared, and Jemmy's cries ceased abruptly, succeeded by loud sucking and slurping noises.

"What is that? It isn't small enough for him to swallow, is it?" I asked anxiously.

"Ah, no. It's a watch chain. Not to worry," Roger assured me, "I've a good grip on the end of it. If he swallows it, I can pull it back out."

"Why would someone not want you to be married?" Jamie said patiently, ignoring the imminent danger to his grandson's digestive system.

"Me?" Roger sounded surprised. "I shouldn't think anyone cares whether I'm married or not, save myself—and you, perhaps," he added, a touch of humor in his voice. "I expect ye'd like the boy to have a name. Speaking of that"—he turned to me, the wind pulling long streamers of his hair loose and turning him into a wild black fiend in silhouette—"what *did* he end up being named? At the christening, I mean."

"Jeremiah Alexander Ian Fraser MacKenzie," I said, hoping I recalled it correctly. "Is that what you wanted?"

"Oh, I didn't mind so much what he was called," Roger said, edging gingerly round a large puddle that spread across the path. It had begun to sprinkle again; I could feel small chilly drops on my face, and see the dimpling of the water in the puddle where the firelight shone across it.

"I wanted Jeremiah, but I told Bree the other names were

up to her. She couldn't quite decide between John for John Grey, and—and Ian, for her cousin, but of course they're the same name in any case."

Again I noticed the faint hesitation, and I felt Jamie's arm stiffen slightly under my hand. Jamie's nephew Ian was a sore point—and fresh in everyone's mind, thanks to the note we had received from him the day before. That must be what had decided Brianna at last.

"Well, if it isna you and my daughter," Jamie pursued doggedly, "then who is it? Jocasta and Duncan? Or the folk from Bremerton?"

"You think someone's out specially to prevent the marriages tonight?" Roger seized the opportunity to talk about something other than Ian Murray. "You don't think it's just general dislike of Romish practices, then?"

"It might be, but it's not. If it were, why wait 'til now to arrest the priest? Wait a bit, Sassenach, I'll fetch ye over."

Jamie let go of my hand and stepped round the puddle, then reached back, grabbed me by the waist, and lifted me bodily across in a swish of skirts. The wet leaves slipped and squelched under my boots as he set me down, but I seized his arm for balance, righting myself.

"No," Jamie continued the conversation, turning back toward Roger. "Lillywhite and Anstruther have no great love of Catholics, I expect, but why stir up a stramash now, when the priest would be gone in the morning, anyway? Do they maybe think he'll corrupt all the God-fearing folk on the mountain before dawn if they dinna keep him in ward?"

Roger gave a short laugh at that.

"No, I suppose not. Is there anything else the priest was meant to do tonight, beyond performing marriages and baptisms?"

"Perhaps a few confessions," I said, pinching Jamie's arm. "Nothing else that I know of." I squeezed my thighs together, feeling an alarming shift in my intimate arrangements. Damn, one of the pins holding the cloth between my legs had come loose when Jamie lifted me. Had I lost it?

"I don't suppose they'd be trying to keep him from hearing someone's confession? Someone in particular, I mean?"

Roger sounded doubtful, but Jamie took the idea and turned it round in his hands, considering.

"They'd no objection to his hearing mine. And I shouldna think they'd care if a Catholic was in mortal sin or not, as by their lights, we're all damned anyway. But if they kent someone desperately needed confession, and they thought there was something to be gained by it . . ."

"That whoever it was might pay for access to the priest?" I asked skeptically. "Really, Jamie, these are Scots. I should imagine that if it were a question of paying out hard money for a priest, your Scottish Catholic murderer or adulterer would just say an Act of Contrition and hope for the best."

Jamie snorted slightly, and I saw the white mist of his breath purl round his head like candle smoke; it was getting colder.

"I daresay," he said dryly. "And if Lillywhite had any thought of setting up in the confession business, he's left it a bit late in the day to make much profit. But what if it wasna a matter of stopping someone's confession—but rather only of making sure that they overheard it?"

Roger uttered a pleased grunt, evidently thinking this a promising supposition.

"Blackmail? Aye, that's a thought," he said, with approval. Blood will out, I thought; Oxford-educated or not, there was little doubt that Roger was a Scot. There was a violent upheaval under his arm, followed by a wail from Jemmy. Roger glanced down.

"Oh, did ye drop your bawbee? Where's it gone, then?" He hoicked Jemmy up onto his shoulder like a bundle of laundry and squatted down, poking at the ground in search of the watch chain, which Jemmy had evidently hurled into the darkness.

"Blackmail? I think that's a trifle far-fetched," I objected, rubbing a hand under my nose, which had begun to drip. "You mean they might suspect that Farquard Campbell, for instance, had committed some dreadful crime, and if they knew about it for sure, they could hold him up about it? Isn't that awfully devious thinking? If you find a pin down there, Roger, it's mine."

"Well, Lillywhite and Anstruther are Englishmen, are they not?" Jamie said, with a delicate sarcasm that made Roger laugh. "Deviousness and double-dealing come naturally to that race, no, Sassenach?"

"Oh, rubbish," I said tolerantly. "Pot calling the kettle black isn't in it. Besides, they didn't try to overhear *your* confession."

"I havena got anything to be blackmailed for," Jamie pointed out, though it was perfectly obvious that he was only arguing for the fun of it.

"Even so," I began, but was interrupted by Jemmy, who was becoming increasingly restive, flinging himself to and fro with intermittent steam-whistle shrieks. Roger grunted, pinched something gingerly between his fingers, and stood up.

"Found your pin," he said. "No sign of the chain, though."

"Someone will find it in the morning," I said, raising my voice to be heard over the increasing racket. "Perhaps you'd better let me take him." I reached for the baby, and Roger surrendered his burden with a distinct air of relief—explained when I got a whiff of Jemmy's diaper.

"Not *again*?" I said. Apparently taking this as a personal reproach, he shut his eyes and started to howl like an air-raid siren.

"Where *is* Bree?" I asked, trying simultaneously to cradle him reassuringly and to keep him at a sanitary distance. "Ouch!" He seemed to have taken advantage of the darkness to grow a number of extra limbs, all of which were flailing or grabbing.

"Oh, she's just gone to run a wee errand," Roger said, with an air of vagueness that made Jamie turn his head sharply. The light caught him in profile, and I saw the thick red brows drawn down in suspicion. Fire gleamed off the long, straight bridge of his nose as he lifted it, questioning. Obviously, he smelled a rat. He turned toward me, one eyebrow lifted. Was I in on it?

"I haven't any idea," I assured him. "Here, I'm going across to McAllister's fire to borrow a clean clout. I'll see you at our camp in a bit."

Not waiting for an answer, I took a firm grasp on the baby and shuffled into the bushes, heading for the nearest campsite. Georgiana McAllister had newborn twins—I'd delivered them four days before—and was happy to provide me with both a clean diaper and a private bush behind which to effect my personal repairs. These accomplished, I chatted with her and admired the twins, all the while wondering about the recent revelations. Between Lieutenant Hayes and his proclamation, the machinations of Lillywhite and company, and whatever Bree and Roger were up to, the mountain seemed a perfect hotbed of conspiracy tonight.

I was pleased that we had managed the christening—in fact, I was surprised to find just how gratified I did feel about it—but I had to admit to a pang of distress over Brianna's canceled wedding. She hadn't said much about it, but I knew that both she and Roger had been looking forward very much to the blessing of their union. The firelight winked briefly, accusingly, off the gold ring on my left hand, and I mentally threw up my hands in Frank's direction.

And just what do you expect me to do about it? I demanded silently, while externally agreeing with Georgiana's opinion on the treatment of pinworms.

"Ma'am?" One of the older McAllister girls, who had volunteered to change Jemmy, interrupted the conversation, dangling a long, slimy object delicately between two fingers. "I found this gaud in the wean's cloot; is it maybe your man's?"

"Good grief!" I was shocked by the watch chain's reappearance, but a moment's rationality corrected my first alarmed impression that Jemmy had in fact swallowed the thing. It would take several hours for a solid object to make its way through even the most active infant's digestive tract; evidently he had merely dropped his toy down the front of his gown and it had come to rest in his diaper.

"Gie it here, lass." Mr. McAllister, catching sight of the watch chain, reached out and took it with a slight grimace. He pulled a large handkerchief from the waist of his breeks and wiped the object carefully, bringing to light the gleam of silver links and a small round fob, bearing some kind of seal.

I noted the fob with some grimness, and made a mental resolve to give Roger a proper bollocking about what he let Jemmy put in his mouth. Thank goodness it hadn't come off.

"Why, that's Mr. Caldwell's wee gaud, surely!" Georgiana leaned forward, peering over the heads of the twins she was nursing.

"Is it?" Her husband squinted at the object, and fumbled in his shirt for his spectacles.

"Aye, I'm sure it is! I saw it when he preached Sunday. The first of my pains was just comin' on," she explained, turning to me, "and I had to come away before he'd finished. He saw me turn to go, and must ha' thought he'd outstayed his welcome, for he pulled the watch from his pocket to have a wee keek, and I saw the glint from that bittie round thing on the chain."

"That's called a seal, *a nighean*," her husband informed her, having now settled a pair of half-moon spectacles firmly atop his nose, and turning the little metal emblem over between his fingers. "You're right, though, it's Mr. Caldwell's, for see?" A horny finger traced the outline of the figure on the seal: a mace, an open book, a bell, and a tree, standing on top of a fish with a ring in its mouth.

"That's from the University of Glasgow, that is. Mr. Caldwell's a scholar," he told me, blue eyes wide with awe. "Been to learn the preachin', and a fine job he makes of it.

"You did miss a fine finish, Georgie," he added, turning to his wife. "He went sae red in the face, talkin' of the Abomination of Desolation and the wrath at world's end, that I thought surely he'd have an apoplexy, and then what should we do? For he wouldna have Murray MacLeod to him, Murray bein' in the way of a heretic to Mr. Caldwell—he's New Light, Murray"—Mr. McAllister explained in an aside to me—"and Mrs. Fraser here a Papist, as well as bein' otherwise engaged wi' you and the bairns."

He leaned over and patted one of the twins gently on its bonneted head, but it paid no attention, blissfully absorbed in its suckling.

"Hmp. Well, Mr. Caldwell could ha' burst himself, for all I cared at the time," his wife said frankly. She hitched up her double armload and settled herself more comfortably. "And for mysel', I shouldna much mind if the midwife was a red Indian or English—oh, I do beg your pardon, Mrs. Fraser—so long as she kent how to catch a babe and stop the bleedin'."

I murmured something modest, brushing away Georgiana's apologies, in favor of finding out more about the watch chain's origins.

"Mr. Caldwell. He's a preacher, you say?" A certain suspicion was stirring in the back of my mind.

"Oh, aye, the best I've heard," Mr. McAllister assured me. "And I've heard 'em all. Now, Mr. Urmstone, he's a grand one for the sins, but he's on in years, and gone a bit hoarse now, so as ye need to be right up front to hear him—and that's a bit dangerous, ye ken, as it's the folk in front whose sins he's likely to start in upon. The New Light fella, though, he's nay much; no voice to him."

He dismissed the unfortunate preacher with the scorn of a connoisseur.

"Mr. Woodmason's all right; a bit stiff in his manner—an Englishman, aye?—but verra faithful about turning up for services, for all he's well stricken in years. Now, young Mr. Campbell from the Barbecue Church—"

"This wean's fair starved, ma'am," the girl holding Jemmy put in. Evidently so; he was red in the face and keening. "Will I give him a bit o' parritch, maybe?"

I gave a quick glance at the pot over the fire; it was bubbling, so likely well-cooked enough to kill most germs. I pulled out the horn spoon I carried in my pocket, which I could be sure was reasonably clean, and handed it to the girl.

"Thank you so much. Now, this Mr. Caldwell—he wouldn't by chance be a Presbyterian, would he?"

Mr. McAllister looked surprised, then beamed at my perceptivity.

"Why, so he is, indeed! Ye'll have heard of him, then, Mrs. Fraser?"

"I think perhaps my son-in-law is acquainted with him," I said, with a tinge of irony.

Georgiana laughed.

"I should say your grandson kens him, at least." She nodded at the chain, draped across her husband's broad palm.

"Bairns that size are just like magpies; they'll seize upon any shiny bawbee they see."

"So they do," I said slowly, staring at the silver links and their dangling fob. That put something of a different complexion on the matter. If Jemmy had picked Mr. Caldwell's pocket, it had obviously been done sometime before Jamie had arranged the impromptu christening.

But Bree and Roger had known about Father Kenneth's arrest and the possible cancelation of their wedding well before that; there would have been plenty of time for them to make other plans while Jamie and I were dealing with Rosamund, Ronnie, and the other assorted crises. Plenty of time for Roger to go and talk to Mr. Caldwell, the Presbyterian minister—with Jemmy along for the ride.

And as soon as Roger had confirmed the unlikelihood of the priest's performing any marriages tonight, Brianna had disappeared on a vague "errand." Well, if Father Kenneth had wanted to interview a Presbyterian groom before marrying him, I supposed Mr. Caldwell might be allowed the same privilege with a prospective Papist bride.

Jemmy was devouring porridge with the single-mindedness of a starving piranha; we couldn't leave quite yet. That was just as well, I thought; let Brianna break the news to her father that she would have her wedding after all—priest or no priest.

I spread out my skirt to dry the damp hem, and the firelight glowed from both my rings. A strong disposition to laugh bubbled up inside me, at the thought of what Jamie would say when he found out, but I suppressed it, not wanting to explain my amusement to the McAllisters.

"Shall I take that?" I said instead to Mr. McAllister, with a nod toward the watch chain. "I think perhaps I shall be seeing Mr. Caldwell a little later."

14

HAPPY THE BRIDE THE MOON SHINES ON

WE WERE LUCKY. The rain held off, and shredding clouds revealed a silver moon, rising lopsided but luminous over the slope of Black Mountain; suitable illumination for an intimate family wedding.

I had met David Caldwell, though I hadn't recalled it until I saw him; a small but immensely personable gentleman, very tidy in his dress, despite camping in the open for a week. Jamie knew him, too, and respected him. That didn't prevent a certain tightness of expression as the minister came into the firelight, his worn prayer book clasped in his hands, but I nudged Jamie warningly, and he at once altered his expression to one of inscrutability.

I saw Roger glance once in our direction, then turn back to Bree. There might have been a slight smile at the corner of his mouth, or it could have been only the effect of the shadows. Jamie exhaled strongly through his nose, and I nudged him again.

"You had your way over the baptism," I whispered. He lifted his chin slightly. Brianna glanced in our direction, looking slightly anxious.

"I havena said a word, have I?"

"It's a perfectly respectable Christian marriage."

"Did I say it was not?"

"Then look *happy*, damn you!" I hissed. He exhaled once more, and assumed an expression of benevolence one degree short of outright imbecility.

"Better?" he asked, teeth clenched in a genial smile. I saw

Duncan Innes turn casually toward us, start, and turn hastily away, murmuring something to Jocasta, who stood near the fire, white hair shining, and a blindfold over her damaged eyes to shield them from the light. Ulysses, standing behind her, had in fact put on his wig in honor of the ceremony; it was all I could see of him in the darkness, hanging apparently disembodied in the air above her shoulder. As I watched, it turned sideways, toward us, and I caught the faint shine of eyes beneath it.

"Who that, *Grand-mère*?"

Germain, escaped as usual from parental custody, popped up near my feet, pointing curiously at the Reverend Caldwell.

"That's a minister, darling. Auntie Bree and Uncle Roger are getting married."

"C'est quoi minster?"

I drew a deep breath, but Jamie beat me to it.

"It's a sort of priest, but not a proper priest."

"Bad priest?" Germain viewed the Reverend Caldwell with substantially more interest.

"No, no," I said. "He's not a bad priest at all. It's only that . . . well, you see, we're Catholics, and Catholics have priests, but Uncle Roger is a Presbyterian—"

"That's a heretic," Jamie put in helpfully.

"It is *not* a heretic, darling, *Grand-père* is being funny—or thinks he is. Presbyterians are . . ."

Germain was paying no attention to my explanation, but instead had tilted his head back, viewing Jamie with fascination.

"Why *Grand-père* is making faces?"

"We're verra happy," Jamie explained, expression still fixed in a rictus of amiability.

"Oh." Germain at once stretched his own extraordinarily mobile face into a crude facsimile of the same expression—a jack-o'-lantern grin, teeth clenched and eyes popping. "Like this?"

"Yes, darling," I said, in a marked tone. "*Just* like that."

Marsali looked at us, blinked, and tugged at Fergus's sleeve. He turned, squinting at us.

"Look happy, Papa!" Germain pointed to his gigantic smile. "See?"

Fergus's mouth twitched, as he glanced from his offspring to Jamie. His face went blank for a moment, then adjusted itself into an enormous smile of white-toothed insincerity. Marsali kicked him in the ankle. He winced, but the smile didn't waver.

Brianna and Roger were having a last-minute conference with Reverend Caldwell, on the other side of the fire. Brianna turned from this, brushing back her loose hair, saw the phalanx of grinning faces, and stared, her mouth slightly open. Her eyes went to me; I shrugged helplessly.

Her lips pressed tight together, but curved upward irrepressibly. Her shoulders shook with suppressed laughter. I felt Jamie quiver next to me.

Reverend Caldwell stepped forward, a finger in his book at the proper place, put his spectacles on his nose, and smiled genially at the assemblage, blinking only slightly when he encountered the row of leering countenances.

He coughed, and opened his Book of Common Worship.

"Dearly beloved, we are assembled here in the presence of God . . ."

I felt Jamie relax slightly, as the words went on, evidencing unfamiliarity, perhaps, but no great peculiarities. I supposed that he had in fact never taken part in a Protestant ceremony before—unless one counted the impromptu baptism Roger himself had conducted among the Mohawk. I closed my eyes and sent a brief prayer upward for Young Ian, as I did whenever I thought of him.

"Let us therefore reverently remember that God has established and sanctified marriage, for the welfare and happiness of mankind . . ."

Opening them, I saw that all eyes now were focused on Roger and Brianna, who stood facing each other, hands entwined. They were a handsome pair, nearly of a height, she bright and he dark, like a photograph and its negative. Their faces were nothing alike, and yet both had the bold bones and clean curves that were their joint legacy from the clan MacKenzie.

I glanced across the fire to see the same echo of bone and flesh in Jocasta, tall and handsome, her blind face turned in absorption toward the sound of the minister's voice. As I watched, I saw her hand reach out and rest on Duncan's arm, the long white fingers gently squeeze. The Reverend Caldwell had kindly offered to perform their marriage as well, but Jocasta had refused, wishing to wait instead for a Catholic ceremony.

"We are in no great hurry, after all, are we, my dear?" she had asked Duncan, turning toward him with an outward exhibition of deference that fooled no one. Still, I thought that Duncan had seemed relieved, rather than disappointed, by the postponement of his own wedding.

"By His apostles, He has instructed those who enter into this relation to cherish a mutual esteem and love . . ."

Duncan had put a hand over Jocasta's, with a surprising air of tenderness. That marriage would not be one of love, I thought, but mutual esteem—yes, I thought there was that.

"I charge you both, before the great God, the Searcher of all hearts, that if either of you know any reason why ye may not lawfully be joined together in marriage, ye do now confess it. For be ye well assured that if any persons are joined together otherwise than as God's Word allows, their union is not blessed by Him."

Reverend Caldwell paused, glancing warningly back and forth between Roger and Brianna. Roger shook his head slightly, his eyes fixed on Bree's face. She smiled faintly in response, and the Reverend cleared his throat and continued.

The air of muted hilarity around the fire had subsided; there was no sound but the Reverend's quiet voice and the crackle of the flames.

"Roger Jeremiah, wilt thou have this Woman to be thy wife, and wilt thou pledge thy troth to her, in all love and honor, in all duty and service, in all faith and tenderness, to live with her, and cherish her, according to the ordinance of God, in the holy bond of marriage?"

"I will," Roger said, his voice deep and husky.

I heard a deep sigh to my right, and saw Marsali lean her head on Fergus's shoulder, a dreamy look on her face. He turned his head and kissed her brow, then leaned his own dark head against the whiteness of her kerch.

"I will," Brianna said clearly, lifting her chin and looking up into Roger's face, in response to the minister's question.

Mr. Caldwell looked benevolently round the circle, firelight glinting on his spectacles.

"Who giveth this Woman to be married to this Man?"

There was the briefest of pauses, and I felt Jamie jerk slightly, taken by surprise. I squeezed his arm, and saw the firelight gleam on the gold ring on my hand.

"Oh. I do, to be sure!" he said. Brianna turned her head and smiled at him, her eyes dark with love. He gave her back the smile, then blinked, clearing his throat, and squeezed my hand hard.

I felt a slight tightening of the throat myself, as they spoke their vows, remembering both of my own weddings. And Jocasta? I wondered. She had been married three times; what echoes of the past did she hear in these words?

"I, Roger Jeremiah, take thee, Brianna Ellen, to be my wedded wife . . ."

The light of memory shone on most of the faces around the fire. The Bugs stood close together, looking at each other with identical gazes of soft devotion. Mr. Wemyss, standing by his daughter, bowed his head and closed his eyes, a look of mingled joy and sadness on his face, no doubt thinking of his own wife, dead these many years.

"In plenty and in want . . ."

"In joy and in sorrow . . ."

"In sickness and in health . . ."

Lizzie's face was rapt, eyes wide at the mystery being carried out before her. How soon might it be her turn, to stand before witnesses and make such awesome promises?

Jamie reached across and took my right hand in his, his fingers linking with mine, and the silver of my ring shone red in the glow of the flames. I looked up into his face and saw the promise spoken in his eyes, as it was in mine.

"As long as we both shall live."

15

THE FLAMES OF DECLARATION

THE GREAT FIRE BELOW was blazing, damp wood snapping with cracks that rang like pistol shots against the mountainside—a distant gunfire, though, and little noticed through the noise of merrymaking.

While she had elected not to be married by the Reverend Caldwell, Jocasta had nonetheless generously provided a lavish wedding feast in honor of Roger and Brianna's nuptials. Wine, ale, and whisky flowed like water under the aegis of Ulysses, whose white wig bobbed through the mob round our family campfire, ubiquitous as a moth round a candle flame.

Despite the chill damp and the clouds that had regathered overhead, at least half the Gathering was here, dancing to the music of fiddle and mouth organ, descending locustlike on the groaning tables of delicacies, and drinking the health of the newlyweds—and the eventually-to-be-wed—with so much enthusiasm that if all such wishes were to take effect, Roger, Bree, Jocasta, and Duncan would each live to be a thousand, at least.

I thought I might be good for a hundred years or so, myself. I was feeling no pain; nothing but an encompassing sense of giddy well-being, and a pleasant sense of impending dissolution.

At one side of the fire, Roger was playing a borrowed guitar, serenading Bree before a rapt circle of listeners. Closer, Jamie sat on a log with Duncan and his aunt, talking with friends.

"Madam?" Ulysses materialized at my elbow, tray in

hand and resplendent in livery, behaving as though he were in the parlor at River Run, rather than on a soggy mountainside.

"Thank you." I accepted a pewter cup full of something, and discovered it to be brandy. Fairly good brandy, too. I took a small sip and let it percolate through my sinuses. Before I could absorb much more of it, though, I became conscious of a sudden lull in the surrounding gaiety.

Jamie glanced around the circle, gathering eyes, then stood and held out his arm to me. I was a little surprised, but hastily replaced the cup on Ulysses's tray, smoothed back my hair, tucked in my kerchief, and went to take my place at his side.

"Thig a seo, a bhean uasa," he said, smiling at me. Come, lady. He turned and raised his chin, summoning the others. Roger put down his guitar at once, covering it carefully with a canvas, then held out a hand to Bree.

"Thig a seo, a bhean," he said, grinning. With a look of surprise, she got to her feet, Jemmy in her arms.

Jamie stood still, waiting, and little by little, the others rose, brushing away pine needles and sand from hems and seats, laughing and murmuring in puzzlement. The dancers, too, paused in their whirling, and came to see what was to do, the fiddle music dying away in the rustle of curiosity.

Jamie led me down the dark trail toward the leaping flames of the great bonfire below, the others following in a murmur of speculation. At the end of the main clearing he stopped and waited. Dark figures flitted through the shadows; a man's shape stood in silhouette before the fire, arm raised.

"The Menzies are here!" the man called, and flung the branch that he carried into the fire. Faint cheers went up, from those of his clan and sept within hearing.

Another took his place—MacBean—and another—Ogilvie. Then it was our turn.

Jamie walked forward alone, into the light of the leaping flames. The fire was built of oak and pinewood, and it burned higher than a tall man, tongues of transparent yellow so pure and ardent as almost to burn white against the blackened sky. The light of it shone on his upturned face, on his head and shoulders, and threw a long shadow that stretched halfway across the open ground behind him.

"We are gathered here to welcome old friends," he said in Gaelic. "And meet new ones—in hopes that they may join us in forging a new life in this new country."

His voice was deep and carrying; the last scraps of conversation ceased as the folk pushing and crowding around the fire hushed and craned to listen.

"We have all suffered much hardship on the road here." He turned slowly, looking from face to face around the fire. Many of the men of Ardsmuir were here: I saw the Lindsay brothers, homely as a trio of toads; Ronnie Sinclair's fox-eyed face, ginger hair slicked up in horns; the Roman-coin features of Robin McGillivray. All looked out from the shadows, ridge of brow and bridge of nose shining in the glow, each face crossed by fire.

Under the influence of brandy and emotion, I could easily see too the ranks of ghosts who stood behind them; the families and friends who remained still in Scotland, whether on the earth . . . or under it.

Jamie's own face was lined with shadow, the firelight showing the mark of time and struggle on his flesh as wind and rain mark stone.

"Many of us died in battle," he said, his voice scarcely audible above the rustle of the fire. "Many died of burning. Many of us starved. Many died at sea, many died of wounds and illness." He paused. "Many died of sorrow."

His eyes looked beyond the firelit circle for a moment, and I thought perhaps he was searching for the face of Abel MacLennan. He lifted his cup then, and held it high in salute for a moment.

"Slàinte!" murmured a dozen voices, rising like the wind.

"Slàinte!" he echoed them—then tipped the cup, so that a little of the brandy fell into the flames, where it hissed and burned blue for an instant's time.

He lowered the cup, and paused for a moment, head bent. He lifted his head then, and raised the cup toward Archie Hayes, who stood across the fire from him, round face unreadable, fire sparking from his silver gorget and his father's brooch.

"While we mourn the loss of those who died, we must also pay tribute to you who fought and suffered with equal valor—and survived."

"Slàinte!" came the salute, louder this time with the rumble of male voices.

Jamie closed his eyes for an instant, then opened them, looking toward Brianna, who stood with Lizzie and Marsali, Jemmy in her arms. The rawness and strength of his features stood out by contrast with the round-faced innocence of the children, the gentleness of the young mothers—though even in their delicacy, I thought, the firelight showed the seams of Scottish granite in their bones.

"We pay tribute to our women," he said, lifting the cup in turn to Brianna, to Marsali, and then, turning, to me. A brief smile touched his lips. "For they are our strength. And our revenge upon our enemies will be at the last the revenge of the cradle. *Slàinte!*"

Amid the shouts of the crowd, he drained the wooden cup, and threw it into the fire, where it lay dark and round for a moment, then burst all at once into brilliant flame.

"Thig a seo!" he called, putting out his right hand to me. *"Thig a seo, a Shorcha, nighean Eanruig, neart mo chridhe." Come to me*, he said. *Come to me, Claire, daughter of Henry, strength of my heart*. Scarcely feeling my feet or those I stumbled over, I made my way to him, and clasped his hand, his grip cold but strong on my fingers.

I saw him turn his head; was he looking for Bree? But no—he stretched out his other hand toward Roger.

"Seas ri mo làmh, Roger an t'òranaiche, mac Jeremiah MacChoinneich!" Stand by my hand, Roger the singer, son of Jeremiah MacKenzie. Roger stood stock-still for a moment, eyes dark on Jamie, then moved toward him, like one sleepwalking. The crowd was still excited, but the shouting had died down, and people craned to hear what was said.

"Stand by me in battle," he said in Gaelic, his eyes fixed on Roger, left hand extended. He spoke slowly and clearly, to be sure of understanding. "Be a shield for my family—and for yours, son of my house."

Roger's expression seemed suddenly to dissolve, like a

face seen in water when a stone is tossed into it. Then it solidified once more, and he clasped Jamie's hand, squeezing hard.

Jamie turned to the crowd then, and began the calling. This was something I had seen him do before, many years before, in Scotland. A formal invitation and identification of tenants by a laird, it was a small ceremony often done on a quarter-day or after the harvest. Faces lighted here and there with recognition; many of the Highland Scots knew the custom, though they would not have seen it in this land before tonight.

"Come to me, Geordie Chisholm, son of Walter, son of Connaught the Red!"

"Stand with me, *a Choinneich*, Evan, Murdo, you sons of Alexander Lindsay of the Glen!"

"Come to my side, Joseph Wemyss, son of Donald, son of Robert!" I smiled to see Mr. Wemyss, flustered but terribly pleased at this public inclusion, make his way toward us, head proudly raised, fair hair flying wild in the wind of the great fire.

"Stand by me, Josiah the hunter!"

Was Josiah Beardsley here? Yes, he was; a slight, dark form slid out of the shadows, to take up a shy place in the group near Jamie. I caught his eye and smiled at him; he looked hastily away, but a small, embarrassed smile clung to his lips, as though he had forgotten it was there.

It was an impressive group by the time he had finished—nearly forty men, gathered shoulder-close and flushed as much with pride as with whisky. I saw Roger exchange a long look with Brianna, who was beaming across the fire at him. She bent her head to whisper something to Jemmy, who was submerged in his blankets, half-asleep in her arms. She picked up one of his wee paws and waved it limply toward Roger, who laughed.

"*. . . Air mo mhionnan . . .*" Distracted, I had missed Jamie's final statement, catching only the last few words. Whatever he had said met with approval, though; there was a low rumble of solemn assent from the men around us, and a moment's silence.

Then he let go my hand, stooped, and picked up a branch from the ground. Lighting this, he held it aloft, then threw the blazing brand high into the air. It tumbled end over end as it fell straight down, into the heart of the fire.

"The Frasers of the Ridge are here!" he bellowed, and the clearing erupted in a massive cheer.

As we made our way back up the slope to resume the interrupted festivities, I found myself next to Roger, who was humming something cheerful under his breath. I put a hand on his sleeve, and he looked down at me, smiling.

"Congratulations," I said, smiling back. "Welcome to the family—son of the house."

He grinned enormously.

"Thanks," he said. "Mum."

We came to a level spot, and walked side by side for a moment, not speaking. Then he said, in a quite different tone, "That was . . . something quite special, wasn't it?"

I didn't know whether he meant historically special, or special in personal terms. In either case, he was right, and I nodded.

"I didn't catch all of the last bit, though," I said. "And I don't know what *earbsachd* means—do you?"

"Oh . . . aye. I know." It was quite dark here between the fires; I could see no more of him than a darker smudge against the black of shrub and tree. There was an odd note in his voice, though. He cleared his throat.

"It's an oath—of a sort. He—Jamie—he swore an oath to us, to his family and tenants. Support, protection, that kind of thing."

"Oh, yes?" I said, mildly puzzled. "What do you mean, 'of a sort'?"

"Ah, well." He was silent for a moment, evidently marshaling his words. "It means a word of honor, rather than just an oath," he said carefully. *"Earbsachd"*—he pronounced it YARB-sochk—"was once said to be the distinguishing characteristic of the MacCrimmons of Skye, and meant basically that their word once given must unfailingly be acted upon at no matter what cost. If a MacCrimmon said he would do something"—he paused and drew breath—"he would do it, though he should burn to death in the doing."

His hand came up under my elbow, surprisingly firm.

"Here," he said quietly. "Let me help; it's slippery underfoot."

16

ON THE NIGHT THAT OUR WEDDING IS ON US

"WILL YOU SING FOR ME, Roger?"

She stood in the opening of the borrowed tent, facing outward. From the back, he could see no more than her silhouette against the gray of the clouded sky, her long hair drifting in the rainy wind. She had worn it unbound to be married—maiden's hair, though she had a child.

It was cold tonight, quite different from that first night together, that hot, gorgeous night that had ended in anger and betrayal. Months of other nights lay between that one and this—months of loneliness, months of joy. And yet his heart beat as fast now as it had on their first wedding night.

"I always sing for you, hen." He came behind her, drew her back against him, so that her head rested on his shoulder, her hair cool and live against his face. His arm curled round her waist, holding her secure. He bent his head, nuzzling for the curve of her ear.

"No matter what," he whispered, "no matter where. No matter whether you're there to hear or not—I'll always sing for you."

She turned into his arms then, with a small hum of content in her throat, and her mouth found his, tasting of barbecued meat and spiced wine.

The rain pattered on the canvas above, and the cold of late autumn curled up from the ground around their feet. The first time, the air had smelled of hops and mudflats; their bower had had the earthy tang of hay and donkeys. Now the air was live with pine and juniper, spiced with the smoke of smoldering fires—and the faint, sweet note of baby shit.

And yet she was once more dark and light in his arms, her face hidden, her body gleaming. Then she had been moist and molten, humid with the summer. Now her flesh was cool as marble, save where he touched it—and yet the summer lived still in the palm of his hand where he touched her, sweet and slick, ripe with the secrets of a hot, dark night. It was right, he thought, that these vows should have been spoken as the first ones had, out of doors, part of wind and earth, fire and water.

"I love you," she murmured against his mouth, and he seized her lip between his teeth, too moved to speak the words in reply just yet.

There had been words between them then, as there had been words tonight. The words were the same, and he had meant them the first time no less than he did now. Yet it *was* different.

The first time he had spoken them to her alone, and while he had done so in the sight of God, God had been discreet, hovering well in the background, face turned away from their nakedness.

Tonight he said them in the blaze of firelight, before the face of God and the world, her people and his. His heart had been hers, and whatever else he had—but now there was no question of him and her, his and hers. The vows were given, his ring put on her finger, the bond both made and witnessed. They were one body.

One hand of their joint organism crushed a breast a little too hard, and one throat made a small sound of discomfort. She drew back from him a little, and he felt rather than saw her grimace. The air came cold between them and his own skin felt suddenly raw, exposed, as though he had been severed from her with a knife.

"I need—" she said, and touched her breast, not finishing. "Just a minute, okay?"

Claire had fed the child while Brianna went to make her overtures to Reverend Caldwell. Bursting with porridge and stewed peaches, Jemmy could scarcely be roused to suckle briefly before relapsing into somnolence and being taken away by Lizzie, his wee round belly tight as a drum. That was as well for their privacy—drugged into such a gluttonous stupor, it was unlikely the bairn would wake before dawn. The price of it, though, was the unused milk.

No one living in the same house with a nursing mother was likely to be unaware of her breasts, let alone her husband. They had a life of their own, those breasts. They changed size from hour to hour, for the one thing, swelling from their normal soft globes into great round hard bubbles that gave him the eerie feeling that if he touched one it would burst.

Now and then, one *did* burst, or at least gave that impression. The ridge of soft flesh would rise like kneaded bread, slowly but surely pushing above the edge of Brianna's bodice. Then suddenly there would be a big, wet circle on the cloth, appearing magically, as though some invisible person had thrown a snowball at her. Or two snowballs—for what one breast did, its fellow rushed at once to follow suit.

Sometimes the Heavenly Twins were foiled, though; Jemmy drained one side, but inconsiderately fell asleep before performing the same service for the other. This left his mother gritting her teeth, gingerly taking the swollen orb in the palm of her hand, pressing the edge of a pewter cup just under the nipple to catch the spray and dribble as she eased the aching fullness, enough to sleep herself.

She was doing it now; modestly turned away from him, an arisaid gathered round her shoulders against the chill. He could hear the hiss of the milk, a tiny chime against the metal.

He was reluctant to drown the sound, which he found erotic, but nonetheless picked up the guitar, and put his thumb to the strings, his hand on the frets. He didn't strum or strike chords, but plucked single notes, small voices to echo his own, the thrum of one string ringing through the chanted line.

A love song, to be sure. One of the very old ones, in the

Gaelic. Even if she didn't know all the words, he thought she'd take the sense of it.

> *"On the night that our wedding is on us,*
> *I will come leaping to thee with gifts,*
> *On the night that our wedding is on us . . ."*

He closed his eyes, seeing in memory what the night now hid. Her nipples were the color of ripe plums and the size of ripe cherries, and Roger had a vivid mental picture of how one would feel in his mouth. He had suckled them once, long before—before the coming of Jemmy—but no more.

> *"You will get a hundred silver salmon . . .*
> *A hundred badger skins . . ."*

She never asked him not to, never turned away—and yet he could tell by the faint intake of her breath that, often, she was bracing herself not to flinch when he touched her breasts.

Was it only tenderness? he wondered. Did she not trust him to be gentle?

He shied away from the thought, drowning it in a small cascade of notes, liquid as a waterfall.

It might not be you, whispered the voice, stubbornly refusing to be distracted. *Perhaps it was* him*—something that he did to her.*

Fuck. Off, he thought succinctly to the voice, marking each word with a sharp-plucked string. Stephen Bonnet would have no place in their wedding bed. None.

He laid a hand on the strings to silence them briefly, and as she slid the arisaid from her shoulders, began again, this time in English. A special song, too—one for the two of them alone. He didn't know whether anyone else might hear, but it made no difference if they did. She stood and slid the shift from her shoulders as his fingers touched the quiet opening of the Beatles' "Yesterday."

He heard her laugh, once, then sigh, and the linen whispered against her skin as it fell.

She came naked behind him as the soft melancholy

yearning of the song filled the dark. Her hand stroked his hair, gathered it tight at the nape of his neck. She swayed, and he felt her press against his back, her breasts soft now, yielding and warm through his shirt, her breath tickling his ear. Her hand rested on his shoulder briefly, then slid down inside his shirt, fingers cool on his chest. He could feel the warm hard metal of her ring on his skin, and felt a surge of possession that pulsed through him like a gulp of whisky, a heat suffusing his flesh.

He ached to turn and take hold of her, but pushed the urge down, heightening anticipation. He bent his head closer to the strings, and sang until all thought left him and there was nothing left but his body and hers. He could not have said when her hand closed over his on the frets, and he rose and turned to her, still filled with the music and his love, soft and strong and pure in the dark.

SHE LAY QUIET in the dark, feeling the thunder of her heart boom slowly in her ears. The throb of it echoed in the pulse of her neck, her wrists, her breasts, her womb. She had lost track of her boundaries; slowly the sense of limbs and digits, head and trunk, of space occupied, returned. She moved the single finger glued between her legs, and felt the last of the tingling shocks run down her thighs as it slid free.

She drew breath slowly, listening.

His breath still came in long, regular exhalations; thank God, he hadn't wakened. She had been careful, moving no more than a fingertip, but the final jolt of climax had struck her so hard that her hips jerked as her belly quivered and convulsed, her heels digging into the pallet with a loud rustling of straw.

He'd had a very long day—they all had. Even so, she could still hear faint sounds of festivity on the mountainside around them. The chance to celebrate like this came so rarely that no one would let something so inconsequential as rain, cold, or tiredness keep them from the revels.

She herself felt like a puddle of liquid mercury; soft and

heavy, shimmering with each heartbeat. The effort of moving was unthinkable; but her final convulsion had pulled the quilt off his shoulders, and the skin of his back lay smooth and bare, dark by contrast with the pale cloth. The pocket of warmth around her was snug and perfect, but she couldn't luxuriate while he lay exposed to the chilly midnight air like that. Tendrils of fog had crept under the tent flap and hung ghostlike and clammy all around them; she could see the faint gleam of moisture on the high curve of his cheekbone.

She summoned back the notion of bones and muscles, found a motor neuron in working order, and sternly ordered it to fire. Embodied once more, she rolled onto her side, facing him, and gently pulled the quilt up around his ears. He stirred and murmured something; she stroked his tumbled black hair and he smiled faintly, eyelids half-opening in the blank stare of one who sees dreams. They dropped again and he took a long, sighing breath and fell back asleep.

"I love you," she whispered, filled with tenderness.

She stroked his back lightly, loving the feel of his flat shoulder blades through the quilt, the solid knob of bone at the nape of his neck, and the long, smooth groove that ran down the center of his spine to arch into the swell of his buttocks. A cold breeze rippled the tiny hairs of her arm, and she pulled it back under the covers, letting her hand rest lightly on Roger's bottom.

The feel of it was no novelty, but thrilled her just the same, with its perfect warm roundness, its coarse curly hair. A faint echo of her solitary joy encouraged her to do it again, and her free hand crept between her legs, but sheer exhaustion stayed her, limp fingers cupped on the swollen flesh, one languid finger tracing the slickness.

She'd hoped it would be different tonight. Without the ever-present danger of waking Jemmy, free to take as much time as they wanted, and riding the waves of emotion from their exchange of vows, she'd thought . . . but it was the same.

It wasn't that she wasn't aroused; quite the contrary. Every movement, each touch, imprinted itself in the nerves of her skin, the crevices of mouth and memory, drowning her with scent, branding her with sensation. But no matter how wonderful the lovemaking, there remained some odd sense of distance, some barrier that she couldn't penetrate.

And so once more she found herself lying beside him as he slept, reliving in memory each moment of the passion they had just shared—and able in memory at last to yield to it.

Perhaps it was that she loved him too much, she thought, was too mindful of his pleasure to take her own. The satisfaction she felt when he lost himself, gasping and moaning in her arms, was far greater than the simple physical pleasure of climax. And yet, there was something darker under that; a peculiar sense of triumph, as though she had won some undeclared and unacknowledged contest between them.

She sighed and butted her forehead against the curve of his shoulder, enjoying the reek of him—a smell of strong and bitter musk, like pennyroyal.

The thought of herbs reminded her, and she reached down again, cautiously so as not to waken him, and slid one slippery finger deep inside to check. No, it was all right; the slip of sponge soaked with tansy oil was still in place, its fragile, pungent presence safeguarding the entrance to her womb.

She moved closer, and he moved unconsciously, his body half-turning to accommodate her, his warmth at once enclosing her, comforting her. His hand groped like a bird flying blind, skimming her hip, her soft belly, in search of a resting place. She seized it in both hands and folded it, secure beneath her chin. His hand curled over hers; she kissed one large, rough knuckle and he sighed deeply, his hand relaxing.

The sounds of revelry on the mountain had faded, as the dancers tired, and the musicians grew hoarse and weary. The rain began again, pattering on the canvas overhead, and gray mist touched her face with cool damp fingers. The smell of wet canvas made her think of camping trips as a child with her father, with their mingled sensations of excitement and safety, and she nestled deeper into the curve of Roger's body, feeling a similar sense of comfort and anticipation.

It was early days, she thought. They had all their lives before them. The time of surrender would surely come.

17

WATCH FIRE

FROM WHERE THEY LAY, he could see down through a gap in the rocks, all the way to the watch fire that burned before Hayes's tent. The great fire of the Gathering had burned itself to embers, the glow of it faint memory of the towering flames of declaration, but the smaller fire burned steady as a star against the cold night. Now and then a dark, kilted figure rose to tend it, stood stark for a moment against the brightness, then faded back again into the night.

He was faintly conscious of the racing clouds that dimmed the moon, the heavy flutter of the canvas overhead, and the rock-black shadows of the mountain slope, but he had no eyes for anything save the fire below, and the white patch of the tent behind it, shapeless as a ghost.

He had slowed his breath, relaxed the muscles of arms and chest, back, buttocks, legs. Not in an attempt to sleep; sleep was far from him, and he had no mind to seek it.

Nor was it an attempt to fool Claire into thinking he slept. So close against his body, so close to his mind as she was, she would know him wakeful. No, it was only a signal to her; an acknowledged pretense that freed her from any need to pay heed to him. She might sleep, knowing him occupied within the walnut shell of his mind, having no immediate demand to make of her.

Few slept on the mountain tonight, he thought. The sound of the wind masked the murmur of voices, the shuffle of movement, but his hunter's senses registered a dozen small stirrings, identifying things half-heard, putting names to moving shadows. A scrape of shoe leather on rock, the flap of a blanket shaken out. That would be Hobson and Fowles, making a quiet departure alone in the dark, fearful of waiting for the morning, lest they be betrayed in the night.

A few notes of music came down on a gust of wind from above; concertina and fiddle. Jocasta's slaves, unwilling to surrender this rare celebration to the needs of sleep or the imperatives of weather.

An infant's thin wail. Wee Jemmy? No, from behind. Tiny Joan, then, and Marsali's voice, low and sweet, singing in French.

". . . Alouette, gentille alouette . . ."

There, a sound he had expected; footsteps passing on the far side of the rocks that bordered his family's sanctuary. Quick and light, headed downhill. He waited, eyes open, and in a few moments heard the faint hail of a sentry near the tent. No figure showed in the firelight below, but the tent flap beyond it stirred, gaped open, then fell unbroken.

As he had thought, then; sentiment lay strong against the rioters. It was not held a betrayal of friends, but rather the necessary giving up of criminals for the protection of those who chose to live by law. It might be reluctant—the witnesses had waited for the dark—but not secretive.

". . . je te plumerai la tête . . ."

It occurred to him to wonder why the songs sung to bairns were so often gruesome, and no thought given to the words they took in with their mothers' milk. The music of the songs was no more to him than tuneless chanting—perhaps that was why he paid more mind than most to the words.

Even Brianna, who came from what was presumably a more peaceable time, sang songs of fearsome death and tragic loss to wee Jem, all with a look on her face as tender as the Virgin nursing the Christ Child. That verse about the miner's daughter who drowned amidst her ducklings . . .

It occurred to him perversely to wonder what awful things the Blessed Mother might have counted in her own repertoire of cradle songs; judging from the Bible, the Holy Land had been no more peaceful than France or Scotland.

He would have crossed himself in penance for the notion, but Claire was lying on his right arm.

"Were they wrong?" Claire's voice came softly from beneath his chin, startling him.

"Who?" He bent his head to hers, and kissed the thick softness of her curls. Her hair smelt of woodsmoke and the sharp, clear tang of juniper berries.

"The men in Hillsborough."

"Aye, I think so."

"What would you have done?"

He sighed, moved one shoulder in a shrug.

"Can I say? Aye, if it was me that was cheated, and no hope of redress, I might have laid hands on the man who'd done it. But what was done there—ye heard it. Houses torn down and set afire, men dragged out and beaten senseless only for cause of the office they held . . . no, Sassenach. I canna say what I might have done—but not that."

She turned her head a little, so he saw the high curve of her cheekbone, rimmed in light, and the flexing of the muscle that ran in front of her ear as she smiled.

"I didn't think you would. Can't see you as part of a mob."

He kissed her ear, not to reply directly. *He* could see himself as part of a mob, all too easily. That was what frightened him. He knew much too well the strength of it.

One Highlander was a warrior, but the mightiest man was only a man. It was the madness that took men together that had ruled the glens for a thousand years; that thrill of the blood, when you heard the shrieks of your companions, felt the strength of the whole bear you up like wings, and knew immortality—for if you should fall of yourself, still you would be carried on, your spirit shrieking in the mouths of those who ran beside you. It was only later, when the blood lay cold in limp veins, and deaf ears heard the women weeping . . .

"And if it wasn't a man who cheated you? If it was the Crown, or the Court? No one person, I mean, but an institution."

He knew where she meant to lead him. He tightened his arm around her, her breath warm on the knuckles of his hand, curled just under her chin.

"It isna that. Not here. Not now." The rioters had lashed out in response to the crimes of men, of individuals; the price of those crimes might be paid in blood, but not requited by war—not yet.

"It isn't," she said quietly. "But it will be."

"Not now," he said again.

The piece of paper was safely hidden in his saddlebag, its damnable summons concealed. He must deal with it, and soon, but for tonight he would pretend it wasn't there. One final night of peace, with his wife in his arms, his family around him.

Another shadow by the fire. Another hail by the sentry, one more to pass through the traitor's gate.

"And are *they* wrong?" A slight tilt of her head toward the tent below. "The ones going to turn in their acquaintances?"

"Aye," he said, after a moment. "They're wrong as well."

A mob might rule, but it was single men would pay the price for what was done. Part of the price was the breaking of trust, the turning of neighbor against neighbor, fear a noose squeezing tight until there was no longer any breath of mercy or forgiveness.

It had come on to rain; the light spatter of drops on the canvas overhead turned to a regular thrum, and the air grew live with the rush of water. It was a winter storm; no lightning lit the sky, and the looming mountains were invisible.

He held Claire close, curving his free hand low over her belly. She sighed, a small sound of pain in it, and settled herself, her arse nesting round as an egg in the cup of his thighs. He could feel the melting begin as she relaxed, that odd merging of his flesh with hers.

At first it had happened only when he took her, and only at the last. Then sooner and sooner, until her hand upon him was both invitation and completion, a surrender inevitable, offered and accepted. He had resisted now and then, only to be sure he could, suddenly fearful of the loss of himself. He had thought it a treacherous passion, like the one that swept a mob of men, linking them in mindless fury.

Now he trusted it was right, though. The Bible did say it, *Thou shalt be one flesh*, and *What God has joined together, let no man put asunder*.

He had survived such a sundering once; he could not stand it twice, and live. The sentries had put up a canvas lean-to near their fire to shelter them from the rain. The flames sputtered as the rain blew in, though, and lit the pale cloth with a flicker that pulsed like a heartbeat. He was not afraid to die with her, by fire or any other way—only to live without her.

The wind changed, carrying with it the faint sound of laughter from the tiny tent where the newlyweds slept—or didn't. He smiled to himself, hearing it. He could only hope that his daughter would find such joy in her marriage as he had—but so far, so good. The lad's face lit when he looked at her.

"What will you do?" Claire said quietly, her words almost lost in the pattering of the rain.

"What I must."

It was no answer, but the only one.

There was no world outside this small confine, he told himself. Scotland was gone, the Colonies were going—what lay ahead he could only dimly imagine from the things Brianna told him. The only reality was the woman held fast in his arms; his children and grandchildren, his tenants and servants—these were the gifts that God had given to him; his to harbor, his to protect.

The mountainside lay dark and quiet, but he could feel them there all round him, trusting him to see them safe. If God had given him this trust, surely He would also grant the strength to keep it.

He was becoming aroused by the habit of close contact, his rising cock uncomfortably trapped. He wanted her, had been wanting for days, the urge pushed aside in the bustle of the Gathering. The dull ache in his balls echoed what he thought must be the ache in her womb.

He had taken her in the midst of her courses now and then, when the two of them had wanted too urgently for waiting. He had found it messy and disturbing, but exciting too, leaving him with a faint sense of shame that was not entirely unpleasant. Now was not the time or place for it, of course, but the memory of other times and other places made him shift, twisting away from her, not to trouble her with the bodily evidence of his thoughts.

Yet what he felt now was not lust—not quite. Nor was it

even the need of her, the wanting of soul's company. He wished to cover her with his body, possess her—for if he could do that, he could pretend to himself that she was safe. Covering her so, joined in one body, he might protect her. Or so he felt, even knowing how senseless the feeling was.

He had stiffened, his body tensing involuntarily with his thoughts. Claire stirred, and reached back with one hand. She laid it on his leg, let it lie for a moment, then reached gently farther up, in drowsy question.

He bent his head, put his lips behind her ear. Said what he was thinking, without thought.

"Nothing will harm ye while there is breath in my body, *a nighean donn*. Nothing."

"I know," she said. Her limbs went slowly slack, her breathing eased, and the soft round of her belly swelled under his palm as she melted into sleep. Her hand stayed on him, covering him. He lay stiff and wide awake, long after the watch fire had been quenched by the rain.

Part Two

The Chieftain's Call

18

NO PLACE LIKE HOME

GIDEON DARTED OUT his head like a snake, aiming for the leg of the rider just ahead.

"Seas!" Jamie wrenched the big bay's head around before he could take a bite. "Evil-minded whoreson," he muttered under his breath. Geordie Chisholm, unaware of his narrow escape from Gideon's teeth, caught the remark, and looked back over his shoulder, startled. Jamie smiled and touched his slouch hat apologetically, nudging the horse past Chisholm's long-legged mule.

Jamie kicked Gideon ungently in the ribs, urging him past the rest of the slow-moving travelers at a speed fast enough to keep the brute from biting, kicking, trampling stray bairns, or otherwise causing trouble. After a week's journey, he was all too well acquainted with the stallion's proclivities. He passed Brianna and Marsali, halfway up the column, at a slow trot; by the time he passed Claire and Roger, riding at the head, he was moving too fast to do more than flourish his hat at them in salute.

"A mhic an dhiobhail," he said, clapping the hat back on and leaning low over the horse's neck. "Ye're a deal too lively for your own good, let alone mine. See how long ye last in the rough, eh?"

He pulled hard left, off the trail, and down the slope, trampling dry grass and brushing leafless dogwood out of the way with a gunshot snapping of twigs. What the seven-sided son of a bitch needed was flat country, where Jamie could gallop the bejesus out of him and bring him back blowing. Given that there wasn't a flat spot in twenty miles, he'd have to do the next best thing.

He gathered up the reins, clicked his tongue, jabbed both heels into the horse's ribs, and they charged up the shrubby hillside as though they had been fired from a cannon.

Gideon was large-boned, well-nourished, and sound of wind, which was why Jamie had bought him. He was also a hard-mouthed, bad-tempered reester of a horse, which was why he hadn't cost much. More than Jamie could easily afford, even so.

As they sailed over a small creek, jumped a fallen log, and hared up an almost vertical hillside littered with scrub oak and persimmon, Jamie found himself wondering whether he'd got a bargain or committed suicide. That was the last coherent thought he had before Gideon veered sideways, crushing Jamie's leg against a tree, then gathered his hindquarters and charged down the other side of the hill into a thicket of brush, sending coveys of quail exploding from under his huge flat hooves.

Half an hour of dodging low branches, lurching through streams, and galloping straight up as many hillsides as Jamie could point them at, and Gideon was, if not precisely tractable, at least exhausted enough to be manageable. Jamie was soaked to the thighs, bruised, bleeding from half a dozen scratches, and breathing nearly as hard as the horse. He was, however, still in the saddle, and still in charge.

He turned the horse's head toward the sinking sun and clicked his tongue again.

"Come on, then," he said. "Let's go home."

They had exerted themselves mightily, but given the rugged shape of the land, had not covered so much ground as to lose themselves entirely. He turned Gideon's head upward, and within a quarter hour, had come out onto a small ridge he recognized.

They picked their way along the ridge, searching for a safe way down through the tangles of chinkapin, poplar, and spruce. The party was not far away, he knew, but it could take some time to cross to them, and he would as soon rejoin them before they reached the Ridge. Not that Claire or MacKenzie could not guide them—but he admitted to himself that he wished very much to return to Fraser's Ridge at the head of the party, leading his people home.

"Christ, man, ye'd think ye were Moses," he muttered, shaking his head in mock dismay at his own pretensions.

The horse was lathered, and when the trees opened out for a space, Jamie halted for a moment's rest—relaxing the reins, but keeping a sufficient grip as to discourage any notions the outheidie creature might still be entertaining. They stood among a grove of silver birch, at the lip of a small rocky outcrop above a forty-foot drop; he thought the horse held much too high an opinion of himself to contemplate self-destruction, but best to be careful, in case he had any thought of flinging his rider off into the laurels below.

The breeze was from the west. Jamie lifted his chin, enjoying the cold touch of it on his heated skin. The land fell away in undulating waves of brown and green, kindled here and there with patches of color, lighting the mist in the hollows like the glow of campfire smoke. He felt a peace come over him at the sight, and breathed deep, his body relaxing.

Gideon relaxed, too, all the feistiness draining slowly out of him like water from a leaky bucket. Slowly, Jamie let his hands drop lightly on the horse's neck, and the horse stayed still, ears forward. Ah, he thought, and the realization stole over him that this was a Place.

He thought of such places in a way that had no words, only recognizing one when he came to it. He might have called it holy, save that the feel of such a place had nothing to do with church or saint. It was simply a place he belonged to be, and that was sufficient, though he preferred to be alone when he found one. He let the reins go slack across the horse's neck. Not even a thrawn-minded creature like Gideon would give trouble here, he felt.

Sure enough, the horse stood quiet, massive dark withers steaming in the chill. They could not tarry long, but he was deeply glad of the momentary respite—not from the battle with Gideon, but from the press of people.

He had learned early on the trick of living separately in a crowd, private in his mind when his body could not be. But he was born a mountain-dweller, and had learned early, too, the enchantment of solitude, and the healing of quiet places.

Quite suddenly, he had a vision of his mother, one of the small vivid portraits that his mind hoarded, producing them unexpectedly in response to God knew what—a sound, a smell, some passing freak of memory.

He had been snaring for rabbits on a hillside then, hot and sweaty, his fingers pricked with gorse and his shirt stuck to him with mud and damp. He had seen a small grove of trees and gone to them for shade. His mother was there, sitting in the greenish shadow, on the ground beside a tiny spring. She sat quite motionless—which was unlike her—long hands folded in her lap.

She had not spoken, but smiled at him, and he had gone to her, not speaking either, but filled with a great sense of peace and contentment, resting his head against her shoulder, feeling her arm go about him and knowing he stood at the center of the world. He had been five, maybe, or six.

As suddenly as it had come, the vision disappeared, like a bright trout vanishing into dark water. It left behind it the same deep sense of peace, though—as though someone had briefly embraced him, a soft hand touched his hair.

He swung himself down from the saddle, needing the feel of the pine needles under his boots, some physical connection with this place. Caution made him tie the reins to a stout pine, though Gideon seemed calm enough; the stallion had dropped his head and was nuzzling for tufts of dried grass. Jamie stood still for a moment, then turned himself carefully to the right, facing the north.

He no longer recalled who had taught him this—whether it was Mother, Father, or Auld John, Ian's father. He spoke the words, though, as he turned himself sunwise, murmuring the brief prayer to each of the four airts in turn, and ended facing west, into the setting sun. He cupped his empty hands and the light filled them, spilling from his palms.

"May God make safe to me each step,
May God make open to me each pass,
May God make clear to me each road,
And may He take me in the clasp of His own two hands."

With an instinct older than the prayer, he took the flask from his belt and poured a few drops on the ground.

Scraps of sound reached him on the breeze; laughter and calling, the sound of animals making their way through brush. The caravan was not far away, only across a small hollow, coming slowly round the curve of the hillside opposite. He should go now, to join them on the last push upward to the Ridge.

Still he hesitated for a moment, loath to break the spell of the Place. Some tiny movement caught the corner of his eye, and he bent down, squinting as he peered into the deepening shadows beneath a holly bush.

It sat frozen, blending perfectly with its dusky background. He would never have seen it had his hunter's eye not caught its movement. A tiny kitten, its gray fur puffed out like a ripe milkweed head, enormous eyes wide open and unblinking, almost colorless in the gloom beneath the bush.

"A Chait," he whispered, putting out a slow finger toward it. "Whatever are ye doing here?"

A feral cat, no doubt; born of a wild mother, fled from some settlers' cabin, and long free of the trap of domesticity. He brushed the wispy fur of its breast, and it sank its tiny teeth suddenly into his thumb.

"Ow!" He jerked away, and examined the drop of blood welling from a small puncture wound. He glowered at the cat for a moment, but it merely stared back at him, and made no move to run. He paused, then made up his mind. He shook the blood drop from his finger onto the leaves, an offering to join the dram he had spilled, a gift to the spirits of this Place—who had evidently made up their minds to offer him a gift, themselves.

"All right, then," he said under his breath. He knelt, and stretched out his hand, palm up. Very slowly, he moved one finger, then the next, and the next and the next, then again, in the undulant motion of seaweed in the water. The big pale eyes fixed on the movement, watching as though hypnotized. He could see the tip of the miniature tail twitch, very slightly, and smiled at the sight.

If he could guddle a trout—and he could—why not a cat?

He made a small noise through his teeth, a whistling hiss, like the distant chittering of birds. The kitten stared, mesmerized, as the gently swaying fingers moved invisibly closer. When at last he touched its fur again, it made no move to escape. One finger edged beneath the fur, another slid under the cold wee pads of one paw, and it let him scoop it gently into his hand and lift it from the ground.

He held it for a moment against his chest, stroking it with one finger, tracing the silken jawline, the delicate ears. The tiny cat closed its eyes and began to purr in ecstasy, rumbling in his palm like distant thunder.

"Oh, so ye'll come away wi' me, will you?" Receiving no demur from the cat, he opened the neck of his shirt and tucked the tiny thing inside, where it poked and prodded at his ribs for a bit before curling up against his skin, purr reduced to a silent but pleasant vibration.

Gideon seemed pleased by the rest; he set off willingly enough, and within a quarter hour, they had caught up with the others. The stallion's momentary docility evaporated, though, under the strain of the final upward climb.

Not that the horse could not master the steep trail; what he couldn't abide was following another horse. It didn't matter whether Jamie wished to lead them home or not—if Gideon had anything to do with the matter, they would be not only in the lead, but several furlongs ahead.

The column of travelers was strung out over half a mile, each family party traveling at its own speed: Frasers, MacKenzies, Chisholms, MacLeods, and Aberfeldys. At every space and widening of the trail, Gideon shouldered his way rudely ahead, shoving past pack mules, sheep, foot-travelers, and mares; he even scattered the three pigs trudging slowly behind Grannie Chisholm. The pigs bolted into the brush in a chorus of panicked oinks as Gideon bore down upon them.

Jamie found himself more in sympathy with the horse than not; eager to be home and working hard to get there, irritated by anything that threatened to hold him back. At the moment, the main impediment to progress was Claire, who had—blast the woman—halted her mare in front of him and slid off in order to gather yet another bit of herbage from the trailside. As though the entire house was not filled from doorstep to rooftree with plants already, and her saddlebags a-bulge with more!

Gideon, picking up his rider's mood with alacrity, stretched out his neck and nipped the mare's rump. The mare bucked, squealed, and shot off up the trail, loose reins dangling. Gideon made a deep rumbling noise of satisfaction and started off after her, only to be jerked unceremoniously to a halt.

Claire had whirled round at the noise, eyes wide. She looked up at Jamie, up the trail after her vanished horse, then back at him. She shrugged apologetically, hands full of tattered leaves and mangy roots.

"Sorry," she said, but he saw the corner of her mouth tuck in and the flush rise in her skin, the smile glimmering in her eyes like morning light on trout water. Quite against his will, he felt the tension in his shoulders ease. He had had it in mind to rebuke her; in fact, he still did, but the words wouldn't quite come to his tongue.

"Get up, then, woman," he said instead, gruffly, with a nod behind him. "I want my supper."

She laughed at him and scrambled up, kilting her skirts out of the way. Gideon, irascible at this additional burden, whipped round to take a nip of anything he could reach. Jamie was ready for that; he snapped the end of the rein sharply off the stallion's nose, making him jerk back and snort in surprise.

"That'll teach ye, ye wee bastard." He pulled his hat over his brow and settled his errant wife securely, fluttering skirts tucked in beneath her thighs, arms round his waist. She rode without shoes or stockings, and her long calves were white and bare against the dark bay hide. He gathered up the reins and kicked the horse, a trifle harder than strictly necessary.

Gideon promptly reared, backed, twisted, and tried to scrape them both off under a hanging poplar bough. The kitten, rudely roused from its nap, sank all its claws into Jamie's midsection and yowled in alarm, though its noise was quite lost in Jamie's much louder screech. He yanked the horse's head halfway round, swearing, and shoved at the hindquarters with his left leg.

No easy conquest, Gideon executed a hop like a

corkscrew. There was a small "eek!" and a sudden feeling of emptiness behind him, as Claire was slung off into the brush like a bag of flour. The horse suddenly yielded to the pull on his mouth, and shot down the path in the wrong direction, hurtling through a screen of brambles and skidding to a halt that nearly threw him onto his hindquarters in a shower of mud and dead leaves. Then he straightened out like a snake, shook his head, and trotted nonchalantly over to exchange nuzzles with Roger's horse, which was standing at the edge of the spring clearing, watching them with the same bemusement exhibited by its dismounted rider.

"All right there?" asked Roger, raising one eyebrow.

"Certainly," Jamie replied, trying to gasp for breath while keeping his dignity. "And you?"

"Fine."

"Good." He was already swinging down from the saddle as he spoke. He flung the reins toward MacKenzie, not waiting to see whether he caught them, and ran back toward the trail, shouting, "Claire! Where are ye?"

"Just here!" she called cheerfully. She emerged from the shadow of the poplars, with leaves in her hair and limping slightly, but looking otherwise undamaged. "Are you all right?" she asked, cocking one eyebrow at him.

"Aye, fine. I'm going to shoot that horse." He gathered her in briefly, wanting to assure himself that she was in fact whole. She was breathing heavily, but felt reassuringly solid, and kissed him on the nose.

"Well, don't shoot him until we get home. I don't want to walk the last mile or so in my bare feet."

"Hey! Let that alone, ye bugger!"

He let go of Claire and turned to find Roger snatching a fistful of ragged-looking plants away from Gideon's questing Roman nose. More plants—what was this mania for gathering? Claire was still panting from the accident, but leaned forward to see them, looking interested.

"What's that you've got, Roger?"

"For Bree," he said, holding them up for her inspection. "Are they the right kind?" To Jamie's jaundiced eye, they looked like the yellowed tops of carrots gone to seed and left too long in the ground, but Claire fingered the mangy foliage, and nodded approval.

"Oh, yes," she said. "*Very* romantic!"

Jamie made a small tactful noise, indicating that they ought perhaps to be making their way, since Bree and the slower-moving tribe of Chisholms would be catching them up soon.

"Yes, all right," Claire said, patting his shoulder in what he assumed she meant to be a soothing gesture. "Don't snort; we're going."

"Mmphm," he said, and bent to put a hand under her foot. Tossing her up into the saddle, he gave Gideon a "Don't try it on, you bastard" look and swung up behind her.

"You'll wait for the others, then, and bring them up?" Without waiting for Roger's nod, Jamie reined around and set Gideon upon the trail again.

Mollified at being far in the lead, Gideon settled down to the job at hand, climbing steadily through the thickets of hornbeam and poplar, chestnut and spruce. Even so late in the year, some leaves still clung to the trees, and small bits of brown and yellow floated down upon them like a gentle rain, catching in the horse's mane, resting in the loose, thick waves of Claire's hair. It had come down in her precipitous descent, and she hadn't bothered to put it up again.

Jamie's own equanimity returned with the sense of progress, and was quite restored by the fortuitous finding of the hat he had lost, hanging from a white oak by the trail, as though placed there by some kindly hand. Still, he remained uneasy in his mind, and could not quite grasp tranquillity, though the mountain lay at peace all round him, the air hazed with blue and smelling of wood-damp and evergreens.

Then he realized, with a sudden jolt in the pit of his stomach, that the kitten was gone. There were itching furrows in the skin of his chest and abdomen, where it had climbed him in a frantic effort to escape, but it must have popped out the neck of his shirt and been flung off his shoulder in the mad career down the slope. He glanced from side to side, searching in the shadows under bushes and trees, but it was a vain hope. The shadows were lengthening, and they were on the main trail now, where he and Gideon had torn through the wood.

"Go with God," he murmured, and crossed himself briefly.

"What's that?" Claire asked, half-turning in the saddle.

"Nothing," he said. After all, it was a wild cat, though a small one. Doubtless it would manage.

Gideon worked the bit, pecking and bobbing. Jamie realized that the tension in his hands was running through the reins once more, and consciously slackened his grip. He loosened his grip on Claire, too, and she took a sudden deep breath.

His heart was beating fast.

It was impossible for him ever to come home after an absence without a certain sense of apprehension. For years after the Rising, he had lived in a cave, approaching his own house only rarely, after dark and with great caution, never knowing what he might find there. More than one Highland man had come home to his place to find it burned and black, his family gone. Or worse, still there.

Well enough to tell himself not to imagine horrors; the difficulty was that he had no need of imagination—memory sufficed.

The horse dug with his haunches, pushing hard. No use to tell himself this was a new place; it was, with its own dangers. If there were no English soldiers in these mountains, there were still marauders. Those too shiftless to take root and fend for themselves, but who wandered the backcountry, robbing and plundering. Raiding Indians. Wild animals. And fire. Always fire.

He had sent the Bugs on ahead, with Fergus to guide them, to save Claire dealing with the simultaneous chores of arrival and hospitality. The Chisholms, the MacLeods, and Billy Aberfeldy, with his wife and wee daughter, would all bide with them at the big house for a time; he had told Mrs. Bug to begin cooking at once. Decently mounted and not hindered by children or livestock, the Bugs should have reached the Ridge two days before. No one had come back to say aught was amiss, so perhaps all was well. But still . . .

He hadn't realized that Claire was tensed, too, until she suddenly relaxed against him, a hand on his leg.

"It's all right," she said. "I smell chimney smoke."

He lifted his head to catch the air. She was right; the tang of burning hickory floated on the breeze. Not the stink of remembered conflagration, but a homely whiff redolent with the promise of warmth and food. Mrs. Bug had presumably taken him at his word.

They rounded the last turn of the trail and saw it, then, the high fieldstone chimney rising above the trees on the ridge, its fat plume of smoke curling over the rooftree.

The house stood.

He breathed deep in relief, noticing now the other smells of home; the faint rich scent of manure from the stable, of meat smoked and hanging in the shed, and the breath of the forest nearby—damp wood and leaf-rot, rock and rushing water, the touch of it cold and loving on his cheek.

They came out of the chestnut grove and into the large clearing where the house stood, solid and neat, its windows glazed gold with the last of the sun.

It was a modest frame house, whitewashed and shingle-roofed, clean in its lines and soundly built, but impressive only by comparison with the crude cabins of most settlers. His own first cabin still stood, dark and sturdy, a little way down the hill. Smoke was curling from that chimney, too.

"Someone's made a fire for Bree and Roger," Claire said, nodding at it.

"That's good," he said. He tightened his arm about her waist, and she made a small, contented noise in her throat, wriggling her bottom into his lap.

Gideon was happy, too; he stretched out his neck and whinnied to the two horses in the penfold, who trotted to and fro in the enclosure, calling greetings. Claire's mare was standing by the fence, reins dangling; she curled her lip in what looked like derision, the wee besom. From somewhere far down the trail behind them came a deep, joyous bray; Clarence the mule, hearing the racket and delighted to be coming home.

The door flew open, and Mrs. Bug popped out, round and flustered as a tumble-turd. Jamie smiled at sight of her, and gave Claire an arm to slide down before dismounting himself.

"All's well, all's well, and how's yourself, sir?" Mrs. Bug was reassuring him before his boots struck ground. She had a pewter cup in one hand, a polishing cloth in the other, and didn't cease her polishing for an instant, even as she turned up her face to accept his kiss on her withered round cheek.

She didn't wait for an answer, but turned at once and stood a-tiptoe to kiss Claire, beaming.

"Oh, it's grand that you're home, ma'am, you and Himself, and I've the supper all made, so you'll not be worrit a bit with it, ma'am, but come inside, come inside, and be takin' off those dusty cloots, and I'll send old Arch along to the mash-hoose for a bit of the lively, and we'll . . ." She had Claire by one hand, towing her into the house, talking and talking, the other hand still polishing briskly away, her stubby fingers dexterously rubbing the cloth inside the cup. Claire gave him a helpless glance over one shoulder, and he grinned at her as she disappeared inside the house.

Gideon shoved an impatient nose under his arm and bumped his elbow.

"Oh, aye," he said, recalled to his chores. "Come along, then, ye prickly wee bastard."

By the time he had the big horse and Claire's mare unsaddled, wiped down, and turned out to their feed, Claire had escaped from Mrs. Bug; coming back from the paddock, he saw the door of the house swing open and Claire slip out, looking guiltily over her shoulder as though fearing pursuit.

Where was she bound? She didn't see him; she turned and hurried toward the far corner of the house, disappearing in a swish of homespun. He followed, curious.

Ah. She had seen to her surgery; now she was going to her garden before it got completely dark; he caught a glimpse of her against the sky on the upward path behind the house, the last of the daylight caught like cobwebs in her hair. There would be little growing now, only a few sturdy herbs and the overwintering things like carrots and onions and turnips, but it made no difference; she always went to see how things were, no matter how short a time she had been gone.

He understood the urge; he would not feel entirely home

himself until he had checked all the stock and buildings, and made sure of matters up at the still.

The evening breeze brought him an acrid hint from the distant privy, suggesting that matters there were shortly going to require his attention, speaking of buildings. Then he bethought him of the new tenants coming, and relaxed; digging a new privy would be just the thing for Chisholm's eldest two boys.

He and Ian had dug this one, when they first came to the Ridge. God, he missed the lad.

"A Mhicheal bheanaichte," he murmured. *Blessed Michael, protect him.* He liked MacKenzie well enough, but had it been his choice, he would not have exchanged Ian for the man. It had been Ian's choice, though, not his, and no more to be said about it.

Pushing away the ache of Ian's loss, he stepped behind a tree, loosened his breeks, and relieved himself. If she saw him, Claire would doubtless make what she considered witty remarks about dogs and wolves marking their home ground as they returned to it. Nothing of the sort, he replied to her mentally; why walk up the hill, only to make matters worse in the privy? Still, if you came down to it, it *was* his place, and if he chose to piss on it . . . He tidied his clothes, feeling more settled.

He raised his head and saw her coming down the path from the garden, her apron bulging with carrots and turnips. A gust of wind sent the last of the leaves from the chestnut grove swirling round her in a yellow dance, sparked with light.

Moved by sudden impulse, he stepped deeper into the trees and began to look about.

Normally, he paid attention only to such vegetation as was immediately comestible by horse or man, sufficiently straight-grained to serve for planks and timbers, or so obstructive as to pose difficulty in passage. Once he began looking with an eye to aesthetics, though, he found himself surprised at the variety to hand.

Stalks of half-ripe barley, the seeds laid in rows like a woman's plait. A dry, fragile weed that looked like the lace edging on a fine handkerchief. A branch of spruce, unearthly green and cool among the dry bits, leaving its fragrant sap on his hand as he tore it from the tree. A twig of glossy dried oak leaves that reminded him of her hair, in shades of gold and brown and gray. And a bit of scarlet creeper, snatched for color.

Just in time; she was coming round the corner of the house. Lost in thought, she passed within a foot or two of him, not seeing him.

"Sorcha," he called softly, and she turned, eyes narrowed against the rays of the sinking sun, then wide and gold with surprise at the sight of him.

"Welcome home," he said, and held out the small bouquet of leaves and twigs.

"Oh," she said. She looked at the bits of leaf and stick again, and then at him, and the corners of her mouth trembled, as though she might laugh or cry, but wasn't sure which. She reached then, and took the plants from him, her fingers small and cold as they brushed his hand.

"Oh, Jamie—they're *wonderful*." She came up on her toes and kissed him, warm and salty, and he wanted more, but she was hurrying away into the house, the silly wee things clasped to her breast as though they were gold.

He felt pleasantly foolish, and foolishly pleased with himself. The taste of her was still on his mouth.

"Sorcha," he whispered, and realized that he had called her so a moment before. Now, that was odd; no wonder she had been surprised. It was her name in the Gaelic, but he never called her by it. He liked the strangeness of her, the Englishness. She was his Claire, his Sassenach.

And yet in the moment when she passed him, she was *Sorcha*. Not only "Claire," it meant—but light.

He breathed deep, contented.

He was suddenly ravenous, both for food and for her, but he made no move to hasten inside. Some kinds of hunger were sweet in themselves, the anticipation of satisfaction as keen a pleasure as the slaking.

Hoofsteps and voices; the others were finally here. He had a sudden urge to keep his peaceful solitude a moment longer, but too late—in seconds, he was surrounded by confusion, the shrill cries of excited children and calls of distracted mothers, the welcoming of the newcomers, the bustle and rush of unloading, turning out the horses and mules, fetching feed and water . . . and yet in the midst of this Babel, he moved as though he were still alone, peaceful and quiet in the setting sun. He had come home.

IT WAS FULL DARK before everything was sorted, the smallest of the wild Chisholm bairns rounded up and sent inside for his supper, all the stock cared for and settled for the night. He followed Geoff Chisholm toward the house, but then held back, lingering for a moment in the dark dooryard.

He stood for a moment, idly chafing his hands against the chill as he admired the look of the place. Snug barn and sound sheds, a penfold and paddock in good repair, a tidy fence of palisades around Claire's scraggly garden, to keep out the deer. The house loomed white in the early dark, a benevolent spirit guarding the ridge. Light spilled from every door and window, and the sound of laughter came from inside.

He sensed a movement in the darkness, and turned to see his daughter coming from the spring house, a pail of fresh milk in her hand. She stopped by him, looking at the house.

"Nice to be home, isn't it?" she said softly.

"Aye," he said. "It is." They looked at each other, smiling. Then she leaned forward, peering closely at him. She turned him, so the light from the window fell on him, and a small frown puckered the skin between her brows.

"What's that?" she said, and flicked at his coat. A glossy scarlet leaf fell free and floated to the ground. Her brows went up at sight of it. "You'd better go and wash, Da," she said. "You've been in the poison ivy."

"YE MIGHT HAVE TOLD ME, Sassenach." Jamie glowered at the table near the bedroom window, where I'd set his bouquet in a cup of water. The bright, blotchy red of the poison ivy glowed, even in the dimness of the firelight. "And ye might get rid of it, too. D'ye mean to mock me?"

"No, I don't," I said, smiling as I hung my apron from the peg and reached for the laces of my gown. "But if I'd told you when you gave it to me, you'd have snatched it back. That's the only posy you've ever given me, and I don't imagine I'll get another; I mean to keep it."

He snorted, and sat down on the bed to take off his stockings. He'd already stripped off coat, stock, and shirt, and the firelight gleamed on the slope of his shoulders. He scratched at the underside of one wrist, though I'd told him it was psychosomatic; he hadn't any signs of rash.

"You've never come home with poison ivy rash," I remarked. "And you're bound to have run into it now and again, so much time as you spend in the woods and the fields. I think you must be immune to it. Some people are, you know."

"Oh, aye?" He looked interested at that, though he went on scratching. "Is that like you and Brianna not catching illness?"

"Something like, but for different reasons." I peeled off the gown of pale green homespun—more than a little grubby, after a week's travel—and stripped off my stays with a sigh of relief.

I got up to check the pan of water I had set to heat in the embers. Some of the newcomers had been sent off to spend the night with Fergus and Marsali, or with Roger and Bree, but the kitchen, the surgery, and Jamie's study below were full of guests, all sleeping on the floor. I wasn't going to bed without washing off the stains of travel, but I didn't care to provide a public spectacle while doing it, either.

The water shimmered with heat, tiny bubbles clinging to the sides of the pot. I put a finger in, just to check—lovely and hot. I poured some into the basin and put the rest back to keep warm.

"We aren't completely immune, you know," I warned him. "Some things—like smallpox—we can't ever catch, Roger and Bree and I, because we've been vaccinated against them, and it's permanent. Other things, like cholera and typhoid, we aren't *likely* to catch, but the injections don't give permanent immunity; it wears off after a time."

I bent to rummage in the saddlebags he had brought up and dumped by the door. Someone at the Gathering had given me a sponge—a real one, imported from the Indies—in payment for my extracting an abscessed tooth. Just the thing for a quick bath.

"Things like malaria—what Lizzie has—"

"I thought ye'd cured her of that," Jamie interrupted, frowning.

I shook my head, regretful.

"No, she'll always have it, poor thing. All I can do is try to lessen the severity of the attacks, and keep them from coming too often. It's in her blood, you see."

He pulled off the thong that bound back his hair, and shook out the ruddy locks, leaving them ruffled round his head like a mane.

"That doesna make any sense," he objected, rising to unfasten his breeks. "Ye told me that when a person had the measles, if he lived, he'd not get it again, because it stayed in the blood. And so I couldna catch pox or measles now, because I'd had them both as a child—they're in my blood."

"Well, it's not quite the same thing," I said, rather lamely. The thought of trying to explain the differences among active immunity, passive immunity, acquired immunity, antibodies, and parasitic infection was more of a challenge than I felt up to, after a long day's ride.

I dipped the sponge into the basin, let it take up water, then squeezed it out, enjoying the oddly silky, fibrous texture. A fine mist of sand floated out of the pores and settled to the bottom of the china basin. The sponge was softening as it took up water, but I could still feel a hard spot at one edge.

"Speaking of riding—"

Jamie looked mildly startled.

"Were we speaking of riding?"

"Well, no, but I was thinking of it." I waved a hand, dismissing the inconsequent distinction. "In any case, what do you mean to do about Gideon?"

"Oh." Jamie dropped his breeks in a puddle on the floor and stretched himself, considering. "Well, I canna afford just to shoot him, I suppose. And he's a braw enough fellow. I'll cut him, to start. That may settle his mind a bit."

"Cut him? Oh, castrate him, you mean. Yes, I suppose that would get his attention, though it seems a bit drastic." I hesitated a moment, reluctant. "Do you want me to do it?"

He stared at me in amazement, then burst out laughing.

"Nay, Sassenach, I dinna think cutting an eighteen-hand stallion is a job for a woman, surgeon or no. It doesna really require the delicate touch, aye?"

I was just as pleased to hear this. I had been working at the sponge with my thumb; it loosened a bit, and a tiny shell popped suddenly out of a large pore. It floated down through the water, a perfect miniature spiral, tinted pink and purple.

"Oh, look," I said, delighted.

"What a bonnie wee thing." Jamie leaned over my shoulder, a big forefinger gently touching the shell at the bottom of the basin. "How did it get into your sponge, I wonder?"

"I expect the sponge ate it by mistake."

"Ate it?" One ruddy eyebrow shot up at that.

"Sponges are animals," I explained. "Or to be more exact, stomachs. They suck in water, and just absorb everything edible as it passes through."

"Ah, so that's why Bree called the bairn a wee sponge. They do that." He smiled at the thought of Jemmy.

"Indeed they do." I sat down and slipped the shift off my shoulders, letting the garment fall to my waist. The fire had taken the chill off the room, but it was still cold enough that the skin of my breasts and arms bloomed into gooseflesh.

Jamie picked up his belt and carefully removed the assorted impedimenta it held, laying out pistol, cartridge box, dirk, and pewter flask on top of the small bureau. He lifted the flask and raised an inquiring eyebrow in my direction.

I nodded enthusiastically, and he turned to find a cup amid the rubble of oddments. With so many people and their belongings stuffed into the house, all of our own saddlebags, plus the bundles and bits acquired at the Gathering, had been carried up and dumped in our room; the humped shadows of the luggage flickering on the wall gave the chamber the odd look of a grotto, lined with lumpy boulders.

Jamie was as much a sponge as his grandson, I reflected, watching him rootle about, completely naked and totally unconcerned about it. He took in everything, and seemed able to deal with whatever came his way, no matter how familiar or foreign to his experience. Maniac stallions, kidnapped priests, marriageable maidservants, headstrong daughters, and heathen sons-in-law . . . Anything he could not defeat, outwit, or alter, he simply accepted—rather like the sponge and its embedded shell.

Pursuing the analogy further, I supposed I was the shell. Snatched out of my own small niche by an unexpected strong current, taken in and surrounded by Jamie and his life. Caught forever among the strange currents that pulsed through this outlandish environment.

The thought gave me a sudden queer feeling. The shell lay still at the bottom of the basin—delicate, beautiful . . . but empty. Rather slowly, I raised the sponge to the back of my neck and squeezed, feeling the tickle of warm water down my back.

For the most part, I felt no regrets. I had chosen to be here; I *wanted* to be here. And yet now and then small things like our conversation about immunity made me realize just how much had been lost—of what I had had, of what I had been. It was undeniable that some of my soft parts had been digested away, and the thought did make me feel a trifle hollow now and then.

Jamie bent to dig in one of the saddlebags, and the sight of his bare buttocks, turned toward me in all innocence, did much to dispel the momentary sense of disquiet. They were gracefully shaped, rounded with muscle—and pleasingly dusted with a red-gold fuzz that caught the light of fire and candle. The long, pale columns of his thighs framed the shadow of his scrotum, dark and barely visible between them.

He had found a cup at last, and poured it half full. He turned and handed it to me, lifting his eyes from the surface of the dark liquid, startled to find me staring at him.

"What is it?" he said. "Is there something the matter, Sassenach?"

"No," I said, but I must have sounded rather doubtful, for his brows drew momentarily together.

"No," I said, more positively. I took the cup from him and smiled, lifting it slightly in acknowledgment. "Only thinking."

An answering smile touched his lips.

"Aye? Well, ye dinna want to do too much of that late at night, Sassenach. It will give ye the nightmare."

"Daresay you're right about that." I sipped from the cup; rather to my surprise, it was wine—and very good wine. "Where did you get this?"

"From Father Kenneth. It's sacramental wine—but not consecrated, aye? He said the Sheriff's men would take it; he would as soon it went with me."

A slight shadow crossed his face at mention of the priest.

"Do you think he'll be all right?" I asked. The Sheriff's men had not struck me as civilized enforcers of an abstruse regulation, but rather as thugs whose prejudice was momentarily constrained by fear—of Jamie.

"I hope so." Jamie turned aside, restless. "I told the Sheriff that if the Father were misused, he and his men would answer for it."

I nodded silently, sipping. If Jamie learned of any harm done to Father Donahue, he would indeed make the Sheriff answer for it. The thought made me a trifle uneasy; this wasn't a good time to make enemies, and the Sheriff of Orange County wasn't a good enemy to have.

I looked up to find Jamie's eyes still fixed on me, though now with a look of deep appreciation.

"You're in good flesh these days, Sassenach," he observed, tilting his head to one side.

"Flatterer," I said, giving him a cold look as I picked up the sponge again.

"Ye must have gained a stone, at least, since the spring," he said with approval, disregarding the look and circling round me to inspect. "It's been a good fat summer, aye?"

I turned round and flung the wet sponge at his head.

He caught it neatly, grinning.

"I didna realize how well ye'd filled out, Sassenach, so bundled as ye've been these last weeks. I havena seen ye naked in a month, at least." He was still eyeing me with an air of appraisal, as though I were a prime entrant in the Silver Medalist Round at the Shropshire Fat Pigs Show.

"Enjoy it," I advised him, my cheeks flushed with annoyance. "You may not see it again for quite some time!" I snatched the top of the chemise up again, covering my—undeniably rather full—breasts.

His eyebrows rose in surprise at my tone.

"You're never angry wi' me, Sassenach?"

"Certainly not," I said. "Whatever gives you an idea like *that*?"

He smiled, rubbing the sponge absently over his chest as his eyes traveled over me. His nipples puckered at the chill, dark and stiff among the ruddy, curling hairs, and the damp gleamed on his skin.

"I like ye fat, Sassenach," he said softly. "Fat and juicy as a plump wee hen. I like it fine."

I might have considered this a simple attempt to remove his foot from his mouth, were it not for the fact that naked men are conveniently equipped with sexual lie detectors. He *did* like it fine.

"Oh," I said. Rather slowly, I lowered the chemise. "Well, then."

He lifted his chin, gesturing. I hesitated for a moment, then stood up and let the chemise fall on the floor, joining his breeks. I reached across and took the sponge from his hand.

"I'll . . . um . . . just finish washing, shall I?" I murmured. I turned my back, put a foot on the stool to wash, and heard an encouraging rumble of appreciation behind me. I smiled to myself, and took my time. The room was getting warmer; by the time I had finished my ablutions, my skin was pink and smooth, with only a slight chill in fingers and toes.

I turned round at last, to see Jamie still watching me, though he still rubbed at his wrist, frowning slightly.

"Did *you* wash?" I asked. "Even if it doesn't trouble you, if you have oil from the poison ivy on your skin, it can get on things you touch—and *I'm* not immune to the stuff."

"I scrubbed my hands with lye soap," he assured me,

putting them on my shoulders in illustration. Sure enough, he smelled strongly of the acrid soft soap we made from suet and wood-ash—it wasn't perfumed toilet soap, but it did get things clean. Things like floorboards and iron pots. No wonder he'd been scratching; it wasn't easy on the skin, and his hands were rough and cracked.

I bent my head and kissed his knuckles, then reached across to the small box where I kept my personal bits and pieces, and took out the jar of skin balm. Made of walnut oil, beeswax, and purified lanolin from boiled sheep's wool, it was pleasantly soothing, green-scented with the essences of chamomile, comfrey, yarrow, and elderflowers.

I scooped out a bit with my thumbnail, and rubbed it between my hands; it was nearly solid to begin with, but liquefied nicely when warmed.

"Here," I said, and took one of his hands between my own, rubbing the ointment into the creases of his knuckles, massaging his callused palms. Slowly, he relaxed, letting me stretch each finger as I worked my way down the joints and rubbed more ointment into the tiny scrapes and cuts. There were still marks on his hands where he had kept the leather reins wrapped tightly.

"The posy's lovely, Jamie," I said, nodding at the little bouquet in its cup. "Whatever made you do it, though?" While in his own way quite romantic, Jamie was thoroughly practical as well; I didn't think he had ever given me a completely frivolous present, and he was not a man to see value in any vegetation that could not be eaten, taken medicinally, or brewed into beer.

He shifted a bit, clearly uncomfortable.

"Aye, well," he said, looking away. "I just—I mean—well, I had a wee thing I meant to give ye, only I lost it, but then you seemed to think it a sweet thing that wee Roger had plucked a few gowans for Brianna, and I—" He broke off, muttering something that sounded like *"Ifrinn!"* under his breath.

I wanted very much to laugh. Instead, I lifted his hand and kissed his knuckles, lightly. He looked embarrassed, but pleased. His thumb traced the edge of a half-healed blister on my palm, left by a hot kettle.

"Here, Sassenach, ye need a bit of this, too. Let me," he said, and leaned to take a dab of the green ointment. He engulfed my hand in his, warm and still slippery with the oil and beeswax mixture.

I resisted for a moment, but then let him take my hand, making deep slow circles on my palm that made me want to close my eyes and melt quietly. I gave a small sigh of pleasure, and must have closed my eyes after all, because I didn't see him move in close to kiss me; just felt the brief soft touch of his mouth.

I raised my other hand, lazily, and he took it, too, his fingers smoothing mine. I let my fingers twine with his, thumbs jousting gently, the heels of our hands lightly rubbing. He stood close enough that I felt the warmth of him, and the delicate brush of the sun-bleached hairs on his arm as he reached past my hip for more of the ointment.

He paused, kissing me lightly once more in passing. Flames hissed on the hearth like shifting tides, and the firelight flickered dimly on the whitewashed walls, like light dancing on the surface of water far above. We might have been alone together at the bottom of the sea.

"Roger wasn't being strictly romantic, you know," I said. "Or maybe he was—depending how one wants to look at it."

Jamie looked quizzical, as he took my hand again. Our fingers locked and twined, moving slowly, and I sighed with pleasure.

"Aye?"

"Bree asked me about birth control, and I told her what methods there are now—which are frankly not all that good, though better than nothing. But old Grannie Bacon gave me some seeds that she says the Indians use for contraception; supposed to be very effective."

Jamie's face underwent the most comical change, from drowsy pleasure to wide-eyed astonishment.

"Birth con—what? She—ye mean he—those clatty weeds—"

"Well, yes. Or at least I think they may help prevent pregnancy."

"Mmphm." The movement of his fingers slowed, and his brows drew together—more in concern than disapproval, I thought. Then he returned to the job of massaging my hands, enveloping them in his much larger grasp with a decided movement that obliged me to yield to him.

He was quiet for a few moments, working the ointment into my fingers more in the businesslike way of a man rubbing saddle soap into harness than one making tender love to his wife's devoted hands. I shifted slightly, and he seemed to realize what he was doing, for he stopped, frowning, then squeezed my hands lightly and let his face relax. He lifted my hand to his lips, kissed it, then resumed his massage, much more slowly.

"Do ye think—" he began, and stopped.

"What?"

"Mmphm. It's only—does it not seem a bit strange to ye, Sassenach? That a young woman newly wed should be thinking of such a thing?"

"No, it doesn't," I said, rather sharply. "It seems entirely sensible to me. And they aren't all that newly wed—they've been . . . I mean, they *have* got a child already."

His nostrils flared in soundless disagreement.

"*She* has a child," he said. "That's what I mean, Sassenach. It seems to me that a young woman well-suited with her man wouldna be thinking first thing how *not* to bear his child. Are ye sure all is well between them?"

I paused, frowning as I considered the notion.

"I think so," I said at last, slowly. "Remember, Jamie—Bree comes from a time where women *can* decide whether or when to have babies, with a fair amount of certainty. She'd feel that such a thing was her right."

The wide mouth moved, pursed in thought; I could see him struggling with the notion—one entirely contrary to his own experience.

"That's the way of it, then?" he asked, finally. "A woman can say, I will, or I won't—and the man has no say in it?" His voice was filled with astonishment—and disapproval.

I laughed a little.

"Well, it's not *exactly* like that. Or not all the time. I mean, there are accidents. And ignorance and foolishness; a lot of women just let things happen. And most women would certainly *care* what their men thought about it. But yes . . . I suppose if you come right down to it, that's right."

He grunted slightly.

"But MacKenzie's from that time, too. So he'll think nothing odd of it?"

"He picked the weeds for her," I pointed out.

"So he did." The line stayed between his brows, but the frown eased somewhat.

It was growing late, and the muffled rumble of talk and laughter was dying down in the house below. The growing quiet of the house was pierced suddenly by a baby's wail. Both of us stood still, listening—then relaxed as the murmur of the mother's voice reached us through the closed door.

"Besides, it's not so unusual for a young woman to think of such a thing—Marsali came and asked me about it, before she married Fergus."

"Oh, did she?" One eyebrow went up. "Did ye not tell her, then?"

"Of course I did!"

"Whatever ye told her didna work all that well, did it?" One corner of his mouth curled up in a cynic smile; Germain had been born approximately ten months following his parents' marriage, and Marsali had become pregnant with Joan within days of weaning him.

I felt a flush rising in my cheeks.

"Nothing works all the time—not even modern methods. And for that matter—nothing works at all if you don't use it." In fact, Marsali had wanted contraception not because she didn't want a baby—but only because she had feared that pregnancy would interfere with the intimacy of her relationship with Fergus. *When we get to the prick part, I want to like it* had been her words on that memorable occasion, and my own mouth curled at the memory.

My equally cynical guess was that she had liked it fine, and had decided that pregnancy was unlikely to diminish her appreciation of Fergus's finer points. But that rather came back to Jamie's fears about Brianna—for surely her intimacy with Roger was well established. Still, that was hardly . . .

One of Jamie's hands remained entwined with mine; the other left my fingers and reached elsewhere—very lightly.

"Oh," I said, beginning to lose my train of thought.

"Pills, ye said." His face was quite close, eyes hooded in thought as he worked. "That's how it's done—then?"

"Um . . . oh. Yes."

"Ye didna bring any with you," he said. "When ye came back."

I breathed deep and let it out, feeling as though I were beginning to dissolve.

"No," I said, a little faintly.

He paused a moment, hand cupped lightly.

"Why not?" he asked quietly.

"I . . . well, I . . . I actually—I thought—you have to keep taking them. I couldn't have brought enough. There's a permanent way, a small operation. It's fairly simple, and it makes one permanently . . . barren." I swallowed. Viewing the prospect of coming back to the past, I had in fact thought seriously about the possibilities of pregnancy—and the risks. I thought the possibility very low indeed, given both my age and previous history, but the risk . . .

Jamie stood stock-still, looking down.

"For God's sake, Claire," he said at last, low-voiced. "Tell me that ye did it."

I took a deep breath, and squeezed his hand, my fingers slipping a little.

"Jamie," I said softly, "if I'd done it, I would have told you." I swallowed again. "You . . . would have wanted me to?"

He was still holding my hand. His other hand left me, touched my back, pressed me—very gently—to him. His skin was warm on mine.

We stood close together, touching, not moving, for several minutes. He sighed then, chest rising under my ear.

"I've bairns enough," he said quietly. "I've only the one life—and that's you, *mo chridhe*."

I reached up and touched his face. It was furrowed with tiredness, rough with whiskers; he hadn't shaved in days.

I *had* thought about it. And had come very close indeed to asking a surgeon friend to perform the sterilization for me.

Cold blood and clear head had argued for it; no sense in taking chances. And yet . . . there was no guarantee that I would survive the journey, would reach the right time or place, would find him again. Still less, a chance that I might conceive again at my age.

And yet, gone from him for so long, not knowing if I might find him—I could not bring myself to destroy any possibility between us. I did not want another child. But if I found him, and *he* should want it . . . then I would risk it for him.

I touched him, lightly, and he made a small sound in his throat and laid his face against my hair, holding me tight. Our lovemaking was always risk and promise—for if he held my life in his hands when he lay with me, I held his soul, and knew it.

"I thought . . . I thought you'd never see Brianna. And I didn't know about Willie. It wasn't right for me to take away any chance of your having another child—not without telling you."

You are Blood of my blood, I had said to him, *Bone of my bone*. That was true, and always would be, whether children came of it or not.

"I dinna want another child," he whispered. "I want you."

His hand rose, as though by itself, touched my breast with a fingertip, left a shimmer of the scented ointment on my skin. I wrapped my hand, slippery and green-scented, round him, and stepped backward, bringing him with me toward the bed. I had just enough presence of mind left to extinguish the candle.

"Don't worry for Bree," I said, reaching up to touch him as he rose over me, looming black against the firelight. "Roger picked the weeds for her. He knows what she wants."

He gave a deep sigh, the breath of a laugh, that caught in his throat as he came to me, and ended in a small groan of pleasure and completion as he slid between my legs, well-oiled and ready.

"I ken what I want, too," he said, voice muffled in my hair. "I shall pick ye another posy, tomorrow."

DRUGGED WITH FATIGUE, languid with love, and lulled by the comforts of a soft, clean bed, I slept like the dead.

Somewhere toward dawn, I began to dream—pleasant dreams of touch and color, without form. Small hands touched my hair, patted my face; I turned on my side, half-conscious, dreaming of nursing a child in my sleep. Tiny soft fingers kneaded my breast, and my hand came up to cup the child's head. It bit me.

I shrieked, shot bolt upright in bed, and saw a gray form race across the quilt and disappear over the end of the bed. I shrieked again, louder.

Jamie shot sideways out of bed, rolled on the floor, and came up standing, shoulders braced and fists half-clenched.

"What?" he demanded, glaring wildly round in search of marauders. "Who? What?"

"A rat!" I said, pointing a trembling finger at the spot where the gray shape had vanished into the crevice between bed-foot and wall.

"Oh." His shoulders relaxed. He scrubbed his hands over his face and through his hair, blinking. "A rat, aye?"

"A rat in our *bed*," I said, not disposed to view the event with any degree of calm. "It bit me!" I peered closely at my injured breast. No blood to speak of; only a couple of tiny puncture marks that stung slightly. I thought of rabies, though, and my blood ran cold.

"Dinna fash yourself, Sassenach. I'll deal with it." Squaring his shoulders once more, Jamie picked up the poker from the hearth and advanced purposefully on the bed-foot. The footboard was solid; there was a space of only a few inches between it and the wall. The rat must be trapped, unless it had managed to escape in the scant seconds between my scream and Jamie's eruption from the quilts.

I got up onto my knees, ready to leap off the bed if necessary. Scowling in concentration, Jamie raised the poker, reached out with his free hand, and flipped the hanging coverlid out of the way.

He whipped the poker down with great force—and jerked it aside, smashing into the wall.

"What?" I said.

"What?" he echoed, in a disbelieving tone. He bent closer, squinting in the dim light, then started to laugh. He dropped the poker, squatted on the floor, and reached slowly into the space between the bed-foot and wall, making a small chirping noise through his teeth. It sounded like birds feeding in a distant bush.

"Are you *talking* to the rat?" I began to crawl toward the foot of the bed, but he motioned me back, shaking his head, while still making the chirping sound.

I waited, with some impatience. Within a minute, he made a grab, evidently catching whatever it was, for he gave a small exclamation of satisfaction. He stood up, smiling, a gray, furry shape clutched by the nape, dangling like a tiny purse from his fingers.

"Here's your wee ratten, Sassenach," he said, and gently deposited a ball of gray fur on the coverlet. Huge eyes of a pale celadon green stared up at me, unblinking.

"Well, goodness," I said. "Wherever did *you* come from?" I extended a finger, very slowly. The kitten didn't move. I touched the edge of a tiny gray-silk jaw, and the big green eyes disappeared, going to slits as it rubbed against my finger. A surprisingly deep purr rumbled through its miniature frame.

"That," Jamie said, with immense satisfaction, "is the present I *meant* to give ye, Sassenach. He'll keep the vermin from your surgery."

"Well, possibly very *small* vermin," I said, examining my new present dubiously. "I think a large cockroach could carry him—is it a him?—off to its lair, let alone a mouse."

"He'll grow," Jamie assured me. "Look at his feet."

He—yes, it was a he—had rolled onto his back and was doing an imitation of a dead bug, paws in the air. Each paw was roughly the size of a broad copper penny, small enough by themselves, but enormous by contrast with the tiny body. I touched the minuscule pads, an immaculate pink in their thicket of soft gray fur, and the kitten writhed in ecstasy.

A discreet knock came at the door, and I snatched the sheet up over my bosom as the door opened and Mr. Wemyss's head poked in, his hair sticking up like a pile of wheat straw.

"Er . . . I hope all is well, sir?" he asked, blinking short-sightedly. "My lass woke me, sayin' as she thought there was a skelloch, like, and then we heard a bit of a bang, like—" His eyes, hastily averted from me, went to the scar of raw wood in the whitewashed wall, left by Jamie's poker.

"Aye, it's fine, Joseph," Jamie assured him. "Only a wee cat."

"Oh, aye?" Mr. Wemyss squinted toward the bed, his thin face breaking into a smile as he made out the blot of gray fur. "A cheetie, is it? Well, and he'll be a fine help i' the kitchen, I've nae doubt."

"Aye. Speakin' of kitchens, Joseph—d'ye think your lassie might bring up a dish of cream for the baudrons here?"

Mr. Wemyss nodded and disappeared, with a final avuncular smile at the kitten.

Jamie stretched, yawned, and scrubbed both hands vigorously through his hair, which was behaving with even more reckless abandon than usual. I eyed him, with a certain amount of purely aesthetic appreciation.

"You look like a woolly mammoth," I said.

"Oh? And what is a mammoth, besides big?"

"A sort of prehistoric elephant—you know, the animals with the long trunks?"

He squinted down the length of his body, then looked at me quizzically.

"Well, I thank ye for the compliment, Sassenach," he said. "Mammoth, is it?" He thrust his arms upward and stretched again, casually arching his back, which—quite inadvertently, I didn't think—enhanced any incidental resemblances that one might note between the half-engorged morning anatomy of a man, and the facial adornments of a pachyderm.

I laughed.

"That's not *precisely* what I meant," I said. "Stop waggling; Lizzie's coming in any minute. You'd better put your shirt on or get back in bed."

The sound of footsteps on the landing sent him diving under the quilts, and sent the little cat scampering up the sheet in fright. In the event, it was Mr. Wemyss himself who had brought the dish of cream, sparing his daughter a possible sight of Himself in the altogether.

The weather being fine, we had left the shutters open the night before. The sky outside was the color of fresh oysters, moist and pearly gray. Mr. Wemyss glanced at it, blinked and nodded at Jamie's thanks, and toddled back to his bed, thankful for a last half hour's sleep before the dawn.

I disentangled the kitten, who had taken refuge in my hair, and set him down by the bowl of cream. I didn't suppose he could ever have seen a bowl of cream in his life, but the smell was enough—in moments, he was whisker-deep, lapping for all he was worth.

"He's a fine thrum to him," Jamie remarked approvingly. "I can hear him from here."

"He's lovely; wherever did you get him?" I nestled into the curve of Jamie's body, enjoying his warmth; the fire had burned far down during the night, and the air in the room was chilly, sour with ash.

"Found him in the wood." Jamie yawned widely, and relaxed, propping his head on my shoulder to watch the tiny cat, who had abandoned himself to an ecstasy of gluttony. "I thought I'd lost him when Gideon bolted—I suppose he'd crept into one of the saddlebags, and came up wi' the other things."

We lapsed into a peaceful stupor, drowsily cuddled in the warm nest of our bed, as the sky lightened, moment by moment, and the air came alive with the voices of waking birds. The house was waking, too—a baby's wail came from below, followed by the stir and shuffle of rising, the murmur of voices. We should rise, too—there was so much to be done—and yet neither of us moved, each reluctant to surrender the sense of quiet sanctuary. Jamie sighed, his breath warm on my bare shoulder.

"A week, I think," he said quietly.

"Before you must go?"

"Aye. I can take that long to settle things here, and speak to the men from the Ridge. A week then, to pass through the country between the Treaty Line and Drunkard's Creek and call a muster—then I'll bring them here to drill. If Tryon should call up the militia, then . . ."

I lay quiet for a moment, my hand wrapped round Jamie's, his loose fist curled against my breast.

"If he calls, I'll go with you."

He kissed the back of my neck.

"D'ye wish it?" he said. "I dinna think there will be need. Neither you nor Bree know of any fighting will be done here now."

"That only means that if anything *will* happen, it won't be a huge battle," I said. "This—the Colonies—it's a big place, Jamie. And two hundred years of things happening—we wouldn't know about the smaller conflicts, especially ones that happened in a different place. Now, in Boston—" I sighed, squeezing his hand.

I wouldn't know a great deal about events in Boston myself, but Bree would; growing up there, she had been exposed in school to a good bit of local and state history. I had heard her telling Roger things about the Boston Massacre—a small confrontation between citizens and British troops that had taken place the past March.

"Aye, I suppose that's true," he said. "Still, it doesna seem as though it will come to anything. I think Tryon only means to frighten the Regulators into good behavior."

This was in fact likely. However, I was quite aware of the old adage—"Man proposes and God disposes"—and whether it was God or William Tryon in charge, heaven only knew what might happen in the event.

"Do you think so?" I asked. "Or only hope so?"

He sighed, and stretched his legs, his arm tightening about my waist.

"Both," he admitted. "Mostly I hope. And I pray. But I do think so, too."

The kitten had completely emptied the dish of cream. He sat down with an audible thump on his tiny backside, rubbed the last of the delicious white stuff from his whiskers, then ambled slowly toward the bed, sides bulging visibly. He sprang up onto the coverlet, burrowed close to me, and fell promptly asleep.

Perhaps not quite asleep; I could feel the small vibration of his purring through the quilt.

"What do you think I should call him?" I mused aloud, touching the tip of the soft, wispy tail. "Spot? Puff? Cloudy?"

"Foolish names," Jamie said, with a lazy tolerance. "Is that what ye were wont to call your pussie-baudrons in Boston, then? Or England?"

"No. I've never had a cat before," I admitted. "Frank was allergic to them—they made him sneeze. And what's a good Scottish cat name, then—Diarmuid? McGillivray?"

He snorted, then laughed.

"Adso," he said, positively. "Call him Adso."

"What sort of name is that?" I demanded, twisting to look back at him in amazement. "I've heard a good many peculiar Scottish names, but that's a new one."

He rested his chin comfortably on my shoulder, watching the kitten sleep.

"My mother had a wee cat named Adso," he said, surprisingly. "A gray cheetie, verra much like this one."

"Did she?" I laid a hand on his leg. He rarely spoke of his mother, who had died when he was eight.

"Aye, she did. A rare mouser, and that fond of my mother; he didna have much use for us bairns." He smiled in memory. "Possibly because Jenny dressed him in baby-gowns and fed him rusks, and I dropped him into the millpond, to see could he swim. He could, by the way," he informed me, "but he didna like to."

"I can't say I blame him," I said, amused. "Why was he called Adso, though? Is it a saint's name?" I was used to the peculiar names of Celtic saints, from Aodh—pronounced OOH—to Dervorgilla, but hadn't heard of Saint Adso before. Probably the patron saint of mice.

"Not a saint," he corrected. "A monk. My mother was verra learned—she was educated at Leoch, ye ken, along with Colum and Dougal, and could read Greek and Latin, and a bit of the Hebrew as well as French and German. She didna have so much opportunity for reading at Lallybroch, of course, but my father would take pains to have books fetched for her, from Edinburgh and Paris."

He reached across my body to touch a silky, translucent ear, and the kitten twitched its whiskers, screwing up its face as though about to sneeze, but didn't open its eyes. The purr continued unabated.

"One of the books she liked was written by an Austrian,

from the city of Melk, and so she thought it a verra suitable name for the kit."

"Suitable . . . ?"

"Aye," he said, nodding toward the empty dish, without the slightest twitch of lip or eyelid. "Adso of Milk."

A slit of green showed as one eye opened, as though in response to the name. Then it closed again, and the purring resumed.

"Well, if he doesn't mind, I suppose I don't," I said, resigned. "Adso it is."

19

THE DEVIL YE KEN

A WEEK LATER, we—that is, the women—were engaged in the backbreaking business of laundry when Clarence the mule let out his clarion announcement that company was coming. Little Mrs. Aberfeldy leaped as though she'd been stung by a bee, and dropped an armload of wet shirts in the dirt of the yard. I could see Mrs. Bug and Mrs. Chisholm opening their mouths in reproach, and took the opportunity to wipe my hands on my apron and hurry round to the front, to greet whatever visitor might be approaching.

Sure enough; a bay mule was coming out of the trees at the head of the trail, followed by a fat brown mare on a leading rein. The mule's ears flicked forward and he brayed enthusiastically in reply to Clarence's greeting. I stuck my fingers in my ears to block the ungodly racket, and squinted against the dazzle of the afternoon sun to make out the mule's rider.

"Mr. Husband!" Pulling my fingers out of my ears, I hurried forward to greet him.

"Mrs. Fraser—good day to thee!"

Hermon Husband pulled off his black slouch hat and gave me a brief nod of greeting, then slid off the mule with a groan that spoke of a good many hours in the saddle. His lips moved soundlessly in the framework of his beard as he straightened stiffly; he was a Quaker, and didn't use strong language. Not out loud, at least.

"Is thy husband at home, Mrs. Fraser?"

"I just saw him heading for the stable; I'll go and find him!" I shouted, above the continued braying of the mules. I took the hat from him, and gestured toward the house. "I'll see to your animals!"

He nodded thanks and limped slowly round the house, toward the kitchen door. From the back, I could see how painfully he moved; he could barely put weight on his left foot. The hat in my hand was covered with dust and mud stains, and I had smelled the odor of unwashed clothes and body when he stood near me. He'd been a long time riding, and not just today—for a week or more, I thought, and sleeping rough for the most of it.

I unsaddled the mule, removing in the process two worn saddlebags half-filled with printed pamphlets, badly printed and crudely illustrated. I studied the illustration with some interest; it was a woodcut of several indignant and righteous-looking Regulators defying a group of officials, among whom was a squat figure I had no trouble identifying as David Anstruther; the caption didn't mention him by name, but the artist had captured the Sheriff's resemblance to a poisonous toad with remarkable facility. Had Husband taken to delivering the bloody things door-to-door? I wondered.

I turned the animals out into the paddock, dumped the hat and saddlebags by the porch, then trekked up the hill to the stable, a shallow cave that Jamie had walled with thick palisades. Brianna referred to it as the maternity ward, since the usual occupants were imminently expectant mares, cows, or sows.

I wondered what brought Hermon Husband here—and

whether he was being followed. He owned a farm and a small mill, both at least two days' ride from the Ridge; not a journey he would undertake simply for the pleasure of our company.

Husband was one of the leaders of the Regulation, and had been jailed more than once for the rabble-rousing pamphlets he printed and distributed. The most recent news I had heard of him was that he had been read out of the local Quaker meeting, the Friends taking a dim view of his activities, which they regarded as incitement to violence. I rather thought they had a point, judging from the pamphlets I'd read.

The door of the stable stood open, allowing the pleasantly fecund scents of straw, warm animals, and manure to drift out, along with a stream of similarly fecund words. Jamie, no Quaker, did believe in strong language, and was using rather a lot of it, albeit in Gaelic, which tends toward the poetic, rather than the vulgar.

I translated the current effusion roughly as, "May your guts twine upon themselves like serpents and your bowels explode through the walls of your belly! May the curse of the crows be upon you, misbegotten spawn of a lineage of dung flies!" Or words to that effect.

"Who are you talking to?" I inquired, putting my head round the stable door. "And what's the curse of the crows?"

I blinked against the sudden dimness, seeing him only as a tall shadow against the piles of pale hay stacked by the wall. He turned, hearing me, and strode into the light from the door. He'd been running his hands through his hair; several strands were pulled from their binding, standing on end, and there were straws sticking out of it.

"Tha nighean na galladh torrach!" he said, with a ferocious scowl and a brief gesture behind him.

"White daughter of a bi—oh! You mean that blasted sow has done it again?"

The big white sow, while possessed of superior fatness and amazing reproductive capacity, was also a creature of low cunning, and impatient of captivity. She had escaped her brood pen twice before, once by the expedient of charging Lizzie, who had—wisely—screamed and dived out of the way as the pig barged past, and again by assiduously rooting up one side of the pen, lying in wait until the stable door was opened, and knocking me flat as she made for the wide-open spaces.

This time, she hadn't bothered with strategy, but merely smashed out a board from her pen, then rooted and dug under the palisades, making an escape tunnel worthy of British prisoners-of-war in a Nazi camp.

"Aye, she has," Jamie said, reverting to English now that his initial fury had subsided somewhat. "As for the curse o' the crows, it depends. It might mean ye want the corbies to come down on a man's fields and eat his corn. In this case, I had in mind the birds pecking out the evil creature's eyes."

"I suppose that would make her easier to catch," I said, sighing. "How near is she to farrowing, do you think?"

He shrugged and shoved a hand through his hair.

"A day, two days, three, maybe. Serve the creature right if she farrows in the wood and is eaten by wolves, her and her piglets together." He kicked moodily at the heap of raw earth left by the sow's tunneling, sending a cascade of dirt down into the hole. "Who's come? I heard Clarence yammering."

"Hermon Husband."

He turned sharply toward me, instantly forgetting the pig.

"Has he, then?" he said softly, as though to himself. "Why, I wonder?"

"So did I. He's been riding for some time—distributing pamphlets, evidently."

I had to scamper after Jamie as I added this; he was already striding down the hill toward the house, tidying his hair as he went. I caught up just in time to brush bits of straw from his shoulders before he reached the yard.

Jamie nodded casually to Mrs. Chisholm and Mrs. MacLeod, who were hoicking steaming bales of wet clothes from the big kettle with paddles and spreading them on bushes to dry. I scuttled along with Jamie, ignoring the women's accusing stares and trying to look as though I had much more important concerns to deal with than laundry.

Someone had found Husband refreshment; a plate of partially eaten bread and butter and a half-full mug of buttermilk lay on the table. So did Husband, who had put his head on his folded arms and fallen asleep. Adso crouched on the table beside him, fascinated by the bushy gray whiskers that quivered like antennae with the Quaker's reverberating snores. The kitten was just reaching an experimental paw toward Husband's open mouth when Jamie nabbed him by the scruff of the neck and dropped him neatly into my hands.

"Mr. Husband?" he said quietly, leaning over the table. "Your servant, sir."

Husband snorted, blinked, then sat up suddenly, nearly upsetting the buttermilk. He goggled briefly at me and Adso, then seemed to recollect where he was, for he shook himself, and half-rose, nodding to Jamie.

"Friend Fraser," he said thickly. "I am—I beg pardon—I have been—"

Jamie brushed away his apologies and sat down opposite him, casually picking up a slice of bread and butter from the plate.

"May I be of service to ye, Mr. Husband?"

Husband scrubbed a hand over his face, which did nothing to improve his looks, but did seem to rouse him more fully. Seen clearly in the soft afternoon light of the kitchen, he looked even worse than he had outside, his eyes pouched and bloodshot and his grizzled hair and beard tangled in knots. He was only in his mid-fifties, I knew, but looked at least ten years older. He made an attempt to straighten his coat, and nodded to me, then Jamie.

"I thank thee for the hospitality of thy welcome, Mrs. Fraser. And thee also, Mr. Fraser. I have come indeed to ask a service of thee, if I may."

"Ye may ask, of course," Jamie said courteously. He took a bite of bread and butter, raising his eyebrows in question.

"Will thee buy my horse?"

Jamie's eyebrows stayed raised. He chewed slowly, considering, then swallowed.

"Why?"

Why, indeed. It would have been a great deal easier for Husband to sell a horse in Salem or High Point, if he didn't want to ride as far as Cross Creek. No one in his right mind would venture to a remote place like the Ridge, simply to sell a horse. I set Adso on the floor and sat down beside Jamie, waiting for the answer.

Husband gave him a look, clear and direct for all its bloodshot quality.

"Thee is appointed a colonel of militia, I'm told."

"For my sins," Jamie said, bread poised in the air. "Do ye suppose the Governor has given me money to provide mounts for my regiment?" He took a bite, half-smiling.

The corner of Husband's mouth lifted briefly in acknowledgment of the joke. A colonel of militia supplied his regiment himself, counting upon eventual reimbursement from the Assembly; one reason why only men of property were so appointed—and a major reason why the appointment was not considered an unalloyed honor.

"If he had, I should be pleased to take some of it." At Jamie's gesture of invitation, Husband reached out and selected another slice of bread and butter, which he munched gravely, looking at Jamie under thick salt-and-pepper brows. Finally, he shook his head.

"Nay, friend James. I must sell my stock to pay the fines levied upon me by the Court. If I do not sell what I can, it may be seized. And if I will not, then I have no choice save to quit the colony and remove my family elsewhere—and if I remove, then I must dispose of what I cannot take—for what price I may get."

A small line formed between Jamie's brows.

"Aye, I see," he said slowly. "I would help ye, Hermon, in any way I might. Ye ken that, I hope. But I have scarce two shillings in cash money—not even proclamation money, let alone sterling. If there is anything I have that would be of use to ye, though . . ."

Husband smiled slightly, his harsh features softening.

"Aye, friend James. Thy friendship and thy honor are of great use to me, indeed. For the rest . . ." He sat back from the table, groping in the small shoulder bag he had set down beside him. He came up with a thin letter, bearing a red wax seal. I recognized the seal, and my chest tightened.

"I met the messenger at Pumpkin Town," Husband said, watching as Jamie took the letter and put his thumb beneath the flap. "I offered to carry the letter to thee, as I was bound here in any case."

Jamie's brows lifted, but his attention was focused on the sheet of paper in his hand. I came close, to see over his shoulder.

November 22, 1770

Colonel James Fraser

Whereas I am informed that those who stile themselves Regulators have gathered together in some force near Salisbury, I have sent word to General Waddell to proceed thither at once with the militia troops at his disposal in hopes of dispersing this unlawful assemblage. You are requested and commanded to gather such men as you judge fit to serve in a Regiment of Militia, and proceed with them to Salisbury with as much despatch as may be managed so as to join the General's troops on or before 15 December, at which point he will march upon Salisbury. So far as possible, bring with you flour and other provision sufficient to supply your men for a space of two weeks.

Your ob't. servant,
William Tryon

The room was quiet, save for the soft rumbling of the cauldron over the coals in the hearth. Outside, I could hear the women talking in short bursts, interspersed with grunts of effort, and the smell of lye soap drifted through the open window, mingling with the scents of stew and rising bread.

Jamie looked up at Husband.

"Ye ken what this says?"

The Quaker nodded, the lines of his face sagging in sudden fatigue.

"The messenger told me. The Governor has no wish to keep his intent secret, after all."

Jamie gave a small grunt of agreement, and glanced at me. No, the Governor wouldn't want to keep it secret. So far as

Tryon was concerned, the more people who knew that Waddell was heading for Salisbury with a large militia troop, the better. Hence also the setting of a specific date. Any wise soldier would prefer to intimidate an enemy rather than fight him—and given that Tryon had no official troops, discretion was certainly the better part of valor.

"What about the Regulators?" I asked Husband. "What are they planning to do?"

He looked mildly startled.

"Do?"

"If your people are assembling, it is presumably to some purpose," Jamie pointed out, a slightly sardonic tone to his voice. Husband heard it, but didn't take exception.

"Certainly there is purpose," he said, drawing himself up with some dignity. "Though thee is mistaken to say these men are mine, in any way save that of brethren, as are all men. But as to purpose, it is only to protest the abuses of power as are all too common these days—the imposition of illegal taxes, the unwarranted seizure of—"

Jamie made an impatient gesture, cutting him off.

"Aye, Hermon, I've heard it. Worse, I've read your writings about it. And if that is the Regulators' purpose, what is yours?"

The Quaker stared at him, thick brows raised and mouth half open in question.

"Tryon has no wish to keep his intentions secret," Jamie elaborated, "but you might. It doesna serve the Regulators' interest that those intentions be carried out, after all." He stared at Husband, rubbing a finger slowly up and down the long, straight bridge of his nose.

Husband raised a hand and scratched at his chin.

"Thee mean why did I bring that"—he nodded toward the letter, which lay open on the table—"when I might have suppressed it?"

Jamie nodded patiently.

"I do."

Husband heaved a deep sigh, and stretched himself, joints cracking audibly. Small white puffs of dust rose from his coat, dissipating like smoke. He settled back into himself then, blinking and looking more comfortable.

"Putting aside any consideration of the honesty of such conduct, friend James . . . I did say that it was thy friendship that would be of most use to me."

"So ye did." The hint of a smile touched the corner of Jamie's mouth.

"Say for the sake of argument that General Waddell does march upon a group of Regulators," Husband suggested. "Is it to the benefit of the Regulators to face men who do not know them, and are inimical to them—or to face neighbors, who know them and are perhaps in some sympathy with their cause?"

"Better the Devil ye ken than the Devil ye don't, eh?" Jamie suggested. "And I'm the Devil ye ken. I see."

A slow smile blossomed on Husband's face, matching the one on Jamie's.

"One of them, friend James. I have been a-horse these ten days past, selling my stock and visiting in one house and another, across the western part of the colony. The Regulation makes no threat, seeks no destruction of property; we wish only that our complaints be heard, and addressed; it is to draw attention to the widespread nature and the justness of these complaints that those most offended are assembling at Salisbury. But I cannot well expect sympathy from those who lack information of the offense, after all."

The smile faded from Jamie's face.

"Ye may have my sympathy, Hermon, and welcome. But if it comes to it . . . I am Colonel of militia. I will have a duty to be carried out, whether that duty is to my liking or no."

Husband flapped a hand, dismissing this.

"I would not ask thee to forsake duty—if it comes. I pray it does not." He leaned forward a little, across the table. "I would ask something of thee, though. My wife, my children . . . if I must leave hurriedly . . ."

"Send them here. They will be safe."

Husband sat back then, shoulders slumping. He closed his eyes and breathed once, deeply, then opened them and set his hands on the table, as though to rise.

"I thank thee. As to the mare—keep her. If my family should have need of her, someone will come. If not—I should greatly prefer that thee have the use of her, rather than some corrupt sheriff."

I felt Jamie move, wanting to protest, and laid a hand on his leg to stop him. Hermon Husband needed reassurance, much more than he needed a horse he could not keep.

"We'll take good care of her," I said, smiling into his eyes. "And of your family, if the need comes. Tell me, what is her name?"

"The mare?" Hermon rose to his feet, and a sudden smile split his face, lightening it amazingly. "Her name is Jerusha, but my wife calls her Mistress Piggy; I am afraid she does possess a great appetite," he added apologetically to Jamie, who had stiffened perceptibly at the word "pig."

"No matter," Jamie said, dismissing pigs from his mind with an obvious effort. He rose, glancing at the window, where the rays of the afternoon sun were turning the polished pinewood of the sills and floors to molten gold. "It grows late, Hermon. Will ye not sup with us, and stop the night?"

Husband shook his head, and stooped to retrieve his shoulder bag.

"Nay, friend James, I thank thee. I have many places still to go."

I insisted that he wait, though, while I made up a parcel of food for him, and he went with Jamie to saddle his mule while I did so. I heard them talking quietly together as they came back from the paddock, voices so low-pitched that I couldn't make out the words. As I came out onto the back porch with the package of sandwiches and beer, though, I heard Jamie say to him, with a sort of urgency, "Are ye sure, Hermon, that what ye do is wise—or necessary?"

Husband didn't answer immediately, but took the parcel from me with a nod of thanks. Then he turned to Jamie, the mule's bridle in his other hand.

"I am minded," he said, glancing from Jamie to me, "of James Nayler. Thee will have heard of him?"

Jamie looked as blank as I did, and Hermon smiled in his beard.

"He was an early member of the Society of Friends, one of those who joined George Fox, who began the Society in

England. James Nayler was a man of forceful conviction, though he was . . . individual in his expression of it. Upon one famous occasion, he walked naked through the snow, whilst shouting doom to the city of Bristol. George Fox inquired of him then, 'Is thee *sure* the Lord told thee to do this?' "

The smile widened, and he put his hat carefully back on his head.

"He said that he was. And so am I, friend James. God keep thee and thy family."

20

SHOOTING LESSONS

BRIANNA GLANCED BACK over her shoulder, feeling guilty. The house below had disappeared beneath a yellow sea of chestnut leaves, but the cries of her child still rang in her ears.

Roger saw her look back down the mountainside, and frowned a little, though his voice was light when he spoke.

"He'll be fine, hen. You know your mother and Lizzie will take good care of him."

"Lizzie will spoil him rotten," she agreed, but with a queer tug at her heart at the admission. She could easily see Lizzie carrying Jemmy to and fro all day, playing with him, making faces at him, feeding him rice pudding with molasses . . . Jemmy would love the attention, once he got over the distress of her leaving. She felt a sudden surge of territorial feeling regarding Jemmy's small pink toes; she hated the very idea of Lizzie playing Ten Wee Piggies with him.

She hated leaving him, period. His shrieks of panic as she pried his grip from her shirt and handed him over to her mother echoed in her mind, magnified by imagination, and his tearstained look of outraged betrayal lingered in her mind.

At the same time, her need to escape was urgent. She couldn't wait to peel Jem's sticky, clutching hands off her skin and speed away into the morning, free as one of the homing geese that honked their way south through the mountain passes.

She supposed, reluctantly, that she wouldn't feel nearly so guilty about leaving Jemmy, had she not secretly been so eager to do it.

"I'm sure he'll be fine," she reassured herself, more than Roger. "It's just . . . I've never really left him for very long before."

"Mmphm." Roger made a noncommittal noise that might have been interpreted as sympathy. His expression, however, made it clear that he personally thought it well past time that she *had* left the baby.

A momentary spurt of anger warmed her face, but she bit her tongue. He hadn't said anything, after all—had clearly made an effort not to say anything, in fact. She could make an effort, too—and she supposed that it was perhaps not fair to quarrel with someone on the basis of what you thought they were thinking.

She choked off the acrimonious remark she'd had in mind, and instead smiled at him.

"Nice day, isn't it?"

The wary look faded from his face, and he smiled, too, his eyes warming to a green as deep and fresh as the moss that lay in thick beds at the shaded feet of the trees they passed.

"Great day," he said. "Feels good to be out of the house, aye?"

She shot a quick look at him, but it seemed to be a simple statement of fact, with no ulterior motives behind it.

She didn't answer, but nodded in agreement, lifting her face to the errant breeze that wandered through the spruce and fir around them. A swirl of rusty aspen leaves blew down, clinging momentarily to the homespun of their breeches and the light wool of their stockings.

"Wait a minute."

On impulse, she stopped and pulled off her leather buskins and stockings, pushing them carelessly into the rucksack on her shoulder. She stood still, eyes closed in ecstasy, wiggling long bare toes in a patch of damp moss.

"Oh, Roger, try it! This is wonderful!"

He lifted one eyebrow, but obligingly set down the gun—he had taken it, when they left the house, and she had let him, despite a proprietorial urge to carry it herself—undid his own footgear, and cautiously slid one long-boned foot into the moss beside hers. His eyes closed involuntarily, and his mouth rounded into a soundless "ooh."

Moved by impulse, she leaned over and kissed him. His eyes flew open in startlement, but he had fast reflexes. He wrapped a long arm around her waist and kissed her back, thoroughly. It was an unusually warm day for late autumn, and he wore no coat, only a hunting shirt. His chest felt startlingly immediate through the woolen cloth of his shirt; she could feel the tiny bump of his nipple rising under the palm of her hand.

God knew what might have happened next, but the wind changed. A faint cry drifted up from the sea of tossing yellow below. It might have been a baby's cry, or perhaps only a distant crow, but her head swiveled toward it, like a compass needle pointing to true north.

It broke the mood, and he let go, stepping back.

"D'ye want to go back?" he asked, sounding resigned.

She pressed her lips together and shook her head.

"No. Let's get a little farther away from the house, though. We don't want to bother them with the noise. Of—of shooting, I mean."

He grinned, and she felt the blood rise hot in her face. No, she couldn't pretend she hadn't realized there was more than one motive for this private expedition.

"No, not that, either," he said. He stooped for his shoes and stockings. "Come on, then."

She declined to put on her own footwear, but took the opportunity to reappropriate the gun. It wasn't that she didn't trust him with it, though he admitted he hadn't fired such a gun before. She just liked the feel of it, and felt secure with its weight balanced on her shoulder, even unloaded. A Land pattern musket, it was more than five feet long, and weighed a good ten pounds or so, but the butt of the polished walnut stock fitted snugly into her hand and the weight of the steel barrel felt right, laid in the hollow of her shoulder, muzzle to the sky.

"You're going to go barefoot?" Roger cast a quizzical glance at her feet, then ahead, up the mountainside, where a faint path wove through blackberry brambles and fallen branches.

"Just for a while," she assured him. "I used to go barefoot all the time when I was little. Daddy—Frank—took us to the mountains every summer, to the White Mountains or the Adirondacks. After a week, the bottoms of my feet were like leather; I could have walked on hot coals and not felt a thing."

"Aye, I did, too," he said, smiling, and tucked his shoes away as well. "Granted," he said, with a nod toward the faint path that wove its way through brush and half-buried granite outcrops, "the walking along the riverbank of the Ness or the shingle by the Firth was a bit easier going than this, stones notwithstanding."

"That's a point," she said, frowning slightly at his feet. "Have you had a tetanus shot recently? In case you step on something sharp and get punctured?"

He was already climbing ahead of her, choosing his footing cautiously.

"I had injections for everything one could possibly have injections for, before I came through the stones," he assured her, over one shoulder. "Typhoid, cholera, dengue fever, the lot. I'm sure tetanus was in there."

"Dengue fever? I thought I'd had shots for everything, too, but not that one." Digging her toes into the cool mats of dead grass, she took a few long strides to catch him up.

"Shouldn't need it up here." The path ambled round the curve of a steep bank overgrown with yellowing pawpaw and vanished under the overhang of a clump of black-green hemlock. He held the heavy branches back for her and she ducked under them into the pungent gloom, gun held carefully crosswise.

"I wasn't sure where I might have to go, see." His voice

came from behind her, casual, damped by the darkened air under the trees. "If it was the coastal towns, or the West Indies . . . there were . . . there *are*," he corrected himself, automatically, "any number of entertaining African diseases, brought in by the slave ships. Thought I'd best be prepared."

She took advantage of the rough terrain not to answer, but was dismayed—and at the same time, rather shamefully pleased—to discover the lengths to which he'd been prepared to go in order to follow and find her.

The ground was covered with the mottled brown of shed needles, but so damp that there was neither crackle nor prick beneath her feet. It felt spongy, cool, and pleasant under her bare soles, with a give to it that made her think the mass of dead needles must be a foot thick, at least.

"Ow!" Roger, not so lucky in his passage, had set his foot on a rotten persimmon and slid, barely catching himself by grabbing hold of a holly bush, which promptly stabbed him with its prickly leaves.

"Shit," he said, sucking the wounded thumb. "Good thing about the tetanus, aye?"

She laughed in agreement, but found herself worrying as they climbed. What about Jemmy, when he began to walk, and clamber over mountains barefoot? She'd seen enough of the small MacLeods and Chisholms—to say nothing of Germain—to realize that small boys punctured, scraped, lacerated, and fractured themselves on a weekly basis, at least. She and Roger were protected against things like diphtheria and typhoid—Jemmy would have no such protection.

She swallowed, remembering the night before. That murderous horse of her father's had bitten him in the arm, and Claire had made Jamie sit down shirtless before the fire while she cleaned and dressed the bite. Jemmy had poked a curious head up from his cradle, and his grandfather, smiling, had scooped him out and taken him upon his knee.

"Gallopy trot, gallopy trot," he'd chanted, bouncing a delighted Jemmy gently up and down. " 'Tis a wicked horse that I have got!/Gallopy trot, gallopy trot/Let's send him to hell and then he'll be hot!"

It wasn't the charming scene of the two redheads giggling at each other that stuck in her mind, though; it was the firelight glowing in her son's translucent, perfect, untouched skin—and shining silver on the webbed scars across her father's back, black-red on the bloody gash in his arm. It was a dangerous time for men.

She couldn't keep Jem safe from harm; she knew that. But the thought of him—or Roger—being injured or ill made her stomach knot and cold sweat come out on the sides of her face.

"Is your thumb all right?" She turned back toward Roger, who looked surprised, having forgotten all about his thumb.

"What?" He looked at it, puzzled. "Aye, of course."

Nonetheless, she took his hand, and kissed the wounded thumb.

"You be *careful*," she said fiercely.

He laughed, and looked surprised when she glared at him.

"I will," he said, sobering a little. He nodded at the gun she carried. "Don't worry; I may not have fired one, but I know a wee bit about them. I won't blow my fingers off. Does this look all right for a bit of practice?"

They had come out into a heath bald, a high meadow thick with grass and rhododendron. There was a stand of aspen at the far side, their pale branches aflutter with a few late tatters of gold and crimson leaves, vivid against the deep blue sky. A stream gurgled downhill, somewhere out of sight, and a red-tailed hawk circled high overhead. The sun was well up now, warm on her shoulders, and there was a pleasant, grassy bank nearby.

"Just right," she said, and swung the gun down from her shoulder.

IT WAS A beautiful gun, more than five feet long, but so perfectly balanced you could rest it across your outstretched arm without a wobble—which Brianna was doing, by way of demonstration.

"See?" she said, pulling her arm in and sweeping the stock up to her shoulder in one fluid movement. "That's the balance point; you want to put your left hand right there, grab the stock by the trigger with your right, and butt it back into your shoulder. Snug it in, really solidly. There's some kick to it." She bumped the burled walnut stock gently into the socket of her buckskinned shoulder in illustration, then lowered the gun and handed it to Roger, with a somewhat more tender caution than she showed when handing him her infant child, he noted wryly. On the other hand, so far as he could tell, Jemmy was much more indestructible than the gun.

She showed him, hesitant at first, reluctant to correct him. He bit his own tongue, though, and imitated her carefully, following the smooth flow of the steps from ripping the cartridge open with his teeth to priming, loading, ramming, and checking, annoyed at his own novice awkwardness, but secretly fascinated—and more than slightly aroused—by the casual ferocity of her movements.

Her hands were nearly as large as his own, though finely boned; she handled the long gun with the familiarity other women showed with needle and broom. She wore breeks of homespun, and the long muscle of her thigh rose up tight and round against the cloth when she squatted beside him, head bent as she groped in her leather bag.

"What, you packed a lunch?" he joked. "I thought we'd just shoot something and eat it."

She ignored him. She pulled out a ragged white kerchief to use as a target, and shook it out, frowning critically. Once he had thought of her scent as jasmine and grass; now she smelled of gunpowder, leather, and sweat. He breathed it, his fingers unobtrusively stroking the wood of the gunstock.

"Ready?" she said, glancing at him with a smile.

"Oh, aye," he said.

"Check your flint and priming," she said, rising. "I'll pin up the target."

Seen from the back, her ruddy hair clubbed tightly back, and clad in a loose buckskin hunting shirt that covered her from shoulder to thigh, her resemblance to her father was intensified to a startling degree. No mistaking the two, though, he thought. Breeks or no, Jamie Fraser had never in life had an arse like *that*. He watched her walk, congratulating himself on his choice of instructor.

His father-in-law would have given him a lesson, willingly. Jamie was a fine shot, and a patient teacher; Roger had seen him taking the Chisholm boys out after supper, to practice blasting away at rocks and trees in the empty cornfield. It was one thing for Jamie to know that Roger was inexperienced with guns; it was another to suffer the humiliation of demonstrating just *how* inexperienced, under that dispassionate blue gaze.

Beyond the matter of pride, though, he had an ulterior motive in asking Brianna to come out shooting with him. Not that he thought said motive was in any way hidden; Claire had glanced from him to her daughter when he had suggested it, and looked amused in a particularly knowing way that had made Brianna frown and say, "Mother!" in an accusatory tone of voice.

Beyond the all-too-brief hours of their wedding night at the Gathering, this was the first—and only—time he'd had Brianna to himself, free from the insatiable demands of her offspring.

He caught the gleam of sun off metal as she lowered her arm. She was wearing his bracelet, he realized with a deep feeling of pleasure. He had given it to her when he'd asked her to marry him—a lifetime ago, in the freezing mists of a winter night in Inverness. It was a simple circlet of silver, engraved with a series of phrases in French. *Je t'aime*, it said: *I love you. Un peu, beaucoup, passionnément, pas du tout: A little, a lot, passionately—not at all.*

"Passionnément," he murmured, envisioning her wearing nothing *but* his bracelet and her wedding ring.

First things first, though, he told himself, and picked up a fresh cartridge. After all, they had time.

SATISFIED THAT HIS loading habits were on the way to being well established, if not yet rapid, Brianna finally allowed him to practice sighting, and at last, to shoot.

It took a dozen tries before he could hit the white square of the kerchief, but the sense of exultation he felt when a dark spot appeared suddenly near the edge of it had him reaching for a fresh cartridge before the smoke of the shot had dissipated. The sense of excited accomplishment took him through another dozen cartridges, scarcely noticing anything beyond the jerk and boom of the gun, the flash of powder, and the breathless instant of realization when he saw an occasional shot go home.

The kerchief hung in tatters by this time, and small clouds of whitish smoke floated over the meadow. The hawk had decamped at the sound of the first shot, along with all the other birds of the neighborhood, though the ringing in his ears sounded like a whole chorus of distant titmice.

He lowered the gun and looked at Brianna, grinning, whereupon she burst into laughter.

"You look like the end man in a minstrel show," she said, the end of her nose going pink with amusement. "Here, clean up a little, and we'll try shooting from farther away."

She took the gun and handed him a clean handkerchief in exchange. He wiped black soot from his face, watching as she swiftly swabbed the barrel and reloaded. She straightened, then heard something; her head rose suddenly, eyes fixing on an oak across the meadow.

Ears still ringing from the roar of the gun, Roger had heard nothing. Swinging round, though, he caught a flicker of movement; a dark gray squirrel, poised on a pine branch at least thirty feet above the ground.

Without the slightest hesitation, Brianna raised the gun to her shoulder and seemed to fire in the same motion. The branch directly under the squirrel exploded in a shower of wood chips, and the squirrel, blown off its feet, plunged to the ground, bouncing off the springy evergreen branches as it went.

Roger ran across to the foot of the tree, but there was no need to hurry; the squirrel lay dead, limp as a furry rag.

"Good shot," he said in congratulation, holding up the corpse as Brianna came to see. "But there's not a mark on him—you must have scared him to death."

Brianna gave him a level look from beneath her brows.

"If I'd meant to hit him, Roger, I'd have hit him," she said, with a slight edge of reproof. "And if I *had* hit him, you'd be holding a handful of squirrel mush. You don't aim right at something that size; you aim to hit just under them and knock them down. It's called barking," she explained, like a kindly kindergarten teacher correcting a slow pupil.

"Oh, aye?" He repressed a small sense of irritation. "Your father teach you that?"

She gave him a slightly odd look before replying.

"No, Ian did."

He made a noncommittal noise in response to that. Ian was a point of awkwardness in the family. Brianna's cousin had been well-loved, and he knew the whole family missed him. Still, they hesitated to speak of Young Ian before Roger, out of delicacy.

It hadn't exactly been Roger's *fault* that Ian Murray had remained with the Mohawk—but there was no denying that he had had a part in the matter. If he hadn't killed that Indian . . .

Not for the first time, he pushed aside the confused memories of that night in Snaketown, but felt nonetheless the physical echoes; the quicksilver rush of terror through his belly and the judder of impact through the muscles of his forearms, as he drove the broken end of a wooden pole with all his strength into a shadow that had sprung up before him out of the shrieking dark. A very solid shadow.

Brianna had crossed the meadow, and set up another target; three irregular chunks of wood set on a stump the size of a dinner table. Without comment, he wiped his sweating hands on his breeks, and concentrated on the new challenge, but Ian Murray refused to leave his mind. He'd barely seen the man, but remembered him clearly; hardly more than a youth, tall and gangly, with a homely but appealing face.

He couldn't think of Murray's face without seeing it as he last had, scabbed with a line of freshly tattooed dots that looped across the cheeks and over the bridge of his nose. His face was brown from the sun, but the skin of his freshly plucked scalp had been a fresh and startling pink, naked as a baby's bum and blotched red from the irritation of the plucking.

"What's the matter?"

Brianna's voice startled him, and the barrel jerked up as he fired, the shot going wild. Or wilder, rather. He hadn't managed to hit any of the wooden blocks in a dozen shots.

He lowered the gun and turned to her. She was frowning, but didn't look angry, only puzzled and concerned.

"What's wrong?" she asked again.

He took a deep breath and rubbed his sleeve across his face, careless of the smears of black soot.

"Your cousin," he said abruptly. "I'm sorry about him, Bree."

Her face softened, and the worried frown eased a little.

"Oh," she said. She laid a hand on his arm and drew near, so he felt the warmth of her closeness. She sighed deeply and laid her forehead against his shoulder.

"Well," she said at last, "I'm sorry, too—but it isn't any more your fault than mine or Da's—or Ian's, for that matter." She gave a small snort that might have been intended for a laugh. "If it's anyone's fault, it's Lizzie's—and nobody blames *her*."

He smiled at that, a little wryly.

"Aye, I see," he answered, and cupped a hand over the cool smoothness of her plait. "You're right. And yet—I killed a man, Bree."

She didn't startle or jerk away, but somehow went completely still. So did he; it was the last thing he'd meant to say.

"You never told me that before," she said at last, raising her head to look at him. She sounded tentative, unsure whether to pursue the matter. The breeze lifted a strand of hair across her face, but she didn't move to brush it away.

"I—well, to tell ye the truth, I've scarcely thought of it." He dropped his hand, and the stasis was broken. She shook herself a little and stood back.

"That sounds terrible, doesn't it? But—" He struggled for words. He'd not meant to say anything, but now he'd started, it seemed urgently necessary to explain, to put it into proper words.

"It was at night, during a fight in the village. I escaped—I'd a bit of broken pole in my hand, and when someone loomed up out of the darkness, I . . ."

His shoulders slumped suddenly, as he realized that there was no possible way to explain, not really. He looked down at the gun he still held.

"I didn't know I'd killed him," he said quietly, eyes on the flint. "I didn't even see his face. I still don't know who it was—though it had to be someone I knew; Snaketown was a small village, I knew all *ne rononkwe*." Why, he wondered suddenly, had he never once thought of asking who the dead man was? Plain enough; he hadn't asked because he didn't want to know.

"Ne rononkwe?" She repeated the words uncertainly.

"The men . . . the warriors . . . braves. It's what they call themselves, the Kahnyen'kehaka." The Mohawk words felt strange on his tongue; alien and familiar at once. He could see wariness on her face, and knew his speaking of it had sounded odd to her; not the way one uses a foreign term, handling it gingerly, but the way her father sometimes casually mingled Gaelic and Scots, mind seizing on the most available word in either language.

He stared down at the gun in his hand, as though he'd never seen one before. He wasn't looking at her, but felt her draw near again, still tentative, but not repulsed.

"Are you . . . sorry about it?"

"No," he said at once, and looked up at her. "I mean . . . aye, I'm sorry it happened. But sorry I did it—no." He had spoken without pausing to weigh his words, and was surprised—and relieved—to find them true. He felt regret, as he'd told her, but what guilt there was had nothing to do with the shadow's death, whoever it had been. He had been a slave in Snaketown, and had no great love for any of the Mohawk, though some were decent enough. He'd not intended killing, but had defended himself. He'd do it again, in the same circumstance.

Yet there was a small canker of guilt—the realization of just how easily he had dismissed that death. The Kahnyen'kehaka sang and told stories of their dead, and kept their memory alive around the fires of the longhouses, naming them for generations and recounting their deeds. Just as the Highlanders did. He thought suddenly of Jamie Fraser, face ablaze at the great fire of the Gathering, calling his people by name and by lineage. *Stand by my hand, Roger the singer, son of Jeremiah MacKenzie*. Perhaps Ian Murray found the Mohawk not so strange, after all.

Still, he felt obscurely as though he had deprived the unknown dead man of name, as well as life, seeking to blot him out by forgetting, to behave as though that death had never happened, only to save himself from the knowledge of it. And that, he thought, was wrong.

Her face was still, but not frozen; her eyes rested on his with something like compassion. Still, he looked away, back at the gun whose barrel he gripped. His fingers, soot-stained, had left greasy black ovals on the metal; she reached out and took it from him, rubbing the marks away with the hem of her shirt.

He let her take it, and watched, rubbing his dirty fingers against the side of his breeches.

"It's just . . . does it not seem that if ye must kill a man, it should be on purpose? Meaning it?"

She didn't answer, but her lips pursed slightly, then relaxed.

"If you shoot someone with this, Roger, it will be on purpose," she said quietly. She looked up at him, then, blue eyes intent, and he saw that what he had taken for compassion was in fact a fierce stillness, like the small blue flames in a burned-out log.

"And if you have to shoot someone, Roger, I want you to mean it."

TWO DOZEN ROUNDS later, he could hit the wooden blocks at least once in six tries. He would have kept it up, doggedly, but she could see the muscles in his forearms beginning to tremble as he lifted the gun, stilled by effort of will. He would begin to miss more often now, out of fatigue, and that would do him no good.

Or her. Her breasts were beginning to ache, engorged with milk. She'd have to do something about it soon.

"Let's go and eat," she said, smiling as she took the musket from him after the last shot. "I'm starving."

The exertion of shooting, reloading, putting up targets, had kept them both warm, but it was nearly winter, and the air was cold; much too cold, she thought regretfully, to lie naked in the dry ferns. But the sun was warm, and with forethought, she had packed two ratty quilts in her rucksack, along with the lunch.

He was quiet, but it was a comfortable quiet. She watched him cut slivers from the chunk of hard cheese, dark lashes lowered, and admired the long-limbed, competent look of him, fingers neat and quick, gentle mouth compressed slightly as he concentrated on his work, a drop of sweat rolling down the high brown curve of his cheekbone, in front of his ear.

She wasn't sure what to make of what he had told her. Still, she knew enough to realize that it was a good thing that he had told her, even though she didn't like to hear or think of his time with the Mohawk. It had been a bad time for her—alone, pregnant, doubting whether he or her parents would ever return—as well as for him. She reached to accept a bit of cheese, brushed his fingers with her own, and leaned forward, to make him kiss her.

He did, then sat back, his eyes gone soft green and clear, free of the shadow that had haunted them.

"Pizza," he said.

She blinked, then laughed. It was one of their games; taking turns to think of things they missed from the other time, the time before—or after, depending how you looked at it.

"Coke," she said promptly. "I think I could maybe do pizza—but what good is pizza without Coca-Cola?"

"Pizza with beer is perfectly fine," he assured her. "And we can have beer—not that Lizzie's homemade hell-brew is quite on a par with MacEwan's Lager, yet. But you really think you could make pizza?"

"Don't see why not." She nibbled at the cheese, frowning. "This wouldn't do"—she brandished the yellowish remnant, then popped it in her mouth—"too strong-flavored. But I think . . ." She paused to chew and swallow, then washed it down with a long drink of rough cider.

"Come to think of it, this would go pretty well with pizza." She lowered the leather bottle and licked the last sweet, semi-alcoholic drops from her lips. "But the cheese—I think maybe sheep's cheese would do. Da brought some from Salem last time he went there. I'll ask him to get some more and see how it melts."

She squinted against the bright, pale sun, calculating.

"Mama's got plenty of dried tomatoes, and tons of garlic. I know she has basil—don't know about the oregano, but I could do without that. And crust—" She waved a dismissive hand. "Flour, water, and lard, nothing to it."

He laughed, handing her a biscuit filled with ham and Mrs. Bug's piccalilli.

"How Pizza Came to the Colonies," he said, and lifted the cider bottle in brief salute. "Folk always wonder where humanity's great inventions come from; now we know!"

He spoke lightly, but there was an odd tone in his voice, and his glance held hers.

"Maybe we do know," she said softly, after a moment. "You ever think about it—why? Why we're here?"

"Of course." The green of his eyes was darker now, but still clear. "So do you, aye?"

She nodded, and took a bite of biscuit and ham, the piccalilli sweet with onion and pungent in her mouth. Of course they thought of it. She and Roger and her mother. For surely it had meaning, that passage through the stones. It must. And yet . . . her parents seldom spoke of war and battle, but from the little they said—and the much greater quantity she had read—she knew just how random and how pointless such things could sometimes be. Sometimes a shadow rises, and death lies nameless in the dark.

Roger crumbled the last of his bread between his fingers, and tossed the crumbs a few feet away. A chickadee flew down, pecked once, and was joined within seconds by a flock that swooped down out of the trees, vacuuming up the crumbs with chattering efficiency. He stretched, sighing, and lay back on the quilt.

"Well," he said, "if you ever figure it out, ye'll be sure to tell me, won't you?"

Her heartbeat was tingling in her breasts; no longer safely contained behind the rampart of her breastbone, but set loose to crackle through her flesh, small jolts of electricity tweaking her nipples. She didn't dare to think of Jem; the barest hint of him and her milk would let down in a gush.

Before she could let herself think too much about it, she pulled the hunting shirt over her head.

Roger's eyes were open, fixed on her, soft and brilliant as the moss beneath the trees. She undid the knot of the linen strip, and felt the cool touch of the wind on her bare breasts. She cupped them in her hands, feeling the heaviness rise, begin to tingle and crest.

"Come here," she said softly, eyes on his. "Hurry. I need you."

THEY LAY HALF-CLOTHED and comfortably tangled beneath the tattered quilt, sleepy and sticky with half-dried milk, the heat of their joining still warm around them.

The sun through the empty branches overhead made black ripples behind the lids of her closed eyes, as though she looked down through a dark red sea, wading in the blood-warm water, seeing black volcanic sand change and ripple round her feet.

Was he awake? She didn't turn her head or open her eyes to see, but tried to send a message to him, a slow, lazy pulse of a heartbeat, a question surging from blood to blood. *Are you there?* she asked silently. She felt the question move up through her chest and out along her arm; she imagined the pale underside of her arm and the blue vein along it, as though she might see some telltale subterranean flash as the impulse threaded through her blood and down her forearm, reached her palm, her finger, and delivered the faintest throb of its pressure against his skin.

Nothing happened at once. She could hear his breathing, slow and regular, a counterpoint to the sough of breeze through trees and grass, like surf coming in upon a sandy shore.

She imagined herself as a jellyfish, he another. She could see them clearly; two transparent bodies, lucent as the moon, veils pulsing in and out in hypnotic rhythm, borne on the tide toward one another, tendrils trailing, slowly touching . . .

His finger crossed her palm, so lightly it might have been the brush of fin or feather.

I'm here, it said. *And you?*

Her hand closed over it, and he rolled toward her.

LATE IN THE YEAR as it was, the light died early. It was still a month 'til the winter solstice, but by mid-afternoon, the sun was already brushing the slope of Black Mountain, and their shadows stretched to impossible lengths before them as they turned eastward, toward home.

She carried the gun; instruction was over for the day, and while they weren't hunting, if the opportunity of game offered, she would take it. The squirrel she had killed earlier was already cleaned and tucked in her sack, but that was barely flavoring for a vegetable stew. A few more would be nice. Or a possum, she thought dreamily.

She wasn't sure of the habits of possum, though; perhaps they hibernated over winter, and if so, they might already be gone. The bears were still active; she'd seen half-dried scat on the trail, and scratches on the bark of a pine, still oozing yellow sap. A bear was good game, but she didn't mean either to look for one, or to risk shooting at one unless it attacked them—and that wasn't likely. Leave bears alone, and they'll generally leave you alone; both her fathers had told her that, and she thought it excellent advice.

A covey of bobwhite blasted out of a nearby bush like exploding shrapnel, and she jerked, heart in her mouth.

"Those are good to eat, aren't they?" Roger nodded at the last of the disappearing gray-white blobs. He had been startled, too, but less than she had, she noticed with annoyance.

"Yeah," she said, disgruntled at being taken unawares. "But you don't shoot them with a musket, unless all you want is feathers for a pillow. You use a fowling piece, with bird shot. It's like a shotgun."

"I know," he said, shortly.

She felt disinclined to talk, jarred out of their peaceful mood. Her breasts were beginning to swell again; it was time to go home, to find Jemmy.

Her step quickened a little at the thought, even as her mind reluctantly surrendered the memory of the pungent smell of crushed dry fern, the glow of sunlight on Roger's bare brown shoulders above her, the hiss of her milk, gilding his chest in a spray of fine droplets, slick and warm and cool by turns between their writhing bodies.

She sighed deeply, and heard him laugh, low in his throat.

"Mmm?" She turned her head, and he motioned to the ground before them. They had begun to move together as they walked, neither noticing the unconscious pull of the gravitational force that bound them. Now their shadows had merged at the top, so an odd, four-legged beast paced spider-like before them, its two heads tilted toward each other.

He put an arm around her waist, and one shadow-head dipped, joining the other in a single bulbous shape.

"It's been a good day, aye?" he said softly.

"Aye, it has," she said, and smiled. She might have spoken further, but a sound came to her above the rattle of tree branches, and she pulled suddenly away.

"What—" he began, but she put a finger to her lips to shush him, beckoning as she crept toward a growth of red oak.

It was a flock of turkeys, scratching companionably in the earth beneath a large oak tree, turning up winter grubs from the mat of fallen leaves and acorns. The late sun shone low, lighting the iridescence in their breast feathers, so the birds' drab black glimmered with tiny rainbows as they moved.

She had the gun already loaded, but not primed. She groped for the powder flask at her belt and filled the pan, scarcely looking away from the birds. Roger crouched beside her, intent as a hound dog on the scent. She nudged him, and held the gun toward him in invitation, one eyebrow up. The turkeys were no more than twenty yards away, and even the smaller ones were the size of footballs.

He hesitated, but she could see the desire to try it in his eyes. She thrust the gun firmly into his hands and nodded toward a gap in the brush.

He shifted carefully, trying for a clear line of sight. She hadn't taught him to fire from a crouch as yet, and he wisely didn't try, instead standing, though it meant firing downward. He hesitated, the long barrel wavering as he shifted his aim from one bird to another, trying to choose the best shot. Her fingers curled and clenched, aching to correct his aim, to pull the trigger.

She felt him draw breath and hold it. Then three things happened, so quickly as to seem simultaneous. The gun went off with a huge *phwoom!*, a spray of dried oak leaves fountained up from the earth under the tree, and fifteen turkeys lost their minds, running like a demented football squad straight at them, gobbling hysterically.

The turkeys reached the brush, saw Roger, and took to the air like flying soccer balls, wings frantically clapping the air. Roger ducked to avoid one that soared an inch above his head, only to be struck in the chest by another. He reeled backward, and the turkey, clinging to his shirt, seized the opportunity to run nimbly up his shoulder and push off, raking the side of his neck with its claws.

The gun flew through the air. Brianna caught it, flipped a cartridge from the box on her belt, and was grimly reloading and ramming as the last turkey ran toward Roger, zigged away, saw her, zagged in the other direction, and finally zoomed between them, gobbling alarms and imprecations.

She swung around, sighted on it as it left the ground, caught the black blob outlined for a split second against the brilliant sky, and blasted it in the tail feathers. It dropped like a sack of coal, and hit the ground forty yards away with an audible thud.

She stood still for a moment, then slowly lowered the gun. Roger was staring at her, openmouthed, pressing the cloth of his shirt against the bloody scratches on his neck. She smiled at him, a little weakly, feeling her hands sweaty on the wooden stock and her heart pounding with delayed reaction.

"Holy God," Roger said, deeply impressed. "That wasn't just luck, was it?"

"Well . . . some," she said, trying for modesty. She failed, and felt a grin blossom across her face. "Maybe half."

Roger went to retrieve her prize while she cleaned the gun again, coming back with a ten-pound bird, limp-necked and leaking blood like a punctured waterskin.

"What a thing," he said. He held it at arm's length to drain, admiring the vivid reds and blues of the bare, warty head and dangling wattle. "I don't think I've ever seen one, save roasted on a platter, with chestnut dressing and roast potatoes."

He looked from the turkey to her with great respect, and nodded at the gun.

"That's great shooting, Bree."

She felt her cheeks flush with pleasure, and restrained the urge to say, "Aw, shucks, it warn't nothin'," settling instead for a simple, "Thanks."

They turned again toward home, Roger still carrying the dripping carcass, held slightly out from his body.

"You haven't been shooting all that long, either," Roger was saying, still impressed. "What's it been, six months?"

She didn't want to lower his estimation of her prowess, but laughed, shrugged, and told the truth anyway.

"More like six years. Really more like ten."

"Eh?"

"Daddy—Frank—taught me to shoot when I was eleven or twelve. He gave me a twenty-two when I was thirteen, and by the time I was fifteen, he was taking me to shoot clay pigeons at ranges, or to hunt doves and quail on weekends in the fall."

Roger glanced at her in interest.

"I thought Jamie'd taught you; I'd no idea Frank Randall was such a sportsman."

"Well," she said slowly. "I don't know that he was."

One black brow went up in inquiry.

"Oh, he knew how to shoot," she assured him. "He'd been in the Army during World War Two. But he never shot much himself; he'd just show me, and then watch. In fact, he never even owned a gun."

"That's odd."

"Isn't it?" She moved deliberately closer to him, nudging his shoulder so that their shadows merged again; now it looked like a two-headed ogre, carrying a gun over one shoulder, and a third head held bloodily in its hand. "I wondered about that," she said, with attempted casualness. "After you told me—about his letter and all that, at the Gathering."

He shot her a sharp look.

"Wondered what?"

She took a deep breath, feeling the linen strips bite into her breasts.

"I wondered why a man who didn't ride or shoot should take such pains to see that his daughter could do both those things. I mean, it wasn't like it was common for girls to do that." She tried to laugh. "Not in Boston, anyway."

There was no sound for a moment but the shuffling of their feet through dry leaves.

"Christ," Roger said softly, at last. "He looked for Jamie Fraser. He said so, in his letter."

"And he found a Jamie Fraser. He said that, too. We just don't know whether it was the right one or not." She kept her eyes on her boots, wary of snakes. There were copperheads in the wood, and timber rattlers; she saw them now and then, basking on rocks or sunny logs.

Roger took a deep breath, lifting his head.

"Aye. And so you're wondering now—what else might he have found?"

She nodded, not looking up.

"Maybe he found me," she said softly. Her throat felt tight. "Maybe he knew I'd go back, through the stones. But if he did—he didn't tell me."

He stopped walking, and put a hand on her arm to turn her toward him.

"And perhaps he didn't know that at all," he said firmly. "He may only have thought ye *might* try it, if you ever found out about Fraser. And if you did find out, and did go . . . then he wanted you to be safe. I'd say no matter what he knew, that's what he wanted; you to be safe." He smiled, a little crookedly. "Like you want me to be safe. Aye?"

She heaved a deep sigh, feeling comfort descend on her with his words. She'd never doubted that Frank Randall had loved her, all the years of her growing up. She didn't want to doubt it now.

"Aye," she said, and tilted up an inch on her toes to kiss him.

"Fine, then," he said, and gently touched her breast, where the buckskin of her shirt showed a small wet patch. "Jem'll be hungry. Come on; it's time we were home."

They turned again and went down the mountain, into the golden sea of chestnut leaves, watching their shadows go before them as they walked, embracing.

"Do you think—" she began, and hesitated. One shadow head dipped toward the other, listening.

"Do you think Ian's happy?"

"I hope so," he replied, and his arm tightened round her. "If he has a wife like mine—then I'm sure he is."

21

TWENTY-TWENTY

NOW, HOLD THIS over your left eye, and read the smallest line you can see clearly."

With a long-suffering air, Roger held the wooden spoon over his right eye and narrowed his left, concentrating on the sheet of paper I had pinned to the kitchen door. He was standing in the front hall, just inside the door, as the length of the corridor was the only stretch of floor within the house approaching twenty feet.

"Et tu Brute?" he read. He lowered the spoon and looked at me, one dark eyebrow raised. "I've never seen a literate eye chart before."

"Well, I always did think the 'f, e, 5, z, t, d' things on the regular charts rather boring," I said, unpinning the paper and flipping it over. "Other eye, please. What's the smallest line you can read easily?"

He reversed the spoon, squinted at the five lines of hand-printing—done in such even decrements of size as I could manage—and read the third one, slowly.

"*Eat no onions*. What's that from?"

"Shakespeare, of course," I said, making a note. "*Eat no*

onions nor garlic, for we are to utter sweet breath. That's the smallest you can read, is it?"

I saw Jamie's expression alter subtly. He and Brianna were standing just behind Roger, out on the porch, watching the proceedings with great interest. Brianna was leaning slightly toward Roger, a faintly anxious expression on her face, as though willing him to see the letters.

Jamie's expression, though, showed slight surprise, faint pity—and an undeniable glint of satisfaction. *He*, evidently, could read the fifth line without trouble. *I honor him*. One from *Julius Caesar: As he was valiant, I honor him; as he was ambitious, I slew him.*

He felt my gaze on him, and the expression vanished, his face instantly resuming its usual look of good-humored inscrutability. I narrowed my eyes at him, with a "You're not fooling *me*" sort of look, and he looked away, the corner of his mouth twitching slightly.

"You can't make out any of the next line?" Bree had moved close to Roger, as though drawn by osmosis. She stared intently at the paper, then at him, with an encouraging look. Obviously she could see the last two lines without difficulty, too.

"No," Roger said, rather shortly. He'd agreed to let me check his eyes at her request, but he obviously wasn't happy about it. He slapped the palm of his hand lightly with the spoon, impatient to be done with this. "Anything else?"

"Just a few small exercises," I said, as soothingly as possible. "Come in here, where the light is better." I put a hand on his arm and drew him toward my surgery, giving Jamie and Bree a hard look as I did so. "Brianna, why don't you go and lay the table for supper? We won't be long."

She hesitated for a moment, but Jamie touched her arm and said something to her in a low voice. She nodded, glanced once more at Roger with a small, anxious frown, and went. Jamie gave me an apologetic shrug, and followed her.

Roger was standing among the litter in my surgery, looking like a bear that hears barking hounds in the distance—simultaneously annoyed and wary.

"There's no need for this," he said, as I closed the door. "I see fine. I just don't shoot very well yet. There's nothing the matter with my eyes." Still, he made no move to escape, and I picked up the hint of doubt in his voice.

"Shouldn't think there is," I said lightly. "Let me have just a quick look, though . . . just curiosity on my part, really. . . ." I got him sat down, however reluctantly, and for lack of the standard small flashlight, lit a candle.

I brought it close to check the dilation of his pupils. His eyes were the most lovely color, I thought; not hazel at all, but a very clear dark green. Dark enough to look almost black in shadow, but a startling color—almost emerald—when seen directly in bright light. A disconcerting sight, to one who had known Geilie Duncan and seen her mad humor laugh out of those clear green depths. I did hope Roger hadn't inherited anything *but* the eyes from her.

He blinked once, involuntarily, long black lashes sweeping down over them, and the memory disappeared. These eyes were beautiful—but calm, and above all, sane. I smiled at him, and he smiled back in reflex, not understanding.

I passed the candle before his face, up, down, right, left, asking him to keep looking at the flame, watching the changes as his eyes moved to and fro. Since no answers were required in this exercise, he began to relax a bit, his fists gradually uncurling on his thighs.

"Very nice," I said, keeping my voice low and soothing. "Yes, that's good . . . can you look up, please? Yes, now look down, toward the corner by the window. Mm-hm, yes . . . Now, look at me again. You see my finger? Good, now close your left eye and tell me if the finger moves. Mm-hmmm . . ."

Finally, I blew out the candle, and straightened up, stretching my back with a small groan.

"So," Roger said lightly, "what's the verdict, Doctor? Shall I go and be making myself a white cane?" He waved away the drifting wisps of smoke from the blown-out candle, making a good attempt at casualness—belied only by the slight tension in his shoulders.

I laughed.

"No, you won't need a Seeing Eye dog for some time yet, nor even spectacles. Though speaking of that—you said you'd never seen a literate eye chart before. But you have seen eye charts, I take it. Did you ever wear glasses as a child?"

He frowned, casting his mind back.

"Aye, I did," he said slowly. "Or rather"—a faint grin showed on his face—"I *had* a pair of specs. Or two or three. When I was seven or eight, I think. They were a nuisance, and gave me a headache. So I was inclined to leave them on the public bus, or at school, or on the rocks by the river . . . I can't recall actually *wearing* them for more than an hour at a time, and after I'd lost the third pair, my father gave up." He shrugged.

"I've never felt as though I needed spectacles, to be honest."

"Well, you don't—now."

He caught the tone of my voice and looked down at me, puzzled.

"What?"

"You're a bit shortsighted in the left eye, but not by enough to cause you any real difficulty." I rubbed the bridge of my nose, as though feeling the pinch of spectacles myself. "Let me guess—you were good at hockey and football when you were at school, but not at tennis."

He laughed at that, eyes crinkling at the corners.

"Tennis? At an Inverness grammar school? Soft Southron sport, we'd have called it; game for poofters. But I take your point—no, you're right, I was fine at the football, but not much at rounders. Why?"

"You don't have any binocular vision," I said. "Chances are that someone noticed it when you were a child, and made an effort to correct it with prismatic lenses—but it's likely that it would have been too late by the time you were seven or eight," I added hastily, seeing his face go blank. "If that's going to work, it needs to be done very young—before the age of five."

"I don't . . . binocular vision? But doesn't everyone? . . . I mean, both my eyes do work, don't they?" He looked mildly bewildered. He looked down into the palm of his hand, closing one eye, then the other, as though some answer might be found among the lines there.

"Your eyes are fine," I assured him. "It's just that they

don't work *together*. It's really a fairly common condition—and many people who have it don't realize it. It's just that in some people, for one reason or another, the brain never learns to merge the images coming in from both eyes in order to make a three-dimensional image."

"I don't see in three dimensions?" He looked at me, now, squinting hard, as though expecting me suddenly to flatten out against the wall.

"Well, I haven't quite got a trained oculist's kit"—I waved a hand at the burned-out candle, the wooden spoon, the drawn figures, and a couple of sticks I had been using—"nor yet an oculist's training. But I'm reasonably sure, yes."

He listened quietly as I explained what I could. His vision seemed fairly normal, in terms of acuity. But since his brain was not fusing the information from his eyes, he must be estimating the distance and relative location of objects simply by unconscious comparison of their sizes, rather than by forming a real 3-D image. Which meant . . .

"You can see perfectly well for almost anything you want to do," I assured him. "And you very likely can learn to shoot all right; most of the men I see shooting close one eye when they fire, anyway. But you might have trouble hitting moving targets. You can see what you're aiming at, all right—but without binocular vision, you may not be able to tell *precisely* where it is in order to hit it."

"I see," he said. "So, if it comes to a fight, I'd best rely on straightforward bashing, is that it?"

"In my humble experience of Scottish conflicts," I said, "most fights amount to no more than bashing, anyway. You only use a gun or arrow if your goal is murder—and in that case, a blade is usually the weapon of preference. So much surer, Jamie tells me."

He gave a small grunt of amusement at that, but said nothing else. He sat quietly, considering what I'd told him, while I tidied up the disorder left by the day's surgery. I could hear thumping and clanging from the kitchen, and the pop and sizzle of fat that went with the tantalizing aroma of frying onions and bacon that floated down the corridor.

It was going to be a hasty meal; Mrs. Bug had been busy all day with the preparations for the militia expedition. Still, even Mrs. Bug's least elaborate spreads were well worth the eating.

Muffled voices came through the wall—Jemmy's sudden wail, a brief exclamation from Brianna, another from Lizzie, then Jamie's deep voice, evidently comforting the baby while Bree and Lizzie dealt with dinner.

Roger heard them, too; I saw his head turn toward the sound.

"Quite a woman," he said, with a slow smile. "She can kill it *and* cook it. Which looks like being a good thing, under the circumstances," he added ruefully. "Evidently I won't be putting much meat on the table."

"Pah," I said briskly, wishing to forestall any attempt on his part to feel sorry for himself. "I've never shot a thing in my life, and I put food on this table every day. If you really feel you must kill things, you know, there are plenty of chickens and geese and pigs. And if you can catch that damnable white sow before she undermines the foundation entirely, you'll be a local hero."

That made him smile, though with a wry twist to it nonetheless.

"I expect my self-respect will recover, with or without the pigs," he said. "The worst of it will be telling the sharpshooters"—he jerked his head toward the wall, where Brianna's voice mingled with Jamie's in muffled conversation—"what the problem is. They'll be very kind—like one is to somebody who's missing a foot."

I laughed, finished swabbing out my mortar, and reached up to put it away in the cupboard.

"Bree's only worrying about you, because of this Regulation trouble. But Jamie thinks it won't amount to anything; the chances of you needing to shoot someone are very small. Besides, birds of prey haven't got binocular vision, either," I added, as an afterthought. "Except for owls. Hawks and eagles can't have; their eyes are on either side of their heads. Just tell Bree and Jamie I said you have eyes like a hawk."

He laughed outright at that, and stood up, dusting off the skirts of his coat.

"Right, I will." He waited for me, opening the door to the

hall for me. As I reached it, though, he put a hand on my arm, stopping me.

"This binocular thing," he said, gesturing vaguely toward his eyes. "I was born with it, I suppose?"

I nodded.

"Yes, almost certainly."

He hesitated, clearly not knowing quite how to put what he wanted to say.

"Is it . . . inherited, then? My father was in the RAF; he can't have had it, surely—but my mother wore spectacles. She kept them on a chain round her neck; I remember playing with it. I might have gotten the eye thing from her, I mean."

I pursed my lips, trying to recall what—if anything—I had ever read on the subject of inherited eye disorders, but nothing concrete came to mind.

"I don't know," I said at last. "It might be. But it might not, too. I really don't know. Are you worried about Jemmy?"

"Oh." A faint look of disappointment crossed his features, though he blotted it out almost at once. He gave me an awkward smile, and opened the door, holding it for me to pass through.

"No, not worried. I was just thinking—if it was inherited, and if the little fella should have it, too . . . then I'd know."

The corridor was full of the savory scents of squirrel stew and fresh bread, and I was starving, but I stood still, staring up at him.

"I wouldn't wish it on him," Roger said hastily, seeing my expression. "Not at all! Just, if it should be that way—" He broke off and looked away, swallowing. "Look, don't tell Bree I thought of it, please."

I touched his arm lightly.

"I think she'd understand. Your wanting to know—for sure."

He glanced at the kitchen door, from which Bree's voice rose, singing "Clementine," to Jemmy's raucous pleasure.

"She might understand," he said. "That doesn't mean she wants to hear it."

22

THE FIERY CROSS

THE MEN WERE GONE. Jamie, Roger, Mr. Chisholm and his sons, the MacLeod brothers . . . they had all disappeared before daybreak, leaving no trace behind save the jumbled remains of a hasty breakfast, and a collection of muddy bootprints on the doorsill.

Jamie moved so quietly that he seldom woke me when he left our bed to dress in the dark predawn. He did usually bend to kiss me goodbye, though, murmuring a quick endearment in my ear and leaving me to carry the touch and scent of him back into dreams.

He hadn't wakened me this morning.

That job had been left to the tender offices of the junior Chisholms and MacLeods, several of whom had held a pitched battle directly under my window, just after dawn.

I had sprung into wakefulness, momentarily confused by the shouts and screams, my hands reaching automatically for sponge and oxygen, syringe and alcohol, visions of a hospital emergency room vivid around me. Then I drew breath, and smelled woodsmoke, not ethanol. I shook my head, blinking at the sight of a rumpled blue and yellow quilt, the peaceful row of clothes on their pegs, and the wash of pure, pale light streaming through half-opened shutters. Home. I was home, on the Ridge.

A door banged open below, and the racket died abruptly, succeeded by a scuffle of flight, accompanied by muffled giggling.

"Mmmphm!" said Mrs. Bug's voice, grimly satisfied at having routed the rioters. The door closed, and the clank of wood and clang of metal from below announced the commencement of the day's activities.

When I went down a few moments later, I found that good lady engaged simultaneously in toasting bread, boiling coffee, making parritch, and complaining as she tidied up the men's leavings. Not about the untidiness—what else could be expected of men?—but rather that Jamie had not waked her to provide a proper breakfast for them.

"And how's Himself to manage, then?" she demanded, brandishing the toasting-fork at me in reproach. "A fine, big man like that, and him out and doing wi' no more to line his wame than a wee sup of milk and a stale bannock?"

Casting a bleary eye over the assorted crumbs and dirty crockery, it appeared to me that Himself and his companions had probably accounted for at least two dozen corn muffins and an entire loaf of salt-rising bread, accompanied by a pound or so of fresh butter, a jar of honey, a bowl of raisins, and all of the first milking.

"I don't think he'll starve," I murmured, dabbing up a crumb with a moistened forefinger. "Is the coffee ready?"

The older Chisholm and MacLeod children had mostly been sleeping by the kitchen hearth at night, rolled in rags or blankets. They were up and out now, their coverings heaped behind the settle. As the smell of food began to permeate the house, murmurous sounds of rising began to come through the walls and down the stairs, as the women dressed and tended the babies and toddlers. Small faces began to reappear from outside, peeking hungrily round the edge of the door.

"Have ye washed your filthy paws, wee heathens?" Mrs. Bug demanded, seeing them. She waved a porridge spoon at the benches along the table. "If ye have, come in and set yourselves doon. Mind ye wipe your muddy feet!"

Within moments, the benches and stools were filled, Mrs. Chisholm, Mrs. MacLeod, and Mrs. Aberfeldy yawning and blinking among their offspring, nodding and murmuring "Good morn" to me and each other, straightening a kerchief here and a shirttail there, using a thumb wet with spittle to plaster down the spiked hair on a little boy's head or wipe a smudge from a little girl's cheek.

Faced with a dozen gaping mouths to feed, Mrs. Bug was in her element, hopping back and forth between hearth and table. Watching her bustle to and fro, I thought she must have been a chickadee in a former life.

"Did you see Jamie when he left?" I asked, as she paused momentarily to refill all the coffee cups, a large uncooked sausage in her other hand.

"No, indeed." She shook her head, neat white in its kerch. "I didna ken a thing about it. I heard my auld lad up and stirring before dawn, but I thought it was only him out to the privy, he not liking to trouble me with the noise o' the pot. He didna come back, though, and by the time I waked myself, they'd all gone off. Ah! None of that, now!"

Catching a movement from the corner of her eye, she dotted a six-year-old MacLeod smartly on the head with her sausage, causing him to snatch his fingers back from the jam jar.

"Perhaps they've gone hunting," Mrs. Aberfeldy suggested timidly, spooning porridge into the little girl she held on her knee. Barely nineteen, she seldom said much, shy of the older women.

"Better they be hunting homesteads, and timber for houses," Mrs. MacLeod said, hoisting a baby onto her shoulder and patting its back. She pushed a strand of graying hair out of her face and gave me a wry smile. "It's nay reflection upon your hospitality, Mrs. Fraser, but I'd as soon not spend the winter under your feet. Geordie! Leave your sister's plaits alone, or ye'll wish ye had!"

Not at my best so early in the day, I smiled and murmured something politely incomprehensible. I would as soon not have five or ten extra people in my house for the winter, either, but I wasn't sure it could be avoided.

The Governor's letter had been quite specific; all able-bodied men in the backcountry were to be mustered as militia troops and to report to Salisbury by mid-December. That left very little time for house-building. Still, I hoped Jamie had some plan for relieving the congestion; Adso the kitten had taken up semipermanent residence in a cupboard in my surgery, and the scene in the kitchen was quickly assuming its usual daily resemblance to one of the paintings of Hieronymus Bosch.

At least the kitchen had lost its early morning chill with so many bodies crowded into it, and was now comfortably warm and noisy. What with the mob scene, though, it was several moments before I noticed that there were four young mothers present, rather than three.

"Where did you come from?" I asked, startled at sight of my daughter, huddled frowsily under a rug in a corner of the settle.

Bree blinked sleepily and shifted Jemmy, who was nursing with single-minded concentration, oblivious of the crowd.

"The Muellers showed up in the middle of the night and pounded on our door," she said, yawning. "Eight of them. They didn't speak much English, but I *think* they said Da sent for them."

"Really?" I reached for a slice of raisin cake, narrowly beating a young Chisholm to it. "Are they still there?"

"Uh-huh. Thanks, Mama." She stretched out a hand for the bit of cake I offered her. "Yes. Da came and hauled Roger out of bed while it was still dark, but he didn't seem to think he needed the Muellers yet. When Roger left, a big old Mueller got up off the floor, said, *'Bitte, Maedle,'* and lay down next to me." A delicate pink flushed her cheeks. "So I thought maybe I'd get up and come up here."

"Oh," I said, suppressing a smile. "That would be Gerhard." Eminently practical, the old farmer would see no reason why he should lay his old bones on a hard plank floor, if there was bed space available.

"I suppose so," she said indistinctly, through a mouthful of cake. "I guess he's harmless, but even so . . ."

"Well, he'd be no danger to *you*," I agreed. Gerhard Mueller was the patriarch of a large German family who lived between the Ridge and the Moravian settlement at Salem. He was somewhere in his late seventies, but by no means harmless.

I chewed slowly, remembering how Jamie had described to me the scalps nailed to the door of Gerhard's barn.

Women's scalps, long hair dark and silken, ends lifting in the wind. *Like live things*, he'd said, his face troubled at the memory, *like birds, pinned to the wood*. And the white one Gerhard had brought to me, wrapped in linen and flecked with blood. No, not harmless. I swallowed, the cake feeling dry in my throat.

"Harmless or not, they'll be hungry," said Mrs. Chisholm practically. She bent and gathered up a corn-dolly, a soggy diaper, and a squirming toddler, contriving somehow to leave a hand free for her coffee. "Best we clear this lot awa, before the Germans smell food and come hammering at the door."

"Is there anything left to feed them?" I said, uneasily trying to remember how many hams were left in the smokeshed. After two weeks of hospitality, our stores were dwindling at an alarming rate.

"Of course there is," Mrs. Bug said briskly, slicing sausage and flipping the slices onto the sizzling griddle. "Let me just ha' done with this lot, and ye can send them along for their breakfasts. You, *a muirninn*—" She tapped a girl of eight or so on the head with her spatula. "Run ye doon the root cellar and fetch me up an apronful of potatoes. Germans like potatoes."

By the time I had finished my porridge and begun to collect up bowls to wash, Mrs. Bug, broom in hand, was sweeping children and debris out of the back door with ruthless efficiency, while issuing a stream of orders to Lizzie and Mrs. Aberfeldy—Ruth, that was her name—who seemed to have been dragooned as assistant cooks.

"Shall I help . . ." I began, rather feebly, but Mrs. Bug shook her head and made small shooing motions with the broom.

"Dinna think of it, Mrs. Fraser!" she said. "You'll have enough to do, I'm sure, and—here now, ye'll no be comin' intae my nice, clean kitchen wi' those mucky boots! Out, out and wipe them off before ye think of setting foot in here!"

Gerhard Mueller, followed by his sons and nephews, stood in the doorway, nonplussed. Mrs. Bug, undeterred either by the fact that he towered over her by more than a foot, or that he spoke no English, screwed up her face and poked fiercely at his boots with her broom.

I waved welcomingly to the Muellers, then seized the chance of escape, and fled.

SEEKING TO AVOID the crowd in the house, I washed at the well outside, then went to the sheds and occupied myself in taking inventory. The situation was not as bad as I'd feared; we had enough, with careful management, to last out the winter, though I could see that Mrs. Bug's lavish hand might have to be constrained a bit.

Besides six hams in the smokeshed, there were four sides of bacon and half another, plus a rack of dried venison and half of a relatively recent carcass. Looking up, I could see the low roof beams, black with soot and thick with clusters of smoked, dried fish, split and bound stiffly in bunches, like the petals of large ugly flowers. There were ten casks of salt fish, as well, and four of salt pork. A stone crock of lard, a smaller one of the fine leaf lard, another of headcheese . . . I had my doubts about that.

I had made it according to the instructions of one of the Mueller women, as translated by Jamie, but I had never seen headcheese myself, and was not quite sure it was meant to look like *that*. I lifted the lid and sniffed cautiously, but it smelled all right; mildly spiced with garlic and peppercorn, and no scent at all of putrefaction. Perhaps we wouldn't die of ptomaine poisoning, though I had it in mind to invite Gerhard Mueller to try it first.

"How can ye bide the auld fiend in your house?" Marsali had demanded, when Gerhard and one of his sons had ridden up to the Ridge a few months earlier. She had heard the story of the Indian women from Fergus, and viewed the Germans with horrified revulsion.

"And what would ye have me do?" Jamie had demanded in return, spoon lifted halfway from his bowl. "Kill the Muellers—all of them, for if I did for Gerhard, I'd have to do for the lot—and nail their hair to *my* barn?" His mouth quirked slightly. "I should think it would put the cow off her milk. It would put me off the milkin', to be sure."

Marsali's brow puckered, but she wasn't one to be joked out of an argument.

"Not that, maybe," she said. "But ye let them into your house, and treat them as friends!" She glanced from Jamie to me, frowning. "The women he killed—*they* were your friends, no?"

I exchanged a look with Jamie, and gave a slight shrug. He paused for a moment, gathering his thoughts, as he slowly stirred his soup. Then he laid down the spoon and looked at her.

"It was a fearful thing that Gerhard did," he said simply. "But it was a matter of vengeance to him; thinking as he did, he couldna have done otherwise. Would it make matters better for me to take vengeance on him?"

"Non," Fergus said positively. He laid a hand on Marsali's arm, putting a stop to whatever she might have said next. He grinned up at her. "Of course, Frenchmen do not believe in vengeance."

"Well, perhaps some Frenchmen," I murmured, thinking of the Comte St. Germain.

Marsali wasn't to be put off so easily, though.

"Hmph," she said. "What ye mean is, they weren't *yours*, isn't it?" Seeing Jamie's brow flick up in startlement, she pressed the point. "The women who were murdered. But if it were your family? If it had been me and Lizzie and Brianna, say?"

"That," said Jamie evenly, "is my point. It *was* Gerhard's family." He pushed back from the table and stood up, leaving half his soup unfinished. "Are ye done, Fergus?"

Fergus cocked a sleek brow at him, picked up his bowl, and drank it down, Adam's apple bobbing in his long brown throat.

"Oui," he said, wiping his mouth on his sleeve. He stood and patted Marsali on the head, then plucked a strand of her straw-pale hair free of her kerch. "Do not worry yourself, *ma douce*—even though I do not believe in vengeance, if anyone should hunt your hair, I promise I will make a tobacco pouch

of his scrotum. And your papa will tie up his stockings with the malefactor's entrails, surely."

Marsali gave a small *pffft!* of irritated amusement and slapped at his hand, and no more was said about Gerhard Mueller.

I lifted the heavy crock of headcheese and set it down by the door of the smokeshed, so as not to forget it when I went back to the house. I wondered whether Gerhard's son Frederick had come with him—likely so; the boy was less than twenty, not an age willing to be left out of anything that promised excitement. It was Frederick's young wife Petronella and her baby who had died—of measles, though Gerhard had thought the infection a deliberate curse put on his family by the Tuscarora.

Had Frederick found a new wife yet? I wondered. Very likely. Though if not . . . there were two teenaged girls among the new tenants. Perhaps Jamie's plans involved finding them fast husbands? And then there was Lizzie . . .

The corncrib was more than three-quarters full, though there were worrying quantities of mouse droppings on the ground outside. Adso was growing rapidly, but perhaps not fast enough; he was just about the size of an average rat. Flour—that was a little low, only eight sacks. There might be more at the mill, though; I must ask Jamie.

Sacks of rice and dried beans, bushels of hickory nuts, butternuts, and black walnuts. Heaps of dried squash, burlap bags of oatmeal and cornmeal, and gallon upon gallon of apple cider and cider vinegar. A crock of salted butter, another of fresh, and a basket of spherical goat cheeses, for which I had traded a bushel of blackberries and another of wild currants. The rest of the berries had been carefully dried, along with the wild grapes, or made up into jam or preserve, and were presently hidden in the pantry, safe—I hoped—from childish depredations.

The honey. I stopped, pursing my lips. I had nearly twenty gallons of purified honey, and four large stone jars of honeycomb, gleaned from my hives and waiting to be rendered and made into beeswax candles. It was all kept in the walled cave that served as stable, in order to keep safe from bears. It wasn't safe from the children who had been deputed to feed the cows and pigs in the stable, though. I hadn't seen any telltale sticky fingers or faces yet, but it might be as well to take some preventative steps.

Between meat, grain, and the small dairy, it looked as though no one would starve this winter. My concern now was the lesser but still important threat of vitamin deficiency. I glanced at the chestnut grove, its branches now completely bare. It would be a good four months before we saw much of fresh greenery, though I did have plenty of turnips and cabbage still in the ground.

The root cellar was reassuringly well-stocked, heady with the earthy smell of potatoes, the tang of onions and garlic, and the wholesome, bland scent of turnips. Two large barrels of apples stood at the back—with the prints of several sets of childish feet leading up to them, I saw.

I glanced up. Enormous clusters of wild scuppernong grapes had been hung from the rafters, drying slowly into raisins. They were still there, but the lower, more reachable bunches had been reduced to sprays of bare stems. Perhaps I needn't worry about outbreaks of scurvy, then.

I wandered back toward the house, trying to calculate how many provisions should be sent with Jamie and his militia, how much left for the consumption of the wives and children. Impossible to say; that would depend in part on how many men he raised, and on what they might bring with them. He was appointed Colonel, though; the responsibility of feeding the men of his regiment would be primarily his, with reimbursement—if it ever came—to be paid later by appropriation of the Assembly.

Not for the first time, I wished heartily that I knew more. How long might the Assembly be a functional body?

Brianna was out by the well, walking round and round it with a meditative look furrowing her brows.

"Pipe," she said, without preliminaries. "Do people make metal piping now? The Romans did, but—"

"I've seen it in Paris and Edinburgh, being used to carry rain off roofs," I offered. "So it exists. I'm not sure I've seen any in the Colonies, though. If there is any, it will be terribly expensive." Beyond the simplest of things, like horseshoes, all ironmongery had to be imported from Britain, as did all other metal goods like copper, brass, and lead.

"Hmm. At least they'll know what it is." She narrowed her eyes, calculating the slope of land between well and house, then shook her head and sighed. "I can make a pump, I think. Getting water into the house is something else." She yawned suddenly, and blinked, eyes watering slightly in the sunlight. "God, I'm so tired, I can't think. Jemmy squawked all night and just when he finally conked out, the Muellers showed up—I don't think I slept at all."

"I recall the feeling," I said, with sympathy—and grinned.

"Was I a very cranky baby?" Brianna asked, grinning back.

"Very," I assured her, turning toward the house. "And where is yours?"

"He's with—"

Brianna stopped dead, clutching my arm.

"What—" she said. "What in the name of God is *that*?"

I turned to look, and felt a spasm of shock, deep in the pit of my stomach.

"It's quite evident *what* it is," I said, walking slowly toward it. "The question is—why?"

It was a cross. Rather a big cross, made of dried pine boughs, stripped of their twigs and bound together with rope. It was planted firmly at the edge of the dooryard, near the big red spruce that guarded the house.

It stood some seven feet in height, the branches slender, but solid. It was not bulky or obtrusive—and yet its quiet presence seemed to dominate the dooryard, much as a tabernacle dominates a church. At the same time, the effect of the thing seemed neither reverent nor protective. In fact, it was bloody sinister.

"Are we having a revival meeting?" Brianna's mouth twitched, trying to make a joke of it. The cross made her as uneasy as it did me.

"Not that I've heard of." I walked slowly round it, looking up and down. Jamie had made it—I could tell that by the quality of the workmanship. The branches had been chosen for straightness and symmetry, carefully trimmed, the ends tapered. The cross piece had been neatly notched to fit the upright, the rope binding crisscrossed with a sailor's neatness.

"Maybe Da's starting his own religion." Brianna lifted a brow; she recognized the workmanship, too.

Mrs. Bug appeared suddenly round the corner of the house, a bowl of chicken feed in her hands. She stopped dead at sight of us, her mouth opening immediately. I braced myself instinctively for the onslaught, and heard Brianna snicker under her breath.

"Och, there ye are, ma'am! I was just sayin' to Lizzie as how it was a shame, a mortal shame it is, that those spawn should be riotin' upstairs and doon, and their nasty leavings scattered all about the hoose, and even in Herself's own still-room, and she said to me, did Lizzie, she said—"

"In my surgery? What? Where? What have they done?" Forgetting the cross, I was already hastening toward the house, Mrs. Bug hard on my heels, still talking.

"I did catch twa o' them wee de'ils a-playin' at bowls in there with your nice blue bottles and an apple, and be sure I boxed their ears sae hard for it I'm sure they're ringin' still, the wicked creeturs, and them a-leavin' bits of good food to rot and go bad, and—"

"My bread!" I had reached the front hall, and now flung open the door of the surgery to find everything within spick-and-span—including the countertop where I had laid out my most recent penicillin experiments. It now lay completely bare, its oaken surface scoured to rawness.

"Nasty it was," Mrs. Bug said from the hall behind me. She pressed her lips together with prim virtue. "Nasty! Covered wi' mold, just covered, all blue, and—"

I took a deep breath, hands clenched at my sides to avoid throttling her. I shut the surgery door, blotting out the sight of the empty counter, and turned to the tiny Scotswoman.

"Mrs. Bug," I said, keeping my voice level with great effort, "you know how much I appreciate your help, but I *did* ask you not to—"

The front door swung open and crashed into the wall beside me.

"Ye wretched auld besom! How dare ye to lay hands on my weans!"

I swung round to find myself nose-to-nose with Mrs. Chisholm, face flushed with fury and armed with a broom, two red-faced toddlers clinging to her skirts, their cheeks smeared with recent tears. She ignored me completely, her attention focused on Mrs. Bug, who stood in the hallway on my other side, bristling like a diminutive hedgehog.

"You and your precious weans!" Mrs. Bug cried indignantly. "Why, if ye cared a stitch for them, ye'd be raisin' them proper and teachin' them right from wrong, not leavin' them to carouse about the hoose like Barbary apes, strewin' wreck and ruin from attic to doorstep, and layin' their sticky fingers on anything as isna nailed to the floor!"

"Now, Mrs. Bug, really, I'm sure they didn't mean—" My attempt at peacemaking was drowned out by steam-whistle shrieks from all three Chisholms, Mrs. Chisholm's being by far the loudest.

"Who are you, to be callin' my bairns thieves, ye maundering auld nettercap!" The aggrieved mother waved the broom menacingly, moving from side to side as she tried to get at Mrs. Bug. I moved with her, hopping back and forth in an effort to stay between the two combatants.

"Mrs. Chisholm," I said, raising a placating hand. "Margaret. Really, I'm sure that—"

"Who am I?" Mrs. Bug seemed to expand visibly, like rising dough. "Who am I? Why, I'm a God-fearin' woman and a Christian soul! Who are *you* to be speakin' to your elders and betters in such a way, you and your evil tribe a-traipsin' the hills in rags and tatters, wi'out sae much as a pot to piss in?"

"Mrs. Bug!" I exclaimed, whirling round to her. "You mustn't—"

Mrs. Chisholm didn't bother trying to find a rejoinder to this, but instead lunged forward, broom at the ready. I flung my arms out to prevent her shoving past me; finding herself foiled in her attempt to swat Mrs. Bug, she instead began poking at her over my shoulder, jabbing wildly with the broom as she tried to skewer the older woman.

Mrs. Bug, obviously feeling herself safe behind the barricade of my person, was hopping up and down like a Ping-Pong ball, her small round face bright red with triumph and fury.

"Beggars!" she shouted, at the top of her lungs. "Tinkers! Gypsies!"

"Mrs. Chisholm! Mrs. Bug!" I pleaded, but neither paid the least attention.

"Kittock! Mislearnit pilsh!" bellowed Mrs. Chisholm, jabbing madly with her broom. The children shrieked and yowled, and Mrs. Chisholm—who was a rather buxom woman—trod heavily on my toe.

This came under the heading of more than enough, and I rounded on Mrs. Chisholm with fire in my eye. She shrank back, dropping the broom.

"Ha! Ye pert trull! You and—"

Mrs. Bug's shrill cries behind me were suddenly silenced, and I whirled round again to see Brianna, who had evidently run round the house and come in through the kitchen, holding the diminutive Mrs. Bug well off the floor, one arm round her middle, the other hand firmly pressed across her mouth. Mrs. Bug's tiny feet kicked wildly, her eyes bulging above the muffling hand. Bree rolled her eyes at me, and retreated through the kitchen door, carrying her captive.

I turned round to deal with Mrs. Chisholm, only to see the flick of her homespun gray skirt, disappearing hastily round the corner of the doorstep, a child's wail receding like a distant siren. The broom lay at my feet. I picked it up, went into the surgery, and shut the door behind me.

I closed my eyes, hands braced on the empty counter. I felt a sudden, irrational urge to hit something—and did. I slammed my fist on the counter, pounded it again and again with the meaty side of my hand, but it was built so solidly that my blows made scarcely any sound, and I stopped, panting.

What on earth was the matter with me? Annoying as Mrs. Bug's interference was, it was not critical. Neither was Mrs. Chisholm's maternal pugnacity—she and her little fiends would be gone from the house sooner or later. Sooner, I hoped.

My heart had begun to slow a little, but prickles of irritation still ran over my skin like nettle rash. I tried to shake it off, opening the big cupboard to assure myself that neither

Mrs. Bug's nor the children's depredations had harmed anything truly important.

No, it was all right. Each glass bottle had been polished to a jewellike gleam—the sunlight caught them in a blaze of blue and green and crystal—but each had been put back exactly in its place, each neatly written label turned forward. The gauzy bundles of dried herbs had been shaken free of dust, but carefully hung back on their nails.

The sight of the assembled medicines was calming. I touched a jar of anti-louse ointment, feeling a miser's sense of gratification at the number and variety of bags and jars and bottles.

Alcohol lamp, alcohol bottle, microscope, large amputation saw, jar of sutures, box of plasters, packet of cobweb—all were arrayed with military precision, drawn up in ranks like ill-assorted recruits under the eye of a drill sergeant. Mrs. Bug might have the flaws of her greatness, but I couldn't help but admit her virtue as a housekeeper.

The only thing in the cabinet that plainly hadn't been touched was a tiny leather bag, the amulet given to me by the Tuscaroran shaman Nayawenne; that lay askew in a corner by itself. Interesting that Mrs. Bug wouldn't touch that, I thought; I had never told her what it was, though it did look Indian, with the feathers—from raven and woodpecker—thrust through the knot. Less than a year in the Colonies, and less than a month in the wilderness, Mrs. Bug regarded all things Indian with acute suspicion.

The odor of lye soap hung in the air, reproachful as a housekeeper's ghost. I supposed I couldn't really blame her; moldy bread, rotted melon, and mushy apple slices might be research to me; to Mrs. Bug, they could be nothing but a calculated offense to the god of cleanliness.

I sighed and closed the cupboard, adding the faint perfume of dried lavender and the skunk scent of pennyroyal to the ghosts of lye and rotted apples. I had lost experimental preparations many times before, and this one had not been either complex or in a greatly advanced state. It would take no more than half an hour to replace it, setting out fresh bits of bread and other samples. I wouldn't do it, though; there wasn't enough time. Jamie was clearly beginning to gather his militiamen; it could be no more than a few days before they would depart for Salisbury, to report to Governor Tryon. Before *we* would depart—for I certainly meant to accompany them.

It occurred to me, quite suddenly, that there hadn't been enough time to finish the experiment when I had set it up to begin with. I had known we would leave soon; even if I got immediate good growth, I would not have had time to collect, dry, purify . . . I'd known that, consciously—and yet I had done it anyway, gone right on with my plans, pursuing my routines, as though life were still settled and predictable, as though nothing whatever might threaten the tenor of my days. As though acting might make it true.

"You really are a fool, Beauchamp," I murmured, pushing a curl of hair tiredly behind one ear. I went out, shutting the door of the surgery firmly behind me, and went to negotiate peace between Mrs. Bug and Mrs. Chisholm.

SUPERFICIALLY, peace in the house was restored, but an atmosphere of uneasiness remained. The women went about their work tense and tight-lipped; even Lizzie, the soul of patience, was heard to say "Tcha!" when one of the children spilled a pan of buttermilk across the steps.

Even outside, the air seemed to crackle, as though a lightning storm were near. As I went to and fro from sheds to house, I kept glancing over my shoulder at the sky above Roan Mountain, half-expecting to see the loom of thunderheads—and yet the sky was still the pale slate-blue of late autumn, clouded with nothing more than the wisps of mare's tails.

I found myself distracted, unable to settle to anything. I drifted from one task to another, leaving a pile of onions half-braided in the pantry, a bowl of beans half-shelled on the stoop, a pair of torn breeks lying on the settle, needle dangling from its thread. Again and again, I found myself crossing the yard, coming from nowhere in particular, bound upon no specific errand.

I glanced up each time I passed the cross, as though expecting it either to have disappeared since my last trip, or to have acquired some explanatory notice, neatly pinned to the wood. If not *Iesus Nazarenus Rex Iudaeorum*, then *something*. But no. The cross remained, two simple sticks of pinewood, bound together by a rope. Nothing more. Except, of course, that a cross is *always* something more. I just didn't know what it might be, this time.

Everyone else seemed to share my distraction. Mrs. Bug, disedified by the conflict with Mrs. Chisholm, declined to make any lunch, and retired to her room, ostensibly suffering from headache, though she refused to let me treat it. Lizzie, normally a fine hand with food, burned the stew, and billows of black smoke stained the oak beams above the hearth.

At least the Muellers were safely out of the way. They had brought a large cask of beer with them, and had retired after breakfast back to Brianna's cabin, where they appeared to be entertaining themselves very nicely.

The bread refused to rise. Jemmy had begun a new tooth, a hard one, and screamed and screamed and screamed. The incessant screeching twisted everyone's nerves to the snapping point, including mine. I should have liked to suggest that Bree take him away somewhere out of earshot, but I saw the deep smudges of fatigue under her eyes and the strain on her face, and hadn't the heart. Mrs. Chisholm, tried by the constant battles of her own offspring, had no such compunction.

"For God's sake, why do ye no tak' that bairn awa to your own cabin, lass?" she snapped. "If he mun greet so, there's no need for us all to hear it!"

Bree's eyes narrowed dangerously.

"Because," she hissed, "your two oldest sons are sitting in my cabin, drinking with the Germans. I wouldn't want to disturb them!"

Mrs. Chisholm's face went bright red. Before she could speak, I quickly stepped forward and snatched the baby away from Bree.

"I'll take him out for a bit of a walk, shall I?" I said, hoisting him onto my shoulder. "I could use some fresh air. Why don't you go up and lie down on my bed for a bit, darling?" I said to Bree. "You look just a little tired."

"Uh-huh," she said. One corner of her mouth twitched. "And the Pope's a little bit Catholic, too. Thanks, Mama." She kissed Jemmy's hot, wet cheek, and vanished toward the stairwell.

Mrs. Chisholm scowled horridly after her, but caught my eye, coughed, and called to her three-year-old twins, who were busily demolishing my sewing basket.

The cold air outside was a relief, after the hot, smoky confines of the kitchen, and Jemmy quieted a little, though he continued to squirm and whine. He rubbed his hot, damp face against my neck, and gnawed ferociously on the cloth of my shawl, fussing and drooling.

I paced slowly to and fro, patting him gently and humming "Lilibuleero" under my breath. I found the exercise soothing, in spite of Jemmy's crankiness. There was only one of him, after all, and he couldn't talk.

"You're a male, too," I said to him, pulling his woolen cap over the soft bright down that feathered his skull. "As a sex, you have your defects, but I will say that catfighting isn't one of them."

Fond as I was of individual women—Bree, Marsali, Lizzie, and even Mrs. Bug—I had to admit that taken en masse, I found men much easier to deal with. Whether this was the fault of my rather unorthodox upbringing—I had been raised largely by my Uncle Lamb and his Persian manservant, Firouz—my experiences in the War, or simply an aspect of my own unconventional personality, I found men soothingly logical and—with a few striking exceptions—pleasingly direct.

I turned to look at the house. It stood serene amid the spruce and chestnut trees, elegantly proportioned, soundly built. A face showed at one of the windows. The face stuck out its tongue and pressed flat against the pane, crossing its eyes above squashed nose and cheeks. High-pitched feminine voices and the sound of banging came to me faintly through the cold, clean air.

"Hmm," I said.

Reluctant as I was to leave home again so soon, and little as I liked the idea of Jamie being involved in armed conflicts of any kind, the thought of going off to live in the company of twenty or thirty unshaven, reeking men for a week or two had developed a certain undeniable attraction. If it meant sleeping on the ground . . .

"Into each life some rain must fall," I told Jemmy with a sigh. "But I suppose you're just learning that now, aren't you, poor thing?"

"Gnnnh!" he said, and drew himself up into a ball to escape the pain of his emergent teeth, his knees digging painfully into my side. I settled him more comfortably on my hip, and gave him an index finger to chew on. His gums were hard and knobbly; I could feel the tender spot where the new tooth was coming in, swollen and hot under the skin. A piercing shriek came from the house, followed by the sound of shouts and running feet.

"You know," I said conversationally, "I think a bit of whisky would be just the thing for that, don't you?" and withdrawing the finger, I tucked Jemmy up against my shoulder. I ducked past the cross and into the shelter of the big red spruce—just in time, as the door of the house burst open and Mrs. Bug's penetrating voice rose like a trumpet on the chilly air.

IT WAS A LONG WAY to the whisky clearing, but I didn't mind. It was blessedly quiet in the forest, and Jemmy, lulled by the movement, finally relaxed into a doze, limp and heavy as a little sandbag in my arms.

So late in the year, all the deciduous trees had lost their leaves; the trail was ankle-deep in a crackling carpet of brown and gold, and maple seeds whirled past on the wind, brushing my skirt with a whisper of wings. A raven flew past, high above. It gave an urgent, raucous cry, and the baby jerked in my arms.

"Hush," I said, hugging him close. "It's nothing, lovey; just a bird."

Still, I looked after the raven, and listened for another. They were birds of portent—or so said Highland superstition. One raven was an omen of change; two were good fortune; three were ill. I tried to dismiss such notions from my mind—but Nayawenne had told me the raven was my guide, my spirit animal—and I never saw the big, black shadows pass overhead without a certain shiver up the spine.

Jemmy stirred, gave a brief squawk, and fell back into silence. I patted him and resumed my climb, wondering as I made my way slowly up the mountain, what animal might be his guide?

The animal spirit chose you, Nayawenne told me, not the other way around. You must pay careful attention to signs and portents, and wait for your animal to manifest itself to you. Ian's animal was the wolf; Jamie's the bear—or so the Tuscarora said. I had wondered at the time what one was supposed to do if chosen by something ignominious like a shrew or a dung beetle, but was too polite to ask.

Only one raven. I could still hear it, though it was out of sight, but no echoing cry came from the firs behind me. An omen of change.

"You could have saved yourself the trouble," I said to it, under my breath so as not to wake the baby. "Hardly as though I needed telling, is it?"

I climbed slowly, listening to the sigh of the wind and the deeper sound of my own breath. At this season, change was in the air itself, the scents of ripeness and death borne on the breeze, and the breath of winter in its chill. Still, the rhythms of the turning earth brought change that was expected, ordained; body and mind met it with knowledge and—on the whole—with peace. The changes coming were of a different order, and one calculated to disturb the soul.

I glanced back at the house; from this height, I could see only the corner of the roof, and the drifting smoke from the chimney.

"What do you think?" I said softly, Jemmy's head beneath my chin, round and warm in its knitted cap. "Will it be yours? Will you live here, and your children after you?"

It would be a very different life, I thought, from the one he might have led. If Brianna had risked the stones to take him back—but she had not, and so the little boy's fate lay here. Had she thought of that? I wondered. That by staying, she chose not only for herself, but him? Chose war and ignorance, disease and danger, but had risked all that, for the sake of his father—for Roger. I was not entirely sure it had been the right choice—but it hadn't been my choice to make.

Still, I reflected, there was no way of imagining beforehand what having a child was like—no power of the mind was equal to the knowledge of just what the birth of a child could do, wresting lives and wrenching hearts.

"And a good thing, too," I said to Jemmy. "No one in their right mind would do it, otherwise."

My sense of agitation had faded by now, soothed by the wind and the peace of the leafless wood. The whisky clearing, as we called it, was hidden from the trail. Jamie had spent days searching the slopes above the Ridge, before finding a spot that met his requirements.

Or spots, rather. The malting floor was built in a small clearing at the foot of a hollow; the still was farther up the mountain in a clearing of its own, near a small spring that provided fresh, clear water. The malting floor was out of direct sight of the trail, but not difficult to get to.

"No point in hiding it," Jamie had said, explaining his choice to me, "when anyone wi' a nose could walk to it blindfolded."

True enough; even now, when there was no grain actively fermenting in the shed or toasting on the floor, a faintly fecund, smoky scent lingered in the air. When grain was "working," the musty, pungent scent of fermentation was perceptible at a distance, but when the sprouting barley was spread on the floor above a slow fire, a thin haze of smoke hung over the clearing, and the smell was strong enough to reach Fergus's cabin, when the wind was right.

No one was at the malting floor now, of course. When a new batch was working, either Marsali or Fergus would be here to tend it, but for the moment, the roofed floor lay empty, smooth boards darkened to gray by use and weather. There was a neat stack of firewood piled nearby, though, ready for use.

I went close enough to see what sort of wood it was; Fergus liked hickory, both because it split more easily, and for the sweet taste it gave the malted grain. Jamie, deeply traditional in his approach to whisky, would use nothing but oak. I touched a chunk of split wood; wide grain, light wood, thin bark. I smiled. Jamie had been here recently, then.

Normally, a small keg of whisky was kept at the malting floor, both for the sake of hospitality and caution. "If someone should come upon the lass alone there, best she have something to give them," Jamie had said. "It's known what we do there; best no one should try to make Marsali tell them where the brew is." It wasn't the best whisky—generally a very young, raw spirit—but certainly good enough either for uninvited visitors or a teething child.

"You haven't got any taste buds yet, anyway, so what's the odds?" I murmured to Jemmy, who stirred and smacked his lips in his sleep, screwing up his tiny face in a scowl.

I hunted about, but there was no sign of the small whisky keg either in its usual place behind the bags of barley or inside the pile of firewood. Perhaps taken away for refilling, perhaps stolen. No great matter, in either case.

I turned to the north, past the malting floor, took ten steps and turned right. The stone of the mountain jutted out here, a solid block of granite thrusting upward from the growth of tupelo and buttonbush. Only it wasn't solid. Two slabs of stone leaned together, the open crack below them masked by holly bushes. I pulled my shawl over Jemmy's face to protect him from the sharp-edged leaves, and squeezed carefully behind them, ducking down to go through the cleft.

The stone face fell away in a crumple of huge boulders on the far side of the cleft, with saplings and undergrowth sprouting willy-nilly in the crevices between the rocks. From below, it looked impassable, but from above, a faint trail was visible, threading down to another small clearing. Hardly a clearing; no more than a gap in the trees, where a clear spring bubbled from the rock and disappeared again into the earth. In summer, it was invisible even from above, shielded by the leafy growth of the trees around it.

Now, on the verge of winter, the white glimmer of the rock by the spring was easily visible through the leafless scrim of alder and mountain ash. Jamie had found a large, pale boulder, and rolled it to the head of the spring, where he had scratched the form of a cross upon it, and said a prayer, consecrating the spring to our use. I had thought at the time of making a joke equating whisky with holy water—thinking of Father Kenneth and the baptisms—but had on second thoughts refrained; I wasn't so sure Jamie would think it a joke.

I made my way cautiously down the slope, the faint trail leading through the boulders, and finally round an outcrop of rock, before debouching into the spring clearing. I was warm from the walking, but it was cold enough to numb my fingers where I gripped the edges of my shawl. And Jamie was standing at the edge of the spring in nothing but his shirt.

I stopped dead, hidden by a scrubby growth of evergreens.

It wasn't his state of undress that halted me, but rather something in the look of him. He looked tired, but that was only reasonable, since he had been up and gone so early.

The ragged breeks he wore for riding lay puddled on the ground nearby, his belt and its impedimenta neatly coiled beside them. My eye caught a dark blotch of color, half-hidden in the grass beyond; the blue and brown cloth of his hunting kilt. As I watched, he pulled the shirt over his head and dropped it, then knelt down naked by the spring and splashed water over his arms and face.

His clothes were mud-streaked from riding, but he wasn't filthy, by any means. A simple hand-and-face wash would have sufficed, I thought—and could have been accomplished in much greater comfort by the kitchen hearth.

He stood up, though, and taking the small bucket from the edge of the spring, scooped up cold water and poured it deliberately over himself, closing his eyes and gritting his teeth as it streamed down his chest and legs. I could see his balls draw up tight against his body, looking for shelter as the icy water sluiced through the auburn bush of his pubic hair and dripped off his cock.

"Your grandfather has lost his bloody mind," I whispered to Jemmy, who stirred and grimaced in his sleep, but took no note of ancestral idiosyncrasies.

I knew Jamie wasn't totally impervious to cold; I could see him gasp and shudder from where I stood in the shelter of the rock, and I shivered in sympathy. A Highlander born and bred, he simply didn't regard cold, hunger, or general discomfort as anything to take account of. Even so, this seemed to be taking cleanliness to an extreme.

He took a deep, gasping breath, and poured water over himself a second time. When he bent to scoop up the third bucketful, it began to dawn on me what he was doing.

A surgeon scrubs before operating for the sake of cleanliness, of course, but that isn't all there is to it. The ritual of soaping the hands, scrubbing the nails, rinsing the skin, repeated and repeated to the point of pain, is as much a mental activity as a physical one. The act of washing oneself in this obsessive way serves to focus the mind and prepare the spirit; one is washing away external preoccupation, sloughing petty distraction, just as surely as one scrubs away germs and dead skin.

I had done it often enough to recognize this particular ritual when I saw it. Jamie was not merely washing; he was cleansing himself, using the cold water not only as solvent but as mortification. He was preparing himself for something, and the notion made a small, cold trickle run down my own spine, chilly as the spring water.

Sure enough, after the third bucketful, he set it down and shook himself, droplets flying from the wet ends of his hair into the dry grass like a spatter of rain. No more than half-dry, he pulled the shirt back over his head, and turned to the west, where the sun lay low between the mountains. He stood still for a moment—very still.

The light streamed through the leafless trees, bright enough that from where I stood, I could see him now only in silhouette, light glowing through the damp linen of his shirt, the darkness of his body a shadow within. He stood with his head lifted, shoulders up, a man listening.

For what? I tried to still my own breathing, and pressed the baby's capped head gently into my shoulder, to keep him from waking. I listened, too.

I could hear the sound of the woods, a constant soft sigh of needle and branch. There was little wind, and I could hear the water of the spring nearby, a muted rush past stone and root. I heard quite clearly the beating of my own heart, and Jemmy's breath against my neck, and suddenly I felt afraid, as though the sounds were too loud, as though they might draw the attention of something dangerous to us.

I froze, not moving at all, trying not to breathe, and like a rabbit under a bush, to become part of the wood around me. Jemmy's pulse beat blue, a tender vein across his temple, and I bent my head over him, to hide it.

Jamie said something aloud in Gaelic. It sounded like a challenge—or perhaps a greeting. The words seemed vaguely familiar—but there was no one there; the clearing was empty. The air felt suddenly colder, as though the light had dimmed; a cloud crossing the face of the sun, I thought, and looked up—but there were no clouds; the sky was clear. Jemmy moved suddenly in my arms, startled, and I clutched him tighter, willing him to make no sound.

Then the air stirred, the cold faded, and my sense of apprehension passed. Jamie hadn't moved. Now the tension went out of him, and his shoulders relaxed. He moved just a little, and the setting sun lit his shirt in a nimbus of gold, and caught his hair in a blaze of sudden fire.

He took his dirk from its discarded sheath, and with no hesitation, drew the edge across the fingers of his right hand. I could see the thin dark line across his fingertips, and bit my lips. He waited a moment for the blood to well up, then shook his hand with a sudden hard flick of the wrist, so that droplets of blood flew from his fingers and struck the standing stone at the head of the pool.

He laid the dirk beneath the stone, and crossed himself with the blood-streaked fingers of his right hand. He knelt then, very slowly, and bowed his head over folded hands.

I'd seen him pray now and then, of course, but always in public, or at least with the knowledge that I was there. Now he plainly thought himself alone, and to watch him kneeling so, stained with blood and his soul given over, made me feel that I spied on an act more private than any intimacy of the body. I would have moved or spoken, and yet to interrupt seemed a sort of desecration. I kept silent, but found I was no longer a spectator; my own mind had turned to prayer unintended.

Oh, Lord, the words formed themselves in my mind,

without conscious thought, *I commend to you the soul of your servant James. Help him, please.* And dimly thought, but help him with what?

Then he crossed himself, and rose, and time started again, without my having noticed it had stopped. I was moving down the hillside toward him, grass brushing my skirt, with no memory of having taken the first step. I didn't recall his rising, but Jamie was walking toward me, not looking surprised, but his face filled with light at sight of us.

"Mo chridhe," he said softly, smiling, and bent to kiss me. His beard stubble was rough and his skin still chilled, fresh with water.

"You'd better put your trousers on," I said. "You'll freeze."

"I'll do. *Ciamar a tha thu, an gille ruaidh?*"

To my surprise, Jemmy was awake and drooling, eyes wide blue in a rose-leaf face, all hint of temper gone without a trace. He leaned, twisting to reach for Jamie, who lifted him gently from my arms and cradled him against a shoulder, pulling the woolly cap down snugly over his ears.

"We're starting a tooth," I told Jamie. "He wasn't very comfortable, so I thought perhaps a bit of whisky on his gums . . . there wasn't any in the house."

"Oh, aye. We can manage that, I think. There's a bit in my flask." Carrying the baby to the spot where his clothes lay, he bent and rummaged one-handed, coming up with the dented pewter flask he carried on his belt.

He sat on a rock, balancing Jemmy on his knee, and handed me the flask to open.

"I went to the mash house," I said, pulling the cork with a soft *pop*, "but the cask was gone."

"Aye, Fergus has it. Here, I'll do it; my hands are clean." He held out his left index finger, and I dribbled a bit of the spirit onto it.

"What's Fergus doing with it?" I asked, settling myself on the rock beside him.

"Keeping it," he said, uninformatively. He stuck the finger in Jemmy's mouth, gently rubbing at the swollen gum. "Oh, there it is. Aye, that hurts a bit, doesn't it? Ouch!" He reached down and gingerly disentangled Jemmy's fingers from their grip on the hairs of his chest.

"Speaking of that . . ." I said, and reached out to take his right hand. Shifting his other arm to keep hold of Jemmy, he let me take the hand and turn his fingers upward.

It was a very shallow cut, just across the tips of the first three fingers—the fingers with which he had crossed himself. The blood had already clotted, but I dribbled a bit more of the whisky over the cuts and cleaned the smears of blood from his palm with my handkerchief.

He let me tend him in silence, but when I finished and looked up at him, he met my eyes with a faint smile.

"It's all right, Sassenach," he said.

"Is it?" I said. I searched his face; he looked tired, but tranquil. The slight frown I had seen between his brows for the last few days was gone. Whatever he was about, he had begun it.

"Ye saw, then?" he asked quietly, reading my own face.

"Yes. Is it—it's to do with the cross in the dooryard, is it?"

"Oh, in a way, I suppose."

"What is it for?" I asked bluntly.

He pursed his lips, rubbing gently at Jemmy's sore gum. At last he said, "Ye never saw Dougal MacKenzie call the clan, did you?"

I was more than startled at this, but answered cautiously. "No. I saw Colum do it once—at the oath-taking at Leoch."

He nodded, the memory of that long-ago night of torches deep in his eyes.

"Aye," he said softly. "I mind that. Colum was chief, and the men would come when he summoned them, surely. But it was Dougal who led them to war."

He paused a moment, gathering his thoughts.

"There were raids, now and again. That was a different thing, and often no more than a fancy that took Dougal or Rupert, maybe an urge born of drink or boredom—a small band out for the fun of it, as much as for cattle or grain. But to gather the clan for war, all the fighting men—that was a rarer thing. I only saw it the once, myself, but it's no a sight ye would forget."

The cross of pinewood had been there when he woke one morning at the castle, surprising him as he crossed the courtyard. The inhabitants of Leoch were up and about their business as usual, but no one glanced at the cross or referred to it in any way. Even so, there were undercurrents of excitement running through the castle.

The men stood here and there in knots, talking in undertones, but when he joined a group, the talk shifted at once to desultory conversation.

"I was Colum's nephew, aye, but newly come to the castle, and they kent my sire and grandsire." Jamie's paternal grandfather had been Simon, Lord Lovat—chief of the Frasers of Lovat, and no great friend of the MacKenzies of Leoch.

"I couldna tell what was afoot, but something was; the hair on my arms prickled whenever I caught someone's eye." At last, he had made his way to the stable, and found Old Alec, Colum's Master of Horse. The old man had been fond of Ellen MacKenzie, and was kind to the son for his mother's sake, as well as his own.

" 'Tis the fiery cross, lad," he'd told Jamie, tossing him a currycomb and jerking his head toward the stalls. "Ye'll not ha' seen it before?"

It was auld, he'd said, one of the ways that had been followed for hundreds of years, no one quite knowing where it had started, who had done it first or why.

"When a Hielan' chief will call his men to war," the old man had said, deftly running his gnarled hand through a knotted mane, "he has a cross made, and sets it afire. It's put out at once, ken, wi' blood or wi' water—but still it's called the fiery cross, and it will be carried through the glens and corries, a sign to the men of the clan to fetch their weapons and come to the gathering place, prepared for battle."

"Aye?" Jamie had said, feeling excitement hollow his belly. "And who do we fight, then? Where do we ride?"

The old man's grizzled brow had crinkled in amused approval at that "we."

"Ye follow where your chieftain leads ye, lad. But tonight, it will be the Grants we go against."

"It was, too," Jamie said. "Though not that night. When darkness came, Dougal lit the cross and called the clan. He doused the burnin' wood wi' sheep's blood—and two men rode out of the courtyard wi' the fiery cross, to take it through the mountains. Four days later, there were three hundred men in that courtyard, armed wi' swords, pistols, and dirks—and at dawn on the fifth day, we rode to make war on the Grants."

His finger was still in the baby's mouth, his eyes distant as he remembered.

"That was the first time I used my sword against another man," he said. "I mind it well."

"I expect you do," I murmured. Jemmy was beginning to squirm and fuss again; I reached across and lifted him into my own lap to check—sure enough, his clout was wet. Luckily, I had another, tucked into my belt for convenience. I laid him out across my knee to change.

"And so this cross in our dooryard . . ." I said delicately, eyes on my work. "To do with the militia, is it?"

Jamie sighed, and I could see the shadows of memory moving behind his eyes.

"Aye," he said. "Once, I could have called, and the men would come without question—because they were mine. Men of my blood, men of my land."

His eyes were hooded, looking out over the mountainside that rose up before us. I thought he did not see the wooded heights of the Carolina wilderness, though; rather, the scoured mountains and rocky crofts of Lallybroch. I laid my free hand on his wrist; the skin was cold, but I could feel the heat of him, just below the surface, like a fever rising.

"They came for you—but you came for them, Jamie. You came for them at Culloden. You took them there—and you brought them back."

Ironic, I thought, that the men who had come then to serve at his summons were for the most part still safe at home in Scotland. No part of the Highlands had been untouched by war—but Lallybroch and its people were for the most part still whole—because of Jamie.

"Aye, that's so." He turned to look at me, and a rueful smile touched his face. His hand tightened on mine for a moment, then relaxed, and the line deepened again between his brows. He waved a hand toward the mountains around us.

"But these men—there is no debt of blood between them and me. They are not Frasers; I am not born either laird or chief to them. If they come to fight at my call, it will be of their own will."

"Well, that," I said dryly, "and Governor Tryon's."

He shook his head at that.

"Nay, not that. Will the Governor ken which men are here, or which ones come to meet his summons?" He grimaced slightly. "He kens me—and that will do nicely."

I had to admit the truth of this. Tryon would neither know nor care whom Jamie brought—only that he appeared, with a satisfactory number of men behind him, ready to do the Governor's dirty work.

I pondered that for a moment, patting Jemmy's bottom dry with the hem of my skirt. All I knew of the American Revolution were the things I had heard at second hand from Brianna's schoolbooks—and I, of all people, knew just how great the gap could be between written history and the reality.

Also, we had lived in Boston, and the schoolbooks naturally reflected local history. The general impression one got from reading about Lexington and Concord and the like was that the militia involved every able-bodied man in the community, all of whom sprang into action at the first hint of alarm, eager to perform their civic duty. Perhaps they did, perhaps not—but the Carolina backcountry wasn't Boston, not by a long chalk.

". . . ready to ride and spread the alarm," I said, half under my breath, *"to every Middlesex village and farm."*

"What?" Jamie's brows shot up. "Where's Middlesex?"

"Well, you'd think it was halfway between male and female," I said, "but it's really just the area round Boston. Though of course that's named after the one in England."

"Yes?" he said, looking bewildered. "Aye, if ye say so, Sassenach. But—"

"Militia." I lifted Jemmy, who was bucking and squirming like a landed fish, making noises of extreme protest at being forcibly diapered. He kicked me in the stomach. "Oh, give over, child, do."

Jamie reached over and took the baby under the arms, hoisting him from my lap.

"Here, I'll have him. Does he need more whisky?"

"I don't know, but at least he can't squawk if your finger's in his mouth." I relinquished Jemmy with some relief, returning to my train of thought.

"Boston's been settled for more than a hundred years, even now," I said. "It *has* villages and farms—and the farms aren't all that far from the villages. People have been living there for a long time; everyone knows each other."

Jamie was nodding patiently at each of these startling revelations, trusting that I would eventually come to some point. Which I did, only to discover that it was the same point he'd been making to me.

"So when someone musters militia there," I said, suddenly seeing what he'd been telling me all along, "they come, because they're accustomed to fighting together to defend their towns and because no man would want to be thought a coward by his neighbors. But here . . ." I bit my lip, contemplating the soaring mountains all around us.

"Aye," he said, nodding, seeing the realization dawn in my face. "It's different here."

There was no settlement large enough to be called a town within a hundred miles, save the German Lutherans at Salem. Bar that, there was nothing in the backcountry but scattered homesteads; sometimes a place where a family had settled and spread, brothers or cousins building houses within sight of one another. Small settlements and distant cabins, some hidden in the mountain hollows, screened by laurels, where the residents might not see another white face for months—or years—at a time.

The sun had sunk below the angled slope of the mountain, but the light still lingered, a brief wash of color that stained the trees and rocks gold around us and flushed the distant peaks with blue and violet. There were living creatures in that cold, brilliant landscape, I knew, habitations nearby and warm bodies stirring; but so far as the eye could see, nothing moved.

Mountain settlers would go without question to help a neighbor—because they might as easily require such help themselves at any moment. There was, after all, no one else to turn to.

But they had never fought for a common purpose, had

nothing in common to defend. And to abandon their homesteads and leave their families without defense, in order to serve the whim of a distant governor? A vague notion of duty might compel a few; a few would go from curiosity, from restlessness, or in the vague hope of gain. But most would go only if they were called by a man they respected; a man that they trusted.

I am not born either laird or chief to them, he'd said. Not born to them, no—but born to it, nonetheless. He could, if he wished, make himself chief.

"Why?" I asked softly. "Why will you do it?" The shadows were rising from the rocks, slowly drowning the light.

"Do you not see?" One eyebrow lifted as he turned his head to me. "Ye told me what would happen at Culloden—and I believed ye, Sassenach, fearful as it was. The men of Lallybroch came home safe as much because of you as because of me."

That was not entirely true; any man who had marched to Nairn with the Highland army would have known that disaster lay somewhere ahead. Still . . . I *had* been able to help in some small way, to make sure that Lallybroch was prepared, not only for the battle, but its aftermath. The small weight of guilt that I always felt when I thought of the Rising lifted slightly, easing my heart.

"Well, perhaps. But what—"

"Ye've told me what will happen here, Sassenach. You and Brianna and MacKenzie, all three. Rebellion, and war—and this time . . . victory."

Victory. I nodded numbly, remembering what I knew of wars and the cost of victory. It was, however, better than defeat.

"Well, then." He stooped to pick up his dirk, and gestured with it to the mountains around us. "I have sworn an oath to the Crown; if I break it in time of war, I am a traitor. My land is forfeit—and my life—and those who follow me will share my fate. True?"

"True." I swallowed, hugging my arms tight around me, wishing I still held Jemmy. Jamie turned to face me, his eyes hard and bright.

"But the Crown willna prevail, this time. Ye've told me. And if the King is overthrown—what then of my oath? If I have kept it, then I am traitor to the rebel cause."

"Oh," I said, rather faintly.

"Ye see? At some point, Tryon and the King will lose their power over me—but I dinna ken when that may be. At some point, the rebels will hold power—but I dinna ken when *that* may be. And in between . . ." He tilted the point of his dirk downward.

"I do see. A very tidy little cleft stick," I said, feeling somewhat hollow as I realized just how precarious our situation was.

To follow Tryon's orders now was plainly the only choice. Later, however . . . for Jamie to continue as the Governor's man into the early stages of the Revolution was to declare himself a Loyalist—which would be fatal, in the long run. In the short run, though, to break with Tryon, forswear his oath to the King, and declare for the rebels . . . that would cost him his land, and quite possibly his life.

He shrugged, with a wry twist of the mouth, and sat back a little, easing Jemmy on his lap.

"Well, it's no as though I've never found myself walking between two fires before, Sassenach. I may come out of it a bit scorched round the edges, but I dinna think I'll fry." He gave a faint snort of what might be amusement. "It's in my blood, no?"

I managed a short laugh.

"If you're thinking of your grandfather," I said, "I admit he was good at it. Caught up with him in the end, though, didn't it?"

He tilted his head from one side to the other, equivocating.

"Aye, maybe so. But do ye not think things perhaps fell out as he wished?"

The late Lord Lovat had been notorious for the deviousness of his mind, but I couldn't quite see the benefit in planning to have his head chopped off, and said so.

Jamie smiled, despite the seriousness of the discussion.

"Well, perhaps beheading wasna quite what he'd planned,

but still—ye saw what he did; he sent Young Simon to battle, and he stayed home. But which of them was it who paid the price on Tower Hill?"

I nodded slowly, beginning to see his point. Young Simon, who was in fact close to Jamie's own age, had not suffered physically for his part in the Rising, overt though it had been. He had not been imprisoned or exiled, like many of the Jacobites, and while he had lost most of his lands, he had in fact regained quite a bit of his property since, by means of repeated and tenacious lawsuits brought against the Crown.

"And Old Simon *could* have blamed his son, and Young Simon would have ended up on the scaffold—but he didn't. Well, I suppose even an old viper like that might hesitate to put his own son and heir under the ax."

Jamie nodded.

"Would ye let someone chop off your head, Sassenach, if it was a choice betwixt you and Brianna?"

"Yes," I said, without hesitation. I was reluctant to admit that Old Simon might have possessed such a virtue as family feeling, but I supposed even vipers had some concern for their children's welfare.

Jemmy had abandoned the proffered finger in favor of his grandfather's dirk, and was gnawing fiercely on the hilt. Jamie wrapped his hand around the blade, holding it safely away from the child, but made no effort to take the knife away.

"So would I," Jamie said, smiling slightly. "Though I do hope it willna come to that."

"I don't think either army was—will be—inclined to behead people," I said. That did, of course, leave a number of other unpleasant options available—but Jamie knew that as well as I did.

I had a sudden, passionate wish to urge him to throw it all up, turn away from it. Tell Tryon to stuff his land, tell the tenants they must make their own way—abandon the Ridge and flee. War was coming, but it need not engulf us; not this time. We could go south, to Florida, or to the Indies. To the west, to take refuge with the Cherokee. Or even back to Scotland. The Colonies would rise, but there were places one could run to.

He was watching my face.

"This," he said, a gesture dismissing Tryon, the militia, the Regulators, "this is a verra little thing, Sassenach, perhaps nothing in itself. But it is the beginning, I think."

The light was beginning to fail now; the shadow covered his feet and legs, but the last of the sun threw his own face into strong relief. There was a smudge of blood on his forehead, where he had touched it, crossing himself. I should have wiped it away, I thought, but made no move to do so.

"If I will save these men—if they will walk wi' me between the fires—then they must follow me without question, Sassenach. Best it begins now, while not so much is at stake."

"I know," I said, and shivered.

"Are ye cold, Sassenach? Here, take the wean and go home. I'll come in a bit, so soon as I'm dressed."

He handed me Jemmy and the dirk, since the two seemed momentarily inseparable, and rose. He picked up his kilt and shook out the tartan folds, but I didn't move. The blade of the knife was warm where I gripped it, warm from his hand.

He looked at me in question, but I shook my head.

"We'll wait for you."

He dressed quickly, but carefully. Despite my apprehensions, I had to admire the delicacy of his instincts. Not his dress kilt, the one in crimson and black, but the hunting kilt. No effort to impress the mountain men with richness; but an oddity of dress, enough to make the point to the other Highlanders that he was one of them, to draw the eye and interest of the Germans. Plaid pinned up with the running-stag brooch, his belt and scabbard, clean wool stockings. He was quiet, absorbed in what he was doing, dressing with a calm precision that was unnervingly reminiscent of the robing of a priest.

It would be tonight, then. Roger and the rest had clearly gone to summon the men who lived within a day's ride; tonight he would light his cross and call the first of his men—and seal the bargain with whisky.

"So Bree was right," I said, to break the silence in the clearing. "She said perhaps you were starting your own religion. When she saw the cross, I mean."

He glanced at me, startled. He looked in the direction where the house lay, then his mouth curled wryly.

"I suppose I am," he said. "God help me."

He took the knife gently away from Jemmy, wiped it on a fold of his plaid, and slid it away into its scabbard. He was finished.

I stood to follow him. The words I couldn't speak—wouldn't speak—were a ball of eels in my throat. Afraid one would slither free and slip out of my mouth, I said instead, "Was it God you were calling on to help you? When I saw you earlier?"

"Och, no," he said. He looked away for a second, then met my eyes with a sudden queer glance. "I was calling Dougal MacKenzie."

I felt a deep and sudden qualm go through me. Dougal was long dead; he had died in Jamie's arms on the eve of Culloden—died with Jamie's dirk in his throat. I swallowed, and my eyes flicked involuntarily to the knife at his belt.

"I made my peace wi' Dougal long ago," he said softly, seeing the direction of my glance. He touched the hilt of the knife, with its knurl of gold, that had once been Hector Cameron's. "He was a chieftain, Dougal. He will know that I did then as I must—for my men, for you—and that I will do it now again."

I realized now what it was he had said, standing tall, facing the west—the direction to which the souls of the dead fly home. It had been neither prayer nor plea. I knew the words—though it was many years since I had heard them. He had shouted *"Tulach Ard!"*—the war cry of clan MacKenzie.

I swallowed hard.

"And will he . . . help you, do you think?"

He nodded, serious.

"If he can," he said. "We will ha' fought together many times, Dougal and I; hand to hand—and back to back. And after all, Sassenach—blood is blood."

I nodded back, mechanically, and lifted Jemmy up against my shoulder. The sky had bleached to a winter white, and shadow filled the clearing. The stone at the head of the spring stood out, a pale and ghostly shape above black water.

"Let's go," I said. "It's nearly night."

23

THE BARD

IT WAS FULL DARK when Roger finally reached his own door, but the windows glowed welcomingly, and sparks showered from the chimney, promising warmth and food. He was tired, chilled, and very hungry, and he felt a deep and thankful appreciation for his home—substantially sharpened by the knowledge that he would leave it on the morrow.

"Brianna?" He stepped inside, squinting in the dim glow, looking for his wife.

"There you are! You're so late! Where have you been?" She popped out of the small back room, the baby balanced on her hip and a heap of tartan cloth clutched to her chest. She leaned over it to kiss him briefly, leaving him with a tantalizing taste of plum jam.

"I've been riding up hill and down dale for the last ten hours," he said, taking the cloth from her and tossing it onto the bed. "Looking for a mythical family of Dutchmen. Come here and kiss me properly, aye?"

She obligingly wrapped her free arm round his waist and gave him a lingering, plum-scented kiss that made him think that hungry as he was, dinner could perhaps wait for a bit. The baby, however, had other ideas, and set up a loud wail that made Brianna hastily detach herself, grimacing at the racket.

"Still teething?" Roger said, observing his offspring's red and swollen countenance, covered with a shiny coating of snot, saliva, and tears.

"How did you guess?" she said caustically. "Here, can

you take him, just for a minute?" She thrust Jemmy, writhing, into his father's arms, and tugged at her bodice, the green linen damply creased and stained with pale splotches of spit-up milk. One of her breasts bobbed into view, and she reached out for Jemmy, sitting down with him in the nursing chair by the fire.

"He's been fussing all day," she said, shaking her head as the baby squirmed and whined, batting at the proffered nourishment with a fretful hand. "He won't nurse for more than a few minutes, and when he does, he spits it up again. He whines when you pick him up, but he screams if you set him down." She shoved a hand tiredly through her hair. "I feel like I've been wrestling alligators all day."

"Oh, mm. That's too bad." Roger rubbed his aching lower back, trying not to be ostentatious about it. He pointed toward the bed with his chin. "Ah . . . what's the tartan for?"

"Oh, I forgot—that's yours." Attention momentarily distracted from the struggling child, she glanced up at Roger, taking in for the first time his disheveled appearance. "Da brought it down for you to wear tonight. You have a big smudge of mud on your face, by the way—did you fall off?"

"Several times." He moved to the washstand, limping only slightly. One sleeve of his coat and the knee of his breeches were plastered with mud, and he rubbed at his chest, trying to dislodge bits of dry leaf that had got down the neck of his shirt.

"Oh? That's too bad. Shh, shh, shh," she crooned to the child, rocking him to and fro. "Did you hurt yourself?"

"Ah, no. It's fine." He shed the coat and turned his back, pouring water from the pitcher into the bowl. He splashed cold water over his face, listening to Jemmy's squeals and privately calculating the odds of being able to make love to Brianna sometime before having to leave next morning. Between Jemmy's teeth and his grandfather's plans, the chances seemed slight, but hope sprang eternal.

He blotted his face with the towel, glancing covertly around in hopes of food. Both table and hearth were empty, though there was a strong vinegar scent in the air.

"Sauerkraut?" he guessed, sniffing audibly. "The Muellers?"

"They brought two big jars of it," Brianna said, gesturing toward the corner where a stone crock stood in the shadows. "That one's ours. Did you get anything to eat while you were out?"

"No." His belly rumbled loudly, evidently willing to consider cold sauerkraut, if that was all that was on offer. Presumably there would be food at the big house, though. Cheered by this thought, he pulled off his breeches and began the awkward business of pleating up the tartan cloth to make a belted plaid.

Jemmy had quieted a little, now making no more than intermittent yips of discomfort as his mother rocked him to and fro.

"What was that about mythical Dutchmen?" Brianna asked, still rocking, but now with a moment's attention to spare.

"Jamie sent me up to the northeast to look for a family of Dutchmen he'd heard had settled near Boiling Creek—to tell the men about the militia summons and have them come back with me, if they would." He frowned at the cloth laid out on the bed. He'd worn a plaid like this only twice before, and both times, had had help to put the thing on. "Is it important for me to wear this, do you think?"

Brianna snorted behind him with brief amusement.

"I think you'd better wear *something*. You can't go up to the big house in nothing but your shirt. You couldn't find the Dutchmen, then?"

"Not so much as a wooden shoe." He had found what he *thought* was Boiling Creek, and had ridden up the bank for miles, dodging—or not—overhanging branches, bramble patches, and thickets of witch hazel, but hadn't found a sign of anything larger than a fox that had slipped across his path, disappearing into the brush like a flame suddenly extinguished.

"Maybe they moved on. Went up to Virginia, or Pennsylvania." Brianna spoke with sympathy. It had been a long, exhausting day, with failure at the end of it. Not a terrible failure; Jamie had said only, "Find them if ye can"—and if he *had* found them, they might not have understood his rudimentary Dutch, gained on brief holidays to the Amsterdam of the 1960s. Or might not have come, in any case. Still, the small failure nagged at him, like a stone in his shoe.

He glanced at Brianna, who grinned widely at him in anticipation.

"All right," he said with resignation. "Laugh if ye must." Getting into a belted plaid wasn't the most dignified thing a man could do, given that the most efficient method was to lie down on the pleated fabric and roll like a sausage on a girdle. Jamie could do it standing up, but then, the man had had practice.

His struggles—rather deliberately exaggerated—were rewarded by Brianna's giggling, which in turn seemed to have a calming effect on the baby. By the time Roger made the final adjustments to his pleats and drapes, mother and child were both flushed, but happy.

Roger made a leg to them, flourishing, and Bree patted her own leg in one-handed applause.

"Terrific," she said, her eyes traveling appreciatively over him. "See Daddy? Pretty Daddy!" She turned Jemmy, who stared openmouthed at the vision of male glory before him and blossomed into a wide, slow smile, a trickle of drool hanging from the pouting curve of his lip.

Roger was still hungry, sore, and tired, but it didn't seem so important. He grinned, and held out his arms toward the baby.

"Do you need to change? If he's full and dry, I'll take him up to the house—give you a bit of time to fix up."

"You think I need fixing up, do you?" Brianna gave him an austere look down her long, straight nose. Her hair had come down in wisps and straggles, her dress looked as though she'd been sleeping in it for weeks, and there was a dark smear of jam on the upper curve of one breast.

"You look great," he said, bending and swinging Jemmy deftly up. "Hush, *a bhalaich*. You've had enough of Mummy, and she's definitely had enough of you for a bit. Come along with me."

"Don't forget your bodhran!" Bree called after him as he headed for the door. He glanced back at her, surprised.

"What?"

"Da wants you to sing. Wait, he gave me a list."

"A list? Of *what*?" To the best of Roger's knowledge, Jamie Fraser paid no attention whatever to music. It rankled him a bit, in fact, though he seldom admitted it—that his own greatest skill was one that Fraser didn't value.

"Songs, of course." She furrowed her brow, conjuring up the memorized list. "He wants you to do 'Ho Ro!' and 'Birniebouzle,' and 'The Great Silkie'—you can do other stuff in between, he said, but he wants those—and then get into the warmongering stuff. That's not what *he* called it, but you know what I mean—'Killiecrankie' and 'The Haughs of Cromdale,' and 'The Sherrifsmuir Fight.' Just the older stuff, though; he says don't do the songs from the '45, except for 'Johnnie Cope'—he wants that one for sure, but toward the end. And—"

Roger stared at her, disentangling Jemmy's foot from the folds of his plaid.

"I wouldn't have thought your father so much as knew the names of songs, let alone had preferences."

Brianna had stood up and was reaching for the long wooden pin that held her hair in place. She pulled it out and let the thick red shimmer cascade over shoulders and face. She ran both hands through the ruddy mass and pushed it back, shaking her head.

"He doesn't. Have preferences, I mean. Da's completely tone-deaf. Mama says he has a good sense of rhythm, but he can't tell one note from another."

"That's what I thought. But why—"

"He may not listen to music, Roger, but he *listens*." She glanced at him, snigging the comb through the tangles of her hair. "And he watches. He knows how people act—and how they feel—when they hear you do those songs."

"Does he?" Roger murmured. He felt an odd spark of pleasure at the thought that Fraser had indeed noticed the effect of his music, even if he didn't appreciate it personally. "So—he means me to soften them up, is that it? Get them in the mood before he goes on for his own bit?"

"That's it." She nodded, busy untying the laces of her bodice. Escaped from confinement, her breasts bobbed suddenly free, round and loose under the thin muslin shift.

Roger shifted his weight, easing the fit of his plaid. She

caught the slight movement and looked at him. Slowly, she drew her hands up, cupping her breasts and lifting them, her eyes on his and a slight smile on her lips. Just for a moment, he felt as though he had stopped breathing, though his chest continued to rise and fall.

She was the first to break the moment, dropping her hands and turning to delve into the chest where she kept her linen.

"Do you know exactly what he's up to?" she asked, her voice muffled in the depths of the chest. "Did he have that cross up when you left?"

"Aye, I know about it." Jemmy was making small huffing noises, like a toy engine struggling up a hill. Roger tucked him under one arm, his hand cradling the fat little belly. "It's a fiery cross. D'ye ken what that is?"

She emerged from the chest, a fresh shift in her hands, looking mildly disturbed.

"A fiery cross? You mean he's going to *burn* a cross in the yard?"

"Well, not burn it all the way, no." Taking down his bodhran with his free hand and flicking a finger against the drum head to check the tautness, he explained briefly the tradition of the fiery cross. "It's a rare thing," he concluded, moving the drum out of Jemmy's grasping reach. "I don't think it was ever done in the Highlands again, after the Rising. Your father told me he'd seen it once, though—it's something really special, to see it done here."

Flushed with historical enthusiasm, he didn't notice at once that Brianna seemed slightly less eager.

"Maybe so," she said uneasily. "I don't know . . . it sort of gives me the creeps."

"Eh?" Roger glanced at her in surprise. "Why?"

She shrugged, pulling the crumpled shift off over her head.

"I don't know. Maybe it's just that I *have* seen burning crosses—on the evening news on TV. You know, the KKK—or do you know? Maybe they don't—didn't—report things like that on television in Britain?"

"The Ku Klux Klan?" Roger was less interested in fanatical bigots than in the sight of Brianna's bare breasts, but made an effort to focus on the conversation. "Oh, aye, heard of them. Where d'you think they got the notion?"

"What? You mean—"

"Sure," he said cheerfully. "They got it from the Highland immigrants—from whom they were descended, by the bye. That's why they called it 'Klan,' aye? Come to think," he added, interested, "it could be this—tonight—that's the link. The occasion that brings the custom from the Old World to the New, I mean. Wouldn't that be something?"

"Something," Brianna echoed faintly. She'd pulled on a fresh shift, and now shook out a clean dress of blue linen, looking uneasy.

"Everything starts somewhere, Bree," he said, more gently. "Most often, we don't know where or how; does it matter if this time we do? And the Ku Klux Klan won't get started for a hundred years from now, at least." He hoisted Jemmy slightly, bouncing him on one hip. "It won't be us who sees it, or even wee Jeremiah here—maybe not even his son."

"Great," she said dryly, pulling on her stays and reaching for the laces. "So our *great*-grandson can end up being the Grand Dragon."

Roger laughed.

"Aye, maybe so. But for tonight, it's your father."

24

PLAYING WITH FIRE

HE WASN'T SURE what he had expected. Something like the spectacle of the great fire at the Gathering, perhaps. The preparation was the same, involving large quantities of food and drink. A huge keg of beer and a smaller one of whisky stood on planks at the edge of the dooryard, and a huge roast pig on a spit of green hickory turned slowly over a bed of coals, sending whiffs of smoke and mouthwatering aromas through the cold evening air.

He grinned at the fire-washed faces in front of him, slicked with grease and flushed with booze, and struck his bodhran. His stomach rumbled loudly, but the noise was drowned beneath the raucous chorus of "Killiecrankie."

"O, I met the De-ev-il and Dundeeee . . .
On the brae-aes o' Killiecrankie-O!"

He would have earned his own supper by the time he got it. He had been playing and singing for more than an hour, and the moon was rising over Black Mountain now. He paused under cover of the refrain, just long enough to grab the cup of ale set under his stool and wet his throat, then hit the new verse fresh and solid.

"I fought on land, I fought on sea,
At hame I fought my auntie, Oh!
I met the Devil and Dundee . . .
On the braes o' Killiecrankie-O!"

He smiled professionally as he sang, meeting an eye here, focusing on a face there, and calculated progress in the back of his mind. He'd got them going now—with a bit of help from the drink on offer, admittedly—and well stuck into what Bree had called "the warmongering stuff."

He could feel the cross standing at his back, almost hidden by the darkness. Everyone had had a chance to see it, though; he'd heard the murmurs of interest and speculation.

Jamie Fraser was away to one side, out of the ring of firelight. Roger could just make out his tall form, dark in the shadow of the big red spruce that stood near the house. Fraser had been working his way methodically through the group all evening, stopping here and there to exchange cordialities, tell a joke, pause to listen to a problem or a story. Now he stood alone, waiting. Nearly time, then—for whatever he meant to do.

Roger gave them a moment for applause and his own refreshment, then launched into "Johnnie Cope," fast, fierce, and funny.

He'd done that one at the Gathering, several times, and knew pretty much how they'd take it. A moment's pause, uncertainty, then the voices beginning to join in—by the end of the second verse, they'd be whooping and shouting ribald remarks in the background.

Some of the men here had fought at Prestonpans; if they'd been defeated at Culloden, they'd still routed Johnnie Cope's troops first, and loved the chance to relive that famous victory. And those Highlanders who hadn't fought had heard about it. The Muellers, who had likely never heard of Charles Stuart and probably understood one word in a dozen, seemed to be improvising their own sort of yodeling chorus round the back, waving their cups in sloshing salute to each verse. Aye, well, so long as they were having a good time.

The crowd was half-shouting the final chorus, nearly drowning him out.

"Hey, Johnnie Cope, are ye walking yet?
And are your drums a-beatin' yet?
If ye were walkin', I wad wait,
Tae gang tae the coals in the mornin'!"

He hit a final thump, and bowed to huge applause. That was the warm-up done; time for the main act to come onstage. Bowing and smiling, he rose from his stool and faded off, fetching up in the shadows near the hacked remains of the huge pork carcass.

Bree was there waiting for him, Jemmy wide-awake and owl-eyed in her arms. She leaned across and kissed him, handing him the kid as she did so, and taking his bodhran in exchange.

"You were great!" she said. "Hold him; I'll get you some food and beer."

Jem usually wanted to stay with his mother, but was too stupefied by the noise and the leaping flames to protest the handover. He snuggled against Roger's chest, gravely sucking his thumb.

Roger was sweating from the exertion, his heart beating fast from the adrenaline of performance, and the air away from the fire and the crowd was cold on his flushed face. The baby's swaddled weight felt good against him, warm and solid in the crook of his arm. He'd done well, and knew it. Let's hope it was what Fraser wanted.

By the time Bree reappeared with a drink and a pewter plate heaped with sliced pork, apple fritters, and roast potatoes, Jamie had come into the circle of firelight, taking Roger's place before the standing cross.

He stood tall and broad-shouldered in his best gray gentleman's coat, kilted below in soft blue tartan, his hair loose and blazing on his shoulders, with a small warrior's plait down one side, adorned with a single feather. Firelight glinted from the knurled gold hilt of his dirk and the brooch that held his looped plaid. He looked pleasant enough, but his manner overall was serious, intent. He made a good show—and knew it.

The crowd quieted within seconds, men elbowing their more garrulous neighbors to silence.

"Ye ken well enough what we're about here, aye?" he asked without preamble. He raised his hand, in which he held the Governor's crumpled summons, the red smear of its official seal visible in the leaping firelight. There was a rumble of agreement; the crowd was still cheerful, blood and whisky coursing freely through their veins.

"We are called in duty, and we come in honor to serve the cause of law—and the Governor."

Roger saw old Gerhard Mueller, leaning to one side to hear the translation that one of his sons-in-law was murmuring in his ear. He nodded his approval, and shouted, *"Ja! Lang lebe* Governor*!"* There was a ripple of laughter, and echoing shouts in English and Gaelic.

Jamie smiled, waiting for the noise to die down. As it did, he turned slowly, nodding as he looked from one face to the next, acknowledging each man. Then he turned to the side and lifted a hand to the cross that stood stark and black behind him.

"In the Highlands of Scotland, when a chieftain would set himself for war," he said, his tone casually conversational, but pitched to be heard throughout the dooryard, "he would burn the fiery cross, and send it for a sign through the lands of his clan. It was a signal to the men of his name, to gather their weapons and come to the gathering place, prepared for battle."

There was a stir in the midst of the crowd, a brief nudging and more cries of approval, though these were more subdued. A few men had seen this, or at least knew what he was talking about. The rest raised their chins and craned their necks, mouths half-open in interest.

"But this is a new land, and while we are friends"—he smiled at Gerhard Mueller—"*Ja, Freunde*, neighbors, and countrymen"—a look at the Lindsay brothers—"and we will be companions in arms, we are not clan. While I am given command, I am not your chief."

The hell you aren't, Roger thought. *Or well on your way to it, anyroad*. He took a last deep swallow of cold beer and put down cup and plate. The food could wait a bit longer. Bree had taken back the baby and had his bodhran tucked under her arm; he reached for it, and she gave him a glancing smile, but most of her attention was fixed on her father.

Jamie bent and pulled a torch from the fire, stood with it in his hand, lighting the broad planes and sharp angles of his face.

"Let God witness here our willingness, and may God strengthen our arms—" He paused, to let the Germans catch up. "But let this fiery cross stand as testament to our honor, to invoke God's protection for our families—until we come safe home again."

He turned and touched the torch to the upright of the cross, holding it until the dry bark caught and a small flame grew and glimmered from the dark wood.

Everyone stood silent, watching. There was no sound but the shift and sigh of the crowd, echoing the sough of the wind in the wilderness around them. It was no more than a tiny tongue of fire, flickering in the breeze, on the verge of going out altogether. No petrol-soaked roar, no devouring conflagration. Roger felt Brianna sigh beside him, some of the tension leaving her.

The flame steadied and caught. The edges of the jigsaw-pieces of pine bark glowed crimson, then white, and vanished into ash as the flame began to spread upward. It was big and solid, and would burn slowly, this cross, halfway through the night, lighting the dooryard as the men gathered beneath it, talking, eating, drinking, beginning the process of becoming what Jamie Fraser meant them to be: friends, neighbors, companions in arms. Under his command.

Fraser stood for a moment, watching, to be sure the flame had caught. Then he turned back to the crowd of men and dropped his torch back into the fire.

"We cannot say what may befall us. God grant us courage," he said, very simply. "God grant us wisdom. If it be His will, may He grant us peace. We ride in the morning."

He turned then and left the fire, glancing to find Roger as he did so. Roger nodded back, swallowed to clear his throat, and began to sing softly from the darkness, the opening to the song Jamie had wanted to finish the proceedings—"The Flower of Scotland."

"Oh flower of Scotland,
When will we see your like again?
That fought and died for
Your wee bit hill and glen . . ."

Not one of the songs Bree called the warmongering ones. It was a solemn song, that one, and melancholy. But not a song of grief, for all that; one of remembrance, of pride and determination. It wasn't even a legitimately ancient song—Roger knew the man who'd written it, in his own time—but Jamie had heard it, and knowing the history of Stirling and Bannockburn, strongly approved the sentiment.

"And stood against him,
Proud Edward's army,
And sent him homeward
Tae think again."

The Scottish members of the crowd let him sing alone through the verse, but voices lifted softly, then louder, in the refrain.

"And sent him ho-omeward . . .
Tae think again!"

He remembered something Bree had told him, lying in bed the night before, during the few moments when both of them were still conscious. They had been talking of the people of the times, speculating as to whether they might one day meet people like Jefferson or Washington face to face; it was an exciting—and not at all impossible—prospect. She had mentioned John Adams, quoting something she had read that he had said—or would say, rather—during the Revolution:

"I am a warrior, that my son may be a merchant—and his son may be a poet."

"The hills are bare now,
And autumn leaves lie thick and still,
O'er land that is lost now,
Which those so dearly held.

And stood against him,
Proud Edward's army,
And sent him homeward
Tae think again."

No longer Edward's army, but George's. And yet the same proud army. He caught a glimpse of Claire, standing with the other women, apart, at the very edge of the circle of light. Her face was remote and she stood very still, hair floating loose around her face, the gold eyes dark with inner shadow—fixed on Jamie, who stood quiet by her side.

The same proud army with which she had once fought; the proud army with which his father had died. He felt a catch at his throat, and forced air from down deep, singing through it fiercely. *I will be a warrior, that my son may be a merchant—and his son may be a poet.* Neither Adams nor Jefferson had fought; Jefferson had no son. He had been the poet, whose words had echoed through the years, raised armies, burned in the hearts of those who would die for them, and for the country founded on them.

Perhaps it's the hair, Roger thought ironically, seeing the gleam of ruddy light as Jamie moved, watching silently over the thing he had started. Some Viking tinge in the blood, that gave those tall fiery men the gift of rousing men to war.

"That fought and died for
Your wee bit hill and glen . . ."

So they had; so they would again. For that was what men always fought for, wasn't it? Home and family. Another glint of red hair, loose in firelight, by the bones of the pig. Bree, holding Jemmy. And if Roger found himself now bard to a displaced Highland chieftain, still he must try also to be a warrior when the time came, for the sake of his son, and those who would come after.

"And sent him homeward
Tae think again.

Tae think . . . again."

25

THE ANGELING OF MY REST

LATE AS IT WAS, we made love by unspoken consent, each wanting the refuge and reassurance of the other's flesh. Alone in our bedroom, with the shutters closed tight against the sounds of the voices in the dooryard—poor Roger was still singing, by popular demand—we could shed the urgencies and fatigues of the day—at least for a little while.

He held me tightly afterward, his face buried in my hair, clinging to me like a talisman.

"It will be all right," I said softly, and stroked his damp hair, dug my fingers deep into the place where neck and shoulder met, the muscle there hard as wood beneath the skin.

"Aye, I know." He lay still for a moment, letting me work, and the tension of his neck and shoulders gradually relaxed, his body growing heavier on mine. He felt me draw breath under him, and moved, rolling onto his side.

His stomach rumbled loudly, and we both laughed.

"No time for dinner?" I asked.

"I canna eat, just before," he answered. "It gives me cramp. And there wasna time, after. I dinna suppose there's anything edible up here?"

"No," I said regretfully. "I had a few apples, but the Chisholms got them. I'm sorry, I should have thought to bring something up for you." I did know that he seldom ate "before"—before any fight, confrontation, or other socially stressful situation, that is—but hadn't thought that he might not have a chance to eat afterward, what with everyone and his brother wanting to "have just a wee word, sir."

"It's not as though ye didna have other things to think of, Sassenach," he answered dryly. "Dinna fash yourself; I'll do 'til breakfast."

"Are you sure?" I put a foot out of bed, making to rise. "There's plenty left; or if you don't want to go down, I could go and—"

He stopped me with a hand on my arm, then dragged me firmly back under the covers, tucking me spoon-fashion into the curve of his body and wrapping an arm over me to insure that I stayed there.

"No," he said definitely. "This may be the last night I spend in a bed for some time. I mean to stay in it—with you."

"All right." I snuggled obediently under his chin, and relaxed against him, just as pleased to stay. I understood; while no one would come to fetch us unless there was some emergency, the mere sight of either of us downstairs would cause an immediate rush of people needing this or that, wanting to ask a question, offer advice, require something . . . much better to stay here, snug and peaceful with each other.

I had put out the candle, and the fire was burning low. I wondered briefly whether to get up and add more wood, but decided against it. Let it burn itself to embers if it liked; we would be gone at daybreak.

Despite my tiredness and the serious nature of the journey, I was looking forward to it. Beyond the lure of novelty and the possibility of adventure, there was the delightful prospect of escape from laundry, cookery, and female warfare. Still, Jamie was right; tonight was likely the last we would have of privacy and comfort for some little time.

I stretched, consciously enjoying the soft embrace of the feather bed, the smooth, clean sheets with their faint scent of rosemary and elderflower. Had I packed sufficient bedding?

Roger's voice reached through the shutters, still strong but beginning to sound a bit ragged with fatigue.

"The Thrush had best get to his bed," Jamie said, with mild disapproval, "if he means to bid his wife a proper farewell."

"Goodness, Bree and Jemmy went to bed hours ago!" I said.

"The wean, perhaps; the lass is still there. I heard her voice, a moment ago."

"Is she?" I strained to listen, but made out no more than a rumble of muted applause as Roger brought his song to a close. "I suppose she wants to stay with him as long as she can. Those men are going to be exhausted in the morning—to say nothing of hung over."

"So long as they can sit a horse, I dinna mind if they slip off to have a vomit in the weeds now and again," Jamie assured me.

I nestled down, covers drawn up warm around my shoulders. I could hear the deep rumble of Roger's voice, laughing, but declining firmly to sing anymore. Little by little, the noises in the dooryard ceased, though I could still hear bumpings and rattlings as the beer keg was picked up and shaken empty of the last few drops. Then a hollow thud as someone dropped it on the ground.

There were noises in the house; the sudden yowl of a wakening baby, footsteps in the kitchen, the sleepy whine of toddlers disturbed by the men, a woman's voice raised in remonstrance, then reassurance.

My neck and shoulders ached, and my feet were sore from the long walk to the whisky spring, carrying Jemmy. Still, I found myself annoyingly wakeful, unable to shut out the noises of the external world as completely as the shutters blocked it from view.

"Can you remember everything you did today?" This was a small game we played sometimes at night, each trying to recall in detail everything done, seen, heard, or eaten during the day, from getting up to going to bed. Like writing in a journal, the effort of recall seemed to purge the mind of the day's exertions, and we found great entertainment in each other's experiences. I loved to hear Jamie's daily accounts, whether pedestrian or exciting, but he wasn't in the mood tonight.

"I canna remember a thing that happened before we closed the chamber door," he said, squeezing my buttock in a companionable way. "After that, though, I expect I could recall a detail or two."

"It's reasonably fresh in my mind, too," I assured him. I curled my toes, caressing the tops of his feet.

We stopped speaking, then, and began to shift and settle toward sleep, as the sounds below ceased, replaced by the buzz and rasp of miscellaneous snores. Or at least I tried to. Late as it was, and exhausted as my body undoubtedly was, my mind appeared determined to stay up and carouse. Fragments of the day appeared behind my eyelids the moment I shut my eyes—Mrs. Bug and her broom, Gerhard Mueller's muddy boots, bare-stemmed grape clusters, blanched tangles of sauerkraut, the round halves of Jemmy's miniature pink bottom, dozens of young Chisholms running amok . . . I resolutely strove to discipline my fugitive mind by turning instead to a mental checklist of my preparations for leaving.

This was most unhelpful, as within moments I was wide awake with suppressed anxiety, imagining the complete destruction of my surgery; Brianna, Marsali, or the children succumbing to some sudden hideous epidemic; and Mrs.

Bug inciting riot and bloodshed from one end of the Ridge to the other.

I rolled onto my side, looking at Jamie. He had rolled onto his back as usual, arms neatly folded across his abdomen like a tomb figure, profile pure and stern against the dying glow of the hearth, tidily composed for sleep. His eyes were closed, but there was a slight frown on his face, and his lips twitched now and then, as though he were conducting some kind of interior argument.

"You're thinking so loudly, I can hear you from over here," I said, in conversational tones. "Or are you only counting sheep?"

His eyes opened at once, and he turned over to smile ruefully at me.

"I was counting pigs," he informed me. "And doing nicely, too. Only I kept catchin' sight of that white creature from the corner of my eye, skippin' to and fro just out of reach, taunting me."

I laughed with him, and scooted toward him. I laid my forehead against his shoulder and heaved a deep sigh.

"We really must sleep, Jamie. I'm so tired, my bones feel as though they're melting, and you've been up even longer than I have."

"Mmm." He put an arm around me, pulling me into the curve of his shoulder.

"That cross—it isn't going to catch the house afire, is it?" I asked after a moment, having thought of something else to worry about.

"No." He sounded slightly drowsy. "It's burnt out long since."

The fire in the hearth had burned down to a bed of glowing embers. I rolled over again and lay watching them for a few minutes, trying to empty my mind of everything.

"When Frank and I were married," I said, "we went to be counseled by a priest. He advised us to begin our married life by saying the rosary together in bed each night. Frank said he wasn't sure whether this was meant to be devotion, an aid to sleep, or only a Church-sanctioned method of birth control."

Jamie's chest vibrated with silent laughter behind me.

"Well, we could try if ye like, Sassenach," he said. "Though ye'll have to keep count of the Hail Marys; you're lyin' on my left hand and my fingers have gone numb."

I shifted slightly to allow him to pull his hand out from under my hip.

"Not that, I don't think," I said. "But perhaps a prayer. Do you know any good going-to-bed prayers?"

"Aye, lots," he said, holding up his hand and flexing his fingers slowly as the blood returned to them. Dark in the dimness of the room, the slow movement reminded me of the way in which he lured trout from under rocks. "Let me think a bit."

The house below was silent now, save for the usual creaks and groans of settling timbers. I thought I heard a voice outside, raised in distant argument, but it might have been no more than the rattle of tree branches in the wind.

"Here's one," Jamie said at last. "I'd nearly forgotten it. My father taught it to me, not so long before he died. He said he thought I might one day find it useful."

He settled himself comfortably, head bent so his chin rested on my shoulder, and began to speak, low and warm-voiced, in my ear.

"Bless to me, O God, the moon that is above me,
Bless to me, O God, the earth that is beneath me,
Bless to me, O God, my wife and my children,
And bless, O God, myself who have care of them;
Bless to me my wife and my children,
And bless, O God, myself who have care of them."

He had begun with a certain self-consciousness, hesitating now and then to find a word, but that had faded with the speaking. Now he spoke soft and sure, and no longer to me, though his hand lay warm on the curve of my waist.

"Bless, O God, the thing on which mine eye doth rest,
Bless, O God, the thing on which my hope doth rest,
Bless, O God, my reason and my purpose,
Bless, O bless Thou them, Thou God of life;
Bless, O God, my reason and my purpose,
Bless, O bless Thou them, Thou God of life."

His hand smoothed the curve of my hip, lifted to stroke my hair.

"Bless to me the bed companion of my love,
Bless to me the handling of my hands,
Bless, O bless Thou to me, O God, the fencing of my defense,
And bless, O bless to me the angeling of my rest;
Bless, O bless Thou to me, O God, the fencing of my defense,
And bless, O bless to me the angeling of my rest."

His hand lay still, curled under my chin. I wrapped my own hand round his, and sighed deeply.

"Oh, I like that. Especially 'the angeling of my rest.' When Bree was small, we'd put her to bed with an angel prayer—'May Michael be at my right, Gabriel at my left, Uriel behind me, Rafael before me—and above my head, the Presence of the Lord.' "

He didn't answer, but squeezed my fingers in reply. An ember in the hearth fell apart with a soft *whuff*, and sparks floated for an instant in the dimness of the room.

Sometime later, I returned briefly to consciousness, feeling him slide out of bed.

"Wha—?" I said sleepily.

"Nothing," he whispered. "Just a wee note I'd meant to write. Sleep, *a nighean donn*. I'll wake beside ye."

Fraser's Ridge, 1 December, 1770
James Fraser, Esq., to Lord John Grey,
Mount Josiah Plantation

My Lord,

I write in hopes that all continues well with your Establishment and its Inhabitants; my particular Regard to your Son.

All are well in my House and—so far as I am aware—at River Run, as well. The Nuptials planned for my Daughter and my Aunt, of which I wrote you, were unexpectedly interfered with by Circumstance (principally a Circumstance by the name of Mr. Randall Lillywhite, whose Name I mention in case it may one Day pass your Cognizance), but my Grandchildren were fortunately christened, and while my Aunt's Wedding has been postponed to a later Season, my Daughter's Union with Mr. MacKenzie was solemnized by the Courtesy of the Reverend Mr. Caldwell, a worthy Gentleman, though Presbyterian.

Young Jeremiah Alexander Ian Fraser MacKenzie (the name "Ian" is of course the Scottish variant of "John"—my Daughter's Compliment to a Friend, as well as her Cousin) survived both the Occasion of his Baptism and the Journey home in good Spirit. His Mother bids me tell you that your Namesake now possesses no fewer than four Teeth, a fearsome Accomplishment which renders him exceeding dangerous to those unwary Souls charmed by his apparent Innocence, who surrender their Digits all unknowing to his pernicious Grasp. The Child bites like a Crocodile.

Our Population here exhibits a gratifying Growth of late, with the addition of some twenty Families since last I wrote. God has prospered our Efforts during the Summer, blessing us with an Abundance of Corn and wild Hay, and an Abundance of Beasts to consume them. I estimate the Hogs running at large in my Wood to number no fewer than forty at present, two Cows have borne Calves, and I have bought a new Horse. This Animal's Character lies in grave Doubt, but his Wind does not.

Thus, my good News.

And so to the bad. I am made Colonel of Militia, ordered to muster and deliver so many Men as I can to the Service of the Governor, by mid-month, this Service to be of Aid in the Suppression of local Hostilities.

You may have heard, during your visit to North

Carolina, of a Group of Men who style themselves "Regulators"—or you may not, as other Matters compelled your Attention on that Occasion (my Wife is pleased to hear good Report of your own Health, and sends with this a Parcel of Medicines, with Instructions for their Administration should you still be plagued with Headache).

These Regulators are no more than Rabble, less disciplined in their Actions even than the Rioters whom we hear have hanged Gov. Richardson in Effigy in Boston. I do not say there is no Substance to their Complaint, but the Means of its Expression seems unlikely to result in Redress by the Crown—rather, to provoke both Sides to further Excess, which cannot fail to end in Injury.

There was a serious outbreak of Violence in Hillsborough on 24 September, in which much Property was wantonly destroyed and Violence done—some justly, some not—to officials of the Crown. One Man, a Justice, was grievously Wounded; many of the Regulation were arrested. Since then, we have heard little more than Murmurs; Winter damps down Discontent, which smolders by the Hearths of Cottages and Pothouses, but once let out with the Spring Airing, it will flee abroad like the foul Odors from a sealed House, staining the Air.

Tryon is an able Man, but not a Farmer. If he were, he would scarce think of seeking to make War in Winter. Still, it may be that he hopes by making Show of Force now—when he is likely sure it will not be needed—so to intimidate the Rapscallions as to obviate its Necessity later. He is a Soldier.

Such remarks bring me to the true Point of this Missive. I expect no evil Outcome of the present Enterprise, and yet—you are a Soldier, too, even as I am. You know the Unpredictability of Evil, and what Catastrophe may spring from trivial Beginnings.

No man can know the Particulars of his own End—save that he will have one. Thus, I have made such Provision as I can, for the Welfare of my Family.

I enumerate them here, as you will not know them all: Claire Fraser, my beloved Wife; my Daughter Brianna and her Husband, Roger MacKenzie, and their Child, Jeremiah MacKenzie. Also my Daughter Marsali and her Husband, Fergus Fraser (who is my adopted Son)—they have now two young ones, Germain and Joan by Name. Wee Joan is named for Marsali's sister, known as Joan MacKenzie, presently abiding still in Scotland. I have not the leisure to acquaint you with the History of the Situation, but I am disposed for good Reason to regard this young Woman likewise as a Daughter, and I hold myself similarly obligated for her Welfare, and that of her Mother, one Laoghaire MacKenzie.

I pray you for the Sake of our long Friendship and for the Sake of your Regard for my Wife and Daughter, that if Mischance should befall me in this Enterprise, you will do what you can to see them safe.

I depart upon the Morrow's Dawn, which is now not far off.

Your most humble and obedient Servant,
James Alexander Malcolm MacKenzie Fraser

Postscriptum: My Thanks for the Intelligence you provide in answer to my earlier Query regarding Stephen Bonnet. I note your accompanying Advice with the greatest Appreciation and Gratitude for its kind Intent—though as you suspect, it will not sway me.

Post-Postscriptum: Copies of my Will and Testament, and of the Papers pertaining to my Property and Affairs here and in Scotland, will be found with Farquard Campbell, of Greenoaks, near Cross Creek.

Part Three

Alarms and Excursions

26

THE MILITIA RISES

THE WEATHER FAVORED US, keeping cold but clear. With the Muellers and the men from the nearby homesteads, we set out from Fraser's Ridge with a party of nearly forty men—and me.

Fergus would not serve with the militia, but had come with us to raise men, he being the most familiar with the nearby settlements and homesteads. As we approached the Treaty Line, and the farthest point of our peripatetic muster, we formed a respectable company in number, if not in expertise. Some of the men had been soldiers once, if not trained infantrymen; either in Scotland, or in the French and Indian Wars. Many had not, and each evening saw Jamie conducting military drills and practice, though of a most unorthodox sort.

"We havena got time to drill them properly," he'd told Roger over the first evening's fire. "It takes weeks, ken, to shape men so they willna run under fire."

Roger merely nodded at that, though I thought a faint look of uneasiness flickered across his face. I supposed he might be having doubts regarding his own lack of experience, and exactly how he himself would respond under fire. I'd known a lot of young soldiers in my time.

I was kneeling by the fire, cooking corn dodgers on an iron griddle set in the ashes. I glanced up at Jamie, to find him looking at me, a slight smile hidden in the corner of his mouth. He'd not only known young soldiers; he'd been one. He coughed, and bent forward to stir the coals with a stick, looking for more of the quails I'd set to bake, wrapped in clay.

"It's the natural thing, to run from danger, aye? The point of drilling troops is to accustom them to an officer's voice, so they'll hear, even over the roar of guns, and obey without thinkin' of the danger."

"Aye, like ye train a horse not to bolt at noises," Roger interrupted, sardonically.

"Aye, like that," Jamie agreed, quite seriously. "The difference being that ye need to make a horse believe ye ken better than he does; an officer only needs to be louder." Roger laughed, and Jamie went on, half-smiling.

"When I went for a soldier in France, I was marched to and fro and up and down, and wore a pair of boots clear through before they gave me powder for my gun. I was sae weary at the end of a day of drilling that they could have shot off cannon by my pallet and I wouldna have turned a hair."

He shook his head a little, the half-smile fading from his face. "But we havena got the time for that. Half our men will have had a bit of soldiering; we must depend on them to stand if it comes to fighting, and keep heart in the others." He glanced past the fire, and gestured toward the fading vista of trees and mountains.

"It's no much like a battlefield, is it? I canna say where the battle may be—if there is one—but I think we must plan for a fight where there's cover to be had. We'll teach them to fight as Highlanders do; to gather or to scatter at my word, and otherwise, to make shift as they can. Only half the men were soldiers, but all of them can hunt." He raised his chin, gesturing toward the recruits, several of whom had bagged small game during the day's ride. The Lindsay brothers had shot the quail we were eating.

Roger nodded, and bent down, scooping a blackened ball of clay out of the fire with his own stick, keeping his face hidden. Almost all. He had gone out shooting every day since our return to the Ridge, and had still to bag even a possum. Jamie, who had gone with him once, had privately expressed the opinion to me that Roger would do better to hit the game on the head with his musket, rather than shoot at it.

I lowered my brows at Jamie; he raised his at me, returning my stare. Roger's feelings could take care of themselves, was the blunt message there. I widened my own eyes, and rose.

"But it isn't really like hunting, is it?" I sat down beside Jamie, and handed him one of the hot corn dodgers. "Especially now."

"What d'ye mean by that, Sassenach?" Jamie broke the corn dodger open, half-closing his eyes in bliss as he inhaled the hot, fragrant steam.

"For one, you don't know that it will come to a fight at all," I pointed out. "For another, if it does, you won't be facing trained troops—the Regulators aren't soldiers, any more than your men are. For a third, you won't really be trying to kill the Regulators; only frighten them into retreat or surrender. And for a fourth"—I smiled at Roger—"the point of hunting is to kill something. The point of going to war is to come back alive."

Jamie choked on a bite of corn dodger. I thumped him helpfully on the back, and he rounded on me, glaring. He coughed crumbs, swallowed, and stood up, plaid swinging.

"Listen to me," he said, a little hoarsely. "Ye're right, Sassenach—and ye're wrong. It's no like hunting, aye. Because the game isna usually trying to kill *you*. Mind me—" He turned to Roger, his face grim. "She's wrong about the rest of it. War is killing, and that's all. Think of anything less—think of half-measures, think of frightening—above all, think of your own skin—and by God, man, ye will be dead by nightfall of the first day."

He flung the remains of his corn dodger into the fire, and stalked away.

I SAT FROZEN for a moment, until heat from the fresh corn dodger I was holding seeped through the cloth round it and burned my fingers. I set it down on the log with a muffled "ouch," and Roger shifted a little on his log.

"All right?" he said, though he wasn't looking at me. His eyes were fixed on the direction in which Jamie had vanished, toward the horses.

"Fine." I soothed my scorched fingertips against the cold, damp bark of the log. With the awkward silence eased by this little exchange, I found it possible to address the matter at hand.

"Granted," I said, "that Jamie has a certain amount of experience from which to speak . . . I do think what he said was rather an overreaction."

"Do you?" Roger didn't seem upset or taken aback by Jamie's remarks.

"Of course I do. Whatever happens with the Regulators, we know perfectly well that it isn't going to be an all-out war. It's likely to be nothing at all!"

"Oh, aye." Roger was still looking into the darkness, lips pursed in thoughtfulness. "Only—I think that's not what he was talking about."

I lifted one eyebrow at him, and he shifted his gaze to me, with a wry half-smile.

"When he went out hunting with me, he asked me what I knew about what was coming. I told him. Bree said he'd asked her, and she told him, too."

"What was coming—you mean, the Revolution?"

He nodded, eyes on the fragment of corn dodger he was crumbling between long, callused fingers.

"I told him what I knew. About the battles, the politics. Not all the detail, of course, but the chief battles I remembered; what a long, drawn-out, bloody business it will be." He was quiet for a moment, then looked up at me, a slight glint of green in his eye.

"I suppose ye'd call it fair exchange. It's hard to tell with him, but I *think* I maybe scared him. He's just returned the favor."

I gave a small snort of amusement, and stood up, brushing crumbs and ashes off my skirt.

"The day you scare Jamie Fraser by telling him war stories, my lad," I said, "will be the day hell freezes over."

He laughed, not discomposed in the slightest.

"Maybe I didn't scare him, then—though he got very quiet. But I tell you what"—he sobered somewhat, though the glint stayed in his eye—"he did scare me, just now."

I glanced off in the direction of the horses. The moon hadn't yet risen, and I couldn't see anything but a vague jumble of big, restless shadows, with an occasional gleam of firelight off a rounded rump or the brief shine of an eye. Jamie wasn't visible, but I knew he was there; there was a subtle shift and mill of movement among the horses, with faint whickers or snorts, that told me someone familiar was among them.

"He wasn't just a soldier," I said at last, speaking quietly, though I was fairly sure Jamie was too far away to hear me. "He was an officer."

I sat down on the log again, and put a hand on the corn dodger. It was barely warm now. I picked it up, but didn't bite into it.

"I was a combat nurse, you know. In a field hospital in France."

He nodded, dark head cocked in interest. The fire threw deep shadows on his face, emphasizing the contrast of heavy brow and strong bones with the gentle curve of his mouth.

"I nursed soldiers. They were *all* scared." I smiled a little, sadly. "The ones who'd been under fire remembered, and the ones who hadn't, imagined. But it was the officers who couldn't sleep at night."

I ran a thumb absently over the bumpy surface of the corn dodger. It felt faintly greasy, from the lard.

"I sat with Jamie once, after Preston, while he held one of his men in his arms as he died. And wept. He remembers that. He doesn't remember Culloden—because he can't bear to." I looked down at the lump of fried dough in my hand, picking at the burned bits with my thumbnail.

"Yes, you scared him. He doesn't want to weep for you. Neither do I," I added softly. "It may not be now, but when the time does come—take care, will you?"

There was a long silence. Then, "I will," he said quietly. He stood up and left, his footsteps fading quickly into silence on the damp earth.

The other campfires burned brightly, as the night deepened. The men still kept to the company of relative and friend, each small group around its own fire. As we went on, they would begin to join together, I knew. Within a few days, there would be one large fire, everyone gathered together in a single circle of light.

Jamie wasn't scared by what Roger had told him, I thought—but by what he himself knew. There were two choices for a good officer: let concern for his responsibilities tear him apart—or let necessity harden him to stone. He knew that.

And as for me . . . I knew a few things, too. I had been married to two soldiers—officers, both; for Frank had been one, too. I had been nurse and healer, on the fields of two wars.

I knew the names and dates of battles; I knew the smell of blood. And of vomit, and voided bowels. A field hospital sees the shattered limbs, the spilled guts, and bone ends . . . but it also sees the men who never raised a gun, but died there anyway, of fever and dirt and sickness and despair.

I knew that thousands died of wounds and killing on the battlefields of two World Wars; I knew that hundreds upon hundreds of thousands died there of infection and disease. It would be no different now—nor in four years.

And that scared me very much indeed.

THE NEXT NIGHT, we made camp in the woods on Balsam Mountain, a mile or so above the settlement of Lucklow. Several of the men wanted to push on, to reach the hamlet of Brownsville. Brownsville was the outer point of our journey, before turning back toward Salisbury, and it held the possibility of a pothouse—or at least a hospitable shed to sleep in—but Jamie thought better to wait.

"I dinna want to scare the folk there," he had explained to Roger, "riding in with a troop of armed men after dark. Better to announce our business by daylight, then give the men a day—and a night—to make ready to leave." He had stopped then, and coughed heavily, shoulders racked with the spasm.

I didn't like either the looks of Jamie or the sound of him. He had the patchy look of a mildewed quilt, and when he came to the fire to fill his dinner bowl, I could hear a faint wheezing sigh in every breath. Most of the men were in similar condition; red noses and coughing were endemic, and the fire popped and sizzled every few moments, as someone hawked and spat into it.

I should have liked to tuck Jamie up in bed with a hot stone to his feet, a mustard plaster on his chest, and a hot tisane of aromatic peppermint and ephedra leaves to drink. Since it would have taken a brace of cannon, leg irons, and several armed men to get him there, I contented myself with fishing up a particularly meaty ladle of stew and plopping it into his bowl.

"Ewald," Jamie called hoarsely to one of the Muellers. He stopped and cleared his throat, with a sound like tearing flannel. "Ewald—d'ye take Paul and fetch along more wood for the fire. It'll be a cold night."

It already was. Men were standing so close to the fire that the fringes of their shawls and coats were singed, and the toes of their boots—those who had boots—stank of hot leather. My own knees and thighs were close to blistering, as I stood perforce near the blaze in order to serve out the stew. My backside was like ice, though, in spite of the old pair of breeks I wore under shift and petticoat—both for insulation and for the avoidance of excessive friction while on horseback. The Carolina backwoods were no place for a sidesaddle.

The last bowl served, I turned round to eat my own stew, with the fire at my back, a grateful bloom of warmth embracing my frozen bottom.

"All right, is it, ma'am?" Jimmy Robertson, who had made the stew, peered over my shoulder in search of compliment.

"Lovely," I assured him. "Delicious!" In fact, it was hot and I was hungry. That, plus the fact that I hadn't had to cook it myself, lent a sufficient tone of sincerity to my words that he retired, satisfied.

I ate slowly, enjoying the heat of the wooden bowl in my chilly hands, as well as the soothing warmth of food in my stomach. The cacophony of sneezing and hacking behind me did nothing to impair the momentary sense of well-being engendered by food and the prospect of rest after a long day in the saddle. Even the sight of the woods around us, bone-cold and black under growing starlight, failed to disturb me.

My own nose had begun to run rather freely, but I hoped it was merely the result of eating hot food. I swallowed experimentally, but there was no sign of sore throat, nor rattling of congestion in my chest. Jamie rattled; he had finished eating and come to stand beside me, warming his backside at the blaze.

"All right, Sassenach?" he asked hoarsely.

"Just vasomotor rhinitis," I replied, dabbing at my nose with a handkerchief.

"Where?" He cast a suspicious look at the forest. "Here? I thought ye said they lived in Africa."

"What—oh, rhinoceroses. Yes, they do. I just meant my nose is running, but I haven't got *la grippe*."

"Oh, aye? That's good. I have," he added unnecessarily, and sneezed three times in succession. He handed me his emptied bowl, in order to use both hands to blow his nose, which he did with a series of vicious honks. I winced slightly, seeing the reddened, raw look of his nostrils. I had a bit of camphorated bear grease in my saddlebag, but I was sure he wouldn't let me anoint him in public.

"Are you sure we oughtn't to push on?" I asked, watching him. "Geordie says the village isn't far, and there is a road—of sorts."

I knew the answer to that; he wasn't one to alter strategy for the sake of personal comfort. Besides, camp was already made and a good fire going. Still, beyond my own longing for a warm, clean bed—well, any bed, I wasn't fussy—I was worried for Jamie. Close to, the sigh in his breath had a deeper, wheezing note to it that troubled me.

He knew what I meant. He smiled, tucking away the sodden kerchief in his sleeve.

"I'll do, Sassenach," he said. "It's no but a wee cold in the neb. I've been a deal worse than this, many times."

Paul Mueller heaved another log onto the fire; a big ember broke and roared up with a flare that made us step away in order to avoid the spray of sparks. Well baked in the rear by this time, I turned to face the fire. Jamie, though, stayed facing outward, a slight frown on his face as he surveyed the shadows of the looming wood.

The frown relaxed, and I turned to see two men emerging from the woods, shaking needles and bits of bark from their clothes. Jack Parker, and a new man—I didn't yet know his name, but he was plainly a recent immigrant from somewhere near Glasgow, judging from his speech.

"All quiet, sir," said Parker, touching his hat in brief salute. "Cold as charity, though."

"Aye, Ah hivny felt ma privates anytime since dinner," the Glaswegian chimed in, grimacing and rubbing himself as he headed for the fire. "Might as well be gone aetegither!"

"I take your meaning, man," Jamie said, grinning. "Went for a piss a moment ago, but I couldna find it." He turned amid the laughter and went to check the horses, a half-finished second bowl of stew in one hand.

The other men were already making ready their bedrolls, debating the wisdom of sleeping with feet or head near the fire.

"It'll scorch the soles o' your boots, and ye get too close," argued Evan Lindsay. "See? Charred the pegs right out, and now look!" He lifted one large foot, exhibiting a battered shoe with a wrapping of rough twine tied round it to hold it together. The leather soles and heels were sometimes stitched, but more often fastened with tiny whittled pegs of wood or leather, glued with pine gum or some other adhesive. The pine gum in particular was flammable; I'd seen occasional sparks burst from the feet of men who slept with their feet too near the fire, when a shoe peg suddenly ignited from the heat.

"Better than settin' your hair on fire," Ronnie Sinclair argued.

"I dinna think the Lindsays need worry about that owermuch." Kenny grinned at his elder brother, and tugged down the knit cap he wore—like his two brothers—over a balding head.

"Aye, headfirst every time," Murdo agreed. "Ye dinna want to chill your scalp; it'll go right to your liver, and then you're a dead man." Murdo was tenderly solicitous of his exposed scalp, being seldom seen without either his knitted nightcap or a peculiar hat made from the hairy skin of a possum, lined and rakishly trimmed with skunk fur. He glanced enviously at Roger, who was tying back his own thick black hair with a bit of leather string.

"MacKenzie needna worry; he's furred like a bear!"

Roger grinned in response. Like the others, he had stopped shaving when we left the Ridge; now, eight days later, a thick scurf of dark stubble did give him a fiercely ursine look. It occurred to me that beyond convenience, a heavy beard undoubtedly kept the face warm on nights like this; I tucked my own bare and vulnerable chin down into the sheltering folds of my shawl.

Returning from the horses in time to hear this, Jamie laughed, too, but it ended in a spasm of coughing. Evan waited 'til it ended.

"How say ye, *Mac Dubh*? Heads or tails?"

Jamie wiped his mouth on his sleeve and smiled. Hairy as the rest, he looked a proper Viking, with the fire glinting red, gold, and silver from his sprouting beard and loosened hair.

"Nay bother, lads," he said. "I'll sleep warm enough nay matter *how* I'm laid." He tilted his head in my direction, and there was a general rumble of laughter, with a spattering of mildly crude remarks in Scots and Gaelic from the Ridge men.

One or two of the new recruits eyed me with a brief, instinctive speculation, quickly abandoned after a glance at Jamie's height, breadth, and air of genial ferocity. I met one man's eyes and smiled; he looked startled, but then smiled back, ducking his head in shyness.

How the hell did Jamie do that? One brief, crude joke, and he'd laid public claim to me, removed me from any threat of unwanted advances, and reasserted his position as leader.

"Just like a bloody baboon troop," I muttered under my breath. "And I'm sleeping with the head baboon!"

"Baboons are the monkeys with no tails?" Fergus asked, turning from an exchange with Ewald about the horses.

"You know quite well they are." I caught Jamie's eye, and

his mouth curled up on one side. I knew what he was thinking, and he knew I did; the smile widened.

Louis of France kept a private zoo at Versailles, among the inhabitants of which were a small troop of mandrill baboons. One of the most popular Court activities on spring afternoons was to visit the baboon quarters, there to admire both the sexual prowess of the male, and his splendidly multicolored bottom.

One M. de Ruvel had offered—in my hearing—to have his posterior similarly tattooed, if it would result in such a favorable reception by the ladies of the Court. He had, however, been firmly informed by Madame de la Tourelle that his physique was in every way inferior to that of the mandrill, and coloring it was unlikely to improve matters.

The firelight made it difficult to tell, but I was reasonably sure that Jamie's own rich color owed as much to suppressed amusement as to heat.

"Speakin' of tails," he murmured in my ear. "Have ye got those infernal breeks on?"

"Yes."

"Take them off."

"What, here?" I gave him a wide-eyed look of mock innocence. "You want me to freeze my arse off?"

His eyes narrowed slightly, with a blue cat-gleam in the depths.

"Oh, it wilna freeze," he said softly. "I'll warrant ye that."

He moved behind me, and the fierce shimmer of the blaze on my flesh was replaced by the cool solidness of his body. No less fierce, though, as I discovered when he put his arms round my waist and drew me back against him.

"Oh, you found it," I said. "How nice."

"Found what? Had you lost something?" Roger paused, coming from the horses with a lumpy roll of blankets under one arm, his bodhran under the other.

"Oh, just a pair of auld breeks," Jamie said blandly. Under cover of my shawl, one hand slid inside the waistband of my skirt. "D'ye mean to give us a song, then?"

"If anyone likes, sure." Roger smiled, the firelight ruddy on his features. "Actually, I'm meaning to learn one; Evan's promised to sing me a silkie-song his grannie knew."

Jamie laughed.

"Oh, I ken that one, I think."

One of Roger's eyebrows shot up, and I twisted slightly round, to look up at Jamie in surprise.

"Well, I couldna *sing* it," he said mildly, seeing our amazement. "I ken the words, though. Evan sang it often and again, in the prison at Ardsmuir. It's a bit bawdy," he added, with that faintly prim tone that Highlanders often adopt, just before telling you something truly shocking.

Roger recognized it, and laughed.

"I'll maybe write it down, then," he said. "For the benefit of future generations."

Jamie's fingers had been working skillfully away, and at this point, the breeks—which were his, and thus about six sizes too large for me—came loose and dropped silently to the ground. A cold draft whooshed up under my skirt and struck my newly bared nether portions. I drew in my breath with a faint gasp.

"Cold, isn't it?" Roger hunched his shoulders, smiling as he shivered exaggeratedly in sympathy.

"Yes, indeed," I said. "Freeze the balls off a brass monkey, wouldn't it?"

Jamie and Roger burst into simultaneous coughing fits.

SENTRY IN PLACE and horses bedded down, we retired to our own resting place, a discreet distance from the circle by the fire. I had dug the largest rocks and twigs out of the leaf mold, cut spruce branches, and spread our blankets over them by the time Jamie finished his last round of the camp. The warmth of food and fire had faded, but I didn't begin to shiver in earnest until he touched me.

I would have moved at once to get under the blankets, but Jamie still held me. His original intent appeared intact—to say the least—but his attention was momentarily distracted. His arms were still clasped round me, but he was standing quite still, head up as though listening, looking into the murk of the wood. It was full dark; no more showed of the trees than the glow of fire reflected from the few trunks that stood nearest the camp—the last shadow of twilight had faded, and everything beyond was a depthless black.

"What is it?" I drew back a little, pressing instinctively against him, and his arms tightened round me.

"I dinna ken. But I do feel something, Sassenach." He moved a little, lifting his head in restless query, like a wolf scenting the wind, but no message reached us save a distant rattling of leafless branches.

"If it's no rhinoceroses, it's something," he said softly, and a whisper of unease raised the hairs on the back of my neck. "A moment, lass."

He left me, the wind blowing suddenly cold about me with the loss of his presence, and went to speak quietly with a couple of the men.

And what might he feel, out there in the dark? I had the greatest respect for Jamie's sense of danger. He had lived too long as hunter and as hunted, not to sense the edgy awareness that lay between the two—invisible or not.

He returned a moment later, and squatted beside me as I burrowed shivering into the blankets.

"It's all right," he said. "I've said we'll have two guards tonight, and each man to keep his piece loaded and to hand. But I think it's all right." He looked beyond me, into the wood, but his face now was merely thoughtful.

"It's all right," he repeated again, more certainly.

"Is it gone?"

He turned his head, his lips curling slightly. His mouth looked soft, tender and vulnerable amid the stiff, ruddy wires of his starting beard.

"I dinna ken if it was ever there, Sassenach," he said. "I thought I felt eyes upon me, but it could have been a passing wolf, an owl—or nay more than a restless *spiorad*, a-roaming in the wood. But aye, it's gone now."

He smiled at me; I saw the flicker of the light that rimmed his head and shoulders as he turned, silhouetted by the fire. Beyond, the sound of Roger's voice drifted to me above the crackle of the fire, as he learned the melody of the silkie-song, following Evan's voice, hoarse but confident. Jamie slid into the blankets beside me and I turned to him, cold hands fumbling to return the favor he had done me earlier.

We shivered convulsively, urgent for each other's warmth. I found him, and he turned me, ruffling up the layers of fabric between us, so that he lay behind me, his arm secure around me, the small secret patches of our nakedness joined in warmth beneath the blankets. I lay facing the darkness of the wood, watching the firelight dance among the trees, as Jamie moved behind me—behind, between, within—warm and big, and so slowly as scarcely to rustle the branches beneath us. Roger's voice rose strong and sweet above the murmur of the men, and the shivering slowly stopped.

I WOKE MUCH LATER beneath a blue-black sky, dry-mouthed, the rasping sigh of Jamie's breath in my ear. I had been dreaming; one of those pointless dreams of uneasy repetition, that fades at once with the waking but leaves a nasty taste in mouth and mind. Needing both water and relief of my bladder, I squirmed carefully out from under Jamie's arm, and slid out from between the blankets. He stirred and groaned slightly, snuffling in his sleep, but didn't wake.

I paused to lay a hand lightly on his forehead. Cool, no fever. Perhaps he was right, then—just a bad cold. I stood up, reluctant to leave the warm sanctuary of our nest, but knowing I couldn't wait until morning.

The songs were stilled, the fire smaller now, but still burning, kept up by the sentry on duty. It was Murdo Lindsay; I could see the white fur of his possum-skin cap, perched atop what looked like a huddled pile of clothing and blankets. The anonymous Glaswegian crouched on the other side of the clearing, musket on his knees; he nodded to me, face shadowed by the brim of his slouch hat. The white cap turned in my direction too, at the sound of my step. I sketched a wave, and Murdo nodded toward me, then turned back toward the wood.

The men lay in a shrouded circle, buried in their blankets. I felt a sudden qualm as I walked between them. With the spell of night and dreams still on me, I shivered at sight of the silent forms, lying so still, side by side. Just so had they laid the bodies at Amiens. At Preston. Still and shrouded, side by side, faces covered and anonymous. War seldom looks on the faces of its dead.

And why should I wake from love's embrace, thinking of war and the sleeping ranks of dead men? I wondered, stepping lightly past the shrouded line of bodies. Well, that was simple enough, given our errand. We were headed for battle—if not now, then soon enough.

One blanket-wrapped form grunted, coughed, and turned over, face invisible, indistinguishable from the others. The movement startled me, but then one big foot thrust free of the blanket, revealing Evan Lindsay's twine-wrapped shoe. I felt the anxious burden of imagination ease, with this evidence of life, of individuality.

It's the anonymity of war that makes the killing possible. When the nameless dead are named again on tombstone and on cenotaph, then they regain the identity they lost as soldiers, and take their place in grief and memory, the ghosts of sons and lovers. Perhaps this journey would end in peace. The conflict that was coming, though . . . the world would hear of that, and I stepped past the last of the sleeping men, as though walking through an evil dream not fully waked from.

I picked up a canteen from the ground near the saddlebags and drank deep. The water was piercingly cold, and my somber thoughts began to dissipate, washed away by the sweet, clean taste of it. I paused, gasping from the coldness, and wiped my mouth.

Best take some back to Jamie; if he wasn't wakened by my absence, he would be by my return, and I knew his mouth would be dry as well, since he was completely unable to breathe through his nose at the moment. I slung the strap of the canteen over my shoulder and stepped into the shelter of the wood.

It was cold under the trees, but the air was still and crystal clear. The shadows that had seemed sinister viewed from the fireside were oddly reassuring, seen from the shelter of the wood. Turned away from the fire's glow and crackle, my eyes and ears began to adapt to the dark. I heard the rustle of something small in the dried grass nearby, and the unexpected distant hooting of an owl.

Finished, I stood still for a few minutes, enjoying the momentary solitude. It was very cold, but very peaceful. Jamie had been right, I thought; whatever might or might not have been here earlier, the wood held nothing inimical now.

As though my thought of him had summoned him, I heard a cautious footfall, and the slow, wheezing rasp of his breath. He coughed, a muffled, strangled noise that I didn't like at all.

"Here I am," I said softly. "How's the chest?"

The cough choked off in a sudden wheeze of panic, and there was a crunch and flurry among the leaves. I saw Murdo start up by the fire, musket in hand, and then a dark shape darted past me.

"Hoy!" I said, startled rather than frightened. The shape stumbled, and by reflex, I swung the canteen off my shoulder and whirled it by the strap. It struck the figure in the back with a hollow *thunk!* and whoever it was—certainly not Jamie—fell to his knees, coughing.

There followed a short period of chaos, with men exploding out of their blankets like startled jack-in-the-boxes, incoherent shouting, and general mayhem. The Glaswegian leaped over several struggling bodies and charged into the wood, musket over his head, bellowing. Barreling into the darkness, he charged the first shape he saw, which happened to be me. I went flying headlong into the leaves, where I ended inelegantly sprawled and windless, the Glaswegian kneeling on my stomach.

I must have given a sufficiently feminine grunt as I fell, for he paused, narrowly checking himself as he was about to club me in the head.

"Eh?" He put down his free hand and felt cautiously. Feeling what was unmistakably a breast, he jerked back as though burned, and slowly edged off me.

"Err . . . hmm!" he said.

"Whoof," I replied, as cordially as possible. The stars were spinning overhead, shining brightly through the leafless branches. The Glaswegian disappeared, with a small Scottish noise of embarrassment. There was a lot of shouting and crashing, off to my left, but I hadn't attention for anything at the moment bar getting my wind back.

By the time I made it back onto my feet, the intruder had been captured and dragged into the light of the fire.

Had he not been coughing when I hit him, he likely would have gotten away. As it was, though, he was hacking and wheezing so badly that he could barely stand upright, and his face was dark with the effort to snatch a breath in passing. The veins on his forehead stood out like worms, and he made an eerie whistling noise as he breathed—or tried to.

"What the hell are *you* doing here?" Jamie demanded hoarsely, then paused to cough in sympathy.

This was a purely rhetorical question, since the boy plainly couldn't talk. It was Josiah Beardsley, my potential tonsillectomy patient, and whatever he'd been doing since the Gathering, it hadn't improved his health to any marked extent.

I hurried to the fire, where the coffeepot sat in the embers. I seized it in a fold of my shawl and shook it. Good, there was some left, and since it had been brewing since supper, it would be strong as Hades.

"Sit him down, loosen his clothes, bring me cold water!" I shoved my way into the circle of men around the captive, forcing them aside with the hot coffeepot.

Within a moment or two, I had a mug of strong coffee at his lips, black and tarry, diluted with no more than a splash of cold water to keep it from burning his mouth.

"Breathe out slowly to the count of four, breathe in to the count of two, breathe out and take a drink," I said. The whites of his eyes showed all round the iris, and spittle had collected at the corners of his mouth. I put a firm hand on his shoulder though, urging him to breathe, to count, to breathe—and the desperate straining eased a little.

One sip, one breath, one sip, one breath, and by the time the coffee was all inside him, his face had faded from its alarming crimson hue to something more approximating fish belly, with a couple of faint reddish marks where the men had hit him. The air still whistled in his lungs, but he *was* breathing, which was a substantial improvement.

The men stood about murmuring and watching with interest, but it was cold, it was late, and as the excitement of the capture faded, they began to droop and yawn. It was, after all, only a lad, and a scrawny, ill-favored one at that. They departed willingly enough to their blankets when Jamie dispatched them, leaving Jamie and me to attend to our unexpected guest.

I had him swaddled in spare blankets, larded with camphorated bear grease, and provided with another cup of coffee in his hands, before I would let Jamie question him. The boy seemed deeply embarrassed at my attentions, shoulders hunched and eyes on the ground, but I didn't know whether he was simply unused to being fussed over, or whether it was the looming presence of Jamie, arms crossed, that discomfited him.

He was small for fourteen, and thin to the point of emaciation; I could have counted his ribs when I opened his shirt to listen to his heart. No beauty otherwise; his black hair had been chopped short, and stood on his head in matted spikes, thick with dirt, grease, and sweat, and his general aspect was that of a flea-ridden monkey, eyes large and black in a face pinched with worry and suspicion.

At last having done all I could, I was satisfied with the look of him. At my nod, Jamie lowered himself to the ground beside the boy.

"So, Mr. Beardsley," he said pleasantly. "Have ye come to join our troop of militia, then?"

"Ah . . . no." Josiah rolled the wooden cup between his hands, not looking up. "I . . . uh . . . my business chanced to take me this way, that's all." He spoke so hoarsely that I winced in sympathy, imagining the soreness of his inflamed throat.

"I see." Jamie's voice was low and friendly. "So ye saw our fire by chance, and thought to come and seek shelter and a meal?"

"I did, aye." He swallowed, with evident difficulty.

"Mmphm. But ye came earlier, no? You were in the wood just after sundown. Why wait 'til past moonrise to make yourself known?"

"I didn't . . . I wasn't . . ."

"Oh, indeed ye were." Jamie's voice was still friendly, but firm. He put out a hand and grasped Josiah's shirtfront, forcing the boy to look at him.

"Look ye, man. There's a bargain between us. You're my tenant; it's agreed. That means you've a right to my protection. It means also that I've a right to hear the truth."

Josiah looked back, and while there was fear and wariness in the look, there was also a sense of self-possession that seemed far older than fourteen. He made no effort to look away, and there was a look of deep calculation in the clever black eyes.

This child—if one could regard him as a child; plainly Jamie didn't—was used to relying on himself alone.

"I said to you, sir, that I would come to your place by the New Year, and so I mean to. What I do in the meantime is my own affair."

Jamie's brows shot up, but he nodded slowly, and released his grip.

"True enough. You'll admit, though, that one might be curious."

The boy opened his mouth as though to speak, but changed his mind and buried his nose instead in his cup of coffee.

Jamie tried again.

"May we offer you help in your business? Will ye travel a ways with us, at least?"

Josiah shook his head.

"No. I am obliged to you, sir, but the business is best managed by myself alone."

Roger had not gone to sleep, but sat a little behind Jamie, watching silently. He leaned forward now, green eyes intent on the boy.

"This business of yours," he said. "It's not by any means connected with that mark on your thumb?"

The cup hit the ground and coffee splashed up, spattering my face and bodice. The boy was out of his blankets and halfway across the clearing before I could blink my eyes to see what was happening—and by then, Jamie was up and after him. The boy had circled the fire; Jamie leaped over it. They disappeared into the wood like fox and hound, leaving Roger and me gaping after them.

For the second time that night, men erupted from their bedrolls, grabbing for their guns. I began to think the

Governor would be pleased with his militia; they were certainly ready to spring into action at a moment's notice.

"What in hell . . . ?" I said to Roger, wiping coffee from my eyebrows.

"Maybe I shouldn't have mentioned it so suddenly," he said.

"Wha? Wha? What's amiss, then?" bellowed Murdo Lindsay, glaring round as he swept his musket barrel past the shadowed trees.

"Are we attacked? Where's the bastards?" Kenny popped up on hands and knees beside me, peering out from under the band of his knitted cap like a toad beneath a watering pot.

"Nobody. Nothing's happened. I mean—it's really quite all right!"

My efforts to calm and explain went largely unnoticed in the racket. Roger, however, being much larger and much louder, succeeded at last in quelling the disturbance and explaining matters—so far as they could be explained. What did a lad more or less matter? With considerable grumbling, the men settled down once more, leaving Roger and me staring at each other over the coffeepot.

"What was it, then?" I asked, a little testily.

"The mark? I'm pretty sure it was the letter 'T'—I saw it when you made him take the coffee and he wrapped his hand round the cup."

My stomach tightened. I knew what that meant; I'd seen it before.

"Thief," Roger said, eyes on my face. "He's been branded."

"Yes," I said unhappily. "Oh, dear."

"Would the folk on the Ridge not accept him, if they knew?" Roger asked.

"I doubt most of them would be much bothered," I said. "It's not that; it's that he ran when you mentioned it. He isn't just a convicted thief—I'm afraid he may be a fugitive. And Jamie called him, at the Gathering."

"Ah." Roger scratched absently at his whiskers. "*Earbsachd*. Jamie will feel obliged to him in some way, then?"

"Something like that."

Roger was a Scot, and—technically, at least—a Highlander. But he had been born long after the death of the clans, and neither history nor heritage could ever have taught him the strength of the ancient bonds between laird and tenant, between chief and clansman. Most likely, Josiah himself had no idea of the importance of the *earbsachd*—of what had been promised and accepted on both sides. Jamie had.

"Do you think Jamie will catch him?" Roger asked.

"I expect he already has. He can't be tracking the boy in the dark, and if he'd lost him, he would have come back already."

There were other possibilities—that Jamie had fallen over a precipice in the dark, tripped on a stone and broken his leg, or met with a catamount or a bear, for instance—but I preferred not to dwell on those.

I stood up, stretching my cramped limbs, and looked into the woods, where Jamie and his prey had disappeared. Josiah might be a good woodsman and hunter; Jamie had been one much longer. Josiah was small, quick, and impelled by fear; Jamie had a considerable advantage in size, strength, and sheer bloody-mindedness.

Roger stood up beside me. His lean face was slightly troubled, as he peered into the encircling trees.

"It's taking a long time. If he's caught the lad, what's he doing with him?"

"Extracting the truth from him, I imagine," I said. I bit my lip at the thought. "Jamie doesn't like being lied to."

Roger looked down at me, mildly startled.

"How?"

I shrugged.

"However he can." I'd seen him do it by reason, by guile, with charm, with threats—and on occasion, by means of brute force. I hoped he hadn't had to use force—though more for his sake than Josiah's.

"I see," Roger said quietly. "Well, then."

The coffeepot was empty; I bundled my cloak round me and went down to the stream to rinse and fill it, hung it to brew once more above the fire, and sat down to wait.

"You should go to sleep," I said to Roger, after a few minutes. He merely smiled at me, wiped his nose, and hunched deeper into his cloak.

"So should you," he said.

There was no wind, but it was very late, and the cold had settled well into the hollow, lying damp and heavy on the ground. The men's blankets had grown limp with condensation, and I could feel the dense chill of the ground seeping through the folds of my skirt. I thought about retrieving my breeches, but couldn't muster the energy to search for them. The excitement of Josiah's appearance and escape had faded, and the lethargy of cold and fatigue was setting in.

Roger poked up the fire a bit, and added a few small chunks of wood. I tucked another fold of skirt beneath my thighs and pulled cloak and shawl close around me, burying my hands in the folds of fabric. The coffeepot hung steaming, the hiss of occasional droplets falling into the fire punctuating the phlegm-filled snores of the sleeping men.

I wasn't seeing the blanket-rolled shapes, though, or hearing the sough of dark pines. I heard the crackle of dried leaves in a Scottish oak wood, in the hills above Carryarrick. We had camped there, two days before Prestonpans, with thirty men from Lallybroch—on our way to join Charles Stuart's army. And a young boy had come suddenly out of the dark; a knife had glinted in the light of a fire.

A different place, a different time. I shook myself, trying to dispel the sudden memories: a thin white face and a boy's eyes huge with shock and pain. The blade of a dirk, darkening and glowing in the embers of the fire. The smell of gunpowder, sweat, and burning flesh.

"I mean to shoot you," he had told John Grey. *"Head, or heart?"* By threat, by guile—by brute force.

That was then; this was now, I told myself. But Jamie would do what he thought he must.

Roger sat quietly, watching the dancing flames and the wood beyond. His eyes were hooded, and I wondered what he was thinking.

"D'you worry for him?" he asked softly, not looking at me.

"What, now? Or ever?" I smiled, though without much humor. "If I did, I'd never rest."

He turned his head toward me, and a faint smile touched his lips.

"You're resting now, are you?"

I smiled again, a real one in spite of myself.

"I'm not pacing to and fro," I answered. "Nor yet wringing my hands."

One dark eyebrow flicked up.

"Might help keep them warm."

One of the men stirred, muttering in his wrappings, and we ceased talking for a moment. The coffeepot was boiling; I could hear the soft rumble of the liquid inside.

Whatever could be keeping him? He couldn't be taking all this time to question Josiah Beardsley—he would either have gotten what answers he required in short order, or he would have let the boy go. No matter what the boy had stolen, it was no concern of Jamie's—save for the promise of the *earbsachd*.

The flames were mildly hypnotic; I could look into the wavering glow and see in memory the great fire of the Gathering, the figures dark around it, and the sound of distant fiddles. . . .

"Should I go to look for him?" Roger asked suddenly, low-voiced.

I jerked, startled out of sleepy hypnosis. I rubbed a hand over my face and shook my head to clear it.

"No. It's dangerous to go into strange woods in the dark, and you couldn't find him anyway. If he isn't back by the morning—that will be time enough."

As the moments wore slowly on, I began to think that the dawn *might* come before Jamie did. I was worried for Jamie—but there was in fact nothing that could be done before the morning. Disquieting thoughts tried to push their way in; did Josiah have a knife? Surely he did. But even if the boy was desperate enough to use it, could he possibly take Jamie by surprise? I pushed aside these anxious speculations, trying to occupy my mind instead with counting the number of coughs from the men around the fire.

Number eight was Roger; a deep, loose cough that shook his shoulders. Was he worried for Bree and Jemmy? I wondered. Or did he wonder whether Bree worried about *him*? I could have told him that, but it wouldn't have helped him to know. Men fighting—or preparing to fight—needed the idea of home as a place of utter safety; the conviction that all was well there kept them in good heart and on their feet, marching, enduring. Other things would make them fight, but fighting is such a small part of warfare. . . .

A damned important part, Sassenach, said Jamie's voice in the back of my head.

I began at last to nod off, waking repeatedly as my head jerked sharply on my neck. The last time, it was the feel of hands on my shoulders that wakened me, but only briefly. Roger eased me to the ground, wadding half my shawl beneath my head for a pillow, tucking the rest of it snug about my shoulders. I caught a brief glimpse of him in silhouette against the fire, black and bearlike in his cloak, and then I knew no more.

I DON'T KNOW how long I slept; I woke quite suddenly, at the sound of an explosive sneeze nearby. Jamie was sitting a few feet away, holding Josiah Beardsley's wrist in one hand, his dirk in the other. He paused long enough to sneeze twice more, wiped his nose impatiently on his sleeve, then thrust the dirk into the embers of the fire.

I caught the stink of hot metal, and raised myself abruptly on one elbow. Before I could say or do anything, something twitched and moved against me. I looked down in astonishment, then up, then down again, convinced in my muddled state that I was still dreaming.

A young boy lay under my cloak, curled against my body, sound asleep. I saw black hair and a scrawny frame, a pallid skin smeared with grime and grazed with scratches. Then there was a sudden loud hiss from the fire and I jerked my gaze back to see Jamie press Josiah's thumb against the searing metal of his blackened dirk.

Jamie glimpsed my convulsive movement from the corner of his eye and scowled in my direction, lips pursed in a silent adjuration to stillness. Josiah's face was contorted, lips drawn back from his teeth in agony—but he made no noise. On the far side of the fire, Kenny Lindsay sat watching, silent as a rock.

Still convinced that I was dreaming—or hoping that I was—I put a hand on the boy curled against me. He moved again, and the feel of solid flesh under my fingers woke me completely. My hand closed on his shoulder, and his eyes sprang open, wide with alarm.

He jerked away, scrambling awkwardly to get to his feet. Then he saw his brother—for plainly Josiah *was* his brother—and stopped abruptly, glancing wildly around the clearing, at the scattered men, at Jamie, Roger, and me.

Ignoring what must have been the frightful pain of a burned hand, Josiah rose from his seat and stepped quick and soft to his brother's side, taking him by the arm.

I got to my feet, moving slowly so as not to frighten them. They watched me, identical looks of wariness on the thin, white faces. Identical. Yes, just the same pinched faces—though the other boy's hair was worn long. He was dressed in nothing but a ragged shirt, and he was barefoot. I saw Josiah squeeze his brother's arm in reassurance, and began to suspect just what it was he had stolen. I summoned a smile for the two of them, then stretched out my hand to Josiah.

"Let me see your hand," I whispered.

He hesitated a moment, then gave me his right hand. It was a nice, neat job; so neat that it made me slightly faint for a moment. The ball of the thumb had been sliced cleanly off, the open wound cauterized with searing metal. A red-black, crusted oval had replaced the incriminating brand.

There was a soft movement behind me; Roger had fetched my medicine box and set it down by my feet.

There wasn't a great deal to do for the injury, save apply a little gentian ointment and bandage the thumb with a clean, dry cloth. I was conscious of Jamie as I worked; he had sheathed his dirk and risen quietly, to go and rummage among the packs and saddlebags. By the time I had finished my brief job, he was back, with a small bundle of food wrapped in a kerchief, and a spare blanket tied in a roll. Over his arm were my discarded breeches.

He handed these to the new boy, gave the food and blanket to Josiah, then clapped a hand on the boy's shoulder, and squeezed hard. He touched the other boy gently, turning him toward the wood with a hand on his back. Then he jerked his head toward the trees, and Josiah nodded. He touched his forehead to me, the bandage glinting white on his thumb, and whispered, "Thank'ee, ma'am."

The two boys disappeared silently into the forest, the twin's bare feet winking pale below the flapping hem of the breeks as he followed his brother.

Jamie nodded to Kenny, then sat down again by the fire, shoulders slumping in sudden exhaustion. I poured him coffee and he took it, his mouth twitching in an attempted smile of acknowledgment that dissipated in a fit of heavy coughing.

I reached for the cup before it could spill, and caught Roger's eye over Jamie's shoulder. He nodded toward the east, and laid a finger across his lips, then shrugged with a grimace of resignation. He wanted as much as I did to know what had just happened—and why. He was right, though; the night was fading. Dawn would be here soon, and the men—all accustomed to wake at first light—would be floating toward the surface of consciousness.

Jamie had stopped coughing, but was making horrible gurgling noises in an attempt to clear his throat—he sounded rather like a pig drowning in mud.

"Here," I whispered, giving him back the cup. "Drink it, and lie down. You should sleep a little."

He shook his head and lifted the cup to his lips. He swallowed, grimacing at the bitterness.

"Not worth it," he croaked. He nodded toward the east, where the tufted pines were now inked black on a graying sky. "And besides, I've got to think what the hell to do now."

27

DEATH COMES CALLING

I COULD SCARCELY CONTAIN my impatience until the men had roused and eaten, broken camp—in an irritatingly leisurely fashion—and mounted. At last, though, I found myself once more on horseback, riding through a morning so crisp and cold, I thought the air might shatter as I breathed it.

"Right," I said without preamble, as my mount nosed her way up next to Jamie's. "Talk."

He glanced back at me and smiled. His face was creased with tiredness, but the brisk air—and a lot of very strong coffee—had revived him. Despite the troubled night, I felt quick and lively myself, blood coursing near the surface of my skin and blooming in my cheeks.

"Ye dinna mean to wait for wee Roger?"

"I'll tell him later—or you can." There was no way of riding three abreast; it was only owing to a washout that had left a fan of gravel down the mountainside that we were able to pick our way side by side for the moment, out of hearing of the others. I nudged my mount closer to Jamie's, my knees wreathed in steam from the horse's nostrils.

Jamie rubbed a hand over his face, and shook himself, as though to throw off fatigue.

"Aye, well," he said. "You'll have seen they were brothers?"

"I did notice that, yes. Where the hell did the other one come from?"

"From there." He lifted his chin, pointing toward the west. Thanks to the washout, there was an unimpeded view of a small cove in the hollow below—one of those natural breaks in the wilderness, where the trees gave way to meadow and stream. From the trees at the edge of the cove, a thin plume of smoke rose upward, pointing like a finger in the still, cold air.

Squinting, I could make out what looked like a small farmhouse, with a couple of rickety outbuildings. As I watched, a tiny figure emerged from the house and headed toward one of the sheds.

"They're just about to discover that he's gone," Jamie said, a trifle grimly. "Though with luck, they'll think he's only gone to the privy, or to milk the goats."

I didn't bother asking how he knew they had goats.

"Is that their home? Josiah and his brother?"

"In a manner of speaking, Sassenach. They were bond servants."

"Were?" I said skeptically. Somehow I doubted that the brothers' terms of indenture had just happened to expire the night before.

Jamie lifted one shoulder in a shrug, and wiped a dripping nose on his sleeve.

"Unless someone catches them, aye."

"You caught Josiah," I pointed out. "What did he tell you?"

"The truth," he said, with a slight twist of the mouth. "Or at least I think so."

He had hunted Josiah through the dark, guided by the sound of the boy's frantic wheezing, and trapped him at last in a rocky hollow, seizing him in the dark. He had wrapped the freezing boy in his plaid, sat him down, and with judicious application of patience and firmness—augmented with sips of whisky from his flask—had succeeded at last in extracting the story.

"The family were immigrants—father, mother, and six bairns. Only the twins survived the passage; the rest perished of illness at sea. There were no relatives here—or none that met the boat, at any rate—and so the ship's master sold them. The price wouldna cover the cost of the family's passage, so the lads were indentured for thirty years, their wages to be put toward the debt."

His voice in the telling was matter-of-fact; these things happened. I knew they did, but was much less inclined to accept them without comment.

"Thirty years! Why, that's—how old were they at the time?"

"Two or three," he said.

I was taken aback at that. Overlooking the basic tragedy, that was some mitigation, I supposed; if the boys' purchaser had been providing for their welfare as children . . . but I remembered Josiah's scrawny ribs, and the bowing of his legs. They hadn't been all that well provided for. But then, neither were a good many children who came from loving homes.

"Josiah's no idea who his parents were, where they came from, nor what their names were," Jamie explained. He coughed briefly, and cleared his throat.

"He kent his own name, and that of his brother—the brother's name is Keziah—but nothing else. Beardsley is the name o' the man who took them, but as for the lads, they dinna ken if they're Scots, English, Irish—with names like that, they likely aren't German or Polish, but even that's not impossible."

"Hmm." I puffed a cloud of thoughtful steam, temporarily obscuring the farmhouse below. "So Josiah ran away. I imagine that had something to do with the brand on his thumb?"

Jamie nodded, eyes on the ground as his horse picked its way down the slope. The ground to either side of the gravel was soft, and clumps of black dirt showed like creeping fungus through the scree.

"He stole a cheese—he was honest enough about that." His mouth widened in momentary amusement. "Took it from a dairy shed in Brownsville, but the dairymaid saw him. In fact, the maid said 'twas the other—the brother—who took it, but . . ." Jamie's ruddy brows drew together for a moment. "Perhaps Josiah wasna so honest about it as I thought. At any rate, one of the boys took the cheese; Beardsley caught the two of them with it and summoned the sheriff, and Josiah took the blame—and the punishment."

The boy had run away from the farm following this incident, which took place two years before. Josiah had—he told Jamie—always intended to return and rescue his brother, so soon as he could contrive a place for them to live. Jamie's offer had seemed a godsend to him, and he had left the Gathering to make his way back on foot.

"Imagine his surprise to find us perched there on the hillside," Jamie said, and sneezed. He wiped his nose, eyes watering slightly. "He was lurking close by, trying to make up his mind whether to wait until we'd gone, or find out whether we were headed for the farm—thinking if so, we might make a fine distraction for him to slip in and steal away his brother."

"So you decided to slip in with him instead, and help with the stealing." My own nose was dripping from the cold. I groped for my handkerchief with one hand, trusting to the horse, Mrs. Piggy, not to catapult us head over heels down the mountain while I blew my nose. I eyed Jamie over the hanky. He still had the clammy, red-nosed look of illness, but his high cheekbones were flushed with the morning sun and he looked remarkably cheerful for a man who'd been out in a cold wood all night. "Fun, was it?"

"Oh, aye, it was. I've not done anything like that in years." Jamie's eyes creased into blue triangles with his grin. "It reminded me o' raiding into the Grants' lands with Dougal and his men, when I was a lad. Creepin' through the dark, stealing into the barn without a sound—Christ, I had to stop myself in time before I took the cow. Or I would have, if they'd had one."

I sniffed, and laughed indulgently.

"You are the most complete bandit, Jamie," I said.

"Bandit?" he said, mildly affronted. "I'm a verra honest man, Sassenach. Or at least I am when I can afford to be," he amended, with a quick glance behind, to be sure we were not overheard.

"Oh, you're entirely honest," I assured him. "Too honest for your own good, in fact. You're just not very law-abiding."

This observation appeared to disconcert him slightly, for he frowned and made a gruff sound in his throat that might have been either a Scottish noise of disagreement or merely an attempt to dislodge phlegm. He coughed, then reined in, and standing up in his stirrups, waved his hat to Roger, who was some distance up the slope. Roger waved back, and turned his horse's nose in our direction.

I pulled my horse in beside Jamie, and dropped the reins on its neck.

"I'll have wee Roger take the men on to Brownsville," Jamie explained, sitting back in his saddle, "while I go and call upon the Beardsleys alone. Will ye come with me, Sassenach, or go on wi' Roger?"

"Oh, I'll come with you," I said, without hesitation. "I want to see what these Beardsleys are like."

He smiled and brushed back his hair with one hand before replacing his hat. He wore his hair loose to cover his neck and ears against the cold, and it shone like molten copper in the morning sun.

"I thought ye might. Mind your face, though," he said, in half-mocking warning. "Dinna go gape-jawed or gooseberry, and they mention their missing servant lad."

"Mind your own face," I said, rather crossly. "Gooseberry, indeed. Did Josiah say that he and his brother were badly treated?" I wondered whether there had been more to Josiah's leaving than the cheese incident.

Jamie shook his head.

"I didna ask, and he didna say—but ask yourself, Sassenach: would ye leave a decent home to go and live in the woods alone, to make your bed in cold leaves and eat grubs and crickets 'til ye learned to hunt meat?"

He nudged his horse into motion, and rode up the slope to meet Roger, leaving me pondering that conjecture. He returned a few moments later, and I turned my mount in beside him, another question in my mind.

"But if things were bad enough here as to force him to leave—why didn't his brother go with him?"

Jamie glanced at me, surprised, but then smiled, a little grimly.

"Keziah's deaf, Sassenach."

Not born deaf, from what Josiah had told him; his twin had lost his hearing as the result of an injury, occurring at the age of five or so. Keziah could therefore speak, but not hear any but the loudest of noises; and unable to perceive the sound of rustling leaves or shuffling feet, could neither hunt nor avoid pursuit.

"He says Keziah understands him, and doubtless he does. When we crept into the barn, I kept watch below while the lad went up the ladder to the loft. I didna hear a sound, but within a minute, both lads were down on the floor beside me, Keziah rubbing the sleep from his eyes. I hadna realized they were twins; gave me a turn to see the two of them, so like."

"I wonder why Keziah didn't bring away his breeches," I said, touching on one thing that had been puzzling me.

Jamie laughed.

"I asked. Seems he'd taken them off the night before, left them in the hay, and one o' the barn cats had kittens on them. He didna want to disturb her."

I laughed too, though with an uneasy memory of pale bare feet, blue-tinged skin showing purple in the firelight.

"Kind lad. And his shoes?"

"He hadn't any."

By now we had reached the bottom of the slope. The horses milled for a moment, turning in a slow gyre round Jamie as directions were decided, rendezvous appointed, farewells taken. Then Roger—with only slight evidence of self-consciousness—whistled through his teeth and waved his hat in the air in summons. I watched him ride away, and noticed him half-turn in the saddle, then turn back, looking straight ahead.

"He's no sure they'll really follow him," Jamie said, watching. He shook his head critically, then shrugged, dismissing it. "Aye, well. He'll manage, or not."

"He'll manage," I said, thinking of the night before.

"I'm glad ye think so, Sassenach. Come on, then." He clicked his tongue and reined his horse's head around.

"If you're not sure Roger can manage, why are you sending him on his own?" I inquired of his back, swaying in the saddle as we turned into the thin copse that lay between us and the now-invisible farm. "Why not keep the men together, and take them into Brownsville yourself?"

"For one thing, he'll no learn, and I dinna give him the chance. For another . . ." He paused, turning to look back at me. "For another, I didna want the whole boiling coming along to the Beardsleys' and maybe hearing of their missing servant. The whole camp saw Josiah last night, aye? If you've a lad missing, and hear of a lad popping up and causing a stir in the forest nearby, conclusions might be drawn, d'ye not think?"

He turned back, and I followed him through a narrow defile between the pine trees. Dew gleamed like diamonds on bark and needle, and small icy drops fell from the boughs above, startling my skin where they fell.

"Unless this Beardsley is old or infirm, though, won't he be joining you?" I objected. "Someone's bound to mention Josiah in his hearing sooner or later."

He shook his head, not turning round.

"And tell him what, if they do? They saw the lad when we dragged him in, and they saw him run away again. For all they ken, he got clear away."

"Kenny Lindsay saw them both when you brought them back."

He shrugged.

"Aye, I had a word wi' Kenny, while we were saddling the horses. He'll say nothing." He was right, I knew. Kenny was one of his Ardsmuir men; he would follow Jamie's orders without question.

"No," Jamie went on, skillfully reining round a large boulder, "Beardsley's not infirm; Josiah told me he's an Indian trader—taking goods across the Treaty Line to the Cherokee villages. What I don't know is if he's to home just now. If he is, though—" He drew breath and paused to cough as the cold air tickled his lungs.

"That's the other reason for sending the men ahead," he continued, wheezing slightly. "We'll not join them again until tomorrow, I think. By that time, they'll have had a night to drink and be sociable in Brownsville; they'll scarce recall the lad, and be the less likely to speak of him in Beardsley's hearing. With luck, we'll be well away before anything's said—no chance of Beardsley leaving us to pursue the lad then."

So he was counting on the Beardsleys being sufficiently hospitable as to put us up for the night. A reasonable expectation, in this neck of the woods. Listening to him cough again, I resolved to sit on his chest this evening, if necessary, and oblige him to be well-greased with camphor, whether he liked it or not.

We emerged from the trees, and I glanced dubiously at the farmhouse ahead. It was smaller than I had thought, and rather shabby, with a cracked step, a sagging porch, and a wide patch of shingles missing from the weathered roof. Well, I had slept in worse places, and likely would again.

The door to a stunted barn gaped open, but there was no sign of life. The whole place seemed deserted, save for the plume of smoke from the chimney.

I had meant what I said to Jamie, though I hadn't been entirely accurate. He *was* honest, and also law-abiding—provided that the laws were those he chose to respect. The mere fact that a law had been established by the Crown was not, I knew, sufficient to make it law in his eyes. Other laws, unwritten, he would likely die for.

Still, while the law of property meant somewhat less to an erstwhile Highland raider than it might to others, it hadn't escaped my attention—and therefore certainly hadn't escaped his—that he was about to claim both hospitality and duty from a man whose property he had just helped to abscond. Jamie had no deep-seated objection to indenture as such, I knew; ordinarily, he would respect such a claim. That he hadn't meant that he perceived some higher law in operation—though whether that was friendship, pity, the claim of his *earbsachd*, or something else, I didn't know. He had paused, waiting for me.

"Why did you decide to help Josiah?" I asked bluntly, as we made our way across the ragged cornfield that lay before the house. Dry stalks snapped beneath the horses' feet, and ice crystals glittered on the litter of dead leaves.

Jamie took off his hat, and set it on the saddle before him, as he tied back his hair in preparation for meeting company.

"Well, I said to him that if he was set on this course, so be it. But if he chose to come to the Ridge—alone or with his brother—then we must rid him of the mark on his thumb, for it would cause talk, and word might get back to yon Beardsley, wi' the devil to pay and a' that."

He took a deep breath and let it out, the smoke of it wisping white around his head, then turned to look at me, his face serious.

"The lad didna hesitate for a moment, though he'd been branded; he knew. And I'll tell ye, Sassenach—while a man may do a desperate thing once from love or courage . . . it takes something more than that, if ye've done it once already, and ye know damn well what it's going to feel like to have to do it again."

He turned away without waiting for my response, and rode into the dooryard, scattering a flock of foraging doves. He sat his horse upright, his shoulders broad and square. There was no hint of the deep-webbed scars that lined his back beneath the homespun cloak, but I knew them well.

So that was it, I thought. *As in water face answereth to face, so the heart of man to man.* And the law of courage was the one he had lived by for the longest.

SEVERAL CHICKENS HUDDLED on the porch, fluffed into balls of yellow-eyed resentment. They muttered balefully among themselves as we dismounted, but were too cold to do more than shuffle away from us, reluctant to abandon their patch of sunshine. Several boards of the porch itself were broken, and the yard nearby was littered with scraps of half-hewn lumber and scattered nails, as though someone had meant to mend it, but had not yet found a moment to attend to the job. The procrastination had lasted for some time, I thought; the nails were rusty, and the newly cut boards had warped and split with damp.

"Ho! The house!" Jamie shouted, stopping in the center of the dooryard. This was accepted etiquette for approaching a strange house; while most people in the mountains were hospitable, there were not a few who viewed strangers warily—and were inclined to make introductions at gunpoint, until the callers' bona fides should be established.

With this in mind, I kept a cautious distance behind Jamie, but made sure I was visible, ostentatiously spreading my skirts and brushing them down, displaying my gender as evidence of our peaceable intent.

Damn, there was a small hole burnt through the brown wool, no doubt from a flying campfire spark. I concealed the burned spot in a fold of skirt, thinking how odd it was that everyone regarded women as inherently harmless. Had I been so inclined, I could easily have burgled houses and murdered hapless families from one end of the Ridge to the other.

Fortunately the impulse to do so hadn't struck me, though it *had* dawned on me now and then that the Hippocratic Oath and its injunction to "Do no harm" might not have strictly to do with medical procedure. I'd had the impulse to dot one of my more recalcitrant patients over the head with a stick of firewood more than once, but had so far managed to keep the urge in check.

Of course, most people hadn't the advantage of a doctor's jaundiced view of humanity. And it was true that women didn't go in so much for the recreational sorts of mayhem that men enjoyed—I rarely found women beating each other into pulp for fun. Give them a good motive, though, and . . .

Jamie was walking toward the barn, shouting at intervals, to no apparent effect. I glanced round, but there were no fresh tracks in the dooryard save our own. A scatter of dung balls lay near the half-hewn log, but those had plainly been left days ago; they were moist with dew, but not fresh—most had crumbled to powder.

No one had come, no one had gone, save on foot. The Beardsleys, whoever and however many of them there were, were likely still within.

Lying low, though. It was early, but not so early that farm people would not already be about their chores; I had seen someone earlier, after all. I stepped back and shaded my eyes against the rising sun, looking for any sign of life. I was more than curious about these Beardsleys—and more than slightly apprehensive about the prospects of having one or more male Beardsleys riding with us, given recent events.

I turned back to the door, and noticed an odd series of notches cut into the wood of the jamb. Each one was small, but there were a great many, running the complete length of one doorpost, and halfway down the other. I looked closer;

they were arranged in groups of seven, a scant width of unscarred wood between the groups, as a prisoner might count, keeping track of the weeks.

Jamie emerged from the barn, followed by a faint bleating. The goats he'd mentioned, of course; I wondered whether it had been Keziah's job to milk them—if it was, his absence was going to become rapidly apparent, if it wasn't already.

Jamie took a few paces toward the house, cupped his hands round his mouth, and shouted again. No answer. He waited a few moments, then shrugged and strode up onto the porch, where he hammered on the door with the hilt of his dirk. It made enough noise to wake the dead, had there been any in the vicinity, and sent the chickens squawking away in a feather-scattering panic, but no one appeared in answer to the thunderous summons.

Jamie glanced back at me, one eyebrow raised. People didn't normally go off and leave their farms untended, not if they had livestock.

"Someone's here," he said, in answer to the unvoiced thought. "The goats are fresh-milked; there are drops still on their teats."

"Do you think they could all be out searching for . . . er . . . you know who?" I murmured, moving closer to him.

"Perhaps." He moved to the side, bending to peer into a window. It had once been glassed, but most of the panes were cracked or missing, and a sheet of ratty muslin had been tacked over the opening. I saw Jamie frown at it, with the craftsman's disdain for a shoddy repair.

He turned his head suddenly, then looked at me.

"D'ye hear something, Sassenach?"

"Yes. I thought it was the goats, but . . ."

The bleat came again—this time unmistakably from the house. Jamie set his hand to the door, but it didn't budge.

"Bolted," he said briefly, and moved back to the window, where he reached carefully into the frame and pulled loose a corner of the muslin cloth.

"Phew," I said, wrinkling my nose at the air that wafted out. I was used to the odors of a winter-sealed cabin, where the scents of sweat, dirty clothes, wet feet, greasy hair, and slop jars mingled with baking bread, stewing meat, and the subtler notes of fungus and mold, but the aroma within the Beardsley residence went well beyond the norm.

"Either they're keeping the pigs in the house," I said, with a glance at the barn, "or there are ten people living in there who haven't come out since last spring."

"It's a bit ripe," Jamie agreed. He put his face into the window, grimacing at the stink, and bellowed, "*Thig a mach!* Come out, Beardsley, or I'm comin' in!"

I peered over his shoulder, to see whether this invitation might produce results. The room within was large, but so crowded that scarcely any of the stained wooden floor was visible through the rubble. Sniffing cautiously, I deduced that the barrels I saw contained—among other things—salt fish, tar, apples, beer, and sauerkraut, while bundles of woolen blankets dyed with cochineal and indigo, kegs of black powder, and half-tanned hides reeking of dog turds lent their own peculiar fragrances to the unique mephitis within. Beardsley's trade goods, I supposed.

The other window had been covered as well, with a tattered wolf hide, so that the interior was dim and shadowy; with all the boxes, bundles, barrels, and bits of furniture lying in heaps, it looked like a poverty-stricken version of Ali Baba's cave.

The sound came again from the back of the house, somewhat louder; a noise midway between a squeal and a growl. I took a step back, sound and acrid smell together vividly recalling an image of dark fur and sudden violence.

"Bears," I suggested, half-seriously. "The people are gone and there's a bear inside."

"Aye, Goldilocks," Jamie said, very dryly. "Nay doubt. Bears or not, there's something wrong. Fetch the pistols and cartridge box from my saddlebag."

I nodded and turned to go, but before I could step off the porch, a shuffling noise came from inside, and I turned back sharply. Jamie had grasped his dirk, but as he saw whatever was inside, his hand relaxed on the hilt. His eyebrows also rose in surprise, and I leaned over his arm to see.

A woman peered out from between two hillocks of goods, looking round suspiciously, like a rat peering out of a garbage dump. She was not particularly ratlike in appearance, being wavy-haired and quite stout, but she blinked at us in the calculating way of vermin, reckoning the threat.

"Go away," she said, evidently concluding that we were not the vanguard of an invading army.

"Good morning to ye, ma'am," Jamie began, "I am James Fraser, of—"

"I don't care who you are," she replied. "Go away."

"Indeed I will not," he said firmly. "I must speak with the man o' the house."

An extraordinary expression crossed her plump face; concern, calculation, and what might have been amusement.

"Must you?" she said. She had a slight lisp; it came out as *mutht you?* "And who says that you must?"

Jamie's ears were beginning to redden slightly, but he answered calmly enough.

"The Governor, madam. I am *Colonel* James Fraser," he said, with emphasis, "charged with the raising of militia. All able-bodied men between the ages of sixteen and sixty are called to muster. Will ye fetch Mr. Beardsley, please?"

"Mili-ish-ia, is it?" she said, handling the word with care. "Why, who will you be fighting, then?"

"With luck, no one. But the call to muster is sent out; I must answer, and so must all able-bodied men within the Treaty Line." Jamie's hand tightened on the crosspiece of the inner frame and rattled it experimentally. It was made of flimsy pine sticks, the wood shrunken and badly weathered; he could plainly rip it out of the wall and step through the opening, if he chose to do so. He met her eyes straight on, and smiled pleasantly.

She narrowed her eyes and pursed her lips, thinking.

"Able-bodied men," she said at last. "Hmp. Well, we've none of those. The bond lad's run off again, but even if he were here, he's not able; deaf as that doorpotht, and quite as dumb." She nodded toward the door in illustration. "If you care to hunt him down, you're welcome to keep him, though."

It didn't look as though there would be any hue and cry after Keziah, then. I took a deep breath, in a sigh of relief, but let it out again, swiftly.

Jamie wasn't giving up easily.

"Is Mr. Beardsley in the house?" he asked. "I wish to see him." He gave an experimental tug on the frame, and the dry wood cracked with a sound like a pistol shot.

"He's thcarce fit for company," she said, and the odd note was back in her voice; wary, but at the same time, filled with something like excitement.

"Is he ill?" I asked, leaning over Jamie's shoulder. "I might be able to help; I'm a doctor."

She shuffled forward a step or two, and peered at me, frowning under a heavy mass of wavy brown hair. She was younger than I'd thought; seen in better light, the heavy face showed no cobweb of age or slackening of flesh.

"A doctor?"

"My wife's well-kent as a healer," Jamie said. "The Indian folk call her White Raven."

"The conjure woman?" Her eyes flew wide in alarm, and she took a step back.

Something struck me odd about the woman, and looking at her, I realized what it was. Despite the reek in the house, both the woman's person and her dress were clean, and her hair was soft and fluffy—not at all the norm at this time of year, when people generally didn't bathe for several months in the cold weather.

"Who are you?" I asked bluntly. "Are you Mrs. Beardsley? Or perhaps Miss Beardsley?"

No more than twenty-five, I thought, in spite of the bulk of her swaddled figure. Her shoulders swelled fatly under her shawl, and the width of her hips brushed the barrels she stood between. Evidently trade with the Cherokee was sufficiently profitable to keep Beardsley's family in adequate food, if not his bond servants. I eyed her with some dislike, but she met my gaze coolly enough.

"I am Mrs. Beardthley."

The alarm had faded; she pursed her lips, and pushed them in and out, regarding me with an air of calculation. Jamie flexed his arm, and the window frame cracked loudly.

"Come you in, then."

The odd tone was still in her voice; half defiance, half eagerness. Jamie caught it and frowned, but released his grip on the frame.

She moved out from between the boxes and turned toward the door. I caught no more than a glimpse of her in motion, but that was enough to see that she was lame; one leg dragged, her shoe scraping on the wooden floor.

There was a bumping and grunting as she fumbled with the bolt; a grating noise, and then a *thunk* as she dropped it on the floor. The door was warped, stuck in its frame; Jamie put his shoulder to it and it sprang loose and swung in, boards quivering with the shock. How long since it had been opened? I wondered.

A good long time, evidently. I heard Jamie snort and cough as he went in, and did my best to breathe through my mouth as I followed. Even so, the smell was enough to knock a ferret over. Beyond the reek of the goods, there was an outhouse smell from somewhere; stale urine and a ripe fecal stench. Rotting food, too, but something else besides. My nostrils twitched cautiously as I tried to inhale no more than a few molecules of air for analysis.

"How long has Mr. Beardsley been ill?" I asked.

I had picked out a distinct stench of sickness amid the general fetor. Not only the ghost of long-dried vomit, but the sweet smell of purulent discharge and that indefinable musty, yeast-rising odor that seems to be simply the smell of illness itself.

"Oh . . . thome time."

She shut the door behind us, and I felt a sudden surge of claustrophobia. Inside, the air seemed thick, both from the stench and from the lack of light. I had a great impulse to rip down the coverings from both windows and let in a little air, and clenched my hands in the fabric of my cloak to keep from doing it.

Mrs. Beardsley turned sideways and scuttled crablike through a narrow passage left between the stacks of goods. Jamie glanced at me, made a Scottish noise of disgust in his throat, and ducked under a jutting bundle of tent poles to follow her. I made my way cautiously after, trying not to notice that my foot fell now and then on objects of an unpleasant squashiness. Rotten apples? Dead rats? I pinched my nose and didn't look down.

The farmhouse was simple in construction; one big room across the front, one behind.

The rear room was a striking contrast to the squalid clutter of the front. There was no ornament or decoration; the room was plain and orderly as a Quaker meeting hall. Everything was bare and spotless, the wooden table and stone hearth scrubbed to rawness, a few pewter utensils gleaming dully on a shelf. One window here had been left uncovered, glass intact, and the morning sun fell across the room in pure white radiance. The room was quiet and the air still, increasing the odd feeling that we had entered a sanctuary of some sort from the chaos of the front room.

The impression of peace was dispelled at once by a loud noise from above. It was the sound we had heard earlier, but close at hand, a loud squeal filled with desperation, like a tortured hog. Jamie started at the sound, and turned at once toward a ladder at the far side of the room, which led upward to a loft.

"He'th up there," Mrs. Beardsley said—unnecessarily, as Jamie was already halfway up the ladder. The squealing noise came again, more urgently, and I decided not to fetch my medicine box before investigating.

Jamie's head appeared at the top of the ladder as I grasped it.

"Bring a light, Sassenach," he said briefly, and his head vanished.

Mrs. Beardsley stood motionless, hands buried in her shawl, making no effort to find a light. Her lips were pressed tight together, her plump cheeks mottled with red. I pushed past her, seized a candlestick from the shelf, and knelt to light it at the hearth before hastening upward.

"Jamie?" I poked my head above the edge of the loft, holding my candle cautiously above my head.

"Here, Sassenach." He was standing at the far end of the loft, where the shadows lay thickest. I scrambled over the top of the ladder and made my way toward him, stepping gingerly.

The stench was much stronger here. I caught the gleam of something in the dark, and brought the candle forward to see.

Jamie drew in his breath, as shocked as I was, but quickly mastered his emotion.

"Mr. Beardsley, I presume," he said.

The man was enormous—or had been. The great curve of his belly still rose whalelike out of the shadows, and the hand that lay slack on the floorboards near my foot could have cupped a cannonball with ease. But the flesh of the upper arm hung slack, white and flabby, the massive chest sunken in the center. What must once have been the neck of a bull had wasted to stringiness, and a single eye gleamed, frantic behind strands of matted hair.

The eye widened, and he made the noise again, his head straining upward urgently. I felt a shudder go through Jamie. It was enough to raise the hair on the back of my own neck, but I disregarded it, pushing the candlestick into Jamie's hands.

"Hold the light for me."

I sank to my knees, too late feeling the liquid ooze through the fabric of my skirt. The man lay in his own filth, and had been lying so for quite some time; the floor was thick with slime and wet. He was naked, covered by no more than a linen blanket, and as I turned it back, I glimpsed ulcerated sores amid the smears of ordure.

It was clear enough what ailed Mr. Beardsley; one side of his face sagged grotesquely, the eyelid drooping, and both the arm and the leg on the near side of his body splayed limp and dead, the joints left knobby and weirdly distorted by the falling away of the muscle around them. He snuffled and bleated, tongue poking and slobbering from the corner of his mouth in his vain but urgent attempts at speech.

"Hush," I said to him. "Don't talk; it's all right now."

I took the wrist to check his pulse; the flesh moved loosely on the bones of his arm, with not the slightest twitch of response to my touch.

"A stroke," I said softly to Jamie. "An apoplexy, you call it." I put my hand on Beardsley's chest, to offer the comfort of touch.

"Don't worry," I said to him. "We've come to help." I

spoke reassuringly, though even as I said the words, I wondered what help was possible. Well, cleanliness and warmth at least; it was nearly as cold in the loft as it was outside, and his chest was chilly and pebbled with gooseflesh among the bushy hair.

The ladder creaked heavily, and I turned to see the outline of Mrs. Beardsley's fluffy head and heavy shoulders, silhouetted by the light from the kitchen below.

"How long has he been like this?" I asked sharply.

"Perhapth . . . a month," she said, after a pause. "I could not move him," she said, defensive. "He ith too heavy."

That was plainly true. However . . .

"Why is he up here?" Jamie demanded. "If ye didna move him, how did he get here?" He turned, shedding the light of the candle over the loft. There was little here that would draw a man; an old straw mattress, a few scattered tools, and bits of household rubbish. The light shone on Mrs. Beardsley's face, turning her pale blue eyes to ice.

"He wath . . . chathing me," she said faintly.

"What?" Jamie strode over to the ladder, and bending down, seized her by the arm, helping her—rather against her will, it seemed—to clamber up the rest of the way into the loft.

"What d'ye mean, chasing you?" he demanded. She hunched her shoulders, looking round and homely as a cookie jar in her bundled shawls.

"He thtruck me," she said simply. "I came up the ladder to get away from him, but he followed. I tried to hide back here in the thadows, and he came, but then . . . he fell. And . . . he could not get up." She shrugged again.

Jamie held the candlestick near her face. She gave a small nervous smile, eyes darting from me to Jamie, and I saw that the lisp was caused by the fact that her front teeth were broken—snapped off at an angle, just beyond the gums. A small scar ran through her upper lip; another showed white in the hairs of one eyebrow.

A horrible noise came from the man on the floor—a furious squeal of what sounded like protest—and she flinched, eyes shut tight in reflexive dread.

"Mmphm," Jamie said, glancing from her to her husband.

"Aye. Well. Fetch up some water, ma'am, and ye will. Another candle and some fresh rags as well," he called after her departing back as she hastened toward the ladder, only too glad to be given an excuse to leave.

"Jamie—bring back the light, will you?"

He came and stood beside me, holding the candle so it shed its glow on the ruined body. He gave Beardsley a dark look of mingled pity and dislike, and shook his head slowly.

"God's judgment, d'ye think, Sassenach?"

"Not entirely God's, I don't think," I said, my voice lowered so as not to carry to the kitchen below. I reached up and took the candlestick from him. "Look."

A flask of water and a plate of bread, hard and tinged with blue mold, stood in the shadows near Beardsley's head; orts and bits of gluey, half-chewed bread covered the floor nearby. She had fed him—enough to keep him alive. Yet I had seen great quantities of food in that front room as we passed—hanging hams, barrels of dried fruit and salt fish and sauerkraut.

There were bundles of furs, jugs of oil, piles of woolen blankets—and yet the master of those goods lay here in the dark, starved and shivering beneath a single sheet of linen.

"Why did she not just let him die, I wonder?" Jamie asked softly, eyes fixed on the moldy bread. Beardsley gargled and growled at this; his open eye rolled angrily, tears running down his face and snot bubbling from his nose. He flailed and grunted, arching his body in frustration, collapsing with a meaty thud that shook the boards of the loft.

"He can understand you, I think. Can you?" I addressed this remark to the sick man, who gobbled and drooled in a manner that made it clear that he understood at least that he was being spoken to.

"As to why . . ."

I gestured toward Beardsley's legs, moving the candle slowly above them. Some of the sores were indeed compression sores, caused by lying helpless for a long time. Others were not. Parallel slashes, clearly made by a knife, showed black and clotted on one massive thigh. The shin was decorated with a regular line of ulcerations, angry red wounds rimmed with black and oozing. Burns, left to fester.

Jamie gave a small grunt at the sight, and glanced over his shoulder, toward the ladder. The sound of a door opening came from below, and a cold draft blew up into the loft, making the candle flame dance wildly. The door shut, and the flame steadied.

"I can make shift to lower him, I think." Jamie lifted the candle, assessing the beams overhead. "A sling, perhaps, with a rope put over yon beam there. Is it all right to move him?"

"Yes," I said, but I wasn't paying attention. Bending over the sick man's legs, I had caught a whiff of something that I hadn't smelled in a long, long time—a very bad and sinister stink.

I hadn't encountered it often, but even once would have been enough; the pungent smell of gas gangrene is strikingly memorable. I didn't want to say anything that might alarm Beardsley—if he was capable of understanding—so instead, I patted him reassuringly and stood up to go and fetch the candle from Jamie for a better look.

He gave it to me, leaning close to murmur in my ear as he did so.

"Can ye do aught for him, Sassenach?"

"No," I said, equally low-voiced. "Not for the apoplexy, that is. I can treat the sores and give him herbs against fever—that's all."

He stood for a moment, looking at the humped figure in the shadows, now quiescent. Then he shook his head, crossed himself, and went quickly down the ladder to hunt a rope.

I went slowly back to the sick man, who greeted me with a thick "Haughhh" and a restless thumping of one leg, like a rabbit's warning. I knelt by his feet, talking soothingly of nothing in particular, while I held the light close to examine them. The toes. All the toes on his dead foot had been burned, some only blistered, others burned nearly to the bone. The first two toes had gone quite black, and a greenish tinge spread over the upper aspect of the foot nearby.

I was appalled—as much by the thought of what might have led to this as by the action itself. The candle wavered; my hands were shaking, and not only with cold. I was not only horrified by what had happened here; I was also worried by the immediate prospects. What on earth were we to do about these wretched people?

Plainly we couldn't take Beardsley with us—just as plainly, he could not be left here, under the care of his wife. There were no near neighbors to look in, no one else on the farm to safeguard him. I supposed we might manage to transport him to Brownsville; there might be a wagon in the barn. But even if so, what then?

There was no hospital to care for him. If one of the homes in Brownsville might take him in for the sake of charity . . . well and good, but seeing Beardsley's state after a month, I thought it unlikely that his condition—in terms either of paralysis or speech—would improve much. Who would keep him, if it meant caring for him day and night for the rest of his life?

The rest of his life, of course, could be rather short, depending on my success in dealing with the gangrene. Worry retreated as my mind turned to the immediate problem. I would have to amputate; it was the only possibility. The toes were easy—but the toes might not be enough. If I had to take off the foot or part of it, we ran a greater risk from shock and infection.

Could he feel it? Sometimes stroke victims retained feeling in an affected limb, but not movement, sometimes movement without feeling—sometimes neither. Cautiously, I touched the gangrenous toe, eyes on his face.

His working eye was open, focused on the beams overhead. He didn't glance at me or make a noise, which answered that question. No, he couldn't feel the foot. That was a relief, in a way—at least he wouldn't suffer pain from the amputation. Nor, it occurred to me, had he felt the damage inflicted on his limb. Had she been aware of that? Or had she chosen to attack his dead side only because he retained some strength on the other, and might still defend himself?

There was a soft rustle behind me. Mrs. Beardsley was back. She set down a bucket of water and a pile of rags, then stood behind me, watching in silence as I began to sponge away the filth.

"Can you cure him?" she asked. Her voice was calm, remote, as though she spoke of a stranger.

The patient's head lolled suddenly back, so his open eye fixed on me.

"I think I can help a bit," I said carefully. I wished Jamie would return. Aside from need of my medical box, I was finding the company of the Beardsleys rather unnerving.

The more so when Mr. Beardsley inadvertently released a small quantity of urine. Mrs. Beardsley laughed, and he made a sound in reply that made the goose bumps rise on my arms. I wiped the liquid off his thigh and went on with my work, trying to ignore it.

"Have you or Mr. Beardsley any kin nearby?" I asked, as conversationally as possible. "Someone who might come to lend you a hand?"

"No one," she said. "He took me from my father's house in Maryland. To thith place." *This place* was spoken as though it were the fifth circle of hell; so far as I could see, there was certainly some resemblance at the present moment.

The door opened below, and a welcome draft of cold air announced Jamie's return. There was a clunking noise as he set my box on the table, and I hastily rose, eager to escape them, if only for a moment.

"There's my husband with my medicines. I'll just . . . er . . . go and fetch . . . um . . ." I edged past Mrs. Beardsley's bulk, and fled down the ladder, sweating in spite of the chill in the house.

Jamie stood by the table, frowning as he turned a length of rope in his hands. He glanced up as he heard me, and his face relaxed a little.

"How is it, Sassenach?" he asked, low-voiced, with a jerk of the chin toward the loft.

"Very bad," I whispered, coming to stand beside him. "Two of his toes are gangrenous; I'll have to take them off. And she says they've no family near to help."

"Mmphm." His lips tightened, and he bent his attention to the sling he was improvising.

I reached for my medical chest, to check my instruments, but stopped when I saw Jamie's pistols lying on the table beside it, along with his powder horn and shot case. I touched his arm and jerked my head at them, mouthing, "What?" at him.

The line between his brows deepened, but before he could answer, a dreadful racket came from the loft above, a great thrashing and thumping, accompanied by a gargling noise like an elephant drowning in a mud bog.

Jamie dropped the rope and shot for the ladder, with me at his heels. He let out a shout as his head topped the ladder, and dived forward. As I scrambled into the loft behind him, I saw him in the shadows, grappling with Mrs. Beardsley.

She smashed an elbow at his face, hitting him in the nose. This removed any inhibitions he might have had about man-handling a woman, and he jerked her round to face him and struck her with a short, sharp uppercut to the chin that clicked her jaws and made her stagger, eyes glazing. I dashed forward to save the candle, as she collapsed on her rump in a pouf of skirts and petticoats.

"God . . . dab . . . that . . . womad." Jamie's voice was muffled, his sleeve pressed across his face to stanch the flow of blood from his nose, but the sincerity in it was unmistakable.

Mr. Beardsley was flopping like a landed fish, wheezing and gurgling. I lifted the candle and found him flailing at his neck with one splayed hand. A linen kerchief had been twisted into a rope and wrapped round his neck, and his face was black, his one eye popping. I hastily seized the kerchief and undid it, and his breathing eased with a great whoosh of fetid air.

"If she'd been faster, she'd have had him." Jamie lowered his blood-streaked arm and felt his nose tenderly. "Christ, I think she broke my dose."

"Why? Why did you thtop me?" Mrs. Beardsley was still conscious, though swaying and glassy-eyed. "He thould die, I want him to die, he mutht die."

"*A nighean na galladh*, ye could ha' killed him at your leisure any time this month past, if ye wanted him dead," Jamie said impatiently. "Why in God's name wait until ye had witnesses?"

She looked up at him, eyes suddenly sharp and clear.

"I did not want him dead," she said. "I wanted him to *die*." She smiled, showing the stubs of her broken teeth. "Thlowly."

"Oh, Christ," I said, and wiped a hand across my face. It was only mid-morning, but I felt as though the day had lasted several weeks already. "It's my fault. I told her I thought I could help; she thought I'd save him, maybe cure him altogether." The curse of a reputation for magic healing! I might have laughed, had I been in the mood for irony.

There was a sharp, fresh stink in the air, and Mrs. Beardsley turned on her husband with a cry of outrage.

"Filthy beast!" She scrambled to her knees, snatched up a hard roll from the plate, and threw it at him. It bounced off his head. "Filthy, thtinking, dirty, wicked . . ." Jamie seized her by the hair as she hurled herself at the prone body, grabbed her arm, and jerked her away, sobbing and shrieking abuse.

"Bloody hell," he said, over the uproar. "Fetch me that rope, Sassenach, before I kill them both myself."

The job of getting Mr. Beardsley down from the loft was enough to leave both Jamie and me sweat-soaked and streaked with filth, reeking and weak in the knees with effort. Mrs. Beardsley squatted on a stool in the corner, quiet and malevolent as a toad, making no effort to help.

She gave a gasp of outrage when we laid the big, lolling body on the clean table, but Jamie glared at her, and she sank back on her stool, mouth clamped to a thin, straight line.

Jamie wiped his bloodstained sleeve across his brow, and shook his head as he looked at Beardsley. I didn't blame him; even cleaned up, warmly covered, and with a little warm gruel spooned into him, the man was in a dreadful state. I examined him once more, carefully, in the light from the window. No doubt about the toes; the stink of gangrene was distinct, and the greenish tinge covered the outer dorsal aspect of the foot.

I'd have to take more than the toes—I frowned, feeling my way carefully around the putrefying area, wondering whether it was better to try for a partial amputation between the metacarpals, or simply to take the foot off at the ankle. The ankle dissection would be faster, and while I would normally try for the more conservative partial amputation, there was really no point to it in this case; Beardsley was plainly never going to walk again.

I gnawed my lower lip dubiously. For that matter, the whole business might be moot; he burned with intermittent fever, and the sores on legs and buttocks oozed with suppuration. What were the chances of his recovering from the amputation without dying of infection?

I hadn't heard Mrs. Beardsley come up behind me; for a heavyset woman, she moved with remarkable silence.

"What do you mean to do?" she asked, her voice sounding neutral and remote.

"Your husband's toes are gangrenous," I said. No point in trying not to alarm Beardsley now. "I'll have to amputate his foot." There was really no choice, though my heart sank at the notion of spending the next several days—or weeks—here, nursing Beardsley. I could hardly leave him to the tender care of his wife!

She circled the table slowly, coming to a stop near his feet. Her face was blank, but a tiny smile appeared at the corners of her mouth, winking on and off, as though quite without her willing it. She looked at the blackened toes for a long minute, then shook her head.

"No," she said softly. "Let him rot."

The question of Beardsley's understanding was resolved, at least; his open eye bulged, and he let out a shriek of rage, thrashing and flailing in an effort to get at her, so that he came perilously near to falling onto the floor in his struggles. Jamie seized him, shoving and heaving to keep his ponderous bulk on the table. As Beardsley at last subsided, gasping and making mewling noises, Jamie straightened up, gasping himself, and gave Mrs. Beardsley a look of extreme dislike.

She hunched her shoulders, pulling her shawl tight around them, but didn't retreat or look away. She raised her chin defiantly.

"I am hith wife," she said. "I thall not let you cut him. It ith a rithk to hith life."

"It's certain death if I don't," I said shortly. "And a nasty one, too. You—" I didn't get to finish; Jamie put a hand on my shoulder, squeezing hard.

"Take her outside, Claire," he said quietly.

"But—"

"Outside." His hand tightened on my shoulder, almost painful in its pressure. "Dinna come back until I call for ye."

His face was grim, but there was something in his eyes that made me go hollow and watery inside. I glanced at the sideboard, where his pistols lay beside my medicine chest, then back at his face, appalled.

"You can't," I said.

He looked at Beardsley, his face bleak.

"I would put down a dog in such case without a second's thought," he said softly. "Can I do less for him?"

"He is not a dog!"

"No, he is not." His hand dropped from my shoulder, and he circled the table, until he stood by Beardsley's side.

"If ye understand me, man—close your eye," he said quietly. There was a moment's silence, and Beardsley's bloodshot eye fixed on Jamie's face—with undeniable intelligence. The lid closed slowly, then rose again.

Jamie turned to me.

"Go," he said. "Let it be his choice. If—or if not—I will call for ye."

My knees were trembling, and I knotted my hands in the folds of my skirt.

"No," I said. I looked at Beardsley, then swallowed hard and shook my head. "No," I said again. "I—if you . . . you must have a witness."

He hesitated a moment, but then nodded.

"Aye, you're right." He glanced at Mrs. Beardsley. She stood stock-still, hands knotted under her apron, eyes darting from me to Jamie to her husband and back. Jamie shook his head briefly, then turned back to the stricken man, squaring his shoulders.

"Blink once for yes, twice for nay," he said. "You understand?"

The eyelid lowered without hesitation.

"Listen, then." Jamie drew a deep breath and began to speak, in a flat, unemotional tone of voice, his eyes steady on the ruined face and the fierce gaze of its open eye.

"Ye ken what has happened to you?"

Blink.

"Ye ken that my wife is a physician, a healer?"

The eye rolled in my direction, then back to Jamie. Blink.

"She says that you have suffered an apoplexy, that the damage canna be mended. You understand?"

A huffing sound came from the lopsided mouth. This was not news. Blink.

"Your foot is putrid. If it is not taken off, you will rot and die. You understand?"

No response. The nostrils flared suddenly, moist, questing; then the air was expelled with a snort. He had smelled the rot; had suspected, perhaps, but not known for sure that it came from his own flesh. Not 'til now. Slowly, a blink.

The quiet litany went on, statements and questions, each a shovelful of dirt, taken from a deepening grave. Each ending with the inexorable words, "You understand?"

My hands and feet and face felt numb. The odd sense of sanctuary in the room had altered; it felt like a church, but no longer a place of refuge. A place now in which some ritual took place, leading to a solemn, predestined end.

And it was predestined, I understood. Beardsley had made his choice long since—perhaps even before we arrived. He had had a month in that purgatory, after all, suspended in the cold dark between heaven and earth, in which to think, to come to grips with his prospects and make his peace with death.

Did he understand?

Oh, yes, very well.

Jamie bent over the table, one hand on Beardsley's arm, a priest in stained linen, offering absolution and salvation. Mrs. Beardsley stood frozen in the fall of light from the window, a stolid angel of denunciation.

The statements and the questions came to an end.

"Will ye have my wife take your foot and tend your wounds?"

One blink, then two, exaggerated, deliberate.

Jamie's breathing was audible, the heaviness in his chest making a sigh of each word.

"Do ye ask me to take your life?"

Though one half of his face sagged lifeless and the other was drawn and haggard, there was enough of Beardsley left to show expression. The workable corner of the mouth turned up in a cynical leer. *What there is left of it*, said his silence. The eyelid fell—and stayed shut.

Jamie closed his own eyes. A small shudder passed over him. Then he shook himself briefly, like a man shaking off cold water, and turned to the sideboard where his pistols lay.

I crossed swiftly to him, laying a hand on his arm. He didn't look at me, but kept his eyes on the pistol he was priming. His face was white, but his hands were steady.

"Go," he said. "Take her out."

I looked back at Beardsley, but he was my patient no longer; his flesh beyond my healing or my comfort. I went to the woman and took her by the arm, turning her toward the door. She came with me, walking mechanically, and did not turn to look back.

THE OUTDOORS SEEMED unreal, the sunlit yard unconvincingly ordinary. Mrs. Beardsley pulled free of my grip and headed toward the barn, walking fast. She glanced back over her shoulder at the house, then broke into a heavy run, disappearing through the open barn door as though fiends were after her.

I caught her sense of panic and nearly ran after her. I didn't, though; I stopped at the edge of the yard and waited. I could feel my heart beating, slowly, thumping in my ears. That seemed unreal, too.

The shot came, finally, a small flat sound, inconsequent amid the soft bleating of goats from the barn and the rustle of chickens scratching in the dirt nearby. Head, I wondered suddenly, or heart, and shuddered.

It was long past noon; the cold, still air of the morning had risen and a chilly breeze moved through the dooryard, stirring dust and wisps of hay. I stood and waited. He would have paused, I thought, to say a brief prayer for Beardsley's soul. A moment passed, two, then the back door opened. Jamie came out, took a few steps, then stopped, bent over, and vomited.

I started forward, in case he needed me, but no. He

straightened and wiped his mouth, then turned and walked across the yard away from me, heading for the wood.

I felt suddenly superfluous, and rather oddly affronted. I had been at work no more than moments before, deeply absorbed in the practice of medicine. Connected to flesh, to mind and body; attentive to symptoms, aware of pulse and breath, the vital signs. I hadn't liked Beardsley in the least, and yet I had been totally engaged in the struggle to preserve his life, to ease his suffering. I could still feel the odd touch of his slack, warm flesh on my hands.

Now my patient was abruptly dead, and I felt as though some small part of my body had been amputated. I thought I was perhaps a trifle shocked.

I glanced at the house, my original sense of caution superseded by distaste—and something deeper. The body must be washed, of course, and decently laid out for burial. I had done such things before—with no great qualms, if without enthusiasm—and yet I found myself now with a great reluctance to go back into the place.

I'd seen death by violence—and many much more distasteful than this was likely to have been. Death was death. Whether it came as passage, as parting, or in some cases, as dearly desired release . . . Jamie had freed Beardsley very suddenly from the prison of his stricken body; did his spirit perhaps still linger in the house, having not yet realized its freedom?

"You are being superstitious, Beauchamp," I said severely to myself. "Stop it at once." And yet I didn't take a step toward the house, but hovered in the yard, keyed up like an indecisive hummingbird.

If Beardsley was beyond my help, and Jamie in no need of it, there was still one who might require it. I turned my back on the house and went toward the barn.

This was no more than a large open shed with a loft, fragrantly dark and filled with hay and moving shapes. I stood in the doorway until my eyes adjusted. There was a stall in one corner, but no horse. A rickety fence with a milking stanchion made a goat pen in the other corner; she was crouched inside it, on a pile of fresh straw. Half a dozen goats crowded and bumped around her, jostling and nibbling at the fringes of her shawl. She was little more than a hunched shape, but I caught the brief shine of a wary eye in the shadows.

"Ith it over?" The question was asked softly, barely audible above the quiet grunting and bleating.

"Yes." I hesitated, but she seemed in no need of my support; I could see better now—she had a small kid curled in her lap, her fingers stroking the small, silky head. "Are you quite all right, Mrs. Beardsley?"

Silence, then the heavy figure shrugged and settled, some tension seeming to leave her.

"I thcarthely know," she said softly. I waited, but she neither moved nor spoke further. The peaceful company of the goats seemed as likely as mine to be a comfort to her, so I turned and left them, rather envying her the warm refuge of the barn and her cheerful companions.

We had left the horses in the dooryard, still saddled, tethered to an alder sapling. Jamie had loosened their girths and removed their saddlebags when he went to fetch my medicine box, but had not taken the time to unsaddle them. I did that now; plainly it would be some time yet before we could leave. I took off the bridles as well, and hobbled them, turning them loose to graze on the winter-brown grass that still grew thickly at the edge of the pines.

There was a hollowed half-log on the western side of the house, plainly meant to serve as a horse trough, but it was empty. Welcoming the chore for the delay it allowed me, I raised water from the well and emptied bucket after bucket into the trough.

Wiping my wet hands on my skirt, I looked round for further useful occupation, but there wasn't any. No choice, then. I braced myself, poured more water into the bucket, dropped in the hollow drinking gourd that stood on the edge of the well, and carried it back around the house, concentrating fiercely on not spilling any, in order to avoid thinking about the prospects within.

When I raised my eyes, I was startled to see that the back door stood open. I was sure it had been closed before. Was Jamie inside? Or Mrs. Beardsley?

Keeping a wary distance, I craned my neck to peep into

the kitchen, but as I sidled closer, I heard the steady *chuff* of a spade shifting dirt. I went around the far corner to find Jamie digging near a mountain-ash tree that stood by itself in the yard, a short distance from the house. He was still in shirtsleeves, and the wind blew the stained white linen against his body, ruffling the red hair over his face.

He brushed it back with one wrist, and I saw with a small sense of shock that he was crying. He wept silently and somehow savagely, attacking the soil as though it were an enemy. He caught my movement from a corner of his eye, and stopped, swiping a blood-smeared shirtsleeve quickly across his face, as though to wipe away sweat from his brow.

He was breathing hoarsely, loud enough to hear from a distance. I came silently and offered him the gourd of water, along with a clean handkerchief. He didn't meet my eyes, but drank, coughed, drank again, handed back the gourd, and blew his nose, gingerly. It was swollen, but no longer bleeding.

"We won't sleep here tonight, will we?" I ventured to ask, seating myself on the chopping block that stood under the ash tree.

He shook his head.

"God, no," he said hoarsely. His face was blotched and his eyes bloodshot, but he had firm hold of himself. "We'll see him decently buried and go. I dinna mind if we sleep cold in the wood again—but not here." I agreed wholeheartedly with that notion, but there was one thing more to be considered.

"And . . . her?" I asked delicately. "Is she in the house? The back door is open."

He grunted, and thrust in his shovel.

"No, that was me. I'd forgot to leave it open when I came out before—to let the soul go free," he explained, seeing my upraised eyebrow.

It was the complete matter-of-factness with which he offered this explanation, rather than the fact that it echoed my own earlier notion, that made the hairs prickle along my neck.

"I see," I said, a little faintly.

Jamie dug steadily for a bit, the shovel biting deep into the dirt. It was loamy soil and leaf mold here; the digging was easy. At last, without breaking the swing of the blade, he said, “Brianna told me a story she’d read once. I dinna recall all about it, quite, but there was a murder done, only the person killed was a wicked man, who had driven someone to it. And at the end, when the teller of the tale was asked what should be done, he said, ‘Let pass the justice of God.’ ”

I nodded. I was in agreement, though it seemed a trifle hard on the person who found himself required to be the instrument of such justice.

“Do you suppose that’s what it was, in this case? Justice?”

He shook his head; not in negation, but in puzzlement, and went on digging. I watched him for a bit, soothed by his nearness and by the hypnotic rhythm of his movements. After a bit, though, I stirred, steeling myself to face the task awaiting me.

“I suppose I’d best go and lay out the body and clear up the loft,” I said reluctantly, drawing my feet under me to rise. “We can’t leave that poor woman alone with such a mess, no matter what she did.”

“No, wait, Sassenach,” Jamie said, pausing in his digging. He glanced at the house, a little warily. “I’ll go in with ye, in a bit. For now”—he nodded toward the edge of the wood—“d’ye think ye could fetch a few stones for the cairn?”

A cairn? I was more than slightly surprised at this; it seemed an unnecessary elaboration for the late Mr. Beardsley. Still, there were undoubtedly wolves in the wood; I’d seen scats on the trail two days before. It also occurred to me that Jamie might be contriving an honorable excuse for me to postpone entering the house again—in which case, hauling rocks seemed a thoroughly desirable alternative.

Fortunately, there was no shortage of suitable rocks. I fetched the heavy canvas apron that I wore for surgery from my saddlebag, and began to trundle to and fro, an ant collecting laborious crumbs. After half an hour or so of this, the thought of entering the house had begun to seem much less objectionable. Jamie was still hard at it, though, so I kept on.

I stopped finally, gasping, and dumped yet another load out of my apron onto the ground by the deepening grave. The shadows were falling long across the dooryard, and the air was cold enough that my fingers had gone numb—a good thing, in view of the various scrapes and nicks on them.

"You look a right mess," I observed, shoving a disheveled mass of hair off my own face. "Has Mrs. Beardsley come out yet?"

He shook his head, but took a moment to get his breath back before replying.

"No," he said, in a voice so hoarse I could scarcely hear him. "She's still wi' the goats. I daresay it's warm in there."

I eyed him uneasily. Grave-digging is hard work; his shirt was clinging to his body, soaked through in spite of the coldness of the day, and his face was flushed—with labor, I hoped, rather than fever. His fingers were white and as stiff as mine, though; it took a visible effort for him to uncurl them from the handle of the shovel.

"Surely that's deep enough," I said, surveying his work. I would myself have settled for the shallowest of gouges in the soft earth, but slipshod work was never Jamie's way. "Do stop, Jamie, and change your shirt at once. You're wringing wet; you'll catch a terrible chill."

He didn't bother arguing, but took up the spade and carefully neatened the corners of the hole, shaping the sides to keep them from crumbling inward.

The shadows under the pine trees were growing thick, and the chickens had all gone to roost, feathery blobs perched in the trees like bunches of brown mistletoe. The forest birds had fallen silent, too, and the shadow of the house fell long and cold across the new grave. I hugged my elbows, and shivered at the quiet.

Jamie tossed the shovel onto the ground with a clunk, startling me. He climbed up out of the hole, and stood still for a minute, eyes closed, swaying with weariness. Then he opened his eyes and smiled tiredly at me.

"Let's finish, then," he said.

WHETHER THE OPEN DOOR had indeed allowed the deceased's spirit to flee, or whether it was only that Jamie was with me, I felt no hesitation in entering the house now. The fire had gone out, and the kitchen was cold and dim, yet there was no sense of anything evil within. It was simply . . . empty.

Mr. Beardsley's mortal remains rested peacefully under one of his own trade blankets, mute and still. Empty, too.

Mrs. Beardsley had declined to assist with the formalities—or even to enter the house, so long as her husband's body remained inside—so I swept the hearth, kindled a new fire, and coaxed it into reluctant life, while Jamie took care of the mess in the loft. By the time he came down again, I had turned to the main business at hand.

Dead, Beardsley seemed much less grotesque than he had in life; the twisted limbs were relaxed, the air of frantic struggle gone. Jamie had placed a linen towel over the head, though when I peeked beneath it, I could see that there was no gory mess to deal with; Jamie had shot him cleanly through the blind eye, and the ball had not burst the skull. The good eye was closed now, the blackened wound left staring. I laid the towel gently back over the face, its symmetry restored in death.

Jamie climbed down the ladder, and came quietly to stand behind me, touching my shoulder briefly.

"Go and wash," I said, gesturing behind me to the small kettle of water I had hung over the fire to heat. "I'll manage here."

He nodded, stripped off his sodden, filthy shirt, and dropped it on the hearth. I listened to the small, homely noises he made as he washed. He coughed now and then, but his breathing sounded somewhat easier than it had outside in the cold.

"I didna ken it might be that way," he said from behind me. "I thought an apoplexy would kill a man outright."

"Sometimes that's so," I said, a little absently, frowning as I concentrated on the job at hand. "Most often that's the way of it, in fact."

"Aye? I never thought to ask Dougal, or Rupert. Or Jenny. Whether my father—" The sentence stopped abruptly, as though he had swallowed it.

Ah. I felt a small jolt of realization in my solar plexus. So that was it. I hadn't remembered, but he had told me of it, years before, soon after we were married. His father had seen Jamie flogged at Fort William, and under the shock of it, had suffered an apoplexy and died. Jamie, wounded and ill, had been spirited away from the Fort and gone into exile. He had not been told of his father's death until weeks later—had no chance of farewell, had been able neither to bury his father nor honor his grave.

"Jenny would have known," I said gently. "She would have told you, if . . ." If Brian Fraser had suffered a death of such lingering ignominy as this, dwindled and shrunken, powerless before the eyes of the family he had striven to protect.

Would she? If she had nursed her father through incontinence and helplessness? If she had waited days or weeks, suddenly bereft of both father and brother, left alone to stare death in the face as it approached, moment by slow moment . . . and yet Jenny Fraser was a very strong woman, who had loved her brother dearly. Perhaps she would have sought to shield him, both from guilt and from knowledge.

I turned to face him. He was half-naked, but clean now, with a fresh shirt from his saddlebag in his hands. He was looking at me, but I saw his eyes slip beyond me, to fasten on the corpse with a troubled fascination.

"She would have told you," I repeated, striving to infuse my voice with certainty.

Jamie drew a deep, painful breath.

"Perhaps."

"She would," I said more firmly.

He nodded, drew another deep breath, and let it out, more easily. I realized that the house was not the only thing haunted by Beardsley's death. Jenny held the key of the only door that could be opened for Jamie, though.

I understood now why he had wept, and had taken such care with the digging of the grave. Not from either shock or charity, let alone from regard for the dead man—but for the sake of Brian Fraser; the father he had neither buried nor mourned.

I turned back and drew the edges of the blanket up, folded them snugly over the cleaned and decent remains, and tied it with twine at head and feet, making a tidy, anonymous package. Jamie was forty-nine; the same age at which his father had died. I stole a quick glance at him, as he finished dressing. If his father had been such a one as he was . . . I felt a sudden pang of sorrow, for the loss of so much. For strength cut off and love snuffed out, for the loss of a man I knew had been great, only from the reflection I saw of him in his son.

Dressed, Jamie circled round the table to help me lift the body. Instead of putting his hands under it, though, he reached across and took my hands in both of his.

"Swear to me, Claire," he said. His voice was nearly gone with hoarseness; I had to lean close to hear it. "If it should one day fall to my lot as it did to my father . . . then swear ye will give me the same mercy I gave this wretched bugger here."

There were fresh blisters on his palms from the digging; I felt the strange softness of them, fluid-filled and shifting as he gripped my hands.

"I'll do what must be done," I whispered back, at last. "Just as you did." I squeezed his hands and let them go. "Come now and help me bury him. It's over."

28

BROWNSVILLE

IT WAS MID-AFTERNOON before Roger, Fergus, and the militia reached Brownsville, having missed their road and wandered in the hills for several hours before meeting two Cherokee who pointed the way.

Brownsville was half a dozen ramshackle huts, strewn among the dying brush of a hillside like a handful of rubbish tossed into the weeds. Near the road—if the narrow rut of churned black mud could be dignified by such a word—two cabins leaned tipsily on either side of a slightly larger and more solid-looking building, like drunkards leaning cozily on a sober companion. Rather ironically, this larger building seemed to operate as Brownsville's general store and tap-room, judging from the barrels of beer and powder and the stacks of drenched hides that stood in the muddy yard beside it—though to apply either term to it was granting that more dignity than it deserved, too, Roger thought.

Still, it was plainly the place to start—if only for the sake of the men with him, who had begun to vibrate like iron filings near a magnet at sight of the barrels; the yeasty scent of beer floated out like a welcome. He wouldn't say no to a pint, either, he thought, waving a hand to signal a halt. It was a numbingly cold day, and a long time since this morning's breakfast. They weren't likely to get anything beyond bread or stew here, but as long as it was hot and washed down with some sort of alcohol, no one would complain.

He slid off his horse, and had just turned to call to the others when a hand clutched his arm.

"Attendez." Fergus spoke softly, barely moving his lips. He was standing beside Roger, looking at something beyond him. "Do not move."

Roger didn't, nor did any of the men still on their horses. Whatever Fergus saw, so did they.

"What is it?" Roger asked, keeping his voice low, too.

"Someone—two someones—are pointing guns at us, through the window."

"Ah." Roger noted Jamie's good sense in not riding into Brownsville after dark the night before. Evidently, he knew something about the suspicious nature of remote places.

Moving very slowly, he raised both his hands into the air, and jerked his chin at Fergus, who reluctantly did the same, his hook gleaming in the afternoon sun. Still keeping his hands up, Roger turned very slowly. Even knowing what to expect, he felt his stomach contract at sight of the two long, gleaming barrels protruding from behind the oiled deerskin that covered the window.

"Hallo the house!" he shouted, with as much authority as could be managed with his hands over his head. "I am

Captain Roger MacKenzie, in command of a militia company under Colonel James Fraser, of Fraser's Ridge!"

The only effect of this intelligence was to cause one gun barrel to swivel, centering on Roger, so that he could look straight down the small, dark circle of its muzzle. The unwelcome prospect did, though, cause him to realize that the other gun had not been trained on him to start with. It had been, and remained, pointing steadily over his right shoulder, toward the cluster of men who still sat their horses behind him, shifting in their saddles and murmuring uneasily.

Great. Now what? The men were waiting for him to do *something*. Moving slowly, he lowered his hands. He was drawing breath to shout again, but before he could speak, a hoarse voice rang out from behind the deerskin.

"I see you, Morton, you bastard!"

This imprecation was accompanied by a significant jerk of the first gun barrel, which turned abruptly from Roger to focus on the same target as the second—presumably Isaiah Morton, one of the militiamen from Granite Falls.

There was a scuffling noise among the mounted men, startled shouts, and then all hell broke loose as both guns went off. Horses reared and bolted, men bellowed and swore, and drifts of acrid white smoke fumed from the window.

Roger had thrown himself flat at the first explosion. As the echoes died away, though, he scrambled up as though by reflex, flung mud out of his eyes, and charged the door, headfirst. To his detached surprise, his mind was working very clearly. Brianna took twenty seconds to load and prime a gun, and he doubted that these buggers were much faster. He thought he had just about ten seconds' grace left, and he meant to use them.

He hit the door with his shoulder, and it flew inward, smashing against the wall inside and causing Roger to rush staggering into the room and crash into the wall on the opposite side. He struck his shoulder a numbing blow on the chimney piece, bounced off, and managed somehow to keep his feet, stumbling like a drunkard.

Several people in the room had turned to gape at him. His vision cleared enough to see that only two of them were in fact holding guns. He took a deep breath, lunged for the nearest of these, a scrawny man with a straggling beard, and seized him by the shirtfront, in imitation of a particularly fearsome third-form master at Roger's grammar school.

"What do you think you are doing, you *wee* man, you!?" he roared, jerking the man up onto his toes. Mr. Sanderson would have been pleased, he supposed, at the thought that his example had been so memorable. Effective, too; while the scrawny man in Roger's grip did not either wet himself or snivel, as the first-form students occasionally had under such treatment, he did make small gobbling sounds, pawing ineffectually at Roger's hand clutching his shirt.

"You, sir! Leave hold of my brother!" Roger's victim had dropped both his gun and powder horn when seized, spilling black powder all over the floor. The other gunman had succeeded in reloading his weapon, though, and was now endeavoring to bring it to bear on Roger. He was somewhat impeded in this attempt by the three women in the room, two of whom were blethering and pulling at his gun, getting in his way. The third had flung her apron over her head and was uttering loud, rhythmic shrieks of hysteria.

At this point, Fergus strolled into the house, an enormous horse pistol in his hand. He pointed this negligently at the man with the gun.

"Be so kind as to put that down, if you will," he said, raising his voice to be heard above the racket. "And perhaps, Madame, you could pour some water upon this young woman? Or slap her briskly?" He gestured toward the screaming woman with his hook, wincing slightly at the noise.

Moving as though hypnotized, one of the women went slowly toward the screeching girl, shook her roughly by the shoulder, and began to murmur in the girl's ear, not taking her eyes off Fergus. The shrieking stopped, replaced by irregular gulps and sobs.

Roger felt an immense relief. Sheer rage, simple panic, and the absolute necessity of doing *something* had got him this far, but he would freely admit that he had not the slightest idea what to do next. He took a deep breath, feeling his legs begin to tremble, and slowly lowered his victim, releasing his grip with an awkward nod. The man took several fast steps backward, then stood brushing at the creases in his shirt, narrowed eyes fixed on Roger in resentment.

"And who in blazes are *you*?" The second man, who had indeed put his weapon down, looked at Fergus in confusion.

The Frenchman waved his hook—which, Roger noticed, seemed to fascinate the women—in a gesture of dismissal.

"That is of no importance," he said grandly, lifting his aristocratically prominent nose another inch. "I require—that is, *we* require"—he amended, with a polite nod toward Roger—"to know who *you* are."

The inhabitants of the cabin all exchanged confused looks, as though wondering who they might in fact be. After a moment's hesitation, though, the larger of the two men thrust out his chin pugnaciously.

"My name is Brown, sir. Richard Brown. This is my brother, Lionel, my wife, Meg, my brother's daughter, Alicia"—that appeared to be the girl in the apron, who had now removed the garment from her head and stood tearstained and gulping—"and my sister, Thomasina."

"Your servant, Madame, Mesdemoiselles." Fergus made the ladies an extremely elegant bow, though taking good care to keep his pistol aimed at Richard Brown's forehead. "My apologies for the disturbance."

Mrs. Brown nodded back, looking a little glazed. Miss Thomasina Brown, a tall, severe-looking person, looked from Roger to Fergus and back with the expression of one comparing a cockroach and a centipede, deciding which to step on first.

Fergus, having managed to transform the atmosphere from an armed confrontation to that of a Parisian *salon*, looked pleased. He glanced at Roger and inclined his head, clearly handing management of the situation over to him.

"Right." Roger was wearing a loose woolen hunting shirt, but he felt as though it were a straitjacket. He took another deep breath, trying to force air into his chest. "Well. As I said, I am . . . ah . . . Captain MacKenzie. We are charged by Governor Tryon with raising a militia company, and have come to notify you of your obligation to provide men and supplies."

Richard Brown looked surprised at this; his brother glowered. Before they could offer objections, though, Fergus moved closer to Roger, murmuring, "Perhaps we should discover whether they have killed Mr. Morton, *mon capitaine*, before we accept them into our company?"

"Oh, mphm." Roger fixed the Browns with as stern an expression as possible. "Mr. Fraser. Will you see about Mr. Morton? I will remain here." Keeping the Browns in his gaze, he held out a hand for Fergus's pistol.

"Oh, yon Morton's still canty, Captain. He isny wae us, forbye, 'cause he's ta'en to the broosh like a bit' moggie wae a scorchit tail, but he wiz movin' a' his limbs when I saw um last." A nasal Glaswegian voice spoke from the doorway, and Roger glanced over to see a cluster of interested heads peering into the cabin, Henry Gallegher's bristly nob among them. A number of drawn guns were also in evidence, and Roger's breath came a little easier.

The Browns had lost interest in Roger, and were staring at Gallegher in sheer bewilderment.

"What did he say?" Mrs. Brown whispered to her sister-in-law. The older lady shook her head, lips drawn in like a pursestring.

"Mr. Morton is alive and well," Roger translated for them. He coughed. "Fortunately for you," he said to the male Browns, with as much menace as he could contrive to put into his voice. He turned to Gallegher, who had now come into the room and was leaning against the doorjamb, musket in hand and looking distinctly entertained.

"Is everyone else all right, then, Henry?"

Gallegher shrugged.

"They crap-bags hivny holed anyone, but they gie'd your saddlebag rare laldy wae a load o' bird shot. Sir," he added as an afterthought, teeth showing in a brief flash through his beard.

"The bag with the whisky?" Roger demanded.

"Get awa!" Gallegher bugged his eyes in horror, then grinned in reassurance. "Nah, t'other."

"Och, well." Roger waved a hand dismissively. "That's only my spare breeks, isn't it?"

This philosophical response drew laughter and hoots of support from the men crammed in the doorway, which heartened Roger enough to round on the smaller Brown.

"And what d'ye have against Isaiah Morton?" he demanded.

"He's dishonored my daughter," Mr. Brown replied promptly, having recovered his composure. He glared at Roger, beard twitching with anger. "I told him I'd see him dead at her feet, if ever he dared show his wretched countenance within ten miles of Brownsville—and damn my eyes if the grass-livered spittle-snake hasn't the face to ride right up to my door!"

Mr. Richard Brown turned to Gallegher.

"You mean to tell me we both *missed* the bastard?"

Gallegher shrugged apologetically.

"Aye. Sorry."

The younger Miss Brown had been following this exchange, mouth hanging slightly open.

"They missed?" she asked, hope lighting her reddened eyes. "Isaiah's still alive?"

"Not for long," her uncle assured her grimly. He reached down to pick up his fowling piece, and all the female Browns burst out in a chorus of renewed screeches, as the guns of the militia at the door all raised simultaneously, trained on Brown. He very slowly put the gun back down.

Roger glanced at Fergus, who lifted one brow and gave the slightest of shrugs. Up to him.

The Browns had drawn together, the two brothers glaring at him, the women huddled behind them, sniffling and murmuring. Militiamen poked their heads curiously through the windows, all staring at Roger, waiting for direction.

And just what was he to tell them? Morton was a member of the militia, and therefore—he assumed—entitled to its protection. Roger couldn't very well turn him over to the Browns, no matter what he'd done—always assuming he could be caught. On the other hand, Roger was charged with enlisting the Browns and the rest of the able-bodied men in Brownsville, and extracting at least a week's supplies from them as well; they didn't look as though such a suggestion would be well received at this point.

He had the galling conviction that Jamie Fraser would have known immediately how best to resolve this diplomatic crisis. He personally hadn't a clue.

He did, at least, have a delaying tactic. Sighing, he lowered the pistol, and reached for the pouch at his waist.

"Henry, fetch in the saddlebag with the whisky, aye? And Mr. Brown, perhaps ye will allow me to purchase some food, and a barrel of your beer, for my men's refreshment."

And with luck, by the time it was all drunk, Jamie Fraser would be here.

29

ONE-THIRD OF A GOAT

IT WASN'T QUITE OVER, after all. It was well past dark by the time we had finished everything at the Beardsley farm, tidied up, repacked the bags, and resaddled the horses. I thought of suggesting that we eat before leaving—we had had nothing since breakfast—but the atmosphere of the place was so disturbing that neither Jamie nor I had any appetite.

"We'll wait," he said, heaving the saddlebags over the mare's back. He glanced over his shoulder at the house. "I'm hollow as a gourd, but I couldna stomach a bite within sight o' this place."

"I know what you mean." I glanced back, too, uneasily, though there was nothing to see; the house stood still and empty. "I can't wait to get away from here."

The sun had sunk below the trees, and a chill blue shadow spread across the hollow where the farmhouse stood. The raw earth of Beardsley's grave showed dark with moisture, a humped mound beneath the bare branches of the mountain ash. It was impossible to look at it without thinking of the weight of wet earth and immobility, of corruption and decay.

You will rot and die, Jamie had said to him. I hoped the reversal of those two events had been of some benefit to Beardsley—it had not, to me. I hugged my shawl tight around my shoulders and breathed out hard, then deeply in, hoping the cold, clean scent of the pines would eradicate the phantom reek of dead flesh that seemed to cling to hands and clothes and nose.

The horses were shifting, stamping, and shaking their manes, eager to be off. I didn't blame them. Unable to stop myself, I looked back once more. A more desolate sight would be hard to imagine. Even harder to imagine was the thought of staying here, alone.

Evidently, Mrs. Beardsley *had* imagined it, and come to similar conclusions. At this point, she emerged from the barn, the kid in her arms, and announced that she was coming with us. So, evidently, were the goats. She handed me the kid, and disappeared back into the barn.

The kid was heavy and half-asleep, flexible little joints folded up into a cozy bundle. It huffed warm air over my hand, nibbling gently to see what I was made of, then made a small "meh" of contentment and relaxed into peaceful inertness against my ribs. A louder "meh!" and a nudge at my thigh announced the presence of the kid's mother, keeping a watchful eye on her offspring.

"Well, she can't very well leave them here," I muttered to Jamie, who was making disgruntled noises in the dusk behind me. "They have to be milked. Besides, it's not a terribly long way, is it?"

"D'ye ken how fast a goat walks, Sassenach?"

"I've never had occasion to time one," I said, rather testily, shifting my small hairy burden. "But I shouldn't think they'd be a lot slower than the horses, in the dark."

He made a guttural Scottish noise at that, rendered more expressive even than usual by the phlegm in his throat. He coughed.

"You sound awful," I said. "When we get where we're going, I'm taking the mentholated goose grease to you, my lad."

He made no objection to this proposal, which rather alarmed me, as indicating a serious depression of his vitality. Before I could inquire further into his state of health, though, I was interrupted by the emergence from the barn of Mrs. Beardsley, leading six goats, roped together like a gang of jovially inebriate convicts.

Jamie viewed the procession dubiously, sighed in resignation, and turned to a consideration of the logistical problems at hand. There was no question of mounting Mrs. Beardsley on Gideon the Man-Eater. Jamie glanced from me to Mrs. Beardsley's substantial figure, then at the small form of my mare, little bigger than a pony, and coughed.

After a bit of contemplation, he had Mrs. Beardsley mounted on Mrs. Piggy, the sleepy kid balanced before her. I would ride with him, on Gideon's withers, theoretically preventing any attempt on that animal's part to fling me off his hindquarters into the underbrush. He tied a rope round the billy goat's neck, and affixed this loosely to the mare's saddle, but left the nannies loose.

"The mother will stay wi' the kid, and the others will follow the billy here," he told me. "Goats are sociable creatures; they'll no be wanting to stray awa by themselves. Especially not at night. Shoo," he muttered, pushing an inquisitive nose out of his face as he squatted to check the saddle girth. "I suppose pigs would be worse. They *will* gang their own way." He stood up, absently patting a hairy head.

"If anything should come amiss, pull it loose at once," he told Mrs. Beardsley, showing her the half-bow loop tied to the saddle near her hand. "If the horse should run away wi' ye all, your wee fellow there will be hangit."

She nodded, a hunched mound atop the horse, then lifted her head and looked toward the house.

"We should go before moonrithe," she said softly. "She cometh out then."

An icy ripple ran straight up my spine, and Jamie jerked, head snapping round to look at the darkened house. The fire had gone out, and no one had thought to close the open door; it gaped like an empty eye socket.

"She *who*?" Jamie asked, a noticeable edge in his voice.

"Mary Ann," Mrs. Beardsley answered. "She was the latht

one." There was no emphasis whatever in her voice; she sounded like a sleepwalker.

"The last *what*?" I asked.

"The latht wife," she replied, and picked up her reins. "She thtands under the rowan tree at moonrithe."

Jamie's head turned toward me. It was too dark to see his expression, but I didn't need to. I cleared my throat.

"Ought we . . . to close the door?" I suggested. Mr. Beardsley's spirit had presumably got the idea by now, and whether or not Mrs. Beardsley had any interest in the house and its contents, it didn't seem right to leave it at the mercy of marauding raccoons and squirrels, to say nothing of anything larger that might be attracted by the scent of Mr. Beardsley's final exit. On the other hand, I really had no desire at all to approach the empty house.

"Get on the horse, Sassenach."

Jamie strode across the yard, slammed the door somewhat harder than necessary, then came back—walking briskly—and swung into the saddle behind me.

"Hup!" he said sharply, and we were off, the glow of a rising half-moon just visible above the trees.

It was perhaps a quarter mile to the head of the trail, the ground rising from the hollow in which the Beardsleys' farmhouse stood. We were moving slowly, because of the goats, and I watched the grass and shrubs as we brushed through them, wondering whether they seemed more visible only because my eyes were adapting to the dark—or because the moon had risen.

I felt quite safe, with the powerful bulk of the horse under me, the sociable natter of the goats around us, and Jamie's equally reassuring presence behind me, one arm clasped about my waist. I wasn't sure that I felt quite safe enough to turn and look back again, though. At the same time, the urge to look was so compelling as almost to counter the sense of dread I felt about the place. Almost.

"It's no really a rowan tree, is it?" Jamie's voice came softly from behind me.

"No," I said, taking heart from the solid arm around me. "It's a mountain ash. Very like, though." I'd seen mountain ash many times before; the Highlanders often planted them near cabins or houses because the clusters of deep orange berries and the pinnate leaves did indeed look like the rowan tree of Scotland—a close botanical relative. I gathered that Jamie's comment stemmed not from taxonomic hairsplitting, though, but rather from doubt as to whether the ash possessed the same repellent qualities, in terms of protection from evil and enchantment. He hadn't chosen to bury Beardsley under that tree from a sense either of aesthetics or convenience.

I squeezed his blistered hand, and he kissed me gently on top of the head.

At the head of the trail, I did glance back, but I could see nothing but a faint gleam from the weathered shingles of the farmhouse. The mountain ash and whatever might—or might not—be under it were hidden in darkness.

Gideon was unusually well-behaved, having made no more than a token protest at being double-mounted. I rather thought he was happy to leave the farm behind, too. I said as much, but Jamie sneezed and expressed the opinion that the wicked sod was merely biding his time while planning some future outrage.

The goats seemed inclined to view this nocturnal excursion as a lark, and ambled along with the liveliest interest, snatching mouthfuls of dry grass, bumping into one another and the horses, and generally sounding like a herd of elephants in the crackling underbrush.

I felt great relief at leaving the Beardsley place at last. As the pines blotted out the last sight of the hollow, I resolutely turned my mind from the disturbing events of the day, and began to think what might await us in Brownsville.

"I hope Roger's managed all right," I said, leaning back against Jamie's chest with a small sigh.

"Mmphm." From long experience, I diagnosed this particular catarrhal noise as indicating a polite general agreement with my sentiment, this overlaying complete personal indifference to the actuality. Either he saw no reason for concern, or he thought Roger could sink or swim.

"I hope he's found an inn of sorts," I offered, thinking this prospect might meet with a trifle more enthusiasm. "Hot food and a clean bed would be lovely."

"Mmphm." That one held a touch of humor, mingled with an inborn skepticism—fostered by long experience—regarding the possible existence of such items as hot food and clean beds in the Carolina backcountry.

"The goats seem to be going along very well," I offered, and waited in anticipation.

"Mmphm." Grudging agreement, mingled with a deep suspicion as to the continuance of good behavior on the part of the goats.

I was carefully formulating another observation, in hopes of getting him to do it again—three times was the record so far—when Gideon suddenly bore out Jamie's original mistrust by flinging up his head with a loud snort and rearing.

I crashed back into Jamie's chest, hitting my head on his collarbone with a thump that made me see stars. His arm crushed the air out of me as he dragged at the reins one-handed, shouting.

I had no idea what he was saying, or even whether he was shouting in English or Gaelic. The horse was screaming, rearing and pawing with his hooves, and I was scrabbling for a grip on anything at all, mane, saddle, reins. . . . A branch whipped my face and blinded me. Pandemonium reigned; there was screeching and bleating and a noise like tearing fabric and then something hit me hard and sent me flying into the darkness.

I wasn't knocked out, but it didn't make much difference. I was sprawled in a tangle of brush, struggling for breath, unable to move, and unable to see anything whatever beyond a few scattered stars in the sky overhead.

There was an ungodly racket going on some little distance away, in which a chorus of panicked goats figured largely, punctuated by what I took to be a woman's screams. Two women's screams.

I shook my head, confused. Then I flung myself over and started crawling, having belatedly recognized what was making that noise. I had heard panthers scream often enough—but always safely far in the distance. This one wasn't far away at all. The tearing-fabric noise I'd heard had been the cough of a big cat, very close at hand.

I bumped into a large fallen log and promptly rolled under

it, wedging myself as far into the small crevice there as possible. It wasn't the best hiding place I'd ever seen, but might at least prevent anything leaping out of a tree onto me.

I could still hear Jamie shouting, though the tenor of his remarks had changed to a sort of hoarse fury. The goats had mostly quit yammering—surely the cat couldn't have killed all of them? I couldn't hear anything of Mrs. Beardsley, either, but the horses were making a dreadful fuss, squealing and stamping.

My heart was hammering against the leafy ground, and a cold sweat tingled along my jaw. There isn't much for invoking raw terror like the primitive fear of being eaten, and my sympathies were entirely with the animals. There was a crashing in the brush near at hand, and Jamie shouting my name.

"Here," I croaked, unwilling to move out of my refuge until I knew for certain where the panther was—or at least knew for certain that it wasn't anywhere near me. The horses had stopped squealing, though they were still snorting and stamping, making enough noise to indicate that neither of them had either fallen prey to our visitor or run away.

"Here!" I called, a little louder.

More crashing, close at hand. Jamie stumbled through the darkness, crouched, and felt under the log until his hand encountered my arm, which he seized.

"Are ye all right, Sassenach?"

"I hadn't thought to notice, but I think so," I replied. I slid cautiously out from under my log, taking stock. Bruises here and there, abraded elbows, and a stinging sensation where the branch had slapped my cheek. Basically all right, then.

"Good. Come quick, he's hurt." He hauled me to my feet and started propelling me through the dark with a hand in the small of my back.

"Who?"

"The goat, of course."

My eyes were well-adapted to the dark by now, and I made out the large shapes of Gideon and the mare, standing under a leafless poplar, manes and tails swishing with agitation. A smaller shape that I took to be Mrs. Beardsley was crouched nearby, over something on the ground.

I could smell blood, and a powerful reek of goat. I squatted and reached out, touching rough, warm hair. The goat jerked at my touch, with a loud "MEHeheh!" that reassured me somewhat. He might be hurt, but he wasn't dying—at least not yet; the body under my hands was solid and vital, muscles tense.

"Where's the cat?" I asked, locating the ridged hardness of the horns and feeling my way hastily backward along the spine, then down the ribs and flanks. The goat had objections, and heaved wildly under my hands.

"Gone," Jamie said. He crouched down, too, and put a hand on the goat's head. "There, now, *a bhalaich*. It's all right, then. *Seas, mo charaid*."

I could feel no open wound on the goat's body, but I could certainly smell blood; a hot, metallic scent that disturbed the clean night air of the wood. The horses did, too; they whickered and moved uneasily in the dark.

"Are we fairly *sure* it's gone?" I asked, trying to ignore the sensation of eyes fastened on the back of my neck. "I smell blood."

"Aye. The cat took one of the nannies," Jamie informed me. He knelt next to me, laying a big hand on the goat's neck.

"Mrs. Beardsley loosed this brave laddie, and he went for the cat, bald-heided. I couldna see it all, but I think the creature maybe slapped at him; I heard it screech and spit, and the billy gave a skelloch just then, too. I think his leg is maybe broken."

It was. With that guidance, I found the break easily, low on the radius of the right front leg. The skin wasn't broken, but the bone was cracked through; I could feel the slight displacement of the raw ends. The goat heaved and thrust his horns at my arm when I touched the leg. His eyes were wild and rolling, the odd square pupils visible but colorless in the faint moonlight.

"Can ye mend him, Sassenach?" Jamie asked.

"I don't know." The goat was still struggling, but the flurries of movement were growing perceptibly weaker, as shock set in. I bit my lip, groping for a pulse in the fold between leg and body. The injury itself was likely repairable, but shock was a great danger; I had seen plenty of animals—and a few people, for that matter—die quickly following a traumatic incident, of injuries that were not fatal in themselves.

"I don't know," I said again. My fingers had found a pulse at last; it was trip-hammer fast, and thready. I was trying to envision the possibilities for treatment, all of them crude. "He may well die, Jamie, even if I can set the leg. Do you think perhaps we ought to slaughter him? He'd be a lot easier to carry, as meat."

Jamie stroked the goat's neck, gently.

"It would be a great shame, and him such a gallant creature."

Mrs. Beardsley laughed at that, a nervous small giggle, like a girl's, coming out of the dark beyond Jamie's bulk.

"Hith name ith Hiram," she said. "He'th a good boy."

"Hiram," Jamie repeated, still stroking. "Well, then, Hiram. *Courage, mon brave.* You'll do. You've balls as big as melons."

"Well, persimmons, maybe," I said, having inadvertently encountered the testicles in question while making my examination. "Perfectly respectable, though, I'm sure," I added, taking shallow breaths. Hiram's musk glands were working overtime. Even the harsh iron smell of blood took second place.

"I was speaking figuratively," Jamie informed me, rather dryly. "What will ye be needing, Sassenach?"

Evidently, the decision had been made; he was already rising to his feet.

"Right, then," I said, brushing back my hair with the back of a wrist. "Find me a couple of straight branches, about a foot long, no twigs, and a bit of rope from the saddlebags. Then you can help here," I added, trying to achieve a good grip on my struggling patient. "Hiram seems to like you. Recognizes a kindred spirit, no doubt."

Jamie laughed at that, a low, comforting sound at my elbow. He stood up with a final scratch of Hiram's ears, and rustled off, coming back within moments with the requested items.

"Right," I said, loosing one hand from Hiram's neck in order to locate the sticks. "I'm going to splint it. We'll have to carry him, but the splint will keep the leg from flexing and doing any more damage. Help me get him onto his side." Hiram, whether from male pride or goat stubbornness—always assuming these to be different things—kept trying to stand up, broken leg notwithstanding. His head was bobbing alarmingly, though, as the muscles in his neck weakened, and his body lurched from side to side. He scrabbled feebly at the ground, then stopped, panting heavily.

Mrs. Beardsley hovered over my shoulder, the kid still clutched in her arms. It gave a faint bleat, as though it had awakened suddenly from a nightmare, and Hiram gave a loud, echoing "Mehh" in reply.

"There's a thought," Jamie murmured. He stood up suddenly, and took the kid from Mrs. Beardsley. Then he knelt down again, pushing the little creature up close to Hiram's side. The goat at once ceased struggling, bending his head around to sniff at his offspring. The kid cried, pushing its nose against the big goat's side, and a long, slimy tongue snaked out, slobbering over my hand as it sought the kid's head.

"Work fast, Sassenach," Jamie suggested.

I needed no prompting, and within minutes, had the leg stabilized, the splinting padded with one of the multiple shawls Mrs. Beardsley appeared to be wearing. Hiram had settled, making only occasional grunts and exclamations, but the kid was still bleating loudly.

"Where is its mother?" I asked, though I didn't need to hear the answer. I didn't know a great deal about goats, but I knew enough about mothers and babies to realize that nothing but death would keep a mother from a child making that sort of racket. The other goats had come back, drawn by curiosity, fear of the dark, or a simple desire for company, but the mother didn't push forward.

"Poor Beckie," said Mrs. Beardsley sadly. "Thuch a thweet goat."

Dark forms bumped and jostled; there was a whuff of hot air in my ear as one nibbled at my hair, and another stepped on my calf, making me yelp as the sharp little hooves scraped the skin. I made no effort to shoo them away, though; the presence of his harem seemed to be doing Hiram the world of good.

I had the leg bones back in place and the splint bandaged firmly round them. I had found a good pulse point at the base of his ear, and was monitoring it, Hiram's head resting in my lap. As the other goats pressed in, nuzzling at him and making plaintive noises, he suddenly lifted his head and rolled up onto his chest, the broken leg awkwardly stuck out before him in its bindings.

He swayed to and fro like a drunken man for a moment, then uttered a loud, belligerent "MEEEEEHHH" and lurched onto three feet. He promptly fell down again, but the action cheered everyone. Even Mrs. Beardsley emitted a faint trill of pleasure at the sight.

"All right." Jamie stood up, and ran his fingers through his hair with a deep sigh. "Now, then."

"Now, then *what*?" I asked.

"Now I shall decide what to do," he said, with a certain edge to his voice.

"Aren't we going on to Brownsville?"

"We might," he said. "If Mrs. Beardsley happens to ken the way well enough to find the trail again by starlight?" He turned expectantly toward her, but I could see the negative motion of her head, even in the shadows.

It dawned on me that we were, in fact, no longer on the trail—which was in any case no more than a narrow deer track, winding through the forest.

"We can't be terribly far off it, surely?" I looked round, peering vainly into the dark, as though some lighted sign might indicate the position of the trail. In fact, I had no idea even in which direction it might lie.

"No," Jamie agreed. "And by myself, I daresay I could pick it up sooner or later. But I dinna mean to go floundering through the forest in the dark with this lot." He glanced round, evidently counting noses. Two very skittish horses, two women—one distinctly odd and possibly homicidal—and six goats, two of them incapable of walking. I rather saw his point.

He drew his shoulders back, shrugging a little, as though to ease a tight shirt.

"I'll go and have a keek round. If I find the way at once, well and good. If I don't, we'll camp for the night," he said.

"It will be a deal easier to look for the trail by daylight. Be careful, Sassenach."

And with a final sneeze, he vanished into the woods, leaving me in charge of the camp followers and wounded.

The orphaned goat was becoming louder and more anguished in its cries; it hurt my ears, as well as my heart. Mrs. Beardsley, though, had become somewhat more animated in Jamie's absence; I thought she was rather afraid of him. Now she brought up one of the other nannies, persuading her to stand still for the orphan to suckle. The kid was reluctant for a moment, but hunger and the need for warmth and reassurance were overwhelming, and within a few minutes, it was feeding busily, its small tail wagging in a dark flicker of movement.

I was happy to see it, but conscious of a small feeling of envy; I was all at once aware that I had eaten nothing all day, that I was very cold, desperately tired, sore in a number of places—and that without the complications of Mrs. Beardsley and her companions, I would long since have been safely in Brownsville, fed, warm, and tucked up by some friendly fireside. I put a hand on the kid's stomach, growing round and firm with milk, and thought rather wistfully that I should like someone simply to take care of *me*. Still, for the moment, I seemed to be the Good Shepherd, and no help for it.

"Do you think it might come back?" Mrs. Beardsley crouched next to me, shawl pulled tight around her broad shoulders. She spoke in a low tone, as though afraid someone might overhear.

"What, the panther? No, I don't think so. Why should it?" Nonetheless, a small shiver ran over me, as I thought of Jamie, alone somewhere in the dark. Hiram, his shoulder firmly jammed against my thigh, snorted, then laid his head on my knee with a long sigh.

"Thome folk thay the catth hunt in pairth."

"Really?" I stifled a yawn—not of boredom, simply fatigue. I blinked into the darkness, a chilled lethargy stealing over me. "Oh. Well, I should think a good-sized goat would do for two. Besides"—I yawned again, a jaw-cracking stretch—"besides, the horses would let us know."

Gideon and Mrs. Piggy were companionably nose-and-tailing it under the poplar tree, showing no signs now of agitation. This seemed to comfort Mrs. Beardsley, who sat down on the ground quite suddenly, her shoulders sagging as though the air had gone out of her.

"And how are you feeling?" I inquired, more from an urge to maintain conversation than from any real desire to know.

"I am glad to be gone from that place," she said simply.

I definitely shared that sentiment; our present situation was at least an improvement on the Beardsley homestead, even with the odd panther thrown in. Still, that didn't mean I was anxious to spend very long here.

"Do you know anyone in Brownsville?" I asked. I wasn't sure how large a settlement it was, though from the conversation of some of the men we had picked up, it sounded like a fair-sized village.

"No." She was silent for a moment, and I felt rather than saw her tilt back her head, looking up at the stars and the peaceful moon.

"I . . . have never been to Brownsville," she added, almost shyly.

Or anywhere else, it seemed. She told the story hesitantly, but almost eagerly, with no more than slight prodding on my part.

Beardsley had—in essence—bought her from her father, and brought her, with other goods acquired in Baltimore, down to his house, where he had essentially kept her prisoner, forbidding her to leave the homestead, or to show herself to anyone who might come to the house. Left to do the work of the homestead while Beardsley traveled into the Cherokee lands with his trade goods, she had had no society but a bond lad—who was little company, being deaf and speechless.

"Really," I said. In the events of the day, I had quite forgotten Josiah and his twin. I wondered whether she had known both of them, or only Keziah.

"How long is it since you came to North Carolina?" I asked.

"Two yearth," she said softly. "Two yearth, three month, and five dayth." I remembered the marks on the doorpost, and wondered when she had begun to keep count. From the very beginning? I stretched my back, disturbing Hiram, who grumbled.

"I see. By the way, what is your Christian name?" I asked, belatedly aware that I had no idea.

"Frantheth," she said, then tried again, not liking the mumbled sound of it. "Fran-*cess*," the end of it a hiss through her broken teeth. She gave a shrug, then, and laughed—a small, shy sound. "Fanny," she said. "My mother called me Fanny."

"Fanny," I said, encouragingly. "That's a very nice name. May I call you so?"

"I . . . would be pleathed," she said. She drew breath again, but stopped without speaking, evidently too shy to say whatever she'd had in mind. With her husband dead, she seemed entirely passive, quite deprived of the force that had animated her earlier.

"Oh," I said, belatedly realizing. "Claire. Do call me Claire, please."

"Claire—how pretty."

"Well, it hasn't any esses, at least," I said, not thinking. "Oh—I do beg your pardon!"

She made a small *pff* sound of dismissal. Encouraged by the dark, the faint sense of intimacy engendered by the exchange of names—or simply from a need to talk, after so long—she told me about her mother, who had died when she was twelve, her father, a crabber, and her life in Baltimore, wading out along the shore at low tide to rake oysters and gather mussels, watching the fishing craft and the warships come in past Fort Howard to sail up the Patapsco.

"It wath . . . peatheful," she said, rather wistfully. "It wath tho open—nothing but the thky and the water." She tilted back her head again, as though yearning for the small bit of night sky visible through the interlacing branches overhead. I supposed that while the forested mountains of North Carolina were refuge and embrace to a Highlander like Jamie, they might well seem claustrophobic and alien to someone accustomed to the watery Chesapeake shore.

"Will you go back there, do you think?" I asked.

"Back?" She sounded slightly startled. "Oh. I . . . I hadn't thought . . ."

"No?" I had found a tree trunk to lean against, and stretched slightly, to ease my back. "You must have seen that your—that Mr. Beardsley was dying. Didn't you have some plan?" Beyond the fun of torturing him slowly to death, that is. It occurred to me that I had been getting altogether too comfortable with this woman, alone in the dark with the goats. She might truly have been Beardsley's victim—or she might only be saying so now, to enlist our aid. It would behoove me to remember the burned toes on Beardsley's foot, and the appalling state of that loft. I straightened up a little, and felt for the small knife I carried at my belt—just in case.

"No." She sounded a little dazed—and no wonder, I supposed. I felt more than a little dazed myself, simply from emotion and fatigue. Enough so that I almost missed what she said next.

"What did you say?"

"I thaid . . . Mary Ann didn't tell me what I wath to do . . . after."

"Mary Ann," I said cautiously. "Yes, and that would be . . . the first Mrs. Beardsley, would it?"

She laughed, and the hair on my neck rippled unpleasantly.

"Oh, no. Mary Ann wath the fourth one."

"The . . . fourth one," I said, a little faintly.

"Thye'th the only one he buried under the rowan tree," she informed me. "That wath a mithtake. The otherth are in the woodth. He got lazy, I think; he did not want to walk tho far."

"Oh," I said, for lack of any better response.

"I told you—sshe thtands under the rowan tree at moonrithe. When I thaw her there at firtht, I thought sshe wath a living woman. I wath afraid of what *he* might do, if he thaw her there alone—tho I sstole from the houthe to warn her."

"I see." Something in my voice must have sounded less than credulous, for her head turned sharply toward me. I took a firmer grip on the knife.

"You do not believe me?"

"Of course I do!" I assured her, trying to edge Hiram's head off my lap. My left leg had gone to sleep from the pressure of his weight, and I had no feeling in my foot.

"I can thow you," she said, and her voice was calm and

certain. "Mary Ann told me where they were—the otherth—and I found them. I can thow you their graveth."

"I'm sure that won't be necessary," I said, flexing my toes to restore circulation. If she came toward me, I decided, I would shove the goat into her path, roll to the side, and make off as fast as possible on all fours, shouting for Jamie. And where in bloody hell *was* Jamie, anyway?

"So . . . um . . . Fanny. You're saying that Mr. Beardsley"—it occurred to me that I didn't know his name either, but I thought I would just as soon keep my relations with his memory formal, under the circumstances—"that your husband *murdered* four wives? And no one knew?" Not that anyone necessarily *would* know, I realized. The Beardsley homestead was very isolated, and it wasn't at all unusual for women to die—of accident, childbirth, or simple overwork. Someone might have known that Beardsley had lost four wives—but it was entirely possible that no one cared how.

"Yeth." She sounded calm, I thought; not incipiently dangerous, at least. "He would have killed me, too—but Mary Ann thtopped him."

"How did she do that?"

She drew a deep breath and sighed, settling herself on the ground. There was a faint, sleepy bleat from her lap, and I realized that she was holding the kid again. I relaxed my grip on the knife; she could hardly attack me with a lapful of goat.

She had, she said, gone out to speak to Mary Ann whenever the moon was high; the ghostly woman appeared under the rowan tree only between half-moon wax and half-moon wane—not in the dark of the moon, or at crescent.

"Very particular," I murmured, but she didn't notice, being too absorbed in the story.

This had gone on for some months. Mary Ann had told Fanny Beardsley who she was, informed her of the fate of her predecessors, and the manner of her own death.

"He choked her," Fanny confided. "I could see the markth of his handth on her throat. Sshe warned me that he would do the thame to me, one day."

One night a few weeks later, Fanny was sure that the time had come.

"He wath far gone with the rum, you thee," she explained. "It wath alwayth worth when he drank, and thith time . . ."

Trembling with nerves, she had dropped the trencher with his supper, splattering food on him. He had sprung to his feet with a roar, lunging for her, and she had turned and fled.

"He wath between me and the door," she said. "I ran for the loft. I hoped he would be too drunk to manage the ladder, and he wath."

Beardsley had stumbled, lurching, and dragged the ladder down with a crash. As he struggled, mumbling and cursing, to put it into place again, there came a knock on the door.

Beardsley shouted to know who it was, but no answer came; only another knock at the door. Fanny had crept to the edge of the loft, to see his red face glaring up at her. The knock sounded for a third time. His tongue was too thick with drink to speak coherently; he only growled in his throat and held up a finger in warning to her, then turned and staggered toward the door. He wrenched it open, looked out—and screamed.

"I have never heard thuch a thound," she said, very softly. "Never."

Beardsley turned and ran, tripping over a stool and sprawling full-length, scrabbling to his feet, stumbling to the foot of the ladder and scrambling up it, missing rungs and clawing for purchase, crying out and shouting.

"He kept thouting to me to help him, help him." Her voice held an odd note; perhaps only astonishment that such a man should have called to her for help—but with a disquieting note that I thought betrayed a deep and secret pleasure in the memory.

Beardsley had reached the top of the ladder, but could not take the final step into the loft. Instead, his face had gone suddenly from red to white, his eyes rolled back, and then he fell senseless onto his face on the boards, his legs dangling absurdly from the edge of the loft.

"I could not get him down; it wath all I could do to pull him up into the loft." She sighed. "And the retht . . . you know."

"Not quite." Jamie spoke from the dark near my shoulder, making me jump. Hiram grunted indignantly, shaken awake.

"How the hell long have *you* been there?" I demanded.

"Long enough." He moved to my side and knelt beside me, a hand on my arm. "And what was it at the door, then?" he asked Mrs. Beardsley. His voice held no more than light interest, but his hand was tight on my arm. A slight shudder went over me. *What*, indeed.

"Nothing," she said simply. "There wath no one there at all, that I could thee. But—you can thee the rowan tree from that door, and there *wath* a half-moon rithing."

There was a marked period of silence at this. Finally, Jamie rubbed a hand hard over his face, sighed, and got to his feet.

"Aye. Well. I've found a spot where we can shelter for the night. Help me wi' the goat, Sassenach."

We were on hilly ground, spiked with rocky outcrops and small tangles of sweet shrub and greenbrier, making the footing between the trees so uncertain in the dark that I fell twice, catching myself only by luck before breaking my neck. It would have been difficult going in broad daylight; by night, it was nearly impossible. Fortunately, it was no more than a short distance to the spot Jamie had found.

This was a sort of shallow gash in the side of a crumbling clay bank, overhung with a tattered grapevine and thatched with matted grasses. At one time, there had been a stream here, and the water had carved away a good-sized chunk of earth from the bank, leaving an overhanging shelf. Something had diverted the flow of water some years ago, though, and the rounded stones of what had been the streambed were scattered and half-sunk in mossy soil; one rolled under my foot and I fell to one knee, striking it painfully on another of the beastly stones.

"All right, Sassenach?" Jamie heard my rude exclamation and stopped, turning toward me. He stood on the hillside just above me, Hiram on his shoulders. From below, silhouetted against the sky, he looked grotesque and rather frightening; a tall, horned figure with hunched and monstrous shoulders.

"Fine," I said, rather breathless. "Just here, is it?"

"Aye. Help me . . . will ye?" He sounded a lot more breathless than I did. He sank carefully to his knees, and I hurried to help him lower Hiram to the ground. Jamie stayed kneeling, one hand on the ground to brace himself.

"I hope it won't be too hard to find the trail in the morning," I said, watching him anxiously. His head was bent with exhaustion, air rattling wetly in his chest with each breath. I wanted him in a place with fire and food, as fast as possible.

He shook his head, and coughed, clearing his throat.

"I ken where it is," he said, and coughed again. "It's only—" The coughing shook him hard; I could see his shoulders braced against it. When he stopped, I put a hand gently on his back, and could feel a fine, constant tremor running through him; not a chill, just the trembling of muscles forced beyond the limits of their strength.

"I canna go any further, Claire," he said softly, as though ashamed of the admission. "I'm done."

"Lie down," I said, just as softly. "I'll see to things."

There was a certain amount of bustle and confusion, but within a half hour or so, everyone was more or less settled, the horses hobbled, and a small fire going.

I knelt to check my chief patient, who was sitting on his chest, splinted leg stuck out in front. Hiram, with his ladies safely gathered behind him in the shelter of the bank, emitted a belligerent "Meh!" and threatened me with his horns.

"Ungrateful sod," I said, pulling back.

Jamie laughed, then broke off to cough, his shoulders shaking with the spasm. He was curled at one side of the depression in the bank, head pillowed on his folded coat.

"And as for you," I said, eyeing him, "I wasn't joking about that goose grease. Open your cloak, lift your shirt, and do it now."

He narrowed his eyes at me, and shot a quick glance in Mrs. Beardsley's direction. I hid a smile at his modesty, but gave Mrs. Beardsley the small kettle from my saddlebag and sent her off to fetch water and more firewood, then dug out the gourd of mentholated ointment.

Jamie's appearance alarmed me slightly, now that I had a good look at him. He was pale and white-lipped, red-rimmed round the nostrils, and his eyes were bruised with fatigue. He looked very sick, and sounded worse, the breath wheezing in his chest with each respiration.

"Well, I suppose if Hiram wouldn't die in front of his nannies, you won't die in front of me, either," I said dubiously, scooping out a thumbful of the fragrant grease.

"I am not dying in the least degree," he said, rather crossly. "I'm only a wee bit tired. I shall be entirely myself in the morn—oh, Christ, I hate this!"

His chest was quite warm, but I thought he wasn't fevered; it was hard to tell, my own fingers being very cold.

He jerked, made a high-pitched "eee" noise, and tried to squirm away. I seized him firmly by the neck, put a knee in his belly, and proceeded to have my way with him, all protests notwithstanding. At length, he gave up struggling and submitted, only giggling intermittently, sneezing, and uttering an occasional small yelp when I reached a particularly ticklish spot. The goats found it all very entertaining.

In a few minutes, I had him well-greased and gasping on the ground, the skin of his chest and throat red from rubbing and shiny with grease, a strong aroma of peppermint and camphor in the air. I patted a thick flannel into place on his chest, pulled down his shirt, drew the folds of his cloak around him, and tucked a blanket up snugly under his chin.

"Now, then," I said with satisfaction, wiping my hands on a cloth. "As soon as I have hot water, we'll have a nice cup of horehound tea."

He opened one eye suspiciously.

"We will?"

"Well, you will. I'd rather drink hot horse piss, myself."

"So would I."

"Too bad; it hasn't any medicinal effects that I know of."

He groaned and shut the eye. He breathed heavily for a moment, sounding like a diseased bellows. Then he raised his head a few inches, opening his eyes.

"Is yon woman back yet?"

"No, I imagine it will take her a little time to find the stream in the dark." I hesitated. "Did you . . . hear everything she was telling me?"

He shook his head.

"Not all—but enough. Mary Ann and that?"

"Yes, that."

He grunted.

"Did ye believe her, Sassenach?"

I didn't reply immediately, but took my time in cleaning the goose grease out from under my fingernails.

"I did at the time," I finally said. "Just now—I'm not sure."

He grunted again, this time with approval.

"I shouldna think she's dangerous," he said. "But keep your wee knife about ye, Sassenach—and dinna turn your back on her. We'll take watch and watch about; wake me in an hour."

He shut his eyes, coughed, and without further ado, fell fast asleep.

CLOUDS WERE BEGINNING to drift across the moon, and a cold wind stirred the grass on the bank above us.

"Wake him in an hour," I muttered, shifting myself in an effort to achieve some minimal level of comfort on the rocky ground. "Ha, bloody ha." I leaned over and hoisted Jamie's head into my lap. He groaned slightly, but didn't twitch.

"Sniffles," I said accusingly to him. "Ha!"

I wriggled my shoulders and leaned back, finding some support against the sloping wall of our shelter. Despite Jamie's warning, it seemed unnecessary to keep an eye on Mrs. Beardsley; she had obligingly built up the fire, then curled up among the goats and—being merely flesh and blood, and therefore exhausted by the day's events—had gone immediately to sleep. I could hear her on the far side of the fire, snoring peacefully among the assorted wheezings and grunts of her companions.

"And what do you think you are, anyway?" I demanded of the heavy head resting on my thigh. "Vulcanized rubber?" My fingers touched his hair, quite without intent, and smoothed it gently. One corner of his mouth lifted suddenly, in a smile of startling sweetness.

It was gone as quickly as it had come, and I stared at him

in astonishment. No, he was sound asleep; his breath came hoarse but even, and the long parti-colored lashes rested dark against his cheeks. Very softly, I stroked his head again.

Sure enough; the smile flickered like the touch of a flame, and disappeared. He sighed, very deeply, bent his neck to nuzzle closer, then relaxed completely, his body going limp.

"Oh, Christ, Jamie," I said softly, and felt tears sting my eyes.

It had been years since I'd seen him smile in his sleep like that. Not since the early days of our marriage, in fact—at Lallybroch.

He'd always do it as a wee lad, his sister Jenny had told me then. *I think it means he's happy.*

My fingers curled into the soft, thick hair at the nape of his neck, feeling the solid curve of his skull, the warm scalp and the hair-thin line of the ancient scar across it.

"Me, too," I whispered to him.

30

SPAWN OF SATAN

MRS. MACLEOD and her two children had gone to stay with Evan Lindsay's wife, and with the leaving of the MacLeod brothers with the militia, plus Geordie Chisholm and his two eldest sons, the congestion in the big house was eased substantially. Not nearly enough, though, Brianna reflected, considering that Mrs. Chisholm remained.

The problem was not Mrs. Chisholm as such; the problem was Mrs. Chisholm's five younger children, all boys, and referred to collectively—by Mrs. Bug—as "the spawn of Satan." Mrs. Chisholm, perhaps understandably, objected to this terminology. While the other inhabitants of the house were less forthright than Mrs. Bug in stating their opinions, there was a remarkable unanimity among them. Three-year-old twin boys *would* have that effect, Brianna thought, eyeing Jemmy with some trepidation as she envisioned the future.

He was at the moment giving no indication of a potential for future rampage, being half-asleep on the rag rug of Jamie's study, where Brianna had retired in the faint hope of fifteen minutes' semi-solitude in which to write. Residual awe of Jamie was sufficient to keep the little warts out of this room, for the most part.

Mrs. Bug had informed eight-year-old Thomas, six-year-old Anthony, and five-year-old Toby Chisholm that Mrs. Fraser was a notable witch; a White Lady, who would undoubtedly turn them into toads on the spot—and no great loss to society, she gave them to understand—should any harm come to the contents of her surgery. That didn't keep them out—quite the opposite; they were fascinated—but it had so far prevented them breaking much.

Jamie's inkstand stood to hand on the table; a hollow gourd, neatly corked with a large acorn, with a pottery jar of neatly sharpened turkey quills beside it. Motherhood had taught Brianna to seize random moments; she seized this one, and a quill, flipping open the cover of the small journal in which she kept what she thought of as her private accounts.

Last night I dreamed about making soap. I haven't made soap yet, myself, but I'd been scrubbing the floor yesterday, and the smell of the soap was still on my hands when I went to bed. It's a nasty smell, something between acid and ashes, with a horrible faint stink from the hog fat, like something that's been dead for a long time.

I was pouring water into a kettle of wood ash, to make lye, and it was turning to lye even as I poured. Big clouds of poisonous smoke were coming up from the kettle; it was yellow, the smoke.

Da brought me a big bowl of suet, to mix with the lye, and there were babies' fingers in it. I don't remember thinking there was anything strange about this—at the time.

Brianna had been trying to ignore a series of crashing noises from upstairs, which sounded like several persons jumping up and down on a bedstead. These ceased abruptly, succeeded by a piercing scream, which in turn was followed by the sound of flesh meeting flesh in a loud slap, and several more screams of assorted pitches.

She flinched and shut her eyes tight, recoiling as the sounds of conflict escalated. A moment more, and they were thundering down the stairs. With a glance at Jemmy, who had been startled awake, but didn't seem frightened—my God, he was getting used to it, she thought—she put down the quill and stood up, sighing.

Mr. Bug was there to tend the farm and livestock and repel physical threats; Mr. Wemyss was there to chop firewood, haul water, and generally maintain the fabric of the house. But Mr. Bug was silent, Mr. Wemyss timid; Jamie had left Brianna formally in charge. She was, therefore, the court of appeal, and judge in all conflicts. Herself, if you would.

Herself flung open the study door and glowered at the mob. Mrs. Bug, red in the face—as usual—and brimming with accusation. Mrs. Chisholm, ditto, overflowing with maternal outrage. Little Mrs. Aberfeldy, the color of an eggplant, clutching her two-year-old daughter, Ruth, protectively to her bosom. Tony and Toby Chisholm, both in tears and covered with snot. Toby had a red handprint on the side of his face; little Ruthie's wispy hair appeared to be oddly shorter on one side than the other. They all began to talk at once.

". . . Red savages!"

". . . My baby's beautiful hair!"

"She started it!"

". . . Dare to strike my son!"

"We was just playin' at scalpin', ma'am . . ."

". . . EEEEEEEEEEE!"

". . . and torn a great hole in my feather bed, the wee spawn!"

"*Look* what she's done, the wicked auld besom!"

"*Look* what they've done!"

"Look ye, ma'am, it's only . . ."

"AAAAAAAAAAA!"

Brianna stepped out into the corridor and slammed the door behind her. It was a solid door, and the resultant boom temporarily halted the outcry. On the other side, Jemmy began to cry, but she ignored him for the moment.

She drew a deep breath, prepared to wade into the melee, but then thought better of it. She couldn't face the thought of the interminable wrangling that would come of dealing with them as a group. Divide and conquer was the only way.

"I am *writing*," she declared instead, and looked narrow-eyed from face to face. "Something important." Mrs. Aberfeldy looked impressed; Mrs. Chisholm affronted; Mrs. Bug astonished.

She nodded coolly to each one in turn.

"I'll talk to each of you about it later. Aye?"

She opened the door, stepped inside, and shut it very gently on the three pop-eyed faces, then pressed her back against it, closed her eyes, and let out the breath she had been holding.

There was silence outside the door, then a distinct "Hmp!" in Mrs. Chisholm's voice, and the noise of footsteps going away—one set up the stairs, another toward the kitchen, and a heavier tread into the surgery across the hall. A rush of small footsteps out the front door announced Tony and Toby making their escape.

Jemmy ceased wailing when he saw her, and started sucking his thumb instead.

"I hope Mrs. Chisholm doesn't know anything about herbs," she told him, whispering. "I'm sure Grandma keeps poisons in there." A good thing her mother had taken the box of saws and scalpels with her, at least.

She stood still a moment, listening. No sounds of breaking glass. Perhaps Mrs. Chisholm had merely stepped into the surgery in order to avoid Mrs. Aberfeldy and Mrs. Bug. Brianna sank down in the straight chair by the small table her father used as a desk. Or maybe Mrs. Chisholm was lying in wait, hoping to snare Brianna to listen to her own grievances, as soon as the others were safely out of the way.

Jemmy was now lying on his back with his feet in the air,

happily mangling a bit of rusk he had found somewhere. Her journal had fallen to the floor. Hearing Mrs. Chisholm come out of the surgery, she hastily seized the quill, and snatched one of the ledger books from the stack on the desk with the other.

The door opened an inch or two. There was a moment's silence, during which she bent her head, frowning in exaggerated concentration at the page before her, scratching with an empty quill. The door closed again.

"Bitch," she said, under her breath. Jemmy made an interrogative noise, and she looked down at him. "You didn't hear that, all right?"

Jemmy made an agreeable noise and crammed the soggy remnant of his toast into his left nostril. She made an instinctive movement to take it away from him, then stopped herself. She wasn't in the mood for any more conflict this morning. Or this afternoon, either.

She tapped the black quill thoughtfully on the ledger page. She'd have to do something, and fast. Mrs. Chisholm might have found the deadly nightshade—and she *knew* Mrs. Bug had a cleaver.

Mrs. Chisholm had the advantage in weight, height, and reach, but Brianna personally would put her money on Mrs. Bug, in terms of guile and treachery. As for poor little Mrs. Aberfeldy, she'd be caught in the crossfire, riddled with verbal bullets. And little Ruthie would likely be bald as an egg before another week was out.

Her father would have sorted them out in nothing flat by the joint exercise of charm and male authority. She gave a small snort of amusement at the thought. Come, he sayeth to one, and she curleth up at his feet, purring like Adso the cat. Go, he sayeth to another, and she goeth promptly out into the kitchen and baketh him a plate of buttered muffins.

Her mother would have seized the first excuse to escape the house—to tend a distant patient or gather medicinal herbs—and left them to fight it out among themselves, returning only when a state of armed neutrality had been restored. Brianna hadn't missed the look of relief on her mother's face as she swung up into her mare's saddle—or the faintly apologetic glance she sent her daughter. Still, neither strategy was going to work for her—though the urge to seize Jemmy and run for the hills was pretty strong.

For the hundredth time since the men had left, she wished passionately that she could have gone with them. She could imagine the bulk of a horse moving under her, the clean, cold air in her lungs, and Roger riding by her side, the sun glowing off his dark hair, and unseen adventure to be faced together, somewhere ahead.

She missed him with a deep ache, like a bruise to the bone. How long might he be gone, if it really came to fighting? She pushed that thought aside, not wanting to look at the thought that came after it; the thought that if it came to fighting, there was a possibility—however faint—that he would come back ill or injured—or wouldn't come back at all.

"It's *not* going to come to that," she said firmly, aloud. "They'll be back in a week or two."

There was a rattling sound as a blast of icy rain struck the window. The weather was turning cold; it would be snowing by nightfall. She shivered, drawing the shawl around her shoulders, and glanced at Jem to see that he was warm enough. His smock was puddled up around his middle, his diaper was plainly damp, and one stocking had fallen off, leaving his small pink foot bare. He appeared not to notice, being absorbed in babbling a song to the bare toes idly flexing overhead.

She looked dubiously at him, but he seemed happy enough—and the brazier in the corner *was* putting out some heat.

"Okay," she said, and sighed. She had Jem, and that was that. That *being* that, the problem was to find some means of dealing with the Three Furies before they drove her crazy or assassinated each other with rolling pin or knitting needle.

"Logic," she said to Jemmy, sitting up straight in the chair and pointing the quill at him. "There must be a logical way. It's like that problem where you have to get a cannibal, a missionary, and a goat across a river in a canoe. Let me think about this."

Jem began trying to get his foot into his crumb-encrusted mouth, despite the clear illogic of the procedure.

"You must take after Daddy," she told him, tolerantly. She put the quill back in its jar, and started to close the ledger, then stopped, attracted by the sprawling entries. The sight of Jamie's characteristically messy writing still gave her a faint thrill, remembering her first sight of it—on an ancient deed of sasine, its ink gone pale brown with age.

This ink had been pale brown to start with, but had now darkened, the iron-gall mixture achieving its typical blue-black with exposure to air over a day or so.

It was not so much a ledger, she saw, as a logbook, recording the daily activities of the farm.

> ***16 July***—*Rec'd six weaned piglets of Pastor Gottfried, in trade for two bottles muscat wine and a goosewing axhead. Have put them in the stable 'til they be grown enough to forage conveniently.*
>
> ***17 July***—*One of the hives commenced to swarm in the afternoon, and came into the stable. My wife fortunately recaptured the swarm, which she housed in an empty churn. She says Ronnie Sinclair must make her a new one.*
>
> ***18 July***—*Letter from my aunt, asking advice re sawmill on Grinder's Creek. Replied, saying I will ride to inspect the situation within the month. Letter sent with R. Sinclair, who goes to Cross Creek with a load of 22 barrels, from which I am to receive half his profit toward payment of debt on cobbler's tools. Have arranged to deduct cost of new churn from this amount.*

The flow of entries was soothing, as peaceful as the summer days they recorded. She felt the knot of tension between her shoulder blades beginning to relax, and her mind began to loosen and stretch, ready to seek a way out of her difficulties.

> ***20 July***—*Barley in the lower field as high as my stocking-tops. A healthy heifer calf born to red cow soon after midnight. All well. An excellent day.*
>
> ***21 July***—*Rode to Muellers'. Exchanged one jar*

honeycomb for leather bridle in poor repair (but can be mended). Home well after dark, in consequence of seeing a twilight hatch rising upon the pond near Hollis's Gap. Stopped to fish, and caught a string of ten fine trout. Six eaten for supper; the rest will do for breakfast.

22 July—*My grandson has a rash, though my wife declares it of no moment. The white sow has broken through her pen again and escaped into the forest. I am in two minds whether I shall pursue her or only express sympathy for the unfortunate predator that first encounters her. Her temper is similar to that of my daughter at the moment, the latter having slept little these past few nights . . .*

Brianna leaned forward, frowning at the page.

. . . in consequence of the infant's screaming, which my wife says is the colic and will pass. I trust she is right. Meanwhile, I have settled Brianna and the child in the old cabin, which is some relief to us in the house, if not to my poor daughter. The white sow ate four of her last litter before I could prevent her.

"Why, you bloody *bastard*!" she said. She was familiar with the white sow in question, and not flattered by the comparison. Jemmy, alarmed by her tone, stopped crooning and dropped his toast, his mouth beginning to quiver.

"No, no, it's all right, sweetie." She got up and scooped him into her arms, swaying gently to soothe him. "Shh, it's all right. Mummy is just talking to Grandpa, that's all. You didn't hear that word either, okay? Shh, shh."

Jemmy was reassured, but leaned out from her arms, reaching after his discarded meal with small grunts of anxiety. She stooped and picked it up, eyeing the half-dissolved object with distaste. The crust was not only stale and wet, but had acquired a light coating of what seemed to be cat hair.

"Ick. You don't really want that, do you?"

Evidently he did, and was persuaded only with difficulty to accept a large iron bull's ring—used for leading male animals by the nose, she noted with some irony—from the shelf in lieu of it. A brief nibble confirmed the desirability of the nose ring, though, and he settled down in her lap to single-minded gnawing, allowing her to reread the conclusion of the offensive entry.

"Hmm." She leaned back, shifting Jemmy's weight more comfortably. He could sit up easily now, though it still seemed incredible that his noodle-neck could support the round dome of his head. She regarded the ledger broodingly.

"It's a thought," she said to Jemmy. "If I shift the old bi—I mean, Mrs. Chisholm—to our cabin, it will get her and her horrible little monsters out of everyone's hair. Then . . . hmm. Mrs. Aberfeldy and Ruthie could go in with Lizzie and her father, if we move the trundle from Mama and Da's room in there. The Bugs get their privacy back, and Mrs. Bug stops being an evil-minded old . . . er . . . anyway, then I suppose you and I could sleep in Mama and Da's room, at least 'til they come back."

She hated to think of moving from the cabin. It was her home, her private place, her family's place. She could go there and close the door, leaving the furor here behind. Her things were there; the half-built loom, the pewter plates, the pottery jug she had painted—all the small, homely objects with which she had made the space her own.

Beyond the sense of possession and peace, she had an uncomfortable sense of something like superstition about leaving it. The cabin was the home Roger had shared with her; to leave it, however temporarily, seemed somehow an admission that he might not return to share it again.

She tightened her grip on Jemmy, who ignored her in favor of concentration on his toy, his fat little fists shiny with drool where he grasped the ring.

No, she didn't want to give up her cabin at all. But it *was* an answer, and a logical one. Would Mrs. Chisholm agree? The cabin was much more crudely built than the big house, and lacking its amenities.

Still, she was pretty sure Mrs. Chisholm would accept the suggestion. If ever she'd seen someone whose motto was, "Better to reign in hell than serve in heaven . . ." Despite her trouble, she felt a small bubble of laughter rise beneath her stays.

She reached out and flipped the ledger closed, then tried to replace it on the stack from which she'd taken it. One-handed, though, and encumbered by Jemmy, she couldn't quite reach, and the book slipped off, falling back onto the table.

"Rats," she muttered, and scooted forward on her chair, reaching to pick it up again. Several loose sheets had fallen out, and she stuffed these back as tidily as she could with her free hand.

One, plainly a letter, had the remnants of its wax seal still attached. Her eye caught the impression of a smiling half-moon, and she paused. That was Lord John Grey's seal. It must be the letter he had sent in September, in which he described his adventures hunting deer in the Dismal Swamp; her father had read it to the family several times—Lord John was a humorous correspondent, and the deer hunt had been beset by the sort of misfortunes that were no doubt uncomfortable to live through, but which made picturesque recounting afterward.

Smiling in memory, she flipped the letter open with her thumb, looking forward to seeing the story again, only to find that she was looking at something quite different.

13 October, Anno Domini 1770

Mr. James Fraser
Fraser's Ridge, North Carolina

My dear Jamie,

I woke this Morning to the sound of the Rain which has beat upon us for the last Week, and to the gentle clucking of several Chickens, who had come to roost upon my Bedstead. Rising under the Stare of numerous beady Eyes, I went to make Inquiry as to this Circumstance, and was informed that the River has risen so far under the Impetus of the recent Rain as to have undermined both the Necessary House and the Chicken Coop. The contents of the latter were rescued by William (my Son, whom you will recall), and two of the Slaves, who swept the dispossessed Fowl out of the passing Floodwaters with Brooms. I cannot say whose was the Notion to sequester the hapless feathered Flood Victims in my Sleeping Chamber, but I hold certain Suspicions in this regard.

Resorting to use of my Chamber Pot (I could wish that the Chickens shared this Facility, they are distressing incontinent Fowl), I dressed and ventured forth to see what might be salvaged. Some few Boards and the shingled Roof of the Chicken Coop remain, but my Privy, alas, has become the Property of King Neptune—or whatever minor water Deity presides over so modest a Tributary as our River.

I pray you will suffer no Concern for us, though; the House is at some distance from the River, and safely placed upon a Rise of Ground, such as to render us quite safe from even the most incommodious flooding. (The Necessary had been dug by the old homestead, and we had not yet attempted a new structure more convenient; this minor disaster, by affording us the Necessary *opportunity for rebuilding, thus may prove a blessing in disguise.)*

Brianna rolled her eyes at the pun, but smiled nonetheless. Jemmy dropped his ring and began at once to whine for it. She stooped to pick it up, but stopped halfway down, riveted by the words at the beginning of the next paragraph.

Your letter mentions Mr. Stephen Bonnet, and inquires whether I have news or knowledge of him. I have met with him, you will collect, but have unfortunately no Memory whatever of the Encounter, not even to Recalling of his Appearance, though as you know, I carry a small Hole in my Head, as a singular Memento of the occasion. (You may inform your Lady Wife that I am healed well, with no further Symptoms of Discomfort than the occasional Headache. Beyond this, the Silver Plate with which the Opening is covered is subject to sudden chill when the Weather is cold, which tends to make my left Eye water, and to cause a great Discharge of Snot, but this is of no consequence.)

As I thus share your Interest in Mr. Bonnet and his Movements, I have long since had Inquiries dispersed among such Acquaintance as I have near the Coast, since the Descriptions of his Machinations cause me to believe the man is most like to be found there (this is a comforting Notion, given the Great Distance between the Coast and your remote Eyrie). The River being navigable to the Sea, however, I had some Thought that the River Captains and Water Scallywags who now and again grace my Dinner Table might at some Point bear me Word of the man.

I am not pleased by the Obligation to report that Bonnet still resides among the Living, but both Duty and Friendship compel me to impart such Particulars of him as I have obtained. These are sparse; the Wretch appears sensible of his criminal Situation, so far as to render him subtle in his Movements until now.

Jemmy was kicking and squawking. As though in a trance, she stooped, holding him, and picked up the ring, her eyes still fixed on the letter.

I had heard little of him, save a Report at one Point that he had repaired to France—good News. However, two Weeks past I had a Guest, one Captain Liston ("Captain" being no more than a title of courtesy; he claims service with the Royal Navy, but I will stake a Hogshead of my best Tobacco [a sample of which you will find accompanying this Missive—and if you do not, I would be obliged to hear of it, since I do not altogether trust the Slave by whom I send it] that he has never so much as smelled the Ink on a

Commission, let alone the Reek of the Bilges) who gave me a more recent—and highly disagreeable—History of the man Bonnet.

Finding himself at large in the Port of Charleston, Liston said that he fell in with some Companions of low Aspect, who invited him to accompany them to a Cockfight, held in the Innyard of an Establishment called the Devil's Glass. Among the Rabble there was a Man notable for the fineness of his Dress, and the Freedom with which he spent his Coin—Liston heard this man referred to as Bonnet, and was told by the Landlord that this Bonnet had the name of a Smuggler upon the Outer Banks, being Popular with the Merchants of the coastal Towns in North Carolina, though much less so with the Authorities, who were Helpless to deal with the Man by reason of his Business and the dependence of the Towns of Wilmington, Edenton, and New Bern upon his Trade.

Liston took little further Note of Bonnet (he said) until an Altercation rose over a Wager upon the Fighting. Hot Words were exchanged, and nothing would do save Honor be satisfied by the drawing of Blood. Nothing loath, the Spectators at once began to wager upon the Outcome of the human Contest, in the same manner as that of the fighting Fowl.

One combatant was the man Bonnet, the other a Captain Marsden, a half-pay Army Captain known to my Guest as a good Swordsman. This Marsden, feeling himself the injured Party, damned Bonnet's eyes, and invited the Smuggler to accommodate him upon the Spot, an Offer at once accepted. Wagers ran heavy upon Marsden, his Reputation being known, but it was soon clear that he had met his Match and more in Bonnet. Within no more than a few moments, Bonnet succeeded in disarming his Opponent, and in Wounding him so grievously in the Thigh that Marsden sank down upon his Knees and yielded to his Opponent—having no Choice in the Matter at that Point, to be sure.

Bonnet did not accept of this Surrender, though, but

instead performed an Act of such Cruelty as made the deepest Impression upon all who saw it. Remarking with great coolness that it was not his own Eyes that would be damned, he drew the Tip of his Weapon across Marsden's Eyes, twisting it in such Fashion as not only to blind the Captain, but to inflict such Mutilation as would make him an Object of the greatest Horror and Pity to all who might behold him.

Leaving his Foe thus mangled and fainting upon the bloody Sand of the Innyard, Bonnet cleansed his Blade by wiping it upon Marsden's Shirtfront, sheathed it, and left—though not before removing Marsden's Purse, which he claimed in payment of his original Wager. None present had any Stomach to prevent him, having so cogent an Example of his Skill before them.

I recount this History both to acquaint you with Bonnet's last known whereabouts, and as warning to his Nature and Abilities. I know you are already well acquainted with the Former, but I draw your Attention to the Latter, out of due Regard for your Well-being. Not that I expect a word of my well-meant Advice will find lodging in your Breast, so filled must it be with animadverse Sentiment toward the Man, but I would beg that you take Notice at least of Liston's Mention of Bonnet's Connexions.

Upon the occasion of my own Meeting with the man, he was a Condemned Felon, and I cannot think he has since performed such Service toward the Crown as would gain him official Pardon. If he is content to flaunt himself thus openly in Charleston—where scant Years ago he escaped the Hangman's Noose—it would seem he is in no great Fears for his Safety—and this can only mean that he now enjoys the Protection and Patronage of powerful Friends. You must discover and beware of these, if you seek to destroy Bonnet.

I will continue my Inquiries in this regard, and notify you at once of any further Particulars. In the meantime, keep you well, and spare a thought now and again to your drenched and shivering Acquaintance in Virginia. I remain, sir, with all good Wishes toward your Wife, Daughter, and Family,

Your ob't. servant,
John William Grey, Esq.
Mount Josiah Plantation
Virginia

Postscriptum: I have been in search of an Astrolabe, per your Request, but so far have heard of nothing that would suit your Purpose. I am sending to London this month for assorted Furnishings, though, and will be pleased to order one from Halliburton's in Green Street, their Instruments are of the highest Quality.

Very slowly, Brianna sat back down on the chair. She placed her hands gently but firmly over her son's ears, and said a very bad word.

31

ORPHAN OF THE STORM

I FELL ASLEEP, leaning against the bank, with Jamie's head on my lap. I dreamed luridly, as one does when cold and uncomfortable. I dreamed of trees; endless, monotonous forests of them, with each trunk and leaf and needle etched like scrimshaw on the inside of my eyelids, each one crystal-sharp, all just alike. Yellow goat-eyes floated in the air between the tree trunks, and the wood of my mind rang with the screams of she-panthers and the crying of motherless children.

I woke suddenly, with the echoes of their cries still ringing in my ears. I was lying in a tangle of cloaks and blankets, Jamie's limbs heavily entwined with my own, and a fine, cold snow was falling through the pines.

Granules of ice crusted my brows and lashes, and my face was cold and wet with melted snow. Momentarily disoriented, I reached out by reflex to touch Jamie; he stirred and coughed thickly, his shoulder shaking under my hand. The sound of it brought back the events of the day before—Josiah and his twin, the Beardsley farm, Fanny's ghosts; the smell of ordure and gangrene and the cleaner reek of gunpowder and wet earth. The bleating of goats, still echoing from my dreams.

A thin cry came through the whisper of snow, and I sat up abruptly, flinging back the blankets in a spray of icy powder. Not a goat. Not at all.

Startled awake, Jamie jerked and rolled instinctively away from the mess of cloaks and blankets, coming up in a crouch, hair in a wild tangle and eyes darting round in search of threat.

"What?" he whispered hoarsely. He reached for his knife, lying nearby in its sheath on the ground, but I lifted a hand to stop him moving.

"I don't know. A noise. Listen!"

He lifted his head, listening, and I saw his throat move painfully as he swallowed. I could hear nothing but the chisping of the snow, and saw nothing but dripping pines. Jamie heard something, though—or saw it; his face changed suddenly.

"There," he said softly, nodding at something behind me. I scrambled round on my knees, to see what looked like a small heap of rags, lying some ten feet away, next to the ashes of the burned-out fire. The cry came again, unmistakable this time.

"Jesus H. Roosevelt Christ." I was scarcely aware of having spoken, as I scrambled toward the bundle. I snatched it up and began to root through the layers of swaddling cloth. It was plainly alive—I had heard it cry—and yet it lay inert, almost weightless in the curve of my arm.

The tiny face and hairless skull were blue-white, the

features closed and sere as the husk of a winter fruit. I laid my palm over nose and mouth and felt a faint, moist warmth against my skin. Startled by my touch, the mouth opened in a mewling cry, and the slanted eyes crimped tighter shut, sealing out the threatening world.

"Holy God." Jamie crossed himself briefly. His voice was little more than a phlegmy crackle; he cleared his throat and tried again, glancing around. "Where's the woman?"

Shocked by the child's appearance, I had not paused to consider its origin, nor was there time to do so now. The baby twitched a little in its wrappings, but the tiny hands were cold as ice, the skin mottled blue and purple with chill.

"Never mind her now—get my shawl, will you, Jamie? The poor thing's nearly frozen." I fumbled one-handed with the lacing of my bodice; it was an old one that opened down the front, worn for ease of dressing on the trail. I pulled loose my stays and the drawstring of my shift and pressed the small icy creature against my bare breasts, my skin still warm from sleep. A blast of wind drove stinging snow across the exposed skin of my neck and shoulders. I pulled my shift hastily up over the child and hunched myself, shivering. Jamie flung the shawl round my shoulders, then wrapped his arms round us both, hugging fiercely as though to force the heat of his own body into the child.

The heat of him was considerable; he was burning with fever.

"My God, are you all right?" I spared a glance up at him; white-faced and red-eyed, but steady enough.

"Aye, fine. Where is she?" he asked again, hoarsely. "The woman."

Gone, evidently. The goats were huddled close together under the shelter of the bank; I saw Hiram's horns bobbing among the nannies' brindled backs. Half a dozen pairs of yellow eyes watched us with interest, reminding me of my dreams.

The place where Mrs. Beardsley had lain was empty, with no more than a patch of flattened grass to testify that she had ever been there. She must have gone some distance away in order to give birth; there was no trace of it near the fire.

"It is hers?" Jamie asked. I could still hear the congestion in his voice, but the small wheezing sound in his chest had eased; that was a relief.

"I suppose it must be. Where else could it have come from?"

My attention was divided between Jamie and the child—it had begun to stir, with little crablike movements against my belly—but I spared a glance around our makeshift camp. The pines stood black and silent under the whispering snow; if Fanny Beardsley had gone into the forest, no trace remained on the matted needles to mark her passage. Snow crystals rimed the trunks of the trees, but not enough had fallen to stick to the ground; no chance of footprints.

"She can't have gone far," I said, craning to peer round Jamie's shoulder. "She hasn't taken either of the horses." Gideon and Mrs. Piggy stood close together under a spruce tree, ears morosely flattened by the weather, their breath making clouds of steam around them. Seeing us up and moving, Gideon stamped and whinnied, big yellow teeth showing in an impatient demand for sustenance.

"Aye, ye auld bugger, I'm coming." Jamie dropped his arms and stepped back, wiping his knuckles beneath his nose.

"She couldna have taken a horse, if she meant to be secret. If she had, the other would have made a fuss and roused me." He laid a gentle hand on the bulge under my shawl. "I'll need to go and feed them. Is he all right, Sassenach?"

"He's thawing out," I assured him. "But he—or she, for that matter—will be hungry, too." The baby was beginning to move more, squirming sluggishly, like a chilled worm, its mouth blindly groping. The feeling was shocking in its familiarity; my nipple sprang up by reflex, the flesh of my breast tingling with electricity as the tiny mouth groped, rooted, found the nipple, and clamped on.

I gave a small yelp of surprise, and Jamie raised one eyebrow.

"It . . . um . . . *is* hungry," I said, readjusting my burden.

"I see that, Sassenach," he said. He glanced at the goats, still snug in their sheltered spot by the bank, but beginning to shift and stir with drowsy grumbles. "He's no the only one starving. A moment, aye?"

We had brought large forage nets of dry hay from the Beardsley farm; he opened one of these and scattered feed for the horses and goats, then returned to me. He stooped to disentangle one of the cloaks from the damp heap of coverings, and put it round my shoulders, then rootled through the pack for a wooden cup, with which he purposefully approached the grazing goats.

The baby was suckling strongly, my nipple pulled deep into its mouth. I found this reassuring so far as the health of the child was concerned, but the sensation was rather unsettling.

"It's not that I mind at all, really," I said to the child, trying to distract both of us. "But I'm afraid I'm *not* your mother, you see? Sorry."

And where in bloody hell *was* its mother, anyway? I turned slowly round in a circle, searching the landscape more carefully, but still discerned no trace of Fanny Beardsley, let alone any reason for her disappearance—or her silence.

What on earth could have happened? Mrs. Beardsley could have—and quite obviously *had*—hidden an advanced pregnancy under that mound of fat and wrappings—but why should she have done so?

"Why not tell us? I wonder," I murmured to the top of the baby's head. It was growing restless, and I rocked from foot to foot to soothe it. Well, perhaps she had feared that Jamie wouldn't take her with us, if he knew she was so far gone with child. I didn't blame her for not wanting to remain in that farmhouse, whatever the circumstance.

But still, why had she now abandoned the child? *Had* she abandoned it? I considered for a moment the possibility that someone, or something—my spine prickled momentarily at the thought of panthers—had come and stolen the woman from the fireside, but my common sense dismissed the notion.

A cat or bear might conceivably have entered the camp without waking Jamie or me, exhausted as we were, but there wasn't a chance that it could have come near without raising alarms from the goats and horses, who had all had quite enough to do with wild beasts by this time. And a wild animal looking for prey would clearly prefer a tender tidbit like this child, to a tough item like Mrs. Beardsley.

But if a human agency had been responsible for Fanny Beardsley's disappearance—why had they left the child?

Or, perhaps, brought it back?

I sniffed deeply to clear my nose, then turned my head, breathing in and out, testing the air from different quarters. Birth is a messy business, and I was thoroughly familiar with the ripe scents of it. The child in my arms smelled strongly of such things, but I could detect no trace at all of blood or birth waters on the chilly wind. Goat dung, horse manure, cut hay, the bitter smell of wood ash, and a good whiff of camphorated goose grease from Jamie's clothes—but nothing else.

"Right, then," I said aloud, gently jiggling my burden, who was growing restless. "She went away from the fire to give birth. Either she went by herself—or someone made her go. But if someone took her and saw that she was about to deliver, why would they have bothered bringing you back? Surely they'd either have kept you, killed you, or simply left you to die. Oh—sorry. Didn't mean to upset you. Shh, darling. Hush, hush."

The baby, beginning to thaw from its stupor, had had time to consider what else was lacking in its world. It had relinquished my breast in frustration, and was wriggling and wailing with encouraging strength by the time Jamie returned with a steaming cup of goat's milk and a moderately clean handkerchief. Twisting this into a makeshift teat, he dipped it in the milk and carefully inserted the dripping cloth into the open maw. The mewling ceased at once, and we both sighed with relief as the noise stopped.

"Ah, that's better, is it? *Seas, a bhalaich, seas*," Jamie was murmuring to the child, dipping more milk. I peered down at the tiny face, still pale and waxy with vernix, but no longer chalky, as it suckled with deep concentration.

"How could she have left it?" I wondered aloud. "And why?"

That was the best argument for kidnapping; what else could have made a new mother abandon her child? To say nothing of making off on foot into a darkened wood immediately after giving birth, heavy-footed and sore, her own flesh still torn and oozing . . . I grimaced at the thought, my womb tightening in sympathy.

Jamie shook his head, his eyes still intent on his task.

"She had some reason, but Christ and the saints only ken what it is. She didna hate the child, though—she might have left it in the wood, and us none the wiser."

That was true; she—or someone—had wrapped the baby carefully, and left it as close to the fire as she could. She wished it to survive, then—but without her.

"You think she left willingly, then?"

He nodded, glancing at me.

"We're no far from the Treaty Line here. It *could* be Indians—but if it was, if someone took her, why should they not capture us as well? Or kill us all?" he asked logically. "And Indians would have taken the horses. Nay, I think she went on her own. But as to why . . ." He shook his head, and dipped the handkerchief again.

The snow was falling faster now, still a dry, light snow, but beginning to stick in random patches. We should leave soon, I thought, before the storm grew worse. It seemed somehow wrong, though, simply to go, with no attempt to determine the fate of Fanny Beardsley.

The whole situation seemed unreal. It was as though the woman had suddenly vanished through some sorcery, leaving this small substitute in exchange. It reminded me bizarrely of the Scottish tales of changelings; fairy offspring left in the place of human babies. I couldn't fathom what the fairies could possibly want with Fanny Beardsley, though.

I knew it was futile, but turned slowly round once more, surveying our surroundings. Nothing. The clay bank loomed over us, fringed with dry, snow-dusted grass. The trickle of a tiny stream ran past a little distance away, and the trees rustled and sighed in the wind. There was no mark of hoof or foot on the layer of damp, spongy needles, and no hint of any trail. The woods were not at all silent, what with the wind, but dark and deep, all right.

"And miles to go before we sleep," I remarked, turning back to Jamie with a sigh.

"Eh? Ah, no, it's no more than an hour's ride to Brownsville," he assured me. "Or maybe two," he amended, glancing up at the white-muslin sky, from which the snow was falling faster. "I ken where we are, now it's light."

He coughed again, a sudden spasm racking his body, then straightened, and handed me the cup and dummy.

"Here, Sassenach. Feed the poor wee *sgaogan* while I tend the beasts, aye?"

Sgaogan. A changeling. So the air of supernatural strangeness about the whole affair had struck him, too. Well, the woman had claimed to see ghosts; perhaps one of them had come for her? I shivered, and cradled the baby closer.

"Is there any settlement near here, besides Brownsville? Anywhere Mrs. Beardsley might have decided to go?"

Jamie shook his head, a line between his brows. The snow melted where it touched his heated skin, and ran down his face in tiny streams.

"Naught that I ken," he said. "Is the wean takin' to the goat's milk?"

"Like a kid," I assured him, and laughed. He looked puzzled, but one side of his mouth turned up nonetheless—he wanted humor just now, whether he understood the joke or not.

"That's what the Americans call—will call—children," I told him. "Kids."

The smile broadened across his face.

"Oh, aye? So that's why Brianna and MacKenzie call wee Jem so, is it? I thought it was only a bit of private fun between them."

He milked the rest of the goats quickly while I dribbled more nourishment into the child, bringing back a brimming bucket of warm milk for our own breakfast. I should have liked a nice hot cup of tea—my fingers were chilled and numb from dipping the false teat over and over—but the creamy white stuff was delicious, and as much comfort to our chilled and empty stomachs as to the little one's.

The child had stopped suckling, and had wet itself copiously; a good sign of health, by and large, but rather inconvenient just at the moment, as both its swaddling cloth and the front of my bodice were now soaked.

Jamie rootled hastily through the packs once again, this

time in search of diapering and dry clothes. Fortunately, Mrs. Piggy had been carrying the bag in which I kept lengths of linen and wads of cotton lint for cleansing and bandaging. He took a handful of these and the child, while I went about the awkward and drafty business of changing my shift and bodice without removing skirt, petticoat, or cloak.

"P-put on your own cloak," I said, through chattering teeth. "You'll die of f-frigging pneumonia."

He smiled at that, eyes focused on his job, though the tip of his nose glowed redly in contrast to his pale face.

"I'm fine," he croaked, then cleared his throat with a noise like ripping cloth, impatient. "Fine," he repeated, more strongly, then stopped, eyes widening in surprise.

"Oh," he said, more softly. "Look. It's a wee lassie."

"Is it?" I dropped to my knees beside him to look.

"Rather plain," he said, critically surveying the little creature. "A good thing she'll have a decent dowry."

"I don't suppose you were any great beauty when you were born, either," I said rebukingly. "She hasn't even been properly cleaned, poor thing. What do you mean about her dowry, though?"

He shrugged, contriving to keep the child covered with a shawl, meanwhile sliding a folded sheet of linen dexterously beneath her miniature bottom.

"Her father's dead and her mother's gone. She's no brothers or sisters to share, and I didna find any will in the house saying that anyone else was to have Beardsley's property. There's a decent farm left, though, and a good bit in trade goods there—to say nothing of the goats." He glanced at Hiram and his family, and smiled. "So they'll all be hers, I expect."

"I suppose so," I said slowly. "So she'll be a rather well-to-do little girl, won't she?"

"Aye, and she's just shit herself. Could ye not have done that before I'd put ye on a fresh clout?" he demanded of the child. Unfazed by the scolding, the little girl blinked sleepily at him and gave a soft belch.

"Oh, well," he said, resigned. He shifted himself to better shelter her from the wind, lifted the coverings briefly, and wiped a smear of blackish slime deftly off the budlike privates.

The child seemed healthy, though rather undersized; she was no bigger than a large doll, her stomach bulging slightly with milk. That was the immediate difficulty; small as she was, and with no body fat for insulation, she would die of hypothermia within a very short time, unless we could keep her warm as well as fed.

"Don't let her get chilled." I put my hands in my armpits to warm them, in preparation for picking up the child.

"Dinna fash yourself, Sassenach. I must just wipe her wee bum and then—" He stopped, frowning.

"What's this, Sassenach? Is she damaged, d'ye think? Perhaps yon silly woman dropped her?"

I leaned close to look. He held the baby's feet up in one hand, a wad of soiled cotton lint in the other. Just above the tiny buttocks was a dark bluish discoloration, rather like a bruise.

It wasn't a bruise. It was, though, an explanation of sorts.

"She isn't hurt," I assured him, pulling another of Mrs. Beardsley's discarded shawls up to shelter her daughter's bald head. "It's a Mongol spot."

"A what?"

"It means the child is black," I explained. "African, I mean, or partly so." Jamie blinked, startled, then bent to peer into the shawl, frowning.

"No, she isn't. She's as pale as ye are yourself, Sassenach."

That was quite true; the child was so white as to seem devoid of blood.

"Black children don't usually look black at birth," I explained to him. "In fact, they're often quite pale. The pigmentation of the skin begins to develop some weeks later. But they're often born with this faint discoloration of the skin at the base of the spine—it's called a Mongol spot."

He rubbed a hand over his face, blinking away snowflakes that tried to settle on his lashes.

"I see," he said slowly. "Aye, well, that explains a bit, does it not?"

It did. The late Mr. Beardsley, whatever else he might have been, had assuredly not been black. The child's father had been. And Fanny Beardsley, knowing—or fearing—that the child she was about to bear would reveal her as an adulteress, had thought it better to abandon the child and flee before the truth was revealed. I wondered whether the mysterious father had had anything to do with what had happened to Mr. Beardsley, for that matter.

"Did she know for sure that the father was a Negro, I wonder?" Jamie touched the small underlip, now showing a tinge of pink, gently with one finger. "Or did she never see the child at all? For after all, she must have given birth in the dark. If she had seen it looked white, perhaps she would ha' chosen to brazen it out."

"Perhaps. But she didn't. Who do you suppose the father can have been?" Isolated as the Beardsleys' farm had been, I couldn't imagine Fanny having the opportunity to meet very many men, other than the Indians who came to trade. Did Indian babies perhaps have Mongol spots? I wondered.

Jamie glanced bleakly around at the desolate surroundings, and scooped the child up into his arms.

"I dinna ken, but I shouldna think he'll be hard to spot, once we've reached Brownsville. Let's go, Sassenach."

JAMIE RELUCTANTLY DECIDED to leave the goats behind, in the interest of reaching shelter and sustenance for the child as quickly as possible.

"They'll be fine here for a bit," he said, scattering the rest of the hay for them. "The nannies willna leave the auld fellow—and ye're no going anywhere for the present, are ye, *a bhalaich*?" He scratched Hiram between the horns in farewell, and we left to a chorus of protesting *meh*s, the goats having grown used to our company.

The weather was worsening by the moment; as the temperature rose, the snow changed from dry powder to large, wet flakes that stuck to everything, dusting ground and trees with icing sugar, and melting down through the horses' manes.

Well-muffled in my thick hooded cloak, with multiple shawls beneath and the child snuggled in a makeshift sling against my stomach, I was quite warm, in spite of the flakes that brushed my face and stuck in my lashes. Jamie coughed now and then, but on the whole, looked much healthier than he had; the need to take charge of an emergency had energized him.

He rode just behind me, keeping an eye out in case of marauding panthers or other menaces. I thought myself that any self-respecting cat—particularly one with a bellyful of goat—would spend a day like this curled up in some cozy den, not out tramping through the snow. Still, it was very reassuring to have him there; I was vulnerable, riding with one hand on the reins, the other wrapped protectively over the bulge under my cloak.

The child was sleeping, I thought, but not quiet; it stretched and squirmed with the slow, languid movements of the water world, not yet accustomed to the freedom of life outside the womb.

"Ye look as though you're wi' child, Sassenach." I glanced back over my shoulder, to see Jamie looking amused under the brim of his slouch hat, though I thought there was something else in his expression; perhaps a slight wistfulness.

"Probably because I *am* with child," I replied, shifting slightly in the saddle to accommodate the movements of my companion. "It's just somebody else's child I'm with." The pressure of small knees and head and elbows shifting against my belly were in fact unsettlingly like the sensations of pregnancy; the fact that they were outside rather than inside made remarkably little difference.

As though drawn to the swelling under my cloak, Jamie nudged Gideon up beside me. The horse snorted and tossed his head, wanting to push ahead, but Jamie held him back with a soft *"Seas!"* of rebuke, and he subsided, huffing steam.

"Ye're troubled for her?" Jamie asked, with a nod toward the surrounding forest.

No need to ask whom he meant. I nodded, my hand on the curled tiny backbone, arched still to fit the curve of the vanished womb. Where was she, Fanny Beardsley, alone in the wood? Crawled off to die like a wounded beast—or making, perhaps, for some imagined haven, floundering blindly through frozen leaf mold and deepening snow, heading back, maybe, toward the Chesapeake Bay and some memory of open sky, of broad waters and happiness?

Jamie leaned over and laid a hand on mine where it curled over the sleeping child; I could feel the chill of his ungloved fingers through the layer of cloth between us.

"She's made her choice, Sassenach," he said. "And she's trusted us wi' the bairn. We'll see the wee lass safe; that's all we can do for the woman."

I couldn't turn my hand to take his, but nodded. He let my hand go with a squeeze and dropped back, and I turned my face toward our destination, my lashes wet and spiky as I blinked away the melting drops.

By the time we came in sight of Brownsville, though, most of my concern for Fanny Beardsley had been subsumed by anxiety for her daughter. The child was awake and bawling, pummeling my liver with tiny fists in search of food.

I lifted myself in the saddle, peering through the curtain of falling snow. How big a place was Brownsville? I could see no more than the roofline of a single cabin peeping through the evergreen of pine and laurel. One of the men from Granite Falls had said it was sizable, though—what was "sizable," here in the backcountry? What were the odds that at least one of the residents of Brownsville might be a woman with a nursing child?

Jamie had emptied out the canteen and filled it with goat's milk, but it was better, I thought, to reach shelter before trying to feed the baby again. If there was a mother who might offer her milk to the child, that would be best—but if not, the goat's milk would need to be heated; cold as it was outside, to give the baby cold milk might lower her body temperature dangerously.

Mrs. Piggy snorted out a great gout of steam, and suddenly picked up her pace. She knew civilization when she smelled it—and other horses. She threw up her head and whinnied piercingly. Gideon joined her, and when the racket stopped, I could hear the encouraging replies of a number of horses in the distance.

"They're here!" I exhaled in a steamy burst of relief. "The militia—they made it!"

"Well, I should hope so, Sassenach," Jamie replied, taking a firm grip to prevent Gideon's bolting. "If wee Roger couldna find a village at the end of a straight trail, I'd have my doubts of his wits as well as his eyesight." But he was smiling, too.

As we came round a curve in the trail, I could see that Brownsville really *was* a village. Chimney smoke drifted up in soft gray plumes from a dozen cabins, scattered over the hillside that rose to our right, and a cluster of buildings stood together by the road, clearly placed for custom, judging from the rubble of discarded kegs, bottles, and other rubbish strewn in the dead weeds of the roadside.

Across the road from this pothouse, the men had erected a crude shelter for the horses, roofed with pine boughs and walled on one side with more branches to break the wind. The militiamen's horses were gathered under this in a cozy knot, hobbled and snorting, wreathed in clouds of their mingled breath.

Spotting this refuge, our own horses were moving at a good clip; I had to pull heavily on the reins one-handed in order to keep Mrs. Piggy from breaking into a trot, which would have seriously jostled my passenger. As I hauled her back to a reluctant walk, a slight figure detached itself from the shelter of a pine tree and stepped into the road before us, waving.

"Milord," Fergus greeted Jamie, as Gideon slewed to a reluctant halt. He peered up at Jamie from beneath the band of an indigo-dyed knitted cap, which he wore pulled down over his brows. It made his head look rather like the top of a torpedo, dark and dangerous. "You are well? I thought perhaps you had encountered some difficulty."

"Och." Jamie waved vaguely at me, indicating the bulge beneath my cloak. "No really a difficulty; it's only—"

Fergus was staring over Gideon's shoulder at the bulge with some bemusement.

"Quelle virilité, Monsieur," he said to Jamie, in tones of deep respect. "My congratulations."

Jamie gave him a scathing look and a Scottish noise that

sounded like boulders rolling underwater. The baby began to cry again.

"First things first," I said. "Are there any women here with babies? This child needs milk, and she needs it now."

Fergus nodded, eyes wide with curiosity.

"*Oui*, milady. Two, at least, that I have seen."

"Good. Lead me to them."

He nodded again, and taking hold of Piggy's halter, turned toward the settlement.

"What's amiss, then?" Jamie inquired, and cleared his throat. In my anxiety for the baby, I hadn't paused to consider what Fergus's presence meant. Jamie was right, though; simple concern for our well-being wouldn't have brought him out on the road in this weather.

"Ah. We appear to have a small difficulty, milord." He described the events of the previous afternoon, concluding with a Gallic shrug and a huff of breath. ". . . and so Monsieur Morton has taken refuge with the horses"—he nodded ahead, toward the makeshift shelter—"while the rest of us enjoy the *hospitalité* of Brownsville."

Jamie looked a trifle grim at this; no doubt from a contemplation of what the *hospitalité* for forty-odd men might cost.

"Mmphm. I take it that the Browns dinna ken Morton is there?"

Fergus shook his head.

"Why *is* Morton there?" I asked, having temporarily stifled the baby by putting it to my own breast. "I should have thought he'd be off away, back to Granite Falls, and pleased to be alive."

"He will not go, milady. He says he cannot forgo the bounty." Word had come just before our departure from the Ridge; the Governor was offering forty shillings per man as an inducement to serve in the militia; a substantial sum, particularly to a new homesteader such as Morton, facing a bleak winter.

Jamie rubbed a hand slowly over his face. This was a dilemma, all right; the militia company needed the men and supplies from Brownsville, but Jamie could scarcely conscript several Browns who would immediately attempt to assassinate Morton. Nor could he afford to pay Morton's bounty himself. Jamie looked as though he were tempted to assassinate Morton personally, but I supposed this wasn't a reasonable alternative.

"Perhaps Morton could be induced to marry the girl?" I suggested delicately.

"I thought of that," Fergus said. "Regretfully, Monsieur Morton is already possessed of a wife in Granite Falls." He shook his head, which was beginning to look like a small snowcapped hillock in his cap.

"Why did the Browns not follow yon Morton?" Jamie asked, apparently following his own train of thought. "If an enemy comes upon your land, and you wi' your kin, ye dinna just let him flee; ye hunt him down and kill him."

Fergus nodded, clearly familiar with this brand of Highland logic.

"I believe that was the intent," he said. "They were distracted, however, by *le petit Roger*."

I could hear a distinct note of amusement in his voice; so could Jamie.

"What did he do?" he asked warily.

"Sang to them," Fergus said, the amusement becoming more pronounced. "He has been singing most of the night, and playing upon his drum. The entire village came to hear—there are six men of suitable age for the militia, and," he added practically, "the two women *avec lait*, as I said, milady."

Jamie coughed, wiped a hand under his nose, and nodded to Fergus, with a wave at me.

"Aye. Well, the wee lass must eat, and I canna stay back or the Browns will tumble to it that Morton's here. Go and say to him that I shall come and speak to him as soon as may be."

He reined his horse's head toward the tavern, and I nudged Mrs. Piggy to follow.

"What are you going to do about the Browns?" I asked.

"Christ," Jamie said, more to himself than to me. "How in hell should I know?" And coughed again.

32

MISSION ACCOMPLISHED

OUR ARRIVAL with the baby created a sufficient sensation to distract everyone in Brownsville from their private concerns, be these practical or homicidal. A look of intense relief crossed Roger's face at sight of Jamie, though this was instantly suppressed, replaced by a bland attitude of square-shouldered self-assurance. I ducked my head to hide a smile, and glanced at Jamie, wondering if he had noted this rapid transformation. He sedulously avoided my eye, indicating that he had.

"Ye've done well," he said in a casual undertone, clapping Roger's shoulder in greeting before turning to receive the salutations of the other men and introductions to our involuntary hosts.

Roger merely nodded in an offhand sort of way, but his face took on a muted glow, as though someone had lit a candle inside him.

Young Miss Beardsley caused a great stir; one of the nursing mothers was fetched and at once put the screeching baby to her breast, hastily handing me her own child in exchange. A three-month-old boy of placid temperament, he looked up at me with mild bewilderment, but seemed not to object to the substitution, merely blowing a few thoughtful spit bubbles in my direction.

A certain amount of confusion ensued, with everyone asking questions and offering speculations at once, but Jamie's story—edited to terseness—of events at the Beardsley farm put a stop to the hubbub. Even the red-eyed young woman whom I recognized from Fergus's story as

Isaiah Morton's inamorata forgot her grief, listening open-mouthed.

"Poor little creature," she said, peering at the baby as it suckled fiercely at her cousin's breast. "So you have no parents at all, it seems." Miss Brown cast a dark look at her own father, apparently thinking orphanhood had its advantages.

"What will become of her?" Mrs. Brown asked, with more practicality.

"Oh, we'll see she's taken good care of, my dear. She'll find a secure place with us." Her husband put a reassuring hand on her arm, at the same time exchanging a glance with his brother. Jamie saw it, too; I saw his mouth twitch as though he might say something, but he shrugged slightly and turned instead to confer with Henry Gallegher and Fergus, his two stiff fingers tapping gently on his leg.

The elder Miss Brown leaned toward me, preparing to ask another question, but was prevented by a sudden blast of arctic wind that blew through the big room, lifting the loose hides over the windows and peppering the room with a spray of snow like frozen bird shot. Miss Brown gave a small whoop, abandoned her curiosity, and ran to fasten down the window coverings; everyone else stopped discussing the Beardsleys and began hastily to batten down hatches.

I caught a quick glimpse outside, as Miss Brown struggled with the unwieldy hides. The storm had arrived now in good earnest. Snow was coming down thick and fast; the black ruts of the road had all but disappeared under a coating of white, and it was obvious that Fraser's Company was going nowhere for the time being. Mr. Richard Brown, looking mildly disgruntled, nonetheless graciously offered us a second night's shelter, and the militiamen settled in for supper among the houses and barns of the village.

Jamie went out to bring in our bedding and provisions from the horses, and see them fed and sheltered. Presumably he would also take the opportunity to speak privately with Isaiah Morton, if the latter was still lurking out there in the blizzard.

I did wonder what Jamie meant to do with his mountain Romeo, but I hadn't time for much speculation. It was getting on now for twilight, and I was sucked into the swirl of activity around the hearth, as the women rose to the fresh challenge of providing supper for forty unexpected guests.

Juliet—that is, the younger Miss Brown—moped sullenly in the corner, refusing to help. She did, though, take over care of the Beardsley baby, rocking the little girl and crooning to her long after it was plain that the child was asleep.

Fergus and Gallegher had been sent off to retrieve the goats, and returned with them just before suppertime, wet and muddy to the knees, their beards and eyebrows frosted with snow. The nannies were wet and snow-caked, too, their chilled udders red with cold, milk-swollen and swinging painfully against their legs. They were enchanted to be back in the bosom of civilization, though, and nattered to each other in cheerful excitement.

Mrs. Brown and her sister-in-law took the goats off to the tiny barn to be milked, leaving me in charge of the stewpot and Hiram, who was installed in solitary majesty near the hearth, contained in a makeshift pen composed of an overturned table, two stools, and a blanket chest.

The cabin was essentially one large, drafty room, with a walled loft above and a small lean-to at the back for storage. Crowded as it was with tables, benches, stools, kegs of beer, bundles of hides, a small handloom in one corner, a chiffonier—with a most incongruous chiming clock, adorned with cupids—in another, a bed against the wall, two settles by the hearth, a musket and two fowling pieces hung above the chimney breast, and various aprons and cloaks on pegs by the door, the presence of a sick goat was surprisingly inconsequential.

I had a look at my erstwhile patient, who *meh*ed ungratefully at me, long blue tongue protruding in derision. Snow was melting from the deep spirals of his horns, leaving them black and shiny, and his coat was soaked into brindled spikes round his shoulders.

"There's gratitude for you," I said rebukingly. "If it weren't for Jamie, you'd be cooking *over* that fire, instead of beside it, and good enough for you, too, you wicked old sod."

"Meh!" he said shortly.

Still, he was cold, tired, and hungry, and his harem wasn't

there to be impressed, so he suffered me to rub his head and scratch his ears, feed him wisps of hay, and—eventually—to step into his pen and run a light hand down his injured leg to check the splinting. I was more than a little tired and hungry, too, having had nothing to eat since a little goat's milk at dawn. Between the smell of the simmering stew and the flickering light and shadows in the room, I felt light-headed, and very slightly disembodied, as though I were floating a foot or two above the floor.

"You're a nice old lad, aren't you?" I murmured. After an afternoon spent in close contact with babies, all in varying stages of moistness and shrieking, the company of the irascible old goat was rather soothing.

"Is he going to die?"

I looked up in surprise, having quite forgotten the younger Miss Brown, who had been overlooked in the shadows of the settle. She was standing by the hearth now, still holding the Beardsley baby and frowning down at Hiram, who was trying to nibble the edge of my apron.

"No," I said, twitching the cloth out of his mouth. "I shouldn't think so." What *was* her name? I groped blearily through my memory, matching up faces and names from the earlier flurry of introductions. Alicia, that was it, though I couldn't help still thinking of her as Juliet.

She wasn't much older than Juliet; barely fifteen, if that. She was a plain child, though, round-jawed and pasty. Narrow in the shoulder and broad through the hip; not much of the jewel in the Ethiop's ear about her. She said nothing more, and to keep the conversation going, I nodded at the baby, still in her arms. "How's the little one?"

"All right," she said listlessly. She stood staring at the goat a moment longer. Then tears suddenly welled in her eyes.

"I wish *I* was dead," she said.

"Oh, really?" I said, taken aback. "Er . . . well . . ." I rubbed a hand over my face, trying to summon enough presence of mind to deal with this. Where was the beastly girl's mother? I cast a quick look at the door, but heard no one coming. We were momentarily alone, the women milking or minding supper, the men all caring for the stock.

I stepped out of Hiram's pen and laid a hand on her arm.

"Look," I said in a low voice. "Isaiah Morton's not worth it. He's married; did you know that?"

Her eyes went wide, then squinted nearly shut, spurting sudden tears. No, evidently she hadn't known.

Tears were pouring down her cheeks and dripping on the baby's oblivious head. I reached out and took the swaddled child gently from her, steering her toward the settle with my free hand.

"H-how did you . . . ? Wh-who . . . ?" She was gurgling and sniffling, trying to ask questions and get control of herself at the same time. A man's voice shouted something outside, and she scrubbed frantically at her cheeks with her sleeve.

The gesture reminded me that while the situation seemed rather melodramatic—not to say slightly comic—in my currently muzzy frame of mind, it was a matter of great seriousness to the principals involved in it. After all, her male relations *had* tried to kill Morton, and would certainly try again, if they found him. I tensed at the sound of approaching feet, and the baby stirred and whined a little in my arms. But the footsteps crunched past in the road, and the sound vanished in the wind.

I sat down beside Alicia Brown, sighing with the sheer pleasure of taking weight off my feet. Every muscle and joint in my body ached from the aftereffects of the previous day and night, though I hadn't had time until now to think about it much. Jamie and I would undoubtedly spend the night wrapped in blankets on someone's floor; I eyed the grimy, firelit boards with an emotion approaching lust.

It was incongruously peaceful in the large room, with the snow whispering down outside, and the stewpot burbling away in the hearth, filling the air with the enticing scents of onion, venison, and turnips. The baby slept on my breast, emanating peaceful trust. I would have liked just to sit and hold her, thinking of nothing, but duty called.

"How do I know? Morton told one of my husband's men," I said. "I don't know who his wife is, though; only that she lives in Granite Falls." I patted the tiny back, and the baby burped faintly and relaxed again, her breath warm beneath my ear. The women had washed and oiled her, and she smelled rather like a fresh pancake. I kept one eye on the door, and the other warily on Alicia Brown, in case of further hysterics.

She sniffed and sobbed, hiccuped once, and then relapsed into silence, staring at the floor.

"I wish I was *dead*," she whispered again, in tones of such fierce despair that I set both eyes on her, startled. She sat hunched, hair hanging limply beneath her cap, her hands fisted and crossed protectively over her belly.

"Oh, dear," I said. Given her pallor, the circumstances, and her behavior toward the Beardsley baby, that particular gesture made it no great leap to the obvious conclusion. "Do your parents know?"

She gave me a quick look, but didn't bother asking how *I* knew.

"Mama and Aunt do."

She was breathing through her mouth, with intermittent wet snuffles.

"I thought—I thought Papa would have to let me wed him, if—"

I never had thought blackmail a very successful basis for marriage, but this seemed the wrong time to say so.

"Mmm," I said instead. "And does Mr. Morton know about it?"

She shook her head, disconsolate.

"Does he—does his wife have children, do you know?"

"I've no idea." I turned my head, listening. I could hear men's voices in the distance, carried on the wind. So could she; she gripped my arm with surprising strength, wet brown eyes spike-lashed and urgent.

"I heard Mr. MacKenzie and the men talking last night. They said you were a healer, Mrs. Fraser—one said you were a conjure woman. About babies. Do you know how—"

"Someone's coming." I pulled away from her, interrupting before she could finish. "Here, take care of the baby. I need to—to stir the stew."

I thrust the child unceremoniously into her arms and rose. When the door opened to admit a blast of wind and snow along with a large number of men, I was standing at the hearth, spoon in hand, eyes fixed on the pot and my mind bubbling as vigorously as the stew.

She hadn't had time to ask explicitly, but I knew what she'd been about to say. *Conjure woman,* she'd called me. She wanted my help to get rid of the child, almost certainly. How? I wondered. How could a woman think of such a thing, with a living child in her arms, less than a day out of the womb?

But she was very young. Very young, and suffering from the shock of hearing that her lover was untrue. Not yet far enough advanced in pregnancy to show, either; if she hadn't yet felt her own child move, no doubt it seemed quite unreal to her. She'd seen it only as a means of forcing her father's consent; now it likely seemed a trap that had closed suddenly upon her.

No wonder if she was distraught, looking frantically for escape. Give her a little time to recover, I thought, glancing at the settle, where the shadows hid her. I should talk to her mother, to her aunt. . . .

Jamie appeared suddenly beside me, rubbing reddened hands over the fire, snow melting from the folds of his clothes. He looked extremely cheerful, in spite of his cold, the complications of Isaiah Morton's love life, and the storm going on outside.

"How is it, Sassenach?" he asked hoarsely, and without waiting for me to reply, took the spoon from my hand, put one hard, cold arm around me, and pulled me off my feet and up into a hearty kiss, made the more startling by the fact that his half-sprouted beard was thickly encrusted with snow.

Emerging slightly dazed from this stimulating embrace, I realized that the general attitude of the men in the room was similarly jolly. Backs were being slapped, boots stamped, and coats shaken to the accompaniment of the sort of hoots and roaring noises men make when feeling particularly exuberant.

"What is it?" I asked, looking round in surprise. To my astonishment, Joseph Wemyss stood in the center of the crowd. The tip of his nose was red with cold, and he was being knocked half off his feet by men smacking him on the back in congratulations. "What's happened?"

Jamie gave me a brilliant smile, teeth gleaming in the frozen wilderness of his face, and thrust a limp crumple of wet paper into my hand, fragments of red wax still clinging to it.

The ink had run with the wet, but I could make out the relevant words. Hearing of General Waddell's intended approach, the Regulators had decided that discretion was the better part of valor. They had dispersed. And as per this order from Governor Tryon—the militia was stood down.

"Oh, *good*!" I said. And flinging my arms round Jamie, kissed him back, snow and ice notwithstanding.

THRILLED WITH THE NEWS of the stand-down, the militia took advantage of the bad weather to celebrate. Equally thrilled not to be obliged to join the militia, the Browns instead joined heartily in the celebration, contributing three large kegs of Thomasina Brown's best home-brewed beer and six gallons of hard cider to the cause—at half-cost.

By the time supper was over, I sat in the corner of a settle with the Beardsley baby in my arms, half-dissolved with weariness, and kept vertical only by the fact that there was no place as yet to lie down. The air shimmered with smoke and conversation, I had drunk strong cider with my supper, and both faces and voices tended to swim in and out of focus, in a way that was not at all disagreeable, though mildly disconcerting.

Alicia Brown had had no further chance to speak with me—but I had had no chance to speak with her mother or her aunt. The girl had taken up a seat by Hiram's pen, and was methodically feeding the goat crusts of corn bread left from supper, her face set in lines of sullen misery.

Roger was singing French ballads, by popular request, in a soft, true voice. A young woman's face floated into view in front of me, eyebrows raised in question. She said something, lost in the babble of voices, then reached gently to take the baby from me.

Of course. Jemima, that was her name. The young mother

who had offered to nurse the child. I stood up to give her room on the settle, and she put the baby at once to her breast.

I leaned against the chimney piece, watching with dim approval as she cupped the child's head, guiding it and murmuring. She was both tender and businesslike; a good combination. Her own baby—little Christopher, that was his name—snored peaceably in his grandmother's arms, as the old lady bent to light her clay pipe from the fire.

I glanced back at Jemima, and had the oddest sense of déjà vu. I blinked, trying to catch the fleeting vision, and succeeded in capturing a sense of overwhelming closeness, of warmth and utter peace. For an instant, I thought it was the sense of nursing a child, and then, odder still, realized that it was not the mother's sense I felt . . . but the child's. I had the very distinct memory—if that's what it was—of being held against a warm body, mindless and replete in the sure conviction of absolute love.

I closed my eyes, and took a firmer grip on the chimney breast, feeling the room begin a slow and lazy spin about me.

"Beauchamp," I murmured, "you are *quite* drunk."

If so, I wasn't the only one. Delighted at the prospect of imminent return to their homes, the militiamen had absorbed most of the drinkables in Brownsville, and were working assiduously on the remainder. The party was beginning to break up now, though, with men stumbling off to cold beds in barns and sheds, others thankfully rolling up in blankets by the fire.

I opened my eyes to see Jamie throw back his head and yawn enormously, gape-jawed as a baboon. He blinked and stood up, shaking off the stupor of food and beer, then glanced toward the hearth and saw me standing there. He was plainly as tired as I was, if not quite as giddy, but he had a sense of deep content about him, apparent in the long-limbed ease with which he stretched and settled himself.

"I'm going to see to the horses," he said to me, voice husky from grippe and much talking. "Fancy a walk in the moonlight, Sassenach?"

THE SNOW HAD STOPPED, and there *was* moonlight, glowing through a haze of vanishing cloud. The air was lung-chillingly cold, still fresh and restless with the ghost of the passing storm, and did much to clear my spinning head.

I felt a childish delight in being the first to mark the virgin snow, and stepped high and carefully, making neat bootprints and looking back to admire them. The line of footprints wasn't very straight, but fortunately no one was testing my sobriety.

"Can you recite the alphabet backward?" I asked Jamie, whose footsteps were wavering companionably along with my own.

"I expect so," he replied. "Which one? English, Greek, or Hebrew?"

"Never mind." I took a firmer grip of his arm. "If you remember all three forward, you're in better condition than I am."

He laughed softly, then coughed.

"You're never drunk, Sassenach. Not on three cups of cider."

"Must be fatigue, then," I said dreamily. "I feel as though my head's bobbing about on a string like a balloon. How do you know how much I drank? Do you notice *everything*?"

He laughed again, and folded a hand round mine where it clutched his arm.

"I like to watch ye, Sassenach. Especially in company. You've the loveliest shine to your teeth when ye laugh."

"Flatterer," I said, feeling nonetheless flattered. Given that I hadn't so much as washed my face in several days, let alone bathed or changed my clothes, my teeth were likely the only things about me that could be honestly admired. Still, the knowledge of his attention was singularly warming.

It was a dry snow, and the white crust compressed beneath our feet with a low crunching noise. I could hear Jamie's breathing, hoarse and labored still, but the rattle in his chest had gone, and his skin was cool.

"It will be fair by morning," he said, looking up at the hazy moon. "D'ye see the ring?"

It was hard to miss; an immense circle of diffuse light that ringed the moon, covering the whole of the eastern sky. Faint stars were showing through the haze; it would be bright and clear within the hour.

"Yes. We can go home tomorrow, then?"

"Aye. It will be muddy going, I expect. Ye can feel the air changing; it's cold enough now, but the snow will melt as soon as the sun's full on it."

Perhaps it would, but it *was* cold enough now. The horses' brushy shelter had been reinforced with more cut branches of pine and hemlock, and it looked like a small, lumpy hillock rising from the ground, thickly covered over with snow. Dark patches had melted clear, though, warmed by the horses' breath, and wisps of steam rose from them, scarcely visible. Everything was quiet, with a palpable sense of drowsy content.

"Morton will be cozy, if he's in there," I observed.

"I shouldna think so. I sent Fergus out to tell him the militia was disbanded, so soon as Wemyss came wi' the note."

"Yes, but if I were Isaiah Morton, I don't know that I would have set straight out on the road home in a blinding snowstorm," I said dubiously.

"Likely ye would, if ye had all the Browns in Brownsville after ye wi' guns," he said. Nonetheless, he paused in his step, raised his voice a little, and called "Isaiah!" in a croaking rasp.

There was no answer from the makeshift stable, and taking my arm again, he turned back toward the house. The snow was virgin no longer, trampled and muddied by the prints of many feet, as the militia dispersed to their beds. Roger had stopped singing, but there were still voices from inside the house; not everyone was ready to retire.

Reluctant to go back at once to the atmosphere of smoke and noise, we walked by unspoken mutual consent round the house and barn, enjoying the silence of the snowy wood and the nearness of each other. Coming back, I saw that the door of the lean-to at the rear of the house stood ajar, creaking in the wind, and pointed it out to Jamie.

He poked his head inside, to see that all was in order, but then, instead of closing the door, he reached back and took my arm, pulling me into the lean-to after him.

"I'd a question to ask ye, Sassenach, before we go in," he said. He set the door open, so the moonlight streamed in, shining dimly on the hanging hams, the hogsheads and burlap bags that inhabited the lean-to with us.

It was cold inside, but out of the wind I at once felt warmer, and put back the hood of my cloak.

"What is it?" I said, mildly curious. The fresh air had cleared my head, at least, and while I knew I would be as good as dead the instant I lay down, for the moment I had that sense of pleasant lightness that comes with the feeling of effort completed, honor satisfied. It had been a terrible day and night, and a long day after, but now it was done, and we were free.

"Do ye want her, Sassenach?" he asked softly. His face was a pale oval, blurred by the mist of his breath.

"Who?" I asked, startled. He gave a small grunt of amusement.

"The child. Who else?"

Who else, indeed.

"Do I want her—to keep her, you mean?" I asked cautiously. "Adopt her?" The notion hadn't crossed my mind consciously, but must have been lurking somewhere in my subconscious, for I was not startled at his question, and at the speaking, the idea sprang into full flower.

My breasts had been tender since the morning, feeling full and engorged, and I felt the demanding tug of the little girl's mouth in memory. I could not feed the baby myself—but Brianna could, or Marsali. Or she could live on cow's milk, goat's milk.

I realized suddenly that I had unconsciously cupped one breast, and was gently massaging it. I stopped at once, but Jamie had seen it; he moved closer and put an arm around me. I leaned my head against him, the rough weave of his hunting shirt cold against my cheek.

"Do *you* want her?" I asked. I wasn't sure whether I was hopeful of his answer, or fearful of it. The answer was a slight shrug.

"It's a big house, Sassenach," he said. "Big enough."

"Hmm," I said. Not a resounding declaration—and yet I knew it was commitment, no matter how casually expressed.

He had acquired Fergus in a Paris brothel, on the basis of three minutes' acquaintance, as a hired pickpocket. If he took this child, he would treat her as a daughter. Love her? No one could guarantee love—not he . . . and not I.

He had picked up my dubious tone of voice.

"I saw ye with the wean, Sassenach, riding. Ye've a great tenderness about ye always—but when I saw ye so, wi' the bairn tumbling about beneath your cloak, it—I remembered, how it was, how ye looked, when ye carried Faith."

I caught my breath. To hear him speak the name of our first daughter like that, so matter-of-factly, was startling. We spoke of her seldom; her death was so long in the past that sometimes it seemed unreal, and yet the wound of her loss had scarred both of us badly.

Faith herself was not unreal at all, though.

She was near me, whenever I touched a baby. And this child, this nameless orphan, so small and frail, with skin so translucent that the blue threads of her veins showed clear beneath—yes, the echoes of Faith were strong. Still, she wasn't *my* child. Though she could be; that was what Jamie was saying.

Was she perhaps a gift to us? Or at least our responsibility?

"Do you think we ought to take her?" I asked cautiously. "I mean—what might happen to her if we don't?"

Jamie snorted faintly, dropping his arm, and leaned back against the wall of the house. He wiped his nose, and tilted his head toward the faint rumble of voices that came through the chinked logs.

"She'd be well cared for, Sassenach. She's in the way of being an heiress, ken."

That aspect of the matter hadn't occurred to me at all.

"Are you sure?" I said dubiously. "I mean, the Beardsleys are both gone, but as she's illegitimate—"

He shook his head, interrupting me.

"Nay, she's legitimate."

"But she can't be. No one realizes it yet except you and me, but her father—"

"Her father was Aaron Beardsley, so far as the law is concerned," he informed me. "By English law, a child born in wedlock is the legal child—*and* heir—of the husband—even if it's known for a fact that the mother committed adultery. And yon woman did say that Beardsley married her, no?"

It struck me that he was remarkably positive about this particular provision of English law. It also struck me—in time, thank God, before I said anything—exactly *why* he was positive.

William. His son, conceived in England, and so far as anyone in England knew—with the exception of Lord John Grey—presumably the ninth Earl of Ellesmere. Evidently, he legally *was* the ninth Earl, according to what Jamie was telling me, whether the eighth Earl had been his father or not. The law really was an ass, I thought.

"I see," I said slowly. "So little Nameless will inherit all Beardsley's property, even after they discover that he can't have been her father. That's . . . reassuring."

His eyes met mine for a moment, then dropped.

"Aye," he said quietly. "Reassuring." There might have been a hint of bitterness in his voice, but if there was, it vanished without trace as he coughed and cleared his throat.

"So ye see," he went on, matter-of-factly, "she's in no danger of neglect. An Orphan Court would give Beardsley's property—goats and all"—he added, with a faint grin—"to whomever is her guardian, to be used for her welfare."

"And her guardians'," I said, suddenly recalling the look Richard Brown had exchanged with his brother, when telling his wife the child would be "well cared for." I rubbed my nose, which had gone numb at the tip.

"So the Browns would take her willingly, then."

"Oh, aye," he agreed. "They kent Beardsley; they'll ken well enough how valuable she is. It would be a delicate matter to get her away from them, in fact—but if ye want the child, Sassenach, then ye'll have her. I promise ye that."

The whole discussion was giving me a very queer feeling. Something almost like panic, as though I were being pushed by some unseen hand toward the edge of a precipice. Whether that was a dangerous cliff or merely a foothold for a larger view remained to be seen.

I saw in memory the gentle curve of the baby's skull, and the tissue-paper ears, small and perfect as shells, their soft pink whorls fading into an otherworldly tinge of blue.

To give myself a little time to organize my thoughts, I asked, "What did you mean, it would be a delicate matter to get her away from the Browns? They've no claim on her, have they?"

He shook his head.

"Nay, but none of them shot her father, either."

"What—oh." That was a potential trap that I hadn't seen; the possibility that Jamie might be accused of killing Beardsley in order to get his hands on the trader's farm and goods, by then adopting the orphan. I swallowed, the back of my throat tasting faintly of bile.

"But no one knows how Aaron Beardsley died, except us," I pointed out. Jamie had told them only that the trader had had an apoplexy and died, leaving out his own role as the angel of deliverance.

"Us and Mrs. Beardsley," he said, a faint tone of irony in his voice. "And if she should come back, and accuse me of murdering her husband? It would be hard to deny, and I'd taken the child."

I forbore from asking why she might do such a thing; in light of what she had already done, it was clear enough that Fanny Beardsley might do anything.

"She won't come back," I said. Whatever my own uncertainties about the rest of it, I was sure that in this respect at least, I spoke the truth. Wherever Fanny Beardsley had gone—or why—I was sure she had gone for good.

"Even if she did," I went on, pushing aside my vision of snow drifting through an empty wood, and a wrapped bundle lying by the burned-out fire, "I was there. I could say what happened."

"If they'd let ye," Jamie agreed. "Which they wouldna. You're a marrit woman, Sassenach; ye couldna testify in a court, even if ye weren't my own wife."

That brought me up short. Living as we did in the wilderness, I seldom encountered the more outrageous legal injustices of the times in a personal way, but I was aware of some of them. He was right. In fact, as a married woman, I had no legal rights at all. Ironically enough, Fanny Beardsley *did*, being now a widow. *She* could testify in a court of law—if she wished.

"Well, bloody hell!" I said, with feeling. Jamie laughed, though quietly, then coughed.

I snorted, with a satisfactory explosion of white vapor. I wished momentarily that I was a dragon; it would have been extremely enjoyable to huff flame and brimstone on a number of people, starting with Fanny Beardsley. Instead, I sighed, my harmless white breath vanishing in the dimness of the lean-to.

"I see what you mean by 'delicate,' then," I said.

"Aye—but not impossible." He cupped a large, cold hand along my cheek, turning my face up to his. His eyes searched my own, dark and intent.

"If ye want the child, Claire, I will take her, and manage whatever comes."

If I wanted her. I could feel the soft weight of the child, sleeping on my breast. I had forgotten the intoxication of motherhood for years; pushed aside the memory of the feelings of exaltation, exhaustion, panic, delight. Having Germain and Jemmy and Joan nearby, though, had reminded me vividly.

"One last question," I said. I took his hand and brought it down, fingers linked with mine. "The baby's father wasn't white. What might that mean to her?"

I knew what it would have meant in Boston of the 1960s, but this was a very different place, and while in some ways society here was more rigid and less officially enlightened than the time I had come from, in others it was oddly much more tolerant.

Jamie considered carefully, the stiff fingers of his right hand tapping out a silent rhythm of contemplation on the head of a barrel of salt pork.

"I think it will be all right," he said at last. "There's no question of her being taken into slavery. Even if it could be proved that her father was a slave—and there's no proof at all—a child takes the mother's status. A child born to a free woman is free; a child born to a slave woman is a slave. And whatever yon dreadful woman might be, she wasna a slave."

"Not in name, at least," I said, thinking of the marks on the doorpost. "But beyond the question of slavery . . . ?"

He sighed and straightened.

"I think not," he said. "Not here. In Charleston, aye, it would likely matter; at least if she were in society. But in the backcountry?"

He shrugged. True enough; so close as we were to the Treaty Line, there were any number of mixed-breed children. It was in no way unusual for settlers to take wives among the Cherokee. It was a good deal rarer to see children born of a black and white liaison in the backcountry, but they were plentiful in the coastal areas. Most of them slaves—but there, nonetheless.

And wee Miss Beardsley would not be "in society," at least, not if we left her with the Browns. Here, her potential wealth would matter a great deal more than the color of her skin. With us, it might be different, for Jamie was—and always would be, despite his income or lack of it—a gentleman.

"That wasn't the last question, after all," I said. I laid a hand over his, cold on my cheek. "The last one is—why are you suggesting the notion?"

"Ah. Well, I only thought . . ." He dropped his hand, and looked away. "What ye said when we came home from the Gathering. That ye could have chosen the safety of barrenness—but did not, for my sake. I thought—" He stopped again, and rubbed the knuckle of his free hand hard along the bridge of his nose. He took a deep breath and tried again.

"For my sake," he said firmly, addressing the air in front of him as though it were a tribunal, "I dinna want ye to bear another child. I wouldna risk your loss, Sassenach," he said, his voice suddenly husky. "Not for a dozen bairns. I've daughters and sons, nieces and nephews, grandchildren—weans enough."

He looked at me directly then, and spoke softly.

"But I've no life but you, Claire."

He swallowed audibly, and went on, eyes fixed on mine.

"I did think, though . . . if ye do want another child . . . perhaps I could still give ye one."

Brief tears blurred my eyes. It was cold in the lean-to, and our fingers were stiff. I fumbled my hand into his, squeezing tight.

Even as we had spoken, my mind had been busy, envisioning possibilities, difficulties, blessings. I did not need to think further, for I knew the decision had made itself. A child was a temptation of the flesh, as well as of the spirit; I knew the bliss of that unbounded oneness, as I knew the bittersweet joy of seeing that oneness fade as the child learned itself and stood alone.

But I had crossed some subtle line. Whether it was that I was born myself with some secret quota embodied in my flesh, or only that I knew my sole allegiance must be given elsewhere now . . . I knew. As a mother, I had the lightness now of effort complete, honor satisfied. Mission accomplished.

I leaned my forehead against his chest and spoke into the shadowed cloth above his heart.

"No," I said softly. "But, Jamie . . . I so love you."

WE STOOD WRAPPED in each other's arms for a time, hearing the rumble of voices from the other side of the wall that separated the house from the lean-to, but silent ourselves, and content with the peace of it. We were at once too exhausted to make the effort to go in, and reluctant to abandon the tranquillity of our rude retreat.

"We'll have to go in soon," I murmured at last. "If we don't, we'll fall down right here, and be found in the morning, along with the hams."

A faint wheeze of laughter ran through his chest, but before he could answer, a shadow fell over us. Someone stood in the open door, blocking the moonlight.

Jamie lifted his head sharply, hands tight on my shoulders, but then he let his breath out, and his grip relaxed, allowing me to step back and turn round.

"Morton," Jamie said, in a long-suffering sort of voice. "What in Christ's name are ye doing here?"

Isaiah Morton didn't much look like a rakish seducer, but then, I supposed tastes must differ. He was slightly shorter than I, but broad through the shoulder, with a barrel-shaped torso and slightly bowed legs. He did have rather pleasant-looking eyes and a nice mop of wavy hair, though I was unable to tell the color of either, in the dim light of the lean-to. I estimated his age at somewhere in the early twenties.

"Colonel, sir," he said in a whisper. "Ma'am." He gave me a quick, brief bow. "Didn't mean to give you fright, ma'am. Only I heard the Colonel's voice and thought I best seize the day, so to speak."

Jamie regarded Morton narrowly.

"So to speak," he repeated.

"Yes, sir. I couldn't make out how I was to get Ally to come forth, and was just a-circling of the house again, when I caught heed of you and your lady talking."

He bowed to me again, as though by reflex.

"Morton," Jamie said, softly, but with a certain amount of steel in his voice, "why have ye not gone? Did Fergus not tell ye that the militia is stood down?"

"Oh, aye, sir, he did, sir." He bowed to Jamie this time, looking faintly anxious. "But I couldn't go, sir, not without seeing Ally."

I cleared my throat and glanced at Jamie, who sighed and nodded to me.

"Er . . . I'm afraid that Miss Brown has heard about your prior entanglement," I said delicately.

"Eh?" Isaiah looked blank, and Jamie made an irritable noise.

"She means the lass kens ye've a wife already," he said brutally, "and if her father doesna shoot ye on sight, she may stab ye to the heart. And if neither of them succeeds," he went on, drawing himself up to his fully menacing height, "I'm inclined to do the job myself, wi' my bare hands. What sort of man would slip round a lass and get her with child, and him with no right to give it his name?"

Isaiah Morton paled noticeably, even in the dim light.

"With child?"

"She is," I said, quite coldly.

"She is," Jamie repeated, "and now, ye wee bigamist, ye'd best leave, before—"

He stopped speaking abruptly, as Isaiah's hand came out

from under his cloak, holding a pistol. Close as he was, I could see that it was both loaded and cocked.

"I'm that sorry, sir," he said apologetically. He licked his lips, glancing from Jamie to me, and back. "I wouldn't do you harm, sir, nor certain sure your lady. But you see, I just got to see Ally." His rather pudgy features firmed a little, though his lips seemed inclined to tremble. Still, he pointed the pistol at Jamie with decision.

"Ma'am," he said to me, "if might be as you'd be so kind, would you go on into the house and fetch Ally out? We'll . . . just wait here, the Colonel and me."

I hadn't had time to feel afraid. I wasn't really afraid now, though I was speechless with astonishment.

Jamie closed his eyes briefly, as though praying for strength. Then he opened them and sighed, his breath a white cloud in the cold air.

"Put it down, idiot," he said, almost kindly. "Ye ken fine ye willna shoot me, and so do I."

Isaiah tightened both his lips and his trigger finger, and I held my breath. Jamie continued to look at him, his gaze a mixture of censure and pity. At last, the finger relaxed, and the pistol barrel sank, along with Isaiah's eyes.

"I just got to see Ally, Colonel," he said softly, looking at the ground.

I drew a deep breath, and looked up at Jamie. He hesitated, then nodded.

"All right, Sassenach. Go canny, aye?"

I nodded, and turned to slip into the house, hearing Jamie mutter something under his breath in Gaelic behind me, to the general effect that he must have lost his mind.

I wasn't sure he hadn't, though I had also felt the strength of Morton's appeal. If any of the Browns happened to discover this rendezvous, though, there would be hell to pay—and it wouldn't be only Morton who paid.

The floor inside was littered with sleeping bodies wrapped in blankets, though a few men still huddled round the hearth, gossiping and passing a jug of something spirituous among themselves. I looked carefully, but fortunately Richard Brown was not among them.

I made my way across the room, carefully stepping

through and over the bodies on the floor, and peered into the bed that stood against the wall as I passed. Richard Brown and his wife were both curled up in it, sound asleep, nightcaps pulled well down over their respective ears, though the house was warm enough, what with all the trapped body heat.

There was only one place that Alicia Brown could be, and I pushed open the door to the loft stair, as quietly as I could. It made little difference; no one by the fire paid the slightest attention. One of the men appeared to be trying to get Hiram to drink from the jug, with some success.

By contrast to the room below, the loft was quite cold. This was because the small window was uncovered, and quite a lot of snow had drifted in, together with a freezing wind. Alicia Brown was lying in the little snowdrift under the window, stark naked.

I walked over and stood looking down at her. She lay stiffly on her back, arms folded over her chest. She was shivering, and her eyes were squinched shut with ferocious concentration. Obviously, she hadn't heard my footsteps, over the noises from below.

"What in God's name are you doing?" I inquired politely.

Her eyes popped open and she gave a small shriek. Then she clapped a hand over her mouth and sat up abruptly, staring at me.

"I've heard of a number of novel ways of inducing miscarriage," I told her, picking up a quilt from the cot and dropping it over her shoulders, "but freezing to death isn't one of them."

"If I'm d-dead, I won't need to m-m-miscarry," she said, with a certain amount of logic. Nonetheless, she drew the quilt around her, teeth chattering.

"Scarcely the best means of committing suicide, either, I shouldn't think," I said. "Though I don't mean to sound critical. Still, you can't do it now; Mr. Morton is out in the lean-to and won't go away until you come down to speak to him, so you'd better get up and put something on."

Her eyes flew wide and she scrambled to her feet, her muscles so stiff with cold that she stumbled awkwardly and would have fallen, had I not grabbed her arm. She said nothing more, but dressed as quickly as her chilled fingers would allow, wrapping a thick cloak around herself.

Bearing in mind Jamie's adjuration to "Go canny," I sent her down the narrow stair alone. Alone, she would be merely assumed to be going to the privy—if anyone even noticed her departure. Both of us together might cause comment.

Left by myself in the darkened loft, I drew my own cloak around me and went to the narrow window to wait for the few minutes necessary before I could leave, too. I heard the soft thump of the door closing below, but couldn't see Alicia from this high angle. Judging from her response to my summons, she didn't intend to stab Isaiah to the heart, but heaven knew what either of them *did* intend.

The clouds were gone now, and the frozen landscape stretched before me, brilliant and ghostly under a setting moon. Across the road, the horses' brushy shelter stood dark, dappled with clumps of snow. The air had changed, as Jamie had said, and warmed by the horses' breath, chunks of melting snow slid free and plopped to the ground.

In spite of my annoyance with the young lovers, and the undertones of comic absurdity attending the whole situation, I couldn't help but feel some sympathy for them. They were so in earnest, so intent on nothing but each other.

And Isaiah's unknown wife?

I hunched my shoulders, shivering slightly inside my cloak. I should disapprove—I did, in fact—but no one knew the true nature of a marriage, save those who made it. And I was too aware of living in a glass house, to think of throwing stones myself. Almost absently, I stroked the smooth metal of my gold wedding ring.

Adultery. Fornication. Betrayal. Dishonor. The words dropped softly in my mind, like the clumps of falling snow, leaving small dark pits, shadows in moonlight.

Excuses could be made, of course. I had not sought what had happened to me, had fought against it, had had no choice. Except that, in the end, one always has a choice. I had made mine, and everything had followed from it.

Bree, Roger, Jemmy. Any children that might be born to

them in the future. All of them were here, in one way or another, because of what I had chosen to do, that far-off day on Craigh na Dun.

You take too much upon yourself. Frank had said that to me, many times. Generally in tones of disapproval, meaning that I did things he would have preferred I did not. But now and then in kindness, meaning to relieve me of some burden.

It was in kindness that the thought came to me now, whether it was truly spoken, or only called forth from my exhausted memory for what comfort the words might hold. Everyone makes choices, and no one knows what may be the end of any of them. If my own was to blame for many things, it was not to blame for everything. Nor was harm all that had come of it.

'Til death us do part. There were a great many people who had spoken those vows, only to abandon or betray them. And yet it came to me that neither death nor conscious choice dissolved some bonds. For better or for worse, I had loved two men, and some part of them both would be always with me.

The dreadful thing, I supposed, was that while I had often felt a deep and searing regret for what I had done, I had never felt guilt. With the choice so far behind me, now, perhaps, I did.

I had apologized to Frank a thousand times, and never once had I asked him for forgiveness. It occurred to me suddenly that he had given it, nonetheless—to the best of his ability. The loft was dark, save for faint lines of light that seeped through the chinks of the floor, but it no longer seemed empty.

I stirred abruptly, pulled from my abstraction by sudden movement below. Silent as flying reindeer, two dark figures darted hand-in-hand across the field of snow, cloaks like clouds around them. They hesitated for a moment outside the horses' shelter, then disappeared inside.

I leaned on the sill, heedless of the snow crystals under my palms. I could hear the noise of the horses rousing; whickers and stamping came clearly to me across the clear air. The sounds in the house below had grown fainter; now a clear, loud *"Meh-eh-eh!"* came up through the floorboards, as Hiram sensed the horses' uneasiness.

There was renewed laughter from below, temporarily drowning the sounds across the road. Where was Jamie? I leaned out, the wind billowing the hood of my cloak, brushing a spray of ice across my cheek.

There he was. A tall dark figure, walking across the snow toward the shelter, but going slowly, kicking up white clouds of dusty ice. What . . . but then I realized that he was following in the lovers' tracks, stamping and floundering deliberately to obliterate a trail that must tell its story clearly to any of the trackers in the house below.

A hole appeared suddenly in the brushy shelter, as a section of the branched wall fell away. Clouds of steam roiled out into the air, and then a horse emerged, carrying two riders, and set off to the west, urged from a walk to a trot and then a canter. The snow was not deep; no more than three or four inches. The horse's hooves left a clear dark trail, leading down the road.

A piercing whinny rose from the shelter, followed by another. Sounds of alarm came from below, scuffling and thuds as men rolled from their blankets or lunged for their weapons. Jamie had disappeared.

All at once, horses burst from the shelter, knocking down the wall and trampling the fallen branches. Snorting, whinnying, kicking, and jostling, they spilled out over the road in a chaos of flying manes and rolling eyes. The last of them sprang from the shelter and joined the runaway, tail whisking away from the switch that landed on its rump.

Jamie flung away the switch and ducked back into the shelter, just as the door below flung open, spilling pale gold light over the scene.

I seized the opportunity of the commotion to run downstairs without being seen. Everyone was outside; even Mrs. Brown had rushed out, nightcap and all, leaving the quilts pulled half off the bed. Hiram, smelling strongly of beer, swayed and *meh*ed tipsily at me as I passed, yellow eyes moist and protuberant with conviviality.

Outside, the roadway was full of half-dressed men,

surging to and fro and waving their arms in agitation. I caught sight of Jamie in the midst of the crowd, gesticulating with the best of them. Among the excited bits of question and comment, I heard scraps of speech—"spooked" . . . "panther?" . . . "goddamn!" and the like.

After a bit of milling around and incoherent argument, it was unanimously decided that the horses would likely come back by themselves. Snow was blowing off the trees in veils of whirling ice; the wind stuck freezing fingers through every crevice of clothing.

"Would *you* stay out on a night like this?" Roger demanded, reasonably enough. It being generally decided that no sane man would—and horses being, if not quite sane, certainly sensible creatures—the party began to trickle back into the house, shivering and grumbling as the heat of excitement began to die down.

Among the last stragglers, Jamie turned toward the house and saw me, still standing on the porch. His hair was loose and the light from the open door lit him like a torch. He caught my eye, rolled his own toward heaven, and raised his shoulders in the faintest of shrugs.

I put cold fingers to my lips and blew him a small frozen kiss.

Part Four

I Hear No Music
But the Sound of Drums

33

HOME FOR CHRISTMAS

"WHAT WOULD YOU HAVE DONE?" Brianna asked. She turned over, moving carefully in the narrow confines of Mr. Wemyss's bed, and parked her chin comfortably in the hollow of Roger's shoulder.

"What would I have done about what?" Warm through for the first time in weeks, filled to bursting with one of Mrs. Bug's dinners, and having finally achieved the nirvana of an hour's privacy with his wife, Roger felt pleasantly drowsy and detached.

"About Isaiah Morton and Alicia Brown."

Roger gave a jaw-cracking yawn and settled himself deeper, the corn-shuck mattress rustling loudly under them. He supposed the whole house had heard them at it earlier, and he didn't really care. She'd washed her hair in honor of his homecoming; waves of it spread over his chest, a silky rich gleam in the dim glow of the hearth. It was only late afternoon, but the shutters were closed, giving the pleasant illusion that they were inside a small private cave.

"I don't know. What your Da did, I suppose; what else? Your hair smells great." He smoothed a lock of it around his finger, admiring the shimmer.

"Thanks. I used some of that stuff Mama makes with walnut oil and marigolds. What about Isaiah's poor wife in Granite Falls, though?"

"What about her? Jamie couldn't force Morton to go home to her—assuming that she wants him back," he added logically. "And the girl—Alicia—was evidently more than willing; your father couldn't very well have made a kerfuffle about Morton leaving with her, unless he wanted the man dead. If the Browns had found Morton there, they would have killed him on the spot and nailed his hide to their barn door."

He spoke with conviction, remembering the pointed guns that had greeted him in Brownsville. He smoothed the hair behind her ear, and lifted his head far enough to kiss her between the eyebrows. He'd been imagining that for days, that smooth pale space between the heavy brows. It seemed like a tiny oasis among the vivid danger of her features; the flash of eyes and blade of nose were more than attractive, to say nothing of a mobile brow and a wide mouth that spoke its mind as much by its shape as by its words—but not peaceful. After the last three weeks, he was in a mood for peace.

He sank back on the pillow, tracing the stern arch of one ruddy brow with a finger.

"I think the best he could do under the circumstances was to give the young lovers a bit of room to get safe away," he said. "And they did. By the morning, the snow was already melting to mud, and with all the trampling, you couldn't have told whether a regiment of bears had marched through, let alone which way they were going."

He spoke with feeling; the weather had turned suddenly to a warm thaw, and the militia had returned to their homes in good spirits, but muddy to the eyebrows.

Brianna sighed, her breath raising a pleasant gooseflesh across his chest. She lifted her own head a little, peering in interest.

"What? Have I got filth stuck to me still?" He had washed, but in haste, eager to eat, more eager to get to bed.

"No. I just like it when you get goose bumps. All the hairs on your chest stand up, and so do your nipples." She flicked one of the objects in question lightly with a fingernail, and a fresh wave of gooseflesh raced across his chest for her entertainment. He arched his back a little, then relaxed. No, he'd have to go downstairs soon, to deal with the evening chores; he'd heard Jamie go out already.

Time for a change of subject. He breathed deep, then

lifted his head from the pillow, sniffing with interest at the rich aroma seeping through the floor from the kitchen below.

"What's that cooking?"

"A goose. Or geese—a dozen of them." He thought he caught an odd undertone in her voice, a faint tinge of regret.

"Well, that's a treat," he said, running a lingering hand down the length of her back. A pale gold down covered her back and shoulders, invisible save when there was candle-light behind her, as there was now. "What's the occasion? For our homecoming?"

She lifted her head from his chest and gave him what he privately classified as A Look.

"For Christmas," she said.

"What?" He groped blankly, trying to count the days, but the events of the last three weeks had completely erased his mental calendar. "When?"

"Tomorrow, idiot," she said with exaggerated patience. She leaned over and did something unspeakably erotic to his nipple, then heaved herself up in a rustle of bedclothes, leaving him bereft of blissful warmth and exposed to chilly drafts.

"Didn't you see all the greenery downstairs when you came in? Lizzie and I made the little Chisholm monsters go out with us to cut evergreens; we've been making wreaths and garlands for the last three days." The words were somewhat muffled, as she wormed her way into her shift, but he thought she sounded only incredulous, rather than angry. He could hope.

He sat up and swung his feet down, toes curling as they came in contact with the cold boards of the floor. His own cabin had a braided rug by the bed—but his cabin was full of Chisholms at the moment, or so he was informed. He rubbed a hand through his hair, groping for inspiration, and found it.

"I didn't see anything when I came in but you."

That was the simple truth, and evidently honesty was the best policy. Her head popped through the neckhole of her shift and she gave him a narrow look, which faded into a slow smile as she saw the evident sincerity stamped on his features.

She came over to the bed and put her arms around him, enveloping his head in a smother of marigolds, butter-soft linen, and . . . milk. Oh, aye. The kid would be needing to eat again soon. Resigned, he put his arms round the swell of her hips and rested his head between her breasts for the few moments that were his own meager share of that abundance.

"Sorry," he said, words muffled in her warmth. "I'd forgotten it entirely. I'd have brought you and Jem something, if I'd thought."

"Like what? A piece of Isaiah Morton's hide?" She laughed and let go, straightening up to smooth her hair. She was wearing the bracelet he'd given her on an earlier Christmas Eve; the hearthlight glinted off the silver as she lifted her arm.

"Aye, ye could cover a book in it, I suppose. Or make a pair of wee boots for Jem." It had been a long ride, men and horses pushing past tiredness, eager for home. He felt boneless, and would have asked no better present himself than to go back to bed with her, pressed tight together in warmth, to drift toward the inviting depths of deep black sleep and amorous dreams. Duty called, though; he yawned, blinked, and heaved himself up.

"Are the geese for our supper tonight, then?" he asked, squatting to poke through the discarded pile of mud-caked garments he'd shucked earlier. He might have a clean shirt somewhere, but with the Chisholms in his cabin, and Bree and Jem temporarily lodged here in the Wemysses' room, he had no idea where his own things were. No sense to put on something clean only to go and muck out a byre and feed horses, anyway. He'd shave and change before supper.

"Uh-huh. Mrs. Bug has half a hog barbecuing in a pit outside for tomorrow's Christmas dinner. I shot the geese yesterday, though, and she wanted to use them fresh. We were hoping you guys would be home in time."

He glanced at her, picking up the same undertone in her voice.

"Ye don't care for goose?" he asked. She looked down at him, with an odd expression.

"I've never eaten one," she answered. "Roger?"

"Aye?"

"I was just wondering. I wanted to ask if you knew . . ."

"If I know what?"

He was moving slowly, still wrapped in a pleasant fog of exhaustion and lovemaking. She had put her gown on, brushed her hair, and put it up neatly in a thick coil on her neck, all in the time it had taken him to disentangle his stockings and breeches. He shook the breeks absentmindedly, sending a shower of dried mud fragments pattering over the floor.

"Don't do that! What's the matter with you?" Flushed with sudden annoyance, she snatched the breeks away from him. She thrust open the shutters and leaned out, flapping the garment violently over the sill. She jerked the shaken breeks back in and threw them in his general direction; he dived to catch them.

"Hey. What's the matter with *you*?"

"Matter? You shower dirt all over the floor and you think there's something wrong with *me*?"

"Sorry. I didn't think—"

She made a noise deep in her throat. It wasn't very loud, but it was threatening. Obeying a deep-seated masculine reflex, he shoved a leg into his breeches. Whatever might be happening, he'd rather meet it with his trousers on. He jerked them up, talking fast.

"Look, I'm sorry I didn't think of it being Christmas. It was—there were important things to deal with; I lost track. I'll make it up to ye. Perhaps when we go to Cross Creek for your aunt's wedding. I could—"

"The hell with Christmas!"

"What?" He stopped, breeks half-buttoned. It was winter dusk, and dark in the room, but even by candlelight, he could see the color rising in her face.

"The hell with Christmas, the hell with Cross Creek—and the fucking hell with you, too!" She punctuated this last with a wooden soap dish from the washstand, which whizzed past his left ear and smacked into the wall behind him.

"Now just a fucking minute!"

"Don't you use language like that to me!"

"But you—"

"You and your 'important things'!" Her hand tightened on

the big china ewer and he tensed, ready to duck, but she thought better of it and her hand relaxed.

"I've spent the last *month* here, up to my eyeballs in laundry and baby shit and screeching women and horrible children while you're out doing 'important things' and you come marching in here covered in mud and tromp all over the clean floors without even noticing they *were* clean in the first place! Do you have any idea what a pain it is to scrub pine floors on your hands and knees? With lye soap!" She waved her hands at him in accusation, but too quickly for him to see whether they were covered with gaping sores, rotted off at the wrist, or merely reddened.

". . . And you don't even want to look at your son or hear anything about him—he's learned to *crawl*, and I wanted to show you, but all *you* wanted was to go to bed, and you didn't even bother to shave first . . ."

Roger felt as though he'd walked into the blades of a large, rapidly whirling fan. He scratched at his short beard, feeling guilty.

"I . . . ah . . . thought you wanted to—"

"I did!" She stamped her foot, raising a small cloud of dust from the disintegrated mud. "That hasn't got anything to do with it!"

"All right." He bent to get his shirt, keeping one eye warily on her. "So—you're mad because I didn't notice you'd washed the floor, is that it?"

"No!"

"No," he repeated. He took a deep breath and tried again. "So, it *is* that I forgot it's Christmas?"

"No!"

"You're angry that I wanted to make love to you, even though you wanted to do it, too?"

"NO! Would you just shut up?"

Roger was strongly tempted to accede to this request, but a dogged urge to get to the bottom of things made him push on.

"But I don't understand why—"

"I know you don't! *That's* the problem!"

She spun on her bare heel and stomped over to the chest that stood by the window. She flung back the lid with a bang, and began rummaging, with a series of small snorts and growls.

He opened his mouth, shut it again, and jerked the dirty shirt on over his head. He felt simultaneously irritated and guilty, a bad combination. He finished dressing in an atmosphere of charged silence, considering—and rejecting—possible remarks and questions, all of which seemed likely to inflame the situation further.

She had found her stockings, yanked them on, and gartered them with small savage movements, then thrust her feet into a pair of battered clogs. Now she stood at the open window, drawing deep breaths of air as though she were about to perform a set of RAF exercises.

His inclination was to escape while she wasn't looking, but he couldn't bring himself simply to leave, with something wrong—whatever in God's name it was—between them. He could still feel the sense of closeness that they had shared, less than a quarter of an hour before, and couldn't bring himself to believe that it had simply evaporated into thin air.

He walked up behind her, slowly, and put his hands on her shoulders. She didn't whirl round and try either to stamp on his foot or to knee him in the stones, so he took the risk of kissing her lightly on the back of the neck.

"You were going to ask me something about geese."

She took a deep breath and let it out in a sigh, relaxing just a little against him. Her anger seemed to have vanished as quickly as it had appeared, leaving him baffled but grateful. He put his arms round her waist, and pulled her back against him.

"Yesterday," she said, "Mrs. Aberfeldy burnt the biscuits for breakfast."

"Oh. Aye?"

"Mrs. Bug accused her of being too taken up with her daughter's hair ribbons to pay attention to what she was doing. And what was she doing—Mrs. Bug said—putting blueberries into buttermilk biscuits in the first place?"

"Why shouldn't one put blueberries into buttermilk biscuits?"

"I have no idea. But Mrs. Bug doesn't think you should.

And then Billy MacLeod fell down the stairs, and his mother was nowhere to be found—she went to the privy and got stuck—and—"

"She *what?*" Mrs. MacLeod was short and rather stout, but had a well-defined rear aspect, with an arse like two cannonballs in a sack. It was all too easy to envision such an accident befalling her, and Roger felt laughter gurgle up through his chest. He tried manfully to stifle it, but it emerged through his nose in a painful snort.

"We shouldn't laugh. She had splinters." Despite this rebuke, Brianna herself was quivering against him, tremors of mirth fracturing her voice.

"Christ. What then?"

"Well, Billy was screaming—he didn't break anything, but he banged his head pretty hard—and Mrs. Bug shot out of the kitchen with her broom, hollering because she thought we were being attacked by Indians, and Mrs. Chisholm went to find Mrs. MacLeod and started yelling from the privy, and . . . well, anyway, the geese came over in the middle of all of it, and Mrs. Bug looked up at the ceiling with her eyes popping, then said 'Geese!' so loud that everybody stopped yelling, and she ran into Da's study and came back with the fowling piece and shoved it at me."

She had relaxed a little with the telling. She snorted, and settled back against him.

"I was so mad, I just really *wanted* to kill something. And there were a lot of them—the geese—you could hear them calling all across the sky."

He had seen the geese, too. Black V-shapes, flexing in the winds of the upper air, arrowing their way through the winter sky. Heard them calling, with a strange feeling of loneliness at the heart, and wished she were beside him there.

Everyone had rushed out to watch; the wild Chisholm children and a couple of the half-wild Chisholm dogs went scampering through the trees with whoops and barks of excitement, to retrieve the fallen birds, while Brianna shot and reloaded, as quickly as she could.

"One of the dogs got one, and Toby tried to wrestle it away, and the dog bit him, and he was running around and around the yard screaming that his finger was bitten off, and there was blood all over him, and nobody could make him stop so we could see whether it was, and Mama wasn't here, and Mrs. Chisholm was down by the creek with the twins . . ."

She was stiffening again, and he could see the hot blood rising once more, flushing the back of her neck. He tightened his hold on her waist.

"Was his finger bitten off, then?"

She stopped and took a deep breath, then looked round at him over her shoulder, the color fading slightly from her face.

"No. The skin wasn't even broken; it was goose blood."

"Well, so. Ye did well, didn't you? The larder full, not a finger lost—and the house still standing."

He'd meant it as a joke, and was surprised to feel her heave a deep sigh, a little of the tension going out of her.

"Yes," she said, and her voice held a note of undeniable satisfaction. "I did. All present and accounted for—and everybody fed. With minimal bloodshed," she added.

"Well, it's true what they say about omelettes and eggs, aye?" He laughed and bent to kiss her, then remembered his beard. "Oh—sorry. I'll go and shave, shall I?"

"No, don't." She turned as he released her, and brushed a fingertip across his jaw. "I sort of like it. Besides, you can do that later, can't you?"

"Aye, I can." He bent his head and kissed her gently, but thoroughly. Was that it, then? She'd only wanted him to say that she'd done well, left on her own to run the place? He was thinking she deserved it, if so. He'd known she hadn't been only sitting by the hearth singing cradle songs to Jemmy in his absence—but he hadn't envisioned the gory details.

The smell of her hair and the musk of her body was all round him, but breathing deep to get more of it, he realized that the room was fragrant with juniper and balsam, too, and the mellow scent of beeswax candles. Not just one; there were three of them, set in candlesticks about the room. Normally, she would have lit a rush dip, saving the valuable candles, but the small room glowed now with soft gold light, and he realized that the bloom of it had lit them through their lovemaking, leaving him with memories of russet and ivory and the gold down that covered her like a lion's pelt, the shadowed crimson and purple of her secret places, the dark of his skin on the paleness of hers—memories that glowed vivid against white sheets in his mind.

The floor *was* clean—or had been—its white-pine boards scrubbed, and the corners strewn with dried rosemary. He could see the tumbled bed past her ear, and realized that she'd made it up with fresh linen and a new quilt. She'd taken trouble for his homecoming. And he'd come barging in, brimming with his adventures, expecting praise for the feat of coming back alive, and seeing none of it—blind to everything in his urgent need to get his hands on her and feel her body under his.

"Hey," he said softly in her ear. "I may be a fool, but I love you, aye?"

She sighed deeply, her breasts pushing against his bare chest, warm even through the cloth of shift and gown. They were firm; filling with milk, but not yet hard.

"Yeah, you are," she said frankly, "but I love you too. And I'm glad you're home."

He laughed and let go. There was a branch of juniper tacked above the window, heavy with its clouded blue-green berries. He reached up and broke off a sprig, kissed it, and tucked it into the neck of her gown, between her breasts, as a token of truce—and apology.

"Merry Christmas. Now, what was it about the geese?"

She put a hand to the juniper sprig, a half-smile growing, then fading.

"Oh. Well. It's not important. It's just . . ." He followed the direction of her eyes, turned, and saw the sheet of paper, propped up behind the basin on the washstand.

It was a drawing, done in charcoal; wild geese against a stormy sky, striving through the air above a lash of wind-tossed trees. It was a wonderful drawing, and looking at it gave him the same odd feeling at the heart that hearing the geese themselves had done—half joy, half pain.

"Merry Christmas," Brianna said softly, behind him. She came to stand beside him, wrapping a hand around his arm.

"Thanks. It's . . . God, Bree, you're good." She was. He bent and kissed her, hard, needing to do something to lessen the sense of yearning that haunted the paper in his hand.

"Look at the other one." She pulled a little away from him, still holding his arm, and nodded at the washstand.

He hadn't realized there were two. The other drawing had been behind the first.

She *was* good. Good enough to chill the blood at his heart. The second drawing was in charcoal, too, the same stark blacks and whites and grays. In the first, she had seen the wildness of the sky, and put it down: yearning and courage, effort enduring in faith amid the emptiness of air and storm. In this, she had seen stillness.

It was a dead goose, hung by the feet, its wings half-spread. Neck limp and beak half-open, as though even in death it sought flight and the loud-calling company of its companions. The lines of it were grace, the details of feather, beak, and empty eyes exquisite. He had never seen anything so beautiful, nor so desolate, in his life.

"I drew that last night," she said quietly. "Everybody was in bed, but I couldn't sleep."

She had taken a candlestick and prowled the crowded house, restless, going outside at last in spite of the cold, seeking solitude, if not rest, in the chill dark of the outbuildings. And in the smokeshed, by the light of the embers there, had been struck by the beauty of the hanging geese, their clear plumage black and white against the sooty wall.

"I checked to be sure Jemmy was sound asleep, then brought my sketch box down and drew, until my fingers were too cold to hold the charcoal anymore. That was the best one." She nodded at the picture, her eyes remote.

For the first time, he saw the blue shadows in her face, and imagined her by candlelight, up late at night and all alone, drawing dead geese. He would have taken her in his arms then, but she turned away, going to the window, where the shutters had begun to bang.

The thaw had faded, to be followed by a freezing wind that stripped the last sere leaves from the trees and sent acorns and chestnut hulls sailing through the air to rattle on the roof like buckshot. He followed her, reached past her to draw in the shutters and fasten them against the bitter wind.

"Da told me stories, while I was—while I was waiting for Jemmy to be born. I wasn't paying close attention"—the corner of her mouth quirked with wryness—"but a bit here and there stuck with me."

She turned around then, and leaned against the shutters, hands gripping the sill behind her.

"He said when a hunter kills a greylag goose, he must wait by the body, because the greylag mate for life, and if you kill only one, the other will mourn itself to death. So you wait, and when the mate comes, you kill it, too."

Her eyes were dark on his, but the candle flames struck glints of blue in their depths.

"What I wondered is—are all geese like that? Not only greylags?" She nodded at the pictures.

He touched her, and cleared his throat. He wanted to comfort her, but not at the price of an easy lie.

"Maybe so. I don't know for sure, though. You're worried, then, about the mates of the birds you shot?"

The soft pale lips pressed tight together, then relaxed.

"Not worried. Just . . . I couldn't help thinking about it, afterward. About them, flying on . . . alone. You were gone—I couldn't help thinking—I mean, I *knew* you were all right, this time, but next time, you might not come—well, never mind. It's just silly. Don't worry about it."

She stood up, and would have pushed past him into the room, but he put his arms around her and held her, close so she couldn't see his face.

He knew that she didn't absolutely require him—not to make hay, to plow, to hunt for her. If needs must, she could do those things herself—or find another man. And yet . . . the wild geese said she needed *him*—would mourn his loss if it came. Perhaps forever. In his present vulnerable mood, that knowledge seemed a great gift.

"Geese," he said at last, his voice half-muffled in her hair. "The next-door neighbors kept geese, when I was a wee lad. Big white buggers. Six of them; they went round in a gang, all high-nosed and honking. Terrorized dogs and children and folk that passed by on the street."

"Did they terrorize you?" Her breath tickled warm on his collarbone.

"Oh, aye. All the time. When we played in the street,

they'd rush out honking and peck at us and beat us with their wings. When I wanted to go out into the back garden to play with a mate, Mrs. Graham would have to come, too, to drive the bastards off to their own yard with a broomstick.

"Then the milkman came by one morning while the geese were in their front garden. They went for him, and he ran for his float—and his horse took fright at all the honking and screeching, and stamped two of the geese flatter than bannocks. The kids on the street were all thrilled."

She was laughing against his shoulder, half-shocked but amused.

"What happened then?"

"Mrs. Graham took them and plucked them, and we had goose pie for a week," he said matter-of-factly. He straightened up and smiled at her. She was flushed and rosy. "That's what I ken about geese—they're wicked buggers, but they taste great."

He turned and plucked his mud-stained coat from the floor.

"So, then. Let me help your Da with the chores, and then I want to see how ye've taught my son to crawl."

34

CHARMS

I TOUCHED A FINGER to the gleaming white surface, then rubbed my fingers together appraisingly.

"There is absolutely nothing greasier than goose grease," I said with approval. I wiped my fingers on my apron and took up a large spoon.

"Nothing better for a nice pastry crust," Mrs. Bug agreed.

She stood on her tiptoes, watching jealously as I divided the soft white fat, ladling it from the kettle into two large stone crocks; one for the kitchen, one for my surgery.

"A nice venison pie we'll have for Hogmanay," she said, eyes narrowing as she envisioned the prospect. "And the haggis to follow, wi' cullen skink, and a bit o' corn crowdie . . . and a great raisin tart wi' jam and clotted cream for sweeties!"

"Wonderful," I murmured. My own immediate plans for the goose grease involved a salve of wild sarsaparilla and bittersweet for burns and abrasions, a mentholated ointment for stuffy noses and chest congestion, and something soothing and pleasantly scented for diaper rash—perhaps a lavender infusion, with the juice of crushed jewelweed leaves.

I glanced down in search of Jemmy; he had learned to crawl only a few days before, but was already capable of an astonishing rate of speed, particularly when no one was looking. He was sitting peaceably enough in the corner, though, gnawing intently at the wooden horse Jamie had carved for him as a Christmas present.

Catholic as many of them were—and nominally Christian as they *all* were—Highland Scots regarded Christmas primarily as a religious observance, rather than a major festive occasion. Lacking priest or minister, the day was spent much like a Sunday, though with a particularly lavish meal to mark the occasion, and the exchange of small gifts. My own gift from Jamie had been the wooden ladle I was presently using, its handle carved with the image of a mint leaf; I had given him a new shirt with a ruffle at the throat for ceremonial occasions, his old one having worn quite away at the seams.

With a certain amount of forethought, Mrs. Bug, Brianna, Marsali, Lizzie, and I had made up an enormous quantity of molasses toffee, which we had distributed as a Christmas treat to all the children within earshot. Whatever it might do to their teeth, it had the beneficial effect of gluing their mouths shut for long periods, and in consequence, the adults had enjoyed a peaceful Christmas. Even Germain had been reduced to a sort of tuneful gargle.

Hogmanay was a different kettle of fish, though. God knew what feverish pagan roots the Scottish New Year's celebration sprang from, but there was a reason why I wanted to have a good lot of medicinal preparations made up in advance—the same reason Jamie was now up at the whisky spring, deciding which barrels were sufficiently aged as not to poison anyone.

The goose grease disposed of, there was a good bit of dark broth left in the bottom of the kettle, aswirl with bits of crackled skin and shreds of meat. I saw Mrs. Bug eyeing it, visions of gravy dancing in her brain.

"Half," I said sternly, reaching for a large bottle.

She didn't argue; merely shrugged her rounded shoulders and settled back on her stool in resignation.

"Whatever will ye do with that, though?" she asked curiously, watching as I put a square of muslin over the neck of the bottle, in order to strain the broth. "Grease, aye, it's a wonder for the salves. And broth's good for a body wi' the ague or a wabbly wame, to be sure—but it willna keep, ye know." One sketchy eyebrow lifted at me in warning, in case I hadn't actually known that. "Leave it more than a day or two, and it'll be blue with the mold."

"Well, I do hope so," I told her, ladling broth into the muslin square. "I've just set out a batch of bread to mold, and I want to see if it will grow on the broth, too."

I could see assorted questions and responses flickering through her mind, all based on a growing fear that this mania of mine for rotten food was expanding, and would soon engulf the entire output of the kitchen. Her eyes darted toward the pie safe, then back at me, dark with suspicion.

I turned my head to hide a smile, and found Adso the kitten balanced on his hind legs on the bench, foreclaws anchored in the tabletop, his big green eyes watching the movements of the ladle with fascination.

"Oh, you want some, too?" I reached for a saucer from the shelf and filled it with a dark puddle of broth, savory with bits of goose meat and floating fat globules.

"This is from my half," I assured Mrs. Bug, but she shook her head vigorously.

"Not a bit of it, Mrs. Fraser," she said. "The bonnie wee laddie's caught *six* mice in here in the past two days." She beamed fondly at Adso, who had leaped down and was lapping broth as fast as his tiny pink tongue could move. "Yon cheetie's welcome to anything he likes from my hearth."

"Oh, has he? Splendid. He can come and have a go at the ones in my surgery, then." We were presently entertaining a plague of mice; driven indoors by cold weather, they skittered along the baseboards like shadows after nightfall, and even in broad daylight, shot suddenly across floors and leaped out of opened cupboards, causing minor heart failure and broken dishes.

"Well, ye can scarcely blame the mice," Mrs. Bug observed, darting a quick glance at me. "They go where the food is, after all."

The pool of broth had nearly drained through the muslin, leaving a thick coating of flotsam behind. I scraped this off and dropped it on Adso's saucer, then scooped up a fresh ladle of broth.

"Yes, they do," I said, evenly. "And I'm sorry about it, but the mold is important. It's medicine, and I—"

"Oh, aye! Of course it is," she assured me hurriedly. "I ken that." There was no tinge of sarcasm in her voice, which rather surprised me. She hesitated, then reached through the slit in her skirt, into the capacious pocket that she wore beneath.

"There was a man, as lived in Auchterlonie—where we had our hoose, Arch and me, in the village there. He was a carline, was Johnnie Howlat, and folk went wary near him—but they went. Some went by day, for grass cures and graiths, and some went by night, for to buy charms. Ye'll ken the sort?" She darted another glance at me, and I nodded, a little uncertainly.

I knew the sort of person she meant; some Highland charmers dealt not only in remedies—the "graiths" she'd mentioned—but also in minor magic, selling lovephilters, fertility potions . . . ill wishes. Something cold slid down my back and vanished, leaving in its wake a faint feeling of unease, like the slime trail of a snail.

I swallowed, seeing in memory the small bunch of thorny plants, so carefully bound with red thread and with black. Placed beneath my pillow by a jealous girl named

Laoghaire—purchased from a witch named Geillis Duncan. A witch like me.

Was that what Mrs. Bug was getting at? “Carline” was not a word I was certain of, though I thought it meant “witch,” or something like it. She was regarding me thoughtfully, her normal animation quite subdued.

“He was a filthy wee mannie, Johnnie Howlat was. He’d no woman to do for him, and his cot smelt of dreadful things. So did he.” She shivered suddenly, in spite of the fire at her back.

“Ye’d see him, sometimes, in the wood or on the moor, pokin’ at the ground. He’d find creatures that had died, maybe, and bring back their skins and their feet, bones and teeth for to make his charms. He wore a wretched auld smock, like a farmer, and sometimes ye’d see him comin’ doon the path wi’ something pooched up under his smock, and stains of blood—and other things—seepin’ through the cloth.”

“Sounds most unpleasant,” I said, eyes fixed on the bottle as I scraped the cloth again and ladled more broth. “But people went to him anyway?”

“There was no one else,” she said simply, and I looked up. Her dark eyes fixed unblinkingly on mine, and her hand moved slowly, fingering something inside her pocket.

“I didna ken at first,” she said. “For Johnnie kept mool from the graveyard and bone dust and hen’s blood and all manner of such things, but you”—she nodded thoughtfully at me, white kerch immaculate in the fire-glow—“ye’re a cleanly sort.”

“Thank you,” I said, both amused and touched. That was a high compliment from Mrs. Bug.

“Bar the moldy bread,” she added, the corners of her mouth primming slightly. “And that heathen wee pooch ye keep in your cabinet. But it’s true, no? Ye’re a charmer, like Johnnie was?”

I hesitated, not knowing what to say. The memory of Cranesmuir was vivid in my mind, as it had not been for many years. The last thing I wanted was for Mrs. Bug to be spreading the rumor that I was a carline—some already called me a conjure-woman. I was not worried about legal prosecution as a witch—not here, not now. But to have a reputation for healing was one thing; to have people come to me for help with the other things that charmers dealt in . . .

"Not exactly," I said, guardedly. "It's only that I know a bit about plants. And surgery. But I really don't know anything at all about charms or . . . spells."

She nodded in satisfaction, as though I had confirmed her suspicions instead of denying them.

Before I could respond, there was a sound from the floor like water hitting a hot pan, followed by a loud screech. Jemmy, tiring of his toy, had cast it aside and crawled over to investigate Adso's saucer. The cat, disinclined to share, had hissed at the baby and frightened him. Jemmy's shriek in turn had frightened Adso under the settle; only the tip of a small pink nose and a flicker of agitated whiskers showed from the shadows.

I picked Jem up and soothed his tears, while Mrs. Bug took over the broth-straining. She looked over the goose debris on the platter and picked out a leg bone, the white cartilage at the end smooth and gleaming.

"Here, laddie." She waved it enticingly under Jemmy's nose. He at once stopped crying, grabbed the bone, and put it in his mouth. Mrs. Bug selected a smaller wing bone, with shreds of meat still clinging to it, and put that down on the saucer.

"And that's for you, lad," she said to the darkness under the settle. "Dinna fill your wame too full, though—stay hungry for the wee moosies, aye?"

She turned back to the table, and began to scoop the bones into a shallow pan.

"I'll roast these; they'll do for soup," she said, eyes on her work. Then without changing tone or looking up, she said, "I went to him once, Johnnie Howlat."

"Did you?" I sat down, Jemmy on my knee. "Were you ill?"

"I wanted a child."

I had no idea what to say; I sat still, listening to the drip of the broth through the muslin cloth, as she scraped the last bit of gristle neatly into the roasting pan, and carried it to the hearth.

"I'd slippit four, in the course of a year," she said, back turned to me. "Ye'd not think it, to look at me now, but I was nay more than skin and bane, the color o' whey, and my paps shrunk awa to nothing."

She settled the pan firmly into the coals and covered it.

"So I took what money we had, and I went to Johnnie Howlat. He took the money, and put water in a pan. He sat me doon on the one side of it and him on the other, and there we sat for a verra long time, him starin' into the water and me starin' at him.

"At last, he shook himself a bit and got up, and went awa to the back of his cot. 'Twas dark, and I couldna see what he did, but he rummaged and poked, and said things beneath his breath, and finally he came back to me, and handed me a charm."

Mrs. Bug straightened up and turned round. She came close, and laid her hand on Jemmy's silky head, very gently.

"He said to me, Johnnie did, that here was a charm that would close up the mouth of my womb, and keep a babe safe inside, until it should be born. But there was a thing he'd seen, lookin' in the water, and he must tell me. If I bore a live babe, then my husband would die, he said. So he would give me the charm, and the prayer that went with it—and then it was my choice, and who could say fairer than that?"

Her stubby, work-worn finger traced the curve of Jemmy's cheek. Engaged with his new toy, he paid no attention.

"I carried that charm in my pocket for a month—and then I put it away."

I reached up and put my hand over hers, squeezing. There was no sound but the baby's slobbering and the hiss and pop of the bones in the coals. She stayed still for a moment, then drew her hand away, and put it back in her pocket. She drew out a small object, and put it on the table beside me.

"I couldna quite bring myself to throw it away," she said, gazing down at it dispassionately. "It cost me three silver pennies, after all. And it's a wee thing; easy enough to carry along when we left Scotland."

It was a small chunk of stone, pale pink in color, and veined with gray, badly weathered. It had been crudely carved into the shape of a pregnant woman, little more than a huge belly, with swollen breasts and buttocks above a pair of stubby legs that tapered to nothing. I had seen such figures before—in museums. Had Johnnie Howlat made it himself? Or perhaps found it in his pokings through wood and moor, a remnant of much more ancient times?

I touched it gently, thinking that whatever Johnnie Howlat might have been, or might have seen in his pan of water, he had no doubt been astute enough to have seen the love between Arch and Murdina Bug. Was it easier for a woman, then, to forswear the hope of children, thinking it a noble sacrifice for the sake of a much-loved husband, than to suffer bitterness and self-blame for constant failure? Carline he may have been, Johnnie Howlat—but a charmer, indeed.

"So," Mrs. Bug said, matter-of-factly, "it may be as ye'll find some lass who's a use for it. Shame to let it go to waste, aye?"

35

HOGMANAY

THE YEAR ENDED clear and cold, with a small, brilliant moon that rose high in the violet-black vault of the sky, and flooded the coves and trails of the mountainside with light. A good thing, as people came from all over the Ridge—and some, even farther—to keep Hogmanay at "the Big House."

The men had cleared the new barn and raked the floor clean for the dancing. Jigs and reels and strathspeys—and a number of other dances for which I didn't know the names, but they looked like fun—were executed under the light of bear-oil lanterns, accompanied by the music of Evan Lindsay's scratchy fiddle and the squeal of his brother Murdo's wooden flute, punctuated by the heartbeat thump of Kenny's bodhran.

Thurlo Guthrie's ancient father had brought his pipes, too—a set of small uilleann pipes that looked nearly as decrepit as did Mr. Guthrie, but produced a sweet drone. The melody of his chanter sometimes agreed with the Lindsays' notion of a particular tune, and sometimes didn't, but the overall effect was cheerful, and sufficient whisky and beer had been taken by this point in the festivities that no one minded in the least.

After an hour or two of the dancing, I privately decided that I understood why the word "reel" had come to indicate drunkenness; even performed without preliminary lubrication, the dance was enough to make one dizzy. Done under the influence of whisky, it made all the blood in my head whirl round like the water in a washing machine. I staggered off at the end of one such dance, leaned against one of the barn's uprights, and closed one eye, in hopes of stopping the spinning sensation.

A nudge on my blind side caused me to open that eye, revealing Jamie, holding two brimming cups of something. Hot and thirsty as I was, I didn't mind what it was, so long as it was wet. Fortunately it was cider, and I gulped it.

"Drink it like that, and ye'll founder, Sassenach," he said, disposing of his own cider in precisely similar fashion. He was flushed and sweating from the dancing, but his eyes sparkled as he grinned at me.

"Piffle," I said. With a bit of cider as ballast, the room had quit spinning, and I felt cheerful, if hot. "How many people are in here, do you think?"

"Sixty-eight, last time I counted." He leaned back beside me, viewing the milling throng with an expression of deep content. "They come in and out, though, so I canna be quite sure. And I didna count the weans," he added, moving slightly to avoid collision as a trio of small boys caromed through the crowd and shot past us, giggling.

Heaps of fresh hay were stacked in the shadows at the sides of the barn; the small bodies of children too wee to stay awake were draped and curled among them like so many barn kittens. The flicker of lantern light caught a gleam of silky red-gold; Jemmy was sound asleep in his blanket, happily lulled by the racket. I saw Bree come out of the dancing and lay her hand briefly on him to check, then turn back. Roger put out a hand to her, dark and smiling, and she took it, laughing as they whirled back into the stamping mass.

People did come in and out—particularly small groups of young people, and courting couples. It was freezing and frost-crisp outside, but the cold made cuddling with a warm body that much more appealing. One of the older MacLeod boys passed near us, his arm round a much younger girl—one of old Mr. Guthrie's granddaughters, I thought; he had three of them, all much alike to look at—and Jamie said something genial to him in Gaelic that made his ears go red. The girl was already pink with dancing, but went crimson in the face.

"What did you say to them?"

"It doesna bear translation," he said, putting a hand in the small of my back. He was pulsing with heat and whisky, alight with a flame of joy; looking at him was enough to kindle my own heart. He saw that, and smiled down at me, the heat of his hand burning through the cloth of my gown.

"D'ye want to go outside for a moment, Sassenach?" he said, his voice pitched low and rich with suggestion.

"Well, since you mention it . . . yes," I said. "Maybe not just yet, though." I nodded past him, and he turned to see a cluster of elderly ladies sitting on a bench against the wall, all viewing us with the bright-eyed curiosity of a flock of crows. Jamie waved and smiled at them, making them all burst into pink-faced giggles, and turned back to me with a sigh.

"Aye, well. In a bit, then—after the first-footing, maybe."

The latest spate of dancing came to an end, and there was a general surge in the direction of the tub of cider, presided over by Mr. Wemyss at the far end of the barn. The dancers clustered round it like a horde of thirsty wasps, so that all that was visible of Mr. Wemyss was the top of his head, fair hair almost white under the glow of the lanterns.

Seeing it, I looked round for Lizzie, to see whether she was enjoying the party. Evidently so; she was holding court on a hay bale, surrounded by four or five gawky boys, who were all behaving very much like the dancers round the cider tub.

"Who's the big one?" I asked Jamie, calling his attention to the small gathering with a nod of my head. "I don't recognize him." He glanced over, squinting slightly.

"Oh," he said, relaxing, "that will be Jacob Schnell. He's ridden over from Salem with a friend; they came with the Muellers."

"Really." Salem was a good long ride; nearly thirty miles. I wondered whether the attraction had been the festivities alone. I looked for Tommy Mueller, whom I had privately marked out as a possible match for Lizzie, but didn't see him in the crowd.

"Do you know anything about this Schnell lad?" I asked, giving the boy in question a critical look. He was a year or two older than the other boys dancing attendance on Lizzie, and quite tall. Plain-featured but good-natured-looking, I thought; heavy-boned, and with a thickness through the middle that foretold the development of a prosperous paunch in middle age.

"I dinna ken the lad himself, but I've met his uncle. It's a decent family; I think his father's a cobbler." We both looked automatically at the young man's shoes; not new, but very good quality, and with pewter buckles, large and square in the German fashion.

Young Schnell appeared to have gained an advantage; he was leaning close, saying something to Lizzie, whose eyes were fixed on his face, a slight frown of concentration wrinkling the skin between her fair brows as she tried to make out what he was saying. Then she worked it out, and her face relaxed in laughter.

"I dinna think so." Jamie shook his head, a slight frown on his face as he watched them. "The family's Lutheran; they wouldna let the lad marry a Catholic—and it would break Joseph's heart to send the lass to live so far away."

Lizzie's father *was* deeply attached to her; and having lost her once, he was unlikely to give her so far away in marriage as to lose sight of her again. Still, I thought that Joseph Wemyss would do almost anything to insure his daughter's happiness.

"He might go with her, you know."

Jamie's expression grew bleak at the thought, but he nodded in reluctant acknowledgment.

"I suppose so. I should hate to lose him; though I suppose Arch Bug might—"

Shouts of *"Mac Dubh!"* interrupted him.

"Come on, *a Sheumais ruaidh*, show him how!" Evan called from the far end of the barn, and jerked his bow authoritatively.

There had been a break in the dancing, to give the musicians time to breathe and have a drink, and in the interim, some of the men had been trying their hand at sword dancing, which could be done with only the accompaniment of pipes or to a single drum.

I had been paying little attention to this, only hearing the shouts of encouragement or derision from that end of the barn. Evidently, most of those present were no great hand at the sport—the latest gentleman to try it had tripped over one of the swords and fallen flat; he was being helped to his feet, red-faced and laughing, returning genial insults with his friends as they beat the hay and dirt from his clothes.

"Mac Dubh, Mac Dubh!" Kenny and Murdo shouted in invitation, beckoning, but Jamie waved them off, laughing.

"Nay, I havena done that in more time than I—"

"Mac Dubh! Mac Dubh! Mac Dubh!" Kenny was thumping his bodhran, chanting in rhythm, and the group of men around him were joining in. *"Mac Dubh! Mac Dubh! Mac Dubh!"*

Jamie cast me a brief look of helpless appeal, but Ronnie Sinclair and Bobby Sutherland were already heading purposefully toward us. I stepped away, laughing, and they seized him each by an arm, smothering his protests with raucous shouts as they hustled him into the center of the floor.

Applause and shouts of approval broke out as they deposited him in a clear space, where the straw had been trampled into the damp earth far enough to make a hard-packed surface. Seeing that he had no choice, Jamie drew himself up and straightened his kilt. He caught my eye, rolled an eye in mock resignation, and began to take off his coat, waistcoat, and boots, as Ronnie scrambled to lay out the two crossed broadswords at his feet.

Kenny Lindsay began to tap gently on his bodhran, hesitating between the beats, a sound of soft suspense. The crowd murmured and shifted in anticipation. Clad in shirt, kilt, and stockinged feet, Jamie bowed elaborately, turning sunwise to dip four times, to each of the "airts" in turn. Then he stood upright, and moved to take his place, standing just above the crossed swords. His hands lifted, fingers pointing stiff above his head.

There was an outburst of clapping nearby, and I saw Brianna put two fingers in her mouth and give an earsplitting whistle of approbation—to the marked shock of the people standing next to her.

I saw Jamie glance at Bree, with a faint smile, and then his eyes found mine again. The smile stayed on his lips, but there was something different in his expression; something rueful. The beat of the bodhran began to quicken.

A Highland sword dance was done for one of three reasons. For exhibition and entertainment, as he was about to do it now. For competition, as it was done among the young men at a Gathering. And as it first was done, as an omen. Danced on the eve of a battle, the skill of the dancer foretold success or failure. The young men had danced between crossed swords, the night before Prestonpans, before Falkirk. But not before Culloden. There had been no campfires the night before that final fight, no time for bards and battle songs. It didn't matter; no one had needed an omen, then.

Jamie closed his eyes for a moment, bent his head, and the beat of the drum began to patter, quick and fast.

I knew, because he had told me, that he had first done the sword dance in competition, and then—more than once—on the eve of battles, first in the Highlands, then in France. The old soldiers had asked him to dance, had valued his skill as reassurance that they would live and triumph. For the Lindsays to know his skill, he must also have danced in Ardsmuir. But that was in the Old World, and in his old life.

He knew—and had not needed Roger to tell him—that the old ways had changed, were changing. This was a new world, and the sword dance would never again be danced in earnest, seeking omen and favor from the ancient gods of war and blood.

His eyes opened, and his head snapped up. The tipper struck the drum with a sudden *thunk!* and it began with a shout from the crowd. His feet struck down on the pounded earth, to the north and the south, to the east and the west, flashing swift between the swords.

His feet struck soundless, sure on the ground, and his shadow danced on the wall behind him, looming tall, long arms upraised. His face was still toward me, but he didn't see me any longer, I was sure.

The muscles of his legs were strong as a leaping stag's beneath the hem of his kilt, and he danced with all the skill of the warrior he had been and still was. But I thought he danced now only for the sake of memory, that those watching might not forget; danced, with the sweat flying from his brow as he worked, and a look of unutterable distance in his eyes.

PEOPLE WERE STILL TALKING of it when we adjourned to the house, just before midnight, for stovies, beer, and cider, before the first-footing.

Mrs. Bug brought out a basket of apples, and gathered all the young unmarried girls together in a corner of the kitchen, where—with much giggling and glancing over shoulders toward the young men—each peeled a fruit, keeping the peeling in one piece. Each girl tossed her peel behind her, and the group all whirled round to cluster and exclaim over the fallen strip and see what was the shape of the letter it made.

Apple peelings being by their nature fairly circular, there were a good many "C"s, "G"s, and "O"s discovered—good news for Charley Chisholm, and Young Geordie Sutherland—and much speculation as to whether "Angus Og" might be the meaning of an "O" or not, for Angus Og MacLeod was a canty lad, and much liked, while the only "Owen" was an elderly widower, about five feet tall, and with a large wen on his face.

I had taken Jemmy up to put him to bed, and after depositing him limp and snoring in his cradle, came down in time to see Lizzie cast her peeling.

"'C'!" chorused two of the Guthrie girls, almost knocking heads as they bent to look.

"No, no, it's a 'J'!"

Appealed to as the resident expert, Mrs. Bug bent down, eyeing the strip of red peel with her head on one side, like a robin sizing up a likely worm.

"A 'J' it is, to be sure," she ruled, straightening up, and the group burst out in giggles, turning as one to stare at John Lowry, a young farmer from Woolam's Mill, who peered over his shoulder at them in total bewilderment.

I caught a flash of red from the corner of my eye, and turned to see Brianna in the doorway to the hall. She tilted her head, beckoning me, and I hurried to join her.

"Roger's ready to go out, but we couldn't find the ground salt; it wasn't in the pantry. Do you have it in your surgery?"

"Oh! Yes, I have," I said guiltily. "I'd been using it to dry snakeroot, and forgot to put it back."

Guests packed the porches and lined the wide hallway, spilling out of the kitchen and Jamie's study, all talking, drinking, and eating, and I threaded my way through the crush after her toward my surgery, exchanging greetings as I ducked brandished cups of cider, stovie crumbs crunching under my feet.

The surgery itself was nearly empty, though; people tended to avoid it, through superstition, painful associations, or simple wariness, and I had not encouraged them to go in, leaving the room dark, with no fire burning. Only one candle was burning in the room now, and the only person present was Roger, who was poking among the bits and pieces I'd left on the counter.

He looked up as we entered, smiling. Still faintly flushed from the dancing, he had put his coat back on and draped a woolen scarf round his neck; his cloak lay over the stool beside him. Custom held that the most fortunate "firstfoot" on a Hogmanay was a tall and handsome dark-haired man; to welcome one as the first visitor across the threshold after midnight brought good fortune to the house for the coming year.

Roger being beyond argument the tallest—and quite the best-looking—dark man available, he had been elected to be firstfoot, not only for the Big House, as folk called it, but for those homes nearby. Fergus and Marsali and the others who lived near had already rushed off to their houses, to be ready to greet their firstfoot when he should come.

A red-haired man, though, was frightful ill luck as a first-foot, and Jamie had been consigned to his study, under the riotous guard of the Lindsay brothers, who were to keep him safely bottled up 'til after midnight. There were no clocks nearer than Cross Creek, but old Mr. Guthrie had a pocket watch, even older than himself; this instrument would declare the mystic moment when one year yielded to the next. Given the watch's propensity for stopping, I doubted that this would be more than a symbolic pronouncement, but that was quite enough, after all.

"Eleven-fifty," Brianna declared, popping into the surgery after me, her own cloak over her arm. "I just checked Mr. Guthrie's watch."

"Plenty of time. Are ye coming with me, then?" Roger grinned at Bree, seeing her cloak.

"Are you kidding? I haven't been out after midnight in years." She grinned back at him, swirling the cloak around her shoulders. "Got everything?"

"All but the salt." Roger nodded toward a canvas bag on the counter. A firstfoot was to bring gifts to the house: an egg, a faggot of wood, a bit of salt—and a bit of whisky, thus insuring that the household would not lack for necessities during the coming year.

"Right. Where did I—oh, Christ!" Swinging open the cupboard door to search for the salt, I was confronted by a pair of glowing eyes, glaring out of the darkness at me.

"Good grief." I put a hand over my chest, to keep my heart from leaping out, waving the other hand weakly at Roger, who had sprung up at my cry, ready to defend me. "Not to worry—it's just the cat."

Adso had taken refuge from the party, bringing along the remains of a freshly killed mouse for company. He growled at me, evidently thinking I meant to snatch this treat for myself, but I pushed him crossly aside, digging the small bag of ground salt out from behind his furry hindquarters.

I closed the cupboard door, leaving Adso to his feast, and handed Roger the salt. He took it, laying down the object he had had in his hand.

"Where did ye get that wee auld wifie?" he asked, nodding toward the object as he put the salt away in his bag. I glanced at the counter, and saw that he had been examining the little pink stone figure that Mrs. Bug had given me.

"Mrs. Bug," I replied. "She says it's a fertility charm—which is certainly what it looks like. It *is* very old, then?" I'd thought it must be, and seeing Roger's interest confirmed the impression.

He nodded, still looking at the thing.

"Very old. The ones I've seen in museums are dated at thousands of years." He traced the bulbous outlines of the stone with a reverent forefinger.

Brianna moved closer to see, and without thinking, I set a hand on her arm.

"What?" she said, turning her head to smile at me. "I shouldn't touch it? Do they work *that* well?"

"No, of course not."

I took my hand away, laughing, but feeling rather self-conscious. At the same time, I became aware that I would really rather she *didn't* touch it, and was relieved when she merely bent down to examine it, leaving it on the counter. Roger was looking at it, too—or rather, he was looking at Brianna, his eyes fixed on the back of her head with an odd intensity. I could almost imagine that he was willing her to touch the thing, as strongly as I was willing her not to.

Beauchamp, I said silently to myself, *you have had much too much to drink tonight.* All the same, I reached out by impulse and scooped the figure up, dropping it into my pocket.

"Come on! We have to go!" The odd mood of the moment abruptly broken, Brianna straightened up and turned to Roger, urging him.

"Aye, right. Let's go, then." He slung the bag over his shoulder and smiled at me, then took her arm and they disappeared, letting the surgery door close behind them.

I put out the candle, ready to follow them, and then stopped, suddenly reluctant to go back at once to the chaos of the celebration.

I could feel the whole house in movement, throbbing around me, and light flowed under the door from the hall. Just here, though, it was quiet. In the silence, I felt the weight of the little idol in my pocket, and pressed it, hard and lumpy against my leg.

There is nothing special about January the first, save the meaning we give to it. The ancients celebrated a new year at Imbolc, at the beginning of February, when the winter slackens and the light begins to come back—or the date of the spring equinox, when the world lies in balance between the powers of dark and light. And yet I stood there in the dark, listening to the sound of the cat chewing and slobbering in the cupboard, and felt the power of the earth shift and stir beneath my feet as the year—or something—prepared to change. There was noise and the sense of a crowd nearby, and yet I stood alone, while the feeling rose through me, hummed in my blood.

The odd thing was that it was not strange in the slightest. It was nothing that came from outside me, but only the acknowledgment of something I already possessed, and recognized, though I had no notion what to call it. But midnight was fast approaching. Still wondering, I opened the door, and stepped into the light and clamor of the hall.

A shout from across the hall betokened the arrival of the magic hour, as announced by Mr. Guthrie's timepiece, and the men came jostling out of Jamie's office, joking and pushing, faces turned expectantly toward the door.

Nothing happened. Had Roger decided to go to the back door, given the crowd in the kitchen? I turned to look down the hall, but no, the kitchen doorway was crowded with faces, all looking back at me in expectation.

Still no knock at the door, and there was a small stir of restiveness in the hallway, and a lull in conversation, one of those awkward silences when no one wants to talk for fear of sudden interruption.

Then I heard the sound of footsteps on the porch, and a

rapid knock, one-two-three. Jamie, as householder, stepped forward to fling the door open and bid the firstfoot welcome. I was near enough to see the look of astonishment on his face, and looked quickly to see what had caused it.

Instead of Roger and Brianna, two smaller figures stood on the porch. Skinny and bedraggled, but definitely dark-haired, the two Beardsley twins stepped shyly in together, at Jamie's gesture.

"A happy New Year to you, Mr. Fraser," said Josiah, in a bullfrog croak. He bowed politely to me, still holding his brother by the arm. "We've come."

THE GENERAL AGREEMENT was that dark-haired twins were a most fortunate omen, obviously bringing twice the luck of a single firstfoot. Nonetheless, Roger and Bree—who had met the twins hesitating in the yard, and sent them up to the door—went off to do their best for the other houses on the Ridge, Bree being severely warned not to enter any house until Roger had crossed the threshold.

Fortunate or not, the appearance of the Beardsleys caused a good deal of talk. Everyone had heard of the death of Aaron Beardsley—the official version, that is, which was that he had perished of an apoplexy—and the mysterious disappearance of his wife, but the advent of the twins caused the whole affair to be raked up and talked over again. No one knew what the boys had been doing between the militia's expedition and New Year's; Josiah said only "wanderin'" in his raspy croak, when asked—and his brother Keziah said nothing at all, obliging everyone to talk about the Indian trader and his wife until exhaustion caused a change of subject.

Mrs. Bug took the Beardsleys at once under her wing, taking them off to the kitchen to be washed, warmed, and fed. Half the partygoers had gone home to be firstfooted; those who would not leave 'til morning split into several groups. The younger people returned to the barn to dance—or to seek a bit of privacy among the hay bales—the older ones sat to talk of memories by the hearth, and those who had overindulged in dance or whisky curled up in any convenient corner—and quite a few inconvenient ones—to sleep.

I found Jamie in his study, leaning back in his chair with his eyes closed, a drawing of some kind on the table before him. He wasn't asleep, and opened his eyes when he heard my step.

"Happy New Year," I said softly, and bent to kiss him.

"A guid New Year to you, *a nighean donn*." He was warm and smelled faintly of beer and dried sweat.

"Still want to go outside?" I asked, with a glance at the window. The moon had set long since, and the stars burned faint and cold in the sky. The yard outside was bleak and black.

"No," he said frankly, rubbing a hand over his face. "I want to go to bed." He yawned and blinked, trying to smooth down the disheveled bits of hair sticking up on the top of his head. "I want you to come, too, though," he added, generously.

"I'd like nothing better," I assured him. "What's that?" I circled round behind him, looking over his shoulder at the drawing, which seemed to be some sort of floor plan, with mathematical calculations scribbled in the margins.

He sat up, looking a trifle more alert.

"Ah. Well, this is wee Roger's gift to Brianna, for Hogmanay."

"He's building her a house? But they—"

"Not her." He grinned up at me, hands flat on either side of the drawing. "The Chisholms."

Roger, with a guile that would have become Jamie himself, had scouted round among the settlers on the Ridge, and engineered an agreement between Ronnie Sinclair and Geordie Chisholm.

Ronnie had a large and commodious cabin next to his cooperage. So the agreement was that Ronnie, who was unmarried, would move into the cooper's shop, where he could easily sleep. The Chisholms would then move into Ronnie's cabin, to which they would at once—weather allowing—add two rooms, as per the plan on Jamie's table. In return, Mrs. Chisholm would undertake to make Ronnie's meals and do his washing. In the spring, when the Chisholms took possession of their own homestead and built a house there, Ronnie would take back his newly enlarged cabin—when the grandness of his improved accommodation might prove sufficient inducement for some young woman to accept his proposal of marriage, he hoped.

"And in the meantime, Roger and Bree get back their cabin, Lizzie and her father stop sleeping in the surgery, and everything is beer and skittles!" I squeezed his shoulders, delighted. "That's a wonderful arrangement!"

"What's a skittle?" he inquired, frowning back at me in puzzlement.

"One of a set of ninepins," I said. "I believe the expression is meant to exemplify a state of general delight with prevailing conditions. Did you do the plan?"

"Aye. Geordie's no carpenter, and I dinna want the place to fall down about his ears." He squinted at the drawings, then took a quill from the jar, flipped open the inkwell, and made a small correction to one of the figures.

"There," he said, dropping the quill. "That'll do. Wee Roger wants to show it to Bree when they come back tonight; I said I'd leave it out for him."

"She'll be thrilled." I leaned against the back of his chair, massaging his shoulders with my hands. He leaned back, the weight of his head warm against my stomach, and closed his eyes, sighing in pleasure.

"Headache?" I asked softly, seeing the vertical line between his eyes.

"Aye, just a bit. Oh, aye, that's nice." I had moved my hands to his head, gently rubbing his temples.

The house had quieted, though I could still hear the rumble of voices in the kitchen. Beyond them, the high sweet sound of Evan's fiddle drifted through the cold, still air.

" 'My Brown-Haired Maid,' " I said, sighing reminiscently. "I do love that song." I pulled loose the ribbon binding his plait, and unbraided the hair, enjoying the soft, warm feel of it as I spread it with my fingers.

"It's rather odd that you don't have an ear for music," I said, making small talk to distract him, as I smoothed the ruddy arcs of his brows, pressing just within the edge of the orbit. "I don't know why, but an aptitude for mathematics often goes along with one for music. Bree has both."

"I used to," he said absently.

"Used to what?"

"Have both." He sighed and bent forward to stretch his neck, his elbows resting on the table. "Oh, Christ. Please. Oh, aye. Ah!"

"Really?" I massaged his neck and shoulders, kneading the tight muscles hard through the cloth. "You mean you used to be able to *sing*?" It was a family joke; while possessed of a fine speaking voice, Jamie's sense of pitch was so erratic that any song in his voice was a chant so tuneless that babies were stunned, rather than lulled, to sleep.

"Well, perhaps not that, so much." I could hear the smile in his voice, muffled by the fall of hair that hid his face. "I could tell one tune from another, though—or say if a song was sung badly or well. Now it's no but noise or screeching." He shrugged, dismissing it.

"What happened?" I asked. "And when?"

"Oh, it was before I kent ye, Sassenach. In fact, quite soon before." He lifted a hand, reaching toward the back of his head. "Do ye recall, I'd been in France? It was on my way back wi' Dougal MacKenzie and his men, when Murtagh came across ye, wanderin' the Highlands in your shift. . . ."

He spoke lightly, but my fingers had found the old scar under his hair. It was no more now than a thread, the welted gash healed to a hairbreadth line. Still, it had been an eight-inch wound, laid open with an ax. It had nearly killed him at the time, I knew; he had lain near death in a French abbey for four months, and suffered from crippling headaches for years.

"It was that? You mean that you . . . couldn't hear music anymore, after you were hurt?"

His shoulders lifted briefly in a shrug.

"I hear no music but the sound of drums," he said simply. "I've the rhythm of it still, but the tune is gone."

I stopped, my hands on his shoulders, and he turned to look back at me, smiling, trying to make a joke of it.

"Dinna be troubled for it, Sassenach; it's no great matter. I didna sing well even when I *could* hear it. And Dougal didna kill me, after all."

"Dougal? You do think it was Dougal, then?" I was surprised at the certainty in his voice. He had thought at the time that it might perhaps have been his uncle Dougal who had made the murderous attack upon him—and then, surprised by his own men before being able to finish the job, had pretended instead to have found him wounded. But there had been no evidence to say for sure.

"Oh, aye." He looked surprised, too, but then his face changed, realizing.

"Oh, aye," he said again, more slowly. "I hadna thought—you couldna tell what he said, could you? When he died, I mean—Dougal." My hands were still resting on his shoulders, and I felt an involuntary shiver run through him. It spread through my hands and up my arms, raising the hairs all the way to the back of my neck.

As clearly as though the scene took place before me now, I could see that attic room in Culloden House. The bits and pieces of discarded furniture, things toppled and rolling from the struggle—and on the floor at my feet, Jamie crouching, grappling with Dougal's body as it bucked and strained, blood and air bubbling from the wound where Jamie's dirk had pierced the hollow of his throat. Dougal's face, blanched and mottled as his lifeblood drained away, eyes fierce black and fixed on Jamie as his mouth moved in Gaelic silence, saying . . . something. And Jamie's face, as white as Dougal's, eyes locked on the dying man's lips, reading that last message.

"What did he say?" My hands were tight on his shoulders, and his face was turned away as my thumbs rose up under his hair to seek the ancient scar again.

"Sister's son or no—I would that I had killed you, that day on the hill. For I knew from the beginning that it would be you or me." He spoke calm and low-voiced, and the very emotionlessness of the words made the shudder pass again, this time from me to him.

It was quiet in the study. The sound of voices in the kitchen had died to a murmur, as though the ghosts of the past gathered there to drink and reminisce, laughing softly among themselves.

"So that was what you meant," I said quietly. "When you said you'd made your peace with Dougal."

"Aye." He leaned back in his chair and reached up, his hands wrapping warmly round my wrists. "He was right, ken. It *was* him or me, and would have been, one way or the other."

I sighed, and a small burden of guilt dropped away. Jamie had been fighting to defend me, when he killed Dougal, and I had always felt that death to be laid at my door. But he was right, Dougal; too much lay between them, and if that final conflict had not come then, on the eve of Culloden, it would have been another time.

Jamie squeezed my wrists, and turned in his chair, still holding my hands.

"Let the dead bury the dead, Sassenach," he said softly. "The past is gone—the future is not come. And we are here together, you and I."

36

WORLDS UNSEEN

THE HOUSEHOLD WAS QUIET; it was the perfect opportunity for my experiments. Mr. Bug had gone to Woolam's Mill, taking the Beardsley twins; Lizzie and Mr. Wemyss had gone to help Marsali with the new mash; and Mrs. Bug, having left a pot of porridge and a platter of toast in the kitchen, was out, too, combing the woods for the half-wild hens, catching them one by one and dragging them in by the feet to be installed in the handsome new chicken coop her husband had built. Bree and Roger sometimes came up to the big house for their breakfast, but more often chose to eat by their own hearth, as was the case this morning.

Enjoying the peace of the empty house, I made up a tray with cup, teapot, cream, and sugar, and took it with me to my surgery, along with my samples. The early morning light was perfect, pouring through the window in a brilliant bar of gold. Leaving the tea to steep, I took a couple of small glass bottles from the cupboard and went outside.

The day was chilly but beautiful, with a clear pale sky that promised a little warmth later in the morning. At the moment, though, it was cold enough that I was glad of my warm shawl, and the water in the horses' trough was frigid, rimmed with sheets of fragile ice. Not cold enough to kill the microbes, I supposed; I could see long strands of algae coating the boards of the trough, swaying gently as I buckled the thin crust of ice and disturbed the water, scraping one of my bottles along the slimy edge of the trough.

I scooped up further samples of liquid from the springhouse and from a puddle of muddy standing water near the privy, then hurried back to the house to make my trials while the light was still good.

The microscope stood by the window where I had set it up the day before, all gleaming brass and bright mirrors. A few seconds' work to place droplets on the glass slides I'd laid ready, and I bent to peer through the eyepiece with rapt anticipation.

The ovoid of light bulged, diminished, went out altogether. I squinted, turning the screw as slowly as I could, and . . . there it was. The mirror steadied and the light resolved itself into a perfect pale circle, window to another world.

I watched, enchanted, as the madly beating cilia of a paramecium bore it in hot pursuit of invisible prey. Then a quiet drifting, the field of view itself in constant movement as the drop of water on my slide shifted in its microscopic tides. I waited a moment more, in hopes of spotting one of the swift and elegant Euglena, or even a hydra, but no such luck; only bits of mysterious black-green, daubs of cellular debris and burst algal cells.

I shifted the slide to and fro, but found nothing else of

interest. That was all right; I had plenty of other things to look at. I rinsed the glass rectangle in a cup of alcohol, let it dry for a moment, then dipped a glass rod into one of the small beakers I had lined up before my microscope, dabbing a drop of liquid onto the clean slide.

It had taken some experimentation to put the microscope together properly; it wasn't much like a modern version, particularly when reduced to its component parts for storage in Dr. Rawlings's handsome box. Still, the lenses were recognizable, and with that as a starting point, I had managed to fit the optical bits into the stand without much trouble. Obtaining sufficient light, though, had been more difficult, and I was thrilled finally to have got it working.

"What are ye doing, Sassenach?" Jamie, with a piece of toast in one hand, paused in the doorway.

"Seeing things," I said, adjusting the focus.

"Oh, aye? What sorts of things?" He came into the room, smiling. "Not ghosties, I trust. I will have had enough o' those."

"Come look," I said, stepping back from the microscope. Mildly puzzled, he bent and peered through the eyepiece, screwing up his other eye in concentration.

He squinted for a moment, then gave an exclamation of pleased surprise.

"I see them! Wee things with tails, swimming all about!" He straightened up, smiling at me with a look of delight, then bent at once to look again.

I felt a warm glow of pride in my new toy.

"Isn't it marvelous?"

"Aye, marvelous," he said, absorbed. "Look at them. Such busy wee strivers as they are, all pushing and writhing against one another—and such a mass of them!"

He watched for a few moments more, exclaiming under his breath, then straightened up, shaking his head in amazement.

"I've never seen such a thing, Sassenach. Ye'd told me about the germs, aye, but I never in life imagined them so! I thought they might have wee teeth, and they don't—but I never kent they would have such handsome, lashing wee tails, or swim about in such numbers."

"Well, some microorganisms do," I said, moving to peer into the eyepiece again myself. "These particular little beasts aren't germs, though—they're sperms."

"They're what?"

He looked quite blank.

"Sperms," I said patiently. "Male reproductive cells. You know, what makes babies?"

I thought he might just possibly choke. His mouth opened, and a very pretty shade of rose suffused his countenance.

"Ye mean seed?" he croaked. "Spunk?"

"Well . . . yes." Watching him narrowly, I poured steaming tea into a clean beaker and handed it to him as a restorative. He ignored it, though, his eyes fixed on the microscope as though something might spring out of the eyepiece at any moment and go writhing across the floor at our feet.

"Sperms," he muttered to himself. "Sperms." He shook his head vigorously, then turned to me, a frightful thought having just occurred to him.

"Whose are they?" he asked, his tone one of darkest suspicion.

"Er . . . well, yours, of course." I cleared my throat, mildly embarrassed. "Who else's would they be?"

His hand darted reflexively between his legs, and he clutched himself protectively.

"How the hell did ye get them?"

"How do you think?" I said, rather coldly. "I woke up in custody of them this morning."

His hand relaxed, but a deep blush of mortification stained his cheeks dark crimson. He picked up the beaker of tea and drained it at a gulp, temperature notwithstanding.

"I see," he said, and coughed.

There was a moment of deep silence.

"I . . . um . . . didna ken they could stay alive," he said at last. "Errrrm . . . outside, I mean."

"Well, if you leave them in a splotch on the sheet to dry out, they don't," I said, matter-of-factly. "Keep them from drying out, though"—I gestured at the small, covered beaker, with its small puddle of whitish fluid—"and they'll do for a few hours. In their proper habitat, though, they can live for up to a week after . . . er . . . release."

"Proper habitat," he repeated, looking pensive. He darted a quick glance at me. "Ye do mean—"

"I do," I said, with some asperity.

"Mmphm." At this point, he recalled the piece of toast he still held, and took a bite, chewing meditatively.

"Do folk know about this? Now, I mean?"

"Know what? What sperm look like? Almost certainly. Microscopes have been around for well over a hundred years, and the first thing anyone with a working microscope does is to look at everything within reach. Given that the inventor of the microscope was a man, I should certainly think that . . . Don't you?"

He gave me a look, and took another bite of toast, chewing in a marked manner.

"I shouldna quite like to refer to it as 'within reach,' Sassenach," he said, through a mouthful of crumbs, and swallowed. "But I do take your meaning."

As though compelled by some irresistible force, he drifted toward the microscope, bending to peer into it once more.

"They seem verra fierce," he ventured, after a few moments' inspection.

"Well, they do need to be," I said, suppressing a smile at his faintly abashed air of pride in his gametes' prowess. "It's a long slog, after all, and a terrific fight at the end of it. Only one gets the honor, you know."

He looked up, blank-faced. It dawned on me that he *didn't* know. He'd studied languages, mathematics, and Greek and Latin philosophy in Paris, not medicine. And even if natural scientists of the time were aware of sperm as separate entities, rather than a homogenous substance, it occurred to me that they probably didn't have any idea what sperm actually did.

"Wherever did you *think* babies came from?" I demanded, after a certain amount of enlightenment regarding eggs, sperms, zygotes, and the like, which left Jamie distinctly squiggle-eyed. He gave me a rather cold look.

"And me a farmer all my life? I ken precisely where they come from," he informed me. "I just didna ken that . . . er . . . that all of this daffery was going on. I thought . . . well, I thought a man plants his seed into a woman's belly, and it . . .

well . . . grows." He waved vaguely in the direction of my stomach. "You know—like . . . seed. Neeps, corn, melons, and the like. I didna ken they swim about like tadpoles."

"I see." I rubbed a finger beneath my nose, trying not to laugh. "Hence the agricultural designation of women as being either fertile or barren!"

"Mmphm." Dismissing this with a wave of his hand, he frowned thoughtfully at the teeming slide. "A week, ye said. So it's possible that the wee lad really *is* the Thrush's get?"

Early in the day as it was, it took half a second or so for me to make the leap from theory to practical application.

"Oh—Jemmy, you mean? Yes, it's quite possible that he's Roger's child." Roger and Bonnet had lain with Brianna within two days of each other. "I told you—and Bree—so."

He nodded, looking abstracted, then remembered the toast and pushed the rest of it into his mouth. Chewing, he bent for another look through the eyepiece.

"Are they different, then? One man's from another, I mean?"

"Er . . . not to look at, no." I picked up my cup of tea and had a sip, enjoying the delicate flavor. "They *are* different, of course—they carry the characteristics a man passes to his offspring. . . ." That was about as far as I thought it prudent to go; he was sufficiently staggered by my description of fertilization; an explanation of genes and chromosomes might be rather excessive at the moment. "But you can't see the differences, even with a microscope."

He grunted at that, swallowed the mouthful of toast, and straightened up.

"Why are ye looking, then?"

"Just curiosity." I gestured at the collection of bottles and beakers on the countertop. "I wanted to see how fine the resolution of the microscope was, what sorts of things I might be able to see."

"Oh, aye? And what then? What's the purpose of it, I mean?"

"Well, to help me diagnose things. If I can take a sample of a person's stool, for instance, and see that he has internal parasites, then I'd know better what medicine to give him."

Jamie looked as though he would have preferred not to

hear about such things right after breakfast, but nodded. He drained his beaker and set it down on the counter.

"Aye, that's sensible. I'll leave ye to get on with it, then."

He bent and kissed me briefly, then headed for the door. Just short of it, though, he turned back.

"The, um, sperms . . ." he said, a little awkwardly.

"Yes?"

"Can ye not take them out and give them decent burial or something?"

I hid a smile in my teacup.

"I'll take good care of them," I promised. "I always do, don't I?"

THERE THEY WERE. Dark stalks, topped with clublike spores, dense against the pale bright ground of the microscope's field of view. Confirmation.

"Got them." I straightened up, slowly rubbing the small of my back as I looked over my preparations.

A series of slides lay in a neat fan beside the microscope, each bearing a dark smear in the middle, a code written on the end of each slide with a bit of wax from a candle stub. Samples of mold, taken from damp corn bread, from spoiled biscuit, and a bit of discarded pastry crust from the Hogmanay venison pie. The crust had yielded the best growth by far; no doubt it was the goose grease.

Of the various test substrates I had tried, those were the three resultant batches of mold that had contained the highest proportion of *Penicillium*—or what I could be fairly sure was *Penicillium*. There were a dismaying number of molds that would grow on damp bread, in addition to several dozen different strains of *Penicillium*, but the samples I had chosen contained the best matches for the textbook pictures of *Penicillium* sporophytes that I had committed to memory, years ago, in another life.

I could only hope that my memory wasn't faulty—and that the strains of mold I had here were among those species that produced a large quantity of penicillin, that I had not inadvertently introduced any virulent bacteria into the meat-broth mixture, and that—well, I could hope for a lot of things, but there came a point when one abandoned hope for faith, and trusted fate for charity.

A line of broth-filled bowls sat at the back of the countertop, each covered with a square of muslin to prevent things—insects, airborne particles, and mouse droppings, to say nothing of mice—from falling in. I had strained the broth and boiled it, then rinsed each bowl with boiling water before filling it with the steaming brown liquid. That was as close as I could come to a sterile medium.

I had then taken scrapings from each of my best mold samples, and swished the knife blade gently through the cooled broth, dissipating the clumps of soft blue as best I could before covering the bowl with its cloth and leaving it to incubate for several days.

Some of the cultures had thrived; others had died. A couple of bowls showed hairy dark green clumps that floated beneath the surface like submerged sea beasts, dark and sinister. Some intruder—mold, bacterium, or perhaps a colonial alga—but not the precious *Penicillium.*

Some anonymous child had spilled one bowl; Adso had knocked another onto the floor, maddened by the scent of goose broth, and had lapped up the contents, mold and all, with every evidence of enjoyment. There obviously hadn't been anything toxic in *that* one; I glanced down at the little cat, curled up in a pool of sunshine on the floor, the picture of somnolent well-being.

In three of the remaining bowls, though, spongy velvet mats of mottled blue covered the surface, and my examination of a sample taken from one of them had just confirmed that I did indeed have what I sought. It wasn't the mold itself that was antibiotic—it was a clear substance secreted *by* the mold, as a means of protecting itself from attack by bacteria. That substance was penicillin, and that was what I wanted.

I had explained as much to Jamie, who sat on a stool watching me as I poured the broth from each live culture through another bit of gauze to strain it.

"So what ye've got there is broth that the mold has pissed in, is that right?"

"Well, if you insist on putting it that way, yes." I gave him an austere glance, then took up the strained solution and began distributing it into several small stoneware jars.

He nodded, pleased to have got it right.

"And the mold piss is what cures sickness, aye? That's sensible."

"It is?"

"Well, ye use other sorts of piss for medicine, so why not that?"

He lifted the big black casebook in illustration. I had left it open on the counter after recording the latest batch of experiments, and he had been amusing himself by reading some of the earlier pages, those recorded by the book's previous owner, Dr. Daniel Rawlings.

"Possibly Daniel Rawlings did—*I* don't." Hands busy, I lifted my chin at the entry on the open page. "What was he using it for?"

"Electuary for the Treatment of Scurvy," he read, finger following the neat small lines of Rawlings's script. *"Two Heads of Garlic, crushed with six Radishes, to which are added Peru Balsam and ten drops of Myrrh, this Compound mixed with the Water of a Man-child so as to be conveniently drunk."*

"Bar the last, it sounds like a rather exotic condiment," I said, amused. "What would it go with best, do you think? Jugged hare? Ragout of veal?"

"Nay, veal's too mild-flavored for radish. Hodgepodge of mutton, maybe," he replied. "Mutton will stand anything." His tongue flicked absentmindedly across his upper lip in contemplation.

"Why a man-child, d'ye think, Sassenach? I've seen the mention of it in such receipts before—Aristotle has it so, and so have some of the other ancient philosophers."

I gave him a look, as I began tidying up my slides.

"Well, it's certainly easier to collect urine from a male child than from a little girl; just try it, sometime. Oddly enough, though, urine from baby boys *is* very clean, if not entirely sterile; it may be that the ancient philosophers noticed they had better results with it in their formulae, because it was cleaner than the usual drinking water, if they were getting that from public aqueducts and wells and the like."

"Sterile meaning that it hasna got the germs in it, not that it doesna breed?" He gave my microscope a rather wary glance.

"Yes. Or rather—it doesn't breed germs, because there aren't any there."

With the countertop cleared, save for the microscope and the jars of penicillin-containing broth—or at least I hoped that's what they were—I began the preparations for surgery, taking down my small case of surgical instruments, and fetching a large bottle of grain alcohol out of the cupboard.

I handed this to Jamie, along with the small alcohol burner I had contrived—an empty ink bottle, with a twisted wick of waxed flax drawn up through a cork stuck into the neck.

"Fill that up for me, will you? Where are the boys?"

"In the kitchen, getting drunk." He frowned in concentration, carefully pouring the alcohol. "Is the urine of wee lassies not clean, then? Or is it only harder to get?"

"No, actually, it isn't as clean as that of boys." I unfolded a clean cloth on the countertop and laid out two scalpels, a pair of long-nosed forceps, and a bunch of small cautery irons. I dug about in the cupboard, unearthing a handful of cotton pledgets. Cotton cloth was hideously expensive, but I had had the good fortune to cajole a sack of raw cotton bolls from Farquard Campbell's wife, in return for a jar of honey.

"The . . . um . . . route to the outside isn't quite so direct, you might say. So the urine tends to pick up bacteria and bits of debris from the skin folds." I looked over my shoulder at him and smiled. "Not that you ought to go feeling superior on that account."

"I shouldna dream of it," he assured me. "Are ye ready, then, Sassenach?"

"Yes, fetch them in. Oh, and bring the basin!"

He went out, and I turned to face the east window. It had snowed heavily the day before, but today was a fine, bright day, clear and cold, with the sun reflecting off the snow-covered trees with the light of a million diamonds. I couldn't have asked for better; I should need all the light I could get.

I set the cautery irons in the small brazier to heat. Then I fetched my amulet from the cabinet, put it round my neck so it hung beneath the bodice of my gown, and took down the heavy canvas apron from its hook behind the door. I put that on, too, then went to the window and looked out at the cold icing-sugar landscape, emptying my mind, steadying my spirit for what I was about to do. It was not a difficult operation, and I had done it many times before. I had not, however, done it on someone who was sitting upright and conscious, and that always made a difference.

I hadn't done it in several years, either, and I closed my eyes in recollection, visualizing the steps to take, feeling the muscles of my hand twitch slightly in echo of my thoughts, anticipating the movements I would make.

"God help me," I whispered, and crossed myself.

Stumbling footsteps, nervous giggles, and the rumble of Jamie's voice came from the hallway, and I turned round smiling to greet my patients.

A month of good food, clean clothes, and warm beds had improved the Beardsleys immensely, in terms of both health and appearance. They were both still small, skinny, and slightly bowlegged, but the hollows of their faces had filled out a bit, their dark hair lay soft against their skulls, and the look of hunted wariness had faded a little from their eyes.

In fact, both pairs of dark eyes were presently a little glazed, and Lizzie was obliged to grab Keziah by the arm in order to prevent his stumbling over a stool. Jamie had Josiah gripped firmly by the shoulder; he steered the boy over to me, then set down the pudding basin he carried under his other arm.

"All right, are you?" I smiled at Josiah, looking deep into his eyes, and squeezed his arm in reassurance. He swallowed hard, and gave me a rather ghastly grin; he wasn't drunk enough not to be scared.

I sat him down, chatting soothingly, wrapped a towel round his neck, and set the basin on his knees. I hoped he wouldn't drop it; it was china, and the only large pudding basin we had. To my surprise, Lizzie came to stand behind him, putting her small hands on his shoulders.

"Are you sure you want to stay, Lizzie?" I asked dubiously. "We can manage all right, I think." Jamie was thoroughly accustomed to blood and general carnage; I didn't think Lizzie could ever have seen anything beyond the common sorts of illness and perhaps a childbirth or two.

"Oh, no, ma'am; I'll stay." She swallowed, too, but set her small jaw bravely. "I promised Jo and Kezzie as I'd stay with them, all through."

I glanced at Jamie, who lifted one shoulder in the hint of a shrug.

"All right, then." I took one of the stoneware jars of penicillin broth, poured it into two cups, and gave one to each of the twins to drink.

Stomach acid would likely inactivate most of the penicillin, but it would—I hoped—kill the bacteria in their throats. Following surgery, another dose washed over the raw surfaces might prevent infection.

There was no way of knowing exactly how much penicillin there might be in the broth; I might be giving them massive doses—or too little to matter. At least I was reasonably sure that whatever penicillin was in the broth was presently active. I had no means of stabilizing the antibiotic, and no notion how long it might be potent—but fresh as it was, the solution was bound to be medicinally active, and there was a good chance that the rest of the broth would remain usable for at least the next few days.

I would make new cultures, as soon as the surgery was complete; with luck, I could dose the twins regularly for three or four days, and—with greater luck—thus prevent any infections.

"Oh, so ye can drink the stuff, can ye?" Jamie was eyeing me cynically over Josiah's head. I had injected him with penicillin following a gunshot injury a few years before, and he obviously now considered that I had done so with purely sadistic intent.

I eyed him back.

"You can. Injectable penicillin is much more effective, particularly in the case of an active infection. However, I haven't any means of injecting it just at present, and this is meant to prevent them getting an infection, not to cure one. Now, if we're *quite* ready . . ."

I had thought that Jamie would restrain the patient, but both Lizzie and Josiah insisted that this was not necessary;

Josiah would sit quite still, no matter what. Lizzie still gripped his shoulders, her face paler than his, and her small knuckles sharp and white.

I had examined both boys at length the day before, but had another quick look before starting, using a tongue depressor made of a slip of ash wood. I showed Jamie how to use this to keep the tongue pressed out of my way, then took up forceps and scalpel and drew a long breath.

I looked deep into Josiah's dark eyes, and smiled; I could see two tiny reflections of my face there, both looking pleasantly competent.

"All right, then?" I asked.

He couldn't speak, with the tongue depressor in his mouth, but made a good-natured sort of grunt that I took for assent.

I needed to be quick, and I was. The preparations had taken hours; the operation, no more than a few seconds. I seized one spongy red tonsil with the forceps, stretched it toward me, and made several small, quick cuts, deftly separating the layers of tissue. A trickle of blood was running out of the boy's mouth and down his chin, but nothing serious.

I pulled the gobbet of flesh free, dropped it into the basin, and shifted my grip to the other tonsil, where I repeated the process, only a trifle more slowly in consequence of working backhanded.

The whole thing couldn't have taken more than thirty seconds per side. I drew the instruments out of Josiah's mouth, and he goggled at me, astonished. Then he coughed, gagged, leaned forward, and another small chunk of flesh bounced into the basin with a small *splat*, together with a quantity of bright red blood.

I seized him by the nose and thrust his head back, stuffed pledgets into his mouth to absorb sufficient blood that I could see what I was doing, then snatched a small cautery iron and took care of the largest vessels; the smaller ones could clot and seal on their own.

His eyes were watering ferociously, and his hands were clamped in a death grip on the basin, but he had neither moved nor made a sound. I hadn't expected that he would, after what I had seen when Jamie removed the brand from his thumb. Lizzie was still gripping his shoulders, her eyes tight shut. Jamie reached up and tapped her on the elbow, and her eyes sprang open.

"Here, *a muirninn*, he's done. Take him and put him to his bed, aye?"

Josiah declined to go, though. Mute as his brother, he shook his head violently, and sat down upon a stool, where he sat swaying and white-faced. He gave his brother a ghastly grin, his teeth outlined in blood.

Lizzie hovered between the two boys, looking back and forth between them. Jo caught her eye, and pointed firmly at Keziah, who had assumed the patient's stool with an outward show of fortitude, chin upraised. She patted Jo gently on the head, and went at once to take hold of Keziah's shoulders. He turned his head and gave her a smile of remarkable sweetness, then bent his head and kissed her hand. Then he turned to me, shutting his eyes and opening his mouth; he looked just like a nestling begging for worms.

This operation was somewhat more complicated; his tonsils and adenoids were terribly enlarged, and badly scarred from chronic infection. It was a bloody business; both the towel and my apron were heavily splattered before I had done. I finished the cautery and looked closely at my patient, who was white as the snow outside, and completely glassy-eyed.

"Are you all right?" I asked. He couldn't hear me, but my concerned expression was clear enough. His mouth twitched in what I thought was a gallant effort to smile. He began to nod; then his eyes rolled up and he slid off the stool, ending with a crash at my feet. Jamie caught the basin, rather neatly.

I thought Lizzie might faint as well; there was blood everywhere. She did totter a little, but went obediently to sit down beside Josiah when I told her to. Josiah sat looking on, squeezing Lizzie's hand fiercely while Jamie and I picked up the pieces.

Jamie gathered Keziah up in his arms; the boy lay limp and bloodstained, looking like a murdered child. Josiah rose to his feet, his eyes resting anxiously on his brother's unconscious body.

"It will be all right," Jamie said to him, in tones of

complete confidence. "I told ye, my wife is a great healer." They all turned then, and looked at me, smiling: Jamie, Lizzie, and Josiah. I felt as though I ought to take a bow, but contented myself with smiling, too.

"It will be all right," I said, echoing Jamie. "Go and rest now."

The small procession left the room, more quietly than they had come in, leaving me to put away my instruments and tidy up.

I felt very happy, glowing with the calm sort of satisfaction that attends successful work. I had not done this sort of thing for a long time; the exigencies and limitations of the eighteenth century precluded most surgeries save those done in emergency. Without anesthesia and antibiotic, elective surgery was simply too difficult and too dangerous.

But now I had penicillin, at least. And it *would* be all right, I thought, humming to myself as I extinguished the flame of my alcohol lamp. I had felt it in their flesh, touching the boys as I worked. No germ would threaten them, no infection mar the cleanliness of my work. There was always luck in the practice of medicine—but the odds had shifted today, in my favor.

"All shall be well," I quoted to Adso, who had silently materialized on the counter, where he was industriously licking one of the empty bowls, "and all shall be well, and all manner of thing shall be well."

The big black casebook lay open on the counter where Jamie had left it. I turned to the back pages, where I had been recording the progress of my experiments, and took up my quill. Later, after supper, I would write down the details of the surgery. For the moment . . . I paused, then wrote *Eureka!* at the bottom of the page.

37

MAIL CALL

FERGUS UNDERTOOK his bimonthly trip to Cross Creek in mid-February, returning with salt, needles, indigo, a few more miscellaneous necessities, and a bag full of mail. He arrived in mid-afternoon, so anxious to get back to Marsali that he stayed only long enough for a quick mug of beer, leaving Brianna and me to sort through the parcels, gloating over the bounty.

There was a thick stack of newspapers from Wilmington and New Bern; a few from Philadelphia and Boston as well, sent by friends in the north to Jocasta Cameron, and thence forwarded on to us. I flipped through these; the most recent was dated three months prior. No matter; newspapers were as good as novels, in a place where reading material was almost literally scarcer than gold.

Jocasta had also sent two issues of *Brigham's Lady's Book* for Brianna, this being a periodical featuring drawings of fashionable London costumes, and articles of interest to women of such tastes.

"How to Clean Gold Lace," Brianna read, arching one eyebrow as she opened one of these at random. "That's something everybody ought to know how to do, for sure."

"Look in the back," I advised her. "That's where they publish the articles about how to avoid catching gonorrhea and what to do about your husband's piles."

The other brow went up, making her look just like Jamie, presented with some highly questionable proposition.

"If my husband gave me gonorrhea, I think he could just worry about his own piles." She turned several pages, and the eyebrows arched higher. *"A Spur to Venus. This being a List of infallible Remedys for Fatigue of the Male Member."*

I peered over her arm, my own eyebrows rising.

"Goodness. *A Dozen of Oysters, soaked overnight in a Mixture of Wine and Milk, to be baked in a Tart with Crushed Almonds and Lobstermeat, and served with Spiced Peppers*. I don't know what it would do for the male member, but it would probably give the gentleman attached to it violent indigestion. Of course, we haven't got any oysters here anyway."

"No loss," she assured me, frowning at the page in concentration. "Oysters remind me of big plugs of snot."

"That's only the raw ones; they're more or less edible when cooked. Speaking of snot, though—where's Jemmy?"

"Asleep, or at least I hope so." She cast a suspicious eye toward the ceiling, but no untoward noises manifested themselves, and she returned to the page.

"Here's one we could do. *The Testicles of a Male Animal*—like you'd get them from a female animal—*taken with six large Mushrooms and boyled in Sour Ale until tender, then both Testicles and Mushrooms to be sliced thin, well-pepper'd and seasoned with Salt, then sprinkl'd with Vinegar and brown'd before the Fire until crusty*. Da hasn't gotten around to castrating Gideon yet, has he?"

"No. I'm sure he'd be happy to give you the objects in question, if you want to try."

She went very pink in the face, and cleared her throat with a noise that reminded me even more of her father. "I—um—don't think we need that *just* yet."

I laughed and left her to her fascinated perusal, turning back to the mail.

There was a wrapped object addressed to Jamie that I knew must be a book, sent from a bookseller in Philadelphia, but with Lord John Grey's seal affixed—a daub of blue wax whimsically marked with a smiling half-moon and a single star. Half our library came from John Grey, who insisted that he sent us books primarily for his own satisfaction, as he knew no one in the Colonies other than Jamie who was capable of carrying on a decent discussion of literature.

There were several letters addressed to Jamie, too; I looked these over carefully, in hopes of seeing his sister's characteristic spiky script, but no such luck. There was a letter from Ian, who wrote faithfully once a month, but nothing from Jenny; there had been no word from her in the past six months; not since Jamie had written reluctantly to tell her of the fate of her youngest son.

I frowned, setting the letters in a small stack at the edge of the desk for Jamie's later attention. I could scarcely blame Jenny, under the circumstances—but I'd been there, after all. It hadn't been Jamie's fault, even though he'd accepted the blame for it. Young Ian had chosen to stay with the Mohawk. He was a man, if a young one, and the decision was his to make. But then, I reflected, he had been still a lad when he left his parents, and likely still was, so far as Jenny was concerned.

I knew that her silence hurt Jamie deeply, though. He continued to write to her, as he always had, stubbornly putting down a few paragraphs most evenings, putting by the pages until someone should be going down from the mountain, to Cross Creek or Wilmington. He was never obvious about it, but I saw the way his eyes flicked across each batch of letters, looking for her writing, and the almost-invisible tightening at the corner of his mouth when he didn't find it.

"Drat you, Jenny Murray," I murmured under my breath. "Forgive him and have done with it!"

"Hmm?" Brianna had put down the periodical and was examining a square letter, frowning as she did so.

"Nothing. What's that you have there?" I put down the letters I had been sorting and came to look.

"It's from Lieutenant Hayes. What do you think he's writing about?"

A tiny spurt of adrenaline tightened my belly. It must also have shown on my unwary face, for Brianna put down the letter and looked at me, brow furrowed.

"What?" she demanded.

"Nothing," I said, but it was too late. She stood looking at me, a fist doubled on her hip, and raised one brow.

"You are the most terrible liar, Mama," she said tolerantly. Without hesitation, she broke the seal.

"That's addressed to your father," I said, though my protest lacked strength.

"Um-hm. So was the other one," she said, head bent over the unfolded sheet of paper.

"What?" But I had come to her side, and was reading over her arm, even as I spoke.

Lieutenant Archibald Hayes
Portsmouth, Virginia

Mr. James Fraser
Fraser's Ridge, North Carolina

January 18, 1771

Sir—

I write to inform you that we are at present in Portsmouth, and like to remain here until Spring. If you are acquainted with any Sea Captains willing to grant Passage to Perth for forty Men, on promise of Recompense from the Army once Port is reached, I should be glad to hear of it at your earliest Convenience.

In the Meantime, we have put our Hands to various Labors, that we might sustain ourselves through the Winter Months. Several of my Men have obtained Work in the Repair of Boats, which are plentiful here. I myself am employed as Cook in a local Tavern, but make shift to visit my Men regularly in the assorted Quarters where they are lodged, to make myself acquainted with their State.

I called upon one such Lodging two Evenings ago. In course of Conversation, one of the Men—a Private Ogilvie, whom I think you will know—mentioned to me a Conversation which he had overheard in the Shipyard. As this pertained to one Stephen Bonnet, who I recollect is of Interest to you, I pass on herewith the Intelligence of the Matter.

Bonnet appears by Report to be a Smuggler, scarce an uncommon Occupation in the Area. Howsoever, he seems to deal in a higher Quality—and Quantity—of

Contraband than is the usual, and in Consequence, the Nature of his Connexions appears also unusual. Which is to say that certain Warehouses on the Carolina Coast periodically contain Goods of a Nature not generally to be found therein, and that such Visitations coincide with Sightings of Stephen Bonnet in the Taverns and "Holes" nearby.

Private Ogilvie has little Recollection of specific Names overheard, as he had no Knowledge that Bonnet was of Interest, and mentioned the Matter to me only as a curious Piece of Information. One Name mentioned was "Butler," he says, but he is uncertain whether this Name had aught to do with Bonnet. Another name was "Karen," but Ogilvie does not know whether this pertained to a Woman or perhaps to a Ship.

A Warehouse which he supposed to be a particular Building indicated in the Conversation—though he freely admits that he is uncertain of this—happened to be at no great Distance from the Shipyard, and when he told me of his Intelligence, I took it upon myself to pass by this Building and make Enquiries concerning its Ownership. The Building is owned jointly by two Partners: one Ronald Priestly and one Phillip Wylie. I have no Information concerning either Man at Present, but will continue my Enquiries as my Time permits.

Having learned the Above, I have made an Effort to solicit Conversation concerning Bonnet in the local Taprooms, but to little Effect. I should say that the Name is known, but few wish to speak of him.

You most obedient servant,
Archibald Hayes, Lieutenant
67th Highland Regiment

All the normal noises of the house were still around us, but Bree and I seemed suddenly to be together in a small, clear bubble of silence, where time had abruptly stopped.

I felt reluctant to put down the letter, for that would mean that time would go on, and something must at that point be done. At the same time, I wanted not merely to put it down but to throw it into the fire, and pretend neither of us had seen it.

Then Jemmy began to cry upstairs, Brianna jerked in response and turned toward the door, and things began to move normally again.

I set the letter down in a space by itself, and returned to the rest of the mail, setting things tidily aside for Jamie's later attention, putting the newspapers and periodicals into a neat stack, untying the string round the parcel; as I had supposed, it was a book—Tobias Smollett's *The Expedition of Humphrey Clinker.* I wound up the string and tucked it into my pocket, while all the time a small "Now-what, now-what" beat in the back of my mind like a metronome.

Brianna came back, carrying Jemmy, who was red and creased from his nap, and obviously in that state of mind where one rouses from sleep to a dazed irritation at the intrusive demands of consciousness. I sympathized.

She sat down, pulled down the neck of her shift, and put the baby to her breast. His cries ceased like magic, and I had a moment of intense wishfulness that I could do something that immediately effective for her. As it was, she looked pale, but composed.

I had to say something.

"I am sorry, sweetheart," I said. "I tried to stop him—Jamie, I mean. I know he didn't mean you to know about it. To worry about it."

"That's okay. I already knew." Reaching across one-handed, she slid one of the ledgers out of the stack Jamie kept on his desk, and holding it by the spine, shook out a folded letter. She nodded over Jemmy's head at it.

"Look at that. I found it while you were gone with the militia."

I read Lord John's account of the duel between Bonnet and Captain Marsden, feeling a coldness gather beneath my breastbone. I hadn't been under any illusions regarding Bonnet's character, but I hadn't known that he had that much skill. I greatly preferred dangerous criminals to be incompetent.

"I thought maybe Lord John was just answering a casual question for Da—but I guess not. What do you think?" Bree asked. Her tone was cool, almost detached, as though she were inquiring my opinion of a hair-ribbon or a shoe-buckle. I looked up at her sharply.

"What do *you* think?" It was Brianna who was important in this—or that was *my* opinion.

"About what?" Her eyes slid away from mine, glancing off the letter, then fastening themselves on the curve of Jemmy's head.

"Oh, the price of tea in China, for starters," I said, with some irritation. "Going on promptly to the topic of Stephen Bonnet, if you like." It felt oddly shocking to say the name out loud; we had all avoided it for months, by unspoken consent.

Her teeth were fastened in her lower lip. She kept her eyes fixed on the floor for a moment, then shook her head, very slightly.

"I don't want to hear about him, or think about him," she said, very evenly. "And if I ever see him again, I might just . . . just . . ." She shuddered violently, then looked up at me, eyes fierce and sudden.

"What's *wrong* with him?" she cried. "How could he do this?" Her clenched fist struck her thigh, and Jemmy, startled, lost his grip and began to wail.

"Your father, you mean—not Bonnet."

She nodded, pressing Jemmy back toward her breast, but he had picked up her agitation, and was squirming and howling. I reached down and took him, hoisting him to my shoulder and patting his back in automatic comfort. Bree's hands, left empty, fastened on her knees, crumpled the cloth of her skirt.

"Why couldn't he leave Bonnet alone?" She had to raise her voice to be heard above the baby's wailing, and the bones of her face seemed to have shifted, so that the skin looked tight-drawn over them.

"Because he's a man—and a bloody Highlander," I said. "'Live and let live' is not in their vocabulary." Milk was dripping slowly from her nipple onto the fabric of her shift; I reached out one-handed and tweaked the cloth up to cover her. She put a hand over her breast and pressed hard to stop the milk.

"What does he mean to do, though? If he finds him."

"*When* he finds him, I'm afraid," I said reluctantly. "Because I don't believe he's going to stop looking until he does. As to what he'll do then . . . well . . . then he'll kill him, I suppose." It sounded oddly offhand, put that way, and yet I didn't see any other way of putting it, really.

"You mean he'll *try* to kill him." She glanced at the letter from Lord John, then away, swallowing. "What if he . . ."

"Your father has a great deal of experience in killing people," I said bleakly. "In fact, he's awfully good at it—though he hasn't done it for some time."

This didn't seem to reassure her to any great extent. It hadn't reassured me, either.

"It's such a big place," she murmured, shaking her head. "America, I mean. Why couldn't he just—go away? Far away?" An excellent question. Jemmy was snorting, rubbing his face furiously in my shoulder, but no longer screaming.

"I was rather hoping that Stephen Bonnet would have the good sense to go and pursue his smuggling in China or the West Indies, but I suppose he has local connections that he didn't want to abandon." I shrugged, patting Jemmy.

Brianna let go of her skirt and reached for the baby, who was still twisting like an eel.

"Well, he doesn't know he has Sherlock Fraser and his sidekick Lord John Watson on his trail, after all." It was a brave try, but her lip trembled as she said it, and she bit the lower one again. I hated to cause her more worry, but there was no point now in avoiding things.

"No, but he very likely will, before too long," I said reluctantly. "Lord John is very discreet—Private Ogilvie isn't. If Jamie goes on asking questions—and he will, I'm afraid—his interest is going to be rather widely known before long." I wasn't sure whether Jamie had hoped to discover Bonnet quickly and take him unawares—or whether his plan was to smoke Bonnet out into the open by means of his inquiries. Or whether he meant in fact to draw Bonnet's attention deliberately, and cause him to come to *us*. The last possibility made me a little weak in the knees, and I sat down heavily on the stool.

Brianna drew a slow, deep breath and let it out through her nose, settling the baby back at her breast.

"Does Roger know? I mean, is he in on this—this—bloody *vendetta*?"

I shook my head.

"I don't think so. I mean, I'm sure not. He would have told you—wouldn't he?"

Her expression eased a little, though a shadow of doubt still darkened her eyes.

"I'd hate to think he'd keep something like that from me. On the other hand," she added, voice sharpening a little in accusation, "*you* did."

I felt the sting of it, and pressed my lips tight together.

"You said that you didn't want to think of Stephen Bonnet," I said, looking away from the turbulence of feeling in her face. "Naturally not. I—we—didn't want you to have to." With a certain feeling of inevitability, I realized that I was being drawn into the vortex of Jamie's intentions, through no consent of my own.

"Now, look," I said briskly, sitting up straight and giving Brianna a sharp look. "*I* don't think it's a good idea to look for Bonnet, and I've done all I could to discourage Jamie from doing it. In fact," I added ruefully, with a nod toward Lord John's letter, "I thought I *had* discouraged him. But apparently not."

A look of determination was hardening Brianna's mouth, and she settled herself more solidly in the chair.

"*I'll* bloody discourage him," she said.

I gave her a look, considering. If anyone had the necessary stubbornness and force of character to sway Jamie from his chosen path, it would be his daughter. That was, however, a very large "if."

"You can try," I said, a little dubiously.

"Don't I have the right?" Her initial shock had vanished, and her features were back under control, her expression cold and hard. "Isn't it for me to say whether I want . . . what I want?"

"Yes," I agreed, a twinge of uneasiness rippling down my back. Fathers were inclined to think they had rights, too. So were husbands. But perhaps that was better left unsaid.

A momentary silence fell between us, broken only by Jemmy's noises, and the calling of crows outside. Almost by impulse, I asked the question that had risen to the surface of my mind.

"Brianna. What do you want? Do you want Stephen Bonnet dead?"

She glanced at me, then away, looking out the window while she patted Jemmy's back. She didn't blink. Finally, her eyes closed briefly, then opened to meet mine.

"I can't," she said, low-voiced. "I'm afraid if I ever let that thought in my mind . . . I'd never be able to think about anything else, I'd want it so much. And I will be *damned* if I'll let . . . him . . . ruin my life that way."

Jemmy gave a resounding belch, and spit up a little milk. Bree had an old linen towel across her shoulder, and deftly wiped his chin with it. Calmer now, he had lost his look of vexed incomprehension, and was concentrating intently on something over his mother's shoulder. Following the direction of his clear blue gaze, I saw the shadow of a spiderweb, high up in the corner of the window. A gust of wind shook the window frame, and a tiny spot moved in the center of the web, very slightly.

"Yeah," Brianna said, very softly. "I do want him dead. But I want Da and Roger alive, more."

38

THE DREAMTIME

ROGER HAD GONE to sing for Joel MacLeod's nephew's wedding, as arranged at the Gathering, and come home with a new prize, which he was anxious to commit to paper before it should escape.

He left his muddy boots in the kitchen, accepted a cup of tea and a raisin tart from Mrs. Bug, and went directly to the study. Jamie was there, writing letters; he glanced up with an absent murmur of acknowledgment, but then returned to his composition, a slight frown between his heavy brows as he formed the letters, hand cramped and awkward on the quill.

There was a small, three-shelf bookcase in Jamie's study, which held the entire library of Fraser's Ridge. The serious works occupied the top shelf: a volume of Latin poetry, Caesar's *Commentaries*, the *Meditations* of Marcus Aurelius, a few other classic works, Dr. Brickell's *Natural History of North Carolina*, lent by the Governor and never returned, and a schoolbook on mathematics, much abused, with *Ian Murray the Younger* written on the flyleaf in a staggering hand.

The middle shelf was given over to more light-minded reading: a small selection of romances, slightly ragged with much reading, featuring *Robinson Crusoe*; *Tom Jones*, in a set of seven small, leather-covered volumes; *Roderick Random*, in four volumes; and Sir Henry Richardson's monstrous *Pamela*, done in two gigantic octavo bindings—the first of these decorated with multiple bookmarks, ranging from a ragged dried maple leaf to a folded penwiper, these indicating the points which various readers had reached before giving up, either temporarily or permanently. A copy of *Don*

Quixote in Spanish, ratty, but much less worn, since only Jamie could read it.

The bottom shelf held a copy of *Dr. Sam. Johnson's Dictionary*, Jamie's ledgers and account books, several of Brianna's sketchbooks, and the slender buckram-bound journal in which Roger recorded the words of unfamiliar songs and poems acquired at ceilidhs and hearthsides.

He took a stool on the other side of the table Jamie used as a desk, and cut a new quill for the job, taking care with it; he wanted these records to be readable. He didn't know precisely what use the collection might be put to, but he had been ingrained with the scholar's instinctive value for the written word. Perhaps this was only for his own pleasure and use—but he liked the feeling that he might be leaving something to posterity as well, and took pains both to write clearly and to document the circumstances under which he had acquired each song.

The study was peaceful, with no more than Jamie's occasional sigh as he stopped to rub the kinks from his cramped hand. After a while, Mr. Bug came to the door, and after a brief colloquy, Jamie put away his quill and went out with the factor. Roger nodded vaguely as they bade him farewell, mind occupied with the effort of recall and recording.

When he finished, a quarter of an hour later, his mind was pleasantly empty, and he sat back, stretching the ache from his shoulders. He waited a few moments for the ink to be thoroughly dry before he put the book away, and while waiting, went to pull out one of Brianna's sketchbooks from the bottom shelf.

She wouldn't mind if he looked; she had told him he was welcome to look at them. At the same time, she showed him only the occasional drawing, those she was pleased with, or had done especially for him.

He turned over the pages of the notebook, feeling the sense of curiosity and respect that attends the prying into mystery, searching for small glimpses of the workings of her mind.

There were lots of portrait sketches of the baby in this one, a study in circles.

He paused at one small sketch, caught by memory. It was a sketch of Jemmy sleeping, back turned, his small sturdy body curled up in a comma. Adso the cat was curled up beside him, in precisely similar fashion, his chin perched on Jemmy's fat little foot, eyes slits of comatose bliss. He remembered that one.

She drew Jemmy often—nearly every day, in fact—but seldom fullface.

"Babies don't really have faces," she had told him, frowning critically at her offspring, who was industriously gnawing on the leather strap of Jamie's powder horn.

"Oh, aye? And what's that on the front of his head, then?" He had lain flat on the floor with the baby and the cat, grinning up at her, which made it easier for her to look down her nose at him.

"I mean, strictly speaking. Naturally they have faces, but they all look alike."

"It's a wise father that kens his own child, eh?" he joked, regretting it instantly, as he saw the shadow cloud her eyes. It passed, quick as a summer cloud, but it had been there, nonetheless.

"Well, not from an artist's point of view." She drew the blade of her penknife at an angle across the tip of the charcoal stick, sharpening the point. "They don't have any bones—that you can see, I mean. And it's the bones that you use to show the shape of a face; without bones, there isn't much there."

Bones or not, she had a remarkable knack for capturing the nuances of expression. He smiled at one sketch; Jemmy's face wore the aloof and unmistakable expression of one concentrating hard on the production of a truly terrible diaper.

Beyond the pictures of Jemmy, there were several pages of what looked like engineering diagrams. Finding these of no great interest, he bent and replaced the book, then drew out another.

He realized at once that it was not a sketchbook. The pages were dense with Brianna's tidy, angular writing. He flipped curiously through the pages; it wasn't really a diary, but appeared to be a sort of record of her dreams.

Last night I dreamed that I shaved my legs. Roger smiled at the inconsequence, but a vision of Brianna's shins, long-boned and glimmering, kept him reading.

> *I was using Daddy's razor and his shaving cream, and I was thinking that he'd complain when he found out, but I wasn't worried. The shaving cream came in a white can with red letters, and it said Old Spice on the label. I don't know if there ever was shaving cream like that, but that's what Daddy always smelled of, Old Spice aftershave and cigarette smoke. He didn't smoke, but the people he worked with did, and his jackets always smelled like the air in the living room after a party.*

Roger breathed in, half-conscious of the remembered scents of fresh baking and tea, furniture polish and ammonia. No cigarettes at the decorous gatherings held in the manse's parlor—and yet his father's jackets too had smelled of smoke.

> *Once Gayle told me that she'd gone out with Chris and hadn't had time to shave her legs, and she spent the whole evening trying to keep him from putting his hand on her knee, for fear he'd feel the stubble. Afterward, I never shaved my legs without thinking of that, and I'd run my fingers up my thigh, to see whether I could feel anything there, or if it was okay to stop shaving at my kneecaps.*

The hair on Brianna's thighs was so fine it could not be felt; and only seen when she rose up naked over him, with the sun behind her gilding her body, gleaming through that delicate nimbus of secrecy. The thought that no one would ever see it but himself gave him a small glow of satisfaction, like a miser counting each hair of gold and copper, enjoying his secret fortune undisturbed by any fear of theft.

He turned the page, feeling unspeakably guilty at this intrusion, yet drawn irresistibly by the urge to penetrate the intimacy of her dreams, to know the images that filled her sleeping mind.

The entries were undated, but each entry began with the same words: *Last night, I dreamed.*

Last night I dreamed that it was raining. Hardly surprising, since it was *raining, and has been for two days. When I went out to the privy this morning, I had to jump over a huge puddle by the door, and sank up to the ankles in the soft spot by the blackberries.*

We went to bed last night with the rain pounding on the roof. It was so nice to curl up with Roger and be warm in our bed, after a wet, chilly day. Raindrops fell down the chimney and hissed in the fire. We told each other stories from our youths—maybe that's where the dream came from, thinking about the past.

There wasn't much to the dream, just that I was looking out a window in Boston, watching the cars go past, throwing up big sheets of water from their wheels, and hearing the swoosh and rush of their tires on the wet streets. I woke up still hearing that sound; it was so clear in my mind that I actually went to the window and peeked out, half expecting to see a busy street, full of cars rushing through the rain. It was a shock to see spruce trees and chestnuts and wild grass and creepers, and hear nothing but the soft patter of raindrops bouncing and trembling on the burdock leaves.

Everything was so vivid a green, so lush and overgrown, that it seemed like a jungle, or an alien planet—a place I'd never been, with nothing I recognized, though in fact I see it every day.

All day, I've heard the secret rush of tires in the rain, somewhere behind me.

Feeling guilty, but fascinated, Roger turned the page.

Last night I dreamed of driving my car. It was my own blue Mustang, and I was driving fast down a winding road, through the mountains—these mountains. I never have driven through these mountains, though I have been through the mountain woodlands in upstate New York. It was definitely here, though; I knew it was the Ridge.

It was so real. I can still feel my hair snapping in the wind, the wheel in my hands, the vibration of the motor and the rumble of tires on the pavement. But that sensation—as well as the car—is impossible. It can't happen now, anywhere but in my head. And yet there it is, embedded in the cells of my memory, as real as the privy outside, waiting to be called back to life at the flick of a synapse.

That's another oddness. Nobody knows what a synapse is, except me and Mama and Roger. What a strange feeling; as though we three share all kinds of secrets.

Anyway, that particular bit—the driving—is traceable to a known memory. But what about the dreams, equally vivid, equally real, of things I do not know of my waking self. Are some dreams the memories of things that haven't happened yet?

Last night I dreamed that I made love with Roger.

He had been about to close the book, feeling a sense of guilt at his intrusion. The guilt was still there—in spades—but totally insufficient to overcome his curiosity. He glanced at the door, but the house was quiet; women were moving about in the kitchen, but no one was near the study.

Last night I dreamed that I made love with Roger.

It was great; for once I wasn't thinking, wasn't watching from the outside, like I always do. In fact, I wasn't even aware of myself for a long time. There was just this . . . very wild, exciting stuff, and I was part of it and Roger was part of it, but there wasn't any him or me, just us.

The funny thing is that it was Roger, but I didn't

think of him like that. Not by his name—not that name. It was like he had another name, a secret, real one—but I knew what it was.

(I've always thought everybody has that kind of name, the kind that isn't a word. I know who I am—and whoever it is, her name isn't "Brianna." It's me, that's all. "Me" works fine as a substitute for what I mean—but how do you write down someone else's secret name?)

I knew Roger's real name, though, and that seemed to be why it was working. And it really was working, too; I didn't think about it or worry about it, and I only thought toward the very end, Hey, it's happening!

And then it did happen and everything dissolved and shook and throbbed—

Here she had blacked out the rest of the line, with a small, cross note in the margin, that said,

Well, none of the books I've ever read could describe it, either!

Despite his shocked fascination, Roger laughed aloud, then choked it off, glancing round hastily to see that he was still alone. There were noises in the kitchen, but no sound of footsteps in the hall, and his eyes went back to the page like iron filings drawn to a magnet.

I had my eyes closed—in the dream, that is—and I was lying there with little electric shocks still going off, and I opened my eyes and it was Stephen Bonnet inside me.

It was such a shock it woke me up. I felt like I'd been screaming—my throat was all raw—but I couldn't have been, because Roger and the baby were sound asleep. I was hot all over, so hot I was sweating, but I was cold, too, and my heart was pounding. It took a long time before things settled down enough for me to go back to sleep; all the birds were carrying on.

That's what finally let me go back to sleep, in fact—

the birds. Da—and Daddy, too, come to think of it—told me that the jays and crows give alarm calls, but songbirds stop singing when someone comes near, so when you're in a forest, you listen for that. With so much racket in the trees by the house, I knew it was safe—nobody was there.

There was a small blank space at the foot of the page. He turned it, feeling his palms sweat and his heartbeat heavy in his ears. The writing resumed at the top of the page. Before, the writing had been fluid, almost hasty, the letters flattened as they raced across the page. Here, they were formed with more care, rounded and upright, as though the first shock of the experience were spent, and she had returned, with a stubborn caution, to think further about it.

I tried to forget it, but that didn't work. It kept coming back and coming back into my mind, so I finally went out by myself to work in the herb shed. Mama keeps Jemmy when I'm there because he gets in things, so I knew I could be alone. So I sat down in the middle of all the hanging bunches and closed my eyes and tried to remember every single thing about it, and think to myself about the different parts, "That's okay," or "That's just a dream." Because Stephen Bonnet scared me, and I felt sick when I thought of the end—but I really wanted to remember how. How it felt, and how I did it, so maybe I can do it again, with Roger.

But I keep having this feeling that I can't, unless I can remember Roger's secret name.

There the entry stopped. The dreams continued on the next page, but Roger didn't read further. He closed the book very carefully and slid it back behind the others on the shelf. He rose to his feet and stood looking out the window for some time, unconsciously rubbing his sweating palms over the seams of his breeches.

Part Five

'Tis Better to Marry Than Burn

39

IN CUPID'S GROVE

DO YE THINK they'll share a bed?"

Jamie didn't raise his voice, but he'd made no effort to lower it, either. Luckily, we were standing at the far end of the terrace, too far away for the bridal couple to hear. A number of heads turned in our direction, though.

Ninian Bell Hamilton was openly staring at us. I smiled brightly and fluttered my closed fan at the elderly Scotsman in greeting, meanwhile giving Jamie a swift nudge in the ribs.

"A nice, respectable sort of thing for a nephew to be wondering about his aunt," I said under my breath.

Jamie shifted out of elbow range and lifted an eyebrow at me.

"What's respectable to do with it? They'll be married. And well above the age of consent, both o' them," he added, with a grin at Ninian, who went bright pink with smothered mirth. I didn't know how old Duncan Innes was, but my best guess put him in his mid-fifties. Jamie's aunt Jocasta had to be at least a decade older.

I could just see Jocasta over the heads of the intervening crowd, graciously accepting the greetings of friends and neighbors at the far end of the terrace. A tall woman gowned in russet wool, she was flanked by huge stone vases holding sprays of dried goldenrod, and her black butler Ulysses stood at her shoulder, dignified in wig and green livery. With an elegant white lace cap crowning her bold MacKenzie bones, she was undeniably the queen of River Run Plantation. I stood on tiptoe, searching for her consort.

Duncan was slightly shorter than Jocasta, but he should still have been visible. I'd seen him earlier in the morning, dressed in an absolute blaze of Highland finery, in which he looked dashing, if terribly self-conscious. I craned my neck, putting a hand on Jamie's arm to keep my balance. He grabbed my elbow to steady me.

"What are ye looking for, Sassenach?"

"Duncan. Shouldn't he be with your aunt?"

No one could tell by looking that Jocasta was blind—that she stood between the big vases to keep her bearings, or that Ulysses was there to whisper in her ear the names of approaching guests. I saw her left hand drift outward from her side, touch empty air, and drift back. Her face didn't change, though; she smiled and nodded, saying something to Judge Henderson.

"Run away before the wedding night?" suggested Ninian, lifting his chin and both eyebrows in an effort to see over the crowd without standing on his toes. "I'd maybe feel a bit nervous at the prospect myself. Your aunt's a handsome woman, Fraser, but she could freeze the ballocks off the King o' Japan, and she wanted to."

Jamie's mouth twitched.

"Duncan's maybe caught short," he said. "Whatever the reason. He's been to the necessary house four times this morning."

My own brows went up at this. Duncan suffered from chronic constipation; in fact, I had brought a packet of senna leaves and coffee-plant roots for him, in spite of Jamie's rude remarks about what constituted a suitable wedding present. Duncan must be more nervous than I'd thought.

"Well, it's no going to be any great surprise to my aunt, and her wi' three husbands before him," Jamie said, in reply to a murmured remark of Hamilton's. "It'll be the first time Duncan's been married, though. That's a shock to any man. I remember my own wedding night, aye?" He grinned at me, and I felt the heat rise in my cheeks. I remembered it, too—vividly.

"Don't you think it's rather warm out here?" I flicked my fan into an arc of ivory lace, and fluttered it over my cheeks.

"Really?" he said, still grinning at me. "I hadna taken notice of it."

"Duncan has," Ninian put in. His wrinkled lips pursed closed, holding in the laughter. "Sweating like a steamed pudding when I saw him last."

It was in fact a little chilly out, in spite of the cast-iron tubs full of hot embers that sent the sweet smell of applewood smoke wisping up from the corners of the stone terrace. Spring had sprung, and the lawns were fresh and green, as were the trees along the river, but the morning air still held a sharp nip of winter's bite. It *was* still winter in the mountains, and we had encountered snow as far south as Guildford on our journey toward River Run, though daffodils and crocuses poked bravely through it.

It was a clear, bright March day now, though, and house, terrace, lawn, and garden were thronged with wedding guests, glowing in their finery like an unseasonable flight of butterflies. Jocasta's wedding was clearly going to be the social event of the year, so far as Cape Fear society was concerned; there must be nearly two hundred people here, from places as far distant as Halifax and Edenton.

Ninian said something to Jamie in low-voiced Gaelic, with a sidelong glance at me. Jamie replied with a remark elegant in phraseology and extremely crude in content, blandly meeting my eye as the older man choked with laughter.

I did in fact understand Gaelic fairly well by now, but there were moments when discretion was the better part of valor. I spread my fan wide, concealing my expression. True, it took some practice to achieve grace with a fan, but it was a useful social tool to someone cursed, as I was, with a glass face. Even fans had their limits, though.

I turned away from the conversation, which gave every promise of degenerating further, and surveyed the party for signs of the absent bridegroom. Perhaps Duncan was truly ill, and not with nerves. If so, I should have a look at him.

"Phaedre! Have you seen Mr. Innes this morning?" Jocasta's body servant was flying past, her arms full of tablecloths, but came abruptly to a halt at my call.

"Ain't seen Mister Duncan since breakfast, ma'am," she said, with a shake of her neatly capped head.

"How did he seem then? Did he eat well?" Breakfast was an ongoing affair of several hours, the resident guests serving themselves from the sideboard and eating as they chose. It was more likely nerves than food poisoning that was troubling Duncan's bowels, but some of the sausage I had seen on the sideboard struck me as highly suspect.

"No, ma'am, nary a bite." Phaedre's smooth brow puckered; she was fond of Duncan. "Cook tried to tempt him with a nice coddled egg, but he just shook his head and looked peaked. He did take a cup of rum punch, though," she said, seeming somewhat cheered at the thought.

"Aye, that'll settle him," Ninian remarked, overhearing. "Dinna trouble yourself, Mrs. Claire; Duncan will be well enough."

Phaedre curtsied and made off toward the tables being set up under the trees, starched apron flapping in the breeze. The succulent aroma of barbecuing pork wafted through the chill spring air, and fragrant clouds of hickory smoke rose from the fires near the smithy, where haunches of venison, sides of mutton, and broiled fowl in their dozens turned on spits. My stomach gurgled loudly in anticipation, despite the tight lacing of my stays.

Neither Jamie nor Ninian appeared to notice, but I took a discreet step away, turning to survey the lawn that stretched from the terrace to the river landing. I wasn't so positive of the virtues of rum, particularly taken on an empty stomach. Granted, Duncan wouldn't be the first groom to go to the altar in an advanced state of intoxication, but still . . .

Brianna, brilliant in blue wool the color of the spring sky, was standing near one of the marble statues that graced the lawn, Jemmy balanced on her hip, deep in conversation with Gerald Forbes, the lawyer. She also had a fan, but at the moment, it was being put to better use than usual—Jemmy had got hold of it and was munching on the ivory handle, a look of fierce concentration on his small pink face.

Of course, Brianna had less need of good fan technique than I did, she having inherited Jamie's ability to hide all thoughts behind a mask of pleasant blandness. She had the mask in place now, which gave me a good idea of her opinion of Mr. Forbes. Where was Roger? I wondered. He'd been with her earlier.

I turned to ask Jamie what he thought of this epidemic of disappearing husbands, only to discover that he had joined it. Ninian Hamilton had turned away to talk to someone else, and the space at my side was now occupied by a pair of slaves, staggering under the weight of a fresh demijohn of brandywine as they headed for the refreshment tables. I stepped hastily out of their way, and turned to look for Jamie.

He had vanished into the crowd like a grouse into heather. I turned slowly, surveying the terrace and lawns, but there wasn't a sign of him among the milling crowd. I frowned against the bright sunlight, shading my eyes with my hand.

It wasn't as though he were inconspicuous, after all; a Highlander with the blood of Viking giants in his veins, he stood head and shoulders above most men, and his hair caught the sun like polished bronze. To add icing to the cake, he was dressed today in his best to celebrate Jocasta's wedding—a belted plaid in crimson and black tartan, with his good gray coat and weskit, and the gaudiest pair of red-and-black Argyle stockings ever to grace a Scotsman's shins. He should have stood out like a splotch of blood on fresh linen.

I didn't find him, but did see a familiar face. I stepped off the terrace and eeled my way through the knots of partygoers.

"Mr. MacLennan!" He turned toward my call, looking surprised, but then a cordial smile spread across his blunt features.

"Mrs. Fraser!"

"How lovely to see you," I said, giving him my hand. "How are you?" He looked much better than when last seen, clean and decent in a dark suit and plain laced hat. There were hollows in his cheeks, though, and a shadow behind his eyes that remained even as he smiled at me.

"Oh . . . I'm well enough, ma'am. Quite well."

"Are you—where are you living, these days?" That seemed a more delicate question than "Why aren't you in jail?" No fool, he answered both questions.

"Och, well, your husband was sae kind as to write to Mr.

Ninian there"—he nodded across the lawn toward the lean figure of Ninian Bell Hamilton, who was in the middle of a heated discussion of some kind—"and to tell him of my trouble. Mr. Ninian's a great friend to the Regulation, ken—and a great friend of Judge Henderson's, forbye." He shook his head, mouth pursed in puzzlement.

"I couldna say quite how it fell out, but Mr. Ninian came and fetched me out of the gaol, and took me into his own household. So I am there, for the present. 'Twas kind—verra kind." He spoke with evident sincerity, and yet with a certain air of abstraction. He fell silent then. He was still looking at me, but his eyes were blank. I groped for something to say, hoping to bring him back to the present, but a shout from Ninian brought him out of his trance, saving me the trouble. Abel excused himself politely to me and went to assist in the argument.

I strolled down the lawn, nodding to acquaintances over my fan. I was glad to see Abel again, and know he was physically well, at least—but I couldn't deny that the sight of him cast a chill over my heart. I had the feeling that in fact, it made little difference to Abel MacLennan where his body resided; his heart still lay in the grave with his wife.

Why had Ninian brought him today? I wondered. Surely a wedding could not but recall his own marriage to him; weddings did that to everyone.

The sun had risen high enough to warm the air, but I shivered. The sight of MacLennan's grief reminded me too much of the days after Culloden, when I had gone back to my own time, knowing Jamie dead. I knew too well that deadness of heart; the sense of sleepwalking through days and lying open-eyed at night, finding no rest, knowing only emptiness that was not peace.

Jocasta's voice floated down from the terrace, calling to Ulysses. She had lost three husbands, and now was fixed to take a fourth. Blind she might be, but there was no deadness in her eyes. Did that mean she had not cared deeply for any of her husbands? I wondered. Or only that she was a woman of great strength, capable of overcoming grief, not once, but over and again?

I had done it once, myself—for Brianna's sake. But Jocasta had no children; not now, at least. Had she once had them, and put aside the pain of a sundered heart, to live for a child?

I shook myself, trying to dispel such melancholy thoughts. It was, after all, a festive occasion, and a day to match. The dogwoods in the grove were in bloom, and courting bluebirds and cardinals shot in and out of the greening trees like bits of confetti, crazed with lust.

"But of course they have," a woman was saying, in an authoritative tone of voice. "My God, they've shared a house for months now!"

"Aye, that's so," one of her companions agreed, sounding doubtful. "But ye wouldna think it from the looks of them. Why, they scarcely glance at each other! Ah . . . I mean—well, of course, she canna be looking at him, blind as she is, but ye'd think . . ."

It wasn't only the birds, I thought, amused. A certain sense of rising sap suffused the whole gathering. Glancing up at the terrace, I could see young women clustered, tittering and gossiping in small groups like hens, while the men strode oh-so-casually up and down in front of them, gaudy as peacocks in their party clothes. I wouldn't be surprised if at least a few engagements resulted from this celebration—and a few pregnancies as well. Sex was in the air; I could smell it, under the heady fragrances of spring flowers and cooking food.

The sense of melancholy had quite left me, though I still had a strong urge to find Jamie.

I had gone down one side of the lawn and up the other, but saw no sign of him anywhere between the big plantation house and the dock, where slaves in livery were still greeting latecomers arriving by water. Among those still expected—and very late indeed—was the priest who was to perform the wedding.

Father LeClerc was a Jesuit, bound from New Orleans to a mission near Quebec, but seduced from the strict path of duty by a substantial donation made by Jocasta to the Society of Jesus. Money might not buy happiness, I reflected, but it was a useful commodity, nonetheless.

I glanced in the other direction and stopped dead. At one

side, Ronnie Campbell caught my eye and bowed; I lifted my fan in acknowledgment, but was too distracted to speak to him. I hadn't found Jamie, but I had just spotted the likely reason for his abrupt disappearance. Ronnie's father, Farquard Campbell, was coming up the lawn from the landing, accompanied by a gentleman in the red and fawn of His Majesty's army, and another in naval uniform—Lieutenant Wolff.

The sight gave me an unpleasant shock. Lieutenant Wolff was not my favorite person. He wasn't all that popular with anyone else who knew him, either.

I supposed it was reasonable for him to have been invited, as His Majesty's navy was the principal buyer of River Run's production of timber, tar, and turpentine, and Lieutenant Wolff was the navy's representative in such matters. And it was possible that Jocasta had invited him for more personal reasons as well—the Lieutenant had at one point asked her to marry him. Not, as she had dryly noted, from any desire for her person, but rather to get his hands on River Run.

Yes, I could see her enjoying the Lieutenant's presence here today. Duncan, less naturally given to ulterior motives and manipulations, might not.

Farquard Campbell had spotted me, and was making for me through the crowd, the armed forces in tow. I got my fan up and made the necessary facial adjustments for polite conversation, but—much to my relief—the Lieutenant spotted a servant carrying a tray of glasses across the terrace and sheared off in pursuit, abandoning his escort in favor of refreshment.

The other military gentleman glanced after him, but dutifully followed Farquard. I squinted at him, but he was no one I'd met before, I was sure. Since the removal of the last Highland regiment in the autumn, the sight of a red coat was unusual anywhere in the colony. Who could this be?

My features fixed in what I hoped was a pleasant smile, I sank into a formal curtsy, spreading my embroidered skirts to best advantage.

"Mr. Campbell." I glanced covertly behind him, but Lieutenant Wolff had fortunately vanished in the pursuit of alcoholic sustenance.

"Mrs. Fraser. Your servant, ma'am." Farquard made me a graceful leg in reply. An elderly, desiccated-looking man, Mr. Campbell was sedate as usual in black broadcloth, a small burst of ruffles at the throat being his only concession to the festivities.

He looked over my shoulder, frowning slightly in puzzlement. "I had seen—I *thought* I had seen your husband with you?"

"Oh. Well, I think he's . . . er . . . gone . . ." I twiddled my fan delicately toward the trees where the necessary facilities lurked, separated from the main house by an aesthetic distance and a screen of small white pines.

"Ah, I see. Just so." Campbell cleared his throat, and gestured to the man who accompanied him. "Mrs. Fraser, may I present Major Donald MacDonald?"

Major MacDonald was a rather hawk-nosed but handsome gentleman in his late thirties, with the weathered face and erect bearing of a career soldier, and a pleasant smile belied by a pair of sharp blue eyes, the same pale, vivid shade as Brianna's dress.

"Your servant, ma'am." He bowed, very gracefully. "May I say, ma'am, how particularly that color becomes you?"

"You may," I said, relaxing a little. "Thank you."

"The Major is but recently arrived in Cross Creek. I assured him he would find no greater opportunity to pursue acquaintance with his countrymen and familiarize himself with his surroundings." Farquard swept a hand around the terrace, encompassing the party—which did indeed comprise a Who's Who of Scottish society along the Cape Fear.

"Indeed," the Major said politely. "I have not heard so many Scottish names since last I was in Edinburgh. Mr. Campbell gives me to understand that your husband is the nephew of Mrs. Cameron—or Mrs. Innes, perhaps I should say?"

"Yes. Have you met Mrs. . . . er . . . Innes yet?" I glanced toward the far end of the terrace. Still no sign of Duncan, let alone Roger or Jamie. Blast it, where *was* everybody? Holding summit conferences in the necessary house?

"No, but I shall look forward to presenting my compliments. The late Mr. Cameron was by way of being an acquaintance of my father, Robert MacDonald of Stornoway." He inclined his wigged head a respectful inch in the direction of the small white marble building at the side of the lawn—the mausoleum that presently sheltered the fleshly remnants of Hector Cameron. "Has your husband any connection with the Frasers of Lovat, by chance?"

With an internal groan, I recognized a Scottish spiderweb in the making. The meeting of any two Scots invariably began with the casting out of skeins of inquiry until enough strands of relation and acquaintanceship had stuck to form a useful network. I tended to become entangled in the sticky strands of sept and clan, myself, ending up like a fat, juicy fly, thoroughly trapped and at the mercy of my questioner.

Jamie had survived the intrigues of French and Scottish politics for years by means of such knowledge, though—skating precariously along the secret strands of such webs, keeping away from the sticky snares of loyalty and betrayal that had doomed so many others. I settled myself to pay attention, struggling to place this MacDonald among the thousand others of his ilk.

MacDonald of Keppoch, MacDonald of the Isles, MacDonald of Clanranald, MacDonald of Sleat. How many kinds of MacDonald were there, anyway? I wondered, a little crossly. Surely one or two should be sufficient to most purposes.

MacDonald of the Isles, evidently; the Major's family hailed from the Isle of Harris. I kept one eye out during the interrogation, but Jamie had safely gone to earth.

Farquard Campbell—no mean player himself—seemed to be enjoying the verbal game of battledore and shuttlecock, his dark eyes flicking back and forth between me and the Major with a look of amusement. The amusement faded into a look of surprise as I finished a rather confused analysis of Jamie's paternal lineage, in response to the Major's expert catechism.

"Your husband's grandfather was Simon, Lord Lovat?" Campbell said. "The Old Fox?" His voice rose slightly with incredulity.

"Well . . . yes," I said, a little uneasily. "I thought you knew that."

"Indeed," said Farquard. He looked as though he had swallowed a brandied plum, noticing too late that the stone was still in it. He'd known Jamie was a pardoned Jacobite, all right, but plainly Jocasta hadn't mentioned his close connection with the Old Fox—executed as a traitor for his role in the Stuart Rising. Most of the Campbells had fought on the Government side of that particular brouhaha.

"Yes," MacDonald said, ignoring Campbell's reaction. He frowned slightly in concentration. "I have the honor to be slightly acquainted with the present Lord Lovat—the title has been restored, I collect?"

He went on, turning to Campbell in explanation. "That would be Young Simon, who raised a regiment to fight the French in . . . '58? No, '57. Yes, '57. A gallant soldier, excellent fighting man. And he would be your husband's . . . nephew? No, uncle."

"Half-uncle," I clarified. Old Simon had been married three times, and made no secret of his extramarital by-blows—of which Jamie's father had been one. No need to point that out, though.

MacDonald nodded, lean face clearing in satisfaction at having got it all neatly sorted. Farquard's face relaxed a little, hearing that the family reputation had gone so far toward rehabilitation.

"Papist, of course," MacDonald added, "but an excellent soldier, nonetheless."

"Speaking of soldiers," Campbell interrupted, "do you know . . ."

I breathed a sigh of relief that made my corset strings creak, as Mr. Campbell smoothly led the Major into an analysis of some past military event. The Major, it seemed, was not on active duty, but like many, presently retired on half-pay. Unless and until the Crown found some further use for his services, he was thus left to mooch round the Colonies in search of occupation. Peace was hard on professional soldiers.

Just wait, I thought, with a small premonitory shiver. Four years, or less, and the Major would be busy enough.

I caught a flash of tartan from the corner of my eye and turned to look, but it was neither Jamie nor Duncan. One less mystery, though; it was Roger, dark-haired and handsome in his kilt. His face lit as he spotted Brianna, and his stride lengthened. She turned her head, as though feeling his presence, and her own face brightened in answer.

He reached her side, and without the least acknowledgment of the gentleman with her, embraced her and kissed her soundly on the mouth. As they drew apart, he held out his arms for Jemmy, and dropped another kiss on the silky red head.

I returned to the conversation at hand, belatedly realizing that Farquard Campbell had been talking for some time without my having any notion what he had said. Seeing my bemusement, he smiled, a little wryly.

"I must go and pay my respects elsewhere, Mrs. Fraser," he said. "If you will pardon me? I shall leave you to the Major's excellent company." He touched his hat courteously, and eeled off toward the house, perhaps intending to track down Lieutenant Wolff and stop him pocketing the silver.

Thus marooned with me, the Major cast about for suitable conversation, and fell back upon the most commonly asked question between new acquaintances.

"Are you and your husband long arrived in the colony, ma'am?"

"Not long," I said, rather wary. "Three years or so. We live in a small settlement in the backcountry—" I waved my closed fan toward the invisible mountains to the west. "A place called Fraser's Ridge."

"Ah, yes. I have heard of it." A muscle twitched near the corner of his mouth, and I wondered uneasily just what he had heard. Jamie's still was an open secret in the backcountry, and among the Scottish settlers of the Cape Fear—in fact, several kegs of raw whisky from the still were sitting in plain sight by the stables, Jamie's wedding present to his aunt and Duncan—but I hoped the secret wasn't quite so open that an army officer newly arrived in the colony would already have heard about it.

"Tell me, Mrs. Fraser . . ." He hesitated, then plunged ahead. "Do you encounter a great deal of . . . factionalism in your area of the colony?"

"Factionalism? Oh, er . . . no, not a great deal." I cast a wary eye toward Hector Cameron's mausoleum, where Hermon Husband's dark Quaker gray showed up like a blot against the pure white marble. Factionalism was a code word for the activities of men like Husband and James Hunter—Regulators.

The Governor's militia action in December had quashed the violent demonstrations, but the Regulation was still a simmering pot under a very tight lid. Husband had been arrested and imprisoned for a short time in February on the strength of his pamphlets, but the experience had in no way softened either his disposition or his language. A boilover could happen at any time.

"I am pleased to hear it, ma'am," Major MacDonald said. "Do you hear much news, remotely situated as you are?"

"Not a great deal. Er . . . nice day, isn't it? We've been so fortunate in the weather this year. Was it an easy journey from Charleston? So early in the year—the mud . . ."

"Indeed, ma'am. We had some small difficulties, but no more than . . ."

The Major was assessing me quite openly as he chatted, taking in the cut and quality of my gown, the pearls at my throat and ears—borrowed from Jocasta—and the rings on my fingers. I was familiar with such a look; there was no hint of lechery or flirtation in it. He was simply judging my social standing and my husband's level of prosperity and influence.

I took no offense. I was busy doing the same thing to him, after all. Well-educated and of good family; that much was plain from his rank alone, though the heavy gold signet on his right hand clinched the matter. Not personally well-off, though; his uniform was worn at the seams, and his boots were deeply scarred, though well-polished.

A light Scots accent with a hint of French gutturality—experience in Continental campaigns. And very newly arrived in the colony, I thought; his face was drawn from recent illness, and the whites of his eyes bore the slight tinge of jaundice common to new arrivals, who tended to contract everything from malaria to dengue fever, when exposed to the seething germ pools of the coastal towns.

"Tell me, Mrs. Fraser—" the Major began.

"You insult not only me, sir, but every man of honor here present!"

Ninian Bell Hamilton's rather high-pitched voice rang out through a lull in the general conversation, and heads turned all over the lawn.

He was face-to-face with Robert Barlow, a man I had been introduced to earlier in the morning. A merchant of some kind, I vaguely recalled—from Edenton? Or possibly New Bern. A heavyset man with the look of one unused to contradiction, he was sneering openly at Hamilton.

"Regulators, you call them? Gaolbirds and rioters! You suggest that such men possess a sense of honor, do you?"

"I do not suggest it—I state it as fact, and will defend it as such!" The old gentleman drew himself upright, hand groping for a sword-hilt. Fortunately for the occasion, he wasn't wearing a sword; none of the gentlemen present were, given the congeniality of the gathering.

Whether this fact affected Barlow's behavior, I couldn't have said, but he laughed contemptuously, and turned his back on Hamilton, to walk away. The elderly Scot, inflamed, promptly kicked Barlow in the buttocks.

Taken unaware and off balance, Barlow pitched forward, landing on hands and knees, his coattails ludicrously up over his ears. Whatever their respective political opinions, all the onlookers burst into laughter. Thus encouraged, Ninian puffed up like a bantam rooster and strutted round his fallen opponent to address him from the front.

I could have told him that this was a tactical error, but then, I had the benefit of seeing Barlow's face, which was crimson with mortified rage. Eyes bulging, he scrambled awkwardly to his feet and launched himself with a roar, knocking the smaller man flat.

The two of them rolled in the grass, fists and coattails flying, to whoops of encouragement from the spectators. Wedding guests came rushing from lawn and terrace to see what was going on. Abel MacLennan pushed his way through the mob, obviously intent on offering support to his patron. Richard Caswell seized his arm to prevent him, and he swung round, pushing Caswell off balance.

James Hunter, lean face alight with glee, tripped Caswell, who sat down hard on the grass, looking surprised. Caswell's son George let out a howl of outrage and punched Hunter in the kidney. Hunter whirled round and slapped George on the nose.

A number of ladies were shrieking—not all with shock. One or two appeared to be cheering on Ninian Hamilton, who had got temporarily atop his victim's chest and was endeavoring to throttle him, though with little success, owing to Barlow's thick neck and heavy stock.

I looked frantically round for Jamie—or Roger, or Duncan. Goddamn it, where were they all?

George Caswell had fallen back in surprise, hands to his nose, which was dribbling blood down his shirtfront. DeWayne Buchanan, one of Hamilton's sons-in-law, was shoving his way purposefully through the gathering crowd. I didn't know whether he meant to get his father-in-law off Barlow, or assist him in his attempt to murder the man.

"Oh, bloody hell," I muttered to myself. "Here, hold this." I thrust my fan at Major MacDonald, and hitched up my skirts, preparing to wade into the melee, and deciding whom to kick first—and where—for best effect.

"Do you want me to stop it?"

The Major, who had been enjoying the spectacle, looked disappointed at the thought, but resigned to duty. At my rather startled nod, he reached for his pistol, pointed it skyward, and discharged it into the air.

The bang was loud enough to temporarily silence everyone. The combatants froze, and in the momentary lull, Hermon Husband shoved his way into the scene.

"Friend Ninian," he said, nodding cordially round. "Friend Buchanan. Allow me." He grabbed the elderly Scot by both arms and lifted him bodily off Barlow. He gave James Hunter a warning look; Hunter gave an audible "Humph!" but retired a few steps.

The younger Mrs. Caswell, a woman of sense, had got her husband off the field of battle already, and was applying a handkerchief to his nose. DeWayne Buchanan and Abel MacLennan had each got hold of one of Ninian Hamilton's arms, and were making a great show of restraining him as they marched him off toward the house—though it was reasonably apparent that either one of them could simply have picked him up and carried him.

Richard Caswell had got up by himself, and while looking rather affronted, was evidently not disposed to hit anyone. He stood brushing dried grass from the back of his coat, lips pressed together in disapproval.

"Your fan, Mrs. Fraser?" Jerked from my appraisal of the conflict, I found Major MacDonald politely offering me back my fan. He looked quite pleased with himself.

"Thank you," I said, taking it and eyeing him with some respect. "Tell me, Major, do you always go about with a loaded pistol?"

"An oversight, ma'am," he replied blandly. "Though perhaps a fortunate one, aye? I had been in the town of Cross Creek yesterday, and as I was returning alone to Mr. Farquard Campbell's plantation after dark, I thought it would be as well to go canny on the road."

He nodded over my shoulder.

"Tell me, Mrs. Fraser, who is the ill-shaven individual? He seems a man of guts, despite his lack of address. Will he take up the cudgels in his own behalf now, do ye think?"

I swung round, to see Hermon Husband nose-to-nose with the risen Barlow, his round black hat thrust down on his head and his beard bristling with pugnacity. Barlow stood his ground, red-faced and thunder-browed, but had his arms folded tightly across his chest as he listened to Husband.

"Hermon Husband is a Quaker," I said, with a slight tone of reproof. "No, he won't resort to violence. Just words."

Quite a lot of words. Barlow kept trying to interject his own opinions, but Husband ignored these, pressing his argument with such enthusiasm that drops of spittle flew from the corners of his mouth.

". . . an heinous miscarriage of justice! Sheriffs, or so they call themselves, who have not been appointed by any legal writ, but rather appoint themselves for the purposes of corruptly enriching themselves and scorn all legitimate . . ."

Barlow dropped his arms, and began to edge backward, in an effort to escape the barrage. When Husband paused momentarily to draw breath, though, Barlow seized the opportunity to lean forward and jab a threatening finger into Husband's chest.

"You speak of justice, sir? What have riot and destruction to do with justice? If you advocate the ruin of property as means to redress your grievances—"

"I do not! But is the poor man to fall a spoil to the unscrupulous, and his plight pass unregarded? I say to you, sir, God will unmercifully requite those who oppress the poor, and—"

"What are they arguing about?" MacDonald asked, viewing the exchange with interest. "Religion?"

Seeing Husband involved, and realizing that no further punch-ups were to be expected, most of the crowd had lost interest, wandering away toward the buffet tables and the braziers on the terrace. Hunter and a few other Regulators hung about to give Husband moral support, but most of the guests were planters and merchants. While they might side with Barlow in theory, in practice most were disinclined to waste a rare festive occasion in controversy with Hermon Husband over the rights of the tax-paying poor.

I wasn't all that eager to examine the rhetoric of the Regulation in detail, either, but did my best to give Major MacDonald a crude overview of the situation.

". . . and so Governor Tryon felt obliged to raise the militia to deal with it, but the Regulators backed down," I concluded. "But they haven't abandoned their demands, by any means."

Husband hadn't abandoned his argument, either—he never did—but Barlow had at last succeeded in extricating himself, and was restoring his tissues at the refreshment tables under the elm trees in company with some sympathetic friends, who all cast periodic glances of disapproval in Husband's direction.

"I see," MacDonald said, interested. "Farquard Campbell did tell me something of this disruptive movement. And the Governor has raised a militia on occasion to deal with it, you say, and may again. Who commands his troops, do you know?"

"Um . . . I believe General Waddell—that's Hugh Waddell—has command of several companies. But the

Governor himself was in command of the main body; he's been a soldier himself."

"Has he indeed?" MacDonald seemed to find this very interesting; he hadn't put away his pistol, but was fondling it in an absentminded sort of way. "Campbell tells me that your husband is the holder of a large grant of land in the backcountry. He is by way of being an intimate of the Governor?"

"I wouldn't put it that strongly," I said dryly. "But he does *know* the Governor, yes."

I felt a trifle uneasy at this line of conversation. It was—strictly speaking—illegal for Catholics to hold Royal land grants in the Colonies. I didn't know whether Major MacDonald was aware of that fact, but he did plainly realize that Jamie was likely a Catholic, given his family background.

"Do you suppose your husband might be prevailed upon for an introduction, dear lady?" The pale blue eyes were bright with speculation, and I realized suddenly what he was after.

A career soldier with no war was at a distinct disadvantage in terms of occupation and income. The Regulation might be a tempest in a teapot, but on the other hand, if there was any prospect of military action . . . After all, Tryon had no regular troops; he might well be inclined to welcome—and to pay—an experienced officer, if the militia were called out again.

I cast a wary eye toward the lawn. Husband and his friends had withdrawn a bit, and were in close conversation in a little knot near one of Jocasta's new statues. If the recent near-brawl was any indication, the Regulation was still dangerously on the boil.

"That might be done," I said cautiously. I couldn't see any reason why Jamie would object to providing a letter of introduction to Tryon—and I did owe the Major something, after all, for having averted a full-scale riot. "You'd have to ask my husband, of course, but I'd be happy to put in a word for you."

"You shall have my utmost gratitude, ma'am." He put away his pistol, and bowed low over my hand. Straightening up, he glanced over my shoulder. "I think I must take my leave now, Mrs. Fraser, but I shall hope to make your husband's acquaintance soon."

The Major marched off toward the terrace, and I turned, to see Hermon Husband stumping toward me, Hunter and a few other men in his wake.

"Mrs. Fraser, I must ask thee to give my good wishes and my regrets to Mrs. Innes, if thee will," he said without preamble. "I must go."

"Oh, must you leave so soon?" I hesitated. On the one hand, I wanted to urge him to stay; on the other, I could foresee further trouble if he did. Barlow's friends had not taken their eyes off him since the near-brawl.

He saw the thought cross my face, and nodded soberly. The flush of debate had faded from his face, leaving it set in grim lines.

"It will be better so. Jocasta Cameron has been a good friend to me and mine; it would ill repay her kindness for me to bring discord to her wedding celebrations. I would not choose that—and yet, I cannot in conscience remain silent, hearing such pernicious opinions as I have received here." He gave Barlow's group a look of cold contempt, which was met in kind.

"Besides," he added, turning his back on the Barlowites in dismissal, "we have business that compels our attention elsewhere." He hesitated, clearly wondering whether to tell me more, but then decided against it. "Thee will tell her?"

"Yes, of course. Mr. Husband—I'm sorry."

He gave me a faint smile, tinged with melancholy, and shook his head, but said no more. As he left, though, trailed by his companions, James Hunter paused to speak to me, low-voiced.

"The Regulators are a-gathering. There's a big camp, up near Salisbury," he said. "You might see fit to tell your husband that."

He nodded, put his hand to his hat-brim, and without waiting for acknowledgment, strode off, his dark coat disappearing in the crowd like a sparrow swallowed by a flock of peacocks.

FROM MY VANTAGE POINT at the edge of the terrace, I could see the whole sweep of the party, which flowed in a stream of festivity from house to river, its eddy-pools obvious to the knowledgeable eye.

Jocasta formed the eye of the largest social swirl—but smaller pools swirled ominously around Ninian Bell Hamilton and Richard Caswell, and a restless current meandered through the party, leaving deposits of conversation along its edges, rich in the fertile silt of speculation. From the things I overheard, the question of our hosts' putative sex life was the predominant subject of conversation—but politics ran a close second.

I still saw no sign either of Jamie or of Duncan. There was the Major again, though. He stopped, a glass of cider in each hand; he had caught sight of Brianna. I smiled, watching.

Brianna often stopped men in their tracks, though not always entirely from admiration. She had inherited a number of things from Jamie; slanted blue eyes and flaming hair, a long straight nose and a wide, firm mouth; the bold facial bones that came from some ancient Norseman. In addition to these striking attributes, though, she had also inherited his height. In a time when the average woman stood a hair less than five feet tall, Brianna reached six. People were inclined to stare.

Major MacDonald was doing so, cider forgotten in his hands. Roger noticed; he smiled and nodded, but took that one step closer to Brianna that said unmistakably, *She's mine, mate.*

Watching the Major in conversation, I noticed how pale and spindly he looked by comparison with Roger, who stood nearly as tall as Jamie. He was broad-shouldered and olive-skinned, and his hair shone black as a crow's wing in the spring sun, perhaps the legacy of some ancient Spanish invader. I had to admit that there was no noticeable resemblance between him and little Jem, ruddy as a fresh-forged brass candlestick. I could see the flash of white as Roger smiled; the Major kept his lips pulled down when smiling, as most people over the age of thirty did, to hide the gaps and decay that were endemic. Perhaps it was the stress of the Major's occupation, I thought; perhaps merely the effects of poor nourishment. Being of good family didn't mean a child in this time ate very well.

I ran my tongue lightly over my own teeth, testing the biting edge of my incisors. Straight and sound, and I took considerable pains to see they would stay that way, given the current state of the art of dentistry.

"Why, Mrs. Fraser." A light voice broke in on my thoughts, and I looked round to find Phillip Wylie at my elbow. "Whatever can you be thinking, my dear? You look positively . . . feral." He took my hand and lowered his voice, baring his own fairly decent teeth in a suggestive smile.

"I am not your dear," I said with some acerbity, jerking my hand out of his. "And as for feral, I'm surprised no one has bitten you in the backside yet."

"Oh, I have hopes," he assured me, eyes twinkling. He bowed, managing in the process to get hold of my hand again. "Might I have the honor to claim a dance later, Mrs. Fraser?"

"Indeed you may not," I said, tugging. "Let go."

"Your wish is my command." He let go, but not before planting a light kiss on the back of my hand. I suppressed the urge to wipe the moist spot on my skirt.

"Go away, child," I said. I flicked my fan at him. "Shoo."

Phillip Wylie was a dandy. I had met him twice before, and on both occasions, he had been got up regardless: satin breeches, silk stockings, and all the trappings that went with them, including powdered wig, powdered face, and a small black crescent beauty mark, stuck dashingly beside one eye.

Now, however, the rot had spread. The powdered wig was mauve, the satin waistcoat was embroidered with—I blinked. Yes, with lions and unicorns, done in gold and silver thread. The satin breeches were fitted to him like a bifurcated glove, and the crescent had given way to a star at the corner of his mouth. Mr. Wylie had become a macaroni—with cheese.

"Oh, I have no intention of deserting you, Mrs. Fraser," he assured me. "I have been searching everywhere for you."

"Oh. Well, you've found me," I said, eyeing his coat, which was velvet, rose in color, and had six-inch cuffs of palest pink silk and button-covers embroidered with scarlet peonies. "Though it's no wonder you had trouble. I expect you were blinded by the glare from your waistcoat."

Lloyd Stanhope was with him, as usual, quite as prosperous, but much more plainly dressed than his friend. Stanhope guffawed, but Wylie ignored him, and bowed low, making me a graceful leg.

"Ah, well, Fortuna has smiled upon me this year. The trade with England has quite recovered, may the gods be thanked—and I have had my share of it, and more besides. You must come with me to see—"

I was saved at this point by the sudden appearance of Adlai Osborn, a well-to-do merchant from somewhere up the coast, who tapped Wylie on the shoulder. Seizing the opportunity afforded by the distraction, I put up my fan and sidled away through a gap in the crowd.

Left momentarily to my own devices, I strolled nonchalantly off the terrace and down the lawn. I still had an eye out for Jamie or Duncan, but this was my first opportunity to examine Jocasta's latest acquisitions, which were causing considerable comment among the wedding guests. These were two statues, carved from white marble, one standing squarely in the center of each lawn.

The one closest to me was a life-size replica of a Greek warrior—Spartan, I assumed, from the fact that the more frivolous items of attire had been omitted, leaving the gentleman clad in a sturdy-looking plumed helmet, with a sword in one hand. A large shield was planted at his feet, strategically placed so as to cover the more glaring deficiencies of his wardrobe.

There was a matching statue on the right lawn, this one of Diana the Huntress. While the lady was rather skimpily draped, and her shapely white marble breasts and buttocks were attracting a certain amount of sidelong appreciation from the gentlemen present, she was no match for her companion, in terms of public fascination. I smiled behind my fan, seeing Mr. and Mrs. Sherston swan past the statue without so much as a glance. After all, their raised noses and bored looks at each other said, such artworks were commonplace in Europe. Only rude Colonials, lacking both experience and breeding, would consider it a *spectacle*, my dear.

Examining the statue myself, I discovered that it was not an anonymous Greek after all, but rather Perseus. From this new angle, I could see that what I had assumed to be a rock resting beside the shield was in fact the severed head of a Gorgon, half its snakes standing on end in shocked dismay.

The evident artistry of these reptiles was affording an excuse for close examination of the statue by a number of ladies, who were brazening it out, pursing their lips knowingly and making sounds of admiration about the sculptor's skillfulness in rendering every scale, just so. Every so often one would allow her eyes to dart upward for a split second, before jerking her gaze back to the Gorgon, cheeks reddened—by the morning air and the mulled wine being served, no doubt.

My attention was distracted from Perseus by a steaming mug of this beverage, thrust beneath my nose in invitation.

"Do have some, Mrs. Fraser." It was Lloyd Stanhope, roundly amiable. "You wouldn't want to take a chill, dear lady."

There was no danger of that, given the increasing warmth of the day, but I accepted the cup, enjoying the scent of cinnamon and honey that wafted from it.

I leaned to one side, looking for Jamie, but he was still nowhere to be seen. A group of gentlemen arguing the merits of Virginia tobacco versus indigo as a crop were clustered round one side of Perseus, while the statue's rear aspect now sheltered three young girls, who were glancing at it from behind their fans, red-faced and giggling.

". . . unique," Phillip Wylie was saying to someone. The eddies of conversation had brought him back to my side. "Absolutely unique! Black pearls, they're called. Never seen anything like them, I'll wager." He glanced round and, seeing me, reached out to touch my elbow lightly. "I collect you have spent some time in France, Mrs. Fraser. Have you seen them there, perhaps?"

"Black pearls?" I said, scrambling to catch hold of the threads of the conversation. "Well, yes, a few. I recall the

Archbishop of Rouen had a small Moorish page boy who wore a very large one in his nose."

Stanhope's jaw sagged ludicrously. Wylie stared at me for a split second, then uttered a whoop of laughter so loud that both the tobacco lobby and the giggling girls stopped dead and stared at us.

"You will be the death of me, my dear lady," Wylie wheezed, as Stanhope declined into choked snorts of mirth. Wylie drew out a lacy kerchief and dabbed delicately at the corners of his eyes, lest tears of merriment blotch his powder.

"Really, Mrs. Fraser, have you not seen my treasures?" He grasped my elbow and propelled me out of the crowd with surprising skill. "Come, let me show you."

He guided me smoothly through the gathering throng and past the side of the house, where a flagged path led toward the stables. Another crowd—mostly men—was clustered round the paddock, where Jocasta's groom was throwing down hay for several horses.

There were five of them—two mares, a couple of two-year-olds, and a stallion. All five black as coal, with coats that gleamed in the pale spring sun, even shaggy as they were with winter hair. I was no expert in horse conformation, but knew enough by now to notice the deep chests, barreled vaults, and sculpted quarters, which gave them a peculiar but deeply appealing look of elegant sturdiness. Beyond the beauties of conformation and coat, though, what was most striking about these horses was their hair.

These black horses had great floating masses of silky hair—almost like women's hair—that rose and fluttered with their movements, matching the graceful fall of their long, full tails. In addition, each horse had delicate black feathers decorating hoof and fetlock, that lifted like floating milkweed seed with each step. By contrast to the usual rawboned riding horses and rough draft animals used for haulage, these horses seemed almost magical—and from the awed comment they were occasioning among the spectators, might as well have come from Fairyland as from Phillip Wylie's plantation in Edenton.

"They're yours?" I spoke to Wylie without looking at him,

unwilling to take my eyes away from the enchanting sight. "Wherever did you get them?"

"Yes," he said, his usual affectations erased by simple pride. "They are mine. They are Friesians. The oldest breed of warm-bloods—their lineage can be traced back for centuries.

"As to where I got them"—he leaned over the fence, extending a hand palm-up and wiggling his fingers toward the horses in invitation—"I have been breeding them for several years. I brought these at Mrs. Cameron's invitation; she has it in mind perhaps to purchase one of my mares, and suggested that one or two of her neighbors might also be interested. As for Lucas, here, though"—the stallion had come over, recognizing his owner, and was submitting gracefully to having his forehead rubbed—"he is not for sale."

Both mares were heavily in foal; Lucas was the sire, and so had been brought, Wylie said, as proof of the bloodlines. That, I thought, privately amused, and for purposes of showing him off. Wylie's "black pearls" were exciting keen interest, and a number of the horse-breeding gentlemen from the neighborhood had gone visibly green with envy at sight of Lucas. Phillip Wylie preened like a cock grouse.

"Oh, there ye are, Sassenach." Jamie's voice came suddenly in my ear. "I was looking for you."

"Were you, indeed?" I said, turning away from the paddock. I felt a sudden warmth under my breastbone at sight of him "And where have *you* been?"

"Oh, here and there," Jamie said, undisturbed by my tone of accusation. "A verra fine horse indeed, Mr. Wylie." A polite nod, and he had me by the arm and headed back toward the lawn before Wylie's murmured "Your servant, sir" had been quite voiced.

"What are ye doing out here wi' wee Phillip Wylie?" Jamie asked, picking his way through a flock of house slaves, who streamed past from the cookhouse with platters of food steaming alluringly under white napkins.

"Looking at his horses," I said, putting a hand over my stomach in hopes of suppressing the resounding borborygmi occasioned by the sight of food. "And what have you been doing?"

"Looking for Duncan," he said, guiding me round a puddle. "He wasna in the necessary, nor yet the smithy, the stables, the kitchen, the cookhouse. I took a horse and rode out to the tobacco-barns, but not a smell of the man."

"Perhaps Lieutenant Wolff has assassinated him," I suggested. "Disappointed rival, and all that."

"Wolff?" He stopped, frowning at me in consternation. "Is yon gobshite here?"

"In the flesh," I replied, waving my fan toward the lawn. Wolff had taken up a station next to the refreshment tables, his short, stout figure unmistakable in its blue and white naval uniform. "Do you suppose your aunt invited him?"

"Aye, I do," he said, sounding grim but resigned. "She couldna resist rubbing his nose in it, I expect."

"That's what I thought. He's only been here for half an hour or so, though—and if he goes on mopping it up at that rate," I added, looking disapprovingly at the bottle clutched in the Lieutenant's hand, "he'll be out cold before the wedding takes place."

Jamie dismissed the Lieutenant with a contemptuous gesture.

"Well, then, let him pickle himself and welcome, so long as he only opens his mouth to pour drink in. Where's Duncan hidden himself, though?"

"Perhaps he's thrown himself in the river?" It was meant as a joke, but I glanced toward the river nonetheless, and saw a boat headed for the landing, the oarsman standing in the prow to throw his mooring rope to a waiting slave. "Look—is that the priest at last?"

It was; a short, tubby figure, black soutane hiked up over hairy knees as he scrambled ignominiously onto the dock, with the help of a push from the boatmen below. Ulysses was already hurrying down to the landing, to greet him.

"Good," Jamie said, in tones of satisfaction. "We've a priest, then, and a bride. Two of three—that's progress. Here, Sassenach, wait a bit—your hair's coming down." He traced the line of a fallen curl slowly down my back, and I obligingly let the shawl fall back from my shoulders.

Jamie put up the curl again, with a skill born of long practice, then kissed me gently on the nape of the neck, making me shiver. He wasn't immune to the prevailing airs of spring, either.

"I suppose I must go on looking for Duncan," he said, with a tinge of regret. His fingers lingered on my back, thumb delicately tracing the groove of my spine. "Once I've found him, though . . . there must be some place here with a bit of privacy to it."

The word "privacy" made me lean back against Jamie, and glance toward the riverbank, where a clump of weeping willows sheltered a stone bench—quite a private and romantic spot, especially at night. The willows were thick with green, but I caught a flash of scarlet through the drooping branches.

"Got him!" I exclaimed, straightening up so abruptly that I trod on Jamie's toe. "Oh—sorry!"

"Nay matter," he assured me. He had followed the direction of my glance, and now drew himself up purposefully. "I'll go and fetch him out. Do ye go up to the house, Sassenach, and keep an eye on my aunt and the priest. Dinna let them escape until this marriage is made."

JAMIE MADE HIS WAY down the lawn toward the willows, absently acknowledging the greetings of friends and acquaintances as he went. In truth, his mind was less on Duncan's approaching nuptials than on thoughts of his own wife.

He was generally aware that he had been blessed in her beauty; even in her usual homespun, knee-deep in mud from her garden, or stained and fierce with the blood of her calling, the curve of her bones spoke to his own marrow, and those whisky eyes could make him drunk with a glance. Besides, the mad collieshangie of her hair made him laugh.

Smiling to himself even at the thought, it occurred to him that he *was* slightly drunk. Liquor flowed like water at the party, and there were already men leaning on old Hector's mausoleum, glaze-eyed and slack-jawed; he caught a glimpse of someone behind the thing, too, having a piss in the shrubbery. He shook his head. There'd be a body under every bush by nightfall.

Christ. One thought of bodies under bushes, and his mind had presented him with a blindingly indecent vision of Claire, lying sprawled and laughing under one, breasts falling out of her gown and the dead leaves and dry grass the same colors as her rumpled skirts and the curly brown hair between her— He choked the thought off abruptly, bowing cordially to old Mrs. Alderdyce, the Judge's mother.

"Your servant, ma'am."

"Good day to ye, young man, good day." The old lady nodded magisterially and passed by, leaning on the arm of her companion, a long-suffering young woman who gave Jamie a faint smile in response to his salute.

"Master Jamie?" One of the maids hovered beside him, holding out a tray of cups. He took one, smiling his thanks, and drank half its contents in a gulp.

He couldn't help it. He had to turn and look after Claire. He caught no more than a glimpse of the top of her head among the crowd on the terrace—she wouldn't wear a proper cap, of course, the stubborn wee besom, but had some foolishness pinned on instead, a scrap of lace caught up with a cluster of ribbons and rose hips. That made him want to laugh, too, and he turned back toward the willows, smiling to himself.

It was seeing her in the new gown that did it. It had been months since he'd seen her dressed like a lady, narrow-waisted in silk, and her white breasts round and sweet as winter pears in the low neck of her gown. It was as though she were suddenly a different woman; one intimately familiar and yet still excitingly strange.

His fingers twitched, remembering that one rebel lock, spiraling free down her neck, and the feel of her slender nape—and the feel of her plump warm arse through her skirts, pressed against his leg. He had not had her in more than a week, what with the press of people round them, and was feeling the lack acutely.

Ever since she had shown him the sperms, he had been uncomfortably aware of the crowded conditions that must now and then obtain in his balls, an impression made forcibly stronger in situations such as this. He kent well enough that there was no danger of rupture or explosion—and yet he couldn't help but think of all the shoving going on.

Being trapped in a seething mass of others, with no hope of escape, was one of his own personal visions of Hell, and he paused for a moment outside the screen of willow trees, to administer a brief squeeze of reassurance, which he hoped might calm the riot for a bit.

He'd see Duncan safely married, he decided, and then the man must see to his own affairs. Come nightfall, and if he could do no better than a bush, then a bush it would have to be. He pushed aside a swath of willow branches, ducking to go through.

"Duncan," he began, and then stopped, the swirl of carnal thoughts disappearing like water down a sewer. The scarlet coat belonged not to Duncan Innes but to a stranger who turned toward him, with surprise equal to his own. A man in the uniform of His Majesty's army.

THE LOOK OF MOMENTARY startlement faded from the man's face, almost as quickly as Jamie's own surprise. This must be MacDonald, the half-pay soldier Farquard Campbell had mentioned to him. Evidently Farquard had described him to MacDonald, as well; he could see the man had put a name to him.

MacDonald held a cup of punch, as well; the slaves had been busy. He drained the cup deliberately, then set it down on the stone bench, wiping his lips on the back of his hand.

"Colonel Fraser, I presume?"

"Major MacDonald," he replied, with a nod that mingled courtesy with wariness. "Your servant, sir."

MacDonald bowed, punctilious.

"Colonel. If I might command a moment of your time?" He glanced over Jamie's shoulder; there were giggles on the riverbank behind them, and the excited small screams of very young women pursued by very young men. "In private?"

Jamie noted the usage of his militia title with a sour amusement, but nodded briefly, and discarded his own cup, still half-full, alongside the Major's.

He tilted his head toward the house in inquiry; MacDonald nodded and followed him out of the willows, as loud rustlings and squealings announced that the bench and its sheltering trees had now become the province of the younger element. He wished them good luck with it, privately noting the location for his own possible use, after dark.

The day was cold but still and bright, and a number of guests, mostly men who found the civilized atmosphere within too suffocating for their tastes, were clustered in argumentative groups in the corners of the terrace, or strolling round the paths of the newly-sprouting garden, where their tobacco pipes might fume in peace. Assessing the latter venue as the best means of avoiding interruption, Jamie led the Major toward the brick-lined path that curved toward the stables.

"Have you seen Wylie's Friesians?" the Major asked as they rounded the house, making casual conversation 'til they should be safely out of earshot.

"Aye, I have. The stallion's a fine animal, is he not?" By reflex, Jamie's eyes turned toward the paddock by the barn. The stallion was browsing, nibbling at the weeds by the trough, while the two mares head-and-tailed it companionably near the stable, broad backs shining in the pale sun.

"Aye? Well, perhaps." The Major squinted toward the paddock, one eye half-shut in dubious agreement. "Sound enough, I daresay. Good chest. All that hair, though—wouldn't do in a cavalry horse, though I suppose if it were proper shaved and dressed . . ."

Jamie suppressed the urge to ask whether MacDonald liked his women shaved as well. The image of the loosened curl spiraling down that bare white neck was still in his mind. Perhaps the stables might afford a better opportunity. . . . He pushed that thought aside, for later reference.

"You had some matter with which ye were concerned, Major?" he asked, more abruptly than he'd meant to.

"Not so much my own concern," MacDonald replied equably. "I had been told that you have some interest in the whereabouts of a gentleman named Stephen Bonnet. Am I reliably informed, sir?"

He felt the name like a blow to the chest; it took his wind for a moment. Without conscious thought, his left hand curled over the hilt of his dirk.

"I—yes. You know his whereabouts?"

"Unfortunately, no." MacDonald's brow lifted, seeing his response. "I ken where he *has* been, though. A wicked lad, our Stephen, or so I gather?" he inquired, with a hint of jocularity.

"Ye might say so. He has killed men, robbed me—and raped my daughter," Jamie said bluntly.

The Major drew breath, face darkening in sudden understanding.

"Ah, I see," he said softly. He lifted his hand briefly, as though to touch Jamie's arm, but let it fall to his side. He walked a few steps further, brows puckered in concentration.

"I see," he said again, all hint of amusement gone from his voice. "I hadn't realized . . . yes. I see." He lapsed into silence once again, his steps slowing as they neared the paddock.

"I trust you do intend to tell me what ye know of the man?" Jamie said politely. MacDonald glanced up at him, and appeared to recognize that regardless of his intentions, Jamie's own intent was to gain what knowledge he had, whether by conversation or more direct methods.

"I have not met the man myself," MacDonald said mildly. "What I know, I learnt in the course of a social evening in New Bern last month."

It was an evening of whist tables hosted by Davis Howell, a wealthy shipowner and a member of the Governor's Royal Council. The party, small but select, had begun with an excellent supper, then moved on to cards and conversation, well marinated with rum punch and brandy.

As the hour grew late and the smoke of cigarillos heavy in the air, the conversation grew unguarded, and there were jocular references to the recent improvement in one Mr. Butler's fortunes, with much half-veiled speculation as to the source of his new riches. One gentleman, expressing envy, was heard to say, “If one could but have a Stephen Bonnet in one’s pocket . . .” before being elbowed into silence by a friend whose discretion was not quite so much dissolved in rum.

“Was Mr. Butler among those present at this soiree?” Jamie asked sharply. The name was unfamiliar, but if Butler was known to members of the Royal Council . . . well, the circles of power in the colony were small; someone in them would be known to his aunt, or to Farquard Campbell.

“No, he wasn’t.” They had reached the paddock; MacDonald rested his folded arms atop the rail, eyes fixed on the stallion. “He resides, I believe, in Edenton.”

As did Phillip Wylie. The stallion—Lucas, that was his name—sidled toward them, soft black nostrils flaring in curiosity. Jamie stretched out his knuckles mechanically and, the horse proving amiable, rubbed the sleek jawline. Beautiful as the Friesian was, he scarcely noticed it, his thoughts spinning like a whirligig.

Edenton lay on the Albemarle Sound, easily accessible by boat. Likely, then, that Bonnet had returned to his sailor’s trade—and with it, piracy and smuggling.

“Ye called Bonnet ‘a wicked lad,’ ” he said, turning to MacDonald. “Why?”

“Much of a hand at whist, Colonel Fraser?” MacDonald glanced at him inquiringly. “I recommend it particularly. It shares some advantage with chess, in terms of discovering the mind of one’s opponent, and the greater advantage, in that it can be played against a greater number.” The hard-bitten lines of his face relaxed momentarily in a faint smile. “And the still greater advantage that it is possible to earn a living by it, which is seldom the case with chess.”

“I am familiar with the game, sir,” Jamie returned, with extreme dryness.

MacDonald was a half-pay officer, with neither official duties nor an active regiment. It was by no means unusual for such men to eke out their meager salary by the acquisition of small bits of intelligence, which might be sold or traded. No price was being asked—now—but that didn’t mean that the debt would not be called in later. Jamie gave a brief nod in acknowledgment of the situation, and MacDonald nodded in turn, satisfied. He would say what he wanted, in good time.

"Well, sir. I was, as ye might suppose, intrigued to learn who this Bonnet might be—and if he were indeed a golden egg, which goose's arse he'd dropped out of."

MacDonald's companions had regained their caution, though, and he could learn nothing further of the mysterious Bonnet—save the effect he had on those who had met him.

"You'll ken that often enough, ye learn as much from what men don't say, as what they do? Or from *how* they say it?" Without waiting for Jamie's nod, he went on.

"There were eight of us at play. Three were making free with their speculations, but I could see they kent nay more of Mr. Bonnet than I did myself. Two more seemed neither to know nor to care, but the last two—" He shook his head. "They became very quiet, sir. Like those who will not speak of the devil, for fear of summoning him."

MacDonald's eyes were bright with speculation.

"You are familiar with the fellow Bonnet yourself?"

"I am. The two gentlemen who knew him?"

"Walter Priestly and Hosea Wright," MacDonald responded promptly. "Both particular friends of the Governor."

"Merchants?"

"Among other things. Both have warehouses; Wright in Edenton and Plymouth, Priestly in Charleston, Savannah, Wilmington, and Edenton. Priestly has business concerns in Boston, as well," MacDonald added as an afterthought. "Though I know little of their nature. Oh—and Wright's a banker."

Jamie nodded. His hands were folded together beneath the tails of his coat as he walked; no one could see how tightly his fingers clenched.

"I believe I have heard of Mr. Wright," he said. "Phillip Wylie mentioned that a gentleman of that name owns a plantation near his own."

MacDonald nodded in affirmation. The end of his nose had gone quite red, and small broken blood vessels stood out in his cheeks, mementoes of years spent campaigning.

"Aye, that would be Four Chimneys." He glanced sidewise at Jamie, tongue probing a back tooth as he thought.

"Ye mean to kill him, then?"

"Of course not," Jamie replied evenly. "A man so well-connected wi' those in high places?"

MacDonald looked at him sharply, then away with a brief snort.

"Aye. Just so."

They paced side by side for several moments without speech, each occupied with his private calculations—and each aware of the other's.

The news of Bonnet's associations cut both ways; on the one hand, it would likely make the man easier to find. On the other, those associations would complicate matters quite a bit, when it came to the killing. It wouldn't stop Jamie—and MacDonald clearly perceived that—but it was a matter for thought, to be sure.

MacDonald himself was a considerable complication. Bonnet's business associates would be interested to hear that someone meant to cut off their source of profit—and would be more than likely to take action to prevent it. They would also pay well for the news that their golden goose was threatened; a prospect MacDonald would naturally appreciate.

There was no immediate way of corking up MacDonald, though; Jamie lacked the means for bribery, and that was a poor recourse in any case, as a man who could be bought once was always for sale.

He glanced at MacDonald, who met his eye, smiled slightly, then turned his head away. No, intimidation wouldn't serve, even had he a mind to threaten one who'd done him a service. What, then? He could scarcely knock MacDonald on the head, only to prevent his spilling to Wright, Priestly, or Butler.

Well, and if it could not be bribery or force, the only thing left to stop the man's mouth was blackmail. Which presented its own complications, insofar as he knew nothing—for the moment—to MacDonald's discredit. A man who lived as the Major did almost certainly had weak spots, but finding them . . . how much time might he have?

That thought triggered another.

"How did ye hear that I sought news of Stephen Bonnet?"

he demanded abruptly, breaking in on MacDonald's own contemplations.

MacDonald shrugged, and settled his hat and wig more firmly.

"I heard it from a half dozen different sources, sir, in places from taverns to magistrates' courts. Your interest is well known, I fear. But not," he added delicately, with a sideways glance, "its reason."

Jamie grunted, deep in his throat. It seemed he had no knife with but a single edge. Casting a wide net had brought him his fish—but without doubt, it had also caused ripples that might warn away the whale. If the whole coast knew he sought Bonnet—then so did Bonnet.

Perhaps this was a bad thing; or perhaps it was not. If Brianna were to hear of it—she had been outspoken in her desire that he leave Bonnet to his own fate. That was nonsense, of course, but he hadn't argued with her; only listened with every appearance of consideration. She need know nothing until the man was safely dead, after all. If an unwary word were to reach her before that, though . . . He had only begun to turn the possibilities over in his mind when MacDonald spoke again.

"Your daughter . . . that would be Mrs. MacKenzie, would it?"

"Does it matter?" He spoke coldly, and MacDonald's lips tightened briefly.

"No. To be sure. 'Twas only—I had some conversation of Mrs. MacKenzie, and found her most . . . charming. The thought of—" He broke off, clearing his throat. "I have a daughter, myself," he said abruptly, stopping and turning to face Jamie.

"Aye?" Jamie had not heard that MacDonald was married. Quite possibly he wasn't. "That would be in Scotland?"

"In England. Her mother's English." The chill had painted streaks of color on the soldier's weathered skin. They deepened, but MacDonald's pale blue eyes stayed steady on Jamie's, the same color as the hazy sky behind him.

Jamie felt the tightness down his backbone ease. He lifted his shoulders in a shrug, and let them fall. MacDonald nodded infinitesimally. The two men turned, without discussion, and started back toward the house, conversing casually of the price of indigo, the latest news from Massachusetts, and the surprising clemency of the weather for the season.

"I had spoken with your wife, a little earlier," MacDonald remarked. "A charming woman, and most amiable—you are a fortunate man, sir."

"I am inclined to think so," Jamie replied, darting a glance at MacDonald.

The soldier coughed, delicately.

"Mrs. Fraser was so kind as to suggest that you might consider providing me with a letter of introduction to his Excellency, the Governor. In light of the recent threat of conflict, she thought that perhaps a man of my experience might be able to provide something in the way of . . . you see?"

Jamie saw fine. And while he doubted that Claire had suggested any such thing, he was relieved to find the price asked so cheap.

"It shall be done at once," he assured MacDonald. "See me after the wedding this afternoon, and I shall have it in hand for ye."

MacDonald inclined his head, looking gratified.

As they reached the path that led to the necessary houses, MacDonald nodded farewell and took his leave with a raised hand, passing by Duncan Innes, who was coming from that direction, looking drawn and haggard as a man will whose bowels are tied in sheepshank knots.

"Are ye well, Duncan?" Jamie asked, eyeing his friend with some concern. Despite the coolness of the day, a faint sheen of sweat shone on Innes's brow, and his cheeks were pale. Jamie hoped that if it were an ague, it wasn't catching.

"No," Innes said, in answer to his question. "No, I am . . . *Mac Dubh*, I must speak to ye."

"Of course, *a charaid*." Alarmed by the man's appearance, he took hold of Duncan's arm, to support him. "Shall I fetch my wife to ye? D'ye need a wee dram?" From the smell of him, he'd had several already, but nothing out of the ordinary for a bridegroom. He didn't appear to be the worse for drink, but was plainly the worse for something. Perhaps a bad mussel at last night's supper. . . .

Innes shook his head. He swallowed, and grimaced, as though something hard was stuck in his throat. He drew air through his nose then, and set his shoulders, steeling himself to something.

"No, *Mac Dubh*, it's yourself I am needing. A bit of counsel, if ye might be so kind . . ."

"Aye, Duncan, surely." More curious than alarmed now, he let go of Duncan's arm. "What is it, man?"

"About—about the wedding night," Duncan blurted. "I—that is, I have—" He broke off abruptly, seeing someone turning into the path before them, heading for the necessary.

"This way." Jamie turned toward the kitchen gardens, which were safely enclosed in sheltering brick walls. Wedding night? he thought, both reassured and curious. Duncan had not been married before, he knew, and when they were in Ardsmuir together, Duncan had never spoken of women as some men did. He had thought it only a modest constraint at the time, but perhaps . . . but no, Duncan was well past fifty; surely the opportunity had occurred.

That left buggery or the clap, he thought, and he'd swear Duncan had no taste for boys. A bit awkward, to be sure, but he had full faith that Claire could deal with it. He did hope it was only drip, and not the French disease, though; that was a cruel plague.

"Here, *a charaid*," he said, drawing Duncan after him into the shelter of the onion beds. "We'll be quite private here. Now, then, what's your trouble?"

40

DUNCAN'S SECRET

FATHER LECLERC SPOKE NO ENGLISH, with the exception of a jolly "Tally-ho!" which he used alternately as a greeting, an interjection of amazement, and an exclamation of approbation. Jocasta was still at her toilette, so I introduced the priest to Ulysses, then escorted him to the main parlor, saw him provided with suitable refreshment, and sat him down to make conversation with the Sherstons, who were Protestant and rather bug-eyed at meeting a Jesuit, but so eager to show off their French that they were willing to overlook Father LeClerc's unfortunate profession.

Mentally wiping my brow after this bit of delicate social rapprochement, I made my excuses and went out to the terrace, to see whether Jamie had succeeded in retrieving Duncan. Neither man was in sight, but I met Brianna, coming up from the lawn with Jemmy.

"Hallo, darling, how are you?" I reached for Jemmy, who seemed restless, squirming and smacking his lips like someone sitting down to a six-course meal after a trek through the Sahara. "Hungry, are we?"

"Hak!" he said, then feeling this perhaps an insufficient explanation, repeated the syllable several times, with increasing volume, bouncing up and down by way of emphasis.

"*He's* hungry; *I'm* about to explode," Brianna said, lowering her voice and plucking gingerly at her bosom. "I'm just going to take him upstairs and feed him. Auntie Jocasta said we could use her room."

"Oh? That's good. Jocasta's just gone up herself—to rest a bit and change, she said. The wedding's set for four o'clock, now the priest is here." I had just heard the case clock in the hall chime noon; I did hope Jamie had got Duncan safely in hand. Perhaps he should be shut up somewhere, to prevent his wandering away again.

Bree reached to take Jemmy back, sticking a prophylactic knuckle in his mouth to muffle his remarks.

"Do you know the Sherstons?" she asked.

"Yes," I replied warily. "Why, what have they done?"

She raised one eyebrow at me.

"They've asked me to paint a portrait of Mrs. Sherston. A commission, I mean. Evidently Auntie Jocasta sang my praises to them, and showed them some of the things I did when I stayed here last spring, and now they want a picture."

"Really? Oh, darling, that's marvelous!"

"Well, it will be if they have any money," she said practically. "What do you think?"

It was a good question; fine clothes and appointments didn't always reflect actual worth, and I didn't know much about the Sherstons' circumstances; they were from Hillsborough, not Cross Creek.

"Well, they're rather vulgar," I said dubiously, "and dreadful snobs, but I think he's legitimately rich. He owns a brewery, I think. But ask Jocasta; she'll know for sure."

"Rah-tha vul-gah," she drawled, mocking my own accent, and grinned. "Who's a snob, then?"

"I am not a snob," I said with dignity. "I am a keen observer of social nuance. Have you seen your father and Duncan anywhere?"

"Not Duncan, but Da's down there by the trees with Mr. Campbell." She pointed helpfully, and I spotted Jamie's bright hair and crimson tartan, a fiery gleam at the bottom of the lawn. Not a sign of Duncan's scarlet coat, though.

"Damn the man," I said. "Where *has* he got to?"

"Went to the necessary, and fell in," Bree suggested. "All right, hold your horses, we're going!" Addressing this last to Jemmy, who was uttering plaintive cries suggestive of imminent starvation, she disappeared into the house.

I settled my shawl and strolled down the lawn to join

Jamie. A picnic lunch was being served to accommodate the guests, and I snatched a biscuit and a slice of ham as I passed the refreshment tables, improvising a hasty snack in order to stave off my own hunger pangs.

The air was still cool, but the sun was high and hot on my shoulders; it was a relief to join the men in the shade of a small grove of oaks that stood near the bottom of the lawn. They were pin oaks, and had begun to leaf out already, the unfolding leaves peeping out like a baby's fingers. What had Nayawenne told me about oaks? Oh, yes; one planted corn when the oak leaves were the size of a squirrel's ear.

Judging by that, the slaves could be planting corn in the River Run kitchen garden any day now. It would be weeks before the oak leaves were out on the Ridge, though.

Jamie had evidently just said something humorous, for Campbell made the low, creaking noise that passed with him for laughter, nodding to me in greeting.

"I shall leave ye to the practice of your own affairs, then," he said to Jamie, recovering his composure. "Call upon me, though, at need." He shaded his eyes, looking up toward the terrace.

"Ah, the prodigal returns. In shillings, sir, or bottles of brandy?"

I turned to look as well, in time to see Duncan crossing the terrace, nodding and smiling shyly to well-wishers as he passed. I must have looked bewildered, for Mr. Campbell bowed to me, dry mouth crooked with amusement.

"I'd laid your husband a small wager, ma'am."

"Five to one on Duncan, the night," Jamie explained. "That he and my aunt will share a bed, I mean."

"Goodness," I said, rather crossly. "Is anyone here talking of anything else? Minds like sewers, the lot of you."

Campbell laughed, then turned aside, distracted by the urgencies of a small grandson.

"Don't tell me ye werena wondering the same thing." Jamie nudged me gently.

"Indeed I was not," I said primly. I wasn't—but only because I already knew.

"Oh, indeed," he said, one corner of his mouth curling up.

"And you wi' lechery as plain on your face as whiskers on a cat."

"Whatever do you mean by that?" I demanded. Just in case he was right, I flicked the fan open and covered the lower half of my face. I peered over its ivory lacework, batting my eyelashes in mock innocence.

He made a derisive Scottish noise in his throat. Then, with a quick glance round, he bent low and whispered in my ear.

"It means ye look as ye do when ye want me to come to your bed." A warm breath stirred the hair over my ear. "Do you?"

I smiled brilliantly at Mr. Campbell, who was viewing us with interest over his grandson's head, snapped the fan open, and using it as a shield, stood on tiptoe to whisper in Jamie's ear. I dropped back on my heels and smiled demurely at him, fanning away for all I was worth.

Jamie looked mildly shocked, but definitely pleased. He glanced at Mr. Campbell, who had fortunately turned away, drawn into conversation elsewhere. Jamie rubbed his nose and regarded me with intense speculation, his dark blue gaze lingering on the scalloped neckline of my new gown. I fluttered the fan delicately over my décolletage.

"Ah . . . we could . . ." His eyes flicked up, assessing our surroundings for possible prospects of seclusion, then down again, ineluctably drawn to the fan as though it were a magnet.

"No we couldn't," I informed him, smiling and bowing to the elderly Misses MacNeil, who were strolling past behind him. "Every nook and cranny in the house is filled with people. So are the barns and stables and outbuildings. And if you had in mind a rendezvous under a bush on the riverbank, think again. This dress cost a bloody fortune." A fortune in illegal whisky, but a fortune nonetheless.

"Oh, I ken that well enough."

His eyes traveled slowly over me, from the coils of upswept hair to the tips of my new calf-leather shoes. The dress was pale amber silk, bodice and hem embroidered with silk leaves in shades of brown and gold, and if I did say so myself, it fit me like a glove.

"Worth it," he said softly, and leaned down to kiss me. A chilly breeze stirred the oak branches overhead, and I moved closer to him, seeking his warmth.

What with the long journey from the Ridge and the crush of guests caused by the impending celebration, we hadn't shared a bed ourselves in more than a week.

It wasn't so much an amorous encounter I wanted—though I would certainly not say no, if the opportunity offered. What I missed was simply the feel of his body next to mine; being able to reach out a hand in the dark and rest it on the long swell of his thigh; to roll toward him in the morning and cup his round, neat buttocks in the curve of thigh and belly; to press my cheek against his back and breathe the scent of his skin as I slipped into sleep.

"Damn," I said, resting my forehead briefly in the folds of his shirt ruffle, and inhaling the mingled scents of starch and man with longing. "You know, if your aunt and Duncan *don't* need the bed, perhaps . . ."

"Oh, so ye *were* wondering."

"No, I wasn't," I said. "Besides, what business is it of yours?"

"Oh, none at all," he said, unperturbed. "Only I've been asked by four men this morning if I think they will—or have done already. Which is rather a compliment to my aunt, no?"

It was true; Jocasta MacKenzie must be well into her sixties, and yet the thought of her sharing a man's bed was by no means unthinkable. I had met any number of women who had gratefully abandoned all notion of sex, directly the cessation of childbearing made it possible—but Jocasta wasn't one of them. At the same time—

"They haven't," I said. "Phaedre told me yesterday."

"I know. Duncan told me, just now." He was frowning slightly, but not at me. Toward the terrace, where the bright splotch of Duncan's tartan showed between the huge stone vases.

"Did he?" I was more than a little surprised at that. A sudden suspicion struck me. "You didn't *ask* him, did you?"

He gave me a slightly reproachful look.

"I did not," he said. "What d'ye take me for, Sassenach?"

"A Scot," I said. "Sex fiends, the lot of you. Or so one

would think, listening to all the talk around here." I gave Farquard Campbell a hard look, but he had turned his back, engrossed in conversation.

Jamie regarded me thoughtfully, scratching the corner of his jaw.

"Sex fiends?"

"You know what I mean."

"Oh, aye, I do. I'm only wondering—is that an insult, would ye say, or a compliment?"

I opened my mouth, then paused. I gave him back the thoughtful look.

"If the shoe fits," I said, "wear it."

He burst out laughing, which made a number of those nearby turn and look at us. Taking my arm, he steered me across the lawn and into the patchy shade of the elms.

"I did mean to ask ye something, Sassenach," he said, checking over his shoulder to be sure we were out of earshot. "Can ye find occasion to speak wi' my aunt, alone?"

"In this madhouse?" I glanced toward the terrace; a swarm of well-wishers surrounded Duncan like bees round a flower patch. "Yes, I suppose I could catch her in her room, before she comes down for the wedding. She's gone up to rest." I wouldn't mind a lie-down, either; my legs ached with hours of standing, and my shoes were new and slightly too tight.

"That'll do." He nodded pleasantly to an approaching acquaintance, then turned his back, shielding us from interruption.

"All right," I said. "Why?"

"Well, it's to do wi' Duncan." He looked at once amused and slightly worried. "There's a wee difficulty, and he canna bring himself to speak to her about it."

"Don't tell me," I said. "He was married before, and he thought his first wife was dead, but he's just seen her here, eating cullen skink."

"Well, no," he said, smiling. "Not so bad as that. And perhaps it's nay so troublesome as Duncan fears. But he's worrit in his mind about it, and yet he canna bring himself to speak to my aunt; he's a bit shy of her, aye?"

Duncan was a shy and modest man altogether; an ex-fisherman pressed into service during the Rising, he had been captured after Culloden, and spent years in prison. He had been released, rather than transported, only because he had contracted blood poisoning from a scratch, and had lost one arm, making him unfit for labor and unsalable as an indenture. I didn't have to wonder whose idea this marriage had been; such lofty aspirations would never have occurred to Duncan in a million years.

"I can see that. What's he worried about, though?"

"Well," he said slowly, "it's true that Duncan hasna been wed before. Did ye not wonder why?"

"No," I said. "I'd just assumed that the Rising had—oh, dear." I stopped, catching a notion of what this might be about. "It's not—goodness. You mean . . . he likes men?" My voice rose involuntarily.

"No!" he said, scandalized. "Christ, ye dinna think I'd let him marry my aunt, and him a sodomite? Christ." He glanced around, to be sure no one had heard this calumny, and shepherded me into the shelter of the trees, just in case.

"Well, you wouldn't necessarily know, would you?" I asked, amused.

"I'd know," he said grimly. "Come along." He lifted an overhanging bough and ushered me beneath it, a hand in the small of my back. The grove was a large one, and it was easy enough to get out of sight of the party.

"No," he said again, reaching a small open space well in among the trunks. "The filthy mind of you, Sassenach! No, it's nothing o' the sort." He glanced behind him, but we were a good distance from the lawn, and reasonably shielded from view. "It's only that he's . . . incapable." He lifted one shoulder slightly, looking profoundly uncomfortable at the thought.

"What—impotent?" I felt my mouth hanging open, and closed it.

"Aye. He was betrothed, as a young man, but there was a dreadful accident; a cart horse knocked him into the street and kicked him in the scrotum." He made a slight motion, as though to touch himself for reassurance, but checked it. "He healed, but it—well, he wasna fit for nuptial rites any longer, so he released the young woman and she marrit elsewhere."

"The poor man!" I said, with a pang of sympathy. "Gracious, poor Duncan's had nothing but bad luck."

"Well, he's alive," Jamie observed. "A good many others aren't. Besides"—he gestured over one shoulder, at the spread of River Run behind him—"I shouldna be inclined to call his present situation precisely unlucky. Bar the one small difficulty, that is," he added.

I frowned, running through the medical possibilities. If the accident had resulted in severe vascular damage, there wasn't much I could do; I was in no way equipped for fine reconstructive surgery. If it were only a hemocoel, though, then perhaps . . .

"When he was a young man, you said? Hmm. Well, it's not promising, after so long, but I can certainly have a look and see whether—"

Jamie stared at me, incredulous.

"A look? Sassenach, the man goes puce when ye inquire after the health of his bowels, and he nearly died o' shame, telling me. He'll have an apoplexy, and ye go pokin' his privates."

A strand of hair had been pulled loose by an oak twig; I pushed it irritably behind my ear.

"Well, what did you expect me to do, then? I can't heal him with spell-casting!"

"Of course not," he said, a little impatiently. "I dinna want ye to do anything to Duncan—only to speak to my aunt."

"What—you mean she doesn't know? But they've been engaged to be married for months, and living together for most of it!"

"Aye, but . . ." Jamie made the odd half-shrugging gesture he used when feeling embarrassed or uncomfortable, as though his shirt were too tight. "D'ye see—when the question of marriage rose, it never occurred to Duncan that it was a matter of . . . mmphm."

"Mmphm," I said, raising one eyebrow. "Doesn't marriage usually involve at least the possibility of mmphm?"

"Well, he didna think my aunt was wanting him for his manly beauty, aye?" Jamie said, raising his own brows back at me. "It seemed only a matter of business and convenience—there are things he could manage as owner of River

Run that he couldna do as overseer. At that, he wouldna have agreed, save she persuaded him."

"And he never thought to mention this . . . this impediment?"

"Oh, he thought. But there wasna any indication that my aunt regarded marriage in any but the sense of business. *She* didna mention the matter of bed; he was too shy to say. And the question didna really arise, ken."

"I gather that it now *has* arisen? What happened? Did your aunt slip her hand under his kilt this morning and make a bawdy remark about the wedding night?"

"He didna happen to say," he replied dryly. "But it wasna until this morning, when he began to hear the jests among the guests, that it occurred to Duncan that perhaps my aunt was expecting him to . . . well."

He lifted one shoulder, and let it fall. "He couldna think what to do, and was in a panic, listening to everyone."

"I see." I rubbed a knuckle across my upper lip, thinking. "Poor Duncan; no wonder he's been nervous."

"Aye." Jamie straightened up, with the air of one having settled something. "So, if ye'll be so kind as to speak wi' Jocasta, and see it's all straight—"

"Me? You want *me* to tell her?"

"Well, I shouldna think she'll mind greatly," he said, looking quizzically down at me. "After all, at her age, I shouldna think—"

I made a rude noise.

"Her age? Your grandfather Simon was well into his seventies and still putting it about, when last seen."

"My aunt is a woman," he said, rather austerely. "If ye hadna noticed it."

"And you think that makes a difference?"

"You don't?"

"Oh, it makes a difference, all right," I said. I leaned back against a tree, arms crossed under my bosom, and gave him a look from under my lashes. "When I am a hundred and one, and you're ninety-six, I'll invite you to my bed—and we'll see which one of us rises to the occasion, hmm?"

He looked at me thoughtfully, a glint in the dark blue of his eyes.

"I've a mind to take ye where ye stand, Sassenach," he said. "Payment on account, hmm?"

"I've a mind to take you up on it," I said. "However . . ." I glanced through the screen of branches toward the house, which was clearly visible. The trees were beginning to leaf out, but the tiny sprays of tender green were by no means sufficient camouflage. I turned back, just as Jamie's hands descended on the swell of my hips.

Events after that were somewhat confused, with the predominant impressions being an urgent rustling of fabric, the sharp scent of trodden onion grass, and the crackling of last year's oak leaves, dry underfoot.

My eyes popped open a few moments later.

"Don't stop!" I said, disbelieving. "Not *now*, for God's sake!"

He grinned down at me, stepping back and letting his kilt fall into place. His face was flushed a ruddy bronze with effort, and his chest heaved under his shirt ruffles.

He grinned maliciously, and wiped a sleeve across his forehead.

"I'll gie ye the rest when I'm ninety-six, aye?"

"You won't live that long! Come here!"

"Oh," he said. "So ye'll speak to my aunt."

"Effing blackmailer," I panted, fumbling at the folds of his kilt. "I'll get you for this, I swear I will."

"Oh, aye. You will."

He put an arm round my waist and swung me off my feet, turning round so that his back was to the house, screening me with his body. His long fingers deftly ruffled up the skirt of my gown, then the two petticoats beneath, and even more deftly, slid between my bare legs.

"Hush," he murmured in my ear. "Ye dinna want folk to hear, do ye?" He set his teeth gently in the curve of my ear, and proceeded about his business in a workmanlike way, ignoring my intermittent—and admittedly rather feeble—struggles.

I was more than ready and he knew what he was doing. It didn't take long. I dug my fingers into his arm, hard as an iron bar across my middle, arched backward for a moment of dizzying infinity, and then collapsed against him, twitching like a worm on the end of a hook. He made a deep chuckling sound, and let go of my ear.

A cold breeze had sprung up, and was wafting the folds of my skirts about my legs. The scent of smoke and food drifted through the cool spring air, along with the rumble of talk and laughter from the lawn. I could dimly hear it, under the slow, loud thumping of my heart.

"Come to think of it," Jamie remarked, releasing me, "Duncan has still got the one good hand." He set me gently on my feet, keeping hold of my elbow, lest my knees give way. "Ye might mention that to my aunt, if ye think it will help."

41

MUSIC HATH CHARMS

ROGER MACKENZIE MADE HIS WAY through the crowd, nodding here and there to a familiar face, but pushing on purposefully, preventing any attempt at conversation. He was not in a talkative mood.

Brianna had gone off to feed the kid, and while he missed her, he was just as pleased that she was out of sight for the moment. He didn't care at all for the sort of looks she'd been getting. Those directed at her face were admiring, but respectful enough; he'd caught that wee bastard Forbes staring at her rear view with an expression similar to the one the gentlemen were using on the undraped marble goddess on the lawn, though.

At the same time, he was more than proud of her. She was gorgeous in her new dress, and he felt a pleasant sense of possession when he looked at her. Still, his pleasure was slightly spoiled by the uneasy thought that she looked as though she belonged here, mistress of all this . . . this . . .

Yet another slave trotted past him, skirts hooped up over one arm as she made for the house, a basin of fresh rolls balanced on her head and another under her arm. How many slaves did Jocasta Cameron keep? he wondered.

Of course, that alone put the notion of Brianna's inheriting River Run out of the question. She wouldn't countenance the notion of slaves, not ever. Nor would he himself; still, it was comforting to think that it wasn't merely his own pride keeping Bree from her rightful inheritance.

He caught the thin wail of a fiddle coming from the house, and felt his ears prick up at the sound. Of course there would be music for the party. And with luck, a few new songs that he didn't know.

He turned across the terrace toward the house. He hadn't a notebook with him, but doubtless Ulysses could provide him with something. He bowed to Mrs. Farquard Campbell, who looked like a particularly horrible but expensive lampshade in pink silk. He paused to let her precede him into the house, biting the inside of his cheek as the four-foot spread of her skirt stuck momentarily in the three-foot doorway. She twitched adroitly sideways, though, and sidled crabwise into the hall, Roger following at a respectful distance.

The fiddle had ceased, but he could hear the twang and throb of instruments being handled and tuned nearby. They were in the big drawing room, whose double doors could be thrown open to allow dancers to spill out across the foyer, when the time came. At the moment, there were only a few guests in the drawing room, engaged in casual conversation.

Roger made his way past Ulysses, who was standing at the hearth, immaculate in wig and green livery, a poker held at the ready as he supervised two maidservants in the making of a gigantic vat of fresh rum punch. His eyes flicked automatically to the door, registered Roger's presence and identity, then returned to his business.

The musicians were huddled at the far end of the room, casting occasional thirsty glances at the hearth as they readied their instruments.

"What will you be giving us the day?" Roger inquired, pausing beside the fiddler. He smiled as the man turned round to him. " 'Ewie wi' the Crooked Horn,' perhaps, or 'Shawn Bwee'?"

"Oh, God love ye, sir, nothin' fancy." The conductor of the small ensemble, a cricketlike Irishman whose bent back was belied by the brightness of his eyes, waved a hand in cordial scorn at his motley crew of musicians.

"They ain't up to more than jigs and reels. No more are the folk as will be dancin', though," he added, practically. " 'Tisn't the Assembly Rooms in Dublin, after all, nor even Edenton; a good fiddler can keep 'em up to snuff."

"And that would be you, I expect?" Roger said with a smile, nodding at the cracked fiddle case the conductor had set on a whatnot, carefully out of the way of being stepped or sat on.

"That would be me," the gentleman agreed, with a graceful bow of acknowledgment. "Seamus Hanlon, sir—your servant."

"I am obliged, sir. Roger MacKenzie, of Fraser's Ridge." He returned the bow, taking pleasure in the old-fashioned formality, and clasped Hanlon's hand briefly, careful of the twisted fingers and knobby joints. Hanlon saw his care of the arthritic hand and gave a brief grimace of deprecation.

"Ah, they'll be fine with a drop of lubrication, so they will." Hanlon flexed one hand experimentally, then flipped the fingers in dismissal, fixing Roger with a bright glance.

"And yourself, sir; I felt the calluses on your fingertips. Not a fiddler, perhaps, but would ye be after playin' some stringed instrument?"

"Only to pass the time of an evening; nothing like you gentlemen." Roger nodded politely toward the ensemble, which, now unpacked, boasted a battered cello, two viols, a trumpet, a flute, and something which he thought might have started life as a hunting horn, though it appeared to have been amended since by the addition of several odd loops of tubing that stuck out in different directions.

Hanlon eyed him shrewdly, taking in his breadth of chest.

"And hark at the voice in him! Sure, and you're a singer, Mr. MacKenzie?"

Roger's reply was interrupted by a loud thump and a dolorous twang behind him. He whirled to see the cello player inflating himself over his instrument in the manner of a hen with a very large chick, to protect it from further injury by the gentleman who had evidently kicked it carelessly in passing.

"Watch yourself, then!" the cellist snapped. "Clumsy sot!"

"Oh?" The intruder, a stocky man in naval uniform, glowered menacingly at the cellist. "You dare . . . dare shpeak to me . . ." His face was flushed an unhealthy red, and he swayed slightly as he stood; Roger could smell the fumes of alcohol from a distance of six feet.

The officer raised a forefinger to the cellist, and appeared to be on the point of speech. A tongue tip showed pinkly between his teeth, but no words emerged. His empurpled jowls quivered for a moment, then he abandoned the attempt, turned on his heel, and made off, swerving narrowly to avoid an incoming footman with a tray of drinks, and caroming off the doorjamb as he passed into the corridor.

" 'Ware, then, Mr. O'Reilly." Seamus Hanlon spoke dryly to the cellist. "Were we near the sea, I should reckon there'd be a press-gang waitin' for ye, the instant ye set foot outside. As it is, I'd put no odds on him layin' for ye with a marlinspike or something of the kind."

O'Reilly spat eloquently on the floor.

"I know him," he said contemptuously. "Wolff, he's called. Dog, more like, and a poor dog at that. He's tight as a tick—he'll not remember me, an hour hence."

Hanlon squinted thoughtfully at the doorway through which the Lieutenant had vanished.

"Well, that's as may be," he allowed. "But I know the gentleman, too, and I do believe his mind may be somewhat sharper than his behavior might suggest." He stood for a moment, tapping the bow of his fiddle thoughtfully against the palm of his hand, then turned his head toward Roger.

"Fraser's Ridge, ye said? Will ye be a kinsman of Mrs. Cameron's—or Mrs. Innes, I should say?" he corrected himself.

"I'm married to Jamie Fraser's daughter," Roger said patiently, having discovered that this was the most efficient description, as most of the county appeared to know who Jamie Fraser was, and it prevented further questions regarding Roger's own family connections.

"Ho-ho," Seamus said, looking visibly impressed. "Well, then. Hum!"

"What's that bladder doing here, anyway?" the cellist demanded, still glaring after the departed officer. He patted his instrument soothingly. "Everyone knows he meant to wed Mrs. Cameron and have River Run for himself. I wonder he's the tripes to show his face today!"

"Perhaps he's come to show there are no hard feelings," Roger suggested. "A civil gesture—best man won and all that, aye?"

The musicians emitted a medley of sniggers and guffaws at this suggestion.

"Maybe," said the flutist, shaking his head over his instrument. "But if you're any friend to Duncan Innes, tell him to watch his back in the dancin'."

"Aye, do that," Seamus Hanlon concurred. "Be off with ye, young man, and speak to him—but see ye come back."

He crooked a finger at the waiting footman, and scooped a cup neatly from the proffered tray. He lifted this in salute, grinning at Roger over its rim. "It may be you'll know a tune or two that's new to me."

42

THE DEASIL CHARM

BRIANNA SAT BACK in the leather wing chair before the hearth, nursing Jemmy as she watched her great-aunt ready herself for the wedding.

"What you think, then?" Phaedre asked, dipping the silver

comb into a small pot of pomade. "Dress it up high, with the curls over the top?" Her voice was hopeful, but wary. She disapproved overtly of her mistress's refusal to wear a wig, and would do her level best to create a similarly fashionable effect with Jocasta's own hair, if allowed.

"Tosh," said Jocasta. "This isn't Edinburgh, child, let alone London." She leaned back, head lifted and eyes closed, basking. Bright spring sunshine poured through the panes, sparking off the silver comb, and making dark shadows of the slave's hands against the nimbus of shining white hair.

"Maybe not, but 'taint the wild Caribee nor the back-country, neither," Phaedre countered. "You the mistress here; this your weddin'. Everybody be lookin' at you—you wantin' to shame me, wear your hair down your shoulders like a squaw, and everybody be thinkin' I don't know my business?"

"Oh, heaven forbid." Jocasta's wide mouth twisted with an irritable humor. "Dress it simply, if you please, swept back and put up with combs. Perhaps my niece will let you show off your skill on her locks."

Phaedre cast a narrow glance over her shoulder at Brianna, who simply smiled and shook her head. She'd worn a lace-edged cap for the sake of public decency, and wasn't disposed to fuss with her hair. The slave snorted, and resumed her attempt to cajole Jocasta. Brianna closed her eyes, letting the amicable bickering recede into the background. Warm sun fell through the casement over her feet, and the fire purred and crackled at her back, embracing her like the old woolen shawl she had wrapped about herself and little Jem.

Beyond the voices of Jocasta and Phaedre, she could hear the thrum of the house below. Every room in the house was bursting with guests. Some were staying at nearby plantations, and had ridden in for the festivities, but enough were staying at River Run overnight that all the bedchambers were full, with guests sleeping five and six to a bed, and more on pallets in the tents by the river landing.

Brianna eyed the expanse of Jocasta's big tester bed enviously. Between the exigencies of travel, Jemmy, and the crowded conditions at River Run, she and Roger hadn't slept together in more than a week, and weren't likely to, until they returned to the Ridge.

Not that sleeping together was the major concern, nice as it was. The tug of the baby's mouth on her breast aroused a number of nonmaternal urges elsewhere, which required both Roger and a little privacy for satisfaction. They had started something promising the night before, in the pantry, but had been interrupted by one of the kitchen slaves, coming in to fetch a cheese. Perhaps the stable? She stretched her legs out, toes curling, and wondered whether the grooms slept in the stable or not.

"Well, I shall wear the brilliants, then, but only to please you, *a nighean.*" Jocasta's humorous voice pulled her out of the alluring vision of a dark, hay-lined stall, and Roger's body, naked limbs half-seen in the gloom.

She glanced up from Jemmy's blissful suckling, to where Jocasta sat upon the window seat, the spring light through the casement falling across her face. She looked abstracted, Bree thought, as though she were listening to something faint and far-off, that only she could hear. Maybe the hum of the wedding guests below.

The murmur in the house below reminded her of her mother's summer hives; a thrum that you could hear if you put your ear against one of the bee gums, a distant sound of busy content. The product of this particular swarm was talk, rather than honey, though the intent was similar—the laying up of reserves to see them through bleak and nectarless days of deprivation.

"That will do, that will do." Jocasta waved Phaedre away, getting to her feet. She shooed the maid out of the room, then stood tapping her fingers restlessly on the dressing table, clearly thinking of further details that should be attended to. Jocasta's brows drew together, and she pressed two fingers against the skin above her eyes.

"Have you got a headache, Auntie?" Brianna kept her voice low, so as not to disturb Jemmy, who was nearly asleep. Jocasta dropped her hand and turned toward her niece with a small, wry smile.

"Och, it's nothing. Whenever the weather turns, my poor head turns with it!"

In spite of the smile, Brianna could see small lines of pain tugging at the corners of Jocasta's eyes.

"Jem's nearly finished. I'll go and fetch Mama, shall I? She could make you a tisane."

Jocasta flapped a hand in dismissal, pushing away the pain with an obvious effort.

"No need, *a muirninn.* It's none so bad as that." She rubbed at her temple, careful of the hairdressing, the gesture belying her words.

Jemmy's mouth released its hold with a small, milky *pop!* and his head lolled back. The crook of Brianna's elbow was hot and sweaty, where his head had rested; his tiny ear was crumpled and crimson. She lifted his inert body and sighed with relief as the cool air struck her skin. A soft belch bubbled out of him with a dribble of excess milk, and he subsided against her shoulder like a half-filled water balloon.

"Full, is he?" Jocasta smiled, blind eyes turned toward them at the faint sound.

"As a drum," Brianna assured her. She patted his small back, to be sure, but heard no more than the soft sigh of sleep-filled breathing. She rose, wiped the milk from his chin, and laid the baby on his stomach in his makeshift cradle, a drawer from Jocasta's mahogany chiffonier, laid on the floor and thickly padded with pillows and quilts.

Brianna hung the shawl over the back of the chair, shivering slightly in a draft that leaked around the window frame. Not wanting to risk her new dress being stained with spit-up milk, she'd been nursing Jemmy in shift and stockings, and her bare forearms were pebbled with gooseflesh.

Jocasta turned her head in answer to the creak of wood and rustle of fabric, as Brianna opened the big armoire and took out two linen petticoats and her dress, smoothing the panels of soft, pale blue wool with satisfaction. She had woven the cloth and engineered the design of the gown herself—though Mrs. Bug had spun the thread, Claire had dyed it with indigo and saxifrage, and Marsali had helped with the sewing.

"Shall I call Phaedre back to dress ye, lass?"

"No, that's all right, I can manage—if you'll help me with

the laces?" She didn't like to call on the services of the slaves, any more than could be helped. The petticoats were no problem; she simply stepped into them, one at a time, and fastened the drawstrings round her waist. The stays needed to be laced up the back, though, and so did the gown itself.

Jocasta's brows were still dark, bronze against the pale apricot hue of her skin. They rose a little at the suggestion that she help to dress her niece, but she nodded, with no more than a brief hesitation. She turned her blind eyes toward the hearth, frowning a little.

"I suppose I can. The laddie's not too near the fire, is he? Sparks can jump, aye?"

Brianna wriggled into the stays, scooping her breasts up into the scalloped hollows that supported them, then pulled the gown on over them.

"No, he's not too near the fire," she said patiently. She'd made the bodice with light boning in the front and sides. Brianna turned slightly to and fro, admiring the effect in Jocasta's looking glass. Catching sight in the mirror of her aunt's slight frown behind her, she rolled her eyes at herself, then bent and pulled the drawer a little farther from the hearth, just in case.

"Thanks to ye for humoring an auld woman," Jocasta said dryly, hearing the scrape of wood.

"You're welcome, Aunt," Brianna replied, letting both warmth and apology show in her voice. She laid a hand on her great-aunt's shoulder, and Jocasta put her own long hand over it, squeezing gently.

"It's no that I think ye're a neglectful mother, aye?" Jocasta said. "But when ye've lived so long as I have, ye may be cautious, too, lass. I have seen dreadful things happen to bairns, ye ken?" she said, more softly. "And I should rather be set afire myself, than see harm come to our bonnie lad."

She moved behind Brianna and ran her hands lightly down her niece's back, finding the lacings without trouble.

"Ye've regained your figure, I see," the old woman said with approval, her hands skimming the sides of Brianna's waist. "What is this—crewelwork? What color is it?"

"Dark indigo blue. Flowering vines done in heavy cotton, to contrast with the pale blue wool." She took one of Jocasta's hands and guided the fingertips lightly over the vines that covered each bone in the bodice, running from the scalloped neck to the V of the waist, dropped sharply in front to show off the trim figure Jocasta had remarked upon.

Brianna drew in her breath as the laces tightened, glancing from her reflection to her son's small head, round as a cantaloupe and heartbreakingly perfect. Not for the first time, she wondered about her great-aunt's life. Jocasta had had children, or at least Jamie thought so—but she never spoke of them, and Brianna hesitated to ask. Perhaps lost in infancy; so many were. Her chest tightened at the thought.

"Dinna fash yourself," her aunt said. Jocasta's face readjusted itself into determined cheerfulness in the mirror. "Yon laddie's born for great things; nay harm will come to him, I'm sure."

She turned, the green silk of her dressing gown rustling over her petticoats, leaving Bree freshly startled at her aunt's ability to divine people's feelings, even without seeing their faces.

"Phaedre!" Jocasta called. "Phaedre! Bring my case—the black one."

Phaedre was nearby, as always, and a brief rustling in the drawers of the armoire produced the black case. Jocasta sat down with it at her secretary.

The black leather case was old and worn, a narrow box covered in weathered hide, unadorned save for its silver hasp. Jocasta kept her best jewels in a much grander case of velvet-lined cedarwood, Brianna knew. What could be in this one?

She moved to stand beside her aunt as Jocasta put back the lid. Inside the case was a short length of turned wood, the thickness of a finger, and on it were ranged three rings: a plain band of gold set with a beryl, another with a large cabochon emerald, and the last with three diamonds, surrounded by smaller stones that caught the light and threw it back in rainbows that danced across the walls and beams.

"What a lovely ring!" Bree exclaimed involuntarily.

"Oh, the diamond one? Well, Hector Cameron was aye a rich man," said Jocasta, absently touching the biggest ring. Her long fingers—unadorned—sorted deftly through a small heap of trinkets that lay in the box beside the rings, and came out with something small and dull.

She handed the tiny object to Brianna, who discovered it to be a small pierced-work tin brooch, rather tarnished, made in the shape of a heart.

"That's a *deasil* charm, *a muirninn*," Jocasta said, with a satisfied nod. "Put it on the wean's skirts, behind."

"A charm?" Brianna glanced at Jemmy's huddled form. "What kind of charm?"

"Against the fairies," Jocasta said. "Keep it pinned to the lad's smock—always to the back, mind—and naught born of the Auld Folk will trouble him."

The hair on Brianna's forearms prickled slightly at the matter-of-factness in the old woman's voice.

"Your mother should ha' told ye," Jocasta went on, with a hint of reproval in her voice. "But I ken as she's a Sassenach, and your father likely wouldna think of it. Men don't," she added, with a hint of bitterness. "It's a woman's job to see to the weans, to keep them from harm."

Jocasta stooped to the kindling basket and groped among the bits of debris, coming up with a long pine twig in her hand, the bark still on it.

"Take that," she commanded, holding it out toward Brianna. "Light the end of it from the hearth, and walk ye round the bairn three times. Sunwise, mind!"

Mystified, Brianna took the stick and thrust it into the fire, then did as she was bid, holding the flaming twig well away from both the makeshift cradle and her blue wool skirts. Jocasta tapped her foot rhythmically on the floor, and chanted, half under her breath.

She spoke in Gaelic, but slowly enough that Brianna could make out most of the words.

"Wisdom of serpent be thine,
Wisdom of raven be thine,
Wisdom of valiant eagle.

Voice of swan be thine,
Voice of honey be thine,
Voice of the Son of the stars.

Sain of the fairy-woman be thine,
Sain of the elf-dart be thine,
Sain of the red dog be thine.

Bounty of sea be thine,
Bounty of land be thine,
Bounty of the Father of Heaven.

Be each day glad for thee,
No day ill for thee,
A life joyful, satisfied."

Jocasta paused for a moment, a slight frown on her face, as though listening for any backtalk from Fairyland. Evidently satisfied, she motioned toward the hearth.

"Throw it into the fire. Then the wean will be safe from burning."

Brianna obeyed, finding to her fascination that she did not find any of this even faintly ridiculous. Odd, but very satisfying to think that she was protecting Jem from harm—even harm from fairies, which she didn't personally believe in. Or she hadn't, before this.

A thread of music drifted up from below; the screek of a fiddle, and the sound of a voice, deep and mellow. She couldn't make out any words, but knew the sound of the song.

Jocasta cocked her head, listening, and smiled.

"He's a good voice, your young man."

Brianna listened, too. Very faintly, she heard the familiar rise and fall of "My Love Is in America," somewhere below. *When I sing, it's always for you*. Her breasts were soft now, drained of milk, but they tingled slightly at the memory.

"You have good ears, Auntie," she said, tucking the thought away with a smile.

"Are ye pleased in your marriage?" Jocasta asked abruptly. "D'ye find yourself well-suited wi' the lad?"

"Yes," Brianna said, a little startled. "Yes—very much."

"That's good." Her great-aunt stood still, head tilted to the side, still listening. "Aye, that's good," she repeated, softly.

Seized by impulse, Brianna laid a hand on the older woman's wrist.

"And you, Auntie?" she asked. "Are you . . . pleased?"

"Happy" seemed not quite the word, in view of that row of rings in the case. "Well-suited" seemed not quite right, either, with her memory of Duncan, skulking in the corner of the drawing room the night before, shy and wordless whenever anyone but Jamie spoke to him, sweating and nervous this morning.

"Pleased?" Jocasta sounded puzzled. "Oh—to be married, ye mean!" To Brianna's relief, her aunt laughed, the lines of her face drawing up in genuine amusement.

"Oh, aye, surely," she said. "Why, it's the first time I shall ha' changed my name in fifty years!"

With a small snort of amusement, the old lady turned toward the window and pressed her palm against the glass.

"It's a fine day out, lass," she said. "Why not take your cloak and have a bit of air and company?"

She was right; the distant river gleamed silver through a lacework of green branches, and the air inside, so cozy a few moments ago, seemed now suddenly stale and frowsty.

"I think I will." Brianna glanced toward the makeshift cradle. "Shall I call Phaedre to watch the baby?"

Jocasta waved a hand at her, shooing.

"Och, away wi' ye. I'll mind the bairnie. I dinna mean to go down yet a while."

"Thanks, Auntie." She kissed the old woman's cheek, and turned to go—then, with a glance at her aunt, took a step back toward the hearth, and unobtrusively slid the cradle a little farther from the fire.

THE AIR OUTSIDE was fresh, and smelled of new grass and barbecue smoke. It made her want to skip down the brick paths, blood humming in her veins. She could hear the strains of music from the house, and the sound of Roger's voice. A quick turn in the fresh air, and then she'd go in; perhaps Roger would be ready for a break by then, and they could—

"Brianna!" She heard her name, hissed from behind the wall of the kitchen garden, and turned, startled, to find her father's head poking cautiously round the corner, like a ruddy snail. He jerked his chin at her and disappeared.

She cast a quick look over her shoulder to be sure no one was watching, and hastily whisked round the wall into the shelter of a sprouting carrot bed, to find her father crouched over the recumbent body of one of the black maids, who was sprawled atop a pile of aging manure with her cap over her face.

"What on earth—" Brianna began. Then she caught a whiff of alcohol, pungent among the garden scents of carrot tops and sun-ripened manure. "Oh." She squatted next to her father, skirts ballooning over the brick path.

"It was my fault," he explained. "Or some of it, at least. I left a cup under the willows, still half-full." He nodded toward the brick path, where one of Jocasta's punch cups lay on its side, a sticky drop of liquid still clinging to its rim. "She must have found it."

Brianna leaned over and sniffed at the edge of the maid's rumpled cap, now fluttering with heavy snores. Rum punch was the prevailing odor, but she also detected the richly sour scent of ale and the smooth tang of brandy. Evidently the slave had been thriftily disposing of any dregs left in the cups she collected for washing.

She lifted the ruffled edge of the cap with a cautious finger. It was Betty, one of the older maids, her face slack-lipped and drop-jawed in alcoholic stupor.

"Aye, it wasna the first half-cup she'd had," Jamie said, seeing her. "She must have been reeling. I canna think how she walked so far from the house, in such condition."

Brianna glanced back, frowning. The brick-walled kitchen garden was near to the cookhouse, but a good three hundred yards from the main house, and separated from it by a rhododendron hedge, and several flower beds.

"Not just how," Brianna said, and tapped a finger against her lip in puzzlement. "Why?"

"What?" He had been frowning at the maid, but glanced up at her tone. She rose, and tilted her head at the snoring woman.

"Why *did* she walk out here? It looks like she's been tippling all day—she can't have been dashing out here with every cup; somebody would have noticed. And why bother? It's not like it would be hard to do without being noticed. If I were drinking leftovers, I'd just stay there under the willows and gulp it."

Her father gave her a startled look, replaced at once with one of wry amusement.

"Would ye, then? Aye, that's a thought. But perhaps there was enough in the cup that she thought to enjoy it in peace."

"Maybe so. But there are surely hiding places nearer the river than this." She reached down and scooped up the empty cup. "What was it you were drinking, rum punch?"

"No, brandy."

"Then it wasn't yours that pushed her over the edge." She held out the cup, tilting it so he could see the dark dregs at the bottom. Jocasta's rum punch was made not only with the usual rum, sugar, and butter but also with dried currants, the whole concoction being mulled with a hot poker. The result not only was dark brown in color but always left a heavy sediment in the cups, composed of tiny grains of soot from the poker and the charred remnants of incinerated currants.

Jamie took the cup from her, frowning. He inserted his nose into the cup and took a deep sniff, then stuck a finger into the liquid and put it in his mouth.

"What is it?" she asked, seeing his face change.

"Punch," he said, but ran the tip of his tongue back and forth over his teeth, as though to cleanse it. "With laudanum, I think."

"Laudanum! Are you sure?"

"No," he said frankly. "But there's something in it beyond dried currants, or I'm a Dutchman." He held the cup out to her, and she took it, sniffing furiously. She couldn't make out much beyond the sweet, burned smell of rum punch. Perhaps there was a sharper tang, something oily and aromatic . . . perhaps not.

"I'll take your word for it," she said, wiping the tip of her nose on the back of her hand. She glanced at the supine maid. "Shall I go look for Mama?"

Jamie squatted beside the maid and inspected her carefully. He lifted a limp hand and felt it, listened to her breathing, then shook his head.

"I canna say whether she's drugged, or only drunk—but I dinna think she's dying."

"What shall we do with her? We can't leave her lie."

He looked down at the slave, frowning.

"No, of course not." He stooped and—quite gently—gathered the woman into his arms. One worn shoe fell off, and Brianna retrieved it from the brick walk.

"D'ye ken where she sleeps?" Jamie asked, gingerly negotiating his stertorous burden round the edge of a cucumber frame.

"She's a house slave; she must sleep in the attics."

He nodded, tossing his head to dislodge a strand of red hair that had blown into his mouth.

"Verra well, then, we'll go round the stables and see can we get up the back stair without bein' seen. Go across, will ye, lass, and signal me when it's clear."

She tucked shoe and cup under her cloak to hide them, then ducked quickly out onto the narrow walk that led past the kitchen garden, branching to cookhouse and necessary. She glanced to and fro, feigning casualness. There were a few people within sight, near the paddock, but that was some distance away—and all of them had their backs to her, engrossed with Mr. Wylie's black Dutch horses.

As she turned to signal to her father, she caught sight of Mr. Wylie himself, escorting a lady into the stable block. A gleam of gold silk—wait, it was her mother! Claire's pale face turned momentarily in her direction, but her attention was fixed on something Wylie was saying, and she didn't notice her daughter on the path.

Bree hesitated, wanting to call to her mother, but couldn't do so without attracting unwanted attention. Well, at least she knew where Claire was. She could come and fetch her mother to help—once they had Betty safely tucked away.

WITH A FEW CLOSE alarms and near-misses, they managed to get Betty up to the long attic room she shared with the other female house servants. Jamie, panting, dumped her unceremoniously on one of the narrow beds, then wiped his sweating brow on his coat sleeve, and, long nose wrinkled, began fastidiously to dust manure crumbs from the skirts of his coat.

"So, then," he said, a little grumpily. "She's safe, aye? If ye tell one of the other slaves she's taken ill, I suppose no one who matters will find out."

"Thanks, Da." She leaned close and kissed his cheek. "You're a sweet man."

"Oh, aye," he said, sounding resigned. "My bones are filled wi' honey, to be sure." Still, he didn't look displeased. "Have ye got that shoe, still?" He took off the maid's remaining shoe, and placed it neatly beside its fellow beneath the bed, then drew the coarse woolen blanket gently over the woman's feet, grimy white in their thick stockings.

Brianna checked the maid's condition; so far as she could tell, everything seemed all right; the woman was still snoring wetly, but in a reassuringly regular manner. As they tiptoed cautiously back down the rear stairs, she gave Jamie the silver cup.

"Here. Did you know this was one of Duncan's cups?"

"No." He arched one brow, frowning. "What d'ye mean, 'Duncan's cups'?"

"Aunt Jocasta had a set of six cups made for Duncan, for a wedding present. She showed them to me yesterday. See?" She turned the cup in her hand, to show him the engraved monogram—"I," for "Innes," with a tiny fish, its scales beautifully detailed, swimming round the letter.

"Does that help?" she asked, seeing his brow crease in interest.

"It may." He pulled out a clean cambric handkerchief and wrapped the cup carefully before putting it in the pocket of his coat. "I'll go and find out. Meanwhile, can ye find Roger Mac?"

"Of course. Why?"

"Well, it does occur to me that if yon Betty drank part of a cup of rum punch and was laid out like a fish on a slab, then I should like to find whoever drank the first part of it, and see if they're in a similar condition." He raised one brow at her.

"If the punch was drugged, then likely it was meant for someone, aye? I thought perhaps you and Roger Mac might look round discreetly for bodies in the shrubbery."

That aspect of the matter hadn't struck her in the rush to get Betty upstairs.

"All right. I should find Phaedre or Ulysses first, though, and tell one of them that Betty's sick."

"Aye. If ye speak with Phaedre, ye might inquire whether yon Betty is an opium-eater as well as a bibber. Though I will say I think it unlikely," he added dryly.

"So do I," she said, matching his tone. She took his point, though; perhaps the punch had not been drugged, but Betty had taken the laudanum herself, on purpose. It was possible; she knew Jocasta kept some in the stillroom. If she had taken it herself, though, was it for recreational use—or had the maid perhaps intended to commit suicide?

She frowned at Jamie's back, as he paused at the foot of the stair, listening before stepping onto the landing. It was easy enough to think that the misery of slavery might dispose one to suicide. At the same time, honesty compelled her to admit that Jocasta's house servants lived reasonably well; better than any number of free individuals—black *or* white—that she'd seen in Wilmington and Cross Creek.

The servants' room was clean, the beds rough but comfortable. The house servants had decent clothes, even to shoes and stockings, and more than enough to eat. As for the sorts of emotional complications that could lead one to contemplate suicide—well, those weren't limited to slaves.

Much more likely that Betty was merely a toper, of the sort who would drink anything even vaguely alcoholic—the reek of her garments certainly suggested as much. But in that case, why take the risk of stealing laudanum, on a day when the wedding party insured there would be an abundance of every kind of drink?

She was reluctantly forced to the same conclusion that she was sure her father had already reached. Betty had taken the laudanum—if that's what it was, she reminded herself—by accident. And if that was so . . . whose cup had she drunk from?

Jamie turned, lips pursed to enjoin silence, and beckoned

to her that the coast was clear. She followed him quickly across the landing and outside, letting out her breath in relief as they arrived on the path unobserved.

"What were you doing there in the first place, Da?" she asked. He looked blank.

"In the kitchen garden," she elaborated. "How did you find Betty?"

"Oh." He took her arm, fetching her away from the house. They walked casually toward the paddock; innocent guests bent on viewing the horses. "I was just havin' a word wi' your mother, over by the grove. I came back through the kitchen garden, and there the woman was, flat on her back on the shit heap."

"That's a point, isn't it?" she asked. "Did she lie down in the garden on purpose, or was it only an accident that you found her there?"

He shook his head.

"I dinna ken," he said. "But I mean to speak to Betty, once she's sober. D'ye ken where your mother is now?"

"Yes, she's with Phillip Wylie. They were headed for the stables, I think." Her father's nostrils flared slightly at mention of Wylie, and she suppressed a smile.

"I'll find her," he said. "Meanwhile, lass, do you go and speak to Phaedre—and, lass—"

She had already turned to go; at this, she looked back, surprised.

"I think perhaps ye should tell Phaedre to say nothing unless someone asks her where Betty is, and if they do, to tell you—or me." He straightened abruptly, clearing his throat. "Go find your husband then, lass—and, lass? Make sure no one kens what you're about, aye?"

He lifted one brow, and she nodded in reply. He turned on his heel then, and strode off toward the stables, the fingers of his right hand tapping gently against his coat as though he were deep in thought.

The chilly wind nipped under her skirts and petticoats, belling them out and sending a deep shiver through her flesh. She understood his implication well enough.

If it was neither attempted suicide nor accident—then it might be intended murder. But of whom?

43

FLIRTATIONS

JAMIE HAD GIVEN ME a lingering kiss for encouragement after our interlude, and crashed off through the underbrush, intending to hunt down Ninian Bell Hamilton and find out just what the Regulators were up to at the camp Hunter had mentioned. I followed, after a moment's interval for decency, but paused at the edge of the grove before emerging back into public view, to be sure I was seemly.

I had a rather light-headed sense of well-being, and my cheeks were very flushed, but I thought that wasn't incriminating in and of itself. Neither would coming out of the wood be inculpatory; women and men alike often simply stepped into the shelter of the trees along the lawn in order to relieve themselves, rather than making their way to the overcrowded and smelly necessaries. Coming out of the wood flushed and breathing heavily, with leaves in my hair and sap stains on my skirt, though, would cause a certain amount of comment behind the fans.

There were a few sandburs and an empty cicada shell clinging to my skirt, a ghostly excrescence that I picked off with a shudder of distaste. There were dogwood petals on my shoulder; I brushed them off and felt carefully over my hair, dislodging a few more that fluttered away like scraps of fragrant paper.

Just as I stepped out from under the trees, it occurred to me to check the back of my skirt for stains or bits of bark, and I was craning my neck to see over my shoulder when I walked slap into Phillip Wylie.

"Mrs. Fraser!" He caught me by the shoulders, to prevent my falling backward. "Are you quite all right, my dear?"

"Yes, certainly." My cheeks were flaming legitimately at this point, and I stepped back, shaking myself back into order. Why did I keep bumping into Phillip Wylie? Was the little pest following me? "I do apologize."

"Nonsense, nonsense," he said heartily. "It was my fault entirely. Deuced clumsy of me. May I get you something to restore your spirits, my dear? A glass of cider? Wine? Rum punch? A syllabub? Applejack? Or—no, brandy. Yes, allow me to bring you a bit of brandy to recover from the shock!"

"No, nothing, thank you!" I couldn't help laughing at his absurdities, and he grinned back, obviously thinking himself very witty.

"Well, if you are quite recovered, then, dear lady, you must come with me. I insist."

He had my hand tucked into the crook of his arm, and was towing me determinedly off in the direction of the stable, despite my protests.

"It will take no more than a moment," he assured me. "I have been looking forward all day to showing you my surprise. You will be utterly entranced, I give you my word!"

I subsided feebly; it seemed less trouble to go and look at the damned horses again than to argue with him—and there was plenty of time to speak with Jocasta before the wedding, in any case. This time, though, we skirted the paddock where Lucas and his companions were submitting tolerantly to inspection by a couple of bold gentlemen who had climbed the fence for a closer look.

"That *is* an amazingly good-tempered stallion," I said with approval, mentally contrasting Lucas's kindly manners with Gideon's rapacious personality. Jamie still had not found time to castrate the horse, who had consequently bitten almost everyone, horse and man alike, on the journey to River Run.

"A mark of the breed," Wylie replied, pushing open the door that led to the main stable. "They are the most amiable of horses, though a gentle disposition does not impair their intelligence, I do assure you. This way, Mrs. Fraser."

By contrast with the brilliant day outside, it was pitch-dark in the stable; so dark that I stumbled over an uneven brick in the floor, and Mr. Wylie seized my arm as I lurched forward with a startled cry.

"Are you all right, Mrs. Fraser?" he asked, setting me upright again.

"Yes," I said, a little breathless. In fact I had both stubbed my toe viciously and turned my ankle; my new morocco-heeled shoes were lovely, but I wasn't used to them yet. "Just let me stand a moment—'til my eyes adjust."

He did, but he didn't let go of my arm. Instead, he pulled my hand through the crook of his elbow and set it solidly, to give me more support.

"Lean on me," he said, simply.

I did, and we stood quietly for a moment, me with my injured foot drawn up like a heron's, waiting for my toes to stop throbbing. For once, Mr. Wylie seemed bereft of quips and sallies; perhaps because of the peaceful atmosphere.

Stables on the whole *are* peaceful, horses and the people who tend them being generally kindly sorts of creatures. This one, though, had a special air, both quiet and vibrant. I could hear small rustlings and stampings, and the contented noise of a horse champing hay close at hand.

So close to Phillip Wylie, I was aware of his perfume, but even the expensive whiff of musk and bergamot was overcome by the stable smells. It smelled of fresh straw and grain, of brick and wood, but there was a faint scent as well of more elemental things—manure and blood and milk; the basic elements of motherhood.

"It's rather womblike in here, isn't it?" I said softly. "So warm and dark, I mean. I can almost feel the heartbeat."

Wylie laughed, but quietly.

"That's mine," he said. He touched a hand briefly to his waistcoat, a dark shadow against the pale satin.

My eyes adapted quickly to the dark, but even so, the place was very dim. The lithe shadow-shape of a stable cat glided past, making me wobble and set down my injured foot. It wouldn't yet bear weight, but I could at least put it to the floor.

"Can you stand for a moment alone?" Wylie asked.

Without waiting for my reply, he detached himself and

went to light a lantern that stood on a nearby stool. There were a few faint chinks of flint and steel, then the wick caught and a soft globe of yellow light ballooned around us. Taking my arm again with his free hand, he led me toward the far end of the stable.

They were in the loose-box at the end. Phillip raised the lantern high, turning to smile at me as he did so. The lantern light gleamed on hide that shone and rippled like midnight water, and glowed in the huge brown eyes of the mare as she turned toward us.

"Oh," I said softly, "how beautiful," and then, a little louder, "Oh!" The mare had moved a little, and her foal peered out from behind her mother's legs. She was long-legged and knob-kneed, her tiny rump and sloping shoulders rounded echoes of her mother's muscular perfection. She had the same large, kind eyes, fringed with long, long lashes—but instead of the sleek hide of rippling black, she was a dark reddish-brown and fuzzy as a rabbit, with an absurd little whisk broom of a tail.

Her dam had the same glorious profusion of flowing mane I had noted on the Friesians in the paddock; the baby had a ridiculous crest of stiff hair, about an inch long, that stuck straight up like a toothbrush.

The foal blinked once, dazzled by the light, then ducked swiftly behind the shelter of her mother's body. A moment later, a small nose protruded cautiously into sight, nostrils twitching. A big eye followed, blinked—and the nose vanished, only to reappear almost instantly, a little further this time.

"Why, you little flirt!" I said, delighted.

Wylie laughed.

"She is indeed," he said, voice filled with pride of ownership. "Are they not magnificent?"

"Well, yes," I said, considering. "They are. Still, I'm not sure that's quite it. 'Magnificent' seems more like what you'd say of a stallion, or a warhorse of some kind. These horses are . . . well, they're *sweet*!"

Wylie gave a small, amused sort of snort.

"Sweet?" he said. *"Sweet?"*

"Well, you know," I said, laughing. "Charming. Good-natured. Delightful."

"All those things," he said, turning to me. "And beautiful, as well." He wasn't looking at the horses, but rather at me, a faint smile on his face.

"Yes," I said, feeling a small, obscure twinge of unease. "Yes, they are very beautiful."

He was standing very close; I took a step to the side and turned away, under the pretext of looking at the horses again. The foal was nuzzling at the mare's swollen udder, scraggy tail waggling with enthusiasm.

"What are their names?" I asked.

Wylie moved to the bar of the loose-box, casually, but in such a way that his arm brushed my sleeve as he reached above me to hang the lantern from a hook on the wall.

"The mare's name is Tessa," he said. "You saw the sire, Lucas. As for the filly . . ." He reached for my hand, and lifted it, smiling. "I thought I might name her La Belle Claire."

I didn't move for a second, stunned by sheer disbelief at the expression that showed quite clearly on Phillip Wylie's face.

"What?" I said blankly. Surely I was wrong, I thought. I tried to snatch my hand away, but I had hesitated one second too long, and his fingers tightened on mine. Surely he wasn't really meaning to . . .

He was.

"Charming," he said softly, and moved closer. "Good-natured. Delightful. And . . . beautiful." He kissed me.

I was so shocked that I didn't move for a moment. His mouth was soft, the kiss brief and chaste. That hardly mattered, though; it was the fact that he had done it.

"Mr. Wylie!" I said. I took a hasty step back, but was brought up short by the rail.

"Mrs. Fraser," he said softly, and took the same step forward. "My dear."

"I am *not* your—" I began, and he kissed me again. Without the least hint of chasteness. Still shocked, but no longer stunned, I shoved him, hard. He wobbled, and lost his grip on my hand, but recovered instantly, seizing me by the arm and slipping his other hand behind me.

"Flirt," he whispered, and lowered his face toward mine. I kicked him. Unfortunately, I kicked him with my injured foot, which deprived the blow of much force, and he ignored it.

I began to struggle in good earnest, as the sense of stunned disbelief faded into the awareness that the young man had one hand firmly on my backside. At the same time, I was aware that there were a good many people in the vicinity of the stable; the last thing I wanted was to attract attention.

"Stop that!" I hissed. "Stop it at once!"

"You madden me," he breathed, pressing me to his bosom and attempting to stick his tongue in my ear.

I certainly thought he was mad, but I declined absolutely to accept any responsibility for the condition. I jerked back as far as I could—not far, with the railing at my back—and fought to get one hand between us. Shock quite gone by now, I was thinking with surprising clarity. I couldn't knee him in the balls; he had one leg thrust between my own, trapping a wodge of skirt in my way. If I could get my hand round his throat and get a sound hold of his carotids, though, he'd drop like a rock.

I did get hold of his throat, but his blasted stock was in the way; my fingers scrabbled at it, and he jerked to the side, grabbing at my hand.

"Please," he said. "I want—"

"I don't give a damn *what* you want!" I said. "Let go of me this instant, you—you—" I groped wildly for some suitable insult. "You—*puppy*!"

Rather to my surprise, he stopped. His face couldn't go pale, being already covered in rice flour—I could taste it on my lips—but his mouth was set, and his expression was . . . rather wounded.

"Is that really what you think of me?" he asked in a low voice.

"Yes, it bloody is!" I said. "What else am I to think? Have you lost your mind, behaving in this—this despicable fashion? What is the matter with you?"

"Despicable?" He seemed quite taken aback to hear his

advances described in this fashion. "But I—that is, you—I thought you were . . . I mean, might be not averse—"

"You can't," I said, positively. "You can't possibly have thought anything of the sort. I've never given you the *slightest* reason to think such a thing!" Nor had I—intentionally. The uneasy thought came to me, though, that perhaps my perceptions of my own behavior were not quite the same as Phillip Wylie's.

"Oh, haven't you?" His face was changing, clouding with anger. "I beg to differ with you, madam!"

I had told him I was old enough to be his mother; it had never for a moment occurred to me that he didn't believe it.

"Flirt," he said again, though in quite a different tone than the first time. "No reason? You have given me every reason, since the first occasion of our meeting."

"What?" My voice went up a tone, in incredulity. "I've never done anything but engage you in civil conversation. If that constitutes flirtation in *your* book, my lad, then—"

"Don't call me that!"

Oh, so he *had* noticed that there was a difference of age. He simply hadn't appreciated the magnitude, I thought. It came to me, with a certain feeling of apprehension, that at Phillip's level of society, most flirtation was indeed conducted under the guise of banter. What in the name of God had I said to him?

I had some dim recollection of having discussed the Stamp Act with him and his friend Stanhope. Yes, taxes, and, I thought, horses—but surely that couldn't have been sufficient to inflame his misapprehensions?

"Thine eyes are like the fishpools in Heshbon," he said, low-voiced and bitter. "Do you not recall the evening when I said that to you? The Song of Solomon is merely 'civil conversation' to you, is it?"

"Good grief." I was, despite myself, beginning to feel slightly guilty; we *had* had a brief exchange along those lines, at Jocasta's party, two or three years ago. And he remembered it? The Song of Solomon was reasonably heady stuff; perhaps the simple reference . . . Then I shook myself mentally, and drew myself up straight.

"Nonsense," I declared. "You were teasing me, and I simply answered you in kind. Now, I really must—"

"You came in here with me today. Alone." He took another step toward me, eyes determined. He was talking himself back into it, the fatheaded popinjay!

"Mr. Wylie," I said firmly, sliding sideways. "I am terribly sorry if you have somehow misunderstood the situation, but I am very happily married, and I have no romantic interest in you whatsoever. And now, if you will excuse me . . ." I ducked past him, and hurried out of the stable, as fast as my shoes would allow. He made no effort to follow me, though, and I reached the outdoors unmolested, my heart beating fast.

There were people near the paddock; I turned in the other direction, going round the end of the stable block before anyone should see me. Once out of sight, I made a swift inventory, checking to be sure that I didn't look too disheveled. I didn't know whether anyone had seen me going into the stable with Wylie; I could only hope no one had seen my hasty exit.

Only one lock of hair had come down in the recent contretemps; I pinned it carefully back, and dusted a few bits of straw from my skirts. Fortunately, he hadn't torn my clothes; a retucked kerchief and I was quite decent again.

"Are ye all right, Sassenach?"

I leaped like a gaffed salmon, and so did my heart. I whirled, adrenaline jolting through my chest like an electric current, to find Jamie standing beside me, frowning slightly as he surveyed me.

"What have ye been doing, Sassenach?"

My heart was still stuck in my throat, choking me, but I forced out what I hoped were a few nonchalant words.

"Nothing. I mean, looking at the horses—horse. The mare. She has a new foal."

"Aye, I know," he said, looking at me oddly.

"Did you find Ninian? What did he have to say?" I groped behind my head, tidying my hair and taking the opportunity to turn away a little, to avoid his eye.

"He says it's true—though I hadna doubted it. There are more than a thousand men, camped near Salisbury. And more joining them each day, he says. The auld mumper is pleased about it!" He frowned, drumming the two stiff fingers of his right hand lightly against his leg, and I realized that he was rather worried.

Not without cause. Putting aside the threat of conflict itself, it was spring. Only the fact that River Run was in the piedmont had allowed us to come to Jocasta's wedding; down here, the woods were cloudy with blossom and crocuses popped through the earth like orange and purple dragon's-teeth, but the mountains were still cloaked in snow, the tree branches sporting swollen buds. In two weeks or so, those buds would burst, and it would be time for the spring planting on Fraser's Ridge.

True, Jamie had provided for such an emergency by finding old Arch Bug, but Arch could manage only so much by himself. And as for the tenants and homesteaders . . . if the militia were raised again, the women would be left to do the planting alone.

"The men in this camp—they're men who've left their land, then?" Salisbury was in the piedmont, as well. It wasn't thinkable for working farmers to abandon their land at this time of year for the sake of protest against the government, no matter how annoyed they were.

"Left it, or lost it," he said briefly. The frown deepened as he looked at me. "Have ye spoken wi' my aunt?"

"Ah . . . no," I said, feeling guilty. "Not yet. I was just going . . . oh—you said there was another problem. What else has happened?"

He made a sound like a hissing teakettle, which for him betokened rare impatience.

"Christ, I'd nearly forgot her. One of the slave women's been poisoned, I think."

"What? Who? How?" My hands dropped from my hair as I stared at him. "Why didn't you tell me?"

"I *am* telling ye, am I not? Dinna fash yourself, she's in no danger. Only stinking drunk." He twitched his shoulders irritably. "The only difficulty is that perhaps it wasna her that was meant to be poisoned. I've sent Roger Mac and Brianna to look, and they've not come back to say anyone's dead, so maybe not."

"*Maybe* not?" I rubbed the bridge of my nose, distracted from the extant worries by this new development. "I grant you, alcohol is poisonous, not that anyone seems ever to realize it, but there's a difference between being drunk and being deliberately poisoned. What do you mean—"

"Sassenach," he interrupted.

"What?"

"What in the name o' God have ye been doing?" he burst out.

I stared at him in bewilderment. His face had been growing redder as we talked, though I had supposed it to be only frustration and worry over Ninian, and the Regulators. It dawned on me, catching a dangerous blue glint in his eye, that there was something rather more personal about his attitude. I tilted my head to one side, giving him a wary look.

"What do you mean, what have I been doing?"

His lips pressed tight together, and he didn't answer. Instead, he extended a forefinger and touched it, very delicately, beside my mouth. He turned his hand over then, and presented me with a small dark object clinging to the tip of his finger—Phillip Wylie's star-shaped black beauty mark.

"Oh." I felt a distinct buzzing in my ears. "That. Er . . ." My head felt light, and small spots—all shaped like black stars—danced before my eyes.

"Yes, that," he snapped. "Christ, woman! I'm deviled to death wi' Duncan's havers and Ninian's pranks—and why did ye not tell me he'd been fighting wi' Barlow?"

"I'd scarcely describe it as a fight," I said, struggling to regain a sense of coolness. "Besides, Major MacDonald put a stop to it since *you* were nowhere to be found. And if you want to be told things, the Major wants—"

"I ken what he wants." He dismissed the Major with a curt flick of his hand. "Aye, I'm up to my ears in Majors and Regulators and drunken maid servants, and *you're* out in the stable, canoodling wi' that fop!"

I felt the blood rising behind my eyes, and curled my fists, in order to control the impulse to slap him.

"I was *not* 'canoodling' in the slightest degree, and you know it! The beastly little twerp made a pass at me, that's all."

"A pass? Made love to ye, ye mean? Aye, I can see that!"

"He did not!"

"Oh, aye? Ye asked him to let ye try his bawbee on for luck, then?" He waggled the finger with the black patch under my nose, and I slapped it away, recalling a moment too late that "make love to" merely meant to engage in amorous flirtation, rather than fornication.

"I *mean*," I said, through clenched teeth, "that he kissed me. Probably for a joke. I'm old enough to be his mother, for God's sake!"

"More like his grandmother," Jamie said brutally. "Kissed ye, forbye—why in hell did ye encourage him, Sassenach?"

My mouth dropped open in outrage—insulted as much at being called Phillip Wylie's grandmother as at the accusation of having encouraged him.

"Encourage him? Why, you bloody idiot! You know perfectly well I didn't encourage him!"

"Your own daughter saw ye go in there with him! Have ye no shame? With all else there is to deal with here, am I to be forced to call the man out, as well?"

I felt a slight qualm at the thought of Brianna, and a larger one at the thought of Jamie challenging Wylie to a duel. He wasn't wearing his sword, but he'd brought it with him. I stoutly dismissed both thoughts.

"*My* daughter is neither a fool nor an evil-minded gossip," I said, with immense dignity. "She wouldn't think a thing of my going to look at a horse, and why ought she? Why ought anyone, for that matter?"

He blew out a long breath through pursed lips, and glared at me.

"Why, indeed? Perhaps because everyone saw ye flirt with him on the lawn? Because they saw him follow ye about like a dog after a bitch in heat?" He must have seen my expression alter dangerously at that, for he coughed briefly and hurried on.

"More than one person's seen fit to mention it to me. D'ye think I like bein' made a public laughingstock, Sassenach?"

"You—you—" Fury choked me. I wanted to hit him, but I could see interested heads turning toward us. "'Bitch in heat'? How dare you say such a thing to me, you bloody bastard?"

He had the decency to look slightly abashed at that, though he was still glowering.

"Aye, well. I shouldna have said it quite that way. I didna mean—but ye *did* go off with him, Sassenach. As though I hadna enough to contend with, my own wife . . . and if ye'd gone to see my aunt, as I asked ye, then it wouldna have happened in the first place. Now see what ye've done!"

I had changed my mind about the desirability of a duel. I wanted Jamie and Phillip Wylie to kill each other, promptly, publicly, and with the maximum amount of blood. I also didn't care who was looking. I made a very serious effort to castrate him with my bare hands, and he grabbed my wrists, pulling them up sharply.

"Christ! Folk are watching, Sassenach!"

"I . . . don't . . . bloody . . . care!" I hissed, struggling to get free. "Let go of me, and I'll fucking give them something to watch!"

I didn't take my eyes off his face, but I was aware of a good many other faces turning toward us in the crowd on the lawn. So was he. His brows drew together for a moment, then his face set in sudden decision.

"All right, then," he said. "Let them watch."

He wrapped his arms around me, pressed me tight against himself, and kissed me. Unable to get loose, I quit fighting, and went stiff and furious instead. In the distance, I could hear laughter and raucous whoops of encouragement. Ninian Hamilton shouted something in Gaelic that I was pleased not to understand.

He finally moved his lips off mine, still holding me tightly against him, and very slowly bent his head, his cheek lying cool and firm next to mine. His body was firm, too, and not at all cool. The heat of him was leaching through at least six layers of cloth to reach my own skin: shirt, waistcoat, coat, gown, shift, and stays. Whether it was anger, arousal, or both, he was fully stoked and blazing like a furnace.

"I'm sorry," he said quietly, his breath hot and tickling in my ear. "I didna mean to insult ye. Truly. Shall I kill him, and then myself?"

I relaxed, very slightly. My hips were pressed solidly against him, and with only five layers of fabric between us there, the effect was reassuring.

"Perhaps not quite yet," I said. I felt light-headed from the rush of adrenaline, and took a deep breath to steady myself. Then I drew back a little, recoiling from the pungent reek that wafted off his clothes. Had I not been so upset, I would have noticed immediately that he was the source of the vile aroma I had been smelling.

"What on earth have you been doing?" I sniffed at the breast of his coat, frowning. "You smell terrible! Like—"

"Manure," he said, sounding resigned. "Aye, I know." His arms relaxed.

"Yes, manure," I said, sniffing further. "And rum punch"—he hadn't been drinking rum punch himself, though; I had tasted nothing but brandy when he kissed me—"and something awful, like old sweat, and—"

"Boiled turnips," he said, sounding more resigned. "Aye, the maid servant I was telling ye about, Sassenach. Betty, she's called." He tucked my hand into the crook of his arm, and with a deep bow of acknowledgment toward the crowd—who all applauded, damn them—turned to steer me toward the house.

"It would be as well if ye can get anything sensible out of her," he said, with a glance toward the sun, which hung in mid-sky above the tops of the willows along the river. "But it's growing late; I think perhaps ye'd best go up and speak to my aunt first, if there's to be a wedding at four o'clock."

I took a deep breath, trying to settle myself. A good deal of unexpended emotion was still sloshing round inside me, but there was plainly work to do.

"Right, then," I said. "I'll see Jocasta, and then have a look at Betty. As for Phillip Wylie . . ."

"As for Phillip Wylie," he interrupted, "dinna give him another thought, Sassenach." A certain look of inward intentness grew in his eyes. "I'll take care of him, later."

44

PRIVATE PARTS

I LEFT JAMIE in the parlor, and made my way up the stairs and along the hall toward Jocasta's room, nodding distractedly to friends and acquaintances encountered along the way. I was disconcerted, annoyed—and at the same time, reluctantly amused. I hadn't spent so much time in bemused contemplation of a penis since I was sixteen or so, and here I was, preoccupied with three of the things.

Finding myself alone in the hall, I opened my fan, peering thoughtfully into the tiny round looking glass that served as a lake in the pastoral scene painted on it. Meant as an aid to intrigue rather than grooming, the glass showed me no more than a few square inches of my face at once—one eye and its arched brow regarded me quizzically.

It was quite a pretty eye, I admitted. There were lines around it, true, but it was nicely shaped, gracefully lidded, and equipped with long, curving lashes whose dark sable complemented the black pupil and contrasted very strikingly with the gold-flecked amber of the iris.

I moved the fan a bit, to get a view of my mouth. Full-lipped, and rather fuller than usual at present, to say nothing of a dark, moist pink. The lips looked as though someone had been kissing them rather roughly. They also looked as though they'd liked it.

"Hm!" I said, and snapped shut the fan.

With my blood no longer boiling, I could admit that Jamie might perhaps be right about Phillip Wylie's intent in making objectionable advances to me. He might not be, too. But regardless of the young man's underlying motives, I did have incontrovertible proof that he had found me physically appealing, grandmother or not. I rather thought I wouldn't mention that to Jamie, though; Phillip Wylie was a very annoying young man, but upon cooler reflection, I had decided that I would prefer not to have him disemboweled on the front lawn, after all.

Still, maturity did alter one's perspective somewhat. For all the personal implications of those male members in an excited state, it was the flaccid one that most interested me at the moment. My fingers itched to get hold of Duncan Innes's private parts—figuratively, at least.

There were not so many kinds of trauma, short of outright castration, that would cause physical impotence. Surgery nowadays being the primitive affair it was, I supposed that it was possible that whatever doctor had attended the original injury—if one did—had in fact simply removed both testicles. If that were the case, though, would Duncan not have said so?

Well, perhaps not. Duncan was an intensely shy and modest man, and even a more extroverted personality might hesitate to confide a misfortune of that extent, even to an intimate friend. Could he have concealed such an injury in the close confines of a prison, though? I drummed my fingers on the inlaid marquetry of the table outside Jocasta's door, considering.

It was certainly possible for men to go for several years without bathing; I'd seen a few who obviously had. On the other hand, the prisoners at Ardsmuir had been forced to work outdoors, cutting peat and quarrying stone; they would have had regular access to open water, and presumably would at least have washed periodically, if only to keep the itching of vermin at bay. I supposed one could wash without necessarily stripping naked, though.

I suspected that Duncan was still more or less intact. It was much more likely, I thought, that his impotence was psychological in origin; having one's testes badly bruised or crushed was bound to give a man pause, after all, and an early experiment might easily have convinced Duncan that all was up with him—or rather, down.

I paused before knocking, but not for long. I had had

some experience of giving people bad news, after all, and the one thing that experience had taught me was that there was no point in preparation, or worry over what to say. Eloquence didn't help, and bluntness was no bar to sympathy.

I rapped sharply on the door, and entered at Jocasta's invitation.

Father LeClerc was present, seated at a small table in the corner, dealing in a workmanlike manner with a large assortment of edibles. Two bottles of wine—one empty—stood on the table as well, and the priest looked up at my entrance with a greasily beaming smile that appeared to go round his face and tie together behind his ears.

"Tally-ho, Madame!" he said cheerfully, and brandished a turkey leg at me in greeting. "Tally-ho, Tally-ho!"

"Bonjour" seemed almost repressive by contrast, so I contented myself with a curtsy and a brief "Cheerio, then!" in reply.

There was clearly no way of dislodging the priest, and nowhere else to take Jocasta, as Phaedre was in the dressing room, making a great to-do with a pair of clothes brushes. Still, given the limits of Father LeClerc's English, I supposed absolute privacy was not a requirement.

I touched Jocasta's elbow, therefore, and murmured discreetly that perhaps we might sit down in the window seat, as I had something of importance to discuss with her. She looked surprised, but nodded, and with a bow of excuse toward Father LeClerc—who didn't notice, being occupied with a stubborn bit of gristle—came to sit down beside me.

"Aye, niece?" she said, having adjusted her skirts over her knees. "What is it, then?"

"Well," I said, taking a deep breath, "it's to do with Duncan. You see . . ."

And she did. Her face grew quite blank with astonishment as I began to talk, but I was conscious of a growing sense of something else in her attitude as she listened—almost . . . relief, I thought, surprised.

Her lips pursed in absorption, the blind blue eyes fixed in her usual unsettling way, a little over my right shoulder. There was concern in her manner, but no great distress. Her expression was altering, in fact, changing from startlement to the look of one who suddenly finds an explanation for a previously troubling circumstance—and is both relieved and satisfied to have discovered it.

It occurred to me that she and Duncan *had* been living under the same roof for more than a year, and had been engaged to be married for months. Duncan's attitude toward her in public was always respectful—even deferential—and thoughtful, but he made no physical gestures of tenderness or possession toward her. That was not unusual in the least, for the times; though some gentlemen were demonstrative toward their wives, others were not. But perhaps he hadn't made such gestures in private, either, and she had expected them.

She had been beautiful, was handsome still, and quite accustomed to the admiration of men; sightless or not, I had seen her flirt skillfully with Andrew MacNeill, Ninian Bell Hamilton, Richard Caswell—even with Farquard Campbell. Perhaps she had been surprised, and even mildly discomfited, to provoke no apparent show of physical interest from Duncan.

Now she knew why, though, and drew in a deep breath, shaking her head slowly.

"My God, the poor man," she said. "To suffer such a thing, and come to terms with it and then, all at once, to have it be dragged up afresh to worry him. Dear Bride, why cannot the past leave us be in what peace we have made with it?" She looked down, blinking, and I was both surprised and touched to see that her eyes were moist.

A large presence loomed up suddenly beyond her, and I glanced up to see Father LeClerc hovering over us, like a sympathetic thundercloud in his black habit.

"Is there trouble?" he said to me, in French. "Monsieur Duncan, he has suffered some injury?"

Jocasta didn't speak more than *"Comment allez-vous?"* French, but was clearly able to understand the tone of the question, as well as to pick out Duncan's name.

"Don't tell him," she said to me, with some urgency, putting her hand on my knee.

"No, no," I assured her. I looked up at the priest, flicking my fingers in indication that there was nothing to worry about.

"Non, non," I said in turn to him. *"Ce n'est rien."* It's nothing.

He frowned at me, uncertain, then glanced at Jocasta.

"A difficulty of the marriage bed, is it?" he asked bluntly, in French. My face must have betrayed dismay at this, for he gestured discreetly downward, toward the front of his habit. "I heard the word 'scrotum,' Madame, and think you do not speak of animals."

I realized—a good bit too late—that while Father LeClerc spoke no English, he most certainly spoke Latin.

"Merde," I said under my breath, causing Jocasta, who had glanced up sharply at the word "scrotum" herself, to turn back toward me. I patted her hand reassuringly, trying to make up my mind what to do. Father LeClerc was regarding us with curiosity, but also with great kindness in his soft brown eyes.

"I'm afraid he's guessed the general shape of things," I said apologetically to Jocasta. "I think perhaps I had better explain."

Her upper teeth fastened over her lower lip, but she made no demur, and I explained matters in French, as briefly as I could. The priest's eyebrows rose, and he clutched automatically for the wooden rosary that hung from his belt.

"Oui, merde, Madame," he said. *"Quelle tragédie."* He crossed himself briefly with the crucifix, then quite unselfconsciously wiped the grease from his beard onto his sleeve, and sat down beside Jocasta.

"Ask her, please, Madame, what is her desire in this matter," he said to me. The tone was polite, but it was an order.

"Her desire?"

"*Oui*. Does she wish still to be married to Monsieur Duncan, even knowing this? For see you, Madame, by the laws of Holy Mother Church, such an impediment to consummation is a bar to true marriage. I ought not to administer the sacrament of matrimony, knowing this. However—" he hesitated, pursing his lips in thought as he glanced at Jocasta. "However, the purpose of such provision is the intent that marriage shall be a fruitful union, if God so wills. In this case, there is no question of God willing such a thing. So, you see . . ." He raised one shoulder in a Gallic shrug.

I translated this question to Jocasta, who had been squinting toward the priest, as though she could divine his meaning by sheer force of will. Enlightened, her face grew blank, and she sat back a little. Her face had assumed a MacKenzie look; that characteristic calm, still mask that meant a great deal of furious thinking was going on behind it.

I was slightly disturbed, and not only on Duncan's behalf. It hadn't occurred to me that this revelation could prevent the wedding. Jamie wanted his aunt protected, and Duncan provided for. The marriage had seemed the perfect answer; he would be perturbed if things should come unstuck at this late date.

After only a moment, though, Jocasta stirred, letting out her breath in a deep sigh.

"Well, thank Christ I'd the luck to get a Jesuit," she said dryly. "One of them could argue the Pope out of his drawers, let alone deal wi' a small matter of reading the Lord's mind. Aye, tell him I do desire to be married, still."

I conveyed this to Father LeClerc, who frowned slightly, examining Jocasta with great attention. Unaware of this scrutiny, she raised one brow, waiting for his reply.

He cleared his throat, and spoke, his eyes still on her, though he was speaking to me.

"Tell her this, Madame, if you please. While it is true that procreation is the basis of this law of the Church, that is not the only matter to consider. For marriage—true marriage of a man and woman—this . . . union of the flesh, it is important of itself. The language of the rite—the two shall become one flesh, it says, and there is reason for that. Much happens between two people who share a bed, and joy in each other. That is not all a marriage is, but it is something, truly."

He spoke with great seriousness, and I must have looked surprised, for he smiled slightly, now looking directly at me.

"I have not always been a priest, Madame," he said. "I was married once. I know what that is, as I know what it is to put aside forever that . . . fleshly . . . part of life." The wooden beads of his rosary clicked softly together as he shifted.

I nodded, took a deep breath, and translated this directly as he had said it. Jocasta listened, but took no time for thought this time; her mind was made up.

"Tell him I thank him for his advice," she said, with only the slightest edge in her voice. "I too have been married before—more than once. And with his help, I shall be married once again. Today."

I translated, but he had already taken her meaning from her upright posture and the tone of her voice. He sat for a moment, rubbing his beads between his fingers, then nodded.

"Oui, Madame," he said. He reached over and squeezed her hand in gentle encouragement. "Tally-ho, Madame!"

45

IF IT QUACKS . . .

WELL, THAT WAS ONE DOWN, I thought, mounting the stairs to the attic. Next on the agenda of pressing affairs, the slave Betty. Had she really been drugged? It had been more than two hours since Jamie had discovered her in the kitchen garden, but I thought I might still be able to discern symptoms, if she had been as badly affected as he had described her. I heard the muffled chime of the grandfather clock far below. One, two, three. An hour left before the wedding—though it could easily be postponed a bit, if Betty required more attention than I expected.

Given the undesirable position of Catholics in the colony, Jocasta would not offend her guests—mostly Protestants of one stripe or another—by obliging them to witness the Popish ceremony itself. The marriage would be performed discreetly, in her boudoir, and then the newlywed couple would descend the stairs arm-in-arm, to celebrate with their friends, all of whom could then diplomatically pretend that Father LeClerc was merely an eccentrically dressed wedding guest.

As I neared the attic, I was surprised to hear a murmur of voices above. The door to the female slaves' dormitory stood ajar; I pushed it open, to discover Ulysses standing at the head of one narrow bed, arms folded, looking like an avenging angel carved in ebony. Obviously, he considered this unfortunate occurrence to be a grave dereliction of duty on Betty's part. A small, dapper man in a frock coat and a large wig stooped by her side, some small object in his hand.

Before I could speak, he pressed this against the maid's limp arm. There was a small, sharp *click!* and he removed the object, leaving a rectangle of welling blood, a rich dark red against the slave's brown skin. The drops bloomed, merged, and began to trickle down her arm and into a bleeding bowl at her elbow.

"A scarificator," the little man explained to Ulysses, with some pride, displaying his object. "A great improvement over such crudities as lancets and fleams. Got it from Philadelphia!"

The butler bent his head courteously, either in acceptance of the invitation to examine the instrument, or acknowledgment of its distinguished provenance.

"I am sure Mistress Cameron is most obliged for your kind condescension, Dr. Fentiman," he murmured.

Fentiman. So, this was the medical establishment of Cross Creek. I cleared my throat and Ulysses lifted his head, eyes alert.

"Mistress Fraser," he said, with a small bow. "Dr. Fentiman has just been—"

"Mistress Fraser?" Doctor Fentiman had swung round, and was eyeing me with the same sort of suspicious interest with which I was viewing him. Evidently he'd been hearing things, too. Manners triumphed, though, and he made me a leg, one hand to the bosom of his satin waistcoat.

"Your servant, ma'am," he said, wobbling slightly as he came upright again. I smelled gin on his breath, and saw it in the blossoms of burst blood vessels in his nose and cheeks.

"Enchanted, I'm sure," I said, giving him my hand to kiss. He looked at first surprised, but then bent over it with a deep flourish. I looked over his powdered head, trying to make out as much as I could in the dim light of the attic.

Betty might as well have been dead for a week, judging from the ashy cast of her skin, but such light as there was in the attic came through thick oiled paper nailed across the tiny gables. Ulysses himself looked gray, like charcoal frosted with ash.

The blood from the slave's arm had already begun to clot; that was good—though I shuddered to think how many people Fentiman might have used his nasty little implement on since acquiring it. His case was open on the floor beside the bed, and I saw no indication that he thought of cleaning his instruments between usages.

"Your kindness does you great credit, Mrs. Fraser," the doctor pronounced, straightening up, but keeping hold of my hand—to steady himself, I thought. "There is no need of your troubling yourself, however. Mrs. Cameron is an old and valued acquaintance; I am quite content to attend her slave." He smiled benignly, blinking in an attempt to bring me into focus.

I could hear the maid's breathing, deep and stertorous, but quite regular. I itched to get my hands on her pulse. I inhaled deeply, as unobtrusively as possible. Above the pungent scent of Dr. Fentiman's wig, which had evidently been treated with nettle powder and hyssop against lice, and a strong fog of ancient sweat and tobacco from the doctor's body, I caught the sharp copper scent of fresh blood, and the older reek of caked, decayed blood from the inside of his case. No, Fentiman didn't clean his blades.

Beyond that, I could easily smell the alcoholic miasma that Jamie and Brianna had described, but I couldn't tell how much of it came from Betty, and how much from Fentiman. If there was any hint of laudanum in the mix, I would have to get closer to detect it, and do it fast, before the volatile aromatic oils could completely evanesce.

"How exceedingly kind of you, Doctor," I said, smiling insincerely. "I'm sure my husband's aunt is most grateful for your efforts. But surely a gentleman such as yourself—I mean, you must have many more important demands upon your attention. I'm sure that Ulysses and I can see to the woman's nursing; you'll surely be missed by your companions." Especially those eager to win a few pounds off you at cards, I thought. They'll want a chance before you sober up!

Rather to my surprise, the doctor did not at once succumb to the flattery of this speech. Releasing my hand, he smiled at me with an insincerity equal to my own.

"Oh, no, not at all, my dear. I assure you, no nursing is required here. It is no more than a simple case of overindulgence, after all. I have administered a strong emetic; as soon as it shall have its effect, the woman may safely be left. Do return to your pleasures, my dear lady; there is no need for you to risk soiling such a lovely gown, no need at all."

Before I could remonstrate, there came a heavy gagging noise from the bed, and Doctor Fentiman turned at once, snatching up the chamber pot from beneath the bed.

In spite of his own impairment, he was commendably attentive to the patient. I would myself have hesitated to administer an emetic to a comatose patient, but I had to admit that it wasn't an unreasonable thing to do in a case of suspected poisoning, even if the poison was something as commonly accepted as alcohol—and if Dr. Fentiman had perhaps detected the same thing Jamie had . . .

The slave had eaten heavily; no surprise, with so much food available for the festivities. That in itself might have saved her life, I thought, slowing the absorption of alcohol—and anything else—into her bloodstream. The vomitus reeked of mingled rum and brandy, but I did think I smelled the ghost of opium as well, faint and sickly sweet, among the other odors.

"What sort of emetic did you use?" I asked, bending over the woman and thumbing open one eye. The iris stared upward, brown and glassy as an agate marble, the pupil shrunk to a pinpoint. Ha, definitely opium.

"Mrs. Fraser!" Dr. Fentiman glared at me in irritation, his wig fallen half askew over one ear. "Do you go, please, and cease interfering! I am greatly occupied, and have no time to indulge your fancies. You, sir—remove her!" He waved a hand at Ulysses and turned back to the bed, shoving his wig into place as he did so.

"Why, you little—" I choked off the intended epithet, seeing Ulysses take an uncertain step toward me. He clearly hesitated to remove me bodily, but it was just as clear that he would obey the Doctor's orders in preference to mine.

Trembling with fury, I swept around and left the room.

Jamie was waiting for me at the foot of the stair. Seeing my face as I descended, he took my arm at once and led me out into the yard.

"That—that—" Words failed me.

"Officious worm?" he supplied helpfully. "Unsonsie sharg?"

"Yes! Did you hear him?! The gall of him, that jumped-up butcher, that bloody little . . . squirt! No time to indulge my fancies! How dare he?"

Jamie made a guttural noise, indicating sympathetic outrage.

"Shall I go up and knivvle him?" he inquired, hand on his dirk. "I could gut him for ye—or just beat his face in, if ye'd rather."

Attractive as this prospect sounded, I was forced to decline.

"Well . . . no," I said, bringing my choler under control with some difficulty. "No, I don't think you'd better do that."

The echo of our similar conversation regarding Phillip Wylie struck me. It struck Jamie, too; I saw one corner of his long mouth curl with wry humor.

"Damn," I said ruefully.

"Aye," he agreed, reluctantly taking his hand off his dirk. "It doesna look as though I shall be allowed to spill anyone's blood today, does it?"

"You want to, do you?"

"Verra much," he said, dryly. "So do you, Sassenach, from the looks of it."

I couldn't argue with that; I should have liked nothing better than to disembowel Dr. Fentiman with a blunt spoon. Instead, I rubbed a hand over my face, and took a deep breath, bringing my feelings back into some semblance of order.

"Is he likely to kill the woman?" Jamie asked, jerking his chin back toward the house.

"Not immediately." Bleeding and purging were highly objectionable and possibly dangerous, but not likely to be instantly fatal. "Oh—you were probably right about the laudanum."

Jamie nodded, pursing his lips thoughtfully.

"Well, then. The important thing is to speak wi' Betty, once she's in a condition to make sense. Ye dinna think Fentiman's the sort to stand watch over a sick slave's bed?"

Now it was my turn to think, but finally I shook my head.

"No. He *was* doing his best for her," I admitted reluctantly. "But so far as I could tell, she's in no great danger. She should be watched, but only in case she should vomit and choke in her sleep, and I doubt he'd hang about to do that, even if he thinks of it."

"Well, then." He stood in thought for a moment, the breeze lifting strands of red hair from the crown of his head. "I've sent Brianna and her man to poke about and see whether any of the guests is snoring in a corner. I'll go and do the same for the slaves. Can ye maybe steal up to the attic when Fentiman's gone, and talk to Betty as soon as she wakes?"

"I imagine so." I would have gone up in any case, if only to assure myself of Betty's welfare. "Don't take too long, though; they're almost ready for the wedding."

We stood for a moment, looking at each other.

"Dinna fash yourself, Sassenach," he said softly, and tucked a wisp of hair behind my ear. "The doctor's a wee fool; dinna mind him."

I touched his arm, thankful for his comfort and wishing to offer him the same solace for bruised feelings.

"I am sorry about Phillip Wylie," I said. I realized at once that no matter what my intentions, the effect of this reminder had not been soothing. The soft curve of his mouth tightened, and he moved back, his shoulders stiffening.

"Dinna fash yourself about him, either, Sassenach," he said. His voice was still soft, but there was nothing even slightly reassuring in it. "I shall settle wi' Mr. Wylie, by and by."

"But—" I broke off, helpless. Evidently there was nothing I could say or do that would make matters right again. If Jamie felt his honor offended—and he plainly did, regardless of what I said—then Wylie would pay for it, and that was all about it.

"You are the most pigheaded man I have ever met," I said crossly.

"Thank you," he said, with a small bow.

"That was not a compliment!"

"Aye, it was." And with another bow, he turned on his heel and strode off on his errand.

46

QUICKSILVER

TO JAMIE'S RELIEF, the wedding went off with no further difficulties. The ceremony—conducted in French—took place in Jocasta's small sitting room upstairs, attended only by the bridal pair, the priest, himself and Claire as witnesses, and Brianna and her young man. Jemmy had been present, too, but scarcely counted, as he had slept through the service.

Duncan had been pale, but composed, and Jamie's aunt had spoken her vows in a firm voice, with no evidence of hesitation. Brianna, recently wed herself and sentimental in consequence, had looked on with misty approbation, squeezing her lad's arm tight, and Roger Mac looking down at her tender-eyed. Even knowing what he did regarding the nature of this particular marriage, Jamie had felt moved himself by the sacrament, and had lifted Claire's fingers to his lips, brushing a brief kiss across them as the fat little priest intoned the blessing.

Then, the formalities concluded and the wedding contracts signed, they had all come down to join the guests at a lavish wedding supper, under the light of torches that lined the terrace, their long flames streaming over tables that groaned with the abundance of River Run.

He took a glass of wine from one of the tables, and leaned back against the low terrace wall, feeling the tension of the day drain away down his spine. One down, then.

The maid Betty was still out like a brained ox, but safe enough for the present. No one else had been found poisoned, so it was likely she'd taken the stuff herself. Auld Ninian and Barlow were both nearly as legless as the maid, and no threat to each other or anyone else. And whatever Husband and his Regulators were up to, they were doing it at a safe distance. Jamie felt pleasantly light, relieved of responsibility, and ready to turn his mind to recreation.

He raised his glass in automatic salute to Caswell and Osborn, who wandered by, heads together in earnest discourse. He had no wish for political conversation, though; he got up and turned aside, making his way through the crowds near the refreshment tables.

What he really wanted was his wife. Early as it was, the sky was already dark, and a sense of reckless festivity was spreading over the house and terrace as the torches flamed high. The air was cold, and with good wine pulsing through his blood, his hands recalled the warm touch of her under her skirt in the grove, soft and succulent as a split peach in his palm, sun-ripe and juicy.

He wanted her badly.

There. At the end of the terrace, torchlight shining on the waves of her hair, where it swooped up under that ridiculous bit of lace. His fingers twitched; once he got her alone, he'd take out her pins, one by one, and pile up her hair on her head with his hands, for the pleasure of letting it fall again, loose down her back.

She was laughing at something Lloyd Stanhope had said, a glass in her hand. Her face was slightly flushed with wine and the sight of it gave him a pleasurable itch of anticipation.

Bedding her could be anything from tenderness to riot,

but to take her when she was a bit the worse for drink was always a particular delight.

Intoxicated, she took less care for him than usual; abandoned and oblivious to all but her own pleasure, she would rake him, bite him—and beg him to serve her so, as well. He loved the feeling of power in it, the tantalizing choice between joining her at once in animal lust, or of holding himself—for a time—in check, so as to drive her at his whim.

He sipped his own wine, savoring the rare pleasure of a decent vintage, and watched her covertly. She was the center of a small knot of gentlemen, with whom she seemed to be enjoying a clash of wits. A glass or two loosened her tongue and limbered her mind, as it did his. A few glasses more, and her glow would turn to a molten heat. It was early yet, and the real feasting not yet started.

He caught her eye briefly on him, and smiled. He held the goblet by its bowl and his fingers curved round the smooth glass as though it were her breast. She saw, and understood. She lowered her lashes in coquetry to him, and turned back to her conversation, color heightened.

The delightful paradox of having her in drink was that, having abandoned consciousness of him as anything save the agent of her own sensation, she would also cease to guard herself in any way, and thus lay entirely open to him. He might tease and caress, or churn her like butter, leading her through frenzy to gasping limpness beneath him, lying at his mercy.

She was using her fan to good effect, opening her eyes wide over the edge of it, in feigned shock at something that sodomite Forbes had said. He ran the tip of his tongue thoughtfully within the tender margin of his lower lip, tasting sweet silver blood in memory. Mercy? No, he would have none.

That decision made, he was turning his mind to the more practical problem of finding a spot sufficiently secluded to carry out this engaging agenda, but was interrupted by the advent of Milford Lyon, looking sleek and full of himself. He had been introduced, but knew little of the man.

"Mr. Fraser. A word with you, sir?"

"Your servant, sir."

He turned aside for a moment to set down his glass, a slight shift of his weight enough to effect discreet adjustment of his plaid, glad that he wasn't wearing tight satin breeks like that fop, Wylie. Indecent, he thought them, and grossly uncomfortable, forbye. Why, a man would be risking slow emasculation in female company, if he were not a natural eunuch—and Wylie clearly wasn't that, for all his powder and patches. A belted plaid, though, could hide a multitude of sins—or at the least, a dirk and pistol—let alone a random cockstand.

"Shall we walk a bit, Mr. Lyon?" he suggested, turning back. If the man had such private business as his manner implied, they had best not stand here, where they might be interrupted at any moment by one of the wedding guests.

They strolled slowly to the end of the terrace, exchanging commonplaces with each other, and pleasantries with passersby, until they had gained the freedom of the yard, where they hesitated for a moment.

"The paddock, perhaps?" Not waiting for Lyon's nod of assent, Jamie turned toward the distant stable yard. He wanted to see the Friesians again, in any case.

"I have heard much of you, Mr. Fraser," Lyon began pleasantly, as they ambled toward the tall clock tower of the stable block.

"Have you, sir? Well, and I trust not a great deal of it was to my discredit, then." He had heard a bit about Lyon; a dealer in what anyone would buy or sell—and maybe not just that bit too scrupulous regarding the provenance of his goods. Rumor had it that he dealt in things less tangible than iron and paper on occasion, too, but that was only rumor.

Lyon laughed, showing teeth that were even enough, but badly stained with tobacco.

"Indeed not, Mr. Fraser. Bar the slight impediment of your familial connections—which can scarcely be held to be your fault, though folk *will* make assumptions—I have heard none but the most glowing encomiums, both of your character and your accomplishments."

A Dhia, Jamie thought, blackmail and butter, all in the first sentence. Was it only that North Carolina was a backwater, and not worth the time of a more competent intriguer?

He smiled politely, with a murmur of modest dismissal, and waited to see what the blockheid wanted.

Not so much, at least to start. The strength of Fraser's militia regiment, and the names of the men. That was interesting, he thought. Lyon was not the Governor's man, then, or he would have such information to hand. Who was behind him, if anyone? Not the Regulation surely; the only one of them with a spare shilling to his name was Ninian Bell Hamilton, and if auld Ninian had wanted to know a thing, he would have come and asked himself. One of the rich planters from the coast, then? Most aristocrats had an interest in the colony that went no further than their pockets.

Which led to the logical conclusion that whoever Lyon's intended market was thought there'd be something either to gain or to lose from the potential disaffections in the colony. Who might that be?

"Chisholm, McGillivray, Lindsay . . ." Lyon was saying reflectively. "So the majority of your men are Scottish Highlanders. The sons of earlier settlers, are they, or perhaps retired soldiers, like yourself, sir?"

"Oh, I should doubt that a soldier is ever truly retired, sir," Jamie said, stooping to let one of the stable dogs smell his knuckles. "Once a man has lived under arms, I suspect he is marked for life. In fact I have heard it remarked that old soldiers never die; they just fade away."

Lyon laughed immoderately at that, declaring it a fine epigram, was it his own? Without stopping to hear the answer, he went on, clearly paddling into well-charted waters.

"I am pleased to hear such a sentiment expressed, Mr. Fraser. His Majesty has always relied upon the stoutness of the Highlanders, and their abilities as fighting men. Did you or your neighbors perhaps serve with your cousin's regiment? The Seventy-eighth Frasers acquitted themselves with great distinction during the recent conflict; I daresay the art of warfare runs in the blood, eh?"

That was a bald enough swipe. Young Simon Fraser was not in fact his cousin, but his half-uncle, son of his grandfather. It was as expiation of the old man's treason and in an effort to retrieve the family fortunes and estates that Young Simon had raised two regiments for the Seven Years' War—

what Brianna persisted in calling the French and Indian Wars, as though Britain had had nothing to do with it.

Lyon was asking now whether Jamie had also sought to establish his credentials as a loyal soldier of the Crown, by taking commission with one of the Highland regiments? He could scarcely believe the flat-footedness of the man.

"Ah, no. I regret that I was unable to serve in such a capacity," Jamie said. "An indisposition from an earlier campaign, you understand?" The minor indisposition of having been a prisoner of the Crown for several years after the Rising, though he did not mention that. If Lyon didn't know it already, there was no sense in telling him.

They had reached the paddock by now, and leaned comfortably upon the split-rail fence. The horses had not yet been put away for the night; the big black creatures moved like shadows, their coats glossy in the torchlight.

"What strange horses, are they not?" He interrupted Lyon's disquisition on the evils of factionalism, watching them move in fascination.

It wasn't just the enormously long, silky manes, rippling like water as they tossed their heads, nor yet the coal-black coats nor the springy arch of the neck, thicker and more muscular than Jocasta's thoroughbreds. Their bodies were thick as well, broad through chest, withers, and barrel so that each one seemed almost blocky—and yet they moved as gracefully as any horse he had ever seen, adroit and light-footed, with a sense of playfulness and intelligence.

"Yes, it is a very old breed," Lyon said, putting aside his inquisitiveness for the moment in order to watch. "I've seen them before—in Holland."

"Holland. Ye will have traveled there a great deal?"

"Not so much. I was there some years ago, though, and chanced to meet a kinsman of yours. A wine merchant named Jared Fraser?"

Jamie felt a jolt of surprise, succeeded by a warm sense of pleasure at the mention of his cousin.

"Did ye indeed? Aye, Jared is my father's cousin. I trust ye found him well."

"Very well indeed." Lyon moved fractionally closer, settling himself on the fence, and Jamie realized that they had now reached the point of the man's business, whatever that might be. He drained the rest of the wine in his glass and set it down, prepared to listen.

"I understand that a . . . talent for liquor runs in the family as well, Mr. Fraser."

He laughed, though he felt no great humor.

"A taste, perhaps, sir. I couldna say, as to talent."

"Couldn't you? Ah, well. I am sure you are too modest, Mr. Fraser. The quality of your whisky is well known."

"Ye flatter me, sir." He knew what was coming now, and settled himself to pretend attention. It wouldn't be the first time someone had suggested a partnership; he to provide the whisky, they to manage the distribution of it to Cross Creek, to Wilmington, even as far as Charleston. Lyon, it seemed, had grander schemes in mind.

The best aged stuff would go by boat up the coast to Boston and Philadelphia, he suggested. The raw whisky, though, could go across the Treaty Line, there to be delivered to the Cherokee villages, in return for hides and furs. He had partners, who would provide . . .

Jamie listened in growing disapproval, then cut Lyon off abruptly.

"Aye. I thank ye for your interest, sir, but I fear I havena anything like sufficient product for what ye suggest. I make whisky only for my family's use, and a few barrels beyond that, now and then, for local trade. No more."

Lyon grunted amiably.

"I am sure you could increase your production, Mr. Fraser, given your knowledge and skill. If it were to be a matter of the materials . . . some arrangement could be made, I am sure . . . I can speak with the gentlemen who would be our partners in the enterprise, and—"

"No, sir. I fear not. If ye will excuse me . . . ?" He bowed abruptly, turned on his heel, and headed back toward the terrace, leaving Lyon in the dark.

He must ask Farquard Campbell about Lyon. The man would bear watching. It was not that Jamie had any great objection to smuggling. He did, however, have a great objection to being caught at it, and could think of few things more dangerous than a large-scale operation of the sort Lyon was suggesting, where he himself would be involved up to the neck, but have no control over the more dangerous parts of the process.

Aye, the thought of the money was attractive, but not so much as to blind him to the risks. If he were to engage in such a trade, he would do it himself, perhaps with the aid of Fergus or Roger Mac—maybe old Arch Bug and Joe Wemyss—but no one else. A great deal safer to keep it small, keep it private . . . though since Lyon had suggested the notion, perhaps it was worth a bit of thought. Fergus was no farmer, that was sure; something must be found for him to do, and the Frenchman was well acquainted with the risky business, as they called it, from their time in Edinburgh. . . .

He strolled back to the terrace, pondering, but the sight of his wife erased all thought of whisky from his mind.

Claire had left Stanhope and his cronies, and stood by the buffet table, looking over the delicacies on display with a faint frown upon her broad clear brow, as though puzzled by such surfeit.

He saw Gerald Forbes's eyes rest on her, alight with speculation, and he moved at once by reflex, interposing himself neatly between his wife and the lawyer. He felt the man's eyes slap against his back, and smiled grimly to himself. *Mine, corbie*, he thought to himself.

"Can ye not decide where to begin, Sassenach?" He reached down and took the empty wineglass from her hand, taking advantage of the movement to come close against her back, feeling the warmth of her through his clothes.

She laughed, and swayed back against him, leaning on his arm. She smelled faintly of rice powder and warm skin, with the scent of rose hips in her hair.

"I'm not even terribly hungry. I was just counting the jellies and preserves. There are thirty-seven different ones—unless I've missed my count."

He spared a glance for the table, which did indeed hold a bewildering array of silver dishes, porcelain bowls, and wooden platters, groaning with more food than would feed a Highland village for a month. He wasn't hungry, either, though. At least not for puddings and savories.

"Well, Ulysses will have seen to that; he wouldna have my aunt's hospitality put to shame."

"No fear of that," she assured him. "Did you see the barbecue pit out back? There are no fewer than three whole oxen roasting on spits out there, and at least a dozen pigs. I didn't even try to count the chickens and ducks. Do you think it's just hospitality, or is your aunt meaning to make a show of what a good job Duncan's done—showing off how profitable River Run is under his management, I mean?"

"I suppose she might," he said, though privately he thought it unlikely that Jocasta's motives were either so thoughtful or so generous in nature. He considered that the lavishness of the present celebration was much more likely owing to her desire to wipe Farquard Campbell's eye, overshadowing the fete he had held at Greenoaks in December, to celebrate his most recent marriage.

And speaking of marriage . . .

"Here, Sassenach." He deposited her empty glass on a passing tray borne by a servant, and took a full one in return, which he set in her hand.

"Oh, I'm not—" she began, but he forestalled her, taking another glass from the proffered tray and lifting it to her in salute. Her cheeks flushed deeper, and her eyes glowed amber.

"To beauty," he said softly, smiling.

I FELT PLEASANTLY liquid inside, as though belly and limbs were filled with quicksilver. It wasn't all to do with the wine, though that was very good. More the release of tension, after all the worries and conflicts of the day.

It had been a quiet, tender wedding, and while the evening's celebration was likely to be noisy in the extreme—I had heard a number of the younger men plotting vulgar hilarities for the later festivities—I needn't worry about any of that. My own intent had been to enjoy the delightful supper that had been laid on, perhaps take a glass or two more of the excellent wine . . . and then find Jamie and go to investigate the romantic potential of the stone bench beneath the willows.

Jamie had appeared a trifle prematurely in the program, insofar as I had not yet eaten anything, but I had no objection to rearranging my priorities. There would be plenty of left-overs, after all.

The torchlight burnished him, making hair and brows and skin glow like copper. The evening breeze had come up, flapping tablecloths and pulling the torch flames into fiery tongues, and it nipped strands of hair from his queue and lashed them across his face. He raised his glass, smiling at me across the rim.

"To beauty," he said softly, then drank, not taking his eyes off me.

The quicksilver shifted, quivering through my hips and down the backs of my legs.

"To . . . ah . . . privacy," I replied, with a slight lift of my own glass. Feeling pleasantly reckless, I reached slowly up, and deliberately pulled the ornamented lace from my hair. Half-unpinned, curls fell loose down my back, and I heard someone draw in his breath in shock behind me.

In front of me, Jamie's face went suddenly blank, his eyes fixed on me like a hawk's on a rabbit. I lifted my glass, holding his eyes with mine, and drank, swallowing slowly as I drained it. The scent of black grapes perfumed the inside of my head and the heat of the wine warmed my face, my throat, my breasts, my skin. Jamie moved abruptly to take the empty glass from my hand, his fingers cold and hard on mine.

And then a voice spoke from the candlelit French doors behind him.

"Mr. Fraser."

We both started, and the glass fell between us, exploding into shards on the flags of the terrace. Jamie whirled round, his left hand going by reflex to the hilt of his dirk. Then it relaxed, as he saw the silhouetted figure, and he stepped back, mouth twisting in a wry grimace.

Phillip Wylie stepped out into the torchlight. His color was high enough to show through the powder, burning in hectic spots across his cheekbones.

"My friend Stanhope has proposed a table or two of whist this evening," he said. "Will you not join us, Mr. Fraser?"

Jamie gave him a long, cool look, and I saw the damaged fingers of his right hand twitch, very slightly. The pulse was throbbing at the side of his neck, but his voice was calm.

"At whist?"

"Yes." Wylie gave a thin smile, sedulously avoiding looking at me. "I hear you are a good hand at the cards, sir." He pursed his lips. "Though of course, we do play for rather high stakes. Perhaps you do not feel that you—"

"I shall be delighted," Jamie said, in a tone of voice that made it perfectly clear that the only thing that would truly have delighted him was the prospect of cramming Phillip Wylie's teeth down his throat.

The teeth in question gleamed briefly.

"Ah. Splendid. I shall . . . look forward to the occasion."

"Your servant, sir." Jamie bowed abruptly, then spun on his heel, seized my elbow, and marched off down the terrace, me decorously in tow.

I marched along, keeping step and keeping silence, until we were safely out of earshot. The quicksilver had shot up out of my lower regions, and was rolling nervously up and down my spine, making me feel dangerously unstable.

"Are you quite out of your mind?" I inquired politely. Receiving nothing but a brief snort in reply, I dug in my heels and pulled on his arm to make him stop.

"That was not a rhetorical question," I said, rather more loudly. "High-stakes whist?"

Jamie was indeed an excellent card player. He also knew most of the possible ways of cheating at cards. However, whist was difficult if not impossible to cheat at, and Phillip Wylie also had the reputation of an excellent player—as did Stanhope. Beyond this, there remained the fact that Jamie didn't happen to possess *any* stakes, let alone high ones.

"Ye expect me to allow yon popinjay to trample my honor, and then insult me to my face?" He swung round to face me, glaring.

"I'm sure he didn't mean—" I began, but broke off. It was quite apparent that if Wylie had not intended outright insult, he had meant it as a challenge—and to a Scot, the two were likely indistinguishable.

"But you don't *have* to do it!"

I would have had a much greater effect had I been arguing with the brick wall of the kitchen garden.

"I do," he said stiffly. "I have my pride."

I rubbed a hand over my face in exasperation.

"Yes, and Phillip Wylie plainly knows it! Heard the one about pride going before a fall, have you?"

"I havena the slightest intention of falling," he assured me. "Will ye give me your gold ring?"

My mouth fell open in shock.

"Will I . . . my ring?" My fingers went involuntarily to my left hand, and the smooth gold of Frank's wedding band.

He was watching me intently, eyes steady on mine. The torches along the terrace had been lit; the dancing light caught him from the side, throwing the stubborn set of his bones into sharp relief, lighting one eye with burning blue.

"I shall need a stake," he said quietly.

"Bloody hell." I swung away from him, and stood staring off the edge of the terrace. The torches on the lawn had been lit, too, and Perseus's white marble buttocks glimmered through the dark.

"I willna lose it," Jamie said behind me. His hand rested on my shoulder, heavy through my shawl. "Or if I do—I shall redeem it. I know ye . . . value it."

I twitched my shoulder out from under his hand, and moved a few steps away. My heart was pounding, and my face felt at once clammy and hot, as though I were about to faint.

He didn't speak, or touch me; only stood there, waiting.

"The gold one," I said at last, flatly. "Not the silver?" Not *his* ring; not *his* mark of ownership.

"The gold is worth more," he said, and then, after the briefest hesitation, added, "in terms of money."

"I know that." I turned round to face him. The torch flames fluttered in the wind and cast a moving light across his features that made them hard to read.

"I meant—hadn't you better take both of them?" My hands were cold and slippery with sweat; the gold ring came off easily; the silver was tighter, but I twisted it past my knuckle. I took his hand and dropped the two rings clinking into it.

Then I turned and walked away.

47

THE LISTS OF VENUS

ROGER MADE HIS WAY from the drawing room out onto the terrace, threading through the gathering crowd that clustered thick as lice round the supper tables. He was hot and sweating and the night air struck coldly refreshing on his face. He paused in the shadows at the end of the terrace, where he could unbutton his waistcoat inconspicuously and flap his shirtfront a bit, letting the cold air inside.

The pine torches that lined the edge of the terrace and the brick paths were flickering in the wind, casting wildly shifting shadows over the mass of celebrants, from which limbs and faces emerged and disappeared in bewildering succession. Fire gleamed off silver and crystal, gold lace and shoebuckles, earrings and coat buttons. From a distance, it looked as though the assembly were lit by fireflies, winking in and out among the dark mass of rustling fabric. Brianna was not wearing anything reflective, he thought, but she should be easy enough to spot, nonetheless, on account of her height.

He had caught no more than tantalizing glimpses of her during the day; she had been dancing attendance on her aunt, or caring for Jemmy, or engaged in conversation with the—apparently—dozens of people she knew from her earlier sojourn at River Run. He didn't begrudge her the opportunity in the least; there was precious little society to be had on

Fraser's Ridge, and he was pleased to see her enjoying herself.

He'd been having a great time himself; his throat had an agreeably raspy feeling now, from the exertion of prolonged singing, and he had learned three new songs from Seamus Hanlon, safely committed to memory. He'd bowed out at last, and left the little orchestra playing in the drawing room, throbbing away in a steamy haze of effort, sweat, and alcohol.

There she was; he caught the glint of her hair as she came out of the parlor doors, turning back to say something to the woman behind her.

She caught sight of him as she turned back, and her face lit up, touching off a complementary warm glow beneath his rebuttoned waistcoat.

"There you are! I've barely seen you all day. Heard you now and then, though," she added, with a nod toward the open drawing-room doors.

"Oh, aye? Sound all right, did it?" he asked casually, shamelessly fishing for compliments. She grinned and tapped his chest with her closed fan, mimicking the gesture of an accomplished coquette—which she wasn't.

"Oh, Mrs. MacKenzie," she said, pitching her voice high and through her nose, "your husband's voice is divinity itself! Were I so fortunate, I am sure I should spend hours just *drrrinking* in the sound of it!"

He laughed, recognizing Miss Martin, old Miss Bledsoe's young and rather plain companion, who had hung about wide-eyed and sighing while he sang ballads in the afternoon.

"You know you're good," she said, dropping back into her own voice. "You don't need me to tell you."

"Maybe not," he admitted. "Doesn't mean I don't like to hear it, though."

"Really? The adulation of the multitudes isn't enough?" She was laughing at him, eyes gone to triangles of amusement.

He didn't know how to answer that, and laughed instead, taking her hand.

"D'ye want to dance?" He cocked his head toward the end

of the terrace where the French doors to the drawing room stood open, letting out the cheerful strains of "Duke of Perth," then back toward the tables. "Or to eat?"

"Neither. I want to get away from here for a minute; I can hardly breathe." A drop of sweat ran down her neck, glinting red in the torchlight before she swiped it away.

"Great." He took her hand and drew it through his arm, turning toward the herbaceous border that lay beyond the terrace. "I know just the place."

"Great. Oh—wait. Maybe I do want something to eat." She lifted a hand and stopped a slave boy, coming up to the terrace from the cookhouse with a small covered tray from which an appetizing steam wafted into the air. "What's that, Tommy? Can I have some?"

"You have all you want, Miss Bree." He smiled, whipping the napkin away to display a selection of savories. She inhaled beatifically.

"I want them all," she said, taking the tray, to Tommy's amusement. Roger, seizing the chance, murmured his own request to the slave, who nodded, disappeared, and returned within moments with an open bottle of wine and two goblets. Roger took these, and together they wandered down the path that led from the house to the dock, sharing tidbits of news along with the pigeon pies.

"Did you find any of the guests passed out in the shrubbery?" she asked, her words muffled by a mouthful of mushroom pasty. She swallowed, and became more distinct. "When Da asked you to go and look this afternoon, I mean."

He snorted briefly, selecting a dumpling made of sausage and dried pumpkin.

"Ken the difference between a Scottish wedding and a Scottish funeral, do ye?"

"No, what?"

"The funeral has one less drunk."

She laughed, scattering crumbs, and took a Scotch egg.

"No," he said, steering her skillfully to the right of the dock, and toward the willows. "Ye'll see a few feet sticking out of the bushes now, but this afternoon, they hadn't had the time to get rat-legged yet."

"You have *such* a way with words," she said appreciatively. "I went and talked to the slaves; all present and accounted for, and mostly sober, too. A couple of the women admitted that Betty does tipple at parties, though."

"To say the least, from what your Da said. Stinking, he described her as, and I gather he didn't mean only drunk." Something small and dark leaped out of his path. Frog; he could hear them piping away in the grove.

"Mmm. Mama said she seemed to be okay later on, in spite of Dr. Fentiman insisting on bleeding her." She gave a small shudder, drawing her shawl round her shoulders one-handed. "He gives me the creeps, the Doctor. He looks like a little goblin or something, and he's got the clammiest hands I ever felt. And he smells terrible, speaking of stinking."

"I haven't had the pleasure yet," Roger said, amused. "Come on." He pushed aside the hanging veil of willow branches, alert lest he disturb some courting couple that had beaten them to the stone bench, but all was well. Everyone was up at the house, dancing, eating, drinking, and planning a later serenade of the wedding pair. Better Duncan and Jocasta than us, he thought, rolling his eyes inwardly at some of the things he'd heard suggested. Another time, he might have been interested to see a shivaree, and trace all the roots of it from French and Highland customs—but not bloody now.

It was suddenly quiet under the willows, most of the noise from the house drowned by the rushing of water and the monotonous chirping of frogs. It was also dark as midnight, and Brianna felt carefully for the bench, in order to set down her tray.

Roger shut his eyes hard and counted to thirty; when he opened them, he could at least make out her form, silhouetted against the dim light that filtered through the willows, and the horizontal line of the bench. He set down the glasses and poured out the wine, the neck of the bottle chinking faintly against the goblets as he felt his way.

He put out a hand and ran it down her arm, locating her hand in order to put the full goblet safely into it. He raised his own glass in salute.

"To beauty," he said, letting the smile show in his voice.

"To privacy," she said, returning the toast, and drank. "Oh, that's good," she said, a moment later, sounding slightly dreamy. "I haven't had wine in . . . a year? No, nearly two. Not since before Jemmy was born. In fact, not since . . ." Her voice stopped abruptly, then resumed, more slowly. "Not since our *first* wedding night. In Wilmington, remember."

"I remember." He reached out and cupped a hand round her cheek, tracing the bones of her face softly with his thumb. It was no wonder that she thought of that night now. They had begun it there, under the drooping branches of a huge horse-chestnut tree, that had sheltered them from the noise and light of a nearby tavern. Their present situation was oddly and movingly reminiscent of that dark and private secrecy, the two of them amid the smell of leaves and nearby water—the nearby racket of lust-crazed tree frogs replacing the tavern noises.

That had been a hot night, though, thick and humid enough that flesh melted to flesh. Now it was cold enough that his body yearned for the warmth of hers, and the scent that enclosed them was the spring smell of green leaves and running river, not the musty smell of leaf-litter and mudflats.

"Do you think they'll sleep together?" Brianna asked. She sounded slightly breathless; perhaps it was the wine.

"Who? Oh, Jocasta, ye mean, and Duncan? Why not? They'll be married." He drained his own glass and set it down, the glass chiming faintly on the stone.

"It was a beautiful wedding, wasn't it?" She didn't resist as he took the glass from her hand and set it down with his own. "Quiet, but awfully nice."

"Aye, very nice." He kissed her, softly, and held her close against him. He could feel the back lacing of her gown, criss-crossed under the thin knitted shawl.

"Mmm. You taste good."

"Oh, aye, like sausages and wine. So do you." His hand twitched up the edge of the shawl, getting beneath and fumbling for the end of the lace, somewhere down near the small of her back. She pressed against him, making it easier.

"Will we still want to make love, do you think, when we're as old as they are?" she murmured in his ear.

"I will," he assured her, getting hold of the small bow that secured the lace. "I hope you will, too; I shouldna like to have to do it alone."

She laughed, and took a deep breath, her back swelling suddenly as the tight lacing came loose. There were the stays underneath, too, though, damn it. He used both hands, looking for the inner lacings, and she arched her back helpfully, which made her breasts swell up into sight just below his chin. The sight made him take one hand off her back, to deal with this new and delightful development.

"I haven't got my . . . I mean, I didn't bring . . ." She pulled back a little, sounding dubious.

"Ye've taken the seeds today, though?" Away to hell with pizza and loo-paper, he thought; at the moment, he'd trade all prospects of indoor plumbing for a rubber condom.

"Yes." She still sounded doubtful, though, and he gritted his teeth, taking a firmer hold on her, as though she might bolt.

"It's all right," he whispered, nuzzling his way down the side of her neck toward that heartbreaking slope where the muscle of her shoulder joined it. She was smooth beneath his lips, her skin cool in the air, warm and scented beneath the fall of her hair. "We needn't . . . I mean . . . I won't . . . just let me . . ."

The neckline of her dress was fashionably low with her kerchief pulled off, still lower, with her gown unlaced, and her breast was heavy and soft in his hand. He felt the nipple big and round as a ripe cherry against his palm, and bent on impulse to put his mouth to it.

She stiffened, then relaxed with an odd little sigh, and he felt a warm sweet taste on his tongue, then a strange pulsing and a flooding of the . . . he swallowed by reflex, shocked. Shocked, and terribly aroused. He hadn't thought; he hadn't meant . . . but she pulled his head hard against her, holding him.

He went on, emboldened, and pushed her gently backward, easing her down onto the edge of the bench, so that he knelt before her. A sudden thought had come to him, prompted by the stinging memory of that entry in her dreambook.

"Don't worry," he whispered to her. "We won't . . . risk anything. Let me do this—just for you."

She hesitated, but let him run his hands under her skirt, up the silken curves of stockinged calf and round, bare thigh, under the flattened curve of her buttocks, cool and bare on the stone, beneath the froth of petticoats. One of Seamus's songs had described a gentleman's exploits "in the lists of Venus." The words drifted through his head with the rushing of the water, and he was determined to acquit himself with honor in those lists.

Maybe she couldn't describe it, but he meant to make sure she knew it had happened. She shivered between his hands, and he cupped one hand between her thighs.

"Miss Bree?"

Both of them jerked convulsively, Roger snatching his hands away as though burned. He could feel the thunder of blood in his ears—and his balls.

"Yes, what is it? Is that you, Phaedre? What's wrong—is it Jemmy?"

He was sitting back on his heels, trying to breathe, feeling dizzy. He caught the brief pale gleam of her breasts above him as she stood up and turned toward the voice, tucking her kerchief hastily back in, pulling the shawl up over her unfastened gown.

"Yes, ma'am." Phaedre's voice came out from under the willow nearest the house; nothing of the slave showed but the whiteness of her cap, floating dimly in the shadows. "Poor child, he woke up hot and fussin', wouldn't take neither mush nor milk, and then he started in to cough, sounded bad enough, Teresa said we best fetch Dr. Fentiman along to him, but I said . . ."

"Dr. Fentiman!"

Brianna disappeared with a ferocious rustling of willow branches, and he heard the hurrying thump of slippered feet on earth as she ran toward the house, Phaedre in her wake.

Roger got to his feet, and paused for a moment, hand on his fly-buttons. The temptation was strong; it wouldn't take more than a minute—less, probably, in his present condition. But no, Bree might need him to deal with Fentiman. The thought of the Doctor using his gory instruments on Jemmy's soft flesh was enough to send him crashing through the willows in hot pursuit. The lists of Venus would have to wait.

HE FOUND BREE and Jemmy in Jocasta's boudoir, the center of a small knot of women, all of whom looked surprised—even mildly scandalized—at his appearance. Disregarding the raised eyebrows and huffing noises, he forged his way through the skirts to Brianna's side.

The little fella did look bad, and Roger felt a clutch of fear in the pit of his stomach. Christ, how could it happen so fast? He'd seen Jem at the wedding only a few hours before, curled up pink and sweet in his makeshift cradle, and before that, being his usual raucously genial self at the party. Now he lay against Brianna's shoulder, flush-cheeked and heavy-eyed, whimpering a little, with a slick of clear mucus dribbling from his nose.

"How is he?" He reached out and touched a flushed cheek gently, with the back of his hand. God, he was hot!

"He's sick," Brianna said tersely. As though in confirmation, Jemmy began to cough, a dreadful noise, loud but half-choked, like a seal choking on its fish. The blood surged into his already flushed face, and his round blue eyes bulged with the effort of drawing breath between the spasms.

"Shit," Roger muttered. "What do we do?"

"Cold water," one of the women standing beside him said, authoritatively. "Put him altogether under a bath of cold water, then make him drink more of it."

"No! Heavens, Mary, you'll kill the child." Another young matron reached out to pat Jemmy's quivering back. "It's the croup; my lot have had it now and again. Sliced garlic, warmed and put to the soles of his feet," she told Brianna. "That works well, sometimes."

"And if it doesn't?" another woman said, skeptical. The first woman's nostrils pinched, and her friend butted in helpfully.

"Johanna Richards lost two babes to the croup. Gone like that!" She snapped her fingers, and Brianna flinched as though the sound were one of her own bones cracking.

"Why are we havering so, and a medico to hand? You, girl, go and fetch Dr. Fentiman! Did I not say so?" One of the women clapped her hands sharply at Phaedre, who stood pressed back against the wall, eyes fixed on Jemmy. Before she could move to obey, though, Brianna's head shot up.

"No! Not him, I won't have him." She glared round at the women, then shot Roger a look of urgent entreaty. "Find Mama for me. Quick!"

He turned and shoved past the women, fear momentarily assuaged by the ability to do something. Where was Claire likely to be? *Help*, he thought, *help me find her, help him be all right*, directing the incoherent prayer toward anyone who might be listening—God, the Reverend, Mrs. Graham, Saint Bride, Claire herself—he wasn't particular.

He thundered down the front stair to the foyer, only to meet Claire hurrying across it toward him. Someone had told her; she gave him one quick look, asked, "Jemmy?" with a lift of her chin, and at his breathless nod, was up the stairs in a flash, leaving a foyer full of people gaping after her.

He caught her up in the hall above and was in time to open the door for her—and to receive an undeserved but much appreciated look of gratitude from Bree.

He stood back out of the way, catching his breath and marveling. The moment Claire stepped into the room, the atmosphere of worry and near-panic changed at once. There was still an air of concern among the women, but they gave way without hesitation, standing back respectfully and murmuring to one another as Claire headed straight for Jemmy and Bree, ignoring everything else.

"Hallo, lovey. What is it, then, are we feeling miserable?" She was murmuring to Jem, turning his head to one side and feeling gently under his flushed chubby jowls and behind his ears. "Poor thing. It's all right, sweetheart, Mummy's here, Grannie's here, everything will be just fine. . . . How long has he been like this? Has he had anything to drink? Yes, darling, that's right. . . . Does it hurt him to swallow?"

She alternated between comforting remarks to the baby and questions to Brianna and Phaedre, all delivered in the same tone of calm reassurance as her hands touched here and there, exploring, soothing. Roger felt it working on him, too, and drew a deep breath, feeling the tightness in his own chest ease a bit.

Claire took a sheet of Jocasta's heavy notepaper from the secretary, rolled it into a tube, and used it to listen intently to Jemmy's back and chest as he made more of the choking-seal noises. Roger noticed dimly that her hair had fallen down somehow; she had to brush it out of the way to listen.

"Yes, of course it's croup," she said absently, in answer to a half-questioning diagnosis offered diffidently by one of the bystanders. "But that's only the cough and the difficult breathing. You can have croup by itself, so to speak, or as an early symptom of various other things."

"Such as?" Bree had a death grip on Jemmy, and her face was nearly as white as her knuckles.

"Oh. . . ." Claire seemed to be listening intently, but not to Bree. More to whatever was happening inside Jemmy, who had quit coughing and was lying exhausted against his mother's shoulder, breathing thickly in steam-engine gasps. "Um . . . coryza—that's only a common cold. Influenza. Asthma. Diphtheria. But it isn't that," she added hurriedly, looking up and catching a glimpse of Brianna's face.

"You're sure?"

"Yes," Claire replied firmly, straightening up and putting aside her makeshift stethoscope. "It doesn't feel at all like diphtheria to me. Besides, there isn't any of that about, or I'd have heard. And he's still being breast-fed; he'll have immunity—" She stopped speaking abruptly, suddenly aware of the women looking on. She cleared her own throat, bending down again, as though to encourage Jemmy by example. He made a small whimper and coughed again. Roger felt it, like a rock in his chest.

"It isn't serious," Claire announced firmly, straightening. "We must put him in a croup tent, though. Bring him down to the kitchen. Phaedre, will you find me a couple of old quilts, please?"

She moved toward the door, shooing the women before her like a flock of hens.

Obeying an impulse that he didn't stop to question, Roger reached for the baby, and after a instant's hesitation, Brianna let him take him. Jemmy didn't fuss, but hung listless and heavy, the limp slackness a terrible change from his normal India-rubber bounce. The baby's cheek burned through the cloth of Roger's shirt as he carried the little boy downstairs, Bree at his elbow.

The kitchen was in the brick-walled basement of the house, and Roger had a brief vision of Orpheus descending into the underworld, Eurydice close behind him, as they made their way down the dark back stair into the shadowy depths of the kitchen. Instead of a magic lyre, though, he bore a child who burned like coal and coughed as though his lungs would burst. If he didn't look back, he thought, the boy would be all right.

"Perhaps a little cold water wouldn't come amiss." Claire put her hand on Jemmy's forehead, judging his temperature. "Have you got an ear infection, sweetheart?" She blew gently into one of the baby's ears, then the other; he blinked, coughed hoarsely, and swiped a chubby hand across his face, but didn't flinch. The slaves were bustling round in a corner of the kitchen, bringing boiling water, pinning the quilts to a rafter to make the tent at her direction.

Claire took the baby out of Roger's arms to bathe him, and he stood bereft, wanting urgently to do something, anything, until Brianna took his hand and clutched it hard, her nails digging into his palm.

"He'll be all right," she whispered. "He will." He squeezed hard back, wordless.

Then the tent was ready, and Brianna ducked under the hanging quilt, turning to reach back for Jemmy, who was alternately coughing and crying, having not liked the cold water at all. Claire had sent a slave to fetch her medicine box, and now rummaged through it, coming up with a vial filled with a pale yellow oil, and a jar of dirty white crystals.

Before she could do anything with them, though, Joshua, one of the grooms, came thumping down the stairs, half-breathless with his hurry.

"Mrs. Claire, Mrs. Claire!"

Some of the gentlemen had been firing off their pistols in celebration of the happy event, it seemed, and one of them had suffered some kind of mishap, though Josh seemed uncertain as to exactly what had happened.

"He isna bad hurt," the groom assured Claire, in the Aberdonian Scots that came so peculiarly from his black face, "but he is bleedin' quite free, and Dr. Fentiman—well, he's maybe no quite sae steady as he might be the noo. Will ye come, Ma'am?"

"Yes, of course." In the blink of an eye, she had thrust vial and jar into Roger's hands. "I'll have to go. Here. Put some in the hot water; keep him breathing the steam until he stops coughing." Quick and neat, she'd closed up her box and handed it to Josh to carry, heading for the stair before Roger could ask her anything. Then she was gone.

Wisps of steam were escaping through the opening in the tent; seeing that, he paused long enough to shed coat and waistcoat, leaving them in a careless heap on the floor as he bent and ducked into the darkness, vial and jar in hand.

Bree was crouched on a stool, Jemmy on her lap, a big white pudding-basin full of steaming water at her feet. A swath of light from the hearth fell momentarily across her face, and Roger smiled at her, trying to look reassuring, before the quilt dropped back into place.

"Where's Mama? Did she leave?"

"Aye, there was some sort of emergency. It'll be fine, though," he said firmly. "She gave me the stuff to put in the water; said just to keep him in the steam until the coughing stops."

He sat down on the floor beside the basin of water. It was very dim in the tent, but not totally dark. As his eyes adjusted, he could see well enough. Bree still looked worried, but not nearly so frightened as she'd been upstairs. He felt better, too; at least he knew what to be doing, and Claire hadn't seemed too bothered about leaving her grandson; obviously she thought he wasn't going to choke on the spot.

The vial contained pine oil, sharp and reeking of resin. He wasn't sure how much to use, but poured a generous dollop into the water. Then he pried the cork out of the jar, and the pungent scent of camphor rose up like a genie from the bottle. Not really crystals, he saw; lumps of some sort of dried resin, grainy and slightly sticky. He poured some into the palm of his hand, then rubbed them hard between his hands before dropping them into the water, wondering even as he did so at the instinctive familiarity of the gesture.

"Oh, that's it," he said, realizing.

"What's it?"

"This." He waved a hand round the snug sanctuary, rapidly filling with pungent steam. "I remember being in my cot, with a blanket over my head. My mother put this stuff in hot water—smelled just like this. That's why it seemed familiar."

"Oh." The thought seemed to reassure her. "Did you have croup when you were little?"

"I suppose so, though I don't remember it. Just the smell." Steam had quite filled the little tent by now, moist and pungent. He drew a deep breath, pulling in a penetrating lungful, then patted Brianna's leg.

"Don't worry; this'll do the trick," he said.

Jemmy promptly started coughing his guts out with more seal noises, but they seemed less alarming now. Whether it was the darkness, the smell, or simply the homely racket of the renewed kitchen noises outside the tent, things seemed calmer. He heard Bree take in a deep breath, too, and let it out, and felt rather than saw the subtle shift of her body as she relaxed a little, patting Jemmy's back.

They sat quietly for a bit, listening to Jemmy cough, wheeze, gasp, cough, and finally catch his breath, hiccupping slightly. He'd stopped whimpering, seeming soothed by the proximity of his parents.

Roger had dropped the cork to the camphor jar; he patted round on the floor until he found it, then pushed it firmly back in.

"I wonder what your mother's done with her rings?" he said, looking for some easy subject of conversation to break the steam-filled silence.

"Why should she have done anything with them?" Brianna brushed back a lock of hair; she'd had it put up for the evening, but it was slipping out of its pins, clinging damply to her face.

"She wasn't wearing them when she gave me the stuff." He nodded at the camphor jar, set out of harm's way near the wall. He had a clear memory of her hands, the fingers long, white, and bare; they'd struck him, since he'd never seen her hands without the gold and silver rings.

"Are you sure? She never takes them off, except to do something really nasty." She giggled, a nervous, unexpected sound. "The last time I remember was when Jem dropped his bawbee in the chamber pot."

Roger gave a brief snort of amusement. A bawbee was any sort of small object, but that's what they'd taken to calling the iron ring—originally meant for leading cattle by the nose—that Jem liked to chew on. It was his favorite toy, and he didn't like to go to bed without it.

"Ba-ba?" Jem raised his head, eyes half-closed. He was still breathing thickly, but beginning to display an interest in something besides his own discomfort. "Ba-ba!"

"Oops, shouldn't have mentioned it." Bree joggled him gently on her knee, and began to sing softly, half under her breath, to distract him.

"In a can-yon, in a cav-ern, exca-va-ting for a mine . . . Dwelt a min-er, forty-nin-er, and his daugh-ter, Clementine . . ."

The dark privacy of the tent reminded Roger of something; he realized that it had something of the same feeling of peaceful enclosure that the bench beneath the willows had had, though the tent was a lot hotter. The linen of his shirt was already limp on his shoulders, and he could feel sweat trickling down his back from under the hair tied at his neck.

"Hey." He nudged Bree's leg. "D'ye maybe want to go up and take off your new dress? It'll be spoilt if ye stay in here for long."

"Oh. Well . . ." She hesitated, biting her lip. "No, I'll stay, it's okay."

He got up, stooping under the quilts, and gathered Jem up off her lap, hacking and gurgling.

"Go," he said firmly. "You can fetch his b—his you-know-what. And don't worry. Ye can tell it's helping, the steam. He'll be right in no time."

It took a bit more argument, but at last she consented, and Roger sat down on the vacated stool, Jemmy cuddled in the crook of his arm. The pressure of the wooden seat reminded him of a certain amount of residual congestion from the encounter under the willows, and he shifted slightly to ease the discomfort.

"Well, it doesn't do ye any lasting harm," he muttered to Jemmy. "Ask any girl; they'll tell ye."

Jemmy snorted, snuffled, said something unintelligible beginning with "Ba—?" and coughed again, but only briefly. Roger put the back of his hand against the soft round cheek. He *thought* it was cooler. Hard to tell, warm as it was in here. The sweat was running freely down his face, and he wiped it with a sleeve.

"Ba-ba?" asked a froggy little voice against his chest.

"Aye, in a bit. Hush, now."

"Ba-ba. Ba-ba!"

"Shhhh."

"Ba—"

"Light she was, and like a fairy—" He groped for the words to the song.

"BA—"

"AND HER SHOES WERE NUMBER NINE!" Roger abruptly raised the volume, causing startled silence both inside the tent and outside, in the kitchen. He cleared his throat and lowered his voice back to lullaby level.

"Erm . . . *Herring boxes without topses . . . Sandals were for Clementine. Oh, my darling, oh, my darling, oh, my darling Clementine . . . Thou art lost, and gone for-ev-er, oh, my dar-ling . . . Clementine."*

The singing seemed to be having an effect. Jemmy's eyelids had dropped to half-mast. He put a thumb in his mouth and began to suck, but plainly couldn't breathe through his clogged nose. Roger gently pulled the thumb away, and held the little fist enclosed in his own. It was wet and sticky, and very small, but felt reassuringly sturdy.

"Fed she duck-lings, by the water, every mor-ning just at nine . . . Hit her foot a-gainst a splin-ter, fell into the foaming brine."

The eyelids fluttered briefly, then gave up the struggle and closed. Jemmy sighed and went completely limp, the heat coming off his skin in waves. Tiny beads of moisture trembled on each lash—tears, sweat, steam, or all three.

"Ruby lips a-bove the wa-ter, blowing bub-bles soft and fine . . . Alas for me, I was no swim-mer, so I lost my Clementine. Oh, my darling, oh, my darling . . ."

He wiped his face again, bent and kissed the soft thatch of damp, silky hair. *Thank you*, he thought with heartfelt sincerity, addressing everyone from God on down the line.

". . . Oh, my darling . . . Clementine."

48

STRANGERS IN THE NIGHT

IT WAS VERY LATE by the time I made my way to bed after a last check on the welfare of all my patients. DeWayne Buchanan had suffered a slight flesh wound in the upper arm when Ronnie Campbell neglected to raise his pistol high enough while carousing on the riverbank, but was in good spirits after having the wound cleaned and dressed. Having been liberally plied with further spirits by a remorseful Ronnie, he was quite literally feeling no pain at present.

One of Farquard Campbell's slaves, a man named Rastus, had been badly burned on the hand when taking grilled fowl off a skewer; all I could do there was to wrap the hand in clean cloth, set it in a bowl of cold water, and prescribe gin, to be taken internally. I had also treated several young men who were considerably the worse for drink, and sporting miscellaneous contusions, abrasions, and missing teeth as the result of a disagreement over dice. Six cases of indigestion, all treated with peppermint tea, and reporting improvement. Betty was in what looked like a deep but natural sleep, snoring loudly in bed. Jemmy was doing likewise, his fever abated.

Most of the loud revelry had died down by now; only the

most die-hard of the card players were still at it, peering red-eyed at their pasteboards through a cloud of tobacco smoke in the small drawing room. I glanced into the other rooms as well, as I made my way across the ground floor to the front stair. A few gentlemen lingered in low-voiced political conversation at one end of the dining room, the table long since cleared and empty brandy glasses forgotten by their elbows. Jamie wasn't one of them.

A heavy-eyed slave in livery bowed as I poked my head in, murmuring to ask whether I wanted food or drink. I hadn't eaten anything since supper, but I waved him away, too tired to think of food.

I paused at the first landing and glanced down the hall toward Jocasta's suite of rooms, but all was quiet there, the charivari and horseplay over. There was a large dent in the linenfold paneling, where a heavy body had struck, and glancing up, I could see several burned spots in the ceiling, where shots had been fired into it.

The butler Ulysses sat guard on a stool by the door, still dressed in wig and formal livery, head nodding over folded arms. A candle guttered and spat in the sconce above him. By its wavering light, I could see that his eyes were closed, but he wore a deep frown; he hunched in his sleep, and his lips moved briefly, as though he dreamed of evil things. I thought to waken him, but even as I moved toward him, the dream passed. He stretched, half-rousing, then fell asleep again, his face relaxing into calm. An instant later, the candle flickered out.

I listened, but heard no sound in the darkness save Ulysses's heavy breathing. Whether Duncan and Jocasta murmured understandings to each other behind the curtains of their bed, or lay silent, side by side and eternally separate, no one would ever know. I sent them a mental wish for happiness, and dragged myself upward, knees and back aching, wishing for my own bed—and my own husband's understanding.

Through an open casement on the second-floor landing, I heard distant whoops, laughter, and the occasional crack of recreational gunfire, borne on the night air. The younger, wilder gentlemen—and a few old enough to know better—

had gone down to the river landing in company with a dozen bottles of whisky and brandy to shoot frogs, or so I was informed.

The ladies, though, were all asleep. The second floor was quiet save for the buzz of muffled snoring. By contrast to the chilly corridor outside, the chamber itself was stifling, though the fire had burned down to a crimson coal bed that shed no more than an eerie red glow across the hearth.

With so many guests in the house, the only people with the luxury of a private bedroom were the bridal pair; everyone else was crammed into the few available rooms, willy-nilly. Two large tester beds and a trundle occupied the room, with straw-tick pallets spread over most of the remaining floor space. Each bed was packed like a sardine tin with shift-clad women lying side by side across the mattress, radiating as much moist heat as a greenhouse full of orchids.

I breathed shallowly—the air was filled with a cloying mixture of stale sweat, barbecue, and fried onions, French perfume, drink-sodden breath, and the sharp, sweet smell of vanilla beans—and shed my gown and shoes as quickly as I could, hoping not to break out into a drenching sweat before I could undress. I was still keyed up from the events of the day, but exhaustion was pulling like lead weights at my limbs, and I was glad enough to tiptoe through the sprawl of bodies and creep into my accustomed space near the foot of one of the big beds.

My mind was still buzzing with speculations of all sorts, and in spite of the hypnotic lull of so much slumber all around me, I lay stiff-limbed and sore, watching the silhouette of my bare toes against the hearth's dying light.

Betty had passed from her stupor into what looked like a normal deep sleep. When she woke in the morning, we would find out who had given her the cup, and—perhaps—what was in it. I hoped that Jemmy would sleep comfortably as well. But what was really on my mind, of course, was Jamie.

I hadn't seen him among the card players, nor yet among the men talking low-voiced of taxes and tobacco.

I hadn't seen Phillip Wylie anywhere on the first floor of the house, either. I could well believe he was out with the revelers by the river landing. That was his set and his style, wealthy young men who would seek diversion in drink and carouse in the dark, careless both of cold and danger, laughing and chasing each other by the light of random gunfire.

That was neither Jamie's set nor his style, but the thought of him among them was what made my feet curl with chill, despite the heat of the room.

He wouldn't do anything stupid, I assured myself, rolling onto my side, knees drawn up as much as possible in the cramped quarters. He wouldn't; but his notion of stupid wasn't always the same as mine, by any means.

Most of the male guests were bedded down in the outbuildings, or in the parlors; as I passed, I had seen anonymous sleeping figures sprawled on the floor of the front parlor, snoring loudly, wrapped in their cloaks before the fire. I had not gone to poke among them, but doubtless Jamie was there—he had had as long a day as I had, after all.

But it was not like him to retire without coming to wish me good night, no matter what the circumstances. Of course, he had been annoyed with me, and despite the promise of our interrupted conversation on the terrace, we had not quite made up the quarrel. Re-inflamed it, rather, with beastly Phillip Wylie's invitation. My hands curled, thumbs rubbing at the slight calluses that marked the spots where my rings normally sat. Effing Scot!

Next to me Jemima Hatfield stirred and murmured, disturbed by my restlessness. I eased myself slowly back onto my side, and stared sightlessly at the oaken footboard in front of me.

Yes, he was undoubtedly still angry about Phillip Wylie's advances. So was I—or I would be, were I not so tired. How dare he—I yawned, nearly dislocating my jaw, and decided that it really wasn't worth the bother of being annoyed, at least not now.

But it wasn't like Jamie to avoid me, angry or not. He wasn't the sort of man to sulk or brood. He would seek a confrontation or provoke a fight, without a moment's hesitation; but I didn't think he had ever let the sun go down on anger—at least not with regard to me.

Which left me to worry about where he was, and what in

bloody hell he was doing. And the necessity of worrying about him was making me *really* angry, if only because that was better than being worried.

But it *had* been a very long day, and as the moments passed, and the faint pops of gunfire from the river landing gradually ceased, languor stole over me, blunting my fears and scattering my thoughts like spilled sand. The gentle breathing of the women all around me lulled me like the sound of wind in the trees, and my grip on reality slackened and at last fell free.

I might have expected dreams of violence or nightmares of dread, but my subconscious had plainly had enough of that. In the contrary way of such things, it instead chose to dwell on another thread of the day's events. Perhaps it was the warmth of the room, or simply the closeness of so many bodies, but I dreamed vividly and erotically, the tides of arousal washing me now and then near to the shores of wakefulness, then once more carrying me out into the deeps of unconsciousness.

There were horses in my dreams; glowing black Friesians with flowing manes that rippled in the wind as the stallions ran beside me. I saw my own legs stretch and leap; I was a white mare, and the ground flew past in a blur of green beneath my hooves, until I stopped and turned, waiting for the one, a broad-chested stallion who came to me, his breath hot and moist against my neck, his white teeth closing on my nape . . .

"I am the King of Ireland," he said, and I came slowly awake, tingling from head to foot, to find that someone was gently stroking the sole of said foot.

Still bemused by the carnal images of my dreams, I was not alarmed by this, but merely muzzily pleased to discover that I had feet after all, and not hooves. My toes curled and my foot flexed, reveling in the delicate touch of the thumb that traced its way from the ball of my foot down the high arch and up into the hollow below my anklebone, managing to stimulate an entire plexus of sensation. Then I came all the way awake, with a small jerk.

Whoever it was plainly sensed my return to consciousness, for the touch left my foot momentarily. Then it came back, this time more firmly, a large warm hand curling quite round my foot, the thumb executing a firm but languid massage at the base of my toes.

By this time, I was quite awake, and mildly startled, but not frightened. I wiggled my foot briefly, as though to throw off the hand, but it squeezed my foot lightly in response, and then its companion gently pinched my great toe.

This little piggy went to market, this little piggy stayed home . . . I could hear the rhyme as clearly as though it had been spoken aloud, as the fingers deftly pinched their way across my toes, one by one.

And this little piggy went weee-weee-weee, all the way home! The touch flicked tickling down the sole of my foot and I jerked, an involuntary giggle caught in my throat.

I lifted my head, but the hand seized my foot again and squeezed in admonition. The fire had gone out altogether and the room was black as velvet; even with eyes completely dark-adapted, I could gain nothing but the sense of a hunched figure near my feet, an amorphous blob that shifted like mercury, its edges blending with and disappearing into the dark of the air.

The hand slid gently up the calf of my leg. I twitched violently, and the woman next to me snorted, reared up with a bleary, "Hnh?" and collapsed again, in a whoosh.

My stomach muscles quivered with suppressed laughter. He must have felt the slight vibration—the fingers left my little toe with a gentle squeeze, and stroked the bottom of my foot, making all my toes curl tight.

The fingers curled into a fist, pressing along the length of my sole, then suddenly opened, cupping my heel. His thumb stroked my ankle, and paused, questioning. I didn't move.

His fingers were getting warmer; there was only a faint sensation of cold as they followed the curve of my calf and sought shelter in the soft place behind my knee. The fingers played a quick tattoo on the sensitive skin there, and I twitched in agitation. They slowed and stopped, settling surely on the artery where my pulse beat fast; I could feel it, blood rushing past where the skin was so thin the veins would show blue beneath it.

I heard a sigh as he shifted his weight; then one hand

cupped the round of my thigh, and slid slowly upward. The other followed, pressing my legs gently, inexorably apart.

My heart was thumping in my ears and my breasts felt swollen, nipples poking hard and round through the thin muslin of my shift. I took a deep breath, and smelled rice powder.

All at once, my heart gave a double-thump and nearly stopped, as the sudden thought sprang to life in my mind—what if it wasn't Jamie?

I lay quite still, trying not to breathe, concentrating on the hands, which were doing something delicate and quite unspeakable. Large hands, they *were* large hands; I could feel the knuckles pressing the soft inner flesh of my thigh. But Phillip Wylie had large hands, too; quite large for his size. I had seen him scoop up a handful of oats for his stallion, Lucas, and the horse bury its big black nose in the palm.

Calluses; the roving hands—oh, God!—were smoothly callused. But so were Wylie's; dandy he might be, but a horseman; his palms were quite as smooth and hard as Jamie's.

It had to be Jamie, I assured myself, lifting my head an inch or so and peering into the black velvet darkness. Ten little pigs . . . of course it was Jamie! Then one of the hands did something quite startling and I gasped out loud and jerked, limbs twitching. My elbow slammed into the ribs of the woman next to me, who snapped upright with a loud exclamation. The hands retreated abruptly, squeezing my ankles in a hasty farewell.

There was a shuffling noise as someone crawled hurriedly across the floor, then a flash of dim light and a breath of cold air from the corridor as the door opened and shut again immediately.

"Wha—?" said Jemima next to me, in woozy astonishment. "Whozat?"

Receiving no answer, she flounced, muttered, and at last lay down again, to fall promptly fast asleep.

I did not.

49

IN VINO VERITAS

I LAY SLEEPLESS for quite a long time, listening to the peaceful snores and rustlings of my bedmates, and to the agitated thump of my own heart. Every nerve in my body felt as though it were sticking out through my skin, and when Jemima Hatfield rolled unconsciously into me, I jabbed her viciously in the ribs with my elbow, so that she uttered a startled "Whoof?" and sat halfway up, blinking and muttering, before collapsing slowly back into the communal sea of sleep.

As for me, my small bark of consciousness was adrift on the flood, spinning rudderless, but without the slightest chance of being pulled under.

I simply couldn't decide how to feel. On the one hand, I was aroused—unwillingly, to be sure, but still most definitely aroused. Whoever my nocturnal visitor had been, he knew his way around a woman's body.

That would argue for its being Jamie, I thought. Still, I had no idea how experienced Phillip Wylie might be in the arts of love—I had spurned his approaches in the stable so promptly that he had had no chance of demonstrating any skills he might possess in that direction.

But my midnight visitor had not used any caress that I could positively identify as being in Jamie's repertoire. Now, if he had used his mouth . . . I shied away from *that* line of thought like a spooked horse, and Jemima gave a muffled grunt as I convulsed slightly, my skin rippling in involuntary response to the images it evoked.

I didn't know whether to feel amused or outraged, seduced or violated. I *was* extremely angry; I was sure of that much, at least, and the surety gave me some small anchor in the maelstrom of emotion. Still, I had no idea as to the correct target of my anger, and with nowhere to aim that particularly destructive emotion, it was simply crashing round inside me, knocking things down and leaving dents.

"Oof," said Jemima, in a pointed—and quite conscious—tone of voice. Evidently I wasn't the only one being dented by my emotions.

"Mmmm?" I murmured, feigning half-sleep. "Glrgl. Bzg."

There was a small tinge of guilt in the mix, as well.

If I were sure it *had* been Jamie, would I be angry?

The worst of it was, I realized, that there was absolutely nothing I could do to find out who it had been. I could scarcely ask Jamie whether he had crept in and fondled me in the darkness—because if he *hadn't*, his immediate response would certainly be to assassinate Phillip Wylie bare-handed.

I felt as though tiny electric eels were squirming under my skin. I stretched as hard as I could, alternately tensed and relaxed every muscle—and still could find no way to keep still.

At last, I slid cautiously off the bed, and made my way to the door, with a glance at my erstwhile bedmates, who lay slumbering peacefully under the quilts like a row of perfumed sausages. Moving with great stealth, I eased the door open and peeked out into the hallway. It was either very late or very early; the tall window at the end of the corridor had gone to gray, but the last of the stars still showed, vanishing pinpoints on the charcoal satin of the sky.

It was cold in the hall, away from the contained body heat of the women, but I welcomed the chill; the blood was pulsing just under my skin, and I bloomed with heat and agitation. A nice cooldown was exactly what I wanted. I made my way quietly to the back stairs, meaning to go down and outside for a breath of air.

I stopped dead at the top of the staircase. A man stood at the foot of the stair, a silhouette tall and black against the panes of the double French doors. I didn't think I had made any sound, but he turned at once, face lifted toward me. Even in the poor light, I knew at once that it was Jamie.

He was still clad in the clothes he had worn the night before—coat and waistcoat, frilled shirt and belted plaid. The shirt was open at the neck, though, coat and weskit unbuttoned and askew. I could see the narrow line of white linen, the flesh of his throat dark against it. His hair was loose; he had been running his hands through it.

"Come down," he said softly.

I hesitated, looking back over my shoulder. A ladylike medley of snores came from the room I had just left. Two slaves were sleeping on the floor in the hall, curled under blankets, but neither moved.

I looked back. He didn't speak again, but lifted two fingers, beckoning. The scent of smoke and whisky filled the stairwell.

The blood was thrumming in my ears—and elsewhere. My face was flushed, my hair damp at the temples and on my neck; cool air rose up under my shift, touched the patch of dampness at the base of my spine, the film of slickness where my thighs brushed together.

I came down slowly, cautiously, trying not to let the stairs creak under my bare feet. It occurred to me belatedly that this was ridiculous; the slaves thundered up and down these stairs hundreds of times a day. Even so, I felt the need for secrecy; the house was still asleep, and the stairwell was filled with a gray light that seemed as fragile as smoked glass. A sudden sound, a move too quick, and something might explode under my feet, with a flash like a lightbulb popping.

His eyes stayed fixed on me, dark triangles in the paler dark of his face. He stared at me with a fierce intensity, as though to drag me down the stairs by the force of his gaze alone.

I stopped, one step from the bottom. There was no blood on his clothes; thank God for that.

It wasn't that I'd never seen Jamie drunk before. No wonder he hadn't come up the stairs to me. I thought he was very drunk now, and yet there was something quite different in this. He stood rock-solid, legs set wide, betrayed only by a certain deliberation in the way he moved his head to look at me.

"What—" I began, whispering.

"Come here," he said. His voice was low, rough with sleeplessness and whisky.

I hadn't time either to reply or to acquiesce; he seized my arm and pulled me toward him, then swept me off the last step, crushed me to him, and kissed me. It was a most disconcerting kiss—as though his mouth knew mine all too well, and would compel my pleasure, regardless of my desires.

His hair smelled of a long night's smoke—tobacco and woodsmoke and the smoke of beeswax candles. He tasted so strongly of whisky that I felt light-headed, as though the alcohol in his blood were seeping into mine through our skins where they touched, through the sealed membranes of our mouths. Something else was seeping into me from him, as well—a sense of overpowering lust, as blind as it was dangerous.

I wanted to remonstrate with him, to push him away. Then I decided that I didn't, but it wouldn't have made any difference if I had. He didn't mean to let go.

One big hand was gripping the back of my neck, warm and hard on my skin, and I thought of a stallion's teeth closing on the neck of the mare he mounts, and shivered from scalp to sole. His thumb accidentally pressed the great artery under my jaw; darkness swam behind my eyes and my knees began to buckle. He felt it and let go, easing me back so that I was almost lying supine upon the stairs, his weight half on me and his hands seeking.

I was naked under my shift, and the thin muslin might as well not have been there.

The hard edge of a stair pressed into my back, and it occurred to me, in the dim way that things do when you're drunk, that he was just about to take me right there on the stairs, and devil take anyone who might see.

I got my mouth free of his long enough to gasp, "Not here!" in his ear. That seemed to bring him momentarily to his senses; he lifted his head, blinking like one roused from a nightmare, eyes wide and blind. Then he nodded once, jerkily, and rose, pulling me to my feet with him.

The maids' cloaks were hanging by the door; he seized one and wrapped it round me, then picked me up bodily and shouldered his way through the door, past a staring housemaid with a slop jar in her hands.

He set me down when he reached the brick path outside; the bricks were cold under my feet. Then we were moving together through the gray light across a landscape of shadow and wind, still entangled with each other, stumbling, jostling, and yet somehow almost flying, clothes fluttering round us and cold air brushing our skins with the rude touch of spring, bound for some vaguely sensed and yet inevitable destination.

The stables. He hit the door and pulled me through with him into the warm dark, thrust me hard against a wall.

"I must have ye now, or die," he said, breathless, and then his mouth was on mine again, his face cold from the air outside, and his breath steaming with mine.

Then he drew abruptly away, and I staggered, pressing my hands against the rough bricks of the wall to keep my balance.

"Hold up your hands," he said.

"What?" I said stupidly.

"Your hands. Put them up."

In complete bewilderment, I held them up, and felt him take hold of the left one, fumbling. Pressure and warmth, and the faint light from the open door shone on my gold wedding ring. Then he seized my right hand, shoved my silver ring onto my finger, the metal warm from the heat of his body. He raised my hand to his mouth, and bit my knuckles, hard.

Then his hand was on my breast, cold air brushed my thighs, and I felt the scratch of the bricks on my bare backside.

I made a noise, and he clapped a hand over my mouth. Speared as neatly as a landed trout, I was just as helpless, pinned flapping against the wall.

He took his hand away and replaced it with his mouth, engulfing mine. I could feel the small urgent growls he was making in his throat, and felt another one, much louder, rising in mine.

My shift was wadded high around my waist, and my bare buttocks smacked rhythmically against the roughened brick, but I felt no pain at all. I gripped him by the shoulders and held on.

His hand skimmed my thigh, pushing at the drifts of linen that threatened to come between us. I remembered, vividly, those hands in the darkness, and bucked convulsively.

"Look." His breath came hot in my ear. "Look down. Watch while I take ye. Watch, damn you!"

His hand pressed my neck, bending my head forward to look down in the dimness, past the folds of sheltering fabric to the naked fact of my possession.

I arched my back and then collapsed, biting the shoulder of his coat to make no noise. His mouth was on my neck, and fastened tight as he shuddered against me.

WE LAY TANGLED together in the straw, watching daylight creep through the half-open door across the red-brick floor of the stable. My heart was still thumping in my ears, blood tingling through skin and temples, thighs and fingers, but I felt somehow detached from such sensations, as though they were happening to someone else. I felt unreal—and slightly shocked.

My cheek lay flat against his chest. Moving my eyes slightly, I could see the fading red flush of his skin in the open neck of his shirt, and the coarse curly hairs, so deep an auburn that they looked nearly black in the shadowed light.

A pulse was throbbing in the hollow of his throat, no more than an inch from my hand. I wanted to lay my fingers on it, feel his heartbeat echo in my blood. I felt oddly shy, though, as though such a gesture were too intimate to contemplate. Which was completely ridiculous, in view of what we had just done with—and to—each another.

I did move my index finger, just a bit, so that my fingertip brushed the tiny three-cornered scar on his throat; a faded white knot, pale against his bronzed skin.

There was a slight catch in the rhythm of his breathing, but he didn't move. His arm was round me, his hand splayed on the small of my back. Two breaths, three . . . and then the faint pressure of a fingertip against my spine.

We lay silent, breathing lightly, both concentrated on the delicate acknowledgment of our connection, but didn't speak or move; slightly embarrassed, with the return of reason, at what we had just done.

The sound of voices coming toward the stable galvanized me into motion, though. I sat up abruptly, yanked my shift up over my shoulders, and began to brush straw from my hair. Jamie rolled up onto his knees, his back to me, and began hastily to tuck in his shirttail.

The voices outside stopped abruptly, and we both froze. There was a brief, charged silence, and then the sound of footsteps, delicately retreating. I let out the breath I had been holding, feeling my racing heart begin to slow. The stable was filled with the rustlings and whickers of the horses, who had heard the voices and footsteps, too. They were getting hungry.

"So you won," I said to Jamie's back. My voice sounded strange to me, as though I hadn't used it in a long time.

"I promised ye I would." He spoke softly, head bent as he rearranged the folds of his plaid.

I stood up, feeling mildly dizzy, and leaned against the wall to keep my balance as I brushed sand and straw from my feet. The rough feel of the bricks behind me was a vivid reminder, and I spread my hands out against them, bracing myself against the rush of recalled sensation.

"Are ye all right, Sassenach?" He turned his head sharply to look up at me, sensing my movement.

"Yes. Yes," I repeated. "Fine. Just . . . I'm fine. And you?"

He looked pale and scruffy, his face stubbled and hollow with strain, eyes smudged black from a long and sleepless night. He met my eyes for a moment, then glanced away. A hint of color showed on his cheekbones, and he swallowed audibly.

"I—" he began, then stopped. He got to his feet and stood before me. His formal queue had come undone, and the tails of his hair splayed over his shoulder, glimmering redly as the bar of light from the door lit him.

"Ye dinna hate me?" he asked abruptly. Taken by surprise, I laughed.

"No," I said. "Do you think I should?"

His mouth twitched a little, and he rubbed his knuckles across it, scraping on the stubble of his beard.

"Well, maybe so," he said, "but I'm glad if ye don't."

He took my hands gently in his own, his thumb rubbing lightly across the interlaced pattern of my silver ring. His hands were cold, chilled by the dawn.

"Whyever do you think I might hate you?" I asked. "Because of the rings, do you mean?" Granted, I would have been upset and furious with him, had he lost either one. Since he hadn't . . . Of course, he *had* caused me to worry all night about where he was and what he was doing, to say nothing of sneaking into my room and making improper advances to my feet. Perhaps I ought to be annoyed with him, after all.

"Well, starting wi' that," he said dryly. "I havena let my pride get the better of me in some time, but I couldna seem to stop myself, what with wee Phillip Wylie preenin' about, smirkin' at your breasts, and—"

"He was?" I hadn't noticed that part.

"He was," Jamie said, glowering momentarily at the thought. Then he dismissed Phillip Wylie, returning to the catalogue of his own sins.

"And then, draggin' ye out of the house in your shift and going after ye like a ravening beast—" He gently touched my neck, where I could still feel the tingling soreness of a bite mark.

"Oh. Well, I quite liked that part, actually."

"You did?" His eyes flicked wide and blue in momentary startlement.

"Yes. Though I rather think I have bruises on my bottom."

"Oh." He looked down, apparently abashed, though the corner of his mouth twitched slightly. "I'm sorry for that. When I'd finished—at the whist, I mean—I couldna think of anything but finding ye, Sassenach. I went up and down that stair a dozen times, going to your door, and back away again."

"Oh, you did?" I was pleased to hear this, as it seemed to increase the odds that he had in fact been my midnight visitor.

He picked up a hank of my rumpled hair and ran his fingers gently through it.

"I kent I couldna sleep, and thought, well, I shall go out and walk in the night for a time, and I would, but then I should find myself again outside your room, not knowing how I'd come there, but only trying to think how I might get to ye—trying to will ye to come out to me, I suppose."

Well, that explained my dreams of wild stallions, I thought. The place where he had bitten my neck throbbed slightly. And where had he brought me? A stable. King of Ireland, forsooth.

He squeezed my hands lightly.

"I thought the force of my wanting must wake ye, surely. And then ye *did* come. . . ." He stopped, looking at me with eyes gone soft and dark. "Christ, Claire, ye were so beautiful, there on the stair, wi' your hair down and the shadow of your body with the light behind ye. . . ." He shook his head slowly.

"I did think I should die, if I didna have ye," he said softly. "Just then."

I reached up to stroke his face, his beard a soft bristle on my palm.

"Wouldn't want you to die," I whispered, tucking back a lock of hair behind his ear.

We smiled at each other then, but whatever else we might have said was interrupted by a loud whinny from one of the horses, followed by stamping noises. We were interfering with their breakfast.

I dropped my hand and Jamie bent to pick up his coat, which lay half-buried in the straw. He didn't lose his balance as he bent, but I saw him wince as the blood went suddenly to his head.

"Did you have a terrible lot to drink last night?" I asked, recognizing the symptoms.

He straightened up with a small grunt of amusement.

"Aye, quarts," he said, ruefully. "Ye can tell?"

A person with much less experience than I had could have told at a distance of roughly half a mile; putting aside the more obvious indications of recent intoxication, he smelled like a distillery.

"It didn't impair your card playing, evidently," I said, being tactful. "Or was Phillip Wylie similarly affected?"

He looked surprised, and slightly affronted.

"Ye dinna think I'd get besotted whilst I was playing, do ye? And with your rings at stake? No, that was after—MacDonald fetched a bottle of champagne and another of whisky, and insisted that we must celebrate our winnings in proper style."

"MacDonald? Donald MacDonald? He was playing with you?"

"Aye, he and I were partnered against Wylie and Stanhope." He shook the coat, sending bits of straw flying. "I couldna say what sort of soldier he was, but the man's a fine hand at the whist, to be sure."

Mention of the words "fine hand" reminded me. He'd come to the door of my room, he said; he hadn't mentioned coming in. Had he, and been too far gone between liquor and longing to recall doing it? Had I, dazed with dreams of equine lust, imagined the whole thing? Surely not, I thought, but shook off the sense of vague disquiet engendered by the memory, in favor of another word from his remark.

"You said winnings?" In the stress of the moment, it had only seemed important that he had kept my rings, but it occurred to me belatedly that those were only his stake. "What did you take off Phillip Wylie?" I asked, laughing. "His embroidered coat buttons? Or his silver shoe buckles?"

His face had an odd expression as he glanced at me.

"Well, no," he said. "I took his horse."

HE SWUNG HIS COAT round my shoulders, put an arm round my waist, and led me down the main aisle of the stable block, past the loose-boxes and stalls.

Joshua had come in quietly, through the other door, and was working at the far end of the stable, silhouetted against the light from the open double-doors as he pitchforked hay into the end stall. As we reached him, he glanced at us and nodded in greeting, his face carefully neutral at the sight of us, bedraggled, barefoot, and prickled with straw. Even in a household with a blind mistress, a slave knew what not to see.

No business of his, his downcast countenance said clearly. He looked nearly as tired as I felt, eyes heavy and bloodshot.

"How is he?" Jamie asked, lifting his chin toward the stall. Josh perked up a bit at the inquiry, putting down his pitchfork.

"Oh, he's bonnie," he said, with an air of satisfaction. "A bonnie lad, Mr. Wylie's Lucas."

"Indeed he is," Jamie agreed. "Only he's mine now."

"He's what?" Josh goggled at him, openmouthed.

"He's mine." Jamie went to the railing and reached out a hand to scratch the ears of the big stallion, busily engaged in eating hay from his manger.

"Seas," he murmured to the horse. *"Ciamar a tha thu, a ghille mhoir?"*

I followed him, peering over his arm at the horse, who lifted his head for a moment, regarded us with a genial eye, snorted, tossed his veil-like mane out of his face, and went back to his breakfast with single-minded intent.

"A lovely creature, is he no?" Jamie was admiring Lucas, a look of distant speculation in his eyes.

"Well, yes, he is, but—" My own admiration was substantially tinged with dismay. If Jamie had set out to avenge his own pride at the cost of Wylie's, he'd done it in spades. Despite my irritation with Wylie, I couldn't help a small pang at the thought of how he must be feeling at the loss of his magnificent Friesian.

"But what, Sassenach?"

"Well, just—" I fumbled awkwardly for words. I could scarcely say I felt sorry for Phillip Wylie, under the circumstances. "Just—well, what do you mean to do with him?"

Even I could see that Lucas was totally unsuited to life on Fraser's Ridge. The thought of plowing or hauling with him seemed sacrilegious, and while I supposed Jamie *could* use him only for riding . . . I frowned dubiously, envisioning the boggy bottoms and rocky trails that would threaten those well-turned legs and splinter the glossy hooves; the hanging boughs and undergrowth that would tangle in mane and tail. Gideon the Man-eater was a thousand times better suited to such rough environs.

"Oh, I dinna mean to keep him," Jamie assured me. He looked at the horse and sighed regretfully. "Though I should dearly love to. But ye're right; he wouldna do for the Ridge. No, I mean to sell him."

"Oh, good." I was relieved to hear this. Wylie would undoubtedly buy Lucas back, no matter what the cost. I found that a comforting thought. And we could certainly use the money.

Joshua had gone out while we were talking. At this point, he reappeared in the doorway, a sack of grain on his shoulder. His previous sluggish air had disappeared, though; his eyes were still bloodshot, but he looked alert, and mildly alarmed.

"Mrs. Claire?" he said. "Beggin' your pardon, ma'am, but I met Teresa by the barn just now; she's says as how there's summat gone amiss wi' Betty. I thought ye'd maybe want to know."

50

BLOOD IN THE ATTIC

THE ATTIC ROOM looked like the scene of a murder, and a brutal one, at that. Betty was struggling on the floor beside her overturned bed, knees drawn up and fists doubled into her abdomen, the muslin of her shift torn and saturated with blood. Fentiman was on the floor with her, dwarfed by her bulk but vainly grappling with her spasming body, nearly as smeared with gore as she was.

The sun was fully up now, and pouring in through the tiny windows in brilliant shafts that spotlighted parts of the chaos, leaving the rest in shadowed confusion. Cots were pushed aside and upset, bedding tangled in mounds, worn shoes and bits of clothing scattered like debris among the splotches of fresh blood on the wooden floor.

I hurried across the attic, but before I could reach her, Betty gave a deep, gurgling cough, and more blood gushed from her mouth and nose. She curled forward, arched back, doubled hard again . . . and went limp.

I fell to my knees beside her, though it was apparent from a glance that her limbs had relaxed into that final stillness from which there could be no hope of revival. I lifted her head and pressed my fingers under her jaw; her eyes had rolled back, only the whites showing. No breath, no sign of a pulse in the clammy neck.

From the quantities of blood spread round the room, I thought there could be very little left in her body. Her lips were blue, and her skin had gone the color of ashes. Fentiman knelt behind her, wigless and white-faced, skinny arms still locked about her heavy torso, holding her slumped body half off the floor.

He was in his nightshirt, I saw, a pair of blue satin breeches hastily pulled on beneath it. The air reeked of blood, bile, and feces, and he was smeared with all those substances. He looked up at me, though he showed no sign of recognition, his eyes wide and blank with shock.

"Dr. Fentiman." I spoke softly; with the noise of struggle ceased, the attic was stricken with that absolute silence that often follows in the wake of death, and it seemed sacrilege to break it.

He blinked, and his mouth worked a little, but he seemed to have no notion how to reply. He didn't move, though the spreading pool of blood had soaked through the knees of his breeches. I put a hand on his shoulder; it was bird-boned, but rigid with denial. I knew the feeling; to lose a patient you have fought for is a terrible thing—and yet one all doctors know.

"You have done all you can," I said, still softly, and tightened my grip. "It is not your fault." What had happened the day before wasn't important. He was a colleague, and I owed him what absolution lay in my power to give.

He licked dry lips, and nodded once, then bent to lay the body gently down. A shaft of light skimmed the top of his head, glowing through the scanty bristles of cropped gray hair, and making the bones of his skull seem thin and fragile.

He seemed suddenly frail altogether, and let me help him to his feet without protest.

A low moan made me turn, still holding his arm. A knot of female slaves huddled in the shadowed corner of the room, faces stark and dark hands fluttering with distress against the pale muslin of their shifts. There were male voices on the stair outside, muted and anxious. I could hear Jamie, low-voiced and calm, explaining.

"Gussie?" I called toward the women in the corner with the first name that came to mind.

The knot of slaves clung together for a moment, then reluctantly unraveled, and Gussie stepped out, a pale brown moth of a girl from Jamaica, small under a turban of blue calico.

"Madam?" She kept her eyes on mine, steadfastly away from the still form on the floor.

"I'm taking Doctor Fentiman downstairs. I'll have some of the men come to . . . to take care of Betty. This . . ." I made a small gesture toward the mess on the floor, and she nodded, still shocked, but obviously relieved to have something to do.

"Yes, Madam. We do that, quick." She hesitated, eyes darting round the room, then looked back at me. "Madam?"

"Yes?"

"Someone must go—tell that girl name Phaedre what's gone with Betty. You tell her, please?"

Startled, I looked, and realized that Phaedre was not among the slaves in the corner. Of course; as Jocasta's body servant, she would sleep downstairs, near her mistress, even on her wedding night.

"Yes," I said, uncertainly. "Of course. But—"

"This Betty that girl's mama," Gussie said, seeing my incomprehension. She swallowed, tears swimming in her soft brown eyes. "Somebody—can I go, Madam? Can I go tell her?"

"Please," I said, and stepped back, motioning her to go. She tiptoed past the body, then darted for the door, callused bare feet thumping softly on the boards.

Dr. Fentiman had begun to emerge from his shock. He pulled away from me and stooped toward the floor, making vague groping gestures. I saw that his medical kit had been upset in the struggle; bottles and instruments were strewn across the floor in a litter of metal and broken glass.

Before he could retrieve his kit, though, there was a brief commotion on the stair, and Duncan came into the room, Jamie on his heels. I noticed with some interest that Duncan was still wearing his wedding clothes, though minus coat and waistcoat. Had he been to bed at all? I wondered.

He nodded to me, but his eyes went at once to Betty, now sprawled on the floor, bloody shift crumpled round her broad, splayed thighs. One breast spilled from the torn fabric, heavy and slack as a half-filled pouch of meal. Duncan blinked several times. Then he wiped the back of his hand across his mustache, and took a visible breath. He bent to pluck a quilt from the carnage and laid it gently over her.

"Help me with her, *Mac Dubh*," he said.

Seeing what he was about, Jamie knelt and gathered the dead woman up into his arms. Duncan drew himself upright, and turned his face toward the women in the corner.

"Dinna fash yourselves," he said quietly. "I shall see her taken care of." There was an unusual note of authority in his voice that made me realize that in spite of his natural modesty, he had accepted the fact that he was master here.

The men left with their burden, and I heard Dr. Fentiman give a deep sigh. It felt as though the whole attic sighed with him; the atmosphere was still thick with stench and sorrow, but the shock of violent death was dissipating.

"Leave it," I said to Fentiman, seeing him move again to pick up a bottle lying on the floor. "The women will take care of it." Not waiting for argument, I took him firmly by the elbow and marched him out the door and down the stair.

People were up; I caught the sounds of rattling dishes from the dining room, and the faint scent of sausages. I couldn't take him through the public rooms in his current state, nor up to the bedrooms; he was undoubtedly sharing a room with several other men, any of whom might still be abed. For lack of a better idea, I took him outside, pausing to snatch another of the maids' cloaks from the pegs by the door and wrap it round his shoulders.

So Betty was—or had been—Phaedre's mother. I hadn't

known Betty well, but I did know Phaedre, and felt grief for her tighten my throat. There was nothing I could do for her just now, though; but perhaps I could help the doctor.

Silent with shock, he followed me obediently as I led him down the side path by the lawns, shielded from view by Hector Cameron's white-marble mausoleum and its growth of ornamental yew bushes. There was a stone bench by the river, half-hidden under a weeping willow. I doubted anyone would be patronizing it at this hour of the morning.

No one was, though two wine goblets sat on the bench, stained red with beeswing, abandoned remnants of the night's festivities. I wondered briefly whether someone had been having a romantic rendezvous, and was reminded suddenly of my own midnight tryst. Damn it, I still didn't know for sure who the owner of those hands had been!

Pushing the nagging question away with the wineglasses, I sat down, gesturing to Doctor Fentiman to join me. It was chilly, but the bench was in full sun at this hour, and the heat was warm and comforting on my face. The Doctor was looking better for the fresh air; vestiges of color had come back into his cheeks, and his nose had resumed its normal roseate hue.

"Feeling a bit better, are you?"

He nodded, hunching the cloak around his narrow shoulders.

"I am, I thank you, Mrs. Fraser."

"Rather a shock, wasn't it?" I asked, employing my most sympathetic bedside manner.

He closed his eyes, and shook his head briefly.

"Shocked . . . yes, very shocked," he muttered. "I would never have . . ." He trailed off, and I let him sit quiet for a moment. He would need to talk about it, but best to let him take it at his own pace.

"It was good of you to come so quickly," I said, after a bit. "I see they called you from your bed. Had she grown suddenly worse, then?"

"Yes. I could have sworn she was on the mend last night, after I bled her." He rubbed his face with both hands, and emerged blinking, eyes very bloodshot. "The butler roused me just before dawn, and I found her once again complaining of griping in the guts. I bled her again, and then administered a clyster, but to no avail."

"A clyster?" I murmured. Clysters were enemas; a favorite remedy of the time. Some were fairly harmless; others were positively corrosive.

"A tincture of nicotiana," he explained, "which I find answers capitally in most cases of dyspepsia."

I made a noncommittal noise in response. Nicotiana was tobacco; I supposed a strong solution of that, administered rectally, would probably dispose promptly of a case of pinworms, but I didn't think it would do much for indigestion. Still, it wouldn't make anyone bleed like that, either.

"Extraordinary amount of bleeding," I said, putting my elbows on my knees and resting my chin in my hands. "I don't think I've ever seen anything like it." That was true. I was curious, turning over various possibilities in my mind, but no diagnosis quite fit.

"No." Doctor Fentiman's sallow cheeks began to show spots of red. "I—if I had thought . . ."

I leaned toward him, and laid a consoling hand on his arm.

"I'm sure you did all that anyone could possibly do," I said. "She wasn't bleeding at all from the mouth when you saw her last night, was she?"

He shook his head, hunching deeper into his cloak.

"No. Still, I blame myself, I really do."

"One does," I said ruefully. "There's always that sense that one should have been able to do *something* more."

He caught the depth of feeling in my voice and turned toward me, looking surprised. The tension in him relaxed a little, and the red color began to fade from his cheeks.

"You have . . . a most remarkably sympathetic understanding, Mrs. Fraser."

I smiled at him, not speaking. He might be a quack, he might be ignorant, arrogant, *and* intemperate—but he had come at once when called, and had fought for his patient to the best of his ability. That made him a physician, in my book, and deserving of sympathy.

After a moment, he put his hand over mine. We sat in silence, watching the river go by, dark brown and turbid with silt. The stone bench was cold under me, and the morning breeze kept sticking chilly fingers under my shift, but I was too preoccupied to take much note of such minor discomforts. I could smell the drying blood on his clothes, and saw again the scene in the attic. What on earth had the woman died of?

I prodded him gently, asking tactful questions, extracting what details he had gleaned, but they were not helpful. He was not an observant man at the best of times, and it had been very early and the attic dark. He grew easier with the talking, though, gradually purging himself of that sense of personal failure that is the frequent price of a physician's caring.

"I hope Mrs. Cameron—Mrs. Innes, I mean—will not feel that I have betrayed her hospitality," he said uneasily.

That seemed a rather odd way to put it. On the other hand . . . Betty *had* been Jocasta's property. I supposed that beyond any sense of personal failure, Dr. Fentiman was also contemplating the possibility that Jocasta might blame him for not preventing Betty's death, and try to claim recompense.

"I'm sure she'll realize that you did all you could," I said soothingly. "I'll tell her so, if you like."

"My dear lady." Doctor Fentiman squeezed my hand with gratitude. "You are as kind as you are lovely."

"Do you think so, Doctor?"

A male voice spoke coldly behind me, and I jumped, dropping Dr. Fentiman's hand as though it were a high-voltage wire. I whirled on the bench to find Phillip Wylie, leaning against the trunk of the willow tree with a most sardonic expression on his face.

" 'Kind' is not the word that springs most immediately to mind, I must say. 'Lewd,' perhaps. 'Wanton,' most certainly. But 'lovely,' yes—I'll give you that."

His eyes raked me from head to toe with an insolence that I would have found absolutely reprehensible—had it not suddenly dawned on me that Dr. Fentiman and I had been sitting hand in hand in what could only be called a compromising state of dishabille, both still in our nightclothes.

I stood up, drawing my cloak round me with great dignity.

His eyes were fixed on my breasts—with a knowing expression? I wondered. I folded my arms under my breasts, lifting my bosom defiantly.

"You forget yourself, Mr. Wylie," I said, as coldly as possible.

He laughed, but not as though he thought anything were funny.

"I forget myself? Have you not forgotten something, Mrs. Fraser? Such as your gown? Do you not find it a trifle cold, dressed like that? Or do the good doctor's embraces warm you sufficiently?"

Doctor Fentiman, as shocked as I was by Wylie's appearance, had got to his feet and now pushed his way in front of me, his thin cheeks mottled with fury.

"How dare you, sir! How do you have the infernal presumption to speak to a lady in such fashion? Were I armed, sir, I should call you out upon the instant, I swear it!"

Wylie had been staring boldly at me. At this, his gaze shifted to Fentiman, and he saw the blood staining the doctor's legs and breeches. His hot-eyed scowl grew less certain.

"I—has something happened, sir?"

"It is none of your concern, I assure you." Fentiman bristled like a banty rooster, drawing himself upright. Rather grandly, he presented me with his arm.

"Come, Mrs. Fraser. You need not be exposed to the insulting gibes of this puppy." He glared at Wylie, red-eyed. "Allow me to escort you back to your husband."

Wylie's face underwent an instant transformation at the word "puppy," turning a deep, ugly red. So early in the morning, he was wearing neither paint nor powder, and the blotches of fury stood out like a rash on his fair skin. He seemed to swell noticeably, like an enraged frog.

I had a sudden urge to laugh hysterically, but nobly suppressed it. Biting my lip instead, I accepted the doctor's proffered arm. He came up roughly to my shoulder, but pivoted on his bare heel and marched us away with all the dignity of a brigadier.

Looking back over my shoulder, I saw Wylie still standing under the willow tree, staring after us. I lifted my hand and gave him a small wave of farewell. The light sparked from my gold ring, and I saw him stiffen further.

"I do hope we'll be in time for breakfast," Doctor Fentiman said cheerfully. "I believe I have quite recovered my appetite."

51

SUSPICION

THE GUESTS BEGAN TO DEPART after breakfast. Jocasta and Duncan stood together on the terrace, the very picture of a happily united couple, bidding everyone farewell, as a line of carriages and wagons made its slow way down the drive. Those folk from down-river waited on the quay, the women exchanging last-minute recipes and bits of gossip, while the gentlemen lit pipes and scratched themselves, relieved of their uncomfortable clothes and formal wigs. Their servants, all looking considerably the worse for wear, sat openmouthed and red-eyed on bundles of luggage.

"You look tired, Mama." Bree looked rather tired herself; she and Roger had both been up 'til all hours. A faint smell of camphor wafted from her clothes.

"Can't imagine why," I replied, stifling a yawn. "How's Jemmy this morning?"

"He's got a sniffle," she said, "but no fever. He ate some porridge for breakfast, and he's—"

I nodded, listened automatically, and went with her to examine Jemmy, who was cheerfully rambunctious, if runny-nosed, all in a slight daze of exhaustion. It reminded me of nothing so much as the sensation I had had now and then when flying from America to England. Jet lag, they called it;

an odd feeling, of being conscious and lucid, and yet not quite solidly fixed within one's body.

The girl Gussie was watching Jemmy; she was as pale and bloodshot as everyone else on the premises, but I thought her air of dull suffering derived from emotional distress rather than hangover. All the slaves had been affected by Betty's death; they went about the chores of clearing up after the wedding festivities in near-silence, their faces shadowed.

"Are you feeling all right?" I asked her, when I had finished looking in Jemmy's ears and down his throat.

She looked startled, then confused; I wondered whether anyone had ever asked her that before.

"Oh. Oh, yes, Madam. Surely." She smoothed down her apron with both hands, clearly nervous at my scrutiny.

"All right. I'll just go and have a look at Phaedre, then."

I had come back to the house with Dr. Fentiman and turned him over to Ulysses, to be fed and tidied up. I had then gone directly to find Phaedre, taking time only to wash and change my clothes—not wanting to come to her so visibly smeared with her mother's blood.

I had found her in Ulysses's pantry, sitting numb and shocked on the stool where he sat to polish silver, a large glass of brandy by her side, undrunk. One of the other slaves, Teresa, was with her; she breathed a short sigh of relief at my appearance and came to greet me.

"She's none sae weel," Teresa muttered to me, shaking her head with a wary glance back at her charge. "She's no said a word, nor wept a drop."

Phaedre's beautiful face might have been carved of fruitwood; normally a delicate cinnamon, her complexion had faded to a pale, ligneous brown, and her eyes stared fixedly through the open door of the pantry at the blank wall beyond.

I put a hand on her shoulder; it was warm, but so motionless that she might have been a stone in the sun.

"I am sorry," I said to her, softly. "Very sorry. Dr. Fentiman came to her; he did all that he could." That was true; no point in giving an opinion of Fentiman's skill—it was irrelevant now, in any case.

No response. She was breathing; I could see the slight rise and fall of her bosom, but that was all.

I bit the inside of my lower lip, trying to think of anything or anyone that might possibly give her comfort. Jocasta? Did Jocasta even know of Betty's death yet? Duncan knew, of course, but he might have chosen not to tell her until after the guests had left.

"The priest," I said, the idea occurring suddenly to me. "Would you like Father LeClerc to—to bless your mother's body?" I thought it rather too late for Last Rites—assuming that Phaedre knew what those were—but I was sure that the priest would not mind offering any comfort he could. He had not left yet; I had seen him in the dining room only a few moments since, polishing off a platter of pork-chops garnished with fried eggs and gravy.

A slight tremor went through the shoulder under my hand. The still, beautiful face turned toward me, dark eyes opaque.

"What good will that do?" she whispered.

"Ah . . . well . . ." Flustered, I groped for a reply, but she had already turned away, staring at a stain in the wood of the table.

What I had done in the end was to give her a small dose of laudanum—an irony I resolutely ignored—and tell Teresa to put her to bed on the cot where she normally slept, in the dressing room off Jocasta's boudoir.

I pushed open the door of the dressing room now, to see how she was. The small room was windowless and dark, smelling of starch and burnt hair and the faint flower fragrance of Jocasta's toilet water. A huge armoire and its matching chiffonier stood at one side, a dressing table at the other. A folding screen marked off the far corner, and behind this was Phaedre's narrow cot.

I could hear her breathing, slow and deep, and felt reassured by that. I moved quietly through the dark room, and pulled back the screen a little; she lay on her side, turned away, curled into a ball with her knees drawn up.

Bree had come into the dressing room behind me; she looked over my shoulder, her breath warm on my ear. I made a small gesture indicating that everything was all right, and pushed the screen back into place.

Just inside the door to the boudoir, Brianna paused. She turned to me suddenly, put her arms about me, and hugged me fiercely. In the lighted room beyond, Jemmy missed her and began to shriek.

"Mama! Ma! Ma-MA!"

I THOUGHT I ought to eat something, but with the smell of the attic and the scent of toilet water still lingering in the back of my sinuses, I had no appetite. A few guests still lingered in the dining room; particular friends of Jocasta's, they would be staying on for a day or two. I nodded and smiled as I passed, but ignored the invitations to come and join them, instead heading for the stairs to the second floor.

The bedroom was empty, the mattresses stripped and the windows opened to air the room. The hearth had been swept and the room was cold, but blessedly quiet.

My own cloak still hung in the wardrobe. I lay down on the bare ticking, pulled the cloak over me, and fell instantly asleep.

I WOKE JUST BEFORE sunset, starving, with an oddly mixed sense of reassurance and unease. The reassurance I understood at once; the scent of blood and flowers had been replaced by one of shaving soap and body-warmed linen, and the pale gold light streaming through the window shone on the pillow beside me, where a long red-gold hair glinted in the hollow left by someone's head. Jamie had come and slept beside me.

As though summoned by my thought, the door opened and he smiled in at me. Shaved, combed, freshly dressed, and clear-eyed, he seemed to have erased all traces of the night before—bar the expression on his face when he looked at me. Frowsy and ill-kempt as I was by contrast with his own neat appearance, the look of tenderness in his eyes warmed me, in spite of the lingering chill in the room.

"Awake at last. Did ye sleep well, Sassenach?"

"Like the dead," I replied automatically, and felt a small internal lurch as I said it.

He saw it reflected on my face, and came swiftly to sit down on the bed beside me.

"What is it? Have ye had an evil dream, Sassenach?"

"Not exactly," I said slowly. In fact, I had no memory of having dreamed at all. And yet, my mind appeared to have been ticking away in the shadows of unconsciousness, making notes and drawing its deductions. Prompted now by the word "dead," it had just presented me with its conclusions, which accounted for the feeling of unease with which I had awoken.

"That woman Betty. Have they buried her yet?"

"No. They've washed the body and put it in a shed, but Jocasta wished to wait until the morning for the burial, so as not to trouble her guests. Some are staying on for another night." He frowned slightly, watching me. "Why?"

I rubbed a hand over my face, less to rouse myself than to collect my words.

"There's something wrong. About her death, I mean."

"Wrong . . . how?" One eyebrow lifted. "It was a fearful way to die, to be sure, but that's not what ye mean, is it?"

"No." My hands were cold; I reached automatically for his, and he took them, engulfing my fingers with warmth. "I mean—I don't believe it was a natural death. I think someone killed her."

Blurted out that way, the words hung cold and stark in the air between us.

His brows drew together, and he pursed his lips slightly, thinking. I noticed, though, that he did not reject the idea out of hand, and that strengthened my conviction.

"Who?" he asked at last. "And are ye sure of it, Sassenach?"

"I have no idea. And I can't be totally sure," I admitted. "It's only—" I hesitated, but he squeezed one of my hands lightly in encouragement. I shook my head. "I've been a nurse, a doctor, a healer, for a long time, Jamie. I've seen a dreadful number of people die, and from all sorts of things. I can't quite put into words what it is here, but now that I've slept on it, I just know—I think—it's wrong," I ended, rather lamely.

The light was fading; shadows were coming down from the corners of the room, and I shivered suddenly, gripping his hands.

"I see," he said softly. "But there's no way ye can tell for sure, is there?"

The window was still half-open; the curtains billowed suddenly into the room with a gust of wind, and I felt the hairs rise on my arms with cold.

"There might be," I said.

52

A HARD DAY'S NIGHT

THE OUTBUILDING where they had put the body was well away from the house—a small toolshed outside the kitchen garden. The waning moon was low in the sky, but still shed light enough to see the brick path through the garden; the espaliered fruit trees spread black as spiderwebs against the walls. Someone had been digging; I could smell the cold damp of recently turned earth, and shivered involuntarily at the hint of worms and mold.

Jamie felt it, and put a light hand on my back.

"All right, Sassenach?" he whispered.

"Yes." I gripped his free hand for reassurance. They would hardly be burying Betty in the kitchen garden; the digging must be for something prosaic, like an onion bed or a trench for early peas. The thought was comforting, though my skin still felt cold and thin, prickling with apprehensions.

Jamie himself was far from easy, though he was outwardly composed, as usual. He was no stranger to death, and had no great fear of it. But he was both Catholic and Celt, with a strong conviction of another, unseen world that lay past the dissolution of the body. He believed implicitly in *tannasgeach*—in spirits—and had no desire to meet one. Still, if I was determined, he would brave the otherworld for my sake; he squeezed my hand hard, and didn't let go.

I squeezed back, deeply grateful for his presence. Beyond the debatable question of how Betty's ghost might feel about my proposed plan of action, I knew that the notion of deliberate mutilation disturbed him deeply, however much his own intelligence might be convinced that a soulless body was no more than clay.

"To see men hacked to death on a battlefield is one thing," he'd said earlier in the evening, still arguing with me. "That's war, and it's honorable, cruel as it may be. But to take a blade and carve up a poor innocent like yon woman in cold blood . . ." He looked at me, eyes dark with troubled thought. "Ye're sure ye must do it, Claire?"

"Yes, I am," I had said, eyes fixed on the contents of the bag I was assembling. A large roll of lint wadding, to soak up fluids, small jars for organ samples, my largest bone saw, a couple of scalpels, a wicked pair of heavy-bladed shears, a sharp knife borrowed from the kitchen . . . it was a sinister-looking collection, to be sure. I wrapped the shears in a towel to prevent them clanking against the other implements, and put them in the bag, carefully marshaling my words.

"Look," I said at last, raising my eyes to meet his. "There's something wrong, I know it. And if Betty was killed, then surely we owe it to her to find that out. If you were murdered, wouldn't you want someone to do whatever they could to prove it? To—to avenge you?"

He stood still for a long moment, eyes narrowed in thought as he looked down at me. Then his face relaxed, and he nodded.

"Aye, I would," he said quietly. He picked up the bone saw, and began wrapping it with cloth.

He hadn't protested further. He hadn't asked me again whether I was sure. He had merely said firmly that if I was going to do it, he was coming with me, and that was all about it.

As for being sure, I wasn't. I did have an abiding feeling that something was very wrong about this death, but I was less confident in my sense of what it was, with the cold moon sinking through an empty sky and wind brushing my cheeks with the touch of icy fingers.

Betty might have died only by accident, not malice. I could be wrong; perhaps it was a simple hemorrhage of an esophageal ulcer, the bursting of an aneurysm in the throat, or some other physiological oddity. Unusual, but natural. Was I doing this, in fact, only to try to vindicate my faith in my own powers of diagnosis?

The wind belled my cloak and I pulled it tighter around me, one-handed, stiffening my spine. No. It wasn't a natural death, I knew it. I couldn't have said *how* I knew it, but fortunately Jamie hadn't asked me that.

I had a brief flash of memory; Joe Abernathy, a jovial smile of challenge on his face, reaching into a cardboard box full of bones, saying, "I just want to see can you do it to a dead person, Lady Jane?"

I could; I had. He had handed me a skull, and the memory of Geillis Duncan shuddered through me like liquid ice.

"Ye needna do it, Claire." Jamie's hand tightened on mine. "I willna think ye a coward." His voice was soft and serious, barely audible above the wind.

"I would," I said, and felt him nod. That was the matter settled, then; he let go of my hand and went ahead of me, to open the gate.

He paused, and my dark-adapted eyes caught the clean sharp line of his profile as he turned his head, listening. The dark-lantern he carried smelled hot and oily, and a faint gleam escaping from its pierced-work panel sprinkled the cloth of his cloak with tiny flecks of dim light.

I glanced round myself, and looked back at the house. Late as it was, candles still burned in the back parlor, where the card games lingered on; I caught a faint murmur of voices as the wind changed, and a sudden laugh. The upper floors were mostly dark—save one window which I recognized as Jocasta's.

"Your aunt's awake late," I whispered to Jamie. He turned and looked up at the house.

"Nay, it's Duncan," he said softly. "My aunt doesna need the light, after all."

"Perhaps he's reading to her in bed," I suggested, trying to leaven the solemnity of our errand. A small derisive huff came from Jamie, but the oppressive atmosphere did lift just a bit. He unlatched the gate and pushed it open, showing a square of utter black beyond. I turned my back on the friendly lights of the house and stepped through, feeling just a bit like Persephone entering the Underworld.

Jamie swung the gate to, and handed me the lantern.

"What are you doing?" I whispered, hearing the rustle of his clothing. It was so dark by the gate that I couldn't see him as more than a dark blur, but the faint sound that came next told me what he was doing.

"Pissing on the gateposts," he whispered back, stepping back and rustling further as he did up his breeks. "If we must, then we will, but I dinna want anything to be following us back to the house."

I made my own small huffing noise at that, but made no demur when he insisted upon repeating this ritual at the door to the shed. Imagination or not, the night seemed somehow inhabited, as though invisible things moved through the darkness, murmuring under the voice of the wind.

It was almost a relief to go inside, where the air was still, even though the scents of death mingled thickly with the dankness of rust, rotted straw, and mildewed wood. There was a faint rasp of metal as the dark-lantern's panel slid back, and a dazzling shaft of light fell over the confines of the shed.

They had laid the dead slave on a board across two trestles, already washed and properly laid out, wrapped in a rough muslin shroud. Beside her stood a small loaf of bread and a cup of brandy. A small posy of dried herbs, carefully twisted into a knot, lay on the shroud, just above the heart. Who had left those? I wondered. One of the other slaves, surely. Jamie crossed himself at the sight, and looked at me, almost accusingly.

"It's ill luck to touch grave goods."

"I'm sure it's only ill luck to take them," I assured him, low-voiced, though I crossed myself before taking the objects and putting them on the ground in a corner of the shed. "I'll put them back when I've finished."

"Mmphm. Wait just a moment, Sassenach. Dinna touch her yet."

He dug in the recesses of his cloak, and emerged with a tiny bottle. He uncorked this, and putting his fingers to the opening, poured out a little liquid, which he flicked over the corpse, murmuring a quick Gaelic prayer that I recognized as an invocation to St. Michael to protect us from demons, ghouls, and things that go bump in the night. Very useful.

"Is that holy water?" I asked, incredulous.

"Aye, of course. I got it from Father LeClerc." He made the sign of the Cross over the body, and laid his hand briefly on the draped curve of the head, before nodding reluctant approval for me to proceed.

I extracted a scalpel from my bag and slit the stitching on the shroud carefully. I'd brought a stout needle and waxed thread, to sew up the body cavity; with luck, I could also repair the shroud sufficiently that no one would realize what I'd been doing.

Her face was almost unrecognizable, round cheeks gone slack and sunken, and the soft bloom of her black skin faded to an ashy gray, the lips and ears a livid purple. That made it easier; it was clear that this was indeed only a shell, and not the woman I had seen before. That woman, if she was still in the vicinity, would have no objections, I thought.

Jamie made the sign of the Cross again and said something soft in Gaelic, then stood still, the lantern held high so that I could work by its light. The light threw his shadow on the wall of the shed, gigantic and eerie in the wavering flicker. I looked away from it, down to my work.

The most formal and sanitary of modern autopsies is simple butchery; this was no better—and worse only in the lack of light, water, and specialized tools.

"You needn't watch, Jamie," I said, standing back for a moment to wipe a wrist across my brow. Cold as it was in the shed, I was sweating from the heavy work of splitting the breastbone, and the air was thick with the ripe smells of an open body. "There's a nail on the wall; you could hang up the lantern, if you want to go out for a bit."

"I'm all right, Sassenach. What is that?" He leaned forward, pointing carefully. The look of disquiet on his features had been replaced by one of interest.

"The trachea and bronchi," I replied, tracing the graceful rings of cartilage, "and a bit of a lung. If you're all right, then can I have the light a little closer here, please?"

Lacking spreaders, I couldn't wrench the rib cage far enough apart to expose the complete lung on either side, but thought I could see enough to eliminate some possibilities. The surfaces of both lungs were black and grainy; Betty was in her forties, and had lived all her life with open wood fires.

"Anything nasty that you breathe in and don't cough up again—tobacco smoke, soot, smog, what-have-you—gradually gets shoved out between the lung tissue and the pleura," I explained, lifting a bit of the thin, half-transparent pleural membrane with the tip of my scalpel. "But the body can't get rid of it altogether, so it just stays there. A child's lung would be a nice clean pink."

"Do mine look like that?" Jamie stifled a small, reflexive cough. "And what is smog?"

"The air in cities like Edinburgh, where you get smoke mixing with fog off the water." I spoke abstractedly, grunting slightly as I pulled the ribs back, peering into the shadowed cavity. "Yours likely aren't so bad, since you've lived out of doors or in unheated places so much. Clean lungs are one compensation to living without fire."

"That's good to know, if ye've got no choice about it," he said. "Given the choice, I expect most folk would rather be warm and cough."

I didn't look up, but smiled, slicing through the upper lobe of the right lung.

"They would, and they do." No indication of hemorrhage in either lung; no blood in the airway; no evidence of pulmonary embolism. No pooling of blood in the chest or abdominal cavity, either, though I was getting some seepage. Blood will clot soon after death, but then gradually reliquefies.

"Hand me a bit more of the wadding, will you, please?" A

little spotting of blood on the shroud likely wouldn't worry anyone, given the spectacular nature of Betty's demise, but I didn't want enough to make anyone sufficiently suspicious to check inside.

I leaned across to take the lint from his hand, inadvertently putting a hand on the corpse's side. The body emitted a low groan and Jamie leaped back with a startled exclamation, the light swinging wildly.

I had jumped, myself, but quickly recovered.

"It's all right," I said, though my heart was racing and the sweat on my face had gone suddenly cold. "It's only trapped gas. Dead bodies often make odd noises."

"Aye." Jamie swallowed and nodded, steadying the lantern. "Aye, I've seen it often. Takes ye a bit by surprise, though, doesn't it?" He smiled at me, lopsided, though a pale sheen of sweat gleamed on his forehead.

"It does that." It occurred to me that he had doubtless dealt with a good many dead bodies, all unembalmed, and was likely at least as familiar with the phenomena of death as I was. I set a cautious hand in the same place, but no further noises resulted, and I resumed my examination.

Another difference between this impromptu autopsy and the modern form was the lack of gloves. My hands were bloody to the wrist, and the organs and membranes had a faint but unpleasant feel of sliminess; cold though it was in the shed, the inexorable process of decomposition had started. I got a hand under the heart and lifted it toward the light, checking for gross discolorations of the surface, or visible ruptures of the great vessels.

"They move, too, now and then," Jamie said, after a minute. There was an odd tone to his voice, and I glanced up at him, surprised. His eyes were fixed on Betty's face, but with a remote look that made it plain he was seeing something else.

"Who moves?"

"Corpses."

Gooseflesh rippled up my forearms. He was right, though I thought he might have kept that particular observation to himself for the moment.

"Yes," I said, as casually as possible, looking back at my

work. "Common postmortem phenomena. Usually just the movement of gases."

"I saw a dead man sit up once," he said, his tone as casual as my own.

"What, at a wake? He wasn't really dead?"

"No, in a fire. And he was dead enough."

I glanced up sharply. His voice was flat and matter-of-fact, but his face bore an inward look of deep abstraction; whatever he'd seen, he was seeing it again.

"After Culloden, the English burned the Highland dead on the field. We smelled the fires, but I didna see one, save when they took me out and put me in the wagon, to send me home."

He had lain hidden under a layer of hay, nose pressed to a crack in the boards in order to breathe. The wagon driver had taken a circuitous route off the field, to avoid any questions from troops near the farmhouse, and at one point, had stopped for a moment to wait for a group of soldiers to move away.

"There was a fresh pyre burning, perhaps ten yards away; they'd set it alight no more than a short time before, for the clothes had only just begun to char. I saw Graham Gillespie lyin' on the heap near me, and he was surely dead, for there was the mark of a pistol shot on his temple."

The wagon had waited for what seemed a long time, though it was hard to tell, through the haze of pain and fever. But as he watched, he had seen Gillespie suddenly sit up amid the flames, and turn his head.

"He was lookin' straight at me," he said. "Had I been in my right mind, I expect I would ha' let out a rare skelloch. As it was, it only seemed . . . friendly of Graham." There was a hint of uneasy amusement in his voice. "I thought he was perhaps tellin' me it wasna so bad, being dead. That, or welcoming me to hell, maybe."

"Postmortem contracture," I said, absorbed in the excavation of the digestive system. "Fire makes the muscles contract, and the limbs often twist into very lifelike positions. Can you bring the light closer?"

I had the esophagus pulled free, and carefully slit the length of it, turning back the flabby tissue. There was some irritation toward the lower end, and there was blood in it, but no sign of rupture or hemorrhage. I bent, squinting up into the pharyngeal cavity, but it was too dark to see much there. I was in no way equipped for detailed exploration, so instead returned my examinations to the other end, slipping a hand under the stomach and lifting it up.

I felt a sharpening of the sense of wrongness that I had had through this whole affair. If there was something amiss, this was the most likely place to find evidence of it. Logic as well as sixth sense said as much.

There was no food in the stomach; after such vomiting that was hardly surprising. When I cut through the heavy muscular wall, though, the sharp scent of ipecac cut through the reek of the body.

"What?" Jamie leaned forward at my exclamation, frowning at the body.

"Ipecac. That quack dosed her with ipecac—and recently! Can you smell it?"

He grimaced with distaste, but took a cautious sniff, and nodded.

"Would that not be a proper thing to do, when you've a person wi' a curdled wame? Ye gave wee Beckie MacLeod ipecacuanha yourself, when she'd drunk your blue stuff."

"True enough." Five-year-old Beckie had drunk half a bottle of the arsenic decoction I made to poison rats, attracted by the pale blue color, and evidently not at all put off by the taste. Well, the rats liked it, too. "But I did that right away. There's no point in giving it hours afterward, when the poison or irritant has already passed out of the stomach."

Given Fentiman's state of medical knowledge, though, would he have known that? He might simply have administered ipecac again because he could think of nothing else to do. I frowned, turning back the heavy wall of the stomach. Yes, this was the source of the hemorrhage; the inner wall was raw-looking, dark red as ground meat. There was a small amount of liquid in the stomach; clear lymph that had begun to separate from the clotted blood left in the body.

"So you're thinking that it was maybe the ipecac that killed her?"

"I was . . . but now I'm not so sure," I murmured, probing

carefully. It had occurred to me that if Fentiman had given Betty a heavy dose of ipecac, the violent vomiting provoked by it might have caused an internal rupture and hemorrhage—but I wasn't finding any evidence of that. I used the scalpel to slit the stomach further open, pulling back the edges, and opening the duodenum.

"Can you hand me one of the small empty jars? And the wash bottle, please?"

Jamie hung the lantern on the nail and obligingly knelt to rummage through the bag, while I rummaged further through the stomach. There was some granular material forming a pale sludge in the furrows of the rugae. I scraped gingerly at it, finding that it came free easily, a thick, gritty paste between my fingertips. I wasn't sure what it was, but a suspicion was growing unpleasantly in the back of my mind. I meant to flush the stomach, collect the residue, and take it back to the house, where I could examine it in a decent light, come morning. If it was what I thought—

Without warning, the door of the shed swung open. A whoosh of cold air made the flame of the lantern burn suddenly high and bright—bright enough to show me Phillip Wylie's face, pale and shocked in the frame of the doorway.

He stared at me, his mouth hanging slightly open, then closed it and swallowed; I heard the sound of it clearly. His eyes traveled slowly over the scene, then returned to my face, wide pools of horror.

I was shocked, too. My heart had leapt into my throat, and my hands had frozen, but my brain was racing.

What would happen if he caused an outcry? It would be the most dreadful scandal, whether I was able to explain what I was doing, or not. If not—fear rippled over me in a chilly wave. I had come close to being burned for witchcraft once before; and that was one time too often.

I felt a slight movement of the air near my feet, and realized that Jamie was crouched in the deep shadow below the table. The light of the lantern was bright, but limited; I stood in a pool of darkness that reached to my waist. Wylie hadn't seen him. I reached out a toe and nudged him, as a signal to stay put.

I forced myself to smile at Phillip Wylie, though my heart

was stuck firmly in my throat, and beating wildly. I swallowed hard and said the first thing that came into my mind, which happened to be "Good evening."

He licked his lips. He was wearing neither patch nor powder at the moment, but was quite as pale as the muslin sheet.

"Mrs. . . . Fraser," he said, and swallowed again. "I—er—what *are* you doing?"

I should have thought that was reasonably obvious; presumably his question had to do with the reasons why I was doing it—and I had no intention of going into those.

"Never you mind that," I said crisply, recovering a bit of nerve. "What are *you* doing, skulking round the place at dead of night?"

Evidently that was a good question; his face shifted at once from open horror to wariness. His head twitched, as though to turn and look over his shoulder. He stopped the motion before it was completed, but my eyes followed the direction of it. There was a man standing in the darkness behind him; a tall man who now stepped forward, his face glimmering pale in the glow of the lantern, sardonic eyes the green of gooseberries. Stephen Bonnet.

"Jesus H. Roosevelt Christ," I said.

A number of things happened at that point: Jamie came out from under the table with a rush like a striking cobra, Phillip Wylie leaped back from the door with a startled cry, and the lantern crashed from its nail to the floor. There was a strong smell of splattered oil and brandy, a soft *whoosh* like a furnace lighting, and the crumpled shroud was burning at my feet.

Jamie was gone; there were shouts from the darkness outside, and the sound of running feet on brick. I kicked at the burning fabric, meaning to stamp it out.

Then I thought better, and instead lunged against the table, knocking it over and dumping its contents. I seized the blazing shroud with one hand and dragged it over corpse and upturned table. The floor of the shed was thick with sawdust, already burning in spots. I kicked the shattered lantern hard, knocking it into the dry boards of the wall, and spilling out the rest of its oil, which ignited at once.

There were shouts from the kitchen garden, voices calling

in alarm; I had to get out. I seized my bag and fled, red-handed, into the night, my fist still clenched tight about the evidence. It was the one point of certainty in the prevailing chaos. I had no notion what was going on, or what might happen next, but at least I knew for sure that I was right. Betty had indeed been murdered.

THERE WERE A PAIR of agitated servants in the kitchen garden, apparently wakened by the disturbance. They were casting round in a haphazard manner, calling out to each other, but with no light but that of the fading moon, it was an easy matter to keep to the shadows and slip past them.

No one had come out of the main house yet, but the shouts and flames were going to attract attention soon. I crouched against the wall, in the shadows of a huge raspberry cane, as the gate flung open and two more slaves came rushing through from the stable, half-dressed and incoherent, shouting something about the horses. The smell of burning was strong in the air; no doubt they thought the stable was on fire, or about to be.

My heart was pounding so hard against the inside of my chest that I could feel it, like a fist. I had an unpleasant vision of the flaccid heart I had just held in my hand, and of what my own must look like now—a dark red knob of slick muscle, pulsing and thumping, battering mindlessly away in its neatly socketed cave between the lungs.

The lungs weren't working nearly so well as the heart; my breath came short and hard, in gasps that I tried to stifle for fear of detection. What if they dragged Betty's desecrated body from the shed? They wouldn't know who had been responsible for the mutilation, but the discovery would cause the most fearful outcry, with resultant wild rumors and public hysteria.

A glow was visible now above the far wall of the kitchen garden; the roof of the shed was beginning to burn, fire-glow showing in brilliant thin lines as the pine shingles began to smoke and curl.

Sweat was prickling behind my ears, but my breath came a little easier when I saw the slaves standing by the far gate in a knot, bunched together in awed silhouette. Of course—they wouldn't try to put it out, well caught as it was. The nearest water was in the horse troughs; by the time buckets were fetched, the shed would be well on its way to ashes. There was nothing near it that would burn. Best to let it go.

Smoke purled up in quickening billows, high into the air. Knowing what was in the shed, it was much too easy to imagine spectral shapes in the transparent undulations. Then the fire broke through the roof, and tongues of flame lit the smoke from below in an eerie, beautiful glow.

A high-pitched wail broke from behind me, and I started back, banging my elbow against the brick wall. Phaedre had come through the gate, Gussie and another female slave behind her. She ran through the garden, screaming "Mama!" as her white shift caught the light of the flames that now burst through holes in the shed's roof, showering sparks.

The men by the gate caught her; the women hurried after, reaching for her, calling out in agitation. I tasted blood in my mouth, and realized that I had bitten my lower lip. I closed my eyes convulsively, trying not to hear Phaedre's frantic cries and the antiphonal babble of her comforters.

A frightful sense of guilt washed over me. Her voice was so like Bree's, and I could imagine so clearly what Bree might feel, were it my own body, burning in that shed. But there were worse things Phaedre might feel, had I not let loose the fire. My hands were shaking from cold and tension, but I groped for my bag, which I had dropped on the ground at my feet.

My hands felt stiff and dreadful, gummy with drying blood and lymph. I mustn't—*mustn't*—be found this way. I fumbled in the sack with my free hand, finally coming up by feel with a lidded jar, normally used to keep leeches, and the small wash bottle of dilute alcohol and water.

I couldn't see, but felt blood crack and flake away as I opened my cramped fingers and gingerly scraped the contents of my hand into the jar. I couldn't grip the cork of the bottle with my shaking fingers; finally I pulled it out with my teeth, and poured the alcohol over my open palm, washing the rest of the grainy residue into the jar.

The house had been roused now; I could hear voices coming from that direction. What was going on? Where was Jamie—and where were Bonnet and Phillip Wylie? Jamie had not been armed with anything save a bottle of holy water; were either of the others? I had heard no shots, at least—but blades made no noise.

I rinsed both hands hastily with the rest of the wash bottle, and dried them on the dark lining of my cloak, where the smears wouldn't show. People were running back and forth through the garden, shadows flitting along the walkways like phantoms, mere feet from my hiding place. Why did they make no noise? Were they truly people, or shades, somehow roused by my sacrilege?

Then one figure shouted; another replied. I realized dimly that the running people made no sound on the bricks because they were barefoot and because my ears were ringing. My face was tingling with cold sweat, my hands far more numb than chill would account for.

You idiot, Beauchamp, I thought to myself. *You're going to faint. Sit down*!

I must have managed to do so, for I came to myself a few moments later, sprawled in the dirt under the raspberry canes, half-leaning against the wall. The kitchen garden seemed full of people by now; jostling pale shapes of guests and servants, indistinguishable as ghosts in their shifts.

I waited for the space of a few breaths, to be sure I was recovered, then lurched awkwardly to my feet and stepped out onto the dark path, bag in hand.

The first person I saw was Major MacDonald, standing on the path watching the shed burn, his white wig gleaming in the light from the fire. I gripped him by the arm, startling him badly.

"What is happening?" I said, not bothering to apologize.

"Where is your husband?" he said in the same moment, peering round me in search of Jamie.

"I don't know," I said, all too truthfully. "I'm looking for him."

"Mrs. Fraser! Are you all right, dear lady?" Lloyd Stanhope popped up by my elbow, looking like a very animated boiled egg in his nightshirt, his polled head startlingly round and pale without his wig.

I assured him that I was quite all right, which I was, by now. It wasn't until I saw Stanhope and noticed that most of the other gentlemen present were in a similar state of dishabille that I realized the Major was fully clothed, from wig to buckled shoes. My face must have changed as I looked at him, for I saw his brows raise and his gaze run from my bound hair to my shod feet, as he quite obviously noticed the same thing about me.

"I heard shouts of 'Fire!' and thought someone might be hurt," I said coolly, lifting the bag. "I've brought my medical kit. Is everyone all right, do you know?"

"So far as I—" MacDonald began, but then sprang back in alarm, grasping my arm and dragging me back, too. The roof gave way with a deep sighing noise, and sparks plumed high, showering down among the crowd in the garden.

Everyone gasped and cried out, falling back. Then there came one of those brief, inexplicable pauses when everyone in a crowd falls suddenly silent at once. The fire was still burning, with a noise like crumpling paper, but over it I could hear a distant shouting. It was a woman's voice, high and cracked, but strong for all that, and full of fury.

"Mrs. Cameron!" Stanhope exclaimed, but the Major was already making for the house at a run.

53

THE FRENCHMAN'S GOLD

WE FOUND JOCASTA CAMERON Innes on the window seat in her room, clad in her chemise, bound hand and foot with strips of bed linen, and absolutely scarlet-faced with fury. I had no time to take further note of her condition, for Duncan Innes, clad for the night in nothing but his shirt, was lying sprawled on his face on the floor near the hearth.

I rushed over and knelt by him at once, searching for a pulse.

"Is he dead?" The Major peered over my shoulder, evidencing more curiosity than sympathy.

"No," I said briefly. "Get these people out of here, will you?" The chamber was crammed with guests and servants, all exclaiming over the newly freed Jocasta, expostulating, speculating, and generally making bloody nuisances of themselves. The Major blinked at my peremptory tone, but retired without demur to deal with the situation.

Duncan was certainly alive, and a cursory examination showed me no injury beyond a large lump behind one ear; evidently, he had been clubbed with the heavy silver candlestick which lay beside him on the floor. He had a nasty color, but his pulse was fairly good, and he was breathing evenly. I thumbed open his eyelids, one at a time, and bent close to check his pupils. They stared back at me, glazed, but the same size and not abnormally dilated. So far, so good.

Behind me, the Major was making good use of his military experience, barking orders in a parade-ground voice.

Since most of those present were not soldiers, this was having a limited effect.

Jocasta Cameron was having a much greater one. Released from her bonds, she staggered across the room, leaning heavily on Ulysses's arm, parting the crowd like the waves of the Red Sea.

"Duncan! Where is my husband?" she demanded, turning her head from side to side, blind eyes fierce. People gave way before her, and she reached my side in seconds.

"Who is there?" Her hand swept in a flat arc before her, searching for position.

"It's me—Claire." I reached up to touch her hand, guiding her down beside me. Her own fingers were chilled and trembling, and there were deep red marks on her wrists from the bonds. "Don't worry; I think Duncan will be all right."

She put out a hand, seeking to see for herself, and I guided her fingers to his throat, setting them on the big vein I could see pulsing at the side of his neck. She uttered a small exclamation and leaned forward, putting both hands on his face, tracing his features with an anxious tenderness that quite moved me, so at odds as it was with her normal autocratic mien.

"They struck him . . . is he badly hurt?"

"I think not," I assured her. "Only a knock on the head."

"Are you quite sure?" Her face turned toward me, frowning, and her sensitive nostrils flared. "I smell blood."

With a small shock, I realized that while my hands were mostly clean, my fingernails were still heavily ringed with dark blood from the impromptu autopsy. I repressed the urge to curl my hands, instead murmuring discreetly, "That's me, I expect; my courses." Major MacDonald was glancing curiously in our direction; had he heard her?

There was a stir at the doorway, and I turned. To my immense relief, it was Jamie. He was disheveled, his coat was torn, and he sported what looked like the beginnings of a black eye, but otherwise appeared undamaged.

My relief must have shown on my face, for his grim look softened a little, and he nodded as he met my eye. Then it hardened again, as he saw Duncan. He dropped to one knee beside me.

"He's all right," I said, before he could ask. "Someone hit him on the head and tied up your aunt."

"Aye? Who?" He glanced up at Jocasta, and laid a hand on Duncan's chest, as though to reassure himself that Duncan was indeed still breathing.

"I havena the slightest notion," she replied crisply. "If I had, I should have sent men to hunt the ill-deedie shargs down by now." Her lips tightened into a thin line, and the high color surged back into her face at thought of the assailants. "Did no one see the rascals?"

"I think not, Aunt," Jamie replied calmly. "With such a boiling in the house, no one kens what to look for, aye?"

I raised one eyebrow at him in silent question. What did he mean by that? Had Bonnet got away? For surely it must have been Bonnet who had invaded Jocasta's chamber; boiling or no, there couldn't be multiple violent criminals at large on the same night in a place the size of River Run.

Jamie shook his head briefly. He glanced at my hands, saw the blood under my nails, and raised an eyebrow of his own. Had I discovered anything? Had there been time for me to be sure? I nodded, and a slight shudder went over me; yes, I knew.

Murder, I mouthed to him.

He squeezed my arm in quick reassurance, and glanced over his shoulder; the Major had at last succeeded in pushing most of the crowd out into the hallway, sending the servants for restoratives and refreshments, a groom for the Sheriff in Cross Creek, the men out to search the grounds for possible miscreants, and the ladies down to the salon in a flutter of excited puzzlement. The Major closed the door firmly behind them, then came briskly over to us.

"Shall we get him onto the bed, then?"

Duncan was beginning to stir and groan. He coughed and gagged a little, but fortunately didn't throw up. Jamie and Major MacDonald got him up and conveyed him to the big four-poster, where they laid him down with complete disregard for the quilted silk coverlet.

With a faint atavistic sense of housewifeliness, I tucked a soft green velvet pillow under his head. It was filled with bran, but crackled faintly under my hand and gave off a strong scent of lavender. Lavender was good for headache, all right, but I wasn't sure it was quite up to this.

"Where is Phaedre?"

Ulysses had guided Jocasta to her chair, and she sank back in its leather depths, looking suddenly exhausted and old. The color had left her face along with her rage, and her white hair was coming down in straggles round her shoulders.

"I sent Phaedre to bed, Auntie." Bree had come in, unnoticed in the scrum, and had resisted removal by the Major. She bent over Jocasta, touching her hand with solicitude. "Don't worry; I'll take care of you."

Jocasta put her own hand over Bree's in gratitude, but sat up straighter, looking puzzled.

"Sent her to bed? Why? And what in God's name is burning?" She jerked bolt upright, alarmed. "Are the stables afire?" The wind had changed, and the night air was streaming in through a broken pane above the window seat, heavy with the scent of smoke and a faint, dreadful smell of burned flesh.

"No, no! The stables are fine. Phaedre was upset," Bree explained, with some delicacy. "The shed by the kitchen garden seems to have burned down; her mother's body . . ."

Jocasta's face went quite blank for a moment. Then she drew herself up, and an extraordinary look came into her face, something almost like satisfaction, though with a tinge of puzzlement.

Jamie was standing behind me. He evidently saw it, too, for I heard him give a soft grunt.

"Are ye somewhat recovered, Aunt?" he asked.

She turned her face toward him, one eyebrow lifted in sardonic reply.

"I shall be the better for a dram," she said, accepting the cup that Ulysses set deftly into her hands. "But aye, nephew, I'm well enough. Duncan, though?"

I was sitting by Duncan on the bed, his wrist in my hand, and could feel him coming toward the surface of consciousness, eyelids fluttering and fingers twitching slightly against my palm.

"He's coming round," I assured her.

"Give him brandy, Ulysses," Jocasta commanded, but I stopped the butler with a shake of my head.

"Not quite yet. He'll choke."

"Do ye feel yourself equal to telling us what happened, Aunt?" Jamie asked, with a noticeable edge to his voice. "Or must we wait for Duncan to come to himself?"

Jocasta sighed, closing her eyes briefly. She was as good as all the MacKenzies at hiding what she thought, but in this case, it was evident at least that she *was* thinking, and furiously, at that. The tip of her tongue flicked out, touching a raw spot at the corner of her mouth, and I realized that she must have been gagged as well as bound.

I could feel Jamie behind me, seething with some strong feeling. Near as he was, I could hear his stiff fingers drumming softly on the bedpost. Much as I wanted to hear Jocasta's story, I wanted even more to be alone with Jamie, to tell him what I had discovered, and to find out what had happened in the darkness of the kitchen garden.

Outside, voices murmured in the hall; not all the guests had dispersed. I caught muffled phrases—"quite burnt up, nothing left but the bones," ". . . stolen? Don't know . . ." ". . . check the stables," "Yes, completely burned . . ." A deep shiver struck me, and I gripped Duncan's hand hard, fighting a panic that I did not understand. I must have looked odd, for Bree said softly, "Mama?" She was looking at me, brow creased with worry. I tried to smile at her, but my lips felt stiff.

Jamie's hands settled on my shoulders, large and warm. I had been holding my breath without realizing it; at his touch, I let it out in a small gasp, and breathed again. Major MacDonald glanced curiously at me, but his attention was at once deflected by Jocasta, who opened her eyes and turned her face in his direction.

"It is Major MacDonald, is it not?"

"At your service, Mum." The Major made an automatic bow, forgetting—as folk often did—that she could not see him.

"I thank ye for your gallant service, Major. My husband and I are most indebted to ye."

The Major made a politely dismissive sound.

"No, no," she insisted, straightening up and brushing back her hair with one hand. "Ye've been put to great trouble on our account, and we must not impose further on your kindness. Ulysses—take the Major down to the parlor and find him proper refreshment."

The butler bowed obsequiously—I noticed for the first time that he was dressed in a nightshirt over unbuckled breeches, though he had clapped his wig on his head—and ushered the Major firmly toward the door. MacDonald looked ludicrously surprised and not a little disgruntled at being given the push in this civilized fashion, he having quite obviously intended to stay and hear all the gory details. Still, there was no graceful way of resisting, and he made the best of it, bowing in a dignified manner as he took his leave.

The panic had begun to recede, as bafflingly as it had come. Jamie's hands radiated a warmth that seemed to spread through my body, and my breath came easily again. I was able to focus my attention on my patient, who had got his eyes open, though he seemed to be regretting it.

"Och, *mo cheann*!" Duncan squinted against the glow of the lamp, focusing with some difficulty on my face, then rising to Jamie's behind me. "*Mac Dubh*—what's come amiss?"

One of Jamie's hands left my shoulder, and reached down to tighten on Duncan's arm.

"Dinna fash yourself, *a charaid*." He glanced meaningfully at Jocasta. "Your wife is just about to tell us what has happened. Are ye not, Aunt?"

There was a slight but definite emphasis on the "not," and Jocasta, thus put on the spot, pursed her lips, but then sighed and sat straight, plainly resigned to the unpleasant necessity of confidence.

"There is no one here but family?"

Being assured that there was not, she nodded, and began.

She had sent away her maid, and been on the point of retiring, she said, when the door from the hall had suddenly opened to admit what she thought were two men.

"I am sure there was more than one—I heard their footsteps, and breathing," she said, frowning in concentration. "There *might* have been three, but I think not. Only one of them spoke, though. I think the other must have been someone I ken, for he stayed far away, quite at the end of the room, as though he were afraid I should recognize him by some means."

The man who had spoken to her was a stranger; she was positive that she had never heard his voice before.

"He was an Irishman," she said, and Jamie's hand tightened abruptly on my shoulder. "Well enough spoken, but not a gentleman, by any means." Her nostrils flared a little, with unconscious disdain.

"No, hardly that," Jamie said, under his breath. Bree had started slightly at the word "Irishman," though her face bore no more than a slight frown of concentration as she listened.

The Irishman had been polite, but blunt in his demands; he wanted the gold.

"Gold?" It was Duncan who spoke, but the question was plain on everyone's face. "What gold? We've no money in the house save a few pounds sterling and a bit of the Proclamation money."

Jocasta's lips pressed tight. There was no help for it, though; not now. She made a small growling noise in her throat, an inarticulate protest at being compelled to give up the secret she had kept for so long.

"The Frenchman's gold," she said, abruptly.

"What?" said Duncan in bewilderment. He touched the lump behind his ear, gingerly, as though convinced it had affected his hearing.

"The French gold," Jocasta repeated, rather irritably. "That was sent, just before Culloden."

"Before—" Bree began, wide-eyed, but Jamie interrupted her.

"Louis's gold," he said softly. "That's what ye mean, Aunt? The Stuarts' gold?"

Jocasta uttered a short laugh, quite without humor.

"Once it was."

She paused, listening. The voices had moved away from the door, though there were still noises in the hallway. She turned toward Bree, and motioned toward the door.

"Go and see that no one's got his lug to the keyhole, lass. I havena held my peace these twenty-five years only to spill it to the whole county."

Bree opened the door briefly, peered out, then closed it, reporting that no one was near.

"Good. Come ye here, lass. Sit by me. But no—first, fetch me the case I showed ye yesterday."

Looking more than puzzled, Bree vanished into the dressing room, returning with a slender case of worn black leather. She laid it in Jocasta's lap and settled onto a stool beside her aunt, giving me a look of faint concern.

I was feeling quite myself again, though a faint echo of that odd fear still rang in my bones. I nodded reassuringly to Bree, though, and bent to give Duncan a sip of watered brandy. I knew what it was now, that ancient distress. It was that phrase overheard, the words by chance the same that a small girl had once heard spoken, whispered in the next room by the strangers who had come to say her mother would not be coming back, that she had died. An accident; a crash; fire. *Burnt to bones,* the voice had said, filled with the awe of it. *Burnt to bones,* and the desolation of a daughter, forever abandoned. My hand trembled, and the cloudy liquid ran in a trickle down Duncan's chin.

But that was long ago, and in another country, I thought, steeling myself against the riptide of memory.

And besides . . .

Jocasta drained her own cup, set it down with a small thump, and opened the case in her lap. A gleam of gold and diamonds showed inside, and she lifted out a slender wooden rod that held three rings.

"I had three daughters, once," she said. "Three girls. Clementina, Seonag, and Morna." She touched one of the rings, a wide band, set with three large diamonds.

"This was for my girls; Hector gave it to me when Morna was born. She was his, Morna—you know it means 'beloved'?" Her other hand left the box and stretched out, groping. She touched Bree's cheek, and Bree took the hand, cradling it between her own.

"I had one living child of each marriage." Jocasta's long fingers probed delicately, touching each ring in turn. "Clementina belonged to John Cameron; him I wed when I myself was little more than a child; I bore her at sixteen. Seonag was the daughter of Black Hugh—she was dark, like her sire, but she had my brother Colum's eyes." She turned her own blind eyes toward Jamie, briefly, then bent her head back, touching the ring with three diamonds again.

"And then Morna, my last child. She was but sixteen when she died."

The old woman's face was bleak, but the line of her mouth softened, speaking the names of her vanished girls.

"I'm sorry, Aunt." Bree spoke softly. She bent her head to kiss the knuckles of the hand she cradled, knobbed with age. Jocasta tightened her hand a little in acknowledgment, but did not mean to be distracted from her story.

"Hector Cameron gave me this," Jocasta said, touching the ring. "And he killed them all. My children, my daughters. He killed them for the Frenchman's gold."

The shock of it took my breath and hollowed my stomach. I felt Jamie go still behind me, and saw Duncan's bloodshot eyes go wide. Brianna didn't change expression. She closed her eyes for a moment, but still held on to the long bony hand.

"What happened to them, Aunt?" she said quietly. "Tell me."

Jocasta was silent for a few moments. So was the room; there was no sound save the hiss of beeswax burning, and the faint asthmatic wheeze of her breath. To my surprise, when she spoke again, it wasn't to Brianna. Instead, she lifted her head and turned again toward Jamie.

"You know about the gold, then, *a mhic mo pheathar*?" she said. If he found this a strange question, he gave no sign of it, but answered calmly.

"I have heard something of it," he said. He moved, coming round the bed to sit beside me, closer to his aunt. "It has been a rumor in the Highlands, ever since Culloden. Louis would send gold, they said, to help his cousin in his holy fight. And then they said the gold had come, yet no man saw it."

"I saw it." Jocasta's wide mouth, so like her nephew's, widened further in a sudden grimace, then relaxed. "I saw it," she repeated.

"Thirty thousand pound, in gold bullion. I was with them the night it came ashore, rowed in from the French ship. It was in six small chests, each one so heavy that only two at a time could be brought, else the boat would sink. Each chest had the fleur-de-lis carved on the lid, each one bound with iron bands and a lock, each lock itself sealed with red wax, and the wax bore the print of King Louis's ring. The *fleur-de-lis*."

A sigh ran through us all at the words, a collective breath of awe. Jocasta nodded slowly, blind eyes open to the sights of that night long past.

"Where was it brought ashore, Aunt?" Jamie asked softly.

She nodded slowly, as though to herself, eyes fixed on the scene her memory painted.

"On Innismaraich," she said. "A tiny isle, just off Coigach."

I had been holding my breath. Now I let it out, slowly, and met Jamie's eyes. Innismaraich. Island of the Sea-people; the silkies' isle, it meant. We knew that place.

"There were the three men trusted with it," she said. "Hector was one, my brother Dougal was another—the third man was masked; they all were, but of course I kent Hector and Dougal. I didna ken the third man, nor did any of them speak his name. I knew his servant, though; a man named Duncan Kerr."

Jamie had stiffened slightly at Dougal's name; at the name of Duncan Kerr he froze.

"There were servants, too?" he asked.

"Two," she said, and a faint, bitter smile twisted her mouth. "The masked man brought Duncan Kerr, as I said, and my brother Dougal had a man with him from Leoch—I kent his face, but not his name. Hector had me to help him; I was a braw, strong woman—like you, *a leannan*, like you," she said softly, squeezing Brianna's hand. "I was strong, and Hector trusted me as he could trust no other. I trusted him, too—then."

The noises from outside had died away, but a breeze through the broken pane stirred the curtains, uneasy as a ghost that hears its name called from a distance.

"There were three boats. The chests were small, but heavy enough that it took two persons to carry one between them. We took two chests into our boat, Hector and I, and we rowed away, into the fog. I could hear the splash of the others' oars, growing fainter as they drew away, and then lost in the night."

"When was this, Aunt?" Jamie asked, his eyes intent on her. "When did the gold come from France?"

"Too late," she whispered. "Much too late. Damn Louis!" she exclaimed, with a sudden fierceness that brought her upright in her seat. "Damn the wicked Frenchman, and may his eyes rot as mine have! To think what might have been, had he been true to his blood and his word!"

Jamie's eyes met mine, sidelong. Too late. Had the gold come sooner—when Charles landed at Glenfinnan, perhaps, or when he took Edinburgh, and for a few brief weeks held the city as a king returned—what then?

The ghost of a smile touched Jamie's lips with ruefulness, and he glanced at Brianna, then back at me, the question asked and answered in his eyes. What, then?

"It was March," Jocasta said, recovering from her outburst. "A freezing night, but clear as ice. I stood upon the cliff and looked far out to sea, and the path of the moon lay like gold on the water. The ship came sailing in upon that golden path, like a king to his coronation, and I did think it a sign." Her head turned toward Jamie, and her mouth twisted abruptly.

"I did think I heard him laughing, then," she said. "Black Brian. Him who took my sister from me. It would have been like him. But he was not there; I suppose it was only the barking of the silkies."

I was watching Jamie as she spoke. He didn't move, but like magic, the reddish hairs on his forearm rose, glinting like wires in the candlelight.

"I didna ken ye knew my father," he said, a faint edge to his voice. "But let that be for now, Aunt. It was March, ye say?"

She nodded.

"Too late," she repeated. "It was meant to have come two months before, Hector said. There were delays . . ."

It *had* been too late. In January, after the victory at Falkirk, such a show of support from France might have been decisive. But in March, the Highland Army was already moving north, turned back at Derby from its invasion of

England. The last slim chance of victory had been lost, and Charles Stuart's men were marching then toward destruction at Culloden.

With the chests safe ashore, the new guardians of the gold had conferred over what to do with the treasure. The army was moving, and Stuart with it; Edinburgh was once more in the hands of the English. There was no safe place to take it, no trustworthy hands into which it could be delivered.

"They didna trust O'Sullivan or the others near the Prince," Jocasta explained. "Irishmen, Italians . . . Dougal said he hadna gone to so much trouble, only to have the gold squandered or stolen by foreigners." She smiled, a little grimly. "He meant he didna want to chance losing the credit for having got it."

The three keepers had been no more willing to trust one another than the Prince's advisers. Most of the night had been spent in argument in the bleak upper room of a desolate tavern, while Jocasta and the two servants slept on the floor, among the red-sealed chests. Finally, the gold had been divided; each man had taken two of the chests, swearing on his blood to keep the secret and hold the treasure faithfully, in trust for his rightful monarch, King James.

"They made the two servants swear as well," Jocasta said. "They cut each man, and the drops of blood shone redder in the candlelight than the wax seals on the chests."

"Did you swear, too?" Brianna spoke quietly, but her eyes were intent on the white-haired figure in the chair.

"No, I didna swear." Jocasta's lips, still finely shaped, curved slightly, as though amused. "I was Hector's wife; his oath bound me. Then."

Uneasy in possession of so much wealth, the conspirators had left the tavern before dawn, bundling the chests in blankets and rags to hide them.

"A pair of travelers rode in, as the last of the chests was brought down. It was their coming that saved the innkeeper's life, for it was a lonely spot, and he the only witness to our presence there that night. I think Dougal and Hector would not have thought to do such a thing—but the third man, he meant to dispose of the landlord; I saw it in his eyes, in the crouch of his body as he waited near the bottom of the stair, his hand on his dirk. He saw me watching—he smiled at me, beneath his mask."

"And did he never unmask, this third man?" Jamie asked. His ruddy brows drew together as though by sheer concentration he could recreate the scene she saw in her mind's eye, and identify the stranger.

She shook her head.

"No. I asked myself, now and then, when I thought of that night, would I know the man again, did I see him. I thought I would; he was dark, a slender man, but with a strength in him like knife steel. Could I see his eyes again, I would be sure of it. But now . . ." She shrugged. "Would I ken him by his voice alone? I canna say, so long ago it was."

"But he wasna by any means an Irishman, this man?" Duncan was still pale and clammy-looking, but had raised himself on one elbow, listening with deep absorption.

Jocasta started a little, as though she had forgotten his presence.

"Ah! No, *a dhuine*. A Scot by his speech—a Highland gentleman."

Duncan and Jamie exchanged glances.

"A MacKenzie or a Cameron?" Duncan asked softly, and Jamie nodded.

"Or perhaps one of the Grants."

I understood their half-voiced speculations. There were—had been—a staggeringly complex array of associations and feuds among the Highland clans, and there were many who would not—could not—have cooperated in an undertaking of such importance and secrecy.

Colum MacKenzie had negotiated a close alliance with the Camerons; in fact, Jocasta herself had been part of that alliance, her marriage to a Cameron chief the token of it. If Dougal MacKenzie was one of the men who had engineered the receipt of the French gold, and Hector Cameron another, it was odds-on that the third man had been someone from one of those clans, or from another trusted by both. MacKenzie, Cameron . . . or Grant. And if Jocasta had not known the man by sight, the odds on his being a Grant improved, for she would have known most high-ranking tacksmen of clans MacKenzie or Cameron.

But there was no time now to consider such things; the story was not finished.

The conspirators had separated then, each going by his own way, each with one-third of the French gold. Jocasta had no knowledge of what Dougal MacKenzie or the unknown man had done with their chests; Hector Cameron had put the two chests he brought away into a hole in the floor of his bedroom, an old hiding place made by his father to conceal valuables.

Hector meant to leave it there until the Prince had reached some place of safety, where he could receive the gold, and use it for the furtherance of his aims. But Charles Stuart was already in flight, and would not find a place to rest for many months. Before he reached his final refuge, disaster intervened.

"Hector left the gold—and me—at home, and went to join the Prince and the army. On the seventeenth of April, he rode back into the dooryard at sunset, his horse lathered to a froth. He swung down and left the poor beast to a groom, while he rushed into the house and bade me pack what valuables I could—the Cause was lost, he said, and we must flee, or die with the Stuarts."

Cameron was wealthy, even then, and canny enough to have kept his coach and horses, rather than giving them to the Stuart cause. Canny enough, too, not to carry two chests of French gold in his flight.

"He took three bars of the gold from one of the chests, and gave them to me. I hid them under the seat of the coach; he and the groom carried the chests awa to the wood—I didna see where they buried them."

It was midday of April 18, when Hector Cameron boarded his coach, with his wife, his groom, his daughter Morna, and three bars of French bullion, and headed hell-for-leather south toward Edinburgh.

"Seonag was married to the Master of Garth—he declared early for the Stuarts; he was killed at Culloden, though of course we didna know it then. Clementina was widowed already, and living with her sister at Rovo."

She took a deep breath, shuddering slightly, unwilling to relive the events she recounted, unable to resist them.

"I begged Hector to go to Rovo. It was only ten miles out of the way—it would have taken no but a few hours—but he wouldna stop. We could not, he said. Too big a risk, to take the time needed to fetch them. Clementina had two children, Seonag the one. Too many people for the coach, he said; it would slow us too much.

"Not to bring them away, then, I said. Only to warn them—only to see them once more."

She paused.

"I kent where we were bound—we had talked of it, though I didna ken he had things in such readiness."

Hector Cameron had been a Jacobite, but was also a keen judge of human affairs, and no man to throw his own life after a lost cause. Seeing how matters were falling out, and fearing some disaster, he had taken pains to engineer an escape. He had quietly put aside a few bags of clothing and necessities, turned what he could of his property into money, and secretly booked three open passages, from Edinburgh to the Colonies.

"Sometimes, I think I canna blame him," Jocasta said. She sat bolt upright, the light of the candles gleaming from her hair. "He thought Seonag wouldna go without her husband, and Clementina wouldna risk her bairns at sea. Perhaps he was right about that. And perhaps it would have made no difference to warn them. But I knew I shouldna see them again. . . ." Her mouth closed, and she swallowed.

In any case, Hector had refused to stop, fearing pursuit. Cumberland's troops had converged upon Culloden, but there were English soldiers on the Highland roads, and word of Charles Stuart's defeat was spreading like ripples near the edge of a whirlpool, moving faster and faster, in a vortex of danger.

As it was, the Camerons were discovered, two days later, near Ochtertyre.

"A wheel came off the coach," Jocasta said with a sigh. "Lord, I can see it now, spinning down the road by itself. The axletree was broke, and we'd no choice but to camp there by the road, while Hector and the groom made shift to mend it."

Repairs had taken the best part of a day, and Hector had

grown more and more edgy as the work went on, his anxiety infecting the rest of the party.

"I didna ken then what he'd seen at Culloden," Jocasta said. "He kent weel enough that if the English took him, it was all up wi' him. If they didna kill him on the spot, he'd be hangit as a traitor. He was sweating as he worked, and more wi' fear than with the heat of his labor. But even so . . ." Her lips pressed tight for a moment, before she went on.

"It was nearly dusk—it was spring, dusk came early—when they got the wheel back on the coach, and everyone got back aboard. The coach had been in a wee hollow when the wheel flew off; the groom urged the horses up a long slope, and just as we reached the crest of the hill, two men with muskets stepped out from the shadows into the road ahead."

It was a company of English soldiers, Cumberland's men. Arriving too late to join in the victory at Culloden, they were inflamed by news of it—but frustrated at not sharing in the battle, and only too ready to wreak what vengeance they could on fleeing Highlanders.

Always a quick thinker, Hector had sunk back in the corner of the coach at sight of them, his head bent and a shawl pulled over it, pretending to be an aged crone, sunk in sleep. Following his hissed instructions, Jocasta had leaned out of the window, prepared to pose as a respectable lady traveling with her daughter and mother.

The soldiers had not waited to hear her speech. One yanked open the door of the coach, and dragged her out. Morna, panicked, had leapt out after her, trying to pull her mother away from the soldier. Another man had grabbed the girl, and dragged her back, so that he stood between Jocasta and the coach.

"Another minute, and they meant to have 'Grannie' out on the ground as well—and then they would find the gold, and it would be all up wi' all of us."

A pistol shot startled all of them into momentary immobility. Leaning from the coach's open door, Hector had fired at the soldier holding Morna—but it was dusk and the light was poor; perhaps the horses had moved, jostling the coach. The shot struck Morna in the head.

"I ran to her," Jocasta said. Her voice was hoarse, her throat gone dry and thick. "I ran to her, but Hector jumped out and seized me. The soldiers were all standing, staring with the shock. He dragged me back, into the coach, and shouted to the groom to drive, drive on!"

She licked her lips and swallowed, once.

" 'She is dead,' he said to me. Over and over, 'She is dead, you cannot help,' he said, and held me tight when I would have thrown myself from the coach in my despair."

Slowly she pulled her hand away from Brianna; she had needed support to begin her story, but needed none to finish it. Her hands folded into fists, pressed hard against the white linen of her shift, as though to stanch the bleeding of a desecrated womb.

"It had gone dark by then," she said, and her voice was remote, detached. "I saw the glow of fires against the sky to the north."

Cumberland's troops were spreading outward, burning and pillaging. They reached Rovo, where Clementina and Seonag were with their families, and set the manor house afire. Jocasta never learned whether they had died in the fire, or later, starved and freezing in the cold Highland spring.

"So Hector saved his life—and mine, for what it was worth then," she said, still detached. "And of course, he saved the gold." Her fingers sought the ring again, and turned it slowly round upon its rod, so the stones caught the lamplight, glimmering.

"Indeed," Jamie murmured. His eyes were fixed on the blind face, watching her intently. It struck me suddenly as unfair that he should watch her so, almost judging, when she could not look back, or even know how he looked at her. I touched him, and he glanced aside at me, then took my hand, squeezing it hard.

Jocasta put aside the rings and rose, restless now that the worst part of the story was told. She moved toward the window seat, knelt there, and brushed back the curtains. It was hard to believe her blind, seeing her move with such purpose—and yet this was her room, her place, and every item in it was scrupulously placed so that she could find her way.

She pressed her hands against the icy glass and the night outside, and a white fog of condensation flared around her fingers like cold flames.

"Hector bought this place with the gold we brought," she said. "The land, the mill, the slaves. To do him credit"—her tone suggested that she was not inclined to do any such thing—"the worth of it now is due in great part to his own work. But it was the gold that bought it, to begin with."

"What of his oath?" Jamie asked softly.

"What of it?" she said, and uttered a short laugh. "Hector was a practical man. The Stuarts were finished; what need had they of gold, in Italy?"

"Practical," I repeated, surprising myself; I hadn't meant to speak, but I thought I had heard something odd in the way she spoke the word.

Evidently, I had. She turned around to face us, turning toward my voice. She was smiling, but a chill ran down my backbone at the sight of it.

"Aye, practical," she said, nodding. "My daughters were dead; he saw no reason to waste tears upon them. He never spoke of them, and would not let me speak, either. He had been a man of worth once, he would be, again—not so easy here, had anyone known." She breathed out, a heavy sound of stifled anger. "I daresay there are none in this land who even ken I was once a mother."

"You still are," said Brianna softly. "That much I know." She glanced at me, and her blue eyes met mine, dark with understanding. I felt the sting of tears behind the smile I gave her back. Yes, that much she knew, as did I.

So did Jocasta; the lines of her face relaxed for a moment, fury and remembered despair displaced for a moment by longing. She walked slowly to where Brianna sat on her stool, and laid her free hand on Bree's head. It rested there for a moment, then slid down, the long, sensitive fingers probing Brianna's strong cheekbones, her wide lips and long, straight nose, tracing the small track of the wetness down her cheek.

"Aye, *a leannan*," she said softly. "Ye ken what I mean. And ye ken now, why I would leave this place to you—or to your blood?"

Jamie coughed, breaking in before Bree could answer.

"Aye," he said, in a matter-of-fact tone. "So that is what ye told the Irishman tonight? Not all the story, to be sure—but that ye have no gold here?"

Jocasta's hands dropped from Brianna's face and she turned to face Jamie.

"Aye, I told them. Him. Told him that for all I kent, those chests were still buried in the wood in Scotland; he was welcome, I said, to go and dig there, and it suited him." One corner of her mouth curled up in a bitter smile.

"He wasna inclined to take your word for it?"

She shook her head, lips pressed together.

"He wasna a gentleman," she said again. "I canna say how it might have fallen out—for I sat near the bed, and I keep a wee knife beneath my pillow; I wouldna have suffered him to lay hands on me unscathed. Before I could reach for it, though, I heard footsteps in the dressing room."

She waved a hand toward the door near the fireplace; her dressing room lay beyond, joining her bedroom to another—the room that had once been Hector Cameron's, and was now presumably Duncan's.

The intruders had heard the footsteps, too; the Irishman hissed something to his friend, then moved away from Jocasta, toward the hearth. The other fellow had come close then, and seized her from behind, a hand across her mouth.

"All I could tell ye from that was that the fellow wore a cap pulled low over his head, and he stank of liquor, as though he'd poured it over himself instead of drinking it." She made a brief grimace of distaste.

The door had opened, Duncan had come in, and the Irishman had apparently leapt from behind the open door and clubbed him over the head.

"I dinna recall a thing," Duncan said ruefully. "I came to bid Miss—that is, my wife—good night. I recall settin' my hand upon the knob of the door, and next thing, I was lyin' here wi' my head split open." He touched the lump tenderly, then looked at Jocasta with an anxious concern.

"You are all right, yourself, *mo chridhe*? The bastards didna offer ye ill use?" He stretched out his hand to her, then, realizing that she could not see him, tried to sit up. He collapsed with a stifled groan, and she stood up at the sound, coming hurriedly to the bedside.

"Of course I am all right," she said, crossly, groping until she found his hand. "Save for the distress of thinking myself about to be a widow for the fourth time." She let out a sigh of exasperation and sat down beside him, smoothing back a swath of loosened hair from her face.

"I couldna tell what had happened; I only heard the thud, and a dreadful groan as ye fell. Then the Irishman came back toward me, and the creature holding me let go."

The Irishman had informed her pleasantly that he did not believe a word of her claim that there was no gold at River Run. He was convinced that the gold was here, and while he would not dream of offering harm to a lady, the same inhibitions did not obtain with respect to her husband.

"If I didna tell him where it was, he said, he and his companion would set in to cut wee bits off Duncan, beginning with his toes, and advancing to his ballocks," Jocasta said bluntly. Duncan hadn't much blood in his face to begin with, but what there was drained away at this. Jamie glanced at Duncan, then away, clearing his throat.

"Ye were convinced he meant it, I suppose."

"He'd a good sharp knife; he ran it across the palm of my hand to show me that he was in earnest." She opened her free hand; sure enough, a hair-thin red line ran across the heel of it.

She shrugged.

"Well, I supposed I couldna have that. So I made pretense of reluctance, until the Irishman went to pick up one of Duncan's feet—then I wept and carried on, in hopes that someone would hear, but the damned servants had gone to bed, and the guests were too busy drinking my whisky and fornicating in the grounds and stables to hear."

At this last remark, Bree's face flamed a sudden crimson. Jamie saw it and coughed, avoiding my eye.

"Aye. So then—"

"So then I told them at last that the gold was buried under the floor of the shed outside the kitchen garden." The look of satisfaction returned briefly to her face. "I thought they would come upon the body and 'twould put them off their stride for a bit. By the time they'd nerved themselves to dig, I hoped I should have found some way to escape or to give the alarm—and so I did."

They had bound and gagged her hastily and gone to the shed, threatening to return and resume operations where they had left off, should they discover she had been lying to them. They had made no great job of the gag, though, and she had soon succeeded in tearing it away and kicking out a window-pane, through which to shout for help.

"So I am thinking that when they opened the door to the shed and saw the corpse, they must have dropped their lantern in shock, and so set fire to the place." She nodded in grim satisfaction. "A small price. I could but wish I thought they had gone up with it!"

"Ye dinna suppose they set the fire on purpose?" Duncan asked. He was looking a little better, though still gray and ill. "To cover any marks of digging?"

Jocasta shrugged, dismissing the notion.

"To what end? There was nothing to be found there, and they dug themselves to China." She was beginning to relax a little, a normal color returning to her face, though her broad shoulders had begun to droop with exhaustion.

Silence fell among us, and I became aware that there had been rising noises downstairs for some minutes now; male voices and footsteps. The various search parties had returned, but it was apparent from the tired, disgruntled tones that no suspects had been apprehended.

The candle on the table had burned very low by now; the flame stretched high near my elbow as the wick reached its last inch. One of the candles on the mantelpiece guttered and went out in a fragrant wisp of beeswax smoke. Jamie glanced automatically at the window; it was still dark outside, but the character of the night had changed, as it does soon before dawn.

The curtains moved silently, a chilly, restless air breathing through the room. Another candle went out. A second sleep-less night was telling on me; I felt cold all over, numb and disembodied, and the various horrors I had seen and heard had begun to fade into unreality in my mind, with nothing save a lingering strong scent of burning to bear witness to them.

There seemed no more to say or to do. Ulysses came back, sliding discreetly into the room with a fresh candlestick and a tray holding a bottle of brandy and several glasses. Major MacDonald reappeared briefly to report that indeed, they had found no sign of the miscreants. I checked both Duncan and Jocasta briefly, and then left Bree and Ulysses to put them to bed.

Jamie and I made our way downstairs in silence. At the bottom of the staircase, I turned to him. He was white with fatigue, his features drawn and set as though he had been carved of marble, his hair and beard stubble dark in the shadowed light.

"They'll come back, won't they?" I said quietly.

He nodded, and taking my elbow, led me toward the kitchen stair.

54

TÊTE-À-TÊTE, WITH CRUMBCAKE

SO EARLY IN THE YEAR, the kitchen in the cellar of the house was still in use, with the summer cookhouse reserved for messier or malodorous preparations. Roused by the commotion, all the slaves were up and working, though a few looked as though they would collapse into the nearest corner and go back to sleep at the first opportunity. The chief cook, though, was wide-awake, and it was clear that no one was sleeping on *her* watch.

The kitchen was warm and welcoming, the windows still

dark, walls red with hearth-glow, and the air suffused with the comforting scents of broth, hot bread, and coffee. I thought this would be an excellent place to sit down and recuperate for a bit before toddling off to bed, but evidently Jamie had other ideas.

He paused in conversation with the cook, just long enough for politeness, acquiring in the process not only an entire fresh crumb cake, dusted with cinnamon and soaked with melted butter, but a large jug of freshly brewed coffee. Then he made his farewells, scooped me up off the stool onto which I had thankfully subsided, and we were off again, into the cool wind of the dying night.

I had a very odd sense of déjà vu as he turned down the brick path toward the stables. The light was just the same as it had been twenty-four hours earlier, with the same pinprick stars just fading from the same blue-gray sky. The same faint breath of spring passed by, and my skin shivered in memory.

But we were walking sedately side by side, not flying—and overlaid on my memories of the day before were the unsettling odors of blood and burning. With each step I felt as though I were about to reach out to push through the swinging doors of a hospital; that the hum of fluorescent light and the subdued reek of medicines and floor polish were about to engulf me.

"Lack of sleep," I murmured to myself.

"Time enough for sleep later, Sassenach," Jamie replied. He shook himself briefly, throwing off tiredness as a dog shakes off water. "There's a thing or two to be done, first." He shifted the paper-wrapped cake, though, and took hold of my elbow with his free hand, in case I was about to fall facefirst into the cabbage bed from fatigue.

I wasn't. I had meant only that it was the lack of sleep that was giving me the mildly hallucinatory feeling of being back in a hospital. For years, as an intern, resident, and mother, I had worked through long sleepless shifts, learning to function—and function well—despite complete exhaustion.

It was that same feeling that was stealing over me now, as I passed through simple sleepiness and out again, into a state of artificially heightened alertness.

I felt cold and shrunken, as though I inhabited only the

innermost core of my body, insulated from the world around me by a thick layer of inert flesh. At the same time, every tiny detail of my surroundings seemed unnaturally vivid, from the delicious fragrance of the food Jamie carried and the rustle of his coat skirts, to the sound of someone singing in the distant slave quarters and the spikes of sprouting corn in the vegetable beds beside the path.

The sense of lucid detachment stayed with me, even as we followed the turn of the path toward the stables. A thing to be done, he'd said. I supposed that he did not mean he intended to repeat yesterday's performance. If he proposed a more sedate form of orgy, though, involving cake and coffee, it seemed peculiar to hold it in the stable, rather than the parlor.

The side door was unbarred; he pushed it open, and the warm scents of hay and sleeping animals rushed out.

"Who is it?" said a soft, deep voice from the shadows inside. Roger. Of course; he hadn't been among the mob in Jocasta's room.

"Fraser," Jamie replied, equally softly, and drew me inside, closing the door behind us.

Roger stood silhouetted against the dim glow of a lantern, near the end of the row of loose-boxes. He was wrapped in a cloak, and the light shone in a reddish nimbus round his dark hair as he turned toward us.

"How is it, *a Smeòraich*?" Jamie handed him the jug of coffee. Roger's cloak fell back as he reached for it, and I saw him thrust a pistol into the waist of his breeches with his other hand. Without comment, he pulled the cork and lifted the jug to his mouth, lowering it several moments later with an expression of sheer bliss. He sighed, breath steaming.

"Oh, God," he said fervently. "That's the best thing I've tasted in months."

"Not quite." Sounding faintly amused, Jamie took the jug back and handed him the wrapped crumb cake. "How is he, then?"

"Noisy at first, but he's been quiet for a bit. I think he may be asleep."

Already tearing at the butter-soaked wrappings, Roger nodded toward the loose-box. Jamie took down the lantern from its hook and held it high over the barred gate. Peering under his arm, I could see a huddled shape, half-buried in the straw at the back of the box.

"Mr. Wylie?" Jamie called, still softly. "Are ye asleep, sir?"

The shape stirred, with a rustling of hay.

"I am not, sir," came the reply, in tones of cold bitterness. The shape began slowly to unfold itself, and Phillip Wylie rose to his feet, shaking straw from his clothes.

I had certainly seen him appear to better advantage. Several buttons were missing from his coat, one shoulder seam was split, and both knees of his breeches hung loose, the buckles burst and his stockings drooping in unseemly fashion about his shins. Someone had evidently hit him in the nose; a trickle of blood had dried on his upper lip, and there was a splotch of crusty brown on the embroidered silk of his waistcoat.

Despite the deficiencies of his wardrobe, his manner was unimpaired, being one of icy outrage.

"You will answer for this, Fraser, by God you will!"

"Aye, I will," Jamie said, unperturbed. "At your pleasure, sir. But not before I've had answers from yourself, Mr. Wylie." He unlatched the gate of the loose-box and swung it open. "Come out."

Wylie hesitated, unwilling either to remain in the box, or to come out of it at Jamie's command. I saw his nostrils twitch, though; evidently he had caught scent of the coffee. That seemed to decide him, and he came out of the box, head held high. He brushed within a foot of me, but kept his eyes straight ahead, affecting not to see me.

Roger had collected two stools and an upturned bucket. I took the latter and shoved it modestly into the shadows, leaving Jamie and Wylie to seat themselves within easy strangling distance of each other. Roger himself retired discreetly into the shadows beside me with the crumb cake, looking interested.

Wylie accepted the jug of coffee stiffly, but a few deep swallows seemed to restore his composure to a noticeable degree. He lowered it at last and breathed audibly, his features a little more relaxed.

"I thank you, sir." He handed the jug back to Jamie with a

small bow and sat bolt upright on his stool, tenderly adjusting his wig, which had survived the evening's adventures, but was much the worse for its experiences. "Now, then. May I inquire the reason for this . . . this . . . unspeakable behavior?"

"Ye may, sir," Jamie replied, drawing himself up straight in turn. "I wish to discover the nature of your associations with a certain Stephen Bonnet, and your knowledge of his present whereabouts."

Wylie's face went almost comically blank.

"Who?"

"Stephen Bonnet."

Wylie began to turn toward me, to ask for clarification, then recalled that he was not acknowledging my presence. He glowered at Jamie, dark brows drawn down.

"I have no acquaintance with any gentleman of that name, Mr. Fraser, and thus no knowledge of his movements—though if I did, I greatly doubt that I should feel myself obliged to inform you of them."

"No?" Jamie took a thoughtful sip of coffee, then handed the jug to me. "What of the obligations of a guest toward his host, Mr. Wylie?"

The dark brows rose in astonishment.

"What do you mean, sir?"

"I take it that you are not aware, sir, that Mrs. Innes and her husband were assaulted last evening, and an attempt at robbery made upon them?"

Wylie's mouth fell open. Either he was a very good actor, or his surprise was genuine. Given my acquaintance with the young man to date, I thought he was no kind of actor.

"I was not. Who—" A thought struck him, and bewilderment vanished in renewed outrage. His eyes bulged slightly. "You think that I was concerned in this—this—"

"Dastardly enterprise?" Roger suggested. He seemed to be enjoying himself, relieved of the boredom of guard duty. "Aye, I expect we do. A bit of crumb cake with your coffee, sir?" He held out a chunk of cake; Wylie stared at it for a moment, then leaped to his feet, striking the cake out of Roger's hand.

"You blackguard!" He rounded on Jamie, fists clenched. "You dare to imply that I am a thief?"

Jamie rocked back a little on his stool, chin lifted.

"Aye, I do," he said coolly. "Ye tried to steal my wife from under my nose—why should ye scruple at my aunt's goods?"

Wylie's face flushed a deep and ugly crimson. Had it not been a wig, his hair would have stood on end.

"You . . . absolute . . . *cunt*!" he breathed. Then he launched himself at Jamie. Both of them went over with a crash, in a flurry of arms and legs.

I leaped back, clasping the coffee jug to my bosom. Roger lunged toward the fray, but I snatched at him, catching his cloak to hold him back.

Jamie had the advantage of size and skill, but Wylie was by no means a novice in the art of fisticuffs, and was in addition propelled by a berserk rage. Given a few moments more, Jamie would have him hammered into submission, but I was not inclined to wait.

Monstrously irritated with the pair of them, I stepped forward and upended the coffee jug. It wasn't boiling, but hot enough. There were simultaneous yelps of surprise, and the two men rolled apart, scrambling and shaking themselves. I thought I heard Roger laugh behind me, but when I whirled on him, he had assumed a look of straight-faced interest. He raised his eyebrows at me, and crammed another chunk of cake into his mouth.

I turned back to find Jamie already on his feet, and Wylie rising from his knees, both soaked with coffee, and both with expressions implying that they intended to resume proceedings at the point where I had interrupted them. I pushed my way between them and stamped my foot.

"I have bloody well had enough of this!"

"I haven't!" Wylie said hotly. "He has impugned my honor, and I demand—"

"Oh, to hell with your beastly honor—and yours, too!" I snarled, glaring from him to Jamie. Jamie, who had evidently been going to say something equally inflammatory, contented himself instead with a resounding snort.

I kicked one of the fallen stools, and pointed at it, still glaring at Jamie.

"Sit!"

Plucking the soaked fabric of his shirt away from his

chest, he righted the stool and sat on it, with immense dignity.

Wylie was less inclined to pay attention to me, and was carrying on with further remarks about his honor. I kicked him in the shin. This time, I was wearing stout boots. He yelped and hopped on one foot, holding his affronted leg. The horses, thoroughly roused by the commotion, were stamping and snorting in their boxes, and the air was full of floating chaff.

"Ye dinna want to trifle with her when she's in a temper," Jamie told Wylie, with a wary glance at me. "She's dangerous, aye?"

Wylie glowered at me, but his scowl altered to a look of uncertainty—whether because of the empty coffee jug, which I was now holding by the neck like a club, or because of his memories of the night before, when he had discovered me in the midst of Betty's autopsy. With an effort, he swallowed whatever he had been going to say, and sat slowly down upon the other stool. He pulled a kerchief from his stained waistcoat pocket, and blotted a trickle of blood that was running down the side of his face from a cut above the brow.

"I would like," he said, with exquisite politeness, "to know what is going on here, please."

He had lost his wig; it was lying on the floor in a puddle of coffee. Jamie bent and picked it up, holding it gingerly, like a dead animal. He wiped a smear of mud off the side of his jaw with his free hand, and held the wig out, dripping, to Wylie.

"We are in agreement, then, sir."

Wylie took the wig with a stiff nod of acknowledgment and laid it on his knee, disregarding the coffee soaking into his breeches. Both men looked at me, with identical expressions of skeptical impatience. Evidently, I had been appointed mistress of ceremonies.

"Robbery, murder, and heaven knows what else," I said firmly. "And we mean to get to the bottom of it."

"Murder?" Roger and Wylie spoke together, both sounding startled.

"Who has been murdered?" Wylie asked, looking wildly back and forth between me and Jamie.

"A slave woman," Jamie said, with a nod toward me. "My wife suspected ill doing in her death, and so we meant to discover the truth of the matter. Thus our presence in the shed when you came upon us last night."

"Presence," Wylie echoed. His face was already pale, but he looked slightly ill at the recollection of what he had seen me doing in the shed. "Yes. I . . . see." He darted a look at me from the corner of his eye.

"So she was killed?" Roger came into the circle of lantern light and set the bucket back in place, sitting down at my feet. He set the remains of the cake on the floor. "What killed her?"

"Someone fed her ground glass," I said. "I found quite a lot of it still in her stomach."

I paid particular attention to Phillip Wylie as I said this, but his face bore the same expression of blank astonishment as did Jamie's and Roger's.

"Glass." Jamie was the first to recover. He sat up on his stool, shoving a disordered hank of hair behind his ear. "How long might that take to kill a body, Sassenach?"

I rubbed two fingers between my brows; the numbness of the early hour was giving way to a throbbing headache, made worse by the rich smell of coffee and the fact that I hadn't gotten to drink any of it.

"I don't know," I said. "It would go into the stomach within minutes, but it might take quite a long time to do enough damage to cause major hemorrhage. Most of the damage would likely be to the small intestine; the glass particles would perforate the lining. And if the digestive system were somewhat impaired—by drink, say—and not moving well, then it might take even longer. Or if she'd taken a lot of food with it."

"Is this the woman that you and Bree found in the garden?" Roger turned to Jamie, inquiring.

"Aye." Jamie nodded, his eyes still fixed on me. "She was insensible wi' the drink then. And when ye saw her later, Sassenach—were there signs of it, then?"

I shook my head.

"The glass might have been working then—but she was out cold. One thing—Fentiman did say she woke in the middle of the night, complaining of griping in her guts. So she was certainly affected by that time. But I can't say for sure whether she'd been given the ground glass before you and Bree found her, or whether perhaps she roused from her stupor in the early evening, and someone gave it to her then."

"Griping in the guts," Roger murmured. He shook his head, mouth grim at the thought. "Christ, what a way to go."

"Aye, it's black wickedness," Jamie agreed, nodding. "But why? Who should wish the woman's death?"

"A good question," Wylie said shortly. "However, I can assure you that it wasn't I."

Jamie gave him a long stare of assessment.

"Aye, maybe," he said. "If not, though—how came ye to the shed last night? What business might ye have there, save perhaps to look upon the face of your victim?"

"*My* victim!" Wylie jerked bolt upright, stiff with renewed outrage. "It was not I in that shed, red to the elbow with the woman's gore and snatching bits of bone and offal!" He snapped his head to the side, glaring up at me.

"My victim, indeed! It is a capital crime to defile a body, Mrs. Fraser. And I have heard things—oh, yes, I have heard things about you! I put it to you that it is *you* who did the woman to death, for the purpose of obtaining—"

His words ended in a gurgle, as Jamie's hand jerked his shirtfront tight and twisted it hard about his neck. He punched Wylie in the stomach, hard, and the young man doubled up, coughed, and spewed coffee, bile, and a few more disagreeable substances all over the floor, his knees, and Jamie.

I sighed wearily. The briefly warming effects of the discussion had faded, and I was feeling cold and mildly disoriented again. The stench didn't help.

"That's not really helpful, you know," I said reprovingly to Jamie, who had released Wylie and was now hastily removing his own outer garments. "Not that I don't appreciate the vote of confidence."

"Oh, aye," he said, voice muffled in the shirt as he pulled

it over his head. He popped out, glaring at me, and dropped the shirt on the floor with a splat. "D'ye think I'm going to sit idle and let this popinjay insult ye?"

"I don't suppose he'll do it again," Roger said. He stood and bent over Wylie, who was still doubled up on his stool, rather green in the face. Roger glanced back over his shoulder at Jamie.

"Is he right, though? About it being a capital crime to tamper with a body?"

"I dinna ken," Jamie said, rather shortly. Stripped to the waist, stained with blood and vomit, and with his red hair wild in the lantern light, he looked a far cry from the polished gentleman who had gone off to play whist.

"It scarcely matters," he added, "as he isna going to tell anyone about it. Because if he does, I shall cut him like a stirk and feed both his ballocks and his lying tongue to the pigs." He touched the hilt of his dirk, as though assuring himself that it was handy if wanted.

"But I am sure ye dinna mean to make any such unfounded accusations regarding my wife, do ye . . . sir?" he said to Wylie, with excessive politeness.

I was not surprised to see Phillip Wylie shake his head, evidently still incapable of speech. Jamie made a noise of grim satisfaction and stooped to pick up the cloak he had dropped earlier.

Feeling rather weak-kneed after this latest exhibition of the male sense of honor, I sat down on the bucket.

"All right," I said, and pushed back a strand of hair. "Fine. If we've got all that settled, then . . . where were we?"

"Betty's murder," Roger prompted. "We don't know who, we don't know when, and we don't know why—though for the sake of argument, might I suggest we assume that no one amongst the present company had anything to do with it?"

"Verra well." Jamie dismissed murder with a brusque gesture and sat down. "What about Stephen Bonnet?"

Roger's expression, hitherto one of interest, darkened at that.

"Aye, what about him? Is he involved in this business?"

"Not in the murder, perhaps—but my aunt and her husband were assaulted in their chamber last evening by two villains. One of whom was an Irishman." Jamie wrapped his cloak about his bare shoulders, bending a sinister glance on Phillip Wylie, who had recovered sufficiently to sit up.

"I repeat," he said coldly, hands still pressed against his stomach, "that I have no acquaintance with a gentleman of that name, whether Irishman or Hottentot."

"Stephen Bonnet is not a gentleman," Roger said. The words were mild enough, but carried an undertone that made Wylie glance up at him.

"I do not know the fellow," he said firmly. He took a shallow breath by way of experiment, and finding it bearable, breathed deeper. "Why do you suppose that the Irishman who committed the outrage upon Mr. and Mrs. Innes should be this Bonnet? Did he leave his card, perchance?"

I laughed, surprising myself. In spite of everything, I had to admit to a certain amount of respect for Phillip Wylie. Held captive, battered, threatened, doused with coffee, and deprived of his wig, he retained a good deal more dignity than would most men in his situation.

Jamie glanced at me, then back at Wylie. I thought the corner of his mouth twitched, but it was impossible to tell in the dim light.

"No," he said. "I *do* claim some acquaintance with Stephen Bonnet, who is a felon, a degenerate, and a thief. And I saw the man with ye, sir, when ye happened upon my wife and myself at the shed."

"Yes," I said. "I saw him, too—standing right behind you. And what were you doing there, anyway?" I asked, this question suddenly occurring to me.

Wylie's eyes had widened at Jamie's accusation. At my statement, he blinked. He took another deep breath and looked down, rubbing his knuckles beneath his nose. Then he looked up at Jamie, the bluster gone.

"I do not know him," he said quietly. "I had some thought that I was followed, but, glancing behind me, I saw no one, and so paid it no great mind. When I . . . saw what lay within the shed"—his eyes flicked toward me, but would not quite meet my own—"I was too much shocked to give heed to aught but what lay before my eyes."

That, I could believe.

Wylie lifted his shoulders, and let them fall.

"If this Bonnet was indeed behind me, then I must take your word for it, sir. And yet I assure you that he was not there by my doing, nor with my recognition."

Jamie and Roger exchanged glances, but they could hear the ring of truth in Wylie's words, just as I could. There was a brief silence, in which I could hear the horses moving in their stalls. They were no longer agitated, but were getting restive, anticipating food. Dawn light was filtering through the cracks beneath the eaves, a soft, smoky radiance that leached the air inside the stable of all color, and yet revealed the dim outlines of harness hanging on the wall, pitchforks and shovels standing in the corner.

"The grooms will be coming soon." Jamie stirred and drew breath, drawing up his shoulders in a half-shrug. He glanced back at Wylie.

"Verra well, sir. I accept your word as a gentleman."

"Do you? I am flattered."

"Still," Jamie went on, pointedly ignoring the sarcasm, "I should like to know what it was that brought ye to the shed last night."

Wylie had half-risen from his seat. At this, he hesitated, then slowly sat again. He blinked once or twice, as though thinking, then sighed, giving up.

"Lucas," he said simply. He didn't look up, but kept his eyes fixed on his hands, hanging limp between his thighs. "I was there, the night he was foaled. I raised him, broke him to the saddle, trained him." He swallowed once; I saw the tremor move beneath the frill at his neck. "I came to the stable to have a few moments alone with him . . . to bid him farewell."

For the first time, Jamie's face lost the shadow of dislike that it bore whenever he looked at Wylie. He breathed deep, and nodded slightly.

"Aye, I see," he said quietly. "And then?"

Wylie straightened a little.

"When I left the stable, I thought I heard voices near the wall of the kitchen garden. And when I came nearer to see what might be afoot, I saw light shining through the cracks of the shed." He shrugged. "I opened the door. And you know better than I what happened then, Mr. Fraser."

Jamie rubbed a hand hard over his face, then shook his head hard.

"Aye," he said. "I do. I went for Bonnet, and ye got in my way."

"You attacked me," Wylie said coldly. He hitched the ruined coat higher up on his shoulders. "I defended myself, as I had every right to do. And then you and your son-in-law seized me between you, frog-marched me in there"—he jerked his chin at the box stall behind him—"and held me captive half the night!"

Roger cleared his throat. So did Jamie, though with more dour intent.

"Aye, well," he said. "We willna argue about it." He sighed and stood back, gesturing to Wylie that he might go. "I suppose ye didna see in which direction Bonnet fled?"

"Oh, yes. Though I did not know his name, of course. I expect he is well beyond reach by now," Wylie said. There was an odd note in his voice; something like satisfaction. Jamie turned sharply.

"What d'ye mean?"

"Lucas." Wylie nodded down the dim aisle of the stable, toward the shadows at the farther end. "His stall is at the far end. I know his voice well, the sound of his movement. And I have not heard him this morning. Bonnet—if that was who it was—fled toward the stable."

Before Wylie had finished talking, Jamie had seized the lantern and was striding down the stable. Horses thrust inquiring noses over their stall doors as he passed, snorting and whuffling in curiosity—but no black nose appeared at the end of the row, no black mane floated out in joyous greeting. The rest of us hastened after him, leaning to see past him as he held the lantern high.

The yellow light shone on empty straw.

We stood silent for a long moment, looking. Then Phillip Wylie sighed and drew himself up.

"If I no longer have him, Mr. Fraser—neither do you." His

eyes rested on me, then, darkly ironic. "But I wish you joy of your wife."

He turned and walked away, stockings sagging, the red heels of his shoes winking in the growing light.

OUTSIDE, DAWN WAS BREAKING, still and lovely. Only the river seemed to move, the spreading light flashing silver on its current beyond the trees.

Roger had gone off to the house, yawning, but Jamie and I lingered by the paddock. People would be stirring within minutes; there would be more questions, speculations, talk. Neither one of us wanted any more talk; not now.

At last, Jamie put his arm about my shoulders, and with an air of decision, turned away from the house. I didn't know where he was going, and didn't much care, though I did hope I could lie down when we got there.

We passed the smithy, where a small, sleepy-looking boy was blowing up the forge with a pair of bellows, making red sparks float and flash like fireflies in the shadows. Past the outbuildings, around a corner, and then we were in front of a nondescript shed with a large double door. Jamie lifted the latch and swung one door open a bit, beckoning me inside.

"I canna think why I never thought of this place," he said, "when I was looking for a spot to be private."

We were in the carriage shed. A wagon and a small buggy stood in the shadows, as did Jocasta's phaeton. An open carriage like a large sleigh on two wheels, it had a bench seat with blue velvet squabs, and a scroll-like front like the prow of a ship. Jamie picked me up by the waist and swung me in, then clambered up after me. There was a buffalo robe lying across the squabs; he pulled this off and spread it on the floor of the phaeton. There was just room for two people to curl up there, if they didn't mind lying close together.

"Come on, Sassenach," he said, sinking to his knees. "Whatever comes next . . . it can wait."

I quite agreed. Though on the verge of unconsciousness, I

couldn't help drowsily asking, "Your aunt . . . do you trust her? What she said, about the gold and all?"

"Oh, aye, of course I do," he mumbled in my ear. His arm was heavy where it lay over my waist. "At least as far as I could throw her."

55

DEDUCTIONS

AT LAST FORCED FROM OUR REFUGE by thirst and hunger, we made our way out of the carriage shed and past the tactfully averted eyes of the yard slaves, still busy clearing up the debris from the wedding feast. At the edge of the lawn, I saw Phaedre, coming up from the mausoleum with her arms full of plates and cups that had been left in the shrubbery. Her face was swollen and blotched with grief, and her eyes were red, but she was not crying.

She saw us, and stopped.

"Oh," she said. "Miss Jo be lookin' for you, Master Jamie."

She spoke dully, as though the words had little meaning for her, and appeared to find nothing odd in our sudden appearance or disheveled dress.

"Oh? Aye." Jamie rubbed a hand over his face, nodding. "Aye, I'll go up to her."

She nodded, and was turning to go when Jamie reached out and touched her shoulder.

"I'm sorry for your trouble, lass," he said quietly.

Sudden tears welled in her eyes and spilled over, but she didn't speak. She dropped a brief curtsy, turned, and hurried away, moving so fast that a knife fell from the stack of crockery, bouncing on the grass behind her.

I stooped and picked it up, the feel of the knife's handle reminding me suddenly and vividly of the blade I had used to open her mother's body. For a disorienting moment, I was no longer on the lawn before the house, but in the dark confines of the shed, the scent of death heavy in the air and the proof of murder gritty in my hand.

Then reality readjusted itself, and the green lawn was covered with flocks of doves and sparrows, foraging peacefully for crumbs at the feet of a marble goddess, bright with sun.

Jamie was saying something.

". . . . go and wash and rest a bit, Sassenach?"

"What? Oh . . . no, I'll come with you." I was suddenly anxious to have this business done with, and go home. I had had enough society for the moment.

WE FOUND JOCASTA, Duncan, Roger, and Brianna all together in Jocasta's sitting room, digging into what looked like a substantial, if very late, breakfast. Brianna cast a sharp look at Jamie's ruined clothes, but said nothing, and went back to sipping tea, her eyebrows still raised. She and Jocasta both wore dressing gowns, and while Roger and Duncan were dressed, they looked pale and scruffy after the adventures of the night. Neither had shaved, and Duncan sported a large blue bruise on the side of his face where he had hit the hearthstone in falling, but he seemed otherwise all right.

I assumed that Roger had told everyone about our tête-à-tête with Phillip Wylie, and the disappearance of Lucas. At least no one asked questions. Duncan silently shoved a platter of bacon in Jamie's direction, and there was no sound for a bit save the musical tinkling of cutlery on plates and the sloshing noises of tea being drunk.

At last, replete and feeling somewhat restored, we sat back and began hesitantly to discuss the events of the day—and night—before. So much had happened that I thought perhaps it might be best to try to reconstruct events in a logical sort of way. I said as much, and while Jamie's mouth twitched in an annoying manner that suggested he found the notion of logic incompatible with me personally, I ignored this and firmly called the meeting to order.

"It begins with Betty, don't you think?"

"Whether it does or not, I suppose that's as good a starting point as any, Sassenach," Jamie agreed.

Brianna finished buttering a final slice of toast, looking amused.

"Carry on, Miss Marple," she said, waving it at me before taking a bite. Roger made a brief choking noise, but I ignored that, too, with dignity.

"Fine. Now, I thought Betty was likely drugged when I saw her, but since Dr. Fentiman stopped me examining her, I couldn't be positive. But we are reasonably sure that Betty did drink drugged punch, is that right?" I looked round the circle of faces, and both Bree and Jamie nodded, adopting solemn expressions.

"Aye, I tasted *something* in the cup that wasna liquor," Jamie said.

"And I talked to the house slaves after I left Da," Brianna added, leaning forward. "Two of the women admitted that Betty tipples—tippled—from the dregs of drinks at parties, but both of them insisted she was no more than what they called 'cheerful' when she helped serve rum punch in the drawing room."

"And I was in the drawing room then, with Seamus Hanlon and his musicians," Roger confirmed. He glanced at Bree and squeezed her knee gently. "I saw Ulysses make the punch himself—that was the first time during the day that you made it, Ulysses?"

All heads swiveled toward the butler, who stood closed-faced behind Jocasta's chair, his neat wig and pressed livery a silent reproach to the general air of exhausted dishevelment.

"No, the second," he said softly. "The first was all drunk at breakfast." His eyes were alert, if bloodshot, but the rest of his face might have been chiseled from gray granite. The household and its servants were his charge, and it was clear that he felt recent events to be a mortifying personal reproach to his stewardship.

"Right." Roger turned back toward me, rubbing a hand over his stubbled face. He might have snatched a nap since the confrontation with Wylie in the stable, but he didn't look it.

"I didn't take any notice of Betty myself, but the point is, I think I *would* surely have noticed, if she were drunk and reeling at that point. So would Ulysses, I expect." He glanced over his shoulder for confirmation, and the butler nodded, reluctantly.

"Lieutentant Wolff *was* drunk and reeling," Roger added. "Everyone noticed that—they all remarked how early it was for anyone to be in that condition."

Jocasta made a rude noise, and Duncan bent his head, hiding a smile.

"The point being," Jamie summed up neatly, "that the second lot of rum punch was served out just past midday, and I found the woman flat on her back in the dung heap, steamin' with drink and a punch cup beside her, nay more than an hour later. I'll no say it couldna be done, but it would be quick work to get mortal in that span of time, especially if it was all done wi' dregs."

"So we assume that she was indeed drugged," I said. "The most likely substance being laudanum. Was there some available in the stillroom here?"

Jocasta caught the lift of my voice and knew the question was addressed to her; she straightened up in her chair, tucking a wisp of white hair back under her ribboned cap. She seemed to have recovered nicely from the night before.

"Oh, aye. But that's naught to go by," she objected. "Anyone might ha' brought it; it's no sae hard to come by, and ye have the price. I ken at least two women among the guests who take the stuff regular. I daresay they'd have brought a bit with them."

I would have loved to know which of Jocasta's acquaintances were opium addicts, and how she knew, but dismissed that point, moving on to the next.

"Well, wherever the laudanum—for the sake of argument—came from, it apparently ended up inside Betty." I turned to Jamie. "Now, you said that it occurred to you when you found her that she might have drunk something—drugged or poisonous—intended for someone else."

He nodded, following me closely.

"Aye, for why would someone seek to harm or kill a slave?"

"I don't know why, but someone *did* kill her," Brianna interrupted, a definite edge in her voice. "I can't see how she could have eaten ground glass meant for someone else, can you?"

"Don't rush me! I'm trying to be logical." I frowned at Bree, who made a rude noise akin to Jocasta's, but not as loud.

"No," I went on, "I don't think she can have taken the ground glass by accident, but I don't know when she *did* take it. Almost certainly, it was sometime after you and Jamie took her up to the attic, though, and after Dr. Fentiman saw her the first time."

Fentiman's emetics and purgatives would have caused extensive bleeding, had Betty already ingested the glass—as indeed they did, when he returned to treat her renewed complaints of internal distress toward dawn.

"I think you're right," I told Brianna, "but just to be tidy—when you went to look round, Roger, you didn't find any of the guests who looked as though they might be drugged?"

He shook his head, dark brows drawn together, as though the sunlight bothered him. I wasn't surprised if he had a headache; the cotton-wool feeling had turned into a throbbing inside my own skull.

"No," he said, and dug a knuckle hard between his brows. "There were at least twenty who were beginning to stagger a bit, but they all seemed just legitimately drunk."

"What about Lieutenant Wolff?" Duncan asked at this point, to everyone's surprise. He blushed slightly, seeing everyone's eyes on him, but doggedly pursued his point.

"*A Smeòraich* said the man was drunk and reeling in the drawing room. Might he have taken the laudanum, or whatever it was, drunk the half, and given the rest to the slave there?"

"I don't know," I said dubiously. "If ever I saw anyone who could have achieved intoxication within an hour, purely on the basis of straight alcohol . . ."

"When I went to check the guests, the Lieutenant was propped up against the wall of the mausoleum with a bottle in his fist," Roger said. "Mostly incoherent, but still conscious."

"Aye, he fell down in the shrubbery later," Jamie put in, looking dubious. "I saw him, in the afternoon. He didna look like yon slave woman, though, only drunk."

"The timing is about right, though," I said thoughtfully. "So it's possible, at least. Did anyone see the Lieutenant later in the day?"

"Yes," Ulysses said, causing everyone to swivel round to look at him again. "He came into the house during the supper, asked me to find him a boat at once, and left by water. Still very drunk," he added precisely, "but lucid."

Jocasta made a small puffing sound with her lips, and muttered, "Lucid, forbye," under her breath. She massaged her temples with both forefingers; evidently she had a headache, too.

"I suppose that puts the Lieutenant out as a suspect? Or is the fact that he left so suddenly suspicious by itself?" Brianna, the only person present who seemed *not* to have a headache, dropped several lumps of sugar into her tea and stirred it vigorously. Jamie shut his eyes, wincing at the noise.

"Are ye no overlooking something?" Jocasta had been following all the arguments intently, a slight frown of concentration on her face. Now she leaned forward, stretching out her hand toward the low table with its breakfast things. She tapped her fingers lightly here and there to locate what she wanted, then picked up a small silver cup.

"Ye showed me the cup from which Betty drank, Nephew," she said to Jamie, holding out the one in her hand. "It was like this, aye?"

The cup was sterling silver, and brand-new, the incised design barely showing. Later, when the metal began to acquire a patina, black tarnish would settle into the lines of the etching and cause it to stand out, but for the moment, the capital letter "I" and the small fish that swam around it were almost lost in the gleam of light off the metal.

"Aye, it was one like that, Aunt," Jamie replied, touching the hand that held the cup. "Brianna says it was one of a set?"

"It was. I gave them to Duncan in the morning of our wedding day, as a bride-gift." She set down the cup, but laid her long fingers across the top of it. "We drank from two of the cups, Duncan and I, with our breakfast, but the other four stayed up here." She waved a hand behind her, indicating the small sideboard against the wall, where the platters of bacon and fried eggs had been placed. Decorated plates were propped upright along the back of the sideboard, interspersed with a set of crystal sherry glasses. I counted; all six of the silver fish cups were on the table now, filled with port, which Jocasta appeared to like with breakfast. There was no indication which of them had held the drugged liquor, though.

"Ye didna take any of these cups down to the drawing room on the wedding day, Ulysses?" she asked.

"No, Madam." He looked shocked at the thought. "Of course not."

She nodded, and turned her blind eyes toward Jamie, then toward me.

"So ye see," she said simply. "It was Duncan's cup."

Duncan looked startled, then uneasy, as the implications of what she had said sank in.

"No," he said, shaking his head. "Ach, no. Couldna be." But tiny droplets of sweat had begun to form a dew across the weathered skin of his jaw.

"Did anyone offer ye a drink day before yesterday, *a charaid*?" Jamie asked, leaning forward intently.

Duncan shrugged helplessly.

"Aye, everyone did!"

And of course they had. He was, after all, the bridegroom. He had accepted none of the proffered refreshment, though, owing to the digestive upset occasioned by his nerves. Nor had he noticed particularly whether any of the drinks on offer had been served in a silver cup.

"I was that distracted, *Mac Dubh*, I shouldna have noticed

if anyone had been offering me a live snake in his hand." Ulysses plucked a linen napkin from the tray and offered it unobtrusively. Blindly, Duncan took it and wiped his face.

"So . . . you think that someone was trying to harm *Duncan*?" The astonishment in Roger's voice might not have been strictly flattering, but Duncan appeared not to take it amiss.

"But why?" he said, bewildered. "Who could hate *me*?"

Jamie chuckled under his breath, and the tension round the table relaxed slightly. It was true; while Duncan was intelligent and competent, he was of so modest a disposition that it was impossible to conceive of his having offended anyone, let alone driven them into a murderous frenzy.

"Well, *a charaid*," Jamie said tactfully, "it might not just be personal, ken?" He caught my eye, and made a wry grimace. More than one attempt had been made on his own life, for reasons having to do only with who he was, rather than anything he had done. Not that people hadn't tried to kill him occasionally for things he'd done, as well.

Jocasta appeared to have been thinking along the same lines.

"Indeed," she said. "I have been thinking, myself. Do ye not recall, nephew, what happened at the Gathering?"

Jamie lifted one eyebrow, and picked up a cup of tea.

"A good many things happened there, Aunt," he said. "But I take it ye mean what happened with Father Kenneth?"

"I do." She reached up a hand automatically, as Ulysses set a fresh cup into it. "Did ye not tell me that yon Lillywhite said something about the priest being prevented from performing ceremonials?"

Jamie nodded, closing his eyes briefly as he took a mouthful of tea.

"Aye, he did. So, ye think it was maybe your marriage with Duncan he meant? That was the 'ceremonial' to be prevented?"

My headache was growing worse. I pressed my fingers between my brows; they were warm from the teacup, and the heat felt good on my skin.

"Wait just one minute," I said. "Are you saying that someone wanted to prevent your aunt's marriage to Duncan, and succeeded in doing so at the Gathering, but then couldn't think of any way of preventing it now, and so tried to murder Duncan, in order to stop it?" My own voice echoed the astonishment on Duncan's features.

"I'm no saying so, myself," Jamie said, eyeing Jocasta with interest, "but I gather that my aunt is suggesting as much."

"I am," she said calmly. She drank off her tea, and set down the cup with a sigh. "I dinna wish to rate myself too high, nephew, but the fact is that I have been courted by this one and that one, ever since Hector died. River Run is a rich property, and I am an auld woman."

There was a moment's silence, as everyone absorbed that. Duncan's face reflected an uneasy horror.

"But—" he said, stuttering slightly, "but—but—if it was that, *Mac Dubh*, why wait?"

"Wait?"

"Aye." He looked around the table, seeking understanding. "See you, if someone meant to stop the marriage at the Gathering, well and good. But it's been four months since then, and no one's lifted a hand against me. I mostly ride alone; 'twould have been a simple matter, surely, to lay for me on the road as I went about my business, and put a bullet through my head." He spoke matter-of-factly, but I saw a small shiver pass through Jocasta at the notion.

"So why wait until almost the hour of the wedding itself, and in the presence of hundreds of people? Aye, well, it's a point, Duncan," Jamie admitted.

Roger had been following all this, elbows propped on his knees, chin resting in his hands. He straightened up at this.

"One reason I can think of," he said. "The priest."

Everyone stared at him, eyebrows raised.

"The priest was here," he explained. "See, if it's River Run that's behind all this, then it isn't only a matter of getting Duncan out of the way. Kill him, and our murderer is right back where he started—Jocasta's not married to Duncan, but she isn't married to *him*, either, and no way to force the issue.

"But," Roger raised a finger, "if the priest is here, and all set to perform a private ceremony . . . then it's simple. Kill Duncan—in a manner that might suggest suicide or accident—and then swoop up to Jocasta's suite, and force the priest to perform the marriage at gunpoint. The servants and guests are all occupied with Duncan, no one to make objections or interfere. There's the bed to hand—" He nodded at the big tester, visible through the doorway into the bedroom. "Take Jocasta straight there and consummate the marriage by force . . . and Bob's your uncle."

At this point, Roger caught sight of Jocasta's dropped jaw and Duncan's stunned look, and it occurred to him that this was not merely an interesting academic proposition. He blushed crimson, and cleared his throat.

"Ah . . . I mean . . . it's been done."

Jamie coughed, and cleared his own throat. It had been done. His own bloody-minded grandfather had begun his social rise by forcibly wedding—and promptly bedding—the elderly and wealthy dowager Lady Lovat.

"What?" Brianna swiveled round to stare at Roger, obviously appalled. "That's the most . . . but they couldn't get away with something like that!"

"I expect they could, really," Roger said, almost apologetically. "See, hen, possession is a lot more than nine-tenths of the law when it comes to women. Marry a woman and take her to bed, and she and all her property are yours, whether she likes it or not. Without another male relative to protest, it's not likely a court would do a thing."

"But she *does* have a male relative!" Brianna flipped a hand toward Jamie—who did have a protest to make, but probably not along the lines Brianna had expected.

"Aye, well, but. Witnesses," he objected. "Ye canna do something like that, without ye have a witness to say it was a valid marriage." He cleared his throat again, and Ulysses reached for the teapot.

Old Simon had had witnesses; two of his friends, plus the two attendants of the dowager. One of whom had later become Jamie's grandmother, though I did trust less force had been involved in that transaction.

"I can't see that that's a difficulty," I said, brushing crumbs off my bosom. "Obviously, this wasn't a one-man show. Whoever the intending bridegroom is—and mind, we don't even know there is one, but for the sake of argument—

anyway, whoever he is, if he exists, plainly he has accomplices. Randall Lillywhite, for one."

"Who wasna here," Jamie reminded me.

"Hm. That's true," I admitted. "But still, the principle holds."

"Yes," Roger said stubbornly, "and if he *does* exist, then the chief suspect is Lieutenant Wolff, isn't he? Everyone knows he's made more than one try to marry Jocasta. And he *was* here."

"But pie-eyed," Jamie added, dubiously.

"Or not. As I said, Seamus and his boys were surprised that anyone could be that drunk so early on, but what if it was a sham?" Roger glanced round the table, one eyebrow lifted. "If he were only pretending to be reeling drunk, no one would pay attention to him or treat him later as a suspect, and yet he could manage to be in position to poison a cup of punch, give it to Betty with instructions to give it to Duncan, then slip away and hang about, ready to nip upstairs the moment word came that Duncan had collapsed. And if Betty then offered it to Duncan, who refused it—well, there she was, with a full cup of fresh rum punch in her hand."

He shrugged.

"Who could blame her for stealing away into the kitchen garden to enjoy it?"

Jocasta and Ulysses snorted simultaneously, making it reasonably clear what they thought of the blameworthiness of Betty's action. Roger coughed and hurried on with his analysis.

"Right. Well. But the dose didn't kill Betty. Either the murderer miscalculated or . . ." Another bright thought occurred to Roger. "Perhaps he didn't intend the drug to kill Duncan. Maybe he only meant to render him unconscious, and then tip him quietly into the river. That would have been even better. Ye can't swim, can you?" he asked, turning to Duncan, who shook his head in a dazed sort of way. His one hand rose, mechanically massaging the stump of his missing arm.

"Aye. So a nice drowning would have passed for accident, no worry." Roger rubbed his hands together, looking pleased. "But then it all went wrong, because the maid drank the drugged punch, not Duncan. And *that's* why she was killed!"

"Why?" Jocasta was looking quite as dazed as Duncan.

"Because she could identify the man who'd given her the cup," Jamie put in. He nodded, lounging thoughtfully back in his chair. "And she would have, the minute folk started in on her about it. Aye, that's sense. But of course he couldna make away with her by violent means; the risk of being seen coming or going to the attic was too great."

Roger nodded approval at this quick appreciation.

"Aye. But it would have been no great trick to get your hands on ground glass—how many goblets and tumblers were floating through this place during the day? Drop one on the bricks and grind the shards under your heel, and there ye are."

Even that might not have been necessary; there had been shattered glass all over the paths and the terrace, after the post-wedding celebrations. I had dropped one glass myself, when surprised by Phillip Wylie.

I turned to address Ulysses.

"There's still the problem of how the ground glass was administered. Do you know what Betty was given to eat or drink, Ulysses?"

A frown rippled over the butler's face, like a stone thrown into dark water.

"Dr. Fentiman ordered her a syllabub," he said slowly. "And a bit of porridge, if she were awake enough to swallow. I made up the syllabub myself, and gave it to Mariah to take up to her. I gave the order for porridge to the cook, but I do not know whether Betty ate it, or who might have carried it."

"Hmm." Jocasta pursed her lips, frowning. "The cookhouse would be madness. And with so many folk about . . . well, we can ask Mariah and the others, but I shouldna be surprised if they dinna recall even carrying the dishes, let alone someone tampering with them. It would take nay more than a moment, ken; distract the girl, whisk in the glass . . ." She waved a hand, indicating the scandalous ease with which murder could be committed.

"Or someone could have gone up to the attic under the pretext of seeing how she was, and given her something to drink, with the glass in it then," I suggested. "A syllabub would be perfect. People were coming and going, but Betty was alone up there for long stretches, between Dr. Fentiman's visit, and the time the other slaves came to bed. It would be quite possible for someone to go up there unseen."

"Very nice, Inspector Lestrade," Brianna said to Roger, *sotto voce*. "But there's no proof, is there?"

Jocasta and Duncan were sitting side by side, rigid as a pair of Toby jugs, carefully not facing each other. At this, Jocasta took a deep and audible breath, obviously forcing herself to relax.

"True," she said. "There's not. Ye dinna recall Betty offering you a cup of punch, *a dhuine*?"

Duncan gnawed fiercely on his moustache for a moment, concentrating, but then shook his head.

"She might have . . . *a bhean*. But she might not, too."

"Well, then."

Everyone fell silent for a moment, during which Ulysses moved silently round the table, clearing things away. At last Jamie gave a deep sigh and straightened up.

"Well, so. Then there's what happened last night. We are agreed that the Irishman who entered your chamber, Aunt, was Stephen Bonnet?"

Brianna's hand jerked, and the cup of tea crashed to the table.

"Who?" she said hoarsely. "Stephen Bonnet—here?"

Jamie glanced at me, frowning.

"I thought ye'd told her, Sassenach."

"When?" I said, with some irritation. "I thought *you'd* told her," I said, turning to Roger, who merely shrugged, stone-faced. Ulysses had swooped down with a cloth and was blotting up the tea. Bree was white-faced, but had regained her self-possession.

"Never mind," she said. "He was here? Last night?"

"Aye, he was," Jamie said reluctantly. "I saw him."

"So he was the thief who came after the gold—or one of them?" Brianna reached for one of the silver cups of port and drank it off as though it were water. Ulysses blinked, but hastened to refill the cup from the decanter.

"It would seem so." Roger reached for a fresh scone, carefully avoiding Brianna's eyes.

"How did he find out about the gold, Aunt?" Jamie leaned back in his chair, eyes half-closed in concentration.

Jocasta gave a small snort, and held out her hand. Ulysses, accustomed to her needs, put a piece of buttered toast into it.

"Hector Cameron told someone; my brother Dougal told someone; or the third man told someone. And knowing them as I did, I should lay odds it wasna either Hector nor Dougal." She shrugged and took a bite of toast.

"But I'll tell ye one thing," she added, swallowing. "The second man in my room, the one who reeked of drink. I said he didna speak, aye? Well, that's plain enough, no? He was someone I ken, whose voice I should have known, if he spoke."

"Lieutenant Wolff?" Roger suggested.

Jamie nodded, a crease forming between his brows.

"Who better than the navy, to find a pirate when one's wanted, aye?"

"*Would* one want a pirate?" Brianna murmured. The port had restored her composure, but she was still pale.

"Aye," Jamie said, paying little attention to her. "No small undertaking, ten thousand pound in gold. It would take more than one man to deal with such a sum—Louis of France and Charles Stuart kent that much; they sent six to deal with thirty thousand." Little wonder, then, if whoever learned of the gold had enlisted the help of Stephen Bonnet—a well-known smuggler and pirate, and one with not only the means of transport but the connections to dispose of the gold.

"A boat," I said slowly. "The Lieutenant left by boat, during the supper. Suppose that he went downriver, and met Stephen Bonnet. They came back together, and waited for the opportunity to sneak into the house and try to terrorize Jocasta into telling them where the gold was."

Jamie nodded.

"Aye, that could be. The Lieutenant has had dealings here for years. Is it possible, Aunt, that he saw something that made him suspect ye had the gold here? Ye said Hector had three bars; is any of it left?"

Jocasta's lips pressed tight, but after a moment's hesitation, she gave a grudging nod.

"He *would* keep a lump of it on his desk, to weight his papers. Aye, Wolff might have seen—but how would he have kent what it was?"

"Perhaps he didn't at the time," Brianna suggested, "but then later heard about the French gold, and put two and two together."

There was a nodding and murmuring at this. As a theory, it fitted well enough. I didn't see quite how one would go about proving it, though, and said so.

Jamie shrugged, and licked a smear of jam off his knuckle.

"I shouldna think proving what's happened is so important, Sassenach. It's maybe what comes next." He looked at Duncan, straight on.

"They'll come back, *a charaid*," he said quietly. "Ye ken that, aye?"

Duncan nodded. He looked unhappy, but determined.

"Aye, I ken." He reached out a hand and took Jocasta's—the first gesture of the sort I had ever seen him make toward her. "We shall be ready, *Mac Dubh*."

Jamie nodded, slowly.

"I must go, Duncan. The planting willna wait. But I shall send word to those I ken, to have a watch of some sort kept upon Lieutenant Wolff."

Jocasta had sat silent, her hand unmoving in Duncan's. She sat up taller in her chair at this.

"And the Irishman?" she said. Her other hand rubbed slowly across her knee, pressing lightly with the heel of her hand, where the knife blade had cut.

Jamie exchanged a glance with Duncan, then with me.

"He'll come back," he said, grim certainty in his voice.

I was looking at Brianna as he said it. Her face was calm, but I was her mother, and I saw the fear move in her eyes, like a snake through water. Stephen Bonnet, I thought, with a sinking heart, was already back.

WE LEFT NEXT DAY for the mountains. We were no more than five miles on our journey, when I caught the sound of hoofbeats on the road behind us, and saw a flash of scarlet, through the spring-green of the chestnut trees.

It was Major MacDonald, and the look of delight upon his face as he spurred toward us told me all I needed to know.

"Oh, bloody *hell*!" I said.

The note bore Tryon's scarlet seal, bloodred as the Major's coat.

"It came this morning to Greenoaks," the Major said, reining up to watch as Jamie broke the seal. "I offered to bring it, as I was bound this way, in any case." He knew already what the note contained; Farquard Campbell would already have opened his.

I watched Jamie's face as he read. His expression didn't change. He finished reading, and handed me the note.

19th March, 1771

To the Commanding Officers of the Militia:

Sirs:

I Yesterday determined by Consent of His Majesty's Council to march with a Body of Forces taken from several Militia Regiments, into the Settlements of the Insurgents to reduce them to Obedience, who by their Rebellious Acts and Declarations have set the Government at defiance and interrupted the Course of Justice by obstructing, overturning and shutting up the Courts of Law. That some of your Regiment therefore may have a Share in the Honor of serving their Country in this important Service, I am to require you to make a choice of thirty men, who shall join the Body of my Force in this Endeavor.

It is not intended to move the Troops before the twentieth of next Month before which time you shall be informed of the day you are to assemble your Men, the time of march and the Road you are to take.

It is recommended as a Christian Duty incumbent on every Planter that remains at Home, to take care of, and assist to the utmost of his Abilities the Families of those Men who go on this Service that neither their Families nor plantations may suffer while they are employed on a Service where the Interest of the whole is concerned.

For the Expenditures ordered on this Expedition I shall give printed Warrants payable to the Bearers, These Warrants will become negotiable, until the Treasury can pay them out of the contingent Fund in case there is not a sufficiency of Money in the Treasury to answer the necessary Services of this Expedition.

I am &c. &c.,
William Tryon

Had Hermon Husband and James Hunter known, when they left River Run? I thought they must. And the Major, of course, was bound for New Bern now, to offer his services to the Governor. His boots were filmed with the dust of his ride, but the hilt of his sword gleamed in the sun.

"Bloody, bloody, fucking hell," I said softly, again, with emphasis. Major MacDonald blinked. Jamie glanced at me, and the corner of his mouth twitched up.

"Aye, well," he said. "Nearly a month. Just time to get the barley in."

Part Six

The War of the Regulation

56

". . . AND FIGHT THEM, SAYING THEY HAD MEN ENOUGH TO KILL THEM, WE CAN KILL THEM"

Deposition of Waightstill Avery, Witness
North Carolina
Mecklenburg County

Waightstill Avery Testifieth and saith that on the sixth Day of March Instant about nine or Ten OClock in the Morning He this Deponent was at the now dwelling house of one Hudgins who lives at the lower end of the long Island.

And He this Deponent there saw Thirty or Forty of those People who style themselves Regulators, and was then and there arrested and forceably detained a prisoner by one of them (who said his Name was James McQuiston) in the Name of them all, and that soon after one James Graham (or Grimes) spoke to this Deponent these Words "You are now a Prisoner and You must not go any where without a Guard." immediately after adding that "You must keep with Your Guard and You shan't be hurt."

This Deponent was then conducted under Guard of two Men to the regulating Camp (as they termed it) about a Mile distant, where were many more persons of the same Denomination and others came there some Hours after, in the whole as this Deponent supposes and imagines about two hundred and Thirty.

That from themselves He this Deponent learned the

Names of five of their Captains or leading Men then present (Viz., Thomas Hamilton and one other Hamilton, James Hunter, Joshua Teague one Gillespie and the aforesaid James Grimes (or Graham)). He this Deponent heard many of them whose Names are to Him unknown say approbrious Things against the Governor, the Judges of the Superior Court, against the House of Assembly and other persons in Office. While a surrounding Crowd were uttering Things still more approbrious the said Thomas Hamilton stood in the Midst and spoke Words of the following Tenor and purport (the Crowd still assenting to and affirming the Truth of what was said):

"What Business has Maurice Moore to be judge, He is no Judge, he was not appointed by the King He nor Henderson neither, They'll neither of them hold Court. The Assembly have gone and made a Riotous Act, and the people are more inraged than ever, it was the best thing that could be for the Country for now We shall be forced to kill all the Clerks and Lawyers, and We will kill them and I'll be damned if they are not put to Death. If they had not made that Act We might have suffered some of them to live. A Riotous Act! there never was any such Act in the Laws of England or any other Country but France, they brought it from France, and they'll bring the Inquisition."

Many of them said the Governor was a Friend to the Lawyers and the Assembly had worsted the Regulators in making Laws for Fees. They shut Husband up in Gaol that He might not see their roguish proceedings and then the Governor and the Assembly made just such Laws as the Lawyers wanted. The Governor is a Friend to the Lawyers, the Lawyers carry on every Thing, they appoint weak ignorant Justices of Peace for their own purposes.

There should be no Lawyers in the province, they damned themselves if there should. Fanning was outlawed as of the Twenty-Second of March and any Regulator that saw Him after that Time would kill him and some said they would not wait for that, wished they could see him, and swore they would kill him before they returned if they could find him at Salisbury—Some wished they could see Judge Moore at Salisbury that they might flog him, others that they might kill him. One Robert Thomson said Maurise Moore was purjured and called him by approbrious Names as Rascal, Rogue, Villian, Scoundral, etc. others assented to it.

When News was brought that Captain Rutherford at the head of His Company was parading in the Streets of Salisbury, this Deponent heard Sundry of them urge very hard and strenuously that the whole Body of the Regulators then present should March into Salisbury with their Arms and fight them saying They had Men enough to kill them, We can kill them We'll teach them to oppose Us.

Taken sworn to & Subscribed this eighth
Day of March 1771 before Me

(signed) Waightstill Avery

(witnessed) Wm. Harris, Justice of the Peace

William Tryon to General Thomas Gage
North Carolina
New Bern ye 19th March 1771

Sir,

It was Yesterday determined in His Majestys Council of this Province to Raise a Body of Forces from the Militia Regiments and Companies to March into the Settlements of the Insurgents, who by their Rebellious Acts and Declarations have set this Government at defiance.

As we have few Military Engines or implements in this Country, I am to request your assistance in procuring me for this Service the Articles (cannon, shot, colours, drums, etc.) listed hereby.

I intend to begin My March from this Town about the Twentieth of next Month, and assemble the Militia as I march through the Counties. My Plan is to form fifteen Hundred Men, though from the Spirit that now appears on the Side of Government that Number may be considerably increased.

I am with much Respect and Esteem
Sir Your Most Obedt. Servt.,
Wm. Tryon

57

NOW I LAY ME DOWN TO SLEEP . . .

Fraser's Ridge
15 April, 1771

ROGER LAY IN BED, listening for the intermittent whine of an invisible mosquito that had squeezed past the hide covering the cabin window. Jem's cradle was covered by gauze netting, but he and Brianna had no such shielding. If the damn thing would just light on him, he'd get it—but it seemed to circle tirelessly above their bed, occasionally swooping down to sing taunting little *neeeee* songs into his ear, before zooming off again into the dark.

He should have been tired enough to fall asleep in the face of an assault by airborne squadrons of mosquitoes, after the last few days of frantic activity. Two days of fast riding through the mountain coves and ridges, spreading the word to the nearer settlements, whose inhabitants would in turn alert those militia members farther away. The spring planting had been accomplished in record time, all the available men spending the hours from dawn to dusk in the fields. His system was still charged with adrenaline, and little jolts of it zapped through mind and muscle, as though he'd been taking coffee intravenously.

He'd spent all day today helping to ready the farm for their departure, and fragmented images of the round of chores scrolled behind his closed lids whenever he shut his eyes. Fence repair, hay hauling, a hasty excursion to the mill for the bags of flour needed to feed the regiment on the march. Fixing a split rim on the wagon's wheel, splicing a broken harness trace, helping to catch the white sow, who had made an abortive escape attempt from the stable, woodchopping, and finally, a brisk hour's digging just before supper so Claire could plant her wee patch of yams and peanuts before they left.

In spite of the hurry and labor, that dusk-lit digging had been a welcome respite in the organized frenzy of the day; the thought of it made him pause now, reliving it in hopes of slowing his mind and calming himself enough to sleep.

It was April, warm for the season, and Claire's garden was rampant with growth: green spikes and sprouting leaves and small brilliant flowers, climbing vines that twisted up the palisades and opened silent white trumpets slowly above him as he worked in the gathering twilight.

The smells of the plants and the fresh-turned earth rose round him as the air cooled, strong as incense. The moths came to the trumpet flowers, soft things drifting out of the wood in mottled shades of white and gray and black. Clouds of midges and mosquitoes came too, drawn to his sweat, and after them, the mosquito-hawks, dark fierce creatures with narrow wings and furry bodies, who whirred through the hollyhocks with the aggressive attitude of football hooligans.

He stretched long toes out against the weight of the quilts, his leg just touching his wife's, and felt in memory the chunk of the spade, hard edge beneath his foot, and the satisfying feeling of cracking earth and snapping roots as another spadeful yielded, the black earth moist and veined with the blind white rhizomes of wild grass and the fugitive gleam of earthworms writhing frantically out of sight.

A huge cecropia moth had flown past his head, lured by the garden scents. Its pale brown wings were the size of his hand, and marked with staring eyespots, unearthly in their silent beauty.

Who makes a garden works with God. That had been written on the edge of the old copper sundial in the garden of the manse in Inverness where he had grown up. Ironic, in view of the fact that the Reverend had neither time nor talent for gardening, and the place was a jungle of unmown grass and ancient rosebushes run wild and leggy with neglect. He smiled at the thought, and made his mental good-night to the Reverend's shade.

Good-night, Dad. God bless you.

It had been a long time since he'd lost the habit of bidding good-night in this fashion to a brief list of family and friends; the hangover of a childhood of nightly prayers that ended with the usual list of, "God bless Nana, and Grandpa Guy in heaven, and my best friend Peter, and Lillian the dog, and the grocer's cat . . ."

He hadn't done it in years, but a memory of the peace of that small ritual made him draw up a new list, now. Better than counting sheep, he supposed—and he wanted the sense of peace he remembered, more than he wanted sleep.

Good-night, Mrs. Graham, he thought, and smiled to himself, summoning a brief, vivid image of the Reverend's old housekeeper, dipping her hand in a bowl and flicking water onto a hot griddle, to see if the drops would dance. *God bless.*

The Reverend, Mrs. Graham, her granddaughter Fiona and Fiona's husband Ernie . . . his parents, though that was a *pro forma* nod toward two faceless shapes. Claire, up at the big house, and, with a slight hesitation, Jamie. Then his own small family. He warmed at the thought of them.

Good night, wee lad, he thought, turning his head in the direction of the cradle where Jemmy slept. *God bless.* And Brianna.

He turned his head the other way, and opened his eyes, seeing the dark oval of her sleeping face turned toward his, no more than a foot away on the pillow. He eased himself as quietly as possible onto his side, and lay watching her. They had let the fire go out, since they would be leaving early in the morning; it was so dark in the room he could make out no more of her features than the faint markings of brows and lips.

Brianna never lay wakeful. She rolled onto her back, stretched and settled with a sigh of content, took three deep breaths and was out like a light. Maybe exhaustion, maybe just the blessings of good health and a clear conscience—but he sometimes thought it was eagerness to escape into that private dreamscape of hers, that place where she roamed free at the wheel of her car, hair snapping in the wind.

What was she dreaming now? he wondered. He could feel the faint warmth of her breath on his face.

Last night, I dreamed I made love with Roger. The memory of that particular entry still rankled, hard as he'd tried to dismiss it. He had been drifting toward sleep, lulled by his litany, but the memory of her dreambook pulled him back to wakefulness. She had damn well better not be dreaming such a thing now! Not after the time he'd just given her.

He closed his eyes again, concentrating on the regular pulse of her breathing. His forehead was mere inches from hers. Perhaps he could catch the echo of her dream, through the bones of her skull? What he felt, though, was the echo of her flesh, and the reverberations of their farewell, with all its doubts and pleasures.

She and the lad would leave in the morning, too; their things were packed and stood with his own bundle beside the door. Mr. Wemyss would drive them to Hillsborough, where she would presumably be safely—and gainfully—employed in painting Mrs. Sherston's portrait.

"You be bloody careful," he'd said to her, for the third time in an evening. Hillsborough was smack in the center of the Regulators' territory, and he had considerable reservations about her going at all. She had dismissed his concern, though, scoffing at the notion that she or Jem might be in any danger. She was likely right—and yet he wasn't so sure that she would act differently if there *was* danger. She was so excited at the prospect of her damn commission, he thought, she'd walk straight through armed mobs to get to Hillsborough.

She was singing softly to herself—"Loch Lomond," of all bloody things. "Oh, you'll take the high road, and I'll take the low road, and I'll be in Scotland aforrrrrrre ye . . ."

"Did ye hear me?" he'd asked, catching hold of her arm as she folded the last of Jemmy's dresses.

"Yes, dear," Bree had murmured, lashes fluttering in mocking submission. That had irritated him into grabbing her wrist and pulling her round to face him.

"I mean it," he said. He stared into her eyes, wide open now, but with a hint of mockery still glinting in dark blue triangles. He tightened his grip on her wrist; tall and well-built as she was, her bones felt delicate, almost frail in his grasp. He had a sudden vision of the bones beneath Brianna's skin—high, wide cheekbones, domed skull, and long white teeth; all too easy to imagine those teeth exposed to the root in a permanent rictus of bone.

He had pulled her to him then with sudden violence, kissed her hard enough to feel her teeth against his own, not caring if he bruised either of them.

She wore only a shift and he hadn't bothered to take it off, merely shoving her backward onto the bed and pushing it above her thighs. She'd lifted her hands toward him, but he hadn't let her touch him; he'd pinned her arms at first, then later, borne her into the hollow of the mattress with the weight of his body, grinding, grasping, seeking reassurance in the thin padding of flesh that kept her bones from his.

They had done it in silence, half-aware of the sleeping child nearby. And yet somewhere in the midst of it, her body had answered him, in some deep and startling way that went beyond words.

"I mean it," he'd repeated, moments later, speaking softly into the tangle of her hair. He lay on her, enclosing her with his arms, keeping her from moving. She twitched, and he tightened his grasp, holding her still. She sighed, and he felt her mouth move, her teeth sink gently into the flesh below his collarbone. She bit him. Not abruptly, but in a slow, sucking bite that made him gasp and lift up to break away.

"I know," she said, and wriggled her arms free, to come round his back and hold him close to her damp, warm softness. "I mean it, too."

"THAT WHAT YOU WANTED?" He whispered the words now, but softly, not to awaken her. The warmth of her body radiated through the bedclothes; she was deep asleep.

If it was what she'd wanted—what, exactly, was it? Was it the brutal nature of his lovemaking that she'd responded to? Or had she sensed the strength of what lay behind it, and acknowledged that—the desperation of his need to keep her safe?

And if it was the roughness . . . he swallowed, clenching a fist against the thought of Stephen Bonnet. She'd never told him what had passed between them, her and Bonnet—and it was unthinkable that he should ask. More unthinkable that he should suspect anything in that encounter might have shamefully stirred her. And yet she did stir visibly on those rare occasions when something led him to take her abruptly, without his usual gentleness.

He was a long way from praying now.

He felt as he had once before, trapped in a rhododendron hell, with the same maze of damp roots and hanging leaves always before him, no matter in which direction he turned. Dim tunnels seemed to offer hope of escape, and yet led only to further tangles.

For me and my true love will never meet again, on the bonnie banks and braes of Loch Lomond . . .

He was wound tight again, skin prickling and his legs twitching with restlessness. The mosquito whined by and he slapped at it—too late, of course. Unable to keep still, he slid quietly out of bed, and did a quick series of deep knee-bends to loosen the cramped muscles.

That brought some relief, and he dropped to the floor to do push-ups, counting silently as he dipped toward the floorboards. One. Two. Three. Four. Concentrating only on the increasing burn in chest and arms and shoulders, the soothing monotony of the count. Twenty-six, twenty-seven, twenty-eight . . .

At last, muscles quivering with temporary exhaustion, he stood up, untacked the hide from the window, and stood naked, letting the damp night air flood in upon him. He might let in more mosquitoes—but the one might go out, too.

The wood was silvered with moonlight, and a faint fire-glow in the darkened heart of it spoke of the militia encamped there. They had been coming in all day, on mules or ragged horses, muskets laid across the bundles of their blankets. He caught the sound of voices and casual laughter, a fragment borne on the breeze. At least he wasn't the only one wakeful; the notion comforted him.

A brighter light glowed at the side of the big house, at the farther side of the clearing. A lantern; two figures walking close together, one tall, one smaller.

The man said something, an interrogative rumble; he recognized Jamie's voice, but couldn't make out the words.

"No," Claire's voice answered, lighter, clear as they came closer. He saw her hands flutter, silhouetted in the lantern's glow. "I'm filthy from the planting. I'm going to wash before I come in. You go up to bed."

The larger figure hesitated, then handed her the lantern. Roger saw Claire's face in the light for a moment, turned upward, smiling. Jamie bent and kissed her briefly, then stepped back.

"Hurry, then," he said, and Roger could hear the answering smile in his voice. "I dinna sleep well without ye beside me, Sassenach."

"You're going to sleep right away, are you?" She paused, a bantering note in her voice.

"Not right away, no." Jamie's figure had melted into the darkness, but the breeze was toward the cabin, and his voice came out of the shadows, part of the night. "But I canna very well do the other unless ye're beside me, either, now can I?"

Claire laughed, though softly.

"Start without me," she said, turning away toward the well. "I'll catch you up."

Roger waited by the window until he saw her come back, the lantern swinging with the haste of her step, and go inside.

The breeze had turned, and he heard no more of the men in the wood, though their fire still burned.

He looked toward the wood, his skin cool now, and goose-flesh rose on his chest. He rubbed absently at it, and felt the tender spot where she had bitten him. It was dark in the moonlight, a faint blotch on his skin; would it still be there come morning? he wondered.

Reaching up to pull the hide back into place, he caught the gleam of moonlight on glass. Brianna's small collection of personal items lay on the shelf by the window: the pair of tortoiseshell combs Jocasta had given her, her silver bracelet. The small glass jar of tansy oil, two or three discreet slips of sponge beside it. And the larger gleam of the jarful of Dauco seeds. She hadn't had time for the tansy oil tonight, but he'd bet his life she'd taken the seeds sometime today.

He tacked down the hide, and made his way back to bed, pausing by the cradle to put down a hand and feel the baby's breath through the mosquito-netting, warm and reassuring on his skin.

Jem had kicked his covers off; Roger lifted the netting and pulled them up by feel, tucking them firmly in. There was something soft . . . oh, Jemmy's rag-doll; the baby was clutching it to his chest. Roger stood for a moment, hand on Jemmy's back, feeling the soothing rise and fall of his breathing.

"Good-night, laddie," he whispered at last, and touched the soft padded round of the little boy's bottom. "God bless you and keep you safe."

58

HAPPY BIRTHDAY TO YOU

May 1, 1771
May Union Camp

I WOKE UP JUST PAST DAWN, roused by an insect of some sort walking up my leg. I twitched my foot and whatever it was scuttled hastily away into the grass, evidently alarmed to discover that I was alive. I wriggled my toes suspiciously, but finding no more intruders in my blanket, drew a deep breath of sap-filled fresh air and relaxed luxuriously.

I could hear faint stirrings nearby, but it was only the stamp and blowing of the officers' horses, who woke long before the men did. The camp itself was still silent—or as silent as a camp containing several hundred men was likely to be at any hour. The sheet of canvas overhead glowed with soft light and leaf-shadows, but the sun was not yet fully up. I closed my eyes half-way, delighted at the thought that I needn't get up for some time yet—and when I did, someone else would have made breakfast.

We had come into camp the night before, after a winding journey down from the mountains and across the piedmont, to arrive at the place of rendezvous, at Colonel Bryan's plantation. We were in good time; Tryon had not yet arrived with his troops from New Bern, nor had the Craven and Carteret County detachments, who were bringing the artillery field pieces and swivel guns. Tryon's troops were expected sometime today; or so Colonel Bryan had told us over supper the night before.

A grasshopper landed on the canvas above with an audible thump. I eyed it narrowly, but it didn't seem disposed to come inside, thank goodness. Perhaps I should have accepted Mrs. Bryan's offer to find me a bed in the house, along with a few other officers' wives who had accompanied their husbands. Jamie had insisted upon sleeping in the field with his men, though, and I had gone with him, preferring a bed involving Jamie and bugs to one with neither.

I glanced sideways, careful not to move in case he was still asleep. He wasn't. He was lying quite still, though, utterly relaxed, save for his right hand. He had this raised, and appeared to be examining it closely, turning it to and fro and slowly curling and uncurling his fingers—as well as he could. The fourth finger had a fused joint, and was permanently stiff; the middle finger was slightly twisted, a deep white scar spiraling round the middle joint.

His hand was callused and battered by work, and the tiny stigma of a nail-wound still showed, pale-pink, in the middle of his palm. The skin of his hand was deeply bronzed and weathered, freckled with sun-blots and scattered with bleached gold hairs. I thought it remarkably beautiful.

"Happy Birthday," I said, softly. "Taking stock?"

He let the hand fall on his chest, and turned his head to look at me, smiling.

"Aye, something of the sort. Though I suppose I've a few hours left. I was born at half-six; I willna have lived a full half-century until suppertime."

I laughed and rolled onto my side, kicking the blanket off. The air was still delightfully cool, but it wouldn't last long.

"Do you expect to disintegrate much further before supper?" I asked, teasing.

"Oh, I dinna suppose anything is likely to fall off by then," he said, consideringly. "As to the workings . . . aye, well . . ." He arched his back, stretching, and sank back with a gratified groan as my hand settled on him.

"It all seems to be in perfect working order," I assured him. I gave a brief, experimental tug, making him yelp slightly. "Not loose at all."

"Good," he said, folding his hand firmly over mine to

prevent further unauthorized experiments. "How did ye ken what I was doing? Taking stock, as ye say?"

I let him keep hold of the hand, but shifted to set my chin in the center of his chest, where a small depression seemed made for the purpose.

"I always do that, when I have a birthday—though I generally do it the night before. More looking back, I think, reflecting a bit on the year that's just gone. But I do check things over; I think perhaps everyone does. Just to see if you're the same person as the day before."

"I'm reasonably certain that I am," he assured me. "Ye dinna see any marked changes, do ye?"

I lifted my chin from its resting place and looked him over carefully. It was in fact rather hard to look at him objectively; I was both so used to his features and so fond of them that I tended to notice tiny, dear things about him—the freckle on his earlobe, the lower incisor pushing eagerly forward, just slightly out of line with its fellows—and to respond to the slightest change of his expression—but not really to look at him as an integrated whole.

He bore my examination tranquilly, eyelids half-lowered against the growing light. His hair had come loose while he slept and feathered over his shoulders, its ruddy waves framing a face strongly marked by both humor and passion—but which possessed a paradoxical and most remarkable capacity for stillness.

"No," I said at last, and set my chin down again with a contented sigh. "It's still you."

He gave a small grunt of amusement, but lay still. I could hear one of the cooks stumbling round nearby, cursing as he tripped over a wagon-tongue. The camp was still in the process of assembling; a few of the companies—those with a high proportion of ex-soldiers among their officers and men—were tidy and organized. A good many were not, and tipsy tents and strewn equipment sprawled across the meadow in a quasi-military hodgepodge.

A drum began to beat, to no apparent effect. The army continued to snooze.

"Do you think the Governor is going to be able to do anything with these troops?" I asked dubiously.

The local avatar of the army appeared to have gone back to sleep as well. At my question, though, the long auburn lashes lifted in lazy response.

"Oh, aye. Tryon's a soldier. He kens well enough what to do—at least to start. It's no so verra difficult to make men march in column and dig latrines, ken. To make them fight is another thing."

"Can he do that?"

The chest under my chin lifted in a deep sigh.

"Maybe so. Maybe no. The question is—will he have to?"

That was the question, all right. Rumors had flown round us like autumn leaves in a gale, all the way from Fraser's Ridge. The Regulators had ten thousand men, who were marching in a body upon New Bern. General Gage was sailing from New York with a regiment of official troops to subdue the Colony. The Orange County militia had rioted and killed their officers. Half the Wake County men had deserted. Hermon Husband had been arrested and spirited onto a ship, to be taken to London for trial on charges of treason. Hillsborough had been taken by the Regulators, who were preparing to fire the town and put Edmund Fanning and all his associates to the sword. I did hope that one wasn't true—or if it was, that Hubert Sherston was not one of Fanning's intimates.

Sorting through the mass of hearsay, supposition, and sheer wild invention, the only fact of which we could be sure appeared to be that Governor Tryon was en route to join the militia. After which, we would just see, I supposed.

Jamie's free hand rested on my back, his thumb idly stroking the edge of my shoulder blade. With his usual capacity for mental discipline, he appeared to have dismissed the uncertainty of the military prospects completely from his mind, and was thinking of something else entirely.

"Do ye ever think—" he began, and then broke off.

"Think what?" I bent and kissed his chest, arching my back to encourage him to rub it, which he did.

"Well . . . I'm no so sure I can explain, but it's struck me that now I have lived longer than my father did—which is not something I expected to happen," he added, with faint wryness. "It's only . . . well, it seems odd, is all. I only wondered, did ye ever think of that, yourself—having lost your mother young, I mean?"

"Yes." My face was buried in his chest, my voice muffled in the folds of his shirt. "I used to—when I was younger. Like going on a journey without a map."

His hand on my back paused for a moment.

"Aye, that's it." He sounded a little surprised. "I kent more or less what it would be like to be a man of thirty, or of forty—but now what?" His chest moved briefly, with a small noise that might have been a mixture of amusement and puzzlement.

"You invent yourself," I said softly, to the shadows inside the hair that had fallen over my face. "You look at other women—or men; you try on their lives for size. You take what you can use, and you look inside yourself for what you can't find elsewhere. And always . . . always . . . you wonder if you're doing it right."

His hand was warm and heavy on my back. He felt the tears that ran unexpectedly from the corners of my eyes to dampen his shirt, and his other hand came up to touch my head and smooth my hair.

"Aye, that's it," he said again, very softly.

The camp was beginning to stir outside, with clangings and thumps, and the hoarse sound of sleep-rough voices. Overhead, the grasshopper began to chirp, the sound like someone scratching a nail on a copper pot.

"This is a morning my father never saw," Jamie said, still so softly that I heard it as much through the walls of his chest, as with my ears. "The world and each day in it is a gift, *mo chridhe*—no matter what tomorrow may be."

I sighed deeply and turned my head, to rest my cheek against his chest. He reached over gently and wiped my nose with a fold of his shirt.

"And as for taking stock," he added practically, "I've all my teeth, none of my parts are missing, and my cock still stands up by itself in the morning. It could be worse."

59

MILITARY ENGINES

Journal of the Expedition against the Insurgents
Kept by William Tryon, Governor

Thursday, May 2nd

The Craven and Carteret Detachments marched out of New Bern with the two Field Pieces, Six Swivel Guns mounted on Carriages, Sixteen Waggons, & four Carts, loaded with Baggage, Ammunition and as much provisions as would supply the several Detachments that were to join them on their Route to Col. Bryan's, the place of General Rendezvous.

The Governor left New Bern the 27th of April, and arrived at Col. Bryan's the 1st of May. Today the Troops from the two Districts joined.

Friday, 3d. of May, Union Camp

The Governor Reviewed at 12 O'Clock the Detachments in the Meadow at Smiths Ferry on the West Side of Neuse River.

Saturday, the 4th of May

The Whole marched to Johnston Court House. Nine Miles.

Sunday, 5th of May

Marched to Major Theophilus Hunter's in Wake County. Thirteen Miles.

Monday, 6th of May

The Army halted, and the Governor reviewed the Wake Regiment at a Genl. Muster. Mr. Hinton Colonel of the Regiment acquainted the Governor that he had got but Twenty two Men of the Company he had received Orders to raise, owing to a Disaffection among the Inhabitants of the County.

The Governor observing a General Discontent in the Wake Regiment as he passed along the Front Rank of the Battalion, seeing that not more than one Man in five had Arms, & finding that upon his calling on them to turn out as Volunteers in the Service, they refused to obey, ordered the Army to surround the Battalion; which being effected he directed three of his Colonels to draft out Forty of the most Sightly & Most active Men, which Manouvre caused no small Panic in the Regiment, consisting at the Time of about four Hundred Men.

During the drafting the Officers of the Army were active in persuading the men to enlist, and in less than two Hours completed the Wake Company to Fifty Men. Night coming on the Wake Regiment was dismissed, much ashamed both of their Disgrace, & their own Conduct which occasioned it. The Army returned to Camp.

Wednesday, the 8th of May

Col. Hinton's Detachment was left behind, with a View to prevent the disaffected in that County from forming into a Body, and joining the Regulators in the adjacent Counties.

This Morning a Detachment marched to the dwelling House of Turner Tomlinson, a Notorious Regulator, and brought him prisoner to Camp, where he was closely confined. He confess'd he was a Regulator, but would make no discoveries.

The Army marched, & incamped near Booth's, on New Hope Creek.

Friday, the 10th of May

Halted, ordered the Waggons to be refitted, Horses to be shod, and every thing put in Repair. Reviewed in Hillsborough two Companies of the Orange Militia.

The Prisoner Tomlinson made his escape this Evening, from the Quarter Guard. Detachments set after him, but without Success.

Sunday, the 12th of May

Marched, and forded Haw River, and encamped on the West Side of the Banks. It was expected the Regulators would have opposed the passages of the Royalists over this River, as it was their Intent, but not suspecting that the Army would move out of Hillsborough till after Monday, they were by this Sudden Movement of the Army defeated in that part of their plan.

Received this Day flying Reports that General Waddell was forced by the Regulators, with the Troops under his Command to repass the Yadkin River.

Divine Service, with Sermon, performed by the Revd. Mr. McCartny. Text: "If You have no Sword Sell your Garment & Buy One."

This Day Twenty Gentlemen Volunteers joined the Army, chiefly from Granville & Bute Counties. They were formed into a Troop of Light Horse under the Command of Major MacDonald. A Regulator taken by the flanking parties laying in ambush with his Gun. The Commissary took out of his House part of a Hogshead of Rum lodged there for the Use of the Regulators. Also some Hogs which were to be accounted to His Family.

Monday, the 13th of May

Marched to O'Neal. At 12 O'Clock an Express rider arrived from General Waddell, with a Verbal Message, the Express not daring to take a Letter for fear of its being intercepted. The Purport of which Message was that on Thursday Evening the 9th Instant the Regulators to the Number of two Thousand surrounded his Camp, and in the most daring & insolent Manner required the General to retreat with the Troops over the Yadkin River, of which he was then within two Miles. He refused to comply, insisting he had the Governor's Orders to proceed. This made them more insolent, and with many Indian shouts they endeavoured to intimidate his Men.

The General finding his Men not exceeding three Hundred, and generally unwilling to engage; and many of his Sentries going over to the Regulators, was reduced to comply with their requisition, & early the next Morning repassed the Yadkin River, with his Cannon and Baggage; the Regulators agreeing to disperse and return to their several Habitations.

A Council of War was held immediately to deliberate on the Subject of the Intelligence brought by the Express, composed of the Honorable John Rutherford, Lewis DeRosset, Robert Palmer, & Sam Cornell, of His Majesty's Council, and the Colonels & Field Officers of the Army, Wherein it was resolved that the Army should change their Route, get into the Road at Captain Holt's that leads from Hillsborough to Salisbury, pass the little and great Alamance Rivers with all possible Expedition, & march without Loss of Time to join General Waddell; accordingly the Army got under March, and before Night encamped on the West Side of little Alamance, a strong Detachment being sent forward to take possession of the West Banks of Great Alamance, to prevent the Enemy's Parties from occupying that strong Post.

This evening received Intelligence that the Regulators were sending Scouts through all their Settlements, and assembling on Sandy Creek, near Hunter's.

Marched and joined the Detachment on the West Banks of Great Alamance where a strong Camp was chosen. Here the Army halted till more provisions could be brought from Hillsborough, for which purpose several Waggons now emptied and sent from Camp to Hillsborough.

Intelligence being brought this Evening into Camp that the Rebels intended to attack the camp in the Night, the Necessary preparations were made for an Engagement, and one third of the Army ordered to remain under Arms all Night, & the Remainder to lay down near their Arms. No Alarm given.

Tuesday, the 14th of May

Halted, the Men ordered to keep in Camp.

The Army lay on their Arms all Night, as in the preceeding. No alarm.

Wednesday, the 15th of May

About 6 O'Clock in the Evening, the Governor received a Letter from the Insurgents which he laid before the Council of War, wherein it was determined that the Army should march against the Rebels early the next Morning, that the Governor should send them a Letter offering them Terms, and in Case of Refusal, should attack them.

The Men remained all Night under Arms. No alarm, tho' the Rebels lay within five Miles of the Camp.

From the Dreambook:
Hillsborough, May 15

"Last night I fell asleep early, and woke up before dawn inside a gray cloud. All day, I've felt like I was walking inside a mist; people talk to me and I don't

hear them; I can see their mouths move, and I nod and smile, and then go away. The air is hot and muggy and everything smells like hot metal. My head aches, and the cook is clanging pans.

I've tried all day to remember what I dreamed of, and I can't. There's only gray, and a feeling of fear. I've never been near a battle, but I have the feeling that what I'm dreaming of is cannon smoke."

60

COUNCIL OF WAR

JAMIE CAME BACK from the Council of War, well after suppertime, and informed the men briefly of Tryon's intent. The general response was approval, if not outright enthusiasm.

"Ist gut we move now," said Ewald Mueller, stretching out his long arms and cracking all his knuckles simultaneously. "Longer we stay, we are growing moss!"

This sentiment was greeted by laughter and nods of agreement. The mood of the company brightened noticeably at the prospect of action in the morning; men settled down to talk around the fires, the rays of the setting sun glinting off tin cups and the polished barrels of the muskets laid carefully by their feet.

Jamie made a quick round of inspection, answering questions and administering reassurances, then came to join me at our smaller fire. I looked at him narrowly; in spite of the stress of the immediate situation, there was a sense of suppressed satisfaction about him that at once excited my suspicions.

"What have you done?" I asked, handing him a large chunk of bread and a bowl of stew.

He didn't bother denying that he'd been doing something.

"Got Cornell alone long enough after the Council, to ask him about Stephen Bonnet." He ripped off a chunk of bread with his teeth and swallowed it with the minimum of chewing. "Christ, I'm starved. I've not eaten all day, what wi' creepin' through the brambles on my belly like a snake."

"Surely Samuel Cornell wasn't hanging about in the brambles." Cornell was one of the Governor's Royal Council, a stout and wealthy merchant from Edenton, and grossly unsuited by position, build, and temperament for snaking through brambles.

"No, that was later." He swabbed the bread through the stew, took another enormous bite, then waved a hand, momentarily speechless. I handed him a cup of cider, which he used to wash down the mess.

"We were searchin' out the Rebel lines," he explained, the obstruction cleared. "They're no far off, ken. Though 'lines' is giving them the benefit of considerable doubt," he added, scooping up more stew. "I've not seen such a rabble since I fought in France, and we took a village where a gang o' wine-smugglers were. Half of them whoring and all of them drunk; we had to pick them up off the ground to arrest them. This lot's little better, from what I could see. Not so many whores, though," he added, to be fair, and shoved the rest of his bread into his mouth.

At least half the Governor's army was slightly the worse for drink at the moment, but that was so usual a condition as not to call for comment. I gave him another piece of bread, concentrating on the important aspect of the conversation.

"So you've found out something about Bonnet, then?"

He nodded, chewed, and gulped.

"Cornell's not met him, but he's heard talk. It seems he works his way up and down the Outer Banks for a bit, and then disappears for three or four months. Then suddenly, one day he'll be there again, drinking in the taverns in Edenton or Roanoke, gold pieces spilling from his pockets."

"So he's bringing in goods from Europe and selling

them." Three or four months was the time it would take to sail a ship to England and back. "Contraband, I suppose?"

Jamie nodded.

"Cornell thinks so. And d'ye ken where he brings the stuff ashore?" He wiped the back of a hand across his mouth, seeming grimly amused. "Wylie's Landing. Or so rumor says."

"What—you don't mean Phillip Wylie is in cahoots with him?" I was shocked—and rather distressed—to hear this, but Jamie shook his head.

"As to that, I couldna say. But the Landing adjoins Phillip Wylie's plantation, to be sure. And the wee shite *was* wi' Bonnet the night he came to River Run, no matter what he may have said about it, later," he added. He flapped a hand, dismissing Phillip Wylie for the moment.

"But Cornell says that Bonnet's disappeared again; he's been gone, this past month. So my aunt and Duncan are likely safe enough, for the moment. That's one thing off my mind—and a good thing; there's enough to worry about without that."

He spoke without irony, glancing round at the encampment that sprawled around us. As the light failed, the fires began to glow through the dimness of twilight, like hundreds of fireflies along the banks of Great Alamance.

"Hermon Husband is here," he said.

I looked up from the fresh bowl of stew I was dishing out. "Did you speak to him?"

He shook his head.

"I couldna go near. He's with the Regulators, aye? I was on a wee hill, lookin' down across the stream, and saw him in the distance; he was in a great mass of men, but I couldna mistake his dress."

"What will he do?" I handed him the full bowl. "Surely he won't fight—or allow them to fight." I was inclined to view Husband's presence as a hopeful sign. Hermon Husband was the closest thing the Regulators had to a real leader; they would listen to him, I was sure.

Jamie shook his head, looking troubled.

"I dinna ken, Sassenach. He willna take up arms himself, no—but as for the rest . . ." He trailed off, thinking. Then his face set in sudden decision. He handed me back the bowl, and turning on his heel, made his way across the camp.

I saw him touch Roger on the shoulder, and draw him aside a little. They spoke together for a few moments, then Jamie reached into his coat, drew out something white, and handed it to Roger. Roger looked at whatever it was for a moment, then nodded, and tucked it away in his own coat.

Jamie clapped him on the shoulder, left him, and came back across the camp, pausing to laugh and exchange rude remarks with the Lindsay brothers.

He came back smiling, and took the bowl from me, seeming relieved.

"I've told Roger Mac to go first thing in the morning, to find Husband," he said, setting about the stew with renewed appetite. "If he can, I've told him to bring Husband here—to speak face to face wi' Tryon. If he canna convince Tryon—which he can't—perhaps Tryon will convince Husband that he's in earnest. If Hermon sees that it will mean bloodshed, then perhaps he will prevail upon his men to stand down."

"Do you really think so?" It had rained lightly in the afternoon, and banks of cloud still covered the eastern sky. The edges of those clouds glowed faintly red—not from the slanting rays of sunset, but from the fires of the Regulators, camped invisibly on the opposite bank of the Alamance.

Jamie wiped his bowl and took a last bite of bread, shaking his head.

"I dinna ken," he said simply. "But there's nothing else to try, is there?"

I nodded, and stooped to put more wood on the fire. No one would sleep early tonight.

The campfires had burned all day, smoking and sputtering in a light rain. Now, though, the drizzle had ceased and the clouds had parted, shredding into long, wispy mare's-tails that glowed like fire across the whole arc of the western sky, eclipsing the puny efforts of the earthbound flames. Seeing it, I put a hand on Jamie's arm.

"Look," I said. He turned, wary lest someone had appeared at his heels with a fresh problem, but his face relaxed as I gestured upward.

Frank, urged to look at some wonder of nature whilst

preoccupied with a problem, would have paused just long enough not to seem discourteous, said, "Oh, yes, lovely, isn't it?" and returned at once to the maze of his thoughts. Jamie lifted his face to the glowing glory of the heavens and stood still.

What is the matter with you? I thought to myself. *Can't you let Frank Randall rest in peace?*

Jamie put an arm about my shoulders, and sighed.

"In Scotland," he said, "the sky would be like lead all day, and even at the twilight, ye'd see no more than the sun sinking into the sea like a red-hot cannonball. Never a sky like this one is."

"What makes you think of Scotland?" I asked, intrigued that his mind should run as mine did, on things of the past.

"Dawn and twilight, and the season of the year," he said, and his wide mouth curled slightly upward in reminiscence. "Whenever there is a change in the air around me, it makes me think of what has been, and what is now. I dinna always do it in a house, but when I'm living rough, I'll often wake dreaming of folk I once knew, and then sit quiet in the twilight, thinking of other times and places." He shrugged a little. "So now the sun is going down, and it is Scotland in my mind."

"Oh," I said, comforted at having such an explanation. "That must be it."

"Must be what?" The setting sun bathed his face in gold, softening the lines of strain as he looked down at me.

"I was thinking of other times and places, too," I said, and leaned my head against his shoulder. "Just now, though . . . I can't think of anything but this."

"Oh?" He hesitated for a moment, but then said, carefully, "I dinna much mention it, Sassenach, for if the answer's 'yes,' there's nay so much I can do to mend it—but do ye often long for . . . the other times?"

I waited for the space of three heartbeats to answer; I heard them, Jamie's heart beating slow under my ear, and I curled my left hand closed, feeling the smooth metal of the gold ring on my finger.

"No," I said, "but I remember them."

61

ULTIMATUMS

Great Alamance Camp
May 16th 1771

To the People now Assembled in Arms, who Style themselves Regulators

In Answer to your Petition, I am to acquaint you that I have ever been attentive to the true Interest of this Country, and to that of every Individual residing within it. I lament the fatal Necessity to which you have now reduced me, by withdrawing yourselves from the Mercy of the Crown, and the Laws of your Country, to require you are assembled as Regulators, to lay down your Arms, Surrender up the outlawed Ringleaders, and Submit yourselves to the Laws of your Country, and then rest on the lenity and Mercy of Government. By accepting these Terms in one Hour from the delivery of this Dispatch, you will prevent an effusion of Blood, as you are at this time in a state of War and Rebellion against your King, your Country, and your Laws.

Wm. Tryon

JAMIE HAD GONE before I woke; his blanket lay neatly folded beside me, and Gideon was gone from the pin-oak to which Jamie had tethered him the night before.

"Colonel's gone to meet with the Governor's Council of War," Kenny Lindsay told me, yawning widely. He blinked, shaking himself like a wet dog. "Tea, ma'am, or coffee?"

"Tea, please." I supposed it was the tenor of current events that was causing me to think of the Boston Tea Party. I couldn't recall for sure when that brouhaha and its subsequent events were due to occur, but had an obscure feeling that I ought to seize every opportunity of drinking tea while it was still obtainable, in hopes of saturating my tissues—like a bear tucking into the grubs and berries in anticipation of winter.

The day had dawned still and clear, and while it was cool for the moment, there was already a hint of mugginess in the air from the rain the day before. I sipped my tea, feeling small tendrils of hair escape from bondage to curl round my face, sticking to my cheeks in the steam from my cup.

Tissues restored for the moment, I fetched a couple of buckets and set off for the stream. I hoped it wouldn't be needed, but it would be as well to have a quantity of boiled sterile water on hand, just in case. And if it wasn't needed for medical purposes, I could rinse my stockings, which were much in need of attention.

Despite its name the Great Alamance was not a particularly impressive river, being no more than fifteen or twenty feet across for most of its length. It was also shallow, mud-bottomed, and kinked like a wool-raveling, with multiple small arms and tributaries that wandered all over the landscape. I supposed it was a decent military demarcation, though; while a body of men could certainly ford the stream without much trouble, there was no chance of them doing so by stealth.

Dragonflies darted over the water, and over the heads of a couple of militia-men, chatting companionably as they relieved themselves into the murky waters of the stream. I paused tactfully behind a bush until they had left, reflecting as I made my way down the sloping bank with my buckets how fortunate it was that most of the troops would consider *drinking* water only if actually dying of dehydration.

When I came back into camp, I found it wide awake, every man alert, if red-eyed. The atmosphere was one of watchfulness, though, rather than immediate battle-readiness, and there was no more than a general stir of interest when Jamie returned, Gideon threading his way past the campfires with surprising delicacy.

"How is it, *Mac Dubh*?" Kenny asked, standing to greet him as Jamie reined up. "Anything ado?"

Jamie shook his head. He was dressed with a neatness approaching severity, hair clubbed back, dirk and pistols fixed on his belt, sword at his side. A yellow cockade fixed to his coat was the only touch of decoration. Battle-ready, and a small *frisson* crept up my spine at the thought.

"The Governor's sent across his wee letter to the Regulators. Four sheriffs each took a copy; they're to read it out to every group they come across. We must just wait, and see what happens."

I followed his glance toward the third campfire. Roger had likely left as soon as it was light, before the camp woke.

I had emptied the buckets into the kettle for boiling. I picked them up for another trip to the stream, when Gideon's ears pricked and he lifted his head suddenly, with a sharp whicker of greeting. Jamie instantly nudged the horse in front of me, and his hand dropped to his sword. My view was blocked by Gideon's enormous chest and withers; I couldn't see who was coming, but I did see Jamie's hand relax its grip on the sword-hilt as whoever it was came in sight. A friend, then.

Or if not precisely a friend, at least someone he didn't mean to run through or hack out of the saddle. I heard a familiar voice, raised in greeting, and peered out from under Gideon's chin to see Governor Tryon riding across the small meadow, accompanied by two aides.

Tryon sat his horse decently, if without great style, and was dressed as usual for campaigning, in a serviceable blue uniform coat and doeskin breeches, a yellow officer's cockade in his hat, and with one of the cavalry cutlasses called a hanger at his side—not for show; the hilt showed nicks and the scabbard was worn.

Tryon pulled up his horse and nodded, touching his hat to Jamie, who did likewise. Seeing me lurking in Gideon's shadow, the Governor politely removed his cocked hat altogether, bowing from the saddle.

"Mrs. Fraser, your servant." He glanced at the pails I held, then turned in his saddle, beckoning to one of the aides. "Mr. Vickers. Kindly help Mrs. Fraser, if you will."

I surrendered the pails gratefully to Mr. Vickers, a pink-cheeked young man of eighteen or so, but instead of going with him, I simply directed him where to take them. Tryon raised one eyebrow at me, but I returned his expression of mild displeasure with a bland smile, and stood my ground. I wasn't going anywhere.

He was wise enough to recognize that, and make no issue of my presence. Dismissing me instead from his cognizance, he nodded again to Jamie.

"Your troops are in order, Colonel Fraser?" He glanced pointedly around. The only troops visible at the moment were Kenny, who had his nose buried in his cup, and Murdo Lindsay and Geordie Chisholm, who were engaged in a vicious game of mumblety-peg in the shadows of the copse.

"Aye, sir."

The Governor raised both brows in patent skepticism.

"Call them, sir. I will inspect their readiness."

Jamie paused for a moment, gathering up his reins. He squinted against the rising sun, evaluating the Governor's mount. "A nice gelding ye have there, sir. Is he steady?"

"Of course." The Governor frowned. "Why?"

Jamie threw back his head and gave a ululating Highland cry, of the sort meant to be heard over several acres of mountainside. The Governor's horse jerked at the reins, eyes rolling back. Militiamen poured out of the thicket, shrieking like banshees, and a black cloud of crows exploded from the trees above them like a puff of cannon smoke, raucous in flight. The horse reared, decanting Tryon in an undignified heap on the grass, and bolted for the trees on the far side of the meadow.

I took several steps backward, out of the way.

The Governor sat up, purple-faced and gasping for breath, to find himself in the center of a ring of grinning militiamen, all pointing their weapons at him. The Governor glared into the barrel of the rifle poking into his face and batted it away with one hand, making small choking noises, like an angry squirrel. Jamie cleared his throat in a meaningful manner, and the men faded quietly back into the copse.

I thought that on the whole, it would be a mistake either to offer the Governor a hand to arise, or to let him get a look at my face. I tactfully turned my back and wandered a few steps away, affecting to have discovered an absorbing new plant springing from the ground near my feet.

Mr. Vickers reappeared from the wood, looking startled, a pail of water in each hand.

"What has happened?" He started toward the Governor, but I put a hand on his sleeve to detain him. Best if Mr. Tryon had a moment to recover both his breath and his dignity.

"Nothing important," I said, recovering my pails before he could spill them. "Er . . . how many militia troops are assembled here, do you know?"

"One thousand and sixty-eight, mum," he said, looking thoroughly bewildered. "That is not accounting for General Waddell's troops, of course. But what—"

"And you have cannon?"

"Oh, yes, several, mum. We have two detachments with artillery. Two six-pounders, ten swivel-guns, and two eight-pound mortars." Vickers stood a little straighter, important with the thought of so much potential destruction.

"There are two thousand men across the creek, sir—but the most of them barely armed. Many carry no more than a knife." Jamie's voice came from behind me, drawing Vickers's attention away. I turned round, to find that Jamie had dismounted, and was standing face to face with the Governor, holding the latter's hat. He slapped it casually against his thigh and offered it back to its owner, who accepted it with as much grace as might be managed under the circumstances.

"I have been told as much, Mr. Fraser," he said dryly, "though I am pleased to hear that your intelligence corroborates my own. Mr. Vickers, will you be so kind as to go and fetch my horse?" The purple hue had faded from Tryon's face, and while his manner still held a certain constraint, he seemed not to be holding a grudge. Tryon had both a sense of fairness, and—more importantly at present—a sense of humor, both of which seemed to have survived the recent demonstration of military readiness.

Jamie nodded.

"I suppose that your agents have also told you that the Regulators have no leader, as such?"

"On the contrary, Mr. Fraser. I am under the impression that Hermon Husband is and has been for some considerable time one of the chief agitators of this movement. James Hunter, too, is a name that I have often seen appended to letters of complaint and the endless petitions that reach me in New Bern. And there are others—Hamilton, Gillespie . . ."

Jamie made an impatient gesture, brushing a hovering cloud of gnats from his face.

"In some circumstances, sir, I should be willing to dispute with ye whether the pen is mightier than the sword—but not on the edge of a battlefield, and that is where we stand. A boldness in writing pamphlets does not fit a man to lead troops—and Husband is a Quaker gentleman."

"I have heard as much," Tryon agreed. He gestured toward the distant creek, one brow raised in challenge. "And yet he is here."

"He is here," Jamie agreed. He paused for a moment, gauging the governor's mood before proceeding. The Governor was tightly wound; there was no missing the tautness in his figure, or the brightness of his eyes. Still, battle was not yet imminent and the tension was well-leashed. He could still listen.

"I have fed the man at my own hearth, sir," Jamie said carefully. "I have eaten at his. He makes no secret either of his views or his character. If he has come here today, I am certain that he has done so in torment of mind." Jamie drew a deep breath. He was on dicey ground here.

"I have sent a man across the creek, sir, to find Husband, and beg him to meet with me. It may be that I can persuade him to use his considerable influence to cause these men—these citizens"—he gestured briefly toward the creek and the invisible myrmidons beyond—"to abandon this disastrous course of action, which cannot but end in tragedy." He met Tryon's eyes straight on.

"May I ask you, sir—may I beg of you—if Husband will come, will you not speak with him yourself?"

Tryon stood silent, oblivious of the dusty tricorne he turned around and around in his hands. The echoes of the recent commotion had faded; a vireo sang from the branches of the elm above us.

"They are citizens of this colony," he said at last, with a nod in the direction of the creek. "I should regret that harm should come to them. Their grievances are not without merit; I have acknowledged as much—publicly!—and taken steps toward redress." He glanced toward Jamie, as though to see whether this statement was accepted. Jamie stood silent, waiting.

Tryon took a deep breath, and slapped the hat against his leg.

"Yet I am Governor of this colony. I cannot see the peace disturbed, the law flouted, riot and bloodshed run rampant and unpunished!" He glanced bleakly at me. "I will not."

He turned his attention back to Jamie.

"I think he will not come, sir. Their course is set"—he nodded once more toward the trees that edged Alamance Creek—"and so is mine. Still . . ." He hesitated for a moment, then made up his mind, and shook his head.

"No. If he *does* come, then by all means reason with him, and if he will agree to send his men home peaceably—at that point, bring him to me and we shall arrange terms. But I cannot wait upon the possibility."

Mr. Vickers had retrieved the Governor's mount. The boy stood a little way apart, holding both horses by their reins, and I saw him nod slightly at this, as though affirming the Governor's words. His own hat shaded him from the sun, yet his face was flushed, and his eyes bright; he was eager for the fight.

Tryon was not; yet he was ready. Neither was Jamie—but he was ready, too. He held the Governor's gaze for a moment, and then nodded, accepting inevitability.

"How long?" he asked quietly.

Tryon glanced upward at the sun, which stood a little

short of mid-morning. Roger had been gone for nearly two hours; how long might it take him to find Hermon Husband and return?

"The companies are in battle order," Tryon said. He glanced at the copse, and the corner of his mouth twitched. Then he returned a dark gaze to Jamie's face. "Not long. Stand ready, Mr. Fraser."

He turned away, and clapping his hat on his head, seized the reins of his horse and swung into the saddle. He rode away without looking back, followed by his aides.

Jamie watched him go, expressionless.

I moved beside him, touching his hand. I didn't need to say that I hoped Roger would hurry.

62

"STRAGLERS AND SUSPECTED PERSONS"

Item #12 *- No Officer or Soldier to go beyond the Limits of the Camp which is within the distance of the Grand Guard.*

Item #63 *- Commanding Officers of Corps are to examine all Straglers and suspected Persons, and those who cannot give a good account of themselves to be confined and Report thereof made to Head Quarters.*

"Camp Duties and Regulations": *Orders Given Out by His Excellency Governor Tryon to the Provincials of North Carolina.*

ROGER TOUCHED THE POCKET of his breeches, where he had tucked away his pewter militia badge. An inch-and-a-half-wide button of metal, pierced round the edges, stamped with a crude "FC" for "Fraser's Company" and meant to be sewn onto coat or hat, such badges—and the cloth cockades—were the sole items of uniform for most of the Governor's foot-troops, and the only means of distinguishing a member of the militia from one of the Regulators.

"And exactly how d'ye know whom to shoot?" he had inquired ironically, when Jamie had handed him the badge at supper, two days before. "If you get close enough to see the badge before ye fire, won't the other bugger get you first?"

Jamie had given him a glance of equal irony, but courteously forbore any observations on Roger's marksmanship and the likelihood—or otherwise—of his doing any damage with his musket.

"I wouldna wait to see, myself," he said. "If anyone runs toward ye with a gun, fire, and hope for the best."

A few men seated around the fire nearby sniggered at this, but Jamie ignored them. He reached for a stick and pulled three roasting yams out of the coals, so they lay side by side, black and steaming in the cool evening air. He kicked one gently, sending it rolling back into the ashes.

"That's us," he explained. He kicked the next yam. "That's Colonel Leech's company, and that"—he booted the third, which rolled erratically after its fellows—"is Colonel Ashe's. D'ye see?" He cocked an eyebrow at Roger.

"Each company will go forward in its own path, so ye're no likely to see any other militia, at least to begin with. Anyone coming toward us is most probably the enemy." Then his long mouth curled up a bit, as he gestured toward the men all round them, busy with their suppers.

"Ye ken every man here well enough? Well, dinna shoot any of them, and ye'll be fine, aye?"

Roger smiled ruefully to himself as he made his way carefully down a slope covered with tiny yellow-flowered plants. It was sound advice; he was much less concerned with the possibility of being shot than with the fear of accidentally harming someone himself—including the not-inconsiderable worry of blowing off a few of his own fingers.

Privately, he was resolved not to fire at anyone, regardless either of circumstance or of the possibility of his hitting them. He'd heard enough of the Regulators' stories—Abel MacLennan, Hermon Husband. Even allowing for the natural hyperbole of Husband's style, his pamphlets burned with a sense of injustice that was inescapable. How could Roger look to kill a man or maim him, only for protesting against abuses and corruption so blatant that they must offend any just-minded person?

A trained historian, he'd seen enough of present circumstances to understand just how widespread the problems were, how they'd come about—and he understood well enough the difficulties of correcting them. He sympathized with Tryon's position—to a point—but his sympathy stopped a good way short of rendering him a willing soldier in the cause of upholding the Crown's authority—still less, the cause of preserving William Tryon's reputation and personal fortune.

He stopped for a moment, hearing voices, and stepped softly behind the trunk of a large poplar.

Three men came in sight a moment later, talking casually amongst themselves. All three had guns and bullet-boxes, but the impression they gave was of three friends on their way to hunt rabbits, rather than grim troopers on the eve of battle.

In fact, this appeared to be exactly what they were—foragers. One had a cluster of furry bodies slung from his belt, and another carried a muslin bag stained with something that might have been fresh blood. As Roger watched from the shelter of the poplar, one man stopped, hand out to check his comrades, who both stiffened like hounds, noses pointing toward a clump of trees some sixty yards distant.

Even knowing something was there, it took a moment before Roger spotted the small deer, standing still against a grove of saplings, a veil of dappled light through the spring leaves overhead masking it almost perfectly from view.

The first man swung his gun stealthily down from his shoulder, reaching for rod and cartridge, but one of the others stopped him with a hand on his arm.

"Hold there, Abram," said the second man, speaking softly but clearly. "You don't want to be firing so close to the crick. You heard what the Colonel said—Regulators are drawn right up to the bank near that point." He nodded toward the heavy growth of alder and willow that marked the edge of the invisible creek, no more than a hundred yards distant. "You don't want to be provokin' them, not just now."

Abram nodded reluctantly, and put up his gun again.

"Aye, I suppose. Will it be today, do you think?"

Roger glanced back at the sapling grove, but the deer had vanished, silent as smoke.

"Can't see how it won't be." The third man pulled a yellow kerchief from his sleeve and wiped his face; the weather was warm and the air muggy. "Tryon's had his guns in place since dawn; he's not the man to let anybody get a jump on him. He might wait for Waddell's men—but he may think he's no need of them."

Abram snorted with mild contempt.

"To crush those rabble? Seen them, have you? A poorer set of soldiers you'd not see in a month of Sundays."

The man with the kerchief smiled cynically.

"Well, that's as may be, Abie. Seen some of the backcountry militia, have you? Speakin' of rabble. And speakin' of the Regulators, there's a lot of 'em, rabble or not. Two to one, Cap'n Neale says."

Abram grunted, casting a last reluctant glance toward the wood and the creek beyond.

"Rabble," he repeated, more confidently, and turned away. "Come along, then, let's have a look upslope."

The foragers were on the same side as himself; they wore no cockades, but he saw the militia badges on breast and hat, glinting silver in the morning sun. Still, Roger remained in the shadows until the men had vanished, talking casually amongst themselves. He was reasonably sure that Jamie had sent him on this mission with no authority beyond his own; best if he were not asked to explain himself.

The attitude amongst most of the militia toward the Regulation was at best scornful. At worst—at the upper levels of command—it was coldly vindictive.

"Crush them once and for all," Caswell had said, over a cup of coffee by the fire the night before. A plantation owner from the eastern part of the colony, Richard Caswell had no sympathy with the Regulators' grievances.

Roger patted his pocket again, considering. No, best leave it. He could produce the badge if he were challenged, and he didn't think anyone would shoot him in the back without at least a shout of warning. Still, he felt oddly exposed as he walked through the lush grass of the river-meadow, and sighed with involuntary relief, as the languishing branches of the creek-side willows enfolded him in cool shadow.

He had, with Jamie's approval, left his musket behind, and come unarmed, save for the knife at his belt that was a normal accoutrement for any man. His only other item of equipment was a large white kerchief, presently folded up inside his coat.

"If ye should be threatened—anywhere—wave it and cry 'Truce,'" Jamie had instructed him. "Then tell them to fetch me, and dinna say more until I come. If no one prevents you, bring me Husband under its protection."

The vision of himself leading Hermon Husband back across the creek, holding the flapping kerchief on a stick above his head like a guide leading tourists through an airport, made him want to hoot with laughter. Jamie hadn't laughed, though, or even smiled, and so he had accepted the cloth solemnly, tucking it away with care. He peered through the screen of drooping leaves, but the creek ran past sparkling in the new day's sun, silent save for the rush of water past stones and clay. No one was in sight, and the noise of the water drowned any sound that might have come from beyond the trees on the other side. While the militia might not shoot him in the back, he wasn't so sanguine about the possibilities of Regulators shooting him from the front, if they saw him crossing from the Government side.

Still, he couldn't skulk in the trees all day. He emerged onto the bank, and made his way downstream toward the point the foragers had indicated, watching the trees carefully for any signs of life. The crossing near the point was better, shallow water and a rocky bottom. Still, if the Regulators were "drawn up" anywhere nearby, they were being damned quiet about it.

A more peaceful scene could scarcely be imagined, and yet his heart was hammering suddenly in his ears. He had again the odd feeling of someone standing near him. He glanced around in all directions, but nothing moved save the rushing water and the trailing willow fronds.

"That you, Dad?" he said softly, under his breath, and at once felt foolish. Still, the feeling of someone near remained strong, though benign.

With a mental shrug, he bent and took off his shoes and stockings. It must be the circumstances, he thought. Not that one could quite compare wading a shallow creek in search of a Quaker rabble-rouser to flying a Spitfire across the night-time Channel on a bombing run to Germany. A mission was a mission, though, he supposed.

He looked round once again, but saw only tadpoles wriggling in the shallows. With a slightly crooked smile, he stepped into the water, sending the tadpoles into frenzied flight.

"Over the top, then," he said to a wood-duck. The bird ignored him, going on with its foraging among the dark-green rafts of floating cress.

No challenge came from the trees on either side; no sounds at all, bar the cheerful racket of nesting birds. It was as he sat on a sunwarmed rock, drying his feet before putting his shoes and stockings back on, that he finally heard some indication that the far side of the creek was populated by humans.

"So what do you want then, sweeting?"

The voice came from the shrubbery behind him, and he froze, blood thundering in his ears. It was a woman's voice. Before he could move or think to answer, though, he heard a laugh, deeper in pitch, and with a particular tone to it that made him relax.

Instinct informed him before his reason did that voices with that particular intonation were not a threat.

"Dunno, hinney, what will it cost me?"

"Ooh, hark at him! Not the time to count your pennies, is it?"

"Don't you worry, ladies, we'll take up a collection amongst us if we have to."

"Oh, is that the way of it? Well and good, sir, but be you aware, in this congregation, the collection comes *before* the singing!"

Listening to this amiable wrangling, Roger deduced that the voices in question belonged to three men and two women, all of whom seemed confident that whatever the financial arrangements, three would go into two quite evenly, with no awkward remainders.

Picking up his shoes, he stole quietly away, leaving the unseen sentries—if that's what they were—to their sums. Evidently, the army of the Regulation wasn't quite so organized as the government troops.

Less organized was putting it mildly, he thought, a little later. He had kept to the creek bank for some distance, unsure where the main body of the army might be. He had walked nearly a quarter-mile, with neither sight nor sound of a soul other than the two whores and their customers. Feeling increasingly surreal, he wandered through small pine groves, and across the edges of grassy meadows, with no company save courting birds and small gossamer butterflies in shades of orange and yellow.

"What the hell sort of way is this to run a war?" he muttered, shoving his way through a blackberry bramble. It was like one of those science fiction stories, in which everyone but the hero had suddenly vanished from the face of the earth. He was beginning to be anxious; what if he didn't manage to find the bloody Quaker—or even the army—before the shooting started?

Then he rounded a bend in the creek, and caught his first glimpse of the Regulators proper; a group of women, washing clothes in the rushing waters by a cluster of boulders.

He ducked back into the brush before they should see him, and turned away from the creek, heartened. If the women were here, the men weren't far away.

They weren't. Within a few more yards, he heard the sounds of camp—casual voices, laughter, the clank of spoons and tea-kettles and the clunk of splitting wood. Rounding a clump of hawthorn, he was nearly knocked over by a gang of young men who ran past, hooting and yelling, as they chased one of their number who brandished a fresh-cut racoon's tail overhead, floating in the breeze as he ran.

They charged past Roger without a second glance, and he went on, a bit less warily. He wasn't challenged; there were no sentries. In fact, a strange face appeared to be neither a novelty nor a threat. A few men glanced casually at him, but then turned back to their talk, seeing nothing odd in his appearance.

"I'm looking for Hermon Husband," he said bluntly to a man roasting a squirrel over the pale flames of a fire. The man looked blank for a moment.

"The Quaker?" Roger amplified.

"Oh, aye, him," the man said, features clearing. "He's a ways beyond—that way, I think." He gestured helpfully with his stick, the charred squirrel pointing the way with the stubs of its blackened forelegs.

"A ways beyond" was some way. Roger passed through three more scattered camps before reaching what looked to be the main body of the army—if one could dignify it by such a term. True, there did seem to be an increasing air of seriousness; there was less of the carefree frolicking he had seen near the creek. Still, it wasn't Strategic Command headquarters, by a long shot.

He began to feel mildly hopeful that violence could still be avoided, even with the armies drawn up face to face and the gun-crews standing by. There had been an air of excited readiness among the militia as he passed through their lines, but no atmosphere of hatred or blood-thirstiness.

Here, the situation was far different than it was among the orderly militia lines, but even less disposed to immediate hostilities. As he pressed on further, though, asking his way at each campfire he passed, he began to feel something different in the air—a sense of increasing urgency, almost of desperation. The horseplay he'd seen in the outer camps had vanished; men clustered talking in close groups, their heads together, or sat by themselves, grimly loading guns and sharpening knives.

As he got closer, the name of Hermon Husband was recognized by everyone, the pointing fingers surer of direction. The name seemed almost a magnet, pulling him farther and farther into the center of a thickening mass of men and boys, all excited—all armed. The noise grew greater all the time, voices beating on his ears like hammers on a forge.

He found Husband at last, standing on a rock like a large gray wolf at bay, surrounded by a knot of some thirty or forty men, all clamoring in angry agitation. Elbows jabbed and feet trampled, without regard to impact on their fellows. Clearly they were demanding an answer, but unable to pause long enough to hear one were it given.

Husband, stripped to his shirtsleeves and red in the face, was shouting at one or two of those closest to him, but Roger could hear nothing of what was said, above the general hubbub. He pushed through the outer ring of spectators, but was stopped nearer the center by the press of men. At least here, he could pick up a few words.

"We must! You know it, Hermon, there's no choice!" shouted a lanky man in a battered hat.

"There's *always* a choice!" Husband bellowed back. "Now is the time to choose, and God send we do it wisely!"

"Aye, with cannon pointed at us?"

"No, no, forward, we must go forward, or all is lost!"

"Lost? We have lost everything so far! We must—"

"The Governor's taken choice from us, we must—"

"We must—"

"We must—!"

All single words were lost in a general roar of anger and frustration. Seeing that there was nothing to be gained by waiting for an audience, Roger shoved his way ruthlessly between two farmers and seized Husband by the sleeve of his shirt.

"Mr. Husband—I must speak with you!" he shouted in the Quaker's ear.

Husband gave him a glazed sort of look, and made to shake him off, but then stopped, blinking as he recognized him. The square face was flushed with color above the sprouting beard, and Husband's coarse gray hair, unbound, bristled out from his head like the quills of a porcupine. He shook his head and shut his eyes, then opened them again, staring at Roger like a man seeking to dispel some impossible vision, and failing.

He grabbed Roger's arm, and with a fierce gesture at the crowd, leaped down from his rock and made off toward the shelter of a ramshackle cabin that leaned drunkenly in the shade of a maple grove. Roger followed, glaring round at those nearest to discourage pursuit.

A few followed, nonetheless, waving arms and expostulating hotly, but Roger slammed the door in their faces, and dropped the bolt, placing his back against the door for good measure. It was cooler inside, though the air was stale and smelt of wood-ash and burnt food.

Husband stood panting in the middle of the floor, then picked up a dipper and drank deeply from a bucket that stood upon the hearth—the only object left in the cabin, Roger saw. Husband's coat and hat hung neatly on a hook by the door, but bits of rubbish were scattered across the packed-earth floor. Whoever owned the cabin had evidently decamped in haste, carrying their portable belongings.

Calmed by the moment's respite, Husband straightened his rumpled shirt and made shift to tidy his hair.

"What does thee here, friend MacKenzie?" he asked, with characteristic mildness. "Thee does not come to join the cause of Regulation, surely?"

"Indeed I do not," Roger assured him. He cast a wary eye at the window, lest the crowd try to gain access that way, but while the rumble of voices outside continued their argument, there was no immediate sound of assault upon the building. "I have come to ask if you will go across the creek with me—under a flag of truce, your safety is assured—to speak with Jamie Fraser."

Husband glanced at the window, too.

"I fear the time for speaking has long passed," he said, with a wry twist of the lips. Roger was inclined to think so, too, but pressed on, determined to fulfill his commission.

"Not so far as the Governor is concerned. He has no wish

to slaughter his own citizenry; if the mob could be convinced to disperse peaceably—"

"Does it seem to thee a likely prospect?" Husband waved at the window, giving him a cynical glance.

"No," Roger was forced to admit. "Still, if you would come—if they could see that there was still some possibility of—"

"If there were possibility of reconciliation and redress, it should have been offered long since," Husband said sharply. "Is this a token of the Governor's sincerity, to come with troops and cannon, to send a letter that—"

"Not redress," Roger said bluntly. "I meant the possibility of saving all your lives."

Husband stood quite still. The ruddy color faded from his cheeks, though he looked still composed.

"Has it come to that?" he asked quietly, his eyes on Roger's face. Roger took a deep breath and nodded.

"There is not much time. Mr. Fraser bid me tell you—if you could not come to speak with him yourself—there are two companies of artillery arrayed against you, and eight of militia, all well-armed. All lies in readiness—and the Governor will not wait past dawn of tomorrow, at the latest."

He was aware that it was treason to give such information to the enemy—but it was what Jamie Fraser would have said, could he have come himself.

"There are near two thousand men of the Regulation here," Husband said, as though to himself. "Two thousand! Would thee not think the sight of it would sway him? That so many would leave home and hearth and come in protest—"

"It is the Governor's opinion that they come in rebellion, therefore in a state of war," Roger interrupted. He glanced at the window, where the oiled parchment covering hung in tatters. "And having seen them, I must say that I think he has reasonable grounds for that opinion."

"It is no rebellion," Husband said stubbornly. He drew himself up, and pulled a worn black silk ribbon from his pocket, with which to tie back his hair. "But our legitimate complaints have been ignored, disregarded! We have no choice but to come as a physical body, to lay our grievances before Mr. Tryon and thus impress him with the rightness of our objection."

"I thought I heard you speak of choice a few moments past," Roger said dryly. "And if now is the time to choose, as you say, it would seem to me that most of the Regulators have chosen violence—judging from such remarks as I heard on my way here."

"Perhaps," Husband said reluctantly. "Yet we—they—are not an avenging army, not a mob . . ." And yet his unwilling glance toward the window suggested his awareness that a mob was indeed what was forming on the banks of the Alamance.

"Do they have a chosen leader, anyone who can speak officially for them?" Roger interrupted again, impatient to deliver his message and be gone. "Yourself, or perhaps Mr. Hunter?"

Husband paused for a long moment, wiping the back of his hand across his mouth as though to expunge some lingering rancid taste. He shook his head.

"They have no real leader," he said softly. "Jim Hunter is bold enough, but he has no gift of commanding men. I asked him—he said that each man must act for himself."

"You have the gift. You can lead them."

Husband looked scandalized, as though Roger had accused him of a talent for card-sharping.

"Not I."

"You have led them here—"

"They have *come* here! I asked none to—"

"You are here. They followed you."

Husband flinched slightly at this, his lips compressed. Seeing that his words had some effect, Roger pressed his case.

"You spoke for them before, and they listened. They came with you, after you. They'll still listen, surely!"

He could hear the noise outside the cabin growing; the crowd was impatient. If it wasn't yet a mob, it was damn close. And what would they do if they knew who he was, and what he had come to do? His palms were sweating; he pressed them down across the fabric of his coat, feeling the small lump of his militia badge in the pocket, and wished he had paused to bury it somewhere when he crossed the creek.

Husband looked at him a moment, then reached out and seized him by both hands.

"Pray with me, friend," he said quietly.

"I—"

"Thee need say nothing," Husband said. "I know thee is Papist, but it is not our way to pray aloud. If thee would but remain still with me, and ask in your heart that wisdom be granted—not only to me, but to all here . . ."

Roger bit his tongue to keep from correcting Husband; his own religious affiliation was scarcely important at the moment, though evidently Husband's was. Instead he nodded, suppressing his impatience, and squeezed the older man's hands, offering what support he might.

Husband stood quite still, his head slightly lowered. A fist hammered on the flimsy door of the cabin, voices calling out.

"Hermon! You all right in there?"

"Come on, Hermon! There's no time for this! Caldwell's come back from the Governor—"

"An hour, Hermon! He's given us an hour, no more!"

A trickle of sweat ran down Roger's back between his shoulder blades, but he ignored the tickle, unable to reach it.

He glanced from Husband's weathered fingers to his face, and found the other man's eyes seemingly fixed on his own—and yet distant, as though he listened to some far-off voice, disregarding the urgent shouts that came through the walls. Even Husband's eyes were Quaker gray, Roger thought—like pools of rainwater, shivering into stillness after a storm.

Surely they would break down the door. But no; the blows diminished to an impatient knocking, and then to random thumps. He could feel the beating of his own heart, slowing gradually to a quiet, even throb in his chest, anxiety fading in his blood.

He closed his own eyes, trying to fix his thoughts, to do as Husband asked. He groped in his mind for some suitable prayer, but nothing save confused fragments of the Book of Common Worship came to hand.

Help us, O Lord . . .

Hear us . . .

Help us, O Lord, his father's voice whispered. His other father, the Reverend, speaking somewhere in the back of his mind. *Help us, O Lord, to remember how often men do wrong through want of thought, rather than from lack of love; and how cunning are the snares that trip our feet.*

Each word flickered briefly in his mind like a burning leaf, rising from a bonfire's wind, and then disappeared away into ash before he could grasp it. He gave it up then and simply stood, clasping Husband's hands in his own, listening to the man's breathing, a low rasping note.

Please, he thought silently, though with no idea what he was asking for. That word too evaporated, leaving nothing in its place.

Nothing happened. The voices still called outside, but they seemed of no more importance now than the calling of birds. The air in the room was still, but cool and lively, as though a draft played somewhere in the corners, not touching them where they stood in the center of the floor. Roger felt his own breath ease, his heart slow its beat still more.

He didn't remember opening his eyes, and yet they were open. Husband's soft gray eyes had flecks of blue in them, and tiny splinters of black. His lashes were thick, and there was a small swelling at the base of one, a healing sty. The tiny dome was smooth and red, fading from a ruby dot at the center through such successions of crimson, pink, and rose red as might have graced the dawn sky on the day of Creation.

The face before him was sculpted with lines that drew rough arcs from nose to mouth, that curved above the heavy, grizzled brows whose every hair was long and arched with the grace of a bird's wing. The lips were broad and smooth, a dusky rose; the white edge of a tooth glistened, strangely hard by contrast with the pliable flesh that sheltered it.

Roger stood without moving, wondering at the beauty of what he saw. The notion of Husband as a stocky man of middle age and indeterminate feature had no meaning; what he saw now was a heartbreaking singularity, a thing unique and wonderful; irreplaceable.

It struck him that this was the same feeling with which he had studied his infant son, marveling at the perfection of each small toe, the curve of cheek and ear that squeezed his heart, the radiance of the newborn skin that let the innocence within shine through. And here was the same creation, no longer new, perhaps less innocent, but no less marvelous.

He looked down and saw his own hands then, still gripping Husband's smaller ones. A sense of awe came on him, with the realization of the beauty of his own fingers, the curving bones of wrist and knuckle, the ravishing loveliness of a thin red scar that ran across the joint of his thumb.

Husband's breath left him in a deep sigh, and he pulled his hands away. Roger felt momentarily bereft, but then felt the peace of the room settle upon him once more, the astonishment of beauty succeeded by a sense of deep calm.

"I thank thee, Friend Roger," Husband said softly. "I had not hoped to receive such grace—but it is welcome."

Roger nodded, wordless. He watched as Husband took down his coat and put it on, his face settled now in lines of calm determination. Without hesitation, the Quaker lifted the bolt from the door and pushed it open.

The crowd of men outside fell back, the surprise on their faces giving way at once to eagerness and irritation. Husband ignored the storm of questions and exhortations, and walked directly to a horse that stood tethered to a sapling behind the cabin. He untied it and swung up into the saddle, and only then looked down into the faces of his fellow Regulators.

"Go home!" he said, in a loud voice. "We must leave this place; each man must return to his own home!"

This announcement was met with a moment of stunned silence, and then by cries of puzzlement and outrage.

"What home?" called a young man with a scraggly ginger beard. "Maybe you got a home to go to—I ain't!"

Husband sat solid in his saddle, unmoved by the outcry.

"Go home!" he shouted again. "I exhort you—nothing but violence remains to be done here!"

"Aye, and we'll bloody do it!" bellowed one thickset man, thrusting his musket overhead, to a ragged chorus of cheers.

Roger had followed Husband, and was largely ignored by the Regulators. He stood at a little distance, watching as the Quaker began slowly to ride away, bending down from his saddle as he did so, to shout and gesture to the men who ran and shoved beside him. One man grabbed Husband by the sleeve, and the Quaker drew up his rein, leaning down to listen to what was obviously an impassioned speech.

At the end of it, though, he straightened up, shaking his head, and clapped his hat on.

"I cannot stay and let blood be shed by my staying. If thee remain here, friends, there will be murder done. Leave! Thee can still go—I pray thee do so!"

He was no longer shouting, but the noise around him had ceased long enough for his words to carry. He raised a face creased with worry, and saw Roger standing in the shadow of a dogwood. The stillness of peace had left him, but Roger saw that the look of determination was still there in his eyes.

"I am going!" he called. "I beg thee all—go home!" He reined his horse round with sudden decision, and kicked it into a trot. A few men ran after him, but soon stopped. They turned back, looking puzzled and resentful, muttering in small groups and shaking their heads in confusion.

The noise was rising again, as everyone talked at once, arguing, insisting, denying. Roger turned away, walking quietly toward the cover of the maple grove. It seemed wiser to be gone as soon as possible, now that Husband had departed.

A hand seized him by the shoulder, and spun him round.

"Who the hell are you? What did you say to Hermon to make him go?" A grimy fellow in a ragged leather vest confronted him, fists clenched. The man looked angry, ready to take out his frustration on the nearest available object.

"I told him that the Governor doesn't want anyone to be harmed, if it can be avoided," Roger said, in what he hoped was a calming tone.

"Do you come from the Governor?" a black-bearded man asked skeptically, eyeing Roger's grubby homespun. "D'ye come to offer different terms than Caldwell has?"

"No." Roger had been still under the effects of the meeting with Husband, feeling sheltered from the currents of anger and incipient hysteria that swirled about the cabin, but the peace of it was fading fast. Others were coming to join his interrogators, attracted by the sound of confrontation.

"No," he said again, louder. "I came to warn Husband—to warn all of you. The Governor wants—"

He was interrupted by a chorus of rude shouts, indicating that what Tryon wanted was a matter of no concern to those present. He glanced around the circle of faces, but saw none that offered any expression of forbearance, let alone friendliness. He shrugged then, and stepped back.

"You'll suit yourselves, then," he said, as coolly as possible. "Mr. Husband gave you his best advice—I second it." He turned to leave, but was gripped by a pair of hands that descended on his shoulders, pulling him forcibly around to face the ring of questioners once more.

"Not so fast, chuck," said the man in the leather vest. He was still flushed with angry excitement, but his fists were no longer clenched. "You've spoke with Tryon, have you?"

"No," Roger admitted. "I was sent—" He hesitated; ought he to use Jamie Fraser's name? No, better not; it was as likely to cause trouble as to save it. "I came to ask Hermon Husband to come across the creek and discover for himself how matters stand. He chose instead to accept my account of the situation. You saw what his response was."

"So *you* say!" A burly man with ginger sidewhiskers raised his chin pugnaciously. "And why should anyone accept your account of the situation?" He mimicked Roger's clipped Scots in a burlesque that brought laughter from his comrades.

The calm he had carried from the cabin had not altogether left him; Roger gathered its remnants about him and spoke quietly.

"I cannot compel you to listen, sir. But for those who have ears—hear this." He looked from one face to another, and reluctantly, one by one, they left off making noise, until he stood as the center of a ring of unwilling attention.

"The Governor's troops stand ready and well-armed." His voice sounded odd to his own ears, calm but somehow muffled, as though someone else were speaking, some distance away. "I have not seen the Governor myself, but I have heard his stated purpose: he does not wish to see blood shed, but he is determined to take such actions as he perceives necessary to disperse this assembly. Yet if you will return peaceably to your homes, he is disposed to leniency."

A moment of silence greeted this, to be broken by a hawking noise. A glob of mucus, streaked brown with tobacco juice, landed with a splat in the mud near Roger's boot.

"That," observed the spitter concisely, "for the Governor's leniency."

"And that for you, fuckwit!" said one of his companions, swinging an open palm toward Roger's face.

He ducked the blow, and lowering his shoulder, charged the man, who staggered off-balance and gave way. There were more beyond him, though; Roger stopped, fists balled, ready to defend himself if need be.

"Don't hurt him, boys," called the man in the leather vest. "Not yet, anyways." He sidled round Roger, keeping well out of range of his fists, and eyed him warily.

"Whether you've seen Tryon's face or not, reckon you've seen his troops, haven't you?"

"I have." Roger's heart was beating fast, and the blood sang in his temples, but oddly enough, he wasn't afraid. The crowd was hostile, but not bloodthirsty—not yet.

"So how many men does Tryon have?" The man was watching him closely, with a glint in his eye. Best to answer honestly; the odds were good that the answer was already known; there was nothing whatever to hinder men of the Regulation from crossing the Alamance and assessing the situation for themselves.

"A few more than a thousand," Roger said, watching the man's face carefully. No surprise; he *had* known. "But they are trained militia," Roger added pointedly, with a glance at a number of the Regulators, who, having lost interest in Roger, had resumed a wrestling match nearby. "And they have artillery. I think you have none, sir?"

The man's face closed like a fist.

"Think what you like," he said shortly. "But you can tell Tryon that we boast twice his number. And be we *trained* or not—" his mouth twisted ironically, "we are all armed, each man with his musket." He tilted back his head, squinting against the light.

"An hour, is it?" he asked, more softly. "Sooner than that, I think." He lowered his gaze, looking Roger in the eye.

"Go you back across the creek, then, sir. Tell Governor Tryon that we mean to have our say, and have our way of it. If he will listen and do as we demand, well and good. If not . . ." He touched the hilt of the pistol in his belt, and nodded once, his face settling into grim lines.

Roger glanced around at the circle of silent faces. Some bore looks of uncertainty, but most were sullen or openly defiant. He turned without a word and walked away, the Reverend's words whispering among the spring leaves as he passed beneath the trees.

Blessed are the peacemakers: for they shall be called the children of God.

He hoped one got credit for trying.

63

THE SURGEON'S BOOK I

Item #28 - *The Surgeons to keep a Book and enter each Man that comes under his care, Vixt. the Mans Name, the Company he belongs to, the Day he comes under his Hands, and the day he discharges him.*

—"*Camp Duties and Regulations*"

I FELT A COOL BREEZE touch my cheek, and shivered, though the day was very warm. I had the sudden absurd thought that it was the glancing touch of a wing-feather, as though the Angel of Death had silently passed by me, intent on his dark business.

"Nonsense," I said aloud. Evan Lindsay heard me; I saw his head turn momentarily, but then turn back. Like all the others, he kept glancing toward the east.

People who don't believe in telepathy have never set foot on a battlefield, nor served with an army. Something passes unseen from man to man when an army is about to move; the air itself is live with feeling. Half dread, half eagerness, it dances over the skin and bores the length of the spine with an urgency like sudden lust.

No messenger had come yet, but one would, I knew it. Something had happened, somewhere.

Everyone stood rooted, waiting. I felt an overwhelming urge to move, to break that spell, and turned abruptly, my hands flexing with the need to stir, to do something. The kettle had boiled, the water sat ready, covered with a piece of clean linen. I had set up my medicine chest on a stump; I put back the lid and began to go mindlessly through its contents yet again, though I knew all was in order.

I touched the gleaming bottles one by one, their names a soothing litany.

Atropine, Belladonna, Laudanum, Paregoric, Oil of Lavender, Oil of Juniper, Pennyroyal, Lady's-vetch, . . . and the squat brown-glass bottle of alcohol. Always alcohol. I had a keg of it, still on the wagon.

Movement caught my eye; it was Jamie, the sun sparking on his hair through the leaves as he moved quietly under the trees, bending here to speak a word in someone's ear, touching there a shoulder, like a magician bringing statues to life.

I stood still, hands twisted in the folds of my apron, not wanting to distract him, yet wanting very much to attract his attention. He moved easily, joking, touching casually—and yet I could see the tension in him. When had he last stood with an army, waiting the order to charge?

At Culloden, I thought, and the hairs rippled erect on my forearms, pale in the spring sun.

Hoofsteps sounded nearby, and the crashing sound of horses moving through brush. Everyone swung round in expectation, muskets held loose in their hands. There was a general gasp and murmur as the first rider came into view, ducking her bright red head beneath the maple boughs.

"Holy Christ," Jamie said, loudly enough to be heard across the clearing. "What in hell is *she* doing here?" There was a ripple of laughter from the men who knew her, fracturing the tension like cracks in ice. Jamie's shoulders relaxed, very slightly, but his face was rather grim as he strode to meet her.

By the time Brianna had pulled up her horse and swung down from her saddle next to him, I had reached them, too.

"What—" I began, but Jamie was already nose to nose with his daughter, his hand on her arm, eyes narrowed and speaking in a rapid torrent of low-voiced Gaelic.

"I'm that sorry, Mum, but she *would* come." A second horse ambled out of the trees, an apologetic-looking young black man on top. It was Joshua, Jocasta's groom. "I couldna prevent her, nor could Missus Sherston. We did try."

"So I see," I said.

Brianna's color had risen in response to whatever Jamie was saying to her, but she showed no sign of getting back on her horse and leaving. She said something to him, also in Gaelic, that I didn't catch, and he reared back as though stung on the nose by a wasp. She nodded sharply once, as though satisfied with the impact of her statement, and turned on her heel. Then she saw me, and a wide smile transformed her face.

"Mama!" She embraced me, her gown smelling faintly of fresh soap, beeswax, and turpentine. There was a small streak of cobalt-blue paint on her jaw.

"Hallo, darling. Wherever did you come from?" I kissed her cheek and stood back, cheered by the sight of her, in spite of everything. She was dressed very plainly, in the rough brown homespun she wore on the Ridge, but the clothes were fresh and clean. Her long red hair was tied back in a plait, and a broad straw hat hung from its strings down her back.

"Hillsborough," she said. "Someone who came to dinner at the Sherstons' last night told us that the militia was camped here—so I came. I brought some food"— she waved at the bulging saddlebags on her horse—"and some herbs from the Sherstons' garden I thought you might use."

"Oh? Oh, yes. Lovely." I was uneasily aware of Jamie's glowering presence somewhere behind me, but didn't look around. "Ah . . . I don't mean to sound as though I'm not pleased to see you, darling, but there is just possibly going to be a fight here before too long, and . . . ."

"I know that." Her color was still high, and it deepened somewhat at this. She raised her voice slightly.

"That's all right; I didn't come to fight. If I had, I would have worn my breeches." She darted a glance over my shoulder, and I heard a loud snort from that direction, followed by guffaws from the Lindsay brothers. She lowered her head to hide a grin, and I couldn't help smiling, too.

"I'll stay with you," she said, lowering her voice as well, and touching my arm. "If there's nursing to be done . . . afterward—I can help."

I hesitated, but there was no question that if things did come to a fight, there would be wounded to treat, and an extra pair of hands would be useful. Brianna wasn't skilled at nursing, but she did understand about germs and antisepsis, knowledge of much more value in its way than a grasp of anatomy or physiology.

Bree had straightened. Her glance flickered over the men who waited in the maples' shade, searching.

"Where's Roger?" she asked, her voice low but level.

"He's all right," I assured her, hoping it was true. "Jamie sent him across the creek this morning, with a flag of truce, to bring back Hermon Husband to talk with the Governor."

"He's over *there*?" Her voice rose involuntarily, and she lowered it, self-conscious. "With the enemy? If that's the right word for them."

"He'll be back." Jamie stood by my elbow, viewing his daughter with no great favor, but obviously resigned to her presence. "Dinna fash, lassie. No one will trouble him, under a flag of truce."

Bree raised her head, looking as far as she could into the distance toward the creek. Her face had drawn in upon itself, a pale knot of apprehension.

“Will a flag of truce help him if he’s still over there when the shooting starts?”

The answer to that—which she obviously knew—was “Probably not.” So did Jamie, who didn’t bother saying it. He also didn’t bother saying that perhaps it wouldn’t come to shooting; the air was thick with anticipation, acrid with the scent of spilled black powder and nervous sweat.

“He’ll be back,” Jamie repeated, though in a gentler tone. He touched her face, smoothing back a random lock of hair. “I promise, lass. He’ll be all right.”

The look of apprehension faded a bit as she searched his face. She seemed to find some reassurance there, for a little of the tension left her, and she nodded, in mute acceptance. Jamie leaned forward and kissed her on the forehead, then turned away to speak to Rob Byrnes.

Bree stood looking after him for a moment, then untied the strings of her bonnet and came to sit down beside me on a rock. Her hands were trembling slightly; she took a deep breath, and clasped her knees to still them.

“Is there anything I can do to help now?” she asked, with a nod toward my open medicine box. “Do you need me to fetch anything?”

I shook my head.

“No, I have everything I need. There isn’t anything to do but wait.” I grimaced slightly. “That’s the hardest part.”

She made a small sound of reluctant agreement, and relaxed, with a visible effort. She assessed the waiting equipment, a slight frown between her brows: the fire, the boiling water, the folding table, the large instrument box, and the smaller pack that held my emergency kit.

“What’s in there?” she asked, poking a boot-shod toe at the canvas sack.

“Alcohol and bandages, a scalpel, forceps, amputation saw, tourniquets. They’ll bring the wounded here, if they can, or to one of the other surgeons. But if I have to go to a man wounded on the field—someone too bad to walk or be carried—I can snatch that up and go at once.”

I heard her swallow, and when I glanced up at her, the freckles stood out on the bridge of her nose. She nodded, and drew a deep breath to speak. Her face changed suddenly, though, switching comically from seriousness to repugnance. She sniffed once, suspiciously, her long nose wrinkling like an anteater's.

I could smell it, too; the stink of fresh feces, coming from the grove directly behind us.

"That's rather common before a battle," I said, low-voiced, trying not to laugh at her expression. "They're caught short, poor things."

She cleared her throat and didn't say anything, but I saw her gaze roam round the clearing, resting now on one man, then another. I knew what she was thinking. How was it possible? How could one look at such an orderly, compact bundle as a man, head bent to catch a friend's words, arm stretched to take a canteen, face moving from smile to frown, eyes lighted and muscles taut—and envision rupture, abrasion, fracture . . . and death?

It couldn't be done. It was an act of the imagination that lay beyond the capability of one who hadn't ever seen that particular obscene transformation.

It could, however, be remembered. I coughed, and leaned forward, hoping to distract us both.

"Whatever did you say to your father?" I asked, out of the side of my mouth. "When you came, when you were speaking Gaelic."

"Oh, that." A slight flush of amusement momentarily relieved her paleness. "He was snarling at me, wanting to know what I thought I was playing at—did I mean to leave my child an orphan, he said, risking my life along with Roger's?" She wiped a strand of red hair away from her mouth, and gave me a small, edgy smile. "So I said to him, if it was so dangerous, where did he get off, risking making *me* an orphan by having you here, hm?"

I laughed, though keeping that, too, under my breath.

"It's not dangerous for you, is it?" she asked, surveying the militia encampment. "Back here, I mean?"

I shook my head.

"No. If the fighting comes anywhere close, we'll move, right away. But I don't think—"

I was interrupted by the sound of a horse, coming fast, and was on my feet, along with the rest of the camp, by the time the messenger appeared; one of Tryon's baby-faced aides, pale with bottled-up excitement.

"Stand ready," he said, hanging out of his saddle, half-breathless.

"And what d'ye think we've been doing since dawn?" Jamie demanded, impatient. "What in God's name is happening, man?"

Very little, apparently, but that little was important enough. A minister from the Regulators' side had come to parley with the Governor.

"A minister?" Jamie interrupted. "A Quaker, do you mean?"

"I do not, sir," said the aide, annoyed at being interrupted. "Quakers have no clergy, anyone knows as much. No, it was a minister named Caldwell, the Reverend David Caldwell."

Regardless of religious affiliation, Tryon had been unmoved by the ambassador's appeal. He could not, would not, deal with a mob, and there was an end to it. Let the Regulators disperse, and he would promise to consider any just complaints laid before him in a proper manner. But disperse they must, within an hour.

"Could you, would you, in a box?" I murmured under my breath, half unhinged by the waiting. "Could you, would you, with a fox?" Jamie had taken off his hat, and the sun shone bright on his ruddy hair. Bree gave a strangled giggle, as much shock as amusement.

"He could not, would not, with a mob," she murmured back. "Could not, would not . . . do the job?"

"He can, though," I said, sotto voce. "And I'm very much afraid he will." For the hundredth time that morning, I glanced toward the scrim of willows through which Roger had disappeared on his errand.

"An hour," Jamie repeated, in answer to the aide's message. He glanced in the same direction, toward the creek. "And how much time is left of that?"

"Perhaps half an hour." The aide looked suddenly much younger even than his years. He swallowed, and put on his hat. "I must go, sir. Listen for the cannon, sir, and luck to you!"

"And with you, sir." Jamie touched the aide's arm in

farewell, then slapped the horse's rump with his hat, sending it off.

As though it had been a signal, the camp sprang into a flurry of activity, even before the Governor's aide had disappeared through the trees. Weapons already primed and loaded were checked and rechecked, buckles unfastened and refastened, badges polished, hats beaten free of dust and cockades affixed, stockings pulled up and tightly gartered, filled canteens shaken for reassurance that their contents had not evaporated in the last quarter-hour.

It was catching. I found myself running my fingers over the rows of glass bottles in the chest yet again, the names murmuring and blurring in my mind like the words of someone telling rosary beads, sense lost in the fervor of petition. *Rosemary, atropine, lavender, oil of cloves . . .*

Bree was notable for her stillness among all this bustle. She sat on her rock, with no movement save the stir of a random breeze in her skirts, her eyes fixed on the distant trees. I heard her say something, under her breath, and turned.

"What did you say?"

"It's not in the books." She didn't take her eyes off the trees, and her hands were knotted in her lap, squeezing together as though she could will Roger to appear through the willows. She lifted her chin, gesturing toward the field, the trees, the men around us.

"This," she said. "It's not in the history books. I read about the Boston Massacre. I saw it *there*, in the history books, and I saw it *here*, in the newspaper. But I never saw this there. I never read a word about Governor Tryon, or North Carolina, or a place called Alamance. So nothing's going to happen." She spoke fiercely, willing it. "If there was a big battle here, someone would have written *something* about it. Nobody did—so nothing's going to happen. Nothing!"

"I hope you're right," I said, and felt a small warming of the chill in the small of my back. Perhaps she was. Surely it couldn't be a major battle, at least. We were no more than four years from the outbreak of the Revolution; even the minor skirmishes preceding that conflict were well-known.

The Boston Massacre had happened a little more than a year before—a street-fight, a clash between a mob and a platoon of nervous soldiers. Shouted insults, a few stones thrown. An unauthorized shot, a panicked volley, and five men dead. It had been reported, with a good deal of fierce editorializing, in one of the Boston newspapers; I had seen it, in Jocasta's parlor; one of her friends had sent her a copy.

And two hundred years later, that brief incident was immortalized in children's textbooks, evidence of the rising disaffection of the Colonists. I glanced at the men who stood around us, preparing to fight. Surely, if there was to be a major battle here, a Royal Governor putting down what was essentially a taxpayer's rebellion, that would have been worth noting!

Still, that was theory. And I was uneasily aware that neither warfare nor history took much account of what *should* happen.

Jamie was standing by Gideon, whom he had tethered to a tree. He would go into battle with his men, on foot. He was taking his pistols from the saddlebag, putting away the extra ammunition in the pouch at his belt. His head was bent, absorbed in the details of what he was doing.

I felt a sudden, dreadful urgency. I must touch him, must say something. I tried to tell myself that Bree was right; this was nothing; likely not even a shot would be fired—and yet there were three thousand armed men here on the banks of the Alamance, and the knowledge of bloodshed hummed and buzzed among them.

I left Brianna sitting on her rock, burning eyes fixed on the wood, and hurried to him.

"Jamie," I said, and put a hand on his arm.

It was like touching a high-voltage wire; power hummed inside the insulation of his flesh, ready to erupt in a burst of crackling light. They say one can't let go of such a line; a victim of electrocution simply freezes to the wire, helpless to move or save himself, as the current burns through brain and heart.

He put his hand on mine, looking down.

"A nighean donn," he said, and smiled a little. "Have ye come to wish me luck, then?"

I smiled back as best I could, though the current sizzled through me, stiffening the muscles of my face as it burned.

"I couldn't let you go without saying . . . something. I suppose 'Good luck' will do." I hesitated, words jamming in my throat with the sudden urge to say much more than there was time for. In the end, I said only the important things. "Jamie—I love you. Be careful!"

He didn't remember Culloden, he said. I wondered suddenly whether that loss of memory extended to the hours just before the battle, when he and I had said farewell. Then I looked into his eyes and knew it did not.

" 'Good luck' will do," he said, and his hand tightened on mine, likewise frozen to the current that surged between us. " 'I love ye' does much better."

He touched my hand, lifted his own and touched my hair, my face, looking into my eyes as though to capture my image in this moment—just in case it should be his last glimpse of me.

"There may come a day when you and I shall part again," he said softly, at last, and his fingers brushed my lips, light as the touch of a falling leaf. He smiled faintly. "But it willna be today."

The notes of a bugle came through the trees, far away, but piercing as a woodpecker's call. I turned, looking. Brianna sat still as a statue on her rock, looking toward the wood.

64

SIGNAL FOR ACTION

Note, when on the March the discharge of three Pieces of Cannon will be the signal to form the line of Battle, and five the signal for Action.

—Order of Battle, Wm. Tryon

ROGER WALKED SLOWLY away from the Regulators' camp, willing himself neither to run nor to look back. A few shouted insults and half-meant threats were hurled in his direction, but by the time he was well into the trees, the crowd had lost interest in him, drawn back into its buzzing controversy. It was past noon, and a hot day for May, but he found his shirt sweat-soaked and clinging to him in a manner more befitting July.

He stopped as soon as he was out of sight. He was breathing fast, and felt dizzy, slightly sick with the aftereffects of adrenaline. In the center of that ring of hostile faces, he hadn't felt a thing—not a thing. Safely away, though, the muscles of his legs were trembling and his fists ached from clenching. He uncurled them, flexed his stiff fingers, and tried to slow his breathing.

Maybe a bit more like the night-time Channel and the anti-aircraft guns than he'd thought, after all.

He'd made it back, though; would be going home to his wife and son. The thought gave him a queer pang; bone-deep relief, and an even deeper grief, quite unexpected, for his father, who hadn't been so lucky.

A slight breeze played about him, lifting the damp hairs on his neck with a breath of welcome coolness. He'd sweated through shirt and coat together, and his damp stock felt suddenly as though it would strangle him. He shucked his coat and pawed at the neckband, jerking it off with shaking fingers, then stood with his eyes closed and the piece of cloth dangling from his hand, breathing great draughts of air, until the momentary sense of nausea subsided.

He called to mind his last sight of Brianna, framed in the doorway, Jemmy in her arms. He saw her lashes wet with tears and the baby's round solemn eyes, and felt a deep echo of the feeling he had experienced in the cabin with Husband; a vision of beauty, a conviction of joy that soothed his mind and eased his soul. He would go back to them; that was all that mattered.

After a moment, he opened his eyes, picked up his coat,

and set off, beginning to feel more settled in body, if not in mind, as he made his way slowly back toward the creek.

He hadn't brought back Husband to Jamie, but he had achieved as much as Jamie himself might have. It was possible that the mob—they were no army, whatever Tryon thought of them—would in fact fall apart, disperse now and go home, deprived of even the faint semblance of leadership Husband had provided. He hoped so.

Or they might not. Another man might rise out of that seething mob, one fit to take command. A thought struck him, with a phrase recalled from the confusion near the cabin.

"D'ye come to offer different terms than Caldwell has?" The man with the black beard had asked him that. And earlier, dimly heard through the pounding at the door of the cabin, as he stood in prayer with Husband—*"There's no time for this!"* someone had shouted. *"Caldwell's come back from the Governor—"* and someone else had added, in tones of desperation, *"An hour, Hermon! He's given us an hour, no more!"*

"Shit," he said, aloud. David Caldwell, the Presbyterian minister who had married him and Bree. It must be. Evidently the man had gone to speak with Tryon on the Regulators' behalf—and been rebuffed, with a warning.

"An hour, no more." An hour to disperse, to leave peaceably? Or an hour to reply to some ultimatum?

He glanced up; the sun stood overhead, just a bit past noon. He pulled on his coat and stuffed the discarded stock in his pocket, next to the unused flag of truce. Whatever it meant, that hour's grace, it was clearly time to be going.

The day was still bright and hot, the smell of grass and tree-leaves pungent with rising sap. Now, though, his sense of urgency and his memory of the Regulators, buzzing like hornets, deprived him of any appreciation of the beauties of nature. Even so, some trace of peace remained deep within him as he made his way quickly toward the creek; a faint echo of what he had felt in the cabin.

That odd sense of awe had stayed with him, hidden but accessible, like a smooth stone in his pocket. He turned it over in his mind as he made his way toward the creek, largely oblivious to clutching brambles and brush in his path.

How peculiar, he thought. Nothing whatever had *happened*, and in fact the entire experience had felt quite ordinary—nothing otherworldly or supernatural about it. And yet, having seen by that particular clear light, he could not forget it. Could he explain it to Brianna? he wondered.

A trailing branch brushed past his face and he reached to push it aside, feeling even as he did so a faint surprise at the cool green gloss of the leaves, the odd delicacy of their edges, jagged as knives but paper-light. An echo, faint but recognizable, of what he had seen before, that piercing beauty. Did Claire see that? he thought suddenly. Did she see the touch of beauty in the bodies beneath her hands? Was that perhaps how—and why—she was a healer?

Husband had seen it, too, he knew; had shared that perception. And seeing it, had been confirmed in his Quaker principles, and had left the field, unable either to do violence or to countenance it.

And what of his own principles? He supposed they were unchanged; if he hadn't meant to shoot anyone before, he could mean it still less, now.

The scents of spring still hung in the air, and a small blue butterfly floated past his knee with no apparent sense of care. It was still a fine spring day, but all illusion of tranquillity had vanished. The smell of sweat, of dirt and fear and anger, that seemed to hang in the air of the encampment, was still in his nostrils, mingling with the cleaner scents of trillium and water.

What about Jamie Fraser's principles? he wondered, turning past the thicket of willow that marked the ford. He often wondered what made Fraser tick, drawn both by a personal liking for the man, and by his colder historian's curiosity. Roger had made his own decision regarding this conflict—or had it made for him. He couldn't in conscience intend harm to anyone, though he supposed he could defend his own life, if needful. But Jamie?

He was fairly sure that Jamie's sympathies, as such, lay with the Regulators. He thought it likely also that his father-in-law had no sense of personal loyalty to the Crown; oath or no oath, surely no man could have lived through Culloden and its aftermath and emerged with any notion that he owed the King of England fealty, let alone anything more substantial. No, not to the Crown, but perhaps to William Tryon?

No loyalty of a personal nature there, either—but there was definitely an obligation felt. Tryon had summoned Jamie Fraser, and he had come. Given conditions as they stood, he had had little choice about that. Having come, though—would he fight?

How could he not? He must lead his men, and if it came to a battle—Roger glanced over his shoulder, as though the cloud of anger that hung over the Regulators' army might be now visible, swelling dark above the treetops—yes, he would have to fight, no matter what his private feelings on the matter might be.

Roger tried to envision himself aiming a musket at a man with whom he had no quarrel and pulling the trigger. Or worse, riding down a neighbor, sword in hand. Smashing in Kenny Lindsay's head, for instance? Imagination failed completely. No wonder that Jamie had sought to enlist Husband's help in ending the conflict before it began!

Still, Claire had told him once that Jamie had fought in France as a mercenary, as a young man. He *had* presumably killed men with whom he had no quarrel. How—

He pushed through the willows, and heard their voices before he saw them. A group of women were working on the near side of the stream; camp-followers. Some crouched bare-legged in the shallows, washing, others were carrying wet laundry up the bank, to be hung from trees and bushes. His eye passed casually beyond them, then jerked back, caught by . . . what? What was it?

There. He couldn't say why he had spotted her at all—there was nothing even faintly distinctive about her. And yet she stood out among the other women as though she had been outlined, drawn with black ink to stand out against the backdrop of stream and budding foliage.

"Morag," he whispered, and his heart thumped suddenly with a small shock of joy. She was alive.

He was halfway through the screen of willows before it occurred to him to wonder what he was doing, let alone why he was doing it. It was too late by then, though; he was already out on the bank, walking openly toward them.

Several of the women glanced at him; a few half-froze, watchful. But he was only one man, unarmed. There were more than twenty women by the river, their own men nearby. They watched him, curious, but not alarmed, as he splashed across the shallow creek.

She stood stock-still, knee-deep in the water, her skirts kirtled high, and watched him come. She knew him, he could see, but she gave him no sign of acknowledgment.

The other women fell back slightly, wary of him. She stood among the darting dragonflies, strands of brown hair poking out from her cap, a wet smock held forgotten in her hands. He stepped up out of the water and stood before her, wet to the knees.

"Mrs. MacKenzie," he said softly. "Well met."

A tiny smile touched the corner of her mouth. Her eyes were brown; he hadn't noticed that before.

"Mr. MacKenzie," she said, and gave him a small nod. His mind was working, thinking what to do. He must warn her, but how? Not before all the other women.

He stood helpless and awkward for a moment, not knowing what to do, then, inspired, he stooped and seized an armload of dripping laundry where it swirled in the water near her legs. He turned and clambered up the bank with it, Morag following in sudden haste.

"What are ye doing?" she demanded. "Here, come back wi' my clothes!"

He carried the wad of wet clothes a short way into the trees, then dropped them casually into a bush, mindful enough of the effort of washing not to let them drag in the dirt. Morag was right behind him, face flushed with indignation.

"What d'ye think you're about, ye thievin' clotheid?" she demanded heatedly. "Give those back!"

"I'm not stealing them," Roger assured her. "I only wanted to talk to you alone for a bit."

"Oh, aye?" She gave him a suspicious glance. "What about, then?"

He smiled at her; she was still thin, he saw, but her arms were brown and her small face a healthy color—she was clean, and she had lost the pallid, bruised look she had had on board the *Gloriana*.

"I wished to ask if you are well," he said softly. "And your child—Jemmy?" To speak the name gave him an odd frisson, and for a split second he saw the image of Brianna in the doorway, her son in her arms, laid over his memory of Morag, holding her baby in the dimness of the hold, ready to kill or die to keep him.

"Oh," she said, and the suspicion faded slightly, replaced by a reluctant acknowledgment of his right to ask. "We're well . . . the both of us. And my husband, too," she added pointedly.

"I'm pleased to hear it," he assured her. "Very pleased." He groped for something else to say, feeling awkward. "I—had thought of you now and then . . . wondered whether—whether everything was all right. When I saw you just now . . . well, I thought I'd ask, that's all."

"Oh, aye. Aye, I see. Well, I do thank ye, Mr. MacKenzie." She looked up and met his eyes directly as she said it, her own gaze brown and earnest. "I ken what ye did for us. I'll not forget; ye're in my prayers each night."

"Oh." Roger felt as though some soft weight had struck him in the breast. "Ahh . . . thank you." He had wondered, now and then, if she ever thought of him. Did she remember the kiss he had given her, there in the hold, seeking the spark of her warmth as some shield against the chill of loneliness? He cleared his throat, flushing at the memory.

"You—live nearby?"

She shook her head, and some thought, some memory, tightened her mouth.

"We did, but now—well, that's no matter." She turned, suddenly businesslike, and began to take her wet clothes from the bush, shaking each one before folding it. "I do thank ye for your concern, Mr. MacKenzie."

He was clearly dismissed. He wiped his hands down his breeks and shifted his feet, not wanting to leave. He must tell her—but having found her again, he was oddly reluctant simply to warn her and leave; curiosity bubbled in him—curiosity and a peculiar sense of connection.

Perhaps not so peculiar; this small brown woman was his

relative, his own family—the only person of his own blood he had known since the death of his parents. At the same time, it was *very* peculiar, he realized, even as his hand reached out and curved around her arm. She was his many-times great-grandmother, after all.

She stiffened, tried to pull away, but he kept hold of her forearm. Her skin was cold from the water, but he felt her pulse throb under his fingers.

"Wait," he said. "Please. Just a moment. I—I need to tell you . . . things."

"No, ye don't. I'd rather ye didn't." She pulled harder, and her hand slid through his, pulled free.

"Your husband. Where is he?" Belated realizations were forming in his brain. If she did not live nearby, then she was what he had first thought when he saw the women—a camp-follower. She was not a whore, he would stake his life on that; so she followed her husband, which meant—

"He is very nearby!" She backed up a step, eyeing the distance between herself and the remnants of her laundry. Roger stood between her and the bush; she would have to pass near him in order to retrieve her petticoats and stockings.

Realizing suddenly that she was slightly afraid of him, he turned hastily, grabbing a handful of things at random.

"I'm sorry. Your laundry . . . here." He thrust them at her, and she reached to take them by reflex. Something fell—a baby's gown—and both ducked to reach for it, cracking foreheads with a solid smack.

"Oh! Oh! Mary and Bride!" Morag clutched her head, though she still clasped the wet clothes against her bosom with one hand.

"Christ, are you all right? Morag—Mrs. MacKenzie—are you all right? I'm very sorry!" Roger touched her shoulder, squinting at her through eyes that watered with pain. He stooped to pick up the tiny gown that had fallen to the ground between them, and made a vain effort to wipe the smears of mud off the wet cloth. She blinked, eyes similarly watering, and laughed at his expression of dismay.

The collision had somehow broken the tension between them; she stepped back, but seemed not to feel threatened now.

"Aye, I'm fine." She sniffed and wiped her eyes, then touched the spot on her forehead gingerly. "I've got a thick skull, my Mam always said. Are you all right yourself, then?"

"Aye, fine." Roger touched his own forehead, suddenly and tinglingly aware that the curve of the browbone under his fingers was precisely echoed on the face before him. Hers was smaller, lighter—but just the same.

"I've a thick skull, too." He grinned at her, feeling ridiculously happy. "It runs in my family."

He handed her the mud-stained shirt, carefully.

"I *am* sorry," he said, apologizing again—and not only for the ruined laundry. "Your husband. I asked about him because—is he one of the Regulators, then?"

She looked at him curiously, one brow lifted.

"Of course. Are ye not with the Regulation yourself?"

Of course. Here on this side of Alamance, what else? Tryon's troops were drawn up in good military order on the field beyond the creek; over here, the Regulators swarmed like bees, without leadership or direction, an angry mass buzzing with random violence.

"No," he said. "I've come with the militia." He waved toward the distant smudge, where the smoke of Tryon's campfires hung, far beyond the creek. Her eyes grew wary again, but not frightened; he was only one man.

"That's the thing I wanted to tell you," he said. "To warn you, and your husband. The Governor is serious this time; he's brought organized troops, he's brought cannon. Lots of troops, all armed." He leaned toward her, holding out the rest of the wet stockings. She reached out a hand to take them, but kept her eyes on his, waiting.

"He means to put down this rebellion, by any means necessary. He has given orders to kill, if there is resistance. Do you understand? You must tell your husband, make him leave before—before anything happens."

She paled, and her hand went reflexively to her belly. The wet from the clothes had soaked through her muslin dress, and he saw the small swelling that had been hidden there, round and smooth as a melon under the damp cloth. He felt the jolt of her fear go through him, as though the wet stockings she held conducted electricity.

"We did, but not now . . ." she had said, when he asked whether they lived nearby. She might mean only that they had moved to some new place, but . . . there were baby's things in her wash; her son was with her here. Her husband was somewhere in this boiling of men.

A single man might pick up his gun and join a mob, for no reason beyond drink or boredom; a married man with a child would not. That spoke of serious disaffection, consequential grievance. And to bring both wife and child to war suggested that he had no safe place to leave them.

Roger thought it likely that Morag and her husband had no home at all now, and he understood her fear perfectly. If her husband should be maimed or killed, how was she to provide for Jemmy, for the new baby swelling under her skirt? She had no one, no family here to turn to.

Except that she did, though she did not know it. He gripped her hand hard, pulling her toward him, overcome with the need somehow to protect her and her children. He had saved them once; he could do it again.

"Morag," he said. "Hear me. If anything should happen—anything—come to me. If you are in need of anything at all. I'll take care of you."

She made no effort to pull away, but searched his face, her eyes brown and serious, a small frown between those curving brows. He had an irresistible urge to make some physical connection between them—this time for her sake, as much as his. He leaned forward and kissed her, very gently.

He opened his eyes then, and lifted his head, to find himself looking over her shoulder, into the disbelieving face of his many-times great-grandfather.

"GET AWAY FROM MY WIFE." William Buccleigh MacKenzie emerged from the shrubbery with a great rustling of leaves and a look of sinister intent upon his face. He was a tall man, close to Roger's own height, and burly through the shoulders. Further personal details seemed inconsequent, given that he also had a knife. It was still sheathed at his belt, but his hand rested on the hilt in a significant manner.

Roger resisted his original impulse, which had been to say, "It's not what you think." It wasn't, but there weren't any plausible alternatives to suggest.

"I meant her no disrespect," he said, instead, straightening up slowly. He felt it would be unwise to make any quick moves. "My apologies."

"No? And just what the hell d'ye mean by it, then?" MacKenzie put a possessive hand on his wife's shoulder, glowering at Roger. She flinched; her husband's fingers were digging into her flesh. Roger would have liked to knock the hand away, but that was likely to cause more trouble than he had already.

"I met your wife—and you—" he added, "on board the *Gloriana*, a year or two ago. When I recognized her here, I thought to inquire as to the family's welfare. That's all."

"He meant nay harm, William." Morag touched her husband's hand, and the painful grip lessened. "It's right, what he says. Do ye not ken the man? It was him that found me and Jemmy in the hold when we hid there—he brought us food and water."

"You asked me to care for them," Roger added pointedly. "During the fight, that night when the sailors threw the sick ones into the sea."

"Oh, aye?" MacKenzie's features relaxed a trifle. "It was you, was it? I didna see your face, in the dark."

"I didn't see yours, either." He could see it clearly now, and despite the awkwardness of the present circumstances, couldn't help studying it with interest.

So this was the son—unacknowledged—of Dougal MacKenzie, erstwhile war chief of the MacKenzies of Leoch. He looked it. His was a rougher, squarer, fairer version of the family face, but looking carefully, Roger could easily spot the broad cheekbones and high forehead that Jamie Fraser had inherited from his mother's clan. That and the family height; MacKenzie stood over six feet tall, nearly eye to eye with Roger himself.

The man turned slightly at a sound in the brush, and the

sun lit those eyes with a flash of bright moss-green. Roger had a sudden urge to shut his own eyes, lest MacKenzie feel the same bolt of recognition.

MacKenzie had other concerns, though. Two men emerged from the bushes, wary-eyed and grimy with long camping. One held a musket; the other was armed with nothing but a rough club cut from a fallen limb.

"Who's this, then, Buck?" the man with the gun asked, eyeing Roger with some suspicion.

"That's what I mean to be finding out." The momentary softening had disappeared, leaving MacKenzie's face grimly set. He turned his wife away from him and gave her a small push. "Go ye back to the women, Morag. I'll deal with this fellow."

"But, William—" Morag glanced from Roger to her husband, face drawn in distress. "He hasna done anything—"

"Oh, ye think it's nothing, do you, that a man should cheek up to ye in public, like a common radge?" William turned a black look on her, and she blushed suddenly crimson, evidently recalling the kiss, but stumbled on.

"I—no, I mean—that is—he was kind to us, we shouldna be—"

"I said go back!"

She opened her mouth as though to protest, then flinched as William made a sudden move in her direction, fist clenched. Without an instant of conscious decision, Roger swung from the waist, his own fist hitting MacKenzie's jaw with a crack that jarred his arm to the elbow.

Caught off-balance, William staggered and fell to one knee, shaking his head like a pole-axed ox. Morag's gasp was drowned by startled exclamations from the other men. Before he could turn to face them, Roger heard a sound behind him—quiet in itself, but loud enough to chill the blood; the small, cold snick of a hammer drawing back.

There was a brief *pst!* of igniting powder, and then a *phfoom!* as the gun went off with a roar and a puff of black smoke. Everyone jerked and stumbled with the noise, and Roger found himself struggling in a confused sort of way with one of the other men, both of them coughing and half-deafened. As he shoved his assailant off, he caught sight of

Morag, kneeling in the leaves, dabbing at her husband's face with a bit of wet laundry. William shoved her roughly away, scrambled to his feet, and headed for Roger, his eyes bulging, face blotched red with fury.

Roger spun on his heel, slipping in the leaves, and shook off the grip of the man with the gun, making for the shelter of the bushes. Then he was into the thicket, twigs and small branches splintering around him, raking face and arms as he thrust his way through. A heavy crashing and the huff of breath came just behind him, and a hand fastened on his shoulder with a grip of iron.

He seized the hand and twisted hard, hearing a crack of joint and bone. The hand's owner yelled and jerked back, and Roger flung himself headlong toward an opening in the scrub.

He hit the ground on one shoulder, half-curled, rolled, broke through a small bush, and tobogganed down a steep clay bank and into the water, where he landed with a splash.

Scrabbling to find a foothold, he plunged and coughed and flapped upright, shaking hair and water from his eyes, only to see William MacKenzie poised at the top of the bank above him. Seeing his enemy thus at a disadvantage, MacKenzie launched himself with a whoop.

Something like a cannonball crashed into Roger's chest and he fell back into the water in a mighty splash, hearing the distant shrieks of women. He couldn't breathe and couldn't see, but grappled with the twisting mess of clothes and limbs and roiling mud, churning the bottom as he strove vainly for footing, lungs bursting for air.

His head broke the surface. His mouth opened and closed like a fish's, gulping air, and he heard the wheeze of his breath, and MacKenzie's, too. MacKenzie broke away, floundering, and stood upright a few feet away, wheezing like an engine as water poured from his clothes. Roger bent, chest heaving, hands braced on his thighs and his arms quivering with effort. With a final gulp of air, he straightened, wiping away the wet hair plastered over his face.

"Look," he began, panting, "I—"

He got no further, for MacKenzie, still breathing heavily himself, was advancing on him through the waist-deep water.

The man's face had an odd, eager look, and the moss-green eyes were very bright.

Belatedly, Roger thought of something else. The man was the son of Dougal MacKenzie. But the son also of Geillis Duncan, witch.

Somewhere beyond the willows, there was a deep booming noise, and flocks of startled birds rose screeching from the trees. The battle had begun.

65

ALAMANCE

The Governor then sent Captain Malcolm, one of his Aides-de-Camp, and the Sherif of Orange, with his Letter, requiring the Rebels, to lay down their Arms, Surrender up their outlawed Ringleaders &c. About half past ten Capt. Malcolm and the Sherif returned with the Information that the Sherif had read the Letter four several Times, to different Divisions of the Rebels, who rejected the Terms offered, with disdain, said they wanted no time to consider of them, & with Rebellious Clamours called out for Battle.

—*"A Journal of the Expedition against the Insurgents," Wm. Tryon*

"YE'LL WATCH FOR MACKENZIE." Jamie touched Geordie Chisholm's shoulder, and Geordie turned his head, acknowledging the message with a slight nod.

All of them knew. They were good lads, they'd be careful. They'd find him, surely, coming back toward them.

He told himself so for the dozenth time, but the reassurance rang as hollow this time as it had before. Christ, what had happened to the man?

He moved up into the lead, shoving aside the brush with as much violence as though it were a personal enemy. If they were watching out, they'd see MacKenzie in time, not shoot him by mistake. Or so he told himself, knowing perfectly well that in the midst of enemies and the heat of battle, one fired at whatever moved, and there was seldom time to check the features of a man who came at you out of the smoke.

Not that it would make so much difference who did for MacKenzie, if anyone did. Brianna and Claire would hold him responsible for the man's life, and rightly so.

Then, to his relief, there was no more time to think. They broke out into open ground and the men spread out and ran, bending low, zigzagging through the grass in threes and fours as he had taught them, one seasoned soldier to each group. Somewhere behind them, the first boom of cannon came like thunder from a sunny sky.

He spotted the first of the Regulators then, a group of men running, as they were, coming from the right across the open ground. They hadn't seen his men yet.

Before they could, he bellowed "Casteal an DUIN!" and charged them, musket raised overhead in signal to the men behind him. Roars and shrieks split the air, and the Regulators, startled and taken unawares, stumbled to an untidy halt, fumbling their weapons and interfering with each other.

"Thugham! Thugham!" To me, to me! Close enough, it was close enough. He dropped to one knee, crouched over the musket, brought it to bear, and fired just over the heads of the milling men.

Behind him, he heard the grunt of his men falling into firing order, the clink of flint and then the deafening noise of the volley.

One or two of the Regulators crouched, returning fire. The rest broke and ran for cover, toward a small rise of grassy ground.

"*A draigha!* Left! *Nach links!* Cut them off!" He heard

himself bellowing, but did it without thought, already running himself.

The small group of Regulators split, a few making off toward the creek, the rest bunching like sheep, galloping for the shelter of the rise.

They made it, disappearing around the curve of the hill, and Jamie called his troops back, with a piercing whistle that would carry over the rising thunder of the guns. He could hear firing now, a rattle of muskets, away to their left. He sheared off in that direction, trusting that they would follow.

A mistake; the land here was marshy, full of boggy holes and clinging mud. He shouted and waved again, back toward the higher ground. Fall back there, let the enemy come to them across the bog, if they would.

The high ground was heavy with brush, but dry, at least. He spread his fingers wide and waved, gesturing the men to spread out, take cover.

The blood was pumping through his veins, and his skin prickled and tingled with it. A puff of gray-white smoke drifted through the nearby trees, acrid with the scent of black powder. The boom of artillery was regular now, as the gun-crews fell into their rhythm, thumping like a huge, slow heart in the distance.

He made his way slowly toward the west, keeping an eye out. The brush here was mostly sumac and redbud, with waist-high tangles of bramble and clumps of pine that rose above his head. Visibility was poor, but he would hear anyone coming, long before he saw them—or they saw him.

None of his own men were in sight. He took cover in a stand of dogwood and gave a sharp call, like a bobwhite quail. Similar calls of "bob-WHITE!" came from behind him, none in front. Good, they knew roughly where one another were. Cautiously, he went forward, pressing through the brush. It was cooler here, with the shade of the trees, but the air was thick and sweat ran down his neck and back.

He heard the thump of feet and pressed back into the branches of a pinetree, letting the dark-needled fans swing over him, his musket raised to sight on an opening in the bushes. Whoever it was was coming fast. A crack of snapping twigs underfoot and the sound of labored breath, and a young man shoved through the shrubbery, panting. He had no gun, but a skinning-knife glinted in his hand.

The lad was familiar, the first glance gave him that, and Jamie's memory put a name to the young man's face before his finger had relaxed upon the trigger.

"Hugh!" he called, low-voiced but sharp. "Hugh Fowles!"

The young man let out a startled yelp, and swung round staring. He saw Jamie and his gun through the screen of needles, and froze like a rabbit.

Then a surge of panicked determination rose in his face, and he launched himself toward Jamie, screaming. Startled, Jamie barely got his musket up in time to catch the knife-blade on its barrel. He forced the knife up and back; it sheared down the barrel with a screech of metal, glancing off Jamie's knuckles. Young Hugh whipped back his arm for a stab, and he kicked the boy briskly in the knee, stepping back out of the way as the lad lost his balance and lurched to one side, knife swinging wildly.

Jamie kicked him again, and he fell down, the knife embedding itself in the ground.

"Will ye stop that?" Jamie said, rather crossly. "For Christ's sake, lad, do ye not know me?"

He couldn't tell whether Fowles knew him or not—nor even whether the boy had heard him. Face white and eyes staring, Fowles was thrashing in a panic, stumbling and gasping as he tried to get up, trying at the same time to wrench his knife free.

"Will you—" Jamie began, and then jerked back as Fowles abandoned the knife and threw himself forward with a grunt of effort.

The boy's weight knocked Jamie backward, and hands scrabbled at him, trying for a grip on his throat. He dropped the musket, turned a shoulder into Fowles's grip, and put a stop to this nonsense with a quick, brutal punch to the lad's midsection.

Hugh Fowles collapsed and lay curled into a ball on the ground, twitching like a wounded centipede, and making the shocked breathless faces of a man whose breakfast has just been knocked up into his lungs.

Jamie put his right hand to his mouth, sucking blood from

his grazed knuckles. The boy's knife had skinned all four, and the punch hadn't helped; they burned like fire, and the blood had the taste of hot silver in his mouth.

More feet, coming fast. He had barely time to seize his musket before the bushes burst open once more, this time to reveal Fowles's father-in-law, Joe Hobson, his own musket held at the ready.

"Stop right there." Jamie crouched behind his gun, training the muzzle on Hobson's chest. Hobson halted as though a puppet-master had jerked his strings.

"What have ye done to him?" Hobson's eyes flicked from Jamie to his son-in-law and back.

"Nothing permanent. Put your gun down, aye?"

Hobson didn't move. He was grimed with filth and sprouting a beard, but the eyes were live and watchful in his face.

"I mean ye nay harm. Set it down!"

"We'll not be taken," Hobson said. His finger rested on the trigger of his gun, but there was a dubious note in his voice.

"Ye already are, fool. Dinna fash yourself, nay harm will come to you or the lad. You're a deal safer in gaol than out here, man!"

A whistling crash punctuated his statement, as something flew through the trees a few feet overhead, shearing branches as it went. Chain shot, Jamie thought automatically, even as he ducked in reflex, bowels clenched.

Hobson jerked in terror, swinging the barrel of his musket toward Jamie. He jerked again, and his eyes went wide with surprise, as a red stain flowered slowly on his breast. He looked down at it in puzzlement, the muzzle of his gun drooping like a wilted stem. Then he dropped the gun, sat down quite suddenly, leaned back against a fallen tree, and died.

Jamie whirled on his heel, still squatting, and saw Geordie Chisholm behind him, face half-black with the smoke of his shot, looking at Hobson's body as though wondering just how *that* had happened.

The boom of artillery came again, and another missile crashed through the branches and landed nearby with a thud Jamie felt through the soles of his boots. He flung himself flat on his belly and writhed toward Hugh Fowles, who had got himself up on hands and knees now, retching.

He grabbed Fowles's arm, disregarding the pool of vomit, and jerked, hard.

"Come on!" He scrambled up, seizing Fowles by waist and shoulder, and dragged him toward the shelter of the copse behind them. "Geordie! Geordie, help me!"

Chisholm was there. Between them, they got Fowles onto his feet and half-dragged, half-carried him, running and stumbling as they went.

The air was filled with the pungent scent of tree-sap, oozing from the severed branches, and he thought fleetingly of Claire's garden, turned earth, churned earth beneath his boots, the fresh-turned earth of furrows and graves, and Hobson sitting in the sun by the log, the look of surprise not yet gone from his eyes.

Fowles stank of vomit and shit. He hoped it was Fowles.

He thought he would vomit himself from sheer nerves, but bit his tongue, tasting blood again, and clenched the muscles of his belly, willing his wame to go back down.

Someone rose from the shrubbery to his left. He held the gun in his left hand, raised it by reflex, fired one-handed. He stumbled through his own smoke, seeing whoever he had fired at turn and run, smashing heedless through the trees.

Fowles had his feet back under him now, and Jamie let go his arm, leaving Geordie to it. He fell to one knee, groping for powder and shot, ripped the cartridge with his teeth and tasted gunpowder tinged with blood, poured and rammed home, filled his priming pan, checked his flint—all the while noticing with a sense of bemusement that his hands were not shaking in the least, but went about their business with a deft calm, as though they knew just what to do.

He raised the barrel and bared his teeth, only half-conscious of doing it. There were men coming, three, and he raised the gun to bear on the first. With a last shred of conscious thought, he jerked it higher and fired above their heads, the musket jolting in his hands. They stopped, and he dropped the gun, ripped the dirk from his belt, and charged them, screaming.

The words seared his throat, raw from the smoke.

"Run!"

As though from a distance, he watched himself, thinking that it was just so that Hugh Fowles had done, and he had thought it foolish then.

"Run!"

The men scattered like fleeing quail. As a wolf might do, he turned at once after the slowest, bounding over the broken ground, a ferocious joy flooding his legs, blooming in his belly. He could run forever, the wind cold on his skin and shrill in his ears, the spring of the earth beneath him lifting his feet so he flew over grass and rock.

The man he pursued heard him coming, glanced back over his shoulder, and with a shriek of terror, ran full-tilt into a tree. He threw himself upon his prey, landing on the man's back and feeling the springy crack of ribs beneath his knee. He gripped a handful of hair, slick and hot with greasy sweat, and jerked back the man's head. He barely stopped himself cutting the naked throat that lay before him, stretched and defenseless. He could feel the shock of the blade on flesh, the hotness of the spurting blood, and wanted it.

He gulped air, panting.

Very slowly, he drew the knife away from the leaping pulse. The movement left him trembling with need, as though he had been dragged from his woman's body on the verge of spilling seed.

"You are my prisoner," he said.

The man stared up at him, uncomprehending. The man was weeping, tears making tracks through the dirt on his face, and trying to speak, sobbing, but unable to draw enough air to make words with his head wrenched back. Vaguely, it occurred to Jamie that he had spoken in Gaelic; the man did not understand.

Slowly, he loosened his grip, made himself release the man's head. He groped for the English words, buried somewhere under the bloodlust that pulsed through his brain.

"You are . . . my . . . prisoner," he managed at last, panting for air between words.

"Yes! Yes! Anything, don't kill me, please don't kill me!" The man huddled under him, sobbing, hands clasped to the back of his neck and shoulders hunched around his ears, as though he feared Jamie would seize his neck in his teeth and snap his spine.

At the thought, he felt a dim desire to do so, but the thrum of his blood was even now dying down. He could hear again, as his heartbeat faded in his ears. The wind no longer sang to him, but made its own way, heedless and alone, through the leaves above. There was a popping of distant gunshots, but the boom of the artillery had ceased.

Sweat dripped from chin and eyebrows, and his shirt was sodden with it, reeking.

He slid slowly off his prisoner, and knelt beside the prone body. The muscles of his thighs trembled and burned from the effort of the chase. He felt a sudden inexpressible tenderness for the man, and reached to touch him, but the feeling was succeeded by a sense of horror, quite as sudden, and as suddenly gone. He closed his eyes and swallowed, feeling sick, the place where he had bitten his tongue throbbing.

The energy the earth had lent him was draining from his body now, flowing out of his legs, going back to the earth. He reached out and patted the prisoner's shoulder, awkwardly, then struggled to his feet against the dead weight of his own exhaustion.

"Get up," he said. His hands were shaking; it took three tries to sheathe his dirk.

"Ciamar a tha thu, Mac Dubh?" Ronnie Sinclair was at his side, asking if he was all right. He nodded, and stood back as Sinclair pulled the man to his feet and made him turn his coat. The others were coming, in ones and twos: Geordie, the Lindsays, Gallegher, catching up and clustering round him like iron filings drawn to a bit of magnet steel.

The others had bagged prisoners, too; six in all, looking sullen, frightened, or simply exhausted, their coats turned lining-out to show their status. Fowles was among them, white and wretched.

His mind had cleared now, though his body felt limp and heavy. Henry Gallegher had a bloody graze across his forehead; one of the men from Brownsville—Lionel, was it?—carried one arm at an awkward angle, obviously broken. Bar that, no one seemed to be injured; that was good.

"Ask if they have seen MacKenzie," he said to Kenny Lindsay in Gaelic, with a small gesture toward the prisoners.

The gunshots had mostly ceased. There was only a random firing now, and a flock of doves passed overhead in a racket of wings, belatedly alarmed.

None had seen Roger MacKenzie, to know him. Jamie nodded, hearing, and wiped the last of the sweat from his face with his sleeve.

"Either he has come back safe, or he has not. But whatever's done is done now. Ye've done brawly, lads—let's go."

66

A NECESSARY SACRIFICE

This Evening the Dead were interred with military Honors; and three Outlaws taken in the Battle were hanged at the Head of the Army. This gave great Satisfaction to the Men & at this Time it was a necessary Sacrifice to appease the Murmurings of the Troops, who were importunate that public Justice should be immediately executed against some of the Outlaws that were taken in the Action and in opposing of whom they had braved so many Dangers, & suffered such Loss of lives and Blood.

—"A Journal of the Expedition against the Insurgents," Wm. Tryon

ROGER JERKED HARD at the rope round his wrists, but succeeded only in digging the rough hemp farther into his flesh. He could feel the burn of abraded skin and a damp feel that he thought was oozing blood, but his hands had gone so numb that he wasn't sure. His fingers felt the size of sausages, the skin stretched tight.

He was lying where Buccleigh and his friends had thrown him, after tying his wrists and ankles, in the shade of a fallen log. Soaked through from the river, he would have been shivering with cold, had he not been struggling so desperately to get loose. Instead, sweat ran down his neck, his cheeks burned, and he felt as though his head would burst from the influx of furious blood.

They'd gagged him with the flag of truce, stuffing the kerchief so deep into his throat that he was close to choking, and knotting his own stock round his mouth. Ancestor or no, he was going to mangle William Buccleigh MacKenzie, if it was the last thing he ever did.

Shots were still being fired nearby; not in volleys, but a ragged popcorn rattle. The air reeked with black powder smoke, and every so often, something came whistling through the trees like a jabberwock, with a tremendous ripping and snapping of branches and leaves. Chain-shot? Cannonballs?

A cannonball had thudded into the riverbank, earlier, burying itself in a small explosion of mud and momentarily interrupting the fight. One of Buccleigh's friends had uttered a cry and run, splashing, for the shelter of the trees, but the other had stayed, grappling and punching, heedless of the shooting and yelling, until he and Buccleigh had managed to press Roger's head beneath the water and overpower him. He could still feel the burn of the river-water in his sinuses.

He'd managed to get to his knees now, hunched like an inch-worm, but didn't dare to raise his head above the log, for fear of having it shot off. Fury was running so strong through his veins that he hadn't really been frightened, even at the realization that the battle was going on round him, but he hadn't lost his mind entirely.

He rubbed his face hard against the crumbling bark of the log, trying to snag the strip of linen tied round his head. It worked; the stub of a twig caught, and he jerked his head up, pulling the stock down below his chin. Grunting with the effort, he shoved the wadded kerchief out a little way, caught it on the same twig, and drew back, the soggy rag pulling out of his throat like a snake-swallower in reverse.

He gagged with reaction, feeling bile rise up the back of his throat. He gulped air, greedy for oxygen, and his stomach settled a bit.

Great, he could breathe, now what? The firing was still going on, and he could hear crashing off to his left, as several men plowed through the bushes, heedless of obstruction.

Running feet were coming toward him; he ducked behind the shelter of the log, just in time to avoid being flattened as a body catapulted over it. His new companion scrambled up onto hands and knees, pressing tight against the log, only then becoming aware of his presence.

"You!" It was Black-beard, from Husband's encampment. He stared at Roger, face suffusing slowly with blood. He could smell the man, a rank, penetrating reek of fear and anger.

Black-beard grabbed him by the shirt-front, jerking him close.

"This is your fault! Bastard!"

With his hands and feet still tied, he had no means of fighting back, but jerked back, trying to free himself.

"Let go, fool!"

Only then did the man realize that he was tied, and in his astonishment, did let go. Off-balance, Roger fell to the side, scraping his face painfully on the rough bark of the log. Black-beard's eyes bulged with amazement, then narrowed in glee.

"By Dad, you been captured! If that ain't luck! Who's got you, fool?"

"He's mine." A low Scottish voice behind him announced the return of William Buccleigh MacKenzie. "What d'ye mean it's his fault? What is?"

"This!" Black-beard flung out an arm, indicating the field around them, and the dying battle. The artillery had ceased, and there were no more than scattered rifle-shots in the distance.

"This damn smooth-talker come unto the camp this morning, asking for Hermon Husband, and took him away for a private word. I don't know what in desolation's name he said, but when he finished it, Husband come out, got straight onto his horse, told us all to go home, and rode off!"

Black-beard glared at Roger, and drawing back his hand, slapped him hard across the face. "What did you say to him, arse-bite?"

Without waiting for an answer, he turned back to Buccleigh, who was glancing back and forth between his captive and his visitor, a look of deep interest furrowing the thick, fair brows. "If Hermon had stuck with us, we might ha' stood," Black-beard raged. "But with him goin' off like that, it cut the ground right from under us—wasn't no one knew quite what to do, and the next thing you know, here's Tryon a-bawling surrender at us—and a course we wasn't goin' to do that, but we wasn't what you'd call prepared to fight neither . . ." He trailed off at this, catching Roger's eye on him, and uncomfortably aware that Roger had seen him fleeing in panic.

There was nothing but silence on the far side of the log; all firing had stopped. It was dawning on Roger that the battle was not only over, but well and truly lost. Which meant in turn that the militia were likely to be swarming over this place in short order. His eyes were still watering from the slap, but he blinked them clear, glaring at Black-beard.

"I said to Husband what I say to you," he said, with as much authority as he could muster, lying trussed on the ground like a Christmas goose. "The Governor is serious. He means to put down this rebellion, and by the looks of things, he's done just that. If you have a care for your skin—and I'd say you do—"

With an inarticulate growl of rage, Black-beard seized Roger by the shoulders and tried to smash his head into the log.

Roger twisted like an eel. He reared back, breaking the man's grip, then threw himself forward, and butted the man squarely, smashing Black-beard's nose with his forehead. He felt the satisfying crunch of bone and cartilage, and the spurt of blood hot and wet against his face, and fell back onto one elbow, panting.

He'd not given anyone a Glasgow kiss before, but it seemed to come natural. The jar of it hurt his wrist badly, but he was beyond caring. Just let Buccleigh come close enough to get the same, that's all he wanted.

Buccleigh eyed him with a mixture of amusement and wary respect.

"Oh, a man of talent, aye? A traitor, a wife-stealer, *and* a bonnie brawler, all in the same wee bundle, is it?"

Black-beard threw up, choking on the blood from his crushed nose, but Roger paid no attention. His vision clear now, he kept his eyes square on Buccleigh. He knew which man of the two was the greater threat.

"A man who's sure of his wife needn't worry that someone else might steal her," he said, anger only slightly tempered with wariness. "I'm sure of my own wife, and have no need of yours, *amadain*."

Buccleigh was sunburned and deeply flushed from fighting, but at this, a darker red crept into his cheeks. Still, he kept his composure, smiling lightly.

"Marrit, are ye? Your wife must be ill-favored, surely, for ye to be sniffing after mine. Or is it only that she's put ye out of her bed, because ye couldna serve her decently?"

The rasp of the rope on his wrists reminded Roger that he was in no position to bandy words. With an effort, he bit back the retort that sat at the tip of his tongue, and swallowed it. It tasted foul, going down.

"Unless ye mean your wife to be a widow, I think it's time ye were going, aye?" he said. He jerked his head toward the far side of the log, where the brief silence had been succeeded by the distant sound of voices.

"The battle's over, your cause is lost. I don't know if they mean to take prisoners—"

"They've taken several." Buccleigh frowned at him, clearly undecided. There weren't that many options, Roger thought; Buccleigh must let him go, leave him tied, or kill him. Either of the first two was acceptable. As for the third, surely if Buccleigh meant to kill him, he'd be already dead.

"You'd best go while ye can," Roger suggested. "Your wife will be worried."

It was a mistake to have mentioned Morag again. Buccleigh's face grew darker, but before he could say anything, he was interrupted by the appearance of the woman herself, in company with the man who had helped Buccleigh tie him earlier.

"Will! Oh, Willie! Thank Christ you're safe! Are ye hurt at all?" She was pale and anxious, and had a small child in her arms, clinging monkeylike to her neck. Despite the burden, she reached out a hand to touch her husband, to assure herself that he was indeed unharmed.

"Dinna fash yourself, Morag," Buccleigh said gruffly. "I've taken no harm." Still, he patted her hand, and kissed her self-consciously on the forehead.

Ignoring this tender reunion, Buccleigh's companion prodded Roger interestedly in the side with the toe of his boot.

"What shall we do with this, then, Buck?"

Buccleigh hesitated, his attention drawn momentarily from his wife. Morag, spotting Roger on the ground, uttered a muffled scream and clapped her hand across her mouth.

"What have ye done, Willie?" she cried. "Let him go, for Bride's sake!"

"I shan't. He's a damned traitor." Buccleigh's mouth set in a grim line, obviously displeased at his wife's taking notice of Roger.

"He's not, he can't be!" Clutching her son tightly to her, Morag stooped to peer at Roger, an anxious crease between her brows. Seeing the state of his hands, she gasped and turned indignantly to her husband.

"Will! How can ye treat this man so, and after he's done such service to your own wife and bairn!"

For God's sake, Morag, back off! Roger thought, seeing Buccleigh's fist clench suddenly. Buccleigh was plainly a jealous bastard to start with, and being on the losing side of the battle just past was doing his temper no good at all.

"Bugger off, Morag," said Buccleigh, echoing Roger's sentiment in less-gallant language. "This is no place for you or the bairn; take him and go."

Black-beard had recovered slightly by this time, and loomed up alongside Buccleigh. He glared down at Roger, hands pressed tenderly to his swollen nose.

"Slit his throat, I say, and good riddance." He emphasized this opinion with a kick in the ribs that curled Roger up like a shrimp.

Morag uttered a fierce cry and kicked Black-beard in the shin.

"Let him alone!"

Black-beard, taken off-guard, let out a yelp and hopped backward. Buccleigh's other companion appeared to find this more than funny, but stifled his hilarity when Buccleigh turned an awful glare on him.

Morag was on her knees, her small belt-knife in her hand, trying one-handed to cut the bonds about Roger's wrists. Much as he appreciated her intent, Roger wished she wouldn't try to help him. It was all too apparent that the original green-eyed monster had firm possession of the soul of William Buccleigh MacKenzie, and was glaring out of his eye-sockets in an emerald fury.

Buccleigh seized his wife by the arm and jerked her to her feet. The baby, startled, began to shriek.

"Leave, Morag!" Buccleigh snarled. "Go, and go now!"

"Yes, go!" Black-beard put in, glowering. "We've no need of your help, you interfering little bizzom!"

"Don't you speak to my wife that way!" Turning on his heel, Buccleigh punched Black-beard swiftly in the stomach. The man sat down hard, his mouth opening and closing in comical astonishment. Roger could almost feel a certain sympathy for Black-beard, who appeared to be faring no better between the two MacKenzies than he was himself.

Buccleigh's other friend, who had been observing the exchange with the fascination of someone watching a close tennis match, seized the opportunity to join the conversation, butting in as Morag tried to soothe her baby's crying.

"Whatever ye mean to do, Buck, best we do it and be gone." He nodded toward the creek, uneasy. There were a number of men coming in their direction, judging from the rumble of voices. Not fleeing Regulators; it was a purposeful sound. Militia, coming in search of prisoners? Roger sincerely hoped so.

"Aye." Buccleigh glanced in the direction of the noises, then turned to his wife. He took her by the shoulders, but gently.

"Go, Morag. I'd have ye safe."

She heard the note of pleading in his voice, and her face softened. Still, she looked from her husband to Roger, who was now trying mental telepathy, beaming thoughts at her in increasing desperation.

Leave, for God's sake, woman, before you get me killed!

Morag turned back to her husband, small jaw set in determination.

"I'll go. But you swear to me, William Buccleigh, that ye willna harm one hair of this man's head!"

Buccleigh's eyes bulged slightly, and his hands curled into fists, but Morag stood her ground, small and fierce.

"Swear it!" she said. "For by the name of Bride, I'll not share the bed of a murderer!"

Clearly torn, Buccleigh glanced from the sullen Blackbeard to his other friend, who was shuffling from one foot to the other like a man in urgent need of a privy. The party of militia was getting closer. Then he looked down into his wife's face.

"All right, Morag," he said gruffly. He gave her a small push. "Go, now!"

"No." She reached out and took her husband's hand, pulling it toward her breast. Little Jemmy had got over his alarm, and was curled into his mother's shoulder, noisily sucking his thumb. Morag placed his father's hand on the little boy's head.

"Swear on your son's head, Will, that ye'll not hurt this man nor see him killed."

Roger mentally applauded the gesture, but was afraid she'd gone too far; Buccleigh stiffened for a moment, and the blood rose in his face again. After a tense moment, though, he nodded, once.

"I swear," he said quietly, and let his hand fall. Morag's face eased, and without a word, she turned then and hurried away, the baby held close to her bosom.

Roger let out the breath he'd been holding. God, what a woman! He hoped passionately that she and her baby *would* be safe—though if her fat-headed husband chose to step in a gopher hole and break his neck . . .

William Buccleigh was looking down at him, green eyes narrowed in contemplation, ignoring the increasing agitation of his friend.

"Come on, Buck!" The man glanced over his shoulder toward the creek, where loud calls to and fro indicated searchers combing the ground. "There's no time to be lost. They did say Tryon means to hang prisoners, and I've no mind to be one!"

"Does he," Buccleigh said softly. He held Roger's eyes with his, and Roger thought for a moment that something familiar stirred in those depths. A chill of unease ran down his spine.

"He's right," he said to Buccleigh, with a jerk of the head toward the other man. "Go. I'll not speak against you—for your wife's sake."

Buccleigh pursed his lips slightly, thinking.

"No," he said at last, "I dinna think ye will. Speak against me, that is." He stooped and picked up the sodden, dirt-smeared ex-flag of truce from the ground. "Go along with ye, Johnny. See to Morag. I'll meet ye later."

"But, Buck . . . "

"Go! I'm safe enough." With a faint smile, his eyes still on Roger, Buccleigh put his hand in his pouch and drew out a small bit of dull silver metal. With a small shock, Roger recognized his own militia badge, the crudely lettered "FC" burned black in the pewter disc.

Tossing the badge lightly in his palm, Buccleigh turned to Black-beard, who was taking a suddenly renewed interest in the proceedings.

"I've a thought, sir, regarding our mutual friend." He nodded toward Roger. "If you're with me?"

Black-beard looked at Roger, back at MacKenzie, and a slow smile began to grow beneath his bulbous, reddened nose. The ripple of unease down Roger's back blossomed suddenly into a full-blown jolt of fear.

"Help!" he roared. "Help, militia! Help!" He rolled, twisting to avoid them, but Black-beard seized him by the shoulders, pulling him back. Calls came from beyond the trees, and the sound of feet, beginning to run.

"No, sir," said William Buccleigh, kneeling down in front of him. He seized Roger's jaw in a grip of iron, strangling his yells and squeezing his cheeks to force open his mouth. "I do not think you'll speak, indeed." With a slight smile, he rammed the sodden cloth down Roger's throat again, and tied the tattered neckcloth fast around it.

He stood up, then, the militia badge held tight in his hand. As the bushes opened, he turned toward them and waved an arm in hearty greeting.

67

AFTERMATH

It being now half past two O'Clock the Enemy entirely dispersed, and the Army five Miles from Camp, it was thought adviseable to lose no Time, but to return immediately to the Camp at Alamance. Empty Waggons were ordered from Camp which took both the killed and wounded of the Loyalists, and even several of the wounded Rebels, who acknowledged had they gained the day no Quarters would have been given but to such as would have turned Regulators, these were nevertheless, taken good Care of, and had their wounds dressed.

—"A Journal of the Expedition against the Insurgents," Wm. Tryon

A MUSKET-BALL had shattered David Wingate's elbow. Bad luck; had it struck an inch higher, it would have broken the bone, but healed cleanly. I'd opened the joint with a semicircular incision across the outer aspect, and dug out both the flattened ball and several bone chips, but the cartilage was badly damaged, and the biceps tendon had been sheared through completely; I could see the silvery gleam of one end, hiding deep in the dark-red meat of the muscle.

I gnawed my lower lip, considering. If I left matters as they were, the arm would be permanently—and badly—crippled. If I could reattach the severed tendon and bring the bone-ends in the joint capsule into good alignment, he might just possibly regain some use of it.

I glanced round the campsite, which now resembled an ambulance depot, littered with bodies, equipment, and blood-stained bandages. Most of the bodies were moving, thank God, if only to curse or moan. One man had been dead when his friends brought him in; he lay quiet in the shade of a tree, wrapped in his blanket.

Most of the injuries I saw had been slight, though there were two men shot through the body; I could do nothing for them but keep them warm and hope for the best. Brianna was checking them every few minutes for signs of shock and fever, in between rounds of administering honeyed water to those suffering more superficial wounds. Best she kept busy, I thought, and she did keep moving, though her face looked like one of the wild morning glories on the vine that climbed the bush behind me—white and puckered, pinched tight closed against the terrors of the day.

I had had to amputate a leg, soon after the battle ended. It was a man from Mercer's Company—camped near to us, and lacking a surgeon of their own—struck by a rebounding chunk of a mortar round that had torn off most of his foot and left the flesh of the lower leg hanging in ribbons from the shattered bone. I'd thought she would faint when the heavy limb thumped into the dirt at her feet, and she'd thought so, too, but had by some miracle stayed upright, supporting the patient—who really *had* fainted, thank the Lord for small mercies—while I cauterized the bleeding vessels and bound the stump with brutal speed.

Jamie was gone; he had brought back his men, hugged me hard and kissed me once, fiercely, then left with the Lindsays to take the prisoners to the Governor—and inquire along the way for any news of Roger.

Relief at Jamie's return buoyed my heart, but fear for Roger was a small heavy counterweight below my breastbone. I could ignore it while I worked, though. No news was good news for a short time yet, and I welcomed the immediate realities of triage and treatment as a refuge from imagination.

Nothing else looked exigent. Men were still straggling in, but Bree looked up at each one, her heart in her eyes. If any of them needed me, she would call. All right, I decided. There was time; I'd try it. There was little to lose, bar a bit more suffering for Mr. Wingate, and I would ask if he were willing.

He was wax-pale and sweating, but still upright. He nodded his permission and I gave him the whisky bottle again; he applied it to his mouth with his sound hand as though it contained the elixir of life. I called one of the other men to hold his arm steady while I worked, and swiftly incised the skin just above the bend of the elbow in an inverted "T," exposing the lower head of the biceps and making the site more accessible. I began to probe with my longest forceps, teasing out the tough silver strand of the sheared tendon, pulling it down as far as I could, until I had a sound spot where I could pierce it with a suture, and set about the delicate work of rejoining the severed ends.

I lost touch then with everything around me, all my attention focused on the problem before me. I was dimly conscious of the *pit! pit! pit!* of drops striking the ground at my feet, but didn't know whether it was the sweat that ran down my arms and face, the patient's oozing blood, or both. I could have used the hands of a trained surgical nurse to help, but didn't have them, so made do with my own. I had a fine surgeon's needle, though, and thin boiled-silk sutures; the stitches showed small and neat, a stark black zigzag that marked a sturdy hold on the slippery, gleaming tissue. I would normally have used the cat-gut sutures for internal work like this, as those would gradually dissolve and be absorbed by the body. Tendons healed so slowly, though—if at all—that I couldn't risk that. The silk stitches would simply stay permanently in place, and I prayed would cause no problems of their own.

Then the hard part was done, and time started again. I was able to talk soothingly to David, who had come through it gallantly; he nodded and made a feeble attempt to smile when I told him it was done, though his teeth were clenched and his cheeks wet with tears. He screamed when I washed the wounds with diluted alcohol—they always did; they couldn't help it, poor things—but then sagged back, trembling, while I stitched the surgical incisions and bandaged the wounds.

That took no great skill, though; I had attention to spare now, and gradually became aware that some of the men behind me were discussing the recent battle, full of praise for Governor Tryon.

"Did you see it, then?" one was asking eagerly. "Did he really do as they said?"

"Hope I may be gutted and fried for breakfast if it ain't so," his companion replied sententiously. "Saw him with my own eyes, didn't I? He rode up within a hundred yards of the swine, and ordered 'em face-to-face to surrender. They wasn't much answer for a minute, only them kind of lookin' to and fro amongst themselves to see who might speak, and then somebody shouts out that no, damn it all, they ain't a-going to surrender nohow. So the Governor, he's a-scowlin' fit to fright a thundercloud, and he rears up and lifts his sword high, then brings it down and shouts, 'Fire on them!' "

"And did they do so straight off?"

"No, we didn't," put in another voice, more educated, and rather dry in tone. "Do you blame us? A forty-shilling bounty for joining the militia is one thing, but to fire in cold blood on folk you know is something else. I looked across and who should I see on the other side but my wife's own cousin, grinning back at me! Now, I'm not saying that the rascal is any great favorite with me or the family, but how am I to go home and tell my Sally as I've just shot her cousin Millard full of holes?"

"Better than Cousin Millard doin' the same service by

you," said the first voice, with an audible grin, and the third man laughed.

"True enough," he said. "But we didn't wait to see if it might come to that. The Governor, he went red as a turkey-cock when the men there with him hesitated. He stood up in his stirrups with his sword held on high, glared round at us all, and he hollered out, 'Fire, Goddamn you! Fire on them, or on me!' "

The narrator put a good deal of enthusiasm into this re-enactment, and there was a murmur of admiration from his hearers.

"Now there's a soldier for ye!" said one voice, followed by a general rumble of agreement.

"So we fired," said the narrator, a faint shrug in his voice. "Didn't take so long, once it started. Cousin Millard is right fast, it seems, once he's started running. Bastard got clean away."

More laughter at this, and I smiled, patting David's shoulder. He was listening, too, the conversation a welcome distraction.

"No sir," another agreed. "I reckon Tryon means to make sure of his victory this time. Heard he's gone to hang the leaders of the Regulation on the field."

"He what?" I whirled round at this, bandage still in hand.

The small group of men blinked up at me, surprised.

"Yes, ma'am," said one man, with an awkward tug at the brim of his hat. "A fellow from Lillington's brigade told me so; he was off to see the fun."

"Fun," muttered another of the men, and crossed himself.

"Shame if he hangs the Quaker," another opined, face shadowed. "Old Husband's a right terror in print, but he ain't a ruffian. Nor are James Hunter or Ninian Hamilton."

"Perhaps he'll hang Cousin Millard," another suggested, nudging his neighbor with a grin. "Then you'll be rid of him and your wife can blame the Governor!"

There was a chorus of laughter at this, but the tone was subdued. I turned back to my work, concentrating fiercely to blot out the picture of what was now happening on the field of war.

War was bad enough, even when it was necessary. Cold-blooded revenge by the victor was one degree beyond. And yet from Tryon's point of view, that might be necessary, too. As battles went, this one had been both quick, and relatively minor in terms of casualty. I had only twenty or so wounded in my keeping, and had seen only one fatality. There would be more elsewhere, of course, yet from the comments of those nearby, it had been a rout, but not a slaughter, the militiamen being largely unenthusiastic about butchering their fellow citizens, cousins or not.

That meant that most of the men of the Regulation survived unharmed. I supposed that the Governor might feel that a drastic gesture was required, to seal his victory, intimidate the survivors, and stamp once and for all on the long-smoldering wick of that dangerous movement.

There was a stir, and the sound of a horse's hooves. I looked up—next to me, Bree's head jerked up, her body tense—to see Jamie returning, riding double with Murdo Lindsay. Both men slid off, and he sent Murdo away with a word to care for Gideon, then came at once to me.

I could see from the anxious look of his face that he had no word of Roger; he glanced at my face and saw the answer to his own question there. His shoulders dropped slightly in discouragement, then straightened, stiffening.

"I will go to search the field," he said to me, low-voiced. "I have sent word already, through the companies. If he is brought in anywhere, someone will bring us word."

"I'm going with you." Brianna was already taking off her grubby apron, wadding it into a ball.

Jamie glanced at her, then nodded.

"Aye, lass, of course. Just a moment, then—I'll fetch wee Josh to help your mother."

"I'll get—get the horses ready." Her movements were quick and jerky, without her usual athletic grace, and she dropped the water bottle she was holding, fumbling several times before she succeeded in retrieving it. I took it from her before she could drop it again, and squeezed her hand, hard.

The corner of her mouth trembled as she looked at me; I thought she meant it for a smile.

"He'll be all right," she said. "We'll find him."

"Yes," I said, and let go her hand. "I know you will."

I watched her hurry across the clearing, hands clenched in her raised skirts, and felt the counterweight of fear come loose, plunging like a stone into my belly.

68

EXECUTION OF ORDERS

ROGER WOKE SLOWLY, to throbbing pain and a sense of dreadful urgency. He had no idea where he was, or how he came to be there, but there were voices, lots of voices, some talking just beyond the range of comprehension, some singing like harpies, in shrill discord. For a moment, he felt the voices were inside his head. He could see them, little brown things with leather wings and sharp teeth, banging into each other in paroxysms of interruption that set off small bombs of light behind his eyes.

He could feel the seam along which his head must surely split under the pressure, a burning streak across the top of his skull. He wanted someone to come and unzip it, to let out all the flying voices and their racket, to leave his skull an empty bowl of shining bone.

He had no real sense of opening his eyes, and stared numbly for some minutes, thinking that the scene on which he looked was still part of the confusion inside his skull. Men swarmed before him in a sea of colors, swirling blues and reds and yellows, mixed with blobs of green and brown.

A defect in his vision deprived him of perspective and caused him to see them in fragments—a distant cluster of heads floating like a bobble of hairy balloons, a waving arm that held a crimson banner, seemingly severed from its body.

Several pairs of legs that must be close by . . . was he sitting on the ground? He was. A fly droned past his ear and landed, buzzing, on his upper lip, and he moved by reflex to swat it, only then realizing that he was indeed awake—and still bound.

His hands had gone numb beyond any sense of pain, but the ache now throbbed through the straining muscles of his arms and shoulders. He shook his head to clear it, a terrible mistake. Blinding pain shot through his head, bringing water to his eyes.

He blinked hard and breathed deep, willing himself to grasp some shred of reality, to come to himself. *Focus*, he thought. *Hold on*. The singing voices had faded away, leaving only a faint ringing in his ears. The others were still talking, though, and now he knew that the sound was real, he was able to seize on a word here and there, and pin it down, flapping, to examine for meaning.

"Example."

"Governor."

"Rope."

"Piss."

"Regulators."

"Stew."

"Foot."

"Hang."

"Hillsborough."

"Water."

"Water." That one made sense. He knew water. He *wanted* water; wanted it badly. His throat was dry, his mouth felt as though it was stuffed with . . . it was stuffed with something; he gagged as his tongue moved in an unconscious attempt at swallowing.

"Governor." The repeated word, spoken just above him, made him look up. He fixed his floating vision on a face. Lean, dark, frowning with a fierce intent.

"You are sure?" the face said, and he wondered dimly, *Sure of what?* He was sure of nothing, save that he was in a bad way.

"Yessir," said another voice, and he saw another face swim into view alongside the first. This one seemed familiar, fringed with thick black beard. "I saw him in Hermon Husband's camp, palavering with Husband. You ask amongst the prisoners, sir—they'll say so."

The first head nodded. It turned to the side, and up, addressing someone taller. Roger's eyes drifted up, seeking, and he jerked upright with a muffled exclamation, as he saw the green eyes looking down on him, dispassionate.

"He's James MacQuiston," said the green-eyed man, nodding confirmation. "From Hudgin's Ferry."

"You saw him in the battle?" The first man was coming into complete focus, a soldierly-looking fellow in his late thirties, dressed in uniform. Something else was coming into focus—James MacQuiston. He'd heard of MacQuiston . . . what . . . ?

"He killed a man in my company," Green-eyes said, his voice rough with anger. "Shot him in cold blood as he lay wounded on the ground."

The Governor—that was who it must be, Governor . . . Tryon! That was the name! The Governor was nodding, the frown etched deep on his face.

"Take him, too, then," he said, and turned away. "Three are enough for now."

Hands gripped Roger's arms and jerked him upright, supporting him for a moment, then pulling him so that he stumbled, off-balance, and found himself half-walking, his weight supported by two men dressed in uniform. He pulled against them, wanting to turn and find Green-eyes—damn, what was the man's name?—but they yanked him round, compelling him to stumble toward a small rise, topped with a huge white oak.

The rise was surrounded by a sea of men, but they fell back, making way for Roger and his escorts. The sense of urgency was back, a feeling like ants beneath the surface of his brain.

MacQuiston, he thought, the name suddenly clear in his memory. *James MacQuiston*. MacQuiston was a minor leader of the Regulation, a rabble-rouser from Hudgin's Ferry whose fiery speech of threat and denunciation had been published in the *Gazette*; Roger had seen it.

Why in hell had Green-eyes—Buccleigh! It was

Buccleigh. His sense of relief at remembering the name was succeeded instantly by shock as he realized that Buccleigh had told them he was MacQuiston. Why—

He had not even time to form the question when the last ranks broke before him, and he saw the horses beneath the tree, the looped nooses hanging above the empty saddles from its branches.

THEY HELD THE horses by the heads, while the men were put upon them. Leaves brushed his cheek; twigs caught in his hair, and he ducked, turning his head by instinct to save his eyes being put out.

Some way across the clearing, he saw a woman's figure, half-hidden in the crowd; indistinct but with the unmistakable curve of a child in her arm, a small brown Madonna. The sight brought him upright with a jolt through chest and belly, the memory of Bree with Jemmy in her arms searing through his mind.

He threw himself to the side, back arched, felt himself slide and had no hands to save himself. Other hands caught him, pushed him back, one struck him hard across the face. He shook his head, eyes watering, and through the blur of tears saw the brown Madonna thrust her burden into someone's hands, pick up her skirts, and run as though the devil chased her.

Something dropped upon his breast with the heavy slither of a serpent. Prickly hemp touched his neck, drew tight about his throat, and he screamed behind the gag.

He struggled without thought for consequence or possibility, impelled by the desperation of the instinct to survive. Heedless of bleeding wrists and wrenching muscle, thighs clenched so hard about the horse's body that it jerked under him in protest, he strained at his bonds with a strength beyond what he had ever imagined he possessed.

Across the clearing, the child had begun to shriek for his mother. The crowd had fallen silent and the baby's cries rang loud. The dark soldier sat on his horse, arm lifted, sword upraised. He seemed to speak, but Roger heard nothing for the roar of blood in his ears.

The bones of his hands popped and a line of liquid heat ran down one arm as a muscle tore. The sword fell, a flash of sunlight from its blade. His buttocks slid back over the horse's rump, legs trailing helpless, and his weight fell free in an empty-bellied plunge.

A wrenching jerk . . .

And he was spinning, choking, fighting for air, and his fingers scrabbled, nails tearing at the rope sunk deep in his flesh. His hands had come loose, but it was too late, he couldn't feel them, couldn't manage. His fingers slipped and slid on the twisted strands, futile, numb, and unresponsive as wood.

He dangled, kicking, and heard a far-off rumble from the crowd. He kicked and bucked, feet pawing empty air, hands clawing at his throat. Chest strained, back arched, and his sight had gone black, small lightnings flickering in the corners of his eyes. He reached for God and heard no plea for mercy deep within himself but only a shriek of *no!* that echoed in his bones.

And then the stubborn impulse left him and he felt his body stretch and loosen, reaching, reaching for the earth. A cool wind embraced him and he felt the soothing warmth of his body's voidings. A brilliant light blazed up behind his eyes, and he heard nothing more but the bursting of his heart and the distant cries of an orphaned child.

69

HIDEOUS EMERGENCY

JAMIE AND BREE were nearly ready to leave. Smoke-stained and weary as they were, a number of the men had offered to join the search-party, an offer that made Bree bite her lip and nod thanks. She was grateful for the offer of help, I knew—but it takes time to move a larger group, and I could see the impatience flare up in red blotches under her skin as weapons were cleaned, canteens refilled, cast-off shoes located.

"Wee Josh" had been mildly apprehensive regarding his new position as surgeon's assistant, but he was a groom, after all, and thus accustomed to tending the ills of horseflesh. The only difference, as I told him—making him grin—was that human patients could tell you where it hurt.

I had paused to wash my hands before stitching a lacerated scalp, when I became aware of some disturbance taking place at the edge of the meadow behind me. Jamie, hearing it too, turned his head—and then came swiftly back across the clearing, eyebrows raised.

"What is it?" I turned to look, and saw a young woman, evidently in a dreadful state, heading toward us at a lopsided trot. She was slight of build and limping badly—she had lost a shoe somewhere—but still half-running, supported on one side by Murdo Lindsay, who seemed to be expostulating with her even as he helped her along.

"Fraser," I heard her gasp. "Fraser!" She let go of Murdo and pushed her way through the waiting men, her eyes raking the faces as she passed, searching. Her brown hair was tangled and full of leaves, her face scratched and bloody.

"James . . . Fraser . . . I must . . . are you . . . ?" She was panting for breath, her chest heaving and her face so red it looked as though she might have an apoplexy on the spot.

Jamie stepped forward and took her by the arm.

"I'm Jamie Fraser, lass," he said. "Is it me ye want?"

She nodded, gasping, but had no breath for words. I hastily poured a cup of water and offered it to her, but she shook her head violently, instead waving her arms in agitation, gesturing wildly toward the creek.

"Rog . . . er," she got out, gulping air like a landed fish. "Roger. MacKen . . . zie." Before the final syllable left her mouth, Brianna was at the young woman's side.

"Where is he? Is he hurt?" She seized the young woman's arm, as much to compel answers as to provide support.

The girl's head bobbed up and down, shook back and forth, and she gasped out, "Hang . . . they . . . they are . . . hanging him! Gov—ner!"

Brianna let go of her and ran for the horses. Jamie was already there, untying reins with the same swift intensity he had shown when the fighting began. Without a word, he stooped, hands cupped; Brianna stepped up and swung into the saddle, kicking the horse into motion before Jamie had reached his own. Gideon caught the mare up within moments, though, and both horses disappeared into the willows, as though swallowed up.

I said something under my breath, with no consciousness of whether I'd uttered a curse or a prayer. I thrust needle and suture into Josh's startled hands, caught up the sack with my emergency kit, and ran for my own horse, leaving the brown-haired woman collapsed on the grass, vomiting from her effort.

I CAUGHT THEM UP within a few moments. We didn't know precisely where Tryon was holding his drumhead court, and valuable time was lost as Jamie was compelled to stop, time and again, and lean from his horse to ask directions—these often muddled and contradictory. Bree was gathered into herself, quivering like a nocked arrow, ready for flight, but lacking direction.

I tried to ready myself for anything, including the worst. I had no idea what preliminaries Tryon might have engaged in, or how much time might elapse between condemnation and execution. Not bloody long, I thought. I'd known Tryon long enough to see that he acted with thought, but also with dispatch—and he would know that if such things were done, 'twas best they were done quickly.

As to the why of it . . . imagination failed completely. I could only hope that the woman was wrong; that she had mistaken someone else for Roger. And yet I didn't think so; neither did Brianna, urging her horse through a boggy patch ahead with an intensity that suggested she would be better pleased to leap off the horse and drag it bodily through the mud.

The afternoon was fading, and clouds of small gnats surrounded us, but Jamie made no move to brush them away. His shoulders were set like stone, braced to bear the burden of knowledge. It was that as much as my own fears that told me Roger was likely dead.

The thought beat against me like a small, sharp hammer, the sort meant for breaking rocks. So far, I felt only brief, recurrent shocks of imagined loss, each time I glanced at Brianna's white face, thought of tiny Jemmy orphaned, heard the echo of Roger's soft, deep voice, laughing in the distance, singing through my heart. I did not try to push the hammering thoughts aside; it would do no good. And I would not truly break, I knew, until I saw his body.

Even then, the break would be internal. Brianna would need me. Jamie would stand like a rock for her, would do what must be done—but he, too, would need me, later. No one could absolve him of the guilt I knew he felt, but I could at least be confessor for him, and his intercessor with Brianna. My own mourning could wait—a long time, I hoped.

The ground opened, flattening into the edge of a wide meadow, and Jamie kicked Gideon into a gallop, the other horses streaming after him. Our shadows flew like bats across the grass, the sound of our hoofbeats lost in the sounds of a crowd of men who filled the field.

On a rise at the far end of the meadow stood a huge white oak, its spring leaves bright in the slanting sun. My horse moved suddenly, dodging past a group of men, and I saw them, three stick-figures, dangling broken in the tree's deep shadow. The hammer struck one final blow, and my heart shattered like ice.

Too late.

IT WAS A BAD HANGING. Without benefit of official troops, Tryon had had no one to hand with a hangsman's gruesome—and necessary—skills. The three condemned men had been sat on horses, the ropes round their necks thrown over tree branches above, and at the signal, the horses had been led out from under them, leaving them dangling.

Only one had been fortunate enough to die of a snapped neck. I could see the sharp angle of his head, the limpness of his limbs in their bonds. It wasn't Roger.

The others had strangled, slowly. The bodies were twisted, held by their bonds in the final postures of their struggle. One man—one body—was cut down as I rode up, and carried past me in the arms of his brother. There was not much to choose between their faces, each contorted, each darkened in its separate agony. They had used what rope was to hand; it was new, unstretched. Roger's toes trailed in the dust; he had been taller than the rest. His hands had come free; he had managed to hook the fingers of one hand beneath the rope. The fingers were nearly black, all circulation cut off. I couldn't look at his face at once. I looked at Brianna's, instead; white and utterly still, each bone and tendon set like death.

Jamie's face was the same, but where Brianna's eyes were blank with shock, Jamie's burned, holes charred black in the bone of his skull. He stood for a moment before Roger, then crossed himself, and said something very quietly in Gaelic. He drew the dirk from his side.

"I'll hold him. Cut him down, lass." Jamie handed the knife to Brianna, not looking at her, and stepping forward, took hold of the body round the middle, lifting slightly to take the strain off the rope.

Roger moaned. Jamie froze, arms wrapped tight, and his eyes flicked to me, huge with shock. It was the faintest of sounds; it was only Jamie's response that convinced me I had indeed heard it—but I had, and so had Brianna. She leapt at the rope, and sawed at it in silent frenzy, and I—stunned into temporary immobility—began to think, as fast as possible.

Maybe not; maybe it was only the sound of the body's residual air escaping with the movement—but it wasn't; I could see Jamie's face, holding him, and I knew it wasn't.

I darted forward, reaching upward as Roger's body fell, to catch and cradle the head in my hands, to steady him as Jamie lowered him to the ground. He was cold, but firm. Of course, if he were alive, he must be, but I had prepared myself for the flaccid-meat touch of dead flesh, and the shock of feeling life under my hands was considerable.

"A board," I said, breathless as though someone had just punched me in the stomach. "A plank, a door, something to put him on. We mustn't move his head; his neck may be broken."

Jamie swallowed once, hard, then jerked his head in an awkward nod, and set off, walking stiffly at first, then faster and faster, past the knots of sorrowing kin and eager gawkers, whose curious gaze was turning now in our direction.

Brianna had the dirk still in her hand. As people began to come toward us, she moved past me, and I caught a glimpse of her face. It was still white, still set—but the eyes burned now with a black light that would sear any soul so reckless as to come too near.

I had no attention to spare for interference—or anything else. I pulled the gag from his mouth but he wasn't breathing visibly; no obvious movement of the chest, no twitch of lips or nostrils. I felt vainly for a pulse in his free wrist—pointless to poke at the mass of swollen tissue in his neck—finally found an abdominal pulse, beating faintly just below the breastbone.

The noose was sunk deep in his flesh; I groped frantically in my pocket for my penknife. It was a new rope, raw hemp. The fibers were hairy, stained brown with dried blood. I registered the fact faintly, in the remote part of my mind that had time for such things while my hands were busy. New ropes stretch. A real hangsman has his own ropes, already stretched and oiled, well-tested for ease of use. The raw hemp jabbed my fingers, stabbed painfully under my nails as I clawed and pried and ripped at it.

The last strand popped and I yanked it free, heedless of laceration—that hardly mattered. I daren't risk tilting his head back; if the cervical vertebrae were fractured, I could cripple or kill him. And if he couldn't breathe, that wouldn't matter, either.

I gripped his jaw, tried to sweep my fingers through his mouth, to clear mucus and obstructions. No good, his tongue was swollen, not sticking out, but in the way. Air takes less room than fingers do, though. I pinched his nose tight, breathed two or three times, as deeply as I could, then sealed my mouth on his and blew.

Had I seen his face as he hung, I would have realized at once that he wasn't dead; his features had gone slack with loss of consciousness and his lips and eyelids were blue—but his face wasn't black with congested blood, and his eyes were closed, not bulging. He'd lost his bowels, but his spinal cord wasn't snapped, and he hadn't strangled—yet.

He was, however, in the process of doing so before my eyes. His chest wasn't moving. I took another breath, and blew, free hand on his breast. Nothing. Blow. No movement. Blow. Something. Not enough. Blow. Air leaking all around the edges of my mouth. Blow. Like blowing up a rock, not a balloon. Blow again.

Confused voices over my head, Brianna shouting, then Jamie at my elbow.

"Here's the board," he said calmly. "What must we do?"

I gasped for breath, and wiped my mouth.

"Take his hips, Bree his shoulders. Move when I tell you, not before."

We shifted him quickly, my hands holding his head like the Holy Grail. There were people all around us now, but I had no time to look or listen; I had eyes only for what must be done.

I ripped off my petticoat, rolled it and used it to brace his neck; I hadn't felt any grinding or crackling in the neck when we lifted him, but I needed all the luck I had for other things.

By stubbornness or sheer miracle, he wasn't dead. But he had hung by the neck for the best part of an hour, and the swelling of the tissues in his throat was very shortly going to accomplish what the rope itself hadn't.

I didn't know whether I had a few minutes or an hour, but the process was inevitable, and there was only one thing to do about it. No more than a few molecules of air were seeping through that mass of crushed and mangled tissue; a bit more swelling would seal it off altogether. If no air could reach his lungs by means of nose or mouth, another channel must be provided.

I turned to look for Jamie, but it was Brianna who knelt beside me. A certain amount of racket in the background indicated that Jamie was dealing with the spectators.

A cricothrotomy? Fast, and requiring no great skill, but difficult to keep open—and it might not be sufficient to relieve the obstruction. I had one hand on Roger's sternum, the soft bump of his heart secure under my fingers. Strong enough . . . maybe.

"Right," I said to Brianna, hoping I sounded quite calm. "I'll need a bit of help."

"Yes," she said—and thank God, *she* sounded calm. "What shall I do?"

In essence, nothing all that difficult; simply hold Roger's head pulled well back, and keep it steady while I slit his throat. Of course, hyperextending the neck could easily sever the spinal cord if there were a fracture, or compress it irreversibly. But Brianna needn't worry about that—or know about it, either.

She knelt by his head and did as I told her, and the mediastinum of the trachea bulged into view as the skin and fascia over it tightened. There it was, neatly lined up—I hoped—between the great vessels on either side. If it wasn't, I could easily lacerate the common carotid or the internal jugular, and he'd bleed to death right under my hands.

The only virtue to hideous emergency is that it gives one license to attempt things that could never be done in cold blood.

I fumbled for the small bottle of alcohol that I carried in my pocket. I nearly dropped it, but by the time I had poured the contents over my fingers and wiped both my scalpel and Roger's neck, the surgeon's trance had come over me, and my hands were once more steady.

I took a moment, hands on his neck, eyes closed, feeling for the faint throb of the artery, the slightly softer mass of the thyroid. I pressed upward; yes, it moved. I massaged the isthmus of the thyroid, pushing it out of the way, hard toward his head, and with my other hand, pressed the knife blade down into the fourth tracheal cartilage.

The cartilage here was U-shaped, the esophagus behind it soft and vulnerable; I must not stab too deeply. I felt the fibrous parting of skin and fascia, resistance, then the soft pop as the blade went in. There was a sudden loud gurgle, and a wet kind of whistling noise; the sound of air being sucked through blood. Roger's chest moved. I felt it, and it was only then that I realized my eyes were still shut.

70

ALL IS WELL

THE BLACKNESS CRADLED HIM, comforting in its warm completeness. He felt some faint stirring of something outside it, a painful, intrusive presence, and shrank back into the shelter of the dark. It was melting away around him, though, slowly exposing parts of him to light and harshness.

He opened his eyes. He couldn't tell what he was looking at, and struggled to understand. His head throbbed and so did a dozen smaller pulses, each one a brilliant, tender burst of pain. He felt the points of pain like pins that nailed him like a butterfly to a board. If he could but pry them free, he might fly away . . .

He closed his eyes again, seeking the comfort of the darkness. He felt a dim recollection of terrible effort, his rib-muscles tearing with the struggle for air. There was water somewhere in his memory, filling his nose, wetness ballooning the hollows of his clothes . . . was he drowning? The idea sent a faint flicker of alarm through his mind. They said it was an easy death, drowning, like falling asleep. Was he sinking, falling into a treacherous and final ease, even as he sought the beguiling dark?

He jerked, flailing with his arms, trying to turn and reach the surface. Pain burst through his chest and burned in his throat; he tried to cough and could not, tried to gulp air and found none, struck something hard—

Something seized him, held him still. A face appeared above him, a blur of skin, a blaze of reddish hair. Brianna? The name floated into his mind like a bright balloon. Then his eyes focused a little, bringing a harsher, fiercer face into view. Jamie. The name hung in front of him, floating, but seeming somehow reassuring.

Pressure, warmth . . . a hand was clasping his arm, another on his shoulder, pressing hard. He blinked, his vision swimming, gradually clearing. He felt no air moving in mouth or nose, his throat was closed and his chest still burned, but he *was* breathing; he felt the soreness of the tiny muscles between his ribs as they moved. He hadn't drowned then; it hurt too much.

"You are alive," Jamie said. Blue eyes stared intently into his, so close he felt warm breath on his face. "You are alive. You are whole. All is well."

He examined the words with a sense of detachment, turning them over like a handful of pebbles, feeling the weight of them in the palm of his mind.

You are alive. You are whole. All is well.

A vague feeling of comfort came over him. That seemed to be all he needed to know just then. Anything else could wait. The waiting black rose up again, with the inviting aspect of a soft couch, and he sank gratefully upon it, still hearing the words like plucked harpstrings.

You are alive. You are whole. All is well.

71

A FEEBLE SPARK

"MRS. CLAIRE?"

It was Robin McGillivray hovering in the doorway of the tent, his dark wiry hair standing up on end like a bottle-brush. He looked like a harried raccoon, the skin round his eyes wiped free of sweat and soot, the rest still blackened with the smoke of battle.

At sight of him, Claire rose at once.

"Coming." She was on her feet, kit in hand and already moving toward the door before Brianna could speak.

"Mother!" It was no more than a whisper, but the tone of panic brought Claire round as though she had stepped on a turntable. The amber eyes fastened on Brianna's face for a moment, flicked to Roger, then back to her daughter.

"Watch his breathing," she said. "Keep the tube clear. Give him honey-water, if he's conscious enough to swallow a bit. And touch him. He can't turn his head to see you; he needs to know you're there."

"But—" Brianna stopped dead, her mouth too dry to speak. *Don't go!* she wanted to cry. *Don't leave me alone! I can't keep him alive, I don't know what to do!*

"They need me," Claire said, very gently. She turned, skirts whispering, to the impatiently waiting Robin, and vanished into the twilight.

"And I don't?" Brianna's lips moved, but she didn't know whether she had spoken aloud or not. It didn't matter; Claire was gone, and she was alone.

She felt light-headed, and realized that she had been holding her breath. She breathed out, and in, deeply, slowly. The fear was a poisonous snake, writhing round her spine, slithering through her mind. Ready to sink its fangs in her heart. She took one more breath through gritted teeth, seized the snake by the head, mentally stuffed it wriggling into a basket, and slammed down the lid. So much for panic, then.

Her mother would not have left, were there any immediate danger, she told herself firmly, nor if there were anything more that could be done medically. So there wasn't. Was there anything *she* could do? She breathed, deep enough to make the boning of her stays creak.

Touch him. Speak to him. Let him know you're with him. That was what Claire had said, speaking urgently but somehow absentmindedly, during the messy proceedings following the impromptu tracheotomy.

Brianna turned back to Roger, looking in vain for something safe to touch. His hands were swollen like inflated gloves, stained purple-red with bruising, the crushed fingers nearly black, raw rope-weals sunk so deep in the flesh of his wrists that she was queasily sure she could see white bone. They looked unreal, badly-done makeup for a horror play.

Grotesque as they were, they were better than his face. That was bruised and swollen, too, with a ghastly ruff of leeches attached beneath his jaw, but it was more subtly deformed, like some sinister stranger pretending to be Roger.

His hands were lavishly decorated with leeches, too. He must be wearing every leech available, she thought. Claire had sent Josh rushing to the other surgeons, to beg their supplies, and then sent him and the two Findlay boys splashing down the creek banks in hasty search of more.

Watch his breathing. That, she could do. She sat down, moving as quietly as she could, from some obscure urge not to wake him. She laid a hand lightly over his heart, so relieved to find him warm to the touch that she gave a great sigh. He grimaced slightly at the feel of her breath on his face, tensed, then relaxed again.

His own breath came so shallowly that she took her hand away, feeling that the pressure of her palm on his chest might be enough to stop its labored rise. He *was* breathing, though; she could hear the faint whistle of air through the tube in his throat. Claire had commandeered Mr. Caswell's imported English pipe, ruthlessly breaking off the amber stem. Rinsed hastily with alcohol, it was still stained with tobacco tar, but seemed to be functioning well enough.

Two fingers of Roger's right hand were broken, all his nails clawed bloody, torn, or missing. Her own throat tightened at this evidence of just how ferociously he had fought to live. His state seemed so precarious that she hesitated to touch him, as though she might startle him over some invisible edge between death and life. And yet she could see what her mother meant; the same touch might hold him back, keep him from stumbling over just such an edge, lost in the dark.

She squeezed his thigh firmly, reassured by the solid feel of the long, curving muscle under the blanket that covered his lower body. He made a small sound, tensed, and relaxed again. She wondered for a surreal moment whether to cup his genitals.

"That would let him know I'm here, all right," she murmured, swallowing a hysterical desire to laugh. His leg quivered slightly at the sound of her voice.

"Can you hear me?" she asked softly, leaning forward. "I'm here, Roger. It's me—Bree. Don't worry, you aren't alone."

Her own voice sounded strange; too loud, stiff and awkward.

"Bi socair, mo chridhe," she said, and relaxed a little. *"Bi samnach, tha mi seo."*

It was easier, somehow, in Gaelic, its formality a thin dam against the intensity of feelings that might swamp her, were they ever set free. Love and fear and anger, swirled together in a mix so strong her hand trembled with it.

She realized suddenly that her breasts were turgid, aching with milk; there had been no time in the last several hours even to think of it, let alone take the time to relieve the pressure. Her nipples stung and tingled at the thought, and she gritted her teeth against the small gush of milk that leaked into her bodice, mingling with her sweat. She yearned toward Roger, wanting suddenly to suckle him, wanting to cradle him against her breast and let life flow into him from her.

Touch him. She was forgetting to touch him. She stroked his arm, squeezed his forearm gently, hoping to distract herself from discomfort.

He seemed to feel her hand on his arm; one eye opened a little, and she thought she saw a consciousness of her flicker in its depths.

"You look like the male version of Medusa," she said, the first thing that popped into her head. One dark eyebrow twitched slightly upward.

"The leeches," she said. She touched one of those on his neck, and it contracted sluggishly, already half-full. "A beard of snakes. Can you feel them? Do they bother you?" she asked before remembering what her mother had said. His lips moved, though, forming a soundless "no," with obvious effort.

"Don't talk." She glanced at the other bed, feeling self-conscious, but the wounded man in it was quiet, eyes closed. She turned back, bent, and quickly kissed Roger, the merest touch of lips. His mouth twitched; she thought he meant to smile.

She wanted to shout at him. *What happened? What in hell did you DO?* But he couldn't answer.

Suddenly, fury overwhelmed her. Mindful of the people passing to and fro nearby, she didn't shout, but instead leaned down and gripped his shoulder—that seeming one of the reasonably undamaged spots—and hissed, "How in God's name did you *do* this?" in his ear.

His eyes rolled slowly toward her, fixing on her face. He made a slight grimace which she couldn't interpret at all, and then the shoulder under her hand began to vibrate. She stared at him in complete perplexity for a few seconds, before she realized that he was laughing. Laughing!

The tube in his throat jiggled, and made a soft wheezing noise, which aggravated her beyond bearing. She stood up, hands pressed against her aching breasts.

"I'll be right back," she said. "Don't you bloody go anywhere, damn you!"

72

TINDER AND CHAR

GERALD FORBES WAS A SUCCESSFUL lawyer, and normally looked the part. Even dressed in his campaigning gear, and with the soot of gunpowder staining his face, he still had an air of solid assurance that served him well as a captain of militia. This air had not quite deserted him, but he seemed visibly uneasy, curling and uncurling the brim of his hat as he stood in the doorway of the tent.

At first I assumed that it was merely the discomfort that afflicts many people in the presence of illness—or perhaps awkwardness over the circumstances of Roger's injury. But evidently it was something else; he barely nodded toward Brianna, who sat by Roger's bed.

"My sympathies for your misfortune, ma'am," he said, then turned at once to Jamie. "Mr. Fraser. If I might—a word? And Mrs. Fraser, too," he added, with a grave bow in my direction.

I glanced at Jamie, and at his nod, got up, reaching by reflex for my medical kit.

There was not a great deal I could do; that much was obvious. Isaiah Morton lay on his side in Forbes's tent, his face dead-white and sheened with sweat. He still breathed, but slowly, and with a horrible gurgling effect that reminded me unpleasantly of the sound when I had pierced Roger's throat. He wasn't conscious, which was a small mercy. I made a cursory examination, and sat back on my heels, wiping sweat from my face with the hem of my apron; the evening had not cooled much, and it was close and hot in the tent.

"Shot through the lung," I said, and both men nodded, though they both clearly knew as much already.

"Shot in the back," Jamie said, a grim tone to his voice. He glanced at Forbes, who nodded, not taking his eyes from the stricken man.

"No," he said quietly, answering an unspoken question. "He wasn't a coward. And it was a clean advance—no other companies in the line behind us."

"No Regulators behind you? No sharpshooters? No ambush?" Jamie asked, but Forbes was shaking his head before the questions were finished.

"We chased a few Regulators as far as the creek, but we stopped there and let them go." Forbes still held the hat between his fingers, and he mechanically rolled and unrolled the brim, over and over. "I had no stomach for killing."

Jamie nodded, silent.

I cleared my throat, and drew the bloody remnants of Morton's shirt gently over him.

"He was shot *twice* in the back," I said. The second bullet had only grazed his upper arm, but I could plainly see the direction of the furrow it had left.

Jamie closed his eyes briefly, then opened them.

"The Browns," he said, in grim resignation.

Gerald Forbes glanced at him, surprised.

"Brown? That's what he said."

"He spoke?" Jamie squatted beside the injured man, a frown drawing his ruddy brows together. He glanced at me, and I shook my head mutely. I was holding Isaiah Morton's wrist, and could feel the flutter and stumble in his pulse. He would not likely speak again.

"When they brought him in." Forbes squatted by Jamie, at last setting down the maltreated hat. "He asked for you, Fraser. And then he said, 'Tell Ally. Tell Ally Brown.' He said that several times, before he—" He gestured mutely at Morton, whose half-closed lids showed slices of white, his eyes rolled up in agony.

Jamie said something obscene, very softly, under his breath in Gaelic.

"Do you really think they did this?" I asked, equally softly. The pulse thumped and shuddered under my thumb, struggling.

He nodded, looking down at Morton.

"I shouldna have let them go," he said, as though to himself. Morton and Alicia Brown, he meant.

"You couldn't have stopped them." I reached my free hand toward him, to touch him in reassurance, but couldn't quite reach him, tethered as I was to Morton's pulse.

Gerald Forbes was looking at me in puzzlement.

"Mr. Morton . . . eloped with the daughter of a man named Brown," I explained delicately. "The Browns weren't happy about it."

"Oh, I see." Forbes nodded understandingly. He glanced down at Morton's body and clicked his tongue, a sound mingling reproof with sympathy. "The Browns—do you know which company they belong to, Fraser?"

"Mine," Jamie said shortly. "Or they did. I havena seen either of them, since the end of the battle." He turned to me. "Is there aught to do for him, Sassenach?"

I shook my head, but didn't let go of his wrist. The pulse hadn't improved, but it hadn't gotten worse, either.

"No. I thought he might be gone already, but he isn't sinking yet. The ball must not have struck a major vessel. Even so . . ." I shook my head again.

Jamie sighed deeply and nodded.

"Aye. Will ye stay with him, then, until . . . ?"

"Yes, of course. Will you go back to our tent, though, and make sure everything's under control there? If Roger—I mean, come and fetch me if I'm needed."

He nodded once more and left. Gerald Forbes came near, and put a tentative hand on Morton's shoulder.

"His wife—I shall see that she has help. If he should come round again, will you tell him that?"

"Yes, of course," I said again, but my hesitation made him look up, brows raised.

"It's just that he . . . um . . . has *two* wives," I explained. "He was already married when he eloped with Alicia Brown. Hence the difficulty with her family, you see."

Forbes's face went comically blank.

"I see," he said, and blinked. "The . . . ah . . . first Mrs. Morton. Do you know her name?"

"No, I'm afraid I—"

"Jessie."

The word was barely more than a whisper, but it might have been a gunshot, for its effect in stopping the conversation.

"What?" My grip on Morton's wrist must have tightened, for he flinched slightly, and I loosened it.

His face was still dead white, but his eyes were open, fogged with pain but definitely conscious.

"Jessie . . ." he whispered again. "Jeze . . . bel. Jessie Hatfield. Water?"

"Wat—oh, yes!" I let go of his wrist and reached at once for the water jug. He would have glugged it, but I let him have only small sips, for the present.

"Jezebel Hatfield, and Alicia Brown," Forbes said carefully, evidently noting the names in his neatly-docketed lawyer's mind. "That is correct? And where do these women live?"

Morton took a breath, coughed, and interrupted the cough abruptly with a gasp of pain. He struggled for a moment, then found speech.

"Jessie—in Granite Falls. Ally's—in Guildford." He breathed very shallowly, gasping between words. And yet I heard no gurgling of blood in his throat, saw none oozing from nose or mouth. I could still hear the sucking sound from the wound in his back, and moved by inspiration, I pulled him slightly forward and jerked back the pieces of his shirt.

"Mr. Forbes, have you a sheet of paper?"

"Why . . . yes. I . . . that is . . ." Forbes had thrust his hand into his coat in automatic response, and come out with a folded sheet of paper. I snatched this from him, unfolded it, poured water over it, and plastered it flat against the small hole beneath Morton's shoulder blade. The ink mixed with blood and ran in little dark runnels over the pasty skin, but the sucking noise abruptly stopped.

Holding the paper in place with my hand, I could feel the

beating of his heart. It was still faint, but steadier—yes, it was steadier.

"I'll be damned," I said, leaning to the side to look at his face. "You aren't going to die, are you?"

Sweat poured from his face, and the rags of his shirt hung dark and sodden against his chest, but the edge of his mouth trembled in an attempt at a smile.

"No, ma'am," he said. "I ain't." He was still breathing in short gasps, but the breaths were deeper. "Ally. Baby's . . . next . . . month. Told her . . . I be there."

I picked up the edge of the blanket with my free hand, and wiped some of the sweat from his face.

"We'll do our best to see that you are," I assured him, then glanced up at the lawyer, who had been watching these proceedings with his mouth hanging slightly open.

"Mr. Forbes. I think perhaps we had better take Mr. Morton back to my tent. Will you find a couple of men to carry him?"

He closed his mouth abruptly.

"Oh. Yes. Of course, Mrs. Fraser. At once." He didn't move right away, though, and I saw his eyes dart toward the wet sheet of paper plastered over Morton's back. I glanced down at it. I could read only a few indistinct words between my fingers, but those were enough to tell me that Jamie's casually insulting references to Forbes as a sodomite were likely inaccurate. "My darling Valencia," the letter began. I knew only one woman named Valencia in the vicinity of Cross Creek—in the colony of North Carolina, for that matter. Farquard Campbell's wife.

"I'm terribly sorry about your paper," I said, looking up at Forbes. Holding his gaze with my own, I carefully rubbed the palm of my hand over the sheet of paper, irrevocably smearing every word on it into a mess of blood and ink. "I'm afraid it's quite ruined."

He took a deep breath, and clapped his hat back on his head.

"That is quite all right, Mrs. Fraser. Perfectly all right. I'll—go and fetch some men."

EVENING BROUGHT RELIEF from the flies, as well as the heat. Drawn by sweat, blood, and manure, they swarmed over the encampment, biting, stinging, crawling, and buzzing in maddening fashion. Even after they had gone, I kept slapping absentmindedly at arms and neck, imagining I felt the tickle of feet.

But they were gone, at last. I glanced round my small kingdom, saw that everyone was breathing—if with an astounding variety of sound effects—and ducked out of the tent for a breath of cool air, myself.

A highly undervalued activity, breathing. I stood for a moment, eyes closed, appreciating the easy rise and fall of my bosom, the soft inrush, the cleansing flux. Having spent the last several hours in keeping air out of Isaiah Morton's chest, and getting it into Roger's, I was inclined to cherish the privilege. Neither of them would draw a single breath without pain for some time—but they *were* both breathing.

They were my only remaining patients; the other seriously wounded had all been claimed by the surgeons of their own companies, or taken to the Governor's tent to be tended by his personal physician. Those with minor injuries had gone back to their fellows, to boast of their scars or nurse their pains with beer.

I heard a ruffle of drums in the distance, and stood still, listening. A solemn cadence played, and stopped abruptly. There was a moment's silence, in which all motion seemed suspended, and then the boom of a cannon.

The Lindsay brothers were nearby, sprawled on the ground by their fire. They too had looked up at the sound of drums.

"What is it?" I called to them. "What's happening?"

"They're bringin' up the dead, Mrs. Fraser," Evan called back. "Ye'll no be worrit, aye?"

I waved to them in reassurance, and began to walk toward the creek. The frogs were singing, a descant to the distant drums. Full military honors for the battle dead. I wondered whether the two hanged ringleaders would be buried in the same place, or whether some separate and less honorable grave would be set aside for them, if their families didn't claim them. Tryon wasn't the sort to leave even an enemy to the flies.

He would know by now, surely. Would he come, to apologize for his mistake? What apology was possible, after all? It was only by the fluke of fortune and a new rope that Roger was alive.

And he might still die.

When I set my hand on Isaiah Morton, I could feel the burning of the bullet lodged in his lung—but I could feel the stronger burning of his ferocious will to live in spite of it, too. When I set my hand on Roger, I felt that same burning . . . but it was a feeble spark. I listened to the whistle of his breath and in my mind I saw charred wood, with a tiny patch of white-hot ember still alight, but trembling on the verge of abrupt extinction.

Tinder, I thought, absurdly. That's what you did with a fire that threatened to go out. You blew on the spark—but then there must be char; something for the spark to catch, to feed on and grow.

A creaking of wagon wheels made me look up from my contemplation of a patch of reeds. It was a small wagon, with a single horse, and a single driver.

"Mrs. Fraser? Is that you?"

It took a moment for me to recognize the voice.

"Mr. MacLennan?" I asked, astonished.

He pulled up alongside me, and touched a hand to his hat. By starlight, his face was dim and grave in its shadow.

"What are you doing here?" I asked, drawing close and lowering my voice, though there was no one anywhere near to hear me.

"I came to find Joe," he replied, with a slight motion of his head toward the wagonbed. It should have been no great shock; I had been seeing death and destruction all day, and I was no more than slightly acquainted with Joe Hobson. I hadn't known he was dead, though, and the hairs rippled on my forearms.

Without speaking further, I went round to the back of the wagon. I felt the small jerk and vibration through the wood as Abel put on the wagon-brake, and got down to join me.

The body wasn't shrouded, though someone had laid a large half-clean kerchief over the face. Three huge black flies rested on it, still and bloated. It made no difference, but I dashed them away with the back of my hand. They drifted up buzzing, and settled again, out of my reach.

"Were you in the fighting?" I asked, not looking at Abel MacLennan. He must have been with the Regulators, but there was no smell of gunpowder on him.

"No," he said softly behind my shoulder. "I'd no wish to fight. I came wi' Joe Hobson, Mr. Hamilton, and the others—but when it looked as though there would be fighting, I came awa'. I walked away, as far as the mill on the other side of the town. And then, when the sun went down, and no sign of Joe . . . I came back," he finished simply.

"What now?" I asked. We both spoke softly, as though we might disturb the dead man's slumber. "Shall we give you help to bury him? My husband—"

"Och, no," he interrupted, still softly. "I'll be takin' him home, Mrs. Fraser. Though I thank ye for the kindness. If ye might spare a bit o' water, though, or food for the way . . ."

"Of course. Wait here—I'll get it."

I hurried back toward our tent, thinking as I went of the distance to Drunkard's Spring from Alamance. Four days, five, six? And the sun so hot, and the flies . . . but I knew the sound of a Scot whose mind was made up, and went without argument.

I took a moment to check the two men; both breathing. Noisily, painfully—but breathing. I had replaced the wet paper on Morton's wound with a bit of oiled linen, stuck down round the edges with honey, which made an excellent seal. No leakage; very good.

Brianna still sat by Roger. She had found a wooden comb, and was combing out his tumbled hair, gently removing burs and twigs, working at the tangles, slowly and patiently. She was singing something under her breath—*"Frère Jacques."* The bodice of her dress showed wet circles. She had gone out once or twice during the day to relieve the growing pressure of milk, but obviously it was time again. The sight made my own breasts ache with remembered strain.

She looked up and I caught her eye. I touched my breast briefly and nodded toward the tent-flap, eyebrow raised. She gave me a nod and a tiny smile, meant to be bravely reassuring, but I could see the bleakness in her eyes. I supposed it had occurred to her that while Roger might live, he would likely never sing—or perhaps even talk—again.

I couldn't speak past the lump in my own throat; only nodded to her and hurried out again, the parcel under my arm.

A figure stepped out of the darkness in front of me, and I nearly ran bang into it. I stopped short with an exclamation, clutching the parcel to my chest.

"My apologies, Mrs. Fraser. I did not realize that you didn't see me." It was the Governor. He took another step, into the glow of light from the tent.

He was alone, and looked very tired, the flesh of his face furrowed and loose. He smelt of drink; his Council and the militia officers would have been toasting his victory, I supposed. His eyes were clear, though, and his step firm.

"Your son-in-law," he said, and glanced toward the tent behind me. "Is he—"

"He is alive," said a soft, deep voice behind the Governor. He whirled round with a smothered exclamation, and my head jerked up.

I saw a shadow move and take shape, and Jamie rose up slowly out of the night; he had been sitting at the base of a hickory tree, invisible in the dark. How long had he been there? I wondered.

"Mr. Fraser." The Governor had been startled, but he firmed his jaw, hands folded into fists at his sides. He was obliged to tilt his head back to look up at Jamie, and I could see that he didn't like it. Jamie could see it, too, and plainly didn't care. He stood close to Tryon, looming over him, with an expression on his face that would have rattled most people.

It appeared to rattle Tryon, too, but he lifted his chin, determined to say whatever he had come to say.

"I have come to make my apologies for the injury done to your son-in-law," he said. "It was a most regrettable error."

"Most regrettable," Jamie repeated, with an ironic intonation. "And would ye care to say, sir, how this . . . error . . . came about?" He took a step forward, and Tryon automatically took a step back. I could see the heat rise in the Governor's face, and his jaw clench.

"It was a mistake," he said, through his teeth. "He was wrongly identified as one of the outlawed ringleaders of the Regulation."

"By whom?" Jamie's voice was polite.

Small hectic spots burned in the Governor's cheeks.

"I do not know. By several people. I had no reason to doubt the identification."

"Indeed. And did Roger MacKenzie say nothing in his own defense? Did he not say who he was?"

Tryon's lower teeth fastened briefly in the flesh of his upper lip, then let go.

"He . . . did not."

"Because he was bloody bound and gagged!" I said. I had pulled the gag from his mouth myself, when Jamie had cut him down from the hanging tree. "You didn't *let* him speak, did you, you—you—"

The lamplight from the tent-flap gleamed off Tryon's gorget, a crescent of silver that hung round his throat. Jamie's hand rose slowly—so slowly that Tryon plainly perceived no threat—and very gently fitted itself around the Governor's throat, just above the gorget.

"Leave us, Claire," he said. There was no particular threat in his voice; he sounded merely matter-of-fact. A flash of panic lit Tryon's eyes, and he jerked backward, gorget flashing in the light.

"You dare to lay hands on me, sir!" The panic subsided at once, replaced by fury.

"Oh, I do, aye. As ye laid hands on my son."

I didn't *think* Jamie actually intended to harm the Governor. On the other hand, this was by no means merely an act of intimidation; I could feel the core of cold rage inside him, and see it like an ice-burn in his eyes. So could Tryon.

"It was a mistake! And one I have come to rectify, so far as I may!" Tryon was standing his ground, jaw tight as he glared upward.

Jamie made a sound of contempt, low in his throat.

"A mistake. And is the loss of an innocent man's life no more than that to ye? You will kill and maim, for the sake of your glory, and pay no heed to the destruction ye leave—save only that the record of your exploits may be enlarged. How will it look in the dispatches ye send to England—sir? That ye brought cannon to bear on your own citizens, armed with no more than knives and clubs? Or will it say that ye put down rebellion and preserved order? Will it say that in your haste to vengeance, ye hanged an innocent man? Will it say there that ye made 'a mistake'? Or will it say that ye punished wickedness, and did justice in the King's name?"

Tryon's jaw muscles bulged, and his limbs trembled, but he kept his temper in check. He breathed deeply through his nose, in and out, before he spoke.

"Mr. Fraser. I will tell you something that is known to a few, but is not yet public knowledge."

Jamie didn't reply, but raised one brow, glinting red in the light. His eyes were cold, dark and unblinking.

"I am made Governor of the colony of New York," Tryon said. "The letter of appointment arrived more than a month past. I shall leave by July to take up the new appointment; Josiah Martin is made Governor here in my room." He glanced from Jamie to me, and back. "So you see. I had no personal stake in this; no need to glorify my exploits, as you put it." His throat moved as he swallowed, but fear had been replaced now by a coldness equal to Jamie's own.

"I have done what I have done as a matter of duty. I would not leave this colony in a state of disorder and rebellion, for my successor to deal with—though I might rightfully have done so."

He took a deep breath, and stepped back, forcing his hands to relax from the fists into which they had been clenched.

"You have experience of war, Mr. Fraser, and of duty. And if you are an honest man, you will know that mistakes are made—and made often—in both realms. It cannot be otherwise."

He met Jamie's eyes straight on, and they stood in silence, looking at each other.

My attention was jerked away from this confrontation quite suddenly, by the distant sound of a baby crying. I turned, head up, just as Brianna emerged from the tent-flap behind me, in a rustle of agitated skirts.

"Jem," she said. "That's Jemmy!"

It was, too. A disturbance of voices at the far side of the camp came closer, resolving itself into the round, flounced shape of Phoebe Sherston, looking frightened but determined, followed by two slaves: a man carrying two huge baskets, and a woman, with a wrapped and squirming bundle in her arms that was making a terrible racket.

Brianna made for the bundle like a compass needle swinging north, and the racket ceased as Jemmy emerged from his blankets, hair sticking up in red tufts and feet churning in paroxysms of joyous relief. Mother and child disappeared promptly into the shadows under the trees, and a certain amount of confusion ensued, with Mrs. Sherston explaining disjointedly to a gathering crowd of interested onlookers that she had just become *so* distraught, hearing reports of the battle, so terrible, and she feared . . . but Mr. Rutherford's slave had come to say all was well . . . and she thought perhaps . . . and so . . . and the child would *not* give over shrieking . . . so . . .

Jamie and the Governor, shaken out of their nose to nose confrontation, had also retired to the shadows; I could see them, two stiff shadows, one tall and one shorter, standing close together. The element of danger had gone out of their *tête-à-tête*, though; I could see Jamie's head bent slightly toward Tryon's shadow, listening.

". . . brought food," Phoebe Sherston was telling me, her round face pink with excited self-importance. "Fresh bread, and butter, and some blackberry jam and cold chicken and . . ."

"Food!" I said, abruptly reminded of the parcel I held under my arm. "Do pardon me!" I gave her a quick, bright smile, and ducked away, leaving her open-mouthed in front of the tent.

Abel MacLennan was where I had left him, waiting patiently under the stars. He brushed aside my apologies, thanking me for the food and jug of beer.

"Is there anything—?" I began, then broke off. What else could I possibly do for him?

And yet it seemed there was something.

"Young Hugh Fowles," he said, tidily tucking the parcel beneath the wagon's seat. "They said he was taken prisoner.

Would—would your husband maybe speak for him, d'ye think? As he did for me?"

"I expect he would. I'll ask him."

It was quiet here, far enough from the camp that the sounds of conversation didn't carry above the song of frogs and crickets, and the rushing of the creek.

"Mr. MacLennan," I said, moved by impulse, "where will you go? After you've taken Joe Hobson back, I mean."

He took off his hat and scratched his balding head, quite unself-consciously, though the gesture was not one of puzzlement, but merely of one preparing to state something already settled in his mind.

"Och," he said. "I dinna mean to go anywhere. There are the women there, aye? And the weans. They've no man, with Joe dead and Hugh prisoner. I shall stay."

He bowed to me then, and put on his hat. I shook his hand—surprising him—and then he climbed aboard his wagon and clicked his tongue to the horse. He lifted his hand to me in farewell, and I waved back, realizing the difference in him as I did so.

There was still grief in his voice, and sorrow on his shoulders; and yet he sat upright on his errand, the starlight shining on his dusty hat. His voice was firm, and his hand likewise. If Joe Hobson had left for the land of the dead, Abel MacLennan had come back from there.

Things had settled somewhat by the time I came back to the tent. The Governor and Mrs. Sherston were gone, with her slaves. Isaiah Morton slept, moaning now and then, but without fever. Roger lay still as a tomb-figure, face and hands black with bruises, the faint whistle of his breathing tube a counterpoint to Brianna's murmured song as she rocked Jemmy.

The little boy's face was slack, mouth pinkly open in the utter abandonment of sleep. With sudden inspiration, I held out my arms, and Bree, looking surprised, let me take him. Very carefully, I laid the limp, heavy little body on Roger's chest. Bree made a small movement, as though to catch the baby and stop him sliding off—but Roger's arm moved up, stiff and slow, and folded across the sleeping child. *Tinder*, I thought, satisfied.

Jamie was outside the tent, leaning against the hickory tree. When I had made sure of things inside, I came out to join him in the shadows. He raised his arms without speaking, and I came inside them.

We stood together in the shadows, listening to the crackle of campfires and the crickets' songs.

Breathing.

Great Alamance Camp
Friday 17th May 1771
Parole - Granville
Countersign - Oxford

The Governor impressed with the most affectionate sense of Gratitude gives Thanks to both Officers and Soldiers of the Army for the Vigorous and Generous support they afforded Him Yesterday in the Battle near Alamance, it was to their Valour and steady Conduct that he owed under the Providence of Almighty God, the signal Victory obtained over obstinate and infatuated Rebels,—His Excellency simpathises with the Loyalists for the brave Men that fell and suffered in the Action, but when he reflects that the fate of Constitution depended on the success of the Day, and the important Services thereby rendered to their King and Country, He considers this Loss (though at present the Cause of Affliction to their Relations and Friends) as a Monument of lasting Glory and Honor to themselves and Families.

The Dead to be interred at five OClock this Evening in the Front of the Park of Artillery, Funeral Service to be performed with Military Honors to the deceased—after the Ceremony, Prayers and Thanksgiving for the signal Victory it has pleased Divine Providence Yesterday to Grant the Army over the Insurgents.

Part Seven

Alarms of Struggle and Flight

73

A WHITER SHADE OF PALE

MRS. SHERSTON, with an unexpected generosity, offered us her hospitality. I moved to the Sherstons' large house in Hillsborough with Brianna, Jemmy, and my two patients; Jamie divided his time between Hillsborough and the militia camp, which remained in place at Alamance Creek while Tryon satisfied himself that the Regulation had indeed been decisively crushed.

While I couldn't reach the bullet lodged in Morton's lung with my forceps, it didn't appear to be troubling him greatly, and the wound had begun to seal itself in a satisfactory fashion. There was no telling exactly where the bullet was, but plainly it hadn't pierced any major vessels; as long as it didn't move further, it was quite possible for him simply to live with the bullet embedded in his body; I had known a good many war veterans who had—Archie Hayes among them.

I was not at all sure how stable my small stock of penicillin might prove to be, but it seemed to work; there was a little redness and seepage at the wound site, but no infection, and very little fever. Beyond penicillin, the appearance a few days after the battle of Alicia Brown, now enormously pregnant, was the most important boost to Morton's recovery. Within an hour of her arrival, he was sitting up in his cot, pale but jubilant, hair sticking up on end and his hand lovingly pressed against the writhing bulges of his unborn child.

Roger was another matter. He was not badly injured, beyond the crushing of his throat—though that was bad enough. The fractures to his fingers were simple; I had set them with splints and they should heal with no trouble. The bruising faded fairly quickly from livid reds and blues into a spectacular array of purple, green, and yellow that made him look as though he had just been exhumed after having been dead for a week or so. His vital signs were excellent. His vitality was not.

He slept a great deal, which should have been good. His slumber wasn't restful, though; it had about it something unsettling, as though he sought unconsciousness with a fierce desire, and once achieved, clung to it with a stubbornness that bothered me more than I wanted to admit.

Brianna, who possessed her own brand of stubbornness, had the job of forcing him back to wakefulness every few hours, to take some nourishment and have the tube and its incision cleansed and tended. During these procedures, he would fix his eyes on the middle distance, and stare darkly at nothing, making the barest acknowledgment of remarks addressed to him. Once finished, his eyes would close again, and he would lie back on his pillow, bandaged hands folded across his chest like a tomb-figure, with no sound save the soft, breathy whistle from the tube in his neck.

Two days after the battle of Alamance, Jamie arrived at the Sherstons' house in Hillsborough just before supper, tired from long riding, and covered with reddish dust.

"I had a wee talk wi' the Governor today," he said, taking the cup of water I had brought out to him in the yard. He drained it in a gulp and sighed, wiping sweat from his face with a coat-sleeve. "He was fashed about wi' all the to-do, and of no mind to think about what happened after the battle—but *I* was of no mind to let it be."

"I don't imagine it was much of a contest," I murmured, helping him to peel off the dusty coat. "William Tryon's not even Scots, let alone a Fraser."

That got me a reluctant half-smile. "Stubborn as rocks," was the succinct description of the Fraser clan I had been given years before—and nothing in the intervening time period had given me cause to think it inaccurate in any way.

"Aye, well." He shrugged and stretched luxuriously, his vertebrae cracking from the long ride. "Oh, Christ. I'm starved; is there food?" He relaxed and lifted his long nose, sniffing the air hopefully.

"Baked ham and sweet potato pie," I told him, unnecessarily, since the honey-soaked fragrances of both were thick on the humid air. "So what did the Governor say, once you'd got him properly browbeaten?"

His teeth showed briefly at that description of his interview with Tryon, but I gathered from his faint air of satisfaction that it wasn't totally incorrect.

"Oh, a number of things. But to begin with, I insisted he recall to me the circumstances when Roger Mac was taken; who gave him up, and what was said. I mean to get to the bottom of it." He pulled the thong from his hair and shook out the damp locks, dark with sweat.

"Did he remember anything when you pressed him?"

"Aye, a bit more. Tryon says there were three men who had Roger Mac captive; one of them had a badge for Fraser's Company, so of course he thought the man was one of mine. He says," he added, with irony.

That would have been a reasonable assumption for the Governor to make, I thought—but Jamie was plainly in no mood to be reasonable.

"It must have been Roger's badge that the man had," I said. "The rest of your company came back with you—all except the Browns, and it wouldn't have been them." The two Browns had vanished, seizing the opportunity of the confusion of battle to take their vengeance on Isaiah Morton and then to escape before anyone discovered the crime. They wouldn't have hung about to frame Roger, even had they some motive for doing so.

He nodded, dismissing the conclusion with a brief gesture.

"Aye. But why? He said Roger Mac was bound and gagged—a dishonorable way to treat a prisoner of war, as I said to him."

"And what did he say to that?" Tryon might be slightly less stubborn than Jamie; he wasn't any more amenable to insult.

"He said it wasna war; it was treasonable insurrection,

and he was justified in taking summary measures. But to seize and hang a man, without allowing him to speak a word in his own behalf—" The color was rising dangerously in his face. "I swear to ye, Claire, if Roger Mac had died at the end of yon rope, I would have snapped Tryon's neck and left him for the crows!"

I hadn't the slightest doubt that he meant it; I could still see his hand, fitting itself so slowly, so gently, about the Governor's neck above the silver gorget. I wondered whether William Tryon had had the slightest notion of the danger in which he had stood, that night after the battle.

"He didn't die, and he isn't going to." I hoped I was right, but spoke as firmly as I could, laying a hand on his arm. The muscles in his forearm bulged and shifted with the restrained desire to hit someone, but stilled under my touch, as he looked down at me. He took a deep breath, then another, drummed his stiff fingers twice against his thigh, then got his anger under control once more.

"Well, so. He said the man identified Roger Mac as James MacQuiston, one of the ring-leaders of the Regulation. I have been asking after MacQuiston," he added, with another glance at me. He was growing slightly calmer, talking. "Would it surprise ye, Sassenach, to discover that no one kens MacQuiston, by his face?"

It would, and I said so. He nodded, the high color receding slightly from his cheeks.

"So it did me. But it's so; the man's words are there in the papers for all to see—but no one has ever seen the man. Not auld Ninian, not Hermon Husband—no one of the Regulators that I could find to speak to—though the most of them are lying low, to be sure," he added.

"I even found the printer who set one of MacQuiston's speeches in type; he said the script of it was left upon his doorstep one morning, with a brick of cheese and two certificates of proclamation money to pay for the printing."

"Well, that *is* interesting," I said. I took my hand gingerly off his arm, but he seemed under control now. "So you think 'James MacQuiston' is likely an assumed name."

"Verra likely indeed."

Pursuing the implications of that line of thought, I had a sudden idea.

"Do you think that perhaps the man who identified Roger to the Governor as MacQuiston might have been MacQuiston himself?"

Jamie's brows went up, and he nodded slowly.

"And he sought to shield himself, by having Roger Mac hanged in his place? Being dead is an excellent protection against arrest. Aye, that's a bonnie idea—if a trifle vicious," he added judiciously.

"Oh, just a trifle."

He seemed less angry with the vicious and fictitious MacQuiston than with the Governor—but then, there was no doubt as to what Tryon had done.

We had moved across the yard to the well. There was a half-filled bucket sitting on the coping, warm and brackish from the day's heat. He rolled up his sleeves, cupped his hands, and dashed water from the bucket up into his face, then shook his head violently, spattering droplets into Mrs. Sherston's hydrangeas.

"Did the Governor recall what any of these men who had Roger looked like?" I asked, handing him a crumpled linen towel from the well-coping. He took it and wiped his face, shaking his head.

"Only the one. The one who had the badge, who did most of the talking. He said it was a fair-haired fellow, verra tall and well set up. Green-eyed, he thought. Tryon wasna taking careful note of his appearance, of course, bein' exercised in his mind at the time. But he recalled that much."

"Jesus H. Roosevelt Christ," I said, struck by a thought. "Tall, fair-haired, and green-eyed. Do you think it could have been Stephen Bonnet?"

His eyes opened wide and he stared at me over the towel for a moment, face blank with astonishment.

"Jesus," he said, and set the towel down absentmindedly. "I never thought of such a thing."

Neither had I. What I knew of Bonnet didn't seem to fit the picture of a Regulator; most of them were poor and desperate men, like Joe Hobson, Hugh Fowles, and Abel

MacLennan. A few were outraged idealists, like Husband and Hamilton. Stephen Bonnet might occasionally have been poor and desperate—but I was reasonably sure that the notion of seeking redress from the government by protest wasn't one that would have occurred to him. Take it by force, certainly. Kill a judge or sheriff in vengeance for some offense, quite possibly. But—no, it was ridiculous. If I was certain of anything regarding Stephen Bonnet, it was that he didn't pay taxes.

"No." Jamie shook his head, having evidently come to the same conclusions. He wiped a lingering droplet off the end of his nose. "There's nay money anywhere in this affair. Even Tryon had to appeal to the Earl of Hillsborough for funds to pay his militia. And the Regulators—" He waved a hand, dismissing the thought of the Regulators paying anyone for anything. "I dinna ken everything about Stephen Bonnet, but from what I've seen of the man, I think that only gold or the promise of it would bring him to a battlefield."

"True." The clink of china and chime of silver came faintly through the open window, accompanying the soft voices of slaves; the table was being set for dinner. "I don't suppose there's any way Bonnet could be James MacQuiston, is there?"

He laughed at that, his face relaxing for the first time.

"No, Sassenach. That I *can* be sure of. Stephen Bonnet canna read, nor write much more than his name."

I stared at him.

"How do you know that?"

"Samuel Cornell told me so. He hasna met Bonnet himself, but he said that Walter Priestly came to him once, to borrow money urgently. He was surprised, for Priestly's a wealthy man—but Priestly told him that he had a shipment coming that must be paid for in gold—for the man bringing it would not take warehouse receipts, proclamation money, or even bank-drafts. He didna trust words on paper that he couldna read himself, nor would he trust anyone to read them to him. Only gold would do."

"Yes, that does sound like Bonnet." I had been holding his coat, folded over one arm. Now I shook it out, and began to beat the red dust from its skirts, averting my face from the resultant clouds. "What you said about gold . . . do you think Bonnet could have been at Alamance by accident? On his way to River Run, perhaps?"

He considered that one for a moment, but then shook his head, rolling down the cuffs of his shirt.

"It wasna a great war, Sassenach—not the sort of thing where a man might be caught up unawares and carried along. The armies faced each other for more than two days, and the sentry lines had holes like a fishing seine; anyone could have left Alamance, or ridden round it. And Alamance is nowhere near River Run. No, whoever it was that tried to kill wee Roger, it was someone who was there on his own account."

"So we're back to the mysterious Mr. MacQuiston—whoever he might be."

"Perhaps," he said dubiously.

"But who else could it be?" I protested. "Surely no one among the Regulators could have had anything personal against Roger!"

"Ye wouldna think so," Jamie admitted. "But we're no going to know until the lad can tell us, aye?"

AFTER SUPPER—during which there was naturally no mention of MacQuiston, Stephen Bonnet, or anything else of an upsetting nature—I went up to check on Roger. Jamie came with me, and quietly dismissed the slave woman who sat by the window, mending. Someone had to stay with Roger at all times, to make sure the tube in his throat didn't become clogged or dislodged, as it was still his only means of breathing. It would be several days yet before the swelling of the mangled tissues in his throat subsided enough for me to risk removing it.

Jamie waited until I had checked Roger's pulse and breathing, then at my nod, sat down by his bedside.

"Do ye ken the names of the men who denounced ye?" he asked without preliminaries. Roger looked up at him, frowning, dark brows drawn together. Then he nodded slowly, and held up one finger.

"One of them. How many were there?"

Three fingers. That agreed with Tryon's recollection, then.

"They were Regulators?"

A nod.

Jamie glanced at me, then back at Roger.

"It wasna Stephen Bonnet?"

Roger sat up bolt upright, mouth open. He clutched at the tube in his throat, struggling vainly to speak, and shaking his head violently.

I grabbed for his shoulder, one hand reaching for the tube; the violence of his movement had jerked it nearly out of the incision, and a trickle of blood ran down his neck where the wound had reopened. Roger himself seemed oblivious; his eyes were fixed on Jamie's and his mouth was working urgently, asking silent questions.

"No, no. If ye didna see him, then he wasna there." Jamie took him firmly by the other shoulder, helping me to ease him back on the pillow. "It was only that Tryon described the man who betrayed ye as a tall, fair-haired fellow. Green-eyed, maybe. We thought perhaps . . ."

Roger's face relaxed at that. He shook his head again and sank back, mouth twisted a little. Jamie pressed on.

"Ye kent the man, though; ye'd met him before?" Roger glanced away, nodded, then shrugged. He looked both irritated and helpless; I could hear his breathing quicken, whistling through the amber tube. I cleared my throat significantly, frowning at Jamie. Roger was out of immediate danger; that didn't mean he was well, or anywhere near it.

Jamie ignored me. He'd picked up Bree's sketching-box on his way upstairs; laying a sheet of paper on it, he put it on Roger's lap, then extended one of the sticks of hardened charcoal to him.

"Will ye try again?" He had been trying to get Roger to communicate on paper ever since he had regained full consciousness, but Roger's hands had been too swollen even to close around a pen. They were still puffed and bruised, but repeated leeching and gentle massage had improved them to the point that they did at least *look* vaguely like hands again.

Roger's lips pressed together momentarily, but he wrapped his hand clumsily around the charcoal. The first two fingers on that hand were broken; the splints stuck out in a crude "V" sign—which I thought rather appropriate, under the circumstances.

Roger frowned in concentration, and began to scrawl something slowly. Jamie watched intently, holding the paper flat with both hands to keep it from sliding.

The stick of charcoal snapped in two, the fragments flying off across the floor. I went to pick them up, while Jamie leaned frowning over the smeared sheet of paper. There was a sprawling "W" and an "M," then a space, and an awkward "MAC."

"William?" He looked up at Roger for verification. Sweat shone on Roger's cheekbones, but he nodded, very briefly.

"William Mac," I said, peering over Jamie's shoulder. "A Scotsman, then—or a Scottish name, at least?" Not that that narrowed down the possibilities a great deal: MacLeod, MacPherson, MacDonald, MacDonnel, Mac . . . Quiston?

Roger raised his hand and thumped it against his chest. He thumped it again, and mouthed a word. Recalling television shows based on charades, I was for once quicker than Jamie.

"MacKenzie?" I asked, and was rewarded with a quick flash of green eyes, and a nod.

"MacKenzie. William MacKenzie." Jamie was frowning, obviously running through his mental roster of names and faces, but not turning up a match.

I was watching Roger's face. Still heavily bruised, it too was beginning to look more normal, despite the livid weal under his jaw, and I thought there was something odd about his expression. I could see physical pain in his eyes, helplessness, and frustration at his immediate inability to tell Jamie what he wanted to know, but I thought there was something else there, too. Anger, certainly, but something like bafflement, as well.

"Do you know any William MacKenzies?" I asked Jamie, who was tapping his fingers lightly on the table as he thought.

"Aye, four or five," he replied, brows still knotted in concentration. "In Scotland. But none here, and none that—"

Roger's hand lifted abruptly at the word "Scotland," and Jamie stopped, fixed on Roger's face like a pointing bird dog.

"Scotland," he said. "Something about Scotland? The man is a new immigrant?"

Roger shook his head violently, then stopped abruptly, grimacing in pain. He squeezed his eyes shut for a moment, then opened them, and waved urgently at the bits of charcoal I still held in my hand.

It took several tries, and at the end of it Roger lay back exhausted on the pillow, the neck of his nightshirt damp with sweat and spotted with blood from his throat. The result of his effort was smeared and straggling, but I could read the word clearly.

Dougal, it said. Jamie's look of interest sharpened into something like wariness.

"Dougal," he repeated carefully. He knew several Dougals as well; a few of them resident in North Carolina. "Dougal Chisholm? Dougal O'Neill?"

Roger shook his head and the tube in his throat wheezed with his exhalation. He lifted his hand and pointed emphatically at Jamie, the splinted fingers jabbing. Getting only a blank look in response, he fumbled for the bit of charcoal again, but it rolled off the sketch-box and shattered on the floor.

His fingers were smeared with charcoal dust. Grimacing, he pressed the tip of his ring finger against the page, and by dint of using all the fingers in turn, produced a faint and ghostly scrawl that sent a small electric shock shooting up from the base of my spine.

Geilie, it said.

Jamie stared at the name for a moment. Then I saw a small shiver move over him, and he crossed himself.

"A Dhia," he said softly, and looked at me. Awareness thickened between us; Roger saw it and fell back on his pillow, exhaling loudly through his breathing-tube.

"Dougal's son by Geillis Duncan," Jamie said, turning to Roger with incredulity writ large on his face. "He was named William, I think. Ye mean it? Ye're sure of it?"

A brief nod, and Roger's eyes closed. Then they opened again; one splinted finger rose wavering, and pointed to his own eye—a deep, clear green, the color of moss. He was white as the linen he lay on, and his charcoal-smeared fingers were trembling. His mouth was twitching; he wanted badly to talk, to explain—but further explanations were going to have to wait, for a little while, at least.

His hand dropped, and his eyes closed again.

THE REVELATION OF William Buccleigh MacKenzie's identity didn't alter Jamie's urgent desire to find the man, but it did change his intention of murdering him immediately, once found. On the whole, I was grateful for small favors.

Brianna, summoned from her painting to consult, arrived in my room in her smock, smelling strongly of turpentine and linseed oil, with a smear of cobalt blue on one earlobe.

"Yes," she said, bewildered by Jamie's abrupt questions. "I've heard of him. William Buccleigh MacKenzie. The changeling."

"The what?" Jamie's brows shot up toward his hairline.

"That's what I called him," I said. "When I saw Roger's family tree, and realized who William Buccleigh MacKenzie must be. Dougal gave the child to William and Sarah MacKenzie, remember? And they gave him the name of the child they'd lost two months before."

"Roger mentioned that he'd seen William MacKenzie and his wife, on board the *Gloriana*, when he sailed from Scotland to North Carolina," Bree put in. "But he said he didn't realize who the man was until later, and didn't have a chance to talk to him. So he is here—William, I mean—but why on earth would he try to kill Roger—and why that way?" She shuddered briefly, though the room was very warm. It was early summer, and even with the windows open, the air was hot and liquid with humidity.

"He's the witch's get," Jamie said shortly, as though that was sufficient answer—as perhaps it was.

"They thought I was a witch, too," I reminded him, a little tartly. That got me a sideways blue glance, and a curve of the mouth.

"So they did," he said. He cleared his throat, and wiped a sleeve across his sweating brow. "Aye, well. I suppose we must just wait and find out. And having a name helps. I shall send to Duncan and Farquard; have them put out word." He drew a deep breath of exasperation, and blew it out again.

"What am I to do when I find him, though? Witch-son or no, he's my own blood; I canna kill him. Not after Dougal—" He caught himself in time, and coughed. "I mean, he's Dougal's son. He's my own cousin, for God's sake."

I knew what he really meant. Four people knew what had happened in that attic room at Culloden House, the day before that distant battle. One of those was dead, the other disappeared and almost certainly dead too, in the tumult of the Rising. Only I was left as the witness to Dougal's blood and the hand that had spilled it. No matter what crime William Buccleigh MacKenzie had committed, Jamie would not kill him, for his father's sake.

"You were going to kill him? Before you found out who he was?" Bree didn't look shocked at the thought. She had a stained paint-rag in her hands, and was twisting it slowly.

Jamie turned to look at her.

"Roger Mac is your man, the son of my house," he said, very seriously. "Of course I would avenge him."

Brianna flicked a glance at me, then looked away. She looked thoughtful, with a certain intentness that gave me a slight chill to see.

"Good," she said, very softly. "When you find William Buccleigh MacKenzie, I want to know about it." She folded up the rag, thrust it into the pocket of her smock, and went back to her work.

BRIANNA SCRAPED a tiny blob of viridian onto the edge of her palette, and feathered a touch of it into the big smear of pale gray she had created. She hesitated a moment, tilting the palette back and forth in the light from the window to judge the color, then added the faintest dab of cobalt to the other side of the smear, producing a range of subtle tones that ran from blue-gray to green-gray, all so faint as scarcely to be distinguishable from white by the uneducated eye.

She took one of the short, thick brushes, and worked the

gray tones along the curve of the jaw on her canvas with tiny overlapping strokes. Yes, that was just about right; pale as fired porcelain, but with a vivid shadow under it—something both delicate and earthy.

She painted with a deep absorption that shut out her surroundings, engrossed in an artist's double vision, comparing the evolving image on the canvas with the one so immutably etched in her memory. It wasn't that she had never seen a dead person before. Her father—Frank—had had an open-casket funeral, and she had been to the obsequies of older family friends in her own time, as well. But the colors of the embalmer's art were crude, almost coarse by comparison with those of a fresh corpse. She had been staggered by the contrast.

It was the blood, she thought, taking a fine two-haired brush to add a dot of pure viridian in the deep curve of the eye socket. Blood and bone—but death didn't alter the curves of the bones, nor the shadows they cast. Blood, though, colored those shadows. In life, you got the blues and reds and pinks and lavenders of moving blood beneath the skin; in death, the blood stilled and pooled and darkened . . . clay-blue, violet, indigo, purple-brown . . . and something new: that delicate, transient green, barely there, that her artist's mind classified with brutal clarity as "early rot."

Unfamiliar voices came from the hall, and she looked up, wary. Phoebe Sherston was fond of bringing in visitors to admire the painting in progress. Normally, Brianna didn't mind being watched, or talking about what she was doing, but this was a tricky job, and one with limited time; she couldn't work with such subtle colors save for a short period just before sunset, when the light was clear but diffuse.

The voices passed on to the parlor, though, and she relaxed, taking up the thicker brush again.

She resummoned the vision in her mind; the dead man they had laid under a tree at Alamance, near her mother's makeshift field hospital. She had expected to be shocked by battle-wounds and death—and was instead shocked by her own fascination. She had seen terrible things, but it wasn't like attending at her mother's normal surgeries, where there was time to empathize with the patients, to take note of all the small indignities and nastinesses of weak flesh. Things happened too fast on a battlefield; there was too much to be done for squeamishness to take hold.

And in spite of the haste and urgency, each time she had passed near that tree, she had paused for an instant. Bent to turn back the blanket over the corpse and look at the man's face; appalled at her own fascination but making no effort to resist it—committing to memory the amazing, inexorable change of color and shadow, the stiffening of muscle and shifting of shape, as skin settled and clung to bone, and the processes of death and decay began to work their awful magic.

She hadn't thought to ask the dead man's name. Was that unfeeling? she wondered. Probably; the fact was that all her feelings had been otherwise engaged at the time—and still were. Still, she closed her eyes for a moment and said a quick prayer for the repose of the soul of her unknown sitter.

She opened her eyes to see that the light was fading. She scraped the palette and began to clean her brushes and hands, returning slowly and reluctantly to the world outside her work.

Jem would have been fed his supper and bathed already, but he refused to go to bed without being nursed and rocked to sleep. Her breasts tingled slightly at the thought; they were pleasantly full, though they seldom became excruciatingly engorged since he had taken to eating solid food and thus decreased his voracious demands on her flesh.

She'd nurse Jem and put him down, and then go have her own belated supper in the kitchen. She had not eaten with the others, wanting to take advantage of the evening light, and her stomach was growling softly, as the lingering smells of food in the air replaced the astringent scents of turps and linseed oil.

And then . . . then she would go upstairs to Roger. Her lips tightened at the thought; she realized it, and forced her mouth to relax, blowing air out so that her lips vibrated with a flatulent noise like a motorboat.

At this unfortunate moment, Phoebe Sherston's capped head popped through the door. She blinked slightly, but had sufficiently good manners to pretend that she hadn't seen anything.

"Oh, my dear, there you are! Do come into the parlor for a moment, won't you? Mr. and Mrs. Wilbur are *so* eager to make your acquaintance."

"Oh—well, yes, of course," Brianna said, with what graciousness she could summon. She gestured at her paint-stained smock. "Let me just go and change—"

Mrs. Sherston waved away the smock, obviously wanting to show off her tame artist in costume.

"No, no, don't trouble about that. We are quite simple this evening. No one will mind."

Brianna moved reluctantly toward the drawing room.

"All right. Only for a minute, though; I need to put Jem to bed."

Mrs. Sherston's rosebud mouth primmed slightly at that; she saw no reason why her slaves could not take care of the child altogether—but she had heard Brianna's opinions on the subject before, and was wise enough not to press the issue.

Brianna's parents were in the parlor with the Wilburs, who turned out to be a nice, elderly couple—what her mother would call a Darby and Joan. They fussed appropriately over her appearance, insisted politely on seeing the portrait, expressed profound admiration for both subject and painter—though blinking slightly at the former—and generally behaved with such kindness that she felt herself relaxing.

She was just on the verge of making her excuses, when Mr. Wilbur took advantage of a lull in the conversation to turn to her, smiling benevolently.

"I understand that congratulations upon your good fortune are in order, Mrs. MacKenzie."

"Oh? Ah . . . thank you," she said, uncertain what she was being congratulated for. She glanced at her mother for some clue; Claire grimaced slightly, and glanced at Jamie, who coughed.

"Governor Tryon has granted your husband five thousand acres of land, in the back-country," he said. His voice was even, almost colorless.

"He has?" She felt momentarily bewildered. "What—why?"

There was a brief stir of embarrassment among the party, with small throat-clearings and marital glances between the Sherstons and the Wilburs.

"Compensation," her mother said tersely, darting a marital glance of her own at Jamie.

Brianna understood then; no one would be so uncouth as to mention Roger's accidental hanging openly, but it was much too sensational a story not to have made the rounds of Hillsborough society. She realized suddenly that Mrs. Sherston's invitation to her parents and Roger had perhaps not been motivated purely by kindness, either. The notoriety of having the hanged man as house-guest would focus the attention of Hillsborough on the Sherstons in a most gratifying way—better, even, than having an unconventional portrait painted.

"I do hope that your husband is much improved, my dear?" Mrs. Wilbur tactfully bridged the conversational gap. "We were so sorry to hear of his injury."

Injury. That was as circumspect a description of the situation as could well be imagined.

"Yes, he's much better, thank you," she said, smiling as briefly as politeness allowed before turning back to her father.

"Does Roger know about this? The land grant?"

He glanced at her, then away, clearing his throat.

"No. I thought perhaps ye might wish to tell him of it yourself."

Her first response was gratitude; she would have something to say to Roger. It was an awkward business, talking to someone who couldn't talk back. She stored up conversational fodder during the day; tiny thoughts or events that she could turn into stories, to tell him when she saw him. Her stock of stories ran out all too soon, though, and left her sitting by his bed, groping for inanities.

Her second response was a feeling of annoyance. Why had her father not told her privately, rather than exposing her family's business to total strangers? Then she caught the subtle interplay of glances between her parents, and realized that her mother had just asked him that, silently—and he had replied, with the briefest flick of the eyes toward Mr. Wilbur, then toward Mrs. Sherston, before the long auburn lashes swept down to hide his gaze.

Better to speak the truth before a reputable witness, his expression said, *than to let gossip spread of its own accord.*

She had no great regard for her own reputation—"notorious" did not begin to encompass it—but she had grasped enough of the social realities to realize that real damage could be done to her father by scandal. If a false report were to get around, for instance, that Roger had really been a Regulation ring-leader, then Jamie's own loyalties would be suspect.

She had begun to realize, listening to the talk in the Sherstons' parlor over the last few weeks, that the Colony was a vast spiderweb. There were innumerable strands of commerce along which a few large spiders—and a number of smaller ones—made their delicate way, always listening for the faint hum of distress made by a fly that had blundered in, always testing for a thinning strand, a broken link.

The smaller entities glided warily along the margins of the web, with an eye out always for the movements of the bigger ones—for spiders were cannibals—and so, she thought, were ambitious men.

Her father's position was prominent—but by no means so secure as to resist the undermining effects of gossip and suspicion. She and Roger had talked about it before, privately, speculating; the fracture-lines were already there, plain enough to someone who knew what was coming; the strains and tensions that would deepen into sudden chasm—one deep enough to sunder the colonies from England.

Let the strain grow too great, too quickly, let the strands between Fraser's Ridge and the rest of the Colony fray too far . . . and they might snap, wrapping sticky ends in a thick cocoon round her family and leaving them suspended by a thread—alone, and prey to those who would suck their blood.

You are *morbid tonight*, she thought to herself, sourly amused at her mind's choice of imagery. She supposed that painting death would do that.

Neither the Wilburs nor the Sherstons appeared to have noticed her mood; her mother had, and gave her a long, thoughtful look—but said nothing. She exchanged a few more pleasantries, then excused herself to the company.

Her mood was not lightened by the discovery that Jemmy had grown tired of waiting for her to come, and fallen asleep, tear-tracks on his cheeks. She knelt by his crib for a minute, one hand laid lightly on his back, hoping that he might sense her nearness and wake up. His small back rose and fell in the warm rhythm of utter peace, but he didn't stir. Perspiration glimmered wetly in the creases of his neck.

The heat of the day rose upward, and the second floor of the house was always stifling by evening. The window, of course, was firmly closed, lest the dangerous night airs get in and do the baby harm. Mrs. Sherston had no children of her own, but she knew what precautions must be taken.

In the mountains, Brianna would not have hesitated to open the window. In a heavily-populated town like Hillsborough, full of strangers from the coast, and rife with stagnant horse troughs and dank wells . . .

Weighing the relative danger of malaria-bearing mosquitoes versus that of suffocation, Brianna finally settled for pulling the light quilt off her son and gently removing his gown, leaving him comfortably sprawled on the sheet in nothing but a clout, his soft skin damp and rosy in the dim light.

Sighing, she put out the candle and left, leaving the door ajar so that she could hear if he woke. It was nearly dark now; light welled up through the bannisters from the floor below, but the upstairs hall lay in deep shadow. Mrs. Sherston's gilded tables and the portraits of Mr. Sherston's ancestors were no more than spectral shapes in the darkness.

There was a light in Roger's room; the door was shut, but a fan of soft candle-glow spread across the polished boards beneath it, just catching the edge of the blue hall-runner. She moved toward the door, thoughts of food subsumed in a greater hunger for touch. Her breasts had begun to ache.

A slave was nodding in the corner, hands slack on the knitting that had fallen to her lap. She jerked, startled, as the door opened, and blinked guiltily at Brianna.

Bree looked at once toward the bed, but it was all right;

she could hear the hiss and sigh of his breath. She frowned a little at the woman, but made a small gesture of dismissal. The woman clumsily gathered up her half-finished stocking and blundered out, avoiding Brianna's eye.

Roger lay on his back, eyes closed, a sheet drawn tidily over the sharp angles of his body. *He's so thin*, she thought, *how did he get so thin, so fast*? He could swallow no more than a few spoonsful of soup and Claire's penicillin broth, but surely two or three days was not enough to leave his bones showing so prominently?

Then she realized that he had likely been thin already, from the stress of campaigning—both her parents were thinner than usual. The prominence of his bones had been disguised by the dreadful swelling of his features; now that that had subsided, his cheekbones were high and gaunt, the hard, graceful line of his jaw once more visible, stark above the white linen of the bandage wrapped around his lacerated throat.

She realized that she was staring at his jaw, appraising the color of the fading bruises. The yellow-green of a healing bruise was different than the delicate gray-green of new death; just as sickly, but withal, a color of life. She took a deep breath, suddenly aware that the window in this room was closed, too, and sweat was trickling down the small of her back, seeping unpleasantly into the crack of her buttocks.

The sound of the sash rising wakened him—he turned his head on the pillow, and smiled faintly when he saw her.

"How are you?" She spoke in a hushed voice, as though in a church. Her own voice always seemed too loud, talking to herself.

He lifted one shoulder in a slight shrug, but mouthed a silent "Okay." He looked wilted and damp, the dark hair at his temples sweat-soaked.

"It's awfully hot, isn't it?" She waved at the window, where warm air—but moving air—came in. He nodded, poking at the collar of his shirt with one bandaged hand. She took the hint and untied it, spreading the slit open as far as it would go, to expose his chest to the breeze.

His nipples were small and neat, the aureoles pinkish-brown under the dark curly hairs. The sight reminded her of her own milk-full breasts, and she had a moment's insane urge to lift his head, pull down her shift, and put his mouth to her breast. She had an instant's vivid recall of the moment when he had done that, under the willows at River Run, and a warm rush spread through her, tingling from breasts to womb. Blood rising in her cheeks, she turned to look over the nourishment available on the bedside table.

There was cold meat-broth—spiked with penicillin—in a covered bowl, and a flask of honey-sweetened tea alongside. She took up the spoon and raised a brow inquiringly, her hand hovering over the table.

He grimaced slightly, but nodded at the broth. She picked up the cup and sat down on the stool beside him.

"Open up the stable-door," she said cheerily, circling the spoon toward his mouth as though he were Jem. "Heeeeere comes the horsie!" He rolled his eyes upward in exasperation.

"When I was little," she said, ignoring his scowl, "my parents said things like, 'Here comes the tugboat, open the drawbridge!' 'Open the garage, here comes the car!'—but I can't use those with Jem. Did your mother do cars and airplanes?"

His lips twisted, but finally settled on a reluctant smile. He shook his head and lifted one hand, pointing toward the ceiling. She turned to see a dark spot on the plaster—looking closer, she could see that it was a vagrant bee, blundered in from the garden during the day, somnolent now in the shadows.

"Yeah? Okay, here comes the honeybee," she said, more softly, slipping the spoon into his mouth. "Bzzz, bzzz, bzzz."

She couldn't keep up the attempted air of playfulness, but the atmosphere had relaxed a little. She talked about Jem, who had a new favorite word—"Wagga"—but no one yet had figured out what he meant by it.

"I thought maybe it meant 'cat,' but he calls the cat 'Mowmow.' " She brushed a drop of sweat from her forehead with the back of her hand, then dipped the spoon again.

"Mrs. Sherston says he should be walking by now," she said, eyes fixed on his mouth. "Her sister's children were both walking at a year old, naturally! I asked Mama, though;

she says he's fine. She says kids walk when they're ready, and it can be any time between ten months and as much as eighteen, but fifteen months is about the usual."

She had to watch his mouth in order to guide the spoon, but was aware of his eyes, watching her. She wanted to look into them, but was halfway afraid of what she might see in those dark green depths; would it be the Roger she knew, or the silent stranger—the hanged man?

"Oh—I almost forgot." She interrupted herself in the middle of an account of the Wilburs. She hadn't forgotten, but hadn't wanted to blurt the news out right away. "Da spoke to the Governor this afternoon. He—the Governor, I mean—is giving you a land grant. Five thousand acres." Even as she said it, she realized the absurdity of it. Five thousand acres of wilderness, in exchange for a life almost destroyed. *Cancel the "almost,"* she thought suddenly, looking at Roger.

He frowned at her in what looked like puzzlement, then shook his head and lay back on the pillow, eyes closing. He lifted his hands and let them fall, as though this was simply too much to be asked to contemplate. Maybe it was.

She stood watching him in silence, but he didn't open his eyes. There were deep creases where his brows drew together.

Moved by the need to touch him, to bridge the barrier of silence, she traced the shadow of the bruise that lay over his cheekbone, her fingers drifting, barely touching his skin.

She could see the oddly blurred edges of the bruise, could almost see the dark clotted blood beneath the skin, where the capillaries had ruptured. It was beginning to yellow; her mother had told her that the body's leukocytes would come to the site of an injury, where they gradually broke down the injured cells, thriftily recycling the spilled blood; the changing colors were the result of this cellular housekeeping.

His eyes opened, fixed on her face, his own expression impassive. She knew she looked worried, and tried to smile.

"You don't look dead," she said. That broke the impassive facade; his eyebrows twitched upward, and a faint gleam of humor came into his eyes.

"Roger—" At a loss for words, she moved impulsively toward him. He stiffened slightly, hunching instinctively to protect the fragile tube in his throat, but she put her arms around his shoulders, careful, but needing desperately to feel the substance of his flesh.

"I love you," she whispered, and her hand tightened on the muscle of his arm, urging him to believe it.

She kissed him. His lips were warm and dry, familiar—and yet a feeling of shock ran through her. No air moved against her cheek, no warm breath touched her from his nose or mouth. It was like kissing a mask. Air, damp from the secret depths of his lungs, hissed cool from the amber tube against her neck, like the exhalation from a cave. Gooseflesh ran down her arms and she stepped back, hoping that neither shock nor revulsion showed on her face.

His eyes were closed, squeezed tight shut. The muscle of his jaw bulged; she saw the shift of the shadow there.

"You . . . rest," she managed, her voice shaky. "I'll—I'll see you in the morning."

She made her way downstairs, barely noticing that the candlestick in the hall was lit now, or that the waiting slave slid silently from the shadows back into the room.

Her hunger had come back, but she didn't go downstairs in search of food. She had to do something about the unused milk, first. She turned toward her parents' room, feeling a faint draft move through the stifling shadows. In spite of the warm, muggy air, her fingers felt cold, as though turpentine was still evaporating from her skin.

Last night I dreamed about my friend Deborah. She used to make money doing Tarot readings in the Student Union; she'd always offer to do one for me, for free, but I wouldn't let her.

Sister Marie Romaine told us in the fifth grade that Catholics aren't allowed to do divination—we weren't to touch Ouija boards or Tarot cards or crystal balls, because things like that are seductions of the D-E-V-I-L—she always spelled it out like that, she'd never say the word.

I'm not sure where the Devil came into it, but

somehow I couldn't bring myself to let Deb do readings for me. She was, last night, though, in my dream.

I used to watch her do it for other people; the Tarot cards fascinated me—maybe just because they seemed forbidden. But the names were so cool—the Major Arcana, the Minor Arcana; Knight of Pentacles, Page of Cups, Queen of Wands, King of Swords. The Empress, the Magician. And the Hanged Man.

Well, what else would I dream about? I mean, this was not a subtle dream, no doubt about it. There it was, right in the middle of the spread of cards, and Deb was telling me about it.

"A man is suspended by one foot from a pole laid across two trees. His arms, folded behind his back, together with his head, form a triangle with the point downward; his legs form a cross. To an extent, the Hanged Man is still earthbound, for his foot is attached to the pole."

I could see the man on the card, suspended permanently halfway between heaven and earth. That card always looked odd to me—the man didn't seem to be at all concerned, in spite of being upside-down and blind-folded.

Deb kept scooping up the cards and laying them out again, and that one kept coming up in every spread.

"The Hanged Man represents the necessary process of surrender and sacrifice," she said. "This card has profound significance," she said, and she looked at me and tapped her finger on it. "But much of it is veiled; you have to figure out the meaning for yourself. Self-surrender leads to transformation of the personality, but the person has to accomplish his own regeneration."

Transformation of the personality. That's what I'm afraid of, all right. I liked Roger's personality just fine the way it was!

Well . . . rats. I don't know how much the D-E-V-I-L has to do with it, but I am sure that trying to look too far into the future is a mistake. At least right now.

74

THE SOUNDS OF SILENCE

IT WAS TEN DAYS before Penelope Sherston's portrait was completed to her satisfaction. By that point, both Isaiah Morton and Roger had recovered sufficiently for travel. Given the imminence of Morton's offspring and the danger to him in coming anywhere near either Granite Falls or Brownsville, Jamie had arranged for him and Alicia to lodge with the brewmaster of Mr. Sherston's brewery; Isaiah would undertake employment as a wagoner for the brewery, as soon as his strength permitted.

"I canna imagine why," Jamie had said to me privately, "but I've grown a bit fond of the immoral wee loon. I shouldna like to see him murdered in cold blood."

Isaiah's spirits had revived spectacularly upon the arrival of Alicia, and within a week, he had made his way downstairs, to sit watching Alicia like a devoted dog as she worked in the kitchen—and to pause on his way back to bed to offer comments on the progress of Mrs. Sherston's portrait.

"Don't it look just like her?" he'd said admiringly, standing in his nightshirt in the door of the drawing-room where the sitting was in progress. "Why, if you was to see that picture, you'd know just who it was."

Given the fact that Mrs. Sherston had chosen to be painted as Salome, I was not positive that this would be considered a compliment, but she flushed prettily and thanked him, evidently recognizing the sincerity in his tone.

Bree *had* done a marvelous job, contriving to portray Mrs. Sherston both realistically and flatteringly, but without overt irony—difficult as that must have been. The only point where she had given in to temptation was in a minor detail; the severed head of John the Baptist bore a striking resemblance to Governor Tryon's saturnine features, but I doubted that anyone would notice, what with all the blood.

We were ready to go home, and the house was filled with a spirit of restless excitement and relief—except for Roger.

Roger was indisputably better, in purely physical terms. His hands were mobile again, bar the broken fingers, and most of the bruising over his face and body had faded. Best of all, the swelling in his throat had subsided enough that he could move air through his nose and mouth again. I was able to remove the tube from his throat, and stitch up the incision—a small but painful operation that he had borne with body stiff and eyes wide open, staring up at the ceiling while I worked.

In mental terms, I was not so sure of his recovery. After stitching his throat, I had helped him sit up, wiped his face, and given him a little water mixed with brandy as a restorative. I had watched carefully as he swallowed, then put my fingers lightly on his throat, felt carefully, and asked him to swallow again. I closed my eyes, feeling the movement of his larynx, the rings of his trachea as he swallowed, assessing as best I could the degree of damage.

At last I opened my eyes, to find his eyes two inches from my own and still wide open, the question in them cold and stark as glacier ice.

"I don't know," I said at last, my own voice no more than a whisper. My fingers still rested on his throat; I could feel the thrum of blood through the carotid under my palm, his life flowing just below the skin. But the angular hardness of his larynx lay still under my fingers, queerly misshapen; I felt no pulsing there, no vibration of air across the vocal cords.

"I don't know," I said again, and drew my fingers slowly away. "Do you—want to try now?"

He had shaken his head then, and risen from the bed, going to the window, facing away from me. His arms were braced against the frame as he looked down into the street, and a faint, uneasy memory stirred in my mind.

It had been a moonlit night, then, not broad day—in Paris. I had waked from sleep to see Jamie standing naked in the window frame, the scars on his back pale silver, arms braced and body gleaming with cold sweat. Roger was sweating, too, from the heat; the linen of his shirt stuck to his body—and the lines of his body were just the same; the look of a man braced to meet fear; one who chose to face his demons alone.

I could hear voices in the street below; Jamie, coming back from the camp, with Jemmy held before him on his saddle. He had formed the habit of taking Jem with him on his daily errands, so that Bree could work without distraction. In consequence, Jemmy had learned four new words—only two of them obscene—and Jamie's good coat sported jam stains and smelled like a soiled diaper, but both of them seemed generally pleased with the arrangement.

Bree's voice floated up from below, laughing as she went out to retrieve her son. Roger stood as though he'd been carved out of wood. He couldn't call to them, but he might have knocked on the window frame, or made some other noise, waved to them. But he didn't move.

After a moment, I rose quietly and left the room, feeling a lump in my throat, hard and unswallowable.

When Bree had carried Jemmy off for his bath, Jamie told me that Tryon had released most of the men captured during the battle. "Hugh Fowles among them." He put aside his coat and loosened the collar of his shirt, raising his face to the slight breeze from the window. "I spoke for him—and Tryon listened."

"As well he might," I said, with an edge to my voice. He glanced at me, and made a noise deep in his throat. It reminded me of Roger, whose larynx was no longer capable of that peculiarly Scottish form of expression.

I must have looked distressed at the thought, for Jamie raised his brows and touched my arm. It was too hot to embrace, but I pressed my cheek against his shoulder briefly, taking comfort from the solidness of his body under the thin, damp linen.

"I sewed up Roger's throat," I said. "He can breathe—but I don't know whether he'll ever be able to talk again." *Let alone sing*. The unvoiced thought floated in the muggy air.

Jamie made another noise, this one deep and angry.

"I spoke to Tryon regarding his promise to Roger Mac, as well. He's given me the document of the land grant—five thousand acres, adjoining my own. His last official act as Governor—almost."

"What do you mean by that?"

"I said he's released most of the prisoners?" He moved away, restless. "All but twelve. He has a dozen men still gaoled, outlawed ringleaders of the Regulation. Or so he says." The irony in his voice was as thick as the dusty air. "He'll hold them for trial in a month, on charges of rebellion."

"And if they're found guilty—"

"At least they'll be able to speak before they hang."

He had stopped in front of the portrait, frowning, though I wasn't sure whether he was actually seeing it or not.

"I willna stay to see it. I told Tryon that we must go, to tend our crops and farms. He has released the militia company from service, on those grounds."

I felt a lightening of the weight on my heart. It would be cool in the mountains, the air green and fresh. It was a good place to heal.

"When will we go?"

"Tomorrow." He *had* noticed the portrait; he nodded at the gape-jawed head on the platter in grim approval. "There's only the one thing to stay for, and I think there's little point to it, now."

"What's that?"

"Dougal's son," he said, turning away from the portrait. "I have been seeking William Buccleigh MacKenzie from one end of the county to the other for the past ten days. I found some who kent him, but none who has seen him since Alamance. Some said perhaps he had left the Colony altogether. A good many of the Regulators have fled; Husband's gone—taken his family to Maryland, they say. But as for William MacKenzie, the man's disappeared like a snake down a rathole; him, and his family with him."

Last night I dreamed that we were lying under a big rowan tree, Roger and I. It was a beautiful summer day, and we were having one of those conversations we used to have all the time, about things we missed. Only the things we were talking about were there on the grass between us.

I said I'd sell my soul for a Hershey bar with almonds, and there it was. I slipped the outer wrapper off, and I could smell the chocolate. I unfolded the white paper wrapper inside and started eating the chocolate, but it was the paper we were talking about, then—the wrapper.

Roger picked it up and said what he missed most was loo-paper; this was too slick to wipe your arse with. I laughed and said there wasn't anything complicated about toilet paper—people could make it now, if they wanted to. There was a roll of toilet paper on the ground; I pointed at it, and a big bumblebee flew down and grabbed the end of it and flew off, unfurling the toilet paper in its wake. It flew in and out, weaving it through the branches overhead.

Then Roger said it was blasphemy to think about wiping yourself with paper—it is, here. Mama writes in tiny letters when she does her case-notes, and when Da writes to Scotland he writes on both sides of the page, and then he turns it sideways and writes across the lines, so it looks like latticework.

Then I could see Da, sitting on the ground, writing a letter to Aunt Jenny on the toilet paper, and it was getting longer and longer and the bee was carrying it up into the air, flying off toward Scotland with it.

I use more paper than anyone. Aunt Jocasta gave me some of her old sketchbooks to use, and a whole quire of watercolor paper—but I feel guilty when I use them, because I know how expensive it is. I have to draw, though. A nice thing about doing this portrait for Mrs. Sherston—since I'm earning money, I feel like I can use a little paper.

Then the dream changed and I was drawing pictures of Jemmy, with a #2B yellow pencil. It said

"Ticonderoga" on it in black letters, like the ones we used to use in school. I was drawing on toilet paper, though, and the pencil kept ripping through it, and I was so frustrated that I wadded up a bunch in my hand.

Then it went into one of those boring, uncomfortable dreams where you're wandering around looking for a place to go to the bathroom and can't find one—and finally you wake up enough to realize that you do have to go to the bathroom.

I can't decide whether I'd rather have the Hershey bar, the toilet paper, or the pencil. I think the pencil. I could smell the freshly-sharpened wood on the point, and feel it between my fingers, and my teeth. I used to chew my pencils, when I was little. I still remember what it felt like to bite down hard and feel the paint and wood give, just a little, and munch my way up and down the length of the pencil, until it looked like a beaver had been gnawing on it.

I was thinking about that, this afternoon. It made me feel sad that Jem won't have a new yellow pencil, or a lunchbox with Batman on it, when he goes to school—if he ever does go to school.

Roger's hands are still too bad to hold a pen.

And now I know that I don't want pencils or chocolate, or even toilet paper. I want Roger to talk to me again.

75

SPEAK MY NAME

OUR JOURNEY BACK to Fraser's Ridge was much quicker than the one to Alamance, for all that the return was uphill. It was late May, and the cornstalks stood already high and green in the fields around Hillsborough, shedding golden pollen on the wind. The grain would just be up, in the mountains, and the newborn stock appearing, calves and foals and lambs needing protection from wolf and fox and bear. The militia company had disbanded at once upon receiving the Governor's dismissal, its members scattering in haste to return to their homesteads and fields.

We were in consequence a much smaller party going back; only two wagons. A few of the men who lived near the Ridge had chosen to travel with us, as had the two Findlay boys, since we would pass by their mother's homestead on our way.

I cast a covert glance at the Findlays, who were helping to unload the wagon and set up our nightly camp. Nice boys, though quiet. They were respectful of—and rather awed by—Jamie, but had developed a peculiar sense of allegiance to Roger over the course of the short-lived campaign, and this odd fidelity had continued, even after the militia's disbanding.

They had come, the two of them, to see him in Hillsborough, wriggling their bare toes in embarrassment on Phoebe Sherston's Turkish carpets. Scarlet-faced and nearly speechless themselves, they had presented Roger with three early apples, lopsided green nubbins obviously stolen from someone's orchard on the way.

He had smiled broadly at them in thanks, picked up one of the apples, and taken a heroic bite from it before I could stop him. He hadn't swallowed anything but soup for a week, and nearly choked to death. Still, he got it down, strangling and gasping, and all three of them had sat there grinning wordlessly at each other, tears standing in their eyes.

The Findlays were usually to be found somewhere near Roger as we traveled, always watchful, leaping to help with anything he couldn't quite manage with his injured hands. Jamie had told me about their uncle, Iain Mhor; plainly they had a good deal of experience in anticipating unspoken needs.

Young and strong, Roger had healed quickly, and the fractures weren't bad ones—but two weeks was not a long time for broken bones to knit. I would have preferred to keep him bandaged for another week, but he was all too plainly chafing at the restraint. I had reluctantly taken the splints off his fingers the day before, warning him to take things easy.

"Don't you *dare*," I said now, seizing his arm as he reached into the wagon for one of the heavy rucksacks of supplies. He looked down at me, one eyebrow raised, then shrugged good-naturedly and stood back, letting Hugh Findlay pull out the sack and carry it away. Roger pointed at the ring of fire-stones Iain Findlay was assembling, then at the woods nearby. Could he gather firewood?

"Certainly not," I said firmly. He pantomimed drinking, and raised his brows. Fetch water?

"No," I said. "All it needs is for a bucket to slip, and . . ."

I looked around, trying to think of something he could safely do, but all camp-making chores involved rough work. At the same time, I knew how galling he found it to stand by, feeling useless. He was bloody tired of being treated like an invalid, and I could see the gleam of incipient rebellion in his eye. One more "no" and he would probably try to pick up the wagon, just to spite me.

"Can he write, Sassenach?" Jamie had paused by the wagon, and noticed the impasse in progress.

"Write? Write what?" I asked in surprise, but he was already reaching past me, digging out the battered portable writing-desk he carried when traveling.

"Love letters?" Jamie suggested, grinning down at me. "Or sonnets, maybe?" He tossed the lap-desk to Roger, who caught it neatly in his arms, even as I yelped in protest. "But perhaps before ye compose an epic in William Tryon's honor, Roger Mac, ye might oblige me wi' the tale of how our mutual kinsman came to try and murder ye, aye?"

Roger stood stock-still for a moment, clutching the desk, but then gave Jamie a lopsided smile, and nodded slowly.

He had begun while the camp was set up, paused to eat supper, and then taken up the task again. It was tiresome work, and very slow; the fractures were mostly healed, but his hands were very stiff, sore, and awkward. He had dropped the quill a dozen times. It made my own finger-joints ache just to watch him.

"Ow! Will you *stop* that?" I looked up from scouring out a pan with a handful of rushes and sand, to find Brianna locked in mortal combat with her son, who was arched backward like a bow over her arm, kicking, squirming, and making the sort of nerve-wracking fuss that makes even devoted parents momentarily contemplate infanticide. I saw Roger's shoulders draw up toward his ears at the racket, but he went doggedly on with his writing.

"What is the *matter* with you?" Bree demanded crossly. She knelt and wrestled Jemmy into a semi-sitting position, evidently trying to make him lie down so she could change his clout for the night.

The diaper in question was much in need of attention, being wet, grimy, and hanging halfway down the little boy's legs. Jem, having slept most of the afternoon in the wagon, had wakened sun-dazed, cranky, and in no mood to be trifled with, let alone changed and put to bed.

"Perhaps he isn't tired yet," I suggested. "He's eaten, though, hasn't he?" This was a rhetorical question; Jemmy's face was smeared with hasty pudding, and he had bits of eggy toast in his hair.

"Yes." Bree ran a hand through her own hair, which was cleaner, but no less disheveled. Jem wasn't the only cranky one in the MacKenzie family. "Maybe *he's* not tired, but *I* am." She was; she had walked beside the wagon most of the day, to spare the horses on the steepening slopes. So had I.

"Leave him here and go have a wash, why don't you?" I said, nobly suppressing a yawn. I picked up a large wooden spoon and waggled it alluringly toward Jem, who was oscillating backward and forward on his hands and knees, emitting horrible whining noises. Spotting the spoon, he stopped making the noise, but crouched in place, glaring suspiciously.

I added an empty tin cup to the lure, setting it on the ground near him. That was enough; he rolled onto his bottom with a squish, picked up the spoon with both hands and began trying to pound the cup into the dirt with it.

Bree cast me a look of profound gratitude, scrambled to her feet, and disappeared into the woods, heading down the slope to the small creek. A quick rinse in cold water, surrounded by dark forest, wasn't quite the sybaritic escape that a fragrant bubble-bath by candlelight might be—but "escape" was the important word here. A little solitude worked wonders for a mother, as I knew from experience. And if cleanliness was not quite next to godliness, having clean feet, face, and hands definitely improved one's outlook on the universe, particularly after a day of sweat, grime, and dirty diapers.

I examined my own hands critically; between horse-leading, fire-starting, cooking, and pot-scouring, my own outlook on the universe could stand a bit of improvement, too.

Still, water was not the only liquid capable of lifting one's spirits. Jamie reached over my shoulder, put a cup of something into my hands, and sat down beside me, his own cup in hand.

"Slàinte, mo nighean donn," he said softly, smiling at me as he lifted his cup in salute.

"Mmm." I closed my eyes, inhaling the fragrant fumes. "Is it proper to say *'Slàinte,'* if it isn't whisky you're drinking?" The liquid in the cup was wine—and a nice one, too, rough but with a good round flavor, redolent of sun and grape leaves.

"I canna see why not," Jamie said logically. "It's only to wish ye good health, after all."

"True, but I think 'Good Health' may be more a practical wish than a figurative one, at least with some whiskies—that you hope the person you're toasting survives the experience of drinking it, I mean."

He laughed, eyes creasing in amusement.

"I havena killed anyone wi' my distilling yet, Sassenach."

"I didn't mean yours," I assured him, pausing for another sip. "Oh, that's nice. I was thinking of those three militiamen from Colonel Ashe's regiment." The three in question had been found blind-drunk—in one case, literally blind—by a sentry, after having indulged in a bottle of so-called whisky, obtained from God knew where.

As Ashe's Company had no surgeon, and we were camped next to them, I had been summoned in the middle of the night to deal with the matter, as best I could. All three men had survived, but one had lost the sight in one eye and another plainly had minor brain-damage—though privately, I had my doubts as to how intelligent he could have been to start with.

Jamie shrugged. Drunkenness was a simple fact of life, and bad brewing was another.

"Thig a seo, a chuisle!" he called, seeing Jemmy, who had lost interest in spoon and cup, making off on hands and knees toward the coffeepot, which had been left to keep hot between the stones of the fire-ring. Jemmy ignored the summons, but was snatched away from danger by Hugh Findlay, who snagged him neatly round the waist and delivered him, kicking, to Jamie.

"Sit," Jamie said firmly to him, and without waiting for a response, parked the child on the ground and handed him his ball of rags. Jemmy clutched this, looking craftily from his grandfather to the fire.

"Throw that in the fire, *a chuisle*, and I'll smack your bum," Jamie informed him pleasantly. Jemmy's brow contorted and his lower lip protruded, quivering dramatically. He didn't throw the ball into the fire, though.

"A chuisle?" I said, trying out the pronunciation. "That's a new one. What's it mean?"

"Oh." Jamie rubbed a finger across the bridge of his nose, considering. "It means 'my blood.' "

"I thought that was *mo fuil*."

"Aye, it is, but that's blood like what comes out when ye

wound yourself. *A chuisle* is more like . . . 'O, thou in whose veins runs my very blood.' Ye only say it to a wee bairn, mostly—one ye're related to, of course."

"That's lovely." I set my empty wine-cup on the ground and leaned against Jamie's shoulder. I still felt tired, but the magic of the wine had smoothed the rough edges of exhaustion, leaving me pleasantly muzzy.

"Would you call Germain that, do you think, or Joan? Or is it meant very literally, *a chuisle*?"

"I should be more inclined to call Germain *un petit emmerdeur*," he said, with a faint snort of amusement. "But Joan—aye, I would call wee Joanie *a chuisle*. It's blood of the heart, ken, not only the body."

Jemmy had let his rag-ball fall to the ground and was staring in openmouthed enchantment at the fireflies, which had begun to blink in the grass as darkness fell. With our stomachs full and cool rest at hand, everyone was beginning to feel the soothing effects of the gathering night.

The men were sprawled in the grassy dark under a sycamore tree, passing the wine bottle from hand to hand and exchanging talk in the easy, half-connected fashion of men who know each other well. The Findlay boys were on the wagon-track, that being the only really clear space, throwing something back and forth, missing half their catches as darkness fell, and exchanging genial shouted insults.

There was a loud rustling of bushes beyond the fire, and Brianna emerged, looking damp, but much more cheerful. She paused by Roger, a hand light on his back, and looked over his shoulder at what he was writing. He glanced up at her, then, with a shrug of resignation, withdrew the finished pages of his opus and handed them to her. She knelt down beside him and began to read, brushing back wet strands of hair and frowning to make out the letters by firelight.

A firefly landed on Jamie's shirt, glowing cool green in the shadowed folds of cloth. I moved a finger toward it, and it flew away, spiraling above the fire like a runaway spark.

"It was a good idea, making Roger write," I said, looking across the fire with approval. "I can't wait to find out what actually happened to him."

"Nor I," Jamie agreed. "Though wi' William Buccleigh vanished, what's happened to Roger Mac is maybe no so important as what *will* happen to him."

I didn't have to ask what he meant by that. More than anyone, he knew what it meant, to have a life kicked out from under one—and what strength was required to rebuild it. I reached for his right hand, and he let me take it. Under cover of darkness, I stroked his crippled fingers, tracing the thickened ridges of the scars.

"So it doesn't matter to you, to find out whether your cousin is a cold-blooded murderer or not?" I asked lightly, to cover the more serious conversation going on silently between our hands.

He made a small, gruff sound that might have been a laugh. His fingers curled over mine, smooth with callus, pressing in acknowledgment.

"He's a MacKenzie, Sassenach. A MacKenzie of Leoch."

"Hm." The Frasers were stubborn as rocks, I'd been told. And Jamie himself had described the MacKenzies of Leoch—*charming as larks in the field—and sly as foxes, with it*. That had certainly been true of his uncles, Colum and Dougal. I hadn't heard anything to indicate that his mother, Ellen, had shared that particular family characteristic—but then, Jamie had been only eight when she died. His aunt Jocasta? No one's fool, certainly, but with a good deal less scope for plotting and scheming than her brothers had had, I thought.

"You *what*?" Brianna's exclamation drew my attention back to the other side of the fire. She was looking at Roger, the pages in her hand, an expression of mingled amusement and dismay on her face. I couldn't see Roger's face; he was turned toward her. One hand rose in a shushing gesture, though, and he turned his head toward the tree where the men sat drinking, to be sure no one had heard her exclamation.

I caught a glimpse of firelight shining on the bones of his face, and then his expression changed in an instant, from wariness to horror. He lunged to his feet, mouth open.

"STOKH!" he roared.

It was a terrible cry, loud and harsh, but with a ghastly

strangled quality to it, like a shout forced out around a fist shoved down his throat. It froze everyone in earshot—including Jemmy, who had abandoned the fireflies and stealthily returned to an investigation of the coffeepot. He stared up at his father, his hand six inches from the hot metal. Then his face crumpled, and he began to wail in fright.

Roger reached across the fire and snatched him up; the little boy screamed, kicking and squirming to get away from this terrifying stranger. Bree hastily took him, clutching him to her bosom and burying his face in her shoulder. Her own face had gone pale with shock.

Roger looked shocked, too. He put a hand to his throat, gingerly, as though unsure he was really touching his own flesh. The ridge of the rope-scar was still dark under his jaw; I could see it, even in the flicker of the firelight, along with the smaller, neater line of my own incision.

The initial shock of his shout had worn off, and the men came scrambling out from under the tree, the Findlays rushing in from the road, to gather round Roger, exclaiming in astonishment and congratulation. Roger nodded, submitting to having his hand shaken and his back pounded, all the while looking as though he would strongly prefer to be elsewhere.

"Say somethin' else," Hugh Findlay coaxed him.

"Yes, sir, you can do it," Iain joined in, round face beaming. "Say . . . say 'She sells sea shells, by the sea-shore'!"

This suggestion was howled down, to be replaced by a rain of other excited proposals. Roger was beginning to look rather desperate, his jaw set tight. Jamie and I had got to our feet; I could feel Jamie setting himself to intervene in some way.

Then Brianna pushed her way through the excited throng, with Jemmy perched on one hip, regarding the proceedings with intense distrust. She took Roger's hand with her free one, and smiled at him, the smile trembling only a little round the edges.

"Can you say my name?" she asked.

Roger's smile matched hers. I could hear the air rasp in his throat as he took a breath.

This time he spoke softly; very softly, but everyone held silence, leaning forward to listen. It was a ragged whisper, thick and painful, the first syllable punched hard to force it through his scarred vocal cords, the last of it barely audible. But,

"BRREEah . . . nah," he said, and she burst into tears.

76

BLOOD MONEY

Fraser's Ridge
June, 1771

I SAT IN THE VISITOR'S CHAIR in Jamie's study, companionably grating bloodroots while he wrestled with the quarterly accounts. Both were slow and tedious businesses, but we could share the light of a single candle and enjoy each other's company—and I found enjoyable distraction in listening to the highly inventive remarks he addressed to the paper under his quill.

"Egg-sucking son of a porcupine!" he muttered. "Look at this, Sassenach—the man's nay more than a common thief! Two shillings, threepence for two loaves of sugar and a brick of indigo!"

I clicked my tongue sympathetically, forbearing to note that two shillings seemed a modest enough price for substances produced in the West Indies, transported by ship to Charleston, and thence carried by wagon, pirogue, horseback, and foot another several hundred miles overland, to be finally brought to our door by an itinerant peddler who did not expect payment for the three or four months until his next visit—and who would in any case likely not get cash, but rather six pots of gooseberry jam or a haunch of smoked venison.

"Look at that!" Jamie said rhetorically, scratching his way down a column of figures and arriving with a vicious stab at the bottom. "A cask of brandywine at twelve shillings, two bolts of muslin at three and ten each, ironmongery—what in the name of buggery is wee Roger wanting wi' an ironmonger, has he thought of a way to play tunes on a hoe?—ironmongery, ten and six!"

"I believe that was a ploughshare," I said pacifically. "It's not ours; Roger brought it for Geordie Chisholm." Ploughshares were in fact rather expensive. Having to be imported from England, they were rare amongst colonial small farmers, many of whom made do with nothing more than wooden dibbles and spades, with an ax and perhaps an iron hoe for ground-clearing.

Jamie squinted balefully at his figures, rumpling a hand through his hair.

"Aye," he said. "Only Geordie hasna got a spare penny to bless himself with, not until next year's crops are sold. So it's me that's paying the ten and six now, isn't it?" Without waiting for an answer, he plunged back into his calculations, muttering "Turd-eating son of a flying tortoise" under his breath, with no indication whether this applied to Roger, Geordie, or the ploughshare.

I finished grating a root and dropped the stub into a jar on the desk. Bloodroot is aptly named; the scientific name is *Sanguinaria*, and the juice is red, acrid, and sticky. The bowl in my lap was full of oozy, moist shavings, and my hands looked as though I had been disemboweling small animals.

"I have six dozen bottles of cherry cordial made," I offered, picking up another root. As though he didn't know that; the whole house had smelled like cough syrup for a week. "Fergus can take those over to Salem and sell them."

Jamie nodded absently.

"Aye, I'm counting on that to buy seedcorn. Have we anything else that can go to Salem? Candles? Honey?"

I gave him a sharp glance, but encountered only the whorled cowlicks on top of his head, bent studiously over his figures. The candles and honey were a sensitive subject.

"I think I can spare ten gallons of honey," I said guardedly. "Perhaps ten—well, all right, twelve dozen candles."

He scratched the tip of his nose with the end of the quill, leaving a blot of ink.

"I thought ye'd had a good year wi' the hives," he said mildly.

I had; my original single hive had expanded, and I now had nine bee-gums bordering my garden. I had taken nearly fifty gallons of honey from them, and enough beeswax for a good thirty dozen candles. On the other hand, I had uses in mind for those things.

"I need some of the honey for the surgery," I said. "It makes a good antibacterial dressing over wounds."

One eyebrow went up, though he kept his eyes on the hen-scratches he was making.

"I should think it would draw flies," he said, "if not bears." He flicked the end of his quill, dismissing the thought. "How much d'ye need then? I shouldna think you've so many wounded coming through your surgery as to require forty gallons of honey—unless you're plastering them with it, head to toe."

I laughed, despite my wariness.

"No, two or three gallons should be enough for dressings—say five, allowing extra to make up electrolytic fluids."

He glanced up at me, both brows raised.

"Electric?" He looked at the candle, its flame wavering in the draft from the window, then back at me. "Did Brianna not say that was something to do wi' lights? Or lightning, at least?"

"No, electrolyte," I amplified. "Sugar-water. You know, when a person is feeling shocked, or is too ill to eat, or has the flux—an electrolytic fluid is one that supports the body by putting back the essential ions they've lost from bleeding or diarrhea—the bits of salt and sugar and other things—which in turn draws water into the blood and restores blood pressure. You've seen me use it before."

"Oh, is that how it works?" His face lighted with interest, and he seemed about to ask for an explanation. Then he caught sight of the stack of receipts and correspondence still waiting on his desk, sighed, and picked up his quill again.

"Verra well, then," he conceded. "Keep the honey. Can I sell the soap?"

I nodded, pleased. I had, with a good deal of cautious experimentation, succeeded at last in producing a soap that did not smell like a dead pig soaked in lye, and that did not remove the upper layer of the epidermis. It required sunflower oil or olive oil in lieu of suet, though; both very expensive.

I had it in mind to trade my spare honey to the Cherokee ladies for sunflower oil with which to make both more soap and shampoo. Those, in turn, would fetch excellent prices almost anywhere—Cross Creek, Wilmington, New Bern—even Charleston, should we ever venture that far. Or so I thought. I was unsure whether Jamie would agree to gamble on that enterprise, though; it would take months to come to fruition, while he could dispose of the honey at an immediate profit. If he saw for sure that the soap would bring much more than the raw honey, though, there would be no difficulty in getting my way.

Before I could expound on the prospects, we heard the sound of light footsteps in the hall, and a soft rap at the door.

"Come," Jamie called, pulling himself up straight. Mr. Wemyss poked his head into the room, but hesitated, looking mildly alarmed at the sight of the sanguinary splotches on my hands. Jamie beckoned him companionably in with a flick of his quill.

"Aye, Joseph?"

"If I might speak a word in your ear, sir?" Mr. Wemyss was dressed casually, in shirt and breeks, but had slicked down his fine, pale hair with water, indicating some formality about the situation.

I pushed back my chair, reaching to gather up my leavings, but Mr. Wemyss stopped me with a brief gesture.

"Oh, no, Ma'am. If ye wouldna mind, I should like ye to stay. It's about Lizzie, and I should value a woman's opinion on the matter."

"Of course." I sat back, brows raised in curiosity.

"Lizzie? Have ye found our wee lass a husband, then, Joseph?" Jamie dropped his quill into the jar on his desk and sat forward, interested, gesturing toward an empty stool.

Mr. Wemyss nodded, the candlelight throwing the bones of his thin face into prominence. He took the proffered seat with a certain air of dignity, quite at odds with his usual attitude of mild discombobulation.

"I am thinking so, Mr. Fraser. Robin McGillivray came to call upon me this morning, to speir for my Elizabeth, to be pledged to his lad, Manfred."

My eyebrows went a little higher. To the best of my knowledge, Manfred McGillivray had seen Lizzie less than half a dozen times, and had not spoken more than the briefest of courtesies to her. It wasn't impossible that he should have been attracted; Lizzie had grown into a delicately pretty girl, and if still very shy, was possessed of nice manners. It scarcely seemed the basis for a proposal of marriage, though.

As Mr. Wemyss laid out the matter, it became a little clearer. Jamie had promised Lizzie a dowry, consisting of a section of prime land, and Mr. Wemyss, freed from his indenture, had a freeman's homestead claim of fifty acres as well—to which Lizzie was heir. The Wemyss land adjoined the McGillivrays' section, and the two together would make a very respectable farm. Evidently, with her three girls now married or suitably engaged, Manfred's marriage was the next step in Ute McGillivray's master plan. Reviewing all of the available girls within a twenty-mile radius of the Ridge, she had settled upon Lizzie as the best prospect, and sent Robin round to open negotiations.

"Well, the McGillivrays are a decent family," Jamie said judiciously. He dipped a finger into my bowl of bloodroot shavings and dotted it thoughtfully on his blotter, leaving a chain of red fingerprints. "They've not much land, but Robin does well enough for himself, and wee Manfred's a hard worker, from all I hear." Robin was a gunsmith, with a small shop in Cross Creek. Manfred had been apprenticed to another gun-maker in Hillsborough, but was now a journeyman himself.

"Would he take her to live in Hillsborough?" I asked. That might weigh heavily with Joseph Wemyss. While he would do anything to insure his daughter's future, he loved Lizzie dearly, and I knew that the loss of her would strike him to the heart.

He shook his head. His hair had dried, and was beginning to rise in its usual fair wisps.

"Robin says not. He says the lad plans to ply his trade in Woolam's Creek—providing he can manage a wee shop. They'd live at the farm." He darted a sideways glance at Jamie, then looked away, blood rising under his fair skin.

Jamie bent his head, and I saw the corner of his mouth tuck in. So this was where he entered the negotiation, then. Woolam's Creek was a small but growing settlement at the base of Fraser's Ridge. While the Woolams, a local Quaker family, owned the mill there, and the land on the far side of the creek, Jamie owned all of the land on the Ridge side.

He had so far provided land, tools, and supplies to Ronnie Sinclair, Theo Frye, and Bob O'Neill, for the building of a cooper's shop, a smithy—still under construction—and a small general store, all on terms that provided us with an eventual share of any profit, but no immediate income.

If Jamie and I had plans for the future, so did Ute McGillivray. She knew, of course, that Lizzie and her father held a place of special esteem with Jamie, and that he would in all likelihood be moved to do what he could for her. And that—of course—was what Joseph Wemyss was very delicately asking now; might Jamie provide premises for Manfred at Woolam's Creek as part of the agreement?

Jamie glanced at me out of the corner of his eye. I lifted one shoulder in the faintest of shrugs, wondering whether Lizzie's physical delicacy had entered into Ute McGillivray's calculations. There were a good many girls sturdier than Lizzie, and better prospects for motherhood. Still, if Lizzie should die in childbirth, then the McGillivrays would be the richer both for her dower-land, and the Woolam's Creek property—and new wives were not so difficult to come by.

"I expect something might be done," Jamie said cautiously. I saw his gaze drift to the open ledger, with its depressing columns of figures, then speculatively to me. Land was not a problem; with no cash and precious little credit, tools and materials would be. I firmed my lips and returned his stare; no, he was not getting his hands on my honey!

He sighed, and sat back, tapping his red-tinged fingers lightly on the blotter.

"I'll manage," he said. "What does the lass say, then? Will she have Manfred?"

Mr. Wemyss looked faintly dubious.

"She says she will. He's a nice enough lad, though his mother . . . a fine woman," he added hurriedly, "verra fine. If just a trifle . . . erhm. But . . ." he turned to me, narrow forehead furrowed. "I am not sure Elizabeth knows her mind, ma'am, to say truly. She kens 'twould be a good match, and that it would keep her near me . . ." His expression softened at the thought, then firmed again. "But I wouldna have her make the match only because she thinks I favor it." He glanced shyly at Jamie, then at me.

"I did love her mother so," he said, the words coming out in a rush, as though confessing some shameful secret. He blushed bright pink, and looked down at the thin hands he had twisted together in his lap.

"I see," I said, tactfully averting my own gaze, and brushing a few bits of stray bloodroot off the desk. "Would you like me to talk to her?"

"Oh, I should be most grateful, Mum!" Lightened by relief, he nearly sprang to his feet. He wrang Jamie's hand fervently, bowed repeatedly to me, and at last made his way out, with much bobbing and murmuring of thanks.

The door closed behind him, and Jamie sighed, shaking his head.

"Christ knows it's trouble enough to get daughters married when they *do* ken their own minds," he said darkly, plainly thinking of Brianna and Marsali. "Maybe it's easier if they don't."

THE SINGLE CANDLE was guttering, casting flickering shadows over the room. I got up and went to the shelf where a few fresh ones lay. To my surprise, Jamie got up and came to join me. He reached past the assortment of half-burned tapers and fresh candles, pulling out the squat clock-candle that sat behind them, hidden in the shadows.

He set it on the desk, and used one of the tapers to light it. The wick was already blackened; the candle had been used before, though it wasn't burned down very far. He looked at me, and I went quietly to shut the door.

"Do you think it's time?" I asked softly, moving back to stand beside him.

He shook his head, but didn't answer. He sat back a little in his chair, hands folded in his lap, watching the flame of the clock-candle take hold and swell into a wavering light.

Jamie sighed and put out a hand to turn his account-book toward me. I could see the state of our affairs laid out there in black and white—dismal, so far as cash went.

Very little business in the Colony was done on a cash basis—virtually none, west of Cross Creek. The mountain homesteaders all dealt in barter, and so far as that went, we managed fairly well. We had milk, butter, and cheese to trade; potatoes and grain, pork and venison, fresh vegetables and dried fruit, a little wine made from the scuppernong grapes of the autumn past. We had hay and timber—though so did everyone else—and my honey and beeswax. And above everything else, we had Jamie's whisky.

That was a limited resource, though. We had fifteen acres in new barley, which—bar hailstones, forest fires, and other Acts of God—would eventually be made into nearly a hundred kegs of whisky, which could be sold or traded for quite a lot, even completely raw and unaged. The barley was still green in the field, though, and the whisky no more than a profitable phantom.

In the meantime, we had used or sold almost all the spirit on hand. True, there were fourteen small kegs of spirit remaining—buried in a small cave above the whisky-spring—but that couldn't be used. From each distilling, Jamie put aside two kegs, to be religiously kept for aging. The eldest barrel in this cache was only two years old; it would stay there for ten more, God willing, to emerge as liquid gold—and almost as valuable as the solid kind.

The immediate financial demands were not going to wait ten years, though. Beyond the possibility of a gunsmith's shop for Manfred McGillivray and a modest dowry for Lizzie, there were the normal expenses of farming, livestock maintenance, and an ambitious plan to provide ploughshares to every tenant—many of whom were still tilling by hand.

And beyond our own expenses, there was one very

burdensome obligation. Bloody Laoghaire MacKenzie damn-her-eyes Fraser.

She wasn't precisely an ex-wife—but she wasn't precisely not an ex-wife, either. Thinking me permanently gone, if not actually dead, Jamie had married her, under the prodding of his sister Jenny. The marriage had rather quickly proved to be a mistake, and upon my reappearance, an annulment had been sought, to the relief—more or less—of all parties.

Generous to a fault, though, Jamie had agreed to pay a large sum to her in annual maintenance, plus a dowry to each of her daughters. Marsali's dowry was being paid gradually, in land and whisky, and there was no news of Joan's impending marriage. But the money to keep Laoghaire in whatever style she kept in Scotland was falling due—and we didn't have it.

I glanced at Jamie, who was brooding, eyes half-closed over his long, straight nose. I didn't bother suggesting that we allow Laoghaire to put in for a gaberlunzie badge and go begging through the parish. No matter what he thought of the woman personally, he considered her his responsibility, and that was that.

I supposed that paying the debt in casks of salt fish and lye-soap was not a suitable option, either. That left us three alternatives: We could sell the whisky from the cache, though that would be a great loss in the long term. We could borrow money from Jocasta; possible, but highly distasteful. Or we could sell something else. Several horses, for instance. A large number of pigs. Or a jewel.

The candle was burning strongly, and the wax around the wick had melted. Looking down into the clear puddle of molten wax, I could see them: three gemstones, dark against the pale gray-gold of the candle, their vivid hues subdued but still visible in the wax. An emerald, a topaz, and a black diamond.

Jamie didn't touch them, but stared at them, thick ruddy brows drawn together in concentration.

Selling a gemstone in colonial North Carolina would not be easy; it would likely require a trip to Charleston or Richmond. It could be done, though, and would result in enough money to pay Laoghaire her blood-money, as well as to meet the other mounting expenses. The gemstones had a value, though, that went beyond money—they were the currency of travel through the stones; protection for the life of a traveler.

What few things we knew about that perilous journey were based largely on the things that Geillis Duncan had written or had told me; it was her contention that gems gave a traveler not only protection from the chaos in that unspeakable space between the layers of time, but some ability to navigate, as it were—to choose the time in which one might emerge.

Moved by impulse, I went back to the shelf, and standing on tiptoe, groped for the hide-wrapped bundle hidden in the shadows there. It was heavy in my hand, and I unwrapped it carefully, laying the oval stone on the desk beside the candle. It was a large opal, its fiery heart revealed within a matrix of dull stone by the carving that covered the surface—a spiral; a primitive drawing of the snake that eats its tail.

The opal was the property of another traveler—the mysterious Indian called Otter-Tooth. An Indian whose skull showed silver fillings in the teeth; an Indian who seemed at one time to have spoken English. He had called this stone his "ticket back"—so it seemed that Geilie Duncan was not the only one who believed that gemstones had some power in that dreadful place . . . between.

"Five, the witch said," Jamie said thoughtfully. "She said ye needed five stones?"

"She thought so." It was a warm evening, but the down hairs on my jaw prickled at the thought of Geilie Duncan, of the stones—and of the Indian I had met on a dark hillside, his face painted black for death, just before I had found the opal, and the skull buried with it. Was it his skull we had buried, silver fillings and all?

"Was it needful for the stones to be polished, or cut?"

"I don't know. I think she said cut ones were better—but I don't know why she thought so—or if she was right." That was always the rub; we knew so little for sure.

He made a little *hmf* noise, and rubbed the bridge of his nose slowly with one knuckle.

"Well, we've these three, and my father's ruby. Those are cut and polished stones, and that makes four. Then that wee bawbee"—he glanced at the opal—"and the stone in your amulet, which are not." The point here being that the cut or polished stones would fetch a great deal more in cash than would the rough opal or the raw sapphire in my medicine bag. And yet—could we risk losing a stone that might be needed, that might someday spell the difference between life and death for Bree or Roger?

"It's not likely," I said, answering his thought, rather than his words. "Bree will stay, certainly until Jemmy's grown; perhaps for good." After all, how could one abandon a child, the possibility of grandchildren? And yet, I had done it. I rubbed a finger absently over the smooth metal of my gold ring.

"Aye. But the lad?" He looked up at me, one eyebrow raised, the candlelight clear in his eyes, blue as sapphires cut and polished.

"He wouldn't," I said. "He wouldn't leave Bree and Jemmy." I spoke stoutly, but there was a thread of doubt in my heart, and it was reflected in my voice.

"Not yet," Jamie said quietly.

I took a deep breath, but did not reply. I knew very well what he meant. Wrapped in silence, Roger seemed to withdraw further day by day.

His fingers had healed; I had suggested to Brianna that perhaps he would find solace in his bodhran. She had nodded, doubtfully. I didn't know whether she had mentioned it to him or not—but the bodhran hung on the wall of their cabin, silent as its owner.

He did still smile and play with Jemmy, and was unfailingly attentive to Brianna—but the shadow in his eyes never lessened, and when he was not required for some chore, he would disappear for hours, sometimes all day, to walk the mountains, returning after dark, exhausted, dirt-stained—and silent.

"He hasna slept with her, has he? Since it happened?"

I sighed, brushing a strand of hair off my forehead.

"A few times. I asked. My guess would be that it hasn't happened lately, though."

Bree was doing her best to keep him close, to draw him out of the depths of his gathering depression—but it was clear to me, as well as to Jamie, that she was losing the battle, and knew it. She too was growing silent, and had shadows in her eyes.

"If he went . . . back . . . might there be a cure for his voice? There in your own time?" Jamie ran a finger over the opal as he spoke, eyes following the spiral as his finger traced it.

I sighed again, and sat down.

"I don't know. There would be help—perhaps surgery, certainly speech therapy. I can't say how *much* it would help; no one can. The thing is . . . he might recover a good deal of his voice naturally, if he'd only work at it. But he isn't going to do that. And of course," honesty compelled me to add, "he might *not* get it back, no matter how hard he worked."

Jamie nodded, silent. Regardless of the possibilities of medical help, the fact was that if the marriage between Roger and Brianna failed, there was nothing whatever to keep him here. Whether he would choose to go back then . . .

Jamie sat up in his chair, and blew the candle out.

"Not yet," he said in the darkness, his voice firm. "We've a few weeks yet before I must send money to Scotland; I'll see what else we might contrive. For now, we'll keep the stones."

Last night I dreamed that I was making bread. Or at least I was trying to make bread. I'd be mixing dough and suddenly realize that I didn't have any flour. Then I'd put the bread in pans and put it in the oven and realize that it hadn't risen, and take it back out. I'd knead it and knead it and then I'd be carrying it around in a bowl under a cloth, looking for a warm place to put it, because you have to keep it warm or the yeast dies, and I was getting frantic because I couldn't find a warm place; there was a cold wind blowing and the bowl was heavy and slippery and I thought I was going to drop it; my hands and feet were freezing and going numb.

Then I woke up and I really was cold. Roger had

pulled all the covers off and rolled himself up in them, and there was a terrible draft blowing in under the door. I nudged him and yanked on the blankets, but I couldn't get them loose and I didn't want to make a lot of noise and wake Jemmy up. Finally, I got up and got my cloak off the peg and went back to sleep under that.

Roger got up before me this morning and went out; I don't think he noticed that he'd left me in the cold.

77

A PACKAGE FROM LONDON

THE PACKAGE ARRIVED in August, by the good offices of Jethro Wainwright, one of the few itinerant peddlers with sufficient enterprise to ascend the steep and winding paths that led to the Ridge. Red-faced and wheezing from the climb and the work of unloading his donkey's pack-frame, Mr. Wainwright handed me the package with a nod, and staggered gratefully off toward the kitchen at my invitation, leaving his donkey to crop grass in the yard.

It was a small parcel, a box of some sort, sewn up carefully in oilskin and tied with twine for good measure. It was heavy. I shook it, but the only sound was a soft clunking, as though whatever lay within was padded. The label read simply "To Mr. James Fraser, Esq., Fraser's Ridge, the Carolinas."

"Well, what do you suppose this is?" I asked the donkey. It was a rhetorical question, but the donkey, an amiable creature, looked up from her meal and hee-hawed in reply, stems of fescue hanging from the corner of her mouth.

The sound set off answering cries of curiosity and welcome from Clarence and the horses, and within seconds, Jamie and Roger appeared from the direction of the barn, Brianna came out of the springhouse, and Mr. Bug rose up from behind the manure pile in his shirtsleeves like a vulture rising from a carcass, all drawn by the noise.

"Thanks," I said to the donkey, who flicked a modest ear at me and went back to the grass.

"What is it?" Brianna stood on her toes to peer over Jamie's shoulder as he took the package from me. "It's not from Lallybroch, is it?"

"No, it's neither Ian's hand . . . nor my sister's," Jamie replied with no more than a brief hesitation, though I saw him glance twice to make sure. "It's come a good way, though—by ship?" He held the parcel under my nose inquiringly. I sniffed and nodded.

"Yes; there's a whiff of tar about it. No documents, though?"

He turned the package over, then shook his head.

"It had a seal, but that's gone." Grayish fragments of wax clung to the twine, but the seal that might have provided a clue to the sender had long since succumbed to the vicissitudes of travel and Mr. Wainwright's pack.

"Ump." Mr. Bug shook his head, squinting dubiously at the package. "Not a mattock."

"No, it's nay a mattock-head," Jamie agreed, hefting the little parcel appraisingly. "Nor yet a book, let alone a quire of paper. I havena ordered anything else that I can think of. D'ye think it might be seeds, Sassenach? Mr. Stanhope did promise to send ye bits from his friend's garden, aye?"

"Oh, it might be!" That was an exciting possibility; Mr. Stanhope's friend Mr. Crossley had an extensive ornamental garden, with a large number of exotic and imported species, and Stanhope had offered to see whether Crossley might be amenable to an exchange; seeds and cuttings of some of the rarer European and Asian herbs from his collection, for bulbs and seeds from what Stanhope described as my "mountain fastness."

Roger and Brianna exchanged a brief look. Seeds were a good deal less intriguing to them than either paper or books would be. Still, the novelty of any letter or package was sufficient that no one suggested opening it until the full measure of enjoyment should have been extracted from speculation about its contents.

In the event, the package was not opened until after supper, when everyone had had a chance to weigh the parcel, poke and sniff at it, and offer an opinion regarding its contents. Pushing his empty plate aside, Jamie finally took up the parcel with all due ceremony, shook it once more, and then handed it to me.

"That knot's a job for a surgeon's hands, Sassenach," he said with a grin. It was; whoever had tied it was no sailor, but had substituted thoroughness for knowledge. It took me several minutes of picking, but I got the knot undone at last, and rolled the twine up tidily for future use.

Jamie then slit the stitching carefully with the point of his dirk, and drew out a small wooden box, to gasps of astonishment. It was plain in design, but elegant in execution, made of a polished dark wood, equipped with brass hinges and hasp, and with a matching small brass plate set into the lid.

"From the Workshop of Messrs. Halliburton and Halliburton, 14 Portman Square, London." Brianna read it out, leaning across the table and craning her neck. "Who on earth are Halliburton and Halliburton?"

"I havena the slightest idea," Jamie replied. He lifted the hasp with one finger, and delicately put back the lid. Inside was a small bag of dark red velvet. He pulled this out, opened its drawstring, and slowly drew out a . . . thing.

It was a flat golden disk, about four inches across. Goggling in astonishment, I could see that the rim was slightly raised, like that of a plate, and printed with tiny symbols of some kind. Set into the central part of the disk was an odd pierced-work arrangement, made of some silvery metal. This consisted of a small open dial, rather like a clock-face, but with three arms connecting its outer rim to the center of the bigger, golden disk.

The small silver circle was also adorned with printed arcana, almost too fine to see, and attached to a lyre-shape which itself rested in the belly of a long, flat silver eel, whose back curved snugly round the inner rim of the golden disk. Surmounting the whole was a gold bar, tapered at the ends like a very thick compass needle, and affixed with a pin that passed through the center of the disk and allowed the bar to revolve. Engraved in flowing script down the center of the bar was the name "James Fraser."

"Why, whatever in the name of Bride will *that* be?" Mrs. Bug, naturally, recovered first from her surprise.

"It's a planispheric astrolabe," Jamie answered, recovered from his surprise, and sounding now almost matter-of-fact.

"Oh, of *course*," I murmured. "Naturally!"

He turned the thing over, displaying a flat surface etched with several concentric circles, these in turn subdivided by hundreds of tiny markings and symbols. This side had a revolving bit like the compass-needle thing on the other side, but rectangular in shape, and with the ends bent upward, flattened and notched so that the notches formed a pair of sights.

Bree reached out a finger and touched the gleaming surface reverently.

"My God," she said. "Is that really *gold*?"

"It is." Jamie placed the object gingerly into her outstretched palm. "And what I should like to know is why?"

"Why gold, or why an astrolabe?" I asked.

"Why gold," he replied, frowning at the thing. "I'd been wanting such an instrument for some time, and couldna find one anywhere between Albany and Charleston. Lord John Grey had promised to have one sent me from London, and I suppose this is it. But why in Christ's name . . ."

Everyone's attention was still riveted by the astrolabe itself, but Jamie glanced away, reaching instead for the box it had come in. Sure enough, at the bottom of the box lay a note, crisply folded and sealed with blue wax. The insignia, though, was not Lord John's customary smiling half-moon-and-stars, but an unfamiliar crest, showing a fish with a ring in its mouth.

Jamie glanced at this, frowning, then broke the seal and opened the note.

Mr. James Fraser, Esq.
at Fraser's Ridge
Royal Colony of North Carolina

My dear sir,

I have the honor to send the enclosed, with the compliments of my father, Lord John Grey. Upon my departure for London, he gave me instructions to obtain the finest instrument possible, and with knowledge of the high esteem in which he holds your friendship, I have taken pains to do so. I hope it will meet with your approval.

Your obdt. servant,
William Ransome, Lord Ellesmere,
Captain, 9th Regiment

"William Ransome?" Brianna had stood up in order to read over Jamie's shoulder. She glanced at me, frowning. "He says his father's Lord John—but isn't Lord John's son still a little boy?"

"He's fifteen." Jamie's voice held an odd note, and I saw Roger glance up abruptly from the astrolabe in his hands, green eyes suddenly intent. His gaze shifted to me, with that odd look he had developed of late, of listening to something no one else could hear. I looked away.

" . . . not Grey," Brianna was saying.

"No." Jamie was still looking at the note in his hand, and sounded a little abstracted. He shook his head briefly, as though dispelling some thought, and returned to the matter at hand.

"No," he repeated more firmly, laying down the note. "The lad is John's stepson—his father was the Earl of Ellesmere; the boy's the ninth of that title. Ransome is Ellesmere's family name."

I kept my eyes fixed sedulously on the table and the empty box, afraid to look up for fear that my transparent face might reveal something—if only the fact that there was something to be revealed.

William Ransome's father had not, in fact, been the eighth Earl of Ellesmere. His father had been James Fraser, and I could feel the tension in Jamie's leg where it touched mine beneath the table, though his face now wore an expression of mild exasperation.

"Evidently the lad's been bought a commission," he said, folding the letter neatly and tucking it back in the box. "So he's gone off to London, and purchased the thing there at John's instruction. But I suppose that to a lad of his background, 'fine' must necessarily mean plated wi' gold!"

He stretched out a hand and Mr. Wainwright, who had been admiring his reflection in the polished golden surface, reluctantly surrendered the astrolabe.

Jamie examined it critically, rotating the inset silver eel with an index finger.

"Aye, well," he said, almost reluctantly. "It *is* verra fine, as to the workmanship of the thing."

"Pretty." Mr. Bug nodded his approval, reaching for one of the hot stovies his wife was offering round. "Survey?"

"Aye, that's right."

"Survey?" Brianna took two of the little potato dumplings and sat down beside Roger, automatically passing him one. "It's for surveying?"

"Among other things." Jamie turned the astrolabe over and gently pushed the flat bar, making the notched sights revolve. "This bit—it's used as a transit. Ye'll ken what that is?"

Brianna nodded, looking interested.

"Sure. I know how to do different sorts of surveying, but we generally used . . ."

I saw Roger grimace as he swallowed, the roughness of the stovie catching at his throat. I lifted my hand toward the water pitcher, but he caught my eye and shook his head, almost imperceptibly. He swallowed again, more easily this time, and coughed.

"I recall ye said ye could survey." Jamie regarded his daughter with approval. "That's why I wanted this"—he hefted the object in his hand—"though I did have something a wee bit less gaudy in mind. Pewter would ha' been more serviceable. Still, so long as I havena got to pay for it . . ."

"Let me see." Brianna extended a hand and took the thing, frowning in absorption as she moved the inner dial.

"Do you know how to use an astrolabe?" I asked her dubiously.

"I do," Jamie said, with a certain degree of smugness. "I was taught, in France." He stood up, and jerked his chin toward the door.

"Bring it outside, lass. I'll show ye how to tell the time."

". . . AYE, JUST THERE." Jamie leaned intently over Bree's shoulder, pointing at a spot on the outer dial. She moved the inner dial carefully to match, looked up at the sun, and twitched the pointer a fraction of an inch.

"Five-thirty!" she exclaimed, flushed with delight.

"Five thirty-five," Jamie corrected, grinning broadly. "See there?" He pointed at one of the tiny symbols on the rim, which at this distance, appeared to be no more than a flyspeck to me.

"Five thirty-five," Mrs. Bug said, in tones of awe. "Think of that, Arch! Why—I havena kent the time for sure, since . . . since . . ."

"Edinburgh," her husband said, nodding.

"Aye, that's right! My cousin Jane had a case-clock, a lovely thing, 'twould chime like a church bell, and its face wi' brass numbers, and a pair of wee cherubs flying right across, so—"

"This is the first time I've known what time it was, since I left the Sherstons' house." Bree was ignoring both Mrs. Bug's raptures and the instrument in her hands. I saw her meet Roger's eyes, and smile—and after a moment, his own lopsided smile in return. How long had it been for him?

Everyone was squinting up at the setting sun, waving clouds of gnats from their eyes and discussing when they had last known the time. How very odd, I thought, with some amusement. Why this preoccupation with measuring time? And yet I had it, too.

I tried to think when the last time had been for me. At Jocasta's wedding? No—on the field near Alamance Creek, just before the battle. Colonel Ashe had had a pocket watch, and—I stopped, remembering. No. It was after the battle. And that was very likely the last time Roger had known what time it was—if he had been sufficiently conscious to hear one of the Army surgeons announce that it was then four o'clock—and to give his considered opinion that Roger would not live to see the hour of five.

"What else can you do with it, Da?"

Bree handed the astrolabe carefully back to Jamie, who took it and at once began polishing away the fingermarks with the tail of his shirt.

"Oh, a great number of things. Ye can find your position, whether on land or at sea, tell the time, find a particular star in the sky . . ."

"Very useful," I observed. "Though perhaps not quite so convenient as a clock. But I suppose telling time wasn't your chief intent?"

"No." He shook his head, stowing the astrolabe tenderly away in its velvet bag. "I must have the land of the two grants properly surveyed—and soon."

"Why soon?" Bree had been turning to go, but turned back at this, one brow raised.

"Because time grows short." Jamie looked up at her, the pleasure of his acquisition subsiding into seriousness. He glanced over his shoulder, but there was no one left on the porch save himself and me, Brianna and Roger.

Mr. Wainwright, uninterested in scientific marvels, had gone down to the yard and was lugging his packs into the house, aided by Mr. Bug, and hindered by Mrs. Bug's running commentary. Everyone on the Ridge would know he was here by tomorrow, and would come to the house to buy, sell, and hear the latest news.

"Ye ken what's coming, the two of ye." Jamie glanced from Bree to Roger. "The King may fall, but the land will stay. And if we are to hold this land through it all, we must have it properly surveyed and registered. When there is trouble, when folk must leave their land or maybe have it seized—it's the devil and all to get back, but it's maybe possible, forbye—and ye have a proper deed to say what was once yours."

The sun sparked gold and fire from the curve of his head as he looked up. He nodded toward the dark line of the mountains, silhouetted by a glorious spray of pink and gold cloud, but I could see from the look of distance in his eyes that he saw something far beyond.

"Lallybroch—we saved it by means of a deed of sasine. And Young Simon, Lovat's son—he fought for his land, after Culloden, and got most of it back at last. But only because he had the papers to prove what had been his. So."

He put back the lid of the box he had brought out, and laid the velvet bag gently in it. "I will have papers. And whether it is one George or the other who rules in time—this land will be ours. And yours," he added softly, raising his eyes to Brianna's. "And your children's after you."

I laid my hand on his, where it rested on the box. His skin was warm with work and the heat of the day, and he smelt of clean sweat. The hairs on his forearm shone red and gold in the sun, and I understood very well just then, why it is that men measure time. They wish to fix a moment, in the vain hope that so doing will keep it from departing.

78

NO SMALL THING

BRIANNA HAD COME UP to the big house to borrow a book. She left Jemmy in the kitchen with Mrs. Bug, and went down the hall to her father's study. He was gone, the room empty, though it smelled faintly of him—some indefinable masculine scent, composed of leather, sawdust, sweat, whisky, manure—and ink.

She rubbed a finger under her nose, nostrils twitching,

and smiled at the thought. Roger smelled of those things, too—and yet he had his own scent, underneath. What was it? she wondered. His hands used to smell slightly of varnish and metal, when he owned a guitar. But that was long ago and far away.

Pushing away the thought, she bent her attention to the books on the shelf. Fergus had brought back three new books from his latest trip to Wilmington: a set of essays by Michel de Montaigne—those were in French, no good—a tattered copy of Daniel Defoe's *Moll Flanders*, and a very thin, paper-covered book by B. Franklin, *The Means and Manner of Obtaining Virtue*.

No contest, she thought, plucking out *Moll Flanders*. The book had seen hard use; the spine was cracked and the pages loose. She hoped they were all there; nothing worse than reaching a good part of the story and discovering that the next twenty pages were missing. She flipped carefully through, checking, but the pages seemed to be complete, if occasionally crumpled or stained with food. The book had a rather peculiar smell, as though it had been dipped in tallow.

A sudden crash from her mother's surgery jerked her from her contemplation of the books. She looked instinctively for Jem—but of course he wasn't there. Shoving the book hastily back into place, she rushed out of the study, only to meet her mother hurrying down the hall from the kitchen.

She beat Claire to the door of the surgery by a scant moment.

"Jem!"

The door of the big standing cupboard stood ajar, and the smell of honey was strong in the air. A broken stoneware bottle lay on the floor in a sticky golden puddle, and Jemmy sat in the middle of it, liberally smeared, his blue eyes absolutely round, mouth open in guilty shock.

Blood surged into her face. Ignoring the stickiness, she grabbed him by the arm and stood him on his feet.

"Jeremiah Alexander MacKenzie," Brianna said, in awful tones, "you are a Bad Boy!" She checked him hastily for blood or injury, found none, and fetched him a smack on the bottom, hard enough to make the palm of her hand sting.

The resulting screech gave her an instant qualm of guilt. Then she saw the rest of the carnage in the surgery, and quelled the impulse to spank him again.

"Jeremiah!"

Bunches of dried rosemary, yarrow, and thyme had been pulled out of the drying rack and shredded. One of the gauze shelves of the rack itself had been pulled loose, the fabric ripped and hanging. Bottles and jars from the cupboards lay tipped and rolling; some of the corks had fallen out, spilling multicolored powders and liquids. A big linen bag of coarse ground salt had been rifled, handsful of the crystals tossed around with abandon.

Worst of all, her mother's amulet lay on the floor, the little leather pouch torn open, flat and empty. Scattered bits of dried plants, a few tiny bones, and other debris lay strewn round it.

"Mama, I'm so sorry—he got away. I wasn't looking—I should have kept a better eye on—" She had nearly to shout her apologies, to be heard above Jemmy's bawling.

Claire, flinching slightly at the noise, looked round the surgery, taking hasty inventory. Then she stooped and picked Jemmy up, disregarding the honey.

"Shhhh," she said, putting a hand lightly over his mouth. This proving ineffective, she patted the hand over the gaping orifice, producing a "wa-wa-wa-wa" sound that made Jemmy stop bellowing at once. He stuck a thumb in his mouth, snuffling loudly round it, and pressed a filthy cheek to Claire's shoulder.

"Well, they do get into things," she said to Bree, looking more amused than upset. "Don't worry, darling, it's only a bit of a mess. He couldn't reach the knives, thank goodness, and I keep the poisons up high, too."

Brianna felt her heart begin to slow down. Her hand felt hot, pulsing with blood.

"But your amulet . . ." She pointed, and saw a shadow cross her mother's face when she saw the desecration.

"Oh." Claire took a deep breath, patted Jemmy's back, and put him down. Her teeth set in her lower lip, she stooped and gingerly picked up the limp pouch with its draggled feathers.

"I'm sorry," Brianna repeated, helplessly.

She could see the effort it cost, but her mother made a small dismissive gesture, before crouching to pick up the bits and pieces from the floor. Her curly hair was untied, and swung forward, hiding her face.

"I always did wonder what was in this thing," Claire said. She gingerly began to pick up the tiny bones, collecting them carefully in the palm of one hand. "What do you think these are from—a shrew?"

"I don't know." Keeping a wary eye on Jemmy, Brianna squatted and began to pick things up. "I thought maybe they were from a mouse or a bat."

Her mother glanced up at her, surprised. "Aren't you clever—look." She plucked a small, papery brown object from the floor and held it out. Bending to look closer, Brianna could see that the thing that looked like a crumpled dried leaf was in fact a fragment of a tiny bat's wing, the fragile leather dried to translucence, a bone slender as a needle curving through it like the central rib of a leaf.

"Eye of newt, and toe of frog / Wool of bat, and tongue of dog," Claire quoted. She spilled the handful of bones onto the counter, looking at them with fascination. "I wonder what she meant by that?"

"She?"

"Nayawenne—the woman who gave me the pouch." Crouching, Claire swept up the crumbled bits of leaf—at least Brianna hoped they were real leaves—into her hand, and sniffed them. There were so many odors in the air of the surgery that she herself couldn't distinguish anything beyond the overwhelming sweetness of honey, but evidently her mother's sensitive nose had no trouble in making out individual scents.

"Bayberry, balsam fir, wild ginger, and Arsesmart," she said, sniffing like a truffle-hound. "Bit of sage, too, I think."

"Arsesmart? Is that a comment on what she thought of you?" In spite of her distress, Brianna laughed.

"Ha bloody ha," her mother replied tartly, dusting the little heap of dried plant matter onto the table with the bones. "Otherwise known as water-pepper. It's a rather irritating little thing that grows near brooks—gives you blisters and smarts the eyes—or other things, I imagine, if you happen to carelessly sit on it."

Jemmy, rebukes forgotten, had got hold of a surgical clamp and was turning it to and fro, evidently trying to decide whether it was edible. Brianna debated taking it away from him, but given that her mother always sterilized her metal implements by boiling, decided to let him keep it for the moment, since it had no sharp edges.

Leaving him with Claire, she went back to the kitchen to fetch hot water and some cloths with which to deal with the honey. Mrs. Bug was there but was sound asleep, snoring gently on the settle, hands folded on her rounded stomach, her kerch comfortably askew over one ear.

Tiptoeing back with the bucket of water and a handful of cloths, she found most of the debris already swept up, and her mother crawling round on hands and knees, peering under things.

"Have you lost something?" She glanced at the bottom shelf of the cupboard, but didn't see anything missing, bar the honey-jar. The other bottles had been neatly stoppered and replaced, and everything looked much as usual.

"Yes." Claire crouched lower, frowning as she peered under the cupboard itself. "A stone. About so big"—she held out a hand, thumb and index finger circled, describing a sphere about the diameter of a small coin—"and a sort of grayish-blue. Translucent in spots. It's a raw sapphire."

"Was it in the cupboard? Maybe Mrs. Bug moved it."

Claire sat back on her heels, shaking her head.

"No, she doesn't touch anything in here. Besides, it wasn't in the cupboard—it was in there." She nodded at the table, where the amulet's empty pouch lay beside the bones and plant debris.

A quick search—and then a slower one—of the surgery revealed no sign of the stone.

"You know," Claire said, running a hand through her hair as she looked thoughtfully at Jemmy, "I hate to suggest this, but do you think . . . ?"

"Shi—I mean rats," Brianna said, concern escalating to mild alarm. She stooped to look at Jemmy, who loftily ignored her, concentrating on the job of inserting the surgical clamp into his left nostril. There *were* crumbs of dried plant matter stuck to the honey around his mouth, but surely that was just rosemary or thyme . . .

Offended at the close scrutiny, he tried to whack her with the clamp, but she seized his wrist in a grip of iron, removing the clamp from his grasp with her other hand.

"Don't hit Mummy," she said automatically, "it's not nice. Jem—did you swallow Grannie's rock?"

"No," he said, just as automatically, grabbing at the clamp. "Mine!"

She sniffed at his face, causing him to lean back at an alarming angle, but couldn't be sure. She didn't think it was rosemary, though.

"Come smell him," she said to her mother, standing up. "I can't tell."

Claire stooped to oblige, and Jemmy shrieked in giggling alarm, preparing for an enjoyable game of "Eat me up." He was disappointed, though; his grandmother merely inhaled deeply, said definitely, "wild ginger," then leaned in for a closer look, seizing a damp cloth to rub away the honey smears, in spite of increasing howls of protest.

"Look." Claire pointed at the soft skin around his mouth. Freshly cleansed, Brianna could see them clearly—two or three tiny blisters, like seed pearls.

"Jeremiah," she said sternly, attempting to look him in the eye. "Tell Mummy. Did you eat Grannie's rock?"

Jeremiah avoided her gaze and wriggled away, putting both hands protectively behind him.

"No hit," he said. "Nod nice!"

"I'm not going to spank you," she assured him, grabbing an escaping foot. "I just want to know. Did you swallow a rock about this big?" She held up thumb and forefinger. Jemmy giggled.

"Hot," he said. That was his new favorite word, applied without distinction to any object he liked.

Brianna closed her eyes, sighing in exasperation, then opened them to look at her mother.

"I'm afraid so. Will it hurt him?"

"Shouldn't think so." Claire regarded her grandson thoughtfully, tapping a finger against her lips. Then she crossed the room, opening one of the high cupboards and withdrawing a large brown-glass bottle.

"Castor-bean oil," she explained, rummaging in a drawer for a spoon. "Not *quite* as tasty as honey," she added, fixing Jemmy with a gimlet eye, "but *very* effective."

CASTOR OIL MIGHT BE effective, but it took a while. Keeping a close eye on Jemmy, who was set down to play with his basket of wooden blocks after being dosed, Brianna and Claire used the waiting time to tidy the surgery, and then turned to the peaceful, but time-consuming, job of compounding medicines. It was some time since Claire had had time to do this, and there was a staggering profusion of leaves and roots and seeds to be shredded, grated, pounded, boiled in water, steeped in oil, extracted with alcohol, strained through gauze, stirred into melted beeswax or bear grease, mixed with ground talc or rolled into pills, then jarred or bottled or bagged for preservation.

It was a pleasantly warm day, and they left the windows open for the breeze, even though this meant constantly swatting flies, shooing gnats, and picking the occasional enthusiastic bumblebee out of some bubbling solution.

"Be careful, sweetie!" Brianna reached hastily to brush away a honeybee that had lighted on one of Jemmy's blocks, just before Jem could grab it. "Bad bug. Ouchie!"

"They smell their honey," Claire said, waving away another. "I'd better give them some of it back." She set a bowl of honey-water on the windowsill, and within moments, bees were thick about the rim of it, drinking greedily.

"Single-minded, aren't they?" Brianna observed, blotting a trickle of sweat that ran between her breasts.

"Well, single-mindedness will get you a long way," Claire murmured absently, frowning slightly as she stirred a solution warming over an alcohol lamp. "Does this look done to you?"

"You know a lot better than I do." Still, she bent obligingly and sniffed. "I think so; it smells pretty strong."

Claire dipped a quick finger into the bowl, then tasted it.

"Mm, yes, I think so." Taking the bowl off the flame, she poured the dark greenish liquid carefully through a gauze strainer into a bottle. Several other tall glass bottles stood in a row on the counter, the sunlight glowing through their contents like red and green and yellow gems.

"Did you always know you were meant to be a doctor?" Brianna asked curiously. Her mother shook her head, skillfully shredding a handful of dogwood bark with a sharp knife.

"Never thought of it when I was young. Girls mostly didn't, then, of course. Growing up, I always assumed that I'd marry, have children, make a home . . . does Lizzie look all right to you? I thought she was looking a bit yellow round the edges last night, but it might only have been the candlelight."

"I think she's all right. Do you think she's really in love with Manfred?" They had celebrated Lizzie's betrothal to Manfred McGillivray the night before, with the entire McGillivray family traveling from their homestead for a lavish supper. Mrs. Bug, who was fond of Lizzie, had given of her best; no wonder she was asleep today.

"No," Claire said frankly. "But as long as she isn't in love with anyone else, it's probably all right. He's a good lad, and quite good-looking. And Lizzie likes his mother, which is also a good thing, under the circumstances." She smiled at the thought of Ute McGillivray, who had taken Lizzie at once under her capacious maternal wing, picking out particularly delicious tidbits and poking them assiduously down Lizzie's gullet, like a robin feeding a puny nestling.

"I think she may like Mrs. McGillivray more than she likes Manfred. She was really young when her own mother died; it's nice for her to sort of have one again." Brianna glanced at her mother from the corner of her eye. She could remember all too well the feeling of being motherless—and the sheer bliss of being mothered once more. By reflex, she glanced at Jemmy, who was holding an animated if mostly unintelligible conversation with Adso the cat.

Claire nodded, rubbing the shredded bark between her hands into a small round jar full of alcohol.

"Yes. Still, I think it's as well they wait a bit—Lizzie and

Manfred, I mean—and get used to each other." It had been agreed that the marriage would take place the next summer, after Manfred had finished setting up his shop in Woolam's Creek. "I hope this will work."

"What?"

"The dogwood bark." Claire stoppered the bottle and put it in the cupboard. "Dr. Rawlings' casebook says it can be used as a substitute for cinchona bark—for quinine, you know. And it's certainly easier to get, to say nothing of less expensive."

"Great—I hope it does work." Lizzie's malaria had stayed in abeyance for several months—but there was always the threat of recurrence, and cinchona bark *was* hideously expensive.

The subject of their earlier conversation lingered in her mind, and she returned to it, as she took a fresh handful of sage leaves for her mortar, bruising them carefully before putting them to steep.

"You didn't plan to be a doctor when you were young, you said. But you seemed pretty single-minded about it, later on." She had scattered, but vivid, memories of Claire's medical training; she could still smell the hospital smells caught in her mother's hair and clothing, and feel the soft cool touch of the green scrubs her mother sometimes wore, coming in to kiss her goodnight when she came in late from work.

Claire didn't answer at once, concentrating on the dried corn silk she was cleaning, plucking out rotted bits and flicking them through the open window.

"Well," she said at last, not taking her eyes off her work. "People—and it's not just women, not by any means—people who know who they are, and what they're meant to be . . . they'll find a way. Your father—Frank, I mean—" She scooped up the cleaned silk and transferred it to a small woven basket, small fragments scattering across the counter as she did so. "He was a very good historian. He liked the subject, and he had the gift of discipline and concentration that made him a success, but it wasn't really a . . . a *calling* for him. He told me himself—he could have done other things just as well, and it wouldn't have mattered a great deal. For some people, one thing *does* matter a great deal, though. And when it does . . . well, medicine mattered a great deal to me. I didn't know, early on, but then I realized that it was simply what I was meant to do. And once I knew that . . ." She shrugged, dusting her hands, and covered the basket with a bit of linen, securing it with twine.

"Yes, but . . . you can't always do what you're meant to, can you?" she said, thinking of the ragged scar on Roger's throat.

"Well, life certainly forces some things on one," her mother murmured. She glanced up, meeting Brianna's eyes, and her mouth quirked in a small, wry smile. "And for the common man—or woman—life as they find it is often the life they lead. Marsali, for instance. I shouldn't think it's ever entered her mind that she might do other than she does. Her mother kept a house and raised children; she sees no reason why she should do anything else. And yet—" Claire lifted one shoulder in a shrug, and reached across the table for the other mortar. "She had one great passion—for Fergus. And that was enough to jar her out of the rut her life would have been—"

"And into another just like it?"

Claire bent her head in a half-nod, not looking up.

"Just like it—except that she's in America, rather than Scotland. And she's got Fergus."

"Like you have Jamie?" She seldom used his given name, and Claire glanced up in surprise.

"Yes," she said. "Jamie's part of me. So are you." She touched Bree's face, quick and light, then turned half away, reaching to take down a tied bundle of marjoram from the array of hanging herbs on the beam above the hearth. "But neither of you is all of me," she said softly, back turned. "I am . . . what I am. Doctor, nurse, healer, witch—whatever folk call it, the name doesn't matter. I was born to be that; I will be that 'til I die. If I should lose you—or Jamie—I wouldn't be quite a whole person any longer, but I would still have that left. For a little time," she went on, so softly that Brianna had to strain to hear her, "after I went . . . back . . . before you came . . . that was all I had. Just the knowing."

Claire crumbled the dried marjoram into the mortar, and

took up the pestle to grind it. The sound of clumping boots came from outside, and then Jamie's voice, a friendly remark to a chicken that crossed his path.

And was loving Roger, loving Jemmy, not enough for her? Surely it should be. She had a dreadful, hollow feeling that perhaps it was not, and spoke quickly, before the thought should find words.

"What about Da?"

"What about him?"

"Does he—is he one who knows what he is, do you think?"

Claire's hands stilled, the clanking pestle falling silent.

"Oh, yes," she said. "He knows."

"A laird? Is that what you'd call it?"

Her mother hesitated, thinking.

"No," she said at last. She took up the pestle and began to grind again. The fragrance of dried marjoram filled the room like incense. "He's a man," she said, "and that's no small thing to be."

79

LONESOME ME

BRIANNA CLOSED THE BOOK, with a mingled sense of relief and foreboding. She hadn't objected to Jamie's notion that she teach a few of the little girls on the Ridge their ABC's. It filled the cabin with cheerful noise for a couple of hours, and Jemmy loved the cosseting of a half-dozen miniature mothers.

Still, she was not a natural teacher, and always felt relieved at the end of a lesson. The foreboding came on its heels, though. Most of the girls came alone, or under the care of an older sister. Anne and Kate Henderson, who lived two miles away, were escorted by their older brother, Obadiah.

She wasn't sure when or how it had started. Perhaps from the first day, when he had looked her in the eye, smiling faintly, and held the glance for a moment too long before patting his sisters' heads and leaving them to her care. But there had been nothing she could reasonably object to. Not then, not in the days since. And yet . . .

Stated bluntly to herself, Obadiah Henderson gave her the creeps. He was a tall lad of twenty or so, heavily muscled and not bad-looking, brown-haired and blue-eyed. But there was something about him that was somehow not right; a sense of something brutal about the mouth, something feral in the deepset eyes. And something very unsettling in the way he looked at her.

She hated going to the door at the end of a lesson. The little girls would scatter in a flutter of dresses and giggles—and Obadiah would be waiting, leaning against a tree, sitting on the well-coping, once even lounging on the bench outside her door.

The constant uncertainty, never knowing where he would be—but knowing that he was there, somewhere, got on her nerves nearly as much as that half-smiling look of his, and the silent smirk as he left her, almost winking, as though he knew some dirty little secret about her, but chose to keep it to himself—for now.

It occurred to her, with a certain sense of irony, that her discomfort near Obadiah was at least partly because of Roger. She had grown accustomed to hearing things that weren't spoken aloud.

And Obadiah didn't speak aloud. He didn't say anything to her, made no improper motions toward her. Could she tell him not to look at her? That was ridiculous. Ridiculous, too, that something so simple could cause her heart to jump into her throat when she opened the door, and make sweat prick beneath her arms when she saw him.

Bracing herself, she opened the door for the girls and called goodbye as they scattered, then stood and looked around. He wasn't there. Not by the well, the tree, the bench . . . nowhere.

Anne and Kate weren't looking; they were already halfway across the clearing with Janie Cameron, all three hand in hand.

"Annie!" she called. "Where's your brother?"

Annie half-turned, pigtails bouncing.

"He's gone to Salem, Miss," she called back. "We're going home to sup with Jane today!" Not waiting for acknowledgment, the girls all skipped away, like a trio of bouncing balls.

The tension melted slowly from her neck and shoulders as she drew a long, deep breath. She felt blank for a moment, as though she weren't quite sure what to do. Then she drew herself up and brushed down her rumpled apron. Jemmy was asleep, lulled by the girls' nasal singing of the alphabet song. She could take advantage of his nap to go and fetch some buttermilk from the springhouse. Roger liked buttermilk biscuits; she'd make them for supper, with a little ham.

The springhouse was cool and dark, and restful with the sound of water running through the stone-lined channel in the floor. She loved going in there, and waiting for her eyes to adjust to the darkness, so she could admire the trailing fronds of dark-green algae that clung to the stone, drifting in the current. Jamie had mentioned that a family of bats had taken up residence in the springhouse, too—yes, there they were, four tiny bundles hung up in the darkest corner, each one barely two inches long, as neat and tidy as a Greek dolmade wrapped in grape leaves. She smiled at the thought, though it was followed by a pang.

She had eaten dolmades with Roger, at a Greek restaurant in Boston. She didn't care all that much for Greek food, but it would have been a memory of their own time to share with him, when she told him about the bats. If she told him now, she thought, he would smile in response—but the smile wouldn't quite reach his eyes, and she would remember alone.

She left the springhouse, walking slowly, the bucket of buttermilk in one hand balanced by a wedge of cheese in the other. A cheese omelette would be good for lunch; quick to cook, and Jemmy loved it. He preferred to use his spoon to kill his prey, then devour it messily with both hands, but he *would* feed himself, and that was progress.

She was still smiling when she looked up from the path to see Obadiah Henderson sitting on her bench.

"What are you doing here?" Her voice was sharp, but higher than she'd intended it to be. "The girls said you'd gone to Salem."

"So I had." He rose to his feet and stepped forward, that knowing half-smile on his lips. "I came back."

She suppressed the urge to take a step back. This was her house; damned if he'd make her back away from her own door.

"Well, the girls have gone," she said, as coolly as she could manage. "They're at the Camerons'." Her heart was thumping heavily, but she moved past him, meaning to put the bucket down on the porch.

She bent, and he put his hand on the small of her back. She froze momentarily. He didn't move his hand, didn't try to stroke or squeeze—but the weight of it lay on her spine like a dead snake. She jerked upright and whirled around, taking a step back, and to hell with not letting him intimidate her. He'd already done that.

"I brought ye something," he said. "From Salem." The smile was still on his lips, but it seemed completely disconnected from the look in his eyes.

"I don't want it," she said. "I mean—thank you. But no. It isn't right for you to—my husband wouldn't like it."

"No need for him to know." He took a step toward her; she took one back, and the smile grew wider.

"I hear your husband's not home much, these days," he said softly. "That sounds lonesome."

He put out a large hand, reaching toward her face. Then there was an odd, small sound, a sort of meaty *tnk!*, and his face went blank, his eyes shocked wide.

She stared at him for a moment, completely unable to grasp what had happened. Then he turned those staring eyes to his outstretched hand, and she saw the small knife stuck in the flesh of his forearm, and the growing stain of red on the shirt around it.

"Leave this place." Jamie's voice was low, but distinct. He stepped out of the trees, eyes fixed on Henderson in a most unfriendly manner. He reached them in three strides, put out his hand, and pulled the knife from Henderson's arm. Obadiah made a small sound, deep in his throat, like a wounded animal might make, baffled and pitiable.

"Go," Jamie said. "Never come here again."

The blood was flowing down Obadiah's arm, dripping from his fingers. A few drops fell into the buttermilk, floating crimson on the rich yellow surface. In a dazed sort of way, she recognized the horrid beauty of it—like rubies set in gold.

Then the boy was going, free hand clamped to his wounded arm, shambling, then running for the trail. He disappeared into the trees, and the dooryard was very still.

"Did you have to do that?" was the first thing she managed to say. She felt stunned, as though she herself had been struck with something. The blood drops were beginning to blur, their edges dissolving into the buttermilk, and she thought she might throw up.

"Should I have waited?" Her father caught her by the arm, pulled her down to sit on the porch.

"No. But you—couldn't you just . . . have *said* something to him?" Her lips felt numb and there were small flashing lights in the periphery of her vision. Remotely, she realized that she was going to faint, and leaned forward, her head between her knees, face buried in the sanctuary of her apron.

"I did. I told him to go." The porch creaked as Jamie sat down beside her.

"You know what I mean." Her voice sounded odd to her own ears, muffled in the folds of cloth. She sat up slowly; the red spruce by the big house wavered slightly in her vision, but then steadied. "What were you *doing*? Showing off? How could you count on sticking somebody with a knife at that distance? And what was that, anyway—a *pen*knife?"

"Aye. It was all I had in my pocket. And in fact, I didna mean to stick him," Jamie admitted. "I meant to throw into the wall o' the cabin, and when he looked to see what made the noise, hit him from behind. He moved, though."

She closed her eyes and breathed deeply through her nose, willing her stomach to settle.

"Ye're all right, *a muirninn*?" he asked quietly. He laid a hand gently on her back—somewhat higher than Obadiah had. It felt good; large, warm and comforting.

"I'm fine," she said, opening her eyes. He looked worried, and she made an effort, smiling at him. "Fine."

He relaxed a bit, then, and his eyes grew less troubled, though they stayed intent on hers.

"Well, then," he said. "It's no the first time, aye? How long has yon gomerel been tryin' it on wi' you?"

She took another breath, and forced her fists to uncurl. She wanted to minimize the situation, moved by a sense of guilt—for surely she should have found some way to stop it? Faced with that steady blue gaze, though, she couldn't lie.

"Since the first week," she said.

His eyes widened.

"So long? And why did ye not tell your man about it?" he demanded, incredulous.

She was startled, and fumbled for a reply.

"I—well—I didn't think . . . I mean, it wasn't his problem." She heard the sudden intake of his breath, no doubt the precursor to some biting remark about Roger, and hurried to defend him.

"It—he—he didn't actually *do* anything. Just looks. And . . . smiles. How could I tell Roger he was *looking* at me? I didn't want to look weak, or helpless." Though she had been both, and knew it. The knowledge burned under her skin like ant bites.

"I didn't want to . . . to have to ask him to defend me."

He stared at her, his face blank with incomprehension. He shook his head slowly, not taking his eyes away from her.

"What in God's name d'ye think a man is *for*?" he asked at last. He spoke quietly, but in tones of complete bewilderment. "Ye want to keep him as a pet, is it? A lapdog? Or a caged bird?"

"You don't understand!"

"Oh. Do I not?" He blew out a short breath, in what might have been a sardonic laugh. "I have been marrit near thirty years, and you less than two. What is it that ye think I dinna understand, lass?"

"It isn't—it isn't the same for you and Mama as it is for me and Roger!" she burst out.

"No, it's not," he agreed, his voice level. "Your mother has regard for my pride, and I for hers. Or do ye maybe think her a coward, who canna fight her own battles?"

"I . . . no." She swallowed, feeling perilously close to tears, but determined not to let them escape. "But, Da—it *is* different. We're from another place, another time."

"I ken that fine," he said, and she saw the edge of his mouth curl up in a wry half-smile. His voice grew more gentle. "But I canna think that men and women are so different, then."

"Maybe not." She swallowed, forcing her voice to steady. "But maybe Roger's different. Since Alamance."

He drew breath as though to speak, but then let it out again slowly, saying nothing. He had taken his hand away; she felt the lack of it. He leaned back a little, looking out over the dooryard, and his fingers tapped lightly on the boards of the porch between them.

"Aye," he said at last, quietly. "Maybe so."

She heard a muffled thump in the cabin behind them, then another. Jem was awake, throwing his toys out of his cradle. In a moment, he would start calling for her to come and pick them up. She stood up suddenly, straightening her dress.

"Jem's up; I have to go in."

Jamie stood up, too, and picking up the bucket, flung the buttermilk in a thick yellow splash across the grass.

"I'll fetch ye more," he said, and was gone before she could tell him not to bother.

Jem was standing up, clinging to the side of his cradle, eager for escape, and launched himself into her arms when she bent to pick him up. He was getting heavy, but she clutched him tightly to her, pressing her cheek against his head, damp with sweaty sleep. Her heart was beating heavily, feeling bruised inside her chest.

"That sounds lonesome," Obadiah Henderson had said. He was right.

80

CREAMED CRUD

JAMIE LEANED BACK from the table, sighing in repletion. As he started to get up, though, Mrs. Bug popped up from her place, wagging an admonitory finger at him.

"Now, sir, now, sir, ye'll be going nowhere, and me left wi' gingerbread and fresh crud to go to waste!"

Brianna clapped a hand to her mouth, with the muffled noise characteristic of one who has just shot milk up one's nose. Jamie and Mr. Bug, to whom "crud" was the familiar Scottish usage for "curds," both looked at her curiously, but made no comment.

"Well, I'll surely burst, Mrs. Bug, but I expect I'll die a happy man," Jamie informed her. "Bring it on, then—but I've a wee thing to fetch whilst ye serve it out." With amazing agility for a man who had just consumed a pound or two of spiced sausage with fried apples and potatoes, he slid out of his chair and disappeared down the hall toward his study.

I took a deep breath, pleased that I had smelled the gingerbread cooking earlier in the afternoon, and had had the foresight to remove my stays before sitting down to supper.

"Wan' crud!" Jemmy crowed, picking up infallibly on the word most calculated to cause maternal consternation. He pounded his hands on the table in ecstasy, chanting, "Crud-crud-crud-crud!" at the top of his lungs.

Roger glanced at Bree with a half-smile, and I was pleased to see that she caught it, smiling back even as she captured Jemmy's hands and started the job of wiping the remains of dinner off his face.

Jamie returned just as the gingerbread and curds—these being sugared and whipped into creamy blobs—made their appearance. He reached over Roger's shoulder as he passed, and deposited a cloth-bound ledger on the table in front of him, topped with the small wooden box containing the astrolabe.

"The weather's good for another two months, maybe," he said casually, sitting down and sticking a finger into the huge dollop of creamed crud on his plate. He stuck the finger in his mouth, closing his eyes in bliss.

"Aye?" The word came out choked and barely audible, but enough to make Jemmy quit babbling and stare at his father open-mouthed. I wondered whether it was the first time Roger had spoken today.

Jamie had opened his eyes and picked up his spoon, eyeing his dessert with the determination of a man who means to die trying.

"Aye, well, Fergus will be going down to the coast just before snowfall—if he can take the surveying reports to be filed in New Bern then, that will be good, no?" He dug into the gingerbread in a businesslike way, not looking up.

There was a silence, filled only with heavy breathing and the clack of spoons on wooden plates. Then Roger, who had not picked up his spoon, spoke.

"I can . . . do that." It might have been no more than the effort it took to force air through his scarred throat, but there was an emphasis on the last word, that made Brianna wince. Only slightly, but I saw it—and so did Roger. He glanced at her, then looked down at his plate, lashes dark against his cheek. His jaw tightened, and he picked up his spoon.

"Good, then," Jamie said, even more casually. "I'll show ye how. Ye can go in a week."

Last night I dreamed that Roger was leaving. I've been dreaming about his going for a week, ever since Da suggested it. Suggested—ha. Like Moses brought down the Ten Suggestions from Mount Sinai.

In the dream, Roger was packing things in a big

sack, and I was busy mopping the floor. He kept getting in my way, and I kept pushing the sack aside to get at another part of the floor. It was filthy, with all sorts of stains and sticky glop. There were little bones scattered around, like Adso had eaten some little animal there, and the bones kept getting caught up in my mop.

I don't want him to go, but I do, too. I hear all the things he isn't saying; they echo in my head. I keep thinking that when he's gone, it will be quiet.

SHE PASSED ABRUPTLY from sleep to instant wakefulness. It was just past dawn, and she was alone. There were birds singing in the wood. One was caroling near the cabin, its notes sharp and musical. Was it a thrush? she wondered.

She knew he was gone, but lifted her head to check. The rucksack was gone from beside the door, as was the bundle of food and bottle of cider she had prepared for him the night before. The bodhran still hung in its place on the wall, seeming to float suspended in the unearthly light.

She had tried to get him to play again, after the hanging, feeling that at least he could still have music, if not his voice. He had resisted, though, and finally she could see that she was angering him with her insistence, and had stopped. He would do things his way—or not at all.

She glanced toward the cradle, but all was quiet, Jemmy still sound asleep. She lay back on her pillow, hands lifting to her breasts. She was naked, and they were smooth, round, and full as gourds. She squeezed one nipple gently, and tiny pearls of milk popped out. One swelled bigger, overflowed, and ran in a tiny, tickling droplet down the side of her breast.

They had made love before sleeping, the night before. At first, she hadn't thought he would, but when she came up to him and put her arms around him, he had clasped her hard against himself, kissed her slowly for a long, long time, and finally carried her to bed.

She had been so anxious for him, wanting to assure him of her love with mouth and hands and body, to give him something of herself to take away, that she had forgotten herself completely, and been surprised when the climax overtook her. She slid one hand down, between her legs, remembering the sense of being caught up suddenly by a great wave, swept helplessly toward shore. She hoped that Roger had noticed; he hadn't said anything, nor opened his eyes.

He had kissed her goodbye in the dark before dawn, still silent. Or had he? She put a hand to her mouth, suddenly unsure, but there was no clue in the smooth, cool flesh of her lips.

Had he kissed her goodbye? Or had she only dreamed it?

81

BEAR-KILLER

August, 1771

THE HORSES NEIGHING from the direction of the paddock announced company. Curious, I abandoned my latest experiment and went to peer out of the window. Neither horse nor man was in evidence in the dooryard, but the horses were still snorting and carrying on as they did when they saw someone new. The company must be afoot, then, and have gone round to the kitchen door—which most people did, this being mannerly.

This supposition was almost instantly borne out by a high-pitched shriek from the back of the house. I poked my head out into the hall just in time to see Mrs. Bug race out of the kitchen as though discharged from a cannon, screaming in panic.

Not noticing me, she shot past and out of the front door,

which she left hanging open, thus enabling me to see her cross the dooryard and vanish into the woods, still in full cry. It came as something of an anticlimax, when I glanced the other way and saw an Indian standing in the kitchen doorway, looking surprised.

We eyed each other warily, but as I appeared indisposed to screaming and running, he relaxed slightly. As he appeared unarmed and lacking paint or any other evidence of malevolent intent, I relaxed slightly.

"Osiyo," I said cautiously, having observed that he was a Cherokee, and dressed for visiting. He wore three calico shirts, one atop the other, homespun breeches, and the odd drooping cap, rather like a half-wound turban, that men favored for formal occasions, plus long silver earrings and a handsome brooch in the shape of the rising sun.

He smiled brilliantly in response to my greeting, and said something I didn't understand at all. I shrugged helplessly, but smiled in return, and we stood there nodding at one another and smiling back and forth for several moments, until the gentleman, struck by inspiration, reached into the neck of his innermost shirt—a dressy number printed with small yellow diamonds on a blue background—and withdrew a leather thong, on which were strung the curved black claws of one or more bears.

He held these up, rattled them gently, and raised his eyebrows, glancing to and fro as though searching for someone under the table or on the cabinet.

"Oh," I said, comprehending immediately. "You want my husband." I mimed someone aiming a rifle. "The Bear-Killer?"

A flash of good teeth in a beaming smile rewarded my intelligence.

"I expect he'll be along any minute," I said, waving first at the window, indicating the path taken by the exiting Mrs. Bug—who had undoubtedly gone to inform Himself that there were red savages in the house, bent on murder, mayhem, and the desecration of her clean floor—and then in the direction of the kitchen. "Come back, won't you, and have a drink of something?"

He followed me willingly, and we were seated at the table,

companionably sipping tea and exchanging further nods and smiles, when Jamie came in, accompanied not only by Mrs. Bug, who stuck close to his coattails, casting suspicious looks at our guest, but by Peter Bewlie.

Our guest was promptly introduced as Tsatsa'wi, the brother of Peter's Indian wife. He lived in a small town some thirty miles past the Treaty Line, but had come to visit his sister, and was staying with the Bewlies for a time.

"We were havin' a wee pipe after our supper last night," Peter explained, "and Tsatsa'wi was a-telling of my wife about a difficulty in their village—and she tellin' it to me, ye see, him havin' no English and me not speakin' so verra much of their tongue, no but the names of things and the odd politeness here and there—but as I say, he was telling of a wicked bear, what's been a-plaguing of them for months past."

"I should think Tsatsa'wi well-equipped to deal wi' such a creature, by the looks of it," Jamie said, nodding at the Indian's necklace of claws, and touching his own chest in indication. He smiled at Tsatsa'wi, who evidently gathered the meaning of the compliment and smiled broadly back. Both men bowed slightly to each other over the cups of tea, in token of mutual respect.

"Aye," Peter agreed, licking droplets of liquid from the corners of his mouth, and smacking his lips in approval. "He's a bonnie hunter, is Tsatsa'wi, and in the usual course o' things, I expect he and his cousins might manage well enough. But it seems as how this particular bear is just that wee bit above the odds. So I says to him as perhaps we'll come and tell *Mac Dubh* about it, and maybe as Himself would spare the time to go and sort the creature for them."

Peter lifted his chin to his brother-in-law, and nodded toward Jamie, with a proprietorial air of pride. *See*, said the gesture. *I told you. He can do it*.

I suppressed a smile at this. Jamie caught my eye, coughed modestly and set down his cup.

"Aye, well. I canna come just yet awhile, but perhaps when the hay is in. D'ye ken what's the nature of this problematical bear, Peter?"

"Oh, aye," Peter said cheerfully. "It's a ghost."

I choked momentarily on my own tea. Jamie didn't seem too shocked, but rubbed his chin dubiously.

"Mmphm. Well, what's it done, then?"

The bear had first made its presence known nearly a year before, though no one had seen it for some time. There had been the usual incidents of depredation—the carrying away of racks of drying fish or strings of corn hung outside houses, the stealing of meat from lean-tos—but at first the townspeople had regarded this merely as the work of a bear slightly more clever than the usual—the usual bear being completely unconcerned as to whether he was observed in the act.

"It would only come at night, ye see," Peter explained. "And it didna make a great deal o' noise. Folk would just come out in the morning and find their stores broken into, and not a sound made to rouse them."

Brianna, who had seen Mrs. Bug's unceremonious exit and come up to investigate the cause, began humming softly under her breath—a song to which memory promptly supplied the words, *"Oh, he'll sleep 'til noon, but before it's dark . . . he'll have every picnic basket that's in Jellystone Park . . ."* I pressed a napkin to my mouth, ostensibly to blot the remains of the tea.

"They kent it was a bear from the first, aye?" Peter explained. "Footprints."

Tsatsa'wi knew that word; he spread his two hands out on the table, thumb to thumb, demonstrating the span of the footprint, then touched the longest of the claws hung round his neck, nodding significantly.

The townspeople, thoroughly accustomed to bears, had taken the usual precautions, moving supplies into more protected areas, and putting out their dogs in the evening. The result of this was that a number of dogs had disappeared—again without sound.

Evidently the dogs had grown warier, or the bear hungrier. The first victim was a man, killed in the forest. Then, six months ago, a child had been taken. Brianna stopped humming abruptly.

The victim was a baby, snatched cradle-board and all from the bank of the river where its mother was washing clothes toward sunset. There had been no sound, and no clue left save a large clawed footprint in the mud.

Four more of the townspeople had been killed in the months since. Two children, picking wild strawberries by themselves in late afternoon. One body had been found, the neck broken, but otherwise untouched. The other had disappeared; marks showed where it had been dragged into the woods. A woman had been killed in her own cornfield, again toward sunset, and partially eaten where she fell. The last victim, a man, had in fact been hunting the bear.

"They didna find anything of *him*, save his bow and a few bits o' bloodied clothes," Peter said. I heard a small thump behind me, as Mrs. Bug sat down abruptly on the settle.

"So they have hunted it themselves?" I asked. "Or tried to, I should say?"

Peter took his eyes off Jamie and looked at me, nodding seriously.

"Oh, aye, Mrs. Claire. That's how they kent what it was, finally."

A small party of hunters had gone out loaded—literally—for bear, armed with bows, spears, and the two muskets the village boasted. They had circled the village in a widening gyre, convinced that since the bear's attentions focused on the town, it would not wander far away. They had searched for four days, now and then finding old spoor, but no trace of the bear itself.

"Tsatsa'wi was wi' them," Peter said, lifting a finger toward his brother-in-law. "He and one of his friends were sittin' up at night, keepin' watch whilst the others slept. 'Twas just past moonrise, he said, when he got up to make water. He turned back to the fire—just in time to see his friend bein' dragged off, stone-dead, wi' his neck crushed in the jaws of the thing itself!"

Tsatsa'wi had been following the tale intently. At this juncture, he nodded, and made a gesture that appeared to be the Cherokee equivalent of the Sign of the Cross—some quick and formal gesture to repel evil. He began to talk himself, then, hands flying as he pantomimed the subsequent events.

He had of course shouted, rousing his remaining comrades, and had rushed at the bear, hoping to frighten it into dropping his friend—though he could see that the man was already dead. He tilted his head sharply to indicate a broken neck, letting his tongue loll in an expression that would have been quite funny under different circumstances.

The hunters were accompanied by two dogs, which had also flown at the bear, barking. The bear had in fact dropped its prey, but instead of fleeing, had charged toward him. He had thrown himself to one side, and the bear had paused long enough to swipe one of the dogs off its feet, and then disappeared into the darkness of the wood, pursued by the other dog, a hail of arrows, and a couple of musket balls—none of which had touched it.

They had chased the bear into the wood with torches, but been unable to discover it. The second dog had returned, looking ashamed of itself—Brianna made a small fizzing noise at Tsatsa'wi's pantomime of the dog—and the hunters, thoroughly unnerved, had gone back to their fire, and spent the rest of the night awake, before returning to their village in the morning. From whence, Tsatsa'wi indicated with a graceful gesture, he had now come to solicit the assistance of the Bear-Killer.

"But why do they think it's a ghost?" Brianna leaned forward, interest displacing her initial horror at the tale.

Peter glanced at her, one eyebrow raised.

"Oh, aye, he didna say—or rather I expect he did, but not so as ye'd understand it. The thing was much bigger than the usual bear, he says—and pure white. He says when it turned to look at him, the beast's eyes glowed red as flame. They kent at once it must be a ghost, and so they werena really surprised that their arrows didna touch it."

Tsatsa'wi broke in again, pointing first at Jamie, then tapping his bear-claw necklace, and then—to my surprise—pointing at me.

"Me?" I said. "What have I got to do with it?"

The Cherokee heard my tone of surprise, for he leaned across the table, took my hand in his own, and stroked it—not in any affectionate manner, but merely as an indication of my skin. Jamie made a small sound of amusement.

"You're verra white, Sassenach. Perhaps the bear will

think ye're a kindred spirit." He grinned at me, but Tsatsa'wi evidently gathered the sense of this, for he nodded seriously. He dropped my hand, and made a brief cawing noise—a raven's call.

"Oh," I said, distinctly uneasy. I didn't know the words in Cherokee, but evidently the people of Tsatsa'wi's town had heard of White Raven as well as the Bear-Killer. Any white animal was regarded as being significant—and often sinister. I didn't know whether the implication here was that I might exert some power over the ghost-bear—or merely serve as bait—but evidently I was indeed included in the invitation.

And so it was that a week later, the hay safely in and four sides of venison peacefully hanging in the smokehouse, we set off toward the Treaty Line, bent on exorcism.

BESIDES JAMIE AND MYSELF, the party consisted of Brianna and Jemmy, the two Beardsley twins, and Peter Bewlie, who was to guide us to the village, his wife having gone ahead with Tsatsa'wi. Brianna had not wanted to come, more for fear of taking Jemmy into the wilderness than from disinclination to join the hunt, I thought. Jamie had insisted that she come, though, claiming that her marksmanship would be invaluable. Unwilling to wean Jemmy yet, she had been obliged to bring him—though he seemed to be thoroughly enjoying the trip, hunched bright-eyed on the saddle in front of his mother, alternately gabbling happily to himself about everything he saw, or sucking his thumb in dreamy content.

As for the Beardsleys, it was Josiah that Jamie wanted.

"The lad's killed two bears, at least," he told me. "I saw the skins, at the Gathering. And if his brother likes to come along, I canna see the harm in it."

"Neither do I," I agreed. "But why are you making Bree come? Can't you and Josiah handle the bear between you?"

"Perhaps," he said, running an oily rag over the barrel of his gun. "But if two heids are better than one, then a third should be better still, no? Especially if it shoots like yon lass can."

"Yes?" I said skeptically. "And what else?"

He glanced up at me and grinned.

"What, ye dinna think I have ulterior motives, do ye, Sassenach?"

"No, I don't think so—I know so."

He laughed and bent his head over his gun. After a few moments' swabbing and cleaning, though, he said, not looking up, "Aye, well. I thought it no bad idea for the lass to have friends among the Cherokee. In case she should need a place to go, sometime."

The casual tone of voice didn't fool me.

"Sometime. When the Revolution comes, you mean?"

"Aye. Or . . . when we die. Whenever that might be," he added precisely, picking the gun up and squinting down the barrel to check the sight.

It was bright Indian summer still, but I felt shards of ice crackle down my back. Most days, I managed to forget that newspaper clipping—the one that reported the death by fire of one James Fraser and his wife, on Fraser's Ridge. Other days, I remembered it, but shoved the possibility to the back of my mind, refusing to dwell on it. But every now and then, I would wake up at night, with bright flames leaping in the corners of my mind, shivering and terrified.

"The clipping said, 'no living children,' " I said, determined to face down the fear. "Do you suppose that means that Bree and Roger will have gone . . . somewhere . . . before then?" To the Cherokee, perhaps. Or to the stones.

"It might." His face was sober, eyes on his work. Neither one of us was willing to admit the other possibility—no need, in any case.

Reluctant though she had been to come, Brianna too seemed to be enjoying the trip. Without Roger, and relieved of the chores of cabin housekeeping, she seemed much more relaxed, laughing and joking with the Beardsley twins, teasing Jamie, and nursing Jemmy by the fire at night, before curling herself around him and falling peacefully asleep.

The Beardsleys were having a good time, too. The removal of his infected adenoids and tonsils had not cured Keziah's deafness, but had improved it markedly. He could understand fairly loud speech now, particularly if you faced him and spoke clearly, though he seemed to make out anything his twin said with ease, no matter how softly voiced. Seeing him look round wide-eyed as we rode through the thick, insect-buzzing forest, fording streams and finding faint deer paths through the thickets, I realized that he had never been anywhere in his life, save the area near the Beardsley farm, and Fraser's Ridge.

I wondered what he would make of the Cherokee—and they of him and his brother. Peter had told Jamie that the Cherokee regarded twins as particularly blessed and lucky; the news that the Beardsleys would be joining the hunt had delighted Tsatsa'wi.

Josiah seemed to be having fun, too—insofar as I could tell, he being a very contained sort of person. As we drew closer to the village, though, I thought that he was becoming slightly nervous.

I could see that Jamie was a trifle uneasy, too, though in his case, I suspected the reason for it. He didn't mind at all going to help with a hunt, and was pleased to have the opportunity to visit the Cherokee. But I rather thought that having his reputation as the Bear-Killer trumpeted before him, so to speak, was making him uncomfortable.

This supposition was borne out when we camped on the third night of our journey. We were no more than ten miles from the village, and would easily make it by mid-day next day.

I could see him making up his mind to something as we rode, and as we all sat down to supper round a roaring fire, I saw him suddenly set his shoulders and stand up. He walked up to Peter Bewlie, who sat staring dreamily into the fire, and faced him with decision.

"There's a wee thing I have to be sayin', Peter. About this ghost-bear we're off to find."

Peter looked up, startled out of his trance. He smiled, though, and slid over to make room for Jamie to sit down.

"Oh, aye, *Mac Dubh*?"

Jamie did so, and cleared his throat.

"Well, ye see—the fact is that I dinna actually ken a great deal about bears, as there havena been any in Scotland for quite some years now."

Peter's eyebrows went up.

"But they say ye killed a great bear wi' naught but a dirk!"

Jamie rubbed his nose with something approaching annoyance.

"Aye, well . . . so I did, then. But I didna hunt the creature down. It came after me, so I hadna got a choice about it, after all. I'm none so sure that I shall be of any great help in discovering this ghost-bear. It must be a particularly clever bear, no? To have been walking in and out of their village for months, I mean, and no one with more than a single glimpse of it?"

"Smarter than the average bear," Brianna agreed, her mouth twitching slightly. Jamie gave her a narrow look, which he switched to me as I choked on a swallow of beer.

"What?" he demanded testily.

"Nothing," I gasped. "Nothing at all."

Turning his back on us in disgust, Jamie suddenly caught sight of Josiah Beardsley, who, while not guffawing, was doing a little mouth-twitching of his own.

"What?" Jamie barked at him. "They're no but loons"—he jerked a thumb over his finger at Brianna and me—"but what's to do wi' *you*, eh?"

Josiah immediately erased the grin from his face and tried to look grave, but the corner of his mouth kept on twitching, and a hot flush was rising in his narrow cheeks, visible even by firelight. Jamie narrowed his eyes and a stifled noise that might have been a giggle escaped Josiah. He clapped a hand across his mouth, staring up at Jamie.

"What, then?" Jamie inquired politely.

Keziah, obviously gathering that something was up, hunched closer to his twin, squaring up beside him in support. Josiah made a brief, unconscious movement toward Kezzie, but didn't look away from Jamie. His face was still red, but he seemed to have got himself under control.

"Well, I suppose I best say, sir."

"I suppose ye had." Jamie gave him a quizzical look.

Josiah drew a deep breath, resigning himself.

" 'Twasn't a bear, always. Sometimes it was me."

Jamie stared at him for a moment. Then the corners of his mouth began to twitch.

"Oh, aye?"

"Not all the time," Josiah explained. But when his wanderings through the wilderness brought him within reach of one of the Indian villages—"Only if I was hungry, though, sir"—he hastened to add—he would lurk cautiously in the forest nearby, stealing into the place after dark and absconding with any easily-reached edibles. He would remain in the area for a few days, eating from the village stores until his strength and his pack were replenished, then move on to hunt, eventually returning with his hides to the cave where he had made a cache.

Kezzie's expression throughout this recital hadn't changed; I wasn't sure how much of it he had heard, but he didn't appear surprised. His hand rested on his twin's arm for a moment, then slid off, reaching for a skewer of meat.

Brianna's laughter had subsided, and she had been listening to Josiah's confession with a furrowed brow.

"But you didn't—I mean, I'm *sure* you didn't take the baby in its cradleboard. And you didn't kill the woman who was partly eaten . . . did you?"

Josiah blinked, though he seemed more baffled than shocked by the question.

"Oh, no. Why'd I do that? You don't think *I* ate 'em, do ye?" He smiled at that, an incongruous dimple appearing in one cheek. "Mind, I been hungry enough now and then as I might consider it, if I happened on somebody dead—providin' it was fairly recent," he added judiciously. "But not hungry enough as I'd kill someone a-purpose."

Brianna cleared her throat, with something startlingly like one of Jamie's Scottish noises.

"No, I didn't think you ate them," she said dryly. "I just thought that if *someone* happened to have killed them—for some other reason—the bear could have come along and gnawed on the bodies."

Peter nodded thoughtfully, seeming interested but unfazed by the assorted confessions.

"Aye, a bear'll do that," he said. "They're no picky eaters, bears. Carrion is fine by them."

Jamie nodded in response, but his attention was still fixed on Josiah.

"Aye, I've heard that, forbye. But Tsatsa'wi said he did see the bear take his friend—so it *does* kill people, no?"

"Well, it killed that one," Josiah agreed. There was an odd tone to his voice, though, and Jamie's look sharpened. He lifted a brow at Josiah, who worked his lips slowly in and out, deciding something. He glanced at Kezzie, who smiled at him. Kezzie, I saw, had a dimple in his left cheek, while Josiah's was in the right.

Josiah sighed and turned back to face Jamie.

"I wasn't a-goin' to say about this part," he said frankly. "But you been straight with us, sir, and I see it ain't right I let you go after that bear not knowin' what else might be there."

I felt the hairs rise on the back of my neck, and resisted the sudden impulse to turn round and look into the shadows behind me. The urge to laugh had left me.

"What else?" Jamie slowly lowered the chunk of bread he had been about to bite into. "And just . . . what else *might* be there, then?"

"Well, 'twas only the once I saw for sure, mind," Josiah warned him. "And 'twas a moonless night, too. But I'd been out all the night, and my eyes was well-accustomed to the starlight—you'll know the way of it, sir."

Jamie nodded, looking bemused.

"Aye, well enough. And ye were where, at the time?"

Near the village we were headed toward. Josiah had been there before, and was familiar with the layout of the place. A house at the end of the village was his goal; there were strings of corn hung to dry beneath the eaves, and he thought he could get away with one easily enough, provided he didn't rouse the village dogs.

"Rouse one, ye've got 'em all a-yowling on your tail," he said, shaking his head. "And it wasn't but a couple of hours before the dawn. So I crept along slow-like, looking to see was one of the rascals curled up asleep by the house I had my eye on." Lurking in the wood, he had seen a figure come out of the house. As no dogs took exception to this, it was a reasonable conclusion that the person belonged to the house. The man had paused to make water, and then, to Josiah's alarm, had shouldered a bow and quiver, and marched directly toward the woods where he lay hidden.

"I didn't think as he could be after me, but I went up a tree quick as a bob-tail cat, and not makin' no more noise than one, neither," he said, not bragging.

The man had most likely been a hunter, making an early start for a distant stream where raccoon and deer would come to drink at dawn. Not seeing any need of caution so near his own village, the man had not displayed any, walking through the forest quietly, but with no attempt at concealment.

Josiah had crouched in his tree, no more than a few feet above the man's head, holding his breath. The man had gone on, disappearing at once into the heavy undergrowth. Josiah had been just about to descend from his perch when he had heard a sudden exclamation of surprise, followed by the sounds of a brief scuffle that concluded with a sickening *thunk!*

"Just like a ripe squash when you chunk it with a rock to break it open," he assured Jamie. "Made my arse-hole draw up like a purse-string, hearin' that noise, there in the dark."

Alarm was no bar to curiosity, though, and he had eased through the wood in the direction of the sound. He could hear a rustling noise, and as he peered cautiously through a screen of cedar branches, he made out a human form stretched upon the ground, and another bending over it, evidently struggling to pull some kind of garment off the prone man's body.

"He was dead," Josiah explained, matter-of-factly. "I could smell the blood, and a shit-smell, too. Reckon the little fella caved in his head with a rock or maybe a club."

"Little fella?" Peter had been following the story with close attention. "How little d'ye mean? Did ye see his face?"

Josiah shook his head.

"No, I saw naught but the shadow of him, movin' about. It was full dark, still; the sky hadn't started to go light yet." He squinted, making a mental estimate. "Reckon he'd be shorter than me; maybe so high." He held out a hand in illustration, measuring a distance some four and a half feet from the ground.

The murderer had been interrupted in his work of plundering the body, though. Josiah, intent on watching, had noticed nothing, until there came a sudden crack from a breaking stick, and the inquiring *whuff* of a questing bear.

"You best believe the little fella run when he heard that," he assured Jamie. "He dashed right past, no further from me than you are now. That was when I got the only good look I had at him."

"Well, don't keep us in suspense," I said, as he paused to take a gulp of his beer. "What *did* he look like?"

He wiped a line of foam from the sparse whiskers on his upper lip, looking thoughtful.

"Well, ma'am, I was pretty near sure he was the devil. Only I did think the devil would be bigger," he added, taking another drink.

This statement naturally caused some confusion. Upon further elucidation, it appeared that Josiah merely meant that the mysterious "little fella" had been black.

"Wasn't 'til I went along to that Gathering of yours that it come to me that some regular folks just *are* black," he explained. "I hadn't never seen anybody who was, nor heard tell of it, neither."

Kezzie nodded soberly at this.

"Devil in the Book," he said, in his odd, gruff voice.

"The Book," it seemed, was an old Bible that Aaron Beardsley had taken somewhere in trade and never found a buyer for. Neither of the boys had ever been taught to read, but they were most entertained by the pictures in the Book, which included several drawings of the devil, depicted as a crouching black creature, going about his sly business of tempting and seduction.

"I didn't see no forked tail," Josiah said, shaking his head, "but then, he went by so fast, stood to reason I might have missed it in the dark and all."

Not wanting to draw the attention of such a person to himself, Josiah had stood still, and thus been in a position to hear the bear giving its attention to the unfortunate inhabitant of the village.

"It's like Mr. Peter says," he said, nodding at Peter Bewlie in acknowledgment. "Bears ain't particular. I never did see this 'un, so I can't say was it the white one or no—but it surely did eat on that Indian. I heard it, chawin' and slobberin' like anything." He seemed untroubled by this recollection, but I saw Brianna's nostrils pinch at the thought.

Jamie exchanged looks with Peter, then glanced back at Josiah. He rubbed a forefinger slowly down the bridge of his nose, thinking.

"Well, then," he said at last. "It seems that not all the evil doings in your brother-in-law's village can be laid at the ghost-bear's door, aye? What wi' Josiah stealin' food, and wee black devils killing folk. What d'ye ken, Peter? Might a bear take a taste for human flesh, once he'd had it, and then maybe go to hunting humans on his own?"

Peter nodded slowly, face creased in concentration.

"That might be, *Mac Dubh*," he allowed. "And if there's a wee black bastard hangin' about in the wood—who's to say how many the bear's killed, and how many the wee black devil's done for, and the bear takin' the blame?"

"But who *is* this wee black devil?" Bree asked. The men looked from one to another, and shrugged, more or less in unison.

"It must be an escaped slave, surely?" I said, lifting my brows at Jamie. "I can't see why a free black in his right mind would go off into the wilderness alone like that."

"Maybe he isn't in his right mind," Bree suggested. "Slave *or* free. If he's going around killing people, I mean." She cast an uneasy look at the wood around us, and put a hand on Jemmy, who was curled in a blanket on the ground beside her, sound asleep.

The men looked automatically to their weapons, and even I reached under my apron to touch the knife I wore at my belt for digging and chopping.

The forest seemed suddenly both sinister and claustrophobic. It was much too easy to imagine lurking eyes in the shadows, ascribe the constant soft rustle of leaves to stealthy footsteps or the brush of passing fur.

Jamie cleared his throat.

"Your wife's not mentioned black devils, I suppose, Peter?"

Bewlie shook his head. The concern with which he had greeted Josiah's tale was still stamped upon his grizzled face, but a small touch of amusement gleamed in his eyes.

"No. I can't say as she has, *Mac Dubh*. The only thing I recall in that regard is the Black Man o' the West."

"And who is that?" Josiah asked, interested.

Peter shrugged and scratched at his beard.

"Aye, well, I shouldna say it's anyone, so to speak. Only that the shamans say there is a spirit who lives in each o' the four directions, and each spirit has a color to him—so when they go to singin' their prayers and the like, they'll maybe call the Red Man o' the East to help the person they're singing for, because Red is the color of triumph and success. North, that's blue—the Blue Man, to give the spirit of the North his right name—that's defeat and trouble. So ye'd call on *him* to come and give your enemy a bit of grief, aye? To the South, that's the White Man, and he's peace and happiness; they sing to him for the women with child, and the like."

Jamie looked both startled and interested to hear this.

"That's verra like the four airts, Peter, is it no?"

"Well, it is, then," Peter agreed, nodding. "Odd, no? That the Cherokee should get hold of the same notions as we Hielanders have?"

"Oh, not so much." Jamie gestured to the dark wood, beyond the small circle of our fire. "They live as we do, aye? Hunters, and dwellers in the mountains. Why should they not see what we have seen?"

Peter nodded slowly, but Josiah was impatient with this philosophizing.

"Well, what's the Black Man o' the West, then?" he demanded. Both Jamie and Peter turned their heads as one to look at him. The two men looked nothing alike—Peter was short, squat, and genially bearded, Jamie tall and elegant, even in his hunting clothes—and yet there was something identical in their eyes, that made little mouse-feet run skittering down my spine. "What we have seen," indeed! I thought.

"The West is the home of the dead," Jamie said softly, and Peter nodded, soberly.

"And the Black Man o' the West is death himself," he added. "Or so say the Cherokee."

Josiah was heard to mutter that he didn't think so very much of *that* idea, but Brianna thought even less of it.

"I do *not* believe that the spirit of the West was out in the woods conking people on the head," she declared firmly. "It was a person Josiah saw. And it was a black person. Ergo, it was either a free black or an escaped slave. And given the odds, I vote for escaped slave."

I wasn't sure it was a matter for democratic process, but I was inclined to agree with her.

"Here's another thought," she said, looking round. "What if it's this little black man who's responsible for some of the half-eaten people? Aren't some of the African slaves cannibals?"

Peter Bewlie's eyes popped at that; so did the Beardsleys'. Kezzie cast an uneasy look over his shoulder and edged closer to Josiah.

Jamie appeared amused at this suggestion, though.

"Well, I suppose ye might get the odd cannibal here and there in Africa," he agreed. "Though I canna say I've heard of one amongst the slaves. I shouldna think they'd be verra desirable as house-servants, aye? Ye'd be afraid to turn your back, for fear of being bitten in the backside."

This remark made everyone laugh, and relieved the tension somewhat. People began to stir and make preparations for going to bed.

We took especial care in putting the food into two of the saddlebags, which Jamie hung up in a tree, a good distance from the camp. Even if the ghost-bear had been revealed to be less powerful than previously supposed, there was an unspoken agreement that there was no sense taking chances.

For the most part, I managed to put aside the knowledge that we lived in a wilderness. Now and then some tangible evidence would shove the fact under my nose: nocturnal visits by foxes, possums, and raccoons, or the occasional unnerving screams of panthers, with their uncanny resemblance to the crying of women or the shrieks of small children. It was quiet now, where we were. But there was no way of standing in the center of those mountains at night, submerged in the absolute black at their feet, listening to the secret murmurs of the great trees overhead, and pretending that one was anywhere but in the grip of the forest primeval—or of doubting that the wilderness could swallow us in one gulp, if it cared to, leaving not a clue behind of our existence.

For all her logic, Brianna was by no means immune to the whispers of the forest—not with a small and tender child to guard. She didn't help with the readying of camp for the night, but instead sat close to Jemmy, loading her rifle.

Jamie, after a quick look at Brianna, announced that he and she would take the first watch; Josiah and I the next, and Peter and Kezzie the last watch of the night. Heretofore, we hadn't kept a watch, but no one complained at this suggestion.

A long day in the saddle is one of the best soporifics, and I lay down beside Jamie with that utter gratitude for being horizontal that compensates for the hardest of beds. Jamie's hand rested gently on my head; I turned my face and kissed his palm, feeling safe and protected.

Peter and the Beardsley twins fell asleep within seconds; I could hear them snoring on the other side of the fire. I was nearly asleep myself, lulled by the quiet, half-heard talk between Jamie and Bree, when I became aware that the tenor of their conversation had changed.

"Are ye worrit for your man, *a nighean*?" he asked softly.

She gave a small, unhappy laugh.

"I've been worrit since they hanged him," she said. "Now I'm scared, too—or should that be 'scairt'?" she asked, trying to make a joke of it.

Jamie made a low noise in his throat, which I think he meant to be soothing.

"He's in no more danger tonight than he was last night, lass—nor any night since he set out."

"True," she answered dryly. "But just because I didn't know about ghost-bears and black murderers last week doesn't mean they weren't out there."

"My point precisely," he replied. "He'll be no safer for your fear, will he?"

"No. You think that's going to stop me worrying?"

There was a low, rueful chuckle in reply.

"I shouldna think so, no."

There was a brief silence, before Brianna spoke again.

"I just—keep thinking. What will I do, if something does happen—if he . . . doesn't come back? I'm all right during the day, but at night, I can't help thinking . . ."

"Och, well," he said softly. I saw him tilt up his head to the stars, blazing overhead. "How many nights in twenty years, *a nighean*? How many hours? For I spent that long in wondering whether my wife still lived, and how she fared. She and my child."

His hand ran smoothly over my head, gently stroking my hair. Brianna said nothing in reply, but made a small, inarticulate sound in her throat.

"That is what God is for. Worry doesna help—prayer does. Sometimes," he added honestly.

"Yes," she said, sounding uncertain. "But if—"

"And if she had not come back to me"—he interrupted firmly—"if you had not come—if I had never known—or if I had known for sure that both of you were dead . . ." He turned his head to look at her, and I felt the shift of his body as he lifted his hand from my hair and reached out his other hand to touch her. "Then I would still have lived, *a nighean*, and done what must be done. So will you."

82

A DARKENING SKY

ROGER PUSHED HIS WAY through a thick growth of sweet gum and pin oak, sweating. He was close to water; he couldn't hear it yet, but could smell the sweet, resinous scent of some plant that grew on streambanks. He didn't know what it was called, or even for sure which plant it was, but he recognized the scent.

The strap of his pack caught on a twig, and he jerked it

free, setting loose a flutter of yellow leaves like a small flight of butterflies. He would be glad to reach the stream, and not only for the sake of water, though he needed that. The nights were growing cold, but the days were still warm, and he had emptied his canteen before noon.

More urgently than water, though, he needed open air. Down here in the bottomland, the stands of dogwood and sweet bay grew so thickly that he could barely see the sky, and where the sun poked through, thick grass sprang up knee-high and the prickly leaves of dahoon caught at him as he passed.

He had brought Clarence the mule, as being better suited than the horses to the rough going in the wilderness, but some places were too rough even for a mule. He had left Clarence hobbled on the higher ground, with his bedroll and saddlebags, while he thrashed his way through the brush to reach the next point for a survey reading.

A wood-duck burst from the brush at his feet, nearly stopping his heart with the drumming of its wings. He stood still, heart thumping in his ears, and a horde of vivid little parakeets came chattering through the trees, swooping down to look at him, friendly and curious. Then something unseen gave them alarm and they rose up in a bright shriek of flight, arrowing away through the trees.

It was hot; he took off his coat and tied the sleeves round his waist, then wiped his face with a shirtsleeve and resumed his shoving, the weight of the astrolabe swinging on a thong round his neck. From the top of a mountain, he could look down on the misty hollows and wooded ridges, and take a certain awed pleasure in the thought that he owned such a place. Down here, come to grips with wild vines, burrowing fox-tails, and thickets of bamboolike cane higher than his head, the thought of ownership was ridiculous—how could something like this—this fucking swamp primeval—possibly be *owned*?

Ownership aside, he wanted to finish with this jungle and get back to higher ground. Even dwarfed by the gigantic trees of the virgin forest, a man could breathe in the space beneath. The limbs of the giant tulip trees and chestnuts stretched in a canopy overhead that shaded the ground beneath, so that only small things grew beneath—mats of delicate wildflowers, lady's slippers, trilliums—and the trees' dead leaves rained down in such profusion that one's feet sank inches into the springy mat.

Incomprehensible that such a place should ever alter—and yet it did, it would. He knew that fine; *knew* it—better than knew it, he'd bloody *seen* it! He'd driven a car down a paved highway, straight through the heart of a place once like this. He knew it could be changed. And yet as he struggled through the growth of sumac and partridgeberry, he knew even better that this place could swallow him without a second's hesitation.

Still, there was something about the sheer awful scale of the wilderness that soothed him. Among the gigantic trees and teeming wildlife, he found some peace; peace from the dammed-up words inside his head, from the unspoken worry in Brianna's eyes, the judgment in Jamie's—judgment withheld, but hanging there like the sword of Damocles. Peace from the glances of pity or curiosity, from the constant slow, aching effort of speech—peace from the memory of singing.

He missed them all, especially Bree and Jem. He seldom dreamed with any coherence; not like Bree—what was she writing now in her book?—but he had wakened this morning from a vivid impression of Jem, crawling over him as he liked to do, poking and prodding inquisitively, then softly patting Roger's face, exploring eyes and ears, nose and mouth, as though searching for the missing words.

He hadn't spoken at all for the first few days of surveying, terribly relieved not to have to. Now he was beginning to talk again, though—disliking the hoarse, mangled sound of the words, but not so bothered, since there was no one else to hear.

He heard the gurgle then of water over stones, and burst through a screen of willow saplings to find the stream at his feet, sun sparking off the water. He knelt and drank and splashed his face, then chose the spots along the bank from which to take his sightings. He dug the ledger book, ink, and quill from the leather bag over his shoulder, and fished the astrolabe out of his shirt.

He had a song in his head—again. They sneaked in when he wasn't looking, melodies singing in his inner ear like sirens from the rocks, ready to dash him in pieces.

Not this one, though. He smiled to himself, as he nudged the bar of the astrolabe and sighted on a tree on the opposite bank. It was a children's song, one of the counting songs Bree sang to Jemmy. One of those terrible songs that got into one's head and wouldn't get out again. As he took his sightings and made the notations in his book, he chanted under his breath, ignoring the cracked distortion of the sounds.

"The . . . ants go . . . mar-shing . . . one . . . by one."

Five thousand acres. What in hell was he to do with it? What in hell was he to do, period?

"Down . . . to . . . the gr-grround . . . to ggetout . . . atha RAIN . . . bum, bum, bum . . ."

I DISCOVERED QUICKLY why my name had appeared to have significance to Tsatsa'wi; the name of the village was Kalanun'yi—Raventown. I didn't see any ravens as we rode in, but did hear one, calling hoarsely from the trees.

The village lay in a charming location; a narrow river valley at the foot of a smallish mountain. The town itself was surrounded by a small spread of fields and orchards. A middling stream ran past it, dropping down a small cataract and flowing off down the valley into what looked from a distance like a huge thicket of bamboo—a canebrake, it was called, the leafy giant canes glowing dusty gold in the sun of early afternoon.

We were greeted with cordial enthusiasm by the residents of the town, lavishly fed and entertained for a day and a night. In the afternoon of the second day, we were invited to join in what I gathered was a petition to whichever Cherokee deity was in charge of hunting, to invoke favor and protection for the expedition against the ghost-bear that was to take place next day.

It had not occurred to me, prior to meeting Jackson Jolly, that there might be as much variance in talent among Indian shamans as there was among the Christian clergy. I had by this time encountered several of both species, but buffered by the mysteries of language, had not previously realized that a calling as shaman did not necessarily guarantee a person the possession of personal magnetism, spiritual power, or a gift for preaching.

Watching a slow glaze spread across the features of the people packed into Peter Bewlie's wife's father's house, I realized now that whatever his personal charm or connections with the spirit world, Jackson Jolly was sadly lacking in the last of these talents.

I had noticed a certain look of resignation on the faces of some of the congregation as the shaman took his place before the hearth, clad in a shawl-like blanket of red flannel, and wearing a mask carved in the semblance of a bird's face. As he began to speak, in a loud, droning voice, the woman next to me shifted her weight heavily from one leg to the other and sighed.

The sighing was contagious, but it wasn't as bad as the yawning. Within minutes, half the people around me were gaping, eyes watering like fountains. My own jaw muscles ached from being clenched, and I saw Jamie blinking like an owl.

Jolly was undoubtedly a sincere shaman; he also appeared to be a boring one. The only person who appeared riveted by his petitions was Jemmy, who perched in Brianna's arms, mouth hanging open in awe.

The chant for bear-hunting was a fairly monotonous one, featuring endless repetitions of *"He! Hayuya'haniwa, hayuya'haniwa, hayuya'haniwa . . ."* Then slight variations on the theme, each verse ending up with a rousing—and rather startling—*"Yoho!"*, as though we were all about to set sail on the Spanish main with a bottle of rum.

The congregation exhibited more enthusiasm during this song, though, and it finally dawned on me that what was wrong was probably not with the shaman himself. The ghost-bear had been plaguing the village for months; they must have gone through this particular ceremony several times, already, with no success. No, it wasn't that Jackson Jolly was a poor preacher; only that his congregation was suffering a lack of faith.

After the conclusion of the song, Jolly stamped fiercely on the hearth as punctuation to something he was saying, then took a sage-wand from his pouch, thrust it into the fire, and began to march round the room, waving the smoke over the congregation. The crowd parted politely as he marched up to Jamie and circled him and the Beardsley twins several times, chanting and perfuming them with wafts of fragrant smoke.

Jemmy thought this intensely funny. So did his mother, who was standing on my other side, vibrating with suppressed giggling. Jamie stood tall and straight, looking extremely dignified, as Jolly—who was quite short—hopped around him like a toad, lifting the tail of his coat to perfume his backside. I didn't dare catch Brianna's eye.

This phase of the ceremony complete, Jolly regained his position by the fire and began to sing again. The woman next to me shut her eyes and grimaced slightly.

My back was beginning to ache. At long last, the shaman concluded his proceedings with a shout. He then retired into the offing and took off his mask, wiping the sweat of righteous labor from his brow and looking pleased with himself. The headman of the village then stepped up to speak, and people began to shift and stir.

I stretched, as unobtrusively as possible, wondering what there might be for supper. Distracted by these musings, I didn't at first notice that the shiftings and stirrings were becoming more pronounced. Then the woman beside me straightened up abruptly and said something loud, in a tone of command. She cocked her head to one side, listening.

The headman stopped talking at once, and all around me people began to look upward. Bodies grew rigid and eyes grew wide. I heard it, too, and a sudden shiver raised gooseflesh on my forearms. The air was filled with a rush of wings.

"What on earth is that?" Brianna whispered to me, looking upward like everyone else. "The descent of the Holy Ghost?"

I had no idea, but it was getting louder—much louder. The air was beginning to vibrate, and the noise was like a long, continuous roll of thunder.

"Tsiskwa!" shouted a man in the crowd, and all of a sudden there was a stampede for the door.

Rushing out of the house, I thought at first that a storm had come suddenly upon us. The sky was dark, the air filled with thunder, and a strange, dim light flickered over everything. But there was no moisture in the air, and a peculiar smell filled my nose—not rain. Definitely not rain.

"Birds, my god, it's birds!" I barely heard Brianna behind me, among the chorus of amazement all around. Everyone stood in the street, looking up. Several children, frightened by the noise and darkness, started to cry.

It *was* unnerving. I had never seen anything like it—nor had most of the Cherokee, judging from their reaction. It felt as though the ground was shaking; the air was certainly shaking, vibrating to the clap of wings like a drum being slapped with frantic hands. I could feel the pulse of it on my skin, and the cloth of my kerchief tugged, wanting to rise on the wind.

The paralysis of the crowd didn't last long. There were shouts here and there, and all of a sudden, people were rushing up and down the street, charging into their houses and racing out again, with bows. Within seconds, a perfect hail of arrows was zipping up into the cloud of birds, and feathered bodies plopped out of the sky to land in limp, blood-soaked blobs, pierced with arrows.

Bodies weren't the only thing plopping out of the sky. A juicy dropping struck my shoulder, and I could see a rain of falling particles, a noxious precipitation from the thundering flock overhead, raising tiny puffs of dust from the street as the droppings struck. Down feathers shed from the passing birds floated in the air like dandelion seeds, and here and there, larger feathers knocked from tails and wings spiraled down like miniature lances, bobbing in the wind. I hastily backed up, taking shelter under the eaves of a house with Brianna and Jemmy.

We watched from our refuge in awe, as the villagers jostled each other in the street, archers shooting as fast as they could, one arrow following on the heels of another. Jamie, Peter Bewlie, and Josiah had all run for their guns, and were among the crowd, blasting away, not even troubling to aim. It wasn't necessary; no one could miss. Children, streaked with bird droppings, dodged and darted through the crowd, picking up the fallen birds, piling them in heaps by the doorsteps of the houses.

It must have lasted for nearly half an hour. We crouched under the eaves, half-deafened by the noise, hypnotized by the unceasing rush overhead. After the first fright, Jemmy stopped crying, but huddled close in his mother's arms, head buried under the drape of her kerchief.

It was impossible to make out individual birds in that violent cascade; it was no more than a river of feathers that filled the sky from one side to the other. Above the thunder of the wings, I could hear the birds calling to each other, a constant susurrus of sound, like a wind storm rushing through the forest.

At last—at long last—the great flock passed, stray birds trailing from the ragged fringe of it as it crossed the mountain and disappeared.

The village sighed as one. I saw people rubbing at their ears, trying to get rid of the clap and echo of the flight. In the midst of the crowd, Jackson Jolly stood beaming, liberally plastered with down feathers and bird droppings, eyes glowing. He spread out his arms and said something, and the people nearby murmured in response.

"We are blessed," Tsatsa'wi's sister translated for me, looking deeply impressed. She nodded at Jamie and the Beardsley twins. "The Ancient White has sent us a great sign. They will find the evil bear, surely."

I nodded, still feeling slightly stunned. Beside me, Brianna stooped and picked up a dead bird, holding it by the slender arrow that pierced it through. It was a plump thing, and very pretty, with a delicate, smoky-blue head and buff-colored breast feathers, the wing plumage a soft reddish-brown. The head lolled limp, the eyes covered by fragile, wrinkled gray-blue lids.

"It is, isn't it?" she said, softly.

"I think it must be," I answered, just as softly. Gingerly, I put out a finger and touched the smooth plumage. As signs and portents went, I was unsure whether this one was a good omen, or not. I had never seen one before, but I was quite sure that the bird I touched was a passenger pigeon.

THE HUNTERS SET FORTH before dawn the next day. Brianna parted reluctantly from Jemmy, but swung up into her saddle with a lightness that made me think she wouldn't pine for him while hunting. As for Jemmy himself, he was much too absorbed in rifling the baskets under the bed platform to take much notice of his mother's leaving.

The women spent the day in plucking, roasting, smoking, and preserving the pigeons with wood-ash; the air was filled with drifting down and the scent of grilled pigeon livers was thick in the air, as the whole village gorged on this delicacy. For my part, I helped with the pigeons, interspersing this work with entertaining conversation and profitable barter, only pausing now and then to look toward the mountain where the hunters had gone, and say a brief silent prayer for their well-being—and Roger's.

I had brought twenty-five gallons of honey with me, as well as some of the imported European herbs and seeds from Wilmington. Trade was brisk, and by the evening, I had exchanged my stocks for quantities of wild ginseng, cohosh, and—a real rarity—a chaga. This item, a huge warty fungus that grows from ancient birch trees, had a reputation—or so I was told—for the cure of cancer, tuberculosis, and ulcers. A useful item for any physician to have on hand, I thought.

As for the honey, I had traded that straight across, for twenty-five gallons of sunflower oil. This was provided in bulging skin bags, which were piled up under the eaves of the house where we were staying, like a small heap of cannon balls. I paused to look at them with satisfaction whenever I went outside, envisioning the soft, fragrant soap to be made from the oil—no more hands reeking of dead pig fat! And with luck, I could sell the bulk of it for a high enough price to make up the next chunk of Laoghaire's blood money, damn her eyes.

The next day was spent in the orchards with my hostess, another of Tsatsa'wi's sisters, named Sungi. A tall, sweet-faced woman of thirty or so, she had a few words of English, but some of her friends had slightly more—and a good thing, my own Cherokee being so far limited to "Hello," "Good," and "More."

In spite of the Indian ladies' increased fluency, I had some difficulty in making out exactly what "Sungi" meant—depending upon whom I was talking to, it seemed to mean either "onion," "mint," or—confusingly—"mink." After a certain amount of cross talk and sorting out, I got it established that the word seemed to mean none of these things precisely, but rather to indicate a strong scent of some kind.

The apple trees in the orchard were young, still slender, but bearing decently, providing a small yellowish-green fruit that wouldn't have impressed Luther Burbank, but which did have a nice crunchy texture and a tart flavor—an excellent antidote to the greasy taste of pigeon livers. It was a dry year, Sungi said, frowning critically at the trees; not so much fruit as the year before, and the corn was not so good, either.

Sungi put her two young daughters in charge of Jemmy, obviously warning them to be careful, with much pointing toward the wood.

"Is good the Bear-Killer come," she said, turning back to me, apple basket on her hip. "This bear not-bear; is not speak us."

"Oh, ah," I said, nodding intelligently. One of the other ladies helpfully amplified this idea, explaining that a reasonable bear would pay attention to the shaman's invocation, which called upon the bear-spirit, so that hunters and bears would meet appropriately. Given the color of this bear, as well as its stubborn and malicious behavior, it was apparent that it was not a real bear, but rather some malign spirit that had decided to manifest itself as a bear.

"Ah," I said, somewhat more intelligently. "Jackson mentioned 'the Ancient White'—was it the bear he meant?" Surely Peter had said that white was one of the favorable colors, though.

Another lady—who had given me her English name of Anna, rather than try to explain what her Cherokee name meant—laughed in shock at that.

"No, no! Ancient White, he the fire." Other ladies chipping in here, I finally gathered that the fire, while obviously powerful and to be treated with deep respect, was a beneficial entity. Thus the atrociousness of the bear's conduct; white animals normally were accorded respect and considered to be carriers of messages from the otherworld—here one or two of the ladies glanced sideways at me—but this bear was not behaving in any manner they understood.

Knowing what I did about the bear's assistance from Josiah Beardsley and the "wee black devil," I could well understand this. I didn't want to implicate Josiah, but I mentioned that I had heard stories—carefully not saying where I had heard them—of a black man in the forest, who did evil things. Had they heard of this?

Oh, yes, they assured me—but I should not be troubled. There was a small group of the black men, who lived "over there"—nodding toward the far side of the village, and the invisible canebrake and bottomlands beyond the river. It was possible that these persons were demons, particularly since they came from the west.

It was possible that they were not. Some of the village hunters had found them, and followed them carefully for several days, watching to see what they did. The hunters reported that the black men lived wretchedly, having barely scraps of clothing and without decent houses. This seemed not how self-respecting demons should live.

However, they were too few and too poor to be worth raiding—and the hunters said there were only three women, and those very ugly—and they might be demons, after all. So the villagers were content to leave them alone for now. The black men never came near the village, one lady added, wrinkling her nose; the dogs would smell them. Conversation lapsed then, as we spread out through the orchard, gathering ripe fruit from the trees, while the younger girls gathered the windfalls from the ground.

We went home in mid-afternoon, tired, sunburnt, and smelling of apples, to find that the hunters had come back.

"Four possums, eighteen rabbits, and nine squirrels," Jamie reported, sponging his face and hands with a damp cloth. "We found a great many birds, too, but what wi' the pigeons, we didna bother, save for a nice hawk that George Gist wanted for the feathers." He was windblown, the bridge of his nose burned red, but very cheerful. "And Brianna, bless her, killed a fine elk, just the other side of the river. A chest shot, but she brought it down—and cut the throat herself, though that's a dicey thing to do, and the beast's still thrashing."

"Oh, good," I said, rather faintly, envisioning a flurry of sharp hooves and lethal antlers in the close vicinity of my daughter.

"Dinna fash yourself, Sassenach," he said, seeing my expression. "I taught her the proper way of it. She came from behind."

"Oh, good," I said, a little more tartly. "I imagine the hunters were impressed?"

"Verra much," he said cheerfully. "Did ye ken, Sassenach, that the Cherokee let their women make war, as well as hunt? Not that they do it so often," he added, "but now and again, one will take it into her head, and go out as what they call a War Woman. The men will follow her, in fact."

"Very interesting," I said, trying to ignore the vision this summoned up, of Brianna being invited to head up a Cherokee raiding party. "Blood will out, I suppose."

"What?"

"Never mind. Did you happen to see any bears, or were you too busy exchanging interesting tidbits of anthropological lore?"

He narrowed one eye at me over the towel with which he was wiping his face, but answered equably enough.

"We found a deal of bear-sign. Josiah's an eye for it. Not only the droppings; he spotted a scratching-tree—one wi' bits of hair caught in the bark. He says that a bear has a favorite tree or two, and will come back to the same one again and again, so if ye're set to kill a particular bear, ye could do worse than camp nearby and wait."

"I gather that strategy didn't answer at present?"

"I daresay it would," he answered, grinning, "save it was

the wrong bear. The hair on the tree was dark brown, not white."

The expedition had not, however, been a failure. The hunters had completed a great semi-circle round the village, casting far out into the wood, then ranging down as far as the river. And in the soft earth of the bottomland near the canebrake, they had found footprints.

"Josiah said they were different than the prints of the bear whose hair we found—and Tsatsa'wi thought they were the same as the prints he'd seen when the white bear killed his friend."

The logical conclusion, agreed upon by all the bear-experts present, was that the ghost-bear had in all probability made its den in the canebrake. Such places were dense, dark, and cool in the heat of summer, and teeming with birds and small game. Even deer would hide there in hot weather.

"You can't get into such a place on horseback, can you?" I asked. He shook his head, combing leaves out of his hair with his fingers.

"No, nor can ye make much headway on foot, either, dense as it is. But we dinna mean to go in after the bear."

Instead, the plan was to set fire to the canebrake, driving the bear—and any other game present—out onto the flat bottomland on the other side, where it could be easily killed. Evidently, this was common practice in hunting, particularly in the fall, when the canebrakes grew dry and flammable. However, the burning would likely drive out a good deal more game than only the bear. That being so, an invitation had been sent to another village, some twenty miles distant, for their hunters to come and join with those of Ravenstown. With luck, enough game would be taken to supply both villages for the winter, *and* the extra hunters would insure that the evil ghost-bear did not escape.

"Very efficient," I said, amused. "I hope they don't smoke out the slaves, too."

"What?" He paused in his tidying.

"Black devils," I said, "or something along those lines." I told him what I had learned about the settlement—if that's what it was—of escaped slaves—if that's what they were.

"Well, I dinna suppose they're demons," he said dryly, sitting down in front of me so that I could braid his hair up neatly into a queue. "But I shouldna think they'll be in danger. They must live on the far side of the canebrake, on the opposite bank o' the river. I'll ask, though. There's time; it will be three or four days before the hunters come from Kanu'gala'yi."

"Oh, good," I said, tying the thong neatly in a bow. "That will give you just about time enough to eat all the leftover pigeon livers."

THE NEXT FEW DAYS PASSED pleasantly, though with a sense of rising anticipation that culminated with the arrival of the hunters from Kanu'gala'yi—Briertown, or so I was told. I wondered whether they had been invited because of a particular expertise in dealing with thorny territory, but forbore asking. Jamie, with his usual spongelike facility, was picking up Cherokee words like headlice, but I didn't want to tax his ability with trying to translate puns, just yet.

Jemmy appeared to have inherited his grandfather's touch with languages, and in the week since our arrival, had roughly doubled his vocabulary, with half his words being now in English and the other half in Cherokee, which rendered him unintelligible to everyone except his mother. My own vocabulary had expanded by the addition of the words for "water," "fire," "food," and "Help!"—for the rest, I depended on the kindness of the English-speaking Cherokee.

After the proper ceremonies and a large welcoming feast—featuring smoked pigeon livers with fried apples—the large party of hunters set off at dawn, equipped with pine torches and firepots, in addition to bows, muskets, and rifles. Having seen them off with a suitable breakfast—cornmeal mush mixed with pigeon livers and fresh apples—those of us not in the hunting party repaired to the houses, to pass the time in basketry, sewing, and talk.

The day was hot, muggy, and still. Not a breeze stirred in the fields, where the dry stalks of harvested corn and sunflowers lay like scattered pick-up sticks. No breath of air moved the dust in the village street. If one was going to set something on fire, I thought, it was a good day for the job. For myself, I was pleased to take refuge in the cool, shadowy interior of Sungi's cabin.

In the course of the day's conversation, I thought to ask about the components of the amulet that Nayawenne had made for me. Granted, she had been a Tuscaroran medicine-woman, so the underlying beliefs might not be the same—but I *was* curious about the bat.

"There is a story about bats," Sungi began, and I hid a smile. The Cherokee were in fact a great deal like the Scottish Highlanders, particularly in terms of liking stories. I had heard several already, in the few days we had spent in the village.

"The animals and the birds decided to play a ball game," Anna said, translating smoothly as Sungi talked. "At this time, bats walked on four feet, like the other animals. But when they came to play in the ball game, the other animals said no, they couldn't play; they were too small, and would surely be crushed. The bats didn't like this." Sungi frowned, with a grimace indicating a displeased bat.

"So the bats went to the birds, and offered to play on their side, instead. The birds accepted this offer, and so they took leaves and sticks, and they made wings for the bats. The birds won the ball game, and the bats liked their wings so much that—"

Sungi stopped talking abruptly. Her head lifted, and she sniffed the air. All around us, the women stopped talking. Sungi rose swiftly and went to the door, hand braced on the doorframe as she looked out.

I could smell the smoke—had been smelling it for the last hour as it came floating in on the wind—but I realized that the reek of burning had indeed gotten much stronger now. Sungi stepped outside; I got up and followed her with the other women, small prickles of unease beginning to nip at the backs of my knees.

The sky was beginning to darken with rain clouds, but the cloud of smoke was darker still, a roiling black smudge that rose above the distant trees. A wind had come up, riding on the edge of the approaching storm, and flurries of dry leaves rolled past us with a sound like small, skittering feet.

Most languages have a few monosyllables suitable for use in situations of sudden dismay, and so does Cherokee. Sungi said something I didn't catch, but the meaning was clear. One of the younger women licked a finger and held it up, but the gesture was unnecessary—I could feel the wind on my face, strong enough to lift the hair from my shoulders, cool on my neck. It was blowing straight toward the village.

Anna drew a long, deep breath; I could see her inflate herself, shoulders squaring to deal with the situation. Then all at once, the women were in motion, hurrying down the street toward their houses, calling for children, stopping to sweep the contents of a rack of drying jerky into a skirt or snatch a string of onions or squash from the eaves in passing.

I wasn't sure where Jemmy was; one of the older Indian girls had taken him to play with, but in the flurry, I couldn't be sure which one it was. I picked up my skirts and hurried down the street, ducking into each house without invitation, looking for him. There was a strong feeling of urgency in the air, but not panic. The sound of the dry leaves seemed constant, though, a faint rustling that followed at my heels.

I found him in the fifth house, sound asleep with several other children of different ages, all nestled like puppies in the folds of a buffalo robe. I would never have spotted him, save for his bright hair, shining like a beacon in the midst of the soft darkness. I woke them as gently as possible, and extricated Jemmy. He came awake at once, though, and was looking round, blinking in confusion.

"Come with Grannie, sweetheart," I said. "We're going to go now."

"Go horsie?" he asked, brightening at once.

"An excellent idea," I replied, hoisting him onto one hip. "Let's go find the horsie, shall we?"

The smell of smoke was much stronger when we emerged into the street. Jemmy coughed, and I could taste something acrid and bitter at the back of my mouth as I breathed. The evacuation was in full progress; people—mostly women—were hurrying in and out of the houses, pushing children before them, carrying hastily wrapped bundles of belongings. Still, there was no sense of panic or alarm in the exodus; everyone seemed concerned, but fairly matter-of-fact about it all. It occurred to me that a wooden village located in a deep forest must now and then be exposed to the risk of fire. No doubt the inhabitants had faced at least the possibility of a forest fire before, and were prepared to deal with it.

That realization calmed me a little—though the further realization that the constant dry-leaf rustling that I was hearing was in fact the crackle of the approaching fire wasn't calming at all.

Most of the horses had gone with the hunters. When I reached the brush pen, there were only three left. One of the older men of the village was mounted on one, and had Judas and the other horse on tethers, ready to lead away. Judas was saddled, and wore his saddlebags, and a rope halter. When the old man saw me, he grinned and called something, gesturing to Judas.

"Thank you!" I called back. The man leaned down and scooped Jemmy deftly from my arms, allowing me to mount Judas and get proper hold of the reins before handing Jemmy carefully back.

The horses were all restless, stamping and shifting. They knew as well as we did what fire was—and liked it even less. I took a firm hold on the halter with one hand, and a firmer hold on Jemmy with the other.

"Right, beast," I said to Judas, with an assumption of authority. "We're going now."

Judas was all in favor of this suggestion; he headed for the open gap in the brush fence as though it were the finish line of a race, snagging my skirts on the thorns of the fence as we passed. I managed to hold him back a little, long enough for the old man and his two horses to emerge from the brushy paddock and catch us up.

The man shouted something to me, and pointed toward the mountain, away from the fire. The wind had picked up; it blew his long gray hair across his face, muffling his words. He shook it away, but didn't bother to repeat himself, instead merely wheeling his mount in the direction he had pointed.

I kneed Judas in the side, turning him to follow, but kept a close rein, hesitating. I looked back over my shoulder toward the village, to see small streams of people trickling out from between the houses, all heading in the general direction the old man had indicated. No one was running, though they were all walking with great purpose.

Bree would be coming for Jemmy, as soon as she realized that the village was in danger. I knew she trusted me to see him safe, but no mother in such circumstances would rest until reunited with her child. We were not in any immediate peril, so I held back, waiting, in spite of Judas's increasing agitation.

The wind was lashing through the trees now, ripping loose billows of green and red and yellow leaves that pelted past us, plastering my skirt and Judas's hide in autumn patchwork. The whole sky had gone a violet-black, and I heard the first grumbles of thunder under the whistle of wind and rustle of fire. I could smell the tang of coming rain, even through the smoke, and felt a sudden hope. A good hard drench seemed just what the situation called for, and the sooner the better.

Jemmy was wildly excited by the atmospherics, and beat his fat little hands on the pommel, shouting a personal war chant toward the heavens that sounded something like "Oogie-oogie-oogie!"

Judas didn't care for this sort of behavior at all. I was having an increasingly hard time keeping him under any sort of control; he kept jerking at the halter while executing a sort of corkscrew maneuver that carried us in erratic circles. The wrapped rope was cutting hard into my hand, and Jemmy's bare heels were drumming a tattoo against my thighs.

I had just decided to give up and let the horse have his head, when he suddenly swung round and flung the head in question up, neighing loudly toward the village.

Sure enough, there were riders coming; I saw several horses coming out of the forest on the far side of the village at a trot. Judas, overjoyed to see other horses, was more than willing to go back into the village, even though it was in the direction of the fire.

I met Brianna and Jamie in the middle of the village, both looking anxiously round as they rode down the street. Jemmy shrieked with delight at sight of his mother, and lunged across into her arms, narrowly missing being dropped under the horses' nervous hooves.

"Did you get the bear?" I called to Jamie.

"No!" he shouted back, over the rising wind. "Come away, Sassenach!"

Bree was already off, heading for the forest, where the last of the villagers were disappearing into the trees. Relieved of my responsibility for Jemmy, though, I had thought of something else.

"Just a minute!" I shouted. I pulled up, and slid off Judas's back, throwing the reins toward Jamie. He leaned out to catch them, and yelled something after me, but I didn't catch it.

We were outside Sungi's house, and I had caught sight of the skins of sunflower oil, piled under the eaves. I risked a glance back in the direction of the canebrake. The fire was definitely coming closer; there were visible wisps of smoke swirling past me, and I *thought* I could see the glimmer of distant flame among the lashing trees. Still, I was fairly sure that we could outrun the fire on horseback—and that was a year's honey-profit lying about on the ground; I wasn't leaving it for the fire to take.

I dashed into the house, ignoring Jamie's infuriated bellows, and scrabbled madly through the scattered baskets, hoping against hope that Sungi hadn't taken . . . she hadn't. I seized a handful of rawhide strips and ran back outside.

Kneeling amid the swirling dust and smoke, I whipped strips of hide around the necks of two of the skin bags, and knotted the long ends of the two strips together, pulling the leather as tight as I could. Gathering the unwieldy pair up into my arms, I staggered back to the horses.

Jamie, seeing what I was about, gathered both sets of reins up one-handed, leaned out, and grabbed the makeshift handle that joined the skins, heaving the contraption over Gideon's withers so that the bags hung on either side.

"Come on!" he shouted.

"One more!" I called back, already running back to the house. From the corner of my eye, I could see him fighting the horses, who were plunging and snorting, anxious to be away. He was yelling uncomplimentary things about me in

Gaelic, but I sensed a certain resignation in his tone, and couldn't help smiling to myself, in spite of the anxiety that tightened my chest and made me fumble with the slippery hide strips.

Judas was snorting and rolling his eyes, baring his teeth intermittently with fear, but Jamie pulled him up close, holding his head tightly while I managed to fling the second pair of oil-filled bags across his saddle, and then mount myself.

The moment Jamie's iron grip on his halter relaxed, Judas was off. The rope was in my hands, but realizing its uselessness, I merely clung to the saddle for dear life, the oil bags bouncing madly against my legs as we hightailed it for the safety of the rising ground.

The storm was a lot closer now; the wind had dropped, but the thunder sounded in a loud clap overhead, which made Judas dig in his heels and bound over the open ground like a jackrabbit. Judas hated thunder. Remembering what had happened the last time I'd ridden him in a rainstorm, I flattened myself along his back and clung like a cocklebur, grimly determined not to be thrown or scraped off in his mad career.

Then we were into the wood, and leafless branches lashed at me like whips. I pressed myself lower against the horse's neck, closing my eyes to avoid having one poked out. Judas was moving more slowly now, by necessity, but was clearly still panicked; I could feel the churn of his hindquarters, driving us upward, and hear the breath whistling through his nostrils.

The thunder came again, and he lost his footing on the slippery leaves, slewing sideways and smashing into a stand of saplings. The springy wood saved us major damage, though, and we stumbled and staggered back upright, still moving upward. Opening one eye cautiously, I could tell that Judas had somehow found a trail—I could see the faint line of it, zigging through the dense growth in front of us.

Then the trees closed in again, and I could see nothing but a claustrophobic array of interwoven trunks and branches, twined with the yellowing remnants of wild honeysuckle and the flash of scarlet creepers. The thick growth slowed the horse still further, and I was at last able to draw a deep breath and wonder where Jamie was.

The thunder cracked again, and in its wake, I heard a high-pitched neigh, not far behind me. Of course—Judas hated thunder, but Gideon hated to follow another horse. He would be close behind, pushing to catch up.

A heavy drop of rain struck me between the shoulder blades, and I heard the rustle of the beginning rain, striking drop by drop by drop on leaves and wood and ground around me. The scent of ozone was sharp in my nostrils, and the whole wood seemed to give a green sigh, opening itself to the rain.

I gave a deep sigh, too, of relief.

Judas took a few steps further, and lurched to a halt, panting and blowing. Not waiting for another clap of thunder to set him off again, I hastily slid to the ground, and seizing his halter-rope, tied him to a small tree—no easy task, with my hands stiff and shaking.

Just in time. The thunder crashed again, a clap so loud that I could feel it on my skin. Judas screamed and reared, jerking at his rope, but I had wrapped it round the tree trunk. I stumbled back to get away from his panic, and Jamie caught me from behind. He started to say something, but the thunder boomed again, drowning him out.

I turned and clung to him, shaking with the adrenaline of delayed shock. The rain began to fall in good earnest now, drops cool on my face. He kissed my forehead, then let go and led me under the overhang of a big hemlock, whose fans of needles broke the rain, providing a fragrant, almost-dry cave beneath.

As the adrenaline surging through my body began to die down, I had a moment to look around, and realized that we were not the first inhabitants of this refuge.

"Look," I said, pointing into the shadows. The traces were slight, but obvious; someone had eaten here, discarding a tidy pile of small bones. Animals were not so tidy. Animals didn't scrape up dead needles into a comfy pillow, either.

Jamie winced at another bang of thunder, but nodded.

"Aye, it's a mankiller's spot, though I dinna think it's been used lately."

"A *what*?"

"Mankiller," he repeated. The lightning flashed behind

him, a vivid sheet that left his silhouette imprinted on my retina. "It's what they call the sentries; the warriors who stay outside the village, to keep watch and stop anyone coming in unaware. D'ye see?"

"I can't see a thing, just yet." I put out a hand, groping, and touched his coatsleeve, moving blindly into the shelter of his arm. I closed my eyes, in hopes of restoring my vision, but even against my sealed lids, I could see the flash and burst of lightning.

The thunder seemed to be moving off a little, or at least growing less frequent. I blinked, and found that I could see again. Jamie moved aside, gesturing, and I saw that we were standing on a sort of ledge, with the face of the mountain rising steeply behind us. Screened from view from below by a row of conifers, there was a narrow clearing—obviously man-made, as that was the only sort of clearing that occurred in these mountains. Looking out through the conifer branches, though, I had a breathtaking view over the small valley where Ravenstown lay.

The rain had slackened. Looking out from this high vantage point, though, I could see that the clouds were not one storm, but several; patches of dark rain hung randomly from the clouds like veils of gray velvet, and silent, jagged forks of lightning lanced suddenly across the black sky above the distant peaks, thunder grumbling in their wake.

Smoke still bloomed from the canebrake, a low flat crown of pale gray, almost white against the darkened sky. Even as high as we were, the smell of burning stung the nose, mingling oddly with the scent of rain. Here and there I could see flame-licks, still burning in the cane, but it was apparent that the fire was mostly out; the next shower of rain would quench it entirely. I could see, too, the people returning to the village, small groups making their way from the wood, bundles and children in tow.

I looked for riders, but saw none, let alone any with red hair. Surely Brianna and Jemmy were safe, though? I shivered suddenly; with the changeableness of mountain weather, the air had gone from smothering blanket to chill within less than an hour.

"All right, Sassenach?" Jamie's hand settled warmly on

my neck, fingers rubbing gently along the tense ridge of my shoulders. I took a deep breath and let them relax, as much as I could.

"Yes. Do you think it's safe to ride down?" My only impression of the trail was that it was both narrow and steep; it would be muddy now, and slippery with wet, dead leaves.

"No," he said, "but I dinna think—" He stopped abruptly, frowning in thought as he gauged the sky. He glanced behind us; I could barely make out the outline of the horses, standing close together under the shelter of the tree where I had tied Judas.

"I was going to say I didna think it particularly safe to stay here," he said at last. His fingers tapped gently on my shoulder as he thought, pattering like raindrops.

"But yon storm is moving fast; ye can see the lightning come across the mountain, and the thunder . . ." With melodramatic timing, a sharp boom of thunder rolled across the valley. I heard a shrill whinny of protest from one of the horses, and the rattle of foliage as he tugged at his halter. Jamie glanced over his shoulder, expression bleak.

"Your mount's got a strong mislike of thunder, Sassenach."

"Yes, I noticed that," I said, huddling closer to him for warmth. The wind was picking up again, as the next storm rolled in.

"Aye, he'll likely break his neck, and yours, too, if ye're so misfortunate as to be on that trail when it—" Another boom of thunder drowned his words, but I took his meaning.

"We'll wait," he said, positively.

He pulled me in front of him, and put his arms round me, sighing as he rested his chin on the top of my head. We stood together in the shelter of the hemlock, waiting for the storm to come.

Far below, the canebrake seethed and hissed, the smoke of the burning beginning to rise and fly with the wind. Away from the village, this time, toward the river. I wondered suddenly where Roger was—somewhere under that murky sky. Had he found safe refuge from the storm?

"I wonder where that bear is, too," I said, voicing half my thoughts. Jamie's chest moved in a rueful laugh, but the thunder drowned his voice.

83

WILDFIRE

ROGER HALF-WOKE with the smell of smoke burning in his throat. He coughed and sank back into sleep, fragmented images of a sooty hearth and burnt sausages fading into mist. Tired from a morning of shoving his way through impenetrable thickets of brush and cane, he had eaten a sparse lunch and lain down for an hour's rest in the shade of a black willow on the river bank.

Lulled by the rushing water, he might have sunk back into solid slumber, but a distant shriek pulled him upright, blinking. The shriek was repeated, far off but loud. The mule!

He was on his feet, stumbling toward the sound, before he remembered the leather bag that held his ink and quills, the half-chain, and the precious surveying records. He lunged back to snatch it, then splashed across the shallows toward Clarence's hysterical braying, the weight of the astrolabe swinging on its thong against his chest. He crammed it inside his shirt to stop it catching on branches, looking desperately for the way by which he had come.

Smoke—he *did* smell smoke. He coughed, half choking as he tried to stifle it. Coughing hurt his throat, with a searing pain as the scar tissue inside seemed to tear.

"Coming," he breathed, in Clarence's direction. It wouldn't have mattered if he could have shouted; even when he'd had a voice, it hadn't the carrying quality of Clarence's. He'd left the mule hobbled in a grassy patch on the edge of the canebrake, but he hadn't come in very far.

"Again," he muttered, throwing his weight against a stand of young cane to force his way through. "Yell . . . again . . .

dammit." The sky was dark. Springing from sleep and blundering off as he had, he had no sense of where he was, save for Clarence.

Shit, what was happening? The smell of smoke was noticeably stronger; as his mind cleared from the muddle of sleep and panic, he realized that something was drastically wrong. The birds, normally somnolent in mid-day, were agitated, fluttering and calling with loud, disjointed screeches past his head. Air moved restless through the canes, fluttering their ragged leaves, and he caught a touch of warmth on his face—not the moist, clinging, all-embracing warmth of the muggy canebrake, but a dry, hot touch that brushed his cheek and sent a paradoxical chill right down his back. Holy Christ, the place was on fire.

He took a deep breath, calming himself deliberately. The canebrake was alive around him; a hot wind was moving, rattling dry canes, driving flocks of songbirds and parakeets before it, flung like handsful of bright confetti through the leaves. The smoke crept into his chest and gripped his lungs, burning, keeping him from drawing a full breath.

"Clarence," he rasped, as loudly as he could. No good; he could scarcely hear himself above the rising agitation of the canebrake. He couldn't hear the mule at all. Surely the fat-headed animal hadn't been burned to a crisp already? No, more likely, he'd broken his rag hobbles and galloped off to safety.

Something brushed his leg and he looked down in time to see the naked, scaly tail of a possum, scampering into the brush. That was as good a direction as any, he thought, and plunged into the growth of buttonbush after it.

There was a grunting somewhere near; a small pig burst out of a patch of yaupon and crossed his path, heading to the left. Pig, possum—was either known to have a good sense of direction? He hesitated for a moment, then followed the pig; it was big enough to help break a path.

A path there seemed to be; small patches of bare earth showed here and there, trampled between the tussocks of grass. Wild orchids winked among them, vivid as small jewels, and he wondered at the delicacy of them—how could he notice such things, at such a time?

The smoke was thicker; he had to stop and cough, bending nearly double and clutching at his throat, as though he could keep the tissue intact, keep it from tearing with his hands. Eyes streaming, he straightened up to find that the trail had disappeared. A thrill of panic squeezed his insides as he saw a wisp of drifting smoke, nosing its way slowly through the undergrowth, delicately questing.

He clenched his fists hard enough to feel the short nails bite into his palms, using the pain to focus his mind. He turned slowly round, eyes closed to concentrate, listening, turning his face from side to side, searching for a draft of fresh air, a sense of heat—anything that would tell him which way to go, away from the fire.

Nothing. Or rather, everything. Smoke was everywhere now, in thickening clouds that crept low across the ground, rolled black out of thickets, choking. He could *hear* the fire now, a chuckling noise, like someone laughing, low down in a scar-choked throat.

Willows. His mind clung to the notion of willows; he could see a growth of them in the distance, barely visible above the waving canes. Willows grow near water; that was where the river was.

A small red and black snake slid across his foot as he reached the water, but he scarcely noticed. There was no time for any fear but the fear of fire. He splashed into the center of the stream and dropped to his knees, bending to get his face as close to the water as he could.

There was moving air, there, cool from the water, and he gulped it, deep enough to make him cough again, shaking his body with a series of racking, tearing spasms. Which way, which way? The stream wound to and fro through acres of cane and river thicket. To follow it one way would lead him toward the bottomland—perhaps, out of the fire, or at least to open country—a place where he could see again to run. To go the other way might take him straight to the heart of the fire. But there was nothing overhead but cloudy darkness, and no way of knowing.

He pressed his arms tight against his body, trying to stifle the coughing, and felt the bulge of his leather bag. The records. Goddamn it, he could countenance the possibility of his own death, but not the loss of those records, made over so many laborious days. Floundering and stumbling, he made his way to the river's edge. He dug frantically with his hands, scrabbling in the soft mud, ripping out handsful of the long, tough grass, yanking horsetails up by the roots. They came apart in his hands and he flung the segments heedless over his shoulder, breath sobbing in his chest as he gasped and dug.

The air was hot all round him, searing in his lungs. He crammed the leather bag into the damp hole he had made, reached out his arms and grasped the dirt, pulling it to him, the mud a comfort on his skin as he scooped it in.

He stopped, panting. He should be sweating, but the sweat dried before it reached the surface of his skin. The fire was close. Rocks, he needed rocks to mark the place—they wouldn't burn. He splashed back into the creek, groped beneath the surface, oh God it was cold, it was wet, thank God, grasped a boulder slick with green slime and threw it toward the bank. Another, a handful of smaller rocks, grasped in desperation, another big one, a flat one, another—enough, it would have to be enough, the fire was coming.

He piled his rocks into a hasty cairn, and commending his soul to the mercy of God, plunged back into the river and fled, stumbling and choking, rocks rolling and sliding under his feet, fled for as long as his trembling legs would carry him, before the smoke seized him by the throat, filled head and nose and chest, and choked him, the band of scarring a hand that squeezed out air and life, and left only blackness behind his eyes, lit by the flickering redness of fire.

HE WAS FIGHTING. Fighting the noose, fighting the bonds on his wrists, fighting most of all the black void that crushed his chest and sealed his throat, fighting for one final sip of precious air. He bucked, straining with every ounce of force, and then was rolling on the ground, arms flying free.

He struck something with one flailing hand. It was soft, and yelped in surprise.

Then there were hands on his shoulders, his legs, and he

was sitting up, vision fractured and chest heaving in the effort to breathe. Something struck him hard in the middle of the back. He choked, coughed, gulped enough air to cough down deep in the charred center of himself, and a huge gobbet of black phlegm rolled up out of his chest, warm and slimy as a rotten oyster on his tongue.

He spat it out, choked and heaved as the bile rose up burning through the raw squeezed channel of his throat. Then spat again, gulped, and sat up, gasping.

He had no attention to spare for anything, lost in the miracle of air and breath. There were voices around him, and vague faces in the dark; everything smelled of burning. Nothing mattered but the oxygen flooding through his chest, plumping up his shriveled cells like raisins soaked in water.

Water touched his mouth, and he looked up, eyes blinking and watering in the effort to see. His eyeballs felt seared; light and shadow smeared together, and he blinked hard, warm tears a balm to the rawness of his eyes, cooling his skin as they ran down his cheeks. Someone held a cup to his lips; a woman, face blackened with soot. No, not soot. He blinked, squinted, blinked. She was black herself. Slave?

He took a brief gulp of water, unwilling to interrupt his breathing even for the pleasure of the coolness on his ravaged throat. It was good, though—very good. His hands rose and wrapped around the cup, surprising him. He had expected the pain of broken fingers, long-numbed flesh . . . but his hands were whole and serviceable. He reached automatically for the hollow of his neck, expecting pain and the whistle of amber—and prodded unbelievingly at the solid flesh there. He breathed, and the air whistled through his nose and down the back of his throat. The world shifted around him, and realigned itself.

He was sitting in a ramshackle hut of some sort. There were several people in the hut, and more peering in at the door. Most of them were black, all were in rags, and none of the faces looked even faintly friendly.

The woman who had given him water looked scared. He tried a smile at her, and coughed again. She looked up at him under the ragged cloth tied round her brows, and he saw that the whites of her eyes were scarlet, the lids red-rimmed and swollen. His must look the same, from the feel of them. The air was still thick with smoke, and he could hear the distant cracks and pops of heat-split cane, the dying rumble of the fire. Somewhere nearby, a bird called once in alarm, then fell abruptly silent.

There was a conversation going on near the door, conducted in sibilant whispers. The men who were talking—no, arguing—glanced at him now and then, their faces masks of fear and distrust. It had begun to rain outside; he couldn't smell it, but cool air struck his face, and he heard the patter of drops on the roof, on the trees outside.

He drained the rest of the water, then offered the woman back the cup. She shrank back, as though he might be contaminated. He set the cup on the ground, nodding to her, and swiped at his eyes with the back of his wrist. The hair on his arm was singed; it crumbled to dust at a touch.

He strained to pick out words, but heard nothing but gabble. The men weren't speaking English, nor yet French or Gaelic. He had heard some of the fresh blackbirds brought up from Charleston for sale in the Wilmington market, talking among themselves in just that sort of husky, secretive murmur. Some African tongue—or more than one.

His skin was blistered, hot and painful in several places, and the air in the hut was so thickly warm that sweat ran down his face with the water from his eyes, but a chill touched the base of his spine at the realization. He was not on a plantation—there were none, so far into the mountains. Such isolated homesteads as there were up here would be too poor to have slaves, let alone such a number. Some of the Indians kept slaves—but not black ones.

Only one answer possible, one confirmed by their behavior. They were maroons, then, his captors—his saviors? Escaped slaves, living here in secrecy.

Their freedom—and perhaps their lives—depended on that secrecy. And here he sat, a living threat to it. His insides gelled as he realized just how tenuous his position was. *Had* they saved him from the fire? If so, they must now be regretting it, judging from the looks of the men by the door.

One of the arguants broke away from the group, came and squatted down before him, pushing the woman out of the way. Narrow black eyes darted over him, from face to chest, then back. "Who you?"

He didn't think the pugnacious questioner wanted his name. Rather, he wanted to know Roger's purpose. Possibilities flickered through Roger's mind—what would be most likely to keep him alive?

Not "hunter"—if they thought him English and alone, they'd kill him for sure. Could he pretend to be French? A Frenchman wouldn't seem so dangerous to them. Perhaps.

He blinked hard to clear his vision, and was opening his mouth to say, *"Je suis Français—un voyageur,"* when he felt a sharp pain in the center of his chest that made him suck breath.

The metal of the astrolabe had seared him in the fire, and quick blisters had risen and burst beneath it, gluing the thing to him with their sticky fluid. As he moved now, the weight of it had torn free, ripping the ragged shreds of skin away, and leaving a throbbing raw patch in the center of his chest.

He dipped two fingers into the neck of his shirt, and carefully pulled up the leather thong.

"Sur . . . vey . . . or," he croaked, forcing the syllables past the knot of soot and scar in his throat.

"Hau!"

His questioner stared at the golden disk, eyes bulging. The men by the door pushed and shoved each other, trying to get close enough to see.

One reached out and snatched the astrolabe, dragging it off over his head. He made no attempt to keep it, but sat back, taking advantage of their preoccupation with the gaudy thing to gather his feet slowly under him. He strained to keep his eyes open, against the nearly irresistible urge to squeeze them shut; even the soft daylight from the door was painful.

One of the men glanced at him, and said something sharp. Two of them moved at once between him and the door, bloodshot eyes fixed on him like basilisks. The man holding the astrolabe called out something, a name, he thought, and there was a movement at the door, someone pushing through the bodies there.

The woman who came in looked much like the others; dressed in a ragged shift, damp with rain, with a square of cloth tied round her head, hiding her hair. One major difference, though; the thin arms and legs protruding from the shift were the weathered, freckled brown of a white person. She stared at Roger, keeping her eyes fixed on him as she moved into the center of the hut. Only the weight of the astrolabe in her hand pulled her gaze away from him.

A tall, rawboned man with one eye shoved forward. He moved close to the woman, poked a finger at the astrolabe, and said something that sounded like a question. She shook her head slowly, tracing the markings round the edge of the disk with puzzled fascination. Then she turned it over.

Roger saw her shoulders stiffen when she saw the engraved letters, and a flicker of hope sprang up in his chest; she knew it. She recognized the name.

He had been gambling that they might know what a surveyor was, might realize that the word implied that there were people awaiting his results—people who would come looking for him, if he did not return. From their point of view, there could be no gain in killing him, if others would come searching. But if the woman knew the name "James Fraser" . . .

The woman shot Roger a sudden, hard look, quite at odds with her earlier hesitation. She approached him, slowly, but without apparent fear.

"You are not Jameth Frather," she said, and he jerked, startled at the sound of her voice, clear but lisping. He blinked and squinted, then rose slowly to his feet, shading his eyes to see her against the glare of light from the door.

She might have been any age between twenty and sixty, though the light brown hair that showed at her temples was unmarked with gray. Her face was lined, but with struggle and hunger, he thought, not age. He smiled at her, deliberately, and her mouth drew back in reflex, a hesitant grimace, but nonetheless enough for him to catch a glimpse of her front teeth, broken off at an angle. Squinting, he made out the thin slash of a scar through one eyebrow. She was much thinner than Claire's description of her, but that was hardly surprising.

"I am not . . . James Fraser," he agreed hoarsely, and had to stop to cough. He cleared his throat, hawking up more soot and slime. He spat, turning politely aside, then turned back to her. "But you are . . . Fanny Beardsley . . . aren't you?"

He hadn't been sure, in spite of the teeth, but the look of shock that crossed her face at his words was solid confirmation. The men knew that name, too. The one-eyed man took a quick step forward and seized the woman by the shoulder; the others moved menacingly closer.

"James Fraser is . . . my wife's father," he said, as quickly as he could, before they could lay hands on him. "Do you want to know—about the child?"

The look of suspicion faded from her face. She didn't move, but a look of such hunger rose in her eyes that he had to steel himself not to step back from it.

"Fahnee?" The tall man still had a hand on her shoulder. He drew closer to her, his one eye flicking back and forth in suspicion, from the woman to Roger.

She said something, almost under her breath, and put up her hand, to cover the man's where it rested on her shoulder. His face went suddenly blank, as though wiped with a slate eraser. She turned to him, looking up into his face, talking in a low tone, quick and urgent.

The atmosphere in the hut had changed. It was still charged, but an air of confusion now mingled with the general mood of menace. There was thunder overhead, much louder than the sound of the rain, but no one took note of it. The men near the door looked at each other, then, frowning, at the couple arguing in whispers. Lightning flashed, silent, framing the people in the door with darkness. There were murmuring voices outside, sounds of puzzlement. Another boom of thunder.

Roger stood motionless, gathering his strength. His legs felt like rubber, and while breathing was still a joy, each breath burned and tickled in his lungs. He wouldn't go fast or far, if he had to run.

The argument stopped abruptly. The tall man turned and made a sharp gesture toward the door, saying something that made the other men grunt with surprise and disapproval. Still, they went, slowly, and with much muttered grumbling. One short fellow with his hair in knots glared back at Roger, bared his teeth, and drew the edge of a hand across his throat with a hiss. With a small shock, Roger saw that the man's teeth were jagged, filed to points.

The ramshackle door had barely closed behind them when the woman clutched his sleeve.

"Tell me," she said.

"Not so . . . fast." He coughed again, wiping spittle from his mouth with the back of his hand. His throat was seared; the words felt like cinders, forced burning from his chest. "You get . . . me . . . out of here. Then . . . I'll tell you. All I know."

"Tell me!"

Her fingers dug hard into his arm. Her eyes were bloodshot from the smoke, and the brown irises glowed like coals. He shook his head, coughing.

The tall man brushed the woman aside, grabbing Roger by a handful of shirt. Something gleamed dully, too close to Roger's eye to see clearly, and amid the stench of burning, he caught the reek of rotting teeth.

"You tell her, man, or I rip you guts!"

Roger brought a forearm up between them, and with an effort, shoved the man back, stumbling.

"No," he said doggedly. "You get . . . me out. Then I tell."

The man hesitated, crouched, the knife blade wavering in a small arc of uncertainty. His one eye flicked to the woman. "You sure he know?"

The woman had not taken her eyes off Roger's face. She nodded slowly, not looking away.

"He knows."

"It was . . . a girl." Roger looked at her steadily, fighting the urge to blink. "You'll know . . . that much . . . yourself."

"Does she live?"

"Get me . . . out."

She was not a tall woman, nor a large one, but her urgency seemed to fill the hut. She fairly quivered with it, hands clenched into fists at her sides. She glared at Roger for a long minute more, then whirled on her heel, saying something violent to the man in the odd African tongue.

He tried to argue, but it was fruitless; the stream of her words struck him like water from a fire hose. He flung up his hands in frustrated surrender, then reached out and snatched the rag from the woman's head. He undid the knots with quick, long fingers, and whipped it into the shape of a blindfold, muttering under his breath.

The last thing Roger saw before the man fastened the cloth round his eyes was Fanny Beardsley, hair in a number of small greasy plaits round her shoulders, her eyes still on him, burning like embers. Her broken teeth were bared, and he thought she would bite him, if she could.

THEY DIDN'T GET OUT without some argument; a chorus of angry voices surrounded them for some way, and hands plucked at his clothes and limbs. But the one-eyed man still had the knife. Roger heard a shout, a scuffling of feet and bodies close by, and a sharp cry. The voices dropped, and the hands no longer snatched at him.

They walked on, his hand on Fanny Beardsley's shoulder for guidance. He thought it was a small settlement; at least, it took very little time before he felt the trees close around him. Leaves brushed his face, and the resin smell of sap was heightened by the hot, smoky air. It was still raining fairly hard, but the smell of smoke was everywhere. The ground was lumpy, layers of leaf-mold punctuated by upthrusting rocks, studded with stumps and fallen branches.

The man and woman exchanged occasional remarks, but soon fell silent. His clothes grew wet and clung to him, the seams of his breeches chafing as he walked. The blindfold was too tight to allow him to see anything, but light leaked under the edge, and from that, he could judge the changing time of day. He thought it was just past mid-afternoon when they left the hut; when they stopped at last, the light had faded almost completely.

He blinked when the blindfold was taken off, the sudden flood of light compensating for its dimness. It was late twilight. They stood in a hollow, already halfway filled with darkness. Looking up, he saw the sky above the mountains blazing with orange and crimson, the smoky haze lit up as though the world itself were still burning. Overhead, the clouds had broken; a slice of pure blue sky shone through, soft, and bright with twilight stars.

Fanny Beardsley faced him, looking smaller beneath the canopy of a towering chestnut tree, but every bit as intent as she had in the hut.

He had had plenty of time to think about it. Ought he to tell her where the child was, or should he claim not to know? If she knew, would she make an attempt to reclaim the little girl? And if so, what might be the fallout—for the child, the escaped slaves—or even for Jamie and Claire Fraser?

Neither of them had said anything about the events that had transpired at the Beardsley farmhouse, beyond the simple fact that Beardsley had died of an apoplexy. Roger was sufficiently familiar with them both, though, to draw silent deductions from Claire's troubled face and Jamie's impassive one. He didn't know what had happened, but Fanny Beardsley did—and it might well be something the Frasers would prefer remain undiscovered. If Mrs. Beardsley reappeared in Brownsville, seeking to reclaim her daughter, questions would certainly be asked—and perhaps it was to no one's benefit that they be answered.

The blazing sky washed her face with fire, though, and faced with the hunger in those burning eyes, he could speak nothing but the truth.

"Your daughter . . . is well," he began firmly, and she made a small strangled noise, deep in her throat. By the time he had finished telling what he knew, the tears were running down her face, making tracks in the soot and dust that covered her, but her eyes stayed wide, fixed on him as though to blink would be to miss some vital word.

The man hung back a little, wary, keeping watch. His attention was mostly on the woman, but he stole occasional glances at Roger as he spoke, and at the end, stood beside the woman, his one eye bright as hers.

"She have de money?" he asked. He had the lilt of the Indies in his speech, and a skin like dark honey. He would have been handsome, save for whatever accident had deprived him of his eye, leaving a pocket of livid flesh beneath a twisted, drooping lid.

"Yes, she's . . . inherited . . . all of Aaron . . . Beardsley's property," Roger assured him, breath rasping in his throat from so much talking. "Mr. Fraser saw . . . to it." He and Jamie had both gone to the hearing of the Orphan's Court, for Jamie to bear witness to the girl's identity. Richard Brown and his wife had been given the guardianship of the child—and her property. They had named the little girl—from what depths of sentiment or outrage, he had no idea—"Alicia."

"No matta she black?" He saw the slave's one eye flick sideways toward Fanny Beardsley, then slide away. Mrs. Beardsley heard the note of uncertainty in the man's voice, and turned on him like a viper striking.

"She is yourss!" she said. "She could not be histh, could not!"

"Yah, you say so," he replied, his face cast down in sullenness. "Dey give money to black girl?"

She stamped her foot, noiseless on the ground, and slapped at him. He straightened up and turned his face aside, but made no other attempt to escape her fury.

"Do you think I would have left her, *ever* left her, if she had been white, if she could posthibly have been white?" she shouted. She punched at him, pummelling his arms and chest with blows. "It wath your fault I had to leave her, yourss! You and that damned black hide, God damn you—"

It was Roger who seized her flailing wrists and held them tight against her straining, letting her shriek herself to hoarseness before she collapsed at last in tears.

The slave, who had watched all this with an expression between shame and anger, lifted his hands a little toward her. It was the slightest of movements, but enough; she turned at once from Roger and flung herself into her lover's arms, sobbing against his chest. He wrapped his arms awkwardly around her and held her close, rocking back and forth on his bare heels. He looked sheepish, but no longer angry.

Roger cleared his throat, grimacing at the soreness. The slave looked up at him, and nodded.

"You go, man," he said softly. Then, before Roger could turn to go, he said, "Wait . . . true, man, de child fix good?"

Roger nodded, feeling unutterably tired. Whatever adrenaline or sense of self-preservation had been keeping him going was all used up. The blazing sky had gone to ashes, and everything in the hollow was fading, blurring into dark.

"She's all . . . right. They'll take . . . good care of her." He groped, wanting to offer something else. "She's . . . pretty," he said at last. His voice was nearly gone, no more than a whisper. "A pretty . . . girl."

The man's face shifted, caught between embarrassment, dismay, and pleasure.

"Oh," he said. "Dat be from de mama, sure." He patted Fanny Beardsley's back, very gently. She had stopped sobbing, but stood with her face pressed against his chest, still and silent. It was nearly full dark; in the deep dusk, all color was leached away; her skin seemed the same color as his.

The man wore nothing but a tattered shirt, wet through, so that his dark skin showed in patches through it. He had a rope belt, though, with a rough cloth bag strung on it. He groped one-handed in this, and drew out the astrolabe, which he extended toward Roger.

"You don't mean . . . to keep that?" Roger asked. He felt as though he was standing inside a cloud; everything was beginning to feel far away and hazy, and words reached him as though filtered through cotton wool.

The ex-slave shook his head.

"No, man, what I do wid dat? Beside," he added, with a wry lift of the mouth, "maybe no one come look you, man, but de masta what own dat ting—he come look, maybe."

Roger took the heavy disk, and put the thong over his neck. It took two tries; his arms felt like lead.

"Nobody . . . will come looking," he said. He turned and walked away, with no idea where he was, or where he might be going. After a few steps, he turned and looked back, but the night had already swallowed them.

84

BURNT TO BONES

THE HORSES SETTLED SLIGHTLY, but were still uneasy, pawing, stamping, and jerking at their tethers, as the thunder rumbled hollowly in the distance. Jamie sighed, kissed the top of my head, and pushed his way back through the conifers to the tiny clearing where they stood.

"Well, if ye dinna like it up here," I heard him say to them, "why did ye come?" He spoke tolerantly, though, and I heard Gideon whinny briefly in pleasure at seeing him. I was turning to go and help with the reassuring, when a flicker of movement caught my eye below.

I leaned out to see it, keeping a tight grip on one of the hemlock's branches for safety, but it had moved. A horse, I thought, but coming from a different direction than that in which the refugees had come. I wove my way down the line of conifers, peeking through the branches, and reached a spot near the end of the narrow ledge where I had a clear view of the river valley below.

Not a horse, quite—it was—

"It's Clarence!" I shouted.

"Who?" Jamie's voice came back from the far end of the ledge, half-drowned by the rustle of the branches overhead. The wind was still rising, damp with returning rain.

"Clarence! Roger's mule!" Not waiting for a reply, I ducked beneath an overhanging branch and balanced myself precariously on the lip of the ledge, clinging to a rocky outcrop that jutted from the cliff where it met the ledge. There were serried ranks of trees below, marching down the slope, their tops no more than a few inches below the level of my feet, but I didn't want to risk falling down into them.

It *was* Clarence, I was sure of it. I was by no means expert enough to recognize any quadruped by its distinctive gait, but Clarence had suffered some form of mange or other skin disease in his youth, and the hair had grown in white over the healed patches, leaving him peculiarly piebald over the rump.

He was lolloping over the stubbled corn fields, ears pointed forward and obviously happy to be rejoining society. He was also saddled and riderless, and I said a very bad word under my breath when I saw it.

"He's broken his hobbles and run." Jamie had appeared at my shoulder, peering down at the small figure of the mule. He pointed. "See?" I hadn't noticed, in my alarm, but there was a small rag of cloth tied round one of his forelegs, flapping as he ran.

"I suppose that's better," I said. My hands had gone sweaty, and I wiped my palms on the elbows of my sleeves, unable to look away. "I mean—if he was hobbled, then Roger wasn't on him. Roger wasn't thrown, or knocked off and hurt."

"Ah, no." Jamie seemed concerned, but not alarmed. "He'll have a long walk back, is all." Still, I saw his gaze shift out, over the narrow river valley, now nearly filled with smoke. He shook his head slightly, and said something under his breath—no doubt a cousin to my own bad word.

"I wonder if this is how the Lord feels," he said aloud, and gave me a wry glance. "Able to see what foolishness men are up to, but canna do a bloody thing about it."

Before I could answer him, lightning flashed, and the thunder cracked on its heels with a clap so loud and sudden that I jumped, nearly losing my grip. Jamie seized my arm to stop me falling, and pulled me back from the edge. The horses were throwing fits again, at the far end of the ledge, and he turned toward them, but stopped suddenly, his hand still on my arm.

"What?" I looked where he was looking, and saw nothing but the wall of the cliff, some ten feet away, festooned with small rock plants.

He let go my arm, and without answering, walked toward the cliff. And, I saw, toward an old fire-blasted snag that stood near it. Very delicately, he reached out and tweaked something from the dead tree's bark. I reached his side and peered into the palm of his hand, where he cradled several long, coarse hairs. White hairs.

Rain began to fall again, settling down in a businesslike way to the job of soaking everything in sight. A piercing pair of whinnies came from the horses, who didn't like being abandoned one bit.

I looked at the trunk of the tree; there were white hairs all over it, caught in the cracks of the ragged bark. *A bear has special scratching trees*, I could hear Josiah saying. *He'll come back to one, again and again*. I swallowed, hard.

"Perhaps," Jamie said very thoughtfully, "it's no just the thunder that troubles the horses."

Perhaps not, but it wasn't helping. Lightning flashed into the trees far down the slope and the thunder sounded with it. Another flash-bang following on its heels, and another, as though an ack-ack gun were going off beneath our feet. The horses were having hysterics, and I felt rather like joining them.

I had put on my hooded cloak when I left the village, but both hood and hair were matted to my skull, the rain pounding down on my head like a shower of nails. Jamie's hair was plastered to his head as well, and he grimaced through the rain.

He made a "stay here" gesture, but I shook my head and followed him. The horses were in a complete state, saturated manes dangling over rolling eyes. Judas had succeeded in half-uprooting the small tree I had tied him to, and Gideon had his ears laid flat, flexing his lip repeatedly over his big yellow teeth, looking for someone or something to bite.

Seeing this, Jamie's lips tightened. He glanced back toward the place where we had found the scratching-tree, invisible from our present position. The lightning flashed, the thunder shuddered through the rock, and the horses both screamed and lunged. Jamie shook his head, making the decision, and grabbed Judas's reins, holding him steady. Evidently we were getting off the mountain, slippery trail or not.

I got into the saddle in a swash of wet skirts, and took a firm grip, trying to shout soothing words into Judas's ear as he skittered and danced, eager to be gone. We were dangerously close to the conifers at the edge, and I leaned hard inward, trying to get him toward the cliff side of the ledge.

An extraordinary prickling sensation ran over my body, as though I were being bitten from head to toe by thousands of tiny ants. I looked at my hands and saw them glowing, limned in blue light. The hairs on my forearms stood straight out, each one glowing blue. My hood had fallen back, and I felt the hair on my head rise all at once, as though a giant hand had gently lifted it.

The air smelled suddenly of brimstone, and I looked about in alarm. Trees, rocks, the ground itself was bathed in blue light. Tiny snakes of brilliant white electricity hissed across the surface of the cliff, a few yards away.

I turned, calling for Jamie, and saw him on Gideon, turning toward me, his mouth open as he shouted, all words lost in the reverberation of the air around us.

Gideon's mane began to rise, as though by magic. Jamie's hair floated up from his shoulders, shot with wires of crackling blue. Horse and rider glowed with hell-light, each muscle of face and limb outlined. I felt a rush of air over my skin, and then Jamie flung himself from his saddle and into me, hurling us both into emptiness.

The lightning struck before we hit the ground.

I came to, smelling burned flesh and the throat-searing sting of ozone. I felt as though I had been turned inside out; all of my organs seemed to be exposed.

It was still raining. I lay still for a while, letting the rain run over my face and soak my hair, while the neurons of my nervous system slowly began to work again. My finger twitched, by itself. I tried to do it on purpose, and succeeded. I flexed my fingers—not so good. A few more minutes, though, and enough circuits were working to allow me to sit up.

Jamie was lying near me, sprawled on his back like a rag doll amid a patch of sumac. I crawled over to him, and found that his eyes were open. He blinked at me, and a muscle twitched at the side of his mouth in an attempt at a smile.

I couldn't see any blood, and while his limbs were thrown awry, they were all straight. The rain pooled in his eye sockets, running into his eyes. He blinked violently, then turned his head to let the water drain off his face. I put a hand on his stomach, and felt the big abdominal pulse beneath my fingers, very slow, but steady.

I didn't know how long we had been unconscious, but this storm too had moved away. Sheet lightning flashed beyond the distant mountains, throwing the peaks into sharp relief.

"Thunder is good," I quoted, watching it in a sort of dreamy stupor, "thunder is impressive; but it is the lightning that does the work."

"It's done a job of work on me. Are ye all right, Sassenach?"

"Splendid," I said, still feeling pleasantly remote. "And you?"

He glanced at me curiously, but seemed to conclude that it was all right. He grasped a sumac bush and dragged himself laboriously to his feet.

"I canna feel my toes just yet," he told me, "but the rest is all right. The horses, though—" He glanced upward, and I saw his throat move as he swallowed.

The horses were silent.

We were some twenty feet below the ledge, among the firs and balsams. I *could* move, but didn't seem able to summon the will to do so. I sat still, taking stock, while Jamie shook himself, then began the climb back up to the mankiller's ledge.

It seemed very quiet; I wondered whether I had been deafened by the blast. My foot was cold. I looked down and discovered that my left shoe was gone—whether knocked off by the lightning or lost in the fall, I had no idea, but I didn't see it anywhere nearby. The stocking was gone, too; there was a small dark starburst of veins, just below the anklebone—a legacy of my second pregnancy. I sat staring at it as though it were the key to the secrets of the universe.

The horses must be dead; I knew that. Why weren't we? I breathed in the stink of burning flesh, and a tiny shudder arose, somewhere deep inside me. Were we alive now, only because we were doomed to die in four years? When it came our turn, would we lie in the burnt ruins of our house, shells of charred and reeking flesh?

Burnt to bones, whispered the voice of my memory. Tears ran down my face with the rain, but they were distant tears—for the horses, for my mother—not for myself. Not yet.

There were blue veins beneath the surface of my skin, more prominent than before. On the backs of my hands, they traced a roadmap . . . in the tender flesh behind my knee, they showed in webs and traceries; along my shin, one large vein swelled snakelike, distended. I pressed a finger on it; it was soft and disappeared, but came back the instant I removed the finger.

The inner workings of my body were becoming slowly more visible, the taut skin thinning, leaving me vulnerable, with everything outside, exposed to the elements, that once was safely sheltered in the snug casing of the body. Bone and blood push through . . . there was an oozing graze on the top of my foot.

Jamie was back, drenched to the skin and breathless from the climb. Both his shoes were gone, I saw.

"Judas is dead," he said, sitting down beside me. He took my cold hand in his own cold hand and pressed it hard.

"Poor thing," I said, and the tears ran faster, warm streams mingling with cold rain. "He knew, didn't he? He always hated thunder and lightning, always."

Jamie put an arm round my shoulders and pressed my head against his chest, making little soothing noises.

"And Gideon?" I asked at last, raising my head and making an effort to wipe my nose on a fold of sodden cloak. Jamie shook his head, with a small, incredulous smile.

"He's alive," he said. "He's burnt down the side of his right shoulder and foreleg and his mane's singed off entirely." He picked up a fold of his own tattered cloak and tried to wipe my face, with no better results than I had had myself. "I expect it will do wonders for his temper," he said, trying to make a joke of it.

"I suppose so." I was too worn out and shaken to laugh, but I managed a small smile, and it felt good. "Can you lead him down, do you think? I—I have some ointment. It's good for burns."

"Aye, I think so." He gave me a hand and helped me stand up. I turned to brush down my crumpled skirts, and as I did so, caught sight of something.

"Look," I said, my voice no more than a whisper. "Jamie—look."

Ten feet away, up the slope from us, stood a big balsam fir, its top sheared cleanly away and half its remaining branches charred and smoking. Wedged between one branch and the stump of the trunk was a huge, rounded mass. It was half black, the tissues turned to carbon—but the hair on the other half lay in sodden white spikes, the cream-white color of trilliums.

Jamie stood looking up at the corpse of the bear, his mouth half open. Slowly he closed it, and shook his head. He turned to me, then, and looked past me, toward the distant mountains, where the retreating lightning flashed silently.

"They do say," he said softly, "that a great storm portends the death of a king."

He touched my face, very gently.

"Wait here, Sassenach, while I fetch the horse. We'll go home."

85

HEARTHFIRE

Fraser's Ridge
October, 1771

THE SEASON CHANGED, from one hour to the next. She had gone to sleep in the cool balm of an Indian summer evening, and wakened in the middle of the night to the sharp bite of autumn, her feet freezing under the single quilt. Still drowsy, she couldn't fall sleep again, not without more covers.

She dragged slit-eyed out of bed, padded over the icy floor to check Jemmy. He was warm enough, sunk deep into his tiny featherbed, the quilt drawn up around his small pink ears. She laid a gentle hand on his back, waiting for the reassurance of the rise and fall of his breath. Once, twice, once more.

She rummaged for an extra quilt and spread it on the bed, reached for a cup of water to ease her dry throat, and realized with a grunt of annoyance that it was empty. She thought with longing of crawling back into bed, sinking into deep, warm slumber—but not dying of thirst.

There was a bucket of well water by the stoop. Yawning and grimacing, she slid the bolt from its brackets and set it gently down—though Jem slept so soundly at night, there wasn't much danger of waking him.

Still, she opened the door with care and stepped out, shivering slightly as the cold air twitched the shift about her legs. She bent and groped in the darkness. No bucket. Where—

She saw a flicker of movement from the corner of her eye and whirled. For an instant, she thought it was Obadiah Henderson, sitting on the bench beside her door, and her heart clenched like a fist as he stood up. Then she realized, and was in Roger's arms before her mind could consciously sort out the details of him.

Pressed against him, speechless, she had time to notice things: the arch of his collarbone against her face, the smell of clothes gone so long worn, so long unwashed that they didn't smell even of sweat any longer, but of the wood he walked through and the earth he slept upon, and mostly of the bitter smoke he breathed. The strength of his arm about her and the rasp of his beard on her skin. The cracked cold leather of his shoes beneath her bare toes, and the shape of the bones of his feet within them.

"It's you," she said, and was crying. "You're home!"

"Aye, I'm home," he whispered in her ear. "You're well? Jem's well?"

She relaxed her hold on his ribs and he smiled at her, so

strange to see his smile through a growth of thick black beard, the curve of his lips familiar in the moonlight.

"We're fine. You're all right?" She sniffed, eyes overflowing as she looked at him. "What are you doing out here, for heaven's sake? Why didn't you knock?"

"Aye. I'm fine. I didn't want to scare ye. Thought I'd sleep out here, knock in the morning. Why are ye crying?"

She realized then that he wasn't whispering from any desire to avoid waking Jem; what voice he had was a ragged husk, warped and breathless. And yet he spoke clearly, the words unforced, without the painful hesitation he had had.

"You can talk," she said, wiping hastily at her eyes with the back of a wrist. "I mean—better." Once, she would have hesitated to touch his throat, fearful of his feelings, but instinct knew better than to waste the sudden intimacy of shock. The strain might come again, and they be strangers, but for a moment, for *this* moment in the dark, she could say anything, do anything, and she put her fingers on the warm ragged scar, touched the incision that had saved his life, a clean white line through the whiskers.

"Does it still hurt to talk?"

"It hurts," he said, in the faint croaking rasp, and his eyes met hers, dark and soft in the moonlight. "But I can. I will—Brianna."

She stepped back, one hand on his arm, unwilling to let go.

"Come in," she said. "It's cold out here."

I HAD ANY NUMBER of objections to hearthfire, ranging from splinters under the fingernails and pitch on the hands to blisters, burns, and the sheer infuriating contrariness of the element. I would, however, say two things in its favor: it was undeniably warm, and it cast the act of love in a light of such dim beauty that all the hesitations of nakedness could safely be forgotten.

Our mingled shadows flowed together on the wall, here a limb, there the curve of back or haunch showed clean, some part of an undulating beast. Jamie's head rose clear, a great maned creature looming over me, back arched in his extremity.

I reached up across the stretch of glowing skin and trembling muscle, brushed the sparking hairs of arms and chest, to bury my hands in the warmth of his hair and pull him down gasping to the dark hollow of my breasts.

I kept my eyes half-closed, my legs as well, unwilling to surrender his body, to give up the illusion of oneness—if illusion it was. How many more times might I hold him so, even in the enchantment of firelight?

I clung with all my might to him, and to the dying pulse of my own flesh. But joy grasped is joy vanished, and within moments I was no more than myself. The dark starburst on my ankle showed clearly, even in firelight.

I slackened my grip on his shoulders and touched the rough whorls of his hair with tenderness. He turned his head and kissed my breast, then stirred and sighed and slid sideways.

"And they say hen's teeth are rare," he said, gingerly touching a deep bite-mark on one shoulder.

I laughed, in spite of myself.

"As rare as a rooster's cock, I suppose." I raised myself on one elbow and peered toward the hearth.

"What is it, wee hen?"

"Just making sure my clothes won't catch fire." What with one thing and another, I hadn't much noticed where he'd thrown my garments, but they seemed to be a safe distance from the flames; the skirt was in a small heap by the bed, the bodice and shift somehow had ended up in separate corners of the room. My brassiere-strip was nowhere to be seen.

Light flickered on the whitewashed walls, and the bed was full of shadows.

"You are beautiful," he whispered to me.

"If you say so."

"Do ye not believe me? Have I ever lied to you?"

"That's not what I mean. I mean—if you say it, then it's true. You make it true."

He sighed and shifted, easing us into comfort. A log cracked suddenly in the hearth, sending up a spray of gold sparks, and subsided, hissing as the heat struck a hidden seam of damp. I watched the new wood turn black, then red, blazing into white-hot light.

"Do ye say it of me, Sassenach?" he asked suddenly. He sounded shy, and I turned my head to look up at him in surprise.

"Do I say what? That you're beautiful?" My mouth curved involuntarily, and he smiled in return.

"Well . . . not that. But that ye can bear my looks, at least."

I traced the faint white line of the scar across his ribs, left by a sword, long ago. The longer, thicker scar of the bayonet that had ripped the length of one thigh. The arm that held me, browned and roughened, the hairs of it bleached white-gold with long days of sun and work. Near my hand, his cock curled between his thighs, gone soft and small and tender now, in its nest of auburn hair.

"You're beautiful to me, Jamie," I said softly, at last. "So beautiful, you break my heart."

His hand traced the knobs of my backbone, one at a time.

"But I am an auld man," he said, smiling. "Or should be. I've white hairs in my head; my beard's gone gray."

"Silver," I said, brushing the soft stubble on his chin, parti-colored as a quilt. "In bits."

"Gray," he said firmly. "And scabbit-looking with it. And yet . . ." His eyes softened as he looked at me. "Yet I burn when I come to ye, Sassenach—and will, I think, 'til we two be burned to ashes."

"Is that poetry?" I asked cautiously. "Or do you mean it literally?"

"Oh," he said. "No. I hadna meant . . . no." He tightened his arm around me and bent his head to mine.

"I dinna ken about that. If it should be—"

"It won't."

A breath of laughter stirred my hair.

"Ye sound verra sure of it, Sassenach."

"The future can be changed; I do it all the time."

"Oh, aye?"

I rolled away a bit, to look at him.

"I do. Look at Mairi MacNeill. If I hadn't been there last

week, she would have died, and her twins with her. But I *was* there, and they didn't."

I put a hand behind my head, watching the reflection of the flames ripple like water across the ceiling beams.

"I do wonder—there are lots I can't save, but some I do. If someone lives because of me, and later has children, and *they* have children, and so on . . . well, by the time you reach my time, say, there are probably thirty or forty people in the world who wouldn't otherwise have been there, hm? And they've all been doing things meanwhile, living their lives—don't you think that's changing the future?" For the first time, it occurred to me to wonder just how much I was single-handedly contributing to the population explosion of the twentieth century.

"Aye," he said slowly. He picked up my free hand and traced the lines of my palm with one long finger.

"Aye, but it's *their* future ye change, Sassenach, and perhaps you're meant to." He took my hand in his and pulled gently on the fingers. One knuckle popped, making a small sound like a log spitting in the hearth. "Physicians have saved a good many folk over the years, surely."

"Of course they do. And not just physicians, either." I sat up, impelled by the force of my argument. "But it doesn't matter—don't you see? You—" I pointed one finger at him, "—you've saved a life now and then. Fergus? Ian? And here they are, both going about the world doing things and procreating and what-not. You changed the future for them, didn't you?"

"Aye, well . . . perhaps. I couldna do otherwise, though, could I?"

That simple statement stopped me, and we lay in silence for a bit, watching the flicker of light on the white-plastered wall. At last he stirred beside me, and spoke again.

"I dinna say it for pity," he said. "But ye ken . . . now and then my bones ache a bit." He didn't look at me, but spread his crippled hand, turning it in the light, so the shadow of the crooked fingers made a spider on the wall.

Now and then. I kent, all right. I knew the limits of the body—and its miracles. I'd seen him sit down at the end of a day's labor, exhaustion written in every line of his body. Seen him move slowly, stubborn against the protests of flesh and bone when he rose on cold mornings. I would be willing to bet that he had not lived a day since Culloden without pain, the physical damages of war aggravated by damp and harsh living. And I would also be willing to bet that he had never mentioned it to anyone. Until now.

"I know that," I said softly, and touched the hand. The twisting scar that runneled his leg. The small depression in the flesh of his arm, legacy of a bullet.

"But not with you," he said, and covered my hand where it lay on his arm. "D'ye ken that the only time I am without pain is in your bed, Sassenach? When I take ye, when I lie in your arms—my wounds are healed, then, my scars forgotten."

I sighed and laid my head in the curve of his shoulder. My thigh pressed his, the softness of my flesh a mold to his harder form.

"Mine, too."

He was silent for a time, stroking my hair with his good hand. It was wild and bushy, freed from its moorings by our earlier struggles, and he smoothed one curly strand at a time, combing down each lock between his fingers.

"Your hair's like a great storm cloud, Sassenach," he murmured, sounding half-asleep. "All dark and light together. No two hairs are the same color."

He was right; the lock between his fingers bore strands of pure white, of silver and blond, dark streaks, nearly sable, and several bits still of my young light brown.

His fingers went under the mass of hair, and I felt his hand cup the base of my skull, holding my head like a chalice.

"I saw my mother in her coffin," he said at last. His thumb touched my ear, drew down the curve of helix and lobule, and I shivered at his touch.

"The women had plaited her hair, to be seemly, but my father wouldna have it. I heard him. He didna shout, though, he was verra quiet. He would have his last sight of her as she was to him, he said. He was half-crazed wi' grief, they said, he should let well alone, be still. He didna trouble to say more to them, but went to the coffin himself. He undid her plaits and he spread out her hair in his two hands across the pillow. They were afraid to stop him."

He paused, his thumb stilled.

"I was there, keepin' quiet in the corner. When they all went out to meet the priest, I crept up close. I hadna seen a dead person before."

I let my fingers curl over the ridge of his forearm, quietly. My mother had left me one morning, kissed my forehead, and slid in the clip that fell out of my curly hair. I had never seen her again. Her coffin had been closed.

"Was it—her?"

"No," he said softly. His eyes were half-lidded as he looked into the fire. "Not quite. The face had the look of her, but no more. Like as if someone had set out to carve her from birch wood. But her hair—that was still alive. That was still . . . her."

I heard him swallow, and half-clear his throat.

"The hair lay down across her breast, so it covered the child who lay with her. I thought perhaps he wouldna like it; to be smothered so. So I lifted up the locks of red to let him out. I could see him—my wee brother, curled up in her arms, wi' his head on her breast, all shadowed and snug under the curtain of her hair.

"So then I thought no, he'd be happier if I left him so—so I smoothed her hair down again, to cover his head." He drew a deep breath, and I felt his chest rise under my cheek. His fingers ran slowly down through my hair.

"She hadna one white hair, Sassenach. Not one."

Ellen Fraser had died in childbirth, aged thirty-eight. My own mother had been thirty-two. And I . . . I had the richness of all those long years lost to them. And more.

"To see the years touch ye gives me joy, Sassenach," he whispered, "—for it means that ye live."

He lifted his hand and let my hair fall slowly from his fingers, brushing my face, skimming my lips, floating soft and heavy on my neck and shoulders, lying like feathers at the tops of my breasts.

"Mo nighean donn," he whispered, "*mo chridhe*. My brown lass, my heart.

"Come to me. Cover me. Shelter me, *a bhean*, heal me. Burn with me, as I burn for you."

I lay on him, covered him, my skin, his bone, and still—still!—that fierce bright core of flesh to join us. I let my hair fall down around us both, and in the fire-shot cavern of its darkness, whispered back.

"Until we two be burned to ashes."

86

THERE'S A HOLE IN THE BOTTOM OF THE SEA

Fraser's Ridge
October, 1771

ROGER WAS INSTANTLY AWAKE, in that way that allowed no transition through drowsiness; body inert, but mind alert, ears tuned to the echo of what had wakened him. He had no conscious recollection of Jemmy's cry, but it echoed in his inner ear, with that combination of hope and resignation that is the lot of the more-easily wakened parent.

Sleep dragged at him, pulling him back under the waves of slumber like a ten-ton boulder chained to his foot. A tiny rustling noise kept his head momentarily above the surface.

"Go back to sleep," he thought fiercely, in the direction of the cradle. *"Shhhhh. Hush. Quiet. Go . . . to . . . sleeeeeep."* This telepathic hypnosis seldom worked, but it delayed for a few precious seconds the necessity of moving. And now and then the miracle happened, and his son actually *did* go back to sleep, relaxing into the warm sogginess of wet diaper and crumb-caked dreams.

Roger held his breath, clinging to the fading edge of sleep, hoarding the cherished seconds of immobility. Then another small sound came, and he was on his feet at once.

"Bree? Bree, what is it?" The "r" in her name fluttered in his throat, not quite there, but he didn't take the time to be troubled by it. All his attention was for her.

She was standing by the cradle, a ghostly column in the dark. He touched her, took her by the shoulders. Her arms were wrapped tight around the little boy, and she was shuddering with cold and fear.

He pulled her close by instinct; her cold infected him at once. He felt the chill on his heart and forced himself to hold tighter, not to look at the empty cradle.

"What is it?" he whispered. "Is it Jemmy? What's . . . happened?"

A shiver rose up the length of her body, and he felt the goosebumps rise under the thin cloth of her shift. Despite the warmth of the room, he felt the hair on his own arms rising.

"Nothing," she said. "He's all right." Her voice was thick, but she was right; Jem, waking to find himself uncomfortably squashed between his parents, let out a sudden yelp of surprised indignation, and began to churn his arms and legs like an eggbeater.

This sturdy battering filled Roger with a flood of warm relief, drowning the cold imaginings that had seized his mind at the sight of her. With a little difficulty, he pried Jemmy from his mother's arms and hoisted him high against his own shoulder.

He patted the solid little back in reassurance—reassurance of himself, as much as Jemmy—and made soft hissing noises through his teeth. Jemmy, finding this accustomed procedure soothing, yawned widely, relaxed into his normal hamlike state, and began to hum drowsily in Roger's ear, with the rising and falling note of a distant siren.

"DadeeDadeeDadee . . ."

Brianna was still standing by the cradle, empty arms wrapped now around herself. Roger reached out with his free hand and stroked her hair, her hard-boned shoulder, and drew her close against him.

"Shhh," he said to them both. "Shhh, shhh. It's all right now, shhh."

Her arms went around him, and he could feel the wetness on her face through the linen shirt. His other shoulder was already damp with Jemmy's sleepy, sweaty warmth.

"Come to bed," he said softly. "Come under the quilt, it's . . . cold out here." It wasn't; the air in the cabin was warm. She came, nonetheless.

Brianna reached for the child, taking him to her breast even before she lay down. Never one to refuse nourishment at any hour, Jemmy accepted the offer with alacrity, curling up into an apostrophe of content against his mother's stomach as she settled on one side.

Roger slid into bed behind her, and echoed his son's posture, bringing up his knees behind Brianna's, curling his body in a protective comma around her. Thus securely punctuated, Brianna began slowly to relax, though Roger could still feel the tension in her body.

"All right now?" he asked softly. Her skin was still clammy to the touch, but warming.

"Yeah." She took in a deep breath and let it out in a shuddering sigh. "Had a bad dream. I'm sorry I woke you."

"It's OK." He stroked the swell of her hip, over and over, like one gentling a horse. "Want to tell me?" He hoped she did, though the sound of Jemmy's suckling was rhythmic and soothing, and he felt sleep stealing over him as the three of them warmed, melting together like candle wax.

"I was cold," she said softly. "I think the quilt must have fallen off. But in the dream, I was cold because the window was open."

"Here? One of these windows?" Roger lifted a hand, indicating the faint oblong of the window in the far wall. Even in the middle of the darkest night, the oiled hide covering the window was very slightly lighter than the surrounding blackness.

"No." She took a deep breath. "It was in the house in Boston; where I grew up. I was in bed, but I was cold, and the cold woke me—in the dream. I got up to see where the draft was coming from."

There were French windows in her father's study. The cold wind came from there, bellying the long white curtains into the room. The cradle stood by the antique desk, the end of a thin white blanket flickering in the draft.

"He was gone." Her voice had steadied, but had a momentary catch in it at the memory of terror. "Jemmy was gone. The cradle was empty, and I knew something came through the window and took him."

She pressed back against him, unconsciously seeking reassurance. "I was afraid of it—whatever it was—but it didn't matter—I had to find Jemmy."

One hand was curled up tight under her chin. He folded it in his, and squeezed lightly, embracing her.

"I threw open the curtains and ran out, and—and there was nothing there. Only water." She was shaking at the memory.

"Water?" He stroked her clenched fist with a thumb, trying to calm her.

"Ocean. The sea. Just—water, lapping up against the edge of the terrace. It was dark, and I knew it went down forever, and that Jemmy was down there, he'd drowned, and I was too late—" She choked, but got her voice back and went on, more steadily. "But I dived in anyway, I had to. It was dark, and there were things in the water with me—I couldn't see them, but they brushed by me; big things. I kept looking and looking but I couldn't see anything, and then the water suddenly got lighter and I—I saw him."

"Jemmy?"

"No. Bonnet—Stephen Bonnet."

Roger forced himself not to move, not to stiffen. She dreamed often; he always imagined that the dreams she would not tell him were of Bonnet.

"He was holding Jemmy, and laughing. I went to take him, and Bonnet held him up away from me. He kept doing that, and I tried to hit him, and he just caught my hand and laughed. Then he looked up and his face changed."

She took a deep breath, and took hold of Roger's fingers, holding on for comfort.

"I never saw a look like that, Roger, never. There was something behind me that he could see, something coming—

and it scared him more than I've ever seen anyone scared. He was holding me; I couldn't turn around to look, and I couldn't get away—I couldn't leave Jemmy. It was coming—and . . . then I woke up."

She gave a small, shaky laugh.

"My friend Gayle's grandmother always said that when you fall off a cliff in a dream, if you hit the bottom, you'll die. Really die, I mean. You figure the same thing goes for getting eaten by a sea monster?"

"No. Besides, you always wake up in time from dreams like that."

"I have so far." She sounded a little dubious. Still, dream told, she was eased of its terror; her body let go its last resistance and she breathed deep and easy against him; he could feel the swell of her rib cage under his arm.

"You always will. Don't be troubled now; Jemmy's safe. I'm here; I'll keep you both safe." He put his arm gently round her, and cupped his hand around Jemmy's fat bottom, warm in its linen clout. Jemmy, all his bodily needs met, had relapsed into a peaceful torpor, contagious in its abandon. Brianna sighed and put her hand over Roger's, squeezing lightly.

"There were books on the desk," she said, beginning to sound drowsy. "On Dad's desk. He'd been working, I could tell—there were open books and scattered papers everywhere. There was a paper lying in the middle of the desk, with writing on it; I wanted to read it, to see what he'd been doing—but I couldn't stop."

"Mm-hm."

Brianna shivered slightly, and the movement rustled the corn shucks in the mattress, a tiny seismic disturbance of their small, warm universe. She tensed, fighting sleep, and then relaxed, as his hand cupped her breast.

Roger lay awake, watching the square of the window grow slowly lighter, holding his family safe in his arms.

IT WAS OVERCAST and morning-cool, but very humid; Roger could feel the sweat film his body like the skin on boiled milk. It was no more than an hour past dawn, they weren't yet out of sight of the house, and his scalp was prickling already, slow droplets gathering under the plait at the base of his skull.

He flexed his shoulders with resignation, and the first trickle crawled tickling down his backbone. At least sweating helped to ease the soreness; his arms and shoulders had been so stiff this morning that Brianna had had to help him dress, pulling his shirt over his head and buttoning his flies with deft fingers.

He smiled inwardly, remembering what else those long fingers had done. It had taken his mind temporarily off the stiffness of his body, and banished the troubling memory of dreams. He stretched, groaning, feeling the pull of muscle on tender joints. The clean linen was already sticking to chest and back.

Jamie was ahead of him on the trail, a damp patch growing visibly between his shoulder blades where the strap of the canteen crossed his back. Roger noted with some consolation that his father-in-law was moving with a good bit less than his usual pantherlike grace this morning, too. He knew the Great Scot was only human, but it was reassuring to have that fact confirmed now and then.

"Think the weather will hold?" Roger said it as much for the sake of speaking as for anything else; Jamie was by no means garrulous, but he seemed abnormally quiet this morning, barely speaking beyond a murmured "Aye, morning," in reply to Roger's earlier greeting. Perhaps it was the grayness of the day, with its threat—or promise—of rain.

The sky overhead curved low and dull as the inside of a pewter bowl. An afternoon indoors, with rain beating on the oiled hides of the windows, and wee Jemmy curled up peaceful as a dormouse for a nap, while his mother shed her shift and came to bed in the soft gray light . . . aye, well, some ways of breaking a sweat were better than others.

Jamie stopped and glanced up at the lowering sky. He flexed his right hand, closing it to an awkward fist, then opening it slowly. The stiff fourth finger made delicate chores such as writing difficult, but did provide one dubious benefit in compensation; the swollen joints signaled rain as reliably as a barometer.

Jamie wiggled the fingers experimentally, and gave Roger a faint smile.

"No but a wee twinge," he said. "Nay rain before nightfall." He stretched, easing his back in anticipation, and sighed. "Let's get to it, aye?"

Roger glanced back; the house and cabin had disappeared. He frowned at Jamie's retreating back, debating. It was nearly half a mile to the new field; ample time for conversation. Not the right time, though, not yet. It was a matter to be addressed face-to-face, and at leisure—later, then, when they paused to eat.

The woods were hushed, the air still and heavy. Even the birds were quiet, only the occasional machine-gun burst of a woodpecker startling the silence. They threaded their way through the forest, silent as Indians on the layer of rotted leaves, and emerged from the scrub-oak thicket with a suddenness that sent a flock of crows shrieking out of the torn earth of the new-cleared field like demons escaping from the netherworld.

"Jesus!" Jamie murmured, and crossed himself involuntarily. Roger's throat closed tight, and his stomach clenched. The crows had been feeding on something lying in the hollow left by an uprooted tree; all he could see above the ragged clods of earth was a pale curve that looked unsettlingly like the round of a naked shoulder.

It *was* a naked shoulder—of a pig. Jamie squatted by the boar's carcass, frowning at the livid weals that marred the thick, pale skin. He touched the deep gouges on the flank with distaste; Roger could see the busy movement of flies inside the black-red cavities.

"Bear?" he asked, squatting beside Jamie. His father-in-law shook his head.

"Cat." He brushed aside the stiff, sparse hairs behind the ear and pointed to the bluish puncture wounds in the folded lard. "Broke the neck wi' one bite. And see the claw marks?" Roger had, but lacked the knowledge to differentiate the marks of a bear's claws from those of a panther's. He looked closely, committing the pattern to memory.

Jamie stood, and wiped a sleeve across his face.

"A bear would ha' taken more of the carcass. This is barely touched. Cats will do that, though—make a kill and leave it, then come back to nibble at it, day after day."

Muggy as it was, the hair pricked with chill on Roger's neck. It was much too easy to imagine yellow eyes in the shadow of the thicket behind him, fixed with cool appraisal on the spot where skull met fragile spine.

"Think it's still close by?" He glanced about, trying to seem casual. The forest was just as it had been, but now the silence seemed unnatural and sinister.

Jamie waved away a couple of questing flies, frowning.

"Aye, maybe. This is a fresh kill; no maggots yet." He nodded at the gaping wound in the pig's flank, then stooped to grasp the stiff trotters. "Come, let's hang it. It's too much meat to waste."

They dragged the carcass to a tree with a low, sturdy limb. Jamie reached into his sleeve and pulled out a grubby kerchief, to tie round his head to keep the sweat from burning into his eyes. Roger groped for his own kerchief—carefully washed, neatly ironed—and did likewise. Mindful of the laundering, they stripped their clean shirts and hung them over an alder bush.

There was rope in the field, left from the stump-pulling of earlier days' work; Jamie whipped a length several times around the pig's forelimbs, then flung the free end over the branch above. It was a full-grown boar, some two-hundredweight of solid flesh. Jamie set his feet and hauled back on the rope, grunting with the sudden effort.

Roger held his breath as he bent to help hoist the stiffened corpse, but Jamie had been right; it was fresh. There was the usual fleshy pig-scent, gone faint with death, and the sharper tang of blood—nothing worse.

Rough hair scraped the skin of his belly as he wrapped his arms around the carcass, and he set his teeth against a grimace of distaste. There are few things deader than a large, dead pig. Then a word from Jamie, and the carcass was secure. He let go, and the pig swung gently to and fro, a meaty pendulum.

Roger was wringing wet; more than the effort of lifting

accounted for. There was a big smudge of brownish blood over his chest and stomach. He rubbed the heel of his hand over the knot in his belly, smearing the blood with sweat. He glanced casually round once more. Nothing moved among the trees.

"The women will be pleased," he said.

Jamie laughed, taking the dirk from his belt.

"I shouldna think so. They'll be up half the night, butchering and salting." He nodded in the direction of Roger's glance.

"Even if it's near, it willna trouble us. Cats dinna hunt large prey unless they're hungry." He looked wryly at the torn flank of the dangling pig. "A half-stone of prime bacon will ha' satisfied it for the moment, I should think. Though if not—" He glanced at his long rifle, leaning loaded against the trunk of a nearby hickory.

He held the pig while Jamie gutted it, then wrapped the stinking mass of intestines in the cloth from their lunch, while Jamie patiently worked at kindling a fire of green sticks that would keep the flies away from the hanging carcass. Streaked and reeking with blood, waste, and sweat, Roger walked across the field to the small stream that ran by the woods.

He knelt and splashed, arms and face and torso, trying to rid himself of the feeling of being watched. More than once, he had crossed an empty moor in Scotland, only to have a full-grown stag erupt from nowhere in front of him, springing by apparent magic from the heather at his feet. Despite Jamie's words, he was all too aware that some piece of quiet landscape could abruptly detach itself and take life in a thunder of hooves or a snarl of sudden teeth.

He rinsed his mouth, spat, and drank deep, forcing water past the lingering tightness in his throat. He could still feel the stiff coldness of the pig's carcass, see the caked dirt in the nostrils, the raw sockets where crows had pecked out the eyes. Gooseflesh prickled over his shoulders, chilled as much by his thoughts as by the cold stream-water.

No great difference between a pig and a man. Flesh to flesh, dust to dust. One stroke, that's all it took. Slowly, he stretched, savoring the last soreness in his muscles.

There was a raucous croaking from the chestnut overhead. The crows, black blotches in the yellow leaves, voicing their displeasure at the robbery of their feast.

"Whaur . . . shall we gang and . . . dine the day?" he murmured under his breath, looking up at them. "Not here . . . you bastards. Get along!" Seized by revulsion, he scooped a stone from the bank and hurled it into the tree with all his might. The crows erupted into shrieking flight, and he turned back to the field, grimly satisfied.

But his belly was still knotted, and the words of the corbies' mocking song echoed in his ears: *"Ye'll sit on his white hause-bane/and I'll pick oot his bonny blue e'en. Wi' ae lock o' his golden hair/we'll theek oor nest when it grows bare."*

Jamie glanced at his face when he came back, but said nothing. Beyond the field, the pig's carcass hung above the fire, its outlines hidden in wreaths of smoke.

They had cut the fencerails already, made from pine saplings they'd uprooted; the rough-barked logs lay ready by the edge of the forest. The fence would have drystone pillars to join the wooden rails, though; not one of the simple rick-rack fences meant to keep out deer or mark boundaries, but one solid enough to withstand the jostling of three- and four-hundred-pound hogs.

Within the month, it would be time to drive in the pigs that had been turned out to live wild in the forest, fattening themselves on the chestnut mast that lay thick on the ground. Some would have fallen prey to wild animals or accident, but there would likely be fifty or sixty left to slaughter or sell.

They worked well together, he and Jamie. Much of a size, each had an instinct for the other's moves. When a hand was needed, it was there. No need for it just now, though—this part of the job was the worst, for there was no interest to soften the tedium, no skill to ease the labor. Only rocks, hundreds of rocks, to be hoisted from the loamy soil and carried, dragged, wrestled to the field, to be piled and fitted into place.

Often they talked as they worked, but not this morning. Each man worked alone with his thoughts, tramping to and fro with the endless load. The morning passed in silence, broken only by the far-off calling of the disgruntled crows, and by the thunk and grate of stones, dropped on the growing pile.

It had to be done. There was no choice. He'd known that for a long time, but now that the dim prospect had hardened into reality . . . Roger eyed his father-in-law covertly. Would Jamie agree to it, though?

From a distance, the scars on his back were barely visible, masked by the gleam of sweat. Constant hard work kept a man trim and taut, and no one seeing Fraser in outline—or close enough to see the deep groove of his backbone, the flat belly and long clean lines of arm and thigh—would have taken him for a man in middle age.

Jamie had showed him the scars, though, the first day they went out to work together, after he had come back from the surveying. Standing by the half-built dairy-shed, Jamie had pulled the shirt off and turned his back, saying casually, "Have a keek, then."

Up close, the scars were old and well-healed, thin white crescents and lines for the most part, with here and there a silvery net or a shiny lump, where a whipstroke had flayed the skin in too wide a patch for the edges of the wound to draw cleanly together. There was some skin untouched, showing fair and smooth among the weals—but not much.

And what was he to say? Roger had wondered. I'm sorry for it? Thanks for the viewing privileges?

In the event, he had said nothing. Jamie had merely turned around, handed Roger an ax with complete matter-of-factness, and they had begun their work, bare-chested. But he had noticed that Jamie never stripped to work, if the other men were with them.

All right. Of all men, Jamie would understand the need, the necessity—the burden of Brianna's dreaming, that lay in Roger's belly like a stone. Certainly he would help. But would he consent to allow Roger to finish it alone? Jamie, after all, had some stake in the matter, too.

The crows were still calling, but farther off, their cries thin and desperate, like those of lost souls. Perhaps he was foolish even to think of acting alone. He flung an armload of stones onto the pile; small rocks clacked and rolled away.

"Preacher's lad." That's what the other lads at school had

called him, and that's what he was, with all the ambiguity the term implied. The initial urge to prove himself manly by means of force, the later awareness of the ultimate moral weakness of violence. But that was in another country—

He choked off the rest of the quotation, grimly bending to lever a chunk of rock free of moss and dirt. Orphaned by war, raised by a man of peace—how was he to set his mind to murder? He trundled the stone down toward the field, rolling it slowly end over end.

"You've never killed anything but fish," he muttered to himself. "What makes you think . . ." But he knew all too well what made him think.

BY MID-MORNING, there were enough rocks collected to begin the first pillar; with a nod and a murmur, they set to work, dragging and heaving, stacking and fitting, with now and then a muffled exclamation at a smashed finger or bruised toes.

Jamie heaved a big stone into place, then straightened up, gasping for breath.

Roger drew his own deep breath. It might as well be now; no better opportunity was likely to come.

"I've a favor to ask," he said abruptly.

Jamie glanced up, breathing heavily, one eyebrow raised. He nodded, waiting for the request.

"Teach me to fight."

Jamie wiped an arm across his streaming face, and blew out a deep breath.

"Ye ken well enough how to fight," he said. One corner of his mouth quirked up. "D'ye mean will I teach ye to handle a sword without cutting off your foot?"

Roger kicked a stone back into the pile.

"That will do, to start."

Jamie stood for a moment, looking him over. It was a thoroughly dispassionate examination, much as he would have given a bullock he thought to buy. Roger stood still, feeling the sweat stream down the groove of his back, and thought that once more, he was being compared—to his disadvantage—with the absent Ian Murray.

"You're auld for it, mind," Jamie said at last. "Most swordsmen start when they're boys." He paused. "I had my first sword at five."

Roger had had a train when he was five. With a red engine that tooted its whistle when you pulled the cord. He met Jamie's eye, and smiled pleasantly.

"Old for it, maybe," he said. "But not dead."

"Ye could be," Fraser answered. "A little learning is a dangerous thing—a fool wi' a blade by his side in a scabbard is safer than a fool who thinks he kens what to do with it."

"A little learning is a dangerous thing," Roger quoted. "*Drink deep, or taste not the Pierian spring.* Do you think me a fool?"

Jamie laughed, surprised into amusement.

"There shallow draughts intoxicate the brain," he replied, finishing the verse. "*And drinking largely sobers us again.* As for foolish—ye'll no just be drunk on the thought of it, I suppose?"

Roger smiled slightly in reply; he had given up being surprised by the breadth of Jamie's reading.

"I'll drink deep enough to stay sober," he said. "Will ye teach me?"

Jamie squinted, then lifted one shoulder slightly. "Ye've size to your credit, and a good reach, forbye." He looked Roger head to toe once more and nodded. "Aye, ye'll maybe do."

He turned and walked away, toward the next heap of stones. Roger followed, feeling oddly gratified, as though he had passed some small but important test.

The test hadn't yet begun, though. It was only partway through the building of the new pillar that Jamie spoke again.

"Why?" he asked, eyes on the huge stone he was slowly heaving into place. It was too heavy to lift, the size of a whisky keg. Knotted clumps of grass roots stuck out from under it, ripped out of the earth by the stone's slow and brutal passage across the ground.

Roger bent to lend his own weight to the task. The lichens

on the rock's surface were rough under his palms, green and scabby with age.

"I've a family to protect," he said. The rock moved grudgingly, sliding a few inches across the uneven ground. Jamie nodded, once, twice; on the silent "three," they shoved together, with an echoed grunt of effort. The monster half-rose, paused, rose altogether and overbalanced, chunking down into place with a *thunk!* that quivered through the ground at their feet.

"Protect from what?" Jamie stood and wiped a wrist across his jaw. He glanced up and away, gesturing with his chin at the hanging pig. "I shouldna care to take on a panther wi' a sword, myself."

"Oh, aye?" Roger bent his knees and maneuvered another large rock into his arms. "I hear you've killed two bears—one with a dirk."

"Aye, well," Jamie said dryly. "A dirk's what I had. As for the other—if it was a sword, it was Saint Michael's, not mine."

"Aye, and if ye'd known ahead of time that you might—ugh—meet it—would you not have armed yourself—better?" Roger bent his knees, lowering the stone carefully into place. He let it drop the last few inches, and wiped stinging hands on his breeks.

"If I'd *known* I should meet a damn bear," Jamie said, grunting as he lifted another stone into place, "I would have taken another path."

Roger snorted and wiggled the new stone, easing its fit against the others. There was a small gap at one side that left it loose; Jamie eyed it, walked to the stone pile, and picked up a small chunk of granite, tapered at one end. It fit the gap exactly, and the two men smiled involuntarily at each other.

"D'ye think there's another path to take, then?" Roger asked.

Fraser rubbed a hand across his mouth, considering.

"If it's the war ye mean—then, aye, I do." He gave Roger a stare. "Maybe I'll find it and maybe I won't—but aye, there's another path."

"Maybe so." He hadn't meant the oncoming war, and he didn't think Jamie had, either.

"As to bears, though . . ." Jamie stood still, eyes steady. "There's a deal of difference, ye ken, between meeting a bear unawares—and hunting one."

THE SUN STILL WASN'T VISIBLE, but it wasn't necessary, either. Noon came as a rumbling in the belly, a soreness of the hands; a sudden awareness of the weariness of back and legs as timely as the chiming of a grandfather's clock. The last large rock fell into place, and Jamie straightened up, gasping for breath.

By unspoken but mutual consent, they sat down with the packet of food, clean shirts draped across bare shoulders, against the chill of drying sweat.

Jamie chewed industriously, washing down a large bite with a gulp of ale. He made an involuntary face, pursed his lips to spit, then changed his mind and swallowed.

"Ach! Mrs. Lizzie's been at the mash again." He grimaced and took a remedial bite of biscuit, to erase the taste.

Roger grinned at his father-in-law's face.

"What's she put in it this time?" Lizzie had been trying her hand at flavored ales—with indifferent success.

Jamie sniffed warily at the mouth of the stone bottle.

"Anise?" he suggested, passing the bottle to Roger.

Roger smelt it, wrinkling up his nose involuntarily at the alcoholic whiff.

"Anise *and* ginger," he said. Nevertheless, he took a cautious sip. He made the same face Jamie had, and emptied the bottle over a compliant blackberry vine.

"Waste not, want not, but . . ."

"It's nay waste to keep from poisoning ourselves." Jamie heaved himself up, took the emptied bottle, and set off toward the small stream on the far side of the field.

He came back, sat down, and handed Roger the bottle of water. "I've had word of Stephen Bonnet."

It was said so casually that Roger didn't register the meaning of the words at first.

"Have you?" he said at last. Piccalilli relish was oozing over his hand. Roger wiped the relish from his wrist with a finger, and put it into his mouth, but didn't take another bite of sandwich; his appetite had vanished.

"Aye. I dinna ken where he is now—but I ken where he'll be come next April—or rather, where I can cause him to be. Six months, and then we kill him. Do ye think that will give ye time?"

He was looking at Roger, calm as though he had suggested an appointment with a banker, rather than an appointment with death.

Roger could believe in netherworlds—and demons, too. He hadn't dreamed last night, but the demon's face floated always at the edge of his mind, just out of sight. Time to summon him, perhaps, and bring him into view. You had to call a demon up, didn't you, before you could exorcise him?

There were preparations to make, though, before that could happen. He flexed his shoulders and his arms once more, this time in anticipation. The soreness had mostly gone.

"There's mony an ane for him maks mane
but nane shall ken where he is gane.
O'er his white banes when they are bare,
The wind shall blaw forever mair, O—
The wind shall blaw forever mair."

"Aye," he said. "That'll do."

87

EN GARDE

FOR A MOMENT, he didn't think he was going to be able to lift his hand to the latch-string. Both arms hung as though weighted with lead, and the small muscles of his forearm jumped and trembled with exhaustion. It took two tries, and even then, he could do no more than catch the string clumsily between two middle fingers; his thumb wouldn't close.

Brianna heard him fumbling; the door opened suddenly and his hand fell nerveless from the latch. He had no more than a glimpse of tumbled hair and a beaming face with a smear of soot down one cheek, and then she had her arms around him, her mouth on his, and he was home.

"You're back!" she said, letting go.

"I am." And glad of it, too. The cabin smelt of hot food and lye soap, with a clean, faint tang of juniper overlaying the smoke of reed candles and the muskier scents of human occupation. He smiled at her, suddenly a little less tired.

"Dadee, Dadee!" Jemmy was bouncing up and down in excitement, clinging to a low stool for balance. "Da—*deeee*!"

"Hallo, hallo," Roger said, reaching down to pat the boy's fluffy head. "Who's a good lad, then?" He missed his mark and his hand brushed a soft cheek instead, but Jemmy didn't care.

"Me! Me!" he shouted, and grinned with a huge expanse of pink gum, showing off all his small white teeth. Brianna echoed the grin, with substantially more enamel but no less delight.

"We have a surprise for you. Watch this!" She went swiftly toward the table, and sank to one knee, a pace from Jemmy. She stretched out her arms, her hands no more than a few inches from his. "Come to Mama, sweetie. Come here, baby, come to Mama."

Jemmy swayed precariously, loosed one hand, reached for his mother, then let go and took one drunken step, then two, and fell shrieking into her arms. She clutched him, giggling in delight, then turned him toward Roger.

"Go to Daddy," Brianna encouraged. "Go on, go to Daddy."

Jemmy screwed up his face in doubtful concentration, looking like a first-time parachutist at the open door of a circling plane. He swayed dangerously to and fro.

Roger squatted, hands held out, tiredness forgotten for the moment.

"Come on, mate, come on, you can do it!"

Jemmy clung a moment, leaning, leaning, then let go his mother's hand and staggered drunkenly toward Roger, faster and faster and faster through three steps, falling headlong into Roger's saving grasp.

He hugged Jemmy tight against him, the little boy wriggling and crowing in triumph.

"Good lad! Be into everything now, won't you?"

"Like he's not already!" Brianna said, rolling her eyes in resignation. As though in illustration, Jemmy wriggled loose from Roger's grasp, dropped to hands and knees, and crawled off at a high rate of speed, heading for his basket of toys.

"And what else have ye been doing today?" Roger asked, sitting down at the table.

"What *else*?" Her eyes went wide, then narrowed. "You don't think learning to walk is enough for one day?"

"Of course; it's wonderful, it's marvelous!" he assured her hastily. "I was only making conversation."

She relaxed, appeased.

"Well, then. We scrubbed the floor—not that anybody could tell the difference—" She glanced down with some distaste at the rough, discolored boards underfoot, "—and we made bread and set it to rise, only it didn't, so that's why you're having flat-bread with your dinner."

"Love flat-bread," he assured her hastily, catching the gimlet gleam in her eye.

"Sure you do," she said, lifting one thick red brow. "Or at least you know which side it's buttered on."

He laughed. Here in the warm, the chill was wearing off, and his hands were starting to throb, but he felt good, nonetheless. Tired enough to fall off his stool, but good. Good and hungry. His stomach growled in anticipation.

"Flat-bread and butter is a start," he said. "What else? I smell something good." He looked at the bubbling cauldron and sniffed hopefully. "Stew?"

"No, laundry." Bree glowered at the kettle. "The third bloody batch today. I can't fit much in that dinky thing, but I couldn't take the wash up to the big kettle at the house, because of washing the floor and spinning. When you do wash outside, you have to stay there, to tend the fire and stir it, so you can't do much else at the same time." Her lips clamped and thinned. "Very inefficient."

"Shame." Roger passed lightly over the logistics of laundry, in favor of more pressing issues. He lifted his chin toward the hearth.

"I do smell meat. You don't think a mouse has fallen into the pot?"

Jemmy, catching this, let go his hold on a rag-ball and crawled eagerly toward the fire. "Mouzee? See mouzee?"

Brianna grabbed the collar of Jemmy's smock and turned the glower on Roger.

"Certainly not. No, baby, no mousie. Daddy's being silly. Here, Jemmy, come eat." Letting go the collar, she seized the little boy by the waist and lifted him—kicking and struggling—into his high chair. "Eat, I said! You stay put." Jemmy arched his back, grunting and squealing in protest, then suddenly relaxed, sliding down out of the chair and disappearing into the folds of his mother's skirt.

Brianna grappled for him, going red in the face with laughter and exasperation.

"All *right*!" she said, hauling him upright. "Don't eat,

then. See if I care." She reached for the litter of toys, spilled out of their basket, and plucked a battered corn-husk doll from the rubble. "Here, see dolly? Nice dolly."

Jemmy clasped the doll to his bosom, sat down abruptly on his bottom, and began to address the doll in earnest tones, shaking it now and then for emphasis.

"Eat!" he said sternly, poking it in the stomach. He laid the doll on the floor, picked up the basket, and carefully turned it over on top of the dolly. "Stay put!"

Brianna rubbed a hand down her face, and sighed. She gave Roger a glance. "And you want to know what I do all day."

The glance sharpened, as she truly looked at him for the first time.

"And what have *you* been doing, Mr. MacKenzie? You look like you've been in the wars." She touched his face gently; there was a knot forming on his forehead; he could feel the skin tightening there, and the tiny stab of pain when she touched it.

"Something like. Jamie's been showing me the rudiments of swordsmanship."

Her brows went up, and he laughed self-consciously, keeping his hands in his lap.

"Wooden swords, aye?"

Several wooden swords. They'd broken three so far, though the makeshift weapons were stout lengths of wood; not twigs, by any means.

"He stabbed you in the *head*?" Brianna's voice had a slight edge, though Roger couldn't tell whether it was meant for him or for her father.

"Ah . . . no. Not exactly."

With hazy memories of swashbuckling films and university fencing matches, he'd been unprepared for the sheer brutal force involved in hand-to-hand combat with swords. Jamie's first blow had knocked Roger's sword from his hand and sent it flying; a later one had split the wood and sent a large chunk of it rocketing past his ear.

"What does 'not exactly' mean?"

"Well, he was showing me something called *corps à corps*—which appears to be French for 'Get your opponent's sword wrapped round your own, then knee him in the balls and punch his head while he's trying to get loose.' "

Brianna gave a brief, shocked laugh.

"You mean he—"

"No, but it was a near thing," he said, wincing at the memory. "I've a bruise on my thigh the size of my hand."

"Are you hurt anywhere else?" Brianna was frowning at him, worried.

"No." He smiled up at her, keeping his hands in his lap. "Tired. Sore. Starving."

The frown eased and her smile flickered back, though a small line stayed between her brows. She reached for the wooden platter on the sideboard, turned, and squatted by the hearth.

"Quail," she said with satisfaction, raking a number of blackened bundles out of the ashes with the poker. "Da brought them this morning. He said not to pluck them; just wrap them in mud and bake them. I hope he knows what he's talking about." She jerked her head toward the boiling cauldron. "Jemmy helped me with the mud; that's why we had to do another pot of laundry. Ouch!" She snatched away her hand and sucked a burned finger, then picked up the platter and brought it to the table.

"Let them cool a little," she instructed him. "I'll get some of those pickles you like."

The quail looked like nothing so much as charred rocks. Still, a tantalizing steam drifted up through cracks in a few of the blackened lumps. Roger felt like picking one up and eating it on the spot, burned mud and all. Instead, he fumbled at the cloth-covered plate on the table, discovering the maligned flat-bread underneath. Stiff-fingered, he managed to tear off a good chunk, and stuffed it silently into his mouth.

Jemmy had abandoned his ball of rags under the bed, and come to see what his father was doing. Pulling himself upright by the table leg, he spotted the bread and reached up, making urgent noises of demand. Roger carefully tore off another bit of bread and handed it to his offspring, nearly dropping it in the process. His hands were cut and battered; the knuckles of his right hand blood-grazed, swollen, and black with fresh bruising. Half his right thumbnail had been knocked away, and the bit of raw nail bed showed red and oozing.

"Ow-ee." Clutching his bread, Jemmy looked at Roger's hands, then up at his face. "Daddy owee?"

"Dad's all right," Roger assured him. "Just tired."

Jemmy stared at the injured thumb, then slowly raised his hand to his mouth and inserted his own thumb, sucking loudly.

It actually looked like a good idea. His thumb stung and ached, where the nail had gone, and all his fingers were cold and stiff. With a quick glance at Brianna's back, he lifted his hand and stuck his thumb in his mouth.

It felt alien, thick and hard and tasting of silvery blood and cold grime. Then suddenly it fit, and tongue and palate closed round the injured digit in a warm and soothing pressure.

Jemmy butted him in the thigh, his usual signal for "up," and he grasped the back of the little boy's clout with his free hand, boosting him up onto his knee. Jemmy made himself at home, rooting and squirming, then relaxed in sudden peace, bread squashed in one hand, sucking quietly on his thumb.

Roger slowly relaxed, one elbow propped on the table, the other arm round his son. Jemmy's heavy warmth and heavy breathing against his ribs were a soothing accompaniment to the homely noises Brianna was making as she dished the supper. To his surprise, his thumb stopped hurting, but he left it where it was, too tired to question the odd sense of comfort.

His muscles were gradually relaxing, too, coming off the state of tensed readiness in which he'd held them for hours.

His inner ear still rang with brisk instruction. *Use your forearm, man—the wrist, the wrist! Dinna move your hand out like that, keep it near the body. It's a sword, aye? Not a bloody club. Use the tip!*

He'd thrown Jamie heavily against a tree, at one point. And Fraser had tripped over a rock and gone down once, Roger on top. As for any actual damage inflicted with a sword, he might as well have been fighting a cloud.

Dirty fighting is the only kind there is, Fraser had told

him, panting, as they knelt at the stream and splashed cold water over sweating faces. *Anything else is no but exhibition.*

His head jerked on his neck and he blinked, coming back abruptly from the grate and crash of wooden swords to the dim warmth of the cabin. The platter was gone; Brianna was cursing softly under her breath at the sideboard, banging the hilt of his dirk against the blackened lumps of clay-baked quail to crack them open.

Watch your footing. Back, back—aye, now, come back at me! No, dinna reach so far . . . keep your guard up!

And the stinging *whap!* of the springy "blade" across arms and thighs and shoulders, the solid thunk of it driven bruising home between his ribs, sunk deep and breathless in his belly. Had it been cold steel, he would have been dead in minutes, cut to bleeding ribbons.

Don't catch the blade on yours—throw it off. Beat, beat it off! Come at me, thrust! Keep it close, keep it close . . . aye, good . . . ha!

His elbow slipped and his hand fell. He jerked upright, barely keeping hold of the sleeping child, and blinked, vision swimming with firelight.

Brianna started guiltily and shut her notebook. Getting to her feet, she thrust it out of sight behind a pewter plate, resting upright on its edge at the back of the sideboard.

"It's ready," she said hurriedly. "I just—I'll get the milk." She disappeared into the pantry in a rustle of skirts.

Roger shifted Jemmy, got a grip, and lifted the small, solid body up to his shoulder, though his arms felt like cooked noodles. The little boy was sound asleep, but kept his thumb plugged firmly into his mouth.

Roger's own thumb was wet with spittle, and he felt a flush of embarrassment. Christ, had she been drawing him that way? No doubt; she must have caught sight of him sucking his thumb and thought it "cute"; it wouldn't be the first time she'd drawn him in what he considered a compromising position. Or was she writing dreams again?

He laid Jemmy gently in his cradle, brushed damp bread crumbs off the coverlet, and stood rubbing his bruised knuckles with the fingers of his other hand. Sloshing noises came from the pantry. Moving quietly, he stepped to the sideboard and extracted the book from its hiding place. Sketches, not dreams.

It was no more than a few quick lines, the essence of a sketch. A man tired to death, still watchful; head on one hand, neck bowed with exhaustion—free arm clamped tight around a treasured, helpless thing.

She'd titled it. *En garde*, it said, in her slanted, spiky script.

He closed the book and slid it back behind the plate. She was standing in the pantry doorway, the milk jug in her hand.

"Come and eat," she said softly, eyes on his. "You need your strength."

88

ROGER BUYS A SWORD

Cross Creek
November, 1771

HE'D HANDLED EIGHTEENTH-CENTURY broadswords before; neither the weight nor the length surprised him. The basket around the hilt was slightly bent, but not enough to interfere with fitting his hand inside the grip. He'd done that before, too. There was a considerable difference, though, beyond reverently placing an antique artifact into a museum display, and picking up a length of sharpened metal with the conscious intent of driving it through a human body.

"It's a bit battered," Fraser had told him, squinting critically down the length of the sword before handing it to him, "but the blade's well-balanced. Try the feel of it, to see if it suits."

Feeling a total fool, he slipped his hand into the basket and struck a fencing pose, based on memories of Errol Flynn films. They were standing in the busy lane outside the smithy in Cross Creek, and a few passersby paused to watch and offer helpful comment.

"What's Moore asking for that bit of pot tin?" someone asked disparagingly. "Anything more than two shillings, and it's highway robbery."

"That's a fine sword," said Moore, leaning over the half-door of his forge and glowering. "I had it from my uncle, who saw service at Fort Stanwyck. Why, that blade's killed a-many Frenchmen, and no but the one wee nick to be seen in it."

"One nick!" cried the disparager. "Why, the thing's bent so, if you went to stick a man, you'd end up cutting off his ear!"

There was a laugh from the gathering crowd that drowned the smith's response. Roger lowered the point of the sword, raised it slowly. How the hell did one road-test a sword? Ought he to wave it to and fro? Stick something with it? There was a cart standing a little way down the lane, loaded with burlap bags of something—raw wool, from the smell.

He looked for the proprietor of the bags, but couldn't pick him out from the growing crowd; the huge draft horse hitched to the cart was unattended, ears twitching sleepily over his dropped reins.

"Ah, if it's a sword the young man's wanting, sure and Malachy McCabe has a better one than that, left from his service. I think he'd part with it for nay more than three shillings." The cobbler from across the lane pursed his lips, nodding shrewdly at the sword.

" 'Tisn't an elegant piece," one middle-aged ex-soldier agreed, head tilted on one side. "Serviceable, though, I grant you that."

Roger extended his arm, lunged toward the door of the smithy, and narrowly missed Moore, coming out to defend the quality of his wares. The smith leaped aside with a startled cry, and the crowd roared.

Roger's apology was interrupted by a loud, nasal voice behind him.

"Here, sir! Let me offer a foe more worthy of your steel than an unarmed smith!"

Whirling round, Roger found himself confronting Dr. Fentiman, who was pulling a long, thin blade from the head of his ornamental cane. The doctor, who was roughly half Roger's size, brandished his rapier with a genial ferocity. Obviously fueled by a liberal luncheon, the tip of his nose glowed like a Christmas bulb.

"A test of skill, sir?" The doctor whipped his sword to and fro, so the narrow blade sang as it cut the air. "First to pink his man, first to draw blood is the victor, what say you?"

"Oh, an unfair advantage to the doctor! And isn't drawing blood your business, then?"

"Ha ha! And if ye run him through instead of pinking him, will ye patch the hole for no charge?" yelled another onlooker. "Or are ye out to drum up business, leech?"

"Watch yourself, young man! Turn your back on him and he's like to give ye a clyster!"

"Better a clyster than a blade up the arse!"

The doctor ignored these and similar vulgar observations, holding his blade upright in readiness. Roger shot a glance at Jamie, who was leaning against the wall, looking amused. Jamie raised one eyebrow and shrugged slightly.

"Try the feel of it," Jamie'd said. Well, and he supposed a duel with a drunken midget was as good a test as any.

Roger raised his blade and fixed the doctor with a menacing look.

"En garde," he said, and the knot of onlookers roared approval.

"Gardez-vous," replied the doctor promptly, and lunged. Roger spun on one heel and the doctor shot past, rapier pointed like a lance. Moore the smith leaped aside just in time to avoid being skewered for the second time, cursing fluently.

"What am I, a friggin' target?" he shouted, shaking a fist.

Disregarding the near miss, the doctor regained his balance and charged back toward Roger, uttering shrill cries of self-encouragement.

It was rather like being attacked by a wasp, Roger thought. If you didn't panic, you found it possible to follow the thing and bat it away. Perhaps the doctor was a decent swordsman when sober; in his current state, his frenzied thrusts and mad flurries were easily fended off—as long as Roger paid attention.

It occurred to him early on that he could end the contest at any time, merely by meeting the doctor's slender rapier edge-on with his own much heavier weapon. He was beginning to enjoy himself, though, and was careful to parry with the flat of the broadsword.

Gradually everything disappeared from Roger's view but the flashing point of the rapier; the shouts of the crowd faded to a bee-buzz, the dirt of the lane and the wall of the smithy were scarcely visible. He grazed his elbow on the wall, moved back, moved in a circle to gain more room, all without conscious thought.

The rapier beat on his wider blade, engaged, and screeched loose with a *whinggg!* of metal. Clang and click and the whish of empty air and the ringing beat that vibrated in his wristbones with every blow of the doctor's sword.

Watch the stroke, follow it, bat it away. He had no idea what he was doing, but did it anyway. The sweat was running in his eyes; he shook his head to fling it away, nearly missed a low lunge toward his thigh, stopped it close, and flung the rapier back.

The doctor staggered, thrown off balance, and feral shouts of *"Now! Take him! Stick him now!"* rang in the dust-filled air. He saw the expanse of the doctor's embroidered waistcoat, unguarded, filled with silken butterflies, and choked back the visceral urge to lunge for it.

Shaken by the intensity of the urge, he took a step back. The doctor, sensing weakness, leapt forward, bellowing, blade pointed. Roger took a half-step sideways, and the doctor shot past, grazing the hock of the draft horse in his path.

The horse emitted an outraged scream, and promptly sent swordsman and sword flying through the air, to crash against the front of the cobbler's shop. The doctor fell to ground like a crushed fly, surrounded by lasts and scattered shoes.

Roger stood still, panting. His whole body was pulsing

with every heartbeat, hot with the fighting. He wanted to go on, he wanted to laugh, he wanted to hit something. He wanted to get Brianna up against the nearest wall, and *now*.

Jamie gently lifted his hand and pried his fingers from the hilt of the sword. He hadn't remembered he was holding it. His arm felt too light without it, as though it might fly up toward the sky, all by itself. His fingers were stiff from gripping so hard, and he flexed them automatically, feeling the tingle as the blood came back.

The blood was tingling everywhere. He hardly heard the laughter, the offers of drinks, or felt the blows of congratulation rained on his back.

"A clyster, a clyster, give him a clyster!" a gang of apprentices was chanting, following along as the doctor was borne off for first-aid in the nearest tavern. The horse's owner was fussing solicitously over the big bay, who looked more bemused than injured.

"I suppose he's won. After all, he drew first blood."

Roger didn't realize that he'd spoken until he heard his own voice, strangely calm in his ears.

"Will it do?" Jamie was looking at him in question, the sword held lightly on the palms of his hands.

Roger nodded. The lane was bright and filled with white dust; it gritted under his eyelids, between his teeth when he closed his mouth.

"Aye," he said. "It will do."

"Good," said Jamie. "So will you," he added casually, turning away to pay the smith.

PART EIGHT

A-Hunting We Will Go

89

THE MOONS OF JUPITER

Late November, 1771

FOR THE FOURTH TIME in as many minutes, Roger assured himself that it was not medically possible to die of sexual frustration. He doubted that it would even cause lasting damage. On the other hand, it wasn't doing him any great good, either, in spite of his efforts to consider it as an exercise in building character.

He eased himself onto his back, careful of the rustling mattress, and stared at the ceiling. No good; from a crack at the edge of the oiled hide covering the window, early morning sun was streaming in across the bed, and from the corner of his eye, he could still see the pure golden haunches of his wife, lit as though spotlighted.

She was lying on her stomach, face buried in the pillow, and the linen sheet had slipped down past the swell of her buttocks, leaving her bare from her nape to the crack of her arse. She lay so close in the narrow bed that his leg touched hers, and the warmth of her breathing brushed his bare shoulder. His mouth was dry.

He closed his eyes. That didn't help; he promptly started seeing images of the night before: Brianna by the dim light of a smothered fire, the flames of her hair sparking in the shadows, light gleaming sudden across the curve of a naked breast as she slipped the butter-soft linen from her shoulders.

Late as it was, tired as he was, he'd wanted her desperately. Someone else had wanted her more, though. He cracked an eyelid and raised himself just slightly, enough to see over Brianna's tumbled red locks, to where the cradle stood against the wall, still in shadow. No sign of movement.

They had a long-standing agreement. He woke instantly when disturbed, she was groggy and maladroit. So when a siren shriek from the cradle jerked him into heart-pounding alertness, it was Roger who would rise, pick up the soggy, yowling bundle, and deal with the immediate necessities of hygiene. By the time he brought Jemmy to his mother, bucking and squirming in the search for sustenance, Brianna would have roused herself far enough to wriggle free of her gown, and would reach up for the child, drawing him down in warm dark to the murmuring, milky refuge of her body.

Now that Jem was older, he seldom woke at night, but when he did, with bellyache or nightmare, it took a lot longer to settle him back to sleep than it had when he was tiny. Roger had fallen back to sleep while Bree was still administering comfort, but woke when she turned in the narrow bed, her buttocks sliding past his thigh. The corn shucks under them crackled loudly with a noise like a thousand distant firecrackers, all going off down the length of his spine, waking him to full awareness of an urgent, nearly painful arousal.

He'd felt the pressure of her arse against him and narrowly restrained himself from rolling over and assaulting her from the rear. Small suckling noises from the other side of her body stopped him. Jem was still in their bed.

He'd lain still, listening, praying that she'd stay awake long enough to return the little bugger to his cradle; sometimes they fell asleep together, mother and child, and Roger would wake in the morning to the confusingly mingled scents of a beddable woman and baby pee. And then in the end, he'd fallen asleep himself, in spite of his discomfort, worn out from a day of felling logs on the mountainside.

He inhaled gently. No, she'd put him back. No scent in his bed now save Brianna's, the earthy smell of woman-flesh, a faint, sweet cloud of sweat and slippery willingness.

She sighed in her sleep, murmured something incomprehensible, and turned her head on the pillow. There were blue smudges under her eyes; she'd been up late making jelly, up again twice more with the little bas—with the baby. How could he wake her, only to gratify his own base urges?

How could he *not*?

He gritted his teeth, torn between temptation, compassion, and the sure conviction that if he yielded to his inclinations, he would get precisely as far as the worst possible moment before an interruption from the vicinity of the cradle compelled him to stop.

Experience had been a harsh teacher, but the urgings of the flesh were louder than the voice of reason. He put out a stealthy hand and gently grasped the buttock nearest. It was cool and smooth and round as a gourd.

She made a small noise deep in her throat and stretched luxuriously. She arched her back, pushing her backside up in a way that convinced Roger that the course of wisdom was to fling back the quilt, roll on top of her, and achieve his goal in the ten seconds flat it was likely to take.

He got as far as flinging back the quilt. As he raised his head from the pillow, a round, pale object rose slowly into view over the rim of the cradle, like one of the moons of Jupiter. A pair of blue eyes regarded him with clinical dispassion.

"Oh, *shit*!" he said.

"Oh, *chit*!" Jemmy said, in happy mimicry. He clambered to his feet and stood, bouncing up and down as he gripped the edge of the cradle he was rapidly outgrowing, chanting *"Chit-chit-chit-chit"* in what he evidently thought was a song.

Brianna jerked into wakefulness, blinking through tangled locks.

"What? What's wrong?"

"Ah . . . something stung me." Roger flipped the edge of the quilt discreetly back in place. "Must be a wasp in here."

She stretched on her pillow, groaning and smoothing her hair out of her face with one hand, then picked up the cup from the table and took a drink; she always woke up thirsty.

Her eyes traveled over him, and a slow smile spread across her wide, soft mouth. "Yeah? Nasty sting you got there. Want me to rub it?" She put down the cup, rolled gracefully up onto an elbow, and reached out a hand.

"Ye're a sadist," Roger said, gritting his teeth. "No doubt about it. Ye must get it from your father."

She laughed, took her hand off the quilt, and stood up, pulling her shift on over her head.

"MAMA! Chit, Mama!" Jemmy informed her, beaming, as she swung him up out of his cradle with a grunt of effort.

"You rat," she said, affectionately. "You aren't very popular with Daddy this morning. Your timing stinks." She wrinkled her nose. "And not only your timing."

"Depends on your perspective, I suppose." Roger rolled onto his side, watching. "I imagine from *his* point of view, the timing was perfect."

"Yeah." Brianna gave him a raised brow. "Hence the new word, huh?"

"He's heard it before," Roger said dryly. "Many times." He sat up, swinging his legs out of bed, and rubbed a hand through his hair and over his face.

"Well, all we have to do now is figure out how to get from the abstract to the concrete, huh?" She put Jemmy on his feet and knelt in front of him, kissing him on the nose, then unpinning his diaper. "Oh, yag. Is eighteen months too soon for toilet-training, do you think?"

"Are ye asking me, or him?"

"Pew. I don't care; whichever one of you has an opinion."

Jemmy plainly didn't; cheerfully stoic, he was ignoring his mother's determined assault on his private parts with a cold, wet cloth, absorbed in a new song of his own composition, which went along the lines of "Pew, pew, chit, chit, PEW, PEW . . ."

Brianna put a stop to this by swinging him up in her arms and sitting down with him in the nursing chair by the hearth.

"Want snackies?" she said, pulling down the neck of her shift invitingly.

"God, yes," Roger said, with feeling. Bree laughed, not without sympathy, as she settled Jemmy on her lap, where he settled happily to suckling.

"Your turn next," she assured Roger. "You want oatmeal porridge, or fried mush for breakfast?"

"Anything else on the menu?" Damn, he'd been nearly ready to stand up. Back to square one.

"Oh, sure. Toast with strawberry jam. Cheese. Eggs, but

you'll have to go get them from the coop; I don't have any in the pantry."

Roger found it hard to concentrate on the discussion, faced with the sight of Brianna in the dim smoky light of the cabin, long thighs spread under her shift, her heels tucked under the chair. She seemed to detect his lack of interest in matters dietary, for she looked up and smiled at him, her eyes taking in his own nakedness.

"You look nice, Roger," she said softly. Her free hand drifted down, resting lightly on the inner curve of one thigh. The long, blunt-nailed fingers made slow circles, barely moving.

"So do you." His voice was husky. "Better than nice."

Her hand rose and patted Jemmy softly on the back.

"Want to go see Auntie Lizzie after breakfast, sweetie?" she asked, not looking at him. Her eyes were fixed on Roger's, and her wide mouth curved in a slow smile.

He didn't think he could wait until after breakfast to touch her, at least. Her shawl was thrown across the foot of the bed; he grabbed it and wrapped it round his hips for the sake of decency as he got out of bed and crossed to kneel beside her chair.

Her hair stirred and lifted in a draft from the window, and he saw the stipple of gooseflesh break out suddenly on her arms. He put his arms around them both. The draft was cold on his bare back, but he didn't care.

"I love you," he whispered in her ear. His hand lay over hers, resting on her thigh.

She turned her head and kissed him, a glancing contact of soft lips.

"I love you, too," she said.

She had rinsed her mouth with water and wine, and tasted of autumn grapes and cold streams. He was just settling down to more serious business when a loud hammering shivered the timbers of the door, accompanied by his father-in-law's voice.

"Roger! Are ye in there, man? Up wi' ye this minute!"

"What does he mean am I in here?" Roger hissed to Brianna. "Where the hell else would I be?"

"Shh." She nipped his neck and reluctantly let go, her eyes traveling over him with deep appreciation.

"He's already up, Da!" she called.

"Aye, it's likely to be a permanent condition, too," Roger muttered. "Coming!" he bellowed. "Where the hell are my clothes?"

"Under the bed where you left them last night." Brianna set down Jemmy, who shrieked ecstatically at the sound of his grandfather's voice and ran to pound on the bolted door. Having finally ventured to walk, he had lost no time with the next stage, moving on to rapid—and perpetual—locomotion within a matter of days.

"Hurry!" Sunlight flooded into the cabin as the hide over the window was thrust aside, revealing Jamie Fraser's broad-boned face, flushed with excitement and morning sun. He lifted an eyebrow at the view of Roger thus revealed, crouched on the floor with a shirt clutched protectively to his midsection.

"Move yourself, man," he said, mildly. "It's no time to be hangin' about bare-arsed; MacLeod says there are beasts just over the ridge." He blew a kiss to Jemmy. *"A ghille ruaidh, a charaid! Ciamar a tha thu?"*

Roger forgot both sex and self-consciousness. He jerked the shirt over his head and stood up.

"What kind? Deer, elk?"

"I dinna ken, but they're meat!" The hide dropped suddenly, leaving the room half in shadow.

The intrusion had let in a blast of cold air, breaking the warm, smoke-laden atmosphere and bringing with it the breath of hunting weather, of crisp wind and crimson leaves, of mud and fresh droppings, of wet wool and sleek hide, all spiced with the imaginary reek of gunpowder.

With a final, longing look at his wife's body, Roger grabbed his stockings.

90

DANGER IN THE GRASS

GRUNTING AND PUFFING, the men pushed into the dark-green zone of the conifers by noon. High on the upper ridges, clusters of balsam fir and hemlock huddled with spruce and pine, over the tumbled rock. Here they stood secure in seasonal immortality, needles murmuring lament for the bright fragility of the fallen leaves below.

Roger shivered in the cold shadow of the conifers, and was glad of the thick wool hunting shirt he wore over the linen one. There was no conversation; even when they paused briefly to draw breath, there was a stillness in the wood here that forbade unnecessary speech.

The wilderness around them felt calm—and empty. Perhaps they were too late, and the game had moved on; perhaps MacLeod had been wrong. Roger had not yet mastered the killing skills, but he had spent a good deal of time alone in sun and wind and silence; he had acquired some of the instincts of a hunter.

The men came out into full sun as they emerged on the far side of the ridge. The air was thin and cold, but Roger felt heat strike through his chilled body, and closed his eyes in momentary pleasure. The men paused together in unspoken appreciation, basking in a sheltered spot, momentarily safe from the wind.

Jamie stepped to the edge of a rocky shelf, sun glinting off his tailed copper hair. He turned to and fro, squinting downward through the trees. Roger saw his nostrils flare, and smiled to himself. Well, then, perhaps he did smell the game.

He wouldn't be surprised. Roger sniffed experimentally, but got nothing but the must of decaying leaves and a strong whiff of well-aged perspiration from the body of Kenny Lindsay.

Fraser shook his head, then turned to Fergus, and with a quiet word, climbed over the edge of the shelf and disappeared.

"We wait," Fergus said laconically to the others, and sat down. He produced a pair of carved stone balls from his bag, and sat rolling them to and fro in his palm, concentrating intently, rolling a sphere out and back along the length of each dexterous finger.

A brilliant fall sun poked long fingers through the empty branches, administering the last rites of seasonal consolation, blessing the dying earth with a final touch of warmth. The men sat talking quietly, reeking in the sun. He hadn't noticed in the colder wood, but here in the sun, the tang of fresh sweat was apparent, overlying the deeper layers of grime and body odors.

Roger reflected that perhaps it was not extraordinary olfactory acuteness on the part of animals, but merely the extreme smelliness of human beings that made it so difficult to get near game on foot. He had sometimes seen the Mohawk rub themselves with herbs, to disguise their natural odor when hunting, but even oil of peppermint wouldn't make a dent in Kenny Lindsay's stench.

He didn't reek like that himself, did he? Curious, he bent his head toward the open neck of his shirt and breathed in. He felt a trickle of sweat run down the back of his neck, under his hair. He blotted it with his collar and resolved to bathe before going back to the cabin, no matter if the creek was crusted with ice.

Showers and deodorants were of more than aesthetic importance, he reflected. One got used to almost any habitual stink in short order, after all. What he'd not realized, secure in his relatively odorless modern environment, were the more intimate implications of smell. Sometimes he felt like a bloody baboon, his most primitive responses unleashed without warning, by some random assault of odor.

He remembered what had happened just the week before, and felt a hot blush creep over him at the memory.

He had walked into the dairy shed, looking for Claire. He'd found her—and Jamie, too. They were both fully clothed, standing well apart—and the air was so filled with the musk of desire and the sharp scent of male completion that Roger had felt the blood burn in his face, the hair on his body prickling erect.

His first instinct had been to turn and leave, but there was no excuse for that. He had given his message to Claire, conscious of Fraser's eyes on him, bland and quizzical. Conscious, too, of the unspoken communication between the two of them, an unseen thrum in the air, as though they were two beads strung on a wire stretched tight.

Jamie had waited until Roger left, before leaving himself. From the corner of his eye, Roger had caught a slight movement, seen the light touch of the hand with which he left her, and even now, felt a queer clutch of his insides at the memory.

He blew out his breath to ease the tightness in his chest, then stretched out in the leaves, letting the sun beat down on his closed eyelids. He heard a muffled groan from Fergus, then the rustle of footsteps as the Frenchman made another hasty withdrawal. Fergus had eaten half-cured sauerkraut the night before—a fact made clear to anyone who sat near him for long.

His thoughts drifted back to that awkward moment in the dairy shed.

It was not prurience, nor even simple curiosity, and yet he often found himself watching them. He saw them from the cabin window, walking together in the evening, Jamie's head bent toward her, hands clasped behind his back. Claire's hands moved when she talked, rising long and white in the air, as though she would catch the future between them and give it shape, would hand Jamie her thoughts as she spoke them, smooth and polished objects, bits of sculptured air.

Once aware of what he was doing, Roger watched them purposefully, and brushed aside any feelings of shame at such intrusion, minor as it was. He had a compelling reason for his curiosity; there was something he needed to know, badly enough to excuse any lack of manners.

How was it done, this business of marriage?

He had been brought up in a bachelor's house. Given all he needed as a boy in terms of affection by his great-uncle and the Reverend's elderly housekeeper, he found himself lacking something as an adult, ignorant of the threads of touch and word that bound a married couple. Instinct would do, for a start.

But if love like that could be learned . . .

A touch on his elbow startled him and he jerked round, flinging out an arm in quick defense. Jamie ducked neatly, eluding the blow, and grinned at him.

Fraser jerked his head toward the edge of the shelf.

"I've found them," he said.

JAMIE RAISED A HAND, and Fergus went at once to his side. The Frenchman came barely to the big Scot's shoulder, but didn't look ridiculous. He shaded his eyes with his one hand, peering down where Fraser pointed.

Roger came up behind them, looking down the slope. A flicker shot through a clearing below, marked by the swooping dip and rise of its flight. Its mate called deep in the wood, a sound like a high-pitched laugh. He could see nothing else remarkable below; it was the same dense tangle of mountain laurel, hickory, and oak that existed on the side of the ridge from which they had come; far below, a thick line of tall leafless trees marked the course of a stream.

Fraser saw him, and gestured downward with a twist of the head, pointing with his chin.

"By the stream; d'ye see?" he said.

At first, Roger saw nothing. The stream itself wasn't visible, but he could chart its course by the growth of bare-limbed sycamore and willows. Then he saw it; a bush far down the slope moved, in a way that wasn't like the wind-blown tossings of the branches near it. A sudden jerk that shook the bush as something pulled at it, feeding.

"Jesus, what's that?"

His glimpse of a sudden dark bulk had been enough only to tell him that the thing was big—very big.

"I dinna ken. Bigger than a deer. Wapiti, maybe." Fraser's eyes were intent, narrowed against the wind. He stood easy, musket in one hand, but Roger could see his excitement.

"A moose, perhaps?" Fergus frowned under his shading hand. "I have not seen one, but they are very large, no?"

"No." Roger shook his head. "I mean yes, but that's not what it is. I've hunted moose—with the Mohawk. They don't move like that at all." Too late, he saw Fraser's mouth tighten briefly, then relax; by unspoken consent, they avoided mention of Roger's captivity among the Mohawk. Fraser said nothing, though, only nodded at the tangle of woodland below.

"Aye, it's not deer or moose, either—but there's more than one. D'ye see?"

Roger squinted harder, then saw what Fraser was doing, and did likewise—swaying from foot to foot, deliberately letting his eyes drift casually across the landscape.

With no attempt to focus on a single spot in the panorama below, he could instead see the whole slope as a blurred patchwork of color and motion—like a Van Gogh painting, he thought, and smiled at the thought. Then he saw what Jamie had seen, and stiffened, all thought of modern art forgotten.

Here and there among the faded grays and browns and the patches of evergreen was a disjunction, a knot in the pattern of nature's weft—strange movements, not caused by the rushing wind. Each beast was invisible itself, but made its presence known, nonetheless, by the twitchings of the bushes nearby. God, how big must they be? There . . . and there . . . he let his eyes drift to and fro, and felt a tightening of excitement through chest and belly. Christ, there were half a dozen, at least!

"I was right! I was right, was I no, *Mac Dubh*?" MacLeod exulted. His round face beamed from one to another, flushed with triumph. "I did say as I'd seen beasts, aye?"

"Jesus, there's a whole herd of them," Evan Lindsay breathed, echoing his thought. The Highlander's face was bright, fierce with anticipation. He glanced at Jamie.

"How will it be, *Mac Dubh*?"

Jamie lifted one shoulder slightly, still peering into the valley. "Hard to say; they're in the open. We canna corner them anywhere." He licked a finger and held it to the breeze, then pointed.

"The wind's from the west; let us come down the runnel there to the foot of the slope. Then wee Roger and I will pass to the side, near that great outcrop; ye see the one?"

Lindsay nodded slowly, a crooked front tooth worrying the thin flesh of his lip.

"They're near the stream. Do you circle about—keep well clear until ye're near to the big cedar tree; ye see it? Aye, then spread yourselves, two to each bank of the stream. Evan's the best marksman; have him stand ready. Roger Mac and I will come behind the herd, to drive them toward ye."

Fergus nodded, surveying the land below.

"I see. And if they shall see us, they will turn into that small defile, and so be trapped. Very good. *Allons-y!*"

He gestured imperiously to the others, his hook gleaming in the sun. Then he grimaced slightly, hand to his belly, as a long, rumbling fart despoiled the silence of the wood. Jamie gave him a thoughtful look.

"Keep downwind, aye?" he said.

IT WAS IMPOSSIBLE to walk silently through the drifts of dry leaves, but Roger stepped as lightly as possible. Seeing Jamie load and prime his own gun, Roger had done likewise, feeling mingled excitement and misgiving at the acrid scent of powder. From his impressions of the size of the beasts they followed, even he might have a chance at hitting one.

Putting aside his doubts, he paused for a moment, turning his head from side to side to listen. Nothing but the faint rush of wind through the bare branches overhead, and the far-off murmur of water. A small *crack* sounded in the underbrush ahead, and he caught a glimpse of red hair. He cupped the gunstock in his hand, the wood warm and solid in his palm, barrel aimed upward over his shoulder, and followed.

Stealing carefully round a sumac bush, Roger felt something give suddenly under his foot, and jerked back to keep his balance. He looked at what he'd stepped on, and in spite of his instant disappointment, felt a strong urge to laugh.

"Jamie!" he called, not bothering any longer about stealth or silence.

Fraser's bright hair appeared through a screen of laurel, followed by the man himself. He didn't speak, but lifted one thick brow in inquiry.

"I'm no great tracker," Roger said, nodding downward, "but I've stepped in enough of these to know one when I see one." He scraped the side of his shoe on a fallen log, and pointed with his toe. "What d'ye think we've been creeping up on, all this time?"

Jamie stopped short, squinting, then walked forward and squatted next to the corrugated brown splotch. He prodded it with a forefinger, then looked up at Roger with an expression of mingled amusement and dismay.

"I will be damned," he said. Still squatting, he turned his head, frowning as he surveyed the wilderness around them. "But what are they doing here?" he murmured.

He stood up, shading his eyes as he looked toward the creek, where the lowering sun dazzled through the branches.

"It doesna make a bit of sense," he said, squinting into the shadows. "There are only three kine on the Ridge, and I saw two of them bein' milked this morning. The third belongs to Bobby MacLeod, and I should think he'd ken if it was his own cow he'd seen. Besides . . ." He turned slowly on his heel, looking up the steep slope they'd just descended.

He didn't have to speak; no cow not equipped with a parachute could have come down that way.

"There's more than one—a lot more," Roger said. "You saw."

"Aye, there are. But where did they come from?" Jamie glanced at him, frowning in puzzlement. "The Indians dinna keep kine, especially not at this season—they'd slaughter any beasts they had, and smoke the meat. And there's no farm in thirty miles where they might have come from."

"Maybe a wild herd?" Roger suggested. "Escaped a long time ago, and wandering?" Speculation sprang up in Jamie's eyes, echoing the hopeful gurgle of Roger's stomach.

"If so, they'll be easy hunting," Jamie said. Skepticism tempered his voice, even as he smiled. He stooped and broke off a small piece of the cow-pat, crushed it with a thumb, then tossed it away.

"Verra fresh," he said. "They're close; let's go."

Within a half-hour's walking, they emerged onto the bank of the stream they had glimpsed from above. It was wide and shallow here, with willows trailing leafless branches in the water. Nothing moved save a sparkle of sun on the riffles, but it was plain that the cows had been there; the mud of the bank was cut and churned with drying hoofprints, and in one place, the dying plants had been pawed away in a long, messy trough where something large had wallowed.

"Why did I not think to bring rope?" Jamie muttered, pushing through the willow saplings on the bank as they skirted the wallow. "Meat's one thing, but milk and cheese would be—" The muttering died away, as he turned from the stream, following a trail of broken foliage back into the wood.

Without speaking, the two men spread out, walking softly. Roger listened with all his might to the quiet of the forest. They had to be nearby; even such an inexperienced eye as Roger's had picked up the freshness of the signs. And yet the wood was autumn-still, the silence broken only by a raven, calling in the distance. The sun was hanging low in the sky, filling the air in the wood with a golden haze. It was getting noticeably colder; Roger passed through a patch of shadow, and shivered, in spite of his coat. They'd have to find the others and make camp soon; twilight was short. A fire would be good. Better, of course, if there were something to cook over it.

They were going down, now, into a small hollow where wisps of autumn mist rose from the cooling earth. Jamie was some distance ahead, walking with as much purpose as the broken ground allowed; evidently the trail was still plain to him, in spite of the thick vegetation.

A herd of cows couldn't just vanish, he thought, even in mist as heavy as this . . . not unless they were faery kine. And that, he wasn't quite prepared to believe, in spite of the unearthly quiet of the woods just here.

"Roger." Jamie spoke very quietly, but Roger had been listening so intently that he located his father-in-law at once, some distance to his right. Jamie jerked his head at something nearby. "Look."

He held aside a large, brambly bush, exposing the trunk of a substantial sycamore tree. Part of the bark had been rubbed away, leaving an oozing whitish patch on the gray bark.

"Do cows rub themselves like that?" Roger peered dubiously at the patch, then picked out a swatch of woolly dark hair, snagged by the roughened bark.

"Aye, sometimes," Jamie replied. He leaned close, shaking his head as he peered at the dark-brown tangle in Roger's hand. "But damned if I've ever seen a cow wi' a coat like that. Why ye'd think it was . . ."

Something moved at Roger's elbow and he turned, to find a monstrous dark head peering over his shoulder. A tiny, blood-dark eye met his own, and he let out a yell and jerked backward. There was a loud bang as his gun went off, and then a rush and a thud, and he was lying wrapped round a tree trunk, the breath knocked out of him, left with no more than a fleeting notion of a hairy dark bulk and a power that had sent him flying like a leaf.

He sat up, fighting for breath, and found Jamie on his knees in the leaves, scrabbling frantically for Roger's gun.

"Up!" he said. "Up, wee Roger! My God, it's buffalo!"

Then he was up, following Jamie. Still half-winded, but running, his gun in his hand with no clear memory of how it got there, powder-horn bumping against his hip.

Jamie was bounding like a deer through bushes, bundled cloak bouncing against his back. The wood wasn't silent any longer; ahead there were crashings and splinterings, and low snorting bellows.

He caught up Jamie on the upward slope; they labored up it, feet sliding on damp leaves, lungs burning from the effort, then topped a rise and came out onto a long downward slope, scattered with spindly pine and hickory saplings.

There they were; eight or nine of the huge, shaggy beasts, clustering together as they thundered down the hill, splitting to go around thickets and trees. Jamie dropped to one knee, sighted, and fired, to no apparent effect.

There was no time to stop and reload; they must keep the herd in sight. A bend of the stream glinted between the trees, below and to the right. Roger charged down the slope in a rush of excitement, canteen and bullet-box flying, heart thundering like the hooves of the buffalo herd. He could hear Jamie bellowing behind him, shouting Gaelic exhortations.

An exclamation in a different tone made Roger glance back. Jamie had stopped, his face frozen in shock. Before Roger could call to him, shock shifted to a look of fury. Teeth bared, he seized his gun by the barrel, and brought down the stock with a vicious *tchunk!* Barely pausing, he lifted the gun and clubbed it down again—and again, shoulders rolling with the effort.

Reluctantly abandoning the chase, Roger turned and bounded up the slope toward him.

"What the hell—?" Then he saw, and felt the hair on his body rise in a surge of revulsion. Brown coils squirmed between the tussocks, thick and scaly. One end of the snake had been battered to pulp, and its blood stained the butt of Fraser's musket, but the body writhed on, wormlike and headless.

"Stop! It's dead. D'ye hear me? Stop, I say!" He grasped Fraser's arm, but his father-in-law jerked free of his hold and brought the gun-butt down once more. Then he did stop, and stood shuddering violently, half-leaning on his gun.

"Christ! What happened? Did it get you?"

"Aye, in the leg. I stepped on it." Jamie's face was white to the lips. He looked at the still-writhing corpse and a deep shudder ran through him again.

Roger repressed his own shudder and grabbed Fraser's arm.

"Come away. Sit down, we'll have a look."

Jamie came, half-stumbling, and collapsed onto a fallen log. He fumbled at his stocking top, fingers shaking. Roger pushed Jamie's hand away and stripped buskin and stocking off the right foot. The fang marks were clear, a double dark-red puncture in the flesh of Fraser's calf. The flesh around the small holes had a bluish tinge, visible even in the late gold light.

"It's poisonous. I've got to cut it." Roger felt dry-mouthed, but oddly calm, with no sense of panic. He pulled the knife from his belt, thought briefly of sterilization, and dismissed the notion. It would take precious minutes to light a fire, and there was no time at all to waste.

"Wait." Fraser was still white, but had stopped shaking. He took the small flask from his belt and trickled whisky over the blade, then poured a few drops on his fingers and rubbed the liquid over the wound. He gave Roger a brief twitch of the mouth, meant as a smile.

"Claire does that, when she sets herself to cut someone." He leaned back, hands braced on the mossy trunk, and nodded. "Go on, then."

Biting his lip in concentration, Roger pressed the tip of the knife into the skin just above one of the puncture marks. The skin was surprisingly tough and springy; the knife dented it, but didn't penetrate. Fraser reached down and clasped his hand around Roger's; he shoved, with a deep, vicious grunt, and the knife sank suddenly in, an inch or more. Blood welled up around the blade; the gripping hand fell away.

"Again. Hard—and quick, man, for God's sake." Jamie's voice was steady, but Roger felt clear droplets of sweat fall onto his hand from Fraser's face, warm and then cold on his skin.

He braced himself to the necessary force, stabbed hard and cut quick—two X marks over the punctures, just as the first-aid guides said. The wounds were bleeding a lot, blood pouring down in thick streams. That was good, though, he thought. He had to go deep; deep enough to get beyond the poison. He dropped the knife and bent, mouth to the wounds.

There was no panic, but his sense of urgency was rising. How fast did venom spread? He had no more than minutes, maybe less. Roger sucked as hard as he could, blood filling his mouth with the taste of hot metal. He sucked and spat in quiet frenzy, blood spattering on the yellow leaves, Fraser's leg hairs scratchy against his lips. With the peculiar diffusion of mind that attends emergency, he thought of a dozen fleeting things at once, even as he bent his whole concentration to the task at hand.

Was the bloody snake really dead?

How poisonous was it?

Had the bison got away?

Christ, was he doing this right?

Brianna would kill him if he let her father die. So would Claire.

He had the devil of a cramp in his right thigh.

Where in hell were the others? Fraser should call for them—no, he *was* calling, was bellowing somewhere outside Roger's ken. The flesh of the leg Roger held had gone rock-hard, muscles rigid under his pressing fingers.

Something grasped the hair on the back of his head and twisted, forcing him to stop. He glanced up, breathing hard.

"That's enough, aye?" Jamie said mildly. "You'll drain me dry." He gingerly wiggled his bared foot, grimacing at his leg. The slashmarks were vivid, still oozing blood, and the flesh around them was swollen from the sucking, blotched and bruised.

Roger sat back on his heels, gulping air.

"I've made more—of a mess—than the snake did."

His mouth filled with saliva; he coughed and spat. Fraser silently offered him the whisky flask; he swirled a mouthful round and spat once more, then drank deep.

"All right?" He wiped his chin with the back of a hand, still tasting iron, and nodded at the lacerated leg.

"I'll do." Jamie was still pale, but one corner of his mouth turned up. "Go and see are the others in sight."

They weren't; the view from the top of the outcrop showed nothing but a sea of bare branches, tossing to and fro. The wind had come up. If the bison still moved along the river, there was no trace visible, either of them or of their hunters.

Hoarse from hallooing into the wind, Roger made his way back down the slope. Jamie had moved a little, finding a sheltered spot among rocks at the foot of a big balsam fir. He was sitting, back against a rock and legs outstretched, a handkerchief bound round his wounded leg.

"No sign of anyone. Can ye walk?" Roger bent over his father-in-law, and was alarmed to see him flushed and sweating heavily, despite the gathering chill of the air.

Jamie shook his head and gestured toward his leg.

"I can—but not for long." The leg was noticeably swollen near the bite, and the blue tinge had spread; it showed like a faint fresh bruise on either side of the encircling handkerchief.

Roger felt the first stab of uneasiness. He had done everything he knew to do; first-aid guides always had as the next step in the treatment of snakebite, "Immobilize limb and get patient to hospital as soon as possible." The cutting and sucking were meant to pull poison from the wound—but clearly there was plenty still left, spreading slowly through Jamie Fraser's body. He hadn't been in time to get it all—if he'd gotten any. And the nearest thing to a hospital—Claire and her herbs—a day's walk away.

Roger sank slowly down onto his haunches, wondering what the hell to do next. Immobilize the limb—well, that was effectively taken care of, for what good it might do.

"Hurt much?" he asked awkwardly.

"Yes."

With this unhelpful response, Jamie leaned back against the rock and closed his eyes. Roger eased himself down onto a sheaf of dry needles, trying to think.

It was getting dark fast; the brief warmth of the day had faded, and the shadows under the trees had taken on the deep blue look of evening, though it couldn't be more than four or so. Plainly they weren't going anywhere tonight; navigation in the mountains was nearly impossible in the dark, even if Fraser could walk. If the others were here, they could make shift to carry him—but would that be any better than leaving him where he was? While he urgently wished Claire were here, sense told him there was little even she could do—except, perhaps, comfort Jamie if he were to die . . .

The thought knotted his belly. Shoving it firmly aside, he reached into his pouch, checking supplies. He had a small quantity of johnny-cake still in his bag; water was never a difficulty in these mountains—through the sound of the trees, he could hear the gurgle of a stream somewhere below, not far off. He'd better be gathering wood while it was still light, though.

"We'd best make a fire." Jamie spoke suddenly, startling Roger with this echo of his thought. Jamie opened his eyes and looked down at one hand, turning it over and back as though he'd never seen it before.

"I've pins and needles in my fingers," he remarked with interest. He touched his face with one hand. "Here, too. My lips have gone numb. Is that usual, d'ye ken?"

"I don't know. I suppose it is, if you've been drinking the whisky." It was a feeble joke, but he was relieved to have it greeted with a faint laugh.

"Nay." Jamie touched the flask beside him. "I thought I might need it more, later."

Roger took a deep breath and stood up.

"Right. Stay there; you shouldn't move. I'll fetch along some wood. The others will likely see the light of the fire." The other men would be of no particular help, at least not until morning—but it would be a comfort not to be alone.

"Fetch the snake, too," Jamie called after him. "Fair's fair; we'll hae a bite of *him* for our supper!"

Grinning in spite of present worry, Roger gave a reassuring wave and turned down the slope.

What were the chances? he asked himself, stooping to wrest a thick pine knot from the soft wood of a rotted log. Fraser was a big man, and in robust health. Surely he would survive.

Yet folk did die of snakebite, and not infrequently; he'd heard only last week of a German woman near High Point; bent to pick up a stick of wood from her woodpile, struck full in the throat by a snake lying hidden there, dead in minutes. Reaching under a bush for a dry branch just as this recollection came to him, he hastily withdrew his bare hand, gooseflesh running up his arm. Berating himself for stupidity, he got a stick and thoroughly stirred the drift of dry leaves before reaching once more cautiously into it.

He couldn't help glancing up the slope every few minutes, feeling a small stab of alarm whenever Fraser was out of sight. What if he should collapse before Roger returned?

Then he relaxed a little as he remembered. No, it was all right. Jamie wasn't going to die tonight, either of snakebite or cold. He couldn't; he was meant to die some years hence, by fire. For once, future doom meant present reassurance. He took a deep breath and let it out in relief, then steeled himself to approach the snake.

It was motionless now, quite obviously dead. Still, it took some effort of will to pick the thing up. It was as thick around as his wrist and nearly four feet long. It had begun to stiffen; in the end, he was obliged to lay it across the armload of firewood, like a scaly branch. Seeing it so, he had no trouble imagining how the snake that had bitten the German woman had escaped notice; the subtle browns and grays of its patterns made it nearly invisible against its background.

Jamie skinned the thing while Roger built the fire. Watching from the corner of his eye, he could see that his father-in-law was making an unusually clumsy job of it; the numbness in his hands must be getting worse. Still, he went on doggedly, hacking at the corpse, stringing chunks of pale raw flesh onto a half-peeled twig with trembling fingers.

The job complete, Jamie extended the stick toward the budding fire and nearly dropped it. Roger grabbed for it, and felt through the stick the tremor that shook Jamie's hand and arm.

"You all right?" he said, and reached automatically to feel Jamie's forehead. Fraser jerked back, surprised and mildly affronted.

"Aye," he said, but then paused. "Aye, well . . . I do feel a bit queer," he admitted.

It was hard to tell in the uncertain light, but Roger thought he looked a good bit more than queer.

"Lie down for a bit, why don't you?" he suggested, trying to sound casual. "Sleep if ye can; I'll wake ye when the food's ready."

Jamie didn't argue, which alarmed Roger more than anything else so far. He curled himself into a drift of leaves, moving his wounded leg with a care that told Roger just how painful it was.

The snakemeat dripped and sizzled, and in spite of a slight distaste at the notion of eating snake, Roger felt his stomach rumble in anticipation; damned if it didn't smell like roasting chicken! Not for the first time, he reflected on the thin line that separated appetite from starvation; give the most finicky gourmand a day or two without food, and he'd be eating slugs and lizards without the least hesitation; Roger had, on the journey back from his surveying trip.

He kept an eye on Jamie; he didn't move, but Roger could see him shiver now and then, in spite of the now-leaping flames. His eyes were closed. His face looked red, but that might be only firelight—no telling his real color.

By the time the meat had cooked through, it was full dark. Roger fetched water, then heaped armloads of dried grass and wood on the fire, making the flames dance and crackle, higher than his head; if the other men were anywhere within a mile, they should see it.

Fraser roused himself with difficulty to eat. It was clear that he had no appetite, but he forced himself to chew and swallow, each bite a dogged effort. What was it? Roger wondered. Simple stubbornness? A notion of vengeance against the snake? Or perhaps some Highland superstition, the idea that consuming the reptile's flesh might be a cure for its bite?

"Did the Indians ken aught to do for snakebite?" Jamie asked abruptly, lending some credence to the last guess.

"Yes," Roger answered cautiously. "They had roots and herbs that they mixed with dung or hot cornmeal, to make a poultice."

"Did it work?" Fraser held a bit of meat in his hand, wrist drooping as though too tired to raise it to his mouth.

"I only saw it done twice. Once, it seemed to work perfectly—no swelling, no pain; the little girl was quite all right by evening of the same day. The other time—it didn't work." He had only seen the hide-wrapped body taken from the longhouse, not witnessed the grisly details of the death. Evidently he was going to get another chance to see the effects of snakebite up close, though.

Fraser grunted.

"And what would they do in your time?"

"Give you an injection of something called antivenin."

"An injection, aye?" Jamie looked unenthusiastic. "Claire did that to me, once. I didna like it a bit."

"Did it work?"

Jamie merely grunted in reply, and tore off another small morsel of meat between his teeth.

In spite of his worry, Roger wolfed his share of the meat, and the uneaten part of Jamie's meal as well. The sky spread black and starry overhead, and a cold wind moved through the trees, chilling hands and face.

He buried the remnants of the snake—all they needed now was for some large carnivore to show up, drawn by the smell of blood—and tended the fire, all the time listening for a shout from the darkness. No sound came but the moaning of wind and cracking of branches; they were alone.

Fraser had pulled off his hunting shirt in spite of the chill, and was sitting with his eyes closed, swaying slightly. Roger squatted next to him and touched his arm. Jesus! The man was blazing hot to the touch.

He opened his eyes, though, and smiled faintly. Roger held up a cup of water; Jamie nodded and took the cup, fumbling. The leg was grotesquely swollen below the knee, nearly twice its normal size. The skin showed irregular dark red blotches, as though some succubus had come to place its hungry mouth upon the flesh, then left unsatisfied.

Roger wondered uneasily whether he might, perhaps, be wrong. He'd been convinced that the past couldn't be changed; ergo, the time and manner of Fraser's death was set—some four years in the future. If it weren't for that certainty, though, he thought, he'd be bloody worried by the look of the man. Just how certain *was* he, after all?

"Ye could be wrong." Jamie had put down the cup and was regarding him with a steady blue gaze.

"About what?" he asked, startled to hear his thought spoken aloud. Had he been muttering to himself, not realizing it?

"About the changing. Ye thought it wasna possible to change history, ye said. But what if ye're wrong?"

Roger bent to poke the fire.

"I'm not wrong," he said firmly, as much to himself as to Fraser. "Think, man. You and Claire—you tried to stop Charles Stuart—change what he did—and ye couldn't. It can't be done."

"That's no quite right," Fraser objected. He leaned back, eyes half-hooded against the fire's brightness.

"What's not right?"

"It's true we failed to keep him from the Rising—but that didna depend only on us and on him; there were a good many other folk had to do wi' that. The chiefs who followed him, the damn Irishmen who flattered him—even Louis; him and his gold."

He waved a hand, dismissing it. "But that's neither here nor there. Ye said Claire and I couldna stop him—and it's true, we couldna stop the beginning. But we might have stopped the end."

"Culloden, you mean?" Roger stared into the fire, remembering dimly that long-ago day when Claire had first told him and Brianna the story of the stones—and Jamie Fraser. Yes, she had spoken of a last opportunity—the chance to prevent that final slaughter of the clans . . .

He glanced up at Fraser.

"By killing Charles Stuart?"

"Aye. If we had done so—but neither she nor I could bring ourselves to it." His eyes were nearly closed, but he turned his head restlessly, clearly uncomfortable. "I have wondered many times since, if that was decency—or cowardice."

"Or maybe something else," Roger said abruptly. "You don't know. If Claire had tried to poison him, I'm betting something would have happened; the dish would have spilled, a dog would have eaten it, someone else would have died—it wouldn't have made a difference!"

Fraser's eyes opened slowly.

"So ye think it's all destined, do ye? A man has no free choice at all?" He rubbed at his mouth with the back of his hand. "And when ye chose to come back, for Brianna, and then again, for her and the wean—it wasna your choice at all, aye? Ye were meant to do it?"

"I—" Roger stopped, hands clenched on his thighs. The smell of the *Gloriana*'s bilges seemed suddenly to rise above the scent of burning wood. Then he relaxed, and gave a short laugh. "Hell of a time to get philosophical, isn't it?"

"Aye, well," Fraser spoke quite mildly. "It's only that I may not have another time." Before Roger could expostulate, he went on. "If there is nay free choice . . . then there is neither sin nor redemption, aye?"

"Jesus," Roger muttered, shoving the hair back from his

forehead. "Come out with Hawkeye and end up under a tree with bloody Augustine of Hippo!"

Jamie ignored him, intent on his point.

"We chose—Claire and I. We wouldna do murder. We wouldna shed the blood of one man; but does the blood of Culloden then rest on us? We wouldna commit the sin—but does the sin find us, still?"

"Of course not." Roger rose to his feet, restless, and stood poking the fire. "What happened at Culloden—it wasn't your fault, how could it be? All the men who took part in that—Murray, Cumberland, all the chiefs . . . it was not any one man's doing!"

"So ye think it is all meant? We're doomed or saved from the moment of birth, and not a thing can change it? And you a minister's son!" Fraser gave a dry sort of chuckle.

"Yes," Roger said, feeling at once awkward and unaccountably angry. "I mean no, I don't think that. It's only . . . well, if something's already happened one way, how can it happen another way?"

"It's only you that thinks it's happened," Fraser pointed out.

"I don't think it, I know!"

"Mmphm. Aye, because ye've come from the other side of it; it's behind you. So perhaps *you* couldna change something—but I could, because it's still ahead of me?"

Roger rubbed a hand hard over his face.

"That makes—" he began, and then stopped. How could he say it made no sense? Sometimes he thought nothing in the world made sense anymore.

"Maybe," he said wearily. "God knows; I don't."

"Aye. Well, I suppose we'll find out soon enough."

Roger glanced sharply at him, hearing a strange note in his voice.

"What d'ye mean by that?"

"Ye think ye ken that I died three years from now," Fraser said calmly. "If I die tonight, then you're wrong, aye? What ye think happened won't have happened—so the past *can* be changed, aye?"

"You're not going to die!" Roger snapped. He glowered at Fraser, daring him to contradict.

"I'm pleased to hear it," Fraser said. "But I think I'll take a bit o' the whisky now. Draw the cork for me, aye? My fingers willna grasp it."

Roger's own hands were far from steady. Perhaps it was only the heat of Fraser's fever that made his own skin feel cold as he held the flask for his father-in-law to drink. He doubted that whisky was recommended for snakebite, but it didn't seem likely to make much difference now.

"Lie down," he said gruffly, when Jamie had finished. "I'll fetch a bit more wood."

He was unable to keep still; there was plenty of wood to hand, yet still he prowled the darkness, keeping just within sight of the blazing fire.

He had had a lot of nights like this; alone under a sweep of sky so vast that it made him dizzy to look up, chilled to the bone, moving to keep warm. The nights when he had wrestled with choice, too restless to lie in a comforting burrow of leaves, too tormented to sleep.

The choice had been clear then, but far from easy to make: Brianna on the one hand, and all that came with her; love and danger, doubt and fear. And on the other, surety. The knowledge of who and what he was—a certainty he had forsaken, for the sake of the woman who was his . . . and the child who might be.

He had chosen. Dammit, he *had* chosen! Nothing had forced him, he had made the choice himself. And if it meant remaking himself from the ground up, then he'd bloody well chosen that, too! And he'd chosen to kiss Morag, too. His mouth twisted at the thought; he'd had even less notion of the consequences of *that* small act.

Some small echo stirred in his mind, a soft voice far back in the shadows of his memory.

". . . what I was born does not matter, only what I will make of myself, only what I will become."

Who'd written that? he wondered. Montaigne? Locke? One of the bloody Enlightenment lads, them and their notions of destiny and the individual? He'd like to see what they had to say about time traveling! Then he remembered where he'd read it, and the marrow of his spine went cold.

"This is the grimoire of the witch, Geillis. It is a witch's

name, and I take it for my own; what I was born does not matter, only what I will make of myself, only what I will become."

"Right!" he said aloud, defiant. "Right, and you couldn't change things either, could you, Grandma?"

A sound came from the forest behind him, and the hair rose on the back of his neck before he recognized it; it wasn't laughter, as he'd thought at first—only a panther's distant cry.

She had, though, he thought suddenly. True, she'd not managed to make a king of Charles Stuart—but she'd done a good number of other things. And now he came to think on the matter . . . She and Claire had both done something guaranteed to change things; they'd borne children, to men of another time. Brianna . . . William Buccleigh—and when he thought of the effect those two births had had on his own life, let alone anything else . . .

That *had* to change things, didn't it? He sat down slowly on a fallen log, feeling the bark cold and damp under him. Yes, it did. To name one minor effect, his own bloody existence was the result of Geilie Duncan's taking charge of her destiny. If Geilie hadn't borne a child to Dougal MacKenzie . . . of course, she hadn't *chosen* to do that.

Did intention make any difference, though? Or was that exactly the point he'd been arguing with Jamie Fraser?

He got up and circled the fire quietly, peering into the shadows. Fraser was lying down, a humped shape in the darkness, very still.

He walked lightly, but his feet crunched on the needles. Fraser didn't twitch. His eyes were closed. The blotchiness had spread to his face. Roger thought his features had a thick, congested look, lips and eyelids slightly swollen. In the wavering light, it was impossible to tell whether he was still breathing.

Roger knelt and shook him, hard.

"Hey! Are ye still alive?" He'd meant to say it jokingly, but the fear in his voice was apparent to his own ears.

Fraser didn't move. Then one eye cracked open.

"Aye," he muttered. "But I'm no enjoying it."

Roger didn't leave again. He wiped Jamie's face with a wet cloth, offered more whisky—which was refused—then sat beside the recumbent form, listening for each rasping breath.

Much against his will, he found himself making plans, proceeding from one unwelcome assumption to the next. What if the worst happened? Against his will, he thought it possible; he had seen several people die who didn't look nearly as bad as Fraser did just now.

If the worst *should* happen, and the others not have returned, he would have to bury Jamie. He could neither carry the body nor leave it exposed; not with panthers or other animals nearby.

His eye roamed uneasily over the surroundings. Rocks, trees, brush—everything looked alien, the shapes half-masked by darkness, outlines seeming to waver and change in the flickering glow, the wind moaning past like a prowling beast.

There, maybe; the end of a half-fallen tree loomed jagged in the darkness, leaning at an angle. He could scrape a shallow trench, perhaps, then lever the tree and let it fall to cover the temporary grave . . .

He pressed his head hard against his knees.

"No!" he whispered. "Please, no!"

The thought of telling Bree, telling Claire, was a physical pain, stabbing him in chest and throat. It wasn't only them, either—what about Jem? What about Fergus and Marsali, Lizzie and her father, the Bugs, the Lindsays, the other families on the Ridge? They all looked to Fraser for confidence and direction; what would they do without him?

Fraser shifted, and groaned with the movement. Roger laid a hand on his shoulder, and he stilled.

Don't go, he thought, the unspoken words balled tight in his throat. *Stay with us. Stay with me.*

He sat for a long time, his hand resting on Fraser's shoulder. He had the absurd thought that he was somehow holding Fraser, keeping him anchored to the earth. If he held on 'til the sunrise, all would be well; if he lifted his hand, that would be the end.

The fire was burning low now, but he put off from moment to moment the necessity of tending it, unwilling to let go.

"MacKenzie?" It was no more than a murmur, but he bent at once.

"Aye, I'm here. Ye want water? A drop of whisky?" He was reaching for the cup even as he spoke, spilling water in his anxiety. Fraser took two swallows, then waved the cup away with a twitch of his hand.

"I dinna ken yet if ye're right or you're wrong," Fraser said. His voice was soft and hoarse, but distinct. "But if you're wrong, wee Roger, and I'm dying, there are things I must say to ye. I dinna want to leave it too late."

"I'm here," Roger repeated, not knowing what else to say.

Fraser closed his eyes, gathering strength, then brought his hands beneath him and rolled halfway over, ponderous and clumsy. He grimaced, and took a moment to catch his breath.

"Bonnet. I must tell ye what I've put in train."

"Aye?" For the first time, Roger felt something other than simple worry for Fraser's welfare.

"There is a man named Lyon—Duncan Innes will ken best how to find him. He works on the coast, buying from the smugglers who run the Outer Banks. He sought me out at the wedding, to see would I deal with him, over the whisky."

The plan in outline was simple enough; Jamie meant to send word—by what route, Roger had no notion—to this Lyon, indicating that he was willing to enter into business, provided that Lyon would bring Stephen Bonnet to a meeting, to prove that he had a man of the necessary reputation and skill to manage the transport up and down the coast.

"Necessary reputation," Roger echoed under his breath. "Aye, he's got that."

Fraser made a sound that might have been a laugh.

"He'll not agree that easily—he'll bargain and set terms—but he'll agree. Tell him ye've got enough whisky to make it worth his while—give him a barrel of the two-year-old to try, if ye must. When he sees what folk will pay for it, he'll be eager enough. The place—" He stopped, frowning, and breathed for a moment before going on.

"I'd thought to make it Wylie's Landing—but if it's you, ye should choose a place to your liking. Take the Lindsays with ye to guard your back, if they'll go. If not, find someone else; dinna go alone. And go ready to kill him at the first shot."

Roger nodded, swallowing heavily. Jamie's eyelids were swollen, but he looked up under them, his eyes glinting sharp in the firelight.

"Dinna let him get close enough to take ye with a sword," he said. "Ye've done well—but ye're not good enough to meet a man like Bonnet."

"And you are?" Roger couldn't stop himself from saying. He thought Fraser was smiling, but it was difficult to tell.

"Oh, aye," he said softly. "If I live." He coughed then, and lifted a hand, dismissing Bonnet for the moment.

"For the rest . . . watch Sinclair. He's a man to be used—he kens everything that passes in the district—but no a man to turn your back on, ever."

He paused, brow furrowed in thought.

"Ye can trust Duncan Innes and Farquard Campbell," he said. "And Fergus—Fergus will help ye, if he can. For the rest—" He shifted again and winced. "Go wary of Obadiah Henderson; he'll try ye. A-many of them will, and ye let them—but dinna let Henderson. Take him at the first chance—ye willna get another."

Slowly, with frequent pauses to rest, he went down the list of the names of the men on the Ridge, the inhabitants of Cross Creek, the prominent men of the Cape Fear valley. Characters, leanings, secrets, obligations.

Roger fought down panic, struggling to listen carefully, commit it all to memory, wanting to reassure Fraser, tell him to stop, to rest, that none of this was necessary—at the same time knowing it was more than necessary. There was war coming; it didn't take a time traveler to know it. If the welfare of the Ridge—of Brianna and Jemmy, of Claire—were to be left in Roger's inexperienced hands, he must take heed of every scrap of information that Fraser could give him.

Fraser's voice trailed off in hoarseness. Had he lost consciousness? The shoulder under Roger's hand was slack, inert. He sat quietly, not daring to move.

It wouldn't be enough, he thought, and a dull fear settled in the pit of his stomach, an aching dread that underlay the sharper pangs of grief. He couldn't do it. Christ, he couldn't even shoot a thing the size of a house! And now he was meant to step into Jamie Fraser's shoes? Keep order with fists and brain, feed a family with gun and knife, tread the tightrope of politics over a lighted powderkeg, tenants and family all balanced on his shoulders? Replace the man they called Himself? Not fucking likely, he thought bleakly.

Fraser's hand twitched suddenly. The fingers were swollen like sausages, the skin stretched red and shiny. Roger laid his free hand over it, and felt the fingers move, trying to curl around his own.

"Tell Brianna I'm glad of her," Fraser whispered. "Give my sword to the bairn."

Roger nodded, unable to speak. Then, realizing that Fraser couldn't see him, cleared his throat.

"Aye," he said gruffly. "I'll tell her." He waited, but Fraser said no more. The fire had burned very low, but the hand in his burned hot as embers. A gust of wind knifed past, whipping strands of his hair against his cheek, sending up a spray of sudden sparks from the fire.

He waited as long as he thought he dared, the cold night creeping past in lonely minutes. Then leaned close, so Fraser could hear him.

"Claire?" he asked quietly. "Is there anything ye'd have me tell her?"

He thought he'd waited too long; Fraser lay motionless for several minutes. Then the big hand stirred, half-closing swollen fingers; the ghost of a motion, grasping after time that slipped away.

"Tell her . . . I meant it."

91

DOMESTIC MANAGEMENT

"I'VE NEVER SEEN ANYTHING like that in my entire life." I leaned closer, peering. "That is absolutely *bizarre*."

"And you a healer half your life," Jamie muttered crossly. "Ye canna tell me they've no got snakes in your time."

"They haven't got many in downtown Boston. Besides, they wouldn't call out a surgeon to deal with a case of snakebite. Closest I came was when a keeper at the zoo was bitten by a king cobra—a friend of mine did the autopsy, and invited me to come and watch."

I refrained from saying that Jamie looked a lot worse at present than the subject of the autopsy had.

I set a hand gingerly on his ankle. The skin was puffy, hot and dry under my hand. It was also red. Bright red. The brilliant color extended from his feet up nearly to his rib cage; he looked as though he'd been dipped in boiling water.

His face, ears, and neck were also flushed the color of a plum tomato; only the pale skin of his chest had escaped, and even that was dotted with pinpricks of red. Beyond the lobsterlike coloration, the skin was peeling from his feet and hands, hanging in wispy shreds like Spanish moss.

I peered closely at his hip. Here, I could see that the redness was caused by a denser version of the rash on his chest; the stipple of tiny dots showed up clearly on the stretched skin over the ilial crest.

"You look like you've been roasted over a slow fire," I said, rubbing a finger over the rash in fascination. "I've never seen anything so red in my life." Not raised; I couldn't feel the individual spots, though I could see them at close range. Not a rash as such; I thought it must be petechiae, pinpoint hemorrhages under the skin. But so many of them . . .

"I shouldna say ye've much room to criticize, Sassenach," he said. Too weak to nod, he cut his eyes at my fingers—stained with huge blotches of yellow and blue.

"Oh, *damn*!" I leaped to my feet, threw the quilts hastily on top of him, and ran for the door. Distracted by Jamie's dramatic arrival, I had left a vat full of dyeing to mind itself in the side yard—and the water had been low. Christ, if it boiled dry and burned the clothes . . .

The hot reek of urine and indigo hit me in the face as I shot out the door. In spite of that, I drew a deep breath of relief, as I saw Marsali, red in the face with the effort of levering a dripping mass from the pot with the big wooden clothes-fork. I went hastily to help her, snatching the steaming garments one by one from the sopping pile and flinging them onto the blackberry bushes to dry.

"Thank goodness," I said, waving my scalded fingers in the air to cool them. "I was afraid I'd ruined the lot."

"Weel, they'll be a bit dark, maybe." Marsali wiped a hand across her face, plastering back the fine blond strands that escaped from her kerch. "If the weather keeps fine, though, ye can leave them in the sun to fade. Here, let's move the pot before it scorches!"

Crusts of indigo had already started to crackle and blacken in the bottom of the pot as we tipped it off the fire, and clouds of acrid smoke rose up around us.

"It's all right," Marsali said, coughing and fanning smoke from her face. "Leave it, Mother Claire; I'll fetch up water so it can soak. Ye'll need to see to Da, aye? I came down at once when I heard; is he verra poorly?"

"Oh, thank you, dear." I was overwhelmed with gratitude; the last thing I had time to do just now was to haul several buckets of water from the spring to soak the pot. I blew on my scalded fingers to cool them; the skin under the splotches of dye was nearly as red as Jamie's.

"I think he'll be all right," I assured her, suppressing my own fears. "He feels dreadful, and looks worse—I've never seen anyone look like that in all my born days—but if the wound doesn't get infected . . ." I crossed my sore fingers in superstitious prophylaxis.

"Ah, he'll do," Marsali said confidently. "Fergus said as they thought he was dead when they found him and Roger Mac, but by the time they crossed the second ridge, he was makin' terrible jokes about the snake, so they didna worry anymore."

I wasn't quite so sanguine myself, having seen the state of his injured leg, but I smiled reassuringly.

"Yes, I think he'll be fine. I'm just going to make an onion poultice and clean out the wound a bit. Go and see him, why don't you, while I fetch the onions?"

Luckily there were plenty of onions; I had pulled them two weeks before, when the first frost came, and dozens of knobbly braided strings hung in the pantry, fragrant and crackling when I brushed against them. I broke off six large onions and brought them into the kitchen to slice. My fingers were tingling, half-burned and stiff from handling the boiling clothes, and I worked slowly, not wanting to slice off a finger accidentally.

"Here, I'll do that, *a leannan*." Mrs. Bug took the knife out of my hand and dealt briskly with the onions. "Is it a poultice? Aye, that'll be the thing. A good onion poultice will mend anything." Still, a worried frown puckered her forehead as she glanced toward the surgery.

"Can I help, Mama?" Bree came in from the hallway, also looking worried. "Da looks awful; is he all right?"

"Ganda full?" Jem popped into the kitchen after his mother, less worried about his grandfather than interested in the knife Mrs. Bug was using. He dragged his little stool toward her, face purposeful under his coppery fringe. "Me do!"

I brushed the hair out of my face with the back of my hand, eyes watering fiercely from the onions.

"I think so." I sniffed and blotted my eyes. "How's Roger?"

"Roger's good." I could hear the small note of pride in her voice; Jamie had told her Roger had saved his life. Possibly he had. I just hoped it *stayed* saved.

"He's asleep," she added. Her mouth curved slightly as

she met my eyes, with complete understanding. If a man was in bed, at least you knew where he was. And that he was safe, for the moment.

"Jem! You leave Mrs. Bug alone!" She scooped him off his stool and whirled him away from the chopping board, feet kicking in protest. "Do you need anything, Mama?"

I rubbed a finger between my brows, considering.

"Yes, can you try to find me some maggots? I'll need them for Jamie's leg." I frowned, glancing out the window at the bright autumn day. "I'm afraid the frost has killed all the flies; I haven't seen one in days. Try the paddock, though; they'll lay eggs in the warm dung."

She made a brief face of distaste, but nodded, setting Jemmy down on the floor.

"Come on, pal, let's go find ickies for Grannie."

"Icky-icky-icky-icky!" Jemmy scampered after her, enchanted at the prospect.

I dropped the sliced onions into a bowl made from a hollowed gourd and scooped a little of the hot water from the cauldron into it. Then I left the onions to stew, and went back to the surgery. In the center of the room was a sturdy pine table, serving as examination table, dentist's chair, drug preparation surface, or auxiliary dining table, depending on medical exigencies and the number of dinner guests. At the moment, it was supporting the supine form of Jamie, scarcely visible under his heap of quilts and blankets. Marsali stood close to the table, head bent toward him as she held a cup of water for him to sip.

"You're sure you're all right, Da?" she said. One hand stole toward him, but she stopped, clearly afraid to touch him in his present condition.

"Oh, aye, I'll do." I could hear the deep fatigue in his voice, but a big hand rose slowly out from under the quilts to touch her cheek.

"Fergus did braw work," he said. "Kept the men together through the night, found me and Roger Mac in the morning, brought everyone home safe across the mountain. He's a fine sense of direction."

Marsali's head was still bent, but I saw her cheek curve in a smile.

"I did tell him so. He'll no give over berating himself for lettin' the beasts get away, though. Just one would ha' fed the whole Ridge for the winter, he said."

Jamie gave a small grunt of dismissal.

"Och, we'll manage."

It was plainly an effort for him to speak, but I didn't try to send Marsali away. Roger told me Jamie had been vomiting blood as they brought him back; I couldn't give him brandy or whisky to ease the pain, and I hadn't any laudanum. Marsali's presence might help to distract him from his wretchedness.

I opened the cupboard quietly and brought out the big lidded bowl where I kept my leeches. The pottery was cold, soothing to my scalded hands. I had a dozen or so big ones; somnolent black blobs, half-floating in their murky brew of water and cattail roots. I scooped three into a smaller bowl full of clear water, and set it by the brazier to warm.

"Wake up, lads," I said. "Time to earn your keep."

I laid out the other things I would need, listening to the murmured conversation behind me—Germain, baby Joan, a porcupine in the trees near Marsali and Fergus's cabin.

Coarse gauze for the onion poultice, the corked bottle with its mixture of alcohol and sterile water, the stoneware jars of dried goldenseal, coneflower, and comfrey. And the bottle of penicillin broth. I cursed silently, looking at the label on it. It was nearly a month old; caught up in the bear hunt and the autumn chores upon our return, I had not made a fresh batch for weeks.

It would have to do. Pressing my lips together, I rubbed the herbs between my hands, into the beechwood brewing cup, and with no more than a faint sense of self-consciousness, silently said the blessing of Bride over it. I'd take all the help I could get.

"Are the cut pine-fans ye find on the ground verra fresh?" Jamie asked, sounding slightly more interested in the porcupine than in Joan's new tooth.

"Aye, green and fresh. I ken weel enough he's up there, the wicked creature, but it's a great huge tree, and I canna spot him from the ground, let alone fire on him." Marsali was no more than a middling shot, but since Fergus couldn't fire a musket at all with his one hand, she did the family's hunting.

"Mmphm." Jamie cleared his throat with an effort, and she hastily gave him more water. "Take a bit o' salted pork rind from the pantry and rub it ower a stick of wood. Set it on the ground, not too far from the trunk of the tree, and let Fergus sit up to watch. Porcupines are gey fond o' the salt, and of grease; they'll smell it and venture down after dark. Once it's on the ground, ye needna waste shot; just bat it ower the head. Fergus can do that fine."

I opened the medical chest and frowned into the tray that held saws and scalpels. I took out the small, curve-bladed scalpel, its handle cool under my fingers. I would have to debride the wound—clean away the dead tissue, the shreds of skin and bits of leaf and cloth and dirt; the men had plastered his leg with mud and wrapped it with a filthy neckerchief. Then I could sprinkle the penicillin solution over the exposed surfaces; I hoped that would help.

"That would be grand," Marsali said, a little wistfully. "I've no had such a beast before, but Ian did tell me they were fine; verra fat, and the quills good for sewing and all manner o' things."

I bit my lip, looking at the other blades. The biggest was a folding saw, meant for field amputation, with a blade nearly eight inches long; I hadn't used it since Alamance. The thought of using it now made cold sweat spring out under my arms and inch down my sides—but I'd seen his leg.

"The meat's greasy," Jamie said, "but that's good—" He stopped abruptly as he shifted his weight, with a muffled groan as he moved his leg.

I could feel the steps of the process of amputation, echoing in the muscles of my hands and forearms; the tensile severing of skin and muscle, the grate of bone, the snap of tendon, and the slippery, rubbery, blood-squirting vessels, sliding away into the severed flesh like . . . snakes.

I swallowed. No. It wouldn't come to that. Surely not.

"Ye need fat meat. You're verra thin, *a muirninn*," Jamie said softly, behind me. "Too thin, for a woman breeding."

I turned round, swearing silently to myself once more. I'd

thought so, but had hoped I was wrong. Three babies in four years! And a one-handed husband, who couldn't manage the man's work of a homestead and wouldn't do the "women's work" of baby-minding and mash-brewing that he could handle.

Marsali made a small sound, half-snort, half-sob.

"How did you know? I havena even told Fergus yet."

"Ye should—though he kens it already."

"He told you?"

"No—but I didna think it only the indigestion that troubled him, whilst we were hunting. Now I see ye, I ken what it is that's weighin' on him."

I was biting my tongue hard enough to taste blood. Did the tansy oil and vinegar mixture I'd given her not work? Or the *dauco* seeds? Or, as I strongly suspected, had she just not bothered to use either one regularly? Well, too late for questions or reproaches. I caught her eye as she glanced up, and managed—I hoped—to look encouraging.

"Och," she said with a feeble smile. "We'll manage."

The leeches were stirring, bodies stretching slowly like animated rubber bands. I turned back the quilt over Jamie's leg, and pressed the leeches gently onto the swollen flesh near the wound.

"It looks nastier than it is," I said reassuringly, hearing Marsali's unguarded gasp at the sight. That was true, but the reality was nasty enough. The slashmarks were crusted black at the edges, but still gaped. Instead of the sealing and granulation of normal healing, they were beginning to erode, the exposed tissues oozing pus. The flesh around the wounds was hugely swollen, black and mottled with sinister reddish streaks.

I bit my lip, frowning as I considered the situation. I didn't know what kind of snake had bitten him—not that it made much difference, with no antivenin for treatment—but it had plainly had a powerful hemolytic toxin. Tiny blood vessels had ruptured and bled all over his body—internally, as well as externally—and larger ones, near the site of the wound.

The foot and ankle on the injured side were still warm and pink—or rather, red. That was a good sign, insofar as it meant the deeper circulation was intact. The problem was to improve circulation near the wound, enough to prevent a massive die-off and sloughing of tissue. The red streaks bothered me very much indeed, though; they *could* be only part of the hemorrhagic process, but it was more likely that they were the early signs of septicemia—blood poisoning.

Roger hadn't told me much of their night on the mountain, but he hadn't had to; I'd seen men before who'd sat through the dark with death beside them. If Jamie had lived a night and a day since then, chances were he would go on surviving—if I could control the infection. But in what condition?

I hadn't treated snakebite injuries before, but I'd seen sufficient textbook illustrations. The poisoned tissue would die and rot; Jamie could easily lose most of the muscle of his calf, which would cripple him permanently—or worse, the wound could turn gangrenous.

I stole a look at him under my lashes. He was covered with quilts and so ill he could barely move—and yet the lines of his body were drawn with grace and the promise of strength. I couldn't bear the thought of mutilating him—and yet I would do it if I must. To cripple Jamie . . . to leave him halt and half-limbed . . . the thought made my stomach clench and sweat break out on my blue-blotched palms.

Would he wish that himself?

I reached for the cup of water by Jamie's head and drained it myself. I wouldn't ask him. The choice was his by right—but he was mine, and I had made my choice. I wouldn't give him up, no matter what I had to do to keep him.

"You're sure you're all right, Da?" Marsali had been watching my face. Her eyes darted from me to Jamie and back, looking scared. I hastily tried to rearrange my features into a look of competent assurance.

Jamie had been watching me, too. One corner of his mouth turned up.

"Aye, well, I did think so. Now I'm none so sure, though."

"What's the matter? Do you feel worse?" I asked anxiously.

"No, I feel fine," he assured me—lying through his teeth. "It's only, when I've hurt myself, but it's all right, ye always scold like a magpie—but if I'm desperate bad, ye're tender as milk. Now, ye havena called me wicked names or uttered a word of reproach since I came home, Sassenach. Does that mean ye think I'm dyin'?"

One eyebrow rose in irony, but I could see a true hint of worry in his eyes. There were no vipers in Scotland; he couldn't know what was happening to his leg.

I took a deep breath and laid my hands lightly on his shoulders.

"Bloody man. Stepping on a snake! Couldn't you have looked where you were going?"

"Not whilst chasing a thousand-weight of meat downhill," he said, smiling. I felt a tiny relaxation in the muscles under my hands, and repressed the urge to smile back. I glared down at him instead.

"You scared bloody hell out of me!" That at least was sincere.

The eyebrow went up again.

"Maybe ye think I wasna frightened, too?"

"You're not allowed," I said firmly. "Only one of us can be scared at a time, and it's my turn."

That made him laugh, though the laughter was quickly succeeded by coughing and a shaking chill.

"Fetch me a hot stone for his feet," I said to Marsali, quickly tucking in the quilts around him. "And fill the teapot with boiling water and bring that, too."

She darted hastily toward the kitchen. I glanced toward the window, wondering whether Brianna was having any luck in finding maggots. They had no equal in cleaning pustulant wounds without damage to the healthy flesh nearby. If I was to save his leg as well as his life, I needed more help than Saint Bride's.

Wondering vaguely if there were a patron saint of maggots, I lifted the edge of the quilt and stole a quick look at my other invertebrate assistants. Good; I let out a small sigh of relief. The leeches worked fast; they were already swelling into plumpness, sucking away the blood that was flooding the tissues of his leg from ruptured capillaries. Without that pressure, healthy circulation *might* be restored in time to keep skin and muscle alive.

I could see his hand clenched on the edge of the table, and could feel the shuddering of his chill through my thighs, pressed against the wood.

I took his head between my hands; the skin of his cheeks was burning hot.

"You are *not* going to die!" I hissed. "You're not! I won't let you!"

"People keep sayin' that to me," he muttered, eyes closed and sunken with exhaustion. "Am I not allowed my own opinion?"

"No," I said. "You're not. Here, drink this."

I held the cup of penicillin broth to his lips, steadying it while he drank. He made faces, squinching his eyes shut, but swallowed it obediently enough.

Marsali had brought the teapot, brimful of boiling water. I poured most of it over the waiting herbs, and left them to steep, while I poured him a cup of cold water to wash away the taste of the penicillin.

He swallowed the water, eyes still shut, then lay back on the pillow.

"What is that?" he asked. "It tastes of iron."

"Water," I replied. "Everything tastes of iron; your gums are bleeding." I handed the empty water jug to Marsali and asked her to bring more. "Put honey in it," I said. "About one part honey to four parts water."

"Beef tea is what he needs," she said, pausing to look at him, brow furrowed with concern. "That's what my Mam did swear by, and her Mam before her. When a body's lost a deal o' blood, there's naught like beef tea."

I thought Marsali must be seriously worried; she seldom mentioned her mother in my hearing, out of a natural sense of tact. For once, though, bloody Laoghaire was right; beef tea would be an excellent thing—if we happened to have any fresh beef, which we didn't.

"Honey water," I said briefly, shooing her out of the room. I went to fetch reinforcements from the leech department, pausing to check on Brianna's progress through the front window.

She was out by the paddock, barefoot, skirts kilted up above the knee, shaking bits of horse dung from one foot. No luck so far, then. She saw me at the window and waved, then motioned to the ax that stood nearby, then to the edge of the wood. I nodded and waved back; a rotted log might be a possibility.

Jemmy was on the ground nearby, his leading-strings securely tied to the paddock fence. He certainly didn't need them to help him stay upright, but they did keep him from escaping while his mother was busy. He was industriously engaged in pulling down the remains of a dried gourd-vine that had grown up over the fence, crowing with delight as bits of crumbled leaf and the dried remains of frostbitten gourds showered over his flaming hair. His round face bore a look of determined intent, as he set about the task of getting a gourd the size of his head into his mouth.

A movement caught the corner of my eye; Marsali, bringing up water from the spring, to fill the crusted cauldron. No, she wasn't showing at all yet—Jamie was right, she was much too thin—but now that I knew, I could see the pallor in her face, and the shadows under her eyes.

Damn. Another glimpse of movement; Bree's long pale legs, flashing under her kilted skirts in the shadow of the big red spruce. And was *she* using the tansy oil? She was still nursing Jemmy, but that was no guarantee, not at his age . . .

I swung around at a sound behind me, to find Jamie climbing slowly back into his nest of quilts, looking like a great crimson sloth, my amputation saw in one hand.

"What the hell are you doing?"

He eased himself down, grimacing, and lay back on the pillow, breathing in long, deep gasps. The folded saw was clasped to his chest.

"I repeat," I said, standing menacingly over him, hands on my hips, "what the hell . . ."

He opened his eyes and lifted the saw an inch or so.

"No," he said positively. "I ken what ye're thinking, Sassenach, and I willna have it."

I took a deep breath, to keep my voice from quivering.

"You know I wouldn't, not unless I absolutely had to."

"No," he said again, and gave me a familiar look of obstinacy. No surprise at all that *he* never wondered who Jemmy looked like, I thought with sour amusement.

"You don't know what may happen—"

"I ken what's happening to my leg better than you do, Sassenach," he interrupted, then paused to breathe some more. "I dinna care."

"Maybe you don't, but *I* do!"

"I'm no going to die," he said firmly, "and I dinna wish to live with half a leg. I've a horror of it."

"Well, I'm not very keen on it myself. But if it's a choice between your leg and your life?"

"It's not."

"It damn well may be!"

"It won't." Age made not the slightest difference, I thought. Two years or fifty, a Fraser was a Fraser, and no rock was more stubborn. I rubbed a hand through my hair.

"All. Right," I said, between clenched teeth. "Give me the bloody thing and I'll put it away."

"Your word."

"My what?" I stared at him.

"Your word," he repeated, giving me back the stare, with interest. "I may be fevered and lose my wits. I dinna want ye to take my leg if I'm in no state to stop it."

"If you're in that sort of state, I'll have no choice!"

"Perhaps ye don't," he said evenly, "but I do. I've made it. Your word, Sassenach."

"You bloody, unspeakable, *infuriating*—"

His smile was startling, a white grin in the ruddy face. "If ye call me a Scot, Sassenach, then I *know* I'm going to live."

A shriek from outside kept me from answering. I swung round to the window, in time to see Marsali drop two pails of water on the ground. The water geysered over her skirt and shoes, but she paid no attention. I glanced hastily in the direction she was looking, and gasped.

It had walked casually through the paddock fence, snapping the rails as though they were matchsticks, and stood now in the midst of the pumpkin patch by the house, vines jerking in its mouth as it chewed. It stood huge and dark and wooly, ten feet away from Jemmy, who stared up at it with round, round eyes and open mouth, his gourd forgotten in his hands.

Marsali let out another screech, and Jemmy, catching her

terror, began to scream for his mother. I turned, and—feeling as though I were moving in slow motion, though I was surely not—snatched the saw neatly from Jamie's hand, went out the door, and headed for the yard, thinking as I did so that buffalo looked so much smaller in zoos.

As I cleared the stoop—I must have leaped; I had no memory of the steps—Brianna came out of the woods. She was running silently, ax in her hand, and her face was set, inward and intent. I had no time to call out before she reached it.

She had drawn back the ax, still running, swung it in an arc as she took the last step, and brought it down with all her strength, just behind the huge beast's ears. A thin spray of blood flew up and spattered on the pumpkins. It bellowed and lowered its head, as though to charge forward.

Bree dodged to one side, dived for Jemmy, was on her knees, tugging at the strings that bound him to the fence. From the corner of my eye, I could see Marsali, yelling Gaelic prayers and imprecations as she seized a newly dyed petticoat from the blackberry bushes.

I had somehow unfolded the saw as I ran; I cut Jemmy's strings with two swipes, then was on my feet and running back across the dooryard. Marsali had thrown the petticoat over the buffalo's head; it stood bewildered, shaking its head and swaying to and fro, blood showing black on the yellow-green of the fresh-dyed indigo.

It stood as tall as I at the shoulder, and it smelt strange; dusty and warm, gamey but oddly familiar, with a barn-smell, like a cow. It took a step, another, and I dug my fingers into its wool, holding on. I could feel the tremors running through it; they shook me like an earthquake.

I had never done it, but felt as though I had, a thousand times. Dreamlike and sure, I ran a hand under slobbering lips, felt warm breath blow down my sleeve. The great pulse throbbed in the angle of the jaw; I could see it in my mind, the big meaty heart and its pumping blood, warm in my hand, cold against my cheek where it pressed the sodden petticoat.

I drew the saw across the throat, cut hard, and felt in hands and forearms the tensile severing of skin and muscle, the grate of bone, the snap of tendon, and the slippery, rubbery, blood-squirting vessels, sliding away.

The world shook. It shifted and slid, and landed with a thud. When I came to myself, I was sitting in the middle of my dooryard, one hand still twisted in its hair, one leg gone numb beneath the weight of the buffalo's head, my skirts plastered to my thighs, hot and stinking, sodden with its blood.

Someone said something and I looked up. Jamie was on his hands and knees on the stoop—mouth open, stark naked. Marsali sat on the ground, legs splayed out in front of her, soundlessly opening and closing her mouth.

Brianna stood over me, Jemmy held against her shoulder. Terror forgotten, he leaned far over, looking down in curiosity at the buffalo.

"Ooo!" he said.

"Yes," I said. "Very well put."

"You're all right, Mama?" Bree asked, and I realized she had asked several times before. She put down a hand and rested it gently on my head.

"I don't know," I said. "I think so."

I took her hand and laboriously worked my leg free, leaning on her as I stood up. The same tremors that had gone through the buffalo were going through her—and me—but they were fading. She took a deep breath, looking down at the massive body. Lying on its side, it rose nearly as high as her waist. Marsali came to stand beside us, shaking her head in awe at its size.

"Mother of God, how on earth are we going to butcher *that*?" she said.

"Oh," I said, and dragged a trembling hand through my hair. "I suppose we'll manage."

92

I GET BY WITH A LITTLE HELP FROM MY FRIENDS

I LEANED MY FOREHEAD against the cool glass of my surgery window, blinking at the scene outside. Exhaustion lent the scene in the dooryard an extra tinge of surrealism—not that it needed much extra.

The sun had all but set, flaming gold in the last ragged leaves of the chestnut trees. The spruces stood black against the dying glow, as did the gibbet in the center of the yard, and the grisly remains that swung from it. A bonfire had been lit near the blackberry bushes, and silhouetted figures darted everywhere, disappearing in and out of flames and shadow. Some attacked the hanging carcass, armed with knives and hatchets; others plodded laden away, carrying slabs of flesh and buckets of fat. Near the fire, the skirted bell-shapes of women showed, bending and reaching in silent ballet.

Dark as it was, I could pick Brianna's tall, pale figure out of the horde of demons hacking at the buffalo—keeping order, I thought. Before being forcibly returned to the surgery, Jamie had estimated the buffalo's weight at something between eighteen hundred and two thousand pounds. Brianna had nodded at this, handed Jemmy to Lizzie, then walked slowly around the carcass, squinting in deep thought.

"Right," she'd said, and as soon as the men began to appear from their homesteads, half-dressed, unshaven, and wild-eyed with excitement, had issued cool directions for the cutting of logs and the building of a pulley-frame capable of hoisting and supporting a ton of meat.

The men, disgruntled at not being in on the kill, hadn't

been inclined to pay attention to her at first. Brianna, however, was large, vivid, strongly-spoken—and stubborn.

"Whose stroke is that?" she'd demanded, staring down Geordie Chisholm and his sons as they started toward the carcass, knives in hand. She pointed at the deep gash across the neck, then wiped her hand slowly down her sleeve, drawing attention to the splashed blood there. "Or that?" One long bare foot pointed delicately at the severed throat, and the pool of blood that soaked the dooryard. My stockings lay at the edge of the congealing puddle where I had stripped them off, limp red rags, but recognizably feminine.

Watching from the window, I had seen more than one face glance toward the house, frowning with the realization that Brianna was Himself's daughter—a fact the wise kept well in mind.

It was Roger who had turned the tide for her, though, with a cool stare that brought the Lindsay brothers to heel behind him, axes in hand.

"It's her kill," he said, in his husking croak. "Do what she says." He squared his shoulders and gave the other men a look that strongly suggested there should be no further controversy.

Seeing this, Fergus had shrugged and bent to seize the beast—one-handed—by its spindly tail.

"Where will you have us put it, Madame?" he asked politely. The men had all laughed, and then with sheepish glances and shrugs of resignation, reluctantly pitched in as well, following her directions.

Brianna had given Roger a look of surprise, then gratitude, and then—the bit firmly between her teeth—had taken charge of the whole enterprise, with remarkable results. It was barely nightfall, and the butchery was almost done, the meat distributed to all the households on the Ridge. She knew everyone, knew the number of mouths in each cabin, and parceled out the meat and sweetbreads as they were cut. Not even Jamie could have managed it better, I thought, feeling a warm swell of pride in her.

I glanced across at the table, where Jamie lay swaddled in blankets. I had wanted to move him upstairs to his bed, but he had insisted on staying downstairs, where he could hear—if not see—what was going on.

"They're nearly finished with the butchering," I said, coming to lay a hand on his head. Still flushed and blazing. "Brianna's done a wonderful job of it," I added, to distract both of us.

"Has she?" His eyes were half-open, but fixed in a fever-stare; that dream-soaked daze where shadows writhe in the wavering hot air over a fire. As I spoke, though, he came slowly back from wherever he had been, and his eyes met mine, heavy-lidded but clear, and he smiled faintly. "That's good."

The hide had been pegged out to dry, the enormous liver sliced for quick searing, intestines taken to soak for cleaning, haunches to the shed for smoking, strips of meat taken off for drying into jerky, fat for rendering into suet and soap. Once stripped bare, the bones would be boiled for soup, salvaged for buttons.

The prized hooves and horns sat bloodily discreet on my counter, brought in by Murdo Lindsay. Tacit trophies, I supposed; the eighteenth-century equivalent of two ears and a tail. I had got the gallbladder, too, though that was simply by default; no one wanted it, but it was popularly assumed that I must have some medicinal use for almost any natural object. A greenish thing the size of my fist, it sat oozing in a dish, looking rather sinister next to the set of detached and muddy hooves.

Everyone on the Ridge had come at the news—even Ronnie Sinclair, from his cooper's shop at the foot of the slope—and little remained of the buffalo now, save a rack of scavenged bones. I caught the faint odor of roasting meat, of burning hickory wood and coffee, and pushed up the window all the way to let in the appetizing smells.

Laughter and the crackle of fire came in on a gust of cold wind. It was warm in the surgery now, and the cold air from the window felt good against my flushed cheeks.

"Are you hungry, Jamie?" I asked. I was starving myself; though I hadn't realized it 'til I smelled food. I closed my eyes and inhaled, buoyed up by the hearty scent of liver and onions.

"No," he said, sounding drowsy. "I dinna fancy anything."

"You should eat a bit of soup, if you can, before you fall asleep." I turned and smoothed the hair off his face, frowning a little as I looked at him. The flush had faded a bit, I thought—hard to tell for sure in the uncertain light of fire and candle. We had got enough honey-water and herb tea into him so that his eyes were no longer sunken with dehydration, but the bones of cheek and jaw were still prominent; he hadn't eaten in more than forty-eight hours, and the fever was consuming an immense amount of energy, consuming his tissues.

"D'ye need more hot water, ma'am?" Lizzie appeared in the doorway, looking more disheveled than usual, Jemmy clutched in her arms. She had lost her kerch and her fine, fair hair had escaped from its bun; Jemmy had a good handful of it in his chubby fist, and was yanking fretfully at it, making her squint with each yank.

"Mama-mama-mama," he said, in an escalating whine that made it obvious that he'd been saying the same thing for quite some time. "Mama-mama-MAMA!"

"No, I have enough; thank you, Lizzie. Stop that, young man," I said, getting hold of Jemmy's hand and forcibly unpeeling his fat little fingers. "We don't pull hair." There was a small chuckle from the nest of blankets on the table behind me.

"Ye'd never ken it to look at ye, Sassenach."

"Mm?" I turned my head and stared blankly at him for a moment, then followed the direction of his glance with my hand. Sure enough, my own cap had somehow disappeared, and my hair was standing out like a bramblebush. Attracted by the word "hair," Jemmy abandoned Lizzie's fine locks, leaned over, and grabbed a fistful of mine.

"Mama-mama-mama-mama . . ."

"Foo," I said, crossly, reaching to disentangle him. "Let go, you little fiend. And why aren't you in bed, anyway?"

"MAMA-MAMA-MAMA . . ."

"He wants his mother," Lizzie explained, rather redundantly. "I've put him in his cot a dozen times, but he'll be climbin' out again, the instant my back's turned. I couldna keep him—"

The outer door opened, letting in a strong draft that made the embers in the brazier glow and smoke, and I heard the pad of bare feet on the oak boards in the hall.

I'd heard the expression, "blood to the eyebrows" before, but I hadn't seen it all that often, at least not outside the confines of a battlefield. Brianna's eyebrows were invisible, being red enough to have blended into the mask of gore over her face. Jemmy took a good look at her, and turned down his mouth in an expression of doubtful distress, just this side of outright wails.

"It's me, baby," she reassured him. She reached a hand toward him, but stopped short of touching him. He didn't cry, but burrowed his face into Lizzie's shoulder, rejecting the notion that this apocalyptic vision had anything at all to do with the mother he'd been fussing for a few minutes earlier.

Brianna ignored both her son's rejection and the fact that she was leaving footprints composed in equal parts of mud and blood all over the floor.

"Look," she said, holding out a closed fist to me. Her hands were caked with dried blood, her fingernails crescents of black. She reverently uncurled her fingers to show me her treasure; a handful of tiny, wriggling white worms that made my heart give a quick bump of excitement.

"Are they the right kind?" she asked anxiously.

"I think so; let me check." I hastily dumped the wet leaves from the herb tea onto a small plate, to give the worms a temporary refuge. Brianna gently deposited them on the mangled foliage and carried the plate to the counter where my microscope stood, as though the plate bore specks of gold dust, rather than maggots.

I picked up one of the worms with the edge of a fingernail, and deposited it on a glass slide, where it writhed unhappily in a futile search for nourishment. I beckoned to Bree to bring me another candle.

"Nothing but a mouth and a gut," I muttered, tilting the mirror to catch the light. It was much too dim for microscopic work, but might just be sufficient for this. "Voracious little buggers."

I held my breath, peering through the fragile eyepiece, straining to see. Ordinary blow-fly and flesh-fly larvae had one line visible on the body; screw-worm larvae had two. The lines were faint, invisible to the naked eye, but very important. Blow-fly maggots ate carrion, and only carrion—dead, decaying flesh. Screw-worm larvae burrowed into the living flesh, and consumed the live muscle and blood of their host. Nothing I wanted to insert into a fresh wound!

I closed one eye, to let the other adapt to the moving shadows in the eyepiece. The dark cylinder of the maggot's body writhed, twisting in all directions at once. One line was clearly visible. Was that another? I squinted until my eye began to water, but could see no more. Letting out the breath I'd been holding, I relaxed.

"Congratulations, Da," Brianna said, moving to Jamie's side. He opened one eye, which passed with a marked lack of enthusiasm down Brianna's figure. Stripped to a knee-length shift for butchering, she was splotched from head to toe with gouts of dark blood, and the muslin had stuck to her in random patches.

"Oh, aye?" he said. "For what?"

"The maggots. You did it," she explained. She opened her other hand, revealing a misshapen blob of metal—a squashed rifle-ball. "The maggots were in a wound in the hindquarters—I dug this out of the hole behind them."

I laughed, as much from relief as from amusement.

"Jamie! You shot it in the arse?"

Jamie's mouth twitched a little.

"I didna think I'd hit it at all," he said. "I was only trying to turn the herd toward Fergus." He reached up a slow hand and took the ball, rolling it gently between his fingers.

"Maybe you should keep it for good luck," Brianna said. She spoke lightly, but I could see the furrow between her invisible brows. "Or to bite on while Mama's working on your leg."

"Too late," he said, with a very faint smile.

It was then she caught sight of the small leather strip that lay on the table near his head, marked with overlapping crescents—the deep imprints of Jamie's teeth. She glanced at me, appalled. I lifted one shoulder slightly. I had spent more than an hour cleaning the wound in his leg, and it hadn't been easy on either of us.

I cleared my throat, and turned back to the maggots. From the corner of my eye, I saw Bree lay the back of her hand gently against Jamie's cheek. He turned his head and kissed her knuckles, blood notwithstanding.

"Dinna fash, lassie," he said. His voice was faint, but steady. "I'm fine."

I opened my mouth to say something, but caught sight of Bree's face and bit my tongue instead. She'd been working hard, and still had Jemmy and Roger to care for; she needn't worry for Jamie, too—not yet.

I dropped the maggots into a small bowl of sterile water and swished them rapidly round, then dumped them back on the bed of wet leaves.

"It won't hurt," I said to Jamie, trying to reassure myself as much as him.

"Oh, aye," he said, with an unbecoming cynicism. "I've heard *that* one before."

"Actually, she's right," said a soft, rasping voice behind me. Roger had already had a quick wash; his dark hair lay damp against his collar, and his clothes were clean. Jemmy, half asleep, lay against his father's shoulder, dreamily sucking his thumb. Roger came over to the table to look down at Jamie.

"How is it, man?" he said quietly.

Jamie moved his head on the pillow, dismissive of discomfort.

"I'll do."

"That's good." To my surprise, Roger grasped Jamie's shoulder in a brief gesture of comfort. I'd never seen him do that before, and once more I wondered just what had passed between them on the mountain.

"Marsali's bringing up some beef tea—or rather, buffalo tea—for him," Roger said, frowning slightly as he looked at me. "Maybe you'd best be having some, too."

"Good idea," I said. I closed my eyes briefly and took a deep breath.

Only when I sat down did I realize that I had been on my feet since the early morning. Pain outlined every bone in my feet and legs, and I could feel the ache where I had broken my left tibia, a few years before. Duty called, though.

"Well, time and tide wait for no maggot," I said, struggling back to my feet. "Best get on with it."

Jamie gave a small snort and stretched, then relaxed, his long body reluctantly readying itself. He watched with resignation while I fetched the plate of maggots and my forceps, then reached for the leather strip by his head.

"You'll not need that," Roger said. He pulled up another stool and sat down. "It's true what she said, the wee beasts don't hurt."

Jamie snorted again, and Roger grinned at him.

"Mind," he said, "they tickle something fierce. That's only if ye think about it, though. If ye can keep all thought of them out of your mind, why, there's nothing to it."

Jamie eyed him.

"Ye're a great comfort, MacKenzie," he said.

"Thanks," said Roger, with a husk of a laugh. "Here, I brought ye something." He leaned forward and deposited a drowsy Jemmy into Jamie's arms. The little boy uttered a small squawk of surprise, then relaxed as Jamie's arms tightened about him in reflex. One chubby hand swung free, seeking anchorage, then found it.

"Hot," he murmured, smiling beatifically. Fist twined in Jamie's ruddy hair, he sighed deeply and went soundly to sleep on his grandfather's fever-warm chest.

Jamie narrowed his eyes at me as I picked up the forceps. Then he gave a slight shrug, laid his stubbled cheek gently against Jemmy's silk-bright hair, and closed his own eyes, though the tenseness in his features was a marked contrast to the rounded peace of Jemmy's.

It couldn't have been easier; I simply lifted away the fresh onion poultice, and tucked the maggots one by one into the ulcerated slashmarks on Jamie's calf. Roger circled behind me to watch.

"It looks almost like a leg again," he said, sounding surprised. "I never thought it would."

I smiled, though I didn't look round at him, too intent on my delicate work. "Leeches are very effective," I said. "Though your rather crude knifework may have been useful, too—you left big enough holes that the pus and fluid were able to drain; that helped."

It was true; while the limb was still hot and grossly discolored, the swelling had subsided markedly. The long stretch of shinbone and the delicate arch of foot and ankle were once more visible. I was under no illusion about the dangers still remaining—infection, gangrene, sloughing—but nonetheless, my heart grew lighter. It was recognizably Jamie's leg.

I pinched another maggot just behind the head with my forceps, careful not to crush it. I lifted the edge of the skin with the slender probe I held in my other hand, and deftly inserted the tiny, wiggling thing into the small pocket thus provided—trying to ignore the nastily spongy feel of the flesh under my fingers, and my memory of Aaron Beardsley's foot.

"Done," I said, a moment later, and gently replaced the poultice. Stewed onion and garlic wrapped in muslin and soaked with penicillin broth would keep the wounds moist and draining. Renewed every hour or so, I hoped that the warmth of the poultices would also encourage circulation in the leg. And then a dressing of honey, to prevent any further bacterial invasions.

Concentration alone had kept my hands steady. Now it was done, and there was nothing more to do but wait. The saucer of wet leaves rattled against the counter as I set it down.

I didn't think I had ever been so tired before.

93

CHOICES

BETWEEN THEM, Roger and Mr. Bug got Jamie up to our bedroom. I hadn't wanted to disturb his leg by moving him from the surgery, but he insisted.

"I dinna want ye to be sleeping on the floor down here,

Sassenach," he said, when I protested. He smiled at me. "Ye should be in your bed—but I ken ye willna leave me alone, and so that means I must go and be in it, too, aye?"

I would have argued further, but in all truth, I was so tired that I wouldn't have complained much if he had insisted we both sleep in the barn.

Once he was settled, though, my doubts returned.

"I'll joggle your leg," I said, hanging up my gown on one of the pegs. "I'll just make up a pallet by the fire here, and—"

"You will not," he said definitely. "Ye'll sleep wi' me." He lay back on the pillows, eyes closed, his hair an auburn tumble against the linen. His skin had begun to fade; it wasn't quite so red. It was, however, alarmingly pale where the tiny hemorrhages didn't stain it.

"You would argue on your deathbed," I said crossly. "You don't *have* to be constantly in charge, you know. You *could* lie still and let other people take care of things, for once. What do you think would happen, if—"

He opened his eyes and gave me a dark blue look.

"Sassenach," he said softly.

"What?"

"I would like ye to touch me . . . without hurting me. Just once before I sleep. Would ye mind much?"

I stopped and drew breath, terribly disconcerted at the realization that he was right. Caught up in the emergency and worry of his condition, everything I had done to him during the day had been painful, intrusive, or both. Marsali, Brianna, Roger, Jemmy—all of them had touched him in gentleness, offering sympathy and comfort.

And I—I had been so terrified at the possibility of what might happen, of what I might be forced to do, that I had taken no time, allowed no room for gentleness. I looked away for a moment, blinking until the tears retreated. Then I stood and walked over to the bed, bent, and kissed him, very softly.

I stroked the hair back from his forehead, smoothed his brows with my thumb. Arch Bug had shaved him; the skin of his cheek was smooth, hot against the side of my hand. His bones were hard under his skin, framing his strength—and yet he seemed suddenly fragile. I felt fragile, too.

"I want ye to sleep beside me, Sassenach," he whispered.

"All right." I smiled at him, my lips trembling only a little. "Let me brush out my hair."

I sat down in my shift, shook out my hair, and took up the brush. He watched me, not speaking, but with a faint smile on his lips, as I worked. He liked to watch me brush my hair; I hoped it was as soothing to him as it was to me.

There were noises downstairs, but they were muffled, safely distant. The shutters were ajar; firelight flickered against the glass of the window from the dying bonfire in the yard. I glanced at the window, wondering if I ought to close the shutters.

"Leave them, Sassenach," he murmured from the bed. "I like to hear the talk." The sound of voices from outside *was* comforting, rising and falling, with small bursts of laughter.

The sound of the brush was soft and regular, like surf on sand, and I felt the stress of the day lessen slowly, as though I could brush all the anxieties and dreads out of my hair as easily as tangles and bits of pumpkin vine. When at last I put down the brush and rose, Jamie's eyes were closed.

I knelt to smoor the fire, rose to blow out the candle, and went at last to bed.

I eased myself gently into the bed beside him, not to jostle. He lay turned away from me, on his side, and I turned toward him, echoing the curve of his body with my own, careful not to touch him.

I lay very quietly, listening. All the house sounds had settled to their night-time rhythm; the hiss of the fire and the rumble of wind in the flue, the sudden startling *crack!* of the stairs, as though some unwary foot had stepped upon a riser. Mr. Wemyss's adenoidal snoring reached me, reduced to a soothing buzz by the thickness of the intervening doors.

There were still voices outside, muffled by distance, disjointed with drink and the lateness of the hour. All jovial, though; no sound of hostility or incipient violence. I didn't really care, though. The inhabitants of the Ridge could hammer each other senseless and dance on the remains, for all I cared. All my attention was focused on Jamie.

His breathing was shallow but even, his shoulders relaxed. I didn't want to disturb him; he needed rest above all things. At the same time, I ached to touch him. I wanted to reassure myself that he was here, alive beside me—but I also needed badly to know how things went with him.

Was he feverish? Had the incipient infection in his leg blossomed in spite of the penicillin, spreading poison through his blood?

I moved my head cautiously, bringing my face within an inch of his shirt-covered back, and breathed in, slow and deep. I could feel the warmth of him on my face, but couldn't tell through the linen nightshirt just how hot he really was.

He smelt faintly of the woods, more strongly of blood. The onions in the dressing gave off a bitter tang; so did his sweat.

I inhaled again, testing the air. No scent of pus. Too early for the smell of gangrene, even if the rot was beginning, invisible under the bandages. I thought there was a strange scent about his skin, though; something I hadn't smelled before. Necrosis of the tissue? Some breakdown product of the snake's venom? I blew a short breath through my nose and took in a fresh one, deeper.

"Do I stink verra badly?" he inquired.

"Uk!" I said, startled into biting my tongue, and he quivered slightly, in what I took to be suppressed amusement.

"Ye sound like a wee truffle-pig, Sassenach, snortling away back there."

"Oh, indeed," I said, a bit crossly. I touched the tender spot on my tongue. "Well, at least you're awake. How do you feel?"

"Like a pile of moldy tripes."

"Very picturesque," I said. "Can you be a trifle more specific?" I put a hand lightly on his side, and he let his breath out in a sound like a small moan.

"Like a pile of moldy tripes . . ." he said, and pausing to breathe heavily, added, " . . . .with *maggots*."

"You'd joke on your deathbed, wouldn't you?" Even as I said it, I felt a tremor of unease. He *would*, and I hoped this wasn't it.

"Well, I'll try, Sassenach," he murmured, sounding drowsy. "But I'm no really at my best under the circumstances."

"Do you hurt much?"

"No. I'm just . . . tired." He sounded as though he were in fact too exhausted to search for the proper word, and had settled for that one by default.

"Little wonder if you are. I'll go and sleep somewhere else, so you can rest." I made to throw back the covers and rise, but he stopped me, raising one hand slightly.

"No. No, dinna leave me." His shoulder fell back toward me, and he tried to lift his head from the pillow. I felt still more uneasy when I realized that he was too weak even to turn over by himself.

"I won't leave you. Maybe I should sleep in the chair, though. I don't want to—"

"I'm cold," he said softly. "I'm verra cold."

I pressed my fingers lightly just under his breastbone, seeking the big abdominal pulse. His heartbeat was rapid, shallower than it should have been. He wasn't feverish. He didn't just feel cold, he *was* cold to the touch, his skin chilled and his fingers icy. I found that very alarming.

No longer shy, I cuddled close against him, my breasts squashing softly against his back, cheek resting on his shoulder blade. I concentrated as hard as I could on generating body heat, trying to radiate warmth through my skin and into his. So often he had enfolded me in the curve of his body, sheltering me, giving me the warmth of his big body. I wished passionately that I were larger, and could do the same for him now; as it was, I could do no more than cling to him like a small, fierce mustard plaster, and hope I had the same effect.

Very gently, I found the hem of his shirt and pulled it up, then cupped my hands to fit the rounds of his buttocks. They tightened slightly in surprise, then relaxed.

It occurred to me to wonder just why I felt I must lay hands on him, but I didn't trouble my mind with it; I had had the feeling many times before, and had long since given up worrying that it wasn't scientific.

I could feel the faintly pebbled texture of the rash upon his skin, and the thought came unbidden of the lamia. A creature smooth and cool to the touch, a shape-shifter, passionately venomous, its nature infectious. A swift bite and the snake's poison spreading, slowing his heart, chilling his warm blood; I could imagine tiny scales rising under his skin in the dark.

I forcibly repressed the thought, but not the shudder that went with it.

"Claire," he said softly. "Touch me."

I couldn't hear his heartbeat. I could hear mine; a thick, muffled sound in the ear pressed to the pillow.

I slid my hand over the slope of his belly, and more slowly down, fingers parting the coarse curly tangle, dipping low to cup the rounded shapes of him. What heat he had was here.

I stroked him with a thumb and felt him stir. The breath went out of him in a long sigh, and his body seemed to grow heavier, sinking into the mattress as he relaxed. His flesh was like candle wax in my hand, smooth and silky as it warmed.

I felt very odd; no longer frightened, but with all my senses at once preternaturally acute and yet . . . peaceful. I was no longer conscious of any sounds save Jamie's breathing and the beating of his heart; the darkness was filled with them. I had no conscious thought, but seemed to act purely by instinct, reaching down and under, seeking the heart of his heat in the center of his being.

Then I was moving—or we were moving together. One hand reached down between us, up between his legs, my fingertips on the spot just behind his testicles. My other hand reached over, around, moving with the same rhythm that flexed my thighs and lifted my hips, thrusting against him from behind.

I could have done it forever, and felt that perhaps I did. I had no sense of time passing, only of a dreamy peace, and that slow, steady rhythm as we moved together in the dark. Somewhere, sometime, I felt a steady pulsing, first in the one hand, then in both. It melded with the beat of his heart.

He sighed, long and deep, and I felt the air rush from my own lungs. We lay silent and passed gently into unconsciousness, together.

I WOKE FEELING utterly peaceful. I lay still, without thought, listening to the thrum of blood through my veins, watching the drift of sunlit particles in the beam of light that fell through the half-opened shutters. Then I remembered, and flung myself over in bed, staring.

His eyes were closed, and his skin was the color of old ivory. His head was turned slightly away from me, so that the cords of his neck stood out, but I couldn't see any pulse in his throat. He was still warm, or at least the bedclothes were still warm. I sniffed the air, urgently. The room was fetid with the scent of onions and honey and fever-sweat, but no stink of sudden death.

I clapped a hand on the center of his chest, and he jerked, startled, and opened his eyes.

"You *bastard*," I said, so relieved to feel the rise of his chest as he drew breath that my voice trembled. "You tried to die on me, didn't you?"

His chest rose and fell, rose and fell, under my hand, and my own heart jerked and shuddered, as though I had been pulled back at the last moment from an unexpected precipice.

He blinked at me. His eyes were heavy, still clouded with fever.

"It didna take much effort, Sassenach," he said, his voice soft and husky from sleep. "Not dying was harder."

He made no pretense of not understanding me. In the light of day, I saw clearly what exhaustion and the aftereffects of shock had stopped me seeing the night before. His insistence on his own bed. The open shutters, so he could hear the voices of his family below, his tenants outside. And me beside him. He had, very carefully, and without saying a word to me, decided how and where he wanted to die.

"You thought you were dying when we brought you up here, didn't you?" I asked. My voice sounded more bewildered than accusing.

It took him a moment to answer, though he didn't look hesitant. It was more as though he was looking for the proper words.

"Well, I didna ken for sure, no," he said slowly. "Though I did feel verra ill." His eyes closed, slowly, as though he were too tired to keep them open. "I still do," he added, in a detached sort of voice. "Ye needna worry, though—I've made my choice."

"What on earth do you mean by that?"

I groped beneath the covers, and found his wrist. He *was* warm; hot again, in fact, and with a pulse that was too fast, too shallow. Still, it was so different from the deathly chill I had felt in him the night before that my first reaction was relief.

He took a couple of deep breaths, then turned his head and opened his eyes to look at me.

"I mean I could have died last night."

He could, certainly—and yet that wasn't what he meant. He made it sound like a conscious—

"What do you mean you've made your choice? You've decided not to die, after all?" I tried to speak lightly, but it wasn't working very well. I remembered all too well that odd sense of timeless stillness that had surrounded us.

"It was verra strange," he said. "And yet it wasna strange at all." He sounded faintly surprised.

"I think," I said carefully, keeping a thumb on his pulse, "you'd better tell me just what happened."

He actually smiled at that, though the smile was more in his eyes than his lips. Those were dry, and painfully cracked in the corners. I touched his lips with a finger, wanting to go and fetch some soothing ointment for him, some water, some tea—but I put aside the impulse, steeling myself to stay and hear.

"I dinna really know, Sassenach—or rather, I do, but I canna think quite how to say it." He still looked tired, but his eyes stayed open. They lingered on my face, a vivid blue in the morning light, with an expression almost of curiosity, as though he hadn't seen me before.

"You are so beautiful," he said, softly. "So verra beautiful, *mo chridhe*."

My hands were covered with fading blue blotches and overlooked smears of buffalo blood, I could feel my hair clinging in unwashed tangles to my neck, and I could smell everything from the stale-urine odor of dye to the reek of fear-sweat on my body. And yet whatever he saw lit his face as though he were looking at the full moon on a summer night, pure and lovely.

His eyes stayed fixed on my face as he talked, absorbed, moving slightly as they seemed to trace my features.

"I felt verra badly indeed when Arch and Roger Mac brought me up," he said. "Terribly sick, and my leg and my head both throbbing with each heartbeat, so much that I began to dread the next. And so I would listen to the spaces between. Ye wouldna think it," he said, sounded vaguely surprised, "but there is a great deal of time between the beats of a heart."

He had, he said, begun to hope, in those spaces, that the next beat would not come. And slowly, he realized that his heart was indeed slowing—and that the pain was growing remote, something separate from himself.

His skin had grown colder, the fever fading from both body and mind, leaving the latter oddly clear.

"And this is where I canna really say, Sassenach." He pulled his wrist from my grip in the intensity of his story, and curled his fingers over mine. "But I . . . saw."

"Saw what?" And yet I already knew that he couldn't tell me. Like any doctor, I had seen sick people make up their minds to die—and I knew that look they sometimes had; eyes wide-fixed on *something* in the distance.

He hesitated, struggling to find words. I thought of something, and jumped in to try to help.

"There was an elderly woman," I said. "She died in the hospital where I was on staff—all her grown children with her, it was very peaceful." I looked down, my own eyes fixed on his fingers, still red and slightly swollen, interlaced with my own stained and bloody digits.

"She died—she was *dead*, I could see her pulse had stopped, she wasn't breathing. All her children were by her bedside, weeping. And then, quite suddenly, her eyes opened. She wasn't looking at any of them, but she was seeing *something*. And she said, quite clearly, 'Oooh!' Just like that—thrilled, like a little girl who's just seen something wonderful. And then she closed her eyes again." I looked up at him, blinking back tears. "Was it—like that?"

He nodded, speechless, and his hand tightened on mine.

"Something like," he said, very softly.

He had felt oddly suspended, in a place he could by no means describe, feeling completely at peace—and seeing very clearly.

"It was as if there was a—it wasna a door, exactly, but a passageway of some kind—before me. And I could go through it, if I wanted. And I did want to," he said, giving me a sideways glance and a shy smile.

He had known what lay behind him, too, and realized that for that moment, he could choose. Go forward—or turn back.

"And that's when you asked me to touch you?"

"I knew ye were the only thing that could bring me back," he said simply. "I didna have the strength, myself."

There was a huge lump in my throat; I couldn't speak, but squeezed his hand very tight.

"Why?" I asked at last. "Why did you . . . choose to stay?" My throat was still tight, and my voice was hoarse. He heard it, and his hand tightened on mine; a ghost of his usual firm grip, and yet with the memory of strength within it.

"Because ye need me," he said, very softly.

"Not because you love me?"

He looked up then, with a shadow of a smile.

"Sassenach . . . I love ye now, and I will love ye always. Whether I am dead—or you—whether we are together or apart. You know it is true," he said quietly, and touched my face. "I know it of you, and ye know it of me as well."

He bent his head then, the bright hair swinging down across his cheek.

"I didna mean only you, Sassenach. I have work still to do. I thought—for a bit—that perhaps it wasna so; that ye all might manage, with Roger Mac and auld Arch, Joseph and the Beardsleys. But there is war coming, and—for my sins—" he grimaced slightly, "I am a chief."

He shook his head slightly, in resignation.

"God has made me what I am. He has given me the duty—and I must do it, whatever the cost."

"The cost," I echoed uneasily, hearing something harsher than resignation in his voice. He looked at me, then glanced, almost off-handed, toward the foot of the bed.

"My leg's no much worse," he said, matter-of-factly, "but it's no better. I think ye'll have to take it off."

I SAT IN MY SURGERY, staring out the window, trying to think of another way. There had to be something else I could do. Had to.

He was right; the red streaks were still there. They hadn't advanced any further, but they were still there, ugly and threatening. The oral and topical penicillin had evidently had some effect on the infection, but not enough. The maggots were dealing nicely with the small abscesses, but they couldn't affect the underlying bacteremia that was poisoning his blood.

I glanced up at the brown glass bottle; only about a third full. It might help him hold his ground for a little longer, but there wasn't enough—and it wasn't likely to have sufficient effect, administered by mouth—to eradicate whatever deadly bacterium was multiplying in his blood.

"Ten thousand to ten million milligrams," I murmured to myself. Recommended dosage of penicillin for bacteremia or sepsis, according to the *Merck Manual*, the physician's basic desk reference. I glanced at Daniel Rawlings' casebook, then back at the bottle. With no way of telling what concentration of penicillin I had, administration was likely still more efficacious than the combination of snakeroot and garlic Rawlings advised—but not enough to matter, I was afraid.

The amputation saw was still lying on the counter, where he had left it the day before. I'd given him my word—and he'd given it back.

I clenched my hands, a feeling of unutterable frustration washing over me, so strongly as almost to overwhelm my sense of despair. Why, why, *why* hadn't I started more penicillin brewing at once? How could I have been so feckless, so careless—so bloody fucking *stupid*?

Why had I not insisted on going to Charleston, or at least Wilmington, in hopes of finding a glassblower who could make me the barrel and plunger for a hypodermic syringe? Surely I could have improvised *something* for a needle. All that difficulty, all that experimentation, to get the precious substance in the first place—and now that I desperately needed it . . .

A tentative movement at the open door made me turn round, struggling to get my face under control. I'd have to tell the household what was happening, and soon. But it would be better to choose my time, and tell them all together.

It was one of the Beardsleys. With their hair grown out and neatly trimmed to the same length by Lizzie, it was increasingly difficult to tell them apart—unless one was close enough to see their thumbs. Once they spoke, of course, it was simple.

"Ma'am?" It was Kezzie.

"Yes?" No doubt I sounded short, but it didn't matter; Kezzie couldn't distinguish nuances of speech.

He was carrying a cloth bag. As he came into the room, I saw the bag twitch and change shape, and a small shudder of revulsion came over me. He saw that, and smiled a little.

"This for Himself," he said, in his loud, slightly flat voice, holding up the bag. "Him—old Aaron—said this works good. A big snake bite you, get you a little 'un, cut his head off, drink his blood." He thrust out the bag, which I very gingerly accepted, holding it as far away from me as I could. The contents of the sack shifted again, making my skin crawl, and a faint buzzing noise issued through the cloth.

"Thank you," I said faintly. "I'll . . . ah . . . do something with it. Thank you."

Keziah beamed and bowed his way out, leaving me in personal custody of a sack containing what appeared to be a small but highly annoyed rattlesnake. I looked round frantically for some place to put it. I didn't dare throw it out of the window; Jemmy often played in the dooryard near the house.

Finally, I pulled the big clear glass jar of salt over to the edge of the counter, and—holding the bag at arm's length—used my other hand to dump the salt out on the counter. I dropped the bag into the jar and slammed the lid on it, then rushed to the other side of the room and collapsed on a stool, the backs of my knees sweaty with dread.

I didn't really mind snakes in theory; in practice, though . . .

Brianna poked her head through the door.

"Mama? How's Da this morning?"

"Not all that well." My face evidently told her just how serious it was, for she came into the room and stood beside me, frowning.

"Really bad?" she asked softly, and I nodded, unable to speak. She let her breath out in a deep sigh.

"Can I help?"

I let out an identical sigh, and made a helpless gesture. I had one vague glimmering of an idea—or rather, the return of an idea I'd had in the back of my mind for some time.

"The only thing I can think of doing is to open the leg—cut down deep through the muscle—and pour what penicillin I have left directly into the wounds. It's much more effective against bacterial infections if you can inject it, rather than give it orally. Raw penicillin like this"—I nodded at the bottle—"is very unstable in the presence of acid. It's not likely enough would make it through the stomach to do any good."

"That's more or less what Aunt Jenny did, isn't it? That's what made that huge scar on his thigh."

I nodded, wiping my palms unobtrusively over my knees. I didn't normally suffer from sweaty hands, but the feel of the amputation saw was much too clear in my memory.

"I'd have to do two or three deep cuts. It would likely cripple him permanently—but it might work." I tried to give her a smile. "I don't suppose MIT taught you how to engineer a hypodermic syringe, did they?"

"Why didn't you say so before?" she said calmly. "I don't know if I can make a syringe, but I'd be really surprised if I can't figure out something that does the same thing. How long have we got?"

I stared at her, my mouth half open, then shut it with a snap.

"A few hours, at least. I thought if we didn't get any improvement with the hot poultices, I'd have to either cut or amputate by this evening."

"Amputate!" All the blood drained out of her face. "You can't do that!"

"I can—but my God, I don't want to." My hands curled hard, denying their skill.

"Let me think, then." Her face was still pale, but the shock was passing as her mind began to focus. "Oh—where's Mrs. Bug? I was going to leave Jemmy with her, but—"

"She's gone? Are you sure she isn't just out in the hen-coop?"

"No, I stopped there when I came up to the house. I didn't see her anywhere—and the kitchen fire is smoored."

That was more than odd; Mrs. Bug had come to the house as usual to make breakfast—what could have induced her to leave again? I hoped Arch hadn't suddenly been taken ill; that would just about put the cocked hat on things.

"Where's Jemmy, then?" I asked, looking round for him. He didn't normally go far away from his mother, though he was beginning to wander a bit, as small boys did.

"Lizzie took him upstairs to see Da. I'll ask her to look after him for a while."

"Fine. Oh!"

My exclamation made her turn back at the door, eyebrows raised in question.

"Do you think you could take that"—I gestured distastefully at the big glass jar—"outside, darling? Dispose of it somewhere?"

"Sure. What is it?" Curious, she walked over to the jar. The little rattlesnake had crawled out of its bag and was coiled up in a suspicious dark knot; as she extended a hand toward the jar, it lunged, striking at the glass, and Brianna jumped back with a yelp.

"Ifrinn!" she said, and I laughed, in spite of the general stress and worry.

"Where did you get him, and what is he for?" she asked. Recovering from the initial shock, she leaned forward cautiously and tapped lightly on the glass. The snake, who appeared irascible in the extreme, struck the side of the jar with an audible thump, and she jerked her hand away again.

"Kezzie brought him in; Jamie is meant to drink his blood as a cure," I explained.

She reached out a cautious forefinger, and traced the path of a small droplet of yellowish liquid, sliding down the glass. Two droplets, in fact.

"Look at that! He tried to bite me right through the glass!

That's a really mad snake; I guess he doesn't think much of the idea."

He didn't. He—if it was a he—was coiled again, tiny rattles vibrating in an absolute frenzy of animosity.

"Well, that's all right," I said, coming to stand beside her. "I'm sure Jamie wouldn't think much of the idea, either. He's rather strongly anti-snake at the moment."

"Mmphm." She was still staring at the little snake, a slight frown drawing down her thick red brows. "Did Kezzie say where he got it?"

"I didn't think to ask. Why?"

"It's getting cold out—snakes hibernate, don't they? In dens?"

"Well, Dr. Brickell says they do," I replied, rather dubiously. The good doctor's *Natural History of North Carolina* made entertaining reading, but I took leave to doubt some of his observations, particularly those pertaining to snakes and crocodiles, of whose prowess he appeared to have a rather exaggerated opinion.

She nodded, not taking her eyes off the snake.

"See, the thing is," she said, sounding rather dreamy, "pit-vipers have beautiful engineering. Their jaws are disarticulated, so they can swallow prey bigger than they are—and their fangs fold back against the roof of their mouth when they aren't using them."

"Yes?" I said, giving her a slightly fishy look, which she ignored.

"The fangs are hollow," she said, and touched a finger to the glass, marking the spot where the venom had soaked into the linen cloth, leaving a small yellowish stain. "They're connected to a venom sac in the snake's cheek, and so when they bite down, the cheek muscles squeeze venom out of the sac . . . and down through the fang into the prey. Just like a—"

"Jesus H. Roosevelt Christ," I said.

She nodded, finally taking her eyes off the snake in order to look at me.

"I was thinking of trying to do something with a sharpened quill, but this would work lots better—it's already designed for the job."

"I see," I said, feeling a small surge of hope. "But you'll need a reservoir of some kind . . ."

"First I need a bigger snake," she said practically, turning toward the door. "Let me go find Jo or Kezzie, and see if that one *did* come from a den—and if so, if there are more of them there."

She set off promptly on this mission, taking the glass jar with her, and leaving me to return to a contemplation of the antibiotic situation with renewed hope. If I was going to be able to inject the solution, it needed to be strained and purified as much as possible.

I would have liked to boil the solution, but didn't dare to; I didn't know whether high temperatures would destroy or inactivate raw penicillin—if, in fact, there still *was* active penicillin in there. The surge of hope I had experienced at Brianna's idea dimmed somewhat. Having a hypodermic apparatus wouldn't help, if I had nothing useful to inject.

Restlessly, I moved around the surgery, picking things up and putting them down again.

Steeling myself, I put my hand on the saw again, and closed my eyes, deliberately reliving the movements and sensations, trying also to recapture the sense of otherworldly detachment with which I had killed the buffalo.

Of course, it was Jamie who'd been talking to the otherworld this time. *Nice of you to give him the choice*, I thought sardonically. *I see you aren't going to make it easy on him, though.*

But he wouldn't have asked for that. I opened my eyes, startled. I didn't know whether that answer came from my own subconscious, or elsewhere—but there it was in my mind, and I recognized the truth of it.

Jamie was accustomed to make his choice and abide by it, no matter the cost. He saw that living would likely mean the loss of his leg and all that that implied—and had accepted that as the natural price of his decision.

"Well, I don't bloody accept it!" I said out loud, chin uplifted toward the window. A cedar waxwing swinging on the end of a tree limb gave me a sharp look through his black robber's mask, decided I was mad but harmless, and went about his business.

I pulled open the cupboard door, threw open the top of my medicine chest, and fetched a sheet of paper, quill, and ink from Jamie's study.

A jar of dried red wintergreen berries. Extract of pipsissewa. Slippery elm bark. Willow bark, cherry bark, fleabane, yarrow. Penicillin was by far the most effective of the antibiotics available, but it wasn't the only one. People had been waging war on germs for thousands of years, without any notion what they were fighting. I knew; that was some slight advantage.

I began to make a list of the herbs I had on hand, and under each name, all the uses that I knew for that herb—whether I had ever made such use of it or not. Any herb used to treat a septic condition was a possibility—cleansing lacerations, treating mouth sores, treatment of diarrhea and dysentery . . . I heard footsteps in the kitchen, and called to Mrs. Bug, wanting her to bring me a kettle of boiling water, so I could set things to steeping at once.

She appeared in the doorway, her cheeks bright pink from the cold and her hair coming down in untidy wisps from under her kerch, a large basket clutched in her arms. Before I could say anything, she came and plunked the basket down on the counter in front of me. Just behind her came her husband, with another basket, and a small open keg, from which came a pungent alcoholic scent. The air around them held a faint ripe smell, like the distant reek of a garbage dump.

"I did hear ye say as how ye'd not enough mold on hand," she started in, anxious but bright-eyed, "so I said to Arch, I said, we must go round to the houses nearabouts, and see what we can fetch back wi' us for Mrs. Fraser, for after all, bread does go bad so quick when it's damp, and the good Lord kens that Mrs. Chisholm is a slattern, for all I'm sure she's a good heart, and what goings-on there may be at her hearth I'm sure I shouldna like even to *think* about, but we—"

I wasn't paying attention, but was staring at the results of the Bugs' morning raid on the pantries and middens of the Ridge. Crusts of bread, spoilt biscuit, half-rotted squash, bits of pie with the marks of teeth still visible in the pastry . . . a hodgepodge of gluey orts and decaying fragments—all sprouting molds in patches of velvet-blue and lichen-green, interspersed with warty blobs of pink and yellow and dustings of splotchy white. The keg was half-filled with decaying corn, the resultant murky liquid rimmed with floating islands of blue mold.

"Evan Lindsay's pigs," Mr. Bug explained, in a rare burst of loquacity. Both Bugs beamed at me, begrimed with their efforts.

"Thank you," I said, feeling choked, and not only from the smell. I blinked, eyes watering slightly from the miasma of the corn liquor. "Oh, thank you."

IT WAS JUST AFTER DARK when I made my way upstairs, carrying my tray of potions and implements, feeling a mixture of excitement and trepidation.

Jamie was propped on his pillows, surrounded by visitors. People had been coming by the house all day to see him and wish him well; a good many of them had simply stayed, and a host of anxious faces turned toward me as I came in, glimmering in the light of the candles.

He looked very ill, flushed and drawn, and I wondered whether I ought to have chased the visitors away. I saw Murdo Lindsay take his hand, though, and squeeze it tight, and realized that the distraction and support of his company through the day was probably much more helpful to him than the rest that he wouldn't have taken in any case.

"Well, then," Jamie said, with a good assumption of casualness, "we're ready, I suppose." He stretched his legs, flexing his toes hard under the blanket. Given the state of his leg, it must have hurt dreadfully, but I recognized that he was taking what he thought would be the last opportunity to move the limb, and bit the inside of my lip.

"Well, we're ready to have a go at something," I said, smiling at him with an attempt at confident reassurance. "And anyone who would like to pray about it, please do."

A rustle of surprise replaced the air of dread that had been sprung up at my appearance, and I saw Marsali, who was holding a sleeping Joan with one hand, grope hastily in her pocket with the other to pull out her rosary.

There was a rush to clear the bedside table, which was littered with books, papers, candle-stubs, various treats brought up to tempt Jamie's appetite—all untouched—and, for some unfathomable reason, the fret-board of a dulcimer and a half-tanned groundhog hide. I set down the tray, and Brianna, who had come up with me, stepped forward, her invention carefully held in both hands, like an acolyte presenting bread to a priest.

"What in the name of Christ is that?" Jamie frowned at the object, then up at me.

"It's sort of a do-it-yourself rattlesnake," Brianna told him.

Everyone murmured with interest, craning their necks to see—though the interest was diverted almost at once as I turned back the quilt and began to unwrap his leg, to a chorus of shocked murmurs and sympathetic exclamations at sight of it.

Lizzie and Marsali had been faithfully applying fresh, hot onion and flaxseed poultices to it all day, and wisps of steam rose from the wrappings as I put them aside. The flesh of his leg was bright red to the knee, at least in those parts that weren't black or seeping with pus. We had removed the maggots temporarily, afraid the heat would kill them; they were presently downstairs on a plate in my surgery, happily occupied with some of the nastier bits of the Bugs' gleanings. If I succeeded in saving the leg, they could help with the tidying-up, later.

I had carefully gone through the detritus bit by bit, examining the blue molds with my microscope, and putting aside everything that could be identified as bearing *Penicillium* into a large bowl. Over this miscellaneous collection I had poured the fermented corn liquor, allowing the whole to steep during the day—and with luck, to dissolve any actual raw penicillin from the garbage into the alcoholic liquid.

Meanwhile, I had made a selection of those herbs with a reputation for the internal treatment of suppurative conditions, and made a stiff decoction of them, steeped in boiling water for several hours. I poured a cup of this highly aromatic solution, and handed it to Roger, carefully averting my nose.

"Make him drink it," I said. "All of it," I added pointedly, fixing Jamie with a look.

Jamie sniffed the proffered cup, and gave me the look back—but obediently sipped, making exaggerated faces for the entertainment of his company, who giggled appreciatively. The mood thus lightened, I proceeded to the main event, turning to take the makeshift hypodermic from Bree.

The Beardsley twins, standing shoulder-to-shoulder in the corner, pressed forward to see, swelling with pride. They had gone out at once at Bree's request, coming back in midafternoon with a fine rattlesnake, nearly three feet long—and fortunately dead, having been cut nearly in half with an ax, so as to preserve the valuable head.

I had dissected out the poison sacs with great caution, detaching the fangs, and then had put Mrs. Bug to the task of rinsing the fangs repeatedly with alcohol, to eradicate any lingering traces of venom.

Bree had taken the oiled silk that had been used to wrap the astrolabe, and stitched part of it into a small tube, gathering one end of this with a draw-stitch, like a purse-string. She had cut a thick segment from a turkey's wing-quill, softened with hot water, and used this to join the gathered end of the silk tube to the fang. Melted beeswax had sealed the joints of tube, quill, and fang, and been spread carefully along the line of the stitching, to prevent leakage. It was a nice, neat job—but it *did* look quite like a small, fat snake with one enormous curved fang, and occasioned no little comment from the spectators.

Murdo Lindsay was still holding one of Jamie's hands. As I motioned to Fergus to hold the candle for me, I saw Jamie reach out the other toward Roger. Roger looked momentarily startled, but grabbed the hand and knelt down by the bed, holding on tight.

I ran my fingers lightly over the leg, selected a good spot, clear of major blood vessels, swabbed it with pure alcohol, and jabbed the fang in, as deeply as I could. There was a gasp from the spectators, and a sharp intake of breath from Jamie, but he didn't move.

"All right." I nodded at Brianna, who was standing by with the bottle of strained corn-alcohol. Teeth sunk in her lower lip, she poured carefully, filling the silk tube as I supported it. I folded the open top tightly over, and with thumb and forefinger, firmly pressed downward, forcing the liquid out through the fang and into the tissues of the leg.

Jamie made a small, breathless noise, and both Murdo and Roger leaned inward instinctively, their shoulders pressing against his, holding on.

I didn't dare go too fast, for fear of cracking the wax seals by exerting too much pressure, though we had a second syringe, made with the other fang, just in case. I worked my way up and down the leg, with Bree refilling the syringe with each injection, and blood rose glistening from the holes as I withdrew the fang, rolling in tiny rivulets down the side of his leg. Without being asked, Lizzie picked up a cloth and blotted it clean, eyes intent on the job.

The room was silent, but I felt everyone's breath held as I chose a new spot, let out in a sigh as the stab was made—and then the unconscious leaning toward the bed as I squeezed the stinging alcohol deep into the infected tissues. The muscles stood out in knots on Jamie's forearms, and sweat ran down his face like rain, but neither he, nor Murdo, nor Roger made a sound or moved.

From the corner of my eye, I saw Joseph Wemyss stroke back the hair from Jamie's forehead, and wipe away the sweat from his face and neck with a towel.

"Because ye need me," he'd said. And I realized then that it wasn't only me that he'd meant.

It didn't take a long time. When it was done, I spread honey carefully over all the open wounds, and rubbed oil of wintergreen into the skin of foot and calf.

"That's a nice job of basting, Sassenach. D'ye reckon it's ready for the oven yet?" Jamie asked, and wiggled his toes, causing the tension in the room to relax into laughter.

Everyone did leave, then, patting Jamie's shoulder or kissing his cheek in farewell, with gruff wishes of good luck. He smiled and nodded, lifting his hand in farewell, exchanging goodbyes, making small jokes.

When the door closed behind the last of them, he lay back on the pillow and closed his eyes, letting all his breath out in a long, deep sigh. I set about tidying my tray, setting the syringe to soak in alcohol, corking bottles, folding bandages. Then I sat down beside him, and he reached out a hand to me, not opening his eyes.

His skin was warm and dry, the hand reddened from Murdo's fierce grip. I traced his knuckles gently with my thumb, listening to the rumble and clatter of the house below, subdued but lively.

"It will work," I said softly, after a minute. "I know it will."

"I know," he said. He took a deep breath, and at last, began to weep.

94

NEW BLOOD

ROGER WOKE ABRUPTLY, out of a black and dreamless sleep. He felt like a landed fish, jerked gasping into an alien and unimagined element. He saw but did not grasp his surroundings; strange light and flattened surfaces. Then his mind made sense of Brianna's touch on his arm, and he was once more inside his skin, and in a bed.

"Hwh?" He sat up suddenly, making a hoarse noise of inquiry.

"I'm sorry to wake you." Brianna smiled, but a line of concern drew her brows together as her eyes searched his face. She smoothed the tangled hair back from his brow, and he reached for her by reflex, falling back against the pillow with her heavy in his arms.

"Hwm." Holding her was an anchor to reality—solid flesh and warm skin, her hair soft as dreams against his face.

"Okay?" she asked softly. Long fingers touched his chest and his nipple puckered, curly hairs around it rising.

"Okay," he said, and sighed deeply. He kissed her forehead briefly, and relaxed, blinking. His throat was dry as sand, and his mouth felt sticky, but he was beginning to think coherently again. "Whatime ist?" He was in his own bed, and it was dim enough in the room to be evening, but that was because the door was closed and the windows covered. Something felt wrong about the light, the air.

She pushed herself up off him, sweeping back the fall of red hair with one hand.

"It's a little past noon. I wouldn't have waked you up, but there's a man, and I don't know what to do about him." She glanced in the direction of the big house, and lowered her voice, though surely no one was near enough to hear her.

"Da's sound asleep, and Mama, too," she said, confirming this impression. "I don't want to wake them—even if I could." She smiled briefly, one corner of her long mouth curling up with her father's irony. "It would take gunpowder, I think. They're dead to the world."

She turned away and reached for the pitcher on the table. The sound of water pouring fell on Roger's ears like rain on parched land, and he drained the offered cup in three gulps and held it out again.

"More. Please. Man?" That was an improvement; he was making complete words again, and his capacity to think coherently was coming back.

"He says his name is Thomas Christie. He's come to see Da; he says he was at Ardsmuir."

"Yeah?" Roger drank the second cup more slowly, assembling his thoughts. Then he put down the cup and swung his legs out of bed, reaching for the discarded shirt that hung from the peg. "Okay. Tell him I'll be there in a minute."

She kissed him briefly and left, pausing long enough to untack the hide over the window and let in a brilliant shaft of light and chilly air.

He dressed slowly, his mind still pleasantly torpid. As he bent to dredge his stockings out from under the bed, though, something in the tumbled bedclothes caught his eye, just under the edge of the pillow. He reached out slowly and picked it up. The "auld wifie"—the tiny fertility charm, its ancient pink stone smooth in the sun, surprisingly heavy in his hand.

"I will be damned," he said, aloud. He stood staring at it for a moment, then bent and tucked it gently back beneath the pillow.

BRIANNA HAD PUT the visitor in Jamie's study—what most of the tenants still called the speak-a-word room. Roger stopped for a moment in the corridor, checking to be sure all his bodily parts were present and attached. There hadn't been time to shave, but he'd combed his hair; there was a limit to what this Christie might expect, under the circumstances.

Three faces turned toward the door as he came in, surprising him. Bree hadn't thought to warn him that Christie had outriders. Still, the elder man, a square-set gentleman with trimly cut black hair streaked with gray, was obviously Thomas Christie; the dark-haired younger man was no more than twenty, and just as obviously Christie's son.

"Mr. Christie?" He offered the older man his hand. "I'm Roger MacKenzie; I'm married to Jamie Fraser's daughter—you've met my wife, I think."

Christie looked mildly surprised, and looked over Roger's shoulder, as though expecting Jamie to materialize behind him. Roger cleared his throat; his voice was still thick from sleep, and thus even more hoarse than it usually was.

"I'm afraid my father-in-law is . . . not available at present. Could I be of service to you?"

Christie frowned at him, assessing his potential, then nodded slowly. He took Roger's hand, and shook it firmly. To his astonishment, Roger felt something both familiar and grossly unexpected; the distinctive pressure against his knuckle of a Masonic greeting. He had not experienced that in years, and it was more reflex than reason that caused him to respond with what he hoped was the proper countersign. Evidently it was satisfactory; Christie's severe expression eased slightly, and he let go.

"Perhaps ye may, Mr. MacKenzie, perhaps ye may," Christie said. He fixed a piercing gaze on Roger. "I wish to find land on which to settle with my family—and I was told that Mr. Fraser might feel himself in a position to put something suitable in my way."

"That might be possible," Roger replied cautiously. *What the hell?* he thought. Had Christie just been trying it on at a venture, or had he reason to expect that sign would be recognized? If he did—that presumably meant that he knew Jamie Fraser would recognize it, and thought his son-in-law might, as well. Jamie Fraser, a Freemason? The thought had never so much as crossed Roger's mind, and Jamie himself had certainly never spoken of it.

"Please—do sit down," he said abruptly, motioning to the visitors. Christie's family—the son and a girl who might be either Christie's daughter or the son's wife—had risen as well when Roger came in, standing behind the paterfamilias like attendants behind some visiting potentate.

Feeling more than slightly self-conscious, Roger waved them back to their stools, and sat down himself behind Jamie's desk. He plucked one of the quills from the blue salt-glazed jar, hoping this would make him seem more businesslike. Christ, what questions ought he to ask a potential tenant?

"Now, then, Mr. Christie." He smiled at them, conscious of his unshaven jaws. "My wife says that you were acquainted with my father-in-law, in Scotland?"

"In Ardsmuir prison," Christie answered, darting Roger a sharp look, as though daring him to make something of this.

Roger cleared his throat again; healed as it was, it tended still to be clogged and rasping for some time after rising. Christie appeared to take it as an adverse comment, however, and bristled slightly. He had thick brows and prominent eyes of a light yellowish-brown color, and this, coupled with feathery, close-clipped dark hair and the lack of any visible neck, gave him the aspect of a large, irascible owl.

"Jamie Fraser was a prisoner there as well," he said. "Surely ye knew as much?"

"Why, yes," Roger said mildly. "I understand that several of the men who are settled here on the Ridge came from Ardsmuir."

"Who?" Christie demanded, increasing the owlish impression.

"Ah . . . the Lindsays—that's Kenny, Murdo, and Evan," Roger said, rubbing a hand over his brow to assist thought. "Geordie Chisholm and Robert MacLeod. I think—yes, I'm fairly sure Alex MacNeill was from Ardsmuir, too."

Christie had been following this list with close attention, like a barn owl keeping track of a rustling in the hay. Now he relaxed, settling his feathers, as Roger thought.

"I know them," he said, with an air of satisfaction. "MacNeill will vouch for my character, if that's needful." His tone strongly suggested that it shouldn't be.

Roger had never seen Jamie interview a potential tenant, but he had heard Fraser talk to Claire about the ones he chose. Accordingly, he posed a few questions regarding Christie's more recent past, trying to balance courtesy with an attitude of authority, and—he thought—managing it none too badly.

Christie had been transported with the other prisoners, he said, but had been fortunate in having his indenture purchased by a plantation owner in South Carolina, who upon finding that Christie possessed some learning, had made him schoolmaster to his own six children, taking fees from the nearby families for the privilege of sending their children also to be tutored by Christie. Once Christie's term of indenture had expired, he had agreed to remain, working for wages.

"Really?" Roger said, his interest in Christie increasing markedly. A schoolmaster, eh? It would please Bree no end, to be able to resign her involuntary position as what she disparagingly termed Bo-Peep. And Christie looked more than capable of dealing with intransigent scholars. "What brings you here, then, Mr. Christie? It's some way from South Carolina."

The man shrugged broad shoulders. He was road-worn and quite dusty, but his coat was of decent cloth, and he had sound shoes.

"My wife died," he said gruffly. "Of the influenza. So did Mr. Everett, the owner. His heir did not require my services, and I did not wish to remain there without employment." He shot Roger a piercing look under shaggy brows. "You said Mr. Fraser is not available. How long will it be until his return?"

"I couldn't say." Roger tapped the end of the quill against his teeth, hesitating. In fact, he couldn't say how long Jamie might be incapacitated; when seen last night, he'd looked barely alive. Even if he recovered uneventfully, he could be ill for some time. And he hated to send Christie away, or make him wait; it was late in the year, and not much time to spare, if the man and his family were to be settled for the winter.

He glanced from Christie to his son. Both sizable men, and strong, from the looks of them. Neither had the look of a drunkard or a lout, and both had the callused palms that bespoke at least familiarity with manual labor. They had a woman to look after their domestic requirements. And after all, Masonic brotherhood quite aside, Christie had been one of Jamie's Ardsmuir men. He knew that Jamie always made a special effort to find such men a place.

Making a decision, Roger pulled out a clean sheet of paper and uncapped the inkwell. He cleared his throat once more.

"Very well, Mr. Christie. I think we can reach some . . . accommodation."

To his pleased surprise, the study door opened, and Brianna came in, carrying a tray of biscuits and beer. She cast down her eyes modestly as she set it on the desk, but he caught the flash of amusement she sent him under her lashes. He bent his head, smiling, and touched her wrist lightly in acknowledgment as she set out the mugs in front of him. The gesture reminded him of Christie's handshake, and he wondered whether Brianna knew anything about Jamie's history in that direction. He rather thought not; surely she would have mentioned it.

"Brianna, say hello to our new tenants," he said, with a nod at the Christies. "Mr. Thomas Christie, and . . ."

"My son, Allan," Christie said, with a jerk of the head, "and my daughter, Malva."

The son had none of his father's owlish look, being much fairer in aspect, with a broad, square, clean-shaven face, though he had the same feathery, tufted dark hair. He nodded in silent acknowledgment of the introduction, eyes fixed on the refreshment.

The girl—Malva?—barely looked up, her hands folded modestly in her lap. Roger had the vague impression of a tallish girl, perhaps seventeen or eighteen, neat in a dark blue dress and white kerch, with a soft frill of black curls just visible around the pale oval of her face. Another point in Christie's favor, Roger thought absently; girls of marriageable age were rare, pretty ones still rarer. Malva Christie would likely have several offers before the spring planting.

Bree nodded to each of them, looking at the girl with particular interest. Then a loud shriek came from the kitchen, and she fled with a murmured excuse.

"My son," Roger said, in apology. He lifted a mug of beer, offering it. "Will you take a bit of refreshment, Mr. Christie?"

The tenant contracts were all kept in the left-hand drawer of the desk; he'd seen them, and knew the general outlines. Fifty acres would be granted outright, more land rented as needed, with provision for payment made according to individual situations. A little discussion over the beer and biscuits, and they had reached what seemed an adequate agreement.

Completing the contract with a flourish, Roger signed his own name, as agent for James Fraser, and pushed the paper across the desk for Christie to sign. He felt a deep, pleasant glow of accomplishment. A sound tenant, and willing to pay half his quitrent by serving as schoolmaster for five months of the year. Jamie himself, Roger thought complacently, would not have done better.

Then he caught himself. No, Jamie would have taken one more step, and seen the Christies offered not only hospitality but lodging, a place to stay until they could achieve some shelter of their own. Not here, though; not with Jamie ill and Claire occupied in nursing him. He thought for a moment, then stepped to the door and called for Lizzie.

"We've a new tenant come, and his family, *a muirninn*," he said, smiling at her anxious, willing mouse-face. "This is Mr. Thomas Christie, and his son and daughter. Can ye ask your Da will he take them up to Evan Lindsay's cabin? It's near where they'll have their own land, and I'm thinking perhaps Evan and his wife have room for them to stay for a bit, until they can get a start on a place of their own."

"Oh, aye, Mister Roger." Lizzie bobbed a quick curtsy toward Christie, who acknowledged her with a small bow. Then she glanced at Roger, thin brows lifted. "Will Himself know about it, then?"

Roger felt a slight flush rise in his cheeks, but gave no sign of discomposure.

"That's all right," he said. "I'll be telling him, so soon as he's feeling better."

"Mr. Fraser is ill? I am sorry to hear it." The unfamiliar soft voice came from behind, startling him, and he turned to find Malva Christie looking up at him in question. He hadn't taken much notice of her, but was now struck by the beauty of her eyes—an odd light gray, almond-shaped and luminous, and thickly fringed with long black lashes. Perhaps sooner than the spring planting, he thought, and coughed.

"Bitten by a snake," he said abruptly. "Not to worry, though; he's mending."

He thrust out a hand to Christie, ready this time for the secret grip.

"Welcome to Fraser's Ridge," he said. "I hope you and your family will be happy here."

JAMIE WAS SITTING UP in bed, attended hand and foot by devoted women, and looking desperate in consequence. His face relaxed a little at sight of a fellow man, and he waved away his handmaidens. Lizzie, Marsali, and Mrs. Bug left reluctantly, but Claire remained, busy with her bottles and blades.

Roger moved to sit down on the bed-foot, only to be shooed off by Claire, who motioned him firmly to a stool before lifting the sheet to check matters beneath and be sure that his ill-advised gesture had caused no damage.

"All right," she said at last, poking at the white cheesecloth dressing with an air of satisfaction. The maggots were back, evidently earning their keep. She straightened up and nodded to Roger—like the Grand Vizier granting an audience with the Caliph of Baghdad, Roger thought, amused. He glanced at Jamie, who rolled his eyes upward, then gave Roger a small, wry smile of greeting.

"How is it?" both of them said at once. Roger smiled, and the corner of Jamie's mouth turned up. He gave a brief shrug.

"I'm alive," he said. "Mind, that doesna prove ye were right. Ye're not."

"Right about what?" Claire asked, glancing up with curiosity from the bowl in her hands.

"Oh, a wee point of philosophy," Jamie told her. "Regarding choice, and chance."

She snorted.

"I don't want to hear a word about it."

"Just as well. I'm no inclined to discuss such matters on nothing but bread and milk." Jamie glanced with mild distaste at a bowl of that nourishing but squashy substance, sitting half-finished on the table at his side. "So, have ye seen to the ulcer on the mule's leg, then, Roger Mac?"

"I did," Claire told him. "It's healing very well. Roger's been busy, interviewing new tenants."

"Oh, aye?" Fraser's brows went up in interest.

"Aye, a man named Tom Christie and his family. He said he was at Ardsmuir with you."

For a split second, Roger felt as though all the air in the room had been removed by a vacuum, freezing everything. Fraser stared at him, expressionless. Then he nodded, his expression of pleasant interest restored as though by magic, and normal time resumed.

"Aye, I mind Tom Christie fine. Where has he been in the last twenty years?"

Roger explained both Tom Christie's account of his wanderings, and what accommodations had been reached for his tenancy.

"That will do verra well," Jamie said approvingly, hearing of Christie's willingness to be schoolmaster. "Tell him he may use any of the books here—and ask him to make up a list of others he might need. I'll tell Fergus to look about, next time he's in Cross Creek or Wilmington."

The conversation moved on to more mundane affairs, and after a few minutes, Roger got up to take his leave.

Everything seemed perfectly all right, and yet he felt obscurely uneasy. Surely he hadn't imagined that instant? Turning to close the door behind him, he saw that Jamie had folded his hands neatly on his chest and closed his eyes; if not yet asleep, effectively forbidding conversation. Claire was looking at her husband, her yellow hawk-eyes narrowed in speculation. No, she'd seen it, too.

So he hadn't imagined it. What on earth was the matter with Tom Christie?

95

THE SUMMER DIM

THE NEXT DAY Roger closed the door behind him and stood on the porch for a moment, breathing the cold bright air of the late morning—late, Christ, it couldn't be more than half seven, but it was a good deal later than he was accustomed to start the day. The sun had already drifted into the chestnut trees on the highest ridge, the curve of its flaming disk visible in silhouette through the last of the yellow leaves.

The air still held the tang of blood, but there was no trace of the buffalo left, beyond a dark patch in the flattened pumpkin vines. He glanced around, taking stock as he mentally made his list of chores for the day. Chickens scratched in the fall-shabby yard, and he could hear a small group of hogs rooting for mast in the chestnut grove.

He had the odd feeling that he had left his work months, or even years, before, not days. The feeling of dislocation—so strong at first—had left him for quite a long time, but now it had come back again, stronger than before. If he closed his eyes for a moment, then opened them again, surely he would find himself on the Broad Street in Oxford, the smell of auto exhaust in his nostrils and the prospect of a peaceful morning's work among the dusty books of the Bodleian ahead.

He smacked a hand against one thigh, to dispel the feeling. Not today. This was the Ridge, not Oxford, and the work might be peaceful, but it would be done with hands, not head. There were trees to be girdled and hay to be gathered; not the field hay, but the small wild patches scattered through the hills that would yield an armload here, an armload there—enough to allow the keeping of an extra cow through the winter.

A hole in the roof of the smoke-shed, made by a falling tree branch. The roof to be mended and re-shingled and the branch itself to be chopped for wood. A fresh privy-hole to be dug, before the ground froze or turned to mud. Flax to be chopped. Fence rails to split. Lizzie's spinning wheel to mend . . .

He felt groggy and stupid, incapable of simple choice, let alone complex thought. He had slept enough—more than enough—to be physically recovered from the exhaustion of the last few days, but Thomas Christie and his family, coming on the heels of the desperate business of getting Jamie safely home, had taken all the mental energy he had.

He glanced at the sky; a low sweep of mare's tails, sketched against the sky. No rain for a bit, the roof could wait. He shrugged and scratched his scalp. Hay, then, and tree-girdling. He stuffed a stone jar of ale and the packet of sandwiches Bree had made for him into his bag, and went to fetch the hand-scythe and hatchet.

Walking began to rouse him. It was cold in the shadows under the pines, but the sun was now high enough to make itself felt whenever he walked through the bright patches. His muscles warmed and loosened with the exercise, and by the time he had climbed to the first of the high meadows, he had begun to feel himself again, solidly embedded in the physical world of mountain and forest. The future had gone back to the world of dreams and memory, and he was once more present and accounted for.

"Good thing, too," he muttered to himself. "Don't want to be cutting off your foot." He dropped the ax under a tree, and bent to cut hay.

It wasn't the soothingly monotonous labor of regular haying, where the big two-handed scythe laid the dry, rich grass in pleasing swathes across a field. This was at once rougher but easier work, that involved grasping a clump of sprouting muhly or blue-stem with one hand, slicing the stalks near the root, and stuffing the handful of wild hay into the burlap sack he had brought.

It took no great strength, but required attention, rather than the mindless muscular effort of field-haying. The grass clumps grew thickly all over this small break in the trees, but were interspersed with outcrops of granite, small bushes, decaying snags, and brambles.

It was soothing labor, and while it did require some watchfulness, soon enough his mind began to stray to other things. The things Jamie had told him, out on the black mountainside, under the stars.

Some he had known; that there was bad feeling between Alex MacNeill and Nelson McIver, and the cause of it; that one of Patrick Neary's sons was likely a thief, and what should be done about it. Which land to sell, when, and to whom. Others, he had had no inkling of. He pressed his lips tight together, thinking of Stephen Bonnet.

And what should be done about Claire.

"If I am dead, she must leave," Jamie had said, rousing suddenly from a feverish stupor. He had gripped Roger's arm with surprising strength, his eyes burning dark. "Send her. Make her go. Ye should all go, if the bairn can pass. But she must go. Make her go to the stones."

"Why?" Roger had asked quietly. "Why should she go?" It was possible that Jamie was deranged by fever, not thinking clearly. "It's a dangerous thing, to go through the stones."

"It is dangerous for her here, without me." Fraser's eyes had momentarily lost their sharp focus; the lines of his face relaxed in exhaustion. His eyes half-closed and he sagged back. Then, suddenly, his eyes opened again.

"She is an Old One," he said. "They will kill her, if they

know." Then his eyes had closed again, and he had not spoken again until the others had found them at daylight.

Viewed now in the clear light of an autumn morning, safely removed from the whining wind and dancing flames of that lost night on the mountain, Roger was reasonably sure that Fraser had only been wandering in the mists of his fever, concern for his wife muddled by phantoms that sprang from the poison in his blood. Still, Roger couldn't help but take notice.

"She is an Old One." Fraser had been speaking in English, which was too bad. Had it been Gaelic, his meaning would have been clearer. Had he said *"She is ban-sidhe,"* Roger would have known whether Jamie truly thought his wife was one of the faery-folk, or only a thoroughly human wisewoman.

Surely he couldn't . . . but he might. Even in Roger's own time, the belief in "the others" ran strongly, if less widely admitted, in the blood of the Highlands. Now? Fraser believed quite openly in ghosts—to say nothing of saints and angels. To Roger's cynical Presbyterian mind, there wasn't a great deal of difference between lighting candles to St. Genevieve and putting out a pan of milk for the faeries.

On the other hand, he was uneasily aware that he would himself never have disturbed milk meant for the Others, nor touched a charm hung over cow-byre or door lintel—and not only from respect for the person who had placed it there.

The work had warmed him thoroughly; his shirt was beginning to stick to his shoulders, and sweat trickled down his neck. He paused for a moment, to drink from his water gourd and tie a rag round his brow as a sweatband.

Fraser might just have a point, he thought. While the notion of himself or Brianna—even of Claire—as being *sìdheanach* was laughable on the face of it . . . there was more than one face to it, wasn't there? They *were* different; not everyone could travel through the stones, let alone did.

And there were others. Geillis Duncan. The unknown traveler she had mentioned to Claire. The gentleman whose severed head Claire had found in the wilderness, silver fillings intact. The thought of that one made the hairs prickle on his forearms, sweat or no.

Jamie had buried the head, with due respect and a brief prayer, on a hill near the house—the first inhabitant of the small, sun-filled clearing intended as the future cemetery of Fraser's Ridge. At Claire's insistence, he had marked the small grave with a rough chunk of granite, unlabeled—for what was there to say?—but marbled with veins of green serpentine.

Was Fraser right? *Ye should all go back, if the bairn can pass.*

And if they didn't go back . . . then someday they might all lie there in the sunny clearing together: himself, Brianna, Jemmy, each under a chunk of granite. The only difference was that each would bear a name. What on earth would they carve for dates? he wondered suddenly, and wiped sweat from his jaw. Jemmy's would be no problem, but for the rest of them . . .

There was the rub, of course—or one of them. *If the bairn can pass*. If Claire's theory was right, and the ability to pass through the stones was a genetic trait, like eye color or blood-type—then fifty/fifty, if Jemmy were Bonnet's child; three chances out of four, or perhaps certainty, if he were Roger's.

He hacked savagely at a clump of grass, not bothering to grasp it, and grain heads flew like shrapnel. Then he remembered the small pink figure underneath his pillow, and breathed deep. And if it worked, if there were to be another child, one that was his for sure, by blood? Odds three out of four—or perhaps another stone, one day, in the family graveyard.

The bag was almost full, and there was no more hay worth the cutting here. Fetching the hatchet, he slung the bag across his shoulder and made his way downhill, to the edge of the highest cornfield.

It bore no more resemblance to the British cornfields he had been used to than did the high meadows to a hayfield. Once a patch of virgin forest, the trees still stood, black and dead against the pale blue sky. They had been girdled and left to die, the corn planted in the open spaces between them.

It was the quickest way to clear land sufficiently for crops.

With the trees dead, enough sunlight came through the leafless branches for the corn below. One or two or three years later, the dead tree roots would have rotted sufficiently to make it possible to push the trunks over, to be gradually cut for wood and hauled away. For now, though, they stood, an eerie band of black scarecrows, spreading empty arms across the corn.

The corn itself had been gathered; flocks of mourning doves foraged for bugs among the litter of dry stalks, and a covey of bobwhite took fright at Roger's approach, scattering like a handful of marbles thrown across the ground. A ladder-backed woodpecker, secure above his head, uttered a brief shriek of startlement and paused in its hammering to inspect him before returning to its noisy excavations.

"You should be pleased," he said to the bird, setting down the bag and unlimbering the hatchet from his belt. "More bugs for you, aye?" The dead trees were infested by myriad insects; several woodpeckers could be found in any field of girdled trees, heads cocked to hear the subterranean scratchings of their burrowing prey.

"Sorry," he murmured under his breath to the tree he had selected. It was ridiculous to feel pity for a tree; the more so in this sprawling wilderness, where saplings sprang out of the thawing earth with such spring vigor as to crack solid rock and the mountains were so thickly blanketed with trees that the air itself was a smoky blue with their exhalations. For that matter, the emotion wouldn't last longer than it took to begin the job; by the time he reached the third tree, he would be sweating freely and cursing the awkwardness of the work.

Still, he always approached the job with a faint reluctance, disliking the manner of it more than the result. Chopping down a tree for timber was straight-forward; girdling it seemed somehow mean-spirited, if practical, leaving the tree to die slowly, unable to bring water from its roots above the ring of bare, exposed wood. It was not so unpleasant in the fall, at least, when the trees were dormant and leafless already; it must be rather like dying in their sleep, he thought. Or hoped.

Chips of aromatic wood flew past his head, as he chopped his way briskly around the big trunk, and went on without pause to the next victim.

Needless to say, he took care never to let anyone hear him apologize to a tree. Jamie always said a prayer for the animals he killed, but Roger doubted that he would regard a tree as anything other than fuel, building material, or sheer bloody obstruction. The woodpecker screeched suddenly overhead. Roger swung round to see what had caused the alarm, but relaxed at once, seeing the small, wiry figure of Kenny Lindsay approaching through the trees. It appeared that Lindsay had come on the same business; he flourished his own girdling knife in cordial greeting.

"Madain mhath, a Smeòraich!" he shouted. "And what's this I hear, that we've a newcomer?"

No longer even faintly surprised at the speed with which news passed over the mountain, Roger offered his ale-jug to Lindsay, and gave him the details of the new family.

"Christie is their name, is it?" Kenny asked.

"Yes. Thomas Christie, and his son and daughter. You'll know him—he was at Ardsmuir."

"Aye? Oh."

There it was again, that faint tremor of reaction at Christie's name.

"Christie," Kenny Lindsay repeated. The tip of his tongue showed briefly, tasting the name. "Mm. Aye, well."

"What's the matter with Christie?" Roger demanded, feeling more uneasy by the minute.

"Matter?" Kenny looked startled. "Nothing's the matter with him—is there?"

"No. I mean—you seemed a bit taken aback to hear his name. I wondered whether perhaps he was a known thief, or a drunkard, or the like."

Enlightenment spread across Kenny's stubbled face like sun on a morning meadow.

"Oh, aye, I take your meaning now. No, no, Christie's a decent enough sort, so far as I ken the man."

"So far as ye ken? Were ye not at Ardsmuir together, then? He said so."

"Och, aye, he was there right enough," Kenny agreed, but

seemed still vaguely hesitant. Additional prodding by Roger elicited nothing, though, save a shrug, and after a few moments, they returned to the cutting, pausing only for the occasional swig of ale or water. The weather was cool, thank God, but working like that made the sweat run free, and at the end of the job, Roger took a last drink, and then poured the rest of his water over his head, gasping with the welcome chill on his heated skin.

"You'll come ben for a bit, *a Smeòraich*?" Kenny laid down his ax and eased his back with a groan. He jerked his head toward the pines on the far side of the meadow. "My wee house is just there. The wife's awa' to sell her pork, but there's fresh buttermilk in the spring."

Roger nodded, smiling.

"I will then, Kenny, thanks."

He went with Kenny to tend his beasts; Lindsay had two milch-goats and a penned sow. Kenny fetched them water from a small nearby creek, while Roger stacked the hay and threw a forkful into the goats' manger.

"Nice pig," Roger said politely, waiting while Kenny poured cracked corn into the trough for the sow, a big mottled creature with one ragged ear and a nasty look in her eye.

"Mean as a viper, and nearly as fast," Kenny said, giving the pig a narrow look. "Near as Godalmighty took my hand off at the wrist yesterday. I meant to take her to *Mac Dubh*'s boar for breeding, but she wasna inclined to go."

"Not much ye can do with a female who's not in the mood," Roger agreed.

Kenny wobbled his head from one side to the other, considering.

"Och, well, that's as may be. There are ways to sweeten them, aye? That's a trick my brother Evan taught me." He gave Roger a gap-toothed grin, and nodded toward a barrel in the corner of the shed, that gave off the sweet pungency of fermenting corn.

"Aye?" Roger said, laughing. "Well, I hope it works, then." He had an involuntary vision of Kenny and his imposing wife, Rosamund, in bed together, and wondered in passing whether alcohol played much part in their unlikely marriage.

"Oh, it'll work," Kenny said with confidence. "She's a terror for the sour-mash, is that one. Trouble is, if ye give her enough to improve her disposition, she canna walk just so verra well. We'll need to bring the boar to her, instead, when *Mac Dubh*'s on his feet."

"Is she in season? I'll bring the boar tomorrow," Roger said, feeling reckless. Kenny looked startled, but then nodded, pleased.

"Aye, that's kind, *a Smeòraich*." He paused a moment, then added casually, "I hope *Mac Dubh* is on his feet soon, then. Will he be well enough to have met Tom Christie?"

"He hasn't met him, no—but I told him."

"Oh? Oh. Well, that's fine, isn't it?"

Roger narrowed his eyes, but Kenny looked away.

His sense of unease about Christie persisted, and seized by a sudden impulse, Roger leaned across the hay and grasped Kenny by the hand, startling the older man considerably. He gave the squeeze, the tap on the knuckle, and then let go.

Kenny gawked at him, blinking in the beam of sunlight from the door. Finally, he set down the empty pail, carefully wiped his hand on his ragged kilt, and offered it formally to Roger.

When he let go, they were still friendly, but the situation between them had altered, very subtly.

"Christie, too," Roger observed, and Kenny nodded.

"Oh, aye. All of us."

"All of you at Ardsmuir? And—Jamie?" He felt a sense of astonishment at the thought.

Kenny nodded again, bending to pick up his bucket.

"Oh, aye, it was *Mac Dubh* started it. Ye didna ken?"

No point in prevarication. He shook his head, dismissing the matter. He'd mention it to Jamie when he saw him—assuming Jamie was in any shape to be questioned then. He fixed Kenny with a direct look.

"So, then. About Christie. Is there anything wrong about the man?"

Lindsay's earlier constraint had disappeared, now that it was no longer a matter of discussing a Masonic brother with an outsider. He shook his head.

"Och, no. It's only I was a bit surprised to see him here. He didna quite get on sae well wi' *Mac Dubh*, is all. If he had another place to go, I wouldna have thought he'd seek out Fraser's Ridge."

Roger was momentarily surprised by the revelation that there was someone from Ardsmuir who didn't think the sun shone out of Jamie Fraser's arse, though on consideration, there was no reason why this shouldn't be so; God knew the man was quite as capable of making enemies as friends.

"Why?"

What he was asking was plain. Kenny looked about the goat-shed, as though seeking escape, but Roger stood between him and the door.

"No great matter," he said, finally, shoulders slumping in capitulation. "Only Christie's a Protestant, see?"

"Aye, I see," Roger said, very dryly. "But he was put in with the Jacobite prisoners. So, was there trouble in Ardsmuir over it, is that what you're telling me?"

Likely enough, he reflected. In his own time, there was no love lost between the Catholics and the stern Scottish sons of John Knox and his ilk. Nothing Scots liked better than a wee spot of religious warfare—and if you got right down to it, that's what the entire Jacobite cause had been.

Take a few staunch Calvinists, convinced that if they didn't tuck their blankets tight, the Pope would nip down the chimney and bite their toes, and bang them up in a prison cheek-by-jowl with men who prayed out loud to the Virgin Mary . . . aye, he could see it. Football riots would be nothing to it, numbers being equal.

"How did he come to be in Ardsmuir, then—Christie, I mean?"

Kenny looked surprised.

"Och, he was a Jacobite—arrested wi' the rest after Culloden, tried and imprisoned."

"A Protestant Jacobite?" It wasn't impossible, or even farfetched—politics made stranger bedfellows than that, and always had. It was unusual, though.

Kenny heaved a sigh, glancing toward the horizon, where the sun was slowly sinking into the pines.

"Come along inside then, MacKenzie. If Tom Christie's

come to the Ridge, I suppose it's best someone tells ye all about it. If I hurry myself, ye'll be in time for your supper."

Rosamund was not at home, but the buttermilk was cool in the well, as advertised. Stools fetched and the buttermilk poured, Kenny Lindsay was good as his word, and started in in businesslike fashion. Christie was a Lowlander, Kenny said; MacKenzie would have gathered as much. From Edinburgh. At the time of the Rising, Christie had been a merchant in the city, with a good business, newly inherited from a hard-working father. Tom Christie was far from lazy, himself, and determined to set up for a gentleman.

With this in mind, and Prince *Tearlach*'s army occupying the city, Christie had put on his best suit of clothes and gone calling on O'Sullivan, the Irishman who had charge of the army commissary. "Naebody kens what passed between them, other than words—but when Christie came out, he had a contract to victual the Highland Army, and an invitation to dance at Holyrood that night." Kenny took a long drink of sweet buttermilk and set down the cup, his mustache thickly coated with white. He nodded wisely at Roger.

"We heard what they were like, those balls at the Palace. *Mac Dubh* told us of them, time and again. The Great Gallery, wi' the portraits of all the kings o' Scotland, and the hearths of blue Dutch tile, big enough to roast an ox. The Prince, and all the great folk who'd come to see him, dressed in silks and laces. And the food! Sweet Jesus, such food as he'd tell about." Kenny's eyes grew round and dreamy, remembering descriptions heard on an empty stomach. His tongue came out and absently licked the buttermilk from his upper lip.

Then he shook himself back to the present.

"Well, so," he said, matter-of-factly. "When the Army left Edinburgh, Christie cam' along. Whether it was to mind his investment, or that he meant to keep himself in the Prince's eye, I canna say."

Roger noted privately that the notion of Christie having acted from patriotic motives wasn't on Kenny Lindsay's list of possibilities. Whether from prudence or ambition, whatever his reasons, Christie had stayed—and stayed too long. He had left the Army at Nairn, the day before Culloden, and started back toward Edinburgh, driving one of the commissary wagons.

"If he'd left the wagon and ridden one o' the horses, he might ha' made it," Kenny said cynically. "But no; he ran smack into a sackful o' Campbells. Government troops, aye?"

Roger nodded.

"I heard tell as he tried to pass himself off as a peddler, but he'd taken a load of corn from a farmhouse on that road, and the farmer swore himself purple that Christie'd been in his yard no more than three days before, wi' a white cockade on his breest. So they took him, and that was that."

Christie had gone first to Berwick Prison, and then—for reasons known only to the Crown—to Ardsmuir, where he had arrived a year before Jamie Fraser.

"I came at the same time." Kenny peered into his empty mug, then reached for the pitcher. "It was an old prison—half-falling down—but they'd not used it for some years. When the Crown decided to reopen it, they brought men from here and from there; maybe a hundred and fifty men, all told. Mostly convicted Jacobites—the odd thief, and a murderer or two." Kenny grinned suddenly, and Roger couldn't help smiling in response.

Kenny was no great storyteller, but he spoke with such simple vividness that Roger had no trouble seeing the scene he described: the soot-streaked stones and the ragged men. Men from all over Scotland, ripped from home, deprived of kin and companions, thrown like bits of rubbish into a heap of compost, where filth, starvation, and close quarters generated a heat of rot that broke down both sensibility and civilness.

Small groups had formed, for protection or for the comfort of society, and there was constant conflict between one group and another. They banged to and fro like pebbles in the surf, bruising each other and now and then crushing some hapless individual who got in between.

"It's food and warmth, aye?" Kenny said dispassionately. "There's naught else to care for, in a place like that."

Among the groups had been a small obdurate knot of Calvinists, headed by Thomas Christie. Mindful of their own, they shared food and blankets, defended each other—and behaved with a dour self-righteousness that roused the Catholics to fury.

"If one of us was to catch afire—and now and then, someone would, bein' pushed into the hearth whilst sleepin'—they wouldna piss on him to put it out," Kenny said, shaking his head. "They wouldna be stealing food, to be sure, but they *would* stand in the corner and pray out loud, rattlin' on and on about whore-mongers and usurers and idolaters and the lot—and makin' damn sure we kent who was meant by it!"

"And then came *Mac Dubh*." The late autumn sun was sinking; Kenny's stubbled face was blurred with shadow, but Roger could see the slight softening that came across it, relaxing the grimness of expression that accompanied Lindsay's reminiscence.

"Something like the Second Coming, was it?" Roger said. He spoke half under his breath, and was surprised when Kenny laughed.

"Only if ye mean some of us kent *Sheumais ruaidh* already. No, man, they'd brought him by boat. Ye'll ken Jamie Roy doesna take to boats, aye?"

"I'd heard something of the sort," Roger answered dryly.

"Whatever ye heard, it's true," Kenny assured him, grinning. "He staggered into the cell green as a lass, vomited in the corner, then crawled under a bench and stayed there for the next day or two."

Upon his emergence, Fraser had kept quiet for a time, watching to see who was who and what was what. But he was a gentleman born, and had been both a laird and a fierce warrior; a man much respected among the Highlanders. The men deferred to him naturally, seeking his opinion, asking his judgment, and the weaker sheltering in his presence.

"And that griped Tom Christie's arse like a saddle-gall," Kenny said, nodding wisely. "See, he'd got to thinking as how he was the biggest frog in the pond, aye?" Kenny ducked his chin and puffed his throat, popping his eyes in illustration, and Roger burst out laughing.

"Aye, I see. And he didn't care for the competition, was that it?"

Kenny nodded, off-hand.

"It wouldna have been so bad, maybe, save that half his wee band of salvationers started creepin' off from their prayers to hear *Mac Dubh* tell stories. But the main thing was the new governor."

Bogle, the prison's original governor, had left, replaced by Colonel Harry Quarry. Quarry was a relatively young man, but an experienced soldier, who had fought at Falkirk and at Culloden. Unlike his predecessor, he viewed the prisoners under his command with a certain respect—and he knew Jamie Fraser by repute, regarding him as an honorable, if defeated, foe.

"Quarry had *Mac Dubh* brought up to see him, soon after he took command at Ardsmuir. I couldna say what happened between them, but soon it was a matter of course; once a week, the guards would come and take *Mac Dubh* off to shave and wash himself, and he would go take a bit of supper with Quarry, and speak to him of whatever was needed."

"And Tom Christie didn't like that, either," Roger guessed. He was forming a comprehensive picture of Christie; ambitious, intelligent—and envious. Competent himself, but lacking Fraser's fortunate birth and skill at warfare—advantages that a self-made merchant with social aspirations might well have resented, even before the catastrophe of Culloden. Roger felt a certain sneaking sympathy for Christie; Jamie Fraser was stiff competition for the merely mortal.

Kenny shook his head, and tilted back to drain his cup. He set it down with a sigh of repletion, raising his brows with a gesture toward the jug. Roger waved a hand, dismissing it.

"No, no more, thanks. But the Freemasons . . . how did that happen? You said it was to do with Christie?" The light was nearly gone. He would have to walk home in the dark—but that was no matter; his curiosity wouldn't let him leave without learning what had happened.

Kenny grunted, rearranging his kilt over his thighs. Hospitality was all very well, but he had chores to do as well. Still, courtesy was courtesy, and he liked the Thrush for himself, not only that he was *Mac Dubh*'s good-son.

"Aye, well." He shrugged, resigning himself. "No,

Christie didna like it a bit, that *Mac Dubh* should be the great one, when he felt it his own place by right." He cast a shrewd glance at Roger, assessing. "I dinna think he kent what it might cost to be chief in a place like that—not 'til later. But that's naught to do with it." He flapped a hand, waving off irrelevancy.

"The thing was, Christie *was* a chief himself; only not just so good at it as was *Mac Dubh*. But there were those who listened to him, and not only the God-naggers."

If Roger was a trifle taken aback at hearing this characterization of his co-religionists, he disregarded it in his eagerness to hear more.

"Aye, so?"

"There was trouble again." Kenny shrugged again. "Small things, aye, but ye could see it happening."

Shifts and schisms, the small faults and fractures that result when two land masses come together, straining and shoving until either mountains rise between them or one is subsumed by the other, in a breaking of earth and a shattering of stone.

"We could see *Mac Dubh* thinking," Kenny said. "But he's no the man to be telling anyone what's in his mind, aye?"

Almost no one, Roger thought suddenly, with the memory of Fraser's voice, so low as barely to be heard beneath the whining autumn wind. *He told me*. The thought was a small sudden warmth in his chest, but he pushed it aside, not to be distracted.

"So one evening *Mac Dubh* came back to us, quite late," Kenny said. "But instead of lying down to his rest, he came and summoned us—me and my brothers, Gavin Hayes, Ronnie Sinclair . . . and Tom Christie."

Fraser had roused the six men quietly from their sleep, and brought them to one of the cell's few windows, where the light of the night sky might shine upon his face. The men had gathered round him, heavy-eyed and aching from the day's labors, wondering what this might mean. Since the last small clash—a fight between two men over a meaningless insult—Christie and Fraser had not exchanged a word, but had kept each man to himself.

It was a soft spring night, the air still crisp, but smelling of fresh green things from the sprouting moor and the salt scent of the distant sea; a night to make a man yearn to run free upon the earth and feel the blood humming dark in his veins. Tired or not, the men roused to it, alive and alert.

Christie was alert; wary-eyed and watchful. Here he was, called face-to-face with Fraser and five of his closest allies—what might they intend? True, they stood in a cell with fifty men sleeping round them, and some of those would come to Christie's aid if he called; but a man could be beaten or killed before anyone knew he was threatened.

Fraser had spoken not a word to start, but smiled and put out his hand to Tom Christie. The other man had hesitated for a moment, suspicious—but there was no choice, after all.

"Ye would have thought *Mac Dubh* held a bolt of lightning in his hand, the way the shock of it went through Christie." Kenny's own hand lay open on the table between them, the palm hard as horn with calluses. The short, thick fingers curled slowly closed, and Kenny shook his head, a broad grin creasing his face.

"I dinna ken how it was *Mac Dubh* found out that Christie was a Freemason, but he knew it. Ye should have seen the look on Tom's face when he realized that Jamie Roy was one besides!

"It was Quarry did it," Kenny explained, seeing the question still on Roger's face. "He was a Master himself, see."

A Master Mason, that was, and head of a small military lodge, composed of the officers of the garrison. One of their members had died recently, though, leaving them one man short of the required seven. Quarry had considered the situation, and after some cautiously exploratory conversation on the matter, invited Fraser to join them. A gentleman was a gentleman, after all, Jacobite or no.

Not precisely an orthodox situation, Roger thought, but this Quarry sounded the type to adjust regulations to suit himself. For that matter, so was Fraser.

"So Quarry made him, and he moved from Apprentice to Fellow Craft in a month's time, and was a Master himself a month after that—and that was when he chose to tell us of it. And so we founded a new lodge that night, the seven of us—Ardsmuir Lodge Number Two."

Roger snorted in wry amusement, seeing it.

"Aye. You six—and Christie." Tom Christie the Protestant. And Christie, stiff-necked but honorable, sworn to the Mason's oaths, would have had no choice, but been obliged to accept Fraser and his Catholics as brethren.

"To start with. Within three months, though, every man in the cells was made Apprentice. And there wasna so much trouble after that."

There wouldn't have been. Freemasons held as basic principles the notions of equality—gentleman, crofter, fisherman, laird; such distinctions were not taken account of in a lodge—and tolerance. No discussion of politics or religion among the brothers, that was the rule.

"I can't think it did Jamie any harm to belong to the officers' lodge, either," Roger said.

"Oh," said Kenny, rather vaguely. "No, I dinna suppose it did." He pushed back his stool and made to rise; the story was done; the dark had come and it was time to light a candle. He made no move toward the clay candlestick that stood on the hearth, but Roger glanced toward the glow of the banked fire, and noticed for the first time that there was no smell of cooking food.

"It's time I was away home for supper," he said, rising himself. "Come with me, aye?"

Kenny brightened noticeably.

"I will, then, *a Smeòraich*, and thanks. Give me a moment to milk the goats, and I'll be right along."

WHEN I CAME BACK upstairs next morning after a delicious breakfast featuring omelettes made with minced buffalo meat, sweet onions, and mushrooms, I found Jamie awake, though not noticeably bright-eyed.

"How are you this morning?" I asked, setting down the tray I had brought him and putting a hand on his forehead. Still warm, but no longer blazing; the fever was nearly gone.

"I wish I were deid, if only so folk would stop asking how am I?" he replied grumpily. I took his mood as an indicator of returning health, and took my hand away.

"Have you used the chamberpot yet this morning?"

He raised one eyebrow, glowering.

"Have you?"

"You know, you are perfectly impossible when you don't feel well," I remarked, rising to peer into the crudely glazed pot for myself. Nothing.

"Does it not occur to ye, Sassenach, that perhaps it's yourself that's impossible when I'm ill? If ye're not feeding me some disgusting substance made of ground beetles and hoof-shavings, you're pokin' my belly and making intimate inquiries into the state of my bowels. Ahh!"

I had in fact pulled down the sheet and prodded him in the lower abdomen. No distention from a swollen bladder; his exclamation appeared to be due entirely to ticklishness. I quickly palpated the liver, but found no hardness—that was a relief.

"Have you a pain in your back?"

"I've a marked pain in my backside," he said, narrowing one eye at me and folding his arms protectively across his middle. "And it's getting worse by the moment."

"I am trying to determine whether the snake venom has affected your kidneys," I explained patiently, deciding to overlook this last remark. "If you can't piss—"

"I can do that fine," he assured me, pulling the sheet up to his chest, lest I demand proof. "Now, just leave me to my breakfast, and I'll—"

"How do you know? You haven't—"

"I have." Seeing my skeptical glance at the chamberpot, he glowered under his brows, and muttered something ending in ". . . window." I swung round to the open window, shutters open and sash raised in spite of the chilly morning air.

"You did what?"

"Well," he defended himself, "I was standing up, and I just thought I would, that's all."

"Why were you standing up?"

"Oh, I thought I would." He blinked at me, innocent as a day-old child. I left the question, going on to more important matters.

"Was there blood in—"

"What have ye brought for my breakfast?" Ignoring my

clinical inquiries, he rolled to one side, and lifted the napkin draped over the tray. He looked at the bowl of bread and milk thus revealed, then turned his head, giving me a look of the most profound betrayal.

Before he could start in on further grievances, I forestalled him by sitting down on the stool beside him and demanding bluntly, “What’s wrong with Tom Christie?”

He blinked, taken by surprise.

“Is something amiss wi’ the man?”

“I wouldn’t know; I haven’t seen him.”

“Well, I havena seen him in more than twenty years myself,” he said, picking up the spoon and prodding the bread and milk suspiciously. “If he’s grown a spare head in that time, it’s news to me.”

“Ho,” I said tolerantly. “You may—and I say *may*—possibly have fooled Roger, but I know you.”

He looked up at that, and gave me a sidelong smile.

“Oh, aye? D’ye know I dinna care much for bread and milk?”

My heart fluttered at sight of that smile, but I maintained my dignity.

“If you’re thinking of blackmailing me into bringing you a steak, you can forget it,” I advised him. “I can wait to find out about Tom Christie, if I have to.” I stood up, shaking out my skirts as though to leave, and turned toward the door.

“Make it parritch with honey, and I’ll tell ye.”

I turned round to find him grinning at me.

“Done,” I said, and came back to the stool.

He considered for a moment, but I could see that he was only deciding how and where to begin.

“Roger told me about the Masonic lodge at Ardsmuir,” I said, to help out. “Last night.”

Jamie shot me a startled look.

“And where did wee Roger Mac find that out? Did Christie tell him?”

“No, Kenny Lindsay did. But evidently Christie gave Roger a Masonic sign of some sort when he arrived. I thought Catholics weren’t allowed to be Masons, actually.”

He raised one eyebrow.

"Aye, well. The Pope wasna in Ardsmuir prison, and I was. Though I havena heard that it's forbidden, forbye. So wee Roger's a Freemason, too, is he?"

"Apparently. And perhaps it isn't forbidden, now. It will be, later." I flapped a hand, dismissing it. "There's something else about Christie, though, isn't there?"

He nodded, and glanced away.

"Aye, there is," he said quietly. "D'ye recall a Sergeant Murchison, Sassenach?"

"Vividly." I had met the Sergeant only once, more than two years previously, in Cross Creek. The name seemed familiar in some other, more recent context, though. Then I recalled where I had heard it.

"Archie Hayes mentioned him—or them. That was it; there were two of them, twins. One of them was the man who shot Archie at Culloden, wasn't he?"

Jamie nodded. His eyes were hooded, and I could see that he was looking back into the time he had spent in Ardsmuir.

"Aye. And to shoot a lad in cold blood was nay more than one could expect from either of them. A crueler pair I hope never to meet." The corner of his mouth turned up, but without humor. "The only thing I ken to Stephen Bonnet's credit is that he killed one o' yon lurdans."

"And the other?" I asked.

"I killed the other."

The room seemed suddenly very quiet, as though the two of us were far removed from Fraser's Ridge, alone together, that bald statement floating in the air between us. He was looking straight at me, blue eyes guarded, waiting to see what I would say. I swallowed.

"Why?" I asked, vaguely surprised at the calmness of my own voice.

He did look away then, shaking his head.

"A hundred reasons," he said softly, "and none." He rubbed absently at his wrist, as though feeling the weight of iron fetters.

"I could tell ye stories of their viciousness, Sassenach, and they would be true. They preyed upon the weak, robbing and beating—and they were the sort who took delight in cruelty for its own sake. There's no recourse against such men, not in a prison. But I dinna say so as an excuse—for there is none."

The prisoners at Ardsmuir were used for labor, cutting peats, quarrying and hauling stone. They worked in small groups, each group guarded by an English soldier, armed with musket and club. The musket, to prevent escape—the club, to enforce orders and ensure submission.

"It was summer. Ye'll ken the summer in the Highlands, Sassenach—the summer dim?"

I nodded. The summer dim was the light of the Highland night, early in summer. So far to the north, the sun barely set on Midsummer's Eve; it would disappear below the horizon, but even at midnight, the sky was pale and milky white, and the air was not dark, but seemed filled with unearthly mist.

The prison governor took advantage of the light, now and then, to work the prisoners into the late hours of the evening.

"We didna mind so much," Jamie said. His eyes were open, but fixed on whatever he was seeing in the summer dim of memory. "It was better to be outside than in. And yet, by the evening, we would be so droukit wi' fatigue that we could barely set one foot before the other. It was like walking in a dream."

Both guards and men were numb with exhaustion, by the time the work of the day was done. The groups of prisoners were collected, formed up into a column, and marched back toward the prison, shuffling across the moorland, stumbling and nodding, drunk with the need to fall down and sleep.

"We were still by the quarry, when they set off; we were to load the wagon wi' the stone-cutting tools and the last of the blocks, and follow. I remember—I heaved a great block up into the wagon bed, and stood back, panting wi' the effort. There was a sound behind me, and I turned to see Sergeant Murchison—Billy, it was, though I didna find that out 'til later."

The Sergeant was no more than a squat black shape in the dim, face invisible against a sky the color of an oyster's shell.

"I wondered, now and then, if I wouldna have done it, had

I seen his face." The fingers of Jamie's left hand stroked his wrist absently, and I realized that he still felt the weight of the irons he had worn.

The Sergeant had raised his club, poked Jamie hard in the ribs, then used it to point to a maul left lying on the ground. Then the Sergeant turned away.

"I didna think about it for a moment," Jamie said softly. "I was on him in two steps, wi' the chain of my fetters hard against his throat. He hadna time to make a sound."

The wagon stood no more than ten feet from the lip of the quarry pool; there was a drop of forty feet straight down, and the water below, a hundred feet deep, black and waveless under that hollow white sky.

"I tied him to one of the blocks and threw him over, and then I went back to the wagon. The two men from my group were there, standing like statues in the dim, watching. They said nothing, nor did I. I stepped up and took the reins, they got into the back of the wagon, and I drove toward the prison. We caught up to the column before too long, and all went back together, without a word. No one missed Sergeant Murchison until the next evening, for they thought he was down in the village, off-duty. I dinna think they ever found him."

He seemed to notice what he was doing, then, and took his hand away from his wrist.

"And the two men?" I asked softly. He nodded.

"Tom Christie and Duncan Innes."

He sighed deeply, and stretched his arms, shifting his shoulders as though to ease the fit of his shirt—though he wore a loose nightshirt. Then he raised one hand and turned it to and fro, frowning at his wrist in the light.

"That's odd," he said, sounding faintly surprised.

"What is?"

"The marks—they're gone."

"Marks . . . from the irons?" He nodded, examining both his wrists in bemusement. The skin was fair, weathered to a pale gold, but otherwise unblemished.

"I had them for years—from the chafing, aye? I never noticed that they'd gone."

I set a hand on his wrist, rubbing my thumb gently over the pulse where his radial artery crossed the bone.

"You didn't have them when I found you in Edinburgh, Jamie. They've been gone a long time."

He looked down at his arms, and shook his head, as though unable to believe it.

"Aye," he said softly. "Well, so has Tom Christie."

Part Nine

A Dangerous Business

96

AURUM

IT WAS QUIET IN THE HOUSE; Mr. Wemyss had gone to the gristmill, taking Lizzie and Mrs. Bug with him, and it was too late in the day for anyone on the Ridge to come visiting—everyone would be at their chores, seeing that the beasts were fed and bedded down, wood and water fetched, the fires built up for supper.

My own beast was already fed and bedded; Adso perched in a somnolent ball in a patch of late sun on the window ledge, feet tucked up and eyes closed in an ecstasy of repletion. My contribution to the supper—a dish Fergus referred to elegantly as *lapin aux chanterelles* (known as rabbit stew to the vulgar among us)—had been burbling cheerfully away in the cauldron since early morning, and needed no attention from me. As for sweeping the floor, polishing the windows, dusting, and general drudgery of that sort . . . well, if women's work was never done, why trouble about how much of it wasn't being accomplished at any given moment?

I fetched down ink and pen from the cupboard, and the big black clothbound casebook, then settled myself to share Adso's sun. I wrote up a careful description of the growth on little Geordie Chisholm's ear, which would bear watching, and added the most recent measurements I had taken of Tom Christie's left hand.

Christie *did* suffer from arthritis in both hands, and had a slight degree of clawing in the fingers. Having observed him closely at dinner, though, I was nearly sure that what I was seeing in the left hand was not arthritis, but Dupuytren's contracture—an odd, hooklike drawing-in of the ring and little fingers toward the palm of the hand, caused by shortening of the palmar aponeurosis.

Ordinarily, I should have been in no doubt, but Christie's hands were so heavily callused from years of labor that I couldn't feel the characteristic nodule at the base of the ring finger. The finger had felt *wrong* to me, though, when I'd first looked at the hand—in the course of stitching a gash across the heel of it—and I'd been checking it, whenever I caught sight of Tom Christie and could persuade him to let me look at it—which wasn't often.

In spite of Jamie's apprehensions, the Christies had been ideal tenants so far, living quietly and keeping largely to themselves, aside from Thomas Christie's schoolmastering, at which he appeared to be strict but effective.

I became aware of a looming presence just behind my head. The sunbeam had moved, and Adso with it.

"Don't even think of it, cat," I said. A rumbling purr of anticipation started up in the vicinity of my left ear, and a large paw reached out and delicately patted the top of my head.

"Oh, all right," I said, resigned. No choice, really, unless I wanted to get up and go write somewhere else. "Have it your way."

Adso could not resist hair. Anyone's hair, whether attached to a head or not. Fortunately, Major MacDonald had been the only person reckless enough to sit down within Adso's reach while wearing a wig, and after all, I *had* got it back, though it meant crawling under the house where Adso had retired with his prey; no one else dared snatch it from his jaws. The Major had been rather austere about the incident, and while it hadn't stopped him coming round to see Jamie now and then, he no longer removed his hat on such visits, but sat drinking chicory coffee at the kitchen table, his tricorne fixed firmly on his head and both eyes fixed firmly upon Adso, monitoring the cat's whereabouts.

I relaxed a bit, not quite purring myself, but feeling quite mellow. It was rather soothing to have the cat knead and comb with his half-sheathed claws, pausing now and then in his delicate grooming to rub his face lovingly against my head. He was only really dangerous if he'd been in the catnip, but that was safely locked up. Eyes half-closed, I contemplated the minor complication of describing Depuytren's contracture without calling it that, Baron Depuytren not having been born yet.

Well, a picture was worth a thousand words, and I thought I could produce a competent line drawing, at least. I did my best, meanwhile wondering how I was to induce Thomas Christie to let me operate on the hand.

It was a fairly quick and simple procedure, but given the lack of anesthesia and the fact that Christie was a strict Presbyterian and a teetotaller . . . perhaps Jamie could sit on his chest, Roger on his legs. If Brianna held his wrist tightly . . .

I gave up the problem for the moment, yawning drowsily. The drowsiness disappeared abruptly, as a three-inch yellow dragonfly came whirring in through the open window with a noise like a small helicopter. Adso sailed through the air after it, leaving my hair in wild disarray and my ribbon—which he appeared to have been quietly chewing—hanging wet and mangled behind my left ear. I removed this object with mild distaste, laid it on the sill to dry, and flipped back a few pages, admiring the neat drawing I had done of Jamie's snakebite, and of Brianna's rattlesnake hypodermic.

The leg, to my amazement, had healed cleanly and well, and while there had been a good bit of tissue sloughing, the maggots had dealt with that so effectively that the only permanent traces were two small depressions in the skin where the original fang marks had been, and a thin, straight scar across the calf where I had made an incision for debridement and maggot-placement. Jamie had a slight limp still, but I thought this would cure itself in time.

Humming in a satisfied sort of way, I flipped back farther, idly browsing through the last few pages of Daniel Rawlings' notes.

> *Josephus Howard . . . chief complaint being a fistula of the rectum, this of so long a standing as to have become badly abscessed, together with an advanced case of Piles. Treated with a decoction of Ale Hoof, mixed with Burnt Alum and small amount of Honey, this boiled together with juice of Marigold.*

A later note on the same page, dated a month later, referred to the efficacy of this compound, with illustrations of the condition of the patient before and after administration. I raised a brow at the drawings; Rawlings was no more an artist than I was, but had succeeded in capturing, to a remarkable degree, the intrinsic discomfort of the condition.

I tapped the quill against my mouth, thinking, then added a careful note in the margin, to the effect that a diet rich in fibrous vegetables should be recommended as an adjunct to this treatment, useful also in preventing both constipation and the more serious complications thereof—nothing like a little object lesson!

I wiped the quill, laid it down, and turned the page, wondering whether Ale Hoof was a plant—and if so, which one—or a suppurative condition of horses' feet. I could hear Jamie rustling about in his study; I'd go ask him in a moment.

I nearly missed it. It had been jotted on the back of the page containing the drawing of Mr. Howard's fistula, evidently added as a casual afterthought on the day's activities.

> *Have spoke with Mr. Hector Cameron of River Run, who begs me come examine his wife's eyes, her sight being sadly affected. It is a far distance to his plantation, but he will send a horse.*

That bit overcame the soporific atmosphere of the afternoon at once. Fascinated, I sat up and turned the page, looking to see whether the doctor had in fact examined Jocasta. I had—with some difficulty—persuaded her to allow me to examine her eyes once, and I was curious as to Rawlings' conclusions. Without an ophthalmoscope, there was no way of making sure of the cause of her blindness, but I had strong suspicions—and I could at least rule out such things as cataracts and diabetes with a fair amount of certainty. I wondered whether Rawlings had seen anything I had missed, or whether her condition had changed noticeably since he had seen her.

Bled the smith of a pint, purged his wife with senna oil (10 minims), and administered 3 minims of same to the cat (gratis), I having observed a swarming of worms in the animal's stool.

I smiled at that; however crude his methods, Daniel Rawlings was a good doctor. I wondered once again what had happened to him, and whether I should ever get the chance to meet him. I had the rather sad feeling that I should not; I couldn't imagine a doctor not returning somehow to claim such beautiful instruments as his, if he was in any condition to do so.

Under the prodding of my curiosity, Jamie had obligingly made inquiries, but with no results. Daniel Rawlings had set out for Virginia—leaving his box of instruments behind—and had promptly vanished into thin air.

Another page, another patient; bleeding, purging, lancing of boils, removal of an infected nail, drawing of an abscessed tooth, cautery of a persistent sore on a woman's leg . . . Rawlings had found plenty of business in Cross Creek. Had he ever made it as far as River Run, though?

Yes, there it was, a week later and several pages on.

Reached River Run after a dire journey, wind and rain fit to sink a ship, and the road washed away entirely in places, so was obliged to ride cross-country, lashed by hail, mud to the eyebrows. Had set out at dawn with Mr. Cameron's black servant, who brought a horse for me—did not reach sanctuary 'til well past dark, exhausted and starving. Made welcome by Mr. Cameron, who gave me brandy.

Having gone to the expense of procuring a doctor, Hector Cameron had evidently decided to make the most of the opportunity, and had had Rawlings examine all the slaves and servants, as well as the master of the house himself.

Aged Seventy-three, of middling height, broad-shouldered, but somewhat bowed in Stature, Rawlings

> had written of Hector, *with hands so gnarled by rheumatism as to make the handling of any implement more subtle than a spoon impossible. Otherwise, is well-preserved, very Vigorous in his age. Complains of rising in the night, painful Micturition. I am inclined to suspect a prurient Distemper of the Bladder, rather than Stone or chronic Disease of the inward male parts, as the complaint is recurrent, but not of long standing on any occasion of its evidence—two weeks being the average duration of each attack and accompanied by Burning in the male Organ. A low fever, tenderness upon palpation of the lower abdomen and a Black Urine, smelling strongly, incline me further to this belief.*
>
> *The household being possessed of a good quantity of dried cranberries, have prescribed a decoction, the inspissated juice to be drunk thrice daily, a cupful at a time. Also recommend infusion of Cleavers, drunk morning and evening, for its cooling Effect, and in case of there being Gravel present in the Bladder, which may aggravate this Condition.*

I found myself nodding approvingly. I didn't always agree with Rawlings, either in terms of diagnosis or treatment, but I thought he was likely spot-on on this occasion. What about Jocasta, though?

There she was, on the next page.

> *Jocasta Cameron, Sixty-four years in age, tri-gravida, well-nourished and in good Health generally, very youthful in Aspect.*

Tri-gravida? I paused for a moment at that matter-of-fact remark. So plain, so stark a term, to stand for the bearing—let alone the loss—of three children. To have raised three children past the dangers of infancy, only to lose them all at once, and in such cruel fashion. The sun was warm, but I felt a chill on my heart, thinking of it.

If it was Brianna? Or little Jemmy? How did a woman bear such loss? I had done it, myself, and still had no idea. It had been a long time, and yet still, now and then, I would wake in the night, feeling a child's warm weight sleeping on my breast, her breath warm on my neck. My hand rose and touched my shoulder, curved as though the child's head lay there.

I supposed that it might be easier to have lost a daughter at birth, without the years of acquaintance that would leave ragged holes in the fabric of daily life. And yet I knew Faith to the last atom of her being; there was a hole in my heart that fit her shape exactly. Perhaps it was that that had been a natural death, at least; it gave me the feeling that she was still with me in some way, was taken care of, and not alone. But to have children slain in blood, butchered in war?

So many things could happen to children in this time. I returned to my perusal of her case history with a troubled mind.

> *No sign of organic Illness, nor external Damage to the Eyes. The White of the Eye is clear, the lashes free of any Matter, no Tumor visible. The Pupils respond normally to a Light passed before them, and to shading of the Light. A candle held close to one side illuminates the vitreous Humor of the Eye, but shows no Defect therein. I note a slight Clouding, indicating incipient Cataract in the lens of the right eye, but this is insufficient to explain the gradual loss of Sight.*

"Hum," I said aloud. Both Rawlings' observations and his conclusions matched mine. He briefly noted the length of time over which sight had failed—roughly two years—and the process of its failure—nothing abrupt, but a gradual shrinking of the field of vision.

I thought it likely had taken longer; sometimes the loss was so gradual that people didn't notice the tiny decrements at all, until the sight was seriously threatened.

> *. . . bits of the vision whittled away like cheese parings. Even the small remnant of sight remaining is of use only in dim light, as patient exhibits great irritation and pain when the eye is exposed to strong sunlight.*

I have seen this condition twice before, always in persons of some age, though not so far advanced. Gave it as my opinion that sight would soon be completely obliterated, with no amelioration possible. Fortunately, Mr. Cameron has a black servant capable of reading, whom he has given to his wife to accompany her and warn her of obstacles, likewise to read to her and apprise her of her surroundings.

It had gone further than that now; the light had gone, and Jocasta was entirely blind. So, a progressive condition—that didn't tell me much, most of them were. When had Rawlings seen her?

It could be any number of conditions—macular degeneration, tumor of the optic nerve, parasitic damage, retinitis pigmentosa, temporal arteritis—probably not retinal detachment, that would have happened abruptly—but my own preliminary suspicion was of glaucoma. I remembered Phaedre, Jocasta's body servant, wringing out cloths in cold tea, observing that her mistress was suffering from headache *"again,"* in a tone of voice that suggested this was a frequent occurrence—and Duncan asking me to make up a lavender pillow, to ease his wife's "megrims."

The headaches might have nothing to do with Jocasta's eyesight, though—and I had not inquired at the time as to the nature of the headaches; they might be simple tension headaches or migraines, rather than the pressure-band type that might—or might not—attend glaucoma. Arteritis would cause frequent headache, too, after all. The frustrating thing about it was that glaucoma by itself had absolutely no predictable symptoms—save eventual blindness. It was caused by a failure of proper drainage of the fluid inside the eyeball, so that pressure inside the eye increased to the point of damage, with no warning at all to the patient or her physician. But other kinds of blindness were largely symptomless as well . . .

I was still contemplating the possibilities, when I became aware that Rawlings had continued his notes onto the back of the page—in Latin.

I blinked at that, a little surprised. I could tell that he had written it as a continuation of the earlier passage; quill-writing shows a characteristic darkening and fading of words, as the ink is renewed with each dip of the pen, and the shading of each passage tended to be different, as different inks were used. No, this had been written at the same time as the passage on the preceding page.

But why drop suddenly into Latin? Rawlings knew some Latin, plainly—which argued some degree of formal education, even if not formal medical education—but he didn't normally use it in his clinical notes, beyond the occasional word or phrase required for the formal description of some condition. Here was a page and a half of Latin, though, and written in scrupulous letters, smaller than his usual writing, as though he had thought carefully about the contents of the passage—or perhaps as though he felt secretive about it, as the Latin itself seemed to argue.

I flipped back through the casebook, checking to verify my impression. No, he had written in Latin here and there—but not often, and always as he did here; as the continuation of a passage begun in English. How odd. I turned back to the passage concerning River Run and began to try to puzzle it out.

Within a sentence or two, I abandoned the effort and went to find Jamie. He was in his own study, across the hall, writing letters. Or not.

The inkstand—made of a small gourd with a cork to keep the ink from drying—stood at hand, freshly filled; I could smell the woody reek of oak galls brewed with iron filings. A new turkey quill lay on the desk, trimmed to a point of such sharpness that it looked more suitable for stabbing than writing, and a fresh sheet of paper lay on the blotter, three words black and lonely at its head. It took no more than a glance at his face to know what they said.

My dear Sister.

He looked up at me, smiled wryly, and shrugged.

"What shall I say?"

"I don't know." At sight of him, I had shut the casebook, clasping it under one arm. I came in and stood behind him, laying a hand on his shoulder. I squeezed gently, and he laid his own hand over mine for a moment, then reached to pick up the quill.

"I canna go on saying that I'm sorry." He rolled the quill slowly to and fro between his thumb and middle finger. "I've said it in each letter. If she was disposed to forgive me . . ."

If she was, Jenny would have replied by now to at least one of the letters that he sent faithfully to Lallybroch each month.

"Ian's forgiven you. And the children." Missives from Jamie's brother-in-law arrived sporadically—but they did come, along with occasional notes from his namesake, Young Jamie, and now and then a line from Maggie, Kitty, Michael, or Janet. But the silence from Jenny was so deafening as to drown out all other communications.

"Aye, it would be worse if . . ." he trailed off, staring at the blank paper. In fact, nothing could be worse than this estrangement. Jenny was closer to him, more important to him, than anyone in the world—with the possible exception of myself.

I shared his bed, his life, his love, his thoughts. She had shared his heart and soul since the day he was born—until the day when he had lost her youngest son. Or so she plainly saw it.

It pained me to see him go on carrying the guilt of Ian's disappearance—and I felt some small resentment toward Jenny. I understood the depth of her loss, and sympathized with her grief, but still, Ian wasn't dead—so far as we knew. She alone could absolve Jamie, and surely she must know it.

I pulled up a stool and sat down by him, laying the book aside. A small stack of papers lay to one side, covered with his labored writing. It cost him dearly to write, wrong-handed, and that hand crippled—and yet he wrote stubbornly, almost every evening, recording the small events of the day. Visitors to the Ridge, the health of the animals, progress in building, new settlers, news from the Eastern counties . . . He wrote it down, one word at a time, to be sent off when some visitor arrived who would take the accumulated pages away, on the first stage of their precarious journey to Scotland. All the letters might not arrive at their destination, but some would. Likewise, most letters from Scotland would reach us, too—if they were sent.

For a time, I had hoped that Jenny's letter had simply been mis-sent, misplaced, lost somewhere in transit. But it had been too long, and I had stopped hoping. Jamie hadn't.

"I thought perhaps I should send her this." He shuffled through the stack of papers at the side of the desk, and withdrew a small sheet, stained and grubby, ragged along one edge where it had been torn from a book.

It was a message from Ian; the only concrete evidence we had that the boy was still alive and well. It had reached us at the Gathering in November, through the agency of John Quincy Myers, a mountain man who roamed the wilderness, as much at home with Indian as with settler, and more at home with deer and possum than with anyone who lived in a house.

Written in clumsy Latin as a joke, the note assured us that Ian was well, and happy. Married to a girl "in the Mohawk fashion" (meaning, I thought, that he had decided to share her house, bed, and hearth, and she had decided to let him), he expected to become a father himself "in the spring." And that was all. Spring had come and gone, with no further word. Ian wasn't dead, but the next thing to it. The chances of us ever seeing him again were remote, and Jamie knew it; the wilderness had swallowed him.

Jamie touched the ratty paper gently, tracing the round, still-childish letters. He'd told Jenny what the note said, I knew—but I also knew why he hadn't sent the original before. It was the only physical link with Ian; to give it up was in some final way to relinquish him to the Mohawk.

"Ave!" said the note, in Ian's half-formed writing. *"Ian salutat avunculus Jacobus."* Ian salutes his uncle James.

Ian was more to Jamie than one of his nephews. Much as he loved all of Jenny's children, Ian was special—a foster-son, like Fergus; but unlike Fergus, a son of Jamie's blood, replacement in a way for the son he had lost. That son wasn't dead, either, but could not ever be claimed. The world seemed suddenly full of lost children.

"Yes," I said, my throat tight. "I think you should send it. Jenny should have it, even if . . ." I coughed, reminded suddenly by the note of the casebook. I reached for it, hoping it would distract him.

"Um. Speaking of Latin . . . there's an odd bit in here. Could you have a look at it, perhaps?"

"Aye, of course." He set Ian's note aside and took the book from me, moving it so the last of the afternoon sun fell across the page. He frowned slightly, a finger tracing the lines of writing.

"Christ, the man's no more grasp of Latin grammar than ye have yourself, Sassenach."

"Oh, thanks. We can't all be scholars now, can we?" I moved closer, peering over his shoulder as he read. I'd been right, then; Rawlings didn't drop casually into Latin for the fun of it, or merely to show off his erudition.

"An oddity . . ." Jamie said, translating slowly as his finger moved across the page. "I am awake—no, he means 'I was wakened,' I think—by sounds in the chamber adjoining that where I lay. I am thinking—'I thought'—that my patient went to make water, and am risen to follow . . . Why should he do that, I wonder?"

"The patient—it's Hector Cameron, by the way—had a problem with his bladder. Rawlings would have wanted to watch him urinate, to see what sort of difficulty he had, whether he had pain, or blood in the urine, that sort of thing."

Jamie gave me a side-long glance, one brow raised, then shook his head and returned to the casebook, murmuring something about the peculiar tastes of physicians.

"*Homo procediente* . . . the man proceeds . . . Why does he call him 'the man,' rather than his name?"

"He was writing in Latin to be secret," I said, impatient to hear what came next. "If Cameron saw his name in the book, he'd be curious, I expect. What happened?"

"The man goes out—outdoors, does he mean, or only out of his chamber?—outdoors, it must be . . . goes out, and I follow. He walks steadily, quickly . . . Why should he not? Oh, here—I am puzzled. I give—have given—the man twelve grains of laudanum . . ."

"Twelve *grains*? Are you sure that's what he says?" I leaned over Jamie's arm, peering, but sure enough—he pointed to the entry, inscribed in clear black and white. "But that's enough laudanum to fell a horse!"

"Aye, 'twelve grains of laudanum to assist sleep,' he says.

No wonder the doctor was puzzled, then, to see Cameron scampering about the lawn in the middle of the night."

I nudged him with an elbow.

"Get on!"

"Mmphm. Well, he says he went to the necessary house—no doubt thinking to find Cameron—but no one was there, and there wasna any smell of . . . er . . . he didna think anyone had been there recently."

"You needn't be delicate on my account," I said.

"I know," he said, grinning. "But my own sensibilities are no quite coarsened yet, in spite of my long association with you, Sassenach. Ow!" He jerked away, rubbing his arm where I had pinched him. I lowered my brows and gave him a stare, though inwardly pleased to have lightened the mood for both of us.

"Less about your sensibilities, *if* you please," I said, tapping my foot. "Besides, you haven't got any in the first place, or you'd never have married me. Where was Cameron, then?"

He scanned the page, lips silently forming words.

"He doesna ken. He prowled about the place until the butler popped out of his wee hole, thinking him a marauder of some sort, and threatened him wi' a bottle of whisky."

"A formidable weapon, that," I observed, smiling at the thought of a nightcapped Ulysses, brandishing his implement of destruction. "How do you say 'bottle of whisky' in Latin?"

Jamie gave the page a glance.

"*He* says *'aqua vitae,'* which is doubtless as close as he could manage. It must have been whisky, though; he says the butler gave him a dram to cure the shock."

"So he never found Cameron?"

"Aye, he did, after he left Ulysses. Tucked up in his wee white bed, snoring. Next morning, he asked, but Cameron didna recall getting up in the night." He flipped the page over with one finger and glanced at me. "Would the laudanum keep him from remembering?"

"It could do," I said, frowning. "Easily. But it's simply incredible that anyone with that much laudanum in him could have been up marching round in the first place . . . unless . . ." I cocked a brow at him, recalling Jocasta's remarks during our discussion at River Run. "Any chance your Uncle Hector was an opium-eater or the like? Someone who took a great deal of laudanum by habit would have a tolerance for it, and might not be really affected by Rawlings' dose."

Never one to be shocked by any intimation of depravity among his relatives, Jamie considered the suggestion, but finally shook his head.

"If so, I've heard naught of it. But then," he added logically, "there's no reason anyone would tell me so."

That was true enough. If Hector Cameron had had the means to indulge in imported narcotics—and he certainly had, River Run being one of the most prosperous plantations in the area—then it would have been no one's business save his own. Still, I did think someone might have mentioned it.

Jamie's mind was running on other lines.

"Why would a man leave his house in dead of night to piss, Sassenach?" he asked. "I *know* Hector Cameron had a chamber pot; I've used it myself. It had his name and the Cameron badge painted on the bottom."

"Excellent question." I stared down at the page of cryptic scratchings. "If Hector Cameron was having great pain or difficulty—passing a kidney stone, for example—I suppose he might have gone out, to avoid waking the house."

"I havena heard my uncle was an opium-eater, but I havena heard he was ower-mindful of his wife or servants' convenience, either," Jamie observed, rather cynically. "From all accounts, Hector Cameron was a bit of a bastard."

I laughed.

"No doubt that's why your aunt finds Duncan so congenial."

Adso wandered in, the remains of the dragonfly in his mouth, and sat down at my feet so I could admire his prize.

"Fine," I told him, with a cursory pat. "Don't spoil your appetite, though; there are a lot of cockroaches in the pantry that I want you to deal with."

"Ecce homo," Jamie murmured thoughtfully, tapping a finger on the casebook. "A French homo, do you think?"

"A what?" I stared at him.

"Does it not occur to ye, Sassenach, that perhaps it wasna Cameron that the doctor followed outside?"

"Not 'til this minute, no." I leaned forward and peered at the page. "Why ought it to be anyone else, though, let alone a Frenchman?"

Jamie pointed to the edge of the page, where there were a few small drawings; doodles, I'd thought. The one under his finger was a fleur-de-lis.

"Ecce homo," he said again, tapping it. "The doctor wasna easy in his mind about the man he followed—that's why he didna call him by name. If Cameron were drugged, then it was someone else who left the house that night—yet he doesna speak of anyone else who was present."

"But he might not mention it, unless he'd examined whoever it was," I argued. "He does put in personal notes, but most of this is strictly his case histories; his observations of his patients and the treatments he was administering. But still . . ." I frowned at the page. "A fleur-de-lis scribbled in the margin doesn't necessarily mean anything at all, let alone that there was a Frenchman there." Save Fergus, Frenchmen were not at all common in North Carolina. There were some French settlements south of Savannah, I knew—but that was hundreds of miles away.

The fleur-de-lis *could* be nothing more than a random doodle—and yet, Rawlings hadn't made such scribbles anywhere else in his book that I recalled. When he added drawings, they were careful and to the point, intended as a reminder to himself, or as a guide to any physician who should come after him.

Above the fleur-de-lis was a figure that looked rather like a triangle with a small circle at the apex and a curved base; below it was a sequence of letters. *Au et Aq*.

"A . . . u," I said slowly, looking at that. "Aurum."

"Gold?" Jamie glanced up at me, surprised. I nodded.

"It's the scientific abbreviation for gold, yes. 'Aurum et aqua.' Gold and water—I suppose he means *goldwasser*, bits of gold flake suspended in an aqueous solution. It's a remedy for arthritis—oddly enough, it often works, though no one knows why."

"Expensive," Jamie observed. "Though I suppose Cameron could afford it—perhaps he saved an ounce or two of his gold bars, eh?"

"He did say Cameron suffered from arthritis." I frowned at the page and its cryptic marginalia. "Maybe he meant to advise the use of *goldwasser* for the condition. But I don't know about the fleur-de-lis or that other thing—" I pointed at it. "It's not the symbol for any medical treatment *I* know of."

To my surprise, Jamie laughed.

"I shouldna think so, Sassenach. It's a Freemason's compass."

"It is?" I blinked at it, then glanced at Jamie. "Was Cameron a Mason?"

He shrugged, running a hand through his hair. Jamie never spoke of his own association with the Freemasons. He had been "made," as the saying went, in Ardsmuir, and beyond any secrecy imposed by membership in the society, he seldom spoke of anything that had happened between those dank stone walls.

"Rawlings must have been one as well," he said, clearly reluctant to talk about Freemasonry, but unable to keep from making logical connections. "Else he'd not have kent what that is." One long finger tapped the sign of the compass.

I didn't know quite what to say next, but was saved from indecision by Adso, who spit out a pair of amber wings, and sprang up onto the desk in search of more hors d'oeuvres. Jamie made a grab for the inkwell with one hand, and seized his new quill protectively in the other. Deprived of prey, Adso strolled to the edge of the desk and sat on the stack of Jamie's letters, tail waving gently as he pretended to admire the view.

Jamie's eyes narrowed at this insolence.

"Take your furry wee arse off of my correspondence, beast," he said, poking at Adso with the sharp end of his quill. Adso's big green eyes widened as they fixed on the tip of the moving feather, and his shoulder blades tensed in anticipation. Jamie twiddled the quill tantalizingly, and Adso made an abortive swipe at it with one paw.

I seized the cat hastily before mayhem could ensue, lifting him off the papers with a surprised and indignant *mirp!* of protest.

"No, that's *his* toy," I said to the cat, and gave Jamie a reproving look. "Come along now; there are cockroaches to attend to."

I reached for the casebook with my free hand, but to my surprise, Jamie stopped me.

"Let me keep it a bit longer, Sassenach," he said. "There's something verra odd about the notion of a French Freemason wandering River Run by night. I should like to see what else Dr. Rawlings might have to say when he's speaking Latin."

"All right." I hoisted Adso, who had begun to purr loudly in anticipation of cockroaches, to my shoulder, and glanced out the window. The sun had set to a burning glow beyond the chestnut trees, and I could hear the noise of women and children in the kitchen; Mrs. Bug was starting to lay the supper, helped by Brianna and Marsali.

"Dinner soon," I said, and bent to kiss the top of Jamie's head, where the last of the light touched his crown with fire. He smiled and touched his fingers to his lips and then to me, but he had already gone back to a perusal of the close-written pages by the time I reached the door. The single sheet with its three black words lay at the edge of the desk, forgotten—for the moment.

97

CONDITIONS OF THE BLOOD

I CAUGHT A FLASH OF BROWN outside the door, and Adso shot off the counter as though someone had shouted "Fish!" The next best thing, evidently; it was Lizzie, on her way back from the dairy shed, a bowl of clotted cream in one hand, a butter dish in the other, and a large jug of milk pressed to her bosom, precariously held in place by her crossed wrists. Adso was twining round her ankles like a furry rope, in obvious hopes of tripping her up and making her drop the booty.

"Think again, cat," I told him, reaching to rescue the milk jug.

"Oh, thank ye, ma'am." Lizzie relaxed, easing her shoulders with a little sigh. "It's only as I didna want to be making two trips." She sniffed and tried to wipe her nose with a forearm, imperiling the butter.

I snatched a handkerchief from my pocket and applied it, repressing the maternal impulse to say, "Now, blow."

"Thank ye, ma'am," she repeated, bobbing.

"Are you quite well, Lizzie?" Without waiting for an answer, I took her by the arm and towed her into my surgery, where the large windows gave me light enough to see by.

"I'm well enough, ma'am. Truly, I'm fine!" she protested, clutching the cream and butter to her as though for protection.

She was pale—but Lizzie was always pale, looking as though she had not a corpuscle to spare. There was an odd pallid look to her skin, though, that gave me an uneasy feeling. It had been nearly a year since her last attack of malarial fever, and she did seem generally well, but . . .

"Come here," I said, drawing her toward a pair of high stools. "Have a seat, just for a moment."

Clearly unwilling, but not daring to protest, she sat down, balancing the dishes on her knees. I took them from her and—after a glance at Adso's unblinkingly predatory green gaze—put them in the cupboard for safekeeping.

Pulse normal—normal for Lizzie, that is; she tended always to be a trifle fast and shallow. Breathing . . . all right, no catch or wheezing. The lymph glands under the jaw were palpable, but that was not unusual; the malaria had left them permanently enlarged, like the curve of a quail's egg under the tender skin. Those in the neck were enlarged now, too, though—and those I generally could *not* feel.

I thumbed an eyelid up, peering closely at the pale gray orb that looked anxiously back. Superficially fine, though slightly bloodshot. Again, though—there was something not quite . . . right . . . about her eyes, though I couldn't put my finger on what that something might be. Could there possibly be a tinge of yellow to the white? I frowned, turning her head to the side with a hand under her unresisting chin.

"Hullo, there. Everything all right?" Roger paused in the doorway, a very large, very dead bird held nonchalantly in one hand.

"A turkey!" I exclaimed, summoning a warm note of admiration. I liked turkeys, all right, but Jamie and Bree had killed five of the enormous birds the week before, introducing a certain note of monotony into dinner of late. Three of the things were hanging in the smoking shed at the moment. On the other hand, wild turkeys were wily and difficult to kill, and so far as I knew, Roger had never managed to bag one before.

"Did you shoot it yourself?" I asked, coming dutifully to admire the thing. He held it by the feet, and the big cupped wings flapped halfway open, the breast-feathers catching sunlight in iridescent patterns of blackish green.

"No." Roger's face was flushed, from sun, excitement, or both, a warm hue spreading under the tanned skin. "I ran it down," he said proudly. "Hit it in the wing with a stone, then chased it and broke its neck."

"Wonderful," I said, with somewhat more genuine enthusiasm. We wouldn't have to pick buckshot out of the flesh while cleaning it, or risk breaking a tooth in the eating.

"It's a lovely bird, Mr. Mac." Lizzie had slid off her stool and come to admire it, too. "Such a fat one as it is! Will I take it and clean it for ye, then?"

"What? Oh, thanks, Lizzie, no—I'll, um, take care of it." The color rose a little higher under his skin, and I suppressed a smile. He meant he wanted to show off his catch to Brianna, in all its glory. He shifted the bird to his left hand, and held out the right to me, wrapped in a bloodstained cloth.

"I had a bit of an accident, wrestling the bird. Do you think perhaps . . . ?"

I unwrapped the cloth, pursing my lips at what lay underneath. The turkey, fighting for its life, had ripped three jagged gashes across the back of his hand with its claws. The blood had mostly clotted, but fresh drops welled up from the deepest puncture, rolling down his finger to drip on the floor.

"Oh, just a bit," I said, glancing up at him with eyebrows raised. "Yes, I do think perhaps. Come over here and sit down. I'll clean it, and—Lizzie! Wait a moment!"

Lizzie, seizing the distraction as an opportunity to escape, was sidling toward the door. She stopped as though shot in the back.

"Really, ma'am, I'm quite all right," she pleaded. "Nothing's wrong, really there isn't."

In fact, I had stopped her only to remind her to retrieve the butter and cream from the cupboard. Too late for the milk; Adso stood on his hind legs, head and shoulders stuck completely into the mouth of the jug, from which came small lapping noises. The sound of it echoed the small splat of Roger's blood dripping on the floor, though, and gave me a sudden thought.

"I've had an idea," I said. "Sit down again, Lizzie—I want just a tiny bit of your blood."

Lizzie looked like a field mouse that has suddenly looked up from its crumb to discover itself in the midst of a meeting of barn owls, but she wasn't the sort to defy an order from anyone. Very reluctantly, she climbed back onto the stool beside Roger, who had laid his turkey on the floor beside him.

"Why do you want blood?" he asked, interested. "You can have all ye want of mine, for free." Grinning, he lifted the injured hand.

"A generous offer," I said, laying out a linen cloth and a handful of clean glass rectangles. "But you haven't had malaria, have you?" I plucked Adso out of the milk jug by the scruff of the neck and dropped him on the floor, before reaching into the cupboard above.

"Not so far as I know." Roger was watching my preparations, deeply interested.

Lizzie gave a small, forlorn sound of mirth.

"Ye'd ken it well enough if ye had, sir."

"I suppose I would." He gave her a look of sympathy. "Very nasty, from all I hear."

"It is that. Your bones ache so ye think they've all broken inside ye, and your eyes flame like a demon's. Then the sweat pours off your skin in rivers, and the chills come on, fit to crack your teeth with the chatterin' . . ." She hunched into herself, shuddering at the memory. "I did think it was gone, though," she said, glancing uneasily at the lancet I was sterilizing in the flame of my alcohol lamp.

"I hope it is," I said, frowning at the tiny blade. I picked up a small cloth and the blue glass bottle that held my distilled alcohol, and thoroughly cleaned the tip of her middle finger. "Some people never have another attack after the first, and I do hope you're one of them, Lizzie. But for most people, it does come back now and then. I'm trying to find out whether yours might be coming back. Ready?"

Without waiting for her nod, I jabbed the lancet swiftly through the skin, then set it down and snatched up a glass slide. I squeezed the fingertip, dotting generous blood drops on each of three slides, then wrapped the cloth round her finger and let go.

Working swiftly, I took up a clean slide and laid it over a blood-drop, then drew it quickly away, smearing the blood thinly across the original slide. Again, and a third, and I laid them down to dry.

"That's all, then, Lizzie," I told her with a smile. "It will take a bit of preparation before these are ready to look at. When they are, I'll call you, shall I?"

"Oh . . . no, that's quite all right, ma'am," she murmured, sliding off the high stool with a fearful look at the blood-smeared slides. "I dinna need to see." She set down the discarded cloth, brushed at her apron, and scampered out of the room—forgetting the butter and cream, after all.

"Sorry to keep you waiting," I apologized to Roger. "I just thought . . ." I reached into the cupboard, withdrew three small earthenware pots, and uncorked them.

"Not a problem," he assured me. He watched with fascination as I checked each slide to be sure the blood-smear was dry, then slid a bit of glass into each of the pots.

"All right, then." Now I could turn my attention to cleaning and dressing his hand—a straightforward-enough process. "Not so bad as I thought," I murmured, wiping caked blood off his knuckles. "It bled quite a bit, which is good."

"Aye, if you say so." He didn't flinch at all, but carefully kept his face turned away from what I was doing, his attention focused out the window.

"Washes out the wounds," I explained, dabbing with alcohol. "I needn't swab so deeply to clean them."

He drew in his breath with a sharp hiss, then, to distract himself, nodded at the pots where the slides were soaking.

"Speaking of blood, what are you doing with Mistress Mousie's?"

"Trying something. I don't know whether it will work or not, but I've made up some experimental stains, using extracts from some of the dyeing-plants. If any of them work on blood, I'll be able to see the red cells clearly under the microscope—and what's in them." I spoke with a mixture of hope and tentative excitement.

Trying to duplicate cellular stains with the materials I had at hand was a long shot—but not totally unfeasible. I had the ordinary solvents—alcohol, water, turpentine and its distillates—and I had a great range of plant pigments to try, from indigo to rosehips, along with a good working knowledge of their dyeing properties.

I hadn't any crystal violet or carbofuchsin, but I had been able to produce a reddish stain that made epithelial cells highly visible, if only temporarily. It remained to be seen whether the same stain would work on red blood cells and their inclusions, or whether I should need to try differential staining.

"What *is* in them?" Roger turned to look at me, interested.

"Plasmodium vivax," I said. "The protozoan that causes malaria."

"You can *see* it? I thought germs were much too small to see, even under a microscope!"

"You're as bad as Jamie," I said tolerantly. "Though I do love to hear a Scotsman say 'gerrrms.' Such a sinister word, spoken in a deep voice with that rolling 'r,' you know."

Roger laughed. The hanging had destroyed much of the power of his voice, but the lower, harsher registers remained.

"Nearly as good as murrrderr," he said, rumbling like a cement mixer.

"Oh, nothing's as good as 'murrrderr' to a Scot," I assured him. "Bloody-minded blokes that you all are."

"What, all of us?" He grinned, plainly not minding this gross generalization in the least.

"To a man," I assured him. "Mild enough to look at, but insult a Scot or trouble his family, and it's up wi' the bonnets of bonnie Dundee. All the blue bonnets are over the border, and next thing you know, it's lances and swords all over the Haughs of Cromdale."

"Remarkable," he murmured, eyeing me. "And you've been married to one for . . ."

"Quite long enough." I finished my sponging and rinsing and blotted the back of his hand, small red patches soaking into the fresh gauze. "Speaking of bloody men," I added casually, "do you happen to know your own blood type?"

One dark brow went up at that. Well, I didn't mean to slip it by him, after all; I'd only wanted a way to broach the question.

"Yes," he said slowly, "I do. It's O-positive."

The dark green eyes were fixed on mine, steady with interest.

"Very interesting," I said. I replaced the gauze square with a fresh one, and started winding a bandage around it.

"Just *how* interesting is it?" he asked. I glanced at him, and met his eyes.

"Moderately." I drew out the slides, dripping pink and blue dyes. One slide I propped against the milk jug to dry, the other two I exchanged, putting the pink slide into the blue stain, and vice-versa.

"There are three main blood groups," I said, blowing gently on the propped-up slide. "More really, but those three are the ones everyone knows about. It's called the ABO grouping, and everyone is said to have type A, type B, or type O blood. The thing is, like all your other traits, it's determined genetically, and—human beings being heterosexual, generally speaking—you have one half your genes for any trait from one parent, the other half from the other."

"I dimly recall that bit from school," Roger said dryly. "All those bloody charts—excuse me—about hemophilia in the Royal Family, and the like. I assume it has a certain amount of personal significance now, though?"

"I don't know," I said. "It might have." The pink slide

looked dry; I laid it gently on the stage of the microscope and bent to adjust the mirror.

"The thing is," I said, squinting through the eyepiece as I twiddled the focusing knob, "those blood groups are to do with antibodies—little odd-shaped things on the surfaces of blood cells. That is, people who are type A have one sort of antibody on their cells, people with type B have a different sort, and people with type O don't have any at all."

The red blood cells showed up suddenly, faintly stained, like round pink ghosts. Here and there a blotch of darker pink indicated what might be a bit of cellular debris, or perhaps one of the larger white blood cells. Not much else, though.

"So," I went on, lifting the other two slides from their baths, "if one of his parents gave a child the gene for type O blood, and the other gave him one for type A, the child's blood will show up as type A, because it's the antibodies that are tested for. The child does still *have* the gene for type O, though."

I waved one of the slides gently in the air, drying it.

"My blood type is A. Now, I happen to know that my father's blood was type O. In order to show up with type O blood, that means that both his genes must have been for O. So whichever of those genes he gave me, it has to have been for O. The A gene therefore came from my mother."

Seeing a familiar glaze come over his features, I sighed and set the slide down. Bree had been drawing pictures of penicillin spores for me, and had left her pad and graphite pencil by the microscope. I took it and flipped to a fresh page.

"Look," I said, and drew a quick chart.

Henry		Julia
OO=Type O		A?=A or AB
	Claire	
	OA=Type A	

"Do you see?" I pointed with the stick of graphite. "I don't know my mother's type for sure, but it doesn't matter;

for me to have type A blood, she must have given me her gene for it, because my father hadn't one."

The next slide was nearly dry; I laid down the pencil, put the slide in place, and bent to look through the eyepiece.

"Can you see blood types—these antibodies—through a microscope?" Roger was quite close behind me.

"No," I said, not looking up. "The resolution's nowhere near good enough. But you can see other things—I hope." I moved the knob a fraction of an inch, and the cells sprang into focus. I let out the breath I had been holding, and a small thrill went through me. There they were; the disc-shaped pinkish blobs of the red blood cells—and here and there, inside a few of the cells, a darkish blob, some rounded, some looking like miniature nine-pins. My heart thumped with excitement, and I made a small exclamation of delight.

"Come look," I said, and stood aside. Roger bent, looking quizzical.

"What am I looking at?" he asked, squinting.

"Plasmodium vivax," I said proudly. "Malaria. The small dark blobs inside the cells." The rounded blobs were the protozoans, the single-celled creatures transferred to the blood in a mosquito's bite. The few that looked like bowling pins—those were protozoa in the act of budding, getting ready to reproduce themselves.

"When they bud," I explained, bending for another look myself, "they multiply until they burst the blood cell, and then they move into new blood cells, multiply, and burst those, too—that's when the patient suffers a malarial attack, with the fever and chills. When the *Plasmodium* are dormant—not multiplying—the patient is all right."

"And what makes them multiply?" Roger was fascinated.

"No one knows, exactly." I drew a deep breath, and corked up my bottles of stain again. "But you can check, to see what's happening, if they *are* multiplying. No one can live on quinine, or even take it for a long period—Jesuit bark is too expensive, and I don't know what the long-term effects on the body might be. And you can't touch most protozoans with penicillin, unfortunately.

"But I'll check Lizzie's blood every few days; if I see the

Plasmodium increasing sharply, then I'll start giving her the quinine at once. With luck, that might prevent an outbreak. Worth a try, certainly."

He nodded, looking at the microscope and the pink-and-blue-splotched slide.

"Well worth it," he said quietly.

He watched me move about, tidying up the small debris of my operations. As I bent to retrieve the bloody cloth in which he'd wrapped his hand, he asked, "And you know Bree's blood type, of course?"

"Type B," I said, eyes on the box of bandages. "Quite rare, particularly for a white person. You see it mostly in small, rather isolated populations—some Indian tribes in the American Southwest, certain black populations; probably they came from a specific area of Africa, but of course by the time blood groups were discovered, that connection had been long lost."

"Small, isolated populations. Scottish Highlanders, perhaps?"

I lifted my eyes.

"Perhaps."

He nodded silently, clearly thinking to himself. Then he picked up the pencil, and slowly drew a small chart of his own on the pad.

Claire	Jamie
AO=Type A	B?=B or AB

Brianna

OB=Type B

"That's right," I said, nodding as he looked up at me in question. "Exactly right."

He gave me a small, wry smile in response, then dropped his eyes, studying the charts.

"Can you tell, then?" he asked finally, not looking up. "For sure?"

"No," I said, and dropped the cloth into the laundry basket with a small sigh. "Or rather—I can't tell for sure whether Jemmy is yours. I *might* be able to tell for sure if he's not."

The flush had faded from his skin.

"How's that?"

"Bree is type B, but I'm type A. That means she'll have a gene for B *and* my gene for O, either of which she might have given Jemmy. You could only have given him a gene for type O, because that's all you have."

I nodded at a small rack of tubes near the window, the serum in them glowing brownish-gold in the late afternoon sun.

"So. If Bree gave him an O gene, and you—his father—gave him an O gene, he'd show up as type O—his blood won't have any antibodies, and won't react with serum from my blood or from Jamie's or Bree's. If Bree gave him her B gene, and you gave him an O, he'd show up as type B—his blood would react with my serum, but not Bree's. In either case, you might be the father—but so might anyone with type-O blood. IF, however—"

I took a deep breath, and picked up the pencil from the spot where Roger had laid it down. I drew slowly as I talked, illustrating the possibilities.

Brianna	Roger
OB=Type B	OO=Type O

Jemmy

OB or OO=Type B or Type O

"But"—I tapped the pencil on the paper—"if Jemmy were to show as type A or type AB—then his father was not homozygous for type O—homozygous means both genes are the same—and you are." I wrote in the alternatives, to the left of my previous entry.

X	Brianna	Roger
AO/AA/AB/BB/BO/OO	BO=Type B	OO=Type O
	Jemmy	Jemmy
	AB=Type AB	BO=Type B
	AO=Type A	OO=Type O
	OB/BO=Type B	
	BB=Type B	
	OO=Type O	

I saw Roger's eyes flick toward that "X," and wondered what had made me write it that way. It wasn't as though the contender for Jemmy's paternity could be just anyone, after all. Still, I could not bring myself to write "Bonnet"—perhaps it was simple superstition; perhaps just a desire to keep the thought of the man at a safe distance.

"Bear in mind," I said, a little apologetically, "that type O is very common, in the population at large."

Roger grunted, and sat regarding the chart, eyes hooded in thought.

"So," he said at last. "If he's type O or type B, he may be mine, but not for sure. If he's type A or type AB, he's not mine—for sure."

One finger rubbed slowly back and forth over the fresh bandage on his hand.

"It's a very crude test," I said, swallowing. "I can't—I mean, there's always the possibility of a mistake in the test itself."

He nodded, not looking up.

"You told Bree this?" he asked softly.

"Of course. She said she doesn't want to know—but that if you did, I was to make the test."

I saw him swallow, once, and his hand lifted momentarily to the scar across his throat. His eyes were fixed on the scrubbed planks of the floor, hardly blinking.

I turned away, to give him a moment's privacy, and bent over the microscope. I would have to make a grid, I thought—a counting grid that I could lay across a slide, to help me estimate the relative density of the *Plasmodium*-infected cells. For the moment, though, a crude eyeball count would have to do.

It occurred to me that now that I had a workable stain, I ought to test the blood of others on the Ridge—those in the household, for starters. Mosquitoes were much rarer in the mountains than near the coast, but there were still plenty, and while Lizzie might be well herself, she was still a sink of potential infection.

". . . four, five, six . . ." I was counting infected cells under my breath, trying to ignore both Roger on his stool behind me, and the sudden memory that had popped up, unbidden, when I told him Brianna's blood type.

She had had her tonsils removed at the age of seven. I still recalled the sight of the doctor, frowning at the chart he held—the chart that listed her blood type, and those of both her parents. Frank had been type A, like me. And two type-A parents could not, under any circumstances, produce a type B child.

The doctor had looked up, glancing from me to Frank and back, his face twisted with embarrassment—and his eyes filled with a kind of cold speculation as he looked at me. I might as well have worn a scarlet "A" embroidered on my bosom, I thought—or in this case, a scarlet "B."

Frank, bless him, had seen the look, and said easily, "My wife was a widow; I adopted Bree as a baby." The doctor's face had thawed at once into apologetic reassurance, and Frank had gripped my hand, hard, behind the folds of my skirt. My hand tightened in remembered acknowledgment, squeezing back—and the slide tilted suddenly, leaving me staring into blank and blurry glass.

There was a sound behind me, as Roger stood up. I turned round, and he smiled at me, eyes dark and soft as moss.

"The blood doesn't matter," he said quietly. "He's my son."

"Yes," I said, and my own throat felt tight. "I know."

A loud crack broke the momentary silence, and I looked down, startled. A puff of turkey-feathers drifted past my foot, and Adso, discovered in the act, rushed out of the surgery, the huge fan of a severed wing-joint clutched in his mouth.

"You *bloody* cat!" I said.

98

CLEVER LAD

A COLD WIND BLEW from the east tonight; Roger could hear the steady whine of it past the mud-chinked wall near his head, and the lash and creak of the wind-tossed trees beyond the house. A sudden gust struck the oiled hide tacked over the window; it bellied in with a *crack!* and popped loose at one side, the whooshing draft sending papers scudding off the table and bending the candle flame sideways at an alarming angle.

Roger moved the candle hastily out of harm's way, and pressed the hide flat with the palm of his hand, glancing over his shoulder to see if his wife and son had been awakened by the noise. A kitchen-rag stirred on its nail by the hearth, and the skin of his bodhran thrummed faintly as the draft passed by. A sudden tongue of fire sprang up from the banked hearth, and he saw Brianna stir as the cold air brushed her cheek.

She merely snuggled deeper into the quilts, though, a few loose red hairs glimmering as they lifted in the draft. The trundle where Jemmy now slept was sheltered by the big bed; there was no sound from that corner of the room.

Roger let out the breath he had been holding, and rummaged briefly in the horn dish that held bits of useful rubbish, coming up with a spare tack. He hammered it home with the heel of his hand, muffling the draft to a small, cold seep, then bent to retrieve his fallen papers.

"O will ye let Telfer's kye gae back?
Or will ye do aught for regard o' me?"

He repeated the words in his mind as he wiped the half-dried ink from his quill, hearing the words in Kimmie Clellan's cracked old voice.

It was a song called "Jamie Telfer of the Fair Dodhead"—one of the ancient reiving ballads that went on for dozens of verses, and had dozens of regional variations, all involving the attempts of Telfer, a Borderer, to revenge an attack upon his home by calling upon the help of friends and kin. Roger knew three of the variations, but Clellan had had another—with a completely new subplot involving Telfer's cousin Willie.

"Or by the faith of my body, quo' Willie Scott.
I'se ware my dame's calfskin on thee!"

Kimmie sang to pass the time of an evening by himself, he had told Roger, or to entertain the hosts whose fire he shared. He remembered all the songs of his Scottish youth, and was pleased to sing them as many times as anyone cared to listen, so long as his throat was kept wet enough to float a tune.

The rest of the company at the big house had enjoyed two or three renditions of Clellan's repertoire, began to yawn and blink through the fourth, and finally had mumbled excuses and staggered glazen-eyed off to bed—*en masse*—leaving Roger to ply the old man with more whisky and urge him to another repetition, until the words were safely committed to memory.

Memory was a chancy thing, though, subject to random losses and unconscious conjectures that took the place of fact. Much safer to commit important things to paper.

"I winna let the kye gae back,
Neither for thy love, nor yet thy fear . . ."

The quill scratched gently, capturing the words one by one, pinned like fireflies to the page. It was very late, and Roger's muscles were cramped with chill and long sitting, but he was determined to get all the new verses down, while they were fresh in his mind. Clellan might go off in the morning to be eaten by a bear or killed by falling rocks, but Telfer's cousin Willie would live on.

"But I will drive Jamie Telfer's kye,
In spite of every Scot that's . . ."

The candle made a brief sputtering noise as the flame struck a fault in the wick. The light that fell across the paper shook and wavered, and the letters faded abruptly into shadow as the candle flame shrank from a finger of light to a glowing blue dwarf, like the sudden death of a miniature sun.

Roger dropped his quill, and seized the pottery candlestick with a muffled curse. He blew on the wick, puffing gently, in hopes of reviving the flame.

"But Willie was stricken owre the head," he murmured to himself, repeating the words between puffs, to keep them fresh. *"But Willie was stricken owre the head/And through the knapscap the sword has gane/And Harden grat for very rage/When Willie on the grund lay slain . . . When Willie on the grund lay slain . . ."*

A ragged corona of orange rose briefly, feeding on his breath, but then dwindled steadily away despite continued puffing, winking out into a dot of incandescent red that glowed mockingly for a second or two before disappearing altogether, leaving no more than a wisp of white smoke in the half-dark room, and the scent of hot beeswax in his nose.

He repeated the curse, somewhat louder. Brianna stirred in the bed, and he heard the corn shucks squeak as she lifted her head with a noise of groggy inquiry.

"It's all right," he said in a hoarse whisper, with an uneasy glance at the trundle in the corner. "The candle's gone out. Go back to sleep."

But Willie was stricken owre the head . . .

"Ngm." A plop and sigh, as her head struck the goose-down pillow again.

Like clockwork, Jemmy's head rose from his own nest of blankets, his nimbus of fiery fluff silhouetted against the hearth's dull glow. He made a sound of confused urgency, not quite a cry, and before Roger could stir, Brianna had shot out of bed like a guided missile, snatching the boy from his quilt and fumbling one-handed with his clothing.

"Pot!" she snapped at Roger, poking blindly backward with one bare foot as she grappled with Jemmy's clothes. "Find the chamber pot! Just a minute, sweetie," she cooed to Jemmy, in an abrupt change of tone. "Wait juuuuust a minute, now . . ."

Impelled to instant obedience by her tone of urgency, Roger dropped to his knees, sweeping an arm in search through the black hole under the bed.

Willie was stricken owre the head . . . And through the . . . kneecap? nobskull? Overwhelmed by the situation, some remote bastion of memory clung stubbornly to the song, singing in his inner ear. Only the melody, though—the words were fading fast.

"Here!" He found the earthenware pot, accidentally struck the leg of the bed with it—thank Christ, it didn't break!—and bowled it across the floor to Bree.

She clapped the now-naked Jemmy down onto it with an exclamation of satisfaction, and Roger was left to grope about in the semi-dark for his fallen candle while she murmured encouragements.

"OK, sweetie, yes, that's right . . ."

Willie was struck about . . . no, stricken . . .

He found the candle, luckily uncracked, and sidled carefully round the drama in progress to kneel and relight the charred wick from the embers of the fire. While he was at it, he poked up the embers and added a fresh stick of wood. The fire revived, illuminating Jemmy, who was making what looked like a very successful effort to go back to sleep, in spite of his position and his mother's urging.

"Don't you need to go potty?" she was saying, shaking his shoulder gently.

"Go potty?" Roger said, this curious locution pushing the remnants of the verse from his mind. "What do you mean, *go* potty?" It was his personal opinion, based on current experience as a father, that small children were *born* potty, and improved very slowly thereafter. He said as much, causing Brianna to give him a remarkably dirty look.

"What?" she said, in an edgy tone. "What do you mean, they're *born potty*?" She had one hand on Jemmy's shoulder, balancing him, while the other cupped his round little belly, an index finger disappearing into the shadows below to direct his aim.

"Potty," Roger explained, with a brief circular gesture at his temple in illustration. "You know, barmy. Daft."

She opened her mouth to say something in reply to this, but Jemmy swayed alarmingly, his head sagging forward.

"No, no!" she said, taking a fresh grip. "Wake up, honey! Wake up and go potty!"

The insidious term had somehow taken up residence in Roger's mind, and was merrily replacing half the fading words of the verse he had been trying to recapture.

Willie sat upon his pot/The sword to potty gane . . .

He shook his head, as though to dislodge it, but it was too late—the real words had fled. Resigned, he gave it up as a bad job and crouched down next to Brianna to help.

"Wake up, chum. There's work to be done." He drew a finger gently under Jemmy's chin, then blew in his ear, ruffling the silky red tendrils that clung to the child's temple, still damp with sleep-sweat.

Jemmy's eyelids cracked in a slit-eyed glower. He looked like a small pink mole, cruelly excavated from its cozy burrow and peering balefully at an inhospitable upper world.

Brianna yawned widely, and shook her head, blinking and scowling in the candlelight.

"Well, if you don't like 'go potty,' what do you say in Scotland, then?" she demanded crabbily.

Roger moved the tickling finger to Jem's navel.

"Ah . . . I seem to recall a friend asking his wee son if he needed to do a poo," he offered. Brianna made a rude noise, but Jemmy's eyelids flickered.

"Poo," he said dreamily, liking the sound.

"Right, that's the idea," Roger said encouragingly. His finger twiddled gently in the slight depression, and Jemmy gave the ghost of a giggle, beginning to wake up.

"Poooooo," he said. "Poopoo."

"Whatever works," Brianna said, still cross, but resigned.

"Go potty, go poo—just get it over with, all right? Mummy wants to go to sleep."

"Perhaps you should take your finger off of his . . . mmphm?" Roger nodded toward the object in question. "You'll give the poor lad a complex or something."

"Fine." Bree took her hand away with alacrity, and the stubby object sprang back up, pointing directly at Roger over the rim of the pot.

"Hey! Now, just a min—" he began, and got his hand up as a shield just in time.

"Poo," Jemmy said, beaming in drowsy pleasure.

"Shit!"

"Chit!" Jemmy echoed obligingly.

"Well, that's not quite—would you stop laughing?" Roger said testily, wiping his hand gingerly on a kitchen rag.

Brianna snorted and gurgled, shaking her head so the straggling locks of hair that had escaped her plait fell down around her face.

"*Good* boy, Jemmy!" she managed.

Thus encouraged, Jemmy took on an air of inner absorption, scrunched his chin down into his chest, and without further ado, proceeded to Act Two of the evening's drama.

"Clever lad!" Roger said sincerely.

Brianna glanced at him, momentary surprise interrupting her own applause.

He was surprised himself. He had spoken by reflex, and hearing the words, just for a moment, his voice hadn't sounded like his own. Very familiar—but not his own. It was like writing the words of Clellan's song, hearing the old man's voice, even as his own lips formed the words.

"Aye, that's clever," he said, more softly, and patted the little boy gently on his silky head.

He took the pot outside to empty it while Brianna put Jemmy back to bed with kisses and murmurs of admiration. Basic sanitation accomplished, he went to the well to wash his hands before coming back inside to bed.

"Are you through working?" Bree asked drowsily, as he slid into bed beside her. She rolled over and thrust her bottom unceremoniously into his stomach, which he took as a gesture of affection, given the fact that she was about thirty degrees warmer than he was after the sortie outside.

"Aye, for tonight." He put his arms round her and kissed the back of her ear, the warmth of her body a comfort and delight. She took his chilly hand in hers without comment, folded it, and tucked it snugly beneath her chin, with a small kiss on the knuckle. He stretched slightly, then relaxed, letting his muscles go slack and feeling the tiny movements as their bodies adjusted, shaping to each other. A faint buzzing snore rose from the trundle, where Jemmy slept the sleep of the righteously dry.

Brianna had freshly smoored the fire; it burned with a low, even heat and the sweet scent of hickory, making small occasional pops as the buried flame reached a pocket of resin or a spot of damp. Warmth crept over him, and sleep tiptoed in its wake, drawing a blanket of drowsiness up round his ears, unlocking the tidy cupboards of his mind, and letting all the thoughts and impressions of the day spill out in brightly colored heaps.

Resisting unconsciousness for a last few moments, he poked desultorily among the scattered riches thus revealed, in the faint hope of finding a corner of the Telfer song poking out; some scrap of word or music that would allow him to seize the vanished verses and drag them back into the light of consciousness. It wasn't the story of the ill-fated Willie that emerged from the rubble, though, but rather a voice. Not his own, and not that of old Kimmie Clellan, either.

Clever lad! it said, in a clear warm contralto, tinged with laughter. Roger jerked.

"Whaju say?" Brianna mumbled, disturbed by the movement.

"Go on—be clever," he said slowly, echoing the words as they formed in his memory. "That's what she said."

"Who?" Brianna turned her head, with a rustle of hair on the pillow.

"My mother." He put his free hand round her waist, resettling them both. "You asked what they said in Scotland. I'd forgotten, but that's what she used to say to me. 'Go on—be clever!' or 'Do ye need to be clever?' "

Bree gave a small grunt of sleepy amusement.

"Well, it's better than poo," she said.

They lay quiet for a bit. Then she said, still speaking softly, but with all traces of sleep gone from her voice, "You talk about your dad now and then—but I've never heard you mention your mother before."

He gave a one-shouldered shrug, bringing his knees up against the yielding backs of her thighs.

"I don't remember a lot about her."

"How old were you when she died?" Brianna's hand floated up to rest over his.

"Oh, four, I think, nearly five."

"Mmm." She made a small sound of sympathy, and squeezed his hand. She was quiet for a moment, alone in private thought, but he heard her swallow audibly, and felt the slight tension in her shoulders.

"What?"

"Oh . . . nothing."

"Aye?" He disengaged his hand, used it to lift the heavy plait aside, and gently massaged the nape of her neck. She turned her head away to make it easier, burying her face in the pillow.

"Just—I was just thinking—if I died now, Jemmy's so young—he wouldn't remember me at all," she whispered, words half-muffled.

"Yes, he would." He spoke in automatic contradiction, wanting to give her reassurance, even knowing that she was likely right.

"You don't remember, and you were lots older when you lost your mother."

"Oh . . . I do remember her," he said slowly, digging the ball of his thumb into the place where her neck joined her shoulder. "Only, it's just in bits and pieces. Sometimes, when I'm dreaming, or thinking of something else, I get a quick glimpse of her, or some echo of her voice. A few things I recall clearly—like the locket she used to wear round her neck, with her initials on it in wee red stones. Garnets, they were."

That locket had perhaps saved his life, during his first ill-fated attempt to pass through the stones. He felt the loss of it now and then, like a small thorn buried beneath the surface of the skin, but pushed the feeling aside, telling himself that after all, it was nothing more than a bit of metal.

At the same time, he missed it.

"That's a *thing*, Roger." Her voice held a hint of sharpness. "Do you remember *her*? I mean—what would Jemmy know about me—about you, for that matter—if all he had left of us was"—she cast about for some suitable object—"was your bodhran and my pocket knife?"

"He'd know his dad was musical, and his mum was bloodthirsty," Roger said dryly. "Ouch!" He recoiled slightly as her fist came down on his thigh, then set his hands placatingly on her shoulders. "No, really. He'd know a lot about us, and not just from the bits and bobs we'd left behind, though those would help."

"How?"

"Well . . ." Her shoulders had relaxed again; he could feel the slender edge of her shoulder blade, hard against the skin—she was too thin, he thought. "You studied history for a time, didn't you? You know how much one can tell from homely objects like dishes and toys."

"Mmm." She sounded dubious, but he thought that she simply wanted to be convinced.

"And Jem would know a lot more than that about you, from your drawings," he pointed out. *And a hell of a lot more than a son ought, if he ever read your dream-book,* he thought. The sudden impulse to say so, to confess that he himself had read it, trembled on his tongue, but he swallowed it. Beyond simple fear of how she might respond if she discovered his intrusion, was the greater fear that she would cease to write in it, and those small secret glimpses of her mind would be lost to him.

"I guess that's true," she said slowly. "I wonder if Jem will draw—or be musical."

If Stephen Bonnet plays the flute, Roger thought cynically, but choked off that subversive notion, refusing to contemplate it.

"That's how he'll know the most of us," he said instead, resuming his gentle kneading. "He'll look at himself, aye?"

"Mmm?"

"Well, look at you," he pointed out. "Everyone who sees

you says, 'You must be Jamie Fraser's lass!' And the red hair isn't the only thing—what about the shooting? And the way you and your mother are about tomatoes . . ."

She smacked her lips reflexively, and giggled when he laughed.

"Yeah, all right, I see," she said. "Mmm. Why did you have to mention tomatoes? I used the last of the dried ones last week, and it'll be six months before they're on again."

"Sorry," he said, and kissed the back of her neck in apology.

"I did wonder," he said, a moment later. "When you found out about Jamie—when we began to look for him—you must have wondered what he was like." He knew she had; *he* certainly had. "When you found him—how did he compare? Was he at all like you thought he'd be, from what you knew about him already? Or—from what you knew about yourself?"

That made her laugh again, a little wryly.

"I don't know," she said. "I didn't know then, and I still don't know."

"What d'ye mean by that?"

"Well, when you hear things about somebody before you meet them, of course the real person isn't just like what you heard, or what you imagined. But you don't forget what you imagined, either; that stays in your mind, and sort of merges with what you find out when you meet them. And then—" She bent her head forward, thinking. "Even if you know somebody *first*, and then hear things about them later—that kind of affects how you see them, doesn't it?"

"Aye? Mmm, I suppose so. Do ye mean . . . your other dad? Frank?"

"I suppose I do." She shifted under his hands, shrugging it away. She didn't want to talk about Frank Randall, not just now.

"What about your parents, Roger? Do you figure that's why the Reverend saved all their old stuff in those boxes? So later you could look through it, learn more about them, and sort of add that to your real memories of them?"

"I—yes, I suppose so," he said uncertainly. "Not that I have any memories of my real dad in any case; he only saw me the once, and I was less than a year old then."

"But you do remember your mother, don't you? At least a little bit?"

She sounded slightly anxious; she wanted him to remember. He hesitated, and a thought struck him with a small shock. The truth of it was, he realized, that he never consciously *tried* to remember his mother. The realization gave him a sudden and unaccustomed feeling of shame.

"She died in the War, didn't she?" Bree's hand had taken up his suspended massage, reaching back to gently knead the tightened muscle of his thigh.

"Yes. She—in the Blitz. A bomb."

"In Scotland? But I thought—"

"No. In London."

He didn't want to speak of it. He never *had* spoken of it. On the rare occasions when memory led in that direction, he veered away. That territory lay behind a closed door, with a large "No Entry" sign that he had never sought to pass. And yet tonight . . . he felt the echo of Bree's brief anguish at the thought that her son might not recall her. And he felt the same echo, like a faint voice calling, from the woman locked behind that door in his mind. But was it locked, after all?

With a hollow feeling behind his breastbone that might have been dread, he reached out and put his hand on the knob of that closed door. How much *did* he recall?

"My Gran, my mother's mum, was English," he said slowly. "A widow. We went south to live with her in London, when my dad was killed."

He had not thought of Gran, any more than his mum, in years. But with his speaking, he could smell the rosewater and glycerine lotion his grandmother had used on her hands, the faintly musty smell of her upstairs flat in Tottenham Court Road, crammed with horsehair furniture too large for it, remnants of a previous life that had held a house, a husband, and children.

He took a deep breath. Bree felt it, and pressed her broad firm back encouragingly against his chest. He kissed the back of her neck. So the door *did* open—just a crack, maybe, but the light of a wintry London afternoon shone through it, lighting up a stack of battered wooden blocks on a threadbare carpet. A woman's hand was building a tower with them, the faint sun scattering rainbows from a diamond on her hand. His own fingers curled in reflex, seeing that slim hand.

"Mum—my mother—she was small, like Gran. That is, they both seemed big, to me, but I remember . . . I remember seeing her stand on her tiptoes to reach things down from the shelf."

Things. The tea-caddy, with its cut-glass sugar bowl. The battered kettle, three mismatched mugs. His had had a panda bear on it. A package of biscuits—bright red, with a picture of a parrot . . . My God, he hadn't seen those kind ever again—did they still make them? No, of course not, not now . . .

He pulled his veering mind firmly back from such distractions.

"I know what she looked like, but mostly from pictures, not from my own memories." And yet he did *have* memories, he realized, with a disturbing sensation in the pit of his stomach. He thought "Mum," and suddenly he didn't see the photos anymore; he saw the chain of her spectacles, a string of tiny metal beads against the soft curve of a breast, and a pleasant warm smoothness, smelling of soap against his cheek; the cotton fabric of a flowered housedress. Blue flowers. Shaped like trumpets, with curling vines; he could see them clearly.

"What did she look like? Do you look like her at all?"

He shrugged, and Bree shifted, rolling over to face him, her head propped upon her outstretched arm. Her eyes shone in the half-dark, sleepiness overcome by interest.

"A little," he said slowly. "Her hair was dark, like mine." *Shiny, curly. Lifting in the wind, sprinkled with white grains of sand. He'd sprinkled sand on her head, and she brushed it from her hair, laughing. A beach somewhere?*

"The Reverend kept some pictures of her, in his study. One showed her holding me on her lap. I don't know what we were looking at—but both of us look as though we're trying hard to keep from laughing. We look a lot alike in that one. I have her mouth, I think—and . . . maybe . . . the shape of her brows."

For a long time he had felt a tightness in his chest

whenever he saw the pictures of his mother. But then it had passed, the pictures lost their meaning and became no more than objects in the casual clutter of the Reverend's house. Now he saw them clearly once again, and the tightness in his chest was back. He cleared his throat hard, hoping to ease it.

"Need water?" She made to rise, reaching for the jug and cup she kept for him on the stool by the bed, but he shook his head, a hand on her shoulder to stop her.

"It's all right," he said, a little gruffly, and cleared his throat again. It felt as tight and painful as it had in the weeks just past the hanging, and his hand involuntarily sought the scar, smoothing the ragged line beneath his jaw with the tip of a finger.

"You know," he said, seeking at least a momentary diversion, "you should do a self-portrait, next time you go to see your aunt at River Run."

"What, me?" She sounded startled, though, he thought—perhaps a bit pleased at the idea.

"Sure. You could, I know. And then there'd be . . . well, a permanent record, I mean." *For Jem to remember, in case anything should happen to you.* The words floated above them in the dark, striking them both momentarily silent. Damn, and he'd been trying to reassure her.

"I'd like a portrait of you," he said softly, and reached out a finger to trace the curve of cheek and temple. "So we can look at it when we're very old, and I can tell ye that you haven't changed a bit."

She gave a small snort, but turned her head and kissed his fingers briefly, before rolling onto her back. She stretched, pointing her toes until her joints cracked, then relaxed with a sigh.

"I'll think about it," she said.

The room was quiet, save for the murmur of the fire and the gentle creak of settling timber. The night was cold, but still; the morning would be foggy—he had felt the damp gathering in the ground when he'd gone outside, breathing from the trees. But it was warm and dry within. Brianna sighed again; he could feel her sinking back toward sleep beside him, could feel it coming for him, too.

The temptation to give in and let it carry him painlessly

away was great. But while Brianna's fears were eased for the moment, he still heard that whisper—"He wouldn't remember me at all." But it came now from the other side of the door in his mind.

Yes, I do, Mum, he thought, and shoved it open all the way.

"I was with her," he said softly. He was on his back, staring up at the pine-beamed ceiling, the joins of the rafters barely visible to his dark-adapted eyes.

"What? With who?" He could hear the lull of sleep in her voice, but curiosity roused her briefly.

"With my mother. And my grandmother. When . . . the bomb."

He heard her head turn sharply toward him, hearing the strain in his voice, but he looked straight upward into the dark roof-beams, not blinking.

"Do you want to tell me?" Brianna's hand found his, curled round it, squeezing. He wasn't sure at all that he did, but he nodded a little, squeezing back.

"Aye. I suppose I must," he said softly. He sighed deeply, smelling the lingering scents of fried corn-mush and onions that hung in the corners of the cabin. Somewhere in the back of his nose, the imagined scents of hot-air registers and breakfast porridge, wet woolens, and the petrol fumes of lorries woke silent guides through the labyrinth of memory.

"It was at night. The air-raid sirens went. I knew what it was, but it scared the shit out of me every time. There wasn't time to dress; Mum pulled me out of bed and put my coat on over my pajamas, then we rushed out and down the stairs—there were thirty-six steps, I'd counted them all that day, coming home from the shops—and we hurried to the nearest shelter."

The nearest shelter for them was the Tube station across the street; grubby white tiles and the flicker of fluorescent lights, the thrilling rush of air somewhere deep below, like the breathing of dragons in nearby caves.

"It was exciting." He could see the crush of people, hear the shouting of the wardens over the noise of the crowd. "Everything was vibrating; the floors, the walls, the air itself."

Feet thundered on the wooden treads as streams of

refugees poured into the bowels of the earth, down one level to a platform, down another, yet another, burrowing toward safety. It was panic—but an orderly panic.

"The bombs could go through fifty feet of earth—but the lower levels were safe."

They had reached the bottom of the first stairway, run jostling with a mass of others through a short, white-tiled tunnel to the head of the next. There was a wide space at the head of the stairway, and the crowd pooled in a swirling eddy into it, swelling with the pressure of refugees pouring from the tunnel behind, draining only slowly as a thin stream crowded onto the stair leading down.

"There was a wall round the head of the stair; I could hear Gran worrying that I'd be crushed against it—people were pouring down from the street, pressing from behind."

He could just see over the wall, standing on his toes, chest pressed against the concrete. Down below, emergency lights shone in interrupted streaks along the walls, striping the milling crowd below. It was late night; most of the people were dressed in whatever they had been able to seize when the siren went, and the light glowed on unexpected flashes of bare flesh and extraordinary garments. One woman sported an extravagant hat, decorated with feathers and fruit, worn atop an ancient overcoat.

He had been watching the crowd below in fascination, trying to see if it was really a whole pheasant on the hat. There was shouting; an air-raid warden in a white helmet with a big black "W," beckoning madly, trying to hasten the already rushing crowd toward the far end of the platform, making room for those coming off the stair.

"There were children crying, but not me. I wasn't really afraid at all." He hadn't been afraid, because Mum was holding his hand. *If she was there, nothing bad could happen.*

"There was a big thump nearby. I could see the lights shake. Then there was a noise like something tearing overhead. Everyone looked up and began to scream."

The crack through the slanted ceiling hadn't looked particularly frightening; just a thin black line that zigzagged back and forth like a jigsaw snake, following the lines of the tiles. But then it widened suddenly, a gaping maw like a dragon's mouth, and dirt and tiles began to pour down.

He had long since thawed, and yet every hair on his body rippled now with gooseflesh. His heart pounded against the inside of his chest, and he felt as though the noose had drawn tight about his neck again.

"She let go," he said, in a strangled whisper. "She let go my hand."

Brianna's hand gripped his in both of hers, hard, trying to save the child he'd been.

"She had to," she said, in an urgent whisper. "Roger, she wouldn't have let go unless she had to."

"No." He shook his head violently. "That's not what—I mean—wait. Wait a minute, OK?"

He blinked hard, trying to slow his breathing, fitting back the shattered pieces of that night. Confusion, frenzy, pain . . . but what had actually *happened*? He had kept nothing save an impression of bedlam. But he had lived through it; he must know what had happened—if he could bring himself to live through it again.

Brianna's hand clutched his, her fingers still squeezing tight enough to stop the blood. He patted her hand, gently, and her grip relaxed a little.

He closed his eyes, and let it happen.

"I didn't remember at first," he said at last, quietly. "Or rather, I did—but I remembered what people told me had happened." He had had no memory of being carried unconscious through the tunnel, and once rescued, he had spent several weeks being shuttled round Aid shelters and foster homes with other orphans, mute with terrified bewilderment.

"I knew my name, of course, and my address, but that didn't help much under the circumstances. My dad had already gone down—anyway, by the time the Aid people located Gran's brother—that was the Reverend—and he came to fetch me, they'd pieced together the story of what happened in the shelter.

"It was a miracle that I hadn't been killed with everyone else on that stair, they told me. They said my mother must somehow have lost hold of me in the panic—I must have been separated from her and carried down the stair by the crowd; that's how I ended on the lower level, where the roof hadn't given way."

Brianna's hand was still curled over his, protective, but no longer squeezing.

"But now you remember what happened?" she asked quietly.

"I did remember her letting go my hand," he said. "And so I thought the rest of it was right, too. But it wasn't.

"She let go my hand," he said. The words came more easily now; the tightness in his throat and chest was gone. "She let go my hand . . . and then she picked me up. That small woman—she picked me up, and threw me over the wall. Down into the crowd of people on the platform below. I was knocked mostly out by the fall, I think—but I remember the roar as the roof went. No one on the stair survived."

She pressed her face against his chest, and he felt her take a deep, shuddering breath. He stroked her hair, and his pounding heart began to slow at last.

"It's all right," he whispered to her, though his voice was thick and cracked, and the firelight burst in starry blurs through the moisture in his eyes. "We won't forget. Not Jem, not me. No matter what. We won't forget."

He could see his mother's face, shining clear among the stars.

Clever lad, she said, and smiled.

99

BROTHER

THE SNOW BEGAN TO MELT. I was torn between pleasure at the thawing of the world and the throb of spring in the ground—and disturbance at the loss of the frozen barrier that shielded us, however temporarily, from the world outside.

Jamie had not changed his mind. He spent an evening in composing a carefully worded letter to Milford Lyon. He was now ready, he wrote, to contemplate the sale of his goods—for which, read illegal whisky—as Mr. Lyon had suggested, and was pleased to say that a substantial quantity was now available. He was, however, concerned lest his goods suffer some misfortune in delivery—i.e., interception by customs authorities or pilferage en route—and wished some assurance that his goods would be handled by a gentleman of known ability in such matters—in other words, a smuggler who knew his way up and down the coast.

He had received assurances from his good friend Mr. Priestly of Edenton (whom he did not, of course, know from a hole in the ground), he wrote, and from Mr. Samuel Cornell, with whom he had had the honor to serve upon the Governor's Council of War, that one Stephen Bonnet was by far the most able in such endeavors, with a reputation for ability unsurpassed by others. If Mr. Lyon would arrange a meeting with Mr. Bonnet, so that Jamie might form his own impressions and assure himself of the safety of the arrangement contemplated, why then . . .

"Do you think he'll do it?" I asked.

"If he knows Stephen Bonnet or can find him, aye, he will."

Jamie pressed his father's cabochon ring into the wax seal. "Priestly and Cornell are names to conjure with, to be sure."

"And if he does find Bonnet—"

"Then I will go and meet with him." He cracked the ring from the hardened wax, leaving a smooth indentation surrounded by the tiny strawberry leaves of the Fraser crest. Constancy, they stood for. In some moods, I was sure this was merely another word for stubbornness.

The letter to Lyon was dispatched with Fergus, and I tried to dismiss it from my mind. It was still winter; with only a little luck, Bonnet's ship might meet with a storm and sink, saving us all a good deal of trouble.

Still, the matter lurked in the recesses of my mind, and when I returned to the house after attending a childbirth to find a pile of letters on the desk in Jamie's study, my heart leaped into my throat.

There was—thank God!—no answer among them from Milford Lyon. Even had such an answer come, though, it would have been promptly eclipsed and forgotten—for among the sheaf of correspondence was a letter bearing Jamie's name, written in his sister's strong black hand.

I could scarcely keep myself from tearing it open at once—and if it were some searing reproach, sticking it directly into the fire before Jamie could see it. Honor prevailed, though, and I managed to contain myself until Jamie arrived from an errand to Salem, plastered with mud from the impassable trails. Informed of the waiting missive, he splashed hands and face hastily with water, and came to the study, carefully shutting the door before breaking the seal of the letter.

His face showed nothing, but I saw him take a deep breath before opening it, as though bracing for the worst. I moved quietly round behind him, and put a hand on his shoulder in encouragement.

He unfolded the pages carefully, and I saw him frown slightly. There was a flattened mass of dried flowers pressed between the pages; a sprig of yellow roses, still faintly fragrant. He separated these carefully from the paper, laid them on the desk, then turned to the letter itself.

Jenny Fraser Murray wrote in a well-schooled hand, the letters round and graceful, the lines straight and easily readable on the page.

September 16, 1771

Brother,

Well. Having taken up my pen and written the single word above, I have now sat here staring at it 'til the candle has burned almost an inch, and me having not one thought what I shall say. It would be a wicked waste of good beeswax to continue so, and yet if I were to put the candle out and go to bed, I should have spoilt a sheet of paper to no purpose—so I see I must go on, in the name of thrift.

I could berate you. That would occupy some space upon the page, and preserve what my husband is pleased to compliment as the most foul and hideous curses he has been privileged to hear in a long life. That seems thrifty, as I was at great pains in the composition of them at the time, and should not like to see the effort wasted. Still, I think I have not so much paper as would contain them all.

I think also that perhaps, after all, I do not wish to rail or condemn you, for you might take this as a just punishment, and so ease your conscience in perceived expiation, so that you leave off your chastising of yourself. That is too simple a penance; I would that if you have wove a hairshirt for yourself, you wear it still, and may it chafe your soul as the loss of my son chafes mine.

In spite of this, I suppose that I am writing to forgive you—I had some purpose in taking up my pen, I know, and while forgiveness seems a doubtful enterprise to me at present, I expect the notion will grow more comfortable with practice.

Jamie's brows rose nearly to his hairline at this, but he continued to read aloud with fascination.

You will be curious to know what has led me to this action, I suppose, so I will tell you.

I rode to visit Maggie early Monday last; she has a new babe, so you are once more an uncle; a bonnie wee lassie called Angelica, which is a foolish name, I think, but she is very fair and born with a strawberry mark on her chest, which is a charm for good. I left them in the evening, and had made some way towards home when my mule chanced to step into a mole's hole and fell. Both mule and I rose up somewhat lamed from this accident, and it was clear that I could not ride the creature nor yet make shift to travel far by foot myself.

I found myself on the road to Auldearn just over the hill from Balriggan. I should not normally seek the society of Laoghaire MacKenzie—for she has resumed that name, I having made plain in the district my dislike of her use of "Fraser," she having no proper claim to that style—but it was the only place where I might obtain food and shelter, for night was coming on, with the threat of rain.

So I unsaddled the mule and left him to find his supper by the road, while I limped off in search of mine.

I came down behind the house, past the kailyard, and so came upon the arbor that you built. The vines are well grown on it now, so I could see nothing, but I could hear that there were folk inside, for I heard voices.

The rain had begun by then. It was not but a smizzle, yet the patter on the leaves must have drowned my voice, for no one answered when I called. I came closer—creeping like a spavined snail, to be sure, for I was gromished from the fall and my right ankle gruppit—and was just about to call once more, when I heard sounds of a rare hochmagandy from inside the arbor.

"Hochmagandy?" I glanced at Jamie, brows raised in question.

"Fornication," he said tersely.

"Oh," I said, and moved to look over his shoulder at the letter.

> *I stood still, of course, thinking what was best to do. I could hear that it was Laoghaire shedding her shanks, but I had no hint who her partner might be. My ankle was blown up like a bladder, so I could not walk much farther, and so I was obliged to stand about in the wet, listening to all this* inhonesté.
>
> *I should have known, had she been courted by a man of the district, and I had heard nothing of her paying heed to any—though several have tried; she has Balriggan, after all, and lives like a laird on the money you pay her.*
>
> *I was filled with outrage at the hearing, but somewhat more filled with amazement to discover the cause. That being a sense of fury on your behalf—irrational as such fury might be, in the circumstances. Still, having discovered such an emotion springing full-blown in my breast, I was reluctantly compelled to the realization that my feelings for you must not in fact have perished altogether.*

Here the text broke off, as Jenny had apparently been called away upon some domestic errand. It resumed, freshly dated, on the next page.

> *September 18, 1771*
>
> *I dream of young Ian now and then. . . .*

"What?" I exclaimed. "To hell with Young Ian—who was with Laoghaire?"

"I should like to know that myself," Jamie muttered. The tips of his ears were dark with blood, but he didn't look up from the page.

> *I dream of Ian now and then. These dreams most often take the shape of daily life, and I see him here at Lallybroch, but now and again I dream of him in his*

life among the savages—if indeed he still lives (and I persuade myself that my heart would by some means know if he did not).

So I see that what it comes to in the end is only the same thing with which I began—that one word, "Brother." You are my brother, as young Ian is my son, the both of you my flesh and my spirit and always shall be. If the loss of Ian haunts my dreams, the loss of you haunts my days, Jamie.

He stopped reading for a moment, swallowing, then went on, his voice steady.

I have been writing letters all the morning, debating with myself whether to finish this one, or to put it into the fire instead. But now the accounts are done, I have written to everyone I can think of, and the clouds have gone away, so the sun shines through the window by my desk, and the shadows of Mother's roses are falling over me.

I have thought to myself often and often that I heard my mother speak to me, through all these years. I do not need to hear her now, though, to ken well enough what she would say. And so I shall not put this in the fire.

You remember, do you, the day I broke the good cream-pitcher, flinging it at your head because you deviled me? I know you recall the occasion, for you once spoke to Claire of it. I hesitated to admit the crime, and you took the blame upon yourself, but Father kent the truth of it, and punished us both.

So now I am a grandmother ten times over, with my hair gone grey, and still I feel my cheeks go hot with shame and my wame shrink like a fist, thinking of Father bidding us kneel down side by side and bend over the bench to be whipped.

You yelped and grunted like a puppy when he tawsed you, and I could scarce breathe and did not dare to look at you. Then it was my turn, but I was so wrought with emotion that I think I barely felt the strokes. No doubt you are reading this and saying indignantly that it was only Father was softer with me because I was a lass. Well, maybe so, and maybe no; I will say Ian is gentle with his daughters.

Jamie snorted at this.

"Aye, ye've got that right," he muttered. He rubbed his nose with one finger and resumed, drumming his fingers on the desk as he read.

But then Father said you would have another whipping, this one for lying—for the truth was the truth, after all. I would have got up and fled away then, but he bade me stay as I was, and he said to me, quiet, that while you would pay the price of my cowardice, he did not think it right for me to escape it altogether.

Do you know that you did not make a sound, the second time? I hope you did not feel the strokes of the tawse on your backside, because I felt each one.

I swore that day that I should not ever be a coward again.

And I see that it is cowardice indeed, that I should go on blaming you for Young Ian. I have always kent what it is to love a man—be he husband or brother, lover or son. A dangerous business; that's what it is.

Men go where they will, they do as they must; it is not a woman's part to bid them stay, nor yet to reproach them for being what they are—or for not coming back.

I knew it when I sent Ian to France with a cross of birchwood and a lock of my hair made into a love knot, praying that he might come home to me, body and soul. I knew it when I gave you a rosary and saw you off to Leoch, hoping you would not forget Lallybroch or me. I knew it when Young Jamie swam to the seal's island, when Michael took ship for Paris, and I should have known it, too, when wee Ian went with you.

But I have been blessed in my life; my men have always come back to me. Maimed, perhaps; a bit singed round the edges now and then; crippled, crumpled, tattered, and torn—but I have always got them back. I grew to expect that as my right, and I was wrong to do so.

I have seen so many widows since the Rising. I cannot say why I thought I should be exempt from their suffering, why I alone should lose none of my men, and only one of my babes, my wee girl-child. And since I had lost Caitlin, I treasured Ian, for I knew he was the last babe I should bear.

I thought him my babe still; I should have kent him for the man he was. And that being so, I know well enough that whether you might have stopped him or no, you would not—for you are one of the damnable creatures, too.

Now I have nearly reached the end of this sheet, and I think it profligate to begin another.

Mother loved you always, Jamie, and when she kent she was dying, she called for me, and bade me care for you. As though I could ever stop.

Your most Affectionate and Loving Sister,
Janet Flora Arabella Fraser Murray

Jamie held the paper for a moment, then set it down, very gently. He sat with his head bent, propped on his hand so that I couldn't see his face. His fingers were splayed through his hair, and kept moving, massaging his forehead as he slowly shook his head, back and forth. I could hear him breathing, with a slight catch in his breath now and then.

Finally he dropped his hand and looked up at me, blinking. His face was deeply flushed, there were tears in his eyes, and he wore the most remarkable expression, in which bewilderment, fury, and laughter were all mingled, laughter being only slightly uppermost.

"Oh, God," he said. He sniffed, and wiped his eyes on the back of his hand. "Oh, Christ. How in *hell* does she do that?"

"Do what?" I pulled a clean handkerchief from my bodice and handed it to him.

"Make me feel as though I am eight years old," he said ruefully. "And an idiot, to boot."

He wiped his nose, then reached out a hand to touch the flattened roses, gently.

I WAS THRILLED with Jenny's letter, and knew that Jamie's heart was substantially lightened by its receipt. At the same time, I remained extremely curious about the incident she had begun to describe—and knew that Jamie was even more interested, though he carefully refrained from saying so.

A letter arrived a week or so later, sent by his brother-in-law Ian, but while this contained the usual news of Lallybroch and Broch Mordha, it made no mention whatever of Jenny's adventure near Balriggan, nor her subsequent discovery in the grape arbor.

"I don't suppose you could ask either of them?" I suggested delicately, perched on the fence as I watched him preparing to castrate a litter of piglets. "Ian or Jenny?"

"I could not," Jamie replied firmly. "And after all, it's no my business, is it? If yon woman was ever my wife, she surely is not now. If she chooses to take a lover, it's her own affair. Surely." He stamped on the foot-bellows, fanning up the small fire in which the cautery iron was heating, and pulled the castrating shears from his belt. "Which end of the business d'ye want, Sassenach?"

It was a choice between the strong possibility of being bitten while clipping the teeth and the certainty of being shitten while assaulting the other end. The unfortunate truth was that Jamie was far stronger than I, and while he could certainly castrate an animal with no difficulty at all, I did have some professional expertise. It was therefore practicality rather than heroism that dictated my choice, and I had prepared for this activity by donning my heavy canvas apron, wooden clogs, and a ragged ex-shirt that had once belonged to Fergus, and was bound from the pigpen straight into the fire.

"You hold; I'll snip." I slid off the fence and took the shears.

There ensued a brief but noisy interlude, after which the five piglets were sent off to a consolatory meal of kitchen scraps, their rear aspects heavily daubed with a tar and turpentine mixture to prevent infection.

"What do you think?" I asked, seeing them settle down to their feeding in an apparent state of content. "If you were a pig, I mean. Would you rather root for your food, but keep your balls, or give them up and wallow in luxurious swill?" These would be kept penned, raised carefully on slops for tender meat, while most of the pigs were routinely turned out into the wood to manage for themselves.

Jamie shook his head.

"I suppose they canna miss what they've never had," he said. "And they've had food, after all." He leaned on the fence for a few moments, watching the curly tails begin to wag and twirl with pleasure, the tiny wounds beneath apparently forgotten.

"Besides," he added cynically, "a pair of ballocks may bring a man more sorrow than joy—though I havena met many who'd wish them gone, for all that."

"Well, priests might find them a burden, I suppose." I pulled the stained shirt gingerly away from my body before lifting it over my head. "Phew. Nothing smells worse than pig excrement—nothing."

"What—not a blackbirder's hold, or a rotting corpse?" he asked, laughing. "Festering wounds? A billy goat?"

"Pig shit," I said firmly. "Hands down."

Jamie took the wadded shirt from me and ripped it into strips, reserving the cleanest ones for jobs like wiping tools and wedging cracks. The rest he consigned to the fire, stepping back as a random breeze blew a plume of reeking smoke in our direction.

"Aye, well, there was Narses. He was a great general, or so they say, in spite of being a eunuch."

"Perhaps a man's mind works better without the distraction," I suggested, laughing.

He gave no more than a brief snort in reply to this, though it was tinged with amusement. He shoveled dirt onto the cinders of the fire, while I retrieved my cautery iron and tar-pot, and we went back to the house, talking of other things.

My mind lingered on that one remark, though—"a pair of ballocks may bring a man more sorrow than joy." Had he been speaking only generally? I wondered. Or had there been some personal allusion lurking in it?

In everything he had ever said to me regarding his brief marriage to Laoghaire MacKenzie—little as that was, by our common consent—there had been no hint that he had felt physically drawn to her. He had wed her from loneliness and a sense of duty, wanting some small anchor in the emptiness his life had been after his return from England. Or so he had said.

And I believed what he'd said. He was a man of honor and duty, and I knew what his loneliness had been—for I had had my own. On the other hand, I knew his body, nearly as well as my own. If it had a great capacity to endure hardship, it had an equal capacity to experience great joy. Jamie could be ascetic from necessity—never from natural temperament.

Most of the time I succeeded in forgetting that he had shared Laoghaire's bed, however briefly and—he said—unsatisfactorily. I did not forget that she had been, and was still, quite an attractive woman.

Which left me rather wishing that Jenny Murray had found some other inspiration for the conversion of her feelings toward her brother.

JAMIE WAS QUIET and abstracted through the rest of the day, though he roused himself to be sociable when Fergus and Marsali arrived with their children for a visit after supper. He taught Germain to play draughts, while Fergus recalled for Roger the words of a ballad he had picked up in the alleys of Paris as a juvenile pickpocket. The women retired to the hearth to stitch baby gowns, knit booties, and—in honor of Marsali's advancing pregnancy and Lizzie's engagement—entertain each other with hair-raising anecdotes of labor and birth.

"Laid sideways, the babe was, and the size of a six-month shoat . . ."

"Ha, Germain had a head like a cannonball, the midwife said, and he was facing *backward*, the wee rattan—"

"Jemmy had a huge head, but it was his shoulders that were the problem. . . ."

". . . *la bourse* . . . the lady's 'purse,' of course, is her—"

"Her means of making a living, aye, I see. Then the next bit, where her customer puts his fingers *in* her purse—"

"No, ye dinna get to move yet, it's still my turn, for I've jumped your man *there*, and so I can go *here*—"

"Merde!"

"Germain!" Marsali bellowed. She glared at her offspring, who hunched his shoulders, scowling at the draughtboard, lower lip thrust out.

"Dinna fash yourself, man, for see? Now it's your turn, ye can go *there*, and *there*, and *there*—"

". . . *Avez-vous été à la selle aujourd'hui?* . . . and what he is asking the whore, of course—"

" 'Have you—been in the saddle today?' Or would it be, 'Have you had a ride today?' "

Fergus laughed, the end of his aristocratic nose pinkening with amusement.

"Well, that is one translation, surely."

Roger lifted a brow at him, half-smiling.

"Aye?"

"That particular expression is also what a French doctor says," I put in, seeing his incomprehension. "Colloquially speaking, it means, 'Have you had a bowel movement today?' "

"The lady in question being perhaps *une spécialiste*," Fergus explained cheerfully. "I used to know one who—"

"Fergus!" Marsali's whole face was pink, though she seemed more amused than outraged.

"I see," Roger murmured, eyebrows still raised as he struggled with the nuances of this bit of sophisticated translation. I did wonder how one would set it to music.

"Comment sont vos selles, Grand-père?" Germain inquired chummily, evidently familiar with this line of social inquiry. And how are your stools, Grandfather?

"Free and easy," his grandfather assured him. "Eat up your parritch every morning, and ye'll never have piles."

"Da!"

"Well, it's true," Jamie protested.

Brianna was bright red, and emitting small fizzing noises. Jemmy stirred in her lap.

"*Le petit rouge* eats parritch," Germain observed, frowning narrowly at Jemmy, who was nursing contentedly at his mother's breast, eyes closed. "He shits stones."

"Germain!" all the women shouted in unison.

"Well, it's true," he said, in perfect imitation of his grandfather. Looking dignified, he turned his back on the women and began building towers with the draughts-men.

"He doesna seem to want to give up the teat," Marsali observed, nodding at Jemmy. "Neither did Germain, but he'd no choice—nor did poor wee Joanie." She glanced ruefully down at her stomach, which was barely beginning to swell with Number Three.

I caught the barest flicker of a glance between Roger and Bree, followed by a Mona Lisa smile on Brianna's face. She settled herself more comfortably, and stroked Jemmy's head. *Enjoy it while you can, sweetheart,* her actions said, more vividly than words.

I felt my own eyebrows rise, and glanced toward Jamie. He'd seen that little byplay, too, and gave me the male equivalent of Brianna's smile, before turning back to the draughts-board.

"I like parritch," Lizzie put in shyly, in a minor attempt to change the subject. "Specially with honey and milk."

"Ah," said Fergus, reminded of his original task. He turned back to Roger, lifting a finger. "Honeypots. The refrain, you see, where *les abeilles* come buzzing—"

"Aye, aye, that's so," Mrs. Bug neatly recaptured the conversation, when he paused to draw breath, "parritch wi' honey is the best thing for the bowels, though sometimes even that fails. Why, I kent a man once, who couldna move his bowels for more than a month!"

"Indeed. Did he try a pellet of wax rolled in goose-grease? Or a tisane of grape leaves?" Fergus was instantly diverted. French to the core, he was a great connoisseur of purges, laxatives, and suppositories.

"Everything," Mrs. Bug assured him. "Parritch, dried apples, wine mixed wi' an ox's gall, water drunk at the dark o' the moon at midnight . . . nothing at all would shift him. 'Twas the talk of the village, wi' folk placing wagers, and the poor man gone quite gray in the face. Nervous spasms, it was, and his bowels tied up like garter strings, so that—"

"Did he explode?" Germain asked, interested.

Mrs. Bug shook briefly with laughter.

"No, that he didna, laddie. Though I did hear as how it was a near thing."

"What was it finally shifted him, then?" Jamie asked.

"She finally said she'd marry me, and not the other fellow." Mr. Bug, who had been dozing in the corner of the settle through the evening, stood up and stretched himself, then put a hand on his wife's shoulder, smiling tenderly down at her upturned face. " 'Twas a great relief, to be sure."

IT WAS LATE when we went to bed, after a convivial evening that ended with Fergus singing the prostitute's ballad in its lengthy entirety to general applause, Jamie and Germain beating time on the table with their hands.

Jamie lay back against the pillow, hands crossed behind his head, chuckling to himself now and then as bits of the song came back to him. It was cold enough that the windowpanes were misted with our breath, but he wore no nightshirt, and I admired the sight of him as I sat brushing my hair.

He had recovered well from the snakebite, but was still thinner than usual, so that the graceful arch of his collarbone was visible, and the long muscles of his arms roped from bone to bone, distinct beneath his skin. The skin of his chest was bronze where his shirt usually lay open, but the tender skin on the underside of his arms was white as milk, a tracery of blue veins showing. The light shadowed the prominent bones of his face and glimmered from his hair, cinnamon and amber where it lay across his shoulders, dark auburn and red-gold where it dusted his bared body.

"The candlelight becomes ye, Sassenach," he said, smiling, and I saw that he was watching me, blue eyes the color of bottomless ocean.

"I was just thinking the same of you," I said, standing up and putting aside my brush. My hair floated in a cloud round my shoulders, clean, soft, and shining. It smelled of marigolds and sunflowers and so did my skin. Bathing and shampooing in winter was a major undertaking, but I had been determined not to go to bed smelling of pig shit.

"Let it burn, then," he said, reaching out to stop me as I bent to blow the candle out. His hand curled round my wrist, urging me toward him.

"Come to bed, and let me watch ye. I like the way the light moves in your eyes; like whisky, when ye pour it on a haggis, and then set it on fire."

"How poetic," I murmured, but made no demur as he made room for me, pulled loose the drawstring of my shift, and slipped it off me. The air of the room was cold enough to make my nipples draw up tight, but the skin of his chest was delightfully warm on my breasts as he gathered me into him, sighing with pleasure.

"It's Fergus's song inspiring me, I expect," he said, cupping one of my breasts in his hand and weighing it with a nice balance between admiration and appraisal. "God, ye've the loveliest breasts. Ye recall that one verse, where he says the lady's tits were so enormous, she could wrap them round his ears? Yours aren't so big as that, of course, but d'ye think ye maybe could wrap them round—"

"I don't think they need to be enormous to do *that*," I assured him. "Move up. Besides, I don't believe it's actually wrapping round, so much as it is squashing together, and they're certainly large enough for . . . see?"

"Oh," he said, sounding deeply gratified and a little breathless. "Aye, ye're right. That's . . . oh, that looks verra beautiful, Sassenach—at least from here."

"It looks very interesting from here, too," I assured him, trying neither to laugh nor go cross-eyed. "Which one of us moves, do you think?"

"Me, for now. I'm no chafing ye, Sassenach?" he inquired.

"Well, just a bit. Wait, though—" I reached out a hand, feeling blindly over the table by the bed. I got hold of the little pot of creamy almond ointment I used for hand lotion, flicked the lid off, and dug a finger into it.

"Yes, that's much better," I said. "Isn't it?"

"Oh. Oh. Aye."

"And then there's that other verse, isn't there?" I said thoughtfully, letting go for a moment, and drawing a slippery finger slowly round the curve of his buttock. "About what the prostitute did to the choirboy?"

"Oh, Christ!"

"Yes, that's what he said. According to the song."

MUCH LATER, in the dark, I roused from sleep to feel his hands on me again. Still pleasantly adrift in dreams, I didn't move, but lay inert, letting him do what he would.

My mind was loosely tethered to reality, and it took some time for me to come to the slow realization that something wasn't quite right. It took even longer to focus my mind and struggle toward the surface of wakefulness, but at last I got my eyes open, blinking away clouds of sleep.

He was crouched half over me, his face half-lit by the dim glow from the smoored hearth. His eyes were closed, and he was frowning a little, his breath coming through half-opened lips. He moved almost mechanically, and I wondered, muzzily astonished, whether he could possibly be doing it in his sleep?

A thin film of sweat gleamed on the high cheekbones, the long straight bridge of his nose, on the slopes and curves of his naked body.

He was stroking me in an odd, monotonous sort of way, like a man working at some repetitive task. The touch was more than intimate, but weirdly impersonal; I might have been anybody—or anything—I thought.

Then he moved, and eyes still closed, flipped back the quilt covering me and moved between my legs, spreading them apart in a brusque fashion that was quite unlike him. His brows were drawn together, knotted in a frown of concentration. I moved instinctively to close my legs, squirming away. His hands clamped down on my shoulders then, his knee thrust my thighs apart, and he entered me roughly.

I made a high-pitched sound of startled protest, and his

eyes popped open. He stared at me, his eyes no more than an inch from mine, unfocused, then sharpening into abrupt awareness. He froze.

"Who the *bloody* hell do you think I am?" I said, low-voiced and furious.

He wrenched himself away and flung himself off the bed, leaving the covers hanging to the floor in disarray. He seized his clothes from the peg, reached the door in two strides, opened it, and disappeared, slamming it behind him.

I sat up, feeling thoroughly rattled. I scrabbled the quilts back up around myself, feeling dazed, angry—and halfway disbelieving. I rubbed my hands over my face, trying to wake up all the way. Surely *I* hadn't been dreaming?

No. He was. He'd been half-asleep—or wholly so—and he'd bloody thought I was bloody Laoghaire! Nothing else could account for the way he had been touching me, with a sense of painful impatience tinged with anger; he had never touched me like that in his life.

I lay back down, but it was patently impossible to go back to sleep. I stared at the shadowy rafters for a few minutes, then rose with decision, and got dressed.

The dooryard was bleak and cold under a high, bright moon. I stepped out, closing the kitchen door softly behind me, and clutched my cloak round me, listening. Nothing stirred in the cold, and the wind was no more than a sigh through the pines. At some distance, though, I heard a faint, regular noise, and turned toward it, making my way carefully through the dark.

The door of the haybarn was open.

I leaned against the doorjamb, and crossed my arms, watching as he stamped to and fro, pitching hay in the moonlight, working off his temper. Mine was still pulsing in my temples, but began to subside as I watched him.

The difficulty was that I did understand, and all too well. I had not met many of Frank's women—he was discreet. But now and then, I would catch a glance exchanged at a faculty party or the local supermarket—and a feeling of black rage would well up in me, only to be followed by bafflement as to what, precisely, I was to do with it.

Jealousy had nothing to do with logic.

Laoghaire MacKenzie was four thousand miles away; likely neither of us would ever see her again. Frank was even farther away, and it was certain neither of us would ever see him again, this side the grave.

No, jealousy had nothing at all to do with logic.

I began to be cold, but went on standing there. He knew I was there; I could see it in the way he kept his head turned toward his work. He was sweating, in spite of the cold; the thin cloth of his shirt stuck to him, making a dark spot on his back. At last, he stabbed the pitchfork into the stack, left it, and sat down on a bench made from half a log. He put his head in his hands, fingers rubbing violently through his hair.

Finally, he looked up at me, with an expression halfway between dismay and reluctant amusement.

"I dinna understand it."

"What?" I moved toward him, and sat down near him, curling my feet under me. I could smell the sweat on his skin, along with almond cream and the ghost of his earlier lust.

He gave me a sidelong glance, and answered dryly, "Anything, Sassenach."

"Can't be that bad, can it?" I reached tentatively for him, and ran a hand lightly down the curve of his back.

He heaved a deep sigh, blowing air through pursed lips.

"When I was three-and-twenty, I didna understand how it was that to look at a woman could turn my bones to water, yet make me feel I could bend steel in my hands. When I was five-and-twenty, I didna understand how I could want both to cherish a woman and ravish her, all at once."

"*A* woman?" I asked, and got what I wanted—the curl of his mouth and a glance that went through my heart.

"One woman," he said. He took the hand I laid on his knee, and held it tightly, as though afraid I might snatch it back. "Just one," he repeated, his voice husky.

It was quiet in the barn, but the boards creaked and settled in the cold. I moved a little on the bench, scooting toward him. Just a little. Moonlight streamed through the wide-open door, glowing dimly off the piled hay.

"And that," he said, squeezing my fingers tighter, "is what I dinna ken now. I love *you, a nighean donn*. I have loved ye from the moment I saw ye, I will love ye 'til time itself is done, and so long as you are by my side, I am well pleased wi' the world."

A flush of warmth went through me, but before I could do more than squeeze his hand in reply, he went on, turning to look at me with an expression of bewilderment so desperate as to be almost comical.

"And that bein' so, Claire—why, in the name of Christ and all his saints—*why* do I want to take ship to Scotland, hunt down a man whose name and face I dinna ken at all, and kill him, for swiving a woman to whom I have nay claim, and who I couldna stand to be in the same room with for more than three minutes at the most?"

He brought his free hand down in a fist, striking the log with a thump that vibrated through the wood under my buttocks.

"I do *not* understand!"

I suppressed the urge to say, "And you think *I* do?" Instead, I merely sat quietly, and after a moment, stroked his knuckles very lightly with my thumb. It was less a caress than a simple reassurance, and he took it so.

After a moment, he sighed deeply, squeezed my hand, and stood up.

"I am a fool," he said.

I sat still for a moment, but he seemed to expect some sort of confirmation, so I nodded obligingly.

"Well, perhaps," I said. "But you aren't going to Scotland, are you?"

Instead of replying, he got to his feet and walked moodily to and fro, kicking clumps of dried mud, which burst like small bombs. Surely he wasn't contemplating . . . he couldn't be. With some difficulty, I kept my mouth shut, and waited patiently, until he came back to stand in front of me.

"All right," he said, in the tone of one stating a declaration of principle. "I dinna ken why it galls me that Laoghaire should seek another man's company—no, that's no the truth, is it? I ken well enough. And it isna jealousy. Or . . . well, it is, then, but that's no the main thing." He shot me a look, as though daring me to contradict this assertion, but I kept my mouth shut. He exhaled strongly through his nose, and took a deep breath, looking down.

"Well, then. If I'm honest about it." His lips pressed tight together for a moment. "Why?" he burst out, looking up at me. "What is it about him?"

"What is what about who? The man she—"

"She hated it, the bedding!" he interrupted me, stamping a clod into powder. "Perhaps I flatter myself, or you flatter me . . ." He gave me a look that wanted to be a glare, but ended in bewilderment. "Am I . . . am I . . . ?"

I wasn't sure whether he wanted me to say, "Yes, you are!" or "No, you're not!" but satisfied myself with a smile that said both.

"Aye. Well," he said reluctantly. "I didna *think* it was me. And before we were wed, even Laoghaire liked me well enough." I must have made a small snort at that, for he glanced at me, but I shook my head, dismissing it.

"I thought it must be a mislike for men in general, or only for the act. And if it was so . . . well, it wasna quite so bad, if it wasna my fault, though I did feel somehow I should be able to mend it. . . ." He trailed off into this thoughts, brow furrowed, then resumed with a sigh.

"But maybe I was wrong about that. Perhaps it *was* me. And that's a thought that sticks in my craw."

I had no real idea what to say to him, but clearly I had to say something.

"I think it was her," I said, firmly. "Not you. Though of course I may be prejudiced. She did try to kill me, after all."

"She what?" He swung round, looking blank.

"You didn't know that? Oh." I tried to think; had I not told him? No, I supposed not. What with one thing and another, it hadn't seemed important at the time; I had never expected to see her again. And later . . . well, it really *wasn't* important then. I explained briefly about Laoghaire's having sent me to join Geillie Duncan that day in Cranesmuir, fully aware that Geillie was about to be arrested for witchcraft, and hoping that I would be taken with her—as indeed I was.

"The wicked wee bitch!" he said, sounding more astonished than anything else. "No, I didna ken that at all—Christ, Sassenach, ye canna think I would have marrit the woman, knowing she'd done such a thing to you!"

"Well, she was only sixteen at the time," I said, able under the circumstances to be tolerantly forgiving. "And she might not have realized that we'd be tried or that the witch-court would try to burn us. She might only have meant mischief—thinking that if I were accused as a witch, it would make you lose interest in me." The revelation of her chicanery seemed at least to have distracted Jamie's mind, which was all to the good.

His only response to this was a snort. He paced restlessly to and fro for a bit, his feet rustling in the spilled straw. He hadn't taken his shoes or stockings, and was barefoot, though the cold seemed not to trouble him.

At last he stopped, heaved a massive sigh, and bent forward, resting a hand on the bench, his head on my shoulder.

"I'm sorry," he whispered.

I put my arms round his shoulders and pulled him close, holding him hard until at last he sighed again, and the knotted strain in his shoulders relaxed. I let go, and he stood up, giving me a hand to rise.

We closed the barn door and walked back to the house in silence, hand in hand.

"Claire," he said suddenly, sounding a little shy.

"Yes?"

"I dinna mean to excuse myself—not at all. It's only I was wondering . . . do ye ever . . . think of Frank? When we . . ." He stopped and cleared his throat. "Does the shadow of the Englishman perhaps cross my face—now and then?"

And what on earth could I say to that? I couldn't lie, surely, but how could I say the truth, either, in a way he would understand, that wouldn't hurt him?

I drew a deep breath and let it out, watching the mist of it purl softly away.

"I don't want to make love to a ghost," I said at last, firmly. "And I don't think you do, either. But I suppose every now and then a ghost might have other ideas."

He made a small sound that was mostly a laugh.

"Aye," he said. "I suppose they might. I wonder if Laoghaire would like the Englishman's bed better than mine?"

"Serve her right if she did," I said. "But if you like mine, I suggest you come and get back into it. It's *bloody* cold out here."

100

DEAD WHALE

BY LATE MARCH, the trails down the mountain were passable. No word had come yet from Milford Lyon, and after some debate on the matter, it was decided that Jamie and I, with Brianna, Roger, and Marsali, would travel to Wilmington, while Fergus took the survey reports to New Bern to be formally filed and registered.

The girls and I would buy supplies depleted over the winter, such as salt, sugar, coffee, tea, and opium, while Roger and Jamie would make discreet inquiries after Milford Lyon—and Stephen Bonnet. Fergus would come to join us, so soon as the surveying reports were taken care of, making his own inquiries along the coast as chance offered.

After which, presumably, Jamie and Roger, having located Mr. Bonnet, would drop round to his place of business and take turns either shooting him dead or running him through with a sword, before riding back into the mountains, congratulating themselves on a job well done. Or so I understood the plan to be.

"The best-laid plans of mice and men gang aft agley," I quoted to Jamie, in the midst of one discussion on the matter. He raised one brow and gave me a look.

"What sorts of plans have mice got?"

"Well, there you have me," I admitted. "The principle holds, though; you haven't any idea what may happen."

"That's true," he agreed. "But whatever *does* happen, I

shall be ready for it." He patted the dirk that lay on the corner of his desk, and went back to making lists of farm supplies.

The weather warmed markedly as we descended from the mountains, and as we drew nearer to the coast, flocks of seagulls and crows wheeled and swarmed over the fresh-plowed fields, shrieking ecstatically in the bright spring sunshine.

The trees in the mountains were barely beginning to leaf out, but in Wilmington, flowers were already glowing in the gardens, spikes of yellow columbine and blue larkspur nodding over the tidy fences on Beaufort Street. We found lodgings in a small, clean inn a little way from the quay. It was relatively cheap and reasonably comfortable, if a trifle crowded and dark.

"Why don't they have more windows?" Brianna grumbled, nursing a stubbed toe after stumbling over Germain in the darkness on the landing. "Somebody's going to burn the place down, lighting candles to see where they're going. Glass can't be *that* expensive."

"Window tax," Roger informed her, picking Germain up and dangling him head-down over the bannister, to Germain's intense delight.

"What? The Crown taxes *windows*?"

"It does. Ye'd think people would care more about that than stamps or tea, but apparently they're used to the window tax."

"No wonder they're about to have a revolu— Oh, good morning, Mrs. Burns! The breakfast smells wonderful."

The girls, the children, and I spent several days in careful shopping, while Roger and Jamie mixed business with pleasure in assorted taprooms and taverns. Most of their errands were completed, and Jamie produced a small but useful subsidiary income from card-playing and betting on horses, but all he was able to hear of Stephen Bonnet was that he had not been seen in Wilmington for some months. I was privately relieved to hear this.

It rained later in the week, hard enough to keep everyone indoors for two days. More than simple rain; it was a substantial storm, with winds high enough to bend the palmetto trees half over and plaster the muddy streets with torn leaves and fallen branches. Marsali sat up late into the night, listening to the wind, alternating between saying the rosary and playing cards with Jamie for distraction.

"Fergus did say it was a large ship he would be coming on from New Bern? The *Octopus*? That sounds good-sized, doesn't it, Da?"

"Oh, aye. Though I believe the packet boats are verra safe, too. No, dinna discard that, lass—throw away the trey of spades instead."

"How do ye know I have the trey of spades?" she demanded, frowning suspiciously at him. "And it's no true about the packet boats. Ye ken that as well as I do; we saw the wreckage of one at the bottom of Elm Street, day before yesterday."

"I know ye've got the trey of spades because I haven't," Jamie told her, tucking his hand of cards neatly against his chest, "and all the other spades have already turned up on the table. Besides, Fergus might come overland from New Bern; he may not be on a boat at all."

A gust of wind struck the house, rattling the shutters.

"Another reason not to have windows," Roger observed, looking over Marsali's shoulder at her hand. "No, he's right, discard the trey of spades."

"Here, you do it. I've got to go and see to Joanie." She rose suddenly, and thrusting the cards into Roger's hand, rustled off to the small room next door that she shared with her children. I hadn't heard Joanie cry.

There was a loud thump and scrape overhead, as a detached tree limb sailed across the roof. Everyone looked up. Below the high-pitched keen of the wind, we could hear the hollow rumble of the surf, boiling across the submerged mudflats, pounding on the shore.

"They that go down to the sea in ships," Roger quoted softly, "that do business in great waters; these see the works of the Lord, and his wonders in the deep. For he commandeth, and raiseth the stormy wind, which lifteth up the waves thereof."

"Oh, you're a big help," Brianna said crossly. Already edgy, her temper had not been improved by the enforced seclusion. Jemmy, terrified by all the racket, had been wrapped around her like a poultice for the better part of two days; both of them were hot, damp, and exceedingly cranky.

Roger appeared not to be put off by her mood. He smiled, and bending down, peeled Jemmy away from her, with some difficulty. He put the little boy on the floor, holding him by the hands.

"They reel to and fro," he said theatrically, pulling Jem's hands so that he lurched, off-balance. "And stagger like a drunken man, and are at their wit's end."

Jemmy was giggling, and even Brianna was beginning to smile, reluctantly.

"Then they cry unto the Lord in their trouble, and he *bringeth* them out of their distresses—" On *"bringeth,"* he swung Jemmy suddenly up in the air, caught him under the arms and whirled him round, making him shriek in delight.

"He maketh the storm a calm, so that the waves thereof are still. Then are they glad because they be quiet—" He pulled Jemmy in close, and kissed him on the head, "—so he bringeth them unto their desired haven."

Bree applauded the performance sarcastically, but smiled nonetheless. Jamie had retrieved the cards, shuffling the deck neatly back together. He stopped, looking up. Caught by his sudden stillness, I turned my head to look at him. He glanced at me and smiled.

"The wind has dropped," he said. "Hear it? Tomorrow, we'll go out."

THE WEATHER HAD CLEARED by morning, and a fresh breeze came in from the sea, bearing with it a tang of the shore, smelling of sea-lavender, pines, and a strong reek of something maritime rotting in the sun. The quay still exhibited a depressing lack of masts; no large ships lay at anchor, not even a ketch or packet boat, though the water in Wilmington harbor swarmed with dinghies, rafts, canoes, and pirettas, the little four-oared boats that flitted across the water like dragonflies, droplets sparkling from their flying oars.

One of these spotted our small party standing disconsolately on the wharf, and darted toward us, its oarsmen calling out to know whether we required transport? As Roger leaned out to shout a polite refusal, the breeze off the harbor whipped away his hat, which whirled giddily out over the brownish waters and lighted on the foam, spinning like a leaf.

The craft sculled at once toward the floating hat, and one of the oarsmen speared it deftly, raising it dripping in triumph on the end of his oar. As the piretta drew up beside the quay, though, the boatman's look of jubilation changed to one of astonishment.

"MacKenzie!" he cried. "Bugger me wi' a silver toothpick if it isn't!"

"Duff! Duff, me auld lad!" Roger leaned down and grabbed his hat, then reached back to give his erstwhile acquaintance a hand up. Duff, a small, grizzled Scot with a very long nose, sparse jowls, and a fine sprout of graying whiskers that made him look as though he'd been thickly dusted in icing sugar, leaped nimbly up onto the quay and proceeded to clasp Roger in a manly embrace, punctuated by fierce thumpings on the back and ejaculations of amazement, all heartily returned by Roger. The rest of us stood politely watching this reunion, while Marsali prevented Germain from jumping off the quay into the water.

"Do you know him?" I asked Brianna, who was dubiously examining her husband's old friend.

"I *think* he might have been on a ship with Roger once," she replied, renewing her grip on Jemmy, who was wildly excited by the sight of seagulls, finding these much more entertaining than Mr. Duff.

"Why, look at him!" Duff exclaimed, finally standing back and wiping a sleeve happily under his nose. "A coat like a lairdie's and buttons to match. And the hat! Christ, lad, ye're so slick these days as shit wouldna stick to ye, would it?"

Roger laughed, and bent to pick up his soggy hat. He slapped it against his thigh to dislodge a strand of bladderwrack, and handed it absently to Bree, who was still viewing Mr. Duff with a rather narrow eye.

"My wife," Roger introduced her, and waved a hand at the

rest of us. "And her family. Mr. James Fraser, Mrs. Fraser . . . and my wife's good-sister, also Mrs. Fraser."

"Your servant, sir—ladies." Duff bowed to Jamie, and put a finger to the disreputable object on his head in brief token of respect. He glanced at Brianna, and a broad grin stretched his lips.

"Oh, so ye married her. Got her out o' the breeks, I see." He nudged Roger familiarly in the ribs, lowering his voice to a hoarse whisper. "Did ye pay her faither for her, or did he pay you to take her?" He emitted a creaking noise, which I took to be laughter.

Jamie and Bree gave Mr. Duff identical cold looks down the bridges of their long, straight noses, but before Roger could reply, the other oarsman shouted something incomprehensible from the boat below.

"Oh, aye, aye, hold your water, man." Mr. Duff waved a quelling hand at his partner. "That's by way of a jest," he explained to me confidentially. "What with us bein' sailors, ken. 'Hold your water,' aye? Forbye ye *don't* hold water, then ye'll be at the bottom o' the harbor, aye?" He quivered with merriment, making the creaking noise again.

"Most amusing," I assured him. "Did he say something about a whale?"

"Oh, to be sure! Was that not why ye've come down to the shore this morning?"

Everyone looked blank.

"No," Marsali said, too bent upon her errand to pay much attention to anything else, including whales. "Germain, come back here! No, sir, we've come to see if there's any word of the *Octopus*. Ye'll not have heard anything, yourself?"

Duff shook his head.

"No, Missus. But the weather's been that treacherous off the Banks for a month past . . ." He saw Marsali's face go pale, and hastened to add, "A good many ships will ha' sheered off, see? Gone to another port, maybe, or lyin' to just off the coast, in hopes of fair skies to make the run in. Ye recall, MacKenzie—we did that ourselves, when we came in wi' the *Gloriana*."

"Aye, that's true." Roger nodded, though his eyes grew

wary at mention of the *Gloriana*. He glanced briefly at Brianna, then back at Duff, and lowered his voice slightly. "You've parted company with Captain Bonnet, I see."

A small jolt shot through the soles of my feet, as though the dock had been electrified. Jamie and Bree both reacted, too, though in different fashion. He took an immediate step toward Duff, she took one back.

"Stephen Bonnet?" Jamie said, eyeing Duff with interest. "Ye'll be acquainted with that gentleman, will ye?"

"I have been, sir," Duff said, and crossed himself.

Jamie nodded slowly, seeing this.

"Aye, I see. And will ye ken somewhat about Mr. Bonnet's present whereabouts, perhaps?"

"Och, well, as to that . . ."

Duff looked up at him speculatively, taking in the details of his clothing and appearance, and obviously wondering exactly how much the answer to that question might be worth. His partner below was growing increasingly restive, though, and shouted impatiently.

Marsali was restive, too.

"Where might they go, then? If they've gone to another port? Germain, stop! Ye'll fall in, next thing!" She bent to retrieve her offspring, who had been hanging over the edge of the wharf, peacefully exploring its underside, and hoicked him up onto one hip.

"Bonnet?" Jamie raised his brows, contriving to look simultaneously encouraging and menacing.

"They gone see da whale or don't they?" yelled the gentleman in the boat, impatient to be off on more profitable ventures.

Duff seemed somewhat at a loss as to whom to reply to first. His small eyes blinked, shifting to and fro between Jamie, Marsali, and his increasingly vociferous partner below. I stepped in to break the impasse.

"What's all this about a whale?"

Compelled to focus on this straightforward question, Duff looked relieved.

"Why, the dead whale, Missus. A big 'un, gone aground on the Island. I thought sure as ye'd all come down to see."

I looked out across the water, and for the first time realized that the boat traffic was not entirely random. While a few large canoes and barges were headed toward the mouth of Cape Fear, most of the smaller craft were plying to and fro, disappearing into the distant haze, or returning from it, bearing small groups of passengers. Linen parasols sprouted like pastel mushrooms from the boats, and there was a sprinkling of what were obviously townspeople on the dock, standing as we were, looking expectantly across the harbor.

"Two shillin's the boatload," Duff suggested ingratiatingly. "Over and back."

Roger, Brianna, and Marsali looked interested. Jamie looked uneasy.

"In *that*?" he asked, with a skeptical glance at the piretta, bobbing gently below. Duff's partner—a gentleman of indeterminate race and language—seemed inclined to take offense at this implied criticism of his craft, but Duff was reassuring.

"Oh, it's dead calm today, sir, dead calm. Why, 'twould be like sittin' on a tavern bench. Congenial, aye? Verra suitable to conversation." He blinked, innocently affable.

Jamie drew a deep breath in through his nose, and I saw him glance once more at the piretta. Jamie hated boats. On the other hand, he would do far more desperate things than get into a boat in pursuit of Stephen Bonnet. The only question was whether Mr. Duff actually had information to that end, or was only inveigling passengers. Jamie swallowed hard and braced his shoulders, steeling himself to it.

Not waiting, Duff reinforced his position by turning craftily to Marsali.

"There's a lighthouse on the Island, ma'am. Ye can see a good ways out to sea from the top o' that. See if any ships should be lyin' off."

Marsali's hand dropped at once to her pocket, fumbling for the strings. I observed Germain solicitously poking a dead mussel over her shoulder toward Jemmy's eagerly open mouth, like a mother bird feeding her offspring a nice juicy worm, and tactfully intervened, taking Jemmy into my own arms.

"No, sweetheart," I said, dropping the mussel off the dock. "You don't want that nasty thing. Wouldn't you like to go see a nice dead whale, instead?"

Jamie sighed in resignation, and reached for his sporran. "Ye'd best call for another boat, then, so as we'll not all drown together."

IT WAS LOVELY out on the water, with the sun covered by a hazy layer of cloud, and a cool breeze that made me take my hat off for the pleasure of feeling the wind in my hair. While not quite flat calm, the rise and fall of the surf was peacefully lulling—to those of us not afflicted by seasickness.

I glanced at Jamie's back, but his head was bent, shoulders moving in an easy, powerful rhythm as he rowed.

Resigned to the inevitable, he had taken brisk charge of the situation, summoning a second boat and herding Bree, Marsali, and the boys into it. Thereupon Jamie had unfastened his brooch and announced that he and Roger would row the remaining piretta, in order that Duff might put himself at ease and thus improve his chances of recollecting interesting facts regarding Stephen Bonnet.

"Less chance of me puking if I've something to do," he muttered to me, stripping off his coat and plaid.

Roger gave a small snort of amusement, but nodded agreeably and shed his own coat and shirt. With Duff and Peter installed at one end of the craft in a state of high hilarity over the turnabout of being paid to be rowed in their own boat, I was told off to sit in the other end, facing them.

"Just to keep a bit of an eye on things, Sassenach." Under cover of the wadded clothes, Jamie wrapped my hand around the stock of his pistol, and squeezed gently. He handed me down into the boat, then climbed down gingerly himself, going only slightly pale as the craft swayed and shifted under his weight.

It *was* a calm day, fortunately. A faint haze hung over the water, obscuring the dim shape of Smith Island in the distance. Kittiwakes and terns wheeled in gyres far above, and a heavy-bodied gull seemed to hang immobile in the air nearby, riding the wind as we sculled slowly out into the harbor mouth.

Seated just before me, Roger rowed easily, broad bare shoulders flexing rhythmically, obviously accustomed to the exercise. Jamie, on the seat in front of Roger, handled the oars with a fair amount of grace, but somewhat less assurance. He was no sailor, and never would be. Still, the distraction of rowing did seem to be keeping his mind off his stomach. For the moment.

"Oh, I could find myself accustomed to this, what d'ye say, Peter?" Duff lifted a long nose into the breeze, half-closing his eyes as he savored the novelty of being rowed.

Peter, who appeared to be some exotic blend of Indian and African, grunted in reply, but lounged on the seat beside Duff, equally pleased. He wore nothing but a pair of stained homespun breeches, tied at the waist with a length of tarred rope, and was burned so dark by the sun that he might have been a Negro, save for the spill of long black hair that fell over one shoulder, decorated with bits of shell and tiny dried starfish tied into it.

"Stephen Bonnet?" Jamie inquired pleasantly, drawing strongly on the oars.

"Oh, him." Duff looked as though he would have preferred to put off this subject of discussion indefinitely, but a glance at Jamie's face resigned him to the inevitable.

"What d'ye want to know, then?" The little man hunched his shoulders warily.

"To begin with, where he is," Jamie said, grunting slightly as he hauled on the oars.

"No idea," Duff said promptly, looking happier.

"Well, where did ye last see the bugger?" Jamie asked patiently.

Duff and Peter exchanged glances.

"Well, noo," Duff began cautiously, "d'ye mean by 'see,' where it was I last clapped een on the captain?"

"What else would he mean, clotheid?" Roger said, grunting with a backward stroke.

Peter nodded thoughtfully, evidently awarding a point to our side, and elbowed Duff in the ribs.

"He was in a pot-house on Roanoke, eatin' fish pie," Duff said, capitulating. "Baked wi' oysters and breadcrumbs on the top, and a pint of dark ale to wash it down. Molasses pudding, too."

"Ye've a keen sense of observation, Mr. Duff," Jamie said. "How's your sense of time, then?"

"Eh? Oh, aye, I tak' your meanin', man. When was it . . . twa month past, aboot."

"And if ye were close enough to see what the man was eating," Jamie observed mildly, "then I expect ye were at table with him, no? What did he speak of?"

Duff looked mildly embarrassed. He glanced at me, then up at one of the circling gulls.

"Aye, well. The shape of the arse on the barmaid, mostly."

"I shouldna think that a topic of conversation to occupy the course of a meal, even if the lassie was particularly shapely," Roger put in.

"Ah, ye'd be surprised how much there is to say about a woman's bum, lad," Duff assured him. "This one was round as an apple, and heavy as a steamed puddin'. 'Twas cold as charity in the place, and the thought of havin' such a plump, hot, wee bridie in your hands—meanin' no offense to ye, ma'am, I'm sure," he added hurriedly, tipping his hat in my direction.

"None taken," I assured him cordially.

"Can you swim, Mr. Duff?" Jamie asked, his tone still one of mild curiosity.

"What?" Duff blinked, taken back. "I . . . ah . . . well . . ."

"No, he can't," Roger said cheerfully. "He told me."

Duff gave him a look of outraged betrayal over Jamie's head.

"Well, there's loyalty!" he said, scandalized. "A fine shipmate *you* are! Givin' me away so—ye should be ashamed of yersel', so ye should!"

Jamie raised his oars, dripping, out of the water, and Roger followed suit. We were perhaps a quarter-mile from shore, and the water beneath our hull was a deep, soft green, portending a bottom several fathoms deep. The boat rocked gently, lifting on the bosom of a long, slow swell.

"Bonnet," Jamie said, still politely, but with a definite edge. Peter folded his arms and closed his eyes, making it clear that the subject had nothing to do with *him*. Duff sighed and eyed Jamie narrowly.

"Aye, well. It's true, I've no notion where the man is. When I saw him on Roanoke, he was makin' arrangements to have some . . . goods . . . brought in. For what that might be worth to ye," he added, rather ungraciously.

"What goods? Brought in where? And going where?" Jamie was leaning on his shipped oars, apparently casual. I could see a certain tension in the line of his body, though, and it occurred to me that while his attention might be fixed on Duff's face, he was of necessity also watching the horizon behind Duff—which was rising and falling hypnotically as the swell lifted the piretta and let it drop. Over and over and . . .

"Tea-chests was what I took in for him," Duff answered warily. "Couldna say, for the rest."

"The rest?"

"Christ, man, every boat on this water brings in the odd bit of jiggery-pokery here and there—surely ye ken that much?"

Peter's eyes had opened to half-slits; I saw them rest on Jamie's face with a certain expression of interest. The wind had shifted a few points, and the smell of dead whale was decidedly stronger. Jamie took a slow, deep breath, and let it out again, rather faster.

"Ye brought in tea, then. Where from? A ship?"

"Aye." Duff was watching Jamie, too, in growing fascination. I shifted uneasily on the narrow seat. I couldn't tell from the back of his neck, but I thought it more than likely that he was beginning to turn green.

"The *Sparrow*," Duff went on, eyes fixed on Jamie. "She anchored off the Banks, and the boats went out to her. We loaded the cargo and came in through Joad's Inlet. Cam' ashore at Wylie's Landing, and handed over to a fellow there."

"What . . . fellow?" The wind was cool, but I could see sweat trickling down the back of Jamie's neck, dampening his collar and plastering the linen between his shoulders.

Duff didn't answer immediately. A look of speculation flickered in his small, deep-set eyes.

"Don't think about it, Duff," Roger said, softly, but with great assurance. "I can reach ye from here with an oar, ken?"

"Aye?" Duff glanced thoughtfully from Jamie, to Roger, and then to me. "Aye, reckon ye might. But allowin' for the sake for argyment as how you can swim, MacKenzie—and even that Mr. Fraser might keep afloat—I dinna think that's true of the lady, is it? Skirts and petticoats . . ." He shook his head, pursing thin lips in speculation as he looked at me. "Go to the bottom like a stone, she would."

Peter shifted ever so slightly, bringing his feet under him.

"Claire?" Jamie said. I saw his fingers curl tight round the oars, and heard the note of strain in his voice. I sighed and drew the pistol out from under the coat across my lap.

"Right," I said. "Which one shall I shoot?"

Peter's eyes snapped open, wide enough that I saw a rim of white show all round his black pupils. He looked at the pistol, then at Duff, then directly at Jamie.

"Give tea to a man name Butlah," he said. "Work for Mist' Lyon." He pointed at me, then at Duff. "Shoot him," he suggested.

The ice thus broken, it took very little time for our two passengers to confide the rest of what they knew, pausing only momentarily for Jamie to be sick over the side between questions.

Smuggling was, as Duff had suggested, so common in the area as to constitute general business practice; most of the merchants—and all of the small boatmen—in Wilmington engaged in it, as did most others on the Carolina coast, in order to avoid the crippling duties on officially imported goods. Stephen Bonnet, however, was not only one of the more successful smugglers, but also rather a specialist.

"Brings in goods to order, like," Duff said, twisting his neck in order to scratch more effectively between his shoulder blades. "And in what ye might call quantity."

"How much quantity?" Jamie's elbows rested on his knees, his head sunk onto his hands. It seemed to be helping; his voice was steady.

Duff pursed his lips and squinted, calculating.

"There was six of us at the tavern on Roanoke. Six wi' small boats, I mean, as could run the inlets. If we were each to be fetchin' along as much as we could manage . . . say, fifty chests of tea all told, then."

"And he brings in such a load how often—every two months?" Roger had relaxed a little, leaning on his oars. I hadn't, and gave Duff a hard eye over the pistol to indicate as much.

"Oh, more often than that," Duff answered, eyeing me warily. "Couldn't say exactly, but you hear talk, aye? From what the other boats say, I reckon he's got a load comin' every two weeks in the season, somewhere on the coast betwixt Virginia and Charleston." Roger gave a brief grunt of surprise at that, and Jamie looked up briefly from his cupped hands.

"What about the Navy?" he asked. "Who's he paying?" That was a good question. While small boats might escape the Navy's eye, Bonnet's operation evidently involved large quantities of contraband, coming in on large ships. It would be hard to hide something on that scale—and the obvious answer was that he wasn't bothering to hide it.

Duff shook his head and shrugged.

"Can't say, man."

"But you haven't worked for Bonnet since February?" I asked. "Why not?"

Duff and Peter exchanged a glance.

"You eat scorpion-fish, you hungry," Peter said to me. "You don' eat dem, iffen you got sumpin' bettah."

"What?"

"The man's dangerous, Sassenach," Jamie translated dryly. "They dinna like to deal with him, save for need."

"Well, see him, Bonnet," Duff said, warming to the topic. "He's no bad at all to deal with—sae long as your interest runs wi' his. Only, if it might be as all of a sudden it *doesna* quite run with his . . ."

Peter solemnly drew a finger across his stringy neck, nodding in affirmation.

"And it's no as if there's warnin' about it, either," Duff added, nodding too. "One minute, it's whisky and segars, the next, ye're on your back in the sawdust, breathin' blood, and happy still to be breathin' at that."

"A temper, has he?" Jamie drew a hand down over his face, then wiped his sweaty palm on his shirt. The linen clung damply to his shoulders, but I knew he wouldn't take it off.

Duff, Peter, and Roger all shook their heads simultaneously at the question.

"Cold as ice," Roger said, and I heard the small note of strain in his voice.

"Kill ye without the turn of an arse-hair," Duff assured Jamie.

"Rip you like dem whale," Peter put in helpfully, with a wave toward the island. The current had carried us a good deal closer to the land, and I could see the whale as well as smell it. Seabirds whirled and screamed in a great cloud over the carcass, swooping down to tear away gobbets of flesh, and a small crowd of people clustered nearby, hands to their noses, clearly clutching handkerchiefs and sachets.

Just then, the wind changed, and a fetid gust of decay washed over us like a breaking wave. I clapped Roger's shirt to my own face, and even Peter appeared to pale.

"Mother of God, have mercy on me," Jamie said, under his breath. "I—oh, Christ!" He leaned to the side and threw up, repeatedly.

I nudged Roger in the buttock with my toe.

"Row," I suggested.

Roger obeyed with alacrity, putting his back into it, and within a few minutes, the keel of the piretta touched sand. Duff and Peter leaped out to run the hull up onto the beach, then gallantly assisted me out of the boat, evidently not holding the pistol against me.

Jamie paid them, then staggered a short distance up the beach and sat down, quite suddenly, in the sand beneath a loblolly pine. He was roughly the same shade as the dead whale, a dirty gray with white blotches.

"Will we wait for ye, sir, and row ye back?" Duff, his purse now bulging healthily, hovered helpfully over Jamie.

"No," Jamie said. "Take them." He waved feebly at me and Roger, then closed his eyes and swallowed heavily. "As for me, I believe . . . I shall just . . . swim back."

101

MONSTERS AND HEROES

THE LITTLE BOYS WERE mad to see the whale, and tugged their reluctant mothers along like kites. I came along, keeping a somewhat more discreet distance from the towering carcass, leaving Jamie on the beach to recover. Roger took Duff aside for a bit of private conversation, while Peter subsided into somnolence in the bottom of the boat.

The carcass was newly washed up on the beach, though it must have been dead for some time before its landing; such an impressive state of decomposition must have taken days to develop. The stench notwithstanding, a number of the more intrepid visitors were standing on the carcass, waving cheerily to their companions on the beach below, and a gentleman armed with a hatchet was employed in hacking chunks of flesh from the side of the animal, dropping these into a pair of large buckets. I recognized him as the proprietor of an ordinary on Hawthorn Street, and made a mental note to strike that establishment from our list of potential eating-places.

Numbers of small crustaceans, not nearly so fastidious in their habits, swarmed merrily over the carcass, and I saw several people, also armed with buckets, picking the larger crabs and crayfish off like ripe fruit. Ten million sand fleas had joined the circus, too, and I retreated to a safe distance, rubbing my ankles.

I glanced back down the beach, seeing that Jamie had risen now and joined the conversation—Duff was looking increasingly restive, glancing back and forth from the whale to his boat. Clearly, he was anxious to return to business, before the attraction should disappear altogether.

At last he succeeded in escaping, and scampered away toward his piretta, looking hunted. Jamie and Roger came toward me, but the little boys were clearly not ready yet to leave the whale. Brianna nobly volunteered to watch them both, so that Marsali could climb the nearby lighthouse tower, to see whether there might be any sign of the *Octopus.*

"What have you been saying to poor Mr. Duff?" I asked Jamie. "He looked rather worried."

"Aye? No need of worry," he said, glancing toward the water, where Duff's piretta was rapidly pulling back to the quay. "I've only put a wee bit of business in his way."

"He knows where Lyon is," Roger put in. He looked disturbed, but excited.

"And Mr. Lyon knows where Bonnet is—or if not where, precisely, at least how to get word to him. Let us go a bit higher, aye?" Jamie was still pale; he gestured toward the stair of the tower with his chin, wiping sweat from the side of his neck.

The air *was* fresher at the top of the tower, but I had little attention to spare for the view out over the ocean.

"And so . . . ?" I said, not sure I wanted to hear the answer.

"So I have commissioned Duff to carry a message to Mr. Lyon. All being agreeable, we will meet with Mr. Bonnet at Wylie's Landing, in a week's time."

I swallowed, feeling a wave of dizziness that had nothing to do with the height. I closed my eyes, clutching the wooden rail that surrounded the tiny platform we stood on. The wind was blowing hard, and the boards of the tower creaked and groaned, feeling frighteningly insubstantial.

I heard Jamie shift his weight, moving toward Roger.

"He is a man, ken?" he said quietly. "Not a monster."

Was he? It was a monster, I thought, who haunted Brianna—and perhaps her father. Would killing him reduce him, make him no more than a man again?

"I know." Roger's voice was steady, but lacked conviction.

I opened my eyes, to see the ocean falling away before me into a bank of floating mist. It was vast and beautiful—and empty. One might well fall off the end of the world, I thought.

"YE SAILED WI' our Stephen, aye? For what, two months, three?"

"Near on three," Roger answered.

Our Stephen, was it? And what did Jamie mean by that homely usage, then?

Jamie nodded, not turning his head. He looked out over the rolling wash of the sea, the breeze whipping strands of hair loose from their binding to dance like flames, pale in daylight.

"Ye'll have kent the man well enough, then."

Roger leaned his weight against the rail. It was solid, but wet and sticky with half-dried spray, where spume from the rocks below had reached it.

"Well enough," he echoed. "Aye. Well enough for what?"

Jamie turned then, to look him in the face. His eyes were narrowed against the wind, but straight and bright as razors.

"Well enough to ken he *is* a man—and no more."

"What else would he be?" Roger felt the edge in his own voice.

Jamie turned back toward the sea, shading his eyes with his hand as he looked toward the sinking sun.

"A monster," he said softly. "Something less than a man—or more."

Roger opened his mouth to reply, but found he could not. For it was a monster that shadowed his own heart with fear.

"How did the sailors see him?" Claire's voice came from Jamie's other side; she leaned over the rail to look around him, and the wind seized her hair and shook it out in a flying cloud, stormy as the distant sky.

"On the *Gloriana*?" Roger took a deep breath, a whiff of dead whale mingling with the fecund scent of the salt marsh behind. "They . . . respected him. Some of them were afraid of him." *Like me*. "He had the reputation of a hard captain, but a good one. Competent. Men were willing to ship with him, because he always came safe into port, his voyages were always profitable."

"Was he cruel?" Claire asked. A faint line showed between her brows.

"All captains are cruel sometimes, Sassenach," Jamie said, with a slight tinge of impatience. "They need to be."

She glanced up at him, and Roger saw her expression change, memory softening her eyes, a wry thought tightening the corner of her mouth. She laid a hand on Jamie's arm, and he saw her knuckles whiten as she squeezed.

"You've never done other than you had to," she said, so quietly that Roger could scarcely hear her. No matter; the words were plainly not meant for him. She raised her voice then, slightly. "There's a difference between cruelty and necessity."

"Aye," Jamie said, half under his breath. "And a thin line, maybe, between a monster and a hero."

102

THE BATTLE OF WYLIE'S LANDING

THE SOUND WAS CALM and flat, the surface barely ruffled by tiny wind-driven waves. And a bloody good thing, too, Roger thought, looking at his father-in-law. Jamie had his eyes open, at least, fixed on the shore with a sort of desperate intensity, as though the sight of solid land, however unreachable, might yet impart some comfort. Droplets of sweat gleamed on his upper lip, and his face was the same nacreous color as the dawn sky, but he hadn't vomited yet.

Roger wasn't seasick, but he felt nearly as ill as Jamie looked. Neither of them had eaten any breakfast, but he felt as though he'd swallowed a large mass of parritch, liberally garnished with carpet-tacks.

"That's it." Duff sat back on his oars, nodding toward the wharf ahead. It was cool on the water—almost cold at this hour—but the air was thick with moisture, and sweat ran down his face from his efforts. Peter sat silent on his own oars, dark face set in an expression indicating that he wanted nothing to do with this enterprise, and the sooner their unwelcome cargo disembarked, the better.

Wylie's Landing seemed like a mirage, floating in a layer of mist above the water amid a thick growth of needlerush and cord grass. Marshland, clumps of stunted coastal forest, and broad stretches of open water surrounded it, under an overwhelming arch of pale gray sky. By comparison to the green enclosures of the mountains, it seemed uncomfortably exposed. At the same time, it was completely isolated, evidently miles from any other sign of human habitation.

That was in part illusion; Roger knew that the plantation house was no more than a mile from the landing, but it was hidden by a dense growth of scraggy-looking forest that sprang from the marshy ground like some misshapen, dwarfish Sherwood, thick with vines and brush.

The landing itself consisted of a short wooden dock on pilings, and a collection of ramshackle sheds adjoining it, weathered to a silver-gray that seemed about to disappear into the lowering sky. A small open boat was drawn up on the shore, hull upturned. A zigzag split-rail fence enclosed a small pen beyond the sheds; Wylie must ship livestock by water now and then.

Jamie touched the cartridge box that hung at his belt, either for reassurance, or perhaps only to insure that it was still dry. His eyes went to the sky, assessing, and Roger realized with a sudden qualm that if it rained, the guns might not be dependable. Black powder clumped in the damp; more than a trace of moisture and it wouldn't fire at all. And the last thing he wanted was to find himself facing Stephen Bonnet with a useless gun.

He is a man, no more, he repeated silently to himself. Let

Bonnet swell to supernatural proportions in his mind, and he was doomed. He groped for some reassuring image, and fastened on a memory of Stephen Bonnet, seated in the head of the *Gloriana*, breeches puddled round his bare feet, blond-stubbled jaw slack in the morning light, his eyes half-closed in the pleasure of taking a peaceful crap.

Shit, he thought. Think of Bonnet as a monster, and it became impossible; think of him as a man, and it was worse. And yet, it had to be done.

His palms were sweating; he rubbed them on his breeks, not even bothering to try to hide it. There was a dirk on his belt, along with the pair of pistols; the sword lay in the bottom of the boat, solid in its scabbard. He thought of John Grey's letter, and Captain Marsden's eyes, and tasted something bitter and metallic at the back of his throat.

At Jamie's direction, the piretta drew slowly nearer the landing, everyone on board alert for any sign of life.

"No one lives here?" Jamie asked, low-voiced, leaning over Duff's shoulder to scan the buildings. "No slaves?"

"No," Duff said, grunting as he pulled. "Wylie doesna use the landing sae often these days, for he's built a new road from his house—goes inland and joins wi' the main road toward Edenton."

Jamie gave Duff a cynical glance.

"And if Wylie doesna use it, there are others who do, aye?"

Roger could see that the landing was well situated for casual smuggling; out of sight from the landward side, but easily accessible from the Sound. What he had at first taken for an island to their right was in fact a maze of sandbars, separating the channel that led to Wylie's Landing from the main sound. He could see at least four smaller channels leading into the sandbanks, two of them wide enough to accommodate a good-sized ketch.

Duff chuckled under his breath.

"There's a wee shell-road as leads to the house, man," he said. "If anyone should come that way, ye'll have fair warnin'."

Peter stirred restively, jerking his head toward the sandbars.

"Tide," he muttered.

"Oh, aye. Ye'll no have long to wait—or ye will, depending." Duff grinned, evidently thinking this funny.

"Why?" Jamie said gruffly, not sharing the amusement. He was looking somewhat better, now that escape was at hand, but was obviously in no mood yet for jocularity.

"The tide's comin' in." Duff stopped rowing and leaned on his oars long enough to remove his disreputable cap and wipe his balding brow. He waved the cap at the sandbars, where a crowd of small shorebirds were running up and down in evident dementia.

"When the tide's out, the channel's too shallow to float a ketch. In two hours"—he squinted at the glow in the east that marked the sun's rising, and nodded to himself—"or a bit more, they can come in. If they're waitin' out there now, they'll come in at once, so as to finish the job and get off again before the tide turns. But if they've not come yet, they'll maybe need to wait for the evening surge. It's a chancy job, to risk the channels by night—but Bonnet's no the lad to be put off by a bit o' darkness. Still, if he's in nay rush, he might well delay 'til next morning. Aye, ye might have a bit of a wait."

Roger realized he had been holding his breath. He let it out and drew a deep, slow breath, smelling of salt and pines, with a faint stink of dead shellfish. So it would be soon—or perhaps not until after nightfall, or not until the next day's dawn. He hoped it would be soon—and hoped at the same time that it wouldn't.

The piretta slid in close to the wharf, and Duff thrust out an oar against one of the barnacle-crusted pilings, swinging the tiny boat deftly alongside. Jamie hoisted himself up onto the dock with alacrity, eager to reach dry land. Roger handed up the swords and the small bundle that contained their canteens and spare powder, then followed. He knelt on the dock, all his senses alert for the slightest sound of human movement, but heard nothing but the liquid singing of blackbirds in the marsh and the cry of gulls on the Sound.

Jamie rummaged in his pouch and pulled out a small purse, which he tossed down to Duff, with a nod. No more need be said; this was a token payment. The rest would be paid when Duff returned for them, in two days.

Jamie had waited to the last possible moment to make the arrangements, ensuring that Bonnet at least would be unreachable until after the meeting—the ambush—had taken place. If it was successful, Jamie would pay the rest of the money agreed; if it was not—Claire would pay.

He had a vision of Claire's face, pale and drawn, nodding in stiff-lipped agreement as Jamie explained the arrangements to Duff. Her eyes had flicked to Duff, then, with the fierce yellow ruthlessness of a hawk about to eviscerate a rat, and he had seen Duff flinch at the implicit threat. He hid a smile at the memory. If friendship and money were insufficient to keep Duff's mouth shut, perhaps fear of the White Lady would suffice.

They stood silently together on the dock, watching the piretta pull slowly away. The knot in Roger's stomach tightened. He would have prayed, but could not. He couldn't ask help for such a thing as he meant now to do—not from God or Michael the archangel; not from the Reverend or his parents. Only from Jamie Fraser.

He wondered now and then how many men Fraser had killed—if he counted. If he knew. It was a different thing, of course, to kill a man in battle or in self-defense, than to lie in ambush for him, planning murder in cold blood. Still, surely it would be easier for Fraser, what they meant to do.

He glanced at Fraser, and saw him watching the boat pull away. He stood still as stone, and Roger saw that his eyes were fixed somewhere far beyond the boat, beyond the sky and water—looking on some evil thing, not blinking. Fraser took a deep breath and swallowed hard. No, it wouldn't be easier for him.

Somehow, that seemed a comfort.

THEY EXPLORED ALL the sheds briefly, finding nothing but scattered rubbish: broken packing crates, heaps of moldy straw, a few gnawed bones left by dogs or slaves. One or two of the sheds had evidently once been used as living quarters, but not recently. Some animal had built a large, untidy nest against the wall of one shed; when Jamie prodded it with a stick, a plump gray rodent-like thing shot out, ran between Roger's feet, and sailed off the dock into the water with an unnerving splash.

They took up quarters in the largest shed, which was built on the wharf itself, and settled down to wait. More or less.

The plan was simplicity itself; shoot Bonnet the instant he appeared. Unless it rained, in which case it would be necessary to employ swords or knives. Stated like that, the procedure sounded altogether straightforward. Roger's imagination, though, was unable to leave it at that.

"Walk about if ye like," Jamie said, after a quarter-hour of watching Roger fidget. "We'll hear him come." He himself sat tranquil as a frog on a lily pad, methodically checking the assortment of weapons laid out before him.

"Mmphm. What if he doesna come alone?"

Jamie shrugged, eyes fixed on the flint of the pistol in his hand. He wiggled it to be sure it was firmly seated, then set the gun down.

"Then he does not. If there are men with him, we must separate him from them. I shall take him into one of the small sheds, on pretext of private conversation, and dispatch him there. You keep anyone from following; I shallna require more than a minute."

"Oh, aye? And then ye come strolling out and inform his men ye've just done for their captain, and then what?" Roger demanded.

Jamie rubbed a hand down the bridge of his nose, and shrugged again.

"He'll be dead. D'ye think he's the man to inspire such loyalty as would make his men seek vengeance for him?"

"Well . . . no," Roger said slowly. "Perhaps not." Bonnet was the type to inspire hard work from his men, but it was labor based on fear and the hope of profit, not love.

"I have discovered a good deal regarding Mr. Bonnet," Jamie observed, laying down the pistol. "He has regular associates, aye, but he doesna have particular friends. He doesna sail always with the same mate, the same crew—which sea captains often do when they find a few men who suit them well. Bonnet picks his crews as chance provides, and he chooses them for strength or skill—not for liking. That being so, I wouldna expect to find any great liking for him among them."

Roger nodded, acknowledging the truth of this observation. Bonnet had run a tight ship on the *Gloriana*, but there had been no sense of camaraderie, even with his mate and bosun. And it was true, what Jamie said; everything they had learned suggested that Bonnet picked up assistants as he required them; if he brought men with him to this rendezvous, they were unlikely to be a devoted lieutenant and crew—more likely sailors picked at random off the docks.

"All right. But if—when—we kill him, any men with him—"

"Will be in need of new employment," Jamie interrupted. "Nay, so long as we take care not to fire upon them, or give them reason to think we threaten them, I dinna think they'll trouble owermuch about Bonnet's fate. Still—" He picked up his sword, frowning slightly, and slid it in and out of the scabbard, to be sure it moved easily.

"I think if that should be the situation, then I will take Bonnet aside, as I said. Give me a minute to deal with him, then make some excuse and come as though to fetch me. Dinna stop, though; go straight through the sheds, and head for the trees. I'll come and meet ye there."

Roger eyed Jamie skeptically. Christ, the man made it sound like a Sunday outing—a turn by the river, and we'll meet in the park, I'll bring ham sandwiches and you fetch the tea.

He cleared his throat, cleared it again, and picked up one of his own pistols. The feel of it was cool and solid in his hand, a reassuring weight.

"Aye, then. Just the one thing. I'll take Bonnet."

Fraser glanced sharply at him. He kept his own eyes steady, listening to the pulse that had begun to hammer hard inside his ears.

He saw Fraser start to speak, then stop. The man stared thoughtfully at him, and he could hear the arguments, hammering on his inner ear with his pulse, as plainly as if they'd been spoken aloud.

You have never killed a man, nor even fought in battle. You are no marksman, and only half-decent with a sword. Worse, you are afraid of the man. And if you try and fail . . .

"I know," he said aloud, to Fraser's deep blue stare. "He's mine. I'll take him. Brianna's your daughter, aye—but she's my wife."

Fraser blinked and looked away. He drummed his fingers on his knee for a moment, then stopped, drawing breath in a deep sigh. He drew himself slowly upright and turned toward Roger once again, eyes straight.

"It is your right," he said, formally. "So, then. Dinna hesitate; dinna challenge him. Kill him the instant ye have the chance." He paused for a moment, then spoke again, eyes steady on Roger's. "If ye fall, though—know I will avenge you."

The nail-studded mass in his belly seemed to have moved upward, sticking in his throat. He coughed to shift it, and swallowed.

"Great," he said. "And if you fall, I'll avenge *you*. A bargain, is it?"

Fraser didn't laugh, and in that moment, Roger understood why men would follow him anywhere, to do anything. He only looked at Roger for a long moment, and then nodded.

"A rare bargain," he said softly. "Thank you." Taking the dirk from his belt, he began to polish it.

THEY HAD NO TIMEPIECE, but they didn't need one. Even with the sky shrouded in low-lying clouds and the sun invisible, it was possible to feel the creep of minutes, the gradual shift of the earth as the rhythms of the day changed. Birds that had sung at dawn ceased singing, and the ones who hunted in morning began. The sound of water lapping against the pilings changed in tone, as the rising tide echoed in the space beneath the wharf.

The time of high tide came and passed; the echo beneath the wharf began to grow hollow, as the water started to drop. The pulse in Roger's ears began to slacken, along with the knots in his gut.

Then something struck the dock, and the vibration juddered through the floor of the shed.

Jamie was up in an instant, two pistols through his belt, another in his hand. He cocked his head at Roger, then disappeared through the door.

Roger jammed his own pistols securely in his belt, touched the hilt of his dirk for reassurance, and followed. He caught a quick glimpse of the boat, the dark wood of its rail just showing above the edge of the wharf, and then was inside the smaller shed to the right. Jamie was nowhere in sight; he'd got to his own post, then, to the left.

He pressed himself against the wall, peering out through the slit afforded between hinge and door. The boat was drifting slowly along the edge of the dock, not yet secured. He could see just a bit of the stern; the rest was out of sight. No matter; he couldn't fire until Bonnet appeared on the wharf.

He wiped his palm on his breeks and drew the better of his two pistols, checking for the thousandth time that priming and flint were in order. The metal of the gun smelled sharp and oily in his hand.

The air was damp; his clothes stuck to him. Would the powder fire? He touched the dirk, for the ten-thousandth time, running through Fraser's instructions on killing with a knife. *Hand on his shoulder, drive it up beneath the breastbone, hard. From behind, the kidney, up from under*. God, could he do it face to face? Yes. He hoped it would be face to face. He wanted to see—

A coil of rope hit the dock; he heard the heavy thump, and then the scramble and thud of someone springing over the rail to tie up. A rustle and a grunt of effort, a pause . . . He closed his eyes, trying to hear through the thunder of his heart. Steps. Slow, but not furtive. Coming toward him.

The door stood half-ajar. He stepped silently to the edge of it, listening. Waiting. A shadow, dim in the cloudy light, fell through the door. The man stepped in.

He lunged out from behind the door and flung himself bodily at the man, knocking him back into the wall with a hollow thud. The man whooped in surprise at the impact, and the sound of the cry stopped him just as he got his hands round a distinctly unmasculine throat.

"Shit!" he said. "I mean, I—I—I beg your pardon, ma'am."

She was pressed against the wall, all his weight on her, and he was well aware that the rest of her was unmasculine, too. Blood hot in his cheeks, he released her and stepped back, breathing heavily.

She shook herself like a dog, straightening her garments, and tenderly touching the back of her head where it had struck the wall.

"I'm sorry," he said, feeling both shocked and a complete prat. "I didn't mean— Are you hurt?"

The girl was as tall as Brianna, but more solidly built, with dark brown hair and a handsome face, broad-boned and deep-eyed. She grinned at Roger and said something incomprehensible, strongly scented with onions. She looked him up and down in a bold sort of way, then, evidently approving, put her hands under her breasts in a gesture of unmistakable invitation, jerking her head toward a corner of the shed, where mounds of damp straw gave off a fecund scent of not-unpleasant decay.

"Ahhh . . ." Roger said. "No. I'm afraid you're mistaken—no, don't touch that. No. *Non! Nein!*" He fumbled with her hands, which seemed determined to unfasten his belt. She said something else in the unfamiliar tongue. He didn't understand a word, but he got the sense of it well enough.

"No, I'm a married man. Would ye stop!"

She laughed, gave him a flashing glance from under long black lashes, and renewed her assault on his person.

He would have been convinced he was hallucinating, were it not for the smell. Engaged at close quarters, he realized that onions were the least of it. She wasn't filthy to look at, but had the deep-seated reek of someone just off a long sea voyage; he recognized that smell at once. Beyond that, though, the unmistakable scent of pigs wafted from her skirts.

"Excusez-moi, Mademoiselle." Jamie's voice came from somewhere behind him, sounding rather startled. The girl was startled, too, though not frightened. She let go of his balls, though, allowing him to step back.

Jamie had a pistol drawn, though he held it by his side. He raised one eyebrow at Roger.

"Who's this, then?"

"How in hell should I know?" Struggling for composure, Roger shook himself back into some kind of order. "I thought she was Bonnet or one of his men, but evidently not."

"Evidently." Fraser seemed disposed to find something humorous in the situation; a muscle near his mouth was twitching fiercely. *"Qui êtes-vous, Mademoiselle?"* he asked the girl.

She frowned at him, clearly not understanding, and said something in the odd language again. Both Jamie's brows rose at that.

"What's she speaking?" Roger asked.

"I've no idea." His look of amusement tinged with wariness, Jamie turned toward the door, raising his pistol. "Watch her, aye? She'll no be alone."

This was clear; there were voices on the wharf. A man's voice, and another woman. Roger exchanged baffled glances with Jamie. No, the voice was neither Bonnet's nor Lyon's—and what in God's name were all these women doing here?

The voices were coming closer, though, and the girl suddenly called out something in her own language. It didn't sound like a warning, but Jamie quickly flattened himself beside the door, pistol at the ready and his other hand on his dirk.

The narrow door darkened almost completely, and a dark, shaggy head thrust into the shed. Jamie stepped forward and shoved his pistol up under the chin of a very large, very surprised-looking man. Seizing the man by the collar, Jamie stepped backward, drawing him into the shed.

The man was followed almost at once by a woman whose tall, solid build and handsome face identified her at once as the girl's mother. The woman was blond, though, while the man—the girl's father?—was as dark as the bear he strongly resembled. He was nearly as tall as Jamie, but almost twice as broad, massive through the chest and shoulders, and heavily bearded.

None of them appeared to be at all alarmed. The man

looked surprised, the woman affronted. The girl laughed heartily, pointing at Jamie, then at Roger.

"I begin to feel rather foolish," Jamie said to Roger. Removing the pistol, he stepped back warily. *"Wer seid Ihr?"* he said.

"I don't think they're German," Roger said. "She"—he jerked a thumb at the girl, who was now eyeing Jamie in an appraising sort of way, as though sizing up his potential for sport in the straw—"didna seem to understand either French or German, though perhaps she was pretending."

The man had been frowning, glancing from Jamie to Roger in an attempt to make out what they were saying. At the word "French," though, he seemed to brighten.

"Comment allez-vous?" he said, in the most execrable accent Roger had ever heard.

"Parlez-vous français?" Jamie said, still eyeing the man cautiously.

The giant smiled and put a callused thumb and forefinger an inch apart.

"Un peu."

A very little *peu*, as they shortly discovered. The man had roughly a dozen words of French, just about enough to introduce himself as one Mikhail Chemodurow, his wife Iva, and his daughter, Karina.

"Rooshki," Chemodurow said, slapping a hand across his beefy chest.

"Russians?" Roger stared at them, flabbergasted, though Jamie seemed fascinated.

"I've never met a Russian before," he said. "What in Christ's name are they doing here, though?"

With some difficulty, this question was conveyed to Mr. Chemodurow, who beamed and flung a massive arm out, pointing toward the wharf.

"Les cochons," he said. *"Pour le Monsieur Wylie."* He looked expectantly at Jamie. *"Monsieur Wylie?"*

Given the eye-watering aroma rising off all three of the Russians, the mention of pigs came as no great surprise. The connection between Russian swineherds and Phillip Wylie was somewhat less obvious. Before the question could be gone into, though, there was a loud thump outside, and a grinding noise, as though some large wooden object had struck the dock. This was succeeded immediately by a piercing chorus of bellows and squeals—mostly porcine, but some of them human—and female.

Chemodurow moved with amazing speed for his size, though Jamie and Roger were on his heels as he shot through the door of the shed.

Roger had barely time to see that there were two boats now tied up at the wharf; the Russian's small bark, and a smaller open boat. Several men, bristling with knives and pistols, were swarming out of the smaller boat onto the dock.

Seeing this, Jamie dived to one side, disappearing out of sight round the edge of a smaller shed. Roger grabbed his pistol, but hesitated, not sure whether to fire or run. Hesitated a moment too long. A musket jammed up under his ribs, knocking out his breath, and hands snatched at his belt, taking pistols and dirk.

"Don't move, mate," the man holding the musket said. "Twitch, and I'll blow your liver out through your backbone."

He spoke with no particular animus, but sufficient sincerity that Roger wasn't inclined to test it. He stood still, hands half-raised, watching.

Chemodurow had waded into the invaders without hesitation, laying about him with hands like hams. One man was in the water, evidently having been knocked off the wharf, and the Russian had another in his grip, throttling him with brutal efficiency. He ignored all shouts, threats, and blows, his concentration fixed on the man he was killing.

Screams rent the air; Iva and Karina had rushed toward their boat, where two of the invaders had appeared on deck, each clutching a slightly smaller version of Karina. One of the men pointed a pistol at the Russian women. He appeared to pull the trigger; Roger saw a spark, and a small puff of smoke, but the gun failed to fire. The women didn't hesitate, but charged him, shrieking. Panicking, he dropped the gun and the girl he was holding, and jumped into the water.

A sickening thud wrenched Roger's attention from this byplay. One of the men, a short, squat figure, had clubbed Chemodurow over the head with the butt of a gun. The Russian blinked, nodded, and his grip on his victim loosened slightly. His assailant grimaced, took a tighter hold on the gun, and smashed him again. The Russian's eyes rolled up into his head and he dropped to the dock, shaking the boards with the impact.

Roger had been looking from man to man, searching urgently amid the melee for Stephen Bonnet. Look as he might, though, there was no trace of the *Gloriana*'s erstwhile captain.

What was wrong? Bonnet was no coward, and he was a natural fighter. It wasn't thinkable that he would send men in, and hang back himself. Roger looked again, counting heads, trying to keep track of men, but the conclusion became stronger, as the chaos quickly died down. Stephen Bonnet wasn't there.

Roger hadn't time to decide whether he was disappointed or relieved by this discovery. The man who had clubbed Chemodurow turned toward him at this point, and he recognized David Anstruther, the sheriff of Orange County. Anstruther recognized him, too—he saw the man's eyes narrow—but didn't seem surprised to see him.

The fight—such as it was—was wrapping up quickly. The four Russian women had all been rounded up and pushed into the largest shed, amid much screaming and shouting of curses, and the fallen Chemodurow was dragged in as well, leaving a disquieting smear of blood along the boards in his wake.

At this point, a pair of well-kept hands appeared on the edge of the dock, and a tall, elegantly lean man pulled himself up from the boat. Roger had no difficulty in recognizing Mr. Lillywhite, one of the Orange County magistrates, even without his wig and bottle-green coat.

Lillywhite had dressed for the occasion in plain black broadcloth, though his linen was as fine as ever and he had a gentleman's sword at his side. He made his way across the dock, in no great hurry, observing the disposition of matters as he went. Roger saw his mouth tighten fastidiously at sight of the trail of blood.

Lillywhite gestured to the man holding Roger, and at last, the bruising pressure of the gun-muzzle eased, allowing him to draw a deep breath.

"Mr. MacKenzie, is it not?" Lillywhite asked pleasantly. "And where is Mr. Fraser?"

He'd been expecting that question, and had had time to contemplate the answer.

"In Wilmington," he said, matching Lillywhite's pleasant tone. "You're rather far afield yourself, are ye not, sir?"

Lillywhite's nostrils pinched momentarily, as though smelling something bad—which he certainly was, though Roger doubted the reek of pigs was causing his disedification.

"Do not trifle with me, sir," the magistrate said curtly.

"Wouldn't dream of it," Roger assured him, keeping an eye on the fellow with the musket, who seemed disposed to resume jabbing. "Though if we're asking that sort of question—where's Stephen Bonnet?"

Lillywhite gave a brief laugh, a sort of wintry amusement coming into his pale gray eyes.

"In Wilmington."

Anstruther appeared at the magistrate's elbow, squat and sweaty. He gave Roger a nod and an ugly grin.

"MacKenzie. Nice to see you again. Where's your father-in-law, and more important—where's the whisky?"

Lillywhite frowned at the sheriff.

"You haven't found it? Have you searched the sheds?"

"Aye, we looked. Nothing there but bits of rubbish." He rocked up onto his toes, menacing. "So, MacKenzie, where'd you hide it?"

"I haven't hidden anything," Roger replied equably. "There isn't any whisky." He was beginning to relax a little. Wherever Stephen Bonnet was, he wasn't here. He didn't expect them to be pleased at discovering that the whisky was a ruse, but—

The Sheriff hit him in the pit of the stomach. He doubled up, his vision went dark, and he struggled vainly to breathe, fighting a flash of panic as he relived his hanging, the black, the lack of air . . .

Bright floating spots appeared at the edges of his vision, and he drew breath, gasping. He was sitting on the dock, legs splayed out before him, the Sheriff clutching a handful of his hair.

"Try again," Anstruther advised him, shaking him roughly by the hair. The pain was irritating, rather than discomfiting, and he swiped a fist at the Sheriff, catching him a solid blow on the thigh. The man yelped and let go, hopping backward.

"Did you look on the other boat?" Lillywhite demanded, ignoring the Sheriff's discomfort. Anstruther glowered at Roger, rubbing his thigh, but shook his head in answer.

"Nothing there but pigs and girls. And where in fuck's name did *they* come from?" he demanded.

"Russia." Roger coughed, clenched his teeth against the resulting burst of pain, and got slowly to his feet, holding an arm across his middle to keep his guts from spilling out. The Sheriff doubled a fist in anticipation, but Lillywhite made a quelling gesture toward him. He looked incredulously at Roger.

"Russia? What have they to do with this business?"

"Nothing, so far as I know. They arrived soon after I did."

The magistrate grunted, looking displeased. He frowned for a moment, thinking, then decided to try another tack.

"Fraser had an arrangement with Milford Lyon. I have now assumed Mr. Lyon's part of the agreement. It is altogether proper for you to deliver the whisky to me," he said, attempting to infuse a note of businesslike politeness into his voice.

"Mr. Fraser has made other arrangements," Roger said, with equal politeness. "He sent me to say as much to Mr. Lyon."

That seemed to take Lillywhite aback. He pursed his lips, and worked them in and out, staring hard at Roger, as though to estimate his truthfulness. Roger stared blandly back, hoping that Jamie wouldn't reappear inopportunely and put paid to his story.

"How did you get here?" Lillywhite demanded abruptly. "If you did not travel on that boat?"

"I came overland from Edenton." Blessing Duff for the information, he waved casually over his shoulder. "There's a shell road back there."

The two of them stared at him, but he stared back, undaunted.

"Something smells fishy, and it isn't the marsh."

Anstruther sniffed loudly in illustration, then coughed and snorted. “Phew! What a stink.”

Lillywhite disregarded this, but went on looking at Roger with a narrowed eye.

“I think perhaps I must inconvenience you for a little longer, Mr. MacKenzie,” he said, and turned to the Sheriff. “Put him in with the Russians—if that’s what they are.”

Anstruther accepted this commission with alacrity, prodding Roger in the buttocks with the muzzle of his musket as he forced him toward the shed where the Russians were imprisoned. Roger gritted his teeth and ignored it, wondering how high the Sheriff might bounce, if picked up and slammed down on the boards of the dock.

The Russians were all clustered in the corner of the shed, the women tending solicitously to their wounded husband and father, but they all looked up at Roger’s entrance, with a babble of incomprehensible greetings and questions. He gave them as much of a smile as he could manage, and waved them back, pressing his ear to the wall of the shed in order to hear what Lillywhite and company were up to now.

He had hoped they would simply accept his story and depart—and they might still do that, once they satisfied themselves that there really was no whisky hidden anywhere near the landing. Another possibility had occurred to him, though; one that was making him increasingly uneasy.

It was clear enough from the behavior of the men that they had intended to take the whisky by force—if there had been any. And the way Lillywhite had held back, concealing himself . . . it wouldn’t do, obviously, for a county magistrate to be revealed as having connections with smugglers and pirates.

As it was, since there was no whisky, Roger could report no actual wrongdoing on Lillywhite’s part—it was illegal to deal in contraband, of course, but such arrangements were so common on the coast that the mere rumor of it wasn’t likely to damage Lillywhite’s reputation in his own inland county. On the other hand, Roger was alone—or Lillywhite thought he was.

There was clearly some connection between Lillywhite and Stephen Bonnet—and if Roger and Jamie Fraser began to ask questions, chances were good that it would come to light. Was whatever Lillywhite was engaged in sufficiently dangerous that he might think it worth killing Roger to prevent his talking? He had the uneasy feeling that Lillywhite and Anstruther might well come to that conclusion.

They could simply take him into the marsh, kill him and sink his body, then return to their companions, announcing that he had gone back to Edenton. Even if someone eventually traced the members of Lillywhite's gang, *and* if they could be persuaded to talk—both matters of low probability—nothing could be proved.

There was a lot of thumping and banging outside, gradually succeeded by more distant calling, as the sheds were re-searched, and the search then spread to the nearby marsh.

It occurred to Roger that Lillywhite and Anstruther might well have intended to kill him and Jamie after taking the whisky. In which case, there was still less to prevent them doing it now; they would be already prepared for it. As for the Russians—would they harm them? He hoped not, but there was no telling.

A light pattering rang on the tin roof of the shed; it was beginning to rain. Fine, if their powder got wet, they wouldn't shoot him; they'd have to cut his throat. He went from hoping that Jamie wouldn't show up too soon, to hoping fervently that he wouldn't show up too late. As to what he might do if and when he *did* show up . . .

The swords. Were the swords still where they had left them, in the corner of the shed? The rain had grown too loud for him to hear anything outside, anyway; he abandoned his listening post and went to look.

The Russians all looked up at him with mingled expressions of wariness and concern. He smiled and nodded, making little shooing gestures to get them out of the way. Yes, the swords were still there—that was something, and he felt a small surge of hope.

Chemodurow was conscious; he said something in a slurred voice, and Karina got up at once and came to stand by Roger. She patted him gently on the arm, then took one of the swords from him. She drew it from its scabbard with a ringing whoosh that made them all jump, then laugh nervously. She wrapped her hands round the hilt and held it over her shoulder, like a baseball bat. She marched over to the door and took up her station beside it, scowling fiercely.

"Great," Roger said, and gave her a broad smile of approval. "Anyone pokes his head in, take it off, aye?" He mimed a chopping motion with the side of his hand, and the Russians all made loud growling sounds of enthusiastic support. One of the younger girls reached for the other sword, but he smiled and indicated that he would keep it, thanks anyway.

To his surprise, she shook her head, saying something in Russian. He raised his eyebrows and shook his head helplessly. She tugged on his arm, and made him come with her, back toward the corner.

They had been busy during the brief period of their captivity. They had moved aside the rubbish, made a comfortable pallet for the injured man—and uncovered the large trapdoor installed in the floor, meant to be used by boats coming under the wharf at low tide, so that cargo could be handed directly up into the shed, rather than unloaded onto the dock.

The tide was going out now; it was a drop of more than six feet to the water's dark surface. He stripped to his breeks and hung by his hands from the edge of the trapdoor before dropping in feetfirst, not wanting to risk a dive into what might be dangerous shallows.

The water was higher than his head, though; he sank in a shower of silver bubbles, then his feet touched the sandy bottom and he launched himself upward, breaking the surface with a whoosh of air. He waved reassuringly at the circle of Russian faces peering down at him through the trapdoor, then struck out for the far end of the wharf.

FROM HIS PERCH on the roof of the shed, Jamie assessed the magistrate's way of moving, and the manner in which he fondled the weapon. Lillywhite turned away, his hand nervously caressing the hilt of his sword. A long reach, and a good bearing; quick, too, if a little jerky. To wear a sword under these circumstances suggested both a habit of familiarity with the weapon and a fondness for it.

He couldn't see Anstruther, who had pressed himself back against the wall of the shed, under the overhang of the roof, but he was less concerned with the Sheriff. A brawler, that one, and short in the arm.

"I say we kill them all. Only way to be safe."

There was a grunt of dubious assent from Lillywhite.

"That may be—but the men? We do not wish to put our fate in the hands of witnesses who may talk. We could have dealt with Fraser and MacKenzie safely out of sight—but so many . . . perhaps we may leave these Russians; they are foreigners and seem not to speak any English. . . ."

"Aye, and how did they come here, I'd like to know? I'll warrant they wasn't caught up in a waterspout and set down here by accident. Someone knows about 'em, someone will come looking for 'em—and whoever that someone is, he's got some means to talk to 'em, I'll be bound. They've seen too much already—and if you mean to go on using this place . . ."

The rain was still light, but coming down steadily. Jamie turned his head to wipe the moisture out of his eyes against his shoulder. He was lying flat, arms and legs outspread like a frog's to keep from sliding down the pitch of the tin roof. He didn't dare to move, just yet. The rain was whispering out on the Sound, though, puckering the water like drawn silk, and making a faint ringing noise on the metal around him. Let it rain just that wee bit harder, and it would cover any noise he made.

He shifted his weight a little, feeling the press of the dirk, hard under his hipbone. The pistols lay beside him on the roof, likely useless in the rain. The dirk was his only real weapon at the moment, and one much better suited to surprise than to a frontal attack.

". . . send the men back with the boat. We can go by the road, after . . ."

They were still talking, low-voiced, but he could tell that the decision had been made; Lillywhite only needed to convince himself that it was a matter of necessity, and that wouldn't take long. They'd send the men away first, though; the magistrate was right to be afraid of witnesses.

He blinked water out of his eyes and glanced toward the larger shed, where Roger Mac and the Russians were. The sheds were close together; the gaps between the staggered tin roofs no more than three or four feet. There was one shed between him and the larger one. Well, then.

He would take advantage of the men leaving to move across the roofs, and trust to luck and the rain to prevent Lillywhite or Anstruther from looking up. Crouch above the door to the shed, and when they came to do the deed, wait just until they'd got the door open, then drop on the magistrate from above and hope to break his neck or at least disable him at once. Roger Mac could be depended on to rush out and help deal with the Sheriff, then.

It was the best plan he could contrive under the circumstances, and not a bad one, he thought. If he didn't slip and break his own neck, of course. Or a leg. He flexed his left leg, feeling the slight stiffness of the muscles in his calf. It was healed, but there was no denying the slight weakness remaining. He could manage well enough, walking, but jumping across rooftops . . .

"Aye, well, needs must when the Devil drives," he muttered. If it came to smash and he ruined the leg again, he'd better hope the Sheriff killed him, because Claire surely would.

The thought made him smile, but he couldn't think about her now. Later, when it was finished. His shirt was soaked through, stuck to his shoulders, and the rain was chiming off the tin roofs like a chorus of fairy-bells. Squirming cautiously backward, he got his knees under him and rose to a crouch, ready to drop flat again if anyone was looking up.

No one was on the dock. There were four men besides Lillywhite and the Sheriff; all of them were out in the soft ground to the south of the landing, poking through the waist-high grass in a desultory fashion. He took a deep breath and got his feet slowly under him. As he swiveled round, though, he caught a flicker of movement from the corner of his eye, and froze.

Holy Christ, there were men coming out of the wood. For an instant, he thought it was more of Lillywhite's doing, and then he realized that the men were black. All but one.

Les Cochons, the Russian had said. *Pour le Monsieur Wylie.* And here was Monsieur Wylie, coming with his slaves to collect his pigs!

He lay down on his belly again and squirmed over the wet metal, eeling toward the back of the shed roof. It was open to question, he thought, whether Wylie would be better disposed to help him or to run him through himself—but he did suppose the man had some stake in preserving his Russians.

THE WATER WAS COLD, but not numbing, and the pull of the tidal current wasn't great yet. Still, the injury to his throat and the searing of the canebrake fire had left him much shorter of breath than he used to be, and Roger found himself obliged to bob to the surface and gasp for air with every three or four strokes.

Ruby lips, above the water, he sang ironically to himself, *blowing bubb-les soft and fine . . .* He drew in a gulp of air, and trod water, listening. He had headed toward the south side of the landing first, but had heard voices above, and so reversed direction. He was just under the north edge of the wharf now, hidden in the deep shadow by the Russians' boat.

The smell of pigs was overwhelming, and he could hear muffled thumps and grunts from the hold, coming through the wood beside him. Christ, had they sailed that tiny craft all the way from Russia? It looked it; the wood was battered and dented.

No sound of voices nearby. It was raining hard, shushing into the Sound; that would help cover any racket he made. Ready, steady, go, then. He took a great lungful of air and launched himself into the rainy light beyond the landing.

He swam desperately, trying not to splash, expecting a musket ball between the shoulder blades every moment. He blundered into the weeds, felt the grasp and slash of saw-grass on arm and leg, rolled half-over, gasping, salt burning in the cuts, and then was on his hands and knees, crawling through the growth of marsh plants, black needlerushes waving over his head, rain pounding on his back, the water lapping just below his chin.

He stopped at last, chest heaving with the need for air, and wondered what in hell to do next. It was good to be out of the shed, but he hadn't a plan for what happened now. Find Jamie, he supposed—if he could, without being caught again.

As though the thought had drawn attention to him, he heard the slosh and swish of someone walking slowly through the marsh nearby. Searching. He froze, hoping the rain would cover the sound of his breath, loud and rasping in his ears.

Closer. Damn, they were coming closer. He fumbled at his belt, but he had lost the dirk, somewhere in his swimming. He got one knee up under his chin, braced himself to spring and run.

The grass above him swept suddenly away, and he leaped to his feet, just in time to avoid the spear that sliced into the water where he'd lain.

The spear quivered in front of him, six inches from his face. On the other side of it, a black man gaped at him, eyes saucered in amazement. The Negro closed his mouth, blinked at him, and spoke in tones of deepest accusation.

"You ain't no possum!"

"No," said Roger, mildly. "I'm not." He brushed a trembling hand down his chest, assuring himself that his heart was still inside it. "Sorry."

PHILLIP WYLIE LOOKED a great deal different at home, Roger thought, than he did in society. Attired for pig-catching in loose breeks and a farmer's smock, damp with rain, and minus any trace of wig, paint, powder, or patches, he was still elegantly slender, but looked quite normal, and reasonably competent. He also looked somewhat more intelligent, though his mouth did tend to keep dropping open, and he did insist on breaking into Jamie's account with questions and expostulations.

"Lillywhite? Randall Lillywhite? But what can he—"

"Concentrate, man," Jamie said impatiently. "I'm telling ye now, and I'll tell ye more later, but he and yon sheriff are like to be carving up your Russians like a set of Christmas hams, and we dinna go and tend to the matter this minute."

Wylie glared at Jamie, then looked suspiciously at Roger, who was standing under the cover of the forest, half-naked, soaking wet, and covered with blood-streaked mud.

"He's right," Roger croaked, then coughed, cleared his throat, and repeated it, more firmly. "He's right; there's not much time."

Wylie's lips compressed into a thin line, and he exhaled strongly through his nose. He looked round at his slaves, as though counting them; a half-dozen men, all carrying stout sticks. One or two had cane-knives at their belts. Wylie nodded, making up his mind.

"Come on, then."

Avoiding the telltale crunching of the shell-road, they made slow but steady progress through the marsh.

"Why pigs?" He heard Jamie ask curiously, as he and Wylie forged ahead of the group.

"Not pigs," Wylie replied. "Russian boars. For sport." He spoke rather proudly, swishing his own stick through the thick grass. "Everyone says that of all game, the Russian boar is the fiercest and most wily opponent. I propose to release them in the woods on my property and allow them to breed."

"Ye mean to hunt them?" Jamie sounded mildly incredulous. "Have ye ever hunted a boar?"

Roger saw Wylie's shoulders stiffen under his damp smock at the question. The rain had slackened, but was still coming down.

"No," he said. "Not yet. Have you?"

"Yes," Jamie said, but wisely didn't amplify the answer.

As they drew near the landing, Roger caught a glimpse of movement beyond. The smaller boat was pulling away.

"They've given up looking for me or the whisky, and sent their men away." Jamie wiped a hand down his face, slicking the rain off. "What say ye, Wylie? There's no time to lose. The Russians are in the main shed, on the wharf."

Once decided, Wylie was no ditherer.

"Storm the place," he said shortly.

He waved a hand, beckoning his slaves to follow, and headed for the landing at a trot. The whole party swerved onto the shell-road, thundering toward the wharf with a noise like an avalanche. That ought to give Lillywhite and Anstruther pause in their murdering, Roger thought. They sounded like an approaching army.

Barefoot, Roger kept to the marshy ground, and was in consequence slower than the rest. He saw a startled face peer out between the sheds, and quickly withdraw.

Jamie saw it too, and gave one of his wild Highland cries. Wylie jerked, startled, but then joined in, bellowing "Get out of it, you bastards!" Thus encouraged, the Negroes all began shouting and bellowing, waving their sticks with enthusiasm as they charged the landing.

It was something of an anticlimax to arrive on the wharf and find no one there save the captive Russians, who narrowly missed beheading Phillip Wylie when he imprudently shoved open the door to their prison without announcing himself.

A brief search of the Russian boat and the surrounding marsh turned up no trace of Lillywhite and Anstruther.

"Most like they swim for it," one of the Negroes said, returning from the search. He nodded across the channel, toward the tangle of the sandbars, and fingered his spear. "We go hunt them?" It was the man who had discovered Roger, evidently still eager to try his luck.

"They didn't swim," Wylie said shortly. He gestured at the tiny beach near the landing, an empty stretch of oyster shells. "They've taken my boat, blast them."

He turned away, disgusted, and began to give orders for unloading and penning the Russian boars. Chemodurow and his family had already been taken off to the plantation house, with the girls alternating between amazement at the black slaves and coy looks at Roger, who had retrieved his shirt and shoes, but whose breeches were still plastered to his body.

One of the slaves appeared from the shed with an armful of discarded weaponry, recalling Wylie temporarily to the duties of a host.

"I am obliged to you for your help in preserving my property, sir," he said to Jamie. He bowed, rather stiffly. "Will you not allow me to offer you and Mr. MacKenzie my hospitality?" He didn't sound thrilled about it, Roger noted, but still, he'd offered.

"I am obliged to you, sir, for your help in preserving our lives," Jamie said with equal stiffness, returning the bow. "And I thank ye, but—"

"We'd be delighted," Roger interrupted. "Thanks." He gave Wylie a firm handshake, surprising him very much, and grabbed Jamie by the arm, steering him toward the shell-road before he could protest. There were times and places to be on your high horse, he supposed, but this wasn't one of them.

"Look, ye havena got to kiss the man's bum," he said, in response to Jamie's mutterings, as they slogged toward the forest. "Let his butler give us a dry towel and a bit of lunch, and we'll be off while he's still busy with his boars. I've had no breakfast, and neither have you. And if we've got to walk to Edenton, I'm no doing it on an empty belly."

The mention of food seemed to go some way toward restoring Jamie's equanimity, and as they reached the semi-shelter of the wood, a mood of almost giddy cheerfulness had sprung up between them. Roger wondered if this was the sort of way you felt after a battle; the sheer relief of finding yourself alive and unwounded made you want to laugh and arse about, just to prove you still could.

By unspoken consent, they left discussion of recent events—and speculation as to the present whereabouts of Stephen Bonnet—for later.

"Russian boars, for Christ's sake," Jamie said, shaking himself like a dog as they paused under the shelter of the wood. "And I doubt the man's ever seen a boar in his life! Ye'd think he could manage to kill himself without going to such expense about it."

"Aye, what d'ye think it must have cost? More money than we'll see in ten years, likely, just to haul a lot of pigs . . . what, six thousand miles?" He shook his head, staggered at the thought.

"Well, to be fair about it, they're more than only pigs," Jamie said tolerantly. "Did ye not see them?"

Roger had, though only briefly. The slaves had been herding one of the animals across the dock as he'd emerged from the shed with his clothes. It was tall and hairy, with long yellow tushes that looked nasty enough.

It was emaciated from the long sea-voyage, though, its ribs showing and half its bristly pelt rubbed bald. It had obviously not got its landlegs yet, staggering and careening drunkenly on its ridiculous small hooves, eyes rolling, grunting in panic as the slaves shouted and poked at it with their poles. Roger had felt quite sorry for it.

"Oh, they're big enough, aye," he said. "And I suppose once they're filled out a bit, they'd be something to see. I wonder how they'll like this, though, after Russia?" He waved a hand at the damp, scrubby wood around them. The air was moist with rain, but the trees blocked most of the downfall, leaving it dark and resin-smelling under the low canopy of scrub oak and scraggy pines. Twigs and acorn caps crunched pleasantly under their boots on the sandy earth.

"Well, there are acorns and roots aplenty," Jamie observed, "and the odd Negro now and then, for a treat. I expect they'll do well enough."

Roger laughed, and Jamie grunted in amusement.

"Ye think I'm jesting, aye? Ye'll not have hunted boar, either, I suppose."

"Mmphm. Well, perhaps Mr. Wylie will invite us to come and—"

The back of his head exploded, and everything disappeared.

AT SOME POINT, he became aware again. Aware mostly of a pain so great that unconsciousness seemed immensely preferable. But aware too of pebbles and leaves pressing into his face, and of noises nearby. The clash and thud and grunt of men fighting in earnest.

He forced himself toward consciousness, and raised his head, though the effort made colored fireworks go off inside his eyes and made him want very badly to throw up. He braced himself on his folded arms, teeth gritted, and after a moment, his vision cleared, though things were still blurred.

It took a moment to make out what was happening; they were ten feet or so beyond the spot where he lay, with bits of tree and brush obscuring the fight. He caught a muttered "*A Dhia!*" though, among the panting and grunting, and felt a sharp pang of relief. Jamie was alive, then.

He got to his knees, swaying, and stayed there for a moment, his vision winking in and out of blackness. When it steadied, his head had fallen forward and he was staring at the ground. His sword lay a few feet away, half-covered with scuffed sand and leaves. One of his pistols was with it, but he didn't bother with that; he couldn't hold it steady, even if the powder were still dry enough to fire.

He scrabbled and fumbled, but once he'd got his hand wedged into the basket of the sword's hilt, he felt a little better; he wouldn't drop it, now. Something wet was running down his neck—blood, rain? It didn't matter. He staggered, clutched a tree with his free hand, blinked away the blackness, took another step.

He felt like the boar, unfamiliar ground shifting and treacherous under his feet. He trod on something that rolled and gave way, and he fell, landing hard on one elbow.

He turned awkwardly over, hampered by the sword, and found that he had stepped on Anstruther's leg. The Sheriff was lying on his back, mouth open, looking surprised. There was a large rip in his neck, and a lot of blood had soaked into the sand around him, rusty and stinking.

He recoiled, and the shock of it got him on his feet, with no memory of having stood up. Lillywhite's back was to him, the linen of his shirt wet and sticking to his flesh. He lunged, grunting, then flung back, beat, riposted . . .

Roger shook his head, trying to clear it of the idiotic terms of swordsmanship, then stopped, gasping with pain. Jamie's face was set in a maniac half-grin, teeth bared with effort as he followed his opponent's weapon. He'd seen Roger, though.

"Roger!" he shouted, breathless with the fight. "Roger, *a charaid*!"

Lillywhite didn't turn, but flung himself forward, feinting, beating away, lunging back in tierce.

"Not . . . stupid . . ." he gasped.

Roger realized dimly that Lillywhite thought Jamie was bluffing, trying to make him turn around. His vision was flickering round the edges again, and he grabbed for a tree, gripping hard to stay upright. The foliage was wet; his grip was slipping.

"Hey . . ." he called hoarsely, unable to think of any words. He raised his sword, the tip trembling. "Hey!"

Lillywhite stepped back and whirled around, eyes wide with shock. Roger lunged blindly, with no aim, but with all the power left in his body behind it.

The sword went into Lillywhite's eye, and a slithering crunch ran up Roger's arm, as metal scraped bone and went through to something softer, where it stuck. He tried to let go, but his hand was trapped in the basket-hilt. Lillywhite went stiff, and Roger could feel the man's life run straight down the sword, through his hand, and up his arm, swift and shocking as an electric current.

Panicked, he jerked and twisted, trying to get the sword free. Lillywhite spasmed, went limp, and fell toward him, flopping like a huge dead fish as Roger wrenched and yanked, vainly trying to free himself from the sword.

Then Jamie seized him by the wrist and got him loose, got an arm around him, and led him away, stumbling and blind with panic and pain. Held his head and rubbed his back, murmuring nonsense in Gaelic while he puked and heaved. Wiped his face and neck with handsful of wet leaves, wiped the snot from his nose with the wet sleeve of his shirt.

"You okay?" Roger mumbled, somewhere in the midst of this.

"Aye, fine," Jamie said, and patted him again. "You're fine, too, all right?"

At length he was on his feet again. His head had gone past the point of pain; it still hurt, but the pain seemed a separate thing from himself, hovering somewhere nearby, but not actually touching him.

Lillywhite lay face-up in the leaves. Roger closed his eyes and swallowed. He heard Jamie mutter something under his breath, and then a grunt, a rustling of leaves, and a small thud. When Roger opened his eyes, Lillywhite was lying facedown, the back of his shirt smeared with sand and acorn hulls.

"Come on." Jamie got him under the arm, pulled the arm over his shoulder. Roger lifted his free hand, waved it vaguely toward the bodies.

"Them. What should we do with . . . them?"

"Leave them for the pigs."

Roger could walk by himself by the time they left the wood, though he had a tendency to drift to one side or the other, unable to steer quite straight as yet. Wylie's house lay before them, a handsome construction in red brick. They picked their way across the lawn, ignoring the stares of several house-servants, who clustered at the upstairs windows, pointing down at them and murmuring to one another.

"Why?" Roger asked, stopping for a moment to shake some of the leaves from his shirt. "Did they say?"

"No." Jamie pulled a soggy wad of cloth that had once been a handkerchief from his sleeve and swished it in the ornamental fountain. He used it to mop his face, looked critically at the resultant streaks of filth, and soused it in the fountain again.

"The first I knew was the thud when Anstruther clubbed ye—here, your head's still bleedin'. I turned round to see ye lyin' on the ground, and the next instant, a sword came at me out o' nowhere, right across my ribs. Look at that, will ye?" He poked his fingers through a large rent in his shirt, wiggling them. "I ducked behind a tree, and barely got my own blade out in time. But neither of them said a word at all."

Roger pressed the proffered handkerchief gingerly to the back of his head. He sucked air through his teeth with a hiss as the cold water touched the wound.

"Shit. Is it only that my head's cracked, or does that make no sense? Why in Christ's name try so hard to kill us?"

"Because they wanted us dead," Jamie said logically, turning up his sleeves to wash his hands in the fountain. "Or someone else does."

The pain had decided to take up residence in Roger's head again. He was feeling sick again.

"Stephen Bonnet?"

"If I were a gambling man, I'd put good odds on it."

Roger closed one eye in order to correct a tendency for there to be two of Jamie.

"You *are* a gambling man. I've seen ye do it."

"Well, there ye are, then."

Jamie ran a hand absently through his matted hair, and turned toward the house. Karina and her sisters had appeared at the window, and were waving ecstatically.

"What I want verra much to know just now is, where *is* Stephen Bonnet?"

"Wilmington."

Jamie swung round, frowning at him.

"What?"

"Wilmington," Roger repeated. He cautiously opened the other eye, but it seemed all right. Only one Jamie. "That's what Lillywhite said—but I thought he was joking."

Jamie stared at him for a moment.

"I hope to Christ he was," he said.

103

AMONG THE MYRTLES

Wilmington

BY CONTRAST WITH FRASER'S RIDGE, Wilmington was a giddy metropolis, and under normal circumstances, the girls and I should have fully enjoyed its delights. Given the absence of Roger and Jamie, and the nature of the errand they were bound upon, though, we were able to find little distraction.

Not that we didn't try. We lived through the creeping minutes of nights broken by crying children and haunted by imaginations worse than nightmare might be. I was sorry that Brianna had seen as much as she had, after the battle at Alamance; vague imaginings based on fear were bad enough; those based on close acquaintance with the look of ruined flesh, of smashed bone and staring eyes, were a good deal worse.

Rising heavy-eyed amid a crumple of discarded clothes and stale linen, we fed and dressed the children and went out to seek what mental respite might be found during the day in the distractions of horse-racing, shopping, or the competing musicales hosted once a week—on successive evenings—by Mrs. Crawford and Mrs. Dunning, the two most prominent hostesses in town.

Mrs. Dunning's evening had taken place the day after Roger and Jamie left. Performances upon the harp, violin, harpsichord, and flute were interspersed with recitations of poetry—at least it was referred to as poetry—and "Songs, both Comick and Tragick," sung by Mr. Angus McCaskill, the popular and courteous proprietor of the largest ordinary in Wilmington.

The Tragick songs were actually much funnier than the Comick ones, owing to Mr. McCaskill's habit of rolling his eyes up into his head during the more lugubrious passages, as though he had the lyrics written on the inside of his skull. I adopted a suitably solemn expression of appreciation, though, biting the inside of my cheek throughout.

Brianna required no such aid to courtesy. She sat staring at all the performances with a countenance of such brooding intensity that it seemed to disconcert a few of the musicians, who eyed her nervously, and edged toward the other side of the room, getting the harpsichord safely between her and them. Her attitude had nothing to do with the performance, I knew, but rather with a reliving of the arguments that had preceded the men's departure.

These had been prolonged, vigorous, and conducted in low voices, as the four of us walked up and down the quay at sunset. Brianna had been impassioned, eloquent, and ferocious. Jamie had been patient, cool, and immovable. I had kept my mouth shut, for once more stubborn than either of them. I could not in conscience side with Bree; I knew what Stephen Bonnet was. I would not side with Jamie; I knew what Stephen Bonnet was.

I knew what Jamie was, too, and while the thought of his going to deal with Stephen Bonnet was enough to make me feel as though I were hanging from a fraying rope over a bottomless pit, I did know that there were few men better equipped for such a task. For beyond the question of deadly skill, which he certainly had, there was the question of conscience.

Jamie was a Highlander. While the Lord might insist that vengeance was His, no male Highlander of my acquaintance had ever thought it right that the Lord should be left to handle such things without assistance. God had made man for a reason, and high on the list of those reasons was the protection of a family and the defense of its honor—whatever the cost.

What Bonnet had done to Brianna was not a crime that Jamie would ever forgive, let alone forget. And beyond simple vengeance, and the continuing threat that Bonnet might pose to Bree or Jemmy, there was the fact that Jamie felt himself responsible, at least in part, for such harm as Bonnet might do in the world—to our family, or to others. He had helped Bonnet to escape the gallows once; he would not be at peace until he had amended that mistake—and said so.

"Fine!" Brianna had hissed at him, fists clenched at her sides. "So you'll be at peace. Just fine! And how peaceful do you think Mama and I will be, if you or Roger is dead?"

"Ye'd prefer me to be a coward? Or your husband?"

"Yes!"

"No, ye wouldn't," he said with certainty. "Ye only think so now, because ye're afraid."

"Of course I'm afraid! So is Mama, only she won't say so, because she thinks you'll go anyway!"

"If she does think so, she's right," Jamie said, giving me a sidelong look, with a hint of a smile. "She's known me a long time, aye?"

I glanced at him, but shook my head and turned away, sealing my lips and staring out at the masts of the ships anchored in the harbor while the argument raged on.

Roger had finally put a stop to it.

"Brianna," he said softly, when she paused for breath. She turned toward him, face anguished, and he touched her shoulder. "I willna have this man in the same world as my children," he said, still softly, "or my wife. Do we go then with your blessing—or without it?"

She had sucked in her breath, bitten her lip, and turned away. I saw the tears brimming in her eyes, and the working of her throat as she swallowed them. She said no more.

Whatever word of blessing she had given him had been spoken in the night, in the quiet of their bed. I had given Jamie blessing and farewell in that same darkness—still without speaking a word. I couldn't. He *would* go, no matter what I said.

Neither of us slept that night; we lay in each other's arms, silently aware of each breath and shift of body, and when the shutters began to show cracks of gray light, we rose—he to make his preparations, I because I could not lie still and watch him go.

As he left, I stood on tiptoe to kiss him, and whispered the only important thing.

"Come back," I'd said. He'd smiled at me, smoothing a curl behind my ear.

"Ye ken what I said at Alamance? Well, it's no today, either, Sassenach. We'll both be back."

MRS. CRAWFORD'S ASSEMBLY, held the next evening, boasted the same performers, for the most part, as had Mrs. Dunning's, but had one novelty; it was there that I smelled myrtle candles for the first time.

"What is that lovely scent?" I asked Mrs. Crawford during the interval, sniffing at the candelabra that decorated her harpsichord. The candles were beeswax, but the scent was something both delicate and spicy—rather like bayberry, but lighter.

"Wax-myrtle," she replied, gratified. "I don't use them for the candles themselves, though one *can*—but it does take such a tremendous quantity of the berries, near eight pound to get only a pound of the wax, imagine! It took my bondmaid a week of picking, and she brought me barely enough as would make a dozen candles. So I rendered the wax, but then I mixed it in with the regular beeswax when I dipped the candles, and I will say I am pleased. It does give such a pleasant aroma, does it not?"

She leaned closer to me, lowering her voice to a confidential whisper.

"*Someone* said to me that Mrs. Dunning's home smelt last night as though the cook had scorched the potatoes at supper!"

And so, on the third day, faced with the alternatives of a day spent cooped up with three small children in our cramped lodgings, or a repeat visit to the much-diminished remains of the dead whale, I borrowed several buckets from our landlady, Mrs. Burns, commissioned a picnic basket, and marshalled my troops for a foraging expedition.

Brianna and Marsali consented to the notion with alacrity, if not enthusiasm.

"Anything is better than sitting around worrying," Brianna said. "Anything!"

"Aye, and anything is better than the stink of filthy clouts and sour milk, too," Marsali added. She fanned herself with a book, looking pale. "I could do wi' a bit of air."

I worried a little about Marsali's ability to walk so far, given her expanding girth—she was in her seventh month—but she insisted that the exercise would benefit her, and Brianna and I could help to carry Joanie.

As is usual in cases of travel with small children, our departure was somewhat prolonged. Joanie spit up mashed sweet potato down the front of her gown, Jemmy committed a sanitary indiscretion of major proportions, and Germain disappeared during the confusion occasioned by these mishaps. He was discovered, at the conclusion of a half-hour search involving everyone in the street, behind the public livery stable, happily engaged in throwing horse dung at passing carriages and wagons.

Everyone forcibly cleaned, redressed, and—in Germain's case—threatened with death and dismemberment, we descended the stairs again, to find that the landlord, Mr. Burns, had helpfully dug out an old goat-cart, with which he kindly presented us. The goat, however, was employed in eating nettles in the next-door garden, and declined to be caught. After a quarter of an hour's heated pursuit, Brianna declared that she would prefer to pull the cart herself, rather than spend any longer playing ring-around-the-rosy with a goat.

"Mrs. Fraser, Mrs. Fraser!" We were halfway down the street, the children, buckets, and picnic basket in the goat-cart, when Mrs. Burns came hurrying out of the inn after us, a jug of small beer in one hand, and an ancient flintlock pistol in the other.

"Snakes," she explained, handing me the latter. "My Annie says she saw at least a dozen adders, last time she walked that way."

"Snakes," I said, accepting the object and its attendant paraphernalia with reluctance. "Quite."

Given that "adder" could mean anything from a water moccasin to the most harmless grass snake, and also given that Annie Burns had a marked talent for melodrama, I was not unduly concerned. I thought of dropping the gun into the picnic basket, but a glance at Germain and Jemmy, pictures of cherubic innocence, decided me of the unwisdom of leaving even an unloaded firearm anywhere near them. I dropped the pistol into my berry-bucket, instead, and put it over my arm.

The day was overcast and cool, with a light breeze off the ocean. The air was damp, and I thought there was a good chance of rain before long, but for the moment, it was very pleasant out, with the sandy earth packed down sufficiently from earlier rains to make the walking easy.

Following Mrs. Crawford's directions, we made our way a mile or so down the beach, and found ourselves at the edge of a thick growth of coastal forest, where scanty-needled pines mingled with mangroves and palmetto in a dense, sun-splintered tangle, twined with vines. I closed my eyes and breathed in, nostrils flaring at the intoxicating mixture of scents: mudflats and wet sand, pine resins and sea air, the last faint whiffs of dead whale, and what I had been looking for—the fresh, tangy scent of wax-myrtles.

"That way," I said, pointing into the tangle of vegetation.

The going was too heavy for the cart now, so we left it, allowing the little boys to run wild, chasing tiny crabs and bright birds, as we made our way slowly into the scrubby forest. Marsali carried Joan, who curled up like a dormouse in her mother's arms and went to sleep, lulled by the sound of ocean and wind.

In spite of the heavy growth, the walking was more pleasant here than on the open beach; the wind-stunted trees were tall enough to give a pleasing sense of secrecy and refuge, and the footing was better, with a thin layer of decaying leaves and needles underfoot.

Jemmy grew tired of walking, and tugged on my skirt, raising both arms to be picked up.

"All right." I hung a berry-bucket from one wrist, and swung him up, with a crackle and pop of vertebrae; he was a very solid little boy. He twined his sandy feet comfortably round my waist and rested his face on my shoulder with a sigh of relief.

"All very well for you," I said, gently patting his back. "Who's going to give Grannie a ride, hey?"

"Grand-da," he said, and giggled. He lifted his head, looking round. "W'ere Grand-da?"

"Grand-da's busy," I told him, taking care to keep my voice light and cheerful. "We'll see Grand-da and Daddy soon."

"Want Daddy!"

"Yes, so does Mummy," I murmured. "Here, sweetie. See that? See the little berries? We're going to pick some, won't that be fun? No, don't eat them! Jemmy, I said *no*, do *not* put them in your mouth, they'll make you sick!"

We had found a luxuriant patch of wax-myrtles, and soon spread out, losing sight of each other amid the bushes as we picked, but calling out every few minutes, in order not to lose each other entirely.

I had put Jemmy down again, and was idly contemplating whether there might be any use for the berry-pulp, once the myrtle berries were boiled to render the wax, when I heard the soft crunch of footsteps on the other side of the bush I was picking from.

"Is that you, darling?" I called, thinking it was Brianna. "Perhaps we ought to have our lunch soon; I think it's maybe coming on to rain."

"Well, it's a kind invitation, sure," said a male voice, sounding amused. "I thank ye, ma'am, but I've made a decent breakfast not long since."

He stepped out from behind the bush, and I stood paralyzed, completely unable to speak. My mind, oddly enough, was not paralyzed in the slightest; my thoughts were running at the speed of light.

If Stephen Bonnet's here, Jamie and Roger are safe, thank God.

Where are the children?

Where is Bree?

Where's that gun, goddamnit?

"Who's that, *Grand-mère*?" Germain, appearing from behind a bush with what appeared to be a dead rat dangling from one hand, approached me warily, blue eyes narrowed at the intruder.

"Germain," I said in a croak, not taking my eyes off Bonnet. "Go find your mother, and stay with her."

"*Grand-mère*, is it? And who will his mother be, then?" Bonnet glanced from me to Germain and back, interested. He tilted back the hat he wore, and scratched at the side of his jaw.

"Never mind that," I said, as firmly as I could. "Germain, go!" I stole a look downward, but the pistol was not in my bucket. There were six buckets, and we had left three on the goat-cart; undoubtedly the gun was in one of those, worse luck.

"Oh, don't be goin' just yet, young sir." Bonnet made a move toward Germain, but the little boy took alarm at the gesture and skittered back, throwing the rat at Bonnet. It hit him in the knee, surprising him and making him hesitate for the split second necessary for Germain to vanish into the myrtles. I could hear his feet chuffing the sand as he ran, and hoped he knew where Marsali was. The last thing we needed was for him to lose himself.

Well, possibly not the very last thing, I amended. The very

last thing we needed was for Stephen Bonnet to lay eyes on Jemmy, which he promptly did, when the latter wandered out of the bushes an instant later, his short gown smeared with mud, more mud oozing through the fingers of his clenched fists.

There was no sun, but Jemmy's hair seemed to blaze with the brilliance of a striking match. Paralysis disappearing in a heartbeat, I grabbed him up, and backed away several steps, knocking over the half-filled bucket of myrtle berries.

Bonnet's eyes were the pale green of a cat's, and they brightened now with the intentness of a cat that spots a creeping mouse.

"And who will this sweet manneen be?" he asked, taking a step toward me.

"My son," I said instantly, and pulled Jem tight against my shoulder, ignoring his struggles. With the natural perversity of small children, he seemed to be fascinated by Bonnet's Irish lilt, and kept turning his head to stare at the stranger.

"Favors his father, I see." Drops of sweat glistened in the heavy blond brows. He smoothed first one, then the other, with the tip of his finger, so the sweat ran in trickles down the sides of his face, but the pale green eyes never wavered in their regard. "As does his . . . sister. And is your lovely daughter anyplace nearby, dear one? I should enjoy to renew our acquaintaince—such a charmin' girl, Brianna." He smiled.

"No doubt you would," I said, making no particular effort to disguise the edge in my voice. "No, she isn't. She's at home—with her husband." I leaned heavily on the word *husband*, hoping that Brianna was near enough to hear me and take warning, but he paid it no mind.

"At home, now. And where do ye call home then, Mum?" He took off the hat and wiped his face with his sleeve.

"Oh . . . in the backcountry. A homestead." I waved vaguely in the direction I thought roughly west. What was this—social conversation? And yet the choices seemed distinctly limited. I could turn and flee—at which point he would catch me handily, burdened as I was with Jemmy. Or I could stand here until he revealed what he wanted. I didn't think he was out for a picnic among the myrtles.

"A homestead," he repeated, a muscle twitching in his

cheek. "What business brings ye so far from home, and I might ask?"

"You might not," I said. "Or rather—you might ask my husband. He'll be along shortly."

I took another step backward as I said this, and he took a step toward me at the same time. A flicker of panic must have crossed my face, for he looked amused, and took another step.

"Oh, I doubt that, Mrs. Fraser dear. For see, the man's dead by now."

I squeezed Jemmy so hard that he let out a strangled squawk.

"What do you mean?" I demanded hoarsely. The blood was draining from my head, coagulating in an icy ball round my heart.

"Well, d'ye see, it was a bargain," he said, the look of amusement growing. "A division of duties, ye might say. My friend Lillywhite and the good Sheriff were to attend to Mr. Fraser and Mr. MacKenzie, and Lieutenant Wolff was to manage Mrs. Cameron's end of the business. That left me with the pleasant task of makin' myself reacquainted with my son and his mother." His eyes sharpened, focusing on Jemmy.

"I don't know what you are talking about," I said, through stiff lips, taking a better grip on Jemmy, who was watching Bonnet, owl-eyed.

He gave a short laugh at that.

"Sure, and ye're no hand at lyin', ma'am; you'll forgive the observation. Ye'd never make a card player. Ye know well enough what I mean—ye saw me there, at River Run. Though I confess as how I should be obliged to hear exactly what you and Mr. Fraser was engaged in, a-butchering that Negro woman that Wolff killed. I did hear as how the picture of a murderer shows in the victim's eyes—but ye didn't seem to be looking at her eyes, from what I could see. Was it magic of a sort ye were after doing?"

"Wolff—it *was* him, then?" Just at the moment, I didn't really care whether Lieutenant Wolff had murdered scores of women, but I was willing to engage in any line of conversation that offered the possibility of distracting him.

"Aye. He's a bungler, Wolff," he said, dispassionately. "But 'twas him that found out about the gold to begin with, so he claimed a part in the doings."

How far away were Marsali and Brianna? Had Germain found them? I could hear nothing over the whine of insects and the distant wash of surf. Surely they must hear us talking, though.

"Gold," I said, raising my voice a little. "Whatever do you mean, gold? There isn't any gold at River Run; Jocasta Cameron told you as much."

He puffed air through his lips in genial disbelief.

"I will say as Mrs. Cameron is a better liar than yourself, dear one, but sure, I didn't believe her, either. The doctor saw the gold, see."

"What doctor?" A baby's high-pitched cry came faintly through the bushes—Joan. I coughed, hoping to drown it out, and repeated, more loudly, "What doctor do you mean?"

"Rawls, I think was his name, or Rawlings." Bonnet was frowning slightly, head turned toward the sound. "I'd not the pleasure of his acquaintance, though; I might be mistaken."

"I'm sorry—I still have no idea what you're talking about." I was trying simultaneously to hold his gaze and to scan the ground nearby for anything that might be used as a weapon. Bonnet had a pistol in his belt, and a knife, but showed no disposition to draw either one. Why should he? A woman with an armload of two-year-old was not any sort of threat.

One thick blond brow flicked up, but he seemed in no great hurry, whatever he was about.

"No? Well, 'twas Wolff, as I was sayin'. It was a tooth to be drawn or somesuch; he met with this sawbones in Cross Creek. Bought the fellow a drink in reward, and spent the evening inside a wine-skin with him, in the end. Ye'll know the Lieutenant's weakness for the drink—the doctor was another sot, I hear, and the two of them thick as thieves before the dawn. Rawlings let out that he'd seen a great quantity of gold at River Run, for he'd just come from there, see?"

Rawlings had either passed out or sobered up enough to say no more, but the revelation had been enough to renew the

Lieutenant's determination to gain the hand—and property—of Jocasta Cameron.

"The lady would be havin' none of him, though, and then she ups and declares as she'll be takin' the one-armed fella instead. 'Twas a cruel blow to the Lieutenant's pride, alas." He grinned at that, showing a missing molar on one side.

Lieutenant Wolff, furious and baffled, appealed to his particular friend, Randall Lillywhite, for advice.

"Why, that—so that's why he arrested the priest at the Gathering? To prevent him marrying Mrs. Cameron to Duncan Innes?"

Bonnet nodded.

"That would be the way of it. A matter of delay, ye might say, so as to be havin' the opportunity of lookin' further into the matter."

Said opportunity had occurred at the wedding. As we had theorized, someone—Lieutenant Wolff—had in fact attempted to drug Duncan Innes with a cup of punch spiked with laudanum. The plan had been to render him insensible and pitch him into the river. During the uproar occasioned by Duncan's disappearance and presumedly accidental death, Wolff would have the chance to search the premises thoroughly for the gold—and eventually, to renew his addresses to Jocasta.

"But the black bitch drank the stuff herself," he said dispassionately. "Didn't die of it, worse luck—but she could have said who gave the cup to her, of course, and so Wolff slipped round and mixed ground glass into the gruel they were after feedin' her."

"What I want to know," I said, "is just how *you* got involved in this. Why were you there at River Run?"

"And isn't the Lieutenant the friend of my bosom these many years past, dear one? He came to me for help in disposing of the one-armed lad, so as he could take care to be seen in the midst of the party, enjoyin' himself in all innocence whilst accident was befallin' his rival." He frowned slightly, tapping a finger on the hilt of his pistol.

"I would have done better to bash the Innes fella on the head and toss him in, once I saw the laudanum had gone astray. Couldn't get at him, though—he spent half the day in the jakes, and someone always in there with him, bad cess to them."

There was nothing on the ground near me that could possibly be used as a weapon. Twigs, leaves, scattered fragments of shell, a dead rat—well, that had worked for Germain, but I didn't think Bonnet could be surprised twice in that fashion. Jemmy was losing his fear of the stranger as we talked, and was beginning to squirm to get down.

I edged backward a little; Bonnet saw it, and smiled. He wasn't bothered. Obviously he didn't think I could escape, and just as obviously, he was waiting for something. Of course—he had told me, himself. He was waiting for Brianna. I realized belatedly that he had clearly followed us out here from town; he knew that Marsali and Brianna were somewhere nearby—much easier simply to wait until they revealed themselves.

My best hope was that someone else would happen along; the weather was muggy and damp, but not raining yet, and this was a well-known spot for picnicking, according to Mrs. Burns. If someone did come along, how could I take advantage of it? I knew that Bonnet would not have the slightest compunction in simply shooting anyone who got in his way—he was boasting about the rest of his bloodthirsty plans.

"Mrs. Cameron—Mrs. Innes, she'll be now—seemed willin' enough to talk, when I suggested that her husband might soon be lackin' a few of his treasured parts, though as it happens, she was lyin', then, too, deceitful old trout. But it came to me, ponderin' the matter afterward, that she might be more obligin', were it a matter of her heir." He nodded toward Jemmy, and clicked his tongue at the boy. "So, lad, will we be goin' to see your great-auntie, then?"

Jemmy looked suspiciously at Bonnet, cuddling back against me.

"Whozat?" he asked.

"Oh, it's a wise child that knows its father, isn't it? I'm your Da, lad—was your mother not after telling you so?"

"Daddy?" Jemmy looked at Bonnet, then at me. "At's not Daddy!"

"No, he isn't your daddy," I assured Jemmy, shifting my hold. My arms were beginning to ache under the strain of holding him. "He's a bad man; we don't like him."

Bonnet laughed.

"Is there no shame with you at all, dear one? Of course he's mine—it's your daughter has said so, to my face."

"Nonsense," I said. I had maneuvered my way into a narrow gap between two of the evergreen wax-myrtle bushes. I'd try to distract him back into conversation, then seize a moment to whirl round, set Jemmy down, and urge him to run. With luck, I could block the gap long enough to prevent Bonnet grabbing him before he could get away—if he *would* run.

"Lillywhite," I said, taking hold of the conversation. "What did you mean, Lillywhite and the Sheriff were going to—to attend to my husband and Mr. MacKenzie?" Merely mentioning the possibility made me feel sick; sweat was running down my sides, but my face felt cold and clammy.

"Oh, that? What I said, Mrs. Fraser. Your husband is dead." He had started looking past me, pale green eyes flicking through the shrubbery. He was clearly expecting Brianna to show up at any moment.

"What happened at the wedding showed us clear enough that it wouldn't do, to leave Mrs. Cameron with so much protection. No, if we meant to try again, the thing to do was to see that she's no manfolks to call upon, either for help, or vengeance. So when your husband suggested to Mr. Lyon that he fetch me along to a private meeting, I thought that might be a suitable opportunity to dispose of him and Mr. MacKenzie—two birds with one whisky keg, as ye might be sayin'—but then I thought best if Lillywhite were the lad to handle that end of things, him and his tame sheriff." He smiled. "I thought best I come to be fetchin' my son and his mother along, so as not to risk anything goin' amiss, ye see. We'll—"

I shifted weight, spun on my heel, and plunked Jemmy on the ground on the far side of the bushes.

"Run!" I said urgently to him. "Run, Jem! Go!" There was a flash of red as he scampered away, whimpering with fear, and then Bonnet crashed into me.

He tried to shove me aside, but I was ready for that, and

grabbed for the pistol at his belt. He felt me snatch, and jerked back, but I had my fingers on the butt. I got it free and flung it behind me, as I fell to the ground with him on top of me.

He rolled off me and up on to his knees, where he froze.

"Stay there, or by the Holy Virgin, I'll blow your head off!"

Gasping from the fall, I sat up slowly, to see Marsali, pale as a sheet, aiming the ancient flintlock at him over the swell of her belly.

"Shoot him, *Maman*!" Germain was behind her, small face alight with eagerness. "Shoot him like a porcupine!"

Joan was somewhere back in the bushes; she began to wail at the sound of her mother's voice, but Marsali didn't take her eyes off Bonnet. Christ, had she loaded and primed the gun? I thought she must have; I could smell a whiff of black powder.

"Well, now," Bonnet said slowly. I could see his eyes trace the distance between him and Marsali—fifteen feet or more, too much to reach her with a dive. He put one foot on the ground, beginning to rise. He could reach her in three strides.

"Don't let him stand up!" I scrabbled up onto my own feet, shoving at his shoulder. He fell to the side, catching himself on one hand, then heaved back, faster than I could have imagined, seizing me round the waist and pulling me back down, this time on top of him.

There were screams from behind me, but I had no attention to spare. I stabbed my fingers at his eye, narrowly missing as he jerked me sideways; my nails slid off his cheekbone, raking furrows in his skin. We rolled in a flurry of petticoats and Irish oaths, me grabbing for his privates, him trying at once to throttle me and protect himself.

Then he squirmed and flipped over like a fish, and we ended with his arm locked tight around my neck, holding me against his chest. There was a whisper of metal on leather, and something cold against my neck. I stopped struggling, and took a deep breath.

Marsali's eyes were the size of saucers, her mouth clamped tight. Her gaze, thank heaven, was still trained on Bonnet, and so was the gun.

"Marsali," I said, very calmly, "shoot him. Right now."

"Be putting the gun down, colleen," Bonnet said, with equal calmness, "or I'll cut her throat on the count of three. One—"

"Shoot him!" I said, with all my force, and took my last deep gulp of air.

"Two."

"Wait!"

The pressure of the blade across my throat lessened, and I felt the sting of blood as I took a breath I had not expected to be given. I hadn't time to enjoy the sensation, though; Brianna stood amid the myrtles, Jemmy clinging to her skirts.

"Let her go," she said.

Marsali had been holding her breath; she let it out with a gasp and sucked air deep.

"He isn't about to let me go, and it doesn't matter," I said fiercely to them both. "Marsali, shoot him. *Now!*"

Her hand tightened on the gun, but she couldn't quite do it. She glanced at Brianna, white-faced, then back, her hand trembling.

"Shoot him, *Maman*," Germain whispered, but the eagerness had gone from his face. He was pale, too, and stood close to his mother.

"You'll come along with me, darlin', you and the lad." I could feel the vibration through Bonnet's chest as he spoke, and sensed the half-smile on his face, though I couldn't see it. "The others can go."

"Don't," I said, trying to make Bree look at me. "He won't let us go, you know he won't. He'll kill me and Marsali, no matter what he says. The only thing to do is shoot him. If Marsali can't do it, Bree, you'll have to."

That got her attention. Her eyes jerked to me, shocked, and Bonnet grunted, half in annoyance, half in amusement.

"Condemn her mother? She's not the girl to be doing such a thing, Mrs. Fraser."

"Marsali—he'll kill you, and the babe with you," I said, straining every muscle to make her understand, to force her to fire. "Germain and Joan will die out here, alone. What happens to me doesn't matter, believe me—for God's sake, *shoot him now!*"

She fired.

There was a spark and puff of white smoke, and Bonnet jerked. Then her hand sagged, the muzzle of the gun tilted down—and the wad and ball fell out on the sand with a tiny plop. Misfire.

Marsali moaned in horror, and Brianna moved like lightning, seizing the fallen bucket and hurling it at Bonnet's head. He yelped and threw himself aside, letting go his grip on me. The bucket struck me in the chest and I caught it, stupidly staring down into it. It was damp inside, with a scattering of the blue-white waxy berries stuck to the wood.

Then Germain and Jemmy were both crying, Joan was shrieking her head off in the wood, and I dropped the bucket and crawled madly for shelter behind a yaupon bush.

Bonnet was back on his feet, face flushed, the knife in his hand. He was clearly furious, but made an effort to smile at Brianna.

"Ah, now, darlin'," he said, having to raise his voice to be heard above the racket. "It's only yourself and my son I'm wanting. I'll not be harming either of you."

"He's not your son," Brianna said, low-voiced and vicious. "He'll never be yours."

He grunted contemptuously.

"Oh, aye? That's not how I heard it, in that dungeon in Cross Creek, sweetheart. And now I see him . . ." He looked at Jemmy again, nodding slowly. "He's mine, darlin' girl. He's the look of me—haven't ye, boyo?"

Jemmy buried his face in Brianna's skirts, howling.

Bonnet sighed, shrugged, and gave up any pretense of cajolement.

"Come on, then," he said, and started forward, obviously intending to scoop Jemmy up.

Brianna's hand rose out of her skirts, and aimed the pistol I had yanked out of his belt back at the place it had come from. Bonnet stopped in mid-step, mouth open.

"What about it?" she whispered, and her eyes were fixed, unblinking. "Do you keep your powder dry, Stephen?"

She braced the pistol with both hands, drew aim at his crotch, and fired.

He was fast, I'd give him that. He hadn't time to turn and run, but was reaching to cover his threatened balls with both hands, even as she pulled the trigger. Blood exploded in a thick spray through his fingers, but I couldn't tell what she'd hit.

He staggered back, clutching himself. He stared wildly round, as though unable to believe it, then sank to one knee. I could hear him breathing, hard and fast.

We all stood paralyzed, watching. One hand scrabbled at the sand, leaving bloody furrows. Then he rose, slowly, doubled over, the other hand pressed into his middle. His face was dead white, green eyes like dull water.

He stumbled round, gasping, and made off like a bug that's been stepped on, leaking and hitching. There was a crashing noise as he blundered through the bushes, and then he was gone. Beyond a palmetto tree, I could see a line of pelicans flying, ungainly and impossibly graceful against the lowering sky.

I was still crouched on the ground, chilled with shock. I felt something warm slide down my cheek, and realized it was a raindrop.

"Is he right?" Brianna was crouching beside me, helping me sit up. "Do you think he's right? Are they dead?" She was white to the lips, but not hysterical. She had Jemmy in the crook of her arm, clinging to her neck.

"No," I said. Everything seemed remote, as though it were happening in slow motion. I stood up slowly, balancing precariously, as though not sure quite how to do it.

"No," I said again, and felt no fear, no panic at the memory of what Bonnet had said; nothing but a certainty in my chest, like a small, comforting weight. "No, they're not." Jamie had told me; this was not the day when he and I would part.

Marsali had vanished into the wood to retrieve Joanie. Germain was bent over the splotches of blood on the sand, studying them with fascination. It occurred to me dimly to wonder what type they were, but then I dismissed the thought from my mind.

"He'll never be yours," she had said.

"Let's go," I said, patting Jemmy gently. "I think we'll make do with unscented candles, for now."

ROGER AND JAMIE appeared at dawn two days later, rousing everyone in the inn by pounding at the door, and causing people in the neighboring houses to throw open their shutters and put their nightcapped heads out in alarm, owing to the resultant whooping and yelling. I was reasonably sure that Roger had a minor concussion, but he refused to be put to bed—though he did allow Bree to hold his head in her lap and make noises of shocked sympathy about the impressive lump on it, while Jamie gave us a terse account of the battle of Wylie's Landing, and we gave a somewhat confused explanation of our adventures in the myrtle groves.

"So Bonnet's not dead?" Roger asked, opening one eye.

"Well, we don't know," I explained. "He got away, but I don't know how badly he was hurt. There wasn't a dreadful lot of blood, but if he was hit in the lower abdomen, that would be a terrible wound, and almost certainly fatal. Peritonitis is a very slow and nasty way to die."

"Good," Marsali said, vindictively.

"Good!" Germain echoed, looking proudly up at her. "*Maman* shot the bad man, *Grand-père*," he told Jamie. "So did Auntie. He was *full* of holes—there was blood everywhere!"

"Holes," Jemmy said happily. "Holes, holes, lotsa holes!"

"Well, maybe one hole," Brianna murmured. She didn't look up from the damp cloth with which she was gently sponging dried blood from Roger's scalp and hair.

"Oh, aye? Well, if ye only took off a finger or one of his balls, lass, he might survive," Jamie observed, grinning at her. "Wouldna improve his temper, though, I dinna suppose."

Fergus arrived on the noon packet boat, triumphantly bearing the registered, stamped, and officially sealed deeds for the two land grants, thus putting the cocked hat on the day's rejoicing. The celebrations were limited, though, owing to the sobering knowledge that one rather major loose end remained.

After a vigorous discussion, it was decided—meaning that Jamie made up his mind and pigheadedly refused to entertain dissenting views—that he and I would ride west at once to River Run. The young families would remain in Wilmington for a few days, to complete business, and to keep an ear out for any report of a wounded or dying man. They would then proceed back to Fraser's Ridge, keeping strictly clear of Cross Creek and River Run.

"Lieutenant Wolff canna be using threats to you or the lad to influence my aunt, if ye're nowhere near him," Jamie pointed out to Brianna.

"And as for you, *mo charadean*," he said to Roger and Fergus, "ye canna be leaving the women and weans to look out for themselves—God kens who they might shoot next!"

It was only as he closed the door on the resulting laughter that he turned to me, ran a fingertip over the scratch on my throat, and then pulled me so hard against himself that I thought my ribs would break. I clung tight to him on the landing, not caring that I couldn't breathe, nor whether anyone might see; happy only to be touching him—and to have him there to touch.

"Ye did right, Claire," he muttered at last, mouth against my hair. "But for God's sake, never do it again!"

So it was that he and I left at dawn next day, alone.

104

SLY AS FOXES

WE ARRIVED AT RIVER RUN near sundown three days later, horses lathered and filthy, and ourselves in no better case. The place seemed peaceful enough, the last of the spring light glowing on green lawns and spotlighting the white marble statues and the stone of Hector's mausoleum among its dark yews.

"What do you think?" I asked Jamie. We had reined up at the foot of the lawn, looking the situation over cautiously before approaching the house.

"Well, no one's burned the place down," he replied, standing in his stirrups to survey the prospect. "And I dinna see rivers of blood cascading down the front stair. Still . . ." He sat down, reached into his saddlebag, and withdrew a pistol, which he loaded and primed as a precaution. With this tucked into the waistband of his breeks and concealed by the skirts of his coat, we rode slowly up the drive to the front door.

By the time we had reached it, I knew something was wrong. There was a sinister air of stillness about the house; no sound of scurrying servants, no music from the parlor, no scents of supper being fetched in from the cookhouse. Most peculiar of all, Ulysses was not there to greet us; our knocking went unanswered for several minutes, and when the door was at last opened, it was Phaedre, Jocasta's body-servant, who appeared.

She had looked dreadful when I had last seen her, nearly a year before, after her mother's death. She didn't look much better now; there were circles under her eyes, and her skin looked bruised and drawn, like a fruit beginning to go bad.

When she saw us, though, her eyes lighted and her mouth relaxed in visible relief.

"Oh, Mr. Jamie!" she cried. "I been prayin' for somebody to come help, ever since yesterday, but I thought for sure it would be Mr. Farquard, and then we maybe be in worse trouble, he such a man for the law and all, even if he is your auntie's friend."

Jamie raised an eyebrow at this rather confused declaration, but nodded reassuringly and squeezed her hand.

"Aye, lass. I dinna believe I've been an answer to prayer before, but I've no objection. Is my aunt . . . well?"

"Oh, yes, sir—*she's* well enough."

Withdrawing before we could ask further questions, she beckoned us toward the stair.

Jocasta was in her boudoir, knitting. She raised her head

at the sound of feet, alert, and before anyone could say anything, asked "Jamie?" in a quavering voice, and stood up. Even at a distance, I could see that there were mistakes in the knitting, missed stitches and open runs; most unlike her usual fastidious needlework.

"Aye, it's me, Aunt. And Claire. What's amiss, then?" Crossing the room in two strides, he reached her side and took her arm, patting her hand in reassurance.

Her face underwent the same transformation of relief that we had seen in Phaedre, and I thought she might give way at the knees. She stiffened her spine, though, and turned toward me.

"Claire? Thank Blessed Bride ye've come, though how—well, never mind it for now. Will ye come? Duncan's hurt."

Duncan lay in bed in the next room, inert under a stack of comforters. At first, I was afraid he might be dead, but he stirred at once at the sound of Jocasta's voice.

"Mac Dubh?" he said, puzzled. He poked his head up from the mound of covers, squinting to see in the dimness of the room. "What in God's name brings you here?"

"Lieutenant Wolff," Jamie said, a little caustically. "Is the name perhaps familiar to ye?"

"Aye, ye might say so." There was a slightly odd tone to Duncan's voice, but I paid it no mind, engaged in lighting candles and in excavating him sufficiently from the bedclothes to find out what the matter was.

I was expecting to find a knife or gunshot wound. At first examination, there was nothing whatever of the sort visible, and it took a few moments' mental regrouping to discover that what he was suffering from was a broken leg. It was a simple fracture of the lower tibia, fortunately, and while undoubtedly painful, it seemed to be no great threat to his health.

I sent Phaedre to find some splinting materials, while Jamie, informed that Duncan stood in no great danger, sat down to get to the bottom of things.

"He has been here? Lieutenant Wolff?" he asked.

"Aye, he has." Again the slight hesitation.

"Has he gone, then?"

"Oh, aye." Duncan shuddered a little, involuntarily.

"Am I hurting you?" I asked.

"Oh, no, Mrs. Claire," he assured me. "I was only—well . . ."

"Ye may as well tell me straight out, Duncan," Jamie said, in a tone of mild exasperation. "I think it'll no be a tale that improves wi' keeping, aye? And if it's the sort of tale I think, then I have a bittie story to tell to you, as well."

Duncan eyed him narrowly, but then sighed, capitulating, and lay back on the pillow.

The Lieutenant had arrived at River Run two days before, but unlike his usual habit, had not come to the front door to be announced. Instead, he had left his horse hobbled in a field a mile from the house, and approached stealthily on foot.

"We only realized as much, because of finding the horse later, ye see," Duncan explained to me, as I bound his leg. "I didna ken he was here at all, until I went out to the necessary after supper, and he leaped at me, out o' the dark. I near died o' fright, and then I near died of being shot, for he fired at me, and if I had had an arm on that side, I daresay he would have struck it. Only I hadna got one, so he didn't."

In spite of his disability, Duncan had fought back ferociously, butting the Lieutenant in the face, charging him, and knocking him backward.

"He staggered and tripped himself on the brick walk, and fell backward so as he hit his head a dreadful smackit." He shuddered again at memory of the sound. "Like a melon hit wi' an ax, it was."

"Och, aye. So, was he killed at once, then?" Jamie asked, interested.

"Well, no." Duncan had grown easier in his manner, telling the tale, but now began to look uneasy again. "Now, see, *Mac Dubh*, here's the pinch of the matter. For I'd gone staggering, too, when I knocked him ower, and I stepped into the stone channel from the necessary and snapped my leg, and there I lay, groaning by the walk. Ulysses heard me callin' at last, and came down, and Jo after him."

Duncan had told Jocasta what had happened, as Ulysses had gone to fetch a couple of grooms to help carry Duncan into the house. And then, between the pain of his broken leg and his habit of leaving difficulties to the butler to be resolved, had likewise left the Lieutenant.

"It was my fault, *Mac Dubh*, and I ken it well," he said, his face drawn and pale. "I ought to have given orders of some kind; though in fact I canna think even now what I ought to have said, and I've had time and plenty enough to think."

The rest of the story, pried out of him with some reluctance, was that Jocasta and Ulysses had evidently conferred on the matter, and concluded that the Lieutenant had gone beyond being a nuisance, and become an outright threat. And that being so . . .

"Ulysses killed him," Duncan said baldly, then stopped, as though appalled afresh. He swallowed, looking deeply unhappy. "Jo says as how she ordered him to do it—and Christ knows, *Mac Dubh*, she might have done so. She's no the woman to be trifled with, let alone to have her servants murdered, herself threatened, and her husband set upon."

I gathered from his hesitance, though, that some small doubt about Jocasta's part in this still lingered in his mind.

Jamie had grasped the main point troubling him, though.

"Christ," he said. "The man Ulysses will be hangit on the spot, or worse, if anyone hears of it. Whether my aunt ordered it, or no."

Duncan looked a little calmer, now that the truth was out. He nodded.

"Aye, that's it," he agreed. "I canna let him go to the gallows—but what am I to do about the Lieutenant? There's the Navy to be considered, to say nothing of sheriffs and magistrates." That was a definite point. A good deal of the prosperity of River Run depended upon its naval contracts for timber and tar; Lieutenant Wolff had in fact been the naval liaison responsible for such contracts. I could see that His Majesty's Navy might just possibly be inclined to look squiggle-eyed at a proprietor who had killed his local naval representative, no matter what the excuse. I imagined that the law, in the person of Sheriff and magistrates, might take a more lenient view of the situation—save for the person of the perpetrator.

A slave who shed the blood of a white person was automatically condemned, regardless of provocation. It would make no difference what had happened—even with a dozen witnesses to testify to Wolff's attack on Duncan, Ulysses would be doomed. If anyone found out about it. I began to understand the air of desperation that hung over River Run; the other slaves were well aware of what might happen.

Jamie rubbed a knuckle over his chin.

"Ah . . . just how did . . . I mean, would it not be possible to say that ye'd done it yourself, Duncan? It was self-defense, after all—and I've evidence that the man did come in order to murder ye, wi' the notion of marrying my aunt then by force, or at least holding her hostage so as she might be threatened into telling about the gold."

"Gold?" Duncan looked blank. "But there isna any gold here. I thought we'd got that straight last year."

"The Lieutenant and his associates thought there was," I told him. "But Jamie can tell you all about that, in a bit. What *did* happen to the Lieutenant, exactly?"

"Ulysses cut his throat," Duncan said, and swallowed, Adam's apple bobbing in his own throat. "I should be pleased enough to say I'd done it, aye, only . . ."

Beyond the simple difficulty of cutting someone's throat with only one hand, it was evidently all too apparent that the Lieutenant's throat had been cut by a left-handed person—and Duncan, of course, lacked a left hand altogether.

I happened to know that Jocasta Cameron—like her nephew—was left-handed, but it seemed more tactful not to mention that at the moment. I glanced at Jamie, who raised both brows at me.

Would she? I asked silently.

A MacKenzie of Leoch? his cynical look said back.

"Where *is* Ulysses?" I asked.

"In the stable, most like, if he hasna already headed west." Knowing that if anyone learned the truth of the Lieutenant's death, Ulysses would be condemned at once, Jocasta had sent her butler to saddle a horse, with instructions to flee into the mountains, should anyone come.

Jamie drew a deep breath and rubbed a hand over his head, thinking.

"Well, then. I should say the best thing, perhaps, is for the Lieutenant to disappear. Where have ye put him for the moment, Duncan?"

A muscle near Duncan's mouth twitched, in an uneasy attempt at a smile.

"I believe he's in the barbecue pit, *Mac Dubh*. Covered over wi' burlap, and piled with hickory wood, disguised as a pork carcass."

Jamie's brows went up again, but he merely nodded.

"Aye, then. Leave it to me, Duncan."

I left instructions for Duncan to be given honeyed water and tea brewed with boneset and cherry bark, and went outside with Jamie to contemplate methods of disappearance.

"The simplest thing would be just to bury him somewhere, I suppose," I said.

"Mmphm," Jamie said. He lifted the pine torch he was carrying, frowning thoughtfully at the humped mound of burlap in the pit. I hadn't liked the Lieutenant in the least, but it looked rather pitiful.

"Maybe. I'm thinkin', though—the slaves all ken what's happened. If we bury him on the place, they'll ken that, too. They wouldna tell anyone, of course—but he'll haunt the place, aye?"

A shiver ran up my spine, engendered as much by the matter-of-factness of his tone as by his words, and I pulled my shawl closer round me.

"Haunt the place?"

"Aye, of course. A murder victim, done to death here, and hidden, unavenged?"

"You mean . . . really haunt the place?" I asked, carefully, "or do you only mean the slaves would think so?"

He shrugged, twitching his shoulders uneasily.

"I dinna think it matters so much, does it? They'll avoid the spot where he's buried, one of the women will see the ghost at night, rumors will get round, as they do—and next thing, a slave at Greenoaks will say something, someone in Farquard's family will hear of it, and before ye know it, someone will be over here, asking questions. Given that the Navy is like to be looking for the Lieutenant before too long anyway . . . what d'ye say to weighting the body and putting it in the river? That's what he had in mind for Duncan, after all."

"Not a bad notion," I said, considering it. "But he meant

Duncan to be found. There's a lot of boat traffic on the river, and it isn't very deep up this far. Even if we weighted the body well, it's possible it would rise, or someone snag it with a pole. Would it matter if someone found it, though, do you think? The body wouldn't be connected with River Run."

He nodded slowly, moving the torch aside to keep the sparks from showering over his sleeve. There was a light wind, and the elms near the barbecue pit whispered restlessly overhead.

"Aye, that's so. Only, if someone does find him, there'll be an inquiry. The Navy will send someone to try to find out the truth of the matter—and they'll come here, asking questions. What d'ye think will happen, if they were to badger the slaves, askin' had they seen the Lieutenant, and so on?"

"Mm, yes." Given the slaves' present acute state of nerves, I imagined that any inquiry would send one or more of them into a state of panic, in which anything might be blurted out.

Jamie was standing quite still, staring at the burlap-draped shape with an expression of deep abstraction. I drew a deep breath, caught a faint scent of decaying blood, and let it out again, quick.

"I suppose . . . we could burn him," I said, and swallowed a sudden taste of bile. "He *is* already in the pit, after all."

"It's a thought," Jamie said, and one corner of his mouth quirked in a faint smile. "But I think I've a better one, Sassenach." He turned to look thoughtfully at the house. A few windows were dimly alight, but everyone was inside, cowering.

"Come on, then," he said, with sudden decision. "There'll be a sledgehammer in the stable, I expect."

THE FRONT OF THE MAUSOLEUM was covered by an ornamental grille of black wrought iron, with an enormous lock, its metal decorated by sixteen-petalled Jacobite roses. I had always considered this to be merely one of Jocasta Cameron's affectations, since I doubted that grave-robbers were a great threat in such a rural setting. The hinges scarcely creaked when Jamie unlocked the grille and swung it open; like everything else at River Run, it was maintained in impeccable condition.

"You really think this is better than burying or burning him?" I asked. There was no one nearby, but I spoke in a near whisper.

"Oh, aye. Auld Hector will take care of him, and prevent him doin' harm," Jamie replied matter-of-factly. "And it's blessed ground, in a manner of speaking. No a matter of leaving his soul to wander about, makin' trouble, aye?"

I nodded, a little uncertainly. He was probably right; in terms of belief, Jamie understood the slaves much better than I did. For that matter, I wasn't sure whether he was speaking only of what the psychological effect on them might be—or whether he was himself convinced that Hector Cameron ought to be capable of dealing with this *ex post facto* threat to his wife and plantation.

I lifted the torch so Jamie could see what he was doing, and set my teeth in my lower lip.

He had wrapped the sledgehammer in rags, so as not to chip the marble blocks. The small blocks of the front wall, inside the grille, had been expertly cut to fit and lightly mortared in place. The first blow knocked two of the blocks a few inches out of place. A few more blows, and a dark space showed, where the blocks had given way enough to show the blackness inside the mausoleum.

Jamie stopped to wipe sweat from his forehead, and muttered something under his breath.

"What did you say?"

"I said, it stinks," he replied, sounding puzzled.

"This is surprising, is it?" I asked, a little testily. "How long has Hector Cameron been dead, four years?"

"Well, aye, but it's no—"

"What are you doing?" Jocasta Cameron's voice rang out behind me, sharp with agitation, and I jumped, dropping the torch.

It flickered, but didn't go out, and I snatched it up again, waving it to encourage the flame. The flame rose and steadied, shedding a ruddy glow on Jocasta, who stood on the path behind us, ghostly in her white nightgown. Phaedre huddled behind her mistress, no more of her face visible than the brief shine of eyes in the darkness. The eyes looked scared, flicking from Jamie and me to the dark hole in the facade of the mausoleum.

"What am I doing? Disposing of Lieutenant Wolff, what else?" Jamie, who had been as startled as I had by his aunt's sudden appearance, sounded a little cross. "Leave it to me, Aunt. Ye needna concern yourself."

"You are not—no, ye mustn't open Hector's tomb!" Jocasta's long nose twitched, obviously picking up the scent of decay—which was faint, but distinct.

"Dinna fash yourself, Aunt," Jamie said. "Go back to the house. I'll manage. It will all be well."

She ignored his soothing words, advancing blindly over the walk, hands groping in the empty air.

"No, Jamie! Ye mustn't. Close it up again. Close it, for God's sake!"

The panic in her voice was unmistakable, and I saw Jamie frown in confusion. He looked uncertainly from his aunt to the hole in the mausoleum. The wind had dropped, but now rose in a small gust, wafting a much stronger scent of death around us. Jamie's face changed, and ignoring his aunt's cries of protest, he knocked loose more blocks with several quick blows of the padded hammer.

"Bring the torch, Sassenach," he said, setting down the hammer, and with a sense of creeping horror, I did so.

We stood shoulder to shoulder, peering through the narrow gap in the blocks. Two coffins of polished wood stood inside, each on a pedestal of marble. And on the floor between them . . .

"Who is he, Aunt?" Jamie's voice was quiet as he turned to speak to her.

She stood as if paralyzed, the muslin of her gown flapping round her legs in the wind, pulling strands of white hair from beneath her cap. Her face was frozen, but the blind eyes darted to and fro, seeking an impossible escape.

Jamie stepped forward and grabbed her fiercely by the arm, making her start from her frozen trance.

"Co a th'ann?" he growled. "Who is he? Who?"

Her mouth worked, trying to form words. She stopped,

swallowed, tried again, eyes still flickering to and fro over his shoulder, looking at God knew what. Had she still been able to see when they put him in there? I wondered. Did she see it now, in memory?

"His name—his name was Rawlings," she said faintly, and something inside my chest fell like an iron weight.

I must have moved or made some sound, for Jamie's eyes went to me. He reached out a hand for mine, and held on tightly, though his eyes went back to Jocasta.

"How?" he asked, calmly, but with a tone that warned that he would brook no evasion.

She closed her eyes then, and sighed, broad shoulders slumping suddenly.

"Hector killed him," she said.

"Oh, aye?" Jamie cast a cynical glance at the coffins inside the mausoleum, and the huddled mass that lay on the floor between them. "A good trick, that. I hadna realized my uncle was so capable."

"Before." Her eyes opened again, but she spoke dully, as though nothing mattered any longer. "He was a doctor, Rawlings. He'd come to look at my eyes, once before. When Hector took ill, he called the man back. I canna say quite what happened, but Hector caught him nosing round where he should not, and smashed his head in. He was a hot-tempered man, Hector."

"I should say so," Jamie said, with another glance at the body of Dr. Rawlings. "How did he get in here?"

"We—he—hid the corpse, meaning to carry it off and leave it in the wood. But then . . . Hector got worse, and couldna leave his bed. Within a day, he was dead, too. And so . . ." She lifted a long white hand, gesturing toward the draft of dank chill that floated from the open tomb.

"Great minds think alike," I murmured, and Jamie gave me a dirty look, letting go my hand. He stood contemplating the stillness inside the violated mausoleum, thick brows drawn down in a frown of concentration.

"Oh, aye?" he said again. "Whose is the second coffin?"

"Mine." Jocasta was recovering her nerve; her shoulders straightened and her chin lifted.

Jamie made a small puffing noise and glanced at me. I

could believe that Jocasta would callously leave a dead man to lie exposed, rather than put him in her own pristine coffin . . . and yet. To do so drastically increased the odds of discovery, slim as those might be.

No one would have opened Jocasta's coffin until it was time to receive her own body; Dr. Rawlings' corpse could have lain there in complete safety, even were the mausoleum to be opened for some reason. Jocasta Cameron was selfish—but by no means stupid.

"Put Wolff in, then, if you must," she said. "He can lie on the floor with the other one."

"Why not put him in your coffin, Aunt?" Jamie asked, and I saw that he was looking at her intently.

"No!" She had begun to turn away, but at this whipped back, her blind face fierce in the torchlight. "He is dung. Let him lie and rot in the open!"

Jamie narrowed his eyes at her response, but didn't reply. Instead, he turned to the tomb and began to shift the loosened blocks.

"What are you doing?" Jocasta could hear the grating noise of the shifting marble, and became agitated anew. She turned round on the walk, but became disoriented, staring off toward the river. I realized that she must now be completely blind, unable even to see the light from the torch.

I had no attention to pay her just then, though. Jamie wedged himself through the gap in the blocks, and stepped inside.

"Light me, Sassenach," he said softly, and his voice echoed slightly in the small stone chamber.

Breathing very shallowly, I followed him. Phaedre had begun to moan in the darkness outside; she sounded like the *ban-sidhe* that howls for approaching death—but this death had come long since.

The coffins were equipped with brass plates, gone slightly green with damp, but still easily readable. "Hector Alexander Robert Cameron," read one, and "Jocasta Isobeail MacKenzie Cameron," the other. Without hesitation, Jamie seized the edges of the lid of Jocasta's coffin and pulled up.

It wasn't nailed; the lid was heavy, but shifted at once.

"Oh," Jamie said softly, looking down.

Gold will never tarnish, no matter how damp or dank its surroundings. It will lie at the bottom of the sea for centuries, to emerge one day in some random fisherman's net, bright as the day it was smelted. It glimmers from a rocky matrix, a siren's song that has called to men for thousands of years.

The ingots lay in a shallow layer over the bottom of the coffin. Enough to fill two small chests, each chest heavy enough to require two men—or a man and a strong woman—to carry it. Each ingot stamped with a fleur-de-lis. One third of the Frenchman's gold.

I blinked at the shimmer, and looked aside, my eyes blurring with fractured light. It was dark on the floor, but I could still make out the huddled form against the pale marble. "Nosing where he should not." And what had he seen, Daniel Rawlings, that had made him draw the fleur-de-lis in the margin of his casebook, with that discreet notation, "Aurum"?

Hector Cameron was still alive, then. The mausoleum had not yet been sealed. Perhaps when Dr. Rawlings rose to follow his wandering patient, Hector had led him here unwitting, going down in the night to view his hoard? Perhaps. Neither Hector Cameron nor Daniel Rawlings could say, now, how it had been, or what had happened.

I felt a thickening in my throat, for the man whose bones lay now at my feet, the friend and colleague whose instruments I had inherited, whose shade had stood at my elbow, lending me both courage and comfort, when I laid hands on the sick and sought to heal them.

"Such a waste," I said softly, looking down.

Jamie lowered the coffin lid, gently, as though the coffin held an occupant whose rest had been disturbed.

Outside, Jocasta stood still on the path. She had an arm round Phaedre, who had stopped whimpering, but it was not clear which of them was supporting the other. Jocasta must know now from the noise where we were, but she faced the river still, eyes fixed, unblinking in the torchlight.

I cleared my throat, hugging the shawl tighter with my free hand.

"What shall we do, then?" I asked Jamie.

He turned and looked back into the tomb for a moment, then shrugged a little.

"We'll leave the Lieutenant to Hector, as we planned. As for the doctor . . ." He drew breath slowly, troubled gaze fixed on the slender bones that lay in a graceful fan, pale and still in the light. A surgeon's hand—once.

"I think," he said, "we will take him home with us—to the Ridge. Let him lie among friends."

He brushed past the two women without acknowledgment or pardon, and went to fetch Lieutenant Wolff.

105

A THRUSH'S DREAM

Fraser's Ridge
May, 1772

THE NIGHT AIR WAS COOL and fresh. So early in the year, the bloodthirsty flies and mosquitoes hadn't started yet; only random moths came in through the open window now and then, to flutter round the smoored hearth like bits of burning paper, brushing past their outflung limbs in brief caress.

She lay as she had fallen, half on top of him, heart thumping loud and slow in her ears. From here, she could see out through the window; the jagged black line of trees on the far side of the dooryard, and beyond them a section of sky, lit with stars, so near and bright that it should be possible to step out among them and walk from one to another, higher and higher, to the hook of the crescent moon.

"You're not mad at me?" he whispered. He spoke more easily now, but lying with her ear on his chest, she could hear the faint catch in his voice, the point where he forced air hard through his scarred throat to form the words.

"No." His hand was on her hair, stroking. "I didn't ever tell you not to read it."

His fingers touched her shoulder, lightly, and her toes curled with pleasure at the feeling. Did she mind? No. She supposed she ought to feel exposed in some way, the privacy of her thoughts and dreams laid bare to him—but she trusted him with them. He would never use those things against her.

Besides, once set down on paper, the dreams became a separate thing from her, herself. Much like the drawings that she made; a reflection of one facet of her mind, a brief glimpse of something once seen, once thought, once felt—but not the same thing as the mind or heart that made them. Not quite.

"Fair's fair, though." Her chin rested in the hollow of his shoulder. He smelled good, bitter and musky with the scent of satisfied desire. "Tell me one of your dreams, then."

A laugh vibrated through his chest, nearly soundless, but she felt it.

"Only one?"

"Yes, but it has to be an important one. Not the flying ones, or the ones where you're being chased by a monster, or the ones where you go to school without your clothes on. Not the ones that everybody has—one that only *you* have."

One of her hands was on his chest, scratching gently to make the dark curly hairs twitch and rise. The other was under the pillow; if she moved her fingers slightly, she could feel the smooth little shape of the ancient wifie, as he called it. She could imagine her own womb swelling, round and hard. She could feel the clutch and soft spasm in her lower belly; aftershocks of their lovemaking. Would it be this time?

He turned his head on the pillow, thinking. Long lashes lay against his cheek, black as the lines of the trees outside. He turned back then, lifting them, and his eyes were the color of moss, soft and vivid in the shadowed light.

"I could be romantic," he whispered, and his fingers

drifted down her back, so that she felt gooseflesh rise in their wake. "I could say this is my dream—you and me, here alone . . . us and our children." He turned his head a little, checking the trundle in the corner, but Jemmy was sound asleep, invisible.

"You could," she echoed, and ducked her head so her forehead pressed against his shoulder. "But that's a waking dream—not a real dream. You know what I mean."

"Aye, I do."

He was quiet for a minute, his hand lying still, broad and warm across the base of her spine.

"Sometimes," he whispered at last, "sometimes, I dream I am singing, and I wake from it with my throat aching."

He couldn't see her face, or the tears that prickled at the corners of her eyes.

"What do you sing?" she whispered back. She heard the *shush* of the linen pillow as he shook his head.

"No song I've ever heard, or know," he said softly. "But I know I'm singing it for you."

106

THE SURGEON'S BOOK II

July 27, 1772

"Was called from churning to attend Rosamund Lindsay, who arrived in late afternoon with a severe laceration to the left hand, sustained with an axe while girdling trees. Wound was extensive, having nearly severed the left thumb; laceration extended from base of index finger to two inches above the styloid process

of the radius, which was superficially damaged. Injury had been sustained approximately three days prior, treated with rough binding and bacon grease. Extensive sepsis apparent, with suppuration, gross swelling of hand and forearm. Thumb blackened; gangrene apparent; characteristic pungent odor. Subcutaneous red streaks, indicative of blood poisoning, extended from site of injury nearly to antecubital fossa.

Patient presented with high fever (est. 104 degrees F., by hand), symptoms of dehydration, mild disorientation. Tachycardia evident.

In view of the seriousness of patient's condition, recommended immediate amputation of limb at elbow. Patient refused to consider this, insisting instead upon application of pigeon poultice, consisting of the split body of a freshly-killed pigeon, applied to wound (patient's husband had brought pigeon, neck freshly wrung). Removed thumb at base of metacarpal, ligated remains of radial artery (crushed in original injury) and superficialis volae. Debrided and drained wound, applied approximately 1/2 oz. crude penicillin powder (source: rotted casaba rind, batch #23, prep. 15/6/72) topically, followed by application of mashed raw garlic (three cloves), barberry salve—and pigeon poultice, at insistence of husband applied over dressing. Administered fluids by mouth; febrifuge mixture of red centaury, bloodroot, and hops; water ad lib. Injected liquid penicillin mixture (batch # 23), IV, dosage 1/4 oz in suspension in sterile water.

Patient's condition deteriorated rapidly, with increasing symptoms of disorientation and delirium, high fever. Extensive urticaria appeared on arm and upper torso. Attempted to relieve fever by repeated applications of cold water, to no avail. Patient being incoherent, requested permission to amputate from husband; permission denied on grounds that death appeared imminent, and patient "would not want to be buried in pieces."

Repeated penicillin injection. Patient lapsed into unconsciousness shortly thereafter, and expired just before dawn.

I DIPPED MY QUILL again, but then hesitated, letting the drops of ink slide off the sharpened point. How much more should I say?

The deeply-ingrained disposition for scientific thoroughness warred with caution. It was important to describe what had happened, as fully as possible. At the same time, I hesitated to put down in writing what might amount to an admission of manslaughter—it wasn't murder, I assured myself, though my guilty feelings made no such distinctions.

"Feelings aren't truth," I murmured. Across the room, Brianna looked up from the bread she was slicing, but I bent my head over the page, and she returned to her whispered conversation with Marsali by the fire. It was no more than midafternoon, but dark and rainy outside. I had lit a candle by which to write, but the girls' hands flickered over the dim table like moths, lighting here and there among the plates and platters.

The truth was that I didn't think Rosamund Lindsay had died of septicemia. I was fairly sure that she had died of an acute reaction to an unpurified penicillin mixture—of the medicine I gave her, in short. Of course, the truth also was that the blood poisoning would certainly have killed her, left untreated.

The truth also was that I had had no way of knowing what the effects of the penicillin would be—but that was rather the point, wasn't it? To make sure someone else *might* know?

I twiddled the quill, rolling it between thumb and forefinger. I had kept a faithful account of my experiments with penicillin—the growing of cultures on media ranging from bread to chewed pawpaw and rotted melon rind, painstaking descriptions of the microscopic and gross identification of the *Penicillium* molds, the effects of—to this point—very limited applications.

Yes, certainly I must include a description of the effects. The real question, though, was—for whom was I keeping this careful record?

I bit my lip, thinking. If it was only for my own reference, it would be a simple matter; I could simply record the symptoms, timing, and effects, without explicitly noting the cause of death; I was unlikely to forget the circumstances, after all. But if this record were ever to be useful to someone else . . . someone who had no notion of the benefits and dangers of an antibiotic . . .

The ink was drying on the quill. I lowered the point to the page.

Age—44, I wrote slowly. In this day, casebook accounts like this often ended with a pious description of the deceased's last moments, marked—presumably—by Christian resignation on the part of the holy, repentance by the sinful. Neither attitude had marked the passage of Rosamund Lindsay.

I glanced at the coffin, sitting on its trestles under the rain-smeared window. The Lindsays' cabin was very small, not suited for a funeral in the pouring rain, where a large number of mourners were expected. The coffin was open, awaiting the evening wake, but the muslin shroud had been drawn up over her face.

Rosamund had been a whore in Boston; growing too stout and too old to ply her trade with much profit, she had drifted south, looking for a husband. "I couldn't bide another of them winters," she had confided to me, soon after her arrival on the Ridge. "Nor yet another of them stinkin' fishermen."

She had found the necessary refuge in Kenneth Lindsay, who was looking for a wife to share the work of homesteading. Not a match born of physical attraction—the Lindsays had had perhaps six sound teeth between them—or emotional compatibility, still it had seemed an amicable relationship.

Shocked rather than grief-stricken, Kenny had been taken off by Jamie for medication with whisky—a somewhat more effective treatment than my own. At least I didn't think it would be lethal.

Immediate cause of death—I wrote, and paused again. I doubted that Rosamund's response to approaching death would have found outlet in either prayer or philosophy, but she had had opportunity for neither. She had died blue-faced, congested, and bulging-eyed, unable to force word or breath past the swollen tissues of her throat.

My own throat felt tight at the memory, as though I were being choked. I picked up the cooling cup of catmint tea and took a sip, feeling the pungent liquid slide soothingly down. It was little comfort that the septicemia would have killed her more lingeringly. Suffocation was quicker, but not much more pleasant.

I tapped the quill point on the blotter, leaving inky pinpoints that spread through the rough fibers of the paper, forming a galaxy of tiny stars. As to that—there was another possibility. Death might conceivably have been due to a pulmonary embolism—a clot in the lung. That would be a not-impossible complication of the septicemia, and could have accounted for the symptoms.

It was a hopeful thought, but not one I placed much credence in. It was the voice of experience, as much as the voice of conscience, that bade me dip the quill and write down "anaphylaxis," before I could think again.

Was anaphylaxis a known medical term yet? I hadn't seen it in any of Rawlings' notes—but then, I hadn't read them all. Still, while death from the shock of allergic reaction was not unknown in any time, it wasn't common, and might not be known by name. Better describe it in detail, for whoever might read this.

And that was the rub, of course. Who *would* read it? I thought it unlikely, but what if a stranger should read this and take my account for a confession of murder? That was far-fetched—but it could happen. I had come perilously close to being executed as a witch, in part because of my healing activities. Once almost burned, twice shy, I thought wryly.

Extensive swelling in affected limb, I wrote, and lifted the quill, the last word fading as the pen ran dry. I dipped it again and scratched doggedly on. *Swelling extended to upper torso, face, and neck. Skin pale, marked with reddish blotches. Respiration increasingly rapid and shallow, heartbeat very fast and light, tending to inaudibility. Palpitations evident. Lips and ears cyanotic. Pronounced exophthalmia.*

I swallowed again, at the thought of Rosamund's eyes, bulging under the lids, rolling to and fro in uncomprehending terror. We had tried to shut them, when we cleansed the body and laid it out for burial. It was customary to uncover the corpse's face for the wake; I thought it unwise in this case.

I didn't want to look at the coffin again, but did, with a small nod of acknowledgment and apology. Brianna's head turned toward me, then sharply away. The smell of the food laid out for the wake was filling the room, mingling with the scents of oak-wood fire and oak-gall ink—and the fresh-planed oak of the coffin's boards. I took another hasty gulp of tea, to stop my gorge rising.

I knew damn well why the first line of Hippocrates' oath was, "First, do no harm." It was too bloody easy to do harm. What hubris it took to lay hands on a person, to interfere. How delicate and complex were bodies, how crude a physician's intrusions.

I could have sought seclusion in surgery or study, to write these notes. I knew why I hadn't. The coarse muslin shroud glowed soft white in the rainy light from the window. I pinched the quill hard between thumb and forefinger, trying to forget the *pop* of the cricoid cartilage, when I had jabbed a penknife into Rosamund's throat in a final, futile attempt to let air into her straining lungs.

And yet . . . there was not one practicing physician, I thought, who had never faced this. I had had it happen a few times before—even in a modern hospital, equipped with every life-saving device known to man—then.

Some future physician here would face the same dilemma; to undertake a possibly dangerous treatment, or to allow a patient to die who *might* have been saved. And that was my own dilemma—to balance the unlikely possibility of prosecution for manslaughter against the unknown value of my records to someone who might seek knowledge in them.

Who might that be? I wiped the pen, thinking. There were as yet few medical schools, and those few, mostly in Europe.

Most physicians gained their knowledge from apprenticeship and experience. I slipped a finger into the casebook, feeling blind between the early pages, kept by the book's original owner.

Rawlings had not gone to a medical school. Though if he had, many of his techniques would still have been shocking by my standards. My mouth twisted at the thought of some of the treatments I had seen described in those closely written pages—infusions of liquid mercury to cure syphilis, cupping and blistering for epileptic fits, lancing and bleeding for every disorder from indigestion to impotence.

And still, Daniel Rawlings had been a doctor. Reading his case notes, I could feel his care for his patients, his curiosity regarding the mysteries of the body.

Moved by impulse, I turned back to the pages containing Rawlings' notes. Perhaps I was only delaying to let my subconscious reach a decision—or perhaps I felt the need of communication, no matter how remote, with another physician, someone like me.

Someone like me. I stared at the page, with its neat, small writing, its careful illustration, seeing none of the details. Who was there, like me?

No one. I had thought of it before, but only vaguely, in the way of a problem acknowledged, but so distant as not to require any urgency. In the colony of North Carolina, so far as I knew, there was only one formally designated "doctor"—Fentiman. I snorted, and took another sip of tea. Better Murray MacLeod and his nostrums—most of those were harmless, at least.

I sipped my tea, regarding Rosamund. The simple truth was that I wouldn't last forever, either. With luck, a good long time yet—but still, not forever. I needed to find someone to whom I could pass on at least the rudiments of what I knew.

A stifled giggle from the table, the girls whispering over the pots of head-cheese, the bowls of sauerkraut and boiled potatoes. No, I thought, with some regret. Not Brianna.

She would be the logical choice; she knew what modern medicine was, at least. There would be no overcoming of ignorance and superstition, no need to convince of the virtues of asepsis, the dangers of germs. But she had no natural inclination, no instinct for healing. She was not squeamish or afraid of blood—she had helped me with any number of childbirths and minor surgical procedures—and yet she lacked that peculiar mixture of empathy and ruthlessness a doctor needs.

She was perhaps Jamie's child more than mine, I reflected, watching the firelight ripple in the falls of her hair as she moved. She had his courage, his great tenderness—but it was the courage of a warrior, the tenderness of a strength that could crush if it chose. I had not managed to give her my gift; the knowledge of blood and bone, the secret ways of the chambers of the heart.

Brianna's head lifted sharply, turning toward the door. Marsali, slower, turned too, listening.

It was barely audible through the thrumming of the rain, but knowing it was there, I could pick it out—a male voice, raised high, chanting. A pause, and then a faint answering rumble that might have been distant thunder, but wasn't. The men were coming down from the shelter on the mountain.

Kenny Lindsay had asked Roger to chant the *caithris* for Rosamund; the formal Gaelic lament for the dead. "She wasna Scots," Kenny had said, wiping eyes bleared from tears and a long night's watching. "Nor even God-fearin'. But she was that fond o' singin', and she fair admired your way o' it, MacKenzie."

Roger had never done a *caithris* before; I knew he had never heard one. "Dinna fash," Jamie had murmured to him, hand on his arm, "all ye need to be is loud." Roger had bent his head gravely in acquiescence, and went with Jamie and Kenneth, to drink whisky by the malting floor and learn what he could of Rosamund's life, the better to lament her passing.

The hoarse chant vanished; the wind had shifted. It was a freak of the storm that we had heard them so soon—they would be headed down the Ridge now, to collect mourners from the outlying cabins, and then to lead them all in procession back up to the house, for the feasting and singing and storytelling that would go on all night.

I yawned involuntarily, my jaw cracking at the thought of it. I'd never last, I thought in dismay. I had had a few hours' sleep in the morning, but not enough to sustain me through a full-blown Gaelic wake and funeral. The floors would be thick with bodies by dawn, all of them smelling of whisky and wet clothes.

I yawned again, then blinked, my eyes swimming as I shook my head to clear it. Every bone in my body ached with fatigue, and I wanted nothing more than to go to bed for several days.

Deep in thought, I hadn't noticed Brianna coming to stand behind me. Her hands came down on my shoulders, and she moved closer, so I felt the warmth of her touching me. Marsali had gone; we were alone. She began to massage my shoulders, long thumbs moving slowly up the cords of my neck.

"Tired?" she asked.

"Mm. I'll do," I said. I closed the book, and leaned back, relaxing momentarily in the sheer relief of her touch. I hadn't realized I was strung so tightly.

THE BIG ROOM was quiet and orderly, ready for the wake. Mrs. Bug was tending the barbecue. The girls had lit a pair of candles, one at each end of the laden table, and shadows flickered over the whitewashed walls, the quiet coffin, as the candle flames bent in a sudden draft.

"I think I killed her," I said suddenly, not meaning to say it at all. "It was the penicillin that killed her."

The long fingers didn't stop their soothing movement.

"Was it?" she murmured. "You couldn't have done any differently, though, could you?"

"No."

A small shudder of relief went over me, as much from the bald confession as from the gradual release of the painful tightness in my neck and shoulders.

"It's okay," she said softly, rubbing, stroking. "She would have died anyway, wouldn't she? It's sad, but you didn't do wrong. You know that."

"I know that." To my surprise, a single tear slid down my cheek and dropped on the page, puckering the paper. I blinked hard, struggling for control. I didn't want to distress Brianna.

She wasn't distressed. Her hands left my shoulders, and I heard the scraping of stool legs. Then her arms came around me, and I let her draw me back, my head resting just under her chin. She simply held me, letting the rise and fall of her breathing calm me.

"I went to dinner with Uncle Joe once, just after he'd lost a patient," she said finally. "He told me about it."

"Did he?" I was a little surprised; I wouldn't have thought Joe would talk about such things with her.

"He didn't mean to. I could see something was bothering him, though, so I asked. And—he needed to talk, and I was there. Afterward, he said it was almost like having you there. I didn't know he called you Lady Jane."

"Yes," I said. "Because of the way I talk, he said." I felt a breath of laughter against my ear, and smiled slightly in response. I closed my eyes, and could see my friend, gesturing in passionate conversation, face alight with the desire to tease.

"He said—that when something like that happened, sometimes there would be a sort of formal inquiry, at the hospital. Not like a trial, not that—but a gathering of the other doctors, to hear exactly what happened, what went wrong. He said it was sort of like confession, to tell it to other doctors, who could understand—and it helped."

"Mm-hm." She was swaying slightly, rocking me as she moved, as she rocked Jemmy, soothing.

"Is that what's bothering you?" she asked quietly. "Not just Rosamund—but that you're alone? You don't have anybody who can really understand?"

Her arms wrapped around my shoulders, her hands crossed, resting lightly on my chest. Young, broad, capable hands, the skin fresh and fair, smelling of fresh-baked bread and strawberry jam. I lifted one, and laid the warm palm against my cheek.

"Apparently I do," I said.

The hand curved, stroked my cheek, and dropped away. The big young hand moved slowly, smoothing the hair behind my ear with soft affection.

"It will be all right," she said. "Everything will be all right."

"Yes," I said, and smiled, despite the tears blurring my eyes.

I couldn't teach her to be a doctor. But evidently I had, without meaning to, somehow taught her to be a mother.

"You should go lie down," she said, taking her hands away reluctantly. "It will be an hour at least, before they get here."

I let my breath go out in a sigh, feeling the peace of the house around me. If Fraser's Ridge had been a short-lived haven for Rosamund Lindsay, still it had been a true home. We would see her safe, and honored in death.

"In a minute," I said, wiping my nose. "I need to finish something, first."

I sat up straight and opened my book. I dipped my pen, and began to write the lines that must be there, for the sake of the unknown physician who would follow me.

107

ZUGUNRUHE

September, 1772

I WOKE DRENCHED in sweat. The thin chemise in which I slept clung to me, transparent with wet; the darkness of my flesh showed in patches through the cloth, even in the dim light from the unshuttered window. I had kicked away sheet and quilt in my disordered sleep, and lay sprawled with the linen shift rucked up above my thighs—but still my skin pulsed with heat, waves of smothering warmth that flowed over me like melted candle wax.

I swung my legs over the side of the bed, and stood up, feeling dizzy and disembodied. My hair was soaked and my neck was slick with perspiration; a trickle of sweat ran down between my breasts and disappeared.

Jamie was still asleep; I could see the humped mound of his upturned shoulder, and the spill of his hair, dark across the pillow. He shifted slightly and mumbled something, but then lapsed into the regular deep breaths of sleep. I needed air, but didn't want to wake him. I pushed away the gauze netting, stepped softly across to the door, and into the small box-room across the hall.

It was a small room, but it had a large window, in order to balance the one in our bedroom. This one had no glass as yet; it was covered only by wooden shutters, and I could feel drafts of night air drifting through the slats, swirling across the floor, caressing my bare legs. Urgent for the coolness of it, I stripped off my wet shift and sighed in relief as the draft skimmed upward over hips and breasts and arms.

The heat was still there, though, hot waves pulsing over my skin with each heartbeat. Fumbling in the dark, I unfastened the shutters and pushed them open, gasping for the great draughts of cool night that flooded in upon me.

From here, I could see above the trees that screened the house, down the slope of the ridge, almost to the faint black line of the river far away. The wind stirred in the treetops, murmuring, and wafted over me with blessed coolness and the pungent green smell of leaves and summer sap. I closed my eyes and stood still; within a minute or two, the heat was gone, vanished like a quenched coal, leaving me damp but peaceful.

I didn't want to go back to bed yet; my hair was damp, and the sheets where I had lain would still be clammy. I leaned naked on the sill, the down-hairs of my body prickling pleasantly as my skin cooled. The peaceful whooshing of the trees was interrupted by the thin sound of a child's wail, and I glanced toward the cabin.

It was a hundred yards from the house; the wind must be toward me, to have carried the sound. Sure enough, the wind changed as I leaned out of the window, and the crying was lost in the flutter of leaves. The breeze passed on, though, and I could hear the screeching, louder now, in the silence.

It was louder because it was getting closer. There was a creak and the groan of wood as the cabin door opened, and someone stepped out. There was no lamp or candle lit in the cabin, and the quick glimpse I had of the emerging figure showed me nothing but a tall form silhouetted against the dim glow of the banked hearth inside. It seemed to have long hair—but both Roger and Brianna slept with their hair untied and capless. It was pleasant to imagine Roger's glossy black locks mingling with the fire of Brianna's on the pillow—did they share a pillow? I wondered suddenly.

The screeching hadn't abated. Fretful and cranky, but not agonized. Not belly-ache. A bad dream? I waited a moment, watching, to see whether whoever it was would bring the child to the house, in search of me, and put out a hand to my crumpled shift, just in case. No—the tall figure had vanished into the spruce grove; I could hear the receding wails. Not fever, then.

I realized that my breasts had begun to tingle and stiffen in response to the crying, and smiled, a little ruefully. Strange, that instinct went so deep and lasted so long—would I come one day to a point when nothing in me stirred to the sound of a crying baby, to the scent of a man aroused, to the brush of my own long hair against the skin of my naked back? And if I did come to such a point—would I mourn the loss, I wondered, or find myself peaceful, left to contemplate existence without the intrusion of such animal sensations?

It wasn't only the glories of the flesh that were the gifts of the world, after all; a doctor sees the plentiful miseries flesh is heir to, as well—and yet . . . standing cool in the flood of late summer's air from the window, the boards smooth under my bare feet and the touch of wind on bare skin . . . I could not wish to be a pure spirit—not yet.

The crying grew louder, and I heard the low murmur of an adult's voice below it, trying unsuccessfully to soothe it. Roger, then.

I cupped my breasts gently, liking the soft, full weight of them. I remembered what they'd been like when I was very young; small hard swellings, so sensitive that the touch of a boy's hand made me weak in the knees. The touch of my own hand, come to that. They were different now—and yet peculiarly the same.

This was not the discovery of a new and unimagined

thing, but rather only a new awareness, the acknowledgment of something that had risen while my back was turned, like a shadow cast upon the wall, its presence unsuspected, seen only when I turned to look at it—but there all the time.

Oh, I have a little shadow that goes in and out with me,
And what can be the use of him, is more than I can see.

And if I turned my back again, the shadow would not leave me. It was irrevocably attached to me, whether I chose to notice it or not, crouched always insubstantial, intangible but *present*, small to vanishing under my feet when the light of other preoccupations shone upon me, blown up to gigantic proportions in the glare of some sudden urge.

Resident demon, or guardian angel? Or only the shadow of the beast, constant reminder of the inescapability of the body and its hungers?

Another noise mingled with the whinging below; coughing, I thought, but it didn't stop, and the rhythm sounded wrong. I put my head out, cautious as a snail after a thunderstorm, and made out a few words in the rasping gurgle.

" . . . excavating for a mine . . . forty-niner . . . da-aughter, Clementine."

Roger was singing.

I felt the tears sting my eyes, and drew my head in hastily, lest I be seen. There was no tune to it—the pitch varied no more than the hooting of wind across the mouth of an empty bottle—and yet it was music. A dogged, ragged gasp of a song, and yet Jemmy's wailing quieted to sniffling sobs, as though he was trying to make out the words, so painfully forced through his father's scarred throat.

"Fed she duck-lings . . . by the wa-ter . . ." He was having to gasp for breath after each whispered phrase, the sound of it like tearing linen. I curled my fingers into fists, as though by sheer force of will I could help him get the words out.

"Herring box-es . . . without top-ses . . . san-dals were for . . . Clementine." The breeze was rising again, stirring in the tops of the trees. The next line was lost in their rustle, and I heard no more for a minute or two, strain my ears as I would.

Then I saw Jamie, standing still.

He made no noise, but I felt him at once; a warmth, a thickening, in the cool air of the room.

"Are ye well, Sassenach?" he asked softly from the doorway.

"Yes, fine." I spoke in a whisper, not to wake Lizzie and her father, who slept in the back bedroom. "Just needed a breath of air; I didn't mean to wake you."

He came closer, a tall naked ghost, smelling of sleep.

"I always wake when you do, Sassenach; I sleep ill without ye by my side." He touched my forehead briefly. "I thought ye were maybe fevered; the bed was damp where ye'd lain. You're sure you're all right?"

"I was hot; I couldn't sleep. But yes, I'm all right. And you?" I touched his face; his skin was warm with sleep.

He came to stand beside me at the window, looking out into the late summer night. The moon was full, and the birds were restless; from near at hand, I heard the faint chirp of a late-nesting warbler, and farther off, the squeak of a hunting saw-whet owl.

"You recall Laurence Sterne?" Jamie asked, evidently reminded of the naturalist by the sounds.

"I doubt anyone who's met him would forget him," I said dryly. "The bag of dried spiders makes rather an impression. To say nothing of the smell." Sterne carried with him a distinctive aroma, composed in equal parts of natural body odor, an expensive cologne that he favored—which was sufficiently strong to compete with—though not to conquer—the pungencies of various preservatives such as camphor and alcohol—and a faint reek of decay from the specimens he collected.

He chuckled softly.

"That's true. He stinks worse than you do."

"I do not stink!" I said indignantly.

"Mmphm." He took my hand and lifted it to his nose, sniffing delicately. "Onions," he said, "and garlic. Something hot . . . peppercorns. Aye, and clove. Squirrel-blood and meat-juice." His tongue flicked out like a snake's, touching my knuckles. "Starch—potatoes—and something woody. Toadstools."

"Not fair at all," I said, trying to get my hand back. "You

know perfectly well what we had for dinner. And they weren't toadstools, they were woodears."

"Mm?" He turned my hand over and sniffed at my palm, then my wrist and up my forearm. "Vinegar and dill; ye've been making cucumber pickles, aye? Good, I like those. Mm, oh, and soured milk here in the fine hairs on your arm—were ye splashed churning butter, or skimming cream?"

"You guess, since you're so good at it."

"Butter."

"Damn." I was still trying to pull away, but only because the stubble on his face tickled the sensitive skin of my upper arm. He smelled his way up my arm into the hollow of my shoulder, making me squeak as the strands of his hair drifted across my skin.

He lifted my arm a bit, touched the damp silky hair there, and ran his fingers under his nose. *"Eau de femme,"* he murmured, and I heard the laughter in his voice. *"Ma petite fleur."*

"And I *bathed*, too," I said ruefully.

"Aye, with the sunflower soap," he said, a slight tone of surprise in his voice as he sniffed at the hollow of my collarbone. I gave a small, high-pitched yelp, and he reached up to lay a large, warm hand across my mouth. *He* smelt of gunpowder, hay, and manure, but I couldn't say so, what with him muffling me.

He straightened a little, and leaned close, so the roughness of his whiskers brushed my cheek. His hand fell away, and I felt the softness of his lips against my temple, the butterfly touch of his tongue on my skin.

"And salt," he said, very softly, his breath warm on my face. "There is salt on your face, and your lashes are wet. D'ye weep, Sassenach?"

"No," I said, though I had a sudden, irrational urge to do just that. "No, I sweat. I was . . . hot."

I wasn't any longer; my skin was cool; cold where the night-draft from the window chilled my backside.

"Ah, but here . . . mm." He was on his knees now, one arm about my waist to hold me still, his nose buried in the hollow between my breasts. "Oh," he said, and his voice had changed again.

I didn't normally wear perfume, but I had a special oil,

sent from the Indies, made with orange flowers, jasmine, vanilla beans, and cinnamon. I had only a tiny vial, and wore a small dab infrequently—for occasions that I thought might perhaps be special.

"Ye wanted me," he said ruefully. "And I fell asleep without even touching you. I'm sorry, Sassenach. Ye should have said."

"You were tired." His hand had left my mouth; I stroked his hair, smoothing the long dark strands behind his ear. He laughed, and I felt the warmth of his breath on my bare stomach.

"Ye could raise me from the dead for that, Sassenach, and I wouldna mind it."

He stood up then, facing me, and even in the dim light I could see that no such desperate measures on my part would be required.

"It's hot," I said. "I'm sweating."

"Ye think I'm not?"

His hands closed on my waist and he lifted me suddenly, setting me down on the broad windowsill. I gasped at contact with the cool wood, reflexively grasping the window frame on either side.

"What on earth are you doing?"

He didn't bother answering; it was an entirely rhetorical question, in any case.

"Eau de femme," he murmured, his soft hair brushing across my thighs as he knelt. The floorboards creaked under his weight. "*Parfum d'amour*, mm?"

The cool breeze lifted my hair, drew it tickling across my back like the lightest of lover's touches. Jamie's hands were firm on the curve of my hips; I was in no danger of falling, and yet I felt the dizzy drop behind me, the clear and endless night, with its star-strewn empty sky into which I might fall and go on falling, a tiny speck, blazing hotter and hotter with the friction of my passage, bursting finally into the incandescence of a shooting . . . star.

"Ssh," Jamie murmured, far off. He was standing now, his hands on my waist, and the moaning noise might have been the wind, or me. His fingers brushed my lips. They might have been matches, striking flames against my skin. Heat danced over me, belly and breast, neck and face, burning in front, cool behind, like St. Lawrence on his gridiron.

I wrapped my legs around him, one heel settled in the cleft of his buttocks, the solid strength of his hips between my legs my only anchor.

"Let go," he said in my ear. "I'll hold you." I did let go, and leaned back on the air, safe in his hands.

"YOU DID START OUT to tell me something about Laurence Sterne," I murmured drowsily, much later.

"So I did." Jamie stretched and settled himself, a hand curved proprietorially over my buttock. My knuckles brushed the hairs on his thigh. It was too hot to lie pressed together, but we didn't want to separate entirely.

"We were talking of birds; he bein' uncommon fond of them. I asked him why it was that in the late summer, the birds sing at night—the nights are shorter then, ye'd think they'd want their rest, but no. There's rustling and twittering and all manner o' carryings-on, all the night long in the hedges and the trees."

"Are there? I hadn't noticed."

"Ye're no in the habit of sleeping in the forest, Sassenach," he said tolerantly. "I have been, and so had Sterne. He'd noticed the same thing, he said, and wondered why."

"And did he have an answer?"

"Not an answer—but a theory, at least."

"Oh, even better," I said, in sleepy amusement.

He gave a soft grunt of agreement and rolled slightly to one side, admitting a little welcome air between our salty skins. I could see the gleam of moisture over the slope of his shoulder, and the prickle of sweat among the dark curly hairs of his chest. He scratched gently at it, with a softly agreeable rasping sound.

"What he did was to capture a number of the birds, and shut them up in cages lined with blotting paper."

"What?" That waked me up a bit, if only to laugh. "Whatever for?"

"Well, not lined entirely, only on the floor," he explained.

"He put out a wee plate on the floor filled with ink and a cup of seed in the middle, so that they couldna feed without getting the ink on their feet. Then as they hopped to and fro, their footprints would show on the blotting paper."

"Umm. And what, precisely, did that show—other than black footprints?"

The insects were beginning to find us, drawn by the musk of our heated flesh. A tiny *zeeeeee* by my ear prompted me to slap at the invisible mosquito, then reach for the gauze-cloth that Jamie had pushed back when he rose to find me. This was fastened to an ingenious mechanism—Brianna's invention—fixed to the beam above the bed, so that when unrolled, the cloth fell down on all sides, shielding us from the bloodthirsty hordes of the summer nights.

I pulled it into place with some regret, for while it excluded mosquitoes, gnats, and the unnervingly large mosquito-hawk moths, it also unavoidably shut out some of the air and all sight of the luminous night sky beyond the window. I lay down again at a little distance on the bed; while Jamie's natural furnace was a great boon on winter nights, it had its drawbacks in the summer. I didn't mind melting in an inferno of blazing desire, if it came to that, but I had no more clean shifts.

"There were a great many footprints, Sassenach—but most of them were on one side of the cage. In all the cages."

"Oh, really? And what did Sterne think that signified?"

"Well, he had the bright thought of putting down a compass by the cages. And it seems that all the night through, the birds were hopping and striving toward the southeast—which is the direction in which they migrate, come the fall."

"That's very interesting." I pulled my hair back into a tail, lifting it off my neck for coolness. "But it's not quite the time to migrate, is it, in late summer? And they don't fly at night, do they, even when they migrate?"

"No. It was as though they felt the imminence of flight, and the pull of it—and that disturbed their rest. The stranger it was, because most of the birds that he had were young ones, who had never yet made the journey; they hadna seen the place where they were bound, and yet they felt it there—calling to them, perhaps, rousing them from sleep."

I moved slightly, and Jamie lifted his hand from my leg.

"Zugunruhe," he said softly, tracing with a fingertip the damp mark he had left on my skin.

"What's that?"

"It's what Sterne called it—the wakefulness of the wee birds, getting ready to leave on their long flight."

"Does it mean something in particular?"

"Aye. 'Ruhe' is stillness, rest. And 'zug' is a journey of some sort. So 'zugunruhe' is a restlessness—the uneasiness before a long journey."

I rolled toward him, butting my forehead affectionately against his shoulder. I inhaled, in the style of one savoring the delicate aroma of a fine cigar.

"Eau d'homme?"

He raised his head and sniffed dubiously, wrinkling up his nose.

"*Eau de chèvre,* I think," he said. "Though it might be something worse. Is there a French word for skunk, I wonder?"

"Le Pew." I suggested, giggling.

The birds sang all night.

108

TULACH ARD

October, 1772

JAMIE NODDED at something behind him, smiling. "I see we've help today."

Roger looked back to see Jemmy stumping along behind them, his small fair brow furrowed in fierce concentration, a fist-sized rock clutched to his chest with both hands. Roger wanted to laugh at the sight, but instead turned and squatted down, waiting for the boy to catch them up.

"Is that for the new hogpen, *a ghille ruaidh*?" he said.

Jemmy nodded solemnly. The morning was still cool, but the little boy's cheeks glowed with effort.

"Thank you," Roger said gravely. He held out his hand. "Shall I take it, then?"

Jemmy shook his head violently, heavy fringe flying.

"Me do!"

"It's a long walk, *a ghille ruaidh*," Jamie said. "And your mother will miss ye, no?"

"No!"

"Grand-da's right, *a bhalaich*, Mummy needs you," Roger said, reaching for the rock. "Here, let me take . . ."

"No!" Jemmy clutched the rock protectively against his smock, mouth set in a stubborn line.

"But ye can't . . ." Jamie began.

"Come!"

"No, I said ye must . . ." Roger began.

"COME!"

"Now, look, lad—" both men began together, then stopped, looked at each other, and laughed.

"Where's Mummy, then?" Roger said, trying another tack. "Mummy will be worried about you, aye?"

The small red head shook in vehement negation.

"Claire said the women meant to be quilting today," Jamie said to Roger. "Marsali's brought a pattern; they'll maybe have started the stitching of it." He squatted down beside Roger, eye to eye with his grandson.

"Have ye got away from your mother, then?"

The soft pink mouth, hitherto clamped tight, twitched, allowing a small giggle to escape.

"Thought so," Roger said in resignation. "Come on, then. Back to the house." He stood up and swung the little boy up into his arms, rock and all.

"No, no! NO!" Jemmy stiffened in resistance, his feet digging painfully into Roger's belly as his body arched backward like a bow. "Me help! Me HELP!"

Trying to make his own arguments heard through Jemmy's roars without shouting, while at the same time keeping the boy from falling backward onto his head, Roger didn't at first hear the cries from the direction of the house. When he finally resorted to clapping a hand over his offspring's wide-open mouth, though, feminine calls of "Jeeeeemmmeeeeeeee!" were clearly audible through the trees.

"See, Mrs. Lizzie's looking for ye," Jamie said to his grandson, jerking a thumb toward the sound.

"Not only Lizzie," Roger said. More women's voices were echoing the chorus, with increasing notes of annoyance. "Mum and Grannie Claire and Grannie Bug and Auntie Marsali, too, from the sounds of it. They don't sound very pleased with you, lad."

"We'd best take him, back, then," Jamie said. He looked at his grandson, not without sympathy. "Mind, you're like to get your bum smacked, laddie. Women dinna like it when ye run off on them."

This threatening prospect caused Jemmy to drop his rock and wrap his arms and legs tightly round Roger.

"Go with YOU, Daddy," he said coaxingly.

"But Mummy—"

"NO MUMMY! Want Daddy!"

Roger patted Jemmy's back, small but solid under his grubby smock. He was torn; this was the first time Jem had so definitely wanted *him* in preference to Bree, and he had to admit to a sneaking feeling of flattery. Even if his son's present partiality sprang as much from an urge to avoid punishment as from a desire for his company, Jem *had* wanted to come with him.

"I suppose we could take him," he said to Jamie, over Jem's head, now nestled trustingly against his collarbone. "Just for the morning; I could fetch him back at noon."

"Oh, aye," Jamie said. He smiled at his grandson, picked up the fallen stone, and handed it back to him. "Building hogpens is proper man's work, aye? None of this prinking and yaffling the ladies are so fond of."

"Speaking of yaffling . . ." Roger lifted his chin in the

direction of the house, where the cries of "JEEMEEEEE!" were now taking on a distinctly irritated tone, tinged with panic. "We'd best tell them we have him."

"I'll go." Jamie dropped the rucksack off his shoulder with a sigh, and raised one eyebrow at his grandson. "Mind, lad, ye owe me. When women are in a fret, they'll take it out on the first man they see, whether he's to blame or not. Like enough I'll get *my* bum smacked." He rolled his eyes, but grinned at Jemmy, then turned and set off for the house at a trot.

Jemmy giggled.

"Smack, Grand-da!" he called.

"Hush, wee rascal." Roger gave him a soft slap on the bottom, and realized that Jem was wearing short breeks under his smock, but no clout under them. He swung the boy down onto his feet.

"D'ye need to go potty?" he asked automatically, falling into Brianna's peculiar idiom.

"No," Jem said, just as automatically, but with a reflexive kneading of his crotch that made his father take him by the arm, firmly steering him off the path and behind a convenient bush.

"Come on. Let's have a try, while we wait for Grand-da."

IT SEEMED RATHER a long time before Jamie reappeared, though the indignant cries of the searchers had been quickly stilled. If Jamie had got his bum smacked, Roger thought cynically, he appeared to have enjoyed it. A slight flush showed on the high cheekbones, and he wore a faint but definite air of satisfaction.

This was explained at once, though, when Jamie produced a small bundle from inside his shirt and unwrapped a linen towel, revealing half a dozen fresh biscuits, still warm, and dripping with melted butter and honey.

"I think perhaps Mrs. Bug meant them for the quilting circle," he said, distributing the booty. "But there was plenty of batter left in the bowl; I doubt they'll be missed."

"If they are, I'll blame it on you," Roger assured him, catching a dribble of warm honey that ran down his wrist. He wiped it off and sucked his finger, eyes closing momentarily in ecstasy.

"What now, ye'd give me up to the Inquisition?" Jamie's eyes creased into blue triangles of amusement as he wiped crumbs from his mouth. "And after I shared my plunder with ye, too—there's gratitude!"

"Your reputation will stand it," Roger said wryly. "Jem and I are *persona non grata* after what happened to her spice cake last week, but Himself can do no wrong, as far as Grannie Bug is concerned. She wouldn't mind if you ate the entire contents of the pantry single-handed."

Jamie licked a smear of honey from the corner of his mouth, with the smug complacency of a man permanently in Mrs. Bug's good books.

"Well, that's as may be," he admitted. "Still, if ye expect to blame it on me, we'd best wipe a bit of the evidence off the laddie before we go home."

Jemmy had been addressing himself to his treat with single-minded concentration, with the result that his entire face gleamed with butter, daubs of honey ran in amber trails down his smock, and what appeared to be several small globs of half-chewed biscuit were stuck in his hair.

"How in hell did you do that so fast?" Roger demanded in amazement. "Look what ye've done to your shirt! Your mother will kill us both." He took the towel and made an abortive attempt to wipe some of the mess off, but succeeded only in spreading it farther.

"Dinna fash," Jamie said tolerantly. "He'll be so covered wi' filth by the end of the day, his mother will never notice a few crumbs extra. Watch out, lad!" A quick grab saved half a biscuit that had broken off as the boy made an attempt to cram the last pastry into his mouth in a single gulp.

"Still," Jamie said, biting thoughtfully into the rescued biscuit-half as he looked at his grandson, "perhaps we'll souse him in the creek a bit. We dinna want the pigs to smell the honey on him."

A faint qualm of unease went over Roger, as he realized that Jamie was in fact not joking about the pigs. It was common to see or hear pigs in the wood nearby, rooting through the leaf-mold under oaks and poplars, or grunting blissfully over a trove of chestnut mast. Food was plentiful at this season, and the pigs were no threat to grown men. A small boy, though, smelling of sweetness . . . you thought of pigs as only eating roots and nuts, but Roger had a vivid memory of the big white sow, seen a few days before, with the naked, blood-smeared tail of a possum dangling from her maw as she champed placidly away.

A chunk of biscuit seemed to be stuck in his throat. He picked Jemmy up, despite the stickiness, and tucked him giggling under one arm, so the little boy's arms and legs dangled in the air.

"Come on, then," Roger said, resigned. "Mummy won't like it a bit, if you get eaten by a pig."

FENCE POLES LAY piled near the stone pillar. Roger dug about until he found a splintered piece short enough for convenience, and used it to lever a big chunk of granite up far enough to get both hands under it. Squatting, he got it onto his thighs, and very slowly stood up, his back straightening one vertebra at a time, fingers digging into the lichen-splotched surface with the effort of lifting. The rag tied round his head was drenched, and perspiration was running down his face. He shook his head to flick the stinging sweat out of his eyes.

"Daddy, Daddy!"

Roger felt a sudden tug at his breeches, blinked sweat out of his eye, and planted his feet well apart to keep his balance without dropping the heavy rock. He tightened his grip and glanced down, annoyed.

"What, lad?"

Jemmy had tight hold of the cloth with both hands. He was looking toward the wood.

"Pig, Daddy," he whispered. "*Big* pig."

Roger glanced in the direction of the little boy's gaze and froze.

It was a huge black boar, perhaps eight feet away. The thing stood more than three feet at the shoulder, and must weigh two hundred pounds or more, with curving yellow tushes the length of Jemmy's forearm. It stood with lifted head, piggy snout moistly working as it snuffed the air for food or threat.

"Shit," Roger said involuntarily.

Jemmy, who would normally have seized on any inadvertent vulgarity and trumpeted it gleefully, now merely clung tighter to his father's leg.

Thoughts raced through Roger's mind like colliding freight cars. Would it attack if he moved? He had to move; the muscles of his arms were trembling under the strain. He'd splashed Jem with water; did the boy still smell—or look—like something on the pig's menu?

He picked one coherent thought out of the wreckage.

"Jem," he said, his voice very calm, "get behind me. Do it *now*," he added with emphasis, as the boar turned its head in their direction.

It saw them; he could see the small dark eyes change focus. It took a few steps forward, its hooves absurdly small and dainty under its menacing bulk.

"Do you see Grand-da, Jem?" he asked, keeping his voice calm. Streaks of fire were burning through his arms, and his elbows felt as though they'd been crushed in a vise.

"No," Jemmy whispered. Roger could feel the little boy crowding close behind him, pressed against his legs.

"Well, look round. He went to the stream; he'll be coming back from that direction. Turn round and look."

The boar was cautious, but not afraid. That was what came of not hunting the things sufficiently, he thought. They ought to be gutting a few in the wood once a week, as an object lesson to the rest.

"Grand-da!" Jemmy's voice rang out from behind him, shrill with fear.

At the sound, the pig's hackles sprang suddenly erect in a ridge of coarse hair down its spine and it lowered its head, muscles bunching.

"Run, Jem!" Roger cried. "Run to Grand-da!" A surge of adrenaline shot through him and suddenly the rock weighed nothing. He flung it at the charging pig, catching it on the shoulder. It gave a *whuff!* of surprise, faltered, then opened its mouth with a roar and came at him, tushes slashing as it swung its head.

He couldn't duck aside and let it go past; Jem was still close behind him. He kicked it in the jaw with all his strength, then flung himself on it, grasping for a hold round its neck.

His fingers slipped and slid, unable to get a firm grip on the wiry hair, stubbing and sliding off the hard rolls of tight-packed flesh. Christ, it was like wrestling an animated sack of concrete! He felt something warm and wet on his hand and jerked it back; had it slashed him? He felt no pain. Maybe only saliva from the gnashing jaws—maybe blood from a gash too deep to feel. No time to look. He thrust the hand back down, flailing blindly, got his fingers round a hairy leg, and pulled hard.

The pig fell sideways with a squeal of surprise, throwing him off its back. He hit the ground on hands and one knee, and his knee struck stone. A bolt of pain shot from ankle to groin, and he curled up involuntarily, momentarily paralyzed from the shock.

The boar was up, shaking itself with a grunt and a rattle of bristles, but facing away from him. Dust rose from its coat and he could see the corkscrew tail, coiled up tight against its rump. A second more, and the pig would turn, rip him from gut to gullet, and stamp on the pieces. He grabbed for a rock, but it burst in his hand, nothing but a clod of dirt.

The gasp and thud of a running man came from his left, and he heard a breathless shout.

"Tulach Ard! Tulach Ard!"

The boar heard Jamie's cry and swung snorting round to meet this new enemy, mouth agape and eyes gone red with rage.

Jamie had his dirk in his hand; Roger saw the gleam of metal as Jamie dropped low and swung it wide, slashing at the boar, then danced aside as it charged. A knife. Fight that thing with a *knife*?

You are out of your fucking mind, Roger thought quite clearly.

"No, I'm not," Jamie said, panting, and Roger realized

that he must have spoken aloud. Jamie crouched, balanced on the balls of his feet, and reached his free hand toward Roger, his eyes still fastened on the pig, which had paused, kneading the ground with its hooves and clashing its teeth, swinging its head back and forth between the two men, estimating its chances.

"Bioran!" Jamie said, beckoning urgently. "Stick, spear—gie it to me!"

Spear . . . the splintered fence-pole. His numbed leg still wouldn't work, but he could move. He threw himself to the side, grabbed the ragged shaft of wood, and fell back on his haunches, bracing it before him like a boar-spear, sharp end pointed toward the foe.

"Tulach Ard!" he bellowed. "Come here, you fat fucker!"

Distracted for an instant, the boar swung toward him. Jamie lunged at it, stabbing down, aiming between the shoulder blades. There was a piercing squeal and the boar wheeled, blood flying from a deep gash in its shoulder. Jamie threw himself sideways, tripped on something, fell, and skidded hard across the mud and grass, the knife spinning from his outflung hand.

Lunging forward, Roger jabbed his makeshift spear as hard as he could just below the boar's tail. The animal uttered a piercing squeal and appeared to rise straight into the air. The spear jerked through his hands, rough bark ripping skin off his palms. He grabbed it hard and managed to keep hold of it as the boar crashed onto its side in a blur of writhing fury, gnashing, roaring, and spraying blood and black mud in all directions.

Jamie was up, mud-streaked and bellowing. He'd got hold of another fence-pole, with which he took a mighty swing at the rising pig, the wood meeting its head with a crack like a well-hit baseball just as the animal achieved its feet. The boar, mildly stunned, gave a grunt and sat down.

A shrill cry from behind made Roger whirl on his haunches. Jemmy, his grandfather's dirk held over his head with both hands and wobbling precariously, was staggering toward the boar, his face beet-red with ferocious intent.

"Jem!" he shouted. "Get back!"

The boar grunted loudly behind him, and Jamie shouted

something. Roger had no attention to spare; he lunged toward his son, but caught a flicker of movement from the wood beyond Jemmy that made him glance up. A streak of gray, low to the ground and moving so fast that he had no more than an impression of its nature.

That was enough.

"Wolves!" he shouted to Jamie, and with a feeling that wolves on top of pigs was patently unfair, reached Jemmy, grabbed the knife, and threw himself on top of the boy.

He pressed himself to the ground, feeling Jemmy squirm frantically under him, and waited, feeling strangely calm. Would it be tusk or tooth? he wondered.

"It's all right, Jem. Be still. It's all right, Daddy's got you." His forehead was pressed against the earth, Jem's head tucked in the hollow of his shoulder. He had one arm sheltering the little boy, the knife gripped in his other hand. He hunched his shoulders, feeling the back of his neck bare and vulnerable, but couldn't move to protect it.

He could hear the wolf now, howling and yipping to its companions. The boar was making an ungodly noise, a sort of long, continuous scream, and Jamie, too short of breath to go on shouting, seemed to be calling it names in brief, incoherent bursts of Gaelic.

There was an odd whirr overhead and a peculiar, hollow-sounding *thump!*, succeeded by sudden and utter silence.

Startled, Roger raised his head a few inches, and saw the pig standing a few feet before him, its jaw hanging open in what looked like sheer astonishment. Jamie was standing behind it, smeared from forehead to knee with blood-streaked mud, and wearing an identical expression.

Then the boar's front legs gave way and it fell to its knees. It wobbled, eyes glazing, and collapsed onto its side, the shaft of an arrow poking up, looking frail and inconsequential by comparison to the animal's bulk.

Jemmy was squirming and crying underneath him. He sat up slowly, and gathered the little boy up into his arms. He noticed, remotely, that his hands were shaking, but he felt curiously blank. The torn skin on his palms stung, and his knee was throbbing. Patting Jemmy's back in automatic comfort, he turned his head toward the wood and saw the Indian standing at the edge of the trees, bow in hand.

It occurred to him, dimly, to look for the wolf. It was nosing at the pig's carcass, no more than a few feet from Jamie, but his father-in-law was paying it no mind at all. He too was staring at the Indian.

"Ian," he said softly, and a look of incredulous joy blossomed slowly through the smears of mud, grass, and blood. "Oh, Christ. It's Ian."

109

THE VOICE OF TIME

AS LIZZIE HAD NO MOTHER to see to her proper "fitting out" for marriage, the women on the Ridge had grouped together to provide things like petticoats, nightgowns, and knitted stockings, with a few of the more talented ladies piecing quilt blocks. When a quilt-top was completed, everyone would come up to the "Big House" to see to the actual quilting—the laborious stitching together of quilt-top and backing, with whatever might be available in the way of batting—worn-out blankets, stitched-together rags, or wool-combings—laid in between quilt-top and backing for warmth.

I had neither great talent nor great patience for sewing generally, but I did have the manual dexterity for small, fine stitches. More importantly, I had a large kitchen with good light and enough room for a quilting-frame, plus the services of Mrs. Bug, who kept the quilters well supplied with mugs of tea and endless plates of apple scones.

We were in the midst of quilting a block pattern Mrs.

Evan Lindsay had pieced out in creams and blues, when Jamie appeared suddenly in the door to the hallway. Caught up in an absorbing conversation about the snoring of husbands in general and theirs in particular, most of the women didn't notice him, but I was facing the door. He seemed not to want to interrupt, or to attract attention, for he didn't come into the room—but once he'd caught my eye, he jerked his head urgently, and disappeared toward his study.

I glanced at Bree, who was sitting next to me. She'd seen him; she raised an eyebrow and shrugged. I popped the knot—jerking the knotted end of my thread up between the layers of fabric, so it wouldn't show—stabbed my needle through the quilt-top, and got up, murmuring an excuse.

"Give him beer to his supper," Mrs. Chisholm was advising Mrs. Aberfeldy. "A great deal of it, and well-watered. That way, he'll have to wake to piss every half-hour, and can't get started wi' the sort of rumption that shakes the shingles loose."

"Oh, aye," Mrs. Aberfeldy objected. "I tried that. But then when he comes back to bed, he's wantin' to . . . mmphm." She flushed red as the ladies all cackled. "I get less sleep than I do with the snorin'!"

Jamie was waiting in the hall. The moment I appeared, he grabbed me by the arm and hustled me out of the front door.

"What—" I began, bewildered. Then I saw the tall Indian sitting on the edge of the stoop.

"What—" I said again, and then he stood up, turned, and smiled at me.

"Ian!" I shrieked, and flung myself into his arms.

He was thin and hard as a piece of sun-dried rawhide, and his clothes smelled of wood-damp and earth, with a faint echo of the smoke and body-smells of a long-house. I stood back, wiping my eyes, to look at him, and a cold nose nudged my hand, making me utter another small shriek.

"You!" I said to Rollo. "I thought I'd never see you again!" Overcome with emotion, I rubbed his ears madly. He uttered a short bark and dropped to his forepaws, wagging equally madly.

"Dog! Dog-dog! Here, dog!" Jemmy burst from the door of his own cabin, running as fast as his short legs would carry him, wet hair standing on end and face beaming. Rollo shot toward him, hitting him amidships and bowling him over in a flurry of squeals.

I had at first feared that Rollo—who was, after all, half-wolf—saw Jemmy as prey, but it was immediately apparent that the two were merely engaged in mutually ecstatic play. Brianna's maternal sonar had picked up the squealing, though, and she came rushing to the door.

"What—" she began, eyes going to the melee taking place on the grass. Then Ian stepped forward, took her in his arms, and kissed her. Her shriek in turn brought the quilting circle boiling out onto the porch, in an eruption of questions, exclamations, and small subsidiary shrieks in acknowledgment of the general excitement.

In the midst of the resulting pandemonium, I suddenly noticed that Roger, who had appeared from somewhere, was sporting a fresh raw graze across his forehead, a black eye, and a clean shirt. I glanced at Jamie, who was standing next to me watching the goings-on, his face wreathed in a permanent grin. His shirt, by contrast, was not only filthy but ripped down the front, and with an enormous rent in one sleeve. There were huge smears of mud and dried blood on the linen, too, though I didn't see any fresh blood showing. Given Jemmy's wet hair and clean shirt—not that it was, anymore—this was all highly suspicious.

"What on earth have you lot been doing?" I demanded.

He shook his head, still grinning.

"It doesna signify, Sassenach. Though I have got a fresh hog for ye to butcher—when ye've the time."

I pushed back a lock of hair in exasperation.

"Is this the local equivalent of killing the fatted calf in honor of the prodigal's return?" I asked, nodding at Ian, who was by now completely submerged in a tide of women. Lizzie, I saw, was clinging to one of his arms, her pale face absolutely ablaze with excitement. I felt a slight qualm, seeing it, but pushed it away for the moment.

"Has Ian brought friends? Or—his family, perhaps?" He had said his wife was expecting, and that was nearly two years back. The child—if all had gone well—must be nearly old enough to walk.

Jamie's smile dimmed a little at that.

"No," he said. "He's alone. Save for the dog, of course," he added, with a nod at Rollo, who was lying on his back, paws in the air, squirming happily under Jemmy's onslaught.

"Oh. Well." I smoothed down my hair and re-tied the ribbon, beginning to think what ought to be done regarding the quilters, the fresh hog, and some sort of celebratory supper—though I supposed Mrs. Bug would deal with that.

"How long is he staying, did he say?"

Jamie took a deep breath, putting a hand on my back.

"For good," he said, and his voice was full of joy—but with an odd tinge of sadness that made me look up at him in puzzlement. "He's come home."

IT WAS VERY LATE indeed before the butchering, the quilting, and the supper were all finished, and the visitors finally left, charged with gossip. Though not so much gossip as all that; Ian had been friendly to everyone, but reticent, saying very little about his journey from the north—and nothing at all about the reasons behind it.

"Did Ian tell you anything?" I asked Jamie, finding him temporarily alone in his study before dinner. He shook his head.

"Verra little. Only that he had come back to stay."

"Do you suppose something dreadful happened to his wife? And the baby?" I felt a deep pang of distress, both for Ian, and for the slight, pretty Mohawk girl called Wakyo'teyehsnonhsa—Works With Her Hands. Ian had called her Emily. Death in childbirth was not uncommon, even among the Indians.

Jamie shook his head again, looking sober.

"I dinna ken, but I think it must be something of the kind. He hasna spoken of them at all—and the lad's eyes are a great deal older than he is."

Lizzie had appeared at the door then, with an urgent message from Mrs. Bug regarding dispositions for supper, and I had to go. Following Lizzie toward the kitchen, though, I couldn't help wondering just what Ian's return might mean to her—particularly if we were right in our suppositions about Ian's Mohawk wife.

Lizzie had been half in love with Ian, before he had left, and had pined for months following his decision to stay with the Kahnyen'kehaka. But that was more than two years ago, and two years can be a very long time, especially in a young person's life.

I knew what Jamie meant about Ian's eyes, and knew for certain that he wasn't the same impulsive, cheerful lad we had left with the Mohawk. Lizzie wasn't quite the timidly adoring girl-mouse she had been, either.

What she *was*, though, was Manfred McGillivray's betrothed. I could only be thankful that neither Ute McGillivray nor any of her daughters had been present at this afternoon's quilting circle. With luck, the glamor of Ian's return would be short-lived.

"Will you be all right down here?" I asked Ian, dubiously. I had put several quilts and a goose-down pillow on the surgery table for him, he having politely rejected Mr. Wemyss's offer of his own bed and Mrs. Bug's desire to make him a comfortable pallet before the kitchen hearth.

"Oh, aye, Auntie," he said, and grinned at me. "Ye wouldna credit the places Rollo and I have been sleeping." He stretched, yawning and blinking. "Christ—I've no been up past sunset anytime this month or more."

"And up at dawn, too, I expect. That's why I thought you might be better in here; no one will disturb you, if you'd like to sleep late in the morning."

He laughed at that.

"Only if I leave the window open, so Rollo can come and go as he likes. Though he seems to think the huntin' might be good enough inside."

Rollo was seated in the middle of the floor, muzzle lifted in anticipation, his yellow wolf-eyes fixed unwaveringly on the upper cupboard door. A low rumbling noise, like water bumping in a kettle, issued from behind the door.

"I'll gie ye odds on the cat, Ian," Jamie observed, coming into the surgery. "He's a verra high opinion of himself, has wee Adso. I saw him chase a fox, last week."

"The fact that you were behind him with a gun had nothing to do with the fox's running away, of course," I said.

"Well, not so far as yon cheetie's concerned," Jamie agreed, grinning.

"Cheetie," Ian repeated softly. "It feels . . . verra good to speak Scots again, Uncle Jamie."

Jamie's hand brushed Ian's arm lightly.

"I suppose it does, *a mhic a pheathar*," he said, just as softly. "Will ye have forgot all your Gaelic, then?"

" 'S beag 'tha fhios aig fear a bhaile mar 'tha fear na mara bèo," Ian replied, without hesitation. It was a well-known saying: "Little does the landsman know how the seaman lives."

Jamie laughed in gratified surprise, and Ian grinned broadly back. His face was weathered to a deep brown, and the dotted lines of his Mohawk tattoos ran in fierce crescents from nose to cheekbones—but for a moment, I saw his hazel eyes dance with mischief, and saw again the lad we had known.

"I used to say things over in my mind," he said, the grin fading a little. "I'd look at things, and say the words in my mind—*'Avbhar,' 'Coire,' 'Skirlie'*—so as not to forget." He glanced shyly at Jamie. "Ye did tell me to remember, Uncle."

Jamie blinked, and cleared his throat.

"So I did, Ian," he murmured. "I'm glad of it." He squeezed Ian's shoulder hard—and then they were embracing fiercely, thumping each other's backs with wordless emotion.

By the time I had wiped my own eyes and blown my nose, they had separated and resumed an air of elaborate casualness, affecting to ignore my descent into female sentiment.

"I kept hold of the Scots and the Gaelic, Uncle," Ian said, clearing his own throat. "The Latin was a bit beyond me, though."

"I canna think ye'd have much occasion to practice your Latin," Jamie said. He wiped his shirtsleeve under his nose, smiling. "Unless a wandering Jesuit happened by."

Ian looked a little queer at that. He glanced from Jamie to me, then at the door to the surgery, to be sure no one was coming.

"Well, it wasna exactly that, Uncle," he said.

He walked quietly to the door, peeked out into the hallway, then closed the door softly, and came back to the table. He had worn a small leather bag tied at his waist, which—aside from knife, bow, and quiver—appeared to contain the whole of his worldly possessions. He had put this aside earlier, but now picked it up and rummaged briefly in it, withdrawing a small book, bound in black leather. He handed this to Jamie, who took it, looking puzzled.

"When I—that is, just before I left Snaketown—the old lady, Tewaktenyonh, gave me that wee book. I'd seen it before; Emily"—he stopped, clearing his throat hard, then went on steadily—"Emily begged a page of it for me, to send ye a note to say all was well. Did ye get that?"

"Yes, we did," I assured him. "Jamie sent it to your mother, later."

"Oh, aye?" Ian's expression lightened at thought of his mother. "That's good. She'll be pleased to hear I've come back, I hope."

"I'll lay ye any odds ye like on that one," Jamie assured him. "But what's this?" He lifted the book, raising a brow in question. "It looks like a priest's breviary."

"So it does." Ian nodded, scratching at a mosquito bite on his neck. "That's not what it is, though. Look at it, aye?"

I moved close to Jamie, looking over his elbow as he opened the book. There was a ragged edge of paper, where the flyleaf had been torn out. There was no title page, though, nor printing. The book appeared to be a journal of some sort; the pages were filled with writing in black ink.

Two words stood alone at the top of the first page, scrawled in large, shaky letters.

Ego sum, they said. *I am.*

"Are you, then?" said Jamie, half under his breath. "Aye, and who will ye be?" Half down the page, the writing continued. Here the writing was smaller, more controlled, though something seemed odd-looking about it.

"Prima cogitatio est . . ."

"This is the first thing that comes into my head," Jamie read softly, translating aloud.

"I am; I still exist. Did I, in that place between? I must have, for I remember it. I will try later to describe it. Now I have no words. I feel very ill."

The letters were small and rounded, each printed singly. The work of a neat and careful writer, but they staggered drunkenly, words slanting up the page. He did feel ill, if the writing were any indication.

When the tidy printing resumed on the next page, it had steadied, along with the writer's nerve.

"Ibi denum locus . . .

It is the place. Of course it would be. But it is the proper time as well, I know it. The trees, the bushes are different. There was a clearing to the west and now it is completely filled with laurels. I was looking at a big magnolia tree when I stepped into the circle, and now it is gone; there is an oak sapling there. The sound is different. There is no noise of highway and vehicles in the distance. Only birds, singing very loudly. Wind.

I am still dizzy. My legs are weak. I cannot stand yet. I woke under the wall where the snake eats its tail, but some distance from the cavity where we laid the circle. I must have crawled, there are dirt and scratches on my hands and clothes. I lay for some time after waking, too ill to rise. I am better now. Still weak and sick, but I am exultant nonetheless. It worked. We have succeeded."

"We?" I said, looking at Jamie with both eyebrows raised. He shrugged and turned the page.

"The stone is gone. Only a smear of soot in my pocket. Raymond was right, then. It was a small unpolished sapphire. I must remember to put down everything, for the sake of others who may come after me."

A small, cold shudder of premonition flowed up my back and over me, making my scalp tingle as the hair on my head began to stand. Others who may come after me. Not meaning to, I reached out and touched the book; an irresistible impulse. I needed to touch him somehow, make some contact with the vanished writer of these words.

Jamie glanced curiously at me. With some effort, I took my hand away, curling my fingers into a fist. He hesitated for a moment, but then looked back at the book, as though the neat black writing compelled his gaze as it did my own.

I knew now what had struck me about that writing. It had not been written with a quill. Quill-writing, even the best, was uneven in color, dark where the quill was freshly dipped, fading slowly through a line of writing. Every word of this was the same—written in a thin, hard line of black ink that slightly dented the fibers of the page. Quills never did that.

"Ball point," I said. "He wrote it with a ball-point pen. My God."

Jamie glanced back at me. I must have looked pale, for he moved as though to close the book, but I shook my head, motioning to him to go on reading. He frowned dubiously, but with one eye still on me, looked back. Then his attention shifted wholly to the book, and his brows rose as he looked at the writing on the next page.

"Look," he said softly, turning the book toward me and pointing to one line. Written in Latin like the others, but there were unfamiliar words mixed into the text—long, strange-looking words.

"Mohawk?" Jamie said. He looked up, into Ian's face. "That is a word in an Indian tongue, surely. One of the Algonquian tongues, no?"

"Rains Hard," said Ian, quietly. "It is the Kahnyen'kehaka—the Mohawk tongue, Uncle. Rains Hard is someone's name. And the others written there, too—Strong Walker, Six Turtles, and Talks With Spirits."

"I thought the Mohawk have no written language," Jamie said, one ruddy eyebrow lifted. Ian shook his head.

"Nor they do, Uncle Jamie. But someone wrote that"—he nodded at the page,—"and if ye work out the sound of the words . . ." He shrugged. "They are Mohawk names. I'm sure of it."

Jamie looked at him for a long moment, then without comment bent his head and resumed his translation.

"I had one of the sapphires, Rains Hard the other. Talks With Spirits had a ruby, Strong Walker took the diamond, and Six Turtles had the emerald. We were not sure of the diagram—whether it should be four points, for the directions of the compass, or five, in a pentacle. But there were the five of us, sworn by blood to this deed, so we laid the circle with five points."

There was a small gap between this sentence and the next, and the writing changed, becoming now firm and even, as though the writer had paused, then taken up his story at a later point.

"I have gone back to look. There is no sign of the circle—but I see no reason why there should be, after all. I think I must have been unconscious for some time; we laid the circle just inside the mouth of the crevice, but there are no marks in the earth there to show how I crawled or rolled to the spot where I woke, and yet there are marks in the dust, made by rain. My clothes are damp, but I cannot tell if this is from rain, from morning dew, or sweat from lying in the sun; it was near midday when I woke, for the sun was overhead, and it was hot. I am thirsty. Did I crawl away from the crevice, and then collapse? Or was I thrown some distance by the force of the transition?"

I had the most curious sense, hearing this, that the words were echoing, somewhere inside my head. It wasn't that I had heard it before, and yet the words had a dreadful familiarity. I shook my head, to clear it, and looked up to find Ian's eyes on me, soft brown and full of speculation.

"Yes," I said baldly, in answer to his look. "I am. Brianna and Roger, too." Jamie, who had paused to disentangle a phrase, looked up. He saw Ian's face, and mine, and reached to put his hand on mine.

"How much could ye read, lad?" he asked quietly.

"Quite a lot, Uncle," Ian answered, but his eyes didn't leave my face. "Not everything"—a brief smile touched his lips—"and I'm sure I havena got the grammar right—but I think I understand it. Do you?"

It wasn't clear whether he addressed the question to me or Jamie; both of us hesitated, exchanged a glance—then I turned back to Ian and nodded, and so did Jamie. Jamie's hand tightened on mine.

"Mmphm," Ian said, and his face lighted with an expression of profound satisfaction. "I *knew* ye weren't a fairy, Auntie Claire!"

UNABLE TO STAY AWAKE much longer, Ian had finally retired, yawning, though pausing in his flight toward bed to seize Rollo by the scruff of the neck and immobilize him while I removed Adso from the cupboard, fluffed to twice his normal size and hissing like a snake. Holding the cat by his own scruff to avoid being disemboweled, I had carried him out of harm's way, up to our bedroom, where I dumped him unceremoniously on the bed, turning at once to Jamie.

"What happened next?" I demanded.

He was already lighting a fresh candle. Unfastening his shirt with one hand and thumbing the book open with the other, he sank down onto the bed, still absorbed in the reading.

"He couldna find any of his friends. He searched the countryside nearby for two days, calling, but there was no trace. He was verra much distraught, but at last he thought he must go on; he was in need of food, and had nothing but a knife and a bit of salt with him. He must hunt, or find people."

Ian said that Tewaktenyonh had given him the book, enjoining him to bring it to me. It had belonged to a man named Otter-Tooth, she said—a member of my family.

An icy finger had touched my spine at that—and hadn't gone away. Little ripples of unease kept tickling over my skin like the touch of ghostly fingers. My family, indeed.

I *had* told her that Otter-Tooth was perhaps one of "my family," unable to describe the peculiar kinship of time-travelers in any other way. I had never met Otter-Tooth—at least not in the flesh—but if he was the man I thought he was, then his was the head buried in our small burying-ground—complete with silver fillings.

Perhaps I was at last going to learn who he had really been—and how on earth he had come to meet such a startling end.

"He wasna much of a hunter," Jamie said critically, frowning at the page. "Couldna catch so much as a ground-squirrel with a snare, and in the middle of summer, forbye!"

Fortunately for Otter-Tooth—if it was indeed he—he had been familiar with a number of edible plants, and seemed extremely pleased with himself for recognizing pawpaw and persimmon.

"Recognizing a persimmon is no great feat, for God's sake," I said. "They look like orange baseballs!"

"And they taste like the bottom of a chamber pot," Jamie added, he not caring at all for persimmons. "Still, he was hungry by that time, and if ye're hungry enough . . ." He trailed off, lips moving silently as he continued his translation.

The man had wandered through the wilderness for some time—though "wandering" seemed not quite right; he had chosen a specific direction, guided by the sun and stars. That seemed odd—what had he been looking for?

Whatever it was, he had eventually found a village. He didn't speak the language of the inhabitants—"Why ought he to think he should?" Jamie wondered aloud—but had become extraordinarily distraught, according to his writing, at the discovery that the women were using iron kettles to cook with.

"Tewaktenyonh said that!" I interrupted. "When she was telling me about him—if it's the same man," I added, *pro forma*, "she said he carried on all the time about the cooking pots, and the knives and guns. He said the Indians were . . . How did she put it?—they needed to 'return to the ways of their ancestors,' or the white man would eat them alive."

"A verra excitable fellow," Jamie muttered, still riveted to the book. "And with a taste for rhetoric, too."

Within a page or two, though, the source of Otter-Tooth's strange preoccupation with cooking pots became somewhat clearer.

"I have failed," Jamie read. "I am too late." He straightened his back, and glanced at me, then went on.

"I do not know exactly when I am, nor can I find out—these people will not reckon years by any scale I know, even had I enough of their tongue to ask. But I know I am too late.

Had I arrived when I meant to, before 1650, there would be no iron in a village so far inland. To find it here in such casual use means that I am at least fifty years too late—perhaps more!"

Otter-Tooth was cast into great gloom by this discovery, and spent several days in utmost despair. But then he pulled himself together, determining that there was nothing to be done but to go on. And so he had set out alone, though with the gift of some food from the villagers—heading north.

"I've no idea what the man thought he was doing," Jamie observed. "But I will say he shows courage. His friends are dead or gone, and he's nothing with him, no notion where he is—and yet he goes on."

"Yes—though in all honesty, I don't suppose he could think of anything else to do," I said. I touched the book again, gently, remembering the first few days after my own passage through the stones.

The difference, of course, was that this man had chosen to come through the stones on purpose. Exactly *why* he had done it—and how—was not revealed just yet.

Traveling alone through the wilderness, with nothing but this small book for company, Otter-Tooth had—he said—decided that he would occupy his mind with setting down an account of his journey, with its motives and intents.

"Perhaps I will not succeed in my attempt—our attempt. In fact, it seems likely at the moment that I will simply perish here in the wilderness. But if that is so, then the thought that some record of our noble

endeavor remains will be some consolation—and it is all the memorial I can provide for those who were my brothers; my companions in this adventure."

Jamie stopped and rubbed his eyes. The candle had burned far down; my own eyes were watering so much from yawning that I could scarcely see the page in the flickering light, and I felt light-headed from fatigue.

"Let's stop," I said, and laid my head on Jamie's shoulder, taking comfort from its warm solidness. "I can't stay awake any longer, I really can't—and it doesn't seem right to rush through his story. Besides"—I stopped, interrupted by a jaw-cracking yawn that left me swaying and blinking—"perhaps Bree and Roger should hear this, too."

Jamie caught my yawn and gaped hugely, then shook his head violently, blinking like a large red owl shaken rudely out of its tree.

"Aye, ye're right, Sassenach." He closed the book, and laid it gently on the table by the bed.

I didn't bother with any sort of bedtime toilette, merely removing my outer clothes, brushing my teeth, and crawling into bed in my shift. Adso, who had been snoozing happily on the pillow, was disgruntled at our appropriation of his space, but grumpily moved at Jamie's insistence, making his way to the foot of the bed, where he collapsed on my feet like a large, furry rug.

After a few moments, though, he abandoned his pique, kneaded the bedclothes—and my feet—gently with his claws, and began to purr in a somnolent fashion.

I found his presence almost as soothing as Jamie's soft, regular snoring. For the most part, I felt at home, secure in the place I had made for myself in this world, happy to be with Jamie, whatever the circumstances. But now and then, I saw suddenly and clearly the magnitude of the gulf I had crossed—the dizzying loss of the world I had been born to—and felt very much alone. And afraid.

Hearing this man's words, his panic and desperation, had brought back to me the memory of all the terror and doubts of my journeys through the stones.

I cuddled close to my sleeping husband, warmed and anchored, and heard Otter-Tooth's words, as though they were spoken in my inner ear—a cry of desolation that echoed through the barriers of time and language.

Toward the foot of that one page, the tiny Latin writing had grown increasingly hasty, some of the letters no more than dots of ink, the endings of words swallowed in a frantic spider's dance. And then the last lines, done in English, the writer's Latin dissolved in desperation.

Oh God, oh God. . . .
Where are they?

IT WAS AFTERNOON of the next day before we managed to collect Brianna, Roger, and Ian and retire privately to Jamie's study without attracting unwanted attention. The night before, the haze of fatigue, following on the heels of Ian's sudden appearance, had combined to make almost anything seem reasonable. But going about my chores in the bright light of morning, I found it increasingly difficult to believe that the journal really existed, and was not merely something I had dreamed.

There it was, though, small, but black and solid on Jamie's desk-table. He and Ian had spent the morning in his study, immersed in translation; when I joined him, I could tell by the way Jamie's hair was sticking up that he had found the journal's account either deeply absorbing, terribly upsetting—or possibly both.

"I've told them what it is," he said without preamble, nodding toward Roger and Bree. The two of them sat close together on stools, looking solemn. Jemmy, having refused to be parted from his mother, was under the table, playing with a string of carved wooden beads.

"Have you read through the whole thing?" I asked, subsiding into the extra chair.

Jamie nodded, with a glance at Young Ian, who stood by the window, too restless to sit. His hair was cropped short, but nearly as disordered as Jamie's.

"Aye, we have. I'm no going to read the whole thing

aloud, but I thought I'd best start wi' the bit where he's made up his mind to put it all down from the beginning."

He had marked the spot with the scrap of tanned leather he customarily used as a bookmark. Opening the journal, he found his spot and began to read.

"The name I was given at birth is Robert Springer. I reject this name, and all that goes with it, because it is the bitter fruit of centuries of murder and injustice, a symbol of theft, slavery, and oppression—"

Jamie looked up over the edge of the book, remarking, "Ye see why I dinna want to read every word; the man's gey tedious about it." Running a finger across the page, he resumed:

"In the year of Our Lord—their lord, that Christ in whose name they rape and pillage and—well, more of the same, but when he gets down to it, it was the year nineteen-hundred-and-sixty-eight. So I suppose ye'll be familiar wi' all this murder and pillage he's talking about?" He raised his eyebrows at Bree and Roger.

Bree sat up abruptly, clutching Roger's arm.

"I know that name," she said, sounding breathless. "Robert Springer. I know it!"

"You knew *him*?" I asked, feeling a thrill of something—excitement, dread, or simple curiosity—run through me.

She shook her head.

"No, I didn't know *him*, but I know the name—I saw it in the newspapers. Did you—?" She turned toward Roger, but he shook his head, frowning.

"Well, maybe you wouldn't, in the UK, but it was a big deal in Boston. I *think* Robert Springer was one of the Montauk Five."

Jamie pinched the bridge of his nose.

"The five what?"

"It was just a—a thing people did to call attention to themselves." Brianna flapped a hand in dismissal. "It's not important. They were AIM activists, or at least they started out that way, only they were even too nuts for AIM, and so—"

"Nuts? W'ere nuts?" Jemmy, picking the only word of

personal interest out of this account, emerged from under the table.

"Not that kind of nuts, baby, sorry." Looking around for some object of interest to distract him, Bree slipped off her silver bracelet and gave it to him. Seeing the puzzled looks on the faces of father and cousin, she took a deep breath and started over, trying—with occasional clarifications from Roger and me—to define things, and give a short, if confused, account of the sad state of the American Indian in the twentieth century.

"So this Robert Springer is—or was—an Indian, of sorts, in your own time?" Jamie tapped his fingers in a brief tattoo on the table, frowning in concentration. "Well, that corresponds wi' his own account; he and his friends apparently took no little exception to the behavior of what they called 'whites.' I would suppose those to be Englishmen? Or Europeans, at least?"

"Well, yes—except that by nineteen sixty-eight, of course they weren't Europeans anymore, they were Americans, only the Indians were Americans first—and so that's when they started calling themselves *native* Americans, and—"

Roger patted her knee, stopping her in mid-flow.

"Perhaps we can do the history a bit later," he suggested. "What was it ye read about Robert Springer in the papers?"

"Oh." Taken aback, she furrowed her brow in concentration. "He disappeared. They disappeared—the Montauk Five, I mean. They were all wanted by the government, for blowing things up or threatening to or something, I forget—and they were arrested, but then they got out on bail, and the next thing you know, they'd all disappeared."

"Evidently so," Young Ian murmured, glancing toward the journal.

"It was a big deal in the papers for a week or so," Brianna went on. "The other activist types were all accusing the government of having done away with them, so that stuff coming out of the trial wouldn't embarrass the government, and of course the government was denying it. So there was a big search on, and I think I remember reading that they found the body of one of the missing men—out in the woods somewhere in New Hampshire or Vermont or someplace—but they couldn't tell how he died—and nobody turned up any trace of the others."

"Where are they?" I quoted softly, the hair rippling on the back of my neck. *"My God, where are they?"*

Jamie nodded soberly.

"Aye, then; I think this Springer may well be your man." He touched the page before him, with something like respect.

"He and his four companions all renounced any association with the white world, taking new names from their real heritage—or so he says."

"That would be the proper thing to do," Ian said softly. He had a new, strange stillness to him, and I was forcibly reminded that he had been a Mohawk for the last two years—washed free of his white blood, renamed Wolf's Brother—one of the Kahnyen'kehaka, the Guardians of the Western Gate.

I thought Jamie was aware of this stillness, too, but he kept his eyes on the journal, flipping pages slowly as he summarized their content.

Robert Springer—or Ta'wineonawira—"Otter-Tooth," as he chose henceforth to call himself, had numerous associations in the shadow world of extremist politics and the deeper shadows of what he called Native American shamanism—I had no notion how much resemblance there was between what he was doing, and the original beliefs of the Iroquois, but Otter-Tooth believed that he was descended from the Mohawk, and embraced such remnants of tradition as he could find—or invent.

It was at a naming ceremony that I first met Raymond. I sat up abruptly, hearing that. He had mentioned Raymond in the beginning, but I had taken no particular note of the name, then.

"Does he describe this Raymond?" I asked urgently.

Jamie shook his head.

"Not in terms of appearance, no. He says only that Raymond was a great shaman, who could transform himself into birds or animals—and who could walk through time," he added delicately. He glanced at me, one eyebrow raised.

"I don't know," I said. "I thought so, once—but now, I don't know."

"What?" Ian was looking back and forth between us, puzzled. I shook my head, smoothing back my hair.

"Never mind. Someone I knew in Paris was named Raymond, and I thought—but what in the name of *anything* would he be doing in America in nineteen sixty-eight?" I burst out.

"Well, you were there, aye?" Jamie pointed out. "But putting that aside for the moment—" He returned to the text, laying it all out in the oddly stilted English of the translation: Intrigued by Raymond, Otter-Tooth had met with the man repeatedly, and brought several of his closest friends to him as well. Gradually, the scheme—*a great, audacious plan, stunning in conception*—"Modest, isn't he?" Roger muttered—*had been conceived.*

> *"There was a test. Many failed, but I did not. There were five of us who passed the test, who heard the voice of time, five of us who swore in our blood and by our blood that we would undertake this great venture, to rescue our people from catastrophe. To rewrite their history and redress their wrongs, to—"*

Roger gave a faint groan.

"Oh, God," he said. "What did they mean to do—assassinate Christopher Columbus?"

"Not quite," I said. "He meant to arrive before 1600, he said. What happened then, do you know?"

"I dinna ken what happened then," Jamie told me, rubbing a hand through his hair, "but I ken well enough what he thought he was doing. His plan was to go to the Iroquois League, and rouse them against the white settlers. He thought that there were few enough settlers then, that the Indians could easily wipe them out, if the Iroquois led the way."

"Perhaps he was right," Ian said softly. "I've heard the old people tell the stories. When the first of the O'seronni came, how they were welcomed, how they brought trade goods. A hundred years ago, the O'seronni were few—and the Kahnyen'kehaka were masters, leaders of the Nations. Aye, they could have done it—had they wished to."

"Well, but he couldn't possibly have stopped the Europeans," Brianna objected. "There were just way too many. He didn't mean to get the Mohawk to invade Europe, did he?"

A broad grin crossed Jamie's face at the thought.

"I should have liked to see that," he said. "The Mohawk would have given the Sassenachs something to think about. But no, alas"—he gave me a sardonic look—"our friend Robert Springer wasna *quite* so ambitious."

What Otter-Tooth and his companions had had in mind was sufficiently ambitious, though—and perhaps . . . just perhaps . . . possible. Their intention was not to prevent white settlement altogether—they were, just barely, sane enough to realize the impossibility of that. What they intended was to put the Indians on their guard against the whites, to establish trade on *their* terms, to deal from a position of power.

Instead of allowing them to settle in great numbers, they might keep the whites bottled up in small towns. Instead of allowing them to build fortifications, demand weapons from the start. Establish trade on their own terms. Keep them outnumbered, and outgunned—and force the Europeans to teach them the ways of metal.

"Prometheus redux," I said, and Jamie snorted.

Roger shook his head, half-admiringly.

"It's a crack-brained scheme," he said, "but ye do have to admire their nerve. It might just possibly have worked—*if* he could convince the Iroquois League, and *if* they acted at the right time, before the balance of power shifted to the Europeans. It all went wrong, though, didn't it? First he comes to the wrong time—much too late—and then he realizes none of his friends have made it with him."

I saw goosebumps rise suddenly on Brianna's arms, and caught the look she sent me—one of sudden understanding. She had abruptly imagined just how it might be, to arrive suddenly out of one's own time . . . alone.

I gave her a small smile, and put my hand on Jamie's arm. Absentmindedly, he put his own hand over mine, and squeezed it gently.

"Aye. He nearly despaired, as he says, when he realized that it had all gone wrong. He thought of going back—but he didna have a gemstone anymore, and this Raymond had said ye must have one, for protection."

"He did find one eventually, though," I said. Getting up, I reached to the top shelf and brought down the big raw opal, its inner fire flickering through the carved spiral on its surface.

"That is—I'm assuming there can't have been multiple Indians named Otter-Tooth, associated with Snaketown." I had found the opal buried with the skull with silver fillings. Tewaktenyonh, leader of the Council of Mothers in Snaketown, had recognized it, and had told me the story of Otter-Tooth, and how he met his death. I shivered, though it was warm in the room.

The big smooth stone felt warm in my hand, too; I rubbed a thumb gingerly over the spiral. *The snake that eats its tail,* he'd said.

"Aye. He doesna mention that, though." Jamie sat back, running both hands through his loosened hair, then rubbing a hand over his face. "The story ends with him deciding that there's no help for it; whatever year it may be—and he had no notion—and whether he was alone or not, he would carry out his plan."

Everyone was silent for a moment, regarding the enormity—and the futility—of such a plan.

"He can't have thought it would work," Roger said, the rasping husk of his voice giving the words a sense of finality.

Jamie shook his head, looking down at the book, though his eyes were clearly looking through it, dark blue and remote.

"Nor he did," he said softly. "What he said, here at the last"—his fingers touched the page, very gently—"was that thousands of his people had died for their freedom, thousands more would die in years to come. He would walk the path they walked, for the honor of his blood, and to die fighting was no more than a warrior of the Mohawk should ask."

I heard Ian draw breath behind me in a sigh, and Brianna bent her head, so the bright hair hid her face. Roger's own face was turned toward her, grave in profile—but it was none of them I saw. I saw a man with his face painted black for death, walking through a dripping forest at night, holding a torch that burned with cold fire.

A yank on my skirt pulled me away from this vision, and I glanced down to find Jemmy standing beside me, pulling on my hand.

"Watsat?"

"What—oh! It's a rock, sweetheart; a pretty rock, see?" I held out the opal, and he seized it with both hands, plumping down on his bottom to look at it.

Brianna wiped a hand underneath her nose, and Roger cleared his throat with a noise like ripping cloth.

"What I want to know," he said gruffly, gesturing toward the journal, "is why in hell did he write that in Latin?"

"Oh. He says that. He'd learnt Latin in school—perhaps that was what turned him against Europeans"—Jamie grinned at Young Ian, who grimaced—"and he thought if he wrote in Latin, anyone who happened to see it would think it only a priest's book of prayers, and pay it no heed."

"They did think that—the Kahnyen'kehaka," Ian put in. "Old Tewaktenyonh kept the book, though. And when I—left, she gave me the wee book, and said as I must bring it back wi' me, and give it to you, Auntie Claire."

"To me?" I felt a sense of hesitation at touching the book, but nonetheless reached out a hand and touched the open pages. The ink, I saw, had begun to run dry toward the end—the letters skipped and stuttered, and some words were no more than indentations on the paper. Had he thrown the empty pen away, I wondered, or kept it, a useless reminder of his vanished future?

"Do you think she knew what was in the book?" I asked. Ian's face was impassive, but his soft hazel eyes held a hint of trouble. When he had been a Scot, he hadn't been one to hide his feelings.

"I dinna ken," he said. "She kent *something*, but I couldna say what. She didna tell me—only that I must bring ye the book." He hesitated, glancing from me to Brianna and Roger, then back. "Is it true?" he asked. "What ye said, cousin—about what will happen to the Indians?"

She looked up, meeting his eyes squarely, and nodded.

"I'm afraid so," she said softly. "I'm sorry, Ian."

He only nodded, rubbing a knuckle down the bridge of his nose, but I wondered.

He hadn't forsaken his own people, I knew, but the Kahnyen'kehaka were his as well. No matter what had happened to cause him to leave.

I was opening my mouth to ask Ian about his wife, when I heard Jemmy. He had retired back under the table with his prize, and had been talking to it in a genially conversational—if unintelligible—manner for several minutes. His voice had suddenly changed, though, to a tone of alarm.

"Hot," he said, "Mummy, HOT!"

Brianna was already rising from her stool, a look of concern on her face, when I heard the noise. It was a high-pitched ringing sound, like the weird singing of a crystal goblet when you run a wet finger round and round the rim. Roger sat up straight, looking startled.

Brianna bent and snatched Jemmy out from under the table, and as she straightened with him, there was a sudden *pow!* like a gunshot, and the ringing noise abruptly stopped.

"Holy God," said Jamie, rather mildly under the circumstances.

Splinters of glimmering fire protruded from the bookshelf, the books, the walls, and the thick folds of Brianna's skirts. One had whizzed past Roger's head, barely nicking his ear; a thin trickle of blood was running down his neck, though he didn't seem to have noticed yet.

A stipple of brilliant pinpoints glinted on the table—a shower of the sharp needles had been thrust upward through the inch-thick wood. I heard Ian exclaim sharply, and bend to pull a tiny shaft from the flesh of his calf. Jemmy began to cry. Outside, Rollo the dog was barking furiously.

The opal had exploded.

IT WAS STILL broad daylight; the candleflame was nearly invisible, no more than a waver of heat in the late afternoon light from the window. Jamie blew out the taper he had used to light it, and sat down behind his desk.

"Ye didna sense anything odd about yon stone when ye gave it to the lad, Sassenach?"

"No." I still felt shaken by the explosion, the echoes of that eerie noise still chiming in my inner ear. "It felt warm—but everything in the room is warm. And it certainly wasn't making that noise."

"Noise?" He looked at me queerly. "When it went bang, d'ye mean?"

Now it was my turn to look askance.

"No—before that. Didn't you hear it?" He shook his head, a small frown between his brows, and I glanced round at the others. Bree and Roger nodded—both of them looked pale and ill—but Ian shook his head, looking interested, but puzzled.

"I didna hear a thing," he said. "What did it sound like?"

Brianna opened her mouth to answer, but Jamie raised a hand to stop her.

"A moment, *a nighean*. Jem, *a ruaidh*—did ye hear a noise before the bang?"

Jemmy had settled down from his fright, but was still crouching in his mother's lap, thumb in his mouth. He looked at his grandfather out of wide blue eyes that had already begun to show a definite slant, and slowly nodded, not removing the thumb.

"And the stone Grannie gave ye—it was hot?"

Jemmy cast a glare of intense accusation in my direction and nodded again. I felt a small surge of guilt—followed by a much larger one, when I thought of what might have happened, had Bree not snatched him up at once.

We had picked most of the splinters out of the woodwork; they lay on the desk in a small heap of brittle fire. One had sliced a tiny flap of skin from my knuckle; I put it in my mouth, tasting silver blood.

"My God, those things are sharp as broken glass."

"They *are* broken glass." Brianna clutched Jem a little closer.

"Glass? You mean it wasn't a real opal?" Roger raised his brows, leaning forward to pick up one of the needlelike shards.

"Sure it is—but opals are glass. Really hard volcanic

glass. Gemstones are gemstones because they have a crystalline structure that makes them pretty; opals just have a really brittle structure, compared to most." The color was beginning to come back into Brianna's face, though she kept her arms wrapped tightly round her son.

"I knew you could break one if you hit with a hammer or something, but I never heard of one doing *that*." She nodded at the pile of glimmering fragments.

Jamie picked a large shard out of the pile with finger and thumb and held it out to me.

"Put it in your hand, Sassenach. Does it feel warm to you?"

I accepted the jagged piece of stone gingerly. It was thin, nearly weightless, and translucent, sparkling with vivid blues and oranges.

"Yes," I said, tilting my palm cautiously to and fro. "Not remarkably hot—just about skin temperature."

"It felt cool to me," Jamie said. "Give it to Ian."

I transferred the bit of opal to Ian, who put it in the palm of his hand and stroked it cautiously with a fingertip, as though it were some small animal that might bite him if annoyed.

"It feels cool," he reported. "Like a bit of glass, like Cousin Brianna says."

A bit more experimentation established that the stone felt warm—though not strikingly so—to Brianna, Roger, and me—but not to Jamie or Ian. By this time, the wax had melted in the top of the big clock candle, allowing Jamie to extract the gemstones hidden there. He fished them out, rubbed the last of the hot wax off on his handkerchief, and laid them out in a row along the edge of the desk to cool.

Jemmy watched this with great interest, his misadventure apparently forgotten.

"D'ye like these, *a ghille ruaidh*?" Jamie asked him, and he nodded eagerly, leaning out of his mother's lap, reaching toward the stones.

"Hot," he said, then, remembering, shrank back a little, a look of doubt crossing his small, blunt features. "Hot?"

"Well, I do hope not," his grandfather said. He took a deep breath and picked up the emerald, a crudely faceted stone the size of his thumbnail. "Put out your hand, *a bhalaich*."

Brianna looked as though she wanted to protest, but bit her lower lip, and encouraged Jemmy to do as his grandfather asked. He took the stone, still looking suspicious, but then the look of wariness faded into a smile as he looked down at the stone.

"Pretty rock!"

"Is it hot?" Brianna asked, poised to snatch it out of his hand.

"Yes, hot," he said, with satisfaction, holding it against his stomach.

"Let Mama see." With a little difficulty, Brianna succeeded in getting her fingers onto the rock, though Jemmy wouldn't surrender it. "It's warm," she said, looking up. "Like the piece of opal—but not way hot. If it gets way hot, you drop it *fast*, OK?" she said to Jemmy.

Roger had been watching this with fascination.

"He's got it, hasn't he?" he said softly. "Fifty/fifty, you said, or three chances in four, depending—but he's got it, doesn't he?"

"What?" Jamie glanced at Roger, then me, one red brow raised in question.

"I think he can . . . travel," I said, feeling a tightening of my chest at the thought. "You know what Otter-Tooth said—" I nodded at the journal, which lay discarded on the desk. "He said they had to take a test—to see if they could hear 'the voice of time.' We know that not everyone can . . . do this." I felt unaccountably shy, talking of it before Ian. "But some can. From what Otter-Tooth said, there was a way of finding out who could and couldn't, ahead of time, without having actually to try."

Jemmy was paying no attention to the grown-up conversation, instead rocking back and forth, humming to the stone clutched in his pudgy hand.

"Do you suppose the 'voice of time' is—Jem, can you *hear* the rock?" Roger leaned forward, taking hold of Jemmy's arm to compel his attention away from the emerald. "Jem, is the rock singing to you?"

Jemmy looked up, surprised.

"No," he said uncertainly. Then, "Yes." He held the rock up to his ear, frowning, then thrust it at Roger. "You sing, Daddy!"

Roger accepted the emerald gingerly, smiling at Jemmy.

"I don't know any rock songs," he said, in his husky rasp of a voice. "Unless ye count the Beatles." He lifted the rock to his own ear, looking self-conscious. He listened intently, frowning, then lowered his hand, shaking his head.

"It's not—I can't—I couldna really say I *hear* anything. And yet—here, you try." He passed the stone to Brianna, and she in turn to me. Neither of us heard anything in particular, and yet I thought I could perceive something, if I listened very hard. Not exactly a sound, more a sense of very, very faint vibration.

"What is it?" Ian asked. He had been following the proceedings with rapt interest. "Ye're no *sìdheanach*, the three of ye—but why is it you can do . . . what ye do, and Uncle Jamie and I canna? Ye can't, can ye, Uncle Jamie?" he asked dubiously.

"No, thank God," his uncle replied.

"It's genetic, isn't it?" Brianna asked, looking up. "It has to be."

Jamie and Ian looked wary at the unfamiliar term.

"Genetic?" Ian asked. His feathery brows drew together in puzzlement.

"Why shouldn't it be?" I said. "Everything else is—blood type, eye color."

"But everyone has eyes and blood, Sassenach," Jamie objected. "Whatever color his eyes may be, everyone can see. This—" He waved at the small collection of stones.

I sighed with impatience.

"Yes, but there are other things that are genetic—everything, if you come right down to it! Look—" I turned to him and stuck out my tongue. Jamie blinked, and Brianna giggled at his expression.

Disregarding this, I pulled in my tongue and put it out again, this time with the edges rolled up into a cylinder.

"What about that?" I asked, popping it back in. "Can you do that?"

Jamie looked amused.

"Of course I can." He stuck out a rolled tongue and wiggled it, demonstrating, then pulled it back. "Everyone can do that, surely? Ian?"

"Oh, aye, of course." Ian obligingly demonstrated. "Anyone can."

"I can't," said Brianna. Jamie stared at her, taken aback.

"What d'ye mean ye can't?"

"Bleah." She stuck out a flat tongue and waggled it from side to side. "I can't."

"Of course ye can." Jamie frowned. "Here, it's simple, lass—anyone can do it!" He stuck out his own tongue again, rolling and unrolling it like a paternal anteater, anxiously encouraging its offspring toward an appetizing mass of insects. He glanced at Roger, brows lifted.

"You'd think so, wouldn't you?" Roger said ruefully. He stuck out his own tongue, flat. "Bleah."

"See?" I said triumphantly. "Some people can roll their tongues, and some simply can't. It can't be learned. You're born with it, or you're not."

Jamie looked from Bree to Roger and back, frowning, then turned to me.

"Allowing for the moment that ye may be right—why can the lass not do it, if you and I both can? Ye did assure me she's my daughter, aye?"

"She is most assuredly your daughter," I said. "As anyone with eyes in their head could tell you." He glanced at Brianna, taking in her lean height and mass of ruddy hair. She smiled at him, blue eyes creasing into triangles. He smiled back and turned to me, shrugging in good-natured capitulation.

"Well, I shall take your word for it, Sassenach, as an honorable woman. But the tongue, then?" He rolled his own again, in doubtful fashion, still not quite believing that anyone couldn't do it if they put their mind to it.

"Well, you do know where babies come from," I began. "The egg and the . . ."

"I do," he said, with a noticeable edge to his voice. The tips of his ears turned slightly pink.

"I mean, it takes something from the mother and something from the father." I could feel my own cheeks pinken slightly, but carried on gamely. "Sometimes the father's influence is more visible than the mother's; sometimes the other way round—but both . . . er . . . influences are still there. We call them genes—the things babies get from their two parents that affect the child's appearance and abilities."

Jamie glanced at Jemmy, who was humming again, engaged in trying to balance one gemstone on top of another, the sunlight glinting off his coppery hair. Looking back, he caught Roger's eye, and quickly turned his attention to me.

"Aye, so?"

"Well, genes affect more than simply hair or eye-color. Now," I warmed to my lecture, "each person has two genes for every trait—one from the father, one from the mother. And when the . . er . . gametes are formed in the ovaries and testes—"

"Perhaps ye should tell me all about it later, Sassenach," Jamie interrupted, with a sidelong glance at Brianna. Evidently he didn't think the word "testes" suitable for his daughter's ears; his own were blazing.

"It's all right, Da. I know where babies come from," Bree assured him, grinning.

"Well, then," I said, taking back command of the conversation. "You have a pair of genes for each trait, one gene from your mother and one gene from your father—but when the time comes to pass these on to your own offspring, you can only pass *one* of the pair. Because the child will get another gene from his other parent, you see?" I raised an eyebrow at Jamie and Roger, who nodded in unison, as though hypnotized.

"Right. Well, then. Some genes are said to be dominant, and others recessive. If a person has a dominant gene, then that's the one that will be expressed—will be visible. They may have another gene that's recessive and so you don't see it—but it can still be passed to the offspring."

My collective audience looked wary.

"Surely you learned this in school, Roger?" Bree asked, amused.

"Well, I did," he muttered, "but I think perhaps I wasna paying proper attention at the time. After all, I wasn't expecting it actually to *matter*."

"Right," I said dryly. "Well, then. You and I, Jamie, evidently each have one of the dominant genes that allows us to roll our tongues. *But*—" I continued, raising a finger, "we must also each have a recessive gene, that *doesn't* allow tongue-rolling. And evidently, each of us gave the recessive gene to Bree. Therefore, she can't roll her tongue. Likewise, Roger must have two copies of the non-rolling recessive gene, since if he had even one of the dominant genes, he could do it—and he can't. Q.E.D." I bowed.

"Wat's tes-tees?" inquired a small voice. Jemmy had abandoned his rocks and was looking up at me in profound interest.

"Er . . ." I said. I glanced round the room in search of aid.

"That's Latin for your balls, lad," Roger said gravely, suppressing a grin.

Jemmy looked quite interested at that.

"I gots balls? W'ere I gots balls?"

"Er . . ." said Roger, and glanced at Jamie.

"Mmphm," said Jamie, and looked at the ceiling.

"Well, ye do have a kilt on, Uncle Jamie," Ian said, grinning. Jamie gave his nephew a look of gross betrayal, but before he could move, Roger had leaned forward and cupped Jemmy gently between the legs.

"Just there, *a bhalaich*," he said.

Jemmy kneaded his crotch briefly, then looked at Roger, small strawberry brows knitted into a puzzled frown.

"Nots a ball. 'Sa willy!"

Jamie sighed deeply and got up. He jerked his head at Roger, then reached down and took Jemmy's hand.

"Aye, all right. Come outside with me and your Da, we'll show ye."

Bree's face was the exact shade of her hair, and her shoulders shook briefly. Roger, also suspiciously pink about the cheeks, had opened the door and stood aside for Jamie and Jem to go through.

I didn't think Jamie paused to think about it; seized by impulse, he turned to Jemmy, rolling up his tongue into a cylinder and sticking it out.

"Can you do that, *a ruaidh*?" he asked, pulling it back in again.

Brianna drew in her breath with a sound like a startled duck, and froze. Roger froze, too, his eyes resting on Jemmy as though the little boy were an explosive device, primed to go off like the opal.

A second too late, Jamie realized, and his cheeks went pale.

"Damn," he said, very quietly under his breath.

Jemmy's eyes grew round with reproach.

"Bad, Granda! At'sa bad word. Mama?"

"Yes," Brianna said, narrowed eyes on Jamie. "We'll have to wash Grand-da's mouth out with soap, won't we?"

He looked very much as though he had already swallowed a good mouthful of soap, and lye-soap, at that.

"Aye," he said, and cleared his throat. The flush had faded entirely from his face. "Aye, that was verra wicked of me, Jeremiah. I must beg pardon o' the ladies." He bowed, very formally, to me and Brianna. *"Je suis navré, Mesdames. Et Monsieur,"* he added softly to Roger. Roger nodded very slightly. His eyes were still on Jemmy, but his lids were lowered and his face carefully blank.

Jemmy's own round face assumed the expression of beatific delight that he wore whenever French was spoken near him, and—as Jamie had clearly intended—broke immediately into his own pet contribution to that language of art and chivalry.

"*Frère Jacques, Frère Jacques. . . .*"

Roger looked up at Bree, and something seemed to pass through the air between them. He reached down and took hold of Jem's other hand, momentarily interrupting his song.

"So, *a bhalaich*, can ye do it, then?"

"*FRÈRE* . . . do whats?"

"Look at Grand-da." Roger nodded at Jamie, who took a deep breath and quickly put out his tongue, rolled into a cylinder.

"Can ye do that?" Roger asked.

"Chure." Jemmy beamed and put out his tongue. Flat. "Bleah!"

A collective sigh gusted through the room. Jemmy, oblivious, swung his legs up, his weight suspended momentarily from Roger's and Jamie's hands, then stomped his feet down on the floor again, recalling his original question.

"Grand-da gots balls?" he asked, pulling on the men's hands and tilting his head far back to look up at Jamie.

"Aye, lad, I have," Jamie said dryly. "But your Da's are bigger. Come on, then."

And to the sound of Jemmy's tuneless chanting, the men trundled him outside, hanging like a gibbon between them, his knees drawn up to his chin.

110

MAN OF BLOOD

I CRUMBLED DRY SAGE LEAVES in my hands, letting the gray-green flakes fall into the burning coals. The sun hung low in the sky above the chestnut trees, but the small burying-ground lay already in shadow, and the fire was bright.

The five of us stood in a circle around the chunk of granite with which Jamie had marked the stranger's grave. *There were five of us, and so we laid the circle with five points.* By common consent, this was not only for the man with the silver fillings, but for his four unknown companions—and for Daniel Rawlings, whose fresh and final grave lay under a mountain-ash, nearby.

The smoke rose up from the small iron fire-pot, pale and fragrant. I had brought other herbs as well, but I knew that for the Tuscarora, for the Cherokee, and for the Mohawk, sage was holy, the smoke of it cleansing.

I rubbed juniper needles between my hands into the fire, and followed them with rue, called herb-of-grace, and rosemary—that's for remembrance, after all.

The leaves of the trees nearby rustled gently in the evening breeze, and the twilight lit the drifting smoke, turning it from gray to gold as it rose up and up into heaven's vault, where the faint stars waited.

Jamie lifted his head, touched with fire as bright as the blaze by his feet, and looked toward the west, where the souls of the dead fly away. He spoke softly, in Gaelic, but all of us knew enough by now to follow.

"Thou goest home this night to thy home of winter,
To thy home of autumn, of spring, and of summer;
Thou goest home this night to thy perpetual home,
To thine eternal bed, to thine eternal slumber.

The sleep of the seven lights be thine, O brother,
The sleep of the seven joys be thine, O brother,
The sleep of the seven slumbers be thine, O brother,
On the arm of the Jesus of blessings, the Christ of grace.

The shade of death lies upon thy face, beloved,
But the Jesus of Grace has His hand round about thee;
In nearness to the Trinity farewell to thy pains,
Christ stands before thee and peace is in His mind."

Ian stood by him, close, but not touching. The fading light touched his face, fierce upon his scars. He said it first in the Mohawk tongue, but then in English, for the rest of us.

"Be the hunt successful,
Be your enemies destroyed before your eyes,
Be your heart ever joyful in the lodge of your brothers."

"Ye're meant to say it over and over again, a good many times," he added, ducking his head apologetically. "Wi' the drums, aye? But I thought once would do, for now."

"That will do fine, Ian," Jamie assured him, and looked then toward Roger.

Roger coughed and cleared his throat, then spoke, the husk of his voice as transparent and as penetrating as the smoke.

"Lord, make me to know mine end,
And the measure of my days, what it is;
That I may know how frail I am.
Behold, Thou has made my days as an hand-breadth;
And mine age is as nothing before Thee.
Hear my prayer, O Lord, and give ear unto my cry;
Hold not Thy peace at my tears:
For I am a stranger with Thee,
And a sojourner, as all my fathers were."

We stood in silence then, as the darkness came quietly around us. As the last of the light faded and the leaves overhead lost their brilliance, Brianna picked up the pitcher of water, and poured it over the pot of coals. Smoke and steam rose up in a ghostly cloud, and the scent of remembrance drifted through the trees.

IT WAS NEARLY DARK as we came down the narrow trail back to the house. I could see Brianna in front of me, though, leading the way; the men were a little behind us. The fireflies were out in great profusion, drifting through the trees, and lighting the grass near my feet. One of the little bugs lighted briefly in Brianna's hair and clung there for a moment, blinking.

A wood at twilight holds a deep hush, that bids the heart be still, the foot step lightly on the earth.

"Have ye thought, then, a *cliamhuinn*?" Jamie said, behind me. His voice was low, the tone of it friendly enough—but the formal address made it clear that the question was seriously meant.

"Of what?" Roger's voice was calm, hushed from the service, the rasp of it barely audible.

"Of what ye shall do—you and your family. Now that ye ken both that the wee lad can travel—and what it might mean, if ye stay."

What it might mean to them all. I drew breath, uneasy. War. Battle. Uncertainty, save for the certainty of danger. The danger of illness or accident, for Brianna and Jem. The danger of death in the toils of childbirth, if she was again with child. And for Roger—danger both of body and soul. His head had healed, but I saw the stillness at the back of his eyes, when he thought of Randall Lillywhite.

"Oh, aye," Roger said, softly, invisible behind me. "I have thought—and am still thinking . . . *m'athair-cèile*."

I smiled a little, to hear him call Jamie "father-in-law," but the tone of his voice was altogether serious.

"Shall I tell ye what I think? And you will tell me?"

"Aye, do that. There is time still, for thinking."

"I have been thinking, lately, of Hermon Husband."

"The Quaker?" Jamie sounded surprised. Husband had left the colony with his family, after the battle of Alamance. I thought I heard that they had gone to Maryland.

"Aye, him. What d'ye think might have happened, had he not been a Quaker? Had he gone ahead, and led the Regulators to their war?"

Jamie grunted slightly, thinking.

"I dinna ken," he said, though he sounded interested. "Ye mean they might have succeeded, with a proper leader?"

"Aye. Or maybe not—they'd no weapons, after all—but they would have done better than they did. And if so—"

We had come within sight of the house, now. Light was glowing in the back windows as the hearth-fire was stoked up for the evening, the candles lit for supper.

"What's going to happen here—I am thinking, had the Regulation been properly led, perhaps it would have started here and then; not three years from now, in Massachusetts."

"Aye? And if so, what then?"

Roger gave a brief snort, the verbal equivalent of a shrug.

"Who knows? I know what's going on in England now—they are not ready, they've no notion of what they're risking here. If war were to break out suddenly, with little warning—if it *had* broken out, at Alamance—it might spread quickly. It might be over before the English had a clue what was happening. It might have saved years of warfare, thousands of lives."

"Or not," Jamie said dryly, and Roger laughed.

"Or not," he agreed. "But the point there is this; I think there are times for men of peace—and a time for men of blood, as well."

Brianna had reached the house, but turned and waited for the rest of us. She had been listening to the conversation, too.

Roger stopped beside her, looking up. Bright sparks flew from the chimney in a firework shower, lighting his face by their glow.

"Ye called me," he said at last, still looking up into the blazing dark. "At the Gathering, at the fire."

"Seas ri mo lâmh, Roger an t'oranaiche, mac Jeremiah mac Choinneich," Jamie said quietly. "Aye, I did. Stand by my side, Roger the singer, son of Jeremiah."

"Seas ri mo lâmh, a mhic mo thaighe," Roger said. "Stand by my side—son of my house. Did ye mean that?"

"Ye know that I did."

"Then I mean it, too." He reached out and rested his hand on Jamie's shoulder, and I saw the knuckles whiten as he squeezed.

"I will stand by you. We will stay."

Beside me, Brianna let out the breath she had been holding, in a sigh like the twilight wind.

111

AND YET GO OUT TO MEET IT

THE BIG CLOCK CANDLE had burned down a little, but there were still a good many of the black rings that marked the hours. Jamie dropped the stones back into the pool of melted wax around the flame: one, two, three—and blew it out. The fourth stone, the big topaz, was ensconced in a small wooden box, which I had sewn up in oiled cloth. It was bound for Edinburgh, consigned to Mrs. Bug's cousin's husband, who, with his banking connections, would manage the sale of the stone, and—with the deduction of a suitable commission for his help—would see the funds transmitted to Ned Gowan.

The accompanying letter, lying sealed in the box with the stone, charged Ned to determine whether one Laoghaire MacKenzie was living with a man in a state tantamount to marriage—and if so, further charged him to declare the contract between one Laoghaire MacKenzie and one James Fraser to be fulfilled, whereupon the funds from the sale of the stone were to be placed on deposit in a bank, to be used for the dowry of one Joan MacKenzie Fraser, daughter of the aforesaid Laoghaire, when she should marry.

"You're sure you don't want to ask Ned particularly to tell you who the man is?" I asked.

He shook his head firmly.

"If he chooses to tell me, that's fine. And if he doesna, that's fine, as well." He looked up at me with a faint, wry look. Unsatisfied curiosity was to be his penance, evidently.

Down the hall, I could hear Brianna simultaneously talking to Mrs. Bug and admonishing Jemmy, then Roger's voice, interrupting, and Jemmy's excited squeal as Roger swept him up into the air.

"Do you think Roger chose well?" I asked quietly. I was very glad of Roger's decision—and knew that Jamie was, as well. But in spite of the peculiar perspective that Brianna, Roger, and I had on coming events, I knew that Jamie had far better an idea of what was truly coming. And if the stone passage had its dangers, so did war.

He paused, thinking, then leaned past me, reaching for a small volume at the end of the bookcase. It was bound cheaply in cloth, and much used; an edition of Thucydides he had acquired in the wildly optimistic hope that Germain and Jemmy might eventually learn sufficient Greek to read it.

He opened the book gently, to keep the pages from falling out. Greek lettering looked to me like the conniptions of an ink-soaked worm, but he found the bit he was looking for with no difficulty.

"The bravest are surely those who have the clearest vision of what is before them, glory and danger alike, and yet notwithstanding go out to meet it."

The words were before him, and yet I thought he was not reading them from the paper, but from the pages of his memory, from the open book of his heart.

The door slammed, and I heard Roger shouting outside now, cracked voice raised in warning, calling out to Jemmy, and then his laugh, deep and half-choked, as Bree said something to him, a lighter sound too far away to hear in words.

Then they moved away, and there was silence, save for the sough of the wind in the trees.

"The bravest are those who have the clearest vision. Well, you'd know about that, wouldn't you?" I said softly. I laid a hand on his shoulder, just where it joined his neck. I traced the powerful cords of his neck with my thumb, looking at the worm-writhings on the page. He would, and so would I; for the vision he had was the one I had shown him.

He kept hold of the book, but tilted his head to one side, so that his cheek brushed my hand, and the thickness of his hair touched my wrist, soft and warm.

"Ah, no," he said. "Not me. It's only brave if there's a choice about it, aye?"

I laughed, sniffed, and wiped the wrist of my free hand across my eyes.

"And you think you haven't a choice?"

He paused for a moment, then shut the book, though he continued to hold it in his hands.

"No," he said at last, with a queer tone in his voice. "Not now."

He turned in his chair, looking through the window. Nothing was visible but the big red spruce at the side of the clearing, and the deep shade of the oak grove behind it, tangled with the brambles of wild blackberry, escaped from the yard. The blackened spot where the fiery cross had stood was overgrown now, covered with thick wild barley.

The air moved and I realized that it was not silent, after all. The sounds of the mountain were all around us, birds calling, water rushing in the distance—and there were voices, too, speaking in the murmured traffic of daily rounds, a word by the pigpen, a call from the privy. And under and over everything, the sound of children, faint shrieks and giggles borne on the restless air.

"I suppose you're right," I said, after a moment. He was; there *was* no choice about it now, and the knowledge gave me a sort of peace. What was coming, would come. We would meet it as best we might, and hope to survive; that was all. If we didn't—perhaps they would. I gathered the tail of his hair in my hand and twined my fingers through it, holding tight, like an anchor's rope.

"What about the other choices, though?" I asked him, looking out with him over the empty dooryard, and into the shades of the forest beyond. "All the ones you made that brought you here? Those were real—and bloody well brave, if you ask me."

Beneath the tip of my index finger, I could feel the hair-thin line of his ancient scar, buried deep beneath the ruddy waves. He leaned back against the pull of my hand, and swiveled round to look up at me, so my hand now cupped the bone of his jaw.

"Oh. Well," he said, smiling slightly. His hand touched mine, and drew my fingers into his. "Ye'd know about that, now, wouldn't ye, Sassenach?"

I sat down beside him, close, my hand on his leg, and his hand on mine. We sat thus for a bit, side by side, watching the rain clouds roll in over the river, like a threat of distant war. And I thought that whether it was choice or no choice, it might be that it came to the same thing in the end.

Jamie's hand still lay on mine. It tightened a little, and I glanced at him, but his eyes were still fixed somewhere past the dooryard; past the mountains, and the distant clouds. His grip tightened further, and I felt the edges of my ring press into my flesh.

"When the day shall come, that we do part," he said softly, and turned to look at me, "if my last words are not 'I love you'—ye'll ken it was because I didna have time."

And don't miss the next installment of the acclaimed OUTLANDER series . . .

DIANA GABALDON'S

A BREATH OF SNOW AND ASHES

Available now from Dell Books!

Read on for a preview . . .

A BREATH OF SNOW AND ASHES

On sale now

March 1773

NO ONE HAD KNOWN the cabin was there, until Kenny Lindsay had seen the flames, on his way up the creek.

"I wouldna ha' seen at all," he said, for perhaps the sixth time. "Save for the dark comin' on. Had it been daylight, I'd never ha' kent it, never." He wiped a trembling hand over his face, unable to take his eyes off the line of bodies that lay at the edge of the forest. "Was it savages, *Mac Dubh?* They're no scalped, but maybe—"

"No." Jamie laid the soot-smeared handkerchief gently back over the staring blue face of a small girl. "None of them is wounded. Surely ye saw as much when ye brought them out?"

Lindsay shook his head, eyes closed, and shivered convulsively. It was late afternoon, and a chilly spring day, but the men were all sweating.

"I didna look," he said simply.

My own hands were like ice; as numb and unfeeling as the rubbery flesh of the dead woman I was examining. They had been dead for more than a day; the rigor of death had passed off, leaving them limp and chilled, but the cold weather of the mountain spring had preserved them so far from the grosser indignities of putrefaction.

Still, I breathed shallowly; the air was bitter with the scent of burning. Wisps of steam rose now and then from the charred ruin of the tiny cabin. From the corner of my eye, I saw Roger kick at a nearby log, then bend and pick up something from the ground beneath.

Kenny had pounded on our door long before daylight, summoning us from warm beds. We had come in haste, even knowing that we were far too late to offer aid. Some of the tenants from the homesteads on Fraser's Ridge had come, too; Kenny's brother Evan stood with Fergus and Ronnie Sinclair in a small knot under the trees, talking together in low-voiced Gaelic.

"D'ye ken what did for them, Sassenach?" Jamie squatted beside me, face troubled. "The ones under the trees, that is." He nodded at the corpse in front of me. "I ken what killed this puir woman."

The woman's long skirt stirred in the wind, lifting to show long, slender feet shod in leather clogs. A pair of long hands to match lay still at her sides. She had been tall—though not so tall as Brianna, I thought, and looked automatically for my daughter's bright hair, bobbing among the branches on the far side of the clearing.

I had turned the woman's apron up to cover her head and upper body. Her hands were red, rough-knuckled with work, and with callused palms, but from the firmness of her thighs and the slenderness of her body, I thought she was no more than thirty—likely much younger. No one could say whether she had been pretty.

I shook my head at his remark.

"I don't think she died of the burning," I said. "See, her legs and feet aren't touched. She must have fallen into the hearth. Her hair caught fire, and it spread to the shoulders of her gown. She must have lain near enough to the wall or the chimney hood for the flames to touch; that caught, and then the whole bloody place went up."

Jamie nodded slowly, eyes on the dead woman.

"Aye, that makes sense. But what was it killed them, Sassenach? The others are singed a bit, though none are burned like this. But they must have been dead before the cabin caught alight, for none o' them ran out. Was it a deadly illness, perhaps?"

"I don't think so. Let me look at the others again."

I walked slowly down the row of still bodies with their cloth-covered faces, stooping over each one to peer again beneath the makeshift shrouds. There were any number of illnesses that could be quickly fatal in these days—with no antibiotics to hand, and no way of administering fluids save by mouth or rectum, a simple case of diarrhea could kill within twenty-four hours.

I saw such things often enough to recognize them easily; any doctor does, and I had been a doctor for more than twenty years. I saw things now and then in this century that I had never encountered in my own—particularly horrible parasitical diseases, brought with the slave trade from the tropics—but it was no parasite that had done for these poor souls, and no illness that I knew, to leave such traces on its victims.

All the bodies—the burned woman, a much older woman, and three children—had been found inside the walls of the flaming house. Kenny had pulled them out, just before the roof fell in, then ridden for help. All dead before the fire started; all dead virtually at the same time, then, for surely the fire had begun to smolder soon after the woman fell dead on her hearth?

The victims had been laid out neatly under the branches of a giant red spruce, while the men began to dig a grave nearby. Brianna stood by the smallest girl, her head bent. I came to kneel by the little body, and she knelt down across from me.

"What was it?" she asked quietly. "Poison?"

I glanced up at her in surprise.

"I think so. What gave you that idea?"

She nodded at the blue-tinged face below us. She had tried to close the eyes, but they bulged beneath the lids, giving the little girl a look of startled horror. The small, blunt features were twisted in a rictus of agony, and there were traces of vomit in the corners of the mouth.

"Girl Scout handbook," Brianna said. She glanced at the men, but no one was near enough to hear. Her mouth twitched, and she looked away from the body, holding out her open hand. *"Never eat any strange mushroom,"* she quoted. *"There are many poisonous varieties, and distinguishing one from another is a job for an expert.* Roger found these, growing in a ring by that log over there."

Moist, fleshy caps, a pale brown with white warty spots, the open gills and slender stems so pale as to look almost phosphorescent in the spruce shadows. They had a pleasant, earthy look to them that belied their deadliness.

“Panther toadstools,” I said, half to myself, and picked one gingerly from her palm. “*Agaricus pantherinus*—or that’s what they *will* be called, once somebody gets round to naming them properly. *Pantherinus,* because they kill so swiftly—like a striking cat.”

I could see the gooseflesh ripple on Brianna’s forearm, raising the soft, red-gold hairs. She tilted her hand and spilled the rest of the deadly fungus on the ground.

“Who in their right mind would eat toadstools?” she asked, wiping her hand on her skirt with a slight shudder.

“People who didn’t know better. People who were hungry, perhaps,” I answered softly. I picked up the little girl’s hand, and traced the delicate bones of the forearm. The small belly showed signs of bloat, whether from malnutrition or postmortem changes I couldn’t tell—but the collarbones were sharp as scythe blades. All of the bodies were thin, though not to the point of emaciation.

I looked up, into the deep blue shadows of the mountainside above the cabin. It was early in the year for foraging, but there was food in abundance in the forest—for those who could recognize it.

Jamie came and knelt down beside me, a big hand lightly on my back. Cold as it was, a trickle of sweat streaked his neck, and his thick auburn hair was dark at the temples.

“The grave is ready,” he said, speaking low, as though he might alarm the child. “Is that what’s killed the bairn?” He nodded at the scattered fungi.

“I think so—and the rest of them, too. Have you had a look around? Does anyone know who they were?”

He shook his head.

“Not English; the clothes are wrong. Germans would have gone to Salem, surely; they’re clannish souls, and no inclined to settle on their own. These were maybe Dutchmen.” He nodded toward the carved wooden clogs on the old woman’s feet, cracked and stained with long use. “No books nor writing left, if there was any to begin with. Nothing that might tell their name. But—”

“They hadn’t been here long.” A low, cracked voice made me look up. Roger had come; he squatted next to Brianna, nodding toward the smoldering remains of the cabin. A small garden plot had been scratched into the earth nearby, but the few plants showing were no more than sprouts, the tender leaves limp and blackened with late frost. There were no sheds, no sign of livestock, no mule or pig.

"New emigrants," Roger said softly. "Not bond servants; this was a family. They weren't used to outdoor labor, either; the women's hands have blisters and fresh scars." His own broad hand rubbed unconsciously over a homespun knee; his palms were as smoothly callused as Jamie's now, but he had once been a tender-skinned scholar; he remembered the pain of his seasoning.

"I wonder if they left people behind—in Europe," Brianna murmured. She smoothed blond hair off the little girl's forehead, and laid the kerchief back over her face. I saw her throat move as she swallowed. "They'll never know what happened to them."

"No." Jamie stood abruptly. "They do say that God protects fools—but I think even the Almighty will lose patience now and then." He turned away, motioning to Lindsay and Sinclair.

"Look for the man," he said to Lindsay. Every head jerked up to look at him.

"Man?" Roger said, and then glanced sharply at the burned remnants of the cabin, realization dawning. "Aye—who built the cabin for them?"

"The women could have done it," Bree said, lifting her chin.

"*You* could, aye," he said, mouth twitching slightly as he cast a sidelong look at his wife. Brianna resembled Jamie in more than coloring; she stood six feet in her stockings and had her father's clean-limbed strength.

"Perhaps they could, but they didn't," Jamie said shortly. He nodded toward the shell of the cabin, where a few bits of furniture still held their fragile shapes. As I watched, the evening wind came down, scouring the ruin, and the shadow of a stool collapsed noiselessly into ash, flurries of soot and char moving ghostlike over the ground.

"What do you mean?" I stood and moved beside him, looking into the house. There was virtually nothing left inside, though the chimney stack still stood, and jagged bits of the walls remained, their logs fallen like jackstraws.

"There's no metal," he said, nodding at the blackened hearth, where the remnants of a cauldron lay, cracked in two from the heat, its contents vaporized. "No pots, save that—and that's too heavy to carry away. Nay tools. Not a knife, not an ax—and ye see whoever built it had that."

I did; the logs were unpeeled, but the notches and ends bore the clear marks of an ax.

Frowning, Roger picked up a long pine branch and began to poke through the piles of ash and rubble, looking to be sure. Kenny Lindsay and Sinclair didn't bother; Jamie had told them to look for a man, and they promptly went to do so, disappearing into the forest. Fergus went with them; Evan Lindsay, his brother Murdo, and the McGillivrays began the chore of collecting stones for a cairn.

"If there *was* a man—did he leave them?" Brianna murmured to me, glancing from her father to the row of bodies. "Did this woman maybe think they wouldn't survive on their own?"

And thus take her own life, and those of her children, to avoid a long-drawn-out death from cold and starvation?

"Leave them and take all their tools? God, I hope not." I crossed myself at the thought, though even as I did so, I doubted it. "Wouldn't they have walked out, looking for help? Even with children . . . the snow's mostly gone." Only the highest mountain passes were still packed with snow, and while the trails and slopes were wet and muddy with runoff, they'd been passable for a month, at least.

"I've found the man," Roger said, interrupting my thoughts. He spoke very calmly, but paused to clear his throat. "Just—just here."

The daylight was beginning to fade, but I could see that he had gone pale. No wonder; the curled form he had unearthed beneath the charred timbers of a fallen wall was sufficiently gruesome as to give anyone pause. Charred to blackness, hands upraised in the boxer's pose so common to those dead by fire, it was difficult even to be sure that it *was* a man—though I thought it was, from what I could see.

Speculation about this new body was interrupted by a shout from the forest's edge.

"We've found them, milord!"

Everyone looked up from contemplation of this new corpse, to see Fergus waving from the edge of the wood.

"Them," indeed. Two men, this time. Sprawled on the ground within the shadow of the trees, found not together, but not far apart, only a short distance from the house. And both, so far as I could tell, probably dead of mushroom poisoning.

"*That's* no Dutchman," Sinclair said, for probably the fourth time, shaking his head over one body.

"He might be," said Fergus dubiously. He scratched his nose with the tip of the hook he wore in replacement of his left hand. "From the Indies, *non*?"

One of the unknown bodies was in fact that of a black man. The other was white, and both wore nondescript clothes of worn homespun—shirts and breeches; no jackets, despite the cold weather. And both were barefoot.

"No." Jamie shook his head, rubbing one hand unconsciously on his own breeches, as though to rid himself of the touch of the dead. "The Dutch keep slaves on Barbuda, aye—but these are better fed than the folk from the cabin." He lifted his chin toward the silent row of women and children. "They didna live here. Besides . . ." I saw his eyes fix on the dead men's feet.

The feet were grubby about the ankles and heavily callused, but basically clean. The soles of the black man's feet showed yellowish pink, with no smears of mud or random leaves stuck between the toes. These men hadn't been walking through the muddy forest barefoot, that much was sure.

"So there were perhaps more men? And when these died, their companions took their shoes—and anything else of value"—Fergus added practically, gesturing from the burned cabin to the stripped bodies—"and fled."

"Aye, maybe." Jamie pursed his lips, his gaze traveling slowly over the earth of the yard—but the ground was churned with footsteps, clumps of grass uprooted and the whole of the yard dusted with ash and bits of charred wood. It looked as though the place had been ravaged by rampaging hippopotami.

"I could wish that Young Ian was here. He's the best of the trackers; he could maybe tell what happened there, at least." He nodded into the wood, where the men had been found. "How many there were, maybe, and which way they've gone."

Jamie himself was no mean tracker. But the light was going fast now; even in the clearing where the burned cabin stood, the dark was rising, pooling under the trees, creeping like oil across the shattered earth.

His eyes went to the horizon, where streamers of cloud were beginning to blaze with gold and pink as the sun set behind them, and he shook his head.

"Bury them. Then we'll go."

One more grim discovery remained. Alone among the dead, the burned man had not died of fire or poison. When they lifted the charred corpse from the ashes to bear him to his grave, something fell free of the body, landing with a small, heavy thunk on the ground. Brianna picked it up, and rubbed at it with the corner of her apron.

"I guess they overlooked this," she said a little bleakly, holding it out. It was a knife, or the blade of one. The wooden hilt had burned entirely away, and the blade itself was warped with heat.

Steeling myself against the thick, acrid stench of burned fat and flesh, I bent over the corpse, poking gingerly at the midsection. Fire destroys a great deal, but preserves the strangest things. The triangular wound was quite clear, seared in the hollow beneath his ribs.

"They stabbed him," I said, and wiped my sweating hands on my own apron.

"They killed him," Bree said, watching my face. "And then his wife—" She glanced at the young woman on the ground, the concealing apron over her head. "She made a stew with the mushrooms, and they all ate it. The children, too."

The clearing was silent, save for the distant calls of birds on the mountain. I could hear my own heart, beating painfully in my chest. Vengeance? Or simple despair?

"Aye, maybe," Jamie said quietly. He stooped to pick up an end of the sheet of canvas they had placed the dead man on. "We'll call it accident."

The Dutchman and his family were laid in one grave, the two strangers in another.

A cold wind had sprung up as the sun went down; the apron fluttered away from the woman's face as they lifted her. Sinclair gave a strangled cry of shock, and nearly dropped her.

She had neither face nor hair anymore; the slender waist narrowed abruptly into charred ruin. The flesh of her head had burned away completely, leaving an oddly tiny, blackened skull, from which her teeth grinned in disconcerting levity.

They lowered her hastily into the shallow grave, her children and mother beside her, and left Brianna and me to build a small cairn over them, in the ancient Scottish way, to mark the place and provide protection from wild beasts, while a more rudimentary resting place was dug for the two barefoot men.

The work finally done, everyone gathered, white-faced and silent, around the new-made mounds. I saw Roger stand close beside Brianna, his arm protectively about her waist. A small shudder went through her, which I thought had nothing to do with the cold. Their child, Jemmy, was a year or so younger than the smallest girl.

"Will ye speak a word, *Mac Dubh*?" Kenny Lindsay glanced inquiringly at Jamie, pulling his knitted bonnet down over his ears against the growing chill.

It was nearly nightfall, and no one wanted to linger. We would have to make camp, somewhere well away from the stink of burning, and that would be hard enough, in the dark. But Kenny was right; we couldn't leave without at least some token of ceremony, some farewell for the strangers.

Jamie shook his head.

"Nay, let Roger Mac speak. If these were Dutchmen, belike they were Protestant."

Dim as the light was, I saw the sharp glance Brianna shot at her father. It was true that Roger was a Presbyterian; so was Tom Christie, a much older man whose dour face reflected his opinion of the proceedings. The question of religion was no more than a pretext, though, and everyone knew it, including Roger.

Roger cleared his throat with a noise like tearing calico. It was always a painful sound; there was anger in it now as well. He didn't protest, though, and he met Jamie's eyes straight on, as he took his place at the head of the grave.

I had thought he would simply say the Lord's Prayer, or perhaps one of the gentler psalms. Other words came to him, though.

"Behold, I cry out of wrong, but I am not heard: I cry aloud, but there is no judgment. He hath fenced up my way that I cannot pass, and He hath set darkness in my paths."

His voice had once been powerful, and beautiful. It was choked now, no more than a rasping shadow of its former beauty—but there was sufficient power in the passion with which he spoke to make all those who heard him bow their heads, faces lost in shadow.

"He hath stripped me of my glory, and taken the crown from my head. He hath destroyed me on every side, and I am gone: and my hope hath He removed like a tree." His face was set, but his eyes rested for a bleak moment on the charred stump that had served the Dutch family for a chopping block.

"He hath put my brethren far from me, and mine acquaintance are verily estranged from me. My kinsfolk have failed, and my familiar friends have forgotten me." I saw the three Lindsay brothers exchange glances, and everyone drew a little closer together, against the rising wind.

"Have pity upon me, have pity upon me, O ye my friends," he said, and his voice softened, so that it was difficult to hear him, above the sighing of the trees. *"For the hand of God has touched me."*

Brianna made a slight movement beside him, and he cleared his throat once more, explosively, stretching his neck so that I caught a glimpse of the rope scar that marred it.

"Oh, that my words were now written! Oh, that they were printed in a book! That they were graven with an iron pen and lead in the rock forever!"

He looked slowly round from face to face, his own expressionless, then took a deep breath to continue, voice cracking on the words.

"For I know that my redeemer liveth, and that He shall stand at the latter day upon the earth: And though after my skin worms destroy this body"—Brianna shuddered convulsively,

and looked away from the raw mound of dirt—*"yet in my flesh shall I see God. Whom I shall see for myself, and mine eyes shall behold."*

He stopped, and there was a brief collective sigh, as everyone let out the breath they had been holding. He wasn't quite finished, though. He had reached out, half-unconsciously, for Bree's hand, and held it tightly. He spoke the last words almost to himself, I thought, with little thought for his listeners.

"Be ye afraid of the sword: for wrath bringeth the punishments of the sword, that ye may know there is a judgment."

I shivered, and Jamie's hand curled round my own, cold but strong. He looked down at me, and I met his eyes. I knew what he was thinking.

He was thinking, as I was, not of the present, but the future. Of a small item that would appear three years hence, in the pages of the *Wilmington Gazette,* dated February 13, 1776.

It is with grief that the news is received of the deaths by fire of James MacKenzie Fraser and his wife, Claire Fraser, in a conflagration that destroyed their house in the settlement of Fraser's Ridge, on the night of January 21 last. Mr. Fraser, a nephew of the late Hector Cameron of River Run Plantation, was born at Broch Tuarach in Scotland. He was widely known in the Colony and deeply respected; he leaves no surviving children.

It had been easy, so far, not to think too much of it. So far in the future, and surely not an unchangeable future—after all, forewarned was forearmed . . . wasn't it?

I glanced at the shallow cairn, and a deeper chill passed through me. I stepped closer to Jamie, and put my other hand on his arm. He covered my hand with his, and squeezed tight in reassurance. No, he said to me silently. No, I will not let it happen.

As we left the desolate clearing, though, I could not free my mind of one vivid image. Not the burned cabin, the pitiful bodies, the pathetic dead garden. The image that haunted me was one I had seen some years before—a gravestone in the ruins of Beauly Priory, high in the Scottish Highlands.

It was the tomb of a noble lady, her name surmounted by the carving of a grinning skull—very like the one beneath the Dutchwoman's apron. Beneath the skull was her motto:

Hodie mihi cras tibi—sic transit gloria mundi.
My turn today—yours tomorrow. Thus passes the glory of the world.

Also by Diana Gabaldon

THE **OUTLANDER** SERIES

DianaGabaldon.com

AuthorDianaGabaldon @Writer_DG

RANDOM HOUSE BALLANTINE • BANTAM • DELL

Also by DIANA GABALDON

THE COMPANION VOLUME

THE OUTLANDER GRAPHIC NOVEL

THE LORD JOHN SERIES

Lord John and the Private Matter
Lord John and the Brotherhood of the Blade
Lord John and the Hand of Devils
The Scottish Prisoner

Continue the saga with original eNovellas, engrossing tales to complement the Outlander series.

A Plague of Zombies

The Custom of the Army

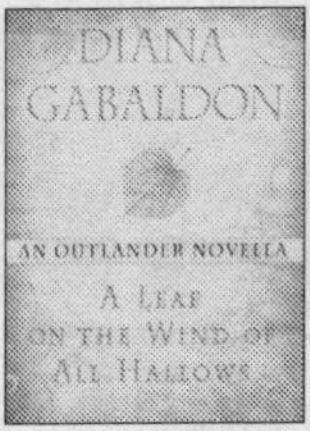

A Leaf on the Wind of All Hallows

The Space Between